S0-BXB-130

LITERARY MARKET PLACE™

LMP
2005

Literary Market Place™
65th Edition

Publisher
Thomas H. Hogan

Vice President, Content
Dick Kaser

Director, ITI Reference Group
Owen O'Donnell

Managing Editor
Karen Hallard

Associate Editors
Kevin Araujo; Kathryn Eaton; Mary-Anne Lutter

Tampa Operations:

Production Manager, Tampa Editoral
Debbie James

Project Coordinator, Tampa Editorial
Lori Mercurio

Data Entry Clerk, Tampa Editorial
Barbara Lauria

LITERARY MARKET PLACE™

LMP 2005

THE DIRECTORY OF THE AMERICAN BOOK PUBLISHING INDUSTRY WITH INDUSTRY YELLOW PAGES

Volume

Published by

Information Today, Inc.
143 Old Marlton Pike
Medford, NJ 08055-8750
Phone: (609) 654-6266
Fax: (609) 654-4309
E-mail (Orders): custserv@infotoday.com
Web site: www.infotoday.com

ISSN 0000-1155
ISBN 1-57387-203-2 (set)
1-57387-201-6 (Vol 1)
1-57387-202-4 (Vol 2)
Library of Congress Catalog Card Number 41-51571

Information Today, Inc.
143 Old Marlton Pike
Medford, NJ 08055-8750
Phone: 800-300-9868 (Customer Service)
          800-409-4929 (Editorial)
Fax: 609-654-4309
E-mail (orders): custserv@infotoday.com
Web Site: www.infotoday.com

Printed in the United States of America

US $299.95

ISBN 1-57387-203-2

59999>

9 781573 872034

CONTENTS

VOLUME 2

ADVERTISING, MARKETING & PUBLICITY

BOOK MANUFACTURING

SALES & DISTRIBUTION

SERVICES & SUPPLIERS

INDEXES

Preface

The year 2005 marks the 65th annual publication of *Literary Market Place*™—the leading directory of the American and Canadian book publishing industry. Covering publishers and literary agents to manufacturers and shipping services, *LMP* is the most comprehensive directory of its kind. Completely revised, *LMP* 2005 contains almost 13,000 entries, of which 592 are listed for the first time. 3,323 of these listings are publishers—including Canadian houses and small presses. Together with its companion publication, *International Literary Market Place*, these directories cover the global book publishing industry.

Organization & Content

Volume 1 covers core publishing industry information: Book Publishers; Editorial Services and Agents; Associations, Events, Courses and Awards; and Books and Magazines for the Trade.

Volume 2 contains information on service providers and suppliers to the publishing industry. Advertising, Marketing and Publicity; Book Manufacturing; Sales and Distribution; and Services and Suppliers can be found in this volume.

Entries generally contain name, address, telephone and other telecommunications data, key personnel, company reportage, branch offices, brief statistics and descriptive annotations. Where applicable, Standard Address Numbers (SANs) have been included. SANs are unique numbers assigned to the addresses of publishers, wholesalers and booksellers. Publishers' entries also contain their assigned ISBN prefixes. Both the SAN and ISBN systems are administered by R.R. Bowker LLC, 630 Central Avenue, New Providence, NJ 07974.

Indexes

In addition to the numerous section-specific indexes appearing throughout, each volume of *LMP* contains four indexes that reference listings appearing in that volume. The Industry Yellow Pages cover two distinct areas of data: a Company Index that includes the name, address, communications information and page reference for company listings and a separate Personnel Index that includes the main personnel associated with each entry as well as the page reference. Other indexes include the Index to Sections for quickly finding specific categories of information and the Index to Advertisers.

A Note to Authors

Prospective authors seeking a publisher should be aware that there are publishers who, as a condition for publishing and marketing an individual's work, may require a significant sum of money be paid to the publisher. This practice is known by a number of terms including author subsidized publishing, author investment, and co-operative publishing. Before entering an agreement involving such a payment, the author is advised to make a careful investigation to determine the standing of the publisher's imprint in the industry. The editors of *LMP* have attempted to exclude from this edition any publishers whom they have determined publish a significant number of titles only when an author pays, contributes or invests a sum of money with the publisher. Such exclusion should not be construed as a judgment on the legitimacy or integrity of any particular publisher.

Similarly, authors seeking literary representation are advised that some agents request a nominal reading fee that may be applied to the agent's commission upon representation. Other agencies may charge substantially higher fees which may not be applicable to a future commission and which are not refundable. The recommended course is to first send a query letter with an outline, sample chapter, and a self-addressed stamped envelope (SASE). Should an agent express interest in handling the manuscript, full details of fees and commissions should be obtained in writing before the complete manuscript is sent. Should an agency require significant advance payment from an author, the author is cautioned to make a careful investigation to determine the agency's standing in the industry before entering an agreement. The author should always retain a copy of the manuscript in his or her possession.

Compilation

LMP is updated throughout the year via a number of methods. A questionnaire is mailed to every current listing at least once each year to corroborate and update the information contained on our database. All returned mailers are edited for the next product release. Those entrants who do not respond to our mailing are verified through telephone interviews. Entrants who cannot be verified or who fall short of entry criteria are dropped from the current edition.

Information on new listings is gathered in a similar method. Possible new listings are identified through ongoing research, or nominations for listing may come from the organization itself or from a third party. A questionnaire is then sent to gather the essential listing information. Unless we receive information directly from the organization, the new listing will not be included in the *LMP* database.

Updated information or suggestions for new listings can also be submitted by using the form that follows this preface. Simply fill in the information requested and send the form to:

Literary Market Place
Information Today, Inc.
630 Central Ave
New Providence, NJ 07974
Fax: 908-219-0192

An updating method using the Internet is also available for *LMP* listings:

Visit the *Literary Market Place* web site to update an *LMP* listing. **Literarymarketplace.com** allows you the opportunity to provide new information for a listing by clicking on the "Update or Correct Your Entry" option. The Feedback option on the home page of the web site can be used to suggest new entries as well.

Once the information regarding a suggested new entry or a correction to an existing listing has been submitted, our editors verify the data with the organization to ensure the accuracy of the update.

Related Services
Literary Market Place, along with its companion volume *International Literary Market Place*, is now available through the World Wide Web at **www.literarymarketplace.com**. Designed to give users simple, logical access to the information they require, the site offers users the choice of searching for data alphabetically, geographically, by type, or by subject. Continuously updated by Information Today's team of editors, this is a truly enhanced version of the *LMP* and *ILMP* databases, incorporating features that make "must-have" information easily available.

Arrangements for placing advertisements in *LMP* can be coordinated through Chuck Fiorello by telephone at 212-689-2855, by fax at 270-738-4305, or by e-mail at cfiorello@infotoday.com.

Your feedback is important to us. We strongly encourage you to contact us with suggestions or comments on the print edition of *LMP*, or its web site. Our editorial office can be reached at 800-409-4929, or by e-mail at khallard@infotoday.com.

The editors would like to thank those entrants who took the time to respond to our questionnaires.

Return this form to:
Literary Market Place
Information Today, Inc.
630 Central Avenue
New Providence, NJ 07974
Fax: 908-219-0192

LITERARY MARKET PLACE™
EDITORIAL REVISION FORM

Company Name:_____

The company listing is found on page number:_____

☐ Please check here if you are nominating this organization for a new listing in the directory

General Information

Address:_____

City:_____ State/Province:_____ Postal Code:_____

Phone:_____ Fax:_____

E-mail:_____ Web Site:_____

Brief Description:_____

Personnel

☐ Addition   ☐ Deletion   ☐ Correction

First Name:_____ Last Name:_____ Title:_____

☐ Addition   ☐ Deletion   ☐ Correction

First Name:_____ Last Name:_____ Title:_____

☐ Addition   ☐ Deletion   ☐ Correction

First Name:_____ Last Name:_____ Title:_____

☐ Addition   ☐ Deletion   ☐ Correction

First Name:_____ Last Name:_____ Title:_____

(continued on back)

Other Information

Indicate other information to be added to or corrected in this listing; please be as specific as possible, noting erroneous data to be deleted.

_____

_____

_____

_____

_____

_____

_____

Verification

Data for this listing will not be updated without the following information (*indicates mandatory information)

*Your First Name:_____ *Your Last Name:_____

Organization Name:_____

*Address:_____

*City:_____ *State/Province:_____ *Postal Code:_____

*Phone:_____ E-mail:_____

*Indicate if you are a: ☐ Representative of this Organization ☐ User of this directory ☐ Other

If other, please specify:_____

Thank you for helping Information Today, Inc. maintain the most up-to-date information available.
Please return by fax to: 908-219-0192, or visit www.literarymarketplace.com and
click on the option to Update or Correct Your Entry under Free Services.

Book Trade Acquisitions & Mergers 2002-2004

The acquisitions & mergers in this edition of LMP cover a two-year period (June 2002 through July 2004). Those that have occurred since the last edition of *LMP* are preceded by an asterisk.

*AARP to publish a line of books in partnership with **Sterling Publishing** under the AARP trademark, *Publishers Weekly*, 7/28/03

Acme Bookbinding has teamed with **Harvard University Press** to create a print-on-demand system, *Publishers Weekly*, 12/2/02

Adams Media Corp acquired by **F+W Publications**, *Publishers Weekly*, 7/14/03

Advanced Marketing Services to acquire **Airlift**, a UK book distributor, *Publishers Weekly*, 11/4/02
—has acquired **H.I. Marketing Ltd**, a UK book distributor, *Publishers Weekly*, 12/9/02
—has acquired **CutSound Ltd**, a UK book distributor, *Publishers Weekly*, 12/9/02
*—combined seven different distribution companies into a new network called **Publishers Group Worldwide (PGW)**, *Publishers Weekly*, 9/29/03

Airlift, a UK book distributor, to be acquired by **Advanced Marketing Services**, *Publishers Weekly*, 11/4/02

Albion Books purchased by **Moyer Bell** from **LPC Group**, *Publishers Weekly*, 10/21/02

Alpha Books, part of Pearson Education's **Pearson Technology Group**, is being moved to **Penguin Putnam**, *Publishers Weekly*, 9/2/02

*Amadeus Press has acquired **Limelight Editions**, *Publishers Weekly*, 4/26/04

American Media Inc, parent company of the *National Enquirer* and *Star* magazine, to form a publishing unit, **AMI Books**, to focus on true crime and celebrity titles, *Publishers Weekly*, 10/7/02

AMI Books, a new publishing company focusing on true crime and celebrity titles, to be formed by **American Media Inc**, parent company of the *National Enquirer* and *Star* magazine, *Publishers Weekly*, 10/7/02

Andrews Publications acquired by **West**, the legal publishing division of Thomson

Corp, from **Haights Cross Communications**, *Publishers Weekly*, 4/7/03

Sherman Asher Publishing has been acquired by **Western Edge Press**, *Publishers Weekly*, 9/30/02

Aspen Publishers, a subsidiary of **Wolters Kluwer**, has sold its healthcare division to **Jones & Bartlett Publishers**, *Publishers Weekly*, 11/18/02

Avalon Publishing Group announced the formation of a new division, **Shoemaker & Hoard**, *Publishers Weekly*, 12/16/02

Axel Springer has sold the **Ullstein Heyne List** publishing group to **Bertelsmann**, *Publishers Weekly*, 2/17/03

Baker & Taylor sold by the **Carlyle Group** to **Willis Stein & Partners**, a private investment group, *Publishers Weekly*, 7/7/03

Baker Book House to acquire **Bethany House Publishers**, *Publishers Weekly*, 12/23/02

Ballantine Books is being combined with **Random House Trade Group** to form the **Random House Ballantine Publishing Group**, *Publishers Weekly*, 1/20/03

Barnes & Noble announced the closing of **eNews**, an online magazine subscription service jointly owned by BarnesandNoble.com and Barnes & Noble Inc, *Publishers Weekly*, 8/26/02
—acquired **Sterling Publishing**, *Publishers Weekly*, 12/16/02
*—has sold its Memphis, TN based print-on-demand facility to **Lightning Source**, *Publishers Weekly*, 9/29/03

*Berkshire House Publishers acquired by **W W Norton** and will become part of Norton's Countryman Press division, *Publishers Weekly*, 8/11/03

Bertelsmann announced it will cease ownership of **BOL**, its online bookselling venture, *Publishers Weekly*, 9/9/02
—has acquired the **Ullstein Heyne List**

publishing group from **Axel Springer**, *Publishers Weekly*, 2/17/03

Bertelsmann Springer acquired by London equity firms Candover and Cinven; the company will be merged with **KAP** to create an international publishing company named **Springer**, *Publishers Weekly*, 5/19/03

Bethany House Publishers to be acquired by **Baker Book House**, *Publishers Weekly*, 12/23/02

Bloomberg Press has signed a deal with **Profile Books**, a UK publisher, to distribute books from the *Economist*, *Publishers Weekly*, 11/18/02

Blue Hen Books, an imprint of **Penguin Putnam**, will be divested, *Publishers Weekly*, 9/30/02

BOL, an online bookselling venture of **Bertelsmann**, will be shut down or sold, *Publishers Weekly*, 9/9/02

*Books On Wings, a wholesaler which stocks Spanish-language titles, acquired by **Brodart**, *Publishers Weekly*, 2/23/04

*Bow Tie Inc has acquired **Doral Publishing**, *Publishers Weekly*, 6/7/04
*—has acquired **Kennel Club Books**, *Publishers Weekly*, 6/7/04

R R Bowker has acquired **PubEasy**, an online book wholesale self-service center, from **Vista International**, *Publishers Weekly*, 2/17/03
*—has acquired **Simba Information**, a publisher of newsletters, from **Primedia Inc**, *Publishers Weekly*, 9/22/03

Bridge Publications has formed a new press, **Galaxy Press**, to handle fiction titles, *Publishers Weekly*, 8/19/02

*Brodart has acquired **Books On Wings**, a wholesaler which stocks Spanish-language titles, *Publishers Weekly*, 2/23/04

*Buckle Down Publishing, a test prep publisher, acquired by **Haights Cross Communications**, *Publishers Weekly*, 4/26/04

Burnham Publishers acquired by **Rowman & Littlefield Publishing Group**, *Publishers Weekly*, 6/16/03

*Career Press to sell 49 career and reference titles to **Delmar Learning**, a Thomson company, *Publishers Weekly*, 4/19/04

Carlyle Group has sold **Baker & Taylor** to **Willis Stein & Partners**, a private investment group, *Publishers Weekly*, 7/7/03

Center for Excellence in Writing at Portland State University (OR) has launched **Ooligan Press**, a general publishing and teaching imprint, *Publishers Weekly*, 1/6/03

*Charis Books, an imprint of **Servant Publications**, sold to **St. Anthony Messenger Press**, *Publishers Weekly*, 10/20/03

*Chicago Review Press Inc has acquired **Zephyr Press**, an educational press located in Phoenix, AZ, *Publishers Weekly*, 10/6/03

Chicago Tribune has bought the **Printers Row Book Fair** from the Near South Planning Board, *Publishers Weekly*, 12/9/02

China's Foreign Language and Research Press has signed a co-publishing deal with **HarperCollins** through the UK Collins reference publishing group to publish bilingual dictionaries, *Publishers Weekly*, 9/23/02

*Chronicle Books LLC acquired **Sea Star Books**, a division of **North-South Books Inc**, *Publishers Weekly*, 1/19/04

City & Co, a small press known for guides to New York City, has sold its backlist to **Rizzoli's Universe** imprint, *Publishers Weekly*, 9/30/02

Clock Tower Press, a new publisher, has been formed as the result of the divestiture of 100 golf, sports, and regional titles to the former shareholders of **Sleeping Bear Press**, *Publishers Weekly*, 8/26/02

*Collegiate Press acquired by **Roman & Littlefield Publishing Group**, *Publishers Weekly*, 9/1/03

*Copperhouse Publishing to sell 44 criminal justice titles to **Thomson**'s higher education unit, *Publishers Weekly*, 4/19/04

*Courier Corp. has agreed to acquire **Research & Education Association** of Piscataway, NJ, a publisher of test prep and study guidebooks and software for the high school, college, graduate school, and professional markets, *Publishers Weekly*, 12/22/03

Course Technology, a subsidiary of Thomson Corp, has acquired **Premier Press**, publisher of computer and technology books from **22nd Century Inc**, *Publishers Weekly*, 8/12/02
—has acquired **Muska & Lipman**, a computer book publisher, *Publishers Weekly*, 8/12/02

CRC Press acquired by **Taylor & Francis Group plc**, *Publishers Weekly*, 3/10/03

Creative will acquire **Two-Can Publishing** the children's book publishing division of **Zenith Entertainment**, *Publishers Weekly*, 9/16/02

Creative Book Group (CBG) formed by **Creative Homeowner** to handle distribution of their own titles as well as titles of other established independent publishers, *Publishers Weekly*, 1/27/03

Creative Homeowner has formed a new unit, **Creative Book Group (CBG)**, to handle distribution of their own titles as well as titles of other established independent publishers, *Publishers Weekly*, 1/27/03

*Creative Publishing International has sold its "how to" line of products to **Rockport Publishers**, *Publishers Weekly*, 7/19/04

*Crown Publishing has signed a three-year deal with the **Wall Street Journal**, *Publishers Weekly*, 3/29/04

CutSound Ltd, a UK book distributor, acquired by **Advanced Marketing Services**, *Publishers Weekly*, 12/9/02

*DaCapo Press forms **DaCapo Lifelong Books** imprint, *Publishers Weekly*, 8/11/03

*Dark Horse Comics has agreed to acquire **Studio Proteus**, *Publishers Weekly*, 2/23/04

*Dekker Group to be acquired by **Taylor & Francis**, *Publishers Weekly*, 11/24/03

*Delmar Learning, a Thomson company, to acquire 49 career and reference titles

from **Career Press**, *Publishers Weekly*, 4/19/04

Distican, the exclusive distributor for **Simon & Schuster** in Canada will be acquired by Simon & Schuster; following the completion of the sale, the company will be renamed **Simon & Schuster Canada**, *Publishers Weekly*, 11/25/02

*R R Donnelley has agreed to acquire **Moore Wallace**, *Publishers Weekly*, 11/17/03

*Doral Publishing acquired by **Bow Tie Inc**, *Publishers Weekly*, 6/7/04

Dun & Bradstreet to acquire **Hoover's Inc**, *Publishers Weekly*, 12/16/02

eNews, an online magazine subscription service jointly owned by BarnesandNoble.com and Barnes & Noble Inc, has closed according to an announcement from **Barnes & Noble**, *Publishers Weekly*, 8/26/02

Entrepreneur Press acquired **Oasis Press** from **Publishing Services Inc**, *Publishers Weekly*, 1/13/03

Everyman Publishers plc, the UK-based publisher of hardcover classics, has been acquired by **Alfred A. Knopf**, an imprint of **Random House**, *Publishers Weekly*, 11/18/02

F+W Publications acquired **Krause Publications**, a book and hobby magazine publisher, *Publishers Weekly*, 9/16/02
—has acquired **Adams Media Corp**, *Publishers Weekly*, 7/14/03

Facts on File has acquired **Ferguson Publishing Co**, a publisher of career education titles, *Publishers Weekly*, 1/13/03

*H B Fenn will buy a controlling interest in **Key Porter Books**, *Publishers Weekly*, 7/5/04

Ferguson Publishing Co, a publisher of career education titles, acquired by **Facts on File**, *Publishers Weekly*, 1/13/03

Sadie Fields Productions Ltd packaging division of **Tango Books** to be acquired by **Intervisual Books Inc** as part of the sale of Tango, *Publishers Weekly*, 6/20/03

Fitzroy Dearborn Publishers acquired by **Taylor & Francis Group plc**, *Publishers Weekly*, 3/10/03

Galaxy Press, a new press fiction imprint,

has been formed by **Bridge Publications**, *Publishers Weekly*, 8/19/02

Gale has acquired a line of children's books from **Sleeping Bear Press**, *Publishers Weekly*, 8/26/02

*****Gospel Light** of Ventura, CA, has acquired **Vine Books**, an imprint of **Servant Publications**, *Publishers Weekly*, 10/20/03

Gotham Books, a new nonfiction imprint, will be launched by **Penguin Putnam** in January 2003, *Publishers Weekly*, 8/12/02

*****Guideposts** has acquired **Williamson Publishing** of Charlotte, VT, *Publishers Weekly*, 2/2/04

H.I. Marketing Ltd, a UK book distributor, acquired by **Advanced Marketing Services**, *Publishers Weekly*, 12/9/02

Haights Cross Communications sold **Andrews Publications** to **West**, the legal publishing division of Thomson Corp, *Publishers Weekly*, 4/7/03
*—has acquired test prep publisher **Buckle Down Publishing**, *Publishers Weekly*, 4/26/04
*—has placed **Oakstone Publishing** for sale, *Publishers Weekly*, 4/26/04

HarperCollins in a new joint venture with **India Today Group** will publish in India, *Publishers Weekly*, 8/5/02
—through its UK Collins reference publishing group has signed a co-publishing agreement with **China's Foreign Language and Research Press** to publish bilingual dictionaries, *Publishers Weekly*, 9/23/02

H.E. Harris acquired the Whitman's line of coin guides and reference works from **St. Martin's Press**, *Publishers Weekly*, 2/3/03

*****Harvard Business School Press** has formed a partnership with **Random House Kodansha** to collaborate on a new imprint that will publish Japanese translations of selected HBS Press title, *Publishers Weekly*, 10/6/03

Harvard Educational Publishing will launch a book imprint aimed primarily at teachers and administrators, *Publishers Weekly*, 9/23/02

Harvard University Press has teamed with **Acme Bookbinding** to create a print-on-demand system, *Publishers Weekly*, 12/2/02

Hatherleigh Press has formed a new imprint, **Healthy Living Books**, *Publishers Weekly*, 10/21/02

Healthy Living Books, a new imprint, formed by **Hatherleigh Press**, *Publishers Weekly*, 10/21/02

*****Henry Holt** has acquired **Roaring Brook Press**, *Publishers Weekly*, 7/26/04

*****Holtzbrinck Publishers** to acquire **Roaring Brook Press** from **Millbrook Press**, *Publishers Weekly*, 4/5/04

Hoover's Inc to be acquired by **Dun & Bradstreet**, *Publishers Weekly*, 12/16/02

Houghton Mifflin sold by Vivendi Universal to an investment group led by **Thomas H. Lee Partners** and **Brian Capital** with additional funds from the **Blackstone Group**, *Publishers Weekly*, 1/6/03

Hydra Publishing, a publisher of illustrated nonfiction titles, founded, *Publishers Weekly*, 12/2/02

India Today Group in a joint venture with **HarperCollins**, *Publishers Weekly*, 8/5/02

Intervisual Books Inc signed a letter of intent to acquire **Sadie Fields Productions Ltd**, the packaging division of **Tango Books** of London, *Publishers Weekly*, 6/20/03

Jones & Bartlett Publishers has acquired the healthcare division of **Aspen Publishers**, a subsidiary of **Wolters Kluwer**, *Publishers Weekly*, 11/18/02
—has acquired a number of healthcare business and management titles from **Management Concepts Inc**, *Publishers Weekly*, 1/27/03

*****Joong Ang Ilbo Publishers** of Korea in a joint venture with **Random House** to publish Korean language titles in adult and children's fiction and nonfiction, *Publishers Weekly*, 1/12/04

KAP merged with **Bertelsmann Springer** to create an international publishing company named **Springer**, *Publishers Weekly*, 5/19/03

*****Kennel Club Books** acquired by **Bow Tie Inc**, *Publishers Weekly*, 6/7/04

*****Key Porter Books** has sold a controlling interest to **H B Fenn**, *Publishers Weekly*, 7/5/04

Alfred A. Knopf, an imprint of **Random House**, has acquired **Everyman Publishers plc**, the UK-based publisher of hardcover classics, *Publishers Weekly*, 11/18/02

Krause Publications, a book and hobby magazine publisher, has been acquired by **F+W Publications**, *Publishers Weekly*, 9/16/02

LPC Group has sold **Albion Books**, **Olmstead Press**, and **Papier-Mache Press** to **Moyer Bell**, *Publishers Weekly*, 10/21/02

*****Lerner Publishing Group** to acquire **Millbrook** and **Twenty-First Century** imprints from **Millbrook Press**, *Publishers Weekly*, 7/26/04

*****Lightning Source** has acquired **Barnes & Noble**'s print-on-demand facility located in Memphis, TN, *Publishers Weekly*, 9/29/03

*****Limelight Editions** acquired by **Amadeus Press**, *Publishers Weekly*, 4/26/04

Management Concepts Inc has sold a number of healthcare business and management titles to **Jones & Bartlett**, *Publishers Weekly*, 1/27/03

*****Mannheim Holdings, LLC** (a subsidiary of Mannheim Trust) has acquired **Springer Publishing Company**, *Publishers Weekly*, 3/22/04

*****McGraw-Hill Companies** has agreed to sell **McGraw-Hill Children's Publishing** unit to **School Specialty Inc** of Columbus, OH, *Publishers Weekly*, 1/26/04

The assets of the **MetaText** division of **OCLC** have been sold to **XanEdu**, the college custom publishing division of **ProQuest Information and Learning**, *Publishers Weekly*, 8/26/02

Microsoft Press has released its first titles in their new Faster Smarter series aimed at the middle ground between computer novices and "geeks," *Publishers Weekly*, 11/18/02

*****Millbrook Press** to sell **Roaring Brook Press** to **Holtzbrinck Publishers**, *Publishers Weekly*, 4/5/04
*—to sell **Millbrook** and **Twenty-First Century** imprints to the **Lerner Publishing Group**, *Publishers Weekly*, 7/26/04

*Moore Wallace to be acquired by **R R Donnelley**, *Publishers Weekly*, 11/17/03

Muska & Lipman, a computer book publisher, has been acquired by **Course Technology**, a subsidiary of Thomson Corp, *Publishers Weekly*, 8/12/02

*Thomas Nelson has acquired certain assets from **World Bible Publishers**, a division of **Riverside World Inc**, *Publishers Weekly*, 10/6/03

New Leaf Distributing Co has been acquired by **Shakti LLC**, *Publishers Weekly*, 2/3/03

*North-South Books Inc has sold **Sea Star Books** to **Chronicle Books LLC**, *Publishers Weekly*, 1/19/04

*W W Norton has acquired the assets of **Berkshire House Publishers**; Berkshire House will become part of Norton's Countryman Press division, *Publishers Weekly*, 8/11/03

*Oakstone Publishing, a unit of **Haights Cross Communications**, placed for sale, *Publishers Weekly*, 4/26/04

Oasis Press acquired by **Entrepreneur Press** from **Publishing Services Inc**, *Publishers Weekly*, 1/13/03

OCLC has sold the assets of its **MetaText** division to **XanEdu**, the college custom publishing division of **ProQuest Information and Learning**, *Publishers Weekly*, 8/26/02

Olmstead Press purchased by **Moyer Bell** from **LPC Group**, *Publishers Weekly*, 10/21/02

Ooligan Press, a general publishing and teaching imprint, launched by the **Center for Excellence in Writing** at Portland State University (OR), *Publishers Weekly*, 1/6/03

Papier-Mache Press purchased by **Moyer Bell** from **LPC Group**, *Publishers Weekly*, 10/21/02

*Pathway Book Service has acquired **Stemmer House Publishers**, *Publishers Weekly*, 9/15/03

Pearson Technology Group's Alpha Books unit is being moved to **Penguin Putnam**, *Publishers Weekly*, 9/2/02

Penguin Group (USA) name changed from **Penguin Putnam** as announced by parent company **Penguin Group**, *Publishers Weekly*, 12/23/02

Penguin Putnam will launch **Gotham Books**, a new nonfiction imprint, in January 2003, *Publishers Weekly*, 8/12/02
—has announced the divestiture of its **Blue Hen Books** imprint, *Publishers Weekly*, 9/30/02
—name changed to **Penguin Group (USA)** as announced by parent company **Penguin Group**, *Publishers Weekly*, 12/23/02

Premier Press, publisher of computer and technology books, has been acquired by **Course Technology**, a subsidiary of Thomson Corp, from **22nd Century Inc**, *Publishers Weekly*, 8/12/02

*Primedia Inc has sold **Simba Information**, a publisher of newsletters, to **R R Bowker**, *Publishers Weekly*, 9/22/03

Printers Row Book Fair acquired by the **Chicago Tribune** from the Near South Planning Board, *Publishers Weekly*, 12/9/02

Profile Books, a UK publisher, has signed a deal allowing **Bloomberg Press** to distribute books from the *Economist*, *Publishers Weekly*, 11/18/02

ProQuest has acquired the assets of the **MetaText** division of **OCLC** through **XanEdu**, its college custom publishing division, *Publishers Weekly*, 8/26/02
—signed a letter of intent to purchase the balance of shares it does not already own in **bigchalk.com**, *Publishers Weekly*, 1/6/03
—acquired the custom publishing assets of **Courier Corp**, *Publishers Weekly*, 1/6/03

PubEasy, an online book wholesale self-service center, has been acquired from **Vista International** by **R R Bowker**, *Publishers Weekly*, 2/17/03

*Publishers Group Worldwide (PGW) formed by the combination of seven different distribution companies by **Advanced Marketing Services**, *Publishers Weekly*, 9/29/03

Publishing Services Inc has sold **Oasis Press** to **Entrepreneur Press**, *Publishers Weekly*, 1/13/03

Random House has acquired **Everyman Publishers plc**, the UK-based publisher of hardcover classics, through its **Alfred A. Knopf** imprint, *Publishers Weekly*, 11/18/02
*—in a joint venture with **Joong Ang Ilbo**

Publishers of Korea to publish Korean language titles in adult and children's fiction and nonfiction, *Publishers Weekly*, 1/12/04

Random House Ballantine Publishing Group formed by the merger of the **Random House Trade Group** with **Ballantine Books**, *Publishers Weekly*, 1/20/03

*Random House Kodansha has formed a partnership with **Harvard Business School Press** to collaborate on a new imprint that will publish Japanese translations of selected HBS Press title, *Publishers Weekly*, 10/6/03

Random House Trade Group is being combined with **Ballantine Books** to form the **Random House Ballantine Publishing Group**, *Publishers Weekly*, 1/20/03

Reed Business Information announced the formation of a new imprint, **Reed Press**, *Publishers Weekly*, 5/19/03

Reed Press, a new imprint for **Reed Business Information**, has signed a distribution agreement with **Sourcebooks**, *Publishers Weekly*, 5/19/03

* **Research & Education Association** of Piscataway, NJ, a publisher of test prep and study guidebooks and software for the high school, college, graduate school, and professional markets, acquired by **Courier Corp.**, *Publishers Weekly*, 12/22/03

*Riverside World Inc has sold certain assets from **World Bible Publishers** to **Thomas Nelson**, *Publishers Weekly*, 10/6/03

Rizzoli's Universe imprint has bought the backlist of **City & Co**, a small press known for guides to New York City, *Publishers Weekly*, 9/30/02

*Roaring Brook Press sold by **Millbrook Press** to **Holtzbrinck Publishers**, *Publishers Weekly*, 4/5/04
*—sold to **Henry Holt**, *Publishers Weekly*, 7/26/04

*Rockport Publishers has acquired the "how to" line of products from **Creative Publishing International**, *Publishers Weekly*, 7/19/04

Rodale has formed an international books group that will be based in London and charged with selling the company's titles worldwide, *Publishers Weekly*, 9/23/02

Rowman & Littlefield Publishing Group has acquired **Burnham Publishers**, *Publishers Weekly*, 6/16/03
*—has acquired the assets of **Collegiate Press**, *Publishers Weekly*, 9/1/03

***St. Anthony Messenger Press** has acquired **Charis Books**, an imprint of **Servant Publications**, *Publishers Weekly*, 10/20/03

St. Martin's Press has sold its Whitman's line of coin guides and reference works to **H.E. Harris**, *Publishers Weekly*, 2/3/03

Scholastic Inc has acquired the majority of assets of **Troll Communications**, *Publishers Weekly*, 7/7/03

***School Specialty Inc** of Columbus, OH, has agreed to acquire **McGraw-Hill Children's Publishing** unit from **McGraw-Hill Companies**, *Publishers Weekly*, 1/26/04

***Sea Star Books**, a division of **North-South Books Inc**, sold to **Chronicle Books, LLC**, *Publishers Weekly*, 1/19/04

***Servant Publications** has gone out of business; **Charis Books** imprint sold to **St. Anthony Messenger Press**; **Vine Books** imprint to be sold to **Gospel Light** of Ventura, CA, *Publishers Weekly*, 10/20/03

Seven Hills Book Distributors has ceased operations, *Publishers Weekly*, 7/29/02

Seybold Seminars has signed an agreement with **John Wiley & Sons** to co-publish a series of software design books, *Publishers Weekly*, 9/16/02

Shakti LLC has acquired **New Leaf Distributing Co**, *Publishers Weekly*, 2/3/03

Shoemaker & Hoard, a new division begun by **Avalon Publishing Group**, *Publishers Weekly*, 12/16/02

***Simba Information**, a publisher of newsletters, acquired by **R R Bowker**, *Publishers Weekly*, 9/22/03

Simon & Schuster will acquire **Distican**, the exclusive distributor for Simon & Schuster in Canada; following the completion of the sale, the company will be renamed **Simon & Schuster Canada**, *Publishers Weekly*, 11/25/02

Simon & Schuster Canada formed from the acquisition by Simon & Schuster of **Distican**, the exclusive distributor for Simon & Schuster in Canada, *Publishers Weekly*, 11/25/02

Sleeping Bear Press has sold its children's division to the **Gale Group**, *Publishers Weekly*, 8/26/02
—has sold most of its turf management and golf architecture titles to **John Wiley & Sons**, *Publishers Weekly*, 8/26/02
—has sold 100 golf, sports, and regional titles as well as 75 books in development to former shareholders who will form a new company, **Clock Tower Press**, *Publishers Weekly*, 8/26/02

Sourcebooks has signed an agreement with *US News & World Report* to publish a college directory based on research conducted by the magazine on America's colleges, *Publishers Weekly*, 5/12/03
—has signed an agreement to distribute titles from **Reed Press**, an imprint of **Reed Business Information**, *Publishers Weekly*, 5/19/03

***South-Western** (a Thompson Corp. subsidiary) has acquired **Texere**, a business book publisher, as a new imprint, *Publishers Weekly*, 8/4/03

Springer, an international publishing company, formed by the merger of **KAP** with **Bertelsmann Springer**, *Publishers Weekly*, 5/19/03

***Springer Publishing Company** acquired by **Mannheim Holdings, LLC** (a subsidiary of Mannheim Trust), *Publishers Weekly*, 3/22/04

***Stemmer House Publishers** acquired by **Pathway Book Service**, *Publishers Weekly*, 9/15/03

Sterling Publishing acquired by **Barnes & Noble**, *Publishers Weekly*, 12/16/02
*—to publish a line of books in partnership with the **AARP** under the AARP trademark, *Publishers Weekly*, 7/28/03

***Studio Proteus** acquired by **Dark Horse Comics**, *Publishers Weekly*, 2/23/04

Tango Books of London's packaging division, **Sadie Fields Productions Ltd**, to be acquired by **Intervisual Books Inc**, *Publishers Weekly*, 6/20/03

Taylor & Francis Group plc has acquired **Fitzroy Dearborn Publishers**, *Publishers Weekly*, 3/10/03
—has acquired **CRC Press** from **Information Holdings**, *Publishers Weekly*, 3/10/03

*—to acquire the **Dekker Group**, *Publishers Weekly*, 11/24/03

***Texere**, a business book publisher, acquired by **South-Western** (a Thompson Corp. subsidiary) as a new imprint, *Publishers Weekly*, 8/4/03

***Thomson**'s higher education unit to buy 44 criminal justice titles from **Copperhouse Publishing**, *Publishers Weekly*, 4/19/04

Thorndike Press, the large print subsidiary of Gale, has acquired a line of large print Christian titles from **Walker Books**, *Publishers Weekly*, 8/5/02

Troll Communications has been sold by investment banking firm **Willis Stein** to **Quad Ventures**, a private equity firm, *Publishers Weekly*, 9/9/02
—will close after the sale of the majority of its assets to **Scholastic**, *Publishers Weekly*, 7/7/03

***Twenty-First Century** and **Millbrook** imprints of **Millbrook Press** sold to the **Lerner Publishing Group**, *Publishers Weekly*, 7/26/04

22nd Century, a holding company, has sold **Premier Press**, publisher of computer and technology books, to **Course Technology**, a subsidiary of Thomson Corp, *Publishers Weekly*, 8/12/02

Two-Can Publishing the children's book publishing division of **Zenith Entertainment** will be sold to **Creative**, *Publishers Weekly*, 9/16/02

Ullstein Heyne List publishing group sold by **Axel Springer** to **Bertelsmann**, *Publishers Weekly*, 2/17/03

Universe, an imprint of **Rizzoli**, has bought the backlist of **City & Co**, a small press known for guides to New York City, *Publishers Weekly*, 9/30/02

***Vine Books**, an imprint of **Servant Publications**, sold to **Gospel Light** of Venura, CA, *Publishers Weekly*, 10/20/03

Vista International has sold **PubEasy**, an online wholesale book distribution self-service center, to **R R Bowker**, *Publishers Weekly*, 2/17/03

Vivendi will put **Houghton Mifflin** up for sale, *Publishers Weekly*, 8/19/02

Walker Books has sold its publishing unit for large print Christian titles to

Thorndike Press, the large print subsidiary of Gale, *Publishers Weekly*, 8/5/02

*The **Wall Street Journal** has signed a three-year deal with **Crown Publishing**, *Publishers Weekly*, 3/29/04

West, the legal publishing division of Thomson Corp, acquired **Andrews Publications** from **Haights Cross Communications**, *Publishers Weekly*, 4/7/03

Western Edge Press has acquired **Sherman Asher Publishing**, *Publishers Weekly*, 9/30/02

John Wiley & Sons has acquired a line of turf management and golf architecture titles from **Sleeping Bear Press**, *Publishers Weekly*, 8/26/02
—has signed an agreement with **Seybold Seminars** to co-publish a series of software design books, *Publishers Weekly*, 9/16/02

***Williamson Publishing** of Charlotte, VT, acquired by **Guideposts**, *Publishers Weekly*, 2/2/04

Willis Stein & Partners, a private investment group, to acquire **Baker & Taylor** from the **Carlyle Group** *Publishers Weekly*, 7/7/03

***World Bible Publishers** assets acquired by **Thomas Nelson** from **Riverside World Inc**, *Publishers Weekly*, 10/6/03

XanEdu, the college custom publishing division of **ProQuest Information and Learning**, has acquired the assets of the **MetaText** division of **OCLC**, *Publishers Weekly*, 8/26/02

Zenith Entertainment will sell its **Two-Can Publishing** children's book publishing division to **Creative**, *Publishers Weekly*, 9/16/02

***Zephyr Press**, an educational press located in Phoenix, AZ, sold to **Chicago Review Press Inc**, *Publishers Weekly*, 10/6/03

Abbreviations & Acronyms

The following is a list of acronyms & abbreviations used throughout *LMP*.

AAP - Association of American Publishers
AAR - Association of Authors' Representatives
AB - Alberta
ABA - American Booksellers Association
Acct(s) - Account(s)
Acctg - Accounting
Acq(s) - Acquisition(s)
Admin - Administrative, Administration
Adv - Advertising
Aff - Affairs
AK - Alaska
AL - Alabama
ALA - American Library Association
ALTA - American Literary Translators Association
APA - Architectural Photographers Association
API - Associated Photographers Interntional
appt - appointment
APS - Alternative Press Syndicate
AR - Arkansas
ASMP - American Society of Media Photographers
ASPP - American Society of Picture Professionals
Assoc(s) - Associate(s)
Asst(s) - Assistant(s)
ATA - American Translators Association
AV - Audiovisual
AZ - Arizona

B&W - Black & White
BC - British Columbia
Bd - Board
bio - biography
BISAC - Book Industry Systems Advisory Committee
BISG - Book Industry Study Group
Bldg - Building
BMI - Book Manufacturers' Institute
Br - Branch
Busn - Business

CA - California
CEO - Chief Executive Officer
CFO - Chief Financial Officer
Chmn - Chairman
Chpn - Chairperson
Circ - Circulation
CN - Canada
CO - Colorado
COO - Chief Operating Officer
Co(s) - Company(-ies)

Co-edns - Co-editions
Coll(s) - College(s)
Comm - Committee
Commun(s) - Communication(s)
Comp - Compiler
Compt - Comptroller
Cons - Consulting
Cont - Controller
Contrib - Contributing
Coord(s) - Coordinator(s)
Corp - Corporate, Corporation
CT - Connecticut
Ct - Court
Curr - Current
Cust - Customer
CZ - Canal Zone

DC - District of Columbia
DE - Delaware
Dept - Department
Devt - Development
Dir(s) - Director(s)
Dist - Distributed, Distribution, Distributor
Div - Division
Dom - Domestic

Ed(s) - Editor(s)
ed - edition
Edit - Editorial
Educ - Education, Educational
El-hi - Elementary-High School
Elem - Elementary
Ency - Encyclopedia
Eng - English
Engg - Engineering
Engr - Engineer
Equip - Equipment
ESL - English as a Second Language
Est - Established
exc - except
Exec(s) - Executive(s)
ext - extension

Fed - Federal
Fin - Finance, Financial
fl - floor
FL - Florida
Freq - Frequency

GA - Georgia
Gen - General
Govt - Government
GU - Guam

HI - Hawaii

HR - Human Resources
HS - High School
Hwy - Highway

IA - Iowa
ID - Idaho
IL - Illinois
Illus - Illustrator
IN - Indiana
indiv(s) - individual(s)
Indus - Industrial, Industry
Info - Information
Instl - Institutional
Instn(s) - Institution(s)
Instrl - Instructional
Intl - International
ISBN - International Standard Book Number
ISSN - International Standard Serial Number

Jt - Joint
Jr - Junior
Juv - Juvenile

K - Kindergarten
KS - Kansas
KY - Kentucky

LA - Louisiana
Lang(s) - Language(s)
Lib(s) - Library(-ies)
Libn(s) - Librarian(s)
Lit - Literature

MA - Massachusetts
Man - Managing
MB - Manitoba
MD - Maryland
Mdse - Merchandise
Mdsg - Merchandising
ME - Maine
Med - Medical
Memb(s) - Member(s)
Metro - Metropolitan
Mfg - Manufacturing
Mgmt - Management
Mgr(s) - Manager(s)
MI - Michigan
Mkt - Market
Mktg - Marketing
MLA - Modern Language Association
MN - Minnesota
MO - Missouri
MS - Mississippi
ms(s) - manuscript(s)
MT - Montana

ABBREVIATIONS & ACRONYMS

Natl - National
NB - New Brunswick
NC - North Carolina
ND - North Dakota
NE - Nebraska
NF - Newfoundland
NH - New Hampshire
NJ - New Jersey
NM - New Mexico
No - Number
NPPA - National Press Photographers Association
NS - Nova Scotia
NT - Northwest Territories
NU - Nunavut
NV - Nevada
NY - New York

Off(s) - Office(s)
OH - Ohio
OK - Oklahoma
ON - Ontario
Oper(s) - Operation(s)
OR - Oregon

PA - Pennsylvania
Pbk(s) - Paperback(s)
PE - Prince Edward Island
Perms - Permissions
Photo - Photograph
Photog - Photography
PIA/GATF - Printing Industries of America/ Graphic Arts Technical Foundation
Pkwy - Parkway
pp - pages
PPA - Professional Photographers of America
PQ - Quebec
PR - Public Relations

PR - Puerto Rico
Pres - President
Proc - Processing
Prod(s) - Product(s)
Prodn - Production
Prof - Professional
Prog(s) - Program(s)
Proj(s) - Project(s)
Promo(s) - Promotion(s)
Prop - Proprietor
PSA - Photography Society of America
Pub Aff - Public Affairs
Publg - Publishing
Publr - Publisher
Pubn(s) - Publication(s)
Purch - Purchasing

R&D - Research & Development
Ref - Reference
Reg - Region
Regl - Regional
Rel - Relations
Rep(s) - Representative(s)
Res - Research
RI - Rhode Island
Rm - Room
Rte - Route
Rts - Rights

SAN - Standard Address Number
SASE - Self-Addressed Stamped Envelope
SATW - Society of American Travel Writers
SC - South Carolina
Sci - Science
SD - South Dakota
Sec - Secretary
Serv(s) - Service(s)
SK - Saskatchewan
SLA - Special Libraries Association

Soc - Social, Sociology
Spec - Special
Sq - Square
Sr - Senior
St - Street
Sta - Station
Subn(s) - Subscription(s)
Subs - Subsidiary
Supv - Supervisor
Synd - Syndicated, Syndication

Tech - Technical
Technol - Technology
Tel - Telephone
Terr - Terrace
TN - Tennessee
Tpke - Turnpike
Treas - Treasurer
TX - Texas

UK - United Kingdom
Univ - University
unsol - unsolicited
UT - Utah

V - Vice
VA - Virginia
VI - Virgin Islands
vol(s) - volume(s)
VP(s) - Vice President(s)
VT - Vermont

WA - Washington
WI - Wisconsin
WV - West Virginia
WY - Wyoming

yr - year
YT - Yukon Territory

Global Publishing Solutions...
Driven by Demand

Lightning Source

Lightning Source
In the US: 615-213-5815
In the UK: 011 44 845 1214567
www.lightningsource.com

* Wholesale Distribution * eBook * Demand Driven Printing *

Book Publishers

U.S. Publishers

Listed in alphabetical order are those U.S. publishers that have reported to *LMP* that they produce an average of three or more books annually. Publishers that have appeared in a previous edition of *LMP*, but whose output currently does not meet our defined rate of activity, will be reinstated when their annual production reaches the required level. It should be noted that this rule of publishing activity does not apply to publishers of dictionaries, encyclopedias, atlases and braille books or to university presses.

The definition of a book is that used for *Books in Print* (R.R. Bowker LLC, 630 Central Avenue, New Providence, NJ 07974) and excludes charts, pamphlets, folding maps, sheet music and material with stapled bindings. Publishers that make their titles available only in electronic or audio format are included if they meet the stated criteria. In the case of packages, the book must be of equal or greater importance than the accompanying piece. With few exceptions, new publishers are not listed prior to having published at least three titles within a year.

§ before the company name indicates publishers involved in electronic publishing.

The following indexes can be found immediately after the publishers' listings:

See **Book Trade Acquisitions & Mergers 2002-2004** and **Imprints, Subsidiaries & Distributors** for additional information on the companies listed herein. Those sections should also be checked for apparently active companies that are no longer listed in the U.S. Publishers section. In many cases, they have been acquired as an imprint or subsidiary of a larger entity and no longer have a discrete listing.

§A & B Publishers Group
Subsidiary of A & B Distributors
223 Duffield St, Brooklyn, NY 11201
Tel: 718-783-7808 *Fax:* 718-783-7267
Web Site: anbdonline.com
Key Personnel
Publr, Ed & Prodn Mgr: Eric Gift
   E-mail: ericgift2002@yahoo.com
Dir: Wendy Gift
Lib Sales Dir: Allison Gift
Prodn Mgr: Eric Gift *E-mail:* ericgift2002@
   yahoo.com
Man Ed: Karen Mitchell
Founded: 1992
Print books full house, comic books, activity books, novels, children's books, history, health, cookery, nutrition, esoteric, video, audio, CD-ROM.
ISBN Prefix(es): 1-881316; 1-886433
Number of titles published annually: 12 Print; 1 CD-ROM; 1 Audio
Total Titles: 88 Print; 1 CD-ROM; 1 Audio
Imprints: Aesop House; Alvin House; Upstream
Branch Office(s)
807 Broad St, Newark, NJ 07102-2803 *Tel:* 973-824-2556
Distributed by African World Press; D & J Books; Lushena Books
Distributor for Random House Inc; Simon & Schuster
Advertising Agency: ACT Communications

A Cappella Books, see Chicago Review Press

A D D Warehouse
Subsidiary of Specialty Press Inc
300 NW 70 Ave, Suite 102, Plantation, FL 33317
SAN: 251-6977
Tel: 954-792-8100 *Toll Free Tel:* 800-233-9273
   Fax: 954-792-8545
E-mail: websales@addwarehouse.com

Web Site: www.addwarehouse.com
Key Personnel
CEO & Intl Rts: Harvey Parker *E-mail:* hparker@
   addwarehouse.com
Founded: 1988
Selections related to children with special needs.
ISBN Prefix(es): 0-9621629; 1-886941
Number of titles published annually: 4 Print
Total Titles: 40 Print
Distributed by American Guidance Service; Boys Town Press; Child Play; Hawthorne Publications; MHS; Thinking Publications
Distributor for Bantam; Guilford Press; Plenum; Simon & Schuster; Slossen; Woodbine House

§A K Peters Ltd
888 Worcester St, Suite 230, Wellesley, MA 02482
Tel: 781-416-2888 *Fax:* 781-416-2889
E-mail: service@akpeters.com
Web Site: www.akpeters.com
Key Personnel
Publr: Alice Peters *E-mail:* alice@akpeters.com;
   Klaus Peters *E-mail:* klaus@akpeters.com
Edit: Charlotte Henderson *E-mail:* charlotte@
   akpeters.com
Mktg Dir: Susannah Sieper *E-mail:* sannie@
   akpeters.com
Founded: 1992
Scientific-technical publisher specializing in mathematics, computer science & robotics from undergraduate textbooks to research monographs & professional books.
ISBN Prefix(es): 1-56881
Number of titles published annually: 25 Print
Total Titles: 160 Print; 2 CD-ROM
Distributor for Association for Symbolic Logic; Canadian Human-Computer Communications Society
Foreign Rep(s): Sunnder Liuhara (India)

Foreign Rights: Modest Agency (Moto Sekino) (Japan)
Warehouse: c/o PSSC, 46 Development Rd, Fitchburg, MA 01420
Distribution Center: Eastern Book Service Inc, 3-1-3 Hongo 3-chome Bunkyo-Ku, Tokyo 13-8480, Japan *Tel:* (03) 3818-0861-3 *Fax:* (03) 818-0864 *E-mail:* k-onaka@sut-cbs.co.jp
Login Brothers Canada, 324 Saulteaux Crescent, Winnipeg, MB R3J 3T2, Canada *Toll Free Tel:* 800-665-1148 *Toll Free Fax:* 800-665-0103 *E-mail:* sales@lb.ca
Transatlantic Publishers Group, c/o Orca Book Services, Stanley House, 3 Fleets Lane, Poole, Dorset BH15 3AJ, United Kingdom *Tel:* (01202) 665432 *Fax:* (01202) 666219 *E-mail:* orders@orcabookservices.co.uk
Woodslane, PO Box 935, Mona Vale, NSW 2107, Australia *Tel:* (02) 9970511 *E-mail:* info@woodslane.com.au

AK Press Distribution
Subsidiary of AK Press Inc
674-A 23 St, Oakland, CA 94612
Tel: 510-208-1700 *Fax:* 510-208-1701
Web Site: www.akpress.org
Key Personnel
Lib Sales Dir & Intl Rts: Ramsey Kanaan
   E-mail: ramsey@akpress.org
Founded: 1991
Specialize in publishing & distribution of radical & small press nonfiction.
ISBN Prefix(es): 1-873176; 1-902593
Number of titles published annually: 25 Print; 3 Audio
Total Titles: 200 Print; 30 Audio
Imprints: AK Press Audio
Distributor for AK Press; Crimethinc; Freedom Press; Payback Press; Phoenix Press; Rebel Inc; Rebel Press

A-R Editions Inc
8551 Research Way, Suite 180, Middleton, WI 53562
Tel: 608-836-9000 *Toll Free Tel:* 800-736-0070 (US book orders only) *Fax:* 608-831-8200
E-mail: info@areditions.com
Web Site: www.areditions.com
Key Personnel
Pres & CEO: Patrick Wall
Dir, Sales & Mktg: James L Zychowicz
E-mail: james.zychowicz@areditions.com
Founded: 1962
Scholarly critical editions of music for performance & study; computer music & digital audio professional books, electronics & Internet technology.
ISBN Prefix(es): 0-89579
Number of titles published annually: 30 Print
Total Titles: 400 Print
Distributor for AIM (American Institute of Musicology)

A R O Publishing Co
398 S 1100 W, Provo, UT 84601
Mailing Address: PO Box 193, Provo, UT 84603-0193
Tel: 801-377-8218 *Fax:* 801-818-0616
E-mail: aro@yahoo.com
Web Site: www.aropublishing.com
Key Personnel
Pres: Bob Reese
Founded: 1973
K-4 beginning to read.
ISBN Prefix(es): 0-89868
Number of titles published annually: 15 Print
Total Titles: 200 Print; 200 Online
Divisions: Reading Research
Distributed by Barnes & Noble; Follett

§AAAI Press
Imprint of American Association for Artificial Intelligence
445 Burgess Dr, Suite 100, Menlo Park, CA 94025-3496
Tel: 650-328-3123 *Fax:* 650-321-4457
E-mail: press@aaai.org
Web Site: www.aaaipress.org
Key Personnel
Exec Dir: Carol Hamilton
Gen Mgr: David Hamilton *Tel:* 650-853-0197
Ed-in-Chief: Kenneth Ford
Founded: 1989
Publishing books on all aspects of artificial intelligence.
ISBN Prefix(es): 0-929280; 1-57735
Number of titles published annually: 30 Print; 2 CD-ROM; 2 Online
Total Titles: 180 Print; 1 CD-ROM; 2 Online; 2 E-Book
Distributed by The MIT Press

AACC, see American Association of Community Colleges (AACC)

§AANS-American Association of Neurological Surgeons
5550 Meadow Brook Dr, Rolling Meadows, IL 60008
Tel: 847-378-0500 *Fax:* 847-378-0600
E-mail: info@aans.org
Web Site: www.neurosurgery.org
Key Personnel
Publr: Kathleen Rynne Craig *E-mail:* ktc@aans.org
Founded: 1931
Medicine, scientific & academic books relating to neurosurgery. Will be co-publishing with Thieme Medical Publishers.
ISBN Prefix(es): 0-9624246; 1-879284; 0-9703144
Number of titles published annually: 5 Print
Total Titles: 80 Print

Distributor for American Medical Association
Foreign Rep(s): Thieme

AAPG (American Association of Petroleum Geologists)
1444 S Boulder Ave, Tulsa, OK 74119
Mailing Address: PO Box 979, Tulsa, OK 74101-0979
Tel: 918-584-2555 *Toll Free Tel:* 800-364-AAPG (364-2274) *Fax:* 918-560-2632
Toll Free Fax: 800-898-2274
E-mail: bookstore@aapg.org
Web Site: www.aapg.org
Key Personnel
Serv & Mktg Asst: Michele Kendrick *Tel:* 918-560-2667 *E-mail:* kendrick@aapg.org
Founded: 1917
Peer-reviewed geological science tomes.
ISBN Prefix(es): 0-89181; 1-58861
Number of titles published annually: 10 Print; 10 CD-ROM
Total Titles: 100 Print; 80 CD-ROM
Distributed by Affiliated East - West Press Private Limited; Canadian Society of Petroleum Geologists; Geological Society of London
Distributor for Geological Society of London

AAVIM, see American Association for Vocational Instructional Materials

§Abacus
5130 Patterson SE, Grand Rapids, MI 49512
Tel: 616-698-0330 *Toll Free Tel:* 800-451-4319
Fax: 616-698-0325
E-mail: info@abacuspub.com
Web Site: www.abacuspub.com
Key Personnel
Pres & Mktg Mgr: Arnie Lee
VP & Sales Dir: James Oldfield, Jr
Founded: 1978
Publish computer books, hardware & software user guides for IBM & compatibles users.
ISBN Prefix(es): 1-55755; 0-916439
Number of titles published annually: 3 Print; 3 E-Book
Total Titles: 3 Print; 7 CD-ROM; 3 E-Book

§Abaris Books
Division of Opal Publishing
64 Wall St, Norwalk, CT 06850
Tel: 203-838-8402 *Fax:* 203-849-9181
E-mail: abarisbooks@abarisbooks.com
Web Site: abarisbooks.com
Key Personnel
Publr: Anthony S Kaufmann
Man Dir: J C West
Gen Ed: John T Spike
Founded: 1973
Art, art history, art reference, classics, facsimile & translation.
ISBN Prefix(es): 0-913870; 0-89835
Number of titles published annually: 7 Print; 1 CD-ROM
Total Titles: 155 Print; 1 CD-ROM
Imprints: The Illustrated Bartsch; Janus Library

Abbeville Publishing Group
116 W 23 St, Suite 500, New York, NY 10011
SAN: 211-4755
Tel: 646-375-2039 *Toll Free Tel:* 800-ART-BOOK (278-2665) *Fax:* 646-375-2040
E-mail: abbeville@abbeville.com
Web Site: www.abbeville.com
Key Personnel
Pres & Publr: Robert E Abrams
Cont & Foreign Rts Mgr: Nadine Winns
E-mail: nwinns@abbeville.com
Edit Dir: Susan Costello
Publicist: Amber Reed
Dir, Fin Analysis: John Olivieri
Warehouse Dir: Arthur Goldberg

Founded: 1977
Publishers of high-quality, fine art books, nonfiction illustrated books, children's books, limited editions, prints, gift line.
ISBN Prefix(es): 0-89659; 1-55859; 0-89660; 0-7892
Number of titles published annually: 30 Print
Imprints: Abbeville; Abbeville Kids; Artabras; Modern Masters
Foreign Rep(s): Bookport Associates (Greece, Italy, Portugal, Spain); Richard Bowen (Scandinavia); Inter-Art (France, Monaco); International Publishers Representatives (Africa, Middle East, Near East); Manda Group (Canada); John Murray Ltd (UK, Ireland); Nationwide Book Distributors (New Zealand); Nilsson & Lamm BV (Belgium, Netherlands, Luxembourg); Onslow Books Ltd (Austria, Scandinavia, Switzerland); Peribo Pty Ltd (Australia); Claus Schmogner, Petra Poker (Central Germany); Ralph & Sheila Summers (Far East, Singapore); Michael Timperley (Eastern Europe); Wolfgang Willmann, Susanne Sieger, c/o Glockenbach Buch Handling (Southern Germany); Yohan/Western Publications (Japan)
Foreign Rights: Bookbank, SA (Latin America, Mexico, Spain); Motovun Tokyo (Japan); Ultreya srl (Italy)
Warehouse: Client Distribution Services, 193 Edwards Dr, Jackson, TN 38301 *Toll Free Tel:* 800-343-4499 *Toll Free Fax:* 800-351-5073
See separate listing for:
Artabras Inc

Abbey Press
One Hill Dr, St Meinrad, IN 47577
SAN: 201-2057
Tel: 812-357-6611 *Toll Free Tel:* 800-962-4760
Fax: 812-357-8388
E-mail: dep@abbeypress.com
Web Site: www.abbeypress.com
Key Personnel
Publr & Dir: Linus Mundy
Gen Mgr: Gerald Wilhite
Prod Mgr: Carol Schipp
Intl Rts & Lib Sales Dir: Phil Etienne
Founded: 1889
Pastoral care, inspiration, self-help & spiritual growth.
ISBN Prefix(es): 0-87029
Number of titles published annually: 25 Print
Total Titles: 70 Print
Imprints: One Caring Place

Abbott, Langer & Associates
548 First St, Crete, IL 60417
Tel: 708-672-4200 *Fax:* 708-672-4674
E-mail: sales@abbott-langer.com
Web Site: www.abbott-langer.com
Key Personnel
Pres: Dr Steven Langer *E-mail:* slanger@abbott-langer.com
Founded: 1967
Full service publisher.
ISBN Prefix(es): 0-916506
Number of titles published annually: 20 Print
Total Titles: 69 Print
Distributor for Aspen; McGraw-Hill; Prentice Hall; John Wiley
Membership(s): Small Publishers Association of North America

§ABC-CLIO
130 Cremona Dr, Santa Barbara, CA 93117
Mailing Address: PO Box 1911, Santa Barbara, CA 93116-1911
Tel: 805-968-1911 *Toll Free Tel:* 800-368-6868
Fax: 805-685-9685
E-mail: sales@abc-clio.com
Web Site: www.abc-clio.com
Key Personnel
CEO & Academic Publr: Ronald Boehm

VP & Publr, School Div: Becky Snyder
CFO: Tony Uhler
Edit Dir, Serials: Vicky Speck
Man Ed, America History & Life: Mary Bagne
Man Ed, Historical Abstracts: Denver Compton
Mgr Adv, Promos & Book Reviews & Publicist:
   Alison Rivers
Exhibits, Coord, Promos: Jenelle Osborn
Founded: 1955
ABC-CLIO is a privately held corporation. It
   has for many years enjoyed an international
   reputation for high quality & innovation. The
   company is headquartered in Santa Barbara,
   California, with offices in Denver, Colorado &
   Oxford, England. As an educational reference
   publisher the company has received critical ac-
   claim for its computer assisted abstracting &
   indexing services, world renowned book pro-
   gram & cutting-edge online products.
ISBN Prefix(es): 0-87436; 1-57607
Number of titles published annually: 100 Print;
   100 Online; 100 E-Book
Total Titles: 500 Print; 50 CD-ROM; 100 Online;
   150 E-Book
Subsidiaries: ABC-CLIO Ltd
Branch Office(s)
501 Cherry St, Suite 350, Denver, CO 80246
   Tel: 303-333-3003 *Fax:* 303-333-4037
Foreign Office(s): ABC-CLIO International Ltd,
   Old Clarendon Ironworks, 35A Great Claren-
   don St, Oxford 0X2 6AT, United Kingdom
   Tel: (0186) 5311-350 *Fax:* (0186) 5311-358
Warehouse: ABC-CLIO Inc, c/o Sheridan Books,
   617 E Industrial Dr, Chelsea, MI 48818

Abdo Publishing
Subsidiary of Abdo Consulting Group Inc (ACGI)
4940 Viking Dr, Suite 622, Edina, MN 55435
Mailing Address: PO Box 398166, Minneapolis,
   MN 55439-8166
Tel: 952-831-2120 (ext 223) *Toll Free Tel:* 800-
   800-1312 *Fax:* 952-831-1632
E-mail: info@abdopub.com
Web Site: www.abdopub.com
Key Personnel
Pres: Jill Hansen *E-mail:* jill@abdopub.com
Ed-in-Chief: Paul Abdo
Natl Sales Mgr: Jim Abdo
Founded: 1985
Children's books for the library market.
ISBN Prefix(es): 1-56239; 1-57765
Number of titles published annually: 320 Print;
   200 Online
Total Titles: 1,600 Print; 1,000 Online; 500 E-
   Book
Imprints: Abdo & Daughters Publishing (Grades
   4-up); Buddy Books (Grades 1-2); The
   Checkerboard Library (Grades 2-4); Sandcas-
   tle (Grades Pre-K to 2)
Distributed by Rockbottom Book Co
Warehouse: 1920 Lookout Dr, North Mankato,
   MN 56003

ABELexpress
601 Beechwood Ave, Carnegie, PA 15106
Tel: 412-279-0672 *Toll Free Tel:* 800-542-9001
   Fax: 412-429-2911
Key Personnel
Owner: Ken Abel *E-mail:* ken.abel@cornell.edu
Founded: 1983
Consumer oriented books on health & healing,
   science, Pennsylvania; wallet size information
   cards.
ISBN Prefix(es): 0-944214
Number of titles published annually: 4 Print
Total Titles: 7 Print
Membership(s): Publishers Marketing Association

ABI Professional Publications
Imprint of Vandamere Press
3580 Morris St N, Saint Petersburg, FL 33713
SAN: 657-3088

Mailing Address: PO Box 149, Saint Petersburg,
   FL 33731
Tel: 727-556-0950 *Toll Free Tel:* 800-551-7776
   Fax: 727-556-2560
E-mail: abipropub@vandamere.com; orders@
   vandamere.com
Web Site: www.abipropub.com
Key Personnel
Publr & Ed-in-Chief: Arthur Brown
   E-mail: abrown@vandamere.com
Sr Book Ed: Pat Berger
Ed, Journal of Facial & Somato Prosthetics:
   Robert McKinstry
Ed, Journal of Opthalmic Prosthetics: James
   Willis
Founded: 1995
Specialize in professional books, dictionaries,
   journals & electronic media in the fields of
   facial prosthetics & dentistry, rehabilitation,
   medical research & allied health.
ISBN Prefix(es): 1-886236
Number of titles published annually: 6 Print; 1
   CD-ROM
Total Titles: 40 Print; 1 CD-ROM
Distributed by Vandamere Press (non-exclusive)
Distributor for Vandamere Press (non-exclusive)
Membership(s): Publishers Association of the
   South

§Abingdon Press
Division of The United Methodist Publishing
House
201 Eighth Ave S, Nashville, TN 37203-3919
SAN: 201-0046
Mailing Address: PO Box 801, Nashville, TN
   37202-0801
Tel: 615-749-6290 (publicist); 615-749-6000;
   615-749-6451 (sales) *Toll Free Tel:* 800-251-
   3320 *Fax:* 615-749-6056
Web Site: www.abingdonpress.com
Key Personnel
Pres & Publr: Neil M Alexander
Sr VP, F&A & Treas: Larry L Wallace
VP, HR: Alyce Meadors
Employment Mgr: Cindy Knight
Sr VP & Edit Dir: Harriett Jane Olson
Sr VP, Sales & Mktg: Edward Kowalski
Royalties Asst: Sandra Lee
Rts & Perms & Lib Mgr: Roslyn Lewis
Unit Dir & Sr Ed, Gen Interest Bks & Resources:
   Mary Catherine Dean
Children's Books Ed: Peggy Augustine
Gen Interest Ed: Joey Crowe
Mature Years Ed: Marvin Cropsey
Prof Prods Sr Ed: Robert Ratcliff
Leader & Circuit Rider Lead Ed: Jill Reddig
Circuit Rider Assoc Ed: Sheila McGee
Newscope Lead Ed: Victoria Rebeck
Prof Ed: Cynthia Gadsen
Prodn Ed: Linda Allen
Music Sr Ed: Gary A Smith
Music Asst: Donna Nowels
Disciple Sr Ed: Nellie M Moser
Copy Edit Mgr: Mada Johnston
Contracts & Documents Admin: Glenda Keef
Exec Dir, Store Sales: Mike Racio
Wholesale Sales Dir: Carol C Williams
Regl Sales Mgr: Bryan C Williams; Hugh Schultz
Publicity Coord: Katrina Fountain
ISBN Contact: Connie Stacy
Dist Serv Dir: Bob Loggins
Unit Dir, Electronic Prods: Paul Franklin
Mgr, Relationship Mktg & Data Base Serv: Alan
   Blair
Founded: 1789
Religion/ecumenical Christianity; general inter-
   est, children's, family, church professional,
   academic, reference, lay spiritual; United
   Methodist history, doctrine, polity.
ISBN Prefix(es): 0-687
Number of titles published annually: 175 Print
Total Titles: 270 Print; 10 CD-ROM; 3 Online

Imprints: Abingdon Press; Cokesbury; Dimen-
   sions for Living; Kingswood Books; The
   United Methodist Publishing House
Branch Office(s)
Academic Books Office, 201 Eighth Ave,
   Nashville, TN 37203 *Tel:* 615-749-6000
   Fax: 615-749-6056
Distributor for Chalice Press; Cokesbury; Dimen-
   sions for Living; Kingswood Books; Presbyte-
   rian Publishing Corp; SPCK
Foreign Rep(s): Alban Books (UK, Ireland, Eu-
   rope); Asian Trading Corp (India); Bethany
   Fellowship Missions (Indonesia); Cross (Hong
   Kong); The Methodist Publishing House (South
   Africa); R G Mitchell Family Books (Canada);
   Omega Distributors (New Zealand); Open Book
   Publishers (Australia); SKS Books (Singapore)
Warehouse: 341 Great Circle Dr, Nashville, TN
   37228-1703

§Abrams & Co Publishers Inc
61 Mattatuck Heights Rd, Waterbury, CT 06705
Mailing Address: PO Box 10025, Waterbury, CT
   06725
Tel: 203-756-6562 *Toll Free Tel:* 800-227-9120
   Fax: 203-756-2895 *Toll Free Fax:* 800-737-
   3322
Key Personnel
CEO: Daniel C Wasp
Pres: Richard I Abrams
Sr VP: Arthur O Peterson
VP, Fin & HR: Judith Maya
VP, Opers: William Thomas
VP, Sales & Mktg: Dan Coakley
VP, Edit Servs: Kathleen Fischer
Founded: 1989
Early childhood reading Pre-K to fourth grade,
   social studies, language arts.
ISBN Prefix(es): 0-7665; 0-7664
Number of titles published annually: 200 Print; 6
   CD-ROM
See separate listing for:
Graphic Learning
The Letter People®

Harry N Abrams Inc
Subsidiary of La Martiniere Groupe
100 Fifth Ave, New York, NY 10011
SAN: 200-2434
Tel: 212-206-7715 *Toll Free Tel:* 800-345-1359
   Fax: 212-645-8437
E-mail: webmaster@abramsbooks.com
Web Site: www.abramsbooks.com
Key Personnel
CEO: Michael Jacobs
Dir, Publicity: Carol Morgan
VP, Prodn: Stanley Redfern
VP, Mktg: Steve Tager
VP, Dist: Ina Raghunandan
VP & Ed-in-Chief: Eric Himmel
VP, Sales & Mktg: Jonathan Stolper
VP, Art & Design: Michael Walsh
VP, Gift & Children's Books: Howard Reeves
Mgr, Ed & ISBN Contact: Marti Malovany
Sr Ed: Richard Olsen; Christopher Sweet
Man Ed: Harriet Whelchel
Ed: Elaine Stainton
Ed, Amulet (Teens): Susan Van Meter
Founded: 1950
Art & architecture, photography, natural sciences,
   performing arts & children's books.
ISBN Prefix(es): 0-8109
Number of titles published annually: 200 Print
Total Titles: 1,200 Print
Imprints: Abradale
Foreign Rep(s): Canadian MANDA; Thames &
   Hudson
Shipping Address: Time Warner Trade Publishing,
   322 S Enterprise Blvd, Lebanon, IN 46052-
   8193
Membership(s): AAP

Absey & Co Inc
23011 Northcrest Dr, Spring, TX 77389
Tel: 281-257-2340 *Toll Free Tel:* 888-412-2739
  Fax: 281-251-4676
E-mail: abseyandco@aol.com
Web Site: www.absey.com
Key Personnel
Publr: Edward E Wilson
Founded: 1996
Small publishing house catering to the author &
  illustrator. We encourage end-to-end participa-
  tion, e.g. author may select his or her illustra-
  tor, type of paper & type style.
ISBN Prefix(es): 1-888842
Number of titles published annually: 8 Print; 1
  CD-ROM
Total Titles: 25 Print
Membership(s): Southwest Booksellers Associa-
  tion

Academic International Press
PO Box 1111, Gulf Breeze, FL 32562-1111
Tel: 850-932-5478 *Fax:* 850-934-0953
E-mail: info@ai-press.com
Web Site: www.ai-press.com
Key Personnel
Lib Sales Dir: A Thompson
Founded: 1965
Reference titles including encyclopedias, statisti-
  cal yearbooks & document collections; subjects
  on Russia & China, US History, sports, religion
  political economy, military affairs, national-
  ism/ethnicity studies.
ISBN Prefix(es): 0-87569
Number of titles published annually: 30 Print; 30
  Online
Total Titles: 75 Print; 75 Online

§Academic Press
Imprint of Elsevier
525 B St, Suite 1900, San Diego, CA 92101
Tel: 619-231-6616 *Toll Free Tel:* 800-321-5068
  (cust serv) *Fax:* 619-699-6715
E-mail: firstinitiallastname@acad.com; firstinitial.
  lastname@elsevier.com
Web Site: www.elsevier.com
Key Personnel
VP & Dir, Journal Publg: Jasna Markovac
VP & Dir, Sales & Mktg: Salvatore Gelardi
ISBN Contact: Connie Smeyres
Perms: Chris Smith
Founded: 1942
Scientific, technical & professional information in
  multiple media formats.
ISBN Prefix(es): 0-12
Number of titles published annually: 375 Print; 8
  E-Book
Total Titles: 4,700 Print; 14 CD-ROM; 175 E-
  Book
Online services available through ScienceDirect.
Imprints: AP Natural World; Morgan Kaufmann
  Publishers; SciVision; T & AD Poyser
Divisions: SciVision
Branch Office(s)
Morgan Kaufmann Publishers, 500 Sansome St,
  Suite 400, San Francisco, CA 94111 *Tel:* 415-
  392-2665 *Fax:* 415-982-2665 *E-mail:* mkp@
  mkp.com
200 Wheeler Rd, Burlington, MA 01803
  Tel: 781-221-2212 *Fax:* 781-221-1615
15 E 26 St, New York, NY 10010 *Tel:* 212-592-
  1000 *Fax:* 212-592-1010
Foreign Office(s): Harcourt (Australia) Pty Ltd,
  30-52 Smidmore St, Locked Bag 16, Mar-
  rickville, NSW 2204, Australia *Tel:* (02) 9517-
  8999 *Fax:* (02) 9517-2249
Harcourt Japan Inc, Ichibancho Central Bldg, 22-
  1 Ichibancho, Chiyoda-Ku, Tokyo 102, Japan
  Tel: (03) 3234-3911; (03) 3234-3915 *Fax:* (03)
  3265-7198
Academic Press Ltd, Harcourt Place, 32
  Jamestown Rd, London NW1 7BY, United

Kingdom *Tel:* (0207) 424-4200 *Fax:* (0207)
  424-4253
Distributor for Harcourt Professional Publishing;
  The Psychological Corp
Warehouse: 465 S Lincoln Dr, Troy, MO 63379
See separate listing for:
Morgan Kaufmann Publishers

Academy Chicago Publishers
363 W Erie St, Chicago, IL 60610
SAN: 213-2001
Tel: 312-751-7300 *Toll Free Tel:* 800-248-7323
  Fax: 312-751-7306
E-mail: info@academychicago.com
Web Site: www.academychicago.com
Key Personnel
Pres & Sr Ed: Anita Miller
VP & Publicity: Jordan Miller
Art & Prodn Dir: Sarah Olson
Founded: 1975
Fiction, nonfiction, history, mysteries, women's
  studies; emphasis on neglected classics &
  books for women.
ISBN Prefix(es): 0-915864; 0-89733
Number of titles published annually: 11 Print
Total Titles: 367 Print
Distributor for Facets Multimedia; Wicker Park
  Press
Foreign Rep(s): Agence Litteraire (France &
  Spain); Agenza Letteraria Internazionale (Italy);
  Transnet Contracts Ltd (Austria, Germany);
  Tuttle-Mori (Japan)
Foreign Rights: Gazelle Book Services (UK &
  the continent); Scholarly Book Services Inc
  (Canada)

**The Academy of Producer Insurance Studies
Inc**
Division of The National Alliance for Insurance
  Education & Research
PO Box 27027, Austin, TX 78755-2027
Tel: 512-346-7050 *Toll Free Tel:* 800-526-2777
  Fax: 512-343-2167 *Fax on Demand:* 800-828-
  8454
E-mail: alliance@scic.com
Web Site: www.thenationalalliance.com
Key Personnel
Res Dir: Jim Cuprisin *E-mail:* jcuprisin@scic.
  com
Founded: 1983
Insurance research & education.
ISBN Prefix(es): 1-878204
Number of titles published annually: 4 Print
Total Titles: 13 Print; 1 CD-ROM; 1 Audio

Accent Publications
Subsidiary of Cook Communications Ministries
4050 Lee Vance View, Colorado Springs, CO
  80918
SAN: 208-5100
Tel: 719-536-0100 *Toll Free Tel:* 800-708-5550;
  800-535-2905 (cust serv) *Fax:* 719-535-2928
  Toll Free Fax: 800-430-0726
Web Site: www.accentpublications.com
Key Personnel
Mktg Mgr: Don Wagner
Founded: 1947
Sunday School curriculum & church resources.
ISBN Prefix(es): 0-89636; 0-916406
Number of titles published annually: 15 Print
Total Titles: 193 Print

ACETO Bookmen
5721 Antietam Dr, Sarasota, FL 34231-4903
Tel: 941-924-9170
Key Personnel
Owner: Charles D Townsend
Founded: 1968
Specialize in publishing & mail order retail ge-
  nealogical books & publications.
ISBN Prefix(es): 0-9607906; 1-878545

Number of titles published annually: 4 Print
Total Titles: 60 Print

Acres USA
Division of Acres USA Inc
PO Box 91299, Austin, TX 78709-1299
SAN: 270-6555
Tel: 512-892-4400 *Toll Free Tel:* 800-355-5313
  Fax: 512-892-4448
E-mail: info@acresusa.com; editor@acresusa.com
Web Site: www.acresusa.com
Key Personnel
Publr: Fred C Walters *E-mail:* fred@acresusa.com
Founded: 1971
Books on eco-agriculture & a monthly periodical.
ISBN Prefix(es): 0-911311
Number of titles published annually: 4 Print; 1
  Audio
Total Titles: 50 Print; 2 Audio
Imprints: Halcyon House Publishers
Divisions: Living Aboard
Shipping Address: 5321 Industrial Oaks Blvd,
  Suite 128, Austin, TX 78735

Acrobat Books
PO Box 870, Venice, CA 90294-0870
Tel: 310-578-1055 *Fax:* 310-823-8447
E-mail: acrobooks@cs.com
Key Personnel
Publr: Tony Cohan
Assoc Publr: Maya Cohan
Lib Sales Dir: Eric Carter
Founded: 1975
Publish & distribute books.
ISBN Prefix(es): 0-918226
Number of titles published annually: 4 Print
Total Titles: 28 Print
Foreign Rep(s): Gazelle/Pandemic Book Svs Ltd
  (Europe); E M Milley (Canada); Tower Books
  (Australia)
Distribution Center: SCB Distributors, 15608 S
  New Century Dr, Gardena, CA 90248, Con-
  tact: Aaron Silverstein *Tel:* 310-532-9400 *Toll
  Free Tel:* 800-729-6432 *Fax:* 310-532-7001
  E-mail: scb@worldnet.att.net

§ACS Publications
Subsidiary of ASTRO Communications Services
  Inc
Affiliate of International Media Holdings (IMH)
5521 Ruffin Rd, San Diego, CA 92123
SAN: 208-5380
Tel: 858-492-9919 *Toll Free Tel:* 800-888-9983
  (orders only) *Fax:* 858-492-9917 (orders only)
E-mail: sales@astrocom.com
Web Site: www.astrocom.com
Key Personnel
Opers Mgr: Jude Curran
Cust Serv: Camille See
Founded: 1973
Astrology: ephemerides, chart interpretation.
ISBN Prefix(es): 0-935127; 0-917086
Number of titles published annually: 8 Print
Total Titles: 71 Print; 1 Audio
Distributed by Llewellyn; New Leaf Distributors
Distributor for Whitford Press
Foreign Rep(s): The Rights Agency (Canada)

ACTA Publications
4848 N Clark St, Chicago, IL 60640-4711
Tel: 773-271-1030 *Toll Free Tel:* 800-397-2282
  Fax: 773-271-7399 *Toll Free Fax:* 800-397-
  0079
E-mail: actapublications@aol.com
Web Site: www.actapublications.com
Key Personnel
Publr & Edit Dir: Gregory Pierce
Founded: 1958
Books, audio & video tapes for the Christian
  market.
ISBN Prefix(es): 0-87946; 0-914070; 0-915388

Number of titles published annually: 15 Print; 2
Audio
Total Titles: 150 Print; 20 Audio
Distributor for Grief Watch; Veritas
Foreign Rep(s): John Garratt Publishing (Australia); Veritas (UK, Ireland)
Advertising Agency: Jim Foster Communications,
45 Staples, San Francisco, CA 94131, Contact:
Jim Foster *Tel:* 415-585-1974 *Fax:* 415-585-
4554
Membership(s): Catholic Book Publishers Association

Action Publishing LLC
PO Box 391, Glendale, CA 91209
Tel: 323-478-1667 *Toll Free Tel:* 800-705-7482
Fax: 323-478-1767
E-mail: info@actionpublishing.com
Web Site: www.actionpublishing.com
Key Personnel
Publr: Michael Metzler *E-mail:* publisher@
actionpublishing.com
Dir: Maaret Schnier *E-mail:* exec@
actionpublishing.com
Founded: 1966
Action publishes values-oriented children's books,
young adult fiction, art & photography & Politicards - a collection of political caricatures
published in the form of collectible playing
cards & sold in both the book & gift markets.
In addition, we distribute fiction & nonfiction
titles from other publishers that align with the
company's purpose to provide innovative books
that educate, entertain & inform our readers.
ISBN Prefix(es): 1-888045; 0-9617199; 1-883649
Number of titles published annually: 4 Print
Total Titles: 14 Print
Distributor for Bamboo Grove; The Unifont Co
Warehouse: Kingsport, TN
Los Angeles, CA
Membership(s): Publishers Marketing Association

ACU Press
Affiliate of Abilene Christian University
1648 Campus Ct, Abilene, TX 79601
SAN: 207-1681
Tel: 325-674-2720 *Toll Free Tel:* 800-444-4228
Fax: 325-674-6471
E-mail: acupress@acu.edu
Web Site: www.acu.edu/acupress
Key Personnel
Man Dir: Thom Lemmons
Founded: 1984
Religion & ethics.
ISBN Prefix(es): 0-915547; 0-89112
Number of titles published annually: 10 Print
Total Titles: 150 Print

Adams & Ambrose Publishing
PO Box 259684, Madison, WI 53725-9684
SAN: 655-5624
Tel: 608-257-5700 *Fax:* 608-257-5719
E-mail: info@adamsambrose.com
Key Personnel
Mktg Dir & Intl Rts: Joyce Harrington
E-mail: jharrington@adamsambrose.com
Edit: Roger B Oakes *E-mail:* rboakes@
adamsambrose.com
Founded: 1983
Publication of nonfiction books, specializing in
academic, professional & how-to books.
ISBN Prefix(es): 0-916951
Number of titles published annually: 6 Print
Total Titles: 6 Print
Returns: c/o United Parcel Service, 8350 Murphy
Dr, Middleton, WI 53562 (hold for pickup)

Adams-Blake Publishing
8041 Sierra St, Suite 102, Fair Oaks, CA 95628
Tel: 916-962-9296
E-mail: info@adams-blake.com
Web Site: www.adams-blake.com

Key Personnel
VP: Alan N Canton
Founded: 1992
Business, career, health, technical.
ISBN Prefix(es): 1-883422
Number of titles published annually: 9 Print; 1
Online; 1 E-Book
Total Titles: 9 Print

§Adams Media, An F+W Publications Co
57 Littlefield St, 2nd fl, Avon, MA 02322
Tel: 508-427-7100 *Fax:* 508-427-6790
Toll Free Fax: 800-872-5628
E-mail: authors@adamsmedia.com; orders@
adamsmedia.com
Web Site: www.adamsmedia.com
Key Personnel
COO: Scott Watrous
Mktg Dir: Karen Cooper
VP, Opers: William Arris, Jr
Publg Dir: Gary M Krebs *Tel:* 508-427-6720
E-mail: gkrebs@adamsmedia.com
Global Sales Dir: Michael Kelly
Mass Merchandise Dir: Matthew Gildea
Spec Sales Dir: Steve Quinn
Subrights: Laura Smith *Tel:* 513-531-2690 ext
1256
Publicity: Beth Gissinger; Gene Molter
Dir, Prod Devt: Paula Munier, V
Man Ed: Kate McBride
Acqs Ed: Jill Alexander; Kate Burgo; Danielle
Chiotti; Kate Epstein; Eric Hall; Gina Marzilli;
Courtney Nolan
Founded: 1980
General nonfiction, including business, self-help,
inspiration, careers, teen nonfiction, women's
issues, cooking, parenting, reference, relationships, weddings, pets.
ISBN Prefix(es): 1-55850; 1-58062; 1-59337
Number of titles published annually: 200 Print
Total Titles: 750 Print; 20 CD-ROM
Foreign Rep(s): Advantage Quest (Malaysia);
Alternative Books (South Africa); David &
Charles (Europe); Manda Group (Canada);
Peribo (Australia); Peribo (Australia & New
Zealand); Marta Schooler Associates (Southeast
Asia); Viva Books (India)
Foreign Rights: Bardon Chinese Media (China,
Hong Kong, Taiwan); The Harris/Elon Agency
(Israel); Imprima Korea Inc (Korea); Michael
Meller Literary Agency (Germany); The Rights
Agency (France); Julio F Yanez Agencia Literaria (Spain)
Warehouse: 1140 Airport Rd, Fall River, MA
02720

ADASI Publishing Co
6 Dover Point Rd, Suite B, Dover, NH 03820-
4698
Tel: 727-488-7353
E-mail: info@adasi.com
Web Site: www.adasi.com
Key Personnel
Mktg Dir: Parvaneh Ghavami
Physics, Math & history of those subjects.
ISBN Prefix(es): 0-9641295
Number of titles published annually: 6 Print
Total Titles: 4 Print

ADC The Map People
Subsidiary of Langenscheidt Publishers
6440 General Green Way, Alexandria, VA 22312
Tel: 703-750-0510 *Toll Free Tel:* 800-232-6277
Fax: 703-750-3092
E-mail: adc@adcmap.com
Web Site: www.adcmap.com
Founded: 1956
Maps & road atlases.
ISBN Prefix(es): 0-87530
Number of titles published annually: 120 Print
Total Titles: 130 Print
Advertising Agency: M Lande Promotions

Addicus Books Inc
PO Box 45327, Omaha, NE 68145
Tel: 402-330-7493 *Toll Free Tel:* 800-352-2873
(orders) *Fax:* 402-330-1707
E-mail: info@addicusbooks.com; addicusbks@
aol.com
Web Site: www.addicusbooks.com
Key Personnel
Pres & Publr: Rod Colvin
Founded: 1994
Independent press, publishing high-quality trade
paperbacks; publish 8-10 titles annually.
ISBN Prefix(es): 1-886039
Number of titles published annually: 10 Print
Total Titles: 50 Print
Foreign Rights: Dieter Hagenbach (Switzerland)
Advertising Agency: C Lewis & Associates
Billing Address: IPG Books, 814 Franklin St,
Chicago, IL 60610 *Tel:* 312-337-0747 *Toll Free
Tel:* 800-888-4741 *Fax:* 312-337-5985 *Web
Site:* ipgbook.com
Returns: IPG Warehouse, 600 N Pulaski,
Chicago, IL 60624, Contact: Tom Green
Distribution Center: IPG Books, 814 Franklin St,
Chicago, IL 60610 *Tel:* 312-337-0747 *Toll Free
Tel:* 800-888-4741 *Fax:* 312-337-5985 *Web
Site:* ipgbook.com
Membership(s): AAP; National Association of
Independent Publishers; Publishers Marketing
Association

Addison Wesley Higher Education Group
Division of Pearson Education
75 Arlington St, Boston, MA 02116
Tel: 617-848-7500 *Fax:* 617-848-6016
E-mail: firstname.lastname@pearsoned.com
Web Site: www.awl.com
Key Personnel
Chmn: William Barke
Branch Office(s)
1301 Sansome St, San Francisco, CA 94111
Tel: 415-402-2500 *Fax:* 415-402-2591

Adenine Press Inc
2066 Central Ave, Schenectady, NY 12304
Mailing Address: PO Box 355, Guilderland, NY
12084
Tel: 518-456-0784 *Fax:* 518-452-4955
E-mail: info@adeninepress.com
Web Site: www.adeninepress.com
Key Personnel
Pres: Mukti H Sarma
Publr: R H Sarma
Founded: 1982
Textbooks & scholarly journals.
ISBN Prefix(es): 0-940030
Number of titles published annually: 15 Print
Total Titles: 47 Print

Adirondack Mountain Club
814 Goggins Rd, Lake George, NY 12845-4117
SAN: 204-7691
Tel: 518-668-4447 *Toll Free Tel:* 800-395-8080
Fax: 518-668-3746
E-mail: adkinfo@adk.org
Web Site: www.adk.org
Key Personnel
Pubns Dir: John Kettlewell *E-mail:* johnk@adk.
org
Founded: 1922
Calendar (wall) - trade, hiking, canoeing, skiing
& climbing guidebooks & maps for New York
State; natural history field guides; cultural &
literary works on the Adirondacks, members
journals, *Adirondac.*
ISBN Prefix(es): 0-935272
Number of titles published annually: 4 Print
Total Titles: 27 Print

Advance Publishing Inc
6950 Fulton St, Houston, TX 77022
SAN: 263-9572

Tel: 713-695-0600 *Fax:* 713-695-8585
E-mail: ap@advancepublishing.com
Web Site: www.advancepublishing.com
Key Personnel
VP: John Sommer
Founded: 1984
Publish children's picture books, junior biographies & general nonfiction, technical books & current events.
ISBN Prefix(es): 1-57537; 0-9610810
Number of titles published annually: 10 Print
Total Titles: 80 Print; 23 CD-ROM; 75 Online
Membership(s): Children's Book Council; Publishers Marketing Association

Advantage Publishers Group
Division of Advanced Marketing Services Inc
5880 Oberlin Dr, San Diego, CA 92121
Tel: 858-457-2500 *Toll Free Tel:* 800-284-3580 *Fax:* 858-812-6476 *Toll Free Fax:* 800-499-3822
E-mail: apgcuserv@advmkt.com
Web Site: www.advantagebooksonline.com
Key Personnel
Publr: Allen Orso *E-mail:* allen@advmkt.com
Officer & VP, Prod Devt: Sydney Stanley
   E-mail: sydney@advmkt.com
Publr, Thunder Bay Press: Ann Ghublikian
   E-mail: anng@advmkt.com
Assoc Dir, Publicity & Mktg: Bernadette M Baillie *Tel:* 858-450-3595 *E-mail:* bernadetteb@advmkt.com
Assoc Publr, Silver Dolphin: Lilian Shia
   E-mail: lilians@advmkt.com
Man Ed: JoAnn Padgett *E-mail:* joannp@advmkt.com
Founded: 1990
ISBN Prefix(es): 1-57145
Number of titles published annually: 170 Print
Total Titles: 520 Print
Imprints: Laurel Glen Publishing; Portable Press; Silver Dolphin Books; Thunder Bay Press
Warehouse: 1809 W Frankford Rd, Suite 160, Carrollton, TX 75007

§Adventure House
914 Laredo Rd, Silver Spring, MD 20901
Tel: 301-754-1589 *Fax:* 978-215-7412
Web Site: www.adventurehouse.com
Key Personnel
Publr & Ed: John P Gunnison *E-mail:* gunnison@adventurehouse.com
Founded: 1985
Special reprints; fiction from the pulp fiction era.
ISBN Prefix(es): 1-886937
Number of titles published annually: 12 Print
Total Titles: 65 Print; 1 CD-ROM

Adventure Publications
820 Cleveland St, Cambridge, MN 55008
SAN: 212-7199
Tel: 763-689-9800 *Toll Free Tel:* 800-678-7006 *Fax:* 763-689-9039
Key Personnel
Pres: Gordon Slabaugh *E-mail:* goslabaugh@aol.com
VP & Gen Mgr: Gerri Slabaugh *E-mail:* gerri@adventurepublications.net
Founded: 1988
General trade & regional.
ISBN Prefix(es): 0-934860; 1-885061; 1-59193
Number of titles published annually: 10 Print
Total Titles: 89 Print
Distributor for Blacklock Nature Photography

Adventures Unlimited Press
One Adventure Place, Kempton, IL 60946
Mailing Address: PO Box 74, Kempton, IL 60946-0074
Tel: 815-253-6390 *Fax:* 815-253-6300
E-mail: auphq@frontiernet.net
Web Site: www.adventuresunlimitedpress.com

Key Personnel
Pres & Intl Rts Contact: David H Childress
Man Dir: Jennifer Bolm
Warehouse Mgr: Brian Lemenager
Founded: 1983
Eclectic variety of books on mysteries of the past, alternative technologies & conspiracy theories.
ISBN Prefix(es): 0-932813
Number of titles published annually: 14 Print
Total Titles: 110 Print
Foreign Office(s): Frontier Sciences Foundation, Netherlands
Distributor for EDFU Books
Foreign Rep(s): Gazelle Books (UK); Gemcraft Books (Australia); Marginal Distribution (Canada)

Aegean Park Press
PO Box 2120, Walnut Creek, CA 94595
Tel: 925-947-2533 *Toll Free Tel:* 800-736-3587 (orders only) *Fax:* 925-947-2144
E-mail: books@aegeanparkpress.com
Web Site: www.aegeanparkpress.com
Key Personnel
Pres: Wayne G Barker
Founded: 1976
Technical books in contract bridges, computers, cryptology, Mayan studies, history, intelligence, communications & genealogy.
ISBN Prefix(es): 0-89412
Number of titles published annually: 10 Print
Total Titles: 145 Print
Shipping Address: 23995 Carrillo Dr, Mission Viejo, CA 92691

The AEI Press
Division of American Enterprise Institute for Public Policy Research
1150 17 St NW, Washington, DC 20036
SAN: 202-4527
Tel: 202-862-5800 *Fax:* 202-862-7177
Web Site: www.aei.org
Key Personnel
Chmn of the Bd: Bruce Kouner
Pres: Christopher C De Muth
Dir, Pubns: Montgomery Brown
Dir, Pubns Mktg & Rts & Perms: Virginia V Bryant
Ed: Samuel Thernstrom
Founded: 1943
Public policy economics, foreign affairs & defense, government & politics, law; research on education, energy, government regulation & tax policy.
ISBN Prefix(es): 0-8447
Number of titles published annually: 22 Print
Total Titles: 298 Print
Distributed by MIT (selected titles)
Foreign Rep(s): Eurospan
Distribution Center: Client Distribution Services, 193 Edwards Dr, Jackson, TN 38301 *Toll Free Tel:* 800-343-4499 *Toll Free Fax:* 800-351-5073 *Web Site:* cdsbooks.com

Aerial Photography Services Inc
2511 S Tryon St, Charlotte, NC 28203
Tel: 704-333-5143 *Fax:* 704-333-5148
   Toll Free Fax: 800-204-4910
E-mail: aps@aps-1.com
Web Site: www.aps-1.com
Key Personnel
Off Mgr: Mary Baker *E-mail:* mbaker@aps-1.com
Founded: 1960
ISBN Prefix(es): 0-933672; 1-880970
Number of titles published annually: 3 Print
Total Titles: 36 Print

Africa World Press Inc
541 W Ingham Ave, Suite B, Trenton, NJ 08638
Tel: 609-695-3200 *Fax:* 609-695-6466

E-mail: awprsp@africanworld.com; awprsp@intar.com
Web Site: africanworld.com
   Telex: 3794257AFRIC
Key Personnel
Pres: Checole Kassahun
Founded: 1983
Latin America, the Caribbean, Afrocentric children's books, Africa.
ISBN Prefix(es): 0-86543; 1-59221
Number of titles published annually: 124 Print
Total Titles: 980 Print; 10 Online; 10 E-Book
Foreign Office(s): East Africa, PO Box 48, Asmara, Eritrea *Tel:* 01-120707 *Fax:* 01-123369
Foreign Rights: Turnaround Publisher Services (Europe, London)
Warehouse: 11 E-F Princess Rd, Lawrenceville, NJ 08648

§African American Images
1909 W 95 St, Chicago, IL 60643
Tel: 773-445-0322 *Toll Free Tel:* 800-552-1991 *Fax:* 773-445-9844
E-mail: customer@africanamericanimages.com
Web Site: africanamericanimages.com
Key Personnel
Pres & Intl Rts: Jawanza Kunjufu
Founded: 1983
Publish & distribute books of an Africentric nature that promote self-esteem, collective values, liberation & skill development.
ISBN Prefix(es): 0-913543
Number of titles published annually: 8 Print
Total Titles: 96 Print; 2 CD-ROM
Online services available through Comtex.
Advertising Agency: Jawanza Kunjufu & Associates

Agathon Press
2741 Arlington Ave, Bronx, NY 10463-4806
Tel: 718-543-6207 (edit & busn); 908-788-5753 (fulfillment) *Toll Free Tel:* 800-488-8040 (orders only) *Fax:* 718-543-6211 (edit & busn); 908-237-2407 (fulfillment)
Web Site: www.agathonpress.com
Key Personnel
Owner & Pres: Burton Lasky *E-mail:* blasky@agathonpress.com
Founded: 1959
Scholarly books in higher education & political science.
ISBN Prefix(es): 0-87586
Number of titles published annually: 1 Print
Total Titles: 6 Print
Billing Address: 1200 Rte 523, Flemington, NJ 08822 *Tel:* 908-788-5753 *Toll Free Tel:* 800-488-8040 *Fax:* 908-237-2407
Orders to: 1200 Rte 523, Flemington, NJ 08822 *Tel:* 908-788-5753 *Toll Free Tel:* 800-488-8040 *Fax:* 908-237-2407
Distribution Center: 1200 Rte 523, Flemington, NJ 08822 *Tel:* 908-788-5753 *Toll Free Tel:* 800-488-8040 *Fax:* 908-237-2407
E-mail: wcbooks@aol.com

§Ageless Press
3759 Collins St, Sarasota, FL 34232
Mailing Address: PO Box 5915, Sarasota, FL 34277-5915 SAN: 297-830X
Tel: 941-365-1367 *Fax:* 941-365-1367
E-mail: irishope@comcast.net
Web Site: irisforrest.com
Key Personnel
Owner: Hope Day
Ed: Iris Forrest
Founded: 1992
Publish short stories by various authors.
ISBN Prefix(es): 0-9635177
Number of titles published annually: 6 Print
Total Titles: 3 Print; 1 Online

§AGS Publishing
4201 Woodland Rd, Circle Pines, MN 55014-1716
Tel: 651-287-7220 *Toll Free Tel:* 800-328-2560 *Toll Free Fax:* 800-471-8457
E-mail: agsmail@agsnet.com
Web Site: www.agsnet.com
Key Personnel
Pres & CEO: Larry Rutkowski
Exec VP & CFO: Joy Hoppe
Rts & Perms Mgr: LeAnn Velde *Tel:* 800-328-2560 ext 7242 *E-mail:* leannv@agsnet.com
Founded: 1957
Standardized tests, textbooks, test preparation & other educational materials for special needs.
ISBN Prefix(es): 0-88671; 0-913476; 0-7854
Number of titles published annually: 25 Print; 3 Audio
Total Titles: 785 Print; 215 CD-ROM; 38 Audio
Warehouse: 22 Village Pkwy, Circle Pines, MN 55014-4401

AGU, see American Geophysical Union (AGU)

AHA Press
Subsidiary of Health Forum Inc
One N Franklin, Suite 2800, Chicago, IL 60606
Tel: 312-893-6800 *Fax:* 312-422-4500
Web Site: www.hospitalconnect.com; www.ahaonlinestore.com (orders)
Key Personnel
Edit Dir: Richard Hill *E-mail:* rhill@healthforum.com
Professional references for healthcare managers.
ISBN Prefix(es): 1-55648
Number of titles published annually: 8 Print
Total Titles: 75 Print
Distributor for American Society for Quality
Membership(s): Society of National Association Publications

Ahsahta Press
Boise State University, Dept of English, Boise, ID 83725
Tel: 208-426-2195 *Fax:* 208-426-4373
Key Personnel
Dir & Ed: Janet Holmes *E-mail:* jholmes@boisestate.edu
Founded: 1974
Trade paperback books. Specialize in American poetry.
ISBN Prefix(es): 0-916272
Number of titles published annually: 3 Print
Total Titles: 56 Print; 1 Audio
Distributed by Small Press Distribution
Shipping Address: Book Store, 1910 University Dr, Boise, ID 83725, Contact: Jan Johns *Tel:* 208-426-1811 *Toll Free Tel:* 800-992-8398 *E-mail:* jholmes@boisestate.edu *Web Site:* english.boisestate.edu/mfa/ahsahta

AIMS Education Foundation
1595 S Chestnut Ave, Fresno, CA 93702-4706
Mailing Address: PO Box 8120, Fresno, CA 93747-8120
Tel: 559-255-4094 *Toll Free Tel:* 888-733-2467 *Fax:* 559-255-6396
E-mail: aimsed@aimsedu.org
Web Site: www.aimsedu.org/
Key Personnel
Systems Admin & Webmaster: Johann Weber *Tel:* 559-255-4049 *E-mail:* jmweber@aimsedu.org
Founded: 1985
Provides educational enrichment for grades K-9 through hands-on activities that integrate mathematics, science, technology & other disciplines; curriculum writing for K-9; music CD-ROM & cassette.
ISBN Prefix(es): 1-881431
Number of titles published annually: 6 Print

Total Titles: 69 Print; 1 CD-ROM; 3 Audio
Shipping Address: 5391 E Home, Fresno, CA 93727

§Aio Publishing Co LLC
PO Box 30788, Charleston, SC 29417
Tel: 843-225-3698 *Toll Free Tel:* 888-287-9888
Web Site: www.aiopublishing.com
Key Personnel
Edit Dir: Tiffany Jonas *E-mail:* trjonas@aiopublishing.com
Acctg & Busn Dir: Amy Redfield
Art Dept Dir: Patrick Jonas
Mktg Dir: Linda Pranger
Founded: 2004
Publisher of adult science fiction books. Produce densely written socological science fiction with deeply developed characters & to present it to the reader as a work of art.
ISBN Prefix(es): 1-933083
Number of titles published annually: 3 Print
Membership(s): Publishers Marketing Association; Speculative Literature Foundation

Airmont Publishing Co Inc
160 Madison Ave, New York, NY 10016
Tel: 212-598-0222 *Fax:* 212-979-1862
Key Personnel
Pres: Wilhelm Mickelsen
Founded: 1956
Reprint classics in mass market form.
ISBN Prefix(es): 0-8049
Number of titles published annually: 86 Print
Total Titles: 86 Print
Warehouse: Offset Paperback Distribution Center, One Passan Dr, Bldg 4, Laflin, PA 18702

Akashic Books
PO Box 1456, New York, NY 10009
Tel: 212-433-1875 *Fax:* 212-414-3199
E-mail: akashic7@aol.com
Web Site: www.akashicbooks.com
Key Personnel
Publr: Johnny Temple
Man Ed: Johanna Ingalls
Founded: 1997
Specialize in urban literary fiction & political nonfiction.
ISBN Prefix(es): 1-888451; 0-9719206
Number of titles published annually: 20 Print
Total Titles: 65 Print
Imprints: RDV Books
Orders to: Consortium Book Sales & Distribution, 1045 Westgate Dr, Saint Paul, MN 55114 *Toll Free Tel:* 800-283-3572
Returns: Consortium Book Sales & Distribution, 1045 Westgate Dr, Saint Paul, MN 55114 *Toll Free Tel:* 800-823-3572
Distribution Center: Consortium Book Sales & Distribution, 1045 Westgate Dr, Saint Paul, MN 55114 *Toll Free Tel:* 800-283-3572

AKTRIN Furniture Information Centre
164 S Main St, Suite 307, High Point, NC 27260
Mailing Address: PO Box 898, High Point, NC 27261-0898
Tel: 336-841-8535 *Fax:* 336-841-5435
E-mail: aktrin@aktrin.com (Canada); aktrinusa@northstate.net (US)
Web Site: www.aktrin.com
Key Personnel
Owner & Pres: Stefan Wille *Tel:* 905-845-3474
Off Mgr: Donna Fincher
Founded: 1985
Specialize in business, industry & statistical reports.
ISBN Prefix(es): 0-921577; 1-894330; 1-894960
Number of titles published annually: 12 Print; 10 Online
Total Titles: 56 Print; 30 Online
Branch Office(s)
151 Randall St, Oakville, ON L6J 1P5, Canada,

Contact: Stefan Wille *Tel:* 905-845-3474 *Fax:* 905-845-7459
Distributor for AMA Research; Business & Research Associates

ALA, see American Library Association (ALA)

Aladdin Paperbacks, see Simon & Schuster Children's Publishing

Alaska Native Language Center
Division of University of Alaska Fairbanks
PO Box 757680, Fairbanks, AK 99775-7680
SAN: 692-9796
Tel: 907-474-7874 *Fax:* 907-474-6586
Web Site: www.uaf.edu/anlc/
Key Personnel
Dir: Lawrence D Kaplan
Ed: Tom Alton *Tel:* 907-474-6577
Founded: 1972
Publish books in & about Alaska's 20 indigenous languages, including dictionaries, grammars & collections of folktales & oral history, language maps.
ISBN Prefix(es): 1-55500; 0-933769
Number of titles published annually: 3 Print
Total Titles: 190 Print; 3 Audio

Alba House
Division of The Society of St Paul
2187 Victory Blvd, Staten Island, NY 10314
SAN: 201-2405
Tel: 718-761-0047 (edit & prodn); 718-698-2759 (mktg & billing) *Toll Free Tel:* 800-343-2522 *Fax:* 718-761-0057
E-mail: albabooks@aol.com
Web Site: www.albahouse.org *Cable:* STPAUL
Key Personnel
Ed-in-Chief, ISBN Contact & Rts & Perms: Fr Anthony Warren
Acqs & Foreign Ed: Victor L Viberti
Man Ed: Edmund C Lane *E-mail:* edmund_lane@juno.com
Copy Ed: Frank Sadowski
Mktg & Sales Mgr: Anthony Warren
Prodn Mgr: James Mann
Art Dir: Edward Donaher
Treas: Lawrence Schubert
Founded: 1961
Religion (Catholic), Bible, education, family life, juvenile, pastoral care, prayer books, sociology, biography, spirituality, psychology, philosophy, theology, cassettes & videos.
ISBN Prefix(es): 0-8189
Number of titles published annually: 30 Print
Foreign Office(s): Edizioni Paoline, Piazza Soncino, 5 20092 Cinisello Balsamo (MI), Italy
Foreign Rep(s): St Paul Publications (Australia, UK, Canada, Ireland, India, Italy, Philippines, South Africa)

The Alban Institute Inc
2121 Cooperative Way, Suite 100, Herndon, VA 20171
Tel: 703-964-2700 *Toll Free Tel:* 800-486-1318 *Fax:* 703-964-0370
E-mail: webmaster@alban.org
Web Site: www.alban.org
Key Personnel
Man Ed: Richard Bass
Lib Sales Dir: Mike O'Connor
Founded: 1974
Ecumenical, research based publications for congregations.
ISBN Prefix(es): 1-56699
Number of titles published annually: 12 Print
Total Titles: 150 Print

The Alexander Graham Bell Association for the Deaf & Hard of Hearing
3417 Volta Place NW, Washington, DC 20007-2778
SAN: 203-6924
Tel: 202-337-5220 *Fax:* 202-337-8314
Web Site: www.agbell.org
Key Personnel
Man Ed, Rts & Perms: Leah Lakins
Dir, Outreach: Gary Yates *Tel:* 201-337-5220 ext 121 *E-mail:* gyates@agbell.org
Orders & Returns: Rachel Reed
Founded: 1890
Resource, support network & advocate for listening, learning, talking & living independently with hearing loss. Through publications, outreach, training, scholarships & financial aid, AG Bell promotes the use of spoken language & hearing technology. Headquarted in Washington DC with chapters located in the US & Canada & a network of international affiliates. AG Bells global presence provides its members & the public with the support they need close to home. With over a century of service, AG Bell supports it's mission, advocating independence through listening & talking.
ISBN Prefix(es): 0-88200
Number of titles published annually: 3 Print
Total Titles: 62 Print
Distributor for Delmar Thomson; Temple University Press; Woodbine Press; York Press

Alexander Street Press LLC
3212 Duke St, Alexandria, VA 22314
Tel: 703-212-8520 *Toll Free Tel:* 800-889-5937 *Fax:* 240-465-0561
E-mail: sales@alexanderstreet.com
Web Site: www.alexanderstreet.com
Key Personnel
Pres: Stephen Rhind-Tutt
CFO: Janice Cronin
VP, Sales & Mktg: Eileen Lawrence
VP, Prodn: Pat Lawry
Founded: 2000
Publish large electronic collections of works in the humanities & social sciences.
Number of titles published annually: 5 CD-ROM; 5 Online; 2,000 E-Book
Total Titles: 20 CD-ROM; 20 Online; 10,000 E-Book
Distributor for Ad Fontes LLC
Membership(s): ALA

§Alfred Publishing Company Inc
PO Box 10003, Van Nuys, CA 91410-0003
Tel: 818-891-5999 *Toll Free Tel:* 800-292-6122 (dealer sales) *Fax:* 818-892-9239 *Toll Free Fax:* 800-632-1928 (dealer sales)
E-mail: customerservice@alfred.com
Web Site: www.alfred.com
Founded: 1922
Publisher of music education; music books & software, performance & instructional.
Number of titles published annually: 500 Print; 4 CD-ROM
Total Titles: 15,000 Print; 20 CD-ROM
Distributor for Dover; Faber Music; Myklas Music Press; National Guitar Workshop
Foreign Rep(s): Dave Bolden (Australia & New Zealand); Larry Bong (Asia); Gerry Mooney (UK); Thomas Petzold (Europe)
Membership(s): Magazine Publishers of America

Algonquin Books of Chapel Hill
Division of Workman Publishing Co Inc
127 Kingston Dr, Suite 105, Chapel Hill, NC 27514
SAN: 282-7506
Mailing Address: PO Box 2225, Chapel Hill, NC 27515-2225
Tel: 919-967-0108 *Fax:* 919-933-0272
E-mail: dialogue@algonquin.com

Web Site: www.algonquin.com
Key Personnel
Publr: Elisabeth Scharlatt *Tel:* 212-254-5900
Assoc Publr: Ina Stern
Exec Ed: Chuck Adams
ISBN Contact & Man Ed: Brunson Hoole *E-mail:* brunson@algonquin.com
Mktg Dir: Craig Popelars
Publicity Dir: Michael Taeckens
Subs Rts: Antonia Fusco *Tel:* 212-254-5900
Design & Prodn: Anne Winslow
Intl Rts: Carolan R Workman
Lib/School Sales: Maribeth Casey *Tel:* 413-346-2135
Founded: 1982
Trade books, fiction & nonfiction.
ISBN Prefix(es): 0-912697; 0-945575; 1-56512
Number of titles published annually: 28 Print
Total Titles: 490 Print
Imprints: Shannon Ravenel Books
Branch Office(s)
708 Broadway, New York, NY 10003 *Tel:* 212-614-7587 *Fax:* 212-614-7783
Sales Office(s): Workman Publishing Co Inc, 708 Broadway, New York, NY 10003 *Tel:* 212-254-5900 *Toll Free Tel:* 800-722-7202 (orders)
Distributed by Workman Publishing Co Inc
Foreign Rep(s): Thomas Allen & Son Ltd (Canada)
Foreign Rights: Big Apple Tuttle-Mori Agency (China, Taiwan); Caroline van Gelderen (Netherlands); Graal Ltd (Poland); Japan UNI Agency (Japan); JLM Literary Agency (Greece); Korea Copyright Ctr (Korea); Kristin Olson (Czech Republic); Julio F Yanez (Latin America, Portugal, Spain)
Billing Address: Workman Publishing Co Inc, 708 Broadway, New York, NY 10003 *Tel:* 212-254-5900
Orders to: Workman Publishing Co Inc, 708 Broadway, New York, NY 10003 *Toll Free Tel:* 800-722-7202
Returns: Workman Publishing Co Inc, c/o George Banta Co, 677 Brighton Beach Rd, Menasha, WI 54952-2998
Warehouse: Workman Publishing Co Inc, c/o George Banta Co, 677 Brighton Beach Rd, Menasha, WI 54952-2998

Algora Publishing
222 Riverside Dr, Suite 16-D, New York, NY 10025-6809
Tel: 212-678-0232 *Toll Free Tel:* 888-405-0689 *Fax:* 212-666-3682 *Fax on Demand:* 917-306-0221
E-mail: editors@algora.com
Web Site: www.algora.com
Key Personnel
Pres: Claudiu A Secara *Tel:* 212-678-0232 *E-mail:* claudiu@algora.com
Dir, Editing & Translation: Andrea L Sengstacken *E-mail:* andrea@algora.com
Ed: Martin DeMers *E-mail:* Martin@algora.com
Founded: 1992
Specializes in books on subjects of history, international affairs, current issues, political economy, philosophy, etc in the tradition of independent progressive thinking.
ISBN Prefix(es): 0-87586; 0-9646073; 1-892941
Number of titles published annually: 25 Print; 25 E-Book
Total Titles: 250 Print; 100 E-Book
Imprints: Agathon Press
Membership(s): AAP; Publishers Marketing Association

§ALI-ABA Committee on Continuing Professional Education
Affiliate of American Bar Association & American Law Institute
4025 Chestnut St, Philadelphia, PA 19104
Tel: 215-243-1600 *Toll Free Tel:* 800-CLE-NEWS *Fax:* 215-243-1664; 215-243-1683

Web Site: www.ali-aba.org
Key Personnel
Dir, Off of Admin Servs: Joseph A Mendicino
Dir, Off of Courses of Study: Alexander Hart
Dir, Off of Periodicals: Mark T Carroll
Dir, Off of R&D: Leslie Belasco
Dir, Off of Audio & Video Law Reviews: Susan Tomita
Adv & Publicity: Kathleen Lawner
Exec Dir: Richard E Carter
Libn: Harry Kyriakodis *Tel:* 215-243-1654
Deputy Exec Dir: Larry Meehan
Founded: 1947
Publish law books & legal periodicals.
ISBN Prefix(es): 0-8318
Number of titles published annually: 4 Print; 2 CD-ROM
Total Titles: 300 Print; 8 CD-ROM; 5 Online; 380 Audio
Online services available through Lexis, Westlaw.

Alice James Books
Division of Alice James Poetry Cooperative Inc
238 Main St, Farmington, ME 04938
SAN: 201-1158
Tel: 207-778-7071 *Fax:* 207-778-7071
E-mail: ajb@umf.maine.edu
Web Site: www.alicejamesbooks.org
Key Personnel
Exec Dir: April Ossmann
Man Ed: Aimee Beal
Founded: 1973
ISBN Prefix(es): 0-914086; 1-882295
Number of titles published annually: 5 Print
Total Titles: 112 Print; 3 Audio
Distribution Center: Consortium Book Sales & Distribution *Toll Free Tel:* 800-283-3572

All About Kids Publishing
117 Bernal Rd, No 70, PMB 405, San Jose, CA 95119
Tel: 408-846-1833 *Fax:* 408-846-1835 (ordering)
Web Site: www.aakp.com
Key Personnel
Ed: Linda Guevara *E-mail:* lguevara99@aol.com
Founded: 1999
Strives to set the standards in children's & educational book publishing by creating innovative books of the highest quality with beautiful art work for children of all walks of life. Encompasses multiculturalism, education & conscience.
ISBN Prefix(es): 0-9700863; 0-9710278
Number of titles published annually: 6 Print
Total Titles: 10 Print; 4 E-Book
Membership(s): Publishers Marketing Association

§All Wild-Up Productions
303 Fourth Ave SE, Puyallup, WA 98372
Mailing Address: PO Box 1354, Puyallup, WA 98371
Tel: 206-457-1949 *Fax:* 206-457-1949
E-mail: mail@allwildup.com
Web Site: www.allwildup.com
Key Personnel
Owner: Chris Ihrig
Founded: 2000
Specializing in historical & entertainment publications focusing on the amusement & theme park industries.
Number of titles published annually: 5 Print

Alleluia Press
672 Franklin Tpke, Allendale, NJ 07401
SAN: 202-3601
Tel: 201-327-3513
Key Personnel
Publr & Owner: Jose M de Vinck
Founded: 1969 (Established by Baron de Vinck)
Quality books, religion, philosophy, poetry; No unsol mss.
ISBN Prefix(es): 0-911726
Total Titles: 22 Print

Allen D Bragdon Publishers Inc
252 Great Western Rd, South Yarmouth, MA
02664-2210
SAN: 208-5623
Tel: 508-398-4440 *Toll Free Tel:* 877-8-SMARTS
(876-2787) *Fax:* 508-760-2397
E-mail: admin@brainwaves.com
Web Site: www.brainwaves.com
Key Personnel
Pres: Allen D Bragdon
Cust Serv & Admin: Donna McGovern
Founded: 1977
Self-improvement, brain development books, puz-
zles, tests, mental exercises.
ISBN Prefix(es): 0-916410
Number of titles published annually: 2 Print; 3 E-
Book
Total Titles: 9 Print; 3 E-Book
Imprints: Brainwaves Books
Divisions: Packaging Division
Branch Office(s)
Brainwaves Books, Tupelo Rd, Bass River, MA
02664 *Tel:* 508-398-4440 *Toll Free Tel:* 877-
876-2787 *Fax:* 508-760-2397
The Brainwaves Research Center, West Coast Fa-
cility, 1846 Ninth Ave, Oakland, CA 94606,
Res Dir: David Gamon, PhD *Tel:* 510-434-
9520 *Fax:* 510-434-9523
Distributed by Walker & Co New York
Foreign Rights: Tuttle Mori (Japan)
Membership(s): ABA; NEBA

Allied Health Publications
Division of California College for Health Sci-
ences
5295 S Commerce Dr, Salt Lake City, UT 84107
SAN: 692-2643
Toll Free Tel: 800-221-7374 (enrollment); 800-
497-7157 *Fax:* 801-263-0345
E-mail: ahp@cchs.edu
Web Site: www.cchs.edu
Founded: 1979
Respiratory care & allied health fields. Offers
books, reference material courses, programs;
CEUs & patient education publications. Spe-
cialize in cardiopulmonary educational & pa-
tient educational materials.
ISBN Prefix(es): 0-931657; 0-933195
Total Titles: 75 Print
Warehouse: 2500 Hoover Ave, Suite A, National
City, CA 91950

Alloy Entertainment
Formerly 17th Street Productions
Division of Alloy Online
151 W 26 St, 11th fl, New York, NY 10001
Tel: 212-244-4307
Key Personnel
Pres: Leslie Morgenstein
Edit Dir: Ben Schrank *Tel:* 212-244-4307 ext
8491 *E-mail:* bschrank@alloy.com
Foreign Rts: Andy Ball *E-mail:* andyb@alloy.com
Founded: 1987
Hardcover, trade, mass market juvenile & young
adult fiction & nonfiction; adult trade fiction &
mass market fiction.
ISBN Prefix(es): 0-533; 0-590; 0-06; 0-14; 0-
931497
Number of titles published annually: 50 Print
Branch Office(s)
17th Street Productions, 33 W 17 St, New York,
NY 10011 *Tel:* 212-645-3865 *Fax:* 212-633-
1236
Distributed by Avon Books; HarperCollins; Hype-
rion; Little, Brown and Co; Millbrook Press;
MTV Books; Penguin Putnam Inc; Pocket
Books; Puffin Books; Random House Inc;
Scholastic Books; Simon & Schuster
Foreign Rep(s): Andy Ball

§Allworth Press
10 E 23 St, Suite 510, New York, NY 10010

Tel: 212-777-8395 *Toll Free Tel:* 800-491-2808
Fax: 212-777-8261
E-mail: pub@allworth.com
Web Site: www.allworth.com
Key Personnel
Mktg Dir: Cynthia Rivelli *Tel:* 212-777-8395 ext
3 *E-mail:* crivelli@allworth.com
Publr: Tad Crawford
Assoc Publr: Robert Porter
Busn Mgr: Gebrina Roberts *E-mail:* groberts@
allworth.com
Ed: Nicole Potter *E-mail:* npotter@allworth.com
Publicity: Michael Madole *E-mail:* mmadole@
allworth.com; Birte Pampel *E-mail:* bpampel@
allworth.com
Founded: 1989
Business & self-help books for artists, designers,
photographers, authors & film & performing
artists; books about business, money & law for
the general public; psychology, sociology &
current affairs (Helios Press).
ISBN Prefix(es): 0-927629; 0-9607118; 1-880559;
1-58115
Number of titles published annually: 40 Print; 2
CD-ROM; 30 E-Book
Total Titles: 219 Print; 10 CD-ROM; 38 E-Book
Imprints: Helios Press
Distributed by Watson-Guptill Publications
Foreign Rep(s): Bookwise International (Aus-
tralia & New Zealand); Geoff Cowen, Windsor
Books (UK, Europe); Theo Philips, CKK Ltd
(Hong Kong, Philippines, Singapore, Thailand)
Foreign Rights: Jean V Naggar Literary Agency;
Jennifer Weltz (foreign lang rts)
Warehouse: Watson-Guptill Publications Distri-
bution Center, 385 Prospect St, Lakewood, NJ
08701 *Tel:* 732-363-5679 *Toll Free Tel:* 800-
451-1741 *Fax:* 732-363-0338 *Web Site:* www.
watsonguptill.com
Membership(s): Publishers Marketing Association

Allyn & Bacon
Division of Pearson Education
75 Arlington St, Suite 300, Boston, MA 02116
Tel: 617-848-6000 *Fax:* 617-848-6016
E-mail: AandBpub@aol.com
Web Site: www.ablongman.com
Key Personnel
Pres: Sandi Kirshner
VP, Mktg: Tim Stookesberry
Fin: Laura Rutherford
Founded: 1868
A college textbook publisher focusing on a select
number of social science, education & humani-
ties disciplines.
ISBN Prefix(es): 0-205
Number of titles published annually: 310 Print
Total Titles: 2,300 Print

Alms House Press
PO Box 218, Woodbourne, NY 12788-0218
Tel: 845-436-0070 *Fax:* 845-436-0099
Key Personnel
Ed & Publr: Alana Sherman *E-mail:* mjslaw@
in4web.com
Founded: 1985
Publish chapbooks of poetry through a submis-
sion, journal (wheatear).
ISBN Prefix(es): 0-939689
Number of titles published annually: 4 Print
Total Titles: 20 Print

Alomega Press
Division of Alomega Services Inc
4601 N Cleveland Ave, Kansas City, MO 64117
Mailing Address: PO Box 901643, Kansas City,
MO 64190-1643
Tel: 816-454-0980 *Fax:* 816-454-0980
Key Personnel
Publr: DeVerne Coleman *E-mail:* deverne-ace@
worldnet.att.net

General trade hardcover & paperback; fiction &
nonfiction books.
ISBN Prefix(es): 0-9661006
Number of titles published annually: 3 Print
Total Titles: 1 Print

ALPHA Publications of America Inc
Affiliate of Alpha Legal Forms & More
4500 E Speedway Blvd, Suite 31, Tucson, AZ
85712-5325
Tel: 520-795-7100 *Toll Free Tel:* 800-528-3494
Toll Free Fax: 800-770-4329
E-mail: alphalegalkits@alphapublications.com
Web Site: www.alphapublications.com
Key Personnel
Pres: Kermit Burton
Founded: 1976
Non-lawyer self-help legal kits (books & pack-
ets).
ISBN Prefix(es): 0-937434; 1-57164
Number of titles published annually: 109 Print
Total Titles: 128 Print; 38 Online; 4 E-Book
Imprints: The Alpha Non-Lawyers A-B Trust
Kit; The Alpha Non-Lawyers Arizona Corpo-
ration Kit; The Alpha Non-Lawyers Arizona
Divorce Kit; The Alpha Non-Lawyers Ari-
zona Limited Liability Company Kit (Arizona
Edition); The Alpha Non-Lawyers California
Divorce Kit (California Edition); The Alpha
Non-Lawyers Chapter 7 Bankruptcy Kit; The
Alpha Non-Lawyers Chapter 13 Bankruptcy
Kit; The Alpha Non-Lawyers Corporation Kit
(National Edition); The Alpha Non-Lawyers
Home Sales Kit; The Alpha Non-Lawyers
Last Will & Testament Kit; The Alpha Non-
Lawyers Limited Liability Company Kit; The
Alpha Non-Lawyers Living Trust Kit; The Al-
pha Non-Lawyers Living Will Kit; The Alpha
Non-Lawyers New Mexico Divorce Kit (New
Mexico Edition); The Alpha Non-Lawyers
Non-Profit Corporation Kit; The Alpha Non-
Lawyers Partnership Kit; The Alpha Non-
Lawyers Pre-Marriage Kit
Branch Office(s)
Alpha Legal Forms & More Inc, 1600 W Camel-
back, Suite 1-L, Phoenix, AZ 85015 *Tel:* 602-
234-0269
Membership(s): Publishers Marketing Association

Alpine Publications Inc
PO Box 7027, Loveland, CO 80537-0027
Tel: 970-667-2017 *Toll Free Tel:* 800-777-7257
(orders only) *Fax:* 970-667-9157
E-mail: alpinecsr@aol.com
Web Site: www.alpinepub.com
Key Personnel
Ed & Publr: Betty McKinney
Founded: 1975
Dog & horse nonfiction titles.
ISBN Prefix(es): 0-931866; 0-87714; 1-57779
Number of titles published annually: 10 Print
Total Titles: 78 Print
Imprints: Blue Ribbon Books
Advertising Agency: Artline
Shipping Address: 225 S Madison, Loveland, CO
80537
Membership(s): ABA; Publishers Marketing As-
sociation; Small Publishers Association of
North America

AltaMira Press
Division of Rowman & Littlefield Publishers Inc
1630 N Main St, No 367, Walnut Creek, CA
94596
Tel: 925-938-7243 *Fax:* 925-933-9720
E-mail: explore@altamirapress.com
Web Site: www.altamirapress.com
Key Personnel
Publr: Mitch Allen *E-mail:* mallen@
altamirapress.com
Founded: 1995

Academic & professional materials, anthropology, museum & cultural studies, religion, archeology, history & humanities.
ISBN Prefix(es): 0-7591; 0-7619 (shared with Sage Publications); 0-930390; 0-910050; 0-942063; 0-7425 (shared with Rowman & Littlefield); 0-8039 (shared with Sage Publications)
Number of titles published annually: 75 Print; 1 CD-ROM
Total Titles: 375 Print; 3 CD-ROM
Distributed by National Book Network/University Press of America
Distributor for American Association for State & Local History
Foreign Rep(s): Oxford Publicity Partnership (Europe & UK)
Shipping Address: National Book Network/University Press of America, 15200 NBN Way, PO Box 191, Blue Ridge Summit, PA 17214 Toll Free Tel: 800-462-6420 Toll Free Fax: 800-538-4550 E-mail: custserv@rowman.com
Distribution Center: National Book Network/University Press of America, 15200 NBN Way, PO Box 191, Blue Ridge Summit, PA 17214 Toll Free Tel: 800-462-6420 Toll Free Fax: 800-338-4550 E-mail: custserv@rowman.com
Membership(s): AAP

§Althos Publishing
106 W Vance St, Fuquay-Varina, NC 27526
Tel: 919-557-2260 Toll Free Tel: 800-227-9681 Fax: 919-557-2261
E-mail: info@althos.com
Web Site: www.althosbooks.com; www.telecomdefinitions.com
Key Personnel
Pres: Lawrence Harte E-mail: lharte@althos.com
Founded: 2002
ISBN Prefix(es): 0-9650658; 0-87288; 0-87288; 0-917845
Number of titles published annually: 50 Print; 45 Online; 45 E-Book
Total Titles: 55 Print; 50 Online; 50 E-Book
Distributed by TMC/Internet Telephony; USTA
Distributor for John-Wiley; McGraw-Hill
Returns: 404 Wake Chappel Rd, Fuquay-Varina, NC 27526
Warehouse: 404 Wake Chappel Rd, Fuquay-Varina, NC 27526

Alyson Publications
Division of LPI Media
6922 Hollywood Blvd, Suite 1000, Los Angeles, CA 90028
Mailing Address: PO Box 4371, Los Angeles, CA 90078
Tel: 323-860-6065 Fax: 323-467-0152
E-mail: mail@alyson.com
Web Site: www.alyson.com
Key Personnel
Ed-in-Chief: Angela Brown Tel: 323-860-6032 E-mail: abrown@alyson.com
Publr: Greg Constante Tel: 323-860-6033 E-mail: gconstan@alyson.com
Founded: 1980
ISBN Prefix(es): 0-932870; 1-55583
Number of titles published annually: 55 Print
Total Titles: 197 Print
Imprints: Advocate Books; Alyson Books; Alyson Wonderland
Foreign Rep(s): Turnaround Publishers Service, London (Europe & UK)

§AMACOM Books
Division of American Management Association
1601 Broadway, New York, NY 10019-7406
SAN: 201-1670
Tel: 212-586-8100; 518-891-5510 (orders)
Toll Free Tel: 800-262-9699 (cust serv)
Fax: 212-903-8168; 518-891-2372 (orders)
Web Site: www.amanet.org

Key Personnel
Pres & Publr: Harold V Kennedy
Exec Ed: Adrienne Hickey
Sr Acqs Ed: Ellen Kadin
Acqs Ed: Jacquie Flynn
Trade Sales: Jenny Wesselmann Tel: 212-586-8100 ext 8448
Dir, Rts & Intl Sales: Therese Mausser
Spec Sales: Renita Hanfling
ISBN Contact: Lydia Lewis
Publicity Dir: Irene Majuk Tel: 212-903-8087
Founded: 1972
Trade books & professional books; nonfiction, management & business, self study courses in loose-leaf & audio formats. Publish practical solutions that are crucial to business communication. Publish books in science, real estate & self-help.
ISBN Prefix(es): 0-8144; 0-7612
Number of titles published annually: 80 Print
Total Titles: 700 Print; 54 Audio
Distributed by McGraw-Hill International
Foreign Rep(s): McGraw Hill International Distribution (International)
Warehouse: PO Box 169, Saranac Lake, NY 12983, Contact: William McIntyre Toll Free Tel: 800-250-5308 E-mail: wmintyre@amanet.org

Amadeus Press
512 Newark Pompton Tpke, Pompton Plains, NJ 07444
Tel: 973-835-6375 Fax: 973-835-6504
Web Site: www.amadeuspress.com
Key Personnel
Publr: John Cerullo
Founded: 1987
Full-service trade publisher that produces books, CDs & DVDs for a wide audience of discerning music lovers & professionals.
ISBN Prefix(es): 1-57467
Number of titles published annually: 15 Print
Total Titles: 120 Print
Foreign Rep(s): Amadeus Press (UK & Europe)

Frank Amato Publications Inc
PO Box 82112, Portland, OR 97282
Tel: 503-653-8108 Toll Free Tel: 800-541-9498 Fax: 503-653-2766
Web Site: www.amatobooks.com
Key Personnel
Publr & Ed: Frank W Amato
Founded: 1967
ISBN Prefix(es): 0-936608; 1-878175; 1-57188
Number of titles published annually: 20 Print; 1 CD-ROM
Total Titles: 325 Print; 1 CD-ROM
Distributed by Anglers Book Supply; Intersports; Partners

Ambassador Books Inc
91 Prescott St, Worcester, MA 01605
Tel: 508-756-2893 Toll Free Tel: 800-577-0909 Fax: 508-757-7055
Web Site: www.ambassadorbooks.com
Key Personnel
Pres: Gerard E Goggins E-mail: ggoggins@ambassadorbooks.com
Edit Dir: Jennifer Conlan E-mail: jconlan@ambassadorbooks.com
Dir, Busn Devt: Kate Conlan
Founded: 1996
Publish books with a Christian/spiritual theme.
ISBN Prefix(es): 0-9646439; 1-929039
Number of titles published annually: 7 Print
Total Titles: 35 Print
Membership(s): Publishers Marketing Association

Amber Lotus
Formerly Bluestar Communication Corp
Strawberry Creek Design Ctr, 1250 Addison St, Studio 214, Berkeley, CA 94702

Tel: 510-225-0149 Toll Free Tel: 800-625-8378 (orders only) Fax: 510-665-6083
E-mail: info@amberlotus.com
Web Site: www.amberlotus.com
Key Personnel
Pres & CEO: Lawson Day
Founded: 1993
New literature, new music, visionary art, divination tools & notecards.
ISBN Prefix(es): 1-885394
Number of titles published annually: 7 Print
Total Titles: 50 Print; 100 Audio
Imprints: Aquamarin; Oreade

Amber Quill Press LLC
PO Box 265, Indian Hills, CO 80454
E-mail: customer_service@amberquillpress.com
Web Site: amberquill.com
Key Personnel
Man Ed & Cust Serv Dir: J L Abbott
Tech Dir: Ingrid Arbogast
Mktg Dir & Man Ed: E J Gilmer E-mail: ej_gilmer@amberquill.com
Mktg Consultant: Josephine Piraneo
Man Ed & Fin Mgr: Karin Story
Edit Dir & Acqs Mgr: Trace Edward Zaber
Founded: 2002
An independent, royalty-paying publisher. Offer a varied list of fiction: young adult, romance (& all sub-genres), science fiction, mystery, thriller, suspense, horror, fantasy, vampire, historical & romantica; e-book or print-on-demand.
ISBN Prefix(es): 1-59279
Number of titles published annually: 72 Print; 120 Online; 135 E-Book
Total Titles: 146 Print; 212 Online; 212 E-Book
Imprints: Amber Heat; Amber Kisses
Membership(s): Publishers Marketing Association

Amboy Associates
620 Venture St, Suite A, Escondido, CA 92029
Toll Free Tel: 800-448-4023 Fax: 760-546-0404
Web Site: www.oshastuff.com
Key Personnel
Pres: Richard Walker E-mail: richard.walker@oshastuff.com
Founded: 1988
Safety & OSHA compliance info.
Number of titles published annually: 6 Print; 2 CD-ROM
Total Titles: 22 Print; 4 CD-ROM

America West Publishers
Subsidiary of Global Insights Inc
PO Box 2208, Carson City, NV 89702-2208
Tel: 775-885-0700 Toll Free Tel: 800-729-4131 Toll Free Fax: 877-726-2632
Key Personnel
Pres: George Green E-mail: geo@nohoax.com
Founded: 1986
Specialize in new science, UFO's, healing, metaphysics, spiritual, political & economic.
ISBN Prefix(es): 0-922356
Number of titles published annually: 10 Print
Total Titles: 35 Print; 1 Audio
Billing Address: Global Insights Inc, 675 Fairview Dr, Suite 246, Carson City, NV 89701
Orders to: Global Insights Inc, 675 Fairview Dr, Suite 246, Carson City, NV 89701
Returns: Global Insights Inc, 675 Fairview Dr, Suite 246, Carson City, NV 89701
Warehouse: 5872 Government Way, Bldg 1, No 10, Dalton Gardens, ID 83815 Toll Free Fax: 877-726-2632 E-mail: geo@nohoax.com

American Academy of Environmental Engineers
130 Holiday Ct, Suite 100, Annapolis, MD 21401
Tel: 410-266-3311 Fax: 410-266-7653
E-mail: academy@aaee.net
Web Site: www.aaee.net

Key Personnel
Pubns Mgr: David A Asselin
Founded: 1955
Journals & textbooks for the environmental engineering & science professions.
ISBN Prefix(es): 1-883767
Number of titles published annually: 5 Print
Total Titles: 37 Print
Distributor for The ABS Group; CRC Press; McGraw-Hill; Pearson Education; Prentice Hall; John Wiley & Sons Inc

§American Academy of Orthopaedic Surgeons
6300 N River Rd, Rosemont, IL 60018-4262
SAN: 228-2097
Tel: 847-823-7186 *Toll Free Tel:* 800-346-2267
  Fax: 847-823-8125 *Toll Free Fax:* 800-999-2939
E-mail: golembiewski@aaos.org
Web Site: www.aaos.org
Key Personnel
Dir, Dept of Pubns: Marilyn L Fox *E-mail:* fox@aaos.org
Fin Analyst: Sharon O'Brien *Tel:* 847-384-4160
  E-mail: sobrien@aaos.org
Founded: 1933
Scientific & technical books, including annual updates on orthopaedic procedures; home study programs & examinations; symposium volumes; monographs on scientific, clinical, practice management & socioeconomic topics in orthopaedics; clinical review journal.
ISBN Prefix(es): 0-89203
Number of titles published annually: 10 Print; 12 CD-ROM; 2 Online; 1 Audio
Total Titles: 90 Print; 38 CD-ROM; 5 Online; 5 Audio
Distributed by Jones & Bartlett Publishers
Foreign Rep(s): Eurospan (Europe, Middle East); Nankodo Co Inc (Japan)
Warehouse: Dearborn Distribution Center, 940 Enterprise St, Aurora, IL 60504 *Toll Free Fax:* 800-823-8025 *E-mail:* custserv@aaos.org
Web Site: aaos.org

American Academy of Pediatrics
141 NW Point Blvd, Elk Grove Village, IL 60007-1098
Tel: 847-434-4000 *Toll Free Tel:* 888-227-1770
  Fax: 847-228-1281
E-mail: pubs@aap.org
Web Site: www.aap.org
Key Personnel
Dir, Mktg & Pubns: Maureen De Rosa
Dir, Mktg & Sales Div: Jill Ferguson *Tel:* 847-434-7922 *E-mail:* jferguson@aap.org
Dir, Prod Devt Div: Mark Grimes *Tel:* 847-434-7822 *E-mail:* mgrimes@aap.org
Founded: 1930
Patient educational material, medical textbooks, professional textbook, patient education & practice management materials; pediatrics; family & emergency medicine.
ISBN Prefix(es): 0-910761; 0-87493; 0-915473; 0-87553; 0-553; 0-89707; 1-56055; 1-58110
Number of titles published annually: 40 Print; 5 CD-ROM; 1 Online
Total Titles: 200 Print; 10 CD-ROM

The American Alpine Club Press
Division of The American Alpine Club
710 Tenth St, Suite 100, Golden, CO 80401
Tel: 303-384-0110 *Fax:* 303-384-0111
E-mail: aacpress@americanalpineclub.org
Web Site: www.americanalpineclub.org
Key Personnel
Deputy Dir: Lloyd Athearn *Tel:* 303-384-0110 ext 13 *E-mail:* lathearn@americanalpineclub.org
Founded: 1902
Mountaineering: general, regional guides, safety, medical & scientific, annual journals & historical.

ISBN Prefix(es): 0-930410
Number of titles published annually: 3 Print
Total Titles: 54 Print
Distributed by Mountaineers Books
Foreign Rep(s): Mountaineers Books (World Rights)

§American Anthropological Association
Publications Dept, 2200 Wilson Blvd, Suite 600, Arlington, VA 22201
Tel: 703-528-1902 ext 3014 *Fax:* 703-528-3546
Web Site: www.aaanet.org
Key Personnel
Dir, Pubns: Susi Skomal
Prodn Ed: David Smith; Sarah Wassell
Man Ed: Stacy Lathrop
Founded: 1902
ISBN Prefix(es): 0-913167
Number of titles published annually: 100 Print
Total Titles: 27 Print
Membership(s): AAP

§American Association for Vocational Instructional Materials
220 Smithonia Rd, Winterville, GA 30683-9527
Tel: 706-742-5355 *Toll Free Tel:* 800-228-4689
  Fax: 706-742-7005
E-mail: sales@aavim.com
Web Site: www.aavim.com
Key Personnel
Dir: Karen S Seabaugh *E-mail:* ksseab@aavim.com
Founded: 1949
Consortium formed for development, publishing & distribution of instructional materials for vocational education.
ISBN Prefix(es): 0-89606
Number of titles published annually: 4 Print
Total Titles: 182 Print; 4 CD-ROM
Distributor for Southeastern Cooperative Wildlife Disease Study

§American Association of Blood Banks
8101 Glenbrook Rd, Bethesda, MD 20814-2749
Tel: 301-907-6977 *Toll Free Tel:* 866-222-2498 (sales) *Fax:* 301-907-6895
E-mail: aabb@aabb.org; sales@aabb.org (ordering)
Web Site: www.aabb.org
Key Personnel
Dir, Pubns: Laurel Munk *Tel:* 301-215-6595
  E-mail: laurie@aabb.org
Founded: 1947
Texts in blood banking standards, transfusion medicine & transplantation.
ISBN Prefix(es): 0-915355
Number of titles published annually: 24 Print; 14 Audio
Total Titles: 89 Print; 2 CD-ROM; 5 Online; 45 Audio
Distributed by Karger; Login Brothers

American Association of Cereal Chemists
3340 Pilot Knob Rd, St Paul, MN 55121-2097
Tel: 651-454-7250 *Toll Free Tel:* 800-328-7560
  Fax: 651-454-0766
E-mail: aacc@scisoc.org
Web Site: www.aaccnet.org *Telex:* 6502439657 (MCI/UW)
Key Personnel
Exec VP: Steven C Nelson
Mktg Dir: Greg Grahek *E-mail:* ggrahek@scisoc.org
Mktg Asst: Michaela DeLong *Tel:* 651-994-3840
  E-mail: mdelong@scisoc.org
Founded: 1920
Source for cereal science information.
ISBN Prefix(es): 1-891127; 0-9624407
Number of titles published annually: 3 Print; 1 CD-ROM
Total Titles: 75 Print; 1 CD-ROM; 1 Online; 1 E-Book

Foreign Office(s): AACC-Europe, Stanislas de Rijcklaan, BE-3001 Heverlee, Belgium, Contact: Hilde Keunen *Tel:* (016) 20 40 35 *Fax:* (016) 20 25 35 *E-mail:* aps@scisoceurope.org
See separate listing for:
Eagan Press

American Association of Colleges for Teacher Education (AACTE)
1307 New York Ave NW, Suite 300, Washington, DC 20005-4701
Tel: 202-293-2450 *Fax:* 202-457-8095
E-mail: aacte@aacte.org
Web Site: www.aacte.org
Key Personnel
CEO & Pres: David G Imig
Mgr & Ed, Pubns: Carol Hamilton
  E-mail: chamilton@aacte.org
Founded: 1948
Teacher education related works.
ISBN Prefix(es): 0-89333
Number of titles published annually: 3 Print
Total Titles: 70 Print

American Association of Collegiate Registrars & Admissions Officers
One Dupont Circle NW, Suite 520, Washington, DC 20036-1135
Tel: 202-293-9161 *Toll Free Tel:* 877-338-3733
  Fax: 202-872-8857
E-mail: info@aacrao.org
Web Site: www.aacrao.org
Key Personnel
Exec Dir: Jerry Sullivan *E-mail:* sullivanj@aacrao.org
Pubns Mgr: Amy Haavik *Tel:* 202-263-0292
  E-mail: haavika@aacrao.org
Founded: 1910
Periodicals, monograph series, higher education-general, international, technology & higher education.
ISBN Prefix(es): 0-929851; 0-910054
Number of titles published annually: 4 Print
Total Titles: 118 Print
Distribution Center: AACRAO Distribution Center, PO Box 231, Annapolis Junction, MD 20701 *Tel:* 301-490-7651 *Fax:* 301-206-9789

American Association of Community Colleges (AACC)
One Dupont Circle NW, Suite 410, Washington, DC 20036
Tel: 202-728-0200; 301-490-8116 (orders)
  Toll Free Tel: 800-250-6557 *Fax:* 202-223-9390 (edit); 301-604-0158 (orders)
E-mail: aaccpub@pmds.com (orders)
Web Site: www.aacc.nche.edu
Key Personnel
VP, Communs: Norma Kent *Tel:* 202-728-0200 ext 209 *E-mail:* nkent@aacc.nche.edu
Founded: 1920
Paperback & hardcover.
ISBN Prefix(es): 0-87117
Number of titles published annually: 10 Print
Total Titles: 100 Print; 5 Audio
Branch Office(s)
Community College Press, PO Box 311, Annapolis Junction, MD 20701
Distributor for ITC; Jossey-Bass Inc, Publishers; Oryx Press; Random House; RTS
Advertising Agency: Ascend Media, 11600 College Blvd, Overland Park, KS 66210 *Tel:* 913-344-1408 *Fax:* 913-469-0806
Membership(s): AAP

American Atheist Press
Affiliate of Charles E Stevens American Atheist Library & Archives Inc
PO Box 5733, Parsippany, NJ 07054-6733
Tel: 908-276-7300 *Fax:* 908-276-7402
E-mail: info@atheists.org
Web Site: www.atheists.org

Key Personnel
Pres: Ellen Johnson
Man Ed: Frank R Zindler *Tel:* 614-299-1036
  Fax: 614-299-3712 *E-mail:* editor@atheists.org
Founded: 1963
Specialize in atheism, religious criticism, atheist
  history, religious intolerance.
ISBN Prefix(es): 0-910309; 0-911826; 1-57884
Number of titles published annually: 5 Print
Total Titles: 40 Print
Imprints: Gustav Broukal Press
Editorial Office(s): American Atheist Press, 1352
  Hunter Ave, Columbus, OH 43201, Man Ed:
  Frank R Zindler *Tel:* 614-299-1036 *Fax:* 614-
  299-3712 *E-mail:* editor@atheists.org
Shipping Address: 225 Cristiani St, Cranford, NJ
  07016-3214

American Bankers Association
1120 Connecticut Ave NW, Washington, DC
  20036
Tel: 202-663-5087 *Toll Free Tel:* 800-BANKERS
  (226-5377) *Fax:* 202-663-5087 (cust serv)
Web Site: www.aba.com
Key Personnel
Pres & CEO: Donald G Ogilvie
Exec Dir, PDG: Doug Adamson
Sr Proj Mgr: George T Martin *Tel:* 202-663-5374
  E-mail: tmartin@aba.com
Founded: 1875
Enhances the role of banks as the nation's preem-
  inent providers of financial services, through
  educational & training programs, federal leg-
  islative & regulatory activities, legal action,
  research & communication; specialize in sales
  & marketing, customer service, small business,
  professional development skills, trust & invest-
  ments, commercial &/or consumer lending.
ISBN Prefix(es): 0-89982
Number of titles published annually: 20 Print
Total Titles: 150 Print
Distribution Center: Professional Book Distributors (PBD), 1650 Bluegrass Lakes Pkwy, Alpharetta, GA 30004, Contact: Julie Goulding
  Tel: 770-442-8633 *Fax:* 770-442-9742

American Bar Association
321 N Clark St, Suite LL-2, Chicago, IL 60610
Tel: 312-988-5000 *Toll Free Tel:* 800-285-2221
  (orders) *Fax:* 312-988-6030
E-mail: askaba@abanet.org
Web Site: www.abanet.org
Key Personnel
Dir, Contracts & Copyrights: Richard Vittenson
Founded: 1878
Books, magazines, journals, newsletters & AV
  materials.
ISBN Prefix(es): 1-57073
Number of titles published annually: 60 Print
Branch Office(s)
1800 "M" St NW, Washington, DC 20036

American Bible Society
1865 Broadway, New York, NY 10023-7505
SAN: 203-5189
Tel: 212-408-1200 *Toll Free Tel:* 800-322-4253
  (orders only) *Fax:* 212-408-1259
E-mail: info@americanbible.org
Web Site: www.americanbible.org
Key Personnel
Pres & CEO: Eugene B Habecker
Sr VP & Publr: John Cruz
Assoc VP, Opers & Dir, Prodn: Gary Ruth
Assoc VP, Prodn Mktg & Mgr, Licensing & Roy-
  alty Properties: Tom Durakis *Tel:* 201-208-2102
Founded: 1816
Publisher, producer & distributor of Bibles,
  books, audio, video & software products em-
  phasizing Christian, inspirational & family val-
  ues.
ISBN Prefix(es): 0-8267; 1-58516
Number of titles published annually: 15 Print

Total Titles: 35 Print
Distribution Center: Wayne Distribution Center,
  186 Parish Dr, Wayne, NJ 07470

American Biographical Institute
Division of Historical Preservations of America
  Inc
5126 Bur Oak Circle, Raleigh, NC 27612
Mailing Address: PO Box 31226, Raleigh, NC
  27622-1226
Tel: 919-781-8710 *Fax:* 919-781-8712
Key Personnel
CEO & VP: Arlene S Calhoun
  E-mail: ascalhoun@abiworldwide.com
Pres & CFO: Janet M Evans *E-mail:* jsmevans@
  abiworldwide.com
Man Ed: Cindy L White *E-mail:* clwhite@
  abiworldwide.com
Founded: 1967
Publish biographical reference books: regional,
  national & international.
ISBN Prefix(es): 0-934544
Number of titles published annually: 6 Print
Total Titles: 170 Print

American Book Publishing
325 E 2400 S, Salt Lake City, UT 84115
Mailing Address: PO Box 65624, Salt Lake City,
  UT 84165-0624
Tel: 801-486-8639
E-mail: info@american-book.com
Web Site: www.american-book.com
Key Personnel
Dir, Opers: C Lee Nunn *E-mail:* operations@
  american-book.com
Ordering Contact: Samantha Harris
  E-mail: orders@american-book.com
Founded: 1985
To support, document & disseminate through
  book publication, great works & teachings of
  talented authors, scholars & professionals.
ISBN Prefix(es): 1-58982
Number of titles published annually: 30 Print
Total Titles: 80 Print
Imprints: American Book Business Press; Amer-
  ican Book Classics; American University &
  Colleges Press; Bedside Books; Millennial
  Mind Publishing

American Catholic Press
16565 S State St, South Holland, IL 60473
SAN: 162-4989
Tel: 708-331-5845 *Fax:* 708-331-5484
E-mail: acp@acpress.org
Web Site: www.acpress.org
Key Personnel
Edit Dir: Michael Gilligan
Mgr: Joan Termini
Mgr, Info Servs: Pat Thompson
Founded: 1967
Christian liturgy, especially in the Roman
  Catholic Church including music resources for
  churches. No poetry or fiction.
ISBN Prefix(es): 0-915866
Number of titles published annually: 3 Print; 1
  Audio
Total Titles: 25 Print; 3 Audio

§The American Ceramic Society
735 Ceramic Place, Westerville, OH 43081-8720
Mailing Address: PO Box 6136, Westerville, OH
  43086-6136
Tel: 614-794-5890 *Fax:* 614-794-5892
E-mail: info@ceramics.org
Web Site: www.ceramics.org
Key Personnel
Exec Dir: Glen F Harvey
Dir, Tech Pubns: Mark Mecklenborg
Prod Mgr, Books: Bill Jones
Promos Proj Coord: Aimee F Zerla *Tel:* 614-794-
  5893 *E-mail:* azerla@ceramics.org
Founded: 1898

Dedicated to the advancement of ceramics, serving more than 8,000 members & subscribers.
  Members include ceramic engineers, scientists,
  researchers & others in the ceramics & materials industry. Provides the latest technical,
  scientific & educational information.
ISBN Prefix(es): 0-944904; 1-57498; 0-916094
Number of titles published annually: 25 Print
Total Titles: 150 Print; 1 CD-ROM

The American Chemical Society
1155 16 St NW, Washington, DC 20036
SAN: 201-2626
Tel: 202-872-4600 *Toll Free Tel:* 800-227-5558
  Fax: 202-872-6067
Web Site: www.acs.org; pubs.acs.org
Key Personnel
Pres, ACS Publns: Robert D Bovenschulte
Chief Info Officer: Marion Mullauer
VP, New Prods: John P Ochs
VP, Sales & Mktg: Dean J Smith
Exec Dir: Madeline Jacobs
Dir, Journals Publns: Mary E Scanlan
Dir, Mktg: Matthew J Price
Busn Opers: William Cook
Mktg Mgr: Crystal C Owens
Founded: 1876
Serials, proceedings, reprint collections, mono-
  graphs & other professional & reference
  books; specializes in food chemistry, environ-
  mental sciences & green chemistry, analyti-
  cal, inorganic, medicinal, organic & physical
  chemistries, biochemistry, polymer & materials
  science & nanotechnology.
ISBN Prefix(es): 0-8412
Number of titles published annually: 31 Print
Total Titles: 500 Print; 1 CD-ROM
Distributed by Oxford University Press
Distributor for Royal Society of Chemistry
Foreign Rep(s): Maruzen Co Ltd (Japan); Sonya
  Nickson (UK); Andrew Pitts (UK)
Membership(s): AAP

American College
270 S Bryn Mawr Ave, Bryn Mawr, PA 19010
SAN: 240-5822
Tel: 610-526-1000 *Fax:* 610-526-1310
Web Site: www.amercoll.edu
Key Personnel
Pres & CEO: Laurence Barton
Exec VP: Roger Vergin
Perms Ed: Patricia Cheers *Tel:* 610-526-1329
  E-mail: patc@amercoll.edu
Founded: 1927
An independent, accredited non-profit educational
  institution offering financial services texts &
  course guides online & life insurance for stu-
  dents in financial services programs at colleges
  & universities including American College
  programs: CLU, ChFC, CLF, LUTCF, RHU,
  REBC, CASL & CFP certification curricu-
  lum & MSFS degree for professionals in the
  financial services industry. Subject specialties:
  business, finance, insurance & securities.
ISBN Prefix(es): 0-943590; 1-57996
Number of titles published annually: 30 Print
Total Titles: 32 Print; 15 CD-ROM

§American College of Physician Executives
4890 W Kennedy Blvd, Suite 200, Tampa, FL
  33609
SAN: 688-7449
Tel: 813-287-2000 *Toll Free Tel:* 800-562-8088
  Fax: 813-287-8993
E-mail: acpe@acpe.org
Web Site: www.acpe.org
Key Personnel
Man Ed & Edit Dir: Bill Steiger
  E-mail: bsteiger@acpe.org
Founded: 1975
Journals.
ISBN Prefix(es): 0-9605218; 0-924674

Number of titles published annually: 6 Print; 1
CD-ROM
Total Titles: 50 Print; 6 CD-ROM; 1 Audio
Distributed by American Hospital Publishing Inc;
Jossey Bass; Health Administration Press
Distributor for American Hospital Publishing Inc;
Aspen Publishers; Jossey Bass; Boland Health-
care; Capitol Publications; Hatherleigh Co;
Health Administration Press
Distribution Center: PMDS, 1780 Crossroads
Dr, Odenton, MD 21113, Contact: Camille
Jones *Tel:* 301-604-3305 *Fax:* 301-543-9052
E-mail: cjones@pmds.com

American College of Surgeons
633 N Saint Clair St, Chicago, IL 60611-3211
Tel: 312-202-5000 *Toll Free Tel:* 800-621-4111
Fax: 312-202-5001
E-mail: postmaster@facs.org
Web Site: www.facs.org
Key Personnel
Mgr, Public Info Electronic Publg Div, Communs
Dept: Sally Garneski
Founded: 1913
Journal of the American College of Surgeons
(monthly); Bulletin of the American College
of Surgeons (monthly); Publications: CD-ROM,
reference books, subscription, manuals. Spe-
cialize in: surgery, trauma, cancer, professional
liability, General (Surgery Reference Textbook)
ACS Surgery: Principals & Practice.
ISBN Prefix(es): 0-9620370
Number of titles published annually: 5 Print
Total Titles: 11 Print; 6 CD-ROM
Distributed by Cine-Med, Inc; Scientific Ameri-
can Medicine

American Correctional Association
4380 Forbes Blvd, Lanham, MD 20706-4322
Tel: 301-918-1800 *Toll Free Tel:* 800-222-5646
Fax: 301-918-1886
Web Site: www.aca.org
Key Personnel
Dir, Pubns: Gabriella Daley *Tel:* 301-918-1801
Mgr, Pubns & Res: Alice Heiserman *Tel:* 301-
918-1894 *E-mail:* aliceh@aca.org
Founded: 1870
Corrections professionals.
ISBN Prefix(es): 1-56991
Number of titles published annually: 12 Print; 1
Audio
Total Titles: 1 Audio

American Council on Education
One Dupont Circle NW, Washington, DC 20036
Tel: 202-939-9380; 202-939-9300 *Fax:* 202-939-
9302
Web Site: www.acenet.edu
Key Personnel
Pres: David Ward
Dir, Pubns: Wendy Bressler
Founded: 1917
Books, directories & handbooks in higher educa-
tion, monographs.
ISBN Prefix(es): 0-8268; 0-89774
Number of titles published annually: 70 Print
Total Titles: 150 Print
Imprints: ACE/Oryx
Distributed by Greenwood

American Counseling Association
5999 Stevenson Ave, Alexandria, VA 22304-3300
Tel: 703-823-9800 *Toll Free Tel:* 800-422-2648
(ext 222 - book orders only) *Fax:* 703-461-
9260 *Toll Free Fax:* 800-473-2329
Web Site: www.counseling.org
Key Personnel
Dir, Pubns: Carolyn C Baker *E-mail:* cbaker@
counseling.org
Perms Ed & Copyright Ed: Cynthia Peay
E-mail: cpeay@counseling.org
Founded: 1952

More than 45,000 members from the school
counseling, mental health & human develop-
ment professions at all educational levels. Pub-
lishes 11 scholarly journals, a newspaper & ap-
proximately 8-10 new professional book titles a
year for members & non-members.
ISBN Prefix(es): 1-55620
Number of titles published annually: 10 Print; 1
CD-ROM
Total Titles: 120 Print; 2 CD-ROM
Imprints: ACA
Distributed by Book Clubs Inc (Behavioral Sciences); Counseling Outfitters; JIST Works Inc;
Mental Health Resources; Paperbacks for Educators; Self-Esteem Shop; Social Sciences
School Services
Distributor for American School Counseling As-
sociation; Association for Assessment in Coun-
seling & Education; Association for Counselor
Education & Supervision; Association for Spir-
itual, Ethical & Religious Values in Counsel-
ing; National Career Development Association
Distribution Center: ACA, PO Box 791019, Baltimore, MD 21279-1019 *Tel:* 703-823-9800 ext
222 *Toll Free Tel:* 800-422-2648 ext 222 *Toll
Free Fax:* 800-347-6647 ext 222

§American Diabetes Association
1701 N Beauregard St, Alexandria, VA 22311
Tel: 703-299-2046 *Toll Free Tel:* 800-232-6733
Fax: 908-806-2301
Web Site: www.diabetes.org *Telex:* 90-1132
Key Personnel
VP, Pubns: Len Boswell
Dir, Mktg: John Fedor
Dir, Rts & Special Mkts: Lee Romano Sequeira
E-mail: lromano@diabetes.org
Acqs: Sherrye Landrum; Christine Welch
Founded: 1945
Books, videos & other materials for patients &
health-care professionals.
ISBN Prefix(es): 0-945448
Number of titles published annually: 22 Print; 10
E-Book; 3 Audio
Total Titles: 62 Print; 5 CD-ROM; 4 Online; 10
E-Book; 3 Audio
Distributed by McGraw-Hill

American Dietetic Association
120 S Riverside Plaza, Suite 2000, Chicago, IL
60606
Tel: 312-899-0040 *Fax:* 312-899-4757
Web Site: www.eatright.org
Key Personnel
Publr: Diana Faulhaber *Tel:* 312-899-4830
E-mail: dfaulhaber@eatright.org
Developmental Ed: Laura Brown
Acqs Ed: Jason Muzinic
Founded: 1917
Information on food, nutrition & fitness for dieti-
cians & other allied health professionals.
ISBN Prefix(es): 0-88091
Number of titles published annually: 12 Print; 1
Online; 4 Audio
Total Titles: 80 Print; 1 Online; 4 Audio

§American Eagle Publications Inc
35610 Highway, Show Low, AZ 85901
Mailing Address: PO Box 1507, Show Low, AZ
85902-1507
Tel: 623-556-2925 *Toll Free Tel:* 866-764-2925
Fax: 623-556-2926
E-mail: custservice@ameaglepubs.com
Web Site: www.ameaglepubs.com
Key Personnel
Pres: Mark A Ludwig
Mktg Ed: Jenny Ludwig
Founded: 1988
Computer & early American literature; current
events nonfiction.
ISBN Prefix(es): 0-929408

Number of titles published annually: 6 Print; 1
CD-ROM
Total Titles: 30 Print; 3 CD-ROM
Distributor for Lexington & Concord Partners
Ltd, Panama

American Federation of Arts
41 E 65 St, New York, NY 10021
Tel: 212-988-7700 *Toll Free Tel:* 800-232-0270
Fax: 212-861-2487
E-mail: publicat@afaweb.org
Web Site: www.afaweb.org
Key Personnel
Dir, Pubn & Design: Michaelyn Mitchell
Tel: 212-988-7700 ext 28
Founded: 1909
Publisher of exhibition catalogues that accompany
art exhibitions organized by the AFA.
ISBN Prefix(es): 0-917418
Number of titles published annually: 4 Print
Total Titles: 47 Print
Distributed by Abbeville Press; Harry N Abrams
Inc; Distributed Art Publishers; Hudson Hills
Press Inc; Scala Publishers; University of
Washington Press

American Federation of Astrologers Inc
6535 S Rural Rd, Tempe, AZ 85283-3746
Tel: 480-838-1751 *Toll Free Tel:* 888-301-7630
Fax: 480-838-8293
E-mail: afa@msn.com
Web Site: www.astrologers.com
Key Personnel
Prodn Mgr: Kris Brandt-Riske
Founded: 1938
Astrology.
ISBN Prefix(es): 0-86690
Number of titles published annually: 15 Print
Total Titles: 421 Print

American Fisheries Society
5410 Grosvenor Lane, Suite 110, Bethesda, MD
20814-2199
Tel: 301-897-8616 *Fax:* 301-897-8096
E-mail: main@fisheries.org
Web Site: www.fisheries.org
Key Personnel
Mktg Coord: Hannelore Quigley
Dir, Admin & Fin: Betsy Fritz
Founded: 1870
Fisheries science, aquaculture & management ma-
terials, aquatic ecology, fisheries law, fisheries
history, conservation biology & publishing.
ISBN Prefix(es): 0-913235; 1-888569
Number of titles published annually: 75 Print
Total Titles: 75 Print
Branch Office(s)
PBD Bluegrass, 1650 Lakes Pkwy, Alpharetta,
GA 20004 *Tel:* 678-366-1411 *Fax:* 770-442-
9742 *E-mail:* afspubs@pbd.com
Foreign Rep(s): USACO (Japan)

**§American Foundation for the Blind (AFB
Press)**
11 Penn Plaza, Suite 300, New York, NY 10001
Tel: 212-502-7600 *Toll Free Tel:* 800-232-3044
(orders) *Fax:* 212-502-7777
E-mail: afbinfo@afb.net
Web Site: www.afb.org
Key Personnel
Ed-in-Chief, Books: Natalie Hilzen *Tel:* 212-502-
7653 *E-mail:* nhilzen@afb.net
Sales & Mktg Mgr: Sharon Baker-Harris
Tel: 212-502-7652 *E-mail:* sharonb@afb.net
Founded: 1921
Text & professional books.
ISBN Prefix(es): 0-89128
Number of titles published annually: 10 Print; 2
Online
Total Titles: 175 Print; 2 Online; 10 Audio
Branch Office(s)
AFB West, 111 Pine St, Suite 725, San Francisco,

CA 94111, Contact: Gil Johnson *Tel:* 415-392-4845 *Fax:* 415-392-0383 *E-mail:* gil@afb.net
Governmental Relations - Washington DC, 820 First St NE, Suite 400, Washington, DC 20002, Contact: Paul Schroeder *Tel:* 202-408-0200 *Fax:* 202-289-7880 *E-mail:* pws@afb.net
AFB Southeast, 100 Peachtree St, Suite 620, Atlanta, GA 30303, Contact: Frances Mary D'Andrea *Tel:* 404-525-2303 *Fax:* 404-659-6957 *E-mail:* fmd@afb.net
AFB Midwest, 401 N Michigan Ave, Suite 308, Chicago, IL 31005, Contact: Jay Stiteley *Tel:* 312-396-4420 *Fax:* 312-527-4660 *E-mail:* stiteley@afb.net
AFB Southwest, 260 Treadway Plaza, Exchange Park, Dallas, TX 75235, Contact: Judy Scott *Tel:* 214-352-7222 *Fax:* 214-352-3214 *E-mail:* jscott@afb.net
Distributed by RNIB National Education Services
Warehouse: Associations Book Distributors International Inc, Buncher Commerce Park, Avenue A, Bldg 16, Leetsdale, PA 15056-1304 *Tel:* 412-741-1398 *Toll Free Tel:* 800-232-3044 *Fax:* 412-741-0609 *E-mail:* afborder@abdintl.com
Membership(s): AAP

§American Geological Institute (AGI)
4220 King St, Alexandria, VA 22302-1507
Tel: 703-379-2480 *Fax:* 703-379-7563
E-mail: pubs@agiweb.org
Web Site: www.agiweb.org
Key Personnel
Exec Dir: Marcus Milling *Tel:* 703-379-2480 ext 202 *E-mail:* mmilling@agiweb.org
Cont: Patrick C Burks *Tel:* 703-379-2480 ext 209 *E-mail:* pburks@agiweb.org
Info Systems Dir: Sharon Tahirkheli *Tel:* 703-379-2480 ext 231 *E-mail:* snt@agiweb.org
Dir, Educ, Outreach & Devt: Ann E Benbow
Environmental Affs Dir: Travis L Hudson *Tel:* 360-582-1844 *Fax:* 360-582-1845 *E-mail:* ageology@olypen.com
Technol & Communs Dir: Christopher Keane *Tel:* 703-379-2480 ext 219 *E-mail:* cmk@agiweb.org
Founded: 1948
Geoscience reference books.
ISBN Prefix(es): 0-922152; 0-913312
Number of titles published annually: 3 Print
Total Titles: 53 Print; 6 CD-ROM; 2 Online; 2 E-Book
Online services available through Dialog, EBSCOhost, OCLC, Ovid, Questel-Orbit, STN.
Distributed by W H Freeman; It's About Time Inc; Prentice Hall
Orders to: AGI Book Center *Web Site:* www.agiweb.org/pubs

American Geophysical Union (AGU)
2000 Florida Ave NW, Washington, DC 20009
SAN: 202-4489
Tel: 202-462-6900 *Toll Free Tel:* 800-966-2481 (North America) *Fax:* 202-328-0566
E-mail: service@agu.org
Web Site: www.agu.org
Key Personnel
Exec Dir: A F Spilhaus, Jr
Mgr, Memb & Pubns Mktg: Barry Pilson
Book Publr: Steve Cole
Founded: 1919
International scientific society with more than 40,000 members in over 115 countries. For over 80 years, AGU researchers, teachers & science administrators have dedicated themselves to advancing the understanding of earth & its environment in space. AGU now stands as a leader in the increasingly interdisciplinary global endeavor that encompasses the geophysical sciences.
ISBN Prefix(es): 0-87590
Number of titles published annually: 20 Print

Foreign Office(s): Max-Planck, 37191 Katlenburg, Lindau, Germany *Tel:* (0555) 6-4706 *Fax:* (0555) 6-1440 *E-mail:* agu@copernicus.org
Membership(s): AAP

American Health Publishing Co
Affiliate of Learn®-The LifeStyle Co
Texas Star Pkwy, Suite 120, Euless, TX 76040
Mailing Address: PO Box 610430, Dept 80, Dallas, TX 75261-0430
Tel: 817-545-4500 *Toll Free Tel:* 800-LEARN41 *Fax:* 817-545-2211
E-mail: contact@thelifestylecompany.com
Web Site: www.thelifestylecompany.com
Key Personnel
Pres: David L Hager *E-mail:* david@thelifestylecompany.com
Founded: 1989
Specialize in journals, self-help books, health professional training & training guides, lifestyle-change programs.
ISBN Prefix(es): 1-878513
Number of titles published annually: 12 Print
Divisions: The Learn Education Center; The Learn Institute, The Lifestyle Company

§American Historical Association
400 "A" St SE, Washington, DC 20003
Tel: 202-544-2422 *Fax:* 202-544-8307
E-mail: aha@historians.org
Web Site: www.historians.org
Key Personnel
Exec Dir: Arnita Jones
Cont: Randy Norell
Dir, Pubns & Prodn Pubns Mgr: Robert B Townsend *Tel:* 202-544-2422 ext 118 *E-mail:* rtownsend@historians.org
Founded: 1884
The umbrella organization for the history profession.
ISBN Prefix(es): 0-87229
Number of titles published annually: 10 Print; 3 Online
Total Titles: 68 Print; 11 Online

American Historical Press
10755 Sherman Way, Suite 2, Sun Valley, CA 91352
Tel: 818-503-0133 *Toll Free Tel:* 800-550-5750 *Fax:* 818-503-9081
E-mail: ahp@amhistpress.com
Web Site: www.amhistpress.com
Key Personnel
Pres: Carolyn Martin
Founded: 1994
Regional & special histories.
ISBN Prefix(es): 0-89781; 1-884166; 0-9654754; 1-892724
Number of titles published annually: 10 Print
Total Titles: 50 Print
Membership(s): Publishers Association of Los Angeles; Publishers Marketing Association; Small Publishers Association of North America

American Indian Studies Center Publications at UCLA
Division of University of California, Los Angeles
3220 Campbell Hall, Los Angeles, CA 90095-1548
Mailing Address: American Indian Studies Ctr, Box 951548, Los Angeles, CA 90095-1548
Tel: 310-825-7315; 310-206-7508 *Fax:* 310-206-7060
E-mail: aiscpubs@ucla.edu; aisc@ucla.edu
Web Site: www.sscnet.ucla.edu
Key Personnel
Dir: Hanay Geiogamah
Pubns Mgr: Pamela Grieman
Founded: 1972
Publish books & quarterly journal on American Indian issues.

ISBN Prefix(es): 0-935626
Total Titles: 30 Print
Distributed by Blackwell
Distributor for Gale Research

American Industrial Hygiene Association
2700 Prosperity Ave, Suite 250, Fairfax, VA 22031-4319
Tel: 703-849-8888 *Fax:* 703-207-3561
E-mail: infonet@aiha.org
Web Site: www.aiha.org
Key Personnel
Sr Mgr: Connie Paradise
Mgr, Prod Devt: Barbara Taylor
Mgr, Design: Jim Myers
Cust Rep: Wanda Barbour
Asst Mgr, Mktg & Prod Devt: Sharon Hammond
Founded: 1939
Industrial marketplace.
ISBN Prefix(es): 1-931504
Number of titles published annually: 15 Print; 1 CD-ROM; 1 Online
Total Titles: 100 Print; 3 CD-ROM

American Institute for CPCU & Insurance Institute of America
720 Providence Rd, Malvern, PA 19355-0716
Mailing Address: PO Box 3016, Malvern, PA 19355-0716
Tel: 610-644-2100 *Toll Free Tel:* 800-644-2101 *Fax:* 610-640-9576; 610-644-7629
E-mail: cserv@cpcuiia.org
Web Site: www.aicpcu.org
Key Personnel
Pres & CEO: Terrie E Troxel
Sr VP, Pubns: Elizabeth A Sprinkel
Lib Dir: Kim R Holston *E-mail:* holston@cpcuiia.org
Mktg & PR Asst: Kathy Myers *Tel:* 610-644-2100 ext 7851 *E-mail:* myers@cpcuiia.org
Founded: 1942
Property & casualty insurance texts & course guides for students in (CPCU) Chartered Property Casualty Underwriters program & the (IIA) Insurance Institute of America programs; Risk Management.
ISBN Prefix(es): 0-89463; 0-89462
Number of titles published annually: 11 Print
Total Titles: 90 Print; 1 CD-ROM
Distribution Center: 420 Eagleview Blvd, Exton, PA 19341-1115
See separate listing for:
Insurance Institute of America Inc

American Institute of Aeronautics & Astronautics
1801 Alexander Bell Dr, Suite 500, Reston, VA 20191
Tel: 703-264-7500 *Toll Free Tel:* 800-639-2422 *Fax:* 703-264-7551
E-mail: custserv@aiaa.org
Web Site: www.aiaa.org
Key Personnel
Exec Dir: Cort Durocher
Journals: Norma Brennan
Edit Prodn Supv, Contact & Gen Cust Serv: Craig Byl
Mgr, Mkt Devt: Janice Saylor
Ed-in-Chief: Elaine Camhi
ISBN Contact: Jennifer Stover
Cust Serv Mgr: Aida Davis
Bk Acqs: Rodger Williams
Electronic Busn Devt: Doug Greevy
Founded: 1963
Professional technical books; archival journals & technical meeting papers in the science & technology of aerospace engineering & systems, print CD-ROMs & online delivery.
ISBN Prefix(es): 0-915928; 0-930403; 1-56347
Number of titles published annually: 50 Print
Total Titles: 600 Print

Foreign Rep(s): D A Direct (Australia); Eurospan (UK)
Distribution Center: Tasco, 9 Jay Gould Ct, Waldorf, MD 20604 *Tel:* 301-645-3651 *Toll Free Tel:* 800-682-2422 *Fax:* 301-843-0159

§American Institute of Certified Public Accountants
Harborside Financial Ctr, 201 Plaza Three, Jersey City, NJ 07311-3881
SAN: 202-4578
Tel: 201-938-3000 *Toll Free Tel:* 888-777-7077 *Fax:* 201-938-3329
Web Site: www.aicpa.org
Key Personnel
VP, Prod Devt: Robert Bouchard
   E-mail: rbouchard@aicpa.org
Mgr, Prod Servs: Peter Tuohy
Publr, Magazines & Newsletters: Colleen Katz
Lib Sales Dir: Edward Novack
Sr Mgr, Specialized Pubns & Subs Rts: Marie Bareille *Tel:* 201-938-3299 *Fax:* 201-938-3780
   E-mail: mbareille@aicpa.org
Publr, Prof Pubns & Tech Prods: Linda P Cohen
Founded: 1959
Professional seminars; accounting, tax, advisory services, management, specialized knowledge & applications.
ISBN Prefix(es): 0-87051
Number of titles published annually: 65 Print
Total Titles: 4 CD-ROM; 4 Online
Distributed by Practitioners Publishing Co

§American Institute of Chemical Engineers (AICHE)
3 Park Ave, New York, NY 10016-5991
Tel: 212-591-7338 *Toll Free Tel:* 800-242-4363 *Fax:* 212-591-8888
E-mail: xpress@aiche.org
Web Site: www.aiche.org
Key Personnel
Pres: Bill Byers
Exec Dir: John A Sofranko
Sr Dir, Publr & Info Tech Serv Mgr: Stephen R Smith *Tel:* 212-591-7335 *E-mail:* steps@aiche.org
Mktg Mgr: Tim McCreight *Tel:* 212-591-7224
Ed, Chemical Engg Progress: Kristina Chin
Ed, AIChE Jl: Stanley Sandler
Ed, Biotechnology Progress: Jerome S Shultz
Ed, Environmental Progress: Gary Bennett
Ed, Process Safety Progress: Ted A Ventrone
Founded: 1908
Chemical engineering books & journals, technical manuals, symposia proceedings, directories, software, CD-ROM.
ISBN Prefix(es): 0-8169
Number of titles published annually: 30 Print; 4 CD-ROM
Total Titles: 300 Print; 4 CD-ROM
Distributed by Dechema (selected titles)
Distributor for ASM International (selected titles); Dechema (selected titles); Engineering Foundation; IchemE (selected titles)
Foreign Rep(s): Ric Bessford (UK, Europe); Patrick Connolly (Belgium, France, Switzerland)
Distribution Center: Institution of Chemical Engineers, Davis Bldg, 165-189 Railway Terr, Rugby CV21 3HQ, United Kingdom

American Institute of Physics
2 Huntington Quadrangle, Suite 1NO1, Melville, NY 11747-4502
Tel: 516-576-2477 *Fax:* 516-576-2474
E-mail: proceedings-mgr@aip.org
Web Site: www.aip.org
Key Personnel
Man Ed: Sabine Kessler
Prodn Ed: Ellen Carrigan
Founded: 1931

Publisher of conference proceedings, professional journals & magazines.
ISBN Prefix(es): 0-88318; 1-56396; 0-7354
Number of titles published annually: 50 Print; 8 CD-ROM; 50 Online
Total Titles: 700 Print; 200 Online
Distributed by Springer-Verlag
Membership(s): AAP

American Institute of Ultrasound in Medicine
14750 Sweitzer Lane, Suite 100, Laurel, MD 20707-5906
Tel: 301-498-4100 *Toll Free Tel:* 800-638-5352 *Fax:* 301-498-4450
E-mail: publications@aium.org
Web Site: www.aium.org
Key Personnel
Communs Asst: Carlos Garcia
Fulfillment Coord: Lu Ann Coelho
Founded: 1953
Ultrasound methods, standards & guidelines.
ISBN Prefix(es): 1-930047
Number of titles published annually: 3 Print
Total Titles: 55 Print

§American Judicature Society
2700 University Ave, Des Moines, IA 50311
Tel: 515-271-2281 *Fax:* 515-279-3090
Web Site: www.ajs.org
Key Personnel
Pubns Dir: David Richert *Tel:* 773-973-0145
   E-mail: drichert@ajs.org
Founded: 1913
Research & educational material.
ISBN Prefix(es): 0-938870; 1-928919
Number of titles published annually: 5 Print
Total Titles: 20 Print; 2 CD-ROM; 1 Audio
Online services available through Westlaw.

§American Law Institute
4025 Chestnut St, Philadelphia, PA 19104-3099
SAN: 204-756X
Tel: 215-243-1600 *Toll Free Tel:* 800-253-6397 *Fax:* 215-243-1664; 215-243-1683
Web Site: www.ali.org
Key Personnel
Pres: Michael Traynor
Dir: Lance Liebman
Treas: Bennett C Boskey
Adv & Publicity: Kathleen H Lawner
Lib Dir: Harry Kyriakodis *Tel:* 215-243-1654
Founded: 1923
Professional & scholarly legal books & treatises.
ISBN Prefix(es): 0-8318
Number of titles published annually: 10 Print
Total Titles: 13 CD-ROM; 13 Online
Online services available through Lexis, Westlaw.

American Library Association (ALA)
50 E Huron St, Chicago, IL 60611
Tel: 312-944-6780 *Toll Free Tel:* 800-545-2433 *Fax:* 312-944-8741
E-mail: editionsmarketing@ala.org
Web Site: www.ala.org
Key Personnel
Mktg Mgr: Catherine English
Founded: 1876
Publisher of titles for librarians & educators; library & information science, professional books.
ISBN Prefix(es): 0-8389
Number of titles published annually: 36 Print; 1 CD-ROM
Total Titles: 375 Print; 2 CD-ROM
Foreign Rep(s): Eurospan (UK, Europe, Israel)
Foreign Rights: Canadian Library Association (Canada); United Publishers Services (Japan)
Orders to: ALA, PO Box 932501, Atlanta, GA 31193-2501 *Toll Free Tel:* 866-746-7252 *Fax:* 770-280-4155 *E-mail:* orders@pbd.com
Web Site: www.alastore.ala.org

Returns: ALA Distribution Center, 3280 Summit Ridge Pkwy, Duluth, GA 30096
Distribution Center: ALA Distribution Center, 3280 Summit Ridge Pkwy, Duluth, GA 30096
See separate listing for:
Association of College & Research Libraries

American Library Publishing Co
PO Box 4272, Sedona, AZ 86340-4272
SAN: 201-9868
Tel: 928-282-4922
E-mail: grace@sedonaarizona.com
Key Personnel
Ed & Publr: Marietta S Chicorel
Founded: 1979
Reference books for the library profession & the book trade.
ISBN Prefix(es): 0-934598
Number of titles published annually: 3 Print
Total Titles: 60 Print
Warehouse: Robert Luce Inc, 2490 Black Rock Tpke, No 342, Fairfax, CT 06430, Contact: Harold Levine

American Map Corp
Subsidiary of Langenscheidt Publishers Inc
46-35 54 Rd, Maspeth, NY 11378
SAN: 202-4624
Tel: 718-784-0055 *Toll Free Tel:* 800-432-MAPS *Fax:* 718-784-0640 (admin); 718-784-1216 (sales & orders) *Telex:* 96-8126
Cable: AMERMAP MSPH
Key Personnel
Pres: Stuart Dolgins *Fax:* 718-784-3294
   E-mail: sdolgins@americanmap.com
Chmn: Andreas Langenscheidt
Dir, Cartography: Vera Benson *E-mail:* vbenson@americanmap.com
Sales Mgr & Intl Rts Contact: Richard Strug
   E-mail: rstrug@americanmap.com
Founded: 1923
Maps & atlases; charts.
ISBN Prefix(es): 0-8416
Total Titles: 1 CD-ROM
Imprints: Cleartype American Map Corp; Colorprint American Map Corp
Subsidiaries: ADC the Map People; Arrow Maps Inc; Creative Sales Corp; Hagstrom Map Co Inc; Hammond World Atlas Corp; Trakker Maps Inc
Distributed by Arrow Maps Inc; Creative Sales Corp
Distributor for DeLorme Atlas; Langenscheidt Publishers Inc; RV Guides; Stubs Magazine
Advertising Agency: ATL/SD, 46-35 54 Rd, Maspeth, NY 11378, Contact: Sara Ascalon *Tel:* 718-784-0555 *Fax:* 718-784-0640 *E-mail:* sascalon@americanmap.com
See separate listing for:
Creative Sales Corp
Hagstrom Map Co Inc

§American Marketing Association
311 S Wacker Dr, Suite 5800, Chicago, IL 60606-2266
Tel: 312-542-9000 *Toll Free Tel:* 800-262-1150 *Fax:* 312-542-9001
E-mail: info@ama.org
Web Site: www.marketingpower.com
Key Personnel
CEO & COO: Dennis Dunlap
Mgr, Electronic Commun: Dimitri Sklyar
Mgr, Membership Mktg: Jennifer Kemper *Tel:* 312-542-9089
Founded: 1937
Professional business books.
ISBN Prefix(es): 0-87757
Number of titles published annually: 9 Print
Total Titles: 75 Print
Distributed by NTC Business Books
Distributor for American Demographics; CRC Press; The Free Press; Irwin Professional Pub-

lications; Jossey-Bass; McGraw-Hill; New Strategist; Kogan Page; Paramount Books; RACOM; Thomson Learning; John Wiley & Sons

§American Mathematical Society
201 Charles St, Providence, RI 02904-2294
SAN: 201-1654
Tel: 401-455-4000 *Toll Free Tel:* 800-321-4267
  Fax: 401-331-3842; 401-455-4046 (cust serv)
E-mail: ams@ams.org
Web Site: www.ams.org
Key Personnel
Exec Dir: John H Ewing
Sales Admin: Lori Sprague
Promos: Ana Jaeger
Prodn Coord: Michelle M Ogilvie
Cust Rel: Janice Clark
Asst, Mktg & Sales: Alyssa D Marinelli *Tel:* 401-455-4117 *E-mail:* axm@ams.org
Founded: 1888
Mathematical books & journals.
ISBN Prefix(es): 0-8218
Number of titles published annually: 100 Print
Total Titles: 2,800 Print; 2 CD-ROM; 28 Online
Imprints: Chelsea Publishing Co Inc
Distributor for Annales de la faculte des sciences de Toulouse mathematiques; Bar-Ilan University; Brown University; European Mathematical Society; Hindustan Book Agency; Independent University of Moscow; International Press; Mathematica Josephina; Mathematical Society of Japan; Narosa Publishing House; Ramanujan Mathematical Society; Science Press New York & Science Press Beijing; Societe Mathematique de France; Tata Institute of Fundamental Research; Theta Foundation of Bucharest; University Press; Vieweg Verlag Publications
Foreign Rep(s): DA Information Services (Australia, New Zealand, Papua New Guinea); Hindustan Book Agency (India); India Book House Ltd (India); Maruzen Co Ltd; Narosa Book Distributors (India); Neutrino Inc (Japan); Oxford University Press (Africa, Europe, Middle East)

American Medical Association
515 N State St, Chicago, IL 60610
Tel: 312-464-5000 *Toll Free Tel:* 800-621-8335
  (cust serv) *Fax:* 312-464-4184
Web Site: www.ama-assn.org
Key Personnel
VP, Busn Prods: Anthony J Frankos *Tel:* 312-464-5000 ext 5488
Publr: Mike Desposito
Dir, Edit: Mary Lou White
Circ Mgr, Journals: Vanessa Hayden
Admin Mgr: Judy Connelly-Clark
Founded: 1847
Medical profession.
ISBN Prefix(es): 1-57947
Number of titles published annually: 30 Print
Total Titles: 85 Print
Advertising Agency: GSP Marketing Services Inc
Warehouse: Catalog Resources Inc, 100 Enterprise Dr, Dover, DE 19901
Membership(s): AAP

American Numismatic Society
26 Fulton St, New York, NY 10038
Tel: 212-571-4470 *Fax:* 212-571-4479
E-mail: info@amnumsoc.org; info@numismatics.org
Web Site: www.amnumsoc.org; www.numismatics.org
Key Personnel
Exec Dir: Ute Wartenberg Kagan
Museum Administrator: Joanne Issac
Founded: 1858
Scholarly materials.
ISBN Prefix(es): 0-89722
Number of titles published annually: 5 Print

Total Titles: 81 Print
Distributed by David Brown Books

American Occupational Therapy Association Inc
4720 Montgomery Lane, Bethesda, MD 20824
Mailing Address: PO Box 31220, Bethesda, MD 20824-1220
Tel: 301-652-2682 *Fax:* 301-652-7711
Web Site: www.aota.org
Key Personnel
Dir, Commns: Audrey Rothstein
Dir, Corp Rel: Jennifer J Jones
Founded: 1918
Single titles, newsletters, journals & magazines.
ISBN Prefix(es): 0-910317; 1-56900
Number of titles published annually: 9 Print
Total Titles: 95 Print

American Oil Chemists' Society, see AOCS Press

American Philosophical Society
104 S Fifth St, Philadelphia, PA 19106
SAN: 206-9016
Tel: 215-440-3425 *Fax:* 215-440-3450
Web Site: www.amphilsoc.org
Key Personnel
Pres: Frank Rhodes
Exec Officers: Mary M Dunn; Richard S Dunn
Ed: Mary McDonald *E-mail:* mmcdonald@amphilsoc.org
Founded: 1743
Private organization for promotion of useful knowledge in humanities & sciences.
ISBN Prefix(es): 0-87169
Number of titles published annually: 15 Print
Total Titles: 150 Print
Imprints: Memoirs; Proceedings; Transactions
Billing Address: PO Box 481, Canton, MA 02021-0481
Orders to: PO Box 481, Canton, MA 02021-0481
Warehouse: Capital City Press, Williamstown Commercial Center, Lot 4, Williamstown, VT 05679

§American Phytopathological Society
3340 Pilot Knob Rd, St Paul, MN 55121-2097
Tel: 651-454-7250 *Toll Free Tel:* 800-328-7560
  Fax: 651-454-0766
E-mail: aps@scisoc.org
Web Site: www.apsnet.org
Key Personnel
Exec VP: Steven Nelson
Mktg Dir: Greg Grahek
Mktg Asst: Michaela DeLong *Tel:* 651-994-3840
  E-mail: mdelong@scisoc.org
Founded: 1908
Scientific materials.
ISBN Prefix(es): 0-89054
Number of titles published annually: 6 Print; 2 CD-ROM; 4 Online
Total Titles: 200 Print; 15 CD-ROM; 2 Online
Foreign Office(s): Stanislas de Rijcklaan, BE-3001 Heverlee, Belgium, Hilde Keunen *Tel:* (016) 20 40 35 *Fax:* (016) 20 25 35 *E-mail:* aps@scisoceurope.org
See separate listing for:
APS Press

American Press
28 State St, Suite 1100, Boston, MA 02109
SAN: 210-7007
Tel: 617-247-0022 *Fax:* 617-247-0022
E-mail: ampress@flash.net
Web Site: www.americanpressboston.com
Key Personnel
Publr: R K Fox
Ed: Marci Taylor
Founded: 1911

College textbooks, study guides, lab manuals & handbooks.
ISBN Prefix(es): 0-89641
Number of titles published annually: 20 Print
Total Titles: 300 Print

§American Printing House for the Blind Inc
1839 Frankfort Ave, Louisville, KY 40206
SAN: 203-5235
Mailing Address: PO Box 6085, Louisville, KY 40206-0085
Tel: 502-895-2405 *Toll Free Tel:* 800-223-1839
  (cust serv) *Fax:* 502-899-2274
E-mail: info@aph.org
Web Site: www.aph.org
Key Personnel
Pres: Tuck Tinsley, III
VP, Pub Aff: Gary Mudd
Dir: Scott Blome
Founded: 1858
Literature & aids for people who are visually impaired: braille text books, magazines & music, large-type textbooks, talking books & magazines, educational & miscellaneous aids, talking PC hardware & software. Publisher of braille & reprints in braille.
Number of titles published annually: 4,500 Print
Total Titles: 6,300 Print

American Products Publishing Co
Division of American Products Corp
10950 SW Fifth St, Suite 155, Beaverton, OR 97005-4782
Tel: 503-672-7502 *Toll Free Tel:* 800-668-8181
  Fax: 503-672-7104
E-mail: info@american-products.com
Web Site: www.american-products.com
Key Personnel
Pres: Robert Shangle
VP: Barbara Shangle
Sales Mgr: David Mulder
Publisher of scenic books & wall calendars for the individual US states.
ISBN Prefix(es): 1-58583; 1-884958; 1-55988
Number of titles published annually: 16 Print; 72 Online
Total Titles: 72 Print; 72 Online
Distribution Center: Book Wholesalers
Membership(s): ABA

§American Psychiatric Publishing Inc
Subsidiary of American Psychiatric Association
1000 Wilson Blvd, Suite 1825, Arlington, VA 22209
SAN: 293-2288
Tel: 703-907-7322 *Toll Free Tel:* 800-368-5777
  Fax: 703-907-1091
E-mail: appi@psych.org
Web Site: www.appi.org
Key Personnel
CEO: Ron McMillen
Edit Dir: John McDuffie
Mktg Dir & Intl Rts Contact: Robert Pursell
Books Man Ed: Greg Kuny
Journals Man Ed: Sandra Patterson
Book Perms: Julia Bozzolo
Oper Mgr: Roger Domras
Acqs Coord: Robin Allan
Busn Mgr: Kathy Stein
Fulfillment Coord: Linda Phillips
Founded: 1981
Professional, reference & general trade books, college textbooks; behavioral & social sciences, psychiatry, medicine.
ISBN Prefix(es): 0-88048; 0-89042; 0-87318; 1-58562
Number of titles published annually: 40 Print
Total Titles: 715 Print; 3 CD-ROM; 3 Online; 1 Audio
Imprints: Group for the Advancement of Psychology; Health Press Intl

Distributor for American Psychiatric Association; Group for the Advancement of Psychiatry
Foreign Rep(s): Blackwell Scientific (Australia, New Zealand); Book Promotion & Service (East Asia); Eurospan (UK, Europe, Middle East); Igaku-Shoin (Japan); Interlivros Editores Ltd (Brazil); Login Brothers (Canada); Oxford University Press (Southern Africa)
Foreign Rights: American Psychiatric Press Inc
Warehouse: PMDS, Arundel Crossing Business Park, 1780 Crossroads Dr, Odenton, MD 21113
Membership(s): AAP; American Association of University Presses

American Psychological Association
750 First St NE, Washington, DC 20002-4242
Tel: 202-336-5500 *Toll Free Tel:* 800-374-2721
  Fax: 202-336-5620
E-mail: order@apa.org
Web Site: www.apa.org/books
Key Personnel
Exec Dir, Pubns & Commun: Gary R VandenBos
Dir, APA Books & Intl Rts: Julia Frank-McNeil
Mgr, Electronic Pubns: Olin Nettles
Mgr, Tech Ed & Prod: Jennifer Macomber
Asst Dir: Mary Lynn Skutley
Founded: 1892
Publish scholarly & professional works including books, journals & related materials; the PsycINFO database & products derived from that database; the *APA Monitor*, a monthly magazine & a variety of other products including brochures & reports.
ISBN Prefix(es): 0-912704; 1-55798
Number of titles published annually: 65 Print
Total Titles: 517 Print
Warehouse: APA Order Dept, PO Box 92984, Washington, DC 20090-2984

American Public Works Association
2345 Grand Blvd, Suite 500, Kansas City, MO 64108-2641
Tel: 816-472-6100 *Fax:* 816-472-1610
E-mail: apwa@apwa.net
Web Site: www.apwa.net
Key Personnel
Man Ed: Kevin Clark *E-mail:* kclark@apwa.net
Founded: 1894
Public work, related publications, Public works magazine, *APWA Reporter.*
ISBN Prefix(es): 0-917084
Number of titles published annually: 11 Print
Total Titles: 85 Print

American Quilter's Society
Subsidiary of Schroeder Publishing Co Inc
5801 Kentucky Dam Rd, Paducah, KY 42002
Mailing Address: PO Box 3290, Paducah, KY 42002-3290
Tel: 270-898-7903 *Toll Free Tel:* 800-626-5420 (orders) *Fax:* 270-898-8890
E-mail: info@aqsquilt.com
Web Site: www.aqsquilt.com
Key Personnel
Pres: Meredith Schroeder *E-mail:* meredith@aqsquilt.com
Assoc Publr: Jay Staten *Tel:* 270-898-7903 ext 157 *E-mail:* jaystaten@aqsquilt.com
Founded: 1984
Publisher of books on quilting in all its forms.
ISBN Prefix(es): 0-89145; 1-57432
Number of titles published annually: 20 Print; 2 CD-ROM
Total Titles: 200 Print; 6 CD-ROM
Imprints: AQS
Distributor for C & T Publishing; Patchwork Place Publishers; Sterling Publishers

American Research Press
Division of Erhus University Press
Subsidiary of Xiquan Publishing House
PO Box 141, Rehoboth, NM 87322

Web Site: www.gallup.unm.edu/~smarandache
Key Personnel
Dir & Publr: Minh L Perez *E-mail:* m_l_perez@yahoo.com
Ed: JoAnne McGray
Intl Rts Contact & Lib Sales Dir: J Castillo
Founded: 1990
Publishers of books, journals, ebooks & ejournals.
ISBN Prefix(es): 1-879585; 1-931233
Number of titles published annually: 10 Print; 10 Online; 40 E-Book
Total Titles: 60 Print; 40 Online; 68 E-Book
Foreign Rep(s): W B Vasantha Kandasami; M Monu
Distribution Center: Pro Quest Inc SAN: 297-5092

American Sciences Press Inc
20 Cross Rd, Syracuse, NY 13224-2104
Key Personnel
Sales Mgr: P Anne
Founded: 1979
ISBN Prefix(es): 0-935950
Number of titles published annually: 3 Print
Total Titles: 52 Print
Imprints: The American Sciences Press Series in Mathematical & Management Sciences

American Showcase Inc
915 Broadway, New York, NY 10010
SAN: 215-0514
Tel: 212-673-6600 *Toll Free Tel:* 800-894-7469
  Fax: 212-673-9795
E-mail: info@amshow.com
Web Site: www.amshow.com *Telex:* 88-0356 AMSHOW P
Key Personnel
Pres & Publr: Ira Shapiro
Exec VP, Mktg: Ann Middlebrook
Prodn Dir: Stan Redfern
Sales Dir: Erica Sturdevant
Circulation Mgr: James Kravitz
Founded: 1977
Annual directories of photography, illustration & advertising; books & periodicals on graphics, photography & design; digital imaging.
ISBN Prefix(es): 0-931144
Number of titles published annually: 3 Print
Total Titles: 3 Print
Foreign Rep(s): Rotovision SA
Foreign Rights: Rotovision SA
Warehouse: c/o Whitehurst & Clark Book Fulfillment, Raritan Industrial Park, 100 Newfield Ave, Edison, NJ 08837

American Society for Nondestructive Testing
1711 Arlingate Lane, Columbus, OH 43228-0518
Mailing Address: PO Box 28518, Columbus, OH 43228-0518
Tel: 614-274-6003 *Toll Free Tel:* 800-222-2768
  Fax: 614-274-6899
E-mail: webmaster@asnt.org
Web Site: www.asnt.org
Key Personnel
Pubns Mgr: Paul McIntire
Founded: 1941
Nonprofit association producing educational materials for members & nonmembers engaged in nondestructive testing.
ISBN Prefix(es): 0-931403
Number of titles published annually: 12 Print
Total Titles: 200 Print
Distributed by American Ceramic Society (ACerS); American Society for Mechanical Engineers (ASME); American Society for Metals (ASM); The American Welding Society (AWS); ASTM; Edison Welding Institute; Mean Free Path

§American Society for Photogrammetry & Remote Sensing
5410 Grosvenor Lane, Suite 210, Bethesda, MD 20814-2160
Tel: 301-493-0290 *Fax:* 301-493-0208
E-mail: asprs@asprs.org
Web Site: www.asprs.org
Key Personnel
Mktg Mgr: AnnaMarie Kianerney
Asst Exec Dir: Kim Tilley
Founded: 1934
Journals, proceedings & manuals.
ISBN Prefix(es): 0-944426; 0-937294; 1-57083
Number of titles published annually: 35 Print
Total Titles: 80 Print; 1 CD-ROM
Distributed by RICS; Space Publication
Distributor for International Geographic Information Foundation; Taylor & Francis; Thomasson Grant; University of Chicago Press; US Geological Survey; Van Nostrand Reinhold; Whittles Publishing; John Wiley & Sons Inc
Foreign Rep(s): RICS Books
Warehouse: ASPRS Distribution Center, PO Box 305, Annapolis Junction, MD 20701-03050
Tel: 301-617-7812 *Fax:* 301-206-9789

§American Society for Quality
Unit of American Society for Quality (ASQ)
600 N Plankinton Ave, Milwaukee, WI 53203
Mailing Address: PO Box 3005, Milwaukee, WI 53201-3005
Tel: 414-272-8575 *Toll Free Tel:* 800-248-1946
  Fax: 414-272-1734
E-mail: cs@asq.org
Web Site: www.asq.org *Telex:* 31-6567
Key Personnel
Acq Ed: Anne Mieke-Koudstaal
Project Ed: Craig Powell
Mktg Admin: Matt Meinholz
Cust Serv: Paula O'Connell *Fax:* 414-272-1734
  E-mail: poconnell@asq.org
Founded: 1983
Publisher of technical books: quality, statistical process control, ISO9000, six sigma, QS9000, ISO14000, statistics, reliability, auditing, sampling, standards' supplier quality & quality costs. Also management topics: Total quality management, human resources & teamwork, health care, government, education & benchmarking, quality tools.
ISBN Prefix(es): 0-87389
Number of titles published annually: 25 Print
Total Titles: 234 Print; 5 CD-ROM
Imprints: Fearon Teacher; Good Apple; Grace Publications; Judy Instructo; Shining Star; Totline Publications
Branch Office(s)
Grace Publications & Shining Star, 13720 Clayton Rd, Chesterfield, MO 63017, Contact: Jane Schmidt *Toll Free Tel:* 800-555-2026 *Fax:* 314-579-9599
Distributed by GOAL/QPC; IEEE Computer Society Press; McGraw-Hill Professional Publishing; Productivity Press
Warehouse: 5131 S Third St, Milwaukee, WI 53207-6028 *Tel:* 414-482-1700 *Fax:* 414-482-1841

American Society for Training & Development (ASTD)
1640 King St, Alexandria, VA 22313-2043
SAN: 224-8972
Mailing Address: PO Box 1443, Alexandria, VA 22313-2043
Tel: 703-683-8100 *Toll Free Tel:* 800-628-2783
  Fax: 703-683-1523
E-mail: publications@astd.org
Web Site: www.astd.org
Key Personnel
Sr Acqs Ed: Mark Morrow *Tel:* 703-683-9205
  Fax: 703-683-9591 *E-mail:* mmorrow@astd.org
Dir, Pubns: Kat Russo *Tel:* 703-683-8136
  Fax: 703-683-9591

Founded: 1944
Professional books for employee learning, training & development, performance, human resource development, organization & career development.
ISBN Prefix(es): 0-201; 0-7755
Number of titles published annually: 25 Print; 4 CD-ROM
Total Titles: 150 Print
Imprints: ASTD Press
Distributor for Jossey Bass; Berrett-Kohler; McGraw-Hill; Random House Inc

§American Society of Agricultural Engineers
2950 Niles Rd, St Joseph, MI 49085-9659
Tel: 269-429-0300 *Fax:* 269-429-3852
E-mail: hq@asae.org
Web Site: www.asae.org
Key Personnel
Books & Journals: Sandy Rutter *E-mail:* rutter@asae.org
Founded: 1907
Agricultural, biological & food systems, books & journals.
ISBN Prefix(es): 0-916150; 0-929355
Number of titles published annually: 4 Print
Total Titles: 150 Print; 2 CD-ROM

American Society of Agronomy
677 S Segoe Rd, Madison, WI 53711-1086
Tel: 608-273-8080 *Fax:* 608-273-2021
E-mail: headquarters@agronomy.org
Web Site: www.agronomy.org
Key Personnel
Exec VP: Ellen Bergfeld
Adv Mgr: Betsy Ahner
Sales & Mktg: Sara Uttech
Founded: 1907
Technical books for professionals in agronomy; crop science, soil science, environmental sciences & related fields.
ISBN Prefix(es): 0-89118
Number of titles published annually: 8 Print
Total Titles: 125 Print

§American Society of Civil Engineers (ASCE)
1801 Alexander Bell Dr, Reston, VA 20191-4400
SAN: 204-7594
Tel: 703-295-6200 *Toll Free Tel:* 800-548-2723
Fax: 703-295-6278
E-mail: marketing@asce.org
Web Site: www.asce.org
Key Personnel
Man Dir, Pubns: Bruce Gossett
Dir, Prodn & Pubns: Charlotte McNaughton
Dir, Mktg: William D Farnam *Tel:* 703-295-6252
E-mail: wfarnam@asce.org
Mgr, Journals: Johanna Reinhart
Div Administrator & Rts & Perms: Karen Ryan
Cust Rel: Clifford Rodin
Founded: 1852
Books, newsletters, journals, CD-ROM journals, magazines & information products on civil engineering & related fields.
ISBN Prefix(es): 0-87262; 0-7844; 0-7277
Number of titles published annually: 50 Print
Total Titles: 1,394 Print; 27 CD-ROM
Distributor for Institution of Civil Engineers (UK); Thomas Telford (UK)
Foreign Rep(s): American Technical Publishers (UK, Western Europe); Book Marketing Services (India, Madras); D A Books (Australia, New Zealand, Papua New Guinea)

American Society of Electroneurodiagnostic Technologists Inc
426 W 42 St, Kansas City, KS 64111
Tel: 816-931-1120 *Fax:* 816-931-1145
E-mail: info@aset.org
Web Site: www.aset.org
Key Personnel
Exec Dir: Sheila Davis

Founded: 1959
Books on EEG, evoked potentials, nerve conduction & polysomnography technology.
ISBN Prefix(es): 1-57797
Number of titles published annually: 20 Print

§American Society of Health-System Pharmacists
7272 Wisconsin Ave, Bethesda, MD 20814
Tel: 301-657-3000 *Toll Free Tel:* 866-279-0681 (orders) *Fax:* 301-664-8867
E-mail: info@ashp.org
Web Site: www.ashp.org
Key Personnel
Exec VP: Henri R Manasse, Jr
Founded: 1943
ISBN Prefix(es): 0-930530; 1-879907; 1-58528
Number of titles published annually: 20 Print
Total Titles: 83 Print
Foreign Rep(s): APAC (Asia); L Horvath (Eastern Europe); LPR (Middle East); LR International (Brazil); R Seshadri (India)
Advertising Agency: Cunningham Associates

American Society of Mechanical Engineers (ASME)
3 Park Ave, New York, NY 10016
SAN: 201-1379
Tel: 212-591-7000 *Toll Free Tel:* 800-843-2763 (cust serv) *Fax:* 212-591-7674; 973-882-1717 (cust serv)
E-mail: infocentral@asme.org
Web Site: www.asme.org
Key Personnel
Exec Dir: Virgil Carter
Mgr, Fulfillment Dept: Wanda Kalgren
Man Dir, Engg Progs: Tom Loughlin
Mktg Dir: Jeff Howitt *Tel:* 212-591-7051
E-mail: howittj@asme.org
Dir, Tech Publg: Philip DiVietro
Special Sales Coord: Craig Backhus
Adv Promo Mgr: Anthony Asiaghi
Founded: 1880
Professional references, codes & standards, special publications, proceedings, transactions journals, technical papers for the mechanical engineer.
ISBN Prefix(es): 0-87053; 0-7918
Number of titles published annually: 185 Print
Total Titles: 873 Print
Imprints: ASME Press
Distributor for Professional Engineering Publishing
Foreign Rep(s): Professional Engineering Publishing LTD (UK)
Warehouse: 22 Law Dr, PO Box 2900, Fairfield, NJ 07007-2900

American Society of Plant Taxonomists
University of Michigan Herbarium, 3600 Varsity Dr, Ann Arbor, MI 48108-2287
SAN: 282-969X
Tel: 734-647-2812 *Fax:* 734-647-5719
Web Site: www.sysbot.org
Key Personnel
Ed: Christiane Anderson *E-mail:* chra@umich.edu
Founded: 1980
Botanical monographs.
ISBN Prefix(es): 0-912861
Number of titles published annually: 3 Print
Total Titles: 68 Print

American Technical Publishers Inc
1155 W 175 St, Homewood, IL 60430-4600
SAN: 206-8141
Tel: 708-957-1100 *Toll Free Tel:* 800-323-3471
Fax: 708-957-1101
E-mail: service@americantech.net
Web Site: www.go2atp.com
Key Personnel
Pres & Treas: Robert D Deisinger *E-mail:* rdd@americantech.net

VP & Mktg Mgr: J David Holloway
E-mail: jdh@americantech.net
Ed-in-Chief & Acqs: Jonathan F Gosse
E-mail: jfg@americantech.net
Mfg Mgr: Christopher Proctor *E-mail:* ctp@americantech.net
Founded: 1898
Technical, industrial & vocational textbooks, reference books & related materials.
ISBN Prefix(es): 0-8269
Number of titles published annually: 8 Print
Total Titles: 200 Print; 2 Online
Distributor for Craftsman Book Co
Foreign Rep(s): Gage Educational Publishing (Canada); Gazelle Book Services Ltd (UK)

American Trust Publications
Affiliate of North American Islamic Trust
745 McClintock Dr, Suite 114, Burr Ridge, IL 60527
Tel: 630-789-9191 *Toll Free Tel:* 888-319-5858
Fax: 630-789-9455
Web Site: www.nait.net
Key Personnel
Gen Mgr: Ali M Naziruddin
Specialize in Islamic literature.
ISBN Prefix(es): 0-89259
Number of titles published annually: 5 Print
Total Titles: 104 Print

§American Water Works Association
6666 W Quincy Ave, Denver, CO 80235
Tel: 303-794-7711 *Toll Free Tel:* 800-926-7337
Fax: 303-347-0804
Web Site: www.awwa.org
Key Personnel
Exec Dir: Jack W Hoffbuhr
Sr Acq Ed: Colin Murcray *Tel:* 303-734-3419
E-mail: cmurcray@awwa.org
Sr Tech Ed: Mindy Burke *Tel:* 303-347-6179
E-mail: mburke@awwa.org
Founded: 1881
Water works technology & management.
ISBN Prefix(es): 0-89867; 1-58321
Number of titles published annually: 75 Print
Total Titles: 500 Print; 12 CD-ROM; 2 Online
Imprints: AWWA; AWWA Research Foundation
Distributor for Fulcrum; McGraw-Hill; Prentice-Hall; Technomic; John Wiley & Sons
Foreign Rep(s): American Technical Publishers Ltd (Africa, European Union, Middle East); Australian Water & Wastewater Association (Australia); Canadian Water & Wastewater Association (Canada)
Warehouse: 3121 S Platte River Dr, Englewood, CO 80110
Membership(s): AAP

America's Health Insurance Plans (AHIP)
Formerly Health Insurance Association of America
South Bldg, 601 Pennsylvania Ave NW, Suite 500, Washington, DC 20004
Tel: 202-778-3200 *Fax:* 202-861-6354
Web Site: www.insuranceeducation.org
Key Personnel
Deputy Dir, Insurance Educ: Joyce C Meals
E-mail: jmeals@ahip.net
Founded: 1948
Specialize in education for the health insurance industry. *Business Health.*
ISBN Prefix(es): 1-879143
Number of titles published annually: 5 Print
Total Titles: 60,000 Print
Distribution Center: Tasco, PO Box 753, Waldorf, MD 20604 *Toll Free Tel:* 800-828-0111

Amherst Media Inc
175 Rano St, Suite 200, Buffalo, NY 14207
Tel: 716-874-4450 *Fax:* 716-874-4508
E-mail: amherstmed@aol.com
Web Site: www.amherstmedia.com

Key Personnel
Pres & Publr: Craig Alesse
Founded: 1979
Specialize in publishing how-to photography books.
ISBN Prefix(es): 0-936262
Number of titles published annually: 24 Print
Total Titles: 180 Print
Distributor for Firefly

Amirah Publishing
Affiliate of IBTS
IBTS, 22-55 31 St, Long Island City, NY 11105
Mailing Address: PO Box 541146, Flushing, NY 11354
Tel: 718-721-4246 (IBTS) *Toll Free Tel:* 800-337-4287 (IBTS) *Fax:* 718-721-6108 (IBTS)
E-mail: amirahpbco@aol.com; information@ibtsonline.com
Key Personnel
Mktg & Adv: Mossadaq Hossain
Founded: 1992
Publishes books related to Islam & Muslim culture, especially children's titles. IBTS is the official outlet for all books by Amirah Publishing.
ISBN Prefix(es): 1-889720
Number of titles published annually: 5 Print; 5 CD-ROM; 15 Audio
Total Titles: 20 Print; 20 Audio
Distributed by IBTS
Orders to: IBTS, PO Box 5153, Long Island City, NY 11105 (contact IBTS for all orders), Contact: M Hossain *Fax:* 718-728-6108 *E-mail:* information@ibtsonline.com

AMS Press Inc
Brooklyn Navy Yard, Bldg 292, Suite 417, 63 Flushing Ave, New York, NY 11205
SAN: 201-1743
Tel: 212-777-4700; 718-875-8100 *Fax:* 212-995-5413
E-mail: amserve@earthlink.net *Cable:* ABMAGSERV
Key Personnel
Contact: Gabriel Hornstein
Founded: 1962
Original publications & reprint editions of scholarly books & periodicals; reference works.
ISBN Prefix(es): 0-404
Number of titles published annually: 65 Print
Total Titles: 6,500 Print

Amsco School Publications Inc
315 Hudson St, New York, NY 10013-1085
SAN: 201-1751
Tel: 212-886-6500; 212-886-6565
Toll Free Tel: 800-969-8398 *Fax:* 212-675-7010
E-mail: info@amscopub.com
Web Site: www.amscopub.com
Key Personnel
Pres: Henry Brun
CEO: Laurence Beller
Pubns Dir, Mfg, Prodn, Design & Editing: Joseph Campanella
Sales Dir: Glen Meloni
Mktg Dir: Irene Rubin
Mfg Mgr: Valerie Mackross
Founded: 1935
El-hi textbooks.
ISBN Prefix(es): 0-87720; 1-56765
Number of titles published annually: 50 Print
Total Titles: 485 Print

The Amwell Press
Subsidiary of National Sporting Fraternity Ltd
Ridge Plaza, 2004 Rte 31 & Cregar Rd, Clinton, NJ 08809
Mailing Address: PO Box 5385, Clinton, NJ 08809
Tel: 908-638-9033 *Fax:* 908-638-4728

Key Personnel
Pres & Publr: James C Rikhoff
VP & Assoc Publr: Monica Sullivan
Corp Sec: Genevieve Symonds
Founded: 1976
Specializes in African big game & upland shooting, sporting (shooting/fishing) limited edition & high-quality trade books; limited edition prints, etchings, artworks, etc, in hunting/fishing genre only; custom-bound; signed & numbered limited edition book & hardcover trade book; no unsol mss.
ISBN Prefix(es): 0-916417
Number of titles published annually: 3 Print
Total Titles: 130 Print
Imprints: National Sporting Fraternity Ltd

Anacus Press
Imprint of Finney Co
3943 Meadowbrook Rd, Minneapolis, MN 55426-4505
Tel: 952-938-9330 *Toll Free Tel:* 800-846-7027 *Fax:* 952-938-7353
E-mail: feedback@finney-hobar.com
Web Site: www.anacus.com
Key Personnel
Pres: Alan Krysan
Founded: 1996
Bicycle related nonfiction & travel guides; tourism in South Florida & coastal areas.
ISBN Prefix(es): 0-933855
Number of titles published annually: 4 Print
Total Titles: 14 Print

The Analytic Press
Division of Lawrence Erlbaum Associates Inc
101 West St, Hillsdale, NJ 07642
SAN: 267-5455
Tel: 201-358-9477; 201-236-9500
Toll Free Tel: 800-926-6579 (orders only); 800-627-0629 (journal orders) *Fax:* 201-358-4700 (edit); 201-760-3735 (orders only)
E-mail: tap@analyticpress.com
Web Site: www.analyticpress.com
Key Personnel
Pres: Lawrence Erlbaum
Man Dir: Paul Stepansky *E-mail:* pstepansky@analyticpress.com
Sr Prodn Mgr: Nancy Liguori *E-mail:* nliguori@analyticpress.com
Man Ed: Eleanor Starke Kobrin
E-mail: ekobrin@analyticpress.com
Promo Mgr & Intl Rts: Joan Riegel
E-mail: jriegel@analyticpress.com
Sales Mgr: Shari Buchwald *E-mail:* sbuchwald@analyticpress.com
Founded: 1982
Professional & academic books & journals in psychoanalysis, psychiatry, psychotherapy & related disciplines.
ISBN Prefix(es): 0-88163
Number of titles published annually: 20 Print
Total Titles: 300 Print
Distributor for Gestalt Institute of Cleveland Press
Foreign Rep(s): DA Information Services (Australia, New Zealand, Papua New Guinea); Eurospan Group (Europe & Middle East)
Billing Address: 10 Industrial Ave, Mahwah, NJ 07430-2262
Orders to: The Analytic Press, 10 Industrial Ave, Mahwah, NJ 07430-2262 *Toll Free Tel:* 800-926-6579 *Fax:* 201-760-3735 *E-mail:* tapbooks@analyticpress.com
Warehouse: TAP/LEA, 10 Maple St, Norwood, NJ 07648, Mgr: Jack Romaine *Tel:* 201-784-5398 *Fax:* 201-784-3591
Distribution Center: 10 Maple St, Norwood, NJ 07648

§Ancestry Publishing
Imprint of MyFamily.com Inc
360 W 4800 N, Provo, UT 84064

SAN: 662-7706
Mailing Address: PO Box 990, Orem, UT 84059-0990
Tel: 801-705-7305 *Toll Free Tel:* 800-262-3787 *Fax:* 801-426-3501
E-mail: editor@ancestry.com; dealersales@ancestry-inc.com
Web Site: www.ancestry.com
Key Personnel
VP, Pubns: Loretto Szucs
Sr Ed: Matt Wright *E-mail:* mwright@ancestry.com
Gen Mgr: Andre Brummer
Dir, Publg: Jennifer Utley
Founded: 1983
ISBN Prefix(es): 0-916489
Number of titles published annually: 8 Print; 50 CD-ROM; 4 Online; 4 E-Book
Total Titles: 72 Print; 120 CD-ROM; 10 Online; 10 E-Book
Warehouse: Ancestry, 193 S Mountain View Dr, Orem, UT 84059

§Anchor Publishing, Virginia
PO Box 9558, Virginia Beach, VA 23450-9558
Tel: 757-431-1366
Web Site: www.antion.com
Key Personnel
Owner: Thomas Antion *E-mail:* tom@antion.com
Mgr: Janet Hall
Founded: 1988
Electronic publishing only, query first.
ISBN Prefix(es): 0-926395
Number of titles published annually: 3 Print
Total Titles: 15 Print

Anchorage Press Plays Inc
PO Box 2901, Louisville, KY 40201-2901
SAN: 203-4727
Tel: 502-583-2288
E-mail: applays@bellsouth.net
Web Site: applays.com
Key Personnel
Owner & Publr: Marilee Miller
Founded: 1935
Publish plays for children's theatre & theatre textbooks; administer production rights; publish texts in field.
ISBN Prefix(es): 0-87602
Number of titles published annually: 10 Print
Total Titles: 300 Print
Foreign Rights: Cressrelles Publishing Co Ltd (UK)

Andrews University Press
Division of Andrews University
Andrews University Press, 213 Information Services Bldg, Berrien Springs, MI 49104-1700
SAN: 241-0958
Tel: 269-471-6915 *Toll Free Tel:* 800-467-6369 (Visa & MC orders only) *Fax:* 269-471-6224
E-mail: aupress@andrews.edu
Web Site: www.andrewsuniversitypress.com; www.ancrews.edu/universitypress
Key Personnel
Dir: Ronald Knott
Selected areas of theology, education, philosophy, science, faith & learning.
ISBN Prefix(es): 0-943872; 1-883925
Number of titles published annually: 6 Print
Total Titles: 100 Print; 1 CD-ROM
Subsidiaries: Oronoko Books
Distributed by Review & Herald Publishing; Pacific Press Publishing

Andujar Communication Technologies Inc
7946 Ivanhoe Ave, Suite 314, La Jolla, CA 92037
Mailing Address: PO Box 2622, La Jolla, CA 92038
Tel: 858-459-2673 *Fax:* 858-459-9768
Key Personnel
Pres: Julio I Andujar
Founded: 1980

English as a foreign language & business education materials for US & overseas markets; computer-assisted language instruction; editorial & consulting services in Spanish; special projects for Japanese & other international publishers.
ISBN Prefix(es): 0-938086
Number of titles published annually: 6 Print

Angel City Press
2118 Wilshire Blvd, No 880, Santa Monica, CA 90403
Tel: 310-395-9982 *Toll Free Tel:* 800-949-8039
Fax: 310-395-3353
E-mail: info@angelcitypress.com
Web Site: www.angelcitypress.com
Number of titles published annually: 8 Print
Total Titles: 50 Print

Angelus Press
2915 Forest Ave, Kansas City, MO 64109
Tel: 816-753-3150 *Toll Free Tel:* 800-966-7337
Fax: 816-753-3557 *Toll Free Fax:* 888-855-9022
E-mail: info@angeluspress.org
Web Site: www.angeluspress.org
Key Personnel
Ed: Kenneth Novak
Opers & Mktg: Christopher McCann *Tel:* 816-753-3150 ext 303 *E-mail:* cmccann@angeluspress.org
Founded: 1978
Monthly journal of Catholic Tradition; traditional Roman Catholic books.
ISBN Prefix(es): 0-935952; 1-892331
Number of titles published annually: 8 Print
Total Titles: 100 Print
Distributed by Catholic Treasures; Fatima Crusader

Anhinga Press
PO Box 10595, Tallahassee, FL 32302-2595
Tel: 850-442-1408 *Fax:* 850-442-6323
E-mail: info@anhinga.org
Web Site: www.anhinga.org
Key Personnel
Dir & Intl Rts: Rick Campbell
Founded: 1974
ISBN Prefix(es): 0-938078
Number of titles published annually: 5 Print
Total Titles: 70 Print
Distributed by Small Press Distribution

§Anker Publishing Co Inc
176 Ballville Rd, Bolton, MA 01740-1255
Mailing Address: PO Box 249, Bolton, MA 01740-0249
Tel: 978-779-6190 *Fax:* 978-779-6366
E-mail: info@ankerpub.com
Web Site: www.ankerpub.com
Key Personnel
Pres & Publr: James D Anker
VP: Susan W Anker
Ed: Carolyn Dumore
Founded: 1990
Publishes professional, scholarly & text books in higher education.
ISBN Prefix(es): 0-9627042; 1-882982
Number of titles published annually: 12 Print
Total Titles: 59 Print; 1 CD-ROM
Warehouse: PO Box 2247, Williston, VT 05495

Annual Reviews
4139 El Camino Way, Palo Alto, CA 94306
SAN: 201-1816
Mailing Address: PO Box 10139, Palo Alto, CA 94303-0139
Tel: 650-493-4400 *Toll Free Tel:* 800-523-8635
Fax: 650-855-9815
E-mail: service@annualreviews.org
Web Site: www.annualreviews.org

Key Personnel
Pres & Ed-in-Chief: Samuel Gubins
Founded: 1932
Scientific review literature, in print & online, in the biomedical, physical & social sciences.
ISBN Prefix(es): 0-8243
Number of titles published annually: 31 Print; 31 Online
Total Titles: 1,100 Print; 1,100 Online
Foreign Rep(s): Gazelle Book Services Ltd (Africa, UK, Continental Europe, Ireland, Middle East); SARAS Books (Bangladesh, India, Pakistan, Sri Lanka)
Returns: National Distribution Services, 6118 Kingsport Hwy, Gray, TN 37615
Membership(s): California Library Association; International Federation of Library Associations & Institutions; MLA; SLA; STM

ANR Publications University of California
6701 San Pablo Ave, 2nd fl, Oakland, CA 94608-1239
Tel: 510-642-2431 *Toll Free Tel:* 800-994-8849
Fax: 510-643-5470
E-mail: danrcs@ucdavis.edu
Web Site: anrcatalog.ucdavis.edu
Key Personnel
Dist Mgr: Jerry Hendrex
Mktg Mgr: Cynthia Kintigh *Tel:* 530-754-5065 *E-mail:* cckintigh@ucdavis.edu
Publications on agriculture, gardening, integrated pest management & biological control, natural resources & nutrition.
ISBN Prefix(es): 0-931876; 1-879906
Number of titles published annually: 5 Print; 20 Online
Total Titles: 700 Print; 100 Online
Editorial Office(s): 1441 Research Park Dr, Suite 110, Davis, CA 95616
Foreign Rights: Bob Sams

Antique Collectors Club Ltd
Division of Antique Collectors Club Ltd (England)
116 Pleasant St, East Hampton, MA 01027
Tel: 413-529-0861 *Toll Free Tel:* 800-252-5231
Fax: 413-297-0862
E-mail: info@antiquecc.com
Web Site: www.antiquecc.com
Key Personnel
Div Dir & Intl Rts: Dan Farrell
Founded: 1966
Books on fine & decorative arts, gardening, architecture & antiques, multicultural.
ISBN Prefix(es): 1-85149; 0-907462; 0-902028; 0-906610; 0-9627359; 0-904017
Number of titles published annually: 300 Print
Total Titles: 1,500 Print
Imprints: Garden Art Press
Foreign Office(s): 5 Church St, Woodbridge, Suffolk 1P12 1DS, United Kingdom
Distributor for Acatos; Adler Planetarium & Astronomy; Umberto Allemandi; Architectura & Natura; Arnoldsche; Arsenale Editrice; Art Price.com; Wadsworth Athenaeum; Bard Graduate Center; Barn Elms Publishing; Beagle Press; Chris Beetles Ltd; Benteli Verlag; Birmingham Museum of Art; Brioni Books; British Museum Press; Canal & Stamperia; Cartago; Colonial Williamsburg; Colophon; Colwood Press Ltd; The William G Congdon Foundation; Conran Octopus; Currier Publications; Alain De Gourcuff Editeur; M H De Young Memorial Museum; Richard Dennis; Detroit Institute of Arts; Editions Vasour; Editoriale Jaca Book; Edizione Press; Elvehjem Museum of Art; Gambero Rosso; Grayson Publishing; Hachette Livre; Robert Hale; Han-Shan Tang Books; Alan Hartman; High Museum of Art; Images Publications; India Book House Ltd; Frances Lincoln; Loft Publications; Lowry Press; Mapin; Marshall Editions; Merrick & Day; Museum of American Folk Art; Na-

tional Galleries of Scotland; National Portrait Gallery; The National Trust; New Architecture Group Ltd; New Cavendish Books Ltd; Newark Museum; Packard Publishing; Peabody Essex Museum; Philadelphia Museum of Art; River Books Co Ltd; Michael Russell; Saigo Trust; Scala Publishers; Superbrands Ltd; Third Millenium Publishing; Ursus Books; Wallace Collection; Watermark Press; Websters International Publishers; Philip Wilson Publishers
Foreign Rep(s): Jenny Gosling (Belgium, Netherlands, London, Luxembourg); Lilian Koe (Malaysia); Clive & Moira Malins (Scotland, Northeast England); Michael Morris (Middle East, Near East); Penny Padovani (Italy, Portugal, Spain); David Pearson (France); Ian Pringle (Brunei, Indonesia, Singapore, Thailand); Ed Summerson (China, Hong Kong, Philippines, South Korea, Taiwan); Ralph & Sheila Sumners (Japan); Robert Towers (Ireland, Northern Ireland)

Antique Trader Books
Division of Krause Publications
c/o Krause Publications, 700 E State St, Iola, WI 54990-0001
Tel: 715-445-2214 *Toll Free Tel:* 888-457-2873
Fax: 715-445-4087
Web Site: www.krause.com
Key Personnel
Publr: Bill Krause *E-mail:* krauseb@krause.com
Collectibles, books, magazines, trades & crafts.
ISBN Prefix(es): 0-930625; 1-58221
Number of titles published annually: 20 Print
Total Titles: 170 Print

Antrim House
21 Goodrich Rd, Simsbury, CT 06070-1804
Mailing Address: PO Box 111, Tariffville, CT 06081
Tel: 860-217-0023 *Fax:* 860-217-0023
E-mail: eds@antrimhousebooks.com
Web Site: www.antrimhousebooks.com
Key Personnel
Ed: Robert McQuilkin
Founded: 2002
Publish cloth bound editions, perfect bound paperbacks & saddle stitched chapbooks by Connecticut poets. On occasion, issue CDs by these poets.
ISBN Prefix(es): 0-9662783
Number of titles published annually: 4 Print; 2 Audio
Total Titles: 4 Print; 1 Audio
Membership(s): Publishers Marketing Association

AOCS Press
Division of American Oil Chemists' Society
2211 W Bradley Ave, Champaign, IL 61821-1827
Mailing Address: PO Box 3489, Champaign, IL 61826-3489
Tel: 217-359-2344 *Toll Free Tel:* 800-336-AOCS (336-2627) *Fax:* 217-351-8091
E-mail: publications@aocs.org; orders@aocs.org
Web Site: www.aocs.org
Key Personnel
Exec VP: Jean Wills
Founded: 1909
Journals & monographs.
ISBN Prefix(es): 0-935315; 1-893997
Number of titles published annually: 10 Print; 2 CD-ROM; 2 Online; 1 E-Book
Total Titles: 100 Print; 7 CD-ROM; 2 Online; 1 E-Book
Distributor for The Oily Press

Aperture Books
Division of Aperture Foundation Inc
20 E 23 St, New York, NY 10010
SAN: 201-1832
Tel: 212-505-5555 *Toll Free Tel:* 800-929-2323
Fax: 212-598-4015
E-mail: info@aperture.org

Web Site: www.aperture.org *Telex:* 85-7718
  Cable: APERTURE NEW YORK
Key Personnel
Exec Dir: Ellen Harris
Dir, Sales & Lib Sales: Chris McLane *Tel:* 212-
  505-5555 ext 346
Sr Ed: Melissa Harris
Exec Ed: Lesley Martin
Intl Rts Contact: Kristian Orozco
Founded: 1952
Quarterly magazine; books on photography as
  fine art, history of photography, photojournal-
  ism, environment.
ISBN Prefix(es): 0-89381
Number of titles published annually: 15 Print
Total Titles: 200 Print
Imprints: Aperture Monographs; Masters of Pho-
  tography; Writers & Artists on Photography
  Series
Distributed by Farrar, Straus & Giroux Inc
Foreign Rep(s): General Publishing (Canada);
  Robert Hale Ltd (UK); InterArt (France); Nils-
  son & Lamm (Belgium, Netherlands); Onslow
  Books Ltd (Western Europe); Penny Padavon
  (Greece, Italy, Portugal & Spain); Southern
  Publisher (New Zealand); Tower (Australia);
  Roger Ward (East Asia)
Shipping Address: Farrar, Straus & Giroux,
  c/o VHPS 16365 James Madison Hwy, Gor-
  donsville, VA 22942

The Apex Press
Affiliate of The Council on International & Public
  Affairs
777 United Nations Plaza, Suite 3-C, New York,
  NY 10017
SAN: 246-2664
Tel: 914-271-6500 *Toll Free Tel:* 800-316-2739
  Fax: 914-271-6500 *Toll Free Fax:* 800-316-
  2739
E-mail: cipany@igc.org
Web Site: www.cipa-apex.org
Key Personnel
Pres: Ward Morehouse *Fax:* 212-972-9878
Pubns Mgr: Judi Rizzi
Founded: 1985
Specialize in books on education, economics, so-
  cial & political issues, human rights, corporate
  power.
ISBN Prefix(es): 0-945257; 0-938960 (CITE); 1-
  891843
Number of titles published annually: 7 Print
Total Titles: 100 Print
Imprints: Center for International Training & Ed-
  ucation/CITE; Policy Studies Associates
Branch Office(s)
PO Box 337, Croton-on-Hudson, NY 10520-
  0337, Contact: Judi Rizzi *Tel:* 914-271-6500
  Toll Free Tel: 800-316-2739 *E-mail:* cipany@
  igc.org
Distributed by Jon Carpenter Publishing (UK); IT
  Pubs (London); Zed Books (London)
Distributor for Bootstrap Press (US); The Labor
  Institute; The Other India Press (India); Zed
  Books (London)
Billing Address: PO Box 337, Croton-on-Hudson,
  NY 10520-0337 *Tel:* 914-271-6500 *Toll Free
  Tel:* 800-316-2739 *Fax:* 914-271-6500 *Toll Free
  Fax:* 800-316-2739
Orders to: PO Box 337, Croton-on-Hudson,
  NY 10520-0337 *Tel:* 914-271-6500 *Toll Free
  Tel:* 800-316-2739 *Fax:* 914-271-6500 *Toll Free
  Fax:* 800-316-2739
Returns: 52 Grand St, Croton-on-Hudson, NY
  10520 *Tel:* 914-271-6500 *Toll Free Tel:* 800-
  316-2739 *Fax:* 914-271-6500 *Toll Free
  Fax:* 800-316-2739
Shipping Address: 52 Grand St, Croton-on-
  Hudson, NY 10520 *Tel:* 914-271-6500 *Toll
  Free Tel:* 800-316-2739 *Fax:* 914-271-6500 *Toll
  Free Fax:* 800-316-2739

Apogee Press
2308 Sixth St, Berkeley, CA 94710
Mailing Address: PO Box 8177, Berkeley, CA
  94707
E-mail: editors@agopeepress.com
Web Site: www.agopeepress.com
Key Personnel
Ed: Alice Jones *Tel:* 510-420-8803; Edward
  Smallfield *Tel:* 510-548-0526
Founded: 1998
Publishes innovative poetry with an emphasis on
  West Coast writers.
ISBN Prefix(es): 0-9669937; 0-9744687
Number of titles published annually: 5 Print; 1
  Audio
Total Titles: 13 Print; 1 Audio
Orders to: Small Press Distribution, 1341 Sev-
  enth St, Berkeley, CA 94710-1409, Contact:
  Laura Moriarty *Toll Free Tel:* 800-869-7553
  Fax: 510-524-1563 *E-mail:* spd@spdbooks.org
Returns: Small Press Distribution, 1341 Sev-
  enth St, Berkeley, CA 94710-1409, Contact:
  Laura Moriarty *Toll Free Tel:* 800-869-7553
  Fax: 510-524-1563 *E-mail:* spd@spdbooks.org
Shipping Address: Small Press Distribution, 1341
  Seventh St, Berkeley, CA 94710-1409, Contact:
  Laura Moriarty *Toll Free Tel:* 800-869-7553
  E-mail: spd@spdbooks.org
Warehouse: Small Press Distribution, 1341 Sev-
  enth St, Berkeley, CA 94710-1409 *Toll Free
  Tel:* 800-869-7553 *E-mail:* spd@spdbooks.org
Distribution Center: Small Press Distribution,
  1341 Seventh St, Berkeley, CA 94710-1409,
  Contact: Laura Moriarty *Toll Free Tel:* 800-
  869-7553 *Fax:* 510-524-1563
Membership(s): Council of Literary Magazines &
  Presses

Apollo Managed Care Consultants
860 Ladera Lane, Santa Barbara, CA 93108
Tel: 805-969-2606 *Fax:* 805-969-3749
E-mail: mail@apollomanagedcare.com
Web Site: www.apollomanagedcare.com
Key Personnel
CEO: Dr Margaret Bischel *E-mail:* mbischel@
  apollomanagedcare.com
Founded: 1987
Publish medical publications.
ISBN Prefix(es): 1-893826
Number of titles published annually: 5 Print; 1
  CD-ROM; 5 Online
Total Titles: 38 Print; 1 CD-ROM; 30 Online

**APPA: The Association of Higher Education
  Facilities Officers**
1643 Prince St, Alexandria, VA 22314-2818
Tel: 703-684-1446 *Fax:* 703-549-2772
Web Site: www.appa.org
Key Personnel
Dir, Communs: Steve Glazner
Dir, Mktg: Francine Moore
Commun Serv Mgr: Cotrenia Aytch
Founded: 1914
All titles seek to enhance the development of
  leadership & professional management appli-
  cable to the planning, design, construction &
  operation of higher education facilities.
ISBN Prefix(es): 0-913359; 1-890956
Number of titles published annually: 3 Print
Total Titles: 50 Print
Branch Office(s)
APPA Publications, PO Box 1201, Alexandria,
  VA 22313-1201
Distribution Center: 13119 Pelfrey Lane, Fairfax,
  VA 22033

Appalachian Mountain Club Books
Division of Appalachian Mountain Club
5 Joy St, Boston, MA 02108
SAN: 203-4808
Tel: 617-523-0655 *Fax:* 617-523-0722
Web Site: www.outdoors.org

Key Personnel
Publr: Beth Krusi *Tel:* 617-523-0655 ext 360
  E-mail: bkrusi@outdoors.org
Ed-in-Chief: Sarah Jane Shangrah *Tel:* 617-523-
  0655 ext 378 *E-mail:* sjshangra@outdoors.org
Ed: Blake Maher
Prodn Mgr: Belinda Thrasher *Tel:* 617-523-0655
  ext 328
Mktg & Publicity Assoc: Katharine Donnelly
  E-mail: kdonnelly@outdoors.org
Founded: 1897
Guidebooks, maps, outdoor recreation & conser-
  vation, mountain history, nature & travel for
  Northeast US.
ISBN Prefix(es): 0-910146; 1-878239; 1-929173
Number of titles published annually: 10 Print
Total Titles: 68 Print
Imprints: A M C Nature Walks Series; A M C
  Quiet Water Guides; A M C River Guides; A
  M C Trail Guides
Distributed by The Globe Pequot Press
Foreign Rep(s): Canadian Manda Group
  (Canada); Windsor Books Ltd (Europe)
Warehouse: The Globe Pequot Press Inc, 246
  Goose Lane, PO Box 480, Guilford, CT 06437-
  0480 *Tel:* 203-455-4547 *Toll Free Tel:* 800-
  962-0973 *Fax:* 860-395-2855 *Web Site:* www.
  globe-pequot.com

Appalachian Trail Conference
PO Box 807, Harpers Ferry, WV 25425
Tel: 304-535-6331 *Toll Free Tel:* 888-287-8673
  (for orders only) *Fax:* 304-535-2667
E-mail: info@atconf.org
Web Site: www.appalachiantrail.org; www.
  atctrailstore.org
Key Personnel
Dir, Pub Aff: Brian B King
Founded: 1925
Books related to the Appalachian Trail.
ISBN Prefix(es): 0-917953; 1-889386
Number of titles published annually: 6 Print
Total Titles: 46 Print
Shipping Address: 799 Washington St, Harpers
  Ferry, WV 25425

§Applause Theatre & Cinema Books
151 W 46 St, New York, NY 10036
Tel: 212-575-9265 *Fax:* 646-562-5852
E-mail: info@applausepub.com
Web Site: www.applausepub.com
Key Personnel
Man Dir: Michael Messina
Publr & Founder: Glenn Young
Exec VP & Assoc Publr: Kay Radtke
Founded: 1983
Plays, theatre books, cinema books, entertain-
  ment, television; including DVDs.
ISBN Prefix(es): 0-936839; 1-55783
Number of titles published annually: 20 Print; 3
  CD-ROM; 6 Audio
Total Titles: 465 Print; 3 CD-ROM; 6 Audio
Sales Office(s): 7777 W Bluemound Rd, Milwau-
  kee, WI 53213
Distributed by Hal Leonard Corp
Foreign Rep(s): The Canconn Group (Canada);
  Roundhouse Publishing Ltd (Europe & UK)
Billing Address: 960 E Mark St, Winona, MN
  55987
Orders to: 7777 W Blue Mound Rd, Milwaukee,
  WI 53213 *Toll Free Tel:* 800-554-0626
Returns: 960 E Mark St, Winona, MN 55987
Warehouse: 960 E Mark St, Winona, MN 55987
  Tel: 507-454-2920 *Fax:* 507-454-8334

Applewood Books Inc
128 The Great Rd, Bedford, MA 01730
Mailing Address: PO Box 365, Bedford, MA
  01730 SAN: 210-3419
Tel: 781-271-0055 *Fax:* 781-271-0056
E-mail: applewood@awb.com
Web Site: www.awb.com

Pres & ISBN Contact: Phil Zuckerman
  E-mail: philz@awb.com
VP, Opers: Sue Cabezas *E-mail:* suec@awb.com
Founded: 1976
Americana reprints.
ISBN Prefix(es): 0-918222; 1-55709
Number of titles published annually: 20 Print
Total Titles: 450 Print
Warehouse: Consortium, 1045 Westgate Dr, St
  Paul, MN 55114-1065

Appraisal Institute
550 W Van Buren St, Suite 1000, Chicago, IL
  60607
Tel: 312-335-4100 *Fax:* 312-335-4400
Web Site: www.appraisalinstitute.org
Key Personnel
Dir, Pubns: Stephanie Shea-Joyce
Founded: 1932
Professional real estate appraisal books, mono-
  graphs, periodicals & videos.
ISBN Prefix(es): 0-911780; 0-922154
Number of titles published annually: 5 Print
Total Titles: 75 Print
Distributed by Dearborn Trade
Foreign Rep(s): Royal Institution of Chartered
  Surveyors (Africa, Caribbean, Commonwealth,
  Europe, Far East, Ethiopia)
Distribution Center: Appraisal Institute, c/o CBI
  Corp, 859 Fiene Dr, Addison, IL 60101 *Toll
  Free Tel:* 888-570-4545 *Fax:* 630-628-1649
  Web Site: www.appraisalinstitute.org

§APS Press
Imprint of The American Phytopathological Soci-
  ety
3340 Pilot Knob Rd, St Paul, MN 55121-2097
Tel: 651-454-7250 *Toll Free Tel:* 800-328-7560
  Fax: 651-454-0766
E-mail: aps@scisoc.org
Web Site: www.shopapspress.org
Key Personnel
VP: Steve Nelson *E-mail:* snelson@scisoc.org
Mktg Dir: Greg Grahek *E-mail:* ggrahek@scisoc.
  org
Founded: 1908
Publishers of key reference books, field guides,
  laboratory manuals & other scientific titles re-
  lated to plant health.
ISBN Prefix(es): 0-89054; 84-7114; 84-8476
Number of titles published annually: 10 Print; 2
  CD-ROM; 4 Online
Total Titles: 200 Print; 15 CD-ROM; 2 Online
Foreign Office(s): Stanislas de Rijcklaan,
  BE-3001 Heverlee, Belgium, Hilde Ke-
  unen *Tel:* (016) 204035 *Fax:* (016) 202535
  E-mail: aps@scisoceurope.org

Aqua Quest Publications Inc
18 Garvies Point Rd, Glen Cove, NY 11542
Mailing Address: PO Box 700, Locust Valley, NY
  11560-0700
Tel: 516-759-0476 *Toll Free Tel:* 800-933-8989
  Fax: 516-759-4519
E-mail: info@aquaquest.com
Web Site: www.aquaquest.com
Key Personnel
Pres: Anthony A Bliss, Jr *E-mail:* tbliss@
  aquaquest.com
Opers Mgr: Josefina A Bliss *E-mail:* josiebliss@
  aquaquest.com
Founded: 1989
Publishes & distributes books on scuba div-
  ing, dive travel destinations, underwater
  photo/video, marine life, technical diving, ma-
  rine related children's books, shipwrecks &
  dive related fiction.
ISBN Prefix(es): 0-9623389; 1-881652; 0-922769
Number of titles published annually: 4 Print; 1 E-
  Book
Total Titles: 39 Print; 1 E-Book

Imprints: Watersport Books
Distributor for J L Publications
Distribution Center: National Book Network,
  15200 NBN Way, Blue Ridge Summit, PA
  17214 *Tel:* 717-794-3800 *Toll Free Tel:* 800-
  462-6420 *Toll Free Fax:* 800-338-4550
Membership(s): Publishers Marketing Association

Arbutus Press
2364 Pinehurst Trail, Traverse City, MI 49686
Tel: 231-946-7240 *Toll Free Tel:* 866-794-8793
  Fax: 231-946-4196
E-mail: info@arbutuspress.com
Web Site: www.arbutuspress.com
Founded: 1998
Midwest regional history & travel related.
ISBN Prefix(es): 0-9665316
Number of titles published annually: 3 Print
Total Titles: 8 Print; 3 Audio
Membership(s): Great Lakes Booksellers Associa-
  tion; Publishers Marketing Association

§Arcade Publishing Inc
141 Fifth Ave, New York, NY 10010
Tel: 212-475-2633 *Fax:* 212-353-8148
E-mail: arcadeinfo@arcadepub.com
Web Site: www.arcadepub.com
Key Personnel
Pres & Ed-in-Chief: Richard Seaver
Publr & Dir, Mktg & Publicity: Jeannette M
  Seaver *E-mail:* publicity@arcadepub.com
Gen Mgr & Sr Ed: Calvert Barksdale *E-mail:* cal.
  barksdale@arcadepub.com
Intl Rts: James Jayo *E-mail:* james.jayo@
  arcadepub.com
Publicity Mgr: Casey Ebro
Asst Ed: Savannah Ashour
Founded: 1988
Sales & distribution handled by Time Warner
  Book Group. For subsidiary rights, including
  foreign rights, address Arcade. Trade fiction &
  nonfiction; adult & juvenile.
ISBN Prefix(es): 1-55970; 1-58996
Number of titles published annually: 45 Print; 5
  E-Book
Total Titles: 506 Print; 12 E-Book; 2 Audio
Distributed by Time Warner Book Group
Foreign Rights: Arcade

Arcadia Enterprises Inc
PO Box 206, Fruitland, MD 21826
Tel: 410-742-2682 *Toll Free Tel:* 877-742-2682
  Fax: 410-742-2708
Web Site: www.buyarcadiabooks.com
Key Personnel
Pres: Elaine Patterson *E-mail:* ehpatterson@
  melleniaisp.com
Founded: 1999
Provide quality books on various topics & by
  various authors to help celebrate America's
  uniqueness...people, events, culture & envi-
  rons. Services provided are publishing services,
  author-subsidy program, consignments, dis-
  tribution services via national company, book
  searches & website exposure through major
  online booksellers.
ISBN Prefix(es): 0-9703802
Number of titles published annually: 3 Print
Total Titles: 3 Print; 3 Online
Distributor for Dogwood Ridge Books; Tapestry
  Press Ltd
Orders to: Biblio Distribution, A Division of Na-
  tional Book Network, 15200 NBN Network,
  Blue Ridge Summit, PA 17214, Contact: Ruth
  Proctor *Tel:* 717-794-3805 ext 3565 *Fax:* 717-
  794-3828 *E-mail:* jwetzel@nbnbooks.com
Returns: Biblio Distribution, A Division of Na-
  tional Book Network, 15200 NBN Network,
  Blue Ridge Summit, PA 17214, Contact: Ruth
  Proctor *Tel:* 717-794-3805 ext 3565 *Fax:* 717-
  794-3828 *E-mail:* jwetzel@nbnbooks.com

Shipping Address: Biblio Distribution, A Divi-
  sion of National Book Network, 15200 NBN
  Network, Blue Ridge Summit, PA 17214, Con-
  tact: Ruth Proctor *Tel:* 717-794-3805 ext 3565
  Fax: 717-794-3828 *E-mail:* jwetzel@nbnbooks.
  com
Warehouse: Biblio Distribution, A Division of
  National Book Network, 15200 NBN Network,
  Blue Ridge Summit, PA 17214, Contact: Ruth
  Proctor *Tel:* 717-794-3805 ext 3565 *Fax:* 717-
  794-3828 *E-mail:* jwetzel@nbnbooks.com
Distribution Center: Biblio Distribution, A Divi-
  sion of National Book Network, 15200 NBN
  Network, Blue Ridge Summit, PA 17214, Con-
  tact: Ruth Proctor *Tel:* 717-794-3805 ext 3565
  Fax: 717-794-3828 *E-mail:* jwetzel@nbnbooks.
  com

Arcadia Publishing
Imprint of Tempus Publishing Group
420 Wando Park Blvd, Mount Pleasant, SC 29464
Tel: 843-853-2070 *Toll Free Tel:* 888-313-2665
  (orders only) *Fax:* 843-853-0044
E-mail: sales@arcadiapublishing.com
Web Site: www.arcadiapublishing.com
Key Personnel
Opers Dir: John Ragland
Sales Dir: Kate Everingham
  E-mail: keveringham@arcadiapublishing.com
Founded: 1992
Local history & vintage images.
ISBN Prefix(es): 0-7524; 0-7385
Number of titles published annually: 550 Print
Total Titles: 1,700 Print; 1,700 Online
Branch Office(s)
Midwest, 3047 N Lincoln Ave, Suite 410,
  Chicago, IL 60657, Publr: John Pearson
  Tel: 773-549-7002 *Fax:* 773-549-7190
  E-mail: jpearson@arcadiapublishing.com
Northeast, 224 State St, Portsmouth, NH
  03801, Publr: Amy Sutton *Tel:* 603-436-7610
  Fax: 603-436-7611
Foreign Office(s): Tempus Publishing Ltd, The
  Mill, Brimscome Port, Stroud, Gloucestershire
  GL5 2QG, United Kingdom, Mgr: Stephen
  Lambe *Tel:* (01453) 883300 *Fax:* (01453)
  883233 *E-mail:* group@tempus-publishing.com
  Web Site: www.tempus-publishing.com
Foreign Rep(s): Tempus Publishing Ltd (UK);
  Vanwell Publishing Ltd (Canada)
Warehouse: North Mill, 100 Main St, 2nd fl,
  Somersworth, NH 03878, Dist Mgr: Cherilynn
  Moulton

Arcana Publishing, see Lotus Press

ArcheBooks Publishing
Division of Gelinas & Wolf Inc
9101 W Sahara Ave, Suite 105-112, Las Vegas,
  NV 89117
Tel: 702-253-1338 *Toll Free Tel:* 800-358-8101
  Fax: 561-868-2127
E-mail: publisher@archebooks.com
Web Site: www.archebooks.com
Key Personnel
Publr: Robert E Gelinas *Tel:* 770-360-9877
  Fax: 770-521-0065 *E-mail:* robert.gelinas@
  archebooks.com
EVP Sales: Ralph C Wolf *E-mail:* ralph.wolf@
  archebooks.com
Founded: 2003
Independent publisher of original fiction; general
  trade books hardcover & electronic books.
ISBN Prefix(es): 1-59507
Number of titles published annually: 40 Print; 40
  E-Book
Total Titles: 7 Print; 7 E-Book
Distribution Center: Baker & Taylor
Ingram Book

Archer Books
PO Box 1254, Santa Maria, CA 93456-1254

Tel: 805-934-9977 *Fax:* 805-934-9977
E-mail: info@archer-books.com
Web Site: www.archer-books.com
Key Personnel
Partner: John Taylor-Conrey *E-mail:* jtc@archer-books.com; Rosemary Tribulato
Founded: 1997
ISBN Prefix(es): 0-9662299; 1-931122
Number of titles published annually: 5 Print
Total Titles: 18 Print
Membership(s): Publishers Marketing Association

Arden Press Inc
PO Box 418, Denver, CO 80201-0418
Tel: 303-697-6766 *Fax:* 303-697-3443
E-mail: ardenpress@msn.com
Key Personnel
Pres, Ed & Intl Rts: Susan Conley
Founded: 1982
Nonfiction & primarily women's studies.
ISBN Prefix(es): 0-912869
Number of titles published annually: 3 Print
Total Titles: 14 Print
Returns: 20723 Seminole Rd, Indian Hills, CO 80454
Shipping Address: 20723 Seminole Rd, Indian Hills, CO 80454
Membership(s): Publishers Marketing Association

§Ardent Media Inc
522 E 82 St, Suite 1, New York, NY 10028
Tel: 212-861-1501 *Fax:* 212-861-0998
E-mail: ivyboxer@aol.com
Key Personnel
Pres & Edit Dir: Irving B Naiburg, Jr
Founded: 1974
Paperbacks, trade, textbooks, professional & reference books, Irvington Reprint Series (article reprints, formerly Bobbs-Merrill Reprint Series).
ISBN Prefix(es): 0-89197; 0-8422; 0-8290
Number of titles published annually: 15 Print
Total Titles: 4,500 Print
Distributor for Cyrco Press; MSS Information Corp
Foreign Rep(s): Gazelle Book Services Ltd (UK, Europe, Former USSR, Turkey)
Shipping Address: ACC Distribution, 91 Market St Industrial Park, Wappingers Falls, NY 12590 *Toll Free Tel:* 800-472-6037 *Toll Free Fax:* 800-455-5520
Warehouse: ACC Distribution, 91 Market St Industrial Park, Wappingers Falls, NY 12590 *Toll Free Tel:* 800-472-6037 *Toll Free Fax:* 800-455-5520

ARE Press
Division of The Association for Research & Enlightenment Inc (ARE)
215 67 St, Virginia Beach, VA 23451
Tel: 757-428-3588 *Toll Free Tel:* 800-333-4499 *Fax:* 757-491-0689
E-mail: are@edgarcayce.org
Web Site: www.edgarcayce.org *Telex:* CAYCE
Key Personnel
Prodn Mgr: Cassie M McQuagge
Sr Ed: Ken Skidmore
Trade Coord: Kathryn Kelly
Founded: 1931
Holistic health & spiritual development, based on Edgar Cayse material.
ISBN Prefix(es): 0-87604
Number of titles published annually: 10 Print
Total Titles: 156 Print; 2 CD-ROM
Divisions: Atlantic University; Edgar Cayce Foundation; Cayce-Reilly School of Massotherapy

Ariadne Press
270 Goins Ct, Riverside, CA 92507
Tel: 951-684-9202 *Fax:* 951-779-0449
E-mail: ariadnepress@aol.com

Web Site: ariadnepress.com
Key Personnel
Partner: Jorun Johns
Founded: 1988
Studies in Austrian literature, culture & thought.
ISBN Prefix(es): 0-929497; 1-57241
Number of titles published annually: 12 Print
Total Titles: 205 Print
Foreign Office(s): Schaden, Sonnenfelsgassde 4, A-1010 Vienna, Austria *Tel:* (01) 512-4856 *Fax:* (01) 512-6028 *E-mail:* buch.schaden@vienna.at
Foreign Rep(s): Schaden (Austria)
Foreign Rights: Gazelle (UK)

Ariel Press
Subsidiary of Light
90 Steve Tate Hwy, Suite 201, Marble Hill, GA 30148
SAN: 652-1363
Mailing Address: PO Box 297, Marble Hill, GA 30148
Tel: 770-894-4226 *Fax:* 706-579-1865 (orders)
Key Personnel
Pres & Publr: Carl Japikse *Tel:* 706-579-1274 *E-mail:* carl@lightariel.com
Art Dir: Nancy Maxwell
Founded: 1975
Nonfiction hardcover & paperbound books; essays & subscription series on personal growth, creativity, holistic health & psychic phenomena; esoteric fiction; reprints.
ISBN Prefix(es): 0-89804
Number of titles published annually: 20 Print
Total Titles: 110 Print
Imprints: Enthea; Kudzu House; Metascience
Distributor for Enthea; Kudzu House

Ariel Starr Productions Ltd
PO Box 17, Demarest, NJ 07627-0017
Tel: 201-784-9148 *Fax:* 201-541-8796
E-mail: darkbird@aol.com
Key Personnel
Pres: Cynthia Soroka
Founded: 1991
Publish any new & innovative projects.
ISBN Prefix(es): 1-889122
Number of titles published annually: 3 Print; 2 Audio
Total Titles: 16 Print; 1 Audio
Foreign Rights: ANU at Atmarr Agency (outside the US)

The Arion Press
Division of Lyra Corp
The Presidio, 1802 Hays St, San Francisco, CA 94129
SAN: 203-1361
Tel: 415-561-2542 *Fax:* 415-561-2545
E-mail: arionpress@arionpress.com
Web Site: www.arionpress.com
Key Personnel
Publr: Andrew Hoyem
Cont: Charles Martin
Founded: 1974
Fine, limited edition illustrated books of fiction, literature & poetry.
ISBN Prefix(es): 0-910457
Number of titles published annually: 3 Print
Total Titles: 68 Print
Divisions: M & H Type

Arjuna Library Press
1025 Garner St D, Space 18, Colorado Springs, CO 80905-1774
Key Personnel
Dir & Ed-in-Chief: Count Joseph Uphoff, Jr
Founded: 1979
Presenting Surrealist Works as experiments in Abstract Realism. The ontology is a study of real shadows from fantasy objects in the con-

text of Visual Poetics, Creative Literature & Differential Logic.
ISBN Prefix(es): 0-943123
Number of titles published annually: 3 Print
Total Titles: 100 Print
Subsidiaries: The Journal of Regional Criticism

Arkansas Research Inc
PO Box 303, Conway, AR 72033-0303
Tel: 501-470-1120 *Fax:* 501-470-1120
Web Site: www.arkansasresearch.com
Key Personnel
Owner & Lib Sales Dir: Ms Desmond Walls Allen *E-mail:* desmond@ipa.net
Founded: 1985
Genealogy & historical material.
ISBN Prefix(es): 1-56546; 0-941765
Number of titles published annually: 20 Print
Total Titles: 290 Print

Arkham House Publishers Inc
PO Box 546, Sauk City, WI 53583-0546
SAN: 206-9741
Tel: 608-643-4500 *Fax:* 608-643-5043
E-mail: sales@arkhamhouse.com
Web Site: www.arkhamhouse.com
Key Personnel
Pres: April Derleth *E-mail:* ard@chorus.net
Founded: 1939
Fantasy fiction; horror, macabre, science fiction.
ISBN Prefix(es): 0-87054
Number of titles published annually: 5 Print
Total Titles: 50 Print; 50 Online; 50 E-Book
Imprints: Mycroft & Moran

Armenian Publishing Shirak, see Shirak

Armenian Reference Books Co
PO Box 231, Glendale, CA 91209
Tel: 818-504-2550 *Toll Free Tel:* 877-504-2550 *Fax:* 818-504-9283
E-mail: info@vassiliansdepot.com
Web Site: www.vassiliansdepot.com/arb
Key Personnel
Pres, Ed & Publr: Hamo Vassilian
Founded: 1983
Armenian.
ISBN Prefix(es): 0-931539
Number of titles published annually: 5 Print
Total Titles: 15 Print
Imprints: Armenian Genocide-Bibliography; Armenian Reference Books; Armenian Wisdom; Armenian Yellow Pages; The Armenians; Armenians & Iran; Ethnic Cuisines: A Comprehensive Biblio

Arnica Publishing Inc
3739 SE Eighth Ave, Portland, OR 97202
Tel: 503-225-9900 *Fax:* 503-225-9901
E-mail: info@arnicapublishing.com
Web Site: www.arnicapublishing.com
Key Personnel
Ed-in-Chief: Gloria Gonzalez
Founded: 2002
Nonfiction publisher with emphasis on health care, self-help & business. Idea development, editing, text formatting & cover design, print management, marketing, warehousing, fulfillment, national distribution, rights sales.
ISBN Prefix(es): 1-58151; 0-9726535
Number of titles published annually: 5 Print
Total Titles: 9 Print; 2 Audio
Distributor for New Leaf

Jason Aronson Inc
Imprint of Rowman & Littlefield Publishing Group
4501 Forbes Blvd, Lanham, MD 20706
SAN: 201-0127

Toll Free Tel: 800-462-6420 (orders) *Fax:* 201-767-4330; 201-767-1576 (orders)
Web Site: www.aronson.com
Founded: 1965
Professional books in psychotherapy, psychoanalysis & Judaica.
ISBN Prefix(es): 0-87668; 1-56821; 0-7657
Number of titles published annually: 30 Print
Total Titles: 1,700 Print
Foreign Rep(s): Baker & Taylor International (all other countries); For Psychotherapy: Astam Books Pty Ltd (Australia)
Foreign Rights: The Marsh Agency

§Arrow Map Inc
Affiliate of Langenscheidt Publishers Inc
58 Norfolk Ave, Unit 4, South Easton, MA 02375
Tel: 508-230-2112 *Toll Free Tel:* 800-343-7500
Fax: 508-230-8186
E-mail: amisales@arrowmap.com
Web Site: www.arrowmap.com
Key Personnel
Sales Dir: Steven T Haringa *E-mail:* sharinga@arrowmap.com
Prodn Dir: Kent Swift *E-mail:* kswift@arrowmap.com
Founded: 1970
Publish & distribute maps, atlases, street guides & zip code directories.
ISBN Prefix(es): 0-913450; 1-55751
Number of titles published annually: 100 Print
Total Titles: 150 Print; 1 CD-ROM

§Art Direction Book Co Inc
456 Glenbrook Rd, Glenbrook, CT 06906
SAN: 208-4023
Tel: 203-353-1441 *Fax:* 203-353-1371
Key Personnel
Pres & Rts & Perms: Don Barron
Prodn Mgr & ISBN Contact: Karyn Mugmon
Founded: 1946
Advertising art & graphic design, book trade reference, crafts, how-to, trademarks & logotypes.
ISBN Prefix(es): 0-910158; 0-88108
Number of titles published annually: 4 Print; 2 CD-ROM
Total Titles: 191 Print; 10 CD-ROM
Imprints: Infosource Publications Inc
Foreign Rep(s): Baker & Taylor International

Art from Latin America
Box 1948, Murray Hill Sta, New York, NY 10156-0612
Tel: 212-683-2136
Key Personnel
Dir & Ed: Gwendolyn K Bennaton *E-mail:* gwenbenn@yahoo.com
Newsletters on Latin American art in New York. Central American writers. Three Mexican Matrons of the Arts. Books on Honduras. Forthcoming issues on museums. Garifuna, Lenca, the Maya culture. Reports on emerging artists.
ISBN Prefix(es): 0-937538
Number of titles published annually: 3 Print
Total Titles: 10 Print

Art Image Publications
Division of GB Publishing Inc
PO Box 160, Derby Line, VT 05830-0160
Toll Free Tel: 800-361-2598 *Toll Free Fax:* 800-559-2598
E-mail: info@artimagepublications.com
Web Site: www.artimagepublications.com
Key Personnel
CEO: Yvan Boulerice
Educ Consultant: Rachel Ross
ISBN Prefix(es): 1-896876; 1-55292
Number of titles published annually: 12 Print
Total Titles: 52 Print

Art Institute of Chicago
111 S Michigan Ave, Chicago, IL 60603-6110

SAN: 204-479X
Tel: 312-443-3600; 312-443-3540 (pubns); 312-443-3533 (sales & orders) *Fax:* 312-443-0849; 312-443-1334 (pubns)
E-mail: webmaster@artic.edu
Web Site: www.artic.edu
Key Personnel
Dir & Pres: James N Wood *Tel:* 312-443-3632 *E-mail:* jwood@artic.edu
Exec Dir, Pubns: Susan F Rossen *Tel:* 312-443-4962
Dir, Pub Aff: Mary Minch *Tel:* 312-443-7263
Founded: 1879
Exhibition catalogues, periodicals, professional & scholarly books; specialize in art & architecture; museum book publishing.
ISBN Prefix(es): 0-86559
Number of titles published annually: 10 Print
Total Titles: 60 Print
Distributed by Abbeville Publishing Group; Harry N Abrams Inc; Bulfinch Press; Chronicle Books; Distributed Art Publishers (DAP); Ernst & Sohn; Editorial Gustavo Gili SA; Grupo Azabache; Hudson Hills Press Inc; Dorling Kindersley Ltd; LTI (Learn Technologies Interactive); Ars Nicolai (Great Britain Scandinavia & Europe; Prestel-Verlag; Princeton Univ Press; Rizzoli International Publications Inc; Thames & Hudson; Thames & Hudson (UK); University of Chicago Press; University of Indiana Press; University of Washington Press; Ernst Wasmuth Verlag

Artabras Inc
Division of Abbeville Publishing Group
116 W 23 St, Suite 500, New York, NY 10011
SAN: 211-349X
Tel: 646-375-2039 *Toll Free Tel:* 800-ART-BOOK *Fax:* 646-375-2040
E-mail: abbeville@abbeville.com
Web Site: www.abbeville.com
Key Personnel
Pres & Publr: Robert E Abrams
Cont & Dir, Fin Analysis: John Olivieri
Publicity Dir: Amber Reed
Edit Dir: Susan Costello
Prodn Mgr: Louise Kurtz
Cust Fulfillment Mgr: Nadine Winns
Warehouse Dir: Arthur Goldberg
Founded: 1974
Publishers of high quality fine art & illustrated books, children's books, reprint promotional books; limited editions, prints, calendars, gift line.
ISBN Prefix(es): 0-89660; 0-7892; 0-55859
Number of titles published annually: 40 Print
Total Titles: 700 Print
Imprints: Abbeville; Abbeville Kids; Artabras; Modern Masters
Foreign Rep(s): Bookport Associates (Greece, Italy, Portugal, Spain); Cameron, Reynolds & Associates (Canada, Western Provinces); Claus Schmogner, Petra Poker (Central Germany); Inter-Art (France, Monaco); International Publishers Representatives (Africa, Middle East, Near East); McLeod, Garner & Associates Ltd (Ontario); John Murray Ltd (UK, Ireland); Nationwide Book Distributors (New Zealand); Nilsson & Lamm BV (Belgium, Netherlands, Luxembourg); Onslow Books Ltd (Austria, Scandinavia, Switzerland); Peribo Pty Ltd (Australia); Ralph Sheila Summers (Asia); Michael Timperley (Eastern Europe); Wolfgang Willmann, Suzanne Sieger, c/o Glockenbach buch handling (Southern Germany); Yohan/Western Publications (Japan)
Foreign Rights: Agence Literaire Alexandra Chapman (Belgium, Denmark, Netherlands, Finland, France, Norway, Sweden); Bookbank, SA (Latin America, Mexico, Spain); Motovun Tokyo (Japan); Ultreya srl (Italy)

Warehouse: Coordinated Systems & Services Corp, Bldg 424, Raritan Ctr, Edison, NJ 08817
Client Distribution Services, 193 Edwards Dr, Jackson, TN 38301

Arte Publico Press
Affiliate of University of Houston
University of Houston, 4800 Calhoun, Houston, TX 77204-2174
Tel: 713-743-2841 *Toll Free Tel:* 800-633-2783 *Fax:* 713-743-2847
Web Site: www.arte.uh.edu
Key Personnel
Publr: Nicolas Kanellos
Publicist: Marina Tristan
Intl Rts: Carmen Pena
Busn Mgr: Patricia Sayles
Sales Mgr: Charles Baker
Founded: 1979
Books by American Hispanic authors.
ISBN Prefix(es): 0-934770; 1-55885
Number of titles published annually: 35 Print
Total Titles: 322 Print
Imprints: Pinata Books
Subsidiaries: The Americas Review
Distributor for Bilingual Review Press; Latin American Review Press
Foreign Rights: Mr Kiyoshi Asano (Japan); Elaine Benisti (France); Raquel de la Concha (Spain); Michael Meller (Germany)
Membership(s): AAP

§Artech House Inc
Subsidiary of Horizon House Publications Inc
685 Canton St, Norwood, MA 02062
SAN: 201-1441
Tel: 781-769-9750 *Toll Free Tel:* 800-225-9977 *Fax:* 781-769-6334
E-mail: artech@artechhouse.com
Web Site: www.artechhouse.com *Telex:* 230-951-659
Key Personnel
COO: Christopher Ernst *E-mail:* cernst@artechhouse.com
Publr: William M Bazzy
Dir, Sales, Mktg & Busn Devt: John W Stone *E-mail:* jwstone@artechhouse.com
Exec Ed: Judi Stone
Sr Acq Ed: Mark Walsh *E-mail:* mwalsh@artechhouse.com
Edit & Prodn Dir: Darrell Judd
Founded: 1970
Technical & engineering.
ISBN Prefix(es): 0-89006; 1-58053
Number of titles published annually: 70 Print; 60 E-Book
Total Titles: 465 Print; 5 CD-ROM; 150 E-Book
Foreign Office(s): 46 Gillingham St, London 5W1V 1AH, United Kingdom *Tel:* (020) 7596 8750 *Fax:* (020) 7630 0166 *E-mail:* artech-uk@artechhouse.com *Web Site:* www.artechhouse.com
Foreign Rep(s): Akateeminen (Finland); Anglo-American Book Co (Italy); Asian Books Pvt Ltd (India, Pakistan); C V Toko Buku Topen (Indonesia); Clarke Associates Ltd (Pacific Basin); Computer Press (Sweden); D A Book Pty Ltd (Australia, New Zealand); Dai-Iti Publications Trading Co Ltd (Japan); Diaz de Santos (Spain); Dietmar Dreier (Germany); DK Book House Co Ltd (Thailand); Freihofer AG (Switzerland); Julio Logrado de Figueiredo Lda (Portugal); Kumi Trading Co Ltd (South Korea); Librairie Lavoisier (France); Login Brothers (Canada); The Modern Book Co (UK); Pak Book Corporation (Pakistan); Polyteknisk (Denmark); Sejong (Korea); Ta Tong Book Co Ltd (Taiwan); Tapir (Norway); Tecmedd (Brazil); UBS Library Services (Singapore); United Publishers Services Ltd (Japan, South Korea); L Wouters (Belgium)
Foreign Rights: ABE Marketing (Poland); BSB Distribution (Germany); Distibuidora Cusipide

(Argentina); Fleet Publications (Chile); Foyles (UK); Hoepli (Italy); Kooy Ker-Ginsberg (Netherlands); Kuwkab (Mideast); Livraria Canuto (Brazil); Papsotiriou (Greece)
Warehouse: Publishers Storage & Shipping (US only), 231 Industrial Park, 46 Development Rd, Fitchburg, MA 01420 *Tel:* 978-345-2121 *Fax:* 978-348-1233

Artisan
Division of Workman Publishing Company Inc
708 Broadway, New York, NY 10003-9555
Tel: 212-254-5900 *Fax:* 212-254-8098
E-mail: artisaninfo@workman.com
Web Site: www.artisanbooks.com
Key Personnel
Publr: Ann Bramson
Exec Ed: Deborah Weiss Geline
Sr Ed: Pamela Cannon
Design Dir: Vivian Ghazarian
Lib Sales Dir: Maribeth Casey
Intl Rts: Carolan R Workman
Founded: 1993
Illustrated books & calendars to the trade.
ISBN Prefix(es): 1-885183; 1-57965
Number of titles published annually: 10 Print
Distributor for Greenwich Workshop Press
Shipping Address: George Banta Co, 677 Brighton Beach Rd, Menasha, WI 54952-2998

Ascension Press
Member of Catholic Word
20 Hagerty Blvd, Suite 3, West Chester, PA 19382
Tel: 610-696-7795 *Toll Free Tel:* 800-376-0520 (sales off) *Fax:* 610-696-7796; 608-565-2025 (sales off)
E-mail: info@ascensionpress.com
Web Site: www.ascensionpress.com
Key Personnel
Dir, Sales: Lynn Kilka *Tel:* 608-565-2020 *E-mail:* lynnklika@tds.net
ISBN Prefix(es): 1-932645; 0-9742238; 0-9659228; 0-9744451; 1-5705848
Number of titles published annually: 5 Print
Total Titles: 33 Online; 40 Online
Sales Office(s): W5180 Jefferson St, Necedah, WI 54646, Contact: Lynn Klika *Tel:* 608-565-2020 *Toll Free Tel:* 800-376-0520 *Fax:* 608-565-5025 *E-mail:* lynnklika@tds.net *Web Site:* www.ascensionpress.com
Orders to: W5180 Jefferson St, Necedah, WI 54646, Lynn Klika *Tel:* 608-565-2020 *Toll Free Tel:* 800-376-0520 *Fax:* 608-565-2025 *E-mail:* lynnklika@tds.net *Web Site:* www.ascensionpress.com
Returns: W5180 Jefferson St, Necedah, WI 54646, Lynn Klika *Tel:* 608-565-2020 *Toll Free Tel:* 800-376-0520 *Fax:* 608-565-2025 *E-mail:* lynnklika@tds.net *Web Site:* www.ascensionpress.com
Warehouse: W5180 Jefferson St, Necedah, WI 54646, Lynn Klika *Tel:* 608-565-2020 *Toll Free Tel:* 800-376-0520 *Fax:* 608-565-2025 *E-mail:* lynnklika@tds.net *Web Site:* www.ascensionpress.com
Distribution Center: W5180 Jefferson St, Necedah, WI 54646, Lynn Klika *Tel:* 608-565-2020 *Toll Free Tel:* 800-376-0520 *Fax:* 608-565-2025 *E-mail:* lynnklika@tds.net *Web Site:* www.ascensionpress.com

ASCP Press
Subsidiary of American Society for Clinical Pathology
2100 W Harrison St, Chicago, IL 60612
SAN: 207-9429
Tel: 312-738-4866; 312-738-1336
Toll Free Tel: 800-621-4142 *Fax:* 312-738-1619
Web Site: www.ascp.org

Key Personnel
Publr: Joshua R Weikersheimer
E-mail: joshuaw@ascp.org
Founded: 1959
Books, multimedia, slide sets, atlases, audiovisual seminars, videotapes, manuals, interactive software & videodiscs for lab professionals. Subjects include continuing education.
ISBN Prefix(es): 0-89189
Number of titles published annually: 15 Print; 13 CD-ROM; 7 Online
Total Titles: 212 Print; 31 CD-ROM; 7 Online

Ashgate Publishing Co
Subsidiary of Ashgate Publishing Ltd
101 Cherry St, Suite 420, Burlington, VT 05401-4405
SAN: 262-0308
Tel: 802-865-7641 *Fax:* 802-865-7847
E-mail: info@ashgate.com
Web Site: www.ashgate.com
Key Personnel
Pres: Barbara J Church *E-mail:* bchurch@ashgate.com
Mktg Mgr: Brandon DeCoff
Fin Cont: Ann Marie Abajian-Harvey
Founded: 1979
Professional, scholarly & reference books, CD-ROMs.
ISBN Prefix(es): 0-566; 1-85742; 0-85967; 1-85628; 0-86078; 0-86127; 0-85331; 0-291; 0-7546; 1-85521; 1-85928; 1-84014; 0-85417
Number of titles published annually: 650 Print
Total Titles: 7,000 Print; 6 CD-ROM
Imprints: Ashgate; Dartmouth Publishing; Gower; Lund Humphries; Gregg Revivals; Scolar; Variorum
Distributor for A A Balkema Publishers; Gower Publishing; Gregg; Lund Humphries; Pickering & Chatto; Swets & Zeitlinger Publishers

Ashland Poetry Press
Affiliate of Ashland University
Ashland University, 401 College Ave, Ashland, OH 44805
Tel: 419-289-5110 *Fax:* 419-289-5638
Web Site: www.ashland.edu/aupoetry
Key Personnel
Ed: Dr Steve Haven *E-mail:* shaven@ashland.edu
Founded: 1969
ISBN Prefix(es): 0-912592
Number of titles published annually: 3 Print
Total Titles: 32 Print

ASIS International
1625 Prince St, Alexandria, VA 22314
Tel: 703-518-1475 *Fax:* 703-518-1517
Key Personnel
Educ Publg Mgr: Evangeline A Pappas
E-mail: epappas@asisonline.org
Founded: 1955
Organization for security professionals, with more than 33,000 members worldwide. Dedicated to increasing the effectiveness & productivy of security professionals by developing educational programs & materials that address broad security interests, such as the annual seminar & exhibits, as well as specific security topics. Also advocates the role & value of the security management profession to business, the media, government entities & the public.
ISBN Prefix(es): 1-887056
Number of titles published annually: 6 Print; 2 CD-ROM; 5 Audio
Total Titles: 17 Print; 2 CD-ROM; 5 Audio

Aslan Publishing
Subsidiary of Renaissance Book Services Corp
2490 Black Rock Tpke, Fairfield, CT 06432
SAN: 242-6129
Tel: 203-372-0300 *Toll Free Tel:* 800-786-5427
Fax: 203-374-4766

E-mail: info@aslanpublishing.com
Web Site: www.aslanpublishing.com
Key Personnel
Pres & Lib Sales Dir: Harold Levine
E-mail: harold@aslanpublishing.com
Pubns Dir: Barbara Levine
Founded: 1987
Publish nonfiction books.
ISBN Prefix(es): 0-944031
Number of titles published annually: 6 Print
Total Titles: 30 Print
Foreign Rep(s): Peaceful Living (New Zealand); Windrush (England)
Billing Address: 1501 County Hospital Rd, Nashville, TN 37218
Orders to: 1501 County Hospital Rd, Nashville, TN 37218
Returns: 1501 County Hospital Rd, Nashville, TN 37218
Warehouse: 1501 County Hospital Rd, Nashville, TN 37218, Contact: Ken Brown *Tel:* 615-254-2433 *Fax:* 615-254-2408

§ASM International
9639 Kinsman Rd, Materials Park, OH 44073-0002
SAN: 204-7586
Tel: 440-338-5151 *Toll Free Tel:* 800-336-5152; 800-368-9800 (Europe) *Fax:* 440-338-4634
E-mail: cust-srv@asminternational.org
Web Site: www.asminternational.org *Telex:* 98-0619 ASMINT
Key Personnel
Dir, Tech Pubns: William Scott
Electronic Publg: Fran Cverna
Founded: 1913
Technical & reference books.
ISBN Prefix(es): 0-87170
Number of titles published annually: 18 Print; 5 CD-ROM; 35 Online
Total Titles: 210 Print; 25 CD-ROM; 1,000 Online
Foreign Rep(s): ATP (Europe); B I Publications (India); Sejong Books Inc (Korea)
Warehouse: 14800 Munnberry Oval, Newbury, OH 44065

§ASM Press
Division of American Society for Microbiology
1752 "N" St NW, Washington, DC 20036-2904
Tel: 202-737-3600 *Toll Free Tel:* 800-546-2416
Fax: 202-942-9342
E-mail: books@asmusa.org
Web Site: www.asmpress.org
Key Personnel
Exec Dir: Michael Goldberg *E-mail:* mgoldberg@asmusa.org
Dir, Books Div: Jeffrey Holtmeier
E-mail: jholtmeier@asmusa.org
Mktg Mgr, Journals: Daphne Greenwood
E-mail: dgreenwood@asmusa.org
Prod Mgr, Books Div: Susan Birch
E-mail: sbirch@asmusa.org
Dir, Journals Div: Linda Illig *E-mail:* lillig@asmusa.org
Mktg Asst, Book Div: Holly L Koppel
E-mail: hkoppel@asmusa.org
Mktg Mgr & Edit Asst, Books Div: Jennifer Adelman *E-mail:* jadelman@asmusa.org
Founded: 1899
Specialize in microbiology, cell biology, medicine, books, journals, proceedings & abstracts.
ISBN Prefix(es): 1-55581; 0-914826
Number of titles published annually: 25 Print; 1 CD-ROM; 1 Online
Total Titles: 120 Print; 3 CD-ROM; 1 Online
Foreign Rep(s): APAC Publishers Services Pte Ltd (Asia exc Korea & China); Blackwell Publishing (Africa, UK, Europe, Middle East); Cassidy & Associates (China); EBS (Japan); Information & Culture Korea (ICK) (Korea); Journal Importacion y Distribucion (Argentina);

Donald MacIvor & Assoc (Canada); R Seshadri (India)
Orders to: PO Box 605, Herndon, VA 20172
Tel: 703-661-1593 *Toll Free Tel:* 800-546-2416
Fax: 703-661-1501
Returns: 2283 Quicksilver Dr, Dulles, VA 20166

Aspatore Books
264 Beacon St, 2nd fl, Boston, MA 02116
Tel: 617-369-7017 *Fax:* 617-249-1970
E-mail: info@aspatore.com
Web Site: www.aspatore.com
Key Personnel
CEO & Publr: Jonathan R Aspatore
Founded: 1999
Publish only the biggest names in the business world, including C-level leaders (CEO, CTO, CFO, COO, CMO, Partner) from over half the world's 500 largest companies & other leading executives. By focusing on publishing only C-Level executives, we provide professionals of all levels with proven business intelligence from industry insiders, rather than relying on the knowledge of unknown authors & analysts.
ISBN Prefix(es): 1-58762
Number of titles published annually: 100 Print; 5 E-Book
Total Titles: 110 Print; 15 E-Book
Imprints: Aspatore Business Reviews; Bigwig Briefs; Brainstormers; Business Travel Bible; CareerJournal; ExecRecs; IdeaJournal; Inside the Minds; What Ifs

§Aspen Publishers, A Wolters Kluwer Company
1185 Avenue of the Americas, New York, NY 10036
SAN: 203-4999
Tel: 212-597-0200 *Toll Free Tel:* 800-234-1660 (cust serv); 800-447-1717 (orders); 800-950-5259 (legal educ); 800-LAW-PLGL (paralegal textbook); 800-317-3113 (bookstore sales); 800-364-2512 (Loislaw)
Web Site: www.aspenpublishers.com
Key Personnel
Pres: Jane Butler
Exec VP: Richard H Kravitz
COO: Gustavo Dobles
CFO: Kevin Entricken
VP, Mktg & Sales: Gerry Centrowitz
VP, HR: Jeanmarie Smith
VP & Publr, Loislaw: Marc Jennings
VP & Publr, Legal: Jon Eldridge
Exec Dir, Cust Care: Judith McRee
Publr, Kluwer Law International: Ashley Fillingham
Founded: 1959
Publisher of legal, business & health care titles for professionals. Publishes more than 500 journals, newsletters, electronic products & loose-leaf manuals & has more than 1000 active professional & textbook titles.
ISBN Prefix(es): 0-89443; 0-912862; 0-912654; 0-8342; 1-56706; 0-87094; 0-87189; 0-471; 0-316
Number of titles published annually: 100 Print; 16 CD-ROM; 55 Online
Total Titles: 1,500 Print; 107 CD-ROM; 55 Online; 1 Audio
Imprints: Panel Publishers
Foreign Rep(s): David Bartolone
Distribution Center: 7201 McKinney Circle, Frederick, MD 21704 *Tel:* 301-698-7100
Fax: 301-695-7931

Associated University Presses
2010 Eastpark Blvd, Cranbury, NJ 08512
Tel: 609-655-4770 *Fax:* 609-655-8366
E-mail: AUP440@aol.com
Key Personnel
Publr: Julien Yoseloff
Founded: 1968

Book distributor.
ISBN Prefix(es): 0-8453
Number of titles published annually: 130 Print
Total Titles: 3,000 Print
Distributor for Balch Institute Press; Bucknell University Press; Fairleigh Dickinson University Press; Lehigh University Press; Susquehanna University Press; University of Delaware Press
See separate listing for:
Bucknell University Press
Fairleigh Dickinson University Press
Lehigh University Press
Susquehanna University Press
University of Delaware Press

§Association for Computing Machinery
1515 Broadway, New York, NY 10036
SAN: 267-7784
Tel: 212-869-7440 *Toll Free Tel:* 800-342-6626
Fax: 212-869-0481
E-mail: acmhelp@acm.org
Web Site: www.acm.org
Key Personnel
Mktg & Commun Mgr: Brian Hebert
Dir, Pubns: Mark Mandelbaum
Publr: Jono Hardjowirogo
Institutional Digital Lib Sales: Tim Bennett
Founded: 1947
Computer science.
ISBN Prefix(es): 0-201; 0-89791; 1-58113
Number of titles published annually: 100 Print
Total Titles: 350 Print
Imprints: ACM Press
Membership(s): AAP

§Association for Supervision & Curriculum Development (ASCD)
1703 N Beauregard St, Alexandria, VA 22311-1453
SAN: 201-1352
Tel: 703-578-9600 *Toll Free Tel:* 800-933-2723
Fax: 703-575-5400
E-mail: member@ascd.org
Web Site: www.ascd.org
Key Personnel
Dir, Publg: Nancy Modrak
Dir, Book Editing: Julie Houtz *Tel:* 703-575-5706
E-mail: jhoutz@ascd.org
Dir, Sales: Joe Elliott *Tel:* 703-575-5634
E-mail: jelliott@ascd.org
Mktg Dir: Ron Miletta
Intl Rts: Tracy Regan *E-mail:* tracyreganascd@hotmail.com
Dir, Acqs: Scott Willis *Tel:* 703-575-5693
E-mail: swillis@ascd.org
Founded: 1943
Professional books for educators.
ISBN Prefix(es): 0-87120; 1-4166
Number of titles published annually: 25 Print; 1 CD-ROM; 1 Online; 20 E-Book; 50 Audio
Total Titles: 220 Print; 14 CD-ROM; 37 Online; 100 E-Book; 300 Audio
Foreign Rights: Ms Tracy Regan (all territories)
Billing Address: PO Box 79760, Baltimore, MD 21279-0760

Association of American University Presses
Formerly University of Chicago Press
1427 E 60 St, Chicago, IL 60637
SAN: 202-5280
Tel: 773-702-7700; 773-702-7600
Toll Free Tel: 800-621-2736 (orders) *Fax:* 773-702-9756 (sales); 773-660-2235 (orders); 773-702-2708
E-mail: general@press.uchicago.edu
Web Site: www.press.uchicago.edu
Key Personnel
Pres: Donald A Collins
CFO: Chris Heiser
Dir: Paula Barker Duffy
Edit Dir: Alan Thomas; John Tryneski

Books Div Mgr: Lain Adkins
Ref Books Dir: Linda J Halvorson
Book Ed: Susan Bielstein; T David Brent; Kathleen Hansell; Christie Henry; Douglas C Mitchell; Catherine Rice; Alex Schwartz
Pbk Ed: Margaret Hivnor
Phoenix Poets Man Ed: Randolph Petilos
Man Ed: Anita Samen
Ms Ed: Erik Carlson; Erin DeWitt; Sandra Hazel; Monica Holliday; Cara Kane; Michael Koplow; Jennifer Moorhouse; Mara Naselli; Maia Rigas; Carol Saller; Yvonne Zipter
Prod Ed: Leslie Keros; Claudia Rex; Christine Schwab
Ed, Amer Hist: Robert Devens
Contracts & Subs Rts: Perry Cartwright
Foreign Rts Mgr: Gretchen Linder
Prodn Dir: Sylvia Hecimovich
Design Mgr: Jill Shimabukuro
Asst Prod Mgr: Phyllis Kingsland
Mktg Dir: Carol Kasper
Publicity Dir: Erin Hogan
Sales Dir: John Kessler
Dir & Mktg Mgr: Joe Weintraub
Assoc Mktg Mgr: Stuart Kisilinsky
Adv Mgr: Levi Stahl
Journals Mgr: Robert Shirrell
Assoc Journals Mgr: Julia Steffen
Chief Ms Ed, Journals: Mary Leas
Biomedical Journals Pubn Mgr: Everett Conner
Prod Mgr, Journals: Teresa Mullen
Assoc Dir, Astronomical Journals: Julia Steffen
HR Mgr, Books & Journals: Onshelle Jackson
Proj Ed: Mary Laur
Dir, Busn Devt & Planning: Mary Summerfield
Info Systems Mgr: Stephen Shaw
Mktg Mgr: June Groppi
Publns Mgr, Astronomical Journals Group: Kerry Kroffe
Founded: 1891
Scholarly, nonfiction, advanced texts, monographs, clothbound & paperback, scholarly & professional journals, reference books & atlases.
ISBN Prefix(es): 0-226
Number of titles published annually: 250 Print
Total Titles: 5,400 Print; 1 E-Book
Distributor for Canadian Museum of Nature; Conservation International; National Bureau of Economic Research; National Gallery of Canada; National Society for the Study of Education; Oriental Institute
Foreign Rep(s): Academic Book Promotions (Benelux, France, Scandinavia); The American University Press Group (Hong Kong, Japan, Korea, Taiwan); Thomas Cassidy (People's Republic of China); Ewa Ledochowicz (Eastern Europe); Uwe Ludemann (Austria, Germany, Italy, Switzerland); Mediamatics (India); Publishers Marketing & Research Associates (Caribbean, Latin America); Arie Ruitenbeek (Portugal, Spain); The University Press Group (Australia, Canada, New Zealand); University Presses Marketing (UK, Ireland, Greece, Israel)
Distribution Center: 11030 S Langley Ave, Chicago, IL 60628
Membership(s): AAP

Association of College & Research Libraries
Division of American Library Association
50 E Huron St, Chicago, IL 60611
Tel: 312-280-2511 *Toll Free Tel:* 800-545-2433 (ext 2517) *Fax:* 312-280-2520
E-mail: acrl@ala.org
Web Site: www.ala.org/acrl
Key Personnel
Contact: Hugh Thompson *E-mail:* hthompson@ala.org
Founded: 1938
ISBN Prefix(es): 0-8389
Number of titles published annually: 8 Print
Total Titles: 60 Print

Association of Research Libraries
21 Dupont Circle NW, Suite 800, Washington, DC 20036
Tel: 202-296-2296 *Fax:* 202-872-0884
E-mail: arlhq@arl.org
Web Site: www.arl.org
Key Personnel
Pubns Prog Officer: Lee Anne George
   E-mail: leeanne@arl.org
Founded: 1932
Serial, occasional paper series & special topics of interest.
ISBN Prefix(es): 0-918006; 1-59407
Number of titles published annually: 30 Print; 10 Online; 2 Audio
Total Titles: 600 Print; 31 Online; 2 Audio
Distribution Center: ARL Publications Distribution Center, PO Box 531, Annapolis Junction, MD 20701-0531 *Tel:* 301-362-8196 *Fax:* 301-206-9789
Membership(s): AAP

Association of School Business Officials International
11401 North Shore Dr, Reston, VA 20190
Tel: 703-478-0405 *Fax:* 703-478-0205
E-mail: asboreq@asbointl.org
Web Site: www.asbointl.org
Key Personnel
Man Ed: Siobhan McMahon
Publg Coord: Mark Aronstein
Founded: 1910
Professional books.
ISBN Prefix(es): 0-910170; 0-810847; 1-1578860
Number of titles published annually: 10 Print
Total Titles: 31 Print

§ASTM International
100 Barr Harbor Dr, West Conshohocken, PA 19428
Mailing Address: PO Box C-700, West Conshohocken, PA 19428
Tel: 610-832-9500 *Fax:* 610-832-9555
E-mail: service@astm.org
Web Site: www.astm.org
Key Personnel
Pres: James A Thomas *Tel:* 610-832-9598 *Fax:* 610-832-9599 *E-mail:* jthomas@astm.org
VP, Pubns & Mktg: John Pace *Tel:* 610-832-9632 *Fax:* 610-832-9635 *E-mail:* jpace@astm.org
Electronic Publg: George Zajdel *Tel:* 610-832-9614 *Fax:* 610-832-9635 *E-mail:* gzajdel@astm.org
AVP & Pubn Serv: Robert Dreyfuss *Tel:* 610-832-9653 *Fax:* 610-832-9635 *E-mail:* rdreyfus@astm.org
Promotional Asst: Jacqueline A Nolden *Tel:* 610-832-9609 *Fax:* 610-832-9623 *E-mail:* jnolden@astm.org
Founded: 1898
Standards, technical publications, data series manuals & journals on engineering, science, materials testing, safety, quality control.
ISBN Prefix(es): 0-8031
Number of titles published annually: 120 Print; 125 CD-ROM
Total Titles: 1,500 Print; 125 CD-ROM; 80 Online
Foreign Office(s): American Technical Publishers Ltd, 27-29 Knowl Piece, Wilbury Way, Hitchin, Herts SG4 OSX, United Kingdom *Tel:* (0462) 437933 *Fax:* (0462) 433678
Foreign Rep(s): American Technical Publishers Ltd (Europe)
Membership(s): AAP

Astragal Press
PO Box 239, Mendham, NJ 07945-0239
Tel: 973-543-3045 *Fax:* 973-543-3044
E-mail: info@astragalpress.com
Web Site: www.astragalpress.com

Key Personnel
Mktg Mgr: Kathryn Bednarz
Pres: Marty Pollak
Founded: 1983
Early tools, trades & technology.
ISBN Prefix(es): 0-9618088; 1-879335; 1-931626
Number of titles published annually: 5 Print
Total Titles: 86 Print; 75 Online

§The Astronomical Society of the Pacific
390 Ashton Ave, San Francisco, CA 94112
Tel: 415-337-1100 *Toll Free Tel:* 800-335-2624 (Cust Serv) *Fax:* 415-337-5205
E-mail: service@astrosociety.org
Web Site: www.astrosociety.org
Key Personnel
Exec Dir: Michael Bennett
Sales Mgr: Joycelin Craig
Founded: 1889
Books, booklets, tapes, slide sets, software & other educational materials about astronomy; a line of conference proceedings. IAU (International Astronomical Union) publications & proceedings. Mercury Magazine.
ISBN Prefix(es): 0-937707
Number of titles published annually: 20 Print; 1 CD-ROM; 4 Online; 1 Audio
Total Titles: 300 Print; 1 CD-ROM; 4 Online; 1 Audio

Atheneum Books for Young Readers, see Simon & Schuster Children's Publishing

Athenos Press, see Stand! Publishing

Athletic Guide Publishing
PO Box 1050, Flagler Beach, FL 32136
Tel: 386-439-2250 *Toll Free Tel:* 800-255-1050 *Fax:* 386-439-6224
E-mail: agp@flaglernet.com
Key Personnel
Publr: Tom Keegan
Founded: 1990
ISBN Prefix(es): 1-880941
Number of titles published annually: 50 Print
Total Titles: 90 Print
Imprints: AGP Publishing; Old Kings Road Press
Membership(s): Publishers Marketing Association

§ATL Press Inc
PO Box 4563 "T" Sta, Shrewsbury, MA 01545-7563
SAN: 297-8334
Tel: 508-898-2290 *Fax:* 508-898-2063
E-mail: atlpress@compuserve.com
Web Site: www.atlpress.com
Key Personnel
Pres: Talieh Keshavarz
Gen Mgr: Paul Lucio
Contact: Tom Kesh
Founded: 1992
Science, technology & business.
ISBN Prefix(es): 1-882360
Number of titles published annually: 12 Print

Atlantic Law Book Co
Division of Peter Kelsey Publishing Inc
22 Grassmere Ave, West Hartford, CT 06110-1215
Tel: 860-231-9300 *Fax:* 860-231-9242
E-mail: atlanticlawbooks@aol.com
Web Site: www.atlntc.com
Key Personnel
Pres: Theodore Epstein
Law books for Connecticut legal practice.
ISBN Prefix(es): 1-878698
Number of titles published annually: 13 Print
Total Titles: 13 Print

Atlantic Publishing Inc
1210 SW 23 Place, Ocala, FL 34474-7014

Toll Free Tel: 800-555-4037 *Fax:* 352-622-5836
E-mail: sales@atlantic-pub.com
Web Site: www.atlantic-pub.com
Key Personnel
Ed: Robert Montgomery
General business, how-to, restaurant management, hospitality training, videos & posters.
ISBN Prefix(es): 0-910627
Number of titles published annually: 25 Print; 30 CD-ROM
Total Titles: 40 Print; 50 CD-ROM

Atria Books
Imprint of Simon & Schuster
1230 Avenue of the Americas, New York, NY 10020
Tel: 212-698-7000 *Fax:* 212-698-7007
Web Site: www.simonsays.com
Key Personnel
Exec VP & Publr: Judith Curr
VP & Dep Publr: Karen Mender
VP & Edit Dir: Tracy Behar
VP & Exec Edit Dir: Emily Bestler
VP & Dir, Mktg: Craig Herman
VP & Dir, Publicity: Justin Loeber
VP & Sr Ed: Greer Kessel-Hendricks
VP & Dir, Art & Design: Paolo Pepe
VP & Dir, Subs Rts: Lisa Keim
Sr Ed: Malaika Adero; Brenda Copeland
Assoc Ed: Sarah Branham; Suzanne O'Neill; Wendy Walker
ISBN Prefix(es): 0-671; 0-7434; 0-7432

Atwood Publishing
2710 Atwood Ave, Madison, WI 53704
Mailing Address: PO Box 3185, Madison, WI 53704-0185
Tel: 608-242-7101 *Toll Free Tel:* 888-242-7101 *Fax:* 608-242-7102
E-mail: customerservice@atwoodpublishing.com
Web Site: www.atwoodpublishing.com
Key Personnel
Publr: Linda Babler *E-mail:* lindab@atwoodpublishing.com
Founded: 1997
Book publishing for higher education market: teaching improvement, distance, education, student affairs, semiotics & administration.
ISBN Prefix(es): 1-891859
Number of titles published annually: 6 Print
Total Titles: 40 Print

Audio Renaissance
Division of Holtzbrinck Publishers Holdings LLC
175 Fifth Ave, New York, NY 10010
Tel: 212-674-5151 *Toll Free Tel:* 888-330-8477 (cust serv) *Fax:* 917-534-0980
E-mail: firstname.lastname@hbpub.com
Web Site: www.audiorenaissance.com
Key Personnel
Pres: Alison Lazarus
VP & Publr: Mary Beth Roche
Assoc Publr: Joe McNeely
Dir, Mktg: Jeanne-Marie Hudson
Dir, Prodn: Laura Wilson
Sr Designer: Margo Goody
Pubn Coord: Lindy Settevendemie
Founded: 1987
ISBN Prefix(es): 1-55927; 0-940687; 1-59397
Number of titles published annually: 60 Audio
Total Titles: 400 Audio
Distributor for Highroads Audio
Orders to: VHPS Order Dept, 16365 James Madison Hwy, Gordonsville, VA 22942-8501 *Toll Free Tel:* 888-330-8477 *Fax:* 540-672-7540 *Toll Free Fax:* 800-672-2054
Returns: VHPS Returns Ctr, 14301 Litchfield Dr, Orange, VA 22960-2570

§Augsburg Fortress Publishers, Publishing House of the Evangelical Lutheran Church in America
100 S Fifth St, Suite 700, Minneapolis, MN 55402
SAN: 169-4081
Tel: 612-330-3300 *Toll Free Tel:* 800-426-0115 (ext 639 subns); 800-328-4648 (orders); 800-421-0239 (perms) *Fax:* 612-330-3455 *Toll Free Fax:* 800-421-0239 (perms & copyrights)
E-mail: customerservice@augsburgfortress.org; copyright@augsburgfortress.org (for reprint permission requests)
Web Site: www.augsburgfortress.org
Key Personnel
Pres & CEO: Beth A Lewis
Sr VP, Mktg: James Donahue
VP, Fin & Info Servs: George Poehlman
VP, Corp Aff: Rachel Riensche
VP, Sales: Tia Simmons
VP, HR: Sandy Middendorf
Gen Mgr, Fortress Press Books & Augsburg Books: Scott Tunseth
Gen Mgr, Worship & Music: Martin Seltz
Gen Mgr, Congregational Life & Learning: Bill Huff
Gen Mgr, Ecclesiastical Arts: D Foy Christopherson
Foreign Rts: Claire Taylor-Sherman
Perms: Esther Diley; Sheo Prasad
Archivist: Lynette Johnson
ISBN Contact & Record Administrator: Judith Hedman *Tel:* 612-330-3402 *E-mail:* hedmanj@augsburgfortress.org
Founded: 1855
Publishing House of the Evangelical Lutheran Church in America.
ISBN Prefix(es): 0-8066; 0-8006
Number of titles published annually: 100 Print
Total Titles: 996 Print; 10 CD-ROM; 5 Audio
Imprints: Augsburg Books; Fortress Press
Branch Office(s)
O'Hara Plaza, 8765 W Higgins Rd, Chicago, IL 60631-4101 *Tel:* 773-380-2424
Seminary Bookstore, Luther Seminary, 2481 Como Ave, St Paul, MN 55108-1445 *Tel:* 651-641-3441
Union Theological Seminary, 3041 Broadway, New York, NY 10027 *Tel:* 212-280-1554
Trinity Lutheran Seminary Bookstore, 2199 E Main St, Columbus, OH 43209-2334 *Tel:* 614-236-3095
Wartbury Theological Seminary, 313 Wartburg Place, Dubuque, OH 52004 *Tel:* 563-588-0200
900 S Arlington Ave, Harrisburg, PA 17109-5024 *Tel:* 717-652-2416
Seminary Bookstore, Lutheran Theological Seminary at Philadelphia, 7301 Germantown Ave, Philadelpia, PA 19119-1794 *Tel:* 215-248-6386
9625 Perry Hwy, Pittsburgh, PA 15237-5590 *Tel:* 412-364-3866
Lutheran Theological Southern Seminary Bookstore, 4201 N Main St, Columbia, SC 29203-5898 *Tel:* 808-691-1118
207 Fourth NE, Edmontron Trail, Calgary, AB T2E 3S1, Canada *Tel:* 403-276-7000 *Toll Free Tel:* 800-661-8379
Box 9940, 500 Trillium Dr, Kitchener, ON N2G 4Y4, Canada *Tel:* 519-748-2200 *Toll Free Tel:* 800-265-6397
Editorial Office(s): PO Box 1209, Minneapolis, MN 55440-1209
Sales Office(s): PO Box 1209, Minneapolis, MN 55440-1209
Foreign Rep(s): Alban Books Ltd (UK); Omega (New Zealand); Open Book Publishers (Australia)
Billing Address: PO Box 1209, Minneapolis, MN 55440-1209
Orders to: PO Box 1209, Minneapolis, MN 55440-1209
Returns: 4001 Gantz Rd, Suite E, Grove City, OH 43123-1891

Warehouse: 4001 Gantz Rd, Suite E, Grove City, OH 43123-1891
Distribution Center: 4001 Gantz Rd, Suite E, Grove City, OH 43123-1891

August House Publishers Inc
201 E Markham, Little Rock, AR 72201
Mailing Address: PO Box 3223, Little Rock, AR 72203-3223 SAN: 223-7288
Tel: 501-372-5450 *Toll Free Tel:* 800-284-8784 *Fax:* 501-372-5579 *Toll Free Fax:* 800-284-8784 (orders)
E-mail: ahinfo@augusthouse.com
Web Site: www.augusthouse.com
Key Personnel
CEO & Publr: Liz Smith Parkhurst
    E-mail: es_parkhurst@augusthouse.com
Pres & Lib Sales Dir: Ted Parkhurst
    E-mail: t_parkhurst@augusthouse.com
Founded: 1979
Folklore, multicultural folktales & storytelling.
ISBN Prefix(es): 0-87483; 0-942303
Number of titles published annually: 9 Print; 4 CD-ROM; 30 Online; 8 Audio
Total Titles: 318 Print; 5 CD-ROM; 254 Online; 70 Audio
Imprints: August House Audio; August House LittleFolk
Distributor for High Windy Audio
Returns: 2400 Cantrell Rd, Space 102, Little Rock, AR 72202 *Tel:* 501-372-1744
Membership(s): Children's Book Council

Augustinian Press
PO Box 476, Villanova, PA 19085-0476
Tel: 610-527-3330 (ext 248) *Fax:* 610-527-0571
E-mail: augustinianpress@augustinian.org
Web Site: www.augustinian.org
Founded: 1983
Publishes or distributes the works of Saint Augustine & other related writings on Augustine, as well as materials on Augustinian spirituality & history.
ISBN Prefix(es): 0-941491
Number of titles published annually: 10 Print
Total Titles: 45 Print; 1 Audio

Aum Publications
86-10 Parsons Blvd, Jamaica, NY 11432
SAN: 201-128X
Tel: 718-291-9757 *Fax:* 718-523-1423
Key Personnel
Pres: Carl Brown
Treas, Busn Mgr & Rts & Perms: Sundar Dalton
Prodn Mgr: Sanatan Curchek
Sales Mgr: Ahuta Markman
Founded: 1973
Trade paperbacks; literature, Eastern philosophy, theology, occult, poetry, meditation; only books on or by Sri Chinmoy.
ISBN Prefix(es): 0-88497
Number of titles published annually: 10 Print
Total Titles: 50 Print; 2 CD-ROM

Authorlink Press
3720 Millswood Dr, Irving, TX 75062
Tel: 972-650-1986 *Fax:* 972-650-1622
Web Site: www.authorlink.com
Key Personnel
Ed-in-Chief: Doris Booth *E-mail:* dbooth@authorlink.com
Founded: 1999
A traditional publisher specializing in true crime, books about the craft of writing, a few children's titles, books on women's issues, & some self-help. Most of our titles are published as traditional runs & not as print on demand. We are an award-winning rights market-place where editors & agents buy & sell unpublished & published mss & screenplays. Provides the serious writer with access exposure to the broadest range of legitimate publishing

professionals. Plus, industry news, information & marketing services for publishers, literary agents, writers & readers.
ISBN Prefix(es): 1-928704
Number of titles published annually: 15 Print
Total Titles: 20 Print
Orders to: Baker & Taylor
Returns: Matrix Digital Technologies, 3522 La Reunion Pkwy, Dallas, TX 75212
Distribution Center: Matrix Digital Technologies, 3522 La Reunion Pkwy, Dallas, TX 75212 *Tel:* 214-252-6370 *Fax:* 214-688-0174
E-mail: dcoach@matrixdt.com

Authors Cooperative
1700 Ben Franklin Dr, Suite 9E, Sarasota, FL 34236-2374
Tel: 941-388-5009
E-mail: authcoop@comcast.net
Web Site: www.authorscooperative.com
Key Personnel
Pres & Intl Rts: Murray Sidman
    E-mail: murraysidman@comcast.net
Fin Officer: May Branagan
Founded: 1989
Books on behavior analysis & related topics in psychology.
ISBN Prefix(es): 0-9623311; 1-888830
Number of titles published annually: 3 Print
Total Titles: 9 Print
Distribution Center: Cambridge Center for Behavioral Studies, 336 Baker Ave, Concord, MA 01742-2107, Contact: Katherine Daugherty *Tel:* 978-369-2227 *Fax:* 978-369-8584 *E-mail:* authorscooperative@behavior.org *Web Site:* www.behavior.org

Auto Book Press, see Coda Publications

Autumn House Press
87 1/2 Westwood St, Pittsburgh, PA 15211
Tel: 412-381-4261
Web Site: www.autumnhouse.org
Key Personnel
Founder & Ed: Michael Simms *E-mail:* simms@dug.edu
Founded: 1998
Non-profit corporation with the mission of publishing poetry.
Number of titles published annually: 4 Print
Total Titles: 14 Print

Avalon Books
Imprint of Thomas Bouregy & Co Inc
160 Madison Ave, 5th fl, New York, NY 10016
Tel: 212-598-0222 *Fax:* 212-979-1862
E-mail: avalon@avalonbooks.com
Web Site: www.avalonbooks.com
Key Personnel
Pres: Wilhelm H Mickelsen
Edit: Erin Cartwright; Abbie Holcomb
Cust Serv: Robert F Hirsch
Contact: Ellen Bouregy Mickelsen
Founded: 1950
ISBN Prefix(es): 0-8034
Number of titles published annually: 60 Print
Total Titles: 400 Print
Foreign Rights: Hansen Literary Agency
Warehouse: Offset Paperback Distribution Ctr, One Passan Dr, Bldg 10, Laflin, PA 18702

Avalon Publishing Group Inc
1400 65 St, Suite 250, Emeryville, CA 94608
Tel: 510-595-3664 *Fax:* 510-535-4228
Web Site: www.avalonpub.com
Key Personnel
Chmn & CEO, Avalon Publishing Group: Charlie Winton
Pres & COO Avalon Publishing Group: Susan Reich
Sr VP & Publicity Dir, Avalon Publishing Group: Michelle Martin

Sr VP & Publr, Avalon Travel Publishing: Bill Newlin
VP & Publr, Thunder's Mouth Press & Nation Books: John Oakes
VP & Publr, Carroll & Graf Publishers: Will Balliett
VP & Assoc Publr, Avalon Travel Publishing: Donna Galassi
VP & Edit Dir, Avalon Travel Publishing: Krista Lyons-Gould
Founded: 1994
One of the leading independent publishers in the U.S. with offices in the San Francisco Bay Area, New York City, & Washington, D.C. Each Avalon imprint has a distinct editorial & marketing focus, combining the vision & commitment of an independent press with the scale & resources of a larger enterprise.
Imprints: Avalon Travel Publishing; Blue Moon Books; Carroll & Graf Publishers; Marlowe & Co; Nation Books; Seal Press; Shoemaker & Hoard; Thunder's Mouth Press
Orders to: Publishers Group West, 1700 Fourth St, Berkeley, CA 94710 *Toll Free Tel:* 800-788-3123 *Fax:* 510-528-3444
Distribution Center: Publishers Group West, c/o Advanced Marketing Services, 5045 W 79 St, Indianapolis, ID 46268
See separate listing for:
Avalon Travel Publishing
Blue Moon Books
Carroll & Graf Publishers
Four Walls Eight Windows
Marlowe & Company
Seal Press
Shoemaker & Hoard, Publishers
Thunder's Mouth Press

Avalon Travel Publishing
Imprint of Avalon Publishing Group - California
1400 65 St, Suite 250, Emeryville, CA 94608
SAN: 202-8522
Tel: 510-595-3664 *Fax:* 510-535-4228
E-mail: info@travelmatters.com
Web Site: www.travelmatters.com
Key Personnel
Sr VP & Publr: Bill Newlin
VP & Assoc Publr: Donna Galassi
VP, Edit: Krista Lyons-Gould
Edit Dir: Kevin McLain
Avalon Travel Publishing, an imprint of Avalon Publishing Group, is the largest independent travel publisher in the United States. Major series include Rick Steves, Moon Handbooks, Moon Metro, Foghorn Outdoors, The Dog Lover's Companion, Living Abroad & Road Trip USA.
ISBN Prefix(es): 1-56261; 1-56691; 1-57354
Number of titles published annually: 100 Print
Total Titles: 352 Print
Orders to: Publishers Group West, 1700 Fourth St, Berkeley, CA 94710 *Toll Free Tel:* 800-788-3123 *Fax:* 510-528-3444
Distribution Center: Publishers Group West, c/o Advanced Marketing Services, 5045 W 79 St, Indianapolis, IN 46268

Ave Maria Press
19113 Douglas Rd, Notre Dame, IN 46556
SAN: 201-1255
Mailing Address: PO Box 428, Notre Dame, IN 46556-0428
Tel: 574-287-2831 *Toll Free Tel:* 800-282-1865 *Fax:* 574-239-2904 *Toll Free Fax:* 800-282-5681
E-mail: avemariapress.1@nd.edu
Web Site: www.avemariapress.com
Key Personnel
Publr: Frank J Cunningham
Dir, Mktg & Sales & Lib Sales Dir: Mary E Andrews *Tel:* 574-287-2831 ext 219 *E-mail:* mary.e.andrews.22@nd.edu

Rts & Perms & Intl Rts Contact: Susana J Kelly *E-mail:* skelly1@nd.edu
Adv Prodn: Kristen Coney *E-mail:* kristen.h.coney.4@nd.edu
Cust Serv: Mary Jo Crandall *E-mail:* mary.j.crandall.6@nd.edu
Edit Dir: Robert Hamma *E-mail:* robert.m.hamma.1@nd.edu
Founded: 1865
Paperback books of religious interest, adult & juvenile; prayer books & religious education materials, programs & textbooks.
ISBN Prefix(es): 0-87793 (Ave Maria Press); 0-939516 (Forest of Peace); 0-88347 (Thomas More); 0-87061 (Christian Classics); 1-893732 (Sorin Books); 1-59471 (Ave Maria Press); 1-932057 (SunCreek Books)
Number of titles published annually: 40 Print
Total Titles: 550 Print; 37 Audio
Imprints: Christian Classics; Forest of Peace; Thomas More; Sorin Books; SunCreek Books
Distributor for Christian Classics; Forest of Peace; Thomas More; Sorin Books; SunCreek Books
Foreign Rep(s): Alban Books Ltd (UK); Catholic Supplies Ltd (New Zealand); John Garratt Publishing (Australia)
See separate listing for:
Sorin Books

Avery
Imprint of Penguin Group (USA) Inc
375 Hudson St, New York, NY 10014
SAN: 282-5074
Tel: 212-366-2000 *Fax:* 212-366-2643
E-mail: online@penguinputnam.com
Web Site: www.penguinputnam.com
Key Personnel
Publr: Megan Newman
Assoc Publr: Kate Stane
Founded: 1976 (acquired by Penguin Putnam Inc in the fall of 1999)
The imprint is dedicated to publishing books on health & nutrition with a complimentary, natural, or alternative focus.
ISBN Prefix(es): 0-89529; 1-58333
Number of titles published annually: 30 Print
Total Titles: 526 Print

Avery Color Studios
511 "D" Ave, Gwinn, MI 49841
Tel: 906-346-3908 *Toll Free Tel:* 800-722-9925 *Fax:* 906-346-3015
E-mail: avery@portup.com
Key Personnel
Pres: Wells Chapin *E-mail:* avery@portup.com
Busn Mgr: Amy Chapin
Founded: 1956
Regional publisher specializing in nautical books.
ISBN Prefix(es): 0-932212; 1-892384
Number of titles published annually: 3 Print
Total Titles: 40 Print
Distributed by Partners Book Distributing

Avid Reader Press
Division of VWI Corp
6705 W Hwy 290, Suite 502-295, Austin, TX 78735
Tel: 512-288-5349 *Fax:* 512-288-0317
E-mail: info@avidreaderpress.com; orders@avidreaderpress.com
Web Site: www.avidreaderpress.com
Key Personnel
Gen Counsel: James Bellevue *E-mail:* jbellevue@avidreaderpress.com
Publr: Elena Lipkowski *E-mail:* elipkowski@avidreaderpress.com
Founded: 1992
Natural health & alternative medicine books & videos which are consumer oriented.
ISBN Prefix(es): 0-9700150
Number of titles published annually: 3 Print

Total Titles: 6 Print; 1 CD-ROM
Membership(s): Publishers Marketing Association; Small Publishers Association of North America

Avisson Press Inc
3007 Taliaferro Rd, Greensboro, NC 27408
Mailing Address: PO Box 38816, Greensboro, NC 27438-8816
Tel: 336-288-6989 *Fax:* 336-288-6989
E-mail: avisson4@aol.com
Key Personnel
Pres & Int Rts Contact: M L Hester
Contact: Michael Blood
Founded: 1994
ISBN Prefix(es): 1-888105
Number of titles published annually: 5 Print
Total Titles: 45 Print
Membership(s): Publishers Marketing Association; Society of Children's Book Writers & Illustrators

AVKO Dyslexia & Spelling Research Foundation Inc
3084 W Willard Rd, Clio, MI 48420
Tel: 810-686-9283 *Toll Free Tel:* 866-285-6612 *Fax:* 810-686-1101
E-mail: avkoemail@aol.com
Web Site: www.avko.org
Key Personnel
Research Dir: Don McCabe *E-mail:* donmccabe@aol.com
Founded: 1974
Tutoring materials & services including teaching others to tutor, spelling & keyboarding.
ISBN Prefix(es): 1-56400
Number of titles published annually: 30 Print
Total Titles: 60 Print
Distributed by Amazon.com; The Distributors

AVKO Foundation, see AVKO Dyslexia & Spelling Research Foundation Inc

Avocet Press Inc
19 Paul Ct, Pearl River, NY 10965-1539
Tel: 845-735-6807 *Toll Free Tel:* 877-428-6238
Key Personnel
Man Ed: Cynthia Webb *E-mail:* cwebb@avocetpress.com
Founded: 1997
Number of titles published annually: 6 Print
Total Titles: 24 Print
Imprints: Ichus Guides; Memento Mori Mysteries
Foreign Rights: Writer's House

Avotaynu Inc
155 N Washington Ave, Bergenfield, NJ 07621
Tel: 201-387-7200 *Toll Free Tel:* 800-286-8296 *Fax:* 201-387-2855
E-mail: info@avotaynu.com
Web Site: www.avotaynu.com
Key Personnel
Publr: Gary Mokotoff *E-mail:* garymokotoff@avotaynu.com
Founded: 1984
Publisher of information & products of interest to persons researching their Jewish family history. This includes the journal, Avotaynu, books & microfiche. Offer books, maps & video tapes published by other companies through catalog.
ISBN Prefix(es): 0-9626373; 1-886223
Number of titles published annually: 5 Print
Total Titles: 28 Print; 1 CD-ROM; 1 Online
Membership(s): Association of Jewish Book Publishers

§Awe-Struck E-Books Inc
2458 Cherry St, Dubuque, IA 52001-5749
E-mail: editor@awe-struckebooks.net; tech@awestruckebooks.net
Web Site: www.awe-struck.net (ordering)

Key Personnel
Pres & Publr: Kathryn D Struck
  E-mail: kdstruck2@yahoo.com
Publ, VP & Webmaster: Dick Claassen *Tel:* 515-964-8518 *E-mail:* dick@awestruckbooks.com
Founded: 1998
Full-service, royalty paying publisher of electronic books in the following formats: html, rocket, Palm, Visor, Pocket PC, Franklin, eBookman, Hiebook, pdf, MS Reader.
Subsidiary, Earthlink Press, publishes trade paperbacks; fiction (romance & science fiction) for disabled readers (Ennoble Line).
ISBN Prefix(es): 1-928670; 1-58749
Number of titles published annually: 12 Print; 42 Online; 42 E-Book
Total Titles: 96 Print; 130 Online; 130 E-Book
Subsidiaries: Earthling Press
Membership(s): Publishers Marketing Association

§Ayer Company, Publishers Inc
One Lower Mill Rd, North Stratford, NH 03590
Mailing Address: 300 Bedford St, Bldg B, Suite 213, Manchester, NH 03101
Tel: 603-669-7032 *Fax:* 603-669-7945
E-mail: ayerpub@yahoo.com
Web Site: www.ayerpub.com
Key Personnel
Pres: Ann Gauntt
Off Mgr & Dist Opers Mgr: Diane Turnbull
  Tel: 603-647-4369
Founded: 1982
Specializes in Black history, classics, Civil War & short stories.
ISBN Prefix(es): 0-405; 0-8369; 0-88143; 0-8337; 0-8434
Number of titles published annually: 200 Print
Total Titles: 13,000 Print; 50 CD-ROM
Imprints: Arno Press; Benjamin Blom; BFL; Burt Franklin
Warehouse: Ayer Rd, North Stratford, NH 03590

Aztex Corp
PO Box 50046, Tucson, AZ 85703-1046
SAN: 210-0371
Tel: 520-882-4656 *Fax:* 520-792-8501
Web Site: www.aztexcorp.com
Key Personnel
Chmn of the Bd & Pres: Elaine C Haessner
Publr: Walter R Haessner
ISBN Contact: Elaine Jordan
Founded: 1976
Transportation, automotive, corporate history; contract publishing.
ISBN Prefix(es): 0-89404
Number of titles published annually: 3 Print
Total Titles: 7 Print
Advertising Agency: ADMAR

Babbage Press
8740 Penfield Ave, Northbridge, CA 91324-3224
Tel: 818-341-3161
E-mail: books@babbagepress.com
Web Site: www.babbagepress.com
Key Personnel
Publr: Lydia C Marano
Ed: Arthur Byron
Founded: 1999
Specialty press publisher; science fiction, fantasy & horror.
ISBN Prefix(es): 1-930235
Number of titles published annually: 10 Print
Total Titles: 22 Print

Back to Eden Books, see Lotus Press

Backbeat Books
Division of CMP Media LLC
Imprint of United Entertainment Media
600 Harrison St, San Francisco, CA 94107

Tel: 415-947-6615 *Toll Free Tel:* 866-222-5232 (orders only) *Fax:* 415-947-6015; 408-848-8294 (orders only)
E-mail: books@musicplayer.com; books@cmp.com
Web Site: www.backbeatbooks.com
Key Personnel
Publr: Matthew Kelsey
Acct Mgr: Susan Fuller
Sales Mgr: Kevin Becketti
Mktg Communs Mgr: Nina Lesowitz
Bk Opers Coord: Jennifer Steele
Founded: 2000
Books about popular music & musical instruments.
ISBN Prefix(es): 0-87930
Number of titles published annually: 35 Print
Total Titles: 160 Print; 20 CD-ROM
Orders to: Backbeat Books Distribution Ctr, 6600 Silacci Way, Gilroy, CA 95020
Returns: Backbeat Books Distribution Ctr, 6600 Silacci Way, Gilroy, CA 95020
Distribution Center: Backbeat Books Distribution Ctr, 6600 Silacci Way, Gilroy, CA 95020
Tel: 408-848-8294; 866-222-5232 *Fax:* 408-848-5784 *E-mail:* books@cmp.com *Web Site:* www.backbeatbooks.com

Baen Publishing Enterprises
PO Box 1403, Riverdale, NY 10471-0605
Tel: 919-570-1640 *Fax:* 919-570-1644
Web Site: baen.com
Key Personnel
Pres & Publr: James P Baen *E-mail:* jim@baen.com
Exec Ed: Toni Weisskopf *E-mail:* toni@baen.com
Founded: 1984
Only science fiction & fantasy.
ISBN Prefix(es): 0-671; 0-7434
Number of titles published annually: 70 Print; 40 Online; 40 E-Book
Total Titles: 500 Print; 200 Online; 200 E-Book
Distributed by Simon & Schuster
Foreign Rep(s): Lona Fountain (France); Alex Korzhenevshi (Russia); Kristin Olson (Czech Republic); Thomas Schlueck (Germany)

Baha'i Publishing Trust
Subsidiary of The National Spiritual Assembly of the Baha'is of the United States
415 Linden Ave, Wilmette, IL 60091
SAN: 213-7496
Tel: 847-425-7950 *Fax:* 847-425-7951
E-mail: bpt@usbnc.org *Telex:* 49000031
  Cable: PUBLITRUST BAHAI
Key Personnel
Gen Mgr & Rts & Perms: Lee Minnerly
Prodn Mgr: Suni Hannan
Acqs Mgr: Terry Cassiday
Founded: 1902
Religion (Baha'i).
ISBN Prefix(es): 0-87743; 1-931847
Number of titles published annually: 40 Print
Total Titles: 200 Print; 8 Audio
Imprints: Baha'i Publishing; Baha'i Publishing Trust; Bellwood Press
Shipping Address: 4703 Fulton Industrial Blvd, Atlanta, GA 30336-2017 *Tel:* 404-472-9019 *Toll Free Tel:* 800-999-9019 *E-mail:* bds@usbnc.org

BajonHouse Publishing
609 Broad Ave, Belle Vernon, PA 15012
Tel: 724-929-5997 *Fax:* 724-929-5997
Key Personnel
Pres: Lynn Williams *E-mail:* lynnlabs@westol.com
Ed: Earl McDaniel
Founded: 1997
Publisher of nonfiction business print, audio & video materials on leadership, business ethics, employee morale & management.

ISBN Prefix(es): 0-9664084
Number of titles published annually: 3 Print
Total Titles: 2 Print; 1 CD-ROM; 2 Audio

§Baker Books
Division of Baker Publishing Group
PO Box 6287, Grand Rapids, MI 49516-6287
SAN: 201-4041
Tel: 616-676-9185 *Toll Free Tel:* 800-877-2665; 800-679-1957 *Fax:* 616-676-9573
  Toll Free Fax: 800-398-3110
Web Site: www.bakerpublishinggroup.com
Key Personnel
Pres: Dwight Baker
CEO & Chmn: Richard Baker
Art Dir: Cheryl Van Andel
Rts & Perms: Marilyn Gordon
Prodn Mgr: Bob Bol
Dist Mgr: Jack Boers
Spec Mkts Mgr: Erik Schmidgal
Sales & Mktg Mgr: Dave Lewis
Dir, Pubns: Don Stephenson
Asst to Edit Dir: Kate Van Noord
Exec Asst: Jessica Miles *E-mail:* jmiles@bakerpublishinggroup.com
Founded: 1939
Religion (Protestant).
ISBN Prefix(es): 0-8010
Number of titles published annually: 75 Print; 1 CD-ROM; 1 Audio
Total Titles: 1,000 Print; 4 CD-ROM; 2 Audio
Imprints: Baker Bytes; Bridgepoint; Hamewith; Hourglass
Foreign Rep(s): Christian Art (South Africa); Family Reading Publications (Australia); R Mitchell (Canada); Omega Distributors (New Zealand); Send The Light (UK, Europe)
Shipping Address: 6030 E Fulton Rd, Ada, MI 49301

Baker's Plays
Division of Samuel French Inc
PO Box 699222, Quincy, MA 02269-9222
Tel: 617-745-0805 *Fax:* 617-745-9891
Web Site: www.bakersplays.com
Key Personnel
Man Dir: Deirdre Shaw
Founded: 1845
Publish exclusively plays & books on theatre.
ISBN Prefix(es): 0-87440
Number of titles published annually: 20 Print
Total Titles: 1,000 Print
Distribution Center: Samuel French Inc

Ball Publishing
Division of Ball Horticultural Co
335 N River St, Batavia, IL 60510
Mailing Address: PO Box 9, Batavia, IL 60510-0009
Tel: 630-208-9080 *Fax:* 630-208-9350
E-mail: info@ballpublishing.com
Web Site: www.ballpublishing.com
Key Personnel
Group Publr: Diane Blazek
Man Ed: Rick Blanchette *Tel:* 630-208-9080 ext 126 *E-mail:* rblanchette@ballpublishing.com
Founded: 1986
Publish titles for professional floriculture growers, retailers & gardeners.
ISBN Prefix(es): 1-883052
Number of titles published annually: 5 Print
Total Titles: 35 Print
Distributed by American Nurserymen
Distributor for AIPH - Association International de Producteurs de l'Horticulture; American Phytopathological Society; Antique Collectors' Club Ltd; DK Publishing Inc; Paul Ecke Ranch; Erdiciones de Horticultura SL; Flora Publications International Pty Ltd; Growers Press Inc; Harcourt Brace & Co and Subsidiaries; HortiTecnia; International Flower Bulb Centre; IPC Plant; ITP Educational Di-

vision - Intl Thomas Publishing; NSW Agriculture; Palmer Publications Inc; Pathfast Publishing; Prentice Hall; The Reference Publishing Co; Seven Hills Book Distributors; Smithmark Publishers, A Division of US Media Holding Inc; Stipes Publishing LLC; Thomson Publications; Timber Press Inc; Truett Software Development; University of Connecticut; John Wiley & Sons Inc; Woodbridge Press
Membership(s): Publishers Marketing Association; Small Publishers Association of North America

Ball-Stick-Bird Publications Inc
PO Box 429, Williamstown, MA 01267-0429
SAN: 222-5565
Tel: 413-664-0002 *Fax:* 413-664-0002
E-mail: info@ballstickbird.com
Web Site: www.ballstickbird.com
Key Personnel
Pres & Rts & Perms: Renee Fuller
Founded: 1975
Children's reading series.
ISBN Prefix(es): 0-917740
Number of titles published annually: 13 Print
Total Titles: 13 Print; 13 Online

Ballinger Publishing
Formerly Burchell Publishing
41 N Jefferson St, Suite 300, Pensacola, FL 32501
Mailing Address: PO Box 12665, Pensacola, FL 32591-2665
Tel: 850-433-1166 *Fax:* 850-435-9174
E-mail: info@ballingerpublishing.com
Web Site: www.ballingerpublishing.com
Key Personnel
Publr: Malcolm Ballinger *Tel:* 850-433-1166 ext 27 *E-mail:* malcolm@ballingerpublishing.com
Founded: 2001
Publishers of local & regional magazines.

The Baltimore Sun
Division of The Tribune Co
501 N Calvert St, Baltimore, MD 21278
Tel: 410-332-6000 *Toll Free Tel:* 800-829-8000
Fax: 410-332-6466
E-mail: sunsource@baltsun.com
Web Site: www.baltimoresun.com
Key Personnel
Public Ed: Paul Moore
Founded: 1837
Publisher of books on Maryland subjects, including history, photography, sports, culture, etc. Compilations of the work of columnists for the Baltimore Sun.
ISBN Prefix(es): 1-893116; 0-9649819
Number of titles published annually: 3 Print

Bancroft-Sage Publishing
Imprint of The Finney Co
3943 Meadowbrook Rd, Minneapolis, MN 55426
Tel: 952-938-9330 *Toll Free Tel:* 800-846-7027
Fax: 952-938-7353
E-mail: feedback@finney-hobar.com
Web Site: www.finney-hobar.com
Key Personnel
Owner & Pres: Allan E Krayson
Founded: 1987
Juvenile books, high interest, low readability, sports, biographies, science, social studies & controlled vocabulary.
ISBN Prefix(es): 0-944280
Number of titles published annually: 4 Print
Total Titles: 16 Print; 24 Online
Distributed by Follett Library Resources; Baker & Taylor Books

Bandanna Books
Affiliate of Sabine Design
1212 Punta Gorda St, Suite 13, Santa Barbara, CA 93103
SAN: 238-7956
Tel: 805-899-2145 *Fax:* 805-899-2145
E-mail: bandanna@cox.net
Web Site: www.beachcollege.net/bookstore
Key Personnel
Pres & Publr: Sasha Briar Newborn
Founded: 1981
Classics of literature & language books.
ISBN Prefix(es): 0-942208
Number of titles published annually: 2 Print
Total Titles: 14 Print; 2 Online
Imprints: Bandanna College classics; Pussywillow
Distribution Center: NACS Corp
Membership(s): Publishers Marketing Association

Bandido Books
9806 Heaton Ct, Orlando, FL 32817
Tel: 407-657-9707 *Toll Free Tel:* 877-814-6824 (pin 1174) *Fax:* 407-677-9796
E-mail: publish@bandidobooks.com
Web Site: www.bandidobooks.com
Key Personnel
Ed-in-Chief: Martin Schiavenato *E-mail:* martin@bandidobooks.com
Sales: Kristy Knowlton *E-mail:* kristy@banditobooks.com
Founded: 1999
Specialize in providing clinical reference titles & other titles of interest to nursing & other healthcare professionals.
ISBN Prefix(es): 1-929693
Number of titles published annually: 5 Print; 2 CD-ROM; 4 E-Book
Total Titles: 16 Print

Banner of Truth
PO Box 621, Carlisle, PA 17013
Tel: 717-249-5747 *Toll Free Tel:* 800-263-8085 (orders) *Fax:* 717-249-0604
E-mail: info@banneroftruth.org
Web Site: www.banneroftruth.co.uk
Key Personnel
Mgr: Jack Smith *E-mail:* jack@banneroftruth.org
Founded: 1957
Not for profit.
ISBN Prefix(es): 0-85151
Total Titles: 506 Print
Shipping Address: 63 E Louther St, Carlisle, PA 17013
Membership(s): Christian Booksellers Association; Evangelical Christian Publishers Association

Bantam Dell Publishing Group
Division of Random House Inc
1745 Broadway, New York, NY 10019
Tel: 212-782-9000 *Toll Free Tel:* 800-223-6834
Fax: 212-302-7985
Web Site: www.randomhouse.com/bantamdell
Key Personnel
Pres & Publr: Irwyn Applebaum
Exec VP & Deputy Publr: Nita Taublib
Sr VP & Dir, Creative Mktg: Betsy Hulsebosch
Sr VP & Dir, Sales Mktg: Cynthia Lasky
Sr VP & Dir, Publicity & PR: Barb Burg
VP & Dir, Cover Art: James Plumeri
VP & Dir, Subs Rts: Sharon Swados
VP & Exec Publg Mgr: Gina Wachtel
VP & Edit Dir, Dial Press: Susan Kamil
VP & Exec Ed: Toni Burbank; Jacqueline Cantor; Kate Miciak
VP & Sr Ed: Ann Harris
VP & Assoc Gen Counsel: Matthew Martin
Dir, Copy - Dell: Elizabeth Kantor
Dir, Copy - Bantam: Michael Cross
Dir, Cover Art: Yook Louie
Assoc Dir, Adv: Melissa Lord
Assoc Dir, Publicity: Susan Corcoran; Theresa Zoro
Assoc Dir, Promo: Sarah Elliott
Asst Dir, Publicity: Christopher Artis
Asst Dir, Subs Rts: Lisa George
Mgr, Subs Rts: Donna Duverglas
Mgr, Copyrights & Perms: Carol Christiansen
Mgr, Contracts: David Sanford
Contracts Assoc: Thomas Dobrowolski
Copy Chief: Margaret Benton; Johanna Tani
Sr Copy Writer: Tracy Marx
Sr Ed: Tracy Devine; Wendy McCurdy; Bill Massey; Anne Groell; Danielle Perez; Beth Rashbaum
Ed: John Flicker; Juliet Ulman
Founded: 1945
General interest fiction & nonfiction, mass market, trade paperbacks & hardcover for adults.
Random House Inc & its publishing entities are not accepting unsol submissions, proposals, mss, or submission queries via e-mail at this time.
ISBN Prefix(es): 0-553; 0-385; 0-440
Imprints: Bantam Books; Bantam Classics; Delacorte Press; Dell Books; Delta Books; Dial Press
Branch Office(s)
Random House Canada Ltd, One Toronto St, Unit 300, Toronto, ON M5C 2V6, Canada *Tel:* 416-364-4449 *Fax:* 416-364-6863
Foreign Office(s): Random House Australia Ltd, 20 Alfred St, Milsons Point, Sydney, NSW 2061, Australia *Tel:* (029) 954-9966 *Fax:* (029) 954-4562
Random House New Zealand, 18 Poland Rd, Glenfield, Auckland, New Zealand *Tel:* (09) 444-7197 *Fax:* (09) 444-7524
Transworld Publishers Ltd UK, 61/63 Uxbridge Rd, Ealing, London W5 5SA, United Kingdom *Tel:* (020) 8579 2652 *Fax:* (020) 8579 5479
Foreign Rep(s): Agence Hoffman (Germany); Agencia Lit BMSR (Brazil); Agencia Literaria Carmen Balcells (Spain); Andrew Nurnberg Associates (Scandinavia, Holland); Andrew Nurnberg Associates (Baltic States); Andrew Nurnberg Literary Agency (Russia); Bantam Nurichan Kesim Literary Agency (Turkey); Bardon Chinese Media Agency (Taiwan); Dell Akcali Copyright Agency (Turkey); Direct/contact Bantam Dell (China); Imprima Korea Agency (Korea); Japan UNI Agency Inc (Japan); JLM Literary Agency (Greece); Lex Copyright Office (Hungary); Luigi Bernabo Assocs (Netherlands); Michelle Lapautre (France); Permissions & Rights Agency (Eastern Europe); Ilana Pikarsky Literary Agency (Israel)

Baptist Spanish Publishing House (d/b/a Casa Bautista de Publicaciones)
Affiliate of Southern Baptist Convention
7000 Alabama St, El Paso, TX 79904
Mailing Address: PO Box 4255, El Paso, TX 79914-4255
Tel: 915-566-9656 *Toll Free Tel:* 800-755-5958 (cust serv & orders); 800-985-9971 (Casa Bautista Miami) *Fax:* 915-562-6502; 915-565-9008 (orders)
E-mail: cbpmail@casabautista.org
Web Site: www.casabautista.org *Cable:* BAPUB
Key Personnel
Gen Dir: Jorge E Diaz
Mktg Sales Dir: Miryam Diaz
Sec: Norma C Armengol *E-mail:* narmengol@casabautista.org
Founded: 1905
Religious publications in Spanish & French. Foreign distributors also located in all latin.
ISBN Prefix(es): 0-311
Number of titles published annually: 20 Print
Total Titles: 895 Print; 895 E-Book; 40 Audio
Imprints: CBP/EMH
Branch Office(s)
Casa Bautista Miami, 12020 NW 40 St, Suite 103, Keith Morris *Tel:* 954-757-9800 *Toll Free Tel:* 800-985-9971 *Fax:* 954-757-9944
E-mail: kmorris@aol.com

Foreign Office(s): Rivadavia 3474, 1203 Buenos Aires, Argentina, Esteban Acuna *Tel:* (01) 4863-6745 *Fax:* (01) 4863-6745
Casilla 2516, Santa Cruz, Bolivia *Tel:* 343-0717 *Fax:* 342-8193
Casilla 1253, Santiago, Chile, Emilio Zapata *Tel:* (02) 672-2114 *Fax:* (02) 695-7145
Apartado Aereo 55294, Bogota 2, DC, Colombia *Tel:* (01) 287-8602 *Fax:* (01) 287-8992
Apartado 285-2050, San Pedro Montes de Oca, San Jose, Costa Rica, Juan Brenes *Tel:* 225-4565 *Fax:* 224-3677
Apartado 880, Santo Domingo, Dominican Republic, Noraima Aquino *Tel:* 565-2282 *Fax:* 565-6944
Casilla 3236, Guayaquil, Ecuador *Tel:* (03) 445-5311 *Fax:* (03) 445-2610
Av Los Andes No J-14 Col Miramonte, San Salvador, El Salvador *Tel:* 260-8658 *Fax:* 260-1730
Apartado 1135, Guatemala 01901, Guatemala *Tel:* (02) 253-0013 *Fax:* (02) 232-5225
Apartado 279, Tegucigalpa, Honduras, Oscar Herrera *Tel:* 238-1481 *Fax:* 237-9909
Independencia 36-B, Col Centro, 06050 Mexico DF, Mexico, Hortencia Vazquez *Tel:* (05) 512-0206 *Fax:* (05) 512-9475
Del Hospital Bautista 2-C, abajo5c. al sur casa No 1206, Managua, Nicaragua, Felix Ruiz Rivera *Tel:* 222-2195 *Fax:* 278-4786
Ave Samuel Lewis No 9 (Ave 2 Sur) entre calles 53 y 54 Urb Obarrio, Panama 5, Panama *Tel:* 264-6469 *Fax:* 264-6736
Casilla 1415, Asuncion, Paraguay, Gail P Joule *Tel:* (021) 21-2952
Francisco Pizarro 388, Trujillo, Peru, Maria Elena Santos *Fax:* 424-5982
Calle San Alegjardro 1825, Urb. San Ignacio, Rio Piedras, Puerto Rico *Tel:* (809) 764-6175
Padre Mendez, No 142-B, 46900 Torrente, Valencia, Spain *Tel:* (06)-156-3578 *Fax:* (06) 156-3579
Distributed by LifeWay Christian Resources
Foreign Rep(s): Guido Picado (Costa Rica)

Barbed Wire Publishing
270 Avenida de Mesilla, Las Cruces, NM 88005
Tel: 505-525-9707 *Toll Free Tel:* 888-817-1990 *Fax:* 505-525-9711
E-mail: thefolks@barbed-wire.net
Web Site: www.barbed-wire.net
Founded: 1998
Number of titles published annually: 12 Print
Total Titles: 92 Print
Imprints: Barbed Wire Publishing; Yucca Tree Press
Distributor for Eakon Press; Kiva Publishers; Texas Technical University Press; Texas Western Press
Membership(s): Mountains & Plains Booksellers Association; New Mexico Book Association; Publishers Marketing Association
See separate listing for:
Yucca Tree Press

Barbour Publishing Inc
1810 Barbour Dr, Uhrichsville, OH 44683
Tel: 740-922-6045 *Fax:* 740-922-5948
E-mail: info@barbourbooks.com
Web Site: www.barbourbooks.com
Key Personnel
Pres & CEO: Tim H Martins *E-mail:* tmartins@barbourbooks.com
Sr Ed: Paul K Muckley
VP, Sales & Mktg: William Westfall
Exec Asst: Michele Clay *Tel:* 740-922-6045 ext 124 *E-mail:* mclay@barbourbooks.com
Founded: 1981
Christian books, Bibles, reference, cards, music, music CDs.
ISBN Prefix(es): 1-57748; 0-929239; 1-57293; 0-916441; 1-55748
Number of titles published annually: 140 Print

Total Titles: 700 Print
Imprints: American Adventure; Barbour Books; The Christian Library; Heartsong Presents; Heroes of the Faith; Inspirational Library; Promise Press; Young Reader's Christian Library
Distributor for Discovery House Publishers
Foreign Rights: Christian Art Wholesale (South Africa); R G Mitchell; Nova Distributors (UK, Canada)

BAR/BRI Group
Division of Thomson Learning
111 W Jackson Blvd, Chicago, IL 60604
Tel: 312-894-1688 *Toll Free Tel:* 800-328-9352 *Fax:* 312-360-1842 *Toll Free Fax:* 800-430-9378 (orders)
Web Site: www.gilbertlaw.com
Key Personnel
Dir, Sales & Mktg: Stephanie Kartofels
Founded: 1953
Number of titles published annually: 15 Print
Total Titles: 145 Print; 22 CD-ROM; 33 Audio
Warehouse: 610 Opperman Dr, Eagan, MN 55123

Barcelona Publishers
Pathway Book Service, 4 White Brook Rd, Gilsum, NH 03448
SAN: 298-6299
Tel: 603-357-0236 *Toll Free Tel:* 800-345-6665 *Fax:* 603-357-2073
E-mail: pbs@pathwaybooks.com
Web Site: barcelonapublishers.com
Key Personnel
Prop: Kenneth E Bruscia *E-mail:* kbruscia@aol.com
Contact: Ernest Peter
Founded: 1991
Music therapy books & materials.
ISBN Prefix(es): 0-9624080; 1-891278
Number of titles published annually: 4 Print
Total Titles: 29 Print
Distributed by General Music Store; MMB Music; West Music

Barefoot Books
Subsidiary of The Barefoot Child
2067 Massachusetts Ave, 5th fl, Cambridge, MA 02140
Tel: 617-576-0660 *Fax:* 617-576-0049
E-mail: ussales@barefootbooks.com; help@barefootbooks.com
Web Site: www.barefootbooks.com
Key Personnel
Pres: Nancy Traversy *E-mail:* nancy@barefootbooks.com
COO: Karen Janson *E-mail:* karen.janson@barefootbooks.com
Publr (UK Office): Tessa Strickland *E-mail:* tessa@barefootbooks.com
Founded: 1993
Publishes high quality picture books for children of all ages specializing in the work of authors & artists from many cultures, wrapping paper, artists prints & cards. All have illustrations from the books.
ISBN Prefix(es): 1-898000; 1-901223; 1-902283; 1-84148
Number of titles published annually: 30 Print; 10 Audio
Total Titles: 175 Print; 10 Audio
Foreign Office(s): Barefoot Books-Bath, 124-126 Walcot St, Bath BA 5 BG, United Kingdom *Tel:* (01225) 322-400
Returns: Distribution Solutions Group, 1120 Rte 22 E, Bridgewater, NJ 08807 *Toll Free Tel:* 888-767-4232
Warehouse: Distribution Solutions Group, 1120 Rte 22 E, Bridgewater, NJ 08807 *Toll Free Tel:* 888-767-4232
Membership(s): ALA; Children's Book Council; EPA

Barnes & Noble Books (Imports & Reprints)
Division of Rowman & Littlefield Publishers Inc
4501 Forbes Blvd, Suite 200, Lanham, MD 20706
SAN: 206-7803
Tel: 301-459-3366 *Toll Free Tel:* 800-462-6420 (orders only) *Fax:* 301-429-5748 *Toll Free Fax:* 800-338-4550 (orders only)
Web Site: www.rowmanlittlefield.com
Key Personnel
Pres, Barnes & Noble Publg Group: Alan Kahn
Publr: Jed Lyons
VP, Mktg: Sheila Burnett
Dir, Rts Ed & ISBN Contact: Kelly Rogers *E-mail:* krogers@rowman.com
Founded: 1873
Imported academic hardbound & paperback.
ISBN Prefix(es): 0-389
Number of titles published annually: 10 Print
Distributed by Rowman & Littlefield Publishers Inc; University Press of America Inc
Distributor for Cooper Square
Warehouse: 15200 NBN Way, Blue Ridge Summit, PA 17215

Barricade Books Inc
185 Bridge Plaza N, Suite 308A, Fort Lee, NJ 07024
Tel: 201-944-7600 *Fax:* 201-944-6363
E-mail: customerservice@barricadebooks.com
Web Site: www.barricadebooks.com
Key Personnel
Pres & Treas: Lyle Stuart
Publr & Subs Rts: Carole Stuart
Dir, Publicity: Jennifer Itskevich
Prodn Mgr: Jeff J Nordstedt
Ed: Allan J Wilson
Off Mgr: Albertha O'Neill
Founded: 1991
ISBN Prefix(es): 0-934878; 0-942637; 0-9623032; 1-56980
Number of titles published annually: 30 Print
Total Titles: 200 Print
Imprints: Barricade Books
Foreign Rep(s): Gordwana Books; Roundhouse Publishing Group (UK, Europe)
Returns: Stackpole Distribution, 7253 Grayson Rd, Harrisburg, PA 17111, Pattie Smith *Tel:* 717-795-8610 *Fax:* 717-564-4479
Warehouse: Stackpole Distribution, 7253 Grayson Rd, Harrisburg, PA 17111, Pattie Smith *Tel:* 717-795-8610 *Fax:* 717-564-4479
Distribution Center: Stackpole Distribution, 7253 Grayson Rd, Harrisburg, PA 17111, Pattie Smith *Tel:* 717-795-8610 *Fax:* 717-564-4479
Membership(s): AAP

Barron's Educational Series Inc
250 Wireless Blvd, Hauppauge, NY 11788
SAN: 201-453X
Tel: 631-434-3311 *Toll Free Tel:* 800-645-3476 *Fax:* 631-434-3723
E-mail: info@barronseduc.com
Web Site: www.barronseduc.com (Books can be purchased online) *Cable:* BARRONS HAUPPAUGE NY
Key Personnel
Chmn & CEO: Manuel H Barron
Pres & Publr: Ellen Sibley
VP, Fin: Nancy Douglas
VP, Sales & Mktg: Alex Hultz
Dir, Mktg: Lonny R Stein
Publicity Mgr: Steve Matteo *E-mail:* steve@barronseduc.com
Acq Ed: Wayne Barr
Subs Rts Mgr & Intl Rts: Patricia Doyle
Dir, School Sales & Lib Sales: Frederick Glasser
Intl Sales Mgr: Jackie Raab
Natl Sales Mgr: Hugh Shiebler
Founded: 1941
El-hi & college education; guidance & test review.
ISBN Prefix(es): 0-8120; 0-7641

Number of titles published annually: 300 Print
Total Titles: 2,000 Print; 125 Audio
Foreign Rep(s): Book Marketing Services Inc
    (Canada)
Foreign Rights: Anthea Literary Agency (Bul-
    garia); Big Apple Tuttle-Mori Inc (China);
    Contacts/The Rights Agency (Canada); DRT
    International (Korea); Lora Fountain Liter-
    ary Agency (France); International Editors Co
    (Latin America, Portugal, Spain); Nurcihan
    Kesim Literary Agency (Turkey); David Mat-
    lock Agency (Russia); Montreal Contacts/The
    Rights Agency (French Canada); OA Liter-
    ary Agency (Greece); Tuttle-Mori Agency Inc
    (Japan)
Advertising Agency: Friedman, Harris & Partners
Warehouse: Barron's Georgetown Book Ware-
    house, 34 Armstrong Ave, Georgetown, ON
    L7G 4R9, Canada

Barrytown/Station Hill Press
120 Station Hill Rd, Barrytown, NY 12507
SAN: 214-1485
Tel: 845-758-5293
E-mail: publishers@stationhill.org
Web Site: www.stationhill.org
Key Personnel
Man Ed: Chip Brill
Pubns & Ed: George Quasha
Founded: 1978
General trade books, quality paperbacks & fine
    editions; poetry, fiction & discourse; visual
    arts; studies in literature & psychology, clas-
    sics, translations, theater, creative nonfiction,
    health/New Age.
ISBN Prefix(es): 0-930794; 0-88268
Number of titles published annually: 6 Print
Total Titles: 300 Print
Divisions: Pulse Books
Foreign Rep(s): Lora Fountain (France); Gara
    Media (Germany); Japanville (Japan); Kerrigan
    (Spain); Living Weary (Italy)
Distribution Center: Consortium Book Sales &
    Distribution, 1045 Westgak Dr, St Paul, MN
    55114-1065 *Tel:* 651-221-3572 *Fax:* 651-221-
    0124

Bartleby Press
Subsidiary of Jackson Westgate Inc
11141 Georgia Ave, Suite A-3, Silver Spring, MD
    20902
SAN: 241-2098
Tel: 301-949-2443 *Fax:* 301-949-2205
E-mail: inquiries@bartlebythepublisher.com
Web Site: www.bartlebythepublisher.com
Key Personnel
Publr: Jeremy Kay
Mktg Dir: Jarom McDonald
Founded: 1981
ISBN Prefix(es): 0-910155; 0-9625963
Number of titles published annually: 15 Print
Total Titles: 40 Print
Imprints: Eshel Books; PS&E Publications
Distributor for BJE Press

Basic Books
Member of The Perseus Books Group
387 Park Ave S, 12th fl, New York, NY 10016-
    8810
Tel: 212-340-8100 *Toll Free Tel:* 800-242-7737
    (orders) *Fax:* 212-340-8135
E-mail: basic.books@perseusbooks.com
Web Site: www.basicbooks.com
Key Personnel
Pres & CEO, Perseus Books Group: Jack McKe-
    own
Sr VP & CFO: John Rogers
VP & Publr: Elizabeth Maguire
VP & Group Dir, Fin & Oper: Robert Mancuso
VP & Group Dir, Sales & Mktg: Matthew Gold-
    berg
VP & Group Rts Dir: Carolyn Savarese

Assoc Publr: John Hughes
Dir, Publicity: Jamie Brickhouse
Exec Man Ed: Steven Bottum
Exec Ed: Jo Ann Miller; William Frucht
Sr Ed: Chip Rosetti
Founded: 1950
Nonfiction only. Subjects include Current Affairs
    & Memoirs.
ISBN Prefix(es): 0-465
Number of titles published annually: 120 Print
Total Titles: 600 Print
Imprints: Basic Civitas; New Republic Books;
    New America Foundation (NAF Basic)
Distributed by HarperCollins
Foreign Rights: Perseus Books Group Subsidiary
    Rights
Advertising Agency: Bennett Books Advertising
Warehouse: HarperCollins Publishers, Order Dept,
    1000 Keystone Park, Scranton, PA 18512-4621

Basic Health Publications Inc
8200 Boulevard E, Suite 25-G, North Bergen, NJ
    07047
Tel: 201-868-8336 *Toll Free Tel:* 800-575-8890
    Fax: 201-868-8335
Key Personnel
Pres & Publr: Norman Goldfind
    E-mail: ngoldfind@basichealthpub.com
Sales Dir: Kenneth Kaiman
Ed: Jack Challem; Stephanie Evans; Cheryl
    Hirsch; Tom Hirsch; Nancy Ringer; Carol A
    Rosenberg; Roberta Waddell
Prodn: Boris Miawer
Design: Mike Stromburg
Publicity: Diana Glynn
Text Design: Gary Rosenberg
Founded: 2001
Health, nutrition, fitness & alternative medicine.
    Publish in trade paperback & mass market for-
    mats.
ISBN Prefix(es): 1-59120
Number of titles published annually: 60 Print
Total Titles: 60 Print
Imprints: Basic Health Guides; Basic Health Pub-
    lications; User's Guides to Nutritional Supple-
    ments
Foreign Rep(s): Athens Productions Inc (World-
    wide)
Foreign Rights: Writers House (Worldwide)
Shipping Address: Mercedes Distribution Ctr,
    Brooklyn Navy Yard, Bldg 3, Brooklyn, NY
    11205, Contact: Joal Savino *Tel:* 718-522-7110
    Fax: 718-935-9647 *E-mail:* jsavino@mdist.com
Warehouse: Mercedes Distribution Ctr, Brooklyn
    Navy Yard, Bldg 3, Brooklyn, NY 11205, Con-
    tact: Joal Savino *Tel:* 718-522-7110 *Fax:* 718-
    935-9647 *E-mail:* jsavino@mdist.com
Distribution Center: Mercedes Distribution Ctr,
    Brooklyn Navy Yard, Bldg 3, Brooklyn, NY
    11205, Contact: Joal Savino *Tel:* 718-522-7110
    Fax: 718-935-9647 *E-mail:* jsavino@mdist.com
Membership(s): Publishers Marketing Association

Battelle Press
Division of Battelle
505 King Ave, Columbus, OH 43201-2693
SAN: 213-4640
Tel: 614-424-6393 *Toll Free Tel:* 800-451-3543
    Fax: 614-424-3819
E-mail: press@battelle.org
Web Site: www.battelle.org/bookstore
Key Personnel
Publr: Joseph E Sheldrick
Busn Mgr: Mashell Roney
Founded: 1980
Professional books & CDs: environmental sci-
    ences, the applied sciences & management for
    engineers & reseachers.
ISBN Prefix(es): 0-935470; 1-57477
Number of titles published annually: 12 Print; 2
    CD-ROM
Total Titles: 150 Print; 6 CD-ROM

Battery Press Inc
1020 Fourth Ave S, Nashville, TN 37210
SAN: 212-5897
Mailing Address: PO Box 198885, Nashville, TN
    37219
Tel: 615-298-1401 *Fax:* 615-298-1401
E-mail: batterybks@aol.com
Web Site: www.batterypress.com
Key Personnel
Pres: Richard S Gardner
Founded: 1976
Military, aviation & naval history; hardcover.
ISBN Prefix(es): 0-89839
Number of titles published annually: 140 Print
Total Titles: 280 Print
Imprints: Battery Classics

Bay/SOMA Publishing Inc
444 De Haro, Suite 130, San Francisco, CA
    94107
Tel: 415-252-4350 *Fax:* 415-252-4352
E-mail: info@baybooks.com
Web Site: www.baybooks.com
Key Personnel
Pres & Publr: James Connolly
Edit Dir: Floyd Yearout
Founded: 1996
Books, video related to public TV & lifestyles,
    interior design.
ISBN Prefix(es): 0-912333; 1-57959
Number of titles published annually: 15 Print
Total Titles: 70 Print
Imprints: Bay Books; KQED Books & Tapes™;
    SOMA Books
Distributed by Publishers Group West
Distribution Center: Publishers Group West, 1700
    Fourth St, Berkeley, CA 94710 *Tel:* 510-528-
    1444 *Toll Free Tel:* 800-788-3123

Baylor University Press
Baylor University, Waco, TX 76798-7363
SAN: 685-317X
Mailing Address: PO Box 97363, Waco, TX
    76798-7363
Tel: 254-710-3164 *Toll Free Tel:* 800-710-3217
    Fax: 254-710-3440
Web Site: www.baylorpress.com
Key Personnel
Dir: Carey C Newman *E-mail:* carey_newman@
    baylor.edu
Prodn Mgr: Diane Smith *E-mail:* diane_smith@
    baylor.edu
Mktg Mgr: Rusty Edwards
    E-mail: rusty_edwards@baylor.edu
Off Mgr: Lorraine Kerr *E-mail:* lorraine_kerr@
    baylor.edu
Founded: 1955
Scholarly books & monographs.
ISBN Prefix(es): 0-918954
Number of titles published annually: 10 Print
Total Titles: 100 Print
Imprints: Markham Press Fund
Distributed by Texas A&M University Press
Distribution Center: Texas A&M University
    Press, College Station, TX 77843-4354 *Toll
    Free Tel:* 800-826-8911 *Toll Free Fax:* 888-
    617-2421
Membership(s): MLA; Society of Bible Litera-
    ture; Society of Scholarly Publishers

Baywood Publishing Co Inc
26 Austin Ave, Amityville, NY 11701
SAN: 206-9326
Mailing Address: PO Box 337, Amityville, NY
    11701
Tel: 631-691-1270 *Toll Free Tel:* 800-638-7819
    Fax: 631-691-1770
E-mail: baywood@baywood.com
Web Site: www.baywood.com
Key Personnel
Pres: Stuart Cohen
Rts & Perms & ISBN Contact: Julie Krempa
Cust Rel: S Edwards

Founded: 1964
Professional journals & textbooks: anthropology, archaeology, education, psychiatry & psychology, health services, health education, labor relations, sociology, mathematics, computers in education, thanatology, imagery, environment, technical writing, gerontology, fire science, employee rights.
ISBN Prefix(es): 0-89503
Number of titles published annually: 25 Print; 21 Online
Total Titles: 250 Print; 21 Online
Foreign Rep(s): Book Representation & Distribution Ltd (UK, England)

BBC Audiobooks America
Subsidiary of BBC AudioBooks Ltd
One Lafayette Rd, Hampton, NH 03842
Mailing Address: PO Box 1450, Hampton, NH 03843-1450
Tel: 603-926-8744 Toll Free Tel: 800-621-0182
Fax: 603-929-3890
E-mail: info@bbcaudiobooksamerica.com
Key Personnel
Pres: Jim Brannigan
Publr: Jennifer Feldman
Cust Rel: Kathie Slattery
Founded: 1976
Popular authors, current fiction & nonfiction on unabridged audiobooks; children's large print books & children's audio books; radio dramatizations.
ISBN Prefix(es): 0-7927; 0-7451
Number of titles published annually: 30 Print; 240 Audio
Total Titles: 30 Print; 3,300 Audio
Imprints: Black Dagger Mysteries; Chivers Audio Books; Chivers Children's Audio Books; Galaxy Large Print Books; Gunsmoke Westerns; Sound Library Audiobooks; Sterling Audio Books

Be Puzzled
Division of University Games
2030 Harrison St, San Francisco, CA 94110
Tel: 415-503-1600 Toll Free Tel: 800-347-4818
Fax: 415-503-0085
E-mail: orders@areyougame.com
Web Site: www.areyougame.com
Key Personnel
Sr Prods Mgr: Connie Gee
Gen Mgr: Moss Kardener
Mystery jigsaw puzzles & mystery games. (Books are included in games & puzzles).
ISBN Prefix(es): 1-57528
Number of titles published annually: 10 Print
Total Titles: 20 Print

Beacham Publishing Corp
PO Box 1810, Nokomis, FL 34274-1810
Tel: 941-480-9644 Toll Free Tel: 800-466-9644
Fax: 941-480-9644
E-mail: beachampub@aol.com
Web Site: www.beachampublishing.com
Key Personnel
Pres & Intl Rts Contact: Walton Beacham
VP, Mktg & Lib Sales Dir: Deborah M Beacham
Ed: Kirk H Beetz
Founded: 1985
Reference books for middle, secondary, college & public libraries; instructional videotapes; business & government.
ISBN Prefix(es): 0-933833
Number of titles published annually: 3 Print
Total Titles: 20 Print
Distributed by The Gale Group
Warehouse: Sheridan Books, 100 N Staebler, Ann Arbor, MI 48103

Beacon Hill Press of Kansas City
Subsidiary of Nazarene Publishing House
PO Box 419527, Kansas City, MO 64141-6527

SAN: 202-9022
Tel: 816-931-1900 Toll Free Tel: 800-877-0700 (retail order) Fax: 816-753-4071
Toll Free Fax: 800-849-9827 (order)
Web Site: www.beaconhillbooks.com
Key Personnel
Dir: Bonnie Perry
Sr Mktg Dir: Barry Russell
Mgr, Rts & Perms: Janet Stapleton
ISBN Contact: Richard Beckner
Founded: 1912
Religion (Nazarene), drama & fiction.
ISBN Prefix(es): 0-83412
Number of titles published annually: 30 Print
Total Titles: 545 Print
Imprints: Crystal Sea Books; Lillenas Publishing Co; Nazarene Publishing House
Branch Office(s)
Church of the Nazarene, 6401 Paseo Blvd, Kansas City, MO 64131, Ed: Judi Perry
Tel: 816-931-1906
Shipping Address: 2923 Troost Ave, Kansas City, MO 64109

Beacon Press
41 Mount Vernon St, Boston, MA 02108
SAN: 201-4483
Mailing Address: 25 Beacon St, Boston, MA 02108
Tel: 617-742-2110 Toll Free Tel: 800-225-3362 (orders only) Fax: 617-723-3097; 617-742-2290
Web Site: www.beacon.org
Key Personnel
Dir: Helene Atwan
Dir, Sales & Mktg & Assoc Publr: Tom Hallock
Exec Ed: Joanne Wyckoff
Prodn Dir: P J Tierney
Creative Dir: Robert Kosturko
Founded: 1854
General nonfiction, religion & theology, current affairs, anthropology, women's studies, history, philosophy, gay & lesbian studies, African-American studies, Native American studies, Latino studies, Asian-American studies, education, hardcover & paperback.
ISBN Prefix(es): 0-8070
Number of titles published annually: 60 Print
Total Titles: 670 Print
Imprints: Bluestreak; Concord Library
Distributed by Houghton Mifflin
Foreign Rep(s): Airlift Book Co (UK, Europe); Fitzhenry & Whiteside (Canada)
Returns: HMCO, Trade & Reference Returns, 2700 N Richardt Ave, Indianapolis, IN 46219
Warehouse: Houghton Mifflin, Trade Customer Service Dept, 181 Ballardvale St, PO Box 7050, Wilmington, MA 01887, Contact: Carol Jones Toll Free Tel: 800-225-3362 Toll Free Fax: 800-634-7568
Distribution Center: HMCO, Trade & Reference Distribution Center, 4925 W 86 St, Indianapolis, IN 46268

Bear & Co Inc
Subsidiary of Inner Traditions International Ltd
One Park St, Rochester, VT 05767
Mailing Address: PO Box 388, Rochester, VT 05767
Tel: 802-767-3174 Toll Free Tel: 800-932-3277
Fax: 802-767-3726
E-mail: orders@InnerTraditions.com
Web Site: InnerTraditions.com
Key Personnel
Pres: Ehud C Sperling E-mail: prez@innertraditions.com
VP, Opers: Pat Harvey E-mail: patty@innertraditions.com
VP & Man Ed: Jeanie Levitan E-mail: jeanie@innertraditions.com
VP, Sales & Mktg: Rob Meadows E-mail: rob@innertraditions.com

Prodn Mgr: Brandi Sargent E-mail: brandi@innertraditions.com
Spec Sales: Nick McDougal E-mail: nick@innertraditions.com
Acqs Ed: Jon Graham E-mail: jon@innertraditions.com
Foreign Rts & Perms: Cynthia Fowles E-mail: cynthia@innertraditions.com
Publicity: Jody Winters E-mail: jody@innertraditions.com
Founded: 1980
Mysticism, philosophy, spirituality & medieval studies, contemporary prophecy, earth sciences, indigenous wisdom, new thought, alternative healing.
ISBN Prefix(es): 1-879181; 0-939680; 1-59143
Number of titles published annually: 22 Print
Total Titles: 145 Print
Imprints: Bear & Co; Bear Cub Books
Foreign Rep(s): Athena Productions (all other countries); Brumby Books Gemcraft (Australia); Michelle Morrow Curreri (Asia); Deep Books (Europe); India Book Distributors (India); India Book House (India); Real Books (South Africa); Southern Publishers Group (New Zealand); Ten Speed Press (Canada)
Foreign Rights: Agenzia Letteraria Internazionale (Italy); Akcali Copyright Agency (Turkey); Big Apple Tuttle-Mori (China & Taiwan); Book Publishers Association of Israel (Israel); Amina Marix Evans (Netherlands); Graal Ltd (Poland); Ilidio da Fonseca Matos (Portugal); International Copyright Agency Ltd (Romania); International Editor's Co SA (Argentina, Spain); Alexander Korzhenevski Agency (Russia); Zvonimir Majdak (Croatia); Montreal - Contacts/The Right Agency (Canada, France); Andrew Nurnberg Associates (Baltic States, Bulgaria, Czech Republic, Hungary); Read n Right Agency (Greece); Karin Schindler, Rights Representative (Brazil); Thomas Schluck Literary & Art Agency (Germany); Tuttle-Mori Agency (Japan); Tuttle-Mori Big Apple Agency (Thailand); Eric Yang Agency (Korea)
Warehouse: Inner Traditions International, Airport Industrial Park, 364 Innovation Dr, North Clarendon, VT 05759 Tel: 802-773-8930 Fax: 802-773-6993

Beard Books Inc
306 N Market St, Frederick, MD 21701-5337
Mailing Address: PO Box 4250, Frederick, MD 21705
Tel: 240-629-3300 Toll Free Tel: 888-563-4573 (book orders) Fax: 240-629-3360
E-mail: info@beardbooks.com; order@beardbooks.com
Web Site: www.beardbooks.com
Key Personnel
Owner & Pres: Chris Beard
Founded: 1988
Publishers of softcover books & electronic newsletters for business & law.

Beautiful America Publishing Co
2600 Progress Way, Woodburn, OR 97071
Mailing Address: PO Box 244, Woodburn, OR 97071
Tel: 503-982-4616 Toll Free Tel: 800-874-1233
Fax: 503-982-2825
E-mail: bapco@beautifulamericapub.com
Web Site: www.beautifulamericapub.com
Key Personnel
Pres: Beverly Paul
Founded: 1987
Nature & scenic regional books & calendars.
ISBN Prefix(es): 0-89802
Number of titles published annually: 5 Print
Total Titles: 28 Print
Imprints: Little America Publishing Co
Membership(s): Pacific Northwest Booksellers Association; Publishers Marketing Association

Bedford/St Martin's
Division of Holtzbrinck Publishers Holdings LLC
75 Arlington St, Boston, MA 02116
Tel: 617-399-4000 *Fax:* 617-426-8582
Web Site: www.bedfordstmartins.com
Key Personnel
Pres: Joan E Feinberg
Ed-in-Chief (Boston Office): Karen Henry
Ed-in-Chief (New York Office): Nancy Perry
Busn Mgr: Jamie Demas
VP, Prod: Marcia Cohen
Edit Dir: Denise Wydra
Adv & Prom Mgr: Tom Macy
Founded: 1981
English history, communications, literature & music.
ISBN Prefix(es): 0-312
Number of titles published annually: 200 Print
Branch Office(s)
33 Irving Place, New York, NY 10003 *Tel:* 212-375-7000 *Toll Free Tel:* 800-375-7000
Warehouse: VHPS Distribution Ctr, 16365 James Madison Hwy (US Rte 15), Gordonsville, VA 22942

Beekman Publishers Inc
2626 Rte 212, Woodstock, NY 12498
Mailing Address: PO Box 888, Woodstock, NY 12498
Tel: 845-679-2300 *Toll Free Tel:* 888-BEEKMAN (orders) *Fax:* 845-679-2301
E-mail: beekman@beekmanpublishers.com
Web Site: www.beekmanpublishers.com
Key Personnel
Chmn of the Bd, Pres & Ed-in-Chief: Stuart A Ober
Mgr: Christina Fendley *E-mail:* christina@beekmanpublishers.com
Founded: 1972
New titles, reprints & imported titles from England, Wales, India & Russia in all subject areas, particularly music, wholistic healing, homeopathic medicine, business, medical & computer books.
ISBN Prefix(es): 0-8464
Number of titles published annually: 5 Print
Total Titles: 3,000 Print; 100 Audio
Distributor for CIPO Chartered Institute for Personnel Development; C W Daniel; Gomer Press; Kogan Page; Music Sales Corp
Shipping Address: 2626 Rte 212, Woodstock, NY 12498

Thomas T Beeler Publisher
710 Main St, Suite 300, Rollinsford, NH 03869
Mailing Address: PO Box 310, Rollinsford, NH 03869-0310
Tel: 603-749-0392 *Toll Free Tel:* 800-818-7574 *Fax:* 603-749-0395 *Toll Free Fax:* 888-222-3396
E-mail: cservice@beelerpub.com
Web Site: www.beelerpub.com
Key Personnel
Chmn & Publr: Thomas T Beeler *E-mail:* tombeeler@beelerpub.com
Pres: David W O'Connor *E-mail:* doconnor@beelerpub.com
Ed: Traci Wason *E-mail:* twason@beelerpub.com
Founded: 1995
Large print.
ISBN Prefix(es): 1-57490
Number of titles published annually: 84 Print
Total Titles: 200 Print
Imprints: Beeler Large Print
Foreign Rep(s): Bolinda Publishing (Australia, New Zealand); Stricker Books (Canada)

Begell House Inc Publishers
145 Madison Ave, Suite 601, New York, NY 10016
Tel: 212-725-1999 *Fax:* 212-213-8368
E-mail: orders@begellhouse.com
Web Site: www.begellhouse.com
Key Personnel
Pres & Intl Rts: William Begell
Publr: Edward M Crane; Yelena Shafeyeva
Journals Mgr: Marsha Pronin
Prod Mgr: Janet Rogers
Book Mgr: Dahlia DeJesus
Founded: 1992
Science books & journals.
ISBN Prefix(es): 1-56700
Number of titles published annually: 5 Print
Total Titles: 200 Print
Subsidiaries: Begell-Atom LLC
Foreign Office(s): 3 Saint Peters St, Wallingford OX14 1GU, United Kingdom, Contact: Mr Ray Johnson *Tel:* (01491) 834930 *Fax:* (01491) 834930 *E-mail:* ray@melbourne-house.demon.co.uk
Membership(s): AAP

Behrman House Inc
11 Edison Place, Springfield, NJ 07081
SAN: 201-4459
Tel: 973-379-7200 *Fax:* 973-379-7280
Web Site: www.behrmanhouse.com
Key Personnel
Pres & Rts & Perms: David Behrman
Sales: Terry Kaye
Founded: 1921
Synagogue school textbooks & trade books (Jewish).
ISBN Prefix(es): 0-87441
Number of titles published annually: 212 Print
Total Titles: 500 Print; 3 CD-ROM
Distributor for Rossel Books

Frederic C Beil Publisher Inc
609 Whitaker St, Savannah, GA 31401
Tel: 912-233-2446 *Fax:* 912-233-6456
E-mail: beilbook@beil.com
Web Site: www.beil.com
Key Personnel
Pres & Publr: Frederic C Beil
Ed: Mary Ann Bowman
Founded: 1982
Fiction & nonfiction, biography, history, regional, the book arts, juveniles.
ISBN Prefix(es): 0-913720; 1-929490
Number of titles published annually: 11 Print
Total Titles: 134 Print
Imprints: Hypermedia Inc; The Sandstone Press
Foreign Office(s): 71 Great Russell St, London WC1B 3BN, United Kingdom
Foreign Rep(s): Gazelle Ltd (UK, Europe)
Warehouse: 711 Wheaton St, Savannah, GA 31401
Distribution Center: 608 Howard St, Savannah, GA 31401

Bell Springs Publishing
PO Box 1240, Willits, CA 95490-1240
SAN: 209-3138
Tel: 707-459-6372 *Toll Free Tel:* 800-515-8050 *Fax:* 707-459-8614
E-mail: info@bellsprings.com
Web Site: bellsprings.com
Key Personnel
Publr: Bernard Bear Kamoroff; Sam Leandro
Founded: 1976
Books, small business, pinball machines.
ISBN Prefix(es): 0-917510
Number of titles published annually: 10 Print; 10 Online; 10 E-Book
Total Titles: 20 Print; 10 Online; 10 E-Book
Foreign Rep(s): James Hitchen (UK)
Shipping Address: 106 State St, Willits, CA 95490

Bellerophon Books
PO Box 21307, Santa Barbara, CA 93121-1307
SAN: 202-392X
Tel: 805-965-7034 *Toll Free Tel:* 800-253-9943 *Fax:* 805-965-8286
E-mail: sales@bellerophonbooks.com
Web Site: www.bellerophonbooks.com
Key Personnel
Pres: Ellen Knill
Founded: 1969
Children's art & history.
ISBN Prefix(es): 0-88388
Number of titles published annually: 6 Print
Total Titles: 138 Print
Foreign Rep(s): St Anne's Books (UK)

Benator Publishing LLC
1240 Johnson Ferry Place, Suite C-5, Marietta, GA 30068
Tel: 770-977-5750 *Fax:* 770-977-8464
E-mail: benpubl2@bellsouth.net
Web Site: benatorpublishing.com
Key Personnel
Pres & Publr: Gene A Benator
Opers Mgr: Robyn Richardson
Founded: 1996
Holds the official license for the NASCAR & PGA Tour.
ISBN Prefix(es): 0-9719035
Number of titles published annually: 4 Print
Total Titles: 5 Print
Membership(s): Publishers Association of the South

BenBella Books
6440 N Central Expressway, Suite 617, Dallas, TX 75206
Tel: 214-750-3600 *Fax:* 214-750-3645
E-mail: editor@benbellabooks.com
Web Site: www.benbellabooks.com
Key Personnel
Publr: Glenn Yeffeth *Tel:* 214-750-3628 *E-mail:* glenn@benbellabooks.com
Ed: Shanna Caughey *E-mail:* shanna@benbellabooks.com
Assoc Ed: Leah Wilson *E-mail:* leah@benbellabooks.com
PR & Mktg: Laura Watkins *E-mail:* laura@benbellabooks.com
Founded: 2001
Specialize in the best of science fiction & pop culture.
ISBN Prefix(es): 1-932100
Number of titles published annually: 25 Print
Distributed by IPG Returns Dept
Orders to: IPG Returns Dept, 814 N Franklin St, Chicago, IL 60610, Mary Rowles *Toll Free Tel:* 800-888-4741 ext 224 *Fax:* 312-337-5985 *E-mail:* frontdesk@ipgbook.com
Returns: IPG Returns Dept, 814 N Franklin St, Chicago, IL 60610, Mary Rowles *Tel:* 312-337-0747 ext 224 *Fax:* 312-337-5985 *E-mail:* frontdesk@ipgbook.com
Shipping Address: 600 N Pulaski Rd, Chicago, IL 60624 *Tel:* 312-337-0747 *Fax:* 312-337-5985
Warehouse: IPG Warehouse, 600 N Pulaski Rd, Chicago, IL 60624 *Tel:* 312-337-0747 *Fax:* 312-337-5985
Membership(s): Publishers Marketing Association

§Matthew Bender & Co Inc
Member of The LexisNexis Group
744 Broad St, 7th fl, Newark, NJ 07102
SAN: 202-330X
Tel: 973-820-2000 *Fax:* 973-820-2007
Web Site: www.bender.com
Key Personnel
Dir, Mktg: Eduardo Gomez
Founded: 1887
Treatises, text & form books, newsletters, periodicals & manuals for the legal, accounting, insurance, banking & related professions, selected libraries on CD-ROM.
Total Titles: 577 Print; 277 CD-ROM; 27 Online; 277 E-Book
Online services available through LexisNexis.

Branch Office(s)
1275 Broadway, Albany, NY 12204 *Toll Free Tel:* 800-424-4200
201 Mission St, San Francisco, CA 94105-1831
Distribution Center: Broome Corp Park, 136 Carlin Rd, Conklin, NY 13748

R James Bender Publishing
PO Box 23456, San Jose, CA 95153-3456
Tel: 408-225-5777 *Fax:* 408-225-4739
E-mail: order@bender-publishing.com
Web Site: www.bender-publishing.com
Key Personnel
Prop & Dir: R J Bender *E-mail:* rbender@best.com
Contact: Roger Bender
Founded: 1967
Military books & magazines.
ISBN Prefix(es): 0-912138
Number of titles published annually: 8 Print
Total Titles: 30 Print

The Benefactory
PO Box 128, Cohasset, MA 02025
Tel: 781-383-8027 *Toll Free Tel:* 800-729-7251
Fax: 781-383-8026
E-mail: thebenefactory@aol.com
Web Site: www.readplay.com
Key Personnel
CEO, Founder & Pres: Randy Houk
Founded: 1990
Books, audio, video for children, read-aloud storytelling kit for stores, schools & libraries, true stories, plush animals, finger puppets & volunteer organizations.
ISBN Prefix(es): 1-882728; 1-58021
Number of titles published annually: 13 Print; 13 Audio
Total Titles: 18 Print; 18 Audio

Benjamin Cummings
Member of Addison Wesley Higher Education Group
1301 Sansome St, San Francisco, CA 94111
Tel: 415-402-2500 *Fax:* 415-402-2591
E-mail: question@aw.com
Web Site: www.aw-bc.com
Key Personnel
Pres: Linda Baron Davis
VP & Dir, Mktg: Stacy Treco
ISBN Prefix(es): 0-201; 0-582; 0-8053; 0-321; 0-8465

Benjamin Scott Publishing
20 E Colorado Blvd, No 202, Pasadena, CA 91105
Tel: 626-449-1339 *Toll Free Tel:* 800-488-4959
Fax: 626-449-1389
E-mail: info@jobsourcenetwork.com
Web Site: www.jobsourcenetwork.com
Key Personnel
Pres: Lisa Kazar
CEO: Peter Kazar
Founded: 1992
Publish career resource directory.
ISBN Prefix(es): 1-891926
Number of titles published annually: 3 Print
Total Titles: 10 Print
Membership(s): Publishers Marketing Association

John Benjamins Publishing Co
Subsidiary of John Benjamins BV (Netherlands)
821 Bethlehem Pike, Erdenheim, PA 19038
SAN: 219-7677
Mailing Address: PO Box 27519, Philadelphia, PA 19118-0519
Tel: 215-836-1200 *Toll Free Tel:* 800-562-5666
Fax: 215-836-1204
E-mail: service@benjamins.com
Web Site: www.benjamins.com

Key Personnel
Gen Man: Paul Peranteau *E-mail:* paul@benjamins.com
Founded: 1981
Linguistics, language studies, English as a second language, terminology & art; translation studies; organizational studies; literacy; scientific study of consciousness & communication.
ISBN Prefix(es): 1-55619; 0-915027; 90-272; 1-58811
Number of titles published annually: 125 Print; 2 CD-ROM; 1 Online; 100 E-Book
Total Titles: 2,200 Print; 10 CD-ROM; 2 Online; 400 E-Book; 3 Audio
Imprints: B R Gruener Publishing Co
Foreign Office(s): John Benjamins BV, Box 36224, 1020 ME Amsterdam, Netherlands

§Bentley Publishers
1734 Massachusetts Ave, Cambridge, MA 02138
SAN: 213-9839
Tel: 617-547-4170 *Toll Free Tel:* 800-423-4595
Fax: 617-876-9235
E-mail: sales@bentleypublishers.com
Web Site: www.bentleypublishers.com
Key Personnel
Chmn & Pres: Michael Bentley
Dir, Publg: Janet Barnes
Founded: 1949
Official automobile service manuals & other automobile manuals, sports car & automobile enthusiast books; hardcover fiction reprints.
ISBN Prefix(es): 0-8376
Number of titles published annually: 15 Print; 20 CD-ROM

R J Berg/Destinations Press Ltd
Formerly R J Berg & Co, Publishers
450 E 96 St, Suite 500, Indianapolis, IN 46290
Mailing Address: PO Box 30225, Indianapolis, IN 46230-0225
Toll Free Tel: 800-638-3909 *Fax:* 317-251-5901
E-mail: r.j.berg@destinationspressltd.com
Web Site: www.destinationspressltd.com
Key Personnel
Pres & Publr: Ray Berg
Exec Ed: Ginny C Berg
Founded: 1978
Specializes in regional & foreign travel, tourism, hospitality, art & language.
ISBN Prefix(es): 0-89730
Number of titles published annually: 16 Print
Total Titles: 38 Print
Imprints: College Days Press; Collegiate Memories Press; Cruise & Resorts Press; Inter American Press Books; Memories Press; Travel Memories Press; Vacation Memories Press
Branch Office(s)
Toronto, ON, Canada
Foreign Office(s): Dublin, Ireland

Berghahn Books
Affiliate of Berghahn Books Ltd (UK)
150 Broadway, Suite 812, New York, NY 10038
Tel: 212-222-6502 *Fax:* 212-222-5209
E-mail: info@berghahnbooks.com
Web Site: www.berghahnbooks.com
Key Personnel
Publr: Marion Berghahn
Founded: 1994
Scholarly books & journals in humanities & social sciences.
ISBN Prefix(es): 1-57181; 1-84545
Number of titles published annually: 80 Print; 1 CD-ROM
Total Titles: 600 Print
Divisions: Berghahn Book Ltd (UK)
Sales Office(s): Books International, PO Box 605, Herndon, VA 20172 *Tel:* 703-661-1500 *Toll Free Tel:* 800-540-8663 *Fax:* 703-661-1501

Foreign Office(s): 3 Newtec Place, Magdalen Rd, Oxford OX4 1RE, United Kingdom
Tel: (01865) 250011 *Fax:* (01865) 250056
Distributor for Yad Vashem
Foreign Rep(s): DA Information Services (Australia); UPS (Japan)
Foreign Rights: Lore Cortis (World)
Billing Address: Books International, PO Box 605, Herndon, VA 20172 *Tel:* 703-661-1500 *Toll Free Tel:* 800-540-8663 *Fax:* 703-661-1501
Orders to: Books International, PO Box 605, Herndon, VA 20172 *Tel:* 703-661-1500 *Toll Free Tel:* 800-540-8663 *Fax:* 703-661-1501
Returns: Books International, PO Box 605, Herndon, VA 20172 *Tel:* 703-661-1500 *Toll Free Tel:* 800-540-8663 *Fax:* 703-661-1501
Warehouse: Books International, PO Box 605, Herndon, VA 20172 *Tel:* 703-661-1500 *Toll Free Tel:* 800-540-8663 *Fax:* 703-661-1501

Berkeley Hills Books
1435 Fourth St, Berkeley, CA 94710
Mailing Address: PO Box 6330, Albany, CA 94706
Tel: 510-559-8650 *Fax:* 510-559-8670
Web Site: www.berkeleyhills.com
Key Personnel
Publr & Pres: Robert Dobbin *E-mail:* rob@berkeleyhills.com
Founded: 1996
Publishers for the trade, with some textbook crossover. Subjects include jazz. Do not accept unsol mss.
ISBN Prefix(es): 1-893163; 0-9653774
Number of titles published annually: 8 Print
Total Titles: 50 Print
Foreign Rep(s): Publishers Group West
Distribution Center: Publisher's Group West, 1700 Fourth St, Berkeley, CA 94710 *Tel:* 510-528-1444

Berkeley Slavic Specialties
PO Box 3034, Oakland, CA 94609-0034
SAN: 212-7245
Tel: 510-653-8048 *Fax:* 510-653-6313
E-mail: 71034.456@compuserve.com
Web Site: www.berkslav.com
Key Personnel
Owner: Gareth K Perkins
Founded: 1971
Slavic culture, literature, language & history.
ISBN Prefix(es): 0-933884; 1-57201; 0-936041
Number of titles published annually: 4 Print
Total Titles: 112 Print
Imprints: Scythian Books
Subsidiaries: Barbary Coast Books

Berkley Books
Imprint of Penguin Group (USA) Inc
375 Hudson St, New York, NY 10014
SAN: 282-5074
Tel: 212-366-2000 *Fax:* 212-366-2666
E-mail: online@penguinputnam.com
Web Site: www.penguin.com
Key Personnel
Pres & Publr: Leslie Gelbman
VP & Sr Exec Ed: Natalee Rosenstein
VP & Edit Dir, Berkley Publishing Group; Ed-in-Chief, Ace Books: Susan Allison
VP, Assoc Publr & Exec Man Ed: Rick Nayer
VP & Exec Art Dir: Rich Hasselberger
VP & Dir, Prodn: Patricia King
VP, Exec Publicity Dir & Mktg Dir: Liz Perl
VP, Adv & Promo Dir: Rick Pascocello
Dir, Contracts: Robin Cooper
Sr Exec Ed & Dir, Mktg, Sci-Fi, Ace/ROC: Mary (Ginger) Buchanan
Exec Ed: Gail Fortune; Denise Silvestro
Sr Ed: Cindy Hwang; Allison McCabe
Founded: 1954
ISBN Prefix(es): 0-425; 0-441; 0-515; 1-57297
Number of titles published annually: 524 Print

Total Titles: 2,145 Print
Imprints: Ace Books; Boulevard Books; Diamond
Books; Jam; Jove; Prime Crime
Advertising Agency: Spier NY

Berkley Publishing Group
Division of Penguin Group (USA) Inc
375 Hudson St, New York, NY 10014
SAN: 282-5074
Tel: 212-366-2000
E-mail: online@penguinputnam.com
Web Site: www.penguin.com
Key Personnel
Pres & Publr: Leslie Gelbman
VP & Sr Exec Ed: Natalee Rosenstein
VP & Edit Dir, The Berkley Publishing Group &
Ed-in-Chief, Ace Books: Susan Allison
VP, Assoc Publr & Exec Man Ed: Rick Nayer
VP & Exec Art Dir: Rich Hasselberger
VP & Dir, Prodn: Patricia King
VP, Exec Publicity Dir & Dir, Mktg: Liz Perl
VP, Adv & Promo Dir: Rick Pascocello
Dir, Contracts: Robin Cooper
Sr Exec Ed & Dir, Mktg, Sci-Fi, Ace/ROC: Mary
(Ginger) Buchanan
Exec Ed: Gail Fortune; Denise Silvestro
Sr Ed: Cindy Hwang; Allison McCabe
Founded: 1954
ISBN Prefix(es): 0-425; 0-515
Number of titles published annually: 562 Print
Total Titles: 3,051 Print
Imprints: Ace Books; Berkley Books; Boulevard;
Diamond Books; HPBooks; Jam; Jove; Perigee;
Prime Crime; Riverhead Books (Paperback)
Advertising Agency: Spier NY

Berkshire House
Imprint of The Countryman Press
1206 Rte 12, Woodstock, VT 05091
Mailing Address: c/o Countryman Press, PO Box
748, Woodstock, VT 05091
Tel: 802-457-4826 *Toll Free Tel:* 800-245-4151
Fax: 802-457-1678
Web Site: www.countrymanpress.com
Key Personnel
Edit Dir: Kermit Hummel *E-mail:* khummel@
wwnorton.com
Prodn Dir: Fred Lee *E-mail:* flee@wwnorton.com
Publicity & Mktg Mgr: David Corey
E-mail: dcorey@wwnorton.com
Founded: 1966
Trade books: travel, American culture (or Ameri-
cana), outdoors, regional interest, cookery.
ISBN Prefix(es): 0-936399; 1-58157
Number of titles published annually: 8 Print
Total Titles: 60 Print
Imprints: Great Destinations
Foreign Rep(s): W W Norton & Co Inc
Foreign Rights: WW Norton & Co Inc
Orders to: W W Norton & Co Inc, c/o National
Book Co Inc, 800 Keystone Industrial Park,
Scranton, PA 18512 *Toll Free Tel:* 800-233-
4830 *Toll Free Fax:* 800-458-6515
Returns: W W Norton & Co Inc, c/o National
Book Co Inc, Key Warehouse, Door No 34,
Reeves St, Dunmore, PA 18512
Distribution Center: W W Norton & Co Inc, c/o
National Book Co, 800 Keystone Industrial
Park, Scranton, PA 18512 *Toll Free Tel:* 800-
245-4151 ext 2 *Toll Free Fax:* 800-458-6515

Bernan
Division of Kraus Organization Ltd
4611-F Assembly Dr, Lanham, MD 20706-4391
Tel: 301-459-2255; 301-459-7666 (cust serv)
Toll Free Tel: 800-274-4447; 800-274-4888
(cust serv) *Fax:* 301-459-9235; 301-459-0056
(cust serv) *Toll Free Fax:* 800-865-3450
E-mail: info@bernan.com
Web Site: www.bernan.com
Key Personnel
Man Dir: Donald H Hagen

Adv & Promos Mgr: Anne Weber *Tel:* 301-459-
2255 ext 277
Dir, Dist: Libby Bauer
Dir, Mktg: Bruce Samuelson
Founded: 1991
Bernan distributes official US government, in-
ternational & intergovernmental publications,
publishes original government-related reference
works & provides a wide range of services to
help librarians build their government informa-
tion collections.
ISBN Prefix(es): 0-89059
Number of titles published annually: 4 Print
Total Titles: 336 Print
Distributor for (Represent) Bernan Press; Bureau
of the Census; Food & Agriculture Organiza-
tion; Government Printing Office; International
Atomic Energy Agency (IAEA); International
Monetary Fund (IMF); Library of Congress;
National Technical Information Service (NTIS);
Office for Official Publications of the European
Communities (EC); UNESCO; United Nations
(UN); World Bank; World Tourism Organiza-
tion (WTO); World Trade Organization (WTO);
Pan American Health Organization (Stationary
Off-UK)

§Berrett-Koehler Publishers Inc
235 Montgomery St, Suite 650, San Francisco,
CA 94104
Tel: 415-288-0260 *Fax:* 415-362-2512
E-mail: bkpub@bkpub.com
Web Site: www.bkconnection.com
Key Personnel
Pres & Publr: Steven Piersanti
VP, Busn Devt: Pat Anderson
VP, Design & Prodn: Rick Wilson
Sr Dir, Subs & Intl Rts: Maria Jesus Aguilo
Dir, Mktg: Kristen Frantz
Dir, Busn & Admin: Bob Liss
Promos Mgr & Electronic Publg: Robin Donovan
Mgr: Ken Lupoff
Mktg & Sales Assoc: Marina Cook
E-mail: mcook@bkpub.com
Founded: 1992
Publications on business, work, stewardship, lead-
ership, management, career development, hu-
man resources, entrepreneurship & global sus-
tainability for the trade, scholarly, text & pro-
fessional reference markets.
ISBN Prefix(es): 1-881052; 1-57675
Number of titles published annually: 33 Print
Total Titles: 200 Print
Distributed by Publishers Group West
Foreign Rep(s): McGraw-Hill Asia (Southeast
Asia); McGraw-Hill Book Co (UK, Europe,
Middle East); McGraw-Hill Ryerson Ltd
(Canada); Woodslane Pty Ltd (Australia &
New Zealand)
Warehouse: 12 Winter Sport Lane, Williston, VT
05495 *Toll Free Tel:* 800-929-2929 *Toll Free
Fax:* 800-864-7626

§Bess Press
3565 Harding Ave, Honolulu, HI 96816
Tel: 808-734-7159 *Toll Free Tel:* 800-910-2377
Fax: 808-732-3627
E-mail: sales@besspress.com
Web Site: www.besspress.com
Key Personnel
Publr: Benjamin E Bess
Ed: Reve Shapard *Tel:* 808-734-7159 ext 14
E-mail: editor@besspress.com
Founded: 1979
Books about the Pacific Islands, with a special
emphasis on Hawaii. Includes elementary &
secondary level textbooks in Hawaiian & Pa-
cific Island history, geography & environment,
Hawaiian & Pacific bilingual language mate-
rials, popular regional trade paperbacks, cook-
books, anthologies, humor, Christmas, guides,
how-to & multicultural children's books.
ISBN Prefix(es): 0-935848; 1-880188; 1-57306

Number of titles published annually: 15 Print
Total Titles: 200 Print; 1 CD-ROM; 12 Audio
Distributor for Kamehameha Schools Press

A M Best Co
Ambest Rd, Oldwick, NJ 08858
Tel: 908-439-2200 *Fax:* 908-439-3385
E-mail: customerservice@ambest.com; sales@
ambest.com
Web Site: www.ambest.com
Key Personnel
Pres: A Snyder
Founded: 1899
Insurance industry statistics & supporting mate-
rial, rate & provide financial information about
insurance companies.
ISBN Prefix(es): 0-89408
Number of titles published annually: 3 Print
Total Titles: 17 Print

Best Publishing Co
PO Box 30100, Flagstaff, AZ 86003-0100
Tel: 928-527-1055 *Toll Free Tel:* 800-468-1055
Fax: 928-526-0370
E-mail: divebooks@bestpub.com
Web Site: www.bestpub.com
Key Personnel
Lib Sales Dir: Sandy Smith
Dir: Susan Joiner
Founded: 1970
Recreational scuba & military diving, commercial
diving, diving history, diving medicine, hyper-
baric medicine.
ISBN Prefix(es): 0-941332; 1-930536
Number of titles published annually: 10 Print
Total Titles: 139 Print
Shipping Address: 2355 N Steves Blvd, Flagstaff,
AZ 86004

Bethany House Publishers/Baker Bookhouse
Division of Baker Bookhouse
PO Box 6287, Grand Rapids, MI 49516-6287
SAN: 201-4416
Tel: 616-676-9185 *Toll Free Tel:* 800-877-2665
Web Site: www.bethanyhouse.com; www.
bakerpublishinggroup.com
Key Personnel
Publr, Bethany House: Gary L Johnson
Publr, Baker Books: Don Stephensen
Edit Dir: Carol Johnson *Tel:* 952-829-2513
Fax: 952-829-2768
Sales Dir: Dave Lewis
Natl Sales Mgr: Steve Holey
Founded: 1956
Religion (Evangelical).
ISBN Prefix(es): 0-87123; 1-55661; 0-7642; 0-
934998; 1-56179; 1-58997; 1-57855; 0-76428;
1-57778; 1-85078-3
Number of titles published annually: 150 Print
Total Titles: 1,400 Print; 1 CD-ROM; 15 Audio
Imprints: Hampshire Books
Foreign Rep(s): Beacon Distribuing Ltd
(Canada); Challenge Bookshops (Nigeria);
Christian Literature Centre (Hong Kong);
Christian Literature Crusade (Japan); Filadelfi-
aforlaget A-S (Norway, Sweden); Glad Sounds
(Malaysia); International Boekencentrum Pel-
grim (Netherlands); Nova Distribution (UK);
Omega Distributors Ltd (New Zealand); Salva-
tion Book Centre (Malaysia); Scripture Union
(Singapore); Word of Life Press (Japan, Korea)
Foreign Rights: Winfried Bluth (Europe)

Bethlehem Books
Affiliate of Bethlehem Community
10194 Garfield St S, Bathgate, ND 58216
Tel: 701-265-3725 *Toll Free Tel:* 800-757-6831
Fax: 701-265-3716
E-mail: help@bethlehembooks.com
Web Site: www.bethlehembooks.com
Key Personnel
Gen Mgr & Publr: Jack Sharpe *E-mail:* jack@
bethlehembooks.com

Mktg Rep: Peter Sharpe *E-mail:* peter@
bethlehembooks.com
Founded: 1993
Children's books.
ISBN Prefix(es): 1-883937
Number of titles published annually: 3 Print; 1
Audio
Total Titles: 49 Print; 2 Audio
Distributed by Ignatius Press
Foreign Rights: Family Publications (UK); John
23 Publications (Australia); St Andrews Church
Supply (Canada)

Betterway Books
Imprint of F & W Publications
4700 E Galbraith Rd, Cincinnati, OH 45236
Tel: 513-531-2690 *Toll Free Tel:* 800-666-0963
Fax: 513-891-7185 *Toll Free Fax:* 888-590-
4082
Web Site: www.fwpublications.com
Key Personnel
Ed-in-Chief: David Lewis
Gen Mgr: Budge Wallis
Dir, Sales: Michael Murphy
Sales Admin Coord: Marcia Jones *Tel:* 513-531-
2690 ext 1288 *E-mail:* marcia.jones@fwpubs.
com
Founded: 1981
Instructional & self help books for creative peo-
ple in the areas of home maintenance, repair,
woodworking, home-based business, sports &
recreation, theater, arts, genealogy.
ISBN Prefix(es): 0-932620; 1-55870
Number of titles published annually: 30 Print
Total Titles: 130 Print
Imprints: Family Tree Books; Horticulture Books;
Popular Woodworking Books
Distributor for Rockport Publishers
Shipping Address: F & W Publications, c/o Aero
Fulfillment Services, 2800 Henkle Dr, Lebanon,
OH 45036

Beyond Words Publishing Inc
20827 NW Cornell Rd, Suite 500, Hillsboro, OR
97124-9808
SAN: 666-4210
Tel: 503-531-8700 *Fax:* 503-531-8773
Web Site: www.beyondword.com
Key Personnel
Publr & Intl Rts: Richard E Cohn
E-mail: richard@beyondword.com
Pres & Ed-in-Chief: Cynthia Black
E-mail: cynthia@beyondword.com
Man Ed: Sarabeth Blakey *E-mail:* sarabeth@
beyondword.com
Man Ed, Children's: Summer Steele
Mktg Dir & Lib Sales Dir: Bernadette Baker
E-mail: bernadette@beyondword.com
Founded: 1983
ISBN Prefix(es): 0-941831; 1-885223; 1-58270
Number of titles published annually: 15 Print
Total Titles: 200 Print; 5 Audio
Imprints: The Earthsong Collection; Kids Books
By Kids
Distributed by Publishers Group West
Foreign Rep(s): Deep Books of London (Eng-
land); Jay Books (New Zealand); PGW
(Canada)
Foreign Rights: Beyond Words Publishing

§Bhaktivedanta Book Publishing Inc
9701 Vencie Blvd, Unit 3, Los Angeles, CA
90034
Tel: 310-559-4455 *Toll Free Tel:* 800-927-4152
Fax: 310-837-1056
E-mail: bbt2@webcom.com
Web Site: www.krishna.com
Key Personnel
Mktg & Dist Mgr: Stuart Kadetz *E-mail:* sura.
acbsp@pamho.net
Warehouse Contact: Efren Gonzalez *Tel:* 310-523-
4533

Founded: 1972
Books of Vedic culture & philosophy, vegetarian-
ism, reincarnation & Karma.
ISBN Prefix(es): 0-89213; 91-7149; 0-912776
Number of titles published annually: 3 Print; 2
CD-ROM
Total Titles: 96 Print; 1 CD-ROM; 2 E-Book; 84
Audio
Distributed by BBT
Billing Address: PO Box 34074, Los Angeles,
CA 90034
Warehouse: BBT, 709 E Gardena Blvd, Los
Angeles, CA 90034, Contact: Efren Gonza-
lez *Tel:* 310-523-4533 *Fax:* 310-523-4258
E-mail: ekaraja@webcom.com

BHB, see BrickHouse Books Inc

Bibliotheca Persica Press
Affiliate of Persian Heritage Foundation
450 Riverside Dr, Suite 4, New York, NY 10027
Tel: 212-851-5723 *Fax:* 212-749-9524
Key Personnel
Publr: Prof Yarshater
Multi-disciplinary humanities/Iranian studies.
ISBN Prefix(es): 0-933273
Number of titles published annually: 2 Print
Total Titles: 10 Print
Sales Office(s): Eisenbrauns Inc, PO Box 275,
Winona Lake, IN 46590-0275
Billing Address: Eisenbrauns Inc, PO Box 275,
Winona Lake, IN 46590-0275 *Tel:* 574-
269-2011 *Toll Free Fax:* 800-736-7921 (US
only) *E-mail:* orders@eisenbrauns.com *Web
Site:* www.eisenbrauns.com
Returns: Eisenbrauns Inc, PO Box 275, Winona
Lake, IN 46590-0275 *Tel:* 574-269-2011
Toll Free Fax: 800-736-7921 (US only)
E-mail: orders@eisenbrauns.com *Web
Site:* www.eisenbrauns.com
Shipping Address: Eisenbrauns Inc, PO Box 275,
Winona Lake, IN 46590-0275
Distribution Center: Eisenbrauns Inc, PO Box
275, Winona Lake, IN 46590-0275 *Tel:* 574-
269-2011 *Toll Free Fax:* 800-736-7921 (US
only) *E-mail:* orders@eisenbrauns.com *Web
Site:* www.eisenbrauns.com

Biblo & Tannen Booksellers & Publishers Inc
Subsidiary of Biblo-Moser
PO Box 302, Cheshire, CT 06410-0302
Tel: 203-250-1647 *Toll Free Tel:* 800-272-8778
Fax: 203-250-1647 *Toll Free Fax:* 800-272-
8778
E-mail: biblo.moser@snet.net
Key Personnel
Owner: Philip Moser
Founded: 1950
Do not accept unsol mss-publish reprint editions.
ISBN Prefix(es): 0-8196
Number of titles published annually: 10 Print
Total Titles: 250 Print
Imprints: Biblo; Biblo-Moser; Biblo-Tannen;
Moser

Bick Publishing House
307 Neck Rd, Madison, CT 06443
Tel: 203-245-0073 *Fax:* 203-245-5990
E-mail: bickpubhse@aol.com
Web Site: www.bickpubhouse.com
Key Personnel
Pres & Publr: Dale Carlson
Exec VP: Hannah Carlson
Edit Dir: Ann Maurer
VP & Dir, Prodn & Design: Jennifer Payne
Dir, Mktg: Dan Carlson
Founded: 1994
Adult & young adult professional information for
general audience & teens on health & recov-
ery, adult & teenage psychology, meditation,
neuroscience, general science, special needs &
wildlife rehabilitation.

ISBN Prefix(es): 1-884158
Number of titles published annually: 4 Print
Total Titles: 26 Print
Foreign Rep(s): Hagenbach-Bender Literary
Agency (World Rights)
Foreign Rights: Hagenbach-Bender (Asia, Europe,
Switzerland, World)
Distribution Center: Bookworld Trade Inc, 1941
Whitfield Park Loop, Sarasota, FL 34243, Con-
tact: Edna Byrd *Toll Free Tel:* 800-444-2524
Toll Free Fax: 800-777-2525
Membership(s): Publishers Marketing Association

Big Guy Books Inc
7750 El Camino Real, Suite F, Carlsbad, CA
92009
SAN: 253-0392
Tel: 760-334-1222 *Toll Free Tel:* 866-210-
5938 (Booksellers cust serv); 800-741-6493
(For parents, teachers, schools & libraries)
Fax: 760-334-1225
E-mail: info@bigguybooks.com; orders@
bigguybooks.com
Web Site: www.bigguybooks.com
Key Personnel
Pres: Robert Gould
Sales & Mktg Asst: John Boaz *E-mail:* john@
bigguybooks.com
Founded: 2000
Publishes high quality adventure stories for chil-
dren. Combine cutting-edge graphics & old
fashioned values to increase literacy as well as
confidence & self respect in young readers.
ISBN Prefix(es): 1-929945
Number of titles published annually: 5 Print
Returns: Big Guy Books c/o One Word Distri-
bution Inc, 1915 Tenth Ave W, Mobridge, SD
57601
Membership(s): ABA; ALA; Publishers Market-
ing Association

Bilingual Press/Editorial Bilingue
Hispanic Research Ctr, Arizona State Univ,
Tempe, AZ 85287-2702
SAN: 208-5526
Mailing Address: PO Box 872702, Tempe, AZ
85287-2702
Tel: 480-965-3867 *Fax:* 480-965-8309
E-mail: brp@asu.edu
Web Site: www.asu.edu/brp/brp
Key Personnel
Man Ed: Karen Van Hooft *E-mail:* kvhbrp@asu.
edu
Ed: Gary D Keller
Assoc Ed: Brian Cassity; Cristina de Isasi; Linda
Thurston
Founded: 1976
Publisher & distributor of US Hispanic creative
literature, literary criticism & scholarship.
ISBN Prefix(es): 0-916950; 0-927534; 1-931010
Number of titles published annually: 8 Print
Total Titles: 154 Print; 2 CD-ROM
Distributor for Dos Pasos Editores; Lalo Press;
Latin American Literary Review Press; Maize
Press; Trinity University Press; Waterfront
Press (selected titles from all)
Shipping Address: University Commons, Suite
212, 215 E Seventh St, Tempe, AZ 85281

Binford & Mort Publishing Inc
5245 NE Elam Young Pkwy, Suite C, Hillsboro,
OR 97124
SAN: 201-4386
Tel: 503-844-4960 *Toll Free Tel:* 888-221-4514
Fax: 503-844-4959
Key Personnel
Pres: Polly Gardenier *E-mail:* polly@binfordmort.
com
Publr & Rts & Perms: Pamela Henningsen
Founded: 1891
Specialize in nonfiction books about the Pacific
Northwest.

ISBN Prefix(es): 0-8323
Number of titles published annually: 10 Print
Total Titles: 200 Print
Orders to: PO Box 91580, Portland, OR 97291-0580

Biographical Publishing Co
35 Clark Hill Rd, Prospect, CT 06712-1011
Tel: 203-758-3661 *Fax:* 253-793-2618
E-mail: biopub@aol.com
Web Site: members.aol.com/biopub
Key Personnel
Ed: John R Guevin
Founded: 1991
ISBN Prefix(es): 0-9637240; 1-929882
Number of titles published annually: 10 Print
Total Titles: 44 Print
Distributor for Eagles Landing Publishing; Spyglass Books LLC

BioTechniques Books
Division of Eaton Publishing
One Research Dr, Suite 400 A, Westborough, MA 01581
Tel: 508-614-1414 *Fax:* 508-616-2930
Web Site: www.biotechniques.com
Key Personnel
Mktg Mgr: Jennifer Fleet
Founded: 1996
Research monographs, laboratory manuals & reference books in biotechnology, medicine & the life sciences.
ISBN Prefix(es): 1-881299
Number of titles published annually: 5 Print
Total Titles: 29 Print

Birch Brook Press
PO Box 81, Delhi, NY 13753
Tel: 607-746-7453 (book sales & prodn)
Fax: 607-746-7453
E-mail: birchbrook@usadatanet.net; birchbrkpr@yahoo.com
Web Site: www.birchbrookpress.info
Key Personnel
Publr & Ed: Tom Tolnay
Art Dir: Frank C Eckmair
Founded: 1982
Popular culture & literary books, printed letterpress at BBP on fine stock, as well as offset trade editions. Books about books, flyfishing, baseball & fine poetry.
ISBN Prefix(es): 0-913559
Number of titles published annually: 6 Print
Total Titles: 80 Print
Imprints: Birch Brook Press; Brief Books; Persephone Press
Subsidiaries: Birch Brook Impressions
Distributor for Abiko Literary Press; Natural Heritage Press; Persephone Press
Foreign Rep(s): Japan UNI Agency (Japan)
Foreign Rights: Chinese Connection (Hong Kong, Taiwan)
Membership(s): Independent Publishers Association

§Birkhauser Boston
Division of Springer-Verlag New York Inc
675 Massachusetts Ave, Cambridge, MA 02139
SAN: 213-2869
Tel: 617-876-2333 *Toll Free Tel:* 800-777-4643 (cust serv) *Fax:* 617-876-1272
E-mail: service@birkhauser.com
Web Site: www.birkhauser.com
Key Personnel
VP, HR: Cathy Adams
Exec Ed, Computational Sci & Engg: Wayne Yubasz
Founded: 1979
Scientific & technical books & journals in physics, mathematics, geology, biology, neuroscience, history of science; scientists' biographies; architecture & design.

ISBN Prefix(es): 0-8176
Number of titles published annually: 260 Print
Total Titles: 2,900 Print; 20 Online
Subsidiaries: Springer Veriag New York Inc
Foreign Office(s): Birkhauser Veriag, Viaduktstrasse 42, CH-4051 Basel, Switzerland
Distributed by Springer-Verlag New York Inc
Advertising Agency: Springer-Verlag
Shipping Address: Springer-Verlag New York Inc, c/o Mercedes Distribution Center, 160 Imlay St, Brooklyn, NY 11231

§George T Bisel Co Inc
710 S Washington Sq, Philadelphia, PA 19106
Tel: 215-922-5760 *Toll Free Tel:* 800-247-3526
Fax: 215-922-2235
E-mail: info@bisel.com
Web Site: www.bisel.com
Key Personnel
Pres: Franklin Jon Zuch *E-mail:* fjzuch@bisel.com
Dir, Sales & Mktg: John Ahrens
Founded: 1876
Pennsylvania, New Jersey, Florida law practice subjects.
ISBN Prefix(es): 1-887024
Number of titles published annually: 4 Print
Total Titles: 75 Print; 10 CD-ROM; 1 Audio

§Bisk Education
9417 Princess Palm Ave, Suite 400, Tampa, FL 33619
Tel: 813-621-6200 *Toll Free Tel:* 800-874-7877
Fax: 813-621-0127 *Toll Free Fax:* 800-345-8273
E-mail: bisk@bisk.com
Web Site: www.bisk.com
Founded: 1971
One of the leading providers of online, interactive continuing professional education, including continuing education for accountants, attorneys, physicians & nurses, CPA Exam preparation materials & web-based certificate, associate's bachelor's & master's degree programs from nationally known, regionally accredited universities, including Villanova University, Regis University, the University of South Florida, Saint Leo University & Jacksonville University.
ISBN Prefix(es): 1-57961
Number of titles published annually: 50 Print
Total Titles: 500 Print; 50 CD-ROM; 150 Online; 9 E-Book; 90 Audio
Imprints: Bisk CPA Review; Bisk CPE; Bisk-Totaltape; Regis External MBA Program
Distributed by Bisk Publishing Co

BizBest Media Corp
860 Via de la Paz, Suite D-4, Pacific Palisades, CA 90272
Tel: 310-230-6868 *Toll Free Tel:* 800-873-5205; 877-424-9237 *Fax:* 310-454-6130
E-mail: info@bizbest.com
Web Site: www.bizbest.com
Key Personnel
CEO: Daniel Kehrer *E-mail:* dan@bizbest.com
Man Ed: Roth Savage *E-mail:* savage@bizbest.com
Exec Ed: Kaye Kittrell *E-mail:* editor@bizbest.com
Founded: 1999
The only integrated media company in America delivering independently researched & rated solution & resource publications for business owners & entrepreneurs across all regions & industries. BizBest books, publications & products meet the expanding information needs of small business owners, startups, consultants, advisors & educators. BizBest is non-commercial & accepts no advertising or sponsorships.
ISBN Prefix(es): 0-9719045

Number of titles published annually: 6 Print; 4 CD-ROM
Subsidiaries: BizBest100.com; Small Business Weekly
Divisions: BizBest Media Features

BKMK Press of the University of Missouri-Kansas City
Division of University of Missouri-Kansas City
5101 Rockhill Rd, Kansas City, MO 64110-2499
Tel: 816-235-2558 *Fax:* 816-235-2611
E-mail: bkmk@umkc.edu
Web Site: www.umkc.edu/bkmk
Key Personnel
Exec Ed: Robert Stewart
Man Ed: Ben Furnish
Assoc Ed: Michelle Boisseau
Founded: 1971
Fine literature & essays.
ISBN Prefix(es): 0-933532; 1-886157
Number of titles published annually: 6 Print
Total Titles: 90 Print

Black Classic Press
PO Box 13414, Baltimore, MD 21203
SAN: 219-5836
Tel: 410-358-0980 *Fax:* 410-358-0987
E-mail: bcp@charm.net
Web Site: www.blackclassic.com
Key Personnel
Pres: W Paul Coates
Founded: 1978
Publishing obscure & significant works by & about people of African descent.
ISBN Prefix(es): 0-933121; 1-57478
Number of titles published annually: 20 Print
Total Titles: 100 Print
Imprints: W M Duforcelf
Distributed by Publishers Group West
Shipping Address: 4701-D Mount Hope Dr, Baltimore, MD 21215 (returns only)

§Black Diamond Book Publishing
PO Box 492299, Los Angeles, CA 90049-8299
SAN: 298-5098
Tel: 310-472-9833 *Toll Free Tel:* 800-962-7622
Fax: 310-472-9833 *Toll Free Fax:* 800-962-7622
Key Personnel
Owner & Publr: Nancy Shaffron *Tel:* 310-472-1050 *E-mail:* nancy_shaffron@compuserve.com
Founded: 1994
Books.
ISBN Prefix(es): 1-886836
Number of titles published annually: 4 Print; 4 E-Book
Total Titles: 4 Print; 4 E-Book

Black Dog & Leventhal Publishers Inc
151 W 19 St, 12th fl, New York, NY 10011
Tel: 212-647-9336 *Fax:* 212-647-9332
E-mail: information@bdlev.com
Web Site: www.bdlev.com
Key Personnel
Publr: J P Leventhal *Tel:* 212-647-9336 ext 101
Sales: Mary Wowk *E-mail:* mary@bdlev.com
Foreign Sales & Rts: Magali Veillon *Tel:* 212-647-9336 ext 114 *E-mail:* magali@bdlev.com
Edit: Laura Ross *E-mail:* laura@bdlev.com
Mktg: Lindley Bogehold
Founded: 1993
Publish general-interest fiction & nonfiction & illustrated books in hardcover & paperback; no unsol mss accepted, send query letter to editorial department.
ISBN Prefix(es): 0-9637056; 1-884822; 1-57912
Number of titles published annually: 40 Print
Total Titles: 260 Print
Imprints: Black Dog & Leventhal; Black Dog Paperbacks; Tess Press
Distributed by Workman Publishing
Foreign Rights: Thomas Allen (Canada); Book Reps (New Zealand); Bookwise (Australia);

Gunnar Lie & Associates (Asia, Europe, South America); Chris Lloyd (UK & Ireland)
Warehouse: c/o Workman Publishing Banta Co, 677 Brighton Beach Rd, Menasha, WI 54952

Black Dome Press Corp
1011 Rte 296, Hensonville, NY 12439
Tel: 518-734-6357 *Fax:* 518-734-5802
E-mail: blackdomep@aol.com
Web Site: www.blackdomepress.com
Key Personnel
Publr: Deborah Allen
Founded: 1990
Regional small press publishing New York State history.
ISBN Prefix(es): 1-883789; 0-9628523
Number of titles published annually: 5 Print
Total Titles: 50 Print

Black Heron Press
PO Box 95676, Seattle, WA 98145-2676
Tel: 206-363-5210 *Fax:* 206-363-5210
Web Site: www.blackheronpress.com
Key Personnel
Publr & Lib Sales Dir: Jerry Gold
    E-mail: jgoldberon@aol.com
Founded: 1984
Literary fiction & nonfiction pertaining to independent publishing & the writing craft; literature, essays, science fiction.
ISBN Prefix(es): 0-930773
Number of titles published annually: 4 Print
Total Titles: 56 Print
Foreign Rep(s): Loris Essay-International Titles (Asia, Austria, Eastern Europe, Germany, Northern Europe, Switzerland); Pina Von Prellwitz-European-Latin Amrecian Literary Agaency (France, Italy, Latin America, Spain)
Foreign Rights: Loris Essay-International Titles
Warehouse: 3032 NE 140 St, Suite 402, Seattle, WA 98125
Distribution Center: Client Distribution Services, 425 Madison Ave, 3rd fl, New York, NY 10017
    Tel: 212-223-2969 *Fax:* 212-223-1504

Blackbirch Press®
Imprint of Gale
27500 Drake Rd, Farmington Hills, MI 48311-3535
Toll Free Tel: 800-877-4253 *Toll Free Fax:* 800-414-5043 (orders)
E-mail: galeord@gale.com; customerservice@gale.com
Web Site: www.gale.com
Key Personnel
Dir, Opers: Pamela S Halvorsen
Dir, Sales & Mktg: Dayna K Burns
Project Ed & Rts & Perms: Emily Kucharczyk
    E-mail: emily@blackbirch.com
Founded: 1979
Specialize in children & young adult; school library books: fiction & nonfiction; exciting new reference biography, world cultures, American history, women.
ISBN Prefix(es): 1-56711
Number of titles published annually: 70 Print
Total Titles: 250 Print; 4 CD-ROM
Imprints: Blackbirch Picturebooks
Foreign Rep(s): PMC International (Asia); Tao Media (Asia); Van Well Book Co (Canada)
Foreign Rights: Lynn Clark Agency (UK)
Distribution Center: Mercedes Distribution Center, 62 Imlay St, Brooklyn, NY 11231

The Blackburn Press
PO Box 287, Caldwell, NJ 07006-0287
Tel: 973-228-7077 *Fax:* 973-228-7276
Web Site: www.blackburnpress.com
Key Personnel
Publr & Edit Dir: Frances Reed *E-mail:* freed@blackburnpress.com

Dir, Order Processing & Cust Serv: Barbara R Chmiel *E-mail:* b.chmiel@blackburnpress.com
Founded: 1999
Book titles, largely reprints, of classics in science, technology & medicine.
ISBN Prefix(es): 1-930665
Number of titles published annually: 50 Print
Total Titles: 50 Print

Blacksmith Corp
PO Box 280, North Hampton, OH 45349-0280
Tel: 937-969-8389 *Toll Free Tel:* 800-531-2665
    Fax: 937-969-8399
E-mail: sales@blacksmithcorp.com
Web Site: www.blacksmithcorp.com
Key Personnel
Sales Mgr: N J Padua
Founded: 1975
Guns, hunting.
ISBN Prefix(es): 0-941540
Number of titles published annually: 4 Print
Total Titles: 25 Print
Membership(s): ABA; Publishers Marketing Association

§Blackwell Publishers
Subsidiary of Blackwell Publishers Ltd (UK)
350 Main St, Malden, MA 02148
Tel: 781-388-8200 *Fax:* 781-388-8210
E-mail: books@blackwellpublishing.com
Web Site: www.blackwellpublishing.com
Key Personnel
Pres: Gordon Tibbitts
VP, Sales & Mktg: Amy Yodanis
Edit Dir: Steve Smith
Journal Publr: Otis Dean
Intl Rts: Karen Gibson
HR: Lisa Bybee
Founded: 1984
General, scholarly, reference & college texts, with an emphasis on the humanities, social sciences & business. Also medical allied health, veterinary, earth & life sciences, environment & engineering.
ISBN Prefix(es): 0-631; 0-85520; 0-86216; 1-55786; 1-57718
Number of titles published annually: 500 Print
Total Titles: 4,500 Print
Imprints: Polity Press
Foreign Office(s): 108 Cowley Rd, Oxford OX4 IJF, United Kingdom
Foreign Rep(s): Academic Marketing Services (South Africa); Allen & Unwin Pty Ltd (Australia); APD Singapore Pte Ltd (SE Asia); Blackwell Publishers Ltd (Scandinavia); Mohamad Dahir (Pakistan); Charles Gibbs Assoc (Greece, Italy, Southern Europe, Spain); Macmillan Publishers (New Zealand); Maya Publishers Pvt Ltd (India); Netwerk Academic Book Agency (Belgium, Netherlands, Luxembourg); Segment Book Distributors (India); United Publishers Services Ltd (Japan); James & Lorin Watt (Middle East); The John Wilde Partnership (Austria, Germany, Switzerland)
Foreign Rights: Blackwell Publishers Ltd (England)
Advertising Agency: Shakespeare Head Advertising Services
Shipping Address: AIDC, 2 Winter Sport Lane, Williston, VT 05495-9703

§Blackwell Publishing/Futura
Imprint of Blackwell Publishing
3 W Main St, Elmsford, NY 10523
SAN: 201-582X
Tel: 914-593-0731 *Toll Free Tel:* 800-759-6102
    Fax: 914-593-0732
E-mail: jbellhouse@ny.blackwellpublishing.com
Web Site: www.blackwellpublishing.com/futura; www.blackwellfutura.com

Key Personnel
Sr VP: Steven E Korn *E-mail:* skorn@blackwellpublishing.com
Exec Dir, Futura Media Servs: Carole Henkin
Founded: 1970
Medical.
ISBN Prefix(es): 0-87993
Number of titles published annually: 15 Print
Total Titles: 150 Print; 5 CD-ROM
Distributed by Blackwell Science
Foreign Rep(s): Blackwell Scientific (World); Igaku Shoin (Japan); Login Bros (Canada); Maruzen International (Japan); Nankodo Co (Japan)

Blackwell Publishing Professional
Formerly Iowa State Press
Subsidiary of Blackwell Publishing
2121 State Ave, Ames, IA 50014
SAN: 202-7194
Tel: 515-292-0140 *Toll Free Tel:* 800-862-6657 (orders only) *Fax:* 515-292-3348
Web Site: www.blackwellprofessional.com
Key Personnel
Publg Dir, Agriculture, Aquaculture/Fisheries: Antonia Seymour *Tel:* 515-292-0140 ext 611 *E-mail:* antonia.seymour@oxon.blackwellpublishing.com
Oper Dir: Brenda O'Neall-Smith *Tel:* 515-292-0140 ext 627 *E-mail:* brenda.oneall@blackwellprofessional.com
Dir, Mktg & Sales: Bray Brockbank *Tel:* 515-292-0140 ext 615 *E-mail:* bray.brockbank@blackwellprofessional.com
Prepress Mgr: Janet Hronek *Tel:* 515-292-0140 ext 614 *E-mail:* janet.hronek@blackwellprofessional.com
Ed, Food Sci & Journalism: Mark Barrett *Tel:* 515-292-0140 ext 613 *E-mail:* mark.barrett@blackwellprofessional.com
Ed, Veterinary Medicine: Jill McDonald *Tel:* 515-292-0140 ext 636 *E-mail:* jill.mcdonald@blackwellprofessional.com
Ed, Applied Chemistry: Joe Eckenrode *Tel:* 717-509-6959 *E-mail:* joe.eckenrode@blackwellprofessional.com
Ed, Dentistry (UK): Caroline Connelly *Tel:* (01865) 47 6504 *E-mail:* caroline.connelly@oxon.blackwellpublishing.com
Founded: 1934
Textbooks, reference books, veterinary medicine, agriculture, journalism, aviation, food science, plant science, fisheries/aquaculture, applied chemistry.
ISBN Prefix(es): 0-8138
Number of titles published annually: 3 CD-ROM
Total Titles: 600 Print; 7 CD-ROM
Distributed by Blackwell Publishing Ltd
Distributor for Blackwell Science Ltd; British Small Animal Veterinary Association; Manson Publishing Ltd
Foreign Rep(s): Blackwell Publishing Ltd; Blackwell Publishing Professional (Canada)
Foreign Rights: Blackwell Publishing Ltd (all territories)

Blade Publishing
4540 Kearny Villa Rd, Suite 103, San Diego, CA 92123
Tel: 619-440-2309 *Fax:* 619-334-7070
E-mail: bladeinternational@yahoo.com
Key Personnel
VP, Mktg: Veronica Gill
Founded: 1999
Publishing house that relentlessly promotes select children's, young adult & adult fiction & nonfiction.
ISBN Prefix(es): 1-929409
Number of titles published annually: 10 Print; 3 CD-ROM; 3 Audio
Total Titles: 25 Print; 6 CD-ROM; 6 Audio

Imprints: Double Dutch Press
Orders to: Quality Books Inc, 1003 W Pines Rd, Oregon, IL 61061-9599 *Toll Free Tel:* 800-323-4241 *Fax:* 815-732-4499

John F Blair Publisher
1406 Plaza Dr, Winston-Salem, NC 27103
SAN: 201-4319
Tel: 336-768-1374 *Toll Free Tel:* 800-222-9796
  Fax: 336-768-9194
E-mail: blairpub@blairpub.com
Web Site: www.blairpub.com
Key Personnel
Pres & Rts & Perms: Carolyn Sakowski
  E-mail: sakowski@blairpub.com
Dir, Mktg & Sales: Anne Waters
Design & Prodn: Debra Hampton
Founded: 1954
General trade.
ISBN Prefix(es): 0-910244; 0-89587
Number of titles published annually: 18 Print
Total Titles: 307 Print
Distributor for Bandit Books; Banks Channel Books; Down Home Press; Novello Festival Press; Pennywell Press; Walkabout Press
Membership(s): Publishers Association of the South

Bloch Publishing Co
118 E 28 St, Suite 501-503, New York, NY 10016-8413
Tel: 212-532-3977 *Fax:* 212-779-9169
E-mail: blochpub@worldnet.att.net
Web Site: www.blochpub.com
Key Personnel
Pres: Charles Bloch
Founded: 1854
Judaica.
ISBN Prefix(es): 0-8197
Number of titles published annually: 8 Print
Total Titles: 80 Print
Distributor for Biblio; Menorah; Scarf Press; Sephardic House; Soncino

Bloomberg Press
Subsidiary of Bloomberg LP
PO Box 888, Princeton, NJ 08542-0888
SAN: 298-6132
Tel: 609-279-4600
E-mail: press@bloomberg.com
Web Site: www.bloomberg.com/books
Key Personnel
Publr: John Crutcher *Tel:* 609-279-4652
  E-mail: jcrutcher@bloomberg.net
Edit Dir: Jared Kieling
Man Ed: Barbara Diez
Subs Rts: Priscilla Treadwell
Ed: Tracy Tait
Dir, Spec Markets: Lisa Goetz *Tel:* 609-279-4494
Founded: 1995
Trade hardcovers & paperbacks on personal finance, businesses & books for financial professionals.
ISBN Prefix(es): 1-57660
Number of titles published annually: 20 Print
Total Titles: 100 Print
Imprints: Bloomberg Personal Bookshelf; Bloomberg Press; Bloomberg Professional Library
Distributed by W W Norton
Foreign Rep(s): Delaney Global Publisher's Service (Guam, Philippines); M K International Ltd (Japan); B.K. Norton Ltd (Korea, Taiwan); W W Norton & Co Ltd (Africa, UK, Ireland, Europe, Middle East); Pearson Education (New Zealand); Penguin Books Canada Ltd (Canada); PTE Ltd (Asia); Transglobal Publishers Service Ltd (Hong Kong); US PubRep, Inc (Caribbean, Mexico, South & Central America); Wiley & Sons, Ltd (Australia)
Foreign Rights: Priscilla Treadwell

Shipping Address: National Book Co, Keystone Industrial Park, Scranton, PA 18512
Warehouse: c/o W W Norton, c/o National Book Co, Keystone Industrial Park, Scranton, PA 18512
Membership(s): AAP

Bloomsbury Publishing
175 Fifth Ave, Suite 300, New York, NY 10010
Tel: 212-674-5151 *Toll Free Tel:* 800-221-7945
  Fax: 212-780-0115
Web Site: www.bloomsbury.com/usa
Key Personnel
Adv Assoc: Alona Fryman
ISBN Prefix(es): 1-58234
Number of titles published annually: 100 Print
Total Titles: 1 Audio
Distributed by Holtzbrink Publishers

Blue Crane Books
PO Box 380291, Cambridge, MA 02238
Tel: 617-926-8989 *Fax:* 617-926-0982
E-mail: bluecrane@arrow1.com
Key Personnel
Publr: Mrs Alvart Badalian
Art Dir: Mr Aramais Andonian
Ed: Ms Salpi H Ghazarian
Founded: 1991
Publish adult trade fiction & nonfiction, history, political & social sciences, culture & art. Special line of adult & children's books in Armenian & English translations of Armenian originals. No unsol mss.
ISBN Prefix(es): 0-9628715; 1-886434
Number of titles published annually: 3 Print
Total Titles: 20 Print

§Blue Dolphin Publishing Inc
12428 Nevada City Hwy, Grass Valley, CA 95945
Mailing Address: PO Box 8, Nevada City, CA 95959
Tel: 530-265-6925 *Toll Free Tel:* 800-643-0765
  Fax: 530-265-0787
E-mail: bdolphin@netshel.net
Web Site: www.bluedolphinpublishing.com
Key Personnel
Pres, Edit & Graphics: Paul M Clemens
  E-mail: clemens@netshel.net
Acct: Josephine L Black
Ed & Edit, Electronic Publg: Linda Maxwell
Founded: 1985
Books & audio tapes on health, psychology, self-help, comparative spiritual traditions, anthropology, education.
ISBN Prefix(es): 0-931892; 0-942444; 1-57733
Number of titles published annually: 20 Print; 20 E-Book
Total Titles: 180 Print; 4 CD-ROM; 85 E-Book; 8 Audio
Imprints: Aura Imaging; Papillion Publishing (Childrens books); Pelican Pond Publishing (fiction); Symposium Publishing (nonfiction)
Foreign Rights: Editions Le Chaos (France); Lucia Riff (Brazil); Singer Media (Pacific Rim)

Blue Dove Press
4204 Sorrento Valley Blvd, Suite K, San Diego, CA 92121
Tel: 858-623-3330 *Toll Free Tel:* 800-691-1008
  (orders) *Fax:* 858-623-3325
E-mail: mail@bluedove.org
Web Site: www.bluedove.org
Key Personnel
Exec Dir & Intl Rts: Jeff Blom
Dir, Opers & Mktg: Eugenia Orlowski
  E-mail: gigi@bluedove.org
Edit: Mary Kowit
Book Design: Tracy DeZenzo
Founded: 1993
Publishes books by & about saints & sages of all religions as well as other spiritually oriented

works. Our Laurel Creek Imprint publishes inspirational & gift books.
ISBN Prefix(es): 1-884997; 1-889606 (Laurel Creek Press)
Number of titles published annually: 3 Print
Total Titles: 26 Print; 3 Audio
Imprints: Laurel Creek Press (Publishes the James Allen Wisdom series)
Distributor for Motilal Banarsidass (Authorized American Distributor for Motilal Banarsidas & other publishers of India)

Blue Moon Books
Imprint of Avalon Publishing Group - New York
245 W 17 St, 11th fl, New York, NY 10011-5300
Tel: 212-981-9898 *Fax:* 646-375-2571
Founded: 1987
Blue Moon Books, an imprint of the Avalon Publishing Group, specializes in erotic fiction writing.

Blue Mountain Arts Inc
PO Box 4549, Boulder, CO 80306
SAN: 169-0477
Tel: 303-449-0536 *Toll Free Tel:* 800-473-2082
  Fax: 303-417-6496 *Toll Free Fax:* 800-256-1213
E-mail: booksbma@mindspring.com; ordersbma@mindspring.com
Web Site: www.sps.com
Key Personnel
Pres: Robert Gall
Edit Mgr: Patricia Wayant
Creative Dir: Clifford Scott
Dir, Books & Mktg: Helene Steinbuck
  E-mail: hsteinbuck@pipeline.com
Founded: 1970
Publisher of trade books: inspirational, poetry, juvenile, young adult & gift books & sidelines.
ISBN Prefix(es): 0-88396; 1-58786
Number of titles published annually: 20 Print; 20 Online
Total Titles: 140 Print; 140 Online
Imprints: Blue Mountain Press®; Rabbit's Foot Press™ (A Division of Blue Mountain Arts)
Editorial Office(s): PO Box 1007, Boulder, CO 80301, Contact: P Wayant
Sales Office(s): 1512 E Broward Blvd, Suite 203, Fort Lauderdale, FL 33301, Contact: Helene Steinbuck *Toll Free Tel:* 800-473-2082 *Fax:* 954-522-0055 *Toll Free Fax:* 800-256-1213 *E-mail:* hsteinbuck@pipeline.com *Web Site:* www.sps.com
Foreign Rights: Mark David Ryan (Worldwide)
Returns: 6455 Spine Rd, Boulder, CO 80301
Shipping Address: 6455 Spine Rd, Boulder, CO 80301, Contact: Wayne Ivers *Tel:* 303-449-0536 SAN: 169-0477
Membership(s): ABA; CBA; National Association of College Stores

Blue Note Books, see Blue Note Publications

Blue Note Publications
Division of Blue Note Publications Inc
400 W Cocoa Beach Causeway, Suite 3, Cocoa Beach, FL 32931
Tel: 321-799-2583 *Toll Free Tel:* 800-624-0401
  Fax: 321-799-1942
E-mail: order@bluenotebooks.com
Web Site: www.bluenotebooks.com
Key Personnel
Pres & Intl Rts Contact: Paul Maluccio
  E-mail: bluenote@bv.net
Founded: 1988
Small press book publishing, production, printing, distribution, marketing.
ISBN Prefix(es): 1-878398
Number of titles published annually: 6 Print
Total Titles: 32 Print; 2 CD-ROM; 2 Audio
Imprints: Blue Note; Blue Note Books; Blue Note Music Manuscript Books
Membership(s): Publishers Marketing Association

§Blue Poppy Press
Division of Blue Poppy Enterprises Inc
5441 Western Ave, No 2, Boulder, CO 80301
Tel: 303-447-8372 *Toll Free Tel:* 800-487-9296
    Fax: 303-245-8362
E-mail: info@bluepoppy.com
Web Site: www.bluepoppy.com
Key Personnel
Ed-in-Chief: Robert Flaws *Fax:* 303-447-0740
    E-mail: bob@bluepoppy.com
Mktg Dir & Busn Mgr: Honora Wolfe
    E-mail: honora@bluepoppy.com
Founded: 1981
Books on acupuncture & Chinese medicine.
ISBN Prefix(es): 0-936185; 1-891845
Number of titles published annually: 3 Print; 2
    CD-ROM; 3 E-Book
Total Titles: 85 Print; 2 CD-ROM; 85 E-Book
Subsidiaries: Blue Poppy Seminars
Divisions: Blue Poppy Herbs
Distributed by New Leaf Books; Redwing Book
    Co
Foreign Rep(s): China Books (Australia); Deep
    Books Ltd (UK); SATAS (Belgium)

Blue Sky Marketing Inc
PO Box 21583, St Paul, MN 55121-0583
SAN: 263-9394
Tel: 651-687-9835 *Fax:* 651-687-9836
Key Personnel
Pres: Vic Spadaccini
Founded: 1982
ISBN Prefix(es): 0-911493
Number of titles published annually: 3 Print
Total Titles: 13 Print
Editorial Office(s): 820 Cleveland St S, Cam-
    bridge, MN 55008 *Tel:* 763-689-9800 *Toll Free
    Tel:* 800-678-7006
Sales Office(s): 820 Cleveland St S, Cambridge,
    MN 55008 *Tel:* 763-689-9800 *Toll Free
    Tel:* 800-678-7006
Distributed by Adventure Publications
Distributor for Lakeland Color Press
Billing Address: 820 Cleveland St S, Cam-
    bridge, MN 55008 *Tel:* 763-689-9800 *Toll Free
    Tel:* 800-678-7006
Shipping Address: 820 Cleveland St S, Cam-
    bridge, MN 55008 *Tel:* 763-689-9800 *Toll Free
    Tel:* 800-678-7006
Membership(s): Minnesota Book Publishers
    Roundtable; Publishers Marketing Association

Blue Unicorn Press Inc
4153 SE 39 Ave, Suite 35, Portland, OR 97202-
    3176
Mailing Address: PO Box 40300, Portland, OR
    97240-0300
Tel: 503-775-9322
E-mail: unicornpress404@aol.com
Key Personnel
Pres: Wanda Z Larson
Bd Member & Contest Chair: L E Stransky
Founded: 1990
ISBN Prefix(es): 0-9628584
Number of titles published annually: 2 Print; 1
    Online; 1 E-Book
Total Titles: 6 Print; 1 Online; 1 E-Book
Distributed by XLIBRIS
Returns: PO Box 40300, Portland, OR 97240-
    0300 (Book must show no wear)

Bluestar Communication Corp, see Amber
    Lotus

Bluestocking Press
3333 Gold Country Dr, El Dorado, CA 95623
SAN: 667-2981
Mailing Address: PO Box 1014, Placerville, CA
    95667-1014
Tel: 530-621-1123 *Toll Free Tel:* 800-959-8586
    Fax: 530-642-9222
E-mail: customerservice@bluestockingpress.com

Web Site: www.bluestockingpress.com
Key Personnel
Owner & Pres: Jane A Williams *Tel:* 530-622-
    8586 *E-mail:* uncleric@jps.net
Founded: 1987
Special reports: The Home School Market Guide,
    Books: home libraries, guidelines for selecting
    books, free market economics, justice, Laura
    Ingalls Wilder, Time Reference, world & US
    history.
ISBN Prefix(es): 0-942617
Number of titles published annually: 3 Print
Total Titles: 15 Print

Bluewood Books
Imprint of The Siyeh Group Inc
38 South "B" St, Suite 202, San Mateo, CA
    94401
Tel: 650-548-0754 *Fax:* 650-548-0654
E-mail: bluewoodb@aol.com
Key Personnel
Publr: Richard Michaels
Ed: Tony Napoli
Founded: 1990
Specialize in adult & young adult nonfiction
    books.
ISBN Prefix(es): 0-912517
Number of titles published annually: 5 Print
Total Titles: 50 Print
Distributed by SCB Distributors
Foreign Rights: Inter License Ltd

Blushing Rose Publishing
29 Katrina Rd, San Anselmo, CA 94960
Mailing Address: PO Box 2238, San Anselmo,
    CA 94979-2238
Tel: 415-458-2090 *Toll Free Tel:* 800-898-2263
    Fax: 415-458-2091
E-mail: info@blushingrose.com
Web Site: www.blushingrose.com
Key Personnel
Publr & Intl Rts: Nancy Cogan Akmon
Founded: 1992
Publish a line of fine gift books including baby
    albums & wedding albums, guest books, chil-
    dren's illustrated classics, illustrated quotation,
    coloring books, gift books, cook books & in-
    spirational children's titles.
ISBN Prefix(es): 1-884807
Number of titles published annually: 40 Print
Total Titles: 40 Print
Distributed by Cogan Books; Folens Ltd (UK);
    Ingram Books
Foreign Rep(s): Folens (UK)

BNA Books
Division of The Bureau of National Affairs Inc
1231 25 St NW, Washington, DC 20037
SAN: 201-4262
Tel: 202-452-4343 *Toll Free Tel:* 800-960-1220
    Fax: 202-452-4997 (editorial off); 732-346-
    1624 (cust serv)
E-mail: books@bna.com
Web Site: www.bnabooks.com
Key Personnel
Pres & Ed-in-Chief: Paul Wojcik
Publr & Exec Ed: Margret S Hullinger *Tel:* 202-
    452-4271 *E-mail:* mhullinger@bna.com
Mktg Mgr: Lois Smith
Acqs Mgr: Timothy Darby; James Fattibene
Founded: 1929
Employment law: labor law, labor relations, em-
    ployee benefits, labor arbitration, intellectual
    property law; health law: legal practice & refer-
    ence.
ISBN Prefix(es): 0-87179; 1-57018
Number of titles published annually: 40 Print
Total Titles: 160 Print; 2 Online
Billing Address: BNA Books, A Division of The
    Bureau of National Affairs, c/o Returns Dept,
    Raritan Ctr, Bldg 424, 80 Northfield Ave, Edi-
    son, NJ 08837-3866

Orders to: BNA Books, A Division of The Bu-
    reau of National Affairs, c/o Returns Dept, Rar-
    itan Ctr, Bldg 424, 80 Northfield Ave, Edison,
    NJ 08837-3866 *Toll Free Tel:* 800-960-1220
    Fax: 732-346-1624
Warehouse: BNA Books, A Division of The Bu-
    reau of National Affairs, c/o Returns Dept, Rar-
    itan Ctr, Bldg 424, 80 Northfield Ave, Edison,
    NJ 08837-3866, Steve Filer *Tel:* 732-225-5555

BNI Publications Inc
1612 S Clementine St, Anaheim, CA 92802
Tel: 714-517-0970 *Toll Free Tel:* 800-873-6397
    Fax: 714-535-8078
Web Site: www.bnibooks.com
Key Personnel
Cont: Peter Barrick *Tel:* 714-517-0970 ext 205
Construction books.
Number of titles published annually: 100 Print
Total Titles: 120 Print
See separate listing for:
Building News

BOA Editions Ltd
260 East Ave, Rochester, NY 14604
Tel: 585-546-3410 *Fax:* 585-546-3913
Web Site: www.boaeditions.org
Key Personnel
Exec Dir: George Wallace
Ed: Thom Ward
Mktg Dir & Assoc Ed: Peter Conners
Devt Dir: Susie Cohen
Founded: 1976
Publication of books of poetry & poetry in trans-
    lation.
ISBN Prefix(es): 0-918526; 1-880238; 1-929918
Number of titles published annually: 10 Print
Total Titles: 150 Print
Orders to: Consortium Book Sales & Distribu-
    tion, 1045 Westgate Dr, St Paul, MN 55114
    Toll Free Tel: 800-283-3572
Distribution Center: Consortium Book Sales &
    Distribution, 1045 Westgate Dr, St Paul, MN
    55114 *Tel:* 612-221-9035 *Toll Free Tel:* 800-
    283-3572 *Fax:* 612-221-0124

§BoardSource
1828 "L" St NW, Suite 900, Washington, DC
    20036-5104
Tel: 202-452-6262 *Toll Free Tel:* 800-883-6262
    Fax: 202-452-6299
E-mail: mail@boardsource.org
Web Site: www.boardsource.org
Key Personnel
Pres & CEO: Judith O'Connor
Gen Counsel & Chief Knowledge Officer: Mari-
    anne Ebby
VP, Busn Opers: Lisa La Montagne
    E-mail: llamontagne@boardsource.org
Founded: 1988
Premier resource for practical information, tools
    & best practices, training & leadership devel-
    opment for board members of nonprofit orga-
    nizations. Enables organizations to fulfill their
    missions by helping build effective nonprofit
    boards, offering credible support in solving
    tough problems.
ISBN Prefix(es): 0-925299; 1-58686
Number of titles published annually: 12 Print; 3
    CD-ROM; 2 E-Book
Total Titles: 115 Print; 8 CD-ROM; 2 Audio
Distributed by American Society of Association
    Executives

Bobley Harmann Corp
311 Crossways Park Dr, Woodbury, NY 11797
SAN: 202-3334
Tel: 516-364-1800 *Fax:* 516-364-1899
E-mail: info@bobley.com
Web Site: www.bobley.com
Key Personnel
Pres: Mark Bobley
VP, Adv: Neal Levin

Publr: Herbert J Cohen; Peter M Bobley; Vincent Harman
Mgr, Sales & Mktg: John Traola
Prodn Mgr: Douglas Bobley
Founded: 1961
Appointment books, fiction.
ISBN Prefix(es): 0-8324
Number of titles published annually: 20 Print
Imprints: Sundial Editions
Subsidiaries: Platinum Press Inc
Divisions: Direct-Mail Division; Special Promotions; Travel & Entertainment
Warehouse: 630 Main St, Westbury, NY 11590

§Bolchazy-Carducci Publishers Inc
1000 Brown St, Unit 101, Wauconda, IL 60084
SAN: 219-7685
Tel: 847-526-4344 *Fax:* 847-526-2867
Web Site: www.bolchazy.com
Key Personnel
Pres, Intl Rts & Treas: Ladislaus J Bolchazy
VP, Sales Dir, Sec & Treas: Marie Carducci Bolchazy *E-mail:* mbolchazy@bolchazy.com
Founded: 1978
Scholarly books, textbooks, language cassettes, CD-ROM Latin series, Latin music CDs, Slovak publications.
ISBN Prefix(es): 0-86516
Number of titles published annually: 15 Print; 5 CD-ROM
Total Titles: 250 Print; 29 CD-ROM
Distributor for Georg Olms Verlag
Advertising Agency: De Chant Hughes
Distribution Center: Partners Book Distributing Co

Bollix Books
1609 W Callender Ave, Peoria, IL 61606
Tel: 309-453-4903 *Fax:* 309-676-6558
E-mail: editor@bollixbooks.com
Web Site: www.bollixbooks.com
Key Personnel
Publ: Staley Krause
Sales & Dist: Mike Krause *Fax:* 309-676-6557
Founded: 2002
ISBN Prefix(es): 9-32188
Number of titles published annually: 6 Print; 1 CD-ROM; 1 Audio
Total Titles: 5 Print
Returns: 1554 Litton Dr, Stone Mountain, GA 30083, Sales: Mike Krause *E-mail:* mkrause@publisherservicesinc.com
Shipping Address: 1554 Litton Dr, Stone Mountain, GA 30083, Sales: Mike Krause *Tel:* 309-676-6558 *Fax:* 309-676-6557
Membership(s): Chicago Book Clinic; Society of Children's Book Writers & Illustrators

Bonus Books Inc
1452 Second St, Santa Monica, CA 90403
Tel: 310-260-9400 *Toll Free Tel:* 800-225-3775
E-mail: webmaster@bonusbooks.com
Web Site: www.bonusbooks.com
Key Personnel
Pres & Publr: Jeffrey Stern *E-mail:* jeff@bonusbooks.com
Man Ed: Devon Freeny *E-mail:* devon@bonusbooks.com
Opers Mgr: Richard T Williams *E-mail:* richard@bonusbooks.com
Publicity & Mktg Mgr: Stephanie Adams *Tel:* 310-260-4443 *E-mail:* stephanie@bonusbooks.com
Founded: 1985
Trade & professional publisher: nonfiction, history, current events, pop culture, gambling, sports, media, journalism, broadcasting, fundraising & direct marketing.
ISBN Prefix(es): 0-933893; 0-929387; 1-56625; 0-944496
Number of titles published annually: 25 Print
Total Titles: 200 Print

Divisions: Precept Press
Editorial Office(s): 875 N Michigan Ave, Suite 1416, Chicago, IL 60611 *Tel:* 312-467-0580 *Fax:* 312-467-9271
Distributor for Precept Press
Warehouse: 350 N Ogden, Lower Level, Chicago, IL 60607
See separate listing for:
Precept Press

§Book Beat Ltd
26010 Greenfield, Oak Park, MI 48237
Tel: 248-968-1190 *Fax:* 248-968-3102
E-mail: bookbeat@aol.com
Web Site: www.thebookbeat.com
Key Personnel
Owner & Art Buyer: Cary Loren
Owner & Sideline Buyer: Colleen Kammer
Founded: 1982
Photography gallery, publisher, bookseller; specialize in children's books, photography. Publish photography & art, surrealist/DADA manner.
Number of titles published annually: 4 Print; 1 CD-ROM; 2 Audio
Total Titles: 4 Print; 1 CD-ROM; 6 Audio

Book East
2330 NE 61 Ave, Portland, OR 97213
SAN: 177-1205
Mailing Address: PO Box 13352, Portland, OR 97213
Tel: 503-287-0974 *Fax:* 503-281-3693
Key Personnel
Owner & Intl Rts Contact: Katsuo Wakiyama *E-mail:* kwakiyama@comcast.net
Founded: 1992
ISBN Prefix(es): 0-9647040
Number of titles published annually: 1 Print
Total Titles: 5 Print
Distributor for Kaibunsha; The Hokuseido Press

Book Marketing Works LLC
50 Lovely St, Avon, CT 06001
Mailing Address: PO Box 715, Avon, CT 06001-0715
Tel: 860-675-1344 *Toll Free Tel:* 800-562-4357
Fax: 203-729-5335
Web Site: www.bookmarketingworks.com
Key Personnel
Pres: Brian Jud *E-mail:* BrianJud@msn.com
Contact: Art Salzfass
Founded: 1990
ISBN Prefix(es): 1-928782
Number of titles published annually: 10 Print
Total Titles: 26 Print
Imprints: Strong Books
Subsidiaries: Book Marketing Works

Book Peddlers
15245 Minnetonka Blvd, Minnetonka, MN 55345-1510
Tel: 952-912-0036 *Toll Free Tel:* 800-255-3379
Fax: 952-912-0105
Web Site: www.bookpeddlers.com; www.practicalparenting.com
Key Personnel
Publr & Owner: Vicki Lansky *E-mail:* vlansky@bookpeddlers.com
Mktg & PR: Abby Lyons-Herstein *E-mail:* abbyherstein@aol.com
Founded: 1987
Nonfiction hardcover & audio tapes; gift-giving occasion books.
ISBN Prefix(es): 0-916773; 1-931863
Number of titles published annually: 5 Print
Total Titles: 40 Print; 4 Audio
Imprints: I N K Books
Distributed by PGW

Membership(s): Minnesota Book Publishers Roundtable; Publishers Marketing Association; Small Publishers Association of North America; Upper Midwest Booksellers Association

Book Publishing Co
415 Farm Rd, Summertown, TN 38483
Mailing Address: PO Box 99, Summertown, TN 38483
Tel: 931-964-3571 *Toll Free Tel:* 888-260-8458
Fax: 931-964-3518
E-mail: info@bookpubco.com
Web Site: www.bookpubco.com
Key Personnel
Pres: Robert Holzapfel
Mgr: Anna Pope *E-mail:* anna@bookpubco.com
Man Ed: Cynthia Holzapfel
Founded: 1984
Community-owned small press publisher committed to promoting books that educate, inspire & empower. Vegetarian cookbooks; Native American titles, health & nutrition titles.
ISBN Prefix(es): 0-913990; 1-57067
Number of titles published annually: 3 Print
Total Titles: 200 Print; 2 Audio
Imprints: Botanica Press; Healthy Living; Native Voices
Distributor for Cherokee Publications; Crazy Crow; CRCS Publications; Critical Path; Gentle World; Magni Co; Sproutman Publications
Foreign Rep(s): Addenda Ltd (New Zealand); Airlift Book Distributor (England); Brumby Books Gemcraft (Australia); Second Story Press (Canada)

Book Sales Inc
Division of The Quarto Group Inc
114 Northfield Ave, Edison, NJ 08837
SAN: 299-4062
Tel: 732-225-0530 *Toll Free Tel:* 800-526-7257
Fax: 732-225-2257
E-mail: sales@booksalesusa.com; customerservice@booksalesusa.com
Web Site: www.booksalesusa.com
Key Personnel
Pres & CEO: Melvin Shapiro
Sales Dir: Joe Fortin
VP, Mktg & Acqs: Frank Oppel
Spec Sales: Daniel Rich
VP, Fin: Lisa Stamets
Credit Mgr: Conny Schoen
Warehouse & Opers Mgr: Deborah Kearney
Founded: 1952
Book Sales Inc has been in the business of publishing & supplying books to wholesalers, mail order companies & retail stores for over 45 years. Imprints include Chartwell, Castle Books, Wellfleet Press, Blue and Grey & Knickerbocker Press, all publishing high quality illustrated books or reprints. In addition to books we publish, we are one of the largest purchasers of other publishers' remainder &/or overstock titles for resale at significantly reduced prices. Categories include novels, cookbooks, history, juvenile, civil war, militaria, fine art, art instruction, how-to craft books, natural history, gardening & more.
ISBN Prefix(es): 0-89009; 1-55521; 0-7858
Number of titles published annually: 300 Print
Total Titles: 2,500 Print
Imprints: Alva Press; Blue & Grey; Castle Books; Chartwell Books; Knickerbocker Press; Poplar Books; Wellfleet Press
Editorial Office(s): 276 Fifth Ave, Suite 206, New York, NY 10001 *Tel:* 212-779-4972 *Fax:* 212-779-6058
Sales Office(s): 276 Fifth Ave, Suite 206, New York, NY 10001 *Tel:* 212-779-4972 *Fax:* 212-779-6058
Membership(s): ABA

The Book Tree
PO Box 16476, San Diego, CA 92176

Tel: 619-280-1263 *Fax:* 619-280-1285
E-mail: booktree1@cs.com
Web Site: www.thebooktree.com
Key Personnel
Owner: Paul Willey
Founded: 1992
ISBN Prefix(es): 1-885395; 1-58509
Number of titles published annually: 20 Print
Total Titles: 155 Print
Editorial Office(s): 3377 Adams Ave, San Diego, CA 92116
Distribution Center: Ingram
Membership(s): Publishers Marketing Association

Book World Inc/Blue Star Productions
9666 E Riggs Rd, No 194, Sun Lakes, AZ 85248
Tel: 480-895-7995 *Fax:* 480-895-6991
E-mail: bsp@bluestarproductions.net
Web Site: www.bluestarproductions.net
Key Personnel
Pres & Ed: Barbara Sue DeBolt
Founded: 1994
Metaphysical, UFOlogy, Atlantis, paranormal, teleportation, Native American, visionary fiction & specialty subjects. No phone queries; SASE only.
ISBN Prefix(es): 1-881542
Number of titles published annually: 4 Print
Total Titles: 60 Print
Imprints: Blue Star Productions
Distributed by Adventures Unlimited; Amazon.com; New Leaf

Bookhaven Press LLC
249 Field Club Circle, McKees Rocks, PA 15136
Mailing Address: PO Box 1243, Moon Township, PA 15108
Tel: 412-494-6926 *Toll Free Tel:* 800-782-7424 (orders only) *Fax:* 412-494-5749
E-mail: bookhaven@aol.com
Web Site: members.aol.com/bookhaven
Key Personnel
Owner: Dennis V Damp
Founded: 1985
ISBN Prefix(es): 0-943641
Number of titles published annually: 3 Print
Total Titles: 7 Print
Distributed by Bookhaus; Planning Communications
Membership(s): Publishers Marketing Association

Books in Motion
Division of Classic Ventures, Ltd
9922 E Montgomery, Suite 31, Spokane, WA 99206
Tel: 509-922-1646 *Toll Free Tel:* 800-752-3199 *Fax:* 509-922-1445
E-mail: sales@booksinmotion.com
Web Site: www.booksinmotion.com
Key Personnel
Pres: Gary Challender
Admin Mgr: Connie Challender
Founded: 1980
Produce fiction books on cassette & compact discs. Does not accept unsol mss. Criteria is exceptionally high for acceptance. There is no cost to the authors. Currently seeking subsidiary audio rights on previously print published titles.
ISBN Prefix(es): 1-55686; 1-58116; 1-59607
Number of titles published annually: 120 Audio
Total Titles: 2,000 Audio
Membership(s): Western Writers of America

Books on Tape®
Division of Random House Inc
Customer Service, 400 Hahn Rd, Westminster, MD 21157
Toll Free Tel: 800-733-3000 *Toll Free Fax:* 800-659-2436
E-mail: botlib@booksontape.com
Web Site: library.booksontape.com

Key Personnel
Pres: Scott Matthews
Pres, Lib Sales: Brian Gurewitz
Mktg Dir: Cheryl Herman
Founded: 1975
In 2005, Books on Tape will celebrate 30 years of offering the best in unabridged audio books. Our best selling & award-winning titles are produced in NY & LA studios & read by the finest narrators in the industry. Select from over 3000 titles available, durable library packaging & delivered with a complement of services tailored to meet special needs of librarians & educators. Flexible standing order plans, featuring the freedom to choose your titles & free lifetime replacement guarantees. Books on Tape® is proud to exclusively have Listening Library® the premier audio book publisher of children's & young adult literature, as its children's imprint.
Number of titles published annually: 300 Audio
Total Titles: 3,000 Audio
Imprints: Listening Library®
Divisions: Listening Library®
Distributor for Listening Library®
Membership(s): AASL; ALA; ALSC; California Library Association; National Council of Teachers of English; Public Library Association; YALSA

§Boson Books
Imprint of C & M Online Media Inc
3905 Meadow Field Lane, Raleigh, NC 27606
Tel: 919-233-8164 *Fax:* 919-233-8578
E-mail: boson@bosonbooks.com
Web Site: www.bosonbooks.com
Key Personnel
Pres & Publr: Nancy McAllister *E-mail:* nancy@cmonline.com
VP & Intl Rts: David McAllister *E-mail:* david@cmonline.com
VP, Mktg: Steve Vivian *E-mail:* steve@cmonline.com
Founded: 1994
Books online. First commercial general online book publisher.
ISBN Prefix(es): 1-886420; 0-917990
Number of titles published annually: 4 Print; 12 Online; 12 E-Book; 4 Audio
Total Titles: 10 Print; 80 Online; 80 E-Book; 4 Audio

Boston America Corp
125 Walnut St, Watertown, MA 02472
Tel: 617-923-1111 (ext 249) *Fax:* 617-923-8839
E-mail: info@bostonamerica.com
Web Site: www.bostonamerica.com
Key Personnel
Pres & Lib Sales Dir: Matthew Kavet
Intl Rts: Herbert Kavet
Founded: 1962
Publisher of humorous books, novelty playing cards, novelty tins, licensed tool items.
ISBN Prefix(es): 1-889647
Number of titles published annually: 5 Print
Total Titles: 80 Print

The Boswell Institute
Affiliate of Credit Card Users of America
PO Box 7100, Beverly Hills, CA 90212-7100
Tel: 818-343-4434
Key Personnel
Pres: Howard Strong
Off Mgr: Joan Bowstrange
Founded: 1986
ISBN Prefix(es): 0-944077
Number of titles published annually: 12 Print
Total Titles: 12 Print
Imprints: Credit Card Users of America Press
Advertising Agency: Strange Advertising
Warehouse: 6923 Geyser Ave, Reseda, CA 91335-4013

Bottom Dog Press
c/o Firelands College of Bowling Green State University, PO Box 425, Huron, OH 44839-0425
SAN: 689-5492
Tel: 419-433-5560 *Fax:* 419-433-9696
Web Site: members.aol.com/lsmithdog/bottomdog
Key Personnel
Dir, Ed & Publr: Larry Smith
  E-mail: lsmithdog@aol.com
Asst Ed: David Shevin; Laura Smith
Founded: 1985
ISBN Prefix(es): 0-933087
Number of titles published annually: 5 Print; 1 Audio
Total Titles: 80 Print; 2 CD-ROM; 4 Audio
Distributor for Collinwood Media; The Firelands Writing Center

Thomas Bouregy & Co Inc
160 Madison Ave, New York, NY 10016
SAN: 201-4173
Tel: 212-598-0222 *Fax:* 212-979-1862
E-mail: customerservice@avalonbooks.com
Web Site: avalonbooks.com
Key Personnel
Pres: Wilhelm Mickelsen
Edit Dir: Erin Cartwright-Niumata
Cust Serv: Robert F Hirsch
Contact: Ellen Bouregy-Mickelsen
Founded: 1950
Fiction: mysteries, romances, westerns, career romances, historical romances.
ISBN Prefix(es): 0-8034
Number of titles published annually: 60 Print
Total Titles: 504 Print
Imprints: Avalon Books
Warehouse: Offset Paperback Distribution Center, One Passan Dr, Bldg 10, Laflin, PA 18702
See separate listing for:
Avalon Books

Eddie Bowers Publishing Inc
PO Box 130, Peosta, IA 52068-0130
Tel: 563-876-3119 *Toll Free Tel:* 800-747-2411 *Fax:* 563-876-3206
E-mail: eddiebowerspub@aol.com
Web Site: www.eddiebowerspublishing.com
Key Personnel
Owner & Publr: Eddie Bowers
Founded: 1981
College textbooks.
ISBN Prefix(es): 0-912855; 0-945483
Number of titles published annually: 20 Print
Total Titles: 75 Print
Foreign Rep(s): Gazelle Book Services (England)

§R R Bowker LLC
Subsidiary of Cambridge Information Group Inc
630 Central Ave, New Providence, NJ 07974
SAN: 214-1191
Tel: 908-286-1090 *Toll Free Tel:* 888-269-5372; 888-269-5372 (cust serv - press 2 for returns) *Fax:* 908-219-0098
E-mail: orderinfo@bowker.com
Web Site: www.bowker.com
Key Personnel
Pres: Michael Cairns
Exec VP: Gary Aiello
VP, Prod Devt & Mktg: Angela D'Agostino
Founded: 1872
As the sole ISBN Agency in the United States, Bowker is the most authoritative source for title & publisher information. Bowker enables & promotes the flow of goods & information through the publishing supply chain with products such as: booksinprint.com; globalbooksinprint.com; ulrichsweb.com; Pubnet EDI-based book ordering service; & PubEasy, web-based book ordering service.
ISBN Prefix(es): 0-8352

Number of titles published annually: 23 Print; 6 CD-ROM; 8 Online
Total Titles: 23 Print; 6 CD-ROM; 8 Online
Online services available through OCLC, OVID.
Foreign Office(s): Thorpe - Bowker, Locked Bag 20, Port Melbourne, Victoria 3207, Australia *Tel:* (03) 8645 0300 *Fax:* 03) 8645 0333 *E-mail:* yoursay@thorpe.com.au *Web Site:* www.thorpe.com.au
Bowker (UK) Ltd, Farringdon House, 3rd fl, Wood St, East Grinstead, West Sussex RH19 1UZ, United Kingdom *Tel:* (0) 1342 310450 *Fax:* (0) 1342 310463 *E-mail:* sales@bowker.co.uk *Web Site:* www.bowker.co.uk
Membership(s): AAP; ALA; BISG
See separate listing for:
Simba Information

BowTie Press
Division of BowTie Inc
3 Burroughs, Irvine, CA 92618
Tel: 949-855-8822 *Toll Free Tel:* 800-426-2516 *Fax:* 949-458-3856
Web Site: www.bowtiepress.com
Key Personnel
Pres: Norman Ridker
ISBN Prefix(es): 0-9629525; 1-889540; 1-931993
Number of titles published annually: 20 Print
Membership(s): AAP

Marion Boyars Publishers Inc
c/o The Feminist, 365 Fifth Ave, Suite 5406, New York, NY 10016
SAN: 200-6049
Tel: 212-697-9676 *Fax:* 212-808-0664
Web Site: www.marionboyars.co.uk
Key Personnel
Dir, Publicity & Subs Rts: Franklin Dennis
Founded: 1978
Fiction, biography, music, theater, literary criticism, drama, travel. All editorial submissions or questions should be directed to the London office. No submissions to the New York office.
ISBN Prefix(es): 0-7145
Number of titles published annually: 20 Print
Total Titles: 250 Print
Foreign Office(s): Marion Boyars Publishers Ltd, 24 Lacy Rd, London SW15 INL, United Kingdom, Man Ed: Catheryn Kilgarriff *Tel:* (020) 8788 9522 *Fax:* (020) 8789 8122
Foreign Rep(s): Peribo Pty Ltd (Australia, New Zealand)
Foreign Rights: Marion Boyars Ltd
Distribution Center: Consortium Book Sales, 1045 Westgate Dr, St Paul, MN 55114-1065, Contact: Julie L Schaper *Fax:* 651-917-6406 *E-mail:* jschaper@cbsd.com

Boydell & Brewer Inc
Affiliate of Boydell & Brewer Ltd (UK)
668 Mount Hope Ave, University of Rochester, Rochester, NY 14620
Tel: 585-275-0419 *Fax:* 585-271-8778
Web Site: www.boydellandbrewer.co.uk
Key Personnel
Dir: Mark Klemens *E-mail:* klemens@boydellusa.net
Mktg Dir: Amy Powers
Intl Rts: Richard Barber *E-mail:* rbarber@boydell.co.uk
Accts Mgr: Eloise Puls
Founded: 1989
Publisher of scholarly books.
ISBN Prefix(es): 0-85115; 0-85991; 0-86193; 0-7293; 0-900411; 1-85566; 1-878822; 1-58046; 1-57113; 1-900639
Number of titles published annually: 200 Print
Total Titles: 3,100 Print
Imprints: Boydell Press; Henry Bradshaw Society; D S Brewer; Camden House; Canterbury & York Society; Lincoln Record Society; Royal Historical Society; Suffolk Records Society;

Tamesis; University of Rochester Press; York Medieval Press
Foreign Office(s): Boydell & Brewer Ltd, PO Box 9, Woodbridge, Suffolk IP12 3DF, United Kingdom
Warehouse: Publishers Storage & Shipping Corp, Fitchburg, MA 01420 *Tel:* 978-345-2121 *Fax:* 978-348-1233
See separate listing for:
University of Rochester Press

Boyds Mills Press
Subsidiary of Highlights for Children Inc
815 Church St, Honesdale, PA 18431
Tel: 570-253-1164 *Toll Free Tel:* 877-512-8366 *Fax:* 570-253-0179
Web Site: www.boydsmillspress.com
Key Personnel
Pres & Intl Rts: Clay Winters
Publr: Kent Brown, Jr
Book Sales Contact: Stan Pratt *Tel:* 570-251-4513
Founded: 1990
Books for children of all ages.
ISBN Prefix(es): 1-56397; 1-878093
Number of titles published annually: 60 Print
Total Titles: 500 Print
Imprints: Bell Books; Calkius Creek Books; Caroline House; Wordsong
Branch Office(s)
4 Hubbell Mountain Rd, Sherman, CT 06784 *Tel:* 203-355-9498
Foreign Rep(s): Clay Winters
Advertising Agency: Bennett Book Advertising

Boys Town Press
Division of Father Flanagan's Boys' Home
14100 Crawford St, Boys Town, NE 68010
Tel: 402-498-1320 *Toll Free Tel:* 800-282-6657 *Fax:* 402-498-1310
E-mail: btpress@boystown.org
Web Site: www.boystownpress.org
Key Personnel
Mgr: Barbara Lonnborg *E-mail:* lonnborgb@boystown.org
Sales & Mktg Coord: Pat Martens *Tel:* 402-498-1334 *E-mail:* martensp@boystown.org
Founded: 1992
Youth care & education books, parenting books, videos & audio, sign language products, inspirational titles.
ISBN Prefix(es): 0-938510; 1-889322
Number of titles published annually: 5 Print
Total Titles: 80 Print; 3 Audio
Distributed by Deep Books (UK); Footprint Books, Australia; Quality Books
Distributor for A D D Warehouse; Character Counts Coalition
Foreign Rights: Evelyn Lee of Amer-Asia Books (China, Japan, Korea & Taiwan)
Warehouse: 250 Monsky Dr, Boys Town, NE 68010
Membership(s): Publishers Marketing Association

BPT, see Baha'i Publishing Trust

§Bradford Publishing Co
1743 Wazee St, Denver, CO 80202
Tel: 303-292-2590 *Toll Free Tel:* 800-446-2831 *Fax:* 303-298-5014
E-mail: marketing@bradfordpublishing.com
Web Site: www.bradfordpublishing.com
Founded: 1881
Specialize in Colorado legal forms & materials.
ISBN Prefix(es): 1-883726
Number of titles published annually: 10 Print
Membership(s): Publishers Association of the West; Publishers Marketing Association

BradyGAMES Publishing
Division of Pearson Technology Group
800 E 96 St, 3rd fl, Indianapolis, IN 46240

Tel: 317-428-3000 *Toll Free Tel:* 800-545-5912; 800-571-5840 (cust serv)
E-mail: bradyquestions@pearsoned.com
Web Site: www.bradygames.com
Key Personnel
Publr: David Waybright
Ed-in-Chief: Leigh Davis
Mktg Mgr: Janet Eshenour
ISBN Prefix(es): 1-56686; 0-7440
Number of titles published annually: 100 Print
Total Titles: 193 Print

Braille Co Inc
65-B Town Hall Sq, Falmouth, MA 02540-2754
Tel: 508-540-0800 *Fax:* 508-548-6116
E-mail: braillinc@capecod.net
Web Site: home.capecod.net/~braillinc
Key Personnel
Pres: Josie Little
VP: Deborah Shearer
Founded: 1971
Professional braille transcription & publishing of contemporary fiction & nonfiction. Publish braille textbooks & vocational materials, including mathematics, computer manuals, music & foreign language materials on order. Price list available in inkprint & braille.

Brainwaves™ Center, see Allen D Bragdon Publishers Inc

Branden Publishing Co Inc
Unit of Branden Books
PO Box 812094, Wellesley, MA 02482-0013
SAN: 201-4106
Tel: 781-235-3634 *Fax:* 781-790-1056
E-mail: branden@branden.com
Web Site: www.branden.com *Cable:* BOSTON BRANDENBOOK
Key Personnel
Pres: Robert Caso
VP: Jerome Frank
Ed & Treas: Adolph Caso
Founded: 1907
ISBN Prefix(es): 0-8283
Number of titles published annually: 15 Print
Total Titles: 300 Print
Imprints: Art Treasures; Brashear Music Co; Four Seas; Bruce Humphries; International Pocket Library; Popular Technology
Distributor for Dante University of America Press Inc
Foreign Rep(s): Amazon.com; Baker & Taylor (Worldwide); Gazelle (England); Ingram
Advertising Agency: ADS-IPL

Brandywine Press
154 General Pulaski Walk, Naugatuck, CT 06770-2978
Mailing Address: 24 Andrea Way, Maplecrest, NY 12454
Tel: 203-729-7556 *Toll Free Tel:* 800-345-1776 *Fax:* 203-729-7567
Web Site: www.brandywinepress.com
Key Personnel
Pres: David Burner *E-mail:* dbburner@aol.com
Cust Rel, Mktg: Sandra Ayers *E-mail:* sjeanayers@aol.com
Pubns Mgr, Orders & Returns Supv: Renzo Melaragno
Founded: 1991
Publish college textbooks in American history & literature; German literature; occasional scholarly monographs.
ISBN Prefix(es): 1-881089
Number of titles published annually: 12 Print
Membership(s): American Historical Association; Organization of American Historians

Brassey's Inc
Subsidiary of Books International
22841 Quicksilver Dr, Dulles, VA 20166

Tel: 703-661-1548 *Toll Free Tel:* 800-775-2518
(orders only) *Fax:* 703-661-1547
E-mail: djacobs@booksintl.com
Web Site: www.brasseysinc.com
Key Personnel
VP & Publr: Don McKeon *Tel:* 703-661-1562
E-mail: don@booksintl.com
Mktg Dir: Sam Dorrance *Tel:* 703-996-1028
E-mail: sam@booksintl.com
Founded: 1984 (Acquired in 1999 by Books International of Dulles, Virginia)
Brassey's, Inc is an American book publisher with a focus on topics of history (especially military history), world & national affairs, foreign policy, defense, intelligence & biography. Additionally, Brassey's Inc is now developing books about transportation (especially automobiles) & about the personalities & events of national & international athletic competition. Based near Washington in Dulles, Virginia.
ISBN Prefix(es): 1-57488
Number of titles published annually: 80 Print
Total Titles: 300 Print
Imprints: Brassey's Sports
Warehouse: PO Box 960, Herndon, VA 20172
Fax: 703-661-1501
Distribution Center: 22883 Quicksilver Dr, Dulles, VA 20166 *Toll Free Tel:* 800-775-2518

George Braziller Inc
171 Madison Ave, Suite 1105, New York, NY 10016
SAN: 201-9310
Tel: 212-889-0909 *Fax:* 212-689-5405
E-mail: georgebraziller@earthlink.net
Web Site: www.georgebraziller.com
Key Personnel
Publr: George Braziller
Prodn Ed: Mary Taveras
Accts: Mary Bryce
Founded: 1955
Publishers of fine illustrated art books.
ISBN Prefix(es): 0-8076
Number of titles published annually: 20 Print
Total Titles: 300 Print
Distributed by Antique Collectors' Club Ltd; W W Norton
Foreign Rep(s): Antique Collectors' Club Ltd (Australia, England, Europe, India, New Zealand); United Publishers Services Ltd (Japan)
Warehouse: National Book Co, 800 Keystone Industrial Park, Scranton, PA 18512 *Toll Free Tel:* 800-233-4830 *Toll Free Fax:* 800-458-6515

Breakaway Books
PO Box 24, Halcottsville, NY 12438-0024
Tel: 607-326-4805 *Toll Free Tel:* 800-548-4348 (voicemail) *Fax:* 212-898-0408
E-mail: mail@breakawaybooks.com; orders@breakawaybooks.com; info@breakawaybooks.com
Web Site: www.breakawaybooks.com
Key Personnel
Publr: Garth Battista *E-mail:* garth@breakawaybooks.com
Founded: 1994
Specialize in sports literature & books.
ISBN Prefix(es): 1-891369; 1-55821
Number of titles published annually: 10 Print
Total Titles: 60 Print; 1 E-Book
Distribution Center: Consortium, 1045 Westgate Dr, St. Paul, MN 55114 *Toll Free Tel:* 800-283-3572

Breakout Productions Inc
PO Box 1643, Port Townsend, WA 98368-0129
Tel: 360-379-1965 *Fax:* 360-379-3794
Key Personnel
Pres: Mike Hoy
Ed: Gia Cosindas

Founded: 1998
Alternative lifestyles, how-to-beat the system, self-sufficiency. General science, computers & Americana.
Number of titles published annually: 2 Print
Total Titles: 150 Print
Distributed by Loompanics Unlimited Ingram
Advertising Agency: Space & Time

Breakthrough Publications Inc
326 Main St, Emmaus, PA 18049
Tel: 610-965-3200 *Toll Free Tel:* 800-824-5000
Fax: 610-965-5836
Web Site: www.booksonhorses.com
Key Personnel
Pres: Peter E Ognibene *E-mail:* peter@booksonhorses.com
Founded: 1980
Career & equestrian.
ISBN Prefix(es): 0-914327
Number of titles published annually: 3 Print
Total Titles: 50 Print
Imprints: Breakthrough Publications; Federal Jobs Digest
Advertising Agency: Peter Ognibene Associates

Nicholas Brealey Publishing
3704 Beard Ave N, Minneapolis, MN 55422
Tel: 763-208-3169 *Toll Free Tel:* 888-BREALEY (273-2539) *Fax:* 763-208-3170
E-mail: booksmatter@earthlink.net
Web Site: www.nbrealey-books.com
Key Personnel
Publr & Foreign Rts: Nicholas Brealey
Tel: (020) 7430 0224 *Fax:* (020) 7404 8311
E-mail: rights@nbrealey-books.com
US Mktg & Sales: Terri Armstrong Welch
Founded: 1992
Professional/trade business book (hardcover & original paperback) publisher. Additional subjects include: international business & culture, training & human resources.
ISBN Prefix(es): 1-85788
Number of titles published annually: 8 Print
Total Titles: 45 Print
Divisions: Intercultural Press Inc
Foreign Office(s): 3-5 Spafield St, Clerkenwell, London EC1R 4QB, United Kingdom *Tel:* (020) 7239 0360 *Fax:* (020) 7239 0370 *E-mail:* sales@nbrealey-books.com *Web Site:* www.nbrealeybooks.com
Distributed by Intercultural Press Inc
Orders to: National Book Network, 15200 NBN Way, Blue Ridge Summit, PA 17214 *Toll Free Tel:* 800-463-6420 *Toll Free Fax:* 800-338-4550
Returns: National Book Network, 15200 NBN Way, Blue Ridge Summit, PA 17214 *Toll Free Tel:* 800-463-6420 *Toll Free Fax:* 800-338-4550
Distribution Center: National Book Network, 15200 NBN Way, Blue Ridge Summit, PA 17214 *Toll Free Tel:* 800-463-6420 *Toll Free Fax:* 800-338-4550
Membership(s): Independent Publisher's Guild; PA
See separate listing for:
Intercultural Press Inc

Brenner Information Group
Division of Brenner Microcomputing Inc
9282 Samantha Ct, San Diego, CA 92129
SAN: 249-6496
Mailing Address: PO Box 721000, San Diego, CA 92172-1000
Tel: 858-538-0093 *Toll Free Tel:* 800-811-4337
Fax: 858-484-2599
E-mail: info@brennerbooks.com; sales@brennerbooks.com (ordering)
Web Site: www.brennerbooks.com
Key Personnel
Publr: Robert Brenner *E-mail:* brenner@brennerbooks.com

CFO: Carol Brenner *Fax:* 858-538-0380
E-mail: carolb@brennerbooks.com
Prodn Mgr: Jenny Hanson *Fax:* 858-538-0380
E-mail: jennyh@brennerbooks.com
Collects, processes, packages & distributes information related to the pricing of desktop computer services.
ISBN Prefix(es): 0-929535; 1-930199
Number of titles published annually: 6 Print; 8 E-Book
Total Titles: 20 Print; 19 E-Book
Distributed by Amazon.com; Publishing Perfection
Distributor for Allworth Press

Brentwood Christian Press
4000 Beallwood Ave, Columbus, GA 31904
Tel: 706-576-5787 *Toll Free Tel:* 800-334-8861
E-mail: brentwood@aol.com
Web Site: www.brentwoodbooks.com
Key Personnel
CEO: Jerry Luquire
Founded: 1982
ISBN Prefix(es): 1-55630
Number of titles published annually: 220 Print
Total Titles: 3,744 Print

Brethren Press
Division of Church of the Brethren General Board
1451 Dundee Ave, Elgin, IL 60120-1694
SAN: 201-9329
Tel: 847-742-5100 *Toll Free Tel:* 800-323-8039
Fax: 847-742-1407
Web Site: www.brethrenpress.com
Key Personnel
Dir & Publr: Wendy McFadden
Founded: 1897
Trade books, church school curriculum, tracts & pamphlets & various media resources. Specialize in Bible study, theology, church history, practical discipleship, personal lifestyle issues, social concerns, peace & justice, devotional life & personal growth.
ISBN Prefix(es): 0-87178
Number of titles published annually: 3 Print
Total Titles: 100 Print
Imprints: faithQuest
Distributed by Spring Arbor

Brewers Publications
Division of Association of Brewers
736 Pearl St, Boulder, CO 80302
Mailing Address: PO Box 1679, Boulder, CO 80306-1679
Tel: 303-447-0816 *Toll Free Tel:* 888-822-6273 (Canada & US) *Fax:* 303-447-2825
Web Site: www.beertown.org
Key Personnel
Publr & Intl Rts: Ray Daniels *Tel:* 773-665-1300 ext 140
Founded: 1986
Not-for-profit educational publishing house & the foremost publisher of books on the art, science, history & culture of beer. Includes nonfiction, sports guidebook, cooking, business, biography, etc.
ISBN Prefix(es): 0-937381
Number of titles published annually: 4 Print
Total Titles: 50 Print
Imprints: Siris Books
Distributed by National Book Network
Foreign Rep(s): Gazelle Book Services Ltd
Foreign Rights: Gazelle Book Services, Ltd (Worldwide exc North America)
Shipping Address: National Book Network, 15200 NBN Way, Blue Ridge Summit, PA 17214 *Toll Free Tel:* 800-462-6420 *Toll Free Fax:* 800-338-4550 *E-mail:* custserv@nbnbooks.com
Warehouse: National Book Network, 15200 NBN Way, Blue Ridge Summit, PA 17214 *Tel:* 717-

794-3800 *Toll Free Tel:* 800-462-6420 *Toll Free Fax:* 800-338-4550 *E-mail:* custserv@ nbnbooks.com

Brick Tower Press
Subsidiary of J T Colby & Co Inc
1230 Park Ave, New York, NY 10128
Tel: 212-427-7139 *Toll Free Tel:* 800-68-BRICK (682-7425) *Fax:* 212-860-8852
E-mail: bricktower@aol.com
Web Site: www.bricktowerpress.com
Key Personnel
Publr: John T Colby, Jr
Founded: 1993
ISBN Prefix(es): 1-883283; 0-9531737; 1-899694
Number of titles published annually: 5 Print
Total Titles: 45 Print
Foreign Office(s): POD Publishing, 24 Tavern Barn, PL 23 1EF Fowey, Cornwall, United Kingdom, Contact: Norman Stobart
Foreign Rep(s): Gazelle Book Services (Europe & UK); INT Press International (Australia & New Zealand)
Foreign Rights: Mia Amato (World)
Warehouse: Brick Tower Press Distribution, 211 Denton Ave, Garden City Park, NY 11040
Distribution Center: Brick Tower Press Distribution, 211 Denton Ave, Garden City Park, NY 11040

BrickHouse Books Inc
306 Suffolk Rd, Baltimore, MD 21218
Tel: 410-704-2869; 410-235-7690 *Fax:* 410-704-3999; 410-235-7690
Web Site: www.towson.edu; www. brickhousebooks.edu
Key Personnel
Ed & Dir: Clarinda Harriss *E-mail:* charriss@ towson.edu
Founded: 1970
Poetry; mixed genres by gay & lesbian (Stonewall only); artistic prose, experimental prose.
ISBN Prefix(es): 0-932616
Number of titles published annually: 4 Print
Total Titles: 61 Print
Imprints: Chesnut Hills Press; New Poets Series; Stonewall
Subsidiaries: Chesnut Hills Press; New Poets Series; Stonewall
Branch Office(s)
English Dept, Towson State Unversity, Towson, MD 21204 *Tel:* 410-704-2869
Distributed by Salmon Publishing
Distributor for Salmon Publishing
Foreign Rep(s): Salmon Publishing (Ireland)

Bridge Learning Systems Inc
351 Los Altos, American Canyon, CA 94589
Tel: 925-228-3177 *Toll Free Tel:* 800-487-9868 *Fax:* 925-372-6099
E-mail: bridge@blsinc.com
Web Site: www.blsinc.com
Key Personnel
Pres, Publr & Co-Owner: Alfred J Garrotto *Fax:* 925-370-6099 *E-mail:* alg@blsinc.com
VP & Co-Owner: James E Potter
Founded: 1991
Books & software.
ISBN Prefix(es): 1-885587; 0-9632069
Number of titles published annually: 3 Print
Total Titles: 15 Print

Bridge-Logos Publishers
17310 NW 32 Ave, Newberry, FL 32669
Mailing Address: PO Box 141630, Gainesville, FL 32614-1630
Tel: 352-472-7900 *Toll Free Tel:* 800-631-5802 *Fax:* 352-472-7908 *Toll Free Fax:* 800-935-6467
E-mail: info@bridgelogos.com
Web Site: www.bridgelogos.com

Key Personnel
Pres: Guy J Morrell *E-mail:* guymorrell@ bridgelogos.com
Dir, Sales & Mktg: Steve Becker *E-mail:* stevebecker@bridgelogos.com
Founded: 1967
Bibles, Christian classics, spirit-filled life, Christian books; parenting, family, Eschatological, evangelism, revival, children's bibles.
ISBN Prefix(es): 0-88270
Number of titles published annually: 25 Print
Total Titles: 216 Print
Imprints: Bridge; Haven; Logos; Open Scroll; Synergy
Distributed by Anchor Distributors; Appalachian Bible; Ingram; MPH Distributors; Riverside Distributors; SSS Distributors
Foreign Rep(s): Winfred Bluth (Germany)
Foreign Rights: W M Bluth (Germany)

§Bridge Publications Inc
4751 Fountain Ave, Los Angeles, CA 90029
SAN: 208-3884
Tel: 323-953-3320 *Toll Free Tel:* 800-722-1733; 800-843-7389 (CA) *Fax:* 323-953-3328
E-mail: info@bridgepub.com
Web Site: www.bridgepub.com
Key Personnel
Pres: Lis Astrupgaard
Exec VP: Ann Arnow *E-mail:* aarnow@ bridgepub.com
Gen Sales Mgr: Don Arnow
VP, Mktg: Victoria Gulierrez
VP, Pub Aff: Blake Silber
Natl Accts Sales Mgr: Barry Fine
Cust Serv: Dave Peters
Founded: 1981
Books on human potential development, self-improvement, education, management technology, children's literary works by L Ron Hubbard.
ISBN Prefix(es): 0-88404; 1-57318; 1-4031
Number of titles published annually: 5 Print; 3 Online; 7 E-Book; 1 Audio
Total Titles: 175 Print; 15 CD-ROM; 3 Online; 7 E-Book; 25 Audio
Imprints: BPI Records; Bridge Audio; Theta Books
Branch Office(s)
Bridge Publications, Canada, 696 Yonge St, Toronto, ON M4Y 2A7, Canada, Contact: Emily Tam *Tel:* 416-964-8927 *Fax:* 416-964-3201
Foreign Office(s): Era Dinamica Editores, SA de CV, Pablo U Cello No 16, Colonia de los Deportes CP 03710, Mexico, Contact: Irma Macias *Tel:* 525-598-4487 *Fax:* 525-598-4624
Distributed by Anchor Bay Entertainment; Cyber-Read; Libronauta
Foreign Rep(s): New Era Publications International (Asia, Copenhagen, Europe)
Foreign Rights: New Era Publications International
Advertising Agency: Gildersleeve, Inc, 3815 Shannon Rd, Los Angeles, CA, Contact: Jan Gildersleeve *Tel:* 323-663-8239 *Fax:* 323-661-8316
Shipping Address: Bridge Publication Distribution Center, 5999 Bandini Blvd, City of Commerce, CA 90040, Returns Contact: Luis Nieto *Tel:* 323-726-7416 *Fax:* 323-726-9323

Bridge Works Publishing
Imprint of Rowman & Littlefield Publishing Group
PO Box 1798, Bridgehampton, NY 11932-1798
Tel: 631-537-3418 *Fax:* 631-537-5092
E-mail: bap@hamptons.com
Key Personnel
Pres & Ed Dir: Barbara Phillips
VP: Warren Phillips
Intl Rts: Maja Nikolic *Tel:* 212-685-2400
Founded: 1992

Quality fiction & nonfiction, mostly hardcover.
ISBN Prefix(es): 1-882593
Number of titles published annually: 13 Print
Total Titles: 90 Print
Subsidiaries: Rowman & Littlefield Publishing Group
Distributed by National Book Network
Foreign Rights: Writers House Inc (Worldwide)
Distribution Center: National Book Network, 15200 NBN Way, Blue Ridge Summit, PA 17214 *Toll Free Tel:* 800-462-6420 *Toll Free Fax:* 800-338-4550

Briefings Publishing Group
Division of Wicks Business Information LLC Co
1101 King St, Suite 110, Alexandria, VA 22314
Tel: 703-548-3800 *Toll Free Tel:* 800-888-2086 *Fax:* 703-684-2136
E-mail: customerservice@briefings.com
Web Site: www.briefings.com
Key Personnel
Pres: Michelle Cox
IT Mgr: Sherry Mullins
Mktg Mgr: Dennis Fyerson
Founded: 1983
Marketing, public relations, business relations, communications & management; books & video cassettes.
Number of titles published annually: 9 Print
Total Titles: 26 Print

Bright Mountain Books Inc
206 Riva Ridge Dr, Fairview, NC 28730
SAN: 289-0674
Tel: 828-628-1768 *Toll Free Tel:* 800-437-3959 *Fax:* 828-628-1755
E-mail: booksbmb@charter.net
Key Personnel
Ed: Cynthia F Bright
Founded: 1983
Nonfiction, regional.
ISBN Prefix(es): 0-914875
Number of titles published annually: 4 Print
Total Titles: 32 Print
Imprints: Historical Images
Membership(s): Publishers Association of the South; Southeast Booksellers Association

Brighton Publications
PO Box 120706, New Brighton, MN 55112-0022
Tel: 651-636-2220 *Toll Free Tel:* 800-536-2665 *Fax:* 651-636-2220
Key Personnel
Pres: Sharon Stueve *E-mail:* sharon@partybooks. com
Founded: 1977
Workable information to help celebrate parties, games & etiquette.
ISBN Prefix(es): 0-918420
Number of titles published annually: 5 Print
Total Titles: 21 Print

§Brill Academic Publishers Inc
Subsidiary of Koninklijke Brill N V
112 Water St, Suite 601, Boston, MA 02109
Tel: 617-263-2323 *Toll Free Tel:* 800-962-4406 *Fax:* 617-263-2324
E-mail: cs@brillusa.com
Web Site: www.brill.nl
Key Personnel
Mktg Dir: Amy Hirschfeld
Founded: 1683
Publishes high level, specialized, academic titles.
ISBN Prefix(es): 90-04
Number of titles published annually: 200 Print
Total Titles: 2,700 Print
Orders to: Toll Free Tel: 800-337-9255
Returns: Brill Academic Publishers Inc Returns Dept, 22883 Quicksilver Dr, Dulles, VA 20166
Warehouse: PO Box 605, Herndon, VA 20172

Brilliance Audio
1704 Eaton Dr, Grand Haven, MI 49417

Tel: 616-846-5256 *Toll Free Tel:* 800-648-2312 (orders only) *Fax:* 616-846-0630
Web Site: www.brillianceaudio.com
Key Personnel
Pres & Publr: R Michael Snodgrass *Tel:* 616-846-5256 ext 701
VP & Assoc Publr: Eileen Hutton *Tel:* 616-846-5256 ext 703
Dir of Sales: Steve Woessner *Tel:* 616-846-5256 ext 705
Studio Mgr: Max Bloomquist *Tel:* 616-846-5256 ext 709
Founded: 1984
Country's leading independent audiobook publisher.
Number of titles published annually: 100 Audio
Total Titles: 600 Audio
Membership(s): Audio Publishers Association

Bristol Fashion Publications Inc
PO Box 4676, Harrisburg, PA 17111-0676
Tel: 772-559-1379 *Toll Free Tel:* 800-478-7147
Fax: 717-564-1711 *Toll Free Fax:* 800-543-9030
E-mail: orders@bfpbooks.com
Web Site: www.bfpbooks.com
Key Personnel
CEO & Publr: John P Kaufman
Founded: 1993
Publish marine books, railroad books & motorcycle books.
ISBN Prefix(es): 1-892216
Number of titles published annually: 20 Print
Total Titles: 60 Print; 60 CD-ROM
Distributed by Lightning Source

Bristol Publishing Enterprises
2714 McCone Ave, Hayward, CA 94545
Tel: 510-783-5472 *Toll Free Tel:* 800-346-4889
Fax: 510-783-5492
Web Site: www.bristolpublishing.com
Key Personnel
Pres: Aidan Wylde *E-mail:* aidan@bristolpublishing.com
Mktg & Sales Mgr: Shaadi Shams
Founded: 1988
Cookbooks, craftbooks.
ISBN Prefix(es): 0-911954; 1-55867
Number of titles published annually: 14 Print
Total Titles: 220 Print
Imprints: Bristol; Magnet Books; Nitty Gritty Cookbooks
Foreign Rep(s): Codasat Distribution, Canada (Canada); Gazelle Book Services Ltd (UK, Europe); Nationwide Book Distributors (New Zealand); Sunstate (Australia)

Broadman & Holman Publishers
127 Ninth Ave N, Nashville, TN 37234-0114
SAN: 201-937X
Tel: 615-251-2520 *Fax:* 615-251-5004
Web Site: www.broadmanholman.com
Key Personnel
Pres: Ken Stephens
Sr VP & Publr: David Shepherd
VP, Sales: John Thompson
Publicity Dir: Heather Hulse
Adv & Art Dir: Paul Mikos
Intl Rts: James Cook
Subs Rts: Sharon Gilbert
Founded: 1934
Religious trade publisher of nonfiction (Christian living, inspirational, devotional, contemporary issues); fiction; children's books; Bibles; Biblical reference; Biblical commentaries.
ISBN Prefix(es): 0-8054
Number of titles published annually: 95 Print
Total Titles: 505 Print; 5 Audio
Imprints: B & H Pub
Foreign Rights: Kathy Perry (outside the US)

Broadway Books, see Doubleday Broadway Publishing Group

§The Bronx County Historical Society
3309 Bainbridge Ave, Bronx, NY 10467
Tel: 718-881-8900 *Fax:* 718-881-4827
Web Site: www.bronxhistoricalsociety.org
Key Personnel
Exec Dir: Dr Gary Hermalyn
Archivist & Ed (The Bronx County Historical Society Journal): Dr Peter Derrick *E-mail:* pderrick@bronzhistoricalsociety.org
Founded: 1897
Bronx history.
ISBN Prefix(es): 0-941980
Number of titles published annually: 3 Print
Total Titles: 85 Print; 1 Online
Distributed by Crown; Grolier; New York University Press
Distributor for College of Mount St Vincent Press

Brooding Heron Press
101 Bookmonger Rd, Waldron Island, WA 98297
Tel: 360-202-6621
Key Personnel
Ed & Intl Rts: Sam Green
Publr: Sally Green
Founded: 1982
Poetry.
ISBN Prefix(es): 0-918116; 1-892275
Number of titles published annually: 2 Print
Total Titles: 35 Print

Brook Street Press LLC
200 Plantation Chase, Saint Simons Island, GA 31522
Mailing Address: PO Box 20284, Saint Simons Island, GA 31522
Tel: 912-638-0264 *Fax:* 912-638-0265
E-mail: info@brookstreetpress.com
Web Site: www.brookstreetpress.com
Key Personnel
Publr: James Pannell *E-mail:* jpannell@brookstreetpress.com
Founded: 2002
Independent publisher of literary fiction & creative nonfiction with a commitment to the patient development of quality writing with shared responsibilities for all parties involved in the publication process.
ISBN Prefix(es): 0-9724295
Number of titles published annually: 5 Print
Total Titles: 3 Print
Distributed by Midpoint Trade Books
Membership(s): Council of Literary Magazines & Presses; Publishers Marketing Association; Small Press Center

§Paul H Brookes Publishing Co
PO Box 10624, Baltimore, MD 21285-0624
SAN: 212-730X
Tel: 410-337-9580 *Toll Free Tel:* 800-638-3775
Fax: 410-337-8539
E-mail: custserv@brookespublishing.com
Web Site: www.brookespublishing.com
Key Personnel
Pres: Paul H Brookes
VP: Melissa A Behm
Mktg Dir: Jessica Reighard
Sales & Textbook Mgr: Michelle L Lauderbaugh
Direct Mail Mgr: Erin M Cahill
Prodn Mgr: Lisa P Rapisarda
IT Mgr: Pat A Perkins
Inventory Mgr: Roslyn A Udris
Publicity Mgr: Anastasia Worcester
Dist Sales Mgr: Jeff Brookes
Exhibits Mgr: Clary Creighton
Digital Book Prodn Supvr: Suzanne Allridge
Fulfillment Dir: Judith A Droege
Cust Care Mgr: Sandy Jensen
Edit Dir: Elaine M Niefeld
Acq Ed: Jessica G Allan; Rebecca Lazo; Heather H Shrestha
Rts Mgr: Lisa M Yurwit
Cont: Howard P Lobl
HR Mgr: Erika Q Kinney
Webmaster: Cathy L Costa
Educ Sales Mgr: Tracy Gray
Publg Asst: Susannah Ray *E-mail:* sray@brookespublishing.com
Founded: 1978
Hardcover, paperback & wire-bound scholarly books in education, psychology & medicine, including special education, early intervention, developmental disabilities, learning disabilities, therapeutic services, early childhood, communication & language, literacy, behavior & mental health.
ISBN Prefix(es): 0-933716; 1-55766
Number of titles published annually: 45 Print; 5 CD-ROM; 1 Online
Total Titles: 330 Print; 10 CD-ROM; 1 Online
Subsidiaries: Health Professions Press
Distributed by Elsevier Australia (New Zealand & Australia); The Eurospan Group (Europe & UK); Unifacmanu Trading Co Ltd (Taiwan)
Foreign Rep(s): STM Publishers Services (China, Hong Kong, Korea, Malaysia, Myanmar, Philippines, Singapore, Thailand, Vietnam)
Warehouse: The Maple Press Distribution Center, 60 Grumbacher Rd, I-83 Industrial Park, PO Box 15100, York, PA 17402
Membership(s): Publishers Marketing Association; Small Publishers Association of North America
See separate listing for:
Health Professions Press

§Brookhaven Press
PO Box 2287, La Crosse, WI 54602-2287
Tel: 608-781-0850 *Toll Free Tel:* 800-236-0850
Fax: 608-781-3883
E-mail: brookhaven@nmt.com
Web Site: www.brookhavenpress.com
Scan & reprint out-of-print county histories & genealogy books.
ISBN Prefix(es): 1-58103; 1-4035
Number of titles published annually: 300 Print

§The Brookings Institution Press
Division of Brookings Institution
1775 Massachusetts Ave NW, Washington, DC 20036-2188
SAN: 201-9396
Tel: 202-797-6000 *Toll Free Tel:* 800-275-1447
Fax: 202-797-6195
E-mail: bibooks@brook.edu
Web Site: www.brookings.edu *Cable:* BROOKINST
Key Personnel
Dir & Intl Rts Contact: Robert L Faherty
Mktg Dir: John Sherer
Rts & Perms: Puja Telikicherla
Man Ed: Janet Walker
Acq Ed: Christopher Kelaher
Ed: Eileen Hughes; Tanjam Jacobson
Lib Mgr: Eric Eisinger
Order Fulfillment Mgr: Terrence Melvin
Program & Web Admin: Renuka Deonarain *Tel:* 202-797-6423 *E-mail:* rdeonarain@brookings.edu
Founded: 1916
Economics, foreign policy & government affairs.
ISBN Prefix(es): 0-8157
Number of titles published annually: 60 Print
Total Titles: 869 Print; 1 CD-ROM; 81 Online
Distributor for Aspen Institute; Bertelsmann Foundation Publishers; Carnegie Endowment for International Peace; Centre for Economic Policy Research; The Century Foundation; Council on Foreign Relations; Economica; Hudson Institute; International Labor Offices; Japan Center for International Exchange; OECD; Royal Institute of International Affairs;

The Trilateral Commission; United Nations University Press; Washington Institute for Near East Policy
Foreign Rep(s): Julio E Emod (South America); Brett Haydon (Australia & New Zealand); Fred Hermans (Benelux, Denmark, Finland, France, Norway, Sweden); Chris Humphrys (Portugal & Spain); Mediamatics (India, Pakistan); Systematics Studies Ltd (Trinadad & Tobago); Taylor & Francis Asia Pacific (Brunei, China & Hong Kong, Korea & Taiwan, Philippines, Singapore & Malaysia); UBC Press, c/o Uni Presses (Canada); UNIREPS (Australia & New Zealand); United Publishing Services Ltd (Japan); University Press Marketing (Greece & Cyprus, Israel, Malta, UK & Ireland); UWE Luedemann (Austria, Germany, Italy, Switzerland)
Foreign Rights: Agency Literaria Internazionale (Italy); Tuttle-Mori Agency (Japan)
Membership(s): AAP; American Association of University Presses

Brookline Books
PO Box 1209, Brookline, MA 02445
Toll Free Tel: 800-666-2665; 800-345-6665 (orders) *Fax:* 617-734-6772
Web Site: www.brooklinebooks.com
Key Personnel
Ed-in-Chief: Milt Budoff *E-mail:* milt@brooklinebooks.com
Founded: 1985
Education, special needs, readings, general trade.
ISBN Prefix(es): 0-914797; 1-57129
Number of titles published annually: 10 Print
Total Titles: 125 Print
Imprints: Lumen
Distributed by Pathway Book Service

Brooklyn Botanic Garden
1000 Washington Ave, Brooklyn, NY 11225-1099
Tel: 718-623-7200 *Toll Free Tel:* 800-367-9692 (orders) *Fax:* 718-622-7839 *Toll Free Fax:* 800-542-7567 (orders)
E-mail: publications@bbg.org
Web Site: www.bbg.org
Key Personnel
Ed: Janet Marinelli
Mktg Dir: Marie Leahy
Founded: 1945
Publishes practical handbooks for gardeners in every region. The titles in the Brooklyn Botanic Garden All-Region Guides Series (formerly 21st Century Gardening Series) are lavishly illustrated & provides a guide to create natural gardens that are both ecologically sensible & beautiful. BBG also publishes a quarterly newsletter.
ISBN Prefix(es): 0-945352
Number of titles published annually: 6 Print
Imprints: Brooklyn Botanic Garden All-Region Guides
Sales Office(s): Sterling Publishing Co, CPO, 387 Park Ave S, New York, NY 10016-8810
Distributed by Sterling Publishing Co Inc
Billing Address: Sterling Publishing Co Inc, PO Box 5078, New York, NY 10087
Warehouse: Sterling Warehouse, 40 Saw Mill Pond Rd, Edison, NJ 08817
Distribution Center: Sterling Publishing Co Inc, 40 Saw Mill Pond Rd, Edison, NJ 08817

Brooks/Cole, see Wadsworth Publishing

Brown Barn Books
Division of Pictures of Record Inc
119 Kettle Creek Rd, Weston, CT 06883
Tel: 203-227-3387 *Toll Free Tel:* 888-227-3308
Fax: 203-222-9673
E-mail: editorial@brownbarnbooks.com
Web Site: www.brownbarnbooks.com

Key Personnel
Pres: Nancy Hammerslough
Founded: 2003
Publisher of young-adult fiction.
ISBN Prefix(es): 0-9746481
Number of titles published annually: 10 Print
Total Titles: 5 Print
Membership(s): NEBA; Publishers Marketing Association; Small Publishers Association of North America

Karen Brown's Guides Inc
PO Box 70, San Mateo, CA 94401-0070
Tel: 650-342-9117 *Fax:* 650-342-9153
E-mail: karen@karenbrown.com
Web Site: www.karenbrown.com
Key Personnel
Owner: Clare Brown; June Brown; Karen A Brown
Founded: 1977
General.
ISBN Prefix(es): 0-930328
Number of titles published annually: 17 Print
Total Titles: 15 Print
Distributed by Random House
Foreign Rep(s): Random House (Australia & New Zealand, Europe)

BrownTrout Publishers Inc
PO Box 280070, San Francisco, CA 94128-0070
SAN: 662-6505
Tel: 650-340-9800 *Toll Free Tel:* 800-777-7812
Fax: 310-316-1138
E-mail: sales@browntrout.com
Web Site: www.browntrout.com
Key Personnel
Pres: Marc Brown
VP, Sales: Mike Brown
VP, Prodn: Wendover Brown
Dir, Books Div: Robert Hutchinson
Founded: 1994
General & regional interest hardcover & trade paperback books focusing on nonfiction in the areas of landscape photography, natural history, dog breeds, poetry, adult & juvenile fiction, self-help, New Age & spirituality.
ISBN Prefix(es): 1-56313; 0-7631
Number of titles published annually: 6 Print
Total Titles: 31 Print
Foreign Rep(s): BrownTrout Publishers Ltd (UK); BrownTrout Publishers Pty Ltd (Australia, New Zealand); Editorial Salmotruti (Mexico); Floyds GmbH (Germany); Paris Southern Lights (Canada)
Warehouse: 4977 Allison Pkwy, Vacaville, CA 95688

Bruccoli Clark Layman Inc
2006 Sumter St, Columbia, SC 29201
SAN: 209-3987
Tel: 803-771-4642 *Fax:* 803-799-6953
Key Personnel
Pres: Matthew J Bruccoli
Exec VP & ISBN Contact: Richard Layman
Founded: 1962
Trade books & literary reference books.
ISBN Prefix(es): 0-89723
Number of titles published annually: 20 Print
Total Titles: 45 Print

Brunner-Routledge
Member of Taylor & Francis Group
270 Madison Ave, New York, NY 10016
SAN: 213-196X
Tel: 212-216-7800 *Toll Free Tel:* 800-634-7064 (orders); 800-797-3803 *Fax:* 212-643-1430
Key Personnel
Mktg Dir: Andrea Ciecierski
Mktg Mgr: Brian Roach
Founded: 1945
Professional books on psychoanalysis & psychiatry, psychology, psychotherapy, child devel-

opment, marriage & family therapy, parenting books, social work & grief counseling.
ISBN Prefix(es): 0-87630; 0-945354; 1-58391
Number of titles published annually: 100 Print
Total Titles: 1,000 Print

Brunswick Publishing Corp
1386 Lawrenceville Plank Rd, Lawrenceville, VA 23868
Tel: 434-848-3865 *Fax:* 434-848-0607
E-mail: brunswickbooks@earthlink.net
Web Site: www.brunswickbooks.com
Key Personnel
Publr: Marianne Salzmann
Autobiographies, poetry, general.
ISBN Prefix(es): 1-55618; 0-931494
Number of titles published annually: 7 Print
Total Titles: 289 Print

Bucknell University Press
Affiliate of Associated University Presses
c/o Associated University Presses, 2010 Eastpark Blvd, Cranbury, NJ 08512
Tel: 609-655-4770 *Fax:* 609-655-8366
E-mail: aup440@aol.com
Key Personnel
Dir: Greg Clingham
Contact: Julien Yoseloff
Founded: 1969
ISBN Prefix(es): 0-8387
Number of titles published annually: 35 Print
Total Titles: 500 Print
Distributed by Associated University Presses
Foreign Rep(s): Eurospan (Europe & UK); Scholarly Book Services (Canada); United Publishers Services (Japan)

BuilderBooks.com
Division of National Association of Home Builders
1201 15 St NW, Washington, DC 20005-2800
SAN: 207-7035
Tel: 202-822-0200; 202-266-8200
Toll Free Tel: 800-223-2665 (orders); 800-368-5242 ext 8368 (editorial) *Fax:* 202-266-8096 (edit); 202-266-5889 (edit)
Web Site: www.builderbooks.com
Key Personnel
Man Ed: Aaron White
Sr Acq Ed: Doris Tennyson *Tel:* 202-266-8638
Asst Staff VP: Lakisha Campbell
Man Dir: Larry Fox
Man Dir, Mktg: Patricia Potts
Affiliate & E-Mktg Mgr: Jacqueline Barnes
Founded: 1943
Publish books about home construction & design, remodeling, land development, housing & construction management, sales & marketing of new homes, safety & seniors housing.
ISBN Prefix(es): 0-86718
Number of titles published annually: 5 Print
Total Titles: 150 Print
Distributor for National Association of Home Builders

Building News
Division of B N I Publications Inc
502 Maple Ave W, Vienna, VA 22180
Tel: 703-319-0498 *Toll Free Tel:* 888-264-2665
Fax: 703-319-9158
E-mail: sales@bnibooks.com
Web Site: www.bnibooks.com
Key Personnel
Regl Mgr: Richard Martinez
Founded: 1946
Construction & engineering.
ISBN Prefix(es): 1-55701
Number of titles published annually: 30 Print
Total Titles: 50 Print
Distributed by Macmillan
Warehouse: 1612 S Clementine St, Anaheim, CA 92802

Bulfinch Press
Subsidiary of Time Warner Book Group
1271 Avenue of the Americas, New York, NY
10020
Tel: 212-522-8700 *Toll Free Tel:* 800-759-0190
Fax: 212-467-2886
Web Site: www.twbookmark.com
Key Personnel
VP & Publr: Jill Cohen
Assoc Publr: Karen Murgolo
Sr VP, Adv & Promo: Martha Otis
VP & Spec Mkts: Jean Griffin
Dir, Publicity: Matthew Ballast
Exec Ed: Michael Sand
Publishers of art, photography, architecture &
interior design, lifestyle, cooking, general illus-
trated books. Also specializes in Ansel Adams
books, calendars & posters.
ISBN Prefix(es): 0-8212
Number of titles published annually: 50 Print
Total Titles: 400 Print
Shipping Address: Time Warner Book Group
Distribution Center, 121 N Enterprise Blvd,
Lebanon, IN 46052 *Tel:* 765-483-9900
Fax: 765-483-0706

Bull Publishing Co
PO Box 1377, Boulder, CO 80306-1377
SAN: 208-5712
Tel: 303-545-6350 *Toll Free Tel:* 800-676-2855
Fax: 303-545-6354
E-mail: bullpublishing@msn.com
Web Site: www.bullpub.com
Key Personnel
Pres & Publr: James Bull
Founded: 1974
Self-care, nutrition & health care, physical fitness,
weight loss, mental health, parenting & child
care, psychology, self-help.
ISBN Prefix(es): 0-915950; 0-923521
Number of titles published annually: 8 Print
Total Titles: 70 Print; 2 Audio
Foreign Rep(s): Publishers Group West (Canada)
Warehouse: A & A Quality Shipping Services,
3623 Munster, Unit B, Hayward, CA 94545
Distribution Center: Publishers Group West,
1700 Fourth St, Berkeley, CA 94710 *Toll Free
Tel:* 800-788-3123

Burchell Publishing, see Ballinger Publishing

§The Bureau For At-Risk Youth
Subsidiary of The Guidance Channel
135 Dupont St, Plainview, NY 11803-0760
Mailing Address: PO Box 9120, Plainview, NY
11803-9020
Tel: 516-349-5520 *Fax:* 516-349-5521
E-mail: info@at-risk.com
Web Site: www.at-risk.com
Key Personnel
Owner & CEO: Edward W Werz
Pres: Kim Lipson
Exec VP: Janice Werz
VP & PR: Sally Germain *Tel:* 516-487-2532 ext
210
Founded: 1988
Educational materials on at-risk children's issues
for educators, counselors, parents & children.
ISBN Prefix(es): 1-56688
Number of titles published annually: 10 Print; 15
CD-ROM
Total Titles: 200 Print; 45 CD-ROM

§Bureau of Economic Geology, University of Texas at Austin
Division of University of Texas at Austin
10100 Burnet Rd, Bldg 130, Austin, TX 78750
Mailing Address: University Sta, Box X, Austin,
TX 78713-8924
Tel: 512-471-7144 *Toll Free Tel:* 888-839-4365
Fax: 512-471-0140 *Toll Free Fax:* 888-839-
6277

E-mail: pubsales@beg.utexas.edu
Web Site: www.beg.utexas.edu
Key Personnel
Ed-in-Chief: Susann Doenges *Tel:* 512-471-0217
E-mail: susie.doenges@beg.utexas.edu
Mgr, Pubn Sales: Amanda Masterson
E-mail: amanda.masterson@beg.utexas.edu
Founded: 1909
Scientific & technical books in geosciences.
Number of titles published annually: 6 Print; 1
CD-ROM
Total Titles: 1,500 Print; 4 CD-ROM
Distributor for Gulf Coast Association of Geolog-
ical Societies
Advertising Agency: Gulf Coast Section-SEPM

Burford Books
32 Morris Ave, Springfield, NJ 07081
Tel: 973-258-0960 *Fax:* 973-258-0113
E-mail: info@burfordbooks.com
Web Site: www.burfordbooks.com
Key Personnel
Pres: Peter Burford
Founded: 1997
Publisher of books on the outdoors: golf, sports,
fitness, nature, travel, fishing, military.
ISBN Prefix(es): 1-58080
Number of titles published annually: 15 Print
Total Titles: 97 Print
Distributed by National Book Network
Foreign Rep(s): Gazelle Book Services Ltd (UK)
Foreign Rights: Tuttle Mori Agency (Japan)

§Burrelle's Information Services
75 E Northfield Rd, Livingston, NJ 07039
Tel: 973-992-6600 *Toll Free Tel:* 800-631-1160
Fax: 973-992-7675 *Toll Free Fax:* 800-898-
6677
E-mail: directory@burrelles.com; directorysales@
burrelles.com
Web Site: www.burrellesluce.com
Key Personnel
Pres & CEO: Robert Waggoner
E-mail: rwaggoner@burrelles.com
Exec VP: Art Wynn
Founded: 1888
Directories of media outlets used to help PR pro-
fessionals place press releases in the media.
Number of titles published annually: 5 Print
Total Titles: 15 Print; 3 CD-ROM; 1 Online; 1 E-
Book
Online services available through FirstSearch.
Advertising Agency: K&H Advertising

§Business & Legal Reports Inc
141 Mill Rock Rd, Old Saybrook, CT 06475-
6001
Tel: 860-510-0100 *Toll Free Tel:* 800-727-5257
Fax: 860-510-7223
E-mail: blrblr@aol.com
Web Site: www.blr.com
Key Personnel
Pres: Robert L Brady *E-mail:* rbrady@blr.com
Exec VP: John F Brady *E-mail:* jbrady@blr.com
VP, Mktg: Kathleen E Long *Tel:* 860-510-0100
ext 2101 *E-mail:* klong@blr.com
Founded: 1977
Specialize in business newsletters, books, book-
lets, films & CD-ROM. Specialize in safety,
human resource & environmental training &
compliance.
Total Titles: 380 Print; 113 CD-ROM; 4 Online;
4 E-Book
Membership(s): NEPA

Business Books Network, see Book Network
International Inc

§Business Research Services Inc
4701 Sangamore Rd, Suite S155, Bethesda, MD
20816

SAN: 691-8522
Tel: 301-229-5561 *Toll Free Tel:* 800-845-8420
Fax: 301-229-6133
E-mail: brspubs@sba8a.com
Web Site: www.sba8a.com; wwww.setasidealert.
com
Key Personnel
Pres & Publr: Thomas D Johnson
Founded: 1984
Directories of minority & women's businesses
& marketing research firms; small business
newsletters.
ISBN Prefix(es): 0-933527
Number of titles published annually: 4 Print; 4
CD-ROM; 1 Online
Total Titles: 7 Print; 4 CD-ROM; 1 Online
Distributed by Gale Research Inc
Distributor for PanOptic; Riley & Johnson
Membership(s): National Directory Publishing
Association

Business/Technology Books (B/T Books)
PO Box 574, Orinda, CA 94563-0526
Tel: 925-299-1829 *Fax:* 925-299-0668
E-mail: btbooks@evinfo.com
Web Site: www.evinfo.com
Key Personnel
Pres: Justin A Bereny
Founded: 1977
Electric vehicles, hybrid vehicles, fuel cells, fly-
wheels, ultracapacitors, hydrogen as a fuel.
ISBN Prefix(es): 0-89934; 0-930978
Number of titles published annually: 12 Print
Total Titles: 90 Print
Imprints: Business/Technology Information Ser-
vices (B/T Info); Electric Vehicle Information
Services (EVINFO); Solar Energy Information
Services (SEIS)

Butte Publications Inc
PO Box 1328, Hillsboro, OR 97123-1328
SAN: 299-8866
Tel: 503-648-9791 *Toll Free Tel:* 866-312-8883
Fax: 503-693-9526
E-mail: service@buttepublications.com
Web Site: www.buttepublications.com
Key Personnel
Pres: Matthew H Brink *E-mail:* mbrink@
buttepublications.com
Founded: 1992
Resources serving the deaf community.
ISBN Prefix(es): 1-884362
Number of titles published annually: 5 Print
Total Titles: 43 Print; 1 CD-ROM
Distributor for Boys Town (selected titles); Gal-
laudet University Press (selected titles); Infant
Hearing Resources (selected titles); Pro Ed (se-
lected titles)
Shipping Address: 149 SE Third, Suite 450, Hills-
boro, OR 97123
Membership(s): AAP

Butternut & Blue
3411 Northwind Rd, Baltimore, MD 21234
Tel: 410-256-9220 *Fax:* 410-256-8423
E-mail: butternutandblue@hotmail.com
Key Personnel
Partner: James L McLean
Founded: 1983
Civil War books & reprints of old titles; also new
titles.
ISBN Prefix(es): 0-935523
Number of titles published annually: 4 Print
Total Titles: 35 Print

By Design Press, see Quite Specific Media
Group Ltd

C A P Publishing & Literary Co LLC
17471 Jefferson Davis Hwy, Dumfries, VA 22026
Tel: 703-441-3500 *Fax:* 301-499-8844
Key Personnel
CEO: Neda Hobbs

Founded: 1989
ISBN Prefix(es): 1-878898
Number of titles published annually: 10 Print; 30 Audio
Total Titles: 20 Print; 30 Audio
Imprints: CAP
Returns: 12138 Central Ave, Suite 152, Mitchelville, MD 20721
Shipping Address: efulfillment Service
Warehouse: efulfillment Service
Distribution Center: Ingram
Membership(s): Small Publishers Association of North America

§C & M Online Media Inc
3905 Meadow Field Lane, Raleigh, NC 27606
Tel: 919-233-8164 *Fax:* 919-233-8578
E-mail: cm@cmonline.com
Web Site: www.cmonline.com
Key Personnel
Pres & Publr: Nancy McAllister *E-mail:* nancy@cmonline.com
VP & Intl Rts: David McAllister *E-mail:* david@cmonline.com
Founded: 1994
Publish books online in electronic editions. Also publish a selection of trade paperbacks.
ISBN Prefix(es): 1-886420; 0-917990
Number of titles published annually: 4 Print; 12 Online; 12 E-Book; 4 Audio
Total Titles: 10 Print; 70 Online; 70 E-Book; 4 Audio
Imprints: Boson Books; Boson Romances; The New South Company
See separate listing for:
Boson Books

C & T Publishing Inc
1651 Challenge Dr, Concord, CA 94520
Tel: 925-677-0377 *Toll Free Tel:* 800-284-1114
Fax: 925-677-0373
E-mail: ctinfo@ctpub.com
Web Site: www.ctpub.com
Key Personnel
CEO: Todd Hensley
Publr: Amy Marson
CFO: Tony Hensley
Edit Dir: Gailen Runge
Intl Rts Contact: John Pilcher *E-mail:* johnp@ctpub.com
Dir, Sales & Mktg: Janet Z Levin *Tel:* 925-677-0377 ext 214 *E-mail:* janetl@ctpub.com
Dir, Prodn: Dave Nash
Founded: 1983
Specialize in fiber & paper craft books.
ISBN Prefix(es): 0-914881; 1-57120
Number of titles published annually: 40 Print; 2 CD-ROM
Total Titles: 265 Print; 5 CD-ROM; 5 Audio
Distributed by Watson-Guptill Publications
Distributor for Rowan UK

C P A Book Publisher
9205 SE Clackamas Rd, Clackamas, OR 97015
Mailing Address: PO Box 596, Boring, OR 97009
Tel: 503-668-4977 *Fax:* 503-668-8614
E-mail: cpabooks@hotmail.com
Key Personnel
Dir: Richard Flowers
Mgr: Jeff Weakley
Founded: 1982
ISBN Prefix(es): 0-944379; 0-9600358
Number of titles published annually: 25 Print
Total Titles: 500 Print

Cache River Press
Imprint of Quick Publishing
1610 Long Leaf Circle, St Louis, MO 63146
Tel: 314-432-3435 *Toll Free Tel:* 888-PUBLISH (782-5474) *Fax:* 314-993-4485
Web Site: www.cacheriverpress.com

Founded: 1994
ISBN Prefix(es): 1-882349; 0-962742; 1-889899
Number of titles published annually: 3 Print
Total Titles: 22 Print; 2 CD-ROM

Caddo Gap Press
3145 Geary Blvd, PMB 275, San Francisco, CA 94118
Tel: 415-666-3012 *Fax:* 415-666-3552
E-mail: caddogap@aol.com
Web Site: www.caddogap.com
Key Personnel
Publr & Intl Rts: Alan H Jones
Founded: 1989
Social foundations of education & teacher education & multicultural education.
ISBN Prefix(es): 0-9625945; 1-880192
Number of titles published annually: 3 Print
Total Titles: 30 Print

Cadence Jazz Books
Division of Cadnor Ltd
Cadence Bldg, Redwood, NY 13679
Tel: 315-287-2852 *Fax:* 315-287-2860
E-mail: cjb@cadencebuilding.com; cadence@cadencebuilding.com
Web Site: www.cadencebuilding.com
Key Personnel
Pres & Intl Rts: Robert D Rusch
Lib Sales Dir: M E Slim
Founded: 1992
Jazz, improvised music & biographies of jazz players.
ISBN Prefix(es): 1-881993
Number of titles published annually: 4 Print
Total Titles: 35 Print
Distributed by North Country Distributors

Cadmus Editions
PO Box 126, Belvedere-Tiburon, CA 94920-0126
SAN: 212-887X
Tel: 707-762-0510
Web Site: www.cadmus-editions.com
Key Personnel
Dir & Ed: Jeffrey Miller *E-mail:* jeffcadmus@aol.com
Founded: 1979
Fine editions & trade paperbacks; fiction, literature, poetry.
ISBN Prefix(es): 0-932274
Number of titles published annually: 3 Print
Total Titles: 29 Print; 1 Audio
Foreign Rep(s): Artellus Ltd (UK, Western Europe)
Foreign Rights: Leslie Gardner
Distribution Center: Publishers Group West

Caissa Editions
Affiliate of Dale A Brandreth Books
PO Box 151, Yorklyn, DE 19736-0151
Tel: 302-239-4608
Key Personnel
Owner & Pres: Dale Brandreth
E-mail: dbrandreth3@comcast.net
Founded: 1971
Publisher of books that are primarily on chess.
ISBN Prefix(es): 0-939433
Number of titles published annually: 3 Print
Total Titles: 20 Print

Calculator Training Center
94 Buckingham Rd, New Milford, CT 06776
Tel: 860-355-8255
E-mail: c-t-c@att.net
Key Personnel
Pres: T Patrick Burke
Founded: 1998
Specialize in remedial algebra texts for colleges.
ISBN Prefix(es): 0-9657238
Number of titles published annually: 3 Print

Total Titles: 3 Print
Membership(s): National Association for Developmental Education

California Journal Press
Division of Information for Public Affairs Inc
2101 "K" St, Sacramento, CA 95816-4920
Tel: 916-444-2840 *Fax:* 916-446-5369
E-mail: edit@statenet.com
Key Personnel
Publr: A G Block
Ed: David Lesher
Founded: 1970
Material covering government operations in California & the other states.
ISBN Prefix(es): 0-930302
Number of titles published annually: 3 Print
Total Titles: 80 Print
Divisions: State Net

Callaway Editions Inc
54 Seventh Ave S, New York, NY 10014
Tel: 212-929-5212 *Fax:* 212-929-8087
Web Site: www.callaway.com
Key Personnel
Pres & Ed-in-Chief: Nicholas D Callaway
Man Ed & Dir, Prodn: George Gould
E-mail: george_gould@callaway.com
Founded: 1980
Producer & publisher of books & multimedia products with a focus on illustrated children's books. Award-winning titles are co-published with major trade houses & distributed in North America & as foreign language editions worldwide.
ISBN Prefix(es): 0-935112
Number of titles published annually: 5 Print
Total Titles: 25 Print
Imprints: BoundSound™; Miss Spider™

Calyx Books
Division of Calyx Inc
PO Box B, Corvallis, OR 97339-0539
Tel: 541-753-9384 *Fax:* 541-753-0515
E-mail: calyx@proaxis.com
Web Site: www.proaxis.com/~calyx
Key Personnel
Dir & Intl Rts: Margarita Donnelly
Sr Ed: Beverly McFarland
Founded: 1976
Publisher of fine literature by women.
ISBN Prefix(es): 0-934971
Number of titles published annually: 4 Print
Total Titles: 42 Print
Imprints: Calyx (a journal of art & literature by women)
Foreign Rights: Elizabeth Wales (Worldwide)

§Cambridge Educational
Division of Films for the Humanities & Sciences
2572 Brunswick Ave, Lawrenceville, NJ 08648-4128
Toll Free Tel: 800-468-4227 *Toll Free Fax:* 800-329-6687
E-mail: custserve@cambridgeeducational.com
Web Site: www.cambridgeeducational.com
Key Personnel
Pres & CEO: Betsy Sherer
VP & Chief Content Officer: Frank Batavick
VP, Busn Devt: Doug Humphrey
Founded: 1980
Produce & distribute educational materials & CD-ROMs. Specialize in crime & legal studies, family & consumer science, health & guidance, social studies & vocational/technical education & career education.
ISBN Prefix(es): 0-927368; 1-56450
Number of titles published annually: 5 Print; 20 CD-ROM
Total Titles: 35 Print; 150 CD-ROM
Foreign Rep(s): Doug Humphrey

§Cambridge University Press
Division of Department of Cambridge University
40 W 20 St, New York, NY 10011-4211
SAN: 200-206X
Tel: 212-924-3900 *Toll Free Tel:* 800-899-5222
   Fax: 212-691-3239
Web Site: www.cambridge.org
Key Personnel
Dir: Richard Ziemacki *Tel:* 212-337-5052
   E-mail: rziemacki@cup.org
Edit Dir, Academic Books: Frank Smith
Busn Devt: Nicholas Reckert
Publg Dir, STM: Kirk Jensen
Assoc Publg Dir, ESL/EFL: Mary Vaughn
Assoc Publg Dir, ESL/EFL: Louisa Hellegers
Press Dist Dir: Ian R Bradie
Dir, Sales & Mktg, Academic Books: Liza Mur-
   phy
Personnel Dir: Carol New
Prodn Dir: Pauline Ireland
Group Dir, ESL/EFL: Richard Milstein
Promo Mgr: Edward Ryan
Academic Mktg Mgr: Catherine Friedl
Mktg Mgr, ESL & Educ: Carine Mitchell
Journal Mgr: Ed Barnas
Journal Mkt Mgr: Susan Soule
Rts & Perms Mgr: Marc Anderson
Cust Serv Mgr & Order Fulfillment Mgr: Lynda
   Di Caprio
MIS Mgr: George Ianello
Inventory Control Mgr: Holly Verrill
Accts Receivable Mgr: Randy Zeitlin
Electronic Prod Devt Mgr: Anna Curry
Electronic Info Mkt Mgr: Jae S Hong
Journals Ed: Mark Zadrozny
Sr Ed, Arts & Classics: Beatrice Rehl
Sr Ed, Economics: Scott Parris
Sr Ed, Engineering: Peter Gordon
Sr Ed, Math Scis: Roger Astley
Sr Ed, Social Sciences: Lewis Bateman
Publg Mgr, ESL/EFL: Deborah Goldblatt
Ed, Biological Sci: Katrina Halliday
Ed, Psychology & Cognitive Sci: Philip G Laugh-
   lin
Ed, Math & Computer Sci: Lauren Cowles
Ed, Social Sci: Edward Parsons
Founded: 1584
Scholarly & trade books, college textbooks &
   journals.
ISBN Prefix(es): 0-521
Number of titles published annually: 2,400 Print
Total Titles: 27,000 Print; 160 Online
Foreign Office(s): The Edinburgh Bldg, Shaftes-
   bury Rd, Cambridge CB2 2RU, United King-
   dom
Warehouse: 100 Brook Hill Dr, West Nyack,
   NY 10994-2133 *Toll Free Tel:* 800-872-7423
   Fax: 845-353-4141
Membership(s): AAP; Association of American
   University Presses; BISG

Cameron & Co
680 Eighth St, Suite 205, San Francisco, CA
   94103
Tel: 415-558-8455 *Toll Free Tel:* 800-779-5582
   Fax: 415-558-8657
Web Site: www.abovebooks.com
Key Personnel
Pres: Anthony Cameron
CEO & Intl Rts: Robert Cameron
Mgr & Corp Sec: Linda Henry
Founded: 1965
Books of aerial photography.
ISBN Prefix(es): 0-918684
Number of titles published annually: 55 Print
Total Titles: 60 Print
Foreign Rep(s): Josabeth Drucker (France);
   Vollmer Communication (Austria, Germany,
   Switzerland)

Camex Books Inc
535 Fifth Ave, New York, NY 10017
Tel: 212-682-8400 *Fax:* 212-808-4669

Key Personnel
Pres: Victor Benedetto
Spec Sales: Jay Columbus
Creative Dir: Alexander Benedetto
Children's books, art, how-to, cookbooks & pho-
   tography.
ISBN Prefix(es): 0-929793
Number of titles published annually: 5 Print
Total Titles: 25 Print

Camino Books Inc
PO Box 59026, Philadelphia, PA 19102-9026
Tel: 215-413-1917 *Fax:* 215-413-3255
E-mail: camino@caminobooks.com
Web Site: www.caminobooks.com
Key Personnel
Pres & Publr: Edward Jutkowitz
Founded: 1987
Regional trade books for the Mid-Atlantic states.
ISBN Prefix(es): 0-940159
Number of titles published annually: 10 Print
Total Titles: 70 Print
Warehouse: Whitehurst & Clark Book Fulfillment
   Inc, 1200 County Rd, Rte 523, Flemington, NJ
   08822 *Tel:* 908-782-2323

Camino E E & Book Co
c/o Jan Linzy, PO Box 6400, Incline Village, NV
   89450
Tel: 530-546-7053 *Fax:* 530-546-7053
E-mail: info@camino-books.com
Web Site: www.camino-books.com
Key Personnel
Owner & Publr: Jan Linzy
Founded: 1985
Dog breed reference books.
ISBN Prefix(es): 0-940808; 1-55893
Number of titles published annually: 24 Print
Total Titles: 227 Print

Candlewick Press
Subsidiary of Walker Books Ltd (London)
2067 Massachusetts Ave, Cambridge, MA 02140
Tel: 617-661-3330 *Fax:* 617-661-0565
E-mail: bigbear@candlewick.com
Web Site: www.candlewick.com
Key Personnel
Pres & Publr: Karen Lotz
Assoc Publr & Edit Dir: Liz Bicknell *Tel:* 617-
   588-4420 *E-mail:* liz.bicknell@candlewick.com
Dir, School & Lib Sales: Elise Supovitz
Cont: Becky S Hemperly
Assoc Dir, Trade Mktg: Lorraine Tauches
Founded: 1991
Children's books.
ISBN Prefix(es): 1-56402; 0-7636
Number of titles published annually: 200 Print
Total Titles: 1,150 Print
Distributed by Penguin Group (USA) Inc
Foreign Rights: Walker Books London
Distribution Center: Penguin Putnam Inc, One
   Grosset Dr, Kirkwood, NY 13795
Membership(s): Children's Book Council

Canon Law Society of America
108 N Payne St, Suite C, Alexandria, VA 22314-
   2906
SAN: 237-6296
Tel: 703-739-2560 *Fax:* 703-739-2562
E-mail: coordinator@clsa.org
Web Site: www.clsa.org
Key Personnel
Exec Coord: Arthur Espelage
Founded: 1938
Books on canon law & marriage.
ISBN Prefix(es): 0-943616
Number of titles published annually: 3 Print
Total Titles: 58 Print

Canyon Country Publications
PO Box 963, Moab, UT 84532-0963

Tel: 435-259-6700
Key Personnel
Publr & Ed: Mary M Barnes
Founded: 1974
Regional guidebooks.
ISBN Prefix(es): 0-9614586; 0-925685
Total Titles: 33 Print
Distributed by Archhunter Publications; Canyon
   Country Distribution

Capital Books Inc
22841 Quicksilver Dr, Sterling, VA 20166
Mailing Address: PO Box 605, Herndon, VA
   20172-0605
Tel: 703-661-1571 *Toll Free Tel:* 800-758-3756
   Fax: 703-661-1547
Web Site: www.capital-books.com
Key Personnel
Pres: Azad Ajamian
Publr: Kathleen Hughes *E-mail:* kathleen@
   booksintl.com
Publicity Mgr: Jennifer Hughes *Tel:* 703-661-
   1533 *E-mail:* jennifer@booksintl.com
Founded: 1998
Publisher of general nonfiction: cookbooks,
   lifestyles, business, how-to, travel, home &
   garden & self-help.
ISBN Prefix(es): 1-892123; 0-931868
Number of titles published annually: 30 Print
Total Titles: 150 Print
Foreign Rep(s): Australian Book Marketing (Aus-
   tralia & New Zealand)
Foreign Rights: Duckworth Publishing (UK &
   Europe); Vanwell Publishing (Canada)
Orders to: International Publishers Market-
   ing, PO Box 605, Herndon, VA 20172-
   0605 *Tel:* 703-661-1586 *Fax:* 703-661-1501
   E-mail: intpubmkt@aol.com
Returns: 22883 Quicksilver Dr, Sterling, VA
   20166
Distribution Center: 22883 Quicksilver Dr, Ster-
   ling, VA 20166 *Tel:* 703-661-1586 *Fax:* 703-
   661-1501 *E-mail:* ipmmail@presswarehouse.
   com
Membership(s): American Publishers Association

Capital Enquiry Inc
1034 Emerald Bay Rd, No 435, South Lake
   Tahoe, CA 96150
Tel: 916-442-1434 *Fax:* 916-244-2704
E-mail: info@capenq.com
Web Site: www.capenq.com
Key Personnel
Owner: Bruce Campbell
Founded: 1973
Legislative directories, information, maps (CA)
   zip code directory, diskette (CA) & US
   Congress Direct.
ISBN Prefix(es): 0-917982
Number of titles published annually: 3 Print
Total Titles: 15 Print
Distributor for Center for Investigative Reporting

Capra Press
155 Canon View Rd, Santa Barbara, CA 93108
Tel: 805-969-0203 *Fax:* 805-565-0724
E-mail: order@caprapress.com
Web Site: www.caprapress.com
Key Personnel
Publr: Robert Bason *E-mail:* robertbason@
   caprapress.com
Founded: 1969
General trade; fiction & nonfiction.
ISBN Prefix(es): 0-9722503; 1-59266
Number of titles published annually: 10 Print
Total Titles: 25 Print
Imprints: Noel Young Books
Distributed by Gem Guides Book Co (selected
   titles)
Foreign Rep(s): Airlift Book Co; BooBooks (Aus-
   tralia); Raincoast Book Distribution Ltd

Foreign Rights: Ursula Bender (Germany);
Georges Hoffman (France)
Distribution Center: Consortium Book Sales &
Distribution, 1045 Westgate Dr, St Paul, MN
55114 *Toll Free Tel:* 800-283-3572

Capstone Press
151 Good Counsel Dr, Mankato, MN 56002
Mailing Address: PO Box 669, Mankato, MN
56002-0669
Toll Free Tel: 800-747-4992 *Toll Free Fax:* 888-
262-0705
Web Site: www.capstonepress.com
Key Personnel
CEO: Robert Coughlan
Pres: John Martin
Edit Dir: Kay Olson
Dist Sales Mgr: Paul Skag
Prod Planning Mgr: Jill Braithwaite
Dist Sale Assoc: Katie Cook *Tel:* 952-224-0582
Founded: 1991
Provides new & struggling readers with a strong
foundation on which to build reading success.
Our broad range of nonfiction titles for grades
pre-K–8 easily blends a world of books with
the world children experience every day.
ISBN Prefix(es): 1-56065; 0-7368
Number of titles published annually: 250 Print
Total Titles: 2,100 Print
Imprints: Bridgestone; Edge Books; Fact Finders;
First Facts; Pebble; Pebble Plus

Captain Fiddle Publications
4 Elm Ct, Newmarket, NH 03857
Tel: 603-659-2658
E-mail: cfiddle@tiac.net
Web Site: www.captainfiddle.com
Key Personnel
Owner: Ryan Thomson
Founded: 1985
Music instruction & audio recording.
ISBN Prefix(es): 0-931877
Number of titles published annually: 3 Print
Total Titles: 21 Print

Aristide D Caratzas, Publisher
Affiliate of Melissa International Publications Ltd
PO Box 344-H, Scarsdale, NY 10583
Tel: 914-725-4847 *Toll Free Tel:* 800-204-2665
Fax: 914-725-4847 (call first)
E-mail: info@caratzas.com
Web Site: www.caratzas.com
Key Personnel
Publr: Aristide D Caratzas
Man Ed: Yvonne Allen
Founded: 1975
Trade, textbooks, fine editions, reprints, paper-
backs, regional, art, book trade, foreign lan-
guage, history, literature, reference, religion &
scholarly.
ISBN Prefix(es): 0-89241
Number of titles published annually: 16 Print
Total Titles: 397 Print
Imprints: Aristide D Caratzas; Melissa Media As-
sociates
Divisions: Melissa Media Associates Inc
Editorial Office(s): 11 Hypatias St, Athens 10557,
Greece *Tel:* (01) 325-7249

Caravan Books
Subsidiary of Academic Resources Corp
PO Box 5934, Carefree, AZ 85377-5934
SAN: 206-7323
Tel: 480-575-9945 *Fax:* 480-575-9451
E-mail: maxinmin@umich.edu
Key Personnel
Publr: Norman Mangouni
Founded: 1972
ISBN Prefix(es): 0-88206
Number of titles published annually: 10 Print
Total Titles: 120 Print

Cardoza Publishing
857 Broadway, 3rd fl, New York, NY 10003
Tel: 212-255-6661 *Fax:* 212-255-6671
E-mail: cardozapub@aol.com
Web Site: www.cardozapub.com
Key Personnel
Publr: Avery Cardoza
Ed: Alixandra Gould
Admin: Mary Grimes
Founded: 1981
An independent publisher specializing in gaming,
gambling, backgammon & chess titles.
ISBN Prefix(es): 1-58042
Number of titles published annually: 40 Print
Total Titles: 100 Print
Imprints: Union Square Publishing
Foreign Office(s): Take That Ltd, 9 Oakdale
Manor, Harrogate, North Yorks HG1 2NA,
United Kingdom, Contact: Chris Brown
Tel: (1423) 507545 *Fax:* (1423) 526035
E-mail: takethat@btinternet.com
Windsor Books, The Boundary, Wheatley Rd,
Garsington, Oxford OX44 9EJ, United King-
dom, Contact: Geoff Cowen *Tel:* (1865)
361122 *Fax:* (1865) 361133 *E-mail:* sales@
windsorbooks.co.uk
Distributed by Simon & Schuster
Foreign Rep(s): Take That Ltd (gaming & gam-
bling only) (UK); Windsor Books (chess only)
(UK)
Orders to: Simon & Schuster, 100 Front St,
Riverside, NJ 08075, Order Processing
Dept *Toll Free Tel:* 800-223-2336 *Toll Free
Fax:* 800-943-9831 *E-mail:* order_desk@
distican.com
See separate listing for:
Union Square Publishing

§Cardweb.com Inc
10 N Jefferson St, Suite 301, Frederick, MD
21701
Mailing Address: PO Box 1700, Frederick, MD
21702-0700
Tel: 301-631-9100 *Fax:* 301-631-9112
E-mail: cardservices@cardweb.com; cardstaff@
cardweb.com
Web Site: www.cardweb.com
Key Personnel
CEO: Robert B McKinley *E-mail:* rbmckinley@
cardweb.com
Electronic Publg: Jason Hipkins
E-mail: jhipkins@cardweb.com
Cust Serv Dir: Tirzah Callahan *E-mail:* tirzahc@
cardweb.com
Founded: 1986
Research & publishing firm focused on the pay-
ment card industry.
ISBN Prefix(es): 0-943329
Number of titles published annually: 5 Print; 1
CD-ROM; 10 Online; 3 E-Book
Total Titles: 10 Print; 1 CD-ROM; 10 Online;
2,000 E-Book

The Career Press Inc
3 Tice Rd, Franklin Lakes, NJ 07417
Mailing Address: PO Box 687, Franklin Lakes,
NJ 07417
Tel: 201-848-0310 *Toll Free Tel:* 800-CAREER-1
(227-3371) *Fax:* 201-848-1727
Web Site: www.careerpress.com
Key Personnel
Pres: Ronald W Fry
VP & Assoc Publr: Anne Brooks
Edit Dir: Stacey Farkas *Tel:* 201-848-0310 ext
523 *E-mail:* sfarkas@careerpress.com
Intl Rts: Allison Olson
Acqs Ed: Michael Lewis
Founded: 1985
Reference books, careers, business & financial
how-to, educational, New Age, weddings &
motivational.
ISBN Prefix(es): 1-56414
Number of titles published annually: 75 Print

Total Titles: 400 Print
Imprints: New Page Books
Foreign Rep(s): Book Representation & Distri-
bution (Europe & UK); Pearson Education
(Australia, Southeast Asia); Southern Publish-
ers Group (New Zealand); Ten Speed Press
(Canada)
Foreign Rights: Karen Wolf (Career Press)

William Carey Library
PO Box 40129, Pasadena, CA 91114-7129
Tel: 626-798-0819 *Toll Free Tel:* 866-732-6657
E-mail: publishing@wclbooks.com
Web Site: www.wclbooks.com
Key Personnel
Owner & Dir: Ralph D Winter
Asst Gen Mgr: Rick Kress
Founded: 1969
Books & studies of church growth & Christian
world missions.
ISBN Prefix(es): 0-87808
Number of titles published annually: 15 Print
Total Titles: 125 Print
Imprints: Mandate Press
Foreign Rep(s): Centre for Mission Awareness
(New Zealand); Koorong Books Ltd (Australia)

§Caribe Betania Editores
Division of Thomas Nelson Inc
501 Nelson Place, Nashville, TN 37214
Mailing Address: PO Box 141000, Nashville, TN
37214-1000
Tel: 615-391-3937 *Toll Free Tel:* 800-322-7426
Fax: 615-883-9376
E-mail: caribe@editorecaribe.com
Web Site: www.caribebetania.com
Key Personnel
Mktg & Adv Mgr: Brooke Del Villar
Publisher of Spanish books & Bibles.
ISBN Prefix(es): 0-88113; 0-89922
Number of titles published annually: 50 Print
Total Titles: 480 Print

Carlisle Press - Walnut Creek
2673 Township Rd 421, Sugarcreek, OH 44681
Tel: 330-852-1900 *Toll Free Tel:* 800-852-4482
Fax: 330-852-3285
Founded: 1992
Amish books, magazines & cookbooks.
ISBN Prefix(es): 1-890050; 0-9642548
Number of titles published annually: 4 Print
Total Titles: 36 Print

Carnegie Mellon University Press
5032 Forbes Ave, Pittsburgh, PA 15289-1021
SAN: 211-2329
Tel: 412-268-2861 *Fax:* 412-268-8706
Web Site: www.cmu.edu/universitypress
Key Personnel
Dir: Gerald Costanzo
Sr Ed: Cynthia Lamb
Founded: 1974
ISBN Prefix(es): 0-915604; 0-88748
Number of titles published annually: 15 Print
Total Titles: 285 Print
Billing Address: PO Box 6525, Ithaca, NY
14850-6525
Orders to: Cornell University Press Services
Returns: Cornell University Press Services
Warehouse: Cornell University Press Services

Carnot USA Books
22 W 19 St, 5th fl, New York, NY 10011
Tel: 212-255-6505 *Fax:* 212-807-8831
E-mail: sales@carnot.fr
Web Site: www.carnotbooks.com
Key Personnel
Dir: Asad Lalljee *E-mail:* asad@carnot.fr
Founded: 1996
ISBN Prefix(es): 1-59209
Number of titles published annually: 20 Print

Total Titles: 30 Print
Membership(s): Publishers Marketing Association

Carolina Academic Press
700 Kent St, Durham, NC 27701
SAN: 210-7848
Tel: 919-489-7486 *Toll Free Tel:* 800-489-7486
  Fax: 919-493-5668
E-mail: cap@cap-press.com
Web Site: www.cap-press.com; www.caplaw.com
Key Personnel
Pres, Intl Rts Contact: Keith R Sipe
  E-mail: ksipe@cap-press.com
Edit Dir: Linda M Lacy *Tel:* 919-489-7486 ext
  128 *E-mail:* linda@cap-press.com
Art Dir & Prodn Mgr: Tim Colton *E-mail:* tim@
  cap-press.com
Founded: 1974
Scholarly books & journals; anthropology, archaeology, economics, government, political science, history, reference, law, social science, middle school textbooks.
ISBN Prefix(es): 0-89089; 1-59460
Number of titles published annually: 60 Print
Total Titles: 600 Print

Carolrhoda Books Inc
Division of Lerner Publishing Group
241 First Ave N, Minneapolis, MN 55401
SAN: 201-9671
Tel: 612-332-3344 *Toll Free Tel:* 800-328-4929
  Fax: 612-332-7615 *Toll Free Fax:* 800-332-
1132
E-mail: info@lernerbooks.com
Web Site: www.lernerbooks.com
Key Personnel
Chmn & CEO: Harry J Lerner
Pres & Publr: Adam Lerner
VP & CFO: Margaret Wunderlich
VP, Lerner Classroom: Gary Tinney
VP & Ed-in-Chief: Mary M Rodgers
VP, Prodn: Gary Hansen
VP, Sales & Mktg: David Wexler
Art Dir: Zach Marell
Mktg Dir: Beth Heiss
Dir, Contracts, Perms & Author Rel: Almena
  Dees
Dir, HR: Cyndi Radant
Subs Rts: Tim Schwarz
Founded: 1969
Juvenile picture story books, fiction & nonfiction, beginning readers, social studies, art, multicultural issues, biography & activity books. We will accept submissions from March 1st through 31st & again from Oct 1st through 31st. Any submissions received at other times of the year will be returned to the sender unopened. We will no longer be answering queries regarding the status of submissions. Submitters will receive a response after their ms or proposal has been considered. We will respond only to those submitters who have included an SASE with their submission.
ISBN Prefix(es): 0-87614; 1-57505
Number of titles published annually: 4 Print
Foreign Rep(s): INT Press Distribution (Australia); Monarch Books of Canada (Canada/Trade); Phambili (Southern Africa); Publishers Marketing Services (Singapore & Malaysia); Saunders Book Co (Canada/Education); Turnaround (UK)
Foreign Rights: Bardon Chinese Media Agency (Taiwan); Japan Foreign Rights Centre (Japan); Korea Copyright Center (Korea); Michelle Lapautre Agence Junior (France); Literarische Agentur Silke Weniger (Germany); Tao Media International (People's Republic of China)
Warehouse: 1251 Washington Ave N, Minneapolis, MN 55401

Carousel Publications Ltd
1304 Rte 42, Sparrowbush, NY 12780

Tel: 212-758-9399 *Fax:* 212-758-6453
E-mail: info@carousel-music.com
Web Site: www.carousel-music.com
Key Personnel
Pres: Carmela Mercuri *E-mail:* cmercuri@
  carousel-music.com
Founded: 1972
ISBN Prefix(es): 0-935474
Number of titles published annually: 4 Print
Total Titles: 60 Print

Carroll & Graf Publishers
Imprint of Avalon Publishing Group - New York
245 W 17 St, 11th fl, New York, NY 10011-5300
Tel: 646-375-2570 *Fax:* 646-375-2571
Web Site: www.carrollandgraf.com
Key Personnel
Sr VP & Publg Dir: Michele Martin
VP & Publr: Will Balliett
Sr Dir & Ed-in-Chief: Philip Turner
Ed: Don Weise
Assoc Ed: Keith Wallman
Founded: 1982
Carroll & Graf Publishers, an imprint of Avalon Publishing Group, is known for history & current affairs titles, as well as high quality fiction & mysteries.
Number of titles published annually: 120 Print
Total Titles: 1,000 Print

Carroll Publishing
4701 Sangamore Rd, Suite S-155, Bethesda, MD 20816
Tel: 301-263-9800 *Toll Free Tel:* 800-336-4240
  Fax: 301-263-9801
E-mail: custsvc@carrollpub.com
Web Site: www.carrollpub.com
Founded: 1973
Number of titles published annually: 21 Print; 4 Online
Total Titles: 21 Print; 4 Online
Membership(s): National Directory Publishing Association

Carson-Dellosa Publishing Co Inc
Subsidiary of Cinar Films
PO Box 35665, Greensboro, NC 27425-5665
Tel: 336-632-0084 *Fax:* 336-632-0087
Web Site: www.carsondellosa.com
Key Personnel
Prod Acqs: Pam Hill
Founded: 1976
Publish supplementary educational materials for elementary & middle grades; teacher idea books, activity books, student workbooks & other classroom resource materials.
Number of titles published annually: 95 Print
Total Titles: 700 Print
Distributor for Kelley Wingate Publications; Mark Twain Media; The Wild Goose Co

Carson Enterprises Inc
PO Box 716, Dona Ana, NM 88032-0716
Tel: 505-541-1732
Key Personnel
Pres: H Glenn Carson *E-mail:* hgcii@zianet.com
Founded: 1971
Materials relating to treasure hunting.
ISBN Prefix(es): 0-941620
Number of titles published annually: 3 Print
Total Titles: 62 Print
Imprints: Carson Enterprises

Carstens Publications Inc
108 Phil Hardin Rd, Newton, NJ 07860
Mailing Address: PO Box 700, Newton, NJ
  07860-0700
Tel: 973-383-3355 *Fax:* 973-383-4064
E-mail: hal@carstens-publications.com
Web Site: www.carstens-publications.com

Key Personnel
Publr: Harold H Carstens *E-mail:* hal@carstens-
  publications.com
Adv Dir: Joan Earley
Founded: 1933
Books & magazines on railroads, railroad modeling & aeronautics.
ISBN Prefix(es): 0-911868; 1-59073
Number of titles published annually: 8 Print
Total Titles: 50 Print
Imprints: Carstens Hobby Books
Advertising Agency: High Point Media Inc
Membership(s): Better Business Bureau; Magazine Publishers of America

CarTech Inc
39966 Grand Ave, North Branch, MN 55056
Tel: 651-277-1200 *Toll Free Tel:* 800-551-4754
  Fax: 651-277-1203
E-mail: info@cartechbooks.com
Web Site: www.cartechbooks.com
Key Personnel
Publr: David Arnold
Mktg & Sales Mgr: Molly Koecher
  E-mail: mollyk@cartechbooks.com
Founded: 1993
Automotive books.
ISBN Prefix(es): 1-884089
Number of titles published annually: 12 Print
Total Titles: 50 Print
Imprints: S-A Design Books
Distributed by Voyageur Press
Distributor for Brooklands Books Ltd; SA Design
Foreign Rights: Brooklands Books Ltd (Australia, England)

Amon Carter Museum
3501 Camp Bowie Blvd, Fort Worth, TX 76107-2631
Tel: 817-738-1933 (ext 625) *Toll Free Tel:* 800-
  573-1933 *Fax:* 817-336-1123
Web Site: www.cartermuseum.org
Key Personnel
Wholesale & Mail Order Mgr: Amy Wisman
  E-mail: amy.wisman@cartermuseum.org
Asst: Amanda Rutland
Founded: 1961
Art & photography.
ISBN Prefix(es): 0-88360
Number of titles published annually: 6 Print
Total Titles: 11 Print
Distributed by Abrams & University of Washington Press
Shipping Address: 222 N University, Fort Worth, TX 76107

§Cascade Pass Inc
4223 Glencoe Ave, Suite C-105, Marina Del Rey, CA 90292
Tel: 310-305-0210 *Toll Free Tel:* 888-837-0704
  Fax: 310-305-7850
Web Site: www.cascadepass.com
Key Personnel
Pres: David Katz *E-mail:* dkatz@cascadepass.com
Proj Mgr: Judith Cohen *E-mail:* jlc@cascadepass.
  com
Founded: 1989
Science career books for children, environmental & sports.
ISBN Prefix(es): 1-880599
Number of titles published annually: 10 Print
Total Titles: 52 Print; 18 CD-ROM; 6 Audio

Casemate Publishers
2114 Darby Rd, Havertown, PA 19083
Tel: 610-853-9131 *Fax:* 610-853-9146
E-mail: casemate@casematepublishing.com
Web Site: www.casematepublishing.com
Key Personnel
CEO & Publr: David Farnsworth
Founded: 2001

Publisher & distributor of military history, defense & travel books.
ISBN Prefix(es): 0-9711709; 1-932033
Number of titles published annually: 10 Print
Total Titles: 40 Print
Distributor for Ian Allan (UK); Amber Books (UK); Arms & Armour Press (UK); Arris Publishing (UK); Birlinn Publishing (UK); Brassey's UK; Casemate (USA); Cassell (UK, military titles only); Compendium Publishing (UK); CondeNast/Johansens (UK); Conway Maritime Press (UK); DACO Publications (Belgium); D-Day Publishing (Belgium); De Krijger (Belgium); Earthbound Publications (South Africa); Editions Charles Herissey (France); Emperor's Press (USA); Formac Publishing (Canada); Front Street Press (USA); Grub Street (UK); Editions Heimdal; Helion & Co Ltd (UK); Histoire & Collections (France); Historical Indexes (USA); Indo Editions (France); Ironclad Publishing (USA); National Maritime Museum (UK); Pen & Sword Books Lrd (UK); Public Record Office (UK); Riebel-Roque; RZM Publishing (USA); Salamander (UK); Savas Beatie (USA); Spellmount Publishers (UK); Travel Publishing Ltd (UK); Vanwell Publishing (Canada); Vegetarian Guides (UK); Weidenfeld & Nicolson (UK, military titles only)
Foreign Rep(s): Greenhill Books (UK & Commonwealth)
Returns: Whitehurst & Clark Book Fulfillment Inc, 1200 Rte 523, Flemington, NJ 08822
Shipping Address: Whitehurst & Clark Book Fulfillment Inc, 1200 Rte 523, Flemington, NJ 08822

Catbird Press
16 Windsor Rd, North Haven, CT 06473-3015
Tel: 203-230-2391 Fax: 203-286-1091
E-mail: info@catbirdpress.com
Web Site: www.catbirdpress.com
Key Personnel
Publr: Robert Wechsler E-mail: rob@catbirdpress.com
Founded: 1987
Czech literature in translation; humor, fiction & general nonfiction.
ISBN Prefix(es): 0-945774
Number of titles published annually: 4 Print
Total Titles: 47 Print
Imprints: Garrigue Books
Foreign Rep(s): Turnaround (UK)
Foreign Rights: Agencia Literaria Transmit (Spain); The English Agency (Japan); Lora Fountain (France); Harris/Elon Agency (Israel); Kristin Olson (Czech Republic); Silke Weniger (Germany)
Warehouse: IPG Warehouse, 600 N Pulaski St, Chicago, IL 60624
Distribution Center: Independent Publishers Group, 814 N Franklin St, Chicago, IL 60610, Contact: Mary Rowles Tel: 312-337-0747 Toll Free Tel: 800-888-4741 Fax: 312-337-5985 E-mail: frontdesk@ipgbooks.com

§Catholic Book Publishing Corp
77 West End Ave, Totowa, NJ 07512
Tel: 973-890-2400 Fax: 973-890-2410
E-mail: cbpcl@bellatlantic.net
Founded: 1911
Publish catechisms, Spanish publications & liturgical books.
ISBN Prefix(es): 0-89942
Number of titles published annually: 3 Print
Total Titles: 25 Print; 9 Audio
Imprints: St Joseph Editions

The Catholic Health Association of the United States
4455 Woodson Rd, St Louis, MO 63134-3797
SAN: 201-968X

Tel: 314-427-2500 Fax: 314-253-3540
Web Site: www.chausa.org
Key Personnel
Sr Dir & Prod Coord: Michele M Oranski E-mail: moranski@chausa.org
Founded: 1915
Catholic health care resources, Catholic ministry, health, labor, medicine & nursing.
ISBN Prefix(es): 0-87125
Number of titles published annually: 3 Print; 1 CD-ROM; 2 Audio
Total Titles: 58 Print; 1 CD-ROM; 4 Audio

Catholic News Publishing Co Inc
210 North Ave, New Rochelle, NY 10801
Tel: 914-632-7771 Toll Free Tel: 800-433-7771 Fax: 914-632-3412
Web Site: www.graduateguide.com
Key Personnel
Pres: Myles Ridder E-mail: mridder@schoolguides.com
Founded: 1886
Directories for institutions & religious communities.
Number of titles published annually: 7 Print
Total Titles: 7 Print
Divisions: School Guide Publications

The Catholic University of America Press
240 Leahy Hall, 620 Michigan Ave NE, Washington, DC 20064
SAN: 203-6290
Tel: 202-319-5052 Fax: 202-319-4985
E-mail: cua-press@cua.edu
Web Site: cuapress.cua.edu
Key Personnel
Dir: David J McGonagle E-mail: mcgonagle@cua.edu
Man Ed: Susan Needham E-mail: needham@cua.edu
Acqs Ed: Gregory F LaNave
Mktg Mgr: Beth A Benevides E-mail: benevides@cua.edu
Founded: 1939
ISBN Prefix(es): 0-8132
Number of titles published annually: 30 Print
Total Titles: 350 Print
Distributor for American Maritain Association
Foreign Rep(s): East West Export Books (Australia, Asia, New Zealand); Eurospan University Press Group (Africa, UK, Europe, Middle East); Scholarly Book Services (Canada)
Orders to: Hopkins Fulfillment Service, PO Box 50370, Baltimore, MD 21211-4370 Toll Free Tel: 800-537-5487 Fax: 410-516-6998
Returns: Hopkins Fulfillment Service, c/o Maple Press Co, Lebanon Distribution Ctr, PO Box 1287, Lebanon, PA 17042-1287
Warehouse: c/o Maple Press Co, Lebanon Distribution Ctr, 704 Legionaire Dr, Fredricksburg, PA 17042
Membership(s): Association of American University Presses

Cato Institute
1000 Massachusetts Ave NW, Washington, DC 20001-5403
Tel: 202-842-0200 Toll Free Tel: 800-767-1241 Fax: 202-842-3490
E-mail: books@cato.org
Web Site: www.cato.org
Key Personnel
Pres: Edward H Crane
Exec VP: David Boaz
Pubns Dir: David Lampo Fax: 202-842-2401
Mktg Mgr: Garrett Brown
Founded: 1977
Non-partisan, public-policy think tank.
ISBN Prefix(es): 0-932790; 1-882577; 1-930865
Number of titles published annually: 15 Print
Total Titles: 150 Print

Foreign Rights: Rights & Distribution Inc (Worldwide)
Warehouse: AGS Custom Graphics Toll Free Tel: 800-669-3658
Distribution Center: National Book Network, 15200 NBN Way, Blue Ridge Summit, PA 17214, Contact: Vicki Metzger Tel: 301-459-3366 Fax: 301-429-5746 E-mail: vmetzger@nbnbooks.com Web Site: www.nbnbooks.com

Cave Books
Affiliate of Cave Research Foundation
277 Clamer Rd, Trenton, NJ 08628
SAN: 216-7220
Mailing Address: 4700 Amberwood Dr, Dayton, OH 45424
Tel: 609-490-6359 (ed); 937-233-3561 (publr); 937-233-3561 (edit)
Web Site: www.cavebooks.com
Key Personnel
Publr & Dist: Roger E McClure E-mail: rogmcclure@aol.com
Ed: Paul J Steward E-mail: pddb@juno.com
Founded: 1957
Books about karst, caves & speleology.
ISBN Prefix(es): 0-939748
Number of titles published annually: 4 Print
Total Titles: 35 Print
Foreign Office(s): 49 Av Jean-Moulin, 75014 Paris, France
Distributor for Zephyrus Press
Foreign Rep(s): Claude Chabert (Europe)

Caxton Press
Division of The Caxton Printers Ltd
312 Main St, Caldwell, ID 83605-3299
SAN: 201-9698
Tel: 208-459-7421 Toll Free Tel: 800-657-6465 Fax: 208-459-7450
E-mail: publish@caxtonpress.com
Web Site: www.caxtonpress.com Cable: CAXTON CALDWELL IDAHO
Key Personnel
VP & Publr: Scott Gipson E-mail: sgipson@caxtonpress.com
Ed: Wayne Cornell E-mail: wcornell@caxtonpress.com
Founded: 1895 (J H Gipson; Still owned & managed by the Gipson family)
Hardcover & paperback.
ISBN Prefix(es): 0-87004
Number of titles published annually: 8 Print
Total Titles: 115 Print
Distributor for University of Idaho Press
Membership(s): AAP

CCC Publications LLC
9725 Lurline Ave, Chatsworth, CA 91311
Tel: 818-718-0507 Toll Free Tel: 800-248-LAFF (248-5233) Fax: 818-718-0655
Web Site: www.whyleavethehouse.com
Key Personnel
Publr & Intl Rts Contact: Mark Chutick E-mail: mchutick@whyleavethehouse.com
Founded: 1983
Humor trade paperback publisher.
ISBN Prefix(es): 0-918259; 1-57644
Number of titles published annually: 6 Print; 6 Online; 30 E-Book
Total Titles: 140 Print; 10 Online; 10 E-Book; 7 Audio
Membership(s): ABA; Publishers Marketing Association

§CCH Inc
Subsidiary of Wolters Kluwer
2700 Lake Cook Rd, Riverwoods, IL 60015
SAN: 202-3504
Tel: 847-267-7000 Toll Free Tel: 888-224-7377
Web Site: www.cch.com
Key Personnel
Pres & CEO: Gene Landoe

VP: James de Gaspe Bonar; Paul Gibson; Jerry Pruitt
PR: Leslie Bonacum
Founded: 1913
Current US International tax law, business, human resources, securities & health care law, tax, small business, home office human resources & health care.
ISBN Prefix(es): 0-8080
Number of titles published annually: 100 Print
Total Titles: 400 Print
Subsidiaries: CCH Peterson; CCH Riverwoods; CCH St Petersburg; CCH Tax Compliance; CCH Washington DC; LIS (Legal Information Services); Washington Service Bureau
Warehouse: 4025 Peterson Ave, Chicago, IL 60646

CDL Press
PO Box 34454, Bethesda, MD 20854
Tel: 301-762-2066 *Fax:* 253-484-5542
E-mail: cdlpress@erols.com
Key Personnel
Pres: Mark E Cohen
Founded: 1981
ISBN Prefix(es): 1-883053
Number of titles published annually: 6 Print
Total Titles: 63 Print
Imprints: CDL Press; University Press of Maryland
Returns: 11903 Reynolds Ave, Potomac, MD 20827

Cedar Fort Inc
925 N Main St, Springville, UT 84663
Tel: 801-489-4084 *Toll Free Tel:* 800-759-2665
Fax: 801-489-1097
E-mail: skybook@cedarfort.com
Web Site: www.cedarfort.com
Key Personnel
Pres: Lyle Mortimer
Dir, Sales & Mktg: Georgia Carpenter
Billing: Cindy Bunce
Founded: 1986
Christian (primarily Latter-Day Saints), inspirational, motivational, LDS fiction & doctrinal.
ISBN Prefix(es): 1-55517
Number of titles published annually: 65 Print
Total Titles: 300 Print
See separate listing for:
Horizon Publishers & Distributors Inc

§Cedco Publishing Co
100 Pelican Way, San Rafael, CA 94901
Tel: 415-451-3000 *Toll Free Tel:* 800-227-6162
Fax: 415-457-4839
E-mail: sales@cedco.com
Web Site: www.cedco.com
Key Personnel
Pres & CEO: Charles E Ditlefsen
COO: Chuck Lesjek
VP, Opers: Shari Lesjek
VP, Licensing & Creative Servs: Mary Sullivan
Founded: 1978
Books & calendars.
ISBN Prefix(es): 1-55912; 0-7683
Number of titles published annually: 300 Print
Total Titles: 1,000 Print; 12 CD-ROM
Foreign Rep(s): Athena Productions (Africa, Caribbean, Latin America, Middle East, Puerto Rico); Pierre Belvedere (Canada); Cedco (Japan); Danilo (UK); Leecom (Southeast Asia); John Sands (Australia, New Zealand); Simplex (Austria, Germany, Switzerland)
Returns: JV West Warehouse, 525 Coney Island Dr, Sparks, NV 89431
Warehouse: JV West Warehouse, 525 Coney Island Dr, Sparks, NV 89431
Distribution Center: JV West Warehouse, 525 Coney Island Dr, Sparks, NV 89431

CEF Press
Subsidiary of Child Evangelism Fellowship Inc
PO Box 348, Warrenton, MO 63383-0348
Tel: 636-456-4380 *Toll Free Tel:* 800-748-7710
Fax: 636-456-4321
Web Site: www.cefonline.com
Key Personnel
VP, Educ: Martha Wright
Exec Dir, Fin, Pubns & Info Servs: Ron Hane
Founded: 1939
Christian education curriculum.
ISBN Prefix(es): 1-55976
Number of titles published annually: 30 Print
Total Titles: 300 Print
Foreign Rep(s): CEFMARK (Australia)

Celebrity Press
Imprint of Hambleton-Hill Publishing
1501 County Hospital Rd, Nashville, TN 37218
Tel: 615-254-2450 *Toll Free Tel:* 800-327-5113
Fax: 615-254-2408
Key Personnel
Pres: Van Hill
Founded: 1995
Adult trade books.
ISBN Prefix(es): 1-55656
Number of titles published annually: 3 Print
Total Titles: 10 Print
Distributed by Associated Publishers Group

Celestial Arts Publishing Co
Imprint of Ten Speed Press
999 Harrison St, Berkeley, CA 94710
Mailing Address: PO Box 7123, Berkeley, CA 94707-0123 SAN: 159-8333
Tel: 510-559-1600 *Toll Free Tel:* 800-841-BOOK
Fax: 510-524-1052
E-mail: order@tenspeed.com
Web Site: www.tenspeed.com
ISBN Prefix(es): 0-89087; 1-58761
Number of titles published annually: 30 Print
Editorial Office(s): 1111 Eighth St, Berkeley, CA 94710
Sales Office(s): 1111 Eighth St, Berkeley, CA 94710
Billing Address: 1111 Eighth St, Berkeley, CA 94710
Orders to: 1201 Ninth St, Berkeley, CA 94710
Returns: 1111 Eighth St, Berkeley, CA 94710
Warehouse: 1201 Ninth St, Berkeley, CA 94710
Distribution Center: 1201 Ninth St, Berkeley, CA 94710

Center for Creative Leadership
One Leadership Place, Greensboro, NC 27438-6300
Mailing Address: PO Box 26300, Greensboro, NC 27438-6300
Tel: 336-288-7210 *Fax:* 336-288-3999
Web Site: www.ccl.org/publications
Key Personnel
Man, Publg Devt: Pete Scisco
Pubns, Sales & Promos: Kelly Lombardino
Tel: 336-286-4095 *Fax:* 336-545-3221
E-mail: lombardinok@leaders.ccl.org
Founded: 1970
Books on leadership & leadership development.
ISBN Prefix(es): 0-912873
Number of titles published annually: 10 Print
Total Titles: 123 Print
Distributed by Jossey Bass/Wiley
Distributor for Free Press; Harvard Business School Press; Jossey Bass/Wiley; Lominger Inc

Center for East Asian Studies (CEAS)
Subsidiary of Western Washington University
Western Washington University, Bellingham, WA 98225-9056
Tel: 360-650-3448 *Fax:* 360-650-7789
Web Site: www.ac.wwu.edu/~eas/publications.html

Key Personnel
Submissions Ed: Edward H Kaplan
E-mail: kaplan@cc.wwu.edu
Founded: 1971
East Asia & Iran; Asia mainly monographs.
ISBN Prefix(es): 0-914584
Number of titles published annually: 3 Print
Total Titles: 30 Print
Imprints: East Asian Research Aids & Translations, Studies on East Asia
Distributed by Amazon.com

§Center for Futures Education Inc
345 Erie St, Grove City, PA 16127
Mailing Address: PO Box 309, Grove City, PA 16127-0309
Tel: 724-458-5860 *Toll Free Tel:* 800-966-2554
Fax: 724-458-5962
E-mail: info@thectr.com
Web Site: www.thectr.com
Key Personnel
Contact: Lyn M Sennholz *E-mail:* lyn@thectr.com
Founded: 1981
Print & online books on commodity futures & securities.
ISBN Prefix(es): 0-915513
Number of titles published annually: 12 Print
Total Titles: 50 Print; 15 E-Book
Foreign Rep(s): Forderverein Warenterminborse (Germany)

The Center for Learning
24600 Detroit Rd, Suite 201, Westlake, OH 44145
Tel: 440-250-9341 *Fax:* 440-250-9715
Web Site: www.centerforlearning.org
Key Personnel
Pres & CEO: Rose Schaffer
VP: Bernadette Vetter
Off Admin: JoAnn Wagner *E-mail:* jwagner@centerforlearning.org
VP, Religion: Mary Jane Simmons
VP, Social Studies: Lora Murphy
Cust Serv Mgr: Margaret Pugh
Founded: 1970
Founded to publish values based curriculum materials. All materials are written by master teachers who integrate academic objectives & ethical values. Non-profit educational publisher of value based curriculum units with reproducible handouts for teachers of English/Language Arts, social studies, novel/dramas, biographies & religion. Specialize in advanced placement, genres; American, British & World novels & literature; skills, supplementary topics, writing; economics, social & global issues, US government & history, world history; Catholic teaching, ministry, retreats, adult faith resources, marriage & parenting, divorce & blended families, abstinence education & chastity.
ISBN Prefix(es): 1-56077
Number of titles published annually: 30 Print
Total Titles: 600 Print
Orders to: PO Box 910, Villa Maria, PA 16155 *Toll Free Tel:* 800-767-9090 *Toll Free Fax:* 888-767-8080 *Web Site:* www.centerforlearning.org
Distribution Center: PO Box 910, Villa Maria, PA 16155, Cust Serv Mgr: Margaret Pugh *Toll Free Tel:* 800-767-9090 *Toll Free Fax:* 888-767-8080

Center for Migration Studies of New York Inc
209 Flagg Place, Staten Island, NY 10304-1199
Tel: 718-351-8800 *Fax:* 718-667-4598
E-mail: cms@cmsny.org
Web Site: www.cmsny.org
Key Personnel
Exec Dir: Rev Joseph Fugolo, c s
E-mail: jfugolo@aol.com

Pubns: Jim McGuire *E-mail:* sales@cmsny.org
Mktg: Carolyn Durante *E-mail:* offices@cmsny.
org
Libn: Diana Zimmerman *E-mail:* library@cmsny.
org
Founded: 1964
Journals & monographs on the sociodemographic,
economic, political & historical aspects of hu-
man migration & refugee movements.
ISBN Prefix(es): 0-913256; 0-934733; 1-57703
Number of titles published annually: 12 Print
Total Titles: 120 Print
Foreign Office(s): CEM, Rua Dr Mario Vicente
1108-CP, 42756-04270 Sao Paulo, Brazil
Tel: (011) 273-9031
CEMLA, Calle Necochea 330, 1158 Buenos
Aires, Argentina *Tel:* (01) 361-7689; (01) 361-
5063
CEPAM, Av Alberto Bins 1026-CP, 1658-90030
Porta Alegre, Brazil *Tel:* (0512) 258-246
CEPAM, Apdo 51480, Caracas 1050-A,
Venezuela *Tel:* (02) 924-463
CIEMI, 46 Rue de Montreuil, 75011 Paris,
France *Tel:* (01) 4372-4934
CMSS, Box 913, Darlinghurst, NSW 2010, Aus-
tralia *Tel:* (02) 212-1606
CSER, Via Dandolo 58, 00153 Rome, Italy
Tel: (06) 580-9764; 589-7664
CSERPE, Oberwilerstr 112, 4054 Basel, Switzer-
land *Tel:* (061) 54-0661
SMC, Broadway Centre, PO Box 10541, Quezon
City, Philippines
Foreign Rep(s): CADEMS (Argentina); CCMS
(Australia); Centro de Estudos Migratorios
(Brazil); CIEM (France); CSER (Italy)

Center For Self Sufficiency
PO Box 416, Denver, CO 80201-0416
Tel: 303-575-5676 *Fax:* 303-575-1187
E-mail: mail@gumbomedia.com
Web Site: www.centerforselfsufficiency.org
Key Personnel
Founder, Intl Rts & Lib Sales Dir: A Doyle
Founded: 1981
Distributors & publishers of self sufficiency titles
& products.
ISBN Prefix(es): 0-910811
Number of titles published annually: 3 Print; 1
CD-ROM; 1 Audio
Total Titles: 28 Print; 1 CD-ROM; 8 Audio
Distributor for Be Somebody Be Yourself Insti-
tute; Center For Self Sufficiency Library

Center for Strategic & International Studies
1800 "K" St NW, Washington, DC 20006
Tel: 202-775-3119 *Fax:* 202-775-3199
E-mail: books@csis.org
Web Site: www.csis.org *Telex:* 710-822-9583
Cable: CENSTRAT
Key Personnel
Dir: James R Dunton *Tel:* 202-775-3160
E-mail: jdunton@csis.org
Mktg & Sales Mgr: Heidi Shinn
Ed-in-Chief, The Washington Quarterly: Alexan-
der Lennon
Man Ed: Roberta Howard; Donna Spitler
Founded: 1962
National & international public policy.
ISBN Prefix(es): 0-89206
Number of titles published annually: 25 Print; 0
E-Book
Total Titles: 250 Print; 0 E-Book
Foreign Rep(s): Books Express (UK, Europe)
Membership(s): AAP

**Center for Thanatology Research & Education
Inc**
391 Atlantic Ave, Brooklyn, NY 11217-1701
Tel: 718-858-3026 *Fax:* 718-852-1846
Web Site: www.thanatology.org

Key Personnel
Dir: Roberta Halporn *E-mail:* rhalporn@pipeline.
com
Sec & Treas: Frank Colonnese
Media Dir: Constance Halporn
Founded: 1982
Deals exclusively with books on dying, death, be-
reavement & recovery from bereavement, as
well as those on life-threatening illness, from
the points of view of psychology & the arts.
We also publish a line of materials on grave-
stone studies & cemeteries. We maintain a
2,500 book library on these subjects; open to
the public.
ISBN Prefix(es): 0-930194
Number of titles published annually: 6 Print; 2
CD-ROM; 1 Online
Total Titles: 65 Print; 2 CD-ROM; 2 Online
Imprints: Foundation Book & Periodical Division;
Foundation of Thanatology & Periodical Div
Distributor for Association for Gravestone Stud-
ies; Calvary Hospital; Greenwood Cemetery
Membership(s): SPA

Center for Urban Policy Research
Affiliate of Rutgers University
33 Livingston Ave, Suite 400, New Brunswick,
NJ 08901-1982
SAN: 206-6297
Tel: 732-932-3133 *Fax:* 732-932-2363
Web Site: www.policy.rutgers.edu/cupr
Key Personnel
Dir: Robert Burchell; David Listokin
Sr Ed & Sales Dir: Arlene Pashman
E-mail: cupr@rci.rutgers.edu
Ed-in-Chief: Robert W Lake *Tel:* 732-932-3133
ext 521 *E-mail:* rlake@rci.rutgers.edu
Founded: 1969
Textbooks: scientific, technical & social sciences.
ISBN Prefix(es): 0-88285
Number of titles published annually: 5 Print
Total Titles: 60 Print

Center for Women Policy Studies
1211 Connecticut Ave NW, Suite 312, Washing-
ton, DC 20036
Tel: 202-872-1770 *Fax:* 202-296-8962
E-mail: cwps@centerwomenpolicy.org
Web Site: www.centerwomenpolicy.org
Key Personnel
Pres: Leslie R Wolfe *E-mail:* lwolfe@
centerwomenpolicy.org
Founded: 1972
Violence against women, education, economic
opportunity, work & family policy, workplace
diversity, womens' health policy, women &
AIDS.
ISBN Prefix(es): 1-877966
Number of titles published annually: 12 Print
Total Titles: 65 Print

Center Press
PO Box 6936, Thousand Oaks, CA 91360-6936
Tel: 818-889-7071 *Fax:* 818-889-7072
Web Site: centerbooks.com
ISBN Prefix(es): 1-889198; 0-9626888
Number of titles published annually: 3 Print
Total Titles: 15 Print
Imprints: Premier Novels (fiction)
Membership(s): Publishers Marketing Association

Centering Corp
7230 Maple St, Omaha, NE 68134
SAN: 298-1815
Tel: 402-553-1200 *Fax:* 402-553-0507
E-mail: j1200@aol.com
Web Site: www.centering.org
Key Personnel
Pres & Co-Founder: Joy Johnson; Dr Marv John-
son
Co-Dir: Ben Sieff; Janet Sieff
Shipping Dir: Nick Sieff

Founded: 1977
Bereavement support; specializes in divorce, grief
& loss. Nonprofit organization.
ISBN Prefix(es): 1-56123
Number of titles published annually: 10 Print
Total Titles: 150 Print
Distributor for Doug Smith

Centerstream Publishing LLC
PO Box 17878, Anaheim Hills, CA 92817-7878
SAN: 683-8022
Tel: 714-779-9390 *Toll Free Tel:* 877-312-8687
Fax: 714-779-9390
E-mail: centerstrm@aol.com
Web Site: www.centerstream-usa.com
Key Personnel
Owner: Ron Middlebrook
Founded: 1980
Music history, bios, music instruction books,
videos & DVDs: all instruments.
ISBN Prefix(es): 0-931759; 1-57424
Number of titles published annually: 20 Print
Total Titles: 250 Print
Subsidiaries: Centerbrook Publishing
Distributed by Booklines Hawaii; Hal Leonard
Corp
Membership(s): Publishers Marketing Association

**Central Conference of American
Rabbis/CCAR Press**
355 Lexington Ave, 18th fl, New York, NY
10017
Tel: 212-972-3636 *Toll Free Tel:* 800-935-2227
Fax: 212-692-0819
E-mail: ccarpress@ccarnet.org
Web Site: www.ccarpress.org
Key Personnel
Pres: Janet Marder
Dir, Pubns: Elliot L Stevens *Tel:* 212-972-3636
ext 242 *E-mail:* estevens@ccarnet.org
Man Ed: Deborah Smilow
Founded: 1889
Books on liturgy & Jewish practices from a lib-
eral point of view.
ISBN Prefix(es): 0-88123; 0-916694
Number of titles published annually: 3 Print
Total Titles: 63 Print
Shipping Address: Mercedes Distribution Center,
Brooklyn Navy Yard, Bldg 3, Brooklyn, NY
11205
Warehouse: Mercedes Distribution Center, 160
Imlay St, Brooklyn, NY 11231

Central European University Press
400 W 59 St, New York, NY 10019
Tel: 212-547-6932 *Fax:* 646-557-2416
Web Site: www.ceupress.com
Key Personnel
Dir & Ed: Istvan Bart
Sales & Mktg Mgr: Peter Inkei
Sales Mgr, US & Canada: Martin Greenwald
E-mail: mgreenwald@sorosny.org
Founded: 1993
Publish topics concerning past & present history
& culture of the peoples living in Central &
Eastern Europe.
ISBN Prefix(es): 1-85866; 963-9116; 963-9241
Number of titles published annually: 20 Print
Total Titles: 135 Print
Foreign Office(s): Szent Istvan tr. 11/b, 2nd fl,
H-1051 Budapest, Hungary, Contact: Peter
Inkei *Tel:* (01) 327-3138 *Fax:* (01) 327-3183
E-mail: ceupress@ceu.hu
Distributor for International Debate Education As-
sociation; Local Government & Public Service
Reform Initiative
Shipping Address: c/o Books International, PO
Box 605, Herndon, VA 20172 *Tel:* 703-661-
1500 *Fax:* 703-661-1501
Warehouse: 22883 Quicksilver Dr, Dulles, VA
20166 *Tel:* 703-661-1500 *Fax:* 703-661-1501

The Century Foundation Press
Division of The Century Foundation Inc
41 E 70 St, New York, NY 10021
Tel: 212-535-4441 *Fax:* 212-535-7534
E-mail: info@tcf.org
Web Site: www.tcf.org
Key Personnel
Pres: Richard C Leone
VP & Dir, Pubns: Beverly Goldberg
Asst VP, Pubns: Jason Renker
Man Ed: Steven Greenfield
Busn Mgr & Cont: Jennifer Grimaldi
Pub Info: Loretta Ahlrich
Founded: 1984
Reports of task forces, papers & books covering
    international & domestic policy issues.
ISBN Prefix(es): 0-87078
Number of titles published annually: 20 Print
Total Titles: 185 Print
Distribution Center: The Brookings Institution,
    1775 Massachusetts Ave NW, Washington, DC
    20036 *Tel:* 202-797-6258 *Toll Free Tel:* 800-
    552-5450

CeShore Publishing Co, see SterlingHouse
    Publisher Inc

§Chain Store Guide
Subsidiary of Lebhar-Friedman Inc
3922 Coconut Palm Dr, Tampa, FL 33619
Tel: 813-627-6800 *Toll Free Tel:* 800-927-9292
    Fax: 813-627-6882
E-mail: info@csgis.com
Web Site: www.csgis.com
Key Personnel
Dir, Res: Michael Jarvis
Dir, Prodn: Jackie Zimmerman
Founded: 1934
Directories of retail & wholesale companies.
ISBN Prefix(es): 0-86730
Number of titles published annually: 3 Print
Total Titles: 21 Print

Chalice Press
Division of Christian Board of Publications
1221 Locust St, Suite 1200, St Louis, MO 63103
SAN: 201-4408
Mailing Address: PO Box 179, St Louis, MO
    63166-0179
Tel: 314-231-8500 *Toll Free Tel:* 800-366-3383
    Fax: 314-231-8524
E-mail: chalicepress@cbp21.com
Web Site: www.cbp21.com; www.chalicepress.
    com
Key Personnel
Chmn of the Bd: Robert Nolan
Pres & Publr: Syrus White
Treas: P J Patterson
Dir, Mktg: Susie Burgess
Founded: 1954
Religion (Protestant) & hymnals.
ISBN Prefix(es): 0-8272
Number of titles published annually: 25 Print
Total Titles: 300 Print
Distributed by Abingdon Press
Warehouse: 303 N 17 St, St Louis, MO 63103-
    1996

§Champion Press Ltd
4308 Blueberry Rd, Fredonia, WI 53021
Tel: 262-692-3897 *Toll Free Tel:* 877-250-3354
    Fax: 262-692-3342
E-mail: info@championpress.com
Web Site: www.championpress.com
Key Personnel
CEO: Brook Noel *E-mail:* brook@championpress.
    com
Acqs Ed: Sara Pattow *E-mail:* sara@
    championpress.com
Dir of Publg: Mike Gulan *E-mail:* michael@
    championpress.com
Founded: 1997

General trade publisher, 95% nonfiction.
ISBN Prefix(es): 1-891400; 1-932783
Number of titles published annually: 50 Print; 8
    CD-ROM; 20 E-Book; 6 Audio
Total Titles: 150 Print; 20 CD-ROM; 12 Audio
Warehouse: 103 E Morgan St, Newton, IL 62448
Distribution Center: 103 E Morgan St, Newton,
    IL 62448

Chandler & Sharp Publishers Inc
11 Commercial Blvd, Suite A, Novato, CA 94949
SAN: 205-6127
Tel: 415-883-2353 *Fax:* 415-440-5004
Web Site: www.chandlersharp.com
Key Personnel
Publr: Edward J Barrett
Founded: 1972
College books.
ISBN Prefix(es): 0-88316
Number of titles published annually: 6 Print
Total Titles: 41 Print
Membership(s): American Anthropological Asso-
    ciation

Charisma House
600 Rinehart Rd, Lake Mary, FL 32746
Tel: 407-333-0600 (all imprints)
    Toll Free Tel: 800-283-8494 (Charisma House,
    Siloam Press, Creation House Press); 800-665-
    1468 *Fax:* 407-333-7100 (all imprints)
E-mail: webmaster@charismahouse.com;
    webmaster@creationhouse.com
Web Site: www.charismamag.com; www.strang.
    com (all imprints)
Key Personnel
Pres & Publr: Stephen Strang
VP, Prod Devt: David W Welday, III
VP, Sales & Mktg: Tom Marin
Natl Sales Dir: Dale Wilsterman
Dir, Intl Sales: Rebeccah Barker
Mgr, Intl: Tessie Devore
Founded: 1970
Christianity.
ISBN Prefix(es): 0-88419
Number of titles published annually: 200 Print
Total Titles: 500 Print; 2 Audio
Imprints: Casa Creation (International Publish-
    ing Group); CharismaLife (Sunday School
    Curriculum Group); Creation House Press
    (Co-Publishing Group); Cross Training (Youth
    Group-Curriculm Group); KIDS Church (Chil-
    dren's Church Curriculum Group); Quest
    (Youth Group-Curriculum Group); Siloam Press
    (Health Publishing Group)
Distributed by Creation House
Foreign Rep(s): Creation House (USA)
Membership(s): Christian Booksellers Associa-
    tion; Evangelical Christian Publishers Associa-
    tion

CharismaLife Publishers
Division of Strang Communications Co
600 Rinehart Rd, Lake Mary, FL 32746
Tel: 407-333-0600 *Toll Free Tel:* 800-451-4598
    Fax: 407-333-7100
E-mail: charismalife@strang.com
Web Site: www.charismamag.com
Key Personnel
Pres: Stephen Strang *E-mail:* steve.strang@strang.
    com
VP, Prod Devt: David Welday *E-mail:* dave.
    welday@strang.com
Acctg: Ken Hartman *E-mail:* ken.hartman@
    strang.com
Natl Sales Dir: Dale Wilsterman
    E-mail: wilsterman@strang.com
Founded: 1990
Christian education materials such as: Sunday
    school curriculum, children's church programs,
    youth resources, training conferences.
ISBN Prefix(es): 1-57405
Number of titles published annually: 20 Print

Total Titles: 40 Print
Distributor for Charisma Life; Cross Training;
    KIDS Church

The Charles Press, Publishers
Subsidiary of Oxbridge Corp
117 S 17 St, Suite 310, Philadelphia, PA 19103
Mailing Address: PO Box 15715, Philadelphia,
    PA 19103
Tel: 215-496-9616; 215-496-9625 *Fax:* 215-496-
    9637
E-mail: mailbox@charlespresspub.com
Web Site: www.charlespresspub.com
Key Personnel
Pres & Publr: Lauren Meltzer *E-mail:* lauren@
    charlespresspub.com
Prodn Mgr: Brad Fisher *E-mail:* brad@
    charlespresspub.com
Founded: 1982
Scholarly, professional & trade books primarily in
    the areas of psychology, criminology, death &
    dying, suicide, bereavement & counseling.
ISBN Prefix(es): 0-914783
Number of titles published annually: 10 Print
Total Titles: 125 Print; 1 CD-ROM

Charles River Media
Division of Books International
10 Downer Ave, Hingham, MA 02043
Tel: 781-740-0400 (edit offices)
    Toll Free Tel: 800-382-8505 (orders) *Fax:* 781-
    740-8816; 703-996-1010 (orders)
E-mail: info@charlesriver.com
Web Site: www.charlesriver.com
Key Personnel
Pres: David F Pallai *E-mail:* dpallai@charlesriver.
    com
Publr: Jenifer L Niles *E-mail:* jniles@charlesriver.
    com
Founded: 1994
Publishing computer books for web development,
    networking, game development & computer
    graphics.
ISBN Prefix(es): 1-886801; 1-58450
Number of titles published annually: 50 Print; 2
    CD-ROM; 1 Online; 25 E-Book
Total Titles: 200 Print; 5 CD-ROM; 1 Online; 25
    E-Book
Foreign Rep(s): Fitzhenry & Whiteside (Canada);
    IPR (Middle East); Thomson Learning (Asia);
    Transatlantic (Europe); Woodslane (Australia)
Foreign Rights: David Pallai

Charles Scribner's Sons
Unit of Thomson Gale
PO Box 9187, Farmington Hills, MI 48333-9187
Toll Free Tel: 800-877-4253 *Toll Free Fax:* 800-
    414-5043
E-mail: galeord@gale.com
Key Personnel
Publr, Scribner Reference: Karen C Day
Founded: 1846
Publishes reference books in fields of history,
    science & literature for audiences ranging
    from high school students to professional re-
    searchers.

Charlesbridge Publishing Inc
85 Main St, Watertown, MA 02472
Tel: 617-926-0329 *Toll Free Tel:* 800-225-3214
    Fax: 617-926-5720
E-mail: books@charlesbridge.com
Web Site: www.charlesbridge.com
Key Personnel
Pres & Publr: Brent Farmer *E-mail:* bfarmer@
    charlesbridge.com
VP & Assoc Publr: Mary Ann Sabia *Tel:* 617-
    926-0329 ext 120 *E-mail:* masabia@
    charlesbridge.com
VP, School Edit: Elena Dworkin Wright
    E-mail: edworkin@charlesbridge.com
VP, Prodn: Brian Walker *E-mail:* bwalker@
    charlesbridge.com

Art Dir: Susan Sherman *E-mail:* ssherman@
charlesbridge.com
Sr Ed: Yolanda LeRoy *E-mail:* yleroy@
charlesbridge.com
Founded: 1980
Children's illustrated picture books, nature & sci-
ence, nonfiction, multicultural, concept & fic-
tion, board books, supplemental educational
materials K-8.
ISBN Prefix(es): 0-88106; 1-57091; 1-879085; 1-
58089
Number of titles published annually: 28 Print
Total Titles: 270 Print; 1 Audio
Foreign Rights: Monarch Books (Canada)
Warehouse: 117 Beaver St, Waltham, MA 02452
Membership(s): Children's Book Council

§Chatelaine Press
Subsidiary of Log Research Ltd
6454 Honey Tree Ct, Burke, VA 22015
SAN: 298-6035
Tel: 703-569-2062 *Toll Free Tel:* 800-249-9527
Fax: 703-569-9610
E-mail: egm-help@enterprise-government.com
Web Site: www.chatpress.com; www.enterprise-
government.com
Key Personnel
Publr: Arlene Forbes *E-mail:* arlene@chatpress.
com
Founded: 1993
Books on public policy, public administration,
education & post modernism.
ISBN Prefix(es): 0-9639824; 1-57420
Number of titles published annually: 4 Print; 1
CD-ROM
Total Titles: 30 Print
Distributor for Law Quest

Chatsworth Press
9135 Alabama Ave, Suite B, Chatsworth, CA
91311
Tel: 818-341-3156 *Toll Free Tel:* 800-262-7367
(US); 800-272-7367 (CA) *Fax:* 818-341-3562
E-mail: info@pac-media.com
Web Site: www.pac-media.com
Key Personnel
Pres: Scott Brastow *E-mail:* scott@pac-media.
com
Founded: 1973
ISBN Prefix(es): 0-917181
Number of titles published annually: 4 Print

Chelsea Green Publishing Co
PO Box 428, White River Junction, VT 05001-
0428
SAN: 669-7631
Tel: 802-295-6300 *Toll Free Tel:* 800-639-4099
(cust serv & consumer orders); 800-807-6726
(trade & wholesale orders) *Fax:* 802-295-6444
Web Site: www.chelseagreen.com
Key Personnel
Publr: Margo Baldwin *E-mail:* mbaldwin@
chelseagreen.com
Assoc Publr: Lynne O'Hara *E-mail:* lohara@
chelseagreen.com
Sr Ed: Ben Watson *E-mail:* bwatson@monad.net
Publicity: Alice Blackmer *E-mail:* blackmer@
chelseagreen.com
Man Ed: Collette Fugere *E-mail:* cfugere@
chelseagreen.com
Publicity: Erin Hanrahan *E-mail:* hanrahan@
chelseagreen.com
Mktg & Sales: Jennifer Nix *E-mail:* jnix@
chelseagreen.com
Founded: 1984
Specialize in books for sustainable living includ-
ing: environment, building, nature, outdoors,
sustainability, organic gardening, home, renewable energy, homesteading, politics & current
events.
ISBN Prefix(es): 0-930031; 1-890132
Number of titles published annually: 20 Print

Total Titles: 250 Print; 1 Audio
Imprints: Good Life Center Books
Distributor for American Council for an Energy
Efficient Economy (ACEEE); Boye Knives
Press; Cal-Earth; Deep Stream Press; Earth
Justice; Ecological Design Press; Good Earth;
Goosefoot Acres; Greenleaf; Jenkins Publish-
ing; Moonsmile Press; Morning Sun Press;
Natural Heritage Books; Ottographics; Out on
Bale; Peregrinzilla; Polyface; Radical Weeds;
Solar Design Association; Spring Wheat; Sus-
sex; Sustainability Press; Trust for Public Land;
Watershed Media
Foreign Rep(s): Codasat: Hargreaves, Fuller, Pa-
ton (Canada); Chandler Crawford; Green Books
(UK)
Foreign Rights: Dieter Hagenboch (Germany);
Green Books (UK)
Warehouse: Business Park, Wellington Dr, Brat-
tleboro, VT 05301, Contact: Rich Norford *Toll
Free Tel:* 877-823-1213 *Fax:* 802-295-6444
Toll Free Fax: 877-823-1213 *E-mail:* seaton@
chelseagreen.com *Web Site:* www.chelseagreen.
com

Chelsea House Publishers LLC
Division of Haights Cross Communications Inc
2080 Cabot Blvd W, Suite 201, Langhorne, PA
19047-1813
SAN: 169-7331
Mailing Address: PO Box 914, Broomall, PA
19008-0914
Tel: 610-353-5166 *Toll Free Tel:* 800-848-
BOOK (848-2665) *Fax:* 610-359-1439
Toll Free Fax: 877-780-7300
E-mail: sales@chelseahouse.com
Web Site: www.chelseahouse.com
Key Personnel
Pres & CEO: Derek Reicherter
CFO: Stephen Seminack *E-mail:* sseminack@
chelseahouse.com
VP, Prod Devt: Sally Cheney *Tel:* 610-353-5191
E-mail: scheney@chelseahouse.com
VP, Sales & Mktg: Randi Misher
E-mail: rmisher@chelseahouse.com
Cust Rel Mgr: Dorothy Navera *E-mail:* dnavera@
chelseahouse.com
Warehouse Mgr: John Woodsmall *Tel:* 508-571-
6701 *E-mail:* jwoodsmall@sundancepub.com
Dir, Dist Sales: Jen Jenson *E-mail:* jjenson@
chelseahouse.com
Dir, HR: Linda Callipari *Fax:* 610-353-6432
E-mail: lcallipari@chelseahouse.com
Founded: 1966
Nonfiction children & young adult titles for the
school & library marketplace.
ISBN Prefix(es): 0-87754; 0-7910
Number of titles published annually: 300 Print
Total Titles: 3,116 Print
Imprints: Bloom Literary Criticism; Chelsea
Clubhouse
Branch Office(s)
Chelsea Clubhouse, 11975 Portland Ave S, Suite
110A, Burnsville, MN 55337
Foreign Rep(s): CIS Educational; Fitzhenry &
Whiteside; James Clarke & Co Ltd; Macro
Distributors; Maruzen Co Ltd; Premier Book
Marketing; Southern Book Publishers
Warehouse: One Beeman Rd, Northborough, MA
01532, Contact: John Woodsmall *Tel:* 508-571-
6701 *E-mail:* jwoodsmall@swundancepub.com
Distribution Center: One Beeman Rd, North-
borough, MA 01532, Contact: John Woods-
mall *Tel:* 508-571-6701 *E-mail:* jwoodsmall@
sundancepub.com
Membership(s): AAP; ALA

Chemical Education Resources Inc
Division of Thomson Learning
c/o Brooks/Cole, Thomson Learning, 3501 Market St, Philadelphia, PA 19104
SAN: 297-1909

Toll Free Tel: 800-523-1850 ext 3781
Toll Free Fax: 800-451-3661
Web Site: www.cerlabs.com
Key Personnel
Busn Center Mgr: Rich Wessler
Founded: 1984
Learning materials for college & university chem-
istry labs.
ISBN Prefix(es): 0-534; 0-87540
Total Titles: 350 Print

Chemical Publishing Co Inc
527 Third Ave, Suite 427, New York, NY 10016
SAN: 203-6444
Tel: 212-779-0090 *Toll Free Tel:* 800-786-3659
Fax: 212-889-1537
E-mail: chempub@aol.com
Web Site: www.chemicalpublishing.com
Key Personnel
Pres & Intl Rts: Silvia Soto-Galicia
Founded: 1934
Technical & professional books; chemical indus-
trial applications; cosmetic chemistry, cooling
& boiler water, cement chemistry, fireworks &
pyrotechnics.
ISBN Prefix(es): 0-8206
Number of titles published annually: 7 Print
Total Titles: 87 Print
Shipping Address: Publishers Storage & Shipping,
46 Development Rd, Fitchburg, MA 01420-
6019
Warehouse: Publishers Storage & Shipping, 46
Development Rd, Fitchburg, MA 01420-6019

§Cheng & Tsui Co Inc
25 West St, 5th fl, Boston, MA 02111-1213
Tel: 617-988-2401 *Toll Free Tel:* 800-554-1963
Fax: 617-426-3669
E-mail: service@cheng-tsui.com
Web Site: www.cheng-tsui.com
Key Personnel
Pres: Jill Cheng
Cust Serv: Lai Kwan
Founded: 1979
Publisher, importer & exporter of Asian books
in English. Publish & distribute Asia related
books & Chinese, Japanese & Korean language
learning textbooks.
ISBN Prefix(es): 0-917056; 0-88727
Number of titles published annually: 8 Print
Total Titles: 200 Print
Distributor for China International Book Trading
Co (Beijing, selected titles only); Commercial
Press (Hong Kong); Renditions Paperbacks;
Wellsweep Press
Warehouse: 46 Development Rd, Fitchburg, MA
01420

Cherokee Publishing Co
1710 Defoor Ave, NW, Atlanta, GA 30318
Mailing Address: PO Box 1730, Marietta, GA
30061 SAN: 201-4432
Tel: 404-467-4189 *Toll Free Tel:* 800-653-3952
Fax: 404-237-1062
E-mail: cherokeepub@defoorcentre.com
Key Personnel
Pres: Kenneth W Boyd
Ed: Alexa Selph
Founded: 1968
Reprints & originals; general trade; biography,
history, Southern Americana, nature, travel.
ISBN Prefix(es): 0-89783; 0-87797; 0-87419; 0-
932419
Number of titles published annually: 5 Print
Total Titles: 100 Print
Subsidiaries: Susan Hunter Publishing; Larlin
Corp; University Press of Washington, DC
Membership(s): ABA; Publishers Association of
the South; Publishers Marketing Association;
Southeast Booksellers Association

Cherry Lane Music Co
6 E 32 St, 11th fl, New York, NY 10016
Tel: 212-561-3000 *Fax:* 212-679-8157
E-mail: publishing@cherrylane.com
Web Site: www.cherrylane.com
Key Personnel
Electronic Publg: Andy Okun
Founded: 1962
Pop & rock song books for guitar keyboard &
    other instruments.
ISBN Prefix(es): 0-89524; 1-57560
Number of titles published annually: 20 Print
Total Titles: 570 Print
Distributed by Hal Leonard Corp

§Chess Combination Inc
PO Box 2423, Noble Sta, Bridgeport, CT 06608-
    0423
Tel: 203-301-0791 *Toll Free Tel:* 800-354-4083
    Fax: 203-301-0792
Web Site: chessNIC.com
Key Personnel
Pres & Publr: Albert Henderson *E-mail:* alh@
    chessnic.com
Founded: 1985
Chess books, magazines & software, electronic
    chess books; databases, indoor recreation, CD-
    ROMs, chess.
ISBN Prefix(es): 0-917237; 1-58863
Number of titles published annually: 8 Print; 4
    CD-ROM
Total Titles: 90 Print; 15 CD-ROM
Imprints: New In Chess

Chess Digest Inc
PO Box 609, Ardmore, TN 38449-0609
Toll Free Tel: 800-524-3527 (orders) *Fax:* 256-
    423-8345
E-mail: info@chessdigest.com
Web Site: www.chessdigest.com
Founded: 1964
Books on chess, exclusively.
ISBN Prefix(es): 0-87568
Number of titles published annually: 3 Print
Total Titles: 200 Print
Distributor for Trends

Chess Enterprises
107 Crosstree Rd, Coraopolis, PA 15108-2607
Tel: 412-262-2138
Key Personnel
Owner: Bobby G Dudley *E-mail:* bgdudley@
    compuserve.com
Founded: 1977
Books on the game of chess.
ISBN Prefix(es): 0-931462; 0-945470
Number of titles published annually: 3 Print
Total Titles: 188 Print
Distributed by Thinkers' Press
Distribution Center: Chessco, 1101 W Fourth St,
    Davenport, IA 52802 *Toll Free Tel:* 800-397-
    7117

Chestnut Hills Press, see BrickHouse Books Inc

Chicago Review Press
Affiliate of Independent Publishers Group
814 N Franklin St, Chicago, IL 60610
Tel: 312-337-0747 *Toll Free Tel:* 800-888-4741
    Fax: 312-337-5110
E-mail: editorial@ipgbook.com
Key Personnel
Publr: Linda H Matthews *E-mail:* lmatthews@
    ipgbook.com
Sales Mgr: Mary Rowles *E-mail:* mrowles@
    ipgbook.com
Ed: Cynthia Sherry *E-mail:* csherry@ipgbook.
    com
Imprints Ed: Yuval Taylor *E-mail:* yuval@
    ipgbook.com
Founded: 1973

ISBN Prefix(es): 1-55652
Number of titles published annually: 40 Print
Total Titles: 250 Print
Imprints: A Cappella Books; Lawrence Hill
    Books

Chicago Spectrum Press
4824 Brownsboro Center Arcade, Louisville, KY
    40207
Tel: 502-899-1919 *Toll Free Tel:* 800-594-5190
    Fax: 502-896-0246
E-mail: evanstonpublish@aol.com
Web Site: www.evanstonpublishing.com
Key Personnel
Off Mgr: Sherry Welch
Founded: 1986
Help authors & companies self-publish books.
    Also do packaging for publishers & maintain a
    catalog of their own publications.
ISBN Prefix(es): 1-886094; 1-58374
Number of titles published annually: 20 Print; 4
    E-Book
Total Titles: 200 Print; 4 E-Book
Membership(s): Better Business Bureau; Publish-
    ers Marketing Association

Child Development Project, see Developmental
    Studies Center

Children's Book Press
2211 Mission St, San Francisco, CA 94110
Tel: 415-821-3080 *Fax:* 415-821-3081
E-mail: info@childrensbookpress.org
Web Site: www.cbookpress.org
Key Personnel
Pres, Publr & Exec Dir: Harriet Rohmer
Exec Dir: Ruth Tobar
Dir, Sales & Mktg: Robert P Langdon
    Tel: 415-821-3080 ext 12 *E-mail:* rlangdon@
    childrensbookpress.org
Cust Serv Mgr: Rod Lowe
Founded: 1975
Multicultural & bilingual picture books for chil-
    dren. Central American, African-American,
    Asian-American, Hispanic-American, Native
    American tales, folklore, contemporary fiction
    & nonfiction.
ISBN Prefix(es): 0-89239
Number of titles published annually: 4 Print
Total Titles: 30 Print
Distributed by Publishers Group West (trade mar-
    ket)
Warehouse: 3602 Munster Ave, Unit B, Hayward,
    CA 94545

Children's Press, see Scholastic Library
    Publishing

Child's Play
Affiliate of Child's Play International, Ltd
67 Minot Ave, Auburn, ME 04210
Toll Free Tel: 800-472-0099; 800-639-6404
    Toll Free Fax: 800-854-6989
E-mail: cplay@earthlink.net
Web Site: www.childs-play.com
Key Personnel
VP, Sales & Mktg: Joe Gardner
Founded: 1972
Children's books, games, toys & AV.
ISBN Prefix(es): 0-85953
Number of titles published annually: 30 Print
Total Titles: 450 Print; 8 Audio
Branch Office(s)
64 Wellington Ave, West Orange, NJ 07052

§The Child's World Inc
PO Box 326, Chanhassen, MN 55317-0326
Tel: 952-906-3939 *Toll Free Tel:* 800-599-READ
    (599-7323) *Fax:* 952-906-3940
E-mail: info@childsworld.com
Web Site: www.childsworld.com

Key Personnel
Pres: Mike Peterson
Founded: 1968
K-8 library books for childhood education; social
    studies.
ISBN Prefix(es): 0-89565; 1-56766
Number of titles published annually: 200 Print;
    100 E-Book
Total Titles: 850 Print; 45 E-Book
Imprints: Tradition Books
Distributor for Tradition Books

Childswork/Childsplay LLC
Subsidiary of Guidance Channel
135 Dupont St, Plainview, NY 11803
Mailing Address: PO Box 760, Plainview, NY
    11803-0760
Tel: 516-349-5520 *Toll Free Tel:* 800-962-
    1141 (cust serv) *Fax:* 516-349-5521
    Toll Free Fax: 800-262-1886 (orders)
E-mail: info@childswork.com
Web Site: www.childswork.com
Key Personnel
CEO: Ed Werz *Tel:* 516-349-5520 ext 200
Pres: Lawrence Shapiro, PhD *Tel:* 516-349-5520
    ext 350
Exec VP: Janice Werz *Tel:* 516-349-5520 ext 202
Ed: Karen Schader *Tel:* 516-349-5520 ext 313
Founded: 1985
Psychological books, toys, games & counseling
    tools to assist counselors, therapists, teachers
    & parents help children cope with emotional &
    behavioral problems.
ISBN Prefix(es): 1-58815; 1-882732
Number of titles published annually: 12 Print
Total Titles: 76 Print

§China Books & Periodicals Inc
Division of Sino United Publications (Holdings)
    Ltd
2929 24 St, San Francisco, CA 94110-4126
SAN: 145-0557
Tel: 415-282-2994 *Toll Free Tel:* 800-818-2017
    Fax: 415-282-0994
E-mail: info@chinabooks.com
Web Site: www.chinabooks.com
Key Personnel
Gen Mgr: Greg Jones *E-mail:* greg@chinabooks.
    com
Mktg Dir: Tracy Lin *E-mail:* tracylin@
    chinabooks.com
Founded: 1960
Fiction, trade, nonfiction, dictionaries, encyclope-
    dias, maps, atlases, periodicals, sidelines, for-
    eign language, secondary textbooks, juvenile &
    young adult, subscription & mail order, hard-
    cover & paperback trade books; government,
    language arts, travel.
ISBN Prefix(es): 0-8351
Number of titles published annually: 10 Print
Total Titles: 750 Print; 20 Audio
Distributor for AsiaPac; CIBTC; Commercial
    Press; Foreign Languages Press; Joint Pub-
    lishers; New World Press; Panda Books; Peace
    Books; Red Mansions Publishing

Chitra Publications
2 Public Ave, Montrose, PA 18801
SAN: 631-0060
Tel: 570-278-1984 *Toll Free Tel:* 800-628-8244
    Fax: 570-278-2223
E-mail: chitra@epix.net
Web Site: www.quilttownusa.com
Key Personnel
Publr: Christiane Meunier
Assoc Publr & Circ Mgr: Twyla Estell
    E-mail: chitrate@epix.net
Founded: 1987
Quilting how-to.
ISBN Prefix(es): 0-9622565; 1-885588
Total Titles: 41 Print

§Chosen Books
Division of Baker Book House Co
PO Box 6287, Grand Rapids, MI 49516-6287
SAN: 203-3801
Tel: 616-676-9185 *Toll Free Tel:* 800-877-2665
  Fax: 616-676-2315
Web Site: www.bakerpublishinggroup.com
Key Personnel
Pres: Dwight Baker
Edit Dir: Jane Campbell
Prodn & ISBN Contact: Robert Bol
Rts & Perms, Intl Rts: Marilyn Gordon
Asst to Edit Dir: Sheila Ingram
Founded: 1971
Religious.
ISBN Prefix(es): 0-8007
Number of titles published annually: 15 Print
Total Titles: 81 Print
Foreign Rep(s): Christian Art (South Africa);
  Family Reading Publications (Australia); R
  G Mitchell (Canada); Omega Distributors (New
  Zealand); STL (UK, Europe)
Shipping Address: 6030 E Fulton Rd, Ada, MI
  49301

Christian Community, see LifeQuest

Christian Fellowship Ministries
915 E Dunlap, Phoenix, AZ 85021
Mailing Address: PO Box 11070, Phoenix, AZ
  85061-1070
Tel: 602-678-1543 *Toll Free Tel:* 888-678-1543
  Fax: 602-678-4196
E-mail: ministry@cfmin.net
Web Site: www.cfmin.net
Key Personnel
Pres: Rev Ronald C Dubrul
Opers Mgr: Rev Robert Brabante, PhD
Founded: 1965
Religious publishers.
ISBN Prefix(es): 1-929138
Number of titles published annually: 12 Print; 12
  Audio
Total Titles: 46 Print; 6 Audio

Christian Liberty Press
502 W Euclid Ave, Arlington Heights, IL 60004
Tel: 847-259-4444 *Fax:* 847-259-2941
Web Site: www.christianlibertypress.com
Key Personnel
Dir: Michael J McHugh *E-mail:* clpmike@
  starnetwx.net
Founded: 1985
ISBN Prefix(es): 1-930092; 1-930367; 1-932971
Number of titles published annually: 6 Print; 3
  CD-ROM; 4 Audio
Total Titles: 150 Print; 8 CD-ROM; 38 Audio
Distributed by Appalachian Distributors

Christian Light Publications Inc
1066 Chicago Ave, Harrisonburg, VA 22802
Mailing Address: PO Box 1212, Harrisonburg,
  VA 22803-1212
Tel: 540-434-0768
Key Personnel
Gen Mgr: John Hartzler
Sec, Bd of Dirs: Merna B Shank
  E-mail: mernas@clp.org
Founded: 1969
Books, booklets, tracts, Sunday school, vacation
  Bible school & Christian day school curricu-
  lum.
ISBN Prefix(es): 0-87813
Number of titles published annually: 9 Print
Total Titles: 130 Print

Christian Literature Crusade Inc
701 Pennsylvania Ave, Fort Washington, PA
  19034-8449
SAN: 169-7358

Mailing Address: PO Box 1449, Fort Washington,
  PA 19034
Tel: 215-542-1242 *Toll Free Tel:* 800-659-1240
  (orders) *Fax:* 215-542-7580
E-mail: clcbooks@safeplace.net
Web Site: www.clcpublications.com
Key Personnel
Pres & Wholesale Mgr: William Almack
Acct Coord: Katy Sherrard
Founded: 1941
Worldwide Christian mission organization.
ISBN Prefix(es): 0-87508
Number of titles published annually: 6 Print
Total Titles: 250 Print
Distributor for Bethany Fellowship; Christian Fel-
  lowship; Christian Publications; Lutterworth
Membership(s): EFMA

Christian Living Books Inc
Imprint of Pneuma Life Publishing Inc
12103 Woodwind Lane, Mitchellville, MD 20721
SAN: 254-2218
Mailing Address: PO Box 7584, Largo, MD
  20792
Tel: 301-218-9092 *Toll Free Tel:* 800-727-3218
  (ordering) *Fax:* 301-218-4943
E-mail: info@christianlivingbooks.com
Web Site: www.christianlivingbooks.com
Key Personnel
Pres: Kimberly Stewart *E-mail:* kimberly@
  christianlivingbooks.com
Founded: 2001
Full-service publisher of Christian living & moti-
  vational books.
ISBN Prefix(es): 0-9716240; 1-56229
Number of titles published annually: 18 Print; 8
  Online; 12 E-Book
Total Titles: 25 Print; 2 Online; 2 E-Book
Distributed by Pneuma Life Publishing
Shipping Address: G L Services, 4588 Interstate
  Dr, Cincinnati, OH 45246 805-677-6815
  E-mail: fulfillment@bookworld.com
Warehouse: BookWorld Services Inc, 1230
  Heil Quaker Blvd, LaVergne, TN 37086
  E-mail: fulfillment@bookworld.com
Distribution Center: BookWorld Services Inc,
  1933 Whitfield Park Look, Sarasota, FL
  34243 *Tel:* 941-758-8094 *Fax:* 941-753-9396
  E-mail: central@bookworld.com
Membership(s): Publishers Marketing Associa-
  tion; Small Publishers Association of North
  America

Christian Publications Inc
3825 Hartzdale Dr, Camp Hill, PA 17011
Tel: 717-761-7044 *Toll Free Tel:* 800-233-4443
  Fax: 717-761-7273
E-mail: editorial@christianpublications.com
Web Site: www.christianpublications.com
Key Personnel
Pres: Ken Paton
Publr: Doug Wicks
Publicist: Tina Weidemann *E-mail:* tweidemann@
  christianpublications.com
Trade Sales Dir & Intl Rts: Drew Park
  E-mail: dpark@christianpublications.com
Mktg Mgr: Rob Billingham *E-mail:* rbillingham@
  christianpublications.com
Founded: 1883
ISBN Prefix(es): 0-87509; 0-88965
Number of titles published annually: 10 Print
Total Titles: 80 Print

Christian Schools International
3350 E Paris Ave SE, Grand Rapids, MI 49512-
  3054
SAN: 204-1804
Mailing Address: PO Box 8709, Grand Rapids,
  MI 49512-8709
Tel: 616-957-1070 *Toll Free Tel:* 800-635-8288
  Fax: 616-957-5022
E-mail: info@csionline.org

Web Site: www.csionline.org
Key Personnel
Dir: Daniel Vander Ark
Prodn Mgr, Ed & Rts & Perms: Judy Bandstra
  Tel: 616-957-1070 ext 243 *E-mail:* judyb@
  csionline.org
Ed: Gordon Bordewyk
Founded: 1920
Teacher resources & aids & curriculum guides.
ISBN Prefix(es): 0-87463
Number of titles published annually: 18 Print; 2
  CD-ROM
Total Titles: 124 Print; 7 CD-ROM
Imprints: CSI Publications

Christopher-Gordon Publishers Inc
1502 Providence Hwy, Suite 12, Norwood, MA
  02062
Tel: 781-762-5577 *Toll Free Tel:* 800-934-8322
  Fax: 781-762-2110
Web Site: www.christopher-gordon.com
Key Personnel
Pres: Hiram G Howard
Sr VP & Treas: Susanne F Canavan
  E-mail: sfcanavan@aol.com
VP, Opers: Linda M Nevins
Founded: 1987
ISBN Prefix(es): 0-926842; 1-929024
Number of titles published annually: 25 Print
Total Titles: 140 Print
Imprints: The Bill Harp Professional Teacher's
  Library

Christopher Publishing House
Member of A T I Group
24 Rockland St, Hanover, MA 02339
SAN: 202-1625
Tel: 781-826-7474; 781-826-5494 *Fax:* 781-826-
  5556
E-mail: cph@atigroupinc.com
Key Personnel
Publr: Harold F Walsh
Man Ed: Nancy Kopp
Founded: 1910
Hardcover & paperback trade books.
ISBN Prefix(es): 0-8158
Number of titles published annually: 6 Print
Total Titles: 50 Print

Chronicle Books LLC
85 Second St, 6th fl, San Francisco, CA 94105
SAN: 202-165X
Tel: 415-537-4200 *Toll Free Tel:* 800-722-
  6657 (cust serv) *Fax:* 415-537-4460
  Toll Free Fax: 800-858-7787 (orders)
E-mail: frontdesk@chroniclebooks.com
Web Site: www.chroniclebooks.com
Key Personnel
Chmn & CEO: Nion McEvoy
Pres & Publr: Jack Jensen
VP, Opers & Fin: Tom Fernald
Exec Dir, Sales & Mktg: Chris Navratil
Mktg Dir: Kendra Kallan
Edit Dir, Cookbooks: Bill LeBlond
Edit Dir, Literature: Jay Schaefer
Dir, Publicity: Andrea Burnett
Dir, Intl Sales & Subsidiary Rts: Sarah Williams
Sr Ed: Susan Pearson
Man Ed: Dean Burrell
Exec Ed, Adult Trade: Alan Rapp
Exec Ed, Gift: Kerry Colburn
Assoc Publr, Adult Trade Div: Christine Carswell
Assoc Publr, Children's Book Div: Victoria Rock
Assoc Publr, Gift Div: Debra Lande
HR Mgr: Joanie Pacheco-Anderson *Tel:* 413-537-
  4200 ext 4255 *E-mail:* jpa@chronbooks.com
Founded: 1966
General nonfiction & fiction, cloth & paperbound:
  fine arts, gift, nature, outdoors, nationwide re-
  gional guidebooks, stationery, calendars & an-
  cillary products.
ISBN Prefix(es): 0-87701; 0-8118

Number of titles published annually: 200 Print
Total Titles: 1,500 Print
Divisions: Adult Trade; Chronicle Books for Children; Chronicle Gift
Distributor for Handprint; Innovative Kids; North/South; Princeton Architectural Press; Ragged Bears
Foreign Rep(s): Critiques Livres (France); Hardie Grant Books (Australia); HI Marketing (UK, Europe); Raincoast Book (Canada); Real Books (South Africa); Marta Schooler (Asia, Middle East); Tandem Press (New Zealand); Cynthia Zimpfer (Latin America)
Foreign Rights: Bettina Nibbe (Germany); Bengt Nordin (Netherlands, Scandinavia); Frederique Porretta (France); Tao Media (China)
Shipping Address: Genco fulfillment West, 545 Coney Island Dr, Sparks, NV 89431

§Chronicle Guidance Publications Inc
66 Aurora St, Moravia, NY 13118
SAN: 202-1641
Tel: 315-497-0330 *Toll Free Tel:* 800-622-7284
   Fax: 315-497-3359
E-mail: customerservice@chronicleguidance.com
Web Site: www.chronicleguidance.com
Key Personnel
Pres: Cheryl Fickeisen *E-mail:* cheryl@chronicleguidance.com
VP & Treas: Gary W Fickeisen
Treas & Asst VP: Christopher D Fickeisen
Founded: 1938
Education materials, kindergarten to higher education. Annual education-oriented directories & guides; career information briefs & reprint articles on occupations, interest inventories & life skills materials.
ISBN Prefix(es): 1-55631
Number of titles published annually: 6 Print; 1 CD-ROM; 2 Online
Total Titles: 25 Print; 1 CD-ROM; 2 Online
Distributed by American Guidance Service (AGS); Cambridge Educational; Communication Skills Inc; Ebsco Subscription Services; EdITS; Educational & Psychological Services International (EPSI); JIST Works Inc; Meridian Education Corp; Nimco Inc; Psychological Assessment Resources Inc (PAR); Southern Media Systems Inc
Advertising Agency: C & G Advertising

Church Growth Institute
Subsidiary of Ephesians Four Ministries
PO Box 7, Elkton, MD 21922-0007
Tel: 434-525-0022 *Toll Free Tel:* 800-553-4769 (orders only) *Fax:* 434-525-0608
   Toll Free Fax: 800-644-4729 (orders only)
E-mail: cgimail@churchgrowth.org
Web Site: www.churchgrowth.org
Key Personnel
Dir: Larry A Gilbert
Resource Dev Dir & Admin: Cindy Spear
   E-mail: cspear@churchgrowth.org
Founded: 1984 (Ephesians Four Ministries 1978, Church Growth Institute 1984)
Create, develop & publish educational materials to help churches & individual Christians reach their potential.
ISBN Prefix(es): 0-941005; 1-57052
Number of titles published annually: 4 Print
Total Titles: 150 Print
Advertising Agency: PO Box 7000, Forest, VA 24551-7000
Orders to: PO Box 9176, Oxnard, CA 93031-9176 *Toll Free Fax:* 800-860-3109
Returns: CGI Insurance, 4588 Interstate Dr, Cincinnati, OH 45246
Distribution Center: CGI Warehouse, 4588 Interstate Dr, Cincinnati, OH 45246

Cinco Puntos Press
701 Texas Ave, El Paso, TX 79901

Tel: 915-838-1625 *Toll Free Tel:* 800-566-9072
   Fax: 915-838-1635
E-mail: info@cincopuntos.com
Web Site: www.cincopuntos.com
Key Personnel
Publr & Acq Ed: Lee Byrd *E-mail:* leebyrd@cincopuntos.com
Publr & Intl Rts: Bobby Byrd *E-mail:* bbyrd@cincopuntos.com
VP, Busn: Edward Holland *E-mail:* bizman@cincopuntos.com
Founded: 1985
Books of the Southwest US & bilingual children's literature.
ISBN Prefix(es): 0-938317
Number of titles published annually: 12 Print
Total Titles: 85 Print; 10 Audio
Distributor for Mariposa Publishing; Trails West Publishing
Distribution Center: Consortium Book Sales & Distribution, 1045 Westgate, St Paul, MN 55114 *Tel:* 651-221-9035 *Fax:* 651-221-0124

Circlet Press Inc
1770 Massachusetts Ave, Suite 278, Cambridge, MA 02140
Tel: 617-864-0492 *Toll Free Tel:* 800-729-6423 (orders) *Fax:* 617-864-0663
E-mail: info@circlet.com
Web Site: www.circlet.com
Key Personnel
Publr & Ed: Cecilia Tan *E-mail:* ctan@circlet.com
Publicist: Ava Perry *E-mail:* avaperry@circlet.com
Founded: 1992
Anthologies of short stories of erotic science fiction/fantasy (a new subgenre) & cutting edge erotica.
ISBN Prefix(es): 0-9633970; 1-885865
Number of titles published annually: 12 Print
Total Titles: 50 Print
Imprints: Circumflex (nonfiction & how-to on sexuality); The Ultra Violet Library (gay & lesbian; science fiction not erotic)
Distributed by SCB Distributors
Foreign Rep(s): Bulldog Books (Australia); Turnaround Ltd (UK, Europe)

CIS Publishers & Distributors
Division of CIS Communications
180 Park Ave S, Lakewood, NJ 08701
Tel: 732-905-3000 *Fax:* 732-367-6666
Key Personnel
Pres: Alexander Z Ellinson
Founded: 1984
Jewish interests including Jewish history & tradition, biographies, Holocaust literature, novels, cookbooks, self-help, children's literature, etc.
ISBN Prefix(es): 0-935063; 1-56062
Number of titles published annually: 7 Print
Total Titles: 218 Print

Cistercian Publications Inc, Editorial Office
WMU, 1903 W Michigan Ave, Kalamazoo, MI 49008
SAN: 202-1668
Tel: 269-387-8920 *Fax:* 269-387-8390
E-mail: cistpub@wmich.edu
Web Site: www.spencerabbey.org/cistpub
Key Personnel
Pres: Ernst Breisach
VP, Ed & Foreign Rts: E Rozanne Elder
Treas: Lowell Rinker
Cust Serv Mgr: Karen Sue McDougall
   E-mail: mcdougall@wmich.edu
Founded: 1969
Religion (Roman Catholic) & history.
ISBN Prefix(es): 0-87907
Number of titles published annually: 15 Print
Total Titles: 212 Print

Distributor for Fairacres Press; Peregrina Press
Shipping Address: St Joseph's Abbey, Spencer, MA 01562, Sales Mgr: Albert James

City Lights Books Inc
261 Columbus Ave, San Francisco, CA 94133
SAN: 202-1684
Tel: 415-362-8193 *Fax:* 415-362-4921
E-mail: staff@citylights.com
Web Site: www.citylights.com
Key Personnel
Publr: Lawrence Ferlinghetti
Exec Ed: Nancy J Peters
Ed & Intl Rts: Robert Sharrard *E-mail:* sharrard@citylights.com
Dir, Mktg: Stacey Lewis
Assoc Dir, Mktg: Elaine Katzenberger
Founded: 1955
Paperbound books; fiction, poetry, literature & criticism.
ISBN Prefix(es): 0-87286
Number of titles published annually: 12 Print
Total Titles: 200 Print
Sales Office(s): Consortium Book Sales & Distribution, 1045 Westgate Dr, Suite 90, St Paul, MN 55114-1065 *Tel:* 612-221-9025 *Toll Free Tel:* 800-283-3572 *Fax:* 612-221-9035
Foreign Rights: Agence Hoffman (France, Germany); Agenzia Letteraria Internazionale (Italy); Carmen Balcells (Spain)
Distribution Center: Consortium Book Sales & Distribution, 1045 Westgate Dr, Suite 90, St Paul, MN 55114-1065 *Tel:* 612-221-9025 *Toll Free Tel:* 800-283-3572 *Fax:* 612-221-9035

Clarion Books
Division of Houghton Mifflin Co
215 Park Ave S, New York, NY 10003
Tel: 212-420-5800 *Toll Free Tel:* 800-225-3362 (orders) *Fax:* 212-420-5855
Web Site: www.clarion.com
Key Personnel
Assoc Publr & Edit Dir: Dinah Stevenson
Mktg Mgr: Marjorie Naughton
Art Dir: Joann Hill
Rts Mgr: Rebecca J Mancini
Founded: 1965
Juvenile & young adult books, audiocassette packages.
ISBN Prefix(es): 0-89919; 0-395; 0-618
Number of titles published annually: 70 Print
Distributed by Houghton Mifflin Co
Membership(s): Children's Book Council

Clarity Press Inc
3277 Roswell Rd NE, Suite 469, Atlanta, GA 30305
SAN: 688-9530
Toll Free Tel: 800-729-6423 (orders); 877-613-1495 *Fax:* 404-231-3899 *Toll Free Fax:* 877-613-7868
E-mail: clarity@islandnet.com; claritypress@usa.net (editorial)
Web Site: www.claritypress.com *Telex:* 650-259-0558
Key Personnel
Edit Dir: Diana G Collier
Busn Mgr: Annette Gordon
Founded: 1984
Scholarly works on political, social, minority & human rights issues.
ISBN Prefix(es): 0-932863
Number of titles published annually: 4 Print
Total Titles: 28 Print
Foreign Rep(s): Fernwood Books (Canada)
Distribution Center: SCB Distributors, 15608 S New Century Dr, Gardena, CA 90248, Contact: Victor Duran *Tel:* 310-532-9400 *Toll Free Tel:* 800-729-6423 *Fax:* 310-532-7001
E-mail: victor@scbdistributors.com
Membership(s): Society for Scholarly Publishing

I E Clark Publications
PO Box 246, Schulenburg, TX 78956
SAN: 282-7433
Tel: 979-743-3232 *Fax:* 979-743-4765
E-mail: ieclark@cvtv.net
Web Site: www.ieclark.com
Key Personnel
Owner: I E Clark; Lila N Clark
Gen Mgr: Donna Cozzaglio
Founded: 1956
Plays of all types for all types of theatre.
ISBN Prefix(es): 0-88680
Number of titles published annually: 10 Print
Total Titles: 280 Print
Foreign Rep(s): J Garnet Miller Ltd (UK); The
Play Bureau Ltd (New Zealand)

Clark Publishing Inc
1000 N Second Ave, Logan, IA 51546
Tel: 712-644-2831 *Toll Free Tel:* 800-845-1916
Fax: 712-644-2392 *Toll Free Fax:* 800-543-2745
E-mail: orders@perfectionlearning.com
Web Site: www.perfectionlearning.com
Small niche publishing company, specializing in
secondary level textbooks in communications
field.
ISBN Prefix(es): 0-931054
Number of titles published annually: 10 Print
Total Titles: 50 Print

Clarkson Potter Publishers
Subsidiary of Crown Publishing Group
1745 Broadway, New York, NY 10019
Tel: 212-782-9000 *Toll Free Tel:* 888-264-1745
Fax: 212-572-6181
Web Site: www.clarksonpotter.com; www.
randomhouse.com/crown/clarksonpotter
Key Personnel
Sr VP & Publr: Lauren Shakely
VP & Edit Dir: Pamela Krauss
Creative Dir: Marysarah Quinn
Mktg Dir: Katherine Dietrich
Publicity Dir: Tammy Blake
Founded: 1959
Illustrated & non-illustrated books on style, de-
sign, architecture, art, cookery, gardening,
crafts, fashion, health, house & home.
Random House Inc & its publishing entities are
not accepting unsol submissions, proposals,
mss or submission queries via e-mail at this
time.
ISBN Prefix(es): 0-609; 0-307; 0-676; 1-4000; 0-517
Number of titles published annually: 60 Print
Total Titles: 900 Print
Imprints: Clarkson Potter; Potter Style
Distributed by Random House
Advertising Agency: Franklin Spier

Classic Books
PO Box 130, Murrieta, CA 92564-0130
Toll Free Tel: 888-265-3547 *Toll Free Fax:* 888-265-3550 *Fax on Demand:* 909-767-0133
E-mail: 4classic@gte.net
Key Personnel
Pres: Michael Frances
Publish reprints of classic books.
ISBN Prefix(es): 1-58201; 0-7426
Number of titles published annually: 1,000 Print
Total Titles: 5,000 Print; 5,000 E-Book

Classroom Connect
8000 Marina Blvd, Suite 400, Brisbane, CA
94005
Tel: 650-351-5100 *Toll Free Tel:* 800-638-1639
(cust support) *Fax:* 650-351-5300
E-mail: connect@classroom.com
Web Site: www.classroom.com
Key Personnel
Pres & CEO: Pat Harrigan
COO: Marc Strohlein

VP, Prod Devt: Micaelia Randolph
VP, Prof Devt: Rem Jackson
VP, Teaching & Learning Initiatives: Scott Noon
VP, Strategic Rel: Jenny House
VP, Sales: Ed Bonessi
Founded: 1994
K-12 educator professional development & online
classroom learning resources.
Branch Office(s)
2221 Rosecrans Ave, Suite 237, El Segundo,
CA 90245 *Tel:* 310-725-0887 *Fax:* 310-725-
0899 *E-mail:* connect@classroom.com *Web
Site:* www.classroom.com
Membership(s): International Society for Tech-
nology in Education; Software & Information
Industry Association

Clear Light Publishers
823 Don Diego, Santa Fe, NM 87505
Tel: 505-989-9590 *Toll Free Tel:* 888-253-2747
(orders) *Fax:* 505-989-9519
E-mail: market@clearlightbooks.com
Web Site: www.clearlightbooks.com
Key Personnel
Publr: Harmon Houghton
Founded: 1981
ISBN Prefix(es): 0-940666; 1-57416
Number of titles published annually: 18 Print
Total Titles: 150 Print
Foreign Rights: Harmon Houghton Clear Light
Books
Membership(s): ABA; ALA; Mountains & Plains
Booksellers Association; New Mexico Book
Association

§Clear View Press
PO Box 11574, Marina del Rey, CA 90295
SAN: 255-934X
Tel: 310-902-0786 *Fax:* 310-821-9007
E-mail: editor@clearviewpress.com
Key Personnel
Ed: Brett Tabin
Founded: 2003
Publishers of books, audio CDs & e-books.
ISBN Prefix(es): 0-9743793
Number of titles published annually: 3 Print; 1
CD-ROM; 1 Audio
Total Titles: 3 Print; 1 CD-ROM; 1 Audio

Cleis Press
PO Box 14684, San Francisco, CA 94114-0684
Tel: 415-575-4700 *Toll Free Tel:* 800-780-2279
(US) *Fax:* 415-575-4705
E-mail: cleis@cleispress.com
Web Site: www.cleispress.com
Key Personnel
Publr: Frederique Delacoste *E-mail:* fdelacoste@
cleispress.com; Felice Newman
E-mail: fnewman@cleispress.com
Dir, Mktg & Publicity: Diane Levinson
E-mail: dlevinson@cleispress.com
Founded: 1980
Lesbian & gay studies; sexuality; Latin & African
American, human rights, gender studies, erot-
ica.
ISBN Prefix(es): 0-939416; 1-57344
Number of titles published annually: 30 Print
Total Titles: 150 Print
Imprints: Midnight Editions
Foreign Rep(s): Banyan Tree (Australia);
Turnaround (UK, Europe)
Distribution Center: Publishers Group West,
1700 Fourth St, Berkeley, CA 94710 *Toll Free
Tel:* 800-788-3123 *Fax:* 510-520-3444

Clock Tower Press
3622 W Liberty Rd, Ann Arbor, MI 48103
SAN: 254-8526
Tel: 734-769-5600 *Toll Free Tel:* 800-956-8999
Fax: 734-769-5607
Web Site: www.clocktowerpress.com;
huronriverpress.com

Key Personnel
Sales & Mktg: Ryan Shuchman
Founded: 2002
Publisher of fine golf books.
ISBN Prefix(es): 1-58536; 1-896947; 1-932202;
1-932399
Number of titles published annually: 7 Print
Total Titles: 100 Print
Imprints: Huron River Press (Publishers of books
about the Great Lakes)
Returns: PSCC, 660 S Mansfield, Ypsilanti, MI
48197, Contact: Paul Was *Tel:* 734-487-9726
Fax: 734-487-1890
Warehouse: PSSC, 660 S Mansfield, Ypsilanti,
MI 48197, Contact: Paul Was *Tel:* 734-487-
9720 *Fax:* 734-487-1890

Close Up Publishing
Division of Close Up Foundation
44 Canal Center Plaza, Alexandria, VA 22314
Toll Free Tel: 800-765-3131 *Fax:* 703-706-3564
E-mail: cup@closeup.org
Web Site: www.closeup.org/publishing
Founded: 1970
Publish supplemental texts, videos, teachers'
guides & simulation activities for secondary
school & college social studies, political sci-
ence, government, economics, international
relations & history courses & for general read-
ership.
ISBN Prefix(es): 0-932765
Number of titles published annually: 5 Print; 3
Audio
Total Titles: 56 Print; 19 Audio

Closson Press
1935 Sampson Dr, Apollo, PA 15613-9208
Tel: 724-337-4482 *Fax:* 724-337-9484
E-mail: clossonpress@comcast.net
Web Site: www.clossonpress.com
Key Personnel
Pres & Owner: Marietta Closson
Founded: 1976
Specialize in history & genealogy.
ISBN Prefix(es): 0-933227; 1-55856
Number of titles published annually: 40 Print
Total Titles: 637 Print
Distributed by Hearthstone Books; Heritage/Wil-
lowbend; Masthof Press
Foreign Rep(s): Cornelia Schrader (Italy); Warner
Hacker (Germany)
Advertising Agency: Retrospect Publishing; Wil-
lowbend/Heritage

Clovernook Printing House for the Blind
Division of The Clovernook Center for the Blind
7000 Hamilton Ave, Cincinnati, OH 45231-5297
Tel: 513-522-3860 *Toll Free Tel:* 888-234-7156
Fax: 513-728-3946 (admin); 513-728-3950
(sales)
Web Site: www.clovernook.org
Key Personnel
VP: Jay Longworth
Mgr, Printing: Charlotte Begley
Braille books & magazines; fiction & nonfiction.
Number of titles published annually: 155 Print
Total Titles: 170 Print

§CMP Books
Division of CMP Media LLC
Imprint of United Business Media
600 Harrison St, San Francisco, CA 94107
Tel: 415-947-6615; 408-848-3854 (orders)
Toll Free Tel: 800-500-6875 (orders) *Fax:* 415-
947-6015; 408-848-5784 (orders)
E-mail: books@cmp.com
Web Site: www.cmpbooks.com
Key Personnel
Publr: Matthew Kelsey
Assoc Publr: Paul Temme
Acctg Mgr: Susan Fuller
Sales Coord: Frank Brogan
Book Opers Coord: Jennifer Steele

Mktg Mgr: Brandy Ernzen
Provides hands-on information for high tech professionals, enabling them to create, develop & implement cutting-edge computing, design & communications solutions. Key markets include software development, embedded applications, telecom, networks, digital video, web development & CAD.
ISBN Prefix(es): 0-87930; 0-936648; 1-57820; 0-923667; 1-929629
Number of titles published annually: 25 Print
Total Titles: 115 Print; 40 CD-ROM; 1 E-Book
Branch Office(s)
1601 W 23 St, Suite 200, Lawrence, KS 66046
Tel: 785-838-7561 *Fax:* 785-841-2047
Sales Office(s): 12 W 21 St, New York, NY 10010-6902
Orders to: Distribution Ctr, 6600 Silacci Way, Gilroy, CA 95020 *Tel:* 408-848-3854 *Fax:* 408-848-5784
Returns: Distribution Ctr, 6600 Silacci Way, Gilroy, CA 95020
Distribution Center: Distribution Ctr, 6600 Silacci Way, Gilroy, CA 95020 *Tel:* 408-848-3854 *Fax:* 408-848-5784

Coaches Choice
4 Justin Ct, Monterey, CA 93940
Mailing Address: PO Box 1828, Monterey, CA 93942-1828
Toll Free Tel: 888-229-5745 *Fax:* 831-372-6075
E-mail: info@coacheschoice.com
Web Site: www.coacheschoice.com
Key Personnel
Pres: James Peterson
VP & Gen Mgr: Susan Peterson
VP, Trade Sales: Weiss Lancaster
Edit Mgr: Kristi Huelsing *Tel:* 831-372-6077
    E-mail: khuelsing@redshift.com
Coaching books & videos, football, basketball, baseball, softball, volleyball, soccer & track & field.
ISBN Prefix(es): 1-57167; 1-58518
Number of titles published annually: 40 Print

Cobblestone Publishing Co
Division of The Cricket Magazine Group
30 Grove St, Suite C, Peterborough, NH 03458
Tel: 603-924-7209 *Toll Free Tel:* 800-821-0115
    Fax: 603-924-7380
E-mail: custsvc@cobblestone.mv.com
Web Site: www.cobblestonepub.com
Key Personnel
Publr: John S Olbrych
Mktg Mgr: Manuela Meier
Children's magazines, occasional educational books & teacher's resources.
Number of titles published annually: 60 Print
Total Titles: 850 Print

Coda Publications
CR A-68, Bldg 92, Raton, NM 87740
Mailing Address: PO Box 71, Raton, NM 87740-0071
Tel: 505-445-4455 *Fax:* 505-445-4455
E-mail: newmexicobooks@bacavalley.com; coda@bacavalley.com
Key Personnel
Man Dir: William Carroll
Founded: 1955
Specialize in books, electronic books, automotive & general trade, New Mexico regional.
ISBN Prefix(es): 0-910390
Number of titles published annually: 3 Print
Total Titles: 40 Print
Imprints: Blue Jeans Poetry; Coda Publications; Funny Farm Books; New Mexico Books

Coffee House Press
27 N Fourth St, Suite 400, Minneapolis, MN 55401
SAN: 206-3883

Tel: 612-338-0125 *Fax:* 612-338-4004
Web Site: www.coffeehousepress.org
Key Personnel
Publr: Allan Kornblum *E-mail:* allan@coffeehousepress.org
Mktg & Sales Dir: Molly Mikolowski *E-mail:* molly@coffeehousepress.org
Sr Ed: Christopher Fischbach *E-mail:* fish@coffeehousepress.org
Subs Rts: Nancy Green Madia *Tel:* 212-864-0425 *Fax:* 212-316-2191 *E-mail:* ngmrights@earthlink.net
Founded: 1984
Fine editions & trade books; contemporary poetry, short fiction, novels, literary essays & memoirs.
ISBN Prefix(es): 0-915124; 0-918273; 1-56689
Number of titles published annually: 14 Print
Total Titles: 200 Print
Distribution Center: Consortium, 1045 Westgate Dr, St Paul, MN 55114

Cognizant Communication Corp
3 Hartsdale Rd, Elmsford, NY 10523-3701
Tel: 914-592-7720 *Fax:* 914-592-8981
E-mail: cogcomm@aol.com
Web Site: www.cognizantcommunication.com
Key Personnel
Chmn & Publr: Bob Miranda
Founded: 1992
STM & social science books & journals. Subjects include: tourism research & leisure studies, medical research, engineering & psychology.
ISBN Prefix(es): 1-882345; 0-971587
Number of titles published annually: 5 Print
Total Titles: 40 Print; 1 CD-ROM; 1 Audio
Online services available through Ingenta.
Imprints: Miranda Press Trade Division; Tourism Dynamic
Foreign Rights: Bob Miranda

Cokesbury, see Abingdon Press

Cold Spring Harbor Laboratory Press
Division of Cold Spring Harbor Laboratory
500 Sunnyside Blvd, Woodbury, NY 11797-2924
SAN: 203-6185
Tel: 516-422-4100 *Toll Free Tel:* 800-843-4388
    Fax: 516-422-4097
E-mail: cshpress@cshl.edu
Web Site: www.cshlpress.com
Key Personnel
Ed & Intl Rts Contact: John Inglis
Book Mktg Mgr & Lib Sales Dir: Ingrid Benirschke *Tel:* 619-275-6021 *Fax:* 619-275-2198 *E-mail:* benirsch@cshl.edu
Prodn Mgr & Rts & Perms: Denise Weiss
Adv Mgr: Marcie Siconolfi
Journal Mktg Mgr & Online Sales Dir: Kathryn Fitzpatrick
Cust Rel: Guy Keyes
Founded: 1933
Scholarly & scientific books; laboratory meeting results, four journals.
ISBN Prefix(es): 0-87969
Number of titles published annually: 20 Print
Total Titles: 220 Print; 2 Audio
Online services available through HighWire Press.
Foreign Rep(s): Maruzen (Japan)
Orders to: 180 Oser Ave, Suite 1000, Hauppauge, NY 11788
Warehouse: 180 Oser Ave, Suite 1000, Hauppauge, NY 11788
Membership(s): AAP

Collectors Press Inc
15655 SW 74 Ave, Suite 200, Tigard, OR 97224
Mailing Address: PO Box 230986, Portland, OR 97281
Tel: 503-684-3030 *Toll Free Tel:* 800-423-1848
    Fax: 503-684-3777
Web Site: www.collectorspress.com

Key Personnel
Pres & Intl Rts: Richard Perry *E-mail:* rperry@collectorspress.com
Owner & Mgr: Lisa Perry *E-mail:* lperry@collectorspress.com
Edit Mgr: Jennifer Weaver-Neist
Founded: 1992
Award winning publishers of pop culture art books.
ISBN Prefix(es): 0-9635202; 1-888054
Number of titles published annually: 12 Print
Total Titles: 90 Print
Divisions: Starbound Publishing
Distributed by Ten Speed Press
Foreign Rights: Sylvia Hayses
Distribution Center: Bridgeport Distribution, 16520 SW 72 Ave, Tigard, OR 97229
Membership(s): Pacific Northwest Booksellers Association; Publishers Association of the West; Publishers Marketing Association

College & University Professional Association for Human Resources
Tyson Place, 2607 Kingston Pike, Suite 250, Knoxville, TN 37919
Tel: 865-637-7673 *Fax:* 865-637-7674
E-mail: communications@cupahr.org
Web Site: www.cupahr.org
Key Personnel
Exec Dir: Stephen Otzenberger
    E-mail: sotzenberger@cupahr.org
Founded: 1946
Serves more than 6,500 human resource administrators at nearly 1,600 colleges & universities.
ISBN Prefix(es): 0-910402
Number of titles published annually: 6 Print
Total Titles: 46 Print

§The College Board
45 Columbus Ave, New York, NY 10023-6992
SAN: 269-0829
Tel: 212-713-8000 *Fax:* 212-713-8143
Web Site: www.collegeboard.com
Key Personnel
Exec Dir, College Planning Servs: Terry Novak
Founded: 1900
Educational & trade books in the fields of college admission, continuing education, guidance, curriculum, financial aid, educational research, college-level & advanced placement examinations & school reform.
ISBN Prefix(es): 0-87447
Number of titles published annually: 7 Print
Total Titles: 100 Print; 7 CD-ROM; 4 E-Book; 1 Audio
Distributed by Henry Holt

College Press Publishing Co
223 W Third St, Joplin, MO 64801
SAN: 211-9951
Mailing Address: PO Box 1132, Joplin, MO 64802
Tel: 417-623-6280 *Toll Free Tel:* 800-289-3300
    Fax: 417-623-8250
E-mail: books@collegepress.com
Web Site: www.collegepress.com
Key Personnel
Pres: Chris De Welt
Exec Ed: Drew Ashwell
Founded: 1959
Religion, theology, Bible study.
ISBN Prefix(es): 0-89900
Number of titles published annually: 20 Print; 2 CD-ROM
Total Titles: 100 Print; 1 Audio
Divisions: Forerunner Books
Distributed by Appalachian; CBD; Midwest Library Service; Riverside; Spring Arbor
Distributor for David C Cook Publishing; Gospel Light
Advertising Agency: Matthewson Advertising

The Colonial Williamsburg Foundation
PO Box 1776, Williamsburg, VA 23187-1776
SAN: 203-297X
Tel: 757-229-1000 *Toll Free Tel:* 800-HISTORY
Fax: 757-220-7325
Web Site: www.colonialwilliamsburg.org/
publications
Key Personnel
Chmn of the Bd & Pres: Colin Campbell
VP, Prod: Richard McCluney
VP & CFO: Katherine H Whitehead
Dir, Pubns & Rts/Perms: Joseph N Rountree
E-mail: jrountree@cwf.org
Founded: 1930
Trade & scholarly nonfiction, children's, young
adult, juveniles & regional books on various
aspects of Williamsburg & Virginia in the colo-
nial period.
ISBN Prefix(es): 0-87935; 0-910412
Number of titles published annually: 4 Print
Total Titles: 100 Print; 28 Audio
Imprints: Colonial Williamsburg
Distributed by Antique Collectors Club; Harry N
Abrams Inc; Ohio University Press; Clarkson
Potter; Scholastic; Stackpole; Quite Specific
Media Ltd; Random House Children's Books;
University Press of New England; Yale Univer-
sity Press
Shipping Address: Colonial Williamsburg, 720
Thimble Shoals Blvd, Suite 108, Newport
News, VA 23606
Distribution Center: 201 Fifth Ave, Williamsburg,
VA 23185

Colorado Geological Survey
Division of Department of Natural Resources
State of Colorado
1313 Sherman St, Rm 715, Denver, CO 80203
Tel: 303-866-2611; 303-866-4762 (pubns)
Fax: 303-866-2461
E-mail: cgspubs@state.co.us
Web Site: www.geosurvey.state.co.us
Key Personnel
Cartographer: Cheryl Brchan
Founded: 1969
Publish books & maps on Colorado geology &
resources.
ISBN Prefix(es): 1-884216
Number of titles published annually: 15 Print
Total Titles: 45 Print

Colorado Railroad Museum
Subsidiary of Colorado Railroad Historical Foun-
dation
17155 W 44 Ave, Golden, CO 80402
Mailing Address: PO Box 10, Golden, CO 80402-
0010
Tel: 303-279-4591 *Toll Free Tel:* 800-365-6263
Fax: 303-279-4229
E-mail: library@crrm.org
Web Site: crrm.org
Key Personnel
Exec Dir: William Gould
Busn Mgr: Jeanine Stahl
Founded: 1959
Railroad history.
ISBN Prefix(es): 0-918654
Number of titles published annually: 3 Print
Total Titles: 29 Print

Columba Publishing Co Inc
2003 W Market St, Akron, OH 44313
Tel: 330-836-2619 *Toll Free Tel:* 800-999-7491
Fax: 330-836-9659
Web Site: www.columbapublishing.com
Key Personnel
Pres & Ed: Vivian Kistler *E-mail:* viviankistler@
columbapublishing.com
VP & Media Specialist: Carli Miller
E-mail: carli@columbapublishing.com
Founded: 1985

Publications for the picture framer & gallery
owner.
ISBN Prefix(es): 0-938655
Number of titles published annually: 6 Print
Total Titles: 16 Print
Imprints: Library of Professional Picture Framing

Columbia Books Inc
1825 Connecticut Ave NW, Suite 625, Washing-
ton, DC 20009
Mailing Address: PO Box 251, Annapolis Junc-
tion, MD 20701-0251
Tel: 202-464-1662 *Toll Free Tel:* 888-265-0600
(cust serv) *Fax:* 202-464-1775; 240-646-7020
(cust serv)
E-mail: info@columbiabooks.com
Web Site: www.columbiabooks.com
Key Personnel
Pres: Debra Mayberry
Busn Mgr: Gino Di Angelo *E-mail:* gdiangelo@
columbiabooks.com
Founded: 1966
ISBN Prefix(es): 0-910416; 1-880873; 0-9715487
Number of titles published annually: 5 Print
Total Titles: 5 Print; 1 E-Book

§Columbia University Press
61 W 62 St, New York, NY 10023
SAN: 212-2472
Tel: 212-459-0600 *Toll Free Tel:* 800-944-8648
Fax: 212-459-3678
Web Site: www.columbia.edu/cu/cup *Cable:*
CUPRESS
Key Personnel
Chmn of the Bd: Alan Brinkley
Dir: Jim Jordan
Mktg & Sales Dir: Helena Schwarz
Sales Dir: Brad Hebel
Publicity Dir: Meredith Howard
Edit Dir: Jennifer Crewe
Man Ed: Anne McCoy
Sr Exec Ed, the Sciences: Robin C Smith
Ed: Peter Dimock; Wendy Lochner; John Michel;
James Warren
Subs Rts Mgr & Intl Rts: Clare Wellnitz
Cust Rel: Janet Kelly
Founded: 1893
Books of scholarly value, including nonfiction,
general interest, scientific & technical books,
textbooks in special fields at the university
level & reference books.
ISBN Prefix(es): 0-231
Number of titles published annually: 4,200 Print
Total Titles: 7 CD-ROM; 4 Online
Foreign Office(s): John Wiley & Sons Ltd, One
Oldlands Way, Bognor Regis, West Sussex
PO22 9SA, United Kingdom
Distributor for Chinese University Press; East
European Monographs; Edinburgh University
Press; Kegan Paul; University of Tokyo Press;
Wallflower Press
Foreign Rep(s): APAC Publishers Services (In-
donesia, Malaysia, Philippines, Singapore, Tai-
wan, Thailand); Book Marketing Services (In-
dia); Cassidy & Associates Inc (China, Hong
Kong); Footprint Books (Australia & New
Zealand); Information & Culture Korea (Ko-
rea); Berj Jamkojian (Africa, Middle East);
Kinokuniya Co Ltd (Japan); Lexa Publishers'
Representatives (Canada); Tahir M Lodhi (Pak-
istan); Maruzen Co Ltd (Japan); United Pub-
lishers Services Ltd; UPCCP (Europe, Israel &
UK)
Foreign Rights: Attila Akcali (Turkey); Asano
Agency (Japan); Bardon Chinese Media
(China); Raquel de la Concha (Spain & Por-
tugal); The English Agency (Japan); Pina von
Prellwitz Eulama Agency (Italy); Peter Fritz
(Germany); Boris Hoffman (France); Japan
UNI Agency (Japan); KCC International (Ko-
rea); Uli Rushby-Smith (UK, Netherlands);
Karin Schindler (Brazil); Maria Strarz-kanska

(Poland); Hanserik Tonnheim (Scandinavia);
Tuttle-Mori Agency (Japan)
Advertising Agency: Columbia Advertising Group
Warehouse: 136 S Broadway, Irvington, NY
10533 *Tel:* 914-591-9111 *Toll Free Tel:* 800-
944-8648 *Fax:* 914-591-9201 *Toll Free
Fax:* 800-944-1844
Membership(s): AAP

**Columbine Communications & Publications
Inc**
1293 Elizabeth Barcus Way, Fortuna, CA 95540
SAN: 246-5345
Tel: 707-726-9200 *Fax:* 707-726-9300
E-mail: cocompub@aol.com
Key Personnel
Pres, Publr & Intl Rts: Bob Erdmann
Lib Sales Dir: David Hermance
Founded: 1978
Publishers of business & personal finance, hobby,
crafts, art & consultants to other publishers.
ISBN Prefix(es): 0-945339
Number of titles published annually: 12 Print
Total Titles: 48 Print
Advertising Agency: Hermance Advertising
Membership(s): Publishers Marketing Association

§Comex Systems Inc
5 Cold Hill Rd, Suite 24, Mendham, NJ 07945
Tel: 973-543-2862 *Toll Free Tel:* 800-543-6959
Fax: 973-543-9644
Web Site: www.comexsystems.com
Key Personnel
VP: Doug Prbylowski *E-mail:* dpryb@
comexsystems.com
Founded: 1973
Publish test preparation & other educational
books.
ISBN Prefix(es): 1-56030
Number of titles published annually: 5 Print; 10
CD-ROM
Total Titles: 30 Print; 50 CD-ROM

Common Courage Press
One Red Barn Rd, Monroe, ME 04951
Mailing Address: PO Box 702, Monroe, ME
04951-0702
Tel: 207-525-0900 *Toll Free Tel:* 800-497-3207
Fax: 207-525-3068
E-mail: orders-info@commoncouragepress.com
Web Site: www.commoncouragepress.com
Key Personnel
Pres: Greg Bates
Founded: 1990
Books on race, feminism, gender issues, class,
media, economics, ecology & foreign policy to
help readers in the struggle for social justice.
ISBN Prefix(es): 0-9628838; 1-56751
Number of titles published annually: 20 Print
Total Titles: 90 Print
Distributor for Odonian Press; Real Story Series
Foreign Rights: James Bier (all other countries)
Distribution Center: LPC Group, 1436 W
Randolph St, Chicago, IL 60607 *Toll Free
Tel:* 800-243-0138 *Toll Free Fax:* 800-334-3892

Commonwealth Business Media
400 Windsor Corporate Center, 50 Millstone Rd,
Suite 200, East Windsor, NJ 08520-1415
Tel: 609-371-7700 *Toll Free Tel:* 800-221-5488;
888-215-6084 (orders) *Fax:* 609-371-7712
Web Site: www.cbizmedia.com
Key Personnel
CEO, Pres & Chmn: Alan Glass
Dir, Creative Servs: Laura Kaiser *Tel:* 609-371-
7854
Magazines, directories & database products.
ISBN Prefix(es): 0-9649630; 1-891131
Number of titles published annually: 63 Print; 1
CD-ROM; 1 E-Book
Total Titles: 50 Print; 4 CD-ROM; 3 E-Book

Commonwealth Editions
Imprint of Memoirs Unlimited Inc
266 Cabot St, Beverly, MA 01915
Tel: 978-921-0747 *Fax:* 978-927-8195
Web Site: www.commonwealtheditions.com
Key Personnel
Publr: Webster Bull *E-mail:* webster b@
  commonwealtheditions.com
VP, Sales: Katie Bull *E-mail:* katieb@
  commonwealtheditions.com
Founded: 1988
Publisher of nonfiction books about New England
  & its historic places.
ISBN Prefix(es): 1-889833
Number of titles published annually: 16 Print
Total Titles: 50 Print
Returns: Publishers Storage & Shipping, 46 De-
  velopment Rd, Fitchburg, MA 01420
Shipping Address: Publishers Storage & Ship-
  ping, 46 Development Rd, Fitchburg, MA
  01420, Contact: Peter Quick *Tel:* 978-345-2121
  Fax: 978-348-1233
Warehouse: Publishers Storage & Shipping, 46
  Development Rd, Fitchburg, MA 01420

Communication Creativity
209 Church St, Buena Vista, CO 81211
SAN: 210-3478
Mailing Address: PO Box 909-LMP, Buena Vista,
  CO 81211
Tel: 719-395-8659 *Toll Free Tel:* 800-331-8355
  Fax: 719-633-1526
Web Site: www.communicationcreativity.com
Key Personnel
Pres: Marilyn Ross *E-mail:* marilyn@
  communicationcreativity.com
Sales & Adv Mgr: Ann Markham *E-mail:* ann@
  communicationcreativity.com
Founded: 1977
Nonfiction & how-to.
ISBN Prefix(es): 0-918880
Number of titles published annually: 3 Print
Total Titles: 13 Print
Membership(s): Publishers Marketing Associa-
  tion; Small Publishers Association of North
  America

Community College Press, see American
  Association of Community Colleges (AACC)

Compass American Guides
Division of Fodors Travel Publications /Random
  House
1745 Broadway, New York, NY 10019
Key Personnel
Edit Dir: Daniel Mangin *E-mail:* editors@fodors.
  com
Founded: 1990
Guides, guidebooks to the USA.
ISBN Prefix(es): 0-679; 0-676
Number of titles published annually: 4 Print
Total Titles: 43 Print
Distributed by Random House Inc (Contact
  Fodor's)
Warehouse: Random House Inc, 400 Hahn Rd,
  Westminster, MD (Orders: 800-733-3000)

Competency Press
PO Box 95, White Plains, NY 10605-0091
Tel: 914-948-6783 *Fax:* 914-761-7179
E-mail: studentcomp@aol.com
Key Personnel
Pres: Sylvia Blake
Partner: Sy Kaufman
Founded: 1979
Textbooks.
ISBN Prefix(es): 0-910307
Number of titles published annually: 4 Print
Total Titles: 25 Print
Warehouse: 2432 Grand Concourse, Bronx, NY
  10458

**Comprehensive Health Education Foundation
(CHEF)**
22419 Pacific Hwy S, Seattle, WA 98198-5104
SAN: 696-3668
Tel: 206-824-2907 *Toll Free Tel:* 800-323-2433
  Fax: 206-824-3072
E-mail: info@chef.org
Web Site: www.chef.org
Key Personnel
Pres: Larry Clark
Off Mgr: Linda Garitone
Founded: 1974
Health education curricula, books, videos & other
  mixed-media materials.
ISBN Prefix(es): 0-935529; 1-57021
Number of titles published annually: 4 Print
Total Titles: 20 Print

Computer Books, Texas Books, see Wordware
  Publishing Inc

§Conciliar Press
Affiliate of Antiochian Archdiocese
10090 "A" Hwy 9, Ben Lomond, CA 95005
Mailing Address: PO Box 76, Ben Lomond, CA
  95005
Tel: 831-336-5118 *Toll Free Tel:* 800-967-7377
  Fax: 831-336-8882
E-mail: marketing@conciliarpress.com
Web Site: www.conciliarpress.com
Key Personnel
Mgr & Assoc Ed: Thomas Zell
Mktg Dir: Shelly Stamps
Prodn Mgr: Carla Zell
Founded: 1978
Books, booklets, brochures, greeting cards, icons,
  liturgical & quarterly magazines.
ISBN Prefix(es): 0-9622713; 0-8821212
Number of titles published annually: 8 Print
Total Titles: 45 Print
Distributed by Light & Life; St Vladimir's
Distributor for Light & Life
Foreign Rep(s): Nicholas Chapman (UK)

Concordia Publishing House
3558 S Jefferson Ave, St Louis, MO 63118-3968
SAN: 202-1781
Tel: 314-268-1000 *Toll Free Tel:* 800-325-3040
  Fax: 314-268-1329 *Toll Free Fax:* 800-490-
  9889
E-mail: cphorder@cph.org
Web Site: www.cph.org
Key Personnel
Pres: Paul T McCain
VP, Opers & COO: Bruce Kintz
Chmn of the Bd: Robert Knox
Prodn Dir: Karen Capps
Dir, Fin: Peggy Anderson
Dir, Mktg & Sales: Richard Johnson
Dir, Graphics & Design: Tim Agnew
Dir, Rts & Perms: Jonathan Schultz
Dir, Music: David Johnson
Dir, Cust Serv: Gerry Puglisi
ISBN Contact: Connie Goodson
Founded: 1869
Theological works, sacred & family, devotional
  music, curriculum, computer software, bul-
  letins, envelopes.
ISBN Prefix(es): 0-570
Number of titles published annually: 150 Print; 2
  CD-ROM
Total Titles: 1,000 Print; 10 CD-ROM
Divisions: Concordia Academic Press; Editorial
  Concordia; Family Films
Membership(s): Christian Booksellers Associa-
  tion; Evangelical Christian Publishers Asso-
  ciation; Protestant Church-Owned Publishers
  Association

Concourse Press
Subsidiary of East-West Fine Arts Corp
PO Box 8265, Philadelphia, PA 19101-8265

SAN: 269-249X
Tel: 610-325-0313 *Fax:* 610-359-1953
Key Personnel
Pres: Chester Daugherty
VP: Shokoofeh Daugherty
Ed-in-Chief: Robert Reed
Ed-at-Large: Thomas West Gregory
Ed, Persian Editions: M R Ghanoon-Parvar
Ed: Joan Smith
Ed, East-West Translation Institute: Bahman
  Sholevar
Ed, German Editions & Foreign Rts: F S Her-
  rmann
Assoc Ed & ISBN Contact: Jody Smith
Founded: 1979
Hardcover & quality paperbacks, periodicals,
  trade books in literary & artistic fields.
ISBN Prefix(es): 0-911323
Number of titles published annually: 3 Print
Total Titles: 25 Print
Imprints: Avesta Fiction Series; Concourse Poetry
  Series
Subsidiaries: East-West Film, Theatre & Art In-
  stitute; East-West Review of Literature & The
  Arts; East-West Translation Institute
Distributor for Hafezieh Publications (Germany)
Foreign Rep(s): F S Herrmann (Western Europe)
Foreign Rights: F S Herrmann
Orders to: Amazon.com, Box 80387, Seattle, WA
  98108-0387
Shipping Address: 1 1/2 Apartments by the Park,
  Suite B, 250 Ann St, Easton, PA 18042-6294
Distribution Center: Baker & Taylor, 652 E Main
  St, PO Box 6920, Bridgewater, NJ 08807-0920

The Conference Board Inc
845 Third Ave, New York, NY 10022
SAN: 202-179X
Tel: 212-759-0900 *Fax:* 212-980-7014
E-mail: info@conference-board.org
Web Site: www.conference-board.org
Key Personnel
Pres: Richard E Cavanagh
Rts & Perms: Yvonne Burnside
ISBN Contact: Linda Saladino
Contact: Ellen Ackerman
Asst Dir, Info Servs: Carol Estoppey
Founded: 1916
Periodic studies in management practices, eco-
  nomics & public affairs.
ISBN Prefix(es): 0-8237
Number of titles published annually: 25 Print; 25
  Online
Foreign Office(s): Chaussee de La Hulpe 130, bte
  11, B-1000 Brussels, Belgium

Congressional Quarterly Press
Division of Congressional Quarterly Inc
1255 22 St NW, Washington, DC 20037
SAN: 202-1803
Tel: 202-729-1800 *Toll Free Tel:* 866-427-7737
  Fax: 202-729-1809 *Toll Free Fax:* 800-380-
  3810
E-mail: customerservice@cqpress.com
Web Site: www.cq.com
Key Personnel
Publr & Ed: Robert Merry
VP & Gen Mgr: John Jenkins
Dir, Lib Pubn: Kathryn C Suazez
Dir, Coll Pubn: Brenda Carter
Natl Sales Mgr: Lonny Merriett *Tel:* 202-729-
  1811 *E-mail:* lmerriett@cqpress.com
Mgr, Lib & Mktg: Nina Tristani
Mgr, Coll Mktg: Rita Matyi
Mgr, Mkt Govt: Christopher Dickinson
Founded: 1945
Hardcover reference; hard & softcover texts; con-
  temporary affairs.
ISBN Prefix(es): 0-87187; 1-56802
Number of titles published annually: 90 Print
Total Titles: 300 Print
Imprints: CQ Inc; CQ Press
Foreign Rights: Charlene Gargosz

Warehouse: Congressional Quarterly Books Returns Dept, 6304 Gravel Ave G&H, Alexandria, VA 22310
Membership(s): AAP

Connecticut Academy of Arts & Sciences
PO Box 208211, New Haven, CT 06520-8211
Tel: 203-432-3113 *Fax:* 203-432-5712
E-mail: caas@yale.edu
Web Site: www.yale.edu/caas
Key Personnel
Pubns Chmn: Catherine Skinner
Pubns Mgr: Sandra Rux
Founded: 1799
A learned society which holds a series of lectures; publisher of academic books.
ISBN Prefix(es): 1-878508
Number of titles published annually: 4 Print

Consortium Publishing
640 Weaver Hill Rd, West Greenwich, RI 02817-2261
Tel: 401-397-9838 *Fax:* 401-392-1926
Key Personnel
Pres & Owner: John M Carlevale
Founded: 1990
Textbooks & self-help books on astronomy, chemistry, counseling/self-help, parenting, early childhood education, English/technical writing, music, child abuse, humor.
ISBN Prefix(es): 0-940139
Number of titles published annually: 20 Print
Total Titles: 77 Print

Consumer Press
13326 SW 28 St, Suite 102, Fort Lauderdale, FL 33330-1102
SAN: 297-7788
Tel: 954-370-9153 *Fax:* 954-472-1008
E-mail: bookguest@aol.com
Web Site: consumerpress.com
Key Personnel
Pres: Diana Gonzalez
Edit Dir: Joseph J Pappas
Publicity Dir: Diana Hunter
Opers Mgr: Linda Muzzarelli
Counsel: Garry Spear
Founded: 1989
Consumer-oriented self-help & how-to titles. Specialize in homeowner issues.
ISBN Prefix(es): 0-9628336; 1-891264
Number of titles published annually: 9 Print
Total Titles: 10 Print
Imprints: Women's Publications
Membership(s): Publishers Marketing Association

Consumertronics
Affiliate of Top Secret Consumertronics Global (TSC-Global)
8400 Menaul NE, Suite A-199, Albuquerque, NM 87112
Mailing Address: PO Box 23097, Albuquerque, NM 87192
Tel: 505-321-1034 *Fax:* 505-257-5637 (orders only)
E-mail: wizguru@consumertronics.net
Web Site: www.consumertronics.net
Key Personnel
Pres & CEO: John J Williams
VP: Laurencia Williams
Founded: 1971
Technical books, manuals & software.
ISBN Prefix(es): 0-934274
Number of titles published annually: 50 Print; 50 CD-ROM
Total Titles: 150 Print; 27 CD-ROM

Contemporary Publishing Co of Raleigh Inc
6001-101 Chapel Hill Rd, Raleigh, NC 27607
Tel: 919-851-8221 *Fax:* 919-851-6666
E-mail: questions@contemporarypublishing.com

Web Site: www.contemporarypublishing.com
Key Personnel
Publr: Charles E Grantham *E-mail:* chuck246cp@aol.com
Lib Sales Dir & Prodn Mgr: Erika Kessler *E-mail:* erikacpc@aol.com
Mktg Dir: Sherri Powell
Founded: 1977
Laboratory textbooks for college.
ISBN Prefix(es): 0-89892
Number of titles published annually: 10 Print
Total Titles: 90 Print; 1 CD-ROM

Continental Afrikan Publishers
Division of Afrikamawu Miracle Mission, AMI Inc
182 Stribling Circle, Spartanburg, SC 29301
Tel: 864-576-7992 *Fax:* 775-295-9699; 864-574-3399
E-mail: afrikalion@aol.com
Web Site: www.bbean.com/afrika/index.html; www.bbean.com/afrika/books.html; www.writers.net/writers/22249; www.freeyellow.com/members3/mike//
Key Personnel
Publr: Prof Afrikadzata Deku, PhD
Founded: 1990
Afrikan-Centric books, booklets, cassettes & video documentaries, calendars, films on Continental Afrikan studies, Afrikan-Centricity, Pan-Continental Afrikanism, Continental Afrikan Government MIRACLE Project of the Century-its what, why, how & when.
ISBN Prefix(es): 1-56454
Number of titles published annually: 30 Print; 152 Online; 20 Audio
Total Titles: 189 Print; 152 Online; 20 Audio
Foreign Office(s): PO Box 209, Dansoman-Accra, Ghana, Chmn: Afrikanenyo Deku
PO Box 773, Belvedere Harare, Zimbabwe, Chmn: Afrikamawuvi Adzakey *Tel:* 011-263-11-403-829
Foreign Rep(s): Continental/Diaspora Afrikan (World)

Continuing Education Press
Affiliate of Portland State University Extended Studies
1633 SW Park, Portland, OR 97201
Mailing Address: PO Box 1394, Portland, OR 97207-1394
Tel: 503-725-4891 *Toll Free Tel:* 866-647-7377 *Fax:* 503-725-4840
E-mail: press@pdx.edu
Web Site: www.cep.pdx.edu
Key Personnel
Mgr: Alba M Scholz
Founded: 1942
ISBN Prefix(es): 0-87678
Number of titles published annually: 3 Print
Total Titles: 17 Print

The Continuum International Publishing Group
15 E 26 St, Suite 1703, New York, NY 10010
SAN: 213-8220
Tel: 212-953-5858 *Toll Free Tel:* 800-561-7704 *Fax:* 212-953-5944
E-mail: info@continuum-books.com
Web Site: www.continuumbooks.com
Key Personnel
Chmn & CEO: Philip Sturrock *E-mail:* psturrock@continuumbooks.com
Pres & CEO: Kenneth Quigley *E-mail:* kquigley@morehousegroup.com
VP, Sales & Mktg: Mary Albi *Tel:* 212-953-5858 ext 106 *E-mail:* mary@continuum-books.com
Exec VP & Gen Mgr: Ulla Schnell *Tel:* 212-953-5858 ext 102 *E-mail:* ulla@continuum-books.com
VP & Sr Ed: Evander Lomke *Tel:* 212-953-5858 ext 104 *E-mail:* evander@continuum-books.

com; Frank Oveis *Tel:* 212-953-5858 ext 103 *E-mail:* frank@continuum-books.com
Commissioning Ed: David Barker *Tel:* 212-953-5858 ext 118 *E-mail:* david@continuum-books.com
Ed-at-Large: J George Lawler *E-mail:* justus@continuum-books.com
Sales Mgr: Kevin Moran *Tel:* 212-953-5858 ext 101 *E-mail:* kevin@continuum-books.com
Rel Mktg Mgr: Claire England *Tel:* 212-953-5858 ext 107 *E-mail:* claire2@continuum-books.com
Academic Mktg Mgr: Emma Cook *Tel:* 212-953-5858 ext 109 *E-mail:* emma@continuum-books.com
Prodn Mgr: Helen Song *Tel:* 212-953-5858 ext 112 *E-mail:* helen@continuum-books.com
Sr Publg Consultant: Werner Mark Linz
Founded: 1999 (result of a merger between The Continuum Publishing Company of NY & the academic & religious publishing programs of Cassell plc in London)
Hardcover & paperbacks; scholary & professional & general interest; music, film, literature, the arts & popular culture; philosophy, religion, biblical studies, theology & spirituality, history, politics & contempory issues, education; women studies & reference.
Number of titles published annually: 150 Print
Total Titles: 5,000 Print
Foreign Office(s): The Continuum International Publishing Group Ltd, The Tower Bldg, 11 York Rd, London SE1 7NX, United Kingdom *Tel:* 011-44-207-922-0880
Distributed by Continuum London
Distributor for Continuum London; Medio Media; Morehouse; Paragon House; Spring Publications
Foreign Rep(s): Elaine Benisti (exclusive French); Liepman AG (exclusive German); Natoli Stefan & Olivia (exclusive Italian)
Foreign Rights: Allen & Unwin Pty Ltd (Australia); APD (Brunei, Indonesia, Malaysia, Singapore, Thailand, Vietnam); APS Ltd (China, Hong Kong, Philippines, South Korea, Taiwan); Robert Barnett (USA); BCR University Bookstore (Jamaica); Elaine Beniste Agent Litteraire (France); Bounty Press Ltd (Nigeria); Georgina Brindley (UK); Codasat Canada Ltd (Canada); Compass Academic (UK); Continuum (Caribbean, Germany & Netherlands, Israel, North America, Africa exc North & South Africa); Cranbury International LLC (Mexico & South & Central America); Durnell Marketing Ltd (Europe); Horizon Books (Botswana, Lesotho, Namibia, Republic of South Africa, Swaziland); IPS (Middle East exc Israel, North Africa); Liepman AG (Switzerland); Richard Lyle (London); Maya Publishers Pvt Ltd (Bangladesh, India, Sri Lanka); Richard McNeace (USA); Novalis (Canada); Nick Pepper (Scotland, Northern England); Publishers Consultants & Representatives (Pakistan); Jonathan Rhodes (England, Midlands); Natoli Stefan & Oliva Agenzia Litteraria (Italy); Andrew Toal (England); United Publishers Services Ltd (Japan)
Billing Address: PO Box 1321, Harrisburg, PA 17105
Orders to: PO Box 1321, Harrisburg, PA 17105
Returns: 3101 N Seventh St, Harrisburg, PA 17110
Shipping Address: 3101 N Seventh St, Harrisburg, PA 17110
Warehouse: 3101 N Seventh St, Harrisburg, PA 17110
Distribution Center: 3101 N Seventh St, Harrisburg, PA 17110

§Cook Communications Ministries
4050 Lee Vance View, Colorado Springs, CO 80918
Tel: 719-536-3271 *Toll Free Tel:* 800-437-4337 *Fax:* 719-536-3269

E-mail: chariotpub@aol.com
Web Site: www.cookministries.com
Key Personnel
VP: Randy Scott Tel: 719-536-3295
E-mail: scottr@cookcommunications.com
Founded: 1875
Christian books, videos, audios, CD-ROM, toys, games.
ISBN Prefix(es): 0-912692; 0-89191; 1-55513; 0-7459; 1-56476; 0-89693
Number of titles published annually: 80 Print
Total Titles: 1,000 Print
Imprints: Faith Kids; Faith Marriage; Faith Parenting; Faithful Woman; Lion; Victor
Foreign Office(s): Cook Communication - Canada Kingsway, UK
Distributor for Lion Publishing
Returns: 850 N Grove, Elgin, IL 60120
Warehouse: 850 N Grove, Elgin, IL 60120

Cooper Publishing Group
2694 Garfield Rd N, No 26, Traverse City, MI 49686
Mailing Address: PO Box 1129, Traverse City, MI 49685
Tel: 231-933-9958 Fax: 231-933-9964
E-mail: icooper100@aol.com
Key Personnel
Publr: I L Cooper
Founded: 1985
College textbooks; health & nutrition books; athletic & sports books, videos, coaching education, trade sports books.
ISBN Prefix(es): 1-884125
Number of titles published annually: 4 Print
Total Titles: 51 Print
Imprints: Biological Sciences Press
Foreign Rep(s): Japan Publications Trading Co Ltd (Japan)

Cooper Square Press
Member of Rowman & Littlefield Publishing Group
5360 Manhattan Circle, Suite 101, Boulder, CO 80303
Tel: 303-543-7835 Fax: 303-543-0043
E-mail: tradeeditorial@rowman.com
Web Site: www.coopersquarepress.com
Key Personnel
Edit Dir: Rick Rinehart E-mail: rrinehart@rowman.com
Publicist: Tracy Miracle E-mail: tmiracle@rowman.com
Founded: 1999
Hardcover & trade paperback publisher in history, the performing arts, biography & literature.
ISBN Prefix(es): 1-56833; 0-8154
Number of titles published annually: 12 Print
Total Titles: 300 Print
Imprints: Madison Books
Branch Office(s)
4501 Forbes Blvd, Lanham, MD 20706 Tel: 301-459-3366 Fax: 301-459-5748
Foreign Rep(s): Oxford Publicity Partnership (UK); Peribo (Australia)
Orders to: National Book Network, 15200 NBN Way, Blue Ridge Summit, PA 17214, Mgr, Cust Serv: Meg Phelps Toll Free Tel: 800-462-6420 Fax: 717-794-3803
Returns: National Book Network, 15200 NBN Way, Blue Ridge Summit, PA 17214, Mgr, Cust Serv: Meg Phelps Toll Free Tel: 800-462-6420 Fax: 717-794-3803
Distribution Center: National Book Network, 15200 NBN Way, Blue Ridge Summit, PA 17214, Mgr, Cust Serv: Meg Phelps Toll Free Tel: 800-462-6420 Fax: 717-794-3803

Copley Publishing Group
Imprint of ProQuest Information & Learning Co
138 Great Rd, Acton, MA 01720

Tel: 978-263-9090 Toll Free Tel: 800-562-2147
Fax: 978-263-9190
E-mail: publish@copleycustom.com; textbook@copleypublishing.com
Web Site: www.copleycustom.com; www.copleypublishing.com; www.copleyeditions.com
Key Personnel
Pres: Ron Klausner
Publr: Lucy Miskin
Prodn Mgr: Susan Myrick
Office Mgr: Bettie Noble
Founded: 1985
Custom publishing & selected academic nonfiction & anthologies.
ISBN Prefix(es): 0-87411; 1-58152; 1-58390
Number of titles published annually: 65 Print
Total Titles: 210 Print
Imprints: Copley Custom Publishing Group; Copley Editions; Copley Publishing Group

Copper Canyon Press
PO Box 271, Port Townsend, WA 98368
SAN: 206-488X
Tel: 360-385-4925 Fax: 360-385-4985
E-mail: poetry@coppercanyonpress.org
Web Site: www.coppercanyonpress.org
Key Personnel
Man Ed & Intl Rts Contact: Michael Wiegers
Ed: Sam Hamill
Mktg Dir: Joseph Bednarik
Assoc Publr: Mary Jane Knecht
Founded: 1972
Hardcover & paperback trade books of poetry.
ISBN Prefix(es): 0-914742; 1-55659
Number of titles published annually: 18 Print; 0 Audio
Total Titles: 300 Print; 5 Audio
Imprints: KAGEAN BOOKS (for translations)
Distributor for American Poetry Review/Honickman
Shipping Address: Bldg 313, Fort Worden State Park, Port Townsend, WA 98368
Distribution Center: Consortium Book Sales & Distribution, 1045 Westgate Dr, St Paul, MN 55114 Toll Free Tel: 800-283-3572

§Copywriter's Council of America (CCA)
Division of The Linick Group Inc
CCA Bldg, 7 Putter Lane, Middle Island, NY 11953-0102
Mailing Address: PO Box 102, Middle Island, NY 11953-0102
Tel: 631-924-3888 Fax: 631-924-3890
E-mail: cca4dmcopy@att.net
Web Site: www.lgroup.addr.com/CCA.htm
Key Personnel
Chmn, Consulting Group: Andrew S Linick, PhD E-mail: linickgrp@att.net
VP: Roger Dextor
Lib Sales Dir: John Kelty
Founded: 1974
Article reprints, monographs; educational, professional & trade, fiction, nonfiction publications in direct response advertising, direct marketing, mail order, sales promotion, measurable response public relations, telemarketing, business-to-business marketing, desktop publishing, internet marketing, e-commerce, e-books, consulting & management. Confidential reports, newsletters, little-known business secrets-library of super money makers you can use tomorrow. Available for e-book licensing.
ISBN Prefix(es): 91-7098
Number of titles published annually: 36 Print; 25 E-Book
Total Titles: 350 Print; 50 E-Book
Imprints: CCA; NAPS; New World Press; Publishers Trade Secrets Library
Subsidiaries: Linick International Programs
Distributor for ASL; Compu-Tek; NAPS; Picture Profits

Advertising Agency: LK Advertising Agency, 7 Putter Lane, Middle Island, NY 11953, VP: Roger Dextor Tel: 631-924-3888 Web Site: lgroup.addr.com

Cornell Maritime Press Inc
PO Box 456, Centreville, MD 21617
SAN: 203-5901
Tel: 410-758-1075 Toll Free Tel: 800-638-7641
Fax: 410-758-6849
E-mail: editor@cornellmaritimepress.com
Web Site: www.cornellmaritimepress.com
Key Personnel
Pres: Joseph Johns
Man Ed & Intl Rts: Charlotte A Kurst
Founded: 1938
Professional, technical books in maritime arts & sciences; boats & boat building; related hobbies & crafts.
ISBN Prefix(es): 0-87033
Number of titles published annually: 6 Print
Total Titles: 76 Print
Imprints: Tidewater Publishers
Distributor for Chesapeake Bay Maritime Museum; Literary House Press; Maryland Historical Trust Press; Maryland Sea Grant Program; Maryland State Archives Publications
Foreign Rep(s): Baker & Taylor International (Australia, Indonesia, Malaysia)
Returns: 101 Water Way, Centerville, MD 21617
Shipping Address: 101 Water Way, Centerville, MD 21617
Warehouse: 101 Water Way, Centerville, MD 21617
Membership(s): AAP; ABA; Midatlantic Publishers Association; Small Publishers Association of North America
See separate listing for:
Tidewater Publishers

Cornell University Press
Division of Cornell University
512 E State St, Ithaca, NY 14850
SAN: 202-1862
Tel: 607-277-2338 Fax: 607-277-2374
E-mail: cupressinfo@cornell.edu
Web Site: www.cornellpress.cornell.edu Cable: CORUPRES ITHACA
Key Personnel
Dir & Ed, European History, Slavic & Medieval Studies: John G Ackerman E-mail: mam278@cornell.edu
CFO & Asst Dir: Roger A Hubbs E-mail: rob9@cornell.edu
Ed Dir, ILR Press, Labor, Bus: Frances Benson E-mail: fgb2@cornell.edu
Man Ed: Priscilla Hurdle E-mail: plh9@cornell.edu
Exec Ed, Classics, Lit, Art History & Archaeology, Drama & Film Studies: Bernhard Kendler E-mail: bk32@cornell.edu
Sr Ed, Philosophy, History of Sci, Political Sci, Intl Rel, Asian Studies: Roger Haydon E-mail: rmhll@cornell.edu
Ed, Amer History, Amer Studies, Native Amer Studies, Anthropology: Sheryl L Englund E-mail: sae7@cornell.edu
Mktg Mgr: Mahinder Kingra
Sales Mgr: Nathan Gemignani E-mail: ndg5@cornell.edu
Subs Rts & Intl Rts: Tonya Cook E-mail: cupsubrights@cornell.edu
ISBN Contact: Michael Morris E-mail: mam278@cornell.edu
Founded: 1869 (reconstituted in 1930)
General nonfiction, scholarly books & monographs; hardcover & paperbacks.
ISBN Prefix(es): 0-8014; 0-87546
Number of titles published annually: 150 Print
Total Titles: 2,200 Print
Imprints: Comstock Publishing Associates; ILR Press

Foreign Rep(s): East-West Export Books (Asia, Pacific); Lexa Publishers' Representatives (Canada); University Presses Marketing (UK, Ireland, Israel); Wolfgang Wingerter (Europe)
Orders to: Cup Services, 750 Cascadilla St, Ithaca, NY 14850 *Tel:* 607-277-2211 *Toll Free Tel:* 800-666-2211 *Toll Free Fax:* 800-688-2877 *E-mail:* orderbook@cupserv.org *Web Site:* cupserv.org
Returns: Cup Services, 750 Cascadilla St, Ithaca, NY 14850 *Tel:* 607-277-2211 *Toll Free Tel:* 800-666-2211 *Toll Free Fax:* 800-688-2877 *E-mail:* orderbook@cupserv.org *Web Site:* cupserv.org
Shipping Address: Cup Services, 750 Cascadilla St, Ithaca, NY 14850 *Tel:* 607-277-2211 *Toll Free Tel:* 800-666-2211 *Toll Free Fax:* 800-688-2877 *E-mail:* orderbook@cupserv.org *Web Site:* cupserv.org
Warehouse: Cup Services, 750 Cascadilla St, Ithaca, NY 14850 *Tel:* 607-277-2211 *Toll Free Tel:* 800-666-2211 *Toll Free Fax:* 800-688-2877 *E-mail:* orderbook@cupserv.org *Web Site:* cupserv.org
Distribution Center: Cup Services, 750 Cascadilla St, Ithaca, NY 14850 *Tel:* 607-277-2211 *Toll Free Tel:* 800-666-2211 *Toll Free Fax:* 800-688-2877 *E-mail:* orderbook@cupserv.org *Web Site:* cupserv.org
Membership(s): AAP; Association of American University Presses

Cornell University Southeast Asia Program Publications

Unit of Cornell University
640 Stewart Ave, Ithaca, NY 14850
Tel: 607-255-8038 *Fax:* 607-277-1904; 607-255-7534
E-mail: seap-pubs@cornell.edu
Web Site: www.einaudi.cornell.edu/southeastasia.publications/SEAP
Key Personnel
Ed: Deborah Homsher *Tel:* 607-255-4359 *E-mail:* dlh10@cornell.edu
Busn Mgr & Intl Rts: Melanie Moss
Founded: 1951
Publish books & one semi-annual journal (Indonesia) on the history, politics, culture & languages of Southeast Asian countries.
ISBN Prefix(es): 0-87727; 0-87763
Number of titles published annually: 3 Print; 1 CD-ROM
Total Titles: 130 Print
Distributor for A U A Language Center
Orders to: SEAP Publications, Cornell University, Box 1004, 95 Brown Rd, Rm 241, Ithaca, NY 14850-2820, Dist Mgr: Denise Rice *Fax:* 607-255-7534 *Toll Free Fax:* 877-865-2432
Shipping Address: SEAP Publications, Cornell University, Box 1004, 95 Brown Rd, Rm 241, Ithaca, NY 14850-2820, Dist Mgr: Denise Rice *Fax:* 607-255-7534 *Toll Free Fax:* 877-865-2432
Warehouse: SEAP Publications, Cornell University, Box 1004, 95 Brown Rd, Rm 241, Ithaca, NY 14850-2820, Dist Mgr: Denise Rice *Fax:* 607-255-7534 *Toll Free Fax:* 877-865-2432
Distribution Center: SEAP Publications, Cornell University, Box 1004, 95 Brown Rd, Rm 241, Ithaca, NY 14850-2820 *Tel:* 607-255-8038 *Fax:* 607-255-7534 *Toll Free Fax:* 877-865-2432

§Cornerstone Productions Inc

Division of Reggae Legends of Trench-Town Jamaica
PO Box 3232, Wilmington, NC 28406
Tel: 910-523-7326 *Fax:* 404-288-8937
Key Personnel
CEO, CFO, Pres, Publicist & Media Consultant: Ricardo A Scott
Assoc: Giancarlo Ryan Tafari Scott

Founded: 1991
Providing authentic source on reggae, reggae music origins & rastafarian spirituality. The true trench-town story. A reggae education.
ISBN Prefix(es): 1-883427; 1-58470
Number of titles published annually: 12 Print; 10 CD-ROM; 10 Audio
Total Titles: 140 Print; 50 CD-ROM; 40 Audio
Imprints: Tafarinri Publishings
Divisions: Reggae Book of Light (Matshafa Berhan)
Foreign Office(s): Kingston, Jamaica
Foreign Rep(s): Rudolph Dennis (Jamaica)
Foreign Rights: Gartie Dennis (Jamaica, West Indies)
Advertising Agency: Cornerstone Productions, Contact: Giancarlo Ryan Tafari Scott

Coronet Books & Publications

PO Box 957, Eagle Point, OR 97524
Tel: 541-858-5585 *Fax:* 541-858-5595
E-mail: lionspaw@country.net
Key Personnel
Publr: Sandy Harding
Founded: 1994
Small publisher of children's fiction.
ISBN Prefix(es): 1-890609
Total Titles: 4 Print
Imprints: Lion's Paw Books
Distributed by Coronet Books & Publications

Cortina Learning International Inc

7 Hollyhock Rd, Wilton, CT 06897-4414
Tel: 203-762-2510 *Toll Free Tel:* 800-245-2145 *Fax:* 203-762-2514
E-mail: info@cortina-languages.com; cortinainc@aol.com
Web Site: www.cortina-languages.com (English language animation & sound); www.cursos-ingles-cortina.com (Spanish language animation & sound)
Key Personnel
Pres: Robert E Livesey *Tel:* 203-762-2510 ext 100
Sec & Man Ed: Magdalen B Livesey *Tel:* 203-762-2510 ext 109
Prodn Mgr: George Bollas *Tel:* 203-762-2510 ext 105
Bookkeeping: Leandro Medalla *Tel:* 203-762-2510 ext 106
Founded: 1882
Foreign languages, English as second language, art instruction, writing instruction.
ISBN Prefix(es): 0-8327; 0-8489
Number of titles published annually: 5 Print
Total Titles: 50 Print
Subsidiaries: Institute for Language Study Inc
Divisions: Cortina Institute of Language, Instituto Linguistico Cortina; Famous Artists School; Famous Writers School
Distributed by Henry Holt and Company Inc
Distributor for Linguaphone Institute Ltd
Foreign Rep(s): Gazelle Book Services (UK)
Advertising Agency: Academic Advertising
Warehouse: 15 Great Pasture Rd, Danbury, CT 06810 *Tel:* 203-778-9639 *Fax:* 203-778-4029
See separate listing for:
Institute for Language Study

Corwin Press

Subsidiary of Sage Publications
2455 Teller Rd, Thousand Oaks, CA 91320
Tel: 805-499-9734 *Fax:* 805-499-5323 *Toll Free Fax:* 800-417-2466
E-mail: info@corwinpress.com
Web Site: www.corwinpress.com *Telex:* 510-1000799 *Cable:* SAGEPUB (7243782)
Key Personnel
Pres: Douglas M Rife *Tel:* 805-499-9734 ext 7753 *E-mail:* douglas.rife@corwinpress.com
Mktg Dir: Kimberly Gonzales
Sales Dir: Anita Linton

Founded: 1990
Offers practical, hands-on books & multimedia resources specifically developed for principals, administrators, teachers, staff developers, curriculum developers, special & gifted educators & other Pre-K–12 education specialists.
ISBN Prefix(es): 0-7591; 1-4129
Number of titles published annually: 125 Print
Total Titles: 1,000 Print; 5 CD-ROM; 8 Audio
Distributor for Paul Chapman Publishing; Sage Ltd; Sage Publications
Foreign Rep(s): ASTAM (Australia); Sage Publications
Foreign Rights: Sage India Pvt (India); Sage Ltd (UK)

Costume + Fashion Press, see Quite Specific Media Group Ltd

Cotsen Institute of Archaeology at UCLA

PO Box 951510, Los Angeles, CA 90095-1510
Tel: 310-825-7411 *Fax:* 310-206-4723
E-mail: ioapubs@ucla.edu
Web Site: www.sscnet.ucla.edu/ioa
Key Personnel
Dir, Pubns: Julia Sanchez
Pubns Asst: Shauna Mecartea
Founded: 1974
Books, monographs & occasional papers in the field of archaeology.
ISBN Prefix(es): 0-917956
Number of titles published annually: 5 Print
Total Titles: 23 Print

Cottonwood Press

University of Kansas, Kansas Union, Rm 400, 1301 Jayhawk Blvd, Lawrence, KS 66045
Tel: 785-864-3777
Key Personnel
Ed: Tom Lorenz *Tel:* 785-864-2516
Founded: 1965
Poetry & fiction.
ISBN Prefix(es): 1-878434
Number of titles published annually: 3 Print
Total Titles: 15 Print
Membership(s): Council of Literary Magazines & Presses

Cottonwood Press Inc

109-B Cameron Dr, Fort Collins, CO 80525
Tel: 970-204-0715 *Toll Free Tel:* 800-864-4297 *Fax:* 970-204-0761
E-mail: cottonwood@cottonwoodpress.com
Web Site: www.cottonwoodpress.com
Key Personnel
Pres & Ed: Cheryl Thurston *E-mail:* cheri@cottonwoodpress.com
Mgr: Mary Gutting
Cust Serv Rep: Sarah Stimely
Prodn & Art Dir: Carli Taylor
Founded: 1986
Supplemental textbooks for language arts teachers, grades 5-12 & instructional materials for senior adults.
ISBN Prefix(es): 1-877673
Number of titles published annually: 3 Print
Total Titles: 41 Print; 1 CD-ROM; 2 Audio
Distributed by Elder Song Publications Inc; Lakeshore Learning; NASCO; PCI; Social Studies School Services; Teacher Discovery
Membership(s): Small Publishers Association of North America

Council for American Indian Education

1240 Burlington Ave, Billings, MT 59102-4224
SAN: 202-2117
Tel: 406-248-3465 (PM); 406-652-7598 (AM) *Fax:* 406-248-1297
E-mail: cie@cie-mt.org
Web Site: www.cie-mt.org
Key Personnel
Pres & Ed: Hap Gilliland *E-mail:* hapcie@aol.com

Lib Sales Dir: Sue Clague
Founded: 1970
Publish only books giving a true picture of American Indian life & culture; for use in schools.
ISBN Prefix(es): 0-89992
Number of titles published annually: 6 Print
Total Titles: 115 Print
Imprints: Indian Culture Series
Editorial Office(s): 2032 Woody Dr, Billings, MT 59102-2852

Council for Exceptional Children
1110 N Glebe Rd, Suite 300, Arlington, VA 22201
Tel: 703-620-3660 *Toll Free Tel:* 888-232-7733 (cust serv) *Fax:* 703-264-9494
E-mail: service@cec.sped.org
Web Site: www.cec.sped.org
Key Personnel
Sr Dir, Pubns & Cont Ed: Kathleen McLane
Sr Prog Dir: Lynn Boyer
Sr Dir, Prof Advancement: Elizabeth Martinez
Founded: 1922
Mail order books & videos.
ISBN Prefix(es): 0-86586
Number of titles published annually: 6 Print
Total Titles: 75 Print
Branch Office(s)
CEC Publications, PO Box 79026, Baltimore, MD 21279-0026
Distributed by Free Spirit Publishing Inc; LMD Inc (selected titles); Orchard House Inc
Distributor for Brooks (selected titles); Longman; Love Publishing; Pearson; Pro Ed; Sopris West

Council for Research in Values & Philosophy (RVP)
Catholic University, Washington, DC 20064
Mailing Address: PO Box 261, Cardinal Sta, Washington, DC 20064-0261
Tel: 202-319-6089 *Fax:* 202-319-6089
Toll Free Fax: 800-659-9962
E-mail: cua-rvp@cua.edu
Web Site: www.crvp.org
Key Personnel
Sec-Treas & Intl Rts: George McLean
E-mail: mclean@cua.edu
Lib Sales Dir: Hu Yeping
Founded: 1982
Works on philosophy, values, education, civil society, culture.
ISBN Prefix(es): 1-56518
Number of titles published annually: 20 Print
Total Titles: 105 Print
Imprints: The Council for Research in Values & Philosophy

Council Oak Books LLC
2105 E 15 St, Suite B, Tulsa, OK 74104
SAN: 689-5522
Tel: 918-743-BOOK (743-2665)
Toll Free Tel: 800-247-8850 *Fax:* 918-743-4288
E-mail: publicity@counciloakbooks.com; orders@counciloakbooks.com
Web Site: www.counciloakbooks.com
Key Personnel
Publr: Paulette Millichap *E-mail:* pmillichap@counciloakbooks.com
Assoc Publr: Ja-lene Clark *E-mail:* jclark@counciloakbooks.com
Sr Ed: Sally Dennison *E-mail:* sdennison@counciloakbooks.com
Founded: 1984
Published books from all over the world, books that cross cultural lines to bring together ancient traditions in new ways. Publish for the future, presenting books that point the way to a richer life & a better world. With a special focus on Native American history & spiritual teachings, we are seeking books in the areas of alternative spirituality, hidden wisdom & esoterica, alternative health for animals, as well as

the spiritual bond between humans & animals & other cutting-edge titles on the relationship between humans & nature; no fiction, poetry, or children's books.
ISBN Prefix(es): 0-933031; 1-57178; 1-88517
Number of titles published annually: 15 Print
Total Titles: 300 Print
Imprints: Wild Canyon Press
Shipping Address: Council Oak Fulfillment Center, 1616 W Airport, Stillwater, OK 74075

Council of State Governments
2760 Research Park Dr, Lexington, KY 40511
Mailing Address: PO Box 11910, Lexington, KY 40578-1910
Tel: 859-244-8000 *Toll Free Tel:* 800-800-1910
Fax: 859-244-8001
Web Site: www.csg.org
Key Personnel
Chief Info Officer: Andrew Teague
Founded: 1935
Nonprofit association representing state government officials in all three branches. Publish reference guides, books, directories, journals, newsletters & conference proceedings & hold major regional & special topical conferences. Will contract or do grant-funded topic research. Specialize in corrections & public safety.
ISBN Prefix(es): 0-87292
Number of titles published annually: 10 Print
Total Titles: 72 Print
Branch Office(s)
121 Second St, 4th fl, San Francisco, CA 94105, Dir: Kent Briggs
444 N Capitol St NW, Suite 401, Washington, DC 20001, Dir: Jim Brown
Lennox Bldg, Suite 810, 3399 Peachtree Rd NE, Atlanta, GA 30326, Dir: Colleen Cousineau
641 E Butterfield Rd, Suite 401, Lombard, IL 60148, Dir: Michael H McCabe
5 World Trade Center, Suite 9241, New York, NY 10048, Dir: Alan Sokolow

Council on Foreign Relations Press
Division of Council on Foreign Relations
58 E 68 St, New York, NY 10021
SAN: 201-7784
Tel: 212-434-9400 *Fax:* 212-434-9859
E-mail: publications@cfr.org; communications@cfr.org
Web Site: www.cfr.org
Key Personnel
Publr: David Kellogg
Dir, Publg: Patricia Dorff
Founded: 1922
Scholarly books on foreign policy, international economics, international affairs.
ISBN Prefix(es): 0-87609
Number of titles published annually: 10 Print
Total Titles: 228 Print
Distributed by Brookings Institution Press
Membership(s): AAP

Council on Social Work Education
1725 Duke St, Suite 500, Alexandria, VA 22314-3457
Tel: 703-683-8080 *Fax:* 703-683-8099
E-mail: webmaster@cswe.org
Web Site: www.cswe.org
Key Personnel
Exec Dir: Julia M Watkins
Founded: 1952 (Professional Association)
Professional books.
ISBN Prefix(es): 0-87293
Number of titles published annually: 5 Print
Total Titles: 54 Print

Counterpoint Press
Member of Perseus Books Group
387 Park Ave S, New York, NY 10016
Tel: 212-340-8100 *Fax:* 212-340-8135 (edit); 212-340-8115

E-mail: counterpointpress@perseusbooks.com
Web Site: www.counterpointpress.com
Key Personnel
Pres & CEO (Perseus Books Group): David Steinberger
Sr VP & CFO: Joe Mangan
VP & Publr: Liz McGuire
VP & Group Dir, Sales & Mktg: Matthew Goldberg
VP & Group Dir, Fin & Opers: Tom Kilkenny
Dir, Intl Pubns: Carolyn Savarese
Ed: Megan Hustad
Publicity Mgr: Jamie Brickhouse
Mktg Assoc: Marty Gonser
Asst Ed: David Shoemaker
Assoc Publr: Jason Brontley
Publicity Assoc: Paul Gilbert
Founded: 1994
Publish literary work with an emphasis on fiction, natural history, philosophy & contemporary thought, history, art, poetry, narrative & non-fiction.
ISBN Prefix(es): 1-887178; 1-58243
Number of titles published annually: 30 Print
Total Titles: 60 Print
Imprints: A Bessie Book
Distributed by HarperCollins
Foreign Rights: Perseus Books Group Subsidiary Rights
Warehouse: HarperCollins, 1000 Keystone Industrial Park, Scranton, PA 08512 *Toll Free Tel:* 800-386-5656 *Toll Free Fax:* 800-822-4090

Country Music Foundation Press
Division of Country Music Hall of Fame® & Museum
222 Fifth Ave S, Nashville, TN 37203
Tel: 615-416-2001 *Fax:* 615-255-2245
Web Site: www.countrymusichalloffame.com
Key Personnel
Dir, Spec Projects: Kira Florita
Founded: 1972
Publish books, calendars & tri-quarterly journals. Also author books for trade publications & co-publish with Vanderbilt University Press.
ISBN Prefix(es): 1-55859; 0-8265; 0-915608
Number of titles published annually: 5 Print
Total Titles: 40 Print; 1 CD-ROM
Distributed by Chronicle; Oxford University Press Inc; Providence Publishing; Universe; Vanderbilt University Press
Membership(s): AAM

The Countryman Press
Division of W W Norton & Co Inc
1206 Rte 12 N, Woodstock, VT 05091
SAN: 206-7401
Mailing Address: PO Box 748, Woodstock, VT 05091-0748
Tel: 802-457-4826 *Toll Free Tel:* 800-245-4151
Fax: 802-457-1678
E-mail: countrymanpress@wwnorton.com
Web Site: www.countrymanpress.com
Key Personnel
Pres: W Drake McFeely
Publicity & Mkt Man: David Corey
Sales Mgr: Dosier D Hammond
Prod Mgr: Fred Lee
Intl Rts: Felice Mello
Lib Sales Dir: Deirdre Dolan
Edit Dir: Kermit Hummel *E-mail:* khummel@wwnorton.com
Founded: 1973
ISBN Prefix(es): 0-88150; 0-942440; 0-912367
Number of titles published annually: 40 Print
Total Titles: 200 Print
Imprints: Backcountry Guides
Distributed by Penguin Books (Canada only); W W Norton & Co Inc
Distributor for Mountain Pond Publishing Corp
Foreign Rep(s): W W Norton & Co Inc
Advertising Agency: Bennett Book Advertising

Warehouse: National Book Co Inc, 800 Keystone Industrial Park, Scranton, PA 18512-4601 *Toll Free Tel:* 800-245-4151
See separate listing for:
Berkshire House

Course Technology
Subsidiary of International Thomson Publishing
25 Thomson Place, Boston, MA 02210
Tel: 617-757-7900 *Toll Free Tel:* 800-881-8922
Fax: 617-757-7969
Web Site: www.course.com
Key Personnel
Pres: Joseph Dougherty
Founded: 1989
Post-secondary educational materials featuring popular commercial software application packages.
ISBN Prefix(es): 0-534; 1-878748; 1-56527; 0-538; 0-7600; 0-7895
Number of titles published annually: 850 Print
Total Titles: 930 Print
Distributed by South-Western Publishing
Foreign Rep(s): Nelson Canada (Canada); Professional Publications (Canada); Times Mirror (Canada)
Advertising Agency: Albuquerque Marketing
Warehouse: 5101 Madison Rd, Cincinnati, OH 45227

§Covenant Communications Inc
920 E State Rd, Suite F, American Fork, UT 84003-0416
Mailing Address: PO Box 416, American Fork, UT 84003-9966
Tel: 801-756-9966 *Toll Free Tel:* 800-662-9545
Fax: 801-756-1049
E-mail: sales@covenant-lds.com
Web Site: www.covenant-lds.com
Key Personnel
Ed, Acqs: Tyler Moulton *Tel:* 801-756-1041 ext 151 *E-mail:* tylerm@covenant-lds.com
Man Ed, Multimedia & Electronic Publg: Phil Reschke
VP, Mktg: Robby Nichols *Tel:* 801-756-1041 ext 106 *E-mail:* robbyn@covenant-lds.com
Founded: 1958
Publish for the LDS (Mormon) marker.
ISBN Prefix(es): 1-55503; 1-57734; 1-59156
Number of titles published annually: 60 Print; 15 CD-ROM; 50 Audio
Total Titles: 300 Print; 50 CD-ROM; 450 Audio

Cowley Publications
Division of Society of St John the Evangelist
4 Brattle St, Cambridge, MA 02138
SAN: 213-9987
Tel: 617-441-0300 *Toll Free Tel:* 800-225-1534
Fax: 617-441-0120 *Toll Free Fax:* 877-225-6675
E-mail: cowley@cowley.org
Web Site: www.cowley.org
Key Personnel
Publr: Curtis Almquist
Ed: Michael Wilt
Mktg & Sales: Jennifer Hopcroft
Founded: 1980
Contemporary spirituality, religion (Episcopalian), pastoral concerns, ethics.
ISBN Prefix(es): 0-936384; 1-56101
Number of titles published annually: 16 Print
Total Titles: 130 Print
Foreign Rep(s): Columba (UK, Ireland, Europe); John Garrett (Australia); Novalis (Canada)
Warehouse: Ware-Pak, 2427 Bond St, University Park, IL 60466

Coyote Press
Affiliate of Archaeological Consulting
PO Box 3377, Salinas, CA 93912-3377
Tel: 831-422-4912 *Fax:* 831-422-4913
E-mail: coyote@coyotepress.com

Web Site: www.coyotepress.com
Key Personnel
Ed: Gary Breschini, PhD
Pubns Tech: Pam Haynes
Archaeology, history, pre-history & ethnography.
ISBN Prefix(es): 1-55567
Number of titles published annually: 50 Print
Total Titles: 3,000 Print

CQ Press
Subsidiary of Congressional Quarterly Inc
1255 22 St NW, Suite 400, Washington, DC 20037
Tel: 202-729-1800 *Toll Free Tel:* 866-427-7737
Fax: 202-729-1923 *Toll Free Fax:* 800-380-3810
E-mail: customerservice@cqpress.com
Web Site: www.cqpress.com
Key Personnel
VP, Congressional Quarterly: John Jenkins
Mgr, Cust Serv: Judy L Plummer
Natl Sales Mgr: Lonny Merriett
Founded: 1959
Directories, data & label products covering the Congressional, Federal & Judicial branches of the federal government.
ISBN Prefix(es): 0-87289; 1-56802
Number of titles published annually: 50 Print
Total Titles: 300 Print; 4 CD-ROM; 1 Online; 3 E-Book

§Crabtree Publishing Co
350 Fifth Ave, Suite 3308, PMB 16-A, New York, NY 10118
Tel: 212-496-5040 *Toll Free Tel:* 800-387-7650
Toll Free Fax: 800-355-7166
E-mail: letters@crabtreebooks.com
Web Site: www.crabtreebooks.com
Key Personnel
Pres: Peter A Crabtree *Tel:* 212-496-5040 ext 225 *E-mail:* peter@crabtreebooks.com
Publr: Ms Bobbie Kalman
Ed: Kathryn Smithyman *Tel:* 212-496-5040 ext 246 *E-mail:* kathryn@crabtreebooks.com
Edit: Ellen Rodger *Tel:* 212-496-5040 ext 233 *E-mail:* ellen@crabtreebooks.com
Mktg Dir: Kathy Middleton *Tel:* 212-496-5040 ext 266 *E-mail:* kathy@crabtreebooks.com
Warehouse Mgr: Jeff Gogo *Tel:* 212-496-5040 ext 237
Cont/Gen Mgr: John Siemens *Tel:* 212-496-5040 ext 229 *E-mail:* jsiemens@crabtreebooks.com
Natl Acct Mgr: Lisa Antonsen *Tel:* 212-496-5040 ext 234 *E-mail:* antonsen@crabtreebooks.com
Sales Mgr: Julie Alguire *Tel:* 212-496-5040 ext 235 *E-mail:* jalguire@crabtreebooks.com
Cust Serv Mgr: Linda Wade *Tel:* 212-496-5040 ext 223 *E-mail:* linda@crabtreebooks.com
Art Dir: Robert Macgregor *Tel:* 212-496-5040 ext 231 *E-mail:* rmacgregor@crabtreebooks.com
Founded: 1978
ISBN Prefix(es): 0-86505; 0-7787
Number of titles published annually: 180 Print; 25 E-Book
Total Titles: 1,042 Print; 2 CD-ROM; 30 E-Book
Subsidiaries: Crabtree Publishing Canada; Crabtree Publishing UK
Foreign Rep(s): Electra Media (Asia); INT Press (Australia); South Pacific Books (New Zealand); Titles (South Africa)
Warehouse: 181 Cooper Ave, Suite 104, Tonawanda, NY 14150

§Craftsman Book Co
6058 Corte Del Cedro, Carlsbad, CA 92009
SAN: 159-7000
Mailing Address: PO Box 6500, Carlsbad, CA 92018
Tel: 760-438-7828 *Toll Free Tel:* 800-829-8123
Fax: 760-438-0398
Web Site: www.craftsman-book.com

Key Personnel
Chmn & Intl Rts: Gary Moselle
Exec VP & Treas: Trudy Moselle
Art Dir & Sales & Adv Mgr: Bill Grote
Edit Man & Rts & Perms: Laurence Jacobs
E-mail: jacobs@costbook.com
Lib Sales Dir: Jennifer Johnson
Founded: 1952
Journal of Light Construction, trade & professional, subscription & mail order, reference; construction industry.
ISBN Prefix(es): 0-934041; 0-910460; 1-57218
Number of titles published annually: 12 Print; 8 CD-ROM; 60 Online; 6 E-Book
Total Titles: 100 Print; 8 CD-ROM; 60 Online; 6 E-Book
Distributed by The Aberdeen Group; American Technical Publishers; Quality Books
Distributor for Building News Inc; Home Builders Press
Foreign Rep(s): Gauge Publications (Canada)
Advertising Agency: Bill Grote Advertising/ Graphics, PO Box 230098, Encinitas, CA 92023-0098, Contact: Bill Grote *Toll Free Tel:* 800-829-8123 ext 311 *E-mail:* grote@ costbook.com

Crane Hill Publishers
3608 Clairmont Ave, Birmingham, AL 35222
Tel: 205-714-3007 *Toll Free Tel:* 800-247-8850
Fax: 205-714-3008
E-mail: cranies@cranehill.com
Web Site: www.cranehill.com
Key Personnel
Pres & Publr: Ellen Sullivan
Prodn, Publicity & Sales: Allison Brown
Tel: 205-714-3007 ext 28 *E-mail:* allison@ cranehill.com
Founded: 1992
Folklore, literary fiction, cookbooks, health & fitness.
ISBN Prefix(es): 1-881548; 1-57587
Number of titles published annually: 10 Print
Total Titles: 150 Print; 40 Online
Imprints: Southern Lights
Divisions: Southern Lights
Distributed by Council Oak Books

§CRC Press LLC
Subsidiary of Taylor & Frances
2000 NW Corporate Blvd, Boca Raton, FL 33431
Tel: 561-994-0555 *Toll Free Tel:* 800-272-7737
Fax: 561-997-7249 (edit); 561-998-8491 (mfg); 561-361-6057 (acctg); 561-994-0313
Toll Free Fax: 800-643-9428 (sales); 800-374-3401 (orders)
E-mail: orders@crcpress.com
Web Site: www.crcpress.com
Key Personnel
Pres: Fenton Markevich
CFO: Emmitt Dages
VP, Sales: Dennis Weiss
VP, Edit: John Lavender
Founded: 1913
ISBN Prefix(es): 0-8493; 0-87371; 1-56670
Number of titles published annually: 400 Print
Total Titles: 6,000 Print
Imprints: Food Chemical News; Interpharm Press; Lewis Publishers; St Lucie Press
Branch Office(s)
St Lucie Press, Publr: Dennis McClellan
Food Chemical News, 1725 "K" St NW, Suite 506, Washington, DC 20006, Publr: Dave Douglas *Tel:* 202-887-6320 *Fax:* 202-887-6339
Lewis Publishers, 535 Fifth Ave, Suite 805, New York, NY 10017, Publr: Bob Hauserman *Tel:* 212-286-1010
Foreign Office(s): Springer-Verlag (CRC/Lewis), Heidelberger Platz 3, 14197 Berlin, Germany
CRC-Press-UK LLC, 235 Southwark Bridge Rd, London SE16LY, United Kingdom

Foreign Rights: CRC Press
Warehouse: Linn Distribution Ctr, Linn, MO 65051

CRC Publications
2850 Kalamazoo Ave SE, Grand Rapids, MI 49560
Tel: 616-224-0819; 616-224-0728
  Toll Free Tel: 800-333-8300 *Fax:* 616-224-0834
E-mail: sales@crcpublications.org
Web Site: www.faithaliveresources.org
Key Personnel
Exec Dir: Gary Mulder
Dir, World Lit Ministries: Alejandro Pimentel
Dir, Faith Alive: Faith Nederveld
Ed-in-Chief: Robert Banner
Founded: 1928
Sunday school curriculum, Bible studies, devotions, hymnals, church resources.
ISBN Prefix(es): 0-933140; 0-930265; 1-56212; 1-59255
Number of titles published annually: 50 Print
Total Titles: 307 Print
Imprints: Faith Alive; Friendship Bible Studies; Libros Desafio; Open Door Books; World Literature Ministries
Branch Office(s)
3475 Mainway, PO Box 5070, Burlington, ON L7R 3Y8, Canada

§Creating Keepsakes Books
14901 S Heritagecrest Way, Bluffdale, UT 84065
Tel: 801-984-2070 *Toll Free Tel:* 800-815-3538
  Fax: 801-984-2080
Web Site: www.creatingkeepsakes.com
Key Personnel
Pres: Lisa Bearnson
Publr & CEO: Mark Seastrand
Publishes books for creative people on photography, lettering, card-making, paper crafts & holidays, as well as on scrapbooking.
ISBN Prefix(es): 1-929180
Number of titles published annually: 6 Print; 2 CD-ROM
Total Titles: 15 Print; 2 CD-ROM
Sales Office(s): Peak View, 2370 Cherry St, Denver, CO 80207, Contact: Polly Wirtz
  Tel: 303-377-9797 *Fax:* 303-377-0770
  E-mail: pollywirtz@aol.com
Billing Address: 624 Maryland Ave NE, Suite 9, Washington, DC 20002
Membership(s): Publishers Association of the West

Creative Arts Book Co
833 Bancroft Way, Berkeley, CA 94710
SAN: 208-4880
Tel: 510-848-4777 *Fax:* 510-848-4844
E-mail: staff@creativeartsbooks.com; capublisher@yahoo.com
Web Site: www.creativeartsbooks.com
Key Personnel
Publr: Donald S Ellis *E-mail:* dellis@creativeartsbooks.com
Ed: George Samsa; Paul Samuelson; Lynn Park
Busn Mgr: Elizabeth M Ellis
Intl Rts: Bobbe Siegel
Sales: Jessica Padilla *E-mail:* jpadilla@creativeartsbooks.com
Founded: 1976
Fiction, literary nonfiction, music, foreign literature in translation, mystery, suspense, Northern California, biography, health, nutrition, how-to, self-help, cookbooks, women, children's reprints, reprints, auto biography, poetry, memoirs.
ISBN Prefix(es): 0-88739; 0-916870
Number of titles published annually: 63 Print; 2 CD-ROM
Total Titles: 492 Print; 165 E-Book; 1 Audio
Imprints: Black River Books; Black Shadow Books; Creative Arts Communications; Cre-

ative Arts Life & Health Books; Donald S Ellis; Saturday Night Specials; Silver Spur Westerns
Divisions: Creative Arts Communications; Gato Negro Books
Distributor for ZYZZYVA First Titles
Foreign Rights: Bobbe Siegel
Membership(s): Antiquarian Booksellers Association of America; BEA; NCBA

The Creative Co
123 S Broad St, Mankato, MN 56001
SAN: 202-201X
Mailing Address: PO Box 227, Mankato, MN 56001
Tel: 507-388-6273 *Toll Free Tel:* 800-445-6209
  Fax: 507-388-2746
E-mail: creativeco@aol.com
Key Personnel
Pres: Tom Peterson
Founded: 1932
Gift books.
ISBN Prefix(es): 0-87191; 0-88682
Number of titles published annually: 80 Print
Total Titles: 550 Print
Imprints: Creative Editions; Creative Education
Foreign Rep(s): Saunders Book Co (Canada)
Warehouse: 1980 Lookout Dr, North Mankato, MN 56003

Creative Homeowner
Division of Federal Marketing Corp
24 Park Way, Upper Saddle River, NJ 07458-9960
SAN: 213-6627
Mailing Address: PO Box 38, Upper Saddle River, NJ 07458-0038
Tel: 201-934-7100 *Toll Free Tel:* 800-631-7795
  Fax: 201-934-8971
E-mail: info@creativehomeowner.com
Web Site: www.creativehomeowner.com
Key Personnel
Chmn: Allan Blair
Pres: Henry Toolan
Sr VP, Sales & Mktg: James Knapp
VP, Busn Devt: Brian Toolan
VP & Edit Dir: Timothy O Bakke
CFO: Richard Weisman
Sr Ed, Home Decor: Kathie Robitz
Sr Ed, Home Improvement: Fran Donegan
Founded: 1978
Quality trade paperbacks for home improvements, home design, decorating, home gardening, landscaping, arts & crafts, hunting & fishing.
ISBN Prefix(es): 0-932944; 1-880029; 1-58011
Number of titles published annually: 40 Print
Total Titles: 120 Print
Imprints: Creative Arts & Crafts; Creative Outdoors
Distributor for Publishing Solutions

Creative Publishing International Inc
18705 Lake Dr E, Chanhassen, MN 55317
SAN: 289-7148
Tel: 952-936-4700 *Toll Free Tel:* 800-328-0590
  (sales) *Fax:* 952-933-1456
Web Site: www.creativepub.com
Key Personnel
Pres: Michael Eleftheriou
VP & Publr: Linda Ball *Tel:* 952-932-0303
  E-mail: lball@creativepub.com
VP, Sales: Kevin Haas
Founded: 1969
Publish & package photograhic how-to books in the areas of do-it-yourself, home improvement, cooking, sewing, crafts, hunting & fishing, weddings, parenting/child development, decorating & entertaining.
ISBN Prefix(es): 0-86573
Number of titles published annually: 50 Print
Total Titles: 275 Print
Imprints: NorthWord Press

Distributed by Contemporary Books
Warehouse: 6007-9 Culligan Way, Minnetonka, MN 55343

Creative Sales Corp
Subsidiary of American Map Corp
780 W Belden, Suite A, Addison, IL 60101
Tel: 630-458-1500 *Fax:* 630-458-1511
Web Site: www.americanmag-csc.com
Key Personnel
Sales Dir: Jerry Killiam
Founded: 1971
Maps, atlases.
ISBN Prefix(es): 0-933162
Number of titles published annually: 30 Print
Total Titles: 60 Print

Cricket Books
Division of Carus Publishing
332 S Michigan Ave, Suite 1100, Chicago, IL 60604
Tel: 312-939-1500 *Fax:* 312-939-8150
Web Site: www.cricketmag.com
ISBN Prefix(es): 0-8126
Number of titles published annually: 20 Print
Total Titles: 40 Print
Distribution Center: Publishers Group West

Criminal Justice Press
Division of Willow Tree Press Inc
PO Box 249, Monsey, NY 10952-0249
SAN: 217-4588
Tel: 845-354-9139 *Toll Free Tel:* 800-914-3379
Web Site: www.criminaljusticepress.com
Key Personnel
Publr: Richard Allinson
Founded: 1983
Independent publisher specializing in books for criminal justice system professionals, criminologists, libraries & students.
ISBN Prefix(es): 0-9606960; 1-881798
Number of titles published annually: 14 Print
Total Titles: 190 Print
Distributed by Federation Press
Distributor for Australian Institute of Criminology; European Institute for Crime Prevention & Control
Foreign Rep(s): Federation Press (Australia & New Zealand); Wasmuth GmbH (Europe)
Billing Address: Library Research Associates Inc, 158 W Main St, Suite 2, Walden, NY 12586 *Tel:* 845-778-6546 *Fax:* 845-778-1864
  E-mail: lrainc@frontier.net
Orders to: Library Research Associates Inc, 158 W Main St, Suite 2, Walden, NY 12586
  Tel: 845-354-9139 *Fax:* 845-778-1864
  E-mail: lrainc@frontier.net
Returns: Library Research Associates Inc, 158 W Main St, Suite 2, Walden, NY 12586 *Tel:* 845-354-9139 *Fax:* 845-778-1864 *E-mail:* lrainc@frontier.net
Distribution Center: Library Research Associates Inc, 158 W Main St, Suite 2, Walden, NY 12586, Contact: Dianne McKinstrie
  Tel: 845-778-6546 *Toll Free Tel:* 800-914-3379
  Fax: 845-778-1864 *E-mail:* lrainc@frontiernet.net

Crop Circle Books Press
1123 N Las Posas Ct, Ridgecrest, CA 93555
Tel: 760-446-1938
E-mail: cropcircles@webtv.net
Web Site: www.cropcirclebooks.com
Key Personnel
Publr & Intl Rts: Steve Canada
  E-mail: stevecanada@webtv.net
Founded: 1990
Specialize in books on crop circles, UFOs, the Sphinx & ancient religions, goddesses & Mars Cydonia structures. Do not accept book proposals or book ideas. No unsol mss. Do not use proof readers or editors.
ISBN Prefix(es): 1-883424

Number of titles published annually: 3 Print
Total Titles: 25 Print

Cross-Cultural Communications
Subsidiary of Cross-Cultural Communications
  Publications Corp
Affiliate of Cross-Cultural Literary Editions Inc
239 Wynsum Ave, Merrick, NY 11566-4725
SAN: 208-6122
Mailing Address: PO Box 383, Merrick, NY
  11566-0383
Tel: 516-868-5635 *Fax:* 516-379-1901
E-mail: cccpoetry@aol.com
Web Site: www.cross-culturalcommunications.com
Key Personnel
Publr & Ed-in-Chief: Stanley H Barkan
Art Ed: Bebe Barkan
Asst Ed: Mia Barkan Clarke
Founded: 1971
Traditionally neglected languages & cultures in
  bilingual format, primarily poetry, some fiction,
  drama, music & art. Cross-cultural review se-
  ries of world literature & art in sound, print &
  motion.
ISBN Prefix(es): 0-89304
Number of titles published annually: 20 Print; 1
  Audio
Total Titles: 350 Print; 11 Audio
Imprints: ARC (Magazine & Press) (Israel);
  Cross-Cultural Prototypes; Expressive Edi-
  tions; Fact Publishers (Ukraine); Inter Esse
  (Poland); Midrashic Editions; Nightingale Edi-
  tions; Ostrich Editions; SAB Konrad Suszczyn-
  ski (Poland)
Subsidiaries: Bulgarian-American Cultural Soci-
  ety ALEKO (Chicago/Sofia (Bulgaria)); Nasha
  Kniga (Macedonia); Varlik (Turkey)
Branch Office(s)
3131 Mott Ave, Far Rockaway, NY 11691, Con-
  tact: Roy Cravzow *Tel:* 718-327-4714
Foreign Office(s): Antigruppo Siciliano, Via Ar-
  genteria Km 4, 91100 Sicily, Italy, Contact:
  Nat Scammacca *Tel:* (0923) 538681
Distributed by Hochelaga (Canada)
Distributor for Ad Infinitum Books (United
  States); Arba Sicula (Magazine); Biblio Press
  (United States); Center of Emigrants from
  Serbia (Serbia); Decalogue Books (United
  States); Greenfield Review Press (United
  States); Hochelaga (Canada); Legas (Publish-
  ers, United States); Lips (Magazine & Press);
  Pholiota Press Inc (England); Shabdaguchha
  (Magazine & Press) (United States); Sicilia
  Parra (Magazine, United States); Word & Quill
  Press (United States)
Foreign Rep(s): Hassan Al Abdullah (Bangladesh,
  USA); Karen Alkalay-Gut (Israel); Vahe Bal-
  adouni (USA, Armenia); Raymond Beau-
  chemin (Canada); Jozo T Boskovski (Mace-
  donia); Bohdan Boychuk (Ukraine); Gaetano
  Cipolla (Italy, USA); Nicolo D'Alessandro
  (Italy); Aleksey Dayen (Russia); Kristine Doll
  (Spain); Talat S Halman (Turkey, USA); Peter
  Thabit Jones (UK); Vladimir Kandelaki (Rus-
  sia); Dovid Katz (UK); Won Ko (Korea, USA);
  Vladimir Levchev (Bulgaria, USA); Beverly
  Matherne (USA); Bijana D Obradovic (Serbia
  and Montenegro, USA); Ritva Poom (Estonia,
  Finland); Stephen A Sadow (Argentina); Marco
  Scalabrino (Italy); Nat Scammacca (Italy);
  Zbigniew Suszcznski (Poland); Adam Szyper
  (Poland); Stoyan "Tchouki" Tchoukanov (Bul-
  garia); Tino Villanueva (Mexico, USA); Daniel
  Weissbort (England); Claire Nicolas White
  (Holland); Sara Wolosker (Brazil)
Membership(s): ALTA; Association of Jewish
  Book Publishers

Cross Cultural Publications Inc
53310 Peggy Lane, South Bend, IN 46635
Mailing Address: PO Box 506, Notre Dame, IN
  46556

Tel: 574-273-6526 *Toll Free Tel:* 800-273-6526
  Fax: 574-273-5973
E-mail: crosscult@aol.com
Web Site: crossculturalpub.com
Key Personnel
Pres: Elizabeth Pullapilly
Intl Rts & Gen Ed: Cyriac K Pullapilly
Lib Sales Dir: Kavita Pullapilly
Founded: 1980
ISBN Prefix(es): 0-940121
Number of titles published annually: 25 Print
Total Titles: 60 Print
Imprints: Cross Roads Books
Divisions: Cross Roads Books

The Crossing Press
Imprint of Ten-Speed Press
PO Box 7123, Berkeley, CA 94707
SAN: 202-2060
Tel: 510-559-1600 *Toll Free Tel:* 800-841-2665
  (orders & cust serv) *Fax:* 510-524-1052
E-mail: publicity@tenspeed.com
Web Site: www.tenspeed.com
Key Personnel
Publr: Jo Ann Deck
Publicity Dir: Kristin Casemore
Mktg: Gonzalo Ferreyra
Founded: 1966
Trade paperbacks; New Age, spirituality, natural
  health & nutrition, cookbooks, pets, self-help,
  personal growth & transformation.
ISBN Prefix(es): 0-89594; 1-58091
Number of titles published annually: 50 Print; 2
  Audio
Total Titles: 400 Print; 5 Audio

Crossquarter Publishing Group
1910 Sombra Ct, Santa Fe, NM 87505
Mailing Address: PO Box 8756, Sante Fe, NM
  87504
Tel: 505-438-9846 *Fax:* 505-438-9846
E-mail: sales@crossquarter.com; info@
  crossquarter.com
Web Site: www.crossquarter.com
Key Personnel
Exec Dir: Therese Francis
Sr Ed: Anthony Ravenscroft
  E-mail: aravenscroft@crossquarter.com
Founded: 1996
Small book press with some sidelines. Publishes
  books, e-books & information packages.
ISBN Prefix(es): 1-890109
Number of titles published annually: 25 Print; 3
  E-Book
Total Titles: 7 Print; 2 E-Book
Imprints: Crossquarter Breeze; CrossTIME; Fenris
  Brothers; Xemplar
Membership(s): Publishers Marketing Associa-
  tion; Small Publishers Association of North
  America

The Crossroad Publishing Company
16 Penn Plaza, Suite 1550, New York, NY 10001
SAN: 287-0118
Tel: 212-868-1801 *Toll Free Tel:* 800-395-0690
  (orders) *Fax:* 212-868-2171 *Toll Free Fax:* 800-
  462-6420 (orders)
E-mail: ask@crossroadpublishing.com
Web Site: www.crossroadpublishing.com
Key Personnel
Pres & CEO: Gwendolin Herder
CFO: James Phillips
Exec Mgr: John Jones *Tel:* 212-868-1801 ext 122
  E-mail: jjones@crossroadpublishing.com
Prodn Mgr: Matthew R Laughlin
Founded: 1980
Independent book publisher in religion, spiritual-
  ity, theology & personal growth.
ISBN Prefix(es): 0-8245
Number of titles published annually: 55 Print; 1
  CD-ROM; 1 Online; 1 Audio

Total Titles: 1,205 Print; 1 CD-ROM; 1 Online; 4
  Audio
Imprints: Crossroad (Catholic & Christian trade);
  Herder & Herder (academic market)
Foreign Rep(s): Alban Books (Europe & UK);
  John Garratt (Australia); Novalis (Canada)
Billing Address: National Book Network, 15200
  NBN Way, Blue Ridge Summit, PA 17214
Membership(s): Catholic Book Publishers Associ-
  ation

Crossway Books
Division of Good News Publishers
1300 Crescent St, Wheaton, IL 60187
SAN: 211-7991
Tel: 630-682-4300 *Fax:* 630-682-4785
E-mail: editorial@goodnews-crossway.org
Web Site: www.crosswaybooks.org
Key Personnel
Pres: Lane T Dennis
VP, Edit: Marvin Padgett
Edit Admin & Perms & ISBN Contact: Jill Carter
  E-mail: jcarter@gnpcb.org
Natl Sales Mgr: Bill Anderson
Publicist: Kathy Jacobs
Dir, Mktg & Sales: Randy Jahns
Founded: 1938
Books with an evangelical Christian perspective
  aimed at the religious market.
ISBN Prefix(es): 0-89107; 1-58134
Number of titles published annually: 80 Print
Total Titles: 354 Print; 9 Audio

§Crown House Publishing
4 Berkely St, Norwalk, CT 06850
SAN: 013-9270
Tel: 203-852-9504 *Toll Free Tel:* 877-925-1213
  (orders) *Fax:* 203-852-9619
Web Site: www.chpus.com
Key Personnel
Dir, American Opers: Mark Tracten
  E-mail: mtracten@chpus.com
Founded: 1996
Publisher of quality books in psychology & edu-
  cation.
ISBN Prefix(es): 1-89983; 1-90442
Number of titles published annually: 40 Print; 1
  CD-ROM; 3 Audio
Total Titles: 200 Print; 1 CD-ROM; 6 Audio
Foreign Rep(s): Footprint Books Pty Ltd (Aus-
  tralia & New Zealand)
Foreign Rights: Ano-Ameerican Book Co Ltd
  (UK/Europe)
Billing Address: PO Box 2223, Williston, VT
  05495
Orders to: PO Box 2223, Williston, VT 05495,
  Laurie Kenyon *Toll Free Tel:* 877-925-1213
  Fax: 802-864-7626 *E-mail:* lkenyon@aidcvt.
  com
Returns: 82 Wintersport Lane, Willis-
  ton, VT 05496, Contact: Laurie Kenyon
  E-mail: lkenyon@aidcvt.com
Shipping Address: PO Box 2223, Williston, VT
  05495, Contact: Laurie Kenyon *Tel:* 802-862-
  0095 ext 113 *Toll Free Tel:* 877-925-1213
  Fax: 802-864-7626 *E-mail:* lkenyon@aidcvt.
  com
Warehouse: PO Box 2223, Williston, VT 05495
Distribution Center: 82 Wintersport Lane, Willis-
  ton, VT 05496, Contact: Laurie Kenyon *Toll
  Free Tel:* 877-925-1213 *Fax:* 802-864-7626
  E-mail: lkenyon@aidcvg.com

Crown Publishing Group
Division of Random House Inc
1745 Broadway, New York, NY 10019
Tel: 212-782-9000 *Toll Free Tel:* 888-264-1745
  Fax: 212-940-7408
Web Site: www.randomhouse.com/crown
Key Personnel
Pres & Publr: Jenny Frost
Sr VP, Publg Opers: Pete Muller

Sr VP & Creative Dir: Whitney Cookman
Sr VP & Publr, Crown, Crown Business, Crown
  Forum & Three Rivers Press: Steve Ross
VP & Publr, Harmony & Shaye Areheart Books:
  Shaye Areheart
VP & Dir, Mktg: Philip Patrick
VP & Exec Dir, Publicity: Tina Constable
VP & Man Ed: Amy Boorstein
VP & Sales Dir: Doug Jones
Edit Dir, Crown: Kristin Kiser
Edit Dir, Three Rivers Press: Becky Cabaza
Mktg Dir, Crown, Crown Business, Crown Forum
  & Three Rivers Press: Jill Flaxman
Mktg Dir, Clarkson Potter, Harmony & Shaye
  Areheart Books: Katherine Dietrich
Dir, Publicity, Crown & Three Rivers Press: Brian
  Belfiglio
Dir, Publicity, Crown Business, Harmony &
  Shaye Areheart Books: Tara Gilbride
Dir, Sub/Foreign Rts: Linda Kaplan
Founded: 1933
Nonfiction & fiction; business books.
Random House Inc & its publishing entities are
  not accepting unsol submissions, proposals,
  mss or submission queries via e-mail at this
  time.
ISBN Prefix(es): 0-307; 0-609; 0-676; 1-4000; 0-
  517
Number of titles published annually: 250 Print
Imprints: Bell Tower; Clarkson Potter; Crown;
  Crown Business; Crown Forum; Harmony
  Books; Shaye Areheart Books; Three Rivers
  Press

Crumb Elbow Publishing
PO Box 294, Rhododendron, OR 97049-0294
Tel: 503-622-4798
Key Personnel
Publr: Michael P Jones
Founded: 1979
ISBN Prefix(es): 0-89904
Number of titles published annually: 20 Print; 5
  Audio
Total Titles: 474 Print
Imprints: Bear Meadows Research Group; Cas-
  cade Expeditions; Cascade Geographic Soci-
  ety; Ecosystem Research Group; Elbow Books;
  The Final Edition; Horse Latitudes Press; Lady
  Fern Press; Meadow Creek Press; Oregon
  Fever Books; Oregon River Watch; Read'n
  Run Books; Research Centrex; Sealife Re-
  search Alliance; Silhouette Imprints; Timer-
  berline Productions; Trillium Productions; Tyee
  Press; Wildlife Research Group; Wild Moun-
  tain Press; Windflower Press
Shipping Address: 73487 E Buggy Trail Dr,
  Rhododendron, OR 97049
Distribution Center: 25580 SE Rebman Rd, Deep
  Creek, OR 97009-9109

Crystal Clarity Publishers
14618 Tyler Foote Rd, Nevada City, CA 95959
Tel: 530-478-7600 *Toll Free Tel:* 800-424-1055
  Fax: 530-478-7610
E-mail: clarity@crystalclarity.com
Web Site: www.crystalclarity.com
Key Personnel
Pres & Publr: Sean Meshorer *Tel:* 530-478-7600
  ext 7606
Founded: 1968
Self-help, psychology, philosophy, religion, busi-
  ness, books, tapes, videos, sidelines, metaphysi-
  cal, health/healing.
ISBN Prefix(es): 0-916124; 1-878265; 1-56589
Number of titles published annually: 12 Print; 4
  Audio
Total Titles: 95 Print; 15 Audio
Imprints: Clarity Sound & Light
Foreign Rep(s): Brumby Books (Australia); Deep
  Books Ltd (England, Europe); National Book
  Network (Canada, New Zealand); New Hori-

zons (South Africa); Pen International (Singapore)
Foreign Rights: Alexandra McGilloway

§Crystal Fountain Publications
Division of Crystal Fountain Ministries Inc
500-A N Golden Springs Dr, Diamond Bar, CA
  91765
Mailing Address: PO Box 4434, Diamond Bar,
  CA 91765
Tel: 909-396-1201 *Fax:* 909-860-7803
Web Site: www.crystalfountain.org
Key Personnel
Pres & Intl Rts: Leonidas Johnson
Founded: 1996
ISBN Prefix(es): 1-889561
Number of titles published annually: 3 Print; 2
  CD-ROM; 4 E-Book; 2 Audio
Total Titles: 11 Print
Distributed by Spring Arbor
Distributor for Judson Press
Membership(s): Publishers Marketing Association

Crystal Productions
1812 Johns Dr, Glenview, IL 60025
Tel: 847-657-8144 *Toll Free Tel:* 800-255-8629
  Fax: 847-657-8149 *Toll Free Fax:* 800-657-
  8149
E-mail: custserv@crystalproductions.com
Web Site: www.crystalproductions.com
Key Personnel
CEO: Thomas N Hubbard
Pres: Amy L Woodworth *E-mail:* alw@
  crystalproductions.com
VP: Loretta W Hubbard
Founded: 1973
Art education & earth science books, CD-ROMs,
  DVDs, posters, prints, videos & timelines.
ISBN Prefix(es): 0-924509; 1-56290
Number of titles published annually: 3 Print; 3
  CD-ROM
Total Titles: 8 Print

Crystal Publishers
3460 Lost Hills Dr, Las Vegas, NV 89122
Tel: 702-434-3037 *Fax:* 702-434-3037
Web Site: www.crystalpub.com
Key Personnel
Pres: Frank Leanza *E-mail:* leanzaent@cox.net
Exec Dir: Inge Allen
Founded: 1985
Music books for schools & professionals.
ISBN Prefix(es): 0-934687
Number of titles published annually: 15 Print
Total Titles: 45 Print

§CSLI Publications
Stanford University, Ventura Hall, 220 Panama St,
  Stanford, CA 94305-4115
Tel: 650-723-1839 *Fax:* 650-725-2166
E-mail: pubs@csli.stanford.edu
Web Site: cslipublications.stanford.edu
Key Personnel
Dir: Dikran Karagueuzian
Ed: Lauri Kanerva
Founded: 1985
Subjects include computer science, computational
  linguistics, linguistics & philosophy.
ISBN Prefix(es): 0-937073; 1-881526; 1-57586;
  0-226
Number of titles published annually: 15 Print
Total Titles: 339 Print; 7 Online
Distributed by University of Chicago Press
Advertising Agency: University of Chicago Press

CTB/McGraw-Hill
Division of The McGraw-Hill Companies
20 Ryan Ranch Rd, Monterey, CA 93940-5703
Tel: 831-393-0700 *Toll Free Tel:* 800-538-9547
  Fax: 831-393-7825
Web Site: www.ctb.com

Key Personnel
Pres: David M Taggart *Fax:* 831-393-7243
Sr VP, Finance: Art Shively *Tel:* 831-393-7848
  Fax: 831-393-7069
VP, Sales & Mktg: Alan Button
VP, Devt & Res: Ellen Haley
VP, Mktg: Linda Cannon
VP, Programs & Busn Transformation: Greg
  Baker *Tel:* 831-393-7466 *Fax:* 831-393-6466
VP, Mfg & Scoring: Doug Hartman *Tel:* 831-393-
  7144
VP & Chief Technol Officer: Curtis Brown
Dir, HR: Monica Casey
Founded: 1926
Publishes nationally standardized tests, provides
  comprehensive scoring & reporting services &
  creates on-line solutions for managing & re-
  porting test scores & student information to
  support sound accountability decisions.
ISBN Prefix(es): 0-9726382

Cumberland House Publishing Inc
431 Harding Industrial Dr, Nashville, TN 37211
Tel: 615-832-1171 *Toll Free Tel:* 888-439-2665
  Fax: 615-832-0633
E-mail: information@cumberlandhouse.com
Web Site: www.cumberlandhouse.com
Key Personnel
Pres & Publr: Ronald E Pitkin *E-mail:* ron@
  cumberlandhouse.com
COO: Julie Jayne *E-mail:* jjayne@
  cumberlandhouse.com
Sales: Chris Bauerle *E-mail:* chris@
  cumberlandhouse.com
Edit Dir: Ed Curtis *E-mail:* edcurtis@
  cumberlandhouse.com
Founded: 1996
Nonfiction books & current subjects include
  cooking, regional topics, humor & lifestyle
  books.
ISBN Prefix(es): 1-888952; 1-58182
Number of titles published annually: 60 Print
Total Titles: 240 Print
Imprints: Cumberland House-Hearthside Books;
  Highland Books
Foreign Rep(s): Gazelle (UK); Jaguar Distribution
  (Canada)
Membership(s): ABA; Publishers Marketing As-
  sociation; Southeast Booksellers Association

Cummings & Hathaway Publishers
395 Atlantic Ave, East Rockaway, NY 11518
Tel: 516-593-3607 *Fax:* 516-593-1401
E-mail: chpublish@aol.com
Key Personnel
Pres: William Burke
Founded: 1980
Publish paperback books only.
ISBN Prefix(es): 1-57981; 0-943025
Number of titles published annually: 3 Print
Total Titles: 48 Print

Curbstone Press
321 Jackson St, Willimantic, CT 06226
SAN: 209-4282
Tel: 860-423-5110 *Fax:* 860-423-9242
E-mail: info@curbstone.org
Web Site: www.curbstone.org
Key Personnel
Dir: Judith Doyle; Alexander Taylor
Founded: 1975
Translations of Vietnamese, Latin American,
  Puerto Rican & Chicano literature; poetry; US
  fiction; photography.
ISBN Prefix(es): 0-915306; 1-880684; 1-931896
Number of titles published annually: 12 Print
Total Titles: 149 Print
Foreign Rights: Raquel de la Concha (Spain);
  Caroline Van Gelderen (Netherlands)
Distribution Center: Consortium, 1045 Westgate
  Dr, St Paul, MN 55114-1065 *Tel:* 651-221-
  9035 *Toll Free Tel:* 800-283-3572 *Fax:* 651-
  221-0124

§Current Clinical Strategies Publishing
27071 Cabot Rd, Suite 126, Laguna Hills, CA 92653-7011
SAN: 298-4490
Tel: 949-348-8404 *Toll Free Tel:* 800-331-8227 *Fax:* 949-348-8404 *Toll Free Fax:* 800-965-9420
E-mail: info@ccspublishing.com
Web Site: www.ccspublishing.com
Key Personnel
Ed: Camille M de Tonnancour
Opers Dir: Vic Summers
Founded: 1988
Medical books & nursing.
ISBN Prefix(es): 1-881528; 1-929622
Number of titles published annually: 6 Print
Total Titles: 19 Print; 4 CD-ROM; 4 Online; 4 E-Book
Foreign Rep(s): Gazelle Book Services (UK); Hipocrates (Portugal); Info Access & Distribution Pte Ltd (China, Korea, Philippines, Thailand); Intersistemas (Mexico); Logan Brothers (Canada); Momento Medico (Italy)

§Current Medicine
Division of Current Science Group
400 Market St, Suite 700, Philadelphia, PA 19106
Tel: 215-574-2266 *Toll Free Tel:* 800-427-1796 *Fax:* 215-574-2270
E-mail: info@phl.curci.com
Key Personnel
Pres: Abe Krieger
Prod Mgr: Lori Holland
Founded: 1990
Medical books & journals.
ISBN Prefix(es): 1-878132; 1-57340
Number of titles published annually: 30 Print
Total Titles: 101 Print; 40 CD-ROM
Imprints: Current Science Inc
Distributed by American Psychology Press; Appleton Lange; Blackwell Science; Butterworth-Heinemann; W B Saunders; Springer Verlag; Thieme; Williams & Wilkins

Cycle Publishing
1282 Seventh Ave, San Francisco, CA 94122-2526
Tel: 415-665-8214 *Toll Free Tel:* 877-353-1207 *Fax:* 415-753-8572
E-mail: pubrel@cyclepublishing.com
Web Site: www.cyclepublishing.com
Key Personnel
Pres & Publr: Rob van der Plas
Founded: 1985 (Formerly Bicycle Books Inc)
Books on sports, fitness, home building & home buying ; Emphasis on cycling.
ISBN Prefix(es): 1-892495
Number of titles published annually: 6 Print
Total Titles: 30 Print
Foreign Office(s): Chris Lloyd, Stanley House, 3 Fleets Lane, Poole, Dorset BH15 3AJ, United Kingdom *Tel:* (01202) 649930
Distributed by Chris Lloyd
Foreign Rights: Orca Books (UK); Tower Books (Australia)
Warehouse: PCFS, 35 Ash Dr, Kimball, MI 48074
Membership(s): Publishers Marketing Association; Small Publishers Association of North America

§CyclopsMedia.com
1076 Eagle Dr, Salinas, CA 93905
Tel: 831-776-9500 *Fax:* 831-422-5915
E-mail: custserv@cyclopsmedia.com
Web Site: www.cyclopsmedia.com
Key Personnel
CEO: David Spiselman *E-mail:* dave-s@ cyclopsmedia.com
COO: Hal Bogner *E-mail:* hal@cyclopsmedia.com

CFO: Jay Glover *E-mail:* jay-g@cyclopsmedia.com
Chief Technol Officer: Gavin Vess *E-mail:* gavin@cyclopsmedia.com
VP, Systems & Opers: Richard Tabor *E-mail:* rich@cyclopsmedia.com
Founded: 2000
Creates & operates private branded eBookstores on behalf of the small & mid-sized presses & for Internet portal eCommerce businesses. Intend to restructure the supply chain for publishing end-to-end, from author to consumer. Publishes quality downloadable eBooks in fiction, nonfiction & children's categories, but only accepts material sponsored by Literary Agents or published (currently or previously) in print. Supplies e-books to Microsoft website that can be bought at mslit.com.
Number of titles published annually: 15 Print; 50 E-Book
Total Titles: 50 Print; 35 E-Book

Cyclotour Guide Books
160 Harvard St, Rochester, NY 14607
Mailing Address: PO Box 10585, Rochester, NY 14610-0585
Tel: 585-244-6157 *Fax:* 585-244-6157
E-mail: cyclotour@cyclotour.com
Web Site: www.cyclotour.com
Key Personnel
Publr & Intl Rts: Harvey Botzman
Founded: 1994
Books, bicycling related, brochures, bicycle travel guides & magazines.
ISBN Prefix(es): 1-889602
Number of titles published annually: 4 Print
Total Titles: 7 Print

Da Capo Press Inc
Member of Perseus Books Group
11 Cambridge Center, Cambridge, MA 02142
SAN: 201-2944
Tel: 617-252-5200 *Toll Free Tel:* 800-242-7737 (orders) *Fax:* 617-252-5285
E-mail: custserve@lrp.com
Web Site: www.dacapopress.com
Key Personnel
Pres & CEO: David Steinberger
Sr VP & CFO: Joe Mangan
VP & Group Dir, Fin & Opers: Tom Kilkenny
VP & Publr: John Radziewicz
VP & Group Dir, Sales & Mktg: Matthew Goldberg
VP, Group Rts Dir: Carolyn Savarese
Dir, Mktg: Kevin Hanover *Tel:* 617-252-5262
Sr Ed: Marnie Cochrane
Ed: Ben Schafer
Founded: 1964
Trade paperbacks & hardcover-trade in music, classical, jazz, blues, popular culture, military history, history, health, fitness, parenting, relationships, pregnancy, sports & biography.
ISBN Prefix(es): 0-201; 0-306; 0-7382
Number of titles published annually: 90 Print
Total Titles: 5,000 Print
Branch Office(s)
387 Park Ave S, New York, NY 10016
Distributed by HarperCollins
Foreign Rights: Perseus Books Group Subsidiary Rights
Warehouse: 1000 Keystone Industrial Park, Scranton, PA 08512

Dalkey Archive Press
Illinois State University 8905, Normal, IL 61790-8905
Tel: 309-438-7555 *Fax:* 309-438-7422
E-mail: contact@dalkeyarchive.com
Web Site: www.dalkeyarchive.com
Key Personnel
Publr & Ed: John O'Brien *E-mail:* obrien@ dalkeyarchive.com

Mktg, Sales & Publicity Dir: Chad Post
Prodn Dir: Nate Furl
Rts Dir: Angela Weaser
Founded: 1984 (Keeping works of literary value in print)
Literary fiction, translations & criticism.
ISBN Prefix(es): 0-916583; 1-56478
Number of titles published annually: 24 Print
Total Titles: 170 Print
Foreign Rep(s): Diane Voight German Language
Distribution Center: University of Nebraska Press, 233 N Eighth St, Lincoln, NE 68588-0255 *Toll Free Tel:* 800-755-1105 *Toll Free Fax:* 800-526-2617

Damron Co
PO Box 422458, San Francisco, CA 94142-2458
Tel: 415-255-0404 *Toll Free Tel:* 800-462-6654 *Fax:* 415-703-9049
E-mail: editor@damron.com
Web Site: www.damron.com
Key Personnel
Publr: Gina Gatta *E-mail:* publisher@damron.com
Man Ed: Ian Philips
Founded: 1964
Annual travel guides.
ISBN Prefix(es): 0-929435
Number of titles published annually: 4 Print
Total Titles: 4 Print
Imprints: AttaGirl Press

Dan River Press
Division of Conservatory of American Letters
PO Box 298, Thomaston, ME 04861
Tel: 207-354-0998
E-mail: cal@americanletter.org
Web Site: www.americanletters.org
Key Personnel
Exec Ed: Richard S Danbury, III
Pres, CAL: Robert W Olmsted
Founded: 1976
ISBN Prefix(es): 0-89754
Number of titles published annually: 4 Print
Total Titles: 35 Print
Divisions: University Press (division for college text books)
Distributor for Century Press; Northwoods Press
Advertising Agency: Creative Images Ad Agency

Dandy Lion Publications
3563 Sueldo, Suite L, San Luis Obispo, CA 93401
Tel: 805-543-3332 *Toll Free Tel:* 800-776-8032 *Fax:* 805-544-2823
E-mail: dandy@dandylionbooks.com
Web Site: www.dandylionbooks.com
Key Personnel
Owner & Intl Rts Contact: Dianne Draze
Off Mgr: Cyndi Wheeler
Founded: 1977
Publish supplementary text books & teacher guides for grades K-8, including gifted educational materials.
ISBN Prefix(es): 1-883055; 0-931724
Number of titles published annually: 4 Print
Total Titles: 140 Print
Membership(s): Publishers Marketing Association

John Daniel & Co, Publishers
Division of Daniel & Daniel, Publishers Inc
PO Box 2790, McKinleyville, CA 95519
SAN: 215-1995
Tel: 707-839-3495 *Toll Free Tel:* 800-662-8351 *Fax:* 707-839-3242
E-mail: dandd@danielpublishing.com
Web Site: www.danielpublishing.com
Key Personnel
Owner & Sales Mgr: Susan Daniel *E-mail:* susan@danielpublishing.com
Publr & Intl Rts: John Daniel *E-mail:* jd@ danielpublishing.com
Founded: 1985

ISBN Prefix(es): 0-936784; 1-880284
Number of titles published annually: 5 Print
Total Titles: 200 Print
Branch Office(s)
2611 Kelly Ave, McKinleyville, CA 95519
Distributor for Fithian Press; Perserverance Press
Foreign Rights: Gaia Media A. G.
Returns: 2611 Kelly Ave, McKinleyville, CA 95519
Distribution Center: SCB Distributors, 15608 S New Century Dr, Gardena, CA 90248, Aaron Silverman *Toll Free Tel:* 800-729-6423
Membership(s): Publishers Marketing Association

Dante University of America Press Inc
PO Box 812158, Wellesley, MA 02482
SAN: 220-150X
Tel: 781-235-3634 *Fax:* 781-790-1056
E-mail: danteu@danteuniversity.org
Web Site: www.danteuniversity.org
Key Personnel
Dir & Pres: Adolph Caso
Founded: 1980
Italian Americana.
Number of titles published annually: 2 Print
Total Titles: 12 Print
Distributed by Branden Publishing Co
Foreign Rep(s): Baker & Taylor (World)
Foreign Rights: Amazon.com; Gazelle (England)

Dark Horse Comics
Affiliate of Dark Horse Entertainment
10956 SE Main St, Milwaukie, OR 97222
Tel: 503-652-8815 *Fax:* 503-654-9440
E-mail: dhcomics@darkhorsecomics.com
Web Site: www.darkhorse.com
Key Personnel
Pres: Michael Richardson
Publicist: Lee Dawson
Mktg Mgr: Sarah McCandless
Founded: 1986
Primary area is graphic novels; pop culture; limited edition hard covers, comics & popculture.
ISBN Prefix(es): 1-56971
Number of titles published annually: 200 Print
Total Titles: 600 Print
Imprints: Dark Horse Books; Dark Horse Comics
Distributed by LPC Group Inc
Foreign Rights: Anita Nelson

§The Dartnell Corp
Subsidiary of LRP Publications
360 Hiatt Dr, Palm Beach Gardens, FL 33418
Mailing Address: PO Box 980, Horsham, PA 19044-0980
Tel: 561-622-6520 *Toll Free Tel:* 800-621-5463
Fax: 561-622-2423
Web Site: www.dartnellcorp.com
Key Personnel
Publr: Kenneth F Kahn
Founded: 1917
Business information, training, motivation.
ISBN Prefix(es): 0-85013
Number of titles published annually: 20 Print
Total Titles: 300 Print

The Darwin Press Inc
280 N Main St, Pennington, NJ 08534
SAN: 201-2987
Mailing Address: PO Box 2202, Princeton, NJ 08543
Tel: 609-737-1349 *Fax:* 609-737-0929
E-mail: books@darwinpress.com
Web Site: www.darwinpress.com
Key Personnel
Man Dir: Ed Breisacher
Info Servs Dir: James Plastine
Lib Sales Dir: Chris Browne
Founded: 1970
Natural & behavioral sciences; world business; Near Eastern studies; technical, scientific, reference.

ISBN Prefix(es): 0-87850
Number of titles published annually: 6 Print
Total Titles: 70 Print
Imprints: Darwin® Books
Foreign Rep(s): Gazelle (Europe)

§Data Trace Publishing Co
110 West Rd, Suite 227, Towson, MD 21204-2316
Mailing Address: PO Box 1239, Brooklandville, MD 21022-9978
Tel: 410-494-4994 *Toll Free Tel:* 800-342-0454 (orders only) *Fax:* 410-494-0515
E-mail: info@datatrace.com
Web Site: www.datatrace.com
Key Personnel
Prodn Mgr: Cindy Lee Floyd
Adv Mgr: Frank Tufariello
Dir, Sales & Mktg: Brian Rohd *E-mail:* b.rohd@datatrace.com
Founded: 1987
Full-service specialty publisher with interest in chemistry, law & medicine.
ISBN Prefix(es): 0-9637468; 1-57400
Number of titles published annually: 20 Print
Total Titles: 100 Print; 15 CD-ROM; 5 Online

Daughters of St Paul, see Pauline Books & Media

May Davenport Publishers
26313 Purissima Rd, Los Altos Hills, CA 94022
Tel: 650-947-1275 *Fax:* 650-947-1373
E-mail: mdbooks@earthlink.net
Web Site: www.maydavenportpublishers.com
Key Personnel
Ed & Publr: May Davenport
Founded: 1975 (Originally created comic tales to read & for the child, 3-4 yrs old, to color the illustrations)
Create & distribute books for children/young adults (ages 15-18). With special grants, we print & distribute literary writings, which counselors at schools give to troubled teens. Books are written by teachers, writers, social workers, mental clinicians & counselors. We sell books by direct mail. Remainders are donated to schools in depressed areas who ask for free copies for their students to take home; to penal institutions who ask for our young adult books for their teenaged inmates & to literacy projects.
ISBN Prefix(es): 0-9603118; 0-943864
Number of titles published annually: 3 Print; 8 Online
Total Titles: 32 Print; 32 Online
Imprints: Md Books

Davies-Black Publishing
Division of CPP Inc
3803 E Bayshore Rd, Palo Alto, CA 94303
Tel: 650-969-8901 *Toll Free Tel:* 800-624-1765
Fax: 650-623-9271
Web Site: www.daviesblack.com
Key Personnel
Publr: Lee Langhammer Law *Tel:* 650-691-9143 *E-mail:* llaw@cpp.com
Dir, Sales & Mktg: Laura Simonds *Tel:* 650-691-9123 *E-mail:* lsimonds@cpp.com
Sr Acqs Ed: Connie Kallback *Tel:* 828-658-9018 *Fax:* 828-658-9017 *E-mail:* ckallback@cpp.com
Founded: 1995
Book publishing in career & organization development, business, management, human resources.
ISBN Prefix(es): 0-89106
Number of titles published annually: 12 Print
Total Titles: 105 Print
Online services available through EBSCOhost.
Distributed by National Book Network
Foreign Rep(s): Eurospan Ltd (UK & Europe)

Orders to: National Book Network, 15200 NBN Way, Blue Ridge Summit, PA *Toll Free Tel:* 800-462-6420
Warehouse: 1150 Hamilton Ct, Menlo Park, CA 94025
Membership(s): BISG; Publishers Marketing Association

The Davies Group Publishers
PO Box 440140, Aurora, CO 80044-0140
Tel: 303-750-8374 *Fax:* 303-337-0952
E-mail: daviesgroup@msn.com
Key Personnel
Publr: Elizabeth B Davies
Founded: 1991
Scholarly publisher; humanities & social sciences.
ISBN Prefix(es): 1-888570; 0-9630076
Number of titles published annually: 6 Print
Total Titles: 33 Print

§Davies Publishing Inc
32 S Raymond Ave, Pasadena, CA 91105-1935
SAN: 217-3255
Tel: 626-792-3046 *Toll Free Tel:* 877-792-0005
Fax: 626-792-5308
E-mail: daviescorp@aol.com
Web Site: www.daviespublishing.com
Key Personnel
Pres & Publr: Michael Davies
Sec & Treas: A L Davies
Opers Mgr: Janet Heard
Systems Design & Support: Steven Beale; Breht Burri
CD-ROM Devt: Christian Jones
Video Prodn: Manny Marquez
Founded: 1981
Ultrasound education & test preparation: books, videos, flashcards, mock examinations & software.
ISBN Prefix(es): 0-941022
Number of titles published annually: 8 Print; 2 CD-ROM
Total Titles: 48 Print; 6 CD-ROM
Imprints: Appleton Davies
Divisions: Davies Direct Booksellers

§F A Davis Co
1915 Arch St, Philadelphia, PA 19103
SAN: 200-2078
Tel: 215-568-2270 *Toll Free Tel:* 800-523-4049
Fax: 215-568-5065
E-mail: info@fadavis.com
Web Site: www.fadavis.com *Telex:* 83-4837
Cable: FADAVCO
Key Personnel
Chmn of the Bd: Robert H Craven, Sr
Pres & Ed-in-Chief: Robert H Craven, Jr
Sr VP: Judith Illov Neely
VP & CFO: Robert B Schenck
Man Ed: Mimi McGinnis
Nursing, Ed-in-Chief: Patti Cleary
Publr, Health Professions/Medicine: Margaret Biblis
Prodn Mgr: Michael Bailey
Dir, Educ Sales: Neil K Kelly
Gen Mgr, Dist Center: John Lancaster
Mgr, MIS: George Ricciardi
Mgr, Electronic Pubns: Ralph Zickgraf
Mgr, Cust Serv: Phyllis Love
Mgr, Mktg: Lynn Borders Caldwell
Founded: 1879
Medical, nursing & allied health professions.
ISBN Prefix(es): 0-8036
Number of titles published annually: 45 Print; 10 CD-ROM; 1 Online; 1 E-Book; 5 Audio
Total Titles: 399 Print; 50 CD-ROM; 2 Online; 1 E-Book; 10 Audio
Distribution Center: F A Davis Co, 404-420 N Second St, Philadelphia, PA 19123, Gen Mgr: John Lancaster *Tel:* 215-440-3001 *Fax:* 215-440-3016

DAW Books Inc
375 Hudson St, 3rd fl, New York, NY 10014
SAN: 282-5074
Tel: 212-366-2096 *Fax:* 212-366-2090
E-mail: daw@us.penguingroup.com
Web Site: www.dawbooks.com
Key Personnel
Publr: Elizabeth R Wollheim; Sheila E Gilbert
Assoc Ed: Peter Stampfel
Dir, Sub Rights/Contracts/Electronic Publg:
   Marsha E Jones *E-mail:* marsha.jones@us.
   penguingroup.com
Founded: 1971
Science fiction; fantasy; paperbound originals &
   reprints; hardcovers & trade paperbacks.
ISBN Prefix(es): 0-8099; 0-88677; 0-7564
Number of titles published annually: 47 Print; 25
   E-Book
Total Titles: 268 Print; 25 E-Book
Imprints: DAW/Fantasy; DAW/Fiction; DAW/Sci-
   ence Fiction
Distributed by Penguin Group (USA) Inc
Foreign Rep(s): Agence Litteraire Hoffman
   (France); GRAAL Ltd (Czech Republic, Hun-
   gary, Poland, Slovak Republic); International
   Editors' Co (Argentina, Spain); Japan UNI
   Agency Inc (Japan); Nurcihan Kesim Liter-
   ary Agency (Turkey); Simona Kessler (Roma-
   nia); Alexander Korzhenevski (Russia); Ulla
   Lohren (Scandinavia); Ilidio de Fonseca Matos
   (Portugal); Andrew Nurnberg Associates Sofia
   Ltd (Bulgaria); O A Literary Agency (Greece);
   Ilana Pikarski (Israel); Karin Schindler (Brazil);
   Thomas Schlueck GmbH (Netherlands, Ger-
   many)
Foreign Rights: Penguin (Australia, UK, Canada,
   India, New Zealand, South Africa); Penguin
   Putnam International Sales (all other territories)

Dawbert Press Inc
PO Box 67, Duxbury, MA 02331
SAN: 667-3449
Tel: 781-934-7202 *Toll Free Tel:* 800-933-2923
   Fax: 781-934-2945
E-mail: info@dawbert.com
Web Site: www.dawbert.com; www.
   familiesonthego.com; www.petsonthego.com
Key Personnel
Pres: Robert P Habgood
Edit Dir: Allison Elliot
Lib Sales Dir: Sarah Carpenter
Dir, Internet Rel: Peter Taylor
   E-mail: petertaylor@dawbert.com
Founded: 1983
Regional & national travel guides & special inter-
   est titles; families.
ISBN Prefix(es): 0-933603
Number of titles published annually: 3 Print; 1
   CD-ROM
Total Titles: 4 Print; 3 E-Book
Membership(s): Publishers Marketing Association

The Dawn Horse Press
Division of Avataric Pan-Communion of Adidam
12040 N Seigler Rd, Middletown, CA 95461
SAN: 201-3029
Mailing Address: 10336 Loch Lomond Rd, Suite
   305, Middletown, CA 95461
Tel: 707-928-6590 *Toll Free Tel:* 877-770-0772
   Fax: 707-928-5068
E-mail: dhp@adidam.org
Web Site: www.dawnhorsepress.com
Key Personnel
Publr: Neil Panico *E-mail:* npanico@adidam.org
Mktg Mgr: David Simon *E-mail:* dsimon@
   adidam.org
Prodn Mgr: Patrick Forristal
Edit: Megan Anderson *E-mail:* megan_anderson@
   adidam.org
Acctg: Christina de Jonge
Sr Designer: Matt Barna *E-mail:* matt_barna@
   adidam.org
Founded: 1972

Produces & markets books, CDs & A/V materi-
   als on every aspect of authentic spiritual life &
   human development based upon the wisdom-
   teaching of Avatar.
ISBN Prefix(es): 0-913922; 0-918801; 0-918801;
   1-57097; 0-929929
Number of titles published annually: 8 Print; 8
   CD-ROM; 12 Online; 4 Audio
Total Titles: 49 Print; 19 CD-ROM; 65 Online; 1
   E-Book; 33 Audio
Distributed by De Vorss, Dempsey & Deep
   Books; Ingram Books; New Leaf Distributing
Shipping Address: 12312 Hwy 175, Cobb Moun-
   tain, CA 95426, Contact: Patrick Forristal
   E-mail: dhp@adidam.org
Membership(s): Publishers Marketing Association

Dawn Publications Inc
12402 Bitney Springs Rd, Nevada City, CA
   95959
Tel: 530-274-7775 *Toll Free Tel:* 800-545-7475
   Fax: 530-274-7778
E-mail: nature@dawnpub.com
Web Site: www.dawnpub.com
Key Personnel
Ed & Intl Rts: Glenn Hovemann
Publr: Muffy Weaver
Mktg Dir: Julie Valin *E-mail:* julie@dawnpub.
   com
Founded: 1979
Nature awareness nonfiction picture books for
   children, teachers, naturalists & parents; char-
   acter value education; natural science.
ISBN Prefix(es): 0-916124; 1-883220; 1-58469
Number of titles published annually: 6 Print
Total Titles: 60 Print; 2 CD-ROM; 3 Audio

DawnSignPress
6130 Nancy Ridge Dr, San Diego, CA 92121-
   3223
Tel: 858-625-0600 *Toll Free Tel:* 800-549-5350
   Fax: 858-625-2336
E-mail: info@dawnsign.com
Web Site: www.dawnsign.com
Key Personnel
Pres & Intl Rts: Joe Dannis
Mktg & Lib Sales Dir: Barry Howland
   E-mail: barryh@dawnsign.com
Founded: 1979
Specialty publisher of instructional sign language
   & educational deaf studies materials for both
   children & adults, deaf & hearing.
ISBN Prefix(es): 0-915035; 1-58121
Number of titles published annually: 5 Print
Total Titles: 51 Print
Distributed by Gryphon House
Distributor for Gallaudet University Press; MIT
   Press; Random House Inc
Foreign Rights: Gloval Interprint (Hong Kong)

DBI Books
Division of Krause Publications Inc
700 E State St, Iola, WI 54990-0001
SAN: 202-9960
Tel: 715-445-2214 *Toll Free Tel:* 888-457-2873
   Fax: 715-445-4087
Web Site: www.krause.com
Key Personnel
Publr: Bill Krause
Ed, Gun Digest: Ken Ramage
Man Ed, Krause Book Div: Debbie Bradley
Acctg: Sharon Rustad
Acqs: Steve Smith
Sales Mgr: Jim Felhofer; Al Frey
Founded: 1943
Books on guns, shooting, fishing, archery, price
   guides, cutlery, hunting.
ISBN Prefix(es): 0-910676; 0-87349; 0-87341
Number of titles published annually: 30 Print
Total Titles: 70 Print
Foreign Rep(s): David Bateman Ltd (New
   Zealand); Book Movers (Canada); David &
   Charles (England)

dbS Productions
University Sta, Charlottesville, VA 22903
Mailing Address: PO Box 1894, Charlottesville,
   VA 22903
Tel: 434-293-5502 *Toll Free Tel:* 800-745-1581
   Fax: 434-293-5502
E-mail: info@dbs-sar.com
Web Site: www.dbs-sar.com
Key Personnel
Intl Rts & Publr: Bob Adams *E-mail:* robert@
   dbs-sar.com
Founded: 1989
Search & rescue.
ISBN Prefix(es): 1-879471
Number of titles published annually: 4 Print; 1
   CD-ROM
Total Titles: 15 Print; 2 CD-ROM
Distributed by ERI Bookstore; NASAR Book-
   store; Oklahoma State University

DC Comics
Division of Warner Bros, A Time Warner Enter-
   tainment Co
1700 Broadway, New York, NY 10019
Tel: 212-636-5400 *Toll Free Tel:* 800-759-0190
   (distribution) *Fax:* 212-636-5481
Web Site: www.dccomics.com; www.madmag.com
Key Personnel
Pres & Publr: Paul Levitz
Sr VP, Creative Aff & Media Devt: Gregory
   Noveck
VP, Busn Devt: John Nee
VP, Sales & Mktg: Bob Wayne
VP & Branch Mgr: Cheryl Rubin
Dir, Publg Opers: Bill Godfrey
Dir, Book Trade Sales: Rich Johnson
Founded: 1935
DC Comics, a division of Warner Bros, has a 60
   year history of innovative comics publishing in
   periodical & book formats. In addition to the
   world's most popular super-heroes - Superman,
   Batman & Wonder Woman - DC publishes cut-
   ting edge fantasy, horror, mystery, adventure,
   humor, nonfiction & general interest titles &
   maintains a 500+ title backlist in print. *MAD*
   Books is based on the classic magazine featuring Alfred E. Neuman, Spy vs Spy & other
   icons. DC/MAD properties are also licensed for
   various publishing formats, as well as media,
   promotions & consumer products.
ISBN Prefix(es): 0-930289; 1-56389
Total Titles: 500 Print
Imprints: America's Best Comics; Cliffhanger;
   Homage; 'MAD' Books; Paradox Press; Vertigo; Wildstorm
Distributed by Time Warner Trade Publishing

DC Press
Division of Diogenes Consortium
2445 River Tree, Sanford, FL 32771
Tel: 407-688-1156 *Toll Free Tel:* 866-602-1476
   Fax: 407-688-1135
E-mail: info@focusonethics.com
Web Site: www.focusonethics.com
Key Personnel
Pres: Dennis McClellan *E-mail:* dennis@
   focusonethics.com
Founded: 2001
Independent niche publisher, producing books
   with emphasis on ethics, character, spirit, en-
   couragement & volition in the area of business,
   careers, health care, self-help & some religious
   areas.
ISBN Prefix(es): 1-929902; 1-932021
Number of titles published annually: 6 Print
Total Titles: 30 Print
Foreign Rights: KNS International
Distribution Center: Midpoint Trade Books
Membership(s): Small Publishers Association of
   North America

§Walter de Gruyter, Inc
Division of Walter de Gruyter GmbH & Co KG
500 Executive Blvd, Ossining, NY 10562
SAN: 201-3088
Tel: 914-762-5866 *Fax:* 914-762-0371
E-mail: info@degruyterny.com
Web Site: www.degruyter.com
Key Personnel
VP & Gen Mgr: Eckart A Scheffler
 E-mail: escheffler@degruyterny.com
Founded: 1971
Scholarly & scientific books, journals, paperbacks
 & hardcover reprints.
ISBN Prefix(es): 0-311; 0-89925
Number of titles published annually: 200 Print; 5
 CD-ROM
Total Titles: 8,500 Print; 20 CD-ROM; 15 Online;
 10 E-Book
Imprints: Evangelisches Verlagswerk; Foris Publi-
 cations
Divisions: Mouton de Gruyter
Foreign Office(s): Walter de Gruyter GmbH & Co
 KG, Genthiner Str 13, 10785 Berlin, Germany
Foreign Rep(s): Allied Publishers (India,
 Nepal, Sri Lanka); Book Club International
 (Bangladesh); Combined Representatives
 Worldwide Inc (Philippines); D A Books &
 Journals (Australia, New Zealand); Kumi Trad-
 ing (South Korea); Kweilin Bookstore (Tai-
 wan); Maruzen Co Ltd (Japan); Pak Book
 Corp (Pakistan); Parry's Book Center Sendjrjan
 Berhad (Brunei, Malaysia, Singapore); Swinden
 Book Co Ltd (Hong Kong); Verlags und Kom-
 missionsbuchhandlung Dr Franz Hain (Austria);
 Walter de Gruyter Inc (Canada, Mexico, USA)
Advertising Agency: de Gruyter-Mouton Advertis-
 ing Agency
Shipping Address: 22883 Quick Silver Dr, Dulles,
 VA 20166-2019
Membership(s): AAP
See separate listing for:
Mouton de Gruyter

De Vorss & Co
553 Constitution Ave, Camarillo, CA 93012-8510
SAN: 168-9886
Tel: 805-322-9010 *Toll Free Tel:* 800-843-5743
 Fax: 805-322-9011
E-mail: service@devorss.com
Web Site: www.devorss.com
Key Personnel
Pres: Gary R Peattie *Tel:* 805-322-9010 ext 14
 E-mail: gpeattie@devorss.com
VP: Melinda Grubbauer
Founded: 1929
Publisher & distributor of metaphysical, spiritual,
 inspirational, self-help, body/mind/spirit & new
 thought books & sidelines since 1929.
ISBN Prefix(es): 0-87516
Number of titles published annually: 10 Print
Total Titles: 270 Print; 4 Audio
Distributor for Science of Mind Publications;
 White Eagle Publishing Trust (England)
Foreign Rights: Banyen Books (Australia); Deep
 Books (UK)
Billing Address: PO Box 1389, Camarillo, CA
 93011-1389

Dealer's Choice Books Inc
PO Box 710, Land O'Lakes, FL 34639
Tel: 813-996-6599 *Fax:* 813-996-5226
E-mail: order@dealerschoicebooks.com
Web Site: www.dealerschoicebooks.com
Key Personnel
Pres: Robert Creps
Founded: 1974
Art reference books & art reference price guides.
 Artist signatures, symbols & monograms, North
 American & European, Old Masters to modern;
 biographical, artist signature & auction price
 guides for results on paintings, prints & sculp-
 ture.

Number of titles published annually: 4 Print; 1
 CD-ROM
Total Titles: 100 Print
Distributor for ArtPrice.com; Art Sales Index; E
 Benezit Librairie
Foreign Rep(s): Art Sales Index Ltd (limited ti-
 tles) (UK)
Distribution Center: Art Sales Index, 16 Ludding
 Ave, Virginia Water, Surrey GU25 4DF, United
 Kingdom

Dearborn Trade Publishing
30 S Wacker Dr, Chicago, IL 60606-1719
Tel: 312-836-4400 *Fax:* 312-836-1021
E-mail: contactus@dearborn.com
Web Site: www.dearborn.com
Key Personnel
Pres: Roy Lipner
VP & Publr: Cynthia Zigmund
Intl Mgr & Subs Rts: Scott Adlington
Mktg Dir: Leslie Banks
Founded: 1967
Trade & professional books, textbooks, subscrip-
 tion & training materials in real estate, finan-
 cial planning, investments, securities, insurance,
 banking, small business careers; sales & mar-
 keting books; general management.
ISBN Prefix(es): 0-88462; 0-7931; 1-57410
Number of titles published annually: 280 Print
Total Titles: 140 Print; 10 Audio
Imprints: Dearborn; R&R Newkirk; Real Estate
 Education Co
Subsidiaries: Dearborn Financial Institute Inc
Divisions: Commodity Trend Service; Dearborn
 Trade
Distributor for National Education Standards
Foreign Rep(s): Advantage Quest SDN
 (Malaysia); Alternative Books (UK, Europe,
 Middle East); BHD (South Africa); Book
 Representation & Distribution Ltd (UK, Eu-
 rope); Jacqueline Gross & Associates (Canada);
 JabCo & Associates; RICS Books (Australia
 & New Zealand); Anthony Rudkin Associates
 (Middle East)
Foreign Rights: Flavia Sala (Brazil, Portugal)
Warehouse: 940 Enterprise St, Aurora, IL 60504

Ivan R Dee Publisher
Member of Rowman & Littlefield Publishing
 Group
1332 N Halsted St, Chicago, IL 60622-2694
SAN: 249-535X
Tel: 312-787-6262 *Toll Free Tel:* 800-462-6420
 (orders) *Fax:* 312-787-6269 *Toll Free Fax:* 800-
 338-4550 (orders)
E-mail: elephant@ivanrdee.com
Web Site: www.ivanrdee.com *Cable:* IVANDEE
 CHICAGO
Key Personnel
Pres: Ivan R Dee *E-mail:* idee@ivanrdee.com
VP, Sales: Alexander Dee *E-mail:* adee@
 ivanrdee.com
Man Ed: Hilary Meyer *E-mail:* hmeyer@ivanrdee.
 com
Publicity Dir: Judith Kelly *E-mail:* jkelly@
 ivanrdee.com
Prodn Ed: Joyce Marcum *E-mail:* jmarcum@
 ivanrdee.com
Opers Mgr: Maureen Ryan *E-mail:* mryan@
 ivanrdee.com
Founded: 1988
ISBN Prefix(es): 0-929587; 1-56663; 1-879941 (J
 S Saunders); 1-56131 (New Amsterdam)
Number of titles published annually: 45 Print
Total Titles: 685 Print
Imprints: Elephant Paperbacks; New Amsterdam
 Books; J S Sanders Books
Foreign Rep(s): Ivan R Dee (all other coun-
 tries); Peter S Fritz (Germany); Monica Heyum
 (Scandinavia); International Editors' Co
 (Spain); Oliva, Stefan & Oliva (Italy)
Foreign Rights: Ivan R Dee (all other coun-
 tries); Peter S Fritz (Germany); Monica Heyum

(Scandinavia); International Editors' Co
 (Spain); Oliva, Stefan & Oliva (Italy); Shei-
 land Assoc (Africa, Eastern Europe & Greece,
 France, Japan, Middle East)
Warehouse: National Book Network, 15200 NBN
 Way, Blue Ridge Summit, PA 17214 *Toll Free
 Tel:* 800-462-6420 *Toll Free Fax:* 800-338-4550
Distribution Center: National Book Network,
 4501 Forbes Blvd, Suite 200, Lanham, MD
 20706 *Tel:* 301-459-3366 *Fax:* 301-429-5748

Marcel Dekker Inc
270 Madison Ave, New York, NY 10016
SAN: 201-3118
Tel: 212-696-9000 *Toll Free Tel:* 800-228-1160
 (outside NY) *Fax:* 212-685-4540
Web Site: www.dekker.com
Key Personnel
Chmn of the Bd & CEO: Marcel Dekker
 E-mail: mdekker@dekker.com
Chief Publg Officer: Russell Dekker
 E-mail: rdekker@dekker.com
COO: David Dekker *E-mail:* ddekker@dekker.
 com
VP, Natl & Intl Sales: Henry Secor
 E-mail: hsecor@dekker.com
VP, Corp Sales/Busn Devt: Marianne Russell
 E-mail: mrussell@dekker.com
Dir, Intellectual Property Mgmt: Julia Mulligan
 E-mail: jmulligan@dekker.com
Founded: 1963
Research, reference & professional books, text-
 books, encyclopedias & journals.
ISBN Prefix(es): 0-8247
Number of titles published annually: 250 Print;
 215 Online
Total Titles: 3,300 Print; 1,281 Online
Foreign Office(s): Marcel Dekker Ag, Hutgasse 4,
 Postfach 812, 4001 Basel, Switzerland
Foreign Rep(s): APAC Publishers Services (Hong
 Kong, Indonesia, Korea, Malaysia, Philippines,
 Singapore, Taiwan, Thailand); Michael Bright-
 more (South Africa); Cassidy & Associates,
 Inc (China); Continental Contacts (Netherlands,
 Germany); D A Book Depot Pty Ltd (Aus-
 tralia); Ms Iwona Drozdowicz (Poland); Hari
 Ganesh (India); IMA - Tony Moggach (Africa
 exc North & South Africa); Bill Kennedy
 (UK); Ms Trinidad Lopez (Spain); Flavio Mar-
 cello (Italy, Portugal); Mediterranean Publish-
 ers Services (Middle East); Jan Norbye (Den-
 mark, Finland, Iceland, Norway, Sweden);
 Linda Sametz (Mexico); Harutoshi Shiohara
 (Japan); Tahir Lodhi (Pakistan); David Towle
 (Baltic States, Russia); Dr Blanka Vlasakova
 (Czech Republic); Mary Waite (France); Katia
 Zevelekakis (Cyprus, Greece)
Warehouse: PO Box 5005, Cimarron Rd, Monti-
 cello, NY 12701

Del Rey Books
Imprint of Random House Publishing Group
1745 Broadway, New York, NY 10019
E-mail: delrey@randomhouse.com
Web Site: www.randomhouse.com
Key Personnel
VP & Ed-in-Chief: Elizabeth Mitchell
Edit Dir: Shelly Shapiro
Edit Dir/Media Projs: Steve Saffel
Ed: Chris Schluep
Publisher of science fiction, fantasy, horror, alter-
 nate history & manga.
ISBN Prefix(es): 0-345

Delirium Books
PO Box 338, North Webster, IN 46555
Tel: 574-594-3200
Web Site: www.deliriumbooks.com
Key Personnel
Ed-in-Chief: Shane Ryan Staley
 E-mail: srstaley@deliriumbooks.com
Founded: 1999

Specialty press focusing on limited edition hard-
covers in the horror genre.
ISBN Prefix(es): 1-929653
Number of titles published annually: 20 Print
Total Titles: 50 Print

Delmar Learning, see Thomson Delmar
Learning

Delorme Publishing Co Inc
2 Delorme Dr, Yarmouth, ME 04096
Mailing Address: PO Box 298, Yarmouth, ME
04096
Tel: 207-846-7000 *Fax:* 207-846-7051
E-mail: reseller@delorme.com
Web Site: www.delorme.com
Key Personnel
Dir, PR: Charlie Connely
Founded: 1976
Digital maps; software; posters.
ISBN Prefix(es): 0-89933
Number of titles published annually: 5 Print
Total Titles: 50 Print

Delta Systems Co Inc
1400 Miller Pkwy, McHenry, IL 60050-7030
Tel: 815-363-3582 *Toll Free Tel:* 800-323-8270
Fax: 815-363-2948 *Toll Free Fax:* 800-909-
9901
E-mail: custsvc@delta-systems.com
Web Site: www.delta-systems.com
Key Personnel
Pres: Richard R Patchin *E-mail:* rrp@delta-
systems.com
Exec Asst: Joanne Frank *E-mail:* joanne@delta-
systems.com
Founded: 1979
Publisher & distribution of English as a second
language (ESL) & foreign language materials.
ISBN Prefix(es): 0-937354; 1-887744
Number of titles published annually: 8 Print
Total Titles: 63 Print

Demos Medical Publishing LLC
386 Park Ave S, Suite 201, New York, NY 10016
Tel: 212-683-0072 *Toll Free Tel:* 800-532-8663
Fax: 212-683-0118
E-mail: info@demospub.com
Web Site: www.demosmedpub.com
Key Personnel
Pres: Dr Diana M Schneider *E-mail:* dschneider@
demospub.com
Mktg Mgr: Reina Zeda
Founded: 1985
Publish medical & nursing text & line of patient
education titles.
ISBN Prefix(es): 0-937957; 1-888799
Number of titles published annually: 16 Print
Total Titles: 72 Print
Returns: Publishers Storage & Shipping
Shipping Address: Publishers Storage & Shipping
Warehouse: Publishers Storage & Shipping
Distribution Center: Publishers Storage & Ship-
ping

The Denali Press
PO Box 021535, Juneau, AK 99802-1535
SAN: 661-8278
Tel: 907-586-6014 *Fax:* 907-463-6780
E-mail: denalipress@alaska.com
Web Site: www.denalipress.com
Key Personnel
Owner, Publr & Edit Dir: Alan Edward Schorr
Mktg Dir: Sally Silvas-Ottumwa
Prodn Mgr: Debra Genner
Founded: 1986
Publish reference, scholarly books & Alaskana,
with emphasis on multicultural reference
books.
ISBN Prefix(es): 0-938737
Number of titles published annually: 5 Print

Total Titles: 35 Print
Distributor for Libris; Meridian Books

Denlinger's Publishers Ltd
PO Box 1030, Edgewater, FL 32132-1030
SAN: 201-3150
Tel: 386-424-1737 *Toll Free Tel:* 800-362-1810
Fax: 386-428-3534 *Toll Free Fax:* 800-589-
1191
E-mail: editor@thebookden.com
Web Site: www.thebookden.com
Key Personnel
Pres: Diane Denlinger Oehms
Exec Ed & Sr VP: Gustav Postreich
Sr Ed: Marcia Buckingham
Acqs Ed: Elizabeth-Anne Rogers
E-mail: acquisitions@thebookden.com
Founded: 1926
ISBN Prefix(es): 0-87714
Number of titles published annually: 25 Print; 25
Online; 25 E-Book
Total Titles: 212 Print; 212 Online; 200 E-Book
Distributor for Atlantis Productions
Membership(s): Publishers Marketing Association

§Deseret Book Co
40 E South Temple, Salt Lake City, UT 84111
SAN: 201-3185
Mailing Address: PO Box 30178, Salt Lake City,
UT 84130
Tel: 801-534-1515 *Toll Free Tel:* 800-453-3876
Fax: 801-517-3199
E-mail: wholesale@deseretbook.com
Web Site: www.deseretbook.com
Key Personnel
Pres & CEO: Sheri L Dew
Founded: 1866
Juveniles & young adults, trade paperbacks; fic-
tion, general nonfiction, religion (Mormon).
ISBN Prefix(es): 0-87747
Number of titles published annually: 150 Print
Total Titles: 1,100 Print; 1 CD-ROM; 120 Audio
Imprints: Bookcraft; Cinnamon Tree; Eagle Gate;
Shadow Mountain
Shipping Address: 2240 W 1500 South, Salt Lake
City, UT 84104

Design Image Group
231 S Frontage Rd, Suite 17, Burr Ridge, IL
60527
Tel: 630-789-8991 *Toll Free Tel:* 800-563-5455
Fax: 630-789-9013
E-mail: dig@designimagegroup.com
Web Site: www.designimagegroup.com
Key Personnel
Intl Rts: Thomas Strauch
Lib Sales Dir & Bookseller Rels: Sarah Stillo
Founded: 1984 (Trade publishing operation
launched 1998)
General trade books, horror, dark fiction & mys-
tery.
ISBN Prefix(es): 1-891946
Number of titles published annually: 6 Print
Total Titles: 20 Print
Branch Office(s)
PO Box 2325, Darien, IL 60561
Membership(s): Horror Writers Association; Mys-
tery Writers of America; Publishers Marketing
Association

Destiny Image
167 Walnut Bottom Rd, Shippensburg, PA 17257-
0310
SAN: 253-4339
Mailing Address: PO Box 310, Shippensburg, PA
17257-0310
Tel: 717-532-3040 *Toll Free Tel:* 800-722-6774
(orders only) *Fax:* 717-532-9291
E-mail: gates@destinyimage.com
Web Site: www.destinyimage.com
Key Personnel
CEO & Pres: Don Nori, Sr

Chief Acqs Ed & VP: Don Milam
Mktg & Sales Dir: Don Nori, Jr
Founded: 1983
Publisher of Christian books.
ISBN Prefix(es): 0-914903; 1-56043; 0-938612;
0-7684
Number of titles published annually: 40 Print; 15
Audio
Total Titles: 300 Print; 5 Audio
Imprints: Destiny Image Fiction; Fresh Bread;
Revival Press; Treasure House
Sales Office(s): 1351 W Nido St, Mesa, AZ
85202, Contact: Mary Moore *Tel:* 480-756-
9163 *Toll Free Tel:* 877-484-8031 *Fax:* 480-
756-9164 *E-mail:* mcm@destinyimage.com
Distributor for Mercy Place
Foreign Rep(s): Koorong (Australia); STL Ltd
(UK); Word Alive (Canada)
Membership(s): ABA; Christian Booksellers As-
sociation; Evangelical Christian Publishers As-
sociation

Developmental Studies Center
2000 Embarcadero, Suite 305, Oakland, CA
94606-5300
Tel: 510-533-0213 *Toll Free Tel:* 800-666-7270
Fax: 510-842-0348
E-mail: pubs@devstu.org
Web Site: www.devstu.org
Key Personnel
Exec VP: Frank Snyder
Publr Liaison: Jennie McDonald
Mktg & Sales Dir & Intl Rts Contact: Jan
Berman
Edit Dir: Elaine Ratner
Dir, Dissemination: Yolanda Peeks
Founded: 1981
Books, teacher-study packages, literature guides,
in-school & after-school curricula in character
education, reading & mathematics.
ISBN Prefix(es): 1-885603; 1-57621; 0-439
Number of titles published annually: 15 Print
Total Titles: 450 Print
Advertising Agency: DSC Direct

§Dewey Publications Inc
2009 N 14 St, Suite 705, Arlington, VA 22201
SAN: 694-1451
Tel: 703-524-1355 *Fax:* 703-524-1463
E-mail: info@deweypub.com
Web Site: www.deweypub.com
Key Personnel
Pres: Peter Broida
Founded: 1984
ISBN Prefix(es): 1-878810; 1-932612
Number of titles published annually: 5 Print; 4
CD-ROM
Total Titles: 36 Print; 8 CD-ROM; 5 Audio

Dharma Publishing
2910 San Pablo Ave, Berkeley, CA 94702
SAN: 201-2723
Tel: 510-548-5407 *Toll Free Tel:* 800-873-4276
Fax: 510-548-2230
E-mail: info@dharmapublishing.com
Web Site: www.dharmapublishing.com *Cable:*
DHARMA
Key Personnel
Pres: Tarthang Tulku
Sales Dir: Rima Tamar *Tel:* 510-548-5407 ext 20
E-mail: rimat@dharmapublishing.com
Ed: Elizabeth Cook
Spec Ed: Debby Black; Jack Petranker
Acctg: Irene Byrne
Founded: 1972
Trade paperbacks, limited editions & mail order,
Asian art, Eastern philosophy & psychology,
scholarly, history, biography, cosmology, juve-
niles, Asian culture.
ISBN Prefix(es): 0-913546; 0-89800
Number of titles published annually: 10 Print
Total Titles: 100 Print

Foreign Rep(s): Ka-Nying (India, Nepal); Nyingma Centrum Nederland (Netherlands); Nyingma Do Brazil (Brazil); Nyingma Gemeinschaft (Germany); Windhorse (Australia, UK)
Membership(s): AAP

Diablo Press Inc
Affiliate of Kensington Book Co
3381-A Vincent Rd, Pleasant Hill, CA 94523-4310
Mailing Address: PO Box 7042, Berkeley, CA 94707-0042 SAN: 201-3223
Toll Free Tel: 800-488-2665 (orders only)
Fax: 510-653-5310
E-mail: info@diablopress.com; diablo1@concentric.net
Web Site: www.diablopress.com
Founded: 1962
History textbooks.
ISBN Prefix(es): 0-87297
Number of titles published annually: 6 Print
Total Titles: 29 Print
Imprints: Kensington
Orders to: PO Box 20, Williston, VT 04595-0020
Tel: 802-862-0095 *Toll Free Tel:* 800-488-2665
Shipping Address: 12 Winter Sport Lane, Williston, VT 05495
Warehouse: 64 Depot Rd, Colchester, VT 05466-0095

Dial Books for Young Readers
Imprint of Penguin Group (USA) Inc
345 Hudson St, New York, NY 10014
SAN: 282-5074
Tel: 212-366-2000 *Fax:* 212-414-3396
E-mail: online@penguinputnam.com
Web Site: www.penguinusa.com
Key Personnel
Pres & Publr: Nancy Paulsen
Art Dir: Lily Malcolm
Assoc Publr: Laura Hornik
Sr Ed: Cecile Goyette
Ed: Nancy Mercado; Rebecca Waugh
Founded: 1961
ISBN Prefix(es): 0-8037
Number of titles published annually: 44 Print
Total Titles: 400 Print

§Diamond Farm Book Publishers
Division of Yesteryear Toys & Books Inc
Bailey Settlement Rd, Alexandria Bay, NY 13607
Mailing Address: PO Box 537, Alexandria Bay, NY 13607
Tel: 613-475-1771 *Toll Free Tel:* 800-481-1353
Fax: 613-475-3748 *Toll Free Fax:* 800-305-5138
E-mail: info@diamondfarm.com
Web Site: www.diamondfarm.com
Key Personnel
Pres: Frank Van Meeuwen
Sales & Mktg: Shawn Van Meeuwen
E-mail: shawn@diamondfarm.com
Founded: 1975
Agricultural textbooks & videos.
ISBN Prefix(es): 0-85236
Number of titles published annually: 4 Print
Total Titles: 7 Print; 1 CD-ROM; 1 Audio
Branch Office(s)
RR 3, Brighton, ON K0K 1H0, Canada
Distributor for Farming Press; Whittet

DIANE Publishing Co
330 Pusey Ave, Suite 3 rear, Collingdale, PA 19023
Mailing Address: PO Box 1428, Collingdale, PA 19023
Tel: 610-461-6200 *Toll Free Tel:* 800-782-3833
Fax: 610-461-6130
E-mail: dianepub@comcast.net
Web Site: www.dianepublishingcentral.com
Key Personnel
Publr: Herman Baron

VP, Edit: Dorothy Perkins
Founded: 1987
Publishes & repackages books, documents & reports in law enforcement, intelligence, security, military, education, biotechnology, medicine & health & high-technology. Most titles were originally prepared by US government agencies. Also distributes 3,000 nonfiction remainder books.
ISBN Prefix(es): 0-941375; 1-56806; 0-7881; 0-7567
Number of titles published annually: 1,800 Print
Total Titles: 15,000 Print
Imprints: Cobra Institute
Membership(s): ABA

Dimension Books Inc
PO Box 9, Starrucca, PA 18462
SAN: 211-7916
Tel: 570-727-2486 *Fax:* 570-727-2813
Key Personnel
Chmn of the Bd & Pres: Thomas P Coffey
Asst to Pres & Intl Rts Contact: Anna McCann
Founded: 1963
Social commentary.
ISBN Prefix(es): 0-87193
Number of titles published annually: 20 Print
Total Titles: 258 Print
Editorial Office(s): RR 1, No 1914, Starrucca Creek Rd, Starrucca, PA 18462
Sales Office(s): RR 1, No 1914, Starrucca Creek Rd, Starrucca, PA 18462
Foreign Rep(s): R P Books (UK)
Distribution Center: RR 1, No 1914, Starrucca Creek Rd, Starrucca, PA 18462, Pres: Tom Coffey *Tel:* 570-727-2486 *Fax:* 570-727-2813

Dine College Press
Affiliate of Navajo Nation
Dine College, Tsaile, AZ 86556
Tel: 928-724-6635 *Fax:* 928-724-6637
Web Site: www.dinecollege.edu
Key Personnel
Mgr: Harrison Blie *Tel:* 928-724-6751 *Fax:* 928-724-6752 *E-mail:* harrison@crystal.ncc.cc.nm.us
College press.
ISBN Prefix(es): 0-912586
Distributed by Book People; Five Star Publications Inc; Territory Titles

The Direct Marketing Association Inc (The DMA)
1120 Avenue of the Americas, New York, NY 10036-6700
SAN: 692-6487
Tel: 212-768-7277 *Fax:* 212-768-4547
Fax on Demand: 212-302-7643 (cust serv)
E-mail: dma@the-dma.org; customerservice@the-dma.org
Web Site: www.the-dma.org
Key Personnel
Pres & CEO: John Greco, Jr
VP, Info & Spec Projs: Ann E Zeller
Dir, Exec Commun: Douglas Berger
Media Dir: Laura Colona
Dir, Public & Intl Aff: Louis Mastria
Dir, Consumer Media Relations: Amy Blankenship
Founded: 1917
Directories, consumer guides, industry resource guides, statistical compilations, newsletter & council publications, quarterly magazine & electronic newsletter.
ISBN Prefix(es): 0-933641
Number of titles published annually: 5 Print
Total Titles: 5 Print
Branch Office(s)
1111 19 St NW, Washington, DC 20036-3603
1430 Broadway St, 4th fl, New York, NY 10018
Tel: 212-768-7277

Discipleship Publications International (DPI)
Division of Boston Church of Christ
2 Sterling Rd, Billerica, MA 01862-2595
Tel: 978-670-8840 *Toll Free Tel:* 888-DPI-Book
Fax: 978-670-8485
E-mail: dpibooks@icoc.org
Web Site: www.dpibooks.org
Key Personnel
Ed-in-Chief: Kelly Petre
Man Ed: Sheila Jones
Founded: 1993
Publishing books & cassette tapes on Biblical topics.
ISBN Prefix(es): 1-884553; 1-57782
Number of titles published annually: 6 Print; 1 CD-ROM; 1 E-Book
Total Titles: 126 Print; 1 CD-ROM; 1 E-Book; 6 Audio
Foreign Rep(s): Book Masters Inc (Worldwide)

DiscoverGuides
631 N Stephanie St, No 138, Henderson, NV 89014
SAN: 666-3192
Tel: 702-407-8777 *Fax:* 209-532-2699
E-mail: discoverguides@earthlink.net
Key Personnel
CEO & Pres: Don W Martin
CFO: Betty Woo Martin
Founded: 1987
Publish primarily western states & cities guidebooks, all researched & written in-house; also books on wine.
ISBN Prefix(es): 0-942053
Number of titles published annually: 4 Print
Total Titles: 24 Print
Sales Office(s): 1700 Fourth St, Berkeley, CA 94710
Orders to: Publishers Group West, 7326 Winton Dr, Indianapolis, IN 46268 *Toll Free Tel:* 800-788-3123
Returns: Publishers Group West, 7326 Winton Dr, Indianapolis, IN 46268
Warehouse: Publishers Group West, 7326 Winton Dr, Indianapolis, IN 46268 *Toll Free Tel:* 800-788-3123
Distribution Center: 1700 Fourth St, Berkeley, CA 94710 *Tel:* 510-658-3453 *Toll Free Tel:* 800-788-3123 *Fax:* 510-528-3444
Membership(s): SATW

Discovery Enterprises Ltd
31 Laurelwood Dr, Carlisle, MA 01741
SAN: 297-2611
Tel: 978-287-5401 *Toll Free Tel:* 800-729-1720
Fax: 978-287-5402
E-mail: ushistorydocs@aol.com
Web Site: www.ushistorydocs.com
Key Personnel
Pres, Exec Dir & Intl Rts: JoAnne W Deitch
Lib Sales Dir: Nancy Myers
Sales: Kenneth M Deitch
Founded: 1990
Young adult nonfiction & curriculum materials; adult history; American history; drama; language arts curriculum.
ISBN Prefix(es): 1-878668; 1-57960; 1-932663
Number of titles published annually: 12 Print
Total Titles: 196 Print
Distributor for National Archives

§Discovery House Publishers
3000 Kraft SE, Grand Rapids, MI 49512
Mailing Address: Box 3566, Grand Rapids, MI 49501-3566
Tel: 616-942-9218; 616-974-2210 (cust serv)
Toll Free Tel: 800-653-8333 *Fax:* 616-957-5741
E-mail: dhp@rbc.org
Web Site: www.gospelcom.net/rbc/dhp/; www.rbc.net
Key Personnel
Sr Publr: Robert K DeVries
Publr: Carol Holquist

Man Ed: Judy Markham
Publicity: Kim Collins *E-mail:* publicity@rbc.org
Founded: 1988
Religious trade books; audio & video cassettes;
    recorded music; magazine.
ISBN Prefix(es): 0-929239; 1-57293
Number of titles published annually: 12 Print; 1
    Audio
Total Titles: 150 Print; 3 CD-ROM; 150 Online;
    1 Audio
Distributed by Barbour Publishing Inc

Disney Press
Division of The Walt Disney Co
114 Fifth Ave, New York, NY 10011
Tel: 212-633-4400 *Fax:* 212-807-5432
Web Site: www.disney.go.com
Key Personnel
Sr VP & Man Dir, Disney Publishing Worldwide:
    Deborah Dugan
VP & Group Publr: Lisa Holton
Ed Dir: Brenda Bower
Prodn Dir: Sue Cole
Subs Rts: Molly Kong
Man Ed: Duryan Bhagat
Intl Rts Contact: Jean McGinley
Founded: 1990
Fiction & fantasy.
ISBN Prefix(es): 1-56282; 0-7868
Number of titles published annually: 55 Print
Total Titles: 1,000 Print
Distributed by Time Warner Publishing
Foreign Rep(s): Little, Brown Canada Ltd; Little,
    Brown International
Foreign Rights: A M Heath (England); ACER
    Agencia Literaria (Spain); Agence Hoffman
    (Germany); Luigi Bernabo Associaes (Italy);
    Big Apple-Tuttle-Mori Agency (China); BMSR
    Agencia Literaria (Brazil); The English Agency
    (Japan); Harris/Elon Agency (Israel); Mon-
    ica Heyum Agency (Denmark, Finland, Ice-
    land, Norway, Sweden); Kooy & van Gelderen
    (Netherlands); Michele Lapautre (France)
Warehouse: 3 Center Plaza, Boston, MA 02108-
    2003

Disney Publishing Worldwide
Subsidiary of Walt Disney Co
500 S Buena Vista, Burbank, CA 91521
Mailing Address: 114 Fifth Ave, New York, NY
    10011
Tel: 212-633-4400 *Fax:* 212-633-4833
Web Site: www.disney.go.com/disneybooks
Key Personnel
Pres: Deborah Dugan
Sr VP & Publr, Global Children's Books: Lisa
    Holton
VP, US Children's Book Publr & Global Assoc
    Publr: Jeanne Mosure
Dir, Sales & Mktg: Lynn Waggoner
Edit Dir, Global Children's Books: Jackie Carter
Book Prodn Dir: Sue Cole
Dir, School & Lib Mktg: Angus Killick
Global Man Ed: Duryan Bhagat
Subs Rts Assoc: Jean McGinley
Man Edit Coord: Jaime Herbeck *Tel:* 212-807-
    5436 *E-mail:* jaime.herbeck@disney.com
Founded: 1990
Fiction & fantasy.
ISBN Prefix(es): 1-56115
Number of titles published annually: 275 Print
Total Titles: 1,000 Print
Divisions: Disney Children's Book Group
Shipping Address: 3900 W Alameda, 29th fl, Bur-
    bank, CA 91505

Dissertation.com
23331 Water Circle, Boca Raton, FL 33486-8540
SAN: 299-3635
Tel: 561-750-4344 *Toll Free Tel:* 800-636-8329
Fax: 561-750-6797

E-mail: publisher4@dissertation.com; orders4@
    dissertation.com
Web Site: www.dissertation.com
Key Personnel
Publr: Jeffrey R Young *E-mail:* jeff.young@
    dissertation.com
Founded: 1997
Academic books.
ISBN Prefix(es): 1-58112; 0-9658564
Number of titles published annually: 50 Print; 50
    Online; 50 E-Book
Total Titles: 300 Print; 300 Online; 300 E-Book
Imprints: Brown Walker Press; Dissertation; Uni-
    versal Publishers; Upublish.com
Subsidiaries: Brown Walker Press
Distributed by Bertrams UK
See separate listing for:
Upublish.com

Dixon Price Publishing
9105 Leprechaun Lane, Kingston, WA 98346
Mailing Address: PO Box 1360, Kingston, WA
    98346
Tel: 360-297-8702 *Fax:* 360-297-1620
E-mail: info@dixonprice.com
Web Site: www.dixonprice.com
Key Personnel
Publr & Man Ed: Kendall Hanson
Founded: 1999
ISBN Prefix(es): 1-929516
Number of titles published annually: 3 Print
Total Titles: 13 Print

DK Publishing Inc
Subsidiary of Pearson plc
375 Hudson St, 2nd fl, New York, NY 10014-
    3672
Tel: 212-213-4800 *Toll Free Tel:* 877-342-5357
    (cust serv) *Fax:* 212-213-5202
Web Site: www.dk.com
Key Personnel
Pres, DK US: William Barry
Sr VP, Sales & Mktg: Therese Burke
VP, Opers: John Ball
Dir, PR: Cathy Melnicki
Dir, Mktg: Carl Raymond
Creative Dir: Tina Vaughan
Mgr, Subs Rts: Audrey Puzzo
Founded: 1990
Illustrated reference books on a wide range of
    topics for adults & children, including travel,
    health, history, sports, pets, atlases, dictionaries,
    music, art, decorating, astrology, sex & cook-
    ing.
ISBN Prefix(es): 1-879431; 1-56458; 0-7894; 0-
    7566
Number of titles published annually: 340 Print
Total Titles: 2,829 Print; 50 CD-ROM
Foreign Rep(s): Dorling Kindersley Ltd (UK)
Advertising Agency: Spier NY
Warehouse: Pearson Education, 135 S Mt Zion
    Rd, Lebanon, IN 46052
Membership(s): ABA; ALA; Children's Book
    Council; International Association of Culinary
    Professionals; International Reading Associa-
    tion; National Council of Teachers of English;
    National Science Teachers Association

Do It Now Foundation
2750 S Hardy Dr, Suite 2, Tempe, AZ 85282
Mailing Address: PO Box 27568, Tempe, AZ
    85285-7568
Tel: 480-736-0599 *Fax:* 480-736-0771
E-mail: doitnow@quest.net
Web Site: www.doitnow.org
Key Personnel
Exec Dir: Jim Parker
Founded: 1968
Drugs, alcohol & health.
ISBN Prefix(es): 0-89230
Number of titles published annually: 50 Print
Total Titles: 200 Print

Do-It-Yourself Legal Publishers
Affiliate of Selfhelper Law Press of America
60 Park Place, Suite 1013, Newark, NJ 07102
SAN: 214-1876
Tel: 973-639-0400 *Fax:* 973-639-1801
E-mail: selfhelp1@yahoo.com
Key Personnel
Sr Ed: Dan Benjamin
Founded: 1978
The simplest problems can be effectively handled
    by anyone with average common sense & a
    competent guidebook. Specialists in self-help,
    how-to law manuals & kits for the non-lawyer.
ISBN Prefix(es): 0-932704
Number of titles published annually: 6 Print
Total Titles: 30 Print
Imprints: The Selfhelper Law Press of America
Distributed by Brodart Co; Midwest Library Ser-
    vice; Quality Books; Unique Books
Foreign Rep(s): Yeh Yeh Book Gallery Ltd (Tai-
    wan)

Dog-Eared Publications
PO Box 620863, Middleton, WI 53562-0863
SAN: 281-6059
Tel: 608-831-1410 *Toll Free Tel:* 888-364-3277
    Fax: 608-831-1410 *Toll Free Fax:* 888-364-
    3277
Web Site: www.dog-eared.com
Key Personnel
Publr: Nancy Field *E-mail:* field@dog-eared.com
Founded: 1976
Nature & environmental books.
ISBN Prefix(es): 0-941042
Number of titles published annually: 3 Print
Total Titles: 32 Print
Subsidiaries: Social Ecology Press
Distributed by Beyda Associates Inc; Booklines
    Hawaii; Common Ground Distributors; Inter-
    state Periodicals; Lone Pine Publishing; Part-
    ners Book Distributing; Partners West
Distributor for ACI Publishing; Earth Heart;
    Nichols Garden Nursery Press
Shipping Address: 4642 Toepfer Rd, Middleton,
    WI 53562

Dogwood Press
HC 53 Box 345, Hemphill, TX 75948-0345
Tel: 409-579-2184 *Fax:* 409-579-2184
Web Site: dogwoodpress.myriad.net/
Key Personnel
Pres: Don C Marler *E-mail:* dcmsmm@inu.net
Founded: 1991
History of Louisiana & East Texas; reprint ap-
    propriate public domain books; publish current
    books by local authors.
ISBN Prefix(es): 1-887745; 0-9646846
Number of titles published annually: 3 Print
Total Titles: 40 Print

Tom Doherty Associates, LLC
Subsidiary of Holtzbrinck Publishers Holdings
    LLC
175 Fifth Ave, 14th fl, New York, NY 10010
Tel: 212-388-0100 *Toll Free Tel:* 800-455-0340
    Fax: 212-388-0191
E-mail: firstname.lastname@tor.com
Web Site: www.tor.com
Key Personnel
Pres & Publr: Tom Doherty
VP & Assoc Publr: Linda Quinton
Dir, Mktg: Kathleen Fogarty
Dir, Publicity: Elena Stokes
Dir, Adv & Promo: Phyllis Azar
Publr, Children & Young Adult Titles: Kathleen
    Doherty
Art Dir: Irene Gallo
Pbk Art Dir: Seth Lerner
Mgr, Edit Prodn: Eric Raab
Sec & Gen Counsel: Paul Sleven
VP & Dir, Sales (Holtzbrinck Publishers): Brian
    Heller

VP & Dir, Field Sales (Holtzbrinck Publishers): Ken Holland
Dir, Subs Rts: Christina Harcar
Dir, Intl Sales: Bill Farricker
Perms: Esther Robinson
Contracts Dir: Holly Bash
Exec Ed: Beth Meacham; Harriet McDougal; Robert Gleason
Sr Ed: Natalia Aponte; Claire Eddy; Patrick Nielsen Hayden; David Hartwell; James Frenkel; Melissa Ann Singer
Ed: James Minz
Ed, Young Adult: Susan Chang
Founded: 1980
Mass market & trade paperbacks; trade hardcover: fiction, horror, science fiction, fantasy, mystery, suspense, techno-thrillers, western fiction, American historicals, nonfiction, paranormal romance, true crime & biography.
ISBN Prefix(es): 0-8125; 0-7653
Number of titles published annually: 425 Print
Total Titles: 2,224 Print
Imprints: Aerie Books; Forge Books; Orb Books; Starscape; Tor; Tor Teen
Distributed by Holtzbrinck Publishers; Warner Publishers Services
Distributor for Wizards of the Coast
Foreign Rights: St Martin's Press
Advertising Agency: Slocum Advertising Agency
Warehouse: Quebecor World Inc, 2073 Evergreen St, Dresden, TN 38225
Distribution Center: VHPS Distribution Center, 16365 James Madison Hwy, Gordonsville, VA 22942-8501 *Tel:* 540-672-7540 (cust serv) *Toll Free Tel:* 888-330-8477; 800-672-2054 (orders)

Domhan Books
9511 Shore Rd, Suite 514, Brooklyn, NY 11209
Tel: 718-680-4362 *Toll Free Fax:* 888-823-4770
E-mail: domhan@att.net
Web Site: www.domhanbooks.com
Key Personnel
CEO: Georgiana Stone
Head of Bus Devt: Siobhan McNally
Sr Ed: Carol Olson
Mktg & Promo: Annabelle Stevens
Founded: 1998 (in Ireland, established USA 2000)
Publisher of high-quality fiction & nonfiction from writers all over the world in paperback & electronic formats.
ISBN Prefix(es): 1-58345
Number of titles published annually: 50 Print
Total Titles: 180 Print
Membership(s): AAP; Publishers Marketing Association

Dominie Press Inc
1949 Kellogg Ave, Carlsbad, CA 92008
Tel: 760-431-8000 *Toll Free Tel:* 800-232-4570
    Fax: 760-431-8777
E-mail: info@dominie.com
Web Site: www.dominie.com
Key Personnel
CEO & Intl Rts: Raymond Yuen
    E-mail: rayuen@dominie.com
Pres: Christine Yuen *E-mail:* christine@dominie.com
Founded: 1987
Educational textbooks, children's books, Spanish books.
ISBN Prefix(es): 1-56270; 0-7685
Number of titles published annually: 240 Print
Total Titles: 2,500 Print
Distributor for Cambridge University Press (limited number of titles)

The Donning Co/Publishers
Subsidiary of Walsworth Publishing Co
184 Business Park Dr, Suite 206, Virginia Beach, VA 23462
SAN: 211-6316
Tel: 757-497-1789; 660-376-3543 (Missouri office) *Toll Free Tel:* 800-296-8572 *Fax:* 757-497-2542
Web Site: www.donning.com
Key Personnel
Gen Mgr: Steve Mull
Mktg Dir & ISBN Contact: Scott Rule
Founded: 1974
Americana, cookbooks & pictorial history.
ISBN Prefix(es): 0-915442; 0-89865
Number of titles published annually: 45 Print
Total Titles: 700 Print
Imprints: Portraits of America
Foreign Rights: Writers House Inc

Doral Publishing, see BowTie Press

Dorchester Publishing Co Inc
200 Madison Ave, Suite 2000, New York, NY 10016
Tel: 212-725-8811 *Toll Free Tel:* 800-481-9191 (order dept) *Fax:* 212-532-1054
E-mail: dorchedits@dorchesterpub.com
Web Site: www.dorchesterpub.com
Key Personnel
Pres & Publr: George Sosson
Sr VP, Sales, Mktg & Dist: Tim De Young
VP & Edit Dir: Alicia Condon
VP, Prodn & Art: Katy Steinhilber
Sr Ed: Don D'Auria; Christopher Keeslar
Ed: Kate Seaver
Dir, Sales & Mktg: Brooke Borneman
Mgr, Adv, PR & Web: Leah Hultenschmidt
    E-mail: lhulten@dorchesterpub.com
Founded: 1970
Mass market paperback originals fiction, hardcover reprints, specialize in romance, horror, thrillers, westerns, teen fiction.
ISBN Prefix(es): 0-8439; 0-505
Number of titles published annually: 180 Print; 75 E-Book
Total Titles: 810 E-Book
Imprints: Love Spell; Smooch; Thriller
Foreign Rights: Rights Unlimited (World)
Warehouse: Offset Paperback Manufacturers Inc, 10 Passan Dr, Bldg 10, Laflin, PA 18702

Dordt College Press
Affiliate of Dordt College
498 Fourth Ave NE, Sioux Center, IA 51250
Tel: 712-722-6420 *Fax:* 712-722-1185
E-mail: dordtpress@dordt.edu
Web Site: www.dordt.edu/dordt_press
Key Personnel
Man Ed: John H Kok
Founded: 1978
Publishes primarily academic books & monographs, plus a quarterly journal.
ISBN Prefix(es): 0-932914
Number of titles published annually: 4 Print
Total Titles: 36 Print

Dorland Healthcare Information
Affiliate of Dorland Data Networks
1500 Walnut St, Suite 1000, Philadelphia, PA 19102
Tel: 215-875-1212 *Toll Free Tel:* 800-784-2332
    Fax: 215-735-3966
E-mail: info@dorlandhealth.com
Web Site: www.dorlandhealth.com
Key Personnel
CEO & Pres: Robert A Graham *Tel:* 215-875-1255
VP, Mktg & Sales: Virginia A Kelly *Tel:* 212-875-1270
Founded: 1950
Directories, market research, databases & mailing lists.
ISBN Prefix(es): 1-880874
Number of titles published annually: 6 Print; 1 CD-ROM; 4 Online
Total Titles: 6 Print; 1 CD-ROM; 4 Online
Imprints: Dorland Biomedical; Dorland Healthcare Information
Divisions: The Retention Solutions Group
Distributor for Health Leaders

Dorling Kindersley Publishing Inc, see DK Publishing Inc

Dorset House Publishing Co Inc
353 W 12 St, New York, NY 10014
SAN: 687-794X
Tel: 212-620-4053 *Toll Free Tel:* 800-DHBOOKS (342-6657 orders only) *Fax:* 212-727-1044
E-mail: info@dorsethouse.com; dhpubco@aol.com
Web Site: www.dorsethouse.com
Key Personnel
Pres, Admin & Gen Mgr, Rts & Perms: Wendy Eakin
VP, Mktg Mgr & Sr Ed: David McClintock
Founded: 1984
Professional books, management, business, consulting, geared to software engineering.
ISBN Prefix(es): 0-932633
Number of titles published annually: 5 Print
Total Titles: 54 Print; 1 Audio
Foreign Rep(s): Aikem Company (S) Private Ltd (Brunei, Burma, Hong Kong, Indonesia, Japan, Korea, Malaysia, Philippines, Singapore, Taiwan, Thailand); Prism Books Pvt Ltd (Bangladesh, India, Nepal, Sri Lanka)
Foreign Rights: The Chinese Connection Agency (China, Taiwan)
Advertising Agency: Faville Graphics, NY 10014-1721, Contact: Jeff Faville *Tel:* 212-989-1566 *Fax:* 212-675-6162
Membership(s): Publishers Marketing Association

Doubleday Broadway Publishing Group
Division of Random House Inc
1745 Broadway, New York, NY 10019
Tel: 212-782-9000 *Toll Free Tel:* 800-223-6834; 800-223-5780 (sales) *Fax:* 212-302-7985 (correspondence); 212-492-9862 (orders)
Key Personnel
Pres & Publr: Stephen Rubin
Pres, Random House Inc Sales Group: Don Weisberg
Pres, Edit Dir & Publr, Nan A Talese Books: Nan A Talese
Exec VP & Deputy Publr: Michael Palgon
VP, Subs/Foreign Rts: Carol Lazare
VP, Assoc Publr & Exec Dir, Mktg: Jacqueline Everly-Warren
VP & Creative Dir: John Fontana
VP & Ed-at-Large, Doubleday Broadway: Gerald Howard
VP & Publr: Amy Hertz
VP & Exec Dir, Publicity & Assoc Publr: Suzanne Herz
VP, Prodn, Design & Title Admin: Kim Cacho
Sr VP & Gen Coun: Katherine Trager
VP & Ed-in-Chief, Doubleday Broadway: William Thomas
VP & Dir, Doubleday Religious Publg: Michelle Rapkin
VP & Deputy Edit Dir: Deb Futter
VP & Exec Ed, Doubleday/Harlem Moon: Janet Hill
VP & Mktg Dir, Doubleday: John Pitts
VP & Exec Ed: Charles Conrad; Jennifer Josephy
VP, Exec Ed & Deputy Edit Dir: Stacy Creamer
Exec Ed, Religious Publg: Trace Murphy
Exec Art Dir & Adv Promo: Ellen Elchlepp
Dir, Adv: Judy Jacoby
VP, Dir, Sales Mgmt & Planning: Janelle Moburg
Edit Dir, Currency, Doubleday & Sr Ed, Doubleday: Roger Scholl
Mktg Dir, Broadway: Catherine Pollock
Dir, Publicity, Doubleday: Alison Rich
Dir, Publicity, Broadway: David Drake
Asst Dir, Subs/Foreign Rts: Claire Roberts

Mgr, Copyrights & Perms: Carol Christiansen
Publg Dir & Exec Man Ed: Rebecca Holland
Sr Ed: Jason Kaufman; Kristine Puopolo; Patricia
Medved; Ann Campbell; Phyllis Grann
Founded: 1897
Hardcover & paperback books for the general
& special interest markets for adults, both
nonfiction & fiction. The nonfiction focus is
in the areas of autobiography, memoirs &
biographies, business, current affairs, cookbooks, golf, history, illustrated books, African-
American, spirituality, religion, Bibles, personal
finance & money management, politics, popular
culture, psychology & women's studies, gay &
lesbian studies, self-help, consumer reference,
science & technology. The fiction focus is in
the areas of commercial, literary, thrillers, historical novels, women's fiction, graphic novels
& science fiction.
Random House Inc & its publishing entities are
not accepting unsol submissions, proposals,
mss, or submission queries via e-mail at this
time.
ISBN Prefix(es): 0-385; 0-7679
Imprints: The Anchor Bible; Anchor Books; Currency; DD Equestrian Library; Galilee Books;
Image Books; Jerusalem Bible; Made Simple
Books; Main Street/Back List; New Jerusalem
Bible; Nan A Talese Books; Outdoor Bible Se-
ries
Branch Office(s)
Doubleday Canada Ltd, One Toronto St, Suite
300, Toronto, ON M5C 2V6, Canada *Tel:* 416-
364-4449 *Fax:* 416-364-6863
Foreign Office(s): Random House Australia Ltd,
20 Alfred St, Milsons Point, Sydney, NSW
2061, Australia *Tel:* (02) 9-954-9966 *Fax:* (02)
9-954-4562
Doubleday New Zealand, 18 Poland Rd, Private
Bag 102940 NSMC, Glenfield, Auckland 10,
New Zealand, Man Dir & CEO: Juliet Rogers
Tel: (09) 444-7197 *Fax:* (09) 444-7524
Random House New Zealand Ltd, 18 Poland Rd,
Private Bag 102950 NSMC, Glenfield, Auck-
land 10, New Zealand, Man Dir: Juliet Rogers
Tel: (09) 444-7197 *Fax:* (09) 444-7524
Doubleday London, 61-63 Uxbridge Rd, Ealing,
London W5 5SA, United Kingdom, Mgr, Rts:
Sarah Birdsey *Tel:* (020) 579 2652 *Fax:* (020)
579 5479
Transworld Publishers Ltd, Century House, 61/63
Uxbridge Rd, Ealing, London W5 5SA, United
Kingdom, Man Dir & CEO: Mark Barty-King
Tel: (020) 8579 2652 *Fax:* (020) 579 5479
Advertising Agency: Bennett Book Advertising;
Spier NY

Douglas Publications Inc
2807 N Parham Rd, Suite 200, Richmond, VA
23294
Tel: 804-762-4455 *Toll Free Tel:* 800-223-1797
Fax: 804-935-0271
E-mail: info@douglaspublications.com
Web Site: www.douglaspublications.com
Key Personnel
Pres: Alan Douglas *E-mail:* adouglas@
douglaspublications.com
Mktg Dir: Curtis Wharton
Founded: 1985
Reference books & directories in the retail, ap-
parel, healthcare, hospitality & incentive indus-
tries.
ISBN Prefix(es): 0-87228
Number of titles published annually: 14 Print; 12
CD-ROM; 12 Online
Total Titles: 30 Print; 12 CD-ROM; 12 Online
Imprints: The Salesman's Guide; US Directory
Service

§Dover Publications Inc
31 E Second St, Mineola, NY 11501

Tel: 516-294-7000 *Toll Free Tel:* 800-223-3130
(orders) *Fax:* 516-742-6953; 516-742-5049 (or-
ders)
Web Site: www.doverpublications.com; www.
doverdirect.com *Telex:* 12-7731
Key Personnel
Pres: Clarence C Strowbridge
Sr VP & Ed-in-Chief: Paul Negri
Compt: Carol Meaney
VP, Prodn: Leonard Roland
VP, Trade Sales: Jerry Meskill
Asst to Pres, Sr Reprint Ed, Rts & Perms &
ISBN Contact: John Grafton
Adv Dir: Tom Crawford
Founded: 1941
Trade, scientific, paperbound books; posters, lan-
guage, literature & children's cassettes, sta-
tionery items.
ISBN Prefix(es): 0-486
Number of titles published annually: 670 Print; 8
CD-ROM
Total Titles: 7,500 Print; 36 CD-ROM; 22 Audio
Foreign Rep(s): David & Charles (UK); Forrester
Books NZ (New Zealand); General Publishing
Co Ltd (Canada); Lothian Books (Australia)
Shipping Address: 11 E Second St, Mineola, NY
11501

Down East Books
Division of Down East Enterprise Inc
PO Box 679, Camden, ME 04843
SAN: 208-6301
Tel: 207-594-9544 *Toll Free Tel:* 800-766-1670
(ME only) *Fax:* 207-594-7215
Web Site: www.downeastbooks.com
Key Personnel
Gen Mgr & Intl Rts: Neil Sweet
Sr Ed: Karin L Womer
Promo-Publicity: Terry Bregy
Ed: Chris Cornell
Man Ed: Michael Steere *Tel:* 207-789-5659
E-mail: msteere@downeast.com
Lib Sales Dir: Cheryl Gerry
Internet & Catalog Mktg Dir: Paula Blanchard
Founded: 1967
Maine & New England related subjects; 3 scenic
Maine calendars; outdoors.
ISBN Prefix(es): 0-89272
Number of titles published annually: 25 Print
Total Titles: 150 Print
Imprints: Countrysport Press (Wingshooting &
flyfishing books)
Distributor for Nimbus Publishing Ltd (selected
titles) (Canadian sales only)
Foreign Rep(s): Nimbus Publishing Ltd (Canada)
Shipping Address: 680 Commercial St, Rockport,
ME 04856

Down The Shore Publishing Corp
638 Teal St, Cedar Run, NJ 08092
SAN: 661-082X
Mailing Address: PO Box 3100, Harvey Cedars,
NJ 08008
Tel: 609-978-1233 *Fax:* 609-597-0422
E-mail: shore@att.net
Web Site: www.down-the-shore.com
Key Personnel
Pres: Raymond G Fisk
Founded: 1984
Regional books, local history; calendars; note
cards.
ISBN Prefix(es): 0-9615208; 0-945582; 1-59322
Number of titles published annually: 6 Print
Total Titles: 31 Print
Imprints: Bufflehead Books; Cormorant Books;
Cormorant Calendars; Terrapin Greetings
Membership(s): Publishers Marketing Association

Down There Press
Division of Open Enterprises Cooperative Inc
938 Howard St, Suite 101, San Francisco, CA
94103

SAN: 212-3312
Tel: 415-974-8985 *Fax:* 415-974-8989
E-mail: downtherepress@excite.com
Web Site: www.goodvibes.com/dtp/dtp.html
Key Personnel
Man Ed & Intl Rts: Leigh Davidson *Tel:* 415-
974-8985 ext 205
Founded: 1975
Trade publisher of sexual health & self awareness
books for women, men & children.
ISBN Prefix(es): 0-940208; 0-9602324
Number of titles published annually: 3 Print; 2
Audio
Total Titles: 24 Print; 15 E-Book; 19 Audio
Imprints: Passion Press; Yes Press
Distributor for Red Alder Books
Orders to: SLB Distributors (Trade)
Membership(s): Northern California Book Public-
ity & Marketing Association; Publishers Mar-
keting Association

Drama Publishers, see Quite Specific Media
Group Ltd

§Dramaline® Publications
36-851 Palm View Rd, Rancho Mirage, CA
92270-2417
SAN: 285-239X
Tel: 760-770-6076 *Fax:* 760-770-4507
E-mail: drama.line@verizon.net
Web Site: dramaline.com
Key Personnel
Owner: Roger Karshner
Gen Mgr & Intl Rts: Courtney Marsh
Founded: 1980
Scene-study books for actors.
ISBN Prefix(es): 0-9611792; 0-949669
Number of titles published annually: 3 Print; 2
CD-ROM; 3 Online; 3 E-Book
Total Titles: 50 Print; 50 Online; 50 E-Book; 3
Audio
Imprints: Noble Porter Press
Distributed by Ingram Book Co
Foreign Rep(s): Gazelle Book Services (British
Commonwealth); Tower Books (Australia)
Returns: Publishers Storage, 660 S Mansfield,
Ypsilanti, MI 48197
Warehouse: Publishers Storage, 660 S Mans-
field, Ypsilanti, MI 48197 *Tel:* 734-487-9720
Fax: 734-487-1890
Distribution Center: Publishers Storage, 660 S
Mansfield, Ypsilanti, MI 48197

Dramatic Publishing Co
311 Washington St, Woodstock, IL 60098
SAN: 201-5676
Mailing Address: PO Box 129, Woodstock, IL
60098-0129
Tel: 815-338-7170 *Toll Free Tel:* 800-448-7469
Fax: 815-338-8981 *Toll Free Fax:* 800-334-
5302
E-mail: plays@dramaticpublishing.com
Web Site: www.dramaticpublishing.com
Key Personnel
Pres: Christopher Sergel
VP: Christopher Sergel, III; Gayle Sergel; Susan
Sergel
Founded: 1885
Plays & musicals.
ISBN Prefix(es): 0-87129; 1-58342
Number of titles published annually: 55 Print
Total Titles: 1,305 Print
Foreign Rep(s): DALRO Pty Ltd (Southern
Africa); The Dominie Pty Ltd (Australia); Nick
Hern Books (England); The Play Bureau NZ
Ltd (New Zealand)

Dramatists Play Service Inc
440 Park Ave S, New York, NY 10016
Tel: 212-683-8960 *Fax:* 212-213-1539
E-mail: postmaster@dramatists.com
Web Site: www.dramatists.com

Key Personnel
Pres & Intl Rts: Stephen Sultan
Pubns Dir: Michael Fellmeth *Tel:* 212-683-8960
  ext 115 *E-mail:* fellmeth@dramatists.com
Founded: 1936
Publisher & licensor of plays & musicals.
ISBN Prefix(es): 0-8222
Number of titles published annually: 60 Print
Total Titles: 3,000 Print

The Drummond Publishing Group
362 N Bedford St, East Bridgewater, MA 02333
Tel: 508-378-1110 *Fax:* 508-378-1105
Web Site: www.drummondpub.com
Key Personnel
Pres: Rick Vayo *E-mail:* r_vayo@drummondpub.
  com
CFO: Charlotte Vayo *E-mail:* c_vayo@
  drummondpub.com
VP: Jack Mitchell *E-mail:* j_mitchell@
  drummondpub.com; Margaret Saunders
  E-mail: m_saunders@drummondpub.com
Mktg Mgr: Frank Allen *E-mail:* f_allen@
  drummondpub.com
Exec Ed: Jennifer Carley *E-mail:* j_carley@
  drummondpub.com; Gordon Law
  E-mail: g_laws@drummondpub.com
Founded: 1999
Publish fiction & nonfiction, including reference
  health, sports, cooking, spirituality, psychology,
  self-help, parenting & how-to; children's fiction
  & nonfiction.
ISBN Prefix(es): 9-05
Number of titles published annually: 20 Print
Imprints: Drummond Children's Books; Drum-
  mond Creative
See separate listing for:
Royalton Press

§Dry Bones Press Inc
PO Box 597, Roseville, CA 95678
Tel: 916-435-8355 *Fax:* 916-435-8355
E-mail: drybones@drybones.com
Web Site: www.drybones.com
Key Personnel
Pres & Publr: Jim Rankin *E-mail:* jrankin@
  drybones.com
Founded: 1991 (changing from sole proprietorship
  to corporation)
Books focus primarily on nursing especially
  nursing education & the "LPR" series, fol-
  lowing themes of books written by patients.
  Like to encourage books by nurses & will help
  bring them to print. The Dry Bones imprint
  is used to create several new authors' series:
  fiction, sci-fi, fantasy & family issues. Books
  may be ordered directly from Ingram books at
  www.ingrambooks.com.
ISBN Prefix(es): 1-883938; 1-931333
Number of titles published annually: 5 Print
Total Titles: 30 Print
Imprints: Dry Bones
Distributed by PublishingOnline.com
Distributor for Simplex Publications; Straight
  From The Heart Press
Distribution Center: Ingram Books, 1136 Heil
  Quaker Blvd, La Vergne, TN 37086, Contact:
  Jim Patterson *Tel:* 615-213-5107 *Fax:* 615-
  213-5114 *E-mail:* jim.patterson@ingrambook.
  com *Web Site:* www.ingrambook.com; www.
  lightningprint.com

Paul Dry Books
117 S 17 St, Suite 1102, Philadelphia, PA 19103
Tel: 215-231-9939 *Fax:* 215-231-9942
E-mail: editor@pauldrybooks.com
Web Site: www.pauldrybooks.com
Key Personnel
Owner: Paul Dry *E-mail:* pdry@pauldrybooks.
  com
Man Ed: John Corenswet *E-mail:* jcorenswet@
  pauldrybooks.com

Ed: William Schofield
Literary publications: fiction, history & essays.
ISBN Prefix(es): 0-9664913; 0-9679675; 1-58988
Number of titles published annually: 6 Print
Total Titles: 6 Print

Dufour Editions Inc
PO Box 7, Chester Springs, PA 19425-0007
SAN: 201-341X
Tel: 610-458-5005 *Toll Free Tel:* 800-869-5677
  Fax: 610-458-7103
E-mail: info@dufoureditions.com
Web Site: www.dufoureditions.com
Key Personnel
Pres & Publr: Christopher May
Mktg Dir: Brad Elliott
Founded: 1948
Literary fiction, general nonfiction, literature, po-
  etry, philosophy, history, drama, criticism.
ISBN Prefix(es): 0-8023
Number of titles published annually: 200 Print
Total Titles: 4,000 Print; 24 Audio
Imprints: Dufour Editions' Distributed Presses
Distributor for Angel Books; Anvil Books
  (Dublin) & The Children's Press; Attic/Atrium;
  Between-the-Lines; Blackstaff Press Ltd;
  Bloodaxe Books Ltd; Carysfort Press; Clo Iar-
  Chonnachta; Collins Press; The Columba Press;
  Dedalus Press; The DO-NOT PRESS; Dolmen
  Press Ltd; Eland Books/Sickle Moon; Enithar-
  mon Press; Forest Books; Gallery Books; Gob-
  linshead; Institute of Irish Studies; Iynx; The
  Liffey Press; Lilliput Press Ltd; Mare's Nest;
  New Island Books; Norvik Press; Peter Owen
  Ltd; Parthian; Salmon Poetry; Colin Smythe
  Ltd; Tindal Street Press; University College
  Dublin Press; The Waywiser Press
Warehouse: 124 Byers Rd, Chester Springs, PA
  19425

Duke University Press
905 W Main St, Suite 18-B, Durham, NC 27701
SAN: 201-3436
Mailing Address: PO Box 90660, Durham, NC
  27708-0660
Tel: 919-687-3600 *Toll Free Tel:* 888-651-
  0122 (orders only) *Fax:* 919-688-4574
  Toll Free Fax: 888-651-0124
Web Site: www.dukeupress.edu
Key Personnel
Ed-in-Chief: Ken Wissoker
CFO: Agnes Wong Nickerson
Dir: Stephen Cohn
Ed: Valerie Millholland; J Reynolds Smith
Design & Prodn Mgr: Deborah Wong
Sales Mgr: Michael McCullough
Assoc Mktg Mgr: H Lee Willoughby-Harris
  Tel: 919-687-3646 *E-mail:* hlwh@dukepress.
  edu
Mktg Mgr, Journals Div: Donna Blagden
Prodn Mgr, Journals Div: Mike Brondoli
Edit Dir, Journals Div: Debra Kaufman
Mktg & ISBN Contact: Emily Young
Founded: 1921
Scholarly, trade & textbooks.
ISBN Prefix(es): 0-8223
Number of titles published annually: 105 Print
Total Titles: 1,300 Print; 1 E-Book
Distributor for Forest History Society
Foreign Rep(s): Combined Academic Publish-
  ers Ltd (UK, Europe, Middle East); East-West
  Export Books (Asia, Pacific); Lexa Publishers
  Representatives (Canada)
Advertising Agency: Unabridged Advertising
Warehouse: 120 Golden Dr, Durham, NC 27705,
  Dist Mgr: Julie Tyson *Tel:* 919-384-0733
  Fax: 919-384-9564

Dumbarton Oaks
1703 32 St NW, Washington, DC 20007
Tel: 202-777-0091 *Fax:* 202-339-6419
E-mail: publications@doaks.org

Web Site: www.doaks.org
Key Personnel
Desktop Pubn Specialist: David Topping
ISBN Prefix(es): 0-88402
Number of titles published annually: 8 Print
Total Titles: 260 Print
Distributed by Harvard University Press
Distribution Center: PO Box 4866, Hampden Sta,
  Baltimore, MD 21211

§Dun & Bradstreet
103 JFK Pkwy, Short Hills, NJ 07078
Tel: 973-921-5500 *Toll Free Tel:* 800-526-0651
E-mail: custserv@dnb.com
Web Site: www.dnb.com
Key Personnel
Chmn & CEO: Allan Loren
Business & business reference; US & interna-
  tional coverage, country information.
ISBN Prefix(es): 1-56203
Total Titles: 31 Print; 20 CD-ROM

Dunhill Publishing
Division of Warwick Associates
18340 Sonoma Hwy, Sonoma, CA 95476
Tel: 707-939-0562 *Fax:* 707-938-3515
E-mail: dunhill@vom.com
Web Site: www.dunhillpublishing.net
Key Personnel
Pres: Cierra Trenery
Publr: Simon Warwick-Smith *E-mail:* warwick@
  vom.com
Founded: 1985
Handles process of editing, pre-press, design,
  printing, distribution, book reviews, book &
  author promotion, media contact, internet sales
  & marketing, retail sales & marketing, fulfill-
  ment & shipping.
ISBN Prefix(es): 1-931501
Number of titles published annually: 10 Print
Total Titles: 10 Print

§Dunwoody Press
Division of McNeil Technologies Inc
6564 Loisdale Ct, Suite 800, Springfield, VA
  22150
Tel: 703-921-1600 *Fax:* 703-921-1610
E-mail: dpadmin@mcneiltech.com
Web Site: www.dunwoodypress.com
Founded: 1980
Foreign language teaching materials & dictionar-
  ies, electronic publishing.
ISBN Prefix(es): 0-931745
Number of titles published annually: 4 Print
Total Titles: 123 Print; 41 Audio

Duquesne University Press
600 Forbes Ave, Pittsburgh, PA 15282
Tel: 412-396-6610 *Toll Free Tel:* 800-666-2211
  Fax: 412-396-5984
Web Site: www.dupress.duq.edu
Key Personnel
Dir: Susan Wadsworth-Booth
  E-mail: wadsworth@duq.edu
Prodn Ed: Kathleen Meyer *E-mail:* meyerk@duq.
  edu
Mktg & Busn Mgr: Lori R Crosby
  E-mail: crosbyl@duq.edu
Founded: 1927
Nonfiction: ethics, philosophy, religion, philology,
  psychology, literature & creative nonfiction.
ISBN Prefix(es): 0-8207
Number of titles published annually: 10 Print
Total Titles: 80 Print
Foreign Rep(s): Gazelle (European Union)
Warehouse: CUP Services, 750 Cascadilla St,
  Ithaca, NY 14851-6525 *Toll Free Tel:* 800-
  666-2211 *Toll Free Fax:* 800-688-2877
  E-mail: orderbook@cupserv.org
Membership(s): Association of American Univer-
  sity Presses; Society for Scholarly Publishing

Sanford J Durst
11 Clinton Ave, Rockville Centre, NY 11570
SAN: 211-6987
Tel: 516-766-4444 *Fax:* 516-766-4520
E-mail: sanfordjdurst@aol.com
Founded: 1975
Numismatics (coins, medals, tokens, paper
money).
ISBN Prefix(es): 0-916710; 0-915262; 0-942666;
0-867230; 0-685955; 1-886720
Total Titles: 260 Print
Imprints: Marathon Press; Obol International
Divisions: Marathon Press; Obol International
Distributor for American Numismatic Society;
Ares Publishing Co; Bowers & Merena Gal-
leries Inc; Krause Publications; Obol Interna-
tional; Seabys Ltd; Spink & Son Ltd; Stanton
Books Numismatics International; Whitman
Publishing Co

§Dustbooks
Affiliate of Associated Writing Programs
PO Box 100, Paradise, CA 95967-0222
SAN: 204-1871
Tel: 530-877-6110 *Toll Free Tel:* 800-477-6110
Fax: 530-877-0222
E-mail: publisher@dustbooks.com
Web Site: www.dustbooks.com
Key Personnel
Publr, Ed & Rts & Perms: Len Fulton
Founded: 1963
Full service publishing company.
ISBN Prefix(es): 0-913218; 0-916685
Number of titles published annually: 6 Print; 1
CD-ROM
Distributed by Pushcart Press; Seventh-Wing Pub-
lications
Distributor for American Dust Publications Inc

Dutton
Division of Penguin Group (USA) Inc
375 Hudson St, New York, NY 10014
SAN: 282-5074
Tel: 212-366-2000 *Fax:* 212-366-2262
E-mail: online@penguinputnam.com
Web Site: www.penguin.com
Key Personnel
Pres: Carole Baron
VP, Publr & Edit Dir: Brian Tart
VP, Prodn: Pat Lyons
VP & Exec Art Dir: Rich Hasselberger
VP, Publicity/Spec Projs: Lisa Johnson
Man Ed: Susan Schwartz
Sr Ed: Laurie Chittenden; Mitch Hoffman
ISBN Prefix(es): 0-525; 0-917657; 1-55611
Number of titles published annually: 41 Print
Total Titles: 114 Print
Imprints: Dutton
Advertising Agency: Spier NY

Dutton Children's Books
Imprint of Penguin Group (USA) Inc
345 Hudson St, New York, NY 10014
SAN: 282-5074
Tel: 212-366-2000
E-mail: online@penguinputnam.com
Web Site: www.penguin.com
Key Personnel
Pres & Publr: Stephanie Lurie
Edit Ed: Maureen Sullivan
Art Dir: Sara Reynolds
Man Ed: Steven Meltzer
Sr Ed: Lucia Monfried
Ed: Meredith (Peggy) Mundy Wasinger; Julie
Strauss-Gabel; Michelle Coppola
Founded: 1852 (as Dutton)
ISBN Prefix(es): 0-525
Number of titles published annually: 102 Print
Total Titles: 714 Print
Imprints: Dutton

Duxbury, see Wadsworth Publishing

§E B P Latin America Group Inc
Subsidiary of Editorial Barsa Planeta Inc
175 E Delaware Place, Suite 8806, Chicago, IL
60611
Tel: 312-397-9590 *Fax:* 312-397-9593
Web Site: www.barsa.com
Key Personnel
Pres: Lanny Passaro *E-mail:* lpassaro@aol.com
Distributor of Spanish language reference prod-
ucts.
ISBN Prefix(es): 1-56409

§E-Digital Books LLC
1155 S Havana St, Suite 11, PMB 364, Aurora,
CO 80012
Tel: 303-745-4997 *Fax:* 303-745-4997
E-mail: edigital@edigitalbooks.com
Web Site: www.edigitalbooks.com
Key Personnel
Mgr: Tina R Allen *E-mail:* manager@
edigitalbooks.com
Founded: 1999
E-publisher & E-bookseller of downloadable digi-
tal books in PDF File Format.
ISBN Prefix(es): 0-9672704; 0-9709364; 1-
931792
Number of titles published annually: 10 Print; 5
CD-ROM; 10 Online; 10 E-Book
Total Titles: 64 Print; 10 CD-ROM; 64 Online;
64 E-Book
Membership(s): National Writers Association

e-Scholastic
Division of Scholastic Inc
568 Broadway, 9th fl, New York, NY 10012
Tel: 212-343-7100 *Fax:* 212-343-4949
Key Personnel
Pres: Donna Iucolano
VP, Corp Graphic Systems: Will Kefauver
VP, Opers: Janet Byrne Smith
VP & Gen Mgr, School & Home-based Online
Customer Segments: Victor Aluise
VP, Technol: Steve Morrissey
Dir, Strategic Mktg: Cynthia Sanner
Dir, Fin, Planning & Admin: David Crumrine
Dir, e-Commerce Clubs & Fairs: Deborah Gaffin
Dir, e-Mail Mktg: Kateria Niambi
Dir, e-Commerce Online Stores: Patricia Gormley
Edit Dir: Sylvia Barsotti

E-Z Products Inc, see Socrates Media

Eagan Press
Imprint of American Association of Cereal
Chemists
3340 Pilot Knob Rd, St Paul, MN 55121-2097
Tel: 651-454-7250 *Toll Free Tel:* 800-328-7560
Fax: 651-454-0766
E-mail: aacc@scisoc.org
Web Site: www.aaccnet.org
Key Personnel
Exec VP: Steve Nelson *E-mail:* snelson@scisoc.
org
Mktg Mgr: Greg Grahek *E-mail:* ggrahek@scisoc.
org
Founded: 1995
Food science publishing.
ISBN Prefix(es): 1-891127
Number of titles published annually: 5 Print; 1 E-
Book
Total Titles: 20 Print
Foreign Office(s): Stanislas de Rijcklaan, BE-
3001 Heverlee, Belgium, Contact: Hilde Ke-
unen *Tel:* (016) 204035 *Fax:* (016) 202535
E-mail: aps@scisoceurope.org

Eagle Publishing Inc
One Massachusetts Ave NW, Washington, DC
20001
Tel: 202-216-0600 *Fax:* 202-216-0612
Web Site: www.regnery.com

Key Personnel
Pres: Jeffrey J Carneal
VP & Gen Mgr, Eagle Book Clubs: J Brinley
Lewis
Pres & Publr, Regnery Publg: Marjory Ross
Ed-in-Chief & Pres, Human Events Publg:
Thomas S Winter
Founded: 1993
Trade books, book clubs, newsletters, a news
weekly & list management subsidiaries or divi-
sions.
ISBN Prefix(es): 0-89526
Number of titles published annually: 35 Print
Total Titles: 250 Print
Imprints: Capital Press; Gateway; LifeLine Press;
Regnery
Subsidiaries: Eagle Book Clubs Inc; Human
Events Publishing LLC; Regnery Publishing
Inc
Divisions: Eagle List Division; Newletter Divi-
sion; Special Products Division

Eagle's View Publishing
Subsidiary of Westwind Inc
168W 12 St, Ogden, UT 84404
SAN: 240-6330
Tel: 801-393-4555; 801-745-0905 (edit)
Toll Free Tel: 800-547-3364 (orders over $100)
Fax: 801-745-0903
E-mail: eglcrafts@aol.com
Web Site: eaglefeathertradingpost.com
Key Personnel
Pres & Publr: Monte Smith
Sales Mgr: Sue Smith *Tel:* 801-393-3991
Ed & Publicity: Denise Knight
Founded: 1982
Books on Indian arts, crafts & culture, mountain
men & the early frontier, beading, historical
clothing patterns, how-to craft books in these
areas.
ISBN Prefix(es): 0-943604
Number of titles published annually: 4 Print
Total Titles: 45 Print

Eakin Press
Division of Sunbelt Media Inc
8800 Tara Lane, Austin, TX 78737
Mailing Address: PO Drawer 90159, Austin, TX
78709-0159
Tel: 512-288-1771 *Toll Free Tel:* 800-880-8642
Fax: 512-288-1813
Web Site: www.eakinpress.com
Key Personnel
Publr: Virginia Messer *E-mail:* virginia@
eakinpress.com
Sales Mgr: Tom Messer *E-mail:* tom@eakinpress.
com
Founded: 1978
Book Publisher.
ISBN Prefix(es): 0-89015; 1-57168
Number of titles published annually: 50 Print
Total Titles: 490 Print; 220 E-Book; 1 Audio
Imprints: Nortex Press; PenPoint Press
Distributor for German Texan Heritage Society;
San Antonio Express-News; Ellen Temple Pub-
lishing

East Asian Legal Studies Program
Affiliate of University of Maryland School of
Law
500 W Baltimore St, Baltimore, MD 21201-1786
Tel: 410-706-3870 *Fax:* 410-706-1516
E-mail: eastasia@law.umaryland.edu
Key Personnel
Gen Ed & Ed-in-Chief: Hungdah Chiu
Exec Ed & Assoc Ed-in-Chief: Chih-Yu T Wu
Assoc Exec Ed: Yufan Li
Founded: 1977
East Asian legal studies, political, economic &
legal.
ISBN Prefix(es): 0-942182; 0-925153

Number of titles published annually: 8 Print
Total Titles: 195 Print

Eastern Washington University Press
Eastern Washington University, 705 W First Ave,
Spokane, WA 99201
Tel: 509-623-4286 *Toll Free Tel:* 800-508-9095
Fax: 509-623-4283
E-mail: ewupress@ewu.edu
Web Site: ewupress.ewu.edu
Key Personnel
Man Ed: Joelean Copeland *Tel:* 509-623-4285
E-mail: jcopeland@ewu.edu
ISBN Prefix(es): 0-910055
Number of titles published annually: 8 Print
Total Titles: 54 Print

Eastland Press
3257 16 Ave W, Suite 2, Seattle, WA 98119
Mailing Address: PO Box 99749, Seattle, WA
98139
Tel: 206-217-0204 *Toll Free Tel:* 800-453-
3278 (orders only) *Fax:* 206-217-0205
Toll Free Fax: 800-241-3329 (orders)
E-mail: info@eastlandpress.com; orders@
eastlandpress.com (orders-credit cards only)
Web Site: www.eastlandpress.com
Key Personnel
Gen Mgr: Patricia O'Connor
Man Ed & Lib Sales Dir: John O'Connor
Medical Ed: Dan Bensky
Prodn Mgr: Lilian Bensky
Founded: 1981
Chinese, alternative, osteopathic & manipulative
medicine. Use Seattle, Washington address for
submitting a ms or inquiring about a publica-
tion. Use Vista, California address for ordering
books.
ISBN Prefix(es): 0-939616
Number of titles published annually: 4 Print
Total Titles: 40 Print
Sales Office(s): 1240 Activity Dr, Suite D, Vista,
CA 92081 *Toll Free Tel:* 800-453-3278 *Toll
Free Fax:* 800-241-3329
Distributed by Elsevier (Great Britain) (2 titles)
Distributor for Journal of Chinese Medicine Pub-
lications
Orders to: 1240 Activity Dr, Suite D, Vista,
CA 92081 *Tel:* 760-598-9695 *Toll Free
Tel:* 800-453-3278 *Fax:* 760-598-6083 *Toll Free
Fax:* 800-241-3329 *SAN:* 216-6216
Warehouse: 1240 Activity Dr, Suite D, Vista, CA
92081 *Toll Free Tel:* 800-453-3278 *Toll Free
Fax:* 800-241-3329 *E-mail:* info@eastlandpress.
com *Web Site:* www.eastlandpress.com
Membership(s): Publishers Association of the
West

Easy Money Press
5419 87 St, Lubbock, TX 79424
Tel: 806-543-5215
E-mail: easymoneypress@yahoo.com
Key Personnel
Creative Dir: Henry Wolford *E-mail:* hcwolford@
yahoo.com
Mktg Dir: Sheri Kephart
Prodn Dir: Bud Bailey
Founded: 1996
ISBN Prefix(es): 0-9654563; 1-929714
Number of titles published annually: 4 Print
Total Titles: 12 Print
Imprints: Big Tree Books; EMP; Haase House

Eaton Publishing, see BioTechniques Books

Ebon Research Systems Publishing LLC
812 Sweetwater Club Blvd, Longwood, FL 32779
Mailing Address: PO Box 915115, Longwood, FL
32791-5115
Tel: 407-786-9200 *Fax:* 407-682-2384
E-mail: ebonrs@prodigy.net

Web Site: ebonresearchsystems.com
Key Personnel
Mgr: Dr Florence Alexander
Founded: 1974
Full service publishing house with writing, edit-
ing, graphics & specialized printing capability.
ISBN Prefix(es): 0-9648313; 0-915960
Number of titles published annually: 12 Print; 12
CD-ROM; 2 Online; 2 E-Book; 12 Audio
Total Titles: 17 Print; 12 CD-ROM; 2 Online; 2
E-Book; 12 Audio
Branch Office(s)
Quality Books Inc, 8850 Grissom Pkwy, Ti-
tusville, FL 32780, Contact: Michael Couch
Tel: 321-267-6560 *Fax:* 321-267-6510
E-mail: ebon@ebonresearchsystems.com
Editorial Office(s): Quality Books Inc, 8850 Gris-
som Pkwy, Titusville, FL 32780, Mgr: Dr Flo-
rence Alexander *Tel:* 321-267-6560 *Fax:* 321-
267-6510 *E-mail:* ebonrs@prodigy.net
Sales Office(s): Quality Books Inc, 8850 Grissom
Pkwy, Titusville, FL 32780, Contact: Michael
Couch *Tel:* 321-267-6560 *Fax:* 321-267-6510
E-mail: ebon@ebonresearchsystems.com
Distributed by Quality Books Inc
Billing Address: 112 Bauer Circle, Daytona
Beach, FL 32124, Contact: Kay Yaeger
Tel: 386-274-0030 *Fax:* 386-274-0037
E-mail: kay1244@aol.com
Orders to: 8850 Grissom Pkwy, Titusville, FL
32780, Contact: Michael Couch *Tel:* 321-
267-6560 *Fax:* 321-267-6510 *E-mail:* ebon@
ebonresearchsystems.com
Returns: 8850 Grissom Pkwy, Titusville, FL
32780, Contact: Michael Couch *Tel:* 321-
267-6560 *Fax:* 321-267-6510 *E-mail:* ebon@
ebonresearchsystems.com
Shipping Address: 8850 Grissom Pkwy, Titusville,
FL 32780, Contact: Michael Couch *Tel:* 321-
267-6560 *Fax:* 321-267-6510 *E-mail:* ebon@
ebonresearchsystems.com
Warehouse: 8850 Grissom Pkwy, Titusville, FL
32780, Contact: Michael Couch *Tel:* 321-
267-6560 *Fax:* 321-267-6510 *E-mail:* ebon@
ebonresearchsystems.com
Distribution Center: 8850 Grissom Pkwy, Titusville, FL 32780, Contact: Michael Couch
Tel: 321-267-6560 *Fax:* 321-267-6510
E-mail: ebon@ebonresearchsystems.com
Membership(s): Small Publishers Association of
North America

Eckankar
PO Box 27300, Minneapolis, MN 55427
Tel: 952-380-2200 *Toll Free Tel:* 866-485-5556
(CN orders); 888-408-0301 (US orders)
Fax: 952-380-2395 *Toll Free Fax:* 866-485-
6665 (CN orders) *Fax on Demand:* 717-564-
8307 (US orders)
E-mail: eckbooks@eckankar.org
Web Site: www.eckankar.org
Key Personnel
Natl Sales Mgr & Intl Rts: John Kulick
Founded: 1965
Titles emphasize the value of personal experience
as a vital & most natural basis for spiritual be-
lief. Each of our titles presents the Eckankar
teachings as practical applications of ancient
wisdom for today's world.
ISBN Prefix(es): 1-57043
Number of titles published annually: 5 Print
Total Titles: 47 Print; 6 Audio
Distributed by Hushion House Publishing, Inc
Shipping Address: Hushion House Publishing
Inc, Stackpole Distribution, 7253 Grayson Rd,
Harrisburg, PA 17111 *Toll Free Tel:* 888-408-
0301 (orders only) *Fax:* 717-564-8307 (orders
only) *E-mail:* bmcnally@hushion.com *Web
Site:* www.hushion.com
Warehouse: Hushion House Publishing Inc,
36 Northline Rd, Toronto, ON M4B 3E2,
Canada *Tel:* 416-285-6100 *Toll Free Tel:* 866-

485-5556 (orders only) *Fax:* 416-285-1777
E-mail: jbeau@hushion.com
Membership(s): ABA; BISG; Midwest Indepen-
dent Publishers Association; Publishers Mar-
keting Association; Upper Midwest Booksellers
Association

§Eclipse Press
Subsidiary of The Blood-Horse Publications Inc
3101 Beaumont Centre Circle, Lexington, KY
40513
Mailing Address: PO Box 919003, Lexington,
KY 40544-4038
Tel: 859-278-2361 *Toll Free Tel:* 800-866-2361
Fax: 859-276-6868
E-mail: editorial@eclipsepress.com; marketing@
eclipsepress.com
Web Site: www.eclipsepress.com
Key Personnel
Pres & Publr: Stacy V Bearse *E-mail:* sbearse@
bloodhorse.com
Ed: Jacqueline Duke *E-mail:* jduke@eclipsepress.
com
Dir, Corp Mktg: Robert Bolson
Mktg Mgr: Gerilyn Parfitt
Founded: 1916
Publications dedicated to the enjoyment, health &
betterment of the equine industry.
ISBN Prefix(es): 0-939049; 1-58150
Number of titles published annually: 15 Print
Total Titles: 83 Print; 5 CD-ROM
Imprints: Eclipse Press; The Horse Health Care
Library
Distributed by National Book Network
Membership(s): Publishers Association of the
South; Publishers Marketing Association

ECS, see The Electrochemical Society Inc

ECS Publishing
138 Ipswich St, Boston, MA 02215
Tel: 617-236-1935 *Toll Free Tel:* 800-777-1919
Fax: 617-236-0261
E-mail: office@ecspub.com
Web Site: www.ecspub.com
Key Personnel
Pres & Intl Rts: Robert Schuneman
Founded: 1921
Music publishing (sheet music).
ISBN Prefix(es): 0-911318
Total Titles: 10 Print
Imprints: Galaxy Music Corp; E C Schirmer Mu-
sic Co
Divisions: Galaxy Music Corp; E C Schirmer
Music Co
Distributor for Wayne Leupold Editions

EDC Publishing
Division of Educational Development Corp
10302 E 55 Place, Tulsa, OK 74146-6515
Tel: 918-622-4522 *Toll Free Tel:* 800-475-4522
Fax: 918-665-7919 *Toll Free Fax:* 800-747-
4509
E-mail: edc@edcpub.com
Web Site: www.edcpub.com
Key Personnel
Pres: Randall White *E-mail:* rwhite@edcpub.com
VP: Ron McDaniel *E-mail:* rmcdaniel@edcpub.
com
Lib Sales Dir: Todd White *E-mail:* twhite@ubah.
com
Cont: Debbie Magnon *Tel:* 918-622-4522 ext 121
E-mail: dmagnon@edcpub.com
Founded: 1961
Children's nonfiction.
ISBN Prefix(es): 0-88110; 0-7460; 0-86020; 0-
7945; 1-58086
Number of titles published annually: 200 Print
Total Titles: 1,600 Print; 6 CD-ROM
Imprints: EDC/Usborne
Distributor for Usborne Publishing

EDCO Publishing Inc
2648 Lapeer Rd, Auburn Hills, MI 48326
Tel: 248-475-4678 *Toll Free Tel:* 888-510-3326
 Fax: 248-475-9122
E-mail: info@edcopublishing.com
Web Site: www.edcopublishing.com
Key Personnel
Pres: Edna C Stephens *E-mail:* edna@
 edcopublishing.com
Mgr: Martha Ruebelman *E-mail:* martha@
 edcopublishing.com
Founded: 1997
Create & produce unique, fun, award winning,
 children's books & programs. Major corpo-
 rations, government agencies & museums
 sponsor our educational programs, which are
 printed & distributed to elementary school
 teachers at no charge; increase public knowl-
 edge & appreciation for Michigan's wonderful
 natural resources.
ISBN Prefix(es): 0-9712692; 0-9749412
Number of titles published annually: 4 Print
Total Titles: 8 Print
Membership(s): Great Lakes Booksellers Association; Michigan Reading Association; Publishers
 Marketing Association; Small Publishers Association of North America

Eden Publishing
PO Box 20176, Keizer, OR 97307-0176
Tel: 503-390-9013 *Fax:* 503-390-9013
E-mail: info@edenpublishing.com
Web Site: www.edenpublishing.com
Key Personnel
Publr & Ed: Barbara Griffin Dan
 E-mail: barbgdan@yahoo.com
Founded: 1994
ISBN Prefix(es): 1-884898
Number of titles published annually: 6 Print
Total Titles: 15 Print
Returns: 1665 Dixon St NE, Keizer, OR 97303-
 2214
Warehouse: 1665 Dixon St NE, Keizer, OR
 97303-2214 *Tel:* 503-390-9013 *Fax:* 503-390-
 9013 - orders

Nellie Edge Resources Inc
PO Box 12399, Salem, OR 97309-0399
Tel: 503-399-0040 *Toll Free Tel:* 800-523-4594
 Fax: 503-399-0435
E-mail: info@nellieedge.com
Web Site: www.nellieedge.com
Key Personnel
Pres: Nellie Edge
Founded: 1984
English & Spanish folk songs, "read & sing"
 books, rhymes & chants, anthologies of poetry,
 teacher resource books.
ISBN Prefix(es): 0-922053
Number of titles published annually: 5 Print
Total Titles: 44 Print; 37 Online; 37 E-Book; 16
 Audio

Edgewise Press
24 Fifth Ave, Suite 224, New York, NY 10011
Tel: 212-982-4818 *Fax:* 212-982-1364
E-mail: epinc@mindspring.com
Web Site: www.edgewisepress.com
Key Personnel
Contact: Richard Milazzo
Founded: 1995
Publisher of serious art & literary books.
ISBN Prefix(es): 0-9646466; 1-893207
Number of titles published annually: 3 Print
Total Titles: 18 Print
Distributor for Editions d'Afrique du Nord

Ediciones Universal
3090 SW Eighth St, Miami, FL 33135
Tel: 305-642-3355 *Fax:* 305-642-7978
E-mail: ediciones@ediciones.com
Web Site: www.ediciones.com

Key Personnel
Gen Mgr: Marta Salvat-Golik *E-mail:* marta@
 ediciones.com
Founded: 1965
Publish Spanish language books, specialize in
 Cuban topics.
ISBN Prefix(es): 0-89729; 1-59388
Number of titles published annually: 20 Print

Editions Orphee Inc
1240 Clubview Blvd N, Columbus, OH 43235
Tel: 614-846-9517 *Fax:* 614-846-9794
Web Site: www.orphee.com
Key Personnel
Pres: Matanya Orphee *E-mail:* m.ophee@orphee.
 com
Classical sheet music, books on music.
ISBN Prefix(es): 0-936186; 1-882612
Number of titles published annually: 5 Print
Total Titles: 5 Print
Distributed by Theodore Presser Co

Editorial Bautista Independiente
Division of Baptist Mid-Missions
3417 Kenilworth Blvd, Sebring, FL 33870
Tel: 863-382-6350 *Toll Free Tel:* 800-398-7187
 Fax: 863-382-8650
E-mail: info@ebi-bmm.org
Web Site: www.ebi-bmm.org
Key Personnel
Gen Dir & Busn Mgr: Marvin Stephens
Founded: 1950
Sunday school materials, extension materials,
 Bible study-all in Spanish.
ISBN Prefix(es): 1-879892
Number of titles published annually: 7 Print
Total Titles: 150 Print
Distributor for Casa Bautista; CLIE; Portavoz

Editorial Portavoz
Division of Kregel Publications
733 Wealthy St SE, Grand Rapids, MI 49503-
 5553
SAN: 298-9115
Mailing Address: PO Box 2607, Grand Rapids,
 MI 49501-2607
Tel: 616-451-4775 *Toll Free Tel:* 800-733-2607
 Fax: 616-451-9330
E-mail: portavoz@portavoz.com
Web Site: www.kregel.com; www.portavoz.com
Key Personnel
Pres: James R Kregel *E-mail:* president@kregel.
 com
Dir: Andres Schwartz
Founded: 1974
Christian products.
ISBN Prefix(es): 0-8254
Number of titles published annually: 40 Print
Total Titles: 450 Print
Membership(s): Christian Booksellers Associa-
 tion; Evangelical Christian Publishers Associa-
 tion; SEPA

Editorial Unilit
Division of Spanish House
1360 NW 88 Ave, Miami, FL 33172
Tel: 305-592-6136 *Toll Free Tel:* 800-767-7726
 Fax: 305-592-0087
Web Site: www.editorialunilit.com
Key Personnel
CEO: David Ecklebarger
Pres: Larry Downs, Jr *E-mail:* larry@
 editorialunilit.com
Founded: 1974
Publishing for the Spanish family.
ISBN Prefix(es): 1-56063; 0-7899
Number of titles published annually: 105 Print
Total Titles: 750 Print
Membership(s): CBA; Evangelical Christian Pub-
 lishers Association; SEPA

§EduCare Press
PO Box 17222, Seattle, WA 98127
Tel: 206-782-4797 *Fax:* 206-782-4802
E-mail: educarepress@hotmail.com
Web Site: www.educarepress.com
Key Personnel
Pres: Timothy K O'Mahony
Publr & Intl Rts Contact: Kieran O'Mahony
 E-mail: kieran@educarepress.com
Founded: 1988
Writing, editing, typesetting, marketing, Specializ-
 ing in memoirs, aging, cats.
ISBN Prefix(es): 0-944638
Number of titles published annually: 20 Online; 5
 E-Book
Total Titles: 25 Print; 20 E-Book; 3 Audio
Imprints: Market House Books (Fiction)
Foreign Rep(s): Hagenbach & Bender (Switzer-
 land)
Foreign Rights: Hagenbach & Bender (all territo-
 ries)
Membership(s): Publishers Marketing Associa-
 tion; Small Publishers Association of North
 America

Educational Communications Inc
1701 Directors Blvd, Suite 920, Austin, TX
 78744
Tel: 512-440-2705 *Fax:* 512-447-1687
Web Site: www.honoring.com
Key Personnel
Gen Mgr: Jefferey J Fix
Founded: 1967
Recognition books.
ISBN Prefix(es): 1-56244
Number of titles published annually: 4 Print
Total Titles: 4 Print
Membership(s): ALA; EPA

Educational Directories Inc
1025 W Wise Rd, Suite 101, Schaumburg, IL
 60193
Mailing Address: PO Box 68097, Schaumburg, IL
 60168-0097
Tel: 847-891-1250 *Toll Free Tel:* 800-357-6183
 Fax: 847-891-0945
E-mail: info@ediusa.com
Web Site: www.ediusa.com
Key Personnel
Publr: Douglas Moody
Founded: 1903
Reference publications in education.
ISBN Prefix(es): 0-910536
Number of titles published annually: 3 Print
Total Titles: 3 Print; 1 CD-ROM

Educational Impressions Inc
116 Washington Ave, Hawthorne, NJ 07507
Tel: 973-423-4666 *Toll Free Tel:* 800-451-7450
 Fax: 973-423-5569
Web Site: www.edimpressions.com; www.
 awpeller.com
Key Personnel
Pres: Allan W Peller *E-mail:* awpeller@optonline.
 net
Dir, Sales & Mktg: Neil Peller
Founded: 1973
Supplemental textbooks, literature guides.
ISBN Prefix(es): 0-910857; 1-56644
Number of titles published annually: 8 Print
Total Titles: 158 Print
Distributed by Amazon.com; Barnes & Noble;
 Newbridge Communications Inc; Scholastic
 Inc; Scholastic-Tab Publications

Educational Insights Inc
18730 S Wilmington Ave, Suite 100, Rancho
 Dominguez, CA 90220
SAN: 282-762X
Tel: 310-884-2000 *Toll Free Tel:* 800-933-3277
 Fax: 310-884-2015
E-mail: service@edin.com
Web Site: www.educationalinsights.com

Key Personnel
CEO: Reid Calott
Pres & COO: Jim Whitney
Founded: 1962
El-hi instructional materials; teacher's aids, teaching machines & games.
ISBN Prefix(es): 0-88672; 1-56767
Number of titles published annually: 4 Print; 2 Audio
Total Titles: 92 Print
Warehouse: 2206 Oakland Pkwy, Columbia, TN 38401

Educational Technology Publications
700 Palisade Ave, Englewood Cliffs, NJ 07632-0564
SAN: 201-3738
Tel: 201-871-4007 *Toll Free Tel:* 800-952-2665
  Fax: 201-871-4009
E-mail: edtecpubs@aol.com
Web Site: www.bookstoread.com/etp
Key Personnel
Chmn of the Bd, Pres & Ed: Lawrence Lipsitz
Treas: Howard Lipsitz
Dist Mgr & Rts & Perms: Charles Renard
Founded: 1969
Educational, scholarly & scientific publications.
ISBN Prefix(es): 0-87778
Number of titles published annually: 10 Print
Total Titles: 300 Print

Educator's International Press
18 Colleen Rd, Troy, NY 12180
Tel: 518-271-9886 *Fax:* 518-266-9422
Web Site: www.edint.com
Key Personnel
Publr: William Clockel
Founded: 1996
Educational foundations, teacher research, curriculum, special education.
ISBN Prefix(es): 0-9658339; 1-891928
Number of titles published annually: 6 Print
Total Titles: 35 Print

Educators Progress Service Inc
214 Center St, Randolph, WI 53956
SAN: 201-3649
Tel: 920-326-3126 *Toll Free Tel:* 888-951-4469
  Fax: 920-326-3127
E-mail: epsinc@centurytel.net
Key Personnel
Pres: Kathy Nehmer
Secy: Gladys Syens
Founded: 1934
Educator guides to free materials in various subject areas; video.
ISBN Prefix(es): 0-87708
Number of titles published annually: 16 Print
Total Titles: 16 Print

Educators Publishing Service Inc
Subsidiary of Delta Education LLC
625 Mount Auburn St, Cambridge, MA 02139-9031
SAN: 201-8225
Mailing Address: PO Box 9031, Cambridge, MA 02138
Tel: 617-547-6706 *Toll Free Tel:* 800-225-5750
  Fax: 617-547-0412 *Toll Free Fax:* 888-440-2665
E-mail: epsbooks@epsbooks.com
Web Site: www.epsbooks.com
Key Personnel
Pres: Nick Gaedhe
VP Fin: Dave Ciommo
VP, Publg: Charles Heinle
Dir, Mktg: Brewster Maule
Man Ed: Sheila Neylon
Prodn Dir: Robert Seamans
Founded: 1952
Educational materials for grades K-12, with particular emphasis on language arts, remedial

reading skills, materials for the child with specific language disability, workbooks - elementary; workbooks - secondary, learning differences.
ISBN Prefix(es): 0-8388
Number of titles published annually: 20 Print
Total Titles: 800 Print
Branch Office(s)
Educators Publishing Service - Canada, PO Box 333, Sta A, Scarborough, ON M1K 5C1, Canada *Toll Free Tel:* 877-471-8123 *Toll Free Fax:* 877-635-0911

Edupress Inc
208 Avenida Fabricante, Suite 200, San Clemente, CA 92672-7538
Tel: 949-366-9499 *Toll Free Tel:* 800-835-7978
  Fax: 949-366-9441
E-mail: info@edupressinc.com
Web Site: www.edupressinc.com
Key Personnel
Owner & Intl Rts Contact: Linda H Milliken
  Tel: 949-366-1205
Founded: 1979
Publisher of teacher resource materials.
ISBN Prefix(es): 1-56472
Number of titles published annually: 20 Print
Total Titles: 220 Print

Wm B Eerdmans Publishing Co
255 Jefferson Ave SE, Grand Rapids, MI 49503
SAN: 220-0058
Tel: 616-459-4591 *Toll Free Tel:* 800-253-7521
  Fax: 616-459-6540
E-mail: sales@eerdmans.com
Web Site: www.eerdmans.com *Cable:* EERDMANS
Key Personnel
Pres: William B Eerdmans, Jr
VP & Treas: Claire Vander Kam
VP & Ed-in-Chief: Jon Pott
Prodn Mgr, New Books: Klaas Wolterstorff
  E-mail: kwolter@eerdmans.com
Prodn Mgr, Reprints: Deb Danowski
  E-mail: danowski@eerdmans.com
VP, Sales & Mktg: Samuel Eerdmans
  E-mail: see@eerdmans.com
Cust Serv & ISBN Contact: Amy Kent
  E-mail: akent@eerdmans.com
Adv Coord: Janice Myers *E-mail:* jmyers@eerdmans.com
Children's Books Ed: Judy Zylstra
  E-mail: jzylstra@eerdmans.com
VP, Publicity & Promos: Anita Eerdmans
  E-mail: aeerd@eerdmans.com
Publicist: Katharyn Vandermolen
  E-mail: kvmolen@eerdmans.com
Sales Dir: Michael Thomsom
  E-mail: mthomson@eerdmans.com
Founded: 1911
Scholarly religious & religious reference, religion & social concerns, children's books.
ISBN Prefix(es): 0-8028
Number of titles published annually: 130 Print
Imprints: Eerdmans Books for Young Readers
Foreign Rep(s): Alban Books (UK & Europe); Jonathan Ball (South Africa); Christian Literature Crusade (Japan); John Garratt Publishing (Australia); ISPCK, Delhi (India); KCBS (Korea); Kyo Bun Kwan Inc (Japan); Lime Grove House Distributors (New Zealand); Novalis (Canada); Tien Dao (Hong Kong)

Effective Learning Systems
805 Ocean Ave, Point Richmond, CA 94801-3735
Tel: 510-232-8218 *Fax:* 510-965-0134
Key Personnel
Pres: Vincent Kafka *E-mail:* jkvin@silcon.com
Founded: 1975
ISBN Prefix(es): 0-913261
Number of titles published annually: 3 Print
Total Titles: 26 Print

Eisenbrauns Inc
PO Box 275, Winona Lake, IN 46590-0275
SAN: 200-7835
Tel: 574-269-2011 *Fax:* 574-269-6788
E-mail: publisher@eisenbrauns.com
Web Site: www.eisenbrauns.com/
Key Personnel
Pres & Publr: James E Eisenbraun
  E-mail: jeisenbraun@eisenbrauns.com
Ed: Beverly McCoy
Founded: 1975
Educational books, books on the Ancient Near East.
ISBN Prefix(es): 0-931464; 1-57506
Number of titles published annually: 14 Print; 1 CD-ROM
Total Titles: 203 Print; 3 CD-ROM

Elder Books
PO Box 490, Forest Knolls, CA 94933
Tel: 415-488-9002 *Toll Free Tel:* 800-909-2673 (orders) *Fax:* 415-354-3306
E-mail: info@elderbooks.com
Web Site: www.elderbooks.com
Key Personnel
Owner: Carmel Sheridan *E-mail:* carmel@elderbooks.com
Dir: Susan Sullivan
Founded: 1987
Human interest & inspirational, health, aging senior issues, Alzheimers.
ISBN Prefix(es): 0-943873
Number of titles published annually: 5 Print
Total Titles: 22 Print

Elderberry Press LLC
1393 Old Homestead Dr, 2nd fl, Oakland, OR 97462-9506
Tel: 541-459-6043 *Fax:* 541-459-6043
Web Site: www.elderberrypress.com
Key Personnel
Exec Ed: David W St John *E-mail:* editor@elderberrypress.com
Founded: 1997
Services your company providing the subjects & types of books in which you specialize. We work closely with our authors to insure the spirit of their work shines through in the published book.
ISBN Prefix(es): 0-9658407; 1-930859; 1-932762
Number of titles published annually: 24 Print; 1 E-Book
Total Titles: 150 Print; 1 E-Book
Imprints: Poison Vine Books; Red Anvil Press
Distributed by Quality Book Co Inc
Distributor for Poison Vine Books; Red Anvil Press
Foreign Rep(s): Ingram Book Co (Worldwide); D W St John (Worldwide)
Foreign Rights: D W St John (Worldwide)
Distribution Center: Ingram Book Co
Membership(s): Publishers Marketing Association

§The Electrochemical Society Inc
65 S Main St, Pennington, NJ 08534-2839
Tel: 609-737-1902 *Fax:* 609-737-2743
E-mail: ecs@electrochem.org
Web Site: www.electrochem.org
Key Personnel
Pubns Dir & Intl Rts Contact: Mary E Yess
Exec Dir: Roque J Calvo
Founded: 1902
Technical journals, members magazine, proceedings volumes, monographs.
ISBN Prefix(es): 1-56677
Number of titles published annually: 30 Print; 1 CD-ROM; 3 Online
Total Titles: 300 Print; 1 CD-ROM; 3 Online
Distributed by American Institute of Physics (AIP) (journals); John Wiley & Sons (monographs); Marcel Dekker Inc (monographs)

Element Books
Imprint of HarperCollins Publishers
535 Albany St, 5th fl, Boston, MA 02118
Tel: 617-451-8984
Web Site: www.thorsons.com
Key Personnel
VP, Sales & Mktg: Greg Brandenburgh
Tel: 617-247-1745 *Fax:* 617-247-1745
E-mail: gregbrandenburgh@attglobal.net
Founded: 1975
Publisher of mind, body, spirit books.
ISBN Prefix(es): 0-00
Foreign Office(s): HarperCollins Publishers,
77985 Fulham Palace Rd, Hammersmith, London W68JB, United Kingdom *Fax:* 208 307
4788
Distributed by National Book Network
Distribution Center: National Book Network,
15200 NBN Way, Blue Ridge Summit, PA
17214 *Tel:* 717-794-3800 *Fax:* 717-794-3828

Edward Elgar Publishing Inc
136 West St, Suite 202, Northampton, MA 01060
SAN: 299-4615
Tel: 413-584-5551 *Toll Free Tel:* 800-390-3149
(orders) *Fax:* 413-584-9933
Web Site: www.e-elgar.com
Key Personnel
VP & Sales Dir: Rick Henning
E-mail: rhenning@e-elgar.com
Intl Rts: Clare Arnold
Founded: 1986
Books.
ISBN Prefix(es): 1-85898; 1-85278; 1-84064; 1-84376; 1-84542
Number of titles published annually: 200 Print; 1
CD-ROM; 80 E-Book
Total Titles: 2,000 Print; 1 CD-ROM; 100 E-Book
Foreign Office(s): Edward Elgar Publishing Ltd,
Glensanda House, Montpellier Parade, Cheltenham, Glos GL50 1UA, United Kingdom
Tel: (01242) 262111 *E-mail:* info@e-elgar.co.
uk *Web Site:* www.e-elgar.co.uk
Distributor for Financial Executives Research
Foundation Inc
Warehouse: American International Distribution
Corp, PO Box 574, Williston, VT 05495, Contact: Laurie Kenyon *Toll Free Tel:* 800-390-3149 *Fax:* 802-864-7626 *E-mail:* eep.orders@
aidcvt.com

Elite Books
Division of Author's Publishing Cooperative
(APC)
10 Hop Ranch Ct, Santa Rosa, CA 95407
Tel: 707-525-9292 *Fax:* 360-362-3634
Web Site: elitebooks.org
Key Personnel
CEO: Dawson Church *E-mail:* dawson@
authorspublishing.com
Number of titles published annually: 12 Print
Membership(s): Publishers Marketing Association

Elliot's Books
PO Box 6, Northford, CT 06472-0006
Mailing Address: 799 Forest Rd, Northford, CT
06472
Tel: 203-484-2184 *Fax:* 203-484-7644
E-mail: outofprintbooks@mindspring.com
Key Personnel
Publr & Owner: Elliot Ephraim
Founded: 1957
Academic.
ISBN Prefix(es): 0-686; 0-911830
Number of titles published annually: 100 Print
Total Titles: 1,150 Print

Ellora's Cave Publishing Inc
1337 Commerce Dr, Suite 13, Stow, OH 44224
Tel: 330-689-1118
E-mail: service@ellorascave.com

Web Site: www.ellorascave.com
Key Personnel
CEO: Patty Marks
COO: Christina Brashear *E-mail:* crissy@
ellorascave.com
Man Ed: Raelene Gorlinsky
Founded: 2000
Publisher of erotic romances.
ISBN Prefix(es): 1-84360
Number of titles published annually: 20 Print
Total Titles: 60 Print
Distributed by Ingrams

Elsevier
Formerly Mosby
Division of Reed Elsevier Inc
11830 Westline Industrial Dr, St Louis, MO
63146
SAN: 200-2280
Tel: 314-872-8370 *Toll Free Tel:* 800-325-4177
Fax: 314-432-1380
Web Site: www.elsevier.com; www.elsevierhealth.
com *Telex:* 44-2402 *Cable:* MOSBYCO
Key Personnel
CEO: Brian Nairin
CFO: Frank Verhagen
Exec VP, Sales & Mktg: Mary Ging
Exec VP, Journals: Kevin Hurley
Exec VP, Nursing & Health Professions & Edit:
Sally Schrefer
Sr VP, Global Medicine: Fiona Foley
Sr VP, Sales: Toni Linstedt
VP & Dir, Global Book Prodn: Alex Watson
VP, Mktg: John Schrefer
VP, Med Educ & Edit: Linda Belfus
Dir, Edit Servs: Philippe Terheggen
Founded: 1906
ISBN Prefix(es): 0-7506; 0-443; 0-8016; 0-8151;
0-7216; 0-7020; 0-7234; 0-323; 0-7236; 1-4160
Imprints: ASVP; B C Decker; Gower; Jems;
PSG; Wolfe; Year Book
Branch Office(s)
Jems Communications, PO Box 2789, Suite 200,
Carlsbad, CA 92018 *Tel:* 760-431-9797 *Toll
Free Tel:* 800-266-5367 *Fax:* 760-431-8176
360 Park Ave S, New York, NY 10010-1710
Tel: 212-989-5800
4 Penn Ctr, Philadelphia, PA 19106 *Tel:* 215-238-7800 *Fax:* 215-238-7362
Foreign Office(s): 30-52 Smidmore St, Marrckville, NSW 2204, Australia
Beilstein Informationssysteme, Theodor-Heuss-Allee 108, 60486 Frankfurt, Germany
2F Higashi Azabu, One Chome Bldg, 1-9-15 Higashi Azabu, Minato-ku 106-0044, Japan
3 Killiney Rd 08-01, Winsland House I, Singapore 239519, Singapore
Linacre House, Jordan Hill, Oxford 0X2 8DP,
United Kingdom
Distributor for G W Medical Publisher
Foreign Rights: John Scott & Co (Jake Scott)
Shipping Address: PO Box 437, Linn, MO
65051-0437
Distribution Center: Hwy 50 & Hwy CC, Linn,
MO 65051
See separate listing for:
Mosby Journal Division

Elsevier
Formerly Elsevier Science
Subsidiary of Reed Elsevier
200 Wheeler Rd, 6th fl, Burlington, MA 01803
Tel: 781-313-4700 *Toll Free Tel:* 800-545-2522 (cust serv) *Fax:* 781-313-4880
Toll Free Fax: 800-535-9935 (cust serv)
Web Site: www.focalpress.com
Key Personnel
VP, Tech Publg: Jim DeWolf *E-mail:* j.dewolf@
elsevier.com
Founded: 1880
Books for professionals, researchers & students in
the sciences, technology, engineering, business

& media. Also research monographs, major
reference works & serials.
ISBN Prefix(es): 0-240
Number of titles published annually: 1,100 Print;
400 E-Book
Total Titles: 13,000 Print
Branch Office(s)
525 "B" St, Suite 1900, San Diego, CA 92101-4495 *Tel:* 619-231-0926
Foreign Office(s): Linacre House, Jordan Hill,
Oxford OX2 8DP, United Kingdom, Contact:
Neil Warnock-Smith *Tel:* (01865) 314516
Foreign Rep(s): Elsevier; Linacre House, Jordan
Hill (Europe)
Foreign Rights: Elsevier; Linacre House (Europe)
Membership(s): AAP

Elsevier Engineering Information Inc (Ei)
Subsidiary of Elsevier Science Inc
One Castle Point Terr, Hoboken, NJ 07030
Tel: 201-356-6800 *Toll Free Tel:* 800-221-1044
Fax: 201-356-6801
Web Site: www.ei.org *Telex:* 4990438
Key Personnel
Sr VP, Sales & Mktg: Peter Katz *Tel:* 201-356-6800 ext 816
Contact: Ross Graber
Founded: 1884
Technical database, print & electronic publisher
of engineering materials. Engineering Village 2
on the Internet.
ISBN Prefix(es): 0-87394
Number of titles published annually: 4 Print
Total Titles: 17 Print; 4 E-Book

Elsevier Science, see Elsevier

Elsevier Science Inc
Subsidiary of Reed Elsevier US Holdings Inc
360 Park Ave S, New York, NY 10010
Tel: 212-989-5800 *Fax:* 212-633-3965; 212-633-3990
Web Site: www.elsevier.com *Telex:* 42-0643
Cable: ELSEVIER NEW YORK
Key Personnel
Asst to Pres: Hanifa Aziz
Founded: 1962
ISBN Prefix(es): 0-444
Foreign Office(s): Sara Burgerharstr 25, 1055 KV
Amsterdam, Netherlands (headquarters)
Distributor for Pergamon Press
Membership(s): AAP
See separate listing for:
Elsevier Engineering Information Inc (Ei)

§Embiid Publishing
Division of Embiid Inc
600 Fouts St, Upham, ND 58789
E-mail: info@embiid.net; us@embiid.net;
submissions@embiid.net
Web Site: www.embiid.net
Key Personnel
Publr: Richard Michaels *E-mail:* richard@embiid.
net
Exec Ed: Melisa Michaels *E-mail:* melisa@
embiid.net
Founded: 1999
ISBN Prefix(es): 1-58787
Number of titles published annually: 40 E-Book
Total Titles: 84 E-Book
Distributor for Meisha Merlin

§EMC/Paradigm Publishing
Division of EMC Corporation
875 Montreal Way, St Paul, MN 55102
SAN: 201-3800
Tel: 651-290-2800 (corp) *Toll Free Tel:* 800-328-1452 *Fax:* 651-290-2899 *Toll Free Fax:* 800-328-4564
E-mail: educate@emcp.com
Web Site: www.emcp.com *Cable:* EMC

Key Personnel
Chmn & CEO: David E Feinberg *Tel:* 651-215-7600 *Fax:* 651-215-7604
Pres & Treas: Paul Winter *Tel:* 651-215-7601 *Fax:* 651-215-7604
VP, Info Tech: Chuck Bratton *Tel:* 651-215-7611
VP, Intl Rts & Secondary School Publr: Wolfgang Kraft *Tel:* 651-215-7650 *Fax:* 651-215-7601
VP, Sales & Mktg School: Paul Michaelson *Tel:* 651-215-7610 *Fax:* 651-290-2828
VP, Sales & Mktg College: Robert Galvin *Tel:* 651-215-7634
VP, Coll Publr: George Provol *Tel:* 651-215-7669 *Fax:* 651-290-2828
ISBN Contact: Glenndell Larry *Tel:* 651-215-7655 *Fax:* 651-290-2828
Cust Care Mgr: Sandy Duffey *Tel:* 651-215-7550
Founded: 1954
Paper & hardbound textbooks, audio, video, online internet, CD-ROM & microcomputer instructional materials in world language, business education, literature & language arts, medical, IT (information technology).
ISBN Prefix(es): 0-8219; 0-7638
Number of titles published annually: 100 Print; 30 CD-ROM; 10 Online; 80 Audio
Total Titles: 2,400 Print; 150 CD-ROM; 50 Online; 1,035 Audio
Subsidiaries: Paradigm Publishing Inc
Distributor for Sybex Inc
Foreign Rep(s): Wolfgang Kraft (World)
Foreign Rights: Wolfgang Kraft (World)

Emerald Books
Division of The Emerald Book Co
PO Box 635, Lynnwood, WA 98046
Tel: 425-771-1153 *Toll Free Tel:* 800-922-2143 *Fax:* 425-775-2383
E-mail: emeraldbooks@seanet.com
Web Site: www.ywampublishing.com
Key Personnel
Publr: Warren Walsh
Intl Rts: Anna Kim
Ed: Marit Newton
Founded: 1992
Christian theme.
ISBN Prefix(es): 1-883002; 1-932096
Number of titles published annually: 10 Print
Total Titles: 69 Print
Distributed by Ywam Publishing
Shipping Address: 7825 230 St SW, Edmonds, WA 98026 *Web Site:* ywampublishing.com

The Emerson Co
12342 Northup Way, Bellevue, WA 98005
Tel: 425-869-0655 *Fax:* 425-869-0746
Web Site: www.emersoncompany.com
Key Personnel
Pres: James C Emerson *E-mail:* jim.emerson@emersoncompany.com
Founded: 1983
Specialize in publications for accounting profession; newsletters, whitepapers, directories & ad career guides.
ISBN Prefix(es): 0-943945
Number of titles published annually: 7 Print
Total Titles: 19 Print

Emmaus Road Publishing Inc
Division of Catholics United for the Faith
827 N Fourth St, Steubenville, OH 43952
Tel: 740-283-2484 *Toll Free Tel:* 800-398-5470 *Fax:* 740-283-4011
Web Site: www.emmausroad.org
Key Personnel
Ed-in-Chief: Regis J Flaherty
Founded: 1998
Bible studies, biblically based apologetics & other materials faithful to the teaching of the Catholic church.
ISBN Prefix(es): 0-9663223; 1-931018

Number of titles published annually: 8 Print
Total Titles: 24 Print; 10 Audio

§Emmis Books
1700 Madison Rd, 2nd fl, Cincinnati, OH 45206
Tel: 513-861-4045 *Toll Free Tel:* 800-913-9563 *Fax:* 513-861-4430
E-mail: info@emmis.com
Web Site: www.emmisbooks.com
Key Personnel
Pres & Publr: Richard Hunt
Edit Dir: Jack Heffron
Publicity Dir: Howard Cohen
Sales Dir: Katie Parker
Design Dir: Dana Boll
Founded: 1987
Regional publisher; specialize in history of the Midwest & American frontier era.
ISBN Prefix(es): 1-878208; 0-9617367; 1-57860
Number of titles published annually: 36 Print
Total Titles: 240 Print; 7 CD-ROM; 2 E-Book
Imprints: Conner Prairie Press
Subsidiaries: Hawthorne

Empire Press Media/Avant-Guide
Unit of Empire Press Media Inc
444 Madison Ave, 35th fl, New York, NY 10122
Tel: 212-563-1003 *Fax:* 212-536-2419
E-mail: info@avantguide.com; editor@avantguide.com
Web Site: www.avantguide.com
Key Personnel
Ed & Publr: Daniel Levine *E-mail:* dlevine@avantguide.com
CEO: Laurie Turner *E-mail:* lturner@avantguide.com
CFO: Peter Zeligman *E-mail:* pzeligman@avantguide.com
VP, Sales & Mktg: Andre Johnson *E-mail:* ajohnson@avantguide.com
VP, Acqs: Miles M Hewett *E-mail:* mhewett@avantguide.com
VP, Promos: Susan Lewis *E-mail:* slewis@avantguide.com
Founded: 1999
Publishers of Avant-Guide travel books the only comprehensive travel guidebook series for adventurers who are too old for urban backpacking, but too young for hemetically-sealed tour buses. Avant-Guide books detail museums & neighborhoods as well as stylish hotels, chic shops & the best restaurants for every budget.
ISBN Prefix(es): 1-891603
Number of titles published annually: 8 Print; 10 Online; 10 E-Book
Total Titles: 24 Print; 20 Online; 20 E-Book
Imprints: Avant-Guide
Distributed by Publishers Group West
Foreign Rep(s): Hi Marketing (UK, Europe)
Foreign Rights: PGW (Canada)

§Empire Publishing Service
PO Box 1344, Studio City, CA 91614-0344
Tel: 818-784-8918
Key Personnel
Dir, Opers: Joseph W Witt
Intl Rts & Lib Sales Dir: David Cole
Founded: 1970
ISBN Prefix(es): 1-58690
Number of titles published annually: 50 Print
Total Titles: 1,400 Print; 12 Audio
Imprints: Classics With a Twist (world); Gaslight Publications (world); Phantom Publications (world); Spotlight Books (world); Jack Spratt Choral Music (world); University of Miami Music Press (world)
Subsidiaries: Best Books International
Foreign Office(s): EPS/Players Press Combined Trade, 20 Park Dr, Romford, Essex RM1 4LH, United Kingdom
Distributor for Arte Publico Press (world); Dramatic Lines (USA & Canada); Ian Henry Pub-

lications (world); ISH Group (world exc Australia); Picadilly Books (world)
Advertising Agency: Empire Enterprises, PO Box 1132, Studio City, CA 91614

Enchanted Lion Books
115 W 18 St, 6th fl, New York, NY 10011
Tel: 212-675-1959 *Fax:* 212-675-2142
E-mail: enchantedlionbooks@yahoo.com
Key Personnel
Publr: Peter Bedrick
Assoc Publr: Muriel Bedrick
Man Ed: Claudia Bedrick
Sales & Mktg Mgr: Abigail Bedrick
Founded: 2002
Publish illustrated nonfiction for adults & children in the categories of art, biography & history.
ISBN Prefix(es): 1-59270
Number of titles published annually: 20 Print
Total Titles: 30 Print
Distributed by Farrar, Straus & Giroux
Orders to: c/o VHPS, 16365 James Madison Hwy, Gordonsville, VA 22942 *Toll Free Tel:* 888-330-8477 ext 6540 *Toll Free Fax:* 800-672-2054
Returns: Enchanted Lion Books, c/o VHPS, 14301 Litchfield Rd, Orange, VA 22960
Shipping Address: c/o VHPS, 16365 James Madison Hwy, Gordonsville, VA 22942 *Toll Free Tel:* 888-330-8477 ext 6540 *Toll Free Fax:* 800-672-2054
Warehouse: c/o VHPS, 16365 James Madison Hwy, Gordonsville, VA 22942 *Toll Free Tel:* 888-330-8477 ext 6540 *Toll Free Fax:* 800-672-2054
Distribution Center: c/o VHPS, 16365 James Madison Hwy, Gordonsville, VA 22942 *Toll Free Tel:* 888-330-8477 ext 6540 *Toll Free Fax:* 800-672-2054

§Encore Performance Publishing
2181 W California Ave, Suite 250, Salt Lake City, UT 84104
Tel: 801-485-5012 *Fax:* 801-485-4365
E-mail: encoreplay@aol.com
Web Site: www.encoreplay.com
Key Personnel
Pres & Owner: Michael C Perry
VP: Nathan J Criman
Founded: 1979
Play & theatre book publishing; drama for all ages & consulting.
ISBN Prefix(es): 1-57514
Number of titles published annually: 30 Print
Total Titles: 500 Print
Shipping Address: 1718 N 1200 W, Pleasant Grove, UT 84062

Encounter Books
665 Third St, Suite 330, San Francisco, CA 94107-1951
Tel: 415-538-1460 *Toll Free Tel:* 800-786-3839 *Fax:* 415-538-1461 *Toll Free Fax:* 877-811-1461
E-mail: read@encounterbooks.com
Web Site: www.encounterbooks.com
Key Personnel
Publr: Peter Collier *E-mail:* peter@encounterbooks.com
Publicity Dir: Amy Packard *Tel:* 415-538-1486 *E-mail:* amy@encounterbooks.com
Acqs & Prodn Dir: Stephen Wiley *E-mail:* steve@encounterbooks.com
Dir, Opers & Foreign Rts: Judy Hardin *E-mail:* judy@encounterbooks.com
Sales, Cust Serv & Subs Rights: Tuan Nguyen
Founded: 1998
Serious nonfiction books about history, culture, religion, politics, social criticism & public policy.
ISBN Prefix(es): 1-893554; 1-59403

Number of titles published annually: 20 Print; 12 E-Book
Total Titles: 70 Print; 8 E-Book
Foreign Rep(s): Gazelle Book Services Ltd (Europe); Kinokuniya Co Ltd (Japan); Wakefield Press Pty Ltd (South Pacific); Kate Walker & CO Ltd
Returns: PSSC-Returns, 660 S Mansfield, Ypsilanti, MI 48197
Membership(s): ABA; ALA; Publishers Marketing Association

§Encyclopaedia Britannica Inc
310 S Michigan Ave, Chicago, IL 60604
Tel: 312-347-7000 *Toll Free Tel:* 800-323-1229
 Fax: 312-347-7399
E-mail: editor@eb.com
Web Site: www.eb.com; www.britannica.com
Key Personnel
Pres: Jorge Cauz
Exec VP & Gen Counsel: William J Bowe
Sr VP & Ed: Dale Hoiberg
Sr VP, Sales & Mktg: Patti Ginnis
Sr VP, Corp Devt: Michael Ross
VP, Fin: Richard Anderson
VP, Intl Opers: Leah Mansoor
Founded: 1768
Reference works, print & online for consumers & institutions.
ISBN Prefix(es): 0-85229
Subsidiaries: Merriam-Webster Inc
See separate listing for:
Merriam-Webster Inc

Energy Information Administration, EI-30 National Energy Information Center
Dept of Energy, 1000 Independence Ave SW, Washington, DC 20585
Tel: 202-586-8800 *Fax:* 202-586-0727
E-mail: infoctr@eia.doe.gov
Web Site: www.eia.doe.gov
Key Personnel
Dir: John Weiner
Founded: 1977
Periodicals, analytical reports, energy statistics.
Number of titles published annually: 37 Print
Distributed by EPO; NTIS

§Enfield Publishing & Distribution Co
234 May St, Enfield, NH 03748
Mailing Address: PO Box 699, Enfield, NH 03748
Tel: 603-632-7377 *Fax:* 603-632-5611
E-mail: info@enfieldbooks.com
Web Site: www.enfielddistribution.com
Key Personnel
Man Dir: Linda Jones
Founded: 1996
Specialize in fulfillment services.
ISBN Prefix(es): 0-9656184; 1-893598
Number of titles published annually: 3 Print
Total Titles: 11 Print
Distributor for Djoef Publishing; Editions Technip; Faculty Ridge Books; Gadsden Publishing; Glad Day Books; Gold Charm Press; Green Lion Press; Hill Winds Press; Letterland International Ltd; Lightning Up Press; Moose Country Press; Publishing Works; Safe Harbor Books; Science Publisher Inc; Secret Passage Press; Star Festival; Trans Tech Publishing; Vermont Schoolhouse Press; Writers Publishing Co-op

Enslow Publishers Inc
40 Industrial Rd, Berkeley Heights, NJ 07922
SAN: 213-7518
Mailing Address: PO Box 398, Berkeley Heights, NJ 07922
Tel: 908-771-9400 *Toll Free Tel:* 800-398-2504
 Fax: 908-771-0925
Web Site: www.myreportlinks.com; www.enslow.com

Key Personnel
Pres & Mktg: Mark Enslow *E-mail:* marke@enslow.com
VP & Publr: Brian D Enslow *E-mail:* briane@enslow.com
Founded: 1976
Juvenile & young adult.
ISBN Prefix(es): 0-89490; 0-7760
Number of titles published annually: 200 Print
Total Titles: 2,000 Print
Imprints: Finding Out Books; MyReportLinks.com Books
Foreign Office(s): Box 38, Aldershot, Hants GU12 6BP, United Kingdom
Advertising Agency: Crescent Place Advertising, PO Box 605, Short Hills, NJ 07078-0605
Membership(s): Children's Book Council

EntertainmentPro, see Quite Specific Media Group Ltd

Entomological Society of America
9301 Annapolis Rd, Lanham, MD 20706-3115
Tel: 301-731-4535 *Fax:* 301-731-4538
E-mail: pubs@entsoc.org
Web Site: www.entsoc.org
Key Personnel
Dir, Pubns: Alan Kahan *E-mail:* alan@entsoc.org
Mktg & Pub Aff Mgr: Christopher Stelzig
Founded: 1889
Professional scientific society for entomologists. Publish research journals on all areas of entomology.
ISBN Prefix(es): 0-938522
Number of titles published annually: 3 Print; 1 CD-ROM; 5 Online
Total Titles: 55 Print; 1 CD-ROM; 5 Online

Environmental Ethics Books
Division of Center for Environmental Philosophy
1704 W Mulberry St, UNT, EESAT Bldg 370, Denton, TX 76201
Mailing Address: PO Box 310980, Denton, TX 76203-0980
Tel: 940-565-2727 *Toll Free Tel:* 800-264-9962
 Fax: 940-565-4439 *Toll Free Fax:* 800-295-0536
E-mail: ee@unt.edu
Web Site: www.cep.unt.edu
Key Personnel
Exec Dir: Jan Dickson
Ed: Eugene C Hargrove
Founded: 1979
Reprint book publisher of important works in environmental philosophy.
Number of titles published annually: 6 Print
Total Titles: 6 Print

§Environmental Law Institute
1616 "P" St NW, Suite 200, Washington, DC 20036
Tel: 202-939-3800 *Fax:* 202-939-3868
E-mail: law@eli.org
Web Site: www.eli.org
Key Personnel
Chmn: Kenneth Berlin
Pres: Leslie Carothers
Ed, The Environmental Forum: Stephen Dujack
VP, Gen Counsel & Asst Sec to Corp: Erik Meyers
Founded: 1969
Environmental studies, references, loose leaf service, monographs, policy studies.
ISBN Prefix(es): 0-911937
Number of titles published annually: 8 Print
Total Titles: 24 Print; 1 CD-ROM

Epicenter Press Inc
PO Box 82368, Kenmore, WA 98028
Tel: 425-485-6822 *Fax:* 425-481-8253
E-mail: info@epicenterpress.com

Web Site: www.epicenterpress.com
Key Personnel
Pres & Publr: Kent Sturgis *E-mail:* gksturgis@earthlink.net
Ed: Lael Morgan *E-mail:* laelmorgan@cs.com
Founded: 1987
All subjects must relate to Pacific Northwest & Alaska.
ISBN Prefix(es): 0-945397; 0-9708493; 0-9724944
Number of titles published annually: 10 Print
Total Titles: 10 Print; 70 Online; 30 E-Book
Divisions: Aftershocks Media
Branch Office(s)
PO Box 60529, Fairbanks, AK 99706
Distributed by Graphic Arts Center Publishing Co
Foreign Rights: Wales Literary Agency

§Epimetheus Books Inc
2711 Centerville Rd, Suite 120-5336, Wilmington, DE 19808-1643
SAN: 218-5466
Tel: 646-345-2030
E-mail: epimetheus@att.net
Web Site: www.epimetheusbooks.com
Key Personnel
Pres & Rts & Perms: Michael Mathis
Exec Dir: Ajoy Mani
Man Ed: Nancy Emery
Mktg Mgr: Faye Dore
Ed: Cecil Wiggins
Art Dir: Daniel Weir
Prodn Mgr: Marvin Sacks
Intl Rts: Douglas Moore
Founded: 1989
Trade hardcover fiction: horror & gothic, Russian hard rock music.
ISBN Prefix(es): 0-88008
Number of titles published annually: 6 Print; 3 CD-ROM; 4 Online; 3 E-Book
Total Titles: 36 Print; 10 CD-ROM; 8 Online; 10 E-Book
Distributed by Barnes & Noble

Ericson Books
1614 Redbud St, Nacogdoches, TX 75965
Tel: 936-564-3625 *Fax:* 936-552-8999
E-mail: info@ericsonbooks.com
Web Site: www.ericsonbooks.com
Key Personnel
Ed, Publr & Owner: Carolyn Ericson
Exec Asst: Kathryn Davis
Founded: 1975
Genealogical & local history.
ISBN Prefix(es): 0-911317
Number of titles published annually: 7 Print
Total Titles: 40 Print
Distributed by Mountain Press; Byron Sistler
Distributor for Clearfield; Dietz Press; GPC Southern History Press

Lawrence Erlbaum Associates Inc
10 Industrial Ave, Mahwah, NJ 07430-2262
SAN: 213-960X
Tel: 201-236-2199 *Toll Free Tel:* 800-9-BOOKS-9 (926-6579) *Fax:* 201-760-3735
E-mail: orders@erlbaum.com
Web Site: www.erlbaum.com
Key Personnel
Pres: Lawrence Erlbaum
Exec VP: Joseph Petrowski *Tel:* 201-258-2241
 E-mail: jpetrowski@erlbaum.com
Sr VP, Prodn: Arthur M Lizza, Jr
 E-mail: alizza@erlbaum.com
VP, Fin: Margaret Mullane *E-mail:* mmullane@erlbaum.com
VP, Cust Rel: Nancy Seitz
Asst VP, Journal Prodn: Steve Cestaro
Edit Dir: Lane Akers *E-mail:* lakers@erlbaum.com
Rts & Perms & ISBN Contact & Translations: Bonita D'Amil *E-mail:* bdamil@erlbaum.com

Lib Sales Dir: Steve Rutberg *E-mail:* srutberg@
erlbaum.com
Founded: 1974
Undergraduate & graduate textbooks, scholarly
& professional books, journals, software &
videos; monographs, treatises, reference works
in the behavioral sciences, communications,
education & related fields.
ISBN Prefix(es): 0-89859; 0-8058; 0-88163;
1-56321; 1-57004; 0-86377; 1-880393; 0-
9611800; 0-7123
Number of titles published annually: 175 Print;
200 E-Book
Total Titles: 4,000 Print; 1,000 E-Book
Distributor for The Analytic Press; Hermagoras
Press; Lea Software & Alternative Media Inc;
Learning Inc
Foreign Rep(s): DA Information Services (Aus-
tralia, New Zealand); Eurospan (Europe); Login
Bros Canada (Canada); Taylor & Francis Asia
Pacific (Southeast Asia); VIVA (Bangladesh,
India, Sri Lanka)
Warehouse: New Concept Press, 10 Maple
St, Norwood, NJ 07648, Contact: Tom
Vargo *Tel:* 201-784-5398 *Fax:* 201-784-3591
E-mail: tom.vargo@erlbaum.com
See separate listing for:
The Analytic Press

Ernst Publishing Company LLC
Affiliate of Legal Publications LLC
1937 Delaware Tpke, Clarksville, NY 12041
Mailing Address: PO Box 318, Clarksville, NY
12041
Toll Free Tel: 800-345-3822 *Toll Free Fax:* 800-
252-0906
Web Site: www.ernst.cc
Key Personnel
Owner & VP: Alex Ernst *Tel:* 518-768-8192
E-mail: aernst@ernst.cc
Founded: 1992
ISBN Prefix(es): 1-881627
Number of titles published annually: 4 Print; 4
Online
Total Titles: 4 Print; 4 Online
Editorial Office(s): PO Box 250, Clarksville, NY
12041
Sales Office(s): PO Box 250, Clarksville, NY
12041
Billing Address: PO Box 250, Clarksville, NY
12041

Eros Books
463 Barlow Ave, Staten Island, NY 10308
Tel: 718-317-7484
Web Site: www.geocities.com/marynicholaou/
classic_blue.html
Key Personnel
Publr: Mary Nicholaou *E-mail:* marynicholaou@
aol.com
Founded: 1997
Produce postmodern fiction & nonfiction artifacts,
including qualitative literary research; newslet-
ter & magazine; memoirs.
ISBN Prefix(es): 1-890812
Number of titles published annually: 3 Print; 3
Online; 3 E-Book
Total Titles: 18 Print; 10 Online; 9 E-Book
Distributed by Ex Libris
Shipping Address: Ingram, One Ingram Blvd,
LaVergne, TN 37086-3650
Warehouse: Ingram, 201 Ingram Dr, Roseburg,
OR 97470
Ingram, One Ingram Blvd, LaVergne, TN 37086-
3650
Distribution Center: Ingram, One Ingram Blvd,
PO Box 3006, LaVergne, TN 37086, Contact:
Adina Wade *Tel:* 615-793-5000
Membership(s): Publishers Marketing Associa-
tion; Small Publishers Association of North
America

eSchool News
7920 Norfolk Ave, Suite 900, Bethesda, MD
20814
Tel: 301-913-0115 *Toll Free Tel:* 800-394-0115
Fax: 301-913-0119
Web Site: www.eschoolnews.com
Key Personnel
CEO: Robert Morrow *Tel:* 301-913-0115 ext 105
E-mail: rmorrow@eschoolnews.com
Publr: Gregg Downey *Tel:* 301-913-0115 ext 107
E-mail: gdowney@eschoolnews.com
Founded: 1986
Maryland-based publisher of school technology
newspaper, newsletters, directories & online
school technology buyers guide. A respected
publisher of K-20 education technology news
& information. Provides ideas, advice & cre-
ative strategies necessary to help the K-20 pro-
fessional become an expert in school technol-
ogy decision making.
ISBN Prefix(es): 0-9703007
Number of titles published annually: 12 Print
Total Titles: 5 Print
Imprints: eSchool News (newspaper); School
Technology Alert (newletter); School Technology Best Practices (newsletter); School Technology Funding Directory (directory); School
Technology One Book (directory)
Membership(s): Newsletter & Electronic Publish-
ers Association

§Essence of Vermont
860 Panton Rd, Panton, VT 05491
Tel: 802-475-2933 *Fax:* 802-475-2933
E-mail: info@essenceofvermont.com
Web Site: www.essenceofvermont.com
Key Personnel
Publr & Ed: Dennis Jay Hall *E-mail:* dhall@
essenceofvermont.com
Ed & Publicist: Mary Ellen Hall
E-mail: maryellen@essenceofvermont.com
Founded: 1998
Publishers & printers of early American history
including reprints & enlargements of works of
early authors, documents & maps. Primarily
focusing on Lake Champlain - its rich history
& natural beauty, including documentation of
environmental changes & wildlife. Publishers
of The Champ Quest Field Guide & Almanac.
ISBN Prefix(es): 1-928837
Number of titles published annually: 4 Print; 6
CD-ROM; 6 Online
Total Titles: 6 Print; 6 CD-ROM; 3 Online
Distributed by Amazon.com
Distribution Center: Barnes & Noble, 100 Middlesex Blvd, Jamesburg, NJ 08831, Contact:
Amy Milstein *Tel:* 732-355-3083 *Fax:* 732-274-
9703 *E-mail:* amilstein@bn.com
Membership(s): Vermont Historical Society

ETC Publications
700 E Vereda del Sur, Palm Springs, CA 92262
SAN: 201-4637
Tel: 760-325-5332 *Toll Free Tel:* 800-382-7869
Fax: 760-325-8841
E-mail: etcbooks@earthlink.net
Key Personnel
Publr & Sr Ed: Richard W Hostrop *Tel:* 760-325-
5352
Ed & Intl Rts: Leeona Hostrop
Founded: 1972
Nonfiction & informational books.
ISBN Prefix(es): 0-88280
Number of titles published annually: 6 Print
Total Titles: 120 Print; 120 E-Book
Advertising Agency: Communigraphics, Contact:
Lee Selland *Tel:* 760-325-3002 *Fax:* 760-325-
8841

Etruscan Press
PO Box 9685, Silver Spring, MD 20916-9685
Tel: 301-946-6228 *Fax:* 301-946-5838

E-mail: info@etruscanpress.org
Web Site: www.etruscanpress.com
Key Personnel
Man Ed: Cathy Jewell
Founded: 2000
ISBN Prefix(es): 0-9718228; 0-9745995
Number of titles published annually: 4 Print
Total Titles: 9 Print
Distribution Center: Mint Publishers *Tel:* 914-
276-6579
Small Press Distribution *Toll Free Tel:* 800-869-
7553
Membership(s): Council of Literary Magazines
& Presses; Publishers Marketing Association;
Small Press Center

Evan-Moor Educational Publishers
18 Lower Ragsdale Dr, Monterey, CA 93940
Tel: 831-649-5901 *Toll Free Tel:* 800-777-4362
Fax: 831-649-6256
E-mail: customerservice@evan-moor.com
Web Site: www.evan-moor.com
Key Personnel
Pres & Intl Rts: William Evans *E-mail:* bill@
evan-moor.com
Assoc Publr: Joy Evans; Jo Ellen Moore
VP, Oper: John Bell
Dir, Fin Serv: Cristine Bell
Natl Sales Mgr: Paula Hunt
Founded: 1979
Supplemental educational materials for parents &
teachers of children ages 3-11. Subjects include
reading, math, writing, science, social studies,
arts & crafts & literature.
ISBN Prefix(es): 1-55799
Number of titles published annually: 40 Print; 6
CD-ROM; 40 Online; 40 E-Book
Total Titles: 450 Print; 18 CD-ROM; 250 Online;
250 E-Book
Membership(s): ABA; ALA; Association of Ed-
ucational Publishers; National School Supply
Educational Association

Evangel Publishing House
Division of Brethren in Christ Board for Media
Ministries Inc
2000 Evangel Way, Nappanee, IN 46550
SAN: 211-7940
Mailing Address: PO Box 189, Nappanee, IN
46550-0189
Tel: 574-773-3164 *Toll Free Tel:* 800-253-9315
(orders) *Fax:* 574-773-5934
E-mail: sales@evangelpublishing.com
Web Site: www.evangelpublishing.com
Key Personnel
Exec Dir: Roger Williams
Fulfillment Coord: Marlene Slabaugh
Founded: 1929
Religious books to serve The Brethren in Christ
Church & Evangelical academic market. We do
not accept unsol mss.
ISBN Prefix(es): 0-916035; 1-928915; 1-891314
Number of titles published annually: 7 Print; 1
CD-ROM
Total Titles: 216 Print; 1 CD-ROM; 2 Audio
Imprints: Francis Asbury Press; Jordan Publishing
Distributed by Appalachian Dist; Ingram/Spring
Arbor
Distributor for Bethel Publishing
Foreign Rep(s): R G Mitchell Family Books
(Canada)
Returns: 160 N Main St, Nappanee, IN 46550
Toll Free Tel: 800-253-9315 ext 239 *Fax:* 574-
773-5934 *E-mail:* sales@evangelpublishing.
com

M Evans & Co Inc
216 E 49 St, New York, NY 10017
SAN: 203-4050
Tel: 212-688-2810 *Fax:* 212-486-4544
E-mail: editorial@mevans.com
Web Site: www.mevans.com

Key Personnel
Dir, Publicity: Dina Jordan *E-mail:* dina@mevans. com
Assoc Publr: Harry McCullough
Busn Mgr & Sec: Natalie Firestein
Man Ed: Rick Lain Schell
Sr Ed: PJ Dempsey
Assoc Ed &Perms: Matthew Harper
Cust Serv: Rosemarie Paulicelli
Founded: 1963
ISBN Prefix(es): 0-87131; 1-59077
Number of titles published annually: 30 Print
Total Titles: 250 Print
Foreign Rights: Rights Unlimited
Advertising Agency: Spier NY, 460 Park Ave S, New York, NY 10016 *Tel:* 212-679-4441 *Fax:* 212-683-0812
Shipping Address: 15200 NBN Way, Blue Ridge Summit, PA 17214
Distribution Center: National Book Network, 4720 Boston Way, Lanham, MD 20706

Evanston Publishing Inc
4824 Brownsboro Ctr, Louisville, KY 40207
Tel: 502-899-1919 *Toll Free Tel:* 888BOOKS80
Fax: 502-896-0246
E-mail: evanstonpublish@aol.com
Web Site: www.evanstonpublishing.com
Key Personnel
Pres & Sr Ed: Dorothy Kavka
Off Mgr: Sherry Welch
Founded: 1987
Production, prepress & printing for other publishers & individual authors. General trade, especially feminist, how-to, biography, history & poetry, consumer Q & A, consumer/legal guides & parenting.
ISBN Prefix(es): 1-879260
Number of titles published annually: 3 Print
Total Titles: 25 Print
Subsidiaries: Chicago Spectrum Press
Distributor for Chicago Spectrum Press

Evergreen Pacific Publishing Ltd
18002 15 Ave NE, Suite B, Shoreline, WA 98155-3838
Tel: 206-368-8157 *Fax:* 206-368-7968
Web Site: www.evergreenpacific.com
Key Personnel
Pres: Judy Reynolds
VP & CEO: Larry Reynolds *E-mail:* lr@ evergreenpacific.com
Founded: 1996
Books, charts & guides for water-related recreations.
ISBN Prefix(es): 0-945265
Number of titles published annually: 2 Print
Total Titles: 13 Print
Imprints: Evergreen Pacific Publishing

Everyday Wisdom Press
11010 Northup Way, Bellevue, WA 98004
Tel: 425-822-1950; 425-827-7120 *Toll Free Tel:* 866-319-5900 *Fax:* 425-828-9659
E-mail: everydaywisdom@everydaywisdom.net
Web Site: everydaywisdom.net
Key Personnel
Pres: Andy Mayer *Tel:* 425-822-1950 ext 112
Founded: 2002
Publisher of inspirational books.
ISBN Prefix(es): 1-931412; 1-59233
Number of titles published annually: 4 Print
Total Titles: 5 Print

Evolutionary Products
1653 N Magnolia Ave, Tucson, AZ 85712-4103
Tel: 520-323-1190 *Toll Free Tel:* 800-777-4751
E-mail: info@evolutionaryproducts.com
Web Site: www.newagemarket.com
Key Personnel
CEO: Patricia Bush
Founded: 1984

Products for the New Age market; business-to-business directory.
ISBN Prefix(es): 0-944773
Number of titles published annually: 3 Print
Total Titles: 3 Print; 1 CD-ROM; 1 Audio

Excalibur Publications
PO Box 89667, Tucson, AZ 85752-9667
Tel: 520-575-9057 *Fax:* 520-575-9068
E-mail: excalibureditor@earthlink.net
Key Personnel
Ed: Alan M Petrillo *E-mail:* apetrillo@earthlink. net
Founded: 1990
ISBN Prefix(es): 1-880677
Number of titles published annually: 4 Print
Total Titles: 21 Print
Distributed by Amazon.com; Barnes & Noble; Borders Books

Excelsior Cee Publishing
1311 Cherry Stone, Norman, OK 73072
SAN: 200-397X
Mailing Address: PO Box 5861, Norman, OK 73070
Tel: 405-329-3909 *Fax:* 405-329-6886
E-mail: ecp@oecadvantage.net
Web Site: www.excelsiorcee.com
Key Personnel
Publr: J C Marshall
Lib Sales Dir: Lynn Baker
Dist: Forrest Martin
Off Admin: Adrian Ray
Founded: 1989
Books that inspire the reader (non-religious). A full service publishing company.
ISBN Prefix(es): 0-9625557
Number of titles published annually: 12 Print
Total Titles: 14 Print
Distributor for Great Thought Books; Heirloom Lifestories

Helen Exley Giftbooks
Subsidiary of Exley Publications Ltd
185 Main St, Spencer, MA 01562
Toll Free Tel: 877-395-3942 *Toll Free Fax:* 800-807-7363
E-mail: helen.exleygiftbooks@verizon.net
Key Personnel
Pres: Richard Exley
VP, Opers: Nancy Begin *Tel:* 508-885-0200 *E-mail:* nkbegin@aol.com
Founded: 1976
Books for every gift-giving occasion as well as address books, journals & record books.
ISBN Prefix(es): 1-85015; 1-86187
Number of titles published annually: 20 Print
Total Titles: 350 Print
Foreign Office(s): Helen Exley Giftbooks, 16 Chalk Hill, Watford, Herts WD1 4BN, United Kingdom
Foreign Rights: Exley Publications Ltd (UK)
Warehouse: CSSC, 80 Northfield Ave, Edison, NJ 08837

Expert Knowledge System Press, see RTP Publishing Group

Explorers Guide Publishing
4843 Apperson Dr, Rhinelander, WI 54501
Tel: 715-362-6029 *Toll Free Tel:* 800-487-6029
E-mail: comment@explorers-guide.com
Web Site: www.explorers-guide.com
Key Personnel
Publr: Gary Kulibert
Dir, Mktg & Sales: Brenda Kulibert
Founded: 1984
Outdoor related publications.
ISBN Prefix(es): 0-9623430; 1-879432
Number of titles published annually: 14 Print
Total Titles: 14 Print

Eye On Education
6 Depot Way W, Larchmont, NY 10538
Tel: 914-833-0551 *Fax:* 914-833-0761
Web Site: www.eyeoneducation.com
Key Personnel
Pres & Publr: Robert Sickles *E-mail:* sickles@ eyeoneducation.com
Founded: 1992
Professional & reference books for educators.
ISBN Prefix(es): 1-883001; 1-930556
Number of titles published annually: 20 Print
Total Titles: 165 Print

Faber & Faber Inc
Affiliate of Farrar, Straus & Giroux LLC
19 Union Sq W, New York, NY 10003
SAN: 218-7256
Tel: 212-741-6900 *Toll Free Tel:* 888-330-8477 *Fax:* 212-633-9385
Web Site: www.fsgbooks.com/faberandfaber.htm
Key Personnel
VP & Dir, Publicity & Mktg: Jeff Seroy *Tel:* 212-206-5323 *E-mail:* jseroy@fsgbooks.com
Dir: Linda Rosenberg *Tel:* 212-206-5312 *E-mail:* lrosenberg@fsgbooks.com
Sr Ed: Denise Oswald *Tel:* 212-206-5349 *E-mail:* doswald@fsgbooks.com
Sr Publicist: Kim Hilario *Tel:* 212-206-5306 *E-mail:* khilario@fsgbooks.com
Founded: 1976
Nonfiction for adults, plus screenplays & plays; subjects include popular culture.
ISBN Prefix(es): 0-571
Number of titles published annually: 25 Print
Total Titles: 132 Print
Foreign Office(s): Faber & Faber Ltd, 3 Queen Sq, London WC1N 3AU, United Kingdom
Foreign Rep(s): Faber & Faber Ltd (UK); Penguin Books (Australia, Canada)
Foreign Rights: Faber & Faber Inc (UK, USA)
Shipping Address: Von Holtzbrinck Publishing Services, 16365 James Madison Hwy, Gordonsville, VA 22942
Warehouse: Von Holtzbrinck Publishing Services, 16365 James Madison Hwy, Gordonsville, VA 22942

Factor Press
5204 Dove Point Lane, Salisbury, MD 21801
Mailing Address: PO Box 222, Salisbury, MD 21803
Tel: 410-334-6111 *Toll Free Tel:* 888-334-6677 *Fax:* 410-334-6111
E-mail: factorpress@earthlink.net
Key Personnel
Pres: Robert Bahr
Intl Rts Contact & Lib Sales Dir: Allen Metzgar
Founded: 1990
Paperback, hardcover, trade-all types; specialties are Southern short fiction & male sexuality.
ISBN Prefix(es): 0-9626531; 1-887650
Number of titles published annually: 4 Print
Total Titles: 58 Print; 1 Audio
Distributed by Gazelle; Marginal
Foreign Rep(s): Gazelle Book (Europe)
Foreign Rights: Dieter Hagenbach (Europe)
Membership(s): Small Publishers Association of North America

§Facts on File Inc
132 W 31 St, 17th fl, New York, NY 10001
SAN: 201-4696
Tel: 212-967-8800 *Toll Free Tel:* 800-322-8755 *Fax:* 212-967-9196 *Toll Free Fax:* 800-678-3633
E-mail: custserv@factsonfile.com
Web Site: www.factsonfile.com
Key Personnel
Chmn: Mark McDonnell
CFO: Jim Housley
Dir, Publicity: Laurie Katz
Dir, Opers: Mark Zielinski

Creative Dir: Zina Scarpulla
Edit Dir: Laurie Likoff
Sales Dir & Online Sales: Paul Conklin
Trade & Spec Sales Mgr: Claire Lynch
Fulfillment Mgr & Cust Serv: Veronica Williams
Natl Sales Mgr: Coreena Schultz
Prodn Mgr: Rachel Berlin
Founded: 1941
Known for authoratative, award-winning & comprehensive reference material, Facts On File provides curriculum-related print & online reference solutions for schools & libraries. Facts On File recently acquired Ferguson Publishing Co, a leading publisher of career guidance materials.
ISBN Prefix(es): 0-8160; 0-87196; 0-89434
Number of titles published annually: 100 Print; 14 Online
Total Titles: 1,000 Print; 14 Online
Imprints: Checkmark Books (Ferguson Publishing)
Returns: c/o Maple Press Dist Ctr, 704 Legionaire Dr, Fredericksburg, PA 17026
Warehouse: c/o Maple Press Dist Ctr, 704 Legionaire Dr, Fredericksburg, PA 17026
Distribution Center: c/o Maple Press Dist Ctr, 704 Legionaire Dr, Fredericksburg, PA 17026

Fair Winds Press
Imprint of Rockport Publications Inc
33 Commercial St, Gloucester, MA 01930
Tel: 978-282-9590 *Fax:* 978-283-2742
Web Site: www.rockpub.com; www.fairwindspress.com
Key Personnel
Publr: Holly Schmidt *E-mail:* holly@rockpub.com
Founded: 2000
Nonfiction publisher specializing in mind, body & spirit titles. Topics include health, spirituality, self-help, weight loss, fitness, alternative medicine & lifestyle.
Number of titles published annually: 60 Print

Fairchild Books
Division of Fairchild Publications Inc
7 W 34 St, New York, NY 10001
SAN: 201-470X
Tel: 212-630-3880 *Toll Free Tel:* 800-932-4724
Fax: 212-630-3868; 212-630-3898
Web Site: www.fairchildbooks.com *Telex:* 12-5308
Cable: NEWSIDEAS
Key Personnel
Exec Ed: Olga T Kontzias *Tel:* 212-630-3853
E-mail: olga.kontzias@fairchildpub.com
Art Dir: Adam B Bohannon *Tel:* 212-630-3878
E-mail: adam.bohannon@fairchildpub.com
Gen Mgr: Bill Andrulevich *Tel:* 212-630-3899
E-mail: bill.andrulevich@fairchildpub.com
Prodn Mgr: Priscilla L Taguer *Tel:* 212-630-3852
E-mail: priscilla.taguer@fairchildpub.com
Sales Mgr: Dana Berkowitz *Tel:* 212-630-4171
E-mail: dana.berkowitz@fairchildpub.com
Cust Serv Mgr (Returns): Sandra Washington
Tel: 212-630-3885
Founded: 1950
Interior design, fashion, merchandising, marketing, management, retailing, careers market research art foundation, clothing, textiles. Other memberships include International Textiles Apparel Association (ITAA) & American Apparel Footwear Association (AAFA), Interior Design Educators Council (IDEC), International Interior Design Association, Center for Retailing at University of South Carolina.
ISBN Prefix(es): 0-87005; 1-56367
Number of titles published annually: 24 Print; 10 CD-ROM
Total Titles: 200 Print; 10 CD-ROM
Foreign Rep(s): Kim Gilde (Canada); Patricia Grealish (all countries outside of Canada)
Warehouse: Lebanon Distribution Center, Legionaire Dr, Fredericksberg, PA 17026

Fairleigh Dickinson University Press
Affiliate of Associated University Presses
c/o Associated University Presses, 2010 Eastpark Blvd, Cranbury, NJ 08512
Tel: 609-655-4770 *Fax:* 609-655-8366
E-mail: aup440@aol.com
Key Personnel
Ed: Harry Keyishian
Dir, Assoc Univ: Julien Yoseloff
Founded: 1966
ISBN Prefix(es): 0-8386
Number of titles published annually: 40 Print
Total Titles: 1,000 Print
Distributed by Associated University Presses
Foreign Rep(s): Eurospan (Europe & UK); Scholarly Book Services (Canada); United Publishers Services (Japan)

The Fairmont Press Inc
700 Indian Trail, Lilburn, GA 30047
SAN: 207-5946
Tel: 770-925-9388 *Fax:* 770-381-9865
Web Site: www.fairmontpress.com
Key Personnel
Pres: Brian Thumann
VP & Edit Mgr: Linda Hutchings
Adv Mgr: Jackie Kurklis
Circ Mgr: Beth Pearce
Book Fulfillment Coord: Christine Maddox
Founded: 1973
Professional & reference books on energy, safety, environment, how-to & noise control.
ISBN Prefix(es): 0-915586; 0-88173
Number of titles published annually: 15 Print; 7 CD-ROM
Total Titles: 225 Print; 7 CD-ROM; 100 E-Book
Distributed by CRC Press
Foreign Rep(s): CRC Press

Fairview Press
Division of Fairview Health System
2450 Riverside Ave, Minneapolis, MN 55454
Tel: 612-672-4180 *Toll Free Tel:* 800-544-8207
Fax: 612-672-4980
Web Site: www.fairviewpress.org
Key Personnel
Dir: Lane Stiles
Sales & Commun Coord: Joel Meyer
Sr Ed: Stephanie Billecke
Sales & Mktg Mgr: Steve Deger
Founded: 1988
Publishes books in medical, health & patient education; grief & bereavement; aging & end-of-life issues; medicine & nursing.
ISBN Prefix(es): 0-925190; 1-57749
Number of titles published annually: 8 Print
Total Titles: 80 Print
Imprints: Center for Spirituality & Healing; Fairview Publications
Foreign Rights: Susan Shulman

Faith & Fellowship Press
Subsidiary of Church of the Lutheran Brethren
1020 Alcott Ave W, Fergus Falls, MN 56537
Mailing Address: PO Box 655, Fergus Falls, MN 56538-0655
Tel: 218-736-7357 *Toll Free Tel:* 800-332-9232
Fax: 218-736-2200
E-mail: ffpress@clba.org
Web Site: www.faithandfellowship.org
Key Personnel
Exec Dir: Brent Juliot
Religious books, newsletters.
ISBN Prefix(es): 0-943167
Total Titles: 5 Print

Faith & Life Resources
Division of Mennonite Publishing Network
616 Walnut Ave, Scottdale, PA 15683-1999
Tel: 724-887-8500 *Toll Free Tel:* 800-245-7894
Fax: 724-887-3111
E-mail: info@mph.org

Web Site: www.mph.org
Key Personnel
Dir, Faith & Life Resources: Eleanor Snyder
Founded: 1878
Small denominational publisher specializing in the production of innovative Christian education resources for children, youth, young adults, adults & intergenerational groups. Topics of interest include materials on peace & justice, evangelism, Christian service & radical Christian discipleship.
ISBN Prefix(es): 0-87303; 0-8361; 2-5008
Branch Office(s)
490 Dutton Dr, Unit C-8, Waterloo, ON N2L 6H7, Canada *Tel:* 519-888-7512 *Fax:* 519-888-7506 *Web Site:* www.mph.org
Distributed by Herald Press

Faith Library Publications
Subsidiary of RHEMA Bible Church
1025 W Kenosha St, Broken Arrow, OK 74012
Mailing Address: PO Box 50126, Tulsa, OK 74150-0126
Tel: 918-258-1588 (ext 2218) *Toll Free Tel:* 888-258-0999 (orders only) *Fax:* 918-251-8016 (orders)
Web Site: www.rhema.org
Key Personnel
Mktg Dir: Don Burns *Tel:* 918-258-1588 ext 2253
E-mail: flp@rhema.org
Founded: 1963
ISBN Prefix(es): 0-89276
Number of titles published annually: 4 Print
Total Titles: 145 Print; 115 Audio
Distributed by Appalachian; Harrison House; Spring Arbor; Whitaker

FaithWalk Publishing
333 Jackson St, Grand Haven, MI 49417
Tel: 616-846-9360 *Toll Free Tel:* 800-335-7177
Fax: 616-846-0072
E-mail: customerservice@faithwalkpub.com
Web Site: www.faithwalkpub.com
Key Personnel
Publr: Dirk Wierenga *E-mail:* dirk@faithwalkpub.com
Acctg: Mark Verstraete
Prodn Mgr: Virginia McFadden *E-mail:* gin@faithwalkerpub.com
Sr Ed: Louann Werksma *E-mail:* lnw@iserv.net
Founded: 2002
ISBN Prefix(es): 0-9724196; 1-932902
Number of titles published annually: 8 Print
Total Titles: 13 Print
Warehouse: Du-All Packaging, 14260 172 Ave, Grand Haven, MI 49417 *Tel:* 616-850-0613 *Fax:* 616-850-9102
Distribution Center: Du-All Packaging, 14260 172 Ave, Grand Haven, MI 49417 *Tel:* 616-850-0613 *Fax:* 616-850-9102
Membership(s): Publishers Marketing Association

Falk Art Reference
Formerly Sound View Press
61 Beekman Place, Madison, CT 06443
SAN: 686-5240
Mailing Address: PO Box 833, Madison, CT 06443-0833
Tel: 203-245-2246
Web Site: www.falkart.com
Key Personnel
Ed-in-Chief: Peter H Falk *Tel:* 203-245-4761
Founded: 1985
Art reference books.
ISBN Prefix(es): 0-932087
Total Titles: 23 Print

§Family Process Institute Inc
Division of Family Process Inc
c/o Eldredge, Fox & Porretti, 180 Canal View Blvd, Suite 100, Rochester, NY 14623
Tel: 716-879-4900 (ext 153) *Fax:* 212-744-0206

E-mail: info@familyprocess.org
Web Site: www.familyprocess.org
Key Personnel
Pres: Beatrice Wood
Ed: Evan Imber-Black
Founded: 1961
Psychology, journals.
ISBN Prefix(es): 0-9615519
Total Titles: 3 Print; 1 CD-ROM; 1 Online

Fantagraphics Books
7563 Lake City Way NE, Seattle, WA 98115
Mailing Address: PO Box 25070, Seattle, WA 98125
Tel: 206-524-1967 *Toll Free Tel:* 800-657-1100
Fax: 206-524-2104
E-mail: ffbicomix@fantagraphics.com
Web Site: www.fantagraphics.com
Key Personnel
Pres: Gary Groth
VP & Intl Rts Contact: Kim Thompson
Promo Dir: Eric Reynolds
Lib Sales Dir: Greg Zura
Founded: 1976
Comics, comic-related magazines, comic related trade paperbacks & hardcovers.
ISBN Prefix(es): 0-930193; 1-56097
Number of titles published annually: 50 Print
Total Titles: 300 Print
Imprints: Eros Comix
Shipping Address: 3667 First Ave S, Seattle, WA 98134

W D Farmer Residence Designer Inc
2007 Montreal Rd, Tucker, GA 30084
Mailing Address: PO Box 450025, Atlanta, GA 31145
Tel: 770-934-7380 *Toll Free Tel:* 800-225-7526; 800-221-7526 (GA) *Fax:* 770-934-1700
E-mail: wdfarmer@wdfarmerplans.com
Web Site: www.wdfarmerplans.com; www. homeplansbyfarmer.com
Key Personnel
Pres & Intl Rts Contact: W D Farmer
Sec & Treas: Annette C Farmer
Asst Sec/Treas & Lib Sales Dir: Vickie F Starkey
Founded: 1961
Residential designer.
ISBN Prefix(es): 0-931518
Number of titles published annually: 3 Print
Total Titles: 15 Print

Farrar, Straus & Giroux Books for Young Readers
19 Union Sq W, New York, NY 10003
Tel: 212-741-6900 *Fax:* 212-633-2427
E-mail: childrens.marketing@fsgbooks.com; childrens.editorial@fsgbooks.com
Web Site: www.fsgkidsbooks.com
Key Personnel
Sr VP & Co-Publr: Margaret Ferguson
Sr VP, Gen Mgr & Co-Publr: Michael Eisenberg
VP & Publr, Frances Foster Books: Frances Foster
Publr, Melanie Kroupa Books: Melanie Kroupa
Dir, Mktg: Jeanne T McDermott
Subs Rts Dir: Maria L Kjoller
Art Dir: Robbin Gourley
Founded: 1946
Preschool through young adult fiction & nonfiction, hardcover & paperback.
Number of titles published annually: 100 Print
Total Titles: 550 Print
Imprints: Aerial Fiction; Frances Foster Books; Melanie Kroupa Books; Mirasol; Sunburst Paperbacks
Membership(s): Children's Book Council

Farrar, Straus & Giroux, LLC
19 Union Sq W, New York, NY 10003
SAN: 206-782X
Tel: 212-741-6900 *Fax:* 212-741-6973

Web Site: www.fsgbooks.com
Key Personnel
Pres & Publr: Jonathan Galassi
Sr VP & CFO: Philip Zweiger
Sr VP, Mktg & Publicity: Jeff Seroy
Sr VP, Sales Dir: Spencer Lee
Exec VP, Opers: Joy Isenberg *Tel:* 212-206-5334
    E-mail: jisenberg@fsgee.com
Exec VP & Ed-in-Chief: John Glusman
VP & Assoc Publr: Linda Rosenberg
VP, Subs Rts: Michael Hathaway
VP, Cont, Rts & Perms: Erika Seidman
Dir, Intl Rts: Kendra Poster
Dir, Publicity: Liz Calamari *Tel:* 212-206-5323
Adv Dir: Victoria Genna
VP & Prodn Dir: Tom Consiglio
Design Dir: Abby Kagan
VP & Art Dir: Susan Mitchell
Copy Chief: Debra Helfand
Founded: 1946
General fiction, nonfiction, poetry & juveniles.
Number of titles published annually: 75 Print
Total Titles: 1,150 Print
Imprints: Faber & Faber; Farrar, Straus & Giroux Books for Young Readers; MIRASOL Libros Juveniles; North Point Press; Sunburst Books
Divisions: Hill & Wang
Distributor for Aperture; Enchanted Lion; Greywolf; R & S Books
Foreign Rep(s): Douglas & McIntyre Ltd (Canada); Pan Macmillan Ltd (UK)
Foreign Rights: Agence Hoffman (Germany); Agence Michelle Lapautre (France); Graal Ltd (Poland); Harris/Elon Agency (Israel); International Editors Co (Latin America, Spain); Katai & Bolza (Hungary); KCC (Korea); Leonhardt & Hier (Scandinavia); Kristin Olson (Czech Republic); Tuttle-Mori Agency (Japan); Van Gelderen Agency (Holland); Agenzia Susanna Zevi (Italy)
Advertising Agency: Bennett Book Advertising
Warehouse: Von Holtzbrinck Publishing Services, 16365 James Madison Highway, Gordonsville, VA 22942 *Tel:* 212-741-6900 *Toll Free Tel:* 888-330-8477 *Fax:* 212-633-9385
Membership(s): Children's Book Council
See separate listing for:
Faber & Faber Inc
Hill & Wang
North Point Press

Father & Son Publishing
Affiliate of Father & Son Associates Inc
4909 N Monroe St, Tallahassee, FL 32303
Tel: 850-562-3927 *Toll Free Tel:* 800-741-2712 (orders only) *Fax:* 850-562-0916
Web Site: www.fatherson.com
Key Personnel
Pres: Lance Coalson *Tel:* 850-562-0907
    E-mail: lance@fatherson.com
Founded: 1982
Publishers of nonfiction, cookbooks, giftbooks & humor titles.
ISBN Prefix(es): 0-942407
Number of titles published annually: 12 Print; 2 CD-ROM; 2 Audio
Total Titles: 65 Print; 2 CD-ROM; 9 Audio
Distributor for BADM Books
Warehouse: 100 Salem Rd, Havana, FL 32333
Membership(s): ABA; Florida Publishers Association; National Association of Independent Publishers

FC&A Publishing
103 Clover Green, Peachtree City, GA 30269
Tel: 770-487-6307 *Toll Free Tel:* 800-537-1275
    Fax: 770-631-4357
E-mail: customer_service@fca.com
Web Site: www.fca.com
Key Personnel
Mktg Assoc: Savannah Rogers *Tel:* 770-487-6307 ext 2323 *E-mail:* savannah_rogers@fca.com
Founded: 1969

ISBN Prefix(es): 0-915099; 1-890957; 1-932470
Number of titles published annually: 21 Print
Total Titles: 21 Print; 21 Online
Distributed by NBN

§Federal Bar Association
2215 "M" St NW, Washington, DC 20037
Tel: 202-785-1614 *Fax:* 202-785-1568
E-mail: fba@fedbar.org
Web Site: www.fedbar.org
Key Personnel
Exec Dir: Jack D Lockridge
Man Ed: Stacy Bernstein *E-mail:* sbernstein@fedbar.org
Founded: 1920
Publishes course materials, newsletters & The Federal Lawyer Magazine.
ISBN Prefix(es): 1-56986
Number of titles published annually: 15 Print; 1 CD-ROM
Total Titles: 350 Print; 1 CD-ROM; 2 Audio

Federal Buyers Guide Inc
718-B State St, Santa Barbara, CA 93101
Tel: 805-963-7470 *Fax:* 805-963-7478
Web Site: www.gov-world.com
Key Personnel
CEO: Stuart Miller
Sales Mgr: David Minor
Founded: 1985
Directories & reference books.
Total Titles: 4 Print

Federal Street Press
Division of Merriam-Webster Inc
2513 Old Kings Hwy N, Darien, CT 06820
Tel: 203-852-1280 *Fax:* 203-852-1389
Key Personnel
Publr: Deborah Hastings *E-mail:* dhastings@federalstreetpress.com
Founded: 1998
Branch Office(s)
c/o Merriam-Webster Inc, PO Box 281, Springfield, MA 01102 *Tel:* 413-734-3134

FedEx Trade Networks
Division of FedEx Corp
220 Montgomery St, Suite 448, San Francisco, CA 94104-3410
Tel: 415-391-7501 *Toll Free Tel:* 800-556-9334
    Fax: 415-391-7537 (Fax/Modem)
E-mail: info@worldtariff.com
Web Site: www.worldtariff.com
Key Personnel
Publr: Scott Morse
Acct Exec & Contact: Ray Brown
Founded: 1961
Publish customs duty & tax information.
ISBN Prefix(es): 1-56745
Number of titles published annually: 100 Print
Total Titles: 22 Online
Foreign Office(s): Eurotariff, National House, 60-66 Wardour St, 6th fl, London W1V 3HP, United Kingdom

Philipp Feldheim Inc
200 Airport Executive Park, Nanuet, NY 10954
SAN: 207-0545
Tel: 845-356-2282 *Toll Free Tel:* 800-237-7149
    Fax: 845-425-1908
E-mail: sales@feldheim.com
Web Site: www.feldheim.com
Key Personnel
Pres: Yitzchak Feldheim
Sales Mgr: Eli Hollander
Founded: 1954
Translations from Hebrew of Jewish classical works & works of contemporary authors in the field of Orthodox Jewish thought & contemporary Jewish literature for ages three & up.
ISBN Prefix(es): 0-87306; 1-58330

Number of titles published annually: 50 Print
Total Titles: 800 Print
Imprints: Feldheim Publishers
Foreign Office(s): Feldheim Publishers Ltd, Box 35002, Jerusalem 91064, Israel
Distributor for Am Yisroel Chai Press; Targum Press
Foreign Rep(s): Feldheim Publishers Ltd; J Lehmann (UK)

The Feminist Press at The City University of New York
365 Fifth Ave, Suite 5406, New York, NY 10016
SAN: 213-6813
Tel: 212-817-7926 *Fax:* 212-817-1593
Web Site: www.feministpress.org
Key Personnel
Publr: Jean Casella *Tel:* 212-817-7918
    E-mail: jcasella@gc.cuny.edu
Edit Dir: Livia Tenzer *Tel:* 212-817-7927
    E-mail: ltenzer@gc.cuny.edu
Assoc Ed: Stacy Malyil *E-mail:* smalyil@gc.cuny.edu
Founded: 1970
African studies, international studies, history of feminism, women's studies, working class studies & women's literature from the Middle East & Africa & US women writers.
ISBN Prefix(es): 0-912670; 0-935312; 1-55861
Number of titles published annually: 20 Print
Total Titles: 220 Print
Imprints: Contemporary Classics by Women; Cross-Cultural Memoir Series; Helen Rose Scheuer Jewish Women's Series; Women Changing the World Series; Women Writers of the Middle East; Women Writing Africa Series; The Women's Stories Project; Women's Studies Quarterly
Foreign Rights: Jean Casella (All other territories); Lora Fountain (France); Japan UNI (Japan); Joanna Kabat-Hyzak (Poland); Robesta Oliva (Italy); Shelley Power (UK, Commonwealth, Netherlands); Helene Rande (France); Anna Soler-Pont (Latin America, Portugal, Spain); Silke Weniger (Germany)
Shipping Address: Consortium Book Sales & Distribution Inc, 1045 Westgate Dr, St Paul, MN 55114 *Toll Free Tel:* 800-283-3572 *Fax:* 651-221-0124
Membership(s): AAP

Feral House
PO Box 39910, Los Angeles, CA 90039
Tel: 323-666-3311 *Fax:* 323-666-3330
E-mail: info@feralhouse.com
Web Site: www.feralhouse.com
Key Personnel
Pres: Adam Parfrey *E-mail:* ap@feralhouse.com
Man Ed: Laura Guerrero
Founded: 1988
Pop culture, alternative, art, humor, nonfiction, religion, sociology & social sciences.
ISBN Prefix(es): 0-922915; 1-932595
Number of titles published annually: 10 Print
Total Titles: 66 Print
Foreign Office(s): c/o Turnaround Distribution, London, United Kingdom *Tel:* (020) 8829-3000
Distribution Center: Publishers Group West, 1700 Fourth St, Berkeley, CA 94710 *Toll Free Tel:* 800-788-3123

Ferguson Publishing Co, see Standard Educational Corp

Howard Fertig Inc, Publisher
80 E 11 St, New York, NY 10003
SAN: 201-4777
Tel: 212-982-7922 *Fax:* 212-982-1099
Key Personnel
Pres & Ed-in-Chief: Howard Fertig
Founded: 1966

Scholarly reprints & originals in history, literature & social sciences.
ISBN Prefix(es): 0-86527
Number of titles published annually: 12 Print
Total Titles: 150 Print

Fiction Collective Two Inc
Florida State University, FC2, Dept of English, Tallahassee, FL 32306-1580
Tel: 850-644-2260 *Fax:* 850-644-6808
E-mail: fc2@english.fsu.edu
Web Site: fc2.org
Key Personnel
Publr: R M Berry
Man Ed: Brenda Mills
Chmn of Bd: Lance Olsen
Bd of Dir: Ronald Sukenick
Founded: 1974
A not-for-profit publisher of formally innovative fiction.
ISBN Prefix(es): 1-57366
Number of titles published annually: 8 Print
Total Titles: 150 Print
Imprints: Black Ice Books
Distributed by Northwestern University Press
Foreign Rights: Macintosh & Otish
Orders to: Northwestern University Press, Chicago Distribution Ctr, 110360 S Langley Ave, Chicago, IL 60628 *Toll Free Tel:* 800-621-2736 *Toll Free Fax:* 800-621-8476
Returns: Northwestern University Press, Chicago Distribution Ctr, 110360 S Langley Ave, Chicago, IL 60628
Membership(s): Council of Literary Magazines & Presses

The Figures
5 Castle Hill, Great Barrington, MA 01230
Tel: 413-528-2552
Web Site: www.geoffreyyoung.com
Key Personnel
Publr & Ed: Geoffrey Young
    E-mail: younggeoffrey@hotmail.com
Founded: 1975
Well designed, inexpensive trade books, perfect-bound.
ISBN Prefix(es): 0-935724; 1-930589
Number of titles published annually: 4 Print
Total Titles: 125 Print
Distribution Center: Small Press Distribution, 1341 Seventh St, Berkeley, CA 94710-1409
    Toll Free Tel: 800-869-7553 *Fax:* 510-524-0852

Film-Video Publications/Circus Source Publications
7944 Capistrano Ave, West Hills, CA 91304
SAN: 211-1527
Tel: 818-340-0175 *Fax:* 818-340-6770
E-mail: circussource@aol.com
Key Personnel
Pres, Publr & Intl Rts Contact: Alan Gadney
    Tel: 818-340-6620
VP & Exec Ed: Carolyn Porter
Ed: Mary M Gadney
Founded: 1974
Reference books, directories & audio/video cassettes on film, video, photography, TV/radio broadcasting, writing, theater, business & finance, sports, circus, clowning, juggling, performing arts.
ISBN Prefix(es): 0-930828
Number of titles published annually: 20 Print; 10 Audio
Total Titles: 24 Print; 14 Audio
Foreign Rep(s): Australia & New Zealand Book Co (Australia); Fitzhenry & Whiteside (Canada); Reed Methuen Publishers (New Zealand)
Advertising Agency: Carolyn Chadwick Advertising
Membership(s): Book Publicists of Southern California; Publishers Marketing Association

Filter Press LLC
PO Box 95, Palmer Lake, CO 80133
SAN: 201-484X
Tel: 719-481-2420 *Toll Free Tel:* 888-570-2663
    Fax: 719-481-2420
E-mail: filter.press@prodigy.net
Web Site: filterpressbooks.com
Key Personnel
Pres: Doris Baker
Founded: 1956
American West or Western expansion movement, Colorado history.
ISBN Prefix(es): 0-910584; 0-86541
Number of titles published annually: 5 Print
Total Titles: 35 Print
Returns: 19980 Top O'Moor W, Monument, CO 80132
Shipping Address: 19980 Top O'Moor W, Monument, CO 80132
Membership(s): Colorado Independent Publishers Association; Publishers Marketing Association

Financial Executives Research Foundation Inc
Affiliate of Financial Executives Institute
200 Campus Dr, Florham Park, NJ 07932
Tel: 973-765-1000 *Fax:* 973-765-1023
Web Site: www.ferf.org
Key Personnel
Mgr Fin Servs: Lorna Raagas
Founded: 1944
Executive reports & full-length monographs of research related to financial topics.
ISBN Prefix(es): 1-885065
Number of titles published annually: 20 Print
Total Titles: 50 Print

Financial Times/Prentice Hall
Imprint of Prentice Hall PTR
One Lake St, Upper Saddle River, NJ 07458
Tel: 201-236-7000 *Toll Free Tel:* 800-922-0579 (orders)
Web Site: www.phptr.com
Key Personnel
VP & Exec Ed: Tim Moore *E-mail:* tim_moore@prenhall.com
Exec Ed: Jim Boyd *E-mail:* jim_boyd@prenhall.com
Publisher of business, management, investment & finance books for professionals & students.
ISBN Prefix(es): 0-13
Foreign Office(s): 128 Long Acre, London WC2E 9AN, United Kingdom *Tel:* (020) 7447 2000 *Fax:* (020) 7240 5771
Orders to: 200 Old Tappan Rd, Old Tappan, NJ 07675

Fine Communications
Division of Fine Creative Media Inc
322 Eighth Ave, 15th fl, New York, NY 10001
Tel: 212-595-3500 *Fax:* 212-595-3779
Key Personnel
Pres & Publr: Michael J Fine *E-mail:* mjf@mjfbooks.com
VP: Kaethe Fine
VP, Prodn: Stanley Last
Dir, Acqs: Roslyn Siegel
Sr Prodn Mgr: Mark Jordan
Dir, Contracts & Acqs Assoc: Scott Messina
Ed: Jeffrey Broesche
Acqs Ed: Marlene Rosen-Fine
Cons Ed: George Stade
Prodn Ed: Kerriebeth Mello
Systems: Anton Fine
Edit Res: Jason Baker
Founded: 1991
Publish hardcover & paperback reprints of fiction & nonfiction; develop & produce Barnes & Noble Classics.
ISBN Prefix(es): 1-56731; 1-59308
Number of titles published annually: 200 Print
Total Titles: 750 Print
Imprints: MJF BOOKS

FineEdge.com
14004 Biz Point Lane, Anacortes, WA 98221
Tel: 360-299-8500 *Fax:* 360-299-0535
Web Site: www.fineedge.com
Key Personnel
Pres: Mark Bunzel
Ed-in-Chief: Reanne Douglass
Founded: 1986
Publishing, wholesaling, outdoor guidebooks &
 maps; specializing in nautical books & moun-
 tain bicycling.
ISBN Prefix(es): 0-938665; 1-932310
Number of titles published annually: 6 Print
Total Titles: 50 Print; 1 CD-ROM; 2 Online
Imprints: Mountain Biking Press/FineEdge.com
Distributed by Heritage House; Sunbelt Publica-
 tions Inc
Foreign Rep(s): David's Marine (New Zealand)
Advertising Agency: Haage Design, 44 Glen Ave,
 Oakland, CA 94661, Contact: Melanie Haage
Membership(s): Pacific Northwest Booksellers
 Association; Publishers Marketing Association

Fire Engineering Books & Videos
Division of PennWell Publishing
1421 S Sheridan Rd, Tulsa, OK 74112
Mailing Address: PO Box 21288, Tulsa, OK
 74121-9971
Toll Free Tel: 800-752-9768 *Fax:* 918-831-9555
E-mail: sales@penwell.com
Web Site: www.fireengineeringbooks.com
Key Personnel
Dir: Paul Westervelt
Founded: 1877
Fire science, suppression & protection, hazardous
 materials books, videos & magazine.
ISBN Prefix(es): 1-57340; 0-912212; 0-87814
Number of titles published annually: 10 Print
Total Titles: 120 Print; 2 CD-ROM
Distributed by David Publishing; Fire Protection
 Publications
Distributor for Brady; IDEA Bank; IFSTA;
 Mosby
Foreign Rep(s): American Technical Publishers
 Ltd (Europe); Ish Dawar (India); Arturo Gutier-
 rez Hernandez (Central America, Mexico);
 Christoper Humphries (Spain); Berj Jamkojian
 (Middle East); JN Publishers Representative
 (Scandinavia); Terry Roberts (South America)

Fireside & Touchstone
Imprint of Simon & Schuster Adult Publishing
 Group
1230 Avenue of the Americas, New York, NY
 10020
Key Personnel
Exec VP & Publr: Mark Gompertz
VP & Publr, S&S Libros en Espanol & Dep
 Publr: Christine Lloreda
VP & Ed-in-Chief: Trish Todd
VP & Publicity Dir: Marcia Burch
VP & Dir, Subs Rts: Marcella Berger
Art Dir: Cherylynne Li
Asst Dir, Subs Rts: Marie Florio
Sr Ed: Nancy Hancock; Doris Cooper; Cherise
 Grant
Ed: Amanda Patten
ISBN Prefix(es): 0-684
Number of titles published annually: 75 Print
Imprints: Fireside; Libros en Espanol; Touchstone

First Avenue Editions
Imprint of Lerner Publishing Group
241 First Ave N, Minneapolis, MN 55401
Tel: 612-332-3344 *Toll Free Tel:* 800-328-4929
 Fax: 612-332-7615 *Toll Free Fax:* 800-332-
 1132
E-mail: info@lernerbooks.com
Web Site: www.lernerbooks.com
Key Personnel
Chmn & CEO: Harry J Lerner
Pres & Publr: Adam Lerner

VP & CFO: Margaret Wunderlich
VP & Ed-in-Chief: Mary Rodgers
VP, LernerClassroom: Gary Tinney
VP, Prodn: Gary Hansen
VP, Sales & Mktg: David Wexler
Art Dir: Zach Marell
Mktg Dir: Beth Heiss
Dir, Contracts, Perms & Author Rel: Almena
 Dees
Dir, HR: Cyndi Radant
Subs Rts: Tim Schwarz
Social studies, picture story books, art, multicul-
 tural issues, activity books & beginning read-
 ers.
ISBN Prefix(es): 0-87614; 0-8225; 1-57505
Number of titles published annually: 200 Print
Total Titles: 1,500 Print
Foreign Rep(s): INT Press Distribution (Aus-
 tralia); Monarch Books of Canada (Canada/
 Trade); Phambili (Southern Africa); Pub-
 lishers Marketing Services (Singapore &
 Malaysia); Saunders Book Co (Canada/Edu-
 cation); Turnaround (UK)
Foreign Rights: Bardon Chinese Media Agency
 (Taiwan); Japan Foreign-Rights Centre (Japan);
 Korea Copyright Center (Korea); Michelle La-
 pautre Agence Junior (France); Literarische
 Agentur Silke Weniger (Germany); Tao Media
 International (People's Republic of China)
Warehouse: 1251 Washington Ave N, Minneapo-
 lis, MN 55401

1st Books Library, see AuthorHouse

The Fisherman Library
1622 Beaver Dam Rd, Point Pleasant, NJ 08742
Tel: 732-295-8600 *Fax:* 732-295-4162
Key Personnel
Assoc Publr: Pete Barrett
Ed: Linda Barrett
Founded: 1983
Publish & produce *The Fisherman Library* series
 of educational fishing books.
ISBN Prefix(es): 0-923155
Number of titles published annually: 4 Print
Total Titles: 16 Print

Five Star Publications Inc
4696 W Tyson St, Dept LM, Chandler, AZ 85226
Tel: 480-940-8182 *Fax:* 480-940-8787
E-mail: info@fivestarpublications.com
Web Site: www.fivestarpublications.com; www.
 authorsandexperts.com; www.youcanpublish.
 com; www.schoolbookings.com
Key Personnel
Pres & Publg Consultant: Linda F Radke
 E-mail: radke@fivestarsupport.com
Project Mgr: Sue De Fabis
Founded: 1985
Children's books & textbooks.
ISBN Prefix(es): 0-9619853; 1-877749; 1-58985
Number of titles published annually: 12 Print
Total Titles: 36 Print; 12 E-Book
Distributor for Dine College Press
Advertising Agency: Publishers Support Services
Membership(s): National Federation of Press
 Women; Publishers Marketing Association;
 Religion Writers Organization

FJH Music Co Inc
2525 Davie Rd, Suite 360, Fort Lauderdale, FL
 33317
Tel: 954-382-6061 *Toll Free Tel:* 800-262-8744
 Fax: 954-382-3073
E-mail: custserv@fjhmusic.com
Web Site: www.fjhmusic.com
Key Personnel
Owner & Pres: Frank Hackinson
VP: Kyle Hackinson
Educational music publications.
Number of titles published annually: 100 Print

Florida Academic Press
Division of FAP Books
PO Box 540, Gainesville, FL 32602-0540
SAN: 299-3643
Tel: 352-332-5104 *Fax:* 352-331-6003
E-mail: fapress@worldnet.att.net
Key Personnel
Publr & Intl Rts: Max Vargas
Man Ed: Sam Decalo
Asst Ed: Florence Dusek
Founded: 1997
ISBN Prefix(es): 1-890357
Number of titles published annually: 4 Print
Total Titles: 12 Print
Distributor for Worsley Press

Florida Funding Publications Inc
Subsidiary of John L Adams & Co Inc
PO Box 561565, Miami, FL 33256
Tel: 305-251-2203 *Fax:* 305-251-2773
E-mail: info@floridafunding.com
Web Site: www.floridafunding.com
Key Personnel
Sales & Dist: Mariha Oliveira
Founded: 1985
Grant & funding reference materials.
ISBN Prefix(es): 1-879543
Number of titles published annually: 3 Print; 1
 CD-ROM; 1 Online
Total Titles: 1 CD-ROM; 1 Online

Flower Valley Press Inc
7851-C Beechcraft Rd, Gaithersburg, MA 20809
Tel: 301-654-1996 *Toll Free Tel:* 800-735-5197
Web Site: www.flowervalleypress.com
Founded: 1987
Crafts, art & nonfiction books, games & hobbies.
ISBN Prefix(es): 0-9623468; 1-886388; 0-
 9620543
Number of titles published annually: 3 Print
Total Titles: 21 Print

Flying Frog Publishing
Division of Allied Publishing Group
107 Nob Hill Park Dr, Reistertown, MD 21136
Tel: 410-833-6261 *Fax:* 410-833-6193
E-mail: allied@allpubmd.com
Key Personnel
Pres: Robert Webster
Founded: 1993
Picture books, novelty, religious, nonfiction.
ISBN Prefix(es): 1-884628
Number of titles published annually: 50 Print
Total Titles: 200 Print

Focus on the Family
8605 Explorer Dr, Colorado Springs, CO 80920
Tel: 719-531-3400 *Fax:* 719-531-3484
Web Site: www.family.org
Key Personnel
VP: Kurt Bruner
VP, Mktg: Paul McCusker
Dir, Liscensing: Shari Martin *E-mail:* martinsh@
 fotf.org
Intl Rts: Larry Weeden
Founded: 1986
Casebound & soft cover (adult & children) deal-
 ing with family relationships & emphasizing
 the importance of values & Christian principles
 in people's lives.
ISBN Prefix(es): 0-929608; 1-56179; 1-58997
Number of titles published annually: 60 Print
Total Titles: 200 Print; 4 CD-ROM; 60 Audio
Imprints: Adventures in Odyssey; Brio Girls; Fo-
 cus on the Family; Heritage Builders; Life on
 the Edge; Radio Theatre; Renewing the Heart;
 Ribbits; That the World May Know
Distributed by Baker Books; Cook Communica-
 tions; Harvest House; Moody Press; Tommy
 Nelson; Standard Publishing Co; Tyndale
 House Publishers; Zondervan
Foreign Rights: Bruce Peppin; Worldwide

Focus Publishing/R Pullins Co Inc
Subsidiary of R Pullins Co
311 Merrimac St, Newburyport, MA 01950
Mailing Address: PO Box 369, Newburyport, MA
01950
Tel: 978-462-7288 (edit) *Toll Free Tel:* 800-848-
7236 (orders) *Fax:* 978-462-9035 (orders)
E-mail: pullins@pullins.com
Web Site: www.pullins.com
Key Personnel
Pres & Intl Rts Contact: Ron Pullins
Cust Serv: Kerri Stewart
Founded: 1987
Classical & modern languages.
ISBN Prefix(es): 0-941051; 1-58510
Number of titles published annually: 30 Print; 1
CD-ROM; 2 Audio
Total Titles: 108 Print; 1 CD-ROM; 2 Audio
Imprints: Focus Classical Library; Focus on Per-
formance; Focus Philosophical Library
Distributed by The Peoples Publishing Group
Distributor for Domus Latina Publishing
Foreign Rep(s): Gazelle Book Services (UK, Eu-
ropean Union)
Returns: PSSC, 231 Industrial Park, 46 Develop-
ment Rd, Fitchburg, MA 01420
Shipping Address: PSSC, 231 Industrial Park, 46
Development Rd, Fitchburg, MA 01420
Warehouse: PSSC, 231 Industrial Park, 46 De-
velopment Rd, Fitchburg, MA 01420 *Toll Free
Tel:* 800-848-7236
Distribution Center: PSSC, 231 Industrial Park,
46 Development Rd, Fitchburg, MA 01420
Membership(s): AAP

Fodor's Travel Publications
Division of Random House Inc
1745 Broadway, New York, NY 10019
SAN: 204-1073
Tel: 212-572-8784 *Toll Free Tel:* 800-733-3000
Fax: 212-572-2248
Web Site: www.fodors.com
Key Personnel
Pres: David Naggar
VP & Publr: Timothy Jarrell
VP, Exec Man Ed & Dir, Database: Denise De-
Gennaro
VP, Creative Dir: Fabrizio LaRocca
VP & Gen Mgr, Fodors.com: Brent Peich
Dir, Mktg: Christine Gillespie
Dir, Busn Opers: Katie Ziga
Dir, Subs/Foreign Rts: Linda Kaplan *Tel:* 212-
572-2060 *E-mail:* lkaplan@randomhouse.com
Dir, Prodn: Nina Frieman
Edit Prodn Mgr: Linda Schmidt
Sr Publicist: Erika Kestenbaum
Sr Mgr, Edit Database: Janet Foley
Sr Map Ed: Robert Blake
Sr Ed: Linda Cabasin; Paul Eisenberg; Laura Kid-
der; Chris Swiac
Founded: 1936
Travel guides, foreign & domestic
Random House Inc & its publishing entities are
not accepting unsol submissions, proposals,
mss, or submission queries via e-mail at this
time.
ISBN Prefix(es): 0-679; 0-676; 1-4000
Total Titles: 440 Print; 4 CD-ROM; 26 E-Book; 4
Audio
Imprints: Fodor's; Compass American Guides
Branch Office(s)
2775 Matheson Blvd E, Mississauga, ON L4W
4P7, Canada
Foreign Office(s): 20 Vauxhall Bridge Rd, London
SWIV 2SA, United Kingdom
Distributed by Baedeker's Guides; Karen Brown
Guides
Distributor for Baedeker's Guides; Karen Brown
Guides
Warehouse: Random House, 400 Hahn Rd, West-
minster, MD 21157

FOG Publications
413 Pennsylvania NE, Albuquerque, NM 87108
SAN: 659-4484
Tel: 505-255-3096
Key Personnel
Owner & Pres: Florencio Oscar Garcia
E-mail: foscarg@unm.edu
Founded: 1986
ISBN Prefix(es): 0-9616535; 0-929928
Number of titles published annually: 4 Print
Total Titles: 23 Print

Fondo de Cultura Economica USA Inc
Subsidiary of Fondo de Cultura Economica (Mex-
ico)
2293 Verus St, San Diego, CA 92154
Tel: 619-429-0455 *Toll Free Tel:* 800-532-3872
Fax: 619-429-0827
E-mail: sales@fceusa.com
Web Site: www.fceusa.com
Key Personnel
Pres & CEO: Ignacio De Echevarria
E-mail: iechevarrio@fceusa.com
Founded: 1934 (Founded in Mexico & in the
USA in 1990)
Distribution of Spanish language children or
scholarly books.
ISBN Prefix(es): 968-16
Number of titles published annually: 500 Print; 5
Audio
Total Titles: 5,500 Print; 2 CD-ROM; 15 Audio
Distributed by Arroyo Books; Bilingual Publica-
tions Co; Books on Wings; Booksource; Con-
tinental Book Co; Girol Books Inc; Hispanic
Books Distributors; Mariuccia Iaconi Book
Imports; Ideal Foreign Books; Latin Trading
Corp; Lectorum Publications Inc; Libreria Mar-
tinez; Libros Sin Fronteras; Los Andes Publish-
ing
Membership(s): ABA; ALA; Children's Literature
Association

Fons Vitae
49 Mockingbird Valley Dr, Louisville, KY 40207-
1366
Tel: 502-897-3641 *Fax:* 502-893-7373
E-mail: fonsvitaeky@aol.com
Web Site: www.fonsvitae.com
Key Personnel
Dir: Gray Henry
Founded: 1997
Fons Vitae is both an academic charity with
501c(3) charitable status, & a refereed publish-
ing house which ensures the highest scholarly
standards for its publications. Authentic text,
impeccably translated & exquisitely produced,
make these volumes useful for both the uni-
versity classroom & for those interested in the
eternal verities with no compromise to a recent
soft focus on spirituality.
ISBN Prefix(es): 1-887752
Number of titles published annually: 10 Print; 1
CD-ROM
Total Titles: 56 Print; 1 CD-ROM
Distributor for Archetype (UK); The Foundation
for Traditional Studies (US); Golganooza (UK);
Islamic Texts Society (UK); Pir Press (NY);
Quilliam Press (UK); Quinta Essentia (UK);
Tradigital (Germany); Turab (Jordan); World
Wisdom (US)
Foreign Rep(s): Airlift (UK); American Univer-
sity Cairo Press (AUC) (Middle East)
Distribution Center: Independent Publishers
Group (IPG)

Food & Nutrition Press Inc (FNP)
6527 Main St, Trumbull, CT 06611
SAN: 221-1475
Mailing Address: PO Box 374, Trumbull, CT
06611
Tel: 203-261-8587 *Fax:* 203-261-9724
E-mail: foodpress@worldnet.att.net

Web Site: www.foodscipress.com
Key Personnel
Pres & Intl Rts Contact: John J O'Neil
Ed, Rts & Perms & Prodn Mgr: Kathryn O Ziko
Cust Serv: Lillian M O'Neil
Electronic Publg: Virginia B Ramirez
Founded: 1976
College textbooks & reference books in food sci-
ence & nutrition & related fields.
ISBN Prefix(es): 0-917678
Number of titles published annually: 5 Print
Total Titles: 40 Print
Imprints: FNP Military Division
Distributor for Academic Press
Shipping Address: Publishers Storage & Shipping
Corp, 231 Industrial Park, 46 Development Rd,
Fitchburg, MA 01420-8215 *Tel:* 978-345-2121
Fax: 978-348-1233
Warehouse: Publishers Storage & Shipping Corp,
231 Industrial Park, 46 Development Rd, Fitch-
burg, MA 01420-8215 *Tel:* 978-345-2121
Fax: 978-348-1233

Fordham University Press
2546 Belmont Ave, Bronx, NY 10458-5172
SAN: 201-6516
Mailing Address: University Box L, Bronx, NY
10458
Tel: 718-817-4780 *Toll Free Tel:* 800-247-6553
(orders) *Fax:* 718-817-4785
Web Site: www.fordhampress.com
Key Personnel
Dir: Robert Oppedisano *E-mail:* roppedisano@
fordham.edu
Mktg Mgr: Kate O' Brien *E-mail:* bkaobrien@
fordham.edu
Off Mgr & ISBN Contact: Margaret Noonan
E-mail: mnoonan@fordham.edu
Prodn Ed: Loomis Mayer
Sales & Intl Rts: Jacqueline Philpotts
E-mail: philpotts@fordham.edu
Founded: 1907
Scholarly books & journals, New York regional
books & general trade books & videos.
ISBN Prefix(es): 0-8232; 0-912882
Number of titles published annually: 50 Print
Total Titles: 400 Print
Imprints: Rose Hill Books
Distributor for Alephoe Books/The Poetry Mis-
sion; Creighton University Press; IASTA Press;
Little Room Press; M & M Maschietto & Di-
tore; The Reconstructionist Press; Rockhurst
University Press; St Bede's; St Louis Univer-
sity Press; Sleepy Hollow Press; Something
More Publications; University of San Fran-
cisco; YMCA of Greater New York
Foreign Rep(s): Cranbury International (India,
Latin America, South America); East-West Ex-
port Books (Asia, Pacific); Eurospan (Africa,
Europe, Middle East); Scholarly Book Services
(Canada)
Warehouse: Fordham University Press, c/o Book-
masters, 30 Amberwood Pkwy, Ashland, OH
44805 *Toll Free Tel:* 800-247-6553 *Fax:* 419-
281-6883
Distribution Center: Fordham University Press,
c/o Bookmasters, 30 Amberwood Pkwy, Ash-
land, OH 44805 *Toll Free Tel:* 800-247-6553
Fax: 419-281-6883
Membership(s): AAP; Association of American
University Presses; Association of Jesuit University Presses

Forest House Publishing Co Inc & HTS Books
PO Box 13350, Chandler, AZ 85248
Tel: 480-802-1955 *Toll Free Tel:* 800-394-READ
(394-7323) *Fax:* 480-802-1957
E-mail: info@forest-house.com
Web Site: www.forest-house.com
Key Personnel
Pres, Owner & Publr: Dianne L Spahr
Pres & Publr: Roy Spahr
Founded: 1989

Pre K-6th grade children's library-bound books.
ISBN Prefix(es): 1-878363; 1-56674
Number of titles published annually: 25 Print
Total Titles: 400 Print
Imprints: Forest House®; HTS Books™
Editorial Office(s): 17719 Palm Ave, Casa Grande, AZ
Sales Office(s): 17719 Palm Ave, Casa Grande, AZ
Distributor for ARO Publishing
Foreign Rep(s): Standard House (Indonesia, Malaysia, Philippines, Thailand)
Foreign Rights: Theo Philips (England)
Warehouse: 17719 Palm Ave, Casa Grande, AZ

Fort Ross Inc
26 Arthur Place, Yonkers, NY 10701
Tel: 914-375-6448 *Fax:* 914-375-6439
E-mail: fort.ross@verizon.net
Web Site: www.fortross.net
Key Personnel
Pres & Exec Dir: Vladimir Kartsev
Founded: 1992
Books in Russian. Russia-related books in English, co-publishing of books of American authors in Russia.
ISBN Prefix(es): 1-57480
Number of titles published annually: 5 Print
Total Titles: 34 Print
Divisions: Fort Ross Inc International Rights; Fort Ross Inc Russian-American Publishing Projects; Fort Ross International Representation for Artists
Distributed by Hippocrene Books Inc
Distributor for MIR (Russia); Yuridicheskaya Literatura (Russia)
Foreign Rep(s): Konstantin Paltchikov (Baltic States, Belarus, Eastern Europe, Russia, Ukraine)
Foreign Rights: Olga Borodyanskaya (Russia); Svetlana Kolmanovskaya (Russia)

Fortress Press, see Augsburg Fortress Publishers, Publishing House of the Evangelical Lutheran Church in America

Forum Press Inc, see Harlan Davidson Inc/Forum Press Inc

§Forum Publishing Co
383 E Main St, Centerport, NY 11721
Tel: 631-754-5000 *Fax:* 631-754-0630
Web Site: www.forumbooks.com
Key Personnel
CEO & Publr: Martin Stevens
Founded: 1981
Business magazines & books.
ISBN Prefix(es): 0-9626141
Number of titles published annually: 3 Print
Total Titles: 15 Print; 6 CD-ROM

Forward Movement Publications
300 W Fourth St, Cincinnati, OH 45202
Tel: 513-721-6659 *Toll Free Tel:* 800-543-1813
Fax: 513-721-0729
E-mail: orders@forwarddaybyday.com
Web Site: www.forwardmovement.org
Key Personnel
Dir & Ed: Edward S Gleason
Busn Mgr: D Jane Paraskevopoulos
Asst Ed: George Allen
Founded: 1934
Founded to help reinvigorate the life of the Episcopal church.
ISBN Prefix(es): 0-88028
Number of titles published annually: 4 Print
Total Titles: 125 Print; 1 Audio
Imprints: FMP
Distributor for Anglican Book Centre
Warehouse: 10001 Alliance Rd, Cincinnati, OH 45242

Walter Foster Publishing Inc
Member of The Quarto Group Inc
23062 La Cadena Dr, Laguna Hills, CA 92653
SAN: 249-051X
Tel: 949-380-7510 *Toll Free Tel:* 800-426-0099
Fax: 949-380-7575
Web Site: www.walterfoster.com
Key Personnel
Pres & CEO: Ross Sarracino
Cont: Mark O'Halloran
Sales Mgr: Nancy Lee
Assoc Publr: Sydney Jae Sprague
Project Ed: Jenna Winterberg *E-mail:* jenna@walterfoster.com
Founded: 1922
Instructional art books, specialty art & creative products.
ISBN Prefix(es): 0-929261; 1-56010
Number of titles published annually: 50 Print
Total Titles: 275 Print
Imprints: My Chaotic Life
Foreign Rep(s): Apple Press
See separate listing for:
My Chaotic Life™

§The Foundation Center
79 Fifth Ave, New York, NY 10003-3076
SAN: 207-5687
Tel: 212-807-3690 *Toll Free Tel:* 800-424-9836
Fax: 212-807-3691
Web Site: www.fdncenter.org
Key Personnel
Pres: Sara L Engelhardt
Mktg Mgr: Beverly McGrath
Founded: 1956
Reference books on US foundations, corporations & their grant-making activities & books about philanthropy & nonprofit management.
Total Titles: 60 Print

The Foundation for Economic Education Inc
30 S Broadway, Irvington-on-Hudson, NY 10533
Tel: 914-591-7230 *Toll Free Tel:* 800-960-4FEE (960-4333) *Fax:* 914-591-8910
E-mail: fee@fee.org
Web Site: www.fee.org
Key Personnel
Man Ed: Beth Hoffman
Founded: 1946
"The Freedom" magazine, also economics/personal freedom books.
ISBN Prefix(es): 1-57246; 0-910614
Number of titles published annually: 4 Print
Total Titles: 87 Print

Foundation Press Inc
Division of Thompson Co
395 Hudson St, New York, NY 10014
SAN: 281-7225
Tel: 212-367-6790 *Fax:* 212-367-6799
Web Site: www.foundation-press.com
Key Personnel
Publr: Steve Errick
Mktg Mgr: Charles Taibi
Founded: 1931
Law, business, political science, criminal justice, curriculum books, graduate & undergraduate primarily in law.
ISBN Prefix(es): 0-88277; 1-56662; 1-58778
Number of titles published annually: 120 Print
Total Titles: 500 Print
Warehouse: Eagan Distribution Center, 525 Wescott Rd, Eagan, MN 55123

Foundation Publications
PO Box 6439, Anaheim, CA 92816
Tel: 714-879-2286 *Toll Free Tel:* 800-257-6272
Fax: 714-535-2164
E-mail: info@foundationpublications.com
Web Site: www.foundationpublications.com

Key Personnel
VP, Opers: Pike Lambeth *E-mail:* pike@foundationpublications.com
Founded: 1971
Publish New American Standard Bible & La Biblia de Las Americas.
ISBN Prefix(es): 0-910618; 1-58135; 1-885217
Number of titles published annually: 20 Print
Total Titles: 120 Print; 3 CD-ROM
Membership(s): Evangelical Christian Publishers Association; SEPA

The Fountain
Imprint of The Light Inc
26 Worlds Fair Dr, Unit C, Somerset, NJ 08873
Tel: 732-808-0210 *Fax:* 732-808-0211
E-mail: contact@fountainmagazine.com
Web Site: www.fountainmagazine.com
Number of titles published annually: 6 Print
Total Titles: 14 Print

Four Paws Press LLC
2460 Garden Rd, Suite B, Monterey, CA 93940
Tel: 831-375-PAWS (375-7297) *Fax:* 831-649-8007
Web Site: www.fourpawspress.com
Key Personnel
Man Memb: Hugo N Gerstl *E-mail:* hugo@fourpawspress.com
Ed-in-Chief: Colleen M Flores *E-mail:* colleen@fourpawspress.com
Natl Sales Mgr: Kristi Padley *E-mail:* kdpadley@hotmail.com
Founded: 2001
Paperbound books, primarily pet travel guides.
ISBN Prefix(es): 1-883214; 1-888820; 0-971008
Number of titles published annually: 3 Print
Total Titles: 8 Print
Sales Office(s): 69 Georgetown Dr, Nashua, NH 03062, Contact: Kristi Padley *Tel:* 603-888-9669
Billing Address: Weatherhill Inc, 411 Monroe Tpke, Trumbull, CT 06611 *Tel:* 203-452-6794
Returns: Weatherhill Inc, 411 Monroe Tpke, Trumbull, CT 06611 *Tel:* 203-452-6794
Distribution Center: Weatherhill Inc, 411 Monroe Tpke, Trumbull, CT 06611 *Tel:* 203-452-6794

Four Walls Eight Windows
Subsidiary of Avalon Publishing Group
245 W 17 St, 11th fl, New York, NY 10011
Tel: 646-375-2570 *Fax:* 646-375-2571
Web Site: www.4w8w.com
Key Personnel
Publr: John Oakes
Founded: 1987
ISBN Prefix(es): 0-941423; 1-56858
Total Titles: 230 Print
Imprints: No Exit Press
Foreign Rep(s): PGW (Canada); Tower Books Ltd (Australia); Turnaround Distribution (Europe)
Foreign Rights: Agence Lenclud (France); Susijn Agency (UK); Writers House (All other territories)
Orders to: Publishers Group West, 1700 Fourth St, Berkeley, CA 94710
Distribution Center: Publishers Group West, 1700 Fourth St, Berkeley, CA 94710 *Toll Free Tel:* 800-788-3123 *Fax:* 510-528-9555

Fox Chapel Publishing Co Inc
1970 Broad St, East Petersburg, PA 17520
Tel: 717-560-4703 *Toll Free Tel:* 800-457-9112
Fax: 717-560-4702
E-mail: custservice@foxchapelpublishing.com
Web Site: www.foxchapelpublishing.com
Key Personnel
Pres & Intl Rts Contact: Alan Giagnocavo *E-mail:* alan@carvingworld.com
Prodn: Jon Deck
Founded: 1991

Books & magazines for woodworkers, wood-carvers & other hobby enthusiast.
ISBN Prefix(es): 1-56523
Number of titles published annually: 25 Print
Total Titles: 175 Print
Imprints: Scroll Saw Workshop Magazine; Wood-carvers Favorite Pattern Series; Woodcarving Illustrated Magazine
Distributor for Reader's Digest; Taunton Sterling Dover

Fox Song Books
2315 Glendale Blvd, Unit B, Los Angeles, CA 90039
SAN: 255-593X
Mailing Address: 8721 Santa Monica Blvd, Suite 619, Los Angeles, CA 90069-4507
Toll Free Tel: 888-369-2769 *Toll Free Fax:* 888-309-5063
E-mail: fox@foxsongbooks.com
Web Site: foxsongbooks.com
Key Personnel
Publr: Vincent Richardson *E-mail:* vincent@foxsongbooks.com; Faith Richardson *E-mail:* faith@foxsongbooks.com
Founded: 2002
Publish quality young adult & children's titles.
ISBN Prefix(es): 0-9744989
Number of titles published annually: 5 Print; 1 Online; 5 E-Book
Total Titles: 5 Print; 1 Online
Membership(s): Children's Literature Council of Southern California; Publishers Marketing Association

FPMI Solutions Inc
4901 University Sq, Suite 3, Huntsville, AL 35816
Tel: 256-539-1850 *Fax:* 256-539-0911
E-mail: books@fpmi.com
Web Site: www.fpmisolutions.com
Key Personnel
Pres: Joe Swerdzewski
Deputy Dir, Communs: Anna Ray *Tel:* 256-539-1839 ext 119 *E-mail:* aray@fpmi.com
Founded: 1985
Government publications.
ISBN Prefix(es): 0-936295; 1-930542
Number of titles published annually: 30 Print
Total Titles: 30 Print

Franciscan Press
Subsidiary of Quincy University
1800 College Ave, Quincy, IL 62301-2699
SAN: 201-6621
Tel: 217-228-5670 *Fax:* 217-228-5672
Web Site: www.franciscanpress.com
Key Personnel
Dir: Ben Cooper
Founded: 1991
Popular & scholarly books on Franciscanism, St Francis of Assisi, medieval philosophy & theology.
ISBN Prefix(es): 0-8199
Number of titles published annually: 10 Print
Imprints: Forum Books; Franciscan Press Books; Herald Books

Franklin, Beedle & Associates Inc
8536 SW St Helens Dr, Suite D, Wilsonville, OR 97070
Tel: 503-682-7668 *Toll Free Tel:* 800-322-2665
Fax: 503-682-7638
Web Site: www.fbeedle.com
Key Personnel
Pres, Intl Rts Contact & Rts Perms: James F Leisy, Jr *E-mail:* jimleisy@fbeedle.com
Prodn Ed: Tom Sumner
Founded: 1985
College textbooks in computer science, information systems & computers in education, educational software, computer engineering, computer information systems, information technology.
ISBN Prefix(es): 0-938661; 1-887902
Number of titles published annually: 10 Print; 5 E-Book
Total Titles: 50 Print; 5 E-Book
Imprints: William, James & Co (humanities publisher)
Foreign Rep(s): Transatlantic Publishers (Middle East, UK & Europe); Woodslane (Australia & New Zealand, Fiji, Papua New Guinea, Solomon Islands)
Membership(s): ACM

Franklin Book Co Inc
7804 Montgomery Ave, Elkins Park, PA 19027
SAN: 121-4160
Tel: 215-635-5252 *Fax:* 215-635-6155
E-mail: service@franklinbook.com
Web Site: www.franklinbook.com
Key Personnel
Pres: Manny Deckter
Founded: 1969
Reprinting, book distributor; all subjects.
ISBN Prefix(es): 0-08
Number of titles published annually: 20 Print
Total Titles: 1,758 Print

Franklin Watts, see Scholastic Library Publishing

Fraser Publishing Co
PO Box 217, Flint Hill, VA 22627
SAN: 213-9537
Tel: 540-675-9976 *Toll Free Tel:* 877-996-3336
Fax: 786-513-2807
E-mail: info@fraserpublishing.com
Web Site: www.fraserpublishing.com
Key Personnel
Mgr: Mark Shepardson
Founded: 1969
Contrary Opinion Books Publisher & Out-of-Print Books Dealer, specializing in reprinting out-of-print investment books.
ISBN Prefix(es): 0-87034
Number of titles published annually: 3 Print
Total Titles: 100 Print

Frederick Fell Publishers Inc
2131 Hollywood Blvd, Suite 305, Hollywood, FL 33020
SAN: 208-2365
Tel: 954-925-5242 *Toll Free Tel:* 800-771-FELL (771-3355) *Fax:* 954-925-5244
E-mail: info@fellpub.com
Web Site: www.fellpub.com
Key Personnel
Publr, Pres & Rts & Perms: Donald L Lessne *E-mail:* donlessne@aol.com
Ed-in-Chief: Barbara Newman
Founded: 1943
An award-winning publisher of general trade books. The series we publish include the Know-it-All Guides, the Top 100 series & Heroes & Heroines series & So You Want To Be series.
ISBN Prefix(es): 0-8119; 0-88391
Number of titles published annually: 24 Print; 2 CD-ROM
Total Titles: 150 Print; 2 CD-ROM; 2 Audio
Distributed by Kensington Publishing Corp
Foreign Rep(s): Book Representation & Distribution Ltd (Europe & UK)
Foreign Rights: Agencia Literaria (Brazil, Portugal); Big Apple Tuttle-Mori Agency (China, Taiwan); Book Publishers Association of Israel (Israel); Bookman (Denmark, Finland, Iceland, Norway & Sweden); Julio F-Yanez Agencia Literaria (Mexico, Spain & Latin America); Hagenbach & Bender GmbH-Literary & Media Agency (Germany); Imprima Korea Agency (Korea); International Copyright Agency Ltd (Romania); Japan UNI Agency (Japan); JS Literary & Media Agency (Thailand); Nurcihan Kesim Literary Agency (Turkey); Living Literary Agency (Italy); La Nouvelle Agency (Belgium, Canada, France, Switzerland); Andrew Nurnberg Associates (Baltic States); Andrew Nurnberg Associates Prague (Czech Republic); Andrew Nurnberg Associates Sofia (Bulgaria); Andrew Nurnberg Associates Warsaw (Poland); Andrew Nurnberg Literary Agency (Russia); OA Literary Agency (Greece); Owl's Agency Inc (Japan); Prava & Prevodi Literary Agency (Croatia & Slovenia, Serbia and Montenegro, Albania); RT Copyright Ltd (Hungary); Shin Won Literary Agency (Korea); Tuttle-Mori Agency Inc (Japan)

Free Press
Imprint of Simon & Schuster Adult Publishing Group
1230 Avenue of the Americas, New York, NY 10020
Tel: 212-698-7000 *Toll Free Tel:* 800-223-2345 (cust serv); 800-223-2336 (orders); 888-866-6631 (fulfillment)
Key Personnel
Exec VP & Publr: Martha K Levin
VP & Assoc Publr: Suzanne Donahue
VP & Edit Dir: Dominick V Anfuso
VP & Sr Ed: Fred W Hills; Leslie Meredith; Bruce Nichols
VP & Dir, Publicity: Carisa Hays
VP & Dir Mktg: Sue Fleming
Mgr, Trade Mktg: Bryan Christian
Dir, Subs Rts: Paul O'Halloran
Subs Rts Mgr: Bob Niegowski
Art Dir: Eric Fuentecilla
Prodn Dir: Olga Leonardo
Sr Ed: Amy Scheibe; Elizabeth Stein; Martin Beiser
Number of titles published annually: 85 Print

§Free Spirit Publishing Inc
217 Fifth Ave N, Suite 200, Minneapolis, MN 55401-1299
Tel: 612-338-2068 *Toll Free Tel:* 800-735-7323
Fax: 612-337-5050
E-mail: help4kids@freespirit.com
Web Site: www.freespirit.com
Key Personnel
Publr: Judy Galbraith
Publicity Dir: Amy Dillahunt
Intl Rts: Sara Hartman-Seeskin
Founded: 1983
SELF-HELP FOR KIDS® & SELF-HELP FOR TEENS®, offer books & learning materials for parents, educators, children & teens. Topics include: self-esteem, stress management, school success, creativity, relationships with friends & family, social action, special needs (i.e. children with LD/learning differences, gifted & talented & at-risk youth), bullying & conflict resolution.
ISBN Prefix(es): 0-915793; 1-57542; 0-9665988
Number of titles published annually: 20 Print; 1 CD-ROM
Total Titles: 150 Print; 2 CD-ROM; 3 Audio
Foreign Rep(s): Educational Distributors (New Zealand); Incentive Plus (UK); Monarch Books (Canada); Willow Connection (Australia)

§W H Freeman and Co
Subsidiary of Holtzbrinck Publishers
41 Madison Ave, 37th fl, New York, NY 10010
SAN: 200-2302
Tel: 212-576-9400 *Fax:* 212-689-2383
Web Site: www.whfreeman.com
Key Personnel
Pres: Elizabeth Widdicombe
Ed: Susan Brennan; Patrick Farace; Sara Tenney
Man Ed: Philip McCaffrey
Busn Mgr: Linda Glover
VP, Prodn Ed: Ellen Cash

Foreign Rts & Intl Rts: Ilene Ellenbogen
Rts & Perms: Nancy Walker
Founded: 1946
Science & mathematics text.
ISBN Prefix(es): 0-7167
Number of titles published annually: 20 Print
Total Titles: 1,200 Print; 5 CD-ROM; 3 E-Book
Foreign Rep(s): W H Freeman at Macmillan
    Press (UK); Macmillan Education Australia;
    Macmillan Publishers China; Macmillan Pub-
    lishers New Zealand; Macmillan Shuppan K K
    (Japan)
Warehouse: VHPS Distribution Center, 16365
    James Madison Hwy (US Rte 15), Gor-
    donsville, VA 22942
Distribution Center: VHPS Distribution Center,
    16365 James Madison Hwy (US Rte 15), Gor-
    donsville, VA 22942

§French & European Publications Inc
Rockefeller Center Promenade, 610 Fifth Ave,
    New York, NY 10020-2497
Tel: 212-581-8810 Fax: 212-265-1094
E-mail: livresny@aol.com
Web Site: www.frencheuropean.com Cable:
    FRANCOPUB NEW YORK
Key Personnel
Pres & Lib Sales Dir: Emanuel Molho
VP: Deborah Molho
Founded: 1928
ISBN Prefix(es): 0-8288; 0-7859; 0-3200
Number of titles published annually: 1,000 Print
Total Titles: 18,000 Print; 150 CD-ROM; 600 Au-
    dio
Imprints: Editions de la Maison Francaise; The
    French & Spanish Book Corp; Librairie de
    France
Membership(s): ABA; National Association of
    College Stores

Samuel French Inc
45 W 25 St, New York, NY 10010-2751
SAN: 206-4170
Tel: 212-206-8990 Fax: 212-206-1429
E-mail: samuelfrench@earthlink.net
Web Site: www.samuelfrench.com Cable:
    THEATRICAL NY
Key Personnel
Pres & Man Dir: Charles R Van Nostrand
Ed: Roxanne Hintz
Adv Mgr & ISBN Contact: Kenneth Dingledine
Founded: 1830
Plays.
ISBN Prefix(es): 0-573
Number of titles published annually: 50 Print
Total Titles: 5,000 Print
Branch Office(s)
7623 Sunset Blvd, Hollywood, CA 90046, Con-
    tact: Leon Embry Tel: 323-876-0570 Fax: 323-
    876-6822
100 Lombard St, Toronto, ON M5C 1M3,
    Canada, Contact: Andrew Shaver Tel: 416-363-
    3536 Fax: 416-363-1108
Foreign Office(s): 52 Fitzroy St, London W1P
    6JR, United Kingdom, Vivian Goodwin
    Tel: (020) 7387 9373 Fax: (020) 7387 2161
Distributed by Samuel French Ltd
Distributor for Baker's Plays; Samuel French Ltd
Foreign Rights: DALRO (South Africa); Do-
    minie Pty Ltd (Australia); Play Bureau (New
    Zealand)
See separate listing for:
Baker's Plays

Frieda Carrol Communications
PO Box 416, Denver, CO 80201-0416
Tel: 303-575-5676 Fax: 303-575-1187
E-mail: mail@gumbomedia.com
Key Personnel
Owner: A Doyle
Founded: 1998
Publishers & distributors.

ISBN Prefix(es): 1-890928
Number of titles published annually: 4 Print; 2
    Audio
Total Titles: 26 Print; 4 Audio
Distributed by Sey Yes Marketing
    (www.seyyesmarketing.com)
Distributor for Gumbo Media
    (www.gumbomedia.com)

Friends United Press
Subsidiary of Friends United Meeting
101 Quaker Hill Dr, Richmond, IN 47374
SAN: 201-5803
Tel: 765-962-7573 Toll Free Tel: 800-537-8839
    Fax: 765-966-1293
E-mail: friendspress@fum.org
Web Site: www.fum.org
Key Personnel
Mgr & Ed: Barbara Mays E-mail: barbaram@
    fum.org
Lib Sales Dir: Kathy Sawyer
Founded: 1969
Paperbound books; religion (Society of Friends-
    Friends United Meeting).
ISBN Prefix(es): 0-913408; 0-944350
Number of titles published annually: 3 Print; 3
    Online
Total Titles: 96 Print; 67 Online
Membership(s): Protestant Church-Owned Pub-
    lishers Association; Publishers Marketing Asso-
    ciation; Quakers Uniting in Publications

Frog Ltd
Imprint of North Atlantic Books
1435 Fourth St, Berkeley, CA 94710
Mailing Address: PO Box 12327, Berkeley, CA
    94712
Tel: 510-559-8277 Toll Free Tel: 800-337-2665
    (book orders only) Fax: 510-559-8279
E-mail: orders@northatlanticbooks.com
Web Site: www.northatlanticbooks.com
Key Personnel
Publr: Richard Grossinger E-mail: chard@lmi.net
Publr & Edit Dir: Lindy Hough Tel: 510-
    559-8277 ext 12 E-mail: lhough@
    northatlanticbooks.com
Publicist: Olivia Ford E-mail: oford@
    northatlanticbooks.com
Art Dir: Paula Morrison
Busn Mgr: Ed Angelillo
Sales, Mktg & Subs Rts: Mark Ouimet
Rts & Perms: Sarah Serafimidis
Founded: 1977
Internal martial arts, alternative medicine, somatic
    psychology, sports, science, women's topics,
    psychology, political/current affairs, Buddhism,
    gay & lesbian, environmental, art books (if
    bought direct), sustainable development, ecol-
    ogy, parenting, popular culture, body work,
    literary nonfiction, memoir, biography & chil-
    dren's picture books.
ISBN Prefix(es): 1-883319; 1-58394
Total Titles: 200 Print; 7 E-Book
Distributed by North Atlantic Books
Foreign Rep(s): Airlift Books (UK, Europe);
    PGW (Canada); John Reed (Australia); Tuttle-
    Mori Agency (Japan)
Foreign Rights: Eliane Benisti (France); Hagen-
    bach & Bender (Germany); Karin Schindler
    (Brazil)
Orders to: Publishers Group West, 1170 Trade-
    mark Dr, Reno, NV 89511
Returns: Publishers Group West, 1700 Fourth St,
    Berkeley, CA 94710; Publishers Group West,
    7326 Winton Dr, Indianapolis, IN 46268 Toll
    Free Tel: 800-788-3123 Fax: 775-850-2501
    E-mail: cole.mclachlan@pgw.com
Shipping Address: Publisher's Group West, Dis-
    tribution Ctr, 5045 W 79 St, Indianapolis, IN
    46268

Distribution Center: Publishers Group West, 1170
    Trademark Dr, Reno, NV 89511
Membership(s): Northern California Book Public-
    ity & Marketing Association

Front Street Inc
862 Haywood Rd, Asheville, NC 28806
Tel: 828-236-3097 Fax: 828-221-2112
E-mail: contactus@frontstreetbooks.com
Web Site: www.frontstreetbooks.com
Key Personnel
Pres & Publr: Stephen Roxburgh
ISBN Prefix(es): 1-886910; 1-932425
Number of titles published annually: 15 Print
Total Titles: 80 Print
Imprints: Front Street; Front Street/Lemniscant
Distributed by Chronicle Books
Foreign Rights: Laura Cecil Literary Agency
    (England); Japan UNI Agency (Japan); Ko-
    rean Copyright Ctr (Korea); Jacqueline Miller
    Agency (France); Ombretta Borgia Presenza
    (Italy)
Membership(s): ALA; Children's Book Council

Fugue State Press
PO Box 80, Cooper Sta, New York, NY 10276
Tel: 212-673-7922 Fax: 208-693-6152
E-mail: info@fuguestatepress.com
Web Site: www.fuguestatepress.com
Key Personnel
Ed-in-Chief: James Chapman E-mail: jim@
    fuguestatepress.com
Prodn Mgr: Randie Lipkin
Publicity: Mihaela Giurglu
Founded: 1993
Specialize in experimental & advanced fiction.
ISBN Prefix(es): 1-879193
Number of titles published annually: 3 Print
Total Titles: 16 Print

Fulcrum Publishing Inc
16100 Table Mountain Pkwy, Suite 300, Golden,
    CO 80403
SAN: 200-2825
Tel: 303-277-1623 Toll Free Tel: 800-992-2908
    Fax: 303-279-7111 Toll Free Fax: 800-726-
    7112
E-mail: fulcrum@fulcrum-books.com
Web Site: www.fulcrum-books.com
Key Personnel
Pres & Publr: Robert C Baron
VP: Dianne Howie E-mail: dianneh@fulcrum-
    books.com; Sam Scinta
Compt: Liz Gosse
Natl Sales Dir: Dianne Chrismer
Natl Special Sales Mgr: Anne De Courcey
Man Ed: Katie Raymond
Ed: Faith Marcovecchio
Rts Mgr: Missy Ramey
Mktg Mgr: Jessica Dyer Tel: 303-277-1623 ext
    235 E-mail: jessica@fulcrum-books.com
Founded: 1984
Nonfiction trade: outdoor, nature, travel, Native
    American studies, gardening, environmen-
    tal issues, history, books for the millennium,
    teacher's resource books, children's books.
ISBN Prefix(es): 1-55591; 1-56373; 0-912347
Number of titles published annually: 35 Print
Total Titles: 650 Print; 5 Audio
Imprints: Fulcrum Resources; Gardener's Book-
    shelf
Foreign Rep(s): Athena Productions (all other
    countries); Fifth House Publishing/Fitzhenry
    & Whiteside (Canada); Lone Pine Publishing
    (Canada)
Warehouse: Fulcrum Publishing, 4425 E 46 Ave,
    Denver, CO 80216
Membership(s): Publishers Association of the
    West; Publishers Marketing Association; Small
    Publishers Association of North America

§Future Horizons Inc
721 W Abram St, Arlington, TX 76013
Tel: 817-277-0727 *Toll Free Tel:* 800-489-0727
    Fax: 817-277-2270
E-mail: info@futurehorizons-autism.com
Web Site: www.futurehorizons-autism.com
Key Personnel
Pres: R Wayne Gilpin
Founded: 1990
Resources on Autism/Asperger's Syndrome, in-
    cluding books, video tapes & a magazine.
ISBN Prefix(es): 1-885477
Number of titles published annually: 6 Print
Total Titles: 65 Print

G W Medical Publishing Inc
77 Westport Plaza, Suite 366, St Louis, MO
    63146-3124
Tel: 314-542-4213 *Toll Free Tel:* 800-600-0330
    Fax: 314-542-4239
E-mail: info@gwmedical.com
Web Site: www.gwmedical.com
Key Personnel
Pres: Marianne Whaley *E-mail:* marianne@
    gwmedical.com
VP: Glenn Whaley *E-mail:* glenn@gwmedical.
    com
Founded: 1993
Medical & legal, nursing & allied health texts &
    references; medical consumer books; child care
    & development, clinical & forensic medical
    references.
ISBN Prefix(es): 1-878060
Number of titles published annually: 6 Print; 3
    CD-ROM
Total Titles: 24 Print
Distributed by Amazon.com; American Medical
    Association; Barnes & Noble; Elsevier Science
    (London, Australia, Asia, Philadelphia, New
    York, St Louis)
Advertising Agency: GW Graphics & Publishing

Gagosian Gallery
980 Madison Ave, New York, NY 10021
Tel: 212-744-2313 *Fax:* 212-772-8696
E-mail: info@gagosian.com
Web Site: www.gagosian.com
Founded: 1989
Publish fine editions & illustrated books on con-
    temporary & modern art.
ISBN Prefix(es): 1-880154
Number of titles published annually: 10 Print
Total Titles: 40 Print
Branch Office(s)
456 N Camden Dr, Beverly Hills, CA 90210
    Tel: 310-271-9400 *Fax:* 310-271-9420

Gail's Guides
PO Box 70323, Bellevue, WA 98005
Tel: 425-917-0737
E-mail: guides@oz.net
Web Site: www.gailsguides.com
Key Personnel
Owner: Gail Folgedalen
Lib Sales Dir & Mktg Mgr: Lee Folgedalen
Founded: 1982
Publish regional events guides.
ISBN Prefix(es): 1-881005
Number of titles published annually: 4 Print
Total Titles: 4 Print
Imprints: Holiday Bazaar Guide-OR; Holiday
    Bazaar Guide-WA; Oregon Events Guide;
    Washington Events Guide
Distributed by The News Group; Partners West
Shipping Address: The News Group, 3400 D In-
    dustry Dr E, Fife, WA 98424 *Tel:* 253-922-
    8011 *Toll Free Tel:* 800-843-2995

§Gallaudet University Press
800 Florida Ave NE, Washington, DC 20002-
    3695
SAN: 205-261X

Tel: 202-651-5488 *Fax:* 202-651-5489
E-mail: gupress@gallaudet.edu
Web Site: gupress.gallaudet.edu
Key Personnel
Dir & Ed-in-Chief: John V Van Cleve
Asst Dir, Acqs: Ivey B Wallace
Asst Dir, Mktg: Dan Wallace *Tel:* 202-651-5661
    E-mail: daniel.wallace@gallaudet.edu
Founded: 1968
Specialize in reference books, scholarly, educa-
    tional & general interest books on deaf studies,
    deaf culture & issues, sign language textbooks.
ISBN Prefix(es): 0-913580; 0-930323; 1-56368
Number of titles published annually: 15 Print
Total Titles: 215 Print; 2 CD-ROM
Imprints: Clerc Books; Kendall Green Publica-
    tions
Distributor for Signum Verlag
Foreign Rep(s): Forest Book Services Inc (Ire-
    land, Europe & UK)
Warehouse: Chicago Distribution Center, 11030
    S Langley Ave, Chicago, IL 60628, Ms Karen
    Hyzy *Toll Free Tel:* 800-621-2736; 800-630-
    9347 *Fax:* 773-660-2235 *Toll Free Fax:* 800-
    621-8476
Membership(s): AAP

§Gallopade International Inc
665 Hwy 74 S, Suite 600, Peachtree City, GA
    30269
SAN: 213-8441
Mailing Address: PO Box 2779, Peachtree City,
    GA 30269
Tel: 770-631-4222 *Toll Free Tel:* 800-536-
    2GET (536-2438) *Fax:* 770-631-4810
    Toll Free Fax: 800-871-2979
E-mail: info@gallopade.com
Web Site: www.gallopade.com
Key Personnel
CEO: Carole Marsh *E-mail:* carole@gallopade.
    com
Pres & Intl Rts: Michele Yother
    E-mail: michele@gallopade.com
VP: Michael Marsh *E-mail:* michael@gallopade.
    com; Sherry Moss *E-mail:* sherry@gallopade.
    com
Founded: 1979
"State stuff" for all 50 states including activity
    books, games, maps, posters, stickies, etc. Sub-
    jects include travel, regional, school travel sup-
    ply, home school, juvenile mysteries, human
    sex education, multicultural, preschool through
    adult.
ISBN Prefix(es): 0-935326; 1-55609; 0-7933; 0-
    635
Number of titles published annually: 500 Print;
    50 CD-ROM; 200 Online; 200 E-Book
Total Titles: 12,500 Print; 200 CD-ROM; 10,050
    Online; 10,050 E-Book; 13 Audio
Imprints: The Day That Was Different; Here &
    Now: Things Kids Want to Learn About To-
    day!; Heroes & Helpers: Those Who Help Us
    in Times of Crises-& Everyday!; History Mys-
    tery; How to Get Money, Now!; How to Make
    a Million; Lifewrite; Carole Marsh Books;
    Carole Marsh Family CD-ROM & Interac-
    tive Multimedia; Mind Your Own Business;
    Naked Gourmet; Sex Stuff for Kids; State Ex-
    perience!; State Facts & Factivities; State Stuff
Subsidiaries: Books on Disk & CD-ROM; Carole
    Marsh Books; Carole Marsh Family Interactive
    Multimedia; Six House; The World's Largest
    Publishing Co
Advertising Agency: Marsh Media Methods
Membership(s): NSSEA; Publishers Association
    of the South

Galt Press
Division of Galt International Inc
1725 Clearwater-Largo Rd S, Clearwater, FL
    33756
SAN: 286-0570

Mailing Address: PO Box 8, Clearwater, FL
    33757
Tel: 727-581-8685 *Fax:* 727-585-8423
E-mail: galt@warda.net
Web Site: www.warda.net/GaltPress.html; www.
    galtpress.com
Key Personnel
Pres: Mark Warda *E-mail:* mark@warda.net
VP: Alexandra Schiller *E-mail:* alex@warda.net
Founded: 1983
ISBN Prefix(es): 1-888699
Number of titles published annually: 3 Print
Total Titles: 5 Print
Imprints: Qoool Press
Distributor for Sphinx Publishing
Membership(s): Publishers Marketing Association

Gareth Stevens Inc
Division of World Almanac Education Group Inc
Subsidiary of WRC Media Inc
330 W Olive St, Suite 100, Milwaukee, WI
    53212
Tel: 414-332-3520 *Toll Free Tel:* 800-542-2595
    Fax: 414-332-3567
E-mail: info@gspub.com; info@
    worldalmanaclibrary.com
Web Site: www.garethstevens.com; www.
    worldalmanaclibrary.com
Key Personnel
Publr: Robert Famighetti *E-mail:* rfamighetti@
    gspub.com
CFO: David Miller
COO: David Press
Art Dir: Tammy West
Edit Dir: Mark Sachner
Prodn Dir: Jessica Morris
Natl Sales Mgr: Ken Katula
Mktg Mgr: Susan Ashley
Founded: 1983
ISBN Prefix(es): 0-918831; 1-55532; 0-8368
Number of titles published annually: 400 Print
Total Titles: 1,200 Print
Divisions: AmericanKids Preview; American Li-
    brary Preview; Books & Libros; Library One
    Direct; World Reference Resources; Young
    Adult Resources

§Garland Science Publishing
Member of Taylor & Francis Books Inc
270 Madison Ave, New York, NY 10016
SAN: 201-5897
Tel: 212-216-7800 *Fax:* 212-947-3027
E-mail: info@garland.com
Web Site: www.garlandscience.com
Key Personnel
Pres: Fenton Markevich *Tel:* 212-216-7814
VP, Sales: Dennis Ibeiss *Tel:* 212-216-7827
VP, Garland Science: D Schanck *Tel:* 917-351-
    7120 *E-mail:* dschanck@taylorandfrancis.com
Founded: 1969
Textbooks & professional books in biology &
    chemistry.
ISBN Prefix(es): 0-8153
Number of titles published annually: 3 Print; 5
    CD-ROM
Total Titles: 15 Print; 5 CD-ROM
Branch Office(s)
4133 Whitney Ave, Hamden, CT 06578 *Tel:* 203-
    281-4487 *Toll Free Tel:* 800-627-6273
    Fax: 203-230-1186
Warehouse: Taylor & Francis/Garland, 10650
    Toebben Dr, Independence, KY 41051 *Toll
    Free Tel:* 800-634-7064 *Toll Free Fax:* 800-
    248-4724 *Web Site:* www.garlandscience.com

Garlinghouse Inc
Subsidiary of Sabot Publishing Inc
174 Oakwood Dr, Glastonbury, CT 06033
Tel: 860-659-5667 *Fax:* 860-659-5692
E-mail: info@garlinghouse.com
Web Site: www.garlinghouse.com

Key Personnel
CEO & Publr: Steve Culpepper
Founded: 1907
ISBN Prefix(es): 0-938708; 1-893536
Number of titles published annually: 35 Print
Total Titles: 45 Print; 12 Online

Gateways Books & Tapes
Division of Institute for the Development of the
    Harmonious Human Being Inc
PO Box 370, Nevada City, CA 95959
SAN: 211-3635
Tel: 530-477-8101 *Toll Free Tel:* 800-869-0658
    Fax: 530-272-0184
E-mail: info@gatewaysbooksandtapes.com
Web Site: www.gatewaysbooksandtapes.com;
    www.retrosf.com
Key Personnel
Sr Ed & Intl Rts: Iven Lourie *E-mail:* iven@
gatewaysbooksandtapes.com
Founded: 1971
Trade & fine art book publisher. Categories in-
    clude psychology, spirituality, metaphysics,
    Judaica, science fiction, limited editions.
ISBN Prefix(es): 0-89556
Number of titles published annually: 6 Print; 4
    CD-ROM; 4 Audio
Total Titles: 28 Print; 8 CD-ROM; 300 Audio
Imprints: Consciousness Classics; Gateways Retro
    SF
Distributor for Cloister Recordings (audio &
    video tapes)
Advertising Agency: Morgan Fox Agency

Gault Millau Inc/Gayot Publications
4311 Wilshire Blvd, Suite 405, Los Angeles, CA
    90010
Tel: 323-965-3529 *Toll Free Tel:* 800-LE BEST 1
    Fax: 323-936-2883
E-mail: info@gayot.com
Web Site: www.gayot.com
Key Personnel
Pres: Andre Gayot
Publr & Intl Rts: Alain Gayot
Founded: 1986
Publish travel guides to world destinations with a
    rating system to the best hotels, restaurants &
    shops.
ISBN Prefix(es): 1-881066
Number of titles published annually: 12 Print
Total Titles: 16 Print; 5 E-Book
Imprints: Gaultmillau; GAYOT
Subsidiaries: Tastes Newsletter
Divisions: The Food Paper
Distributed by Publishers Group West

Gauntlet Press
5307 Arroyo St, Colorado Springs, CO 80922
Tel: 719-591-5566 *Fax:* 719-591-6676
E-mail: info@gauntletpress.com
Web Site: www.gauntletpress.com
Key Personnel
Pres: Barry Hoffman
"Classic-revised" books (signed limited) for col-
    lectors. Only publishes established authors. No
    unsol mss. Closed to submissions for the next
    three years.
ISBN Prefix(es): 1-887368
Number of titles published annually: 6 Print
Total Titles: 40 Print

Gay Sunshine Press/Leyland Publications
PO Box 410690, San Francisco, CA 94141
Tel: 415-626-1935 *Fax:* 415-626-1802
Web Site: www.gaysunshine.com
Key Personnel
Publr: Winston Leyland
Founded: 1975
Gay fiction & nonfiction, history, poetry, music &
    dance.
ISBN Prefix(es): 0-943595; 0-940567; 0-917342
Number of titles published annually: 6 Print

Total Titles: 90 Print
Foreign Rep(s): Bulldog Books (Australia & New
    Zealand); Turnaround (Europe)
Distribution Center: Bookazine, 75 Hook Rd,
    Bayonne, NJ 07002, Contact: Ron Hanby *Toll
    Free Tel:* 800-221-8112
Koen Book Distributors, 10 Twosome Dr,
    Moorestown, NJ 08057 *Toll Free Tel:* 800-257-
    8481

§Gazelle Publications
11560 Red Bud Trail, Berrien Springs, MI 49103
Tel: 269-471-4717 *Toll Free Tel:* 800-650-5076
E-mail: info@gazellepublications.com
Web Site: www.gazellepublications.com
Founded: 1976
ISBN Prefix(es): 0-930192
Number of titles published annually: 1 Print; 1
    CD-ROM; 1 Online
Total Titles: 7 Print; 2 CD-ROM; 1 Online
Distributed by FaithWorks/NBN

Gefen Books
600 Broadway, Lynbrook, NY 11563
Tel: 516-593-1234 *Toll Free Tel:* 800-477-5257
    Fax: 516-295-2739
E-mail: gefenny@gefenpublishing.com
Web Site: www.israelbooks.com
Key Personnel
Dir & Lib Intl Rts Contact Israel: Ilan Greenfield
    Tel: (02) 538-0247 *Fax:* (02) 538-8423
    E-mail: ilan@gefenpublishing.com
Sales Mgr: Maury Storch
Mktg Dir Israel: Michal Avrahami *Tel:* (02) 538-
    0247 *E-mail:* michal@gefenpublishing.com
Founded: 1981
General interest, mainly books from Israel. Spe-
    cialize in Judaic interest, Israel, art, Holocaust
    & Jewish history. Can supply any books pub-
    lished in Israel &/or in the Hebrew language.
ISBN Prefix(es): 965-229
Number of titles published annually: 25 Print
Total Titles: 425 Print; 400 Online; 400 E-Book
Imprints: Gefen Publishing Ltd
Subsidiaries: IsraBook
Divisions: Medical Publishing (Gefen)
Foreign Office(s): Gefen Publishing House Ltd, 6
    Hatzvi St, Jerusalem 94386, Israel
Distributor for Bar Ilan; Magnes Press

Gem Guides Book Co
315 Cloverleaf Dr, Suite F, Baldwin Park, CA
    91706
Tel: 626-855-1611 *Fax:* 626-855-1610
E-mail: gembooks@aol.com
Key Personnel
Ed: Kathy Mayerski
Gen Mgr: Alfred Mayerski
Founded: 1965
Publisher & distributor of regional & specialty
    trade books; rocks, minerals, crystals, Old
    West, western & southwestern region & local
    interests.
ISBN Prefix(es): 0-935182; 1-889786
Number of titles published annually: 7 Print
Total Titles: 80 Print
Imprints: Gembooks
Distributed by Nevada Publications
Distributor for Boze Books; Brynmorgen Press;
    Clear Creek Publishing; Earth Love Publish-
    ing; Geoscience Press; Golden Hands Press;
    Grand Canyon Association; Historical Society
    of Southern California; Cy Johnson & Son; KC
    Publications Inc; Natureraph; Nevada Pub-
    lications; Old El Toro Press; Pinyon Publish-
    ing; Primer Publications; Ram Publishing; L
    R Ream Publishing; Recreation Sales; Sierra
    Press; La Siesta Press; To the Point Press;
    Treasure Chest; Trees Company; Weseanne
    Publications; Western Trails Publications
Membership(s): ABA; Northern California Inde-
    pendent Booksellers Association; Publishers
    Marketing Association; PubWest

§GEM Publications
411 Mallalieu Dr, Hudson, WI 54016
Tel: 715-386-7113 *Toll Free Tel:* 800-290-6128
    Fax: 715-386-7113
E-mail: gem@spacestar.net
Web Site: www.spacestar.com/users/gem
Key Personnel
Publr: Marnie McCuen
Off Mgr & Lib Sales Dir: Marie Romsos
Founded: 1981
Publish books that present debates & symposiums
    on moral & social issues for school libraries,
    public libraries & college libraries; also used in
    school & college classrooms.
ISBN Prefix(es): 0-86596
Number of titles published annually: 4 Print
Total Titles: 31 Print; 3 CD-ROM
Imprints: Editorial Forum; Ideas in Conflicts

GemStone Press
Division of Longhill Partners Inc
Sunset Farm Offices, Rte 4, Woodstock, VT
    05091
SAN: 134-5621
Mailing Address: PO Box 237, Woodstock, VT
    05091
Tel: 802-457-4000 *Toll Free Tel:* 800-962-4544
    Fax: 802-457-4004
E-mail: sales@gemstonepress.com
Web Site: www.gemstonepress.com
Key Personnel
Pres, Publr & Intl Rts: Stuart M Matlins
VP, Mktg & Sales: Jon Sweeney
VP & Ed: Emily Wichland
VP, Fin & Admin: Amy Wilson
Founded: 1987
Books on buying, enjoying, identifying & selling
    jewelry & gems for the consumer, collector,
    hobbyist, investor & jewelry trade.
ISBN Prefix(es): 0-943763
Number of titles published annually: 4 Print
Total Titles: 18 Print
Distributed by Bayard (Canada); Pleroma (New
    Zealand); Rainbow Book Agencies (Australia)
Foreign Rep(s): Gazelle (UK, Europe)
Foreign Rights: Andreas Brunner (Germany);
    Harris/Elon (Israel); Judit Hermann (Hun-
    gary); A Korzhenevski (Russia); Isabel Mon-
    teagudo (Spain); Katia Schumer (Brazil); L
    Strakova Nurnberg Associates (Czech Repub-
    lic); Raduslav Trenev (Eastern Europe); Su-
    sanna Zevi (Italy)

§Genealogical Publishing Co Inc
Subsidiary of Chodak Inc
1001 N Calvert St, Baltimore, MD 21202
Tel: 410-837-8271 *Toll Free Tel:* 800-296-6687
    Fax: 410-752-8492
E-mail: orders@genealogical.com
Web Site: www.genealogical.com
Key Personnel
VP, Ed-in-Chief & Rts & Perms: Michael Tepper
Mgr, Book Dept: Roger Sherr *E-mail:* rsherr@
    genealogical.com
Mktg Dir: Joe Garonzik *E-mail:* jgaronzi@
    genealogical.com
Founded: 1959
Genealogy, local history, immigration history &
    source records.
ISBN Prefix(es): 0-8063
Number of titles published annually: 50 Print; 5
    CD-ROM
Total Titles: 352 Print; 84 CD-ROM
Subsidiaries: Clearfield Co Inc

Genesis Press Inc
PO Box 101, Columbus, MS 39703
Tel: 662-329-9927 *Toll Free Tel:* 888-463-4461
    (orders only) *Fax:* 662-329-9399
E-mail: books@genesis-press.com
Web Site: www.genesis-press.com

Key Personnel
Publr & CEO: Nyani Colom
Founded: 1993
ISBN Prefix(es): 1-885478; 1-58571
Number of titles published annually: 30 Print
Total Titles: 160 Print
Imprints: INDIGO; Kid Genesis; Love Spectrum; Pen & Ink; Red Slipper; Tango 2
Membership(s): AAP

Genesis Publishing Co Inc
36 Steeple View Dr, Atkinson, NH 03811
SAN: 298-6159
Tel: 603-362-4121 *Fax:* 603-362-4121
E-mail: genesis@genesisbook.com
Web Site: genesispc.com
Key Personnel
Pres: Gerard M Verschuuren
Sales Mgr: Trudy Doucette
Founded: 1994
Science, Philosophy & Religion.
ISBN Prefix(es): 1-886670
Number of titles published annually: 3 Print
Total Titles: 10 Print
Membership(s): Publishers Marketing Association

Geological Society of America (GSA)
3300 Penrose Place, Boulder, CO 80301
SAN: 201-5978
Mailing Address: PO Box 9140, Boulder, CO 80301-9140
Tel: 303-447-2020 *Toll Free Tel:* 800-472-1988
Fax: 303-357-1070
E-mail: pubs@geosociety.org
Web Site: www.geosociety.org
Key Personnel
Pubns Dir: Jon Olsen
Mktg & Adv: Ann Crawford
Founded: 1888
General earth sciences, cover such areas as geology, economic geology, engineering geology, geochemistry, geomorphology, marine geology, mineralogy, paleontology, petrology, seismology, solid earth geophysics, structural geology, tectonics & environmental geology.
ISBN Prefix(es): 0-8137
Number of titles published annually: 15 Print
Total Titles: 200 Print
Foreign Rep(s): Geological Society of London (UK)

§Geolytics Inc
PO Box 10, East Brunswick, NJ 08816
Tel: 732-651-2000 *Toll Free Tel:* 800-577-6717
Fax: 732-651-2721
E-mail: support@geolytics.com
Web Site: www.geolytics.com
Key Personnel
Mktg Dir: Katia Segre Cohen
Founded: 1987
ISBN Prefix(es): 1-892445
Number of titles published annually: 4 Print; 4 CD-ROM
Total Titles: 22 Print; 22 CD-ROM

Georgetown University Press
3240 Prospect St NW, Washington, DC 20007
SAN: 203-4247
Tel: 202-687-6251 (acq); 202-687-5889 (busn); 202-687-5641 (mktg); 410-516-6956 (orders)
Toll Free Tel: 800-537-5487 *Fax:* 202-687-6340 (edit); 410-516-6998 (orders)
E-mail: gupress@georgetown.edu
Web Site: www.press.georgetown.edu
Key Personnel
Dir: Richard Brown *Tel:* 202-687-5912
Busn Mgr: Christine Quigley *E-mail:* quigley@georgetown.edu
Edit & Prodn Mgr: Deborah Weiner
Mktg Dir: David M Perkins
Founded: 1966

Linguistics, languages, ethics, bioethics, theology, education & public policy.
ISBN Prefix(es): 0-87840
Number of titles published annually: 40 Print; 2 Audio
Total Titles: 500 Print; 9 Audio
Orders to: PO Box 50370, Hampden Sta, Baltimore, MD 21211-4370 *Fax:* 410-516-6998
Warehouse: c/o Maple Press Co, Lebanon Distribution Ctr, 704 Legionaire Dr, Fredericksburg, PA 17026

Geoscience Press Inc
PO Box 42948, Tuscon, AZ 85733-2948
Tel: 520-529-1567 *Fax:* 520-529-1567
E-mail: geobook@ix.netcom.com
Key Personnel
Publr: Charles Hutchinson
Founded: 1988
Popular books about rocks, minerals, gems, fossils, geology & other earth science topics.
ISBN Prefix(es): 0-945005
Number of titles published annually: 3 Print
Total Titles: 19 Print
Warehouse: Fulfillment Services Inc, 526 E 16 St, Tucson, AZ 85701
Membership(s): Publishers Association of the West

Gestalt Journal Press
Division of The Center For Gestalt Development Inc
PO Box 278, Gouldsboro, ME 04607-0278
Tel: 845-691-7192 *Fax:* 775-254-1855
E-mail: tgjournal@gestalt.org
Web Site: www.gestalt.org
Key Personnel
Exec Ed: Molly Rawle
Publr & Intl Rts Contact: Joe Wysong
Founded: 1977
Mental health, gestalt therapy specifically.
ISBN Prefix(es): 0-939266
Number of titles published annually: 3 Print; 1 CD-ROM
Total Titles: 33 Print; 2 CD-ROM

§Getty Publications
1200 Getty Center Dr, Suite 500, Los Angeles, CA 90049-1682
SAN: 208-2276
Mailing Address: PO Box 49659, Los Angeles, CA 90049-0659
Tel: 310-440-7365 *Fax:* 310-440-7758
E-mail: pubsinfo@getty.edu
Web Site: www.getty.edu/bookstore
Key Personnel
Publr: Christopher Hudson *E-mail:* chudson@getty.edu
Gen Mgr: Kara Kirk *Tel:* 310-440-6506 *E-mail:* kkirk@getty.edu
Ed-in-Chief: Mark Greenberg *Tel:* 310-440-7097 *E-mail:* mgreenberg@getty.edu
Head, Dept of Pubns, Getty Research Institute: Julia Bloomfield *Tel:* 310-440-7446 *E-mail:* jbloomfield@getty.edu
Man Ed: Ann Lucke *Tel:* 310-440-6525 *E-mail:* alucke@getty.edu
Design Mgr: Deenie Yudell *Tel:* 310-440-6508 *E-mail:* dyudell@getty.edu
Prodn Mgr: Karen Schmidt *Tel:* 310-440-6504 *E-mail:* kschmidt@getty.edu
Rts Mgr: Leslie Rollins *Tel:* 310-440-7102 *E-mail:* lrollins@getty.edu
Mktg Mgr: Patrick Callahan *Tel:* 310-440-6536 *E-mail:* pcallahan@getty.edu
Founded: 1982
Scholarly works on the visual arts: architecture, conservation, history of art & the humanities. Publishes in areas related to its collections specifically: antiquities, decorative arts, drawings, mss, paintings, photographs & sculpture.
ISBN Prefix(es): 0-89236

Number of titles published annually: 45 Print; 2 CD-ROM; 1 Online
Total Titles: 434 Print; 3 CD-ROM; 1 Online
Imprints: Getty Conservation Institute; Getty Research Institute; J Paul Getty Museum
Distributed by Oxford University Press Inc (US only)
Distributor for Edizioni Quasar; Visions SrL
Foreign Rep(s): Julio E Emod/HARBRA (South America); EWEB (Asia, Pacific Rim); Windsor Books International (UK, Europe)
Membership(s): AAP; Association of American University Presses; CAA; International Association of Museum Publishers; International Association of Scholarly Publishers; International Group of Publishing Libraries; Society of Scholarly Publishers

GIA Publications, Inc
7404 S Mason Ave, Chicago, IL 60638
Tel: 708-496-3800 *Toll Free Tel:* 800-442-1358 *Fax:* 708-496-3828
E-mail: custserv@giamusic.com
Web Site: www.giamusic.com
Key Personnel
Pres: Alec Harris *E-mail:* alech@giamusic.com
Founded: 1941
Publish sacred choral music, hymnals, books & recordings. Also publish music education materials.
Number of titles published annually: 200 Print
Total Titles: 6,000 Print; 250 Audio

Gibbs Smith Publisher
1877 E Gentile, Layton, UT 84040
Mailing Address: PO Box 667, Layton, UT 84041-0667 SAN: 201-9906
Tel: 801-544-9800 *Toll Free Tel:* 800-748-5439 (orders only) *Fax:* 801-544-5582
Toll Free Fax: 800-213-3023 (orders only)
E-mail: info@gibbs-smith.com
Web Site: www.gibbs-smith.com
Key Personnel
Gen Mgr: Christopher Robbins *Tel:* 801-544-9800 ext 104 *E-mail:* ccr@gibbs-smith.com
Dir, Mktg & Pub Rel: Alison Einerson *Tel:* 801-544-9800 ext 142 *E-mail:* alison@gibbs-smith.com
Cust Serv Mgr: Cortney Nessen *Tel:* 801-544-9800 ext 144 *E-mail:* cnessen@gibbs-smith.com
Founded: 1969
ISBN Prefix(es): 0-87905; 1-58685
Number of titles published annually: 80 Print; 50 Online
Total Titles: 350 Print; 200 Online
Foreign Rep(s): Athena; Ken Kaimen
Returns: 570 N Sportsplex Dr, Kaysville, UT 84037
Shipping Address: 570 N Sportsplex Dr, Kaysville, UT 84037
Membership(s): AAP

Gifted Education Press
10201 Yuma Ct, Manassas, VA 20109
Mailing Address: PO Box 1586, Manassas, VA 20109
Tel: 703-369-5017
Web Site: www.giftedpress.com; www.giftedpress.com
Key Personnel
Publr & Dir: Maurice D Fisher *E-mail:* mfisher345@comcast.net
Founded: 1981
Books, quarterly newsletter, bimonthly newsletter, teaching guides & supplemental materials for students. Education of gifted children.
ISBN Prefix(es): 0-910609
Number of titles published annually: 10 Print
Total Titles: 50 Print

Gingerbread House
602 Montauk Hwy, Westhampton Beach, NY
11978-1806
SAN: 217-0760
Tel: 631-288-5119 *Fax:* 631-288-5179
E-mail: ghbooks@optonline.net
Web Site: gingerbreadbooks.com
Key Personnel
Publr: Josephine Nobisso
VP & Opers Mgr: Maria Nicotra
   E-mail: iapmaria@optonline.net
Founded: 2000
Publish fine, trade quality, full-color picture books
   in both hard & soft covers in English & Span-
   ish languages, for USA & foreign markets.
ISBN Prefix(es): 0-940112
Number of titles published annually: 3 Print
Total Titles: 16 Print; 3 E-Book
Foreign Rep(s): IPG
Membership(s): ABC; Children's Book Coun-
   cil; NAIBA; Publishers Marketing Association;
   Small Publishers Association of North Amer-
   ica; Society of Children's Book Writers & Il-
   lustrators

Girl Scouts of the USA
420 Fifth Ave, New York, NY 10018-2798
Tel: 212-852-8000 *Toll Free Tel:* 800-478-7248
   Fax: 212-852-6511
Web Site: www.girlscouts.org
Key Personnel
Dir, Publg: Suzanna Penn *Tel:* 212-852-6530
   E-mail: spenn@girlscouts.org
Sr Ed: Susan Kantor; Ed Levy; Janet Lombardi;
   David Sahatdjian
Founded: 1912
Non profit educational publisher of books, maga-
   zines, newsletters, catalogs, kits, annual reports,
   handbooks & activity books. Subjects covered
   in materials for girls 5-17 & in corporate ma-
   terials. Accept mss from outside our member-
   ship.
ISBN Prefix(es): 0-88441
Number of titles published annually: 70 Print
Total Titles: 500 Print
Distribution Center: 100 Canfield Ave, Randolph,
   NJ 07869-1106

Gival Press LLC
PO Box 3812, Arlington, VA 22203
Tel: 703-351-0079 *Fax:* 703-351-0079
E-mail: givalpress@yahoo.com
Web Site: www.givalpress.prodigybiz.com; www.
   givalpress.com
Key Personnel
Publr: Robert L Giron
Founded: 1998
ISBN Prefix(es): 1-928589
Number of titles published annually: 5 Print; 5 E-
   Book
Total Titles: 19 Print; 15 E-Book
Membership(s): AAP; Council of Literary Maga-
   zines & Presses; Publishers Marketing Associ-
   ation; Publishing Triangle; Small Press Center;
   Small Publishers Association of North America

GLB Publishers
1028 Howard St, No 503, San Francisco, CA
94103
Tel: 415-621-8307 *Toll Free Tel:* 800-452-6119
E-mail: glbpubs@mindspring.com
Web Site: www.glbpubs.com
Key Personnel
Owner, Ed & Publr: W L Warner
Founded: 1990
Books by & for gays, lesbians & bisexuals.
ISBN Prefix(es): 1-879194; 0-9717800
Number of titles published annually: 6 Print; 10
   Online; 10 E-Book
Total Titles: 55 Print; 50 Online; 50 E-Book

Imprints: GLB
Billing Address: PO Box 78212, San Francisco,
   CA 94107-8212

Glenbridge Publishing Ltd
19923 E Long Ave, Centennial, CO 80016-1969
SAN: 243-5403
Tel: 720-870-8381 *Toll Free Tel:* 800-986-4135
   (orders) *Fax:* 720-870-5598
E-mail: glenbr@eazy.net
Web Site: www.glenbridgepublishing.com
Key Personnel
Pres & Intl Rts: Mary B Keene
VP & Ed: James A Keene
Founded: 1986
Publish nonfiction, hardcover originals, reprints &
   paperback originals.
ISBN Prefix(es): 0-944435
Number of titles published annually: 7 Print
Total Titles: 55 Print

Glencoe/McGraw-Hill
Division of McGraw-Hill Education
8787 Orion Place, Columbus, OH 43240
Tel: 614-430-4000 *Toll Free Tel:* 800-848-1567
Web Site: www.glencoe.com
Key Personnel
Pres: Steven E McClung
   E-mail: steven_mcclung@mcgraw-hill.com
Sr VP, Fin: Jody R Bender
Sr VP & Publr: Richard C Brommer
   E-mail: richard_brommer@mcgraw-hill.com
VP & Dir, Adv: Michael Hopkins
   E-mail: michael_hopkins@mcgraw-hill.com
VP & Dir, Sales: Thomas Bruce *Tel:* 803-732-
   2365 ext 12 *E-mail:* thomas_bruce@mcgraw-
   hill.com
Founded: 1971
Educational materials for middle school & high
   school.
ISBN Prefix(es): 0-02 (Glencoe); 0-07 (Glencoe);
   0-31 (Tribune/NTC); 0-39 (Houghton Mifflin);
   0-53 (Tribune/NTC); 0-65 (Tribune/NTC);
   0-67 (Merrill); 0-80 (Jamestown); 0-84 (Tri-
   bune/NTC); 0-89 (Jamestown); 0-93 (Tri-
   bune/NTC); 0-96 (Meeks Heit); 1-57 (Everyday
   Math); 1-58 (Meeks Heit); 1-88 (Meeks Heit)
Imprints: Gregg; Merrill
Branch Office(s)
21600 Oxnard St, 5th fl, Woodland Hills, CA
   91367 *Tel:* 818-615-2600 *Fax:* 818-615-2699
One Prudential Plaza, 130 E Randolph St, Suite
   900, Chicago, IL 60601 *Tel:* 312-233-6500
Peoria Editorial Ctr, 3008 W Willow Knolls Dr,
   Peoria, IL 61614 *Tel:* 309-689-3200
Foreign Rep(s): McGraw-Hill Ryerson Ltd
   (Canada); The McGraw-Hill Companies (In-
   ternational)
Orders to: PO Box 543, Blacklick, OH 43004-
   0543 *Toll Free Tel:* 800-334-7344
Returns: 860 Taylor Station Rd, Blacklick, OH
   43004
Warehouse: PO Box 543, Blacklick, OH 43004-
   0543 *Toll Free Tel:* 800-334-7344 *Fax:* 614-
   860-1877
Distribution Center: 860 Taylor Station Rd,
   Blacklick, OH 43004 *Toll Free Tel:* 800-334-
   7344

Peter Glenn Publications
Division of Blount Communications
6040 NW 43 Terr, Boca Raton, FL 33496
Tel: 561-999-8930 *Toll Free Tel:* 888-332-6700
   Fax: 561-999-8931
E-mail: lynn@pgdirect.com
Web Site: www.pgdirect.com
Key Personnel
CEO & Publr: Gregory James *E-mail:* gjames@
   pgdirect.com
VP: Tricia Mazzilli-Blount
Dir: L Chip Brill; Umberto Guido, III

Licensing Agent: Christine Annechino
   E-mail: acalicensing@att.net
Founded: 1956
Directories for the world of advertising, TV &
   film publicity; directories for performing arts,
   fashion & modeling industry.
ISBN Prefix(es): 0-87314
Number of titles published annually: 9 Print
Total Titles: 9 Print; 6 E-Book
Distribution Center: SCB Distributors

Glimmer Train Press Inc
1211 NW Glisan St, No 207, Portland, OR 97209
Tel: 503-221-0836 *Fax:* 503-221-0837
E-mail: info@glimmertrain.com
Web Site: www.glimmertrain.com
Key Personnel
Contact: Linda Swanson-Davies
Founded: 1990
Quarterly short story magazine.
ISBN Prefix(es): 1-880966
Number of titles published annually: 4 Print
Total Titles: 52 Print
Distributor for Glimmer Train Stories

Global Training Center Inc
7801 N Dixie Dr, Dayton, OH 45414-2779
Tel: 937-454-5044 *Toll Free Tel:* 800-860-5030
   Fax: 937-454-5099
E-mail: xportnow@aol.com
Web Site: www.globaltrainingcenter.com
Key Personnel
Pres: Gloria Klopfenstein
Founded: 1992
Training seminar/workshops covering Interna-
   tional Documentation, NAFTA, Importing, etc.
ISBN Prefix(es): 1-891249
Number of titles published annually: 13 Print
Total Titles: 13 Print

Globe Fearon
Imprint of Pearson Learning Group
299 Jefferson Rd, Parsippany, NJ 07054
Tel: 973-739-8000
Key Personnel
Dir, Mktg: Rebecca Powell
Busn Mgr: Randi Goldberg

The Globe Pequot Press
Division of Morris Book Publishing LLC
246 Goose Lane, Guilford, CT 06437
SAN: 201-9892
Mailing Address: PO Box 480, Guilford, CT
   06437-0480
Tel: 203-458-4500 *Toll Free Tel:* 800-243-
   0495 (cust serv) *Fax:* 203-458-4601
   Toll Free Fax: 800-820-2329 (orders & cust
   serv)
E-mail: info@globepequot.com
Web Site: www.globepequot.com
Key Personnel
Pres & Publr: Linda Kennedy *E-mail:* linda.
   kennedy@globepequot.com
Dir, Mktg: Shana Capozza *Tel:* 203-458-4534
   Fax: 203-458-4603 *E-mail:* shana.capozza@
   globepequot.com
Exec Ed: Mary Norris *Tel:* 203-458-4520
   E-mail: mary.norris@globepequot.com; Laura
   Strom *Tel:* 203-458-4506 *E-mail:* laura.strom@
   globepequot.com; Erin Turner *Tel:* 406-442-
   6597 *E-mail:* erin.turner@globepequot.com
Edit Dir, Lyons Press: Jay Cassell *Tel:* 203-458-
   4631 *E-mail:* jay.cassell@lyonspress.com
Edit Dir, Globe-Falcon: Jeff Serena *Tel:* 203-458-
   4556 *E-mail:* jeff.serena@globepequot.com
Sr Ed, Lyons Press: Tom McCarthy *Tel:* 203-458-
   4652 *E-mail:* tom.mccarthy@lyonspress.com;
   Ann Tristman *Tel:* 203-458-3644 *E-mail:* ann.
   tristman@lyonspress.com
VP, Trade Sales: Larry Dorfman *Tel:* 203-458-
   4532 *E-mail:* larry.dorfman@globepequot.com

VP, Sales: Lee Miller *Tel:* 203-458-4537
  E-mail: lee.miller@globepequot.com
Dir, Spec Sales: Max Phelps *Tel:* 203-458-4551
  E-mail: max.phelps@globepequot.com
Dir, Prodn: Kevin Lynch *Tel:* 203-458-4507
  E-mail: kevin.lynch@globepequot.com
Dir, E-Business Devt: Patty Gallagher *Tel:* 203-458-4535 *E-mail:* patricia.gallagher@
  globepequot.com
Dir, Subs Rts: Gail Blackhall *Tel:* 203-458-4540
  E-mail: gail.blackhall@globepequot.com
Mgr, Cust Serv: Marcia Bird *Tel:* 203-458-4561
  E-mail: marcia.bird@globepequot.com
Mgr, Dist Busn: Andrea Jacobs *Tel:* 203-458-4552 *E-mail:* andrea.jacobs@globepequot.com
Founded: 1947
Travel guidebooks, regional books, sports, how-to, outdoor recreation, personal finance, sports, cooking, entertaining, military history, fishing, hunting, gift books.
ISBN Prefix(es): 0-937959; 1-56044; 1-57380; 1-57540; 1-882997; 0-87842; 0-87106; 0-7511; 0-7627; 0-89933; 0-934641; 1-56440; 0-912367; 0-933469; 0-934802; 0-934318; 1-57034
Number of titles published annually: 600 Print; 600 E-Book
Total Titles: 3,500 Print; 1,000 E-Book
Imprints: Cadogan Guides; Falcon®; FalconGuide®; Fun with the Family; Illustrated Living History Series; Insiders' Guides®; The Lyons Press; Off The Beaten Path®; On My Mind Series; Outside America; Recommended Country Inns®; ThreeForks; Travelers Companion; TwoDot®; Voyager Books
Foreign Office(s): Cadogan Guides, Network House, One Ariel Way, London W12 7SL, United Kingdom *Tel:* (020) 8740-2050 *Fax:* (020) 8740-2059 *E-mail:* info@ cadoganguides.com *Web Site:* www. cadoganguides.com
Distributor for Alastair Sawday Publishing; Appalachian Mountain Club; Boone & Crockett Club; Cadogan Guides; Day Hikes Books Inc; Ducks Unlimited; Earthbound Sports; Everyman Chess; Menasha Ridge Press; Mobil Travel Guide; Montana Historical Society Press; New Holland Publishers Ltd; Oval Books; Thomas Cook Publishing; Trailblazer Publications; Vacation Work Publications; Waterford Press; Western Horseman; Woodall Publications
Foreign Rep(s): Athena Productions (International); Canadian Manda Group (Canada); Peribo (Australia); Windsor Publications International (UK)
Distribution Center: 128 Pinnacle Dr, Springfield, TN 37172, Dist Ctr Mgr: Mark Love *Tel:* 615-382-3983 *Toll Free Tel:* 800-955-3983 *Fax:* 615-382-6952 *E-mail:* mark.love@ globepequot.com
Membership(s): AAP; ABA; BISG; NEBA
See separate listing for:
The Lyons Press

Glory Bound Books
6642 Marlette St, Suite 101, Marlette, MI 48453
Mailing Address: PO Box 278, Cass City, MI 48726
Tel: 989-635-7520
E-mail: info@gloryboundenterprises.com
Web Site: www.thegloryboundbookcompany.com
Key Personnel
Publr & Fiction Ed: Leah M Berry
Poetry Ed: Cindy Knowlton
Founded: 1996
Mid-sized Christian publisher of paperback & e-book originals. Books: digital press, perfect binding, photos, line art, illustrations; average print order 500-1000 copies. Do not accept agented submissions, phone or e-mail queries. Additional information available on the website.

ISBN Prefix(es): 0-9743192
Number of titles published annually: 10 Print; 10 Online; 4 E-Book
Total Titles: 5 Print; 5 Online; 3 E-Book

David R Godine Publisher Inc
9 Hamilton Place, Boston, MA 02108
SAN: 213-4381
Tel: 617-451-9600 *Fax:* 617-350-0250
E-mail: info@godine.com
Web Site: www.godine.com
Key Personnel
Pres: David R Godine
Publicity Dir: Carl W Scarbrough
Prodn Mgr: Jennifer De Lancy
Subs & Foreign Rts: Robert Charlton
Founded: 1969
Fiction & nonfiction, history, biography, typography, art & photography, poetry, horticulture, Americana, cooking, regional, mysteries, juveniles.
ISBN Prefix(es): 0-87923; 1-56792
Number of titles published annually: 25 Print
Total Titles: 400 Print
Imprints: Imago Mundi; Nonpareil Books; Pocket Paragon; Verba Mundi
Editorial Office(s): 9 Hamilton Place, Boston, MA 02108 SAN: 213-4381
Sales Office(s): 426 Nutting Rd, PO Box 450, Jaffrey, NH 03452
Distributor for Black Sparrow Books
Foreign Rep(s): Airlift Book Co (UK, Europe); Hushion House Publishing (Canada)
Foreign Rights: Mercedes Casanovas (Spain); The English Agency (Japan); Paul & Peter Fritz (Germany); Caroline van Gelderen Literary Agency (Netherlands); Harris/Elon Agency (Israel); Korea Copyright Center (Korea); Catherine Lapautre (France); Michelle Lapautre (France); Natoli, Stefan & Oliva (Italy); Sheil Land Associates (UK); Transnet Contracts Ltd (Central Europe)
Orders to: 426 Nutting Rd, PO Box 450, Jaffrey, NH 03452
Warehouse: 426 Nutting Rd, PO Box 450, Jaffrey, NH 03452 *Tel:* 603-532-4100 *Toll Free Tel:* 800-344-4771 *Fax:* 603-532-5940 *Toll Free Fax:* 800-226-0934 *E-mail:* order@godine.com
Web Site: www.godine.com
Membership(s): AAP

Golden Educational Center
857 Lake Blvd, Redding, CA 96003
Tel: 530-244-0101 *Toll Free Tel:* 800-800-1791
  Fax: 530-244-5939
E-mail: info@goldened.com
Web Site: goldened.com
Key Personnel
Pres: Randy L Womack *E-mail:* randy@goldened.com
VP: Theresa J Womack *E-mail:* terry@goldened.com
Founded: 1985
Textbooks, Reproducible workbooks.
ISBN Prefix(es): 1-56500
Number of titles published annually: 3 Print
Total Titles: 43 Print
Divisions: A Plus Discounted Materials

Golden Gryphon Press
3002 Perkins Rd, Urbana, IL 61802
Tel: 217-840-0672 *Fax:* 217-384-4205; 217-352-9748
E-mail: gryphon@goldengryphon.com
Key Personnel
Publr: Gary Turner
Founded: 1997
ISBN Prefix(es): 1-930846
Number of titles published annually: 6 Print
Total Titles: 30 Print

Golden West Books
Division of Pacific Railroad Publications Inc
525 N Electric Ave, Alhambra, CA 91801
SAN: 201-6400
Mailing Address: PO Box 80250, San Marino, CA 91118-8250
Tel: 626-458-8148 *Fax:* 626-458-8148
Key Personnel
Pres, Publr & Rts & Perms: Donald Duke
Treas & Cust Rel: Ruth Rodgers
Sales Mgr: Raymond C Geyer
Art Dir: Harlan Hiney
Founded: 1954
ISBN Prefix(es): 0-87095
Number of titles published annually: 4 Print
Total Titles: 50 Print
Imprints: Athletic Press

Golden West Publishers
4113 N Longview, Phoenix, AZ 85014
Tel: 602-265-4392 *Toll Free Tel:* 800-658-5830
  Fax: 602-279-6901
Web Site: www.goldenwestpublishers.com
Key Personnel
Ed: Hal Mitchell
Pres: Lee Fischer
Founded: 1973
Cookbooks & books on Southwest nonfiction.
ISBN Prefix(es): 0-914846; 1-885590
Number of titles published annually: 15 Print
Total Titles: 125 Print

Gollehon Press Inc
6157 28 St SE, Grand Rapids, MI 49546
Tel: 616-949-3515 *Fax:* 619-949-8674
Key Personnel
Pres: John T Gollehon *E-mail:* john@ gollehonbooks.com
Publr: Kathy Gollehon
Ed: Becky A Anderson
Sales Mgr: Jerome K Smith
Founded: 1983
Books related to health, how-to, reference, antiques, collectibles & gaming. Gollehon does not accept unsol mss. Brief book proposals are reviewed. Simultaneous submissions are encouraged.
ISBN Prefix(es): 0-914839
Number of titles published annually: 10 Print
Total Titles: 79 Print
Imprints: Gollehon Books; GPC/Gollehon
Warehouse: Offset/Gollehon Distribution Center, 10 Passan Dr, Bldg 10, Laflin, PA 18702

Good Books
Subsidiary of Good Enterprises Ltd
3510 Old Philadelphia Pike, Intercourse, PA 17534
SAN: 693-9597
Mailing Address: PO Box 419, Intercourse, PA 17534
Tel: 717-768-3008 *Toll Free Tel:* 800-762-7171 *Fax:* 717-768-3433 *Toll Free Fax:* 888-768-3433
E-mail: custserv@goodbks.com
Web Site: www.goodbks.com
Key Personnel
Publr, Mktg Mgr & Intl Rts Contact: Merle Good
Sr Ed: Phyllis Good
Founded: 1979
Trade hardcover & paperback books: Americana, cookbooks, crafts, general nonfiction, children's, how-to, family/parenting, notebooks, inspirational, calendars.
ISBN Prefix(es): 0-934672; 1-56148
Number of titles published annually: 20 Print
Total Titles: 280 Print
Foreign Rights: Kenneth Pellman
Advertising Agency: Good Advertising

Goodheart-Willcox Publisher
18604 W Creek Dr, Tinley Park, IL 60477-6243
SAN: 203-4387

Tel: 708-687-5000 *Toll Free Tel:* 800-323-0440
Fax: 708-687-0315 *Toll Free Fax:* 888-409-
3900
E-mail: custserv@g-w.com
Web Site: www.g-w.com
Key Personnel
Pres & CEO: John F Flanagan
VP, Admin & Treas: Robert Kelly
VP, Sales: Todd Scheffers
Adv Dir: Brenda Bothwell *Tel:* 708-687-5000 ext
1126 *E-mail:* bbothwell@goodheartwillcox.com
Sales Mgr: Chris Hegg
Founded: 1921
Industrial technical; family & consumer sciences
& career textbooks.
ISBN Prefix(es): 0-87006; 1-56637
Number of titles published annually: 25 Print
Total Titles: 150 Print; 100 CD-ROM; 150 Online
Foreign Rep(s): Baker & Taylor International
(Europe)

GoodSAMARitan Press
PO Box 803282, Santa Clarita, CA 91380
Tel: 661-799-0694
Key Personnel
Man Ed: Jerome Brooke *E-mail:* jeromebrooke@
sbcglobal.net
Sr Ed: Jovita Ador Lee
Founded: 1996
Publisher of poetry chapbooks, paperbacks & lit-
erary journals.
ISBN Prefix(es): 1-930714
Number of titles published annually: 7 Print
Total Titles: 70 Print

Gordian Press
37 Crescent Ave, Staten Island, NY 10301
SAN: 201-6389
Mailing Address: PO Box 40304, Staten Island,
NY 10304
Tel: 718-273-4700 *Fax:* 718-273-4700
Key Personnel
Pres, Ed & Rts & Perms: Roger Texier
E-mail: roger.texier@verizon.net
Founded: 1964
Reprints & original titles.
ISBN Prefix(es): 0-87752; 0-87753
Number of titles published annually: 5 Print
Total Titles: 275 Print
Imprints: Phaeton Press
Distributor for Phaeton Press

Gospel Publishing House
Division of General Council of the Assemblies of
God
1445 Boonville Ave, Springfield, MO 65802-1894
SAN: 206-8826
Tel: 417-831-8000 *Toll Free Tel:* 800-641-4310
Fax: 417-863-1874; 417-862-7566
Web Site: www.gospelpublishing.com
Key Personnel
Natl Dir & Gen Mgr: Arlyn Pember *Tel:* 417-
831-8000 ext 4200
Founded: 1914
Religion (Assemblies of God); sign-language text-
books & curricular materials.
ISBN Prefix(es): 0-88243
Number of titles published annually: 6 Print
Total Titles: 250 Print
Imprints: Logion Press; Radiant Books; Radiant
Life Curricular
Distributed by Spring Arbor

Gossamer Books LLC
2112 Gossamer Ave, Redwood Shores, CA 94065
Tel: 650-257-4058 *Fax:* 650-257-4058
E-mail: info@gossamerbooks.com
Web Site: www.gossamerbooks.com
Key Personnel
Pres: Angel Oberoi
Founded: 2003

Brings history alive through high quality educa-
tional graphic novels.
ISBN Prefix(es): 0-9742502
Number of titles published annually: 6 Print
Total Titles: 1 Print
Membership(s): Publishers Marketing Association

§Gould Publications Inc
1333 N US Hwy 17-92, Longwood, FL 32750-
3724
SAN: 201-6354
Tel: 407-695-9500 *Toll Free Tel:* 800-717-7917
Fax: 407-695-2906
E-mail: info@gouldlaw.com
Web Site: www.gouldlaw.com
Key Personnel
VP: Jeffrey S Gould *E-mail:* jsg@gouldlaw.com
Founded: 1953
Multimedia publisher of law & secondary & col-
lege textbooks. Online catalog & ordering.
ISBN Prefix(es): 0-87526
Number of titles published annually: 200 Print
Total Titles: 353 Print; 61 CD-ROM

Grade Finders Inc
662 Exton Commons, Exton, PA 19341
Mailing Address: PO Box 944, Exton, PA 19341
Tel: 610-524-7070 *Fax:* 610-524-8912
E-mail: info@gradefinders.com
Web Site: www.gradefinders.com
Key Personnel
CEO: William A Subers *Tel:* 610-524-7500
E-mail: bill@gradefinders.com
Pres: Mark Subers
Prodn Mgr: Kris Danato
Founded: 1967
Producer of paper buyers guides (USA & Eu-
rope); publish 3 business directories on paper
grades on the Internet.
ISBN Prefix(es): 0-929502
Number of titles published annually: 3 Print; 3
Online; 3 E-Book
Total Titles: 3 Print; 3 Online; 3 E-Book
Distributed by Graphic Arts Association; National
Paper Trade Assoc

The Graduate Group/Booksellers
86 Norwood Rd, West Hartford, CT 06117-2236
Mailing Address: PO Box 370351, West Hartford,
CT 06137-0351
Tel: 860-233-2330 *Toll Free Tel:* 800-484-7280
ext 3579 *Fax:* 860-233-2330
E-mail: graduategroup@hotmail.com
Web Site: www.graduategroup.com
Key Personnel
Partner: Amy Gibson *E-mail:* agibson@
graduategroup.com; Mara Whitman
Lib Sales Dir: Robert Whitman *Tel:* 860-232-
3100
Founded: 1964
Publish career oriented reference books & self-
help books for libraries, career & placement
offices in the US & abroad, law enforcement,
career series, exam preparation.
ISBN Prefix(es): 0-938609
Number of titles published annually: 20 Print; 1
Online
Total Titles: 100 Print; 2 Online
Orders to: Web Site: www.graduategroup.com

Grafco Productions Inc
291 Pat Mell Rd, Suite 101, Marietta, GA 30060
Tel: 770-436-1500 *Toll Free Tel:* 888-656-1500
Fax: 770-444-9357
E-mail: jabo@rightconnections.net
Web Site: www.jackwboone.com
Key Personnel
Publr & Intl Rts: Anne Q Boone
Founded: 1964
General trade.
ISBN Prefix(es): 1-880719
Number of titles published annually: 4 Print

Total Titles: 16 Print
Imprints: Grafco Rock Books
Membership(s): Publishers Marketing Association

Donald M Grant Publisher Inc
PO Box 187, Hampton Falls, NH 03844-0187
Tel: 603-778-7191 *Fax:* 603-778-7191
E-mail: grantbooks@aol.com
Web Site: www.grantbooks.com
Key Personnel
Pres: Robert K Wiener *E-mail:* robert@
grantbooks.com
VP: Donald M Grant
Dir, Opers: KelLee Larson *E-mail:* kellee@
grantbooks.com
Oper Asst: Kate Clark *E-mail:* kate@grantbooks.
com
Founded: 1964
Horror, science fiction, art & fantasy illustrated
books.
ISBN Prefix(es): 0-937986; 1-880418
Number of titles published annually: 3 Print
Total Titles: 55 Print
Distributor for Archival; Oswald Train

Graphic Arts Center Publishing Co
3019 NW Yeon Ave, Portland, OR 97210
SAN: 201-6338
Mailing Address: PO Box 10306, Portland, OR
97296-0306
Tel: 503-226-2402 *Toll Free Tel:* 800-452-3032
Fax: 503-223-1410 *Toll Free Fax:* 800-355-
9685
E-mail: editorial@gacpc.com; sales@gacpc.com
Web Site: www.gacpc.com
Key Personnel
Pres: Mike Hopkins *Tel:* 800-452-3032 ext 250
E-mail: mikeh@gacpc.com
VP: Douglas A Pfeiffer *Tel:* 800-452-3032 ext
282 *E-mail:* dougp@gacpc.com
Dir, Sales & Mktg: Mike Jones *E-mail:* mikej@
gacpc.com
Exec Ed: Tim Frew *Tel:* 800-452-3032 ext 280
E-mail: timf@gacpc.com
Proj Ed: Jean Andrews *Tel:* 800-452-3032 ext 284
E-mail: jeana@gacpc.com
Acq Ed: Tricia Brown *Tel:* 800-452-3032 ext 234
E-mail: triciab@gacpc.com
Prodn Mgr: Dick Owsiany *Tel:* 800-452-3032 ext
259 *E-mail:* dicko@gacpc.com
MIS Mgr: Steve Anderson
Founded: 1968
International, state & regional photographic
books, illustrated history books, electronic
books, cookbooks, travel guides, calendars,
children's books, juvenile fiction, natural his-
tory, almanacs, field guides, native heritage,
aviation & art.
ISBN Prefix(es): 0-912856; 0-932575; 1-55868;
0-88240
Number of titles published annually: 40 Print
Total Titles: 475 Print
Imprints: Alaska Northwest Books®; Graphic
Arts Books; WestWinds Press®
Branch Office(s)
203 W 15 Ave, No 108, Anchorage, AK 99501,
Contact: Sara Juday *Tel:* 907-278-8838
Fax: 907-278-8839 *E-mail:* saraj@gacpc.com
Distributor for AMES (automotive); Epicenter
Press (Alaskan history & travel); Harbour Pub-
lishing; Roundup Press (aviation); Stoecklein
Publishing; Whitecap Books (cookbooks); Wolf
Creek Books
Foreign Rep(s): Ted Dougherty APS (Europe);
Vollmer Communications (Germany); Whitecap
Books (Canada)
Warehouse: 2619 NW Industrial St, Portland, OR
97210
Membership(s): Publishers Association of the
West

Graphic Arts Publishing Inc
3100 Bronson Hill Rd, Livonia, NY 14487-9716

Tel: 716-346-6978 *Toll Free Tel:* 800-724-9476
Fax: 716-346-2276
Key Personnel
Pres: Miles F Southworth *E-mail:* mfsouth@aol.
com
VP & Sec-Treas: Donna K Southworth
Founded: 1979
Books relating to printed color reproduction &
quality control; journals, mail order books, dic-
tionaries.
ISBN Prefix(es): 0-933600
Number of titles published annually: 1 Print
Total Titles: 9 Print

Graphic Learning
Division of Abrams & Co Publishers Inc
61 Mattatuck Heights Rd, Waterbury, CT 06705
Mailing Address: PO Box 10025, Waterbury, CT
06725
Tel: 203-756-6562 *Toll Free Tel:* 800-874-
0029; 800-227-9120 *Fax:* 203-756-2895
Toll Free Fax: 800-737-3322
Key Personnel
Pres: Daniel Wasp
Sr VP: Arthur O Peterson
VP, Opers: William Thomas
VP, Mktg: Daniel Coakley
CFO & VP, Fin & HR: Judith Maya
VP, Edit Servs: Kathleen Fischer
Cust Serv: Bill Thomas
Founded: 1970
Social studies.
ISBN Prefix(es): 0-87746; 0-07665
Total Titles: 20 Print

Gray & Company Publishers
1588 E 40 St, Cleveland, OH 44103
Tel: 216-431-2665 *Toll Free Tel:* 800-915-3609
E-mail: info@grayco.com
Web Site: www.grayco.com
Key Personnel
Pres: David Gray
Man Ed: Karen Fuller *E-mail:* editorial@grayco.
com
Mktg: Chris Andrikanich *E-mail:* promotions@
grayco.com
Founded: 1991
Books about Cleveland & Northeast Ohio &
Ohio.
ISBN Prefix(es): 1-886228
Number of titles published annually: 10 Print
Total Titles: 44 Print

Graywolf Press
2402 University Ave, Suite 203, St Paul, MN
55114
Tel: 651-641-0077 *Fax:* 651-641-0036
E-mail: wolves@graywolfpress.org
Web Site: www.graywolfpress.org
Key Personnel
Publr: Fiona McCrae
Man Dir: Janna Rademacher
Exec Ed: Anne Czarniecki
Poetry Ed: Jeffrey Shotts
Ed: Katie Dublinski *E-mail:* dublinsk@
graywolfpress.org
Founded: 1974
Poetry, fiction, essays, memoir.
ISBN Prefix(es): 0-915308; 1-55597
Number of titles published annually: 20 Print
Total Titles: 122 Print; 1 E-Book
Distributed by Farrar, Straus & Giroux
Distributor for Aperture
Foreign Rights: Michael Meller Agency (West
Germany)
Billing Address: Von Holtzbrinck Publishing
Services, 16365 James Madison Hwy, Gor-
donsville, VA 22942
Returns: Farrar, Straus & Giroux, c/o VHPS,
14301 Litchfield Rd, Orange, VA 22960
Shipping Address: Farrar, Straus & Giroux, c/o
VHPS, 14301 Litchfield Rd, Orange, VA 22960

Warehouse: Farrar, Straus & Giroux, c/o VHPS,
16365 James Madison Hwy, Gordonsville, VA
22942
Distribution Center: Von Holtzbrinck Publishing
Services, 16365 James Madison Hwy, Gordonsville, VA 22942 *Tel:* 212-206-5311 *Toll
Free Tel:* 888-330-8477 *Fax:* 540-672-7540

Great Potential Press
Division of Anodyne Inc
PO Box 5057, Scottsdale, AZ 85261
Tel: 602-954-4200 *Toll Free Tel:* 877-954-4200
Fax: 602-954-0185
E-mail: info@giftedbooks.com
Web Site: www.giftedbooks.com
Key Personnel
Pres: James T Webb
Founded: 1986
Books relating to social/emotional needs & other
characteristics of gifted children. Types of Pub-
lications: Educational Guide Books & books
for parents & adults.
ISBN Prefix(es): 0-910707
Number of titles published annually: 8 Print; 4
Audio
Total Titles: 35 Print
Distributed by Dandy Lion Press; KIDPROV;
Zephyr Press Inc
Foreign Rights: Hans Huber AG; Liepman AG;
Psychological Publishing Co Inc
Returns: 5223 N 41 Place, Phoenix, AZ 85018
Membership(s): Arizona Book Publishing Associ-
ation; Publishers Marketing Association

Great Quotations Inc
8102 Lemont Rd, Suite 300, Woodridge, IL
60517
Tel: 630-390-3580 *Toll Free Tel:* 800-830-3020
Fax: 630-390-3585
E-mail: greatquotations@yahoo.com
Key Personnel
Pres: Ringo Suek
Founded: 1984
Motivation, inspiration & humor titles, also gifts.
ISBN Prefix(es): 1-56245; 0-931089
Number of titles published annually: 30 Print
Total Titles: 500 Print
Imprints: G Q Publishing

Great Source Education Group
Subsidiary of Houghton Mifflin Co
181 Ballardvale St, Wilmington, MA 01887
Tel: 978-661-1300 *Toll Free Tel:* 800-289-4490
(orders)
Key Personnel
Pres: Steven Zukowski
VP & Dir, Devt: Tina Miller
VP & Natl Sales Dir: Linda Schilling
VP & Dir, Adv & Promos: Andrea Burr
VP & Dir, Mktg: Lisa Bingen
VP & Dir, Info Tech: Carl Saslow
Supplemental school instructional materials.

Great White Dog Picture Co, see Light-Beams
Publishing

Green Knight Publishing
360 Chiquita Ave, No 4, Mountain View, CA
94041
Tel: 650-964-4276 *Fax:* 650-964-4276
E-mail: gawaine@greenknight.com
Web Site: www.greenknight.com
Key Personnel
Publr: Peter Corless
Exec Ed, Fiction: James Lowder *Tel:* 262-821-
1134
Founded: 1998
Home of the Pendragon fiction line which
presents the best of modern Arthurian litera-
ture, from reprints of long unavailable classics
of the early 20th century to new works by to-

day's most exciting & inventive fantasists; also
producers of Pendragon Online; use the follow-
ing address for fiction submission only: 15120
W Mayflower Ct, New Berlin, WI 53151.
ISBN Prefix(es): 1-928999
Number of titles published annually: 8 Print
Total Titles: 4 Print
Distribution Center: Osseum Entertainment, 410
E Denny Way, PMB 19, Seattle, WA 98122-
2124 *Tel:* 206-568-6700 *Fax:* 206-374-2955

Green Nature Books
5290 SE 11 Dr, Bushnell, FL 33585
Mailing Address: PO Box 105, Sumterville, FL
33585
Tel: 352-793-5496
E-mail: info@greennaturebooks.com
Web Site: www.greennaturebooks.com
Key Personnel
Publr: Richard Cary Paull
E-mail: richardcarypaull@aol.com
Founded: 1995
ISBN Prefix(es): 1-888089
Number of titles published annually: 5 Print; 1
CD-ROM
Total Titles: 20 Print; 1 CD-ROM
Imprints: Our Orchids
Foreign Rep(s): Joanna Kabat-Hyzah (Poland)

Warren H Green Inc
8356 Olive Blvd, St Louis, MO 63132
SAN: 201-4939
Tel: 314-991-1335 *Toll Free Tel:* 800-537-0655
Fax: 314-997-1788
E-mail: whgreen@inlink.com
Web Site: www.whgreen.com
Key Personnel
Pres & Ed: Joyce R Green
Assoc Ed: Lucy Knapp *E-mail:* lucyknapp@
whgreen.com
Founded: 1966
ISBN Prefix(es): 0-87527
Number of titles published annually: 50 Print
Total Titles: 300 Print
Imprints: Epoch Press; Greenart Books
Foreign Office(s): White Cross Mills, High Town,
Lancaster LA1 4XS, United Kingdom
Foreign Rights: China Books (Australia); Literary
Services (South Africa)

Greene Bark Press Inc
PO Box 1108, Bridgeport, CT 06601-1108
Tel: 203-372-4861 *Fax:* 203-371-5856
E-mail: greenebark@aol.com
Web Site: www.greenebarkpress.com
Key Personnel
Publr & Intl Rts: Thomas J Greene
Founded: 1991
Children books; fictions ages 3-8; CD-ROMs.
ISBN Prefix(es): 1-880851
Number of titles published annually: 4 Print; 4
Online
Total Titles: 38 Print; 20 CD-ROM; 58 Online
Divisions: Greene Bark Press Music Co; T J
Greene Associates
Distributor for Pumpkin Patch Publishing
Shipping Address: 225 Research Dr, Unit 10/
11, Milford, CT 06460, Contact: Thomas J
Greene *Tel:* 203-877-6772 *Fax:* 203-371-5856
E-mail: greenebark@aol.com *Web Site:* www.
greenebarkpress.com
Warehouse: 225 Research Dr, Unit 10/11, Mil-
ford, CT 06460
Distribution Center: 225 Research Dr, Unit 10/11,
Milford, CT 06460
Membership(s): ABC; Independent Publishers of
New England; Publishers Marketing Associ-
ation; Small Publishers Association of North
America

Greenhaven Press®
Imprint of Thomson Gale

15822 Bernardo Center Dr, Suite C, San Diego, CA 92127
Tel: 858-485-7424 *Toll Free Tel:* 800-877-4253 (cust serv & orders) *Fax:* 858-485-9549; 248-699-8051 (cust serv) *Toll Free Fax:* 800-414-5043 (orders only)
E-mail: customerservice@gale.com; galeord@gale.com (orders)
Web Site: www.gale.com/greenhaven
Key Personnel
Publr: Bonnie Szumski
Office Mgr: Sonya Parker
Founded: 1970
High school, college & secondary nonfiction social studies & debate books for classrooms & libraries: social studies reference series; library & paper bound books in area studies, criminal justice, the environment, health, Literary Companion & American History series & AT Issues series.
ISBN Prefix(es): 0-89908; 1-56510; 0-7377
Number of titles published annually: 500 Print
Total Titles: 3,000 Print

Delano Greenidge Editions
14 Mount Morris Park W, Suite 7, New York, NY 10027-6317
Tel: 917-492-8014 *Fax:* 917-492-0966
E-mail: dge@thing.net
Key Personnel
CEO: Delano Greenidge
Art Dir: Enzo Cornacchione *E-mail:* enzoc@boutique-creativa.com
Founded: 1997
Visual books in the areas of art, photography, design & architecture.
ISBN Prefix(es): 0-929445
Number of titles published annually: 20 Print
Total Titles: 15 Print
Returns: Weatherhill, 41 Monroe Tpke, Trumbull, CT 06611-1315 *Toll Free Tel:* 800-437-7840 *Fax:* 203-459-5095
Distribution Center: CDS Books, 1094 Flex Dr, Jackson, TN 38301 *Toll Free Tel:* 800-343-4499

Greenleaf Book Group LLC
Division of Greenleaf Enterprises Inc
Longhorn Bldg, Suite 600, 3rd fl, 4425 Mopac S, Austin, TX 78735
Tel: 512-891-6100 *Toll Free Tel:* 800-932-5420
Fax: 512-891-6150
E-mail: email@greenleafbookgroup.com
Web Site: www.greenleafbookgroup.com
Key Personnel
CEO & Chmn: Clinton T Greenleaf, III *E-mail:* clint@greenleafbookgroup.com
Exec VP: Meg La Borde *E-mail:* meg@greenleafbookgroup.com
Founded: 1997
Provides new publishers & authors with expert book production, nationwide distribution, comprehensive marketing & consulting services. Work with virtually every category of nonfiction. Publishes, distributes & markets approximately 20 new books each season. Our goal is to strengthen the voices of talented authors & publishers by escalating their influence in the industry & in the marketplace.
ISBN Prefix(es): 0-9665319; 1-929774
Number of titles published annually: 100 Print
Total Titles: 350 Print
Imprints: Conation Press; Greenleaf Enterprises Inc
Membership(s): Publishers Marketing Association; Small Publishers Association of North America

Greenleaf Press
3761 Hwy 109 N, Unit D, Lebanon, TN 37087
SAN: 297-8555
Tel: 615-449-1617 *Fax:* 615-449-4018

E-mail: info@greenleafpress.com
Web Site: www.greenleafpress.com
Key Personnel
Pres: Robert G Shearer
Founded: 1988
History, biography & historical fiction for children.
ISBN Prefix(es): 1-882514
Number of titles published annually: 16 Print
Total Titles: 30 Print

§Greenwich Publishing Group Inc
929 Boston Post Rd, Suite 9, Old Saybrook, CT 06475
Tel: 860-388-9941
E-mail: info@greenwichpublishing.com
Web Site: www.greenwichpublishing.com
Key Personnel
Publr: W John Hostnik, Jr *E-mail:* john@greenwichpublishing.com
Sr Ed: Peter Hawes *E-mail:* peter@greenwichpublishing.com
Sr Proj Mgr: Kathryn Anderson *E-mail:* kathy@greenwichpublishing.com
Founded: 1987
Corporate histories & biographies.
ISBN Prefix(es): 0-944641
Number of titles published annually: 7 Print
Total Titles: 63 Print
Imprints: Bellemore Books

§Greenwood Publishing Group Inc
Division of Reed Elsevier
88 Post Rd W, Westport, CT 06880-4208
SAN: 213-2028
Mailing Address: PO Box 5007, Westport, CT 06881-5007
Tel: 203-226-3571 *Toll Free Tel:* 800-225-5800 *Fax:* 203-222-1502
E-mail: bookinfo@greenwood.com (general); firstintial&fulllastname@greenwood.com (individuals)
Web Site: www.greenwood.com
Key Personnel
Pres: Wayne Smith
CFO: Jim Masullo
VP, Opers: Bob Chase
VP, Mktg: Linda May
VP, Planning: Ron Maas
VP, Edit: Gary Kuris
VP, Sales: Bob Cate
Dir, Prod: Lisa Rowe
Dir, Mktg: Karin Cholak
Dir, Devt: Vince Burns
Edit Dir, Praeger: Peter Kracht
Natl Accts Mgr: Susie Stroud
Mgr, Ed Admin: Margaret Maybury
Lib Systems Sales: Mary Marshall
Founded: 1967
Original general nonfiction & reference, text & professional books, hardback & paperback, in social & behavioral sciences, humanities, business & law.
ISBN Prefix(es): 0-8371; 0-313; 0-89930; 0-275; 0-89789; 0-86569; 1-56720
Number of titles published annually: 800 Print; 3 Online; 250 E-Book
Total Titles: 20,000 Print; 15 Online; 4,000 E-Book
Imprints: GP Subscription Publications; Greenwood Electronic Media; Greenwood Press; Libraries Unlimited
Divisions: Heinemann
Foreign Office(s): Greenwood International, Halley Ct, Jordan Jill, Oxford OX2 PEJ, United Kingdom
Foreign Rep(s): APD Singapore Pte Ltd (Brunei, Cambodia, Indonesia, Laos, Malaysia, Puerto Rico, Philippines, Singapore, Thailand, Vietnam); Asia Publishers Services (Hong Kong, Korea, People's Republic of China, Taiwan); Avicenna Partnership (Bill Kennedy) (Egypt, Gulf States, Iran, Lebanon, Syria, Iraq, Libya);

Avicenna Partnership (Claire de Gruchy) (Cyprus, Jordan, Malta, Morocco, Turkey, Tunisia, Algeria, Palestine); Cranbury International LLC (Caribbean, Central America, Mexico, South America); DA Information Services (Australia, New Zealand); Rodney Franklin Agency (Israel); Heinemann International Southern Africa (South Africa); Overleaf (Bangladesh, India, Pakistan, Sri Lanka); Kelvin Van Hasselt (Africa, Ethiopia, Cote d'Ivoire (Ivory Coast), Eritrea, Rwanda); Yushodo Co Ltd (Japan)
Shipping Address: Greenwood-Heinemann, 300 Exchange Dr, Suite B, Crystal Lake, IL 60014
See separate listing for:
Heinemann
Heinemann/Boynton Cook Publishers Inc

§Greenwood Research Books & Software
Division of Greenwood Research
PO Box 12102, Wichita, KS 67277-2102
Tel: 316-214-5103
E-mail: grnwdrsch@hotmail.com
Web Site: grnwd.tripod.com
Key Personnel
Intl Rts, Lib Sales Dir & Gen Mgr: James A Green *E-mail:* jim_green_himself@yahoo.com
Founded: 1990 (In Clearwater, FL; moved to Wichita, KS in 1991)
Science & Engineering emphasis: Medical Image Processing.
ISBN Prefix(es): 1-890121
Number of titles published annually: 6 Print
Total Titles: 20 Print
Imprints: Greenwood Research
Distributed by Greenwood Research; Midwest Library Service
Membership(s): Publishers Marketing Association

Grey House Publishing Inc
185 Millerton Rd, Millerton, NY 12546
Mailing Address: PO Box 860, Millerton, NY 12546
Tel: 518-789-8700 *Toll Free Tel:* 800-562-2139 *Fax:* 518-789-0556
E-mail: books@greyhouse.com
Web Site: www.greyhouse.com
Key Personnel
Pres: Richard Gottlieb *Fax:* 518-789-0544 *E-mail:* rhg@greyhouse.com
Publr: Leslie Mackenzie *E-mail:* lmackenzie@greyhouse.com
Edit Dir: Laura Mars *E-mail:* lmars@greyhouse.com
VP, Mktg: Jessica Moody *Tel:* 518-789-8700 ext 101 *E-mail:* jmoody@greyhouse.com
Founded: 1979
Specialize in directories & reference books for business, health & demographic areas.
ISBN Prefix(es): 1-930956; 1-891482; 0-939300; 1-59237
Number of titles published annually: 35 Print
Total Titles: 35 Print; 25 Online
Imprints: Grey House; Sedgwick Press; Universal Reference

Griffin Publishing Group
18022 Cowan, Suite 202, Irvine, CA 92614
Tel: 949-263-3733 *Toll Free Tel:* 800-472-9741 *Fax:* 949-263-3734
Web Site: www.griffinpublishing.com
ISBN Prefix(es): 1-882180; 1-58000
Number of titles published annually: 15 Print
Total Titles: 112 Print
Foreign Rep(s): Gazelle (Europe)

Grolier, see Scholastic Library Publishing

Grolier Online, see Scholastic Library Publishing

Grosset & Dunlap
Imprint of Penguin Group (USA) Inc

345 Hudson St, New York, NY 10014
SAN: 282-5074
Tel: 212-366-2000
E-mail: online@penguinputnam.com
Web Site: www.penguin.com
Key Personnel
Pres & Publr: Debra Dorfman
VP & Ed-at-Large: Jane O'Connor
Edit Dir: Bonnie Bader
Exec Man Ed: Nadine Topalian
Art Dir: Rosanne Guararra
Ed: Micol Ostow
Founded: 1898
ISBN Prefix(es): 0-448; 1-58184
Number of titles published annually: 162 Print
Total Titles: 1,336 Print
Imprints: Planet Dexter; Platt & Munk; PSS;
  Somerville House USA

§Group Publishing Inc
1515 Cascade Ave, Loveland, CO 80538
Mailing Address: PO Box 481, Loveland, CO
  80538
Tel: 970-669-3836 *Toll Free Tel:* 800-447-1070
  Fax: 970-678-4392
E-mail: innovatr@grouppublishing.com
Web Site: www.grouppublishing.com
Key Personnel
Publr: Thom Schultz
Lib Sales Dir: Dayle Davidson
Dir, Prod Devt & Intl Rts: David Thornton
Database Mgr: Eric Dowdy
Founded: 1974
Books, magazines, video & audio tapes, computer
  online service, curriculum.
ISBN Prefix(es): 1-55945; 0-7644; 0-931529
Number of titles published annually: 40 Print
Total Titles: 400 Print; 2 CD-ROM; 15 Audio
Imprints: Faith Weaver Bible Curriculum™;
  FW Friends™; Group Workcamps™; Group's
  Hands-On Bible Curriculum™; Kids Own Wor-
  ship™
Shipping Address: 1515 Cascade Ave, Loveland,
  CO 80538
Membership(s): CBA; Evangelical Christian Pub-
  lishers Association

Grove/Atlantic Inc
841 Broadway, 4th fl, New York, NY 10003-4793
SAN: 201-4890
Tel: 212-614-7850 *Toll Free Tel:* 800-521-0178
  Fax: 212-614-7886
Web Site: www.groveatlantic.com
Key Personnel
Pres & Publr: Morgan Entrekin
  E-mail: mentrekin@groveatlantic.com
Exec VP, Assoc Publr & COO: Eric Price
  E-mail: eric.price@groveatlantic.com
VP, Dir, Subs Rts & Sr Exec: Elisabeth Schmitz
  E-mail: eschmitz@groveatlantic.com
VP & Exec Ed: Joan Bingham
  E-mail: jbingham@groveatlantic.com
VP & Assoc Publr: Judy Hottensen
  E-mail: jhottensen@groveatlantic.com
Man Ed: Michael Hornburg *E-mail:* mhornburg@
  groveatlantic.com
Ed: Amy Hundley *E-mail:* ahundley@
  groveatlantic.com; Brando Skyhorse
  E-mail: bskyhorse@groveatlantic.com
Art Dir: Charles Woods *E-mail:* cwoods@
  groveatlantic.com
Contract & Perms: Mary Flower
  E-mail: mflower@groveatlantic.com
Dir, Acctg & Royalties: Virginia Ferrara
  E-mail: vferrara@groveatlantic.com
Subs Rts Mgr & Intl Rts: Lauren Wein
  E-mail: lauren.wein@groveatlantic.com
Subs Rts Assoc: Dara Hyde *E-mail:* dhyde@
  groveatlantic.com
Prodn Dir: Muriel Jorgensen *E-mail:* mjorgens@
  groveatlantic.com
Assoc Publr, Canongate US: Tad Floridis
  E-mail: tad.floridis@groveatlantic.com

Founded: 1952
General fiction & nonfiction, hardcover & paper-
  bound.
ISBN Prefix(es): 0-8021; 0-87113
Number of titles published annually: 150 Print; 5
  E-Book
Total Titles: 1,200 Print; 15 E-Book
Imprints: Atlantic Monthly Press; Canongate US;
  Grove Press
Sales Office(s): Publishers Group West, 1700
  Fourth St, Berkeley, CA 94710 *Tel:* 510-528-
  1444
Distributed by Publishers Group West
Distributor for Open City Books
Foreign Rep(s): Baker & Taylor Intl; Publishers
  Group Canada (Canada)
Foreign Rights: Antonella Antonelli Agenzia
  Letteraria (Italy); Carmen Balcells Agency
  (Mexico, Portugal, South America, Spain);
  Eliane Benisti Agency (France); Big Apple
  Tuttle-Mori Agency (China); BMSR (Brazil);
  Paul & Peter Fritz AG (Germany); Graal Ltd
  (Poland); International Copyright Agency (Ro-
  mania); Japan Uni Agency Inc (Japan); Katai
  & Bolza (Hungary); Korea Copyrights Center
  (Korea); Andrew Nurnberg Associates (Esto-
  nia, Latvia, Lithuania); Kristin Olson Agency
  (Czech Republic); Owl's Agency (Japan); I
  Pikarski Literary Agency (Israel); Synopsis Lit-
  erary Agency (Russia); Sane Toregard Agency
  (Netherlands, Scandinavia)
Billing Address: Publishers Group West, 1700
  Fourth St, Berkeley, CA 94710 *Tel:* 510-528-
  1444
Returns: Publishers Group West, 7326 Winton Dr,
  Indianapolis, IN 46268
Shipping Address: Publishers Group West,
  7326 Winton Dr, Indianapolis, IN 46268
  Tel: 510-528-1444 *Toll Free Tel:* 800-788-3123
  Fax: 510-528-3444 *Web Site:* www.pgw.com
Warehouse: Publishers Group West, 7326 Winton
  Dr, Indianapolis, IN 46268
Distribution Center: Publishers Group West, 7326
  Winton Dr, Indianapolis, IN 46268
Membership(s): AAP

Gryphon Books
PO Box 209, Brooklyn, NY 11228
Web Site: www.gryphonbooks.com
Key Personnel
Pres & Owner: Gary Lovisi
Founded: 1983
Book Shows, NY Collectible PB & Pulp Fiction
  Expo (annual trade show & exhibit). No mss
  accepted, only query letters with SASE.
ISBN Prefix(es): 0-936071
Number of titles published annually: 20 Print
Total Titles: 150 Print
Imprints: Gryphon Crime Series; Gryphon Dou-
  bles; Gryphon Gangster Series; Gryphon SF
  Rediscovery Series; Paperback Parade Collector
  Specials
Distributor for PPC; Zeon

Gryphon Editions
515 Madison Ave, Suite 3200, New York, NY
  10022
Tel: 212-750-1048 *Toll Free Tel:* 800-633-8911
  Fax: 212-644-6828
E-mail: gryphonnyc@aol.com
Web Site: www.gryphoneditions.com
Key Personnel
Pres: Richard G Ritter
Edit Dir: Christine Valentine
Founded: 1977
Reprints: medicine, law, political philosophy, sci-
  ence; fine editions.
Distribution Center: 801 Burlington Ave, Suite K,
  Delanco, NJ 08075

Gryphon House Inc
10726 Tucker St, Beltsville, MD 20704

Mailing Address: PO Box 207, Beltsville, MD
  20704-0207
Tel: 301-595-9500 *Toll Free Tel:* 800-638-0928
  Fax: 301-595-0051
E-mail: info@ghbooks.com
Web Site: www.gryphonhouse.com
Key Personnel
Pres: Larry Rood *E-mail:* larry@ghbooks.com
Ed-In-Chief: Kathleen Charner *E-mail:* kathyc@
  ghbooks.com
Dir, Mktg & Sales: Catherine Calliotte *Tel:* 301-
  595-9500 ext 301 *E-mail:* cathy@ghbooks.com
Publicity: Jenny Groves *E-mail:* jenny@ghbooks.
  com
Mktg Coord: Kelly Anderson *E-mail:* kelly@
  ghbooks.com
Founded: 1971
Publishes & distributes books for teachers, chil-
  dren & parents.
ISBN Prefix(es): 0-87659
Number of titles published annually: 20 Print
Total Titles: 100 Print
Imprints: Robins Lane Press
Distributed by Consortium Book Sales (Gryphon
  House & Robins Lane press titles only)
Distributor for Aha Communications; Book Ped-
  dlers; Bright Ring Publishing; Building Blocks;
  Center For The Child Care Workforce; Chat-
  terbox Press; Chicago Review Press; Children's
  Resources International; Circle Time Publish-
  ers; Sydney Gurewitz Clemens; Conari Press;
  Council Oak Books; Dawn Sign Press; Delmar
  Publishers Inc; Deya Brashears; Early Educa-
  tor's Press; Education Equity Concepts; Educa-
  tors for Social Responsibility; Family Center of
  Nova University; Jean Feldman; Floris Books;
  Hawthorne Press; Highscope; Hunter House
  Publishers; Independent Publishers Group; Ka-
  plan Press; Loving Guidance Inc; Miss Jackie
  Inc; Monjeu Press; National Association for
  the Education of Young Children; National
  Center Early Childhood Workforce; New Eng-
  land AEYC; New Horizons; Nova Southeastern
  University; Pademelon Press; Partner Press;
  Pollyanna Productions; Redleaf Press; Robins
  Lane Press; School Age Notes; School Renais-
  sance; Southern Early Childhood Association;
  Steam Press; Syracuse University Press; Teach-
  ing Strategies; Telshare Publishing
Foreign Rep(s): Monarch Books (Canada);
  Pademelon Press (Australia)
Shipping Address: Consortium Book Sales, 1045
  Westgate Dr, Saint Paul, MN 55114-1065
  (Gryphon House & Robins Lane press titles
  only) *Tel:* 651-221-9035 *Fax:* 651-221-0124
Membership(s): BEA; NACCRRA; NSSEA

Guernica Editions Inc
2250 Military Dr, Tonawanda, NY 14150
Tel: 716-693-2768 *Toll Free Tel:* 800-565-9523
  (orders) *Fax:* 716-692-7479 *Toll Free Fax:* 800-
  221-9985 (orders)
E-mail: guernicaeditions@cs.com
Web Site: www.guernicaeditions.com
Key Personnel
Pres & Publr: Antonio D'Alfonso
Lib Sales Dir: Halli Villegas
Founded: 1978
Translation into English.
ISBN Prefix(es): 0-919349; 0-920717; 2-89135;
  1-55071
Number of titles published annually: 28 Print
Total Titles: 320 Print; 1 Audio
Foreign Office(s): PO Box 117, Sta P, Toronto,
  ON M5S 2S6, Canada *Tel:* 416-658-9888
  Fax: 416-657-8885
Foreign Rights: Independent Publishers Group
  (USA); Paul & Company

**Guideposts Book & Inspirational Media
Division**
16 E 34 St, New York, NY 10016
Tel: 212-251-8100 *Fax:* 212-684-0679

Web Site: www.guidepostsbooks.com
Key Personnel
Man Ed: Elizabeth Gold *E-mail:* egold@
  guideposts.org
Ed: David Morris
Inspirational books & videos.
Number of titles published annually: 20 Print

Guild Publishing
Affiliate of Guild Inc
931 E Main St, Madison, WI 53703-2955
SAN: 697-2799
Tel: 608-257-2590 *Toll Free Tel:* 800-930-1856
  Fax: 608-257-2690
E-mail: artinfo@guild.com
Web Site: www.guild.com
Key Personnel
CEO: Toni Fountain Sikes
Pres: Michael Baum
Chief Edit Officer: Jill Schaefer
  E-mail: jschaefer@guild.com
Founded: 1986
Artists sourcebooks & other books about con-
  temporary art & artists for architects, interior
  designers, gallery & retail stores & for general
  public.
ISBN Prefix(es): 0-9616012; 1-880140; 1-893164
Number of titles published annually: 3 Print
Total Titles: 20 Print
Distributed by BHB International; F & W Publi-
  cations

§The Guilford Press
Division of Guilford Publications Inc
72 Spring St, New York, NY 10012
SAN: 212-9442
Tel: 212-431-9800 *Toll Free Tel:* 800-365-7006
  (orders) *Fax:* 212-966-6708
E-mail: orders@guilford.com
Web Site: www.guilford.com
Key Personnel
Pres & Gen Mgr: Robert Matloff *E-mail:* bob.
  matloff@guilford.com
Ed-in-Chief: Seymour Weingarten
  E-mail: seymour.weingarten@guilford.com
Man Ed: Judith Grauman *E-mail:* judith.
  grauman@guilford.com
Mktg Dir: Marian Robinson *E-mail:* marian.
  robinson@guilford.com
Prodn Mgr: Katya Edwards *E-mail:* katya.
  edwards@guilford.com
Sales Mgr & Lib Sales Dir: Anne Patota
  Tel: 212-431-9800 ext 217 *E-mail:* anne.
  patota@guilford.com
Intl Rts, Perms & ISBN Contact: Kathy Kuehl
  E-mail: kathy.kuehl@guilford.com
Fulfillment Mgr: William McEvoy
  E-mail: william.mcevoy@guilford.com
Busn Mgr: David Mitchell *E-mail:* david.
  mitchell@guilford.com
Credit Mgr: Vernita Hurston *E-mail:* vernita.
  hurston@guilford.com
Founded: 1978
Professional & reference books, videos, journals
  & software in psychology, psychiatry & the be-
  havioral sciences, neuroscience, research meth-
  ods, education & literacy & geography.
ISBN Prefix(es): 0-89862; 1-57230; 1-59385
Number of titles published annually: 75 Print
Total Titles: 825 Print; 2 CD-ROM; 16 Audio
Imprints: The Clinician's Toolbox
Foreign Office(s): Brunner-Routledge UK, 27
  Church Rd, Hove, East Sussex BN3 2FA,
  United Kingdom
Foreign Rep(s): Astam (Australia, New Zealand);
  Brunner-Routledge UK (UK, Europe); Cran-
  bury International (Caribbean, Pakistan, South
  America); Disvan Enterprises (India); Hori-
  zon Books (South Africa); International Pub-
  lisher Representatives (Middle East); Taylor &

Francis Asia Pacific (Asia, China); Unifacmanu
  (Taiwan); United Publishers Services (Japan)
Warehouse: Guilford Press, Maple Press Distribu-
  tion Ctr, I-83 Industrial Park, 60 Grumbacher
  Rd, York, PA 17402

H & M Productions II Inc
226-06 56 Ave, Bayside, NY 11361
Mailing Address: PO Box 640696, Oakland Gar-
  dens, NY 11364
Tel: 718-357-6707 *Fax:* 718-357-8920
E-mail: handm@mft.com
Key Personnel
Pres: John Henderson
Founded: 1990
Books on transportation, New York City history
  & sports.
ISBN Prefix(es): 0-9629037; 1-882608
Number of titles published annually: 5 Print
Total Titles: 20 Print

H D I Publishers
2424 Elmen St, Houston, TX 77019-6710
Mailing Address: PO Box 131401, Houston, TX
  77219-1401
Tel: 713-526-6900 *Toll Free Tel:* 800-321-7037
  Fax: 713-526-7787
Web Site: www.hdipub.com
Key Personnel
Pres: J Charles Haynes *E-mail:* chaynes@hdipub.
  com
Intl Rts & Lib Sales Dir: Joyce Parker
Founded: 1986
Books about brain injury rehabilitation & spinal
  cord injury.
ISBN Prefix(es): 1-882855
Number of titles published annually: 5 Print
Total Titles: 41 Print

Hachai Publications Inc
156 Chester Ave, Brooklyn, NY 11218
SAN: 251-3749
Tel: 718-633-0100 *Toll Free Tel:* 800-50-
  HACHAI (504-2424) *Fax:* 718-633-0103
E-mail: info@hachai.com
Web Site: www.hachai.com
Key Personnel
Pres: Yerachmiel Binyominson
Ed: Dina Rosenfeld *E-mail:* dlr@hachai.com
Publr & Sales: Yossi Leverton *E-mail:* yossi@
  hachai.com
Founded: 1988
Full color children's Judaica books.
ISBN Prefix(es): 0-922613; 1-929628
Number of titles published annually: 5 Print
Total Titles: 58 Print
Imprints: Jewish Reader Press
Distributor for Kerem
Membership(s): Association of Jewish Book Pub-
  lishers; Association of Jewish Libraries; Pub-
  lishers Marketing Association

Hackett Publishing Co Inc
PO Box 44937, Indianapolis, IN 46244-0937
SAN: 201-6044
Tel: 317-635-9250; 617-497-6306 *Fax:* 317-635-
  9292 *Toll Free Fax:* 800-783-9213
E-mail: customer@hackettpublishing.com
Web Site: www.hackettpublishing.com
Key Personnel
Chair/Publr: James Hullett
VP & Mktg Dir: John Pershing *Tel:* 617-234-
  0371 *Fax:* 617-661-8703 *E-mail:* johnp@
  hackettpublishing.com
Sec/Treas: Cheri Brown
Rts: Jenevieve Maerker
Founded: 1972
College textbooks & scholarly books; emphasis
  on philosophy, political theory, political sci-
  ence, classics, history & literature.
ISBN Prefix(es): 0-915144; 0-915145; 0-87220
Number of titles published annually: 30 Print

Total Titles: 370 Print
Editorial Office(s): PO Box 390007, Cambridge,
  MA 02139-0001 (also marketing) *Tel:* 617-
  497-6303 *Fax:* 617-661-8703 *Web Site:* www.
  hackettpublishing.com
Distributor for Bryn Mawr Commentaries
Foreign Rep(s): Combined Representatives World-
  wide (Asia, Pacific); Gazelle Book Services
  Ltd (UK, Europe); UNIREPS (Australia &
  New Zealand)
Foreign Rights: Eulama
Billing Address: 832 N Pierson St, Indianapolis,
  IN 46244-0937
Orders to: 832 N Pierson St, Indianapolis, IN
  46244-0937
Returns: 832 N Pierson St, Indianapolis, IN
  46244-0937
Shipping Address: 832 N Pierson St, Indianapolis,
  IN 46204 *Tel:* 317-635-9250 *Fax:* 317-635-
  9292
Warehouse: 832 N Pierson St, Indianapolis, IN
  46244-0937

Hadronic Press Inc
35246 US 19 N, No 215, Palm Harbor, FL 34684
Tel: 727-934-9593 *Fax:* 727-934-9275
E-mail: hadronic@tampabay.rr.com
Web Site: www.hadronicpress.com
Key Personnel
Pres: Carla G Gandiglio
Founded: 1978
Mathematics & physics; theoretical biology &
  chemistry.
ISBN Prefix(es): 1-57485
Number of titles published annually: 10 Print
Total Titles: 92 Print

§Hagstrom Map Co Inc
Subsidiary of American Map Corp
46-35 54 Rd, Maspeth, NY 11378
SAN: 203-543X
Tel: 718-784-0055 *Toll Free Tel:* 800-432-MAPS
  (432-6277) *Fax:* 718-784-0640 (admin); 718-
  784-1216 (sales & orders)
Web Site: www.americanmap.com *Telex:* 96-8126
  Cable: AMERMAP MSPH
Key Personnel
Pres: Stuart Dolgins *Fax:* 718-784-3294
  E-mail: sdolgins@americanmap.com
Chmn: Andreas Langenscheidt
Sales Mgr & Intl Rts: Richard Strug
  E-mail: rstrug@americanmap.com
Dir, Cartography: Vera Benson *E-mail:* vbenson@
  americanmap.com
Founded: 1916
Maps, atlases, guides.
ISBN Prefix(es): 0-88097
Total Titles: 1 CD-ROM
Distributor for ADC The Map People; American
  Map Corp; Arrow Maps Inc; Creative Sales
  Corp; DeLorme Atlas; Hammond World Atlas
  Corporation; Langenscheidt; RV International
  Maps & Atlases; Stubs Guides; Trakker Maps
  Inc
Advertising Agency: ATL/SD, Sara Ascalon
  E-mail: sascalon@americanmap.com

§Haights Cross Communications Inc
10 New King St, White Plains, NY 10604
Tel: 914-289-9400 *Fax:* 914-289-9401
E-mail: info@haightscross.com
Web Site: www.haightscross.com
Key Personnel
Chmn & CEO: Peter Quandt *Tel:* 914-289-
  9410 *Fax:* 914-289-9411 *E-mail:* pjquandt@
  haightscross.com
COO: Tim McEwen *Tel:* 914-289-9490 *Fax:* 914-
  289-9491 *E-mail:* tjmcewen@haightscross.com
CFO: Paul Crecca *Tel:* 914-289-9420 *Fax:* 914-
  289-9421 *E-mail:* pjcrecca@haightscross.com

Pres & CEO, Triumph Learning: Kevin McAliley *Tel:* 212-652-0222 *E-mail:* kmcaliley@ triumphlearning.com

Pres & CEO, Sundance/Newbridge: Robert Laronga *Tel:* 508-571-6525 *E-mail:* blaronga@ sundancepub.com

Pres & CEO, Recorded Books: David Berset *Tel:* 410-535-5590 ext 1110 *E-mail:* bersetd@ aol.com

Gen Mgr, Audio Adventures: Scott Williams *Tel:* 410-535-5590 ext 1214 *E-mail:* swilliams@recordedbooks.com

Pres & CEO, Chelsea House: Richard Blumenthal *Tel:* 610-353-5166 ext 118 *E-mail:* rich_blumenthal@chelseahouse.com

Pres & CEO, Oakstone: Nancy McMeekin *Tel:* 205-437-3003 *E-mail:* nwilkins@ oakstonepub.com

Founded: 1996

Educational & professional publisher creating books, audio products, periodicals, software & online services, serving the following markets: K-12 supplemental education, public & school library publishing, audiobooks, legal & medical publishing.

Number of titles published annually: 856 Print; 10 CD-ROM; 50 Online; 10 E-Book; 787 Audio

Total Titles: 6,200 Print; 20 CD-ROM; 50 Online; 10 E-Book; 5,808 Audio

Imprints: Audio Adventures; Bloom Literary Criticism (Chelsea House Publishers LLC); Chapter by Chapter® (Sundance Publishing); Chelsea House; Chelsea Clubhouse (Chelsea House Publishers LLC); Clipper Audio; Clipper Audio (UK) (Recorded Books); Discovery Links (Newbridge Educational Publishing); Early Math (Newbridge Educational Publishing); Early Science (Newbridge Educational Publishing); Early Social Studies (Newbridge Educational Publishing); Fact Meets Fiction (Sundance Publishing); Go Facts Guided Writing (Newbridge Educational Publishing); Grammar with a Grin (Sundance Publishing); Griot Audio (Recorded Books); Kid-to-Kid Books (Sundance Publishing); Kids Corner (Sundance Publishing); Landmark Audio; LEAP® (Literature Enrichment Activities for Paperbacks) (Sundance Publishing); LIFT® (Literature is for Thinking) (Sundance Publishing); Little Blue Readers (Sundance Publishing); Little Green Readers (Sundance Publishing); Little Red Readers (Sundance Publishing); Lone Star Audio (Recorded Books); Newbridge; Novel Ideas Plus (Sundance Publishing); Novel Ideas Skills (Sundance Publishing); Oakstone Medical (Oakstone Publishing); Oakstone Publishing; Oakstone Wellness (Oakstone Publishing); Ranger Rick Science Program (Newbridge Educational Publishing); ReAct (Sundance Publishing); The Real Deal (Sundance Publishing); Reading Power Works™ (Sundance Publishing); Recorded Books; Recorded Books Audiolibros (Recorded Books); Recorded Books Development (Recorded Books); Recorded Books Inspirational (Recorded Books); Recorded Books Large Print (Recorded Books); Recorded Books Publishing (Recorded Books); Romantic Sounds Audio (Recorded Books); Second Chance Reading® (Sundance Publishing); Smithsonian College Lecture Series (Recorded Books); Sniffen Court (Triumph Learning); Southern Voices (Recorded Books); Sparklers (Sundance Publishing); Sundance; Sundance Phonics Readers (Sundance Publishing); SunLit Fluency Readers (Sundance Publishing); Supa Doopers (Sundance Publishing); Supa Doopers Plus (Sundance Publishing); Thinking Like a Scientist (Newbridge Educational Publishing); Thrillogy (Sundance Publishing); Triple Play (Sundance Publishing); Triumph Learning; Turman Publishing (Triumph Learning); Twin Texts™ (Sundance Publishing)

Subsidiaries: Audio Adventures; Chelsea House; Newbridge Publishing; Oakstone Medical Publishing; Recorded Books; Sundance Publishing; Triumph Learning

Foreign Office(s): Recorded Books/W F Howes, Victoria Mills, Unit 3, Fowke St, Rothley, Leics LE7 7PJ, United Kingdom, Man Dir: Ron Moody *Tel:* (011) 0016-230-1144 *Fax:* (011) 0016-230-1155

Membership(s): AAP; ALA; Audio Publishers Association; International Reading Association; Newsletter & Electronic Publishers Association

See separate listing for:
Recorded Books LLC

§Hal Leonard Corp

7777 W Bluemound Rd, Milwaukee, WI 53213

Mailing Address: PO Box 13819, Milwaukee, WI 53213-0819

Tel: 414-774-3630 *Toll Free Tel:* 800-524-4425 *Fax:* 414-774-3259

E-mail: halinfo@halleonard.com

Web Site: www.halleonard.com

Key Personnel

Chmn & CEO: Keith Mardak

Publicity Mgr: Lori Hagopian *Tel:* 414-479-8406 *E-mail:* lhagopian@halleonard.com

Sr Sales & Mktg Mgr, Book Trade: Brad Smith *E-mail:* bsmith@halleonard.com

Consumer Products Accts Mgr: Joel Aldinger

Founded: 1947

The world's largest music print publisher, with an incomparable selection of sheet music, songbooks, music related books, self-instruction books, CD packs & videos, music reference & special interest titles, music biographies, children's music products; CD-ROMs, DVDs, performance videos & more.

ISBN Prefix(es): 1-57424; 1-57560; 0-88188; 0-7935; 0-634

Number of titles published annually: 2,000 Print

Total Titles: 60,000 Print; 15 CD-ROM

Imprints: Berklee Press; Centerstream Publications; Cherry Lane Music Co; Ashley Mark Publishing Co; Musicians Institute Press; G Shirmer; Vintage Guitar

Distributor for Amadeus Press; Applause Theatre & Cinema Books; Artistpro; Ashley Music; Backbeat Books; Beacon Music; Berklee Press; Fred Bock Music Company; Boosey & Hawkes; Centerstream Publications; Cherry Lane Music Co; Cinema Books; Community Music Videos; Creative Concepts; DC Publications; Devine Entertainment Corp; Editions Durand; Editions Max Eschig; Editions Salabert; EM Books; EMI Christian; Faber Music Ltd; Guitar One; Guitar World; Home Recording; Homespun Tapes; Houston Publications; Hudson Music; iSong CD-ROMs; Kenyon Publications; Limelight Editions; Ashley Mark Publishing Co; Edward B Marks Music; Meredith Music; Modern Drummer Publications; Musicians Institute Press; Musikverlage Han Sikorski; Christopher Parkening; Reader's Digest; Record Research; Ricordi; Lee Roberts Publications; Rubank Publications; G Schirmer Inc (Associated Music Publishers); Second Floor Music; Sing Out Corporation; Star Licks Videos; Bernard Stein Music Co; String Letter Press; Tara Publications; Transcontinental Music; 21st Century Publications; Vintage Guitar; Word Music; Writer's Digest

Shipping Address: 960 E Mark St, Winona, MN 55987

Warehouse: 960 E Mark St, Winona, MN 55987

Distribution Center: 960 E Mark St, Winona, MN 55987

Half Halt Press Inc

20042 Benevola Church Rd, Boonsboro, MD 21713

Mailing Address: PO Box 67, Boonsboro, MD 21713

Tel: 301-733-7119 *Toll Free Tel:* 800-822-9635 (orders only) *Fax:* 301-733-7408

E-mail: gem@halfhaltpress.com

Web Site: www.halfhaltpress.com

Key Personnel

Publr: Elizabeth Carnes

VP, Opers: James P Farber, Jr

Founded: 1985

Publish own equestrian titles exclusively & distribute for British equestrian publisher. Horses & horsemanship & equestrian related topics.

ISBN Prefix(es): 0-939481; 1-872082; 1-872119

Number of titles published annually: 6 Print

Total Titles: 135 Print

Distributor for The Kenilworth Press Ltd

Alexander Hamilton Institute

70 Hilltop Rd, Ramsey, NJ 07446-1119

Tel: 201-825-3377 *Toll Free Tel:* 800-879-2441 *Fax:* 201-825-8696

E-mail: editorial@ahipubs.com

Web Site: www.ahipubs.com

Key Personnel

Ed-in-Chief: Brian L P Zevnik *E-mail:* blpz@ ahipubs.com

Ed: Ms Gloria Ju

Founded: 1908

Business books, newsletters, videos in personnel & legal field.

ISBN Prefix(es): 0-86604

Number of titles published annually: 4 Print; 5 CD-ROM; 5 Online

Total Titles: 50 Print; 10 CD-ROM; 10 Online

Hamilton Books

Imprint of University Press of America

4501 Forbes Blvd, Suite 200, Lanham, MD 20706

Tel: 301-459-3366

Key Personnel

VP & Dir: Judith Rothman *Tel:* 301-459-3366 ext 5303 *Fax:* 301-429-5749 *E-mail:* jrothman@ rowman.com

Dir, Mktg: Dean Roxanis *Tel:* 301-459-3366 ext 5614

Mktg Mgr: Laura McLean *Tel:* 301-459-3366 ext 5603

Mktg Coord: Markus Townsend *Tel:* 301-459-3366 ext 5620

Ed: David Chao *Tel:* 310-459-3366 ext 5327; Nicole Caddigan *Tel:* 301-459-3366 ext 5318; Joseph Parry *Tel:* 301-459-3366 ext 5316

Founded: 2002

Serious nonfiction: Memoirs, biographies, autobiographies, religious perspectives.

Number of titles published annually: 50 Print

Total Titles: 15 Print

Membership(s): AAP

§Hammond World Atlas Corp

Division of Langenscheidt Publishing Group

95 Progress St, Union, NJ 07083

Tel: 908-206-1300 *Toll Free Tel:* 800-526-4953 *Fax:* 908-206-1104

E-mail: customerservice@hammondmap.com; feedback@hammondmap.com

Web Site: www.hammondmap.com

Key Personnel

Pres & COO: Stuart Dolgins

VP: Richard Strug

Dir, Database Resources: Theophrastos Giouvanos

Dir, Sales Admin: Charles Koch

Dir, Digital Cartography: Vera Benson

Founded: 1900

Maps, atlases, books, education products, general reference, multimedia products.

ISBN Prefix(es): 0-8437

Number of titles published annually: 5 Print

Total Titles: 66 Print; 1 CD-ROM

Distributor for HarperCollins Cartographic

Foreign Rep(s): Thomas Allen & Son Ltd (Canada); Baker & Taylor International (Australia, Africa, Asia, Europe, Latin America)
Warehouse: HarperCollins Cartographic
Distribution Center: HarperCollins Cartographic
Membership(s): AAP

Hampton-Brown Co Inc
26385 Carmel Rancho Blvd, Carmel, CA 93923
Mailing Address: PO Box 223220, Carmel, CA 93923
Tel: 831-625-3666 *Toll Free Tel:* 800-933-3510
Fax: 831-625-8619
E-mail: customerservice@hampton-brown.com
Web Site: www.hampton-brown.com
Key Personnel
CEO & Publr: Sherry Long
Pres: Samuel Gesumaria
VP, Sales & Mktg: John Pichel
VP, Prodn: Curtis Spitler
Founded: 1980
Complete development, marketing & production services for el-hi educational materials, Spanish & English.
ISBN Prefix(es): 0-917837; 1-56334
Number of titles published annually: 50 Print
Total Titles: 3,000 Print
Branch Office(s)
405 N Saint Mary's St, Suite 800, San Antonio, TX 78205 *Tel:* 210-212-6799 *Toll Free Tel:* 800-299-8799
1033 University Place, Suite 110, Evanston, IL 60201 *Tel:* 847-733-4680 *Toll Free Tel:* 800-816-9511 *Fax:* 847-733-1304
Shipping Address: PO Box 369, Marina, CA 93933
Warehouse: 503 Reservation Rd, Marina, CA 93933
Membership(s): AAP

Hampton Press Inc
23 Broadway, Cresskill, NJ 07626
Tel: 201-894-1686 *Toll Free Tel:* 800-894-8955
Fax: 201-894-8732
E-mail: hamptonpr1@aol.com
Web Site: www.hamptonpress.com
Key Personnel
Pres: Barbara Bernstein
Founded: 1992
ISBN Prefix(es): 1-881303; 1-57273
Number of titles published annually: 35 Print
Total Titles: 325 Print
Imprints: Hampton Press
Foreign Rep(s): D & A Information Services (Australia); Eurospan Group (UK)
Returns: c/o Mercedes Distribution Ctr, Brooklyn Navy Yard, Bldg 3, Door 13, Brooklyn, NY 11205 *Tel:* 718-534-3000
Warehouse: c/o Mercedes Distribution Ctr, Brooklyn Navy Yard, Bldg 3, Door 13, Brooklyn, NY 11205 *Tel:* 718-534-3000 *Fax:* 718-935-9647

Hampton Roads Publishing Co Inc
1125 Stoney Ridge Rd, Charlottesville, VA 22902
Tel: 434-296-2772 *Toll Free Tel:* 800-766-8009 (orders) *Fax:* 434-296-5096 *Toll Free Fax:* 800-766-9042
E-mail: hrpc@hrpub.com
Web Site: www.hrpub.com
Key Personnel
Pres: Robert S Friedman
Chmn: Frank De Marco
Sales Dir: Lisette Larkins *Tel:* 434-296-2772 ext 49 *E-mail:* lisette@hrpub.com
Publicity Dir: Grace Pedalino *Tel:* 434-296-2772 ext 20 *E-mail:* oracle@hrpub.com
Lib Servs: Kathy Cooper *Tel:* 434-296-2772 ext 16 *E-mail:* kcooper@hrpub.com
Prodn: Cynthia Mitchell *Tel:* 434-296-2772 ext 21
Founded: 1989

Trade publishing, specialize in Metaphysics, self-help, integrative medicine, visionary fiction, paranormal phenomena.
ISBN Prefix(es): 1-878901; 1-57174
Number of titles published annually: 30 Print
Total Titles: 350 Print; 2 Audio
Foreign Rights: Writers House LLD (World)
Membership(s): Children's Book Council

§Hancock House Publishers
1431 Harrison Ave, Blaine, WA 98230-5005
Tel: 604-538-1114 *Toll Free Tel:* 800-938-1114
Fax: 604-538-2262 *Toll Free Fax:* 800-983-2262
E-mail: sales@hancockhouse.com
Web Site: www.hancockhouse.com
Key Personnel
Publr & Intl Rts: David Hancock
Founded: 1975
Natural History (world); regional NW history.
ISBN Prefix(es): 0-88839
Number of titles published annually: 15 Print
Total Titles: 240 Print
Branch Office(s)
19313 Zero Ave, Surrey, BC V4P 1M7, Canada

Handprint Books Inc
413 Sixth Ave, Brooklyn, NY 11215-3310
Tel: 718-768-3696 *Fax:* 718-369-0844
E-mail: publisher@handprintbooks.com
Web Site: www.handprintbooks.com
Key Personnel
Pres & Publr: Christopher Franceschelli
 E-mail: cmf@handprintbooks.com
Exec Ed: Ann Tobias *Tel:* 718-768-1414
 E-mail: anntobias@handprintbooks.com
Man Ed: Lissa Fox *Tel:* 718-768-1414
 E-mail: lissafox@handprintbooks.com
Founded: 2000
Publisher of high-quality books for children.
ISBN Prefix(es): 1-929766; 1-59354
Number of titles published annually: 20 Print
Distributed by Chronicle Books
Returns: Chronicle Books, c/o Genco Fullfillment, 1585 Linda Way, Door 1, Sparks, NV 89431

Hanging Loose Press
231 Wyckoff St, Brooklyn, NY 11217
SAN: 206-4960
Tel: 212-206-8465 *Fax:* 212-243-7499
E-mail: print225@aol.com
Web Site: www.hangingloosepress.com
Key Personnel
Ed & Intl Rts: Robert Hershon
Ed: Dick Lourie; Mark Pawlak; Ron Schreiber
Founded: 1966
Poetry & short fiction.
ISBN Prefix(es): 0-914610; 1-882413; 1-931236
Number of titles published annually: 8 Print
Total Titles: 150 Print
Returns: 9 Reed St, Cambridge, MA 02140 (Returns Only)
Membership(s): Council of Literary Magazines & Presses

§Hanley & Belfus
Imprint of Elsevier Health Sciences
170 S Independence Mall W, Suite 300 E, Philadelphia, PA 19106-3399
Tel: 215-238-7800 *Toll Free Tel:* 800-545-2522 (orders) *Fax:* 215-238-7883
Web Site: www.elsevierhealth.com
Key Personnel
VP, Med Educ: Linda C Belfus *Tel:* 215-238-7710 *Fax:* 215-238-2237 *E-mail:* l.belfus@elsevier.com
Founded: 1984
Medical books & journals.
ISBN Prefix(es): 0-932883; 1-56053
Number of titles published annually: 1 Print; 2 CD-ROM; 2 Online; 1 E-Book; 1 Audio

Total Titles: 1 Print; 2 CD-ROM; 2 Online; 1 E-Book; 1 Audio
Foreign Rights: John Scott & Co (International)

Hanley-Wood LLC
Division of Hanley-Wood Inc
426 S Westgate St, Addison, IL 60101
Tel: 630-543-0870 *Toll Free Tel:* 800-837-0870
Fax: 630-543-3112
Web Site: www.hanleywood.com
Key Personnel
Books Coord: Sharon Perry
Founded: 1956
Books & trade magazines on concrete construction, masonry construction & concrete production.
ISBN Prefix(es): 0-924659
Number of titles published annually: 10 Print
Total Titles: 40 Print; 1 CD-ROM

Hannacroix Creek Books Inc
1127 High Ridge Rd, PMB 110, Stamford, CT 06905-1203
SAN: 299-9560
Tel: 203-321-8674 *Fax:* 203-968-0193
E-mail: hannacroix@aol.com
Web Site: www.hannacroixcreekbooks.com
Key Personnel
Pres & CEO: Dr Jan Yager
Founded: 1996
Trade publisher of quality & innovative fiction & nonfiction books that entertain, educate & inform.
ISBN Prefix(es): 1-889262
Number of titles published annually: 4 Print; 2 Audio
Total Titles: 20 Print; 1 E-Book; 2 Audio
Foreign Rep(s): Living Literary Agency (Italy)
Foreign Rights: Bookman (Scandinavia); Lora Fountain Agency (France); A Kerrigan (Latin America, Spain); Michael Meller (Netherlands, Germany, Greece); Prava/Prevodi (Eastern Europe)
Membership(s): AAP; Publishers Marketing Association; Publishers' Publicity Association; Women's Media Group; Women's National Book Association

§Hanser Gardner Publications
Affiliate of Gardner Publications Inc & Carl Hanser Verlag
6915 Valley Ave, Cincinnati, OH 45244-3029
Tel: 513-527-8977 *Toll Free Tel:* 800-950-8977
Fax: 513-527-8801 *Toll Free Fax:* 800-527-8801
E-mail: hgfeedback@gardnerweb.com
Web Site: www.hansergardner.com
Key Personnel
Pres: Melissa Kline Skavlem
Exec VP: Barbara Kothe
Mktg Mgr: Julie Angus
Edit Dir & Intl Rts: Woodrow Chapman
Edit Dir: Christine Strohm
Founded: 1993
Technical & reference books & related products in manufacturing, metalworking & products finishing. Hanser Publishers: technical, engineering & science reference books, monographs, textbooks & journals in plastics technology, polymer & materials science.
ISBN Prefix(es): 1-56990
Number of titles published annually: 15 Print
Total Titles: 210 Print; 250 Online
Foreign Office(s): Carl Hanser Verlag GmbH & Co, Postfach 860 420, 81631 Munich, Germany, Pres/Publr: Wolfgang Beisler *Tel:* 89-99830 *Fax:* 89-98 1264
Foreign Rep(s): Allied Publishers Pvt (India, Nepal, Sri Lanka); D A Book Depot Pty (Australia, New Zealand, Papua New Guinea); East-

ern Book Services (Japan); Michael Goh (Singapore)
Warehouse: 7007 Valley Ave, Cincinnati, OH 45244

Harbor House
111 Tenth St, Augusta, GA 30901
Tel: 706-738-0354 *Fax:* 706-738-0354
E-mail: harborbook@knology.net
Web Site: harborhousebooks.com
Key Personnel
Pres & Publr: Randall Floyd
Lib Sales Dir: Anne Shelander
Dir, Creative Serv: Jane Carter
Dir, Mktg: Carrie McCullough
Founded: 1997
Book publishing.
ISBN Prefix(es): 1-891799
Number of titles published annually: 10 Print
Total Titles: 33 Print
Imprints: Batwing Press
Distributed by National Book Network
Advertising Agency: New Millennium Entertainment, 3010 Stratford Dr, Augusta, GA 30909, Contact: Anne Shelonder *Tel:* 706-738-0354 *Fax:* 706-738-0354 *E-mail:* harborbook@knology.net
Orders to: National Book Network, Returns Dept, 15200 NBN Way, Bldg B, Blue Ridge Summit, PA 17214 *Tel:* 717-794-3800 *Toll Free Tel:* 800-462-6420 *Toll Free Fax:* 800-338-4550 *Web Site:* www.nbnbooks.com
Returns: National Book Network, Returns Dept, 15200 NBN Way, Bldg B, Blue Ridge Summit, PA 17214 *Tel:* 717-794-3800 *Toll Free Tel:* 800-462-6420 *Toll Free Fax:* 800-338-4550 *Web Site:* www.nbnbooks.com
Warehouse: National Book Network, Returns Dept, 15200 NBN Way, Bldg B, Blue Ridge Summit, PA 17214 *Tel:* 717-794-3800 *Toll Free Tel:* 800-462-6420 *Fax:* 717-794-3828 *Toll Free Fax:* 800-338-4550 *Web Site:* www.nbnbooks.com
Distribution Center: National Book Network, Returns Dept, 15200 NBN Way, Bldg B, Blue Ridge Summit, PA 17214
Membership(s): Publishers Association of the South; Publishers Marketing Association

Harbor Lights Press (HLP)
Affiliate of Harbor Lights Navigation
PO Box 505, Gloucester City, NJ 08030-0505
Tel: 856-742-5810
E-mail: harborlightspress@yahoo.com
Web Site: www.harborlightspress.com
Key Personnel
Mktg Dir: Paul Drake
PR Dir: Beth McNamee
Affiliate Dir: John W Steel
Founded: 2001
ISBN Prefix(es): 0-911006
Number of titles published annually: 10 Print
Total Titles: 6 Print

Harbor Press Inc
5713 Wollochet Dr NW, PO Box 1656, Gig Harbor, WA 98335
SAN: 696-8953
Tel: 253-851-5190 *Fax:* 253-851-5191
E-mail: info@harborpress.com
Web Site: harborpress.com
Key Personnel
Pres & Publr: Harry R Lynn
Sr Ed: Debby Young *Tel:* 516-931-7099 *Fax:* 516-937-5028 *E-mail:* submissions@harborhealth.com
Foreign Rts: Paula Litzky
Publicity Dir: Sandy McWilliams *E-mail:* smcwilliams@harborpress.com
Founded: 1985
Consumer health books, with emphasis on alternative & natural approaches to health & healing. Also, self-improvement, self-help & how-

to titles. Marketing-oriented publisher looking for promotable titles with both mail order & trade sale potential & authors with credentials & the ability to promote their books on television & radio.
Please send ms submissions to: Debby Young, Sr Ed, 5 Glen Dr, Plainview, NY 11803.
ISBN Prefix(es): 0-936197
Total Titles: 15 Print
Imprints: Harbor Press
Distributed by National Book Network (NBN)
Orders to: National Book Network, 15200 NBN Way, Blue Ridge Summit, PA 17214 *Toll Free Tel:* 800-462-6420 *Web Site:* www.nbnbooks.com
Returns: National Book Network, 15200 NBN Way, Blue Ridge Summit, PA 17214 *Toll Free Tel:* 800-462-6420 *Web Site:* www.nbnbooks.com
Warehouse: National Book Network, 15200 NBN Way, Blue Ridge Summit, PA 17214 *Tel:* 717-794-3800 *Toll Free Tel:* 800-462-6420 *Toll Free Fax:* 800-338-4550
Membership(s): Book Publishers of the Northwest; The Direct Marketing Association; Publishers Marketing Association

§Harcourt Achieve
Formerly Harcourt Supplemental Publishers
Division of Harcourt Education
10801 N MoPac Expressway, Austin, TX 78759
Mailing Address: PO Box 27010, Austin, TX 78755
Tel: 512-343-8227 *Toll Free Tel:* 800-531-5015 *Toll Free Fax:* 800-699-9459
E-mail: ecare@harcourt.com
Web Site: www.harcourtachieve.com
Key Personnel
Pres & CEO: Tim McEwen
Sr VP, Sales: Joe McHale
VP, Fin: Martijn Tel
VP, Devt: Lynelle Morgenthaler
VP, Mktg: Carol Wolf
VP, HR: Gabriele Madison
VP, Mfg: David Lindley
Founded: 2001
Educational materials for Pre-K, elementary, secondary, adult GED, test preparation, ESL & professional development for educators.
ISBN Prefix(es): 0-8172; 0-8114; 0-7312; 0-7327; 0-7901; 0-7578; 0-7635; 1-4189; 0-7398; 1-4190; 1-5574; 0-4350; 0-9473
Total Titles: 6,000 Print; 64 CD-ROM

Harcourt Assessment Inc
Formerly The Psychological Corporation
Division of Reed Elsevier Group, plc
19500 Bulverde Rd, San Antonio, TX 78259
Tel: 210-339-5000 *Toll Free Tel:* 800-211-8378
Web Site: www.harcourtassessment.com
Key Personnel
Chmn: John R Dilworth
Pres & CEO: Jeffrey Galt
Publr: Dr Aurelio Prifiteria
Founded: 1921
Educational, psychological, clinical & industrial tests & scoring services & books on learning disabilities.
Branch Office(s)
55 Horner Ave, Toronto, ON M8Z 4X6, Canada
Foreign Office(s): 30-52 Smidmore St, Locked Bag 16, Marrickville. NSW 2204, Australia
32 Jamestown Rd, Harcourt Place, London NW1 7BY, United Kingdom

§Harcourt Inc
6277 Sea Harbor Dr, Orlando, FL 32887
SAN: 200-2736
Tel: 407-345-2000 *Toll Free Tel:* 800-225-5425 (cust serv) *Fax:* 407-352-3445 (cust serv)
Telex: 56-8373 HBJ ORL UD *Cable:* HBOFA ORLANDO

Key Personnel
Pres & CEO: Pat Tierney
CFO: Ray Fagan
Sr VP, HR: LaBron Chance
VP, Opers: Mike Allsup
VP & Publr, Adult Trade Div: Andre Bernard
Perms & Copyrights: June Neal
Gen Counsel: Henry Horbaczewski
Founded: 1919
ISBN Prefix(es): 0-15
Subsidiaries: Harcourt Canada (Toronto & Montreal); Harcourt Achieve; Harcourt Assessment
Divisions: Harcourt School Publishers; Harcourt Trade Publishers; HRW School
Branch Office(s)
55 Horner Ave, Toronto, ON M8Z 4X6, Canada
955 rue Bergar, Laval, PQ H7L 4Z6, Canada
Membership(s): AAP; BISG; Children's Book Council; Software & Information Industry Association
See separate listing for:
BAR/BRI Group
Harcourt Assessment Inc
Harcourt School Publishers
Harcourt Trade Publishers
Holt, Rinehart and Winston

Harcourt Interactive Technology
99 Powerhouse Rd, Suite 106, Roslyn Heights, NY 11577
Tel: 516-625-6755 *Toll Free Tel:* 800-745-3276 *Fax:* 516-625-6789
E-mail: hit@harcourt.com
Web Site: www.hit.iloli.com
Key Personnel
Pres & CEO: Howard Berrent
VP, Edit & Educ Technol: Karen Bischoff
VP, Mktg: Margaret Ricke
VP, Technol: Adam Rodriguez
Founded: 2001
Online classroom-based instructional assessment, diagnosis & prescription, aligned to state standards.
Membership(s): ASCD

§Harcourt School Publishers
Division of Harcourt Inc
6277 Sea Harbor Dr, Orlando, FL 32887
Tel: 407-345-2000 *Toll Free Tel:* 800-225-5425 (cust serv) *Fax:* 407-352-3445 *Toll Free Fax:* 800-874-6418
E-mail: hbspcs@hbschool.com
Web Site: www.harcourtschool.com *Telex:* 56-8373 *Cable:* HBJOFA ORLANDO
Key Personnel
Pres & CEO: Jan Spalding
Exec VP, Opers & Fin: Robert Hassel
VP & Dir, Mktg: Katie Crowe-Lile
VP, Sales Admin: Karen Bennett
VP, New Media: Nancy Lockwood
VP & Ed-in-Chief, Math: Patricia Brill
VP Ed-in-Chief, Reading/Language Arts: Diane Thomas-Pittari
VP Ed-in-Chief, Social Studies: Bob Keller
VP, Ed-in-Chief, Science & Health: Peggy Smith Herbst
VP, Design & Prodn: Carole Uettwiller
VP, HR: Connie Alden
Pres, Harcourt International Education Group (HIEG): Joan Lucas
Pres, Harcourt Canada: Wendy Cochran
ISBN Prefix(es): 0-15
Total Titles: 20,000 Print; 43 CD-ROM; 3,500 E-Book; 466 Audio
Warehouse: Interstate Industrial Park, 151 Heller & Benigno Blvd, Bellmawr, NJ 08031-2515
1175 N Stemmons Freeway, Lewisville, TX 75067

Harcourt Supplemental Publishers, see
Harcourt Achieve

Harcourt Trade Publishers
Division of Harcourt Inc
525 "B" St, Suite 1900, San Diego, CA 92101
Tel: 619-231-6616 *Toll Free Tel:* 800-543-1918
(cust serv) *Toll Free Fax:* 800-235-0256 (cust serv)
Web Site: www.harcourtbooks.com *Telex:* 18-1726
Cable: HB COSD SANDIEGO
Key Personnel
Pres & CEO (San Diego): Dan Farley
Sr VP & CFO (San Diego): Steve Torres
Sr VP & Dir, Sales & Mktg (New York): Laurie Brown
VP & Publr, Children's Books (New York): Lori Benton
VP & Publr, Adult & Harvest Books (New York): Andre Bernard
VP & Dir Strategic Opers (San Diego): Tim Cooper
VP & Dir, Prod & Design (San Diego): Sandy Grebenar
Exec Dir, Special Mkts & Internet (San Diego): Kira Glass
Edit Dir, Gulliver Books (New York): Liz Van Doren
Dir, Children's Mktg (San Diego): Steven Kasdin
Dir, Adult Mktg (New York): Patty Berg
Edit Dir, Children's Books (San Diego): Allyn Johnston
Ed-in-Chief, Adult & Harvest Books (New York): Rebecca Saletan
ISBN Prefix(es): 0-15
Number of titles published annually: 300 Print
Total Titles: 3,000 Print
Imprints: Green Light Readers; Gulliver Books; Harcourt Children's Books; Harcourt Paperbacks; Harcourt Yours Classics; Harvest Books; Libros Viajeros; Magic Carpet Books; Odyssey Classics; Red Wagon Books; Silver Whistle Books; Voyager Books
Branch Office(s)
15 E 26 St, 15th fl, New York, NY 10010
  Tel: 212-592-1000 *Fax:* 212-592-1010
Sales Office(s): 5 E 26 St, New York, NY 10010
  Tel: 212-592-1118 *Fax:* 212-592-1011
Orders to: 6277 Sea Harbor Dr, Orlando, FL 32887 *Toll Free Tel:* 800-543-1918 *Toll Free Fax:* 800-235-0256
Returns: Harcourt Inc, 465 S Lincoln Dr, Troy, MO 63379
Warehouse: 465 S Lincoln Dr, Troy, MO 63379
Distribution Center: 6277 Sea Harbor Dr, Orlando, FL 32887-4300

Harian Creative Books
Division of Harian Creative Enterprises
47 Hyde Blvd, Ballston Spa, NY 12020-1607
SAN: 204-0255
Tel: 518-885-6699; 518-885-7397
Key Personnel
CEO & Publr: Harry Barba
Mktg Consultant: Shirley Stone Garrett; Penny Gates; John Luther; Mary Peyton
Rep, European Off: Greg Barba
Founded: 1967
Fiction, poetry, plays & monographs on education, culture & art.
ISBN Prefix(es): 0-911906
Number of titles published annually: 5 Print
Total Titles: 37 Print; 20 Audio
Imprints: Barba-Cue Specials; The Harian Press; What's Cooking In...?
Subsidiaries: Harian Creative Enterprises; Harian Creative Associates
Foreign Rights: European American Information Services Inc
Advertising Agency: Harian Creative Associates
Membership(s): Authors Guild; The Authors Guild Inc

Harlan Davidson Inc/Forum Press Inc
773 Glenn Ave, Wheeling, IL 60090-6000
SAN: 201-2375

Tel: 847-541-9720 *Fax:* 847-541-9830
E-mail: harlandavidson@harlandavidson.com
Web Site: www.harlandavidson.com
Key Personnel
Chmn of the Bd & Pres: Angela E Davidson
Prodn Ed: Lucy A Herz
VP & Ed: Andrew J Davidson
VP & Cont: Dorothy Kopf
Founded: 1972
College & secondary textbooks, classics, bibliographies.
ISBN Prefix(es): 0-88295; 0-88273
Number of titles published annually: 6 Print
Total Titles: 226 Print
Imprints: American Biographical History Series; American History Series; Crofts Classics Series; Goldentree Bibliographies
Foreign Rep(s): Gazelle Book Services (Europe, Near East)
Membership(s): National Association of College Stores

Harlequin Enterprises Ltd
Subsidiary of Torstar Corp
233 Broadway, Suite 1001, New York, NY 10279
SAN: 200-2450
Tel: 212-553-4200 *Fax:* 212-227-8969
E-mail: customer.ecare@harlequin.ca
Web Site: www.eharlequin.com; www.luna-books.com; www.mirabooks.com; www.reddressink.com; www.steeplehill.com
Key Personnel
VP, Author & Asset Devt: Isabel Swift
Edit Dir, Next: Tara Gavin
Exec Ed: Tracy Farrell; Mary Theresa Hussey; Leslie Wainger; Margaret Marbury; Joan Marlow Golan
Sr Ed: Gail Chasan; Melissa Jeglinski; Denise O'Sullivan
Man Ed: Pamela Lawson
Assoc Sr Ed: Mavis Allen; Patience Smith; Natashya Wilson
Founded: 1980
Adult contemporary, historical romance novels & women's fiction.
ISBN Prefix(es): 0-373
Number of titles published annually: 400 Print
Imprints: Harlequin; HQN Books; Luna Books; MIRA Books; Red Dress Ink; Silhouette; Steeple Hill
Distributed by Simon & Schuster Mass Merchandise Sales Co
Distribution Center: 3010 Walden Ave, Depew, NY 14043

§Harmonie Park Press
23630 Pinewood, Warren, MI 48091
SAN: 206-7641
Tel: 586-755-3080 *Toll Free Tel:* 800-886-3080
  Fax: 586-755-4213
E-mail: info@harmonieparkpress.com
Web Site: harmonieparkpress.com
Key Personnel
Pres, Busn Mgr, Rts & Perms: Elaine Gorzelski
  E-mail: egorzelski@harmonieparkpress.com
VP: Sonja Hempseed
Data Proc Mgr: Darlene Brown
Ed: Jennifer Burke; Patricia O'Connor; Claire Ann Selestow; Karen Simmons; Randi Vincent; Samuel Wiersma; Barbara Williams
Founded: 1948
Music reference works, original monographs in musicology.
ISBN Prefix(es): 0-911772; 0-89990
Number of titles published annually: 10 Print; 1 CD-ROM
Total Titles: 60 Print; 1 CD-ROM; 1 Online
Membership(s): Music Library Association

Harmony House Publishers - Louisville
1008 Kent Rd, Goshen, KY 40026
SAN: 298-5446

Mailing Address: PO Box 90, Prospect, KY 40059
Tel: 502-228-2010; 502-228-4446 *Fax:* 502-228-2010
E-mail: harmonypub@aol.com
Key Personnel
Pres: William Strode
Sr VP: Joe Paul Pruett
Founded: 1984
Publishers.
ISBN Prefix(es): 0-916509; 1-56469
Number of titles published annually: 12 Print
Total Titles: 201 Print
Distributor for Classic Publishers
Membership(s): Publishers Marketing Association; Small Publishers Association of North America

HarperCollins Children's Books Group
Division of HarperCollins
1350 Sixth Ave, New York, NY 10019
SAN: 202-5760
Tel: 212-261-6500
Web Site: www.harperchildrens.com
Key Personnel
Pres & Publr: Susan Katz *Tel:* 212-307-3610
  E-mail: Susan.Katz@harpercollins.com
VP & Dir, Fin: Randy Rosema *Tel:* 212-307-3616
  E-mail: Randy.Rosema@harpercollins.com
Sr VP, Assoc Publr & Ed-in-Chief: Kate Jackson
  Tel: 212-307-3620 *E-mail:* Kate.Jackson@harpercollins.com
VP, Children's Mktg: Diane Naughton
  Tel: 212-307-3671 *E-mail:* Diane.Naughton@harpercollins.com
VP & Dir, Subs Rts: Joan Rosen *Tel:* 212-307-3606 *E-mail:* Joan.Rosen@harpercollins.com
Picture books, juvenile fiction & nonfiction, young adult novels.
ISBN Prefix(es): 0-06; 0-688; 0-380; 0-694; 0-690
Imprints: Amistad; Avon; Joanna Cotler Books; Eos; Laura Geringer Books; Greenwillow Books; HarperCollins Children's Books; HarperFestival; HarperKids Entertainment; HarperTempest; HarperTrophy; Rayo; Katherine Tegen Books
Membership(s): Children's Book Council

HarperCollins General Books Group
Division of HarperCollins Publishers
10 E 53 St, New York, NY 10022
Tel: 212-207-7000 *Fax:* 212-207-7633
Key Personnel
Sr VP, Fin & Publg Opers: Len Marshall
  Tel: 212-207-7254 *E-mail:* Len.Marshall@harpercollins.com
Exec VP & Publr, Morrow/Avon: Michael Morrison *Tel:* 212-207-7813 *E-mail:* Michael.Morrison@harpercollins.com
Sr VP & Creative Dir: Laurie Rippon
  Tel: 212-207-7250 *E-mail:* Laurie.Rippon@harpercollins.com
VP & Dir, Dom & Foreign Rts: Brenda Segel
  Tel: 212-207-7252 *E-mail:* Brenda.Segel@harpercollins.com
ISBN Prefix(es): 0-06
Imprints: Access; Amistad; Avon; Caedmon; Ecco; Eos; Fourth Estate; HarperAudio; HarperBusiness; HarperCollins; HarperDesign; HarperEntertainment; HarperLargePrint; HarperResource; HarperSanFrancisco; HarperTorch; PerfectBound; Perennial; Perennial Currents; Perrenial Dark Alley; Rayo; ReganBooks; William Morrow; William Morrow Cookbooks

HarperCollins General Books Sales Group, see
HarperCollins Publishers Sales

§HarperCollins Publishers
Subsidiary of News Corporation
10 E 53 St, New York, NY 10022

SAN: 200-2086
Tel: 212-207-7000 *Fax:* 212-207-7145
Web Site: www.harpercollins.com
Key Personnel
Pres & CEO: Jane Friedman *Tel:* 212-207-7166
   E-mail: Jfriedman@harpercollins.com
COO & Exec VP: Glenn D'Agnes *Tel:* 212-207-
   7782 *E-mail:* Glenn.D'Agnes@harpercollins.
   com
Group Pres: Brian Murray *Tel:* 212-207-7690
   E-mail: Brain.Murray@harpercollins.com
CFO: Janet Gervasio *Tel:* 212-207-7688
   E-mail: Janet.Gervasio@harpercollins.com
Chief Info Officer: Rick Schwartz *Tel:* 212-207-
   7174 *E-mail:* Rick.Schwartz@harpercollins.
   com
Sr VP & Gen Counsel: Jim Fox *Tel:* 212-207-
   7118 *E-mail:* Jim.Fox@harpercollins.com
Sr VP, HR: Greg Giangrande *Tel:* 212-207-7251
   E-mail: Greg.Giangrande@harpercollins.com
Pres, Sales: Josh Marwell *Tel:* 212-207-7780
   E-mail: Josh.Marwell@harpercollins.com
Sr VP & Dir, Corp Communs: Lisa Herling
   Tel: 212-207-7583 *E-mail:* Lisa.Herling@
   harpercollins.com
Founded: 1817
HarperCollins is one of the leading English-
   language publishers in the world & is a sub-
   sidiary of News Corp (NYSE: NWS, NWS.A;
   ASX: NCP, NCPDP). Headquartered in New
   York, the company has publishing groups in
   the US, Canada, the UK & Australasia. Its
   publishing groups include the HarperCollins
   General Books Group, HarperCollins Chil-
   dren's Books Group. Zondervan, Harper-
   Collins UK, HarperCollins Canada & Harper-
   Collins Australia/New Zealand. You can visit
   HarperCollins Publishers on the Internet at
   http://www.harpercollins.com & HarperCollins
   UK at http://www.harpercollins.co.uk.
ISBN Prefix(es): 0-06; 0-688; 0-380; 0-694
Number of titles published annually: 1,700 Print
Imprints: Beech Tree Books; Greenwillow Books;
   HarperCollins; Hearst Books; Lothrop, Lee &
   Shepard Books; Morrow Junior Books; Mul-
   berry Books; Quill Trade Paperbacks
Distributed by Cynthia Publishing Co
Distributor for Perseus (Addison Wesley Trade);
   Basic Books; Civitas; Counterpoint; GT Pub-
   lishing; Public Affairs; TV Books
Foreign Rep(s): Publishers International Market-
   ing Services
Foreign Rights: Agence Elaine Benisti (France);
   Antonella Antonelli Agenzia Letteraria (Italy);
   Bardon, Far Eastern Agents (China, Taiwan);
   Gerd Plessl Agency (Czech Republic, Greece,
   Hungary, Poland, Serbia and Montenegro);
   June Hall Literary Agency; Kezban Akcali
   Agency (Turkey); Kooy & Van Gerderen
   Agency (Netherlands); Licht & Licht Agency
   (Denmark, Finland, Norway, Sweden); Lynn
   Franklin (Russia); Mercedes Casanovas Agency
   (Spain); Rogan-Pikarski Agency (Israel);
   Tuttle-Mori Agency (Japan)
Advertising Agency: Franklin Spier Inc
Shipping Address: Wilmor Data & Customer Ser-
   vice Center, 39 Plymouth St, Suite 1219, Fair-
   field, NJ 07007, VP, Data Proc: Paul Pearson
Warehouse: Wilmor Distribution Center, 2912
   Reach Rd, Williamsport, PA 17701, VP & Gen
   Mgr: Mike Ficacci
Distribution Center: 2912 Reach Rd,
   Williamsport, PA 17701, VP & Gen Mgr: Mike
   Ficacci
Membership(s): AAP; BISG
See separate listing for:
Element Books

HarperCollins Publishers Sales
Formerly HarperCollins General Books Sales
   Group
Division of HarperCollins Publishers
10 E 53 St, New York, NY 10022

Fax: 212-207-7826
Web Site: www.harpercollins.com
Key Personnel
Pres, Sales: Josh Marwell *Tel:* 212-207-7780
   E-mail: Josh.Marwell@harpercollins.com
Sr VP, Sales: George Bick *Tel:* 212-207-7725
   E-mail: George.Bick@harpercollins.com
Sr VP, Sales (Children's Div): Andrea Pappen-
   heimer *Tel:* 212-207-7716 *E-mail:* Andrea.
   Pappenheimer@harpercollins.com
Group members include: HarperCollins Trade,
   HarperPerennial, HarperCollins Children's
   Books, HarperPaperbacks, HarperPrism,
   HarperHorizon, HarperSanFrancisco; Harper
   Reference & HarperBusiness.
Imprints: Access; Amistad; Avon Books; Cade-
   mon; Ecco; Eos; Fourth Estate; HarperAudio;
   HarperBusiness; HarperCollins; HarperDe-
   sign; HarperEntertainment; HarperLarge Print;
   HarperResource; HarperSanFrancisco; Harper-
   Torch; Perennial; Perennial Currents; Peren-
   nial Dark Alley; PerfectBound; Rayo; Regan
   Books; William Morrow; William Morrow
   Cookbooks
Shipping Address: 1000 Keystone Industrial Park,
   Scranton, PA 18512 *Tel:* 570-343-4761 *Toll
   Free Tel:* 800-242-7737 *Toll Free Fax:* 800-
   822-4090

Harper's Magazine Foundation
Division of Franklin Square Press
666 Broadway, New York, NY 10012
Tel: 212-420-5720 *Fax:* 212-228-5889
Web Site: www.harpers.org
Key Personnel
VP: Lynn Carlson
General trade.
ISBN Prefix(es): 1-879957
Number of titles published annually: 10 Print
Total Titles: 30 Print

Denis J Harrington Publishers
6207 Fushsimi Ct, Burke, VA 22015-3451
Mailing Address: PO Box 439, Fairfax Station,
   VA 22039-0439
Tel: 703-440-8920 *Fax:* 703-440-8929
Key Personnel
Pres & Publr: Denis J Harrington
VP, Opers: Mary A Harrington
Exec Dir, Graphics: John P Harrington
Art Dir: Sean P Harrington
Founded: 1999
Small publisher of primarily soft cover books for
   both commercial & library trade.
ISBN Prefix(es): 0-9672290
Number of titles published annually: 5 Print
Total Titles: 3 Print

Harris InfoSource
2057 E Aurora Rd, Twinsburg, OH 44087
Tel: 330-425-9000 *Toll Free Tel:* 800-888-5900
   Fax: 330-425-7150 *Toll Free Fax:* 800-643-
   5997
Web Site: www.harrisinfo.com
Key Personnel
Gen Mgr: Kevin Herendeen
Founded: 1971
Database publishing in directory, Internet, CD-
   ROM, media & mail list services.
ISBN Prefix(es): 1-55600
Number of titles published annually: 90 Print
Total Titles: 38 Print
Divisions: IDC
Foreign Rep(s): Elsevier Data Services (England);
   Southam (Canada)

Harrison House Publishers
2448 E 81 St, Suite 4800, Tulsa, OK 74137-4256
SAN: 208-676X
Mailing Address: PO Box 35035, Tulsa, OK
   74153-1035

Tel: 918-523-5700 *Toll Free Tel:* 800-888-4126
   Fax: 918-494-5688 (sales) *Toll Free Fax:* 800-
   830-5688
Web Site: www.harrisonhouse.com
Key Personnel
Pres: Keith Provance
VP & Publr: Bill Fowler
VP, Mktg: Susan Janos
Founded: 1976
Charismatic/Christian publishing house.
ISBN Prefix(es): 0-89275; 1-57794
Number of titles published annually: 50 Print
Total Titles: 400 Online
Foreign Rights: Diana Erwin (International)
Warehouse: GLS/Harrison House, 4588 Interstate
   Dr, Cincinnati, OH 45246 *Tel:* 513-874-0880
Distribution Center: GLS/Harrison House, 4588
   Interstate Dr, Cincinnati, OH 45246, Bart
   Clemon *Tel:* 513-874-0880

Hartman Publishing Inc
8529 Indian School Rd NE, Albuquerque, NM
   87112
Tel: 505-291-1274 *Toll Free Tel:* 800-999-9534
   Fax: 505-291-1284 *Toll Free Fax:* 800-474-
   6106
E-mail: orders@hartmanonline.com
Web Site: www.hartmanonline.com
Key Personnel
Publr: Mark Hartman
Man Ed: Susan Alvare
Founded: 1994
Publish a variety of in-service training materi-
   als & textbooks for certified nursing assis-
   tants & home health aides. Subjects include
   Alzheimer's disease, infection control, body
   mechanics, abuse & neglect, AIDS/HIV &
   communication skills.
ISBN Prefix(es): 1-888343
Number of titles published annually: 12 Print; 1
   CD-ROM; 1 Audio
Total Titles: 40 Print; 1 CD-ROM; 1 Audio
Imprints: Care Spring
Distributor for Beverly Foundation
Membership(s): New Mexico Book Association

Hartmore House Inc
Affiliate of Media Judaica Inc
304 E 49 St, New York, NY 10017
Mailing Address: 1363 Fairfield Ave, Bridgeport,
   CT 06605
Tel: 203-384-2284; 212-319-6666 *Fax:* 203-579-
   9109
Key Personnel
Pres & Ed: Jonathan D Levine
VP & Prodn Mgr: Andrew Amsel
Sales Mgr & Intl Rts: Walter B Stern
Founded: 1956
Inspirational, academic & religious (Jewish).
ISBN Prefix(es): 0-87677
Number of titles published annually: 3 Print
Total Titles: 32 Print; 4 Audio

§Harvard Business School Press
Division of Harvard Business School Publishing
300 N Beacon St, Watertown, MA 02472
SAN: 202-277X
Tel: 617-783-7400 *Toll Free Tel:* 888-500-1016
   Fax: 617-783-7664
E-mail: bookpublisher@mail1.hbsp.harvard.edu
Web Site: www.hbsp.harvard.edu
Key Personnel
Assoc Publr & Edit Dir: Hollis Heimbouch
Communs Dir: Sarah McConville
Mktg Dir: Gayle Treadwell
Foreign Rts & Intl Sales Dir: Leslie Zheutlin
Mktg Mgr: Zeenat Potia *Tel:* 617-783-7671
   E-mail: fpotia@hbsp.harvard.edu
Man Ed: Constance Devanthery-Lewis
Exec Ed: Kirsten Sandberg
Ed at Large: Carol Franco
Founded: 1984

Trade & professional books for the business & academic communities: strategy, organizational behavior/human resource management, finance management, marketing, production & operations management, accounting, business history, business-government relations; Harvard Business Review & Reference books & Internet/New economy strategy.
ISBN Prefix(es): 0-87584; 1-57851
Number of titles published annually: 20 Print
Total Titles: 340 Print; 12 Audio
Imprints: Harvard Business Reference
Distributed by Client Distribution Services
Foreign Rep(s): McGraw-Hill Book Co (Europe); McGraw-Hill International; United Publishers Services Ltd (Japan)

The Harvard Common Press
535 Albany St, Boston, MA 02118
SAN: 208-6778
Tel: 617-423-5803 *Toll Free Tel:* 888-657-3755
Fax: 617-695-9794
E-mail: orders@harvardcommonpress.com
Web Site: www.harvardcommonpress.com
Key Personnel
Pres & Rts & Perms: Bruce P Shaw
Dir, Mktg & Publg: Skye Stewart
Exec Ed: Valerie Cimino
Founded: 1976
General nonfiction: cookbooks, small business guides, travel guides, child care & parenting.
ISBN Prefix(es): 0-916782; 0-87645; 1-55832
Number of titles published annually: 15 Print
Total Titles: 160 Print
Imprints: Gambit Books
Foreign Rep(s): Gazelle; Southern Publishing Group
Foreign Rights: Dan Bial
Distribution Center: National Book Network, 15200 NBN Way, Blue Ridge Summit, PA 17214 *Tel:* 717-794-3800 *Toll Free Tel:* 800-462-6420 *Toll Free Fax:* 800-338-4550

Harvard Education Publishing Group
Division of Harvard University
8 Story St, 1st fl, Cambridge, MA 02138
Tel: 617-495-3432 *Toll Free Tel:* 800-513-0763
Fax: 617-496-3584
E-mail: hepg@harvard.edu
Web Site: gseweb.harvard.edu/hepg
Key Personnel
Publr: Douglas Clayton
Mktg Mgr: Alexandra Merceron *Tel:* 617-384-7249
Ed: Michael Sadowski
Publisher of books & journals on education practice, research & policy.
ISBN Prefix(es): 1-891792; 1-883433; 0-916690
Number of titles published annually: 8 Print
Total Titles: 28 Print
Imprints: Harvard Education Letter; Harvard Education Press; Harvard Educational Review Reprint Series

Harvard Ukrainian Research Institute
Subsidiary of Harvard University
1583 Massachusetts Ave, Cambridge, MA 02138
SAN: 208-967X
Tel: 617-496-8768 *Fax:* 617-495-8097
E-mail: huri@fas.harvard.edu
Web Site: www.huri.harvard.edu
Key Personnel
Mgr, Pubns: G Patton Wright *E-mail:* gpwright@fas.harvard.edu
Founded: 1973
ISBN Prefix(es): 0-916458; 1-932650
Number of titles published annually: 5 Print; 3 Online
Total Titles: 85 Print; 6 Online
Distributed by Harvard University Press

Harvard University Art Museums
32 Quincy St, Cambridge, MA 02138
Tel: 617-495-8286 *Fax:* 617-495-9985
Web Site: www.artmuseums.harvard.edu
Key Personnel
Staff Asst: Dan Wuenschel *E-mail:* wuensch@fas.harvard.edu
Founded: 1901
Art History.
ISBN Prefix(es): 0-916724
Number of titles published annually: 5 Print
Total Titles: 70 Print
Distributed by Arthur Schwartz & Co Inc

Harvard University Press
79 Garden St, Cambridge, MA 02138-1499
SAN: 200-2043
Tel: 617-495-2600; 401-531-2800 (international orders) *Toll Free Tel:* 800-405-1619 (orders) *Fax:* 617-495-5898 (general); 617-496-4677 (edit & rts); 401-531-2801 (international orders) *Toll Free Fax:* 800-406-9145 (orders)
E-mail: firstname_lastname@harvard.edu
Web Site: www.hup.harvard.edu
Key Personnel
Dir: William P Sisler
Sr Ed, History & Social Sciences: Kathleen McDermott
Asst Dir & CFO: William A Lindsay
Asst Dir, Design & Prodn: John Walsh
Sr Exec Ed, Hist & Cont Aff: Joyce Seltzer
Exec Ed, Sci & Med: Michael G Fisher
Exec Ed, Humanities: Lindsay Waters
Sr Acq Ed, Social Sciences: Michael A Aronson
Gen Ed, Humanities: Margaretta Fulton
Sr Acq Ed, Behavorial Sciences: Elizabeth Knoll
Mktg Dir: Paul Adams
Sales Dir: Susan Donnelly
Mgr, Cust Serv & ISBN Contact: Joan O'Donnell
Promo Mgr: Sheila Barrett
Adv Mgr & Web Administrator: Denise Waddington
Mgr, Intellectual Prop: Melinda Koyanis
Exhibits & Internet Sales Mgr: Vanessa Vinarub
Exec Admin Off, Dir & HR: Susan J Seymour *Tel:* 617-495-2602 *E-mail:* susan_seymour@harvard.edu
Intl Rts Mgr: Stephanie Vyce
Man Ed: Mary Ann Lane
Founded: 1913
General scholarly, medical, scientific.
ISBN Prefix(es): 0-674
Number of titles published annually: 130 Print
Total Titles: 2,800 Print
Imprints: Belknap Press
Foreign Office(s): Fitzroy House, 11 Chenies St, London WC1E 7ET, United Kingdom
Distributor for Harvard Center for Middle Eastern Studies; Harvard Center for Population Studies; Harvard Center for the Study of World Religions; Harvard College Library (Including Houghton Library Judaica Division); Harvard Department of Sanskrit & Indian Studies; Harvard Department of The Classics; Harvard Ukrainian Research Institute; Harvard University Asia Center; Harvard University David Rockefeller Center for Latin American Studies; Harvard-Yenching Institute; Peabody Museum of Archaeology & Ethnology
Foreign Rep(s): Academic Book Promotions (Benelux, France, Scandinavia); Alkem Co (Southeast Asia); Aromix Books (Hong Kong); Cassidy & Associates Inc (China); Cory Voight Palgrave (Southern Africa); The Rodney Franklin Agency (Israel); Harba International (South America); Harvard University Press London (UK, Ireland, Greece); Chris Humphrys (Portugal, Spain); Information & Culture, Korea (South Korea); IPR (Middle East exc Israel); Ewa Ledochiwicz (Croatia, Czech Republic, Hungary, Poland, Slovak Republic, Slovenia); Uwe Ludemann (Austria, Germany, Italy, Switzerland); Mediamatics

(India); B K Norton (Taiwan); Rockbook Inc (Japan); World Press (Pakistan); Yuha Associates (Malaysia)
Foreign Rights: International Editors (Spain); Michelle Lapautre (France); Liepman Ag (Germany); Suzanna Zevi Agencia LeHeraria (Italy)
Shipping Address: Triliteral LLC, 100 Maple Ridge Dr, Cumberland, RI 02864-1769
Membership(s): AAP; BISG

Harvest Hill Press
PO Box 55, Salisbury Cove, ME 04672
Tel: 207-288-8900 *Toll Free Tel:* 888-288-8900
Fax: 207-288-3611
Key Personnel
Pres: Sherri Eldridge *E-mail:* sherri@qwi.net
Founded: 1994
Cookbooks & printed kitchen stationery for gift, children's & book markets.
ISBN Prefix(es): 1-886862
Number of titles published annually: 5 Print
Total Titles: 36 Print
Imprints: Coastal New England Publications
Membership(s): Publishers Marketing Association

Harvest House Publishers Inc
990 Owen Loop N, Eugene, OR 97402
SAN: 207-4745
Tel: 541-343-0123 *Toll Free Tel:* 800-547-8979
Fax: 541-342-6410
E-mail: admin@harvesthousepublishers.com
Web Site: www.harvesthousepublishers.com
Key Personnel
Treas: Shirley J Hawkins
Edit VP: Carolyn McCready
Intl Rts: Sharon Burke
Edit Sec: Kimberly Shumate
Founded: 1974
Evangelical Christian books.
ISBN Prefix(es): 0-89081; 1-56507; 0-7369
Number of titles published annually: 190 Print; 3 Audio
Total Titles: 650 Print; 3 Audio
Foreign Rights: Sharon Burke (Worldwide)
Membership(s): BISG

Hastings House/Daytrips Publishers
Subsidiary of Lini LLC
2601 Wells Ave, Suite 161, Fern Park, FL 32730
Tel: 407-339-3600 *Toll Free Tel:* 800-206-7822
Fax: 407-339-5900
E-mail: hastings_daytrips@earthlink.net
Web Site: www.hastingshousebooks.com; www.daytripsbooks.com
Key Personnel
Publr: Peter Leers *E-mail:* pleers@aol.com
Travel Ed: Earl Steinbicker *E-mail:* esteinbicker@erols.com
Founded: 1936
Our additional website, www.booksurge.com, helps customers find Hastings House titles (by author, title, etc) which they can purchase using various credit cards.
ISBN Prefix(es): 0-8038
Number of titles published annually: 5 Print
Total Titles: 60 Print
Warehouse: Midpoint Trade Books, 1263 Southwest Blvd, Kansas City, KS 66103, Contact: Julie Borgelt *Tel:* 913-831-2233 ext 109 *Fax:* 913-362-7401 *E-mail:* julie@midpt.com
Distribution Center: Midpoint Trade Books, 1263 Southwest Blvd, Kansas City, KS 66103, Contact: Julie Borgelt *Tel:* 913-831-2233 ext 109 *Fax:* 913-362-7401 *E-mail:* julie@midpt.com

Hatherleigh Press
Subsidiary of Hatherleigh Co Ltd
5-22 46 Ave, Suite 200, Long Island City, NY 11101
Tel: 718-786-5338 *Toll Free Tel:* 800-528-2550
Fax: 718-706-6087
E-mail: info@hatherleigh.com

Web Site: www.getfitnow.com; www.
hatherleighpress.com
Key Personnel
Chmn: Frederic Flach
Pres: Andrew Flach
Publr: Kevin J Moran *E-mail:* kevin@
hatherleighpress.com
Founded: 1995
Paper & hardbound books, audio, video, CD-
ROM, CE courses in mental health, psychol-
ogy, psychiatry, health & fitness.
ISBN Prefix(es): 1-886330; 1-57826
Number of titles published annually: 20 Print; 1
Audio
Total Titles: 160 Print; 4 Audio
Imprints: getfitnow.com Books; Healthy Living
Books
Distributed by W W Norton & Company Inc
Foreign Rep(s): W W Norton & Co

HAWK Publishing Group
7107 S Yale Ave, Suite 345, Tulsa, OK 74136-
6308
SAN: 299-9293
Tel: 918-492-3677 *Fax:* 918-492-2120
E-mail: hawkpub@cox.net
Web Site: www.hawkpub.com
Founded: 1999
Publishing new fiction & nonfiction.
ISBN Prefix(es): 1-930709
Number of titles published annually: 6 Print
Total Titles: 63 Print
Distribution Center: National Book Network
- NBN Biblio Division, 15200 NBN Way,
Blue Ridge Summit, PA 17214 *Toll Free
Tel:* 800-462-6420 *Toll Free Fax:* 800-338-
4550 *E-mail:* custserv@nbnbooks.com *Web
Site:* www.bibliodistribution.com
Membership(s): Publishers Marketing Association

The Haworth Press Inc
10 Alice St, Binghamton, NY 13904-1580
SAN: 211-0156
Tel: 607-722-5857 *Toll Free Tel:* 800-429-6784
Fax: 607-722-1424 *Toll Free Fax:* 800-895-
0582
E-mail: getinfo@haworthpressinc.com
Web Site: www.haworthpress.com
Key Personnel
Pres & Publr: Bill Cohen *E-mail:* mkoch@
haworthpress.com
Sr VP: Roger Hall *E-mail:* rhall@haworthpress.
com
VP, Edit Devt: Kathryn Rutz *Tel:* 607-656-
7981 *Fax:* 607-656-7876 *E-mail:* krutz@
haworthpress.com
VP, Digital & Electronic Resources: Karen An-
drews *E-mail:* kandrews@haworthpress.com
VP, Mktg: Sandra Jones Sickels *Tel:* 607-
722-5857 ext 345 *Fax:* 607-722-3487
E-mail: ssickels@haworthpress.com
VP, Book Div & Pubns Dir: William Palmer
Fax: 607-722-8465 *E-mail:* bpalmer@
haworthpress.com
VP, Print Prodn: Andrew Cary *Tel:* 607-775-
3372 *Fax:* 607-775-2908 *E-mail:* acary@
haworthpress.com
Personnel Dir: Patricia Iadanza
Intl Sales Dir: Beth Arnold *Tel:* 607-722-5857
ext 397 *Fax:* 607-722-6362 *E-mail:* barnold@
haworthpress.com
Adv Mgr: Rebecca Miller-Baum *Fax:* 607-722-
3487 *E-mail:* bbaum@haworthpress.com
Subs Mgr: Lori Beagell *E-mail:* lbeagell@
haworthpress.com
Accts Payable Mgr: Corey Bliss *E-mail:* cbliss@
haworthpress.com
Sales Mgr: Margaret Tatich *Fax:* 607-722-6362
E-mail: mtatich@haworthpress.com
Foreign Rts Consultant: Anu Hansen *Tel:* 201-
242-5548 *Fax:* 201-242-9446 *E-mail:* anuh8@
aol.com

Microforms Contact: Janette Kemmerer
E-mail: jkemmer@haworthpress.com
Founded: 1973
Scientific & professional journals & books in the
social & behavioral sciences, pharmaceutical
sciences, library science, marketing, health care
& medicine, pastoral care, agriculture & food
science, food & nutrition. Also a trade line.
Periodicals in microfiche.
ISBN Prefix(es): 0-86656; 0-917724; 0-918393;
1-56022; 1-56023; 1-56024; 0-7890
Number of titles published annually: 230 Print
Total Titles: 2,940 Print; 40 E-Book
Online services available through EBSCOhost,
OCLC.
Imprints: Best Business Books; Food Products
Press; Harrington Park Press; The Haworth
Clinical Practice Press; The Haworth Herbal
Press; The Haworth Hispanic/Latino Press; The
Haworth Hospitality Press; The Haworth Infor-
mation Press; The Haworth Integrative Healing
Press; The Haworth Judaica Practice Press; The
Haworth Medical Press; The Haworth Pastoral
Press; The Haworth Political Press; The Ha-
worth Reference Press; The Haworth Trauma
& Maltreatment Press; International Business
Press; Internet Practice Press; Pharmaceutical
Products Press; The Social Work Practice Press
Divisions: Haworth Customized Textbook Ser-
vice; Haworth Document Delivery Service
Branch Office(s)
37 W Broad St, West Hazleton, PA 18202
Foreign Rep(s): Academic Circle (Middle East);
Nicholas H Altwerger (USA); Ian Booth
(USA); Luis Borella (USA); Nathan Carter
(USA); Thomas V Cassidy (China); Sean Con-
cannon (USA); Dipak Guha (India); Tiffany
Eager (USA); Bernd Feldmann (Austria, Ger-
many, Switzerland); Colin Fuller; Steven
Goh (Asia & the Pacific); Sandra Hargraves
(Canada); Eric Hedin (USA); Henry Hubert
(USA); Frans Janssen (Belgium, Netherlands);
Se-Yung Jun (Korea); Barbara Keene (Zim-
babwe); Cameron Kernohan (Australia & New
Zealand); Christopher R Kerr (USA); Masako
Kitamura (Japan); Marek Lewinson (Eastern
Europe); Tahir M Lodhi (Pakistan); Flavio
Marcello (Italy); Glen McHaney (USA); Tom
Murphy (USA); Jan Norbye (Netherlands);
Robert Obudho (Africa); Peter Prout (Spain &
Portugal); Evan Ramer (USA); Howard Ramer
(USA); Elaine Rathgeber (USA); Jan Reineri
(USA); Jose Rios (Central America); I J Sagun
(Asia, Philippines); Linda Sametz (Mexico); R
Seshadri (India); Lee Shedden (Canada); Russ
Sheldrick (Australia & New Zealand); Richard
Sherman (Israel); Anne Shulenberger (USA);
Nancy Suib (USA); Katia Zevelekakis (Greece)
Foreign Rights: Anu Hanson (all territories)
Returns: 72 Grosset Dr, Kirkwood, NY 13795
Shipping Address: 72 Grosset Dr, Kirkwood,
NY 13795, Marie Sbarra *Tel:* 607-775-
3323 *Fax:* 607-725-2908 *E-mail:* msbarra@
haworthpress.com

§Hay House Inc
2776 Loker Ave W, Carlsbad, CA 92008
SAN: 630-477X
Mailing Address: PO Box 5100, Carlsbad, CA
92018-5100
Tel: 760-431-7695 *Toll Free Tel:* 800-650-5115;
800-654-5126 (orders) *Fax:* 760-431-6948
E-mail: info@hayhouse.com
Web Site: www.hayhouse.com
Key Personnel
Founder & Chmn: Louise L Hay
Pres & CEO: Reid Tracy
VP: Ron Tillinghast
Sales Dir: Jeannie Liberati
Edit Dir: Jill Kramer *Tel:* 760-431-7695 ext 112
E-mail: jkramer@hayhouse.com
Intl Rts Contact: Manfred Mroczkowski
Founded: 1985

Self-help/New Age, health, philosophy, spiritual
growth & awareness, mental & environmental
harmony books; also self-healing; biography,
producers & distributors of recordings & video
pertaining to health of mind, body & spirit.
Accept agented submissions; SASE required.
ISBN Prefix(es): 0-937611; 1-56170; 1-4019
Number of titles published annually: 45 Print; 36
Audio
Total Titles: 250 Print; 350 Audio
Imprints: Lifestyles; Smiley Books
Foreign Rights: Inter License Ltd
Warehouse: 2750 Progress St, Suite B, Vista,
CA 92081-8449 *Tel:* 760-431-7695 ext 159
Fax: 760-431-6948 *E-mail:* jcoburn@hayhouse.
com

Haynes Manuals Inc
Division of The Haynes Publishing Group
861 Lawrence Dr, Newbury Park, CA 91320
Tel: 805-498-6703 *Toll Free Tel:* 800-442-9637
Fax: 805-498-2867
E-mail: info@haynes.com
Web Site: www.haynes.com
Key Personnel
Pres: Eric Oakley
Mktg Mgr: Mickee Ferrell
Founded: 1960
Publisher & importer of books on domestic &
foreign autos & motorcycles & historical &
technical motoring.
ISBN Prefix(es): 0-946609; 1-56392
Number of titles published annually: 13 Print
Total Titles: 690 Print
Distributed by Motorbooks International
Distributor for G T Foulis; Haynes Owners Work-
shop Manuals; Oxford Illustrated Press
Warehouse: Eastern Warehouse, 1299 Bridgestone
Pkwy, La Vergne, TN 37086 *Fax:* 615-793-
5325

§Hazelden Publishing & Educational Services
Division of Hazelden Foundation
15251 Pleasant Valley Rd, Center City, MN
55012-0176
SAN: 125-1953
Mailing Address: PO Box 176, Center City, MN
55012-0176
Tel: 651-213-4470 *Toll Free Tel:* 800-328-9000
Web Site: www.hazelden.org
Key Personnel
Exec VP, Publg & Educ: Nick Motu
Prodn & Mfg: Don Freeman
Fin Mgr: Brenda Rausch
Mgr, Oper: Lenny Peterson
Trade Sales & Mktg Mgr & Subs & Intl Rts:
Constance Carlson *Tel:* 651-213-4470
E-mail: ccarlson@hazelden.org
Founded: 1954
Adult trade hardcover & paperbacks; curriculum,
workbooks, giftbooks, video & audio; self-
help, addiction & recovery, personal & spiri-
tual growth; computer based products, wellness
products, young adult nonfiction.
ISBN Prefix(es): 0-89486; 1-56838; 0-89638; 0-
942421; 0-935908; 1-56246; 0-934125
Number of titles published annually: 12 Print
Total Titles: 500 Print; 500 E-Book; 10 Audio
Imprints: Hazelden/Johnson Institute; Hazelden/
Keep Coming Back; Hazelden-Pittman
Archives Press
Distributed by Health Communications Inc (trade)
Distributor for Obsessive Anonymous
Foreign Rep(s): Airlift (UK); Living Solutions
Bookstore (Australia, Ireland, Europe); South-
ern Publishers Group (New Zealand)

§HCPro
200 Hoods Lane, Marblehead, MA 01945
Mailing Address: PO Box 1168, Marblehead, MA
01945

Tel: 781-639-1872 *Toll Free Tel:* 800-650-6787
Fax: 781-639-2982 *Toll Free Fax:* 800-639-8511
E-mail: customer_service@hcpro.com
Web Site: www.hcpro.com
Key Personnel
CEO: Bruce Guzowski
Chmn: James B Flanagan
VP, Sales: David Miller
VP, Mktg: Rob Stuart
Publr: Suzanne Perney
Founded: 1986
Healthcare administration & management. Specialize medicine, nursing, newsletters.
ISBN Prefix(es): 1-885829
Number of titles published annually: 110 Print; 4 CD-ROM; 30 Online; 5 E-Book; 60 Audio
Total Titles: 125 Print; 5 CD-ROM; 40 Online; 25 E-Book; 75 Audio
Imprints: Opus Communications
Subsidiaries: The Greeley Co
Orders to: 100 Hoods Lane, Marblehead, MA 01945
Warehouse: 100 Hoods Lane, Marblehead, MA 01945
Distribution Center: 100 Hoods Lane, Marblehead, MA 01945
Membership(s): NEPA

Health Administration Press
Division of Foundation of the American College of Healthcare Executives
One N Franklin St, Suite 1700, Chicago, IL 60606-3491
SAN: 207-0464
Tel: 312-424-2800 *Fax:* 312-424-0014
E-mail: hap@ache.org
Web Site: www.ache.org
Key Personnel
Dir: Maureen Glass *Tel:* 312-424-9450
E-mail: mglass@ache.org
Mktg Mgr: Kaye Humbert *Tel:* 312-424-9470
E-mail: khumbert@ache.org
Ed: Jane Williams *Tel:* 312-424-9473
Founded: 1972
Health administration, health care, law & medicine, medical care organization; books & journals.
ISBN Prefix(es): 0-910701; 1-56793
Number of titles published annually: 20 Print
Total Titles: 1 E-Book
Imprints: Academy Health Services & Health Policy Research/Health Administration Press; American College of Healthcare Executives Management Series; AUPHA Press/Health Administration Press; Executive Essentials
Branch Office(s)
PO Box 75145, Annapolis Junction, MD 21275, Tammy Preston *Tel:* 301-362-6905 *Fax:* 301-206-9789
Foreign Rep(s): Login Bros (Canada)
Billing Address: 9050 Junction Dr, Annapolis Junction, MD 20701
Orders to: 9050 Junction Dr, Annapolis Junction, MD 20701 *Web Site:* www.ache.org/hap.cfm
Returns: 9050 Junction Dr, Annapolis, MD 20701
Shipping Address: 9050 Junction Dr, Annapolis Junction, MD 20701
Warehouse: 9050 Junction Dr, Annapolis Junction, MD 20701, Contact: Tammy Preston *Tel:* 301-362-6905 *Fax:* 301-206-9789
Distribution Center: 9050 Junction Dr, Annapolis Junction, MD 20701

Health Communications Inc
3201 SW 15 St, Deerfield Beach, FL 33442-8190
SAN: 212-100X
Tel: 954-360-0909 *Toll Free Tel:* 800-851-9100 (cust serv); 800-441-5569 (order entry)
Fax: 954-360-0034
Web Site: www.hcibooks.com
Key Personnel
Pres & Publr: Peter Vegso

Sr VP & Publr: Thomas Sand
VP, Sales: Terry Burke
Art Dir: Larissa Henoch
Mktg Dir: Kelly Maragni
Edit Dir: Bret Witter
Communs Dir: Kim Weiss
Gen Mgr, Sales: Lori Golden
Natl Accts Mgr: Tom Galvin
Spec Sales: Stephanie Frohman
Foreign Rts Agent: Claude Cloquette; Luc Jutras
Perms: Kathy Grant
Founded: 1976
Publishers of nonfiction paperbacks & hardcover books on self-help, personal growth, inspiration, health, parenting, women's issues, teens, religion, psychology, addiction & recovery.
ISBN Prefix(es): 0-932194; 1-55874; 0-75730
Number of titles published annually: 50 Print
Total Titles: 500 Print; 36 Audio
Imprints: Faith Communications; HCI Books; HCI Espanol; HCI Teens; Simcha Press (Judaica)
Distributor for Hazelden Books
Foreign Rights: Claude Choovette (Montreal)
See separate listing for:
Simcha Press

§Health Forum Inc
Subsidiary of American Hospital Association
One N Franklin St, 28th fl, Chicago, IL 60606
SAN: 216-5872
Tel: 312-893-6884 *Toll Free Tel:* 800-242-2626
Fax: 312-422-4600
Web Site: www.ahaonlinestore.com
Key Personnel
Mktg Dir, Periodicals: Pat Foy *E-mail:* pfoy@healthforum.com
Edit Dir, Books: Rick Hill *Tel:* 312-893-6863 *E-mail:* rhill@healthforum.com
Founded: 1936
Publisher of professional books & textbooks for health care professionals. Specialize in books that help hospital executives & department heads manage their business better & achieve improved patient satisfaction. We also provide data information from the American Hospital Association annual survey of hospitals & classroom training books for ICD-9-CM coding.
ISBN Prefix(es): 1-55648; 0-87258
Number of titles published annually: 10 Print; 2 CD-ROM; 1 E-Book
Total Titles: 13 Print; 2 CD-ROM
Imprints: AHA (American Hospital Association); AHA Press
Orders to: AHA Services Inc, PO Box 92683, Chicago, IL 60675-2683, Contact: Jeri Luga *Toll Free Tel:* 800-242-2626 *Fax:* 312-422-4505 *E-mail:* jluga@aha.org
Returns: AHA Services Inc, PO Box 92683, Chicago, IL 60675-2683, Contact: Jeri Luga *Toll Free Tel:* 800-242-2626 *Fax:* 312-422-4505 *E-mail:* jluga@aha.org
Distribution Center: Rittenhouse Book Distributors, 511 Feheley Dr, King of Prussia, PA 19406, Contact: Nicole Gallo *Toll Free Tel:* 800-345-6425 *Fax:* 610-277-0390 *E-mail:* n.gallo@rittenhouse.com *Web Site:* www.rittenhouse.com
Ingram Book Co, 14 Ingram Blvd, LaVergne, TN 37086-1986, Contact: Renee Wilson *Tel:* 615-213-5163 *Fax:* 615-213-5430 *E-mail:* renee.wilson@ingrambook.com *Web Site:* www.ingrambook.com
J A Majors, 1401 Lakeway Dr, Lewisville, TX 75057, Contact: Kelly Thomas *Tel:* 972-353-1125 *Fax:* 972-353-1300 *E-mail:* kthomas@majors.com *Web Site:* www.majors.com
Membership(s): American Hospital Association; Publishers Marketing Association; Small Publishers Association of North America
See separate listing for:
AHA Press

Health InfoNet Inc
231 Market Place, No 331, San Ramon, CA 94583
Tel: 925-358-4370 *Toll Free Tel:* 800-446-1947
Fax: 925-358-4377
Web Site: hinbooks.com
Key Personnel
VP: Lois Kamoroff *E-mail:* logo47@aol.com
Founded: 1993
Medical patient information materials (including booklets & web).
ISBN Prefix(es): 1-885274
Number of titles published annually: 3 Print
Total Titles: 50 Print; 50 Online; 50 E-Book

Health Information Network HIN, see Health InfoNet Inc

Health Insurance Association of America, see America's Health Insurance Plans (AHIP)

§Health Press NA Inc
2920 Carlisle Blvd NE, Albuquerque, NM 87110
Mailing Address: PO Box 37470, Albuquerque, NM 87176-7470
Tel: 505-888-1394 *Fax:* 505-888-1521
E-mail: goodbooks@healthpress.com
Web Site: www.healthpress.com
Key Personnel
Publr & Pres: Kathleen Frazier
Dir, Mktg & Sales: Corie Conwell
Founded: 1988
Health & patient education books for the whole family.
ISBN Prefix(es): 0-929173
Number of titles published annually: 5 Print
Total Titles: 35 Print

§Health Professions Press
Division of Paul H Brookes Publishing Co
PO Box 10624, Baltimore, MD 21285-0624
SAN: 297-7338
Tel: 410-337-9585 *Toll Free Tel:* 888-337-8808
Fax: 410-337-8539
E-mail: custserv@healthpropress.com
Web Site: www.healthpropress.com
Key Personnel
Pres: Melissa A Behm
Dir, Pubns: Mary H Magnus
Publicity Mgr: Anastasia Worcester
Rts Mgr: Lisa M Yurwit
Prodn Mgr: Lisa Rapisarda
Accountant: Susan T Dwyer
Publg Asst: Susannah Ray *E-mail:* sray@brookespublishing.com
Founded: 1989
Hardcover, paperback & wire-bound professional resources & textbooks in aging, long-term care & health administration.
ISBN Prefix(es): 1-878812; 1-932529
Number of titles published annually: 10 Print; 2 CD-ROM
Total Titles: 72 Print; 2 CD-ROM
Distributed by Elsevier Australia; The Eurospan Group; Login Brothers; Unifacmanu Trading Co Ltd
Foreign Rep(s): STM Publishers Services (China, Hong Kong, Malaysia, Myanmar, Philippines, Singapore, Thailand, Vietnam)
Warehouse: The Maple Press Distribution Center, 60 Grumbacher Rd I-83 Industrial Park, PO Box 15100, York, PA 17402
Membership(s): Publishers Marketing Association

Health Research
62 Seventh St, Pomeroy, WA 99347
Mailing Address: PO Box 850, Pomeroy, WA 99347
Tel: 509-843-2385 *Toll Free Tel:* 888-844-2386
Fax: 509-843-2387
E-mail: publish@pomeroy-wa.com
Web Site: www.healthresearchbooks.com

Key Personnel
Mgr: Shirley Elliott
Founded: 1952
Publish reprints of rare, hard to find, out-of-print books. Subjects include mysticism, Egyptology, divination, UFOs, hypnotism, mental & spiritual healing, acupuncture, metaphysical, palmistry & many, many more.
ISBN Prefix(es): 0-7873
Number of titles published annually: 30 Print
Total Titles: 1,400 Print

Health Resources Press Inc
8609 Second Ave, Suite 405B, Silver Spring, MD 20910
Tel: 301-565-2494 *Fax:* 301-565-2494
Web Site: www.healthresourcespress.com
Key Personnel
Owner: Dr Harold Goodman *E-mail:* hrpharold@erols.com
Founded: 1996
Books on alternative medicine.
ISBN Prefix(es): 1-890708
Total Titles: 3 Print
Imprints: Zanzibar Press

Healthy Healing Publications
PO Box 436, Carmel Valley, CA 93924
Tel: 831-659-8324 *Fax:* 831-659-4044
E-mail: customerservice@healthyhealing.com
Web Site: www.healthyhealing.com
Key Personnel
Owner: Linda Page
VP, Mktg, Sales & Intl Rts: Leah Thomson
Founded: 1993
Publish & distribute health related books including herbal healing.
ISBN Prefix(es): 1-884334
Number of titles published annually: 3 Print
Total Titles: 23 Print; 19 Online
Distributed by Crystal Star/Jones Products; Words Distributors
Foreign Rep(s): BNI Inc (Worldwide exc Canada)
Foreign Rights: Book Network International (Worldwide exc Canada)
Shipping Address: Words Distributors, 7900 Edgewater Dr, Oakland, CA 94621, Contact: Lisa Mack *Tel:* 510-553-9673 *Fax:* 510-553-0729

Healthy Learning, see Coaches Choice

§Heart Math
14700 W Park Ave, Boulder Creek, CA 95006
Mailing Address: PO Box 66, Boulder Creek, CA 95006
Tel: 831-338-2161 *Toll Free Tel:* 800-450-9111
Fax: 831-338-9861
Web Site: www.heartmath.com
Key Personnel
Natl Sales Dir & Intl Rts: Lisa Lehnhoff
E-mail: lehnhoff@planetarypub.com
Founded: 1998 (as an independent limited liability company)
Publishers of The HeartMath System.
ISBN Prefix(es): 1-879052
Number of titles published annually: 16 Print
Total Titles: 2 CD-ROM; 7 Audio

Hearts & Tummies Cookbook Co
Division of Quixote Press
1854 345 Ave, Wever, IA 52658
Tel: 319-372-7480 *Toll Free Tel:* 800-571-BOOK
Fax: 319-372-7485
E-mail: heartsntummies@hotmail.com
Key Personnel
Pres & Intl Rts: Bruce Carlson
Founded: 1982
Cookbooks.
ISBN Prefix(es): 1-878488; 1-57166
Number of titles published annually: 24 Print

Total Titles: 250 Print
Imprints: Black Iron Cooking Co; PYO (Publish Your Own) Co; Quixote Press

Hebrew Union College Press
Division of Hebrew Union College
3101 Clifton Ave, Cincinnati, OH 45220
Tel: 513-221-1875 *Fax:* 513-221-0321
E-mail: hucpress@huc.edu
Web Site: www.huc.edu
Key Personnel
Chmn Pubns Comm: Michael A Meyer
Man Ed: Barbara Selya
Founded: 1921
Scholarly Jewish books.
ISBN Prefix(es): 0-87820
Number of titles published annually: 3 Print
Total Titles: 100 Print
Distributed by Wayne State University Press

Heian International Inc
20655 S Western Ave, Suite 105, Torrance, CA 90501
SAN: 213-2036
Tel: 310-328-7200 *Fax:* 310-328-7676
E-mail: heianemail@earthlink.net
Web Site: heian.com
Key Personnel
Pres & Intl Rts: Ted Yukawa
Ed: Diane Ooka
Founded: 1973
General trade, juvenile; languages, dictionaries & literature, Oriental culture, customs, philosophy & religion; classic Japanese art calendars & books.
ISBN Prefix(es): 0-89346
Number of titles published annually: 10 Print
Total Titles: 200 Print

Heimburger House Publishing Co
7236 W Madison St, Forest Park, IL 60130
Tel: 708-366-1973 *Fax:* 708-366-1973
Web Site: www.heimburgerhouse.com
Key Personnel
Publr: Donald J Heimburger
Founded: 1962
Publish books & magazines on railroad & other transportation subjects; list includes more than 300 book titles.
ISBN Prefix(es): 0-911581
Number of titles published annually: 5 Print
Total Titles: 75 Print
Distributor for Harry N Abrams Inc; Acorn Media Publishing; Black Dog & Leventhal; Book Sales Inc; Canadian Caboose Press; Cedco Publishing Co; Child's Play; Deskmap Systems; Douglas & McIntyre Ltd; Evergreen Press; Firefly Books; Footprint Publishing; Fordham University Press; Friedman/Fairfax; The Globe Pequot Press; Golden Hill Press; Harbour Publishing; HarperCollins; Highland Station Inc; Hot Box Press; Howling at the Moon Press; Iconografix Inc; Indiana University Press; Johns Hopkins University Press; Judson Press; Kansas City Star Books; Krause Publications; Motorbooks Intl; Omega Innovative Marketing; Penquin Putman Inc; Pictorial Histories; Publishers Group West; Running Press; Smithmark Publishers; Sono Nis Press; Stackpoole Books; Sterling Publishing; Syracuse University Press; Thunder Bay Press; Voyageur Press; Walker & Co; Westcliffe Publishing; John Wiley & Sons

§William S Hein & Co Inc
1285 Main St, Buffalo, NY 14209-1987
Tel: 716-882-2600 *Toll Free Tel:* 800-828-7571
Fax: 716-883-8100
E-mail: mail@wshein.com
Web Site: www.wshein.com
Key Personnel
Chmn of the Bd: William S Hein, Jr

Pres: Kevin M Marmion
Mktg Mgr: Brian Jablonski *Tel:* 800-828-7571 ext 141 *E-mail:* b_jablonski@wshein.com
Sec to VP: Susan McClinton
Treas: Bonnie L Morton
Ed, Electronic Publg: Daniel Rosati
VP Sales & Mktg: Richard J Spinelli
Founded: 1961
Publish & reprint law & related materials, hard copy, micro, CDs & online products.
ISBN Prefix(es): 0-8377; 0-89941; 1-57588
Number of titles published annually: 30 Print; 2 CD-ROM; 1 Online
Total Titles: 5,000 Print; 5 CD-ROM; 2 Online
Imprints: Fred B Rothman Publications
Distributor for Ashgate; Aspen; Butterworths; Sweet & Maxwell; John Wiley & Sons Inc
Membership(s): American Association of Law Libraries; Canadian Association of Law Libraries; Library Binding Institute

§Heinemann
Division of Greenwood Publishing Group Inc
361 Hanover St, Portsmouth, NH 03801-3912
SAN: 210-5829
Mailing Address: PO Box 5007, Westport, CT 06881-5007
Tel: 603-431-7894 *Toll Free Tel:* 800-225-5800
Fax: 603-431-4971; 603-431-7840
E-mail: info@heinemann.com
Web Site: www.heinemann.com
Key Personnel
Gen Mgr: Lesa Scott
Publg Dir: Leigh Peake
Electronic Publg: Jeffrey Northrop
Intl Rts: Roberta Lew
Contact: Ron Maas
Founded: 1977
Education - professional books for teachers K-College. Literacy, Math, Social Studies, Drama, Art & English teaching. Hardcover & paperbound. Trade - Drama, World Literature, Education, African Studies. Hardcover & paperbound.
ISBN Prefix(es): 0-86709; 0-435; 0-325
Number of titles published annually: 115 Print
Total Titles: 1,500 Print
Imprints: African Writers Series; Boynton/Cook; Caribbean Writers Series; Mandarin; Methuen Drama; Minerva
Foreign Rep(s): Butterworth-Heinemann Publishers (England); Eleanor Curtain; Eurospan; Irwin (Canada)
Warehouse: 300 Exchange Dr, Suite B, Crystal Lake, IL 60014

Heinemann/Boynton Cook Publishers Inc
Division of Heinemann
361 Hanover St, Portsmouth, NH 03801-3912
SAN: 210-5829
Tel: 603-431-7894 *Toll Free Tel:* 800-541-2086
Fax: 603-431-7840
E-mail: custserv@heinemann.com
Web Site: www.boyntoncook.com
Key Personnel
Gen Mgr: Lesa Scott
Founded: 1981
College composition & rhetoric textbooks.
ISBN Prefix(es): 0-86709
Number of titles published annually: 25 Print
Total Titles: 250 Print
Orders to: Greenwood-Heinemann, PO Box 6926, Portsmouth, NH 03802-6926 *Toll Free Tel:* 800-225-5800
Warehouse: Greenwood-Heinemann, 300 Exchange Dr, Suite B, Crystal Lake, IL 60014

Helgate Press
PO Box 3727, Central Point, OR 97502
Tel: 541-855-5566 *Toll Free Tel:* 800-795-4059
Fax: 541-855-1360
Web Site: www.hellgatepress.com

Founded: 1975
ISBN Prefix(es): 1-55571
Number of titles published annually: 10 Print
Total Titles: 58 Print
Distributed by Midpoint Trade Books

§Hellgate Press
Imprint of PSI Research
1375 Upper River Rd, Gold Hill, OR 97525
Mailing Address: PO Box 3727, Central Point, OR 97502
Tel: 541-855-5566 *Toll Free Tel:* 800-795-4059 *Fax:* 541-855-1360
E-mail: info@psi-research.com
Web Site: www.psi-research.com
Key Personnel
Pres, Ed & Intl Rts: Emmett Ramey
   E-mail: eramey@starband.net
VP, Mktg: Ardella R Ramey *E-mail:* aramey@starband.net
Founded: 1975
History; travel, military history.
ISBN Prefix(es): 1-55571
Number of titles published annually: 20 Print; 1 CD-ROM
Total Titles: 60 Print; 50 E-Book
Imprints: Hellgate Press
Distributed by Midpoint Trade Books
Foreign Rep(s): Midpoint Trade Books
Shipping Address: Midpoint Trade Books, 1263 Southwest Blvd, Kansas City, KS 66103, Contact: Eric Campman *Tel:* 913-362-7400

Hemingway Western Studies Series
Boise State University, 1910 University Dr, Boise, ID 83725
Tel: 208-426-1999 *Toll Free Tel:* 800-992-TEXT (992-8398) *Fax:* 208-426-4373
Web Site: www.boisestate.edu/hemingway/series.htm
Key Personnel
Ed: Tom Trusky *E-mail:* ttrusky@boisestate.edu
Founded: 1986
Specialize in artists' books on Rocky Mountain issues.
ISBN Prefix(es): 0-932129
Number of titles published annually: 3 Print
Total Titles: 12 Print
Shipping Address: Book Store, Contact: Jan Johns *Tel:* 208-426-2665 *E-mail:* jjohns@boisestate.edu *Web Site:* www.boisestatebooks.com

Hendrick-Long Publishing Co
10635 Tower Oaks, Suite D, Houston, TX 77070
Tel: 832-912-READ (912-7323) *Fax:* 832-912-7353
E-mail: hendrick-long@worldnet.att.net
Web Site: www.hendricklongpublishing.com
Key Personnel
VP & Ed: Vilma Long
Publr: Michael Long
Founded: 1969
Texas & Southwest material for juveniles & young adults.
ISBN Prefix(es): 0-937460; 1-885777
Number of titles published annually: 8 Print
Total Titles: 113 Print
Distributor for NES, The Official Tasp Study Guide
Membership(s): Publishers Association of the West

Hendrickson Publishers Inc
PO Box 3473, Peabody, MA 01961-3473
Tel: 978-532-6546 *Toll Free Tel:* 800-358-3111 *Fax:* 978-531-8146
E-mail: orders@hendrickson.com
Web Site: www.hendrickson.com
Key Personnel
Pres: Stephen J Hendrickson
Dir Edit: Shirley Decker-Lucke
Sales Dir: Joe Suter

Prodn Mgr: Michael Baranofsky
Assoc Ed & Intl Rts, Rts & Perms: Dawn Harrell *Tel:* 978-573-2275 *E-mail:* rights@hendrickson.com
Assoc Ed: Allan Emery
Cont: Robert Walker
Author Rel: Sara Scott
Founded: 1978
Religious reference, language, history & theology.
ISBN Prefix(es): 0-913573; 0-943575; 0-917006; 1-56563
Number of titles published annually: 20 Print; 3 CD-ROM
Total Titles: 450 Print
Imprints: Prince Press
Foreign Rep(s): Alban Books (UK/Europe)
Warehouse: 140 Summit St, Peabody, MA 01960

Hensley Publishing
6116 E 32 St, Tulsa, OK 74135
Tel: 918-664-8520 *Toll Free Tel:* 800-288-8520 (orders only) *Fax:* 918-664-8562
E-mail: customerservice@hensleypublishing.com
Web Site: www.hensleypublishing.com
Key Personnel
Dir, Publg: Terri Kalfas
Founded: 1965
Bible studies.
ISBN Prefix(es): 1-56322
Number of titles published annually: 5 Print
Total Titles: 27 Print
Membership(s): CBA

Her Own Words
PO Box 5264, Madison, WI 53705-0264
Tel: 608-271-7083 *Fax:* 608-271-0209
E-mail: herownword@aol.com
Web Site: www.herownwords.com
Key Personnel
Producer: Jocelyn Riley
Founded: 1986
Women's history, literature, arts & women in non-traditional careers.
ISBN Prefix(es): 1-877933
Number of titles published annually: 6 Print; 6 Audio
Total Titles: 35 Print; 35 Audio
Imprints: Women In Nontraditional Careers

Herald Press
Subsidiary of Mennonite Publishing House Inc
616 Walnut Ave, Scottdale, PA 15683-1999
SAN: 202-2915
Tel: 724-887-8500 *Toll Free Tel:* 800-245-7894 *Fax:* 724-887-3111
E-mail: hp@mph.org
Web Site: www.heraldpress.com
Key Personnel
Ed: Levi Miller
Mktg Mgr: Patricia Weaver
Libn: Michelle Quinn
Intl Rts: Winfried Bluth
Founded: 1908
General Christian trade books, family, devotional, cookbooks, juveniles, adult fiction, Bible study, theology, peace & social concerns, missions, Amish & Mennonite history & culture, songbooks.
ISBN Prefix(es): 0-8361
Number of titles published annually: 17 Print
Total Titles: 350 Print
Branch Office(s)
Herald Press Canada, 490 Dutton Dr, Unit C8, Waterloo, ON N2L 6H7, Canada, Mgr: Kathy Shantz *Tel:* 519-747-5722 *Fax:* 519-747-5721 *E-mail:* hpcan@mph.org
Foreign Rep(s): Winifried Bluth (Australia, Asia, UK, Europe, Hong Kong, Indonesia, Korea, Lithuania, New Zealand, Poland, Russia, South Africa, Scandinavia, Taiwan)
Foreign Rights: Winfried Bluth

Herald Publishing House
Division of Community of Christ
1001 W Walnut, Independence, MO 64051
SAN: 202-2907
Mailing Address: PO Box 390, Independence, MO 64051
Tel: 816-521-3015 *Toll Free Tel:* 800-767-8181 *Fax:* 816-521-3066
E-mail: marketing@heraldhouse.org
Web Site: www.heraldhouse.org
Key Personnel
Edit Dir & ISBN Contact: Linda Booth
Gen Mgr, Busn: Steven McCrosson *Tel:* 816-521-3074 *E-mail:* smccrosson@cofchrist.org
Dir, Mktg & Mdse: Nancy Vreeland
Founded: 1860
Religion (Community of Christ).
ISBN Prefix(es): 0-8309
Number of titles published annually: 4 Print
Total Titles: 360 Print
Imprints: Graceland Press; Herald Publishing House; Independence Press
Foreign Rep(s): Steve Weber (Canada)

Heritage Books Inc
65 E Main St, Westminster, MD 21157
Tel: 410-876-0371 *Toll Free Tel:* 866-282-2689 *Fax:* 410-871-2674
E-mail: info@heritagebooks.com
Web Site: www.heritagebooks.com
Key Personnel
CEO: Craig R Scott *Tel:* 410-876-6101 *E-mail:* crscott@heritagebooks.com
Edit Dir: Corrine Will
Founded: 1978
Books on local history, genealogy & Americana.
ISBN Prefix(es): 0-917890; 1-55613; 0-7884; 1-58549; 0-940907; 1-888265
Number of titles published annually: 240 Print; 80 CD-ROM
Total Titles: 2,500 Print; 734 CD-ROM

§The Heritage Foundation
214 Massachusetts Ave NE, Washington, DC 20002-4999
Tel: 202-546-4400 *Toll Free Tel:* 800-544-4843 *Fax:* 202-543-9647
E-mail: pubs@heritage.org
Web Site: www.heritage.org
Key Personnel
Dir, Publg Servs: Jonathan Larsen
Founded: 1973
Domestic policy, foreign policy & defense.
ISBN Prefix(es): 0-89195
Number of titles published annually: 7 Print; 2 CD-ROM
Total Titles: 19 Print; 2 CD-ROM; 8 E-Book

Heritage House, see Ye Olde Genealogie Shoppe

Hermitage Publishers
PO Box 310, Tenafly, NJ 07670-0310
SAN: 239-4413
Tel: 201-894-8247 *Fax:* 201-894-5591
Web Site: www.hermitagepublishers.com
Key Personnel
Dir: Igor Yefimov *E-mail:* yefimovim@aol.com
Founded: 1981
Scholarly & Russian-language books.
ISBN Prefix(es): 0-938920; 1-55779
Number of titles published annually: 10 Print
Total Titles: 112 Print

Herzl Press
Subsidiary of W Z O
633 Third Ave, 21st fl, New York, NY 10017
Tel: 212-339-6020 *Fax:* 212-318-6176
E-mail: midstreamthf@aol.com
Web Site: www.midstreamthf.com
Key Personnel
Chmn, Theodore Herzl Found: Kalman Sultanik
Busn Mgr: Sam Bloch

Founded: 1954
Dictionaries, encyclopedias, fine editions, paper-
backs, journals, translations.
ISBN Prefix(es): 0-930830
Number of titles published annually: 2 Print
Total Titles: 50 Print
Distributed by Associated University Presses;
Cornwal Books

Heuer Publishing LLC
211 First Ave SE, Cedar Rapids, IA 52401
Tel: 319-368-8008 *Toll Free Tel:* 800-950-7529
Fax: 319-364-1771
E-mail: editor@hitplays.com
Web Site: www.hitplays.com
Key Personnel
Publr: Steven S Michalicek
Ed: Ms Geri Albrecht
Founded: 1928
Play & musical publisher; Publishes plays, musicals, operas/opperettas & guides (choreography,
costume, production/staging) for amateur &
professional markets including junior & senior
high schools, college/university & community
theatres. Focus includes comedy, drama, fan-
tasy, mystery & holiday with special interest
focus in multicultural, historic, classic literature, Shakespearian theatre, interactive, teen
issues & biographies. Pays by percentage royalty or outright purchase.
Number of titles published annually: 7 Print
Total Titles: 150 Print

Hewitt Homeschooling Resources
Division of Hewitt Research Foundation
2103 "B" St, Washougal, WA 98671
Mailing Address: PO Box 9, Washougal, WA
98671
Tel: 360-835-8708 *Toll Free Tel:* 800-348-1750
Fax: 360-835-8697
E-mail: info@hewitthomeschooling.com
Web Site: hewitthomeschooling.com
Key Personnel
Pres: April Purtell
Founded: 1964
Homeschooling, curriculum.
ISBN Prefix(es): 0-913717; 1-57896
Number of titles published annually: 6 Print
Total Titles: 129 Print

Heyday Books
2054 University Ave, Berkeley, CA 94704
SAN: 207-2351
Mailing Address: PO Box 9145, Berkeley, CA
94709-0145
Tel: 510-549-3564 *Fax:* 510-549-1889
E-mail: heyday@heydaybooks.com
Web Site: www.heydaybooks.com
Key Personnel
Publr: Malcolm Margolin *E-mail:* malcolm@
heydaybooks.com
Sales Mgr: Joanne Chan
Mktg & Publicity Dir: Zachary Nelson
Founded: 1974
Nonprofit company that specializes in California
Indians, California history & literature, regional
conservation & ecology; women of California;
literary anthologies; Asian-American; art &
photography.
ISBN Prefix(es): 0-930588; 1-890771; 0-9666691
Number of titles published annually: 20 Print
Total Titles: 110 Print
Imprints: California Legacy Books (Reprints);
Great Valley Books (Books by Central Valley
authors)
Returns: Heyday Books c/o Fulfillco, 601 Parr
Blvd, Richmond, CA 94801
Warehouse: Heyday Books c/o Fulfillco, 601 Parr
Blvd, Richmond, CA 94801

Hi Willow Research & Publishing
312 S 1000 East, Salt Lake City, UT 84102

Toll Free Tel: 800-873-3043 *Fax:* 936-271-4560
E-mail: sales@lmcsource.com
Web Site: www.lmcsource.com
Key Personnel
Owner: David V Loertscher
Founded: 1978
Books for schools & libraries.
ISBN Prefix(es): 0-931510
Number of titles published annually: 8 Print
Total Titles: 35 Print
Distributed by LMC Source

Higginson Book Co
148 Washington St, Salem, MA 01970
Mailing Address: PO Box 778, Salem, MA 01970
Tel: 978-745-7170 *Fax:* 978-745-8025
E-mail: orders@higginsonbooks.com; higginson@
cove.com
Web Site: www.higginsonbooks.com
Key Personnel
Mgr: Lawrence Young
Founded: 1970
Reprints & new material.
ISBN Prefix(es): 0-8328; 0-7404
Number of titles published annually: 200 Print
Total Titles: 14,000 Print
Distributor for Genealogical Publishing Co

High/Coo Press
Affiliate of Brooks Books
3720 N Woodridge Dr, Decatur, IL 62526-1117
Tel: 217-877-2966
E-mail: brooksbooks@q-com.com
Web Site: www.family-net.net/~brooksbooks
Key Personnel
Publr: Randy Brooks
Founded: 1976
Books of haiku poetry.
ISBN Prefix(es): 0-913719; 1-929820
Number of titles published annually: 3 Print; 3 E-
Book
Total Titles: 62 Print
Distributed by Charles E Tuttle Shokai

High Country Publishers Ltd
197 New Market Center, No 135, Boone, NC
28607
SAN: 254-3753
Tel: 828-964-0590 *Fax:* 828-262-1973
E-mail: editor@highcountrypublishers.com
Web Site: www.highcountrypublishers.com
Key Personnel
Sr & Man Ed: Judith Geary *E-mail:* editor@
highcountrypublishers.com
Exec Ed: Barbara Ingalls *E-mail:* barbingalls@
aol.com
Publr: Robert Ingalls
Opers & Sales Mgr: Wendy Dingwall
Founded: 2001
Small publishing company focusing on fiction &
memoir. Dedicated to discovering the truly ex-
cellent mss overlooked by other houses due to
changing literary fashion or a narrowly focused
target audience.
ISBN Prefix(es): 0-9713045; 1-932158
Number of titles published annually: 6 Print
Total Titles: 16 Print
Shipping Address: Biblio Distribution, A Division
of NBN Books, 15200 NBN Way, Blue Ridge
Summit, PA 17214
Warehouse: Biblio Distribution, A Division of
NBN Books, 15200 NBN Way, Blue Ridge
Summit, PA 17214
Distribution Center: Biblio Distribution, A Di-
vision of NBN Books, 15200 NBN Way,
Blue Ridge Summit, PA 17214 *Toll Free
Tel:* 800-462-6420 *Toll Free Fax:* 800-338-4550
E-mail: custserv@nbnbooks.com
Membership(s): Appalachian Writers Association;
Publishers Association of the South; Publishers
Marketing Association; Southeast Booksellers
Association

High Plains Press
539 Cassa Rd, Glendo, WY 82213
Mailing Address: PO Box 123, Glendo, WY
82213
Tel: 307-735-4370 *Toll Free Tel:* 800-552-7819
Fax: 307-735-4590
E-mail: editor@highplainspress.com
Web Site: www.highplainspress.com
Key Personnel
Publr: Nancy Curtis *E-mail:* nancy@
highplainspress.com
Founded: 1986
Books about Wyoming & the West.
ISBN Prefix(es): 0-931271
Number of titles published annually: 4 Print
Total Titles: 40 Print

High Tide Press
3650 W 183 St, Homewood, IL 60430
Tel: 708-206-2054 *Fax:* 708-206-2044
Web Site: www.hightidepress.com
Key Personnel
Man Ed: Monica Regan *E-mail:* managing.
editor@hightidepress.com
Founded: 1995
Full-service publisher of hardcover & paperback
books & magazines for the book trade & pro-
fessional niche markets. Specializes in the
fields of Psychology, developmental & men-
tal disabilities & nonprofit leadership.
ISBN Prefix(es): 0-9653744; 1-892696
Number of titles published annually: 6 Print
Total Titles: 27 Print
Membership(s): Publishers Marketing Association

Hill & Wang
Division of Farrar, Straus & Giroux LLC
19 Union Sq W, New York, NY 10003
SAN: 201-9299
Tel: 212-741-6900 *Fax:* 212-206-5340
E-mail: fsg.publicity@fsgbooks.com
Web Site: www.fsgbooks.com
Key Personnel
Publr: Elisabeth Sifton
Sr VP, Mktg & Publicity: Jeff Seroy
Adv Dir: Vicki Genna
Publicity Mgr: Cary Goldstein
Contracts & Perms Dir: Erika Seidman
Ed: Thomas LeBien
Founded: 1956
General nonfiction, history & drama.
ISBN Prefix(es): 0-8090
Number of titles published annually: 20 Print
Warehouse: Von Holt & Brinck Publishing
Services, 16365 James Madison Hwy, Gor-
donsville, VA 22942 *Toll Free Tel:* 888-330-
VHPS

Lawrence Hill Books, see Chicago Review Press

Hill Street Press LLC
191 E Broad St, Suite 209, Athens, GA 30601-
2848
Tel: 706-613-7200 *Fax:* 706-613-7204
Web Site: www.hillstreetpress.com
Key Personnel
Pres & Publr: Thomas Payton *E-mail:* payton@
hillstreetpress.com
Ed-in-Chief: Judy Long *E-mail:* long@
hillstreetpress.com
Sr Ed: Patrick Allen *Tel:* 706-613-7200 ext 1
E-mail: allen@hillstreetpress.com
Design & Prodn Mgr: Ann Boston *E-mail:* arb@
hillstreetpress.com
Founded: 1998
Independent small press.
ISBN Prefix(es): 1-58818
Number of titles published annually: 15 Print
Total Titles: 75 Print
Imprints: Hill Street Books; Hill Street Classics;
Hot Cross Books

Foreign Rep(s): Gazelle House (Australia); Hagreaves Fuller (Canada)
Foreign Rights: AmeriAsia; BPA; Peter Fritz Agency; Piergiorgio Nicolazzini; Tuttle-Mori (Asia, China, Japan, Korea)
Distribution Center: CDS

Hillsdale College Press
Division of Hillsdale College
33 E College St, Hillsdale, MI 49242
Tel: 517-437-7341 *Toll Free Tel:* 800-437-2268
  Fax: 517-437-3923
E-mail: news@hillsdale.edu
Web Site: www.hillsdale.edu
Key Personnel
Ed & VP, External Aff: Douglas A Jeffrey
  E-mail: douglas.jeffrey@hillsdale.edu
Founded: 1974
Single author books & collected essays of historical, political & economic interest.
ISBN Prefix(es): 0-916308

Hillsdale Educational Publishers Inc
39 North St, Hillsdale, MI 49242
SAN: 159-8759
Mailing Address: PO Box 245, Hillsdale, MI 49242
Tel: 517-437-3179 *Fax:* 517-437-0531
E-mail: davestory@aol.com
Web Site: hillsdalepublishers.com; michbooks.com
Key Personnel
Pres & Intl Rts: David McConnell
Founded: 1965
Publish & distribute regional titles for schools & libraries.
ISBN Prefix(es): 0-910726; 1-931466
Number of titles published annually: 4 Print; 1 CD-ROM
Total Titles: 18 Print; 1 CD-ROM

Himalayan Institute Press
Division of Himalayan International Institute of Yoga Science and Philosophy
952 Bethany Tpke, Honesdale, PA 18431-9706
Tel: 570-253-5551 *Toll Free Tel:* 800-822-4547
  Fax: 570-253-9078
E-mail: hibooks@himalayaninstitute.org
Web Site: www.himalayaninstitute.org
Key Personnel
Mktg Mgr: Alena Miles *E-mail:* alena@himalayaninstitute.org
Founded: 1971
Publish audio, video & books on yoga, meditation, holistic health, philosophy, psychology & stress management.
ISBN Prefix(es): 0-89389
Number of titles published annually: 5 Print; 2 Audio
Total Titles: 60 Print; 10 Audio
Imprints: Yoga International
Foreign Rights: Hagenbach & Bender (all territories)

Hippocrene Books Inc
171 Madison Ave, New York, NY 10016
Tel: 212-685-4371 (edit); 718-454-2366 (sales & cust serv) *Fax:* 718-454-1391 (cust serv); 212-779-9338 (edit) *Toll Free Fax:* 800-809-3855 (sales)
E-mail: orders@hippocrenebooks.com
Web Site: www.hippocrenebooks.com
Key Personnel
Pres & Edit Dir: George Blagowidow
VP, Treas, Contacts, Royalty & Perms: Ludmilla Blagowidow *E-mail:* ludmilla@hippocrenebooks.com
Cust Serv & Spec Sales: Nicholas Blagowidow
Credit Mgr: Paul Stero
Founded: 1971
Foreign language dictionaries & studies, international cookbooks, international literary classics, love poetry, concise illustrated histories of countries.
ISBN Prefix(es): 0-87052; 0-7818
Number of titles published annually: 30 Print
Total Titles: 600 Print; 25 Audio
Foreign Rights: A B E Marketing (Poland); Gazelle Book Services (England); E A Milley Enterprises (Canada)
Shipping Address: W A Book Service Inc, 26 Ranick Rd, Hauppauge, NY 11788

The Historic New Orleans Collection
533 Royal St, New Orleans, LA 70130
Tel: 504-523-4662 *Fax:* 504-598-7108
E-mail: hnocinfo@hnoc.org
Web Site: www.hnoc.org
Key Personnel
Exec Dir: Priscilla Lawrence
Dir, Pubns: Jessica Dorman *Tel:* 504-598-7174
Founded: 1966
Publications related to Louisiana history & to the holdings of the Historic New Orleans Collection; preservation manuals for family papers, photographs, etc.
ISBN Prefix(es): 0-917860
Total Titles: 32 Print

W D Hoard & Sons Co
28 W Milwaukee Ave, Fort Atkinson, WI 53538-0801
Mailing Address: PO Box 801, Fort Atkinson, WI 53538-0801
Tel: 920-563-5551 *Fax:* 920-563-7298
E-mail: hoards@hoards.com
Web Site: www.hoards.com
Key Personnel
Book Ed: Elvira Kau *E-mail:* hdbooks@hoards.com
Founded: 1870
Dairy oriented & some agricultural, regional books.
ISBN Prefix(es): 0-932147
Number of titles published annually: 3 Print
Total Titles: 18 Print
Imprints: Hoard's Dairyman

Hobby House Press Inc
One Corporate Dr, Grantsville, MD 21536
Tel: 301-895-3792 *Toll Free Tel:* 800-554-1447
  Fax: 301-895-5029
E-mail: email@hobbyhouse.com
Web Site: www.hobbyhouse.com
Key Personnel
Pres, Publr & Intl Rts: Gary Ruddell
Sales & Mktg Mgr: Kathy Trenter
Founded: 1942
Collector's books on dolls, teddy bears, other collectibles & antiques; price & identification guides along with how-to books for artists, plus gift books.
ISBN Prefix(es): 0-87588
Number of titles published annually: 20 Print
Total Titles: 175 Print
Distributed by Hobby House Press
Foreign Rep(s): Boekhand Van de Moosdijk (Netherlands, Europe); Craft Book Wholesalers (Australia); Macedo Books (Australia, New Zealand)

Hogrefe & Huber Publishers
875 Massachusetts Ave, 7th fl, Cambridge, MA 02139
SAN: 293-2792
Toll Free Tel: 800-228-3749; 866-823-4726
  Fax: 617-354-6875
E-mail: hh@hhpub.com
Web Site: www.hhpub.com
Key Personnel
Dir & Intl Rts: Christine Hogrefe
Founded: 1978
Specialize in books & journals in the fields of medicine, neurosciences, psychiatry, psychology.
ISBN Prefix(es): 0-88937; 0-920887
Foreign Office(s): Hogrefe Verlag, Rohnsweg 25, 37085 Goettingen, Germany, Contact: Robert Dimbleby *Tel:* (0551) 49 6090 *Fax:* (0551) 49 60988 *E-mail:* hhpub@hogrefe.de
Distributor for Hans Huber AG (Switzerland); Hogrefe Verlag fur Psychologie (Germany)
Orders to: BookMasters Inc, 30 Amberwood Pkwy, Ashland, OH 44805, Cheryl Householder *Tel:* 419-281-1802 *Toll Free Tel:* 800-228-3749 *Fax:* 419-281-6883
Returns: BookMasters Inc, 30 Amberwood Pkwy, Ashland, OH 44805, Cheryl Householder *Tel:* 419-281-1802 *Toll Free Tel:* 800-228-3749 *Fax:* 419-281-6883
Distribution Center: BookMasters Inc, 30 Amberwood Pkwy, Ashland, OH 44805, Contact: Cheryl Householder *Tel:* 419-281-1802 *Toll Free Tel:* 800-228-3749 *Fax:* 419-281-6883

Hohm Press
Subsidiary of HSM LLC
PO Box 2501, Prescott, AZ 86302
Tel: 928-778-9189 *Toll Free Tel:* 800-381-2700
  Fax: 928-717-1779
E-mail: hppublisher@cableone.net
Web Site: www.hohmpress.com
Key Personnel
Gen Mgr & Sales Dir: Dasya Anthony Zuccarello
Man Ed: Regina Sara Ryan
Prodn: Joe Bala Zuccarello
Mktg & Prom: Tom Shelby
Founded: 1975
Natural health, nutrition & religious studies.
ISBN Prefix(es): 0-934252; 1-890772
Number of titles published annually: 10 Print
Total Titles: 125 Print; 2 CD-ROM; 62 E-Book; 6 Audio
Foreign Rep(s): Business Book Network (World); Gazelle (Europe)
Foreign Rights: Hagenbach & Bender (world exc USA & Canada); Writers House (USA)
Shipping Address: 2508 Shadow Valley Ranch Rd, Prescott, AZ 86305
Distribution Center: SCB Distributors, 15608 S New Century Dr, Gardena, CA 90248

Holiday House Inc
425 Madison Ave, New York, NY 10017
SAN: 202-3008
Tel: 212-688-0085 *Fax:* 212-421-6134
Key Personnel
Pres: John H Briggs, Jr
VP & Ed-in-Chief: Regina Griffin
VP: Kate H Briggs
VP, Sales: Barbara A Walsh
Exec Ed: Mary Cash
Dir, Art & Design: Claire Counihan
Dir, Prodn: Virginia Weinstein
Dir, Mktg: Victoria Tisch
Cont: Judith Ang
Dir, Oper: Lisa Morales
Cust Rel: Dorothy Broshack
Founded: 1935
Juvenile & young adult books.
ISBN Prefix(es): 0-8234
Number of titles published annually: 70 Print
Total Titles: 700 Print
Foreign Rep(s): Thomas Allen & Son Ltd (Canada)
Foreign Rights: Big Apple Tuttle-Mori Agency (China); KCC International (Korea); Lora Fountain (Belgium, Netherlands, France, Italy, Russia, Spanish & Portuguese); Silke Weniger (Germany); Tuttle-Mori (Japan)
Shipping Address: WA Book Service, 26 Ranick Rd, Hauppauge, NY 11788
Membership(s): Children's Book Council

Holloway House Publishing Co

8060 Melrose Ave, Los Angeles, CA 90046-7082
Tel: 323-653-8060 *Fax:* 323-655-9452
E-mail: info@hollowayhousebooks.com
Web Site: www.hollowayhousebooks.com
Key Personnel
Pres & Intl Rts: Bentley Morriss
Mktg Mgr: Mitchell Neal
Exec Ed: Neal Colgrass
Lib Sales Dir: Rita Vega
Founded: 1960
Black, American Indian & Hispanic literature, games & gambling books; premiere trade editions.
ISBN Prefix(es): 0-87067
Number of titles published annually: 16 Print
Total Titles: 405 Print
Imprints: Avanti; Heartline Romances; Mankind; Melrose Square; Premiere
Distributed by All America Distributors Corp
Distributor for Avanti; Mankind; Melrose Square; Premiere
Foreign Rep(s): National Shopper Inc (North America, Orient)
Returns: 8431 Melrose Place, Los Angeles, CA 90069-5382, Lib Sales Dir: Rita Vega *Tel:* 323-653-8060
Warehouse: 8431 Melrose Place, Los Angeles, CA 90069-5382, Contact: Marc Morriss *Tel:* 323-651-2650 *Fax:* 323-655-9452 *E-mail:* info@hollowayhousebooks.com *Web Site:* www.hollowayhousebooks.com

Hollym International Corp

18 Donald Place, Elizabeth, NJ 07208
SAN: 211-0172
Tel: 908-353-1655 *Fax:* 908-353-0255
E-mail: hollym2@optonline.net
Web Site: www.hollym.com
Key Personnel
Pres: Gene S Rhie
Founded: 1976
Korea related books.
ISBN Prefix(es): 0-930878; 1-56591
Number of titles published annually: 10 Print
Total Titles: 155 Print
Foreign Office(s): Hollym Corp, 13-13 Kwancholdong, Chongroku, Seoul, Republic of Korea, Contact: Kim-Man Ham *Tel:* (02) 735-7551 *Fax:* (02) 730-5149 *E-mail:* hollym@chollian.net

Hollywood Creative Directory

Affiliate of Lone Eagle Publishing
1024 N Orange Dr, Hollywood, CA 90038
Tel: 323-308-3490 *Toll Free Tel:* 800-815-0503
Fax: 323-308-3493
Web Site: www.hcdonline.com
Key Personnel
Sr VP, Publg: Jeff Black *E-mail:* jblack@hcdonline.com
Founded: 1987
Specialize in directories on executives in the film, TV & music industries.
ISBN Prefix(es): 1-92893
Number of titles published annually: 5 Print
Total Titles: 8 Print; 6 E-Book
Distribution Center: National Book Network *Tel:* 301-459-3366 *Web Site:* www.hbnbooks.com
Membership(s): Publishers Association of Los Angeles
See separate listing for:
Lone Eagle Publishing

Hollywood Film Archive

8391 Beverly Blvd, PMB 321, Hollywood, CA 90048
Tel: 323-655-4968
Key Personnel
Pres & Dir: D Richard Baer
Busn Mgr: Howard Schiller

Founded: 1972
Publication, sales & distribution of comprehensive movie, video & TV reference books.
ISBN Prefix(es): 0-913616
Number of titles published annually: 3 Print
Total Titles: 34 Print
Subsidiaries: Cinema Book Society
Distributor for R R Bowker
Advertising Agency: Tartan Advertising

Holmes & Meier Publishers Inc

160 Broadway, East Bldg, New York, NY 10038
SAN: 201-9280
Tel: 212-374-0100 *Fax:* 212-374-1313
E-mail: info@holmesandmeier.com
Web Site: www.holmesandmeier.com
Key Personnel
Publr: Miriam H Holmes
Founded: 1969
Scholarly & trade hardcover & paperbacks; general nonfiction & fiction, reference, biography, autobiography & history. Jewish studies, cultural studies, ethnic & immigration studies, area studies, international affairs, women's studies, art, architecture, costume & theatre.
ISBN Prefix(es): 0-8419
Number of titles published annually: 8 Print
Total Titles: 600 Print
Subsidiaries: Africana Publishing Co
Foreign Office(s): Book Representation & Distribution (BRAD), 244 A London Rd, Hadleigh, Essex SS7 2DE, United Kingdom
Distributor for Biblio Press
Foreign Rep(s): Dan Levey (UK)
Warehouse: H&M Distribution, 41 Monroe Tpke, Trumbull, CT 06611
Membership(s): Publishers Marketing Association

Holmes Publishing Group

PO Box 623, Edmonds, WA 98020-0623
Tel: 425-771-2701 *Fax:* 425-771-5651
Key Personnel
Pres & CEO: J D Holmes *E-mail:* jdh@jdholmes.com
Founded: 1983
Religions of the world, New Age, occult, orientalia, metaphysical, philosophy, astrology & theology.
ISBN Prefix(es): 1-55818; 0-916411
Number of titles published annually: 8 Print
Total Titles: 360 Print
Imprints: Alchemical Press; Alexandrian Press; Contra/Thought; Near Eastern Press; Sure Fire Press
Foreign Rep(s): Mandrake Press Ltd (UK)

Henry Holt and Company, LLC

Unit of Holtzbrinck Publishing Holdings
115 W 18 St, New York, NY 10011
SAN: 200-2108
Tel: 212-886-9200 *Toll Free Tel:* 888-330-8477 (orders) *Fax:* 212-633-0748
E-mail: publicity@hholt.com
Web Site: www.henryholt.com
Key Personnel
Pres & Publr: John Sterling
VP & Dir, Fin: Thomas Cronin
VP & Dir, Opers & Admin: Deborah Valcourt
VP & Dir, Sales & Mktg: Maggie Richards
VP & Dir, Intl & Subs Rts: Denise Cronin
VP & Creative Dir, Adult Trade: Raquel Jaramillo
VP & Dir, Publicity: Elizabeth Shreve
VP & Publr, Books for Young Readers: Laura Godwin
Dir, Adv & Promos: Lucille Rettino
Dir, Spec Mkts: Judith Sisko
Dir, Perms: Mimi Ross
Ed-in-Chief, Adult Trade: Jennifer Barth
Exec Ed, Adult Trade: George Hodgman
Exec Ed, Books for Young Readers: Christy Ottaviano

Man Ed, Adult Trade: Kenn Russell
Edit Dir, Times Books: Paul Golob
Assoc Publr, John Macrae Books: John Macrae
Assoc Publr, Metropolitan Books: Sara Bershtel
Sr Ed, Adult Trade: Lisa Considine
Sr Ed, Metropolitan Books: Riva Hocherman
Founded: 1866
ISBN Prefix(es): 0-8050
Number of titles published annually: 250 Print
Total Titles: 3,000 Print
Imprints: Books for Young Readers; John Macrae Books; Metropolitan Books; Owl Books; Times Books
Distributor for The College Board; Cortina Learning International Inc; Slack Inc; Viceroy Press
Foreign Rep(s): H B Fenn & Co Ltd (Canada)
Foreign Rights: A/S Bookman Literary Agency (Denmark, Finland, Iceland, Norway, Sweden); Agence Jacqueline Miller (France); Agencia Literaria BMSR (Brazil); Agencia Literaria Carmen Barcells (Mexico, Portugal, Spain); Bardon-Chinese Media Agency (Mainland China, Taiwan); David Grossman Literary Agency (UK); English Agency (Japan); Frederique Porretta (France); Graal Ltd (Poland); Harris/Elon Agency (Israel); International Copyright Agency (Romania); Interrights (Bulgaria); Japan UNI Agency Inc (Japan); Katia & Bolza (Hungary); KCC (Korea); Kristin Olson Literary Agency (Czech Republic, Slovak Republic); Liepman Agency (Germany); Nurcihan Kesim LA (Turkey); Susanna Zevi (Italy); Tuttle-Mori Agency (Japan); Zvonimir Majdak (Croatia, Slovenia)
Advertising Agency: Bennett Book Advertising
Warehouse: 16365 James Madison Hwy, Gordonsville, VA 22942
Membership(s): AAP; Children's Book Council

§Holt, Rinehart and Winston

Division of Harcourt Inc
10801 N MoPac Expy, Bldg 3, Austin, TX 78759
Tel: 512-721-7000 *Toll Free Tel:* 800-225-5425 (cust serv) *Fax:* 512-721-7833 (mktg); 512-721-7898 (edit)
Web Site: www.hrw.com
Key Personnel
Pres: Judy Fowler *Tel:* 512-721-7700 *Fax:* 512-721-7703
Exec VP, Sales: David Irons *Tel:* 512-721-7600
Sr VP & Publr: Don Lankiewicz *Tel:* 512-721-7900
VP, HR: Julie Smith *Tel:* 512-721-7570
VP, Prof Devt: Bridget Hadley *Tel:* 508-644-2416
VP, Mktg: Greg Long *Tel:* 572-721-7800
Perms: Cathy Pare *Tel:* 512-721-7241
Founded: 1866
Textbooks & related learning materials in language arts, math, science, social studies & world languages for grades 6-12.
ISBN Prefix(es): 0-03
Total Titles: 1,408 Print; 1,511 CD-ROM; 159 Online; 135 E-Book; 66 Audio
Warehouse: 151 Benigno Blvd, Interstate Industrial Park, Bellmawr, NJ 08031-2515
1175 N Stemmons Freeway, Lewisville, TX 75067

Holtzbrinck Publishers

Subsidiary of Verlagsgruppe Georg von Holtzbrinck GmbH
175 Fifth Ave, New York, NY 10010
Tel: 212-674-5151 *Fax:* 212-420-9314
E-mail: firstname.lastname@hbpub.com
Web Site: www.holtzbrinck.com
Key Personnel
CEO: John Sargent *Tel:* 212-674-5151, ext 600 *E-mail:* john.sargent@hbpub.com
COO: Peter Garabedian *Tel:* 212-367-0101 *E-mail:* peter.garabedian@hbpubny.com
Pres, Sales: Alison Lazarus *Tel:* 212-674-5151, ext 602 *Fax:* 212-598-0270 *E-mail:* alison.lazarus@hbpub.com

Sr VP, VHPS: Michael Shareck *Tel:* 540-672-7698 *Fax:* 540-672-7052 *E-mail:* mshareck@vhpsva.com

VP, Acctg & Fin: Peter De Giglio *Tel:* 212-367-0103 *E-mail:* peter.degiglio@hbpubny.com

Sr VP, Info & Tech: Fritz Foy *Tel:* 212-367-0129 *Fax:* 212-691-6682 *E-mail:* fritz.foy@hbpubny.com

Sr VP, Legal Aff: David Kaye *Tel:* 212-654-5151, ext 741 *Fax:* 212-529-0594 *E-mail:* david.kaye@hbpub.com

Founded: 1986

Holtzbrinck Publishers is the administrative, sales, distribution & information technology arm of the Holtzbrinck publishing group in the United States, which includes Audio Renaissance; Bedford, Freeman & Worth Publishing Group LLC (W H Freeman/Worth Publishers & Bedford/St Martin's); Faber & Faber Inc; Farrar, Straus & Giroux LLC; Henry Holt and Company LLC; Nature America Inc; Palgrave Macmillan; Picador; Roaring Brook Press; St Martin's Press LLC; Scientific American Inc & Tom Doherty Associates LLC (Tor & Forge Books).

Branch Office(s)
123 W 18 St, New York, NY 10011 (branch mailing address: 115 W 18 St, New York, 10011) *Tel:* 212-367-0100 *Fax:* 212-367-7245 *E-mail:* firstname.lastname@hbpubny.com

Distribution Center: VHPS Distribution Center, 16365 James Madison Hwy, Gordonsville, VA 22942-8501 *Toll Free Tel:* 888-330-8477 *Fax:* 540-672-7540 (cust serv) *Toll Free Fax:* 800-672-2054 (orders) *E-mail:* firstinitial.lastname@vhpsva.com

See separate listing for:
W H Freeman and Co

Holy Cow! Press
Mount Royal Sta, Duluth, MN 55803
Mailing Address: PO Box 3170, Duluth, MN 55803
Tel: 218-724-1653 *Fax:* 218-724-1653
E-mail: holycow@cpinternet.com
Web Site: www.holycowpress.org
Key Personnel
Ed & Publr: Jim Perlman
Founded: 1977
ISBN Prefix(es): 0-930100
Number of titles published annually: 6 Print
Total Titles: 56 Print
Distribution Center: Consortium Book Sales & Distribution, 1045 Westgate Dr, St Paul, MN 55114 *Tel:* 651-221-9085 *Fax:* 651-221-0124

Holy Cross Orthodox Press
Division of Hellenic College Inc
50 Goddard Ave, Brookline, MA 02445
Tel: 617-731-3500 *Fax:* 617-850-1460
E-mail: press@hchc.edu
Web Site: www.hchc.edu
Key Personnel
Edit Mgr: Tanya Contos
Founded: 1974
Books on Orthodox Christian religion.
ISBN Prefix(es): 0-917651; 1-885652
Number of titles published annually: 10 Print
Total Titles: 120 Print

Home Planners LLC
Subsidiary of Hanley-Wood Inc
3275 W Ina Rd, Suite 220, Tucson, AZ 85741
SAN: 201-5382
Tel: 520-297-8200 *Toll Free Tel:* 800-322-6797 *Fax:* 520-297-6219 *Toll Free Fax:* 800-531-2555
E-mail: customerservice@eplans.com
Web Site: www.eplans.com
Key Personnel
CEO: Joe Carroll
Pres: Jayne Fenton

Publr: Eric Karaffi
Lib Sales Dir: Joanne Ravielli
Exec Ed: Linda Bellamy
Natl Sales Mgr: Julie Marshall *Tel:* 520-544-8240 *E-mail:* jmarshall@homeplanners.com
Architectural Mgr: Marc Wheeler
Fin & Mgmt Info: Joe Carroll
Founded: 1946
Designer of home & landscape plans, publisher of home plans & books, landscape, interior design books & magazines & construction blueprints.
ISBN Prefix(es): 0-918894; 1-881955; 1-931131
Number of titles published annually: 10 Print
Total Titles: 60 Print
Distributed by Creative Homeowner Press; H B Fenn & Co
Advertising Agency: Home Plans Advertising
Distribution Center: Home Planners Distribution Center, 29333 Lorie Lane, Wixom, MI 48393

Home Plans by Farmer, see W D Farmer Residence Designer Inc

Homestead Publishing
Affiliate of Book Design
PO Box 193, Moose, WY 83012-0193
Tel: 307-733-6248 *Fax:* 307-733-6248
Web Site: www.homesteadpublishing.net
Key Personnel
Publr: Carl Schreier *Tel:* 415-487-1331
Contact: Diane Henderson
Founded: 1980
Book publisher.
ISBN Prefix(es): 0-943972
Number of titles published annually: 6 Print; 100 Online
Total Titles: 108 Print; 1,500 Online; 6 E-Book
Subsidiaries: Book Design
Branch Office(s)
1068 14 St, San Francisco, CA 94114 *Tel:* 415-621-5039 *Fax:* 415-621-5039
Warehouse: 4030 W Lake Creek Dr, Wilson, WY 83014

§Homestore Plans & Publications
Division of Homestore Inc
213 E Fourth St, Suite 400, St Paul, MN 55101
Tel: 651-602-5000 *Toll Free Tel:* 888-626-2026 *Fax:* 651-602-5001
Web Site: homeplans.com
Key Personnel
Gen Manager: Wayne Ramaker
Lib Sales Dir & Mktg Assoc: Bruce Krause *Tel:* 651-602-5135
Founded: 1946
House plan books.
ISBN Prefix(es): 1-56547
Number of titles published annually: 44 Print; 1 CD-ROM
Total Titles: 3 CD-ROM
Distributed by HomeStyles Only

Honor Books
Imprint of Cook Communications Ministries
4050 Lee Vance View, Colorado Springs, CO 80918
Tel: 719-536-0100 *Toll Free Tel:* 800-708-5550
Web Site: www.cookministries.com
Key Personnel
Corp Publicity Mgr: Michele Tennesen
Specialize in portable & devotional books which inspire, encourage & motivate readers; gifts.
ISBN Prefix(es): 1-56292
Number of titles published annually: 30 Print
Total Titles: 315 Print
Imprints: RiverOak Publishing

Hoover Institution Press
Subsidiary of Hoover Institution on War, Revolution & Peace
424 Galvez Mall, Stanford, CA 94305-6010

SAN: 202-3024
Tel: 650-723-3373 *Toll Free Tel:* 800-935-2882 *Fax:* 650-723-8626
E-mail: digest@hoover.stanford.edu; hooverpress@hoover.stanford.edu
Web Site: www.hoover.org
Key Personnel
Exec Ed: Patricia Baker *Tel:* 650-725-3464 *E-mail:* baker@hoover.stanford.edu
Sr Ed: E Ann Wood *Tel:* 650-725-3462
Design Prod: Marshall Blanchard *Tel:* 650-725-3460
Founded: 1962
Studies on domestic & international policy, studies of nationalities in Central & Eastern Europe, history & political science; bibliographies & surveys of Hoover Institution's resources.
ISBN Prefix(es): 0-8179
Number of titles published annually: 25 Print
Total Titles: 675 Print; 3 Online
Foreign Rep(s): East-West Export Books (Asia, Hawaii, Pacific)

Hoover's, Inc
5800 Airport Blvd, Austin, TX 78752
Tel: 512-374-4500 *Toll Free Tel:* 800-486-8666 (orders only) *Fax:* 512-374-4538
E-mail: info@hoovers.com
Web Site: www.hoovers.com
Key Personnel
Dir, Print Prods: Dana Smith *E-mail:* dsmith@hoovers.com
Founded: 1990
Business reference books & online services.
ISBN Prefix(es): 1-878753; 1-57311
Number of titles published annually: 7 Print
Total Titles: 7 Print; 3 Online
Imprints: Hoover's Business Press; Hoover's Handbooks
Foreign Office(s): William Snyder Publishing Assoc, 5 Five Mile Dr, Oxford 0X2 8HT, United Kingdom
Foreign Rep(s): William Snyder Publishing Associates (England)

Hope Publishing Co
380 S Main Place, Carol Stream, IL 60188
Tel: 630-665-3200 *Toll Free Tel:* 800-323-1049 *Fax:* 630-665-2552
E-mail: hope@hopepublishing.com
Web Site: www.hopepublishing.com
Key Personnel
Pres: John Shorney *E-mail:* john@hopepublishing.com
VP: Scott Shorney; Steve Shorney
Founded: 1892
Choir music, hymnals, instrumental music books & hand bell music.
ISBN Prefix(es): 0-916642
Number of titles published annually: 5 Print
Total Titles: 15 Print
Divisions: Agape; Providence Press; Somerset Press; Tabernacle Publishing
Advertising Agency: Lamplighter Agency

Horizon Publishers & Distributors Inc
Imprint of Cedar Fort Inc
50 S 500 W, Bountiful, UT 84010
SAN: 159-4885
Tel: 801-295-9451 *Toll Free Tel:* 800-759-2665 *Fax:* 801-489-1096
E-mail: horizonp@burgoyne.com
Web Site: www.horizonpublishersbooks.com
Key Personnel
Pres, Owner & Sr Ed: Duane S Crowther
Founded: 1971
Christian (primarily Latter Day Saints), inspirational, health foods, self-sufficient living, music, marriage & family, children's activities, needlework, nonfiction, biography paperbacks & hardbound.
ISBN Prefix(es): 0-88290

Number of titles published annually: 12 Print
Total Titles: 388 Print; 1 CD-ROM; 40 Audio

Hospital & Healthcare Compensation Service
Subsidiary of John R Zabka Associates Inc
PO Box 376, Oakland, NJ 07436
Tel: 201-405-0075 *Fax:* 201-405-2110
E-mail: allinfo@hhcsinc.com
Web Site: www.hhcsinc.com
Key Personnel
Dir: Rosanne Cioffe
Client Servs: Sophia Molendyk
Founded: 1971
Specialize in salaries in hospital, nursing home, assisted living, CCRC, home care, hospice & healthcare/management company employees.
ISBN Prefix(es): 0-939326
Number of titles published annually: 9 Print

Host Publications
2717 Wooldridge Dr, Austin, TX 78703
Tel: 512-482-8229 *Fax:* 512-482-0580
Web Site: www.hostpublications.com
Founded: 1988
ISBN Prefix(es): 0-924047
Number of titles published annually: 3 Print
Total Titles: 18 Print
Membership(s): Publishers Marketing Association

§Hot House Press
760 Cushing Hwy, Cohasset, MA 02025
Tel: 781-383-8360 *Toll Free Tel:* 866-331-8360
  Fax: 781-383-8346
Web Site: www.hothousepress.com
Key Personnel
Pres & Publr: David Replogle
  E-mail: drreplogle@aol.com
Assoc Publr & Sr Ed: Sally Weltman
Founded: 2000
Publish deserving new authors who find it increasingly difficult to overcome the effects of consolidation & bestseller myopia in the industry.
ISBN Prefix(es): 0-9700476; 0-9755245
Number of titles published annually: 6 Print; 1 CD-ROM; 2 Online; 2 E-Book
Total Titles: 12 Print; 1 CD-ROM; 2 Online; 2 E-Book; 1 Audio
Sales Office(s): National Book Network, 4501 Forbes Blvd, Suite 200, Lanham, MD 20706 *Tel:* 301-459-3366 *Fax:* 301-459-1705 *E-mail:* mcozy@nbnbooks.com *Web Site:* www.nbnbooks.com
Orders to: NBN *Toll Free Tel:* 800-462-6420
Returns: National Book Network, Attn: Returns Dept, 15200 NBN Way, Bldg B, Blue Ridge Summit, PA 17214
Shipping Address: National Book Network, 15200 NBN Way, Blue Ridge Summit, PA 17214 *Tel:* 717-794-3800 *Toll Free Tel:* 800-462-6420 *Toll Free Fax:* 800-338-4550 *E-mail:* custserv@nbnbooks.com *Web Site:* www.nbnbooks.com
Warehouse: National Book Network, 15200 NBN Way, Blue Ridge Summit, PA 17214 *Tel:* 717-794-3800 *Toll Free Tel:* 800-462-6420 *Toll Free Fax:* 800-338-4550 *Web Site:* www.nbnbooks.com
Distribution Center: National Book Network, 15200 NBN Way, Blue Ridge Summit, PA 17214

Houghton Mifflin College Division
Division of Houghton Mifflin Co
222 Berkeley St, Boston, MA 02116-3764
Tel: 617-351-5000 *Toll Free Tel:* 800-225-1464 (orders)
Web Site: www.college.hmco.com
Key Personnel
Exec VP, Coll Div: June Smith
VP & Dir, Planning, Fin & Opers: Clifford M Manko

VP & Dir, Partnerships & Strategic Devt: David Serbun
VP & Edit Dir: Kristine Clerkin
VP & Dir, Sales & Mktg: Garret J White
VP & Dir, Publg Servs: Jane Muse
Sr Man Ed: Terry Wilton
Rts & Perms: Craig Mertens
College textbooks, educational materials & services.
ISBN Prefix(es): 0-395

§Houghton Mifflin Co
222 Berkeley St, Boston, MA 02116-3764
Tel: 617-351-5000 *Toll Free Tel:* 800-225-3362 (trade books); 800-733-2828 (text books); 800-225-1464 (college texts) *Fax:* 617-351-1125
Web Site: www.hmco.com *Telex:* 4430255 HMHQ UI *Cable:* HOUGHTON
Key Personnel
Exec VP & CFO: Steve Richards
Exec VP, Coll Div: June Smith
Exec VP & Pres, McDougal Littell: Rita H Schaefer
Exec VP, Houghton Mifflin Assessment Group: Sylvia Metayer
Sr VP, Trade & Ref Div: Theresa Kelly
Sr VP & Pres, Great Source Educ Group: Steven Zukowski
Sr VP: David Caron
Sr VP, Chief Information Officer: Patrick Meehan
Sr VP & Gen Counsel: Paul D Weaver
Sr VP, Educ & Govt Aff: Maureen DiMarco
Sr VP, HR: Gerald T Hughes, Jr
VP, Communs: Collin Earnst
VP & Gen Mgr: Steven Tapp
VP, Dist: William Brown
Pres, Riverside Publg Co: Lee Jones
Founded: 1832
ISBN Prefix(es): 0-395
Subsidiaries: Clarion Books; Cognitive Concepts Inc; Edusoft; Great Source Education Group; McDougal Littell; Promissor Inc; The Riverside Publishing Co
Distributor for Beacon Press
Membership(s): AAP; BISG; Children's Book Council
See separate listing for:
Clarion Books
Great Source Education Group
Houghton Mifflin College Division
Houghton Mifflin School Division
Houghton Mifflin Trade & Reference Division
McDougal Littell
Promissor Inc
The Riverside Publishing Co

Houghton Mifflin School Division
Division of Houghton Mifflin Co
222 Berkeley St, Boston, MA 02116-3764
Key Personnel
Sr VP & Publr: Donna Lucki
Sr VP & Dir, Fin, Planning & Opers: Steve Zukowski
VP & Natl Sales Mgr: Sue Schulz
VP, Mktg: Mary Anne Kennedy
VP & Man Ed: Marilyn R Stevens
VP & Edit Dir, Reading/Lang Arts & Bilingual Ed: Alice Sullo
VP & Edit Dir, Math, Science, Social Studies & Instructional Technol: Kirby Mansfield
Elementary school textbooks, educational materials & services.
Sales Office(s): 2001 Gateway Place, Suite 750 W, San Jose, CA 95110, VP & Regl Mgr: James Vandiver *Tel:* 972-458-5712
5555 Triangle Pkwy, Suite 150, Norcross, GA 30092, VP & Regl Mgr: Deborah Sanders *Tel:* 404-449-5881
1900 S Batavia Ave, Geneva, IL 60134 *Tel:* 630-232-2550
307 Fellowship Rd, Suite 104, Mt Laurel, NJ 08054, VP & Regl Mgr: Gwen Durden-Simmons *Tel:* 609-452-0200

13400 Midway Rd, Dallas, TX 75244, VP & Regl Mgr: Mary Lytle *Tel:* 972-980-1100
8400 E Prentice Ave, Denver, CO 80232-2550, VP & Regl Mgr: Deborah Lehman

Houghton Mifflin Trade & Reference Division
Division of Houghton Mifflin Co
222 Berkeley St, Boston, MA 02116-3764
SAN: 200-2388
Tel: 617-351-5000 *Toll Free Tel:* 800-225-3362
Web Site: www.houghtonmifflinbooks.com
Key Personnel
Sr VP: Theresa Kelly
Corp VP & Dir, Mktg: Bridget Marmion
VP & Dir, Spec Sales & Merchandise Licensing: Maire Gorman
VP & Exec Dir, Publicity: Lori Glazer
VP & Dir, Subs Rts: Deborah Engel
VP & Dir, Mktg for Dictionaries, Children's & Guide Books & VP & Man Dir, Kingfisher: Nancy Grant
VP & Publr, Walter Lorraine Books: Walter Lorraine
VP, Publr & Ed-in-Chief, Adult Trade Bks: Janet Silver
VP & Publr, Dictionaries & Dir, Prod & Mgmt Servs: Margery Berube
VP & Publr, Children's Books: Andrea Pinkney
VP, Assoc Publr & Edit Dir, Clarion Bks: Dinah Stevenson
VP & Exec Man Ed: Rebecca Saikia-Wilson
VP & Dir, Electronic Publg & Gen Ref: Gordon Hardy
VP & Dir, Cust Serv & Opers: Marilyn Harris
Man Dir, Trade Pbks: Susan Canavan
Dir, Trade Sales: Ken Carpenter
General literature, fiction, nonfiction, biography, autobiography, history, poetry & juvenile publications, dictionary, reference books, cookbooks & guidebooks.
ISBN Prefix(es): 0-89919; 0-395; 1-85697; 0-7534; 0-618; 1-88152
Number of titles published annually: 400 Print; 1 CD-ROM; 1 Online; 14 Audio
Total Titles: 3,300 Print; 2 CD-ROM; 2 Online; 110 Audio
Imprints: Houghton Mifflin; Mariner Books; Houghton Mifflin Books for Children; Walter Lorraine Books; Clarion Books; Kingfisher Publications; American Heritage Dictionary
Editorial Office(s): 215 Park Ave S, New York, NY 10003 *Tel:* 212-420-5800
Distributor for Beacon Press; Larausse; Old Farmers Almanac
Orders to: Houghton Mifflin Trade Customer Service, 181 Ballardvale St, PO Box 705, Wilmington, MA 01887 *Toll Free Tel:* 800-225-3362 *Toll Free Fax:* 800-634-7568
Returns: Houghton Mifflin Company, Trade Returns Department, 2700 N Richard Ave, Indianapolis, IN 46219

House of Collectibles
Imprint of Random House Information Group
1745 Broadway, New York, NY 10019
Tel: 212-782-9000 *Fax:* 212-572-4997
E-mail: houseofcollectibles@randomhouse.com
Web Site: www.houseofcollectibles.com; www.randomhouse.com
Key Personnel
Ed: Dorothy Harris *Tel:* 212-572-6170
  E-mail: dharris@randomhouse.com
Publisher that collectors, dealers & investors around the world turn to for detailed reference information & current market values on all antiques & collectibles-whether they want to know the history of Gustav Stickley furniture, buy a Chinese vase, sell their grandmother's depression glass or evaluate the worth of their Star Wars memorabilia. The House of Collectibles books are compiled by experts, renowned for accuracy & completeness & profusely illustrated, many with full color. Accept

unsol proposals & mss from authors who are experts in the antiques & collectibles areas, also accept mss & proposals from agents.
ISBN Prefix(es): 0-609; 0-676; 1-4000; 0-87637
Number of titles published annually: 20 Print

House to House Publications
Division of DOVE Christian Fellowship International
1924 W Main St, Ephrata, PA 17522
Tel: 717-738-3751 *Toll Free Tel:* 800-848-5892
Fax: 717-738-0656
E-mail: H2HP@dcfi.org
Web Site: www.dcfi.org
Key Personnel
Pubns Ed: Karen Ruiz *E-mail:* karenr@dcfi.org
Founded: 1997
Provide resources for the body of Christ worldwide.
ISBN Prefix(es): 1-886973
Number of titles published annually: 4 Print
Total Titles: 37 Print; 18 Audio

Housing Assistance Council
1025 Vermont Ave NW, Suite 606, Washington, DC 20005
Tel: 202-842-8600 *Fax:* 202-347-3441
E-mail: hac@ruralhome.org
Web Site: www.ruralhome.org
Key Personnel
Dir, Commun: Leslie R Strauss *E-mail:* leslie@ruralhome.org
Founded: 1971
Provides technical housing services, loans, program & policy assistance, training, research & information. Specializes in research reports, technical manuals & information pieces, all exclusively about low-income rural housing in the US.
ISBN Prefix(es): 1-58064
Number of titles published annually: 15 Print; 15 Online
Total Titles: 80 Print; 50 Online

Howard Publishing
3117 N Seventh St, West Monroe, LA 71291
SAN: 298-7597
Tel: 318-396-3122 *Toll Free Tel:* 800-858-4109
Fax: 318-397-1882
E-mail: info@howardpublishing.com
Web Site: howardpublishing.com
Key Personnel
Pres & Intl Rights: John Howard *Tel:* 318-396-3122 ext 101 *E-mail:* john@howardpublishing.com
VP: Gary Myers *E-mail:* gary@howardpublishing.com
Founded: 1969
Religious books & music.
ISBN Prefix(es): 1-878990
Number of titles published annually: 50 Print; 2 Audio
Total Titles: 170 Print; 6 Audio
Foreign Rights: Glint (World)
Returns: 317 Kings Lane, West Monroe, LA 71291
Warehouse: 117 Kings Lane, West Monroe, LA 71291, Contact: David Owen *Tel:* 318-387-2998
Membership(s): Christian Booksellers Association; Evangelical Christian Publishers Association

Howard University Press
2225 Georgia Ave NW, Suite 718, Washington, DC 20059
SAN: 202-3067
Tel: 202-238-2570 *Fax:* 202-588-9849
E-mail: howardupress@howard.edu
Web Site: www.hupress.howard.edu
Key Personnel
Dir: D Kamili Anderson *Tel:* 202-238-2575
E-mail: danderson@howard.edu
Founded: 1972
Scholarship that addresses the contributions, conditions & concerns of African Americans, other people of African descent & people of color around the world in a broad array of disciplines.
ISBN Prefix(es): 0-88258
Number of titles published annually: 3 Print
Total Titles: 130 Print
Foreign Rights: The Permissions Company
Billing Address: PO Box 50283, Hampden Sta, Baltimore, MD 21211
Orders to: PO Box 50283, Hampden Sta, Baltimore, MD 21211 *Tel:* 410-516-6947 *Toll Free Tel:* 800-537-5487
Returns: c/o Maple Press Company, Lebanon Distribution Ctr, 704 Legionnaire Dr, Frederick, PA 17026
Warehouse: c/o Maple Press Company, Lebanon Distribution Ctr, 704 Legionnaire Dr, Frederick, PA 17026 *Tel:* 410-516-6965 *Toll Free Tel:* 800-537-5487 *Fax:* 410-516-6998
Membership(s): AAP; American Association of University Presses

Howell Press Inc
1713-2D Allied Lane, Charlottesville, VA 22903
SAN: 661-6607
Tel: 434-977-4006 *Toll Free Tel:* 800-868-4512 *Fax:* 434-971-7204 *Toll Free Fax:* 888-971-7204
E-mail: custserv@howellpress.com
Web Site: www.howellpress.com
Key Personnel
Pres & Sales: Ross A Howell, Jr *E-mail:* rhowell@howellpress.com
Sales Dir: Elinor Howell *E-mail:* ehowell@howellpress.com
Man Ed & Mktg: Dara P Parker *E-mail:* editorial@howellpress.com
Warehouse Mgr: Jacob Kemper *E-mail:* warehouse@howellpress.com
Acctg: Patrick Otto
Founded: 1985
Subjects include regional (mid-Atlantic & South) gourmet, gift books & quilts.
ISBN Prefix(es): 0-914440; 0-939009; 1-889324; 1-55209; 0-9616878; 0-943231; 1-57427; 1-883522; 0-932664; 1-873376; 0-9519899; 0-920718; 1-887911
Number of titles published annually: 7 Print
Total Titles: 100 Print
Imprints: EPM (Mid-Atlantic regional, quilts & crafts); Rockbridge Publishing (Civil War)
Distributed by Vanwell Publishing (Canada); Spellmount Publishers (UK)
Distributor for Vefa Alexiadou; Art Global; Top Ten Publishing; Vanwell Publishing
Returns: 1741 Allied St, Charlottesville, VA 22903 (Returns after 90 days after purchase but before 12 mos after purchase date. Item must be in resaleable condition)
Warehouse: 1741 Allied St, Charlottesville, VA 22903 (Returns after 90 days after purchase but before 12 mos after purchase date. Item must be in resaleable condition)

Howells House
PO Box 9546, Washington, DC 20016-9546
Tel: 202-333-2182 *Fax:* 202-333-2184
E-mail: hhi@ix.netcom.com
Key Personnel
Pres & Publr: W D Howells
Man Ed: Mellen Candage
Founded: 1988
Adult nonfiction book publishing.
ISBN Prefix(es): 0-929590
Number of titles published annually: 4 Print; 2 Online
Total Titles: 2 Online

Imprints: The Compass Press (current affairs, contemporary history, biography); Whalesback Books
Foreign Rep(s): Gazelle Book Services Ltd (Europe, London); Tuttle-Mori (Asia, Japan)
Foreign Rights: Norman Franklin (Europe, London); Tuttle-Mori (Japan)
Returns: Independent Publishing Group, 814 N Franklin St, Chicago, IL 60610 (For labels call or write) *Tel:* 312-337-0747 *Toll Free Tel:* 800-888-4741 *Fax:* 312-337-5985 *E-mail:* frontdesk@ipgbook.com *Web Site:* www.ipgbook.com
Shipping Address: Independent Publishing Group, 814 N Franklin St, Chicago, IL 60610 (For labels call or write) *Toll Free Tel:* 800-888-4741 *Fax:* 312-337-5985
Distribution Center: Independent Publishing Group, 814 N Franklin St, Chicago, IL 60610 (For labels call or write) *Tel:* 312-337-0747 (returns) *Toll Free Tel:* 800-888-4741 *Fax:* 312-337-5985
Membership(s): Independent Publisher's Guild

HPBooks
Imprint of Penguin Group (USA) Inc
375 Hudson St, New York, NY 10014
SAN: 282-5074
Mailing Address: 1631 Irvine Ave, Suite A, Costa Mesa, CA 92627
Tel: 212-366-2000
E-mail: online@penguinputnam.com
Web Site: www.penguin.com
Key Personnel
VP, Publr & Sr Ed: John Duff
Edit Dir, Auto: Michael Lutfy *Tel:* 949-722-8062 *Fax:* 949-645-8429 *E-mail:* mlutfy@aol.com
Auto Sales Mgr: Jerry Hatch *Tel:* 805-492-5218; 800-541-9325 *Fax:* 805-492-5318 *E-mail:* jhatch@penguin.com
Founded: 1964
Automotive book publisher. High performance, restoration & racing how-to books for automotive enthusiasts. Cover domestic & foreign vehicles. Also publishes cookbooks.
ISBN Prefix(es): 0-89586; 0-912656; 1-55788
Number of titles published annually: 14 Print
Total Titles: 169 Print
Branch Office(s)
3138 Starling Ave, Thousand Oaks, CA 91360 (auto sales), Auto Sales Mgr: Jerry Hatch *Tel:* 805-492-5218 *Fax:* 805-493-5550 *E-mail:* jhatch@penguinputnam.com
Editorial Office(s): 1631 Irvine Ave, Suite A, Costa Mesa, CA 92627, Edit Dir: Michael Lufty *Tel:* 949-722-8062 *Fax:* 949-645-8429 *E-mail:* mlutfy@aol.com
Advertising Agency: Spier NY

§HRD Press
22 Amherst Rd, Amherst, MA 01002
SAN: 201-9213
Tel: 413-253-3488 *Toll Free Tel:* 800-822-2801 *Fax:* 413-253-3490
E-mail: info@hrdpress.com; orders@hrdpress.com
Web Site: www.hrdpress.com
Key Personnel
Pres, Edit Mgr & Publr: R W Carkhuff
Cust Rel: Donna Long
Founded: 1972
Textbooks & off-the-shelf workshops on human resource development, management & training. Packaged training materials & assessments.
ISBN Prefix(es): 0-914234; 0-87425
Number of titles published annually: 25 Print
Total Titles: 600 Print; 20 E-Book

HSC Publications
360-A W Merrick Rd, Suite 40, Valley Stream, NY 11580
Tel: 516-256-0223

E-mail: hscpub@aol.com
Web Site: www.hscpub.com
Key Personnel
Publr: Alex Hammer *Fax:* 425-799-9038
Founded: 1996
Subject specialities include spirituality & collectibles.
Total Titles: 5 Print

Hudson Hills Press LLC
74-2 Union St, Manchester, VT 05254
SAN: 213-0815
Mailing Address: PO Box 205, Manchester, VT 05254
Tel: 802-362-6450 *Fax:* 802-362-6459
E-mail: artbooks@hudsonhills.com
Web Site: www.hudsonhills.com
Key Personnel
Exec: Randall Perkins; Leslie vanBreen
Founded: 1978
Renowned titles on fine art, photography, decorative arts & architecture.
ISBN Prefix(es): 0-933920; 1-55595
Number of titles published annually: 25 Print
Total Titles: 150 Print
Distributed by National Book Network
Foreign Rights: Peribo (Australia); Windsor Books International (Europe & UK)

Hudson Institute
1015 18 St NW, Suite 300, Washington, DC 20036
Tel: 202-223-7770 *Fax:* 202-223-8537
E-mail: info@hudson.org
Web Site: www.hudson.org
Key Personnel
Pres: Dr Herb London
Founded: 1961
Books, monographs, briefing papers, newsletters.
ISBN Prefix(es): 1-55813
Number of titles published annually: 10 Print
Total Titles: 60 Print

Hudson Park Press
Johnny Cake Hollow Rd, Pine Plains, NY 12567
Mailing Address: PO Box 774, Pine Plains, NY 12567-0774
Tel: 212-929-8898 *Fax:* 212-242-6137
E-mail: hudpark@aol.com
Web Site: www.hudsonpark.com
Key Personnel
Pres: Gilman Park *E-mail:* gpark@hudsonpark.com
Mktg Dir & Intl Rts: C B Sayre
Edit Dir: Adele Ursone *E-mail:* ajursone@aol.com
Man Ed: Dorothy Caeser *E-mail:* drcaeser@aol.com
Spec Sales Mgr: Martha Moran
  E-mail: mmoran@hudsonpark.com
Founded: 1995
Publishing & custom packaging of art & photography books, calendars, record books, social stationery, related sidelines.
ISBN Prefix(es): 1-57461
Number of titles published annually: 20 Print
Total Titles: 80 Print
Distributed by Publishers Group West

Hugh Lauter Levin Associates Inc
9 Burr Rd, Westport, CT 06880
Tel: 203-227-6422 *Fax:* 203-227-6717
E-mail: inquiries@hlla.com
Web Site: www.hlla.com
Key Personnel
Pres: Hugh Levin *E-mail:* hugh@hlla.com
Ed: Leslie Carola *E-mail:* leslie@hlla.com; James Muschett *E-mail:* jim@hlla.com; Ellin Yassky *E-mail:* ellin@hlla.com
Founded: 1973
Publish illustrated books & calendars.
ISBN Prefix(es): 0-88363

Number of titles published annually: 15 Print
Total Titles: 70 Print
Imprints: Beaux Arts Editions
Distributed by Publishers Group West
Distributor for Hugh Lauter Levin Assoc, Inc
Foreign Rep(s): Gazelle (UK, Europe)
Warehouse: 1170 Trademark Dr, Reno, NV 89511
  Tel: 775-850-2501 *Fax:* 775-850-2500

Human Kinetics Inc
PO Box 5076, Champaign, IL 61825-5076
SAN: 211-7088
Tel: 217-351-5076 *Toll Free Tel:* 800-747-4457
  Fax: 217-351-1549 (orders/cust serv)
E-mail: info@hkusa.com
Web Site: www.humankinetics.com
Key Personnel
CEO: Brian Holding
Exec VP: Julie S Martens
Publr & Pres: Rainer Martens
VP, Fin: Gayle S Wheeler
VP, Pubn Devt & Rts & Perms: Holly Gilly
VP, Sales & Mktg: Robert Fox
Mktg Dir: Bill Bowman
Prodn Dir: Keith Blomberg
Academic Sales Dir: Cheri Scott
Founded: 1974
Scholarly books, college textbooks & trade books in physical education, sports medicine & science, coaching, sport technique & fitness.
ISBN Prefix(es): 0-931250; 0-87322; 0-88011; 0-918438; 0-7360; 0-912781
Number of titles published annually: 50 Print
Total Titles: 200 Print
Imprints: YMCA of the USA
Subsidiaries: Human Kinetics Australia; Human Kinetics Canada; Human Kinetics Europe; Human Kinetics New Zealand
Foreign Rep(s): Flo Enterprise Sdn Bnd (Malaysia); HK Australia, HK Canada, HK Europe, HK New Zealand, I J Sagun Enterprises (Hong Kong, Korea, Philippines); Berj Jamkojain Associates (Middle East); Japan Publications Trading (Japan); Real Books (South Africa); Unifacmanu (Taiwan); Vigor Book Agents (South Africa); Viva Books (India)
Shipping Address: 1607 N Market St, Champaign, IL 61820-2200

§Human Rights Watch
350 Fifth Ave, 34th fl, New York, NY 10118
Tel: 212-290-4700 *Fax:* 212-736-1300
E-mail: hrwnyc@hrw.org
Web Site: www.hrw.org
Key Personnel
Pubns Mgr: Sobeira Genao
Founded: 1978
Nonprofit human rights organization publishing books & newsletters on human rights practices in more than 70 countries worldwide; documents arbitrary imprisonment, censorship, disappearances, due process of law, murder, prison conditions, torture, violations of laws of war & other abuses of internationally recognized human rights.
ISBN Prefix(es): 0-938579; 0-929692; 1-56432
Number of titles published annually: 67 Print
Total Titles: 1,000 Print; 60 E-Book
Imprints: Human Rights Watch Books
Warehouse: Bookmart Press, 2001 42 St, North Bergen, NJ 07047

§Humana Press
999 Riverview Dr, Suite 208, Totowa, NJ 07512
SAN: 212-3606
Tel: 973-256-1699 *Fax:* 973-256-8341
E-mail: humana@humanapr.com
Web Site: humanapress.com
Key Personnel
Pres & Ed-in-Chief: Thomas Lanigan, Sr
VP, Mktg & Sales: Thomas B Lanigan, Jr
  E-mail: tbhumana@humanapr.com

Treas: Julia Lanigan
Art Dir: Patricia Cleary
Dir, Edit Servs: Robin Weisberg
Edit Dir: Paul Dolgert
Prodn Mgr & ISBN Contact: Frances Lipton
Assoc Dir, Mktg: Richard Hruska
Mktg Specialist: Ron Epstein
Cust Serv: Victor Lao
Founded: 1976
Books & periodicals; specialize in medicine & biomedical science.
ISBN Prefix(es): 0-89603; 1-58829
Number of titles published annually: 120 Print; 15 CD-ROM; 100 Online; 120 E-Book
Total Titles: 1,000 Print; 61 CD-ROM; 100 Online; 500 E-Book
Imprints: Vox Humana
Distributed by Blackwell Science
Foreign Rep(s): Blackwell Science (Australia); Blackwell Science Ltd (Africa, Europe & UK, Middle East); Cassidy & Associates (China); Kay Kato (Japan); John Lee (SE Asia); Maruzen Co Ltd (Japan); Kino Runiya (Japan)
Foreign Rights: John Scott & Co (Worldwide)
Returns: Maple-Vail Distribution Center, 704 Legionaire Dr, Fredericksburg, PA 17026
  Tel: 717-865-7600 *Fax:* 717-865-7800
Warehouse: Maple-Vail Distribution Center, 704 Legionaire Dr, Fredericksburg, PA 17026
  Tel: 717-865-7600 *Fax:* 717-865-7800
Membership(s): American Medical Publishers Association

Humanics Publishing Group
12 S Dixie Hwy, Suite 203, Lake Worth, FL 33460
SAN: 159-2637
Tel: 561-533-6231 *Toll Free Tel:* 800-874-8844
  Toll Free Fax: 888-874-8844
E-mail: humanics@mindspring.com
Web Site: humanicspub.com; humanicslearning.com; humanicsdealer.com
Key Personnel
Chmn: Gary B Wilson
Dir, Opers: Chris Walker
Exec Ed: Geoffrey Select
Prodn Mgr: Jennifer Hall
Fulfillment Mgr: Kevin Hooper
Acqs Ed: Arthur Bligh
Cust Support: Robert G Hall
Founded: 1976
Paperback trade & college textbooks, elementary & child development; teachers' resource books, New Age, Taoism & Zen, self-help, psychology, fine editions, art, child care crafts, education, health & nutrition, how-to, human relations, humor, children's, spirituality & psychological tests.
ISBN Prefix(es): 0-89334
Number of titles published annually: 40 Print
Total Titles: 570 Print; 2 Audio
Imprints: Humanics; Humanics Audio; Humanics Learning; Humanics New Age; Humanics Psychological Test Corp; Humanics Trade Paperback
Divisions: Humanics Training Institute
Distributed by New Leaf; Emery Pratt
Advertising Agency: Wilson Advertising Agency, 147 15 St, Suite 12-F, Atlanta, GA 30361
Membership(s): AAP; Publishers Marketing Association

Hunter House Publishers
1515 1/2 Park St, Alameda, CA 94501
Mailing Address: PO Box 2914, Alameda, CA 94501-0914 SAN: 281-7969
Tel: 510-865-5282 *Toll Free Tel:* 800-266-5592
  Fax: 510-865-4295
E-mail: acquisitions@hunterhouse.com
Web Site: www.hunterhouse.com/

Key Personnel
Pres & Publr: Kiran S Rana *E-mail:* kiran@
  hunterhouse.com
Acqs Ed: Jeanne Brondino *E-mail:* acquisitions@
  hunterhouse.com
Ed Assoc: Alexandra Mummery
  E-mail: editorial@hunterhouse.com
Cust Serv Mgr & Orders Contact: Christina Sver-
  drup *E-mail:* ordering@hunterhouse.com
Founded: 1978
Self-help health, fitness, sexuality, personal
  growth, relationships, violence prevention &
  intervention, life skills, specialized teaching &
  counseling resources.
ISBN Prefix(es): 0-89793
Number of titles published annually: 21 Print
Total Titles: 230 Print
Imprints: Sufi Publishing
Foreign Rep(s): Alternative Books (South Africa);
  Astam books (Australia); Deep Books (UK,
  Europe); PGW (Canada)
Warehouse: 2324 Times Way, Alameda, CA
  94501
Membership(s): Publishers Marketing Association

Hunter Publishing Inc
130 Campus Dr, Edison, NJ 08818
SAN: 695-3425
Mailing Address: PO Box 746, Walpole, MA
  02081
Tel: 732-225-1900 (orders) *Toll Free Tel:* 800-
  255-0343 *Fax:* 732-417-1744
E-mail: comments@hunterpublishing.com
Web Site: www.hunterpublishing.com
Key Personnel
Pres: Michael Hunter
Founded: 1985
Books for travelers.
ISBN Prefix(es): 0-935161; 1-55650; 0-85039; 0-
  681; 0-929756; 0-85285; 3-259; 3-88989
Number of titles published annually: 100 Print;
  50 E-Book
Total Titles: 500 Print; 150 E-Book
Imprints: Adventure Guides; Alive Guides;
  Charming Small Hotel Guides; Nelles Guides;
  Visitor's Guides
Warehouse: Bldg 424, 80 Northfield Ave, Edison,
  NJ 08818

Huntington House Publishers
104 Row 2, Suite A-1 & A-2, Lafayette, LA
  70508
Mailing Address: Box 53788, Lafayette, LA
  70505-3788
Tel: 337-237-7049; 337-749-4009 (sales); 337-
  237-3082 (opers) *Toll Free Tel:* 800-749-4009
  (sales) *Fax:* 337-237-7060
E-mail: admin@alphapublishingonline.com;
  sales@alphapublishingonline.com
Web Site: www.alphapublishingonline.com
Key Personnel
Publr: Mark Anthony *E-mail:* manthony@
  alphapublishingonline.com
VP, Opers: Donald Gaspard *E-mail:* donaldg@
  alphapublishingonline.com
Publicist: Joyce Dwyer
Founded: 1982
Publish books on current events & political top-
  ics, biographies, how-to books, children's
  books, novels, political science. inspirational,
  education & homeschooling. Produce & dis-
  tribute to retail bookstores, wholesalers & rack
  jobbers.
ISBN Prefix(es): 0-910311; 1-56384
Number of titles published annually: 20 Print
Total Titles: 200 Print; 50 Online; 50 E-Book
Imprints: Huntington House Publishers Vital Is-
  sues Press
Distributor for Vital Issues Press
Foreign Rep(s): Baker & Taylor; W A Buchannan
  (Australia); Instate Distributors; Nova Distrib-
  utors Ltd (England); Riverside Book & Bible;
  Spring Arbor Distributors; Whittaker House

Foreign Rights: Winfried Bluth (Europe)
Advertising Agency: Huntington Advertising
  Agency, PO Box 53788, Lafayette, LA 70505-
  3788 *Tel:* 337-237-7049 *Fax:* 337-247-7060
Distribution Center: Book World Services Inc,
  1933 Whitfield Park Loop, Sarasota, FL
  34243 *Tel:* 941-788-8094 *Toll Free Tel:* 800-
  444-2524 *Toll Free Fax:* 800-941-753-9396
  E-mail: bookworld@gnn.com

Huntington Library Press
Division of Huntington Library Art Collections &
  Botanical Gardens
1151 Oxford Rd, San Marino, CA 91108
SAN: 202-313X
Tel: 626-405-2138 *Fax:* 626-585-0794
E-mail: booksales@huntington.org
Web Site: www.huntington.org/HLPress/
  HEHPubs.html
Key Personnel
Dir: Peggy Park Bernal *E-mail:* pbernal@
  huntington.org
Ed: Susan E Green *Tel:* 626-405-2174
  E-mail: sgreen@huntington.org
Founded: 1920
Scholarly nonfiction in English & American his-
  tory, literature & art.
ISBN Prefix(es): 0-87328
Number of titles published annually: 6 Print
Total Titles: 86 Print
Distributed by University of California Press
Membership(s): Publishers Marketing Association

Huntington Press Publishing
3687 S Procyon Ave, Las Vegas, NV 89103
Tel: 702-252-0655 *Toll Free Tel:* 800-244-2224
  Fax: 702-252-0675
E-mail: books@huntingtonpress.com
Web Site: www.huntingtonpress.com
Key Personnel
Mktg Dir, Intl Rts & Lib Sales Dir: Bethany Cof-
  fey Rihel *E-mail:* marketing@huntingtonpress.
  com
Founded: 1983
Books relating to gambling & Las Vegas.
ISBN Prefix(es): 0-929712
Number of titles published annually: 10 Print
Total Titles: 31 Print; 1 E-Book

G F Hutchison Press
319 S Block Ave, Suite 17, Fayetteville, AR
  72701
Tel: 479-587-1726
E-mail: drwriterguy@netscape.net
Web Site: www.familypress.com
Key Personnel
Ed-in-Chief: Garrison Flint Hutchison
Founded: 1953
Mental health, family life, self-improvement, chil-
  dren's fiction, senior citizen fiction, folklore,
  mystery, suspense; use only in-house authors.
ISBN Prefix(es): 1-885631
Number of titles published annually: 10 Print
Total Titles: 68 Print; 1 Online
Imprints: Family of Man Press

Hyperion
Division of ABC Inc
77 W 66 St, 11th fl, New York, NY 10023-6298
Tel: 212-456-0100 *Toll Free Tel:* 800-759-0190
  (cust serv) *Fax:* 212-456-0157
Web Site: hyperionbooks.com
Key Personnel
Pres: Robert Miller
VP & Publr: Ellen Archer
VP & Ed-in-Chief: Will Schwalbe
Assoc Publr, Trade Pbks & Dir, Mktg & Adv:
  Jane Comins
Fin Dir: Terri Lombardi
Creative Dir: Phil Rose
Dir of Subs Rts: Jill Sansone
Sales Dir: Candice Chaplin

Contracts Dir: Dierdre Smerillo
Dir, Pre-prodn/Prodn: Linda Prather
Publicity Dir: Katie Wainwright
Opers Dir: Sharon Kitter
Man Ed: Navorn Johnson
Exec Ed: Mary Ellen O'Neill; Bill Strachan; Pe-
  ternelle van Arsdale; Leslie Wells; Gretchen
  Young
Founded: 1990
General trade books in hardcover & trade paper-
  back, nonfiction, mass market.
ISBN Prefix(es): 1-56282; 0-7868; 1-4013
Number of titles published annually: 120 Print;
  35 E-Book; 12 Audio
Total Titles: 1,370 Print; 113 E-Book; 36 Audio
Distributed by Time Warner Book Group
Distributor for ESPN Books; Wenner Books
Foreign Rep(s): Little, Brown Canada Ltd; Little,
  Brown International
Foreign Rights: A M Heath (England); Agence
  Hoffman (Germany); Luigi Bernabo Associates
  (Italy); Big Apple Tuttle-Mori Agency (Tai-
  wan); The English Agency (Japan); Michelle
  Lapautre Agency (France); Caroline van
  Gelderen Literary Agency (Netherlands)
Warehouse: Time Warner Book Group, 121 N
  Enterprise Blvd, Lebanon, IN 46052
Membership(s): AAP

Hyperion Books for Children
Division of Disney Publishing Worldwide Inc
114 Fifth Ave, New York, NY 10011
Tel: 212-633-4400 *Fax:* 212-807-5880
Web Site: www.hyperionbooksforchildren.com
Key Personnel
Sr VP & Publr: Lisa Holton
VP & Ed-in-Chief: Brenda Bowen
Founded: 1991
Publish high quality picture books, young adult
  fiction & nonfiction.
ISBN Prefix(es): 0-7868
Number of titles published annually: 150 Print
Total Titles: 575 Print
Imprints: Jump at the Sun; Michael di Capua
  Books; Volo
Foreign Rep(s): Little, Brown Canada Ltd; Little,
  Brown International
Foreign Rights: ACER Agencia Literaria (Spain);
  Agence Hoffman (Germany); Luigi Bernabo
  Assocs (Italy); Big Apple Tuttle-Mori Agency
  (China); BMSR Agencia Literaria (Brazil); The
  English Agency (Japan); Harris/Elon Agency
  (Israel); Kooy & van Gelderen (Netherlands);
  Jacqueline Miller (France)
Membership(s): Children's Book Council
See separate listing for:
Jump at the Sun
Michael di Capua Books

Ibex Publishers
8014 Old Georgetown Rd, Bethesda, MD 20814
SAN: 696-866X
Mailing Address: PO Box 30087, Bethesda, MD
  20824
Tel: 301-718-8188 *Toll Free Tel:* 888-718-8188
  Fax: 301-907-8707
E-mail: info@ibexpub.com
Web Site: www.ibexpub.com
Key Personnel
Publr: Farhad Shirzad *E-mail:* farhad@ibexpub.
  com
Founded: 1979
Persian language books & English language
  books concerning Iran.
ISBN Prefix(es): 0-936347; 1-58814
Number of titles published annually: 12 Print
Total Titles: 140 Print; 1 CD-ROM; 1 Audio
Imprints: IBEX Press; Iranbooks Press
Distributor for Iranian Oral History Project at
  Harvard University

§IBFD Publications USA Inc (International Bureau of Fiscal Documentation)
Subsidiary of IBFD Publications B V
PO Box 805, Valatie, NY 12184
Tel: 518-758-2245 *Fax:* 518-784-2963
E-mail: info@ibfd.org
Web Site: www.ibfd.org
Key Personnel
Off Mgr: Tammy MacLean *E-mail:* maclean@ ibfdusa.com
Founded: 1938
Specialize international taxation & investment & tax law.
Number of titles published annually: 17 Print
Total Titles: 25 Print; 5 CD-ROM; 1 Online
Foreign Office(s): HJE Wenckebachweg 210, 1096 AS Amsterdam, Netherlands *Tel:* (20) 554 0100

ibooks Inc
24 W 25 St, 11th fl, New York, NY 10010
Tel: 212-645-9870 *Fax:* 212-645-9874
Web Site: www.bpvp.com; www.ibooks.net
Key Personnel
Pres: Byron Preiss *E-mail:* bpreiss@aol.com
VP & Man Ed: Clarice Levin
Founded: 1974
Number of titles published annually: 200 Print
Total Titles: 350 Print
Distributed by Simon & Schuster

ICC Publishing Inc
Subsidiary of International Chamber of Commerce (ICC)
156 Fifth Ave, Suite 417, New York, NY 10010
Tel: 212-206-1150 *Fax:* 212-633-6025
E-mail: info@iccpub.net
Web Site: www.iccbooksusa.com
Key Personnel
VP & Dir: Rachelle Bijou
Off Mgr: Jonathan Ringel
Founded: 1980
International trade including commerce & transport, banking, law & arbitration.
ISBN Prefix(es): 92-842
Number of titles published annually: 5 Print
Total Titles: 80 Print; 10 CD-ROM
Warehouse: Mercedes Distribution Center, 62 Imlay St, Brooklyn, NY 11231

ICMA, see International City/County Management Association

Iconografix Inc
1830-A Hanley Rd, Hudson, WI 54016
Mailing Address: PO Box 446, Hudson, WI 54016
Tel: 715-381-9755 *Toll Free Tel:* 800-289-3504 (orders only) *Fax:* 715-381-9756
E-mail: iconogfx@spacestar.net
Key Personnel
Pres & Publr: Richard M Seymour
Edit Dir: Dylan Frautshi
Founded: 1992
Publish special historical interest photographic books.
ISBN Prefix(es): 1-882256; 1-58388
Number of titles published annually: 24 Print
Total Titles: 190 Print
Distributed by Motorbooks International
Shipping Address: Motorbooks International, 729 Prospect Ave, Osceola, WI 54020

ICS Press
Division of Institute for Contemporary Studies (ICS)
3100 Harrison St, Oakland, CA 94611
Tel: 510-238-5010 *Toll Free Tel:* 800-326-0263
Fax: 510-238-8440
E-mail: mail@icspress.com
Web Site: www.icspress.com

Key Personnel
Pres & CEO: Robert B Hawkins, Jr
COO: P Fleming
Edit Dir: James Wakeman *Tel:* 510-238-5010
E-mail: jim@icspress.com
Founded: 1974
Current events, international affairs & public policy.
ISBN Prefix(es): 0-917616; 1-55815
Number of titles published annually: 3 Print
Total Titles: 8 Print
Imprints: Center for Self-Governance
Returns: Penny Fulfilment, 151 W Broadway, Jim Thorpe, PA 18229
Distribution Center: Penny Fulfilment, 151 W Broadway, Jim Thorpe, PA 18229 *Toll Free Tel:* 800-326-0263

Idaho Center for the Book
Affiliate of Library of Congress
1910 University Dr, Boise, ID 83725
Tel: 208-426-1999 *Toll Free Tel:* 800-992-8398
Fax: 208-426-4373
Web Site: www.lili.org/icb
Key Personnel
Ed: Tom Trusky *E-mail:* ttrusky@boisestate.edu
Founded: 1993
Idaho book history & culture.
ISBN Prefix(es): 0-932129
Number of titles published annually: 3 Print
Total Titles: 25 Print
Editorial Office(s): ICB, MS 1525 BSU, Boise, ID 83725

Ide House Inc
Affiliate of Publisher's Associates
c/o Publishers Associates, PO Box 408, Radcliffe, IA 50230-0408
SAN: 216-146X
Tel: 515-899-2300 *Fax:* 515-899-2315
E-mail: orders@publishers-associates.com
Web Site: www.publishers-associates.com
Key Personnel
Dir: Art James
Lib Sales Dir: Bobby John Jensen
Founded: 1979
Academic books; behavioral sciences, Black Americans, education, history & women's studies.
ISBN Prefix(es): 0-86663
Number of titles published annually: 20 Print; 2 CD-ROM; 20 Online
Total Titles: 215 Print; 1 CD-ROM; 100 Online
Distributed by Publisher's Associates
Foreign Rep(s): Stobart & Son Ltd (UK)
Advertising Agency: Publisher's Associates
Tel: 515-899-2300 *Fax:* 515-899-2315
E-mail: info@publishers-associates.com *Web Site:* www.publishers-associates.com

Ideals Publications Inc
535 Metroplex Dr, Suite 250, Nashville, TN 37211
SAN: 213-4403
Tel: 615-781-1427 *Toll Free Tel:* 800-558-4343 (customer service) *Fax:* 615-781-1447
Web Site: www.idealsbooks.com
Key Personnel
Publr: Patricia Pingry *Tel:* 615-781-1427 ext 420
Mktg Dir: Deborah Timson *Tel:* 615-781-1427 ext 427
Gen Mgr: Marty Flanagan
Founded: 1944
Ideals magazine, gift books, cookbooks.
ISBN Prefix(es): 0-8249; 0-89542
Number of titles published annually: 60 Print
Total Titles: 107 Print
Distributed by Associated Publishers Group
Distributor for Ideals Gift Books; Ideals Magazine; Smart Squares Games Sets
Warehouse: Mid South Pick 'n Pack Warehouse, 1501 County Hospital Rd, Nashville, TN 37218

Idyll Arbor Inc
25119 SE 262 St, Ravensdale, WA 98051
Mailing Address: PO Box 720, Ravensdale, WA 98051
Tel: 425-432-3231 *Fax:* 425-432-3726
E-mail: sales@idyllarbor.com
Web Site: www.idyllarbor.com
Key Personnel
Pres & Intl Rts: Tom Blaschko *E-mail:* tom@ idyllarbor.com
Publish dictionaries, reference books.
ISBN Prefix(es): 1-882883; 0-937663; 1-930461
Number of titles published annually: 6 Print
Total Titles: 43 Print
Imprints: Issues Press; Pine Winds; Sports Athletics
Membership(s): Book Publishers of the Northwest; Pacific Northwest Booksellers Association; Publishers Association of the West

IEE
c/o Inspec, 379 Thornall St, Edison, NJ 08837-2225
Tel: 732-321-5575 *Fax:* 732-321-5702
E-mail: iee@inspecinc.com
Web Site: www.iee.org/publishing
Key Personnel
Man Dir: Steven Mair
Commissioning Ed: Sarah Kramer
Mktg Mgr, Americas: Michael McCabe
Global Sales Mgr: Sharon Horn
Promos Mgr: Nilu Bharj
Prodn Mgr: Diana Levy
Electronic Journals Exec: Neil Dennis
Edit Asst: Wendy Hiles
Founded: 1871
Professional books, journals, magazines & conference proceedings in many areas of electrical & electronic engineering, including telecommunications, computing, power, control, radar, circuits, materials & more.
ISBN Prefix(es): 0-85296; 0-906048; 0-86341
Number of titles published annually: 30 Print
Total Titles: 500 Print
Imprints: IEE; Inspec; Peter Peregrinus Ltd
Foreign Office(s): IEE, Michael Faraday House, 6 Hills Way, Stevenage SG1 2AY, United Kingdom (Journal & magazine sales) *Tel:* (0440) 1438 31331 *Fax:* (0440) 1438 360079
E-mail: sales@iee.org
Foreign Rep(s): Cranbury International (Latin America, Mexico, South America)
Orders to: IEE, c/o Books International, PO Box 605, Herndon, VA 20172 *Tel:* 703-661-1573 *Toll Free Tel:* 800-230-7286 (US & Canada) *Fax:* 703-661-1501 *E-mail:* ieemail@ presswarehouse.com
Distribution Center: IEE, c/o Books International, PO Box 605, Herndon, VA 20172 *Tel:* 703-661-1500 *Fax:* 703-661-1501
Membership(s): Association of Learned & Professional Society Publishers; STM

§IEEE Computer Society
10662 Los Vaqueros Circle, Los Alamitos, CA 90720-1314
SAN: 264-620X
Mailing Address: PO Box 3014, Los Alamitos, CA 90720-1264
Tel: 714-821-8380 *Toll Free Tel:* 800-272-6657
Fax: 714-821-4010
E-mail: csbooks@computer.org
Web Site: www.computer.org
Key Personnel
Publr & Intl Rts Contact: Angela Burgess
Acct Mgr: John Reimer
Proceedings Mgr: Tom Fink
Founded: 1980
Tutorials, reports, reprint collections, conference proceedings, textbooks & CD-ROM.
ISBN Prefix(es): 0-8186; 0-7695
Number of titles published annually: 155 Print
Total Titles: 808 Print; 5 CD-ROM

Foreign Office(s): 13 Ave de l'Aquilon, B-1200 Brussels, Belgium
2-19-1 Minami Aoyama, Minato-Ku, Tokyo 107, Japan

§IEEE Press
Division of Institute of Electrical & Electronics Engineers Inc
445 Hoes Lane, Piscataway, NJ 08854
Tel: 732-981-3418 *Fax:* 732-981-8062
E-mail: ieeepress@ieee.org
Web Site: www.ieee.org/pubs/press/ *Telex:* 237-936
Key Personnel
Dir, Books & Info Servs: Kenneth Moore
Sr Acqs Ed: Catherine Faduska *E-mail:* c.faduska@ieee.org
Dir, Mktg Proj & Proc: William OConnor
Founded: 1971
Professional books & texts in electrical & computer engineering, computer science, electrotechnology, general engineering, applied mathematics. Tutorials in technical subjects.
ISBN Prefix(es): 0-87942; 0-7803; 0-471
Number of titles published annually: 40 Print
Total Titles: 350 Print; 2 E-Book
Imprints: Wiley-IEEE Press
Distributed by John Wiley & Sons Inc
Foreign Rep(s): John Wiley & Sons Inc
Foreign Rights: John Wiley & Sons Inc
Membership(s): AAP

IFPRI, see International Food Policy Research Institute

Ignatius Press
Division of Guadalupe Associates Inc
2515 McAllister St, San Francisco, CA 94118
SAN: 214-3887
Tel: 415-387-2324 *Toll Free Tel:* 877-320-9276 (book orders) *Fax:* 415-387-0896
E-mail: info@ignatius.com
Web Site: www.ignatius.com
Key Personnel
COO: Mark Brumley
Ed: Joseph Fessio
Prodn Ed: Carolyn Lemon
Mktg Dir: Anthony J Ryan
Art Dir: Roxanne Lum
Sales Dir: Eva Mutean
Intl Rts Contact & Asst Ed: Penelope Boldrick
Asst Ed: Nellie Boldrick *E-mail:* nellie@ignatius.com
Founded: 1978
Religion (Catholic).
ISBN Prefix(es): 0-89870
Number of titles published annually: 30 Print
Total Titles: 510 Print; 55 Audio
Imprints: Ignatius
Subsidiaries: Catholic Dossier; Catholic Faith; The Catholic World Report; Homiletic & Pastoral Review
Distributor for Bethlehem Books; Veritas
Foreign Rep(s): Asian Trading Corp (India); B Broughton Co; Baker & Taylor Intl Ltd; Catholic Supplies Ltd (New Zealand); Ignatius Press (Australia, England); Veritas (Ireland); Words Ink (England, Scotland)
Orders to: PO Box 1339, Ft Collins, CO 80522, Contact: Neil McCaffrey *Toll Free Tel:* 877-320-9276
Warehouse: McCaffrey Enterprises, 1331 Red Cedar Circle, Fort Collins, CO 80522

§Illinois State Museum Society
Affiliate of Illinois State Museum
502 S Spring St, Springfield, IL 62706-5000
Tel: 217-782-7387 *Fax:* 217-782-1254
E-mail: editor@museum.state.il.us
Web Site: www.museum.state.il.us
Key Personnel
Museum Dir: R Bruce McMillan

Assoc Museum Dir, Sci & Educ: Bonnie Styles
Assoc Museum Dir, Policy & Planning: Karen Witter
Museum Ed: Faye Andrashko *Tel:* 217-782-6700
Founded: 1877
Softcover texts, quarterly magazines, quarterly newsletters, quarterly calendars of events & activities brochures, educational posters & CD-ROM, braille magazine.
ISBN Prefix(es): 0-89792
Number of titles published annually: 4 Print
Total Titles: 1 CD-ROM

§Illuminating Engineering Society of North America
120 Wall St, 17th fl, New York, NY 10005-4001
Tel: 212-248-5000 *Fax:* 212-248-5017; 212-248-5018
Web Site: www.iesna.org
Key Personnel
Mktg Mgr: Sue Foley
Founded: 1906
ISBN Prefix(es): 0-87995
Number of titles published annually: 5 Print
Total Titles: 90 Print
Distributed by Thompson/Delmar Learning
Distributor for Elsevier; McGraw-Hill; John Wiley & Sons Inc

Illumination Arts Publishing
13256 Northup Way, Suite 9, Bellevue, WA 98005
Mailing Address: PO Box 1865, Bellevue, WA 98009
Tel: 425-644-7185 *Toll Free Tel:* 888-210-8216 *Fax:* 425-644-9274
E-mail: liteinfo@illumin.com
Web Site: www.illum.com
Key Personnel
Contact: John Thompson
Founded: 1987
ISBN Prefix(es): 0-935699; 0-9740190; 0-9701907
Number of titles published annually: 4 Print
Total Titles: 28 Print

Images from the Past Inc
155 W Main St, Bennington, VT 05201-2105
Mailing Address: PO Box 137, Bennington, VT 05201-0137
Tel: 802-442-3204 *Toll Free Tel:* 888-442-3204 *Fax:* 802-442-3204
E-mail: info@imagesfromthepast.com; sales@imagesfromthepast.com
Web Site: www.imagesfromthepast.com
Key Personnel
Pres & Publr: Tordis Ilg Isselhardt *E-mail:* tordis@imagesfromthepast.com
Founded: 1984
Combines regional history, cultural history & historical images in richly illustrated books.
ISBN Prefix(es): 1-884592
Number of titles published annually: 3 Print
Total Titles: 18 Print
Imprints: Beech Seal Press
Foreign Rep(s): Gazelle (Ireland, Europe & UK)

ImaJinn Books
Division of ImaJinn
PO Box 545, Canon City, CO 81215
Tel: 719-275-0060 *Toll Free Tel:* 877-625-3592 *Fax:* 719-276-0741
E-mail: orders@imajinnbooks.com
Web Site: www.imajinnbooks.com
Key Personnel
Contact: Linda Kichline
Founded: 1998
Specialize in publishing & selling New Age & other worldly romance novels.
ISBN Prefix(es): 1-893896; 0-9759653
Number of titles published annually: 24 Print

Total Titles: 75 Print
Membership(s): Publishers Marketing Association; Small Publishers Association of North America

§Impact Publications
Division of Development Concepts Inc
9104 Manassas Dr, Suite N, Manassas Park, VA 20111-5211
Tel: 703-361-7300 *Fax:* 703-335-9486
E-mail: info@impactpublications.com
Web Site: www.impactpublications.com; www.ishoparoundtheworld.com
Key Personnel
Pres: Ronald Krannich
Founded: 1981
Career & travel publications.
ISBN Prefix(es): 1-57023
Number of titles published annually: 25 Print
Total Titles: 147 Print
Distributed by National Book Network

Impact Publishers Inc
PO Box 6016, Atascadero, CA 93423-6016
SAN: 202-6864
Tel: 805-466-5917 (opers & admin); 805-461-5911 (edit) *Toll Free Tel:* 800-246-7228 (orders) *Fax:* 805-466-5919 (opers & admin offices); 805-461-0554 (edit offices)
E-mail: info@impactpublishers.com
Web Site: www.impactpublishers.com; www.bibliotherapy.com
Key Personnel
Pres & Ed: Robert E Alberti
Publr: Melissa Froehner
Cust Serv Mgr: Lori Bickel
Mktg & Spec Projs: Connie Magee
Prodn: Sharon Skinner
Intl Rts: Jean Trumbull
Founded: 1970
Self-help, relationships, divorce recovery, health, families & parenting, juvenile nonfiction & American Guidance Service.
ISBN Prefix(es): 0-915166; 1-886230
Number of titles published annually: 10 Print; 1 Audio
Total Titles: 40 Print; 3 Audio
Imprints: Little Imp Books
Foreign Rep(s): Airlift Books (UK); Astam Books Ltd (Australia, New Zealand)
Foreign Rights: Bardon Agency (Chinese); BMSR Agency (Brazil); Bookbank SA (Spain & Latin America); Literary Agency Andreas Brunner (Germany); Japan UNI Agency (Japan); Montreal Contacts (Canada, France); O A Literary Agency (Greece); Tonnheim Literary Agency (Scandinavia, Sweden)
Advertising Agency: IMP Ad
Membership(s): AAP; Publishers Marketing Association

Imperium Proviso Publishing
814 E Platte Ave, Colorado Springs, CO 80903
Tel: 719-473-2765
E-mail: imppropub@hotmail.com
Web Site: www.imperiumproviso.com
Founded: 1981
A small press specializing in book length fiction/nonfiction in English, all major foreign languages & braille.
Number of titles published annually: 30 Print; 30 CD-ROM; 30 Online; 14 Audio
Total Titles: 120 Print; 120 CD-ROM; 120 Online; 40 Audio
Imprints: IPP
Distributed by IPP
Membership(s): International Publishers Association

Imprint Publications Inc
230 E Ohio St, Suite 300, Chicago, IL 60611-3705

Tel: 312-337-9268 *Fax:* 312-337-9622
E-mail: imppub@aol.com
Key Personnel
Pres & Publr: Anthony Cheung
Founded: 1990
Scholarly & trade books. Subject specialties: social sciences & humanities.
ISBN Prefix(es): 1-879176
Number of titles published annually: 8 Print
Total Titles: 19 Print

In Audio
Imprint of Sound Room Publishers Inc
PO Box 3168, Falls Church, VA 22043
Tel: 540-722-2535 *Toll Free Tel:* 800-643-0295
Fax: 540-722-0903
E-mail: commuterslib@worldnet.att.net
Web Site: inaudio.biz
Key Personnel
Pres: Joseph Langenfeld
Fullfilment & Cust Serv: Katherine Kwoleck
Founded: 1992
ISBN Prefix(es): 1-58472
Number of titles published annually: 20 Audio
Total Titles: 180 Audio
Sales Office(s): 100 Weems Lane, Winchester, VA 22601
Distributed by Follett Audiovisual Resources
Shipping Address: 100 Weems Lane, Winchester, VA 22601

§IN-D Press
PO Box 642556, Los Angeles, CA 90064
Tel: 310-445-9326 *Fax:* 310-694-0222
E-mail: info@in-d.com
Web Site: www.in-d.com
Key Personnel
Publr: Tim Sakamoto *E-mail:* timsakamoto@in-d.com
Founded: 1998
Architectural & educational media on CD-ROM.
ISBN Prefix(es): 1-893801
Number of titles published annually: 6 CD-ROM
Total Titles: 10 CD-ROM; 10 Online

Incentive Publications Inc
3835 Cleghorn Ave, Nashville, TN 37215
SAN: 203-8005
Tel: 615-385-2934 *Toll Free Tel:* 800-421-2830
Fax: 615-385-2967
E-mail: comments@incentivepublications.com
Web Site: www.incentivepublications.com
Key Personnel
Pres: Imogene Forte
Exec VP: Henry S Forte
VP, Opers: Mike Patenaude
VP, Mktg & Sales: Blake Parker
Founded: 1969
Preschool through high school supplementary educational materials for students, parents & teachers.
ISBN Prefix(es): 0-913916; 0-86530
Number of titles published annually: 25 Print
Total Titles: 400 Print; 1 CD-ROM
Imprints: A-To-Z Series; Basic/Not Boring K-8 Grades; Belair Books; Integrating Instruction Series; Kids' Stuff; Language Literacy Lessons; Learning Fun; Ready to Learn; Table Top Series
Distributor for Belair Publications Ltd
Foreign Rights: Hawker Brownlow (Australia)
Warehouse: 811 Cowan St, Nashville, TN 37207

Independent Information Publications
Division of Computing!
3357 21 St, San Francisco, CA 94110
Tel: 415-643-8600 *Fax:* 415-643-6100
E-mail: orders@movedoc.com
Web Site: www.movedoc.com
Key Personnel
Opers: Linda Tan *E-mail:* linda@movedoc.com
Founded: 1982

ISBN Prefix(es): 0-913733
Number of titles published annually: 4 Print; 6 Online
Total Titles: 4 Print; 4 Online
Imprints: IIP Consumers Series
Branch Office(s)
IIP, 500 Kentucky Ave, Savannah, GA 31404, Contact: Cima Star *Tel:* 912-233-8873
Distributed by BookWorld
Orders to: BookWorld, 1230 Heil Quaker Blvd, La Vergne, TN 37086 *Tel:* 615-793-5983 ext 505
Returns: BookWorld, 1230 Heil Quaker Blvd, La Vergne, TN 37086
Shipping Address: BookWorld, 1230 Heil Quaker Blvd, La Vergne, TN 37086
Warehouse: Ingram
Membership(s): Publishers Marketing Association

Indiana Historical Society Press
450 W Ohio St, Indianapolis, IN 46202-3269
SAN: 201-5234
Tel: 317-233-9557 (sales); 317-234-2716 (editorial) *Toll Free Tel:* 800-447-1830 (orders only) *Fax:* 317-234-0562 (sales); 317-233-0857 (editorial)
E-mail: ihspress@indianahistory.org; orders@indianahistory.org
Web Site: www.indianahistory.org; shop.indianahistory.org (orders)
Key Personnel
Pres: Salvatore G Cilella, Jr *E-mail:* scilella@indianahistory.org
VP: Thomas A Mason *Tel:* 317-232-6546 *E-mail:* tmason@indianahistory.org
Sales Coord: Rachel Vaught *E-mail:* rvaught@indianahistory.org
Founded: 1830
Books, journals & newsletters on Indiana history, including an illustrated history magazine & a family history magazine. Also offers videos, recordings, prints, note cards & other gift items.
ISBN Prefix(es): 0-87195
Number of titles published annually: 9 Print; 1 Online
Total Titles: 80 Print; 1 Online; 3 Audio

Indiana University African Studies Program
Indiana University, 221 Woodburn Hall, Bloomington, IN 47405
Tel: 812-855-8254 *Fax:* 812-855-6734
E-mail: afrist@indiana.edu
Web Site: www.indiana.edu/~afrist
Key Personnel
Dir: John Hanson
Assoc Dir: Maria Grosz-Ngate
Prog Asst: Sue Hanson
Monograph & working papers, humanities, interdisciplinary study of Africa.
ISBN Prefix(es): 0-941934
Number of titles published annually: 50 Print
Total Titles: 52 Print

§Indiana University Press
601 N Morton St, Bloomington, IN 47404-3797
SAN: 202-5647
Tel: 812-855-8817 *Toll Free Tel:* 800-842-6796 (orders only) *Fax:* 812-855-7931 (orders only); 812-855-8507
E-mail: iupress@indiana.edu; iuorder@indiana.edu (orders)
Web Site: www.iupress.indiana.edu *Cable:* INDIANA U BLOM
Key Personnel
Dir: Janet Rabinowitch *Tel:* 812-855-4773, 812-855-5063 *E-mail:* jrabinow@indiana.edu
Dir, Sales & Mktg: Bryan Gambrel *Tel:* 812-855-6553 *E-mail:* bpgambre@indiana.edu
Sales Mgr: Mary Beth Haas *Tel:* 812-855-9440 *E-mail:* mbhaas@indiana.edu
Mktg Mgr: Marilyn Breiter

Direct Mail Promo Mgr: Deborah Rush *Tel:* 812-855-4415 *E-mail:* drush@indiana.edu
ISBN Contact & Edit Staff: Marvin Keenan *Tel:* 812-855-5428
Dir, Prodn & Design: Emmy Ezzell *Tel:* 812-855-5563 *E-mail:* ezzell@indiana.edu
Edit Dir: Robert Sloan *Tel:* 812-855-7561 *E-mail:* rjsloan@indiana.edu
Sponsoring Ed: Michael Lundell *Tel:* 812-855-6803 *E-mail:* mlundell@indiana.edu; Dee Mortensen *Tel:* 812-855-0268 *E-mail:* mortense@indiana.edu
Edit Staff: Linda Oblack *Tel:* 812-855-2175 *E-mail:* loblack@indiana.edu; Rebecca Tolen *Tel:* 812-855-2756 *E-mail:* retolen@indiana.edu
Dir, Opers: Jan Jenkins *Tel:* 812-855-4901 *E-mail:* janjenki@indiana.edu
Dir, Electronic & Serials Publg: Kathryn Caras *Tel:* 812-855-3830 *E-mail:* kcaras@indiana.edu
Cust Serv: Kimberly B Childers *Tel:* 812-855-4134 *E-mail:* kchilder@indiana.edu
Man Ed: Jane Lyle *Tel:* 812-855-9686 *E-mail:* jlyle@indiana.edu
Founded: 1950
Trade & scholarly nonfiction; film & media studies, literature & music, African studies, backlist, classical studies, contemporary issues, cultural studies, folklore, international studies, Jewish studies, journals, Middle East studies, paleontology, philanthropy, politics/political science, railroads & transportation, Russian studies.
ISBN Prefix(es): 0-253
Number of titles published annually: 160 Print; 2 CD-ROM; 5 Audio
Total Titles: 2,500 Print; 8 CD-ROM
Imprints: Quarry Books (Regional imprint for Midwest)
Foreign Rep(s): Agenzia Letteraria Internazionale (Italy); Carmen Balcells Agnecia (Spain); Paul & Peter Fritz Ag (Germany); La Nouvelle Agence (France); Balcells Mello e Souza Riff Agencia Literaria (Brazil)
Foreign Rights: Affiliated East-West Press Pvt Ltd (India); Book Promotions Pty Ltd (South Africa); Nicholas Esson (Europe, Ireland & UK, Middle East, North Africa); EWEB (Asia, Hong Kong, Indonesia, Japan, Korea & Taiwan, Malaysia & Singapore, Philippines, Thailand); Indiana University Press (Caribbean & Latin America, Central America, Mexico); Lynn McClory (Canada); Elise Moser (Canada); UniReps (Australia & New Zealand); United Publishers Services Ltd (Japan)
Shipping Address: 802 E 13 St, Bloomington, IN 47408-2101 *Tel:* 812-855-4362 *Fax:* 812-855-8507
Warehouse: 802 E 13 St, Bloomington, IN 47408-2101, Contact: Mark Kelly *Tel:* 812-855-4362 *Fax:* 812-855-8507 *E-mail:* markkell@indiana.edu

§Industrial Press Inc
200 Madison Ave, 21st fl, New York, NY 10016-4078
SAN: 202-6945
Tel: 212-889-6330 *Toll Free Tel:* 888-528-7852 *Fax:* 212-545-8327
E-mail: info@industrialpress.com
Web Site: www.industrialpress.com
Key Personnel
Pres: Alex Luchars
Edit Dir: John F Carleo *Tel:* 212-889-6330 ext 19 *E-mail:* carleoip@aol.com
Prodn & Art Dir: Janet Romano
Cont: Peter Burri
Mktg Dir: Patrick V Hansard *Tel:* 212-889-6330 ext 20 *E-mail:* phansard@industrialpress.com
Founded: 1883
Scientific & technical handbooks, professional & reference books.
ISBN Prefix(es): 0-8311

Number of titles published annually: 15 Print; 2
CD-ROM
Total Titles: 150 Print; 10 CD-ROM
Foreign Rep(s): American Technical Publishers
Ltd (Europe & Middle East); Elsevier Pty
Ltd (Australia); Techbooks Wholesale (New
Zealand); Thompson Nelson (Canada)
Advertising Agency: Flamm Advertising Inc
Warehouse: c/o Mercedes Distribution Center,
Brooklyn Navy Yard, Bldg 3, Brooklyn, NY
11205 *Tel:* 718-534-3000 *Fax:* 718-935-9647
Membership(s): AAP

The Info Devel Press
Division of The Info Devels Inc
32 Reilly Rd, Lagrangeville, NY 12540
SAN: 242-696X
Tel: 845-223-3269
Key Personnel
Man Dir: Robert Haiber *E-mail:* roblbbc@
earthlink.net
Dir, Mktg: William P Haiber *E-mail:* whaiber@
frontiernet.net
Founded: 1988
Military & brewing history.
ISBN Prefix(es): 0-944089
Number of titles published annually: 10 Print; 8
Online; 5 E-Book
Total Titles: 13 Print
Divisions: The Info Devel Press/Book Premium
Division
Branch Office(s)
3107 W Folkstone, Raleigh, NC 27605, VP,
Southern Oper: Louise Haiber *Tel:* 919-876-
3011 *E-mail:* L111@aol.com
Distributed by Brodart; Motorbooks International;
Zenith Books
Membership(s): Small Publishers Association of
North America

InfoBooks
PO Box 1018, Santa Monica, CA 90406
Tel: 310-394-4102 *Toll Free Tel:* 800-669-0409
Fax: 310-394-2603
Key Personnel
Publr: Gerald P Rafferty, PhD *E-mail:* gerald@
commcoach.com
Founded: 1984
Self improvement in the workplace, personal rela-
tionships & communication.
ISBN Prefix(es): 0-931137
Number of titles published annually: 5 Print
Total Titles: 9 Print
Shipping Address: 1021 Lincoln Blvd, Suite 214,
Santa Monica, CA 90403

INFORM Inc
120 Wall St, 14th fl, New York, NY 10005-4001
SAN: 210-4423
Tel: 212-361-2400 *Fax:* 212-361-2412
Web Site: www.informinc.org
Key Personnel
Pres: Joanna Underwood *E-mail:* underwood@
informinc.org
Founded: 1973
Environmental research in waste management,
chemical hazards prevention, urban air pollu-
tion.
ISBN Prefix(es): 0-918780
Number of titles published annually: 4 Print
Total Titles: 19 Print
Warehouse: Whitman Communications Inc, 10
Water St, PO Box 1220, Lebanon, NH 03766-
4220

Information Age Publishing Inc
80 Mason St, Greenwich, CT 06830
Mailing Address: PO Box 4967, Greenwich, CT
06831
Tel: 203-661-7602 *Fax:* 203-661-7952
E-mail: infoage@infoagepub.com
Web Site: www.infoagepub.com

Key Personnel
Pres & Publr: George F Johnson
E-mail: george@infoagepub.com
Founded: 1999
Social science publisher of academic & scholarly
book series & journals.
ISBN Prefix(es): 1-930608; 1-931576; 1-59311
Number of titles published annually: 40 Print; 9
Online; 5 E-Book
Foreign Rep(s): James Bennett Pty Ltd (Aus-
tralia); DA Information Services (Australia &
New Zealand); The Eurospan Group; Informa-
tion Age Publishing (Europe); Taylor & Francis
Asia Pacific (East Asia, Southeast Asia)

§Information Gatekeepers Inc
320 Washington St, Suite 302, Boston, MA
02135
Tel: 617-782-5033 *Toll Free Tel:* 800-323-1088
Fax: 617-782-5735
E-mail: info@igigroup.com
Web Site: www.igigroup.com
Key Personnel
CEO: Paul Polishuk
Founded: 1977
Fiber optics, optical networks, wireless, ATM,
XDSL & telecommunications, trade shows,
conferences, newsletters, market studies & con-
sulting.
Number of titles published annually: 15 Print
Total Titles: 542 Print
Foreign Office(s): IPI Services Pty Ltd, 128
Chalmers St, Surry Hills NSW 2010, Aus-
tralia *Tel:* 612-9319-7933 *Fax:* 612-9319-3408
E-mail: ipi@ipi.com
Global Informaton Inc, A Sahi Bank Bldg, 4th
fl, 151 Kamiasao, A Sno-ku, Kawasaki 215,
Japan *Tel:* (044) 952 0102 *Fax:* (044) 952 0109
E-mail: k.endo@gii.co.jp
OIC, 3rd fl, Sam Hwam Bldg 38-1, Wonhyoru 1-
9a, Yongsan-Ku, Seoul, Korea *Tel:* 27 49 86 40
Fax: 27 49 86 41
IGI Inc, c/o CMS, 122 High St, Chesham Berks
HP5-1EB, United Kingdom *Tel:* 44 1494 771
734 *Fax:* 44 1494 779 994
Foreign Rep(s): Chiltern Magazine Services (Eng-
land); Chongno Book Center Co Ltd (Korea);
Createk Products cc (South Africa); Investment
Publications Information Service (Australia);
Lavoisier Abonnements (France); Overseas In-
formation Services (Korea)

Information Publications
3790 El Camino Real, PMB 162, Palo Alto, CA
94306
Tel: 650-851-4250 *Toll Free Tel:* 877-544-4636
Fax: 650-529-9980 *Toll Free Fax:* 877-544-
4635
E-mail: info@informationpublications.com
Web Site: www.informationpublications.com
Key Personnel
Contact: Eric Weiner
Founded: 1983
Statistical reference books; profiles statistics on
cities & states.
ISBN Prefix(es): 0-931845; 0-911273; 0-941391
Number of titles published annually: 10 Print
Total Titles: 11 Print

Information Today, Inc
143 Old Marlton Pike, Medford, NJ 08055-8750
Tel: 609-654-6266 *Toll Free Tel:* 800-300-9868
(cust serv) *Fax:* 609-654-4309

E-mail: custserv@infotoday.com
Web Site: www.infotoday.com
Key Personnel
Pres: Thomas H Hogan
VP, Admin: John Yersak
VP, Content: Richard T Kaser
Mktg Dir: Thomas Hogan, Jr
Advtg: Michael Zarrello
Ed-in-Chief: John Bryans *E-mail:* jbryans@
infotoday.com
Mktg Mgr: Heather Rudolph *E-mail:* hrudolph@
infotoday.com
Founded: 1980
Books, newspapers, journals, newsletters, pro-
ceedings, directories, conferences.
ISBN Prefix(es): 0-938734; 0-904933; 1-57387;
0-910965
Number of titles published annually: 15 Print
Total Titles: 200 Print
Imprints: CyberAge Books
Shipping Address: Independent Publishers Group
(IPG)

§Infosential Press
1162 Dominion Dr W, Mobile, AL 36695
Tel: 251-776-5656 *Fax:* 251-460-7181
Web Site: www.infosentialpress.com
Key Personnel
Pres: Dr Richard J Wood *E-mail:* rwood@bbl.
usouthal.edu
Founded: 1997
ISBN Prefix(es): 1-930852
Number of titles published annually: 1 Print; 2
CD-ROM; 1 Online
Total Titles: 1 Print; 7 CD-ROM; 4 Online; 4 E-
Book
Distributed by netLibrary

§InfoServices International Inc
313 Main St, Huntington, NY 11743
Tel: 631-549-0064 *Fax:* 631-549-6663
E-mail: typ@infoservices.com
Web Site: www.infoservices.com
Key Personnel
Ed & Publr: Michael R Dohan
VP, Sales & Mktg: Blanche B Dohan
Founded: 1992
Internet directory & marketing company special-
izing in directories & websites for towns &
local business.
ISBN Prefix(es): 1-881832
Number of titles published annually: 4 Print; 8
Online
Total Titles: 10 Print
Foreign Office(s): Noroe Vremiya Bldg, GSP, 2/1
Putinkovskiy per, K6, Moscow 103782, Rus-
sian Federation
64 Moyka Embankment, Saint Petersburg 190000,
Russian Federation

Infosources Publishing
140 Norma Rd, Teaneck, NJ 07666
Tel: 201-836-7072
Web Site: www.infosourcespub.com
Key Personnel
Publr: Arlene Eis *E-mail:* aeis@carroll.com
Founded: 1981
Legal reference books; newsletters; online
databases. Publisher of the Informed Librarian
Online.
ISBN Prefix(es): 0-939486
Number of titles published annually: 5 Print; 4
Online

§Ingenix Inc
2525 Lake Park Blvd, Salt Lake City, UT 84120
Tel: 801-982-3000 *Toll Free Tel:* 800-765-6014
Web Site: www.ingenix.com
Key Personnel
Edit Dir: Lynn Speirs
Founded: 1983
Books & software for health-care professionals.

ISBN Prefix(es): 1-56337; 1-56329
Number of titles published annually: 90 Print; 5 Online
Total Titles: 90 Print; 8 CD-ROM; 5 Online
Distributed by American Medical Association; Mosby
Distributor for American Medical Association; Medical Economics; Mosby
Warehouse: 3687 W Great Lake Dr, Suite C, Salt Lake City, UT 84120

Inner Ocean Publishing Inc
1037 Makawao Ave, Makawao, Maui, HI 96768-1239
Mailing Address: PO Box 1239, Makawao, Maui, HI 96768
Tel: 808-573-8000 *Toll Free Tel:* 800-863-1449 *Fax:* 808-573-0700 *Toll Free Fax:* 800-755-4118
E-mail: info@innerocean.com
Web Site: www.innerocean.com
Key Personnel
Publr & Edit Dir: Karen Bouris
Exec Publr: John B Elder
Sales Dir: Mark Kerr
Founded: 1999
Publish books that expand consciousness, present alternative philosophies & explore our vast inner human potential.
ISBN Prefix(es): 1-930722
Number of titles published annually: 20 Print
Total Titles: 40 Print
Sales Office(s): 580 California St, Suite 500, San Francisco, CA 94104, Dir, Sales & Mktg: Mark Kerr *Tel:* 415-283-3216 *Toll Free Tel:* 866-731-2216 *Fax:* 415-283-3316 *Toll Free Fax:* 866-944-1212 *E-mail:* sales@innerocean.com *Web Site:* www.innerocean.com
Foreign Rights: Susan Schulman Literary Agency
Shipping Address: Publishers Group West (PGW), 1700 Fourth St, Berkeley, CA 94710 *Toll Free Tel:* 800-788-3123 *Fax:* 510-528-3614
Warehouse: Publishers Group West (PGW), 1700 Fourth St, Berkeley, CA 94710 *Toll Free Tel:* 800-788-3123 *Fax:* 510-528-3614
Membership(s): Publishers Marketing Association

Inner Traditions International Ltd
One Park St, Rochester, VT 05767
SAN: 208-6948
Mailing Address: PO Box 388, Rochester, VT 05767
Tel: 802-767-3174 *Toll Free Tel:* 800-246-8648 *Fax:* 802-767-3726
E-mail: orders@InnerTraditions.com
Web Site: www.InnerTraditions.com
Key Personnel
Pres: Ehud C Sperling *E-mail:* prez@innertraditions.com
VP, Opers: Pat Harvey *E-mail:* patty@innertraditions.com
Prodn Mgr: Brad Sargent *E-mail:* brandi@innertraditions.com
VP & Man Ed: Jeanie Levitan *E-mail:* jeanie@innertraditions.com
VP, Sales & Mktg: Rob Meadows *E-mail:* rob@innertraditions.com
Acqs Ed: Jon Graham *E-mail:* jon@innertraditions.com
Spec Sales: Nick McDougal *E-mail:* nick@innertraditions.com
Foreign Rts & Perms: Cynthia Fowles *E-mail:* cynthia@innertraditions.com
Publicity: Jody Winters *E-mail:* jody@innertraditions.com
Founded: 1975
Nonfiction cloth & quality trade paperbacks; audio cassettes & CDs (ethnic music & meditation aids).
ISBN Prefix(es): 0-89281; 1-59477
Number of titles published annually: 44 Print
Total Titles: 744 Print; 17 Audio

Imprints: Bear & Co; Bear Cub Books; Bindu Books; Destiny Books; Healing Arts Press; Inner Traditions; Inner Traditions en espanol; Inner Traditions India; Park Street Press; Destiny Recordings
Foreign Rep(s): Athena Productions (all other countries); Brumby Books Gencraft (Australia); Deep Books (Europe); India Book Distributors (India); India Book House Ltd (India); Michelle Morrow Curreri (Asia); Real Books (South Africa); Southern Publishers Group (New Zealand); Ten Speed Press (Canada)
Foreign Rights: Agenzia Letteraria Internazionale (Italy); Akcali Copyright Agency (Turkey); Amina Marix Evans (Netherlands); Big Apple Tuttle-Mori (China & Taiwan); Book Publishers Association of Israel (Israel); Graal Ltd (Poland); Ilidio da Fonseca Matos (Portugal); International Copyright Agency Ltd (Romania); International Editor's Co SA (Argentina, Spain); Simona Kessler International Copyright Agency Ltd (Romania); Alexander Korzhenevski Agency (Russia); Zvonimir Majdak (Croatia); Montreal-Contacts/The Rights Agency (Canada, France); Andrew Nurnberg Associates (Baltic States, Bulgaria, Czech Republic, Hungary); Read n Right Agency (Greece); Karin Schindler, Rights Representative (Brazil); Thomas Schluck Literary & Art Agency (Germany); Tuttle-Mori Agency (Japan); Tuttle-Mori Big Apple Agency (Thailand); Eric Yang Agency (Korea)
Warehouse: Inner Traditions International - Bear & Co, Airport Industrial Park, 364 Innovation Dr, North Clarendon, VT 05759, Contact: Michael Ascoli *Tel:* 802-773-8930 *Fax:* 802-773-6993
See separate listing for:
Bear & Co Inc

innovative Kids™
Division of Innovative USA® Inc
18 Ann St, Norwalk, CT 06854
Tel: 203-838-6400 *Fax:* 203-855-5582
E-mail: info@innovativekids.com
Web Site: www.innovativekids.com
Key Personnel
CEO: Michael Levins *E-mail:* mlevins@innovativekids.com
Pres & Publr: Shari Kaufman *E-mail:* skaufman@innovativekids.com
Founded: 1999
Publishing interactive, tactile books for preschool through elementary school age children - unusual formats that foster the growth of essential learning skills. No story books.
ISBN Prefix(es): 1-58476
Number of titles published annually: 25 Print
Distributed by Chronicle Books
Foreign Rep(s): ALC (Australia); Bounce Sales & Marketing (UK)
Membership(s): ABA; American Book Producers Association; NSSEA; Publishers Marketing Association; TMA

Inscape Publishing
6465 Wayzata Blvd, Suite 800, St Louis Park, MN 55426
Tel: 763-765-2222 *Fax:* 763-765-2277
Web Site: www.inscapepublishing.com
Key Personnel
Pres: Jeff Sugarman
VP, Publg & Rts Mgr: Susie Kukkonen
Founded: 1978
Publish personal & organizational learning resources that help people understand themselves & relate effectively to others. Titles include the DISC© *Personal Profile System®*, which has been used by over 30 million people worldwide.
ISBN Prefix(es): 1-56774
Number of titles published annually: 5 Print

Institute for Byzantine & Modern Greek Studies Inc
115 Gilbert Rd, Belmont, MA 02478-2200
Tel: 617-484-6595 *Fax:* 617-876-3600
Key Personnel
Pres: Constantine Cavarnos
Founded: 1956
ISBN Prefix(es): 1-884729
Number of titles published annually: 6 Print
Total Titles: 89 Print

§Institute for International Economics
1750 Massachusetts Ave NW, Washington, DC 20036
SAN: 293-2865
Tel: 202-328-9000 *Toll Free Tel:* 800-522-9139 *Fax:* 202-328-5432
E-mail: orders@iie.com
Web Site: www.iie.com
Key Personnel
Dir: C Fred Bergsten
Dir, Mktg, Foreign Rts: Ed Tureen *E-mail:* etureen@iie.com
Dir, Pubns: Valerie Norville *E-mail:* vnorville@iie.com
Founded: 1981
Trade & textbooks on key economic, monetary, trade & investment issues.
ISBN Prefix(es): 0-88132
Number of titles published annually: 15 Print; 14 Online
Total Titles: 105 Print; 50 Online; 22 E-Book
Distributed by DA Information Services (Handles Australia, New Zealand & Papua New Guinea); The Eurospan Group (Handles Western & Eastern Europe, Russia, Turkey, Israel & Iran); Renouf Bookstore (Handles Canada); Taylor & Francis Asia Pacific (Covers Singapore, Thailand, China, Taiwan, Philippines, Malaysia, Indonesia, Canbodia & Vietnam); United Publishers Services Ltd (Japan & the Republic of Korea); Viva Books PVT (India, Bangladesh, Nepal & Sri Lanka)
Distributor for Center for Global Development
Foreign Rights: Anu Hansen
Returns: IIE, 22883 Quicksilver Dr, Dulles, VA 20166
Distribution Center: IIE Distribution Center, PO Box 960, Herndon, VA 20172 *Toll Free Tel:* 800-522-9139 *Fax:* 703-661-1501 *E-mail:* orders@iie.com *Web Site:* www.iie.com
Membership(s): AAP; Society for Scholarly Publishing; Washington Book Publishers

Institute for Language Study
Affiliate of Cortina Learning International Inc
7 Hollyhock Rd, Wilton, CT 06897
Tel: 203-762-2510 *Toll Free Tel:* 800-245-2145 *Fax:* 203-762-2514
E-mail: cortinainc@aol.com
Web Site: www.cortina-languages.com; members.aol.com/cortinainc
Key Personnel
Pres: Robert E Livesey
VP & Man Ed: Magdalen B Livesey
Art Ed: Howell Dodd
Asst Art Ed: Hank McLaughlin
Prodn Mgr: George Bollas
Treas: M F Brown
Retail Sales Mgr: Katherine R Whitman
Foreign Sales Mgr: Robert Ellis
Founded: 1958
Lerarning foreign languages for English speakers; English as a second language
See Cortina Learning International Inc. Commercial illustration. Painting: oil & water color.
ISBN Prefix(es): 0-8489
Number of titles published annually: 10 Print
Total Titles: 283 Print
Distributed by Henry Holt & Co Inc
Foreign Rep(s): Gazelle Book Services (UK)

Advertising Agency: Academic Advertising
Warehouse: Cortina Warehouse, 15 Great Pasture
Rd, Danbury, CT 06810 *Fax:* 203-778-4029

Institute for the Study of Man Inc
1133 13 St NW, Suite C-2, Washington, DC
20005-4298
Tel: 202-371-2700 *Fax:* 202-371-1523
E-mail: iejournal@aol.com
Web Site: www.jies.org
Key Personnel
Publr: Roger Pearson
Founded: 1975
Specialize in Indo-European studies.
ISBN Prefix(es): 0-941624
Number of titles published annually: 4 Print
Total Titles: 57 Print

§Institute of Continuing Legal Education
1020 Greene St, Ann Arbor, MI 48109-1444
Tel: 734-764-0533 *Toll Free Tel:* 877-229-4350
Fax: 734-763-2412 *Toll Free Fax:* 877-229-
4351
E-mail: icle@umich.edu
Web Site: www.icle.org/
Key Personnel
Exec Dir: Lynn Chard *E-mail:* lchard@umich.edu
Admin Dir: Karen Brown
Pubns Dir: Mary Hiniker
Educ Dir: Sheldon Stark
Founded: 1959
Books, supplements, disk products, audio, web-
site.
Number of titles published annually: 7 Print
Total Titles: 50 Print
Imprints: ICLE

**Institute of East Asian Studies, University of
California**
Unit of University of California
IEAS Publications, 2223 Fulton St, Berkeley, CA
94720-2318
Tel: 510-643-6325 *Fax:* 510-643-7062
E-mail: easia@uclink.berkeley.edu
Web Site: ieas.berkeley.edu/publications
Key Personnel
Dir: T J Pempel *Tel:* 510-642-2809
Man Ed: Joanne Sandstrom
Founded: 1978
ISBN Prefix(es): 0-912966; 1-55729
Number of titles published annually: 4 Print
Total Titles: 116 Print

**Institute of Electrical & Electronics Engineers
Inc**
445 Hoes Lane, Piscataway, NJ 08854
SAN: 203-8064
Tel: 732-981-0060 *Toll Free Tel:* 800-678-4333
Fax: 732-981-9334
E-mail: c.fadvska@ieee.org
Web Site: www.ieee.org
Key Personnel
Dir, IEEE Book & Info Servs: Kenneth Moore
Staff Exec, Pubns: Tony Durniak
Number of titles published annually: 30 Print
Imprints: Wiley-IEEE Press
Membership(s): AAP

**§Institute of Environmental Sciences and
Technology - IEST**
5005 Newport Dr, Suite 506, Rolling Meadows,
IL 60008
Tel: 847-255-1561 *Fax:* 847-255-1699
E-mail: publicationsales@iest.org
Web Site: iest.org
Key Personnel
Edit Asst: Linda Gadja
A multidisciplinary, international society whose
members are recognized worldwide for their
contributions to the environmental sciences in
the area of contamination control in electron-

ics manufacturing & pharmaceutical processes;
design, test & evaluation of commercial & military equipment; product reliability issues associated with commercial & military systems.
Number of titles published annually: 5 Print
Total Titles: 100 Print; 26 CD-ROM

Institute of Governmental Studies
Subsidiary of University of California, Berkeley
102 Moses Hall, Berkeley, CA 94720-2370
Tel: 510-642-1428 *Fax:* 510-642-5537
E-mail: igspress@uclink2.berkeley.edu
Web Site: www.igs.berkeley.edu
Key Personnel
Sr Ed: Maria Wolf *E-mail:* mariaw@uclink.
berkeley.edu
Public policy issues.
ISBN Prefix(es): 0-87772
Number of titles published annually: 6 Print
Total Titles: 54 Print

§Institute of Jesuit Sources
3601 Lindell Blvd, St Louis, MO 63108
Tel: 314-977-7257 *Fax:* 314-977-7263
E-mail: ijs@slu.edu
Web Site: www.jesuitsources.com
Key Personnel
Dir: John W Padberg
Assoc Ed: Martin O'Keefe
Founded: 1961
Books on history & spirituality of society of
Jesus (Jesuits) translated from non-English
sources & originally in English.
ISBN Prefix(es): 0-912422; 1-880810
Number of titles published annually: 8 Print
Total Titles: 94 Print; 1 CD-ROM

§Institute of Mathematical Geography
1964 Boulder Dr, Ann Arbor, MI 48104
Tel: 734-975-0246
Web Site: www.instituteofmathematicalgeography.
org
Key Personnel
Founding Dir & Electronic Publg: Sandra Lach
Arlinghaus *E-mail:* sarhaus@umich.edu
Founded: 1985
Publish scholarly books & college text books;
also publish electronic journal.
ISBN Prefix(es): 1-877751
Number of titles published annually: 5 Print
Total Titles: 34 Print; 10 E-Book

Institute of Mediaeval Music
PO Box 295, Henryville, PA 18332-0295
Tel: 570-629-1278 *Fax:* 613-225-9487
Web Site: members.rogers.com/mediaeval1
Key Personnel
Pres: Luther A Dittmer *E-mail:* cdittmer@
compuserve.com; Brian Gillingham
Founded: 1957
Facsimiles of medieval musical mss, musical the-
orists in translations, collected editions, studies
of music in the Middle Ages, scientific studies,
medicine.
ISBN Prefix(es): 0-912024; 0-931902; 1-8926926
Number of titles published annually: 6 Print
Total Titles: 242 Print
Imprints: IMM
Branch Office(s)
Institut de Musique Medievale, 1270 Lampman
Crescent, Ottawa, ON K2C 1P8, Canada, Con-
tact: Prof Bryan Gillingham *Tel:* 613-225-9487
Fax: 613-225-9487 *Web Site:* members.rogers.
com/mediaeval1
Foreign Office(s): Institut fur Mittelalter-
liche Musikforschung, Melchtalstr 11,
4102 Binningen, Switzerland, Contact:
Prof Luther A Dittmer *Tel:* (061) 421 8078
E-mail: institutme@cs.com
Shipping Address: 1270 Lampman Crescent, Ot-
tawa, ON K2C 1P8, Canada, Contact: Prof
Bryan Gillingham *Tel:* 613-225-9487 *Fax:* 613-

225-9487 *E-mail:* bryan_gillingham@carleton.
ca; Institut fur Mittelalterliche Musikforschung,
Melchtalstr 11, 4102 Binningen, Switzerland,
Contact: Prof Luther A Dittmer *Tel:* (061) 421
8078 *E-mail:* institutme@cs.com

§Institute of Police Technology & Management
Division of University of North Florida
University Ctr, 12000 Alumni Dr, Jacksonville,
FL 32224-2678
Tel: 904-620-4786 *Fax:* 904-620-2453
Key Personnel
Dir: Everett James
Ed: Richard C Hodge *E-mail:* rhodge@unf.edu
Founded: 1980
In-service training for law enforcement, civilian
personnel; marketing of publications, templates
& videos. Specialize in traffic crash investiga-
tion & reconstruction; law enforcement man-
agement & supervision; criminal investigation;
DUI & drug law enforcement; radar/laser speed
enforcement; law enforcement computer train-
ing; gangs & other specialized subjects.
ISBN Prefix(es): 1-884566
Number of titles published annually: 6 Print; 1
CD-ROM
Total Titles: 55 Print; 2 CD-ROM
Foreign Rep(s): Paul Feenan (Australia, South
Pacific)
Foreign Rights: Pacific Traffic Education Centre
(Canada)

Instructional Fair Group
Affiliate of Frank Schaffer Publications
3195 Wilson Dr NW, Grand Rapids, MI 49544
Tel: 616-802-3000 *Toll Free Tel:* 800-417-3261
Fax: 616-802-3007 *Toll Free Fax:* 888-203-
9361
Web Site: elementary-educators.teacherspecialty.
com/Instructional_Fair/
Key Personnel
Subs Ed: Mary Hassinger
Founded: 1876
Educational resources materials, Christian re-
source material; Teacher Resource Book-all
curriculum areas; Life Science.
ISBN Prefix(es): 0-513; 0-7424; 1-56822; 0-
88012
Number of titles published annually: 80 Print

Insurance Institute of America, see American
Institute for CPCU & Insurance Institute of
America

Insurance Institute of America Inc
Affiliate of American Institute for CPCU
720 Providence Rd, Malvern, PA 19355
Tel: 610-644-2100 *Toll Free Tel:* 800-644-2101
Fax: 610-640-9576
E-mail: cserv@cpcuiia.org
Web Site: www.aicpcu.org
Key Personnel
Pres & CEO: Terrie Troxel
Prodn Mgr: Kathy Spicciati
Prod Design Mgr: Joanne Scanlon
Founded: 1909
Specialize in property-liability continuing insur-
ance education.
ISBN Prefix(es): 0-89462
Number of titles published annually: 22 Print; 22
CD-ROM
Total Titles: 82 Print

Inter-American Development Bank
Division of Multilateral Development Bank
1300 New York Ave NW, Washington, DC 20577
Tel: 202-623-1000 *Fax:* 202-623-3096
E-mail: idb-books@iadb.org; idbcc@iadb.org
Web Site: www.iadb.org/pub
Key Personnel
Chief, Public Info & Publg Section: Daniel B
Martin *Tel:* 202-623-1397
Founded: 1959

Economic development, Latin America & the Caribbean.
ISBN Prefix(es): 0-940602; 1-886938; 1-931003
Number of titles published annually: 30 Print
Total Titles: 120 Print
Distributed by Johns Hopkins University Press

§Inter-University Consortium for Political & Social Research
Affiliate of University of Michigan Institute for Social Research
PO Box 1248, Ann Arbor, MI 48106-1248
Mailing Address: 426 Thompson St, Ann Arbor, MI 48104-2321
Tel: 734-647-5000 Fax: 734-647-8200
E-mail: netmail@icpsr.umich.edu
Web Site: www.icpsr.umich.edu
Key Personnel
Exec Dir: Myron Gutmann Tel: 734-615-8400
  E-mail: gutman@umich.edu
Dir, Educ Resources: Henry Heitowit Tel: 734-763-7400 E-mail: hank@icpsr.edu
Dir, Archival Devt: Erik Austin Tel: 734-615-7652 E-mail: erik@icpsr.umich.edu
Tech Dir: Janet Vavra Tel: 734-647-2000
  E-mail: jan@icpsr.umich.edu
Dir: Mary Vardigan Tel: 734-615-7908
  E-mail: maryv@icpsr.umich.edu
Founded: 1962
Provides access to social science data collections & documentation.
ISBN Prefix(es): 0-89138
Number of titles published annually: 10 Print; 5 CD-ROM; 200 Online
Total Titles: 25 CD-ROM; 4,000 Online
Shipping Address: 311 Mayhard St, Ann Arbor, MI 48104

§Interchange Inc
14025 23 Ave N, Suite B, Plymouth, MN 55447
SAN: 250-0094
Mailing Address: PO Box 47596, Plymouth, MN 55447
Tel: 763-694-7596 Toll Free Tel: 800-669-6208
  Fax: 763-694-7117 Toll Free Fax: 800-729-0395
E-mail: sales@interchangeinc.com
Web Site: www.interchangeinc.com
Key Personnel
Pres: Sy H Friedman
Founded: 1966
Specialize in cross-reference guides for industrial, agricultural, commercial & automotive parts (bearings, seals, drive belts & filters); automotive cross-referenced part numbers.
ISBN Prefix(es): 0-916966
Number of titles published annually: 6 Print; 6 CD-ROM; 6 Online
Total Titles: 9 Print; 6 CD-ROM; 6 Online
Advertising Agency: S H Friedman Assoc

Intercultural Development Research Association (IDRA)
5835 Callaghan Rd, Suite 350, San Antonio, TX 78228-1190
Tel: 210-444-1710 Fax: 210-444-1714
E-mail: contact@idra.org
Web Site: www.idra.org
Key Personnel
Exec Dir: Maria Robledo Montecel
Commun Mgr: Christie L Goodman
  E-mail: cgoodman@idra.org
Communs Specialist: Sherry Carr Deer
Founded: 1973
Independent, non-profit organization dedicated to creating schools that work for all children; works with people to create & apply cutting-edge educational policies & practices that value & empower all children, families & communities. Conducts research & development activities, creates, implements & administers innovative education programs & provides teacher,

administrator, parent training & technical assistance.
ISBN Prefix(es): 1-878550
Number of titles published annually: 4 Print

Intercultural Press Inc
Division of Nicholas Brealey Publishing
PO Box 700, 374 US Rte One, Yarmouth, ME 04096
SAN: 212-6699
Tel: 207-846-5168 Toll Free Tel: 866-372-2665
  Fax: 207-846-5181
E-mail: books@interculturalpress.com
Web Site: www.interculturalpress.com
Key Personnel
Publr: Patricia A O'Hare
Man Ed: Judy Carl-Hendrick
Mktg & Translation Rts: Stephanie L Cheney
  E-mail: stephanie@interculturalpress.com
Founded: 1980
Books, training & educational materials on international, cross-cultural & diversity subjects, including reference books, bibliographies, manuals, handbooks, nonfiction.
ISBN Prefix(es): 0-933662; 1-877864; 1-931930
Number of titles published annually: 11 Print
Total Titles: 98 Print
Distributor for Nicholas Brealey Publishing

§Interlingua Publishing
423 S Pacific Coast Hwy, No 208, Redondo Beach, CA 90277
Tel: 310-792-3636 Fax: 509-479-8935
E-mail: interlingua@aol.com
Key Personnel
Pres & Intl Rts: Jack Bernstein
Founded: 1986
Publisher of books, manipulatives & electronic materials in the areas of science & technology from Asia; K-12 education with emphasis on math & GED programs; travel-related materials used by hotel, car rental, restaurant & retail personnel when communicating with non English-speaking clients; medical related materials used by doctors, nurses & hospital administrators when communicating with non English-speaking patients.
ISBN Prefix(es): 0-9616226; 1-884730
Number of titles published annually: 35 Print; 10 CD-ROM
Total Titles: 40 Print; 20 CD-ROM
Imprints: Interlingua; Selling Space
Advertising Agency: Interlingua Advertising

Interlink Publishing Group Inc
46 Crosby St, Northampton, MA 01060
SAN: 664-8908
Tel: 413-582-7054 Toll Free Tel: 800-238-LINK
  (238-5465) Fax: 413-582-7057
E-mail: info@interlinkbooks.com
Web Site: www.interlinkbooks.com
Key Personnel
Publr & Ed: Michel Moushabeck Tel: 413-582-7054 ext 204 E-mail: michel@interlinkbooks.com
Assoc Publr: Pam Thompson
Lib Sales Dir: Brenda Eaton
Publicity Dir: Moira Megargee
Founded: 1987
World travel, world literature, world history & politics, cooking, traditional crafts & illustrated children's books from around the world.
ISBN Prefix(es): 0-940793; 1-56656
Number of titles published annually: 50 Print
Total Titles: 400 Print
Imprints: Crocodile Books; Interlink Books; Olive Branch Press
Distributor for Birlinn Ltd UK; Black & White Publishing UK; Macmillan Caribbean (UK); Mercat Press (UK); Neal Wilson Publishing (UK); Polygon (UK); Quartet Books (UK); Rudisack Readers (UK); Serif Publishing Ltd

(UK); Sheldrake Press (UK); Stacey International (UK); Wolfhound Press (Ireland)
Foreign Rep(s): Electra Media Group (Southeast Asia); Hargreaves, Fuller & Co (Canada); Milley Associates (Eastern Canada); PDS Promotions (South Africa); Publishers Int'l Marketing (Middle East); Roundhouse Publishing (Europe & UK); Tower Books (Australia)

International Book Centre Inc
2391 Auburn Rd, Shelby Township, MI 48317
SAN: 208-7022
Tel: 248-879-8436; 586-254-7230 Fax: 586-254-7230; 248-879-8436
E-mail: ibc@ibcbooks.com
Web Site: www.ibcbooks.com
Key Personnel
Pres & Owner: Claudette Mukalla
Founded: 1974
Publisher of foreign language books.
ISBN Prefix(es): 0-86685
Number of titles published annually: 3 Print; 2 Audio
Total Titles: 24 Print; 5 Audio
Distributor for Library du Liban (Lebanon); Stacey Intl Ltd (London); University of Michigan

International Broadcasting Services Ltd
825 Cherry Lane, Penns Park, PA 18943
SAN: 289-2553
Mailing Address: PO Box 300, Penns Park, PA 18943
Tel: 215-598-3298 Fax: 215-598-3794
E-mail: hq@passband.com; mktg@passband.com
Web Site: www.passband.com
Key Personnel
Ed-in-Chief & Intl Rts Contact: Lawrence Magne
VP & Mktg Mgr: Jane Brinker E-mail: acct@passband.com
Ed (Paraguay): Tony Jones Tel: (021) 481-766
Founded: 1973
Publishers of world band radio & trade paperback references for the general public & professionals.
ISBN Prefix(es): 0-914941
Number of titles published annually: 6 Print
Total Titles: 19 Print
Imprints: Passport; Passport to World Band Radio; Radio Database International
Foreign Office(s): IBS Australia, PO Box 2145, Malaga WA 6062, Australia, Contact: Craig Tyson Tel: (08) 9342-9158 Fax: (08) 9342-9158 E-mail: addresses@passband.com
IBS Japan, 5-31-6 Tamanawa, Kamakura 247, Japan, Contact: T Ohtake Tel: (0467) 43-2167 Fax: (0467) 43-2167 E-mail: ibsjapan@passband.com
IBS Paraguay, Casilla 1844, Asuncion, Paraguay, Contact: Tony Jones Tel: (021) 481-766 E-mail: schedules@passband.com
Foreign Rep(s): Gazelle Book Services Ltd (Europe); National Book Network (Canada)
Advertising Agency: Lightkeeper Communications, 29 Pickering Lane, Troy, NY 12180, Contact: Jock Elliott Tel: 518-271-1761 Fax: 518-271-6131 E-mail: media@passband.com
Orders to: National Book Network, 15200 NBN Way, Blue Ridge Summit, PA 17214 Toll Free Tel: 800-462-6420 Toll Free Fax: 800-338-4550 E-mail: custserv@nbnbooks.com
Distribution Center: National Book Network, 4720-A Boston Way, Lanham, MD 20706, Contact: Eileen Judd Tel: 301-459-3366 Toll Free Tel: 800-462-6420 Fax: 301-459-1705 E-mail: ejudd@nbnbooks.com

§International City/County Management Association
777 N Capitol St NE, Suite 500, Washington, DC 20002

Tel: 202-289-4262 *Fax:* 202-962-3500
Fax on Demand: 732-578-4642
E-mail: pubs@icma.org
Web Site: icma.org
Key Personnel
Exec Dir: Robert J O'Neill, Jr
Dir, Pubns: Barbara H Moore *Tel:* 202-962-3643
E-mail: bmoore@icma.org
Founded: 1914
Textbooks, monthly magazine, newsletter, management information reports, data reports & yearbook.
ISBN Prefix(es): 0-87326
Number of titles published annually: 40 Print; 2 CD-ROM; 25 Online
Total Titles: 275 Print; 7 CD-ROM; 85 Online
Warehouse: PBD, 1650 Bluegrass Lakes Pkwy, Alpharetta, GA 30004 *Tel:* 770-442-8633
Distribution Center: PBD, 1650 Bluegrass Lakes Pkwy, Alpharetta, GA 30004

International Code Council Inc
Formerly International Conference of Building Officials
5360 Workman Mill Rd, Whittier, CA 90601-2298
Tel: 562-699-0541 *Toll Free Tel:* 800-423-6587
Web Site: www.iccsafe.org
Key Personnel
Pres: James L Witt
Founded: 1922
Publisher of construction codes & regulations used in US & abroad.
Number of titles published annually: 50 Print; 8 CD-ROM
Total Titles: 150 Print; 20 CD-ROM

International Conference of Building Officials, see International Code Council Inc

International Council of Shopping Centers
1221 Avenue of the Americas, 41st fl, New York, NY 10020-1099
Tel: 646-728-3800 *Fax:* 646-728-3800; 212-588-5555
Web Site: www.icsc.org
Key Personnel
Dir, Pubns: Patricia Wolf Montagni *Tel:* 646-728-3494 *E-mail:* pmontagni@icsc.org
Founded: 1957
Books, cassettes & CD-ROMs.
ISBN Prefix(es): 0-927547; 0-913598; 1-58268
Number of titles published annually: 12 Print
Total Titles: 75 Print; 15 Audio
Warehouse: Professional Mailing & Distribution Services, 9050 Junction Dr, Annapolis Junction, MD 20701
Distribution Center: Professional Mailing & Distribution Services, 9050 Junction Dr, Annapolis Junction, MD 20701 *Tel:* 301-362-6900

International Evangelism Crusades Inc
21601 Devonshire St, Suite 217, Chatsworth, CA 91311-8415
Tel: 818-882-0039 *Fax:* 818-989-2165
Key Personnel
Pres: Dr Frank E Stranges *E-mail:* drfes@earthlink.net
Founded: 1959
Number of titles published annually: 3 Print
Total Titles: 26 Print
Distributed by Universe Publishing

International Food Policy Research Institute
Member of Consultative Group on International Agricultural Research (CGIAR)
2033 "K" St NW, Washington, DC 20006-1002
Tel: 202-862-5600 *Fax:* 202-467-4439
E-mail: ifpri@cgiar.org
Web Site: www.ifpri.org

Key Personnel
Dir Gen: Joachian Von Braun
Founded: 1975
Research reports, occasional papers & newsletter series, books, briefs, abstracts.
ISBN Prefix(es): 0-89629
Number of titles published annually: 10 Print; 3 CD-ROM; 10 Online
Total Titles: 49 Print; 6 CD-ROM; 200 Online
Distributed by Johns Hopkins University Press

International Foundation for Election Systems
1101 15 St NW, 3rd fl, Washington, DC 20005
Tel: 202-828-8507 *Fax:* 202-822-9744
Web Site: www.ifes.org
Key Personnel
Ed-in-Chief: Dorin Tudoran
Founded: 1987
Non-profit organization promoting democracy; pre & post-election country reports.
ISBN Prefix(es): 1-879720
Number of titles published annually: 15 Print
Total Titles: 500 Print
Imprints: IFES

International Foundation of Employee Benefit Plans
18700 W Bluemound Rd, Brookfield, WI 53045
Mailing Address: PO Box 69, Brookfield, WI 53008-0069
Tel: 262-786-6700 *Toll Free Tel:* 888-334-3327
Fax: 262-786-8780
E-mail: books@ifebp.org
Web Site: www.ifebp.org
Key Personnel
CEO: Michael Wilson
Sr Dir, Info Svcs & Pubns: Dee Birschel
E-mail: deeb@ifebp.org
Founded: 1954
Books, periodicals.
ISBN Prefix(es): 0-89154
Number of titles published annually: 10 Print
Total Titles: 58 Print
Membership(s): Publishers Marketing Association; SNAP

The International Institute of Islamic Thought
500 Grove St, Suite 200, Herndon, VA 20170
Tel: 703-471-1133 *Fax:* 703-471-3922
E-mail: iiit@iiit.org
Web Site: www.iiit.org
Key Personnel
Pres: Abusolayman Abdulhamid
Exec Dir: Sathi Malkawi
Dir, Pubns: Dr Jaman Barzinji
Founded: 1981
Books, books on tape, video cassettes.
ISBN Prefix(es): 0-912463; 1-56564
Number of titles published annually: 15 Print

International Intertrade Index
Division of Printing Consultants Publishers
Subsidiary of Russia China Travel News
636 Buchanan St, Hillside, NJ 07205
Mailing Address: PO Box 636, Federal Sq, Newark, NJ 07101
Tel: 908-686-2382 *Fax:* 908-686-2382
Key Personnel
VP: John E Felber
Founded: 1950
Publishers of business & travel directory containing new imported products, worldwide, in Russia, China, Vietnam, Cuba & North Korea, travel, transport, hotel etc, marketing, sales offices, joint ventures with US firms.
ISBN Prefix(es): 0-910794
Total Titles: 10 Print

International Linguistics Corp
12220 Blue Ridge Blvd, Suite G, Grandview, MO 64030

Tel: 816-765-8855 *Toll Free Tel:* 800-237-1830
Fax: 816-765-2855
E-mail: info@learnables.com
Web Site: www.learnables.com
Key Personnel
Gen Mgr: Jennifer Elliott
Founded: 1976
Foreign & English language materials, language teaching materials.
ISBN Prefix(es): 0-939990; 1-887371
Number of titles published annually: 4 Print
Total Titles: 50 Print; 50 Audio

International Marine Publishing
Division of McGraw-Hill Education
485 Commercial St, Rockport, ME 04856
Mailing Address: PO Box 220, Camden, ME 04843
Tel: 207-236-4837 *Fax:* 207-236-6314
Web Site: www.internationalmarine.com/im
Key Personnel
Edit Dir: Jonathan Eaton
Founded: 1969
Leading publisher of boating, sailing & maritime books. Publishes how-to titles to narratives & action/adventure titles.
ISBN Prefix(es): 0-07
Number of titles published annually: 45 Print
Total Titles: 400 Print
Foreign Rep(s): McGraw-Hill/Ryerson (Canada)

International Medical Publishing Inc
1313 Dolly Madison Blvd, Suite 302, McLean, VA 22101
Tel: 703-356-2037 *Toll Free Tel:* 800-530-3142
Fax: 703-734-8987
E-mail: contact@medicalpublishing.com
Web Site: www.medicalpublishing.com
Key Personnel
Ed: Dr Thomas Masterson *E-mail:* masterson@medicalpublishing.com
Lib Sales Dir: Jonmana Bizri
VP, Mktg: Ben Boccuzzi
Opers: Karen Halladay
Founded: 1991
Medical handbooks for professionals; healthcare planners.
ISBN Prefix(es): 0-9634063; 1-883205
Number of titles published annually: 4 Print
Total Titles: 44 Print

International Monetary Fund (IMF)
Division of International Org (IGO)
700 19 St NW, Suite 12-607, Washington, DC 20431
SAN: 203-8188
Tel: 202-623-7430 *Fax:* 202-623-7201
E-mail: publications@imf.org
Web Site: www.imf.org
Key Personnel
Chief, Pubn Servs: Lori Michele Newsom
Founded: 1946
Reference & professional books & periodicals in economics, business & government, monetary studies, subscription & mail order.
ISBN Prefix(es): 0-939934; 1-55775
Number of titles published annually: 80 Print; 3 CD-ROM; 200 E-Book
Total Titles: 500 Print; 10 CD-ROM; 800 E-Book

§International Press of Boston Inc
PO Box 43502, Somerville, MA 02143
Tel: 617-623-3016 *Fax:* 617-623-3101
E-mail: orders@intlpress.com; journals@intlpress.com
Web Site: www.intlpress.com
Key Personnel
Gen Mgr: Hugh Rutledge *Tel:* 617-623-2033
E-mail: hugh@intlpress.com
Cust Serv Rep: Ivy Mar
Founded: 1992

Publish books, monographs, conference proceedings in advanced mathematics.
ISBN Prefix(es): 1-57146
Number of titles published annually: 12 Print
Total Titles: 80 Print; 3 CD-ROM
Distributed by AMS

International Publishers Co Inc
239 W 23 St, 5th fl, New York, NY 10011
SAN: 202-5655
Tel: 212-366-9816 *Fax:* 212-366-9820
E-mail: service@intpubnyc.com
Web Site: www.intpubnyc.com
Key Personnel
Pres & Ed: Betty Smith *E-mail:* bsmith@intpubnyc.com
Founded: 1924
Short discount titles & Marxist Classics. Trade in cloth & paperback, general nonfiction, social sciences, classic & contemporary Marxism-Leninism, literature, poetry & biography, labor, women's studies.
ISBN Prefix(es): 0-7178
Number of titles published annually: 5 Print
Total Titles: 201 Print
Imprints: New World Paperbacks
Foreign Rep(s): Global Book Marketing (London); Nauka Ltd (Far East)
Warehouse: WA Book Service, 26 Ranick Rd, Hauppauge, NY 11788, Contact: Stephen DiStefano *Tel:* 631-234-2255 *Fax:* 631-234-2268
Membership(s): ABA; National Association of College Stores; Publishers Marketing Association

International Reading Association
800 Barksdale Rd, Newark, DE 19714
Mailing Address: PO Box 8139, Newark, DE 19714-8139
Tel: 302-731-1600 *Fax:* 302-731-1057
E-mail: books@reading.org
Web Site: www.reading.org
Founded: 1956
Books & journals related to reading instruction & literary education.
ISBN Prefix(es): 0-87207
Number of titles published annually: 20 Print
Total Titles: 200 Print

International Research Center for Energy & Economic Development
850 Willowbrook Rd, Boulder, CO 80302
Tel: 303-442-4014 *Fax:* 303-442-5042
E-mail: iceed@colorado.edu
Web Site: www.iceed.org
Key Personnel
Dir: Dorothea H El Mallakh
Lib Sales Dir: Tita Young
Founded: 1973
Monographs & hardcover; public policy; journal.
ISBN Prefix(es): 0-918714
Number of titles published annually: 4 Print
Total Titles: 70 Print

§International Risk Management Institute Inc
12222 Merit Dr, Suite 1450, Dallas, TX 75251-2276
Tel: 972-960-7693 *Toll Free Tel:* 800-827-4242
Fax: 972-371-5120
E-mail: info@irmi.com
Web Site: www.irmi.com
Key Personnel
Owner: William S McIntyre
Publish both print & online books.
ISBN Prefix(es): 1-886813
Number of titles published annually: 5 Print
Total Titles: 41 Print; 1 CD-ROM

International Society for Technology in Education
480 Charnelton St, Eugene, OR 97401-2626
Tel: 541-302-3777 *Toll Free Tel:* 800-336-5191 (orders only) *Fax:* 541-302-3778
E-mail: iste@iste.org
Web Site: www.iste.org
Key Personnel
CEO: Don Knezek
COO: John Ragsdale *Tel:* 541-434-8902
Asst Deputy CEO: Leslie Conery *Tel:* 541-302-3776
Dir, Publg: Jean Hall *Tel:* 541-434-8922
Founded: 1979
Pre-college technology in education on books, journals, newsletters & courseware packages.
ISBN Prefix(es): 0-924667; 1-56484
Number of titles published annually: 12 Print
Total Titles: 60 Print

International Students Inc
7222 Commerce Center Dr, Suite 200, Colorado Springs, CO 80919
Mailing Address: PO Box C, Colorado Springs, CO 80901
Tel: 719-576-2700 *Toll Free Tel:* 800-474-4147 ext 111 (orders) *Fax:* 719-576-5363
E-mail: information@isionline.org
Web Site: www.isionline.org
Key Personnel
Pres: Doug Shaw
Dir, Opers: Denny Yoder *E-mail:* dyoder@isionline.org
Founded: 1953
Books on religion.
ISBN Prefix(es): 0-910796
Number of titles published annually: 15 Print
Total Titles: 12 Print

§International Universities Press Inc
59 Boston Post Rd, Madison, CT 06443
Mailing Address: PO Box 389, Guilford, CT 06437-0389
Tel: 203-245-4000 *Toll Free Tel:* 800-835-3487
Fax: 203-245-0775
E-mail: orders@iup.com
Web Site: www.iup.com
Key Personnel
Exec VP, Ed-in-Chief & Book & Journal Procurement Mgr: Margaret Emery *Tel:* 203-245-4000 ext 116 *E-mail:* office@iup.com
Subs Rts & Adv: Michael Toye
Orders & Cust Serv: Amy L Colter
Founded: 1943
Psychoanalysis, psychology, psychiatry, medicine, social sciences, college textbooks, periodicals & paperbacks.
ISBN Prefix(es): 0-8236; 1-887841
Number of titles published annually: 60 Print
Total Titles: 907 Print; 1 CD-ROM; 1 Audio
Imprints: Psychosocial Press
Subsidiaries: Sphinx Press Inc
Distributor for Psychosocial Press; Sphinx Press
Foreign Rep(s): Mark Paterson & Associates (World)
Foreign Rights: Mark Paterson & Associates (World)
Advertising Agency: Sphinx Press

International Wealth Success Inc
PO Box 186, Merrick, NY 11566-0186
Tel: 516-766-5850 *Toll Free Tel:* 800-323-0548
Fax: 516-766-5919
E-mail: admin@iwsmoney.com
Web Site: www.iwsmoney.com
Key Personnel
Pres & Ed: Tyler G Hicks *E-mail:* tyghicks@aol.com
Founded: 1967
Publish a variety of business & financial titles in the fields of small business, real estate, mail order, import-export & financing.
ISBN Prefix(es): 0-934311; 0-914306; 1-56150
Number of titles published annually: 10 Print; 3 CD-ROM; 1 E-Book; 2 Audio

Total Titles: 105 Print; 2 CD-ROM; 2 E-Book; 1 Audio
Membership(s): ABA; Newsletter & Electronic Publishers Association

InterVarsity Press
Division of InterVarsity Christian Fellowship of the USA
430 E Plaza Dr, Westmont, IL 60559-1234
SAN: 202-7089
Mailing Address: PO Box 1400, Downers Grove, IL 60515-1426
Tel: 630-734-4000 *Toll Free Tel:* 800-843-7225
Fax: 630-734-4200
E-mail: mail@ivpress.com
Web Site: www.ivpress.com
Key Personnel
Publr: Robert A Fryling *Tel:* 630-734-4001
E-mail: bfryling@ivpress.com
Busn Mgr: James Hagen *Tel:* 630-734-4005
E-mail: jhagen@ivpress.com
Edit Dir: Andrew T Le Peau *Tel:* 630-734-4036
E-mail: alepeau@ivpress.com
Sales & Mktg Mgr: Jeff Crosby *Tel:* 630-734-4017 *E-mail:* jcrosby@ivpress.com
Rts & Perms: Ellen Hsu *Tel:* 630-734-4034
E-mail: ehsu@ivpress.com
Art Dir: Cindy Kiple *Tel:* 630-734-4024
E-mail: ckiple@ivpress.com
Sr Ed: Cindy Bunch *Tel:* 630-734-4078
E-mail: cbunch@ivpress.com; Daniel Reid *Tel:* 425-391-0466 *E-mail:* dgreid@ivpress.com
Prodn Mgr & ISBN Contact: Anne Gerth *Tel:* 630-734-4027 *E-mail:* agerth@ivprss.com
Assoc Edit Dir: James Hoover *Tel:* 630-734-4037
E-mail: jhoover@ivpress.com
Founded: 1947
Religion (interdenominational); textbooks.
ISBN Prefix(es): 0-87784; 0-8308
Number of titles published annually: 90 Print; 1 CD-ROM; 2 E-Book; 1 Audio
Total Titles: 800 Print; 2 CD-ROM; 5 E-Book; 6 Audio
Imprints: LifeGuide Bible Studies
Branch Office(s)
16736 235 Ave SE, Issaquah, WA 98027, Contact: Dan Reid *Tel:* 425-391-0466 *Fax:* 425-391-0466 *E-mail:* dgreid@ix.netcom.com
Editorial Office(s): 16736 235 Ave, SE, Issaquah, WA 98027, Contact: Dan Reid *Tel:* 425-391-0466 *Fax:* 425-391-0466 *E-mail:* dgreid@ix.netcom.com
Foreign Office(s): 38 De Montfort St, Leicester LE1 7GP, United Kingdom, Contact: Brian Wilson *E-mail:* ivp@uccf.org.uk
Foreign Rep(s): Inter-Varsity Press - UK (Africa, Asia, Europe)
Foreign Rights: Winfried Bluth (Europe)
Membership(s): Evangelical Christian Publishers Association

Interweave Press
201 E Fourth St, Loveland, CO 80537
Tel: 970-669-7672 *Toll Free Tel:* 800-272-2193
Fax: 970-667-8317
E-mail: customerservice@interweave.com
Web Site: www.interweave.com
Key Personnel
Pres & COO: Marilyn Murphy
CEO & Creative Dir: Linda Ligon
VP, Mktg & Sales: Linda Stark
Founded: 1975
ISBN Prefix(es): 0-934026; 1-883010; 1-931499
Number of titles published annually: 18 Print
Total Titles: 160 Print
Distributed by Keith Ainsworth Pty Ltd, Australia; Independent Publishers Group; Search Press, UK
Membership(s): Publishers Association of the West

The Intrepid Traveler
371 Walden Green Rd, Branford, CT 06405

Tel: 203-488-5341 *Fax:* 203-488-7677
E-mail: info@intrepidtraveler.com
Web Site: www.intrepidtraveler.com
Key Personnel
Publr: Kelly Monaghan
Assoc Publr: Sally Scanlon *E-mail:* sscanlon@
  intrepidtraveler.com
Founded: 1990
Publish travel-related titles.
ISBN Prefix(es): 0-9627892; 1-887140
Number of titles published annually: 3 Print
Total Titles: 12 Print
Distributed by National Book Network Inc (NBN)
Billing Address: PO Box 531, Branford, CT
  06405
Membership(s): Publishers Marketing Association

Intrigue Press, see Speck Press

Investor Responsibility Research Center
1350 Connecticut Ave NW, Suite 700, Washington, DC 20036
Tel: 202-833-0700 *Fax:* 202-833-3555
E-mail: sales@irrc.com
Web Site: www.irrc.com
Key Personnel
Pres & CEO: Linda Crompton
Founded: 1972
Impartial research on proxy voting & company
  profile/portfolio screening, analysis, software &
  consulting to institutional investors. Research
  & expertise also serves corporations, law firms,
  boards of directors, government offices, boards
  of trustees, the media & others who need to
  track & comprehend the ebbs & flows of share-
  holder activism & proxy voting.
ISBN Prefix(es): 0-931035; 1-879775
Number of titles published annually: 10 Print
Total Titles: 200 Print
Distributed by Academic Book Center; Ama-
  zon.com; Blackwell Northamerica Inc; The
  Book House; Coutts Library Service; Dawson
  France; Dawson UK Ltd; Eastern Book Co;
  Ebsco Subscription Services; Emery Pratt Co;
  Faxon Canada; The Faxon Co Inc; Franklin
  Book Co Inc; William S Hein & Co Inc; Hey-
  den & Son; Midwest Library Serv; Readmore;
  Rowe Com; Swets Subscription Serv; Swets &
  Zeitlinger; Yankee Book Peddler

The Invisible College Press LLC
3703 Del Mar Dr, Woodbridge, VA 22193-0209
Mailing Address: PO Box 209, Woodbridge, VA
  22194
Tel: 703-590-4005
E-mail: sales@invispress.com
Web Site: www.invispress.com
Key Personnel
Busn Mgr: Paul Mossinger *Tel:* 703-403-0247
  E-mail: manager@invispress.com
Ed: Phillip Reynolds *E-mail:* editor@invispress.
  com
Founded: 2001
Small, independent publisher dedicated to bring-
  ing literary-quality works in the fields of
  UFOs, conspiracies, secret societies, the para-
  normal, anarchism & other non-traditional,
  subversive topics that are underrepresented by
  mainstream, corporate media. Titles are a blend
  of new, original fiction & reprints of hard-to-
  find classics.
ISBN Prefix(es): 1-931468
Number of titles published annually: 10 Print
Total Titles: 20 Print
Imprints: Fleur de Luce Books

Iowa State Press, see Blackwell Publishing
  Professional

Iron Gate Publishing
PO Box 999, Niwot, CO 80544

Tel: 303-530-2551 *Fax:* 303-530-5273
E-mail: editor@irongate.com; booknews@
  reunionsolutions.com
Web Site: www.irongate.com; www.
  reunionsolutions.com
Key Personnel
Publr: Dina C Carson
Founded: 1990
Genealogy, self-publishing, reference, reunion
  planning how-to.
ISBN Prefix(es): 1-879579; 0-9724975
Number of titles published annually: 10 Print; 6
  CD-ROM; 25 Online; 25 E-Book
Total Titles: 17 Print; 6 CD-ROM; 17 Online; 25
  E-Book
Imprints: KinderMed Press; Reunion Solutions
  Press
Membership(s): Colorado Independent Publishers
  Association; Publishers Marketing Associa-
  tion; PubWest; Small Publishers Association of
  North America

Irvington Publishers Inc, see Ardent Media Inc

§ISA
67 Alexander Dr, Research Triangle Park, NC
  27709
Mailing Address: PO Box 12277, Research Trian-
  gle Park, NC 27709
Tel: 919-549-8411 *Fax:* 919-549-8288
E-mail: info@isa.org
Web Site: www.isa.org
Key Personnel
Exec Dir: Robert Renner
Dir, Conferences & Exhibits: Alan Wagner
Dir, Journals Servs: George Davis
Ed, Member Servs: Dale Lee
Founded: 1945
Technical books, references, journals, video-based
  training programs, directories, software, stan-
  dards, proceedings, CD-ROM, electronic refer-
  ences.
ISBN Prefix(es): 1-55617
Number of titles published annually: 5 Print
Total Titles: 198 Print; 3 CD-ROM; 2 E-Book
Subsidiaries: ISA Services Inc
Foreign Rep(s): ATP (England); COMLINE
  (England); I & C (Australia); ISA/India Re-
  gion; ISA/Latin American Region (Mexico);
  ISA/South American Region (Brazil); Power
  Engineering Books (Canada)

ISI Books
Imprint of Intercollegiate Studies Institute Inc
PO Box 4431, 3901 Centerville Rd, Wilmington,
  DE 19807
Tel: 302-652-4600 *Toll Free Tel:* 800-526-7022
  Fax: 302-652-1760
E-mail: bookstore@isi.org
Web Site: www.isibooks.org
Key Personnel
Dir, Mktg: Douglas Schneider *Tel:* 302-652-4600
  ext 164 *E-mail:* dschneider@isi.org
Sr Ed: Jeremy Beer
Publr: Jeffrey O Nelson
Founded: 1993
ISI Books is a publisher of serious, but accessible
  interdisciplinary books & journals, focused on
  the liberal arts.
ISBN Prefix(es): 1-882926; 1-932236
Number of titles published annually: 20 Print
Total Titles: 100 Print

Island Press
Subsidiary of Center for Resource Economics
1718 Connecticut Ave NW, Suite 300, Washing-
  ton, DC 20009
SAN: 212-5129
Tel: 202-232-7933 *Toll Free Tel:* 800-828-1302
  Fax: 202-234-1328; 707-983-6414 (orders
  only)
E-mail: info@islandpress.org

Web Site: www.islandpress.org
Key Personnel
Pres: Charles C Savitt
VP & Publr: Dan Sayre
Dir, Communs: Amelia Durand
Dir, Mktg & Sales: Christine Dunn
Exec Ed: Jonathan Cobb; Barbara Dean
Founded: 1979
Books about the environment for professionals,
  students & general readers, autobiography-
  scientific; land use; planning; environmental
  economics; nature essays.
ISBN Prefix(es): 0-933280; 1-55963
Number of titles published annually: 50 Print
Total Titles: 400 Print
Imprints: Shearwater Books
Branch Office(s)
PO Box 7, Covelo, CA 95428-0007 *Tel:* 707-
  983-6432 *Fax:* 707-983-6414 *E-mail:* orders@
  islandpress.org
Distributor for IUCN
Foreign Rights: Alexander Hoyt Associates
Shipping Address: 76381 Commercial St, Covelo,
  CA 95428 (deliveries only) *Tel:* 707-983-6432
  Toll Free Tel: 800-828-1302 *Fax:* 707-983-6414
  E-mail: orders@islandpress.org
Membership(s): BISG

ISTE, see International Society for Technology in
  Education

ITA Institute
PO Box 281, Grand Blanc, MI 48439
Tel: 810-232-6482
E-mail: hq@itatkd.com
Web Site: www.itatkd.com
Key Personnel
Pres: James S Benko *Fax:* 810-235-8594
Founded: 1974
ISBN Prefix(es): 0-937314
Number of titles published annually: 12 Print
Total Titles: 17 Print; 64 Online; 64 E-Book; 28
  Audio

§Italica Press
595 Main St, Suite 605, New York, NY 10044
SAN: 695-1805
Tel: 212-935-4230 *Fax:* 212-838-7812
E-mail: inquiries@italicapress.com
Web Site: www.italicapress.com
Key Personnel
Pres & Co-Publr, Electronic Publg: Eileen Gar-
  diner *E-mail:* egardiner@italicapress.com
Sec & Co-Publr, Electronic Publg: Ronald G
  Musto *E-mail:* rgmusto@italicapress.com
Founded: 1985
English translations of Latin & Italian works from
  the Middle Ages to the present.
ISBN Prefix(es): 0-934977
Number of titles published annually: 7 Print; 4
  CD-ROM; 4 E-Book
Total Titles: 100 Print; 16 CD-ROM; 10 E-Book

iUniverse
**2021 Pine Lake Rd, Suite 100, Lincoln, NE
  68512**
Tel: **402-323-7800** *Toll Free Tel:* **877-288-4737**
  Fax: **402-323-7824**
E-mail: **firstname.lastname@iuniverse.com;
  general.inquiries@iuniverse.com**
Web Site: www.iuniverse.com

Key Personnel
CEO: Susan Driscoll *E-mail:* susan.driscoll@
iuniverse.com
iUniverse helps individuals publish, market &
sell fiction & nonfiction books. The company
is the largest independent publisher in the
U.S. & publishes more than 5,000 new titles
per year. Our publishing programs are en-
dorsed by industry leading author organizations, including the Authors Guild, ASJA &
the Mystery Writers of America. The company's major investors include Warburg
Pincus & Barnes & Noble. Our extensive
distribution network includes leading wholesalers like Ingram Book Group & Baker &
Taylor. Books published by iUniverse are
available from online retailers like Barnes &
Noble.com & Amazon.com plus thousands of
traditional booksellers worldwide.
Number of titles published annually: 5,000
Print; 1,000 E-Book
Total Titles: 14,000 Print
See Ad on Inside Back Cover

J & S Publishing Co Inc
1300 Bishop Lane, Alexandria, VA 22302
Tel: 703-823-9833 *Fax:* 703-823-9834
E-mail: jandspub@hotmail.com
Web Site: www.jandspub.com
Key Personnel
Pres, Lib Sales Dir & Intl Rts: Kurt Johnson
Founded: 1992
ISBN Prefix(es): 0-9632873; 1-888308
Number of titles published annually: 4 Print
Total Titles: 30 Print
Foreign Rep(s): Gazelle Book Service (Europe);
International Publishers Representatives (Mid-
dle East); LR International (Latin America)

Lee Jacobs Productions
PO Box 362, Pomeroy, OH 45769-0362
Tel: 740-992-5208 *Fax:* 740-992-0616
E-mail: ljacobs@frognet.net
Web Site: www.leejacobsproductions.com
Key Personnel
Pres: Robert Lee Jacobs *E-mail:* ljacobs@frognet.
net
Intl Rts & Lib Sales Dir: Ramona Compton
Founded: 1966
Books on magic & related subjects for perform-
ers.
Number of titles published annually: 5 Print
Total Titles: 230 Print; 4 Audio

Jade Rabbit, see Quite Specific Media Group
Ltd

Jain Publishing Co
PO Box 3523, Fremont, CA 94539
SAN: 213-6503
Tel: 510-659-8272 *Fax:* 510-659-0501
E-mail: mail@jainpub.com
Web Site: www.jainpub.com
Key Personnel
Pres & Publr: Mukesh Jain
Founded: 1989
General interest trade books, college textbooks,
professional & scholarly books.
ISBN Prefix(es): 0-89581; 0-87573
Number of titles published annually: 8 Print
Total Titles: 120 Print
Imprints: Asian Humanities Press

Jalmar Press
Subsidiary of The B L Winch Group Inc
1050 Canyon Rd, Fawnskin, CA 92333
SAN: 281-8302
Mailing Address: PO Box 370, Fawnskin, CA
92333
Tel: 909-866-2912 *Fax:* 909-866-2961
E-mail: jalmarpress@att.net

Web Site: www.jalmarpress.com *Telex:* 20-9039
WINCH
Key Personnel
Pres & Intl Rts: Bradley L Winch
E-mail: blwjalmar@worldnet.att.net
Gen Mgr: Cathy Winch
Founded: 1971
Trade & educational books for families, caregivers, counselors & teachers psychological; self-help; creative parenting; personal
development; positive self-esteem; right-
brain/whole-brain learning; transactional anal-
ysis; peacemaking skills; conflict resolution;
cross-correlated self-esteem related activities in
teaching elementary curriculum content; presentation skills & inspirational fables; emotional intelligence, character education; anger
management; virtues education. We do not publish children's story books at this time.
ISBN Prefix(es): 0-915190; 0-935266; 1-880396
Number of titles published annually: 12 Print
Total Titles: 150 Print; 150 Online
Imprints: Innerchoice Publishing; Personhood
Press; B L Winch & Associates
Foreign Rights: Anne-Christine Danielssen (Scandinavia); Imprima Korea Agency (Korea); Frederique Porretta (France); Tuttle-Mori Agency
(Japan, Thailand); Cristiana Viacano (Spanish
languages)

§Jane's Information Group
Subsidiary of Jane's Information Group (England)
110 N Royal St, Suite 200, Alexandria, VA
22314-1651
SAN: 286-357X
Tel: 703-683-3700 *Toll Free Tel:* 800-824-0768
(sales) *Fax:* 703-836-0297 *Toll Free Fax:* 800-
836-0297
E-mail: info.us@janes.com
Web Site: www.janes.com
Key Personnel
VP, Sales: Robert Laughman
Dir, Mktg: Alexa Thomas
Founded: 1897
Hard copy, on-line services, magazines, CD-
ROM, electronic databases on defense
aerospace & transportation subjects.
ISBN Prefix(es): 0-7106
Number of titles published annually: 110 Print
Total Titles: 171 Print
Online services available through Dialog, Factiva,
FirstSearch, LexisNexis.
Branch Office(s)
17310 Red Hill Ave, Suite 370, Irvine, CA 92714
Foreign Office(s): 163 Brighton Rd, Coulsdon,
Surrey CR5 2NH, United Kingdom
Warehouse: ITP Distribution Center, 7625 Empire
Dr, Florence, KY 41042

JayJo Books
Subsidiary of Guidance Channel
135 Dupont St, Plainview, NY 11803
Mailing Address: PO Box 9120, Plainview, NY
11803-9020
Tel: 516-349-5520 *Fax:* 516-349-5521
E-mail: jayjobooks@guidancechannel.com
Web Site: www.guidancechannel.com
Key Personnel
CEO: Ed Werz *Tel:* 516-349-5520 ext 200
Exec VP: Janice Werz *Tel:* 516-349-5520 ext 202
Ed-in-Chief: Sally Germain *Tel:* 516-349-5520
ext 210 *E-mail:* sallyg@guidancechannel.com
Founded: 1994
Educational books to help parents, teachers &
children cope with chronic illness, special
needs & health education.
ISBN Prefix(es): 0-9639449; 1-891383
Number of titles published annually: 4 Print
Total Titles: 26 Print

JB Communications Inc
101 W 55 St, Suite 2-D, New York, NY 10019

Tel: 212-246-0900 *Fax:* 212-246-2114
Key Personnel
Pres: Raymond Kurman
Founded: 1989
Children's books.
Number of titles published annually: 15 Print
Total Titles: 45 Print
Imprints: Sunny Books

Jelmar Publishing Co Inc
PO Box 488, Plainview, NY 11803-0488
Tel: 516-822-6861 *Fax:* 516-822-6861
Key Personnel
Pres: Joel J Shulman
Founded: 1986
Publish books for the packaging, package print-
ing & printing industries, with major emphasis
upon package printing & corrugated packag-
ing; products are designed for professional use
by people in the field, ranging from novices to
experts.
ISBN Prefix(es): 0-9616302; 1-885067
Number of titles published annually: 3 Print
Total Titles: 20 Print
Distributed by Flexographic Technical Associ-
ation; GATF (Graphic Arts Technical Foun-
dation); Institute of Packaging Profession-
als; NAPLL (National Association of Printing
Leadership); TAPPI (Technical Association of
the Pulp & Paper Industry)
Distributor for FTA; TAPPI (Technical Associa-
tion of the Pulp & Paper Industry)
Foreign Rep(s): Graphic Arts Books International
(South Africa); Supack International (India)
Warehouse: Publishers Storage & Shipping, 660 S
Mansfield, Ypsilanti, MI 48197

Jewish Lights Publishing
Division of Longhill Partners Inc
Sunset Farm Offices, Rte 4, Woodstock, VT
05091
SAN: 134-5621
Mailing Address: PO Box 237, Woodstock, VT
05091
Tel: 802-457-4000 *Toll Free Tel:* 800-962-4544
Fax: 802-457-4004
E-mail: sales@jewishlights.com
Web Site: www.jewishlights.com
Key Personnel
Pres, Publr, Intl Rts: Stuart M Matlins
VP, PR & Mktg: Jon M Sweeney
VP, Fin & Admin: Amy Wilson
Lib Sales Dir: Shelly Angers
Founded: 1990
General trade adult & children's books on spiritu-
ality, theology, philosophy, mysticism, women's
studies, recovery/self-help/healing & history for
people of all faiths & backgrounds.
ISBN Prefix(es): 1-879045; 1-58023
Number of titles published annually: 15 Print
Total Titles: 175 Print; 3 Audio
Distributor for Jewish Thought Series/Israel Mod
Books
Foreign Rep(s): Deep Books (Europe & UK); Ju-
daica Direct (Australia & New Zealand)
Foreign Rights: Harris/Elon (Israel); Alex Ko-
rzhenevski (Russia); Andrew Nurnberg Asso-
ciates (Czech Republic, Hungary); Frederique
Porretta (France); H Katia Schumer (Brazil);
Diana Voigt Literature Agentur (Germany); Su-
sanna Zevi (Italy)

Jewish New Testament Publications Inc
PO Box 615, Clarksville, MD 21029
Tel: 410-764-6144 *Fax:* 410-764-1376
E-mail: jntp@messianicjewish.net;
rightsandpermissions@messianicjewish.net
(rights & perms)
Web Site: www.messianicjewish.net/jntp
Key Personnel
Pres: Barry Rubin

Man Ed: Janet Chaiet *E-mail:* editor@
  messianicjewish.net
Founded: 1989
Publish books authored by Dr David Stern, emi-
  nent theologian.
ISBN Prefix(es): 965-359
Number of titles published annually: 1 Print
Total Titles: 5 Print; 1 CD-ROM; 1 Audio
Distributed by Messianic Jewish Resources
Foreign Rep(s): Winfried Bluth (Europe)
Membership(s): Christian Booksellers Association

Jewish Publication Society
2100 Arch St, 2nd fl, Philadelphia, PA 19103
SAN: 201-0240
Tel: 215-832-0600 *Toll Free Tel:* 800-234-3151
  Fax: 215-568-2017
E-mail: jewishbook@jewishpub.org
Web Site: www.jewishpub.org
Key Personnel
CEO & Ed-in-Chief: Ellen Frankel
Publg Dir: Carol Hupping *Tel:* 215-832-0605
  E-mail: chupping@jewishpub.org
Mgr, Prodn: Robin Norman
Sr Mgr, Sales & Mktg: Laurie Schlesinger
Sales: Dolores Verbit
Mgr, Mktg: Helene Bludman
Founded: 1888
Books of Jewish interest.
ISBN Prefix(es): 0-8276
Number of titles published annually: 15 Print
Total Titles: 250 Print; 1 Audio
Foreign Rep(s): Eurospan (Commonwealth, Eu-
  rope & UK, Latin America, Middle East)
Shipping Address: Books International, 22883
  Quicksilver Dr, Dulles, VA 20166 *Tel:* 703-
  661-1512 *Toll Free Tel:* 800-355-1165
  Fax: 703661-1501
Membership(s): Association of American Uni-
  versity Presses; Association of Jewish Book
  Publishers

§JHPIEGO
Affiliate of Johns Hopkins University
1615 Thames St, Suite 200, Baltimore, MD
  21231-3492
Tel: 410-537-1825 *Fax:* 410-537-1474
E-mail: info@jhpiego.net; orders@jhpiego.net
Web Site: www.jhpiego.org
Key Personnel
CEO: Leslie Mancuso
Founded: 1973
Reproductive health, medical texts, family plan-
  ning, maternal health, AIDS testing & preven-
  tion & cervical cancer prevention.
ISBN Prefix(es): 0-929817
Number of titles published annually: 5 Print
Total Titles: 80 Print; 4 CD-ROM

Jim Henson Publishing/Muppet Press
Affiliate of The Jim Henson Co
117 E 69 St, New York, NY 10021
Tel: 212-794-2400 *Fax:* 212-794-5157
Web Site: www.henson.com
Key Personnel
Pres & CEO: Charles Rivkin
CFO: Paul Eskenazi
Exec VP & Gen Counsel: Peter Schube, Esq
Art Dir: Lauren Attinello
Founded: 1979
Humor, craft, coffee table, children's concept &
  storybooks, comic books, novelty books, ac-
  tivity & coloring books, children's book clubs,
  movie & TV tie-ins.
Number of titles published annually: 50 Print
Total Titles: 400 Print
Imprints: Muppet Press
Distributed by At a Glance; Walter Foster;
  Golden Books Family Entertainment; Grolier;
  KidsBooks; Penguin Putnam; PK; Random

House; Readers Digest/Childrens Press; Running Press; Simon & Schuster
Foreign Rep(s): Bi Plano (Spain); Design Rights
  International (UK); Gaffney (Australia); Publishing Partner (Germany)

§JIST Publishing Inc
8902 Otis Ave, Indianapolis, IN 46216
SAN: 240-2351
Tel: 317-613-4200 *Toll Free Tel:* 800-648-5478
  Fax: 317-613-4304 *Toll Free Fax:* 800-547-
  8329
E-mail: info@jist.com
Web Site: www.jist.com
Key Personnel
Pres: Michael Farr
COO: Janet Banks
Assoc Publr: Sue Pines
VP, Mktg: Tom Abeel
Lib Sales Mgr: Bob Grilliot
Publicist: Acacia Martinez
Dir, Sales: Barry Newborn
Founded: 1981
Job search, career planning, job retention, refer-
  ence, assessment, business, self-help, career
  exploration, occupational information, charac-
  ter education, life skills, CD-ROM & reference
  books.
ISBN Prefix(es): 0-94278; 1-56370; 1-57112; 1-
  930780; 1-55864; 1-59357
Number of titles published annually: 50 Print; 20
  E-Book
Total Titles: 300 Print; 5 CD-ROM; 20 E-Book
Imprints: JIST Works; JIST Life; Kidsrights; Park
  Avenue Productions; Your Domain Publishing
Warehouse: 2521 Planes Dr, Indianapolis, IN
  46219, Sherry Locke *Tel:* 317-869-0564

JMW Group Inc
5 W Cross St, Hawthorne, NY 10532
Tel: 914-769-6400 *Fax:* 914-769-0250
Key Personnel
Dir: Brice Diedrick *E-mail:* bdiedrick@att.net
Founded: 1950
Publishers of self help, business books & con-
  densed classic fiction.
Number of titles published annually: 5 Print
Total Titles: 80 Print
Imprints: ICCT; The Lifetime Series; LTE Clas-
  sics
Branch Office(s)
International Center for Creative Thinking (ICCT)
Membership(s): Publishers Marketing Association

John Deere Publishing
Division of Deere & Co
5440 Corporate Park Dr, Davenport, IA 52807
Toll Free Tel: 800-522-7448 *Fax:* 563-355-3690
E-mail: johndeerepublishing@johndeere.com
Web Site: www.deere.com
Key Personnel
Publr & Info Tech Analyst: Sharon Clapp
Founded: 1967
ISBN Prefix(es): 0-86691
Number of titles published annually: 15 Print
Total Titles: 250 Print
Advertising Agency: Osborn & Barr
Warehouse: 200 S Bellingham, Bettendorf, IA
  52722

John Milton Society for the Blind
475 Riverside Dr, Rm 455, New York, NY 10027
SAN: 208-3019
Tel: 212-870-3335 *Fax:* 212-870-3229
E-mail: order@jmsblind.org
Web Site: www.jmsblind.org
Key Personnel
Pres: Robert R Pegg
Exec Dir, Discovery Magazine & John Milton
  Magazine: Darcy Quigley *E-mail:* dquigley@
  jmsblind.org

Asst Ed: Jennifer Glover *E-mail:* jglover@
  jmsblind.org
Founded: 1928
Braille magazines, large-type magazine, braille
  & cassette Bible study, braille magazine for
  youth. Distributed free to the blind & visually impaired throughout the world (English
  only). Magazines are religious material, nondenominational & Christian.
Total Titles: 1 Audio
Distributed by Citrus Publishing; Magnetix Corp;
  National Braille Press

§The Johns Hopkins University Press
Affiliate of The Johns Hopkins University
2715 N Charles St, Baltimore, MD 21218-4363
SAN: 202-7348
Tel: 410-516-6900 *Toll Free Tel:* 800-537-5487
  Fax: 410-516-6968
Web Site: www.press.jhu.edu
Key Personnel
Dir: Kathleen Keane
Exec Ed: Henry Tom; Jacqueline C Wehmueller
Ed-in-Chief: Trevor C Lipscombe
Sr Acqs Ed: Robert J Brugger; Wendy A Harris
Journals Mgr: William F Breichner
Mgr, Fulfillment Opers: William F Bishop
Mgr, Info Systems: Stacey L Armstead
Subs Rights Mgr: Heather Lengyel
Sales Mgr: Melanie Schaffner
Adv Mgr & Publicity Coord: Karen L Willmes
Journals Subn: Alta H Anthony
Publicist & Promo Coord: Mahinder Kingra
Founded: 1878
Scholarly books, nonfiction of general interest,
  paperbacks, scholarly journals. Publishers for
  the World Bank & International Food Policy
  Research Institute.
ISBN Prefix(es): 0-8018
Number of titles published annually: 200 Print
Total Titles: 2,000 Print; 1 CD-ROM; 15 Online;
  15 E-Book
Imprints: Robert G Merrick Editions
Subsidiaries: The Johns Hopkins Press Ltd (Lon-
  don)
Distributor for The Inter-American Development
  Bank; Performing Arts Publications; Resources
  for the Future Inc; The Woodrow Wilson Cen-
  ter Press
Foreign Rep(s): Academic Book Promotions
  (Benelux, Denmark, France, Iceland, Scandi-
  navia); Cambridge University Press (Australia,
  New Zealand); Information Publications Pte
  Ltd (SE Asia, including China); Arie Ruiten-
  beek (Portugal, Spain); Trevor Brown Asso-
  ciates (Austria, Germany, Italy, Switzerland);
  United Publishers Services Ltd (Japan); Univer-
  sity Presses Marketing (UK, Ireland, Greece,
  Israel)
Foreign Rights: Agenzia Letteraria Internazionale
  (Italy); International Editors' Co (Portu-
  gal, Spain); La Nouvelle Agence Litteraire
  (France); Lennart Sane Agency (Netherlands,
  Norway, Sweden); Paul & Peter Fritz AG (Ger-
  many)
Advertising Agency: Welch, Mirabile & Co Inc
Warehouse: 2200 Girard Ave, Baltimore, MD
  21211
Membership(s): AAP; BISG

Johnson Books
Division of Johnson Printing Co
1880 S 57 Ct, Boulder, CO 80301
SAN: 201-0313
Tel: 303-443-9766 *Toll Free Tel:* 800-258-5830
  Fax: 303-998-7594
E-mail: books@jpcolorado.com
Web Site: www.jpcolorado.com; www.
  johnsonbooks.com
Key Personnel
Publr & Man Ed: Mira Perrizo *Tel:* 303-998-7585
  E-mail: mperrizo@jpcolorado.com

Edit Dir & Rts & Perms: Stephen Topping
Tel: 303-998-7581 *E-mail:* stopping@
jpcolorado.com
Mktg Dir: Robert Sheldon *Tel:* 303-998-7582
E-mail: rsheldon@jpcolorado.com
Busn Mgr & ISBN Contact: Stephanie White
Tel: 303-998-7587 *E-mail:* swhite@jpcolorado.
com
Founded: 1978
Hardcover & paperbound originals & reprints:
nonfiction history, nature, archaeology, guide-
books, outdoors, travel, astronomy, American
West, environment, Native American.
ISBN Prefix(es): 0-933472; 1-55566
Number of titles published annually: 15 Print
Total Titles: 120 Print
Imprints: Spring Creek Press
Distributor for Cowboy Artists of America; High
Lonesome Press; Woodlands Press

Jonathan David Publishers Inc
68-22 Eliot Ave, Middle Village, NY 11379
SAN: 169-5274
Tel: 718-456-8611 *Fax:* 718-894-2818
E-mail: info@jdbooks.com; jondavpub@aol.com
Web Site: www.jdbooks.com
Key Personnel
Pres & Ed-in-Chief: Alfred J Kolatch
E-mail: editorial@jdbooks.com
VP, Mktg & Rts & Perms: Marvin Sekler
E-mail: m.sekler@aol.com
Treas: Thelma R Kolatch
Edit Dir: David Kolatch
Prodn Coord: Rachel Taller
Website Coord: Allison G Mastropieri
E-mail: info@activenature.com
Cust Rel: Diane Purr
Assoc Ed: Barbara Burke
Founded: 1948
Judaica reference & general.
ISBN Prefix(es): 0-8246
Number of titles published annually: 25 Print
Total Titles: 130 Print
Imprints: PenQuill Press

§Jones & Bartlett Publishers Inc
40 Tall Pine Dr, Sudbury, MA 01776
Tel: 978-443-5000 *Toll Free Tel:* 800-832-0034
Fax: 978-443-8000
E-mail: info@jbpub.com
Web Site: www.jbpub.com
Key Personnel
CEO: Clayton E Jones
COO: Donald W Jones, Jr *E-mail:* djones@jbpub.
com
Founded: 1983
Life science, health science, first aid, EMS &
emergency care.
ISBN Prefix(es): 0-86720; 0-7637
Number of titles published annually: 200 Print
Total Titles: 3 CD-ROM
Foreign Office(s): Barb House, Barb News, Lon-
don W6 7PA, United Kingdom
Warehouse: Publishers Storage & Shipping, 231
Industrial Park, 46 Development Rd, Fitchburg,
MA 01420

§Bob Jones University Press
Unit of Bob Jones University
1700 Wade Hampton Blvd, Greenville, SC 29614
SAN: 223-7512
Tel: 864-242-5100 *Toll Free Tel:* 800-845-5731
(orders only) *Fax:* 864-298-0268
E-mail: asmith@bju.edu
Web Site: www.bjup.com
Key Personnel
Dir, Press: Bill Apelian
Dir, Sales & Mktg: John L Cross
Dir, Prod Devt: Steve Skaggs
Dir, Mktg Communs: Dawn L Watkins
Prodn Mgr: David Harris
Perms Coord: E Anne Smith

Founded: 1974
El-hi textbooks & trade paperbacks; earth sci-
ences, history, language arts, literature, mathe-
matics.
ISBN Prefix(es): 0-89084; 1-57924; 1-59166
Imprints: Textbooks for Christian Schools; Un-
usual Publications
Divisions: ShowForth Videos; SoundForth Music;
Journey Books
Distributed by Spring Arbor Distributors; Ap-
palachian Bible Co Inc
Warehouse: 134 White Oak, Greenville, SC
29607-1218

Jones McClure Publishing Inc
1113 Vine St, Suite 240, Houston, TX 77002
Mailing Address: PO Box 3348, Houston, TX
77253-3343
Tel: 713-223-2727 *Toll Free Tel:* 800-626-6667
Fax: 713-223-9393
E-mail: comments@jonesmcclure.com
Web Site: www.jonesmcclure.com
Key Personnel
Pres: Baird Craft
Founded: 1993
Provides a comprehensive desk reference to the
trial lawyer, through codes, commentaries &
form covering several areas of Texas law &
federal litigation, written in an easy to follow,
plain English format.
ISBN Prefix(es): 1-884554
Number of titles published annually: 5 Print
Total Titles: 20 Print; 3 CD-ROM

Jossey-Bass
Imprint of John Wiley & Sons Inc
989 Market St, San Francisco, CA 94103-1741
Tel: 415-433-1740 *Toll Free Tel:* 800-956-7739
Fax: 415-433-0499 (edit/mktg)
Web Site: www.josseybass.com; www.pfeiffer.com
Cable: JOSSEYBASS
Key Personnel
Pres & VP, P/T: Debra S Hunter
Asst to the Pres & VP, P/T: Catherine Miller
VP & Publr, Busn, Mgmt & Training: Cedric
Crocker
VP & Publr, NPM, HAE, Educ, Religion, Health,
Psychology: Paul Foster
VP & Publr, Periodicals & P/T Journals: Sue
Lewis
VP, HR & Admin: Susan Call
Dir, IT: James Hopkin
Budget Dir: Larry Ishii
Founded: 1966
General education, higher & adult education,
management & business, human resources,
training, health & health administration, so-
cial & behavioral sciences, psychology, conflict
resolution, mediation & negotiation, religion,
nonprofit & public management.
ISBN Prefix(es): 1-55542; 0-87589; 0-7879; 0-
88390; 0-89384
Total Titles: 5,000 Print
Imprints: Jossey-Bass; Pfeiffer
Orders to: John Wiley & Sons Inc, Customer Ser-
vice, One Wiley Dr, Somerset, NJ 08875-1272
Returns: John Wiley & Sons Inc, Customer Service, One Wiley Dr, Somerset, NJ 08875-1272
Tel: 732-469-4400 *Fax:* 732-302-2300

Journal of Regional Criticism, see Arjuna
Library Press

Journal of Roman Archaeology LLC
95 Peleg Rd, Portsmouth, RI 02871
Tel: 401-683-1955 *Fax:* 401-683-1975
E-mail: jra@journalofromanarch.com
Web Site: www.journalofromanarch.com
Key Personnel
Ed & Intl Rts: John H Humphrey
Founded: 1988
Annual journal & six supplements.

ISBN Prefix(es): 1-887829
Number of titles published annually: 6 Print
Total Titles: 75 Print

Journey Editions
Division of Periplus Editions
153 Milk St, Boston, MA 02109
Tel: 617-951-4080 *Fax:* 617-951-4045
Web Site: www.tuttlepublishing.com
Key Personnel
Publg Dir: Ed Walters
Founded: 1994
ISBN Prefix(es): 1-885203; 1-58290
Number of titles published annually: 5 Print
Total Titles: 125 Print
Distributed by Charles E Tuttle Co Inc
Warehouse: Airport Business Park, 364 Innova-
tion Dr, North Clarendon, VT 05759-9436

§Joy Publishing
Division of California Clock Co
PO Box 9901, Fountain Valley, CA 92708
SAN: 663-3544
Tel: 714-545-4321 *Toll Free Tel:* 800-454-8228
Fax: 714-708-2099
Web Site: www.joypublishing.com; www.kit-cat.
com
Key Personnel
Pres: Woody Young *E-mail:* woody@
joypublishing.com
Founded: 1986
Publish spiritual books.
ISBN Prefix(es): 0-939513
Number of titles published annually: 10 Print
Total Titles: 70 Print; 3 CD-ROM; 3 Online; 3
Audio
Shipping Address: 16060 Abajo Circle, Fountain
Valley, CA 92708

Joyce Media Inc
2654 Diamond St, Rosamond, CA 93560
Mailing Address: PO Box 848, Rosamond, CA
93560-0848
Tel: 661-269-1169 *Fax:* 661-269-2139
E-mail: joycemed@pacbell.net
Web Site: www.joycemediainc.com
Key Personnel
Pres: John Joyce
Founded: 1968
General interest publications; specialize in sign
language & newspapers.
ISBN Prefix(es): 0-913072
Number of titles published annually: 10 Print
Total Titles: 35 CD-ROM; 2 Online; 2 E-Book; 2
Audio
Imprints: Joyce Media Inc

Judaica Press Inc
123 Ditmas Ave, Brooklyn, NY 11218
SAN: 204-9856
Tel: 718-972-6200 *Toll Free Tel:* 800-972-6201
Fax: 718-972-6204
E-mail: info@judaicapress.com
Web Site: www.judaicapress.com
Key Personnel
Pres: Gloria Goldman
Man Ed: Norman Shapiro *E-mail:* nshapiro@
judaicapress.com
Sr Ed: Bonnie Goldman
Founded: 1963
Classic & contemporary Jewish literature in He-
brew & English.
ISBN Prefix(es): 0-910818; 1-880582
Number of titles published annually: 20 Print
Total Titles: 250 Print
Imprints: Zahava Publications
Foreign Rep(s): Lehmanns (UK/Europe)

Judson Press
Division of American Baptist Churches in the
USA
Subsidiary of National Ministries
588 N Gulph Rd, King of Prussia, PA 19406

Mailing Address: PO Box 851, Valley Forge, PA 19482-0851 SAN: 201-0348
Tel: 610-768-2118 *Toll Free Tel:* 800-458-3766
Fax: 610-768-2441
Web Site: www.judsonpress.com
Key Personnel
Assoc Publr: Linda Peavy *Tel:* 610-768-2114
Man Ed & Rts, Perms & ISBN: Randy Frame *Tel:* 610-768-2109 *E-mail:* randy.frame@abc-usa.org
Founded: 1824
Religion (Baptist & nondenominational Christian), African American, women & multicultural; cloth & paperback.
ISBN Prefix(es): 0-8170
Number of titles published annually: 20 Print; 2 Audio
Total Titles: 330 Print; 2 Audio
Foreign Rep(s): Christian Resources Wholesale (New Zealand); Openbook Publishers (Australia); Sperling Church Supply (Canada); Sperling Church Supply
Foreign Rights: Christian Resources Wholesale (New Zealand); OpenBook Publishers (Australia); Sperling Church Supply (Canada)

§Juice Gallery Multimedia
Box 151, Chino Hills, CA 91709
Tel: 909-597-0791 *Fax:* 909-597-0791
E-mail: info@juicegallery.com
Web Site: www.juicegallery.com
Key Personnel
Pres: Dan Titus
Founded: 1992
Business opportunity programs for people wishing to start a restaurant; smoothies, gourmet coffee, wraps, bagels & tea.
ISBN Prefix(es): 1-58291
Number of titles published annually: 4 Print; 3 CD-ROM
Total Titles: 16 Print; 8 CD-ROM
Imprints: Venture Marketing
Membership(s): Publishers Marketing Association; Small Publishers Association of North America

Jump at the Sun
Imprint of Hyperion Books for Children
114 Fifth Ave, New York, NY 10011
Tel: 212-633-4400 *Fax:* 212-633-4809
Web Site: www.disney.com
Key Personnel
Exec Ed: Garen Thomas
Edit Dir: Jackie Carter
Books celebrating the African-American experience & culture.
ISBN Prefix(es): 0-7868
Number of titles published annually: 15 Print
Total Titles: 100 Print
Divisions: The Walt Disney Co

Justin, Charles & Co, Publishers
20 Park Plaza, Suite 909, Boston, MA 02116
Tel: 617-426-4406 *Fax:* 617-426-4408
E-mail: info@justincharlesbooks.com
Web Site: www.justincharlesbooks.com
Key Personnel
Publr: Stephen P Hull
Assoc Ed: Carmen Mitchell *E-mail:* carmen@justincharlesbooks.com
Field Ed (UK): Kim Hjelmgaard *Tel:* (011) 781-205-4592
Mktg & Publicity Coord: Karen Conner
Founded: 2002
Adult trade fiction & nonfiction.
ISBN Prefix(es): 1-932112
Number of titles published annually: 13 Print
Total Titles: 7 Print
Imprints: Kate's Mystery Books
Sales Office(s): National Book Network, 4501 Forbes Blvd, Suite 200, Lanham, MD 20706
Tel: 301-459-3366 *Fax:* 301-429-5746

Foreign Office(s): BCM Box 6913, London WC1N 3XX, United Kingdom, Contact: Kim Hjelmgaard *Tel:* (011) 781-205-4592 *E-mail:* kim@justincharlesbooks.com
Foreign Rights: Steve Hull
Orders to: National Book Network, PO Box 190, Blue Ridge Summit, PA 17214 *Toll Free Tel:* 800-462-6420
Returns: National Book Network, PO Box 190, Blue Ridge Summit, PA 17214
Shipping Address: National Book Network *Toll Free Tel:* 800-462-6420
Warehouse: National Book Network, PO Box 190, Blue Ridge Summit, PA 17214 *Toll Free Tel:* 800-462-6420

JustUs & Associates
1420 NW Gilman, No 2154, Issaquah, WA 98027-7001
Tel: 425-391-8371 *Fax:* 425-392-1919
E-mail: justus@speakeasy.org
Web Site: www.horary.com
Key Personnel
Pres: Carol A Wiggers
Founded: 1983
Periodicals & journals on astrology.
ISBN Prefix(es): 1-878935
Number of titles published annually: 50 Print
Total Titles: 150 Print

§Kabbalah Publishing
155 E 48 St, New York, NY 10017
Tel: 212-644-0025 *Toll Free Tel:* 866-524-8723 *Fax:* 212-317-1264
E-mail: ny@kabbalah.com
Web Site: www.kabbalah.com
Key Personnel
President: Rav S P Berg
VP: Karen Berg
Dir: Michael Berg
Mktg Dir: Ruth Wagner *E-mail:* ruth.wagner@kabbalah.com
Founded: 1972
Dedicated to bringing the world's oldest & deepest treasury of spiritual wisdom.
Number of titles published annually: 5 Print; 2 CD-ROM; 2 Online; 2 E-Book; 2 Audio
Total Titles: 20 Print; 3 CD-ROM; 2 Online; 4 E-Book; 4 Audio
Branch Office(s)
1062 S Robertson Blvd, Los Angeles, CA 90035, Contact: Michal Berg *Tel:* 310-657-5404 *Fax:* 310-657-7774 *E-mail:* michal.berg@kabbalah.com
Foreign Rights: Linda Michaels Ltd
Billing Address: 1062 S Robertson Blvd, Los Angeles, CA 90035, Contact: Leah Arnan *Tel:* 310-657-5404 *Fax:* 310-657-7774 *E-mail:* leah.arnan@kabbalah.com

Kabel Publishers
11225 Huntover Dr, Rockville, MD 20852
Tel: 301-468-6463 *Toll Free Tel:* 800-543-3167 *Fax:* 301-468-6463
E-mail: kabelcomp@erols.com
Web Site: www.erols.com/kabelcomp/index2.html
Key Personnel
Pres: K B Absolon
VP: J Aker
Founded: 1985
Publish primarily scholarly books. Among those considered for publication; history, textbooks, poetry, medical, art, philosophy, science, statistics & foreign language.
ISBN Prefix(es): 1-57529; 0-930329
Number of titles published annually: 6 Print
Total Titles: 150 Print

Kaeden Corp
PO Box 16190, Rocky River, OH 44116-0190
Tel: 440-617-1400 *Toll Free Tel:* 800-890-7323
Fax: 440-617-1403

E-mail: info@kaeden.com
Web Site: www.kaeden.com
Key Personnel
Pres: Craig Urmston *E-mail:* curmston@kaeden.com
Sales Mgr: Linda Smalley *E-mail:* lsmalley@kaeden.com
Founded: 1990
Books for emergent, early & fluent readers, Pre-K, grades 1 & 2 including ESL, reading recovery & guided reading programs.
ISBN Prefix(es): 1-879835; 1-57874
Number of titles published annually: 8 Print
Total Titles: 126 Print
Imprints: Kaeden Books
Membership(s): AAP; International Reading Association; National Council of Teachers of English; Reading Recovery Council of North America

Kalimat Press
1600 Sawtelle Blvd, Suite 310, Los Angeles, CA 90025
Tel: 310-479-5668 (edit) *Fax:* 310-477-2840
E-mail: kalimatp@aol.com
Web Site: www.kalimat.com
Key Personnel
Man Ed: Anthony Lee *E-mail:* member700@aol.com
Founded: 1978
Baha'i books, academic books.
ISBN Prefix(es): 0-9933770; 1-890688
Number of titles published annually: 6 Print
Total Titles: 90 Print
Imprints: Highborn Lady Press
Distributed by Baha'i Distribution Service
Distributor for Century Press; Oneworld; George Ronald
Billing Address: Ware-Pak, 2427 Bond St, University Park, IL 60466, Contact: Rhonda Bouchard *Toll Free Tel:* 800-788-4067 *Fax:* 708-534-7803 *E-mail:* orders@kalimat.com
Orders to: Ware-Pak, 2427 Bond St, University Park, IL 60466, Contact: Rhonda Bouchard *Toll Free Tel:* 800-788-4067 *Fax:* 708-534-7803 *E-mail:* orders@kalimat.com
Returns: Ware-Pak, 2427 Bond St, University Park, IL 60466 *Toll Free Tel:* 800-788-4067 *Fax:* 708-534-7803 *E-mail:* orders@kalimat.com
Shipping Address: Ware-Pak, 2427 Bond St, University Park, IL 60466
Warehouse: Ware-Pak, 2427 Bond St, University Park, IL 60466 *Tel:* 708-587-4118; 708-534-2600 *Fax:* 708-534-7803 *E-mail:* orders@kalimat.com
Distribution Center: Ware-Pak, 2427 Bond St, University Park, IL 60466 *Tel:* 708-587-4118; 708-534-2600 *Fax:* 708-534-7803 *E-mail:* orders@kalimat.com
Membership(s): Publishers Marketing Association; Society for Scholarly Publishing

Kalmbach Publishing Co
Division of The Writer Inc
21027 Crossroads Circle, Waukesha, WI 53187
Mailing Address: PO Box 1612, Waukesha, WI 53187-1612
Tel: 262-796-8776 *Toll Free Tel:* 800-533-6644 *Fax:* 262-796-1615 (sales & cust serv)
Web Site: www.kalmbach.com
Key Personnel
Pres: Gerald Boettcher
VP, Mktg: Michael R Stephens
Publr: James J Slocum
Ed-in-Chief: Dick Christianson
Circ Mgr: Michael Barbee; Cathy Cramer
Libn: Nancy Bartol
Founded: 1934
Special interest books, calendars & magazines in the astronomy, hobby & collectibles market.

ISBN Prefix(es): 0-89024; 0-913135; 0-89778; 0-933168
Number of titles published annually: 20 Print
Total Titles: 200 Print
Imprints: Greenberg Books; Kalmbach Books
Foreign Rep(s): Fortress Publications (Canada)

Kamehameha Schools Press
Division of Kamehameha Schools
1887 Makuakane St, Honolulu, HI 96817-1887
Tel: 808-842-8719 *Fax:* 808-842-8895
E-mail: kspress@ksbe.edu
Web Site: kspress.ksbe.edu
Key Personnel
Dir: Henry Bennett *E-mail:* hebennet@ksbe.edu
Ed: Waimea Williams *E-mail:* wawillia@ksbe.edu
Prog Admin: Lani Abrigana *E-mail:* laabriga@ksbe.edu
Founded: 1933
Book & poster publishing in the areas of Hawaiian history, Hawaiian studies, Hawaiian language & Hawaiian culture.
ISBN Prefix(es): 0-87336
Number of titles published annually: 5 Print
Total Titles: 35 Print; 1 CD-ROM; 1 Audio
Imprints: Kamehameha Schools; Kamehameha Schools Bishop Estate; Kamehameha Schools Press
Distributed by Bess Press; University of Hawaii Press
Membership(s): Hawaii Book Publishers Association; Publishers Marketing Association; Small Publishers Association of North America

Kane/Miller Book Publishers
PO Box 8515, La Jolla, CA 92038-8515
SAN: 295-8945
Tel: 858-456-0540 *Toll Free Tel:* 800-968-1930
Fax: 858-456-9641
E-mail: info@kanemiller.com
Web Site: www.kanemiller.com
Key Personnel
Publr: Kira Lynn
Mktg Mgr: Sandra La Brie
Sales Mgr: Byron Parnell
Founded: 1984
Translated foreign juvenile picture books: fiction & nonfiction.
ISBN Prefix(es): 0-916291; 1-929132
Number of titles published annually: 20 Print
Total Titles: 80 Print
Imprints: Cranky Nell Books; Creative Nell Books; Curious Nell Books
Distributed by Georgetown Publications Inc (Canada)
Foreign Rep(s): Athena Productions (Central America, Latin America, South America, Southeast Asia)
Shipping Address: 7946 Ivanhoe Ave, Suite 203, La Jolla, CA 92037, Contact: Sandra La Brie
Warehouse: Mercedes Distribution Center, Brooklyn Navy Yard, Bldg 3, Brooklyn, NY 11205
Membership(s): ABA; ALA; Association of Booksellers for Children; United States Board on Books for Young People

The Kane Press
240 W 35 St, Suite 300, New York, NY 10001-2506
Tel: 212-268-1435 *Fax:* 212-268-2044
Web Site: www.kanepress.com
Key Personnel
Publr: Joanne Kane
Edit Dir: Patricia Boudreau
Sales Dir: Margo Gunsser *E-mail:* mgunsser@kanepress.com
Founded: 1996
ISBN Prefix(es): 1-57565
Number of titles published annually: 12 Print
Total Titles: 70 Print
Warehouse: W A Book Service, 26 Ranick Rd, Hauppauge, NY 11788

Kaplan Publishing
Affiliate of Simon & Schuster Adult Publishing Group
1230 Avenue of the Americas, New York, NY 10020
Fax: 212-632-4973
Web Site: www.simonsays.com
Key Personnel
VP & Publr: Maureen McMahon *Tel:* 212-698-7077 *Fax:* 212-632-4973
Publg Mgr: Beth Grupper *Tel:* 212-698-7406 *Fax:* 212-632-4973
Kaplan Publishing provides a complete range of test preparation & study guides as well as college & graduate school admissions, career development & parent involvement books.
ISBN Prefix(es): 0-684; 0-7432
Number of titles published annually: 90 Print; 9 CD-ROM; 5 E-Book
Total Titles: 180 Print; 10 CD-ROM; 9 E-Book

Kar-Ben Publishing
Division of Lerner Publishing Group
1251 Washington Ave N, Minneapolis, MN 55401
Tel: 612-332-3344 *Toll Free Tel:* 800-4-KARBEN (452-7236) *Toll Free Fax:* 800-332-1132
E-mail: kar-ben@lernerbooks.com
Web Site: www.karben.com
Key Personnel
Edit: Judyth Groner
Dir: Madeline Wikler
Founded: 1976
Jewish books, calendars & cassettes; preschool & primary, activity books, holiday books, folktales, services.
ISBN Prefix(es): 0-930494; 0-929371; 1-58013
Number of titles published annually: 12 Print
Total Titles: 100 Print; 3 Audio
Foreign Rep(s): Bravo (UK); Mazeltov Books (Australia)

Kazi Publications Inc
3023 W Belmont Ave, Chicago, IL 60618
Tel: 773-267-7001 *Fax:* 773-267-7002
E-mail: info@kazi.org
Web Site: www.kazi.org/
Key Personnel
Pres: Liaquat Ali
Mktg Dir: Mary Bakhtiar
Founded: 1976
Non-profit organization; print, publish & distribute; Islamic books in Arabic, English & Urdu language.
ISBN Prefix(es): 0-935782; 1-56744; 0-933511; 1-871031
Number of titles published annually: 30 Print
Total Titles: 400 Print
Imprints: Abjad Books; Library of Islam
Distributor for ABC Intl Group Inc; Foundation for Traditional Studies; Great Books of the Islamic World; QIBLAH Books; Zero Productions

KC Publications Inc
PO Box 94558, Las Vegas, NV 89193-4558
SAN: 201-0364
Tel: 702-433-3415 *Toll Free Tel:* 800-626-9673
Fax: 702-433-3420
E-mail: kcp@kcpublications.com
Web Site: www.kcpublications.com
Key Personnel
Pres: Dennis Harper
Publr: K C Den Dooven
Founded: 1964
Books on national parks, monuments & recreation areas, other scenic areas, southwestern Indian arts & crafts, tribes & ceremonials, western pioneers; mail order books.
ISBN Prefix(es): 0-916122; 0-88714
Number of titles published annually: 8 Print

Total Titles: 130 Print; 11 Audio
Shipping Address: 3245 E Patrick Lane, Suite A, Las Vegas, NV 89120-3416

§J J Keller & Associates, Inc
3003 W Breezewood Lane, Neenah, WI 54957
Mailing Address: PO Box 368, Neenah, WI 54957-0368
Tel: 920-722-2848 *Toll Free Tel:* 800-327-6868
Toll Free Fax: 800-727-7516
E-mail: sales@jjkeller.com
Web Site: www.jjkeller.com/jjk
Key Personnel
Pres: Robert L Keller
Exec VP: James J Keller
Sr VP, Pubns & Prods: Terence J Quirk
VP, Sales: Mark Tremble
Corp Edit Mgr: Webb Shaw
Mktg Communs Mgr: Jean Bilitz *E-mail:* jbilitz@jjkeller.com
Publish regulatory compliance, "best practices" & training products dealing with occupational safety, job safety, environment & industry & motor-carrier (trucking) operations. On demand, we publish in print, CD-ROM, intranet & Internet formats.
ISBN Prefix(es): 1-57943; 0-934674; 1-877798
Number of titles published annually: 7 Print
Total Titles: 194 Print; 96 CD-ROM; 1 Online
Distributed by Amacom Division of American Management Division
Distributor for Chilton Book Co; International Air Transport Association; National Archives & Records Administration; National Institute of Occupational Safety & Health; Office of the Federal Register; Research & Special Programs Administration of the US Department of Transportation; John Wiley & Sons Inc

Kelsey Street Press
50 Northgate, Berkeley, CA 94708
Tel: 510-845-2260 *Fax:* 510-548-9185
E-mail: info@kelseyst.com
Web Site: www.kelseyst.com
Key Personnel
Dir: Rena Rosenwasser
Founded: 1974
Nonprofit press, publish poetry & short fiction by women & collaborations between poets & artists.
ISBN Prefix(es): 0-932716
Number of titles published annually: 4 Print
Total Titles: 48 Print
Orders to: Small Press Distribution, 1341 Seventh St, Berkeley, CA 94710 *Tel:* 510-524-1668 *E-mail:* orders@spdbook.org
Membership(s): Council of Literary Magazines & Presses

Kendall/Hunt Publishing Co
Subsidiary of Westmark Enterprises Inc
4050 Westmark Dr, Dubuque, IA 52002
SAN: 203-9184
Mailing Address: PO Box 1840, Dubuque, IA 52004-1840
Tel: 563-589-1000 *Toll Free Tel:* 800-228-0810 (orders only) *Fax:* 563-589-1114
Toll Free Fax: 800-772-9165
Web Site: www.kendallhunt.com
Key Personnel
Pres: Mark C Falb
Prodn Ed & ISBN Contact: Alfred C Grisanti
Dist Mgr: Tim Beitzel
Sr VP, Coll Div & Prof, Educ Div: Thomas W Gantz
Div Exec VP, K-12: Chad Chandler
Founded: 1969
ISBN Prefix(es): 0-8403; 0-7872
Number of titles published annually: 1,500 Print
Total Titles: 5,000 Print; 8 CD-ROM; 5,000 Online; 5,000 E-Book; 7 Audio
Warehouse: 1111 Purina Dr, Dubuque, IA 52001

Kennedy Information
Division of Kennedy Information LLC
One Phoenix Mill Lane, 5th fl, Peterborough, NH 03458
Tel: 603-924-0900 *Toll Free Tel:* 800-531-0007
Fax: 603-924-4460
E-mail: office@kennedyinfo.com
Web Site: www.kennedyinfo.com
Key Personnel
Pres & CEO: Joseph Bremner *E-mail:* jbremner@kennedyinfo.com
Exec VP: Marshall Cooper *E-mail:* mcooper@kennedyinfo.com
Dir, Mktg & Conference Planning: Carolyn Edwards *Tel:* 603-924-0900 ext 612 *E-mail:* cedwards@kennedyinfo.com
Group Publr: David Beck *E-mail:* dbeck@kennedyinfo.com
Founded: 1970
Newsletters, special reports, books, directories of management consultants, executive recruiters & outplacement consultants.
ISBN Prefix(es): 0-916654; 1-885922
Number of titles published annually: 20 Print; 1 CD-ROM; 3 Online
Total Titles: 50 Print; 1 CD-ROM
Imprints: Consultants News; Consulting Magazine; Executive Recruiter News; Global IT Services; Investor Relations Newsletter; Management Consultant International; Recruiting Trends

Kensington Publishing Corp
850 Third Ave, New York, NY 10022
SAN: 207-9860
Tel: 212-407-1500 *Toll Free Tel:* 800-221-2647
Fax: 212-935-0699
Web Site: www.kensingtonbooks.com
Key Personnel
Chmn of the Bd: Walter Zacharius
Pres: Steven Zacharius
VP & Publr: Laurie Parkin
VP & Dir, Fin: Michael Rosamilia
Ed-in-Chief, Citadel Press: Gene Brissie
Ed-in-Chief, Kensington: Michaela Hamilton
MIS Dir: Jonathan Cohen
Creative Dir: Janice Rossi
Edit Dir: Kate Duffy; John Scognamiglio; Karen Thomas
Prodn Dir: Joyce Kaplan
Dir, Publicity & PR: Joan Schulhafer
Gen Counsel: Barbara Bennett
Cust Serv: Jessica McLean
Subs Rts Mgr: Meryl Earl
Founded: 1975
Mass market paperback originals: romance, fiction, westerns, espionage, general nonfiction, men's adventure, hardcover reprints, fiction & nonfiction, trade paperbacks, hardcovers & originals.
ISBN Prefix(es): 0-89083; 0-8217
Number of titles published annually: 600 Print
Total Titles: 9,000 Print
Imprints: Brava; Citadel; Da Fina; Kensington Books; Pinnacle Books; Lyle Stuart; Zebra Books
Foreign Rep(s): Time Warner
Warehouse: Penguin Putnam

Kent State University Press
PO Box 5190, Kent, OH 44242-0001
SAN: 201-0437
Mailing Address: 307 Lowry Hall, Terrace Dr, Kent, OH 44242
Tel: 330-672-7913; 330-672-8097 (sales office)
Toll Free Tel: 800-247-6553 (orders) *Fax:* 330-672-3104
Web Site: www.kentstateuniversitypress.com
Key Personnel
Dir & Rts & Perms: Will Underwood
Acqs Ed: Joanna Craig
Mktg Mgr: Susan L Cash *E-mail:* scash@kent.edu

Sec & Journals Circ Mgr: Sandra Clark
Founded: 1965
Scholarly nonfiction, with emphasis on Civil War, military history, literary studies, archaeology, biography & Midwest regional.
ISBN Prefix(es): 0-87338
Number of titles published annually: 30 Print
Total Titles: 360 Print
Imprints: Black Squirrel Books
Foreign Rep(s): East-West Export Books (Australia, Asia, Pacific); Eurospan Ltd (Africa, UK, Europe, Middle East); Scholarly Book Services (Canada)
Warehouse: Bookmasters Inc, 30 Amberwood Pkwy, Ashland, OH 44805, Contact: Beth Boeh *Tel:* 419-281-1802 *Toll Free Tel:* 800-247-6553 *Fax:* 419-281-6883

Kessinger Publishing Co
PO Box 4587, Whitefish, MT 59937
E-mail: message@kessinger.net
Web Site: www.kessinger.net
Key Personnel
Pres: Roger A Kessinger
Founded: 1988
Alchemy, free masonry, ancient civilization, astrology, Bible study, comparative religion, Egyptology, esotericism, gnosticism, health, hermetics, magic, metaphysical, mysticism, Rosicrucian; publish only own work.
ISBN Prefix(es): 0-922802; 1-56459; 0-7661; 1-4192; 1-4191
Number of titles published annually: 5,000 Print; 5,000 E-Book

§Key Curriculum Press
Affiliate of Springer Science & Business Media
1150 65 St, Emeryville, CA 94608
Tel: 510-595-7000 *Toll Free Tel:* 800-995-6284
Fax: 510-595-7040 *Toll Free Fax:* 800-541-2442
E-mail: customer.service@keypress.com
Web Site: www.keypress.com
Key Personnel
Pres: Steve Rasmussen
CFO: Joel A Gingold *E-mail:* jgingold@keypress.com
Exec Asst: Michelle Kolota *Tel:* 510-595-7000 ext 136 *E-mail:* mkolota@keypress.com
Founded: 1971 (Founded as Key Curriculum Project; In 1988 changed to Key Curriculum Press)
High school math textbooks.
ISBN Prefix(es): 0-913684; 1-55953
Number of titles published annually: 140 Print; 20 CD-ROM
Total Titles: 450 Print; 20 CD-ROM; 6 Online
Imprints: Key College Publishing
Subsidiaries: KCP Technologies Inc
Divisions: Key College Publishing
Distributor for Key College Publishing
Foreign Rep(s): Business Advantage Development (Denmark, Finland, Norway & Sweden); Chartwell-Yorke Mathematics Software & Books (England, Northern Ireland, Scotland); Creative Learning Systems (South Africa); Michael deVilliers (South Africa); Dreyfous & Association (Dominican Republic, Puerto Rico); EdSoft (Australia, New Zealand); Grupo Editorial Iberoamerica (Latin America); Instituto Tecnologico de Costa Rica (ITCR) (Costa Rica); Learning Interactive Pte Ltd (Brunei, Indonesia, Malaysia, Singapore, Thailand); McGraw-Hill Ryerson Ltd (Canada); Media Direct (Italy); QED Books (England, Northern Ireland, Scotland); Rhombus (Belgium); Sigma Communications (West Indies); Spectrum Educational Supplies Ltd (Canada); Springer-Verlag GmbH & Co (Europe exc UK, India, Middle East); Springer-Verlag H K Ltd (Brunei, Indonesia, Malaysia, People's Republic of China, Philippines, South Korea, Thailand, Vietnam); Springer-Verlag Iberia SA (Por-

tugal, Spain); Springer-Verlag Tokyo/Eastern Book Service (Japan); Tec-Quest SA (Mexico); Virtual Image (Australia, New Zealand); W&G Australia Pty Ltd
Foreign Rights: Centre for Educational Technology (Israel); Cheneliere/McGraw-Hill (French Canada); Institute of New Technologies in Education (Russia); JasonTech Inc (Korea); L&R Uddannelse (Denmark); Mathlove (Korea); People's Education Press (People's Republic of China); Pliroforiki Technognosia (Greece); Yano Electric Co Ltd (Japan)
Membership(s): National Council of Teachers of Mathematics

Kids Can Press Ltd
Subsidiary of Corus Entertainment
2250 Military Rd, Tonawanda, NY 14150
SAN: 115-4001
Tel: 416-925-5437 (Toronto, ON, Canada)
Toll Free Tel: 800-265-0884; 866-481-5827 (orders) *Fax:* 416-960-5437 (Toronto, ON, Canada)
E-mail: info@kidscan.com; lfyman@kidscan.com (orders)
Web Site: www.kidscanpress.com
Key Personnel
Publr: Valerie Hussey *E-mail:* vhussey@kidscan.com
VP & Assoc Publr: Karen Boersma *E-mail:* kboersma@kidscan.com
VP, Rts & Licensing: Barbara Howson *E-mail:* bhowson@kidscan.com
US Sales: Rick Walker *E-mail:* rwalker@kidscan.com
US Mktg: Fred Horler *E-mail:* fhorler@kidscan.com
Founded: 1976
Children's & young adult books.
ISBN Prefix(es): 0-919964; 1-55074; 1-55337
Number of titles published annually: 70 Print
Total Titles: 472 Print
Branch Office(s)
29 Birch Ave, Toronto, ON M4V 1E2, Canada
Tel: 416-925-5437 *Toll Free Tel:* 800-265-0884 *Fax:* 416-960-5437 *E-mail:* info@kidscan.com
Web Site: www.kidscanpress.com
Membership(s): Children's Book Council

Kidsbooks Inc
230 Fifth Ave, Suite 1710, New York, NY 10001
SAN: 666-3729
Tel: 212-685-4444 *Fax:* 212-889-1122
Web Site: www.kidsbooks.com
Key Personnel
CEO: Vic Cavallaro *E-mail:* vcavallaro@kidsbooks.com
Founded: 1986
Juvenile & young adult trade & mass market paperback & hardcover.
ISBN Prefix(es): 0-942025; 1-56156
Number of titles published annually: 75 Print
Total Titles: 700 Print
Imprints: Masterwork Books; Tiger Books
Foreign Rep(s): Booklink (Europe)
Foreign Rights: Booklink Ltd (England)

Kinship Books
781 Rte 308, Rhinebeck, NY 12572
Tel: 845-876-4200 (orders); 845-876-4592
Toll Free Tel: 800-249-1109 (orders)
E-mail: kinshipbooks@cs.com
Web Site: www.kinshipny.com
Key Personnel
Bookkeeping & Cust Sales: Susan Kelly Fitzgerald
Founded: 1967
Books of geneological source information, directory & journals.
ISBN Prefix(es): 1-56012
Number of titles published annually: 40 Print
Total Titles: 202 Print

§Kirkbride Bible Co Inc
335 W Ninth St, Indianapolis, IN 46202
Mailing Address: PO Box 606, Indianapolis, IN 46206-0606
Tel: 317-633-1900 *Toll Free Tel:* 800-428-4385
Fax: 317-633-1444
E-mail: sales@kirkbride.com
Web Site: www.kirkbride.com
Key Personnel
Pres: J Marshall Gage *E-mail:* marshall@kirkbride.com
Founded: 1915
Bible publisher, also children's Bible.
ISBN Prefix(es): 0-88707
Number of titles published annually: 7 Print
Total Titles: 3 CD-ROM
Advertising Agency: Canal Advertising

Kirkland's Press
101 Mount Rock Rd, Newville, PA 17241
SAN: 152-6324
Tel: 717-776-4232
Web Site: www.kirklandspress.com
Key Personnel
Dir: Ronald R Seagrave *E-mail:* seagraver@earthlink.net
Ed: Pia S Seagrave, PhD
Founded: 1995
Non-profit academic book publisher.
ISBN Prefix(es): 1-887901
Number of titles published annually: 14 Print
Total Titles: 54 Print

Kitemaug Press
229 Mohawk Dr, Spartanburg, SC 29301-2827
SAN: 166-395X
Tel: 864-576-3338
E-mail: kitemaugpresswhq@msn.com
Key Personnel
Prop: Frank J Anderson
Founded: 1965
Printer, binder, publisher & distributor of miniature books.
Number of titles published annually: 4 Print
Total Titles: 36 Print
Membership(s): Amalgamated Printers' Association; American Printing History Association; Guild of Bookworkers; Miniature Book Society

Kiva Publishing Inc
21731 E Buckskin Dr, Walnut, CA 91789
Tel: 909-595-6833 *Toll Free Tel:* 800-634-5482
Fax: 909-860-5424
E-mail: kivapub@aol.com
Web Site: www.kivapub.com
Key Personnel
Publr: Stephen W Hill
Founded: 1993
Publish Native American & Southwest regional books & cards.
ISBN Prefix(es): 1-885772
Number of titles published annually: 5 Print
Total Titles: 25 Print
Distributor for Clear Light Books; Petrified Forest Museum Association; San Diego Museum of Man
Membership(s): New Mexico Publishers Association; Publishers Association of the West; Publishers Marketing Association

B Klein Publications
6037 W Atlantic Ave, Delray Beach, FL 33482
SAN: 210-7554
Tel: 561-496-3316 *Fax:* 561-496-5546
Key Personnel
Pres & Rts & Perms: Bernard Klein
Founded: 1953
Subscription & mail order; business & educational reference books & directories.
ISBN Prefix(es): 0-87340
Number of titles published annually: 6 Print
Total Titles: 12 Print

Klutz
Division of Scholastic Corp
455 Portage Ave, Palo Alto, CA 94306
Tel: 650-857-0888 *Fax:* 650-857-9110
Web Site: www.klutz.com
Key Personnel
VP, Sales: Kevin Hunt
VP, Mktg: Kathleen Watson
Chief Creative Officer: John Cassidy
Founded: 1977
Creator of innovative activity products for kids that stimulate growth through creativity. Klutz products combine clear instructions with everything you need to give kids a hands-on experience ranging from the artistic to the scientific & beyond.
ISBN Prefix(es): 0-932592; 1-57054; 1-878257; 1-59174
Number of titles published annually: 20 Print
Total Titles: 130 Print
Foreign Rep(s): Blue Opal (Australia); Catapulta Childrens Entertainment (South America); Novelty Corp (Central America); Scholastic (Australia & New Zealand, UK, Canada, Hong Kong)
Warehouse: 2850 Kifer Rd, Santa Clara, CA 95051

Kluwer Academic Publishers
101 Philip Dr, Assinippi Park, Norwell, MA 02061
SAN: 211-481X
Tel: 781-871-6600 *Fax:* 781-871-6528; 781-681-9045 (cust serv)
E-mail: kluwer@wkap.com
Web Site: www.wkap.nl
Key Personnel
CEO: Peter Hendriks
Dir, Lib Rel: Susan Pastore
Dir, Trade Rel: M Stephen Dane *E-mail:* steve.dane@wkap.com
Publg Dir, Physical Sciences: Zvi Ruder
Publg Dir, Engg: Carl Harris
Man Ed: Claire Stanton
Cont & Busn Mgr: Edward F Woods
Cust Serv Dir: Heather Dana
HR Mgr: Mary Morris
Founded: 1972
Scientific, technical, medical, scholarly, business & professional books & journals, materials science.
ISBN Prefix(es): 0-306; 0-7923; 1-402
Number of titles published annually: 1,200 Print
Total Titles: 18,000 Print; 12 CD-ROM; 1,200 Online; 600 E-Book
Imprints: Kluwer Academic/Plenum Publishers; Kluwer Academic/Plenum Publishers/New York
Divisions: Kluwer Academic Publishers/Boston; Kluwer Academic Publishers/Dordrecht; Kluwer Academic/Plenum Publishers/New York

Kluwer Law International (KLI), see Aspen Publishers, A Wolters Kluwer Company

Allen A Knoll Publishers
200 W Victoria St, 2nd fl, Suite A, Santa Barbara, CA 93101-3627
SAN: 299-0539
Tel: 805-564-3377 *Toll Free Tel:* 800-777-7623
Fax: 805-966-6657
E-mail: bookinfo@knollpublishers.com
Web Site: www.knollpublishers.com
Key Personnel
Lib Sales & Mktg Dir: Abby Schott
Shipping & Receiving Mgr: Rose Mary Smith
Accts: Solera Duguid
Founded: 1991
Books for intelligent people who read for fun. No unsol mss.
ISBN Prefix(es): 0-9627297; 1-888310
Number of titles published annually: 5 Print
Total Titles: 37 Print

Returns: 777 Silver Spur Rd, No 116, Rolling Hills Estates, CA 90274 SAN: 299-0520
Shipping Address: 777 Silver Spur Rd, No 116, Rolling Hills Estates, CA 90274 SAN: 299-0520

Alfred A Knopf
Subsidiary of Random House Inc
1745 Broadway, New York, NY 10019
SAN: 202-5825
Tel: 212-751-2600 *Toll Free Tel:* 800-638-6460
Fax: 212-572-2593
Web Site: www.randomhouse.com/knopf
Cable: KNOPF NEW YORK
Key Personnel
Pres & Ed-in-Chief, Knopf Publg Group: Sonny Mehta
Exec VP & COO, Knopf Publg Group: Anthony Chirico
Exec VP, Publg: Patricia Johnson
Sr VP & Exec Dir, Publicity, Promo & Media: Paul Bogaards
VP, Assoc Publr & Sr Ed: Victoria Wilson
VP & Sr Ed: Judith Jones
VP & Ed-at-Large: Gary Fisketjon
VP & Sr Ed: Jonathan Segal; Ashbel Green; Robin Desser
VP, Sr Ed & Dir, Intl Rts: Carol B Janeway
VP, Prodn: Andrew Hughes
VP & Dir, Art Jacket: Carol Carson
VP & Dir, Interior Design & Desktop: Peter Andersen
VP, Adv: Nina Bourne
VP & Dir, Publicity: Nicholas Latimer
VP & Dir, Sales Promos/Series Publicity: Anne Lise Spitzer
Dir, Promo: Gabrielle T Brooks
Dir, Sales Mktg: Amanda Kauff
Assoc Dir, Publicity: Kathryn Zuckerman
Man Ed: Katherine Hourigan
Dir, Foreign & Dom Subs Rts: Sean Yule
Subs Rts (Book Club, Serial & Performance): Victoria Gerken
Mgr, Foreign Rts: Suzanne Smith
Asst Mgr, Foreign Rts: Stephanie Katz
Sr Ed, Poetry: Deborah Garrison
Sr Ed: Jane Garrett
Ed: Ann Close; Jordan Pavlin; George Andreou
Dir, Busn Opers: Justine LeCates
ISBN Contact: Brigid Wry
Founded: 1915
Fiction, nonfiction, poetry, cookbooks & illustrated books.
Random House Inc & its publishing entities are not accepting unsol submissions, proposals, mss, or submission queries via e-mail at this time.
ISBN Prefix(es): 0-02; 0-679; 1-4000
Imprints: Everyman's Library; Knopf Travel Guides; National Audubon Guides
Foreign Rights: Arts & Licensing International Inc (China); Caroline van Gelderen Agency (Netherlands); DRT International (Korea); Graal Ltd (Poland); Harris/Elon Agency (Israel); JLM Literary Agency (Greece); Karin Schindler (Brazil); Katai & Bolza (Hungary); Licht & Licht (Scandinavia); Literarni Agentura (Czech Republic); Michelle Lapautre (France); Roberto Santachiara (Italy); The English Agency (Japan)
Advertising Agency: Bennett Book Advertising Inc
Warehouse: 400 Hahn Rd, Westminster, MD 21157

Kodansha America Inc
Affiliate of Kodansha Ltd (Japan)
575 Lexington Ave, 23rd fl, New York, NY 10022
SAN: 201-0526
Tel: 917-322-6200 *Fax:* 212-935-6929
E-mail: info@kodanshaamerica.com
Web Site: www.kodansha-intl.com

Key Personnel
Sr VP: Yoichi Kimata
Dir, Mktg & Sales: Sydney Webber
Founded: 1966
Publishes hardcover & paperback books in English on international cultures, history, anthropology, science, religion, health, language, cookbooks, travel & memoir.
ISBN Prefix(es): 0-87011; 0-87040; 1-56836; 4-88996; 4-81709; 0-47700
Number of titles published annually: 75 Print
Total Titles: 800 Print
Imprints: Kodansha Globe
Foreign Office(s): Kodansha International Ltd, 1-17-14 Otowa, Bunkyo-ku, Tokyo 112-8652, Japan, Pres: Sawako Noma *Tel:* 03-944-6493 *Fax:* 03-944-6394
Distributed by Oxford University Press
Distributor for Japan Publications Inc; Japan Publications Trading Co Inc; Nihon/Vogue
Foreign Rep(s): Bookwise International (Australia, New Zealand); Fitzhenry & Whiteside (Canada); Kinokuniya Book Stores Co Ltd (Thailand); Kinokuniya Book Stores of Singapore PTE Ltd (Singapore); Kinokuniya Bookstore Kuala Lumpur SDN BHD (Malaysia); Kinokuniya Lestari Indonesia Plaza Indonesia Store (Indonesia); Kodansha Europe Ltd (Europe)
Warehouse: Oxford University Press, 2001 Evans Rd, Cary, NC 27513 *Toll Free Tel:* 800-451-7556 *Fax:* 919-677-1303

William S Konecky Associates Inc
72 Ayers Pt Rd, Old Saybrook, CT 06475
Tel: 860-388-0878 *Fax:* 860-388-0273
Key Personnel
Publr: Sean Konecky *E-mail:* seankon@comcast.net
Founded: 1982
Hardcover art books & Civil War history, military history, biography.
ISBN Prefix(es): 1-56852
Number of titles published annually: 50 Print
Total Titles: 125 Print
Imprints: Konecky & Konecky; Tabard Press

KotaPress
PO Box 514, Vashon Island, WA 98070-0514
Tel: 206-251-6706
E-mail: editor@kotapress.com
Web Site: www.kotapress.com
Key Personnel
Ed-in-Chief: Kara L C Jones
Creative Dir: Hawk Jones
Founded: 1999
Expressive arts, small press, organization supporting authors exploring grief & healing thru poetry, prose, art, nonfiction & memoir.
ISBN Prefix(es): 1-929359
Number of titles published annually: 4 Print; 12 Online; 2 E-Book
Total Titles: 14 Print; 4 Online; 3 E-Book

H J Kramer Inc
PO Box 1082, Tiburon, CA 94920-7002
Tel: 415-435-5367 *Fax:* 415-435-5364
E-mail: hjkramer@jps.net
Web Site: www.newworldlibrary.com
Key Personnel
Pres: H J Kramer
Exec VP & Intl Rts: Linda Kramer
Mktg & Publicity: Monique Muhlenkamp
 E-mail: monique@newworldlibrary.com
Founded: 1984
Personal growth, self-help, spiritual growth, trade paperbacks & hardcovers; fully illustrated clothbound children's books (Starseed Press). Any correspondence regarding mss must be accompanied by an appropriately sized SASE.
ISBN Prefix(es): 0-915811; 1-932073
Number of titles published annually: 4 Print

Total Titles: 70 Print
Imprints: Starseed Press
Foreign Rep(s): Airlift Books (UK); Gemcraft Books (Australia); New Horizons (South Africa); Peaceful Living Publications (New Zealand); Publishers Group West Canada (Canada)
Orders to: Publisher Group West, 1700 Fourth St, Berkeley, CA 94710 *Toll Free Tel:* 800-788-3123 *Fax:* 510-528-3444
Distribution Center: Publishers Group West, 1170 Trademark Dr, Reno, NV 89511 *Tel:* 775-850-2500 *Fax:* 775-850-2501

Krause Publications
700 E State St, Iola, WI 54990
SAN: 202-6554
Tel: 715-445-4612 ext 365 *Toll Free Tel:* 800-258-0929; 888-457-2873 *Fax:* 715-445-4087
Web Site: www.krause.com *Telex:* 55-6461 KRAUSEPUB
Key Personnel
Founder: Chester L Krause
Pres: Roger Case
Exec VP, Sales: James Gleim
VP, Fin: Mark Arnett
Publr, Toys, Comics & Games: Mark Williams
Publr, Auto & Collector's Mart: Greg Smith
Publr, Sports & Outdoors: Hugh McAloon
Publr, Numis Trade: Rick Groth
Book Publr: Bill Krause
Lib Sales Dir: Phil Sexton
Book Sales Mgr: Michael Murphy
Promo: D'Ann Jackson
Prodn: Mary Lou Marshall
Intl Rts Contact: Laura Smith
Book Sales Asst: Betty Aanstad
Founded: 1952
Periodicals & books for collectors & hobbyists: numismatics, sports, old cars, outdoor, toys, comics, firearms, records, hunting, fishing, Wisconsin regional antiques, sewing, crafts, ceramics, quilting, stamps, antiques & model railroading.
ISBN Prefix(es): 0-930625; 0-87349; 0-87341; 0-87069; 0-89689; 1-58221; 0-8019
Number of titles published annually: 200 Print
Total Titles: 860 Print
Imprints: Antique Trader Books; Books Americana; Chilton Books; DBI Books; Quarto; Warman's
Distributor for AD Publishing; Antique Trader Books; Books Americana; DBI Books; Francis-Joseph Publications; Wallace-Homestead; Warman's
Foreign Rep(s): Bookmovers (Canada); Capricorn Link (Australia); David & Charles (UK & Europe); Forrester Books NZ Ltd (New Zealand); Phambili Agencies CC (South Africa); Marta Schooler (Asia, Latin America, Middle East)
See separate listing for:
Antique Trader Books
DBI Books

Kregel Publications
Division of Kregel Inc
733 Wealthy St SE, Grand Rapids, MI 49503-5553
SAN: 298-9115
Mailing Address: PO Box 2607, Grand Rapids, MI 49501-2607
Tel: 616-451-4775 *Toll Free Tel:* 800-733-2607 *Fax:* 616-451-9330
E-mail: kregelbooks@kregel.com
Web Site: www.kregelpublications.com
Key Personnel
Pres: James R Kregel *E-mail:* president@kregel.com
VP, Opers: Jerold W Kregel
Publr, Rts & Perms & Intl Rts: Dennis Hillman
Exec Dir, Sales & Mktg: David Hill *Tel:* 616-451-4775 ext 235 *E-mail:* dave@kregel.com
Mktg Mgr: Janyre Tromp

Founded: 1949
Evangelical Christian publications including devotionals, Bible study & reference.
ISBN Prefix(es): 0-8254
Number of titles published annually: 75 Print
Total Titles: 600 Print
Imprints: Editorial Portavoz; Kregel Academic & Professional; Kregel Classics; Kregel Kidzone
Distributor for Candle Books; Monarch Books
Foreign Rep(s): Christian Art Wholesale (South Africa); Christian Literature Crusade (Japan); R G Mitchell Family Books Ltd (Canada); Omega Distrib (New Zealand); John Ritchie Ltd (UK); Word of Life Press (Korea)
Membership(s): Evangelical Christian Publishers Association
See separate listing for:
Editorial Portavoz

Krieger Publishing Co
PO Box 9542, Melbourne, FL 32902-9542
SAN: 202-6562
Tel: 321-724-9542 *Toll Free Tel:* 800-724-0025 *Fax:* 321-951-3671
E-mail: info@krieger-publishing.com
Web Site: www.krieger-publishing.com *Cable:* KRIEGPUB MALABAR FLORIDA
Key Personnel
Pres: Donald E Krieger
CEO: Robert E Krieger
VP: Maxine D Krieger
Cust Serv: Dianne Struckmann
Founded: 1969
A scientific-technical publisher serving the college textbook market. Reprints & new titles: technical, science, psychology, geology, humanities, ecology, history, social sciences, engineering, mathematics, chemistry, adult educational, herpetology, space science.
ISBN Prefix(es): 0-88275; 0-89464; 0-89874; 1-57524
Number of titles published annually: 30 Print
Total Titles: 1,000 Print; 2 CD-ROM
Imprints: Anvil Series; Exploring Community History Series; Open Forum; Orbit Series; Professional Practices; Public History
Foreign Rep(s): DA Information Systems (Australia, New Zealand, Papua New Guinea); Eurospan (UK, Middle East)
Advertising Agency: Krieger Enterprises Inc
Shipping Address: 1725 Krieger Dr, Malabar, FL 32950

KTAV Publishing House Inc
930 Newark Ave, Jersey City, NJ 07306
Tel: 201-963-9524 *Fax:* 201-963-0102
E-mail: orders@ktav.com
Web Site: www.ktav.com
Key Personnel
Pres: Sol Scharfstein
Man Ed: Adam Bengal *E-mail:* adam@ktav.com
Sec, Rts & Perms: Bernard Scharfstein
Founded: 1924
Books of Jewish interest; juvenile, textbooks; scholarly Judaica & interfaith issues.
ISBN Prefix(es): 0-87068; 0-88125
Number of titles published annually: 18 Print
Total Titles: 840 Print
Divisions: KTAV Holiday Products Inc
Distributor for Yeshiva University Press
Membership(s): Association of Jewish Book Publishers

Kumarian Press Inc
1294 Blue Hills Ave, Bloomfield, CT 06002
SAN: 212-5978
Tel: 860-243-2098 *Toll Free Tel:* 800-289-2664 (orders only) *Fax:* 860-243-2867
E-mail: kpbooks@kpbooks.com
Web Site: www.kpbooks.com
Key Personnel
Publr & Intl Rts: Krishna Sondhi

Ed & Assoc Publr: Jim Lance *E-mail:* jlance@kpbooks.com
Prodn Ed: Erin Brown
Founded: 1977
Academic, professional books, college textbooks in social sciences: international development, international relations, political science, political economy, economics, globalization, women & gender studies, conflict resolution, environment, sustainability, civil society & NGO's.
ISBN Prefix(es): 0-931816; 1-56549; 1-887208
Number of titles published annually: 16 Print
Total Titles: 80 Print
Imprints: Frog Books
Foreign Rep(s): Alkem Co; Anglia Book & Freight Consolidations (Southern Africa); Bush Books (Australia & New Zealand); Eurospan (Europe & UK, Middle East, North Africa); Everest Media International Services (Nepal); Legacy Book (Eastern Africa); Viva Books (India)

George Kurian Reference Books
PO Box 519, Baldwin Place, NY 10505-0519
Tel: 914-962-3287 *Fax:* 914-962-3287
Web Site: www.encyclopediasociety.com
Key Personnel
Pres: George Kurian *E-mail:* gtkurian@aol.com
Founded: 1972
Reference books for libraries, schools, colleges.
ISBN Prefix(es): 0-914746
Number of titles published annually: 7 Print
Total Titles: 84 Print
Imprints: Foreign Affairs Information Service
Foreign Rights: Gazelle Book Services (UK, London)
Shipping Address: 3689 Campbell Ct, Yorktown Heights, NY 10598

Labyrinthos
3064 Holline Ct, Lancaster, CA 93535-4910
Tel: 661-946-2726 *Fax:* 661-946-2726
Key Personnel
Owner & Dir: Frank E Comparato
Founded: 1979
Original monographs & translations of archival materials on pre-Columbian & colonial life in the New World; Sephardic classics in Ladino.
ISBN Prefix(es): 0-911437
Number of titles published annually: 5 Print
Total Titles: 60 Print

Lacis Publications
3163 Adeline St, Berkeley, CA 94703
Tel: 510-843-7178 *Fax:* 510-843-5018
E-mail: staff@lacis.com
Web Site: www.lacis.com
Key Personnel
Owner: Jules Kliot *E-mail:* jules@lacis.com
Founded: 1965
Publishing & distribution of books relating to the textile arts (lace, embroidery, costume, knitting, needlepoint, etc).
ISBN Prefix(es): 0-916896; 1-891656
Number of titles published annually: 20 Print
Total Titles: 160 Print
Distributed by Unicorn
Distributor for Armand Colin; Gorse; Little Hills; Mani di Fata

LadybugPress
16964 Columbia River Dr, Sonora, CA 95370
SAN: 299-0377
Tel: 209-694-8340 *Toll Free Tel:* 888-892-5000
Fax: 209-694-8916
E-mail: ladybugpress@ladybugbooks.com
Web Site: www.ladybugbooks.com
Key Personnel
Publr: Georgia Jones
Founded: 1996
Specialize in books & audio books.
ISBN Prefix(es): 1-889409

Number of titles published annually: 10 CD-ROM; 4 Audio
Total Titles: 3 Print; 12 CD-ROM; 5 Audio
Membership(s): Publishers Marketing Association

Lake Claremont Press
4650 N Rockwell St, Chicago, IL 60625
Tel: 773-583-7800 *Fax:* 773-583-7877
E-mail: lcp@lakeclaremont.com
Web Site: www.lakeclarmont.com
Key Personnel
Publr: Sharon Woodhouse *E-mail:* sharon@lakeclaremont.com
Founded: 1994
Guidebooks by locals & specialized topics in regional history, especially for Chicago & Midwest.
ISBN Prefix(es): 1-893121; 0-9642426
Number of titles published annually: 6 Print
Total Titles: 30 Print
Membership(s): Chicago Women in Publishing; Publishers Marketing Association

Lake View Press
Box 578279, Chicago, IL 60657-8279
Tel: 773-935-2694
Web Site: www.lakeviewpress.com
Key Personnel
Pres & Dir: Paul Elitzik
Founded: 1982
ISBN Prefix(es): 0-941702
Number of titles published annually: 6 Print
Total Titles: 60 Print; 1 Audio
Distributor for Anthropos Publishers; Ravenswood Books

LAMA Books
Subsidiary of Leo A Meyer Associates
2381 Sleepy Hollow Ave, Hayward, CA 94545
Tel: 510-785-1091 *Toll Free Tel:* 888-452-6244
Fax: 510-785-1099
E-mail: lama@lamabooks.com
Web Site: www.lamabooks.com
Key Personnel
Mktg Asst: Barbara Ragusa
Founded: 1970
Develop & publish books for occupational trades, reading development, teacher preparation; directories-occupational programs in California community colleges; HVAC.
ISBN Prefix(es): 0-88069
Number of titles published annually: 4 Print
Total Titles: 25 Print

Lanahan Publishers Inc
324 Hawthorn Rd, Baltimore, MD 21210
Tel: 410-366-2434 *Toll Free Tel:* 866-354-1949
Fax: 410-366-8798 *Toll Free Fax:* 888-345-7257
E-mail: lanahan@aol.com
Web Site: www.lanahanpublishers.com
Key Personnel
Pres: Donald W Fusting
Founded: 1995
ISBN Prefix(es): 0-9652687; 1-930398
Number of titles published annually: 4 Print
Total Titles: 8 Print
Membership(s): Small Press Center

Landauer Books
12251 Maffitt Rd, Cumming, IA 50061
Tel: 515-287-2144 *Toll Free Tel:* 800-557-2144
Fax: 515-287-1530
E-mail: landaucor@aol.com
Key Personnel
Pres & Publr: Jeramy Landauer
Opers Mgr: Kathryn Jacobson
Edit Consultant: Becky Johnston
Founded: 1991
Publishing & licensing for the home arts working with leading designers & artists.

ISBN Prefix(es): 1-890621; 0-9646870
Number of titles published annually: 15 Print
Total Titles: 47 Print
Sales Office(s): 12251 Maffitt Rd, Cumming, IA 50061, Contact: Kitty Jacobson *Tel:* 515-287-2144
Distributor for Debbie Mumm® Inc
Foreign Rep(s): Dayview Textiles (Australia); Fabco (New Zealand); FJR Fabrics (Europe); Via Nova (Netherlands); Virka (Iceland); Windsor Books (England)
Returns: Landauer/United Warehousing, c/o Landauer, 5804 Enterprise Dr, Grimes, IA 50111 *Tel:* 515-986-4333
Warehouse: United Warehousing, 5804 Enterprise Dr, Grimes, IA 50111 (Bulk returns) *Tel:* 525-986-4333
Membership(s): ABA; Publishers Marketing Association

Landes Bioscience
810 S Church St, Georgetown, TX 78626
Tel: 512-863-7762 *Toll Free Tel:* 800-736-9948
Fax: 512-863-0081
Web Site: www.landesbioscience.com
Key Personnel
Pres: Ronald Landes *E-mail:* rgl@eurekah.com
Sales: Sara Lord *E-mail:* sara@eurekah.com
Founded: 1990
Bioscience & medical books for researchers, clinicians & students.
ISBN Prefix(es): 1-57059
Number of titles published annually: 70 Print
Total Titles: 700 Print
Imprints: Vademecum
Foreign Rights: John Scott & Co

Landmark Editions Inc
1402 Kansas Ave, Kansas City, MO 64127
Mailing Address: PO Box 270169, Kansas City, MO 64127-0169
Tel: 816-241-4919 *Fax:* 816-483-3755
E-mail: l_m_e@swbell.net
Web Site: www.landmarkeditions.com
Key Personnel
Edit Coord: Nan Thatch
Pub Liaison: Traci Symon
Founded: 1985
Books for children by children. Specialize in teachers' manuals, plus emotional impact series (5 books).
ISBN Prefix(es): 0-933849
Number of titles published annually: 5 Print
Total Titles: 45 Print

§Peter Lang Publishing Inc
Subsidiary of Verlag Peter Lang AG (Switzerland)
275 Seventh Ave, 28th fl, New York, NY 10001-6708
SAN: 241-5534
Tel: 212-647-7700 *Toll Free Tel:* 800-770-5264 (cust serv) *Fax:* 212-647-7707
Web Site: www.peterlangusa.com
Key Personnel
Sr VP & Man Dir: Christopher S Myers *E-mail:* chrism@plang.com
Sr Ed: Heidi Burns
Sr Acqs Ed: Phyllis Korper
Mktg Dir & Lib Sales Dir: Patricia Mulrane
Founded: 1982
Scholarly monographs & textbooks in the humanities, social sciences, media studies, Festschriften & conference proceedings.
ISBN Prefix(es): 0-8204
Total Titles: 150 E-Book
Branch Office(s)
PO Box 1246, Bel Air, MD 21014-1246 *Tel:* 410-879-6300
Foreign Office(s): Verlag Peter Lang GmbH, Eschborner-Landstr 42-50, 60460 Frankfurt/Main, Germany

Verlag Peter Lang GmbH, Augustenstr 44, 80333 Munich, Germany
Verlag Peter Lang GmbH, Gotzkowskystr 21, 10555 Berlin, Germany
Verlag Peter Lang AG, Jupiterstr 15, CH-3015 Bern, Switzerland
Verlag Peter Lang Lager, c/o Mobelfabrik Cuenin, Solothurn Str 24, CH-3400 Kirchberg 3422, Switzerland
Foreign Rep(s): Verlag Peter Lang GmbH (Germany)

Langdon Enterprises
16902 N Hardesty, Colbert, WA 99005
Tel: 509-238-4745 *Fax:* 509-238-1181
Key Personnel
Owner & Pres: Chic Langdon
Founded: 1964
Publish eight books authored by William G Langdon, Jr on polo, horse training, horse bits, saddles & horse rider skills.
ISBN Prefix(es): 1-883714
Number of titles published annually: 8 Print
Total Titles: 8 Print

§Langenscheidt Publishers Inc
46-35 54 Rd, Maspeth, NY 11378
SAN: 276-9441
Tel: 718-784-0055 *Toll Free Tel:* 800-432-MAPS (732-6277) *Fax:* 718-784-0640
Toll Free Fax: 888-773-7979
E-mail: sales@langenscheidt.com
Web Site: www.langenscheidt.com *Telex:* 96-8126
Cable: AMERMAP MSPH
Key Personnel
Chmn: Andreas Langenscheidt
Pres: Stuart Dolgins
VP, Trade Sales: Sue Pohja
VP, Map Publg: Richard Strug
Founded: 1983
Bilingual dictionaries, textbooks for Spanish, German & French as a foreign language, language learning cassette packs, travel guides, phrasebooks & cassette packs, maps & world atlases.
ISBN Prefix(es): 0-7511; 3-526; 981-234; 0-887; 1-585; 0-841; 0-843; 0-875; 1-557; 1-877; 981-246; 1-58573; 0-88729; 981-4120; 1-56331
Number of titles published annually: 150 Print; 25 CD-ROM; 20 Audio
Total Titles: 1,000 Print; 50 CD-ROM; 800 Online
Imprints: ADC Map; Arrow Map; Berlitz Publishing; Creative Map; Hagstrom Map; Insight Travel Guides; Langenscheidt Dictionary
Divisions: American Map Corp; Arrow Map; Creative Sales
Foreign Office(s): Langenscherdt Publishers, Postfach 401120, 80711 Munich, Germany
Distributor for Delorme Maps
Foreign Rights: Thomas Allen Sons (Canada)
Shipping Address: Langenscheidt KG, Neusser Strasse 3, 80807 Munich, Germany
Membership(s): AAP
See separate listing for:
Arrow Map Inc
Trakker Maps Inc

LangMarc Publishing
Subsidiary of North Sea Press
PO Box 90488, Austin, TX 78709-0488
SAN: 297-519X
Tel: 512-394-0989 *Toll Free Tel:* 800-864-1648
Fax: 512-394-0829
E-mail: langmarc@booksails.com
Web Site: www.langmarc.com; www.booksails.com
Key Personnel
Pres & Lib Sales Dir: Lois Qualben
VP: Susan Reue
Prodn Mgr: Michael Qualben
Founded: 1991
Inspirational.

ISBN Prefix(es): 1-880292
Number of titles published annually: 7 Print
Total Titles: 40 Print
Imprints: Booksails Press; NorthSea Press
Distributed by LangMarc
Distributor for Langmarc & North Sea Press
Shipping Address: 7500 Shadow Ridge Run, No 28, Austin, TX 70749, Contact: Lois Quallen *Tel:* 512-394-0989 *Toll Free Tel:* 800-864-1648 *Fax:* 512-394-0829 *E-mail:* langmarc@booksails.com *Web Site:* langmarc.com

Lantern Books
One Union Square W, Suite 201, New York, NY 10003
Tel: 212-414-2275 *Toll Free Tel:* 800-856-8664
Fax: 212-414-2412
E-mail: editorial@lanternbooks.com
Web Site: www.lanternbooks.com
Key Personnel
Pres: Gene Gollogly *E-mail:* gene@booklightinc.com
Publg Dir: Martin Rowe *E-mail:* martin@booklightinc.com
Founded: 1999
Publishes books for all wanting to live with greater spiritual depth & commitment to the preservation of the natural world.
ISBN Prefix(es): 1-59056; 1-930051; 1-57582; 1-929297
Distributor for Findhorn Press
Foreign Rep(s): Ceres Books (New Zealand); Deep Books (Europe & UK); Gemcraft Books (Austria); Hushion House Publishing (Canada)
Foreign Rights: Findhorn Publishing Services
Billing Address: Steiner Books, 22883 Quicksilver Dr, Sterling, VA 20166 *E-mail:* anthroposophicmail@presswarehouse.com
Orders to: Steiner Books, 22883 Quicksilver Dr, Sterling, VA 20166 *E-mail:* anthroposophicmail@presswarehouse.com
Returns: Steiner Books, 22883 Quicksilver Dr, Sterling, VA 20166
Shipping Address: Steiner Books, 22883 Quicksilver Dr, Sterling, VA 20166 *E-mail:* ipmmail@presswarehouse.com
Warehouse: Steiner Books, 22883 Quicksilver Dr, Sterling, VA 20166 *E-mail:* anthroposophicmail@presswarehouse.com
Distribution Center: Steiner Books, 22883 Quicksilver Dr, Sterling, VA 20166 *E-mail:* anthroposophicmail@presswarehouse.com
Membership(s): ABA

Laredo Publishing Company Inc
9400 Lloydcrest Dr, Beverly Hills, CA 90210
Tel: 310-860-9930 *Toll Free Tel:* 800-547-5113
Fax: 310-860-9902
E-mail: info@laredopublishing.com
Key Personnel
Pres: Sam Laredo *E-mail:* laredo@laredopublishing.com
ISBN Prefix(es): 1-56492
Number of titles published annually: 25 Print
Total Titles: 121 Print
Imprints: Renaissance House
Distributed by McGraw-Hill SRA
See separate listing for:
Renaissance House

Large Print
Division of Lutheran Braille Workers Inc
PO Box 5000, Yucaipa, CA 92399-1450
Tel: 909-795-8977 *Fax:* 909-795-8970
E-mail: lbw@lbwinc.org
Web Site: www.lbwinc.org
Key Personnel
Exec Dir: Loyd Coppenger

Founded: 1943
Produce & distribute free braille & large print biblical & Christian literature in more than 30 languages for the blind & visually impaired in over 120 countries.
Number of titles published annually: 5 Print
Total Titles: 200 Print

Lark Books
Division of Sterling Publishing Co Inc
67 Broadway, Asheville, NC 28801
Tel: 828-253-0467 *Toll Free Tel:* 800-284-3388 (cust serv) *Fax:* 828-253-7952
E-mail: info@larkbooks.com
Web Site: www.larkbooks.com
Key Personnel
Pres: Carol Taylor
Dir, Mktg, Sterling Publishing Co Inc: Ronni Stolzenberg *Tel:* 212-532-7160 *E-mail:* rstolzenberg@sterlingpub.com
Founded: 1979
Fine craft & how-to books.
ISBN Prefix(es): 0-937274; 1-887374; 1-57990
Number of titles published annually: 70 Print
Total Titles: 400 Print
Foreign Rights: Sterling Publishing Co Inc
Shipping Address: Sterling Publishing Co Inc, 40 Saw Mill Pond Rd, Edison, NJ 08837 *Toll Free Tel:* 800-367-9692 *Toll Free Fax:* 800-542-7567

Larson Publications
4936 Rte 414, Burdett, NY 14818
Tel: 607-546-9342 *Toll Free Tel:* 800-828-2197
Fax: 607-546-9344
E-mail: larson@lightlink.com
Web Site: www.larsonpublications.org
Key Personnel
Dir: Paul Cash
Mktg Dir: Amy Opperman Cash
Founded: 1982
Specialized philosophy & spirituality.
ISBN Prefix(es): 0-943914
Number of titles published annually: 5 Print; 1 CD-ROM; 1 Online
Total Titles: 76 Print; 1 CD-ROM; 1 E-Book; 3 Audio
Distributed by Bookpeople; National Book Network; New Leaf; Reo Wheel/Weiser
Foreign Rep(s): Airlift Book Co (UK); Bokforlaget Robert Larson (Sweden); Specialist Publications (Australia)

Latin American Literary Review Press
176 Penhurst Dr, Pittsburgh, PA 15235
Mailing Address: PO Box 17660, Pittsburgh, PA 15235
Tel: 412-824-7903 *Fax:* 412-824-7909
E-mail: latin@angstrom.net
Web Site: www.lalrp.org
Key Personnel
Pres: Yvette E Miller
Founded: 1980
Publish Latin American literature in English translation; distributes Spanish books on social sciences, history & art. Publish Latin American Literary Review, a semi-annual journal of scholarly essays & book reviews on the literatures of Spanish America & Brazil.
ISBN Prefix(es): 0-935480; 1-891270
Number of titles published annually: 5 Print
Total Titles: 103 Print
Imprints: Discoveries; Explorations
Distributed by Bilingual Review Press; Small Press Distribution
Distributor for Biblioteca Quinto Centenario; LALRP
Membership(s): Council of Literary Magazines & Presses

Laughing Elephant
3645 Interlake Ave N, Seattle, WA 98103

Tel: 206-447-9229 Toll Free Tel: 800-354-0400
Fax: 206-447-9189
E-mail: mail@laughingelephant.com
Web Site: www.laughingelephant.com
Key Personnel
Pres & Publr: Harold Darling
Founded: 1986
Publish books, cards & printed gifts with an emphasis on imagery, especially from antique children's books.
ISBN Prefix(es): 1-883211; 0-9621131; 1-5958
Number of titles published annually: 20 Print
Total Titles: 70 Print
Imprints: Darling & Co; Green Tiger Press
Editorial Office(s): Blue Lantern Studio, 4649 Sunnyside Ave N, Seattle, WA 98103 Tel: 206-632-7075 Fax: 206-632-0466
Distributed by Abingdon Press

Laura Geringer Books
Imprint of HarperCollins Publishers
1350 Avenue of Americas, 4th fl, New York, NY 10019
Tel: 212-261-6500
Web Site: www.harpercollins.com
Key Personnel
Sr VP & Publr: Laura Geringer
Founded: 1991
Number of titles published annually: 10 Print

Laureate Press
PO Box 8125, Bangor, ME 04402-8125
SAN: 298-0770
Toll Free Tel: 800-946-2727 Fax: 207-884-8095
Key Personnel
Ed: Robyn Beck
Ed-in-Chief: Lance C Lobo Tel: 207-884-8093
Founded: 1992
All aspects of the sport of fencing.
ISBN Prefix(es): 1-884528
Number of titles published annually: 3 Print
Total Titles: 13 Print

§Law School Admission Council
662 Penn St, Newtown, PA 18940
Mailing Address: PO Box 40, Newtown, PA 18940
Tel: 215-968-1101 Fax: 215-968-1159
E-mail: wmargolis@lsac.org
Web Site: www.lsac.org
Key Personnel
Dir, Commns: Wendy Margolis Tel: 215-968-1219 E-mail: wmargolis@lsac.org
Pubns & Dist Coord: Linda Lee E-mail: llee@lsac.org
Founded: 1947
Legal education & law school admission activities & law school admission test preparations.
ISBN Prefix(es): 0-942639
Number of titles published annually: 4 Print; 1 CD-ROM; 2 Online
Total Titles: 18 Print; 1 CD-ROM; 2 Online

Law Tribune Books
Division of American Lawyer Media
201 Ann St, 4th fl, Hartford, CT 06103
Tel: 860-527-7900 Fax: 860-527-7815
E-mail: lawtribune@amlaw.com
Web Site: www.law.com/ct
Key Personnel
Publr & Ed: Vince Valvo E-mail: vvalvo@amlaw.com
Mktg Dir: Beth Coleman E-mail: bcoleman@amlaw.com
Founded: 1974
Publisher of books, newspapers & other materials for the legal community & the public.
ISBN Prefix(es): 0-910051
Number of titles published annually: 8 Print; 5 E-Book
Total Titles: 20 Print; 20 E-Book

Imprints: The Connectcut Law Tribune; Law Tribune Newspapers
Shipping Address: Baker & Taylor, 1120 Rte 22 E, Bridgewater, NJ 08807-2944, Contact: Paul Debraski Tel: 908-541-7459 Fax: 908-541-7862 E-mail: debrasp@btol.com

The Lawbook Exchange Ltd
33 Terminal Ave, Clark, NJ 07066-1321
Tel: 732-382-1800 Toll Free Tel: 800-422-6686 Fax: 732-382-1887
E-mail: law@lawbookexchange.com
Web Site: www.lawbookexchange.com
Key Personnel
Sales Mgr: Greg Talbot
Man Ed: Valerie Horowitz
Founded: 1981
Reprints of legal classics.
ISBN Prefix(es): 1-886363; 1-58477; 0-9630106
Number of titles published annually: 100 Print
Total Titles: 520 Print
Membership(s): Antiquarian Booksellers Association of America; International League of Antiquarian Booksellers

Lawells Publishing
PO Box 1338, Royal Oak, MI 48068-1338
Tel: 248-543-5297 Fax: 248-543-5683
Web Site: www.lawells.net
Key Personnel
Publr: Sherry A Wells
Founded: 1984
Law for consumers, juvenile & young adult nonfiction. Request writer's guidelines.
ISBN Prefix(es): 0-934981
Number of titles published annually: 5 Print
Total Titles: 1 Audio
Imprints: Law for Laypersons; Secret Language Press

Merloyd Lawrence Inc
102 Chestnut St, Boston, MA 02108
Tel: 617-523-5895 Fax: 617-252-5285
Key Personnel
Pres & Ed: Merloyd Ludington Lawrence E-mail: merloyd.lawrence@perseusbooks.com
Clerk of Corp: Gerald Gillerman
Intl Rts, Perseus Books Group: Carolyn Savarese
Founded: 1982
Co-publisher with Perseus Publishing Books Group.
Number of titles published annually: 8 Print
Total Titles: 63 Print
Distributed by Perseus Books Groups

Lawrenceville Press Inc
PO Box 704, Pennington, NJ 08534
Tel: 609-737-1148 Fax: 609-737-8564
E-mail: custserv@lvp.com
Web Site: www.lvp.com
Key Personnel
Pres: Bruce W Presley E-mail: bpresley@lrp.com
VP, Intl Rts: Heidi T Crane E-mail: hcrane@lvp.com
Dir, Devt: Beth A Brown E-mail: bbrown@lvp.com
Founded: 1981
ISBN Prefix(es): 0-931717; 1-879233; 1-58003
Number of titles published annually: 22 Print
Total Titles: 75 Print
Branch Office(s)
528 NE Second St, Delray Beach, FL 33483, Dir, Devt: Beth A Brown Tel: 561-265-0033 Fax: 561-265-4664 E-mail: bbrown@lvp.com
Warehouse: 635 J-Gator Dr, Lantana, FL, Contact: Rich Guarascio Tel: 561-582-2259

§Lawyers & Judges Publishing Co Inc
917 N Swan Rd, Tucson, AZ 85711-1213
Mailing Address: PO Box 30040, Tucson, AZ 85751-0040

Tel: 520-323-1500 Fax: 520-323-0055
E-mail: sales@lawyersandjudges.com
Web Site: www.lawyersandjudges.com
Key Personnel
Pres & Publr: Steve Weintraub E-mail: steve@lawyersandjudges.com
Founded: 1963
Professional, text & reference materials in law, accident reconstruction, legal economics & taxation, forensics, medicine.
ISBN Prefix(es): 0-88450; 0-913875; 1-930056
Number of titles published annually: 20 Print; 8 CD-ROM
Total Titles: 84 Print; 15 CD-ROM
Advertising Agency: Global Sales Network
Warehouse: GENCO, 545 Coney Island Dr, Sparks, NV 89431

LDA Publishers
42-46 209 St, Bayside, NY 11361-2747
SAN: 221-4423
Tel: 718-224-9484 Toll Free Tel: 888-388-9887 Fax: 718-224-9487
Web Site: www.ldapublishers.com
Key Personnel
Publr & Intl Rts Contact: Andrew V Ippolito E-mail: andy.ippolito@verizon.net
Ed: Elaine Sprance E-mail: elaine@ldadirect.com
Edit & Mktg: Margaret Riconda
Contact: Emily Dale
Lib Sales Dir: Alan Dale
Founded: 1974
Regional directories for resource sharing & directories for academic, corporate, government, public & school libraries. Premier directory for those librarians & information professionals seeking a wide range of local information for products & services in market place.
ISBN Prefix(es): 0-935912
Number of titles published annually: 3 Print
Membership(s): ALA; SLA

Leadership Directories Inc
104 Fifth Ave, New York, NY 10011
Tel: 212-627-4140 Fax: 212-645-0931
E-mail: info@leadershipdirectories.com
Web Site: www.leadershipdirectories.com
Key Personnel
Pres & Publr: David J Hurvitz
Cont: Catherine Meisterich
Founded: 1969
Personnel directories of government, business, professional organizations & nonprofit organizations.
Number of titles published annually: 14 Print
Total Titles: 14 Print; 1 CD-ROM; 1 Online
Imprints: Leadership Directories; Yellow Book Directories
Branch Office(s)
1001 "G" St NW, Suite 200E, Washington, DC 20001 Tel: 202-347-7757 Fax: 202-628-3430

Leadership Ministries Worldwide
515 Airport Rd, Suite 111, Chattanooga, TN 37421
Mailing Address: PO Box 21310, Chattanooga, TN 37424-0310
Tel: 423-855-2181 Toll Free Tel: 800-987-8790 Fax: 423-855-8616 Toll Free Fax: 800-987-8790
E-mail: info@outlinebible.org
Web Site: www.outlinebible.org
Key Personnel
Dir, Devt & Intl Ministries: Jack D Walker
Gen Dir: John W Burkett
Commentaries.
ISBN Prefix(es): 1-57407; 0-945863
Number of titles published annually: 5 Print
Total Titles: 275 Print

Leadership Publishers Inc
PO Box 8358, Des Moines, IA 50301-8358

Tel: 515-278-4765 *Toll Free Tel:* 800-814-3757
Fax: 515-270-8303
Key Personnel
Pres & Owner: Lois Roets
Founded: 1982
Publish educational books for gifted & talented
students, their parents & teachers; also Biblical
study guides.
ISBN Prefix(es): 0-911943
Number of titles published annually: 4 Print; 2
Audio
Total Titles: 32 Print
Distributed by Amazon.com; Barnes & Noble

§Leading Edge Reports
Affiliate of Business Trend Analysts Inc
2171 Jericho Tpke, Suite 200, Commack, NY
11725
Tel: 631-462-5454 *Toll Free Tel:* 800-866-4648
Fax: 631-462-1842
E-mail: sales@bta-ler.net
Web Site: www.bta-ler.com
Key Personnel
Exec VP: Charles Ritchie
Founded: 1987
Market research.
ISBN Prefix(es): 0-945235
Number of titles published annually: 50 Print
Total Titles: 100 Print
Online services available through Dialog, Lexis-
Nexis, Markintel.
Foreign Rep(s): Adkit Ltd (Israel)

Leapfrog Press
95 Commercial St, Wellfleet, MA 02667-1495
Tel: 508-349-1925 *Fax:* 508-349-1180
E-mail: info@leapfrogpress.com
Web Site: www.leapfrogpress.com
Key Personnel
Man Ed: Ira Wood *E-mail:* ira@leapfrogpress.
com
Founded: 1996
Publisher of quality fiction, literary nonfiction &
poetry.
ISBN Prefix(es): 0-9654578; 0-9679520; 0-
9728984
Number of titles published annually: 8 Print; 2
Audio
Total Titles: 20 Print; 1 E-Book; 2 Audio
Distributed by Consortium Book Sales & Distri-
bution
Foreign Rights: Andreas Brunner Literary Agency
(German Language); Chandler Crawford
Agency (World Rights)
Billing Address: Consortium Book Sales & Distri-
bution, 1045 Westgate Dr, St Paul, MN 55114-
1065 *Tel:* 651-221-9035 *Toll Free Tel:* 800-
283-3572 *Fax:* 651-221-0124 *Web Site:* cbsd.
com
Membership(s): Authors Guild; PEN Interna-
tional; Publishers Marketing Association

Leaping Dog Press
PO Box 3316, San Jose, CA 95156-3316
Toll Free Tel: 877-570-6873 *Toll Free Fax:* 877-
570-6873
E-mail: editor@leapingdogpress.com; sales@
leapingdogpress.com
Web Site: www.leapingdogpress.com
Key Personnel
Ed & Publr: Jordan Jones
Founded: 2000
Publishers of contemporary literature.
ISBN Prefix(es): 1-58775
Number of titles published annually: 4 Print; 4 E-
Book
Total Titles: 4 Print; 4 E-Book
Membership(s): Council of Literary Magazines &
Presses

Learnables Foreign Language Courses, see
International Linguistics Corp

§The Learning Connection (TLC)
1901 Longleaf Blvd, Suite 300, Lake Wales, FL
33859
Mailing Address: PO Box 518, Frostproof, FL
33843
Tel: 863-676-4246 *Toll Free Tel:* 800-218-8489
Fax: 863-676-5216
E-mail: tlc@tlconnection.com
Web Site: www.tlconnection.com
Key Personnel
Pres & Chmn: Irene Handberg Sasman
Gen Mgr: Ryan Handberg
Founded: 1991
Thematic Literacy Centers & teacher's guides for
early childhood & middle school; parent in-
volvement & family literacy; bilingual, math,
science, multicultural, manipulatives, technol-
ogy.
ISBN Prefix(es): 1-56831
Number of titles published annually: 50 Print; 15
CD-ROM; 5 Audio
Total Titles: 1,000 Print; 15 CD-ROM; 50 Audio
Imprints: Computer Connections; PAKS-Parents
& Kids
Membership(s): International Reading Association

Learning Links Inc
2300 Marcus Ave, New Hyde Park, NY 11042
SAN: 175-081X
Tel: 516-437-9071 *Toll Free Tel:* 800-724-2616
Fax: 516-437-5392
E-mail: learning1x@aol.com
Web Site: www.learninglinks.com
Key Personnel
Pres: Rikki Kessler
Chmn: Joyce Friedland
Off Mgr: Susan Nevo
Cust Serv: Georgette De Pasquale
Founded: 1976
Publish study guides for novels for school use,
grades 1-12. Distribute paperback books, au-
dios, videos, craft kits, book-related toys, CD-
ROMs.
ISBN Prefix(es): 0-88122; 1-56982; 0-7675
Number of titles published annually: 25 Print
Total Titles: 625 Print
Imprints: Novel-Ties Study Guides
Divisions: Swan Books
Distributor for Harcourt; HarperCollins; Houghton
Mifflin; Little Brown; Penguin Putnam; Ran-
dom House Inc; Scholastic; Simon & Schuster
Membership(s): International Reading Association

Learning Resources Network (LERN)
208 S Main St, River Falls, WI 54022
Mailing Address: PO Box 9, River Falls, WI
54022-0009
Tel: 715-426-9777 *Toll Free Tel:* 800-678-5376
Fax: 715-426-5847 *Toll Free Fax:* 888-234-
8633
E-mail: info@lern.org
Web Site: www.lern.org
Key Personnel
Pres: William A Draves
VP: Greg Marsello
Founded: 1974
Professional books; business, marketing, man-
agement & administration, education; life-long
learning marketing for continuing educators.
ISBN Prefix(es): 0-914951
Number of titles published annually: 4 Print
Total Titles: 200 Print
Foreign Rep(s): LERN Australia (Australia);
LERN Canada (Canada); LERN UK (UK)
Shipping Address: 1130 Hostetler Dr, Manhattan,
KS 66502

LearningExpress LLC
55 Broadway, 8th fl, New York, NY 10006
Tel: 212-995-2566 *Toll Free Tel:* 800-295-9556
Fax: 212-995-5512

E-mail: customerservice@learnatest.com (cust
serv)
Web Site: www.learnatest.com
Key Personnel
Pres & CEO: Barry Lippman
Mktg Dir: Mark Santee
Founded: 1995
Publishes print & online test-preparation re-
sources, skill building tools, study guides &
career guidance materials for the trade, library,
school & consumer markets.
ISBN Prefix(es): 1-57685
Number of titles published annually: 30 Print; 50
Online
Total Titles: 200 Print; 250 Online; 50 E-Book
Distributed by Delmar (a division of Thomson
Learning)
Foreign Rep(s): Thomson Learning International

§La Leche League International Inc
1400 N Meacham Rd, Schaumburg, IL 60173
Tel: 847-519-7730 *Fax:* 847-519-0035
E-mail: llli@llli.org
Web Site: www.lalecheleague.org
Key Personnel
Exec Dir: Hedy Nuriel
Exec Dir, Pubns: Judy Torgus
Books on parenting & breast feeding.
ISBN Prefix(es): 0-912500
Number of titles published annually: 4 Print
Total Titles: 41 Print

Lectorum Publications Inc
Subsidiary of Scholastic Inc
524 Broadway, New York, NY 10012
Toll Free Tel: 800-853-3291 (admin, mktg &
sales); 800-345-5946 (orders) *Fax:* 212-727-
3035 *Toll Free Fax:* 877-532-8676
E-mail: lectorum@scholastic.com
Web Site: www.lectorum.com
Key Personnel
Pres: Teresa Mlawer *E-mail:* t.mlawer@
scholastic.com
Opers Mgr: Luis Petrillo
Sales Mgr, Trade: Carmen Rivera
Prod Mgr: Marjorie Samper
Founded: 1960
Publisher of children's books in Spanish. Distrib-
utor of children's & adult literature in Spanish.
ISBN Prefix(es): 1-880507; 1-930332
Number of titles published annually: 12 Print
Total Titles: 100 Print
Warehouse: 205 Chubb Ave, Lyndhurst, NJ 07071

Lederer Books
Division of Messianic Jewish Publishers
6204 Park Heights Ave, Baltimore, MD 21215-
3600
Tel: 410-358-6471 *Toll Free Tel:* 800-773-6574
Fax: 410-764-1376
E-mail: lederer@messianicjewish.net;
rightsandpermissions@messianicjewidh.net
(rights & perms)
Web Site: messianicjewish.net
Key Personnel
Pres: Barry Rubin *Tel:* 410-358-6471 ext 205
E-mail: president@messianicjewish.net
Man Ed: Janet Chaiet *Tel:* 410-358-6471 ext 206
E-mail: editor@messianicjewish.net
Founded: 1949
Publish & distribute Messianic Jewish books &
other products.
ISBN Prefix(es): 1-880226
Number of titles published annually: 12 Print
Total Titles: 55 Print; 1 CD-ROM; 1 Audio
Distributor for Chosen People Ministries; First
Fruits of Zion; Jewish New Testament Publica-
tions
Foreign Rep(s): Winfried Bluth (Europe)
Foreign Rights: Winfried Bluth (Europe)
Membership(s): Christian Booksellers Associa-
tion; Evangelical Christian Publishers Associa-
tion

Lee & Low Books Inc
95 Madison Ave, New York, NY 10016
Tel: 212-779-4400 *Toll Free Tel:* 888-320-3190
    ext 25 (orders only) *Fax:* 212-683-1894 (orders
    only); 212-532-6035
E-mail: info@leeandlow.com
Web Site: www.leeandlow.com
Key Personnel
Publr: Philip Lee
Exec Ed: Louise May
VP, Mktg & Webmaster: Jason Low
VP, Sales & Opers: Craig Low *E-mail:* clow@
    leeandlow.com
Founded: 1991
Birthdays, civil rights, coping with death, early
    childhood, fathers, Holocaust, imagination, in-
    ternational, mothers, multiethnic, neighbors,
    quilting/textiles, remarkable women, self-
    esteem/identity, sharing/giving, siblings, single
    parents & war.
ISBN Prefix(es): 1-880000; 1-58430
Number of titles published annually: 11 Print
Total Titles: 250 Print
Imprints: Bebop Books

J & L Lee Co
Box 5575, Lincoln, NE 68505
SAN: 127-3264
Tel: 402-488-4416 *Toll Free Tel:* 888-665-0999
    Fax: 402-489-2770
E-mail: info@leebooksellers.com
Web Site: www.leebooksellers.com
Key Personnel
Pres: James L McKee
Founded: 1979
ISBN Prefix(es): 0-934904
Number of titles published annually: 3 Print
Total Titles: 50 Print
Imprints: Salt Creek Press; Young Hearts

Legacy Press, see Rainbow Publishers

Legal Education Publishing
Division of State Bar of Wisconsin
5302 Eastpark Blvd, Madison, WI 53718
Mailing Address: PO Box 7158, Madison, WI
    53707-7158
Toll Free Tel: 800-957-4670 *Fax:* 608-257-5502
E-mail: service@wisbar.org
Web Site: www.wisbar.org
Key Personnel
Dir: Jacki Gerbitz
Mktg Mgr: Scott Robillard
Founded: 1999
Specialize in academic, professional books &
    how-to guides for the legal profession & lay
    people.
ISBN Prefix(es): 1-57862
Number of titles published annually: 3 Print
Total Titles: 3 Print

Legend Books, College Division
Division of Legend Books
69 Lansing St, Auburn, NY 13021
Tel: 315-258-8012
Key Personnel
Ed & Publr: Joseph P Berry
Founded: 1999
Scholarly works & books of general interest, in-
    cluding biography, communications, govern-
    ment, health, history, journalism, media studies,
    novels, philosophy, political science, psychol-
    ogy, public relations, sociology, sports, televi-
    sion. No mathematics or hard sciences.
ISBN Prefix(es): 0-9657898
Number of titles published annually: 10 Print
Total Titles: 35 Print

Lehigh University Press
Affiliate of Associated University Presses

Linderman Library, 30 Library Dr, Bethlehem, PA
    18015-3067
Tel: 610-758-3933 *Fax:* 610-758-6331
E-mail: inlup@lehigh.edu
Web Site: fp1.cc.lehigh.edu/inlup
Key Personnel
Dir: Philip A Metzger
Founded: 1985
Specialize in 18th century studies, history & tech-
    nology, scholarly hardcover books on business,
    economics, science, sociology, literature, 18th
    century studies & East Asia. We welcome sub-
    missions on any topic that is intellectually sub-
    stantive.
ISBN Prefix(es): 0-934223
Number of titles published annually: 5 Print
Total Titles: 75 Print
Orders to: Associated University Presses, 2010
    Eastpark Blvd, Cranbury, NJ 08512
Distribution Center: Associated University
    Presses, 2010 Eastpark Blvd, Cranbury, NJ
    08512, Contact: Julien Yoseloff

Leisure Arts Inc
5701 Ranch Dr, Little Rock, AR 72223
SAN: 666-9565
Tel: 501-868-8800 *Toll Free Tel:* 800-643-8030
    Fax: 501-868-8937
Web Site: www.leisurearts.com
Key Personnel
VP, Retail Mktg: Bob Humphrey
Publr: Rick Barton
Founded: 1972
Hard & soft cover books featuring instructions for
    needlework, crafts, cooking & gardening.
ISBN Prefix(es): 0-942237; 1-57486
Number of titles published annually: 150 Print
Total Titles: 2,000 Print

Leisure Books, see Dorchester Publishing Co Inc

Leonardo Press
PO Box 1326, Camden, ME 04843-1326
Tel: 207-236-8649 *Fax:* 207-236-8649
E-mail: leonardo@spellingdoctor.com
Web Site: www.spellingdoctor.com
Key Personnel
Pres: Raymond Laurita
Man Ed: Bernice Michaels
Founded: 1980
Spelling programs, all grades as well as ESL, re-
    medial, vocabulary enrichment & scholarly &
    professional books pertaining to language struc-
    ture & teaching.
ISBN Prefix(es): 0-914051
Total Titles: 23 Print

Lerner Publications
Division of Lerner Publishing Group
241 First Ave N, Minneapolis, MN 55401
SAN: 201-0828
Tel: 612-332-3344 *Toll Free Tel:* 800-328-4929
    Fax: 612-332-7615 *Toll Free Fax:* 800-332-
    1132
E-mail: info@lernerbooks.com
Web Site: www.lernerbooks.com
Key Personnel
Chmn & CEO: Harry J Lerner
Pres & Publr: Adam Lerner
VP & CFO: Margaret Wunderlich
VP, LernerClassroom: Gary Tinney
VP & Ed-in-Chief: Mary Rodgers
VP, Prodn: Gary Hansen
VP, Sales & Mktg: David Wexler
Art Dir: Zach Marell
Mktg Dir: Beth Heiss
Dir, HR: Cyndi Radant
Subs Rts: Tim Schwarz
Founded: 1959
Juveniles: science, history, sports, fiction, art, ge-
    ography, aviation, environment, ethnic, multi-
    cultural issues & activity books. We will ac-

cept submissions from March 1 through 31 &
    again from October 1 through 31. Any submis-
    sions received at other times of the year will
    be returned to the sender unopened. We will
    no longer be answering queries regarding the
    status of submissions. Submitters will receive
    a response after their ms or proposal has been
    considered. We will respond only to those sub-
    mitters who have included an SASE with their
    submission.
ISBN Prefix(es): 0-8225
Total Titles: 1,500 Print
Foreign Rep(s): INT Press Distribution (Aus-
    tralia); Monarch Books of Canada (Canada/
    Trade); Phambili (Southern Africa); Publishers
    Marketing Service (Singapore & Malaysia);
    Saunders Book Co (Canada/Education);
    Turnaround (UK)
Foreign Rights: Bardon Chinese Media Agency
    (Taiwan); Japan Foreign-Rights Centre (Japan);
    Korea Copyright Center (Korea); Michelle La-
    pautre Agence Junior (France); Literarische
    Agentur Silke Weniger (Germany); Tao Media
    International (People's Republic of China)
Warehouse: 1251 Washington Ave N, Minneapo-
    lis, MN 55401
Membership(s): Children's Book Council

Lerner Publishing Group
241 First Ave N, Minneapolis, MN 55401
SAN: 201-0828
Tel: 612-332-3344 *Toll Free Tel:* 800-328-4929
    Fax: 612-332-7615 *Toll Free Fax:* 800-332-
    1132
E-mail: info@lernerbooks.com
Web Site: www.lernerbooks.com
Key Personnel
Chmn & CEO: Harry J Lerner
Pres & Publr: Adam Lerner
VP & CFO: Margaret Wunderlich
VP & Edit-in-Chief: Mary Rodgers
VP, Prodn: Gary Hansen
VP, Sales & Mktg: David Wexler
VP, LernerClassroom: Gary Tinney
Dir, HR: Cyndi Radant
Mktg Dir: Beth Heiss
Dir, Contracts, Perms & Author Rel: Almena
    Dees
Art Dir: Zach Marell
Rts & Perms Mgr: Tim Schwarz
School & Lib Sales Mgr: Brad Richason
Founded: 1959
ISBN Prefix(es): 0-87614; 1-58013; 0-8225; 1-
    57505; 0-92937; 0-93049
Number of titles published annually: 200 Print
Total Titles: 1,500 Print
Imprints: Carolrhoda Books Inc; First Avenue
    Editions; Lerner Publications; LernerClass-
    room; LernerSports; Runestone Press
Divisions: Kar-Ben Publishing
Distributor for Darby Creek
Foreign Rep(s): Int Press Distribution (Australia);
    J Appleseed, A Division of Saunders (Canada);
    Mazeltov Books (Australia); Monarch Books
    of Canada (Canada/Trade); Phambili Agencies
    (Botswana, Lesotho, Namibia, South Africa,
    Zimbabwe, Swaziland); Publishers Marketing
    Services (Brunei, Malaysia, Singapore); Saun-
    ders Book Co (Canada/Education); Turnaround
    Distribution (UK)
Foreign Rights: Bardon Chinese Media Agency
    (Taiwan); Japan Foreign-Rights Center (Japan);
    Korea Copy-right Center (Korea); Literarische
    Agentur Silke Weniger (Germany); Michelle
    Lapautre Agence Junior (France); Tao Media
    International (People's Republic of China)
Warehouse: 1251 Washington Ave N, Minneapo-
    lis, MN 55401
See separate listing for:
Carolrhoda Books Inc
First Avenue Editions
Kar-Ben Publishing
Lerner Publications

LernerClassroom
LernerSports
Runestone Press

LernerClassroom
Imprint of Lerner Publishing Group
241 First Ave N, Minneapolis, MN 55401
Tel: 612-332-3344 *Toll Free Tel:* 800-328-4929
Fax: 612-332-7615 *Toll Free Fax:* 800-332-
1132
E-mail: info@lernerbooks.com
Web Site: www.lernerbooks.com
Key Personnel
Chmn & CEO: Harry J Lerner
Pres & Publr: Adam Lerner
VP & CFO: Margaret Wunderlich
VP & Ed-in-Chief: Mary Rodgers
VP, LernerClassroom: Gary Tinney
VP, Prodn: Gary Hansen
Art Dir: Zach Marell
Mktg Mgr: Amanda Wold
Dir, HR: Cyndi Radant
Nonfiction publications with teaching guides.
ISBN Prefix(es): 0-8225
Number of titles published annually: 10 Print
Total Titles: 400 Print
Foreign Rep(s): Monarch Books of Canada
(Canada)
Warehouse: 1251 Washington Ave N, Minneapo-
lis, MN 55401

LernerSports
Imprint of Lerner Publishing Group
241 First Ave N, Minneapolis, MN 55401
Tel: 612-332-3344 *Toll Free Tel:* 800-328-4929
Fax: 612-332-7615 *Toll Free Fax:* 800-332-
1132
E-mail: info@lernerbooks.com
Web Site: www.lernerbooks.com
Key Personnel
Chmn & CEO: Harry J Lerner
Pres & Publr: Adam Lerner
VP & CFO: Margaret Wunderlich
VP & Ed-in-Chief: Mary Rodgers
VP, LernerClassroom: Gary Tinney
VP, Prodn: Gary Hansen
VP, Sales & Mktg: David Wexler
Art Dir: Zach Marell
Mktg Dir: Beth Heiss
Dir, Contracts, Perms & Author Rel: Almena
Dees
Dir, HR: Cyndi Radant
Subs Rts: Tim Schwarz
Founded: 1999
ISBN Prefix(es): 0-8225
Foreign Rep(s): INT Press Distribution (Aus-
tralia); Monarch Books of Canada (Canada/
Trade); Phambili (Southern Africa); Pub-
lishers Marketing Services (Singapore &
Malaysia); Saunders Book Co (Canada/Edu-
cation); Turnaround
Foreign Rights: Bardon Chinese Media Agency
(Taiwan); Japan Foreign-Rights Centre (Japan);
Korea Copyright Center (Korea); Michelle La-
pautre Agence Junior (France); Literarische
Agentur Silke Weniger (Germany); Tao Media
International (People's Republic of China)
Warehouse: 1251 Washington Ave N, Minneapo-
lis, MN 55401

Lessiter Publications
PO Box 624, Brookfield, WI 53008-0624
Tel: 262-782-4480 *Fax:* 262-782-1252
E-mail: lessiter@lesspub.com
Web Site: www.lesspub.com
Key Personnel
Pres: Frank Lessiter
Founded: 1981
ISBN Prefix(es): 0-944079
Number of titles published annually: 3 Print
Total Titles: 30 Print

§The Letter People®
Division of Abrams & Co Publishers Inc
61 Mattatuck Heights Rd, Waterbury, CT 06705
Mailing Address: PO Box 10025, Waterbury, CT
06725-0025
Tel: 203-756-6562 *Toll Free Tel:* 800-227-
9120; 800-874-0029 *Fax:* 203-756-2895
Toll Free Fax: 800-737-3322
Web Site: letterpeople.com
Key Personnel
CEO: Richard I Abrams
CFO & VP, Fin & HR: Judith Maya
Pres: Daniel C Wasp
Sr VP: Arthur O Peterson
Exec VP, Sales & Mktg: Daniel Coakley
VP, Opers: William D Thomas
VP, Edit Servs: Kathleen Fischer
Founded: 1969
Books for early childhood reading Pre-K to first
grade; read-along & music audio cassettes; ed-
ucational games & activities; teachers' guides
& materials.
ISBN Prefix(es): 0-89796; 0-7665
Number of titles published annually: 75 Print; 6
CD-ROM

Lexington Books
Member of Rowman & Littlefield Publishing
Group
4501 Forbes Blvd, Lanham, MD 20706
Tel: 301-459-3366 *Fax:* 301-429-5748
Web Site: www.lexingtonbooks.com
Key Personnel
Dir: Judith Rothman *E-mail:* jrothman@rowman.
com
Dir, Acqs & Edit: Serena Leigh Kromback
Mktg Dir: Dean Roxanis
Sr Acqs Ed: Jason Hallman *E-mail:* jhallman@
rowman.com.com
Premier publisher of scholarly monographs &
textbooks. Subjects include classics, political
science, political theory, philosophy, history,
international, literary studies, public policy.
ISBN Prefix(es): 0-7391
Number of titles published annually: 150 Print
Total Titles: 700 Print
Foreign Rep(s): Oxford Publicity Partnership,
London
Foreign Rights: Kelly Rogers
Orders to: National Book Network, 15200
NBN Way, Blue Ridge Summit, PA 17214
Tel: 717-794-3800 *Toll Free Tel:* 800-462-6420
Fax: 717-794-3803 *E-mail:* custserv@rowman.
com
Membership(s): AAP

§LexisNexis®
Member of Reed Elsevier plc
701 E Water St, Charlottesville, VA 22902
SAN: 202-6317
Mailing Address: PO Box 7587, Charlottesville,
VA 22906-7587
Tel: 434-972-7600 *Toll Free Tel:* 800-446-3410;
800-828-8341 (orders)
E-mail: customer.support@lexisnexis.com
Web Site: www.lexisnexis.com
Key Personnel
CEO, REI Global: Andy Prozes
Pres & CEO, North American Legal Markets:
Lou Andreozzi
CFO, LexisNexis Group: Carolyn Ullerick
Founded: 1897
Multivolume legal reference works, state codes
& single-volume legal texts, treatises & case-
books, Law on Disc for most states.
ISBN Prefix(es): 0-87215; 0-672; 0-87473
Imprints: Michie
Shipping Address: 1317 Carlton Ave, Char-
lottesville, VA 22901

LexisNexis Academic & Library Solutions
Member of The LexisNexis Group

7500 Old Georgetown Rd, Suite 1300, Bethesda,
MD 20814-3389
SAN: 206-345X
Tel: 301-654-1550 *Toll Free Tel:* 800-638-8380
Fax: 301-654-4033; 301-657-3203 (sales)
E-mail: academicinfo@lexisnexis.com
Web Site: www.lexisnexis.com/academic
Key Personnel
Sr Dir, Edit: Diane Smith
Dir, Mktg: Barbara Barclay
Dir, Electronic Sales Support: Katie Culliton
Dir, IT: Andy M Ross
Founded: 1969
Government information, statistical data & histor-
ical research collections. Indexes, abstracts &
full text documents offered in electronic print,
microfiche & microfilm formats.
ISBN Prefix(es): 0-912380; 0-88692; 0-89093; 1-
55655
Total Titles: 409 Print; 8 Online
Online services available through LexisNexis.
Imprints: Clearwater; Congressional Information
Service; University Publications of America
Warehouse: 403 Cottonwood Pkwy, California,
MD 20619
Membership(s): ALA

Leyerle Publications
28 Stanley St, Mount Morris, NY 14510
Mailing Address: PO Box 384, Geneseo, NY
14454-0384
Tel: 585-658-2193 *Fax:* 585-658-3298
Web Site: www.leyerlepublications.com
Key Personnel
Owner & Pres: William D Leyerle
E-mail: leyerlew@rochester.rr.com
Founded: 1977
Vocal music; vocal music translations (opera &
art song); books about singing.
ISBN Prefix(es): 1-878617
Number of titles published annually: 5 Print
Total Titles: 60 Print

Liberty Fund Inc
8335 Allison Pointe Trail, Suite 300, Indianapolis,
IN 46250-1684
SAN: 202-6740
Tel: 317-842-0880 *Toll Free Tel:* 800-955-8335
Fax: 317-579-6060
E-mail: books@libertyfund.org
Web Site: www.libertyfund.org
Key Personnel
VP, Publg: Patricia Gallagher
Mktg Dir: Kristen Beach
Prodn Mgr: Shannon Bahler
Man Ed: Dan Kirklin
Mktg Coord: Heather Probala *Tel:* 317-842-0880
ext 6407
Founded: 1960
A publisher of print & electronic scholarly re-
sources including new editions of classic works
in American constitutional history, European
history, natural law, law, modern political
thought, economics & education.
ISBN Prefix(es): 0-913966; 0-86597
Number of titles published annually: 20 Print
Total Titles: 300 Print
Foreign Rep(s): Eleanor Brasch Enterprises
(Australia & New Zealand); Brookside Pub-
lishing Services (Ireland); Compass Aca-
demic Ltd (UK & Ireland); Claire de Gruchy
(Cyprus, Malta); Everybodys Book's (Southern
Africa); Export Sales Agency (Austria, Ger-
many, Switzerland); Charles Gibbes (Greece);
Iberian Book Services (Gibraltar, Portugal,
Spain); Edwin Makabenta (China, Malaysia,
Philippines); Maya Publishers Pvt Ltd (In-
dia); David Pickering (Italy); Publishers In-
ternational Marketing (Southeast Asia, North-
east Asia); Jonathan Rhodes (UK & Ireland);
Sabrina Righi (France); Anthony Rudkin As-
sociates (Middle East); David Towle (Baltic
States, Northern Europe, Scandinavia)

Warehouse: Total Response, 3131 N Franklin Rd, Suite H, Indianapolis, IN 46219
Distribution Center: Total Response, 3131 N Franklin Rd, Suite H, Indianapolis, IN 46219
Membership(s): AAP; ALA

Libra Publishers Inc
3089-C Clairemont Dr, PMB 383, San Diego, CA 92117
SAN: 201-0909
Tel: 858-571-1414 *Fax:* 858-571-1414
Key Personnel
Pres, Ed & Rts & Perms: William Kroll
VP, Sales & Adv Mgr: Jonathan Kroll
Founded: 1960
Behavioral & social sciences, medical & general nonfiction, some fiction & poetry; professional journals.
ISBN Prefix(es): 0-87212
Number of titles published annually: 8 Print
Total Titles: 180 Print
Foreign Rights: Mary Jane Ross; Bobbe Siegel

Libraries Unlimited
Member of Greenwood Publishing Group
88 Post Rd W, Westport, CT 06881
Toll Free Tel: 800-225-5800 *Fax:* 203-222-1502; 603-431-2214 (orders)
E-mail: lu-books@lu.com
Web Site: www.lu.com
Key Personnel
Gen Mgr: Ron Maas
Founded: 1964
Library science textbooks, annotated bibliographies, reference books, professional books for school media specialists as well as resource & activity books for librarians & teachers; storytelling resources & collections.
ISBN Prefix(es): 0-87287; 1-56308
Number of titles published annually: 60 Print
Total Titles: 400 Print; 5 Audio
Divisions: Teacher Ideas Press
Foreign Rep(s): APD Singapore Pte Ltd (Indonesia, Malaysia, Philippines, Singapore, Thailand); Asia Publishers Services (Hong Kong, Korea, People's Republic of China, Taiwan); Avicenna Partnership (Bill Kennedy) (Egypt, Gulf States, Iran, Lebanon, Syria, Iraq, Libya); Avicenna Partnership (Claire de Gruchy) (Cyprus, Jordan, Malta, Middle East, Morocco, Turkey, Tunisia, Algeria, Palestine); Cranbury International (Caribbean, Central & South America, Mexico); Franklins International (Israel); Greenwood International (UK, Europe); James Bennett Pty Ltd (Australia, New Zealand); OLA Store/Ontario Library Association (Canada); United Publishers Series Ltd (Japan); Kelvin van Hasselt (Africa, Ethiopia, Cote d'Ivoire (Ivory Coast), Eritrea, Rwanda); Viva Books Private Ltd (India)
Orders to: PO Box 6926, Portsmouth, NH 03802-6926
Returns: Greenwood Publishing Group/Libraries Unlimited, 300 Exchange Dr, Suite B, Crystal Lake, IL 60014
Warehouse: Greenwood Publishing Group/Libraries Unlimited, 300 Exchange Dr, Suite B, Crystal Lake, IL 60014

The Library of America
14 E 60 St, New York, NY 10022
SAN: 286-9918
Tel: 212-308-3360 *Fax:* 212-750-8352
E-mail: info@loa.org
Web Site: www.loa.org; www.loaacademic.org
Key Personnel
Pres: Cheryl Hurley
Publr: Max Rudin
CFO: Daniel W Baker
Ed-in-Chief: Geoffrey O'Brien
Man Ed: Sharon Graham
Ed: Derick Schilling

Cust Serv Mgr: Laura Gazlay
Trade & Academic Mktg Mgr: Brian McCarthy
Tel: 212-308-3360 ext 212 *E-mail:* bmccarthy@loa.org
Dir, Mktg: David Smith
Founded: 1979
Collected editions of classic American authors; literature, history, philosophy, poetry & journalism.
ISBN Prefix(es): 0-940450; 1-883011; 1-931082
Number of titles published annually: 15 Print
Total Titles: 138 Print
Distributed by Penguin Putnam Inc
Foreign Rep(s): United Publishers Service (Japan)
Advertising Agency: Franklin Spier Inc
Warehouse: Viking Penguin Inc, 405 Murray Hill Pkwy, East Rutherford, NJ 07073

Library of Virginia
800 E Broad St, Richmond, VA 23219-8000
Tel: 804-692-3999 *Fax:* 804-692-3736
Web Site: www.lva.lib.va.us
Key Personnel
Dir, Pubns: Gregg Kimball *Tel:* 804-692-3722
Founded: 1823
Monographs & reference works on Virginia history.
ISBN Prefix(es): 0-88490
Number of titles published annually: 3 Print
Total Titles: 75 Print

Libros Para Ninos, see Simon & Schuster Children's Publishing

Mary Ann Liebert Inc
2 Madison Ave, Larchmont, NY 10538
Tel: 914-834-3100 *Toll Free Tel:* 800-654-3237
Fax: 914-834-3771
Web Site: www.mliebert.com; www.liebertpub.com
Key Personnel
Sr VP: Harriet I Matysko *E-mail:* hmatysko@liebertpub.com
Founded: 1980
Medical & sci-tech journals, books & newspapers.
ISBN Prefix(es): 0-913113
Number of titles published annually: 10 Print
Total Titles: 73 Print
Divisions: Genetic Engineering News
Advertising Agency: Valerie Taylor Assocs

Life Cycle Books
Division of Life Cycle Books Ltd (Canada)
LPO Box 1008, Niagara Falls, NY 14304-1008
SAN: 692-7173
Tel: 416-690-5860 *Toll Free Tel:* 800-214-5849
Fax: 416-690-8532
E-mail: orders@lifecyclebooks.com
Web Site: www.lifecyclebooks.com
Key Personnel
Gen Mgr: Paul Broughton
Founded: 1973
Books, pamphlets, brochures & audiovisuals on human life issues.
ISBN Prefix(es): 0-919225
Number of titles published annually: 6 Print
Total Titles: 32 Print
Branch Office(s)
421 Nugget Ave, Unit 8, Toronto, ON M1S 4L8, Canada

LifeQuest
6404 S Calhoun St, Fort Wayne, IN 46807
Toll Free Tel: 800-774-3360
E-mail: dadoftia@aol.com
Key Personnel
Pres: Steve Clapp
Mktg Dir: Kristen Leverton Helbert
Founded: 1991

Research & publishing on issues in Protestant congregations. Subject specialties include church growth, stewardship, evangelism & sexuality.
ISBN Prefix(es): 1-893270; 0-9637206
Number of titles published annually: 8 Print
Total Titles: 40 Print
Imprints: Christian Community
Branch Office(s)
Christian Community, 26530 N Dixie Hwy, No 8-230, Perrysburg, OH 43551, Contact: Kristen Helbert *Tel:* 419-872-7448
Distributed by Brethren Press
Distributor for New Life Ministries

Light-Beams Publishing
Formerly Great White Dog Picture Co
10 Toon Lane, Lee, NH 03824
Tel: 603-659-1300 *Toll Free Tel:* 800-397-7641
Fax: 603-659-3399
Web Site: www.light-beams.com
Key Personnel
Mktg/Partner: Barry Kane
Producer/Partner: Kathy Secrest
Dir/Partner: Mark Forman
Creative/Partner: Tracy Kane
Founded: 1997
Specialize & publishes award-winning children's books & videos for children ages 3 & up.
ISBN Prefix(es): 0-9708104
Number of titles published annually: 10 Print

The Light Inc
26 Worlds Fair Dr, Unit C, Somerset, NJ 08873
Tel: 732-868-0210 *Fax:* 732-868-0211
E-mail: info@thelightinc.com
Web Site: www.thelightinc.com
Founded: 2001
Publishing, printing, export-import, international trade.
ISBN Prefix(es): 975-7388; 0-9704370; 0-9720654; 1-932099
Number of titles published annually: 10 Print
Total Titles: 19 Print
Imprints: The Fountain
Distributor for Gonca; ISIK; Kaynak; Nil; Selt; Zambak

Light Technology Publishing
4030 E Huntington Dr, Flagstaff, AZ 86004
Mailing Address: PO Box 3870, Flagstaff, AZ 86003
Tel: 928-526-1345 *Toll Free Tel:* 800-450-0985
Fax: 928-714-1132
E-mail: publishing@lighttechnology.net
ISBN Prefix(es): 1-891824; 1-929385
Number of titles published annually: 15 Print
Total Titles: 150 Print
Editorial Office(s): PO Box 3540, Flagstaff, AZ 86003
Sales Office(s): PO Box 3540, Flagstaff, AZ 86003
Foreign Rights: Hagenbach & Bender GmbH (world exc USA & Canada)
Billing Address: PO Box 3540, Flagstaff, AZ 86003
Membership(s): AAP

§Liguori Publications
One Liguori Dr, Liguori, MO 63057-9999
SAN: 202-6783
Tel: 636-464-2500 *Toll Free Tel:* 800-464-2555
Fax: 636-464-8449
Web Site: www.liguori.org
Key Personnel
Chmn of the Bd & Pres: Harry Grile
E-mail: hgrile@liguori.org
Edit Dir: Hans Christoffersen *E-mail:* hchris@liguori.org
Ed-in-Chief: William Parker *E-mail:* bparker@liguori.org

Man Ed, Trade: Judith A Bauer *E-mail:* jbauer@liguori.org
Man Ed: Cheryl Plass *E-mail:* cplass@liguori.org
Rts & Perms & Intl Rts: Alicia von Stamwitz
 E-mail: avonstamwitz@liguori.org
Dir, Art: Pam Hummelsheim
 E-mail: phummelsheim@liguori.org
Trade Mktg Consultant: Bob Byrns
 E-mail: bobbyrns@bestweb.net
Founded: 1947
Books on religion (Catholic) & spirituality, inspirational & educational resources for parishes & schools, devotional music, bulletins, online subscription service, magazine.
ISBN Prefix(es): 0-89243; 0-7648
Number of titles published annually: 60 Print
Total Titles: 14 CD-ROM
Imprints: Libros Liguori; Liguori/Triumph
Distributor for Redemptorist Publications
Foreign Rep(s): Redemptorist Publications Book Services (England)

Limelight Editions
Subsidiary of Proscenium Publishers Inc
512 Newark Pompton Tpke, Pompton Plains, NJ 07444
Tel: 973-835-6375; 908-788-5753 (orders only) *Fax:* 973-835-6504; 908-237-2407 (orders only)
E-mail: info@limelighteditions.com
Web Site: www.limelighteditions.com
Key Personnel
Pres: Melvyn B Zerman
Asst Publr: Jenna Young
Founded: 1983
Publish paperback reprints & original books in the field of the performing arts. Do original publishing in hardcover & paperback. Specialize in instructional books, criticism & essays, film, theatre.
ISBN Prefix(es): 0-87910
Number of titles published annually: 16 Print
Total Titles: 150 Print
Foreign Rep(s): Gazelle (England, Europe); Scholarly Book Services (Canada); Tower Books (Australia)
Orders to: Proscenium Publishers/Limelight Editions, c/o Whitehurst & Clark Fulfillment, 1200 Rte 523, Flemington, NJ 08822
Returns: Proscenium Publishers/Limelight Editions, c/o Whitehurst & Clark Fulfillment, 1200 Rte 523, Flemington, NJ 08822
Warehouse: Proscenium Publishers/Limelight Editions, c/o Whitehurst & Clark Fulfillment, 1200 Rte 523, Flemington, NJ 08822
Distribution Center: Proscenium Publishers/Limelight Editions, c/o Whitehurst & Clark Fulfillment, 1200 Rte 523, Flemington, NJ 08822

Limulus Books Inc
13742 Callington Dr, Wellington, FL 33414-8579
SAN: 298-4105
Tel: 561-793-3010 *Fax:* 561-793-0460
Key Personnel
Pres: Joseph M Katz
Founded: 1992
Business directories, market research off the shelf, general business & marketing how-to.
ISBN Prefix(es): 1-885177
Number of titles published annually: 4 Print
Total Titles: 35 Print

Linden Publishing Company Inc
2006 S Mary, Fresno, CA 93721
Tel: 559-233-6633 *Toll Free Tel:* 800-345-4447 (orders only) *Fax:* 559-233-6933
Web Site: lindenpub.com
Key Personnel
Pres & Publr: Richard Sorsky *E-mail:* richard@lindenpub.com
Founded: 1977
ISBN Prefix(es): 0-941936

Number of titles published annually: 5 Print
Total Titles: 50 Print
Imprints: Craven Street Books
Membership(s): ABA; Publishers Marketing Association

Lindisfarne Books
Imprint of Anthroposophic Press
PO Box 58, Hudson, NY 12534
Tel: 413-528-8233 *Toll Free Tel:* 800-856-8664 (orders) *Fax:* 413-528-8826; 703-661-1501 (orders)
E-mail: service@lindisfarne.org
Web Site: www.lindisfarne.org
Key Personnel
CEO & Pres: Gene Gollogly
Ed-in-Chief: Chris Bamford
Founded: 1979
Fine quality books in the areas of philosophy, psychology, new sciences, comparative theology, art & literature, emphasizing the synthesis of science, religion & art.
ISBN Prefix(es): 0-940262; 1-58420
Number of titles published annually: 12 Print
Total Titles: 150 Print
Distributed by Floris Books
Foreign Rep(s): Floris Books (UK)
Orders to: PO Box 960, Herndon, VA 20172
 Tel: 703-661-1594 *Toll Free Tel:* 800-856-8664 (orders)
Warehouse: PO Box 960, Herndon, VA 20172
 Tel: 703-661-1594 *Toll Free Tel:* 800-856-8664 (orders)

LinguiSystems Inc
3100 Fourth Ave, East Moline, IL 61244
Tel: 309-755-2300 *Toll Free Tel:* 800-776-4332 *Fax:* 309-755-2377
E-mail: service@linguisystems.com
Web Site: www.linguisystems.com
Key Personnel
Owner: Linda Bowers *E-mail:* lbowers@linguisystems.com; Rosemary Huisingh
Prod Devt: Carolyn Logiudice
Founded: 1977
Acquisition, editing, manufacturing, marketing & fulfillment; educational books, tapes & games for speech therapy, special education & regular education.
ISBN Prefix(es): 1-55999; 0-7606
Number of titles published annually: 50 Print
Total Titles: 137 Print
Foreign Rights: Rights Unlimited Inc (Worldwide)

§The Linick Group Inc
Linick Bldg, 7 Putter Lane, Middle Island, NY 11953
Mailing Address: PO Box 102, Middle Island, NY 11953-0102
Tel: 631-924-3888 *Fax:* 631-924-3890
E-mail: linickgrp@att.net
Web Site: www.lgroup.addr.com
Key Personnel
Lib Sales Dir: Jill Reynolds
Founded: 1968
Specialized health titles, health care, weight loss, exercise, fitness, martial arts/self-defense, wine & spirits, mature market, multicultural & bilingual picture; multi-media, workbooks & instructional material, public relations, restaurants & travel & tourism; confidential reports, foreign countries, newsletters, business & direct response advertising & marketing, communications, subscription & mail order, photography, psychology, e-commerce, e-books, e-publishing, internet interactive campaigns, targeted e-public relations.
ISBN Prefix(es): 0-917098
Number of titles published annually: 25 Print; 10 CD-ROM; 450 Online; 50 E-Book

Total Titles: 125 Print; 120 CD-ROM; 950 Online; 350 E-Book
Imprints: CCA; Isshin-Ryu Productions; LKA Inc; NAPS; New World Press (NWP)
Distributed by Bookmasters; New World Press
Distributor for Linick International; LKA Inc; NAPS
Advertising Agency: L K Advertising Agency, 7 Putter Lane, Middle Island, NY 11953
 Tel: 631-924-3888 *Web Site:* lgroup.addr.com
See separate listing for:
Copywriter's Council of America (CCA)

Linns Stamp News-Ancillary Division
Division of AMOS Hobby Publishing
PO Box 29, Sidney, OH 45365-0029
Tel: 937-498-0801 (ext 197) *Fax:* 937-498-0807
 Toll Free Fax: 800-488-5349
E-mail: cuserv@amospress.com
Web Site: www.amosadvantage.com
Key Personnel
Ancilliary Div Mgr: Donna Houseman
Founded: 1928
Books on stamps & stamp collecting.
ISBN Prefix(es): 0-940403
Number of titles published annually: 3 Print
Total Titles: 67 Print

Linworth Publishing Inc
480 E Wilson Bridge Rd, Suite L, Worthington, OH 43085-2372
Tel: 614-436-7107 *Toll Free Tel:* 800-786-5017 *Fax:* 614-436-9490
E-mail: linworth@linworthpublishing.com
Web Site: www.linworth.com
Key Personnel
Pres & Publr: Marlene Woo-Lun
Founded: 1982
Professional book & magazine publishing for school library media specialists.
ISBN Prefix(es): 0-938865; 1-58683
Number of titles published annually: 20 Print
Total Titles: 50 Print
Imprints: Linworth Learning

Lion Books Publisher
Division of Sayre Publishing Inc
210 Nelson Rd, Scarsdale, NY 10583
SAN: 201-0925
Tel: 914-725-2280 *Fax:* 914-725-3572
Key Personnel
Prop: Sayre Ross
Ed & VP: Harriet Ross
Mktg & Publicity: Bette Callet
Prodn: Nancy Ross
Founded: 1967
Library binding nonfiction; young adult, sports instruction, craft activity books, black studies, biographies & juvenile hardcovers for libraries & schools.
ISBN Prefix(es): 0-87460
Number of titles published annually: 12 Print
Total Titles: 90 Print
Imprints: Sayre Ross Co
Distribution Center: Innovative Packaging, 200 N 12 St, Newark, NJ 07107, Contact: J Schottmuller *Tel:* 973-482-7765 *Fax:* 973-482-0035

LionHearted Publishing Inc
PO Box 618, Zephyr Cove, NV 89448-0618
Tel: 775-588-1388 *Toll Free Tel:* 888-546-6478
 Toll Free Fax: 888-546-6478
E-mail: admin@lionhearted.com
Web Site: www.lionhearted.com
Key Personnel
Pres & CEO: Mary Ann Heathman
CFO & COO: Kim A Heathman
Founded: 1994
Publisher of single title romance.
ISBN Prefix(es): 1-57343

Number of titles published annually: 30 Print; 30 Online; 30 E-Book
Total Titles: 30 Print; 30 Online; 30 E-Book

§Lippincott Williams & Wilkins
Subsidiary of Wolters Kluwer Health
530 Walnut St, 7th fl, Philadelphia, PA 19106
SAN: 201-0933
Tel: 215-521-8300 *Toll Free Tel:* 800-638-3030 (cust serv) *Fax:* 215-521-8902; 301-824-7390 (cust serv)
E-mail: orders@lww.com
Web Site: www.lww.com *Telex:* 83-4566
Cable: LIPPCOT PHILADELPHIA
Key Personnel
Contact: Jean Rodenberger *Tel:* 215-521-8750
Founded: 1792
Medicine, dentistry life sciences, nursing, allied health, veterinary medicine books, journals, textbooks, looseleaf, newsletters & media.
ISBN Prefix(es): 0-397; 0-316; 0-87434; 1-58255; 0-683; 0-7817; 1-5877
Number of titles published annually: 125 Print
Total Titles: 4,000 E-Book
Branch Office(s)
351 W Camden St, Baltimore, MD 21201 *Tel:* 410-528-4000 *Fax:* 410-528-4414
345 Hudson St, 16th fl, New York, NY 10014 *Tel:* 212-886-1200 *Fax:* 212-886-1215
323 Norristown Rd, Suite 200, Ambler, PA 19002 *Tel:* 215-646-8700
Foreign Office(s): LWW Ltd Australia/New Zealand, 22-36 Mountain St, Suite 4, Level 2, Broadway, NSW 2007, Australia *Tel:* 02-9212-5955 *Fax:* 02-9212-6966
LWW Asia Pty Ltd, Suite 907-910, New T & T Centre, Harbour City, 7 Canton Rd, Tsimshatsu, Kowloon, Hong Kong *Tel:* 852-2610-2339 *Fax:* 852-2421-1123
LWW, Europe, 250 Waterloo Rd, London SE1 8RD, United Kingdom *Tel:* (020) 7981 0500 *Fax:* (020) 7981 0501
Warehouse: 16522 Hunters Green Pkwy, Hagerstown, MD 21740 *Tel:* 301-223-2300 *Fax:* 301-223-2398
Distribution Center: 16522 Hunters Green Pkwy, Hagerstown, MD 21740 *Tel:* 301-223-2300 *Fax:* 301-223-2398

Listen & Live Audio Inc
PO Box 817, Roseland, NJ 07068-0817
Tel: 973-781-1444 *Toll Free Tel:* 800-653-9400 *Fax:* 973-781-0333
Web Site: www.listenandlive.com
Key Personnel
Pres & Lib Sales Dir: Alfred Martino *E-mail:* alfred@listenandlive.com
Publr: Alisa Weberman *E-mail:* alisa@listenandlive.com
Founded: 1995
Strictly audio books, motivational & men's adventure.
ISBN Prefix(es): 1-885408; 1-931953; 1-59316
Number of titles published annually: 20 Audio
Total Titles: 200 Audio
Imprints: Appleseed Audio; DeFiance Audio; South Bay Entertainment
Membership(s): Audio Publishers Association; Publishers Marketing Association

Literacy Institute for Education (LIFE) Inc
Subsidiary of B K Nelson Inc
84 Woodland Rd, Pleasantville, NY 10570
Tel: 914-741-1322 *Fax:* 914-741-1324
Web Site: bknelson.com
Key Personnel
CEO: Bonita K Nelson *E-mail:* bknelson4@cs.com
VP: Erv Rosenfeld
Founded: 1994

Publish books for special children. Books, audio cassettes & CDs for special children. Adult training programs for teachers & volunteers.
ISBN Prefix(es): 0-9622627
Number of titles published annually: 12 Print
Total Titles: 5 Print; 5 CD-ROM; 2 Online; 2 E-Book; 5 Audio
Imprints: Regency
Branch Office(s)
1565 Paseo Vida, Palm Springs, CA 92264, Contact: Ellen Rosenfeld *Tel:* 760-778-8800 *Fax:* 760-778-0034

Little, Brown and Company Adult Trade Division
Subsidiary of Time Warner Book Group
1271 Avenue of the Americas, New York, NY 10020
Tel: 212-522-8700 *Fax:* 212-522-2067
Web Site: www.twbookmark.com
Key Personnel
Sr VP & Publr, Adult: Michael Pietsch
Sr VP, Adv & Promo: Martha Otis
VP & Assoc Publr: Sophie Cottrell
VP & Dir, Trade Pbks: Terry Adams
VP, Spec Mkts: Jean Griffin
VP & Creative Dir: Mario Pulice
VP, Sub Rts: Nancy Wiese
VP & Ed-in-Chief: Geoff Shandler
VP, Publicity Dir: Heather Rizzo
Sr Man Ed (Boston Office): Mary Tondorf-Dick
Mgr, Dom Subs Rts: Laura Quinn
Unsol/unagented mss not accepted.
ISBN Prefix(es): 0-316
Number of titles published annually: 100 Print
Total Titles: 850 Print
Imprints: Back Bay Books
Foreign Rights: Agencia Literaria Balcells (Portugal, Spain); Andrew Nurnberg Assoc (Baltic States, Bulgaria, Croatia, Czech Republic, Hungary, Poland, Romania, Russia & former USSR); Bardon Chinese Media (China, Taiwan); BMSR Ag Literaria (Brazil); Eric Yang Agency (Korea); I Pitarski Ltd Literary Agency (Israel); JLM Literary Agency (Greece); The KM Agency (Netherlands); Luigi Bernabo Assoc (Italy); Michelle Lapautre Agency (France); Mohrbooks Agency (Germany); Nurcihan Kesim Literary Agency (Turkey); Sane Toregard Agency (Scandinavia); Tuttle-Mori Agency (Japan)

Little, Brown and Company Books for Young Readers
Formerly Little, Brown and Company Children's Publishing
Subsidiary of Time Warner Book Group
1271 Avenue of the Americas, New York, NY 10020
SAN: 200-2205
Tel: 212-522-8700 *Toll Free Tel:* 800-759-0190 *Fax:* 212-522-7997
Web Site: www.twbookmark.com
Key Personnel
VP & Publr, Children's: David Ford
VP, Assoc Publr & Ed-in-Chief: Megan Tingley
VP, Children's Mktg & Assoc Publr: Bill Boedeker
Dir, Children's Subs Rts: Stephanie Voros
Man Ed: Alex Novak
Sr Mgr, Children's Mktg: Karin Holmgren
Founded: 1837
Specialize in children's books, bilingual books, juvenile & young adult books & reprints. Unsol/unagented mss not accepted.
ISBN Prefix(es): 0-316
Number of titles published annually: 150 Print
Total Titles: 700 Print
Imprints: Megan Tingley Books
Shipping Address: Time Warner Group Distribution Center, 121 N Enterprise Blvd, Lebanon,

IN 46052 *Tel:* 765-483-9900 *Fax:* 765-483-0706
Membership(s): AAP; ALA; Children's Book Council; Women's National Book Association

Little, Brown and Company Children's Publishing, see Little, Brown and Company Books for Young Readers

Little Simon, see Simon & Schuster Children's Publishing

Little Simon Inspirations, see Simon & Schuster Children's Publishing

§Liturgical Press
Division of The Order of St Benedict Inc
St John's Abbey, Collegeville, MN 56321
SAN: 202-2494
Mailing Address: PO Box 7500, Collegeville, MN 56321-7500
Tel: 320-363-2213 *Toll Free Tel:* 800-858-5450 *Fax:* 320-363-3299 *Toll Free Fax:* 800-445-5899
E-mail: sales@litpress.org
Web Site: www.litpress.org
Key Personnel
Dir: Peter Dwyer
Sales & Mktg Dir: Joe Riley
Fin Mgr: Jerry Furst
Mktg Mgr: Michelle Verkuilen *Tel:* 320-363-2220 ext 2227 *E-mail:* mverkuilen@osb.org
Man Ed & Intl Rts Contact: Mark Twomey
Founded: 1926
Pastoral & professional books, college textbooks, paperback & trade, AV materials; religion.
ISBN Prefix(es): 0-8146
Number of titles published annually: 85 Print
Total Titles: 1,200 Print; 5 CD-ROM; 25 Audio
Imprints: Michael Glazier Books; Liturgical Press Books; Pueblo Books
Foreign Rep(s): B Broughton Co Ltd (Canada, non-exclusive); The Catholic Bookshop (South Africa); Claretian Publications (Philippines); Columba Book Service (UK, Ireland, European Union); John Garratt Publishing (Australia); Katong Catholic Book Centre, Pt Ltd (Malaysia, Singapore)
Advertising Agency: Liturgical Advertising Agency

Liturgy Training Publications
Subsidiary of Archdiocese of Chicago
1800 N Hermitage Ave, Chicago, IL 60622-1101
SAN: 670-9052
Tel: 773-486-8970 *Toll Free Tel:* 800-933-1800 (US & Canada only) *Fax:* 773-486-7094 *Toll Free Fax:* 800-933-7094 (US & Canada only)
E-mail: orders@ltp.org
Web Site: www.ltp.org
Key Personnel
Dir: John Thomas *E-mail:* jthomas@ltp.org
Ed: Lorie Simmons *E-mail:* lsimmons@ltp.org
Gen Mgr & Intl Rts: Maureen Como *E-mail:* mcomo@ltp.org
Prepress Mgr: Theresa Pincich *E-mail:* tpincich@ltp.org
Trade Coord & Libr Sales Dir: Louise Griffin *E-mail:* lgriffin@ltp.org
Cust Serv: Timothy Quinn *E-mail:* tquinn@ltp.org
Founded: 1964
Books & periodicals on Roman Catholic liturgy, worship & prayer in the home & church.
ISBN Prefix(es): 0-930467; 0-929650; 1-56854
Number of titles published annually: 40 Print; 2 CD-ROM
Total Titles: 550 Print; 6 CD-ROM; 7 Audio
Imprints: Catechesis of the Good Shepherd Publications; Hillenbrand Books

Distributed by Oregon Catholic Press
Distributor for United States Catholic Conference Publications
Foreign Rep(s): The Catholic Bookshop (South Africa); Catholic Supplies Ltd (New Zealand); Katong Catholic Book Centre (Malaysia); Mc-Crimmons Bookstore/Publisher (UK exc Ireland); Veritas Co Ltd (Ireland); Word of Life Distributors (Australia)
Shipping Address: Tom & Mae Dore Distribution Center (LTP Warehouse), 4251 N Knox Ave, Chicago, IL 60641-1904, Contact: Jesse Rodriguez
Warehouse: 4251 N Knox, Chicago, IL 60641
Membership(s): Catholic Book Publishers Association

Living Language
Division of Random House
1745 Broadway, New York, NY 10019
Tel: 212-572-6148 *Toll Free Tel:* 800-726-0600 (orders) *Fax:* 212-940-7400 *Toll Free Fax:* 800-659-2436
E-mail: livinglanguage@randomhouse.com
Web Site: www.livinglanguage.com
Key Personnel
Pres: David Naggar
Publr, Living Language: Tom Russell
VP & Exec Man Ed: Denise Gennaro
Dir, Busn Opers: Katie Ziga
Dir, Sub/Foreign Rts: Linda Kaplan
Founded: 1946
Self-study foreign language; ESL audio/text programs; sign language & dictionaries
Random House Inc & its publishing entities are not accepting unsol submissions, proposals, mss, or submission queries via e-mail at this time.
ISBN Prefix(es): 0-609; 0-609
Number of titles published annually: 50 Print; 35 Audio
Total Titles: 200 Print; 150 Audio

§Living Stream Ministry (LSM)
2431 W La Palima Ave, Anaheim, CA 92801
Tel: 714-991-4681 *Fax:* 714-991-4685
E-mail: books@lsm.org
Web Site: www.lsm.org
Key Personnel
Intl Rts Contact: Yorke Warden
Lib Sales Dir: John Pester
Founded: 1963
Religious publications.
ISBN Prefix(es): 0-87083; 1-57593; 0-7363
Number of titles published annually: 100 Print
Total Titles: 1,000 Print

Livingston Press
Division of University of West Alabama
University of West Alabama, Sta 22, Livingston, AL 35470
Tel: 205-652-3470 *Fax:* 205-652-3717
Web Site: www.livingstonpress.uwa.edu
Key Personnel
Dir: Debbie Davis; Tina Jones; Joe Taylor
E-mail: jwt@uwa.edu
Founded: 1984
ISBN Prefix(es): 0-942979; 0-930501; 1-931982
Number of titles published annually: 10 Print
Total Titles: 80 Print
Subsidiaries: Swallow's Tale Press
Distributor for Swallow's Tale Press
Membership(s): Council of Literary Magazines & Presses; Publishers Association of the South

Llewellyn Publications
Division of Llewellyn Worldwide Ltd
PO Box 64383, St Paul, MN 55164-0383
SAN: 201-100X
Tel: 651-291-1970 *Toll Free Tel:* 800-843-6666
Fax: 651-291-1908
E-mail: lwlpc@llewellyn.com

Web Site: www.llewellyn.com
Key Personnel
Pres: Carl L Weschcke
Dir, Publicity: Alison Aten
ISBN Contact: Greg Sundem
Dir, Sales: Rhonda Ogren
Founded: 1901
Astrology, occult & New Age sciences; Thoreau.
ISBN Prefix(es): 0-87542; 1-56718
Number of titles published annually: 110 Print
Total Titles: 700 Print
Foreign Rep(s): Airlift (UK)
Shipping Address: 84 S Wabasha St, St Paul, MN 55107

The Local History Co
112 N Woodland Rd, Pittsburgh, PA 15232
Tel: 412-362-2294 *Toll Free Tel:* 866-362-0789
Fax: 412-362-8192
E-mail: info@thelocalhistorycompany.com
Web Site: www.thelocalhistorycompany.com
Key Personnel
CEO: Harold T Maguire, Jr
Chief Content Officer: Cheryl R Towers
E-mail: editor@thelocalhistorycompany.com
Founded: 2001
Publishers of history & heritage.
ISBN Prefix(es): 0-9711835; 0-9744715
Number of titles published annually: 6 Print
Total Titles: 10 Print
Membership(s): Publishers Marketing Association

Locks Art Publications/Locks Gallery
Division of Locks Gallery
600 Washington Sq S, Philadelphia, PA 19106
Tel: 215-629-1000 *Fax:* 215-629-3868
E-mail: info@locksgallery.com
Web Site: www.locksgallery.com
Key Personnel
Pres: Sueyun Locks
Contact: Doug Schaller
Founded: 1969
Exhibition catalogue, monographs on contemporary art.
ISBN Prefix(es): 1-879173; 0-9623799
Number of titles published annually: 4 Print
Total Titles: 42 Print

Loft Press Inc
181 Myra Lane, Fort Valley, VA 22652
Mailing Address: PO Box 150, Fort Valley, VA 22652
Tel: 540-933-6210 *Fax:* 540-933-6523
Key Personnel
Pres & Publr: Stephen R Hunter
Ed-in-Chief: Ann A Hunter
Founded: 1987
Books.
ISBN Prefix(es): 0-9630797; 1-893846
Number of titles published annually: 5 Print
Total Titles: 63 Print
Imprints: Eschat Press; Far Muse Press; Merry Muse Press; Punch Press
Advertising Agency: AAH Advertising *Tel:* 540-933-6211 *Fax:* 540-933-6523
Shipping Address: 187 Myra Lane, Fort Valley, VA 22652
Membership(s): Washington Book Publishers

§Logos Bible Software
1313 Commercial St, Bellingham, WA 98225-4372
Tel: 360-527-1700 *Toll Free Tel:* 800-875-6467
Fax: 360-527-1707
E-mail: info@logos.com
Web Site: www.logos.com
Founded: 1991
Electronic & e-book publisher & technology provider.
ISBN Prefix(es): 1-57799
Number of titles published annually: 6 CD-ROM; 200 E-Book

Total Titles: 100 CD-ROM; 3,800 E-Book
Membership(s): CBA; Evangelical Christian Publishers Association; Society of Bible Literature

Lone Eagle Publishing
Affiliate of Hollywood Creative Directory
1024 N Orange Dr, Los Angeles, CA 90038
Tel: 323-308-3411 *Toll Free Tel:* 800-815-0503
Fax: 323-468-7689
Web Site: www.hcdonline.com
Key Personnel
Sr VP, Publg: Jeffrey Black *E-mail:* jblack@hcdonline.com
Founded: 1982
Broad-based, trade reference & professional books on the entertainment industry.
ISBN Prefix(es): 0-943728; 1-58065; 1-928936
Number of titles published annually: 10 Print
Total Titles: 60 Print; 3 Online
Foreign Rep(s): Gazelle (UK, Europe)
Distribution Center: National Book Network (NBN), 4720 Boston Way, Lanham, MD 20706 *Tel:* 301-459-3366 *Web Site:* www.nbnbooks.com
Membership(s): Publishers Association of Los Angeles; Publishers Marketing Association
See separate listing for:
Hollywood Creative Directory

Lonely Planet Publications
150 Linden St, Oakland, CA 94607
Tel: 510-893-8555 *Toll Free Tel:* 800-275-8555 (orders) *Fax:* 510-893-8972
E-mail: info@lonelyplanet.com
Web Site: www.lonelyplanet.com
Key Personnel
Sales Mgr: Heather Harrison
Publicity Mgr: Cindy Cohen
Acctg: Denise Driscoll
Founded: 1972
Travel guidebooks & phrasebooks, videos, restaurant guides, diving guides, bicycling guides, maps & atlases & hiking guides.
ISBN Prefix(es): 0-908086; 0-86442
Number of titles published annually: 100 Print
Total Titles: 700 Print; 1 CD-ROM; 20 Online; 10 E-Book; 2 Audio
Foreign Office(s): Box 617, Hawthorn, Victoria 3122, Australia
71 bis rue du Cardinal-Lenoine, 75005 Paris, France
10 Barley Mow Passage, Chiswick, London W4, United Kingdom
Foreign Rep(s): A B E Marketing (Poland); Altair (Spain); Asia Books Co Ltd (Thailand); Asia Publishers' Services Ltd (China & Hong Kong, Taiwan); David Bateman Ltd (New Zealand); The Book Centre (Pakistan); Booktraders Ltd (Cyprus, Czech Republic, Greece, Israel, Malta, Middle East, Turkey); Brettschneider (Germany); CDE (Sales- Eng & Fr eds) (France); Centralivros (Portugal); CLB Marketing Services (Croatia, Hungary, Romania, Slovenia, Serbia and Montenegro); CV Java Books (Indonesia); Dinternal (Russia); Electra Media Group Pty Ltd (Guam, Micronesia, Philippines); Eleftheroudakis SA (Greece); Faradawn (South Africa); Freytag & Berndt U Artaria KG (Austria); Geocentre ILH (Germany); Geographical Tours Ltd (Israel); IMA Distribution (East Asia); India Book Distributors (Bombay) Ltd (India, Nepal); Intercontinental Marketing Corp (Japan); International Educational Library (Greece); Kartbutiken (Sweden); Lannoo Publishers (Belgium); Logos Art Srl (Italy); MPH Distributors (Malaysia & Singapore); Nilsson & Lamm Bv (Netherlands); Olf SA (Switzerland); Raincoast Books (Canada); Cav Giovanni Russano SAS (Italy); Scanvik Books Aps (Denmark, Finland, Iceland, Norway); Jana Seta (Latvia); Shoestring International (Korea); Sklep Podroznika (Poland); SODIS (distribution) (France); TB Clarke (Overseas Pty Ltd)

(Fiji); Text Book Centre Ltd (Kenya); Trak Trade Centre (Estonia); The Travel Bookshop (Switzerland); Vijitha Yapa Bookshop (Pvt) Ltd (Sri Lanka); Westland Sundries Ltd (Kenya); Yab Yay Yayimcilik Sanayi (Turkey)
Shipping Address: 112 Linden St, Oakland, CA 94607

Longman Publishers
Division of Pearson Education
1185 Avenue of the Americas, New York, NY 10036
Tel: 212-782-3300 *Fax:* 212-782-3311
Web Site: www.ablongman.com
Key Personnel
Pres: Roth Wilkofsky

Longstreet Press
325 N Milledge Ave, Athens, GA 30601
Tel: 706-543-5999 *Fax:* 706-543-5946
Web Site: www.longstreetpress.net
Key Personnel
Pres & Publr: Scott Bard
Dist Mgr: Joe Pruss
Founded: 1988
General fiction & nonfiction, including humor, cookbooks, photography, sports, art & children.
ISBN Prefix(es): 1-56352
Number of titles published annually: 15 Print
Total Titles: 500 Print

Loompanics Unlimited
Division of Loompanics Enterprises Inc
PO Box 1197, Port Townsend, WA 98368-0997
SAN: 206-4421
Tel: 360-385-5087 *Toll Free Tel:* 800-380-2230
(orders only) *Fax:* 360-385-7785

E-mail: editorial@loompanics.com; service@loompanics.com
Web Site: www.loompanics.com
Key Personnel
Pres & Edit Dir: Michael Hoy
Ed: Gia Cosindas
Founded: 1973
Outrageous subjects treated as matter-of-fact & with authority, as well as how-to books sometimes on obscure but useful technology.
ISBN Prefix(es): 0-915179; 1-55950
Number of titles published annually: 15 Print
Total Titles: 85 Print
Sales Office(s): PO Box 447, Port Townsend, WA 98368
Distributor for Breakout Productions Inc
Advertising Agency: Space & Time, PO Box 447, Port Townsend, WA 98368, Contact: Gia Cosindas
Billing Address: PO Box 447, Port Townsend, WA 98368

Looseleaf Law Publications Inc
Division of Wardean Corp
43-08 162 St, Flushing, NY 11358
Mailing Address: PO Box 650042, Fresh Meadows, NY 11365-0042
Tel: 718-359-5559 *Toll Free Tel:* 800-647-5547
Fax: 718-539-0941
E-mail: llawpub@erols.com
Web Site: www.LooseleafLaw.com
Key Personnel
Owner: Michael L Loughrey
VP & Edit: Mary Loughrey
Sales Dir: Hilary McKeon
Founded: 1967
Law books; study aids for law enforcement, students, attorneys & court personnel.
ISBN Prefix(es): 0-930137; 1-889031; 1-932777

Number of titles published annually: 6 Print; 3 CD-ROM
Total Titles: 116 Print; 23 CD-ROM

Lord John Press
19073 Los Alimos St, Northridge, CA 91326
SAN: 213-6333
Tel: 818-363-6621 *Fax:* 818-366-6674
Web Site: lordjohnpress.com; lordjohnpress.net
Key Personnel
Publr: Herb Yellin *Tel:* 818-360-5804
E-mail: herby11230@aol.com
Founded: 1977
Trade books, signed limited editions.
ISBN Prefix(es): 0-935716
Number of titles published annually: 4 Print
Total Titles: 68 Print
Foreign Rights: Kirby M Cauley
Advertising Agency: PS Design

Lorenz Educational Publishers
PO Box 146340, Chicago, IL 60614-6340
Tel: 773-929-9847 *Fax:* 501-423-4158
Web Site: www.shkspr.com
Key Personnel
Publr: Irene Walters
Founded: 1994
ISBN Prefix(es): 1-885564
Number of titles published annually: 3 Print
Total Titles: 13 Print
Returns: 3100 N Lake Shore Dr, Suite 608, Chicago, IL 60657

Lost Classics Book Co
PO Box 3429, Lake Wales, FL 33859-3429
Tel: 863-676-1920 *Toll Free Tel:* 800-283-3572
(wholesale orders); 888-211-2665 (educational)
Fax: 863-676-1707

E-mail: mgeditor@lostclassicsbooks.com
Web Site: www.lostclassicsbooks.com (retail site); www.lcbcbooks.com (wholesale site)
Key Personnel
Pres: George D O'Neill, Jr
Man Ed: Michael Alan Fitterling
Founded: 1996
Republish late 19th & early 20th century literature & textbooks to aid parents & teachers in educating children.
ISBN Prefix(es): 0-9652735; 1-890623
Number of titles published annually: 6 Print
Total Titles: 20 Print
Sales Office(s): Lost Classics Book Co, PO Box 1756, Fort Collins, CO 80522-1756 *Toll Free Tel:* 888-211-2665, 888-611-2665 *Fax:* 970-493-8781 *E-mail:* lostclassics@intrepidgroup.com
Distributed by Applewood Books
Membership(s): Publishers Marketing Association; Southeast Booksellers Association

Lost Horse Press
105 Lost Horse Lane, Sandpoint, ID 83864
Tel: 208-255-4410 *Fax:* 208-255-1560
E-mail: losthorsepress@mindspring.com
Web Site: losthorsepress.org
Founded: 1998
Non-profit independent press that publishes poetry, fiction & creative nonfiction titles of high literary merit. Makes available fine contemporary literature through it's cultural, educational & publishing programs & activities.
Number of titles published annually: 6 Print
Total Titles: 19 Print
Branch Office(s)
High Hopes Project, 620 Wellington Place, Hope, ID 83836
Distribution Center: Small Press Distribution
Membership(s): Council of Literary Magazines & Presses; Publishers Marketing Association; Small Publishers Association of North America

Lotus Light Publications, see Lotus Press

Lotus Press
Division of Lotus Brands Inc
PO Box 325, Twin Lakes, WI 53181-0325
Tel: 262-889-8561 *Toll Free Tel:* 800-824-6396 (orders only) *Fax:* 262-889-8591
E-mail: lotuspress@lotuspress.com
Web Site: www.lotuspress.com
Key Personnel
Pres: Santosh Krinsky *E-mail:* santosh@lotuspress.com
Founded: 1981
Health, yoga, Native American & New Age metaphysics.
ISBN Prefix(es): 0-941524; 0-910261; 0-914955; 0-940985; 0-940676
Number of titles published annually: 30 Print; 2 CD-ROM; 3 Audio
Total Titles: 300 Print; 4 CD-ROM; 40 Audio
Imprints: Arcana Publishing; DIPTI; Shangri-La; Specialized Software
Distributor for Back to Eden Books; Dipti; Inner Worlds Music; Les Editions E T C; November Moon; S A B D A; Sadhana Publications; Samata Books; Sri Aurobindo Ashram; Star Sounds
Warehouse: 1100 Lotus Dr, Bldg 3, Silver Lake, WI 53170
Membership(s): Network of Alternatives for Publishers, Retailers & Artists Inc

Louisiana State University Press
PO Box 25053, Baton Rouge, LA 70894-5053
SAN: 202-6597
Tel: 225-578-6294 *Toll Free Tel:* 800-861-3477 *Fax:* 225-578-6461 *Toll Free Fax:* 800-305-4416

E-mail: lsupress@lsu.edu
Web Site: www.lsu.edu/guests/lsupress
Key Personnel
Dir: MaryKatherine Calloway
Asst Dir & Prodn Mgr: Laura Gleason
Assoc Dir & Busn Mgr: William Bossier
Sales Mgr: Rebekah Brown
Mktg Mgr: Margaret Hart
Man Ed: Lee Campbell Sioles
Perms: Deborah Carter
Adv: Lauren Cavanaugh
Publicity: Barbara Outland
Asst Busn Mgr: Patrick Reynolds
Founded: 1935
Scholarly, regional, general; humanities & social sciences; southern history & literature; poetry; government & political science; music; paperbacks.
ISBN Prefix(es): 0-8071
Number of titles published annually: 80 Print
Total Titles: 4 CD-ROM
Subsidiaries: McIntosh & Otis
Foreign Rep(s): East-West Export Books (Australia, Asia, Japan, New Zealand, Pacific); Eurospan (Africa, UK, Europe, Middle East); LSU Press Sales Dept (Caribbean & Latin America, Puerto Rico); Scholarly Book Services (Canada)
Warehouse: Printing Bldg, 3555 River Rd, Baton Rouge, LA 70803
Membership(s): AAP; American Association of University Presses

Love Publishing Co
9101 E Kenyon Ave, Suite 2200, Denver, CO 80237
SAN: 205-2482
Tel: 303-221-7333 *Fax:* 303-221-7444
E-mail: lpc@lovepublishing.com
Web Site: www.lovepublishing.com
Key Personnel
Chmn of the Bd, Pres & Publr: Stanley F Love
Cust Rel: Amber Tadych
Founded: 1968
College textbooks, journals & professional books in counseling, social work & special education.
ISBN Prefix(es): 0-89108
Number of titles published annually: 12 Print
Total Titles: 110 Print
Foreign Rep(s): Incentive Plus Ltd (UK/Europe)

Loyola Press
3441 N Ashland Ave, Chicago, IL 60657
SAN: 211-6537
Tel: 773-281-1818; 773-244-4429 *Toll Free Tel:* 800-621-1008 *Fax:* 773-281-0555; 773-281-0152 (trade)
E-mail: editorial@loydapress.com
Web Site: www.loyolapress.org
Key Personnel
Pres: George A Lane
Sr VP Fin: Trudy Weisel
VP: Terry Locke
Edit Dir, Trade Div: Jim Manney
Dir, Catechetical Servs: Barbara Campbell
Trade Div, Mktg Mgr: Merissa Crane
Sr Acq Ed, Trade Books: Joseph Durepos *E-mail:* durepos@loyolapress.com
Man Ed, Trade Books: Matthew S Diener *Tel:* 773-281-1818 ext 278 *E-mail:* diener@loyolapress.com
Founded: 1912
Catholic publisher of books for elementary schools, parishes & the general trade.
ISBN Prefix(es): 0-8294
Number of titles published annually: 50 Print
Total Titles: 50 Print
Imprints: Jesuit Way
Distributor for Biblical Institute Press; Gregorian University Press; Jesuit Historical Institute; Oriental Institute Press

LPD Press
925 Salamanca NW, Albuquerque, NM 87107-5647
Tel: 505-344-9382 *Fax:* 505-345-5129
E-mail: info@nmsantos.com
Web Site: www.nmsantos.com
Key Personnel
Sr Partner: Barbe Awalt; Paul Rhetts
Founded: 1984
Publisher of books on the Hispanic Southwest & a quarterly magazine on the art & culture of the Hispanic American Southwest.
ISBN Prefix(es): 0-9641542; 1-890689
Number of titles published annually: 4 Print; 1 CD-ROM
Total Titles: 20 Print; 1 CD-ROM
Membership(s): New Mexico Book Association; Publishers Marketing Association

§LRP Publications
360 Hiatt Dr, Palm Beach Gardens, FL 33418
Tel: 215-784-0860 *Toll Free Tel:* 800-341-7874 *Fax:* 215-784-9639
E-mail: custserve@lrp.com
Web Site: www.lrp.com
Key Personnel
Pres: Kenneth F Kahn *Tel:* 561-622-6520
Founded: 1978
Legal & general nonfiction in the areas of personal education, health, bankruptcy, employment, disability, workers compensation & personal injury, human resources, international & European coverage, arbitration, corrections, customer service, leadership, teamwork & sales.
ISBN Prefix(es): 0-934753
Number of titles published annually: 580 Print; 20 CD-ROM; 48 Online; 10 Audio
Total Titles: 4,200 Print; 25 CD-ROM; 65 Online; 15 Audio
Online services available through Lexis, Westlaw.
Subsidiaries: The Dartnell Corp; LRP Magazine Group
Divisions: Jury Verdict Research; LRP Magazine Group
Membership(s): NEPA

LRS
Division of Library Reproduction Service
14214 S Figueroa St, Los Angeles, CA 90061-1034
Tel: 310-354-2610 *Toll Free Tel:* 800-255-5002 *Fax:* 310-354-2601
E-mail: lrsprint@aol.com
Web Site: lrs-largeprint.com
Key Personnel
Pres: Joan Hudson-Miller
VP & Gen Mgr: Peter Jones
Founded: 1946
Adult & children's titles-classics-just fiction.
ISBN Prefix(es): 1-58118
Number of titles published annually: 20 Print
Total Titles: 91 Print

Lucent Books Inc
Imprint of The Gale Group
15822 Bernardo Center Dr, Suite C, San Diego, CA 92127
Tel: 858-485-7424 *Fax:* 858-485-9549
E-mail: info@gale.com
Web Site: www.gale.com/lucent
Key Personnel
Pres: Bruce Glassman
Publr: Bonnie Szumski
Man Ed: Lori Shein
Acqs Ed: Chandra Howard *Tel:* 858-485-7424, ext 2956 *E-mail:* chandra.howard@thomson.com
Promos Coord: Nancy Stetzinger
Office Mgr: Sonya Parker
Founded: 1988
Nonfiction books aimed at the upper elementary & junior high level which explore current is-

sues & social studies. *New World Histories* series & *The Way People Live* series. Overview series for high interest topics for reports & informative reading: *Biography, Famous Trials, Building History, Great Religions, Heroes & Villains, Diseases & Disorders, Science & Technology* series.
ISBN Prefix(es): 1-56006; 1-59018
Number of titles published annually: 150 Print
Total Titles: 900 Print
Distributed by Greenhaven Press Inc; Lucent
Distributor for Greenhaven Press Inc; Kidhaven; Lucent; Sleeping Bear Press; Thorndike (Young Adult)

Lucky Press LLC
126 S Maple St, Lancaster, OH 43130
Tel: 740-689-2950 (orders & editorial) *Fax:* 740-689-2951 (orders & editorial)
E-mail: books@luckypress.com
Web Site: www.luckypress.com
Key Personnel
Ed-in-Chief: Janice Phelps
VP: Joan E Phelps
Founded: 1999
Trade publisher specializing in: alternative health, aviation & history.
ISBN Prefix(es): 0-9676050; 0-9706377; 0-9713318
Number of titles published annually: 3 Print
Total Titles: 15 Print
Imprints: Sleepy Dog
Warehouse: 507 E Chestnut St, Lancaster, OH 43130 *Tel:* 740-689-2950 *Fax:* 740-689-2951 *E-mail:* books@luckypress.com *Web Site:* luckypress.com
Membership(s): Publishers Marketing Association

Ludwig von Mises Institute
518 W Magnolia Ave, Auburn, AL 36832
Tel: 334-321-2100 *Fax:* 334-321-2119
Web Site: www.mises.org
Key Personnel
Pres: Llewellyn H Rockwell, Jr
Membership Servs Dir: Susan Thomas
E-mail: susan@mises.org
Founded: 1982
Nonprofit educational organization devoted to the Austrian School of Economics.
ISBN Prefix(es): 0-945466
Number of titles published annually: 4 Print
Total Titles: 28 Print

Luna Bisonte Prods
137 Leland Ave, Columbus, OH 43214
Tel: 614-846-4126
Key Personnel
Head & Intl Rts: John M Bennett
Founded: 1974
Avant-garde to experimental literature & poetry.
ISBN Prefix(es): 0-935350; 1-892280
Number of titles published annually: 4 Print; 1 Audio
Total Titles: 160 Print; 26 Audio
Subsidiaries: Lost & Found Times

Lyceum Books Inc
5758 S Blackstone Ave, Chicago, IL 60637
Tel: 773-643-1902 *Fax:* 773-643-1903
E-mail: lyceum@lyceumbooks.com
Web Site: www.lyceumbooks.com
Key Personnel
Pres & Intl Rts: David C Follmer
Founded: 1988
Provide full services for other publishers.
ISBN Prefix(es): 0-925065
Number of titles published annually: 7 Print
Total Titles: 28 Print
Warehouse: c/o Ware-Pak Inc, 2427 Bond St, University Park, IL 60466

Lyndon B Johnson School of Public Affairs
University of Texas Austin, 2316 Red River St, Austin, TX 78705
Mailing Address: Office of Communications, PO Box Y, Austin, TX 78713-8925
Tel: 512-471-4218 *Fax:* 512-475-8867
E-mail: pubsinfo@uts.cc.utexas.edu
Web Site: www.utexas.edu/lbj/pubs/
Key Personnel
Sales & Accts Mgr: Karen Love
E-mail: karenlove@mail.utexas.edu
Founded: 1972
Working papers; public service handbooks; monographs; periodicals on public affairs topics; policy research projects.
ISBN Prefix(es): 0-89940
Number of titles published annually: 10 Print
Total Titles: 330 Print
Returns: (No refunds; replace damaged books only. All sales are final. Prepayment usually required.)

Lynx House Press
420 W 24 St, Spokane, WA 99203
Tel: 509-624-4894 *Fax:* 509-623-4238
Key Personnel
Dir & Ed-in-Chief: Christopher Howell
E-mail: cnhowell@mail.ewu.edu
Prodn Mgr: Barbara Anderson
Dist Coord: David Luckert
Intl Rts: John Orr
Founded: 1972
Fiction & poetry.
ISBN Prefix(es): 0-89924
Number of titles published annually: 7 Print
Total Titles: 120 Print
Imprints: Anderson Northstar Editions
Branch Office(s)
9305 SE Salmon Ct, Portland, OR 97216
Distributed by Michigan State University Press; Small Press Distribution
Advertising Agency: Arrested Image
Distribution Center: SPD, 1341 Seventh St, Berkeley, CA 94710

The Lyons Press
Imprint of The Globe Pequot Press
246 Goose Lane, Guilford, CT 06437
Tel: 203-458-4500 *Toll Free Tel:* 800-243-0495 *Fax:* 203-458-4668
Web Site: www.lyonspress.com; www.globepequot.com
Key Personnel
Edit Dir: Jay Cassell *E-mail:* jay.cassell@lyonspress.com
Publr: Tony Lyons *E-mail:* tlyons4808@aol.com
Man Ed: Alicia Solis *Tel:* 206-458-4668 *E-mail:* alicia.solis@lyonspress.com
Off-site Ed: Enrica Gadler *E-mail:* gadlertlp@aol.com
Sr Ed: Tom McCarthy *E-mail:* tom.mccarthy@lyonspress.com; Ann Treistman *E-mail:* ann.treistman@lyonspress.com
Sr Acqs Ed: George Donahue *E-mail:* george.donahue@lyonspress.com
Ed: Jay McCullough *E-mail:* jay.mccullough@lyonspress.com
Asst Ed: Christine Duffy *E-mail:* christine.duffy@lyonspress.com
Prodn Ed: Holly Rubino *E-mail:* holly.rubino@lyonspress.com
Ed-at-Large: Lilly Golden *E-mail:* golden@catskill.net; Steve Price *E-mail:* sdprice@aol.com
Prodn Coord: Chris Mongillo *E-mail:* chris.mongillo@lyonspress.com
HR Mgr: Valerie Brown *E-mail:* valerie.brown@globe-pequot.com
Founded: 1978
Outdoors, natural history, sports, fitness, cooking, military history, fishing, hunting, equine, nonfiction, fiction, practical, Americana, outdoor skills, pets, nautical, survival & adventure.

ISBN Prefix(es): 1-55821; 0-8329; 0-8052; 0-89933; 1-58574; 1-59228; 0-936644
Number of titles published annually: 275 Print; 100 E-Book
Total Titles: 1,500 Print
Distributor for Design Books
Foreign Rep(s): Windsor Publications Intl (UK)
Foreign Rights: Gail Blackhall
Warehouse: The Globe Pequot Press Distribution Ctr, 128 Pinnacle Dr, Springfield, TN 37172

M R T S
Imprint of ACMRS
PO Box 874402, Tempe, AZ 85287-4402
Tel: 480-727-6503 *Toll Free Tel:* 800-666-2211 *Fax:* 480-727-6505 *Toll Free Fax:* 800-688-2877
E-mail: mrts@asu.edu
Web Site: www.asu.edu/clas/acmrs/mrts
Key Personnel
Man Ed: Roy Rukkila *Tel:* 480-727-6503
Scholarly/academic press specializing in medival & Renaissance texts & studies.
ISBN Prefix(es): 0-86698
Number of titles published annually: 18 Print
Total Titles: 275 Print
Sales Office(s): Cornell University Press Services, PO Box 6525, Ithaca, NY 14851 *Tel:* 607-277-2211 *Toll Free Tel:* 800-666-2211 *Toll Free Fax:* 800-688-2877 *E-mail:* orderbook@cupserv.org
Billing Address: Cornell University Press Services, PO Box 6525, Ithaca, NY 14851 *Tel:* 607-277-2211 *Toll Free Tel:* 800-666-2211 *Toll Free Fax:* 800-688-2877 *E-mail:* orderbook@cupserv.org
Orders to: Cornell University Press Services, PO Box 6525, Ithaca, NY 14851 *Tel:* 607-277-2211 *Toll Free Tel:* 800-666-2211 *Toll Free Fax:* 800-688-2877 *E-mail:* orderbook@cupserv.org
Returns: Cornell University Press Services, PO Box 6525, Ithaca, NY 14851 *Tel:* 607-277-2211 *Toll Free Tel:* 800-666-2211 *Toll Free Fax:* 800-688-2877 *E-mail:* orderbook@cupserv.org
Distribution Center: Cornell University Press Services, PO Box 6525, Ithaca, NY 14851 *Tel:* 607-277-2211 *Toll Free Tel:* 800-666-2211 *Toll Free Fax:* 800-688-2877 *E-mail:* orderbook@cupserv.org

M S G-Haskell House Publishers Ltd
Subsidiary of M S G
PO Box 190420, Brooklyn, NY 11219-0420
SAN: 202-2818
Tel: 718-435-7878 *Fax:* 718-633-7050
Key Personnel
Acqs Ed, Sales Mgr & Rts & Perms: H Smith
Prodn Mgr: John Arnold
Adv Mgr: Gabriel Yearwood
Founded: 1964
Scholarly reprints.
ISBN Prefix(es): 0-8383
Number of titles published annually: 50 Print; 120 CD-ROM
Total Titles: 1,600 Print

M U Press, see Marquette University Press

MacAdam/Cage Publishing Inc
155 Sansome St, Suite 550, San Francisco, CA 94104
SAN: 299-9730
Tel: 415-986-7502 *Toll Free Tel:* 866-986-7470 *Fax:* 415-986-7414
E-mail: info@macadmcage.com
Web Site: www.macadamcage.com
Key Personnel
Pres: Scott Allen *Tel:* 415-986-7502 ext 15 *E-mail:* scott@macadamcage.com
Publr: David Poindexter *Tel:* 415-986-7502 ext 12 *E-mail:* david@macadamcage.com

Sales & Mktg Mgr: Melanie Mitchell
Tel: 303-753-7565 *Fax:* 303-753-7566
E-mail: melanie@macadamcage.com
Opers Mgr: Avril Sande *Tel:* 415-986-7502 ext 10
E-mail: avril@macadamcage.com
Ed: Anika Streitfeld *Tel:* 415-986-7502 ext 26
E-mail: anika@macadamcage.com; Pat Walsh
Tel: 415-986-7502 ext 13 *E-mail:* pat@
macadamcage.com
Art Dir: Dorothy Carico Smith *Tel:* 415-397-8808
Fax: 415-397-8809 *E-mail:* carico@pacbell.net
Publicist: Tasha Kepler *Tel:* 303-753-7565
E-mail: tasha@macadamcage.com
Publicity Coord: Julie Burton *E-mail:* julie@
macadamcage.com
Ordering: J P Moriarty *Tel:* 415-986-7502 ext 17
E-mail: jp@macadamcage.com
Founded: 1998
Publishers of fiction & nonfiction.
ISBN Prefix(es): 1-878448; 0-9673701; 1-931561
Number of titles published annually: 36 Print
Total Titles: 154 Print
Imprints: MacAdam/Cage Publishing Children's
Sales Office(s): 1900 Wazee St, Suite 210, Denver, CO 80202 *Tel:* 303-753-7565 *Fax:* 303-753-7566
Foreign Rights: Agence Eliane Benisiti (France); Akcali Copyright Agency (Turkey); BMSR (Brazil); Chandler Crawford Agency; Harris/Elon Agency (Israel); International Editors' Co (Spain); Licht & Burr Literary Agency (Scandinavia); Literarische Agentur Andreas Brunner (Austria, Germany, Switzerland); Piergiorgio Nicolazzini Literary Agency (Italy); Prava/Prevodi Permissions & Rights (Eastern Europe); Abner Stein (UK); Synopsis Literary Agency (Russia); Tuttle-Mori Agency (Japan); Eric Yang Agency (Korea)
Warehouse: The Intrepid Group, 1331 Red Cedar Circle, Fort Collins, CO 80524 *Tel:* 970-493-3793 *Fax:* 970-493-8781
Distribution Center: Maple Vail Distribution Center, 704 Legionaire Dr, Lebanon, PA 17402 *Tel:* 717-865-7600 *Fax:* 717-865-7800
Membership(s): AAP; NEBA; Northern California Independent Booksellers Association; Southeast Booksellers Association

Macalester Park Publishing Co
Division of Beard Communications
7317 Cahill Rd, Minneapolis, MN 55439-2067
Tel: 952-562-1234 *Toll Free Tel:* 800-407-9078
Fax: 952-941-3010
E-mail: publisher@mcchronicle.com
Web Site: www.mcchronicle.com
Key Personnel
Pres: Michael Beard
Founded: 1947
Publisher of books to an interdenominational main line Protestant market. Topics include prayer, inspirational literature, books on racial & relationship reconciliation.
ISBN Prefix(es): 0-910924; 1-881158
Number of titles published annually: 60 Print
Total Titles: 45 Print
Imprints: Clear Horizon Books; Las Brisas Research Press
Distributor for Priority Multimedia

Macmillan/McGraw-Hill
Division of McGraw-Hill Education
2 Penn Plaza, New York, NY 10121
Tel: 212-904-2000
Key Personnel
Pres: Sari Factor
Founded: 1989
Print & electronic elementary school instructional materials.
ISBN Prefix(es): 0-02
Number of titles published annually: 7,300 Print; 75 CD-ROM; 75 Audio
Total Titles: 35,000 Print; 815 CD-ROM; 50 Online; 700 Audio

Imprints: Benziger
Warehouse: Desoto Distribution Center, 220 E Danieldale Rd, DeSoto, TX 75115-8815 *Toll Free Tel:* 800-442-9685 *Fax:* 972-224-5444

§Macmillan Reference USA™
Imprint of Thomson Gale
12 Lunar Dr, Woodbridge, CT 06525
Tel: 203-397-2600 *Toll Free Tel:* 800-444-0799
Fax: 203-392-3095
Web Site: www.gale.com
Key Personnel
Publr: Frank Menchaca
ISBN Prefix(es): 0-02; 0-7838; 0-13; 0-7862
Total Titles: 47 CD-ROM

Madison House Publishers
Member of Rowman & Littlefield Publishing Group
4501 Forbes Blvd, Lanham, MD 20706
SAN: 247-4433
Tel: 301-459-3366 *Toll Free Tel:* 800-462-6420
Fax: 301-429-5748
Web Site: www.rowmanlittlefield.com
Key Personnel
Pres: Jed Lyons
Founded: 1988
American history & culture.
ISBN Prefix(es): 0-945612; 0-7425
Number of titles published annually: 10 Print
Total Titles: 50 Print
Distributor for Center for Study of American Constitution

Madison Square Press
10 E 23 St, New York, NY 10010
Tel: 212-505-0950 *Fax:* 212-979-2207
Key Personnel
Owner: Gerald McConnell
Founded: 1982
ISBN Prefix(es): 0-942604
Number of titles published annually: 10 Print

Mage Publishers Inc
1032 29 St NW, Washington, DC 20007
Tel: 202-342-1642 *Toll Free Tel:* 800-962-0922
Fax: 202-342-9269
E-mail: info@mage.com
Web Site: www.mage.com
Key Personnel
Publr & Ed: Mohammad Batmanglij
E-mail: mb@mage.com
Art Dir: Najmieh Batmanglij *E-mail:* nb@mage.com
Asst to Publr & Rts Contact: Amin Sepehri
E-mail: as@mage.com
Founded: 1985
Persian literature, art & culture in English; poetry, fiction, art & history.
ISBN Prefix(es): 0-934211
Number of titles published annually: 4 Print
Total Titles: 34 Print
Imprints: Jefferson Editions
Distributed by University of Toronto Press
Foreign Rights: Gazelle Book Services (UK)
Warehouse: Tasco, 9 Jay Gould Ct, Waldorf, MD 20601
Membership(s): AAP

The Magni Co
Subsidiary of The Magni Group Inc
7106 Wellington Point Rd, McKinney, TX 75070
Tel: 972-540-2050 *Fax:* 972-540-1057
E-mail: sales@magnico.com; info@magnico.com
Web Site: www.magnico.com
Key Personnel
Pres: Evan B Reynolds
VP: Darlene Reynolds
Dir, Mktg: Lindsay Kirk
Founded: 1982

Health books, weight loss books, informative books, organizer books.
ISBN Prefix(es): 1-882330
Number of titles published annually: 5 Print; 2 Audio
Total Titles: 43 Print; 45 Online; 8 Audio
Membership(s): ABA

Maharishi University of Management Press
Subsidiary of Maharishi University of Management
1000 N Fourth St, Dept 1155, Fairfield, IA 52557-1155
Tel: 641-472-1101 *Toll Free Tel:* 800-831-6523
Fax: 641-472-1122
E-mail: mumpress@mum.edu
Web Site: www.mumpress.com
Key Personnel
Dir: Harry Bright
Mgr, Press Mktg & Dist: Richard Andrews
Founded: 1974
Specialize in books about transcendental meditation.
ISBN Prefix(es): 0-9616944; 0-923569
Number of titles published annually: 3 Print
Total Titles: 50 Print; 4 Audio
Distributed by Fairfield Press; Penguin Group (USA) Inc

Maisonneuve Press
Division of Institute for Advanced Cultural Studies
PO Box 2980, Washington, DC 20013-2980
Tel: 301-277-7505 *Fax:* 301-277-2467
Web Site: www.maisonneuvepress.com
Key Personnel
Dir: Robert Merrill
Assoc Ed: Dennis Crow; Thomas Wilkinson
Founded: 1986
Publish books for academic market.
ISBN Prefix(es): 0-944624
Number of titles published annually: 8 Print
Total Titles: 32 Print
Distributed by Merlin Press (London, England)
Membership(s): Publishers Marketing Association

Management Advisory Services & Publications (MASP)
PO Box 81151, Wellesley Hills, MA 02481-0001
SAN: 203-8692
Tel: 781-235-2895 *Fax:* 781-235-5446
Web Site: www.masp.com
Key Personnel
Ed: Jay Kuong *E-mail:* jaykmasp@aol.com; Richard Kuong *Tel:* 215-855-4465; N Lagos
Founded: 1972
A well established publications & advisory & training services company with a concentration in information technology reference books, journals & practitioners' manuals. Additionally, we are currently product diversifying into the literary fiction book market as it is publishing its first title in this category.
ISBN Prefix(es): 0-940706
Number of titles published annually: 10 Print
Total Titles: 50 Print
Branch Office(s)
10 Winterfrost Dr, Brunswick, ME 04011, Contact: M Rushin *Tel:* 207-729-1462 *Fax:* 207-729-1462
202 Hopkins Ct, North Wales, PA 19454, Contact: R Kuong *Tel:* 215-855-4465
E-mail: rich_kuong@merck.com
Foreign Office(s): Santa Fe Ave, Buenes Aires, Argentina, Contact: D Ramos
E-mail: dramos@satlink.com

§Management Concepts Inc
8230 Leesburg Pike, Suite 800, Vienna, VA 22182
Tel: 703-790-9595 *Fax:* 703-790-1930
E-mail: publications@managementconcepts.com
Web Site: www.managementconcepts.com

Key Personnel
Pres: Tom Dungan III
Publr: Jack W Knowles
Mktg Dir: Cynthia Smith
Ed: Steven Simpson
Sales: Cheryl Fine
Founded: 1981
Books, newsletters, looseleafs & electronic products serving the information needs of acquisition & federal financial management professionals.
ISBN Prefix(es): 1-56726
Number of titles published annually: 20 Print; 5 CD-ROM
Warehouse: PMDS Inc, 9060 Junction Dr, Annapolis Junction, MD 20701, Mike Elam
Tel: 301-604-3305
Membership(s): AAP

§Management Sciences for Health
165 Allandale Rd, Boston, MA 02130-3400
Tel: 617-524-7799 *Fax:* 617-524-2825
E-mail: bookstore@msh.org
Web Site: www.msh.org
Key Personnel
Dir of Publns: Janice Miller *Tel:* 617-942-9312
  E-mail: jmiller@msh.org
Deputy Dir of Publns: Barbara K Timmons
  Tel: 617-942-9291 *E-mail:* btimmons@msh.org
Sr Ed: Claire Bahamon *Tel:* 617-942-9212
  E-mail: cbahamon@msh.org
Sr Writer-Ed: Laura Lorenz *Tel:* 617-942-9300
  E-mail: llorenz@msh.org
Founded: 1971
Established to "assist, promote, evaluate, manage & perform research on the delivery of health care," establish "methods & procedures leading to the improvement of health & social services," & conduct education & publishing in these areas. MSH's Publications Unit develops & distributes books & a quarterly periodical to further MSH's mission, which is to help close the gap between knowledge about public health problems & action to solve them.
MSH currently stocks about three dozen products, most of which are books (including monographs, manuals, & handbooks, some of which are available on CD-ROM). Many are available in languages other than English. Major products are The Manager continuing education quarterly; Managing Drug Supply (first published in 1981); instructional manuals (CORE, MOST, HOSPICAL, FIMAT); the Lessons from MSH & Stubbs monograph series; the series of "success stories" (20-page color booklets that present the highlights of successful programs) & books ranging from textbooks to syntheses of research.
MHS has offices in Afghanistan, Angola, Guinea, Haiti, Indonesia, Malawi, the Philippines & Senegal.
ISBN Prefix(es): 0-913723
Number of titles published annually: 2 Print; 1 CD-ROM
Total Titles: 28 Print; 3 CD-ROM
Branch Office(s)
891 Centre St, Boston, MA 02130-3400, Contact: Mike Paydos *Tel:* 617-524-7766 *Fax:* 617-524-1363 *E-mail:* mpaydos@msh.org
4301 N Fairfax Dr, Suite 400, Arlington, VA 22203-1627, Contact: Keith Johnson *Tel:* 703-524-6575 *Fax:* 703-524-7898 *E-mail:* kjohnson@msh.org
Foreign Office(s): MSH Europe, 13, Chemin du Levant, 01210 Ferney-Voltaire, France, Contact: Denis Broun *Tel:* (04) 50 40 22 75 *Fax:* (04) 50 42 98 74 *E-mail:* dbroun@msh.org
Distributed by Kumarian Press
Foreign Rep(s): Last-First Networks (Asia-Pacific); Teaching Aids at Low Cost (TALC) (World)
Billing Address: MSH Bookstore, 165 Allandale Rd, Boston, MA 02130, Contact: Sherry Co-

taco *Tel:* 617-942-9234 *Fax:* 617-524-2825
  E-mail: scotaco@msh.org
Orders to: MSH Bookstore, 165 Allandale Rd, Boston, MA 02130, Contact: Sherry Cotaco *Tel:* 617-942-9316 *Fax:* 617-524-2825
  E-mail: bookstore@msh.org
Returns: MSH Bookstore, 165 Allandale Rd, Boston, MA 02130, Contact: Sherry Cotaco *Tel:* 617-942-9316 *Fax:* 617-524-2825
  E-mail: bookstore@msh.org
Shipping Address: MSH Bookstore, 165 Allandale Rd, Boston, MA 02130, Contact: Sherry Cotaco *Tel:* 617-942-9316 *Fax:* 617-524-2825
  E-mail: bookstore@msh.org
Warehouse: The Field Companies, 108 Clematis Ave, No 8, Waltham, MA 02453, Contact: David O Wilson *Tel:* 781-893-0994 *Fax:* 781-893-1227 *E-mail:* davew@fieldcompanies.com
Distribution Center: The Field Companies, 108 Clematis Ave, No 8, Waltham, MA 02453, Contact: David O Wilson *Tel:* 781-893-0994 *Fax:* 781-893-1227 *E-mail:* davew@fieldcompanies.com
Membership(s): Publishers Marketing Association

Manatee Publishing
Subsidiary of Four Seasons Publishers
176 Fairview Ave, Cocoa, FL 32927
Mailing Address: PO Box 6467, Titusville, FL 32782-6467
Tel: 321-632-2932 *Fax:* 321-632-2935
E-mail: fseasons@bellsouth.net
Key Personnel
Publr: Frank Hudak
Founded: 1997
Fiction, nonfiction, poetry, young adult.
ISBN Prefix(es): 1-891929; 1-932497
Number of titles published annually: 6 Print
Total Titles: 4 Print
Membership(s): Southeast Booksellers Association

Mandala Publishing
Affiliate of Palace Press International
17 Paul Dr, San Rafael, CA 94903
Tel: 415-883-4055 *Toll Free Tel:* 800-688-2218 (orders only) *Fax:* 415-884-0500
E-mail: mandala@mandala.org
Web Site: www.mandala.org
Key Personnel
CEO: Raoul Goff *Tel:* 415-526-1370 ext 1370
  E-mail: raoul@palacepress.com
Publr: Peter Beren *Tel:* 415-526-1370 ext 205
  E-mail: peter@palacepress.com
Edit Dir: Lisa Fitzpatrick *Tel:* 415-526-1380 ext 245 *E-mail:* lisa@mandala.com
Founded: 1987
Full color coffee table books & minibooks, as well as decks, calendars, journals, greeting cards, art prints & incense. Topics include: environmental issues, women's studies, Asian art, music, philosophy, cross-cultural issues & Hinduism.
ISBN Prefix(es): 1-886069; 1-932771
Number of titles published annually: 15 Print; 2 Audio
Total Titles: 75 Print; 200 Online; 10 Audio
Distributed by Ten Speed Press
Shipping Address: Ten Speed Press Warehouse, 1111 Eighth St, Berkeley, CA 94710
Warehouse: Ten Speed Press Warehouse, 1111 Eighth St, Berkeley, CA 94710
Distribution Center: Ten Speed Press Warehouse, 1111 Eighth St, Berkeley, CA 94710
Membership(s): Bookbuilders West; Northern California Book Publicity & Marketing Association; Publishers Association of the West; Publishers Marketing Association

Manhattan Publishing Co
Division of US & Europe Books Inc
PO Box 850, Croton-on-Hudson, NY 10520-0850

Tel: 914-271-5194 *Toll Free Tel:* 888-686-7066
  Fax: 914-271-5856
Web Site: www.manhattanpublishing.com
Key Personnel
Pres: Thomas A Johnson
Lib Sales Dir: Theresa Gibson
Founded: 1938
Import sales for Council of Europe, European Court of Human Rights.
Number of titles published annually: 200 Print
Total Titles: 3,000 Print; 20 CD-ROM
Editorial Office(s): 468 Albany Post Rd, Croton-on-Hudson, NY 10520
Sales Office(s): 468 Albany Post Rd, Croton-on-Hudson, NY 10520
Distributor for Assembly of Western European Union; Council of Europe; European Court of Human Rights
Billing Address: 468 Albany Post Rd, Croton-on-Hudson, NY 10520
Orders to: 468 Albany Post Rd, Croton-on-Hudson, NY 10520
Returns: 468 Albany Post Rd, Croton-on-Hudson, NY 10520

Manic D Press
250 Banks St, San Francisco, CA 94110
Mailing Address: PO Box 410804, San Francisco, CA 94141
Tel: 415-648-8288 *Fax:* 415-648-8288
E-mail: info@manicdpress.com
Web Site: www.manicdpress.com
Key Personnel
Publr & Intl Rts: Jennifer Joseph
Founded: 1984
Poetry & unusual fiction & alternative travel books, emphasis on innovative, new & established styles, writers & artists, paperbacks, general adult books.
ISBN Prefix(es): 0-916397
Number of titles published annually: 10 Print
Total Titles: 60 Print
Distributed by Publishers Group West
Foreign Rep(s): PGW (Australia, Asia); Publishers Group West (Canada); Turnaround Distribution (England)
Membership(s): Council of Literary Magazines & Presses

Manning Publications Co
209 Bruce Park Ave, Greenwich, CT 06830
Tel: 203-629-2211 *Fax:* 203-661-9018
E-mail: orders@manning.com
Web Site: www.manning.com
Key Personnel
Publr: Marjan Bace *Tel:* 203-629-2028 *Fax:* 203-629-8535 *E-mail:* maba@manning.com
Busn Mgr: Lee Fitzpatrick *Tel:* 203-629-2078
  E-mail: lee@manning.com
Founded: 1990
Full-scale company whose titles are distributed in the US, Europe & Asia.
ISBN Prefix(es): 1-884777; 1-930110
Number of titles published annually: 20 Print; 10 E-Book
Total Titles: 130 Print; 20 CD-ROM; 25 E-Book
Distributed by IPG; Pearson Education; Prentice Hall; TransQuest Publishers Pte Ltd; Woodslane Pty Ltd

MapEasy Inc
PO Box 80, Wainscotte, NY 11975-0080
Tel: 631-537-6213 *Toll Free Tel:* 888-627-3279
  Fax: 631-537-4541
E-mail: info@mapeasy.com
Web Site: www.mapeasy.com
Key Personnel
Owner: Gary Bradherrding *Tel:* 631-537-6213 ext 160; Chris Harris *Tel:* 631-537-6213 ext 150
Founded: 1989
Guidemaps & location guides.
ISBN Prefix(es): 1-878979

Number of titles published annually: 50 Print
Total Titles: 64 Print

Mapletree Publishing Co
6233 Harvard Lane, Highlands Ranch, CO 80130-3773
Tel: 303-791-9024 *Toll Free Tel:* 800-537-0414
Fax: 303-791-9028
E-mail: mail@mapletreepublishing.com
Web Site: www.mapletreepublishing.com
Key Personnel
Pres: David A Hall *E-mail:* dave@
mapletreepublishing.com
Prodn & Mktg Mgr: Sue Collier *E-mail:* sue@
mapletreepublishing.com
Fiction Acqs Ed: Kenya Transtrum
E-mail: kenya@mapletreepublishing.com
Nonfiction Developmental Ed: Deniece Schofield
E-mail: deniece@mapletreepublishing.com
Submissions Coord: Liz Lyman *E-mail:* liz@
mapletreepublishing.com
Founded: 2002
ISBN Prefix(es): 0-9728071
Number of titles published annually: 10 Print; 10
E-Book
Total Titles: 3 Print; 2 E-Book
Orders to: Biblio, 15200 NBN Way, Blue
Ridge Summit, PA 17214 *Toll Free Tel:* 800-
462-6420 *Toll Free Fax:* 800-338-4550
E-mail: custserv@nbnbooks.com
Warehouse: Biblio, 15200 NBN Way, Blue Ridge
Summit, PA 17214, Contact: Karen Mattscheck
Tel: 717-794-3800 *E-mail:* kmattscheck@
nbnbooks.com
Distribution Center: Biblio Distribution Inc,
4501 Forbes Blvd, Suite 200, Lanham, MD
20706, Contact: David Breier *Tel:* 301-459-
3366 *Fax:* 301-429-5746 *E-mail:* dbreier@
bibliodistribution.com
Membership(s): Colorado Independent Publish-
ers Association; Latter Day Saints Booksellers
Association; Publishers Marketing Association;
Small Publishers Association of North America

MAR*CO Products Inc
1443 Old York Rd, Warminster, PA 18974
Tel: 215-956-0313 *Toll Free Tel:* 800-448-2197
Fax: 215-956-9041
E-mail: marcoproducts@comcast.net
Web Site: www.marcoproducts.com; www.store.
yahoo.com/marcoproducts
Key Personnel
Pres: Arden Martenz
VP: Cameon Funk
Opers Mgr: Barbara Wetzel
Founded: 1973
Educational guidance materials for elementary &
secondary counselors, psychologists & social
workers.
ISBN Prefix(es): 1-884063; 1-57543
Number of titles published annually: 12 Print; 25
E-Book
Total Titles: 300 Print; 300 Online
Distributed by ACCT FOR KIDS; ASCA; Barnes
& Noble; Jean Barnes Books; The Bookies;
Boulden Publishing; Burnell books; Career
Kids FYI; Carr Peer Resources; CFKR Career;
Community Intervention; Cress Productions
Co; Educational Esteem; Educational Media;
Eight Street Alano; Genesis Book I; Incen-
tive Plus; Jist; Logos Bookstore; M & B Dis-
tributors; Mental Health Resources; National
Professional Resources; National Resource
Center Youth Services; NIMCO Bookstore;
Pale House Publishers; Paperbacks for Educa-
tors; PCI; R & K Bookstore; SourceResource;
STARS; Teachers Gear; UMICOM Education;
US Book Distributor; YOUTHLIGHT
Distributor for Boulden; Center for Youth Issues
Stars; Educational Media; HarperCollins

Marathon Press
PO Box 407, Norfolk, NE 68702-0407

Tel: 402-371-5040 *Toll Free Tel:* 800-228-0629
Fax: 402-371-9382
Web Site: www.marathonpress.com
Key Personnel
Owner: Rex Alewel
Pres: Bruce Price
Founded: 1974
Professional photographers.
ISBN Prefix(es): 0-934420
Number of titles published annually: 5 Print
Distributed by Amherst Media
Shipping Address: 1500 Square Turn Blvd, Nor-
folk, NE 68701

MARC Publications
Subsidiary of World Vision International
800 W Chestnut Ave, Monrovia, CA 91016-3198
Tel: 626-303-8811 *Toll Free Tel:* 800-777-7752
(US only) *Fax:* 626-301-7786
E-mail: marcpubs@wvi.org
Web Site: www.worldvisionresources.com
Key Personnel
Ed-in-Chief: Edna Valdez
Founded: 1968
Books & other products promoting strategies for
the mission activities of the Christian churches.
ISBN Prefix(es): 0-912552; 1-887983
Number of titles published annually: 20 Print

March Street Press
3413 Wilshire Dr, Greensboro, NC 27408
Tel: 336-282-9754 *Fax:* 336-282-9754
Web Site: www.marchstreetpress.com
Key Personnel
Publr & Ed: Robert Bixby *E-mail:* rbixby@aol.
com
Founded: 1988
ISBN Prefix(es): 1-882983
Number of titles published annually: 18 Print
Total Titles: 120 Print; 2 CD-ROM; 4 Online

Margaret K McElderry, see Simon & Schuster
Children's Publishing

Marine Education Textbooks Inc
124 N Van Ave, Houma, LA 70363-5895
SAN: 215-9651
Tel: 985-879-3866 *Fax:* 985-879-3911
E-mail: namenet@triparish.net
Web Site: www.marineeducationtextbooks.com
Key Personnel
Pres: Gwen M Block
VP: Richard A Block
Founded: 1970
Training & educational books for preparation of
USCG Exams. Marine safety signs, nautical
charts.
ISBN Prefix(es): 0-934114; 1-879778
Number of titles published annually: 3 Print
Total Titles: 30 Print
Imprints: Marine Survey Press

Marine Techniques Publishing Inc
126 Western Ave, Suite 266, Augusta, ME 04330-
7252
SAN: 298-7805
Tel: 207-622-7984 *Fax:* 207-621-0821
E-mail: promariner@midmaine.com;
marinetechniques@midmaine.com
Web Site: www.groups.yahoo.com/group/
marinetechniquespublishing
Key Personnel
Pres & CEO: James L Pelletier
Lib Sales Dir: Christopher Pelletier
Founded: 1993
Specialize in industry specific directories; mar-
itime/worldwide merchant marine; Naval ar-
chitecture; marine biology, chemistry, geology;
civil, marine engineering; electrical, electronic
marine engineering; energy, oil & gas offshore;

mechanical marine engineering; transportation,
marine.
ISBN Prefix(es): 0-9644915
Number of titles published annually: 5 Print; 5 E-
Book
Total Titles: 10 Print; 10 E-Book
Foreign Rep(s): Chapters Inc (Canada, Ontario);
W H Everett & Sons Ltd (UK, England, Lon-
don); Lavoisier (France)
Membership(s): American Maritime Association;
American Society of Naval Engineers; Associ-
ation of Marine Engineers; Lloyd's Maritime
Information Register

Marion Street Press
106 S Oak Park Ave, Oak Park, IL 60302
Mailing Address: PO Box 2249, Oak Park, IL
60303
Tel: 708-445-8330 *Toll Free Tel:* 866-443-7987
Fax: 708-445-8648
Web Site: www.marionstreetpress.com
Key Personnel
Publr: Ed Avis *E-mail:* edavis@marionstreetpress.
com
Founded: 1993
Books for writers & journalists.
ISBN Prefix(es): 0-9665176; 0-9729937
Number of titles published annually: 6 Print
Total Titles: 11 Print
Foreign Rep(s): Gazelle (Europe); Hushion House
(Canada)
Membership(s): National Association of Indepen-
dent Publishers; Small Publishers Association
of North America

§Market Data Retrieval
Division of The Dun & Bradstreet Corp
One Forest Pkwy, Shelton, CT 06484
Mailing Address: PO Box 907, Shelton, CT
06484-0947
Tel: 203-926-4800 *Toll Free Tel:* 800-333-8802
Fax: 203-926-0784
E-mail: mdrinfo@dnb.com
Web Site: www.schooldata.com
Key Personnel
Gen Mgr: Sharon Sanford
VP, Systems & Opers: Tom Brady
Dir, Mktg: Mike Subrizi *Tel:* 203-225-4737
E-mail: msubrizi@dnb.com
Founded: 1969
Annual state by state school directories; annual
national school enrollment report; research re-
ports on the education market.
ISBN Prefix(es): 1-57953
Number of titles published annually: 51 Print
Total Titles: 55 Print; 1 CD-ROM
Branch Office(s)
475 Sansome St, Suite 1700, San Francisco, CA
94111 *Tel:* 415-732-5100 *Fax:* 415-732-5151
55 W Monroe St, Suite 2550, Chicago, IL 60603
Tel: 312-263-4169 *Fax:* 312-345-4360
Membership(s): AAP

Marketscope Books, see Marketscope Group
Books LLC

Marketscope Group Books LLC
Formerly Marketscope Books
PO Box 3118, Huntington Beach, CA 92605-
3118
Tel: 714-375-9888 *Fax:* 714-375-9898
Key Personnel
Publr: Matt Graninger
Opers Mgr: Maile Kahaunaele
E-mail: mkahaunaele@marketscopegroup.com
Founded: 1985
Books on recreational fishing.
ISBN Prefix(es): 0-934061
Number of titles published annually: 5 Print
Total Titles: 5 Print

Markowski International Publishers
One Oakglade Circle, Humelstown, PA 17036-9525
Tel: 717-566-0468 *Toll Free Tel:* 800-566-0534 (orders only) *Fax:* 717-566-6423
E-mail: posspress@aol.com; possibilitypress@aol.com
ISBN Prefix(es): 0-938716
Number of titles published annually: 4 Print
Total Titles: 35 Print
See separate listing for:
Possibility Press

Marlor Press Inc
4304 Brigadoon Dr, St Paul, MN 55126
SAN: 240-7140
Tel: 651-484-4600 *Toll Free Tel:* 800-669-4908
Fax: 651-490-1182
E-mail: marlor@minn.net
Key Personnel
Ed: Marlin Bree
Mktg Dir: Loris Theovin Bree
Founded: 1982
Paperback, trade books, children's books, maritime & travel nonfiction only.
ISBN Prefix(es): 0-943400; 1-892147
Number of titles published annually: 3 Print
Total Titles: 20 Print
Distributed by Independent Publishers Group
Foreign Rights: Susan Sewall (World)
Returns: c/o Independent Publishers Group, 814 N Franklin St, Chicago, IL 60610
Tel: 312-337-0747 *Toll Free Tel:* 800-888-4741 *Fax:* 312-337-5985 *E-mail:* frontdesk@ipgbook.com *Web Site:* ipgbook.com
Distribution Center: c/o Independent Publishers Group, 814 N Franklin St, Chicago, IL 60610
Tel: 312-337-0747 *Toll Free Tel:* 800-888-4741 *Fax:* 312-337-5985 *E-mail:* frontdesk@ipgbook.com *Web Site:* ipgbook.com
Membership(s): Minnesota Book Publishers Roundtable; MIP; Publishers Marketing Association

Marlowe & Company
Imprint of Avalon Publishing Group - New York
245 W 17 St, 11th fl, New York, NY 10011-5300
Tel: 646-375-2570 *Fax:* 646-375-2571
Web Site: www.marlowepub.com
Key Personnel
Sr VP & Publg Dir: Michele Martin
VP & Publr: Matthew Lore
Assoc Ed: Sue McCloskey
Founded: 1993
Marlowe & Company, an imprint of the Avalon Publishing Group, publishes in the area of personal growth, psychology, self-help, health & healthy cooking.
ISBN Prefix(es): 1-56924

Marquette University Press
Memorial Library, Rm 116, 1415 W Wisconsin Ave, Milwaukee, WI 53233
Tel: 414-288-1564 *Toll Free Tel:* 800-247-6553
Fax: 414-288-7813
Web Site: www.marquette.edu/mupress/
Key Personnel
Dir: Andrew Tallon
Lib Sales Dir & Intl Rts: Maureen Kondrick
E-mail: maureen.kondrick@marquette.edu
Founded: 1916
Publications by scholars of international reputation. Specializing in philosophy & theology.
ISBN Prefix(es): 0-87462
Number of titles published annually: 16 Print; 1 CD-ROM
Total Titles: 285 Print; 3 CD-ROM
Editorial Office(s): PO Box 3141, Milwaukee, WI 53201-3141
Returns: 30 Amberwood Pkwy, Ashland, OH 44805

Warehouse: 30 Amberwood Pkwy, Ashland, OH 44805
Distribution Center: 30 Amberwood Pkwy, Ashland, OH 44805, Contact: Beth Boeh *Tel:* 419-281-1802 ext 1408
Membership(s): American Association of University Presses; Association of Jesuit University Presses

Marquis Who's Who
562 Central Ave, New Providence, NJ 07974
SAN: 202-6120
Tel: 908-673-1001 *Toll Free Tel:* 800-473-7020
Fax: 908-673-1189
Web Site: www.marquiswhoswho.com
Key Personnel
CEO: Gene McGovern
Sr Man Dir: Fred Marks
Sr Dir, Sales: Susan Towne
Founded: 1899
Publisher of comprehensive biographical references available in print, online & tape. Major Marquis Who's Who publications include *Who's Who in America*, *Who's Who in the World* & *Who's Who of American Women*.
ISBN Prefix(es): 0-8379
Number of titles published annually: 15 Print
Total Titles: 1 Online

Marshall & Swift
911 Wilshire Blvd, Suite 1800, Los Angeles, CA 90017
Tel: 213-683-9000 *Toll Free Tel:* 800-544-2678
Fax: 213-683-9043 (orders)
Web Site: www.marshallswift.com
Key Personnel
Pres: Bob Dowdell
Chief Man Ed: Richard Vishanoff *Tel:* 213-683-9000 ext 2797
Founded: 1932
Building cost databases for the construction market & insurance industry.
ISBN Prefix(es): 1-56842
Number of titles published annually: 10 Print
Total Titles: 21 Print
Imprints: Valuation Press
Distributed by McGraw-Hill Book Co
Warehouse: 1625 W Temple, Los Angeles, CA 90026

Marshall Cavendish Corp
Member of Times Publishing Group
99 White Plains Rd, Tarrytown, NY 10591-9001
Tel: 914-332-8888 *Fax:* 914-332-1888
E-mail: mcc@marshallcavendish.com
Web Site: www.marshallcavendish.com
Key Personnel
Pres: Albert F Lee
VP, Mktg, Opers & Intl Rts: Richard Farley
E-mail: rfarley@marshallcavendish.com
Fin Cont: Michele Noone
Mktg Mgr, Benchmark/Reference/Spec Sales: Geraldine Curran
Mktg Mgr, Wholesalers & Cavendish Children's Books: Dierdre Langeland
Art Dir: Anahid Hamparian
Sr Ed, Ref: Thomas McCarthy
Sr Ed, Benchmark: Joyce Stanton
Edit Dir, Marshall Cavendish Reference Books: Paul Bernabeo
Edit Dir, Benchmark Books: Michelle Bisson
Edit Dir, Cavendish Children's Books: Margery Cuyler
Prodn Mgr: Michael Esposito; Alan Tsai
Subs Rts: Steven Chudney
Founded: 1970
Encyclopedias, curriculum-oriented juvenile reference, children's books & on-line reference.
ISBN Prefix(es): 1-85435; 0-7614
Number of titles published annually: 170 Print; 3 Online
Total Titles: 800 Print; 12 Online

Imprints: Benchmark Books; Marshall Cavendish Children's Books; Marshall Cavendish Online; Marshall Cavendish Reference
Distributed by Peter Pal Library Supplier
Warehouse: Swan Packaging, 415 Hamburg Turnpike, Wayne, NJ 07470
Membership(s): ALA; Children's Book Council

§Martindale-Hubbell
Member of The Reed Elsevier Group
121 Chanlon Rd, New Providence, NJ 07974
SAN: 205-8863
Mailing Address: PO Box 1001, Summit, NJ 07902-1001
Tel: 908-464-6800 *Toll Free Tel:* 800-526-4902
Fax: 908-464-3553
E-mail: info@martindale.com
Web Site: www.martindale.com
Key Personnel
Pres & CEO: John A Lawler, IV
COO: Paul Gazzolo
Sr VP, Sales & Cust Serv: Bob Hopen
Sr VP & CIO of Info Technol: John Roney
VP, Database Prodn: Dean Hollister
Founded: 1868
Publisher of the *Martindale-Hubbell Law Directory* in hardcopy, on CD-ROM & available through LexisNexis & on the Internet; containing listings of over 1 million lawyers & law firms worldwide. Other publications include *Law Digest*, a summary of laws from each of the 50 states & over 60 countries; *Martindale-Hubbell Law Directory International Edition*, designed for the international legal community & *Martindale-Hubbell Bar Register of Preeminent Lawyers*, listing of 10,000 law practices designated as outstanding by members of the legal community.
ISBN Prefix(es): 1-56160
Number of titles published annually: 5 Print; 1 CD-ROM; 1 Online
Total Titles: 5 Print; 1 CD-ROM; 1 Online
Online services available through LexisNexis.

Martingale & Co
20205 144 Ave NE, Woodinville, WA 98072
Mailing Address: Box 118, Bothell, WA 98041-0118
Tel: 425-483-3313 *Toll Free Tel:* 800-426-3126
Fax: 425-486-7596
E-mail: info@martingale-pub.com
Web Site: www.martingale-pub.com
Key Personnel
CFO: Ted S Hartshorn
Dir, Sales & Mktg: John Bjerke
Publr: Jane Hamada
Edit Dir: Mary Green
Mktg Mgr: Donna Lever
Mgr, Trade Sales: Shelley Santa
Founded: 1976
Quilting, knitting, crafting & collecting.
ISBN Prefix(es): 1-56477
Number of titles published annually: 40 Print
Total Titles: 175 Print
Imprints: Fiber Studio Press; Pastimes
Distributor for That Patchwork Place

Maryland Historical Society
201 W Monument St, Baltimore, MD 21201
Tel: 410-685-3750 *Fax:* 410-385-2105
Web Site: www.mdhs.org
Key Personnel
Publr & Intl Rts: Robert Cottom
E-mail: rcottom@mdhs.org
Founded: 1844
Publish historical books.
ISBN Prefix(es): 0-938420
Number of titles published annually: 6 Print
Total Titles: 30 Print
Distributor for Alan C Hood & Co Inc

Orders to: Alan C Hood & Co Inc, PO Box 775, Chambersburg, PA 17201, Contact: Alan Hood *Tel:* 717-267-0867 *Fax:* 717-267-0572
Returns: Maple Press Distribution Ctr, I-83 Industrial Park, York, PA 17405
Shipping Address: Maple Press Distribution Ctr, I-83 Industrial Park, York, PA 17405, Contact: Alan C Hood *Tel:* 717-267-0867 *Fax:* 717-267-0572
Warehouse: Maple Press Distribution Ctr, I-83 Industrial Park, York, PA 17405
Distribution Center: Maple Press Distribution Ctr, I-83 Industrial Park, York, PA 17405

Mason Crest Publishers
370 Reed Rd, Suite 302, Broomall, PA 19008
Tel: 610-543-6200 *Toll Free Tel:* 866-MCP-BOOK (627-2665) *Fax:* 610-543-3878
Web Site: www.masoncrest.com
Key Personnel
CEO: Philip Cohen *E-mail:* pcohen@masoncrest.com
Pres: Daniel Hilferty *E-mail:* dhilferty@masoncrest.com
Dir, Sales & Mktg: Stacy Lineman
Cont: Diana Daniels *E-mail:* ddaniels@masoncrest.com
Sales Coord: Linda McGee *E-mail:* lmcgee@masoncrest.com
Opers Mgr: Lee Wark *Tel:* 610-583-0211 *Fax:* 610-583-0212 *E-mail:* lee6250@aol.com
Cust Serv: Grace Baffa *E-mail:* gbaffa@masoncrest.com
Founded: 2001
Mason Crest Publishers is committed to publishing the finest nonfiction school, library & curriculum products available today. Our titles are full-color & include a glossary, index, further reading section, Internet resources & are library bound.
ISBN Prefix(es): 1-59084
Number of titles published annually: 150 Print
Total Titles: 750 Print
Returns: 701 Ashland Ave, Bays 1 & 2, Folcroft, PA 19032, Opers Mgr: Lee Wark *Tel:* 610-583-0211 *Fax:* 610-583-0212 *E-mail:* lee6250@aol.com
Shipping Address: 701 Ashland Ave, Bays 1 & 2, Folcroft, PA 19032, Opers Mgr: Lee Wark *Tel:* 610-583-0211 *Fax:* 610-583-0212 *E-mail:* lee6250@aol.com
Warehouse: 701 Ashland Ave, Bays 1 & 2, Folcroft, PA 19032, Opers Mgr: Lee Wark *Tel:* 610-583-0211 *Fax:* 610-583-0212 *E-mail:* lee6250@aol.com
Distribution Center: 701 Ashland Ave, Bays 1 & 2, Folcroft, PA 19032, Opers Mgr: Lee Wark *Tel:* 610-583-0211 *Fax:* 610-583-0212 *E-mail:* lee6250@aol.com
Membership(s): Friends of Libraries of USA; Publishers Marketing Association

Massachusetts Historical Society
1154 Boylston St, Boston, MA 02215
Tel: 617-536-1608 *Fax:* 617-859-0074
E-mail: publications@masshist.org
Web Site: www.masshist.org
Key Personnel
Assoc Ed: Ondine E Le Blanc *Tel:* 617-646-0524 *Fax:* 617-859-7400 *E-mail:* oleblanc@masshist.org
Founded: 1792
Historical regional publications.
ISBN Prefix(es): 0-934909; 0-9652584
Number of titles published annually: 3 Print
Total Titles: 77 Print
Distributed by Northeastern University Press
Warehouse: CUP Services, 740 Cascadilla St, Ithaca, NY 14850

Massachusetts Institute of Technology Libraries
77 Mass Ave, Bldg 14, Rm 0551, Cambridge, MA 02139-4307
Tel: 617-253-7059 *Fax:* 617-253-1690
E-mail: docs@mit.edu
Web Site: libraries.mit.edu/docs
Key Personnel
Head: Keith Glavash *E-mail:* kglavash@mit.edu
Founded: 1863
MIT theses, dissertations, technical reports & working papers.
ISBN Prefix(es): 0-911379
Number of titles published annually: 2,000 Print
Total Titles: 15,000 Print

§Master Books
Subsidiary of New Leaf Press
PO Box 726, Green Forest, AR 72638-0726
Tel: 870-438-5288 *Fax:* 870-438-5120
E-mail: nlp@newleafpress.net
Web Site: www.masterbooks.net
Key Personnel
Pres: Tim Dudley
Founded: 1975
Publish Biblically-based, scientifically sound creation materials.
ISBN Prefix(es): 0-89051
Number of titles published annually: 20 Print
Total Titles: 165 Print; 3 CD-ROM; 2 Audio
Shipping Address: 3142 Hwy 103 N, Green Forest, AR 72638

Materials Research Society
506 Keystone Dr, Warrendale, PA 15086
SAN: 686-0125
Tel: 724-779-3003 *Fax:* 724-779-8313
E-mail: info@mrs.org
Web Site: www.mrs.org
Key Personnel
Dir, Membership Affairs: Gail A Oare
Founded: 1973
Scientific reports on leading edge topics.
ISBN Prefix(es): 0-931837; 1-55899
Number of titles published annually: 40 Print
Total Titles: 800 Print

Math Teachers Press Inc
4850 Park Glen Rd, Minneapolis, MN 55416
Tel: 952-545-6535 *Toll Free Tel:* 800-852-2435 *Fax:* 952-546-7502
Web Site: www.movingwithmath.com
Key Personnel
Pres: Caryl K Pierson
Founded: 1985
Pre K-12 manipulative-based math curriculum.
Number of titles published annually: 13 Print
Total Titles: 63 Print

The Mathematical Association of America
1529 18 St NW, Washington, DC 20036
SAN: 203-9737
Tel: 202-387-5200 *Toll Free Tel:* 800-331-1622 (orders) *Fax:* 202-265-2384
E-mail: ldouglas@pmds.com
Web Site: www.maa.org
Key Personnel
Pres: Ronald Graham
Treas: John Kenelly
Assoc Sec: James Tattersall
Sec: Martha Siegel
Exec Dir: Tina H Straley
Pubns Dir: Donald J Albers
Fin Dir: Eugene Darrell
Edit Mgr: Harry Waldman
Mktg & Prod Mgr: Elaine Pedreira *E-mail:* epedreira@maa.org
Membership Dir: James Gandorf
Dir, Memb Servs: Michael Pearson
Dir, Info Servs: Roseana Brown
Founded: 1915
Mathematical books & journals.

ISBN Prefix(es): 0-88385
Number of titles published annually: 20 Print; 2 CD-ROM
Total Titles: 200 Print; 2 CD-ROM
Distributed by Cambridge University Press
Foreign Rep(s): Cambridge University Press (Africa, Europe, Middle East)
Warehouse: PMDS MAA Service Center, 9050 Junction Dr, Annapolis Junction, MD 20701, Contact: Mary Ann Rice *Toll Free Tel:* 800-331-1622 *Fax:* 301-206-9789 *E-mail:* mrice@pmas.com
Distribution Center: PMDS MAA Service Center, 9050 Junction Dr, Annapolis Junction, MD 20701

Maupin House Publishing
4445 SW 35 Terr, Suite 200, Gainesville, FL 32608
Mailing Address: PO Box 90148, Gainesville, FL 32607-0148 SAN: 250-7684
Tel: 352-373-5588 *Toll Free Tel:* 800-524-0634 (orders only) *Fax:* 352-373-5546
E-mail: sales@maupinhouse.com
Web Site: www.maupinhouse.com
Key Personnel
Pres: Julia Graddy *E-mail:* jgraddy@maupinhouse.com
VP: Robert Graddy
Sales: Joanna Neville
Prodn: Mark Devish
Founded: 1989
Publish professional resources for K-12 teachers in field of writing education & language arts. Video distance learning professional training music audio CDs.
ISBN Prefix(es): 0-929895
Number of titles published annually: 9 Print; 2 Audio
Total Titles: 42 Print; 1 Audio
Warehouse: 4460 SW 35 Terr, Suite 106, Gainesville, FL 32608, Contact: Robert Graddy *Tel:* 352-373-5588 *Toll Free Tel:* 800-524-0634 *Fax:* 352-373-5546 *E-mail:* info@maupinhouse.com
Membership(s): Association of Educational Publishers; National School Supply Educational Association; Publishers Marketing Association

Maval Publishing Inc
Subsidiary of Editora Maval Ltda
567 Harrison St, Denver, CO 80206-4534
Mailing Address: PO Box 6672, Denver, CO 80206-0672
Tel: 303-338-8725 *Fax:* 303-745-6215
E-mail: maval@maval.com
Web Site: www.maval.com
Key Personnel
Pres: George Waintrub
Founded: 1978
Publish medical books & a line of children's books.
ISBN Prefix(es): 1-884083
Number of titles published annually: 25 Print
Total Titles: 72 Print; 9 Audio
Foreign Office(s): Editora Maval, Piramide 521, Santiago, Chile, Maria Luder *Tel:* 362-552-1527 *E-mail:* mavalimp@ctcreuna.cl
Distributed by Benjamin & Matthew Book Co; Login Brothers; Rittenhouse Book Distributors

Maverick Publications Inc
63324 Nels Anderson Rd, Bend, OR 97701
SAN: 208-7634
Tel: 541-382-6978 *Fax:* 541-382-4831
E-mail: customerservice@maverickbooks.com
Web Site: www.mavbooks.com
Key Personnel
Owner & Publr: Gary Asher *E-mail:* gmasher@mavbooks.com
Founded: 1968

Trade paperbacks, cookbooks, Pacific Northwest region, history & historical fiction.
ISBN Prefix(es): 0-89288
Number of titles published annually: 5 Print
Total Titles: 18 Print
Subsidiaries: Maverick Distributors

Maximum Press
605 Silverthorn Rd, Gulf Breeze, FL 32561
Tel: 850-934-0819 *Toll Free Tel:* 800-989-6733
Fax: 850-934-9981
E-mail: moreinfo@maxpress.com
Web Site: www.maxpress.com
Key Personnel
Publr & Intl Rts Contact: Jim Hoskins
E-mail: jimh@maxpress.com
Founded: 1985
Books about the Internet.
ISBN Prefix(es): 0-9633214; 1-885068
Number of titles published annually: 20 Print; 6 E-Book
Total Titles: 24 Print; 6 E-Book

Maxit Publishing Inc
PO Box 700, Lompoc, CA 93438-0700
Tel: 805-686-5100 *Toll Free Tel:* 866-686-5100
Fax: 805-686-5102
Web Site: www.maxitpublishing.com
Key Personnel
VP, Opers: Wil Simon *E-mail:* wsimon@maxitpublishing.com
Dir, Online Opers: Ferris Eanfar
Sr Mktg & Sales Rep: Connie Butcher
Founded: 2000
Publishers of award winning books.
ISBN Prefix(es): 0-9700
Number of titles published annually: 1 Print; 1 E-Book
Total Titles: 4 Print; 3 E-Book

Mazda Publishers Inc
2182 Dupont Dr, Suite 216, Irvine, CA 92612
SAN: 658-120X
Mailing Address: PO Box 2603, Costa Mesa, CA 92626-2603
Tel: 714-751-5252 *Fax:* 714-751-4805
E-mail: hello@mazdapub.com
Web Site: www.mazdapub.com
Key Personnel
Publr: Ahmad Jabbari
Chief Ed: Ann West
Founded: 1980
Publishes scholarly books dealing with the Middle East & North Africa; critical reviews of poetry; Central Asia including art & architecture.
ISBN Prefix(es): 1-56859
Number of titles published annually: 20 Print
Total Titles: 210 Print
Distributor for Bibliotheca Persica (Co-Publishers)
Foreign Rep(s): Otto Harrassowitz

McBooks Press Inc
520 N Meadow St, Ithaca, NY 14850
Tel: 607-272-2114 *Toll Free Tel:* 888-266-5711
Fax: 607-273-6068
E-mail: mcbooks@mcbooks.com
Web Site: www.mcbooks.com
Key Personnel
Publr & Intl Rts Contact: Alexander Skutt
Edit Dir: Jackie Swift
Sales & Mktg Dir: Christopher Carey
E-mail: chris@mcbooks.com
Founded: 1979
Trade books; specialize in vegetarianism, regional books, period nautical, military fiction & literature.
ISBN Prefix(es): 0-935526; 1-59013
Number of titles published annually: 25 Print
Total Titles: 95 Print

Foreign Rep(s): Gazelle Book Servcies Ltd (Europe)
Distribution Center: National Book Network Inc, 15200 NBN Way, Blue Ridge Summit, PA 17214 *Toll Free Tel:* 800-462-6420 *Toll Free Fax:* 800-338-4550

Roger A McCaffrey Publishing
PO Box 1209, Ridgefield, CT 06877
Key Personnel
Pres: Roger A McCaffrey
Founded: 1997
ISBN Prefix(es): 0-9742098; 0-9717721; 0-9661325
Number of titles published annually: 4 Print
Total Titles: 21 Print
Sales Office(s): 1331 Red Cedar Circle, Fort Collins, CO 80524 *Tel:* 970-490-2735 *Fax:* 970-493-8781
Billing Address: 1331 Red Cedar Circle, Fort Collins, CO 80524 *Tel:* 970-490-2735 *Fax:* 970-493-8781
Orders to: 1331 Red Cedar Circle, Fort Collins, CO 80524 *Tel:* 970-490-2735 *Fax:* 970-493-8781
Returns: 1331 Red Cedar Circle, Fort Collins, CO 80524 *Tel:* 970-490-2735 *Fax:* 970-493-8781
Shipping Address: 1331 Red Cedar Circle, Fort Collins, CO 80524 *Tel:* 970-490-2735 *Fax:* 970-493-8781
Warehouse: 1331 Red Cedar Circle, Fort Collins, CO 80524 *Tel:* 970-490-2735 *Fax:* 970-493-8781
Distribution Center: 1331 Red Cedar Circle, Fort Collins, CO 80524 *Tel:* 970-490-2735 *Fax:* 970-493-8781

McClanahan Publishing House Inc
PO Box 100, Kuttawa, KY 42055-0100
Tel: 270-388-9388 *Toll Free Tel:* 800-544-6959
Fax: 270-388-6186
E-mail: books@kybooks.com
Web Site: www.kybooks.com
Key Personnel
Pres & Exec Ed: Paula Cunningham
Art Dir: James Asher
Busn Mgr: Michelle Stone
Sales: Jo Doty
Founded: 1983
Art services & artist illustration, jacket design, book design & layout.
ISBN Prefix(es): 0-913383
Number of titles published annually: 8 Print
Total Titles: 85 Print
Imprints: Commonwealth Book Co
Warehouse: Kuttawa Ctr, 88 Cedar St, Kuttawa, KY 42055

McCormack's Guides Inc
1734 Alhambra Ave, Martinez, CA 94553
Mailing Address: PO Box 190, Martinez, CA 94553-0190
Tel: 925-229-3581 *Toll Free Tel:* 800-222-3602
Fax: 925-228-7223
E-mail: bookinfo@mccormacks.com
Web Site: www.mccormacks.com
Key Personnel
Publr & Ed: Don McCormack *Tel:* 925-229-3581 ext 105 *E-mail:* donmc@mccormacks.com
Founded: 1984
California schools & regional relocation guides.
ISBN Prefix(es): 0-931299; 1-929365
Number of titles published annually: 11 Print
Total Titles: 12 Print
Returns: PO Box 1728, 827 Arnold Dr, Suite 160, Martinez, CA 94533-0728

Gary E McCuen Publications Inc, see GEM Publications

McCutchan Publishing Corp
3220 Blume Dr, Suite 197, Richmond, CA 94806

SAN: 203-9486
Tel: 510-758-5510 *Toll Free Tel:* 800-227-1540
Fax: 510-758-6078
E-mail: mccutchanpublish@aol.com
Web Site: www.mccutchanpublishing.com
Key Personnel
Pres & Publr: Nancy Runyon
ISBN Contact & Rts & Perms: Kim Sharrar
Founded: 1963
College textbooks & professional books in education, hotel & restaurant management & law enforcement education.
ISBN Prefix(es): 0-8211

The McDonald & Woodward Publishing Co
431-B E College St, Granville, OH 43023
Tel: 740-321-1140 *Toll Free Tel:* 800-233-8787
Fax: 740-321-1141
E-mail: mwpubco@mwpubco.com
Web Site: www.mwpubco.com
Key Personnel
Publr & Intl Rts Mgr: Jerry N McDonald
E-mail: jmcd@mwpubco.com
Mktg & Sales: Trish Newcomb
Founded: 1986
Books (primarily adult) in natural history & cultural history; co-publish with educational & governmental entities.
ISBN Prefix(es): 0-939923
Number of titles published annually: 5 Print
Total Titles: 38 Print

McDougal Littell
Subsidiary of Houghton Mifflin Co
909 Davis St, Evanston, IL 60201
Tel: 847-869-2300 *Toll Free Tel:* 800-462-6595 (orders) *Toll Free Fax:* 888-872-8380
Web Site: www.mcdougallittell.com
Key Personnel
Pres: Rita H Schaefer
VP & Ed-in-Chief: Susan D Schaffrath
VP & Natl Sales Mgr: Larry Hoce
VP & Dir, Planning, Fin & Opers: Thomas Deming
VP & Dir, Tech Devt: Sue Cowden
VP & Dir, Mktg: Dave Pieklo
Secondary school textbooks & educational materials.

McFarland & Co Inc Publishers
960 Hwy 88 W, Jefferson, NC 28640
Mailing Address: PO Box 611, Jefferson, NC 28640-0611
Tel: 336-246-4460 *Toll Free Tel:* 800-253-2187 (orders only) *Fax:* 336-246-5018; 336-246-4403 (orders)
E-mail: info@mcfarlandpub.com
Web Site: www.mcfarlandpub.com
Key Personnel
Pres: Robert Franklin *E-mail:* rfranklin@mcfarlandpub.com
Exec VP: Rhonda Herman *E-mail:* rherman@mcfarlandpub.com
Man Ed: Lisa Camp *E-mail:* lcamp@mcfarlandpub.com
Edit Devt Chief: Virginia Tobiassen
E-mail: vtobiassen@mcfarlandpub.com
Exec Ed: Steve Wilson *E-mail:* swilson@mcfarlandpub.com
Dir, Fin & Admin: Margie Turnmire
E-mail: mturnmire@mcfarlandpub.com
Sales Mgr: Karl-Heinz Roseman
E-mail: kroseman@mcfarlandpub.com
Intl Rts: Beth Cox *E-mail:* bcox@mcfarlandpub.com
Acqs Ed: Gary Mitchem *E-mail:* gmitchem@mcfarlandpub.com
Founded: 1979
Reference books, scholarly monographs, professional works for librarians. Subjects include chess, world history & Civil War history.
ISBN Prefix(es): 0-89950; 0-7864

Number of titles published annually: 275 Print
Total Titles: 2,500 Print
Subsidiaries: McFarland & Co Ltd, Publishers
(London, UK)
Foreign Rep(s): DA Information Services (Australia, New Zealand, Papua New Guinea);
Eurospan (UK, Europe, Middle East, North
Africa); Viva Books (India)
Returns: 961 Hwy 88 W, Jefferson, NC 28640
Shipping Address: 961 Hwy 88 W, Jefferson, NC
28640

§The McGraw-Hill Companies Inc
1221 Avenue of the Americas, 50th fl, New York,
NY 10020
SAN: 200-2248
Tel: 212-512-2000
E-mail: webmaster@mcgraw-hill.com
Web Site: www.mcgraw-hill.com *Telex:* 12-7960
Cable: MCGRAWHILL NY
Key Personnel
Chmn, Pres & CEO: Harold W (Terry) McGraw,
III
Pres, McGraw-Hill Education: Henry Hirschberg
Pres, Standard & Poors: Kathleen A Corbet
Pres, Info & Media Servs: Scott C Marden
Exec VP Fin & CFO: Robert J Bahash
Exec VP & Gen Coun: Kenneth M Vittor
Exec VP & Chief Info Officer: Mostafa Mehrabani
Exec VP, HR: David L Murphy
Sr VP, Corp Aff & Asst to the Chmn: Glenn S
Goldberg
Sr VP, Investor Rels: Donald S Rubin
Founded: 1888
A global information services provider for the
financial services, education & business information markets.
ISBN Prefix(es): 0-8385; 0-07; 0-83
Divisions: Information & Media Services; Standard & Poor's
Membership(s): AAP; American Business Media;
Association of Test Publishers; Better Business Bureau; Brookings Institution; Business
Roundtable; Conference Board; Copyright
Clearance Center; Council for the Americas;
Council of Foreign Relations; The Direct Marketing Association; Emergency Committee for
American Trade; Entertainment Software Rating Board; European Institute; Magazine Publishers of America; NAB; National Governor's
Association; Private Sector Council; Software
& Information Industry Association; United
States Chamber of Commerce; United States
Council for International Business; US-ASEAN
Business Council; US-China Business Council
See separate listing for:
McGraw-Hill/Dushkin
McGraw-Hill Education

McGraw-Hill/Dushkin
2460 Kerper Blvd, Dubuque, IA 52001
SAN: 201-3460
Toll Free Tel: 800-243-6532
Web Site: www.dushkin.com
Key Personnel
Man Ed: Larry Loeppke
Dir, Mktg: Julie Keck
Dir, Prodn: Beth Kundert
Rts & Perms: Leonard Behnke
Founded: 1971
Thought-provoking series of supplements & online websites appropriate for college-level
courses or for library purchase. Materials span
over 20 disciplines & cover compelling, current topics & issues. The publications include
annual discipline readers, debate style readers,
online readers, geographic/atlas readers & college textbooks.
ISBN Prefix(es): 0-07; 0-697; 0-87967; 1-56134;
0-7024; 0-7235
Number of titles published annually: 90 Print; 85
Online

Total Titles: 1,275 Print; 85 Online; 40 E-Book
Divisions: McGraw-Hill Higher Education

§McGraw-Hill Education
Division of The McGraw-Hill Companies
2 Penn Plaza, New York, NY 10121
Tel: 212-904-2000
E-mail: customer.service@mcgraw-hill.com
Web Site: www.mheducation.com; www.
mheducation.com/custserv.html
Key Personnel
Pres, McGraw-Hill Education: Henry Hirschberg
Exec VP, School Educ Group: William F Oldsey
Pres, Higher Educ, Professional & Intl Group:
Brian Heer
Sr VP & Chief Info Officer: Mark Mooney
Sr VP, GTP Program Mgmt: Kenneth J Michaels
Sr VP, Fin & Opers: Joseph Micallef
Sr VP, Media Technology: Grace Walkus
Sr VP, Pub & Govt Aff: Rosemarie Cappabianca
Sr VP, Res & Devt: Charlotte Frank
VP, Commun: April L Hattori
VP, Busn Devt: Michael Bijaoui
Founded: 1989
A global leader in educational materials & professional information.
ISBN Prefix(es): 0-07
Imprints: CTB/McGraw-Hill; McGraw-Hill Professional Development; Glencoe/McGraw-Hill;
Macmillan/McGraw-Hill; McGraw-Hill Digital
Learning; McGraw-Hill/Dushkin; McGraw-Hill Education - Australia, New Zealand and
South Africa; McGraw-Hill Education Europe, Middle East and Africa; McGraw-Hill
Education Latin America; McGraw-Hill Education - Spain; McGraw-Hill Humanities, Social Sciences and World Languages; McGraw-Hill/Irwin; McGraw-Hill Osborne; McGraw-Hill Custom Publishing; McGraw-Hill Professional; McGraw-Hill Ryerson; McGraw-Hill
Science, Engineering, Mathematics; McGraw-Hill Science, Technical & Medical; McGraw-Hill Trade; SRA/McGraw-Hill (A division of
McGraw-Hill Learning Group); Tata/McGraw-Hill; The Wright Group/McGraw-Hill (A division of McGraw-Hill Learning Group)
Branch Office(s)
Canada
Puerto Rico
Foreign Office(s): Argentina
Asia
Australia
Brazil
Chile
China
Germany
India
Indonesia
Italy
Japan

Malaysia
Mexico
New Zealand
Philippines
Portugal
South Africa
Spain
Taiwan, Province of China
United Kingdom
Distribution Center: McGraw-Hill Education Distribution Center: Norcross, 26510 Jimmy Carter
Blvd, Norcross, GA 30071 *Tel:* 404-442-3347
McGraw-Hill Education Distribution Centers: Gahanna, 860 Taylor Station Rd, Blacklick, OH
43004 *Tel:* 614-755-4151
McGraw-Hill Education Distribution Center: DeSoto, 220 E Danieldale Rd, DeSoto, TX 75115-
2490 *Tel:* 214-224-1111
Membership(s): AAP
See separate listing for:
CTB/McGraw-Hill
Glencoe/McGraw-Hill

International Marine Publishing
Macmillan/McGraw-Hill
McGraw-Hill Higher Education
McGraw-Hill International Publishing Group
McGraw-Hill Learning Group
McGraw-Hill/Osborne
McGraw-Hill Professional
McGraw-Hill Trade
Ragged Mountain Press

§McGraw-Hill Higher Education
Division of McGraw-Hill Education
1333 Burr Ridge Pkwy, Burr Ridge, IL 60527
Tel: 630-789-4000 *Toll Free Tel:* 800-338-3987
(cust serv) *Fax:* 614-755-5645 (cust serv)
Web Site: www.mhhe.com
Key Personnel
Pres: Edward Stanford *Tel:* 630-789-5077
Fax: 630-789-6942 *E-mail:* ed_stanford@
mcgraw-hill.com
Pres, McGraw-Hill, Humanities, Social Sciences, Lang: Steve Debow *Tel:* 212-904-4761
Fax: 212-904-3813 *E-mail:* steve_debow@
mcgraw-hill.com
Pres, McGraw-Hill/Irwin (Business & Economics): Kevin Kane *Tel:* 630-789-5046
Fax: 630-789-5547 *E-mail:* kevin_kane@
mcgraw-hill.com
Pres, McGraw-Hill, Science, Engineering, Math:
Kurt Strand *Tel:* 563-589-2806 *Fax:* 563-589-
1319 *E-mail:* kurt_strand@mcgraw-hill.com
Pres, Online Learning: John Paul Lenney
Tel: 630-789-5071 *Fax:* 630-789-5547
E-mail: john_paula_lenney@mcgraw-hill.com
Sr VP, Fin: Ruth Berke *Tel:* 630-789-5063
Fax: 630-789-5060 *E-mail:* ruth_berke@
mcgraw-hill.com
VP, eProduct/Business Devt: Michael Junior
Tel: 630-789-5227 *Fax:* 630-789-6944
E-mail: mike_junior@mcgraw-hill.com
VP, eLearning: Jim Kelly *Tel:* 757-564-0595
Fax: 757-564-0593 *E-mail:* jim_kelly@
mcgraw-hill.com
VP, Course Content Delivery: Virginia Moffat *Tel:* 630-789-5073 *Fax:* 630-789-6942
E-mail: ginny_moffat@mcgraw-hill.com
Founded: 1996
College texts.
ISBN Prefix(es): 0-07; 0-697; 0-256
Number of titles published annually: 1,379 Print;
580 CD-ROM; 489 Online; 53 Audio
Total Titles: 13,130 Print; 2,252 CD-ROM; 2,431
Online; 423 Audio
Imprints: McGraw-Hill/Dushkin; McGraw-Hill
Humanities, Social Sciences, Languages;
McGraw-Hill/Irwin; McGraw-Hill Custom Publishing; McGraw-Hill Science, Engineering,
Mathematics
Branch Office(s)
2640 Kerper Blvd, Dubuque, IA 52001 (Location of McGraw-Hill Science, Engineering &
Mathematics Co) *Tel:* 563-588-1451 *Fax:* 563-
589-2955
1285 Fern Ridge Pkwy, Suite 200, St Louis, MO
63141 *Toll Free Tel:* 800-992-9553 *Fax:* 314-
439-6848
420 Boylston Street, 2nd fl, Boston, MA 02116
(SEM, HSSL), Contact: Lyn Uhl *Tel:* 617-262-
1160 *Toll Free Tel:* 800-338-3987 (cust serv)
Fax: 617-375-2285
160 Spear St, Suite 700, San Francisco, CA
94105 (Location of McGraw-Hill Humanities,
Social Sciences, Languages & McGraw-Hill/Irwin), Contact: Linda Toy *Tel:* 415-357-8100
Toll Free Tel: 800-435-2665 *Fax:* 415-357-8085
2 Penn Plaza, 20th fl, New York, NY 10121 (Location of McGraw-Hill Humanities, Social
Sciences, Languages), Contact: Steve Debow
Tel: 212-904-2000 *E-mail:* steve_debow@
mcgraw-hill.com
Orders to: The McGraw-Hill Companies, Distribution Center, 860 Taylor Station Rd, Blacklick, OH 43004-0539 *Toll Free Tel:* 800-338-
3987 *Fax:* 614-755-5654

Returns: The McGraw-Hill Companies, Distribution Center, 860 Taylor Station Rd, Blacklick, OH 43004-0539 *Toll Free Tel:* 800-338-3987 *Fax:* 614-755-5654
Shipping Address: The McGraw-Hill Companies, Distribution Center, 860 Taylor Station Rd, Blacklick, OH 43004-0539 *Toll Free Tel:* 800-338-3987 *Fax:* 614-755-5654
Warehouse: The McGraw-Hill Companies, Distribution Center, 860 Taylor Station Rd, Blacklick, OH 43004-0539 *Toll Free Tel:* 800-338-3987 *Fax:* 614-755-5654
Distribution Center: The McGraw-Hill Companies, Distribution Center, 860 Taylor Station Rd, Blacklick, OH 43004-0539 *Toll Free Tel:* 800-338-3987 *Fax:* 614-755-5654
See separate listing for:
McGraw-Hill Humanities, Social Sciences, Languages
McGraw-Hill/Irwin
McGraw-Hill Primis Custom Publishing
McGraw-Hill Science, Engineering, Mathematics

McGraw-Hill Humanities, Social Sciences, Languages
Division of McGraw-Hill Higher Education
2 Penn Plaza, 20th fl, New York, NY 10121
Tel: 212-904-2000 *Toll Free Tel:* 800-338-3987 (cust serv) *Fax:* 614-755-5645 (cust serv)
E-mail: first name_last name@mcgraw-hill.com
Web Site: www.mhhe.com
Key Personnel
Pres: Steve Debow *Tel:* 212-904-4761 *Fax:* 212-904-3813 *E-mail:* steve_debow@mcgraw-hill.com
VP & Ed-in-Chief: Emily Barrosse *Tel:* 212-904-4872 *Fax:* 212-904-3813 *E-mail:* emily_barrosse@mcgraw-hill.com
VP, EDP: Linda Toy *Tel:* 415-357-8145 *Fax:* 415-357-8181 *E-mail:* linda_toy@mcgraw-hill.com
Founded: 1944
Publishes college textbook & numerous e-books.
ISBN Prefix(es): 0-07; 0-697
Number of titles published annually: 476 Print; 255 CD-ROM; 225 Online; 32 Audio
Total Titles: 5,367 Print; 924 CD-ROM; 933 Online; 314 Audio
Branch Office(s)
160 Spear St, Suite 700, San Francisco, CA 94105 *Tel:* 415-357-8100 *Toll Free Tel:* 800-435-2665 *Fax:* 415-357-8085
420 Boylston St, 2nd fl, Boston, MA 02116, Contact: Lyn Uhl *Tel:* 617-262-1160 *Fax:* 617-867-9849
Returns: 860 Taylor Station Rd, Blacklick, OH 43004-0539
Distribution Center: 860 Taylor Station Rd, Blacklick, OH 43004-0539

McGraw-Hill International Publishing Group
Division of McGraw-Hill Education
2 Penn Plaza, New York, NY 10121
Tel: 212-904-2000
Web Site: www.mcgrawhill.com
Key Personnel
Group Pres, Higher Educ, Prof & Intl: Brian Heer
Sr VP, Fin & Opers: Jeremy Moss
Sr VP, Intl Eng Lang Publg: Simon Allen
Sr VP, Latin/Hispanic Lang Publg: Carlos Davis
VP, Fin & Opers: Matthew Wyatt
Pres, M-H Ryerson: John Dill
Exec VP & CFO: Gordon Dyer
ISBN Prefix(es): 0-8126

§McGraw-Hill/Irwin
Division of McGraw-Hill Higher Education
1333 Burr Ridge Pkwy, Burr Ridge, IL 60527
Tel: 630-789-4000 *Toll Free Tel:* 800-338-3987 (cust serv) *Fax:* 630-789-6942; 614-755-5645 (cust serv)
Web Site: www.mhhe.com

Key Personnel
Pres: Kevin Kane *Tel:* 630-789-5046 *Fax:* 630-789-5547 *E-mail:* kevin_kane@mcgraw-hill.com
VP & Ed-in-Chief: Rob Zwettler *Tel:* 630-789-5136 *Fax:* 630-789-5218 *E-mail:* rob_zwettler@mcgraw-hill.com
VP & Natl Sales Mgr: David Littlehale *Tel:* 630-789-5521 *Fax:* 630-789-6946 *E-mail:* david_littlehale@mcgraw-hill.com
VP & Dir, Mktg: Jim Kourmadas *Tel:* 630-789-5257 *Fax:* 630-789-6945 *E-mail:* james_kourmadas@mcgraw-hill.com
VP, Editing, Design & Prodn: Merrily Mazza *Tel:* 630-789-5174 *Fax:* 630-789-5160 *E-mail:* merrily_mazza@mcgraw-hill.com
Founded: 1933
College textbooks & numerous E-book titles.
ISBN Prefix(es): 0-07; 0-697; 0-256
Number of titles published annually: 354 Print; 148 CD-ROM; 131 Online
Total Titles: 3,294 Print; 789 CD-ROM; 774 Online; 13 Audio
Branch Office(s)
Spear St, Suite 700, San Francisco, CA 94105 *Tel:* 415-357-8100 *Toll Free Tel:* 800-435-2665 *Fax:* 415-357-8085
Returns: 860 Taylor Station Rd, Blacklick, OH 43004-0539
Distribution Center: 860 Taylor Station Rd, Blacklick, OH 43004-0539

§McGraw-Hill Learning Group
Division of McGraw-Hill Education
8787 Orion Place, Columbus, OH 43240
Tel: 614-430-4000 *Fax:* 614-430-6621
Key Personnel
Pres: Peter F Sayeski
VP, Fin: Robert R Simons
VP, Technol & Database Mtg: Randall Reina
VP, Urban Accts: Jeffrey B Livingston
VP, Fed Mktg: David Whiting
ISBN Prefix(es): 0-8126; 0-675; 0-574; 0-88120
Imprints: American School Publishers; Barnell-Loft; McGraw-Hill; Merrill; National Textbook Co; Open Court; Optical Data Co; Random House; RBL; SRA
See separate listing for:
SRA/McGraw-Hill, a Division of McGraw-Hill Learning Group
The Wright Group/McGraw-Hill, a Division of McGraw-Hill Learning Group

§McGraw-Hill/Osborne
Division of McGraw-Hill Education
2100 Powell St, 10th fl, Emeryville, CA 94608
SAN: 274-3450
Tel: 510-420-7700 *Toll Free Tel:* 800-227-0900 *Fax:* 510-420-7703
Web Site: shop.osborne.com/cgi-bin/osborne
Key Personnel
VP & Assoc Publr: Scott Rogers
Territory Mgr: Katherine Loch *E-mail:* katherine_loch@mcgraw-hill.com; Jill Salkanskas
Founded: 1970
A leading provider of computer & software reference guides.
ISBN Prefix(es): 0-07
Number of titles published annually: 150 Print; 150 E-Book
Total Titles: 350 Print; 25 CD-ROM; 100 Online; 300 E-Book
Imprints: Certification Press; CorelPRESS; Oracle Press™; Quicken Press; RSA PRESS
Foreign Rights: Editora McGraw-Hill de Portugal Ltd (Portugal); McGraw-Hill Book Co Australia Pty Ltd (Australia, New Zealand); McGraw-Hill Book Co Europe (Africa, UK, Europe, Middle East, Southern Africa); McGraw-Hill Education (Asia, China, Hong Kong); McGraw-Hill-Interamerican de Espana SA (Spain); McGraw-Hill Interamericana SA

(Argentina, Caribbean, Central America, Chile, Colombia, Mexico, Peru, Venezuela, Ecuador, Paraguay, Uruguay); McGraw-Hill Ryerson (Canada)

McGraw-Hill Primis Custom Publishing
Division of McGraw-Hill Higher Education
2460 Kerper Blvd, Dubuque, IA 52001
Tel: 563-588-1451 *Fax:* 563-589-4700
E-mail: first_last@mcgraw-hill.com
Web Site: www.mhhe.com
Key Personnel
Sr Dushkin/Custom Mktg Mgr: Julie Keck *Tel:* 563-589-2895 *Fax:* 563-589-4704 *E-mail:* julie_keck@mcgraw-hill.com
Sr Dushkin/Custom Prodn Mgr: Beth Kundert *Tel:* 563-589-1834 *Fax:* 563-589-4657 *E-mail:* beth_kundert@mcgraw-hill.com
Sr Dushkin/Custom Opers Mgr: Pat Koch *Tel:* 609-426-5721 *Fax:* 609-426-7099 *E-mail:* pat_koch@mcgraw-hill.com
Sr Custom Publ Rep Mgr: Shirley Grall *Tel:* 563-589-4793 *Fax:* 563-589-4766 *E-mail:* shirley_grall@mcgraw-hill.com
Sr Spons Ed, Primis Custom Publg: Dudley Land *Tel:* 530-621-3976 *Fax:* 775-525-9197 *E-mail:* dudley_land@mcgraw-hill.com
VP: Virginia Moffat *Tel:* 630-789-5073 *Fax:* 630-789-6942 *E-mail:* ginny_moffat@mcgraw-hill.com
Mgr, Primis Systems: Cat Mattura *Tel:* 212-904-3559 *Fax:* 212-904-2340 *E-mail:* cat_mattura@mcgraw-hill.com
Dushkin Man Ed: Larry Loeppke *Tel:* 563-589-1315 *Fax:* 563-589-4704 *E-mail:* larry_loeppke@mcgraw-hill.com
Custom products derived from McGraw-Hill copyrighted material; college textbook & electronic book adaptations; supplemental materials.
ISBN Prefix(es): 0-07
Number of titles published annually: 1,400 Print
Total Titles: 4,800 Print
Branch Office(s)
1333 Burr Ridge Pkwy, Burr Ridge, IL 60527
2 Penn Plaza, 20th fl, New York, NY 10121
148 Princeton-Hightstown Rd, Hightstown, NJ 08520
Distribution Center: The McGraw-Hill Companies, Distribution Center, 860 Taylor Station Rd, Blacklick, OH 43004

§McGraw-Hill Professional
Division of McGraw-Hill Education
2 Penn Plaza, New York, NY 10121
Tel: 212-904-2000
Web Site: www.books.mcgraw-hill.com
Key Personnel
Pres: Keith Fox
VP & Group Publr, Trade: Philip Ruppel
VP & Group Publr, Sci, Tech & Med: Michael Hays
VP & Dir, Sales: Michael Rovins
Sci, Tech, Med & Subs Rts: Mary Murray
Trade & Subs Rts: Allyson Gonzalez
Publishes "need-to-know" books & other products for a broad range of professional, technical & consumer/reference markets. Key subject areas include business, computing, medicine, technical & consumer reference including foreign languages, dictionaries & self-help. The company also provides online information services to the medical & other markets.
ISBN Prefix(es): 0-07
Number of titles published annually: 1,100 Print; 5 Online; 500 E-Book
Total Titles: 12,500 Print; 43 Online; 2,000 E-Book
Imprints: Certification Press; International Marine Publishing; Irwin Professional; Lange Medical Books; NTC Contemporary Books; Oracle Press; Osborne; Ragged Mountain Press; Schaum

Branch Office(s)
McGraw-Hill/Osborne, 2100 Powell St, Emeryville, CA 94608 *Tel:* 510-420-7700 *Toll Free Tel:* 800-227-0900 *Web Site:* www. osborne.com
Irwin Professional, 1333 Burr Ridge Pkwy, Burr Ridge, IL 60521 *Tel:* 630-789-4000 *Fax:* 630-789-6933
Shipping Address: 7500 Chavenelle Rd, Dubuque, IA 52002
Warehouse: 7500 Chavenelle Rd, Dubuque, IA 52002
Distribution Center: 7500 Chavenelle Rd, Dubuque, IA 52002
Membership(s): AAP; American Medical Publishers Association; International Association of Scientific, Technical & Medical Publishers

§McGraw-Hill Science, Engineering, Mathematics
Division of McGraw-Hill Higher Education
2460 Kerper Blvd, Dubuque, IA 52001
Tel: 563-588-1451 *Toll Free Tel:* 800-338-3987 (cust serv) *Fax:* 563-589-4700; 614-755-5645 (cust serv)
E-mail: firstname_lastname@mcgraw-hill.com
Web Site: www.mhhe.com
Key Personnel
Pres: Kurt strand *Tel:* 563-589-2806 *Fax:* 563-589-1319 *E-mail:* kurt_strand@mcgraw-hill.com
VP & Ed-in-Chief: Michael Lange *Tel:* 563-589-2980 *Fax:* 563-589-1319 *E-mail:* michael_lange@mcgraw-hill.com
VP & Natl Sales Mgr: Doug DiNardo *E-mail:* doug_dinardo@mcgraw-hill.com
VP, Editing, Design & Prodn: Janice Roerig-Blong *Tel:* 563-589-2830 *Fax:* 563-589-1366 *E-mail:* janice_roerig-blong@mcgraw-hill.com
Founded: 1944
College textbook publisher.
ISBN Prefix(es): 0-07; 0-697
Number of titles published annually: 349 Print; 158 CD-ROM; 129 Online
Total Titles: 2,338 Print; 497 CD-ROM; 714 Online
Imprints: McGraw-Hill
Branch Office(s)
1333 Burr Ridge Pkwy, Burr Ridge, IL 60527 *Tel:* 630-789-4000 *Fax:* 630-789-5030
420 Boylston St, 2nd fl, Boston, MA 02116 *Tel:* 617-262-1160 *Fax:* 617-867-9847
1285 Fern Ridge Pkwy, Suite 200, St Louis, MO 63141 *Toll Free Tel:* 800-992-9553 *Fax:* 314-439-6848
Returns: 860 Taylor Station Rd, Blacklick, OH 43004-0539
Distribution Center: 860 Taylor Station Rd, Blacklick, OH 43004-0539

McGraw-Hill Trade
Division of McGraw-Hill Education
2 Penn Plaza, New York, NY 10121
Key Personnel
VP & Group Publr: Philip Ruppel
ISBN Prefix(es): 0-07; 0-658

Wil McKnight Associates Inc
1801 W Hovey Ave, Suite A, Normal, IL 61761
Tel: 309-451-0000 *Fax:* 309-451-0000
E-mail: info@hardhatonline.com
Web Site: www.hardhatonline.com
Key Personnel
Pres: Wil McKnight
Acctg: Cheryl Kelley
Founded: 1983
Supervisory training programs for the construction industry; self-study books for construction foremen.
ISBN Prefix(es): 1-56067
Number of titles published annually: 5 Print
Total Titles: 20 Print

Andrews McMeel Publishing
Division of Andrews McMeel Universal
4520 Main St, Suite 700, Kansas City, MO 64111-7701
Tel: 816-932-6700 *Toll Free Tel:* 800-851-8923
Web Site: www.universal.com/amp
Key Personnel
Chmn of the Bd: John P McMeel
VChmn: Kathleen W Andrews
Pres & CEO: Thomas N Thornton
VP & Edit Dir: Chris Schillig
VP & Man Dir: Dorothy O'Brien
VP, Sales & Mktg: Hugh Andrews
Asst VP, Client Publrs: Lynne McAdoo
Edit Dir, Gift Books & Sr Ed, Book Div: Patty Rice
Dir, Dom & Subs Rts: Kathy Viele
Mgr, Intl Rts: Suzanne Garrett
Founded: 1973
Specialize in calendars & gift books.
ISBN Prefix(es): 0-7407
Number of titles published annually: 249 Print; 6 CD-ROM
Distributor for Carlton Books; Diamond Select; Melcher Media; Michael O'Mara Books (North America only); National Geographic Calendars; Signatures Network; Sporting News; Universe Publishing Calendars; Welcome Books
Foreign Rights: Agence Hoffman (Germany); Agenzia Letteraria Internazionale (Italy); The Book Publishers Association of Israel (Israel); DS Druck und Verlag (Eastern Europe); Europa Press (Scandinavia); Gamma Medya (Turkey); Japan Uni Agency (Japan); JLM Literary Agents (Greece); Korea Copyright Center (Korea); Lijnkamp Literary Agency (Netherlands); Andrew Nurnberg Associate (Bulgaria); Abner Stein Literary Agency (Australia, UK); The Big Apple Tuttle-Mori (Mainland China, Taiwan); Tuttle Mori Big Apple Agency (Thailand); VVV Agency (France); Julio F Yanez Agencia Literaria SL (Brazil, Latin America, Portugal, Spain)
Distribution Center: Simon & Schuster Inc, 100 Front St, Riverside, NJ 08075 *Toll Free Tel:* 800-223-2336 *Web Site:* www.amuniversal. com/amp

McPherson & Co
148 Smith Ave, Kingston, NY 12401
SAN: 203-0632
Mailing Address: PO Box 1126, Kingston, NY 12402-1126
Tel: 845-331-5807 *Toll Free Tel:* 800-613-8219 *Fax:* 845-331-5807 *Toll Free Fax:* 800-613-8219
Web Site: www.mcphersonco.com
Key Personnel
Ed-in-Chief, Publr & ISBN Contact: Bruce R McPherson *E-mail:* mcpherson@mcphersonco. com
Founded: 1973
Fiction, anthropology, belles lettres & avant-garde art.
ISBN Prefix(es): 0-914232; 0-929701
Number of titles published annually: 6 Print
Total Titles: 117 Print; 2 Audio
Imprints: Documentext; McPherson & Co; Recovered Classics; Treacle Press
Foreign Office(s): c/o Central Books, 99 Wallis Rd, London E9 5LN, United Kingdom
Distributor for Raymond Saroff Editions
Foreign Rights: Agenzia Letteraria (Italy); Agnese Incisa (Italy); Kerigan-Moro Literary (Portugal & Spain); Lijnkamp Literary Agents (Netherlands); Literarische Agentur Simon (Germany); La Nouvelle Agence (France)

§MDRT Center for Productivity
Division of Million Dollar Round Table
325 W Touhy Ave, Park Ridge, IL 60068-4265
Tel: 847-692-6378 *Toll Free Tel:* 800-879-6378 *Fax:* 847-518-8921

E-mail: orders@mdrt.org
Web Site: www.mdrt.org
Key Personnel
Publr: Ileo Lott *E-mail:* ilott@mdrt.org
Exec VP: John Prast
Founded: 1996
Publishing, consulting & marketing services in the life insurance & financial services industries. Products & services include books, audio, video & electronic media.
ISBN Prefix(es): 1-891042
Number of titles published annually: 3 Print; 2 Online; 50 Audio
Total Titles: 80 Print; 15 CD-ROM; 2 Online; 500 Audio
Distributed by John Wiley & Sons; Nightingale-Conant

me+mi publishing inc
128 S County Farm Rd, Wheaton, IL 60187
Tel: 630-752-9951 *Toll Free Tel:* 888-251-1444 *Fax:* 630-588-9804
E-mail: rw@rosawesley.com
Web Site: www.memima.com
Key Personnel
Contact: Mark Wesley
Founded: 2002
Independent publisher dedicated to creating the highest quality books available in two or more languages for infants & toddlers.
ISBN Prefix(es): 0-9679748; 1-931398
Number of titles published annually: 8 Print
Imprints: The English Spanish Foundation Series
Membership(s): Association of Educational Publishers; Publishers Marketing Association; Small Press Center

Meadowbrook Press
5451 Smetana Dr, Minnetonka, MN 55343
SAN: 207-3404
Tel: 952-930-1100 *Toll Free Tel:* 800-338-2232 *Fax:* 952-930-1940
Web Site: www.meadowbrookpress.com
Key Personnel
Pres, Publr & Edit Mgr: Bruce Lansky
Prodn Mgr: Paul Woods
Sales Mgr: Mike Ballard
Intl Rts Contact: Polly Andersen
Founded: 1975
Trade paperbacks; baby & child care, parenting, health, children's activities, humor, parties & games, children's poetry, adult light verse, travel, chapter book for children age 8-12.
Number of titles published annually: 12 Print
Total Titles: 80 Print
Distributed by Simon & Schuster (book trade only)
Foreign Rep(s): Electra Media Group Pty Ltd (Southeast Asia); IPR (Cyprus, Greece, Malta, Turkey); Chris Lloyd Sales & Marketing (UK); Monarch Books of Canada (Canada); PSD Promotions (South Africa)
Foreign Rights: Big Apple Tuttle-Mori Agency (China & Taiwan); The Book Publishers Association of Israel (Israel); Bridge Communications Co (Thailand); Iris Literary Agency (Greece); Japan Uni Agency (Japan); Alexander Korzhenevski Agency (Russia); Majdak Zvonimir (Croatia, Slovenia, Serbia and Montenegro); Kristin Olson Literary Agency (Czech Republic); RDC Agencia Literaria (Latin America, Portugal, Spain); The Rights Agency (France, French Canada, Serbia and Montenegro); RT Copyright Ltd (Bulgaria, Serbia and Montenegro, Hungary, Poland, Romania, Turkey); Shin Won Agency Co (Korea); Transnet Contracts Ltd (Austria, Germany); Eric Yang Agency (Korea)

§R S Means Co Inc
Subsidiary of Construction Market Data Group
63 Smiths Lane, Kingston, MA 02364-0800

Tel: 781-585-7880 *Toll Free Tel:* 800-448-8182 *Fax:* 781-585-8814 *Toll Free Fax:* 800-632-6732
Web Site: www.rsmeans.com
Key Personnel
VP, Sales: John Shea
Ed, Ref: Mary Greene
Founded: 1942
Books, electronic data: construction cost data, engineering, how-to.
ISBN Prefix(es): 0-911950; 0-87629
Number of titles published annually: 24 Print
Total Titles: 101 Print
Divisions: Cost Annuals
Advertising Agency: The Stancliff Agency

Medals of America Press
Division of Medals of America Ltd
114 Southchase Blvd, Fountain Inn, SC 29644
Tel: 864-862-6051 *Toll Free Tel:* 800-308-0849 *Fax:* 864-862-0256 *Toll Free Fax:* 800-407-8640
E-mail: press@usmedals.com
Web Site: www.moapress.com
Key Personnel
Publr: Frank Foster *Fax:* 864-601-1108 *E-mail:* ffoster@usmedals.com
Gen Mgr: Steve Russ *Tel:* 864-601-1112 *E-mail:* russ@usmedals.com
Founded: 1992
Offer complete illustrated guides to United States military medals, decorations & insignia of the Army, Navy, Marines, Air Force, Coast Guard & Merchant Marines, United Nations & Vietnam.
ISBN Prefix(es): 1-884452
Number of titles published annually: 8 Print; 1 Audio
Total Titles: 13 Print; 15 Online; 2 Audio
Foreign Rep(s): Greenhill Books (UK)
Membership(s): Publishers Marketing Association

MedBooks
Division of Professional Education Workshops & Seminars
101 W Buckingham Rd, Richardson, TX 75081
Tel: 972-643-1802 *Toll Free Tel:* 800-443-7397 *Fax:* 972-994-0215
E-mail: medbooks@medbooks.com
Web Site: www.medbooks.com
Key Personnel
Owner: Trish Morin-Spatz
Pres: Patrice Morin-Spatz
Founded: 1985
Specialize in books on health insurance coding & processing for medical offices, insurance companies & other health professions.
ISBN Prefix(es): 0-923369
Number of titles published annually: 5 Print
Total Titles: 5 Print
Distributed by JA Majors
Membership(s): American Health Information Management Association

§Media & Methods
Subsidiary of American Society of Educators
1429 Walnut St, 10th fl, Philadelphia, PA 19102
Tel: 215-563-6005 *Toll Free Tel:* 800-555-5657 *Fax:* 215-587-9706
Web Site: www.media-methods.com
Key Personnel
Publr: Michele Sokoloff *Tel:* 215-241-9200 ext 200 *E-mail:* michelesok@aol.com
VP, Sales: Caliann Mitoulis
Founded: 1964
Educational focus devoted to hands-on uses of multimedia educational technologies. Readers include Library & Media Specialist & curriculum directors & administrators. Readers are buyers of educational resources & equipment K-12 schools nationwide.

Number of titles published annually: 7 Print
Total Titles: 1 E-Book

§Media Associates
Subsidiary of Archives Publications
PO Box 46, Wilton, CA 95693-0046
SAN: 657-3207
Toll Free Tel: 800-373-1897 (orders) *Fax:* 916-687-8711; 916-687-8711
E-mail: carlya777@hotmail.com
Web Site: www.media-associates.co.nz
Key Personnel
Founder, Man Ed & Intl Rts: G H Harrison
Ed: Triona Watson
Founded: 1965
Specialize in multi-media, Internet, mass media, children's books & paperbacks, equestrian, grail & tarot.
ISBN Prefix(es): 0-918501
Number of titles published annually: 17 Print; 3 CD-ROM; 2 Online; 1 E-Book
Total Titles: 130 Print; 11 CD-ROM; 14 Online; 4 E-Book
Imprints: Arkives Books; Arkive.com; Archives Press; BookProcessor; Epona Books; Homemade Books; X Press
Foreign Office(s): One Vondel Park, Amsterdam, Netherlands, Rep: Dan Aeyelts
Distributed by Airlift; Editions France; Equestrian Distribution; Inland; New Leaf; Samuel Weiser
Foreign Rep(s): Gerard Van Eynden (Netherlands)
Foreign Rights: Dan Aeyelts (World Rights)

Medical Group Management Association
104 Inverness Terr E, Englewood, CO 80112
Tel: 303-799-1111 *Toll Free Tel:* 888-608-5601 *Fax:* 303-643-4439
Web Site: www.mgma.com
Key Personnel
Lib Dir: Carolyn Lyons
Founded: 1926
Specialize in medical practice management.
ISBN Prefix(es): 0-8273
Number of titles published annually: 8 Print; 2 CD-ROM
Total Titles: 150 Print; 2 CD-ROM
Branch Office(s)
Govt Affairs, 1717 Pennsylvania Ave NW, No 600, Washington, DC 20006, Contact: Patrick Smith *Tel:* 202-293-3450 *Fax:* 202-293-2787
Distributed by American Academy of Family Physicians
Distributor for Aspen Publishers; Jossey Bass; McGrawHill

Medical Physics Publishing Corp
4513 Vernon Blvd, Madison, WI 53705-4964
Tel: 608-262-4021 *Toll Free Tel:* 800-442-5778 *Fax:* 608-265-2121
E-mail: mpp@medicalphysics.org
Web Site: www.medicalphysics.org
Key Personnel
Pres: John Cameron
Man Ed, Electronic Publg: Betsey Phelps *E-mail:* betsey@medicalphysics.org
Gen Mgr & Intl Rts: June Johnson *E-mail:* junej@medicalphysics.org
Cust Serv Mgr: Dorothy Gable
Founded: 1985
Publish & distribute books & CD-ROMs in medical physics & related fields; two series of books for the public on health & science issues (focus on health & science issues).
ISBN Prefix(es): 0-944838; 1-930524
Number of titles published annually: 6 Print
Total Titles: 55 Print; 1 CD-ROM
Imprints: Cogito Books

Medieval Institute Publications
Division of Medieval Institute of Western Michigan University

1903 W Michigan Ave, Kalamazoo, MI 49008-5432
Tel: 269-387-8755 (orders); 269-387-8754 *Fax:* 269-387-8750
Web Site: www.wmich.edu/medieval/mip
Key Personnel
Man Ed: Patricia Hollahan *E-mail:* patricia.hollahan@wmich.edu
Publish 110 book titles, 3 journals.
ISBN Prefix(es): 1-918720; 1-879288; 1-58044
Number of titles published annually: 14 Print
Total Titles: 110 Print

MedMaster Inc
3337 Hollywood Oaks Dr, Fort Lauderdale, FL 33312
Tel: 954-962-8414 *Toll Free Tel:* 800-335-3480 *Fax:* 954-962-4508
E-mail: mmbks@aol.com
Web Site: www.medmaster.net
Key Personnel
Pres: Stephen Goldberg *E-mail:* stgoldberg@aol.com
VP: Harriet Goldberg
Founded: 1978
Medical book & software publishers; medical subjects for education of medical students & other health professionals.
ISBN Prefix(es): 0-940780
Number of titles published annually: 2 Print; 1 CD-ROM
Total Titles: 28 Print; 3 CD-ROM
Billing Address: PO Box 640028, Miami, FL 33164-0028
Orders to: PO Box 640028, Miami, FL 33164-0028
Returns: 360 NE 191 St, Miami, FL 33179
Warehouse: 360 NE 191 St, Miami, FL 33179

The Russell Meerdink Co Ltd
1555 S Park Ave, Neenah, WI 54956
SAN: 249-1680
Tel: 920-725-0955 *Toll Free Tel:* 800-635-6499 *Fax:* 920-725-0709
Web Site: www.horseinfo.com
Key Personnel
Man Dir & Intl Rts Contact: Jan Meerdink *E-mail:* jmeerdink@horseinfo.com
Founded: 1980
Equine titles & thoroughbred data services. Distribution & mail order sales of equine titles.
ISBN Prefix(es): 0-929346
Number of titles published annually: 4 Print; 2 CD-ROM
Total Titles: 25 Print; 4 CD-ROM

§Mega Media Press
1121 Hub Ct, El Cajon, CA 92020
SAN: 298-7678
Tel: 619-588-6846 *Toll Free Tel:* 800-803-9416 *Fax:* 619-588-6846
Web Site: www.imagetics.com
Key Personnel
Pres: Ray Payn *E-mail:* raypayn@imagetics.com
Founded: 1991
Consulting specializing in motivation, spirituality, aids for everyday living & self development; multimedia.
ISBN Prefix(es): 1-887834
Number of titles published annually: 10 Print
Total Titles: 20 Print; 3 CD-ROM; 3 E-Book; 20 Audio
Advertising Agency: Mega Media Agency
Membership(s): National Speakers Association

Mehring Books Inc
PO Box 48377, Oak Park, MI 48237-5977
Tel: 248-967-2924 *Fax:* 248-967-3023
E-mail: inquiry@mehring.com; sales@mehring.com
Web Site: www.mehring.com

Key Personnel
Pres: Helen Haylard
Sales Rep: Esther Galen
Founded: 1973
Books & journals on contemporary events, history, political economy, Trotsky's writings.
ISBN Prefix(es): 0-929087; 1-893638
Number of titles published annually: 5 Print
Total Titles: 49 Print
Foreign Rep(s): Arbeiterpresse Verlag (Germany); Mehring Books (Australia, England)

§Mel Bay Publications Inc
4 Industrial Dr, Pacific, MO 63069-0066
Mailing Address: PO Box 66, Pacific, MO 63069-0066
Tel: 636-257-3970 *Toll Free Tel:* 800-863-5229 *Fax:* 636-257-5062 *Toll Free Fax:* 800-660-9818
E-mail: email@melbay.com
Web Site: www.melbay.com
Key Personnel
Pres: William A Bay *E-mail:* bill@melbay.com
Cust Serv Rep: Julie Simpson *E-mail:* jsimpson@melbay.com
Founded: 1947
Innovative instructional & performance material for most instruments.
ISBN Prefix(es): 0-7866; 0-87166; 1-56222; 8-83206
Number of titles published annually: 500 Print; 5 CD-ROM
Total Titles: 4,500 Print; 20 CD-ROM
Imprints: Building Excellence; Cathedral Music Press; Creative Keyboard; Editions Classicae; You Can Teach Yourself
Divisions: Cathedral Music Press; Creative Keyboard Publications
Distributed by International Print Edition
Distributor for AMA; Chanterelle; Hardie Press; Konemann; Malley's; Kevin Mayhew Ltd; Voggenreiter Publishers; Walton's
Foreign Rep(s): Allan's Music Group (Australia); Carisch (Italy); Kevin Mayhew (UK)
Advertising Agency: Mel Bay Creative Services

The Edwin Mellen Press
415 Ridge St, Lewiston, NY 14092
SAN: 207-110X
Mailing Address: PO Box 450, Lewiston, NY 14092-0450
Tel: 716-754-2266 (mgr acqs); 716-754-8566 (mktg); 716-754-2788 (order fulfillment) *Fax:* 716-754-4056; 716-754-1860 (order fulfillment)
E-mail: mellen@wzrd.com; cs@wzrd.com (customer service, fulfillment)
Web Site: www.mellenpress.com
Key Personnel
Founder & CEO: Herbert Richardson
Dir: John Rupnow *E-mail:* jrupnow@mellenpress.com
Prodn Mgr & Perms Ed: Patricia Schultz
Mktg Dir: Barbara Vollick
Fulfillment Dir: Irene Miller
Founded: 1974
International scholarly publisher of advanced research.
ISBN Prefix(es): 0-88946; 0-7734
Number of titles published annually: 400 Print; 2 CD-ROM
Total Titles: 5,500 Print; 7 CD-ROM
Imprints: Mellen Poetry Press
Divisions: Edwin Mellen, (Canada, UK)
Branch Office(s)
Box 67, Queenston, ON L0S 1L0, Canada
Foreign Office(s): Mellen House, 17 Llambed Ind Est, Lampeter, Ceredigion SA48 8LT, United Kingdom, Mgr, Wales/UK Off: Mrs Iona Williams *Tel:* 011 44 1570 423 356 *Fax:* 011 44 1570 423 775 *E-mail:* emp@mellen.demon.o.uk *Web Site:* www.mellenpress.com

Foreign Rep(s): Edwin Mellen (UK)
Advertising Agency: Lewiston Business Services

Menasha Ridge Press Inc
2204 First Ave S, Suite 102, Birmingham, AL 35233
Tel: 205-322-0439 *Fax:* 205-326-1012
E-mail: info@menasharidge.com
Web Site: www.menasharidge.com
Key Personnel
Pres: Molly B Merkle *Tel:* 205-322-0439 ext 106 *E-mail:* mmerkle@menasharidge.com
Publr: Robert W Sehlinger *Tel:* 205-322-0439 ext 104 *E-mail:* bsehlinger@menasharidge.com
Ed & Prodn Mgr: Gabriela Oates *Tel:* 205-322-0439 ext 143 *E-mail:* goates@menasharidge.com
Acqs Ed: Russell Helms *Tel:* 205-322-0439 ext 111 *E-mail:* rhelms@menasharidge.com
Sales & Mktg: Tricia Parks *Tel:* 205-322-0439 ext 102 *E-mail:* tparks@menasharidge.com
Founded: 1982
Books & maps.
ISBN Prefix(es): 0-89732
Number of titles published annually: 20 Print; 15 E-Book
Total Titles: 200 Print; 50 E-Book
Distributed by The Globe Pequot Press
Orders to: PO Box 480, Guilford, CT 06437-0480 *Toll Free Tel:* 800-243-0495 *Toll Free Fax:* 800-820-2329 *E-mail:* info@globepequot.com *Web Site:* www.globepequot.com
Returns: The Globe Pequot Press, 128 Pinnacle Dr, Springfield, TN 37172 *Toll Free Tel:* 800-243-0495 *Toll Free Fax:* 800-820-2329 *Web Site:* www.globepequot.com
Membership(s): Publishers Association of the South

§MENC - The National Association for Music Education
1806 Robert Fulton Dr, Reston, VA 20191
Tel: 703-860-4000 *Fax:* 703-860-9443
E-mail: franp@menc.org
Web Site: www.menc.org
Key Personnel
Exec Dir: John J Mahlmann *Fax:* 703-860-1531
Asst Exec Dir, Pubns: Ardene Shafer *Fax:* 703-860-1531
Founded: 1907
Books, brochures & audiovisual materials on all phases of music education in schools & communities; professional philosophy & practical techniques, the arts & art education as a whole; current issues in music teaching & learning; music education advocacy.
ISBN Prefix(es): 0-940796; 1-56545
Number of titles published annually: 12 Print; 3 Online
Total Titles: 110 Print; 10 Online
Distributor for American String Teachers Association

MEP Publications
Division of Marxist Educational Press
University of Minnesota, Physics Bldg, 116 Church St SE, Minneapolis, MN 55455-0112
SAN: 276-9727
Tel: 612-922-7993
E-mail: marqu002@tc.umn.edu
Web Site: umn.edu/home/marqu002
Key Personnel
Pres: Harold L Schwartz
Man Ed: Doris G Marquit
Treas & Intl Rts: Erwin Marquit
Founded: 1977
Nature Society & Thought: a quarterly interdisciplinary scholarly journal; cloth & paperback academic books.
ISBN Prefix(es): 0-930656
Number of titles published annually: 2 Print
Total Titles: 50 Print

Mercer University Press
1400 Coleman Ave, Macon, GA 31207
SAN: 220-0716
Tel: 478-301-2880 *Toll Free Tel:* 800-637-2378 (ext 2880, outside GA); 800-342-0841 (ext 2880, GA) *Fax:* 478-301-2585
E-mail: mupressorders@mercer.edu
Web Site: www.mupress.org *Cable:* MERUNIPRES
Key Personnel
Dir: Marc Jolley, Jr *E-mail:* jolley_ma@mercer.edu
Sr Ed: Edmon L Rowell, Jr *E-mail:* rowell_el@mercer.edu
Dir, Mktg: Barbara Keene *E-mail:* keene_b@mercer.edu
Busn Mgr: James Golden, Jr *E-mail:* golden_jw@mercer.edu
Founded: 1979
History, philosophy, religion, Southern studies, Southern literature, literary studies, regional interest.
ISBN Prefix(es): 0-86554
Number of titles published annually: 40 Print
Total Titles: 900 Print
Foreign Rights: East-West Export Books; Gracewing Books Ltd (England)
Membership(s): American Association of University Presses

Merit Publishing International Inc
5840 Corporate Way, Suite 200, West Palm Beach, FL 33407-2040
Tel: 561-637-1116 *Fax:* 561-477-4961
E-mail: meritpi@aol.com
Web Site: www.meritpublishing.com
Key Personnel
Pres: Gene Evans
VP: Marta Garrido *Tel:* 561-697-1116
Founded: 1986 (Founded in UK 1986, US 1992)
Medical publishing & marketing in all clinical areas. Questions & answers series, visual diagnosis self-tests series, customized books, slide kits, newsletters, proceedings & monographs.
ISBN Prefix(es): 1-873413
Number of titles published annually: 13 Print
Total Titles: 65 Print; 3 CD-ROM; 3 Online
Foreign Office(s): 50 Highpoint Heath Rd, Weybridge, Surrey KT13 8TP, United Kingdom *Tel:* (01932) 844526 *Fax:* (01932) 820419 *E-mail:* merituk@aol.com *Web Site:* www.meritpublishing.com
Foreign Rep(s): Atlas Medical Books (Greece, Italy, Turkey); Benalux (Scandinavia); Gazelle (UK)
Foreign Rights: J & C Ediciones Medicas (Spain & Latin America)
Returns: 22396 Waterside Dr, Boca Raton, FL 33428
Membership(s): Publishers Marketing Association

Meriwether Publishing Ltd/Contemporary Drama Service
885 Elkton Dr, Colorado Springs, CO 80907-3557
SAN: 208-4716
Mailing Address: PO Box 7710, Colorado Springs, CO 80933-7710
Tel: 719-594-4422 *Toll Free Tel:* 800-937-5297 *Fax:* 719-594-9916 *Toll Free Fax:* 888-594-4436
E-mail: merpcds@aol.com
Web Site: www.meriwether.com
Key Personnel
Pres & Intl Rights: A Mark Zapel *Tel:* 719-594-4422 ext 127 *E-mail:* mzapel@aol.com
Ed & Publr: Arthur L Zapel *E-mail:* alzapel@meriwetherpublishing.com
Assoc Ed: Ted Zapel *E-mail:* tzapel@meriwetherpublishing.com
Electronic Publg Mgr: Dianne Bundt
Founded: 1967

Books on theater, performing arts, costuming, stagecraft, clown & mime, play anthologies, plays, musicals, videos, games, general interest how-to books & wedding books.
ISBN Prefix(es): 0-916260; 1-56608
Number of titles published annually: 35 Print
Total Titles: 975 Print
Imprints: Contemporary Drama Service
Subsidiaries: Contemporary Drama Service
Foreign Rep(s): Fitzhenry & Whiteside (Canada); Gazelle Book Service (UK & Europe); Hanbury Plays (UK); Mentone Educational Centre (Australia)
Membership(s): Christian Booksellers Association

Meisha Merlin Publishing Inc
1702 Ronald Rd, Tucker, GA 30084
Mailing Address: PO Box 7, Decatur, GA 30031-0007
Tel: 770-414-4365 *Fax:* 770-414-4365
E-mail: email@meishamerlin.com; orders@meishamerlin.com
Web Site: www.meishamerlin.com
Key Personnel
Pres & Sr Ed: Stephen Pagel
VP & Art Dir: Kevin Murphy
Founded: 1997
Science fiction, fantasy & horror titles & limited signed editions.
ISBN Prefix(es): 0-9658345; 1-892060
Number of titles published annually: 15 Print
Total Titles: 48 Print
Foreign Rights: Joshua Bilmes (World)
Membership(s): Association of Science Fiction Fantasy Artists; Horror Writers Association; Science Fiction & Fantasy Writers of America

§Merriam Press
218 Beech St, Bennington, VT 05201-2611
Tel: 802-447-0313 *Fax:* 802-217-1051
Web Site: www.merriam-press.com
Key Personnel
Owner & Intl Rts: Ray Merriam *E-mail:* ray@merriam-press.com
Founded: 1987
WW II military history & memoirs.
ISBN Prefix(es): 1-57638
Number of titles published annually: 20 Print; 20 CD-ROM
Total Titles: 90 Print; 90 CD-ROM
Imprints: WW II Journal (Historical, scholarly, memoir articles on WW II); WW II Memoirs (Memoirs by WW II Veterans); World War II Monographs (Historical, scholarly books)

§Merriam-Webster Inc
Subsidiary of Encyclopaedia Britannica
47 Federal St, Springfield, MA 01102
Mailing Address: PO Box 281, Springfield, MA 01102-0281
Tel: 413-734-3134 *Toll Free Tel:* 800-828-1880 (orders & cust serv) *Fax:* 413-731-5979
E-mail: merriam_webster@merriam-webster.com
Web Site: www.merriam-webster.com
Key Personnel
Pres & Publr: John M Morse
VP & Assoc Publr: James W Withgott
Dir, Mktg: Hillary Hoffman
Art Dir: Lynn Stowe Tomb
Sr Publicist: Arthur J Bicknell
Founded: 1831
Dictionaries & language reference products.
ISBN Prefix(es): 0-87779
Number of titles published annually: 4 Print
Total Titles: 104 Print; 7 CD-ROM; 2 Online; 2 E-Book
Imprints: Federal Street Press
Divisions: Federal Street Press
See separate listing for:
Federal Street Press

Merryant Publishers Inc
7615 SW 257 St, Vashon, WA 98070
Tel: 206-463-3879 *Toll Free Tel:* 800-228-8958 *Fax:* 206-463-1604
Key Personnel
CEO & Author: Mary Null Boule
Mktg Dir: H James Boule *E-mail:* jmboule@aol.com
Founded: 1988
Self-authored book series.
ISBN Prefix(es): 1-877599
Number of titles published annually: 13 Print
Total Titles: 59 Print

Mesorah Publications Ltd
4401 Second Ave, Brooklyn, NY 11232
SAN: 213-1269
Tel: 718-921-9000 *Toll Free Tel:* 800-637-6724 *Fax:* 718-680-1875
E-mail: artscroll@mesorah.com
Web Site: www.artscroll.com; www.mesorah.com
Key Personnel
Pres & Int Rts Contact: Meir Zlotowitz
Prodn Mgr: Jacob Brander
Dir, Sales: Shneur Groner
Ed-in-Chief & Exec VP: Nosson Scherman
Mktg Dir & Lib Sales Dir: Efraim Perlowitz *Tel:* 718-765-9216 *E-mail:* efraim@mesorah.com
Founded: 1976
Judaica, Bible study, liturgical materials, juvenile, history, Holocaust, Talmud, novels.
ISBN Prefix(es): 0-89906
Number of titles published annually: 50 Print
Total Titles: 700 Print
Imprints: Art Scroll Series; Shaar Press; Tamar Books
Distributor for Mesorah Publications Ltd; NCSY Publications
Foreign Rep(s): Stephen Blitz (Israel)

Messianic Jewish Publishers
Division of Messianic Jewish Communications
6204 Park Heights Ave, Baltimore, MD 21215-3600
Tel: 410-358-6471 *Toll Free Tel:* 800-773-6574 *Fax:* 410-764-1376
E-mail: lederer@messianicjewish.net; rightsandpermissions@messianicjewish.net (rights & perms)
Web Site: messianicjewish.net
Key Personnel
Pres: Barry Rubin *Tel:* 410-358-6471 ext 205 *E-mail:* president@messianicjewish.net
Man Ed: Janet Chaiet *Tel:* 410-358-6471 ext 206 *E-mail:* editor@messianicjewish.net
Founded: 1949
Publish & distribute Messianic Jewish books & other products.
ISBN Prefix(es): 1-880226
Number of titles published annually: 12 Print
Total Titles: 55 Print; 1 CD-ROM; 1 Audio
Distributor for Chosen People Ministries; First Fruits of Zion; Jewish New Testament Publications
Foreign Rep(s): Winfried Bluth (Europe)
Foreign Rights: Winfried Bluth (Europe)
Membership(s): Christian Booksellers Association; Evangelical Christian Publishers Association
See separate listing for:
Lederer Books

META Publications Inc
PO Box 1910, Capitola, CA 95010-1910
Tel: 831-464-0254 *Fax:* 831-464-0517
E-mail: metapub@prodigy.net
Web Site: www.meta-publications.com
Key Personnel
Mgr & Treas: Fred Tapella
Founded: 1976
Neuro-linguistic programming books.

ISBN Prefix(es): 0-916990
Number of titles published annually: 1 Print
Total Titles: 36 Print
Warehouse: Maple Press Distribution Center, 60 Grumbacher Rd, York, PA 17405

Metal Bulletin Inc
Subsidiary of Metal Bulletin PLC (UK)
1250 Broadway, 26th fl, New York, NY 10001
Tel: 212-213-6202 *Toll Free Tel:* 800-638-2525 *Fax:* 212-213-6273
Web Site: www.metbul.com
Key Personnel
Pres: Greg Newton
Founded: 1915
International directories & journals for international steel & metals industry.
ISBN Prefix(es): 0-947671
Number of titles published annually: 8 Print
Total Titles: 26 Print; 2 CD-ROM
Imprints: Metal Bulletin Books
Foreign Office(s): 16 Lower Marsh, London SE1 7RJ, United Kingdom *Tel:* (020) 7827 9977 *Fax:* (020) 7982 6892 *E-mail:* editorial@metalbulletin.com
Park House, Park Terr, Worcester Park, Surrey KT4 7HY, United Kingdom *Tel:* (020) 7827 9977 *Fax:* (020) 8337 8943

§Metal Powder Industries Federation
105 College Rd E, Princeton, NJ 08540-6692
Tel: 609-452-7700 *Fax:* 609-987-8523
E-mail: info@mpif.org
Web Site: www.mpif.org
Key Personnel
Pubns Mgr & Intl Rts: Cindy Jablonowski *E-mail:* jablonow@mpif.org
Founded: 1946
ISBN Prefix(es): 0-918404; 1-878954
Number of titles published annually: 125 Print
Total Titles: 250 Print
Distributor for ASM International (selected titles); Butterworth-Heinemann; DGM Informationsgesellschaft (selected titles); Adam Hilger (selected titles); Institute of Materials (selected titles); MPR Publishing (selected titles); Plenum Publishing Corp (selected titles); Prentice Hall (selected titles); TMS (selected titles); Verlag Schmid (selected titles)
Foreign Rep(s): European Powder Metallurgy Association (Europe); Multi-Tech Research Corp (Japan)
Advertising Agency: Century Graphics

Metamorphous Press
Division of Metamorphous Press Inc
265 N Hancock St, Portland, OR 97227
Mailing Address: PO Box 10616, Portland, OR 97296-0616 SAN: 264-2077
Tel: 503-228-4972 *Toll Free Tel:* 800-937-7771 (orders only) *Fax:* 503-223-9117
E-mail: metabooks@metamodels.com
Web Site: www.metamodels.com
Key Personnel
Publr: David Balding
Dir, Rts & Perms: Candice Martin
Promos & Mktg: David Cottrell
Ed & Prodn Mgr: Courtenay Kelley
Acqs Ed: Nancy Wyatt-Kelsey
Founded: 1982
Neurolinguistic programming, linguistics, workbooks, enneagram & hypnosis.
ISBN Prefix(es): 0-943920; 1-55552
Number of titles published annually: 4 Print
Total Titles: 50 Print
Imprints: Grinder & Associates
Divisions: Metamorphous Advanced Product Services
Distributor for Exclusive: Anue Productions; Facticity; M Grinder & Associates
Membership(s): ABA

Metro Creative Graphics Inc
519 Eighth Ave, New York, NY 10018
Tel: 212-947-5100 *Toll Free Tel:* 800-223-1600
Web Site: www.metrocreativegraphics.com
Key Personnel
Contact: Robert Zimmerman *Tel:* 212-947-5100
   ext 285 *E-mail:* rszmetro@aol.com

§The Metropolitan Museum of Art
1000 Fifth Ave, New York, NY 10028
SAN: 202-6279
Tel: 212-879-5500; 212-535-7710 *Fax:* 212-396-
5062
E-mail: info@metmuseum.org
Web Site: www.metmuseum.org *Telex:* 66-6676
   Cable: METMUSART
Key Personnel
Pres: David McKinney
CEO & Dir: Philippe de Montebello
Ed-in-Chief: John P O'Neill
Man Ed: Ann Lucke
Sr Ed & Mktg Mgr: Susan E Chun
Sr Ed: Margaret Aspinwall; Jane Bobko; Carol
   Fuerstein; Kathleen Howard; Ruth Kozodoy;
   Emily Walter
Ed: Pamela Barr; Jennifer C Bernstein; Sue Pot-
   ter; Ellen Shultz; Dale Tucker
Ed-in-Chief, Bulletin: Joan K Holt
Assoc Gen Mgr, Pubns: Gwen Roginsky
Mgr, Spec Pubns: Robie Rogge
Chief Prodn Mgr: Peter Antony
Mktg Consultant: Harold Holzer
Chief Libn, Art Ref Lib: Kenneth Soehner
Chief Libn, Photo & Slide Lib: Priscilla Farah
Founded: 1870
Art books, exhibition catalogs, quarterly bulletin,
   annual journal.
ISBN Prefix(es): 0-87099
Number of titles published annually: 25 Print
Total Titles: 250 Print; 5 CD-ROM
Distributed by Yale University Press
Foreign Rep(s): Yale University Press
Warehouse: Middle Village, Queens, NY 11381-
0001

Meyerbooks Publisher
235 W Main St, Glenwood, IL 60425
SAN: 208-998X
Mailing Address: PO Box 427, Glenwood, IL
   60425-0427
Tel: 708-757-4950
Key Personnel
Publr & Intl Rts: David Meyer
Founded: 1976
Herbs & herbal recipes; performing arts; stage
   magic, history & technique.
ISBN Prefix(es): 0-916638
Number of titles published annually: 4 Print
Total Titles: 45 Print
Imprints: David Meyer Magic Books; Waltham
   Street Press

MFA Publications
Division of Museum of Fine Arts Boston
465 Huntington Ave, Boston, MA 02115
Tel: 617-369-3438 *Fax:* 617-369-3459
Web Site: www.mfa-publications.org
Key Personnel
Publr: Mark Polizzotti *E-mail:* mp@mfa.org
Ed: Sarah McGanghey; Emiko Usui
Prod Mgr: Terry McAweeney
Sales & Mktg: Kimberly Mullins-Mitchell
Founded: 1877
Exhibition & collection catalogues; general inter-
   est & trade arts publications, children's books.
ISBN Prefix(es): 0-87846
Number of titles published annually: 15 Print
Total Titles: 93 Print
Imprints: ArtWorks
Distributed by D A P
Warehouse: c/o PSSC, 46 Development Rd, Fitch-
   burg, MA 01420 *Tel:* 978-345-2121 *Fax:* 978-
348-1233

MGI Management Institute Inc
701 Westchester Ave, Suite 308W, White Plains,
   NY 10604
Tel: 914-428-6500 *Toll Free Tel:* 800-932-0191
   Fax: 914-428-0773
E-mail: mgiusa@aol.com
Web Site: www.mgi.org
Key Personnel
Pres: Henry Oppenheimer
Founded: 1968
Job improvement books & guides.
Number of titles published annually: 60 Print
Total Titles: 60 Print; 5 Online; 5 E-Book

Michael di Capua Books
Imprint of Hyperion Books for Children
114 Fifth Ave, New York, NY 10011
Tel: 212-633-4400 *Fax:* 212-807-5880
Web Site: www.hyperionbooks.com
Key Personnel
Publr: Michael di Capua
Asst to Publr: Adam Rau *Tel:* 212-633-4418
Founded: 1987
ISBN Prefix(es): 0-7868
Number of titles published annually: 3 Print
Total Titles: 8 Print
Foreign Rights: ACER Agencia Literaria (Spain);
   Agence Hoffman (Germany); Luigi Bernabo
   Assocs (Italy); Big Apple Tuttle-Mori Agency
   (China); BMSR Agencia Literaria (Brazil); The
   English Agency (Japan); Harris/Elon Agency
   (Israel); Kooy & van Gelderen (Netherlands);
   Jacqueline Miller (France)

Michelin Travel Publications
Division of Michelin North America Inc
PO Box 19001, Greenville, SC 29602-9001
Tel: 864-458-5127 *Toll Free Tel:* 800-423-
   0485; 800-223-0987 *Fax:* 864-458-6674
   Toll Free Fax: 866-297-0914
E-mail: michelin.travel-publications-us@us.
   michelin.com
Web Site: www.viamichelin.com
Key Personnel
VP: Robin Bird
Dir, Sales: Jeff Jacobs
Mktg Dir: Saskia Damen
Commercial Sales & Admin Asst: Hellan
   Mitchell *E-mail:* hellan.mitchell@us.michelin.
   com
Founded: 1900
Specialize in travel publications; guides.
ISBN Prefix(es): 2-06; 4-408; 0-600
Number of titles published annually: 800 Print;
   800 Online
Total Titles: 800 Print; 800 Online
Branch Office(s)
710 Kimberly Dr, Carol Stream, IL 60188, Cen-
   tral Natl Accts Mgr: Carol Severson *Tel:* 630-
   690-5048
300 Rector Place, Suite 3C, New York, NY
   10280, Key Acct Mgr: Sue Burke
2208 18 Ave S, Nashville, TN 37212, Natl Acct
   Mgr: Chelle Cox
Shipping Address: One Pkwy S, Greenville, SC
   29615
Warehouse: 3088 S Hwy 14, Greer, SC 29650

Michigan Municipal League
Affiliate of National League of Cities
1675 Green Rd, Ann Arbor, MI 48105
Mailing Address: Box 1487, Ann Arbor, MI
   48106-1487
Tel: 734-662-3246 *Toll Free Tel:* 800-653-2483
   Fax: 734-663-4496
Web Site: www.mml.org
Key Personnel
Ed: Judi Lintott *Tel:* 734-669-6325
   E-mail: jlintott@mml.org
Founded: 1899
Municipal topics & newsletters, services & publi-
   cations for local governments in Michigan.

ISBN Prefix(es): 1-929923
Total Titles: 9 Print
Distributor for Crisp Books

§Michigan State University Press (MSU Press)
Division of Michigan State University
1405 S Harrison Rd, Suite 25, East Lansing, MI
   48823
SAN: 202-6295
Tel: 517-355-9543 *Fax:* 517-432-2611
   Toll Free Fax: 800-678-2120
E-mail: msupress@msu.edu
Web Site: www.msupress.msu.edu
Key Personnel
Dir: Fredric C Bohm
Ed-in-Chief: Julie L Loehr
Journals Mgr: Margot Kielhorn
Busn & Fin: Laura Carantza
Founded: 1947
Scholarly works & general nonfiction trade
   books.
ISBN Prefix(es): 1-882997; 0-916418; 0-944311;
   0-88406; 0-937191; 1-55238
Number of titles published annually: 40 Print; 2
   CD-ROM; 15 Online; 10 E-Book
Total Titles: 380 Print; 4 CD-ROM; 95 Online;
   59 E-Book
Imprints: Colleagues Books; Red Cedar Classics
Distributed by Raincoast; UBC Press, Canada
Distributor for Colleagues Books; Kresge Art
   Museum; Lotus Press; Mackinad Historic
   Parks; MSU Museum; National Museum of
   Science & Industry UK; University of Calgary
   Press
Foreign Rep(s): Foot Print Books (Australia);
   Gazelle Book Services Ltd (England); Rain-
   coast Books (Canada)

MicroMash
Subsidiary of Thomson
6402 S Troy Circle, Englewood, CO 80111-6424
Tel: 303-799-0099 *Toll Free Tel:* 800-823-6039
   Fax: 303-799-1425
E-mail: info@micromash.com
Web Site: www.micromash.net
Key Personnel
Mktg Dir: Mary Howard
VP, Sales: Sam Goble
Edit Dir: Kathryn Quam
Founded: 1984
The leading provider of online CPE to big four &
   major firms; over 150 computer-based continu-
   ing professional education courses.
ISBN Prefix(es): 0-926709

§Microsoft Press
Division of Microsoft Corp
One Microsoft Way, Redmond, WA 98052-6399
SAN: 264-9969
Tel: 425-882-8080 *Toll Free Tel:* 800-677-7377
   Fax: 425-936-7329
Web Site: www.microsoft.com/presspass/exec/
   default.asp#qt
Key Personnel
Publr: Don Falley
Dir, Worldwide Sales: Ed Belleba
Assoc Publr: Jim LeValley
Assoc Publr & Developer: Al Valvano
Edit Dir: Kim Field
Founded: 1983
Computing, technical, professional & chess.
ISBN Prefix(es): 1-55615; 1-57231; 0-7356
Number of titles published annually: 160 Print
Total Titles: 400 Print; 20 CD-ROM; 100 Online;
   1 E-Book
Subsidiaries: Microsoft Press France; Microsoft
   Press Germany
Foreign Rep(s): ITP Nelson (div of Thomson
   Canada Ltd)
Warehouse: 121 N Enterprise Blvd, Lebanon, IN
   46052

Mid-List Press
4324 12 Ave S, Minneapolis, MN 55407-3218
Tel: 612-822-3733 *Fax:* 612-823-8387
E-mail: guide@midlist.org
Web Site: www.midlist.org
Key Personnel
Publr: Lane Stiles
Exec Dir: Marianne Nora
Founded: 1989
Fiction, creative nonfiction, poetry & first novels.
ISBN Prefix(es): 0-922811
Number of titles published annually: 6 Print
Total Titles: 42 Print

Midmarch Arts Press
300 Riverside Dr, New York, NY 10025-5239
SAN: 200-8882
Tel: 212-666-6990
Key Personnel
Mgr: Lynda Hulkower
Ed: Sylvia Moore; Judy Seigel
Founded: 1975
Books & periodicals.
ISBN Prefix(es): 1-877675
Number of titles published annually: 4 Print
Total Titles: 65 Print
Subsidiaries: Women Artists News Book Review
Distributor for N Paradoxa
Returns: 19 Deep Six Dr, East Hampton, NY 11937
Warehouse: 19 Deep Six Dr, East Hampton, NY 11937

Midnight Marquee Press Inc
9721 Britinay Lane, Baltimore, MD 21234
Tel: 410-665-1198 *Fax:* 410-665-9207
E-mail: mmarquee@aol.com
Web Site: www.midmar.com
Key Personnel
Pres: Gary Svehla
VP, Intl Rts Contact & Lib Sales Dir: Susan Svehla
Founded: 1995
Books on film.
ISBN Prefix(es): 1-887664
Number of titles published annually: 6 Print
Total Titles: 32 Print
Foreign Rep(s): Worldwide Media Service

§MidWest Plan Service
Affiliate of Iowa State University
122 Davidson Hall, Iowa State University, Ames, IA 50011-3080
Tel: 515-294-4337 *Toll Free Tel:* 800-562-3618
Fax: 515-294-9589
E-mail: mwps@iastate.edu
Web Site: www.mwpshq.org
Key Personnel
Mgr & Intl Rts: Jack Moore
Founded: 1929
Agricultural handbooks on structures & livestock environment issues, handbooks on agricultural economics & farm management.
ISBN Prefix(es): 0-89373
Number of titles published annually: 6 Print; 2 CD-ROM; 2 Online; 1 E-Book
Total Titles: 60 Print; 4 CD-ROM; 10 Online; 1 E-Book
Distributed by Natural Resource Agriculture & Engineering Service
Distributor for Natural Resource Agriculture & Engineering Service

Midwest Traditions Inc
3147 S Pennsylvania Ave, Milwaukee, WI 53207
Tel: 414-294-4319 *Toll Free Tel:* 800-736-9189
Fax: 414-962-3579
Key Personnel
Exec Dir & Intl Rts: Philip Martin
Founded: 1993
Publish books on regional heritage, with a focus books for children, fiction & nonfiction.

ISBN Prefix(es): 1-883953
Number of titles published annually: 3 Print
Total Titles: 15 Print
Imprints: Face to Face Books
Foreign Rights: Linda Michaels Ltd
Membership(s): Publishers Marketing Association

Mike Murach & Associates Inc
3484 W Gettysburg Ave, Suite 101, Fresno, CA 93722-7801
SAN: 264-2255
Tel: 559-440-9071 *Toll Free Tel:* 800-221-5528
Fax: 559-440-0963
E-mail: murachbooks@murach.com
Web Site: www.murach.com
Key Personnel
Mktg: Georgia Murach *E-mail:* georgia@murach.com
Founded: 1972
Computer books.
ISBN Prefix(es): 0-911625; 1-890774
Number of titles published annually: 5 Print
Total Titles: 50 Print
Foreign Rep(s): BPB Publications Ltd (India); Camelot; Gazelle Book Services Ltd (UK, Continental Europe); Woodslane Pty Ltd (Australia & New Zealand)

Milady Publishing
Division of Thomson Learning
Subsidiary of Delmar Learning
Executive Woods, 5 Maxwell Dr, Clifton Park, NY 12065-2919
Tel: 518-348-2300 (ext 2409) *Toll Free Tel:* 800-998-7498 *Fax:* 518-348-7000
Web Site: www.delmar.com; www.milady.com
Key Personnel
Pres: Dawn Gerrain
Channel Mgr: Sandra Bruce *Tel:* 518-348-2300 ext 2378
Founded: 1928
Textbooks, workbooks, exam reviews, AV materials & instructional software, newsletters, cosmetology & beauty education.
ISBN Prefix(es): 1-56253; 0-87350
Number of titles published annually: 220 Print
Total Titles: 288 Print
Branch Office(s)
NP Group, 1220 Ellesmere Rd, Unit 19, Scarborough, ON M1P 2X5, Canada
Foreign Office(s): Nelson Australia, 102 Dodds St, South Melbourne, Victoria 3205, Australia
Chapman & Hall, 2-6 Boundary Row, London SE1 8HN, United Kingdom
Distribution Center: 7453 Empire Dr, Florence, KY 41042

Military Info Publishing
PO Box 27640, Golden Valley, MN 55427
Tel: 763-533-8627 *Fax:* 763-533-8627
E-mail: publisher@military-info.com
Web Site: www.military-info.com
Key Personnel
Publr: Bruce A Hanesalo
Founded: 1987
Reprint historical military technology, including 34 books, 5,000 photocopies & 400 other items.
ISBN Prefix(es): 1-886848
Number of titles published annually: 4 Print
Total Titles: 34 Print

Military Living Publications
Division of Military Marketing Services Inc
PO Box 2347, Falls Church, VA 22042-0347
Tel: 703-237-0203 *Fax:* 703-237-2233
E-mail: militaryliving@aol.com
Web Site: www.militaryliving.com
Key Personnel
Pres: William R Crawford, Sr
Founded: 1968

Publisher of military travel atlases, maps & directories; for military only.
ISBN Prefix(es): 0-914862
Total Titles: 7 Print
Foreign Rep(s): US Forces Exchanges
Warehouse: 900 S Washington St, Unit G-8, Falls Church, VA 22046

Milkweed Editions
1011 Washington Ave S, Suite 300, Minneapolis, MN 55415
Tel: 612-332-3192 *Toll Free Tel:* 800-520-6455
Fax: 612-215-2550
E-mail: editor@milkweed.org
Web Site: www.milkweed.org; www.worldashome.org
Key Personnel
Ed: Emerson Blake *Tel:* 612-332-3192 ext 551
Man Ed: Laurie Buss *Tel:* 612-332-3192 ext 555
Man Dir: Hilary Reeves *Tel:* 612-332-3192 ext 553
Publicist: Elizabeth Cooper
Fin Dir: Anita Moulton *Tel:* 612-310-7538
Art & Design Coord: Christian Fuenfhausen *Tel:* 612-332-3192 ext 562
Devt Dir: Mary Rondeau Westra
Devt Assoc: Katie Clymer *Tel:* 612-332-3192 ext 561
Cust Serv Asst: Kelly Wavrin *Tel:* 612-332-3192 ext 560
Founded: 1984
Literary nonfiction, children's novels, essays & natural world.
ISBN Prefix(es): 0-915943; 1-57131
Number of titles published annually: 15 Print
Total Titles: 185 Print
Foreign Rights: Nancy Madia
Distribution Center: Publishers Group West, 1700 Fourth St, Berkeley, CA 94710 *Toll Free Tel:* 800-788-3123 *Fax:* 510-528-3444
Membership(s): ABA; Children's Book Council; Council of Literary Magazines & Presses; Publishers Marketing Association; Southeast Booksellers Association; Upper Midwest Booksellers Association

The Millbrook Press Inc
2 Old New Milford Rd, Brookfield, CT 06804
Tel: 203-740-2220 *Toll Free Tel:* 800-462-4703
Fax: 203-740-2526
Key Personnel
Pres: David Allen
Exec VP & Publr: Jean E Reynolds
Man Ed: Colleen Seibert
Founded: 1989
ISBN Prefix(es): 0-8050; 1-56294; 1-878841; 0-7613; 1-57513
Number of titles published annually: 125 Print
Total Titles: 1,400 Print
Imprints: Copper Beech
Divisions: Twenty-First Century Books
Foreign Rep(s): Fitzhenry & Whiteside (Canada)
Warehouse: Simon & Schuster, 100 Front St, Riverside, NJ 08075
Membership(s): BISG; Children's Book Council

Richard K Miller Associates Inc
4132 Atlanta Hwy, Suite 110-366, Loganville, GA 30052
Tel: 770-416-0006 *Fax:* 770-416-0052
Key Personnel
Pres: Richard K Miller
Founded: 1972
Market forecasting & assessments. Subjects include market research handbooks, leisure, hospitality, entertainment & travel.
ISBN Prefix(es): 1-881503
Number of titles published annually: 8 Print; 8 CD-ROM
Total Titles: 8 Print; 8 CD-ROM

Robert Miller Gallery
524 W 26 St, New York, NY 10001
Tel: 212-366-4774 *Fax:* 212-366-4454
E-mail: rmg@robertmillergallery.com
Web Site: www.robertmillergallery.com
Key Personnel
Dir: Betsy Miller
Archivist: Amy Young
Founded: 1977
Art books on artwork by represented artists.
ISBN Prefix(es): 0-944680
Number of titles published annually: 3 Print
Distributed by D A P

§Milliken Publishing Co
11643 Lilburn Park Dr, St Louis, MO 63146
Tel: 314-991-4220 *Toll Free Tel:* 800-325-4136
Fax: 314-991-4807 *Toll Free Fax:* 800-538-
1319
E-mail: mpwebmaster@millikenpub.com
Web Site: www.millikenpub.com
Key Personnel
Pres: Thomas M Moore
Dir, Mktg & Intl Rts: Hawkie Moore *Tel:* 314-
991-4220 ext 23
Founded: 1960
Educational publishing & computer software divi-
sions. Educational publishing division includes
visual resources, instructional guides & repro-
ducibles; elementary supplementals. Computer
software division includes all major curriculum
areas from pre-school to the adult level, in-
volving comprehensive packages & networking
versions for Windows & Macintosh.
ISBN Prefix(es): 0-88335; 1-55863
Number of titles published annually: 50 Print
Total Titles: 400 Print; 20 CD-ROM

**§The Minerals, Metals & Materials Society
(TMS)**
Affiliate of AIME
184 Thorn Hill Rd, Warrendale, PA 15086
Tel: 724-776-9000 *Toll Free Tel:* 800-759-4867
Fax: 724-776-3770
E-mail: publications@tms.org (orders)
Web Site: www.tms.org (orders); www.tms.
org/pubs/publications.html
Key Personnel
Dir, Corp Communs: Robert Makowski *Tel:* 724-
776-9000 ext 217 *E-mail:* makowski@tms.org
Founded: 1871
The Minerals, Metals & Materials Society (TMS)
is a leading professional society dedicated to
the development & dissemination of scientific & engineering knowledge for materials-
centered technology. The society is the only
professional organization that encompasses the
entire spectrum of materials & engineering,
from minerals processing through the advanced
applications of materials.
ISBN Prefix(es): 0-87339
Number of titles published annually: 30 Print
Foreign Rep(s): D A Books & Journals (Australia, New Zealand, Papua New Guinea); Neutrino Inc (Japan); Panima Educational Book
Agency (India)

Minnesota Historical Society Press
Division of Minnesota Historical Society
345 Kellogg Blvd W, St Paul, MN 55102-1906
SAN: 202-6384
Tel: 651-296-2264 *Toll Free Tel:* 800-621-2736
Fax: 651-297-1345 *Toll Free Fax:* 800-621-
8476
Web Site: www.mnhs.org/mhspress
Key Personnel
Man Ed: Ann Regan *Tel:* 651-297-4457
E-mail: ann.regan@mnhs.org
Dir & Intl Rts: Gregory M Britton *Tel:* 651-297-
4463 *E-mail:* greg.britton@mnhs.org
Design & Prod Mgr: Will Powers *Tel:* 651-296-
1448

Publicity & Exhibits Mgr: Alison Vandenberg
Tel: 651-296-2939 *E-mail:* alison.vandenberg@
mnhs.org
Sales & Mktg Mgr: Kevin Morrissey *Tel:* 651-
296-7539 *E-mail:* kevin.morrissey@mnhs.org
Perms: Sally Rubenstein *Tel:* 651-297-4459
E-mail: sally.rubenstein@mnhs.org
Founded: 1849
Scholarly & trade books on Upper Midwest his-
tory & prehistory.
ISBN Prefix(es): 0-87351
Number of titles published annually: 24 Print
Total Titles: 251 Print; 6 Audio
Imprints: Borealis Books
Foreign Rep(s): Gazelle Books Services Ltd (UK,
Europe)
Warehouse: Chicago Distribution Center, 11030
S Langley Ave, Chicago, IL 60628 *Toll Free
Tel:* 800-621-2736 (orders) *Toll Free Fax:* 800-
621-8476 (orders) *Web Site:* www.mnhs.
org/mhspress
Membership(s): American Association of Univer-
sity Presses

Mint Publishers Group
62 June Rd, North Salem, NY 10560
Mailing Address: PO Box 339, North Salem, NY
10560-0339
Tel: 914-276-6576 *Fax:* 914-276-6579
E-mail: info@mintpub.com
Web Site: www.mintpub.com
Key Personnel
CEO & Pres: Morton Mint *E-mail:* morty@
mintpub.com
VP, Mktg & Publicity US: Maryann Palumbo
VP, Mktg & Publicity Canada: Joann Moyle
Busn Mgr: Cindy Russell *E-mail:* cindy@
mintpub.com
Book Club Sales & Consultant: Thomas Woll
Founded: 1989
Publisher & distributor to the trade & mass mar-
ket channels of North America. Specialize in
building brands & creating value.
ISBN Prefix(es): 1-86351; 1-57859; 1-86343; 0-
81039; 0-78760; 0-97182; 0-97459; 0-91259;
0-96633; 0-96852; 0-96936; 0-97297; 0-96835;
1-89395; 0-97307; 1-90363; 0-97453; 1-87708;
0-97316; 0-97354; 1-84236; 1-90294; 1-84229;
1-84510; 1-90474
Number of titles published annually: 550 Print
Total Titles: 524 Print
Distributor for The Catherine Collective Corp
(Canada only); Continental Atlantic (US only);
Cooking for the Rushed (US & Canada); Cre-
ative House (US & Canada); Etruscan Press
(US & Canada); Feather Books (Canada only);
Gallery Six (US & Canada); Gift of Time
(US & Canada); Grownup's Guides (US &
Canada); Hayden Publishing (US & Canada);
Miles Kelly Publishing (Canada only); Open
Door Publishing (US & Canada); Patron's Pick
(US only); Ripley Entertainment Inc (US &
Canada); Top That! Publishing (Canada only);
Visible Ink Press (US & Canada)
Advertising Agency: Marketing Concepts, 340
Hudson St, Suite 700, New York, NY 10013,
Contact: Maryann Palumbo *Tel:* 212-645-8642
Fax: 212-645-5880 *E-mail:* mpmarkcon@aol.
com; J E Moyle Consultants, 46 Loch Erne
Lane, Box 394, Nobleton, ON L0G 1N0,
Canada, Contact: Joanne Moyle *Tel:* 905-859-
0467 *Fax:* 905-859-6888 *E-mail:* jemoyle@
sympatico.ca
Shipping Address: Client Distribution Services,
193 Edward S Dr, Jackson, TN 38301 (US
shipments & orders) *Toll Free Tel:* 800-343-
4499 *Toll Free Fax:* 800-351-5073; Canbook
Distribution Services, c/o Pearson Canada, 195
Harry Walker Pkwy N, PO Box 335, Newmarket, ON L3Y 4X7, Canada (Canada shipments & orders), Contact: Kim Bible *Toll Free
Tel:* 800-399-6858 ext 228 *Toll Free Fax:* 800-
363-2665 *E-mail:* kim.bible@canbook.com

Missouri Historical Society Press
Division of Missouri Historical Society
PO Box 11940, St Louis, MO 63112-0040
Tel: 314-454-3150 *Fax:* 314-454-3162
E-mail: dtz@mohistory.org
Web Site: www.mohistory.org
Key Personnel
Sr Ed: Josh Stevens *E-mail:* jstevens@mohistory.
org
Founded: 1991
ISBN Prefix(es): 1-883982
Number of titles published annually: 4 Print
Total Titles: 34 Print
Distributed by University of Missouri Press; Uni-
versity of New Mexico Press; University of
Southern Illinois; Wayne State University Press
Shipping Address: 225 S Skinker, St Louis, MO
63105
Membership(s): Association of American Univer-
sity Presses

MIT List Visual Arts Center
MIT E 15-109, 20 Ames St, Cambridge, MA
02139
Tel: 617-253-4680; 617-253-4400 (admission to
exhibits) *Fax:* 617-258-7265
E-mail: hiroco@mit.edu
Web Site: web.mit.edu/lvac *Telex:* 17-194 MIT-
CAM
Key Personnel
Dir: Jane Farver *Tel:* 617-253-4425
E-mail: jfarver@mit.edu
Admin Asst: Barbra Pine *Tel:* 617-253-9479
E-mail: barbra@media.mit.edu
Admin Officer: David Freilach *Tel:* 617-253-5076
E-mail: freilach@mit.edu
Founded: 1966
Contemporary art.
ISBN Prefix(es): 0-938437
Number of titles published annually: 6 Print
Distributed by DAP Distributed Art Publishers

§The MIT Press
5 Cambridge Ctr, Cambridge, MA 02142
SAN: 202-6414
Tel: 617-253-5646 *Toll Free Tel:* 800-405-1619
(orders only) *Fax:* 617-258-6779
Web Site: mitpress.mit.edu
Key Personnel
Dir: Ellen W Faran *E-mail:* ewfaran@mit.edu
Assoc Dir, Opers: Michael Leonard *Tel:* 617-253-
5250 *E-mail:* leonardm@mit.edu
Mktg Dir: Vicki Jennings
Acq Ed: Roger L Conover; John Covell; Barbara
Murphy; Elizabeth Murry; Robert Prior; Dou-
glas Sery; Tom Stone
Man Ed: Michael Sims
Ed: Matthew Abbate; Katherine Almeida; Dana
Andrus; Paul Bethge; Sandra Minkkinen
Ed & ISBN Contact: Deborah Cantor-Adams
Journals Mgr: Rebecca McLeod *Tel:* 617-258-
0596 *E-mail:* mcleod@mit.edu
Promo Mgr: Gita Manaktala
Asst Promos Mgr: Astrid Baehrecke
Texts Mgr: Marjorie Hardwick
Mgr, Intl Sales: Tom Clerkin
Subs Rts Mgr & Intl Rts: Cristina Sanmartin
Design Mgr: Yasuyo Iguchi
Adv Mgr: Vincent Scorziello
Prodn Mgr: Terry Lamoureux
Journals Circ Mgr: Lori White
Journals Prodn Mgr: Rachel Besen
Bookstore Mgr: John Jenkins; Maureen Zioc-
houski
Exhibits Mgr: John Costello
Electronic Mktg Mgr: Eric Maki
Founded: 1961
Scholarly & professional books, advanced text-
books, nonfiction trade books & reference
books; architecture & design, cognitive sci-
ences & linguistics, computer science & arti-
ficial intelligence, economics & management
sciences, environmental studies; philosophy,

neuroscience; technology studies; paperbacks, journals.
ISBN Prefix(es): 0-262
Number of titles published annually: 220 Print
Total Titles: 3,000 Print; 5 CD-ROM; 2 Online; 1 E-Book
Imprints: Bradford Books
Foreign Office(s): The MIT Press Ltd, Fitzroy House, 11 Chenies St, London WC1E 7ET, United Kingdom, Contact: Ann Sexsmith
Tel: (020) 7306 0603 *Fax:* (020) 7306 0604
Distributor for AAAI Press; Canadian Centre for Architecture; Zone Books
Foreign Rep(s): Academic Book Promotions (France, Scandinavia); American University Press Group (Hong Kong, Japan, Korea, Taiwan); Apac Publishers Services Pte Ltd; Cassidy & Associates (People's Republic of China); Rodney Franklin Agency (Israel); Christopher Humphrys; Humphrys Roberts Assoc (Latin America); Uwe Ludemann (Austria, Germany, Italy, Switzerland); Mediamatics (India); MIT Press Ltd (UK, Ireland, Greece); David Stimpson (Australia, Canada, New Zealand); Cory Voigt Associates (South Africa)
Foreign Rights: Agencia Literaria Balcells Mecco & Souza Riff (Brazil); Kiyoshi Asano (Japan); Carmen Bacells Agencia Literaria (South America, Spain); Big Apple Tuttle Mori (Mainland China, Taiwan); DRT International (Korea); The English Agency (Japan); Japan UNI Agency (Japan); La Nouvelle Agence (France); Orion Literary Agency (Japan); Tuttle-Mori Agency (Japan); Susanna Zevi Agenzia Letteraria (Italy)
Warehouse: Triliteral LLC, 100 Maple Ridge Dr, Cumberland, RI 02864
Membership(s): AAP; Association of American University Presses

Mitchell Lane Publishers Inc
1104 Kelly Dr, Newark, DE 19711
Mailing Address: PO Box 196, Hockessin, DE 19707
Tel: 302-234-9426 *Toll Free Tel:* 800-814-5484
Fax: 302-234-4742 *Toll Free Fax:* 866-834-4164
E-mail: mitchelllane@mitchelllane.com
Web Site: www.mitchelllane.com
Key Personnel
Pres & Publr: Barbara J Mitchell
    E-mail: barbaramitchell@mitchelllane.com
VP, Sales & Mktg: Robert P Mitchell
    E-mail: robertmitchell@mitchelllane.com
Founded: 1993
Nonfiction for children & young adults.
ISBN Prefix(es): 1-883845; 1-58415
Number of titles published annually: 60 Print
Total Titles: 250 Print
Warehouse: 147 Rickey Blvd, Bear, DE 19701

MMB Music Inc
Contemporary Arts Bldg, 3526 Washington Ave, St Louis, MO 63103-1019
SAN: 210-4601
Tel: 314-531-9635 *Toll Free Tel:* 800-543-3771
Fax: 314-531-8384
E-mail: info@mmbmusic.com
Web Site: www.mmbmusic.com
Key Personnel
Chmn: Norman A Goldberg *E-mail:* normg@mmbmusic.com
Pres: Marcia Lee Goldberg *E-mail:* mlg@mmbmusic.com
Sales Mat Ed: Gary Lee
Founded: 1964
Sheet music & books.
ISBN Prefix(es): 0-918812
Number of titles published annually: 4 Print
Total Titles: 100 Print

Mobile Post Office Society
Affiliate of American Philatelic Society
PO Box 427, Marstons Mills, MA 02648-0427
Tel: 508-428-9132 *Fax:* 508-428-2156
E-mail: dnc@math.uga.edu
Web Site: www.eskimo.com/~rkunz/mposhome. html
Key Personnel
Pres: Thomas J Post
Lib Sales Dir: Fred MacDonald
Founded: 1949
Railroads, philately.
ISBN Prefix(es): 1-175
Number of titles published annually: 8 Print
Total Titles: 4 Print

Mobility International USA
45 W Broadway, Eugene, OR 97401
Mailing Address: PO Box 10767, Eugene, OR 97440-2767
Tel: 541-343-1284 *Fax:* 541-343-6812
E-mail: info@miusa.org
Web Site: www.miusa.org
Key Personnel
CEO: Susan Sygall
Founded: 1981
The mission of Mobility International USA (MIUSA) is to empower people with disabilities through international exchange & international development to achieve their human rights.
MIUSA manages the National Clearinghouse on Disability & Exchange (NCDE), a project sponsored by the bureau of Educational & Cultural Affairs of the US Department of State.
ISBN Prefix(es): 1-880034
Number of titles published annually: 3 Print
Total Titles: 6 Print

Modern Curriculum Press
Imprint of Pearson Learning Group
299 Jefferson Rd, Parsippany, NJ 07054-0480
Tel: 973-739-8000 *Fax:* 973-739-8635
Web Site: www.pearsonlearning.com
Key Personnel
Pres: Dan Caton
Busn Mgr: Al Meese
VP & Natl Sales Dir: Jeff Vohden
VP, Publg: Celia Argiriou
Phonics & supplemental educational materials.
ISBN Prefix(es): 0-8136; 0-7652; 0-87895
Total Titles: 367 Print
Imprints: Silver Burdett Press

§Modern Language Association of America (MLA)
26 Broadway, 3rd fl, New York, NY 10004-1789
Tel: 646-576-5000 *Fax:* 646-458-0030
E-mail: info@mla.org
Web Site: www.mla.org
Key Personnel
Dir, Conventions: Maribeth T Kraus
Exec Dir: Rosemary Feal
Dir, Book Publg & Intl Rts Contact: David Nicholls
Mktg Dir: Kathleen Hansen *Tel:* 646-576-5018
    E-mail: khansen@mla.org
Opers Dir: Regina Mawn Vorbeck
Dir, Acqs & Devt: Joseph Gibaldi
Man Ed: Judy Goulding
Prodn Mgr: Judith Altreuter
Founded: 1883
Research & teaching tools in languages & literature; professional publications for college teachers.
ISBN Prefix(es): 0-87352
Number of titles published annually: 10 Print
Total Titles: 300 Print; 1 CD-ROM; 1 Online
Online services available through GaleNet, OCLC, Ovid.
Shipping Address: 81 New St, 3rd fl, New York, NY 10004

Modern Publishing
Division of Unisystems Inc
155 E 55 St, New York, NY 10022
Tel: 212-826-0850 *Fax:* 212-759-9069
Web Site: www.modernpublishing.com
Key Personnel
Pres: Lawrence Steinberg
VP, Dom & Foreign Rts: Edward D Lenk
VP, Fin: Warren Cohen
VP, Edit: Kathy O'Hehir
Founded: 1969
Juvenile, reference books; general nonfiction, humor, puzzle books.
ISBN Prefix(es): 0-7666
Number of titles published annually: 180 Print
Total Titles: 357 Print
Imprints: All-in-One Books; Bubble Books; Clever Kids; Detect-A-Word; Doggone Days; Early Learners; Flip N Fun; The G A T Abouts; The Gillemajigs; Honey Bear Books; Honey Bear Video; Itsy-Bitsy Story Books; Legendary Books; Looking Glass Preschool Board Books; Lullabies; Modern Pictures; Nice Books; Pajama Party Gang; The Pen Pals; Ready Reader Storybooks; Ready Set Go; Ready Teddy; Rock A Bye Preschool Board Book; Sunshine; Triviagrams; Tot Shots; Whodunits; Who's Who Preschool Board Book; World of Knowledges; World of Wildlife
Warehouse: 2410 Brodhead Rd, Lehigh Valley Industrial Park, Bethlehem, PA 18020

Modern Radio Laboratories
PO Box 14902, Minneapolis, MN 55414-0902
Web Site: www.modernradiolabs.com
Key Personnel
Contact: Paul L Nelson *E-mail:* paul@modernradiolabs.com; Elmer G Osterhoudt
Manufacturing, printing & publishing for small set radio building.
ISBN Prefix(es): 1-891501
Number of titles published annually: 31 Print
Total Titles: 31 Print

Moment Point Press Inc
65 Rivard Rd, Needham, MA 02492
SAN: 299-724X
Mailing Address: PO Box 920287, Needham, MA 02492-0004
Tel: 781-449-9398 *Toll Free Tel:* 800-423-7087 (orders) *Fax:* 781-449-9397
E-mail: info@momentpoint.com
Web Site: www.momentpoint.com
Key Personnel
Pres: Susan Ray *E-mail:* susan@momentpoint.com
VP: Randy Ray *E-mail:* randy@momentpoint.com
Publisher of tools that help people consciously create limitless lives in a limitless world; metaphysical; New Age & personal growth. Also have a book series *Classics in Consciousness.*
ISBN Prefix(es): 0-9661327; 1-930491
Number of titles published annually: 4 Print
Total Titles: 20 Print
Imprints: Woodbridge Group
Distributed by Red Wheel/Weiser
Shipping Address: Red Wheel/Weiser, PO Box 612, York, ME 03910-0612 *Tel:* 617-542-1324 *Toll Free Tel:* 800-423-7087 *Web Site:* redwheelweiser.com
Warehouse: 22883 Quicksilver Dr, Dulles, VA 20166
Membership(s): Publishers Marketing Association

MomsGuide.com Inc
30 Doaks Lane, Marblehead, MA 01945
Tel: 781-639-7088 *Fax:* 781-639-7703
E-mail: mail@momsguide.com
Web Site: www.momsguide.com; www.gametimeguides.com
Key Personnel
VP, Fin: Gayle Grader

Founded: 1996
Publish Game-Time reference guides on the rules of sports.
ISBN Prefix(es): 1-889706
Number of titles published annually: 11 Print
Total Titles: 12 Print
Imprints: Mom's Guide to Sports
Divisions: Mom's Guide to Sports

The Monacelli Press
902 Broadway, 18th fl, New York, NY 10010
Tel: 212-777-0504 *Toll Free Tel:* 800-631-8571 (cust serv) *Fax:* 212-777-0514; 201-256-0000 (cust serv)
E-mail: info@monacellipress.com; production@monacellipress.com; customerservice@penguinputnam.com
Web Site: www.monacellipress.com
Key Personnel
Pres & Publr: Gianfranco Monacelli *Tel:* 212-777-0504 ext 206
Prodn Dir: Steven Sears
Ed: Andrea Monfried *Tel:* 212-777-0504 ext 202
Mkt & Publicity Mgr: Susan Enochs *Tel:* 212-777-0504 ext 203
Founded: 1994
Illustrated books.
ISBN Prefix(es): 1-58093; 1-885254
Number of titles published annually: 24 Print
Total Titles: 202 Print
Distributed by Penguin Putnam
Foreign Rep(s): Bookwise International (Australia, New Zealand); Michael Geoghegan (Austria, Germany, Switzerland); Tom Moggach/IMA (Eastern Europe, Israel); Penny Padovani (Greece, Italy, Portugal, Spain); Penguin Books Canada (Canada); Penguin Netherlands (Netherlands); Anselm Robinson/European Marketing Services (Belgium, France); Hans Rotovnik (Scandinavia); Anthony Rudkin Associates (Cyprus, Malta, Middle East, Turkey); John Rule Sales & Marketing (UK); United Publishers Services ltd (Japan); Roger Ward (Far East excluding Japan); David Williams/IMA (Caribbean, Central America, Eastern Europe, Israel, South America)
Warehouse: Penguin Putnam Distribution Ctr, One Gosset Dr, Kirkwood, NY 13795
Marston Book Services, 160 Milton Park, Abingdon, Oxon OX14 4SD, United Kingdom
Distribution Center: Penguin Putnam Distribution Ctr, One Gosset Dr, Kirkwood, NY 13795
Marston Book Services, 160 Milton Park, Abingdon, Oxon OX14 4SD, United Kingdom

Monday Morning Books Inc
PO Box 1134, Inverness, CA 94937-0034
Tel: 650-327-3374 *Toll Free Tel:* 800-255-6049 *Toll Free Fax:* 800-255-6048
E-mail: MMBooks@aol.com
Web Site: www.mondaymorningbooks.com
Key Personnel
Pres: Roberta Suid *Fax:* 650-328-1638
Founded: 1983
Educational materials.
ISBN Prefix(es): 1-878279; 1-57612
Number of titles published annually: 20 Print
Total Titles: 93 Print
Foreign Rep(s): Dominie (Australia); Vanwell (Canada)
Shipping Address: 30 Amberwood Pkwy, Ashland, OH 44805
Warehouse: 30 Amberwood Pkwy, Ashland, OH 44805

Mondo Publishing
980 Avenue of the Americas, New York, NY 10018
Tel: 212-268-3560 *Toll Free Tel:* 800-242-3650 *Fax:* 212-268-3561
E-mail: mondopub@aol.com
Web Site: www.mondopub.com

Key Personnel
Pres: Mark Vineis
Dir, Sales & Mktg: Antoinette Fleming
Dir, Mktg: Randi Machado
Edit Dir: Susan Eddy
Ed: Susan Derkazarian
Founded: 1986
ISBN Prefix(es): 1-879531; 1-57255; 1-58653
Number of titles published annually: 200 Print
Total Titles: 300 Print
Imprints: Mondo
Warehouse: 113 Amfesco Dr, Plainview, NY 11803
Membership(s): Children's Book Council

Money Market Directories
Unit of Standard & Poor's
320 E Main St, Charlottesville, VA 22902
Mailing Address: PO Box 1608, Charlottesville, VA 22902-1608
Tel: 434-977-1450 *Toll Free Tel:* 800-446-2810 *Fax:* 434-979-9962
Web Site: www.mmdwebaccess.com
Key Personnel
Publr: Thomas Lupo
Man Ed: Jesse Noel
Prodn Mgr: Jehu Martin
Direct Mktg Specialist: Evelyn Inskeep
    E-mail: evelyn-inskeep@standardandpoors.com
Founded: 1970
Financial directories & guides, annuals, pension funds, investment management, non-profits.
ISBN Prefix(es): 0-939712
Number of titles published annually: 6 Print; 2 CD-ROM; 1 Online
Total Titles: 6 Print; 2 CD-ROM; 1 Online

The Mongolia Society Inc
Indiana University, 322 Goodbody Hall, Bloomington, IN 47405-7005
Tel: 812-855-4078 *Fax:* 812-855-7500
E-mail: monsoc@indiana.edu
Web Site: www.indiana.edu/~mongsoc
Key Personnel
Mgr & Treas: Susie Drost
Founded: 1961
Interests, culture & language of Mongolia.
ISBN Prefix(es): 0-910980
Number of titles published annually: 4 Print
Total Titles: 55 Print

Monogram Aviation Publications
PO Box 223, Sturbridge, MA 01566
Tel: 508-347-5574 *Fax:* 508-347-5772
E-mail: monogram@meganet.net
Web Site: www.monogramaviation.com
Key Personnel
Gen Mgr: Barbara W Hitchcock
Publr: Thomas H Hitchcock
Founded: 1972
Military colors, markings; American, British, German, Japanese & Italian aviation subjects.
ISBN Prefix(es): 0-914144
Number of titles published annually: 3 Print
Total Titles: 9 Print
Distributed by Military Model Distributors; Motorbooks International
Shipping Address: 290 Leadmine Rd, Sturbridge, MA 01566

Montana Historical Society Press
225 N Roberts St, Helena, MT 59620
Mailing Address: PO Box 201201, Helena, MT 59620-1201
Tel: 406-444-4741 (editorial); 406-444-2890 (ordering/marketing) *Toll Free Tel:* 800-243-9900 *Fax:* 406-444-2696 (ordering/marketing)
Web Site: www.montanahistoricalsociety.org
Key Personnel
Ed: Clark Whitehorn
Number of titles published annually: 4 Print

Total Titles: 45 Print; 1 Online
Distributed by Globe Pequot Press

Monterey Pacific Publishing, see Robert D Reed Publishers

Monthly Review Press
Division of Monthly Review Foundation Inc
122 W 27 St, New York, NY 10001
SAN: 202-6481
Tel: 212-691-2555 *Toll Free Tel:* 800-670-9499 *Fax:* 212-727-3676
E-mail: mreview@igc.org
Web Site: www.MonthlyReview.org
Key Personnel
Man Dir: Martin Paddio
Promo & Publg: Renee Pendergrass
Founded: 1949
Economics, politics, history, sociology & world affairs.
ISBN Prefix(es): 0-85345; 1-58367
Number of titles published annually: 15 Print
Total Titles: 400 Print
Imprints: Cornerstone Books; New Feminist Library; Voices of Resistance
Distributed by New York University Press
Billing Address: New York University Press, 838 Broadway, 3rd fl, New York, NY 10003
Orders to: New York University Press, 838 Broadway, 3rd fl, New York, NY 10003 *Toll Free Tel:* 800-996-6987 *Fax:* 212-995-4798
Returns: Maple Press Distribution Ctr Lebanon, 704 Legionaire Dr, Fredericksburg, PA 17026
Warehouse: Maple Press Distribution Ctr Lebanon, 704 Legionaire Dr, Fredericksburg, PA 17026

§Moo Press Inc
PO Box 54, Warwick, NY 10990-0054
SAN: 254-8631
Tel: 845-987-7750 *Fax:* 845-987-7845
E-mail: info@moopress.com
Web Site: www.moopress.com
Key Personnel
Publr & Pres: Diane Tinney *E-mail:* dtinney@moopress.com
Founded: 2002
Everyone has something to share; something to pass onto others. Books provide everyone with an opportunity to learn, to share, to grow. At Moo Press, Inc we provide authors & readers with the ability to make dreams come true & we have fun doing it.
ISBN Prefix(es): 0-9724853
Number of titles published annually: 6 Print; 1 E-Book; 1 Audio
Total Titles: 7 Print; 1 E-Book; 1 Audio
Online services available through Content Reserve.
Distributed by Biblio; NBN
Membership(s): AAP; Photo Marketing Association

Moody Press
Affiliate of Ministry of Moody Bible Institute
820 N La Salle Blvd, Chicago, IL 60610
SAN: 202-5604
Tel: 312-329-2111 *Toll Free Tel:* 800-678-8812 *Fax:* 312-329-2019
Web Site: www.moodypress.org *Cable:* BIBLE CHICAGO ILLINOIS
Key Personnel
VP & Exec Ed: Greg Thornton
Gen Mgr: William Thrasher
Prodn Mgr & ISBN Contact: Dave DeWit
Mktg Mgr: John Hinkley
Adv Mgr: Rhonda Elfstrand
Publicist: Janis Backing
Intl Rts Contact: Pam Pugh
Founded: 1894
Religion (interdenominational).
ISBN Prefix(es): 0-8024; 1-881273

Number of titles published annually: 100 Print
Total Titles: 800 Print; 10 Audio
Imprints: Lift Every Voice; Northfield Publishing
Foreign Rep(s): Biblicum AS (Norway); Book-
house Australia Ltd (Australia); Challenge
Bookshops (Nigeria); Christian Art Wholesale
(South Africa); Christian Literature Crusade
(Hong Kong); Editeurs de Litterature Biblique
(Germany); Euro-Outreach Ministries (East
Africa, Kenya, Nairobi); Hong Kong Tien Dao
Publishing House Ltd (Belgium); Kesho Pub-
lications (Zimbabwe); Matopo Book Room
(Philippines); R G Mitchell Family Books Ltd
(Netherlands); Overseas Missionary Fellowship
(Canada); Rhema Boekimport (Singapore); S
& U Book Centre (New Zealand); S-U Whole-
sale; Sent the Light (England)
Shipping Address: 215 W Locust St, Chicago, IL
60610

Moon Lady Press
Formerly Vermilion Inc
PO Box 83, Marshfield Hills, MA 02051
Tel: 781-837-1618 *Toll Free Tel:* 800-840-0205
Fax: 781-837-7249
Web Site: www.donnagreen.com
Key Personnel
Owner & Pres: Donna Green
Illustrated books, art prints, note cards by Donna
Green.
Number of titles published annually: 3 Print
Total Titles: 19 Print
Distributor for The Country Cottage
Shipping Address: 575 Summer St, Suite 90-104,
Marshfield, MA 02050

Moon Mountain Publishing
80 Peachtree Rd, North Kingstown, RI 02852
Tel: 401-884-6703 *Toll Free Tel:* 800-353-5877
Fax: 401-884-7076
E-mail: hello@moonmountainpub.com
Web Site: www.moonmountainpub.com
Key Personnel
Pres & Publr: Cathy A Monroe *E-mail:* cate@
moonmountainpub.com
VP, Sales & Mktg: Bob Holtzman *E-mail:* bob@
moonmountainpub.com
Founded: 1999
Illustrated children's books with positive themes,
affirming the beauty & value of life. Children's
picturebook fiction for all ages up to 12. Books
about Rhode Island.
ISBN Prefix(es): 0-9677929; 1-931659
Number of titles published annually: 4 Print
Total Titles: 14 Print
Foreign Rights: Luigi Bernabo Assistants (Italy);
Big Apple Tuttle-Mori (China, Hong Kong,
Taiwan); Book Publishers Association of Is-
rael (Israel); Imprima Korea Agency (Korea);
International Literatuur Bureau BV (Belgium,
Netherlands); Nurcihan Kesim Literary Agency
(Turkey); Michael Meller Literary Agency
(Austria, Germany, Switzerland); Motovun
Tokyo (Japan); La Nouvelle Agence (France);
Pollinger Ltd (UK, Commonwealth); Sigma TR
Literary Agency (Korea); THE Agency (Korea)
Orders to: National Book Network (NBN)
Returns: National Book Network (NBN)
Membership(s): Independent Publishers of New
England; Publishers Marketing Association

Morehouse Publishing Co
PO Box 1321, Harrisburg, PA 17105-1321
Tel: 717-541-8130 *Toll Free Tel:* 800-877-0012
(orders only) *Fax:* 717-541-8136; 717-541-
8128 (orders only)
E-mail: morehouse@morehousegroup.com
Web Site: www.morehousegroup.com
Key Personnel
Pres: Kenneth Quigley *E-mail:* kquigley@
morehousegroup.com

Publr & Edit Dir: Debra Farrington
E-mail: dfarring@morehousegroup.com
Perms: Cheryl Johnston
Founded: 1884
Spirituality, religious, lay ministry, liturgy, church
supplies, music cassettes & CDs, all from an
Episcopal/Anglican perspective.
ISBN Prefix(es): 0-8192
Number of titles published annually: 40 Print
Total Titles: 462 Print
Editorial Office(s): 4775 Linglestown Rd, Harris-
burg, PA 17112 SAN: 202-6511
Distributor for Canterbury Press Norwich (UK);
Eagle (UK, music audio); Gracewing (UK);
Pendle Hill (US)
Foreign Rep(s): Novalis (Canada)
Foreign Rights: The Continuum International
Publishing Group (outside the US)
Warehouse: Morehouse Distribution Center, 3101
N Seventh St, Harrisburg, PA 17110

Moreland Press Inc
827 Christina Circle, Oldsmar, FL 34677
Mailing Address: PO Box 15123, Clearwater, FL
33766-5123
Tel: 813-891-0568 *Fax:* 813-891-0428
E-mail: morelandpress@aol.com
Web Site: www.morelandpress.com
Key Personnel
Pres: Janet Mathews
Founded: 2000
Independent publisher of fiction & novels.
ISBN Prefix(es): 0-9706677
Number of titles published annually: 3 Print

Morgan Kaufmann Publishers
Imprint of Elsevier
500 Sansome, Suite 400, San Francisco, CA
94111
Tel: 415-392-2665 *Fax:* 415-982-2665
E-mail: mkp@mkp.com
Web Site: www.mkp.com
Key Personnel
Publr: Diane Cerra
Mktg Mgr: Georgina Edwards
Intl Rts: Edna Lopez-Franco *Tel:* 619-699-6717
Lib Sales: Tom Rosenthal *Tel:* 619-699-6806
Nat Acct Sales: Peg O'Malley *Tel:* 415-647-7867
Founded: 1984
Computer science book publishers including
database, networking, architecture, engineer-
ing, graphics & artificial intelligence.
ISBN Prefix(es): 1-55860
Number of titles published annually: 60 Print
Total Titles: 1,500 Print
Orders to: Harcourt Inc, 11830 W Line Industrial
Dr, St Louis, MS 63146 (Attn: Order Fulfill-
ment Dept)
Returns: Troy Distribution Center, 465 S Lincoln
Dr, Troy, MO 63379 (Attn: Returns Dept)
Warehouse: Troy Distribution Center, 465 S Lin-
coln Dr, Troy, MO 63379

Morgan Quitno Corp
PO Box 1656, Lawrence, KS 66044-8656
Tel: 785-841-3534 *Toll Free Tel:* 800-457-0742
Fax: 785-841-3568
E-mail: info@morganquitno.com
Web Site: www.morganquitno.com
Key Personnel
Owner & Officer: Kathleen Morgan
Ed & Publr: Scott E Morgan
Founded: 1989
State statistical reference books & city/metro ref-
erence books.
ISBN Prefix(es): 0-9625531; 1-56692; 0-7401
Number of titles published annually: 211 Print; 5
CD-ROM; 5 Online
Total Titles: 473 Print; 25 CD-ROM; 10 Online
Shipping Address: 512 E Ninth, Lawrence, KS
66044

Morgan Reynolds Publishing
620 S Elm St, Suite 223, Greensboro, NC 27406
Tel: 336-275-1311 *Toll Free Tel:* 800-535-1504
Fax: 336-275-1152 *Toll Free Fax:* 800-535-
5725
E-mail: editorial@morganreynolds.com
Web Site: www.morganreynolds.com
Key Personnel
Publr & Founder: John Riley
Mktg Dir: Anita Richardson *E-mail:* anita@
morganreynolds.com
Ed: Casey Cornelius *E-mail:* casey@
morganreynolds.com; Angie DeCola
E-mail: angie@morganreynolds.com
Founded: 1993
Hardcover trade & library-bound editions.
ISBN Prefix(es): 1-883846; 1-931798
Number of titles published annually: 40 Print
Total Titles: 145 Print

Morning Glory Press Inc
6595 San Haroldo Way, Buena Park, CA 90620-
3748
SAN: 211-2558
Tel: 714-828-1998 *Toll Free Tel:* 888-612-8254
Fax: 714-828-2049 *Toll Free Fax:* 888-327-
4362
E-mail: info@morningglorypress.com
Web Site: www.morningglorypress.com
Key Personnel
Pres: Jeanne Lindsay *E-mail:* jwl@
morningglorypress.com
Dir, Mktg: Eve Wright
Founded: 1977
Publisher of books for young adults with an em-
phasis on resources for teenage parents.
ISBN Prefix(es): 0-930934; 1-885356
Number of titles published annually: 3 Print
Total Titles: 78 Print
Membership(s): Publishers Marketing Association

Morning Sun Books Inc
9 Pheasant Lane, Scotch Plains, NJ 07076
Tel: 908-755-5454 *Fax:* 908-755-5455
Web Site: www.morningsunbooks.com
Key Personnel
Intl Rts: Robert J Yanosey
Color photography of railroads during 1940-1970
period.
ISBN Prefix(es): 1-878887; 1-58248
Number of titles published annually: 24 Print
Total Titles: 265 Print

§Morningside Bookshop
Division of Morningside House Inc
260 Oak St, Dayton, OH 45410
SAN: 202-2206
Mailing Address: PO Box 1087, Dayton, OH
45401-1087
Tel: 937-461-6736 *Toll Free Tel:* 800-648-9710
Fax: 937-461-4260
E-mail: msbooks@erinet.com
Web Site: www.morningsidebooks.com
Key Personnel
Pres: Mary E Younger
VP: Bob Younger
Founded: 1969
New publications & reprint editions of books re-
lating to the Civil War.
ISBN Prefix(es): 0-89029
Number of titles published annually: 10 Print; 10
E-Book
Total Titles: 100 Print; 104 E-Book
Imprints: Morningside House Inc; Morningside
Press; Press of Morningside Bookshop
Billing Address: PO Box 1087, Dayton, OH
45401-1087
Orders to: PO Box 1087, Dayton, OH 45401-
1087

William Morrow & Co Inc, see HarperCollins
Publishers

Morton Publishing Co
925 W Kenyon Ave, Unit 12, Englewood, CO
80110
Tel: 303-761-4805 *Fax:* 303-762-9923
E-mail: morton@morton-pub.com
Web Site: www.morton-pub.com
Key Personnel
Pres & Intl Rts: Doug Morton
Founded: 1977
Allied health, biology, pharmacy, computer infor-
mation technology, speech & educational.
ISBN Prefix(es): 0-89582
Number of titles published annually: 40 Print
Total Titles: 40 Print

Mosaic Press
DMB 145, 4500 Witmer Industrial Estates, Nia-
gara Falls, NY 14305-1386
Mailing Address: 1252 Speers Rd, Units 1 & 2,
Oakville, ON L6L 5N9, Canada
Tel: 905-825-2130 *Toll Free Tel:* 800-387-8992
Fax: 905-825-2130
E-mail: mosaicpress@on.aibn.com
Web Site: www.mosaic-press.com
Key Personnel
Pres: Howard Aster
Founded: 1974
Literary scholarly books.
ISBN Prefix(es): 0-88962
Number of titles published annually: 15 Print
Total Titles: 500 Print
Distributed by Midpoint; Round House Group;
SCB Distributors; Wakefield Press
Warehouse: 1252 Speers Rd, Units 1 & 2,
Oakville, ON L6L 5N9, Canada

Mosaic Press
358 Oliver Rd, Cincinnati, OH 45215
SAN: 219-6077
Tel: 513-761-5977 *Fax:* 513-761-5977
Web Site: www.mosaicpress.com
Key Personnel
Publr: Miriam Irwin *E-mail:* mirwin@cinci.rr.com
Founded: 1977
Books - including miniature.
Not related to Mosaic Press, Ontario, Canada.
ISBN Prefix(es): 0-88014
Number of titles published annually: 1 Print
Total Titles: 35 Print
Membership(s): Miniature Book Society

Mosby, see Elsevier

Mosby Journal Division
Division of Mosby
11830 Westline Industrial Dr, St Louis, MO
63146
Tel: 314-872-8370 *Toll Free Tel:* 800-325-4177
Web Site: www.elsevierhealth.com
Key Personnel
Pres & CEO, Health Science Div: Brian Nairin
CFO: Menno Tas
Exec VP, Sales & Mktg: Mary Ging
Exec VP, Journals: Kevin Hurley
Professional journals, software & standardized
tests for the health sciences & health-related
books for the general market.

Mount Ida Press
152 Washington Ave, Albany, NY 12210-2203
Tel: 518-426-5935 *Fax:* 518-426-4116
E-mail: info@mtidapress.com
Web Site: www.mountidapress.com
Key Personnel
Pres: Diana S Waite
Founded: 1985
Complete book production & marketing plans for
associations, corporations, universities, govern-
ment agencies, public relations firms & small
presses. Trade & scholarly books, guides, di-
rectories, conference proceedings, journals,

premiums, corporate histories, local histories,
calendars, commemorative publications.
ISBN Prefix(es): 0-9625368
Number of titles published annually: 5 Print
Total Titles: 5 Print

Mount Olive College Press
Affiliate of Mount Olive College
634 Henderson St, Mount Olive, NC 28365
Tel: 919-658-2502 *Toll Free Tel:* 800-653-0854
Fax: 919-658-7180
Web Site: www.mountolivecollege.edu
Key Personnel
Edit Dir: Pepper Worthington *Tel:* 252-523-8659
Founded: 1990
Poetry, drama, biography, devotional, travel, es-
say, novel, cookbook, photography, children's
books, literary criticism.
ISBN Prefix(es): 0-9627087; 1-880994
Number of titles published annually: 5 Print
Total Titles: 75 Print

Mountain n' Air Books
2947-A Honolulu Ave, La Crescenta, CA 91214
Mailing Address: PO Box 12540, La Crescenta,
CA 91224-5540
Tel: 818-248-9345 *Toll Free Tel:* 800-446-9696
Fax: 818-248-6516 *Toll Free Fax:* 800-303-
5578
Web Site: www.mountain-n-air.com
Key Personnel
Pres: Gilberto d'Urso *E-mail:* gilberto@mountain-
n-air.com
Publr & Ed: Mary K d'Urso
Founded: 1985
Outdoor guides, nonfiction, cookbooks & travel
adventures.
ISBN Prefix(es): 1-879415
Number of titles published annually: 10 Print
Total Titles: 69 Print
Imprints: Bearly Cooking; Mountain Air Books
Distributor for Tom Harrison Cartography

Mountain Press Publishing Co
1301 S Third W, Missoula, MT 59801
SAN: 202-8832
Mailing Address: PO Box 2399, Missoula, MT
59806-2399
Tel: 406-728-1900 *Toll Free Tel:* 800-234-5308
Fax: 406-728-1635
E-mail: info@mtnpress.com
Web Site: www.mountain-press.com
Key Personnel
Gen Mgr: John Rimel *E-mail:* johnargyle@aol.
com
Mktg: Ingrid Estell
Busn Mgr: Rob Williams
Roadside Geology Series Ed: Jennifer Carey
Natural History Ed: Jennifer Carey
Prod Designs: Jean Nuckolls
Graphic Design: Kim Pryhorocki
History Ed: Gwen McKenna
Founded: 1948
ISBN Prefix(es): 0-87842; 0-9632562; 0-9626999;
1-886370; 1-889921; 1-892784; 0-9676747; 0-
9717748; 0-9724827
Number of titles published annually: 20 Print
Total Titles: 150 Print
Imprints: Geology Underfoot Series; Mountain
Sports Press; Roadside Geology Series; Road-
side History Series; Tumbleweed Series
Distributor for Bear Print; Cottonwood Publish-
ing; Goals Unlimited Press; Hops Press; John
McQuarrie Books; Western Edge Press
Foreign Rep(s): Herron

§Mountain View Press
Division of Epsilon Lyra Corp
19500 Skyline Blvd, La Honda, CA 94020
Mailing Address: Rte 2, RR Box 429, La Honda,
CA 94020-0429
Tel: 650-747-0760

Web Site: www.theforthsource.com
Key Personnel
Pres: Glen Haydon *E-mail:* ghaydon@
theforthsource.com
Founded: 1982
Specialize in desktop publishing & research &
development in software & hardware.
ISBN Prefix(es): 0-914699
Number of titles published annually: 20 Print
Total Titles: 20 Print

The Mountaineers Books
Subsidiary of The Mountaineers
1001 SW Klickitat Way, Suite 201, Seattle, WA
98134
Tel: 206-223-6303 *Toll Free Tel:* 800-553-4453
Fax: 206-223-6306 *Toll Free Fax:* 800-568-
7604
E-mail: mbooks@mountaineers.org
Web Site: www.mountaineersbooks.org
Key Personnel
Dir, Sales & Mktg: Doug Canfield
Cust Rel: Tim Warne
Rts Mgr: Mary Metz *Tel:* 206-223-6303 ext 119
E-mail: marym@mountaineersbooks.org
Publicist: Alison Koop
Founded: 1961
Mountaineering, backpacking, hiking, cross-
country skiing, bicycling, canoeing, kayaking,
trekking, nature & conservation; outdoor how-
to, guidebooks & maps; nonfiction adventure-
travel accounts; biographies of outdoor people;
reprint editions of mountaineering classics; ad-
venture narratives.
ISBN Prefix(es): 0-89886; 0-916890
Number of titles published annually: 60 Print
Total Titles: 650 Print
Distributor for American Alpine Club Press; Col-
orado Mountain Club Press
Foreign Rep(s): Cordee Publishing (UK)

§Mouton de Gruyter
Division of Walter de Gruyter GmbH & Co KG
500 Executive Blvd, Ossining, NY 10562
SAN: 210-9239
Tel: 914-762-5866 *Fax:* 914-762-0371
E-mail: info@degruyterny.com
Web Site: www.degruyter.com
Key Personnel
VP & Gen Mgr: Eckart A Scheffler
E-mail: escheffler@degruyterny.com
Founded: 1956
Scholarly books & journals.
ISBN Prefix(es): 0-311; 90-279
Number of titles published annually: 75 Print; 2
Online
Total Titles: 2,500 Print; 3 CD-ROM; 10 Online
Imprints: Foris Publications
Foreign Office(s): Walter de Gruyter GmbH &
Co. KG, Genthinerstr 13, 10785 Berlin, Ger-
many
Distributed by Walter de Gruyter Inc
Foreign Rep(s): Allied Publishers Ltd (India,
Nepal, Sri Lanka); Book Club International
(Bangladesh); Combined Representatives
Worldwide Inc (Philippines); D A Books &
Journals (Australia, New Zealand); Kumi Trad-
ing (South Korea); Kweilin Bookstore (Tai-
wan); Maruzen Co Ltd (Japan); Pak Book
Corp (Pakistan); Parry's Book Center Sendjrjan
Berhad (Brunei, Malaysia, Singapore); Swinden
Book Co Ltd (Hong Kong); Verlags und Kom-
missionsbuchhandlung Dr Franz Hain (Austria);
Walter de Gruyter Inc (Canada, Mexico)
Foreign Rights: Mouton de Gruyter (Germany)
Advertising Agency: de Gruyter-Mouton Advertis-
ing, Hawthorne, NY
Billing Address: 22803 Quick Silver Sr, Dulles,
VA 20166-2019
Orders to: 22803 Quick Silver Sr, Dulles, VA
20166-2019
Returns: 22803 Quick Silver Sr, Dulles, VA
20166-2019

Shipping Address: 22803 Quick Silver Sr,
VA 20166-2019
Warehouse: 22803 Quick Silver Sr, Dulles, VA
20166-2019
Distribution Center: 22803 Quick Silver Sr,
Dulles, VA 20166-2019

Andrew Mowbray Inc Publishers
PO Box 460, Lincoln, RI 02865-0460
Tel: 401-726-8011 *Toll Free Tel:* 800-999-4697
Fax: 401-726-8061
E-mail: service@manatarmbooks.com
Web Site: www.manatarmbooks.com
Key Personnel
Pres: Stuart Mowbray
Adv Dir: Kate Tompkins
Book Designer: Joanne Langlois
Founded: 1964
Antique arms & armor for the historian, reseacher
& collector.
ISBN Prefix(es): 0-917218
Number of titles published annually: 4 Print
Total Titles: 50 Print

Moyer Bell Ltd
549 Old North Rd, Kingston, RI 02881
Tel: 401-783-5480 *Fax:* 401-284-0959
E-mail: acornalliance@yahoo.com
Web Site: www.acornalliance.com
Key Personnel
Publr: Britt Bell
Founded: 1984
New books & reprints, cloth & paperback; fiction,
poetry, art, travel, general nonfiction, reference
books, consumer books.
ISBN Prefix(es): 0-918825; 1-55921
Number of titles published annually: 12 Print
Total Titles: 150 Print
Imprints: Albion Press; Asphodel Press; Olmstead
Press; Papier-Mache Press
Foreign Office(s): Gazelle Book Service, Falcon
House, Queen Sq, Lancaster LA1 1RN, United
Kingdom
Distributor for Asphodel Press
Foreign Rep(s): Gazelle (Europe)

Moznaim Publishing Corp
4304 12 Ave, Brooklyn, NY 11219
SAN: 214-4123
Tel: 718-438-7680 *Toll Free Tel:* 800-364-5118
Fax: 718-438-1305
Key Personnel
Pres: Menachem Wagshal
VP: Moshe Sternlicht
Sales: Isaac Wolpin
Founded: 1981
Judaica books in Hebrew & English.
ISBN Prefix(es): 0-940118; 1-885220
Number of titles published annually: 10 Print
Total Titles: 160 Print
Foreign Office(s): 10 Telmie Yosef St, Mishor
Adumim, Israel *Tel:* (02) 5333441 *Fax:* (02)
5354345
Distributor for Breslov Research Institute; Red
Wheel-Weiser Inc

§Multicultural Publications
936 Slosson Ave, Akron, OH 44320
Mailing Address: PO Box 8001, Akron, OH
44320-0001
Tel: 330-865-9578 *Toll Free Tel:* 800-238-0297
Fax: 330-865-9578
E-mail: info@multiculturalpub.net
Web Site: www.multiculturalpub.net
Key Personnel
Publr & CEO: Bobby L Jackson
Dir, Mktg & Promos & Intl Rts: James Lynell
Lib Sales Dir: Rae Neal
Founded: 1992
Books, greeting cards, dolls & stuffed toys, multi-
media.
ISBN Prefix(es): 0-9634932; 1-884242

Number of titles published annually: 3 Print; 1
CD-ROM; 1 Audio
Total Titles: 25 Print; 2 CD-ROM; 25 Online; 2
Audio
Branch Office(s)
1907 Massillon Rd, Akron, OH 44312
Returns: 1907 Massillon Rd, Akron, OH 44312
Shipping Address: 1907 Massillon Rd, Akron,
OH 44312

Multnomah Publishers Inc
204 W Adams Ave, Sisters, OR 97759
SAN: 210-4679
Mailing Address: PO Box 1720, Sisters, OR
97759-1720
Tel: 541-549-1144 *Toll Free Tel:* 800-929-0910
Fax: 541-549-2044 (sales); 541-549-0432 (ad-
min); 541-549-0260 (ed/prod); 541-549-8048
(mktg)
E-mail: information@multnomahbooks.com
Web Site: www.multnomahbooks.com
Key Personnel
Pres: Donald C Jacobson
CFO & VP: Doug Gabbert
COO: Kevin Marks
Sr Dir, Sales: Jay Echternach
Intl Rts Contact: Joel Horning
Founded: 1987
Books on Christian living & family enrichment;
devotional & gift books; fiction.
ISBN Prefix(es): 0-88070; 1-57673; 1-59052
Number of titles published annually: 75 Print
Total Titles: 850 Print
Imprints: Multnomah Books
Subsidiaries: Multnomah Gift
Foreign Rep(s): Crossroads (Australia); R G
Mitchell (Canada); Send The Light (England)
Foreign Rights: David Sheets
Distribution Center: Gospel Light

Munchweiler Press
14217 Gale Dr, Victorville, CA 92394-7353
Mailing Address: PO Box 2529, Victorville, CA
92393-2529
Tel: 760-245-9215 *Fax:* 760-245-9418
E-mail: publisher@munchweilerpress.com
Web Site: www.munchweilerpress.com
Key Personnel
Pres & Publr: Theo E Lish *E-mail:* tedlish@
munchweilerpress.com
Founded: 1999
Children's book publisher.
ISBN Prefix(es): 0-7940
Number of titles published annually: 4 Print
Total Titles: 4 Print
Imprints: Tres Duendes (Spanish language im-
print)
Advertising Agency: Uber Advertising & Public
Relations
Membership(s): Association of Booksellers for
Children; Publishers Marketing Association

§Mundania Press
Imprint of Mundania Press LLC
6470A Glenway Ave, Suite 109, Cincinnati, OH
45211-5222
SAN: 255-013X
Tel: 513-574-8902 *Fax:* 513-598-6800
E-mail: books@mundania.com
Web Site: www.mundania.com
Key Personnel
CEO: Bob Sanders *Tel:* 513-404-7357
E-mail: bob@mundania.com
Sr Ed: Daniel J Reitz, Sr *E-mail:* dan@mundania.
com
Founded: 2002
Publisher of select novels & anthologies from tal-
ented authors. Specialize in the science fiction,
fantasy, horror, mystery, romance & paranor-
mal genres as well as cross-genre (i.e. horror-
fantasy, science fiction-mystery).
ISBN Prefix(es): 0-9723670; 1-59426

Number of titles published annually: 35 Print; 35
CD-ROM; 35 E-Book
Total Titles: 21 Print; 15 CD-ROM; 15 E-Book
Foreign Rep(s): Booksurge (UK, USA); Lightning
Source (UK, USA)
Distribution Center: Baker & Taylor SAN: 255-
013X
Ingram's (Distribute also in the UK)
Membership(s): Electronically Published Internet
Connection; Publishers Marketing Association

Municipal Analysis Services Inc
PO Box 13453, Austin, TX 78711-3453
Tel: 512-327-3328 *Fax:* 413-740-1294
E-mail: munilysis@hotmail.com
Key Personnel
Pres: Greg Michels *E-mail:* gregmichels@
hotmail.com
Founded: 1983
ISBN Prefix(es): 1-55507
Number of titles published annually: 40 Print
Total Titles: 1,200 Print

The Museum of Modern Art
11 W 53 St, New York, NY 10019
SAN: 202-5809
Tel: 212-708-9443 *Fax:* 212-333-6575
E-mail: moma_publications@moma.org
Web Site: www.moma.org *Telex:* 6-2370
Cable: MODERNART NY
Key Personnel
Man Ed: David Frankel
Promos & Mktg Coord, Pubns: Rebecca Zimmer-
man *E-mail:* rebecca_zimmerman@moma.org
Prodn Dir: Marc Sapir
Publr: Michael Maegraith
Publg Mgr: Lawrence Allen
Founded: 1929
Art, architecture, design, photography, film.
ISBN Prefix(es): 0-87070
Number of titles published annually: 10 Print
Total Titles: 140 Print
Distributed by Distributed Art Publishers (DAP)
Foreign Rep(s): Thames & Hudson Ltd (London,
outside US & Canada)
Warehouse: South River Distribution, South
River, NJ 08882

Museum of New Mexico Press
Unit of New Mexico State Office of Cultural Af-
fairs
725 Camino Lejo, Santa Fe, NM 87501
SAN: 202-2575
Mailing Address: Box 2087, Santa Fe, NM
87504-2087
Tel: 505-476-1158 *Toll Free Tel:* 800-249-7737
(orders) *Fax:* 505-476-1156 *Toll Free Fax:* 800-
622-8667 (orders)
E-mail: mnmpress@aol.com
Web Site: www.mnmpress.org
Key Personnel
Dir: Anna Gallegos *Tel:* 505-476-1154
E-mail: agallegos@oca.state.nm.us
Edit Dir: Mary Wachs *Tel:* 505-476-1161
E-mail: mwachs@oca.state.nm.us
Art Dir & Prodn Mgr: David Skolkin *Tel:* 505-
476-1159
Sales & Mktg Dir: Daniel Kosharek
Founded: 1909
Publications related to Native America, Hispanic
Southwest, 20th century art, folk art & folk-
lore, nature & gardening, architecture & the
Americas.
ISBN Prefix(es): 0-89013
Number of titles published annually: 12 Print
Total Titles: 150 Print
Warehouse: University of New Mexico Press,
3721 Spirit Dr, Albuquerque, NM 87106
Distribution Center: University of New Mexico
Press, 3721 Spirit Dr, Albuquerque, NM 87106

Muska & Lipman Publishing
Division of Thomson Course Technology

25 Thomson Place, Boston, MA 02210
Tel: 617-757-7900 *Fax:* 513-924-9333
Web Site: www.muskalipman.com
Key Personnel
Publr: Andy Shafran *E-mail:* andy@
muskalipman.com
Founded: 1997
Computer books about digital media topics.
ISBN Prefix(es): 1-929685; 0-992889
Number of titles published annually: 25 Print; 25
E-Book
Total Titles: 60 Print; 50 E-Book
Membership(s): Publishers Marketing Association

Mustang Publishing Co Inc
PO Box 770426, Memphis, TN 38177-0426
SAN: 289-6702
Tel: 901-684-1200 *Toll Free Tel:* 800-250-8713
Fax: 901-684-1256
E-mail: info@mustangpublishing.com
Web Site: www.mustangpublishing.com
Key Personnel
Pres: Rollin A Riggs
Founded: 1983
General trade, hardcover & paperback; how-to,
humor, outdoor recreation, sports & travel.
ISBN Prefix(es): 0-914457
Number of titles published annually: 4 Print
Total Titles: 30 Print
Foreign Rights: Gazelle Book Services (UK, Eu-
rope)
Shipping Address: 442 Wellington Cove,
Memphis, TN 38117, Contact: Rollin
Riggs *Tel:* 901-684-1200 *E-mail:* info@
mustangpublishing.com
Warehouse: National Book Network, 15200 NBN
Way, Blue Ridge Summit, PA 17214 *Toll Free
Tel:* 800-462-6420 *Web Site:* www.nbnbooks.
com
Distribution Center: National Book Network,
4720 Boston Way, Lanham, MD 20706 *Toll
Free Tel:* 800-462-6420 *Fax:* 301-459-1705
Web Site: www.nbnbooks.com
Membership(s): Publishers Marketing Association

My Chaotic Life™
Division of Walter Foster Publishing Inc
23062 La Cadena Dr, Laguna Hills, CA 92653
Tel: 949-380-7510 *Toll Free Tel:* 800-426-0099
Fax: 949-380-7575
Web Site: www.mychaoticlife.com
Key Personnel
Pres & CEO: Ross Sarracino
Cont: Mark O'Halloran
Assoc Publr: Sydney Sprague
Sales Mgr: Nancy Lee
Founded: 2000
Sassy & trendy interactive journals, gift books &
memory books.
ISBN Prefix(es): 0-929261; 1-56010
Number of titles published annually: 20 Print
Total Titles: 16 Print
Distributor for Quarto
Foreign Rep(s): Apple Press

§Mystic Ridge Books
Subsidiary of Mystic Ridge Productions Inc
PO Box 66930, Albuquerque, NM 87193
Tel: 505-899-2121
E-mail: publisher@mysticridgebooks.com
Web Site: www.mysticridgebooks.com
Key Personnel
Pres: Richard Brown
Founded: 1998
Publish books & related audio books, DVDs &
other porducts. Also sponsor author seminars,
public speaking engagements & column syndi-
cation.
ISBN Prefix(es): 0-9672182; 0-9742845
Number of titles published annually: 6 Print; 2
Audio
Total Titles: 12 Print; 2 Audio

Returns: SCB Distributors, 15608 S New Cen-
tury Dr, Gardena, CA 902458, Contact: Aaron
Silverman *Tel:* 310-532-9400 *E-mail:* aaron@
scbdistributors.com
Shipping Address: SCB Distributors, 15608 S
New Century Dr, Gardena, CA 902458, Con-
tact: Aaron Silverman *Tel:* 310-532-9400
E-mail: aaron@scbdistributors.com
Warehouse: SCB Distributors, 15608 S New Cen-
tury Dr, Gardena, CA 902458, Contact: Aaron
Silverman *Tel:* 310-532-9400 *E-mail:* aaron@
scbdistributors.com
Distribution Center: SCB Distributors, 15608
S New Century Dr, Gardena, CA 902458,
Contact: Aaron Silverman *Tel:* 310-532-9400
E-mail: aaron@scbdistributors.com

Mystic Seaport
PO Box 6000, Mystic, CT 06355-0990
SAN: 213-7550
Tel: 860-572-0711 *Fax:* 860-572-5321
Web Site: www.mysticseaport.org
Key Personnel
Dir: Andrew German
Pubns Asst: Constance Stein *E-mail:* connie.
stein@mystic.org
Founded: 1929
Scholarly & trade books on American maritime
history & art.
ISBN Prefix(es): 0-913372
Number of titles published annually: 14 Print
Total Titles: 84 Print
Imprints: American Maritime Library
Distributor for Balsam Abrams; Glencannon; Ten
Pound Island Books
Foreign Rep(s): Dalton Young Assoc (UK); Nim-
bus (Canada)

NACE International
1440 S Creek Dr, Houston, TX 77084-4906
Tel: 281-228-6223 *Fax:* 281-228-6300
E-mail: pubs@mail.nace.org
Web Site: www.nace.org
Key Personnel
Exec Dir: Jeff Littleton
Mgr: Neil Vaughan
Founded: 1943
NACE Press publishes technical books on cor-
rosion control & prevention & materials se-
lection, design & degradation issues. Books
are developed by individual authors/editors
utilizing corrosion experts to contribute text.
Compilations of technical papers from NACE
conferences & symposia are also issued on an
annual basis.
ISBN Prefix(es): 1-877914; 0-915567; 1-57590
Number of titles published annually: 50 Print
Total Titles: 400 Print; 30 CD-ROM; 4 Online;
80 Audio
Distributed by Australasian Corrosion Association
Distributor for ASM International; ASTM; AWS;
Butterworth-Heinemann; Cambridge University
Press; CASTI Publishing; Compass Publica-
tions; CRC Press; Marcel Dekker Inc; E&FN
Spon; Elsevier Science Publishers; Gulf Pub-
lishing; Industrial Press; Institute of Materials;
ISO; McGraw-Hill; MTI; Prentice Hall; Profes-
sional Publications; SSPC; Swedish Corrosion
Institute; John Wiley & Sons Inc
Foreign Rep(s): ABI (India); ATP (Europe); BI
Publications (Asia); IBS (India)

NACE Press, see NACE International

**NAFSA: Association of International
Educators**
1307 New York Ave NW, 8th fl, Washington, DC
20005-4701
Tel: 202-737-3699 *Toll Free Tel:* 800-836-4994
(Book orders only) *Fax:* 202-737-3657
E-mail: inbox@nafsa.org
Web Site: www.nafsa.org

Key Personnel
Sr Dir, Pubns: Christopher Murphy
E-mail: chrism@nafsa.org
Founded: 1948
Magazine (bi-monthly), bound & spiral books;
international education, federal regulations af-
fecting foreign students, electronic newsletter,
web site.
ISBN Prefix(es): 0-912207
Number of titles published annually: 2 Print
Total Titles: 45 Print
Orders to: PO Box 1020, Sewickley, PA 15143-
0920
Warehouse: PO Box 1020, Sewickley, PA 15143-
0920

NAL
Division of Penguin Group (USA) Inc
375 Hudson St, New York, NY 10014
SAN: 282-5074
Tel: 212-366-2000
E-mail: online@penguinputnam.com
Web Site: www.penguin.com
Key Personnel
VP & Publr: Kara Welsh
VP, Prodn: Pat Lyons
VP & Executive Art Dir: Rich Hasselberger
VP & Exec Publicity Dir: Liz Perl
VP & Dir, Adv & Promo: Rick Pascocello
VP & Exec Man Ed: Rick Nayer
Edit Dir: Claire Zion
Man Ed: Frank Walgren
Exec Ed: Ellen Edwards; Tracy Bernstein
Sr Ed: Douglas Grad; Daniel Slater; Kara Cesare;
Laura Cifelli
Exec Ed & Assoc Publr: Jennifer Long
Founded: 1948
ISBN Prefix(es): 0-451
Number of titles published annually: 353 Print
Total Titles: 1,550 Print
Imprints: Mentor; Meridian; New American Li-
brary; Onyx; Roc; Signet; Signet Classics;
Topaz
Advertising Agency: Spier NY

NAR Publications
State Rte 55, Barryville, NY 12719
Mailing Address: PO Box 233, Barryville, NY
12719-0233
Tel: 845-557-8713
E-mail: narpubs@aol.com
Key Personnel
Dir: Nancy Bennett
Sales Mgr: Ed Guild
Founded: 1977
Publisher of home study courses & books for Ad-
diction Professionals.
ISBN Prefix(es): 0-89780
Number of titles published annually: 12 Print
Total Titles: 75 Print

The Narrative Press
319 Salida Del Sol, Santa Barbara, CA 93109
Mailing Address: PO Box 2487, Santa Barbara,
CA 93120-2487
Tel: 805-966-2186 *Fax:* 805-456-3915
E-mail: admin@narrativepress.com
Web Site: www.narrativepress.com
Key Personnel
Pres: Sara Ellsworth
Ed: William Urschel
Founded: 2001
Publishes true first person accounts of adventure
& exploration.
ISBN Prefix(es): 1-58976
Number of titles published annually: 20 Print; 20
E-Book
Total Titles: 78 Print; 78 E-Book
Distributed by Stackpole Publishing
Foreign Rep(s): Stackpole Publishing (Canada)

Nataraj Books
7073 Brookfield Plaza, Springfield, VA 22150

Tel: 703-455-4996 *Fax:* 703-912-9052
E-mail: nataraj@erols.com
Web Site: www.natarajbooks.com
Key Personnel
Pres: Vinnie Mahajan
Books from India.
ISBN Prefix(es): 1-881338
Number of titles published annually: 6 Print
Total Titles: 70 Print

Nation Books
Imprint of Avalon Publishing Group - New York
245 W 17 St, 11th fl, New York, NY 10011-5300
SAN: 216-4663
Tel: 646-375-2570 *Fax:* 646-375-2571
Web Site: www.nationbooks.org
Key Personnel
Sr VP & Publg Dir: Michele Martin
VP & Publr: John Oakes
Ed: Jofie Ferrari-Adler
Founded: 2000
Nation Books, an imprint of Avalon Publishing Group, specializes in publishing books on social & political writings on issues of the day.
ISBN Prefix(es): 1-56025

§National Academies Press
Division of National Academy of Sciences
500 Fifth St NW, Washington, DC 20001
SAN: 202-8891
Tel: 202-334-3313 *Toll Free Tel:* 800-624-6242
Fax: 202-334-2451 (orders)
Web Site: www.nap.edu *Telex:* 24-8664 NASW
UR *Cable:* NARECO
Key Personnel
Dir: Barbara Kline Pope
Mktg & Outreach Dir: Ann Merchant *Tel:* 202-334-3117 *E-mail:* amerchan@nas.edu
Exec Ed: Stephen Mautner
Prodn Mgr: Dorothy Lewis
Art Dir: Francesca Moghari
Dir, Data Imaging: Jim Gormley
Founded: 1863
Science, technology & health, scholarly & trade books.
ISBN Prefix(es): 0-309
Number of titles published annually: 175 Print
Total Titles: 3,500 Print; 1,000 E-Book
Imprints: Joseph Henry Press
Foreign Office(s): Cumnor Hill, 12 Hid's Copse Rd, Oxford 0X2 9JJ, United Kingdom
Foreign Rep(s): Durnell Marketing Ltd (Europe); Footprint Books Pty Ltd (Australia & New Zealand); Kinokuniya (Japan); Maruzen Co Ltd (Japan); Quantum (UK)
Warehouse: 8700 Jericho City Dr, Landover, MD 20785
Membership(s): AAP

National Association of Broadcasters (NAB)
1771 "N" St NW, Washington, DC 20036
Tel: 202-429-5300 *Toll Free Tel:* 800-368-5644
Fax: 202-775-3515
Web Site: www.nab.org
Key Personnel
Pres & CEO: Edward O Fritts
Trade association representing radio & television stations & companies that serve the broadcasting industry.
ISBN Prefix(es): 0-89324
Number of titles published annually: 15 Print
Total Titles: 71 Print
Distributed by Allyn & Bacon; Lawrence Erlbaum Assoc; Focal Press; Macmillan Publishing Co; Tab Books; Wadsworth Inc

§National Association of Insurance Commissioners
2301 McGee, Suite 800, Kansas City, MO 64108
Tel: 816-842-3600; 816-783-8300 (Pubns)
Fax: 816-471-7004
Web Site: www.naic.org

Key Personnel
Publg Mgr: Bill Maher
Ed: Karen Montalto
Founded: 1871
ISBN Prefix(es): 0-89382
Number of titles published annually: 150 Print
Total Titles: 356 Print; 4 Online; 4 E-Book
Branch Office(s)
NAIC Hall of States, Washington, DC 20001-1512, Dir: David Wetmore *Fax:* 202-624-8579
Securities Valuation Office, 195 Broadway, New York, NY 10007-0007, Acting Dir: Robert Carcano *Fax:* 212-285-0073

National Association of Secondary School Principals
1904 Association Dr, Reston, VA 20191
Tel: 703-860-0200 *Toll Free Tel:* 800-253-7746
Fax: 703-476-5432
Web Site: www.principals.org
Founded: 1916
Journals, magazines, monographs, newsletters, videos & software.
ISBN Prefix(es): 0-88210
Number of titles published annually: 5 Print
Total Titles: 69 Print
Imprints: NASSP
Advertising Agency: Publishers Associates

NASW PRESS

National Association of Social Workers (NASW)
750 First St NE, Suite 700, Washington, DC 20002-4241
SAN: 202-893X
Tel: 301-317-8688 *Toll Free Tel:* 800-227-3590
Fax: 301-206-7989
E-mail: nasw@pmds.com
Web Site: www.socialworkers.org
Key Personnel
Publr: Cheryl Bradley
Man Ed & ISBN Contact: Paula Delo
Mktg Mgr: Beth Ledford
Abstracts Mgr: Alfredda Payne
Sr Ed: Marcia Roman
Founded: 1955
Professional & scholarly books & journals in the social sciences.
ISBN Prefix(es): 0-87101
Total Titles: 80 Print; 5 Online; 6 Audio
Foreign Rep(s): Gazelle Book Services (Europe)
Distribution Center: PMDS, PO Box 431, Annapolis Junction, MD 20701-0431 *Toll Free Tel:* 800-227-3590 *Fax:* 301-206-7989 *E-mail:* nasw@pmds.com *Web Site:* www.naswpress.org

National Book Co
Division of Educational Research Associates
PO Box 8795, Portland, OR 97207-8795
SAN: 212-4661
Tel: 503-228-6345 *Fax:* 810-885-5811
E-mail: info@eralearning.com
Web Site: www.eralearning.com
Key Personnel
Chmn of the Bd & Pres: Carl W Salser
VP, Halcyon House: Vernon S White
VP, SE Reg: Richard R Gallagher
Sci Ed, Dir, Spec Materials & ISBN Contact: Mark R Salser
Compt: Kerry L Erickson
Prodn Mgr: Ward J Stroud
Shipping Mgr: Sandor Mayer
Founded: 1960

Individualized mastery learning programs for elementary, secondary & college levels, consisting of multimedia materials in business education, home economics, language skills, mathematics, science, shorthand skills, social studies, general & vocational education; special trade publications, particularly in subjects relating to education. Computer software; reference books; Black/Afro-American history; English as a second language.
ISBN Prefix(es): 0-89420
Number of titles published annually: 25 Print
Total Titles: 175 Print; 100 Audio
Imprints: Halcyon House

National Braille Press
88 Saint Stephen St, Boston, MA 02115
SAN: 273-0944
Tel: 617-266-6160 *Toll Free Tel:* 800-548-7323 (cust serv) *Fax:* 617-437-0456
E-mail: orders@nbp.org
Web Site: www.nbp.org
Key Personnel
Man Dir: William M Raeder *E-mail:* braeder@nbp.org
Dir, Mktg: Diane Croft *E-mail:* dcroft@nbp.org
Mktg Mgr: Tony Grima *E-mail:* agrima@nbp.org
Founded: 1929
Braille books & magazines.
ISBN Prefix(es): 0-939173
Number of titles published annually: 30 Print; 5 E-Book; 5 Audio
Total Titles: 50 Print; 1 CD-ROM; 14 E-Book; 12 Audio
Distributed by Library of Congress

National Bureau of Economic Research Inc
1050 Massachusetts Ave, Cambridge, MA 02138-5398
SAN: 203-7114
Tel: 617-868-3900 *Fax:* 617-868-2742
E-mail: op@nber.org
Web Site: www.nber.org
Key Personnel
Chmn & Dir-at-Large: Carl F Christ
VChmn & Dir-at-Large: Kathleen B Cooper
Pres, CEO & Dir-at-Large: Martin Feldstein, PhD
Treas: Robert Mednick
Dir-at-Large: Peter C Aldrich; Elizabeth E Bailey; John H Biggs; Andrew Brimmer; Don R Conlan; George C Eads; Steven Friedman; George Hatsopoulos; Karen N Horn; Judy C Lewent; John Lipsky; Michael H Moskow; Rudolph A Oswald; Robert T Parry; Peter G Peterson; Richard N Rosett; Kathleen P Utgoff; Marina V N Whitman; Martin B Zimmerman
Corp Sec: Susan Colligan
Cont & Asst Corp Sec: Kelly Horak
Asst Corp Sec: Gerardine Johnson
Public Info: Donna Zorwitz
Founded: 1920
Economics.
ISBN Prefix(es): 0-87014
Number of titles published annually: 550 Print; 550 Online
Total Titles: 10,000 Print; 2,500 Online
Distributed by Ballinger Publishing Co; Columbia University Press; MIT Press; Princeton University Press; University Microfilms International; University of Chicago Press

National Catholic Educational Association
1077 30 St NW, Suite 100, Washington, DC 20007-3852
Tel: 202-337-6232 *Fax:* 202-333-6706
Web Site: www.ncea.org
Key Personnel
Pres: Michael Guerra
Ed, Momentum: Brian Gray
Nonfiction: educational trends, methodology, innovative programs, teacher education & inservice, research, technology, financial & pub-

lic relations programs, management systems all applicable to nonpublic education.
ISBN Prefix(es): 1-55833
Number of titles published annually: 20 Print
Total Titles: 200 Print

§National Center for Children in Poverty
Division of Columbia University School of Public Health
215 W 125 St, 3rd fl, New York, NY 10027
Tel: 646-284-9600 *Fax:* 646-284-9623
E-mail: nccp@columbia.edu
Web Site: www.nccp.org
Key Personnel
Interim Dir, Communs & Pubns: Jane Knitzer
Dir: J Lawrence Aber
Mgr, Pubns & Info Resources: Carole Oshinsky
Founded: 1989
Nonprofit publisher of monographs, reports, statistical updates, working papers & issue briefs concerning children under six who live in poverty in the US. Topics cover impact of poverty on child health & development; statistical profiles of poor children & their families; research programs on the effects of poverty; research on policies that could reduce the young child poverty rate; integrated social & human services (private & public) for low-income families. Welfare reform & children, research forum on children, families & the new federalism.
ISBN Prefix(es): 0-926582
Number of titles published annually: 24 Print
Total Titles: 40 Print; 20 E-Book

National Center For Employee Ownership (NCEO)
1736 Franklin St, 8th fl, Oakland, CA 94612-3445
Tel: 510-208-1300 *Fax:* 510-272-9510
E-mail: nceo@nceo.org
Web Site: www.nceo.org
Key Personnel
Exec Dir: Corey Rosen *E-mail:* crosen@nceo.org
Founded: 1981
Employee ownership books, pamphlets & newsletter.
ISBN Prefix(es): 0-926902
Number of titles published annually: 15 Print
Total Titles: 50 Print

National Conference of State Legislatures
7700 E First Place, Denver, CO 80230
Tel: 303-364-7700 *Fax:* 303-364-7812
E-mail: books@ncsl.org
Web Site: www.ncsl.org
Key Personnel
Exec Dir: William Pound
Dir, Pubns: Karen Hansen
Cust Serv Mgr: Rita Morris
Founded: 1975
Books, magazines & series of papers, periodicals & report survey.
ISBN Prefix(es): 1-55516; 1-58024
Number of titles published annually: 30 Print
Total Titles: 330 Print

National Council of Teachers of English (NCTE)
1111 W Kenyon Rd, Urbana, IL 61801-1096
SAN: 202-9049
Tel: 217-328-3870 *Toll Free Tel:* 800-369-6283; 877-369-6283 (cust serv) *Fax:* 217-328-0977
E-mail: orders@ncte.org
Web Site: www.ncte.org
Key Personnel
Man Ed: Kurt Austin *Tel:* 217-278-3619
    Fax: 217-328-0977 *E-mail:* kaustin@ncte.org
Exec Dir: Kent Williamson *Tel:* 217-278-3601
    Fax: 217-328-0977

Dir, Book Publications & Sr Ed: Zarina M Hock
    Tel: 217-278-3616 *Fax:* 217-328-0977
    E-mail: zhock@ncte.org
Ed: Bonny Graham *Tel:* 217-278-3618 *Fax:* 217-328-0977 *E-mail:* bgraham@ncte.org
Prodn Mgr: Patricia Austin *Tel:* 217-278-3664
    Fax: 217-328-3762 *E-mail:* paustin@ncte.org
Perms: Barbara Lamar *Tel:* 217-278-3621
    Fax: 217-328-0977 *E-mail:* blamar@ncte.org
Books Prog Asst: Kim Black *Tel:* 217-278-3620
    E-mail: kblack@ncte.org
Founded: 1911
Nonprofit professional association of educators in English Studies, Literacy & Language Arts. Specialize in the teaching of English & the language arts at all grade levels; research reports; guidelines & position statements; journals.
ISBN Prefix(es): 0-8141
Number of titles published annually: 15 Print
Total Titles: 240 Print; 1 CD-ROM

§National Council of Teachers of Mathematics
1906 Association Dr, Reston, VA 20191-1502
SAN: 202-9057
Tel: 703-620-9840 *Toll Free Tel:* 800-235-7566
    Fax: 703-476-2970
E-mail: orders@nctm.org
Web Site: www.nctm.org
Key Personnel
Pres: Cathy L Seeley
Exec Dir: Jim Rubillo
Dir, Pubns: Harry B Tunis
Pubns Mgr: Nancy Busse
Founded: 1920
Professional publications, including books (printed & online), monographs & yearbooks. Members include individuals, institutions, students, teachers & educators. Multiyear plans available to individual & institutional members.
ISBN Prefix(es): 0-87353
Number of titles published annually: 15 Print
Total Titles: 200 Print
Distributed by Eric Armin Inc Education Ctr; Delta Education; Didax Educational Resources; Educators Outlet; ETA Cuisenaire; Lakeshore Learning Materials; NASCO; Spectrum

National Council on Radiation Protection & Measurements (NCRP)
7910 Woodmont Ave, Suite 400, Bethesda, MD 20814
Tel: 301-657-2652 *Toll Free Tel:* 800-229-2652
    Fax: 301-907-8768
E-mail: ncrp@ncrp.com
Web Site: www.ncrp.com
Key Personnel
Pres: Thomas Tenforde
Exec Dir: David A Schauer
Founded: 1928
NCRP reports, statements, proceedings, commentaries, news; Taylor lectures.
ISBN Prefix(es): 0-913392; 0-929600
Number of titles published annually: 5 Print
Total Titles: 150 Print

National Crime Prevention Council
1000 Connecticut Ave NW, 13th fl, Washington, DC 20036-5325
Tel: 202-466-6272 *Toll Free Tel:* 800-627-2911 (orders only) *Fax:* 202-296-1356
Web Site: www.ncpc.org
Key Personnel
Pres: Alfonso Lenhardt
Dir, Pubns: Judy Kirby *E-mail:* kirby@ncpc.org
Founded: 1982
Crime prevention publications, training & technical assistance; McGruff public service advertising campaign, conferences & on-site training & technical assistance.
ISBN Prefix(es): 0-934513; 1-929888
Number of titles published annually: 5 Print

Total Titles: 90 Print
Shipping Address: NCPC Fulfillment Ctr, 100 Church St, PO Box 1, Amsterdam, NY 12010
Toll Free Tel: 800-627-2911

National Education Association (NEA)
1201 16 St NW, Washington, DC 20036
SAN: 203-7262
Tel: 202-833-4000; 202-822-7207 (ed office)
    Fax: 202-822-7206
Web Site: www.nea.org *Cable:* EDUCATION
Key Personnel
Exec Dir: John Wilson
Mgr, NEA Member Pubns: Marilyn Milloy
Founded: 1857
Professional development publications for K-12 & higher education & AV materials for educators. Website with resources & general information for educators & the general public.
ISBN Prefix(es): 0-8106
Number of titles published annually: 10 Print; 2 CD-ROM; 2 Online
Total Titles: 189 Print; 2 CD-ROM; 9 Online
Imprints: NEA Professional Library

§National Gallery of Art
Fourth St & Constitution Ave, Landover, MD 20565
Tel: 202-842-6200 *Fax:* 202-408-8530
Web Site: www.nga.gov
Key Personnel
Ed-in-Chief: Judy Metro
Sr Ed: Karen Sagstetter
Prodn Mgr: Chris Vogel
Web Mgr: Phyllis Hecht
Design Mgr: Margaret Bauer
Founded: 1941
Exhibition catalogues, catalogues of the collection & scholarly monographs.
ISBN Prefix(es): 0-89468
Number of titles published annually: 12 Print
Total Titles: 100 Print; 2 CD-ROM; 1 Online
Distributed by Abrams; Bulfinch/Little; Cambridge University Press; Hudson Hills; Lund Humphries/Ashgate; OAP; Princeton University Press; Thames & Hudson; Yale University Press

National Geographic Books
Division of National Geographic Society
1145 17 St NW, Washington, DC 20036
Tel: 202-857-7000 *Fax:* 202-857-7670
Web Site: www.nationalgeographics.com
Key Personnel
Pres, Books & Educ Publg & Exec VP, NGS: Nina Hoffman *E-mail:* nhoffman@ngs.org
Pres, Children's Books & Educ Publg Group: Ericka Markman *E-mail:* emarkman@ngs.org
VP & Ed-in-Chief, Natl Geographic Books: Kevin Mulroy *E-mail:* kmulroy@ngs.org
VP, Retail & Spec Sales, Natl Geographic Books: Linda Howey *E-mail:* lhowey@ngs.org
VP & Ed-in-Chief, Natl Geographic Children's Books: Nancy Laties Feresten *E-mail:* nfereste@ngs.org
Sr VP, Busn Mgmt, Books & Educ Publg: Hector Sierra *E-mail:* hsierra@ngs.org
Dir, Fin & Opers, Children's Books & Educ Publg Group: Jody Giblin *E-mail:* jgiblin@ngs.org
Founded: 1888
Nonfiction general reference, travel & photography. children's nonfiction with emphasis on library market.
ISBN Prefix(es): 0-7922; 0-87044
Number of titles published annually: 120 Print
Total Titles: 700 Print
Imprints: National Geographic Adventure Classics; National Geographic Adventure Press; National Geographic Books; National Geographic Children's Books; National Geographic Directions

Distributed by Hi Marketing (UK); Simon & Schuster (adult & children's titles, US & other markets)
Membership(s): AAP

National Geographic Society
1145 17 St NW, Washington, DC 20036
SAN: 202-8956
Tel: 202-857-7000 *Fax:* 202-429-5727
Web Site: www.nationalgeographic.com *Cable:* NATGEOSOC WASHINGTON
Key Personnel
Pres & CEO: John Fahey
VP & Dir, Book Div: Kevin Mulroy
Pres, Books & Exec VP: Nina Hoffman
Pres, Magazines: Robert B Sims
Sr VP, TV: Timothy T Kelly
Ed: William L Allen
Intl Rts: Robert Hernandez
Founded: 1888
Books for adults; nonfiction.
ISBN Prefix(es): 0-87044
Number of titles published annually: 75 Print
Total Titles: 450 Print
Distributed by Simon & Schuster
Membership(s): AAP; Children's Book Council
See separate listing for:
National Geographic Books

§National Golf Foundation
1150 S US Hwy One, Suite 401, Jupiter, FL 33477
Tel: 561-744-6006 *Toll Free Tel:* 800-733-6006
Fax: 561-744-6107
E-mail: ngf@ngf.org
Web Site: www.ngf.org
Key Personnel
Mktg Mgr: Jennifer Amos
Founded: 1936
Premier publisher of research & information for the business of golf. Over 200 publications are offered on golf consumer research, industry & market trends, golf facility development & operations, golf range development, instruction & player development.
ISBN Prefix(es): 0-9638647; 1-57701
Number of titles published annually: 5 Print
Total Titles: 110 Print; 1 CD-ROM; 1 Online; 1 Audio

National Information Services Corp (NISC)
Wyman Towers, 3100 Saint Paul St, Baltimore, MD 21218
Tel: 410-243-0797 *Fax:* 410-243-0982
E-mail: info@nisc.com; editor@nisc.com (comments); sales@nisc.com (sales); support@nisc.com (cust support)
Web Site: www.nisc.com
Key Personnel
Directories Mgr: Debbie Durr
Founded: 1988
Specialize in abstract & indexing services of huge databases covering various disciplines on Internet & CD-ROM online databases.
Number of titles published annually: 3 Online
Total Titles: 2 Print
Foreign Office(s): NISC SAARC, S-1, Ballad Estates, Saint Ann's School Rd, Tarnaka, Hyderabad, 500 017 Andhra Pradesh, India, Man Dir: Sarath Modali *Tel:* (040) 7001517 *Fax:* (040) 7002538 *E-mail:* sales@nisc.co.in *Web Site:* www.nisc.co.in
NISC South Africa, 19 Worcester St, Grahamstown 6139, South Africa, Man Dir: Margaret Crampton *Tel:* (046) 6229698 *Fax:* (046) 6229550 *E-mail:* sales@nisc.co.za *Web Site:* www.nisc.co.za

National Information Standards Organization
4733 Bethesda Ave, Suite 300, Bethesda, MD 20814
Tel: 301-654-2512 *Fax:* 301-654-1721

E-mail: nisohq@niso.org
Web Site: www.niso.org
Key Personnel
Exec Dir: Patricia Harris
Maintain & develop technical standards for libraries, publishers & information services.
ISBN Prefix(es): 1-880124
Number of titles published annually: 5 Print
Total Titles: 35 Print
Distributor for Niso Press

National Institute for Trial Advocacy
Affiliate of Notre Dame Law School
University of Notre Dame, Notre Dame, IN 46556-6500
Mailing Address: 53550 Generations Dr, South Bend, IN 46635
Tel: 574-271-8370 *Toll Free Tel:* 800-225-6482
Fax: 574-271-8375
E-mail: nita.1@nd.edu
Web Site: www.nita.org
Key Personnel
COO: Raymond M White
Founded: 1970
Legal & litigation training.
ISBN Prefix(es): 1-55681
Number of titles published annually: 40 Print; 1 CD-ROM
Total Titles: 350 Print; 2 CD-ROM; 12 Audio

National League of Cities
1301 Pennsylvania Ave NW, Washington, DC 20004-1763
Tel: 202-626-3000 *Fax:* 202-626-3043
Web Site: www.nlc.org
Key Personnel
Dir, Center for Member Progs: Cathy Spain
Mktg Assoc: Mae Davis *E-mail:* mdavis@nlc.org
Founded: 1924
ISBN Prefix(es): 0-933729; 1-886152
Number of titles published annually: 5 Print
Total Titles: 90 Print; 1 CD-ROM
See separate listing for:
Michigan Municipal League

National Learning Corp
212 Michael Dr, Syosset, NY 11791
SAN: 206-8869
Tel: 516-921-8888 *Toll Free Tel:* 800-645-6337
Fax: 516-921-8743
Web Site: www.passbooks.com
Key Personnel
Pres & Ed-in-Chief: Michael P Rudman
VP: Frances Rudman
Rts & Perms: John Ryan
Founded: 1967
Basic competency tests for college, high school & occupations; functional literacy; career, general, vocational & technical, adult & continuing, special, cooperative & community education; professional licensure; test preparation books for civil service, postal service, government careers, armed forces, high school & college equivalency; college, graduate & professional school enhancement; certification & licensing in engineering & technical careers, teaching, law, dentistry, medicine & allied health professions.
ISBN Prefix(es): 0-8373
Number of titles published annually: 3 Print
Total Titles: 5,000 Print
Imprints: ACT Proficiency Examination Program; Admission Test Series; Career Examination Series; Certified Nurse Series (CN); College Level Examination Series; College Proficiency Examination Series; Dante Series; Graduate Record Examination Series; National Teacher Examination Series; Occupational Competency Examination Series; Passbooks; Regents External Degree Series; Teachers License Examination Series; Test Your Knowledge Books;

Undergraduate Program Field Test Series; What Do You Know About Books
Subsidiaries: Delaney Books Inc; Frank Merriwell Inc
Membership(s): AAP

The National Museum of Women in the Arts
1250 New York Ave NW, Washington, DC 20005
Tel: 202-783-5000 *Toll Free Tel:* 800-222-7270
Fax: 202-393-3234
Web Site: www.nmwa.org
Key Personnel
Dir: Dr Judy L Larson
Dir, Pubns: Sarah Stump
Dir, Retail Opers: Linda Marks
Founded: 1981
Art catalogs, magazine (4/yr) & exhibition brochures.
ISBN Prefix(es): 0-940979
Number of titles published annually: 2 Print
Total Titles: 10 Print
Distributed by Northeastern University Press; University of Washington Press

National Notary Association
9350 De Soto Ave, Chatsworth, CA 91311
Mailing Address: PO Box 2402, Chatsworth, CA 91313-2402
Tel: 818-739-4000 *Toll Free Tel:* 800-876-6827
Fax: 818-700-0920
E-mail: nna@nationalnotary.org
Web Site: www.nationalnotary.org
Key Personnel
Pres & Intl Rts: Milton G Valera
Educ Prog Mgr: Stacy Peterson
Founded: 1957
Publish books, periodical, videos, seminars.
ISBN Prefix(es): 0-9600158; 0-933134; 1-891133
Number of titles published annually: 15 Print
Total Titles: 40 Print

National Park Service Media Production
Subsidiary of US Department of the Interior
Harpers Ferry Ctr, Harpers Ferry, WV 25425
Mailing Address: PO Box 50, Harpers Ferry, WV 25425-0050
Tel: 304-535-6018 *Fax:* 304-535-6144
Web Site: www.nps.gov/hfc
Key Personnel
Printing Specialist: Donna Huffer
Founded: 1965
Official National Park Service, handbooks, maps & brochures.
ISBN Prefix(es): 0-912627
Number of titles published annually: 3 Print
Total Titles: 43 Print
Warehouse: US Govt Printing Office, Superintendent of Documents, Washington, DC 20402

National Publishing Co
Subsidiary of Courier Corp
11311 Roosevelt Blvd, Philadelphia, PA 19154-2105
Mailing Address: PO Box 16234, Philadelphia, PA 19114-0234
Tel: 215-676-1863 *Toll Free Tel:* 888-333-1863
Fax: 215-673-8069
Web Site: www.courier.com
Key Personnel
Chmn & CEO: George Q Nichols
Acting Pres & Exec VP: Peter Tobin
E-mail: ptobin@courier.com
Dir, Sales & Servs: Mike Lorusso
Opers Mgr: Rob Chilton
Founded: 1863
Publish Bibles & Testaments (King James Version); foreign language scriptures.
ISBN Prefix(es): 0-8340
Number of titles published annually: 3 Print
Total Titles: 65 Print
Distributed by Broadman & Holman Publishers

Membership(s): AAP; BISG; BMI; Christian Booksellers Association; Evangelical Christian Publishers Association; National Bible Association

National Register Publishing
562 Central Ave, New Providence, NJ 07974
Tel: 908-673-1001 *Toll Free Tel:* 800-473-7020
 Fax: 909-673-1189
Web Site: www.nationalregisterpub.com
Key Personnel
CEO: Gene McGovern
Sr Man Dir: Fred Marks
Sr Dir, Sales: Susan Towne
Founded: 1915
Publisher of business information directories available in print, online & tape for commercial & reference use. Titles include *American Art Directory, Co-op Advertising Source Directory, Corporate Finance Sourcebook, Direct Marketing Market Place,* Official Catholic Directory & *Official Museum Directory.*
ISBN Prefix(es): 0-87217
Number of titles published annually: 6 Print

National Resource Center for Youth Services (NRCYS)
Division of University of Oklahoma-Outreach
Schusterman Center, 4502 E 41 St, Bldg 4W, Tulsa, OK 74135-2512
Tel: 918-660-3700 *Toll Free Tel:* 800-274-2687
 Fax: 918-660-3737
Web Site: www.nrcys.ou.edu
Key Personnel
Dir: Peter R Correia, III
Mktg Mgr: Rhoda Baker *E-mail:* rbaker@ou.edu
Asst Dir: Dorothy I Ansell; Teressa Kaemmerling; Kristi Charles
Founded: 1985
Curricula & resource manuals for professionals & volunteers who work with foster care & at-risk teenagers.
ISBN Prefix(es): 1-878848
Number of titles published annually: 3 Print
Total Titles: 20 Print

National Science Teachers Association (NSTA)
1840 Wilson Blvd, Arlington, VA 22201-3000
Tel: 703-243-7100 *Toll Free Tel:* 800-722-NSTA (sales) *Fax:* 703-243-7177
Web Site: www.nsta.org
Key Personnel
Assoc Exec Dir & Publr: David Beacom
 Tel: 703-312-9207 *Fax:* 703-526-9754
 E-mail: dbeacom@nsta.org
Founded: 1944
Periodicals & books.
ISBN Prefix(es): 0-87355
Number of titles published annually: 12 Print; 1 CD-ROM
Total Titles: 100 Print; 3 CD-ROM
Membership(s): AAP

National Underwriter Co
5081 Olympic Blvd, Erlanger, KY 41018
Tel: 859-692-2100 *Toll Free Tel:* 800-543-0874
 Fax: 859-692-2289
E-mail: customerservice@nuco.com
Web Site: www.nationalunderwriter.com
Key Personnel
Dir, Mktg: Christine Oldenbrook
Founded: 1897
ISBN Prefix(es): 0-87218
Number of titles published annually: 3 Print
Total Titles: 15 Print
Branch Office(s)
43-47 Newark St, Hoboken, NJ 07030 (Newsmagazine office)

Native American Book Publishers
PO Box 510, Hamburg, MI 48139-0510

Tel: 810-231-3728 *Fax:* 810-231-3728
Founded: 1989
Reprints of books on Native Americans.
ISBN Prefix(es): 1-878592
Number of titles published annually: 20 Print
Total Titles: 34 Print

Naturegraph Publishers Inc
3543 Indian Creek Rd, Happy Camp, CA 96039
SAN: 220-9217
Mailing Address: PO Box 1047, Happy Camp, CA 96039
Tel: 530-493-5353 *Toll Free Tel:* 800-390-5353
 Fax: 530-493-5240
E-mail: nature@sisqtel.net
Web Site: www.naturegraph.com
Key Personnel
Owner, Pres & Ed, Rts & Perms: Barbara Brown
Electronic Publg: Albert Vanderhoof
Founded: 1946
ISBN Prefix(es): 0-911010; 0-87961
Number of titles published annually: 3 Print
Total Titles: 110 Print; 5 E-Book
Distributed by Dakota West Books; Gem Guides Book Co; Treasure Chest Books; Maverick; Museum Products; New Leaf; Partners West; Sunbelt; Bahai Distribution Service
Foreign Rights: International Titles
Membership(s): ABA; Publishers Marketing Association

The Nautical & Aviation Publishing Co of America Inc
2055 Middleburg Lane, Mount Pleasant, SC 29464
SAN: 213-3431
Tel: 843-856-0561 *Fax:* 843-856-3164
E-mail: nauticalaviationpublishing@att.net
Web Site: www.nauticalaviation.com
Key Personnel
Pres: Jan W Snouck-Hurgronje
Founded: 1979
Military history & aviation.
ISBN Prefix(es): 1-877853; 0-933852
Number of titles published annually: 10 Print; 2 Audio
Total Titles: 94 Print; 2 Audio
Imprints: N & A
Warehouse: 1741 Allied St, Charlottesville, VA 22903

§Naval Institute Press
Division of US Naval Institute
291 Wood Rd, Annapolis, MD 21402-5034
SAN: 202-9006
Tel: 410-268-6110 *Toll Free Tel:* 800-233-8764
 Fax: 410-295-1084; 410-571-1703 (customer service)
E-mail: webmaster@navalinstitute.org; customer@navalinstitute.org (cust serv)
Web Site: www.navalinstitute.org *Telex:* 18-7114 ACI PHX
Key Personnel
CEO & Publr: Thomas Wilkerson
Press Dir: Mark Gatlin
Exec Ed: Paul Wilderson
Web Administrator: Matt Brook
Edit Mgr: Linda O Doughda
Art Dir: Jim Bricker
Mfg Supv: Charles E Vance
Sales & Mktg Mgr: Tom Harnish
Publicity Mgr: Susan Artigiani *Tel:* 410-295-1081
 E-mail: sartigiani@usni.org
Photo Archivist & Lib Servs Mgr: Dewitt Roseborough
Cust Servs Mgr: Debbie Wienecke
ISBN Contact: Peggy Wooldridge
Intl Rts: Susan T Brook
Founded: 1873
Naval & maritime subjects: professional, biography, science, history, ship & aviation references, US Naval Institute magazines; literature.

ISBN Prefix(es): 0-87021; 1-55750; 1-59114
Number of titles published annually: 80 Print
Total Titles: 1,000 Print; 1 CD-ROM; 9 Audio
Foreign Rep(s): Greenhill Books (Caribbean, Europe, India, Middle East, Pacific Region, South Africa); Peribo Pty Ltd (Australia, New Zealand, Papua New Guinea); Vanwell Publishing Ltd (Canada)
Advertising Agency: Donovan/Burke Inc, 230 Park Ave, Suite 1509, New York, NY 10169
 Tel: 212-682-1421 *E-mail:* advdpt@aol.com
Warehouse: US Naval Institute, 2062 Generals Hwy, Annapolis, MD 21401 *Tel:* 410-224-3378
 Fax: 410-571-1703
Membership(s): Association of American University Presses

NavPress Publishing Group
Division of The Navigators
3820 N 30 St, Colorado Springs, CO 80904
SAN: 211-5352
Mailing Address: PO Box 6000, Colorado Springs, CO 80934-6000
Tel: 719-548-9222 *Toll Free Tel:* 800-366-7788
 Fax: 719-260-7223 *Toll Free Fax:* 800-343-3902
Web Site: www.navpress.com
Key Personnel
Publr: Kent Wilson
Edit Dir: Dan Rich
Author Rel: Lisa Marshall
Sales & Trade Mktg Dir: Sarah Snelling
Founded: 1975
Paperbacks, mass market & trade, hardcovers, periodicals; religious (Protestant) materials, video.
ISBN Prefix(es): 0-89109; 1-57683
Number of titles published annually: 45 Print
Total Titles: 380 Print; 2 Audio
Imprints: NavPress; Pinon Press

NBM Publishing Inc
555 Eighth Ave, Suite 1202, New York, NY 10018
SAN: 210-0835
Tel: 212-643-5407 *Toll Free Tel:* 800-886-1223
 Fax: 212-643-1545
E-mail: admin@nbmpub.com
Web Site: www.nbmpub.com
Key Personnel
Pres & Publr: Terry Nantier *E-mail:* tnantier@nbmpub.com
Compt: May Wong
Founded: 1976
Graphic novels.
ISBN Prefix(es): 0-918348; 1-56163
Number of titles published annually: 30 Print
Total Titles: 200 Print
Imprints: Amerotica; ComicsLit; Eurotica
Distributor for Plymptoon Books
Foreign Rights: Isaac Pradel Leal (Spain)
Warehouse: Whitehurst & Clark, 1200 Rte 523, Flemington, NJ 08822, Contact: Brad Searles
 Tel: 908-782-2323 *Fax:* 908-782-5013
Membership(s): Children's Book Council; Publishers Marketing Association

§NCCLS
940 W Valley Rd, Suite 1400, Wayne, PA 19087-1898
Tel: 610-688-0100 *Fax:* 610-688-0700
E-mail: exoffice@nccls.org
Web Site: www.nccls.org
Key Personnel
Ed: Donna Wilhelm
Dir, Publns Servs: Colleen Bergan
Asst Exec Dir, Mktg: Louise A Ciccarelli
 E-mail: louisec@nccls.org
Asst Exec Dir, Quality & Educ: Jennifer McGeary
Founded: 1968

Voluntary consensus standards & guidelines for medical testing & in vitro diagnostic products & healthcare services.
ISBN Prefix(es): 1-56238
Number of titles published annually: 3 Print
Total Titles: 164 Print

NCRP, see National Council on Radiation Protection & Measurements (NCRP)

§Neal-Schuman Publishers Inc
100 William St, Suite 2004, New York, NY 10038
SAN: 210-2455
Tel: 212-925-8650 *Toll Free Tel:* 866-672-6657
Toll Free Fax: 866-209-7932
E-mail: orders@neal-schuman.com
Web Site: www.neal-schuman.com
Key Personnel
Pres: Patricia Glass Schuman
VP & ISBN Contact: John Vincent Neal
Dir, Publg: Charles T Harmon *E-mail:* charles@neal-schuman.com
Sales & Opers Mgr: Michelle Rivera Rodriguez *E-mail:* michelle@neal-schuman.com
Devt Ed: Michael G Kelley *E-mail:* michael@neal-schuman.com
Asst Dir, Publg: Miguel A Figueroa *E-mail:* miguel@neal-schuman.com
Founded: 1976
How-to manuals, technology, library & information science texts.
ISBN Prefix(es): 0-918212; 1-55570
Number of titles published annually: 30 Print
Total Titles: 300 Print; 25 CD-ROM
Foreign Office(s): 3 Henrietta St, London WC2E 8LU, United Kingdom
Distributor for Facet

Foreign Rep(s): DA Books Pty Ltd (Australia, New Zealand)
Foreign Rights: Eurospan (Europe & UK)
Warehouse: 1200 County Rd, Rte 523, Flemington, NJ 08822
Membership(s): ALA

E T Nedder Publishing
Subsidiary of Kan Distributing
9121 E Tanque Verde, Suite 105, PMB 299, Tucson, AZ 85749-8390
Tel: 520-760-2742 *Toll Free Tel:* 877-817-2742
Fax: 520-760-5883
E-mail: enedder@hotmail.com
Web Site: nedderpublishing.com
Key Personnel
Publr: Ernie Nedder *E-mail:* ernie@nedder.com
CFO: Kathy Nedder *E-mail:* kathynedder@hotmail.com
Edit Dir: Kate Harrison
Theological Ed: Rev Thomas Santa
Founded: 1999
Publisher of religious education materials. Reproducible activity books, books on Saints & adult books. Mainly publisher for the Catholic market but also does custom publishing. Religious music both books & CDs.
ISBN Prefix(es): 1-893757
Number of titles published annually: 10 Print
Total Titles: 45 Print
Returns: 526 E 16 St, Tucson, AZ 85701-2861
Tel: 526-798-1530 *Toll Free Tel:* 800-795-1513
Warehouse: 526 E 16 St, Tucson, AZ 85701-2861
Tel: 526-798-1530 *Toll Free Tel:* 800-795-1513
Distribution Center: 526 E 16 St, Tucson, AZ 85701-2861 *Tel:* 526-798-1530 *Toll Free Tel:* 800-795-1513

Neibauer Press
Division of Louis Neibauer Co Inc
20 Industrial Dr, Warminster, PA 18974
Tel: 215-322-6200 *Toll Free Tel:* 800-322-6203
Fax: 215-322-2495
E-mail: sales@neibauer.com
Web Site: www.churchstewardship.com
Key Personnel
Pres: Nathan Neibauer *E-mail:* nathan@neibauer.com
Founded: 1967
Church administration & stewardship; no fiction.
ISBN Prefix(es): 1-878259
Number of titles published annually: 5 Print
Total Titles: 30 Print

Nelson Information
Division of Thomson Financial Publishing
195 Broadway, 5th fl, New York, NY 10007
Mailing Address: PO Box 591, Port Chester, NY 10573-0591
Tel: 646-822-2000 *Toll Free Tel:* 888-371-4575; 888-280-4864 (orders) *Fax:* 914-937-8590
Web Site: www.nelsoninformation.com
Key Personnel
Acctg: Lisa Gambardella
Founded: 1974
Publish directories/databases of institutional investment market.
ISBN Prefix(es): 0-922460
Number of titles published annually: 6 Print
Total Titles: 5 Print

§Nemmar Real Estate Training
15 E Putnam Ave, Suite 151, Greenwich, CT 06830
Fax: 212-937-2122
E-mail: info@nemmar.com
Web Site: www.nemmar.com

Key Personnel
Pres: Guy Cozzi
Founded: 1988
Ranked as the most exclusive real estate appraiser training, home inspection training & real estate investor consulting service. Our real estate books, DVDs, CDs & videos are rated number one in their real estate categories nationwide. Our products have taught thousands of home buyers, sellers & real estate professionals worldwide.
ISBN Prefix(es): 1-887450
Number of titles published annually: 3 Print; 2 CD-ROM; 4 Online; 2 E-Book
Total Titles: 12 Print; 4 CD-ROM; 8 Online; 4 E-Book

§Neo-Tech Publishing
Affiliate of Neo-Tech International
PO Box 60906, Boulder City, NV 89006-0906
Tel: 702-293-5552 *Fax:* 702-293-4342
Web Site: www.neo-tech.com *Telex:* 750805
Key Personnel
Ed-in-Chief: John Flint
Ed: Mark Hamilton; Drew Ellis
Ed & Intl Rts: Eric Savage
Dir, Spec Projs & Lib Sales Dir: Gary Twitchell
Founded: 1968
Philosophical-based literature that collapses the 2000-year hoax of mysticism & neocheating in all areas of life. Publish books, consultant reports, newsletter, audio & video tapes, also produce art products & offer seminars. Reach market through direct mail & media advertising.
ISBN Prefix(es): 0-911752
Number of titles published annually: 5 Print
Total Titles: 20 Print; 5 CD-ROM; 5 E-Book; 5 Audio
Imprints: Black & White Publishing; Cosmic-World Publishing; Zon Association
Foreign Rights: Eric Savage (Hong Kong)
Advertising Agency: L Faire Associates

Neshui Publishing
2838 Cherokee, St Louis, MO 63118
Tel: 314-772-3090
E-mail: neshui62@hotmail.com
Key Personnel
Pres: Mr Neshui
Founded: 1995
Publisher of fiction & nonfiction books in all categories except poetry, cookbooks, children's or coffee table books, film & video. Send full ms with a SASE or your ms will be recycled. Reports promptly.
ISBN Prefix(es): 0-9652528; 1-931190
Number of titles published annually: 25 Print; 6 CD-ROM; 20 Online; 20 E-Book; 3 Audio
Total Titles: 100 Print; 15 CD-ROM; 10 Online; 20 E-Book; 3 Audio
Imprints: Neshui
Orders to: Baker & Taylor, TN
 E-mail: neshui62@hotmail.com
Returns: Baker & Taylor, TN *E-mail:* neshui62@hotmail.com
Shipping Address: Baker & Taylor, TN
 E-mail: neshui62@hotmail.com

Nevraumont Publishing Co
71 Broadway, New York, NY 10006
Tel: 212-425-3270 *Fax:* 212-425-1818
E-mail: nevpub@cs.com
Key Personnel
Pres & Intl Rts: Ann J Perrini
Publr: Peter N Nevraumont
Founded: 1989
Natural history.
ISBN Prefix(es): 0-945223
Number of titles published annually: 10 Print
Total Titles: 25 Print

Distributed by Abrams; Crown Publishing Group; Henry Holt; W W Norton & Co; Princeton University Press; University of California Press; John Wiley; Yale University Press
Foreign Rights: Birkhauser Verlag (Switzerland); Edicions Proa (Spain); Julio Einaudi (Italy); Hainan (China); Dina Livro (Portugal); Sejong (Korea); Selica Shobo (Japan); Shidosha (Japan); Spektrum (Germany); TusQuets (Spain); Weidenfeld & Nicolson (UK); Witwatersrand University Press (England); Jorge Zahar Ediciones (Brazil)

§New Age World Publishing
8345 NW 66 St, Suite 6344, Miami, FL 33166-2626
Tel: **305-735-8064** *Toll Free Fax:* **888-739-6129**
E-mail: **info@NAWPublishing.com**
Web Site: **www.NAWPublishing.com**
Key Personnel
Dir of Acqs: Steve Silver, PhD
Sr Exec Ed: Benjamin Gold, PhD
Founded: 1999
General publishing: fiction, nonfiction, religious, New Age; submission by disk preferred. Accept unsol ms; handle film rights. See www.nawpublishing.com for submission requirements. Also internet bookseller.
Number of titles published annually: 500 Print; 600 CD-ROM; 250 E-Book
Total Titles: 2,100 CD-ROM; 3,200 E-Book
Branch Office(s)
New York
Membership(s): AAP; ABA; Northern California Independent Booksellers Association; Publishers Marketing Association
See Ad in this Section and on Book Publishers Tab Side(s) 1 and in Literary Agents section(s)

New American Library, see NAL

New Century Books
213 Bay Club Dr, Santa Teresa, NM 88008
Mailing Address: PO Box 1205, Santa Teresa, NM 88008-1205
Tel: 505-589-1967 *Fax:* 505-589-1967
E-mail: newcentbks@elp.rr.com
Key Personnel
Publr, ISBN Contact & Rts & Perms: Thomas Fensch
Founded: 2000
Autobiographies, memoirs & biographies; "Top Secret" declassified government documents never before published; communication, culture, literature & mysteries; women's issues, Holocaust, Sports, government, WWII, Vietnam. All electronic, all titles are print-on-demand in hardcover or trade paperback, plus e-books. The Sharon Books imprint publishes in the areas of women's studies, parenting, women's memoirs, multi-cultural, hispanic, anything for an audience of women.
ISBN Prefix(es): 0-930751
Number of titles published annually: 10 Print; 10 E-Book
Total Titles: 30 Print; 30 E-Book
Imprints: Sharon's Books
Distribution Center: Ingrams, Ingram Blvd, La Vergne, TN 37086

New City Press
Division of Focolare Movement
202 Cardinal Rd, Hyde Park, NY 12538
SAN: 203-7335
Tel: 845-229-0335 *Toll Free Tel:* 800-462-5980 (orders only) *Fax:* 845-229-0351
E-mail: info@newcitypress.com
Web Site: www.newcitypress.com
Key Personnel
Gen Mgr & Intl Rts Contact: Gary Brandl
 E-mail: GaryBrandl@newcitypress.com
Busn Mgr: Debbie D'Anna
Founded: 1964
Spirituality, family life, biographies, theology, philosophy, patristics.
ISBN Prefix(es): 0-911782; 1-56548
Number of titles published annually: 12 Print
Total Titles: 135 Print
Imprints: NCP
Distributed by Riverside Distributors; Spring Arbor Distributors
Distributor for Ciudad Nueva (Spain/Argentina); New City (Great Britain)
Foreign Rep(s): Catholic Supplies (New Zealand); Examiner Bookshop (India); John Garratt Books (Australia); New City (China); New City (Philippines); New City (Ireland, England); Novalis (Canada); Preca Bookshop (Malta)

§New Concepts Publishing
5202 Humphreys Blvd, Lake Park, GA 31636
Tel: 229-257-0367 *Fax:* 229-219-1097
E-mail: newconcepts@newconceptspublishing.com
Web Site: www.newconceptspublishing.com
Key Personnel
Ed-in-Chief: Madris De Pasture *E-mail:* madris@newconceptspublishing.com
Founded: 1996
ISBN Prefix(es): 1-58608
Number of titles published annually: 60 Print; 240 CD-ROM; 240 E-Book
Total Titles: 240 Online

New Dimensions Publishing
11248 N 11 St, Phoenix, AZ 85020
Tel: 602-861-2631 *Toll Free Tel:* 800-736-7367 *Fax:* 602-944-1235
E-mail: info@thedream.com
Web Site: www.thedream.com
Key Personnel
Pres: Keith Varnum *E-mail:* keith@thedream.com
Founded: 1989
Book & audio tape publisher.
ISBN Prefix(es): 0-9722699
Number of titles published annually: 4 Print; 5 Audio
Total Titles: 6 Print; 5 Audio
Membership(s): Publishers Marketing Association; Small Publishers Association of North America

New Directions Publishing Corp
80 Eighth Ave, New York, NY 10011
SAN: 202-9081
Tel: 212-255-0230 *Toll Free Tel:* 800-233-4830 (PA) *Fax:* 212-255-0231
E-mail: newdirections@ndbooks.com
Web Site: www.ndpublishing.com *Cable:* NEWBOOKS NY
Key Personnel
Pres & Publr: Peggy L Fox *E-mail:* pfox@ndbooks.com
VP & Ed-in-Chief: Barbara Epler
 E-mail: bepler@ndbooks.com
Publicity Dir: Laurie Callahan *E-mail:* lcallahan@ndbooks.com
Prodn Mgr: Daniel J Allman *E-mail:* dallman@ndbooks.com
Perms Mgr: Dennis O Palmore
 E-mail: dpalmore@ndbooks.com

Founded: 1936
Modern literature, poetry, criticism & belles lettres.
ISBN Prefix(es): 0-8112
Number of titles published annually: 30 Print
Total Titles: 900 Print
Distributed by W W Norton Co
Foreign Rep(s): APAC Pubs Svces Pte Ltd (Indonesia, Malaysia, Singapore, Thailand); Delaney Global Pubs Svcs (Guam, Philippines); MK International Ltd (Japan); B K Norton Ltd (Korea, Taiwan); W W Norton & Co, Inc; W W Norton Ltd (Africa, UK, Ireland, Europe, Middle East); Pearson Education (New Zealand); Penguin Books Canada Ltd (Canada); Transglobal Publishers Services Ltd (Hong Kong); US Pub Rep Inc (Caribbean, Mexico, South & Central America); John Wiley & Sons (Australia)
Foreign Rights: Agence Hoffman (Germany); Agencia Literaria Carmen Balcells (Spain); Agenzia Letteraria Internazionale (Italy); Georges Hoffman (France); Laurence Pollinger Ltd (British Commonwealth)
Advertising Agency: Mort Junger Advertising, 708 Third Ave, New York, NY 10017 Tel: 212-867-1737 Fax: 212-599-4677 E-mail: mju2586@aol.com
Warehouse: National Book Co, 800 Keystone Industrial Park, Scranton, PA 18512 Tel: 212-790-9453 Toll Free Tel: 800-233-4830 Toll Free Fax: 800-458-6515
Distribution Center: W W Norton Co, 500 Fifth Ave, New York, NY 10110

The New England Press Inc
PO Box 575, Shelburne, VT 05482-0575
SAN: 213-6376
Tel: 802-863-2520 Fax: 802-863-1510
E-mail: nep@together.net
Web Site: www.nepress.com
Key Personnel
Pres: Alfred Rosa
Fin Officer: Margaret Rosa
Founded: 1978
Nonfiction books on various aspects of life in New England.
ISBN Prefix(es): 0-933050; 1-881535
Number of titles published annually: 4 Print
Total Titles: 75 Print
Shipping Address: 41 IDX Dr, Suite 245, South Burlington, VT 05403
Warehouse: VT Commercial Warehouse, 166 Boyer Circle, Williston, VT 05495

New Falcon Publications/Falcon
Subsidiary of J W Brown Inc
1739 E Broadway Rd, No 1-277, Tempe, AZ 85282
Tel: 602-708-1409 Fax: 602-708-1410
E-mail: info@newfalcon.com
Web Site: www.newfalcon.com
Key Personnel
Pres: Alan Miller
VP & Intl Rts: Nicholas Tharcher
E-mail: nicktharcher@newfalcon.com
Founded: 1982
Books, audio tapes, video tapes.
ISBN Prefix(es): 0-941404; 1-56184
Number of titles published annually: 10 Print; 5 Audio
Total Titles: 125 Print; 10 Audio
Imprints: Falcon Press; Golden Dawn Publications; New Falcon Publications
Distributed by New Leaf Distributing Co
Returns: Falcon Returns, c/o Genco, 1575 Linda Way, Sparks, NV 89431
Warehouse: New Falcon Publications, c/o Genco West, 1585 Linda Way, Sparks, NV 89431
Distribution Center: Genco West, 1545 Linda Way, Sparks, NV 89104

New Forums Press Inc
1018 S Lewis St, Stillwater, OK 74074
Mailing Address: PO Box 876, Stillwater, OK 74076-0876
Tel: 405-372-6158 Toll Free Tel: 800-606-3766 Fax: 405-377-2237
E-mail: info@newforums.com
Web Site: www.newforums.com
Key Personnel
Pres: Douglas Dollar E-mail: dougdollar@newforums.com
Founded: 1981
Practical & innovative academic journals, newsletters & books for educators in two & four year colleges & universities. Textbooks are also a primary interest.
ISBN Prefix(es): 0-913507; 1-58107
Number of titles published annually: 20 Print
Total Titles: 150 Print; 1 Online
Advertising Agency: Copy & Art, 219 E Greenvale Ct, Stillwater, OK 74075, Gayla Tel: 405-377-8224

New Harbinger Publications Inc
5674 Shattuck Ave, Oakland, CA 94609
Tel: 510-652-0215 Toll Free Tel: 800-748-6273 (orders only) Fax: 510-652-5472
E-mail: nhhelp@newharbinger.com
Web Site: www.newharbinger.com
Key Personnel
Gen Mgr: Matt McKay E-mail: matt@newharbinger.com
Acq Ed: Catherine Sutker E-mail: catherine@newharbinger.com
Publicist: Lorna Garano E-mail: lorna@newharbinger.com
Intl Rts: Dorothy Smyk E-mail: dorothy@newharbinger.com
Founded: 1979
We offer the best in self-help psychology & health publications for tackling real problems.
ISBN Prefix(es): 1-57224
Number of titles published annually: 45 Print; 1 E-Book; 1 Audio
Total Titles: 200 Print; 1 E-Book; 46 Audio

New Horizon Press
PO Box 669, Far Hills, NJ 07931-0669
SAN: 677-119X
Tel: 908-604-6311 Toll Free Tel: 800-533-7978 (orders only) Fax: 908-604-6330
E-mail: nhp@newhorizonpressbooks.com
Key Personnel
Pres & Ed-in-Chief: Joan S Dunphy E-mail: nhp@newhorizon.pressbooks.com
VP, Fin & Mktg: JoAnne Thomas
Founded: 1982
True stories of uncommon heroes, true crime issue oriented, social issues, behavioral, political science & psychologically-oriented nonfiction, trade paper, children's self-help, helping children deal with crisis.
ISBN Prefix(es): 0-88282
Number of titles published annually: 12 Print
Total Titles: 149 Print
Imprints: Small Horizons
Distributor for Kensington Publishing Corp
Foreign Rights: Bobbe Siegel
Orders to: Kensington Publishing Corp, c/o Penguin Group (USA) Inc, 405 Murray Hill Pkwy, East Rutherford, NJ 07073-2136 Toll Free Tel: 800-462-6420; 800-526-0275; 800-631-8571 (Cust Serv) Fax: 201-256-0000 (Cust Serv)
Returns: Penguin Group (USA) Inc, One Commerce Rd, Pittston Township, PA 18640
Distribution Center: Kensington Publishing Corp, c/o Penguin Group (USA) Inc, 405 Murray Hill Pkwy, East Rutherford, NJ 07073-2136 Toll Free Tel: 800-526-0275 Toll Free Fax: 800-227-9604

New Issues Poetry & Prose
Western Michigan University, Dept of English, 1903 W Michigan Ave, Kalamazoo, MI 49008-5331
Tel: 269-387-8185 Fax: 269-387-2562
Web Site: www.wmich.edu/newissues
Key Personnel
Ed: Herbert Scott E-mail: herbert.scott@wmich.edu
Founded: 1996
ISBN Prefix(es): 1-930974
Number of titles published annually: 12 Print
Total Titles: 80 Print
Distribution Center: Partners, 2325 Jarco Dr, Holt, MI 48842 Toll Free Tel: 800-336-3137 Fax: 517-694-0617
Small Press Distribution Toll Free Tel: 800-869-7553 Web Site: www.spdbooks.org

New Leaf Press Inc
PO Box 726, Green Forest, AR 72638-0726
Tel: 870-438-5288 Toll Free Tel: 800-643-9535 Fax: 870-438-5120
E-mail: nlp@newleafpress.net
Web Site: www.newleafpress.net
Key Personnel
Ed: Jim Fletcher
Founded: 1975
Christian living & creation books; evangelical, devotionals.
ISBN Prefix(es): 0-89221
Number of titles published annually: 30 Print
Total Titles: 300 Print

New Mexico Books, see Coda Publications

New Past Press Inc
PO Box 558, Friendship, WI 53934-0558
Tel: 608-339-7191
E-mail: newpast@maqs.net
Web Site: www.newpastpress.com
Key Personnel
Publr: Michael J Goc
Publg Asst: Carol Ann Podoll
Founded: 1985
History books-regional.
ISBN Prefix(es): 0-938627
Number of titles published annually: 8 Print
Total Titles: 65 Print; 1 CD-ROM
Shipping Address: 201 West St, Friendship, WI 53934

New Poets Series, see BrickHouse Books Inc

The New Press
Division of W W Norton & Co Inc
38 Greene St, 4th fl, New York, NY 10013
Tel: 212-629-8802 Toll Free Tel: 800-233-4830 (orders) Fax: 212-629-8617 Toll Free Fax: 800-458-6515
E-mail: newpress@thenewpress.com
Web Site: www.thenewpress.com
Key Personnel
Publr: Colin Robinson
Dir: Andre Schiffrin
Prodn Dir: Fran Forte
Exec Dir: Diane Wachtell E-mail: dwachtell@thenewpress.com
Fin Dir: Mary Colman St John E-mail: mcstjohn@thenewpress.com
Publicity Mgr: Daniel Ricciato
Man Ed: Maury Botton E-mail: mbotton@thenewpress.com
Ed, Devt: Marc Favreau E-mail: mfavreau@thenewpress.com
Ed: Andy Hsiao E-mail: ahsiao@thenewpress.com
Academic Mktg: Natalie Graham
Off Mgr: Linda Chavers Tel: 212-714-0487
Founded: 1990
Nonprofit publisher in the public interest; international fiction, general nonfiction & foreign translation.

ISBN Prefix(es): 1-56584
Number of titles published annually: 50 Print
Total Titles: 650 Print
Distributed by W W Norton & Co Inc
Foreign Rep(s): MK Intl Ltd (Japan); W W Norton & Co Ltd (USA); I B Taurus & Co Ltd (Australia, UK, World); University of Toronto Press (Canada)
Foreign Rights: Carmen Balcells (Spain); Ursula Bender (Germany); Ann Christine Danielsson (Scandinavia); Cristina de Mello e Souza; Beth Elon (Israel); Mary Kling (France); William Miller (Japan); Susanna Zevi (Italy)
Warehouse: National Book Co Inc, Keystone Industrial Park, Scranton, PA 18512
Membership(s): AAP

New Readers Press
Division of Pro Literacy Worldwide
1320 Jamesville Ave, Syracuse, NY 13210
SAN: 202-1064
Mailing Address: PO Box 35888, Syracuse, NY 13235-5888
Tel: 315-422-9121 *Toll Free Tel:* 800-448-8878
Fax: 315-422-5561
E-mail: nrp@proliteracy.org
Web Site: www.newreaderspress.com
Key Personnel
Exec Dir, Publg: Dennis Cook
Sales & Mktg Dir: Mary MacKay
Edit Dir: Ruth Ann Hayward
ISBN Contact: Mike Shaffer
Mktg Mgr: Elaine Wackerow
Founded: 1965
Books & periodical for adults, young adult reading at a 0-8 reading level; basic reading & writing program; English as a second language; mathematics.
ISBN Prefix(es): 0-88336; 1-56420; 1-56853; 0-929631
Number of titles published annually: 50 Print
Total Titles: 423 Print; 41 Audio
Distributed by People's Publishing Group
Foreign Rep(s): The Bookery (Australia); Laubach Literacy of Canada (Canada)

New Rivers Press
Minnesota State University Moorhead, 1104 Seventh Ave S, Moorhead, MN 56563
Tel: 218-477-5870 *Fax:* 218-477-2236
E-mail: nrp@mnstate.edu
Web Site: www.newriverspress.com; www.mnstate.edu/newriverspress
Key Personnel
Dir: Wayne Gudmundson *E-mail:* gudmund@mnstate.edu
Sr Ed: Alan Davis *E-mail:* davisa@mnstate.edu
Founded: 1968
Books of poetry, short stories & novellas, creative nonfiction, memoir.
ISBN Prefix(es): 0-912284; 0-89823
Number of titles published annually: 5 Print
Total Titles: 312 Print
Distribution Center: Consortium Books Sales, 1045 W Westgate Dr, Suite 90, St Paul, MN 55114 *Tel:* 651-221-9035 *Toll Free Tel:* 800-283-3572 *Fax:* 651-221-0124 *Web Site:* www.cbsd.com

New Strategist Publications Inc
120 W State St, 4th fl, Ithaca, NY 14850
Mailing Address: PO Box 242, Ithaca, NY 14851-0242
Tel: 607-273-0913 *Toll Free Tel:* 800-848-0842
Fax: 607-277-5009
E-mail: demographics@newstrategist.com
Web Site: newstrategist.com
Key Personnel
Pres & Publr: Penelope Wickham
Ed-in-Chief: Cheryl Russell
Founded: 1990

Publish reference books; demographics & consumer spending.
ISBN Prefix(es): 1-885070
Number of titles published annually: 7 Print; 7 Online
Total Titles: 18 Print; 18 Online

New Victoria Publishers
513 New Boston Rd, Norwich, VT 05055
Mailing Address: PO Box 27, Norwich, VT 05055-0027
Tel: 802-649-5297 *Toll Free Tel:* 800-326-5297
Fax: 802-649-5297 *Toll Free Fax:* 800-326-5297
E-mail: newvic@aol.com
Web Site: www.newvictoria.com
Key Personnel
Ed: Claudia Lamperti
Publr & Intl Rts: Beth Dingman
Founded: 1976
Specialize in feminist & lesbian fiction & nonfiction books.
ISBN Prefix(es): 0-934678; 1-892281
Number of titles published annually: 4 Print
Total Titles: 91 Print
Editorial Office(s): Bookworld Companies, 1941 Whitfield Park Loop, Sarasota, FL 34243 *Toll Free Tel:* 800-444-2524 *Toll Free Fax:* 800-777-2525 *E-mail:* info@bookworld.com *Web Site:* www.bookworld.com
Sales Office(s): Bookworld Companies, 1941 Whitfield Park Loop, Sarasota, FL 34243 *Toll Free Tel:* 800-444-2524 *Toll Free Fax:* 800-777-2525 *E-mail:* info@bookworld.com *Web Site:* www.bookworld.com
Billing Address: Bookworld Companies, 1941 Whitfield Park Loop, Sarasota, FL 34243 *Toll Free Tel:* 800-444-2524 *Toll Free Fax:* 800-777-2525 *E-mail:* info@bookworld.com *Web Site:* www.bookworld.com
Shipping Address: Bookworld Companies, 1941 Whitfield Park Loop, Sarasota, FL 34243 *Toll Free Tel:* 800-444-2524 *Toll Free Fax:* 800-777-2525 *E-mail:* info@bookworld.com *Web Site:* www.bookworld.com
Distribution Center: 1230 Heil Quaker Blvd, La Vergne, TN 37086
Membership(s): Vermont Book Professionals Association

New Voices Publishing
34 Salem St, Wilmington, MA 01887
Mailing Address: PO Box 560, Wilmington, MA 01887-0560
Tel: 508-347-5669; 978-658-2131 *Fax:* 508-347-5669; 978-988-8833
Web Site: www.kidsterrain.com
Key Personnel
Publr: Ellen Gilmartin
Exec Ed: Rita Schiano *E-mail:* rschiano@newvoicespublishing.com
Founded: 2001
Publish children's books (including picture books) & monthly educational newspaper "KidsGazette" for 7-10 years of age.
ISBN Prefix(es): 1-931642
Number of titles published annually: 5 Print
Total Titles: 6 Print
Membership(s): Publishers Marketing Association

New Win Publishing Inc
9682 Telstar Ave, Suite 110, El Monte, CA 91731
SAN: 217-1201
Tel: 626-448-4422 *Fax:* 626-602-3817
Web Site: www.newwinpublishing.com
Founded: 1988
General nonfiction: crafts, reference, health & nutrition, gourmet cooking, career development, religious & inspirational, outdoor sports, hunting, shooting, fishing, decoys & dogs.
ISBN Prefix(es): 0-8329
Number of titles published annually: 3 Print

Total Titles: 43 Print
Imprints: Winchester Press

New World Library
Division of Whatever Publishing Inc
14 Pamaron Way, Novato, CA 94949
SAN: 211-8777
Tel: 415-884-2100 *Toll Free Tel:* 800-227-3900 (ext 52, retail orders) *Fax:* 415-884-2199 (ext 52, retail orders)
E-mail: escort@newworldlibrary.com
Web Site: www.newworldlibrary.com
Key Personnel
Pres: Marc Allen *E-mail:* marc@nwlib.com
Mktg Dir & Subs Rts: Munro Magruder *Tel:* 415-884-2100 ext 21 *E-mail:* munro@nwlib.com
CFO: Victoria Williams-Clarke *E-mail:* victoria@nwlib.com
Edit Dir: Georgia Hughes *E-mail:* georgia@nwlib.com
Publicity Mgr & Rts & Perms: Marjorie Conte *E-mail:* marjorie@nwlib.com
Wholesale Accts Mgr: Ami Parkerson *E-mail:* ami@nwlib.com
Prodn Mgr: Tona Pierce Meyers *E-mail:* tona@nwlib.com
Founded: 1977
Self-improvement, personal growth & spirituality.
ISBN Prefix(es): 0-915811; 0-931432; 1-880032; 0-945934; 1-57731; 1-882591
Number of titles published annually: 40 Print; 2 E-Book; 2 Audio
Total Titles: 250 Print; 50 E-Book; 28 Audio
Imprints: Amber-Allen Publishing; Nataraj
Divisions: H J Kramer
Foreign Rep(s): Airlift Books Ltd (England); Brumbry Books (Australia); Dempsey-Your Distributor (Canada); Peaceful Living Publications (New England); Publishers Group Canada (Canada); Real Books (South Africa)
Foreign Rights: InterLicense Ltd (World)
Distribution Center: Publishers Group West, 5045 W 79 St, Indianapolis, IN 46268 *Toll Free Tel:* 800-788-3123 *Fax:* 510-528-3444 *Web Site:* www.pgw.com

New York Academy of Sciences
2 E 63 St, New York, NY 10021
SAN: 203-753X
Tel: 212-838-0230 *Toll Free Tel:* 800-843-6927
Fax: 212-888-2894
E-mail: publications@nyas.org
Web Site: www.nyas.org
Key Personnel
Man Ed: Wendy Caruso
Mktg Dir: Rich Kelley
Dir, Communs: Fred Moreno
Founded: 1817
Annals & transactions of the New York Academy of Sciences; also publish *Update Magazine.*
ISBN Prefix(es): 0-89072; 0-89766; 1-57331
Number of titles published annually: 28 Print
Total Titles: 305 Print
Branch Office(s)
655 Madison Ave, New York, NY 10021
Foreign Rep(s): The Eurospan Group (Africa, Europe, Middle East); USACO (Japan)
Membership(s): AAP

The New York Botanical Garden Press
Division of The New York Botanical Garden
200 St & Kazimiroff Blvd, Bronx, NY 10458-5126
Tel: 718-817-8721 *Fax:* 718-817-8842
E-mail: nybgpress@nybg.org
Web Site: www.nybg.org
Key Personnel
Dir, NYBG Press: Sandi Frank *Tel:* 718-817-8957 *E-mail:* sfrank@nybg.org
Cust Serv: Maria Toro *Tel:* 718-817-8918 *E-mail:* mtoro@nybg.org
Founded: 1896

Dissemination of information on the scientific study of plants.
ISBN Prefix(es): 0-89327
Number of titles published annually: 15 Print
Total Titles: 244 Print
Warehouse: Allen Press, 810 E Tenth St, Lawrence, KS 66044-8897, Contact: Kerry Collins *Tel:* 785-843-1234 ext 228 *E-mail:* kcollins@allenpress.com
Distribution Center: Allen Press, 810 E Tenth St, Lawrence, KS 66044-8897, Contact: Kerry Collins *Tel:* 785-843-1234 ext 228 *E-mail:* kcollins@allenpress.com
Membership(s): AAP

New York Public Library
Publications Office, Fifth Ave & 42 St, New York, NY 10018
Tel: 212-512-0202; 212-512-0201 *Fax:* 212-704-8620
Web Site: www.nypl.org
Key Personnel
Dir, Pubns: Karen Van Westering *E-mail:* kvanwestering@nypl.org
Founded: 1895
Reference books, exhibition catalogs, literature & humanities; hardcover & softcover.
ISBN Prefix(es): 0-87104
Number of titles published annually: 5 Print
Total Titles: 60 Print
Membership(s): BISG

New York State Bar Association
One Elk St, Albany, NY 12207
SAN: 226-1952
Tel: 518-463-3200 *Toll Free Tel:* 800-582-2452 *Fax:* 518-463-8844
Web Site: www.nysba.org
Key Personnel
CLE (Continuing Legal Educ) Pubns Dir: Daniel McMahon *E-mail:* dmcmahon@nysba.org
Founded: 1985
Legal publications, including hardbound, loose-leaf, softbound & diskettes.
ISBN Prefix(es): 0-942954
Number of titles published annually: 30 Print; 6 CD-ROM
Total Titles: 80 Print; 50 Online

New York University Press
838 Broadway, New York, NY 10003
SAN: 658-1293
Tel: 212-998-2575 (edit) *Toll Free Tel:* 800-996-6987 (orders) *Fax:* 212-995-3833 (orders)
E-mail: feedback@nyupress.nyu.edu
Web Site: www.nyupress.org *Telex:* 23-5128 *Cable:* NYU UR
Key Personnel
Dir: Steve Maikowski
Man Ed: Despina P Gimbel
Ed-in-Chief: Eric Zinner
Sales & Mktg Mgr: Fredric Nachbaur *E-mail:* fredric.nachbaur@nyu.edu
Prodn Mgr: Charles Hames
Publicist: Amanda Davis
Info Systems Specialist: Stephen Kaldon
Exec Ed: Ilene Kalish
Ed: Deborah Gershenowitz; Jennifer Hammer
Cust Serv: Jesse Henderson
Founded: 1916
ISBN Prefix(es): 0-8147
Number of titles published annually: 100 Print
Total Titles: 2,200 Print
Foreign Office(s): Eurospan, 3 Henrietta St, Covent Garden, London WC2 E8LU, United Kingdom
Distributor for Monthly Review Press
Foreign Rights: Diana Voigt (Germany)
Warehouse: c/o Maple Press Distribution Center, Legionaire Dr, Lebanon, PA 17042 *Tel:* 717-865-7600 *Fax:* 717-865-7800
Membership(s): AAP

Newbridge Educational Publishing
Division of Haights Cross Communications Inc
One Beeman Rd, Northborough, MA 01532
Mailing Address: PO Box 800, Northborough, MA 01532-0800
Tel: 508-571-6500 *Toll Free Tel:* 800-867-0307 *Fax:* 508-571-6502 *Toll Free Fax:* 800-456-2419
E-mail: info@newbridgeonline.com
Web Site: www.newbridgeonline.com; www.newbridgepub.com
Key Personnel
Pres: Robert Laronga *Tel:* 508-571-6525 *Fax:* 508-571-6503 *E-mail:* blaronga@sundancepub.com
CFO: Logan Wai *Tel:* 508-571-6650 *Fax:* 508-571-6508 *E-mail:* lwai@sundancepub.com
Sr VP, Opers: Jay Shenk *Tel:* 508-571-6715 *E-mail:* jshenk@sundancepub.com
Sr VP & Dir, Publg: Linda Sanford *Tel:* 212-478-1713 *Fax:* 212-478-1771 *E-mail:* lsanford@newbridgeeducational.com
Dir, Prodn: Anne Brown *Tel:* 212-478-1704 *Fax:* 212-478-1772 *E-mail:* abrown@newbridgeeducational.com
Sr VP, Sales & Mktg: Ed Rock *Tel:* 508-571-6750 *E-mail:* erock@sundancepub.com
VP, Mktg: Katherine Jasmine *Tel:* 508-571-6765 *E-mail:* kjasmine@sundancepub.com
Founded: 1981
Publishes Pre-K through middle school supplementary educational materials for classroom instruction. The major focus is on shared reading instruction through science, social studies & mathematics content & guided reading instruction in science & social studies with performance based assessment tied to national & state curriculum standards.
ISBN Prefix(es): 1-56784; 1-58273; 1-4007
Number of titles published annually: 150 Print; 36 Audio
Total Titles: 680 Print; 118 Audio
Imprints: Early Math; Early Science; Early Social Studies; GoFacts Guided Writing; Newbridge Discovery Links; Ranger Rick Science Program; Thinking Like a Scientist
Editorial Office(s): 11-13 E 26 St, 16th fl, New York, NY 10010, Contact: Linda Sanford *Tel:* 212-478-1713 *Fax:* 212-478-1771 *E-mail:* lsanford@newbridgeeducational.com
Foreign Rep(s): Schmelzer PSI
Orders to: PO Box 800, Northborough, MA 01532-0800, Contact: Sharon Mosbrucker *Toll Free Tel:* 800-867-0307 *Toll Free Fax:* 800-456-2419 *E-mail:* smosbrucker@sundancepub.com
Membership(s): AAP; International Reading Association; National Science Teachers Association

Newbury Street Press
Imprint of New England Historic Genealogical Society
101 Newbury St, Boston, MA 02116
Tel: 617-536-5740 *Fax:* 617-536-7307
Web Site: www.newenglandancestors.org
Key Personnel
Edit Dir: Christopher Hartman *Tel:* 617-536-5740 ext 211 *E-mail:* chartman@nehgs.org
Founded: 1845
The New England Historic Genealogical Society publishes a variety of material including books, CD-ROMs & a scholarly journal. The Society also publishes a members' magazine. Through its special publications division, Newbury Street Press, the Society publishes scholarly books & compiled genealogies.
ISBN Prefix(es): 0-88082
Number of titles published annually: 12 Print
Total Titles: 67 Print
Sales Office(s): One Watson Place, Framingham, MA 01701 *Toll Free Tel:* 888-296-3447 *E-mail:* sales@nehgs.org

NewLife Publications
Affiliate of A Ministry of Campus Crusade for Christ
375 Hwy 74 S, Peachtree City, GA 30269
Tel: 770-631-9940 *Toll Free Tel:* 800-235-7255 *Toll Free Fax:* 800-514-7072
Web Site: www.nlpdirect.com
Key Personnel
Dir, Creative: Michelle Treiber
Founded: 1991
Religious books, video & audio ministry tools for evangelism, discipleship & training.
ISBN Prefix(es): 1-56399
Number of titles published annually: 20 Print
Total Titles: 160 Print
Imprints: LifeSounds Audio Library
Distributed by Appalachian Distributors
Foreign Rep(s): John Crone (Worldwide)

Newmarket Publishing & Communications
Division of Newmarket Publishing & Communications Co
18 E 48 St, New York, NY 10017
SAN: 217-2585
Tel: 212-832-3575 *Toll Free Tel:* 800-669-3903 *Fax:* 212-832-3629
E-mail: mailbox@newmarketpress.com
Web Site: www.newmarketpress.com
Key Personnel
Pres & Publr: Esther Margolis
Exec Asst to Pres: Ann C Lee; Kelli Taylor
Cont: Maina Lopotukhin
Ed: Shannon Berning; Keith Hollaman
Dir, Prodn & Dist: Frank De Maio
Sales & Mktg Dir: Heidi Sachner
Publicity Dir: Harry Burton
Contracts Mgr & Subs Rts: Yulia Borodyanskaya; Tracey Bussell
Founded: 1981
Hardcover, trade paperbacks, fiction & general nonfiction.
ISBN Prefix(es): 0-937858; 1-55704
Number of titles published annually: 35 Print
Total Titles: 260 Print; 1 Audio
Imprints: Newmarket Medallion
Distributed by W W Norton
Foreign Rep(s): Abner Stein Agency (Italy); Gabriella Ambrosioni Agency (Italy); Bardon-Chinese Media Agency (China); Elaine Benisti (France); Raquel de la Concha (Portugal & Spain); Harris/Elon Agency (Israel); KCC International (Korea); Nurcihan Kesim (Turkey); Lex Copyright Office (Hungary); Owl's Agency, Inc (Japan); Prava I Prevodi (Eastern Europe); Read 'n Right Agency (Greece); Karin Schindler (Brazil); Thomas Schluck (Germany); Synopsis Literary Agency (Russia); Caroline Van Gelderen (Netherlands)
Shipping Address: National Book Co Inc, Keystone Industrial Park, Scranton, PA 18512, Contact: B Mecca *Toll Free Tel:* 800-233-4830
Distribution Center: Georgetown Publications, 34 Armstrong Ave, Georgetown, ON L7G 4R9, Canada *Tel:* 905-873-8498 *Toll Free Tel:* 888-595-3008 *Fax:* 905-873-6170 *Toll Free Fax:* 888-595-3009 *E-mail:* orders@gtwcanada.com
Membership(s): AAP; Publishers Marketing Association; Publishers' Publicity Association

NewSouth Books
Imprint of NewSouth Inc
105 S Court St, Montgomery, AL 36104
Mailing Address: PO Box 1588, Montgomery, AL 36102
Tel: 334-834-3556 *Fax:* 334-834-3557
E-mail: info@newsouthbooks.com
Web Site: www.newsouthbooks.com
Key Personnel
Ed-in-Chief & Founder: H Randall Williams
Publr & Founder: Suzanne La Rosa
Founded: 1999

Small independent book publisher, publishing 20-30 titles per year, including literary fiction & non-fiction, with a special emphasis on books about the history & culture of the south.
ISBN Prefix(es): 1-58838
Number of titles published annually: 30 Print
Total Titles: 150 Print
Editorial Office(s): 1406 Plaza Dr, Winston-Salem, SC 27103
Sales Office(s): 1406 Plaza Dr, Winston-Salem, SC 27103
Distributed by John F Blair Publisher
Billing Address: 1406 Plaza Dr, Winston-Salem, SC 27103
Returns: 1406 Plaza Dr, Winston-Salem, SC 27103
Shipping Address: 1406 Plaza Dr, Winston-Salem, SC 27103
Warehouse: 1406 Plaza Dr, Winston-Salem, SC 27103
Distribution Center: 1406 Plaza Dr, Winston-Salem, SC 27103
Membership(s): Publishers Association of the South; Southeast Booksellers Association

NewSouth Inc
105 S Court St, Montgomery, AL 36104
Mailing Address: PO Box 1588, Montgomery, AL 36102-1588
Tel: 334-834-3556 *Fax:* 334-834-3557
E-mail: info@newsouthbooks.com
Web Site: www.newsouthbooks.com
Key Personnel
Pres & Publr: Suzanne LaRosa *E-mail:* suzanne@ newsouthbooks.com
VP & Ed-in-Chief: Randall Williams
   E-mail: randall@newsouthbooks.com
Founded: 1999
Independent book publisher of literary fiction & nonfiction with a special emphasis on books that explore the history & culture of the South.
ISBN Prefix(es): 1-58838
Number of titles published annually: 30 Print
Total Titles: 150 Print
Imprints: Court Street Press; Junebug Books; NewSouth Books
Membership(s): AAP; Publishers Association of the South; Publishers Marketing Association
See separate listing for:
NewSouth Books

Next Decade Inc
39 Old Farmstead Rd, Chester, NJ 07930
Tel: 908-879-6625 *Fax:* 908-879-2920
E-mail: info@nextdecade.com
Web Site: www.nextdecade.com
Key Personnel
Publr & Pres: Barbara Kimmel *E-mail:* barbara@ nextdecade.com
Acqs Ed: Carol Rose
Founded: 1994
Award winning publisher of books that simplify complex subjects.
ISBN Prefix(es): 0-9626003; 0-9700908; 1-932919
Number of titles published annually: 4 Print
Total Titles: 9 Print
Orders to: IPG, 814 N Franklin St, Chicago, IL 60610 (trade sales) *Toll Free Tel:* 800-888-4741
Membership(s): Publishers Marketing Association

Nexus Press
Division of Atlanta Contemporary Art Center
535 Means St, Atlanta, GA 30318
Tel: 404-577-3579 *Fax:* 404-577-5856
E-mail: nexusbooks@thecontemporary.org
Web Site: www.thecontemporary.org
Key Personnel
Dir, Nexus Press: Brad Freeman
Asst Dir: Mandy Mastarovitz
Founded: 1977
Nonprofit visual arts press. Artist books.

ISBN Prefix(es): 0-932526
Number of titles published annually: 10 Print
Total Titles: 100 Print

§Nightingale-Conant
6245 W Howard St, Niles, IL 60714
Tel: 847-647-0306; 847-647-0300
   Toll Free Tel: 800-572-2770 *Fax:* 847-647-7145
Web Site: www.nightingale.com
Key Personnel
Pres: Vic Conant
Sr VP, Mktg & Publg: Gary Chapell
Founded: 1960
Audio, video books & CD-ROMs in the areas of sales, skills, wealth building, spiritual growth, foreign language & personal development.
ISBN Prefix(es): 1-55525
Number of titles published annually: 40 Print; 16 Audio
Total Titles: 190 Print; 500 Audio
Subsidiaries: Nightingale-Conant (UK)
Distributed by William Morrow; Simon & Schuster

§Nilgiri Press
Division of Blue Mountain Center of Meditation
3600 Tomales Rd, Tomales, CA 94971
Mailing Address: PO Box 256, Tomales, CA 94971-0256 SAN: 207-6853
Tel: 707-878-2369 *Toll Free Tel:* 800-475-2369
   Fax: 707-878-2375
E-mail: info@nilgiri.org
Web Site: www.nilgiri.org
Key Personnel
Publicist: Gale E Zimmerman *E-mail:* gale@ nilgiri.org
Intl Rts: Jennifer Jones *E-mail:* jennifer@nilgiri. org
Founded: 1972
Meditation & practical spirituality books, video & audio.
ISBN Prefix(es): 0-915132; 1-888314; 1-58638
Number of titles published annually: 3 Print; 1 CD-ROM, 16 Audio
Total Titles: 28 Print; 1 CD-ROM; 3 Online; 50 Audio
Foreign Rep(s): Bill Bailey (Europe); Hi Marketing (UK); Publishers Group West
Foreign Rights: Bookwise International (Australia, New Zealand); Jerry Carrillo (Latin America); Michelle Morrow Curreri (Asia, Middle East); Publishers Group West (Canada)
Membership(s): Publishers Marketing Association

No Starch Press Inc
555 De Haro St, Suite 250, San Francisco, CA 94107-2192
Tel: 415-863-9900 *Toll Free Tel:* 800-420-7240
   Fax: 415-863-9950
E-mail: info@nostarch.com
Web Site: www.nostarch.com
Key Personnel
Pres: William Pollock
Founded: 1994
Specialize in general computer trade; Linux.
ISBN Prefix(es): 1-886411; 1-593270
Number of titles published annually: 11 Print; 6 CD-ROM; 3 E-Book
Total Titles: 43 Print; 12 CD-ROM
Imprints: Linux Journal Press
Membership(s): Publishers Marketing Association

§Noble Publishing Corp
Division of Eagle Ware Corp
630 Pinnacle Ct, Norcross, GA 30071
Tel: 770-449-6774 *Fax:* 770-448-2839
E-mail: editor@noblepub.com; orders@noblepub. com
Web Site: www.noblepub.com
Key Personnel
COO & Publ: Dennis Ford
Founded: 1994

Specializes in RF, microwave & wireless design books, software & CD-ROM courses for students & professionals in the field.
ISBN Prefix(es): 1-884932
Number of titles published annually: 5 Print; 10 CD-ROM
Total Titles: 60 Print; 12 CD-ROM
Distributed by Amazon.com; BarnesandNoble.com; RFCafe.com; Yankee Book Peddlers
Foreign Rep(s): American Technical Publishers (Europe)

§Nolo
950 Parker St, Berkeley, CA 94710
Tel: 510-549-1976 *Fax:* 510-548-5902
E-mail: info@nolo.com
Web Site: www.nolo.com
Key Personnel
CEO: David Rothenberg
Man Ed: Janet Portman
Lib Sales Mgr: Bill Richter
Dir, Bkstore Sales: Susan McConnell
Dir, Software Devt: Natalie Dejarlais
Intl Rts: Linda Hanger
Web Master: Laurie Briggs
Founded: 1971
Self-help law & business books & software; personal finance books.
ISBN Prefix(es): 0-87337
Number of titles published annually: 200 Print
Total Titles: 300 Print; 8 CD-ROM; 40 E-Book
Warehouse: 932 Parker St, Suite 4, Berkeley, CA 94710

The Noontide Press
Imprint of Legion for the Survival of Freedom
PO Box 2719, Newport Beach, CA 92659-1319
Tel: 949-631-1490 *Fax:* 949-631-0981
E-mail: orders@noontidepress.com
Web Site: www.noontidepress.com
Key Personnel
Pres: Mark Weber
Founded: 1968
Mail-order sales of politically incorrect books.
ISBN Prefix(es): 0-939482; 0-911038
Number of titles published annually: 2 Print; 2 Online
Total Titles: 20 Print; 2 CD-ROM; 5 Online; 1 E-Book; 100 Audio
Shipping Address: 1650 Babcock St, Costa Mesa, CA 92627

Norman Publishing
Division of Jeremy Norman & Co Inc
936-B Seventh St, PMB 238, Novato, CA 94945-3000
SAN: 122-3380
Mailing Address: PO Box 867, Novato, CA 94948-0867
Tel: 415-892-3181 *Toll Free Tel:* 800-544-9359
   Fax: 208-692-7446
E-mail: orders@jnorman.com
Web Site: www.normanpublishing.com
Key Personnel
Pres: Jeremy Norman
Ed: Diana H Hook
Founded: 1987
Medical history, Civil War medicine, history of science. Copy editing & proofreading, production management.
ISBN Prefix(es): 0-930405
Number of titles published annually: 3 Print
Total Titles: 60 Print

North Atlantic Books
Division of Society for the Study of Native Arts & Sciences
1435 Fourth St, Berkeley, CA 94710
SAN: 203-1655
Mailing Address: PO Box 12327, Berkeley, CA 94712-3327
Tel: 510-559-8277 *Toll Free Tel:* 800-337-2665 (book orders only) *Fax:* 510-559-8279

E-mail: orders@northatlanticbooks.com
Web Site: www.northatlanticbooks.com
Key Personnel
Publr: Richard Grossinger
Publr & Edit Dir: Lindy Hough *Tel:* 510-559-8277 ext 12
Publicist: Olivia Ford
Art Dir: Paula Morrison
Sales, Subs Rts & Mktg: Mark Ouimet
Contracts: Susan Bumps
Rts & Perms: Sarah Serafimidis
Founded: 1964
Trade books in the niches of alternative health, body work somatics, martial arts, Buddhism & spirituality & politics/current affairs. Also children's picture books, parenting, books for women & girls.
ISBN Prefix(es): 1-883319; 0-913028; 0-938190; 1-55643
Number of titles published annually: 50 Print
Total Titles: 700 Print; 7 E-Book
Imprints: Frog LTD
Distributor for Frog Ltd
Foreign Rep(s): Airlift Books (UK, Europe); Asia Publications (Asia); PGW (Canada); John Reed (Australia)
Foreign Rights: Eliane Benisti (France); Hagenbach & Bender (Germany); Imprima (Korea); Karin Schindler (Brazil); Tuttle-Mori Agency (Japan)
Orders to: PO Box 12327, Berkeley, CA 94712 (individuals or small orders, less than case quantity), Cust Serv: Erin Lewis *Toll Free Tel:* 800-337-2665 (orders only) *E-mail:* orders@northatlanticbooks.com; Publishers Group West, 1700 Fourth St, Berkeley, CA 94710 (bookstore orders) *Toll Free Tel:* 800-788-3123 *E-mail:* orders@pgw.com
Returns: Publishers Group West, 7326 Winton Dr, Indianapolis, IN 46268 *Toll Free Tel:* 800-788-3123 *E-mail:* returns@pgw.com
Distribution Center: Publisher's Group West, 5045 W 79 St, Indianapolis, IN 46268
Membership(s): Northern California Book Publicity & Marketing Association
See separate listing for:
Frog Ltd

North Bay Books
3110 Whitecliff Ct, Richmond, CA 94803
Mailing Address: PO Box 21234, El Sobrante, CA 94820-1234
Tel: 510-758-4276 *Toll Free Tel:* 800-870-3194 *Fax:* 510-758-4659
Web Site: www.northbaybooks.com
Key Personnel
Publr: John Strohmeier *E-mail:* john@northbaybooks.com
Founded: 2002
Independent publisher of books on Christianity, social change, American history & Hinduism.
ISBN Prefix(es): 0-9725200; 0-9749098
Number of titles published annually: 6 Print
Total Titles: 4 Print
Orders to: Publishers Group West, 1700 Fourth St, Berkeley, CA 94710 *Tel:* 510-528-1444
Returns: Publishers Group West, 5045 W 79 St, Indianapolis, IN 46268 *Tel:* 317-872-5826
Warehouse: Publishers Group West, 5045 W 79 St, Indianapolis, IN 46268 *Tel:* 317-872-5826
Distribution Center: Publishers Group West, 5045 W 79 St, Indianapolis, IN 46268 *Tel:* 317-872-5826

§North Books
PO Box 1277, Wickford, RI 02852
Tel: 401-294-3682 *Fax:* 401-294-9491
Key Personnel
Pres: Jane Sexton
Ed & Electronic Publg: Jim Sexton
Founded: 1986

Electronic books, large & standard print fiction & nonfiction, reprints & public domain material only.
ISBN Prefix(es): 0-939495; 1-58287
Number of titles published annually: 75 Print
Total Titles: 300 Print

North Carolina Office of Archives & History
Historical Publ Sect, 4622 Mail Service Ctr, Raleigh, NC 27699-4622
Tel: 919-733-7442 *Fax:* 919-733-1439
Web Site: www.ncpublications.com
Key Personnel
Mktg Mgr: Frances W Kunstling *E-mail:* frances.kunstling@ncmail.net
Administrator: Donna E Kelly *E-mail:* donna.kelly@ncmail.net
Founded: 1903
State government agency that publishes nonfiction hardcover & trade paperback books relating to North Carolina; publishes maps, posters, facsimile documents & the *North Carolina Historical Review*, a scholarly journal of history.
ISBN Prefix(es): 0-86526
Number of titles published annually: 4 Print
Total Titles: 160 Print

North Country Books Inc
311 Turner St, Utica, NY 13501-1729
Tel: 315-735-4877 *Fax:* 315-738-4342
E-mail: ncbooks@usadatanet.net
Web Site: www.northcountrybooks.com
Key Personnel
Pres, Publr & Ed: Sheila Orlin *E-mail:* sorlin@usadatanet.net
VP, Sales Mgr & Lib Sales Dir: Robert B Igoe, Jr
Founded: 1965
Only New York State related titles.
ISBN Prefix(es): 0-932052; 0-925168; 0-9629159
Number of titles published annually: 10 Print
Total Titles: 130 Print
Imprints: North Country Books; North Country Classics

North Country Press
Division of Maine Fulfillment Corp
RR1, Box 1395, Unity, ME 04988-1395
SAN: 247-9680
Tel: 207-948-2208 *Fax:* 207-948-9000
E-mail: info@ncpbooks.com
Web Site: www.ncpbooks.com
Key Personnel
Publr: Mary Kenney *E-mail:* mkp@uninets.net; Patricia Newell
Founded: 1977
Regional press dealing with New England (specializing in Maine) subjects. Three lines: outdoor (hunting, fishing, etc); humor, lore; literature (mysteries, essays, poetry).
ISBN Prefix(es): 0-945980
Number of titles published annually: 3 Print
Total Titles: 40 Print
Warehouse: Maine Fulfillment Corp, Rte 202, Unity, ME 04988

North Light Books
Imprint of F & W Publications
4700 E Galbraith Rd, Cincinnati, OH 45236
Tel: 513-531-2690 *Toll Free Tel:* 800-666-0963 *Fax:* 513-891-7185 *Toll Free Fax:* 888-590-4082
Web Site: www.fwpublications.com
Key Personnel
Gen Mgr: Budge Wallis
Ed-in-Chief: David Lewis
Dir, Sales: Michael Murphy
Sales Admin Coord: Marcia Jones *Tel:* 513-531-2690 ext 1288 *E-mail:* marcia.jones@fwpubs.com
Founded: 1958

Top-quality instructional books to help fine artists & graphic designers find personal satisfaction & professional success.
ISBN Prefix(es): 0-89134; 1-58180
Number of titles published annually: 80 Print
Total Titles: 550 Print
Imprints: HOW Design Books; Impact
Distributor for Rockport Publishers
Shipping Address: F & W Publications, c/o Aero Fulfillment Services, 2800 Henkle Dr, Lebanon, OH 45036

North Point Press
Division of Farrar, Straus & Giroux LLC
19 Union Sq W, New York, NY 10003
Tel: 212-741-6900 *Toll Free Tel:* 888-330-8477 *Fax:* 212-741-6973
Web Site: www.fsgbooks.com
Key Personnel
Sr VP, Mktg: Jeff Seroy
Dir, Publicity & Promo: Sarita Varma
VP, Contracts & Perms: Erika Seidman
Founded: 1981
Nonfiction, environment, nature, design, food, spirituality.
ISBN Prefix(es): 0-86547
Number of titles published annually: 20 Print
Foreign Rep(s): HarperCollins Publishers (Canada); Jacaranda Wiley Ltd (Australia); Orion Ltd (Australia, New Zealand, World)
Foreign Rights: A/S Bookman; Agence Hoffman; Mercedes Casanovas Agency; DRT International; International Editors Co; International Press Agency (Africa); Japan Uni Agency; Katalin Katai, Artisjus Agency (Hungary); Michelle Lapautre; Jovan Milenkovic; Andrew Nurnberg Associates; Pikarski Literary Agency; Richard Scott Simon; Tuttle-Mori Agency; Agenzia Susanna Zevi

North River Press Publishing Corp
321 Main St, Great Barrington, MA 01230
SAN: 202-1048
Mailing Address: PO Box 567, Great Barrington, MA 01230-0567
Tel: 413-528-0034 *Toll Free Tel:* 800-486-2665 *Fax:* 413-528-3163 *Toll Free Fax:* 800-BOOK-FAX (266-5329)
E-mail: info@northriverpress.com
Web Site: www.northriverpress.com
Key Personnel
Pres: Laurence Gadd
VP: Amy Gallagher
Founded: 1971
General nonfiction hardcovers & paperbacks.
ISBN Prefix(es): 0-88427
Number of titles published annually: 6 Print
Total Titles: 40 Print; 1 Audio

North-South Center Press at the University of Miami
Division of The Dante B Fascell North-South Center at the University of Miami
1500 Monza Ave, Coral Gables, FL 33146
Tel: 305-284-6868 *Fax:* 305-284-6370
Web Site: www.miami.edu/nsc
Key Personnel
Ed Dir: Kathleen Hamman *E-mail:* khamman@miami.edu
Publns Dir: Mary M Mapes *Tel:* 305-284-8912 *E-mail:* mmapes@miami.edu
Dir, Res & Studies: Jeffrey Stark
Founded: 1984
Academic books related to contemporary Latin American issues, sustainable development, trade & investment, inter-American security, democratic governance, civil society participation, migration.
ISBN Prefix(es): 0-935501; 1-57454
Number of titles published annually: 5 Print
Total Titles: 90 Print

Distribution Center: Lynne Rienner Publishers Inc, 1800 30 St, Suite 314, Boulder, CO 80301, Contact: Martha Peacock *Tel:* 303-444-6684 *Fax:* 303-444-0824 *E-mail:* cservice@rienner. com

North Star Press of Saint Cloud Inc
PO Box 451, St Cloud, MN 56302-0451
Tel: 320-558-9062 *Fax:* 320-558-9063
E-mail: nspress@cloudnet.com
Key Personnel
Busn Mgr: Cecelia Dwyer
Publr: Corinne A Dwyer
Founded: 1969
Regional, women's issues, Minnesota history & fiction, Finnish ethnic, nature.
ISBN Prefix(es): 0-87839
Number of titles published annually: 11 Print
Total Titles: 200 Print
Shipping Address: 19485 Estes Rd, Clearwater, MN 55320
Membership(s): MLA; Upper Midwest Booksellers Association

Northeast Midwest Institute
Affiliate of Northeast Midwest Congressional & Senate Coalitions
218 "D" St SE, Washington, DC 20003
Tel: 202-544-5200 *Fax:* 202-544-0043
Web Site: www.nemw.org
Key Personnel
Exec Dir: Richard Munson
Contact: Joanna Stover
Founded: 1976
Energy, environment, economic development, human resources.
ISBN Prefix(es): 1-882061
Number of titles published annually: 6 Print
Total Titles: 50 Print

Northern Illinois University Press
310 N Fifth St, De Kalb, IL 60115
SAN: 202-8875
Tel: 815-753-1826; 815-753-1075 *Fax:* 815-753-1845
E-mail: bberg@niu.edu
Web Site: www.niu.edu/univ_press
Key Personnel
Dir: Mary L Lincoln
Man Ed, Perms: Susan Bean
Prodn & Design: Julia Fauci
Busn Mgr: Barbara Berg
Mktg Mgr: Sarah Atkinson
Founded: 1965
History, literature, philosophy, political science, regional nonfiction, anthropology, railroad history, Civil War history.
ISBN Prefix(es): 0-87580
Number of titles published annually: 20 Print
Total Titles: 250 Print
Foreign Rep(s): Eurospan (Africa, Europe, Middle East); United Publishers Services Ltd (Japan, South Korea)

Northland Publishing Co
2900 N Fort Valley Rd, Flagstaff, AZ 86001
SAN: 202-9251
Mailing Address: PO Box 1389, Flagstaff, AZ 86002-1389
Tel: 928-774-5251 *Toll Free Tel:* 800-346-3257
Fax: 928-774-0592
E-mail: info@northlandpub.com; design@ northlandpub.com; editorial@northlandpub.com
Web Site: www.northlandpub.com
Key Personnel
Publr: David Jenney
Mktg Dir: Eric Howard
Adult Ed: Tammie Gales
Children's Ed: Theresa Howell
Founded: 1958
Trade publisher of adult (nonfiction only) & children's. Adult titles focusing on Southwest arts,

crafts & culture, western life & lore, cookbooks, fine art, natural history, popular culture, bilingual books (Spanish/English only).
ISBN Prefix(es): 0-87358
Number of titles published annually: 13 Print
Total Titles: 107 Print
Imprints: Rising Moon (children's books) (Illustrated children's)
Foreign Rights: Mary Laychak
Membership(s): Publishers Association of the West; Society of Children's Book Writers & Illustrators

Northwestern University Press
625 Colfax St, Evanston, IL 60208
SAN: 202-5787
Tel: 847-491-2046 *Toll Free Tel:* 800-621-2736 (orders only) *Fax:* 847-491-8150
E-mail: nupress@northwestern.edu
Web Site: www.nupress.northwestern.edu
Key Personnel
Acting Dir: Donna Shear
Prodn & Design Mgr: Michael Brooks
Publicity Mgr: Laura Leichum *Tel:* 847-491-5315
E-mail: lleichum@northwestern.edu
Ms Edit: Susan Betz
Asst Acqs Ed: Rachel Delaney
Founded: 1958
Scholarly books, with emphasis on literature & language, philosophy, works in translation, theatre.
ISBN Prefix(es): 0-8101
Total Titles: 968 Print
Imprints: Hydra Books; The Marlboro Press; TriQuarterly Books
Distributor for FC2/Black Ice Books; Butterworth (Law in Context series); Glas; Jannes Art Press; Paper Mirror Press; Tia Chucha Press
Distribution Center: Chicago Distribution Center, 11030 S Langley, Chicago, IL 60628 *Toll Free Fax:* 800-621-8476
Membership(s): Association of American University Presses
See separate listing for:
TriQuarterly Books

Northwoods Press
Division of Conservatory of American Letters
PO Box 298, Thomaston, ME 04861-0298
Tel: 207-354-0998
E-mail: cal@americanletters.org
Web Site: www.americanletters.org
Key Personnel
Ed: Richard S Danbury, III; Robert W Olmsted
Founded: 1971
Poetry & family/local history & quarterly literary journal "The Northwood Journal", writers' conference, workshops; textbooks.
ISBN Prefix(es): 0-89002
Number of titles published annually: 5 Print; 4 CD-ROM; 4 Audio
Total Titles: 20 Print; 8 CD-ROM; 8 Audio
Divisions: American History Press
Distributor for American History Press; Century Press; Dan River Press (textbook div)
Advertising Agency: Creative Images

Jeffrey Norton Publishers Inc
One Orchard Park Rd, Madison, CT 06443
Tel: 203-245-0195 *Toll Free Tel:* 800-243-1234
Fax: 203-245-0769 *Toll Free Fax:* 888-453-4329
E-mail: info@audioforum.com
Web Site: www.audioforum.com
Key Personnel
Pres & Intl Rts: Jeffrey Norton *E-mail:* jnorton@ audioforum.com
VP & Busn Mgr: Bruce Salender
E-mail: bsalender@audioforum.com
Founded: 1972

Adult & children's self-help books, including foreign language & book audio-cassette program.
ISBN Prefix(es): 0-88432; 1-57970
Number of titles published annually: 10 Print; 5 CD-ROM; 10 Audio
Total Titles: 400 Print; 25 CD-ROM; 3,850 Audio
Imprints: Audio-Forum; Sound Seminars; Video-Forum
Divisions: Audio-Forum
Distributor for BBC (selected titles); Cambridge University Press; Insight Travel Guides
Foreign Rep(s): Audio-Forum (Australia, England, South Africa)
Advertising Agency: Media Development Advertising

§W W Norton & Company Inc
500 Fifth Ave, New York, NY 10110-0017
SAN: 202-5795
Tel: 212-354-5500 *Toll Free Tel:* 800-233-4830 (orders & cust serv) *Fax:* 212-869-0856
Toll Free Fax: 800-458-6515
Web Site: www.wwnorton.com
Key Personnel
Pres & Chmn: W Drake McFeely
Vice Chmn, VP & Ed-in-Chief: Starling R Lawrence
CFO: Stephen King
Exec VP, National Book Co: Michael Charnogursky
VP & Dir, Coll Dept: Roby Harrington
VP & Publg Dir, Trade Dept: Jeannie Luciano
VP & Dir, Prodn Dept: Julia Reidhead
VP, Treas & Gen Mgr: Warren Tiley
VP & Mgr, Intl Sales: Dorothy M Cook
VP & Man Ed: Nancy K Palmquist
VP & Art Dir: Debra Morton Hoyt
VP, HR: Lisa Gaeth
Cust Serv Mgr: Flossie Hallett
Assoc Dir, Subs Rights: Felice Mello
Foreign Rts Mgr: Elisabeth Kerr
Perms Mgr: Sandra Chin
Perms & Copyright Mgr: Claire Reinertsen
Contracts Mgr: Sarah Feider
VP & Ed, Coll Dept: Stephen A Forman; Stephen P Dunn
Distance Edit Mgr, Coll Dept: Fred W McFarland
Ed, Coll Dept: Carol Stiles Bemis; Vanessa Drake-Johnson; Jon Durbin; Marilyn Moller; Maribeth Payne; Jack Repcheck; Melea Seward; Peter J Simon; Leo Weigman
Ancillary Ed, Coll Dept: April Lange
VP & Natl Sales Mgr, Coll Dept: Dan Bartell
Busn Mgr, Coll Dept: Richard L Rivellese
Admin Mgr, Coll Dept: Brian Baker
Adv & Conventions Mgr, Coll Dept: Mandy Brown
VP & Exec Ed, Trade Dept: Robert Weil
VP & Ed, Trade Dept: Jill Bialosky; Maria Guarnaschelli
Ed, Trade Dept: Edwin Barber; John Barstow; Amy Cherry; Alane Mason; Angela von der Lippe
Ed-at-Large, Trade Dept: Carol H Smith
VP & Dir, Sales & Mktg, Trade Dept: William F Rusin
Natl Field Sales Mgr & Dir, Promo & Spec Sales: Deirdre F Dolan
Sales & Affiliate Mgr, Trade Dept: Dosier D Hammond
Natl Accts Mgr, Trade Dept: Chris Ippolito
Natl Field Sales Mgr, Trade Dept: Rick Raeber
Internet Acct Mgr: John DiBello
VP & Publicity Dir, Trade Dept: Louise Brockett
Assoc Dir, Publicity, Trade Dept: Elizabeth Riley
Adv Mgr, Trade Dept: Nomi Victor
Edit Dir, Prof Books Dept: Deborah A Malmud
Ed, Prof Books in Architecture & Design: Nancy N Green
Man Ed, Prof Books Dept: Michael McGandy
Mktg Dir, Prof Books Dept: Kevin Olsen
Dir, Electronic Media: Cliff Landesman
E-mail: c.landesman@wwnorton.com

Assoc Dir, Electronic Media: Steve Hoge
Cont: Jorie Krumpfer
Dir, Info Technol: Ray Worrell
Founded: 1923
General nonfiction & fiction; trade paperbacks; college texts, professional books, architecture & interior design.
ISBN Prefix(es): 0-393; 0-87140
Number of titles published annually: 400 Print
Total Titles: 4,400 Print; 75 CD-ROM; 10 E-Book; 16 Audio
Imprints: Backcountry Publications; Countryman Press; Foul Play Press
Subsidiaries: Liveright Publishing Corp
Foreign Office(s): W W Norton & Company Ltd, Castle House, 75/76 Wells St, London W1T 3QT, United Kingdom, Man Dir & VP: Alan Cameron *Tel:* (020) 7323 1579 *Fax:* (020) 7436 4553
Distributor for Albatross Publishing House; Airphoto International Ltd; Bloomberg Press; George Braziller Inc; Chess Information & Research Center; Fantagraphics Books; The Hatherleigh Company Ltd; Kales Press; New Directions Publishing Corp; The New Press; Newmarket Press; Ontario Review; Peace Hill Press; Persea Books Inc; Pushcart Press; Quantuck Lane Press; Rio Nuevo; Smithsonian Books; Thames & Hudson; Verso
Foreign Rep(s): APAC Publishers Services (Indonesia, Malaysia, Singapore, Thailand); Delaney Global Publishers Service (Guam, Philippines); M K International Ltd (Japan); B K Norton Ltd (Korea, Taiwan); W W Norton & Co Ltd (Africa, UK, Ireland, Europe, Middle East); Pearson Education (New Zealand); Penguin Books Canada Ltd (Canada); Transglobal Publishers Services Ltd (Hong Kong); US Pub Rep Inc (Caribbean, Central America, Mexico, South America); John Wiley & Sons Australia Ltd (Australia)
Foreign Rights: Agencia Literaria Carmen Balcells (Portugal, Spain); Balcells Mello e Souza Riff (Brazil); Bardon Chinese Media Agency (China, Taiwan); Japan UNI Agency (Japan); Katai & Bolza (Hungary); Nurcihan Kesim (Turkey); Simona Kessler (Romania); Michelle Lapautre Agency (France); Marijke Lijnkamp (Netherlands); Mohrbooks (Germany); Andrew Nurnberg Associates (Baltic States, Bulgaria, Russia); Kristin Olson (Czech Republic); Roberto Santachiara (Italy); Maria Strarz-Kanska (Poland); Eric Yang Agency (Korea)
Advertising Agency: Bennett Book Advertising
Shipping Address: National Book Company Inc, Keystone Industrial Park, Scranton, PA 18512
See separate listing for:
The Countryman Press
The New Press

Nova Press
11659 Mayfield Ave, Suite 1, Los Angeles, CA 90049
Tel: 310-207-4078 *Toll Free Tel:* 800-949-6175
Fax: 310-571-0908
E-mail: novapress@aol.com
Web Site: www.novapress.net
Key Personnel
Pres & Electronic Publg: Jeff Kolby
Founded: 1993
Test prep books & software; SAT, GRE, LSAT, GMAT & MCAT.
ISBN Prefix(es): 0-9637371; 1-889057
Total Titles: 11 Print; 1 CD-ROM

Nova Publishing Co
1103 W College St, Carbondale, IL 62901
Tel: 618-457-3521 *Toll Free Tel:* 800-748-1175
Fax: 618-457-2541
E-mail: info@novapublishing.com
Web Site: www.novapublishing.com
Key Personnel
CEO: Dan Sitarz *E-mail:* dansitarz@earthlink.net

CFO: Janet Sitarz
Mgr: Melanie Bray
Founded: 1986
Publisher of small business & consumer legal books & software.
ISBN Prefix(es): 0-935755; 1-892949
Number of titles published annually: 4 Print
Total Titles: 25 Print
Imprints: Earthpress
Shipping Address: National Book Network, 15200 NBN Way, Blue Ridge Summit, PA 17214 *Tel:* 717-394-3800 *Toll Free Tel:* 800-462-6420 *Toll Free Fax:* 800-338-4550 *Web Site:* www.nbnbooks.com
Membership(s): Publishers Marketing Association

Nova Science Publishers Inc
400 Oset Ave, Suite 1600, Hauppauge, NY 11788
Tel: 631-231-7269 *Fax:* 631-231-8175
E-mail: novaeditorial@earthlink.net
Web Site: www.novapublishers.com
Key Personnel
Pres: Frank Columbus
Founded: 1985
Scientific, technical, medical & social sciences publishing; trade books - hardcover & softcover.
ISBN Prefix(es): 0-941743
Number of titles published annually: 450 Print; 10 CD-ROM
Total Titles: 2,380 Print
Imprints: Kroshka Books; Nova Science Books; Nova Social Science Books; Troitsa Books

§NovelBooks Inc
PO Box 661, Douglas, MA 01516-0661
Tel: 508-476-1611 *Fax:* 508-476-3866
E-mail: publisher@novelbooksinc.com
Web Site: www.novelbooksinc.com
Key Personnel
Pres & CEO: Penny Hussey *Fax:* 508-476-3866 *E-mail:* publisher@novelbooksinc.com
Prodn Dir: Gail McAbee *E-mail:* gail@novelbooksinc.com
Sales & Dist: April Welsh *E-mail:* sales@novelbooksinc.com
Founded: 2001
A print-on-demand & electronic book publisher that combines the best traditional publishing values with current & emerging technology & trends. We never charge any author fees. All submissions are reviewed with acceptance based on quality of writing. Accepted mss receive comprehensive editing, cover art, formattiing & layout. We provide both company level marketing efforts & assisting our authors with their promotional efforts.
ISBN Prefix(es): 1-931696; 1-59105
Number of titles published annually: 52 Print; 52 Online; 52 E-Book
Total Titles: 90 Print; 52 Online; 90 E-Book
Membership(s): Electronically Published Internet Connection; Electronically Published Professionals; National Foundation of Independent Businesses

NPS, see BrickHouse Books Inc

nursesbooks.org, The Publishing Program of ANA
Division of American Nurses Association
600 Maryland Ave SW, Suite 100-W, Washington, DC 20024-2571
Tel: 202-651-7000 *Toll Free Tel:* 800-637-0323 *Fax:* 202-651-7001
E-mail: anp@ana.org
Web Site: www.nursesbooks.org
Key Personnel
Publr: Rosanne Roe
Ed & Project Mgr: Eric Wurzbacher *Tel:* 202-651-7212 *E-mail:* ewurzbach@ana.org
Health care & nursing.

ISBN Prefix(es): 1-55810
Number of titles published annually: 15 Print
Total Titles: 90 Print

NYBG Press, see The New York Botanical Garden Press

§Nystrom
Division of Herff Jones
3333 Elston Ave, Chicago, IL 60618
SAN: 203-5529
Tel: 773-463-1144 *Toll Free Tel:* 800-621-8086 *Fax:* 773-463-0515
E-mail: info@nystromnet.com
Web Site: www.nystromnet.com
Key Personnel
Pres: Walt Cichy
Mktg Mgr: Don Rescigno
Founded: 1903
Social studies, history & geography programs, maps, globes, atlases & multimedia.
ISBN Prefix(es): 0-7825; 0-88463
Number of titles published annually: 3 Print
Total Titles: 30 Print; 5 CD-ROM; 1 E-Book

§OAG Worldwide
3025 Highland Pkwy, Suite 200, Downers Grove, IL 60515
Tel: 630-515-5300 *Fax:* 630-515-5301
Web Site: www.oag.com
Key Personnel
Sr Exec VP: Bill Andres
Founded: 1929
Supplier of independent travel info.
Total Titles: 14 CD-ROM; 1 Online; 20 Audio
Foreign Office(s): OAG Worldwide, Unit 8C, 2 Arbuthnot, Central Hong Kong, Hong Kong *Tel:* 2965 1700 *Fax:* 2965 1777 *E-mail:* hfong@oag.com
OAG Worldwide, 9 F Toranomon, 40 MT Bldg, 5-13-1 Toranomon, Minato-ku, Tokyo 105-0001, Japan *Tel:* (081) 36402 7301 *Fax:* (081) 36402 7302 *E-mail:* anakano_oag@hotmail.com
OAG Worldwide, 300 Beach Rd, Suite 35-01, The Concourse, Singapore 199555, Singapore *Tel:* 6395-5868 *Fax:* 6293-6566 *E-mail:* custsvcs@oagsin.com.sg
OAG Worldwide, Church St, Dunstable, Bedfordshire LU5 4HB, United Kingdom (headquarters) *Tel:* (01582) 695040 *Fax:* (01582) 695230 *E-mail:* customers@oag.com

Oak Knoll Press
310 Delaware St, New Castle, DE 19720
Tel: 302-328-7232 *Toll Free Tel:* 800-996-2556 *Fax:* 302-328-7274
E-mail: oakknoll@oakknoll.com
Web Site: www.oakknoll.com
Key Personnel
Pres: Robert D Fleck *E-mail:* bob@oakknoll.com
Intl Rts Contact & Dir, Publg & Lib Sales: John von Hoelle *E-mail:* john@oakknoll.com
Dir, Publicity & Mktg: John Laird *E-mail:* johnlaird@oakknoll.com
Founded: 1976
Publish scholarly books (books about books), bibliographies, book arts & book history.
ISBN Prefix(es): 1-884718; 1-58456
Number of titles published annually: 35 Print; 40 Online
Total Titles: 900 Print; 1 CD-ROM; 900 Online
Distributor for American Antiquarian Society; Bibliographical Society of America; The Bibliographical Society (UK); Bibliographical Society of University of Virginia; Bookplate Society; John Carter Brown Library; Catalpa Press; Chapin Library; Edinburgh Bibliographical Society; Martino Fine Books; Private Libraries Association; St Paul's Bibliographies;

Typophiles; University of Pittsburgh Press
(Pittsburgh Biblio Series)
Membership(s): AAP; Antiquarian Booksellers
Association of America; International League
of Antiquarian Booksellers

Oak Tree Publishing
2743 S Veterans Pkwy, Suite 135, Springfield, IL
64704-6402
Tel: 217-879-2822 *Fax:* 217-879-2844
E-mail: oaktreepub@aol.com
Web Site: www.oaktreebooks.com
Key Personnel
Publr: Billie Johnson
Founded: 1998
Independent small press that publishes fiction &
nonfiction. First time authors are welcome.
ISBN Prefix(es): 1-892343
Number of titles published annually: 10 Print
Total Titles: 28 Print
Imprints: Coptales; Dark Oak Mysteries; Oaktree
Books; Timeless Love
Advertising Agency: Captive Additions
Billing Address: 105 N Locust St, Owaneco, IL
62555
Returns: 105 N Locust St, Owaneco, IL 62555

Oaklea Press
Unit of S H Martin LLC
6912 Three Chopt Rd, Suite B, Richmond, VA
23226
Tel: 804-281-5872 *Toll Free Tel:* 800-295-4066
Fax: 804-281-5686
E-mail: info@oakleapress.com
Web Site: oakleapress.com
Key Personnel
Publr: S H Martin *Tel:* 804-281-5685
E-mail: shmartin@oakleapress.com
Ed: John David *E-mail:* jdavid@oakleapress.com
Founded: 1995
Tradebook publisher.
ISBN Prefix(es): 1-892538; 0-9646601; 0-
9664098
Number of titles published annually: 6 Print
Total Titles: 24 Print; 1 Audio
Imprints: New Marketplace; Oaklea Press
Sales Office(s): Midpoint Trade Books, 27 W 20
St, Suite 1102, New York, NY 10011, Contact:
Gail Kump *Tel:* 212-727-0190 *Fax:* 210-727-
0195 *E-mail:* gail@midpointtrade.com
Distribution Center: Midpoint Trade Books,
1263 Southwest Blvd, Kansas City, KS 66103,
Contact: Julie Hardison *Tel:* 913-831-2233
Fax: 913-362-7401 *E-mail:* julie@mipt.com
Membership(s): Publishers Marketing Association

§Oakstone Medical Publishing
Division of Oakstone Publishing, A Haights
Cross Co
6801 Cahaba Valley Rd, Birmingham, AL 35242
Tel: 205-991-5188 *Toll Free Tel:* 800-952-0690
Fax: 205-995-4656
E-mail: service@oakstonemedical.com
Web Site: www.oakstonemedical.com
Key Personnel
Pres: Nancy McMeekin *Tel:* 205-437-3003
Fax: 205-995-4650 *E-mail:* nmcmeekin@
oakstonepub.com
CFO: Charles Dismuke *Tel:* 205-437-3005
Fax: 205-995-4650 *E-mail:* cdismuke@
oakstonepub.com
Publr: Dean Celia *Tel:* 205-437-3004
E-mail: dcelia@oakstonepub.com
VP, Opers: Connie Epperson *Tel:* 205-437-3015
Fax: 205-995-4650 *E-mail:* cepperson@
oakstonepub.com
Dir, Mktg: Mary Hoffman *Tel:* 205-437-3055
Fax: 205-995-5210 *E-mail:* mhoffman@
oakstonepub.com
Dir, Cust Servs: Laura Barnett *Tel:* 205-437-
3042 *Fax:* 205-995-4650 *E-mail:* lbarnett@
oakstonepub.com

Man Ed: Cathy Wesler *Tel:* 205-437-3053
E-mail: cwesler@oakstonepub.com
Founded: 1975
Creates summaries & critical reviews of medical
journal articles, providing audio, print, elec-
tronic, & online products in more than 30 med-
ical, dental, & allied health specialties.
Number of titles published annually: 5 CD-ROM;
4 Online; 5 Audio
Total Titles: 46 CD-ROM; 12 Online; 42 Audio
Imprints: Clinical Advances; Inservice Reviews;
Journalbytes; MKSAP Audio Companion;
MultiMedia Reviews; Practical Reviews;
QuickScan Reviews; Select; SESAP Audio
Companion; Topic Series
Membership(s): NEPA

Oberlin College Press
Subsidiary of Oberlin College
50 N Professor St, Oberlin, OH 44074-1095
Tel: 440-775-8408 *Fax:* 440-775-8124
E-mail: oc.press@oberlin.edu
Web Site: www.oberlin.edu/ocpress
Key Personnel
1st Ed: David Young
Ed: Pamela Alexander; Martha Collins; David
Walker
Man Ed & Intl Rts Contact: Linda Slocum
Founded: 1969
Poetry in translation; contemporary American po-
etry.
ISBN Prefix(es): 0-932440
Number of titles published annually: 3 Print
Total Titles: 37 Print
Distributed by Cornell University Press Services
Orders to: Cornell University Press Services,
PO Box 6525, 750 Cascadilla St, Ithaca, NY
14851-6525
Returns: Cornell University Press Services, PO
Box 6525, 750 Cascadilla St, Ithaca, NY
14851-6525
Membership(s): Council of Literary Magazines &
Presses

Ocean Press
PO Box 1186, Old Chelsea Sta, New York, NY
10113-1186
Tel: 718-246-4160
E-mail: info@oceanbookscom.au
Web Site: www.oceanbooks.com.au
Key Personnel
Contact: Dan Georgakas
Founded: 1990
ISBN Prefix(es): 1-875284; 1-876175
Number of titles published annually: 16 Print
Total Titles: 54 Print
Foreign Office(s): GPO 3279, Melbourne, Victoria
3001, Australia *Tel:* (03) 9326 4280 *Fax:* (03)
9329 5040 *E-mail:* edit@oceanpress.com.au
Calle 21, No 406, Vedado, Havana, Cuba
Tel: (07) 666 082 *Fax:* (07) 666 082
E-mail: edit@oceanpress.com.au
Pluto Press, 345 Archway Rd, London N6
5AA, United Kingdom *Tel:* (020) 834802724
Fax: (020) 8348 9133 *E-mail:* pluto@
plutobooks.com *Web Site:* www.plutobooks.
com
Distributed by Consortium Book Sales & Distri-
bution Inc

Ocean Publishing
Division of The Gromling Group Inc
PO Box 1080, Flagler Beach, FL 32136-1080
SAN: 254-8755
Tel: 386-517-1600 *Fax:* 386-517-2564
E-mail: publisher@cfl.rr.com
Web Site: www.ocean-publishing.com
Key Personnel
Publr: Frank Gromling
Founded: 2002
Traditional publisher of quality books in several
genre's.

ISBN Prefix(es): 0-9717
Number of titles published annually: 10 Print
Total Titles: 10 Print
Membership(s): Florida Publishers Association;
Florida Writers Association; Publishers Market-
ing Association; Small Publishers Association
of North America

Ocean Tree Books
1325 Cerro Gordo Rd, Santa Fe, NM 87501
Mailing Address: PO Box 1295, Santa Fe, NM
87504 SAN: 241-0478
Tel: 505-983-1412 *Fax:* 505-983-0899
E-mail: oceantree@earthlink.net
Web Site: www.oceantree.com
Key Personnel
Dir: Richard Polese *Tel:* 505-982-4980
Publicity & Mktg: Hudson White
Off Mgr: Martin Burch
Founded: 1983
General trade with emphasis on Southwestern &
Southern travel, faith & spirit & peacemaking.
ISBN Prefix(es): 0-943734; 0-9712548
Number of titles published annually: 5 Print
Total Titles: 45 Print
Imprints: Adventure Roads Travel; OTB Legacy
Editions; Peacewatch Editions
Branch Office(s)
Ocean Tree Books Legacy Editions, 2508
Chippewa St, New Orleans, LA 70130
Distributed by Books West LLC; Clear Light Dis-
tribution; New Leaf; Treasure Chest Books
Distributor for Liberty Literary Works; Sunlit
Hills Press
Foreign Rep(s): Blessingway Author Services (In-
ternational)
Foreign Rights: Blessingway Author Services
Membership(s): New Mexico Book Association

Ocean View Books
PO Box 9249, Denver, CO 80209-0246
SAN: 299-0318
Tel: 303-756-5222 *Toll Free Tel:* 800-848-6222
(orders only) *Fax:* 303-756-3208
E-mail: ocean@probook.net
Web Site: www.probook.net/ocean.html
Key Personnel
Pres & Ed: Lee Ballentine
Man Ed: Jennifer MacGregor
Founded: 1981
Poetry, surrealism, regional art & history.
ISBN Prefix(es): 0-938075
Number of titles published annually: 4 Print
Total Titles: 70 Print
Imprints: The Documents of Colorado Art; The
Ocean View Doubles
Foreign Rep(s): Chris Reed (Australia, Europe)

Oceana Publications Inc
75 Main St, Dobbs Ferry, NY 10522-1601
SAN: 202-5744
Tel: 914-693-8100 *Toll Free Tel:* 800-831-0758
(orders only) *Fax:* 914-693-0402
E-mail: info@oceanalaw.com
Web Site: www.oceanalaw.com
Key Personnel
Pres: David R Cohen
Exec VP: Lois Cohen
Sr VP & Gen Counsel: M C Susan DeMaio
Sr VP & CFO: Stephen Nussbaum
VP, Mktg & Sales: Larry Selby
VP, Admin Servs: Louise Ciero
VP, Prodn & Oper Servs: James F Newman
VP, Technol: Michael Peterfreund
MIS Mgr: David Roider
Man Ed: JoAnn Mitchell
Founded: 1946
Legal publisher of international business & trade;
investments & banking; arbitration & litigation;
intellectual property; comparative law; consti-
tutional law; environmental law; legal research
& reference tools, legal history, law for the
layperson, treaties, white collar crime; looseleaf

& online services; monographs & multi-volume reference sets.
ISBN Prefix(es): 0-379
Number of titles published annually: 30 Print; 2 Online
Total Titles: 195 Print; 8 Online; 1 E-Book

Octameron Associates
1900 Mount Vernon Ave, Alexandria, VA 22301
SAN: 209-2751
Mailing Address: PO Box 2748, Alexandria, VA 22301-2748
Tel: 703-836-5480 *Fax:* 703-836-5650
E-mail: info@octameron.com
Web Site: www.octameron.com
Key Personnel
Publr: Anna Leider *E-mail:* anna@octameron.com
Founded: 1976
Educational directories & reference books.
ISBN Prefix(es): 0-917760; 0-945981; 1-57509
Number of titles published annually: 9 Print
Total Titles: 19 Print; 1 CD-ROM
Imprints: Octameron Press

OECD Washington Center, see Organization for Economic Cooperation & Development

Off the Page Press
PO Box 4880-J, Buena Vista, CO 81211
SAN: 298-9220
Tel: 719-395-9450 *Toll Free Tel:* 888-852-6402
Fax: 719-395-9453
E-mail: editor@yellowpagesage.com
Web Site: www.yellowpagesage.com
Key Personnel
Contact: Sydney Miles *E-mail:* sydney@giantpotatoes.com
Founded: 1995
Publisher of books that help you surge past business & personal limitations; "Turning Notions into Motions".
ISBN Prefix(es): 1-888739
Number of titles published annually: 3 Print
Total Titles: 6 Print; 1 Online
Imprints: Quick & Painless

Ohio Genealogical Society
713 S Main St, Mansfield, OH 44907-1644
Tel: 419-756-7294 *Fax:* 419-756-6861
E-mail: ogs@ogs.org
Web Site: www.ogs.org
Key Personnel
Pres: Diane Gagel
Libn Dir: Thomas Stephen Neel
Founded: 1959
Family history library & society.
ISBN Prefix(es): 0-935057
Number of titles published annually: 4 Print
Total Titles: 25 Print

Ohio State University Foreign Language Publications
Division of Foreign Language Center
198 Hagerty Hall, 1775 College Rd, Columbus, OH 43210-1340
Tel: 614-292-3838 *Toll Free Tel:* 800-678-6999
Fax: 614-688-3355
E-mail: flpubs@osu.edu
Web Site: nealrc.osu.edu/flpubs
Key Personnel
Pubns Mgr: Gregory Wilson
Founded: 1972
Foreign language individualized instruction materials for less commonly taught languages.
ISBN Prefix(es): 0-87415
Number of titles published annually: 3 Print
Total Titles: 260 Print

Ohio State University Press
180 Pressey Hall, 1070 Carmack Rd, Columbus, OH 43210-1002
Tel: 614-292-6930 *Toll Free Tel:* 800-621-2736
Fax: 614-292-2065 *Toll Free Fax:* 800-621-8476
E-mail: ohiostatepress@osu.edu
Web Site: ohiostatepress.org
Key Personnel
Dir: Malcolm Litchfield
Man Ed, Journals: Lee Mobley
Acqs Ed: Heather Miller
Lib Sales Dir & Mktg Mgr: Laurie Avery
   Tel: 614-292-1462 *E-mail:* avery.21@osu.edu
Busn Mgr: Kathy Edwards
Founded: 1957
General scholarly & trade nonfiction & fiction; classics.
ISBN Prefix(es): 0-8142
Number of titles published annually: 30 Print
Total Titles: 270 Print
Imprints: Sandstone
Distributor for Western Reserve Historical Society
Foreign Rep(s): East-West Export Books
Distribution Center: University of Chicago Distribution Center, 11030 S Langley Ave, Chicago, IL 60628 *Tel:* 773-568-1550

Ohio University Press
One Ohio University, Scott Quadrangle, Athens, OH 45701
SAN: 282-0773
Tel: 740-593-1155 *Toll Free Tel:* 800-621-2736
Fax: 740-593-4536
Web Site: www.ohio.edu/oupress/
Key Personnel
Dir: David Sanders *Tel:* 740-593-1157
   E-mail: dsanders1@ohio.edu
Sr Ed: Gillian Berchowitz *Tel:* 740-593-1159
   E-mail: gillianberchowitz@ohio.edu
Busn Mgr & Foreign Rts: Bonnie Rand *Tel:* 740-593-1156 *E-mail:* rand@oak.cats.ohio.edu
Ms Ed: Nancy Basmajian *Tel:* 740-593-1161
   E-mail: nbasmajia1@ohio.edu
Mktg Mgr: Richard Gilbert *Tel:* 740-593-1160
   E-mail: gilbert@ohio.edu
Cust Serv Mgr: Judy Wilson *Tel:* 740-593-1154
   E-mail: jwilson1@ohio.edu
Founded: 1964
Victorian studies, African studies, ecology, migration, Polish studies, frontier Americana.
ISBN Prefix(es): 0-8214; 0-8040; 0-89680
Total Titles: 600 Print
Imprints: Swallow Press
Distributor for Center for International Studies; Swallow Press
Foreign Rep(s): East-West Export Books (Australia, Asia, New Zealand, Pacific Region); Eurospan (Africa, UK, Continental Europe, Middle East)
Warehouse: Chicago Distribution Center, 11030 S Langley Ave, Chicago, IL 60628 *Toll Free Tel:* 800-621-2736 *Toll Free Fax:* 800-621-8476
Membership(s): American Association of University Presses
See separate listing for:
Swallow Press

Old Barn Enterprises Inc
600 Kelly Rd, Carthage, NC 28327
Tel: 910-947-2587 *Fax:* 910-947-5112
Key Personnel
Pres: Jeff Farr
Founded: 1992
Publish archival softbound, fine editions; poetry chapbooks, professional books, home study courses, photography & marketing.
ISBN Prefix(es): 1-879009
Number of titles published annually: 7 Print
Total Titles: 23 Print
Imprints: Old Barn Publishing; Scots Plaid Press

§Olde & Oppenheim Publishers
3219 N Margate Place, Chandler, AZ 85224
Tel: 480-839-2280 *Fax:* 480-839-0241
E-mail: olde_oppenheim@hotmail.com
Key Personnel
Dir, Mktg: Mike Gratz
Software manuals, computer how-to, internet sites.
ISBN Prefix(es): 0-944861
Number of titles published annually: 3 Print; 2 CD-ROM; 2 Online; 2 E-Book
Total Titles: 9 Print

The Oliver Press Inc
Charlotte Sq, 5707 W 36 St, Minneapolis, MN 55416-2510
Tel: 952-926-8981 *Fax:* 952-926-8965
Web Site: www.oliverpress.com
Key Personnel
Publr & Intl Rts Contact: Mark Lerner
Ed & Publicity: Charles Helgesen
   E-mail: charles@oliverpress.com
Ed: Mark Lerner *E-mail:* mark@oliverpress.com
Founded: 1991
Nonfiction children's books.
ISBN Prefix(es): 1-881508
Number of titles published annually: 12 Print
Total Titles: 76 Print
Imprints: Clara House Books
Foreign Rights: EDU Reference; John Reed Book Distribution

Omni Publishers Inc
29131 Bulverde Rd, San Antonio, TX 78260
Mailing Address: PO Box 408, Bulverde, TX 78163
Tel: 830-438-7110 *Fax:* 830-438-4645
E-mail: omnipub@gvtc.com
Web Site: www.webbookstore.net
Key Personnel
Pres: Ruth Lansing
Founded: 1986
Books on law & real estate, national education products, Texas law.
Number of titles published annually: 8 Print
Total Titles: 65 Print

Omnibus Press
Division of Music Sales Corp
257 Park Ave S, 20th fl, New York, NY 10010
Tel: 212-254-2100 *Toll Free Tel:* 800-431-7187
   Fax: 212-254-2013 *Toll Free Fax:* 800-345-6842
E-mail: info@musicsales.com
Web Site: www.musicsales.com
Key Personnel
Pres: Barrie Edwards
Dir, Opers: Kim Rabaglia
Founded: 1975
Pop culture, music & film books.
ISBN Prefix(es): 0-8256; 0-7119; 0-86001; 1-84449
Number of titles published annually: 100 Print
Total Titles: 433 Print
Distributor for Big Meteor; Blue Book; Gramophone
Distribution Center: Music Sales Distribution Ctr, 445 Bellvale Rd, Chester, NY 10918
Tel: 845-469-4699 *Toll Free Tel:* 800-431-7187 *Fax:* 845-469-7544 *Toll Free Fax:* 800-345-6842 *E-mail:* info@musicsales.com *Web Site:* www.musicsales.com

Omnidawn Publishing
1632 Elm Ave, Richmond, CA 94805-1614
SAN: 299-3236
Tel: 510-237-5472 *Toll Free Tel:* 800-792-4957
   Fax: 510-232-8525
Web Site: www.omnidawn.com
Key Personnel
Pres & Treas: Ken Keegan *Tel:* 510-610-3763
   E-mail: kkeegan@omnidawn.com
VP & Sec: Rusty Morrison *E-mail:* rusty@omnidawn.com
Founded: 1996
Publishers of poetry & literary fiction.

ISBN Prefix(es): 1-890650
Number of titles published annually: 3 Print
Total Titles: 13 Print
Distributed by Small Press Distribution

Omnigraphics Inc
615 Griswold St, Detroit, MI 48226
SAN: 249-2520
Tel: 313-961-1340 *Toll Free Tel:* 800-234-
   1340 (cust serv) *Fax:* 313-961-1383
   Toll Free Fax: 800-875-1340 (cust serv)
E-mail: info@omnigraphics.com
Web Site: www.omnigraphics.com
Key Personnel
Chmn: Frederick G Ruffner
Pres & Publr: Peter E Ruffner *E-mail:* pruffner@
   omnigraphics.com
Sr VP: Matthew Barbour *E-mail:* mbarbour@
   omnigraphics.com
VP, Directories: Kay Gill *E-mail:* kgill@
   omnigraphics.com
Res & Mktg Consultant: David Bianco
   Tel: 313-961-1340 ext 515 *E-mail:* dbianco@
   omnigraphics.com
Devt Mgr: Leif Gruenberg
Opers Mgr: Kevin Hayes
Founded: 1985
Reference books, periodicals & journals for li-
   braries & schools, directories.
ISBN Prefix(es): 1-55888; 0-7808
Number of titles published annually: 50 Print; 1
   Online
Total Titles: 400 Print; 1 Online
Advertising Agency: Marley & Cratchit
Orders to: PO Box 625, Holmes, PA 19043 *Toll
   Free Tel:* 800-234-1340 *Toll Free Fax:* 800-
   875-1340 *Web Site:* www.omnigraphics.com
Returns: 2050 Elmwood Ave, Sharon Hill, PA
   19079

**Omohundro Institute of Early American
   History & Culture**
109 Cary St, Williamsburg, VA 23185
Mailing Address: PO Box 8781, Williamsburg,
   VA 23187-8781 SAN: 201-5161
Tel: 757-221-1114 *Fax:* 757-221-1047
E-mail: ieahc1@wm.edu
Web Site: www.wm.edu/oieahc
Key Personnel
Dir: Ronald Hoffman *Tel:* 757-221-1133
Sec to Dir: Beverly Smith
Ed: Fredrika J Teute *Tel:* 757-221-1118
   E-mail: fjteut@wm.edu
Man Ed: Gilbert B Kelly *Tel:* 757-221-1117
   E-mail: gbkell@wm.edu
Founded: 1943 (Founded & still sponsored jointly
   by the College of William & Mary & the Colo-
   nial Williamsburg Foundation)
Scholarly books on early American history cul-
   ture & literature 1500-1815.
ISBN Prefix(es): 0-910776
Number of titles published annually: 5 Print
Total Titles: 180 Print
Distributed by The University of North Carolina
   Press

§One Planet Publishing House
PO Box 19840, Seattle, WA 98109-1840
SAN: 253-9438
Tel: 206-282-9699 *Toll Free Tel:* 877-526-
   3814 (87-PLANET-14) *Fax:* 206-282-9699
   Toll Free Fax: 877-526-3814 (87-PLANET-14)
E-mail: info@oneplanetpublishinghouse.com
Web Site: www.oneplanetpublishinghouse.com
Key Personnel
CEO & Pres: Tommie L Jones *E-mail:* media@
   oneplanetpublishinghouse.com
Sr VP, Mktg: Daniela E Schreier
VP, Design: Ken Clark
Founded: 2000
Founded with the mission of publishing books
   on lifestyle, inspiration & self-discovery. Ded-

icated to promoting timely & innovative books
   that focus on spiritual growth & inspiration for
   all people in the world family. Emphasize in-
   spirational books in personal empowerment,
   self-help & stress & life management.
ISBN Prefix(es): 0-9710099
Number of titles published annually: 5 Print; 2
   CD-ROM; 3 Online; 5 E-Book
Total Titles: 1 Print; 1 Online; 1 E-Book
Sales Office(s): Book World Services Inc, 1230
   Heil Quaker Blvd, LaVergne, TN 34086 (Aus-
   tralia, Canada, Europe, New Zealand & US)
STD Distributors Pte Ltd, Pasir Panjang Distri-
   centre, Black 1, No 03-01A, Singapore 118480,
   Singapore *Tel:* (276) 7626 *Fax:* (276) 7119
Distributed by The Bookman Inc; Book World
   Services Inc (Australia, Canada, Europe, New
   Zealand & US); STD Distributors Pte Ltd
   (Brunei, Singapore/Malaysia)
Foreign Rep(s): Book World Services Inc (Aus-
   tralia, Canada, Europe, New Zealand, USA);
   STD Distributors Pte Ltd (Brunei, Malaysia &
   Singapore)
Billing Address: Book World Services Inc, 1230
   Heil Quaker Blvd, LaVergne, TN 34086
   (Australia, Canada, Europe, New Zealand &
   US); STD Distributors Pte Ltd, Pasir Pan-
   jang Districentre, Black 1, No 03-01A, Sin-
   gapore 118480, Singapore (Brunei, Singa-
   pore/Malaysia) *Tel:* (0276) 7626 *Fax:* (0276)
   7119 *E-mail:* clum@tpl.com.sg;sitizahmad@tpl.
   com.sg
Orders to: Book World Services Inc, 1230 Heil
   Quaker Blvd, LaVergne, TN 34086 (Australia,
   Canada, Europe, New Zealand & US); STD
   Distributors Pte Ltd, Pasir Panjang Districentre,
   Black 1, No 03-01A, Singapore 118480, Singa-
   pore (Brunei, Singapore/Malaysia) *Tel:* (0276)
   7626 *Fax:* (0276) 7119
Returns: Book Work Services Inc, 1230 Heil
   Quaker Blvd, LaVergne, TN 34086 (Australia,
   Canada, Europe, New Zealand & US); STD
   Distributors Pte Ltd, Pasir Panjang Districen-
   tre, Block 1, No 03-01A, Pasir Panjang Rd,
   Singapore 118480, Singapore (Brunei, Singa-
   pore/Malaysia) *Tel:* (0276) 7626 *Fax:* (0276)
   7119 *E-mail:* clum@tpl.com.sg
Shipping Address: Book World Services Inc, 1230
   Heil Quaker Blvd, LaVergne, TN 34086 (Aus-
   tralia, Canada, Europe, New Zealand & US);
   STD Distributors Pte, Pasir Panjang Districentre, Block 1, No 03-01A, Pasir Panjang Rd,
   Singapore 118480, Singapore (Brunei, Sin-
   gapore/Malaysia) *Tel:* (276) 7626 *Fax:* (276)
   7119 *E-mail:* clum@tpl.com.sg; sitizahmad@
   tpl.com.sg
Warehouse: Book World Services Inc, 1230
   Quaker Blvd, LaVergne, TN 34086 (Australia,
   Canada, Europe, New Zealand & US)
STD Distributors Pte Ltd, Pasir Panjang Districentre, Block 1, No 03-01A, Pasir Panjang Rd 118480, Singapore (Brunei, Singa-
   pore/Malaysia) *Tel:* (276) 7626 *Fax:* (276)
   7119 *E-mail:* clum@tpl.com.sg; sitizahmad@
   tpl.com.sg
Membership(s): Publishers Marketing Association

§OneOnOne Computer Training
Division of Mosaic Media Inc
2055 Army Trail Rd, Suite 100, Addison, IL
   60101
Tel: 630-628-0500 *Toll Free Tel:* 800-424-8668
E-mail: oneonone@protrain.com
Web Site: www.oootraining.com
Key Personnel
Pres: Lee McFadden *Tel:* 630-628-0500 ext 238
   E-mail: leemcf@protrain.com
Intl Rts Contact: Tom Lydon
Mgr Electronic Media: Larry Janis
Founded: 1976
Training publisher.
ISBN Prefix(es): 0-917792; 1-56562

Number of titles published annually: 2 Print; 2
   Online; 2 E-Book
Total Titles: 25 Print; 10 CD-ROM; 4 Online; 5
   E-Book; 10 Audio
Imprints: Marketing Smarter; Professional Train-
   ing Association; Working Smarter
Foreign Office(s): 11-16 The Bardfield Centre,
   Great Bardfield, Essex CM7 4SL, United King-
   dom
Membership(s): Newsletter & Electronic Publish-
   ers Association

§OneSource
300 Baker Ave, Concord, MA 01742
Tel: 978-318-4300 *Toll Free Tel:* 800-554-5501
   (sales) *Fax:* 978-318-4690
E-mail: sales@onesource.com
Web Site: www.onesource.com
Key Personnel
Pres & CEO: Yvonne Cekel
Sr VP, Sales Support & Solutions: Phil Garlick
Founded: 1984
Database of approximately 50,000 US Techni-
   cians Manufacturers, Developers & Services.
ISBN Prefix(es): 1-57114
Number of titles published annually: 5 Online
Total Titles: 5 CD-ROM; 5 Online

Online Training Solutions Inc
PO Box 2224, Redmond, WA 98073-2224
Tel: 425-885-1441 *Toll Free Tel:* 800-854-3344
   Fax: 425-881-1642; 425-671-0640
E-mail: customerservice@otsi.com
Web Site: www.otsi.com
Key Personnel
Pres: Steve Lambert
VP, Prodn & Publg: Joyce Cox
VP, Opers: Joan Preppernau
Founded: 1987
Educational & professional book publisher.
ISBN Prefix(es): 1-879399; 1-58278
Number of titles published annually: 12 Print
Total Titles: 60 Print

Open Court
SRA/McGraw-Hill, 332 S Michigan, Suite 1100,
   Chicago, IL 60604
Tel: 312-939-1500 *Toll Free Tel:* 800-815-2280
   (orders only) *Fax:* 312-939-8150
E-mail: opencourt@caruspub.com
Web Site: www.opencourtbooks.com
Founded: 1887
ISBN Prefix(es): 0-87548; 0-912050; 0-89688; 0-
   8126
Number of titles published annually: 15 Print
Total Titles: 300 Print

Open Horizons Publishing Co
PO Box 205, Fairfield, IA 52556-0205
SAN: 265-170X
Tel: 641-472-6130 *Toll Free Tel:* 800-796-6130
   Fax: 641-472-1560
E-mail: info@bookmarket.com
Web Site: www.bookmarket.com
Key Personnel
Publr & Author: John Kremer
   E-mail: johnkremer@bookmarket.com
Assoc Publr: Gail Berry
Mktg Dir: Bob Sanny
Lib Sales Dir: Paula Fritchen
Founded: 1982
Books for publishers & direct marketers.
ISBN Prefix(es): 0-912411
Number of titles published annually: 3 Print; 3
   CD-ROM; 3 Online; 3 E-Book; 1 Audio
Total Titles: 21 Print; 10 CD-ROM; 3 Online; 10
   E-Book; 2 Audio
Distributed by National Book Network
Warehouse: 1200 S Main St, Fairfield, IA
   52556, Assoc Publr: Gail Berry *Tel:* 641-472-

6130 *Fax:* 641-472-1560 *E-mail:* orders@bookmarket.com
Membership(s): Publishers Marketing Association; Small Publishers Association of North America

Open Road Publishing
PO Box 284, Cold Spring Harbor, NY 11724-0284
Tel: 631-692-7172 *Fax:* 631-692-7193
E-mail: jopenroad@aol.com
Key Personnel
Publr: Jonathan Stein
Assoc Publr: Avery Cardoza
Acqs Ed: Faith Stanhope
Founded: 1993
Travel, domestic & foreign, how-to, biographies, current events, sports, fantasy & commentary.
ISBN Prefix(es): 1-892975; 1-59360
Number of titles published annually: 22 Print
Total Titles: 62 Print
Imprints: Cold Spring Press
Distributed by Quality Books; Simon & Schuster
Foreign Rep(s): Windsor Books (UK)

§OPIS/STALSBY Directories & Databases
Division of United Communications Group
Parkway 70 Plaza, 1255 Rt 70, Suite 32N, Lakewood, NJ 08701
Tel: 732-901-8800 *Toll Free Tel:* 800-275-0950
Fax: 732-901-9632
Web Site: www.opisnet.com
Key Personnel
Dir, Prodn: Renee Ortner *Tel:* 732-901-8800 ext 162 *E-mail:* rortner@opisnet.com
Sr Ed: Karen England *E-mail:* kengland@opisnet.com
Assoc Ed: Trish Gallotta *E-mail:* tgallotta@opisnet.com
Founded: 1980
ISBN Prefix(es): 0-911299
Number of titles published annually: 4 Print
Total Titles: 4 Print; 4 CD-ROM

§Optical Society of America
2010 Massachusetts Ave NW, Washington, DC 20036-1023
Tel: 202-223-8130 *Fax:* 202-223-1096
E-mail: custserv@osa.org
Web Site: www.osa.org
Key Personnel
Dir, Pubns: John S Childs *Tel:* 202-416-1906 *E-mail:* jchild@osa.org
Assoc Publr: Alan N Tourtlotte *Tel:* 202-416-1908 *Fax:* 202-416-6129 *E-mail:* atourt@osa.org
Dir, IT: Deborah Herrin *Tel:* 202-416-1472 *E-mail:* dherri@osa.org
Manuscripts Dir: Kelly Cohen *Tel:* 202-416-1917 *Fax:* 202-416-6129 *E-mail:* kcohen@osa.org
Rts & Perms: Susannah Lehman *Tel:* 202-416-1901 *Fax:* 202-416-6129 *E-mail:* slehma@osa.org
Founded: 1916
Book & journal publishing, meetings, technical membership.
ISBN Prefix(es): 1-55752
Number of titles published annually: 15 Print; 3 CD-ROM; 9 Online
Total Titles: 250 Print; 3 CD-ROM; 9 Online
U.S. Rep(s): PBD
Foreign Rep(s): Kinokuniya (Japan)
Membership(s): American Institute of Physics

Optimization Software Inc
10800 Savona Rd, Los Angeles, CA 90077
Tel: 310-472-2910 *Fax:* 310-472-2910
E-mail: aries@optipub.bizland.com
Web Site: www.optipub.bizland
Key Personnel
Man Ed: A B Aries *E-mail:* aries@bizland.com
Founded: 1983
Publishing.

ISBN Prefix(es): 0-911575
Number of titles published annually: 2 Print
Total Titles: 32 Print

Optometric Extension Program Foundation
1921 E Carnegie Ave, Suite 3-L, Santa Ana, CA 92705-5510
Tel: 949-250-8070 *Fax:* 949-250-8157
E-mail: oep1@oep.org
Web Site: www.oep.org
Key Personnel
Man Ed & Dir, Pubns: Sally Marshall Corngold *E-mail:* smcorngold@oep.org
Exec Dir & Intl Rts Contact: Robert Williams *E-mail:* rwilliams@oep.org
Lib Sales Dir: Kathleen Patterson *E-mail:* kpatterson@oep.org
Founded: 1928
Books, journals, pamphlets, catalogs & directories.
ISBN Prefix(es): 0-943599; 0-929780
Number of titles published annually: 8 Print; 1 CD-ROM
Total Titles: 130 Print; 1 CD-ROM

Orange Frazer Press Inc
37 1/2 W Main St, Wilmington, OH 45177
Mailing Address: PO Box 214, Wilmington, OH 45177-0214
Tel: 937-382-3196 *Toll Free Tel:* 800-852-9332
Fax: 937-383-3159
E-mail: ofrazer@erinet.com
Web Site: www.orangefrazer.com
Key Personnel
Publr: Marcy Hawley
Ed: John Baskin
Cust Serv & Shipping: Tammy McKay
Tech & Design: Tim Fauley
Mktg: Sarah Hawley *E-mail:* shawley@orangefrazer.com
Founded: 1987
Regional book publisher specializing in Ohio nonfiction (reference, sports, commentary, travel, nature, etc). Production & design is considered "high-end". Recent winner of the Ohioana 2000 Citation Award for Excellence in Publishing.
ISBN Prefix(es): 1-882203; 0-9619637
Number of titles published annually: 7 Print
Total Titles: 50 Print

Orbis Books
Division of Maryknoll Fathers & Brothers
Walsh Bldg, 75 Ryder Rd, Ossining, NY 10562
Mailing Address: PO Box 308, Maryknoll, NY 10545-0308 SAN: 202-828X
Tel: 914-941-7636 *Toll Free Tel:* 800-258-5838 (orders) *Fax:* 914-941-7005 (orders); 914-945-0670 (office)
E-mail: orbisbooks@maryknoll.org
Web Site: www.orbisbooks.com
Key Personnel
Publr: Michael Leach *E-mail:* mleach@maryknoll.org
Ed-in-Chief: Robert Ellsberg *E-mail:* rellsberg@maryknoll.org
Rts & Perms: Doris Goodnough *E-mail:* dgoodnough@maryknoll.org
Man Ed: William R Burrows *E-mail:* bburrows@maryknoll.org
Sr Mktg Mgr: Bernadette Price *E-mail:* bprice@maryknoll.org
Busn Mgr: William Medeot *E-mail:* bmedeot@maryknoll.org
Sales Assoc: Mary Ann Ferrara *E-mail:* mferrara@maryknoll.org
Mktg Assoc: Kim Briggs *E-mail:* kbriggs@maryknoll.org
Cust Serv: Jim Schlesinger *E-mail:* jschlesinger@maryknoll.org
Founded: 1970
ISBN Prefix(es): 0-88344; 1-57075

Number of titles published annually: 50 Print
Total Titles: 480 Print
Foreign Rep(s): Alban Books (UK, Europe); Bayard Distribution (Canada); Catholic Book Shop (South Africa); Rainbow Books (Australia)
Advertising Agency: Roth Advertising, PO Box 96, Sea Cliff, NY 11579-0096, Contact: Charles Roth *Tel:* 516-674-8603 *Fax:* 516-674-8606
Warehouse: Maryknoll Center Warehouse, 55 Ryder Rd, Ossining, NY 10562, Warehouse Mgr: Dave Agosta *Tel:* 914-941-7636 ext 2493
Membership(s): ABA; Catholic Book Publishers Association

Orca Book Publishers
PO Box 468, Custer, WA 98240-0468
Tel: 250-380-1229 *Toll Free Tel:* 800-210-5277
Fax: 250-380-1892
E-mail: orca@orcabook.com
Web Site: www.orcabook.com
Key Personnel
Publr & Intl Rts: Robert Tyrrell *E-mail:* tyrrell@orcabook.com
Mktg Dir & Lib Sales Dir: Andrew Wooldridge *E-mail:* andrew.wooldridge@orcabook.com
Founded: 1984
Children & young adult literature.
ISBN Prefix(es): 1-55143; 0-920501
Number of titles published annually: 45 Print
Total Titles: 250 Print
Branch Office(s)
PO Box 5626, Victoria, BC V8R 6S4, Canada
Distributor for Formac; Grasshopper Books; James Lorimer & Co; Polestar Calendars; Roussand Press; Second Story Press; Sono Nis Pres; Sygnet Publications; Theytus Books; Walrus Publications
Warehouse: Bldg E, 7056 Portal Way, Ferndale, WA 98248

Orchises Press
PO Box 20602, Alexandria, VA 22320-1602
Tel: 703-683-1243 *Fax:* 703-993-1161
Web Site: mason.gmu.edu/~rlathbur/
Key Personnel
Pres & Ed-in-Chief: Roger Lathbury *E-mail:* lathbury@gmu.edu
Founded: 1983
ISBN Prefix(es): 0-914061; 1-932535
Number of titles published annually: 5 Print
Total Titles: 103 Print

Order of the Cross
PO Box 2472, La Grange, IL 60525-8572
Toll Free Tel: 800-611-1361 *Toll Free Fax:* 800-611-1361
E-mail: meditate@interaccess.com
Key Personnel
Lit Sec: Loralee Holton
Number of titles published annually: 1 Print

§Oregon Catholic Press
5536 NE Hassalo, Portland, OR 97213
Tel: 503-281-1191 *Toll Free Tel:* 800-548-8749
Fax: 503-282-3486 *Toll Free Fax:* 800-843-8181
E-mail: liturgy@ocp.org
Web Site: www.ocp.org
Key Personnel
Mktg: David J Island *E-mail:* davei@ocp.org
Founded: 1922
Books of music & liturgy.
ISBN Prefix(es): 0-915531
Number of titles published annually: 25 Print
Total Titles: 500 Print; 1 CD-ROM; 1 Online; 3 Audio
Distributed by Spring Arbor
Foreign Rights: Decani Music; Rainbow Book Agencies (Australia); Universal Songs (UK, Ireland, England, Europe)
Membership(s): CBA; CMPA

Oregon Historical Society Press
Affiliate of Oregon Historical Society
1200 SW Park Ave, Portland, OR 97205-2483
SAN: 202-8301
Tel: 503-222-1741 *Fax:* 503-221-2035
E-mail: press@ohs.org
Web Site: www.ohs.org
Key Personnel
Dir, Press: Marianne Keddington-Lang
Founded: 1873
Trade & scholarly books on Oregon & the Pacific Northwest, with emphasis on exploration & early Oregon, natural history & environment, Oregon & local history & reference. Also publishes historical vehicle plans, maps, posters & the *Oregon Historical Quarterly, the journal of record for Oregon history.*
ISBN Prefix(es): 0-87595
Number of titles published annually: 3 Print
Total Titles: 102 Print
Distributed by University of Washington Press

Oregon State University Press
102 Adams Hall, Corvallis, OR 97331
SAN: 202-8328
Tel: 541-737-3166 *Toll Free Tel:* 800-426-3797 (orders) *Fax:* 541-737-3170 *Toll Free Fax:* 800-426-3797 (orders)
E-mail: osu.press@oregonstate.edu
Web Site: oregonstate.edu/dept/press
Key Personnel
Dir: Karen Orchard
Man Ed: Jo Alexander
Busn Mgr: Pennie Coe
Mktg Mgr & Intl Rts Contact: Tom Booth *Tel:* 503-796-0547 *Fax:* 503-796-0549 *E-mail:* tbooth@teleport.com
Acqs Ed: Mary Elizabeth Braun
Founded: 1961
ISBN Prefix(es): 0-87071
Number of titles published annually: 20 Print
Total Titles: 225 Print
Distributed by University of Arizona Press

O'Reilly & Associates Inc
1005 Gravenstein Hwy N, Sebastopol, CA 95472
SAN: 133-9788
Tel: 707-827-7000 *Toll Free Tel:* 800-998-9938 *Fax:* 707-829-0104
E-mail: info@oreilly.com
Web Site: www.oreilly.com
Key Personnel
Pres: Tim O'Reilly
Corp Sales: Leslie Crandell
Dir, Sales & Mktg: Mark Brokering
Dir, PR: Sara Winge *Tel:* 707-827-7109 *E-mail:* sara@oreilly.com
Founded: 1978
Technical computer books.
ISBN Prefix(es): 0-937175; 1-56592; 0-596
Number of titles published annually: 120 Print
Total Titles: 350 Print
Branch Office(s)
90 Sherman St, Cambridge, MA 02140 *Tel:* 617-354-5800
Foreign Office(s): Sigma Bldg, Suite B809, No 49 Zhichun Rd, Beijing 100080, China, Contact: Heather Cai *Tel:* (010) 88097475;(10) 88097476 *Fax:* (010) 88097463 *E-mail:* orb@oreilly.com.cn *Web Site:* www.oreilly.com.cn
O'Reilly France, Editions O'Reilly, 18 rue Seguier, Paris, France *Tel:* (01) 40-51-52-30 *Fax:* (01) 40-51-52-31 *Web Site:* www.editions-oreilly.fr
O'Reilly Germany, O'Reilly Verlag, Bathasarstr 81, 50670 Cologne, Germany *Tel:* (0221) 9731600 *Fax:* (0221) 973160-8 *Web Site:* www.oreilly.de
O'Reilly Japan, Kiyoshige Bldg 2F 12-Banchi, Sanei-cho, Shinjuki-ku, Tokyo 160-0008, Japan *Tel:* (03) 3356-5227 *Fax:* (03) 335-5261 *Web Site:* www.oreilly.co.jp

Yotsuya Y's Bldg, 7 6 Honshio Cho, Shinjuku-ku Tokyo 160-0003, Japan, Contact: Kenji Watari *Tel:* (03) 3356 5227 *Fax:* (03) 3356 5261 *E-mail:* kenji@oreilly.com *Web Site:* www.oreilly.co.jp
1FL, No 21, Lane 295, Section 1, Fu-Shing South Rd, Taipei, Taiwan, Province of China, Contact: Mori Su *Tel:* (02) 27099669 *Fax:* (02) 27038802 *E-mail:* mori@oreilly.com *Web Site:* www.oreilly.com.tw
O'Reilly Taiwan, 1F, No 3, Lane 131, Section 1, Hang Chow South Rd, Taipei, Taiwan, Province of China *Tel:* (02) 23968990 *Fax:* (02) 23968916
O'Reilly UK Limited, Cheriton House North Way, Andover SP10 5BE, United Kingdom *Tel:* (01264) 342988 *Fax:* (01264) 342732 *Web Site:* www.oreilly.co.uk
4 Castle St, Farnham, Surrey GU9 7HS, United Kingdom *Tel:* (01252) 711776 *Fax:* (01252) 734211 *E-mail:* information@oreilly.co.uk *Web Site:* www.oreilly.uk
Foreign Rep(s): WoodsLane (Australia, New Zealand)

§Organization for Economic Cooperation & Development
Division of Organization for Economic Cooperation & Development (France)
2001 "L" St NW, Suite 650, Washington, DC 20036-4922
Tel: 202-785-6323 *Toll Free Tel:* 800-456-6323 *Fax:* 202-785-0350
Web Site: www.oecdwash.org; www.sourceoecd.org
Key Personnel
Head, Mktg: Matthew E Brosius *Tel:* 202-822-3870 *E-mail:* matt.brosius@oecd.org
Founded: 1960
Periodicals, books, magnetic tapes, diskettes & microfiche, CD-ROM, online services.
ISBN Prefix(es): 92-64; 92-821
Number of titles published annually: 200 Print; 50 CD-ROM; 250 Online; 200 E-Book
Total Titles: 1,000 Print; 50 CD-ROM; 1,200 Online; 1,200 E-Book
Foreign Office(s): 2 rue Andre-Pascal, 75775 Paris Cedex 16, France
Distributor for European Conference of Ministries of Transport (Imprint); International Energy Agency (Imprint); Nuclear Energy Agency (Imprint)
Orders to: OECD Distribution Ctr, c/o Extenza-Turpin, 56 Industrial Park Dr, Pembroke, MA 02359 *Toll Free Tel:* 800-456-6323 *Fax:* 781-829-9052
Distribution Center: OECD Distribution Ctr, c/o Extenza-Turpin, 56 Industrial Park Dr, Pembroke, MA 02359 *Toll Free Tel:* 800-456-6323 *Fax:* 781-829-9052

Oriental Institute Publications Sales
Division of University of Chicago
1155 E 58 St, Chicago, IL 60637
Tel: 773-702-9514 *Fax:* 773-702-9853
E-mail: oi-publications@uchicago.edu; oi-museum@uchicago.edu; oi-administration@uchicago.edu
Web Site: oi.uchicago.edu *Cable:* ORINST CHICAGO
Key Personnel
Pubns Coord: Tom Holland *Tel:* 773-702-1240 *E-mail:* t-holland@uchicago.edu
Ed: Thomas Urban
Founded: 1919
Academic publications.
ISBN Prefix(es): 0-918986; 1-885923
Number of titles published annually: 3 Print
Total Titles: 105 Print; 2 Online
Orders to: The David Brown Book Co, PO Box 511, Oakville, CT 06779 *Tel:* 860-945-9329 *Toll Free Tel:* 800-791-9354 *Fax:* 860-945-9468

Distribution Center: The David Brown Book Co, PO Box 511, Oakville, CT 06779 *Tel:* 860-945-9329 *Toll Free Tel:* 800-791-9354 *Fax:* 860-945-9468

Original Publications
22 E Mall, Plainview, NY 11803
SAN: 133-0225
Tel: 516-454-6809 *Fax:* 516-454-6829
E-mail: originalpub@aol.com
Key Personnel
Publr & Dist: Mark Benezra
Founded: 1962
African religion, New Age, spirituality & occult books.
ISBN Prefix(es): 0-942272
Number of titles published annually: 12 Print
Total Titles: 45 Print
Distributed by Azure Green; Book People; New Leaf

Osprey Publishing Ltd
443 Park Ave S, New York, NY 10016
Tel: 212-685-5560 *Fax:* 212-685-5836
E-mail: ospreyusa@aol.com
Web Site: www.ospreypublishing.com
Key Personnel
Dir: Bill Corsa
Founded: 1969
Special interest, nonfiction, series publishing in history.
ISBN Prefix(es): 1-85532; 0-85045; 1-84176
Number of titles published annually: 120 Print
Total Titles: 1,200 Print
Imprints: Aircraft of the Aces; Aviation Elite Units; Battle Orders; Campaign; Combat Aircraft; Elite; Essential Histories; Fortress; Men at Arms; Modelling Musterclass; New Vanguard; Osprey Modelling; Warrior
Distributed by Motorbooks International

Other Press LLC
307 Seventh Ave, Suite 1807, New York, NY 10001
Tel: 212-414-0054 *Toll Free Tel:* 877-843-6843 *Fax:* 212-414-0939
E-mail: editor@otherpress.com; orders@otherpress.com
Web Site: www.otherpress.com
Key Personnel
Publr: Judith Feher-Gurewich
CEO: Ellen Vanook
Mktg Dir: Juliet Barnes
Dir, Sales & Publg: Ann Blasberg *E-mail:* ann@otherpress.com
Edit Dir, Handsel Books: Harry Thomas
Ed: Blake Radcliffe *E-mail:* blake@otherpress.com; Stacy Hague
Founded: 1998
Publish books & journals in psychoanalysis, cultural & gender studies, psychotherapy & related areas, also fiction, literary, trade.
ISBN Prefix(es): 1-892746; 1-59051
Number of titles published annually: 60 Print
Total Titles: 300 Print
Imprints: Handsel Books
Foreign Office(s): Eurospan, 3 Henrietta St, Covent Garden, London WC2E 8LU, United Kingdom *Tel:* (020) 7845-0811 *Fax:* (020) 7379-3313
Foreign Rep(s): Eurospan (UK)
Returns: Maple-Vail, 704 Legionaire Dr, Lebanon, PA 17042 *Tel:* 717-764-5911
Membership(s): Publishers Marketing Association

§Our Sunday Visitor Publishing
Division of Our Sunday Visitor Inc
200 Noll Plaza, Huntington, IN 46750
SAN: 202-8344
Tel: 260-356-8400 *Toll Free Tel:* 800-348-2440 (orders) *Fax:* 260-356-8472 *Toll Free Fax:* 800-498-6709

E-mail: osvbooks@osv.com
Web Site: www.osv.com
Key Personnel
Chmn: Rev John M D'Arcy
Dir, Mktg: Jill M Kurtz *Tel:* 260-359-2547
    E-mail: jkurtz@osv.com
Dir, Strategic Mktg: John Christensen
Art Mgr: Eric E Schoening *Tel:* 260-359-2569
    E-mail: eschoening@osv.com
Periodicals Mktg Coord: Amy Thomas
Founded: 1912
Religious books: trade, adult & juvenile general
    interest & reference, hardcover & paperback
    early childhood school; religious magazines &
    newspapers, audiocassettes, videocassettes &
    CD-ROM.
ISBN Prefix(es): 0-87973; 1-931709; 0-9707756
Number of titles published annually: 40 Print
Total Titles: 600 Print; 6 CD-ROM; 8 Audio
Foreign Rep(s): Baker & Taylor (Worldwide exc
    UK, Malta, Canada, South Africa, France &
    New Zealand); B Broughton (Canada); Catholic
    Supplies (New Zealand); Preca (Malta); Veri-
    tas (UK); Veritas Co Ltd (Ireland); Grace Wing
    (UK, Canada, Worldwide exc Australia); Word
    of Life (Australia)

Outcomes Unlimited Press Inc
75 Cambridge Rd, Asheville, NC 28804
Tel: 828-712-1311 *Fax:* 828-258-1311
Web Site: www.drdossey.com
Key Personnel
Pres: Dr Donald Dossey *E-mail:* drdossey@
    drdossey.com
Intl Rts & Lib Sales Dir: Lois Elon
Founded: 1987
Self-help, motivational publications, seminars,
    publicity & public relations & hiking. A pro-
    duction company that specializes in stress &
    phobia management, media presentation skills,
    sales, relationship & management training sem-
    inars.
ISBN Prefix(es): 0-925640
Number of titles published annually: 3 Print
Total Titles: 12 Print
Distributed by Bookworld Services Inc

Outdoor Empire Publishing Inc
424 N 130 St, Seattle, WA 98133
SAN: 207-1312
Mailing Address: PO Box 19000, Seattle, WA
    98109-1000
Tel: 206-624-3845 *Toll Free Tel:* 800-645-5489
    Fax: 206-695-8512
E-mail: hjudeh@outdoorempire.com
Web Site: www.outdoorempire.com
Key Personnel
Pres: William J Farden
Pubns Dir: Maureen Liang
Founded: 1955
How-to books for outdoor recreational activities,
    safety education textbooks & workbooks; cus-
    tomized creative book publishing services.
ISBN Prefix(es): 0-916682
Number of titles published annually: 5 Print; 1
    Audio
Total Titles: 305 Print; 70 Online; 70 E-Book; 1
    Audio
Divisions: Outdoor Publications

The Overlook Press
Subsidiary of Peter Mayer Publishers Inc
141 Wooster St, New York, NY 10012
SAN: 202-8360
Tel: 212-965-8400 *Fax:* 212-965-9834
Web Site: www.overlookny.com
Key Personnel
CEO & Pres: Peter Mayer
Assoc Publr: Tracy Carns
Mgr, Publicity: Corrie Schoenberg
Prodn: George Davidson
Spec Sales Mgr: Maureen Nagy

Direct Mail & Overstocks: Janelle Perry
Dir, Mktg: Paul Williams
Founded: 1971
Fiction, general nonfiction, theatre, biography,
    art, architecture, history, design, film, popular
    culture, hardcover reprints & trade paperbacks.
ISBN Prefix(es): 0-87951
Number of titles published annually: 90 Print
Total Titles: 750 Print
Imprints: Elephant's Eye; Tusk Paperbacks
Distributed by Penguin Putnam Inc
Foreign Rights: Agencia Literaria Carmen Bal-
    cells (Portugal, South America, Spain); Agen-
    zia Letteraria (Italy); BMSR Agency (Brazil);
    The Harris/Elon Agency (Israel); Michelle La-
    pautre (Belgium, France); Licht & Burr Liter-
    ary Agency APS (Scandinavia); Dr Ruth Liep-
    man Agency (Germany, Switzerland); Lijnkamp
    Literary Agents (Netherlands); Nurcihan Kesim
    Literary Agency Inc (Turkey); Andrew Nurn-
    berg Associates Baltic (Estonia, Latvia, Lithua-
    nia); Andrew Nurnberg Associates Beijing
    (China, Taiwan); Andrew Nurnberg Associates
    Bucharest (Romania); Andrew Nurnberg As-
    sociates Budapest (Croatia, Hungary); Andrew
    Nurnberg Associates Prague (Czech Republic);
    Andrew Nurnberg Associates Sofia (Bulgaria,
    Serbia and Montenegro); Andrew Nurnberg
    Associates Taiwan (China, Taiwan); Andrew
    Nurnberg Associates Warsaw (Poland); Andrew
    Nurnberg Literary Agency (Russia); The Over-
    look Press Subsidiary Rights Department (UK
    & Commonwealth); Tuttle-Mori Agency Inc
    (Japan); Eric Yang Agency (Korea)
Orders to: One Overlook Dr, Woodstock,
    NY 12498 *Tel:* 845-679-6838 *Toll Free
    Tel:* 800-473-1312 *Fax:* 845-679-8571
    E-mail: sales@overlookpress.com *Web
    Site:* www.overlookpress.com
Distribution Center: One Overlook Dr, Wood-
    stock, NY 12498 *Tel:* 845-679-6838
Membership(s): AAP

The Overmountain Press
Division of Sabre Industries Inc
PO Box 1261, Johnson City, TN 37605-1261
SAN: 687-6641
Tel: 423-926-2691 *Toll Free Tel:* 800-992-2691
    Fax: 423-929-2464
Web Site: www.overmountainpress.com
Key Personnel
Pres & Intl Rts Contact: Elizabeth Wright
    E-mail: beth@overmtn.com
Mktg: Heather Richardson
Sr Ed: Sherry Lewis *E-mail:* sherry@overmtn.
    com
Founded: 1970
Exhibit at trade shows, festivals, conventions.
    Subjects include Southern Appalachian non-
    fiction, history & children.
ISBN Prefix(es): 0-932807; 1-57072
Number of titles published annually: 25 Print
Total Titles: 375 Print
Imprints: Silver Dagger Mysteries
Distributor for John F Blair Publisher

Richard C Owen Publishers Inc
PO Box 585, Katonah, NY 10536-0585
Tel: 914-232-3903 *Toll Free Tel:* 800-336-5588
    Fax: 914-232-3977
E-mail: richardowen@rcowen.com
Web Site: www.rcowen.com
Key Personnel
Pres & Publr: Richard C Owen
Founded: 1982
Education, language arts.
ISBN Prefix(es): 0-913461; 1-878450; 1-57274
Number of titles published annually: 28 Print
Total Titles: 350 Print
Distributor for Horwitz Martin Education
Warehouse: 245 Rte 100, Somers, NY 10589

§Oxbridge Communications Inc
186 Fifth Ave, 6th fl, New York, NY 10010
Tel: 212-741-0231 *Toll Free Tel:* 800-955-0231
    Fax: 212-633-2938
E-mail: info@oxbridge.com; custserv@oxbridge.
    com
Web Site: www.mediafinder.com
Key Personnel
CEO: Louis Hagood
Publr: Patricia Hagood
Edit Dir: Deborah Striplin
Founded: 1964
Over the last 40 years, Oxbridge has built the
    largest database of information on US & Cana-
    dian periodicals & catalogs with a total of
    72,000 titles. Data is available online, on CD
    & in print. Oxbridge publishes the *Standard
    Periodical Directory,* the *National Directory of
    Magazines,* the *National Directory of Catalogs
    & the Oxbridge Directory of Newsletters.*
ISBN Prefix(es): 1-891783
Number of titles published annually: 4 Print; 1
    CD-ROM; 1 Online
Total Titles: 4 Print; 1 CD-ROM; 1 Online

§Oxford University Press, Inc
Division of University of Oxford
198 Madison Ave, New York, NY 10016-4314
SAN: 202-5892
Tel: 212-726-6000 *Toll Free Tel:* 800-451-7556
    (orders)
Web Site: www.oup.com/us
Key Personnel
Pres: Laura N Brown
Exec VP & COO: Barbara Wasserman
Sr VP & CFO: Ellen Taus
VP & Publr, Academic, Prof & Med: Niko Pfund
VP & Dir, Online Devt: Evan Schnittman
Dir, Mfg & Prodn: Dennis Teston
Sr Ed, Medicine: Marion Osmun
VP & Assoc Publr, Ref Div: Karen Day
Sr VP & Publr, Trade Div & Trade Pbks: Ellen
    Chodosh
Sr VP, Dist: Brinton Strode
Ed, Music: Kim Robinson
VP & Assoc Publr, Busn, Sci & Medicine: Joan
    Bossert
Dir, Higher Educ Sales & Mktg: Scott Burns
Mktg Dir, Academic Humanities & Soc Sci:
    Michael Groseth
Mktg Dir, Academic Sciences: Mike Seiden
VP & Edit Dir, Young Adult Books: Nancy Toff
Dir, Scholarly Reference & Lib Mkt & Sales: Re-
    becca Seger
Exec Ed, Bibles: Donald Kraus
Mktg Dir, Paperbacks: Kurt Hettler
Dir, Bible Sales & Mktg: Hargis Thomas
Dir, Book Club & Reprint Sales, Perms & Sub
    Rts: Marjorie Mueller
Dir, ELT: Neil Butterfield
US Edit Mgr, ELT: Janet Aitchison
E Asia Edit Mgr, ELT: Nancy Leonhardt
Libn: Keith Uhlich
Latin American Edit, ELT: Judith Cunningham
Art Dir, ELT: Lynn Luchetti
Dir, Info Systems: Lee West
Credit Mgr: Banks Honeycutt
Cust Serv Mgr: Donna Jones
Warehouse Mgr: Cameron Shaw
HR Mgr: Helene Klappert
Intl & Electronic Rts: Ashley Mabbitt
Off Servs Mgr: Terese Dickerson *Tel:* 212-726-
    6256 *E-mail:* terese.dickerson@oup.com
Prin Ed, OED (N Amer): Jesse Sheidlower
Chief Ed, OED (UK): John Simpson
VP & Publr, Higher Educ Div: Chris Rogers
Dir, Publicity: Sara Leopold
Dir, Sales & Mktg, Medicine NY: Greg Bussy
Founded: 1896
Scholarly, professional & reference books in the
    humanities, science, medicine & social studies;
    nonfiction trade, Bibles, college textbooks, mu-
    sic, English as a second language, paperbacks,

children's books, journals, online reference &
online scholarly.
ISBN Prefix(es): 0-19
Number of titles published annually: 2,500 Print;
3 CD-ROM; 10 Online; 400 E-Book; 23 Audio
Total Titles: 23,000 Print; 27 CD-ROM; 10 On-
line; 200 E-Book; 220 Audio
Imprints: Clarendon Press
Branch Office(s)
70 Wynford Dr, Don Mills, ON M3C 1J9,
Canada
Foreign Office(s): Walton St, Oxford OX2 6DP,
United Kingdom
Distributor for The American Chemical Society;
CABI; Arnold Clarendon; Engineering Press;
Getty; Greenwich Medical Media; Grove Dic-
tionaries; IRL; Kodansha
Returns: 2001 Evans Rd, Cary, NC 27513
Warehouse: 2001 Evans Rd, Cary, NC 27513
Distribution Center: 2001 Evans Rd, Cary,
NC 27513 *Toll Free Tel:* 800-451-7556 *Web
Site:* www.oup-usa.org
Membership(s): AAP; American Association of
University Presses; BISG

Oxmoor House Inc
Subsidiary of Southern Progress Corp
2100 Lakeshore Dr, Birmingham, AL 35209
SAN: 205-3462
Tel: 205-445-6000; 205-445-6560
Toll Free Tel: 800-366-4712 *Fax:* 205-445-6078
Web Site: www.oxmoorhouse.com
Key Personnel
CEO & Pres: Tom Angelillo
VP & Publr: Brian Carnahan
VP & Ed-in-Chief: Nancy Wyatt
Dir, Busn Devt: Gary Wright *Tel:* 205-445-6562
E-mail: gary_wright@timeinc.com
ISBN Contact: Kay Bryant
Mgr, Acctg: Dani Berryhill
Mgr, Mktg: Linda Gilmer
Mgr, R&D: Jon Williams
Founded: 1968
General interest books; cooking, gardening, deco-
rating, home improvement, travel, entertaining,
health, motion film companions, custom prod-
ucts, celebrity how-to, crafts, art, hobbies; book
& binder programs.
ISBN Prefix(es): 0-8487
Number of titles published annually: 200 Print
Total Titles: 329 Print
Imprints: Coastal Living Books; Cooking Light
Books; Health Books; Southern Living Books
Distributed by Leisure Arts Inc
Foreign Rep(s): Beckett Sterling (New Zealand);
General Publishing Co (Canada); Little, Brown
& Co, UK (UK, Europe); Struik Book Dis-
tributers (South Africa); Transworld Publishers
(Australia)

Oyster River Press
20 Riverview Rd, Durham, NH 03824-3313
Tel: 603-868-5006
E-mail: oysterriverpress@comcast.net
Web Site: www.oysterriverpress.com
Key Personnel
Publr & Intl Rts Contact: Cicely Buckley
E-mail: wbuckley@hopper.unh.edu
Ed: Tanya Gold
Founded: 1989
Specializes in literature & essays.
ISBN Prefix(es): 0-9617481; 1-882291
Number of titles published annually: 3 Print
Total Titles: 33 Print; 1 Audio
Distribution Center: Amazon.Com
Baker & Taylor

Ozark Mountain Publishing Inc
276 Madison 2337, Huntsville, AR 72740
Mailing Address: PO Box 754, Huntsville, AR
72740-0754

Tel: 479-738-2348 *Toll Free Tel:* 800-935-
0045; 800-230-0312 *Fax:* 479-738-2348
Toll Free Fax: 800-935-0045; 800-230-0312
Web Site: www.ozarkmt.com
Key Personnel
Pres: Dolores Cannon *E-mail:* decannon@msn.
com
Off Mgr: Nancy Garrison *E-mail:* nancy@
ozarkmt.com
Founded: 1992
Publish nonfiction New Age/metaphysical & spir-
itual type books.
ISBN Prefix(es): 0-9632776; 1-886940
Number of titles published annually: 3 Print
Total Titles: 24 Print
Foreign Rights: Ajatus Publishing Co (Fin-
land); Gill & Macmillan (Ireland); Helfa A
W (Poland); Jaico (India); Luciernaga Oceano
(Spain); Lyubka Mihailova (Bulgaria); Schriwer
Forlag (Norway)
Distribution Center: Book World Service Inc,
1941 Whitfield Park Loop, Sarasota, FL 34243
Toll Free Tel: 800-444-2524 ext 218 *Fax:* 941-
758-8094 *Toll Free Fax:* 800-777-2525

Ozark Publishing Inc
PO Box 228, Prairie Grove, AR 72753-0228
Tel: 479-846-2793 *Toll Free Tel:* 800-321-5671
Fax: 479-846-2843
E-mail: msworkal@pgtc.net
Key Personnel
Man Ed: Dave Sargent
Mgr: Dai Sargent
Founded: 1990
Children & young adult books. All books have a
moral; the children's books include both fact &
fiction.
ISBN Prefix(es): 1-56763
Number of titles published annually: 75 Print
Total Titles: 400 Print; 21 Audio
Distributed by Gumdrop
Shipping Address: 13060 Butler, Prairie Grove,
AR 72753

Jerome S Ozer Publisher Inc
340 Tenafly Rd, Englewood, NJ 07631
SAN: 202-8395
Tel: 201-567-7040 *Fax:* 201-567-8134
Key Personnel
Pres, Rts & Perms: Jerome S Ozer
E-mail: jerryozer@aol.com
Treas: Harriet Ozer
Founded: 1970
Scholarly reprints.
ISBN Prefix(es): 0-89198
Number of titles published annually: 5 Print
Total Titles: 201 Print
Imprints: Film Review Publications
Distributor for The Center for Migration Studies

P & R Publishing Co
1102 Marble Hill Rd, Phillipsburg, NJ 08865
SAN: 205-3918
Mailing Address: PO Box 817, Phillipsburg, NJ
08865
Tel: 908-454-0505 *Toll Free Tel:* 800-631-0094
Fax: 908-859-2390
E-mail: per@prpbooks.com
Web Site: prpbooks.com
Key Personnel
Pres: Bryce H Craig *E-mail:* bryce@prpbooks.
com
Mktg & Promos: Jesse Hillman
E-mail: marketing@prpbooks.com
Dir, Pubns: Allan Fisher *E-mail:* afisher@
prpbooks.com
Founded: 1931
Books on religion (Protestant) & philosophy.
ISBN Prefix(es): 0-87552
Number of titles published annually: 40 Print
Total Titles: 340 Print; 1 CD-ROM; 340 Online
Imprints: P&R Publishing

Distributor for Evangelical Press; Free Presbyte-
rian Publications
Membership(s): Evangelical Christian Publishers
Association

P R B Productions
963 Peralta Ave, Albany, CA 94706-2144
Tel: 510-526-0722 *Fax:* 510-527-4763
E-mail: prbprdns@aol.com
Web Site: www.prbmusic.com; www.prbpro.com
Key Personnel
Prop & Publr: Peter R Ballinger
Founded: 1989
Jobbing music engraving; performing editions.
ISBN Prefix(es): 1-56571
Number of titles published annually: 15 Print
Total Titles: 185 Print

P S M J Resources Inc
10 Midland Ave, Newton, MA 02458
Tel: 617-965-0055 *Toll Free Tel:* 800-537-7765
Fax: 617-965-5152
E-mail: info@psmj.com
Web Site: www.psmj.com
Founded: 1980
Books, survey reports & audio cassette programs
for architects, engineers, interior designers, ur-
ban designers, planners, landscape architects on
business & financial management; marketing;
time & personnel management; legal topics;
project management; human resources; newslet-
ters; consulting & educational seminars.
ISBN Prefix(es): 1-55538
Number of titles published annually: 6 Print
Total Titles: 50 Print

Pace University Press
Unit of Pace University
41 Park Row, Rm 1510, New York, NY 10038
Tel: 212-346-1405 *Fax:* 212-661-8169
Web Site: www.pace.edu/press
Key Personnel
Dir: Sherman Raskin *E-mail:* sraskin@pace.edu
Chmn, Edit Comm: Mark Hussey
E-mail: mhussey@pace.edu
Founded: 1988
Academic books in the humanities.
ISBN Prefix(es): 0-944473
Number of titles published annually: 4 Print
Total Titles: 40 Print

Pacific Books, Publishers
3427 Cork Oak Way, Palo Alto, CA 94303
Mailing Address: PO Box 558, Palo Alto, CA
94302-0558 SAN: 202-8468
Tel: 650-856-6400 *Fax:* 650-856-6400
Key Personnel
Publr, Pres, Rts & Perms: Henry Ponleithner
Founded: 1945
General & scholarly nonfiction; Western Amer-
icana, Hawaiiana & Oceania; professional &
technical reference & college, el-hi texts, in-
cluding paperbacks.
ISBN Prefix(es): 0-87015
Number of titles published annually: 6 Print
Total Titles: 98 Print
Billing Address: PO Box 558, Palo Alto, CA
94302-0558 SAN: 202-8468
Orders to: PO Box 558, Palo Alto, CA 94302-
0558 SAN: 202-8468
Returns: 999 Independence Ave, Unit 424, Moun-
tain View, CA 94043
Warehouse: 999 Independence Ave, Unit 424,
Mountain View, CA 94043

Pacific Press Publishing Association
1350 N Kings Rd, Nampa, ID 83687-3193
Mailing Address: PO Box 5353, Nampa, ID
83653-5353
Tel: 208-465-2500 *Toll Free Tel:* 800-447-7377
Fax: 208-465-2531
Web Site: www.pacificpress.com

Key Personnel
Pres & Gen Mgr: Robert Kyte *Tel:* 208-465-2501
    E-mail: bobkyte@pacificpress.com
Chief Info Officer: Ed Bahr *Tel:* 208-465-2630
    E-mail: edubah@pacificpress.com
VP, Fin: Martin Ytreberg *Tel:* 208-465-2536
VP, Mktg: Susan Harvey *Tel:* 208-465-2505
    E-mail: sushar@pacificpress.com
VP, Prodn: Chuck Bobst *Tel:* 208-465-2611
    E-mail: chubob@pacificpress.com
VP, Edit Devt, Eng: Russell Holt *Tel:* 208-465-
    2595 *E-mail:* russhol@pacificpress.com
Magazine Sr Ed: Marvin Moore *Tel:* 208-465-
    2577 *E-mail:* marmoo@pacificpress.com
Acqs Ed: Tim Lale *Tel:* 208-465-2570
    E-mail: timlal@pacificpress.com
Magazine Juv Ed: A Sox *Tel:* 208-465-2580
    E-mail: ailsox@pacificpress.com
Adv: Virginia Sherman *Tel:* 208-465-2524
    E-mail: virshe@pacificpress.com
Sales: Rhea Harvey *Tel:* 208-465-2605
    E-mail: rhehar@pacificpress.com
Libn: Bonnie Tyson-Flyn *Tel:* 208-465-2582
    E-mail: bontys@pacificpress.com
Intl Rts: Peggy Pottle *Tel:* 208-465-2511
    E-mail: pegpot@pacificpress.com
Founded: 1875
Religion (Seventh-day Adventist).
ISBN Prefix(es): 0-8163
Number of titles published annually: 39 Print
Total Titles: 350 Print; 2 CD-ROM; 675 Online;
    2 Audio
Foreign Rep(s): R Harvey

Pacifica Military History
1149 Grand Teton Dr, Pacifica, CA 94044
Tel: 650-355-6678 *Toll Free Tel:* 800-453-3152
    (orders & inquiries)
E-mail: mail@pacificamilitary.com
Web Site: www.pacificamilitary.com
Key Personnel
Publr: Eric Hammel *E-mail:* hammel@
    pacificamilitary.com
Military history.
ISBN Prefix(es): 0-935553
Number of titles published annually: 3 Print
Total Titles: 30 Print
Foreign Rep(s): Crusade Trading (Asia, Australia
    & New Zealand); Midland Counties Publica-
    tions (Europe)

Pact Publications
Division of Pack Inc
1200 18 St NW, Suite 350, Washington, DC
    20036
Tel: 202-466-5666 *Fax:* 202-466-5669
E-mail: books@pacthq.org
Web Site: www.pactpublications.org
Key Personnel
Admin Officer, Mktg: Margaret Johnson
    E-mail: mjohnson@pacthq.org
Busn Devt Officer & Edit: Sue Bloom
Founded: 1984
ISBN Prefix(es): 1-88753
Number of titles published annually: 8 Print; 1
    Online
Total Titles: 150 Print; 1 CD-ROM; 1 Online
Imprints: Impact Alliance Press
Distributor for VITA
Membership(s): ABA

Paladin Press
Division of Paladin Enterprises Inc
7077 Winchester Circle, Boulder, CO 80301
SAN: 212-0305
Tel: 303-443-7250 *Toll Free Tel:* 800-392-2400
    Fax: 303-442-8741
E-mail: service@paladin-press.com
Web Site: www.paladin-press.com
Key Personnel
Pres & Publr: Peder C Lund

Edit Dir: Jon Ford *E-mail:* editorial@paladin-
    press.com
Sr Ed & ISBN Contact: Karen Petersen
Promo Mgr, Intl Rts & Lib Sales Dir: Michael
    Rigg
Art Dir: Fran Milner
Cust Rel, Trade & Mail Order Sales: Jeanne
    Vaughn
Founded: 1970
New titles & reprints on military science & his-
    tory, weaponry, martial arts & self-defense,
    survival, police science, terrorism & general
    interest.
ISBN Prefix(es): 0-87364; 1-58160
Number of titles published annually: 60 Print
Total Titles: 800 Print
Imprints: C E P Inc; Flying Machines Press;
    Sycamore Island Books
Distributed by Amazon.com; Barnes & Noble;
    Borders
Advertising Agency: J S O Advertising Inc
    Tel: 303-443-7250 *Fax:* 303-442-8741
Membership(s): Publishers Marketing Association

Palgrave Macmillan
Division of St Martin's Press LLC
175 Fifth Ave, New York, NY 10010
Tel: 212-982-3900 *Fax:* 212-777-6359
E-mail: firstname.lastname@palgrave-usa.com
Web Site: www.palgrave.com
Key Personnel
Pres & Publr: Garrett Kiely
Sales Dir: Leonard Allen
Edit Dir: Airie Stuart
Mktg Servs Dir: Carol St Thomasino
Prodn Dir: Alan Bradshaw
Sr Ed: Anthony Wahl
Ed: Brendan O'Malley; Farideh Koohi-Kamali;
    Amanda Johnson; David Pervin
Joint publishing venture between St Martin's
    Press & Macmillan.
ISBN Prefix(es): 0-312; 0-333; 1-4039
Number of titles published annually: 700 Print; 2
    CD-ROM; 1 Online; 50 E-Book
Total Titles: 5,000 Print; 5 CD-ROM; 1 Online;
    150 E-Book
Membership(s): AAP PSP

Palindrome Press
PO Box 65991, Washington, DC 20036-5991
Tel: 703-242-1734 *Fax:* 703-242-1734
E-mail: freedom@palindromepress.com
Web Site: www.palindromepress.com
Key Personnel
Publr: Patrick G Finegan, Jr
Founded: 1990
Subject specialties include finance, film scripts &
    screenplays.
ISBN Prefix(es): 1-878905
Number of titles published annually: 4 Print
Total Titles: 5 Print

Palladium Books Inc
12455 Universal Dr, Taylor, MI 48180-4077
SAN: 294-9504
Tel: 734-946-2900 *Fax:* 734-946-1238
Web Site: www.palladiumbooks.com
Key Personnel
Pres: Kevin Siembieda *E-mail:* ksiembieda@
    palladiumbooks.com
Founded: 1981
Role-playing game books & supplements.
ISBN Prefix(es): 0-916211; 1-57457
Number of titles published annually: 15 Print
Total Titles: 120 Print

Palm Island Press
411 Truman Ave, Key West, FL 33040
SAN: 298-4024
Tel: 305-294-7834 *Fax:* 305-296-3102
E-mail: pipress@earthlink.net
Web Site: junekeith.com

Key Personnel
Dir: Donald Langille
Founded: 1994
ISBN Prefix(es): 0-9643434
Number of titles published annually: 3 Print
Total Titles: 15 Print
Distributed by Independent Publishers Group
Membership(s): Florida Publishers Association;
    Publishers Marketing Association

Pangaea Publications
226 Wheeler St S, St Paul, MN 55105-1927
Tel: 651-690-3320 *Fax:* 651-690-3320
E-mail: info@pangaea.org
Web Site: pangaea.org
Key Personnel
Pres: Bonnie Hayskar *E-mail:* bonzi@pangaea.org
Founded: 1991
Publisher for nature & peoples of the earth.
ISBN Prefix(es): 0-9630180; 1-929165
Number of titles published annually: 4 Print
Total Titles: 22 Print
Imprints: Palm Books
Distributor for Marcelo D Beccaceci
Distribution Center: Baker & Taylor
Follett Library Services
IndyBook.com-Wholesalers
Membership(s): AAP; SATW

Panoply Press Inc
PO Box 1885, Lake Oswego, OR 97035-0611
Tel: 503-697-7964 *Fax:* 503-636-5293
E-mail: panoplypress@aol.com
Key Personnel
Pres: H Kibbey
Mktg Dir: Lee Jewell
Sales: Diane Gronholm
Founded: 1985
Real estate, house & home; regional journals &
    notebooks; illustrated journals & blank books.
ISBN Prefix(es): 0-9615067; 1-882877
Number of titles published annually: 3 Print
Total Titles: 42 Print

§Panoptic Enterprises
PO Box 11220, Burke, VA 22009-1220
SAN: 265-3141
Tel: 703-451-5953 *Toll Free Tel:* 800-594-4766
    Fax: 703-451-5953
Web Site: www.fedgovcontracts.com
Key Personnel
Pres & Intl Rts: Vivina H McVay
    E-mail: blmcvay@erols.com
VP: Barry McVay
Founded: 1982
Books on how-to obtain & administer federal
    contracts.
ISBN Prefix(es): 0-912481
Number of titles published annually: 4 Print
Total Titles: 11 Print
Returns: 6055 Ridge Ford Dr, Burke, VA 22015,
    Vivina McVay *Tel:* 703-451-5953
Shipping Address: 6055 Ridge Ford Dr, Burke,
    VA 22015, Vivina McVay *Tel:* 703-451-5953
Warehouse: 6055 Ridge Ford Dr, Burke, VA
    22015 *Tel:* 703-451-5953 *Fax:* 703-451-5953
Membership(s): Publishers Marketing Associa-
    tion; Washington Book Publishers

Pantheon Books/Schocken Books
Division of Random House Inc
1745 Broadway, New York, NY 10019
SAN: 202-862X
Tel: 212-751-2600 *Toll Free Tel:* 800-638-
    6460 *Fax:* 212-572-6030 *Telex:* 12-6575
    Cable: RANDOM NYK
Key Personnel
VP & Dir, Edit: Daniel Frank
VP & Dir, Publg: Janice Goldklang
VP & Exec Ed: Erroll McDonald
Art Dir: Archie Ferguson
Dir, Publicity: Suzanne Williams

Dir, Edit & Man Ed, Schocken Books: Altie Karper
Sr Ed, Pantheon Books: Shelley Wanger
Dir, Foreign & Dom Rts (Reprint Rts): Sean Yule
Asst Mgr, Subs Rts (Book Club, Serial & Performance): Victoria Gerken
Asst Mgr, Foreign Rts: Suzanne Smith; Stephanie Katz
Ed: Deborah Garrison
Founded: 1942
Fiction & nonfiction.
Random House Inc & its publishing entities are not accepting unsol submissions, proposals, mss, or submission queries via e-mail at this time.
ISBN Prefix(es): 0-02; 0-679; 0-8052
Imprints: Schocken Books
Foreign Rep(s): Century Hutchinson Group (South America); Colt Associates (Africa exc South Africa); India Book Distributors (India); International Publishers Representatives (Middle East exc Israel); Pandemic Ltd (Continental Europe exc Scandinavia); Periodical Management Group Inc (Mexico); Random Century (Australia); Random House New Zealand Ltd (New Zealand); Random House of Canada Ltd (Canada); Random House UK Ltd (UK); Saga Books ApS (Scandinavia); Sonrisa Book Service (Latin America exc Mexico); Steve Franklin (Israel); Yohan (Japan)
Foreign Rights: Agencia Literaria BMSR (Brazil); Arts & Licensing International (China); Carmen Balcells Agencia (Spain); Caroline van Gelderen Agency (Netherlands); DRT International (Korea); Graal Ltd (Poland); JLM Literary Agency (Greece); Katai & Bolza (Hungary); Licht & Licht Agency (Scandinavia); Literarni Agentura (Czech Republic); Michelle Lapautre Agency (France); Roberto Santachiara (Italy); The English Agency (Japan)
Advertising Agency: Sussman Zacardi
Warehouse: Random House, 400 Hahn Rd, Westminster, MD 21157

Panther Creek Press
116 Tree Crest, Spring, TX 77393
SAN: 253-8520
Mailing Address: PO Box 130233, Panther Creek Sta, Spring, TX 77393
Tel: 281-298-5772
E-mail: panthercreek3@hotmail.com
Web Site: www.panthercreekpress.com
Key Personnel
Publr: Guida M Jackson
Ed: Ted Walthen
Founded: 1999
ISBN Prefix(es): 0-9678343; 0-9718361; 0-9747839
Number of titles published annually: 7 Print
Total Titles: 30 Print

Papyrus & Letterbox of London Publishers
10501 Broom Hill Dr, Las Vegas, NV 89134-7339
Tel: 702-256-3838
E-mail: LB27383@earthlink.net
Web Site: booksbyletterbox.com
Key Personnel
Ed-in-Chief: Geoffrey Hutchinson-Cleaves
Man Dir: Anthony Wade
Fin Officer: Josef Kase E-mail: jfkase@earthlink.net
Rts & Perms: Mrs H Neubauer
Founded: 1946
Also mail order books.
ISBN Prefix(es): 0-943698
Number of titles published annually: 3 Print
Total Titles: 117 Print; 2 Audio
Foreign Rights: Mrs H Neubauer (Worldwide)
Advertising Agency: ShowKase Advertising Public Relations

Para Publishing
PO Box 8206-R, Santa Barbara, CA 93118-8206
Tel: 805-968-7277 Toll Free Tel: 800-727-2782
Fax: 805-968-1379
E-mail: orders@parapublishing.com
Web Site: www.parapublishing.com
Key Personnel
Owner & Publr: Dan Poynter
E-mail: danpoynter@parapublishing.com
Office Mgr: Becky Carbone
Founded: 1969
Illustrated nonfiction trade books; parachutes, skydiving & aspects of book publishing; book marketing, promotion & distribution.
ISBN Prefix(es): 0-915516; 1-56860
Number of titles published annually: 6 Print; 3 CD-ROM; 6 Online; 6 E-Book; 1 Audio
Total Titles: 31 Print; 3 CD-ROM; 55 Online; 55 E-Book; 9 Audio
Imprints: Parachuting Publications
Divisions: Para Publishing Seminars; Paralists; Poynter Consulting; Publishing Poynters Newsletter
Foreign Rep(s): Cordee Publishing (UK); PGW (Canada); Technical Book Co (Australia)
Foreign Rights: Bob Erdmann
Advertising Agency: Chadwick Advertising, Dan Poynter Tel: 805-968-7277 Toll Free Tel: 800-727-2782 Fax: 805-968-1379 E-mail: danpoynter@parapublishing.com Web Site: parapublishing.com
Shipping Address: 530 Ellwood Ridge, Santa Barbara, CA 93117-1407
Membership(s): Publishers Marketing Association

Parabola Books
Subsidiary of Society for the Study of Myth & Tradition
656 Broadway, Suite 615, New York, NY 10012
Tel: 212-505-6200 Toll Free Tel: 800-560-6984
Fax: 212-979-7325
E-mail: parabola@panix.com
Web Site: www.parabola.org
Key Personnel
Publr: Joseph Kulin E-mail: joekulin@aol.com
Ed: Lorraine Kisly E-mail: editors@parabola.org
Adv & Publicity: Carrington Morris E-mail: adspromo@parabola.org
Founded: 1976
Classic & contemporary works exploring the human search for meaning through story, art, psychology, science, etc. Subject specialties include essays, literary analysis, interviews, mythology & multiculturalism.
ISBN Prefix(es): 0-930407
Number of titles published annually: 3 Print
Total Titles: 21 Print; 13 Audio
Imprints: Parabola Storytime Series
Distribution Center: Independent Publishers Group, 814 N Franklin St, Chicago, IL 60610, Contact: Curt Matthews Tel: 312-337-0747 Fax: 312-337-5985 E-mail: frontdesk@ipgbook.com

§Parachute Entertainment LLC
Division of Parachute Properties
156 Fifth Ave, Suite 302, New York, NY 10010
Tel: 212-691-1422 Fax: 212-645-8769
Web Site: www.parachutepublishing.com
Key Personnel
Chmn & CEO: Joan Waricha
Chmn: Jane Stine
Founded: 1997
Audio books, media-related licensing & production of television, motion picture, stage, performance & media rights of Parachute Publishing LLC.
Number of titles published annually: 9 Print; 2 CD-ROM; 12 Audio
Total Titles: 12 Print; 4 CD-ROM; 2 E-Book

Parachute Publishing LLC
Division of Parachute Properties
156 Fifth Ave, Suite 302, New York, NY 10010
Tel: 212-691-1422 Fax: 212-645-8769
Web Site: www.parachutepublishing.com
Key Personnel
Chmn & CEO: Joan Waricha
Chmn: Jane Stine
Sr VP & Publr: Susan Lurie
Sr VP & Dir, Mktg & Devt: Susan Knopf
Founded: 1983
Children's fiction: original books & series, books from licensed properties & adult.
ISBN Prefix(es): 0-938753
Number of titles published annually: 100 Print; 2 E-Book
Total Titles: 850 Print; 2 CD-ROM; 12 E-Book; 12 Audio
Distributed by Bantam; Golden Books; Grosset; Harper Entertainment; HarperCollins; Pocket; Scholastic
Membership(s): American Book Producers Association; Children's Book Council

Paraclete Press
Division of Creative Joys Inc
PO Box 1568, Orleans, MA 02653-1568
SAN: 282-1508
Tel: 508-255-4685 Toll Free Tel: 800-451-5006
Fax: 508-255-5705
Web Site: www.paracletepress.com
Key Personnel
CEO & Publr: Lillian Miao E-mail: lillianmiao@paracletepress.com
Founded: 1981
Spirituality, personal testimonies, devotionals, literary fiction, new editions of classics, CDs & videos.
ISBN Prefix(es): 1-55725; 0-941478
Number of titles published annually: 22 Print
Total Titles: 100 Print; 3 Audio
Distributor for Abbey of Saint Peter of Solesmes; Gloriae Dei Cantores
Shipping Address: Southern Eagle Cartway, Brewster, MA 02631
Membership(s): CBA; Evangelical Christian Publishers Association

§Paradigm Publications
Division of Redwing Book Co
202 Bendix Dr, Taos, NM 87571
Tel: 505-758-7758 Toll Free Tel: 800-873-3946
Fax: 505-758-7768
Web Site: www.paradigm-pubs.com; www.redwingbooks.com
Key Personnel
Publr: Robert L Felt E-mail: bob@paradigm-pubs.com
Founded: 1980
Scholarly books on traditional Chinese medicine & acupuncture.
ISBN Prefix(es): 0-912111
Number of titles published annually: 5 Print
Total Titles: 40 Print; 12 E-Book; 1 Audio
Foreign Rights: R Felt

Paradise Cay Publications Inc
550 S "G" St, No 12, Arcata, CA 95521
Mailing Address: PO Box 29, Arcata, CA 95518-0029
Tel: 707-822-9063 Toll Free Tel: 800-736-4509
Fax: 707-822-9163
E-mail: paracay@humboldt1.com
Web Site: www.paracay.com
Key Personnel
Owner & Publr: Matt Morehouse
E-mail: mattm@humboldt1.com
Intl Rts & Lib Sales Dir: Jim Morehouse
Founded: 1977
Nautical books, videos, art prints & software.
ISBN Prefix(es): 0-939837; 0-9646036
Number of titles published annually: 5 Print

Total Titles: 50 Print; 4 Audio
Imprints: Pardey Publications
Distributed by Robert Hale & Co
Distributor for Pardey Publications
Foreign Rep(s): Boat Books (Australia); Islamorado Internacional (Panama); The Nautical Mind (Canada); Transpacific Marine (New Zealand)

Paragon House
2285 University Ave W, Suite 200, St Paul, MN 55114-1635
Tel: 651-644-3087 *Toll Free Tel:* 800-447-3709 *Fax:* 651-644-0997 *Toll Free Fax:* 800-494-0997
E-mail: paragon@paragonhouse.com
Web Site: www.paragonhouse.com
Key Personnel
Exec Dir & VP: Gordon L Anderson
Opers Coord & Acqs Mgr: Rosemary Yokoi
Founded: 1982
Nonfiction; reference, academic/scholarly monographs, trade & college paperbacks. History, religion, philosophy, New Age & Jewish interest, reference.
ISBN Prefix(es): 1-55778; 0-913729; 0-913757; 0-89226; 0-943852; 0-88702; 1-885118; 9966-835
Number of titles published annually: 12 Print
Total Titles: 400 Print
Imprints: Athena Books Trade Paperbacks; IRF Books; Paragon House Hardcovers; PWPA Books
Distributed by Continuum International Publishing
Distributor for International Conferences on the Unity of the Sciences; Professors World Peace Academy
Foreign Rep(s): Baker & Taylor International; Round House Publishing
Foreign Rights: Baker & Taylor International (Canada, Europe, outside the US); McClellan & Stewart (Canada); Round House Publishing (UK, Europe)
Shipping Address: Continuum International Publishing Group, PO Box 1321, Harrisburg, PA 17105 *Tel:* 717-541-8130 *Toll Free Tel:* 800-561-7704 *Fax:* 717-541-8128

§Parallax Press
Division of Unified Buddhist Church
PO Box 7355, Berkeley, CA 94707-0355
SAN: 663-4494
Tel: 510-525-0101 *Fax:* 510-525-7129
E-mail: parallax@parallax.org
Web Site: www.parallax.org
Key Personnel
Man Ed: Rachel Neumann
COO: Travis Masch
Founded: 1986
Trade paperbacks; audio cassettes; subscription & mail-order books.
ISBN Prefix(es): 0-938077; 1-888375
Number of titles published annually: 6 Print
Total Titles: 15 Audio
Foreign Rights: Dieter Hagenbach (Switzerland)
Shipping Address: 850 Talbot Ave, Albany, CA 94706
Distribution Center: 15608 S New Century Dr, Gardena, CA 90248-2129

Paraview Publishing
191 Seventh Ave, Suite 2F, New York, NY 10011
Tel: 212-989-3616 *Fax:* 212-989-3662
E-mail: info@paraview.com; publisher@paraview.com
Web Site: www.paraview.com
Key Personnel
Ed-in-Chief: Patrick Huyghe *Tel:* 845-528-7234 *Fax:* 209-396-9145 *E-mail:* patrick@paraview.com
Founded: 2000

Books appear in two formats: high quality & print-on-demand trade paperbacks ordered from any bookstore & as e-books & traditional books. Specialize in astrology, spirituality, responsible business & parapsychology. Reprints for authors as well as selected original publications.
ISBN Prefix(es): 1-931044
Number of titles published annually: 10 Print; 10 E-Book
Total Titles: 60 Print; 10 E-Book
Distributed by Bertrams (UK); iPublish (ebooks)
Shipping Address: Lightning Source, Lavergne, Mary Gnetz *Tel:* 615-213-4437 *E-mail:* mary.gnetz@lightningsource.com
Membership(s): Publishers Marketing Association

Parenting Press Inc
11065 Fifth Ave NE, Suite F, Seattle, WA 98125
SAN: 215-6938
Mailing Address: PO Box 75267, Seattle, WA 98175-0267
Tel: 206-364-2900 *Toll Free Tel:* 800-99-BOOKS (992-6657) *Fax:* 206-364-0702
E-mail: office@parentingpress.com
Web Site: www.parentingpress.com
Key Personnel
Pres: Elizabeth Crary
Publr & Intl Rts: Carolyn Threadgill *Tel:* 206-364-2900 ext 107 *E-mail:* office@parentingpress.com
Off Mgr: Homer Henderson *Tel:* 206-364-2900 ext 101
Publicity: Kirstin Vorhes *Tel:* 206-364-2900 ext 102
Mktg: Linda Carlson *Tel:* 206-364-2900 ext 105
Founded: 1979
Parenting, social skill building, personal safety for children, discipline, feelings, temperament, development, boundaries, problem solving, social relations.
ISBN Prefix(es): 0-943990; 0-9602862; 1-884734
Number of titles published annually: 6 Print
Total Titles: 86 Print
Distributor for Raefield-Roberts, Publishers
Membership(s): Book Publishers of the Northwest; Publishers Marketing Association

Park Genealogical Books
PO Box 130968, Roseville, MN 55113-0968
Tel: 651-488-4416 *Fax:* 651-488-2653
Web Site: www.parkbooks.com
Key Personnel
Owner: Mary Hawker Bakeman *E-mail:* mbakeman@parkbooks.com
Founded: 1974
ISBN Prefix(es): 0-915709
Number of titles published annually: 6 Print
Total Titles: 60 Print

Park Place Publications
591 Lighthouse Ave, No 22, Pacific Grove, CA 93950
Mailing Address: PO Box 829, Pacific Grove, CA 93950-0829 SAN: 297-5238
Tel: 831-649-6640 *Toll Free Tel:* 888-702-4500 *Fax:* 831-649-6649
E-mail: publisher@parkplace-publications.com; info@parkplace-publications.com
Web Site: www.parkplace-publications.com
Key Personnel
Publr: Patricia Hamilton *E-mail:* patricia@parkplace-publications.com
Book Promo: Pat Murray *E-mail:* promotion@parkplace-publications.com
Admin Asst: Kathy Slarrow *E-mail:* office@parkplace-publications.com
Founded: 1991 (Founded on the premise that "Books make a world of difference." Company slogan)
Book publishing, Graphic Design, Pre-press.
ISBN Prefix(es): 1-877809

Number of titles published annually: 5 Print
Total Titles: 20 Print; 14 Online
Distributed by Manzanila Books.com

§Parkway Publishers Inc
421 Fairfield Lane, Blowing Rock, NC 28605
Mailing Address: PO Box 3678, Boone, NC 28607
Tel: 828-265-3993 *Toll Free Tel:* 800-821-9155 *Fax:* 828-265-3993 *Toll Free Fax:* 800-821-9155
E-mail: parkwaypub@hotmail.com
Web Site: www.parkwaypublishers.com
Key Personnel
Pres: Rao Aluri
Founded: 1993
Publishes original titles pertaining to the history of western North Carolina.
ISBN Prefix(es): 1-887905
Number of titles published annually: 10 Print; 1 E-Book
Total Titles: 80 Print; 1 CD-ROM; 2 E-Book; 2 Audio
Membership(s): Boone Chamber of Commerce

Parlay International
5835 Doyle St, Suite 111, Emeryville, CA 94608
Mailing Address: PO Box 8817, Emeryville, CA 94662-0817
Tel: 510-601-1000 *Toll Free Tel:* 800-457-2752 *Fax:* 510-601-1008
E-mail: info@parlay.com
Web Site: www.parlay.com
Key Personnel
Pres: Bob Lester
Founded: 1987
Provides health, safety, patient education, training & communication resources.
ISBN Prefix(es): 0-945100
Number of titles published annually: 3 Print
Total Titles: 300 Print

Parlay Press
PO Box 894, Superior, WI 54880
Tel: 218-834-2508
E-mail: mail@parlaypress.com
Web Site: www.parlaypress.com
Key Personnel
Publr: Peyton Parker
Founded: 1988
Publishes textbooks on language & writing.
Number of titles published annually: 4 Print

Passeggiata Press Inc
420 W 14 St, Pueblo, CO 81003-2708
Tel: 719-544-1038 *Fax:* 719-544-7911
E-mail: passegpress@cs.com
Key Personnel
Pres & Ed: Donald E Herdeck
VP: Rosemarie Ames
VP, Ed & Busn Mgr: Margaret Herdeck *E-mail:* mherdeck@aol.com
Assoc Publr & Accts Off: Judith F Fodor
Founded: 1973 (Began as Three Contenents Press; in Oct 1997 sold the name & logo to Lynne Rienner Publishers, Boulder, CO; continued as Passeggiata Press Inc)
Caribbean, Asian, Pacific, Black & African studies, literature, poetry, Latin American, Maghrebian (French), Middle Eastern (Arabic & Persian), architecture, some poetry titles of Russia, Hungary & Bulgaria.
ISBN Prefix(es): 1-57889
Number of titles published annually: 10 Print
Total Titles: 70 Print

Passport Press Inc
Imprint of Travel Line Press
PO Box 2543, Champlain, NY 12919-1346
SAN: 211-7533
Tel: 801-504-4385 *Fax:* 801-504-4385
E-mail: travelbook@yahoo.com

Key Personnel
Publr: Paul Glassman; B Houghton
Founded: 1974
Travel books.
ISBN Prefix(es): 0-930016
Number of titles published annually: 4 Print
Total Titles: 8 Print; 1 Online; 1 E-Book

§Pastoral Press
Imprint of OCP Publications Inc
5536 NE Hassalo, Portland, OR 97213-3638
Tel: 503-281-1191 *Toll Free Tel:* 800-548-8749
Fax: 503-282-3486 *Toll Free Fax:* 800-462-7329
E-mail: liturgy@ocp.org
Web Site: www.ocp.org
Key Personnel
Publr: John Limb
Ed: Dr Glen Byer, PhD
Mktg: David Island MBA *E-mail:* davei@ocp.org
Founded: 1985
Association presses, professional books & scholarly books, books on religion & theology.
ISBN Prefix(es): 0-915531; 0-9602378; 0-912405; 1-56929
Number of titles published annually: 8 Print
Total Titles: 172 Print
Foreign Rep(s): Decani Music Ltd (UK); Rainbow Book Agencies (Australia)

Patchwork Press
PO Box 183, Bemidji, MN 56619-0183
Tel: 218-751-0759
Key Personnel
Owner: Ione McIntyre *E-mail:* mc300@charter.net
Founded: 1981
Bilingual children's books & books on quilting & crafts.
ISBN Prefix(es): 0-9607484; 1-892067
Number of titles published annually: 3 Print
Total Titles: 12 Print

Path Press Inc
1229 Emerson St, Evanston, IL 60201
SAN: 630-2041
Mailing Address: PO Box 2925, Chicago, IL 60690-2925
Tel: 847-424-1620 *Fax:* 847-424-1623
E-mail: pathpressinc@aol.com
Key Personnel
Pres: Bennett J Johnson *E-mail:* evnaacp@aol.com
Founded: 1982
Books for African-American & Third World people.
ISBN Prefix(es): 0-910671
Total Titles: 43 Print
Subsidiaries: African-American Book Distributors Inc
Advertising Agency: R J Dale Advertising Inc, 211 E Ontario St, Chicago, IL 60611 *Tel:* 312-644-2316

Pathfinder Press
Subsidiary of Anchor Foundation
4794 Clark Howell Hwy, College Park, GA 30349
Mailing Address: PO Box 162767, Atlanta, GA 30321-2767
Tel: 404-669-0600 (voice mail only) *Fax:* 707-667-1141
E-mail: pathfinder@pathfinderpress.com (edit); orders@pathfinderpress.com; permissions@pathfinderpress.com (permissions & copyright)
Web Site: www.pathfinderpress.com
Key Personnel
Pres: Stephen Clark
Busn Mgr: Holly Harkness
Founded: 1973

Books & pamphlets by revolutionary leaders in the fight against capitalism. Orders accepted online only; no faxed or mail orders accepted.
ISBN Prefix(es): 0-87348; 0-913460; 0-937091
Number of titles published annually: 6 Print
Total Titles: 350 Print
Editorial Office(s): 305 Seventh Ave, 18th fl, New York, NY 10001, Contact: Stephen Clark
Membership(s): AAP

Pathfinder Publishing Inc
3600 Harbor Blvd, Suite 82, Oxnard, CA 93035
SAN: 694-2571
Tel: 805-984-7756 *Toll Free Tel:* 800-977-2282
Fax: 805-985-3267
Web Site: www.pathfinderpublishing.com
Key Personnel
CEO, Pres & Ed: Bill Mosbrook
E-mail: bmosbrook@earthlink.net
Treas: Evelyn Mosbrook *E-mail:* evelyn@pathfinderpublishing.com
Founded: 1985
Books & audiotape books; specialize in music, psychology & military.
ISBN Prefix(es): 0-934793
Number of titles published annually: 3 Print; 1 Audio
Total Titles: 50 Print; 3 Audio
Membership(s): Publishers Marketing Association

Pathways Publishing
183 Guggins Lane, Boxborough, MA 01719
Tel: 978-264-4060 *Toll Free Tel:* 888-333-7284
Fax: 978-264-4069
Web Site: www.pathwayspub.com
Key Personnel
Pres: Susan A Blair *E-mail:* sblair@pathwayspub.com
Founded: 1996
Specialize in supplemental educational materials, juvenile & young adult teaching resources; also distribute paperback books.
ISBN Prefix(es): 1-58303
Number of titles published annually: 25 Print
Total Titles: 160 Print

Patient-Centered Guides
1005 Gravenstein Hwy N, Sebastopol, CA 95472
Tel: 707-829-0515 *Toll Free Tel:* 800-998-9938
Fax: 707-829-0104
Key Personnel
Edit Asst & ISBN Contact: Shawnde Paull
E-mail: shawnde@oreilly.com
Founded: 1997
Health books & e-content for patients, families & healthcare professionals.
ISBN Prefix(es): 1-56592
Number of titles published annually: 8 Print
Total Titles: 25 Print
Subsidiaries: O'Reilly & Associates Inc
Warehouse: Publishers Resources Inc, 1224 Heil Quaker Blvd, Lavergne, TN 37086-7001

Patrick's Press
2218 Wynnton Rd, Columbus, GA 31906
Mailing Address: PO Box 5189, Columbus, GA 31906
Tel: 706-322-1584 *Toll Free Tel:* 800-654-1052
Fax: 706-322-5806
E-mail: quizbowl@aol.com
Web Site: www.patrickspress.com
Founded: 1981
Specialize in excellent selection of weekly academic & current events publications, quiz books, lockout machines, computer software, cassette tapes & competition questions.
ISBN Prefix(es): 0-9609412; 0-944322
Number of titles published annually: 16 Print; 1 CD-ROM
Total Titles: 16 Print; 1 CD-ROM

Paul & Company
Division of Independent Publishers Group
140 Union St, Marshfield, MA 02050-6273
Tel: 781-834-9830 *Toll Free Tel:* 800-888-4741 (orders) *Fax:* 781-837-9996
Web Site: www.ipgbook.com
Key Personnel
Dir, Academic Markets: Jeremy Soldevilla
E-mail: jsold@ipgbook.com
Founded: 1990
Number of titles published annually: 500 Print
Total Titles: 4,500 Print
Distributor for AA Publishing; Allen & Unwin; Asian Development Bank; Auckland U Press; Aurora Press; Battlebridge Publications; Blackhall Publishing; Boheme Press; Bold Strummer; Carcanet Press; Jon Carpenter; Claridge Press; Clinamen Press; Compass Press; DNA Press; Eothen Press; 5 Continents; Guernica Editions; Higganum Hill Books; High Sierra Books; Horwood Publishing; House of Anansi; IHS Press; Independent Institute; India Research Press; International Books; International IDEA; ISH Institut des Sciences de l'Homme; Janus Publishing; Juta Academic & Cape Town University Press; Kahn & Averill Publishers; Karnak House; Kwela Books; Lawrence & Wishart; Libris; Lingua Forum; Maisonneuve Press; Mango Publishing; Media Action International; Melbourne University Press; Merlin Press; Minority Rights Group; Net Biblio; New Clarion Press; New Dawn Press; New School University Graduate Program in Global Affairs; Olive Press; Open Gate Press; Orchard Publications; OSB Publishers; Palgrave Macmillan Academic; Peepal Tree Press; Rivers-Oram Press/Pandora; Saxe Coburg Publications; Scribe Publications; Seren; Shepheard-Walwyn Publishers; Soar Dime; Society for Human Resource Management; Sun Tree; Temenos Press; Toccata Press; Tuckwell Press Ltd; University of Hertfordshire Press; University of Luton Press; University of Wales Press; Victoria University Press; VU University Press; VUB University Press; White Cockade Publishing; White Horse Press; Whiting & Birch; Who's Who in Italy; Bridget Williams Books; Wolf Den Books; Jerome Wycoff
Orders to: c/o Publishers Storage & Shipping Corp, 600 N Polaski Rd, Chicago, IL 60624
Returns: c/o Publishers Storage & Shipping Corp, 600 N Polaski Rd, Chicago, IL 60624
Warehouse: c/o Publishers Storage & Shipping Corp, 600 N Polaski Rd, Chicago, IL 60624

§Pauline Books & Media
Division of Daughters of Saint Paul
50 St Paul's Ave, Jamaica Plain, Boston, MA 02130
SAN: 203-8900
Tel: 617-522-8911 *Toll Free Tel:* 800-876-4463 (orders only) *Fax:* 617-541-9805
E-mail: businessoffice@pauline.org; orderentry@pauline.org
Web Site: www.pauline.org
Key Personnel
Publr & Edit Dir: Sr Donna William Giamo
E-mail: publisher@pauline.org
Mktg: Sr Roberta Hummel
E-mail: publicrelations@pauline.org
Intl Rts: Sr Bernadette Reis
Acqs Ed: Sr Madonna Ratliff *E-mail:* mratliff@pauline.org
Children's Ed: Sr Patricia Edward Jablonski
E-mail: patjab@juno.com
Founded: 1932
Spirituality, prayerbooks, teachers' resources for religious education, liturgical books, church documents, adult religious instruction, saints lives, faith & culture, music.
ISBN Prefix(es): 0-8198
Number of titles published annually: 50 Print; 1 CD-ROM; 1 Audio
Total Titles: 400 Print; 3 CD-ROM; 72 Audio

Imprints: Cardinal Van Thuan Series; Encounter the Saints Series; Faith & Culture; Pauline Comics Series; Poetry as Prayer Series; The Saints Series; Weaver Books

§Paulist Press
997 Macarthur Blvd, Mahwah, NJ 07430
SAN: 202-5159
Tel: 201-825-7300 *Toll Free Tel:* 800-218-1903
Fax: 201-825-8345 *Toll Free Fax:* 800-836-3161 (orders)
E-mail: info@paulistpress.com
Web Site: www.paulistpress.com
Key Personnel
VP & Gen Mgr: Kevin Maguire
Publr & Edit Dir: Lawrence Boadt
Mktg Dir: Steve Arkin *Tel:* 201-825-7300 ext 231 *E-mail:* sarkin@paulistpress.com
Man Ed: Paul McMahon
Prodn Mgr: Theresa Sparacio
Publicity Coord: Jill Gleichman
General Trade Sales Coord: Mindy Barry
Ed: Roberta L LaVorne
Rts & Intl Rts: Milla Vasilaky
Academic Ed: Christopher Bellitto
Founded: 1866
Resources with emphasis on Biblical studies, Christian, Catholic & Ecumenical formation & education, ethics & social issues, pastoral ministry, personal growth, spirituality, philosophy, theology.
ISBN Prefix(es): 0-8091
Number of titles published annually: 90 Print
Total Titles: 1,600 Print
Imprints: HiddenSpring; The Newman Press; Stimulus Books
Foreign Rep(s): BAYARD & B Broughton Co Ltd (Canada); Catholic Supplies NZ Ltd (New Zealand); Columba Book Service (Europe); Katong Book Centre (Singapore); KCBS Inc (Korea); Rainbow Book Agencies/Word of Life (Australia); St Pauls Libreria (India, Philippines)
Warehouse: 39 Ramapo Valley Rd, Mahwah, NJ 07430

Peabody Museum of Archaeology & Ethnology
Unit of Harvard Univ
Peabody Museum Press, 11 Divinity Ave, Cambridge, MA 02138
Tel: 617-495-3938 (Production); 617-496-9922 (Sales) *Fax:* 617-495-7535
E-mail: peapub@fas.harvard.edu
Web Site: www.peabody.harvard.edu/publications
Key Personnel
Prodn & Project Mgr: Donna Dickerson *E-mail:* ddickers@fas.harvard.edu
Founded: 1888
ISBN Prefix(es): 0-87365
Number of titles published annually: 9 Print
Total Titles: 118 Print
Distribution Center: Publications Dept

Peace Hill Press
18101 The Glebe Lane, Charles City, VA 23030
Tel: 804-829-5043 *Toll Free Tel:* 877-322-3445 (orders) *Fax:* 804-829-5704
E-mail: info@peacehillpress.net
Web Site: www.peacehillpress.com
Key Personnel
CEO: Jay Wise
Ed-in-Chief: Susan Wise Bauer
Dir, Sales & Busn Devt: Charlie Park
Asst Ed: Sara Buffington
Sr Classical Tutor: Peter Buffington
Founded: 2001
Publish educational books for home school families & schools & books for the well-trained mind.
ISBN Prefix(es): 0-9714129
Number of titles published annually: 12 Print
Total Titles: 16 Print

Distributed by W W Norton & Co
Foreign Rights: Richard Henshaw (South & Central America)

Peachpit Press
Division of Pearson Technology Group
1249 Eighth St, Berkeley, CA 94710
Tel: 510-524-2178 *Fax:* 510-524-2221
E-mail: firstname.lastname@peachpit.com
Web Site: www.peachpit.com
Key Personnel
VP & Publr: Nancy Ruenzel *Tel:* 510-524-2178, ext 124 *Fax:* 510-524-2385 *E-mail:* nancy.ruenzel@peachpit.com
Assoc Publr: Keasley Jones; Stephanie Wall; Paula Baker
ISBN Prefix(es): 0-201; 1-56609; 0-938151
Number of titles published annually: 180 Print
Total Titles: 400 Print

Peachtree Publishers Ltd
1700 Chattahoochee Ave, Atlanta, GA 30318
SAN: 212-1999
Tel: 404-876-8761 *Toll Free Tel:* 800-241-0113 *Fax:* 404-875-2578 *Toll Free Fax:* 800-875-8909
E-mail: hello@peachtree-online.com
Web Site: www.peachtree-online.com
Key Personnel
Pres & Publr: Margaret M Quinlin
Sales & Mktg Dir: Barbara Witke
Founded: 1978
Children's fiction & nonfiction, self-help & health/parenting & regional guides.
ISBN Prefix(es): 0-931948; 0-934601; 1-56145
Number of titles published annually: 35 Print
Total Titles: 200 Print
Imprints: Freestone; Peachtree Jr
Foreign Rep(s): Jacqueline Miller Agency (France)
Foreign Rights: Kathy Landwehr (World)
Advertising Agency: PPL Agency

Peanut Butter & Jelly Press LLC
PO Box 590239, Newton, MA 02459-0002
SAN: 299-7444
Tel: 617-630-0945 *Fax:* 617-630-0945
E-mail: info@pbjpress.com
Web Site: www.publishinggame.com
Key Personnel
Owner: Elizabeth Harris
Mgr: Alyza Harris *E-mail:* alyza@publishinggame.com
Publicist: Dena Posner
Founded: 1998
General Trade Books - hardcover & softcover, including our best selling "The Infertility Diet: Get Pregnant and Prevent Miscarriage" now in it's 12th printing; BookSense selection: "Terrorism & Kids: Comforting Your Child" & "The Publishing Game" series.
ISBN Prefix(es): 1-893290
Number of titles published annually: 5 Print
Total Titles: 11 Print
Foreign Rep(s): Hasenbach & Bender (World)
Foreign Rights: Gaia Media (World)
Membership(s): ABA; Great Lakes Booksellers Association; NEBA; Pacific Northwest Booksellers Association; Publishers Marketing Association; Small Publishers Association of North America; Southeast Booksellers Association

§Pearson
Member of Pearson Technology Group
800 E 96 St, Indianapolis, IN 46240
Tel: 317-428-3000 *Toll Free Tel:* 800-545-5914 *Fax:* 317-581-4675
Web Site: www.macdigital.com
Key Personnel
Pres: Douglas S Bennett
VP, Busn: Douglas Mills
VP: Mr Lyn Zingraf

Dir, Mktg: Paula Garrett
Dir, Corp: Tanya Neimark-Hussain; Jeanine Connolly
Total Titles: 80 CD-ROM; 35 Online; 35 E-Book

Pearson Custom Publishing
Unit of Pearson Higher Education Division
75 Arlington St, Suite 300, Boston, MA 02116
SAN: 214-0225
Tel: 617-848-6300 *Toll Free Tel:* 800-428-4466 (orders) *Fax:* 617-848-6358
E-mail: pcp@pearsoncustom.com
Web Site: www.pearsoned.com
Key Personnel
Pres: Donald Kilburn
ISBN Prefix(es): 0-8087; 0-536
Branch Office(s)
Pearson Custom Publishing, 7110 Ohms Lane, Edina, MN 55439-2143 *Tel:* 952-831-1881 *Toll Free Tel:* 800-922-2579 *Fax:* 952-831-3167

Pearson Education
One Lake St, Upper Saddle River, NJ 07458
Tel: 201-236-7000 *Fax:* 201-236-3400
E-mail: firstname.lastname@pearsoned.com; communications@pearson.ed
Web Site: www.pearsoned.com
Key Personnel
Pres: Peter Jovanovich
ISBN Prefix(es): 0-582

Pearson Education - Elementary Group
Division of Pearson Education School Group
299 Jefferson Rd, Parsippany, NJ 07054-0480
Tel: 973-735-8000
Key Personnel
Pres: Martha Smith
Imprints: Silver Burdett Ginn Religion
Branch Office(s)
160 Gould St, Needham Heights, MA 02194 *Tel:* 781-455-1200

Pearson Education/ELT
Division of Pearson Education
10 Bank St, 9th fl, White Plains, NY 10606
Tel: 914-993-5000 *Fax:* 914-993-8115
E-mail: firstname.lastname@pearsoned.com
Key Personnel
Pres: Joanne Dresner
Sr VP & Gen Mgr: Anne Boynton-Trigg
VP, Fin & Opers: Paul Kohn
VP & Dir, Publg: Allen Ascher
VP, Design & Prodn: Rhea Banker
VP, Opers: Rick Altman
Dir, Mktg: Kate McLoughlin
Foreign Office(s): Harlow Office, Edinburgh Gate, Harlow, Essex CM20 2JE, United Kingdom *Tel:* (01279) 623623 *Fax:* (01279) 431059

§Pearson Education International Group
One Lake St, Upper Saddle River, NJ 07458
Tel: 201-236-7000
Key Personnel
Pres: William Oldsey
Sr VP, Fin: John LaVacca

Pearson Higher Education Division
Division of Pearson Education
One Lake St, Upper Saddle River, NJ 07458
Tel: 201-236-7000 *Fax:* 201-236-3381
Key Personnel
Pres: Will Ethridge
COO: George Werner
Sr VP, Systems & Technol: Jack Reilly
Sr VP & Dir, Publg Servs: Logan Campbell
ISBN Prefix(es): 0-13; 0-205; 0-8428; 0-87618; 0-87619; 0-87628; 0-89303
Imprints: Alemany Press; Allyn & Bacon; Brady; Cambridge; Fairmount Press; Family Album; Ellis Horwood; Longwood; Merrill; Prentice

Hall; Prentice Hall Canada; Prentice Hall Career & Technology; Prentice Hall Regents; SPSS; Yourdon Press

§Pearson Professional Development
Division of Pearson Education Inc
1900 E Lake Ave, Glenview, IL 60025
Tel: 847-657-7450 *Toll Free Tel:* 800-348-4474
Fax: 847-486-3183
E-mail: info@pearsonpd.com
Web Site: www.skylightedu.com; www.pearsonpd.com
Key Personnel
Man Ed & Intl Rts: Chris Jaeggi
University Relations: Donna Nygren
Cust Serv: Cindy Brettrager
ISBN Prefix(es): 0-932935; 1-57517
Number of titles published annually: 13 Print
Total Titles: 120 Print
Warehouse: 145 S Mount Zion Rd, Lebanon, IN 46052

§Pearson Technology Group (PTG)
201 W 103 St, Indianapolis, IN 46290
Tel: 317-581-3500 *Toll Free Tel:* 800-545-5914
Fax: 317-581-4675
E-mail: firstname.lastname@pearsoned.com
Web Site: www.mcp.com
Key Personnel
Pres: Gary June
Dir, Intl Sales, Mktg & Opers: Alan Bower
Total Titles: 80 CD-ROM; 35 E-Book
See separate listing for:
Macmillan Reference USA™

T H Peek Publisher
PO Box 50123, Palo Alto, CA 94303-0123
SAN: 693-9708
Tel: 650-962-1010 *Toll Free Tel:* 800-962-9245
Fax: 650-962-1211
E-mail: thpeek@aol.com
Web Site: www.thpeekpublisher.com
Key Personnel
Publr & Intl Rts: Trueman H Peek
Ed & Electronic Publg: Barbara Coulson
Founded: 1966
Ms acquisition, editorial, art, design, distribution, advertising & promotion.
ISBN Prefix(es): 0-917962
Number of titles published annually: 3 Print
Total Titles: 12 Print
Warehouse: 897 Independence Ave, Suite 1-A, Mountain View, CA 94043, Owner: T H Peek *Tel:* 650-962-1010 *Fax:* 650-962-1211
E-mail: thpeek@aol.com

Peel Productions Inc
PO Box 546, Columbus, NC 28722-0546
Tel: 828-859-3879 *Toll Free Tel:* 800-345-6665
Fax: 603-719-0067
E-mail: lmp@peelbooks.com
Web Site: www.peelbooks.com
Key Personnel
Publr & Mktg Dir: Douglas C DuBosque
Ed: Susan Joyce DuBosque
Founded: 1985
ISBN Prefix(es): 0-939217
Number of titles published annually: 6 Print
Total Titles: 45 Print
Membership(s): Children's Book Council

Pelican Publishing Co Inc
1000 Burmaster, Gretna, LA 70053
Mailing Address: PO Box 3110, Gretna, LA 70054-3110 SAN: 212-0623
Tel: 504-368-1175 *Toll Free Tel:* 800-843-1724
Fax: 504-368-1195
E-mail: sales@pelicanpub.com (sales); office@pelicanpub.com (permission); promo@pelicanpub.com (publicity)
Web Site: www.pelicanpub.com

Key Personnel
Publr: Milburn Calhoun
Ed & ISBN Contact: Nina Kooij
E-mail: editorial@pelicanpub.com
Promo & Mktg Dir & Intl Rts: Kathleen Calhoun Nettleton *E-mail:* promo@pelicanpub.com
Rts & Perms: Sally Boitnott
Founded: 1926
General, motivational, inspirational, nostalgia, note cards, almanacs, business & children's.
ISBN Prefix(es): 0-911116; 0-88289; 1-56554; 1-58980
Number of titles published annually: 70 Print; 5 Audio
Total Titles: 1,500 Print; 1 CD-ROM; 35 Audio
Imprints: Robert L Crager & Co; Dixie Press; Jackson Square Press; Louisiana Book Distributors
Subsidiaries: Pelican International Corp
Distributor for Hope Publishing House; Marmac Publishing Co
Foreign Rights: Fitzhenry & Whiteside Publishers (Canada); Gazella (Europe & UK); Little Hills Pty Ltd (Australia)
Advertising Agency: Bayou Advertising
Membership(s): AAP; Children's Book Council; Great Lakes Booksellers Association; Jewish Book Publishers Association; Mid-South Booksellers Association; Museum Store Association; Publishers Association of the South; Publishers Association of the West; Southeast Booksellers Association; Upper Midwest Booksellers Association

Pencil Point Press Inc
PO Box 634, New Hope, PA 18938
Tel: 215-862-8855 *Toll Free Tel:* 800-356-1299
Fax: 215-862-8857
E-mail: penpoint@ix.netcom.com
Web Site: pencilpointpress.com
Key Personnel
Pres & Publr: Eugene A Garone
VP & Opers Mgr: John M Moore
Supplemental college, elementary & secondary.
ISBN Prefix(es): 1-881641; 1-58108
Number of titles published annually: 6 Print
Total Titles: 106 Print

Pendragon Press
Subsidiary of Camelot Publishing Co Inc
52 White Hill Lane, Hillsdale, NY 12529-5839
Tel: 518-325-6100 *Fax:* 518-325-6102
E-mail: penpress@taconic.net
Web Site: www.pendragonpress.com
Key Personnel
Pres & Rts & Perms: Robert J Kessler
Founded: 1972
Reference works on books & musicology including music/aesthetics, biographies, music theory, organ, harpsichord, historic brass, 20th century music, french opera, music & religion.
ISBN Prefix(es): 0-918728; 0-945193; 1-57647
Number of titles published annually: 12 Print
Total Titles: 220 Print
Distributed by LIM Editrice SRL (Italy); G Ricordi
Distributor for Croatian Musicological Society
Foreign Rep(s): RMS Dooley (England)

Penfield Books
215 Brown St, Iowa City, IA 52245
SAN: 221-6671
Tel: 319-337-9998 *Toll Free Tel:* 800-728-9998
Fax: 319-351-6846
E-mail: penfield@penfieldbooks.com
Web Site: www.penfieldbooks.com
Key Personnel
Publr & Intl Rts Contact: Joan Liffring-Zug Bourret
Founded: 1979
Ethnic (Scandinavian, Italian, Polish, German, Dutch & Slavic); cookbooks; crafts & folk art;

history; ethnic cultural cookbooks, cookbooks of the states. No unsol mss.
ISBN Prefix(es): 0-941016; 1-932043; 1-57216
Number of titles published annually: 8 Print
Total Titles: 100 Print; 65 E-Book
Distributed by Bergquist; Book Marketing Plus; Partners
Advertising Agency: Joan Liffring - Zug & Associates

Penguin Audiobooks
Imprint of Penguin Group (USA) Inc
375 Hudson St, New York, NY 10014
SAN: 282-5074
Tel: 212-366-2000
E-mail: online@penguin.com
Web Site: www.penguin.com
Key Personnel
Exec Producer: Patti Pirooz *Tel:* 212-366-2402
E-mail: patti.pirooz@us.penguingroup.com
Founded: 1990
Abridged, unabridged formats; simultaneous release with hardcover.
ISBN Prefix(es): 0-14; 0-453; 0-942110; 1-56511
Number of titles published annually: 24 Print
Total Titles: 210 Print; 339 Audio
Imprints: Arkangel Shakespeare; Penguin*HighBridge Audio
Distributor for Highbridge Audio; Arkangel Complete Shakespeare
Advertising Agency: Spier NY
Returns: Penguin Group (USA) Inc, 405 Murray Hill Pkwy, East Rutherford, NJ 07073, Contact: Kathy Green *Toll Free Tel:* 800-788-6262
Warehouse: Penguin Group (USA) Inc, One Grosset Dr, Kirkwood, NY 13795 *Tel:* 607-775-5586
Membership(s): Audio Publishers Association

Penguin Books
Imprint of Penguin Group (USA) Inc
375 Hudson St, New York, NY 10014
SAN: 282-5074
Tel: 212-366-2000
E-mail: online@penguinputnam.com
Web Site: www.penguin.com; www.penguinclassics.com
Key Personnel
Pres & Publr, Penguin Books, Publr, Plume & VP, Penguin Group (USA) Inc: Kathryn Court
VP, Assoc Publr & Ed-in-Chief: Jane von Mehren
Dir, Mktg: John Fagan
VP, Publicity: Maureen Donnelly
Dir, Adv & Promo: Julie Shiroish
Man Ed: Matt Giarratano
Sr Ed, Penguin & Exec Ed, Penguin Classics: Michael Millman
VP, Viking Penguin Publicity & Assoc Publr & Sr Ed, Viking Penguin: Paul Slovak
Sr Ed, Penguin Classics: Caroline White
Sr Ed: Steve Morrison
Founded: 1935
ISBN Prefix(es): 0-14
Number of titles published annually: 232 Print
Total Titles: 3,062 Print
Imprints: Penguin; Penguin Classics; Penguin Compass; Penguin 20th Century Classics
Distributor for Pearson Technology Group Canada
Advertising Agency: Spier NY

Penguin Group (USA) Inc Sales
375 Hudson St, New York, NY 10014
SAN: 282-5074
Tel: 212-366-2000
E-mail: online@penguinputnam.com
Web Site: www.penguin.com
Key Personnel
Pres, Sales, Adult HC/YR: Dick Heffernan
Pres, Pbk Sales: Norman Lidofsky
Pres, Non-Trade Sales & New Busn Devt: Barbara O'Shea
Sr VP & Dir, Child Sales & Mktg: Mariann Donato Caraballo

VP & Dir, Natl Accts, Adult Div: Michael Brennan

VP & Dir, Dist Sales: Ken Kaye

VP & Dir, Field District Sales: Ernest Petrillo

VP & Dir, Academic Mktg: Daniel Lundy

Exec Dir, Natl Accts & Pbk Sales: Don Redpath

Dir, Adult Hardcover, Field Sales: Katya Shannon

Dir, Mass Mdse Sales: Corrine Van Natta

Dir, Natl Accts, Gift: Fran Corea

Field Sales Dir, Children's Div: Jacqueline Engel

Natl Accts Dir, Children's Div: Jennifer O'Donohue

Dir, Jobber Sales, Pbk: Richard Adamonis

Dir, Field Sales, Pbk: Patricia Weyenberg

Dir, Premium Sales: Lisa Vitelli

Dir, Spec Mkts: Laura Koch; Jennifer Schwabinger

Dir, Intl Sales & Mktg: Valentia Rice

Dir, Trade Pbk Sales: Pat Nolan

Dir, Custom Prod & Intercompany Sales: Mary Berger

Dir, Dist Client Sales: Jennifer Trzaska

Online Sales Mktg Dir: John Lawton

Assoc Dir, Online Servs: Timothy McCall

Natl Accts Mgr, Adult Div: Michael Burke; Paul Deykerhoff; Fred Huber; Glenn Timony; Mark McDiarmid; Christine Mosley; Phil Budnick

Natl Accts Mgr, Children's Div: Nancy Feldman; Allan Winebarger

Natl Accts Mgr, Mass Mdse: Robin Fink; Christina Meyer; Patricia Madson

Natl Accts Mgr, Pbk: Mary Margaret Callahan; Hank Cochrane; Sharon Gamboa; Donald Rieck

Educ Sales Mgr: Mary Raymond

Intl Sales Mgr - Europe: Kristen Liedloff

Penguin Group (USA) Inc

Subsidiary of Pearson plc
375 Hudson St, New York, NY 10014
SAN: 282-5074
Tel: 212-366-2000 *Fax:* 212-366-2666
E-mail: online@uspenguingroup.com
Web Site: www.penguin.com
Key Personnel
Chmn & CEO, The Penguin Group & Chmn, Penguin Group (USA): John Makinson
CEO, Penguin Group (USA): David Shanks
CFO: Anthony J Laurino
Pres, G P Putnam's Sons & Dutton Books: Carole Baron
Pres, Penguin Group (USA): Susan Petersen Kennedy
Pres, Penguin Group (USA) Books for Young Readers: Douglas Whiteman
Pres, Mass Market Pbks: Leslie Gelbman
Pres & Publr, Penguin & Publr, Plume: Kathryn Court
Pres & Publr, Penguin Press: Ann Godoff
Pres, Viking Plume: Clare Ferraro
Publr, Gotham Books: William Shinker
Sr VP, Legal Aff & Corp Counsel: Alex Gigante
Sr VP, Warehousing & Fulfillment: Gil Harper
Sr VP, Penguin Group (USA) & Pres, Sales, Adult Hardcover/Young Readers: Dick Heffernan
Sr VP, Penguin Group (USA) & Pres, Sales, Pbk: Norman Lidofsky
Sr VP & Corp Dir, PR: Marilyn Ducksworth
Sr VP & Dir, Subs Rts: Leigh Butler
VP, Sec & Gen Counsel: Karen Mayer
VP & Corp Dir, Busn Aff: John Schline
VP & Dir, Opers, Adult Hardcover/Children's: Nancy Perlman
VP & Dir, Opers, Pbk: Yvette Dano
VP & Dir, Order Fulfillment: James C Clark
VP & Dir, Corp Transportation: Andrew Orlando
VP & Corp Dir, Dist: Carl Jolley
VP, Info Technol: Eric Brooks
VP, Busn Processes & Analysis: Lisa Latoni
VP & Exec Dir, Publicity, Berkley Publg & NAL Books, Man Dir, Berkley, Riverhead & Perigee Trade Pbk, Assoc Publr, Riverhead: Liz Perl

VP & Dir, Bldg Admin: Heidi Kagan

VP & Corp Dir, HR: Carol Peterson

VP & Exec Dir, PPI Online: Peter McCarthy

Print Prodn Dir: Vincenzo Ruggiero

Founded: 1996

Customer Service: 405 Murray Hill Pkwy, East Rutherford, NJ 07073. Tel: 800-631-8571; Fax: 201-933-2903

Inside Sales: Tel: 800-847-5515; Fax: 607-775-4829

Publisher of consumer books in both hardcover & paperback for adults & children. Also produces maps, calendars, audiobooks & mass merchandise products. Adult - hardcover, trade paperbacks & mass market paperbacks (originals & reprints) Children - hardcover picture books, paperback picture books; board & novelty books; young adult books (hardcover & trade paperback); mass merchandise products.

ISBN Prefix(es): 0-201; 0-89529; 0-425; 0-441; 0-515; 1-57297; 0-14; 0-8037; 0-525; 0-452; 0-917657; 1-55611; 0-7232; 0-399; 0-698; 0-448; 1-58184; 0-89586; 0-912656; 1-55788; 0-87477; 0-451; 0-453; 0-670; 0-7860; 0-8431; 1-57395; 1-55773; 1-57322; 1-58333

Number of titles published annually: 2,904 Print; 25 E-Book; 46 Audio

Total Titles: 19,799,278 Print; 25 E-Book; 392 Audio

Imprints: Ace (Paperback); Ace/Putnam (Hardcover); Allen Lane The Penguin Press (Hardcover); Avery; Alpha Books; Berkley Books (Paperback); Boulevard (Hardcover & Paperback); DAW (Hardcover & Paperback); Dial Books for Young Readers (Children's); Dutton (Hardcover); Dutton Children's Books (Children's); Frederick Warne (Children's); Gotham; Grosset & Dunlap (Children's); Grosset/Putnam (Hardcover); HPBooks (Paperbacks); Hudson Street Press (Paperback); Jove (Paperback); Marian Wood Books (Hardcover); Mentor (Paperback); Meridian (Paperback); Onyx (Paperback); PaperStar (Children's); Penguin (Paperback); Penguin Classics (Paperback); Penguin Compass (Paperback); Penguin Press; Perigee (Paperback); Philomel Books (Children's); Planet Dexter (Children's); Plume (Paperback); Portfolio; Prime Crime (Paperback); Price Stern Sloan Inc (Hardcover, Paperback & Children's); Puffin (Children's); Putnam (Hardcover); G P Putnam's Sons (Hardcover & Children's); Razorbill; Riverhead Books (Hardcover & Paperback); ROC (Paperback); Signet (Paperback); Signet Classics (Paperback); Jeremy P Tarcher (Hardcover & Paperback); Topaz (Paperback); Viking (Hardcover); Viking Children's Books (Children's); Viking Compass (Hardcover); Viking Studio (Hardcover); Wee Sing (Children's)

Subsidiaries: Frederick Warne; Heritage Pittston Realty Company Inc; Grosset & Dunlap

Distributor for Arkangel; Bibli O'Phile; Candlewick Press; Consumer Guide/PIL; DAW Books Inc; Dream Works; Granta; HighBridge Audio; Kensington Publishing Corp; The Library of America; The Monacelli Press; The Overlook Press; Reader's Digest

Foreign Rights: Penguin (UK); Penguin (Canada); Penguin (India); Penguin (Australia); Penguin (New Zealand); Penguin (South Africa); Penguin Putnam International Sales (all other territories)

Advertising Agency: Spier NY, Mesa Group (see individual imprints)

Distribution Center: Penguin Putnam HC & Juvenile and Audio Imprints, One Grosset Dr, Kirkwood, NY 13795 *Tel:* 607-775-1740 *Fax:* 607-775-5586

Penguin Putnam Mass Market and Trade Paperback Imprints, One Commerce Rd, Pittston Township, PA 18640 *Tel:* 570-655-5965 *Fax:* 570-655-3907

Membership(s): AAP

See separate listing for:
Avery
Berkley Books
Berkley Publishing Group
DAW Books Inc
Dial Books for Young Readers
Dutton
Dutton Children's Books
Grosset & Dunlap
HPBooks
NAL
Penguin Audiobooks
Penguin Books
Penguin Young Readers Group
Perigee Books
Price Stern Sloan
Puffin Books
Putnam Berkley Audio
The Putnam Publishing Group
G P Putnam's Sons (Hardcover)
Riverhead Books (Hardcover)
Riverhead Books (Trade Paperback)
Jeremy P Tarcher
Viking
Viking Children's Books
Viking Penguin
Viking Studio
Frederick Warne

Penguin Young Readers Group

Division of Penguin Group (USA) Inc
345 Hudson St, New York, NY 10014
SAN: 282-5074
Tel: 212-366-2000
E-mail: online@penguinputnam.com
Web Site: www.penguin.com
Key Personnel
Pres & Publr: Douglas Whiteman
Sr VP, Mktg & Sales: Mariann Donato
VP & Dir of Mfg: Ginny Anson-Turturro
Dir, Prodn & Mass Mdse: Nadine Britt
Dir, Contracts & Busn Aff: George Schumacher
Dir, School Book Trade Sales: Tanni Tytel
Dir, Consumer Prods: Diane Cain
Dir, Subs Rts (Putnam): Camilla Sanderson
Dir, Subs Rts (Penguin): Leigh Butler
Founded: 1997
Children's hardcover picture books; fiction & nonfiction; trade paperbacks; picture book paperbacks; board & novelty books; calendars.
ISBN Prefix(es): 0-201; 0-14; 0-8037; 0-525; 0-7232; 0-399; 0-698; 0-448; 1-58184; 0-670; 0-8431
Number of titles published annually: 645 Print
Total Titles: 10,851 Print
Imprints: Dial Books for Young Readers; Dutton Children's Books; Dutton Interactive; Phyllis Fogelman Books; Grosset & Dunlap; Paperstar; Philomel; Planet Dexter; Platt & Munk; Playskool; Price Stern Sloan; PSS; Puffin Books; G P Putnam's Sons; Viking Children's Books; Frederick Warne
Distribution Center: Penguin Group (USA) Juvenile Imprints, One Grosset Dr, Kirkwood, NY 13795 *Tel:* 607-775-1740 *Fax:* 607-775-5586
See separate listing for:
G P Putnam's Sons (Children's)

Penmarin Books Inc

1044 Magnolia Way, Roseville, CA 95661
Tel: 916-771-5869 *Fax:* 916-771-5879
E-mail: penmarin@penmarin.com
Web Site: www.penmarin.com
Key Personnel
Pres: Hal Lockwood
Prodn Mgr: Connie Hathaway
Mktg & Publicity: Valerie Smith
Founded: 1987
Publisher of adult trade books & packager of adult college textbooks.
ISBN Prefix(es): 1-883955
Number of titles published annually: 4 Print
Total Titles: 22 Print; 1 Audio

Sales Office(s): Midpoint Trade Books, 27 W 20 St, Suite 1102, New York, NY 10011 *Tel:* 212-727-0190 *Fax:* 212-727-0195
Distributed by Hushion House Publishing Ltd; Midpoint Trade Books
Shipping Address: Midpoint Trade Books, 1263 Southwest Blvd, Kansas City, KS 66103, Contact: Julie Borgeldt *Tel:* 913-831-2233, ext 109 *Fax:* 913-362-7401 *E-mail:* julie@midpt.com
Web Site: www.midpointtradebooks.com

Pennsylvania Historical & Museum Commission
Subsidiary of The Commonwealth of Pennsylvania
Commonwealth Keystone Bldg, 400 North St, Harrisburg, PA 17120-0053
SAN: 282-1532
Tel: 717-783-2618 *Toll Free Tel:* 800-747-7790 *Fax:* 717-787-8312
Web Site: www.phmc.state.pa.us
Key Personnel
Chief, Pubns: Diane B Reed *Tel:* 717-787-8099 *E-mail:* direed@state.pa.us
Sales Mgr: Susan Lindeman *E-mail:* slindeman@state.pa.us
Founded: 1913
Books, booklets & references on Pennsylvania prehistory, history, culture & natural history, both scholarly & popular.
ISBN Prefix(es): 0-911124; 0-89271
Number of titles published annually: 7 Print
Total Titles: 125 Print

§Pennsylvania State Data Center
Subsidiary of Institute of State & Regional Affairs
Penn State Harrisburg, 777 W Harrisburg Pike, Middletown, PA 17057-4898
Tel: 717-948-6336 *Fax:* 717-948-6754
E-mail: pasdc@psu.edu
Web Site: pasdc.hbg.psu.edu
Key Personnel
Dir: Susan Copella *Tel:* 717-948-6427 *E-mail:* sdc3@psu.edu
Mgr, Data Servs: Mike De Frank
Founded: 1981
Policy, demographical analytical reports, hard copy & computer discs.
ISBN Prefix(es): 0-939667; 1-58036
Number of titles published annually: 5 Print; 5 CD-ROM
Total Titles: 110 Print; 50 CD-ROM; 1 E-Book

The Pennsylvania State University Press
Division of The Pennsylvania State University
820 N University Dr, University Support Bldg 1, Suite C, University Park, PA 16802-1003
SAN: 213-5760
Tel: 814-865-1327 *Toll Free Tel:* 800-326-9180 *Fax:* 814-863-1408 *Toll Free Fax:* 877 7782665
Web Site: www.psupress.org
Key Personnel
Dir & Foreign Rts: Sanford G Thatcher *E-mail:* sgt3@psu.edu
Ed-in-Chief, History & Social Science: Peter Potter *E-mail:* pjp8@psu.edu
Art History & Humanities Ed: Gloria Kury *E-mail:* gxk17@psu.edu
Busn Mgr & Cust Serv: Clifford Way *Tel:* 814-863-5993 *E-mail:* cgw3@psu.edu
Sales & Mktg Mgr: Tony Sanfilippo *Tel:* 814-863-5994 *E-mail:* ajs23@psu.edu
Publicity Mgr: Anne Davis *Tel:* 814-863-0524 *E-mail:* akd115@psu.edu
Prodn Mgr: Jennifer Norton *Tel:* 814-863-8061 *E-mail:* jsn4@psu.edu
Info Systems Mgr: Ed Spicer *E-mail:* res122@psu.edu
Chief Designer: Steven Kress *E-mail:* srk5@psu.edu
Man Ed: Cherene Holland *E-mail:* cah8@psu.edu

Ms Ed: Patricia Mitchell *E-mail:* pam18@psu.edu; Laura Reed-Morrisson *Tel:* 814-863-8061 *E-mail:* lxr168@psu.edu
Journals Mgr: Mary Lou McMurtrie *Tel:* 814-863-5992 *E-mail:* mlm2@psu.edu
Founded: 1956
Scholarly books & journals; art & architectural history; literature & literary criticism, philosophy, religion, social sciences, law, history, Latin American studies, regional books on mid-Atlantic area; Special Series: Literature & Philosophy; Penn State Series in the History of the Book; Re-Reading the Canon: Feminist Interpretation of Major Philosophers; Keystone Books (regional); American & European Philosophy; Magic in History; Rural Studies.
ISBN Prefix(es): 0-271
Number of titles published annually: 55 Print
Total Titles: 1,000 Print
Imprints: Keystone Books
Foreign Rep(s): East-West Export Books (Asia, Pacific); European University Press Group (Africa, UK, Central America, Europe, Middle East, South America); University of Toronto Press (Canada)
Membership(s): AAP; Association of American University Presses

PennWell Books & More
Division of PennWell
1421 S Sheridan, Tulsa, OK 74112
Mailing Address: Box 21288, Tulsa, OK 74121-1288
Tel: 918-831-9421 *Toll Free Tel:* 800-752-9764 *Fax:* 918-832-9319
E-mail: sales@penwellbooks.com
Web Site: www.penwellbooks.com *Telex:* 211012 *Cable:* PENBK
Key Personnel
Pres & CEO: Bob Biolchini
Prodn Ed: Jay Kilburn
Mktg Mgr: Mary McGee
Mktg Coord: Julie Simmons
Cust Serv: Jeff Crisp *Tel:* 918-831-9449 *Fax:* 918-831-9555 *E-mail:* sales@pennwell.com
Founded: 1973
Petroleum, laser, computer, high technology, software & business, environmental, electric power, firefighting.
ISBN Prefix(es): 0-912212; 0-87814; 1-59370
Number of titles published annually: 20 Print
Total Titles: 350 Print; 5 Audio
Foreign Rep(s): American Technical Publishers Ltd (Europe & UK); Berj Jamkojian Associates (Middle East); DA Book Depot (Australia); Arturo Gutierrez Hernandez (Central America, Mexico); Christopher Humphrys (Spain); Humphrys-Roberts Associates (South America); Intercontinental Marketing (Japan, South Korea); Ish Dawar (India); JN Publishers Representatives (Scandinavia); Smartpetro Ltd (Brazil)

Penrose Press
1333 Gough, Suite 8B, San Francisco, CA 94109
Mailing Address: PO Box 470925, San Francisco, CA 94147
Tel: 415-567-4157 *Fax:* 415-567-4165
E-mail: info@penrose-press.com
Web Site: www.penrose-press.com
Key Personnel
Pubns Dir & Lib Sales Dir: Raymond Lauzzana *E-mail:* rlauzzana@penrose-press.com
Edit Dir & Intl Rts Contact: Denise Penrose *E-mail:* dpenrose@penrose-press.com
Founded: 1992
Serving arts & technology community, higher education, professional organization. Online directory publisher: schools, professional organizations, journals, conference & trade shows.
Number of titles published annually: 1 E-Book

Total Titles: 1 E-Book
Imprints: International Directory of Design

§Pentecostal Publishing House
Subsidiary of United Pentecostal Church International
8855 Dunn Rd, Hazelwood, MO 63042
SAN: 219-3817
Tel: 314-837-7300 *Fax:* 314-837-6574
E-mail: pphordersdept@upci.org (orders)
Web Site: www.pentecostalpublishing.com *Cable:* UNIPEN
Key Personnel
Gen Mgr: Marvin Curry *E-mail:* mcurry@upci.org
Promo Pubns: Mark Christian *E-mail:* mchristian@upci.org
Purch: Jerry McNall *E-mail:* jmcnall@upci.org
Edit/Design: Margie McNall *Tel:* 314-837-7300 ext 460 *E-mail:* mmcnall@upci.org
Founded: 1945
Trade paperbacks, periodicals, bibliographies; religion (Protestant), Bibles, foreign languages, crafts, self-help.
ISBN Prefix(es): 0-912315; 0-932581; 1-56722; 0-7577
Number of titles published annually: 10 Print; 1 CD-ROM
Total Titles: 180 Print; 5 CD-ROM
Imprints: Word Aflame Press
Subsidiaries: Word Aflame Press
Distributed by Spring Arbor

Penton Overseas Inc
2470 Impala Dr, Carlsbad, CA 92008-7226
Tel: 760-431-0060 *Toll Free Tel:* 800-748-5804 *Fax:* 760-431-8110
E-mail: info@pentonoverseas.com
Web Site: www.pentonoverseas.com
Key Personnel
Chmn: Hugh V Penton, Sr
CEO: Hugh V Penton, Jr
Founded: 1986
Publisher & distributor of audio books & videos & printed books specializing in language, travel, business, scientific, self-help, health & wellness, literature classics, writing, parenting & children's titles. Produce popular language learning audio & video programs for worldwide markets since 1986. Major presence in the fields of language, travel & special interest publishing. Expanded into fields of education & entertainment as both publisher & distributor.
ISBN Prefix(es): 1-56015; 0-939001; 1-891100; 1-59125
Number of titles published annually: 45 Print; 40 Audio
Total Titles: 290 Print; 1,016 Audio
Imprints: Penton Kids Press™; Penton Overseas Inc; Smart Kids™; Wiley Audio ™
Distributor for The Book Co Publishing Pty Ltd; Cassidy Video (Little Explorers); Cliffs Notes; Cruise Concepts Inc (Licensor) Cruise Control; Hinkler Books Pty Ltd; Holt Concepts; Kids Creative Classics; Kidzup Entertainment; Maui Media LLC; The Musical Linguist; Production Associates; Relax...Intuit; Rivertree Production; Sound Beginnings; Teach Me Tapes Inc; John Wiley & Sons (Wiley Audio)
Foreign Rep(s): Electra Media Group Pty Ltd (Indonesia, Philippines, Singapore & Malaysia); Faradawn C C (Republic of South Africa); H B Fenn & Co Ltd (Canada); Gazelle Book Service Ltd (UK); Niger R Kahn (Caribbean); Little Hills Press Pty Ltd (Australia & New Zealand); MyCarlSoft (Colombia); B K Norton Ltd (Taiwan); Peter Ward Book Exports (Gulf States, Middle East, North Africa)
Membership(s): American Publishers Association; Network of Alternatives for Publishers, Retailers & Artists Inc; NSSEA; Publishers Marketing Association

Per Annum Inc
48 W 25 St, 10th fl, New York, NY 10010
SAN: 289-3673
Tel: 212-647-8700 *Toll Free Tel:* 800-548-1108
 Fax: 212-647-8716
E-mail: info@perannum.com
Web Site: www.perannum.com
Key Personnel
Pres: Alicia B Settle
Acct Exec: Alixandre M Settle *Tel:* 212-647-8700
 ext 118 *E-mail:* retail@perannum.com
Founded: 1979
Guide books, agendas.
ISBN Prefix(es): 0-914975; 1-57499
Number of titles published annually: 16 Print; 7
 CD-ROM; 7 Online
Total Titles: 16 Print
Distributor for New Yorker Desk Diary

Peradam Press
Subsidiary of The Center for Cultural & Natural-
 ist Studies
PO Box 6, North San Juan, CA 95960-0006
Tel: 530-292-4266 *Toll Free Tel:* 800-241-8689
 Fax: 530-292-4266 *Toll Free Fax:* 800-241-
 8689
E-mail: peradam@earthlink.net
Key Personnel
Pres & Sr Ed: Linda Birkholz
Exec Ed: Dan Cronin
Ed: Patricia Hicks
Founded: 1993
General trade books hardcover & paperbacks.
ISBN Prefix(es): 1-885420
Number of titles published annually: 6 Print
Total Titles: 31 Print
Shipping Address: 19074 Oak Tree Rd, North San
 Juan, CA 95959

Perfection Learning Corp
10520 New York Ave, Des Moines, IA 50322
Tel: 515-278-0133 *Toll Free Tel:* 800-762-2999
 Fax: 515-278-2980
E-mail: orders@perfectionlearning.com
Web Site: perfectionlearning.com
Key Personnel
Art Dir: Randy Messer *E-mail:* rmesser@
 plconline.com
Adv Mgr: John Richards *E-mail:* jrichards@
 plconline.com
Mktg Prod Mgr: Marsha James *E-mail:* mjames@
 plconline.com
Sr Ed (Elementary): Sue Thies *E-mail:* sthies@
 plconline.com
Sr Ed (Secondary): Rebecca Christian
Title Selection: Vicki Cooper *Tel:* 303-467-
 9247 *Fax:* 303-467-9247 *E-mail:* vlcooper@
 plconline.com
Founded: 1926
Elementary & secondary teacher guides, posters,
 workbooks, study guides & hi-lo fiction & non-
 fiction.
ISBN Prefix(es): 0-89598
Number of titles published annually: 30 Print
Total Titles: 500 Print
Imprints: Cover Craft; Cover-to-Cover; Literature
 & Thought; Passages; Retold Classics; Summit
 Books; Tale Blazers
Distributor for Abrams; Ace Books; Airmont; An-
 nick Press; Archway; Atheneum; Baker Books;
 Ballantine; Bantam; Barrons; Berkley; Blake
 Books; Candlewick Press; Charlesbridge Press;
 Chelsea House; Children's Press; Chronicle
 Books; Crabtree Publishing; Crown; Disney
 Press; Distri Books; DK Publishing; Dou-
 bleday; Dutton; Farrar, Straus & Giroux Inc;
 Fawcett; Firefly; First Avenue; Free Spirit;
 Fulcrum; F&W Publications; Golden Books;
 Greenhaven Press Inc; Hammond Pub; Har-
 court Brace & Co; Hayes; Gareth Stevens;
 Frederick Warne
Foreign Rep(s): Ron Grant, School Book Fairs
 Ltd (Canada)

Warehouse: 1000 N Second Ave, PO Box 500,
 Logan, IA 51546-0500, Contact: Ben Norris
Toll Free Tel: 800-831-4190 *Fax:* 712-644-2392
E-mail: orders@perfectionlearning.com

Perigee Books
Imprint of Penguin Group (USA) Inc
375 Hudson St, New York, NY 10014
SAN: 282-5074
Tel: 212-366-2000 *Fax:* 212-366-2365
E-mail: online@penguinputnam.com
Web Site: www.penguin.com
Key Personnel
VP & Publr: John Duff
Art Dir: Charles Bjorklund
Sr Ed: Marian Lizzi
Founded: 1980
Focus on prescriptive nonfiction.
ISBN Prefix(es): 0-399
Number of titles published annually: 70 Print
Total Titles: 317 Print
Advertising Agency: Spier NY

The Permanent Press
4170 Noyac Rd, Sag Harbor, NY 11963
SAN: 212-2995
Tel: 631-725-1101 *Fax:* 631-725-8215
Web Site: www.thepermanentpress.com
Key Personnel
Publr & Ed-in-Chief: Judith Shepard
 E-mail: shepard@thepermanentpress.com
Publr: Martin Shepard
Assoc Publr: Elise D'Haene
Man Ed: Maureen D'Haene *E-mail:* maureen@
 thepermanentpress.com
The Alpern Group Film Rts: Jeff Aghassi
Founded: 1978
Literary fiction.
ISBN Prefix(es): 1-877946; 0-932966; 1-57962
Number of titles published annually: 12 Print
Total Titles: 300 Print
Imprints: Second Chance Press
Foreign Rights: Lora Fountain (France); Jane
 Judd (UK); Jennifer Luithlen (Baltic States,
 Poland); Mercedes Casanovas (Latin Amer-
 ica, Portugal, Spain); Jan Michael (Nether-
 lands & Scandinavia); Read n' Write Agency
 (Greece); Thomas Schluck (Germany); Tuttle
 Mori (Japan); Rita Vivian (Italy); Eric Yang
 (Korea)
See separate listing for:
Second Chance Press

Persea Books Inc
853 Broadway, Suite 604, New York, NY 10003
SAN: 212-8233
Tel: 212-260-9256 *Fax:* 212-260-1902
E-mail: info@perseabooks.com
Web Site: www.perseabooks.com
Key Personnel
Pres & Publr: Michael Braziller
VP & Edit Dir: Karen Braziller
Mkt Consultant: Gayle Greeno
Ed & Perms: Gabriel Fried
Founded: 1975
Literature, poetry, biography, social sciences, mul-
 ticultural fiction & nonfiction, women's studies,
 fiction, anthologies.
ISBN Prefix(es): 0-89255
Number of titles published annually: 12 Print
Total Titles: 100 Print
Imprints: Karen & Michael Braziller Books
Distributed by W W Norton & Co
Distributor for Ontario Review Press
Distribution Center: W W Norton c/o National
 Book Co, Keystone Industrial Park, Scranton,
 PA 18512 *Toll Free Fax:* 800-233-4830

The Perseus Books Group
387 Park Ave S, 12th fl, New York, NY 10016
Tel: 212-340-8100 *Toll Free Tel:* 800-386-5656
 (cust serv) *Fax:* 212-340-8115

Web Site: www.perseusbooksgroup.com
Key Personnel
Chmn: Frank H Pearl
Pres & CEO, Perseus Books Group: David Stein-
 berger
COO: Joseph Mangar
Chief Info Officer: Mark Mareval
VP & Dir, Prodn: Melissa Serdinsky
VP & Group Dir, Sales & Mktg: Matthew Gold-
 berg
Cont: Pam Bayley
Dir, Special Sales: J McCrary
Dir, Intl Publg & Export Sales: Carolyn Savarese
Natl Acct Dir: Elizabeth Tzetzo
Intl Rts Mgr: Isabelle Bleecker
Academic Mktg Mgr: Michelle Mallin
Corp Admin: Michael Stewart
Group Planning Analyst: Gary Farber
Legal Counsel (Coudert Brothers): Kevin Goering
Founded: 1997
Number of titles published annually: 50 Print
Total Titles: 530 Print
Imprints: Basic Books; Basic Civitas Books;
 Combined Publishing; Counterpoint Press;
 Courage Books; Da Capo Press; Fisher Books;
 Perseus Running Press; PublicAffairs; Running
 Press-Kids; Running Press-Miniature Editions;
 Westview Press
Distributed by HarperCollins Publishers
Orders to: 5500 Central Ave, Boulder, CO 80301
 Toll Free Tel: 800-386-5656 *Fax:* 720-406-7336
 E-mail: westview.orders@perseusbooks.com
See separate listing for:
Basic Books
Counterpoint Press
Da Capo Press Inc
PublicAffairs
Running Press Book Publishers
Westview Press

Perseus Publishing, see Da Capo Press Inc

**Perspectives Press Inc: The Infertility &
 Adoption Publisher**
PO Box 90318, Indianapolis, IN 46290-0318
Tel: 317-872-3055
Web Site: www.perspectivespress.com
Key Personnel
Publr: Patricia Irwin Johnston
 E-mail: patjohnston@perspectivespress.com
Founded: 1982
Books for adults & children related to infertil-
 ity, adoption, foster care, reproductive health &
 alternative family building.
ISBN Prefix(es): 0-9609504; 0-944934
Number of titles published annually: 2 Print
Total Titles: 22 Print
Membership(s): Publishers Marketing Association

Peter Pauper Press Inc
202 Mamaroneck Ave, White Plains, NY 10601-
 5376
SAN: 204-9449
Tel: 914-681-0144 *Toll Free Tel:* 800-833-2311
 Fax: 914-681-0389
E-mail: customerservice@peterpauper.com
Web Site: www.peterpauper.com
Key Personnel
Pres: Laurence Beilenson *E-mail:* lbeilenson@
 peterpauper.com
Publr: Evelyn L Beilenson *E-mail:* Ebeilenson@
 peterpauper.com
Edit Dir: Nick Beilenson *E-mail:* nbeilenson@
 peterpauper.com
Dir, Natl Accts: John Hartley *E-mail:* jhartley@
 peterpauper.com
Art Dir: Heather Zschock *E-mail:* hzschock@
 peterpauper.com
Founded: 1928
Decorated hardcover gift, inspirational; women's
 quotations, miniatures, journals, photo albums.
ISBN Prefix(es): 0-88088; 1-59359
Number of titles published annually: 40 Print

Total Titles: 300 Print
Imprints: Inspire Books
Foreign Rep(s): For Arts Sake (Australia & New
Zealand); Phambili (Southern Africa); Power-
fresh (UK)
Shipping Address: Conri Services Inc, 250 Clear-
brook Rd, Elmsford, NY 10523, Contact: Con-
nie Levene *Tel:* 914-592-2300 *Fax:* 914-592-
2455
Warehouse: Conri Services Inc, 250 Clearbrook
Rd, Elmsford, NY 10523, Contact: Connie
Levene *Tel:* 914-592-2300 *Fax:* 914-592-2455

Gerald Peters Gallery
Division of The Peters Corp
1011 Paseo De Peralta, Santa Fe, NM 87501
Tel: 505-954-5700 *Fax:* 505-954-5754
E-mail: bookstore@gpgallery.com
Web Site: www.gpgallery.com
Key Personnel
Owner: Gerald P Peters
Bookstore Mgr, Publications: John Macker
Lib Sales Dir: Dara Doolittle
Founded: 1976
Artbooks, exhibition catalogues, posters, note-
cards, postcards & sidelines.
ISBN Prefix(es): 0-935037; 0-931717
Number of titles published annually: 3 Print; 65
Online
Total Titles: 65 Print; 65 Online

Petroleum Extension Service (PETEX)
Division of University of Texas, Petroleum Exten-
sion Service
University of Texas, One University Sta, R8100,
Austin, TX 78712-1100
Tel: 512-471-5940 *Toll Free Tel:* 800-687-4132
Fax: 512-471-9410 *Toll Free Fax:* 800-687-
7839
E-mail: rbpetex@mail.utexas.edu
Web Site: www.utexas.edu/cee/petex
Key Personnel
Pubns Coord: Debbi Caples
Founded: 1944
Training materials for oilfield personnel.
ISBN Prefix(es): 0-88698
Number of titles published annually: 5 Print
Total Titles: 300 Print
Branch Office(s)
PETEX, 2700-W W Thorne Dr, Houston, TX
77073
PETEX, 1100 Broadway, Kilgore, TX 75662
Shipping Address: 10100 Burnet Rd, Austin, TX
78758

Peytral Publications Inc
PO Box 1162, Minnetonka, MN 55345-0162
SAN: 298-4733
Tel: 952-949-8707 *Toll Free Tel:* 877-PEYTRAL
(739-8725) *Fax:* 952-906-9777
E-mail: help@peytral.com
Web Site: www.peytral.com
Key Personnel
VP: Peggy A Hammeken *E-mail:* peggy@peytral.
com
Intl Rts: Roberto Hammeken *E-mail:* roberto@
peytral.com
Founded: 1995
Special education, inclusion of students with dis-
abilities, fiction & nonfiction.
ISBN Prefix(es): 0-9644271; 1-890455
Number of titles published annually: 3 Print
Total Titles: 15 Print
Distributor for Free Spirit; NPR; Woodbine
Returns: 5901 Whited Ave, Minnetonka, MN
55345, VP: Peggy Hammeken *E-mail:* peggy@
peytral.com

Pflaum Publishing Group
Imprint of Peter Li Education Group
2621 Dryden Rd, Dayton, OH 45439

Tel: 937-293-1415 *Toll Free Tel:* 800-543-4383
Fax: 917-293-1310 *Toll Free Fax:* 800-370-
4450
Web Site: www.pflaum.com
Key Personnel
Edit Dir: Karen A Cannizzo *Tel:* 262-502-4222
E-mail: kcannizzo@pflaum.com; Jean Larkin
Tel: 314-638-6811 *E-mail:* jeanlarkin@pflaum.
com
VP, Catechetical Prods & Servs: Annie Galvin
Teich *Tel:* 336-273-0714 *E-mail:* ateich@
pflaum.com
Founded: 1885
Weekly lectionary-based magazines for Pre-K
through 8. Sacramental preparation for children
& teens, catechetical resources for Pre-K-12,
religious educators & youth ministers.
ISBN Prefix(es): 0-937997; 0-89837
Number of titles published annually: 12 Print
Total Titles: 92 Print; 16 E-Book
Branch Office(s)
N90 W16890 Roosevelt Dr, Menomonee Falls,
WI 53051, Co-Publr: Karen A Cannizzo
Tel: 262-502-4222 *E-mail:* kcannizzo@pflaum.
com

Phaidon Press Inc
Subsidiary of Phaidon Press Ltd
180 Varick St, 14th fl, New York, NY 10014
Tel: 212-652-5400 *Toll Free Tel:* 800-759-
0190 (cust serv) *Fax:* 212-652-5410
Toll Free Fax: 800-286-9471 (cust serv)
E-mail: ussales@phaidon.com
Web Site: www.phaidon.com
Key Personnel
Edit Dir, Archit: Karen Stein
Dir, Dist & Opers: Ken Woidill
Publicity & Mktg Mgr: Caroline Green
Mgr, North American Sales: Nat Green
Sales Rep, Pacific Northwest: Christa Grenawalt
Sales Rep, New York Metro, Northeast: Catherine
Thomas
Sales Rep, Northeast: Melanie Spencer
Sales Rep, Midwest: Jay Gesin
Sales Rep, Latin America: Ana Henriquez
Sales Rep, Natl Chain: James Whittaker
Sales Mktg Asst: Kevin O'Rourke
Sales, Southern CA & Southwest: Tricia Gabriel
Founded: 1923
Illustrated books on fine art, architecture, design,
photography, decorative arts, film & music.
ISBN Prefix(es): 0-7148
Number of titles published annually: 70 Print
Total Titles: 525 Print
Foreign Office(s): Phaidon, 2 rue de la Roquette,
Cour Ste Margueritte, Escu, Paris 75011,
France *Tel:* (01) 55283838 *Fax:* (01) 55283839
Phaidon Verlag, Oranienburger Strasse 27,
Berlin 10117, Germany *Tel:* (030) 2888 640
Fax: (030) 2804 4879
Phaidon Press Ltd, 18 Regents Wharf, All
Saints St, London N1 9PA, United Kingdom
Tel: (020) 7843 1000 *Fax:* (020) 7843 1010
E-mail: sales@phaidon.com *Web Site:* www.
phaidon.com
Distributor for Mitchell Beazley; Electa

Phi Delta Kappa International
Division of Phi Delta Kappa International Inc
408 N Union, Bloomington, IN 47401
Mailing Address: PO Box 789, Bloomington, IN
47402-0789
Tel: 812-339-1156 *Toll Free Tel:* 800-766-1156
Fax: 812-339-0018
E-mail: information@pdkintl.org
Web Site: www.pdkintl.org
Key Personnel
Dir, Pubns & Res: Donovan R Walling
E-mail: dwalling@pdkintl.org
Man Ed: David Ruetschlin
Founded: 1906
Books & monographs in education.
ISBN Prefix(es): 0-87367

Number of titles published annually: 30 Print
Total Titles: 220 Print; 1 CD-ROM
Foreign Rep(s): Unifacmann Trading Co (Taiwan)

Philadelphia Museum of Art
2525 Pennsylvania Ave, Philadelphia, PA 19130
Tel: 215-684-7250 *Fax:* 215-235-8715
Web Site: www.philamuseum.org
Key Personnel
Ed: Kathleen Krattenmaker
Dir, Publg: Sherry Babbitt *Tel:* 215-684-7242
E-mail: sbabbitt@philamuseum.org
Prod Mgr: Rich Bonk
Assoc Edit: Nicole Amoroso; David Updike
Founded: 1901
Illustrated scholarly works on the permanent col-
lection & exhibitions at the museum.
ISBN Prefix(es): 0-87633
Number of titles published annually: 6 Print
Total Titles: 50 Print
Distributed by Antique Collector's Club (ACC);
Distributed Art Publishers (DAP); Penn State
Press; Yale University Press

§Philosophy Documentation Center
PO Box 7147, Charlottesville, VA 22906-7147
Toll Free Tel: 800-444-2419
E-mail: order@pdcnet.org
Web Site: www.pdcnet.org
Key Personnel
Dir: George Leaman *E-mail:* leaman@pdcnet.org
Assoc Dir: Pamela K Swope *E-mail:* pkswope@
pdcnet.org
Founded: 1966
ISBN Prefix(es): 0-912632; 1-889680
Number of titles published annually: 10 Print; 1
CD-ROM; 2 Online
Total Titles: 8 CD-ROM; 51 Online
Distributor for Agora Publications; Imprint Aca-
demic; InteLex Corp; Routledge; KG Saur Ver-
lag

Phobos Books
Imprint of Phobos Entertainment Holdings Inc
200 Park Ave S, Suite 1109, New York, NY
10003
Tel: 212-477-3225 *Fax:* 212-529-4223
E-mail: info@phobosweb.com
Web Site: phobosweb.com
Key Personnel
Chmn of the Bd: Stanley Plotnick
CEO & Pres: Sandra Schulberg *Tel:* 212-529-
3888 ext 311 *E-mail:* sschulberg@aol.com
VP: Moon Cho
Chief Technol Officer: Rajesh Raichoudhury
Creative Consultant: James C Shooter
Book & Web Ed: Keith Olexa *Tel:* 212-529-3888
ext 306 *E-mail:* olexa@phobosweb.com
Creative Dir: Christian O'Toole *Tel:* 212-529-
3888 ext 303 *E-mail:* otoole@phobosweb.com
Founded: 2001
Dedicated to publishing the best new authors
writing quality science fiction. In addition to
new novels & classic reprints, the company
publishes the annual *Phobos Science Fiction
Anthology*, 12 short stories selected through the
Phobos Fiction Contest by celebrated science
fiction authors. The Phobos Fiction Contest
was created in 2003.
ISBN Prefix(es): 0-9720026
Number of titles published annually: 6 Print
Total Titles: 3 Print
Orders to: National Book Network, 15200 NBN
Way, Blue Ridge Summit, PA 17214 *Tel:* 717-
794-3800 *Toll Free Fax:* 800-338-4550
Returns: National Book Network, 15200 NBN
Way, Blue Ridge Summit, PA 17214 *Tel:* 717-
794-3800 *Toll Free Fax:* 800-338-4550
E-mail: custserv@nbnbooks.com
Shipping Address: National Book Network, 15200
NBN Way, Blue Ridge Summit, PA 17214
Tel: 717-794-3800 *Toll Free Fax:* 800-338-4550
E-mail: custserv@nbnbooks.com

Warehouse: National Book Network, 15200 NBN Way, Blue Ridge Summit, PA 17214 *Tel:* 717-794-3800 *Toll Free Fax:* 800-338-4550 *E-mail:* custserv@nbnbooks.com
Distribution Center: National Book Network, 15200 NBN Way, Blue Ridge Summit, PA 17214 *Tel:* 717-794-3800 *Toll Free Fax:* 800-338-4550 *E-mail:* custserv@nbnbooks.com
Membership(s): Science Fiction & Fantasy Writers of America

Phoenix Learning Resources
Division of The Phoenix Learning Group
25 Third St, 2nd fl, Stamford, CT 06905
Tel: 203-353-1665 *Toll Free Tel:* 800-526-6581
  Fax: 212-629-5648
Web Site: www.phoenixlr.com
Key Personnel
Chmn: Heinz Gelles
Pres: Alexander Burke *Tel:* 516-365-9018
  E-mail: ajburkejr@aol.com
VP & Ed: John A Rothermich
Mktg Mgr: Joan Pinkerton
Founded: 1987
Supplementary & remedial materials in reading, language arts, mathematics, social studies. Texts for early childhood through 12th grade & adult learning skills.
ISBN Prefix(es): 0-7915
Number of titles published annually: 90 Print
Total Titles: 675 Print; 42 Audio
Distributed by Nelson Educational Publishing; McGraw-Hill
Distributor for ECI; Galvin Publications; Kane Publishing; Sterling
Foreign Rep(s): McGraw-Hill International; Nelson Educational Publishing (Canada)
Warehouse: 2349 Chaffee Dr, St Louis, MO 63146

Phoenix Society for Burn Survivors
2153 Wealthy SE, Suite 215, E Grand Rapids, MI 49506
Tel: 616-458-2773 *Toll Free Tel:* 800-888-BURN (888-2876) *Fax:* 616-458-2831
E-mail: info@phoenix-society.org
Web Site: www.phoenix-society.org
Key Personnel
Exec Dir: Amy Acton *E-mail:* amy@phoenix-society.org
Founded: 1977
Books regarding burns.
Number of titles published annually: 4 Print
Total Titles: 35 Print; 35 E-Book

§PIA/GATF (Graphic Arts Technical Foundation)
200 Deer Run Rd, Sewickley, PA 15143-2600
Tel: 412-741-6860 *Toll Free Tel:* 800-910-4283
  Fax: 412-741-2311
E-mail: info@gain.net
Web Site: www.gain.net
Key Personnel
VP: Peter M Oresick *E-mail:* poresick@gatf.org
Ed-in-Chief: Thomas M Destree
  E-mail: tdestree@gatf.org
Man Ed: Amy H Woodall *Tel:* 412-741-6860 ext 413 *E-mail:* awoodall@gatf.org
Founded: 1924
Textbooks & reference books on graphic communications techniques & technology.
ISBN Prefix(es): 0-88362
Number of titles published annually: 20 Print; 5 CD-ROM
Total Titles: 110 Print; 6 CD-ROM; 3 Audio
Imprints: Printing Industries of America
Distributor for Printing Industries of America

Piano Press
1425 Ocean Ave, Suite 6, Del Mar, CA 92014
Mailing Address: PO Box 85, Del Mar, CA 92014-0085

Tel: 619-884-1401 *Fax:* 858-459-3376
E-mail: pianopress@aol.com
Web Site: www.pianopress.com
Key Personnel
Owner & Ed: Elizabeth C Axford
  E-mail: eaxford@aol.com
Ed Asst: Carol Buckley; Katie Cook; Gay Salo
Music Typesetter: Liz Axford; David Murray
Webmaster & Mktg: Nicole Roberts
Audio Engr: John Dawes; Denny Martin; Peter Sprague; Kris Stone
Founded: 1998
Piano Press publishes songbooks & CDs as well as music-related coloring books & poetry for the educational & family markets.
ISBN Prefix(es): 0-9673325; 1-931844
Number of titles published annually: 1 Audio
Total Titles: 25 Print; 3 Audio
Membership(s): ASCAP; NARAS; Society of Children's Book Writers & Illustrators

Picador
Subsidiary of Holtzbrinck Publishers Holdings LLC
175 Fifth Ave, New York, NY 10010
Tel: 212-674-5151 *Fax:* 212-253-9627
E-mail: firstname.lastname@picadorusa.com
Web Site: www.picadorusa.com
Key Personnel
VP & Publr: Frances Coady
Publicity Dir: Tanya Farrell
Mktg Dir: Darin Keesler
Man Ed: Leia Vandersnick
Sr Publicist: Katherine Monaghan
Publicist: James Meader
Assoc Publicist: Emily Haile
Ed: Joshua Kendell
Assoc Ed: Amber Qureshi
Founded: 1995
ISBN Prefix(es): 0-312
Total Titles: 120 Print

Picasso Project
Division of Alan Wofsy Fine Arts
1109 Geary Blvd, San Francisco, CA 94109
Tel: 415-292-6500 *Fax:* 415-292-6594
E-mail: editeur@earthlink.net (editorial); picasso@art-books.com (orders)
Web Site: art-books.com
Key Personnel
Mgr: Adios Butler
Ed: Alan Hyman
Founded: 1990
ISBN Prefix(es): 1-55660
Number of titles published annually: 4 Print
Total Titles: 20 Print
Distributed by Alan Wofsy Fine Arts
Distributor for Cramer (Switzerland); Kornfeld (Switzerland); Ramie (France)
Billing Address: PO Box 2210, San Francisco, CA 94126-2110
Warehouse: Ashland, OH 44805
Distribution Center: Ashland, OH 44805

Piccadilly Books Ltd
PO Box 25203, Colorado Springs, CO 80936-5203
SAN: 665-9969
Tel: 719-550-9887
E-mail: orders@piccadillybooks.com
Web Site: www.piccadillybooks.com
Key Personnel
Publr: Bruce Fife *E-mail:* bruce@piccadillybooks.com
Founded: 1985
Health & nutrition, entertainment, performing arts, humorous skits & sketches, writing.
ISBN Prefix(es): 0-941599
Number of titles published annually: 3 Print
Total Titles: 50 Print; 2 Audio
Foreign Rep(s): Empire Publishing Service

Foreign Rights: Empire Publishing Service
Membership(s): Publishers Marketing Association

Pickwick Publications
215 Incline Way, San Jose, CA 95139-1526
SAN: 210-1319
Tel: 408-224-6777 *Fax:* 408-224-6686
Web Site: www.pickwickpublications.com
Key Personnel
Mgr & Libr Sales Dir: Jean W Hadidian
Gen Ed & Intl Rts Contact: Dikran Y Hadidian
  E-mail: dyh1@aol.com
Founded: 1982
Trade paperbacks, scholarly books, subscription & mail order books; philosophy, religion, theology.
ISBN Prefix(es): 0-915138; 1-55635
Number of titles published annually: 3 Print
Total Titles: 110 Print
Distributor for Darton Longman & Todd Ltd (selected titles); Gomer Press (selected titles); Macmillan Press Ltd (selected titles); SPCK (selected titles)

Picton Press
PO Box 250, Rockport, ME 04856-0250
Tel: 207-236-6565 *Fax:* 207-236-6713
E-mail: sales@pictonpress.com (orders)
Web Site: www.pictonpress.com
ISBN Prefix(es): 0-89725
Number of titles published annually: 21 Print
Imprints: Penobscot Press

Pictorial Histories Publishing Co
521 Bickford St, Missoula, MT 59801
Mailing Address: 713 S Third St, Missoula, MT 59801
Tel: 406-549-8488 *Toll Free Tel:* 888-763-8350
  Fax: 406-728-9280
E-mail: phpc@montana.com
Web Site: www.pictorialhistoriespublishing.com
Key Personnel
Pres, Publr & Intl Rts: Stan Cohen
Founded: 1976
History books.
ISBN Prefix(es): 0-933126; 0-929521; 1-57510
Number of titles published annually: 6 Print
Total Titles: 180 Print

Pie in the Sky Publishing
2511 S Dawson Way, Aurora, CO 80014
Mailing Address: Box 316, 16731 E Iliff Ave, Aurora, CO 80013
Tel: 303-751-2672 *Fax:* 303-751-2672
E-mail: pieintheskypublishing@msn.com
Web Site: www.pieintheskypublishing.com
Key Personnel
Pres: Ann Simmons
Publr: Nancy L Mills *Tel:* 303-671-6776
Founded: 1998
Publishers of high quality, brightly illustrated children's picture books. Most stories are written for both the reader & listener.
ISBN Prefix(es): 1-893815
Number of titles published annually: 3 Print; 1 Audio
Total Titles: 8 Print; 1 Audio
Distribution Center: Partners, 1901 Raymond Ave SW, Suite C, Renton, WA 98055 *Tel:* 425-227-8486 *Toll Free Tel:* 800-563-2385

Pieces of Learning
Division of Creative Learning Consultants Inc
1990 Market Rd, Marion, IL 62959-8976
SAN: 298-461X
Tel: 618-964-9426 *Toll Free Tel:* 800-729-5137
  Toll Free Fax: 800-844-0455
E-mail: polmarion@midamer.net
Web Site: www.piecesoflearning.com
Key Personnel
Pres: Kathy Balsamo
Busn Mgr: Stan Balsamo *Tel:* 618-964-9426
Founded: 1989

Teacher supplementary educational books, parenting books; mail order.
ISBN Prefix(es): 1-880505; 0-9623835; 0-945799; 0-913839; 1-931334
Number of titles published annually: 18 Print
Total Titles: 100 Print
Distributed by ALPS Publishing; A W Peller & Associates; Professional Associate Publishing; Prufrock Press Inc
Membership(s): National School Supply Educational Association

Pig Out Publications Inc
207 E Gregory Blvd, Kansas City, MO 64114
Tel: 816-531-3119 *Fax:* 816-531-6113
Web Site: www.pigoutpublications.com
Key Personnel
Pres: Karen Adler *E-mail:* kadler@ pigoutpublications.com
Founded: 1988
Publisher, distributor & wholesaler of BBQ & grill books.
ISBN Prefix(es): 0-925175
Number of titles published annually: 3 Print
Total Titles: 21 Print
Imprints: Two Lane Press

The Pilgrim Press/United Church Press
700 Prospect Ave, Cleveland, OH 44115-1100
Tel: 216-736-3761 *Toll Free Tel:* 800-537-3394 (cust serv) *Fax:* 216-736-2207
E-mail: thepilgrimpress@thepilgrimpress.com
Web Site: www.thepilgrimpress.com; www.theunitedchurchpress.com
Key Personnel
Publr: Timothy G Staveteig *Tel:* 216-736-3755 *E-mail:* tstaveteig@thepilgrimpress.com
Dir, Mktg & Trade Sales: Michael E Lawrence *Tel:* 216-736-3759 *E-mail:* mlawrence@ thepilgrimpress.com
Edit Dir, Church & Educ: Kim Martin Sadler *Tel:* 216-736-3756 *E-mail:* ksadler@ thepilgrimpress.com
Edit Dir, Prof & Academic: Pamela J Johnson *Tel:* 608-455-1741 *E-mail:* pjj14@rconnect.com
Edit Prodn Dir: Janice W Brown *Tel:* 216-736-3763 *E-mail:* jbrown@thepilgrimpress.com
Edit Dir, Prof & Academic Pubs: Ulrike Guthrie *Tel:* 207-942-0968 *E-mail:* ulrikeguthrie@ verizon.net
Dist Servs Mgr: Marie Tyson *Tel:* 216-736-3777 *Fax:* 216-736-2206 *E-mail:* tysonm@ucc.org
Designer: Robyn Henderson *Tel:* 216-736-3758 *E-mail:* rhenderson@thepilgrimpress.com
Assoc Ed: Monitta Lowe *Tel:* 216-736-3764 *E-mail:* mlowe@thepilgrimpress.com
Prod Mgmt Assoc: Said Mougrabi *Tel:* 216-736-3760 *E-mail:* smougrabi@thepilgrimpress.com
Mktg Communs Assoc: Aimee Jannsohn *E-mail:* ajannsohn@thepilgrimpress.com
Mktg Asst: Juliet Dombos *Tel:* 216-736-3766 *E-mail:* jdombos@thepilgrimpress.com
Founded: 1608
Alternative spiritualities; peace & justice; world religions; contemporary ministry.
ISBN Prefix(es): 0-8298
Number of titles published annually: 50 Print
Total Titles: 435 Print
Distributor for Northstone Publishing; SPCK; Wood Lake Books
Foreign Rep(s): Baker & Taylor Intl (World)

Pilgrim Publications
PO Box 66, Pasadena, TX 77501-0066
Tel: 713-477-4261; 713-477-2329 *Fax:* 713-477-7561
E-mail: pilgrimpub@aol.com
Web Site: members.aol.com/pilgrimpub/; www.pilgrimpublications.com
Key Personnel
Dir: Bob Ross
Founded: 1969

The works & sermons of Charles H Spurgeon (1834-1892).
ISBN Prefix(es): 1-56186
Number of titles published annually: 6 Print
Total Titles: 200 Print
Distributor for Ages Software; Ambassador-Emerald; Christian Focus; Fox River Press; Hess Publications; Soli Deo Gloria Publications
Warehouse: 1609 Preston, Pasadena, TX 77503
Membership(s): Christian Booksellers Association

Pine Barrens Press
Division of Barnegat Light Press
3959 Rte 563, Chatsworth, NJ 08019
Mailing Address: PO Box 607, Chatsworth, NJ 08019-0667
Tel: 609-894-4415 *Fax:* 609-894-2350
E-mail: pbp@verizon.net
Key Personnel
Publr: R Marilyn Schmidt
Founded: 1980
Regional books, gardening, cookbooks on regional products, primarily mail order sales. Retail outlet at the Cheshire Cat in Buzby's Chatworth General Store.
ISBN Prefix(es): 0-937996
Number of titles published annually: 4 Print
Total Titles: 30 Print

Pine Forge Press
Subsidiary of SAGE Publications Inc
2455 Teller Rd, Thousand Oaks, CA 91320
Tel: 805-499-4224 *Fax:* 805-499-0721
E-mail: info@sagepub.com
Web Site: www.sagepub.com
Key Personnel
Pres: Blaise Simqu
Sales: Jan Sather *Tel:* 805-499-4224 ext 7128
Founded: 1991
Texts & software for use in graduate & undergraduate social & behavioral science courses.
ISBN Prefix(es): 0-7591
Number of titles published annually: 25 Print
Total Titles: 150 Print

Pineapple Press Inc
PO Box 3889, Sarasota, FL 34230-3889
SAN: 285-0869
Tel: 941-359-0886 *Toll Free Tel:* 800-746-3275 (orders) *Fax:* 941-351-9988
E-mail: info@pineapplepress.com
Web Site: www.pineapplepress.com
Key Personnel
Pres: David M Cussen *E-mail:* david@ pineapplepress.com
Exec Ed: June Cussen
Founded: 1982
ISBN Prefix(es): 0-910923; 1-56164
Number of titles published annually: 25 Print
Total Titles: 200 Print
Foreign Rights: Evan Marshall Agency
Warehouse: 7127 24th Court East, Sarasota, FL 34243

Pinnacle Books, see Kensington Publishing Corp

Pioneer Publishing Co
Hwy 82 E, Carrolton, MS 38917
Mailing Address: PO Box 408, Carrolton, MS 38917-0408
Tel: 662-237-6010
E-mail: pioneerse@tecinfo.com
Web Site: www.pioneersoutheast.com
Key Personnel
Owner: Betty C Wiltshire
Number of titles published annually: 10 Print
Total Titles: 74 Print

Pippin Press
229 E 85 St, New York, NY 10028

Mailing Address: Gracie Sta, PO Box 1347, New York, NY 10028
Tel: 212-288-4920 *Fax:* 908-237-2407
Key Personnel
Pres & Publr: Barbara Francis
Sr Ed: Joyce Segal
Man Ed & Rts Dir: Gregory Filling
Sales Mgr & Lib Sales Dir: Alan Frese
Founded: 1987
Small chapter books for ages 7-10, humorous fiction for all ages, novels for ages 8-12 & unusual nonfiction for ages 6-12.
ISBN Prefix(es): 0-945912
Number of titles published annually: 4 Print
Total Titles: 46 Print
Foreign Rep(s): Baker & Taylor Books (Canada); Baker & Taylor International (Worldwide exc Canada)
Orders to: Whitehurst & Clark Book Fulfillment Inc, 1200 Old County Rd, Rte 523, Flemington, NJ 08822 *Tel:* 908-788-5753 *Fax:* 908-237-2407
Returns: Whitehurst & Clark Book Fulfillment Inc, 1200 Old County Rd, Rte 523, Flemington, NJ 08822 *Tel:* 908-788-5753 *Fax:* 908-237-2407
Shipping Address: Whitehurst & Clark Book Fulfillment Inc, 1200 Old County Rd, Rte 523, Flemington, NJ 08822 *Tel:* 908-788-5753 *Fax:* 908-237-2407
Warehouse: Whitehurst & Clark Book Fulfillment Inc, 1200 Old County Rd, Rte 523, Flemington, NJ 08822 *Tel:* 908-788-5753 *Fax:* 908-237-2407
Distribution Center: Whitehurst & Clark Book Fulfillment Inc, 1200 Old County Rd, Rte 523, Flemington, NJ 08822 *Tel:* 908-788-5753 *Fax:* 908-237-2407
Membership(s): ALA

Pir Publications Inc
227 W Broadway, New York, NY 10013
Tel: 212-334-5212 *Fax:* 212-334-5214
E-mail: pirpress@ulster.net
Web Site: www.sufibooks.com
Key Personnel
Ed: Matthew Brown *Tel:* 212-334-3582
Founded: 1988
Publisher of books & music CDs.
ISBN Prefix(es): 1-879708
Number of titles published annually: 2 Print
Total Titles: 18 Print; 2 Audio
Imprints: Pir Press
Subsidiaries: Sufi Books

Pitspopany Press
40 E 78 St, Suite 16-D, New York, NY 10021
Tel: 212-472-4959 *Toll Free Tel:* 800-232-2931 *Fax:* 212-472-6253
E-mail: pitspop@netvision.net.il; pitspopany@aol.com
Key Personnel
Publr & Intl Rts Contact: Yaacov Peterseil
Mktg Mgr: Dorothy Tananbaum
Founded: 1993
Jewish children's books, young adult titles, self-help, self awareness on Jewish topics, sci-fi, religion, education.
ISBN Prefix(es): 0-943706; 965-483; 965-465
Number of titles published annually: 18 Print
Imprints: Devora Publishing (Adult line of publishing)
Foreign Office(s): PO Box 4636, Jerusalem 91044, Israel *Tel:* (02) 563-7155 *Fax:* (02) 563-7156 *E-mail:* pop@netvision.net.il
Distributor for Simcha Publishing
Distribution Center: Stackpole, 5067 Ritter Rd, Mechanicsburg, PA 17055 *Tel:* 717-795-8610 *Fax:* 717-796-9441

Pittenbruach Press
PO Box 553, Northampton, MA 01061-0553

Tel: 413-584-8547
Key Personnel
Pres: Teddy Milne *E-mail:* teddym@crocker.com
Founded: 1986
Mostly Quaker books. No unsol mss.
ISBN Prefix(es): 0-938875
Number of titles published annually: 3 Print
Total Titles: 40 Print
Foreign Rep(s): Timmon Wallis (UK)

PJD Publications Ltd
PO Box 966, Westbury, NY 11590-0966
SAN: 202-0068
Tel: 516-626-0650 *Fax:* 516-626-5546
E-mail: pjdsankar@msn.com
Web Site: www.pjdonline.com; www.
pjdpublications.com
Key Personnel
CEO, Pres & Ed-in-Chief: Siva Sankar
Tech: Barbara Kelly
Founded: 1968
Biomedical & educational books, philosophy,
scholarly, science & social sciences, books &
journals.
ISBN Prefix(es): 0-9600290; 0-915340
Number of titles published annually: 18 Print
Total Titles: 25 Print
Divisions: Institute for Research Information; Of-
fice & Print Technologies; PJD Electronic Pub-
lishing

Planners Press
Division of American Planning Association
122 S Michigan Ave, Suite 1600, Chicago, IL
60603
Tel: 312-431-9100 *Fax:* 312-431-9985
Web Site: www.planning.org
Key Personnel
Dir, Pubns: Sylvia Lewis *E-mail:* slewis@
planning.org
Founded: 1978
Books on city planning.
ISBN Prefix(es): 0-918286; 1-884829; 1-932364
Number of titles published annually: 4 Print
Total Titles: 110 Print; 15 Audio
Distributed by University of Chicago Press

Planning/Communications
7215 Oak Ave, River Forest, IL 60305-1935
Tel: 708-366-5200 *Toll Free Tel:* 888-366-5200
Fax: 708-366-5280
E-mail: info@planningcommunications.com
Web Site: www.jobfindersonline.com
Key Personnel
Pres & Intl Rts: Daniel Lauber *E-mail:* dl@
planningcommunications.com
Mktg Dir: Jennifer Atkin *E-mail:* jatkin@
planningcommunications.com
Founded: 1979
Publish books on careers, current issues, dream
fulfillment.
ISBN Prefix(es): 1-884587
Number of titles published annually: 4 Print
Total Titles: 10 Print
Distributed by SCB Distributors (paperback edi-
tions only)
Membership(s): Publishers Marketing Association

Platinum Press Inc
311 Crossways Park Dr, Woodbury, NY 11797
Tel: 516-364-1800 *Fax:* 516-364-1899
Key Personnel
Pres: Herbert J Cohen *E-mail:* hcohen@bobley.
com
VP: Peter M Bobley
Founded: 1990
Publish nonfiction; book producer & packager;
appointment books, diaries, date books, jour-
nals & blankbooks.
ISBN Prefix(es): 1-879582
Number of titles published annually: 20 Print

Total Titles: 75 Print; 2 E-Book
Distributed by Barnes & Noble Books

Platypus Media LLC
627 "A" St NE, Washington, DC 20002
Tel: 202-546-1674 *Toll Free Tel:* 877-872-8977
Fax: 202-546-2356
E-mail: info@platypusmedia.com
Web Site: www.platypusmedia.com
Key Personnel
Pres: Dia L Michels
Founded: 2000
An independent publisher creating books for fam-
ilies, teachers & parenting professionals.
ISBN Prefix(es): 1-930775
Number of titles published annually: 4 Print; 2
Audio
Total Titles: 12 Print; 2 Audio
Distributed by Pharmasoft
Membership(s): Children's Book Council; Pub-
lishers Marketing Association; Small Publishers
Association of North America; Washington
Book Publishers

§Players Press Inc
PO Box 1132, Studio City, CA 91614-0132
Tel: 818-789-4980
Key Personnel
Pres & CEO: Robert Gordon
VP, Ed: David Wainright
VP, Opers: Chris Cordero
Sales Mgr: M Cohen
Intl Rts & Lib Sales Dir: Sam Diamond
Founded: 1965
Publisher of plays, musicals & performing arts
textbooks & Sherlock Holmes. Represents
world rights for other publishers of performing
arts books (film, theater, television). Distributes
English Speaking World for other publishers of
entertainment books & Sherlockian. Publishes
costume books in English & German.
ISBN Prefix(es): 0-88734
Number of titles published annually: 40 Print
Total Titles: 2,025 Print; 62 CD-ROM; 4 Audio
Imprints: Healthwatch; Players Press; Showcase
Divisions: Players Press (Canada); Player Press
Ltd (UK); Player Press A/Z Ltd
Foreign Office(s): 20 Park Dr, Romford, Essex,
United Kingdom
Distributor for Garland-Clark Editors; Macmillan
Education (UK); Organica; Preston Editions
Foreign Rep(s): Players Press Germany GMBH;
Players Press UK Ltd (UK)
Foreign Rights: Players Press International (Eu-
rope)
Advertising Agency: Empire Enterprises, PO Box
1344, Studio City, CA 91614-0344 *Tel:* 818-
784-8918
Membership(s): ABA

Playhouse Publishing
1566 Akron-Peninsula Rd, Akron, OH 44313
Tel: 330-926-1313 *Toll Free Tel:* 800-762-6775
Fax: 330-926-1315
E-mail: info@playhousepublishing.com
Web Site: www.playhousepublishing.com
Key Personnel
Pres: Deborah D'Andrea
Dir, Sales: Michelle Varvaro *Tel:* 330-
926-1313 ext 203 *E-mail:* m.varvaro@
playhousepublishing.com
Sales Mgr: Jennifer Cmich *Tel:* 330-926-1313 ext
204 *E-mail:* j.cmich@playhousepublishing.com
Man Ed: Jackie Wolf
Founded: 1989
Children's book publisher of interactive titles.
ISBN Prefix(es): 1-878338; 1-57151
Number of titles published annually: 15 Print
Total Titles: 130 Print

Imprints: Little Lucy & Friends™; Nibble Me
Books™; Picture Me Books™; Picture, Play &
Tote™; Playhouse Publishing; Sparkle Shapes
Membership(s): ABA; Publishers Marketing As-
sociation

Playmore Inc, Publishers
230 Fifth Ave, Suite 711, New York, NY 10001
SAN: 205-1257
Tel: 212-251-0600 *Fax:* 212-251-0966
Web Site: playmorebooks.com *Telex:* TWY 23-
8198
Key Personnel
Pres, Ed & ISBN Contact: Jon Horwich *Tel:* 212-
251-0600 ext 240
VP, Sales: John Barbour
Founded: 1942
Hardcover & softcover children's books.
ISBN Prefix(es): 0-86611
Number of titles published annually: 50 Print
Total Titles: 200 Print
Imprints: Baronet Books; Creative Child Press;
Fun Pads; Magnum Books; Moby Books; Pre
School Press
Foreign Rights: Rights Unlimited (World)

Pleasant Company Publications
Subsidiary of Mattel
8400 Fairway Place, Middleton, WI 53562
Tel: 608-836-4848 *Fax:* 608-257-3865
Web Site: www.americangirl.com
Key Personnel
Pres: Ellen Brothers
Intl Rts: Menzi Behrnd-Klodt
Founded: 1986
Children's fiction & nonfiction.
ISBN Prefix(es): 0-937295; 1-56247; 1-58485
Number of titles published annually: 40 Print; 1
CD-ROM; 6 Audio
Total Titles: 285 Print; 3 CD-ROM; 18 Audio
Imprints: A G Fiction™; American Girl Li-
brary®; The American Girls Collection®; His-
tory Mysteries®
Membership(s): Children's Book Council

Pleasure Boat Studio: A Literary Press
201 W 89 St, Suite 6F, New York, NY 10024-
1848
Tel: 212-362-8563 *Toll Free Tel:* 888-810-5308
Fax: 212-874-1158 *Toll Free Fax:* 800-810-
5308
E-mail: pleasboat@nyc.rr.com
Web Site: www.pbstudio.com
Key Personnel
Publr: Jack Estes
Founded: 1996
ISBN Prefix(es): 0-9651413; 1-929355; 0-912887
Number of titles published annually: 3 Print
Total Titles: 20 Print
Distributor for Empty Bowl Press
Shipping Address: 312 Gehrke Rd, Port Angeles,
WA 98362
Membership(s): Publishers Marketing Association

Plexus Publishing Inc
143 Old Marlton Pike, Medford, NJ 08055
Tel: 609-654-6500 *Fax:* 609-654-4309
E-mail: info@plexuspublishing.com
Web Site: www.plexuspublishing.com
Key Personnel
Intl Rts: Thomas Hogan
Lib Sales Dir: Thomas Hogan, Jr
E-mail: thoganjr@infotoday.com
Edit Dir: Mary S Hogan
Book Mgr & Asst to Pres: Pat Palatucci
E-mail: patp@plexuspublishing.com
Founded: 1977
Publisher of books in the life sciences, in the area
of science career education & the New Jersey
Pinelands.
ISBN Prefix(es): 0-937548; 0-9666748
Number of titles published annually: 3 Print

Total Titles: 33 Print
Imprints: Medford Press
Distributed by Independent Publishers Group
(IPG)

§The Plough Publishing House
Subsidiary of The Bruderhof Foundation Inc
Spring Valley, Rte 381 N, Farmington, PA 15437
SAN: 202-0092
Tel: 724-329-1100
E-mail: contact@bruderhof.com
Web Site: www.plough.com
Key Personnel
Mgr: Detlef Manke
Intl Rts: Anna Tietze
Founded: 1920
Religion (Anabaptist) Bruderhof communities,
church history, children's education, Christian
communal living; music; social justice, radical
Christianity; social issues.
ISBN Prefix(es): 0-87486
Number of titles published annually: 5 Online; 5
E-Book
Total Titles: 42 Online; 42 E-Book
Foreign Office(s): Darvell Bruderhof Plough UK,
Robertsbridge, East Sussex TN32 5DR, United
Kingdom
Foreign Rep(s): Darvell Bruderhof

Ploughshares
Subsidiary of Ploughshares Inc
Emerson College, 120 Boylston St, Boston, MA
02116
Tel: 617-824-8753
E-mail: pshares@emerson.edu
Web Site: www.pshares.org
Key Personnel
Dir & Ed: Don Lee
Founded: 1971
Journal publishing.
ISBN Prefix(es): 0-933277
Number of titles published annually: 3 Print
Total Titles: 93 Print
Online services available through EBSCOhost,
GaleNet, H W Wilson, ProQuest.
Membership(s): Combined Book Exhibit

Plume
Division of Penguin Group (USA) Inc
375 Hudson St, New York, NY 10014
SAN: 282-5074
Tel: 212-366-2000 *Fax:* 212-366-2666
E-mail: online@penguinputnam.com
Web Site: www.penguin.com
Key Personnel
Pres: Clare Ferraro
Publr: Kathryn Court
VP, Prodn: Pat Lyons
Ed-in-Chief: Trena Keating
Dir, Publicity & Publg: Brant Janeway
Dir, Art: Melissa Jacoby
Man Ed: Jeffrey Freiert
Sr Ed: Gary Brozak; Julie Saltman
ISBN Prefix(es): 0-452
Number of titles published annually: 68 Print
Total Titles: 783 Print

§Plunkett Research Ltd
PO Drawer 541737, Houston, TX 77254-1737
Tel: 713-932-0000 *Fax:* 713-932-7080
E-mail: sales@plunkettresearch.com
Web Site: www.plunkettresearch.com
Key Personnel
Publr & CEO: Jack W Plunkett
 E-mail: jack_plunkett@plunkettresearch.com
Founded: 1985
Provider of business & industry information to
corporate, library, academic & government
markets. Plunkett's unique reference books are
the only complete sources written in lay lan-
guage for readers of all types. In many cases,
these valuable resources are the only compre-

hensive guides covering the specific industries
involved. Publish in print & electronic formats.
ISBN Prefix(es): 0-9638268; 1-891775
Number of titles published annually: 29 Print; 29
CD-ROM; 30 Online; 30 E-Book
Total Titles: 30 Print; 30 CD-ROM; 30 Online;
30 E-Book

Plymouth Press/Plymouth Books
PO Box 2044, Miami Beach, FL 33140
Tel: 305-673-0771 *Fax:* 305-673-1014 (call first)
Key Personnel
Ed & Intl Rts: Henry Denton
Founded: 1975
Books especially successful for mail order & re-
tail. Subjects include miracle exercises & super
potency.
ISBN Prefix(es): 0-935540
Number of titles published annually: 6 Print; 2
Audio
Total Titles: 18 Print; 2 Audio
Foreign Rep(s): Henry Denton (World)

Pocket Books
Division of Simon & Schuster Adult Publishing
Group
1230 Avenue of the Americas, New York, NY
10020
Toll Free Tel: 800-456-6798 *Fax:* 212-698-7284
E-mail: consumer.customerservice@
 simonandschuster.com
Web Site: www.simonsays.com
Key Personnel
Exec VP & Publr: Louise Burke
VP & Assoc Publr: Liate Stehlik
VP & Edit Dir: Maggie Crawford
VP & Dir, Mktg: Craig Herman
VP & Man Ed: Donna O'Neill
VP & Assoc Publr, Media: Scott Shannon
VP & Dir, Rts: Lisa Keim
VP & Dir, Publicity: Hillary Schupf
VP & Exec Dir, Art & Design: Paolo Pepe
Art Dir: Lisa Litwack
Mktg Mgr: Barry Porter
Exec Ed, Media: Margaret Clark
Sr Ed, Media: Marco Palmieri
Ed, Media: Jennifer Heddle; Edward Schlesinger
Sr Ed: Mitchell Ivers; Amy Pierpont; Micki Nud-
 ing; Kevin Smith; Lauren McKenna
Assoc Ed: Christina Boys; Selena James
Founded: 1939
Trade paperbacks & hardcovers; mass market,
reprints & originals.
ISBN Prefix(es): 0-671; 0-7434
Imprints: Downtown Press; MTV Books; Pocket
Star; Pocket Books Trade Paperback; Star
Trek®; VH-1; World Wrestling Entertainment
Foreign Rights: Andrew Nurnberg Associates
(Bulgaria, Croatia, Czech Republic, Estonia,
Hungary, Latvia, Lithuania, Poland, Romania,
Russia, Serbia and Montenegro, Slovak Re-
public, Slovenia); Antonella Antonelli Agenzia
(Italy); Arts & Licensing International (Main-
land China, Taiwan); Big Apple Tuttle-Mori
Agency (Thailand); Book Publishers Associa-
tion of Israel (Israel); Eric Yang Agency (Ko-
rea); Caroline van Gelderen Literary Agency
(Netherlands); Japan UPI Agency (Japan); JLM
Literary Agency (Greece); Nurcihan Kesim Lit-
erary Agency (Turkey); La Nouvelle Agence
(France); Mohrbooks Literary Agency (Ger-
many); Sane Toregard Agency (Denmark, Finland, Iceland, Norway, Sweden)
Shipping Address: Total Warehouse Services,
Radcliffe St, Bristol, PA 19007

Pocket Press Inc
PO Box 25124, Portland, OR 97298
Toll Free Tel: 888-237-2110 *Toll Free Fax:* 877-
643-3732
E-mail: sales@pocketpressinc.com
Web Site: www.pocketpressinc.com

Key Personnel
Pres: Bruce Coorpender
Sales & Mktg: Bob Born
Founded: 1991
Reference books for law enforcement.
ISBN Prefix(es): 1-884493
Number of titles published annually: 4 Print
Total Titles: 40 Print

Pocol Press
6023 Pocol Dr, Clifton, VA 20124-1333
SAN: 253-6021
Tel: 703-830-5862
E-mail: chrisandtom@erols.com
Web Site: www.pocolpress.com
Key Personnel
Publr: J Thomas Hetrick
Founded: 1999
Fiction & baseball history from first-time non-
agented authors. Expert storytellers welcome.
ISBN Prefix(es): 1-929763
Number of titles published annually: 4 Print
Total Titles: 17 Print

Pogo Press Inc
4 Cardinal Lane, St Paul, MN 55127
SAN: 665-2107
Tel: 651-483-4692 *Fax:* 651-483-4692
E-mail: pogopres@minn.net
Web Site: www.pogopress.com
Key Personnel
Pres & CEO: Moira F Harris
VP & Intl Rts: Leo J Harris
Founded: 1986
Popular culture.
ISBN Prefix(es): 0-9617767; 1-880654
Number of titles published annually: 4 Print
Total Titles: 41 Print
Distributed by SCB Distributors

Poisoned Pen Press Inc
6962 E First Ave, Suite 103, Scottsdale, AZ
85251
Tel: 480-945-3375 ext 210 *Fax:* 480-949-1707
E-mail: info@poisonpenpress.com
Web Site: www.poisonpenpress.com
Key Personnel
Pres: Robert Rosenwald *E-mail:* robert@
perfectniche.com
Sr Ed: Barbara Peters *E-mail:* barbara@
poisonedpenpress.com
Ed: Jennifer Semon *E-mail:* jennifer@
poisonedpenpress.com
Bookeeper: Marilyn Pizzo *E-mail:* marilyn@
poisonedpenpress.com
Contact: Monty Montee *E-mail:* monty@
poisonedpenpress.com
Founded: 1996
Publishing high quality works in the field of mys-
tery. Interested in publishing books that we
think booksellers everywhere & especially in-
dependent mystery booksellers would want to
have available to sell.
ISBN Prefix(es): 1-890208; 1-59058
Number of titles published annually: 40 Print
Total Titles: 190 Print
Distributor for Sibling Press
Foreign Rep(s): Baror International (World)
Foreign Rights: Danny Baror (World)
Membership(s): Arizona Book Publishing Asso-
ciation; Publishers Association of the West;
Publishers Marketing Association

Polar Bear & Co
The Cascades, 8 Brook St, Solon, ME 04979
Mailing Address: PO Box 311, Solon, ME
04979-0311
Tel: 207-643-2795
E-mail: polarbear@necsys.net
Web Site: www.polarbearandco.com
Key Personnel
Publr & Consultant: Ramona du Houx
Lib Sales Dir: Paul du Houx

Asst Dir: Vance Cornell
Founded: 1991 (To publish high quality works that grow with the readership in time)
Rebuilding our cultural heritage with words & art. We are a publisher of high quality fiction & nonfiction who provide consultancy services for writers, artists & photographers who wish to bring out that spark in us all. We produce quality books & art, highlighting social & environmental issues.
ISBN Prefix(es): 1-882190
Number of titles published annually: 6 Print; 1 E-Book; 1 Audio
Total Titles: 21 Print; 1 Online; 1 E-Book; 2 Audio
Foreign Office(s): 22-12 Miyamotocho Itabashiku, T174 Tokyo, Japan, Takafumi Suzuki
Distribution Center: Bilbio National Book Network, 15200 NBN Way, Blue Ridge Summit, PA 17214, Contact: Mandy Harnish *Tel:* 717-794-3800 *Toll Free Tel:* 800-462-6420 *Fax:* 717-794-3828 *E-mail:* mharnish@nbnbooks.com
Ingram Book Co, PO Box 3500, La Vergne, TN 37086

Police Executive Research Forum
1120 Connecticut Ave NW, Suite 930, Washington, DC 20036
Tel: 202-466-7820 *Toll Free Tel:* 888-202-4563 (cust serv) *Fax:* 202-466-7826
E-mail: perf@policeforum.org
Web Site: www.policeforum.org
Key Personnel
Dir, Pubns: Martha Plotkin *Tel:* 202-466-7820 *E-mail:* mplotkin@policeforum.org
Opers Admin: Rebecca Neuburger *Tel:* 202-454-8300 *E-mail:* rneuburger@policeforum.org
Founded: 1977
Community policing, POP, police research & management, police & criminal justice.
ISBN Prefix(es): 1-878734
Number of titles published annually: 3 Print
Total Titles: 70 Print
Distributor for Anderson; Criminal Justice Press; McGraw-Hill; Sage Publications
Distribution Center: Whitehurst & Clark, 1200 Rte 523, Flemington, NJ 08822, Contact: Brad Searles *Toll Free Tel:* 888-202-4563 *Fax:* 908-237-2407 *E-mail:* wcbooks@aol.com

Polychrome Publishing Corp
4509 N Francisco Ave, Chicago, IL 60625
Tel: 773-478-4455 *Fax:* 773-478-0786
E-mail: info@polychromebooks.com
Web Site: www.polychromebooks.com
Key Personnel
Pres: Sandra S Yamate
Founded: 1990
Multicultural, particularly Asian American children's books.
ISBN Prefix(es): 1-879965
Number of titles published annually: 4 Print
Total Titles: 16 Print

Pomegranate Communications
775-A Southpoint Blvd, Petaluma, CA 94954-1495
Mailing Address: PO Box 808022, Petaluma, CA 94975-8022
Tel: 707-782-9000 *Toll Free Tel:* 800-227-1428 *Toll Free Fax:* 800-848-4376
Web Site: www.pomegranate.com
Key Personnel
Pres & Intl Rts: Thomas F Burke
Publr: Katie Burke
Opers Dir: Joyce Ulrich
Intl Sales Dir: Josh Rifkin
Man Ed: Eva Strock
Founded: 1969
Fine art publisher of books, calendars, posters, notecards, postcards & journals.

ISBN Prefix(es): 0-87654; 1-56640; 0-7649
Number of titles published annually: 13 Print
Total Titles: 136 Print
Foreign Rep(s): Canadian Manda (Canada); Hardie Grant Books (Australia); Pomegranate Europe Ltd (UK, Europe); Pomegranate International Sales (Africa, Asia, Central America, Middle East, South America); Southern Publishers Group (New Zealand)

Popular Culture Inc
PO Box 110, Harbor Springs, MI 49740-0110
Tel: 231-439-9767 *Toll Free Tel:* 800-678-8828 *Fax:* 231-439-9767 *Toll Free Fax:* 800-678-8828
Key Personnel
Pres: Tom Schultheiss
Founded: 1989
Directories, reference books, music, radio & TV.
ISBN Prefix(es): 1-56075
Total Titles: 25 Print
Foreign Rep(s): Eurospan (England)

Porter Sargent Publishers Inc
11 Beacon St, Suite 1400, Boston, MA 02108
SAN: 208-8142
Tel: 617-523-1670 *Toll Free Tel:* 800-342-7470 *Fax:* 617-523-1021
E-mail: info@portersargent.com
Web Site: www.portersargent.com
Key Personnel
Gen Mgr: John Yonce *E-mail:* jyonce@portersargent.com
Sr Ed: Daniel P McKeever *E-mail:* dmckeever@portersargent.com
Founded: 1914
Black studies, education, history, sociology texts, philosophy, reference & social sciences, databases. Directories of private schools, special education & special needs. Also summer camps, summer schools, schools abroad & sociology texts.
ISBN Prefix(es): 0-87558
Number of titles published annually: 3 Print
Total Titles: 27 Print
Imprints: Extending Horizons Books; Handbook Series; Special Education Series
Orders to: 300 Bedford St, Suite 213, Manchester, NH 03101 *Tel:* 603-647-4383; 603-626-1510 *Toll Free Tel:* 800-342-7470 *Fax:* 603-669-7945 *E-mail:* orders@portersargent.com
Web Site: www.portersargent.com
Returns: By permission only

Possibility Press
Imprint of Markowski International Publishers
One Oakglade Circle, Hummelstown, PA 17036
Tel: 717-566-0468 *Toll Free Tel:* 800-566-0534 *Fax:* 717-566-6423
E-mail: posspress@aol.com
Key Personnel
Owner, Publr & Intl Rts: Michael A Markowski
Ed-in-Chief: Marjorie L Markowski
Off Mgr: Janet Althouse
Founded: 1981
Human development, personal growth, sales & marketing, leadership training, network marketing, motivational & success, aviation, model aviation, instructional.
ISBN Prefix(es): 0-938716
Number of titles published annually: 5 Print
Total Titles: 36 Print; 1 Audio
Imprints: Aeronautical Publishers; American Aeronautical Archives; Possibility Press
Sales Office(s): Motorbooks Intl, Galtier Plaza, 380 Jackson St, Suite 200, St Paul, MN 55101 *Tel:* 651-287-5000 *Toll Free Tel:* 800-458-0454
Distributed by Midpoint Trade Books; Motorbooks Intl
Advertising Agency: Media Responce Service
Web Site: www.possibilitypress.com

Billing Address: Motorbooks Intl, Galtier Plaza, 380 Jackson St, Suite 200, St Paul, MN 55101 *Tel:* 651-287-5000 *Toll Free Tel:* 800-458-0454
Orders to: Motorbooks Intl, Galtier Plaza, 380 Jackson St, Suite 200, St Paul, MN 55101 *Tel:* 651-287-5000 *Toll Free Tel:* 800-458-0454
Returns: Motorbooks Intl, Galtier Plaza, 380 Jackson St, Suite 200, St Paul, MN 55101 *Tel:* 651-287-5000 *Toll Free Tel:* 800-458-0454
Warehouse: Banta Book Group Warehouse M, Harrisonburg, VA 22801
Distribution Center: Banta Book Group Warehouse M, Harrisonburg, VA 22801
Membership(s): Publishers Marketing Association

powerHouse Books
Division of powerHouse Cultural Entertainment Inc
68 Charlton St, New York, NY 10014-4601
Tel: 212-604-9074 *Fax:* 212-366-5247
E-mail: info@powerhousebooks.com
Web Site: www.powerhousebooks.com
Key Personnel
Publr: Daniel Power
Assoc Publr: Craig Cohen *E-mail:* craig@powerhousebooks.com
Founded: 1995
Contemporary art, photography & image-based cultural books.
ISBN Prefix(es): 1-57687
Number of titles published annually: 37 Print
Total Titles: 1 Audio
Distributor for Dakini Books; From Here to Fame; Glitterati Inc; Juno Books; 6x6.com; Testify Books; True Agency; Umbrage Editions
Foreign Rep(s): Athena Productions Inc (Asia, Latin America); Bill Bailey (Europe); Bookwise International Pty Ltd (Australia); Critiques Livres (France); Manda Group; Turnaround (UK); Roger Ward (Asia)
Foreign Rights: Athena Productions Inc (Asia, Latin America); Bookwise International Pty Ltd (Australia); Plroska Boros (Switzerland); Canadian Manda Group (Canada); Critiques Livres (France); GVA (Europe); Judith Heckel (Germany); Peter Hyde Associates (South Africa); Seth Meyer-Bruhns (Austria); Susanne Sleger (Germany); Murray Sutton; Turnaround (UK); Visual Books (Germany); Gerd Wagner (Germany)
Warehouse: Mercedes Distribution Center, Brooklyn Navy Yard, Bldg 3, Brooklyn, NY 11205

Practice Management Information Corp (PMIC)
4727 Wilshire Blvd, Suite 300, Los Angeles, CA 90010
SAN: 139-438X
Tel: 323-954-0224 *Fax:* 323-954-0253
E-mail: orders@medicalbookstore.com
Web Site: www.pmiconline.com
Key Personnel
Publr & Pres: James B Davis
Assoc Ed: Carrie Hyatt
Founded: 1986
Books & software for physicians, hospitals, insurance companies & other healthcare professionals on medical coding, reimbursement, practice management, financial management & medical risk management.
ISBN Prefix(es): 1-878487 (Health Info); 1-57066
Number of titles published annually: 50 Print
Total Titles: 300 Print
Imprints: Health Information Press (HIP)
Branch Office(s)
PMIC Sales Off, 2001 Butterfield Rd, Suite 850, Downers Grove, IL 60515 *Tel:* 630-964-7800 *Toll Free Tel:* 800-MEDSHOP *Fax:* 630-964-8873

§Practising Law Institute
810 Seventh Ave, New York, NY 10019
SAN: 203-0136

Tel: 212-824-5700 *Toll Free Tel:* 800-260-4PLI
(260-4754 customer service) *Fax:* 212-265-
4742 *Toll Free Fax:* 800-321-0093
E-mail: info@pli.edu
Web Site: www.pli.edu
Key Personnel
Exec Dir: Victor J Rubino
Cust Servs Mgr: Phillip Friedman
Assoc Dir: William Cubberley
Publg Coord: Todd Warner
Founded: 1933
Professional books for lawyers; audiocassettes,
videocassettes; CD-ROMs, programs.
ISBN Prefix(es): 0-87224; 1-4024
Number of titles published annually: 181 Print
Total Titles: 233 Print; 4 CD-ROM; 206 Online;
308 Audio
Online services available through Lexis, Westlaw.
Imprints: PLI
Distributed by PLI
Shipping Address: PMDS, 1780A Crossroads Dr,
Odenton, MD 21113 *Tel:* 301-604-3305

§Prakken Publications Inc
832 Phoenix Dr, Ann Arbor, MI 48108
Mailing Address: PO Box 8623, Ann Arbor, MI
48107-8623
Tel: 734-975-2800 *Toll Free Tel:* 800-530-9673
(orders only) *Fax:* 734-975-2787
E-mail: tdbooks@techdirections.com
Web Site: www.techdirections.com; www.eddigest.
com
Key Personnel
Publr & Intl Rts: George Kennedy
E-mail: publisher@techdirections.com
Book Sales & Mktg Mgr: Matthew Knope
E-mail: tdbooks@techdirections.com
Founded: 1934
Educational magazines & journals; texts & refer-
ence books, software, video, CD-ROM, posters,
on-line projects.
ISBN Prefix(es): 0-911168
Number of titles published annually: 4 Print; 2
CD-ROM; 20 Online
Total Titles: 20 Print; 5 CD-ROM; 75 Online
Online services available through EBSCOhost,
ProQuest.
Imprints: The Education Digest; Tech Directions;
Tech Directions Books & Media

Prayer Book Press Inc
Subsidiary of Media Judaica Inc
1363 Fairfield Ave, Bridgeport, CT 06605
SAN: 282-1796
Tel: 203-384-2284 *Fax:* 203-579-9109
Key Personnel
Pres & Ed: Jonathan D Levine
VP & Prodn Mgr: Andrew Amsel
VP & Sales & Dist Mgr: Walter B Stern
Compt: Sharon Dworkin
Founded: 1933
Religion (Jewish); prayer books, textbooks, gift
editions & reference.
ISBN Prefix(es): 0-87677
Number of titles published annually: 5 Print; 1
Audio
Total Titles: 50 Print; 5 Audio
Imprints: Center for Contemporary Judaica

Precept Press
Division of Bonus Books Inc
1452 Second St, Santa Monica, CA 90401
SAN: 238-8413
Tel: 310-260-9400 *Fax:* 310-260-9494
E-mail: webmaster@bonusbooks.com
Web Site: www.bonusbooks.com
Key Personnel
CEO & Publr: Jeffrey Stern
Man Ed: Devon Freeny
Assoc Ed: Caralyn Bialo
Founded: 1970

Specialize in medical clinical books & fund rais-
ing research books.
ISBN Prefix(es): 0-944496; 0-931028
Number of titles published annually: 3 Print; 1
CD-ROM
Total Titles: 35 Print; 1 CD-ROM
Distribution Center: National Book Network

Prentice Hall Business Publishing
Unit of Pearson Higher Education Division
One Lake St, Upper Saddle River, NJ 07458
Tel: 201-236-7000
Key Personnel
Pres: Jerome Grant
Dir, Mktg: Anne Todd

**Prentice Hall Career, Health, Education &
Technology**
Division of Pearson Education
One Lake St, Upper Saddle River, NJ 07458
Tel: 201-236-7000 *Fax:* 201-236-7755
Key Personnel
Pres: Robin Baliszewsky
Fin Mgr: Santos Shih

Prentice Hall Engineering/Science & Math
Unit of Pearson Higher Education Division
One Lake St, Upper Saddle River, NJ 07458
Tel: 201-236-7000
Key Personnel
Pres: Paul Corey
VP & Busn Mgr: Brian McGraw
Dir, Mktg, Math & Engg: John Tweeddale

Prentice Hall Humanities & Social Sciences
Unit of Pearson Higher Education Division
One Lake St, Upper Saddle River, NJ 07458
Tel: 201-236-7000
Key Personnel
Pres: Yolanda deRooy
VP & Busn Mgr: Robert Santini
Asst VP & Dir, Prodn: Barbara Kittle
Asst VP & Dir, Mktg: Bess Mejia
EIC & Edit Dir, Humanities & Eng: Charlyce
Jones Owen
EIC, Soc Sci & Psychology: Nancy Roberts
EIC, Devt: Susanna Lesan
EIC, Modern Langs: Rosemary Bradley

Prentice Hall Press
Division of Penguin Group (USA) Inc
375 Hudson St, New York, NY 10014
Tel: 212-366-2000
Key Personnel
Publr, Busn: Adrian Zackheim
Publr, Self-help & Health: John Duff
Exec Ed, Medical: Laura Sheppard
Number of titles published annually: 40 Print
Total Titles: 196 Print

Prentice Hall School
Unit of Pearson Education
One Lake St, Upper Saddle River, NJ 07458
Tel: 201-236-7000
Key Personnel
Pres: Rick Culp
Sr VP, Prod Devt: Jeffrey Ikler
ISBN Prefix(es): 0-13; 0-205; 0-556; 0-8224
Branch Office(s)
160 Gould St, Needham Heights, MA 02194
Tel: 781-455-1200

PREP Publishing
Subsidiary of PREP Inc
1110 1/2 Hay St, Fayetteville, NC 28305
Tel: 910-483-6611 *Toll Free Tel:* 800-533-2814
Fax: 910-483-2439
E-mail: preppub@aol.com
Web Site: www.prep-pub.com
Key Personnel
Publr: Anne McKinney

Lib Sales Dir: Frances Sweeney
Founded: 1994
Books designed to enrich people's lives & help
optimize the human experience. Publisher of
general trade books, fiction & nonfiction, es-
pecially books related to careers, job hunting,
government jobs & business planning, market-
ing & entreprenership. Fiction titles include
mysteries, Christian fiction & romance.
ISBN Prefix(es): 1-885288
Number of titles published annually: 10 Print
Total Titles: 40 Print
Imprints: Business Success Series; Government
Jobs Series; Judeo Christian Ethics Series;
Anne McKinney Career Series (also, Real-
Resumes Series)
Foreign Rep(s): Husion House (Canada)
Advertising Agency: McKinney Communica-
tions, PO Box 66, Fayetteville, NC 28302-
0066, Contact: Pat Mack *Tel:* 910-483-6611
Fax: 910-483-2439 *E-mail:* preppub@aol.com
Web Site: www.prep-pub.com
Warehouse: 435 W Russell St, Fayetteville, NC
28301 *Tel:* 910-483-6611 *E-mail:* preppub@
aol.com *Web Site:* www.prep-pub.com
Membership(s): Council of Literary Magazines &
Presses; Publishers Association of the South;
Publishers Marketing Association; Southeast
Booksellers Association

Presbyterian Publishing Corp
100 Witherspoon St, Louisville, KY 40202
Tel: 502-569-5052 *Toll Free Tel:* 800-227-
2872 (US only) *Fax:* 502-569-8308
Toll Free Fax: 800-541-5113 (US only)
E-mail: ppcmail@presbypub.com
Web Site: www.ppcpub.com
Key Personnel
Pres & Publr: Davis Perkins
Edit Dir: Jack Keller
Events & Author Rel: Sandy Lucas *Tel:* 502-569-
5096 *E-mail:* slucas@presbypub.com
Events & Author Rel Mgr: Mary Bright
Founded: 1838
Biblical studies, academic & scholarly textbooks,
general trade religious books.
ISBN Prefix(es): 0-664; 0-8042
Number of titles published annually: 80 Print
Total Titles: 1,250 Print
Imprints: Geneva Press
Divisions: Westminster John Knox Press
Distributed by Spring Arbor Distributors
Distributor for Deo; Epworth; SCM
See separate listing for:
Westminster John Knox Press

**The Press at California State University,
Fresno**
Unit of California State University, Fresno
2380 E Keats, MB99, Fresno, CA 93740-8024
Tel: 559-278-3056 *Fax:* 559-278-6758
E-mail: press@csufresno.edu
Key Personnel
Man Ed, Adv & Sales: Carla Millar
Founded: 1982
Art, architecture, drama, music, film & the me-
dia, New Age politics, business, autobiography,
Armenian history & Fresno history.
ISBN Prefix(es): 0-912201
Total Titles: 17 Print
Distributed by Southern Illinois University Press
Foreign Rights: Scott Meredith Literary Agency
Membership(s): International Association of
Scholarly Publishers

Prestel Publishing
900 Broadway, Suite 603, New York, NY 10003
Tel: 212-995-2720 *Toll Free Tel:* 888-463-6110
(cust serv) *Fax:* 212-995-2733
E-mail: sales@prestel-usa.com
Web Site: www.prestel.com

Key Personnel
Sales & Mktg Dir: Stephen Hulburt
  E-mail: shulburt@prestel-usa.com
Sales & Mktg Coord: Raya Raitcheva
  E-mail: rraitcheva@prestel-usa.com
Publicist: Evelya Lee Schwarz *E-mail:* elee@
  prestel-usa.com
Founded: 1999
ISBN Prefix(es): 3-7913
Number of titles published annually: 75 Print
Total Titles: 400 Print
Distributor for Die Gestalten Verlag (DGV);
  Schirmer/Mosel
Warehouse: 575 Prospect St, Lakewood, NJ
  08701 *Tel:* 732-363-5679 *Toll Free Tel:* 888-
  463-6110 *Fax:* 732-363-0338 *Toll Free
  Fax:* 877-227-6564

Prestwick House Inc
PO Box 246, Cheswold, DE 19936-0246
SAN: 154-5523
Tel: 302-736-2665 *Fax:* 302-734-0549
E-mail: info@prestwickhouse.com
Web Site: www.prestwickhouse.com
Key Personnel
VP, Opers: Jason Scott
Founded: 1982
Publisher & distributor of materials for use in the
  English & language arts classroom; workbooks,
  tests, study guides & teaching guides.
ISBN Prefix(es): 1-85049
Number of titles published annually: 112 Print
Total Titles: 855 Print
Distributor for Dover Publications; Prentice Hall;
  Westin Walch
Membership(s): ABA

Price Stern Sloan
Imprint of Penguin Group (USA) Inc
345 Hudson St, New York, NY 10014
SAN: 282-5074
Tel: 212-366-2000
E-mail: online@penguin.com
Web Site: www.penguinputnam.com
Key Personnel
Pres & Publr: Debra Dorfman
Founded: 1963
ISBN Prefix(es): 0-201; 0-8431
Number of titles published annually: 75 Print
Total Titles: 744 Print
Imprints: Crazy Games; Doodle Art; Planet Dex-
  ter; Serendipity; Troubador Press; Wee Sing

Prima Games
Imprint of Random House Information Group
3000 Lava Ridge Ct, Roseville, CA 95661
SAN: 289-5609
Tel: 916-787-7000 *Toll Free Tel:* 800-632-8676
  Fax: 916-787-7001
Web Site: www.primagames.com
Key Personnel
Pres: Debra Kempker
Founded: 1984
Computer & video game books.
Random House Inc & its publishing entities are
  not accepting unsol submissions, proposals,
  mss, or submission queries via e-mail at this
  time.
ISBN Prefix(es): 0-7615
Number of titles published annually: 150 Print
Total Titles: 1,100 Print

Primary Research Group
224 W 30 St, Suite 802-1, New York, NY 10001
Tel: 212-736-2316 *Fax:* 212-412-9097
E-mail: primarydat@aol.com
Web Site: www.primaryresearch.com
Key Personnel
Pres: James Moses
Founded: 1989

Research reports on industry, economics, publishing (book, electronic & magazine), telecommunication, entertainment & higher education.
ISBN Prefix(es): 1-57440
Number of titles published annually: 40 Print
Total Titles: 105 Print
Distributed by Academic Impressions; Ambassador Books; The Book House; Coutts Library Service; Global Research Inc; MarketRe-
  search.com; Midwest Library Service; Mindbranch; Research & Markets; Yankee Book
  Peddler

PRIMEDIA Business Directories & Books
Division of Primedia Inc
9800 Metcalf Ave, Overland Park, KS 66212
SAN: 204-3416
Mailing Address: PO Box 12901, Overland Park,
  KS 66282-2901
Tel: 913-967-1719 *Toll Free Tel:* 800-453-9620;
  800-262-1954 (cust serv) *Fax:* 913-967-1901
  Toll Free Fax: 800-633-6219
E-mail: bookorders@primediabooks.com
Web Site: www.primediabooks.com
Key Personnel
Publr: Shawn Etheridge
Sales Mgr, Motorcycle: Matt Tusken
Sales Mgr & I&T Manuals: Ted Metzger
Sales Mgr, Marine: Dutch Sadler
Publisher of repair manuals for motorcycles,
  ATV, PWC, boats, outdoor power equipment,
  snowmobiles & tractors, as well as navigation
  guides & valuation guides.
ISBN Prefix(es): 0-89287; 0-87288
Number of titles published annually: 25 Print
Total Titles: 400 Print
Imprints: Ac-u-Kwik; Clymer ProSeries; Clymer
  Publications; EC&M Books; Electrical Whole-
  saling; The Electronics Source Book; Equip-
  ment Watch; I&T Shop Service; Primedia Price
  Digests
Shipping Address: Wagner Industries, 1201 E 12
  Ave, North Kansas City, MO 64116

Primedia Business Magazine & Media
Division of Primedia Inc
9800 Metcalf Ave, Overland Park, KS 66212
Mailing Address: PO Box 12901, Overland Park,
  KS 66282-2901 SAN: 670-8463
Tel: 913-341-1300 *Toll Free Tel:* 800-262-1954
  Fax: 913-967-1898
Web Site: www.primemediabusiness.com
Key Personnel
Mktg: Karen Garrison
Founded: 1886
ISBN Prefix(es): 0-87288; 0-918371
Number of titles published annually: 12 Print
Total Titles: 520 Print

**Primedia Consumer Magazine & Internet
Group**
Formerly Primedia Special Interest Publications
Division of Primedia Inc
260 Madison Ave, New York, NY 10016
Tel: 212-726-4300 *Toll Free Tel:* 800-521-2885
  Fax: 212-726-4310
E-mail: sgnews@primediasi.com
Web Site: www.primediainc.com
Key Personnel
Pres & CEO: Dan McCarthy
Chief Operating Officer: Dan Aks
Exec VP, Consumer Mktg: Steve Aster
VP, Fin: Linda Jenkins
Interim Sr VP, HR: David Kaupt
Founded: 1961
Consumer magazines, special interest publications
  & related Internet sites.
ISBN Prefix(es): 1-881657
Subsidiaries: Symbol of Excellence Publishers Inc
Distributed by Oxmoor House; Sterling
Shipping Address: 2 New Plaza, Peoria, IL 61614

Primedia Special Interest Publications, see
  Primedia Consumer Magazine & Internet
  Group

Princeton Architectural Press
37 E Seventh St, New York, NY 10003
Tel: 212-995-9620 *Toll Free Tel:* 800-722-6657
  (dist) *Fax:* 212-995-9454
E-mail: sales@papress.com
Web Site: www.papress.com
Key Personnel
Pres: Kevin C Lippert
Edit Dir: Clare Jacobson *E-mail:* clare@papress.
  com
Dir, Sales: Nettie Aljian *E-mail:* nettie@papress.
  com
Dir, Publicity: Katharine Myers
  E-mail: katharine@papress.com
Founded: 1981
Publisher of high quality books in architecture,
  graphic design & popular culture.
ISBN Prefix(es): 0-910413; 1-878271; 1-56898
Number of titles published annually: 100 Print
Total Titles: 700 Print
Distributed by Chronicle Books
Distributor for Balcony Press; Birkhauser Verlag;
  dot dot dot; Hyphen Press; Springer Vienna
Foreign Rep(s): Birkauser V/A (Asia, Europe);
  Chronicle Books (Central/South America); Hi
  Marketing (UK); Manic Ex-Poseur Pty Ltd
  (Australia, New Zealand); Raincoast Books
  (Canada)
Distribution Center: Chronicle Books, 85 Sec-
  ond St, San Francisco, CA 94105 *Toll Free
  Tel:* 800-722-6657

§Princeton Book Co Publishers
PO Box 831, Hightstown, NJ 08520-0831
Tel: 609-426-0602 *Toll Free Tel:* 800-220-7149
  Fax: 609-426-1344
E-mail: pbc@dancehorizons.com; elysian@aosi.
  com
Web Site: www.dancehorizons.com
Key Personnel
Pres & Rts & Perms: Charles Woodford
Dir: Connie Woodford
Compt: Michele Coffey
Cust Serv: Elaine Cinque
Adv & Internet: John McMenamin
Founded: 1975
Specialize in dance, new imprint, Elysian edi-
  tions; adult nonfiction; including DVDs.
ISBN Prefix(es): 0-916622; 0-87127; 0-903102;
  0-85418; 0-932582; 0-7121; 0-8463; 0-340
Number of titles published annually: 6 Print; 11
  E-Book
Total Titles: 150 Print; 11 E-Book; 3 Audio
Imprints: Dance Horizons; Dance Horizons
  Video; Elysian Editions
Divisions: Dance Horizons Video; Elysian Edi-
  tions
Editorial Office(s): 614 Rte 130, Hightstown,
  NJ 08520 *Toll Free Tel:* 800-220-7149
  E-mail: pbc@dancehorizons.com
Distributor for Dance Books Ltd; Dance Notation
  Bureau
Foreign Rep(s): Astam Books (Australia, New
  Zealand); Dance Books Ltd (UK)
Shipping Address: 614 Rte 130, Hightstown,
  NJ 08520 *Toll Free Tel:* 800-220-7149
  E-mail: pbc@dancehorizons.com

§The Princeton Review
Imprint of Random House Information Group
1745 Broadway, New York, NY 10019
Tel: 212-829-6928 *Toll Free Tel:* 800-733-3000
  Fax: 212-940-7400
E-mail: princetonreview@randomhouse.com
Web Site: www.princetonreview.com
Key Personnel
Pres: David Naggar
Publr: Tom Russell

VP & Exec Man Ed: Denise DeGennaro
Dir, Busn Opers: Katie Ziga
Dir, Sub/Foreign Rts: Linda Kaplan
Test preparation, college & graduate school guides, career guides & general study aids.
Random House Inc & its publishing entities are not accepting unsol submissions, proposals, mss, or submission queries via e-mail at this time.
Number of titles published annually: 75 Print; 12 CD-ROM
Total Titles: 230 Print; 15 CD-ROM

Princeton University Press
41 William St, Princeton, NJ 08540
Tel: 609-258-4900 *Toll Free Tel:* 800-777-4726
Fax: 609-258-6305 *Toll Free Fax:* 800-999-1958
E-mail: orders@cpfsinc.com
Web Site: www.pup.princeton.edu
Key Personnel
Dir: Walter Lippincott
Ed-in-Chief: Sam Elsworthy
Assoc Dir & Cont: Patrick M Carroll
Mktg & Asst Dir: Adam Fortgang *Tel:* 609-258-4896 *E-mail:* adam_fortgang@pupress.princeton.edu
Sales Dir & Lib Sales Dir: Eric Rohmann *Tel:* 609-4898 *E-mail:* eric_rohmann@pupress.princeton.edu
Adv Mgr: Ray Potter *Tel:* 609-258-4924 *E-mail:* ray_potter@pupress.princeton.ed
Publicity Mgr: Kathryn Rosko
Exhibits: Melissa Burton *Tel:* 609-258-4915 *E-mail:* melissa_burton@pupress.princeton.edu
ISBN Contact: Bonnie Bole
Founded: 1905
Scholarly & scientific books on all subjects.
ISBN Prefix(es): 0-691
Number of titles published annually: 280 Print
Total Titles: 3,500 Print; 425 E-Book
Imprints: Bollingen Series
Foreign Office(s): c/o John Wiley & Sons Dist Ctr, One Oldlands Way, Bognor Regis, West Sussex PO22 9SA, United Kingdom
3 Market Place, Woodstock, Oxfordshire OX20 1SY, United Kingdom, Publg Dir, Europe: Richard Baggaley *Tel:* (01993) 814500 *Fax:* (01993) 814504 *E-mail:* rbaggaley@pupress.co.uk
Foreign Rep(s): APAC Publishers Servs (Singapore, Southeast Asia); Aromix Books Co Ltd (Hong Kong); Book Promotions Ltd (South Africa); Cassidy & Associates (China); ICK (Information & Culture) (Korea); S Janakiraman, Book Marketing Services (India, Pakistan); B K Norton (Taiwan); Rockbook (Japan); University Press Group (Australia, Canada); The University Presses of California, Columbia & Princeton (Africa, Europe & UK, Israel, Middle East)
Orders to: California/Princeton Fulfillment Services Inc, 1445 Lower Ferry Rd, Ewing, NJ 08618, Contact: Andrew Tunick *E-mail:* orders@cpfsinc.com
Warehouse: California/Princeton Fulfillment Services Inc, 1445 Lower Ferry Rd, Ewing, NJ 08618 *Tel:* 609-883-1759 *Fax:* 609-883-7413 *E-mail:* orders@cpfsinc.com
Membership(s): AAP; American Association of University Presses; BISG

Printlink Publishers Inc
755 Main St, Monroe, CT 06468
Tel: 203-261-2977 *Fax:* 203-261-4331
Key Personnel
Pres: Leonard M Fernandes
Founded: 1991
Juvenile, adult & religious books.
Number of titles published annually: 3 Print
Distributed by Tyndale House Publishers; World Wide Features

PRO-ED Inc
8700 Shoal Creek Blvd, Austin, TX 78757-6897
SAN: 222-1349
Tel: 512-451-3246 *Toll Free Tel:* 800-897-3202 *Fax:* 512-451-8542 *Toll Free Fax:* 800-397-7633
E-mail: info@proedinc.com
Web Site: www.proedinc.com
Key Personnel
VP: Steven C Mathews *Tel:* 512-451-3246 ext 624
Founded: 1977
College & professional reference books, tests, student materials, journals in education & psychology.
ISBN Prefix(es): 0-936104; 0-89079
Number of titles published annually: 50 Print; 2 CD-ROM
Total Titles: 800 Print; 5 CD-ROM

Pro Lingua Associates Inc
74 Cotton Mill Hill, Suite A-315, Brattleboro, VT 05301
Mailing Address: PO Box 1348, Brattleboro, VT 05302-1348 SAN: 216-0579
Tel: 802-257-7779 *Toll Free Tel:* 800-366-4775 *Fax:* 802-257-5117
E-mail: orders@prolinguaassociates.com
Web Site: www.prolinguaassociates.com
Key Personnel
Publr, Pres & Intl Rts: Arthur A Burrows
VP & Ed: Raymond C Clark
Sec: Patrick R Moran
Treas & Libr Sales Dir: Elise C Burrows
Founded: 1980
Teacher resource handbooks, language teacher training handbooks, English language & foreign language texts.
ISBN Prefix(es): 0-86647
Number of titles published annually: 10 Print
Total Titles: 79 Print; 8 Online; 11 Audio
Foreign Rep(s): Attica LaLibrarie des Langues (France); Foreign Language Ltd (Korea); Independent Publishers International (Japan); B K Norton/Bookman Books (Taiwan); The Resource Centre (Canada)
Membership(s): Children's Book Council; Teachers of English to Speakers of Other Languages

Pro Quest Information & Learning
Division of Pro Quest Co
300 N Zeeb Rd, Ann Arbor, MI 48106-1346
SAN: 212-2464
Mailing Address: PO Box 1346, Ann Arbor, MI 48106-1346
Tel: 734-761-4700 *Toll Free Tel:* 800-521-0600 *Fax:* 734-975-6486 *Toll Free Fax:* 800-864-0019
E-mail: info@il.proquest.com
Web Site: www.il.proquest.com
Key Personnel
Pres: Ron Klausner
Sr VP: Carolyn Dyer; Rod Gauvin
Sr VP, Busn Devt: James D Barcelona
Dir, Mktg Communs: Tina Creguer
Mgr, Mktg Communs: Mary K Murray
Publisher distributor & aggregator of value-added information to libraries, government, universities & schools in over 160 countries. Access to information in periodicals, newspapers, doctoral dissertations & out-of-print books (retrospective scholarly works). Produce & publish Dissertation Abstracts International.
ISBN Prefix(es): 0-8357
Number of titles published annually: 56 Print
Total Titles: 56 Print
Online services available through DataStar, Dialog, Ovid, ProQuest.

§Productivity Press
444 Park Ave S, Suite 604, New York, NY 10016
SAN: 290-036X

Tel: 212-686-5900 *Toll Free Tel:* 888-319-5852 *Fax:* 212-686-5411 *Toll Free Fax:* 800-394-6286
E-mail: info@productivitypress.com
Web Site: www.productivitypress.com
Key Personnel
Publr: Maura May
Dir, Sales: Ed Hanus
Publicist: Karen Gaines
Acqs Ed: Michael Sinocchi
Mgr, Mktg: Leon Carter
Founded: 1983
Books & AV programs. Publishes & distributes materials on productivity, quality improvement, product development, corporate management, profit management & employee involvement for business & industry. Many products are direct source materials from Japan that have been translated into English for the first time. The Spanish imprint offers many of the same products in Spanish language version.
ISBN Prefix(es): 0-915299; 1-56327; 0-915801
Number of titles published annually: 15 Print
Total Titles: 160 Print; 4 CD-ROM
Imprints: Productivity Press Spanish Imprint
Foreign Rep(s): American Technical Publishers (UK); Asia Pacific Research Center (Singapore); Books Aplenty (South Africa); Learning & Productivity (Australia); OCAPT Inc (Canada); Prism Books Private Ltd (India); Productivity Editorial Consultores SPD CV (Mexico)

Professional Communications Inc
20968 State Rd 22, Caddo, OK 74729
Mailing Address: PO Box 10, Caddo, OK 74729-0010
Tel: 580-367-9838 *Toll Free Tel:* 800-337-9838 *Fax:* 580-367-9989
E-mail: info@pcibooks.com
Web Site: www.pcibooks.com
Key Personnel
Pres: Malcolm Beasley *Tel:* 631-661-2852 *Fax:* 631-661-2167
VP: Phyllis Jones Freeny
Founded: 1992
Medicine.
ISBN Prefix(es): 1-884735; 0-9632400
Number of titles published annually: 7 Print
Total Titles: 35 Print
Branch Office(s)
Bulk Sales only, 400 Center Bay Dr, West Islip, NY 11795, Contact: Malcolm Beasley *Tel:* 631-661-2852 *Fax:* 631-661-2167 *E-mail:* jmbpci@earthlink.net

The Professional Education Group Inc
12401 Minnetonka Blvd, Minnetonka, MN 55305-3994
Tel: 952-933-9990 *Toll Free Tel:* 800-229-2531 *Fax:* 952-933-7784
E-mail: orders@proedgroup.com
Web Site: www.proedgroup.com
Key Personnel
Pres: Paul A Fogelberg *E-mail:* paul@proedgroup.com
VP: Henry Lake *E-mail:* henry@proedgroup.com
Founded: 1981
Continuing legal education materials for lawyers; audio compact discs & video books.
ISBN Prefix(es): 0-943380
Number of titles published annually: 6 Print; 1 CD-ROM; 5 Audio
Total Titles: 40 Print; 2 CD-ROM; 31 Audio

Professional Publications Inc
1250 Fifth Ave, Belmont, CA 94002
SAN: 264-6315
Tel: 650-593-9119 *Toll Free Tel:* 800-426-1178 *Fax:* 650-592-4519
E-mail: info@passthatexam.com
Web Site: www.passthatexam.com

Key Personnel
Pres: Michael Lindeburg *E-mail:* mlindeburg@passthatexam.com
Mktg Mgr: Matt Brault *Tel:* 650-593-9119 ext 118 *E-mail:* mbrault@passthatexam.com
Prodn Mgr: Cathy Schrott *E-mail:* cschrott@passthatexam.com
Founded: 1981
Engineering, land surveying, architecture & interior design books, video, software.
ISBN Prefix: 0-932276; 0-912045; 1-888577; 1-59126
Number of titles published annually: 10 Print
Total Titles: 160 Print

Professional Publishing
Division of Professional Book Group of McGraw-Hill
1333 Burr Ridge Pkwy, Burr Ridge, IL 60527
SAN: 220-0236
Tel: 630-789-4000; 630-789-5500
  Toll Free Tel: 800-2McGraw (262-4729)
  Fax: 630-789-6933
Web Site: www.books.mcgraw-hill.com
Key Personnel
Ed-in-Chief: Jeffrey Krames
Exec Ed: Stephen Isaacs *Tel:* 630-789-5516
Ed: Kelli Christianson; Catherine Dassopoulos; Dan Silverburg
Founded: 1965
Nonfiction books for the business community.
ISBN Prefix(es): 1-55623; 1-55738; 0-7863
Total Titles: 700 Print
Imprints: McGraw-Hill Professional Publishing
Distributed by Macmillan of Canada (Toronto)
Distributor for Dartnell
Foreign Rep(s): Chitra Bopardikar
Advertising Agency: Ridge Associates
Distribution Center: WCB, 2460 Kerper Blvd, Dubuque, IA 52001

Professional Resource Exchange Inc
1891 Apex Rd, Sarasota, FL 34240
SAN: 240-1223
Mailing Address: PO Box 15560, Sarasota, FL 34277-1560
Tel: 941-343-9601 *Toll Free Tel:* 800-443-3364
  Fax: 941-343-9201
Web Site: www.prpress.com
Key Personnel
Pres: Lawrence G Ritt
VP: Judith W Ritt
Man Ed: Debra Fink *Tel:* 941-343-9403
Mktg & Lib Sales Dir: Judy Warinner
Founded: 1979
Books, audio & video cassettes, CD-ROM, continuing education programs & forensic tests for mental health & health care professionals. Includes medicine & nursing.
ISBN Prefix(es): 0-943158; 1-56887
Number of titles published annually: 15 Print; 1 CD-ROM; 3 Audio
Total Titles: 140 Print; 1 CD-ROM; 14 Audio
Imprints: Professional Resource Press
Advertising Agency: Ashley Ball Group, 510 N Brink Ave, Sarasota, FL 34237 *Tel:* 941-951-6930
Membership(s): Small Publishers Association of North America

Prometheus Books
59 John Glenn Dr, Amherst, NY 14228
SAN: 202-0289
Tel: 716-691-0133 *Toll Free Tel:* 800-421-0351
  Fax: 716-691-0137
E-mail: marketing@prometheusbooks.com; editorial@prometheusbooks.com
Web Site: www.Prometheusbooks.com
Key Personnel
Pres & Ed: Paul Kurtz
Ed-in-Chief: Steven L Mitchell
VP, Busn & Admin Dir: Lynette Nisbet

VP, Mktg: Jonathan Kurtz
Exec Ed: Linda Greenspan Regan
Art Dir: Jacqueline Cooke
Sales Mgr: Marcia Rogers *Tel:* 716-691-0133 ext 214
Intl Rts Contact: Gretchen Kurtz *E-mail:* rights@prometheusmail.com
Mgr, Print-on-Demand Div: Shawn Rucci
Founded: 1969
Adult nonfiction, literary classics, young readers.
ISBN Prefix(es): 0-87975; 1-57392; 1-59102
Number of titles published annually: 125 Print
Total Titles: 2,100 Print; 6 Audio
Imprints: Humanity Books
Foreign Office(s): Lavis Marketing, 10 Crescent View, Loughton, Essex IG10 4PZ, United Kingdom
Foreign Rep(s): Alternative Books (South Africa); CKK Ltd (Southeast Asia); Lavis Marketing (UK & Europe); E A Milley Enterprises (Canada); Tower Books (Australia); United Publisher Services (Japan)
Advertising Agency: University Advertising

Promissor Inc
Subsidiary of Houghton Mifflin Co
1007 Church St, Evanston, IL 60201
Tel: 847-866-2001 *Toll Free Tel:* 800-255-1312
  Fax: 847-866-2002
E-mail: marketing@promissor.com
Web Site: www.promissor.com
Key Personnel
VP & Gen Mgr: Steve Tapp
VP, Solutions Integration: Betty Bergstrom
VP, Technol Solutions: Paul Wilcox
Computerized testing solutions for corporations & organizations.
Branch Office(s)
3 Bala Plaza W, Suite 300, Bala Cynwyd, PA 19004

ProStar Publications Inc
3 Church Circle, Suite 109, Annapolis, MD 21401
SAN: 210-525X
Mailing Address: 8643 Hayden Place, Culver City, CA 90232
Tel: 310-280-1010 *Toll Free Tel:* 800-481-6277
  Fax: 310-280-1025 *Toll Free Fax:* 800-487-6277
E-mail: editor@prostarpublications.com
Web Site: www.prostarpublications.com; www.nauticalbooks.com
Key Personnel
Pres & Publr: Peter L Griffes
Ed: Diana Hunter
Dir, Mktg & Sales: Ron Ligrano
Founded: 1965
Books about boating: regional guides, planning, navigation data, nautical charts, marine fauna, how-to, travel, technical, general fiction & music.
ISBN Prefix(es): 0-930030; 1-57785
Number of titles published annually: 120 Print
Total Titles: 425 Print; 30 CD-ROM
Imprints: Atlantic Boating Almanac; Lighthouse Press; Pacific Boating Almanac; US Coast Pilot

Protea Publishing
5456 Peachtree Industrial Blvd, Suite 648, Atlanta, GA 30341
E-mail: southsky@earthlink.net
Web Site: www.proteapublishing.com
Key Personnel
Publr & Owner: Johan du Toit
ISBN Prefix(es): 1-883707; 1-931768
Number of titles published annually: 100 Print
Total Titles: 92 Print
Distributed by Bertrams; Gardners; Lightning Source Inc; Replica Books

§Providence Publishing Corp
238 Seaboard Lane, Franklin, TN 37067
Tel: 615-771-2020 *Toll Free Tel:* 800-321-5692
  Fax: 615-771-2002
E-mail: books@providencehouse.com
Web Site: www.providencehouse.com
Key Personnel
Pres & Publr: Andrew Miller
Man Ed: Kelly Bainbridge
Fin & Admin: Mark Jacobs
Prod Coord: Holly Jones
Dir, Busn Devt & Mktg: Michael Van Hook
Founded: 1990
Emphasis include regional histories, church-related histories, biographies & memoirs, fiction, inspirational & theological writings, missionary stories, as well as other trade-oriented works such as cookbooks, corporate business issues.
ISBN Prefix(es): 1-57736; 1-881576
Number of titles published annually: 45 Print
Total Titles: 400 Print
Imprints: Hillsboro Press; Providence House Publishers; Sage Hill Resources
Distributor for Guild Bindery Press
Warehouse: 320 Premier Ct, Suite 208, Franklin, TN 37067

Provincetown Arts Inc
Affiliate of Provincetown Arts Press Inc
650 Commercial St, Provincetown, MA 02657
SAN: 298-2641
Mailing Address: PO Box 35, Provincetown, MA 02657-0035
Tel: 508-487-3167
Web Site: www.provincetownarts.org
Key Personnel
Publr & Edit Dir: Christopher Busa
  E-mail: cbusa@attbi.com
Art Dir: Irene Lipton
Founded: 1985
Magazine: art, writing & theater; books: poetry & art.
ISBN Prefix(es): 0-944854
Number of titles published annually: 3 Print
Total Titles: 42 Print
Membership(s): Council of Literary Magazines & Presses

§The PRS Group Inc
6320 Fly Rd, East Syracuse, NY 13057
Tel: 315-431-0511 *Fax:* 315-431-0200
E-mail: custserv@prsgroup.com
Web Site: www.prsgroup.com
Key Personnel
Pres: Mary Lou Walsh
Lib Sales Dir: Patti Davis
Admin Asst: Dianna Spinner *E-mail:* dspinner@prsgroup.com
Founded: 1979
Over 100 reports, newsletters, journals & volumes per year for international business.
ISBN Prefix(es): 1-85271
Total Titles: 20 Print; 100 CD-ROM; 100 Online; 100 E-Book
Online services available through LexisNexis.
Imprints: International Country Risk Guide; Political Risk Services

Pruett Publishing Co
7464 Arapahoe Rd, Unit A-9, Boulder, CO 80303
SAN: 205-4035
Tel: 303-449-4919 *Toll Free Tel:* 800-247-8224
  Fax: 303-443-9019 *Toll Free Fax:* 800-527-9727
E-mail: pruettbks@aol.com
Web Site: www.pruettpublishing.com
Key Personnel
Publr: Jim Pruett *E-mail:* jtpruett@indra.com
Busn Mgr: Mary Pruett
Founded: 1954

Trade; Western Americana, outdoor recreation, fly fishing, US travel, nature & natural history.
ISBN Prefix(es): 0-87108
Number of titles published annually: 10 Print
Total Titles: 70 Print; 0 E-Book
Foreign Rep(s): Gazelle Book Services Ltd (UK)
Membership(s): AAP; Publishers Association of the West

PSI Research, see Hellgate Press

§Psychological Assessment Resources Inc (PAR)
16204 N Florida Ave, Lutz, FL 33549
Tel: 813-968-3003 *Toll Free Tel:* 800-331-8378 *Fax:* 813-968-2598 *Toll Free Fax:* 800-727-9329
Web Site: www.parinc.com
Key Personnel
Chmn & CEO: R Bob Smith, III
   E-mail: bsmith@parinc.com
Pres & COO: Serje G Seminoff
   E-mail: sseminof@parinc.com
Intl Rts & Perms: Patty Drexler
   E-mail: pdrexler@parinc.com
VP, Lib & Book Store Sales Dir: Cynthia Lumpee *E-mail:* clumpee@parinc.com
VP, Mktg & Prod Acq: Jim Gyurke
   E-mail: jgyurke@parinc.com
VP, R&D: Travis White *E-mail:* twhite@parinc.com
Founded: 1978
Career, psychological, neuropsychology, educational & clinical assessments products; software.
ISBN Prefix(es): 0-911907
Number of titles published annually: 20 Print; 2 CD-ROM; 1 Online
Total Titles: 130 Print; 20 CD-ROM; 3 Online; 5 Audio
Distributed by ACER; Pro-Ed; The Psychological Corp; Riverside Publishing; Western Psychological Service
Distributor for American Guidance Service; Pro-Ed; The Psychological Corp; Riverside Publishing Co; Rorschach Workshops
Foreign Rep(s): ACER (Australia); Manasayan (India); Multi-Health (Canada); NFER-Nelson (UK); Psykologiforlaget (Sweden); Swets & Zeitlinger (Netherlands); Tea Ediciones (Spain); Testzentrale (Germany); Unifacmaner (Taiwan)
Warehouse: 16130 N Florida Ave, Lutz, FL 33549 *Tel:* 813-968-3003 *Fax:* 813-968-2598 *E-mail:* gpresson@parinc.com

The Psychological Corporation, see Harcourt Assessment Inc

Psychology Press
Division of Taylor & Francis Publishers Inc
29 W 35 St, New York, NY 10001
Tel: 212-216-7800 *Fax:* 215-643-1430
Web Site: www.psypress.com
Key Personnel
Acqs Ed: Paul Dukes *Tel:* 917-351-7103
Founded: 1983 (Created to serve the needs of researchers, students & professionals concerned with the science of human & animal behavior)
Publish at all levels, including student texts, professional books, reference books, primary research & scientific journals. Specializes in encompassing work of psychological significance by people in related areas such as biology, neuroscience, linguistics, sociology & artificial intelligence, as well as the work of mainstream psychologists.
ISBN Prefix(es): 0-86377; 1-84169
Number of titles published annually: 102 Print; 4 CD-ROM
Total Titles: 450 Print; 6 CD-ROM
Foreign Office(s): 27 Church Rd, Hove, E Sussex BN3 2FA, United Kingdom, Man Dir: Michael

Forster *Tel:* (01273) 207411 *Fax:* (01273) 205612 *E-mail:* info@psypress.co.uk
Distribution Center: ITPS, 10650 Toebben Dr, Independence, KY 41051 *Toll Free Tel:* 800-634-7064 *Toll Free Fax:* 800-248-4724 *E-mail:* bkorders@taylorandfrancis.com

The Psychology Society
100 Beekman St, New York, NY 10038-1810
SAN: 274-8746
Tel: 212-285-1872 *Fax:* 212-285-1872
Key Personnel
Dir: Pierre C Haber
Founded: 1960
Psychology, criminology, drug use, domestic & marital problems, therapeutic practice.
Number of titles published annually: 10 Print
Total Titles: 15 Print
Imprints: PS Press

§PTG Software
Member of Pearson Technology Group
201 W 103 St, Indianapolis, IN 46920-1097
Tel: 317-581-3500; 317-581-3837 (tech support) *Toll Free Tel:* 800-858-7674 *Fax:* 317-581-3611
Web Site: www.macmillansoftware.com
Key Personnel
Dir: Mr Lyn Zingraf
Mktg Mgr: Paula Garrett
Total Titles: 68 Print; 60 CD-ROM

Public Citizen
1600 20 St NW, Washington, DC 20009
Tel: 202-588-1000 *Fax:* 202-588-7798
E-mail: public_citizen@citizen.org
Web Site: www.citizen.org
Key Personnel
Dir, Devt & Mktg: Lane Brooks
Founded: 1971
Books & reports; consumer advocacy organization.
ISBN Prefix(es): 0-937188; 1-58231
Number of titles published annually: 50 Print
Total Titles: 48 Print
Divisions: Congress Watch; Critical Mass Energy Project; Global Trade Watch; Health Research GP Buyers UP; Litigation GP
Distributed by Addison Wesley; Simon & Schuster Pocket Books
Foreign Rights: Random House-Pantheon

§Public Utilities Reports Inc
8229 Boone Blvd, Suite 400, Vienna, VA 22182
Tel: 703-847-7720 *Toll Free Tel:* 800-368-5001 *Fax:* 703-847-0683
E-mail: pur@pur.com
Web Site: www.pur.com
Key Personnel
Publr, PUR Press: Bruce Radford *Tel:* 703-847-7733
Publr, Electronic Publg: J B Yowell *Tel:* 703-847-7746 *E-mail:* jby@pur.com
Founded: 1915
Public utilities case law; books & periodicals on regulation of utilities; training courses on utility management & operation.
ISBN Prefix(es): 0-910325
Number of titles published annually: 4 Print
Total Titles: 1 CD-ROM; 3 Online
Online services available through LexisNexis, ProQuest, Westlaw.

PublicAffairs
Member of Perseus Books Group
250 W 57 St, Suite 1321, New York, NY 10107
Tel: 212-397-6666 *Toll Free Tel:* 800-242-7737 (orders) *Fax:* 212-397-4267
E-mail: publicaffairs@perseusbooks.com
Web Site: www.publicaffairsbooks.com
Key Personnel
Publisher & CEO: Peter Osnos

VP, Group Rts Dir: Carolyn Savarese
VP, Group Dir of Sales & Mktg: Matthew Goldberg
Exec Ed: Clive Priddle
Man Ed: Robert Kimzey
Edit: Kate Darnton
Dir, Publicity: Gene Taft *E-mail:* genetaft@interport.net
Publicist: Kasey Pfaff
Mktg Dir: Lisa Kaufman
Off Admin: Darrell Jonas *Tel:* 212-397-6666 ext 235 *E-mail:* darrell.jonas@perseusbooks.com
Founded: 1997
Current affairs, history, biography, journalism & social criticism.
ISBN Prefix(es): 1-891620; 1-58648
Number of titles published annually: 55 Print
Total Titles: 250 Print
Distributed by HarperCollins
Foreign Rights: Perseus Book Group Subsidiary Rights
Warehouse: HarperCollins, 1000 Keystone Industrial Park, Scranton, PA 18512

PublishAmerica
PO Box 151, Frederick, MD 21705-0151
Tel: 240-529-1031 *Fax:* 301-631-9073
E-mail: writers@publishamerica.com
Web Site: www.publishamerica.com
Key Personnel
Exec Dir: Miranda N Prather
Founded: 1999
A traditional, royalty paying publisher. All accepted authors are offered a standard contract that includes a typical production environment, from editing to cover art design to full retail availability. Do not charge or accept fees or payments of any kind from authors or agents. Books are sold through all major book distributors to all major book retailers.
ISBN Prefix(es): 1-58851; 1-59129; 1-59286; 1-4137
Number of titles published annually: 1,100 Print; 1,100 Online
Total Titles: 3,500 Print; 3,500 Online
Imprints: America House
Distributed by Ingram
Membership(s): AAP; Publishers Marketing Association

Puckerbrush Press
76 Main St, Orono, ME 04473
SAN: 202-0327
Tel: 207-866-4868; 207-581-3832
Key Personnel
Publr & Ed: Constance Hunting
Founded: 1971
Literature, poetry, criticism. Publications: Literary.
ISBN Prefix(es): 0-913006
Number of titles published annually: 3 Print
Total Titles: 80 Print

Pudding House Publications
Affiliate of Pudding House Innovative Writers Programs
81 Shadymere Lane, Columbus, OH 43213
Tel: 614-986-1881
E-mail: info@puddinghouse.com
Web Site: www.puddinghouse.com
Key Personnel
Pres & Dir: Jennifer Bosveld
Founded: 1979
Literary journal, chapbooks, anthologies, educational books on the writing process, literature/poetry publishing, workshops, seminars, retreats, website, posters, broadsides, magazines.
ISBN Prefix(es): 0-944754; 1-930755; 1-58998
Number of titles published annually: 100 Print; 1 Online
Total Titles: 550 Print; 1 Online

Puffin Books
Imprint of Penguin Group (USA) Inc
345 Hudson St, New York, NY 10014
SAN: 282-5074
Tel: 212-366-2000
E-mail: online@penguinputnam.com
Web Site: www.penguin.com
Key Personnel
VP & Publr: Eileen Kreit
Man Ed, Assoc Publr: Gerard Mancini
Exec Dir: Kristin Gilson
Art Dir: Deborah Kaplan
Man Ed: Philip Airoldi, Jr
Sr Ed: Sharyn November
Founded: 1935
ISBN Prefix(es): 0-14
Number of titles published annually: 175 Print
Total Titles: 1,576 Print
Membership(s): Children's Book Council

Purdue University Press
S Campus Courts-E, 509 Harrison St, West
   Lafayette, IN 47907-2025
SAN: 203-4026
Tel: 765-494-2038 *Toll Free Tel:* 800-247-6553
   (orders) *Fax:* 765-496-2442
E-mail: pupress@purdue.edu
Web Site: www.thepress.purdue.edu
Key Personnel
Man Ed: Margaret Hunt
Dir & Mktg Mgr: Thomas Bacher
Intl Rts: Anu Hansen
Prodn Mgr: Bryan Shaffer
Founded: 1960
Publisher of scholarly titles with emphasis on
   business, veterinary medicine, health issues &
   the humanities.
ISBN Prefix(es): 0-911198; 1-55753
Number of titles published annually: 25 Print; 3
   E-Book
Total Titles: 350 Print; 10 E-Book
Imprints: Digital-I Books; Ichor Business Books;
   Nota Bell Books; PUP Books
Distributor for Lemma Publishers; Rosenberg/
   Thela Thesis; Wageningen Pers
Foreign Rep(s): APAC Publishers Servides Pty
   Ltd (Asia, Hawaii, Pacific Islands); Cranbury
   International (Africa, India, Latin America,
   South America); The Eurospan Group (UK,
   Continental Europe, Israel, Middle East); Foot-
   print Books Pty Ltd (Australia, New Zealand);
   Scholarly Book Services Inc (Canada)
Foreign Rights: Atmarr Agency Services; Global
   Rights Agent; Anu Hansen
Returns: Bookmasters Inc
Warehouse: Bookmasters Inc
Distribution Center: Bookmasters Inc
Membership(s): American Association of Univer-
   sity Presses

Pureplay Press
11353 Missouri Ave, Los Angeles, CA 90025
Tel: 310-479-8773 *Toll Free Tel:* 800-247-6553
   (orders only) *Fax:* 310-473-9384
E-mail: info@cubanovel.com
Web Site: www.pureplaypress.com
Key Personnel
Publr: David Landau *E-mail:* davidkaori@
   earthlink.net
Assoc Publr: Wakeford Gong *E-mail:* wclr@ix.
   netcom.com
Ed: Benigno Dou *E-mail:* bdou@elherald.com;
   Nestor Diaz *E-mail:* nchinatown@yahoo.com
Founded: 2001
Publish books in English & Spanish about the
   history & culture of Cuba.
ISBN Prefix(es): 0-9714366
Number of titles published annually: 5 Print
Total Titles: 6 Print
Advertising Agency: Margaret S Keller Publish-
   ing (MSK), 8231 Del Oro Lane, La Palma,
   CA 90623, Contact: Peggy Keller *Tel:* 714-

821-3369 *Fax:* 714-821-3832 *E-mail:* pkeller@
   earthlink.net
Orders to: Bookmasters, 30 Amberwood Pkwy,
   Ashland, OH 44805, Contact: Dannette Her-
   rmann *Tel:* 419-281-1802 *Fax:* 419-281-6883
   E-mail: bmassie@bookmasters.com
Returns: Bookmasters, 30 Amberwood Pkwy,
   Ashland, OH 44805, Contact: Dannette Her-
   rmann *Tel:* 419-281-1802 *Fax:* 419-281-6883
   E-mail: bmassie@bookmasters.com
Shipping Address: Bookmasters, 30 Amberwood
   Pkwy, Ashland, OH 44805, Contact: Dannette
   Herrmann *Tel:* 419-281-1802 *Fax:* 419-281-
   6883 *E-mail:* bmassie@bookmasters.com
Warehouse: Bookmasters, 30 Amberwood Pkwy,
   Ashland, OH 44805, Contact: Dannette Her-
   rmann *Tel:* 419-281-1802 *Fax:* 419-281-6883
   E-mail: bmassie@bookmasters.com
Distribution Center: Bookmasters, 30 Am-
   berwood Pkwy, Ashland, OH 44805, Con-
   tact: Dannette Herrmann *Tel:* 419-281-
   1802 *Fax:* 419-281-6883 *E-mail:* bmassie@
   bookmasters.com

Purple House Press
8138 US Hwy 62 E, Cynthiana, KY 41031
Tel: 859-235-9970 *Fax:* 859-235-9970
E-mail: phpress@earthlink.net
Web Site: www.purplehousepress.com
Key Personnel
Publr: Jill Morgan *E-mail:* jimorgan@earthlink.
   net
Dir, Cust Fulfillment, Managed Info Servs: Ray
   Sanders
Founded: 2000
Reissue of children's classics from the 1920s-
   1970s.
ISBN Prefix(es): 1-930900
Number of titles published annually: 8 Print
Total Titles: 25 Print
Warehouse: Purple House Press c/o Associates
   Warehouse, 251 Price Rd, Lexington, KY
   40511 *Tel:* 859-235-9970

Purple Mountain Press Ltd
PO Box 309, Fleischmanns, NY 12430-0309
SAN: 222-3716
Tel: 845-254-4062 *Toll Free Tel:* 800-325-2665
   Fax: 845-254-4476
E-mail: purple@catskill.net
Web Site: www.catskill.net/purple
Key Personnel
Pres, Publr & Intl Rts: Wray Rominger
Publr: Loni Rominger
Founded: 1973
Publish adult nonfiction books about New York
   State; history, natural history, folklore, the arts,
   outdoor recreation, a few regional mysteries,
   also maritime books.
ISBN Prefix(es): 0-935796; 0-916346; 1-930098
Number of titles published annually: 10 Print
Total Titles: 96 Print
Divisions: Harbor Hill Books
Distributor for Carmania Press, London (North
   America only)
Shipping Address: 1060 Main St, Fleischmanns,
   NY 12430

Purple People Inc
PO Box 3194, Sedona, AZ 86340-3194
Tel: 928-204-6400 *Toll Free Tel:* 866-787-7535
   Fax: 928-282-1662
E-mail: info@purplepeople.com; sales@
   purplepeople.com (sales & orders); admin@
   purplepeople.com (billing)
Web Site: www.purplepeople.com
Key Personnel
Pres: Susan Broude *E-mail:* susan@purplepeople.
   com
VP, Prodn: Tami Aileen *E-mail:* tami@
   purplepeople.com
Founded: 1997

Promote equality among all humans & respect
   for all living creatures. Our primary focus is
   on publishing books to inspire children which
   are consistent with our purpose. Specialize
   in books that present challenging topics in a
   thought-provoking, creative way that spurs con-
   versation between adult & child. Part of the
   proceeds of the books will be donated to char-
   ities that benefit children, animals & the environment. Services: provide inspirational speakers for events, author signings & publishing
   consultation.
ISBN Prefix(es): 0-9707793
Number of titles published annually: 5 Print; 2
   CD-ROM; 3 Audio
Total Titles: 1 Print
Membership(s): American Book Producers Association; CBE; Network of Alternatives for
   Publishers, Retailers & Artists Inc; Publishers
   Marketing Association; Small Publishers Asso-
   ciation of North America; Society of Children's
   Book Writers & Illustrators

Purple Pomegranate Productions
Division of Jews for Jesus
84 Page St, San Francisco, CA 94102-5914
Tel: 415-864-2600 *Fax:* 415-864-3995
E-mail: info@jewsforjesus.org
Web Site: www.jewsforjesus.org
Key Personnel
CSR Mgr: Shamilla Singh
Proj Mgr: Janna Sanders
Jewish evangelism, books, pamphlets, music.
ISBN Prefix(es): 0-9616148; 1-881022
Number of titles published annually: 3 Print
Total Titles: 45 Print; 8 CD-ROM; 5 E-Book; 19
   Audio

Pushcart Press
PO Box 380, Wainscott, NY 11975-0380
SAN: 202-9871
Tel: 631-324-9300
Key Personnel
Pres: Bill Henderson
Founded: 1972
Trade books, literary anthologies.
ISBN Prefix(es): 0-916366; 1-888889
Number of titles published annually: 6 Print
Total Titles: 65 Print
Distributed by W W Norton & Co Inc
Distribution Center: 500 Fifth Ave, New York,
   NY 10110

Putnam Berkley Audio
Imprint of Penguin Group (USA) Inc
375 Hudson St, New York, NY 10014
SAN: 282-5074
Tel: 212-366-2000 *Fax:* 212-366-2666
E-mail: online@penguinputnam.com
Web Site: www.penguin.com
Key Personnel
Exec Producer: Patti Pirooz *Tel:* 212-366-2402
   Fax: 212-366-2643 *E-mail:* patti.pirooz@us.
   penguingroup.com
Founded: 1996
Abridged, unabridged formats; simultaneous re-
   lease with hardcover.
ISBN Prefix(es): 0-399
Total Titles: 53 Audio
Distributor for Arkangel
Orders to: Penguin Group (USA) Inc, 405 Mur-
   ray Hill Pkwy, East Rutherford, NJ 07073 *Toll
   Free Tel:* 800-788-6262
Returns: Penguin Group (USA) Inc, 405 Murray
   Hill Pkwy, East Rutherford, NJ 07073
Warehouse: Penguin Group (USA) Inc, One
   Grosset Dr, Kirkwood, NY 13795 *Fax:* 607-
   775-5586

The Putnam Publishing Group
Division of Penguin Group (USA) Inc
375 Hudson St, New York, NY 10014
SAN: 282-5074

Tel: 212-366-2000 *Toll Free Tel:* 800-631-8571
  Fax: 212-366-2643
E-mail: online@penguinputnam.com
Web Site: www.penguin.com *Telex:* 422386
  Cable: PUTNAM NY
Number of titles published annually: 289 Print
Total Titles: 1,617 Print; 53 Audio
Imprints: Avery; BlueHen; Coward-McCann; G
  P Putnam's Sons; Riverhead Books; Jeremy
  P Tarcher; Tarcher/Penguin; Putnam Berkley
  Audio; Marian Wood Books
Advertising Agency: Mesa Group

G P Putnam's Sons (Children's)
Member of Penguin Young Readers Group
345 Hudson St, New York, NY 10014
SAN: 282-5074
Tel: 212-366-2000
E-mail: online@penguinputnam.com
Web Site: www.penguin.com
Key Personnel
Pres & Publr, Putnam Books for Young Readers:
  Nancy Paulsen
VP & Art Dir, Putnam & Philomel: Cecilia Yung
Exec Ed: Kathryn Dawson
Exec Man Ed: David Briggs
Sr Ed: Susan Kochan
Ed: John Rudolph
Ed-at-Large: Margaret Frith
Founded: 1838
ISBN Prefix(es): 0-399; 0-698
Number of titles published annually: 84 Print
Total Titles: 655 Print
Imprints: PaperStar
Membership(s): Children's Book Council

G P Putnam's Sons (Hardcover)
Imprint of Penguin Group (USA) Inc
375 Hudson St, New York, NY 10014
SAN: 282-5074
Tel: 212-366-2000
E-mail: online@penguinputnam.com
Web Site: www.penguin.com
Key Personnel
Pres: Carol Baron
Sr VP & Publr: Neil Nyren
Sr VP, Corp Dir, PR, Assoc Publr & Exec Dir,
  Publicity: Marilyn Ducksworth
Sr VP & Publg Dir: Daniel Harvey
VP & Edit Dir: Jennifer Hershey
VP & Sr Ed: John Duff
VP & Ed: Marian Wood
VP & Assoc Publr: Catharine Lynch
VP & Prodn Dir: William Peabody
VP & Dir of Publicity: Steve Oppenheim
Sr Publicity Dir: Mih-Ho Cha
VP & Exec Ed: Christine Pepe
Dir, Copy Ed: Elizabeth Wagner
Dir, Art Interiors: Claire Vaccaro
Dir, Contracts & Copyrights: Jean Marie Pierson
Dir, Religious Pubns: Joel Fotinos
Exec Art Dir: Lisa Amoroso
Exec Ed: Leslie Gelbman
Sr Ed: David Highfill
Founded: 1838
Fiction & general nonfiction.
ISBN Prefix(es): 0-399
Number of titles published annually: 114 Print
Total Titles: 333 Print; 53 Audio
Imprints: Ace/Putnam; Blue Hen Putnam; Gros-
  set/Putnam; Putnam; Putnam Berkley Audio;
  Marian Wood Books
Advertising Agency: Mesa Group

Pyncheon House
6 University Dr, Suite 105, Amherst, MA 01002
SAN: 297-6269
Key Personnel
Ed: David R Rhodes
Founded: 1991

Fine editions & trade books; contemporary po-
  etry, short fiction, novels & essays; member of
  Library of Congress CIP Program.
ISBN Prefix(es): 1-881119
Number of titles published annually: 4 Print
Total Titles: 14 Print

QED, see Quality Education Data, Inc

Quail Ridge Press
101 Brooks Dr, Brandon, MS 39042
Mailing Address: PO Box 123, Brandon, MS
  39043 SAN: 214-2201
Tel: 601-825-2063 *Toll Free Tel:* 800-343-1583
  Fax: 601-825-3091
E-mail: info@quailridge.com
Web Site: quailridge.com
Key Personnel
Dir: Gwen McKee *E-mail:* gmckee@quailridge.
  com
Publr: Barney McKee *E-mail:* bmckee@
  quailridge.com
Dir, Sales & Mktg: Terresa Ray *E-mail:* tray@
  quailridge.com
Founded: 1978
Cookbooks, general interest, regional, health.
ISBN Prefix(es): 0-937552
Number of titles published annually: 4 Print
Total Titles: 132 Print

QualHealth Inc
PO Box 6539, Lawrenceville, NJ 08648-0539
Key Personnel
VP: Ms Reshmi M Siddique, PhD *Tel:* 609-658-
  9917
Founded: 2003
Publish information products in the health care
  field.
ISBN Prefix(es): 1-932
Number of titles published annually: 4 Print
Total Titles: 4 Print
Branch Office(s)
3 Fairview Terr, Lawrenceville, NJ 08648
Shipping Address: BookMasters Inc, 2541 Ash-
  land Rd, Mansfield, OH 44905 *Toll Free
  Tel:* 888-537-6727
Warehouse: BookMasters Inc, 2541 Ashland Rd,
  Mansfield, OH 44905
Membership(s): Publishers Marketing Associa-
  tion; Small Publishers Association of North
  America

Quality Education Data, Inc
Subsidiary of Scholastic Inc
1625 Broadway, Suite 250, Denver, CO 80202
Tel: 303-209-9400 *Toll Free Tel:* 800-525-5811
  Fax: 303-209-9444
E-mail: info@qeddata.com
Web Site: www.qeddata.com
Key Personnel
Pres, QED & VP, Mktg Devt: Jeanne Hayes
Dir, Sales: Larry Sanek
Gen Mgr: Andy Lacy
Founded: 1981
Research & database company focused exclu-
  sively on the education market & is a wholly
  owned subsidiary of Scholastic Inc, the global
  children's publishing & media company. In
  2002, QED purchased Nelson B Heller & Associates, now The Heller Reports, a leading
  provider of competitive intelligence & networking opportunities for education marketers.
Together with Scholastic & The Heller Reports,
  QED provides unparalleled services & opportunities for companies marketing to K-12,
  pre-school & higher education institutions &
  educators, as well as libraries & Canadian institutions. From keeping you on top of market
  developments that affect your business to helping you formulate & implement targeted &
  effective sales & marketing strategies, we offer

a comprehensive solution to help you achieve
  maximum success in the education market.
QED's National Education Database™ is comprised of more than 200,000 educational institutions. QED offers a wide range of selection
  options as well as an E-mail Marketing Service
  & Educator at Home database with educators'
  home addresses & demographics linked to their
  school addresses & demographics.
ISBN Prefix(es): 0-88747
Number of titles published annually: 57 Print
Total Titles: 57 Print

§Quality Medical Publishing Inc
2248 Welsch Industrial Ct, St Louis, MO 63146-
  4222
Tel: 314-878-7808 *Toll Free Tel:* 800-423-6865
  Fax: 314-878-9937
E-mail: qmp@qmp.com
Web Site: www.qmp.com
Key Personnel
Pres: Karen Berger *E-mail:* kberger@qmp.com
Founded: 1987
Medical books (especially surgery); plastic, neu-
  rological, spine & general surgery, urology &
  orthopaedics.
ISBN Prefix(es): 0-942219; 1-57626
Number of titles published annually: 16 Print
Total Titles: 145 Print; 2 CD-ROM
Imprints: QMP

§Quantum Leap SLC Publications
Affiliate of Anasazi Foundation for Indigenous
  Americans
2740 Greenbriar Pkwy, Suite 201, Atlanta, GA
  30308
Toll Free Fax: 877-571-9788
E-mail: distribution@blackamericanhandbook.com
Web Site: www.blackamericanhandbook.com
Key Personnel
CEO: RaDine Amen-ra
Founded: 2000
Produces educational books for the Black,
  Caribbean, Latin American & American In-
  dian/Amerindian civilizations community deal-
  ing with history, heritage & culture in America
  before & after European discovery. Publishes
  authors of indigenous American heritage books
  & American Indian/American Indian civiliza-
  tions.
ISBN Prefix(es): 0-9705455
Number of titles published annually: 5 Print; 3
  CD-ROM; 3 Online; 3 E-Book; 3 Audio
Total Titles: 3 Print; 10 Online; 9 Audio

Quarterly Review of Literature
26 Haslet Ave, Princeton, NJ 08540
Fax: 609-258-2230
E-mail: qrl@princeton.edu
Web Site: www.princeton.edu/~qrl
Key Personnel
Man Ed: Renee Weiss
Founded: 1943
Poetry books.
ISBN Prefix(es): 1-888545
Number of titles published annually: 6 Print
Total Titles: 70 Print

Quick Publishing
Formerly Studio 4 Productions
1610 Long Leaf Circle, St Louis, MO 63146
SAN: 299-5123
Tel: 314-432-3435 *Toll Free Tel:* 888-782-5474
  Fax: 314-993-4485
E-mail: quickpublishing@sbcglobal.net
Web Site: www.quickpublishing.com
Key Personnel
Pres: Angie Quick
Founded: 1972
Aging, seniors & parenting.
ISBN Prefix(es): 1-882349
Number of titles published annually: 3 Print

Total Titles: 12 Print
Distribution Center: Partners Book Distributing, 2325 Jarco Dr, Holt, MI 48842 *Fax:* 517-694-3205

Quicksilver Productions
PO Box 340, Ashland, OR 97520-0012
Tel: 541-482-5343 *Fax:* 541-482-0960
E-mail: celestialcalendars@e-mail.com
Web Site: www.quicksilverproductions.com
Key Personnel
Prop: Jim Maynard
Exec Asst: Jane Maynard
Founded: 1972
Publishers of calendars.
ISBN Prefix(es): 0-930356
Number of titles published annually: 3 Print
Total Titles: 8 Print

Quincannon Publishing Group
PO Box 8100, Glen Ridge, NJ 07028-8100
Tel: 973-669-8367
E-mail: editors@quincannongroup.com
Web Site: www.quincannongroup.com
Key Personnel
Ed-in-Chief: Alan Quincannon
Ed: Holly Benedict
Admin Asst & Lib Sales Dir: Patricia Drury
Publicity: Loretta Bolger
Cons Ed: Jeanne Wilcox
Intl Rts: Loris Essary
Founded: 1990
Regional mystery novels made unique by involving some element of a region's history (i.e. the story's setting & time frame or the mystery's origin); custom tailored books for local & regional museums.
ISBN Prefix(es): 1-878452
Number of titles published annually: 5 Print
Total Titles: 10 Print; 10 Online
Imprints: Compass Point Mysteries; Jersey Yarns; Learning & Coloring Books; Rune-Tales; ToryCorner Editions
Foreign Rep(s): International Titles

§Quintessence Publishing Co Inc
551 Kimberly Dr, Carol Stream, IL 60188
SAN: 215-9783
Tel: 630-682-3223 *Toll Free Tel:* 800-621-0387
Fax: 630-682-3288
E-mail: contact@quintbook.com
Web Site: www.quintpub.com
Key Personnel
Pres: H W Haase
VP, Edit & Intl Rts: Tomoko Tsuchiya
E-mail: tomoko@quintbook.com
VP, Oper & Lib Sales Dir: William Hartman
Founded: 1972
Professional & scholarly books, journals, medicine, dentistry, health & nutrition, medical history.
ISBN Prefix(es): 0-931386; 0-86715
Number of titles published annually: 20 Print; 2 CD-ROM
Total Titles: 330 Print; 4 CD-ROM
Imprints: Quintessence Books; Quintessence of Dental Technology; Quintessence Pockets
Subsidiaries: Quintessence Editora Ltda (Brazil)
Foreign Office(s): 2-4 Ifenpfad, D-1000 Berlin 42, Germany
Quint House Bldg, 326 Hongo, Bunkyo-ku Tokyo, Japan
2 Blagden Rd, New Malden, Surrey KT2 4AD, United Kingdom
Distributor for Quintessence Publishing Co Ltd (Japan); Quintessence Publishing Ltd (London); Quintessence Verlags GmbH
Advertising Agency: QPC Advertising Inc

Quirk Books
215 Church St, Philadelphia, PA 19106
Tel: 215-627-3581 *Fax:* 215-627-5220

E-mail: general@quirkbooks.com
Web Site: www.quirkbooks.com
Key Personnel
Publr: David Borgenicht
Edit Dir: Mindy Brown
Sr Ed: Jason Rekulak
Ed: Erin Slonaker; Melissa Wagner
Design Dir: Michael Rogalski
Prodn Dir: Emily Betsch
Mktg Dir: Jason Mitchell
Opers Mgr: Brett Cohen
Subsidiary Rts Mgr: Reka Rubin
Founded: 2001
Publishing list focuses on irreverent pop-culture, humor, gift, self-help & "impractical" reference books. The actual subject matter of our books is quite diverse. Publish everything from childcare tips & magic tricks to advice on stain removal. All our books have a distinct sense of style, a refreshing sense of humor & innovative production values.
ISBN Prefix(es): 1-931686
Number of titles published annually: 25 Print
Total Titles: 25 Print
Distributed by Chronicle Books

Quite Specific Media Group Ltd
7373 Pyramid Place, Hollywood, CA 90046
Tel: 323-851-5797 *Fax:* 323-851-5798
E-mail: info@quitespecificmedia.com
Web Site: www.quitespecificmedia.com
Key Personnel
Publr: Ralph Pine *E-mail:* rpine@quitespecificmedia.com
Man Ed & ISBN Contact: Ina Kohler *Tel:* 718-237-0264 *E-mail:* ikohler@quitespecificmedia.com
Founded: 1967
Publish original books as well as co-publish with foreign publishers, Specialize in costumes, fashion & theatre.
ISBN Prefix(es): 0-89676
Number of titles published annually: 12 Print
Total Titles: 70 Print; 1 Audio
Imprints: By Design Press; Costume & Fashion Press; Drama Publishers; EntertainmentPro; Jade Rabbit
Foreign Rep(s): Nick Hern Books (UK)
Orders to: 7 Old Fulton St, Brooklyn Heights, NY 11201 *Tel:* 718-237-0264 *Fax:* 718-237-1623

Quixote Press
1854 345 Ave, Wever, IA 52658
Tel: 319-372-7480 *Toll Free Tel:* 800-571-BOOK
Fax: 319-372-7485
E-mail: heartsntummies@hotmail.com
Key Personnel
Pres: Bruce Carlson
Founded: 1985
Regional paperback books of humor or folklore & cookbooks.
ISBN Prefix(es): 1-878488; 1-57166
Number of titles published annually: 15 Print
Total Titles: 315 Print
Imprints: Black Iron Cookin' Co; Hearts & Tummies Cookbook Co
Divisions: Hearts & Tummies Cookbook Co
See separate listing for:
Hearts & Tummies Cookbook Co

R D R Books
2415 Woolsey St, Berkeley, CA 94705
Tel: 510-595-0595 *Fax:* 510-228-0300
E-mail: info@rdrbooks.com
Web Site: www.rdrbooks.com
Key Personnel
Publr: Roger Rapoport
Lib Sales Dir: Linda Cohen
Publicity: Bryon Knopp
Intl Rts: Ana Hansea
Founded: 1993

Publish mostly travel books & children's books.
ISBN Prefix(es): 1-57143; 0-9636161
Number of titles published annually: 6 Print
Total Titles: 58 Print
Foreign Office(s): Roundhouse Distribution, United Kingdom
Distributed by Fraser Direct (Jaguar)
Distributor for Wakefield Press Australia
Foreign Rights: Atmar Agency (all territories)

R J Berg & Co, Publishers, see R J Berg/Destinations Press Ltd

§R S V Products
PO Box 26, Hopkins, MN 55343-0026
Tel: 952-936-0400 *Fax:* 952-936-0400
Key Personnel
Prop: Mark Johnson *E-mail:* johnson@net-info.com
Founded: 1992
Mixed-media packages (audio/book); historical re-enactments.
ISBN Prefix(es): 1-883988
Number of titles published annually: 3 Print
Total Titles: 23 Print; 7 Audio
Imprints: Bugling-The Complete Bugler Series; RSV Publishing; Sing-Along Series
Subsidiaries: Nature's Neighborhood

rada press inc
715 Third Ave, Mendota Heights, MN 55118
Tel: 651-455-9695 *Fax:* 651-455-9675
Key Personnel
Ed: Daisy Pellant *E-mail:* daisy@radapress.com
Prodn Head: Ron-Michael Pellant *E-mail:* rm@radapress.com
Asst Ed: Irving Fang *Tel:* 651-645-3304
E-mail: irv@radapress.com
Founded: 1975
ISBN Prefix(es): 0-9604212; 1-933011
Number of titles published annually: 8 Print
Total Titles: 7 Print
Imprints: tree frog publications

§Radix Press
Subsidiary of UGF/OR
2314 Cheshire Lane, Houston, TX 77018-4023
Tel: 713-683-9076
Key Personnel
Dir: Stephen Sherman
Founded: 1983
Directories, reference books. All unauthorized mss sent will be discarded.
ISBN Prefix(es): 0-9624009; 0-9623992; 1-929932
Number of titles published annually: 3 Print
Total Titles: 35 Print; 6 CD-ROM
Imprints: Electric Strawberry Press

Ragged Bears
Division of Ragged Bears Publishing Ltd (UK)
413 Sixth Ave, Brooklyn, NY 11215-3310
Tel: 718-768-3696 *Fax:* 718-369-0844
E-mail: publisher@raggedbears.com
Web Site: www.raggedbears.com
Key Personnel
US Publg Dir: Christopher Franceschelli
E-mail: cmf@raggedbears.com
Founded: 2000
Publisher of high quality books for children.
ISBN Prefix(es): 1-929927
Number of titles published annually: 7 Print
Total Titles: 35 Print
Distributed by Chronicle Books
Foreign Rep(s): Ragged Bears Publishing Ltd (UK)
Returns: Chronicle Books, c/o Genco Fulfillment, 1585 Linda Way, Door 1, Sparks, NV 89431

Ragged Edge Press
Division of White Mane Publishing Co Inc
63 W Burd St, Shippensburg, PA 17257

SAN: 667-1934
Mailing Address: PO Box 708, Shippensburg, PA 17257
Tel: 717-532-2237 *Toll Free Tel:* 888-948-6263
Fax: 717-532-6110
E-mail: marketing@whitemane.com
Key Personnel
Acqs & Subs Rts & Cust Serv Mgr: Harold E Collier
Founded: 1994
ISBN Prefix(es): 0-942597; 1-57249
Number of titles published annually: 40 Print
Total Titles: 300 Print

Ragged Mountain Press
Division of The McGraw-Hill Companies Inc
485 Commercial St, Rockport, ME 04856
Mailing Address: PO Box 220, Camden, ME 04843
Tel: 207-236-4837 *Fax:* 207-236-6314
Web Site: www.raggedmountainpress.com
Key Personnel
Edit Dir: Jonathan Eaton
Man Ed: Deborah Oliver
Edit, Design & Prodn Dir: Molly Mulhern
Founded: 1969
Publishes nonfiction outdoor & environmental issues books of literary merit or unique appeal. Outdoor related how-to subjects include: nature/environment, recreation, sports, adventure, camping, fly-fishing, snowshoeing, backpacking, natural history, climbing, cycling, running, scuba diving.
ISBN Prefix(es): 0-07
Number of titles published annually: 45 Print
Total Titles: 400 Print
Foreign Rep(s): McGraw-Hill/Ryerson (Canada)

Rainbow Books Inc
PO Box 430, Highland City, FL 33846-0430
SAN: 221-9859
Tel: 863-648-4420 *Toll Free Tel:* 800-431-1579 (orders only); 888-613-2665 *Fax:* 863-647-5951
E-mail: rbibooks@aol.com
Web Site: www.rainbowbooksinc.com
Key Personnel
Publr: Betty Wright
Opers Dir: C Marzen Lampe
Edit Dir: Betsy Lampe
Asst to Sr Ed: Jamie Peters
Prodn Mgr: Marilyn Ratzlaff
Prod Ed: Peggy Bryant; Virginia Condello
Founded: 1979
How-to both for the adult layman & the juvenile markets, self-help, reference, resource & general books; parenting; nonfiction; also package books for other publishers & act as consultants, mystery fiction at 50,000 or 75,000 words.
ISBN Prefix(es): 0-935834; 1-56825
Number of titles published annually: 20 Print
Total Titles: 141 Print
Foreign Rep(s): Hagenbach & Bender (all other countries)
Foreign Rights: Hagenbach & Bender (Switzerland)
Warehouse: Publishers Storage & Shipping Corp, Ypsilanti, MI
Membership(s): AAP; Florida Publishers Association; National Association of Independent Publishers; Publishers Association of the South

Rainbow Publishers
PO Box 261129, San Diego, CA 92196-1129
Tel: 858-668-3260
Web Site: www.rainbowpublishers.com
Key Personnel
Gen Mgr: Daniel Miley
Sales Mgr: Chuck Anderson
Edit Dir: Christy Scannell *E-mail:* rainbowed@earthlink.net
Founded: 1951

Christian education books.
ISBN Prefix(es): 0-937282; 1-885358; 1-58411
Number of titles published annually: 10 Print
Total Titles: 190 Print
Imprints: Legacy Press; Rainbow Publishers
Shipping Address: 13691 Danielson St, Suite E, Poway, CA 92064

§Rainbow Studies International
1950 S Shepard Ave, El Reno, OK 73036
Mailing Address: PO Box 759, El Reno, OK 73036-0759
Tel: 405-262-6826 *Toll Free Tel:* 800-242-5348
Fax: 405-262-7599
E-mail: rsimail@rainbowstudies.com
Web Site: www.rainbowstudies.com
Key Personnel
VP & Gen Mgr: Jeff Koos *E-mail:* jeff@rainbowstudies.com
VP, Sales & Mktg: Mike Howard *E-mail:* mikeh@rainbowstudies.com
Founded: 1986
All areas dealing with Christian inspirational materials; CD-ROMs & gift books.
ISBN Prefix(es): 1-58170; 0-933657
Total Titles: 79 Print; 3 CD-ROM; 82 Online
Divisions: Arco Iris Internacional; RainbowSoft
Shipping Address: 319 E Elm St, El Reno, OK 73036

Ram Publishing Co
1881 W State St, Garland, TX 75042-6797
Tel: 972-494-6151 *Fax:* 972-494-1881
Web Site: www.garrett.com
Key Personnel
Ed: Hal Dawson
Founded: 1967
Nonfiction on treasure hunting with a metal detector & metal detector security.
ISBN Prefix(es): 0-915920
Number of titles published annually: 3 Print
Total Titles: 15 Print

§RAND Corp
1776 Main St, Santa Monica, CA 90407
Tel: 310-393-0411 *Fax:* 310-451-6996
E-mail: jane_ryan@rand.org
Web Site: www.rand.org
Key Personnel
Dir, Pubns: Jane Ryan *Tel:* 310-393-0411 ext 7260 *E-mail:* ryan@rand.org
Mktg Dir: John Warren
Man Ed: Peter Hoffman
Prodn Mgr: David Bolhuis
Busn Mgr: Erin Miller
Cust Serv Mgr: Bob Hazzard *Tel:* 310-451-7002 *Fax:* 310-451-6915 *E-mail:* hazzard@rand.org
Founded: 1948
Public policy research.
ISBN Prefix(es): 0-8330
Number of titles published annually: 125 Print; 250 Online; 80 E-Book
Total Titles: 12,000 Print; 5 CD-ROM; 2,000 Online; 500 E-Book
Foreign Rep(s): Eurospan (Europe & Middle East); Unifacmanu Trading Co (Taiwan); United Publishers Services (Japan, Korea)
Foreign Rights: ATMARR (world rights agent); Anu Hansen (world rights agent)
Distribution Center: National Book Network, 4720 Boston Way, Lanham, MD 20706, Mark Cozy *Tel:* 301-459-3366 *Fax:* 301-459-2118 *E-mail:* mcozy@nbnbooks.com
Membership(s): AAP; American Association of University Presses; Society for Scholarly Publishing

§Rand McNally
8255 Central Park Ave N, Skokie, IL 60076
SAN: 203-3917
Mailing Address: PO Box 7600, Chicago, IL 60680

Tel: 847-329-8100 *Toll Free Tel:* 800-333-0136
Fax: 847-673-0539
Web Site: www.randmcnally.com
Key Personnel
Pres & CEO: Rob Apatoff
Sr VP & Chief Mktg Officer: Norm Smagley
Exec VP, Sales & Merchandising: Betsy Owens
VP, Natl Travel: Kendra Ensor
Secy, Mktg: Gabriela Lambesis *Tel:* 847-329-8100 ext 6211
Founded: 1856
Road atlases & maps; world atlases; mileage & routing publications & software; educational maps, atlases; children's atlases, maps, books; electronic multimedia products; retail & online stores; online travel services, travel software.
ISBN Prefix(es): 0-528
Number of titles published annually: 20 Print
Total Titles: 100 Print; 5 CD-ROM
Imprints: Rand McNally for Kids
Subsidiaries: Allmaps
Divisions: Consumer Software; Educational Publishing; Map & Atlas Publishing; Retail; Transportation Data Management (TDM)
Warehouse: 106 Hi-Lane, Richmond, KY 40475

Random House Audio Publishing Group
Subsidiary of Random House Inc
1745 Broadway, New York, NY 10019
Tel: 212-782-9720 *Fax:* 212-782-9600
Key Personnel
Pres, Audio & Diversified Publg Group: David Naggar
VP & Publr, RH Adult Audio, LP: Scott Matthews
VP & Publr, Listening Lib Imprint: Tim Ditlow
Dir Mktg: Sara Schober
Dir, Audio & Mktg Prodn: Helen Kilcullen-Schulter
Dir, Publicity: Amanda D'Acierno
Sr Ed: Amy Metsch
Random House Inc & its publishing entities are not accepting unsol submissions, proposals, mss, or submission queries via e-mail at this time.
ISBN Prefix(es): 0-553; 1-4000
Total Titles: 475 Audio

Random House Children's Books
Division of Random House Inc
1745 Broadway, New York, NY 10019
Tel: 212-782-9000 *Toll Free Tel:* 800-200-3552
Fax: 212-782-9452
Web Site: www.randomhouse.com/kids
Key Personnel
Pres & Publr: Chip Gibson
Exec VP, Publg Opers: Rich Romano
Sr VP & Dir, Sales: Joan DeMayo
VP & Sales Dir, Mass Merchandise: Tom Cox
VP & Sales Dir, National Book Chains: Al Greco
VP, Mktg: Daisy Kline
VP & Exec Dir, Publicity: Judith Haut
VP, Subs Rts Mkts: Pam White
VP & Publr, Bantam Delacorte Dell: Beverly Horowitz
VP & Edit Dir, Pbks: Michelle Poploff
VP & Exec Dir, Mass Mkt Mktg: John Adamo
VP & Publg Dir, Wendy Lamb Books: Wendy Lamb
VP & Publr, Random House/Golden Books Young Readers Group: Kate Klimo
VP, Assoc Publr & Art Dir, Random House/Golden Books Young Readers Group: Cathy Goldsmith
VP & Ed-in-Chief, Random House Books for Young Readers: Mallory Loehr
VP & Publg Dir, David Fickling Books: David Fickling
VP, Field & Educ Sales: Glenn Ellis
VP, Brand/Category Mgmt: Felicia Frazier
Exec Dir, Creative Servs: Mary Beth Kilkelly
Exec Dir, School & Library Mktg: Theresa Borzumato

Exec Dir, Art & Design, Knopf Delacorte Dell Young Readers Group: Isabel Warren-Lynch
Assoc Publg Dir & Exec Ed, Knopf/Crown: Nancy Siscoe
Prodn Dir: Linda Palladino
Art Dir, Random House Books for Young Readers: Jan Gerardi
Art Dir, Mass Mkt, Random House/Golden Books Young Readers Group: Tracy Tyler
Sr Exec Ed, Knopf/Crown: Joan Slattery
Ed-at-Large, Knopf/Crown: Janet Schulman
Exec Ed, Doubleday: Francoise Bui
Exec Ed, Media & Series, Bantam Delacorte Dell: Wendy Loggia
Assoc Dir, Publicity: Melanie Chang
Assoc Dir, Subs Rts: Kim Probeyahn
Assoc Dir, Foreign Rts: Ellen Greenberg
Edit Dir, Mass Mkt, Random House Books for Young Readers: Courtney Devon Silk
Edit Dir, Sesame Workshop, Random House Books for Young Readers: Naomi Kleinberg
Edit Dir, Disney Books for Young Readers: Chris Angellili
Exec Ed, Disney Books for Young Readers: Andrea Posner-Sanchez
Exec Ed, Random House Books for Young Readers: Heidi Kilgras
Edit Dir, Novelty, Random House/Golden Books Young Readers Group: Dennis Shealy
Publg Dir, Knopf/Crown: Nancy Hinkel
Assoc Publr, Golden Books: Amy Jarashow
Assoc Dir, Online Mktg: Linda Leonard
Random House Inc & its publishing entities are not accepting unsol submissions, proposals, mss, or submission queries via e-mail at this time.
ISBN Prefix(es): 0-679; 0-307; 0-676; 0-375; 1-4000; 1-58836
Imprints: Beginner Books; Crown Books for Young Readers; Delacorte Books for Young Readers; Doubleday Books for Young Readers; Dragonfly; David Fickling Books for Young Readers; Golden Books; Alfred A Knopf Books for Young Readers; Laurel-Leaf; Random House Books for Young Readers; Wendy Lamb Books; Yearling
Divisions: Random House/Golden Books Young Readers Group; Knopf Delacorte Dell Young Readers Group
Warehouse: Crawfordsville Distribution Center, 1019 N State Rd 47, Crawfordsville, IN 47933
Distribution Center: Crawfordsville Distribution Center, 1019 N State Rd 47, Crawfordsville, IN 47933
Membership(s): Association of Booksellers for Children; Children's Book Council

Random House Direct Inc
Affiliate of Random House Inc
1745 Broadway, New York, NY 10019
Tel: 212-572-2604 *Fax:* 212-572-6018
Key Personnel
VP & Gen Mgr: Lisa Faith Phillips
Dir: Tom Downing
Mktg Mgr: Lyn Barris Hastings
Random House Inc & its publishing entities are not accepting unsol submissions, proposals, mss, or submission queries via e-mail at this time.

§Random House Inc
Division of Bertelsmann AG
1745 Broadway, New York, NY 10019
SAN: 202-5507
Tel: 212-782-9000 *Toll Free Tel:* 800-726-0600
Web Site: www.randomhouse.com *Cable:* RANDOM NY
Key Personnel
Chmn & CEO, Random House Inc: Peter Olson
Deputy Chmn, Chief Admin Officer & CFO: Edward Volini
Exec VP & COO, Random North America: Don Weisberg

Chmn, Random House Asia: Y S Chi
Exec VP & Publr-at-Large, Random House Worldwide: Bonnie Ammer
Pres & Publr, Bantam Dell Publishing Group: Irwyn Applebaum
Pres & Publr, Random House Publg Group: Gina Centrello
Pres & Publr, Crown Publg Group & Pres & Publr, Random House Audio & Diversified Group: Jenny Frost
Pres & Publr, Random House Children's Books: Chip Gibson
Pres, Knopf Publg Group: Sonny Mehta
Pres & Publr, Doubleday Broadway Publg Group: Stephen Rubin
Pres, Corp Devt & Random House Ventures: Richard Sarnoff
Sr VP, Opers & Technol: Andrew Weber
Exec VP, Communs: Stuart Applebaum
Sr VP & Gen Counsel, Random House Inc: Katherine Trager
Sr VP, Fulfillment: Phyllis Mandel
Pres, Audio, Diversified, Info & Travel: David Naggar
VP Client Rel: John Groton
Sr VP & Dir, RH Adult Sales: Madeline McIntosh
Dir, Independent Bookselling: Ruth Liebmann
VP & Dir, Special Mkts: Andrew Stanley
Pres, Random House Dist Serv & VP, Publg Opers: Josh Wright
Random House Inc & its publishing entities are not accepting unsol submissions, proposals, mss, or submission queries via e-mail at this time.
ISBN Prefix(es): 0-02; 0-679; 0-676; 0-375; 0-87665
Imprints: Anchor Bible Commentary; Anchor Bible Dictionary; Anchor Bible Reference Library; Anchor Books; AtRandom.com; Ballantine Books; Ballantine Wellspring; Bantam Books; Bantam Hardcover; Bantam Mass Market; Bantam Skylark; Bantam Starfire; Bantam Trade Paperback; BDD Audio Publishing; Bell Tower; Children's Classics; Children's Media; Clarkson Potter; Crescent Books; Crimeline; Crown Books for Young Readers; Crown Publishers Inc; CTW Publishing; Currency; Del Rey; Delacorte Press; Dell; Dell Laurel Leaf; Dell Yearling; Delta; Derrydale; The Dial Press; Discovery Books; Domain; Doubleday; Doubleday Bible Commentary; Doubleday/Galilee; Doubleday/Image; Dragonfly Books; DTP; Everyman's Library; Fanfare; Fawcett; First Choice Chapter Books; Fodor's; Gramercy Books; Harmony Books; House of Collectibles; Island; Ivy; Alfred A Knopf Inc; Knopf Books for Young Readers; Knopf Paperbacks; Library of Contemporary Thought; Living Language; Main Street Books; Modern Library; The New Jerusalem Bible; One World; Pantheon Books; Picture Yearling; The Princeton Review; Random House; Random House Children's Publishing; Random House Large Print Publishing; Random House Reference & Information Publishing; Schocken Books; Shaye Areheart Books; Sierra Club Adult Books; Spectra; Nan A Talese; Testament Books; Three Rivers Press; Times Books; Villard Books; Vintage Books; Wings Books
Branch Office(s)
Bantam Books Canada Inc, One Toronto St, Suite 300, Toronto, ON M5C 2V6, Canada *Tel:* 416-364-4449 *Fax:* 416-364-6863
Doubleday Canada, One Toronto St, Suite 300, Toronto, PE M5C 2V6, Canada *Tel:* 416-364-4449 *Fax:* 416-364-6863
Random House of Canada Ltd, 2775 Matheson Blvd East, Mississauga, ON L4W 4P7, Canada *Tel:* 905-624-0672 *Fax:* 905-624-6217
Random House of Canada Ltd, One Toronto St, Suite 300, Toronto, ON M5C 2V6, Canada *Tel:* 416-364-4449 *Fax:* 416-364-6863

WaterBrook Press, 5446 N Academy, Suite 200, Colorado Springs, CO 80918 *Tel:* 719-590-4999 *Fax:* 719-590-8977
Editorial Office(s): One Toronto St, Suite 300, Toronto, ON M5C 2V6, Canada *Tel:* 416-777-9477 *Fax:* 416-777-9470
Foreign Office(s): Random House Australia Pty Ltd, 16 Dalmore Dr, Scoresby, Victoria 3153, Australia *Tel:* (03) 9753-4511 *Fax:* (03) 9753-3944
Random House Australia Pty Ltd, 20 Alfred St, Milsons Point, Sydney, NSW 2061, Australia *Tel:* (02) 9954-9966 *Fax:* (02) 9954-4562
Random House UK Ltd, 20 Vauxhall Bridge Rd, London SW1V 2SA, United Kingdom *Tel:* (020) 7840 8400 *Fax:* (020) 7233 8791
Transworld Publishers Ltd, 61-63 Uxbridge Rd, Ealing, London W5 5SA, United Kingdom *Tel:* (020) 8-579-2652 *Fax:* (020) 8-579-5479
Transworld Publishers Ltd, Sanders Rd, Finedon Rd Industrial Estate, Wellingborough, Northamptonshire NN8 4BU, United Kingdom (Distribution Center) *Tel:* (0193) 322-5761 *Fax:* (0193) 327-1235
Tiptree Book Services, Colchester Rd, Frating Green, Colchester, Essex C07 7DW, United Kingdom *Tel:* (01206) 256000 *Fax:* (01206) 255916
Grantham Book Services, Alma Park Industrial Estate, Isaac Newton Way, Grantham, Lincs NG31 9SD, United Kingdom *Tel:* (01476) 541000 *Fax:* (01476) 590223
Doubleday London, 61-63 Uxbridge Rd, Ealing, London W5 5SA, United Kingdom *Tel:* (020) 8231 6717 *Fax:* (020) 8231 6718
Random House New Zealand Ltd, 18 Poland Rd, Glenfield, Auckland 10, New Zealand (Private Bag 102950 NSMC) *Tel:* (09) 444-7197 *Fax:* (09) 444-7524
Random House South Africa Pty Ltd, Endulini, East Wing, 5A Jubilee Rd, Parktown, Sandton 2193, South Africa *Tel:* (011) 484-3538 *Fax:* (011) 484-6180
Distributor for American Guidance Service; Anness Publishing Inc: Hermes House, Lorenz Books; Becket Publications; Karen Brown Guides; Learning Express; NY Review of Books; Princeton Review; Rebus; Shambhala Publications Inc; Sierra Club Books; Storey Books
Shipping Address: Westminster Distribution Center, 400 Hahn Rd, Westminster, MD 21157 *Tel:* 410-848-1900 *Fax:* 410-386-7013
Membership(s): AAP; BISG
See separate listing for:
Bantam Dell Publishing Group
Books on Tape®
Clarkson Potter Publishers
Crown Publishing Group
Doubleday Broadway Publishing Group
Fodor's Travel Publications
Alfred A Knopf
Pantheon Books/Schocken Books
Random House Audio Publishing Group
Random House Children's Books
Random House Direct Inc
Random House International
Random House Large Print
Random House New Media Division
Random House Publishing Group
Random House Reference
Random House Sales & Marketing
Random House Value Publishing
Vintage & Anchor Books
WaterBrook Press

Random House International
Division of Random House Inc
1745 Broadway, New York, NY 10019
Tel: 212-572-6106 *Fax:* 212-572-6045
Key Personnel
Exec VP, COO, North America: Don Weisberg
VP & Sales Dir, Intl, Spec Mkts & Sales Admin: Reed Boyd

Sr Dir, Sales: Emily Feffer *Tel:* 212-572-6084
E-mail: efeffer@randomhouse.com; Kathryn
Wiess *Tel:* 212-572-2488 *E-mail:* kweiss@
randomhouse.com
Random House Inc & its publishing entities are
not accepting unsol submissions, proposals,
mss, or submission queries via e-mail at this
time.

Random House Large Print
Division of Random House Inc
1745 Broadway, New York, NY 10019
Tel: 212-782-9720 *Fax:* 212-782-9600
Key Personnel
Pres, Audio & Diversified Publg Group: David
Naggar
VP & Publr, RH Adult Audio, LP: Scott
Matthews
Sr Ed: Amy H Metsch *Tel:* 212-782-9716
E-mail: ametsch@randomhouse.com
Founded: 1990
Acquires & publishes general interest fiction &
nonfiction in large print editions.
Random House Inc & its publishing entities are
not accepting unsol submissions, proposals,
mss, or submission queries via e-mail at this
time.
ISBN Prefix(es): 0-679
Number of titles published annually: 60 Print
Total Titles: 200 Print

§Random House New Media Division
Unit of Random House Inc
1745 Broadway, New York, NY 10019
Tel: 212-782-9000
Key Personnel
VP, New Media: Keith Titan
Founded: 1993
Specialize in electronic books.
Random House Inc & its publishing entities are
not accepting unsol submissions, proposals,
mss, or submission queries via e-mail at this
time.

Random House Publishing Group
Division of Random House Inc
1745 Broadway, New York, NY 10019
SAN: 214-1175
Toll Free Tel: 800-200-3552 *Toll Free Fax:* 800-
200-3552
Web Site: www.randomhouse.com
Key Personnel
Exec VP & Exec Ed, Random House: Kate Med-
ina
Exec VP & Exec Ed, Modern Library/Random
House: Bob Loomis
Sr VP & Dir, Creative: Gene Mydlowski
Sr VP & Dir, Sales & Mktg: Anthony Ziccardi
Sr VP & Dir, Publg Opers: Lisa Feuer
Sr VP & Dir, Busn Opers: Bill Takes
Sr VP & Exec Ed-in-Chief: Dan Menaker
Sr VP, Ed-in-Chief & Exec Ed, Ballantine: Nancy
Miller
Sr VP & Ed-in-Chief, Random House: Jonathan
Karp
Sr VP & Assoc Publr: Libby McGuire
VP & Sr Ed, Random House: Ileene Smith
VP & Exec Dir, Publicity & PR: Carol Schneider
VP & Dir, Edit, Ballantine: Linda Marrow
VP & Dir, Subs Rts: Claire Tisne
VP & Dir, Publicity: Thomas Perry
VP & Dir, Mktg, Ballantine: Kimberly Hovey
VP & Exec Ed, Ballantine: Joe Blades
VP & Dir, Edit, Ballantine: Maureen O'Neal
VP & Ed-in-Chief, Del Rey/Ballantine: Betsy
Mitchell
Sr Dir, Art/Design: Beck Stvan; Carl Galian;
Robbin Schiff
Dir, Publg, Modern Library/Random House:
David Ebershoff
Dir, Edit, Villard/Random House: Bruce Tracy
Dir, Edit, Del Rey/Ballantine: Shelly Shapiro

Dir, Edit-Media Projs, Del Rey/Ballantine: Steve
Saffel
Dir, Adv & Promo, Random House: Magee Finn
Dir, Adv & Promo, Ballantine: Stacey Witcraft
Dir, Interior Design: Carole Lowenstein
Dir, Mktg, Random House: Sanyu Dillon
Dir, Dom Rts: Rachel Bernstein
Assoc Dir, Prodn: Alexandra Rudd
Deputy Dir, Publicity, Random House: Sally Mar-
vin
Man Ed: Alexandra Krijgsman
Man Ed & Copy Chief: Benjamin Dreyer
Mgr, Subs/Foreign Rts: Rachel Kind
Exec Ed, Ballantine: Elisabeth Dyssegaard
Sr Ed, Random House: Lee Boudreaux; Susanna
Porter
Sr Ed, Modern Library/Random House: Will
Murphy
Sr Ed, Presidio Press/Random House: Ron Doer-
ing
Sr Ed, One World/Ballantine: Melody Guy
Sr Ed, Random House: Caroline Sutton
Assoc Ed, Random House: Stephanie Higgs;
Jonathan Jao; Frankie Jones
Ed, Del Rey/Ballantine: Christopher Schluep
Ed, Ballantine: Allison Dickens; Charlotte Her-
scher; Mark Tavani; Dana Isaacson
Ed, Random House: Ben Loehnen
Ed, Modern Library/Random House: Judith Stern-
light
Jr Copywriter: Molly Houlihan
Founded: 1952
General fiction & nonfiction hardcover, trade &
mass market paperbacks.
ISBN Prefix(es): 0-02; 0-679; 0-89141; 0-345; 0-
449; 0-8129; 0-375; 1-4000; 1-58836; 0-8041
Number of titles published annually: 700 Print;
225 E-Book
Total Titles: 5,500 Print; 850 E-Book
Imprints: Ballantine Books; Del Rey; Modern
Library; One World; Presidio Press; Random
House; Random House Trade Paperbacks; Vil-
lard
Warehouse: 400 Hahn Rd, Westminster, MD
21157
See separate listing for:
Del Rey Books

Random House Reference
Imprint of Random House Information Group
1745 Broadway, New York, NY 10019
Toll Free Tel: 800-733-3000
E-mail: words@random.com; puzzles@random.
com
Key Personnel
Pres, RH Info Publg: David Naggar
Sr VP, Publg Opers: Peter Muller
VP & Publr: Sheryl Stebbins
VP & Exec Man Ed: Denise DeGennaro
Dir, Sub/Foreign Rts: Linda Kaplan
Dir, Prodn: Nina Frieman
Dir, House of Collectibles: Dorothy Harris
Ed: Jena Puncott
Publishes reference, crossword puzzle books &
chess books.
Random House Inc & its publishing entities are
not accepting unsol submissions, proposals,
mss, or submission queries via e-mail at this
time.
ISBN Prefix(es): 0-679; 0-8129; 0-375
Number of titles published annually: 80 Print; 2
E-Book
Total Titles: 510 Print; 2 CD-ROM; 2 E-Book
Imprints: Boston Globe Puzzle Books; Chicago
Tribune Crosswords; House of Collectibles;
Los Angeles Times Crosswords; McKay Chess
Library; Random House Websters; Washington
Post Crosswords

Random House Sales & Marketing
Division of Random House Inc
1745 Broadway, New York, NY 10019
Fax: 212-782-9000

Key Personnel
Exec VP, COO, North America: Don Weisberg
VP & Sales Dir, Intl, Special Markets & Sales
Admin: Reed Boyd
VP & Sales Dir, Strategic Planning & Busn Op-
ers: Julie Black
VP Client Rel, RH Dist Servs: John Groton
VP & Sales Dir, Special Mkts: Andrew Stanley
Sr VP & Sales Dir (Adult): Madeline McIntosh
VP & Sales Dir, Mass Mdse Sales (Adult):
George Fisher
VP & Deputy Dir, Sales (Adult): Marty McGrath
VP & Sales Dir, B&N Sales: Jaci Updike
VP & Sales Dir, BGI: Lauren Monaco
VP & Sales Dir, BGI & Natl Acct Mktg Reps:
Beryl Needham
VP & Sales Dir, Independent Retail Field Sales
(Adult): Paul Kozlowski
VP & Deputy Dir, Independent Retail Field Sales
(Adult): Christian Waters
Sr VP & Sales Dir (Children's): Joan DeMayo
VP & Sales Dir, Brand Mgmt: Felicia Frazier
VP & Sales Dir, Independent Retail Field Sales,
Educ & Sales Libr, Resupply Jobbers, AMS,
AWBC - RH Children's: Glenn Ellis
VP & Sales Dir, Mass Mdse Sales (Children's):
Tom Cox
VP & Sales Dir, Natl Bookstore Chains (Chil-
dren's): Al Greco
Random House Inc & its publishing entities are
not accepting unsol submissions, proposals,
mss, or submission queries via e-mail at this
time.
Distributor for American Medical Associa-
tion; Karen Brown; Mondadori Spanish Lan-
guage; Old Farmers Almanac; Real V; Rizzoli;
Rugged Land; Shambhala; Steerforth Press
Orders to: Random House, Inc, Distribution
Center, 400 Hahn Rd, Westminister, MD
21157 *Toll Free Tel:* 800-726-0600 *Toll Free
Fax:* 800-659-2436
Returns: Random House Inc Returns Dept, 1019
N State Rd 47, Crawfordsville, IN 47933

Random House Value Publishing
Affiliate of Random House Inc
1745 Broadway, New York, NY 10019
Tel: 212-940-7422 *Fax:* 212-572-2114
Key Personnel
Pres, Audio & Diversified Publishing Group:
David Naggar
VP & Publr, Value Publishing: Sheryl Stebbins
Ed: Celeste Sollod
Founded: 1933
Hardcover & illustrated & non-illustrated, nonfic-
tion, adult fiction & gift.
Random House Inc & its publishing entities are
not accepting unsol submissions, proposals,
mss, or submission queries via e-mail at this
time.
ISBN Prefix(es): 0-609
Total Titles: 750 Print
Imprints: Children's Classics; Crescent;
Gramercy; Testament; Wings

Rapids Christian Press Inc
Division of Gunderson Publications
5777 Vista Dr, Ferndale, WA 98248
Mailing Address: PO Box 717, Ferndale, WA
98248-0717
Tel: 360-384-1747 *Fax:* 360-384-1747
Key Personnel
Pres, Gunderson Publications: Bob Hong
Tel: 360-738-1530 *E-mail:* bob.hong@sim.org
VP: Robert L Samms *Tel:* 360-392-0338
Treas, Gunderson Publications: David Hung
Tel: 360-734-1124
Ed: Wilfred E Gunderson *E-mail:* gundersonwv@
aol.com
Founded: 1960 (by Clifford & Carol Miller. 1995
became div of nonprofit Gunderson Publica-
tions Inc)

Prepare, translate & distribute religious & educational materials.
ISBN Prefix(es): 0-915374
Number of titles published annually: 3 Print; 4 Audio
Total Titles: 60 Print; 6 Audio

Rational Island Publishers
719 Second Ave N, Seattle, WA 98109
Mailing Address: Main Office Sta, PO Box 2081, Seattle, WA 98111-2081
Tel: 206-284-0311 *Fax:* 206-284-8429
E-mail: ircc@rc.org
Web Site: www.rc.org
Key Personnel
Contact: Karen Slaney
Founded: 1954
Articles about re-evaluation counseling (co-counseling) - the theory, the practice, the applications & implications.
ISBN Prefix(es): 0-911214; 0-913937; 1-885357
Number of titles published annually: 6 Print
Total Titles: 257 Print

§Rattapallax Press
532 LaGuardia Place, Suite 353, New York, NY 10012
Tel: 212-560-7459
Web Site: www.rattapallax.com
Key Personnel
Publr: Ram Devineni *E-mail:* devineni@rattapallax.com
Founded: 2000
ISBN Prefix(es): 1-892494
Number of titles published annually: 4 Print; 1 CD-ROM; 15 Online; 15 E-Book; 15 Audio
Total Titles: 15 Print; 1 CD-ROM; 15 Online; 15 E-Book; 15 Audio
Distributed by Biblo Distribution; Ingram Periodicals
Membership(s): Council of Literary Magazines & Presses

Raven Tree Press LLC
200 S Washington St, Suite 306, Green Bay, WI 54301
SAN: 253-6005
Tel: 920-438-1605 *Toll Free Tel:* 877-256-0579
Fax: 920-438-1607
E-mail: raven@raventreepress.com
Web Site: www.raventreepress.com
Key Personnel
Man Partner: Dawn Jeffers *Tel:* 920-438-1605 ext 442 *E-mail:* dawn@raventreepress.com
Art Dir: Rob Kruszynski *Tel:* 920-438-1605 ext 441 *E-mail:* rob@raventreepress.com
Ed: Amy Crane Johnson *Tel:* 920-438-1605 ext 444 *E-mail:* amy@raventreepress.com
Founded: 2000
Specialize in bilingual children's picture books. Also offers services for self-publishing.
ISBN Prefix(es): 0-9701107; 0-9720192; 0-9724973
Number of titles published annually: 10 Print
Total Titles: 20 Print
Distributed by BWI; Follett; Quality Books
Membership(s): Children's Book Council; Publishers Marketing Association; Society of Children's Book Writers & Illustrators; Upper Midwest Booksellers Association

§Ravenhawk™ Books
Division of The 6DOF Group
7739 E Broadway Blvd, No 95, Tucson, AZ 85710
Tel: 520-296-4491 *Fax:* 520-296-4491
E-mail: ravenhawk6dof@yahoo.com
Web Site: ravenhawk.biz
Key Personnel
Publr: Carl Lasky
Sales: Hans B Shepherd, Jr
Founded: 1998

Royalty publisher specializing in general trade, hard/softcover, fiction, nonfiction, self-help, teaching texts for professionals, crime, mystery & suspense fiction. E-books, CD/DVD audio books (audiobooks available late December 2001). Ms submissions are by invitation only through acknowledged literary agents.
ISBN Prefix(es): 1-893660
Number of titles published annually: 6 Print; 4 CD-ROM; 4 Online; 6 E-Book; 4 Audio
Total Titles: 8 Print; 1 Online; 2 E-Book
Imprints: Ravenhawk AudioBooks; RavenhawkCD/DVD; Ravenhawk VideoBooks
Editorial Office(s): 999 N Via Zahara del sol, Tucson, AZ 85748
Distributed by Lightning Source Inc
Advertising Agency: Gordley Design Group Inc, 2540 N Tucson Blvd, Tucson, AZ 85716, Contact: Jan Gordley *Tel:* 520-327-6077 *Fax:* 520-327-4687
Membership(s): Interactive Creative Artists Network; National Writers Association; Small Publishers Association of North America; Society of Southwestern Authors

Rayve Productions Inc
PO Box 726, Windsor, CA 95492
SAN: 248-4250
Tel: 707-838-6200 *Toll Free Tel:* 800-852-4890
Fax: 707-838-2220
E-mail: rayvepro@aol.com
Web Site: www.rayveproductions.com; www.foodandwinebooks.com
Key Personnel
Pres: Norm Ray
VP & Ed-in-Chief: Barbara F Ray
Founded: 1989
Business guidebooks, quality children's books & music, history books, counseling, parenting, caregiving & cook books.
ISBN Prefix(es): 1-877810; 1-893718; 0-9629927
Number of titles published annually: 5 Print
Total Titles: 37 Print; 1 CD-ROM; 1 Audio
Imprints: Hoffman Press Division (food & wine cookbooks); LifeTimes; Minimed Series; Toucan Tales
Divisions: Rayve Fulfillment
Distributed by Lippincott, Williams & Wilkins
Advertising Agency: Windsor Advertising, PO Box 1013, Windsor, CA, Contact: Cynthia Thomas
Returns: Rayve Fulfillment, 7836 Bell Rd, Windsor, CA 95492, Contact: Tom Novak *Tel:* 707-838-2740 *Fax:* 707-838-2740 *E-mail:* fulfrayve@sbcglobal.net
Shipping Address: 7836 Bell Rd, Windsor, CA 95492, Contact: Tom Novak *Tel:* 707-838-2740 *E-mail:* fulfrayve@sbcglobal.net
Membership(s): Publishers Marketing Association

RCL Resources for Christian Living
Division of RCL Enterprises, Inc
200 E Bethany, Allen, TX 75002
SAN: 298-7104
Tel: 972-390-6300 *Toll Free Tel:* 800-527-5030
Fax: 972-390-6560 *Toll Free Fax:* 800-688-8356
E-mail: cservice@rcl-enterprises.com
Web Site: www.rclweb.com
Key Personnel
Publr: Mary Ann Nead *Tel:* 972-390-6891
VP, Dir, Sales & Mktg: Mike Raffio *Tel:* 877-755-6614 *E-mail:* mraffio@rcl-enterprises.com
Founded: 1970
ISBN Prefix(es): 0-7829
Number of titles published annually: 20 Print
Total Titles: 80 Print
Foreign Rep(s): B Broughton (Canada); Charles Payne (Australia); Redemptorist (UK)

§Read Only Productions
Division of Ropes LLC

399 Alameda de la Loma, Novato, CA 94947
Mailing Address: PO Box 1535, Novato, CA 94948-1535
Tel: 415-883-7583
Key Personnel
Mgr: Harlan Cain *E-mail:* harlan@comprend.com
Producer: Mike Campos *Tel:* 415-892-1573 *E-mail:* mikec@comprend.com
Founded: 1995
Full-service integrated design, development & production of e-books, print books & audio books for publishers & authors for all current & future delivery media & platforms: traditional print, Adobe Reader, Microsoft Reader, Palm, CD, tape & MP3.
Number of titles published annually: 7 E-Book; 5 Audio

Reader's Digest Association Inc
Reader's Digest Rd, Pleasantville, NY 10570-7000
SAN: 212-4416
Tel: 914-238-1000 *Toll Free Tel:* 800-431-1726
Fax: 914-238-4559
Web Site: www.rd.com *Telex:* 42-1171 *Cable:* READIGEST PLVE NY
Key Personnel
Chmn & CEO: Thomas Ryder
Sr VP & Gen Coun: Michael A Brizel
Sr VP & Pres, Intl: Tom Gardner
Sr VP & CFO: Michael S Geltzeiler
VP & Circ Dir: Dawn Zier
VP & Treas: William H Magill
VP & Publg Dir: Laura McEwen
Membership(s): AAP
See separate listing for:
Reader's Digest General Books
Reader's Digest Trade Books
Reader's Digest USA Select Editions

Reader's Digest Children's Books
Subsidiary of Reader's Digest USA
Reader's Digest Rd, Pleasantville, NY 10570-7000
SAN: 283-2143
Tel: 914-244-4800 *Toll Free Tel:* 800-934-0977
Key Personnel
Chmn & CEO: Thomas O Ryder
Sr VP & Gen Coun: Michael A Brizel
Sr VP & CFO: Michael S Geltzeiler
VP & Treas: William H Magill
VP & Publg Dir: Laura McEwen
VP & Publr: Harold Clarke
Dir, Sales & Mktg: Debra Polansky
Assoc Publr: Roseanne McManus
Founded: 1994
Publishers & direct marketers of children's fiction & nonfiction.
ISBN Prefix(es): 1-57584
Number of titles published annually: 75 Print
Total Titles: 300 Print

Reader's Digest General Books
Division of Reader's Digest Association Inc
Reader's Digest Rd, Pleasantville, NY 10570-7000
SAN: 240-9720
Tel: 914-238-1000 *Toll Free Tel:* 800-431-1726 *Fax:* 914-244-7436 *Telex:* 42-1171 *Cable:* READIGEST PLVE NY
Key Personnel
Chmn & CEO: Thomas O Ryder
Sr VP & Gen Coun: Michael A Brizel
Sr VP & Pres, Intl: Thomas D Gardner
Sr VP & CFO: Michael S Geltzeiler
VP & Circ Dir: Dawn Zier
VP & Treas: William H Magill
VP & Exec Publr, Reader's Digest U.S. Magazines: Dominick F Rossi, Jr
Sr VP & Pres, North America & Global Ed-in-Chief: Eric Schrier
VP, Gen Mgr, Home & Health: Keira Krausz

Mgr, Rts & Perms: Lisa Garrett Smith
Founded: 1961
Direct marketed reference books on home maintenance & repair, health & fitness, crafts & hobbies, history, cooking, travel, geography, religion, nature, law, medicine, gardening, English usage & vocabulary.
ISBN Prefix(es): 0-89577

Reader's Digest Trade Books
Division of Reader's Digest Association Inc
Reader's Digest Rd, Pleasantville, NY 10570-7000
SAN: 240-9720
Tel: 914-244-7445 *Fax:* 914-244-7605 *Cable:* READIGEST NY
Key Personnel
Chmn & CEO: Thomas O Ryder
Sr VP & Gen Coun: Michael A Brizel
Sr VP & Pres, Intl: Thomas D Gardner
Sr VP & CFO: Michael S Geltzeiler
VP & Circ Dir: Dawn Zier
VP & Treas: William H Magill
VP & Publg Dir: Laura McEwen
VP & Publr: Harold Clarke
Dir, Trade Publg: Chris Reggio
Mgr, Mktg: Marina Shults
Mgr, Rts & Perms: Lisa Garrett Smith
Man Ed: Dolores York
Founded: 1971
Illustrated trade (retail) reference books on home maintenance & repair, gardening, home decorating, crafts, art instruction, cooking & health, parenting & family reference, religion & inspiration, science & nature, travel & atlases, humor.
ISBN Prefix(es): 0-7621
Number of titles published annually: 50 Print
Total Titles: 300 Print
Distributed by Penguin Putnam Inc

Reader's Digest USA Select Editions
Division of Reader's Digest Association Inc
Reader's Digest Rd, Pleasantville, NY 10570-7000
SAN: 212-4416
Tel: 914-238-1000 *Toll Free Tel:* 800-310-6261 *Fax:* 914-238-4559 *Telex:* 42-1171 *Cable:* READIGEST PLVE NY
Key Personnel
Chmn & CEO: Thomas O Ryder
Sr VP & Gen Coun: Michael A Brizel
Sr VP & Pres, Intl: Thomas D Gardner
Sr VP & CFO: Michael S Geltzeiler
VP & Circ Dir: Dawn Zier
VP & Treas: William H Magill
VP & Publg Dir: Laura McEwen
VP & Global Ed-in-Chief: Laura Kelly
Mktg Dir: Kathy Haggerty
Founded: 1950
Publishers of current fiction & general nonfiction in condensed form.
ISBN Prefix(es): 0-89577

Record Research Inc
PO Box 200, Menomonee Falls, WI 53052
Tel: 262-251-5408 *Toll Free Tel:* 800-827-9810 *Fax:* 262-251-9452
E-mail: books@recordresearch.com
Web Site: www.recordresearch.com
Key Personnel
Pres: Joel Whitburn
1st VP: Bill Hathaway
VP: Kim Bloxdorf *Tel:* 262-251-9212
Founded: 1970
Publish reference books authored by Joel Whitburn based on Billboard magazine's music & videocassette chart data.
ISBN Prefix(es): 0-89820
Number of titles published annually: 4 Print
Total Titles: 44 Print

Recorded Books LLC
Division of Haights Cross Communications Inc
270 Skipjack Rd, Prince Frederick, MD 20678
SAN: 677-8887
Tel: 410-535-5590 *Toll Free Tel:* 800-638-1304 *Fax:* 410-535-5499
E-mail: recordedbooks@recordedbooks.com
Web Site: www.recordedbooks.com
Key Personnel
Pres: David Berset *Tel:* 410-535-5590 ext 1110 *E-mail:* bersetd@aol.com
COO: Scott Williams *Tel:* 410-535-5590 ext 1214 *E-mail:* swilliams@recordedbooks.com
Publr: Brian Downing *Tel:* 410-535-5590 ext 1142 *E-mail:* bdowning@recordedbooks.com
Natl Sales Dir: Jim Peterson *Tel:* 410-535-5590 ext 1301 *E-mail:* jpete90184@aol.com
Natl Training Dir: Jim Schmidt *Tel:* 410-535-5590 ext 1305 *E-mail:* james.schmidt7@gte.net
VP, Opers: Edward Longo *Tel:* 410-535-5590 ext 1180 *E-mail:* elongo@recordedbooks.com
Founded: 1979
Premier publisher of unabridged audiobooks. Provides unabridged books on cassette, CD & web for consumer markets, libraries & schools. Also publishes 100 books in large print.
ISBN Prefix(es): 0-7887; 1-4025
Number of titles published annually: 100 Print; 250 CD-ROM; 100 Online; 50 E-Book; 787 Audio
Total Titles: 100 Print; 1,000 CD-ROM; 100 Online; 50 E-Book; 5,808 Audio
Imprints: Clipper Audio (UK); Griot Audio; Lone Star Audio; Recorded Books Audiolibros; Recorded Books Development; Recorded Books Inspirational; Recorded Books Large Print; Recorded Books Publishing; Romantic Sounds Audio; Smithsonian College Lecture Series; Southern Voices
Branch Office(s)
Audio Adventures, 200 Skipjack Rd, Prince Frederick, MD 20678, Contact: Scott Williams *Toll Free Tel:* 800-580-2989 *Fax:* 303-443-3775 *Web Site:* www.landmarkaudio.com
Foreign Office(s): WF Howes (Recorded Books), Unit 3, Victoria Mills, Fowke St, Rothley, Leics LE7 7PJ, United Kingdom, Man Dir: Ron Moody *Tel:* (011) 0016-230-1144 *Fax:* (011) 0016-230-1155
Distributor for Buena Vista DVDs; The Film Movement DVDs
Distribution Center: Audio Adventures, 200 Shipjack Rd, Prince Frederick, MD 20678, Contact: Scott Williams *Toll Free Tel:* 800-580-2989 *Fax:* 303-443-3775 *Web Site:* www.landmarkaudio.com
Membership(s): Audio Publishers Association

Red Crane Books Inc
PO Box 33950, Santa Fe, NM 87594-3950
Tel: 505-988-7070 *Fax:* 505-989-7476
E-mail: publish@redcrane.com
Web Site: www.redcrane.com
Key Personnel
Publr & Intl Rts: Michael O'Shaughnessy *Fax:* 505-986-1325 *E-mail:* michael@redcrane.com
Edit: Marianne O'Shaughnessy *E-mail:* marianne@redcrane.com
Founded: 1989
Books which explore the cultures of the Americas & bring the voice of the people to a broad readership.
ISBN Prefix(es): 1-878610
Number of titles published annually: 3 Print
Total Titles: 46 Print
Warehouse: Consortium Book Sales & Distribution, 1045 Westgate Dr, Suite 90, St Paul, MN 55114-1065 *Toll Free Tel:* 800-283-3572 *Fax:* 651-912-6406 *E-mail:* mcashin@cbsd.com

Red Dust Inc
Box 630, Gracie Sta, New York, NY 10028

SAN: 203-3860
Tel: 212-348-4388
E-mail: reddustjg@aol.com
Key Personnel
Pres & Publr: Joanna Gunderson
Founded: 1963
Works by new writers; fiction, poetry, nonsequential poetic texts.
ISBN Prefix(es): 0-87376
Number of titles published annually: 4 Print
Total Titles: 84 Print

Red Hen Press
PO Box 3537, Granada Hills, CA 91394-0537
Tel: 818-831-0649 *Fax:* 818-831-6659
E-mail: editors@redhen.org
Web Site: www.redhen.org
Key Personnel
Pres: Mark E Cull *E-mail:* mark@redhen.org
Ed: Kate Gale *E-mail:* kate@redhen.org; Peter Pryor
Founded: 1994
Publish perfect bound collections of poetry, short stories & books of a literary nature. Also sponser several literary awards, along with the literary journal "The Los Angeles Review".
ISBN Prefix(es): 0-9639528; 1-888996
Number of titles published annually: 10 Print
Total Titles: 57 Print
Distributed by Small Press Distribution
Membership(s): AWP; Council of Literary Magazines & Presses

Red Moon Press
PO Box 2461, Winchester, VA 22604-1661
Tel: 540-722-2156 *Fax:* 708-810-8992
E-mail: redmoon@shentel.net
Key Personnel
Owner & Publr: Jim Kacian
Founded: 1993
Largest & most prestigious publisher of English-language haiku & related forms in the world.
ISBN Prefix(es): 1-9657818; 1-893959
Number of titles published annually: 10 Print
Total Titles: 60 Print
Imprints: Pond Frog Editions; Soffietto Editions
Distributed by John Weatherhill Inc

Red River Press
Imprint of Archival Services Inc
3900 Roy Rd, Suite 37, Shreveport, LA 71107
Tel: 318-929-4196 *Fax:* 318-929-5125
E-mail: redriverpresskws@yahoo.com
Web Site: www.achivalservices.com
Key Personnel
Pres & CEO: Kevin Sandifer
VP: Glen Sandifer
Publr: Susan Gross
Sr Ed: Shaun Grimshaw
Founded: 1980
ISBN Prefix(es): 0-910653
Number of titles published annually: 21 Print
Total Titles: 60 Print

Red Rock Press
459 Columbus Ave, Suite 114, New York, NY 10024
Tel: 212-362-6216 *Fax:* 212-362-6216
E-mail: info@redrockpress.com
Web Site: www.redrockpress.com
Key Personnel
Creative Dir: Ilene Barth
Founded: 1998
ISBN Prefix(es): 0-97143; 0-96695
Number of titles published annually: 5 Print
Total Titles: 16 Print
Foreign Rep(s): Lora Fountain Association (France & Spain, Russia); E A Milley (Canada)
Distribution Center: Whitehurst & Clark, Flemington, NJ
Membership(s): AAP; Publishers Marketing Association

Red Sea Press Inc

541 W Ingham Ave, Suite B, Trenton, NJ 08638
Mailing Address: PO Box 1892, Trenton, NJ 08607
Tel: 609-695-3200 *Fax:* 609-695-6466
E-mail: awprsp@africanworld.com; awprsp@intac.com
Web Site: www.africanworld.com
Key Personnel
Publr & Pres: Checole Kassahun
Opers Mgr: Senait Kassahun
Founded: 1985
Publisher of books on the Horn of Africa, Latin America; distributor of books on the Third World.
ISBN Prefix(es): 0-932415; 1-56902
Number of titles published annually: 20 Print
Total Titles: 200 Print; 10 Online; 10 E-Book
Imprints: Karnak House
Branch Office(s)
East Africa, PO Box 48, Asmara, Eritrea
Tel: 291-1-120707 *Fax:* 291-1-123369
Foreign Rights: Turnaround Publisher Services (Europe, London)

Red Wheel/Weiser/Conari

368 Congress St, 4th fl, Boston, MA 02210
SAN: 202-9588
Tel: 617-542-1324 *Toll Free Tel:* 800-423-7087
Fax: 617-482-9676
Web Site: www.redwheelweiser.com
Key Personnel
Pres & CEO: Michael Kerber *Tel:* 617-542-1324 ext 101
Publr: Jan Johnson *Tel:* 617-542-1324 ext 102
Founded: 1956
Self-help & spirituality, inspiration, gift books, wicca, tarot, magic & esoteric & occult subjects from many traditions.
ISBN Prefix(es): 0-943233 (Conari); 0-87728 (Weiser); 1-57863 (Weiser); 1-59003 (Red Wheel); 1-57324 (Conari)
Number of titles published annually: 80 Print
Total Titles: 700 Print
Distributor for Nicolas Hays Inc
Foreign Rep(s): Airlift Book Co (UK); Bookwise (Australia); Raincoast (Canada)
Foreign Rights: Bookbank SA (Spain); English Agency (Japan); Karin Schindler (Brazil)
Warehouse: Books International, 22883 Quicksilver Dr, Dulles, VA 20166
Distribution Center: PO Box 612, York Beach, ME 03910-0612 *Tel:* 207-363-4393 SAN: 202-9588
Membership(s): ABA

Redleaf Press

Division of Resources for Child Caring Inc
10 Yorkton Ct, St Paul, MN 55117
SAN: 212-8691
Tel: 651-641-0305 *Toll Free Tel:* 800-423-8309
Toll Free Fax: 800-641-0115
Web Site: www.redleafpress.org
Key Personnel
Dir: Eileen M Nelson
Prodn Mgr: James Cihlar
Opers Mgr: Paul Bloomer
Mkt Mgr: Lisa Bayer
Founded: 1978
Early childhood curriculum, development & professionalism, family day care business & record keeping.
ISBN Prefix(es): 0-934140; 1-884834; 1-929610
Number of titles published annually: 9 Print
Total Titles: 91 Print
Distributed by Consortium Book Sales & Distribution (Trade Market); Gryphon House (Education Market); Monarch Books of Canada (Canadian Market)
Foreign Rep(s): Monarch Books (Canada); Pademelon Press (Australia)

Robert D Reed Publishers

Formerly Monterey Pacific Publishing
PO Box 1992, Brandon, OR 97411-1192
Tel: 541-347-9882 *Fax:* 541-347-9883
E-mail: 4bobreed@msn.com
Web Site: www.rdrpublishers.com
Key Personnel
Publr: Robert D Reed
Founded: 1977
All types of publications for trade, educational institutions, individuals & corporations.
ISBN Prefix(es): 1-889710; 1-885003; 1-931741
Number of titles published annually: 15 Print
Total Titles: 120 Print
Foreign Rep(s): Harry Smith

Thomas Reed Publications Inc

398 Columbus Ave, Box 302, Boston, MA 02116
Tel: 617-236-0465 *Toll Free Tel:* 800-995-4995 (customer service)
E-mail: info@reedsalmanac.com; order@reedsalmanac.com
Web Site: www.reedsalmanac.com
Key Personnel
Pres: Jerald D Knopf *E-mail:* jdk@reedsalmanac.com
Founded: 1782
Publisher & distributor of nautical books.
ISBN Prefix(es): 1-884666
Number of titles published annually: 4 Print
Total Titles: 8 Print

Reedswain Inc

562 Ridge Rd, Spring City, PA 19475
Tel: 610-469-6911 *Toll Free Tel:* 800-331-5191
Fax: 610-495-6632
Web Site: www.reedswain.com
Key Personnel
Pres & For Rts: Richard Kentwell
Founded: 1987
Soccer coaching books.
ISBN Prefix(es): 1-8909
Number of titles published annually: 23 Print
Total Titles: 146 Print
Foreign Rights: Richard Kentwell (World)

Referee Books

Imprint of Referee Enterprises Inc
2017 Lathrop Ave, Racine, WI 53405
Mailing Address: PO Box 161, Franksville, WI 53401-0161
Tel: 262-632-8855 *Toll Free Tel:* 800-733-6100
Fax: 262-632-5460
E-mail: questions@referee.com
Web Site: www.referee.com
Key Personnel
Adv & Group Sales Mgr: Patrick Miles
E-mail: pmiles@referee.com
Founded: 1975
Publish sports officiating publications; magazines, books, manuals & booklets on officiating, umpiring, baseball, basketball, football, soccer, softball & athletics referee books.
ISBN Prefix(es): 1-58208; 0-9660209
Number of titles published annually: 6 Print
Total Titles: 45 Print

Referee Magazine, see Referee Books

Reference Publications Inc

218 Saint Clair River Dr, Algonac, MI 48001
SAN: 208-4392
Mailing Address: PO Box 344, Algonac, MI 48001-0344
Tel: 810-794-5722 *Fax:* 810-794-7463
E-mail: referencepub@sbcglobal.com
Key Personnel
Pres, Ed & Rts & Perms: Marie Aline Irvine
Dir, Mktg: Dominique Irvine
Legal Counsel: John Somers
Founded: 1975

Mail order & reference books. Specialize in botanical & medicinal plants, Americana, Amerindian & African reference books & botanical works.
ISBN Prefix(es): 0-917256
Number of titles published annually: 2 Print
Total Titles: 25 Print
Imprints: Encyclopaedia Africana
Divisions: Encyclopaedia Africana

§Reference Service Press

5000 Windplay Dr, Suite 4, El Dorado Hills, CA 95762-9600
Tel: 916-939-9620 *Fax:* 916-939-9626
E-mail: findaid@aol.com
Web Site: www.rspfunding.com
Key Personnel
Pres: Gail Schlachter
Founded: 1975
ISBN Prefix(es): 0-918276
Number of titles published annually: 15 Print; 3 CD-ROM; 1 Online; 10 E-Book
Total Titles: 25 Print; 3 CD-ROM; 1 Online; 15 E-Book

Reformation Heritage Books

2919 Leonard St NE, Grand Rapids, MI 49525
Tel: 616-977-0599 *Fax:* 616-285-3246
E-mail: orders@heritagebooks.org
Web Site: www.heritagebooks.org
Key Personnel
Chmn: Joel R Beeke
Pres: Gary Swets
Founded: 1993
Sell new & used religious books with emphasis on experiential religion. Also republish out-of-print Puritan works.
ISBN Prefix(es): 1-892777
Number of titles published annually: 4 Print
Total Titles: 20 Print; 6 E-Book

§Regal Books

Division of Gospel Light
1957 Eastman Ave, Ventura, CA 93003
SAN: 203-3852
Mailing Address: PO Box 3875, Ventura, CA 93006
Tel: 805-644-9721 *Toll Free Tel:* 800-446-7735 (orders) *Fax:* 805-644-9728 (editorial); 805-644-4729 (purchasing); 805-650-8713 (sales & corp serv); 805-658-3388 (orders)
Toll Free Fax: 800-860-3109 (orders)
E-mail: info@regalbooks.com
Web Site: www.gospellight.com
Key Personnel
Chmn of the Bd: William T Greig, Jr
Pres: Bill T Greig, III
Prodn Mgr: Nola Grunden
Sales Mgr: Bill Schultz
Dir, Publicity: Marlene Baer
Perms: Hilary Young
Ed: Deena Davis; Steven Lawson
Edit Asst: Amy Simpson
Founded: 1933
Religion, education for church leaders.
ISBN Prefix(es): 0-8307
Number of titles published annually: 35 Print
Foreign Rep(s): African Christian Literature Advance (South Africa); S John Bacon Pty Ltd (Australia, South Pacific); Christian Literature Crusade (Japan); Gospel Light Publishers (Europe); Libreria Betania (Puerto Rico); R G Mitchell Family Books Ltd (Canada); G W Moore Ltd (New Zealand); OMF Publishers (Philippines); S & U Book Centre (Singapore)
Foreign Rights: GLINT (World)
Advertising Agency: Light Advertising

Regatta Press Ltd

750 Cascadilla St, Ithaca, NY 14851
SAN: 202-1862
Mailing Address: PO Box 6525, Ithaca, NY 14851

Tel: 607-277-2211 *Fax:* 607-277-6292
Toll Free Fax: 800-688-2877
E-mail: info@regattapress.com
Web Site: www.regattapress.com
Key Personnel
Publr: Sean M Culhane *E-mail:* smc@
regattapress.com
Dir, Sales & Mktg: William Tautkus *E-mail:* bt@
regattapress.com
Founded: 1999
Publishers of high-quality works in maritime
studies.
ISBN Prefix(es): 0-9674826
Number of titles published annually: 2 Print
Total Titles: 8 Print
Editorial Office(s): PO Box 17408, Arling-
ton, VA 22216-7408, Contact: Sean Culhane
E-mail: smc@regattapress.com
Sales Office(s): PO Box 17408, Arlington, VA
22216-7408, Contact: Bill Tautkus *E-mail:* bt@
regattapress.com
Membership(s): AAP; Independent Publisher's
Guild

Reggae Original Foundation International, see
Cornerstone Productions Inc

Regnery Publishing Inc
Subsidiary of Eagle Publishing
One Massachusetts Ave, NW, Suite 600, Wash-
ington, DC 20001
Tel: 202-216-0600 *Toll Free Tel:* 888-219-4747
Fax: 202-216-0612
E-mail: editorial@regnery.com
Web Site: www.regnery.com
Key Personnel
Pres & Publr: Marji Ross
Exec Ed: Harry Crocker
Publicity Dir: Kelly Keeler
Foreign Rts: Alex Hoyt *Tel:* 212-663-7089
Founded: 1947
Nonfiction trade; college paperbound classics.
ISBN Prefix(es): 0-89526
Number of titles published annually: 30 Print
Imprints: Gateway Editions
Foreign Rep(s): Les Petriw & Assoc (Canada)

Regular Baptist Press
Division of General Association of Regular Bap-
tist Churches
1300 N Meacham Rd, Schaumburg, IL 60173-
4806
Tel: 847-843-1600 *Toll Free Tel:* 800-727-4440
(orders only); 888-588-1600 *Fax:* 847-843-
3757
E-mail: rbp@garbc.org
Web Site: www.regularbaptistpress.org
Key Personnel
Exec Dir: David Gower
Book Ed & Intl Rts Contact: Norman A Olson
Founded: 1932
Curriculum & Christian books.
ISBN Prefix(es): 0-87227
Number of titles published annually: 4 Print

Rei America Inc
10049 NW 89 Ave, No 13-14, Miami, FL 33178
Tel: 305-805-0771 *Toll Free Tel:* 800-726-5337
Fax: 305-887-4138
Web Site: www.reiamericainc.com
Key Personnel
Pres: Francisco C Castro
Mktg Mgr: Javier Castro *E-mail:* jcastro@
reiamericainc.com
Founded: 1988
Software & educational textbooks for Spanish
speakers, Spanish as a second language.
ISBN Prefix(es): 1-56340
Number of titles published annually: 3 Print

Renaissance Alliance Publishing Inc
8691 Ninth Ave, PMB 210, Port Arthur, TX
77642-8025
Fax: 409-727-4824
E-mail: regalcrest@gt.rr.com
Web Site: www.rapbooks.biz; www.regalcrest.biz
Key Personnel
Owner & Mgr: Cathy Lenoir *Tel:* 409-727-4824
Pres: B Coles
Founded: 1999
ISBN Prefix(es): 1-932300
Number of titles published annually: 16 Print
Total Titles: 13 Print
Membership(s): Better Business Bureau

Renaissance House
Imprint of Laredo Publishing Co
9400 Lloydcrest Dr, Beverly Hills, CA 90210
Tel: 310-860-9930 *Toll Free Tel:* 800-547-5113
Fax: 310-860-9902
Web Site: renaissancehouse.net
Key Personnel
Pres: Sam Laredo *E-mail:* laredo@
renaissancehouse.net
Edit Dir: Raquel Benatar *E-mail:* raquel@
renaissancehouse.net
Founded: 1991
Publisher of high quality & highly illustrated
children's books. Specialize in Spanish bilin-
gual books.
ISBN Prefix(es): 1-56492
Number of titles published annually: 30 Print
Total Titles: 70 Print
Distributed by SRA/McGraw-Hill

Reprint Services Corp
PO Box 890820, Temecula, CA 92589-0820
Toll Free Tel: 800-273-6635 *Fax:* 909-767-0133
Key Personnel
Owner: Mike Kelly
Founded: 1988
Reprint of scholarly books.
ISBN Prefix(es): 0-7812
Number of titles published annually: 1,000 Print
Total Titles: 9,000 Print

Research & Education Association
61 Ethel Rd W, Piscataway, NJ 08854
Tel: 732-819-8880 *Fax:* 732-819-8808
E-mail: info@rea.com
Web Site: www.rea.com
Key Personnel
Pres: Max Fogiel
VP, Opers: Carl Fuchs *E-mail:* c.fuchs@rea.com
Cust Serv Mgr: Pamela Weston *E-mail:* p.
weston@rea.com
Founded: 1959
Professional books, secondary & college study
guides & test preparation books, biology, busi-
ness, engineering, mathematics, general sci-
ence, history, social sciences, accounting &
computer science.
ISBN Prefix(es): 0-87891; 0-7386
Number of titles published annually: 50 Print; 10
CD-ROM; 5 Audio
Total Titles: 600 Print; 26 CD-ROM; 7 Audio
Foreign Rep(s): Gage Distribution Co (Canada);
Plymbridge Distributors Ltd (UK, Spain, Swe-
den, Switzerland)

Research Press
2612 N Mattis Ave, Champaign, IL 61822
SAN: 203-381X
Mailing Address: PO Box 9177, Champaign, IL
61826-9177
Tel: 217-352-3273 *Toll Free Tel:* 800-519-2707
Fax: 217-352-1221
E-mail: rp@researchpress.com
Web Site: www.researchpress.com
Key Personnel
Chmn of the Bd: Judy Vacanti
Pres: Ann Wendel

Man Ed & Rts & Perms: Karen Steiner
VP, Mktg: Russell E Pence *E-mail:* rpence@
researchpress.com
Prodn Mgr: Jeff Helgesen
Intl Rts: Gail Salyards
Sec: A O Parkinson
Founded: 1969
ISBN Prefix(es): 0-87822
Number of titles published annually: 12 Print; 2
CD-ROM
Total Titles: 160 Print; 2 CD-ROM; 2 Audio
Foreign Rep(s): Astam Books (Australia); Incen-
tive Plus (UK)
Foreign Rights: Writer's House

§Resource Publications Inc
160 E Virginia St, Suite 290, San Jose, CA
95112-5876
SAN: 209-3081
Tel: 408-286-8505 *Fax:* 408-287-8748
E-mail: orders@rpinet.com
Web Site: www.rpinet.com
Key Personnel
Pres: William Burns *E-mail:* wjb@rpinet.com
Edit Mgr: Helen St Paul
Opers Busn Mgr: Mary J Dent *E-mail:* maryd@
rpinet.com
Mktg Dir, Electronic Publg & Intl Rts: Kathy
Truman
Prepress Mgr: Liz Asborno *E-mail:* liza@rpinet.
com
Founded: 1973
Hardcover & paperback, reference, religious trade
& general trade books, textbooks & periodi-
cals with emphasis on peer counseling, applied
storytelling, recovery & personal growth & on
imagination & creative resources for leaders &
artists.
ISBN Prefix(es): 0-89390
Number of titles published annually: 12 Print; 2
CD-ROM; 3 Online; 3 Audio
Total Titles: 245 Print; 2 CD-ROM; 3 Online; 10
Audio
Foreign Rep(s): Catholic Supplies (New Zealand);
Columba Book Service (Europe); Preca Library
(Malta); St Pauls India (India); Word of Life
Books (Australia)

Resources for Rehabilitation
22 Bonard Rd, Winchester, MA 01890
Tel: 781-368-9094 *Fax:* 781-368-9096
E-mail: info@rfr.org
Web Site: www.rfr.org
Key Personnel
Dir: Susan L Greenblatt *E-mail:* slg@rfr.org
Founded: 1987
Nonprofit publisher of resource guides (directo-
ries) & anthologies in disability & health.
ISBN Prefix(es): 0-929718
Number of titles published annually: 4 Print; 4 E-
Book
Total Titles: 10 Print; 10 E-Book; 2 Audio

§Resources for the Future
1616 "P" St NW, Washington, DC 20036-1400
SAN: 213-1544
Tel: 202-328-5086 *Fax:* 202-328-5137
E-mail: rffpress@rff.org
Web Site: www.rffpress.org
Key Personnel
Dir, Intl Rts: Don Reisman
Mktg Mgr: Meg Keller *E-mail:* keller@rff.org
Prodn Mgr: John Deever
Founded: 1952
ISBN Prefix(es): 0-915707; 0-8018; 1-891853
Number of titles published annually: 20 Print
Total Titles: 110 Print; 17 E-Book
Imprints: RFF Press
Distributed by The Johns Hopkins University
Press
Foreign Rep(s): Academic Book Promotions
(Benelux, Denmark, France, Iceland, Scandi-

navia); Arie Ruitenbeek (Spain & Portugal); Cambridge University Press (Australia & New Zealand); Information Publications Pte Ltd (SE Asia, including China); Trevor Brown Associates (Austria, Germany)
Orders to: RFF Press Customer Service, c/o Johns Hopkins University Press Fulfillment Services, PO Box 50370, Baltimore, MD 21211-4370 *Tel:* 410-516-6965 *Toll Free Tel:* 800-537-5487 *Fax:* 410-516-6998 *E-mail:* rffpress@rff.org
Returns: Hopkins Fulfillment Services c/o Maple Press Co, Lebanon Distribution Center, 704 Legionnaire Dr, Fredricksburg, PA 17026 *Tel:* 410-516-6955
Shipping Address: RFF Press Customer Service, c/o Johns Hopkins University Press Fulfillment Services, PO Box 50370, Baltimore, MD 21211-4370 *Tel:* 410-516-6965 *Toll Free Tel:* 800-537-5487 *Fax:* 410-516-6998 *E-mail:* rffpress@rff.org
Warehouse: RFF Press Customer Service, c/o Johns Hopkins University Press Fulfillment Services, PO Box 50370, Baltimore, MD 21211-4370 *Tel:* 410-516-6965 *Toll Free Tel:* 800-537-5487 *Fax:* 410-516-6998 *E-mail:* rffpress@rff.org
Distribution Center: RFF Press Customer Service, c/o Johns Hopkins University Press Fulfillment Services, PO Box 50370, Baltimore, MD 21211-4370 *Tel:* 410-516-6965 *Toll Free Tel:* 800-537-5487 *Fax:* 410-516-6998 *E-mail:* rffpress@rff.org
Membership(s): AAP; American Association of University Presses; Society for Scholarly Publishing

§Fleming H Revell
Division of Baker Book House Co
PO Box 6287, Grand Rapids, MI 49516-6287
SAN: 203-3801
Tel: 616-676-9185 *Toll Free Tel:* 800-877-2665 *Fax:* 616-676-9573
Web Site: www.bakerbooks.com
Key Personnel
Pres: Dwight Baker
Ed: Lonnie Hull-Du Pont
Prodn & ISBN Contact: Robert Bol
Publicity Dir: Twila Bennett
Rts & Perms & Intl Rts: Marilyn Gordon
Asst to Edit Dir: Sheila Ingram
    E-mail: singram@bakerhooks.com
Founded: 1870
Religious.
ISBN Prefix(es): 0-8007
Number of titles published annually: 100 Print
Total Titles: 65 Print; 5 Audio
Imprints: Spire Books
Foreign Rep(s): Christian Art (South Africa); Family Reading Publication (Australia); R G Mitchell (Canada); Omega Distributors (New Zealand); Send The Light (UK, Europe)
Shipping Address: 6030 E Fulton Rd, Ada, MI 49301

§Review & Herald Publishing Association
55 W Oak Ridge Dr, Hagerstown, MD 21740
Tel: 301-393-3000 *Toll Free Tel:* 800-234-7630 *Fax:* 301-393-4055 (periodicals); 301-393-3222
E-mail: editorial@rhpa.org
Web Site: www.reviewandherald.com *Telex:* 70-5600 *Cable:* RANDH HAGERSTOWN MARYLAND
Key Personnel
Chmn of the Bd: Don Schneider
VChmn: Gerry D Karst
Pres: Robert S Smith
VP, Books: Mark B Thomas *E-mail:* mthomas@rhpa.org
VP, Graphics: Robert L Essex
Acqs Ed: Jeanette Johnson *Tel:* 301-393-4050 *E-mail:* jjohnson@rhpa.org
Founded: 1861

Religion (Seventh-day Adventist), health, nutrition & education.
ISBN Prefix(es): 0-8280
Number of titles published annually: 43 Print
Total Titles: 750 Print; 2 CD-ROM; 10 Audio
Foreign Rep(s): Stanborough Press Ltd (England)

RFF Press, see Resources for the Future

The RGU Group
560 W Southern Ave, Tempe, AZ 85282
SAN: 299-9366
Tel: 480-736-9862 *Toll Free Tel:* 800-266-5265 *Fax:* 480-736-9863 *Toll Free Fax:* 800-973-6694
E-mail: info@thergugroup.com
Web Site: www.thergugroup.com
Key Personnel
Publr: Todd Atkins
Natl Sales Director: Karen Atkins
Commns Dir: Denise Young
Publg Contact: Laura Nero
Off Mgr: Michelle Pagonzzi
Founded: 1992
Regional publisher of children's books & region specific bookstores; regional plush toys.
ISBN Prefix(es): 1-891795
Number of titles published annually: 4 Print
Total Titles: 10 Print; 6 Online; 6 E-Book
Distributed by Sunbelt
Membership(s): Arizona Book Publishing Association; International Reading Association; Museum Store Association; Publishers Marketing Association

Lynne Rienner Publishers Inc
1800 30 St, Suite 314, Boulder, CO 80301
SAN: 683-1869
Tel: 303-444-6684 *Fax:* 303-444-0824
E-mail: cservice@rienner.com
Web Site: www.rienner.com
Key Personnel
CEO, Pres & Ed Dir: Lynne Rienner
Mgr, Cust Serv: Sheila Peck *E-mail:* speck@rienner.com
Mgr, Mktg & Sales: Sally Glover
    E-mail: sglover@rienner.com
Rights: Lisa Tulchin *E-mail:* ltulchin@rienner.com
Founded: 1984
Scholarly & reference books & journals, college textbooks; comparative politics, US politics, international relations, sociology, Third World literature & literary criticism.
ISBN Prefix(es): 0-931477; 1-55587; 1-56000; 1-57454; 1-57454; 0-89410; 1-58826
Number of titles published annually: 65 Print
Total Titles: 700 Print
Foreign Office(s): 3 Henrietta St, Covent Garden, London WC2E 8LU, United Kingdom (Marketing & orders, UK & Europe), Promo Mgr: Imogen Adams *Tel:* (0207) 845 0803 *Fax:* (0207) 845-0802
30 Lake Rd, Wimbledon, London SW19 7EX, United Kingdom (UK editorial office), Ed: Elizabetta Linton *Tel:* (0208) 286-0803 *Fax:* (0208) 286-0803 *E-mail:* elinton@rienner.com
Distributor for North-South Center Press
Foreign Rep(s): Apac (Asia, Pacific); Eurospan (Europe); Palgrave Macmillan (Australia); Viva (India)
Warehouse: 22883 Quicksilver Dr, Dulles, VA 20166, Contact: Vartan Ajamian
Membership(s): AAP

§Rigby
Imprint of Harcourt Achieve
10801 N MoPac Expressway, Austin, TX 78759
Mailing Address: PO Box 27010, Austin, TX 78755

Tel: 512-343-8227 *Toll Free Tel:* 800-531-5015 *Toll Free Fax:* 800-699-9459
E-mail: ecare@harcourt.com
Web Site: www.harcourtachieve.com
Key Personnel
Pres & CEO: Tim McEwen
Sr VP, Sales: Joe McHale
VP, Fin: Martijn Tel
VP, Devt: Lynelle Morgenthaler
VP, Mktg: Carol Wolf
VP, HR: Gabrielle Madison
VP, Mfg: David Lindley
Founded: 1987
Educational materials for Pre-K, elementary, secondary, Adult GED, test preparation, ESL & professional development for educators.
Total Titles: 4,000 Print

Rising Sun Publishing
PO Box 70906, Marietta, GA 30007-0906
Tel: 770-518-0369 *Toll Free Tel:* 800-524-2813 *Fax:* 770-587-0862
E-mail: info@rspublishing.com
Web Site: www.rspublishing.com
Key Personnel
CFO: Mychal Wynn
Founded: 1990
Primary focus is educational training & materials.
ISBN Prefix(es): 1-880463
Number of titles published annually: 3 Print
Total Titles: 16 Print; 4 Audio

Rising Tide Press
526 E 16 St, Tucson, AZ 85701
Toll Free Tel: 800-311-3565
Key Personnel
Owner & Pres: Jean Reehl *E-mail:* jean@fillorders.com
Founded: 1991
Publish books for, by & about women; fiction & nonfiction.
ISBN Prefix(es): 0-9628938; 1-883061
Number of titles published annually: 10 Print
Total Titles: 35 Print
Distributed by Alamo Square; Amazon.com; Baker & Taylor; Banyan Tree; Turnaround (London)

River City Publishing, LLC
1719 Mulberry St, Montgomery, AL 36106
Tel: 334-265-6753 *Toll Free Tel:* 877-408-7078 *Fax:* 334-265-8880
E-mail: web@rivercitypublishing.com
Web Site: www.rivercitypublishing.com
Key Personnel
Owner & Publr: Dr Al Newman; Carolyn Newman
Ed: Ashley Gordon
Prodn & Design: Lissa Monroe
Publicity: Lovelace Cook
Cust Serv: William Hicks
Founded: 1989
Acquisition, editing, design, composition, marketing & sales. Regional fiction & nonfiction, especially books about the South, civil rights, folk art, contemporary Southern fiction, regionally related travel, history & biography/memoir.
ISBN Prefix(es): 1-881320; 0-9622815; 1-57966; 0-913515
Number of titles published annually: 15 Print
Total Titles: 150 Print
Imprints: Elliott & Clark Publishing; River City Kids; Starrhill Press
Membership(s): Southeast Booksellers Association

Riverhead Books (Hardcover)
Imprint of Penguin Group (USA) Inc
375 Hudson St, New York, NY 10014
SAN: 282-5074
Tel: 212-366-2000
E-mail: online@penguinputnam.com
Web Site: www.penguin.com

Key Personnel
Pres & Publr: Susan Petersen Kennedy
VP & Co-Edit Dir: Julie Grau; Cindy Spiegel
Exec Ed: Jake Morrissey
Sr Ed: Wendy Carlton; Sean McDonald
Founded: 1995
ISBN Prefix(es): 1-57322
Number of titles published annually: 23 Print
Total Titles: 61 Print
Advertising Agency: Mesa Group

Riverhead Books (Trade Paperback)
Imprint of Penguin Group (USA) Inc
375 Hudson St, New York, NY 10014
SAN: 282-5074
Tel: 212-366-2000
E-mail: online@penguinputnam.com
Web Site: www.penguin.com
Key Personnel
Art Dir: Charles Bjorklund
Founded: 1995
ISBN Prefix(es): 1-57322
Number of titles published annually: 31 Print
Total Titles: 171 Print
Advertising Agency: Spier NY

RiverOak Publishing
Imprint of Cook Communications Ministries
4050 Lee Vance View, Colorado Springs, CO
80918
Tel: 719-536-0100 *Toll Free Tel:* 800-323-7543
Web Site: www.cookministries.com
Key Personnel
Corp Publicity Mgr: Michele Tennesen
RiverOak Publishing's mission is to inspire, challenge & entertain readers with the truth of God's word.
ISBN Prefix(es): 1-58919
Number of titles published annually: 35 Print
Total Titles: 100 Print

Riverside Book Co Inc
150 W End Ave, No 11-H, New York, NY 10023
Mailing Address: PO Box 237043, New York, NY 10023-0028
Tel: 212-595-0700 *Fax:* 212-559-0780
Web Site: www.riversidebook.com
Key Personnel
Pres: Victor Eskenazi
Publr: Brian Eskenazi *E-mail:* eskenazi@riversidebook.com
Founded: 1987
Publish art books & distribute remainders; Spanish-language publishing.
ISBN Prefix(es): 1-878351
Number of titles published annually: 3 Print
Total Titles: 56 Print
Membership(s): Bookbinders Guild of New York

The Riverside Publishing Co
Subsidiary of Houghton Mifflin Co
425 Spring Lake Dr, Itasca, IL 60143-2079
SAN: 213-554X
Tel: 630-467-7000 *Toll Free Tel:* 800-323-9540
Fax: 630-467-7192 (cust serv)
Web Site: www.riverpub.com
Key Personnel
Pres: Lee Jones
VP, Fin & Opers: James G Nicholson
VP & Dir, Devt: Anita Constant
VP & Natl Sales Mgr: Ellis Tesh
VP, Tech Prod & Servs: Stuart Davidson
Founded: 1979
Develops & sells educational & psychological tests & scoring services as well as software for the school guidance market.
ISBN Prefix(es): 0-8292
Imprints: Wintergreen/Orchard House Inc
Foreign Rep(s): ACER (Australia); Artsberg (Hong Kong); Camera-Mundi (Puerto Rico); Nelson Canada (Canada); NFER-Nelson (UK);

NZCER (New Zealand); Psicologiay Material-Tecnico (Spain); Taskmaster (UK)
Foreign Rights: The Riverside Publishing Co, Intl Dept, 425 Spring Lake Dr, Itaska, IL 60143

Rizzoli International Publications Inc
Subsidiary of R C S Rizzoli Corp New York
300 Park Ave S, 3rd fl, New York, NY 10010-5399
Tel: 212-387-3400 *Toll Free Tel:* 800-522-6657 (orders only) *Fax:* 212-387-3535
Key Personnel
Pres & CEO: Marco Ausenda
VP & Publr: Charles Miers
VP & Dir, Mktg & Sales: Jennifer Pierson
Prodn Mgr: Jacquie Byrnes
Sales Mgr: John Dean
Publicity Dir: Pam Sommers
Mgr, Spec Mkts: Tracey Petitt
Sr Ed, Architecture: David Morton
VP, Admin & Fin: Alan Rutsky
Dist Coord: Jerry Hoffnagle
Founded: 1976
Fine arts, architecture, photography, decorative arts, cookbooks, gardening & landscape design, fashion & sports.
ISBN Prefix(es): 0-8478
Number of titles published annually: 100 Print
Imprints: Rizzoli, New York; Universe
Distributed by Holtzbrinck
Distributor for Editions Flammarion; Skira Editore; Villegas Editores; White Star
Advertising Agency: Rizzoli Graphic Studios
Orders to: VHPS Order Dept, 16365 James Madison Hwy, Gordonsville, VA 22942-8501
See separate listing for:
Universe Publishing

James A Rock & Co Publishers
9710 Traville Gateway Dr, No 305, Rockville, MD 20850
Toll Free Tel: 800-411-2230 *Fax:* 301-294-1683
E-mail: jarock@sprintmail.com
Web Site: rockpublishing.com
Founded: 1977
ISBN Prefix(es): 0-918736
Number of titles published annually: 12 Print
Imprints: Aonian Press; Castle Keep Books; Sense of Wonder Press
Membership(s): Publishers Marketing Association

Rockefeller University Press
Unit of Rockefeller University
1114 First Ave, New York, NY 10021
Tel: 212-327-8572 *Fax:* 212-327-7944
E-mail: rupcd@rockefeller.edu
Web Site: www.rupress.org
Key Personnel
Exec Dir: Michael J Held
Fin Dir: Ray Fastiggi
Founded: 1906
Currently publishes biomedical journals & books.
ISBN Prefix(es): 0-87470
Number of titles published annually: 1 Print
Total Titles: 10 Print; 3 Online; 6 Audio
Online services available through HighWire Press.
Foreign Rep(s): iGroup Asia Pacific Ltd (Asia-Pacific)
Membership(s): AAP; Association of American University Presses; CSE; Society for Scholarly Publishing

Rockport Publishers
33 Commercial St, Gloucester, MA 01930
Tel: 978-282-9590 *Fax:* 978-283-2742
Web Site: www.rockpub.com
Key Personnel
Pres: Ken Fund
Dir, Mktg & PR: Dalyn A Miller
Publr: Winnie Prentiss *E-mail:* winnie@rockpub.com
Intl Sales Dir: Helgard K Krause

Website Mgr: Kim Shea
Prodn Mgr: Barbara States
Founded: 1983
Publisher of high-quality books on graphic design; crafts, architecture, interior design & photography.
ISBN Prefix(es): 1-59253; 1-59233; 2-88046
Number of titles published annually: 75 Print
Total Titles: 300 Print
Imprints: Fair Winds Press; Quarry Books; Rockport; RotoVision
Distributed by F & W Publications

Rocky Mountain Mineral Law Foundation
9191 Sheridan Blvd, Suite 203, Westminister, CO 80031
Tel: 303-321-8100 *Fax:* 303-321-7657
E-mail: info@rmmlf.org
Web Site: www.rmmlf.org
Key Personnel
Exec Dir: David P Phillips
Sr Attorney: Mark Holland *Tel:* 303-321-8100 ext 106 *E-mail:* mholland@rmmlf.org
Founded: 1955
Natural resources & legal education.
ISBN Prefix(es): 0-929047; 0-882047
Number of titles published annually: 5 Print
Total Titles: 30 Print; 1 CD-ROM

Rocky River Publishers LLC
PO Box 1679, Shepherdstown, WV 25443-1679
Tel: 304-876-2711 *Toll Free Tel:* 800-343-0686
Fax: 304-263-2949
E-mail: rockyriverpublishers@citlink.net
Web Site: www.rockyriver.com
Key Personnel
Pres: Miriam J Wilson
Founded: 1987
High quality books & materials with creative approaches to help children deal with problems & needs they may have from infancy to adulthood.
ISBN Prefix(es): 0-944576
Number of titles published annually: 4 Print
Total Titles: 20 Print
Distributed by Academic Book Center; Brodart; Follett Library Resources

Rod & Staff Publishers Inc
Hwy 172, Crockett, KY 41413-0003
Mailing Address: PO Box 3, Crockett, KY 41413-0003
Tel: 606-522-4348 *Toll Free Tel:* 800-643-1244
Fax: 606-522-4896 *Toll Free Fax:* 800-643-1244 (ordering in US)
Web Site: www.anabaptistis.org
Key Personnel
Busn Mgr: Timothy Shenk
Founded: 1958
Religious-story books; church, Sunday & Christian school materials & tracts.
ISBN Prefix(es): 0-7399
Number of titles published annually: 20 Print
Total Titles: 600 Print

Rodale Books
Subsidiary of Rodale Inc
400 S Tenth St, Emmaus, PA 18098-0099
Tel: 610-967-5171 *Fax:* 610-967-8961
Web Site: www.rodale.com
Key Personnel
Pres & CEO: Steven Pleshette Murphy
VP & Publr, Trade Books: Amy Rhodes *Tel:* 212-573-0230
VP, Rodale Books: Cindy Ratzlaff *Tel:* 610-967-8545 *Fax:* 610-967-9312 *E-mail:* cindy.ratzlaff@rodale.com
Dir, Publicity: Cathy Lee Gruhn
Dir, Trade Sales: Leslie Schneider
Dir, Spec Sales: Lisa Dolin *Tel:* 610-967-8148
Dir, Mktg: Dana Bacher *Tel:* 610-967-8754
Dir, Intl Sales: Jane Tappuni

VP & Ed-in-Chief, Women's Health Books: Tami Booth *Tel:* 610-967-7870
Exec Ed, Rodale General Books: Stephanie Tade *Tel:* 610-967-7783
Exec Ed, Lifestyle Books: Margot Schupf
Exec Ed, Men's Health Books: Jeremy Katz
Founded: 1932
Adult trade & mail order titles including health & fitness, gardening, cooking, spirituality, pet care & general nonfiction.
ISBN Prefix(es): 1-57954
Number of titles published annually: 110 Print
Total Titles: 827 Print
Distributed by St Martin's Press

Rodale Inc
33 E Minor St, Emmaus, PA 18098-0099
SAN: 200-2477
Tel: 610-967-5171 *Fax:* 610-967-8962
Web Site: www.rodale.com
Key Personnel
Pres, Rodale Intl: Gianni Crespi
Pres, Rodale Interactive Chief Mktg Off: Thomas Harbeck *Tel:* 212-573-0242
Chmn of the Bd: Ardath Rodale *Tel:* 610-967-8300
V Chmn of the Bd & Pres, Organic Living: Maria Rodale *Tel:* 610-967-8550
CEO & Pres: Steven Murphy *Tel:* 212-573-0304
Pres, Women's Group: Sara Levinson *Tel:* 212-573-0226
Exec VP & COO: Steven Kalin
Pres, Sports & Fitness: Tom Beusse *Tel:* 212-573-0259
Sr VP, Cust Rel & Mktg: Bill Ostroff
Exec VP & Exec Advisor: Benjamin Roter *Tel:* 610-967-7840
VP, Corp Communs: Camille Johnston
Sr VP & CFO: Lester Rackoff *Tel:* 610-967-8587
Founded: 1932 (Founded by J I Rodale)
Adult trade titles in health & fitness, gardening, cooking, spirituality & pet care.
ISBN Prefix(es): 0-87857; 1-57954; 0-87596
Number of titles published annually: 100 Print
Branch Office(s)
733 Third Ave, 15th fl, New York, NY 10017-3204
Distributed by St Martin's Press Inc
Foreign Rep(s): HB Fenn & Co Ltd (Canada)
Foreign Rights: Dr J E Bloch Literary Agency (Brazil); Book Publishers Association of Israel (Israel); Monica Heyum Agency (Sweden); Inter-Ko Copyright Agency Corp (Korea); Japan UNI Agency Inc (Japan); Montreal-Contacts (Canada); Tipress (Italy); Julio F Yanez Agencia Literaria (Spain)
Shipping Address: VHPS Distribution Center, 16365 James Madison Hwy, Gordonsville, VA 22942-8477 *Toll Free Tel:* 888-330-8477 *Toll Free Fax:* 800-672-2054
See separate listing for:
Rodale Books

Rodopi
One Rockefeller Plaza, Rm 1420, New York, NY 10020-2002
Tel: 212-265-6560 *Toll Free Tel:* 800-225-3998 (US only) *Fax:* 212-265-6402
E-mail: info@rodopi.nl
Web Site: www.rodopi.nl
Founded: 1966
Independent academic publishing house.
ISBN Prefix(es): 90-6203; 90-5183; 90-420
Number of titles published annually: 170 Print; 70 E-Book
Total Titles: 2,500 Print; 2 CD-ROM; 60 Online; 100 E-Book
Online services available through Ingenta.
Foreign Office(s): Tijnmuiden 7, 1046 AK Amsterdam, Netherlands *Tel:* (020) 611 4821 *Fax:* (020) 447 2979

Roman Catholic Books
Division of Catholic Media Apostolate
PO Box 2286, Fort Collins, CO 80522-2286
Tel: 970-490-2735 *Fax:* 970-493-8781
Web Site: www.booksforcatholics.com
Key Personnel
Pres: Roger McCaffrey
Prom & Rts & Intl Rts: Maureen Williamson *E-mail:* maureen@intrepidgroup.com
Prodn: Arthur Maranjian
Founded: 1985
Traditional Catholic books.
ISBN Prefix(es): 0-912141; 1-929291
Number of titles published annually: 12 Print
Total Titles: 170 Print
Warehouse: c/o Intrepid, 1331 Red Cedar Circle, Fort Collins, CO 80524

Roncorp Inc
732 Cascade Dr N, Mount Laurel, NJ 08054
Mailing Address: PO Box 724, Cherry Hill, NJ 08003-0724
Tel: 856-722-5993 *Fax:* 856-722-9252
E-mail: roncorp@comcast.net
Key Personnel
Pres: Bruce Ronkin
Treas & Secy: Flora Ronkin
Founded: 1978
Music & music texts.
ISBN Prefix(es): 0-939103
Number of titles published annually: 3 Print
Total Titles: 97 Print; 1 Audio
Imprints: Roncorp Publications
Distributed by Northeastern Music Publications Inc (exclusive)
Orders to: Northeastern Music Publications Inc, PO Box 517, Glenmoore, PA 19343

Ronin Publishing Inc
PO Box 22900, Oakland, CA 94609-5900
Tel: 510-420-3669 *Fax:* 510-420-3672
E-mail: askronin@roninpub.com
Web Site: www.roninpub.com
Key Personnel
Publr: Beverly Potter *E-mail:* beverly@roninpub.com
Founded: 1983
Trade paperbacks on life & work skills, psychedelic references, Leary Library, UFO, pop culture.
ISBN Prefix(es): 0-914171; 1-57951
Number of titles published annually: 8 Print
Total Titles: 90 Print; 2 E-Book; 2 Audio
Imprints: And/Or Books; Books for Independent Minds
Distributed by Homestead Book Co; New Leaf; Publr Group West
Foreign Rep(s): Airlift (UK); Banyan Tree (Australia); PGW (Canada)
Foreign Rights: Interlicense (World)
Membership(s): ABA; Northern California Book Publicity & Marketing Association; Publishers Marketing Association

The Rosen Publishing Group Inc
29 E 21 St, New York, NY 10010
SAN: 203-3720
Tel: 212-777-3017 *Toll Free Tel:* 800-237-9932 *Fax:* 212-777-0277
E-mail: info@rosenpub.com
Web Site: www.rosenpublishing.com
Key Personnel
Pres: Roger Rosen

VP: Gina Strazzabosco-Hayn
Art Dir: Sam Jordan
Founded: 1950
Hardcover, library editions, vocational guidance; personal guidance; music & art catalogs; drug abuse prevention, self-esteem development, values & ethics, new international writing, multicultural, African heritage.
ISBN Prefix(es): 0-8239
Number of titles published annually: 500 Print
Total Titles: 1,387 Print
Imprints: Pelion Press
Divisions: ICARUS
Warehouse: Maple Press Distribution, 60 Grumbacher Rd, York, PA 17405

§Ross Books
PO Box 4340, Berkeley, CA 94704-0340
Tel: 510-841-2474 *Toll Free Tel:* 800-367-0930 *Fax:* 510-841-2695
E-mail: staff@rossbooks.com
Web Site: www.rossbooks.com
Key Personnel
Pres: Franz Ross *E-mail:* franzross@rossbooks.com
Sales: Benny Juarez *E-mail:* sales@rossbooks.com
Founded: 1977
Tradebooks, software, general trade books & CDs, books on holograms.
ISBN Prefix(es): 0-89496
Number of titles published annually: 6 Print; 1 CD-ROM; 1 E-Book; 1 Audio
Total Titles: 26 Print; 2 CD-ROM; 2 Online; 2 E-Book; 2 Audio
Imprints: Baldar (computer programming books & electronic media)
Shipping Address: 1735 MLK Way, Berkeley, CA 95709 *E-mail:* sales@rossbooks.com *Web Site:* www.rossbooks.com

Ross Publishing Inc
330 W 58 St, Suite 306, New York, NY 10019-1827
SAN: 201-8969
Tel: 212-765-8200 *Fax:* 212-765-8296
E-mail: info@rosspub.com
Web Site: www.rosspub.com
Key Personnel
Chmn of the Bd & Pres: Norman A Ross *E-mail:* norman@rosspub.com
Founded: 1972
Publisher of reference books such as US Census Report reprints; Slavica; AV materials.
ISBN Prefix(es): 0-88354
Number of titles published annually: 25 Print
Total Titles: 240 Print; 30 Audio
Distributor for Archival Publications International; Foleor Editions

§Rothstein Associates Inc
4 Arapaho Rd, Brookfield, CT 06804-3104
Tel: 203-740-7444 *Toll Free Tel:* 888-768-4783 *Fax:* 203-740-7401
E-mail: info@rothstein.com
Web Site: www.rothstein.com
Key Personnel
Pres: Philip Jan Rothstein *Tel:* 203-740-7400 *E-mail:* pjr@rothstein.com
Founded: 1985
Publish books & software for business.
ISBN Prefix(es): 0-9641648; 1-931332
Number of titles published annually: 15 Print; 5 CD-ROM
Total Titles: 52 Print; 14 CD-ROM

Rough Guides
Subsidiary of Pearson PLC
345 Hudson St, New York, NY 10014
SAN: 282-5074
Tel: 212-414-3635 *Fax:* 212-414-3352
E-mail: mail@roughguides.com
Web Site: www.roughguides.com

Key Personnel
Dir & Mgr (US): Kevin Fitzgerald
Mktg Dir, North America: Geoff Colquitt
Tel: 212-414-3636 *E-mail:* geoff.colquitt@
roughguides.com
Man Ed (US): Andrew Rosenberg
Dir, New Media (US): Jennifer Gold
Mktg Mgr (US): Megan Kennedy
Publicist (US): Milena Perez
Mktg & Rts Dir (UK): Richard Trillo
Prodn Dir (UK): Julia Bovis
Publr (UK): Mark Ellingham
Travel Publr (UK): Martin Dunford
Founded: 1982
Travel guides; phrasebooks, music reference;
pocket histories; city & country maps; music
CDs; world & internet reference.
ISBN Prefix(es): 1-85828; 1-84353
Number of titles published annually: 50 Print; 30
E-Book
Total Titles: 450 Print; 30 E-Book
Foreign Office(s): 80 Strand, London WC2R
0RL, United Kingdom *Tel:* (020) 7010-3700
Fax: (020) 7010-6767
Distributed by Penguin Group USA
Orders to: 405 Murray Hill Pkwy, East Ruther-
ford, NY 07073 *Toll Free Tel:* 800-526-0275
Toll Free Fax: 800-227-9604
Warehouse: 135 S Mount Zion Rd, Lebanon, IN
46052

§The Rough Notes Co Inc
Subsidiary of Insurance Publishing Plus Corp
11690 Technology Dr, Carmel, IN 46032-5600
Tel: 317-582-1600 *Toll Free Tel:* 800-428-4384
Fax: 317-816-1000 *Toll Free Fax:* 800-321-
1909
Web Site: www.roughnotes.com
Key Personnel
Opers Mgr: Sam Berman
Founded: 1878
Technical/educational reference material specific
to the property/casualty insurance industry.
ISBN Prefix(es): 1-56461
Number of titles published annually: 10 Print
Total Titles: 20 Print; 4 Online
Advertising Agency: AdCom Group

§Routledge
Subsidiary of Taylor & Francis Book Inc
29 W 35 St, New York, NY 10001-2299
SAN: 213-196X
Tel: 212-216-7800 *Fax:* 212-564-7854 (main)
E-mail: info@taylorandfrancis.com
Web Site: www.routledge-ny.com
Key Personnel
Pres: Fenton Markevich
COO & Fin Analyst: Len Cornacchia
VP & Publr: Linda Hollick
VP & Publg Dir: William P Germano
Publg Dir, Social Sciences: Karen A Wolny
Mktg Dir, Acad & Libr Dir: Ande Ciecierski
Mktg Dir & Social Sciences: Ron Longe
Prodn Dir: Dennis Teston
Dir Opers: Jason Cruz
Rts & Perms Mgr: Jeffrey Aristy
Publg Dir, Ref: Sylvia Miller
Natl Field Mgr Trade: Donald O'Connor
Mktg Dir, Humanities: Frederic Nachbaur
Mktg Dir, Ref: Elizabeth Sheehan
Founded: 1836
Hardcover & paperback; scholarly, professional
& trade; adult nonfiction in the humanities, be-
havioral & social sciences.
ISBN Prefix(es): 0-415; 0-87830
Number of titles published annually: 1,800 Print
Total Titles: 6,300 Print; 6 CD-ROM; 1 Online
Imprints: Theatre Arts Books
Foreign Office(s): Routledge Ltd, 11 New Fetter
Lane, London EC4P 4EE, United Kingdom
Foreign Rep(s): Routledge Ltd, London
Advertising Agency: Arch Advertising

Billing Address: Routledge Orders & Customer
Service, 10650 Toebben Dr, Independence, KY
41051 *Toll Free Tel:* 800-634-7064 *Toll Free
Fax:* 800-248-4724
Orders to: Routledge Orders & Customer Ser-
vice, 10650 Toebben Dr, Independence, KY
41051 *Toll Free Tel:* 800-634-7064 *Toll Free
Fax:* 800-248-4724
Returns: Routledge Orders & Customer Ser-
vice, 10650 Toebben Dr, Independence, KY
41051 *Toll Free Tel:* 800-634-7064 *Toll Free
Fax:* 800-248-4724
Warehouse: Routledge Orders & Customer Ser-
vice, 10650 Toebben Dr, Independence, KY
41051 *Toll Free Tel:* 800-634-7064 *Toll Free
Fax:* 800-248-4724
Distribution Center: Routledge Orders & Customer Service, 10650 Toebben Dr, Independence, KY 41051 *Toll Free Tel:* 800-634-7064
Toll Free Fax: 800-248-4724

Rowman & Littlefield Publishers Inc
Subsidiary of Rowman & Littlefield Publishing
Group
4501 Forbes Blvd, Lanham, MD 20706
SAN: 208-5143
Tel: 301-459-3366 *Toll Free Tel:* 800-462-6420
Fax: 301-429-5748
Web Site: www.rowmanlittlefield.com
Key Personnel
Publr: Jonathan Sisk
ISBN Contact & Rts & Perms: Kelly Rogers
VP, Mktg: Sheila Burnett
Coord, Adv & Mktg: Alla Corey
Founded: 1969
Policy studies; supplemental books & mono-
graphs, academic publisher.
ISBN Prefix(es): 0-8476; 0-7425
Number of titles published annually: 350 Print
Total Titles: 2,000 Print
Imprints: Barnes & Noble Books; Littlefield,
Adams Quality Paperbacks
Foreign Rep(s): Baker & Taylor International
(South Korea, World); Plymbridge Distribu-
tors (UK, Europe); United Publishers Service
(Japan, South Korea)
Warehouse: 15200 NBN Way, Blue Ridge Sum-
mit, PA 17215
See separate listing for:
AltaMira Press
Barnes & Noble Books (Imports & Reprints)

Roxbury Publishing Co
2034 Cotner Ave, Los Angeles, CA 90025
Mailing Address: PO Box 491044, Los Angeles,
CA 90049-9044 SAN: 213-6422
Tel: 310-473-3312 *Fax:* 310-473-4490
E-mail: roxbury@roxbury.net
Web Site: www.roxbury.net
Key Personnel
Publr: Claude Teweles
Founded: 1981
College textbooks & supplements, criminal jus-
tice, corrections, family studies.
ISBN Prefix(es): 0-935732; 1-931719; 1-891487
Number of titles published annually: 20 Print
Total Titles: 125 Print
Foreign Rep(s): Cassidy & Associates (China &
Hong Kong, Taiwan); Cranbury International
LLC (Mexico & South & Central America);
CRW Books (Pacific Islands); Publishers Con-
nection (Canada); Roundhouse Publishing (Eu-
rope)
Foreign Rights: Anu Hansen

Royal Fireworks Press
First Ave, Unionville, NY 10988
SAN: 212-4637
Mailing Address: PO Box 399, Unionville, NY
10988-0399
Tel: 845-726-4444 *Fax:* 845-726-3824
E-mail: mail@rfwp.com

Web Site: www.rfwp.com
Key Personnel
Chmn: T M Kemnitz
VP, Mktg & Lib Sales Dir: M Kaye *Tel:* 845-783-
2999 *Fax:* 845-782-6359
Dir, Order Dept & Cust Rel: Margaret Foley
Mgr & Intl Rts Contact: T M Kemnitz *Tel:* 845-
783-2999 *Fax:* 845-782-6359
Founded: 1977
Educational materials for gifted children, their
parents & teachers; reading materials; adult
literacy/education materials; fiction series for
middleschool: mystery & adventure; novels of
growing up; young adult science fiction; youth
against violence early childhood program (K-
3).
ISBN Prefix(es): 0-89824; 0-88092
Number of titles published annually: 75 Print; 10
CD-ROM; 10 Audio
Total Titles: 950 Print; 10 CD-ROM; 12 Audio
Distributor for KAV Books; Silk Label Books;
Trillium Press

Royalton Press
362 N Bedford St, East Bridgewater, MA 02333
Tel: 508-378-1110 *Fax:* 508-378-1105
Web Site: www.drummondpub.com
Key Personnel
Pres: Rick Vayo *E-mail:* f_allen@drummondpub.
com
CFO: Charlotte Vayo *E-mail:* c_vayo@
drummondpub.com
VP: Jack Mitchell *E-mail:* j_mitchell@
drummondpub.com; Margaret Sounders
E-mail: m_saunders@drummondpub.com
Mktg Mgr: Frank Allen *E-mail:* f_allen@
drummondpub.com
Exec Ed: Jennifer Carley *E-mail:* j_carley@
drummondpub.com; Gordon Law
E-mail: g_laws@drummondpub.com
Publish fiction & nonfiction for the LDS
market.
Number of titles published annually: 20 Print

Royalty Publishing Co
1440 Church Camp Rd, Bedford, IN 47421
Mailing Address: PO Box 2125, Bedford, IN
47421
Tel: 812-278-8785 *Fax:* 812-278-8785
E-mail: neeto@admete.net
Web Site: www.v-maximum-zone.com
Key Personnel
Pres: Nita L Scoggan *E-mail:* nitamotivates@
hotmail.com
VP: Stephen L Witt
Founded: 1982
Specialize in health & nutrition, US history, gov-
ernment, education, military, Christian & inspi-
rational.
ISBN Prefix(es): 0-910487
Number of titles published annually: 3 Print
Total Titles: 61 Print; 12 Audio
Advertising Agency: Steve Witt Associates, PO
Box 7386, North Augusta, GA 29861-7386
Tel: 803-819-3493

RSG Publishing
217 County Hwy 1, Bainbridge, NY 13733-9307
SAN: 242-0449
Tel: 607-563-9000 *Fax:* 607-563-9000
Key Personnel
CEO: Shirley B Goerlich
Founded: 1984
Original titles & reprints; do not accept unsol
mss. New York State history, local history,
Americana, regional & genealogy. Rare & used
books as, as well as new.
ISBN Prefix(es): 0-9614858; 1-887530
Number of titles published annually: 3 Print
Total Titles: 25 Print

RT Edwards Inc
PO Box 27388, Philadelphia, PA 19118
Tel: 215-233-5046 *Fax:* 215-233-2421
E-mail: info@edwardspub.com
Web Site: www.rtedwards.com
Key Personnel
Publr: James H Edwards
Founded: 1999
International scholarly publisher.
ISBN Prefix(es): 1-930217
Number of titles published annually: 20 Print

RTP Publishing Group
Formerly Expert Knowledge System Press
Subsidiary of Rocky Top Books
PO Box 4501, Clifton Park, NY 12065
Tel: 518-383-6414 *Fax:* 518-383-6414
E-mail: rockytopbooks@aol.com
Web Site: member.aol.com/rockytopbooks
Key Personnel
Publg Coord: Linda Goss
Founded: 1983
Technical publications, manuals & pharmaceutical.
ISBN Prefix(es): 0-937317
Number of titles published annually: 6 Print; 3 Online
Total Titles: 127 Print; 6 Online

Runestone Press
Imprint of Lerner Publishing Group
241 First Ave N, Minneapolis, MN 55401
SAN: 201-0828
Tel: 612-332-3344 *Toll Free Tel:* 800-328-4929; 800-332-1132 *Fax:* 612-332-7615
E-mail: info@lernerbooks.com
Web Site: www.lernerbooks.com
Key Personnel
Chmn & CEO: Harry J Lerner
Pres & Publr: Adam Lerner
VP & CFO: Margaret Wunderlich
VP & Edit-in-Chief: Mary Rodgers
VP, LernerClassroom: Gary Tinney
VP, Prodn: Gary Hansen
VP, Sales & Mktg: David Wexler
Art Dir: Zach Marell
Mktg Dir: Beth Heiss
Dir, Contracts, Perms & Author Rel: Almena Dees
Dir, HR: Cyndi Radant
Subs Rts: Tim Schwarz
Founded: 1993
Juveniles: science, history, archaeology, fiction, art, geography, multicultural issues, biography & ethnic.
ISBN Prefix(es): 0-8225
Foreign Rep(s): INT Press Distribution (Australia); Phambili (Southern Africa); Publishers Marketing Services (Singapore & Malaysia); Saunders Book Co (Canada); Turnaround (UK)
Foreign Rights: Bardon Chinese Media Agency (Taiwan); Japan Foreign Rights Centre (Japan); Korea Copyright Center (Korea); Michelle Lapautre Agence Junior (France); Literarische Agentur Silke Weniger (Germany); Tao Media International (People's Republic of China)
Warehouse: 1251 Washington Ave N, Minneapolis, MN 55401

§Running Press Book Publishers
Member of The Perseus Books Group
125 S 22 St, Philadelphia, PA 19103-4399
SAN: 204-5702
Tel: 215-567-5080 *Toll Free Tel:* 800-345-5359 (cust serv & orders) *Fax:* 215-568-2919
Toll Free Fax: 800-453-2884
Web Site: www.runningpress.com
Key Personnel
Dir, Opers & CEO: Al Struzinski
Publr: John Whalen
Publisher, Courage Books: Don McGee
VP, Sales: Matty Goldberg

Dir, Prodn: Joanne Casetti
Dir, European Sales & Intl Rts: Moira McCann
Dir, Spec Sales: Sarah Wolf
Publicity Dir: Sam Caggiula
Edit Dir: Ellen Beal
Dir, Design: Bill Jones
Mktg: Rick Joyce
Cust Serv Mgr: Karen Noble
Natl Accts Mgr, Gift Div: Jim Cook
Children's Ed: Andra Serlin
Picture Researcher: Susan Oyama
Founded: 1972
Hardcover & paperback trade books; art, craft/how-to, general nonfiction, children's books, promotional books, notebooks, journals & Miniature Editions™, cookbooks, books & products.
ISBN Prefix(es): 0-89471; 1-56138; 0-7624
Number of titles published annually: 220 Print
Total Titles: 6 CD-ROM
Imprints: Courage Books (illustrated gift books, promotional titles); Running Press Kids; Running Press Miniature Editions
Distributor for Cigar Aficionado; Jim Henson's Muppets; Star Wars; Wine Spectator Press
Foreign Rep(s): Baker & Taylor; General Publishing Co (Canada)
Foreign Rights: International Editors Co (Latin America, Portugal, Spain)

Russell Sage Foundation
112 E 64 St, New York, NY 10021-7383
SAN: 201-4521
Tel: 212-750-6000 *Toll Free Tel:* 800-524-6401
Fax: 212-371-4761
E-mail: pubs@rsage.org
Web Site: www.russellsage.org
Key Personnel
Pres: Eric Wanner
Dir, PR: David Haproff *Tel:* 212-750-6037
E-mail: david@rsage.org
Dir, Pubns: Suzanne Nichols
Founded: 1907
Sociology, economics, political science, history.
ISBN Prefix(es): 0-87154
Number of titles published annually: 25 Print
Total Titles: 680 Print
Foreign Office(s): Plymbridge Distributors Ltd, Plymbridge House, Estover Rd, Plymouth PL6 7PZ, United Kingdom
Foreign Rep(s): University Presses Marketing (UK, Continental Europe, Ireland, Israel)
Foreign Rights: Agence Letteraire (France); Agenzia Litteraria Internazionale (Italy); Paul & Peter Fritz AG (Switzerland); International Editor's Co (Argentina, Brazil, Spain); Coen Rombach (Netherlands); Tuttle-Mori Agency (Japan)
Advertising Agency: Bennett Book Advertising Inc
Shipping Address: CUP Services, 750 Cascadilla St, Ithaca, NY 14851

Russian Information Service Inc
PO Box 567, Montpelier, VT 05601
Tel: 802-223-4955 *Fax:* 802-223-6105
Web Site: www.rispubs.com
Key Personnel
Pres & Publr: Paul E Richardson
Founded: 1990
Publish magazines, books, info, maps for business & independent travel to Russia.
ISBN Prefix(es): 1-880100
Number of titles published annually: 3 Print
Total Titles: 5 Print

Russian Life Magazine, see Russian Information Service Inc

Rutgers University Press
Division of Rutgers, The State University

100 Joyce Kilmer Ave, Piscataway, NJ 08854-8099
SAN: 203-364X
Tel: 732-445-7762 (edit); 732-445-7762 (ext 627, sales) *Toll Free Tel:* 800-446-9323 (orders only) *Fax:* 732-445-7039 (acqs, edit, mktg, perms, prodn); 732-445-1974 (fulfillment)
E-mail: garyf@rci.rutgers.edu
Web Site: rutgerspress.rutgers.edu
Key Personnel
Dir: Marlie Wasserman *E-mail:* marlie@rci.rutgers.edu
Assoc Dir & Ed-in-Chief: Leslie Mitchner
COO: Molly Venezia
Mktg & Sales Dir: Gary Fitzgerald
Pre-press Dir: Marilyn A Campbell
Publicity Mgr: Jonathan Reilly
Promo Mgr: Donna Liese
Acq Ed Sciences: Audra Wolfe
Edit Prodn Coord: Ann Hegeman
Mktg Asst Exhibits: Arlene Bacher
Mktg Assoc: Jessica Pellien
Intl Rts & Asst: Michele Gisbert
E-mail: mgisbert@rci.rutgers.edu
Founded: 1936
Scholarly, but accessible mss in the social sciences, sciences, humanities & regional books.
ISBN Prefix(es): 0-8135
Number of titles published annually: 85 Print; 35 E-Book
Total Titles: 880 Print; 130 Online
Online services available through Questia.
Foreign Rep(s): East-West Export Books (Australia, Far East, New Zealand); Eurospan (Europe); Rutgers University Press (Africa, Latin America, Mideast); Scholarly Book Services Inc (Canada)
Foreign Rights: Daniel Doglioli (Italy)
Returns: J & S Warehouse (Rutgers), 40-D Cotter's Lane, East Brunswick, NJ 08816
Warehouse: J & S Warehouse (Rutgers), 40-D Cotter's Lane, East Brunswick, NJ 08816
Membership(s): American Association of University Presses

Rutledge Hill Press
Division of Thomas Nelson Publishers
c/o Thomas Nelson Publishers, PO Box 141000, Nashville, TN 37214-1000
Tel: 615-902-2703 *Toll Free Tel:* 800-251-4000 (ext 2703) *Fax:* 615-902-2340
Web Site: www.rutledgehillpress.com
Key Personnel
Assoc Publr: Pamela Clements
Mktg VP: Byran Curtis *Tel:* 615-902-2336
Admin Asst: Tina Goodrow *E-mail:* tgoodrow@thomasnelson.com
Founded: 1982
General trade publisher of market specific books; reference books.
ISBN Prefix(es): 0-934395; 1-55853; 1-40160
Number of titles published annually: 35 Print
Total Titles: 287 Print
Returns: Nelson/Word Returns Center, 825 Sixth Ave S, Nashville, TN 37203
Warehouse: Thomas Nelson Warehouse 1, 506 Nelson Place, Nashville, TN 37214-1000

Sable Publishing
365 N Saturmino Dr, Suite 21, Palm Springs, CA 92262
Mailing Address: PO Box 4496, Palm Springs, CA 92263
Tel: 760-408-1881
E-mail: sablepublishing@aol.com
Web Site: www.sablepublishing.com
Key Personnel
CEO: Ed Baron *E-mail:* edbaron@sablepublishing.com
Ed-in-Chief: Glory Harley *Tel:* 760-320-4760
E-mail: gloryharley@sablebooks.com
Founded: 2000

Full publishing & distribution featuring fine art covers.
ISBN Prefix(es): 0-9741776; 0-9754354
Number of titles published annually: 25 Print
Total Titles: 10 Print

William H Sadlier Inc
9 Pine St, New York, NY 10005
SAN: 204-0948
Tel: 212-227-2120 *Toll Free Tel:* 800-221-5175
Fax: 212-312-6080
Web Site: www.sadlier.com; www.sadlier-oxford. com
Key Personnel
Chmn of the Bd: Frank S Dinger
Pres: William S Dinger
VP, Natl Field Sales Mgr: John Bonenberger
VP, Pubns, Sadlier: Rosemary Calicchio
VP, Treas: Henry E Christel
VP, Publg Opers: Deborah Jones
VP, Natl Sales Administrator: Kevin O'Donnell
VP, Pubns, Sadlier-Oxford: Robert Richards
VP, Mktg: Maureen Wales
Gen Counsel: Angela Dinger
Creative Dir: Vincent Gallo
Cust Serv: Gloria Gaudioso
Founded: 1832
Pre-school, elementary & secondary textbooks on catechetics, sacraments, reading/language arts, mathematics; adult catechetical programs.
ISBN Prefix(es): 0-8215
Number of titles published annually: 4 Print
Divisions: Sadlier; Sadlier-Oxford
Shipping Address: 812 Jersey Ave, Jersey City, NJ 07310

§SAE (Society of Automotive Engineers International)
400 Commonwealth Dr, Warrendale, PA 15096-0001
SAN: 216-0811
Tel: 724-776-4841 *Toll Free Tel:* 877-606-7323 (cust serv) *Fax:* 724-776-0790
E-mail: publications@sae.org
Web Site: www.sae.org
Key Personnel
Pres: Dr Jack Thompson
Exec VP: Raymond A Morris
Treas: Karl Goering
Exec Dir: Antenor R Willems *Tel:* 724-776-4841 ext 7125 *E-mail:* will@sae.org
Graphics & Prod Mgr: Michael C Schindel
Prod Devt: LaVerne Winkowski
Founded: 1905
Scientific & technical publications.
ISBN Prefix(es): 0-89883; 1-56091; 0-7680
Number of titles published annually: 9 Print
Total Titles: 650 Print; 23 CD-ROM; 1 Online; 15 E-Book; 1 Audio
Online services available through FIZ Technik, Questel-Orbit, STN.
Imprints: STS Service Technicians Society
Branch Office(s)
Automotive Headquarters, 755 W Big Beaver Rd, Suite 1600, Troy, MI 48084 *Tel:* 248-273-2455 *Fax:* 248-273-2494
Distributor for Coordinating Research Council Inc
Foreign Rep(s): Allied Publishers Pvt Ltd (India); American Bookstore (Argentina); American Technical Publishers Ltd (Europe, Middle East); D A Information Center (Australia, New Zealand, Papua New Guinea); SAE Australasia (Australia); SAE Brasil (Brazil); SAE of Japan (Japan); Sejong Books (South Korea)

Safari Press
15621 Chemical Lane, Bldg B, Huntington Beach, CA 92649
Tel: 714-894-9080 *Toll Free Tel:* 800-451-4788
Fax: 714-894-4949
E-mail: info@safaripress.com
Web Site: www.safaripress.com

Key Personnel
Pres: Ludo J Wurfbain
Chief Ed: J Neufeld
Founded: 1984
Specializes in big-game hunting, firearms, wing-shooting, Africana & sporting; hardcover trade & limited editions.
ISBN Prefix(es): 0-924357; 0-940143; 1-57157
Number of titles published annually: 37 Print
Total Titles: 180 Print
Distributor for Peterson Publishing Co; Quiller; Sportsman's Press

Safer Society Foundation Inc
8-10 Conant Sq, Brandon, VT 05733
Mailing Address: PO Box 340, Brandon, VT 05733-0340
Tel: 802-247-3132 *Fax:* 802-247-4233
E-mail: ssfi@sover.net
Web Site: www.safersociety.org
Key Personnel
Pubns Spec: Stephen Zeoli
Founded: 1985
Specializes in titles relating to the treatment of sexual abuse.
ISBN Prefix(es): 1-884444
Number of titles published annually: 4 Print
Total Titles: 80 Print; 4 Audio
Foreign Rep(s): Bookstall Services Inc (England); Feminist Bookshop (Australia); Visions Book Store Ltd (Canada)
Membership(s): Publishers Marketing Association

Sagamore Publishing LLC
804 N Neil St, Champaign, IL 61820
SAN: 292-5788
Mailing Address: PO Box 647, Champaign, IL 61824-0647
Tel: 217-359-5940 *Toll Free Tel:* 800-327-5557 (orders) *Fax:* 217-359-5975
E-mail: books@sagamorepub.com
Web Site: www.sagamorepub.com
Key Personnel
Pres & Intl Rts: Peter L Bannon
Publr: Joseph J Bannon, Sr
Gen Mgr: Doug Sanders *E-mail:* dsanders@ sagamorepub.com
Founded: 1974
ISBN Prefix(es): 0-915611; 1-57167
Number of titles published annually: 15 Print
Total Titles: 210 Print; 6 Online
Distributor for American Academy for Park & Recreation Admin
Foreign Rep(s): Creative & More (Taiwan); Gazelle Book Services Ltd (UK, Continental Europe, Ireland); HM Leisure Planning (Australia & New Zealand); Japan Publications Trading Co Ltd (Japan); Login Brothers (Canada); Vigor Book Agents (South Africa); World Universities Press (India); Y D Trading (Korea)

Sage Publications
2455 Teller Rd, Thousand Oaks, CA 91320
Tel: 805-499-0721 *Fax:* 805-499-0871
E-mail: info@sagepub.com
Web Site: www.sagepub.com
Key Personnel
Chmn: Sara Miller McCune
Pres & CEO: Mike Melody
Sr VP & CFO: Michael Graves
Exec VP & Publr, Sage Periodicals Press: Blaise Simqu
VP & Edit Dir, Journals: Susan Hanscom
VP & Edit Dir, Books: Alison Mudditt
VP, Book Publg & Ref: Rolf Janke
Exec Ed & Publr, Journals: Elizabeth Haigh
Exec Ed, Books: Margaret Seawall
Sr Ed, Acqs: Catherine Rossbach
Ed: Al Bruckner
Circ Mgr: Mary Nugent
Founded: 1964

Professional & reference books, supplementary texts, journals, papers & newsletters in the social & behavioral sciences.
ISBN Prefix(es): 0-7591
Number of titles published annually: 275 Print
Total Titles: 5,731 Print
Subsidiaries: Corwin Press Inc; Pine Forge Press; Scolari
Divisions: Sage Publications; Scolari
Foreign Office(s): Sage Publications India Pvt Ltd, No 32, M Block Mkt, 2nd fl, Greater Kailash Part I, New Delhi 110 048, India
Sage Publications Ltd, 6 Bonhill St, London EC2A 4PU, United Kingdom
Foreign Rep(s): Astam Books Pty Ltd (Australia, New Zealand); Sage Publications India Private Ltd (India); Sage Publications Ltd (Africa, UK, Europe, Middle East); United Publishers Services Ltd (Japan, Korea)
See separate listing for:
Corwin Press

Saint Aedan's Press & Book Distributors Inc
PO Box 385, Hillsdale, NJ 07642-0385
Tel: 201-664-0127
E-mail: junius1920@yahoo.com
Web Site: www.greatoldebooks.com; www. juniusbooks.com
Key Personnel
Pres: Michael V Cordasco
Founded: 1975
Reference books, scholarly monographs; Shakespeare theatre & folklore; all subjects.
ISBN Prefix(es): 0-940198
Number of titles published annually: 3 Print
Total Titles: 17 Print
Imprints: Junius Vaughn Press Inc

Saint Andrews College Press
Subsidiary of Saint Andrews Presbyterian College
1700 Dogwood Mile, Laurinburg, NC 28352-5598
Tel: 910-277-5310 *Toll Free Tel:* 800-763-0198
Fax: 910-277-5020
E-mail: press@sapc.edu
Web Site: www.sapc.edu
Key Personnel
Ed: Peter Dulgar *E-mail:* dulgarpe@sapc.edu
Founded: 1968
ISBN Prefix(es): 0-932662; 1-879934
Number of titles published annually: 4 Print
Total Titles: 82 Print

St Anthony Messenger Press
28 W Liberty St, Cincinnati, OH 45202
SAN: 204-6237
Tel: 513-241-5615 *Toll Free Tel:* 800-488-0488
Fax: 513-241-0399
E-mail: books@americancatholic.org
Web Site: www.AmericanCatholic.org
Key Personnel
Pres: Rev Fred Link, OFM
Publr: Rev Jeremy Harrington, OFM
E-mail: jeremyh@americancatholic.org
Promo Dir: Thomas Bruce *E-mail:* tomb@ americancatholic.org; John Koize
E-mail: johnpk@americancatholic.org
Edit Dir & Intl Rts: Lisa A Biedenbach
Tel: 513-241-5615 ext 123 *E-mail:* lisab@ americancatholic.org
Prodn Dir: Br Robert A Lucero, OFM
E-mail: robertl@americancatholic.org
Art Dir: Jeanne A Kortekamp *E-mail:* jeannek@ americancatholic.org
Busn & Adv Mgr: Thomas Shumate
E-mail: toms@americancatholic.org
Rts & Perms: Diane Houdek *Tel:* 513-241-5615 ext 151 *E-mail:* dianeh@americancatholic.org
Founded: 1970
Religion (Catholic); inspirational resources for parishes, schools & individuals; books, videos, audiocassette tapes, weekly & Sunday homily programs; monthly subscription newsletters,

monthly magazine; American Catholic (web site).
ISBN Prefix(es): 0-912228; 0-86716
Number of titles published annually: 25 Print; 25 Audio
Total Titles: 256 Print; 92 Audio
Imprints: Fischer Productions; Franciscan Communications; Ikonographics; Servant Books
Distributor for Franciscan Communications (books & videos); Ikonographics (videos)
Foreign Rep(s): Catholic Supplies Ltd (New Zealand); Rainbow/Word of Life (Australia); Redemptorist Publications Book Service (UK)
Membership(s): Canadian Booksellers Association; Catholic Book Publishers Association

St Augustine's Press Inc
PO Box 2285, South Bend, IN 46680-2285
Tel: 773-702-7248 *Toll Free Tel:* 888-997-4994
Fax: 773-702-9756
Web Site: www.staugustine.net
Key Personnel
Pres & Intl Rts: Bruce Fingerhut *E-mail:* bruce@staugustine.net
Prod Mgr: Benjamin Fingerhut
E-mail: bfingerhut@hotmail.com
Founded: 1996
Scholarly & trade publishing in humanities.
ISBN Prefix(es): 1-890318; 1-58731
Number of titles published annually: 30 Print
Total Titles: 200 Print
Imprints: Carthage Reprints; William of Moerbeke Translation Services
Sales Office(s): 1429 E 60 St, Chicago, IL 60637-2954 *Tel:* 773-702-7248 *Fax:* 773-702-9756
Distributed by University of Chicago Press
Distributor for Dumb Ox Books; The Linacre Centre; St Michael's Abbey Press; Sapientia Pres
Orders to: Chicago Distribution Center, 11030 S Langley Ave, Chicago, IL 60628, Karen Hyzy *Toll Free Tel:* 800-621-2736 *Toll Free Fax:* 800-621-8471 *E-mail:* kh@press.uchicago.edu
Shipping Address: Chicago Distribution Center, 11030 S Langley Ave, Chicago, IL 60628 *Toll Free Tel:* 800-621-2736 *Toll Free Fax:* 800-621-8471 *E-mail:* kh@press.uchicago.edu
Warehouse: Chicago Distribution Center, 11030 S Langley Ave, Chicago, IL 60628
University of Chicago Press, 5801 S Ellis Ave, Chicago, IL 60637 *Toll Free Tel:* 800-621-2736 *Toll Free Fax:* 800-621-8471 *E-mail:* kh@press.uchicago.edu
Distribution Center: Chicago Distribution Center, 11030 S Langley Ave, Chicago, IL 60628 *Toll Free Tel:* 800-621-8471 *Toll Free Fax:* 800-621-8471 *E-mail:* kh@press.uchicago.edu

St Bede's Publications
271 N Main St, Box 545, Petersham, MA 01366-0545
SAN: 222-9692
Tel: 978-724-3213 *Fax:* 978-724-3216
Key Personnel
Pres: Mother Mary Clare Vincent
E-mail: smclare@one800.net
Founded: 1977
Christian spirituality.
ISBN Prefix(es): 0-932506; 1-879007
Total Titles: 97 Print; 5 Audio
Distributed by Charismatic Renewal Services; Paulist Press; Cistercian Publications
Foreign Rep(s): Fowler Wright Books Ltd (Europe); Charles Paine Ltd (Australia)

St Herman Press
Subsidiary of Brotherhood of St Herman of Alaska
10 Beegum Gorge Rd, Platina, CA 96076
SAN: 661-583X

Mailing Address: PO Box 70, Platina, CA 96076-0070
Tel: 530-352-4430 *Fax:* 530-352-4432
E-mail: stherman@stherman.com
Web Site: www.stherman.com
Key Personnel
CFO: Nicholas Liebmann
Pres: Gerasim Eliel
Sec: Paisius Bjerke
Founded: 1963
Publisher of books about the Orthodox Christian faith & Orthodox monasticism. Special emphasis on recent saints & spirituality, curriculum & textbooks.
ISBN Prefix(es): 0-938635; 1-887904
Number of titles published annually: 5 Print
Total Titles: 60 Print
Imprints: Brotherhood of St Herman of Alaska; Fr Seraphim Rose Foundation; St Herman Press; St Paisius Abbey; St Paisius Missionary School; St Xenia Skete; Valaam Society of America
Branch Office(s)
Valaam Society of America, PO Box 70, Platina, CA 96076-0070
Foreign Office(s): V Ivlenkov, Box 1854 Q, Melbourne VIC 3001, Australia
Nicholas Chapman, CEO Orthodox Christian Books Ltd, Townhouse Farm, Studio 7, Alsager Rd, Audley, Staffordshire ST7 8JQ, United Kingdom *Fax:* (011)178-272-3930 *E-mail:* 101600.262@compuserve.com
Distributed by Light & Life Publishing Co
Foreign Rep(s): Nicholas Chapman, Orthodox Christian Books Ltd (England); Vladimir Ivlenkov (Australia)
Shipping Address: 4430 Hwy 36 W, Platina, CA 96076

St James Press
Division of Gale
27500 Drake Rd, Farmington Hills, MI 48331-3535
Tel: 248-699-4253 *Toll Free Tel:* 800-877-4253 *Fax:* 248-699-8061 *Toll Free Fax:* 800-414-5043
Web Site: www.gale.com
Key Personnel
Man Ed: Peter Gareffa *E-mail:* peter.gareffa@gale.com
Founded: 1968
ISBN Prefix(es): 1-55862
Total Titles: 303 Print
Online services available through GaleNet.

St Johann Press
315 Schraalenburgh Rd, Haworth, NJ 07641
Tel: 201-387-1529 *Fax:* 201-501-0698
Key Personnel
Pres: David Biesel *E-mail:* d.biesel@worldnet.att.net
VP: Diane Biesel
VP, Edit: Tom Wright
Founded: 1990
Began as book packager & consultant in 1990 & became a full-time publisher in 1998.
ISBN Prefix(es): 1-878282
Number of titles published annually: 7 Print
Total Titles: 33 Print
Distributor for Ramsey Chair of Private Enterprise (Georgia State University)

St Joseph's University Press
5600 City Ave, Philadelphia, PA 19131
SAN: 240-8368
Tel: 610-660-3400 *Fax:* 610-660-3410
E-mail: sjupress@sju.edu
Web Site: www.sju.edu
Key Personnel
Dir: Mr Carmen R Croce *E-mail:* ccroce@sju.edu
Ed Dir of the Press: Rev Joseph F Chorpenning
Tel: 610-660-1214 *E-mail:* jchorpen@sju.edu

Tech & Res Asst: Mr William Conway
E-mail: wconway@sju.edu
Founded: 1971
Scholarly books on literature, religion (Catholic), religious art & religious iconography.
ISBN Prefix(es): 0-916101
Number of titles published annually: 5 Print
Total Titles: 35 Print
Distributor for The Americas Society; The National Museum of Women in the Arts
Membership(s): Association of Jesuit University Presses

St Jude's ImPress
5537 Waterman Blvd, Suite 2W, St Louis, MO 63112
Tel: 314-454-0064
E-mail: stjudes1@mindspring.com
Founded: 1989
Historical novels, socio-economic studies & religious history.
ISBN Prefix(es): 0-9722149
Number of titles published annually: 3 Print
Total Titles: 17 Print

St Martin's Press College Division, see Bedford/St Martin's

St Martin's Press LLC
Subsidiary of Holtzbrinck Publishers Holdings LLC
175 Fifth Ave, New York, NY 10010
SAN: 200-2132
Tel: 212-674-5151 *Fax:* 212-420-9314
E-mail: firstname.lastname@stmartins.com
Web Site: www.stmartins.com
Key Personnel
Pres (Holtzbrinck Publishers): John Sargent
Pres, Priddy Books: Steve Cohen
Treas: Michael Ross
Sr VP for Legal Aff & Sec (Holtzbrinck Publishers): David Kaye
Sr VP & Pres, Trade Div, Pbk & Ref Group: Sally Richardson
Sr VP & COO: Steve Cohen
Sr VP & Chief Info Officer, (Holtzbrinck Publishers): Fritz Foy
Sr VP & Pres, Sales Div (Holtzbrinck Publishers): Alison Lazarus
Exec VP: Philip Schwartz
VP, Fin & Acctg: John Cusack
VP, Admin (Holtzbrinck Publishers): Roy Gainsburg
VP & Gen Counsel: Paul Sleven
VP & Dir, HR (Holtzbrinck Publishers): Helaine Ohl
VP & Dir Prodn & Mfg: Karen Gillis
VP, Fulfillment & Opers: Sidney Conde
Publr, Priddy Books: Roger Priddy
VP & Dir, Sales, Broadway Sales Div (Holtzbrinck Publishers): Jeff Capshew
VP & Dir, Sales, Fifth Ave Sales Div (Holtzbrinck Publishers): Brian Heller
VP & Sr Dir, Spec Mkts & Intl Sales (Holtzbrinck Publishers): Judy Sisko
VP, Sales, Children's Mdse Div (Holtzbrinck Publishers): Bill Kelly
VP & Dir, Dist Sales & Mktg (Holtzbrinck Publishers): Patricia Hughes
VP & Dir, Field Sales (Holtzbrinck Publishers): Ken Holland
Dir, Sales, Trade Merchandise Div: Mike Rohrig
Dir, Sales, Planning & Opers: Tom Stouras
Dir, Intl Sales: Bill Farricker
Dir, Sales, Analysis & Admin: Janet Wagner
Dir, Specialty Retail/Wholesale: Alice Baker
Mgr, Premium Sales: Nicole Vines
Dir, Dist Mktg: Nora Flaherty
Mgr, Tel Sales: Jo Skipwith
Cust Promo Mgr: Tom Gilmore
Backlist Sales Mgr: Martin Quinn
Catalog Sales Mgr: Kristin Greene

Dir, Warehouse Clubs: Merrill Bergenfield
Dir, Subs Rts: Christina Harcar
Perms, Trade: Esther Robinson
Contracts Dir: Holly Bash
Conference Dir: Lisa Sitjar
Office Servs: Helen Plog
Founded: 1952
General nonfiction, fiction, reference, scholarly, mass market, travel, children's books.
ISBN Prefix(es): 0-312
Imprints: Thomas Dunne Books; Griffin; Minotaur; Priddy Books; Truman Talley Books
Distributor for Audio Renaissance Tapes; Berg Publishers; Bloomsbury USA; Consumer Reports; Edmunds; Forge Books; Hambledon; Manchester University Press; Palgrave Macmillan; Picador; Rodale Press; I B Tauris; Tor Books; World Almanac Books; Zed Books
Foreign Rep(s): Athena Productions (Caribbean, Latin America); H B Fenn & Co Ltd (Canada); Macmillan India (India); Macmillan New Zealand (New Zealand); Melia UK (UK, Ireland); Pan Macmillan Australia (Australia); Pan Macmillan-Hong Kong (Asia, Middle East); Pan Macmillan South Africa (South Africa); Pan Macmillan UK (Europe, Israel)
Foreign Rights: Big Apple Tuttle-Mori (China, Taiwan, Thailand); The Book Publishers Association of Israel (Israel); Elaine Benisti (France); International Editors' Co (Portugal, South America, Spain); Lex Copyright Office (Hungary); Literary Services (Italy); Nurcihan Kesim Literary Agency Inc (Turkey); Prava I Prevodi (Eastern Europe, Greece); Sane Toregard Agency (Denmark, Finland, Iceland, Norway, Sweden); Thomas Schlueck GmbH (Germany)
Distribution Center: VHPS Distribution Center, 16365 James Madison Hwy, Gordonsville, VA 22942-8501 *Toll Free Tel:* 888-330-8477 *Fax:* 540-672-7540 (cust serv) *Toll Free Fax:* 800-672-2054 (orders)
Membership(s): AAP
See separate listing for:
Palgrave Macmillan
St Martin's Press Paperback and Reference Group
St Martin's Press Trade Division

St Martin's Press Paperback and Reference Group
Division of St Martin's Press LLC
175 Fifth Ave, New York, NY 10010
Fax: 212-995-2488
E-mail: firstname.lastname@stmartins.com
Key Personnel
Pres: Sally Richardson
Sr VP & Publr: Matthew Shear
VP & Assoc Publr, Ref: Lisa Senz
VP & Publicity Dir: John Murphy
VP & Assoc Publr, Paperbacks: Jennifer Enderlin
Exec Art Dir: Jerry Todd
Mktg Dir, Paperbacks: Anne Marie Tallberg
Dir, Wholesale Sales: Edward Gabrielli
Exec Man Ed: John Rounds
Publicity Mgr: John Karle
Sr Ed: Heather Jackson
Ed: Marc Resnick; Monique Patterson
Also publishes Let's Go Guides & New York Times Crossword Puzzle Books.

St Martin's Press Trade Division
Division of St Martin's Press LLC
175 Fifth Ave, New York, NY 10010
E-mail: firstname.lastname@stmartins.com
Web Site: www.stmartins.com; www.minotaurbooks.com
Key Personnel
Pres & Publr: Sally Richardson
VP & Assoc Publr: John Cunningham
Dir, Subs Rts: Christina Harcar
Mktg Dir: Matthew Baldacci

VP, Exec Ed & Publr, Thomas Dunne Books: Thomas L Dunne
Assoc Publr, Thomas Dunne Books: Peter Wolverton; Ruth Cavin
VP & Ed-in-Chief: George Witte
Publr, Truman Talley Books: Truman Talley
Exec Ed: Jennifer Enderlin; Elizabeth Beier; Jennifer Weis; Hope Dellon; Charles Spicer; Diane Reverand; Sheila Curry Oakes; Michael Flamini
Sr Ed: Keith Kahla; Diane Higgins
Ed: Kelley Ragland
Ed, Thomas Dunne Books: Sean Desmond; Marcia Markland
Exec Man Ed: Amelie Littell
VP & Publicity Dir: John Murphy
Assoc Publicity Dir: Dori Weintraub
VP & Creative Dir: Steve Snider
Sr Art Dir: Michael Storrings; Henry Yee

Saint Mary's Press
Subsidiary of Christian Brothers Publications
702 Terrace Heights, Winona, MN 55987-1318
SAN: 203-073X
Tel: 507-457-7900 *Toll Free Tel:* 800-533-8095 *Toll Free Fax:* 800-344-9225
E-mail: smpress@smp.org
Web Site: www.smp.org
Key Personnel
CEO: Damian Steger
Pres: John M Vitek
Dir, Mktg, Sales & Cust Serv: Beverley J De George *E-mail:* bdegeorge@smp.org
Edit Mgr: Lorraine Kilmartin
Busn Mgr: Dave Coron
Mktg Mgr: Heather Sutton
Prodn Mgr: Caren Yang
Libn & ISBN Contact: Connie Jensen
Trade Sales: Debbie Schoener
Founded: 1943
Paperbound high school textbooks; religion (Catholic); paperbound professional religion resources.
ISBN Prefix(es): 0-88489
Number of titles published annually: 25 Print
Total Titles: 762 Print
Distributor for Group Publishing
Foreign Rep(s): B Broughton Ltd (Canada); Catholic Supplies Ltd (New Zealand); Columba Book Service (Ireland); John Garratt Publishing (Australia)

Saint Nectarios Press
10300 Ashworth Ave N, Seattle, WA 98133-9410
SAN: 159-0170
Tel: 206-522-4471 *Toll Free Tel:* 800-643-4233 *Fax:* 206-523-0550
E-mail: orders@stnectariospress.com
Web Site: www.stnectariospress.com
Key Personnel
Dir: Neketas S Palassis *E-mail:* fatherneketas@orthodoxpress.org
Busn Mgr: Nina S Seco *E-mail:* seco@orthodoxpress.org
Founded: 1977
Traditional Eastern Orthodox books.
ISBN Prefix(es): 0-913026
Number of titles published annually: 3 Print
Total Titles: 47 Print

Salem Press Inc
2 University Plaza, Suite 121, Hackensack, NJ 07601
SAN: 208-838X
Tel: 201-968-9899 *Toll Free Tel:* 800-221-1592 *Fax:* 201-968-1411
E-mail: csr@salempress.com
Web Site: www.salempress.com
Key Personnel
Pres: James L Magill *Tel:* 626-584-0106 *Fax:* 626-584-1525

Exec VP: Kenneth T Burles *Tel:* 626-584-0106 *Fax:* 626-584-1525
VP, Edit & Prodn: Dawn Dawson *Tel:* 626-584-0106 *Fax:* 626-584-1525
VP, Sales & Mktg: Shirley Sarris *E-mail:* ssarris@salempress.com
Inside Sales Mgr: Pamela Brunke *E-mail:* pbrunke@salempress.com
Publicist & Sales & Mktg Mgr: Luisa Torres *E-mail:* ltorres@salempress.com
Founded: 1949
Reference books & online products for middle school, secondary school, colleges & public libraries.
ISBN Prefix(es): 0-89356; 1-58765
Number of titles published annually: 11 Print; 2 Online
Total Titles: 150 Print; 2 CD-ROM; 2 Online
Online services available through EBSCOhost.
Imprints: Magill's Choice
Branch Office(s)
131 N El Molino Ave, Suite 350, Pasadena, CA 91101, Ken Burles *Tel:* 626-584-0106 *Fax:* 626-584-1525
Foreign Rep(s): Aditya Books Pvt Ltd (India); Alkem Co (Singapore, Taiwan); The Eurospan Group (UK, England); C Kirkness Press (Canada); Somohano Express (Mexico); Warner Books Pty Ltd (Australia); Yushodo Co Ltd (Japan)
Billing Address: 131 N El Molino Ave, Suite 350, Pasadena, CA 91101, Sherri Schaeffer *Tel:* 626-584-0106 *Fax:* 626-584-1525
Shipping Address: Quebecor, Hwy 11, W Kingsport Press Rd, Church Hill, TN 37642, Kay Yontis *Tel:* 423-357-2089

San Diego State University Press
Division of San Diego State University Foundation
San Diego State University, 5500 Campanile Dr, San Diego, CA 92182-8141
Tel: 760-768-5536; 619-594-6220 (orders only) *Fax:* 760-768-5631
Web Site: www.rohan.sdsu.edu/dept/press/
Key Personnel
Dir: Harry Polkinhorn
Assoc Dir & Off Mgr: Sheila Dollente *E-mail:* sheila.d@sdsu.edu
Founded: 1959
Scholarly & trade, monographs.
ISBN Prefix(es): 0-916304; 1-879691
Number of titles published annually: 10 Print; 2 Online
Total Titles: 70 Print
Imprints: Binational Press; Campanile Press; Fiction International (Journal); San Diego State College Press
Branch Office(s)
SDSU Press, San Diego State University, Imperial Valley Campus, 720 Heber Ave, Calexico, CA 92231 *Tel:* 760-768-5536
Distributed by UPA (selected titles only)
Distributor for Institute for Regional Studies of the Californias

J S Sanders & Co Inc, see Ivan R Dee Publisher

Sandlapper Publishing Inc
PO Drawer 730, Orangeburg, SC 29116-0730
SAN: 203-2678
Tel: 803-531-1658 *Toll Free Tel:* 800-849-7263 (orders only) *Fax:* 803-534-5223
Web Site: www.sandlapperpublishing.com
Key Personnel
Pres & Owner: Amanda Gallman *E-mail:* agallman1@mindspring.com
Prodn & Mktg: Barbara Stone
Founded: 1982
Nonfiction material about South Carolina only. Submit query letter.
ISBN Prefix(es): 0-87844

Number of titles published annually: 6 Print
Total Titles: 80 Print
Shipping Address: 1281 Amelia St NE, Orangeburg, SC 29115

Santa Monica Press LLC
513 Wilshire Blvd, No 321, Santa Monica, CA 90401
SAN: 298-1459
Mailing Address: PO Box 1076, Santa Monica, CA 90406-1076
Tel: 310-230-7759 *Toll Free Tel:* 800-784-9553
Fax: 310-230-7761
E-mail: books@santamonicapress.com
Web Site: www.santamonicapress.com
Key Personnel
Publr: Jeffrey Goldman *E-mail:* jgoldman@santamonicapress.com
Founded: 1991
Modern how-to books, offbeat looks at popular culture, film history & literature.
ISBN Prefix(es): 0-9639946; 1-891661; 1-59580
Number of titles published annually: 14 Print
Total Titles: 50 Print
Foreign Rep(s): Turnaround Publisher Services Ltd (Africa, Asia, UK/Europe); Wakefield Press (Australia & New Zealand)
Foreign Rights: Susan Sewall Independent Publishers Group
Orders to: 814 N Franklin St, Chicago, IL 60610
Toll Free Tel: 800-888-4741
Returns: I P G Warehouse, 600 N Pulanski Rd, Chicago, IL 60624
Warehouse: I P G Warehouse, 600 N Pulaski Rd, Chicago, IL 60624, Contact: Mark Noble *Tel:* 312-337-0747 *Fax:* 312-337-5985 *Web Site:* www.ipgbook.com

Santillana USA Publishing Co Inc
Imprint of The Richmond Publishing Co Inc
2105 NW 86 Ave, Miami, FL 33122
SAN: 205-1133
Tel: 305-591-9522 *Toll Free Tel:* 800-245-8584
Fax: 305-591-9145 *Toll Free Fax:* 888-248-9518
E-mail: customerservice@santillanausa.com
Web Site: www.santillanausa.com; www.alfaguara.net
Key Personnel
Pres, CEO & Intl Rts Contact: Carlos A Davis
VP, School Div: Stephen Marban
Dir, Gen Books Div: Silvia Matut
Founded: 1972
Educational & Spanish language trade books; English as a second language & bilingual textbooks; Spanish as a foreign language.
ISBN Prefix(es): 0-88272; 1-56014; 1-58105; 1-58986; 1-59437
Number of titles published annually: 50 Print; 3 CD-ROM; 5 Audio
Total Titles: 1,000 Print; 3 CD-ROM; 15 Audio
Imprints: Aguilar; Alfaguara; Santillana; Taurus
Membership(s): AAP

Sarabande Books Inc
2234 Dundee Rd, Suite 200, Louisville, KY 40205
Tel: 502-458-4028 *Fax:* 502-458-4065
E-mail: info@sarabandebooks.org
Web Site: www.sarabandebooks.org
Key Personnel
Pres: Sarah Gorham
Man Ed: Kirby Gann
Founded: 1994
Short fiction, poetry & literary nonfiction collections.
ISBN Prefix(es): 1-889330
Number of titles published annually: 10 Print
Total Titles: 81 Print
Foreign Rep(s): Nancy Green Madia
Foreign Rights: Nancy Green Madia
Distribution Center: Consortium Book Sales

1045 Westgate Dr, St Paul, MN 55114-1065
Membership(s): ABA

SAS Publishing
SAS Campus Dr, Cary, NC 27513
Tel: 919-531-7447 *Fax:* 919-677-4444
E-mail: sasbbu@sas.com
Web Site: www.sas.com
Key Personnel
Ed-in-Chief: Julie M Platt *E-mail:* julie.platt@sas.com
Founded: 1976
Books about SAS or JMP software.
ISBN Prefix(es): 1-55544; 0-917382
Number of titles published annually: 50 Print
Distributed by John Wiley & Sons Inc
Distributor for Amacon; Breakfast Communications; CRC Press; Duxbury; Harcourt; Harvard Business School Press; McGraw-Hill; Oxford; Prentice-Hall; John Wiley & Sons Inc

Sasquatch Books
119 S Main, Suite 400, Seattle, WA 98104
SAN: 289-0208
Tel: 206-467-4300 *Toll Free Tel:* 800-775-0817
Fax: 206-467-4301
E-mail: books@sasquatchbooks.com
Web Site: www.sasquatchbooks.com
Key Personnel
Publr: Chad Haight
VP, Sales & Mktg: Susan Quinn *Tel:* 206-467-4300 ext 314
Sales & Mktg Dir: Sarah Hanson
Man Ed: Heidi Schuessler
Edit Dir: Gary Luke
Design Dir & Rts: Kate Basart
Busn Mgr: JoAnn Diep-Lang
Founded: 1986
Regional books (Pacific Northwest & California).
ISBN Prefix(es): 0-934007; 0-912365; 1-57061
Number of titles published annually: 40 Print
Total Titles: 240 Print; 3 Audio
Imprints: Best Places® Guidebooks Series; Paws IV
Foreign Rep(s): Publishers Group Canada (Canada)
Distribution Center: Publishers Group West, 1700 Fourth St, Berkeley, CA 94710 *Toll Free Tel:* 800-788-3123 *Fax:* 510-528-3444

§Saunders College Publishing
Imprint of Thomson Learning
The Public Ledger Bldg, 150 S Independence Mall W, Suite 1250, Philadelphia, PA 19106-3412
Tel: 215-238-5500 *Fax:* 215-238-5660
Web Site: www.hbcollege.com *Telex:* 17-3146
Key Personnel
Pres: Theodore O Buchholz
Sr VP, Prodn: Tim Frelick
Sr VP, Sales: Scott Stewart
Sr VP & CFO: Ray Vales
Sr VP, Edit: Chris Klein
VP, Publr: Emily Barrosse
ISBN Prefix(es): 0-03
Total Titles: 14 CD-ROM

§W B Saunders Ltd
Imprint of Elsevier Health Sciences
170 S Independence Mall W, Suite 300 E, Philadelphia, PA 19106-3399
Tel: 215-238-7800 *Toll Free Tel:* 800-545-2522 (cust serv) *Fax:* 215-238-7883
Web Site: www.elsevierhealth.com
Key Personnel
CEO, Health Sci Div: Brian Nairin
CFO: Menno Tas
Dir, Edit Servs: Philippe Terheggen
Sr VP: Craig Samios
VP, Mktg: John Schrefer
Sr VP, Sales: Toni Linstedt

Ed-in-Chief, Health Related Professions: Andrew Allen
Exec VP, Nursing & Health Professions: Sally Schrefer
Exec VP, Global Medicine: Fiona Foley
Exec VP, Sales & Mktg: Mary Ging
Exec VP, Journals: Kevin Hurley
Founded: 1888
Books, journals, clinic series & electronic services in medicine, dentistry, nursing, allied health & veterinary medicine.
ISBN Prefix(es): 0-7216
Total Titles: 150 Print; 3 CD-ROM
Foreign Office(s): 55 Horner Ave, Toronto, ON M8Z 4X6, Canada
24-28 Oval Rd, London NW1 7DX, United Kingdom
Ichibancho Central Bldg, 22-1 Ichibancho, Chiyoda-Ku, Tokyo 102, Japan *Tel:* 81-3-3234-3911/5
Distributor for Bailliere-Tindall (UK)
Warehouse: 465 S Lincoln Dr, Troy, MO 63379
Interstate Industrial Park, Heller & Benigno Blvd, Bellmawr, NJ 08031

Savage Press
1209 Lincoln St, Superior, WI 54880
Mailing Address: PO Box 115, Superior, WI 54880
Tel: 715-394-9513 *Toll Free Tel:* 800-732-3867
Fax: 715-394-9513
E-mail: mail@savpress.com
Web Site: www.savpress.com
Key Personnel
Contact: Michael P Savage
Founded: 1989
ISBN Prefix(es): 1-886028
Number of titles published annually: 10 Print
Total Titles: 90 Print

Saxon
Imprint of Harcourt Achieve
10801 N MoPac Expressway, Austin, TX 78759
Mailing Address: PO Box 27010, Austin, TX 78755
Tel: 512-343-8227 *Toll Free Tel:* 800-531-5015
Toll Free Fax: 800-699-9459
E-mail: ecare@harcourt.com
Web Site: www.harcourtachieve.com
Founded: 1981
Educational materials for K-12.

§Scarecrow Press/Government Institutes Div
Division of Rowman & Littlefield
4501 Forbes Blvd, Suite 200, Lanham, MD 20706
SAN: 214-3801
Tel: 301-921-2300 *Fax:* 301-429-5747
Web Site: govinst.scarecrowpress.com
Key Personnel
VP & Publr: Edward Kurdyla *Tel:* 301-459-3366
Dir, Mktg: Janet Wolfe *Tel:* 301-921-2313
E-mail: jwolfe@absconsulting.com
Founded: 1973
Law, regulatory & technical books & environmental safety, code of federal regulations, quality, risk, industrial hygiene & internet; CD-ROM & electronic products.
ISBN Prefix(es): 0-86587
Number of titles published annually: 30 Print; 4 CD-ROM
Total Titles: 240 Print; 11 CD-ROM

Scarecrow Press Inc
Member of The Rowman & Littlefield Publishing Group Inc
4501 Forbes Blvd, Suite 200, Lanham, MD 20706
Tel: 301-459-3366 *Toll Free Tel:* 800-462-6420
Fax: 301-429-5747 *Toll Free Fax:* 800-338-4550
Web Site: www.scarecrowpress.com

Key Personnel
Pres: Jed Lyons *Tel:* 301-731-9538
  E-mail: jlyons@rowman.com
VP & Publr: Edward Kurdyla
Mktg Mgr: Mary Jo Godwin
Intl Rts Contact: Kelly Rogers
Lib Sales Dir: Lita Orner
Founded: 1950
Reference books & texts in music, film, information technology, theater, performing arts, history, religion & cultural studies. Professional & reference books in library & information sciences & government regulatory areas. Co-publishing with Rutgers Jazz Institute, Music Library Association, American Theological Library Association & Children's Literature Association.
ISBN Prefix(es): 0-8108; 1-57886
Number of titles published annually: 200 Print; 2 CD-ROM; 10 Online; 5 E-Book
Total Titles: 2,500 Print; 6 CD-ROM; 100 Online; 30 E-Book
Imprints: Falling Leaf; Government Institutes; Scarecrow Trade
Divisions: VOYA (Voice of Youth Advocates) Magazine
Foreign Office(s): 67 Mowat Ave, Suite 241, Toronto, ON M6K 3E3, Canada, Contact: Les Petriw *Tel:* 416-543-1660
Foreign Rep(s): Oxford Publicity Partnership (UK & Europe)
Advertising Agency: ABC Marketing
Distribution Center: 15200 NBN Way, Blue Ridge Summit, PA 17214, Contact: Meg Phelps *Toll Free Tel:* 800-462-6420 *Toll Free Fax:* 800-338-4550
Membership(s): AAP; ALA; Music Library Association

Scepter Publishers
8 W 38 St, New York, NY 10018
SAN: 207-2858
Mailing Address: PO Box 211, New York, NY 10018
Tel: 212-354-0670 *Toll Free Tel:* 800-322-8773
  Fax: 212-354-0736
Web Site: www.scepterpublishers.org
Key Personnel
Pres, Publr & Ed-in-Chief: John G Powers
  E-mail: jgp@scepterpublishers.org
Founded: 1954
Catholic Book Publishing including doctrinal works, theology & liturgy.
ISBN Prefix(es): 0-933932; 0-1889334; 1-594170
Number of titles published annually: 15 Print
Total Titles: 140 Print
Distribution Center: Maple-Vail Distribution, Fredericksburg, PA 17026

Robert Schalkenbach Foundation
149 Madison Ave, Suite 601, New York, NY 10016-6713
Tel: 212-683-6424 *Toll Free Tel:* 800-269-9555
  Fax: 212-683-6454
E-mail: staff@schalkenbach.org
Web Site: www.schalkenbach.org
Key Personnel
Exec Dir: Mark A Sullivan
Founded: 1925
Founded to promote the ideas of & publish the works of Henry George. Also publishes other authors' writings on George, land value taxation & related subjects. Sponsors American Journal of Economics & Sociology.
ISBN Prefix(es): 0-911312
Number of titles published annually: 3 Print
Total Titles: 28 Print; 1 CD-ROM; 4 Online
Subsidiaries: American Journal of Economics & Sociology
Orders to: New York, NY, Ms Sonny Rivera

Warehouse: Publishers Storage & Shipping Corporation, 42 Development Rd, Fitchbury, MA 01420
Distribution Center: New York, NY, Ms Sonny Rivera

Schiffer Publishing Ltd
4880 Lower Valley Rd, Atglen, PA 19310
SAN: 208-8428
Tel: 610-593-1777 *Fax:* 610-593-2002
E-mail: schifferbk@aol.com; schifferii@aol.com
Web Site: schifferbooks.com
Key Personnel
Pres & Ed-in-Chief: Peter Schiffer
Exec VP: Nancy Schiffer
Cust Rel: Pamela Braceland
Spec Sales: Joe Langman
Founded: 1974
Collecting, art books, antiques, architecture, toys, woodcarving, hobbies, weaving, color, metaphysics, aviation, military books, automotive books, design & fashion.
ISBN Prefix(es): 0-916838; 0-88740; 0-7643
Number of titles published annually: 300 Print
Total Titles: 2,000 Print
Imprints: Canal Press; Kaiser-Barlow; Para Research; Whitford Press
Divisions: Whitford Press
Distributor for The Donning Co
Foreign Rights: Bushwood Books (Europe)

Schirmer, see Wadsworth Publishing

Schirmer Trade Books
Imprint of Music Sales Corp
25 Park Ave S, New York, NY 10010
Tel: 212-254-2100 *Toll Free Tel:* 800-431-7187
  Fax: 212-254-2013 *Toll Free Fax:* 800-345-6842
Web Site: www.musicsales.com
Key Personnel
Pres: Barrie Edwards *E-mail:* be@musicsales.com
Man Ed: Andrea Rotondo *E-mail:* ar@schirmertradebooks.com
Founded: 1935
Committed to intelligent, educational & entertaining books about all aspects of music, especially the recording arts, music business, genre histories & musician biographies.
ISBN Prefix(es): 0-8256; 0-7119
Number of titles published annually: 15 Print
Total Titles: 133 Print
Sales Office(s): 445 Bellvale Rd, Chester, NY 10918-0572, Contack: Steve Wilson *Toll Free Tel:* 800-431-7187 *Toll Free Fax:* 800-345-6842 *E-mail:* sw@musicsales.com
Foreign Office(s): Lisgar House, 4th fl, 30-32 Carrington, NSW 2000 Sydney, Australia *Tel:* (29) 299-8877 *Fax:* (29) 299-6564
8/9 Frith St, London W1D 3JB, United Kingdom *Tel:* (207) 434-0066 *Fax:* (207) 734-2246
Distributor for Big Meteor Publishing; Independent Music Press
Billing Address: 445 Bellvale Rd, Chester, NY 10918-0572 *Toll Free Tel:* 800-431-7187 *Toll Free Fax:* 800-345-6842 *E-mail:* info@musicsales.com
Orders to: 445 Bellvale Rd, Chester, NY 10918-0572 *Toll Free Tel:* 800-431-7187 *Toll Free Fax:* 800-345-6842 *E-mail:* info@musicsales.com
Returns: 445 Bellvale Rd, Chester, NY 10918-0572 *Toll Free Tel:* 800-431-7187 *Toll Free Fax:* 800-345-6842 *E-mail:* info@musicsales.com
Shipping Address: 445 Bellvale Rd, Chester, NY 10918-0572 *Toll Free Tel:* 800-431-7187 *Toll Free Fax:* 800-345-6842 *E-mail:* info@musicsales.com
Warehouse: 445 Bellvale Rd, Chester, NY 10918-0572 *Toll Free Tel:* 800-431-7187 *Toll Free

Fax: 800-345-6842 *E-mail:* info@musicsales.com
Distribution Center: 445 Bellvale Rd, Chester, NY 10918-0572
Membership(s): ABA; American Society of Journalists & Authors; Publishers Marketing Association; Women's National Book Association

Scholars' Facsimiles & Reprints
Subsidiary of Academic Resources Corp
PO Box 5934, Carefree, AZ 85377-5934
SAN: 203-2627
Tel: 480-575-9945 *Fax:* 480-575-9451
E-mail: maxinmin@umich.edu
Key Personnel
Publr: Norman Mangouni
Founded: 1936
Facsimile reprints of rare books of scholarly interest, microforms, occasional originals.
ISBN Prefix(es): 0-8201
Number of titles published annually: 20 Print
Total Titles: 546 Print

Scholastic Education
Division of Scholastic Inc
524 Broadway, New York, NY 10012
Tel: 212-343-6100 *Fax:* 212-343-6189
Web Site: www.scholastic.com
Key Personnel
Pres, Scholastic Education: Margery Mayer
Pres, Scholastic Library: Greg Worrell
Chief Administrative Officer & VP: Francie Alexander
Sr VP, Mktg: Mary Mitchell
Publishing group comprised of ten divisions.
Divisions: Business Development; Finance & Operations; Lectorum Publications Inc; Primary Publishing; Professional Development; Publishing Services; Sales & Marketing; Teaching Resources; Technology; Upper Elementary/Secondary & Magazines Publishing

Scholastic Education Curriculum Publishing
Division of Scholastic Inc
524 Broadway, New York, NY 10012
Tel: 212-343-6100
Web Site: www.scholastic.com
Key Personnel
Pres, Scholastic Education: Margery Mayer
VP & Publr, Upper Elementary/Secondary & Classroom Magazines: David Goddy
VP & Chief Academic Officer: Francie Alexander
Publish for early childhood, classroom magazines, erading improvement, supplementary reading, instructional programs & technology, & language arts for grades Pre-K through grades 12.

Scholastic Entertainment Inc
Division of Scholastic Inc
524 Broadway, New York, NY 10012
Tel: 212-343-7500 *Fax:* 212-965-7448
Key Personnel
Pres: Deborah Forte
Sr VP, Programming & Dist: Linda Kahn
Sr VP, Mktg & Consumer Prods: Leslye Schaefer
VP, Creative Prod Devt: Sharon Lisman
VP, Fin: Ginger McGuire
VP, Licensing: Peter Van Raalte
VP, Brand Mktg, TV/Broadcast Rel: Cheryl Gotthelf

Scholastic Inc
557 Broadway, New York, NY 10012
Tel: 212-343-4469 *Toll Free Tel:* 800-scholastic
  Fax: 212-343-6930
Web Site: www.scholastic.com
Key Personnel
Chmn of the Bd, Pres & CEO: Richard Robinson
Exec VP & CFO: Mary Winston
Exec VP: Richard M Spaulding

Exec VP & Pres, Scholastic Book Clubs: Judy
  Newman
Exec VP, Mktg: Linda Keene
Pres & Div Head, Scholastic Entertainment: Deb-
  orah A Forte
Pres, Internet Group: Donna Iucolano
Pres, Children's Book Publg & Dist: Barbara A
  Marcus
Pres, Scholastic Education: Margery Mayer
Pres, Intl: Hugh Roome
Pres, Scholatic Book Fairs: David Krishock
Pres, Scholastic Library Publishing: Greg Worrell
Sr VP, Corp Communs & Media Rel: Judith A
  Corman
Sr VP, Gen Counsel & Sec: Charles B Deull
Sr VP, Educ & Corp Rel: Ernest B Fleishman
Sr VP & Publr, Children's Book Publg: Jean Fei-
  wel
Sr VP, Global Opers: Beth Ford
Sr VP: Heather Myers
Sr VP, Corp HR & Employee Servs: Larry V
  Holland
VP, Corp Comms & Media Rel: Kyle Good
VP, Internal Communs: Claudia H Cohl
VP, Fin & Investor Rel: Raymond Marchuck
VP & Corp Cont: Karen A Maloney
VP & Treas: Vincent M Marzano
VP & Deputy Publr: Ellie Berger
Founded: 1920
Scholastic Corp (NMS: SCHL) is the world's
  largest publisher & distributor of children's
  books. Scholastic creates quality educational
  & entertaining materials & products for use
  in school & at home, including children's
  books, textbooks, magazines, technology-
  based products, teacher materials, television
  programming, videos & toys. The company
  distributes its products & services through
  a variety of channels, including proprietary
  school-based book clubs, school-based book
  fairs, school-based & direct-to-home continuity programs; retail stores, schools, libraries &
  television networks; & the company's internet
  site, www.scholastic.com.
ISBN Prefix(es): 0-590
Number of titles published annually: 600 Print; 3
  CD-ROM; 20 E-Book
Total Titles: 6,000 Print; 29 CD-ROM; 21 E-
  Book
Distribution Center: 2931 E McCarty St, Jeffer-
  son City, MO 65101
100 Plaza Drive W, Secaucus, NJ 07094
Membership(s): AAP; ALA; Children's Book
  Council
See separate listing for:
e-Scholastic
Lectorum Publications Inc
Quality Education Data, Inc
Scholastic Education
Scholastic Education Curriculum Publishing
Scholastic Entertainment Inc
Scholastic International
Scholastic Library Publishing
Scholastic Paperbacks, Teaching Resources &
  Reading Counts
Scholastic Trade Division

Scholastic International
Division of Scholastic Inc
557 Broadway, New York, NY 10012
Tel: 212-343-6100 *Fax:* 212-343-4712
Key Personnel
Pres, Intl Group: Hugh Roome
VP & Dir, Intl Sales & Mktg: Seth Russo
VP, New Busn Devt: Carol Sakoian
VP, Spanish Publg: Mauricio Sabene
Dir, Intl Licensing: Linda Biagi
Instructional materials for early childhood, ele-
  mentary, middle & HS. Classroom magazines;
  classroom paperback book clubs; book fairs;
  juvenile & young adult hardcover & trade pa-
  perbacks; software for three-12 year olds &
  parents. Direct-to-home educational book clubs

for children. Online & print publisher of refer-
  ence products.
Subsidiaries: Scholastic Argentina SA; Scholas-
  tic Australia Pty Ltd; Scholastic Canada Ltd;
  Scholastic Hong Kong Ltd; Scholastic India
  Private Ltd; Scholastic Mexico SA; Scholastic
  New Zealand Ltd; Scholastic Publications Ltd
  (UK)

Scholastic Library Publishing
Division of Scholastic Inc
90 Old Sherman Tpke, Danbury, CT 06816
Tel: 203-797-3500 *Toll Free Tel:* 800-621-1115
  Fax: 203-797-3657
Web Site: www.scholasticlibrary.com
Key Personnel
Pres: Greg Worrell
VP, Fin: Allison Henderson
VP, Mktg: Pam Sader
VP & Publr: Phil Friedman
VP & Publr, Specialty Ref, Grolier: Joe Hollan-
  der
VP & Publr, Grolier Online & Major Reference:
  Mark Cummings
Assoc VP, Opers: Toni Abrahams
Ed-in-Chief, Children's Press & Franklin Watts:
  Kate Nunn
Publishers of juvenile nonfiction, encyclopedias,
  specialty reference sets, young adult & online
  databases.
ISBN Prefix(es): 0-516; 0-531; 0-7172
Number of titles published annually: 500 Print;
  10 Online
Total Titles: 3,000 Print; 8 Online
Divisions: Children's Press; Franklin Watts;
  Grolier Educational; Grolier Online
Warehouse: 2931 E McCarty St, Jefferson City,
  MO 65101 (Free shipping)

**Scholastic Paperbacks, Teaching Resources &
  Reading Counts**
Division of Scholastic Inc
557 Broadway, New York, NY 10012-3999
Tel: 212-965-7241 *Fax:* 212-965-7487
Web Site: www.scholastic.com
Key Personnel
Sr VP & Gen Mgr: Judy DeTuncq
VP & Publr: Terry Cooper
VP, Mktg, Pbk: Cathy Toohey
Edit Dir: Virginia Dooley; Deborah Schecter
Art Dir: Jay Lucero
Ed & Prod Coord: Adriane Rozier
Mktg, Teaching Resources: Eileen Hillebrand
Founded: 1989
Professional development books, project, activity,
  resource & reference books for teachers of el-
  ementary & middle school grades, classroom
  libraries for schools, reading counts program.
Number of titles published annually: 2,000 Print
Total Titles: 10,000 Print
Distribution Center: 2931 E McCarty St, Jeffer-
  son City, MO 65102 *Tel:* 573-636-5271

Scholastic Trade Division
Division of Scholastic Inc
557 Broadway, New York, NY 10012
Tel: 212-343-6100; 212-343-4685 (export sales)
  Fax: 212-343-4714 (export sales)
Web Site: www.scholastic.com
Key Personnel
Pres, Children's Books: Barbara A Marcus
Sr VP & Publr: Jean Feiwel
Sr VP, Fin & Opers: Ed Monagle
Sr VP, Trade Publg: Ellie Berger
Sr VP, Book Clubs: Judith Newman
VP & Edit Dir, The Blue Sky Press: Bonnie Ver-
  burg
VP & Edit Dir, Arthur A Levine Books: Arthur A
  Levine
VP & Edit Dir, Trade Pbks: Craig Walker
VP, Special Sales: John Illingworth
VP, Trade Mktg: Jennifer Pasanen

VP, Direct Mail: Betsy Poris
VP, Fin & Opers: Peggy Sharpe
VP, Book Clubs: David Vozar
VP, Creative Dir, Edit: David Saylor
VP, Trade Sales: Gary Gentel
VP, Mass Sales: Michelle Lewy
VP, Trade Fin: Mia Camacho
Edit Dir, Scholastic Reference: Ken Wright
Edit Dir, Cartwheel Books & Orchard Books:
  Ken Geist
Edit Dir, Scholastic Press: Liz Szabla
Dir, Trade Opers: Ed Swart
Dir, Mass Sales: Lola Valenciaro; Doug Hender-
  son
Dir, Foreign Rts: Linda Biagi
Dir, Conventions & Events: Jacquelin Harper
Dir, Promo Prods: David Cohen
Dir, Channel Mktg & Mktg Opers: Leslie Garych
Dir, Lib Mktg & Sr Mktg Mgr, Lib Sales: John
  Mason
Publicity Dir: Kris Moran
Dir, Trade Sales & Natl Accts: Chris Murphy
Dir, Field Sales: Margaret Coffee
Assoc Dir, Mktg, Hardcover: Rachel Coun
Assoc Dir, Natl Accts: Simon Tasker
Exec Ed: Diane Hess; Grace Maccarone
Author Visits: Stephanie Wimmer
Hardcover & paperback children's books, licensed
  publishing & children's merchandise.
ISBN Prefix(es): 0-590; 0-439
Number of titles published annually: 650 Print
Total Titles: 6,000 Print
Imprints: Arthur A Levine Books; The Blue
  Sky Press; Cartwheel Books; The Chicken
  House; Orchard Books; Scholastic Non-Fiction;
  Scholastic Paperbacks; Scholastic Press;
  Scholastic Reference
Distribution Center: 2931 E McCarty St, Jeffer-
  son City, MO 65102 *Tel:* 573-635-5881

§Scholium International Inc
PO Box 1519, Port Washington, NY 11050-7519
SAN: 164-744X
Tel: 516-767-7171 *Fax:* 516-944-9824
E-mail: info@scholium.com; artcandido@cs.com
Web Site: www.scholium.com
Key Personnel
Pres: Arthur A Candido *E-mail:* aacandido@
  scholium.com
Exec VP, Juv Ed & Dist Mgr: Elena M Candido
  E-mail: emcandido@scholium.com
Founded: 1973
Science, medicine & technology.
ISBN Prefix(es): 0-87936
Number of titles published annually: 10 Print; 1
  CD-ROM
Total Titles: 300 Print; 5 CD-ROM
Distributor for Chalcombe Publications (UK);
  Dechema Series; International Ediemme Rome;
  Macmillan (UK); Micelle Press; Palladian
  Books Ltd; Piccin Nuova Libraria SPA (Padua
  Italy); Royal Society of London; Sita Technol-
  ogy (UK); Viewpoint; Zuckschwerdt Verlag
  (Munich, Germany)

Schonfeld & Associates Inc
2830 Blackthorn Rd, Riverwood, IL 60015
SAN: 255-2361
Tel: 847-948-8080 *Toll Free Tel:* 800-205-0030
  Fax: 847-948-8096
E-mail: saiinfo@saibooks.com
Web Site: www.saibooks.com
Key Personnel
Pres: Carol Greenhut *E-mail:* cgreenhut@
  saibooks.com
Founded: 1977
Author statistical reference works.
ISBN Prefix(es): 1-878339; 1-932024
Number of titles published annually: 9 Print; 9
  CD-ROM; 1 E-Book
Total Titles: 10 Print; 9 CD-ROM; 1 E-Book

School of American Research Press
660 Garcia St, Santa Fe, NM 87505
Tel: 505-954-7206 *Toll Free Tel:* 888-390-6070
Fax: 505-954-7241
E-mail: bkorders@sarsf.org
Web Site: www.sarweb.org
Key Personnel
Pubns Assoc: Jason S Ordaz
Founded: 1979
Southwestern Indian arts & popular southwestern literature.
ISBN Prefix(es): 1-930618; 0-933452
Number of titles published annually: 16 Print
Total Titles: 102 Print
Foreign Rep(s): Codasat (Canada); James Currey Publishers (Africa, UK, Europe)

School of Government
Division of The University of NC at Chapel Hill
University of North Carolina, CB 3330, Chapel Hill, NC 27599-3330
Tel: 919-966-4119 *Fax:* 919-962-2707
E-mail: khunt@iogmail.iog.unc.edu
Web Site: www.sog.unc.edu
Key Personnel
Mktg & Sales Mgr: Katrina W Hunt
 E-mail: khunt@iogmail.iog.unc.edu
Founded: 1931
Textbooks, casebooks, manuals & guidebooks, monographs, reports, bulletins & two quarterly magazines.
ISBN Prefix(es): 1-56011
Total Titles: 400 Print; 2 CD-ROM; 14 Online

§School Zone Publishing Co
1819 Industrial Dr, Grand Haven, MI 49417
Mailing Address: PO Box 777, Grand Haven, MI 49417
Tel: 616-846-5030 *Toll Free Tel:* 800-253-0564
 Fax: 616-846-6181
Web Site: www.schoolzone.com
Key Personnel
Pres & Intl Rts Contact: Joan Hoffman
VP, Books & Educ: Sharon Winningham
 Tel: 616-846-5030 ext 117 *E-mail:* sharonw@schoolzone.com
Founded: 1979
Instructional materials for early childhood, pre-school - 6; educational workbooks, flashcards & software.
ISBN Prefix(es): 0-88743; 0-938256; 1-58947
Number of titles published annually: 12 Print; 12 CD-ROM
Total Titles: 300 Print; 50 CD-ROM

Schreiber Publishing Inc
51 Monroe St, Suite 101, Rockville, MD 20850
SAN: 203-2465
Tel: 301-424-7737 *Toll Free Tel:* 800-822-3213 (sales) *Fax:* 301-424-2518
E-mail: books@schreibernet.com
Web Site: schreiberpublishing.com
Key Personnel
Pres & Rts & Perms: Mordecai Schreiber
 Tel: 301-424-7737 ext 28
Ed/Off Asst: Jackie Cullerton
Busn Mgr: Marla Schulman
Founded: 1954 (as Shengold Publishers)
Books on language & translation, Judaica history, Holocaust memoirs, juveniles, reference books, fiction, art books.
ISBN Prefix(es): 0-88400; 1-887563
Number of titles published annually: 12 Print
Total Titles: 131 Print
Imprints: Shengold Books
Foreign Rights: Bet Alim (Israel); Gazelle (UK, Europe); Importadora Agrimen (Latin America)
Shipping Address: National Book Network, 15200 NBN Way, Blue Ridge Summit, PA 17214, Contact: Christine Wolf *Tel:* 717-794-3800
 Fax: 717-794-3804

Warehouse: National Book Network, 15200 NBN Way, Blue Ridge Summit, PA 17214, Contact: Christine Wolf *Tel:* 717-794-3800 *Fax:* 717-794-3804
Distribution Center: National Book Network, 4720 Boston Way, Lanham, MD 20706, Contact: Eileen Judd *Tel:* 301-459-3366 *Toll Free Tel:* 800-462-6420 *Fax:* 301-459-1705
 E-mail: vmetzger@nbnbooks.com

§Science & Humanities Press
1023 Stuyvesant Lane, Manchester, MO 63011-3601
Mailing Address: PO Box 7151, Chesterfield, MO 63006-7151
Tel: 636-394-4950
E-mail: publisher@sciencehumanitiespress.com
Web Site: sciencehumanitiespress.com; beachhousebooks.com; macroprintbooks.com; earlyeditionsbooks.com; heuristicsbooks.com
Key Personnel
Publr & CEO: Robert J Banis *E-mail:* banis@sciencehumanitiespress.com
Founded: 1994
Quality books with a mission. Titles include adapting to living with a disability, computer capabilities, education & specialized medical/wellness topics. Most interested in books that have enduring human value, promoting the kind of world we all want to live in. Prefer inquiries by e-mail. No unsol mss; author guidelines on website (sciencehumanitiespress.com).
ISBN Prefix(es): 1-888725; 1-59630
Number of titles published annually: 40 Print; 1 E-Book
Total Titles: 100 Print; 1 E-Book; 1 Audio
Imprints: BeachHouse Books; Early Editions Books; Heuristic Books; MacroPrintBooks
Membership(s): Publishers Marketing Association; St Louis Publisher's Association

Science Publishers Inc
234 May St, Enfield, NH 03748
Mailing Address: PO Box 699, Enfield, NH 03748-0699
Tel: 603-632-7377 *Fax:* 603-632-5611
E-mail: info@scipub.net
Web Site: www.scipub.net
Key Personnel
Pres & Intl Rts: Vijay Primlani
Sales Exec & Lib Sales Dir: Linda Jones
Founded: 1992
Publish scholarly & scientific books.
ISBN Prefix(es): 1-886106; 1-57808; 1-881570
Number of titles published annually: 35 Print; 1 CD-ROM
Total Titles: 300 Print
Foreign Office(s): c/o Plymbridge Distributors Ltd, Estover Rd, Plymouth PL6 7PY, United Kingdom *E-mail:* orders@plymbridge.com
Foreign Rep(s): Academic Marketing Services Pty Ltd (South Africa); James Benson (UK & Ireland); Paulo Ceschi (Brazil); Jim Chalmers (UK & Ireland); D A Information Services (Australia); MICHAEL GOH (Southeast Asia); IMA (North Africa); International Publishers Representatives Ltd (Middle East, North Africa); Ben Kato (Japan); Kemper Conseil Publishing (Benelux, Switzerland); Mark Latcham (UK & Ireland); Livraria Polytechnica Ltda (Brazil); Marcello s.a.s (France, Spain, Italy & Portugal); Minimax SAS (Italy); P B Foreign Book Centre LP (Cambodia, Thailand, Vietnam); P F Books (Indonesia); SHS Publishers' Consultants & Representatives (Austria, Germany & Switzerland); David Towle (Scandinavia)

Scientific Publishers Inc
4460 SW 35 Terr, Suite 305, Gainesville, FL 32608
SAN: 247-0101

Mailing Address: PO Box 15718, Gainesville, FL 32608
Tel: 352-373-5630 *Fax:* 352-373-3249
E-mail: scipub@aol.com
Web Site: www.scipub.com
Key Personnel
CEO & Publr: John B Heppner
Opers Mgr: M Rojas
Founded: 1989
Natural history & scientific books & reprints; worldwide.
ISBN Prefix(es): 0-945417
Total Titles: 31 Print
Divisions: Flora & Fauna Books
Orders to: Flora & Fauna Books/Nature World, PO Box 15718, Gainesville, FL 32604
 Tel: 352-335-5011 *E-mail:* ffbks@aol.com *Web Site:* www.ffbooks.com

SciTech Publishing, Inc
7474 Creedmoor Rd, Raleigh, NC 27613
Tel: 919-866-1501 *Fax:* 919-844-5809
E-mail: info@scitechpub.com
Web Site: www.scitechpub.com
Key Personnel
Pres & Edit Dir: Dudley R Kay *E-mail:* dkay@scitechpub.com
VP, Fin: Teresa H Kay
Founded: 1997
Publisher & packager of books & software on engineering & technology topics for professional & graduate level audiences with an emphasis on electrical engineering.
ISBN Prefix(es): 1-891121
Number of titles published annually: 10 Print
Total Titles: 15 Print
Foreign Rep(s): DA Information Services
Foreign Rights: Applied Media (India); DA Information Services (Australia, New Zealand)
Shipping Address: Publishers Shipping & Storage Corp, Fitchburg, MA
Membership(s): Publishers Marketing Association

Scott Foresman
1900 E Lake Ave, Glenview, IL 60025
Tel: 847-729-3000 *Toll Free Tel:* 800-535-4391 (Midwest) *Fax:* 847-729-8910
E-mail: firstname.lastname@scottforesman.com
Web Site: www.scottforesman.com
Key Personnel
Pres: Paul McFall *E-mail:* paul.mcfall@pearsoned.com
VP & COO: Allen Wheatcroft
VP, HR: Stuart G Cohn *E-mail:* stuart.cohn@pearsoned.com
VP & Busn Mgr: Chet Lucido
VP & Publr: Susanne Singleton
VP & Dir of Mktg: Cindy Lamir
VP & Natl Sales Mgr, Open Terr: Rich Fabrizi
VP, Technol: Brian Parker

Scott Jones Inc
PO Box 696, El Granada, CA 94018
Tel: 650-726-2436 *Fax:* 650-726-4693
Web Site: www.scottjonespub.com
Key Personnel
Pres: Richard Jones *Tel:* 650-726-8361 *Fax:* 650-726-8361 *E-mail:* scottjones1@aol.com
Busn Mgr: Michelle Robelet
 E-mail: scottjones2@aol.com
Founded: 1988
ISBN Prefix(es): 1-881991; 1-57676
Number of titles published annually: 8 Print
Total Titles: 60 Print; 2 CD-ROM
Foreign Rights: Book Network International (Australia, England, Europe, India, South Africa)

Scott Publications Inc
801 W Norton, Suite 200, Muskegon, MI 49441
Tel: 231-733-9382 *Toll Free Tel:* 866-733-9382
Fax: 231-733-7635

E-mail: contactus@scottpublications.com
Web Site: www.scottpublications.com
Key Personnel
Publr: Robert Keessen
Dist Mgr: Jeanette Foxe *Tel:* 248-477-6650
   E-mail: jfoxe@scottpublications.com
Founded: 1955
Magazines & books for the doll crafter, doll collector, miniature hobbyists, stamping enthusiast, soft doll & animal maker.
ISBN Prefix(es): 0-916809
Total Titles: 50 Print

§Scott Publishing Co
Division of Amos Press Inc
911 Vandemark Rd, Sidney, OH 45365
Mailing Address: PO Box 828, Sidney, OH 45365
Tel: 937-498-0802 *Toll Free Tel:* 800-572-6885
   Fax: 937-498-0807
E-mail: ssm@amospress.com
Web Site: www.amosadvantage.com
   Telex: 6502840879
Key Personnel
Ed: James E Kloetzel *E-mail:* ssm@amospress.com
Mktg Dir & Lib Sales Dir: Bill Fay
Promos Mgr: Tim Wagner *Tel:* 937-498-0867
   E-mail: twagner@amospublishing.com
Founded: 1863
Stamp collecting catalogs, reference books & stamp collecting accessories.
ISBN Prefix(es): 0-89487
Number of titles published annually: 8 Print; 7 CD-ROM
Total Titles: 8 Print

Scribner
Imprint of Simon & Schuster Adult Publishing Group
1230 Avenue of the Americas, New York, NY 10020
Key Personnel
Exec VP & Publr: Susan Moldow
VP & Ed-in-Chief: Nan Graham
VP & Publr, Lisa Drew Books: Lisa Drew
VP, Assoc Publr: Rosalind Lippel
VP & Sr Ed: Colin Harrison
VP & Dir, Mktg: Sue Fleming
Dir, Subs Rts: Paul O'Halloran
Subs Rts Mgr: Bob Niegowski
Art Dir: John Fulbrook
Dir, Prodn: Olga Leonardo
Dir, Cookbook & Lifestyle Publg: Beth Wareham
Asst Dir, Publicity: Lucy Kenyon; Erin Cox
Sr Ed: Sarah McGrath
Ed: Brant Rumble
ISBN Prefix(es): 0-684; 0-7432
Number of titles published annually: 70 Print
Imprints: Lisa Drew Books; Scribner Classics; Scribner Poetry

Scripta Humanistica Publishing International
Subsidiary of Brumar Communications
1383 Kersey Lane, Potomac, MD 20854
Tel: 301-294-7949 *Fax:* 301-424-9584
E-mail: scripta@aol.com
Web Site: www.scriptahumanistica.com *Telex:* 21-1515 BDUR
Key Personnel
Pres: Bruno M Damiani *Tel:* 301-340-1095
Founded: 1984
ISBN Prefix(es): 0-916379
Number of titles published annually: 4 Print
Total Titles: 151 Print; 151 Online
Editorial Office(s): 512 Williams Hall, Philadelphia, PA 19104-6305 *Tel:* 215-898-5124
   Fax: 215-898-0933 *E-mail:* jrequeir@sas.upenn.edu
Foreign Rep(s): Grant & Cutler Ltd (UK, Northern Europe); Scripta Humanistica (Caribbean,

Latin America); Solochek Libros (Africa, Southern Europe, Spain); Spain Shobo Co Inc (Australia, Asia, New Zealand)

Scriptural Research Center
PO Box 725, New Britain, CT 06050-0725
Tel: 203-272-1780 *Fax:* 203-272-2296
E-mail: scriptpublish@snet.net
Web Site: www.scripturalresearch.com
Key Personnel
Admin: Joseph Poulin
Founded: 1972
Religious, scripturally-based books & audio book tapes.
ISBN Prefix(es): 1-57277
Number of titles published annually: 7 Print; 1 E-Book
Total Titles: 45 Print; 3 Audio
Imprints: Tampco; Truth Center
Distributor for Scriptural Research & Publishing Co Inc; Truth Center
Shipping Address: 344 E Johnson Ave, Cheshire, CT 06410

Scurlock Publishing Co Inc
1293 Myrtle Springs Rd, Texarkana, TX 75503
Tel: 903-832-4726 *Toll Free Tel:* 800-228-6389
   Fax: 903-831-3177
E-mail: scurlockpubl@txk.net
Web Site: www.muzzmag.com; muzzleloadermag.com
Key Personnel
Ed-in-Chief: Bill Scurlock
Man Ed: Linda Scurlock
Founded: 1974
Historical nonfiction, early American nonfiction, hunting nonfiction, muzzleloading arms & shooting.
ISBN Prefix(es): 0-9605666; 1-880655
Number of titles published annually: 3 Print
Total Titles: 16 Print

Seal Press
Imprint of Avalon Publishing Group - California
1400 65 St, Suite 250, Emeryville, CA 94608
SAN: 215-3416
Tel: 510-595-3664 *Fax:* 510-595-4228
Web Site: www.sealpress.com
Key Personnel
VP & Edit Dir: Krista Lyons-Gould
Assoc Publr: Ingrid Emerick
Sr Ed: Leslie Miller
Founded: 1976
Seal Press, an imprint of the Avalon Publishing Group, publishes books on a broad range of subjects by & for women.
ISBN Prefix(es): 0-931188; 1-878067; 1-58005

Second Chance Press
Imprint of The Permanent Press
4170 Noyac Rd, Sag Harbor, NY 11963
SAN: 213-1633
Tel: 631-725-1101 *Fax:* 631-725-8215
E-mail: info@thepermanentpress.com
Web Site: www.thepermanentpress.com
Key Personnel
Publr: Judith Shepard; Martin Shepard
Assoc Publr: Elise D'Haene
Exec Ed: Maureen D'Haene *E-mail:* maureen@thepermanentpress.com
Founded: 1977
Originals of literary works in hardcover & paperback.
ISBN Prefix(es): 0-933256; 1-877946; 0-932966; 1-57962
Number of titles published annually: 12 Print
Total Titles: 400 Print
Foreign Rights: Nike Davarinou (Greece); Lora Fountain Agency (France, Portugal, Russia, Spain); Jane Judd (UK); Jan Michael (Nether-

lands & Scandinavia); Thomas Schluck (Germany); Tuttle Mori (Japan); Rita Vivian (Italy); Eric Yang (Korea)

See Sharp Press
PO Box 1731, Tucson, AZ 85702-1731
Tel: 520-628-8720 *Fax:* 520-628-8720
E-mail: info@seesharppress.com
Web Site: www.seesharppress.com
Key Personnel
Publr & Sr Ed: Charles Bufe
Founded: 1984
Iconoclastic trade paperbacks & pamphlets on a wide variety of nonfiction topics.
ISBN Prefix(es): 1-884365
Number of titles published annually: 6 Print; 1 CD-ROM
Total Titles: 55 Print; 2 CD-ROM
Distributed by Freedom Press (London)
Foreign Rights: Independent Publishers Group (World)
Distribution Center: Independent Publishers Group, 814 N Franklin, Chicago, IL 60610
   Tel: 312-337-0747 *Toll Free Tel:* 800-888-4741
   Fax: 312-337-5985 *Web Site:* www.ipgbook.com
Membership(s): Publishers Marketing Association

Seedling Publications Inc
520 E Bainbridge St, Elizabethtown, PA 17022
Tel: 614-267-7333 *Toll Free Tel:* 800-233-0759
   Fax: 614-267-4205 *Toll Free Fax:* 888-834-1303
E-mail: sales@seedlingpub.com
Web Site: www.seedlingpub.com
Key Personnel
Publr: Lynn Salem *Tel:* 614-888-4140
Founded: 1992
Books for beginning readers in 8-16 page format.
ISBN Prefix(es): 1-880612; 1-58323
Number of titles published annually: 12 Print
Total Titles: 102 Print
Distributed by Kendall Hunt Publishing
Foreign Rep(s): Irwin Publishing (Canada)

§The SeedSowers
Subsidiary of Christian Books Publishing House
PO Box 3317, Jacksonville, FL 32206-0317
Tel: 904-598-2345 *Toll Free Tel:* 800-228-2665
   Fax: 904-598-3456
E-mail: books@seedsowers.com
Web Site: seedsowers.com
Key Personnel
Busn Mgr & Electronic Publg: Kathy McGraw
   E-mail: kathy@seedsowers.com
Founded: 1972
Publish books on church history, deeper Christian life, Christian classics.
ISBN Prefix(es): 0-940232
Number of titles published annually: 4 Print
Total Titles: 45 Print; 4 Audio
Foreign Rep(s): W A Buchanan & Co (Australia); Christian Art (South Africa); Omega Distributors (New Zealand); Perivale Christian Center (England)
Shipping Address: 4003 N Liberty St, Jacksonville, FL 32206
Membership(s): CBA

SelectiveHouse Publishers Inc
PO Box 10095, Gaithersburg, MD 20898
SAN: 299-3694
Tel: 301-990-2999 *Toll Free Tel:* 888-256-6399 (orders only) *Fax:* 301-990-2998
E-mail: sr@selectivehouse.com
Web Site: www.selectivehouse.com
Key Personnel
Pres & Intl Rts: James B Seigneur
Ed: Gerilynne Seigneur
Artist: Christopher Chon
Founded: 1997

Mainstream fiction with science fiction &/or spiritual overtones, nonfiction spiritual, jacket design.
ISBN Prefix(es): 0-9656948
Number of titles published annually: 4 Print
Total Titles: 4 Print

§Self-Counsel Press Inc
Subsidiary of International Self-Counsel Press Ltd
1704 N State St, Bellingham, WA 98225
SAN: 240-9925
Tel: 360-676-4530 *Toll Free Tel:* 877-877-6490
Fax: 360-676-4549
E-mail: service@self-counsel.com
Web Site: www.self-counsel.com
Key Personnel
Pres: Diana R Douglas *E-mail:* drdouglas@self-counsel.com
Man Ed & ISBN Contact: Richard Day
Gen Mgr: Roy Pattrick
Publicist: Roger Kettyls
Foreign Rts & Mktg Coord: Aaron Morris
  Tel: 604-986-3366 *E-mail:* amorris@self-counsel.com
Founded: 1977
Legal, business & reference books.
ISBN Prefix(es): 0-88908; 1-55180
Number of titles published annually: 12 Print
Total Titles: 201 Print; 2 CD-ROM; 4 Audio
Imprints: Self-Counsel Series
Branch Office(s)
4 Bram Ct, Brampton, ON L6W 3R6, Canada
1481 Charlotte Rd, North Vancouver, BC V7J 1H1, Canada *Tel:* 604-986-3366 *Toll Free Tel:* 800-663-3007 SAN: 115-0545
Foreign Rights: Atmarr Agency Services (China, France & Germany, Japan, Korea & Taiwan, Philippines, Thailand)
Membership(s): AAP; ALA

Sentient Publications LLC
1113 Spruce St, Boulder, CO 80302
Tel: 303-443-2188 *Fax:* 303-381-2538
E-mail: contact@sentientpublications.com; salesmanager@sentientpublications.com
Web Site: www.sentientpublications.com
Key Personnel
Publr: Connie Shaw *E-mail:* cshaw@sentientpublications.com
Gen Mgr: Fred Taylor *E-mail:* fred@sentientpublications.com
Founded: 2001
Ecology, education, health, science, spirituality. Publish quality nonfiction books that arise from the spirit of inquiry & the richness of the inherent dialogue between writer & reader.
ISBN Prefix(es): 0-9710786; 1-59181
Number of titles published annually: 15 Print; 2 Audio
Total Titles: 40 Print; 3 Audio
Foreign Rights: Hagenbach & Bender (Worldwide)
Shipping Address: National Book Network, 4720 Boston Way, Lanham, MD 20706 *Tel:* 301-459-3366 *Fax:* 301-459-1705 *Web Site:* www.nbnbooks.com
Membership(s): Publishers Marketing Association

Sepher-Hermon Press
1153 45 St, Brooklyn, NY 11219
SAN: 169-5959
Tel: 718-972-9010 *Fax:* 718-972-6935
Key Personnel
Mgr: Samuel Gross
Secy & Lib Sales Dir: Margaret Gross
Adv Mgr & Art Dir: Jacob Gross
Founded: 1964
Publishing original nonfiction works on Jewish subjects; reprinting out-of-print books of Judaica.
ISBN Prefix(es): 0-87203
Number of titles published annually: 6 Print

Total Titles: 58 Print
Imprints: Hermon Press Books
Distributor for Bar-Ilan University Press; Vallentine, Mitchell & Co Ltd
Foreign Rep(s): Judaica Book Center (Israel)
Advertising Agency: J J Gross Associates
Returns: Whitehurst & Clark, Book Fulfillment, Inc, 1200 County Rd, Flemington, NJ 08822
Shipping Address: Whitehurst & Clark, Book Fulfillment, Inc, 1200 County Rd, Flemington, NJ 08822
Warehouse: Whitehurst & Clark, Book Fulfillment, Inc, 1200 County Rd, Flemington, NJ 08822

Serindia Publications
PO Box 10335, Chicago, IL 60610-0335
Tel: 312-664-5531 *Fax:* 312-664-4389
E-mail: info@serindia.com
Web Site: www.serindia.com
Key Personnel
Man Dir: Anthony Aris
Founded: 1976 (Established in London)
Number of titles published annually: 3 Print
Total Titles: 60 Print
Distributed by Art Media Resources Inc; Paragon Asia Co Ltd (Thailand, Singapore & Southeast Asia); Thames & Hudson (Europe & United Kingdom); Wisdom Books (Backlist titles)

Seven Stories Press
140 Watts St, New York, NY 10013
Tel: 212-226-8760 *Toll Free Tel:* 800-283-3572
  Fax: 212-226-1411
E-mail: info@sevenstories.com
Web Site: www.sevenstories.com
Key Personnel
Publr: Daniel Simon *E-mail:* dan@sevenstories.com
Sr Ed: Greg Ruggiero *E-mail:* greg@sevenstories.com
Man Ed: India Amos *E-mail:* india@sevenstories.com
Assoc Ed, Open Media: Ria Julien *E-mail:* ria@sevenstories.com
Assoc Ed, Siete Cuentos Editorial: Sara Villa *E-mail:* sara@sevenstories.com
Foreign Rts Dir: Violaine Huisman *E-mail:* violaine@sevenstories.com
Opers Dir: Jon Gilbert *E-mail:* jon@sevenstories.com
Publicity Dir: Ruth Weiner *E-mail:* ruth@sevenstories.com
Publicist: Phoebe Hwang *E-mail:* phoebe@sevenstories.com
Academic Sales & Mktg: Tara Parmiter *E-mail:* tara@sevenstories.com
Founded: 1995
Publish original hardcover & paperback books for the general reader in the area of literature, literature in translation, popular culture, politics, media studies, health & nutrition & sports. No unsol mss.
ISBN Prefix(es): 1-58322; 1-888363
Number of titles published annually: 50 Print; 15 E-Book
Total Titles: 269 Print; 36 E-Book
Foreign Rep(s): Hushion House Publishing (Canada); Liberty Books Pte Ltd (Pakistan); Macmillan (New Zealand); Palgrave Macmillan (Australia); Pen International Pte Ltd (Singapore); Stephan Phillips Pty Ltd (Southern Africa); Turnaround Distribution (UK)
Foreign Rights: I Pikarki Ltd (Israel); Japan Uni Agency Inc (Japan); Duran Kim Agency (Korea); Paul Marsh Agency (UK)
Warehouse: Alianza Distribution Services, 5514 Emile Rd, Levittown, PA 19057
Distribution Center: Consortium Book Sales & Distribution, 1045 Westgate Dr, Saint Paul, MN 55114 *Toll Free Tel:* 800-283-3572

17th Street Productions, see Alloy Entertainment

Severn House Publishers Inc
Subsidiary of Severn House Publishers Ltd
595 Madison Ave, 15th fl, New York, NY 10022
Tel: 212-888-4042 *Fax:* 212-759-5422
E-mail: editorial@severnhouse.com; sales@severnhouse.com
Web Site: www.severnhouse.com
Key Personnel
Chmn & Publr: Edwin Buckhalter
Edit Dir: Amanda Stewart *E-mail:* info@severnhouse.com
Founded: 1974
First hardcover editions of mass market paperbacks/hardcover originals for library market. Growing number of first world publications from multi popular library authors.
ISBN Prefix(es): 0-7278
Number of titles published annually: 140 Print
Total Titles: 770 Print
Imprints: Severn House
Foreign Office(s): 9-15 High St, Sutton, Surrey SM1 1DF, United Kingdom
Warehouse: Chivers North America, PO Box 1450, Hampton, NH 03843-1450 *Toll Free Tel:* 800-830-3044 *Fax:* 603-929-3890
Distribution Center: Grantham Book Services CTP, Alma Park Industrial Estate, Isaac Newton Way, Grantham, Lincs NG31 9SD, United Kingdom *Tel:* (1476) 541080 *Fax:* (1476) 541068

§Shambhala Publications Inc
Horticultural Hall, 300 Massachusetts Ave, Boston, MA 02115
SAN: 203-2481
Mailing Address: PO Box 308, Boston, MA 02117-0308
Tel: 617-424-0030 *Toll Free Tel:* 888-424-2329 (orders only) *Fax:* 617-236-1563; 303-665-5292 (orders only)
E-mail: editors@shambhala.com
Web Site: www.shambhala.com
Key Personnel
Chmn & Ed-in-Chief: Samuel Bercholz *E-mail:* sbercholz@shambhala.com
Pres & Exec Edit: Peter Turner *Tel:* 617-424-0030 ext 238 *E-mail:* pturner@shambhala.com
Cont: Diane McCormick *E-mail:* dmccormick@shambhala.com
VP & Assoc Publ: Jonathan Green *E-mail:* jgreen@shambhala.com
Man Ed & ISBN Contact: David O'Neal *E-mail:* doneal@shambhala.com
Cons Ed: Larry Mermelstein *E-mail:* lmermelstein@shambhala.com
VP, Prodn & Design: Hazel Bercholz *E-mail:* hbercholz@shambhala.com
Prodn Assoc: Jim Zaccaria *E-mail:* jzaccaria@shambhala.com
Systems Mgr: Carin Allen *E-mail:* callen@shambhala.com
Prodn Mgr: Ginny Chang *E-mail:* gchang@shambhala.com
Ed: Emily Bower *E-mail:* ebower@shambhala.com; Kendra Crossen *E-mail:* kendra@shambhala.com; Eden Steinberg *E-mail:* esteinberg@shambhala.com
Assoc Ed: Beth Frankl *E-mail:* bfrankl@shambhala.com
Edit Asst: Liz Shaw *E-mail:* lshaw@shambhala.com
Founded: 1969
Trade books; art, literature, comparative religion, philosophy, science, psychology & related subjects.
ISBN Prefix(es): 0-02; 0-87773; 1-56957; 1-57062; 1-59030
Number of titles published annually: 85 Print; 50 Online
Total Titles: 600 Print; 50 Online

Distributed by Random House Inc
Foreign Rep(s): Airlift Books (UK); Random House Australia Ltd (Australia); Random House of Canada Ltd (Canada); Random House of New Zealand (New Zealand)
Foreign Rights: ACER (Spain); Agency Hoffman (Germany); The English Agency (Japan); Frederique Porretta Agency (France); Random House of South Africa (Southern Africa); Karen Schindler (Brazil)
Advertising Agency: Vermillion Graphics, Boulder, CO 80302
Returns: Random House Returns Dept, 400 Bennett Dr, Westminster, MD 21157
Shipping Address: Random House Distribution Center, 400 Hahn Rd, Westminster, MD 21157

M E Sharpe Inc
80 Business Park Dr, Suite 202, Armonk, NY 10504
SAN: 202-7100
Tel: 914-273-1800 *Toll Free Tel:* 800-541-6563 *Fax:* 914-273-2106
E-mail: info@mesharpe.com
Web Site: www.mesharpe.com
Key Personnel
Pres & CEO: Myron E Sharpe
Sr VP & COO: Vincent Fuentes
VP, Mktg & Sales & Lib Sales Dir: Diana McDermott *E-mail:* dmcdermott@mesharpe.com
VP, Man Ed: Carmen Chetti
VP, Edit Dir: Patricia A Kolb
Exec Ed, Sharpe Ref: Todd Hallman
Exec Ed, History & Political Sci: Niels Aaboe
Exec Ed, Economics: Lynn Taylor
Exec Ed, Mgmt: Harry Briggs
Assoc Ed, Asian Studies: Patricia Loo
MIS: Tom Salvatorelli
Contracts, Rts & Perms: Elizabeth Granda
Fulfillment Mgr: Sorina Pop
Founded: 1958
Scholarly books in social sciences, international relations, area studies, management. College texts, reference, trade, business & professional books. Scholarly & professional journals.
ISBN Prefix(es): 0-87332; 1-56324; 0-7656
Number of titles published annually: 100 Print; 50 E-Book
Total Titles: 800 Print; 3 CD-ROM; 37 Online; 150 E-Book
Imprints: East Gate Books; Sharpe Reference
Foreign Rep(s): APAC Publishers (Indonesia, Korea, Malaysia, Singapore, Taiwan, Thailand); Applied Media (India); Cassidy & Associates (Hong Kong, People's Republic of China); J Coutts Library Services Ltd (Canada); DA Information Services (Australia, New Zealand, Pacific Basin); Eurospan (UK, Europe, Israel); Kinokuniya Co Ltd (Japan); PAK Book Corp (Pakistan); I J Sagun (American Samoa, Brunei, Cambodia, Guam, Laos, Micronesia, Papua New Guinea, Philippines, Solomon Islands, Vietnam); United Publishers Services Ltd (Japan)
Warehouse: Maple Press Distribution Ctr, Legionaire Dr, Fredericksburg, PA 17026
Distribution Center: Maple Press Distribution Ctr, Legionaire Dr, Fredericksburg, PA 17026
Membership(s): ALA; Society for Scholarly Publishing

Shearwater Books, see Island Press

The Sheep Meadow Press
PO Box 1345, Riverdale-on-Hudson, NY 10471
SAN: 669-2648
Tel: 718-548-5547 *Fax:* 718-884-0406
E-mail: poetry@sheepmeadowpress.com
Key Personnel
Publr & Man Ed: Stanley Moss
Founded: 1976

Poetry & contemporary translations. No unsol mss.
ISBN Prefix(es): 0-935296; 1-878818; 0-8180; 1-931357
Number of titles published annually: 7 Print
Total Titles: 160 Print
Distributed by The New England University Press
Distributor for Carcanet

Sheffield Publishing Co
Subsidiary of Waveland Press Inc
9009 Antioch Rd, Salem, WI 53168
Mailing Address: PO Box 359, Salem, WI 53168-0359
Tel: 262-843-2281 *Fax:* 262-843-3683
E-mail: info@spcbooks.com
Web Site: www.spcbooks.com
Key Personnel
Man Ed: Stephen R Nelson
Busn Mgr: Jodi R Jacobsen
Founded: 1984
Publisher of college texts & supplements.
ISBN Prefix(es): 0-88133; 1-879215
Number of titles published annually: 1 Print
Total Titles: 25 Print

Shengold Publishers Inc, see Schreiber Publishing Inc

Sheridan House Inc
145 Palisade St, Dobbs Ferry, NY 10522
SAN: 204-5915
Tel: 914-693-2410 *Fax:* 914-693-0776
E-mail: info@sheridanhouse.com
Web Site: www.sheridanhouse.com
Key Personnel
Pres: Lothar Simon
Gen Mgr & Rts & Perms: J R Simon
Founded: 1940
Nonfiction & fiction trade, boating, marine. Distribute books published abroad.
ISBN Prefix(es): 0-911378; 0-924486; 1-57409
Number of titles published annually: 25 Print
Total Titles: 200 Print
Distributor for Adlard Coles Nautical; Seafarer Books
Membership(s): AAP

Sherman Asher Publishing
PO Box 31725, Santa Fe, NM 87594-1725
Tel: 505-988-7214 *Fax:* 505-988-7214
E-mail: westernedge@santa-fe.net
Web Site: www.shermanasher.com
Key Personnel
Owner & Publr: James Mafchir
Founded: 1995
Literary books that include bilingual memoirs & Judaica.
ISBN Prefix(es): 0-9644196; 1-890932
Number of titles published annually: 4 Print
Total Titles: 24 Print
Distribution Center: SCB

Sheron Enterprises Inc
1035 S Carley Ct, North Bellmore, NY 11710
Tel: 516-783-5885
Key Personnel
Pres: Sheryl Perry
Secy: Ronald Perry
Founded: 1996
Publish college textbooks, lab manuals & study aids for college professors with small & large print runs as well as helping unknown authors get published.
ISBN Prefix(es): 1-891877
Number of titles published annually: 4 Print
Total Titles: 15 Print

Shields Publications
PO Box 669, Eagle River, WI 54521-0669
Tel: 715-479-4810 *Fax:* 715-479-3905

E-mail: shields@nnex.net
Web Site: www.wormbooks.com
Key Personnel
Owner: Patrick Shields
Founded: 1951
Publisher of books about earthworms, vermiculture, vermicomposting, commercial worm production.
ISBN Prefix(es): 0-914116
Number of titles published annually: 22 Print
Total Titles: 22 Print; 1 CD-ROM

Shirak
PO Box 414, Glendale, CA 91209-0414
Tel: 818-240-6540 *Fax:* 818-240-1295
E-mail: hratchh@yahoo.com
Key Personnel
Owner: Sossie Hannessian
Purch Mgr: Harry Hannessian *Tel:* 818-618-6245 *E-mail:* harry@mbsg.net
Founded: 1984 (Also, founded in 1952 in Beruit, Lebanon)
Are retail, wholesale, distributor, manufacturer, & publisher of books relating to the Armenian culture & literature.
ISBN Prefix(es): 1-58253
Number of titles published annually: 3 Print
Total Titles: 200 Print; 2 Audio
Membership(s): ABA

The Shoe String Press Inc
2 Linsley St, North Haven, CT 06473
SAN: 213-2079
Tel: 203-239-2702 *Fax:* 203-239-2568
E-mail: info@shoestringpress.com; books@shoestringpress.com
Web Site: www.shoestringpress.com *Cable:* ARCHON
Key Personnel
Pres, Edit & Mktg Dir: Diantha C Thorpe
VP & Lib Sales Dir: Nancy C McGrath
Secy: John Barnett
Founded: 1952
Nonfiction for children & young adults; serious & scholarly nonfiction in humanities; professional literature; reference.
ISBN Prefix(es): 0-208
Number of titles published annually: 12 Print
Total Titles: 200 Print
Imprints: Archon Books; Linnet Books; Linnet Professional Publications
Foreign Rep(s): East-West Export Books (Australia, Asia, Pacific); Gazelle Book Services Ltd (UK, Europe)

Shoemaker & Hoard, Publishers
Division of Avalon Publishing Group, Inc
3704 Macomb St NW, Suite 4, Washington, DC 20016
Tel: 202-364-4464 *Fax:* 202-364-4484
Web Site: www.shoemakerhoard.com
Key Personnel
Publr: Jack Shoemaker
Assoc Publr: Trish Hoard
Founded: 2003
Shoemaker & Hoard, a division of Avalon Publishing Group, is a small literary book publishing house.
ISBN Prefix(es): 1-59376

Show What You Know® Publishing
Division of Englefield & Associates Inc
6344 Nicholas Dr, Columbus, OH 43234
Mailing Address: PO Box 341348, Columbus, OH 43234-1348
Tel: 614-764-1211 *Toll Free Tel:* 877-PASSING (727-7464) *Fax:* 614-764-1311
E-mail: swyk@eapublishing.com
Web Site: www.eapublishing.com
Key Personnel
Pres: Cynthia Englefield

Educational publisher of K-12 supplemental test-preparation books & other materials.
ISBN Prefix(es): 1-884183; 1-59230
Number of titles published annually: 40 Print
Total Titles: 180 Print
Membership(s): Publishers Marketing Association

Siddha Yoga Publications
Unit of Syda Foundation
371 Brickman Rd, South Fallsburg, NY 12747
Mailing Address: PO Box 600, South Fallsburg, NY 12747
Tel: 845-434-2000 *Toll Free Tel:* 888-422-3334 (bookstore) *Fax:* 845-436-2131 *Toll Free Fax:* 888-422-3339
Fax on Demand: 845-436-2135 (mktg)
E-mail: info@siddhayoga.org; ebookstoreorders@syda.org
Web Site: www.siddhayoga.org
Key Personnel
Ed: Anne Malcolm *Tel:* 845-434-2000 ext 1852
Trade Acct Mgr: Jan Van Zanten *Tel:* 845-434-2000 ext 2839 *E-mail:* jmvanzanten@syda.org
Founded: 1981
Books on the practices & philosophy of Siddha Yoga meditation.
ISBN Prefix(es): 0-914602; 0-911307
Number of titles published annually: 10 Print
Total Titles: 60 Print
Imprints: A Siddha Yoga Publication
Distribution Center: Words Distributing Co (Main Distributor), 7900 Edgewater Dr, Oakland, CA 94621, Contact: Leisa Mock *Toll Free Tel:* 800-593-9673 *Fax:* 510-632-1281
New Leaf Distribution Co, 401 Thornton Rd, Lithia Springs, GA 30122-1557, Contact: Lisa Roggow *Toll Free Tel:* 800-326-2665 *Toll Free Fax:* 800-326-1066
Ingram Book Co, One Ingram Blvd, La Vergne, TN 37086 *Toll Free Tel:* 800-937-8000 *Toll Free Fax:* 800-876-0186

Sierra Club Books
85 Second St, 2nd fl, San Francisco, CA 94105
SAN: 203-2406
Tel: 415-977-5500 *Fax:* 415-977-5792
E-mail: books.publishing@sierraclub.org
Web Site: www.sierraclub.org/books
Key Personnel
Publr: Helen Sweetland
Ed-in-Chief: Danny Moses
Co-published with Univ of California Press. General titles on environment & ecology, natural history & sciences, outdoors & travel.
ISBN Prefix(es): 0-87156; 1-57805
Number of titles published annually: 15 Print
Total Titles: 125 Print
Sales Office(s): Univ of California Press, 2120 Berkeley Way, Berkeley Way, CA 94720 *Tel:* 510-642-4247 *Toll Free Tel:* 800-822-6657
Distributed by University of California Press
See separate listing for:
Sierra Club Books Adult Trade Division

Sierra Club Books Adult Trade Division
Division of Sierra Club Books
85 Second St, 2nd fl, San Francisco, CA 94105
Tel: 415-977-5500 *Fax:* 415-977-5792
E-mail: books.publishing@sierraclub.org
Web Site: ww.sierraclub.org/books
Key Personnel
Publr: Helen Sweetland
Ed-in-Chief: Daniel Moses
Co-published with University of California Press. General titles on environment & ecology, natural history & sciences, outdoors, travel.
ISBN Prefix(es): 0-87156; 1-57805
Number of titles published annually: 15 Print
Total Titles: 125 Print
Distributed by University of California Press

Sierra Press
Subsidiary of Panorama International Productions Inc
4988 Gold Leaf Dr, Mariposa, CA 95338
Tel: 209-966-5071 *Toll Free Tel:* 800-745-2631 *Fax:* 209-966-5073
E-mail: siepress@sti.net
Web Site: www.nationalparksusa.com
Key Personnel
Pres & Publr: Jeff Nicholas
Sales Mgr: Kevin Poulson
Opers Mgr: Kathy Gregory
Founded: 1985
Color photography books on America's National Parks & scenic areas.
ISBN Prefix(es): 0-939365; 1-58071
Number of titles published annually: 5 Print
Total Titles: 94 Print
Distributed by American West Books; Canyonlands Publications; Gem Guides
Distributor for Double Decker Press
Membership(s): APPL; Publishers Association of the West

Signature Books Publishing LLC
564 W 400 N, Salt Lake City, UT 84116-3411
SAN: 217-4391
Tel: 801-531-1483 *Toll Free Tel:* 800-356-5687 (orders) *Fax:* 801-531-1488
E-mail: people@signaturebooks.com
Web Site: www.signaturebooks.com
Key Personnel
Pres: George D Smith
VP, Sec & Treas: Ronald L Priddis
Prodn & Design: Connie Disney
Admin Asst: Jani Fleet
Busn Mgr: Keiko Jones *Tel:* 801-531-1483 ext 102 *E-mail:* keiko@signaturebooks.com
Shipping Mgr: Greg Jones
Mktg: Tom Kimball
Founded: 1981
Western Americana.
ISBN Prefix(es): 0-941214; 1-56085
Number of titles published annually: 12 Print
Total Titles: 175 Print; 1 CD-ROM
Imprints: Smith Research Associates
Distributor for Dialogue Foundation; Mormon History Association; Charles Redd Center; Sunstone Foundation; Tanner Trust

Signpost Books
8912 192 St SW, Edmonds, WA 98026
Tel: 425-776-0370
Key Personnel
Publr: Clifford Cameron *E-mail:* ccameron@oz.net
Founded: 1974
Trade paperbacks for the Pacific Northwest.
ISBN Prefix(es): 0-913140
Number of titles published annually: 3 Print
Total Titles: 7 Print

§SIL International
7500 W Camp Wisdom Rd, Dallas, TX 75236
Tel: 972-708-7404 *Fax:* 972-708-7363
E-mail: academic_books@sil.org
Web Site: www.ethnologue.com
Key Personnel
Gen Mgr: Brian Homoleski
Founded: 1942
Books.
ISBN Prefix(es): 0-88312; 1-55671
Number of titles published annually: 20 Print
Total Titles: 2 CD-ROM; 3 Online; 3 E-Book

Silhouette Books, see Harlequin Enterprises Ltd

Silicon Press
25 Beverly Rd, Summit, NJ 07901
Tel: 908-273-8919 *Fax:* 908-273-6149
E-mail: info@silicon-press.com

Web Site: www.silicon-press.com
Key Personnel
CEO: Narain Gehani *E-mail:* nhg@silicon-press.com
Founded: 1987
Books about computers & technology/fiction.
ISBN Prefix(es): 0-929306
Number of titles published annually: 10 Print; 3 Audio
Total Titles: 28 Print

Silman-James Press
3624 Shannon Rd, Los Angeles, CA 90027
Tel: 323-661-9922 *Toll Free Tel:* 877-SJP-BOOK (757-2665) *Fax:* 323-661-9933
E-mail: silmanjamespress@earthlink.net
Web Site: www.silmanjamespress.com
Key Personnel
Publr: Gwen Feldman *E-mail:* ghfeldman@earthlink.net; Jim Fox *E-mail:* jfcoldblue@worldnet.att.net
Dir, Sales & Mktg: Tom Rusch *E-mail:* tom@silmanjamespress.com
Founded: 1990
Publishers of books on film, filmmaking, the motion picture industry & the performing arts.
ISBN Prefix(es): 1-879505
Number of titles published annually: 7 Print
Total Titles: 62 Print
Divisions: Siles Press (Chess & nonfiction titles)

§Silver Lake Publishing
11 S Mansfield Rd, Lansdowne, PA 19050
Tel: 610-626-8446
E-mail: publisher@silverlakepublishing.com; slp@silverlakepublishing.com
Web Site: www.silverlakepublishing.com
Key Personnel
Owner, Pres & Publr: Stephanie Weidner
Founded: 2000
Publishes primarily novels & anthologies in both electronic & print format, allowing the reader to chose their favored format.
ISBN Prefix(es): 1-931095
Number of titles published annually: 20 Print; 20 CD-ROM; 20 E-Book
Total Titles: 38 Print; 33 CD-ROM; 33 E-Book

§Silver Lake Publishing
3501 W Sunset Blvd, Los Angeles, CA 90026
Tel: 323-663-3082 *Fax:* 323-663-3084
E-mail: theeditors@silverlakepub.com; results@silverlakepub.com
Web Site: www.silverlakepub.com
Key Personnel
Publr: James Walsh *E-mail:* jwalsh@silverlakepub.com
Ed: Kristin Loberg *E-mail:* kristinloberg@silverlakepub.com; Megan Thorpe *E-mail:* mthorpe@silverlakepub.com
Publicist: Daniela Cendron *E-mail:* publicity@silverlakepub.com
Founded: 1998
Provides tools for making smart, aggressive decisions on risk & financial matters. Focuses on personal finance, small business management, consumer reference & popular economics.
ISBN Prefix(es): 1-56343
Number of titles published annually: 15 Print; 10 Online; 10 E-Book; 2 Audio
Total Titles: 62 Print
Distributed by SCB Distributors

Silver Moon Press
160 Fifth Ave, New York, NY 10010
Tel: 212-242-6499 *Toll Free Tel:* 800-874-3320 *Fax:* 212-242-6799
E-mail: mail@silvermoonpress.com
Web Site: www.silvermoonpress.com
Key Personnel
Publr: David Katz
Mktg Coord: Karin Lillebo

Man Ed: Hope Killcoyne
Founded: 1992
Publish juvenile titles for library, elementary & middle school markets; three historical fiction series specializing in Colonial America. Also develops titles for English language arts test preparation.
ISBN Prefix(es): 1-881889; 1-893110
Number of titles published annually: 5 Print
Warehouse: c/o The Oliver Press, 5707 W 36 St, Minneapolis, MN 55416

Silver Pixel Press
Division of The Tiffen Co
90 Oser Ave, Hauppauge, NY 11788
Tel: 631-645-2522 *Toll Free Tel:* 800-645-2522
   Fax: 631-273-2557
Web Site: www.tiffen.com
Key Personnel
Prod Mgr: Jeff Cohen *Tel:* 631-645-2522 ext 1222 *E-mail:* jcohen@tiffen.com
Founded: 1947
ISBN Prefix(es): 1-883403; 0-87985
Number of titles published annually: 10 Print
Total Titles: 100 Print
Imprints: Kodak Books
Distributed by Sterling Publishing Co Inc
Distributor for Focal Press; Little, Brown & Co; Peachpit Press; Sterling Publishing Co Inc
Foreign Rep(s): Sterling Publishing Co

Silverback Books Inc
55 New Montgomery St, Suite 503, San Francisco, CA 94105
Tel: 415-348-8595 *Toll Free Tel:* 866-348-8595
   Fax: 415-348-8592
E-mail: info@silverbackbooks.com
Web Site: www.silverbackbooks.com
Key Personnel
Pres: Peter Dombrouski *E-mail:* peter2@ silverbackbooks.com
Founded: 1999
ISBN Prefix(es): 1-930603
Number of titles published annually: 30 Print
Total Titles: 70 Print
Branch Office(s)
Silverback Communications, 1161 Wilshire Blvd, Los Angeles, CA 90028 *Tel:* 310-479-1555 *Fax:* 310-479-1561
Warehouse: Silverback Fulfillment, Strouther Field, 22167 "C" St, Windfield, KS 67156
Membership(s): ABA; NAIPR; Publishers Marketing Association

Simba Information
Unit of R R Bowker LLC
60 Long Ridge Rd, Suite 300, Stamford, CT 06902
SAN: 210-2021
Tel: 203-325-8193 *Fax:* 203-325-8915
E-mail: info@simbanet.com
Web Site: www.simbanet.com
Key Personnel
Edit Dir: Linda Kopp
Mktg Mgr: Paul Ringer
Founded: 1989
Newsletters & research reports for information companies. Subject specialties: publishing & media.
ISBN Prefix(es): 0-918110
Number of titles published annually: 15 Print; 15 Online
Total Titles: 75 Print; 75 Online
Membership(s): AAP; BISG; Software & Information Industry Association

Simcha Press
Imprint of Health Communications Inc
3201 SW 15 St, Deerfield Beach, FL 33442-8190
Tel: 954-360-0909 ext 212 *Toll Free Tel:* 800-851-9100 ext 212 *Toll Free Fax:* 800-424-7652
E-mail: simchapress@hcibooks.com

Web Site: www.simchapress.com
Key Personnel
Dir, Communs & Mgr: Kim Weiss
   E-mail: kimw@hcibooks.com
Founded: 1999
Nonfiction titles for those on the path of Jewish enrichment. Jewish interest, spirituality, inspirational, mysticism & recovery.
ISBN Prefix(es): 1-55874; 0-7573
Number of titles published annually: 4 Print; 4 Online; 4 E-Book
Total Titles: 13 Print; 13 Online; 8 E-Book
Foreign Rights: Claude Choquette

Simon & Schuster
Imprint of Simon & Schuster Adult Publishing Group
1230 Avenue of the Americas, New York, NY 10020
Tel: 212-698-7000 *Toll Free Tel:* 800-223-2348 (cust serv); 800-223-2336 (orders)
   Toll Free Fax: 800-943-9831 (orders)
Web Site: www.simonsays.com
Key Personnel
Exec VP & Publr: David Rosenthal
Sr VP & Ed-in-Chief: Michael V Korda
VP & Edit Dir: Alice E Mayhew
VP & Exec Dir, Publicity: Victoria Meyer
VP & Exec Man Ed: Irene Kheradi
VP & Ed-at-Large: Rob Weisbach
VP & Dir, Mktg: Craig Herman
VP & Dir, Subs Rts: Marcella Berger
VP & Dir, Art & Design: Jackie Seow
VP & Sr Ed: Robert Bender; Sydny Miner
Assoc Publr: Aileen Boyle; Deb Darrock
Art Dir: Michael Accordino
Asst Dir, Subs Rts: Marie Florio
Publg Assoc: Leigh Lloyd
Exec Ed: Geoff Kloske
Sr Ed: Ruth Fecych; Amanda Murray; Marysue Rucci; Denise Roy
Assoc Ed: Roger Labrie; Emily Takoudes
ISBN Prefix(es): 0-684
Number of titles published annually: 125 Print

Simon & Schuster Adult Publishing Group
Division of Simon & Schuster Inc
1230 Avenue of the Americas, New York, NY 10020
Tel: 212-698-7000 *Toll Free Tel:* 800-223-2336 (orders); 800-223-2348 (cust serv)
Key Personnel
Pres: Carolyn K Reidy
Sr VP & Gen Mgr: Dennis Eulau
Sr VP & Exec Dir, Mktg: Michael Selleck
VP & Dir, Mktg: Sue Fleming; Craig Herman
VP, Prodn: Karen Romano
VP & Copy Chief: Marcia Peterson
VP & Busn Mgr: Craig Mandeville
VP & Exec Man Ed: Irene Kheradi
ISBN Prefix(es): 0-671; 0-02; 0-609; 0-684; 0-7434; 0-7432
Imprints: Atria; Downtown Press; Lisa Drew Books; Fireside; Free Press; Kaplan; MTV Books; Pocket Books; Pocket Star; Scribner; Scribner Classics; Scribner Paperback Fiction; Scribner Poetry; S&S - Libros en Espanol; Simon & Schuster; Simon & Schuster Classic Editions; Simon & Schuster Source; Star Trek®; Touchstone; VH-1; Wall Street Journal Books; WWE Books
Warehouse: Riverside Distribution Center, 100 Front St, Box 300, Riverside, NJ 08075-7500
Tel: 856-461-6500
See separate listing for:
Fireside & Touchstone
Free Press
Kaplan Publishing
Pocket Books
Scribner
Simon & Schuster

Simon & Schuster Audio
1230 Avenue of the Americas, New York, NY 10020
Tel: 212-698-7664
E-mail: audiopub@simonandschuster.com
Web Site: www.simonsaysaudio.com
Key Personnel
Exec VP & Publr: Chris Lynch
VP & Exec Producer: Sandy Moore
Pimsleur Dir: Whit Waterbury
Publicity Mgr: Theresa Pantazopoulos
VP, Mktg: Gavin Caruthers
Ed: Honour Kane
Pimsleur Language Programs.
ISBN Prefix(es): 0-609; 0-7435
Number of titles published annually: 100 Audio
Imprints: AUDIOWORKS; Encore; Pimsleur; Simon & Schuster Audioworks; Simon & Schuster Sound Ideas; Sound Ideas; Success
Distributor for Franklin Covey Audiobooks; The Relaxation Co
Shipping Address: Total Warehouse Services, 2207 Radcliffe St, Bristol, PA 19007

Simon & Schuster Books for Young Readers, see Simon & Schuster Children's Publishing

Simon & Schuster Children's Publishing
Division of Simon & Schuster Inc
1230 Avenue of the Americas, New York, NY 10020
Tel: 212-698-7000
Web Site: www.simonsayskids.com
Key Personnel
Pres & Publr: Rich Richter
Sr VP & Publr, Hardcover: Suzanne Harper
Exec VP & Publr, Novelty, Media Tie-Ins & Teen: Robin Corey
VP & Assoc Publr, Atheneum Books for Young Readers: Ginee Seo
VP & Edit Dir, Atheneum/Anne Schwartz Books: Anne Schwartz
VP & Assoc Publr, Paperback Div: Ellen Krieger
VP & Publr, Simon Spotlight & Simon Spotlight Entertainment: Jen Bergstrom
VP & Edit Dir, Margaret K McElderry Books: Emma Dryden
VP & Gen Mgr: Frank Totaro
VP & Creative Dir: Lee Wade
VP, Mktg & Publicity: Suzanne Murphy
VP & Man Ed: Lisa Donovan
VP & Dir, Prodn: Lottie Gooding
VP, Sales, Sobrights: Bill Gaden
VP & Edit Dir, Little Simon: Cindy Alvarez
VP & Edit Dir, Simon Pulse: Bethany Buck
VP & Assoc Publr, Simon & Schuster Books for Young Readers: Elizabeth Law
Edit Dir, Paula Wiseman Books/Simon & Schuster Books for Young Readers: Paula Wiseman
Edit Dir, Simon & Schuster Books for Young Readers: David Gale
Edit Dir, Atheneum/Richard Jackson Books: Richard Jackson
Exec Art Dir, Paperbacks: Russell Gordon
Exec Art Dir, Atheneum/McElderry: Ann Bobco
Exec Art Dir, Little Simon/Simon Spotlight: Channi Yammer
Exec Dir, Publicity: Tracy van Straaten
Assoc Mktg Dir, Mass Mkt: Julie Amitie
Dir, Creative Servs: Francine Kass
Exec Ed, Paperbacks: Julia Richardson
Mktg Dir, Trade/Retail-Hardcover: Michelle Montague
Exec Ed, Atheneum: Caitlyn Dlouhy
Exec Ed, Simon & Schuster Books for Young Readers: Kevin Lewis
Exec Ed, Simon Spotlight: Sheri Tan
Exec Ed, Simon Spotlight Entertainment: Tricia Boczkowski
Dir, Retail Mktg: Elke Villa
Assoc Mktg Dir, Educ & Lib: Michelle Fadlalla

Preschool through young adult, hardcover & paperback fiction, nonfiction, trade, library, mass market titles & novelty.
ISBN Prefix(es): 0-02; 0-609; 0-689; 0-7434; 1-4169
Number of titles published annually: 700 Print
Total Titles: 4,329 Print; 21 Audio
Imprints: Aladdin Paperbacks; Atheneum Books for Young Readers; Libros Para Ninos; Little Simon; Little Simon Inspirations; Margaret K McElderry Books; Simon & Schuster Books for Young Readers; Simon Pulse; Simon Spotlight; Simon Spotlight Entertainment

§Simon & Schuster Inc
Division of Viacom
1230 Avenue of the Americas, New York, NY 10020
SAN: 200-2450
Tel: 212-698-7000 *Fax:* 212-698-7007
Web Site: www.simonsays.com *Cable:* ESSANDESS NY
Key Personnel
Pres & CEO: Jack Romanos
Pres, Simon & Schuster Adult Publg Group: Carolyn K Reidy
Pres & Publr, Children's Publg Div: Rick Richter
Exec VP & Publr, Simon & Schuster Audio: Chris Lynch
Pres, Simon & Schuster Sales & Dist Div: Lawrence Norton
Sr VP & CFO: David England
Sr VP & Chief Info Officer: Anne Lloyd Davies
Sr VP, HR: Mark Zulli
Sr VP & Gen Coun: Elisa Rivlin
Sr VP, Supply Chain Opers: Joe D'Onofrio
Sr VP & Cont: Dave Upchurch
VP, Simon & Schuster Online: Kate Tentler
VP, Corp Communs: Adam Rothberg
VP, Prodn - Adult: Karen Romano
VP, Prodn - Children's: Lottie Gooding
VP, Facilities: Lee Kartsaklis
VP, Dist & Fulfillment: Dave Schaeffer
VP, Fin Mgmt: Karen Fetty
VP & Exec Dir, Contracts: Joyce Andes
Dir, Order Mgmt: Francine Leinheiser
Mgr, Perms: Agnes Fisher
Man Dir & Chief Exec, Simon & Schuster UK: Ian Chapman
Man Dir, Simon & Schuster Australia: Jon Attenborough
Pres, Simon & Schuster Canada: Deb Woods
Founded: 1924
ISBN Prefix(es): 0-671; 0-689; 0-684; 0-7434; 0-7432; 0-7435; 1-4169; 1-4165
Branch Office(s)
Pimsleur, 30 Monument Sq, Concord, MA 01742 *Tel:* 978-369-7525
Simon & Schuster Canada, 625 Cochrane Dr, Suite 600, Markham, ON L3R 9R9, Canada *Tel:* 905-943-9942 *Fax:* 905-943-9026
Foreign Office(s): Simon & Schuster Australia Pty Ltd, 14-16 Suakin St, Pymble, NSW 2073, Australia *Tel:* (029) 983 6600
Simon & Schuster UK Ltd, Africa House, 4th fl, 64-78 Kingsway, London WC2B 6AH, United Kingdom *Tel:* (020) 7316-1900 *Fax:* (020) 7316-0332
Distributor for AAA Publishing; Andrews McMeel Publishing (fulfillment & billing); Baen Books; Baseball America; Cardoza; Games Workshop; Harlequin (billing only); Hodder Headline USA; ibooks; Meadowbrook Press; National Geographic Society; Open Road; Reader's Digest Children's Books; VIZ (fulfillment & billing)
Returns: c/o Arnold Logistics, 4406 Industrial Park Rd, Bldg 7, Camp Hill, PA 17011 (By appt; to schedule call 717-730-5212 ext 5316)
Shipping Address: Riverside Customer Center, 100 Front St, Riverside, NJ 08075 (trade & children's) *Tel:* 856-461-6500; Bristol Distribution Center, 2207 Radcliffe St, Bristol, PA

19007 (Pocket Books & audio & distribution clients) *Tel:* 215-785-0531
Membership(s): AAP; BISG
See separate listing for:
Simon & Schuster Adult Publishing Group
Simon & Schuster Children's Publishing
Simon & Schuster Online
Simon & Schuster Sales & Distribution

Simon & Schuster Online
Division of Simon & Schuster Inc
1230 Avenue of the Americas, New York, NY 10020
Tel: 212-698-7547 *Fax:* 212-632-8070
E-mail: ssonline@simonsays.com
Web Site: www.simonsays.com; www.simonsayskids.com; www.simonsaysshop.com
Key Personnel
VP & Publr: Kate Tentler
Assoc Publr: Matt Davie
Edit Dir: Kathryn B Gordon
Dir, e-Publg: Claire Israel
Founded: 1996
Manages company website, SimonSays.com & oversees e-book operations for Simon & Schuster, Inc.
Number of titles published annually: 400 E-Book
Total Titles: 2,000 E-Book
Imprints: SimonSays.com

Simon & Schuster Sales & Distribution
Division of Simon & Schuster Inc
1230 Avenue of the Americas, New York, NY 10020
Tel: 212-698-7000
Key Personnel
Pres, Sales & Dist: Lawrence Norton
VP & Dir, Natl Accts: B J Gabriel
VP & Dir, Field & Online Sales & Dist Client Servs: Michael Burkin
VP & Dir, Dist Sales & Retail Mktg: Gary Urda
VP & Dir, Special Sales & Custom Publg: Frank Fochetta
VP & Group Dir, Intl Sales: Cyrus Kheradi
VP & Dir, Sales & Client Communs: Eileen Gentillo

Simon Pulse, see Simon & Schuster Children's Publishing

Simon Spotlight, see Simon & Schuster Children's Publishing

Simon Spotlight Entertainment, see Simon & Schuster Children's Publishing

§Sinauer Associates Inc
23 Plumtree Rd, Sunderland, MA 01375-0407
SAN: 203-2392
Tel: 413-549-4300 *Fax:* 413-549-1118
E-mail: publish@sinauer.com
Web Site: www.sinauer.com
Key Personnel
Pres & Ed: Andrew D Sinauer
VP & Dir, Mktg & Dist: Dean Scudder
Man Ed: Carol J Wigg
Psychology Ed: Graig Donini
Prodn Mgr: Christopher Small
ISBN Contact: Marie Scavotto *E-mail:* scavotto@sinauer.com
Rts & Perms: Linda VandenDolder
Busn Mgr: Penny Grant
Founded: 1969
College textbooks & reference works in the biological & behavioral sciences.
ISBN Prefix(es): 0-87893
Number of titles published annually: 11 Print
Total Titles: 97 Print; 7 CD-ROM
Foreign Rep(s): Alkem (Singapore); Eastern Book Service Inc (Japan); FUNPEC-Editora (Brazil); Maruzen Co (Japan); Palgrave Macmillan

(Australia, Africa, UK, Europe, India, Latin America, Middle East, New Zealand); Shinil Books Co Ltd (Korea); World Science Publishing Co (Korea)
Warehouse: c/o Publishers Storage & Shipping Corp, 46 Development Rd, Fitchburg, MA 01420 *Tel:* 978-345-2121 *Fax:* 978-348-1233

Six Gallery Press
4620 Los Feliz Blvd, Suite 1, Los Angeles, CA 90027
E-mail: sgpwc@yahoo.com
Web Site: www.sixgallerypress.com
Key Personnel
Ed: Tim Miller *E-mail:* tim@sixgallerypress.com
Promo Advisor: Pat Lawrence
Founded: 2000
Independend press producing & marketing experimental literature. We promote these books through reviews in journals, online & through author readings as well as special events including bookfairs.
ISBN Prefix(es): 0-9703840; 0-9726301
Number of titles published annually: 6 Print
Total Titles: 30 Print
Imprints: Replenishment
Distributed by Booksurge

Six Strings Music Publishing
PO Box 7718-151, Torrance, CA 90504-9118
Toll Free Tel: 800-784-0203 *Fax:* 310-362-8864
Web Site: www.sixstringsmusicpub.com
Key Personnel
Pres & Publr: Yoichi Arakawa
Founded: 1997
Publish music/guitar instruction, general music books.
ISBN Prefix(es): 1-891370
Number of titles published annually: 5 Print
Total Titles: 11 Print
Distributed by Music Sales Corp
Membership(s): Publishers Marketing Association

§SkillPath Publications
Division of The Graceland College Center for Professional Development & Lifelong Learning Inc
6900 Squibb Rd, Mission, KS 66202
Mailing Address: PO Box 2768, Mission, KS 66201
Tel: 913-362-3900 *Toll Free Tel:* 800-873-7545 *Fax:* 913-362-4264
E-mail: bookstore@skillpath.net
Web Site: www.ourbookstore.com
Key Personnel
VP, Pubns: William R Cowles *Tel:* 913-362-3900 ext 1355 *E-mail:* bcowles@skillpath.net
Founded: 1989
Books, audio programs, computer based training.
ISBN Prefix(es): 1-878542; 1-57294
Number of titles published annually: 4 Print
Total Titles: 150 Print; 30 Audio
Divisions: CompuMaster
Distributor for Franklin Covey; Glencoe/McGraw-Hill; Impact Publishers; Pearson Technology; Simon & Schuster; Thomson Publishing; John Wiley

Skinner House Books
Division of Unitarian Universalist Association
25 Beacon St, Boston, MA 02108-2800
Tel: 617-742-2100 *Fax:* 617-742-7025
E-mail: skinner_house@uua.org
Web Site: www.uua.org/skinner/index.html
Key Personnel
Publg Dir: Patricia Frevert *Tel:* 617-948-4605 *E-mail:* pfrevert@uua.org
Contact: Ari McCarthy *Tel:* 617-948-4601 *E-mail:* amccarthy@uua.org
Founded: 1975
Specializing in spirituality, inspirational literature, books on church resources for religious liberals.

ISBN Prefix(es): 0-933840; 1-55896
Number of titles published annually: 12 Print
Total Titles: 85 Print
Sales Office(s): Red Wheel/Weiser, PO Box 612, York Beach, ME 03910 *Toll Free Tel:* 800-423-7087
Returns: Red Wheel/Weiser, PO Box 612, York Beach, ME 03910 *Toll Free Tel:* 800-423-7087 ext 22 *E-mail:* orders@redwheelweiser.com
Distribution Center: Red Wheel/Weiser, PO Box 612, York Beach, ME 03910 *Toll Free Tel:* 800-423-7087

Sky Oaks Productions Inc
19544 Sky Oaks Way, Los Gatos, CA 95030
Mailing Address: PO Box 1102, Los Gatos, CA 95031
Tel: 408-395-7600 *Fax:* 408-395-8440
E-mail: tprworld@aol.com
Web Site: www.tpr-world.com
Key Personnel
Pres: Virginia Lee Asher
Founded: 1973
ISBN Prefix(es): 0-940296; 1-56018
Number of titles published annually: 40 Print
Total Titles: 200 Print; 40 Online; 40 E-Book; 7 Audio

Sky Publishing Corp
49 Bay State Rd, Cambridge, MA 02138-1200
Tel: 617-864-7360 *Toll Free Tel:* 800-253-0245
Fax: 617-864-6117
Web Site: skyandtelescope.com
Key Personnel
Pres & Publr: Susan B Lit
Pubn Mgr: Sean Ryan
Mktg Coord: Kerri Williams *E-mail:* kwilliams@skyandtelescope.com
Founded: 1941
Astronomy books & software, maps, posters, globes, sidelines.
ISBN Prefix(es): 0-933346
Number of titles published annually: 13 Print
Total Titles: 20 Print

SkyLight Paths Publishing
Division of LongHill Partners Inc
Sunset Farm Offices, Rte 4, Woodstock, VT 05091
SAN: 134-5621
Mailing Address: PO Box 237, Woodstock, VT 05091-0237
Tel: 802-457-4000 *Toll Free Tel:* 800-962-4544
Fax: 802-457-4004
E-mail: editorial@skylightpaths.com
Web Site: www.skylightpaths.com
Key Personnel
Pres, Publr & Intl Rts: Stuart M Matlins
Exec VP & Assoc Publr: Jon M Sweeney
E-mail: jsweeney@skylightpaths.com
Exec VP, Admin & Fin: Amy M Wilson
E-mail: awilson@longhillpartners.com
Ed: Maura Shaw
Founded: 1999
General trade books for seekers & believers of all spirituality & religion. Subject areas include spirituality, children's, self-help, eastern & western religion.
ISBN Prefix(es): 1-893361
Number of titles published annually: 25 Print
Total Titles: 125 Print
Foreign Rep(s): Harris/Elon (Israel); Frederique Porretta (France); H Katia Schumer (Brazil); Diana Voight Literature Agentur (Germany); Susanna Zevi (Italy)
Foreign Rights: Deep Books (Europe & UK); Novalis (Canada); Willow Connection (Australia)
Returns: 28 River St, Windsor, VT 05089

§Slack Incorporated
6900 Grove Rd, Thorofare, NJ 08086-9447
SAN: 201-8632

Tel: 856-848-1000 *Toll Free Tel:* 800-257-8290
Fax: 856-853-5991
Web Site: www.slackbooks.com
Key Personnel
VP, Book Publg: John H Bond *Tel:* 856-848-1000 ext 294 *Fax:* 856-845-2211 *E-mail:* jbond@slackinc.com
Edit Dir: Amy McShane *E-mail:* amcshane@slackinc.com
Mktg Mgr: Michelle Gatt *E-mail:* mgatt@slackinc.com
Founded: 1960
Academic textbooks & professional reference books: medicine, occupational therapy, physical therapy, ophthalmology, gastroenterology, orthopedics, athletic training, nursing & other areas.
ISBN Prefix(es): 1-55642
Number of titles published annually: 40 Print; 2 CD-ROM; 1 E-Book
Total Titles: 225 Print; 15 CD-ROM; 1 E-Book
Divisions: Journal Publishing; Professional Book Publishing; Trade Book Publishing
Foreign Rep(s): DA Information Services (Australia); Distribuidora Intersistemas (Mexico); EuroSpan (Europe); Igaku Shoin Ltd (Japan); Jaypee Brothers (India); Login Brothers (Canada); McGraw-Hill (Asia); Tecmedd Distribuidora E Importadora de Livros Ribeirao Pretol Ltda (Brazil)
Foreign Rights: John Scott & Associates
Advertising Agency: Alcyon Advertising
Distribution Center: Bldg B, 200 Richardson Ave, Swedesboro, NJ 08085
Membership(s): American Medical Publishers Association; Publishers Marketing Association; Small Publishers Association of North America

Sleeping Bear Press™
Imprint of Thomson Gale
310 N Main St, Suite 300, Chelsea, MI 48118
Tel: 734-475-4411 *Toll Free Tel:* 800-487-2323
Fax: 734-475-0787
E-mail: sleepingbear@thomson.com
Web Site: www.sleepingbearpress.com
Key Personnel
Gen Mgr: Margaret Erdman
Edit Dir: Heather Hughes
Dir, Sales & Mktg: David Swan *E-mail:* swand@thomson.com
Mktg Coord: Amy Patrick
Creative Dir: Jennifer Lundahl
Publicity Dir: Adam Rifenberick *E-mail:* rifenbericka@thomson.com
Founded: 1995
Publisher of children's books K-6.
ISBN Prefix(es): 1-886947; 1-58536
Number of titles published annually: 40 Print
Total Titles: 77 Print
Foreign Rep(s): H B Fenn & Co Inc (Canada); Thomson International (outside the US)
Returns: Thomson Distribution Center, 10650 Toebben Dr, Independence, KY 41051
Shipping Address: Thomson Distribution Center, 10650 Toebben Dr, Independence, KY 41051
Warehouse: Thomson Distribution Center, 10650 Toebben Dr, Independence, KY 41051
Distribution Center: Thomson Distribution Center, 10650 Toebben Dr, Independence, KY 41051
Membership(s): ALA; Association of Children's Booksellers; BookSense Publisher Partner; International Reading Association

Smith & Kraus Inc Publishers
177 Lyme Rd, Hanover, NH 03755
Mailing Address: PO Box 127, Lyme, NH 03768-0127
Tel: 603-643-6431 (edit); 603-669-7032 (cust serv) *Toll Free Tel:* 800-288-2881 (orders only)
Fax: 603-643-1831
E-mail: sandk@sover.net
Web Site: www.smithkraus.com

Key Personnel
Pres: Marisa Smith Kraus
Founded: 1990
Drama books, monologues, books of interest to our theatrical community, play anthologies. Smith & Kraus Global: religious/political.
ISBN Prefix(es): 0-9622722; 1-880399; 1-57525
Number of titles published annually: 35 Print
Total Titles: 50 Print
Imprints: Smith & Kraus Books For Kids (young adult fiction)
Subsidiaries: Smith & Kraus Global (world affairs)
Distributor for Smith & Kraus Inc
Foreign Rep(s): Agnes Krup Literary Agency

§M Lee Smith Publishers LLC
5201 Virginia Way, Brentwood, TN 37027
Mailing Address: PO Box 5094, Brentwood, TN 37024-5094
Tel: 615-373-7517 *Toll Free Tel:* 800-274-6774
Fax: 615-373-5183
Web Site: www.mleesmith.com
Key Personnel
Pres: Dan Oswald
VP, Fin & Admin: Orin Crouch
VP, Human Resources: Marilyn Willis
VP, Content: Brad Forrister
Publr: M Lee Smith
Circ Mgr: Kim Mesecher
Founded: 1975
Legal newsletters/legal book related titles.
ISBN Prefix(es): 0-925773
Number of titles published annually: 130 Print
Total Titles: 2 CD-ROM; 60 Online

Peter Smith Publisher Inc
5 Lexington Ave, Magnolia, MA 01930
SAN: 206-8885
Tel: 978-525-3562 *Fax:* 978-525-3674
Key Personnel
Pres: MaryAnn Lash
Exec VP & Treas: Michael E Smith
ISBN Contact: Carolyn Edwards
Founded: 1929
Hardcover reprints of out-of-print & rare books (adult & junior), hardcover editions of selected paperbacks.
ISBN Prefix(es): 0-8446
Number of titles published annually: 35 Print
Total Titles: 1,200 Print

The Smith Publishers
Subsidiary of The Generalist Association Inc
69 Joralemon St, Brooklyn, NY 11201-4003
Tel: 718-834-1212 *Fax:* 718-834-1212
E-mail: thesmith1@aol.com; artsend@ma.ultranet.com
Web Site: members.aol.com/thesmith1
Key Personnel
Ed & Publr: Harry Smith
Sales: Marshall Brooks *Tel:* 802-464-5584
Founded: 1964
Poetry, fiction, drama, commentary.
ISBN Prefix(es): 0-912292; 1-882986
Number of titles published annually: 4 Print
Total Titles: 76 Print; 76 Online; 76 E-Book
Distributed by Arts End Books
Foreign Rights: International Titles
Orders to: PO Box 162, Newton, MA 02468
Warehouse: Express Industries, Pier 1, Brooklyn, NY 11201

Steve Smith Autosports
PO Box 11631, Santa Ana, CA 92711-1631
Tel: 714-639-7681 *Fax:* 714-639-9741
E-mail: sales@ssapubl.com
Web Site: www.ssapubl.com
Key Personnel
Pres: Steve Smith *E-mail:* steve@ssapubl.com
Founded: 1971
Specialize in auto racing technical books.
ISBN Prefix(es): 0-936834

Number of titles published annually: 5 Print
Total Titles: 200 Print

Smithsonian Federal Series Section
Division of Smithsonian Books
750 Ninth St NW, Suite 4300, Washington, DC
20560-0950
Tel: 202-275-2233 *Fax:* 202-275-2274
Key Personnel
Man Ed: Diane Tyler
Ed: Jack Korytowski; Merideth McQuoid
Founded: 1846
Nine series of scholarly monographs reporting
Smithsonian Institute research.
Number of titles published annually: 10 Print
Total Titles: 500 Print
Shipping Address: Federal Series Pubns, 1111 N
Capitol St NW, Washington, DC 20560

Smithsonian Institution Press
Division of Smithsonian Institution
750 Ninth St NW, Suite 4300, Washington, DC
20560-0950
Tel: 202-275-2300 *Fax:* 202-275-2274
E-mail: inquiries@sipress.si.edu
Web Site: www.sipress.si.edu
Key Personnel
Dir: Don Fehr *E-mail:* dfenr@sipress.si.edu
Busn Mgr: Prospero Hernandez
E-mail: phernandez@sipress.si.edu
Publicity: Matt Litts *E-mail:* mlitts@sipress.si.edu
Foreign Rts: Jenny Meyer *E-mail:* jenny@
meyerlit.com
Prodn: Carolyn Gleason *E-mail:* cgleason@
sipress.si.edu
Design: Janice Wheeler *E-mail:* jwheeler@
sipress.si.edu
Fed Contributions Series: Diane Tyler
E-mail: dtyler@sipress.si.edu
Founded: 1966
General trade & adult nonfiction.
ISBN Prefix(es): 0-87474; 1-56098; 1-58834
Number of titles published annually: 70 Print
Total Titles: 800 Print
Imprints: Smithsonian Books
Distributor for Biological Diversity Handbook
Series; Handbook of North American Indi-
ans; Smithsonian Library of the Solar Sys-
tem; Smithsonian Series in Archaeological
Inquiry; Smithsonian Series in Comparative
Evolutionary Biology; Smithsonian Series in
Ethnographic Inquiry
Distribution Center: WW Norton

§Smyth & Helwys Publishing Inc
6316 Peake Rd, Macon, GA 31210
Tel: 478-757-1305 *Toll Free Tel:* 800-747-3016;
800-568-1248 *Fax:* 478-757-0564
E-mail: market@helwys.com
Web Site: www.helwys.com
Key Personnel
Publr: David Cassady
Intl Rts & Book Ed: Keith Gammons
Founded: 1990
Christian books, literature, Sunday School books
(curriculum).
ISBN Prefix(es): 1-57312
Number of titles published annually: 30 Print
Total Titles: 330 Print
Foreign Rep(s): Grace Wing Publishers (England)

Snow Lion Publications Inc
605 W State St, Ithaca, NY 14850
SAN: 281-7292
Mailing Address: PO Box 6483, Ithaca, NY
14851-6483
Tel: 607-273-8519 *Toll Free Tel:* 800-950-0313
Fax: 607-273-8508
E-mail: tibet@snowlionpub.com
Web Site: www.snowlionpub.com
Key Personnel
Pres, Intl Rts & Lib Sales Dir: Jeffrey Cox

Tel: 607-273-8506 *E-mail:* jeffcox@
snowlionpub.com
Founded: 1980
Trade & scholarly books on Tibetan Buddhism &
Tibet & books by the Dalai Lama.
ISBN Prefix(es): 0-937938; 1-55939
Number of titles published annually: 18 Print
Total Titles: 180 Print; 1 Audio
Imprints: Snow Lion
Distributed by National Book Network
Foreign Rep(s): The Buddhist Merit & Wisdom
Service (Hong Kong); Mandala Books (Aus-
tralia); Stichting Maitreya Institute (Nether-
lands); TBI Publishers Distributor (India); Wis-
dom Books (England)
Foreign Rights: Bardon-Chinese Media Agency
(Chinese); Eliane Benisti (France); Best Liter-
ary & Rights Agency (Korea); Julio F-Yanez
Agencia Literaria (Spain & Portugal); Paul &
Peter Fritz AG Literary Agency (Germany);
Graal Ltd (Poland); Katai & Bolza Literary
Agents (Hungary); Kristin Olson Literary
Agency (Czech Republic); Tuttle-Mori (Japan);
Susanna Zevi Agenzia Letteraria (Italy)
Membership(s): Publishers Marketing Association

§Tom Snyder Productions
Subsidiary of Scholastic Inc
80 Coolidge Hill Rd, Watertown, MA 02472-
5003
Tel: 617-926-6000 *Toll Free Tel:* 800-342-0236
Fax: 617-926-6222
E-mail: ask@tomsnyder.com
Web Site: www.tomsnyder.com
Key Personnel
Gen Mgr: Rick Abrams *E-mail:* abramsr@
tomsnyder.com
Founded: 1980
Educational software publisher.
ISBN Prefix(es): 0-926891; 1-55998; 1-57809; 1-
59009
Number of titles published annually: 20 CD-
ROM; 1 Online
Total Titles: 100 CD-ROM; 20 Online

**Society for Human Resource Management
(SHRM)**
1800 Duke St, Alexandria, VA 22314
Mailing Address: PO Box 930132, Atlanta, GA
31193
Tel: 703-548-3440 *Toll Free Tel:* 800-444-5006
(orders) *Fax:* 703-836-0367; 770-442-9742 (or-
ders)
E-mail: shrm@shrm.org; shrmstore@shrm.org
Web Site: www.shrm.org
Key Personnel
Mgr: Brian Weese
SHRM Store Coord: Vince Caldwell *Tel:* 703-
535-6137 *E-mail:* vcaldwell@shrm.org
Trade organization of human resource profes-
sional with over 170,000 members.
ISBN Prefix(es): 0-939900; 1-58644; 1-932132
Number of titles published annually: 20 Print
Total Titles: 100 Print

§Society for Industrial & Applied Mathematics
3600 University City Science Ctr, Philadelphia,
PA 19104-2688
Tel: 215-382-9800 *Toll Free Tel:* 800-447-7426
Fax: 215-386-7999
E-mail: siam@siam.org
Web Site: www.siam.org
Key Personnel
Exec Dir: James M Crowley
Man Ed: Kelly Thomas
Cont: Lauren Steidel
Pubns Mgr: Mitchell Chernoff
Journals Publr: Mary Muccie
Prodn Mgr: Donna Witzleben
Mktg Mgr: Michelle Montgomery *Tel:* 215-382-
9800 ext 368
Acqs Ed: Elizabeth Greenspan; Linda Thiel

Cust Serv Mgr: Arlette Liberatore
Founded: 1952
Journals, books, conferences & reprints in math-
ematics/computer science/statistics/physical
science.
ISBN Prefix(es): 0-89871
Number of titles published annually: 25 Print
Total Titles: 325 Print; 35 CD-ROM; 2 E-Book

**§Society for Mining, Metallurgy & Exploration
Inc**
PO Box 277002, Littleton, CO 80127-7002
Tel: 303-973-9550 *Toll Free Tel:* 800-763-3132
Fax: 303-973-3845
E-mail: sme@smenet.org
Web Site: www.smenet.org
Key Personnel
Ed: Tim O'Neil
Founded: 1871
Also publishes monthly magazine, quarterly jour-
nal, trade books, hardbound & paperback. Ev-
erything is mining related.
ISBN Prefix(es): 0-87335
Number of titles published annually: 12 Print
Total Titles: 80 Print; 15 CD-ROM
Foreign Rep(s): Affiliated East-West Press (India);
Australian Mineral Foundation (Australia)

Society for Protective Coating
40 24 St, 6th fl, Pittsburgh, PA 15222-4656
Tel: 412-281-2331 *Fax:* 412-281-9992
E-mail: books@sspc.org
Web Site: www.sspc.org
Key Personnel
Exec Dir: William Shoup *Tel:* 412-281-2331 ext
230
Mktg/Pubns Prodn Specialist: Russell Davison
Tel: 412-281-2331 ext 216 *E-mail:* davison@
sspc.org
Info Resources Specialist: Marge Sroka *Tel:* 412-
281-2331 ext 224 *E-mail:* sroka@sspc.org
Founded: 1950
Technical publications; video tapes, standards for
industry.
ISBN Prefix(es): 0-938477; 1-889060
Number of titles published annually: 5 Print
Total Titles: 80 Print
Advertising Agency: Technical Publishing Co

Society of American Archivists
527 S Wells St, 5th fl, Chicago, IL 60607
SAN: 211-7614
Tel: 312-922-0140 *Fax:* 312-347-1452
E-mail: info@archivists.org
Web Site: www.archivists.org
Key Personnel
Exec Dir: Nancy Beaumont *E-mail:* nbeaumont@
archivists.org
Man Ed & Dir Publns: Teresa Brinati
E-mail: tbrinati@archivists.org
Founded: 1936
Archival literature; preservation.
ISBN Prefix(es): 0-931828; 1-931666
Number of titles published annually: 5 Print
Total Titles: 72 Print

Society of Biblical Literature
The Luce Ctr, Suite 350, 825 Houston Mill Rd,
Atlanta, GA 30329
Mailing Address: PO Box 2243, Williston, VT
05495-2243
Tel: 404-727-2325 *Fax:* 802-864-7626
E-mail: sbl@sbl-site.org
Web Site: www.sbl-site.org
Key Personnel
Exec Dir: Kent H Richards
Edit Dir: Rex Matthews
Prodn Mgr: Leigh Anderson
Mktg Mgr: Kathie Klein *E-mail:* kathie.klein@
sbl-site.org
Founded: 1880
A learned society whose purpose is to stimulate
the critical investigation of Biblical literature.

ISBN Prefix(es): 0-89130; 0-7885; 0-88414; 1-58983
Number of titles published annually: 25 Print; 1 Online
Total Titles: 425 Print; 1 Online
Distributor for Brown Judaic Studies; Journal of Feminist Studies in Religion
Warehouse: 82 Winter Sport Lane, Williston, VT 05495 *Tel:* 802-864-6185 *Toll Free Tel:* 877-725-3334 *Fax:* 802-864-7626

Society of Environmental Toxicology & Chemistry
1010 N 12 Ave, Pensacola, FL 32501-3370
Tel: 850-469-9777; 850-469-1500 *Fax:* 850-469-9778
E-mail: setac@setac.org
Web Site: www.setac.org
Key Personnel
Exec Dir: Rodney Parrish *Tel:* 850-469-9777 ext 17
Pubns Asst: Mimi Meredith *Tel:* 850-469-9777 ext 28 *E-mail:* mmeredith@setac.org
Founded: 1991
Supports publications of scientific value relating to environmental topics. Proceedings of technical workshops that explore current & prospective environmental issues are published as peer-reviewed technical documents. Publications are used by scientists, engineers & managers because of their technical basis & comprehensive, state-of-the-science reviews; association press; nonprofit, professional society.
ISBN Prefix(es): 1-880611
Number of titles published annually: 10 Print; 1 CD-ROM
Total Titles: 85 Print; 5 CD-ROM
Imprints: SETAC Press

§Society of Exploration Geophysicists
8801 S Yale, Tulsa, OK 74137
Mailing Address: PO Box 702740, Tulsa, OK 74170-2740
Tel: 918-497-5500 *Fax:* 918-497-5557
Web Site: www.seg.org
Key Personnel
Dir, Pubns: Ted Bakamjian *E-mail:* tbakamjian@seg.org
Founded: 1930
Types of publications: textbooks; videos; technical Journals & Web site.
ISBN Prefix(es): 1-56080; 0-931839
Number of titles published annually: 8 Print
Total Titles: 100 Print; 3 CD-ROM

§Society of Manufacturing Engineers
One SME Dr, Dearborn, MI 48121
SAN: 203-2376
Mailing Address: PO Box 930, Dearborn, MI 48121
Tel: 313-271-1500 *Toll Free Tel:* 800-733-4763 (cust serv) *Fax:* 313-271-2861
Web Site: www.sme.org
Key Personnel
Dir, Membership: Mark Tomlinson *Tel:* 313-425-3060 *E-mail:* mtomlinson@sme.org
SME Resource Center: Margaret Satoh
Web Ed: Karen Wilhelm
Mktg Mgr: Denise Leipold
Founded: 1932
Professional engineering books, periodicals & DVDs.
ISBN Prefix(es): 0-87263
Number of titles published annually: 5 Print
Total Titles: 150 Print; 3 CD-ROM
Distributed by American Technical Publishers; ASME; McGraw-Hill
Distributor for Free Press Division of MacMillan; Industrial Press; McGraw-Hill; Prentice Hall; John Wiley & Sons Inc
Foreign Rights: American Technical Publishers (UK); DA Book Pty Ltd (Australia); Elsevier Science Publishers (Netherlands)

The Society of Naval Architects & Marine Engineers
601 Pavonia Ave, Jersey City, NJ 07306-2907
SAN: 202-0572
Tel: 201-798-4800 *Toll Free Tel:* 800-798-2188 *Fax:* 201-798-4975
Web Site: www.sname.org
Key Personnel
Pubns Mgr: Susan Evans *E-mail:* sevans@sname.org
Reference books, directories, periodicals on naval architecture, marine engineering & ocean engineering.
ISBN Prefix(es): 0-87033; 0-9603048; 0-939773; 0-7698
Number of titles published annually: 3 Print
Total Titles: 29 Print

Society of Spanish & Spanish-American Studies
Univ Colorado, Society for Spanish & Spanish American Studies, Dept Spanish & Portuguese, Boulder, CO 80309-0278
Tel: 303-492-5900 *Fax:* 303-492-3699
E-mail: sssas@colorado.edu
Web Site: www.colorado.edu/spanish/fpubs.html
Key Personnel
Dir: Luis T Gonzalez-del-Valle
Founded: 1976
Spanish, Cuban & Spanish-American literature.
ISBN Prefix(es): 0-89295
Number of titles published annually: 10 Print
Total Titles: 100 Print

§Socrates Media
Formerly E-Z Products Inc
227 W Monroe St, Suite 500, Chicago, IL 60606
Tel: 312-762-5600 *Toll Free Tel:* 800-822-4566
Web Site: www.socrates.com
Key Personnel
Sr VP, Sales: Paul Barrett
VP, Mktg: Janette Barslin
Founded: 1987
Publisher of self-help books, software, forms & kits dealing with legal, financial & business.
ISBN Prefix(es): 1-56382
Number of titles published annually: 12 Print; 8 CD-ROM
Total Titles: 100 Print; 35 CD-ROM

Soho Press Inc
853 Broadway, New York, NY 10003
SAN: 202-5531
Tel: 212-260-1900 *Fax:* 212-260-1902
E-mail: editor@sohopress.com
Web Site: sohopress.com
Key Personnel
Publr & Intl Rts Contact: Juris Jurjevics *E-mail:* sohojj@sohopress.com
VP: Laura M C Hruska *E-mail:* lhruska@sohopress.com
Assoc Ed: Bryan Devendorf *E-mail:* bdevendorf@sohopress.com
Publicity: Sally Ann McCartin Associates *E-mail:* samccartin@aol.com
Founded: 1986
Hard & softcover trade books: mysteries; general nonfiction, history & fiction.
ISBN Prefix(es): 0-939149; 1-56947
Number of titles published annually: 45 Print
Total Titles: 300 Print; 4 E-Book
Imprints: Hera; Soho Crime
Foreign Rights: ACER Agencia Literaria (Latin America, Portugal, Spain); Agence Hoffman (France); Hadary & Associates (Israel); Johnson & Alcock (UK); Leonardt & Hoier Literary Agency (Scandinavia); Meller Literary Agency (Germany); Jan Michael (Netherlands); Daniela Micura (Italy); Synopsis (Russia)
Warehouse: Consortium Book Sales & Distribution, 1045 Westgate Dr, St Paul, MN 55114-

1065 *Tel:* 651-379-5321 *Toll Free Tel:* 800-283-3572
Distribution Center: Consortium Book Sales & Distribution, 1045 Westgate Dr, St Paul, MN 55114-1065 *Toll Free Tel:* 800-283-3572

Soil Science Society of America
677 S Segoe Rd, Madison, WI 53711-1086
Tel: 608-273-8095 *Fax:* 608-273-2021
E-mail: headquarters@soils.org
Web Site: www.soils.org
Key Personnel
Assoc Exec VP: David M Kral
Dir, Meetings & Conventions: Keith Schlesinger *Tel:* 608-273-8090 ext 322 *E-mail:* kschlesinger@agronoma.org
Mktg Mgr: Betsy Ahner
Founded: 1936
Technical books for professionals in soil science.
ISBN Prefix(es): 0-89118
Number of titles published annually: 6 Print
Total Titles: 80 Print

Solano Press Books
PO Box 773, Point Arena, CA 95468
Tel: 707-884-4508 *Toll Free Tel:* 800-931-9373 *Fax:* 707-884-4109
E-mail: spbooks@solano.com
Web Site: www.solano.com
Key Personnel
Pres & Publr: Warren W Jones *E-mail:* wjones@solano.com
Founded: 1984
Professional books: law, public administration, real estate, land use, environment, urban planning, environmental analysis & management.
ISBN Prefix(es): 0-9614657; 0-923956
Number of titles published annually: 4 Print
Total Titles: 22 Print

Soli Deo Gloria Publications
Subsidiary of Soli Deo Gloria Ministries Inc
451 Millers Run Rd, Morgan, PA 15064
Mailing Address: PO Box 451, Morgan, PA 15064-0451
Tel: 412-221-1901 *Toll Free Tel:* 888-266-5734 *Fax:* 412-221-1902
Web Site: www.sdgbooks.com
Key Personnel
Pres: Don Kistler *E-mail:* don@sdgbooks.com
Founded: 1988
Religious books, especially Puritan reprints.
ISBN Prefix(es): 1-877611; 1-57358
Number of titles published annually: 15 Print
Total Titles: 170 Print; 1 Audio
Membership(s): CBA; Evangelical Christian Publishers Association

Solucient
10007 Church St, Suite 700, Evanston, IL 60201
Tel: 847-424-4400 *Toll Free Tel:* 800-366-7526 *Fax:* 847-332-1768
E-mail: pubs@solucient.com
Web Site: www.solucient.com
Key Personnel
VP, Mktg: Chris Clemmensen
Founded: 1985
Analyze, measure & compare the financial, operational & clinical performance of the nation's healthcare system.
ISBN Prefix(es): 1-880678; 1-57372
Number of titles published annually: 5 Print
Total Titles: 177 Print

SOM Publishing
Subsidiary of School of Metaphysics
163 Moon Valley Rd, Windyville, MO 65783
SAN: 159-5423
Tel: 417-345-8411 *Fax:* 417-345-6668 (call 417-345-8411 before faxing)
E-mail: som@som.org
Web Site: www.som.org

Key Personnel
CEO: Dr Barbara Condron
Pres: Dr Pam Blosser *Tel:* 847-991-0140
Dist & Mktg: Paul Blosser
Founded: 1973
Publish books in the fields of dream interpretation, Kundalini, holistic health, visualization, interfaith studies, meditation, Religious-Christian, past life recall & spiritual enlightenment.
ISBN Prefix(es): 0-944386
Number of titles published annually: 4 Print
Total Titles: 25 Print
Distributed by Devores; New Leaf Distributing

Soncino Press
123 Ditmas Ave, Brooklyn, NY 11218
Tel: 718-972-6200 *Toll Free Tel:* 800-972-6201
Fax: 718-972-6204
E-mail: info@soncino.com
Web Site: www.soncino.com
Key Personnel
Mgr: Norman Shapiro *E-mail:* nshapiro@soncino.com
Bible, Talmud & Judaism.
ISBN Prefix(es): 1-871055
Number of titles published annually: 4 Print

Mark Sonnenfeld
Member of Marymark Press
45-08 Old Millstone Dr, East Windsor, NJ 08520
Tel: 609-443-0646
Web Site: experimentalpoet.com
Key Personnel
Ed, Publr & Writer: Mark Sonnenfeld
Founded: 1994
Independent small press publishing vehicle; various size chapbooks, broadsides, writing samplers, give-out sheets, single sheets, audio sound collages. Experimental writing. Prefer automatic writing/avant-garde genre.
ISBN Prefix(es): 0-9632820; 1-887379
Number of titles published annually: 70 Print; 6 Audio
Total Titles: 300 Print; 30 Audio

Sophia Institute Press
PO Box 5284, Manchester, NH 03108
SAN: 657-7172
Tel: 603-641-9344 *Toll Free Tel:* 800-888-9344
Fax: 603-641-8108 *Toll Free Fax:* 888-288-2259
E-mail: orders@sophiainstitute.com
Web Site: www.sophiainstitute.com
Key Personnel
Publr: John L Barger
Prodn Mgr: Sheila M Perry
Acq Ed: Todd Aglialoro *Tel:* 603-641-9344 ext 311
Dir, Sales: Jack Barger
Founded: 1983
Books & sell artworks.
ISBN Prefix(es): 0-918477; 1-928832
Number of titles published annually: 24 Print
Total Titles: 60 Print
Foreign Rep(s): Family Publications (UK); Chawton Alton Hants (UK); John XXIII Fellowship (Australia); Redemptorist Publications Alphonsus House (UK)
Shipping Address: 300 Bedford St, 5th fl, Manchester, NH 03101

§Sopris West Educational Services
Imprint of Cambium Learning
4093 Specialty Place, Longmont, CO 80504
Mailing Address: PO Box 1809, Longmont, CO 80502-1809
Tel: 303-651-2829 *Toll Free Tel:* 800-547-6747
Fax: 303-776-5934
E-mail: customerservice@sopriswest.com
Web Site: www.sopriswest.com

Key Personnel
Pres: Stuart Horsfall
Man Ed: Lynne Stair *E-mail:* lynnes@sopriswest.com
VP, Mktg: Chet Foraker
VP, Acqs: Steve Mitchell *E-mail:* stephenm@sopriswest.com
Founded: 1978
Training, development materials for educators.
ISBN Prefix(es): 0-944584; 1-57035; 1-59318
Number of titles published annually: 50 Print
Total Titles: 350 Print

Sorin Books
Imprint of Ave Maria Press
19113 Douglas Rd, Notre Dame, IN 46556
SAN: 201-1255
Mailing Address: PO Box 428, Notre Dame, IN 46556-0428
Tel: 574-287-2831 *Toll Free Tel:* 800-282-1865
Fax: 574-239-2904 *Toll Free Fax:* 800-282-5681
E-mail: sorinbk@nd.edu
Web Site: www.sorinbooks.com
Key Personnel
Publr: Frank J Cunningham
Dir, Mktg & Sales & Lib Sales Dir: Mary E Andrews *Tel:* 574-287-2831 ext 219 *E-mail:* mary.e.andrews.22@nd.edu
Cust Serv: Mary Jo Crandall *E-mail:* mary.j.crandall.6@nd.edu
Rts & Perms: Susana Kelly *E-mail:* susana.j.kelly.140@nd.edu
Edit Dir: Robert Hamma *E-mail:* robert.m.hamma.1@nd.edu
Founded: 1999
Specialize in the categories of spirituality, marriage, parenting, living simply, transitional moments, wellness, family life, inspiration.
ISBN Prefix(es): 1-893732
Number of titles published annually: 15 Print
Total Titles: 76 Print
Distributed by Ave Maria Press
Foreign Rep(s): Vanwell Publishing Ltd (Ontario)

SOS Publications
43 De Normandie Ave, Fair Haven, NJ 07704-3303
Tel: 732-530-5896; 732-530-3199 *Fax:* 732-530-5896
Web Site: www.netlabs.net/hp/sosjs
Key Personnel
Dir: Dr Joanne Stolen *E-mail:* sosjs@netlabs.net
Founded: 1986
ISBN Prefix(es): 0-9625505; 1-887062
Number of titles published annually: 3 Print
Total Titles: 13 Print

Sound View Press, see Falk Art Reference

Soundprints
Division of Trudy Corp
353 Main Ave, Norwalk, CT 06851
Tel: 203-846-2274 *Toll Free Tel:* 800-228-7839; 800-577-2413, ext 118 (orders) *Fax:* 203-846-1776
E-mail: Soundprints@soundprints.com
Web Site: www.soundprints.com
Key Personnel
Pres: Bill Burnham *E-mail:* bill.burnham@soundprints.com
Publr: Ashley Andersen *E-mail:* ashley.andersen@soundprints.com
VP, Sales: John Sullivan *E-mail:* john.sullivan@soundprints.com
Ed: Laura Galvin *E-mail:* laura.galvin@soundprints.com; Ben Nussbaum *E-mail:* ben.nussbaum@soundprints.com
Edit Asst: Brian Giblin *E-mail:* brian.giblin@soundprints.com
Founded: 1988

Board books, picture books, treasuries, early reading chapter books, nature, environment & children's classics. Age group: pre-school, ages 5-10. Soundprints produces realistic storybooks, audiobooks & toys authenticated by the Smithsonian Institution & other education & conservation programs. Subjects include natural history, science & social studies for ages 3-10. Little Soundprints imprint produces wildlife stories, nursery rhymes & children's classics. Most titles available with audio & toys.
ISBN Prefix(es): 0-924483; 1-56899; 1-931465; 1-59249
Number of titles published annually: 30 Print; 20 Audio
Total Titles: 105 Print; 98 Audio
Imprints: Little Soundprints
Subsidiaries: Studio Mouse LLC
Distributed by H B Fenn; INT Press (Australia & New Zealand)
Distributor for Edimat Libros sa
Foreign Rep(s): Bookwise (Australia, New Zealand, Southeast Asia); H B Fenn (Canada)
Foreign Rights: Jacqueline Miller (France, Germany)
Membership(s): ABA; Museum Store Association; NSSEA; Publishers Marketing Association; Toy International Association

Sourcebooks Inc
1935 Brookdale Rd, Suite 139, Naperville, IL 60563
SAN: 666-7864
Mailing Address: PO Box 4410, Naperville, IL 60567-4410
Tel: 630-961-3900 *Toll Free Tel:* 800-432-7444
Fax: 630-961-2168
E-mail: info@sourcebooks.com
Web Site: www.sourcebooks.com
Key Personnel
Pres & Publr: Dominique Raccah
Edit Dir: Todd Stocke *Tel:* 630-961-3900 ext 243 *E-mail:* todd.stocke@sourcebooks.com
Hysteria Div Mgr: Deborah Werksman
Sphinx Div Mgr: Dianne Wheeler
Founded: 1987
General trade & gift books.
ISBN Prefix(es): 0-942061; 1-57071; 1-57248; 0-913825; 1-883518; 0-9629162; 1-887166; 1-4022
Number of titles published annually: 120 Print
Total Titles: 300 Print
Imprints: Sourcebooks Casablanca; Sourcebooks Hysteria; Sourcebooks Landmark; Sourcebooks MediaFusion; Sphinx Publishing
Branch Office(s)
Sourcebooks Hysteria, 955 Connecticut Ave Suite 1209, Bridgeport, CT 06600, Contact: Deborah Werksman *Tel:* 203-333-9399 *Fax:* 203-367-7188 *E-mail:* laugh@hysteriabooks.com
Foreign Rep(s): Ursula Bender (Germany); Elaine Benisti (France); Big Apple Tuttle-Mori Agency Inc (Thailand); Harris/Elon Agency (Israel); Inter-Ko (Korea); Piergiorgio Nicolazzini (Italy); Prava I Prevodi (Eastern Block, Slovak Republic); Karen Schindler (Brazil); Tuttle-Mori Agency Inc (Japan); Yanez Agencia Literaria (Spain)
Warehouse: Dearborn Dist, 940 Enterprise St, Aurora, IL 60504 *Tel:* 630-851-7666 *Fax:* 630-851-8188

South Carolina Bar
Continuing Legal Education Div, 950 Taylor St, Columbia, SC 29201
Mailing Address: PO Box 608, Columbia, SC 29202-0608
Tel: 803-771-0333 *Toll Free Tel:* 800-768-7787
Fax: 803-252-8427
E-mail: scbar-info@scbar.org
Web Site: www.scbar.org
Key Personnel
Pubns Dir: Alicia Hutto

Continuing Legal Educ Dir: Terry Burnette
E-mail: terry.burnette@scbar.org
Founded: 1979
Law materials.
ISBN Prefix(es): 0-943856
Number of titles published annually: 15 Print
Total Titles: 73 Print

§South Carolina Dept of Archives & History
8301 Parklane Rd, Columbia, SC 29223
Tel: 803-896-6100 *Fax:* 803-896-6198
Web Site: www.state.sc.us/scdah/
Key Personnel
Dir: Rodger E Stroup
Finding Aids, educational books, archives, etc.
ISBN Prefix(es): 1-880067
Number of titles published annually: 5 Print
Imprints: Commons House Journal; Educational
Packets 1-7
Warehouse: State Records Center, 1942-A Lau-
rel St, Columbia, SC 29201 (records storage)
Tel: 803-898-9936 *Fax:* 803-898-9981

South End Press
Affiliate of Institute for Social & Cultural Change
7 Brookline St, No 1, Cambridge, MA 02139-
4146
SAN: 211-979X
Tel: 617-547-4002 *Fax:* 617-547-1333
E-mail: southend@southendpress.org
Web Site: www.southendpress.org
Key Personnel
Ed & Publr, Rts & Perms: Joey Fox
E-mail: joeyfox@southendpress.org
Ed, Publr & Promos Mgr: Jill Petty
Ed, Publr & Prod Coord Mgr: Loie Hayes
Adv: Alyssa Hassan
Founded: 1977
Collectively managed nonprofit publisher of orig-
inal trade paperbacks offering nonfiction anal-
yses of politics, culture, ecology & feminism,
race & sexuality from a progressive perspec-
tive.
ISBN Prefix(es): 0-89608; 1-878825
Number of titles published annually: 14 Print
Total Titles: 250 Print
Distributor for Odonian Press (The Real Story
Series)
Foreign Rep(s): Consortium Book Sales & Distri-
bution (Canada); Pluto Books (UK)
Foreign Rights: Gilly Duff (Worldwide)
Distribution Center: Consortium Book Sales &
Distribution, 1045 Westgate Dr, Suite 90, St
Paul, MN 55114-1065 *Toll Free Tel:* 800-283-
3572 *Fax:* 651-221-0124 *E-mail:* consortium@
cbsd.com *Web Site:* www.cbsd.com SAN: 200-
6049

South Platte Press
PO Box 163, David City, NE 68632-0163
Tel: 402-367-3554
E-mail: railroads@alltel.net
Web Site: www.southplattepress.net
Key Personnel
Publr: James J Reisdorff
Founded: 1982
Railroad related titles.
ISBN Prefix(es): 0-942035
Number of titles published annually: 4 Print
Total Titles: 20 Print

§South-Western, A Thomson Business
Division of Thomson
5191 Natorp Blvd, Mason, OH 45040
Tel: 513-229-1000 *Toll Free Tel:* 800-543-0487
Fax: 513-229-1025
Web Site: www.thomson.com
Key Personnel
Pres & CEO: Robert D Lynch *Tel:* 513-229-1600
E-mail: boblynch@swlearning.com
CFO: Sue Martin *Tel:* 513-229-1651 *E-mail:* sue.
martin@swlearning.com

VP & Dir, Mktg: Lise Johnson *E-mail:* lise.
johnson@swcollege.com
VP, Mkt Devt: Rosemarie Console
VP, Prodn & Mfg: Charles Hess *Tel:* 513-229-
1529 *Fax:* 513-229-1021 *E-mail:* charlie.hess@
swlearning.com
VP & Edit Dir: Jack Calhoun *Tel:* 513-229-1614
Fax: 513-229-1025 *E-mail:* jack.calhoun@
swlearning.com
VP & Ed-in-Chief: Dave Shaut *Tel:* 513-229-
1574 *Fax:* 513-229-1020 *E-mail:* dave.shaut@
swlearning.com
VP, EIC: Michael Roche *Tel:* 513-229-
1671 *Fax:* 513-229-1028 *E-mail:* mike.
roche@swlearning.com; George Werthman
E-mail: george.werthman@swlearning.com
VP & Chief Technol Officer: Thomas Downey
Tel: 513-229-1518 *Fax:* 513-229-1019
E-mail: tom.downey@swlearning.com
Natl Sales Mgr: Bill Hendee *Tel:* 513-229-1634
E-mail: bill.hendee@swlearning.com
Sr Publg & Mktg Mgr: Melissa Acuna *Tel:* 513-
229-1603 *Fax:* 513-229-1029 *E-mail:* melissa.
acuna@swlearning.com
HR Mgr: Michelle Bonomini *Tel:* 513-229-
1340 *Fax:* 513-229-1011 *E-mail:* michelle.
bonomini@swlearning.com
Founded: 1903
Business publisher of college & professional busi-
ness textbooks, training material & general ref-
erence, keyboarding, office technology, business
communications. Material available in print as
well as CD-ROM & on the web.
ISBN Prefix(es): 0-538; 0-324
Number of titles published annually: 250 Print; 5
CD-ROM; 10 Online; 40 E-Book; 2 Audio
Total Titles: 1,175 Print; 30 CD-ROM; 50 Online;
150 E-Book; 5 Audio
Imprints: Dame Publications Inc; West/Thomson
Learning
Sales Office(s): Thompson Learning, 10650
Toebben Dr, Independence, KY 41051, Dir,
Cust Servs: Renee Sparks *Tel:* 859-647-5014
Foreign Rep(s): Thomson Learning International
Division (world exc USA & Canada)
Billing Address: Thompson Learning, 10650
Toebben Dr, Independence, KY 41051, Dir,
Cust Servs: Renee Sparks *Tel:* 859-647-5014
Orders to: Thompson Learning, 10650 Toebben
Dr, Independence, KY 41051, Dir, Cust Servs:
Renee Sparks *Tel:* 859-647-5014
Returns: Thompson Learning, 10650 Toebben
Dr, Independence, KY 41051, Dir, Cust Servs:
Renee Sparks *Tel:* 859-647-5014
Shipping Address: Thompson Learning, 10650
Toebben Dr, Independence, KY 41051, Con-
tact: Mike Ballachino *Tel:* 859-282-5762
Fax: 859-282-5701 *E-mail:* mike.ballachino@
thomsonlearning.com
Warehouse: Thompson Learning, 10650
Toebben Dr, Independence, KY 41051, Con-
tact: Mike Ballachino *Tel:* 859-282-5762
Fax: 859-282-5701 *E-mail:* mike.ballachino@
thomsonlearning.com
Distribution Center: Thompson Learning,
7625 Empire Dr, Florence, KY 41042, Con-
tact: Mike Ballachino *Tel:* 859-282-5762
Fax: 859-282-5701 *E-mail:* mike.ballachino@
thomsonlearning.com
Thompson Learning, 10650 Toebben Dr, In-
dependence, KY 41051, Contact: Mike Ballachino *Tel:* 859-282-5762 *Fax:* 859-282-5701
E-mail: mike.ballachino@thomsonlearning.com
Membership(s): AAP

§Southeast Asia Publications
Northern Illinois University, Center for Southeast
Asian Studies, Adams 412, DeKalb, IL 60115
Tel: 815-753-5790 *Fax:* 815-753-1776
E-mail: seap@niu.edu
Web Site: www.niu.edu/cseas/seap
Key Personnel
Dir: Susan Russell *Tel:* 815-753-1771

Founded: 1963
Scholarly journals & monographs; foreign lan-
guage texts.
ISBN Prefix(es): 1-877979; 1-891134
Number of titles published annually: 3 Print
Total Titles: 35 Print; 8 Audio
Foreign Rep(s): APD Ltd (Singapore &
Malaysia); The Asian Experts (Australia); Bay
Foreign Language Books (UK); White Lotus
(Thailand)
Membership(s): Publishers Marketing Associa-
tion; Small Publishers Association of North
America

Southern Historical Press Inc
275 W Broad St, Greenville, SC 29601-2634
Mailing Address: PO Box 1267, Greenville, SC
29602-1267
Tel: 864-233-2346 *Fax:* 864-233-2349
Key Personnel
Pres: LaBruce M S Lucas
Founded: 1967
Historical & genealogical.
ISBN Prefix(es): 0-89308
Number of titles published annually: 15 Print
Total Titles: 350 Print
Shipping Address: 375 W Broad St, Greenville,
SC 29601

Southern Illinois University Press
Division of Southern Illinois University
PO Box 3697, Carbondale, IL 62902-3697
SAN: 203-3623
Tel: 618-453-2281 *Toll Free Tel:* 800-346-2680
Fax: 618-453-1221 *Toll Free Fax:* 800-346-
2681
E-mail: jstetter@siu.edu
Web Site: www.siu.edu/~siupress
Key Personnel
Dir: John F Stetter *Tel:* 618-453-6615
E-mail: jstetter@siu.edu
Dir, Sales, Mktg & Lib Sales: Larry Townsend
Tel: 618-453-6623 *E-mail:* townsend@siu.edu
Edit Dir: Karl Kageff *Tel:* 618-453-6629
Asst Dir, Budget & Opers: Susan Wilson
Tel: 618-453-6617
Man Ed: Carol Ann Burns *Tel:* 618-453-6627
E-mail: cburns@siu.edu
ISBN Contact: Lisa Falaster *Tel:* 618-453-6610
E-mail: lisafala@siu.edu
Publicity Mgr: Jane Carlson *Tel:* 618-453-6633
E-mail: jcarlson@siu.edu
Intl Rts: Mona Ross *Tel:* 618-453-6616
E-mail: monasiu@siu.edu
Prodn Mgr: Barbara Martin *Tel:* 618-453-6614
E-mail: bbmartin@siu.edu
Founded: 1956
Scholarly nonfiction; educational material rhetoric
& composition; aviation; First Amendment
studies; social studies; history; film & theatre;
speech communication; regional history; media
studies; women's studies; poetry; baseball.
ISBN Prefix(es): 0-8093
Number of titles published annually: 50 Print
Total Titles: 850 Print; 1 CD-ROM; 17 Audio
Online services available through netLibrary,
Questia.
Editorial Office(s): 1915 University Press Dr,
Carbondale, IL 62901
Sales Office(s): 1915 University Press Dr, Car-
bondale, IL 62901
Foreign Rep(s): Baker & Taylor International
(World); Eurospan (Europe, Middle East);
EWEB (East West Export Books) (Australia,
Asia, Pacific Rim); Scholarly Book Services
Inc (Canada)
Billing Address: 1915 University Press Dr, Car-
bondale, IL 62901
Orders to: 1915 University Press Dr, Carbondale,
IL 62901
Returns: 1915 University Press Dr, Carbondale,
IL 62901

Shipping Address: 1915 University Press Dr, Carbondale, IL 62901
Warehouse: 1915 University Press Dr, Carbondale, IL 62901
Distribution Center: 1915 University Press Dr, Carbondale, IL 62901

Southern Methodist University Press
314 Fondren Library W, 6404 Hill Top Lane, Dallas, TX 75275
SAN: 203-3615
Mailing Address: PO Box 750415, Dallas, TX 75275-0415
Tel: 214-768-1430; 214-768-1432 *Fax:* 214-768-1428
Key Personnel
Dir: Keith Gregory
Sr Ed: Kathryn Lang
Mktg & Prodn Mgr: George Ann Goodwin
Tel: 214-768-1434 *E-mail:* ggoodwin@mail.smu.edu
Founded: 1937
Fiction & general scholarly nonfiction: ethics & human values, film & theatre, medical humanities, regional (Southwest) studies.
ISBN Prefix(es): 0-87074
Number of titles published annually: 12 Print
Total Titles: 169 Print; 4 Audio
Distributed by Texas A&M University Press
Warehouse: c/o Texas A&M University Press, John H Lindsey Bldg, Lewis St, College Station, TX 77843

Southfarm Press, Publisher
Division of Haan Graphic Publishing Services Ltd
PO Box 1296, Middletown, CT 06457-1296
SAN: 283-4146
Tel: 860-346-8798 *Fax:* 860-347-9931
E-mail: southfarm@ix.netcom.com
Web Site: www.war-books.com; www.wandahaan.com
Key Personnel
Publr: Walter J Haan
Founded: 1983
Trade & special sales hardbacks & paperbacks; children's books, history, military science & audio books.
ISBN Prefix(es): 0-913337
Number of titles published annually: 3 Print; 2 Audio
Total Titles: 17 Print; 2 Audio
Advertising Agency: Haan Graphic Publishing Services Ltd

Soyfoods Center
PO Box 234, Lafayette, CA 94549-0234
SAN: 212-8411
Tel: 925-283-2991
Key Personnel
Pres & Ed-in-Chief: William Shurtleff
Founded: 1976
Books & bibliographies about soy, including tofu, soymilk, tempeh & miso; industry & marketing studies.
ISBN Prefix(es): 0-933332; 1-928914
Number of titles published annually: 4 Print
Total Titles: 62 Print
Shipping Address: 1021 Dolores Dr, Lafayette, CA 94549

§Specialized Systems Consultants Inc
PO Box 55549, Seattle, WA 98155-0549
Tel: 206-782-7733 *Fax:* 206-782-7191
E-mail: sales@ssc.com; info@ssc.com
Web Site: www.ssc.com
Key Personnel
Prod Mgr: Clarica Grove
Group Publr: Phil Hughes
Founded: 1968
Publish Linux Journal, a computer magazine.
ISBN Prefix(es): 0-916151; 1-57831
Number of titles published annually: 4 Print

Total Titles: 29 Print; 1 CD-ROM; 1 Online
Imprints: Linux Journal Press

Speck Press
Formerly Intrigue Press
Imprint of Corvus Publishing Group
1635 S Fairfax St, Denver, CO 80222
Mailing Address: PO Box 102004, Denver, CO 80250
Tel: 303-777-0539 *Toll Free Tel:* 800-996-9783
Fax: 303-756-8011
E-mail: books@speckpress.com
Web Site: www.speckpress.com
Key Personnel
Publr: Derek Lawrence
Publishers of popular culture & crime fiction.
ISBN Prefix(es): 0-9725776
Number of titles published annually: 15 Print
Total Titles: 45 Print

The Speech Bin Inc
1965 25 Ave, Vero Beach, FL 32960
SAN: 630-1657
Tel: 772-770-0007 *Toll Free Tel:* 800-4-SPEECH (477-3324) *Fax:* 772-770-0006
Toll Free Fax: 888-FAX-2-BIN (329-2246)
E-mail: info@speechbin.com
Web Site: www.speechbin.com
Key Personnel
Sr Ed: Jan J Binney
Founded: 1984
Educational materials, textbooks, manuals, instructional games for rehabilitation professionals, allied health, particularly speech-language pathologists, occupational therapists & special educators.
ISBN Prefix(es): 0-937857
Number of titles published annually: 10 Print; 1 Audio
Total Titles: 100 Print
Distributed by Rompa Ltd (UK)
Advertising Agency: Spoke Media

Robert Speller & Sons, Publishers Inc
Times Sq Sta, New York, NY 10108-0461
SAN: 203-2295
Mailing Address: PO Box 461, New York, NY 10108-0461
Tel: 212-473-0333
Key Personnel
Pres & ISBN Contact: Robert E B Speller, Sr
VP & Rts & Perms: Robert E B Speller, Jr
Founded: 1930
Government & scholarly.
ISBN Prefix(es): 0-8315
Number of titles published annually: 8 Print
Total Titles: 174 Print

Spence Publishing Co
111 Cole St, Dallas, TX 75207
Tel: 214-939-1700 *Fax:* 214-939-1800
Web Site: www.spencepublishing.com
Key Personnel
Intl Rts & Publr: Thomas Spence
Ed-in-Chief: Michell Muncy
Trade Sales: William Tierney
Founded: 1995
Serious nonfiction trade books on cultural & social issues.
ISBN Prefix(es): 0-9653208; 1-890626
Number of titles published annually: 8 Print
Total Titles: 40 Print

Sphinx Publishing
Division of Sourcebooks Inc
1935 Brookdale Rd, Suite 139, Naperville, IL 60563
Mailing Address: PO Box 4410, Naperville, IL 60567-4410
Tel: 630-961-3900 *Toll Free Tel:* 800-43-bright
Fax: 630-961-2168

E-mail: info@sourcebooks.com
Web Site: www.sourcebooks.com
Key Personnel
Lib Liaison: Jeff Tegge *E-mail:* info@sourcebooks.com
Edit Dir: Todd Stocke *Tel:* 630-961-3900 ext 243 *E-mail:* todd.stocke@sourcebooks.com
Edit Mgr: Diane Wheeler *Tel:* 630-961-3900 ext 245 *E-mail:* diane.wheeler@sourcebooks.com
Self-help law books (trade).
ISBN Prefix(es): 1-57071; 1-57248; 0-913825
Number of titles published annually: 60 Print
Total Titles: 120 Print
Warehouse: 940 Enterprise St, Aurora, IL 60504
Tel: 630-851-7666

§SPIE, International Society for Optical Engineering
1000 20 St, Bellingham, WA 98225
Mailing Address: PO Box 10, Bellingham, WA 98227-0010
Tel: 360-676-3290 *Fax:* 360-647-1445
E-mail: spie@spie.org
Web Site: www.spie.org
Key Personnel
Pres: James Bilbro
Exec Dir: Eugene Arthurs
Dir, Pubns & Intl Rts Contact: Eric Pepper
Conf Exhibit Dir: Janice Walker
Founded: 1955
Scientific, technical books & journals, proceedings of symposia.
ISBN Prefix(es): 0-8194
Number of titles published annually: 375 Print; 20 CD-ROM
Total Titles: 5,500 Print; 150 CD-ROM
Imprints: SPIE Press

Spinsters Ink
Division of Spinsters Ink Publishing Co
191 University Blvd, Suite 300, Denver, CO 80206
SAN: 212-6923
Tel: 303-761-5552 *Toll Free Tel:* 800-301-6860; 800-729-6423 (orders)
E-mail: spinster@spinstersink.com
Web Site: www.spinsters-ink.com
Key Personnel
Publr & Ed: Sharon Silvas
Founded: 1978
Novels & nonfiction by women about women, including social justice.
ISBN Prefix(es): 0-933216; 1-883523
Number of titles published annually: 4 Print
Total Titles: 70 Print
Imprints: Grave Issues
Sales Office(s): SBC Distributors, 15608 S New Century Dr, Gardena, CA 90248
Foreign Rep(s): Airlift Book Co (Europe); Stilone Pty Ltd (Australia)
Billing Address: SBC Distributors, 15608 S New Century Dr, Gardena, CA 90248
Returns: SBC Distributors, 15608 S New Century Dr, Gardena, CA 90248
Shipping Address: SBC Distributors, 15608 S New Century Dr, Gardena, CA 90248

SPIRAL Books
Division of SPIRAL Communications Inc
70 Cider Mill Rd, Bedford, NH 03110-4200
SAN: 298-1130
Mailing Address: PO Box 1020, Amherst, NH 03031-1020
Tel: 603-471-1917 *Fax:* 603-471-1977
E-mail: order@spiralbooks.com
Web Site: www.spiralbooks.com
Key Personnel
Pres: Pamela Roth *E-mail:* pjr@spiralbooks.com
Founded: 1979
High technology, business, healthcare & electronics.
ISBN Prefix(es): 1-57109

Number of titles published annually: 7 Print
Total Titles: 3 Print
Divisions: The Spiral Group
Advertising Agency: The SPIRAL Group
Orders to: Amherst, NH *E-mail:* orders@
spiralbooks.com

Spizzirri Press Inc
PO Box 9397, Rapid City, SD 57709-9397
Tel: 605-348-2749 *Toll Free Tel:* 800-325-9819
Fax: 605-348-6251 *Toll Free Fax:* 800-322-
9819
E-mail: spizzpub@aol.com
Web Site: www.spizzirri.com
Key Personnel
Pres: Linda Spizzirri
Founded: 1978
Educational coloring books, book-cassette pack-
ages, activity books, work books & how-to-
draw books. Ages, pre-school thru 5th grade
featuring realistic illustrations & museum cu-
rator approved texts on topics, including every-
thing from dinosaurs to space.
ISBN Prefix(es): 0-86545
Number of titles published annually: 3 Print
Total Titles: 150 Print

**The Sporting News Publishing Co, A Vulcan
Sports Media Company**
10176 Corporate Square Dr, Suite 200, St Louis,
MO 63132
SAN: 203-2260
Tel: 314-997-7111 *Fax:* 314-993-7726
Web Site: www.sportingnews.com
Key Personnel
Pres: C Richard Allen
Dir, Sales & Mktg: Greg Wiley
Prodn Dir: Marilyn H Kasal
Adv Prod Coord: Denise Douglas
Founded: 1886
Publisher of sports books.
ISBN Prefix(es): 0-89204
Number of titles published annually: 15 Print
Total Titles: 30 Print
Distributed by McGraw-Hill

§Sports Publishing LLC
804 N Neil St, Champaign, IL 61820
Mailing Address: PO Box 647, Champaign, IL
61824-0647
Tel: 217-363-2072 *Toll Free Tel:* 877-424-BOOK
(424-2665) *Fax:* 217-363-2073
E-mail: marketing@sportspublishingllc.com
Web Site: www.sportspublishingllc.com
Key Personnel
Pres & Intl Rts: Peter L Bannon
  E-mail: pbannon@sportspublishingllc.com
VP, Mktg: David Kasel *E-mail:* dkasel@
  sportspublishingllc.com
Publr: Joseph J Bannon, Sr *E-mail:* jbannon@
  sportspublishingllc.com
Founded: 1977
Trade: sports books, team histories & autobiogra-
phies.
ISBN Prefix(es): 1-57167; 1-58261; 1-58382
Number of titles published annually: 100 Print;
100 Online; 100 E-Book
Total Titles: 300 Print; 300 Online; 275 E-Book;
2 Audio

Springer Publishing Co Inc
11 W 42 St, New York, NY 10036
SAN: 203-2236
Tel: 212-431-4370 *Toll Free Tel:* 877-687-7476
  Fax: 212-941-7842
E-mail: springer@springerpub.com
Web Site: www.springerpub.com
Key Personnel
Pres & Edit Dir: Dr Ursula Springer
Edit Dir: Sheri Sussman *E-mail:* swsussman@
  springerpub.com
Journals Ed: Matt Fenton

Ed, Nursing Prog: Ruth Chasek
Sales & Mktg Dir: Annette Imperati
  E-mail: aimperati@springerpub.com
Prodn Mgr: Matt Fenton
Foreign & Subs Rts & Intl Mktg: Dorothy
  Kouwenberg
Busn Mgr: Lynn Poggie Chin
Founded: 1950
Professional books, encyclopedias, college text-
books & journals; psychology, psychiatry,
gerontology/geriatrics, nursing, medical edu-
cation, public health, rehabilitation, social work
& scholarly health sciences.
ISBN Prefix(es): 0-8261
Number of titles published annually: 65 Print
Total Titles: 720 Print
Foreign Rep(s): APAC Publishers Services
  (Singapore & Malaysia); Jaypee Brothers
  (Bangladesh, India, Nepal, Pakistan & Sri
  Lanka); MacLennan & Petty (Australia & New
  Zealand); Medicus Media (UK)
Advertising Agency: Springer Advertising Co
Shipping Address: 85 Spring St, 11th fl, New
  York, NY 10012-3955
Warehouse: 85 Spring St, 11th fl, New York, NY
  10012-3955
Membership(s): AAP; STM

§Springer-Verlag New York Inc
Subsidiary of Springer-Verlag GmbH & Co KG
175 Fifth Ave, New York, NY 10010
SAN: 203-2228
Tel: 212-460-1500 *Toll Free Tel:* 800-777-4643
  Fax: 212-473-6272
Web Site: www.springer-ny.com *Cable:*
  BOOKSPRI NYK
Key Personnel
Pres, CEO & Man Dir, Springer Intl: Rudiger
  Gebauer
Sr VP & CFO: Dennis Looney
Dir, HR: Ellen Singer
Edit Dir, Med & Life Sci: William Curtis
Dir, Electronic Publ & Prod: Henry Krell
Dir, Sales & Mktg: Paul Manning
Dir, Fin Opers: Daisy Francisco
Dir, Info Technol: Joan Petersen
Sr Ed, Med: Laura Gillan
Sr Man Ed, Med & Life Sci Journals: Antoinette
  Cimino
Man Ed, Life Sci Journals: Herb Niemirow
Exec Ed, Math, Physics & Engg: Han S Koelsch
Exec Ed, Math: Ina Lindemann
Sr Ed, Math: Achi Dosanjh
Exec Ed, Statistics & Comp Sci: John Kimmel
Lib Sales Dir: Jerry Curtis
Natl Sales Mgr: Matt Conmy
Founded: 1964
Scientific, medical, technical, research, reference
books & periodicals.
ISBN Prefix(es): 0-387
Number of titles published annually: 2,600 Print
Total Titles: 19,000 Print; 468 Online
Imprints: Birkhauser Boston; Copernicus; TELOS
  (The Electronic Library of Science); TIMS
  (Textbooks in Mathematical Sciences)
Branch Office(s)
Birkhauser Boston, 675 Massachusetts Ave, Cam-
  bridge, MA 02139
Foreign Office(s): Heidelberger Platz 3, D-14197
  Berlin, Germany
Tiergartenstrasse 17, D-69121 Heidelberg, Ger-
  many
Sachsenplatz 4-6, PO Box 89, A-1201 Vienna,
  Austria
Distributor for Birkhauser Boston; Copernicus;
  Springer-Verlag GmbH & Co KG; TELOS
Shipping Address: Springer-Verlag New York Inc,
  c/o Mercedes Distribution Center, 160 Imlay
  St, Brooklyn, NY 11231
Membership(s): AAP

Square One Publishers
115 Herricks Rd, Garden City Park, NY 11040

Tel: 516-535-2010 *Fax:* 516-535-2014
E-mail: sq1info@aol.com
Web Site: squareonepublishers.com
Key Personnel
Pres & Publr: Rudy Shur
Busn Mgr: Robert Love
Man Ed: Elaine Kennedy
Art Dir: Phaedra Mastrocola *E-mail:* sq1publish@
  aol.com
Exec Ed: Joanne Abrams
Sr Ed: Marie Caratozzolo
Sales Dir: Ken Kaiman
Mktg & PR: Anthony Pomes
Founded: 2000
Specialize in adult nonfiction books. Topics cov-
ered include collectibles, cooking, general in-
terest, history, how-to, parenting, self-help &
health.
ISBN Prefix(es): 0-7570
Number of titles published annually: 25 Print
Total Titles: 100 Print
Foreign Rep(s): J C Carrillo Inc (Caribbean &
  Latin America); Cassidy & Assoc (China);
  Deep Books (UK & Europe); Georgetown Pub-
  lications (Canada); Pen International (Singa-
  pore); Peribo (Australia & New Zealand); R
  & S Summers (Southeast Asia); Trinity Books
  (South Africa); Yasmy International Marketing
  (Japan)
Membership(s): ABA; ALA; Publishers Market-
  ing Association; Small Publishers Association
  of North America

Squarebooks Inc
PO Box 6699, Santa Rosa, CA 95406
SAN: 209-1062
Tel: 707-545-1221 *Toll Free Tel:* 800-345-6699
  Fax: 707-545-0909
E-mail: sales@fotobaron.com
Web Site: fotobaron.com/squarebooks
Key Personnel
Pres: Baron Wolman *E-mail:* bwolman@
  fotobaron.com
Founded: 1974
High quality illustrated books, calendars & other
  book-related items. Also specialize in classic
  rock & roll & the Golden Gate Bridge.
ISBN Prefix(es): 0-916290
Number of titles published annually: 6 Print
Total Titles: 6 Print
Imprints: California From The Air
Distribution Center: Publishers Group West,
  1700 Fourth St, Berkeley, CA 94710 *Toll Free
  Tel:* 800-788-3123 *Fax:* 510-528-3444

**§SRA/McGraw-Hill, a Division of
  McGraw-Hill Learning Group**
Division of McGraw-Hill Learning Group
8787 Orion Place, Columbus, OH 43240
Tel: 614-430-4000 *Fax:* 614-430-6621
E-mail: sra@mcgraw-hill.com
Web Site: www.sra-4kids.com
Key Personnel
VP, Natl Sales Mgr State Adoption: Lori A
  Holmes
VP, Natl Sales Mgr Open Territory: Michael C
  Walker
VP, Mktg: John P McHale
VP & Publr: Ruth B Cochrane
Founded: 1938
Supplemental & curriculum materials for kinder-
garten through high school & direct instruction
programs. Online instruction & assessment.
ISBN Prefix(es): 0-02; 0-8126; 0-383
Number of titles published annually: 1,200 Print;
5 CD-ROM
Total Titles: 25,000 Print; 30 CD-ROM; 4 Online;
800 Audio

§ST Publications Book Division
Division of ST Publications Inc
407 Gilbert Ave, Cincinnati, OH 45202
SAN: 204-5974

Tel: 513-421-2050 *Toll Free Tel:* 800-925-1110
Fax: 513-421-5144
E-mail: books@stpubs.com
Web Site: www.stpubs.com
Key Personnel
Assoc Publr & Intl Rts Contact: Mark Kissling
Tel: 800-925-1110 ext 399 *E-mail:* mark.
kissling@stmediagroup.com
Cust Servs: Leslie Newman *Tel:* 800-925-1110
ext 356 *E-mail:* leslie.newman@stmediagroup.
com
Founded: 1906
Books, magazines, buyers' guides: sign, screen
printing, visual merchandising & store design
industries & corporate identity.
ISBN Prefix(es): 0-911380; 0-944094
Number of titles published annually: 3 Print
Total Titles: 50 Print

Stackpole Books
5067 Ritter Rd, Mechanicsburg, PA 17055
SAN: 202-5396
Tel: 717-796-0411 *Toll Free Tel:* 800-732-3669
Fax: 717-796-0412
Web Site: www.stackpolebooks.com
Key Personnel
Pres: David Ritter
VP, Dir Creative & Mktg Servs: Tracy Patterson
VP & Edit Dir: Judith Schnell
Ed: Mark Allison; Chris Evans; Edward Skender;
Kyle Weaver
Fulfillment Mgr: Susan Drexler
Rts: Chris Chappell
Sales: Pat Moran
Warehouse Supv: Adrian Fleming
Founded: 1933
ISBN Prefix(es): 0-8117
Number of titles published annually: 100 Print; 1
CD-ROM
Total Titles: 800 Print; 1 CD-ROM
Distributor for Aerial Perspective Publishing; Air-
life Books; The Army War College Foundation
Press; BMC Publications; Capitol Preservation
Committee; Greenhill Books; Proctor Jones;
Pulgas Ridge Press; Quiller Press Ltd; Rank &
File; RKT Trade Publishing; Swan Hill
Foreign Rights: Phillip Chen/Bardon (China); Iza
Garztecka/HELFA (Poland); Alex Korzheneuski
(Russia); PubHub (Korea)

Stairway Publications
PO Box 518, Huntington, NY 11743-0518
SAN: 255-3422
Tel: 631-423-4050 *Fax:* 631-351-2142
E-mail: publisher@stairwaypub.com
Web Site: www.stairwaypub.com
Key Personnel
Publr: Madeline Arroyo
Media Liason: Julie G Fehring *Tel:* 631-224-8801
Founded: 2003
Publisher of books for children.
ISBN Prefix(es): 0-9740061
Number of titles published annually: 3 Print
Total Titles: 1 Print
Sales Office(s): Faithworks, Contact: David Trout-
man *Tel:* 615-895-8706
Foreign Rights: Faithworks/NBN (UK)
Orders to: Faithworks *Toll Free Tel:* 877-323-
4550
Distribution Center: Faithworks/NBN, Blue Ridge
Summit, PA
Membership(s): Publishers Marketing Association

Stand! Publishing
Formerly Athenos Press
2744 Seneca St, No T-12, Wichita, KS 67207
SAN: 254-2110
Tel: 316-265-2880
E-mail: standbooks@yahoo.com
Web Site: www.standbooks.com
Key Personnel
CEO & Pres: Aubrey Shayler

Ed: Quinn Aubrey
Founded: 1999
Publishing service company that includes book &
author promotion & marketing.
ISBN Prefix(es): 0-9716222
Number of titles published annually: 100 Print;
100 E-Book
Shipping Address: Lightning Source, 1246 Heil,
Quaker Blvd, La Vergne, TN 37086 *Tel:* 615-
213-5815 *Fax:* 615-213-4426 *E-mail:* inquiry@
lightningsource.com
Warehouse: Lightning Source, 1246 Heil, Quaker
Blvd, La Vergne, TN 37086 *Tel:* 615-213-
5815 *Fax:* 615-213-4426 *E-mail:* inquiry@
lightningsource.com
Membership(s): Publishers Marketing Association

§Standard Educational Corp
200 W Jackson, 7th fl, Chicago, IL 60606
SAN: 207-1363
Tel: 312-692-1000
Key Personnel
Pres & CEO: Peter Ewing
Prodn Mgr: Tom Myles
Edit Dir: David Hayes
Founded: 1940
Premium & reference sets; career guidance publi-
cations.
ISBN Prefix(es): 0-89434; 0-87392
Number of titles published annually: 10 Print
Total Titles: 3 CD-ROM
Distributed by Brodart; The Frontier Press Co
(selected titles)
See separate listing for:
The United Educators Inc

Standard Publications Inc
903 Western Ave, Urbana, IL 61801
Mailing Address: PO Box 2226, Champaign, IL
61825-2226
Tel: 217-898-7825
E-mail: spi@standardpublications.com
Web Site: www.standardpublications.com
Founded: 2001
ISBN Prefix(es): 0-9709788; 0-9722691
Number of titles published annually: 4 Print
Total Titles: 7 Print

Standard Publishing Co
Division of Standex International
8121 Hamilton Ave, Cincinnati, OH 45231
SAN: 110-5515
Tel: 513-931-4050 *Toll Free Tel:* 800-543-1301
Fax: 513-931-0950 *Toll Free Fax:* 877-867-
5751
E-mail: customerservice@standardpub.com
Web Site: www.standardpub.com
Key Personnel
Pres: Randy Scott
Publr: Mark A Taylor
VP, Mktg & Sales: Darrell Lewis
Exec Dir, Curriculum Devt: Paul Learned
Dir, New Prod Devt: Diane Stortz
Dir, Trade Sales: Les Jones
Dir, Church Resources: Ruth Frederick
Asst Dir, New Prod Devt: Jennifer Holder
Sr Ed: Jim Eichenberger; F Dale Reeves; Jon Un-
derwood
Rts & Perms Mgr: Joann Van Meter
Sr Designer: Sandy Wimmer
Ed: Kelly Carr; Ruth Davis; Cathy Griffith; Greg
Holder; Marcy Levering; Dawn Medill; Elaina
Meyers; Rosemary Mitchell; Jim Nieman; Ron
Nickelson; Margie Redford; Karen Roth; Robin
Stanley; Bruce Stoker
Ed & Asst Dir, Curriculum Devt: Carla Crane
Ed, Christian Standard: Mark Taylor
Man Ed, The Lookout: Shawn McMullen
Exec Ed, The Lookout: David Faust
Dir, Vacation Bible School: Kay Moll
Asst Dir, Vacation Bible School: Donna Fehl
Dir, Creative Servs: Coleen Davis

Designer: Rob Glover
Founded: 1866
Religious children's books, Sunday School lit-
erature & supplies, helps for Sunday School
teachers.
ISBN Prefix(es): 0-87239; 0-87403; 0-7847
Number of titles published annually: 50 Print
Total Titles: 700 Print; 12 CD-ROM
Imprints: Happy Day Books
Foreign Rights: Foundation Distributing Inc
(Canada); Omega (New Zealand); Salvation
Book Centre (Malaysia); Scripture Press Foun-
dation Ltd (UK)

§Standard Publishing Corp
155 Federal St, 13th fl, Boston, MA 02110
Tel: 617-457-0600 *Toll Free Tel:* 800-682-5759
Fax: 617-457-0608
E-mail: info@spcpub.com
Web Site: spcpub.com
Key Personnel
Pres & Publr: John C Cross
Treas: Gorham L Cross
Edit Dir: Robert Montgomery
Prod Mgr & Rts & Perms: Julie Reilly
Mktg Mgr: Susanne Edes
Circ Mgr & Cust Serv: Kelly Cotter
Adv Sales Mgr: Barbara Crockett
Founded: 1865
Insurance.
ISBN Prefix(es): 0-923240
Number of titles published annually: 18 Print
Total Titles: 18 Print; 3 CD-ROM
Subsidiaries: John Liner Organization
Branch Office(s)
Insurance Record, 9601 White Rock Trail, Suite
213, Dallas, TX 75238
Distributed by LexisNexis; Silverplume

Stanford University Press
1450 Page Mill Rd, Palo Alto, CA 94304-1124
SAN: 203-3526
Tel: 650-723-9434 *Fax:* 650-725-3457
Web Site: www.sup.org
Key Personnel
Dir: Geoffrey R H Burn *Tel:* 650-736-1942
E-mail: grhburn@stanford.edu
COO: John Zotz
Dir, Sales & Mktg: David B Jackson
Publg Dir: Alan Harvey
Edit Dir: Norris Pope
Prodn Mgr: Harold Moorehead
Perms, Foreign Rts & Contracts Mgr: Ariane de
Pree *E-mail:* arianep@stanford.edu
Mktg Mgr: Lowell Britson; Puja Sangar
Mgr, Editing & Design: Patricia Myers
Ed: Muriel Bell; Martha Cooley; Amanda Moran;
Kate Wahl
Exhibits Mgr: Christie Cochrell
Art & Design Mgr: Robert Ehle
Acct Mgr: Jean Kim
Founded: 1925
ISBN Prefix(es): 0-8047
Number of titles published annually: 125 Print
Total Titles: 1,500 Print
Foreign Rep(s): East-West Export Books (Asia);
Eurospan (UK, Europe & Middle East)
Warehouse: Chicago Distribution Center, 11030 S
Langley Ave, Chicago, IL 60628
Distribution Center: Chicago Distribution Center,
11030 S Langley Ave, Chicago, IL 60628
Membership(s): AAP; Association of American
University Presses

Star Bright Books
The Star Bldg, Suite 2B, 42-26 28 St, Long Is-
land City, NY 11101
Tel: 718-784-9112 *Toll Free Tel:* 800-788-4439
Fax: 718-784-9012
E-mail: info@starbrightbooks.com; orders@
starbrightbooks.com
Web Site: www.starbrightbooks.com

Key Personnel
Publr: Deborah Shine
Ed: Christina Trent *E-mail:* ttrent@
    starbrightbooks.com
Founded: 1995
Independent children's book publisher.
ISBN Prefix(es): 1-887734; 1-932065; 1-59572
Number of titles published annually: 40 Print
Total Titles: 168 Print
Distributor for Happy Cat Books; Lothian Books
Membership(s): ABA; ALA; Association of
    Booksellers for Children; Publishers Market-
    ing Association

Star Publishing Co
Division of Star Business Group Inc
940 Emmett Ave, Belmont, CA 94002
SAN: 212-6958
Mailing Address: PO Box 68, Belmont, CA
    94002
Tel: 650-591-3505 *Fax:* 650-591-3898
E-mail: mail@starpublishing.com
Web Site: www.starpublishing.com
Key Personnel
Publr: Stuart A Hoffman *E-mail:* stuart@
    starpublishing.com
Founded: 1978
Textbooks; reference books; professional books;
    graphic arts/computer-desktop publishing.
ISBN Prefix(es): 0-89863
Number of titles published annually: 12 Print
Total Titles: 100 Print
Imprints: Encore Editions
Advertising Agency: SBG Inc

Starbooks Press
Affiliate of Florida Literary Foundation
1391 Blvd of the Arts, Sarasota, FL 34236-2904
Tel: 941-957-1281 *Fax:* 941-955-3829
Key Personnel
Ed: Michael Huxley
Inventory Mgr: Paul Marquis
Founded: 1980
ISBN Prefix(es): 1-877978
Number of titles published annually: 8 Print
Total Titles: 30 Print; 1 Audio
Imprints: Florida Literary Foundation Press
    (FLF); Starbooks
Shipping Address: FLF, 1391 Sixth St, Sarasota,
    FL 34236

Starlite Inc
Subsidiary of Viva Ltd
PO Box 20004, St Petersburg, FL 33742-0004
Tel: 727-392-2929 *Toll Free Tel:* 800-577-2929
    Fax: 727-392-6161
E-mail: starlite@citebook.com
Web Site: www.starlite-inc.com; www.citebook.
    com
Key Personnel
Pres: Tony Darwin
Gen Mgr: S Lewis
Exec Asst: S Allen
Founded: 1983
Provide a full range of publishing services.
ISBN Prefix(es): 0-9628328
Number of titles published annually: 25 Print
Total Titles: 800 Print
Imprints: Citebook
Foreign Office(s): 15 Glenbrook Ave, Benowa
    Waters QLD 4217, Australia
210 Hillcross Ave, Morgen, Surrey SM4 4BU,
    United Kingdom
Advertising Agency: Darwin Enterprises
Warehouse: 2280 Tenth St SE, Largo, FL 34641

State Mutual Book & Periodical Service Ltd
PO Box 1199, Bridgehampton, NY 11932-1199
SAN: 212-5862
Tel: 631-537-1104 *Fax:* 631-537-0412 *Cable:*
    RCA BOOKLUXE

Key Personnel
Gen Mgr: Peter Bentley
Founded: 1976
ISBN Prefix(es): 0-89771
Number of titles published annually: 39 Print
Total Titles: 5,100 Print
Warehouse: Gleichen-House, PO Box 1199, 2183
    Main St, Bridgehampton, NY 11932

State University of New York Press
90 State St, Suite 700, Albany, NY 12207-1707
SAN: 203-3488
Tel: 518-472-5000 *Toll Free Tel:* 800-666-2211
    (orders) *Fax:* 518-472-5038 *Toll Free Fax:* 800-
    688-2877 (orders)
E-mail: orderbook@cupserv.org; info@sunypress.
    edu
Web Site: www.sunypress.edu
Key Personnel
Dir: Priscilla Ross *Tel:* 518-472-5026
    E-mail: rosspr@sunypress.edu
Dir, Electronic Sales, Mktg & Prod Dev: Dana
    Yanulavich
Sales Mgr: Dan Flynn *Tel:* 518-472-5036
    E-mail: flynnda@sunypress.edu
Busn Mgr: Frank Mahar
Review Copies: Trisha Smith
Rts & Perms: Jennie Doling *Tel:* 518-472-5024
Founded: 1966
Scholarly nonfiction, especially works in philos-
    ophy, religion, public policy, Asian studies,
    Middle East studies, Jewish studies, psychol-
    ogy, women's studies, education, film, literature
    & political science.
ISBN Prefix(es): 0-87395; 0-88706; 0-7914
Number of titles published annually: 180 Print
Total Titles: 3,488 Print
Distributor for Rockefeller Institute Press
Foreign Rep(s): Eleanor Brasch Enterprises (Aus-
    tralia, New Zealand); Cassidy & Associates
    Inc (China & Hong Kong); Lexa Publishers'
    Representatives (Canada); Mediamatics (In-
    dia); Transdex International PTE Ltd (SE Asia,
    South Asia); United Publishers Services Ltd
    (Japan); University Presses Marketing (UK, Ire-
    land, Europe, Middle East); US Pub Rep Inc
    (Caribbean, Central America, Mexico, Puerto
    Rico, South America)
Shipping Address: c/o CUP Services, 750 Cas-
    cadilla St, Ithaca, NY 14850 *Tel:* 607-277-2211
    Fax: 607-277-6292
Warehouse: c/o Cup Services, Box 6525, Ithaca,
    NY 14851 *Tel:* 607-277-2211 *Fax:* 607-277-
    6292
NBN International, Estover Rd, Plymouth PL6
    7PY, United Kingdom *Tel:* (44) 1752-202-
    301 *Fax:* (44) 1752-202-333 *E-mail:* cservs@
    nbnplymbridge.com;orders@nbnplymbridge.
    com
Membership(s): ABA; Association of American
    University Presses

§Steck-Vaughn
Imprint of Harcourt Achieve
10801 N MoPac Expressway, Austin, TX 78759
SAN: 210-5624
Mailing Address: PO Box 27010, Austin, TX
    78755
Tel: 512-343-8227 *Toll Free Tel:* 800-531-5015
    Toll Free Fax: 800-699-9459
E-mail: ecare@harcourt.com
Web Site: www.harcourtachieve.com
Key Personnel
Pres & CEO: Tim McEwen
Sr VP, Sales: Joe McHale
VP, Fin: Martijn Tel
VP, Mktg: Carol Wolf
VP, HR: Gabriele Madison
VP, Mfg: David Lindley
VP, Devt: Lynelle Morgenthaler
Founded: 1936

Educational materials for Pre-K, elementary, sec-
    ondary, adult GED, test preparation, ESL &
    professional development for educators.
Total Titles: 2,000 Print; 64 CD-ROM

Steeple Hill Books
Imprint of Harlequin Enterprises
233 Broadway, Suite 1001, New York, NY 10279
SAN: 200-2450
Tel: 212-553-4200 *Fax:* 212-227-8969
E-mail: customer_service@harlequin.ca
Web Site: www.steeplehill.com
Key Personnel
Pres & Publr: Donna Hayes
Edit Dir, Harlequin Core Series: Tara Gavin
Exec Ed: Joan Marlow Golan *Tel:* 212-553-4240
    E-mail: joanmarlow_golan@harlequin.ca
PR Mgr: Heather Gilman
Founded: 1997
Specialize in inspirational romance novels, ro-
    mantic suspense & women's fiction.
ISBN Prefix(es): 0-373
Number of titles published annually: 112 Print
Imprints: Steeple Hill Love Inspired; Steeple Hill
    Women's Fiction
Branch Office(s)
Harlequin Enterprises Ltd, 225 Duncan Mill Rd,
    Don Mills, ON M3B 3K9, Canada
Distributed by Simon & Schuster Mass Merchan-
    dise Sales Co
Distribution Center: 3010 Walden Ave, Depew,
    NY 14043

Steerforth Press
25 Lebanon St, Hanover, NH 03755
Tel: 603-643-4787 *Fax:* 603-643-4788
E-mail: info@steerforth.com
Web Site: www.steerforth.com
Key Personnel
Publr: Chip Fleischer *E-mail:* chip@steerforth.
    com
Man Ed: Kristin Camp
Ed: Alan Lelchuk; Michael Moore; Thomas Pow-
    ers
Intl Rts: Helga Schmidt *E-mail:* helga@steerforth.
    com
Founded: 1993
ISBN Prefix(es): 1-883642; 0-944072; 1-58195;
    1-58642
Number of titles published annually: 20 Print
Total Titles: 125 Print
Imprints: Steerforth Italia; Zoland Books
Foreign Rights: Agence Bookman (Scandinavia);
    Agence Hoffman (Germany); Artisjus (Hun-
    gary); Big Apple Tuttle Mori Agency (Tai-
    wan); The English Agency (Japan); Harris-Elon
    Agency (Israel); International Editors Co, SA
    (Argentina, Brazil, Latin America, Portugal,
    Spain); Katai & Bolza (Hungary); Lijnkamp
    Literary Agents (Netherlands); Daniela Micura
    (Italy); Laura Morris (UK, British Common-
    wealth); Onk Agency (Turkey)
Distribution Center: Random House Distribu-
    tion Center, 400 Hahn Rd, Westminster, MD
    21157 *Toll Free Tel:* 800-733-3000 *Toll Free
    Fax:* 800-659-2436
Membership(s): ABA; NEBA; Publishers Market-
    ing Association

§Steiner Books
PO Box 799, Great Barrington, MA 01230-0799
Tel: 413-528-8233 *Fax:* 413-528-8826
E-mail: service@anthropress.org
Web Site: www.anthropress.org
Key Personnel
CEO: Gene Gollogly
Man Ed: Mary Giddens *Tel:* 413-528-8233 ext
    201
Ed: Christopher Bamford
Founded: 1928
American & English editions of works by Rudolf
    Steiner & related authors.

ISBN Prefix(es): 0-910142; 0-88010
Number of titles published annually: 20 Print
Total Titles: 451 Print
Imprints: Bell Pond Books; Lindisfarne Books
Distributed by Rudolf Steiner Press UK
Distributor for Bell Pond Books; Chiron Publications; Clairview Books; Codhill Press; Findhorn Press; Floris Books; Hawthorn Press; Lantern Books; Swedenborg Foundation; Temple Lodge Publishing
Foreign Rep(s): Ceres (New Zealand); Hushion House (Canada); Peter Hyde & Associates (South Africa); Rudolf Steiner Press (UK)
Orders to: PO Box 960, Herndon, VA 20172-0960 Tel: 703-661-1594 Toll Free Tel: 800-856-8664 Fax: 703-661-1501 Toll Free Fax: 800-277-9747 SAN: 201-1824

Stemmer House Publishers Inc
4 White Brook Rd, Gilsum, NH 03448
SAN: 207-9623
Tel: 603-357-0236 Toll Free Tel: 800-345-6665
Fax: 603-357-2073
E-mail: pbs@pathwaybook.com
Web Site: www.stemmer.com
Key Personnel
Pres & Ed: Ernest Peter
Founded: 1975
Books in the arts & humanities, gardening books, children's books, audiocassettes, illustrated books, natural history & multicultural studies.
ISBN Prefix(es): 0-916144; 0-88045
Number of titles published annually: 6 Print
Total Titles: 125 Print; 5 Audio
Imprints: BEDE Productions (audiocassettes & book/cassettes); Curious Little Critters Series; Great Architectural Replica Series; International Design Library; NaturEncyclopedia Series
Divisions: BEDE Productions
Foreign Rep(s): Gazelle Ltd (Europe & UK); Peaceful Living (New Zealand); John Reed Books (Australia)
Advertising Agency: Helleau Ad Agency
Orders to: Stemmer House Publishers
Returns: Pathway Book Service, Gilsum, NH
Shipping Address: Pathway Book Service, Gilsum, NH
Warehouse: Pathway Book Service, Gilsum, NH
Distribution Center: Pathway Book Service, Gilsum, NH
Membership(s): Children's Book Council

Stenhouse Publishers
Subsidiary of Teacher's Publishing Group
477 Congress St, Suite 4B, Portland, ME 04101-3451
Tel: 207-253-1600 Toll Free Tel: 888-363-0566
Fax: 207-253-5121 Toll Free Fax: 800-833-9164
E-mail: info@stenhouse.com
Web Site: www.stenhouse.com
Key Personnel
Ed-in-Chief: Philippa Stratton E-mail: philippa@stenhouse.com
Mktg Dir: Tom Seavey E-mail: tseavey@stenhouse.com
Founded: 1993
Professional books for teachers.
ISBN Prefix(es): 1-57110
Number of titles published annually: 20 Print
Total Titles: 168 Print
Distributor for Pembroke Publishers
Foreign Rep(s): Curriculum Corp (Australia & New Zealand); Pembroke Publishers (Canada); Publishers Marketing Services (SE Asia)
Warehouse: 3880 Zane Trace Dr, Columbus, OH 43228, Bob Waldon Tel: 614-529-1435 Fax: 614-529-0670

Sterling Publishing Co Inc
387 Park Ave S, 5th fl, New York, NY 10016-8810

SAN: 211-6324
Tel: 212-532-7160 Toll Free Tel: 800-367-9692
Fax: 212-213-2495
Web Site: www.sterlingpub.com
Key Personnel
Pres: Charles Nurnberg
Sr VP, New Busn Devt: Martin Schamus
VP & Publr: Andrew Martin
VP, Fin & Opers: Joe Guadango
VP, Sales: Jason Prince
VP, Edit: Steve Magnuson
VP, Sales Admin & Corp Servs: Adria Dougherty Tel: 212-532-7160 ext 131 E-mail: adougherty@sterlingpub.com
VP, Rts & Export Sales: Marilyn Kretzer
VP & Creative Dir: Karen Nelson
VP, Prodn: Rick Willett
Edit Dir: John Woodside
Dir, Mktg: Ronni Stolzenberg
Dir, Trade Sales & Natl Accts: Jeremy Nurnberg
Founded: 1949
Nonfiction, including reference & information books, science activities, nature, arts & crafts, home improvement, history, photography, juvenile humor, health, wine & food, sports, music, psychology, occult, woodworking, pets, hobbies, business, military, puzzles & gardening.
ISBN Prefix(es): 0-88029; 1-56619; 0-7607; 0-945352; 0-88365; 0-88394; 0-304; 0-87192; 0-688; 0-937274; 1-887374; 1-57990; 1-56799; 0-600; 0-915801; 1-883403; 0-87985; 0-7137; 0-8069; 0-912355; 1-85238; 0-7063; 0-903505; 0-946819; 0-289; 1-86351; 1-85368; 0-943822; 1-86108; 1-895569; 0-7134; 0-575; 1-85029; 0-460; 0-297; 1-85799; 0-540; 1-84091; 1-57389; 1-85585; 1-85974; 1-84188; 1-84202; 1-85028; 1-85648; 0-75283; 0-75284; 0-75370; 0-75380; 0-916103; 0-967784; 1-4027; 1-58816; 1-84212; 1-84330; 1-84333; 1-84340; 1-85152; 1-86436; 1-86872; 1-889538; 1-931543; 2-88479; 1-58663; 1-59308; 0-75381; 0-929837; 1-84403; 1-84411; 1-904322; 0-75285; 0-75286; 0-9731651; 1-57866
Number of titles published annually: 1,000 Print
Total Titles: 4,500 Print
Imprints: Hearst Books; Lark Books; Sterling/Balloon; Sterling/Chapelle; Sterling/Pinwheel; Sterling/Tamos; Sterling/Zambezi
Distributor for AAPPL; American Express (selected titles); AVA Publishing (selected titles); Batsford (selected titles); Blandford Press Ltd (selected titles); Brooklyn Botanic Garden (selected titles); Cassell (selected titles); Cassell Illustrated (selected titles); Chancellor Press (selected titles); Collins & Brown (selected titles); Conran (selected titles); Cookworks (selected titles); Davis (selected titles); Expert (selected titles); Galahad Books (selected books); Gollancz (selected titles); Guild of Mastercraftsman (selected titles); Hamlyn (selected titles); Kodak (selected titles); League of Hard of Hearing (selected titles); New Holland (selected titles); Orion (selected titles); Paper Tiger (selected titles); Phoenix Illustrated (selected titles); Phoenix Press (selected titles); PRC Publishing (selected titles); Promontory Press (selected titles); Rudra (selected titles); Sally Milner (selected titles); Seven Dials (selected titles); Silver Lining (selected titles); Sixth & Spring (selected titles); Studio Vista (selected titles); Sun Designs (selected titles); Vega (selected titles); Ward Lock (selected titles); Weidenfeld & Nicolson (selected titles)
Foreign Rep(s): BookPort Associates (Southern Europe); Capricorn Link Ltd (Australia); Chrysalis Books Group Plc (UK); Ted Dougherty (Austria, Belgium, Netherlands, Germany, Luxembourg, Switzerland); European Marketing Services (France); Guild of Master Craftsman (UK); Pernille Larsen (Scandinavia); Chris Lloyd Sales & Marketing Services (juvenile titles only) (Europe & UK); Phambili Agencies (adult titles only) (South Africa); Publishers International Marketing (Asia, Middle East); South Pacific Books (Imports) Ltd (New Zealand)
Foreign Rights: Graal Ltd (Poland); Katai & Bolza Literary Agents; Ute Korner Literary Agent (Spain); Alexander Korzhenevski (Russia); Agence Litteraire Lora Fountain (France); Kristin Olson Literary Agency (Czech Republic); Literarische Agentur Silke Weniger
Warehouse: Sterling Warehouse, 40 Saw Mill Pond Rd, Edison, NJ 08817 Tel: 732-248-6563 Toll Free Fax: 800-775-8736
See separate listing for:
Lark Books

SterlingHouse Publisher Inc
Division of CyntoMedia Corp
7436 Washington Ave, Suite 200, Pittsburgh, PA 15218
Tel: 412-271-8800 Toll Free Tel: 888-542-2665
Fax: 412-271-8600
E-mail: info@sterlinghousepublisher.com
Web Site: www.sterlinghousepublisher.com
Key Personnel
Pres & CEO: Cynthia Sterling E-mail: csterling@sterlinghousepublisher.com
Man Ed: Jason Henze E-mail: jhenze@sterlinghousepublisher.com
Founded: 1988
Nonfiction areas include general trade, trade paperbacks, business & finance, metaphysical, how-to, self-help, fitness, philosophy, religion, esoteric knowledge, political, social, inner development, autobiography, biography, memoir, true stories, humor & satire. Fiction areas include science fiction, mystery, detective, romance, horror, supernatural, mainstream, medical thriller, suspense, adventure, young adult, poetry & audiocassettes.
ISBN Prefix(es): 1-56315 (SterlingHouse); 1-58501 (CeShore)
Number of titles published annually: 35 Print; 10 Audio
Total Titles: 250 Print; 10 Audio
Imprints: CeShore Publishing Co; Sounds of SterlingHouse
Distributed by Partners Publishers Group
Foreign Rep(s): Agencia Literaria (Brazil, Portugal); Amer-Asia Books Inc (Japan); The Asano Agency Inc; Big Apple Tuttle-Mori Agency (China, Thailand); The Book Publishers Assn of Israel (Israel); Julio F-Yanez Agencia Literaria (Latin America, Mexico, Spain); Imprima Korea Agency (Korea); International Copywrite Agency (Romania); Japan UNI Agency (Japan); Living Literary Agency (Italy); Michael Meller Agency (France & Germany); La Nouvelle Agency (Belgium, Canada, France, Switzerland); Andrew Numberg Assoc (Czech Republic, Estonia, Hungary, Latvia, Lithuania, Poland); Andrew Numberg Assoc Sofia Ltd (Bulgaria); Nurchihan Kesim Literary Inc (Turkey); OA Literary Agency (Greece); Sane Toregard Agency (Denmark, Finland, Iceland, Norway & Sweden); Tuttle-Mori Agency Inc (China, Thailand)
Foreign Rights: Rights & Distribution Inc
Membership(s): Publishers Marketing Association

Stewart, Tabori & Chang
Division of La Martiniere Groupe
115 W 18 St, 5th fl, New York, NY 10011
SAN: 239-0361
Tel: 212-519-1200 Fax: 212-519-1210
Web Site: www.abramsbooks.com
Key Personnel
CEO: Steve Parr
Pres & Publr: Leslie Stoker
VP, Mktg: Steve Tager
VP, Publicity & Mktg: Jack Lamplough

Sr Prodn Mgr: Kim Tyner
Art Dir: Galen Smith
Sr Ed: Marisa Bulzone; Sandra Gilbert
Asst Ed: Beth Huseman; Elaine Schiebel
Tel: 212-519-1207 *E-mail:* elaine@stcbooks.
com
Sr Design: Larissa Nowicki
Founded: 1981
Art, illustrated gift books, gardening, cookbooks,
giftline, African American history, interior de-
sign, New Age, photography, popular culture,
humor.
ISBN Prefix(es): 1-55670; 0-941434; 1-58479
Number of titles published annually: 80 Print
Total Titles: 250 Print
Foreign Rep(s): Ralph & Sheila Summers (SE
Asia); Paul Walton (South Africa); David
Williams (South America)
Foreign Rights: David W Niams (South Amer-
ica); General Publishing (Canada); Hi Mar-
keting UK (UK, Europe); New Holland (Aus-
tralia); Onslow Books Ltd (Europe); Southern
Publishers Group (New Zealand)
Distribution Center: Time Warner Trade Pub-
lishing *Toll Free Tel:* 800-759-0190 *Toll Free
Fax:* 800-286-1219

Jeff Stewart's Teaching Tools
PO Box 15308, Seattle, WA 98115
Tel: 425-486-4510 *Fax:* 425-486-4510
Key Personnel
Contact: Jeff Stewart
Founded: 1981
Text & professional books; special education.
ISBN Prefix(es): 1-877866
Number of titles published annually: 5 Print
Total Titles: 7 Print

H Stillman Publishers Inc
21405 Woodchuck Lane, Boca Raton, FL 33428
Tel: 561-482-6343
Key Personnel
Pres: Herbert Stillman
Founded: 1984
Scientific books & journals.
ISBN Prefix(es): 0-917257
Number of titles published annually: 10 Print
Total Titles: 100 Print

§Stipes Publishing LLC
204 W University, Champaign, IL 61820
Mailing Address: PO Box 526, Champaign, IL
61824
Tel: 217-356-8391 *Fax:* 217-356-5753
E-mail: stipes@soltec.net
Web Site: www.stipes.com
Key Personnel
Partner & Publr: Robert A Watts
Partner: John Hecker
Partner & Electronic Publg: Benjamin Watts
Founded: 1927
Primarily educational, some overlap trade publish-
ing in music & horticulture.
ISBN Prefix(es): 0-87563; 1-58874
Number of titles published annually: 30 Print
Total Titles: 450 Print; 2 CD-ROM; 1 Online; 1
E-Book; 2 Audio

Stoeger Publishing Co
Subsidiary of Stoeger Industries
17603 Indian Head Hwy, Suite 200, Accokeek,
MD 20607
SAN: 206-118X
Tel: 301-283-6300 *Fax:* 301-283-6986
Key Personnel
Publr: Jay Langston *E-mail:* stoegeindustries@
msn.com
Founded: 1918
Hunting, fishing, camping & general sports
books.
ISBN Prefix(es): 0-88317

Number of titles published annually: 10 Print
Total Titles: 85 Print

Stone Bridge Press LLC
PO Box 8208, Berkeley, CA 94707-8208
Tel: 510-524-8732 *Toll Free Tel:* 800-947-7271
Fax: 510-524-8711
E-mail: sbp@stonebridge.com; sbpedit@
stonebridge.com
Web Site: www.stonebridge.com
Key Personnel
Publr: Peter Goodman
Founded: 1989
Books on Japan & Asia.
ISBN Prefix(es): 1-880656; 0-9628137
Number of titles published annually: 6 Print
Total Titles: 75 Print
Imprints: Impromptu Journaling Books; Michi
Japanese Arts and Ways; The Rock Spring Col-
lection of Japanese Literature
Distributed by Consortium Book Sales & Distri-
bution
Shipping Address: 1393 Solano Ave, Suite C, Al-
bany, CA 94706
Membership(s): Bay Area Independent Publishers
Association; Publishers Marketing Association

Stonewall, see BrickHouse Books Inc

Stoneydale Press Publishing Co
523 Main St, Stevensville, MT 59870
Mailing Address: PO Box 188, Stevensville, MT
59870-2839
Tel: 406-777-2729 *Toll Free Tel:* 800-735-7006
Fax: 406-777-2521
E-mail: stoneydale@montana.com
Web Site: www.stoneydale.com
Key Personnel
Publr: Dale A Burk *E-mail:* daleburk@montana.
com
Founded: 1976
Outdoor recreation, regional history & reminisces
of Northern Rockies region.
ISBN Prefix(es): 0-912299; 1-931291
Number of titles published annually: 8 Print
Total Titles: 70 Print
Membership(s): Pacific Northwest Booksellers
Association

Storey Books
210 Mass MoCA Way, North Adams, MA 01247
SAN: 203-4158
Tel: 413-346-2100 *Toll Free Tel:* 800-793-9396
Fax: 413-346-2253
E-mail: info@storey.com
Web Site: www.storey.com
Key Personnel
Pres: Pamela Art *E-mail:* pam.art@storey.com
Publr: Janet Harris
COO & VP, Sales & Mktg: Dan Reynolds
Publicity: Diane Cutillo
Intl & Subs Rts: Mary Edgerton
Trade Sales Mgr: Elinor Goodwin
Edit Dir: Deborah Balmuth
Lib & School Sales: Maribeth Casey
Founded: 1983
How-to books on country living, gardening, cook-
ing, natural health, home building, country
business, crafts, small-scale livestock, pets, beer
& wine, children's nonfiction.
ISBN Prefix(es): 0-945352; 0-88266; 1-58017
Number of titles published annually: 40 Print
Total Titles: 450 Print
Imprints: Storey Kids
Distributed by Workman Publishing Co Inc
Foreign Rep(s): Thomas Allen & Son Ltd
(Canada); Bookreps NZ Ltd (New Zealand);
Capricorn Link Ltd (Australia); Michelle Mor-
row Curreri (Asia, Middle East); Media Pub-

lishing Services Ltd (UK); Trinity Books CC
(South Africa)
Foreign Rights: Random House International;
Random House of Canada

Story Line Press
2091 Suncrest Rd, Talent, OR 97540
Mailing Address: PO Box 1240, Ashland, OR
97520-0055
Tel: 541-512-8792 *Fax:* 541-512-8793
E-mail: mail@storylinepress.com
Web Site: www.storylinepress.com
Key Personnel
Publr & Ed: Robert McDowell *E-mail:* robert@
storylinepress.com
Prodn Dir: Sharon McCann *E-mail:* sharon@
storylinepress.com
Founded: 1985
ISBN Prefix(es): 0-934257; 1-885266
Number of titles published annually: 15 Print
Total Titles: 250 Print
Distributor for Kayak Press
Distribution Center: Consortium Book Sellers,
1045 Westgate Dr, St Paul, MN 55114-1065
Toll Free Tel: 800-283-3572

Story Time Stories That Rhyme
PO Box 416, Denver, CO 80201-0416
Tel: 303-575-5676 *Fax:* 303-575-1187
E-mail: mail@storytimestoriesthatrhyme.org
Web Site: www.storytimestoriesthatrhyme.org
Key Personnel
Founder, Pres & Lib Sales Dir: A Doyle
Founded: 1989
ISBN Prefix(es): 1-56820
Number of titles published annually: 3 Print; 5
Audio
Total Titles: 17 Print; 12 Audio
Distributor for Story Time Stories Without
Rhyme; Tapestry Collage Lesson Plans

Strata Publishing Inc
PO Box 1303, State College, PA 16804
SAN: 298-9794
Tel: 814-234-8545; 814-234-2150 (sales)
Fax: 814-238-7222
E-mail: editorial@stratapub.com
Web Site: www.stratapub.com
Key Personnel
Publr: Kathleen Domenig *E-mail:* kmdomenig@
stratapub.com
Founded: 1990
Books in communication & journalism for mid-
level & advanced college courses, scholars &
professionals. Return authorization required.
ISBN Prefix(es): 0-9634489; 1-891136
Number of titles published annually: 3 Print
Total Titles: 8 Print

The Jesse Stuart Foundation
PO Box 669, Ashland, KY 41105-0669
SAN: 245-8837
Tel: 606-326-1667 *Fax:* 606-325-2519
Web Site: www.jsfbooks.com
Key Personnel
CEO & Sr Ed: James M Gifford *E-mail:* jfs@
jsfbooks.com
Dir, Mktg & Fin: Brett Nance
Founded: 1979
Appalachia-Kentuckiana. Not accepting mss at
this time.
ISBN Prefix(es): 0-945084
Number of titles published annually: 12 Print
Total Titles: 75 Print
Shipping Address: 1645 Winchester Ave, Ashland,
KY 41101

Studio 4 Productions, see Quick Publishing

§Stylewriter Inc
4395 N Windsor Dr, Provo, UT 84604-6301

Tel: 801-235-9462 *Toll Free Tel:* 866-997-9462
E-mail: customerservice@swinc.org; query@
swinc.org
Web Site: www.swinc.org; www.stylewriterinc.org
Key Personnel
Admin, Bd of Dirs: Cherrie Floyd
Acqs Ed: William Floyd
Admin, Graphics Design Dept: Andrew Knaupp
Founded: 2001
Nonprofit literary corporation. Publishing activities include printing, publication, graphics design, webmastering & distribution of materials whether in electronic or printed format. Fiction, nonfiction, children's or educational material that is deemed advantageous to the general public.
ISBN Prefix(es): 0-9742376
Number of titles published annually: 30 Print; 30 Online; 5 E-Book
Total Titles: 75 Print; 200 Online; 12 E-Book
Imprints: The Early Years (children's); Expose Press (nonfiction); Illumination (spiritual); Imagine (general fiction, other); Saga (romance); Silhouette (horror)

Stylus Publishing LLC
22883 Quicksilver Dr, Sterling, VA 20166-2012
SAN: 299-1853
Tel: 703-661-1504 (edit & sales)
    Toll Free Tel: 800-232-0223 *Fax:* 703-661-1547
E-mail: stylusmail@presswarehouse.com; stylusinfo@styluspub.com
Web Site: styluspub.com
Key Personnel
Pres: John von Knorring *E-mail:* jvk@styluspub. com
Mktg Mgr: Rachel Necker *E-mail:* rachel@ styluspub.com
Publicity Mgr: Jen Lofquist *E-mail:* jen.lofquist@ styluspub.com
Opers: Robin von Knorring *E-mail:* robin@ styluspub.com
Founded: 1996
Publish books for faculty & administrators in higher education. Distributes books in the areas of art, business, training, psychology & psychotherapy as well as educational & scholarly titles & books on Third World development & the environment.
ISBN Prefix(es): 1-57922
Number of titles published annually: 15 Print
Total Titles: 3,000 Print; 2 CD-ROM
Branch Office(s)
PO Box 605, Herndon, VA 20172-0605
Distributor for Anthem Press; The Commonwealth Secretariat; Cork University Press; Earthscan; Hotei Publishing; IDRC; ITDG Publishing; James & James (Science) Ltd; Karnac Books; Kogan Page Ltd; Nordic Africa Institute; Oxfam Publishing; Trentham Books Ltd; Women, Law & Development International (WLDI)
Distribution Center: Books International

Success Advertising & Publishing
Division of The Success Group
3419 Dunham Rd, Warsaw, NY 14569
SAN: 678-9501
Tel: 585-786-5663
Key Personnel
Pres: Allan H Smith *E-mail:* allan33001@aol.com
VP: Ginger B Smith
Book Ed: Robin Garretson
Founded: 1978
How-to, self-help, crafts, business, home-based business.
ISBN Prefix(es): 0-931113
Number of titles published annually: 12 Print
Total Titles: 35 Print
Divisions: Academy of Continuing Education; National Doll Society of America; Success Advertising
Advertising Agency: Success Advertising

Sherwood Sugden & Co
315 Fifth St, Peru, IL 61354
SAN: 210-5659
Tel: 815-224-6651 *Fax:* 815-223-4486
E-mail: philomon1@netscape.net
Web Site: monist.buffalo.edu
Key Personnel
Publr: Sherwood Sugden
Founded: 1975
Religion (Roman Catholic) & books of Christian apologetics of particular interest to Catholics. Some titles on American literature, political science, world history, education & philosophy.
ISBN Prefix(es): 0-89385
Number of titles published annually: 3 Print
Total Titles: 33 Print
Distributed by Open Court Publishing Co
Distributor for The Monist (An International Philosophical Quarterly)

Summa Publications
PO Box 660725, Birmingham, AL 35266-0725
Tel: 205-822-0463 *Fax:* 205-822-0463
Key Personnel
Publr: Thomas M Hines *E-mail:* tmhines@ samford.edu
Founded: 1983
Critical works, scholarly publications in French & English; no fiction.
ISBN Prefix(es): 0-917786; 1-883479
Number of titles published annually: 6 Print
Total Titles: 103 Print

Summer Institute of Linguistics International Academic Publications, see SIL International

Summit Publications
Division of Ye Olde Genealogie Shoppe
PO Box 39128, Indianapolis, IN 46239
Tel: 317-862-3330 *Toll Free Tel:* 800-419-0200
    Fax: 317-862-2599
E-mail: yogs@iquest.net
Web Site: www.yogs.com
Key Personnel
Pres: Patricia Gooldy
Founded: 1973
Genealogy (local history records).
ISBN Prefix(es): 1-878311
Number of titles published annually: 10 Print
Total Titles: 10 Print
Shipping Address: 9605 Vandergriff Rd, Indianapolis, IN 46239

Summit University Press
558 Old Yellowstone Trail S, Corwin Springs, MT 59030-5000
Tel: 406-848-9295 *Toll Free Tel:* 800-245-5445
    Fax: 406-848-9290
E-mail: info@summituniversitypress.com
Web Site: www.hostmontana.com/supress; www. summituniversitypress.com
Key Personnel
Dir, Global Rts & Dist: Norman N Millman
Founded: 1958
Global publisher of fine books since 1975, spirituality; very active foreign rights sales. Specializes in: spirituality, New Age & mind, body & spirit.
ISBN Prefix(es): 0-916766; 0-922729
Number of titles published annually: 5 Print
Total Titles: 100 Print; 14 CD-ROM; 3 E-Book; 70 Audio
Distributed by New Leaf
Membership(s): Publishers Marketing Association

Summy-Birchard Inc
Division of Warner/Chappell Inc
15800 NW 48 Ave, Miami, FL 33014
Tel: 305-620-1500 *Toll Free Tel:* 800-327-7643
    Fax: 305-621-1094

Key Personnel
Ed & Lib Sales Dir: Judi Gowe Bagnato
    Tel: 305-521-1711 *E-mail:* judi.gowe@ warnerchappell.com
Intl Rts Contact: David Olsen
Founded: 1872
Educational music books.
ISBN Prefix(es): 0-87487; 1-58951
Number of titles published annually: 25 Print; 8 Audio
Total Titles: 495 Print; 120 Audio
Divisions: Suzuki Method International
Distributed by Warner Bros Publications
Distributor for Carisch SPA; IMP
Foreign Rep(s): Warner/Chappell

Sun & Moon Press
Affiliate of Contemporary Arts Educational Project Inc
6026 Wilshire Blvd, Suite 200A, Los Angeles, CA 90036
SAN: 216-3063
Tel: 323-857-1115 *Fax:* 323-857-0143
E-mail: sales@consortium.com
Web Site: www.greeninteger.com
Key Personnel
Dir & Intl Rts Contact: Douglas Messerli
Founded: 1978
Contemporary fiction, criticism, drama & poetry.
ISBN Prefix(es): 0-940650; 1-55713
Number of titles published annually: 25 Print
Total Titles: 300 Print
Imprints: New American Fiction Series; New American Poetry Series; Sun & Moon Classics
Foreign Rights: Elaine Benesti (France); Bookbank (Spain); Paul & Peter Fritz (Germany, Switzerland); Leonhardt Literary Agency (Scandinavia); Natoli, Stefan & Oliva (Italy); Rogan Pikarski Literary Agency (Israel); UNI (Japan)
Distribution Center: Consortium Book Sales & Distribution, 1045 Westgate Dr, Suite 90, Saint Paul, MN 55114-1065 *Tel:* 612-221-9025 *Toll Free Tel:* 800-283-3572 *Fax:* 612-221-9035

Sun Books - Sun Publishing
Division of The Sun Companies
PO Box 5588, Santa Fe, NM 87502-5588
SAN: 206-1325
Tel: 505-471-5177; 505-471-6151 *Fax:* 505-473-4458
E-mail: info@sunbooks.com
Web Site: www.sunbooks.com
Key Personnel
Pres, ISBN Contact & Rts & Perms: Skip Whitson
Lib Sales Dir: Robyn Covelli-Hunt
Founded: 1973
Motivational, success, business, recovery, astrology, metaphysics, inspirational, New Age, occult, history, self-help, new thought, art, philosophy, numerology, earth changes, western mysticism, scholarly; oriental philosophy & studies. No unsol mss.
ISBN Prefix(es): 0-89540
Number of titles published annually: 12 Print
Total Titles: 360 Print
Imprints: Sun Books
Subsidiaries: Far West Publishing Co
Divisions: Sun Books; Sun Cards
Distributor for Far West Publishing Co; Sun Books
Foreign Rights: Skip Whitson
Advertising Agency: Sun Agency

Sun Publishing, see Sun Books - Sun Publishing

Sunbelt Publications Inc
1250 Fayette St, El Cajon, CA 92020-1511
SAN: 630-0790
Mailing Address: PO Box 191126, San Diego, CA 92159

Tel: 619-258-4911 *Toll Free Tel:* 800-626-6579
  Fax: 619-258-4916
E-mail: mail@sunbeltpub.com
Web Site: www.sunbeltbooks.com
Key Personnel
Pres: Diana Lindsay *E-mail:* dlindsay@
  sunbeltpub.com
CEO: Lowell Lindsay *Tel:* 619-258-4911 ext 111
  E-mail: llindsay@sunbeltpub.com
Founded: 1984
Publisher of natural history, science & pictorial
  travel books on Alta & Baja, California.
ISBN Prefix(es): 0-932653; 0-916251
Number of titles published annually: 8 Print
Total Titles: 30 Print
Imprints: First Choice
Distributor for Dawsons Book Shop

Sunburst Technology
400 Columbus Ave, Suite 160E, Valhalla, NY
  10595
Tel: 914-747-3310 *Toll Free Tel:* 800-338-3457
  Fax: 914-747-4109
Web Site: www.sunburst.com
Key Personnel
CEO: Mark Sotir
VP & CFO: Morton Cohen
VP, Software Devt: David Wolff
VP, Sales: Daniel Figurski
Founded: 1972
Developer & publisher of award-winning, multi-
  media educational software, videos & printed
  supplements for use in schools. Publishes
  school products for grades K to 12 under the
  teachers' favorite Sunburst brand & distributes
  the popular Knowledge Adventure® brand
  school products.
ISBN Prefix(es): 0-395; 0-89466
Branch Office(s)
1550 Executive Dr, Elgin, IL 60123 (cust serv)

Sundance Publishing
Division of Haights Cross Communications Inc
One Beeman Rd, Northborough, MA 01532
Mailing Address: PO Box 800, Northborough,
  MA 01532-0800
Tel: 508-571-6500 *Toll Free Tel:* 800-343-8204
  Fax: 508-571-6510 *Toll Free Fax:* 800-456-
  2419
E-mail: info@sundancepub.com
Web Site: www.sundancepub.com
Key Personnel
Pres: Robert Laronga *Tel:* 508-571-6525
  Fax: 508-571-6503 *E-mail:* blaronga@
  sundancepub.com
CFO: Logan Wai *Tel:* 508-571-6650 *Fax:* 508-
  571-6508 *E-mail:* lwai@sundancepub.com
Sr VP, Opers: Jay Shenk *Tel:* 508-571-6715
  E-mail: jshenk@sundancepub.com
VP, Prod Devt: Sherry Litwack *Tel:* 508-571-6580
  E-mail: slitwack@sundancepub.com
Sr VP, Sales & Mktg: Edward A Rock
  E-mail: erock@sundancepub.com
VP, Mktg: Katherine Jasmine *Tel:* 508-571-6765
  E-mail: kjasmine@sundancepub.com
VP, Dist Prods: Anne Sterling *Tel:* 508-571-6760
  E-mail: asterling@sundancepub.com
Dir, Prodn: Marc Brindisi *Tel:* 508-571-6770
  E-mail: mbrindisi@sundancepub.com
Warehouse Dir, HCC Shared Servs: John Woods-
  mall *E-mail:* jwoodsmall@sundancepub.com
Mgr, Cust Serv: Sharon Mosbrucker
  E-mail: smosbrucker@sundancepub.com
Founded: 1971
Supplementary educational publisher of instruc-
  tional materials for shared reading, guided
  reading, independent reading, phonics & com-
  prehension skills for students in K-9, as well as
  a below-level reading program for grades 2-9.
  Also publishes K-12 supplementary materials
  & Teacher Resources for best-selling paperback
  literature for grades 2-12.

ISBN Prefix(es): 0-940146; 0-7608; 1-56801; 0-
  88741
Number of titles published annually: 244 Print;
  36 Audio
Total Titles: 1,250 Print; 36 Audio
Imprints: AlphaKids® Guided Readers; Al-
  phaKids® Plus Guided Readers; Chapter by
  Chapter®; Fact Meets Fiction; Grammar with a
  Grin; Kid-to-Kid Books; Kids Corner; LEAP®
  (Literature Enrichment Activities for Paper-
  backs); LIFT® (Literature is for Thinking);
  Little Blue Readers; Little Green Readers; Lit-
  tle Red Readers; Novel Ideas Plus; Novel Ideas
  Skills; ReAct; The Real Deal; Reading Power-
  Works™; Second Chance Reading®; Sparklers;
  Sundance Phonics Readers; SunLit Fluency
  Readers; Supa Doopers; Supa Doopers Plus;
  Thrillogy; Triple Play; Twin Texts®
Distributor for Aladdin Books; Associated Pub-
  lisher's Group; Avon; Ballantine Books; Ban-
  tam; Barron's Educational Publishers; Berkley;
  Boyds Mill Press; Candlewick Press; Charles
  McCann; Charlesbridge Publishing; Children's
  Book Press; Children's Press; Chronicle Books;
  Crown Publishers; Dutton; Farrar Straus &
  Giroux; Fawcett Books; Firefly Ltd; Folger;
  Groundwood; Harcourt Brace & Co; Harper-
  Collins; Henry Holt; Holiday House; Houghton
  Mifflin Co; Hyperion; Kane Miller; Lee & Low
  Books; Little Brown & Co; Merriam-Webster;
  Millbrook Press; Morrow; New American
  Library; New Directions; Newmarket Press;
  North South Books; Orca Book Publishers; Or-
  chard Books; Owl Books; Oxford University
  Press; Peachtree Publishers; Penguin Books;
  Persea; Pocket Books; Preservation Press; Put-
  nam Publishing Co; Rand McNally; Random
  House; Scholastic Books; Secret Passage Press;
  Silver Press; Simon & Schuster; Steck-Vaughn;
  Stoddart; TOR Books; Troll Books; Univer-
  sity of Nebraska; Usborne; Walker Publishers;
  Warner Paperback Library; Washington Square
  Press
Foreign Rep(s): Schmelzer PSI
Orders to: Newbridge Educational Publishing, PO
  Box 800, Northborough, MA 01532, Cust Serv
  Mgr: Sharon Mosbrucker *Toll Free Tel:* 800-
  867-0307 *Toll Free Fax:* 800-456-2419
Returns: Newbridge Educational Publishing, One
  Beeman Rd, Northborough, MA 01532, Con-
  tact: John Woodsmall *Toll Free Tel:* 800-867-
  0307 *Toll Free Fax:* 800-456-2419
Membership(s): AAP; Association of Educational
  Publishers; Educational Paperback Association;
  International Reading Association

Sunset Books/Sunset Publishing Corp
80 Willow Rd, Menlo Park, CA 94025-3691
Tel: 650-321-3600 *Toll Free Tel:* 800-227-7346;
  800-321-0372 (California only) *Fax:* 650-324-
  1532
Web Site: sunset.com
Key Personnel
VP & Edit Dir: Robert Doyle
VP & Gen Mgr: Richard Smeby
Publish home & garden & lifesytle books.
ISBN Prefix(es): 0-376
Number of titles published annually: 15 Print
Total Titles: 95 Print; 95 Online
Distributed by Leisure Arts Inc
Membership(s): Publishers International Market-
  ing Group

Sunstone Press
Subsidiary of Sunstone Corp
PO Box 2321, Santa Fe, NM 87504-2321
SAN: 214-2090
Tel: 505-988-4418 *Fax:* 505-988-1025 (orders
  only)
Web Site: www.sunstonepress.com
Key Personnel
Pres & Treas: James Clois Smith, Jr
  E-mail: jsmith@sunstonepress.com

Founded: 1971
Southwestern titles, general fiction & how-to craft
  books.
ISBN Prefix(es): 0-913270; 0-86534
Number of titles published annually: 30 Print
Total Titles: 400 Print
Imprints: Sundial Books
Foreign Rights: Daniel Bial Literary Agency
Membership(s): New Mexico Book Association

SUNY Press, see State University of New York
  Press

Superintendent of Documents, see US
  Government Printing Office

Surrey Books
230 E Ohio St, Suite 120, Chicago, IL 60611
SAN: 275-8857
Tel: 312-751-7330 *Toll Free Tel:* 800-326-4430
  Fax: 312-751-7334
E-mail: surreybk@aol.com
Web Site: www.surreybooks.com
Key Personnel
Publr & Mktg Mgr: Susan H Schwartz
Founded: 1982
Trade books. Specialize in nonfiction: cooking,
  health & lifestyle.
ISBN Prefix(es): 0-940625; 1-57284
Number of titles published annually: 10 Print
Total Titles: 40 Print
Distributed by Publishers Group West (contact
  customer service)
Foreign Rep(s): Hi Marketing (UK)
Membership(s): AAP; ABA; International Asso-
  ciation of Culinary Professionals; Publishers'
  Publicity Association

Susquehanna University Press
Affiliate of Associated University Presses
Associated University Presses, 2010 Eastpark
  Blvd, Cranbury, NJ 08512
Tel: 609-655-4770 *Fax:* 609-655-8366
E-mail: aup440@aol.com
Key Personnel
Ed: Rachana Sachdev
Man Ed: Sarah Bailey
Contact: Julien Yoseloff
Founded: 1983
ISBN Prefix(es): 0-941664; 0-945636; 1-57591
Number of titles published annually: 15 Print
Total Titles: 200 Print
Distributed by Associated University Presses
Foreign Rep(s): Eurospan (Europe & UK); Schol-
  arly Book Services (Canada); United Publishers
  Services (Japan)

Swagman Publishing Inc
PO Box 519, Castle Rock, CO 80104
Tel: 303-660-3307 *Toll Free Tel:* 800-660-5107
  Fax: 303-688-4388
E-mail: mail@4wdbooks.com
Web Site: www.4wdbooks.com
Key Personnel
Publr: Peter Mossey
Mktg Dir: Jeanne Mossey *E-mail:* jwm@
  4wdbooks.com
Founded: 1999
ISBN Prefix(es): 0-930657; 0-9665675; 1-930193
Number of titles published annually: 10 Online
Total Titles: 50 Online
Imprints: Outdoor Books & Maps
Membership(s): American Book Producers As-
  sociation; Bookbuilders West; Colorado In-
  dependent Publishers Association; Publishers
  Marketing Association; PubWest

Swallow Press
Scott Quadrangle, Athens, OH 45701

Tel: 740-593-1155 *Toll Free Tel:* 800-621-2736 (orders only) *Fax:* 740-593-4536 *Toll Free Fax:* 800-621-8476 (orders only)
Web Site: www.ohiou.edu/oupress/
Key Personnel
Dir: David Sanders *Tel:* 740-593-1157 *E-mail:* dsanders1@ohiou.edu
Man Ed: Nancy Basmajian *Tel:* 740-593-1161 *E-mail:* nbasmajia1@ohiou.edu
Sr Ed: Gillian Berchowitz *Tel:* 740-593-1159 *E-mail:* gillian.berchowitz@ohiou.edu
Busn Mgr: Bonnie Rand *Tel:* 740-593-1156 *E-mail:* rand@oak.cats.ohiou.edu
Mktg Mgr: Richard Gilbert *Tel:* 740-593-1160 *E-mail:* gilbert@ohiou.edu
Perms: Judy Wilson *Tel:* 740-593-1154 *E-mail:* jwilson@ohiou.edu
Founded: 1964
Frontier Americana, poetry, literature, general interest.
ISBN Prefix(es): 0-8214; 0-8040; 0-89680
Number of titles published annually: 50 Print
Total Titles: 600 Print
Imprints: Ohio University Press
Foreign Rep(s): Eurospan (Europe); EWEB (Pacific Rim)
Warehouse: 11030 S Langley Ave, Chicago, IL 60628 *Toll Free Tel:* 800-621-2736 *Toll Free Fax:* 800-621-8476
Membership(s): American Association of University Presses

Swan Isle Press
11030 S Langley Ave, Chicago, IL 60628
Tel: 773-568-1550 *Toll Free Tel:* 800-621-2736 *Fax:* 773-660-2235 *Toll Free Fax:* 800-621-8476
E-mail: info@swanislepress.com
Web Site: www.swanpress.com
Key Personnel
Dir & Ed: David Rade
ISBN Prefix(es): 0-9678808; 0-9748881
Number of titles published annually: 3 Print
Editorial Office(s): PO Box 408790, Chicago, IL 60640-8790
Distributed by University of Chicago Press

Swedenborg Association
Division of The Lord's New Church
278-A Meeting St, Charleston, SC 29401
Tel: 843-853-6211 *Fax:* 843-853-6226
E-mail: arcana@swedenborg.net; assn@swedenborg.net
Key Personnel
Chmn, Pubns & Intl Rts: Leonard Fox
Lib Sales Dir: Drake H M Kaiser *E-mail:* drake@swedenborg.net
Founded: 1993
Publishes books related to Emanuel Swedenborg.
ISBN Prefix(es): 1-883270
Number of titles published annually: 3 Print
Total Titles: 16 Print
Distributed by Swedenborg Foundation

Swedenborg Foundation Publishers/Chrysalis Books
320 N Church St, West Chester, PA 19380
SAN: 202-7526
Tel: 610-430-3222 *Toll Free Tel:* 800-355-3222 (cust serv) *Fax:* 610-430-7982
E-mail: info@swedenborg.com
Web Site: www.swedenborg.com
Key Personnel
Exec Dir, Publr & Mktg: Deborah Forman
Sr Ed: Mary Lou Bertucci *E-mail:* editor@swedenborg.com
Founded: 1849
Books & videos by, or relating to, the theological works & spiritual insights of Emanuel Swedenborg & related literature.
ISBN Prefix(es): 0-87785
Number of titles published annually: 6 Print

Total Titles: 120 Print; 1 Audio
Imprints: Chrysalis Books; Chrysalis Reader
Distributed by Steiner Books
Distributor for J Appleseed & Co; Swedenborg Scientific Assoc; Swedenborg Society

Sweetgrass Press LLC
PO Box 1862, Merrimack, NH 03054-1862
Tel: 603-883-7001 *Fax:* 603-883-7001 *Toll Free Fax:* 866-727-7757
E-mail: info@sweetgrasspress.com
Web Site: www.sweetgrasspress.com
Key Personnel
CEO: Michelle Wedel *E-mail:* mwedel@sweetgrasspress.com
Founded: 2000
Publisher & publishers service company via Write to Print.
ISBN Prefix(es): 0-9702630; 0-974272
Number of titles published annually: 4 Print
Total Titles: 9 Print
Imprints: Sweetgrass Fiction; Write to Print
Subsidiaries: The Electric Wigwam
Distributor for Greatdream Publications

§SYBEX Inc
1151 Marina Village Pkwy, Alameda, CA 94501
SAN: 211-1667
Tel: 510-523-8233 *Toll Free Tel:* 800-227-2346 *Fax:* 510-523-2373
E-mail: pressinfo@sybex.com
Web Site: www.sybex.com
Key Personnel
Pres & Rts & Perms: Rodnay Zaks
VP, Intl Sales: Bill Marciniak
Founded: 1976
For beginning, intermediate & advanced users of all types of software & hardware, including how-to books on various networking, word processing, database, graphics & spreadsheet software, certification, as well as computer games & Internet books, graphics & programming.
ISBN Prefix(es): 0-89588; 0-7821
Number of titles published annually: 150 Print
Total Titles: 601 Print; 2 CD-ROM

§Synapse Information Resources Inc
1247 Taft Ave, Endicott, NY 13760
Tel: 607-748-4145 *Toll Free Tel:* 888-SYN-CHEM *Fax:* 607-786-3966
E-mail: salesinfo@synapseinfo.com
Web Site: www.synapseinfo.com
Key Personnel
Owner: Irene Ash *E-mail:* iash@synapseinfo.com; Michael Ash
Founded: 1981
Chemical database references for industry. Publish both books & CD-ROMs in industrial chemistry. Reference books & software serving the industrial chemical market.
ISBN Prefix(es): 1-890595
Number of titles published annually: 4 Print; 4 CD-ROM
Total Titles: 18 Print; 20 CD-ROM
Distributor for Ashgate Publishing Co

§SynergEbooks
1235 Flat Shoals Rd, King, NC 27021
SAN: 254-4962
Tel: 336-994-2405 *Toll Free Tel:* 888-812-2533 *Fax:* 336-994-2405 *Fax on Demand:* 336-994-8403
E-mail: inquiries@synergebooks.com; synergebooks@aol.com
Web Site: www.synergebooks.com
Key Personnel
Publr & Exec Ed: Debra Staples
Founded: 1999
Publishing & bookstore.
ISBN Prefix(es): 0-9702; 0-7443; 1-931540
Number of titles published annually: 30 Print; 50 Online; 50 E-Book

Total Titles: 16 Print; 172 CD-ROM; 172 Online; 172 E-Book
Distributed by Amazon.com; Barnes & Noble; Bookbooters; CyberRead; Eloka.com; Fictionwise; Mobipocket; W H Smith UK
Membership(s): Electronically Published Internet Connection; Publishers Marketing Association

Syracuse University Press
621 Skytop Rd, Syracuse, NY 13244-5290
SAN: 206-9776
Tel: 315-443-5534 *Toll Free Tel:* 800-365-8929 (orders only) *Fax:* 315-443-5545
E-mail: supress@syr.edu
Web Site: syracuseuniversitypress.syr.edu
Key Personnel
Dir: Peter B Webber *Tel:* 315-443-5535
Exec Ed, Acqs: Mary Selden Evans *Tel:* 315-443-5543
Mktg Mgr & Lib Sales Dir: Theresa A Litz *Tel:* 315-443-1975 *E-mail:* talitz@syr.edu
Compt: Alice Randel Pfeiffer *Tel:* 315-443-5536
Mgr of Design & Prodn Mgr: Mary Peterson Moore *Tel:* 315-443-5540
Orders Supv: Carol Holava *Tel:* 315-443-2597
Founded: 1943
Scholarly, general & regional nonfiction; Middle East; Irish studies; medieval; women studies; Iroquois studies; television; religion & politics; geography; sports & leisure; space, place & society; literature; Jewish studies (fiction & nonfiction).
ISBN Prefix(es): 0-8156
Number of titles published annually: 50 Print
Total Titles: 1,025 Print
Imprints: Adirondack Museum
Distributor for American University of Beirut; Colgate University Press; Moshe Dayan Center for Middle Eastern & African Studies; National Library of Ireland; Munson Williams Proctor Institute; St Lawrence University; Syracuse University Lightworks
Foreign Rights: Eurospan Services (UK, Europe, Middle East, Scandinavia); EWEB, c/o University of Hawaii Press (Australia, Asia, Far East, India, Pakistan); Rex Williams, Cariad Ltd (Canada)

The Systemsware Corp
973 Russell Ave, Suite D, Gaithersburg, MD 20879
Mailing Address: PO Box 2635, Kensington, MD 20891
Tel: 301-948-4890 *Fax:* 301-926-4243
Web Site: www.systemswarecorp.com
Key Personnel
Publr: Patricia White
Founded: 1981
ISBN Prefix(es): 0-938801
Total Titles: 7 Print
Imprints: Software Engineering Press

T & T Clark International
Formerly Trinity Press International
Division of Continuum
PO Box 1321, Harrisburg, PA 17105
Tel: 717-541-8130 *Toll Free Tel:* 800-877-0012 *Fax:* 717-541-8136
Web Site: www.tandtclarkinternational.com
Key Personnel
Man Ed: Amy Wagner *E-mail:* awagner@morehousegroup.com
Edit Dir: Henry Carrigan *E-mail:* hcarriga@morehousegroup.com
Founded: 1989
Religion, Biblical studies, theology & ethics, scripture, religious education, reference works & paperbacks, religion & culture, religion & science.
ISBN Prefix(es): 0-8264; 1-56338; 0-334; 0-7162; 0-567
Number of titles published annually: 35 Print
Total Titles: 500 Print

Foreign Rep(s): Continuum International (Australia, Europe & UK, New Zealand); Novalis (Canada)
Warehouse: 301 N Seventh St, Harrisburg, PA 17110

Tafnews Press
Division of Track & Field News
2570 El Camino Real, No 606, Mountain View, CA 94040
Tel: 650-948-8188 *Fax:* 650-948-9445
E-mail: biz@trackandfieldnews.com
Web Site: www.trackandfieldnews.com
Key Personnel
Pubr & Intl Rts: Ed Fox *E-mail:* ef@trackandfieldnews.com
Founded: 1948
Track & Field, athletics.
ISBN Prefix(es): 0-911521
Number of titles published annually: 4 Print
Total Titles: 23 Print

§Tahrike Tarsile Qur'an Inc
80-08 51 Ave, Elmhurst, NY 11373
Tel: 718-446-6472 *Fax:* 718-446-4370
E-mail: orders@koranusa.org
Web Site: www.koranusa.org
Key Personnel
Pres: Aunali M Khalfan
Publishers & distributors of the Holy Quran & other Islamic books, videos & CDs.
Number of titles published annually: 5 Print
Total Titles: 27 Print

Talisman House Publishers
PO Box 3157, Jersey City, NJ 07303-3157
Tel: 201-938-0698 *Fax:* 201-938-1693
E-mail: talismaned@aol.com
Web Site: www.talismanpublishers.com
Key Personnel
Pres: Edward Foster
Founded: 1993
Fiction, poetry, literary criticism.
ISBN Prefix(es): 1-883689
Number of titles published annually: 10 Print
Total Titles: 90 Print
Foreign Rep(s): Paul Green (England)
Warehouse: LPC Group/InBook, 4029 W George St, Chicago, IL 60641

TAN Books & Publishers Inc
2020 Harrison Ave, Rockford, IL 61104
Mailing Address: PO Box 424, Rockford, IL 61105-0424
Tel: 815-226-7777 *Fax:* 815-226-7770
E-mail: tan@tanbooks.com; taneditor@tanbooks.com
Web Site: www.tanbooks.com
Key Personnel
Ed: Mary Frances Lester
Founded: 1967
Publish traditional Catholic books, especially reprint classic works.
ISBN Prefix(es): 0-89555
Number of titles published annually: 23 Print
Total Titles: 490 Print

Tapestry Press Ltd
19 Nashoba Rd, Littleton, MA 01460
Tel: 978-486-0200 *Toll Free Tel:* 800-535-2007
Fax: 978-486-0244
E-mail: publish@tapestrypress.com
Web Site: www.tapestrypress.com
Key Personnel
Pres: Michael J Miskin
VP & Ed-in-Chief: Sara E Hofeldt
Publr: Elizabeth A Larsen *E-mail:* liz@tapestrypress.com
Founded: 1988
College textbooks, journals; language arts & psychology.

ISBN Prefix(es): 0-924234; 1-56888
Number of titles published annually: 120 Print
Total Titles: 150 Print
Imprints: Tapestry Press
Membership(s): AAP

Taplinger Publishing Co Inc
PO Box 175, Marlboro, NJ 07746-0175
SAN: 213-6821
Tel: 646-215-9003 *Fax:* 646-215-9560 *Cable:* TAPLINPUB
Key Personnel
Pres: Louis Strick
VP & Treas: Theodore D Rosenfeld
Founded: 1955
General nonfiction, including art, biography, calligraphy, graphic arts, history, music.
ISBN Prefix(es): 0-8008
Number of titles published annually: 4 Print
Total Titles: 150 Print
Imprints: Crescendo
Distributed by Parkwest Publications Inc
Foreign Rep(s): Baker & Taylor International (Africa, Asia, Europe, South Africa, South America)
Returns: Parkwest Publications, c/o Pathway Book Service, 4 White Book Rd, Gilsum, NH 03448
Warehouse: Parkwest Publications Inc, PO Box 20261, New York, NY 10025-1512, Contact: Brian Squire *Tel:* 646-215-9003 *Fax:* 646-215-9560
Distribution Center: Parkwest Publications, c/o Pathway Book Service, 4 White Brook Rd, Gilsum, NH 03448

Tarascon Publishing
1015 W Central Ave, Lompoc, CA 93436
Mailing Address: PO Box 517, Lompoc, CA 93438
Tel: 805-736-7000 *Toll Free Tel:* 800-929-9926
Fax: 805-736-6161 *Toll Free Fax:* 877-929-9926
E-mail: info@tarascon.com
Web Site: www.tarascon.com
Key Personnel
VP: Elizabeth Green *E-mail:* beth@tarascon.com
Sales Mgr: Linda Menzies *E-mail:* linda@tarascon.com
Founded: 1987
Publishers of pocket-sized medical reference books.
ISBN Prefix(es): 1-882742
Number of titles published annually: 3 Print; 7 Online; 2 E-Book
Total Titles: 7 Print; 2 CD-ROM; 7 Online; 2 E-Book
Distributed by J A Majors; Matthews Medical; Rittenhouse
Membership(s): Publishers Marketing Association

Jeremy P Tarcher
Imprint of Penguin Group (USA) Inc
375 Hudson St, New York, NY 10014
SAN: 282-5074
Tel: 212-366-2000
E-mail: online@penguinputnam.com
Web Site: www.penguin.com
Key Personnel
Pres: Jeremy P Tarcher
VP & Publr: Joel Fotinos
VP & Publicity Dir: Ken Siman
Sr Ed: Mitchell Horowitz
Ed: Sarah Carder
Founded: 1965
Nonfiction: cookbooks, crafts, humor, music & dance, health, nutrition, psychology, self-help, social sciences & sociology, biography, child care & development, behavioral sciences, business, human relations, education.
ISBN Prefix(es): 0-87477

Number of titles published annually: 46 Print
Total Titles: 319 Print

Taschen America
6671 Sunset Blvd, Suite 1508, Los Angeles, CA 90028
Tel: 323-463-4441 *Toll Free Tel:* 888-TASCHEN (827-2436) *Fax:* 323-463-4442
Web Site: www.taschen.com
Key Personnel
Busn Mgr: Paul Norton *E-mail:* p.norton@taschen-america.com
Founded: 1996
Publishers of high-quality, reasonably priced illustrated books on the subjects of art, architecture, design, photography, erotica, gay interest & popular culture.
ISBN Prefix(es): 3-8228
Number of titles published annually: 60 Print
Total Titles: 400 Print
Imprints: Evergreen; Taschen
Subsidiaries: Taschen GMBH
Distribution Center: Client Distribution Services, 193 Edwards Dr, Jackson, TN 38301

The Taunton Press Inc
63 S Main St, Newtown, CT 06470
SAN: 210-5144
Mailing Address: PO Box 5506, Newtown, CT 06470-0921
Tel: 203-426-8171 *Toll Free Tel:* 800-283-7252; 800-888-8286 (orders) *Fax:* 203-426-3434
Web Site: www.taunton.com
Key Personnel
Pres & CEO: John Lively
Publr, Trade Book Div: Jim Childs
Publr, Finewoodworking & Finehomebuilding: Tim Schreiner
Publr, Fine Homebuilding: John Miller
Publr, Fine Cooking & Threads: Sarah Roman
Publr, Fine Gardening & Kitchen Gardening: Elizabeth Conklin
Founded: 1975
Woodworking, home building, fiber & gardening books, cooking, magazines & videos; also on the web.
ISBN Prefix(es): 0-918804; 0-942391; 1-56158
Number of titles published annually: 55 Print
Total Titles: 330 Print
Distributed by Publishers Group West
Foreign Rep(s): Guild of Master Craftsman (Europe); Lothian Books (Australia); Publishers Group West (Canada)
Warehouse: 4 Tinkerfield Rd, Newtown, CT 06470

Taylor & Francis Editorial, Production & Manufacturing Division
Division of Taylor & Francis Inc
325 Chestnut St, Philadelphia, PA 19106
Tel: 215-625-8900 *Toll Free Tel:* 800-354-1420 *Fax:* 215-625-2940
E-mail: info@taylorandfrancis.com
Web Site: www.taylorandfrancis.com
Key Personnel
VP, Prodn: Corey Gray
VP, Sales & Mktg: Robert Rooney
Dir, Mktg: Deborah Lovell
Number of titles published annually: 100 Print
Total Titles: 3,324 Print
Imprints: Hemisphere Pub Corp; Crane Russak
Foreign Rep(s): Taylor & Francis Ltd (UK)
Orders to: Taylor & Francis, 7625 Empire Dr, Florence, KY 41042 *Toll Free Tel:* 800-634-7064 *Toll Free Fax:* 800-248-4724

§Taylor & Francis Inc
325 Chestnut St, Philadelphia, PA 19106
Tel: 215-625-8900 *Toll Free Tel:* 800-354-1420 *Fax:* 215-625-2940
E-mail: info@taylorandfrancis.com
Web Site: www.taylorandfrancis.com

Key Personnel
Pres: Kevin J Bradley
VP, Prodn: Corey Gray
VP, Sales & Mktg: Robert Rooney
Dir, Mktg: Deborah Lovell
Sales Mgr: Jim Cook
Founded: 1974
College textbooks, professional & reference books & journals in engineering, physical science, medicine, nursing, psychology, sociology, toxicology & physics.
ISBN Prefix(es): 1-56032; 0-87630; 0-86377; 0-8448; 0-85066; 0-85109; 0-905273; 1-85000
Number of titles published annually: 2,000 Print
Total Titles: 50,000 Print; 4 CD-ROM; 56 E-Book; 10 Audio
Imprints: Psychology Press
Subsidiaries: Brunner/Routledge
Foreign Office(s): 21 New Feter Lane, London EC4A 3DE, United Kingdom
Distributor for Brunner/Routledge; Falmer Press; Psychology Press
Foreign Rep(s): Taylor & Francis Ltd (UK)
Warehouse: 7625 Empire Dr, Florence, KY 41042 *Toll Free Tel:* 800-634-7064 *Toll Free Fax:* 800-248-4724
See separate listing for:
Taylor & Francis Editorial, Production & Manufacturing Division

TCU Press, see Texas Christian University Press

Teach Me Tapes Inc
6016 Blue Circle Dr, Minnetonka, MN 55343
Tel: 952-933-8086 *Toll Free Tel:* 800-456-4656
Fax: 952-933-0512
E-mail: marie@teachmetapes.com
Web Site: www.teachmetapes.com
Key Personnel
Owner, Pres & Publr: Judy Mahoney
E-mail: judy@teachmetapes.com
Founded: 1985
ISBN Prefix(es): 0-934633
Number of titles published annually: 5 Print
Total Titles: 59 Print; 22 Audio
Distributed by Follett; Penton Overseas Inc

Teacher Created Materials Inc
6421 Industry Way, Westminster, CA 92683
Mailing Address: PO Box 1040, Huntington Beach, CA 92647-1040
Tel: 714-891-7895 *Toll Free Tel:* 800-662-4321
Fax: 714-892-0283 *Toll Free Fax:* 800-525-1254
E-mail: tcminfo@teachercreated.com
Web Site: www.teachercreated.com
Key Personnel
Pres: Rachelle Cracchiolo; Mary Dupuy Smith
COO: Rich Levitt
Founded: 1979
Publishes Pre-K to 12 curriculum programs, supplemental resource materials & technology products. Also, provides professional staff development for teachers.
ISBN Prefix(es): 1-55734
Number of titles published annually: 250 Print
Total Titles: 1,000 Print

Teacher Ideas Press
Division of Greenwood Publishing Group
361 Hanover St, Portsmouth, NH 03801-3912
Mailing Address: PO Box 6926, Portsmouth, NH 03802-6926
Toll Free Tel: 800-225-5800 *Fax:* 603-431-2214
Toll Free Fax: 800-354-2004 (perms & foreign rts)
E-mail: custserv@teacherideaspress.com; permissions@teacherideaspress.com; foreignrights@teacherideaspress.com
Web Site: www.teacherideaspress.com
Key Personnel
Pres: Wayne Smith

Acq Ed: Suzanne Barchers
Mktg Dir: Debby Mattil
Art Dir: Joan Garner
Founded: 1964
Books written by educators for educators. Innovative ideas, practical lessons & classroom-tested activities in all areas of discipline. Resource & activity books.
ISBN Prefix(es): 0-87287; 1-56308
Foreign Rep(s): Eurospan (Africa, UK, Europe); Good Faith Worldwide International Co Ltd (Taiwan); James Bennett Pty Ltd (Australia, New Zealand, Papua New Guinea); Taylor & Francis (Asia & the Pacific); United Publishers Services Ltd (Japan)
Orders to: Greenwood International, Linacre House, Oxford OX2 8DP, United Kingdom (European orders) *Tel:* (01865) 888181 *Fax:* (01865) 314981 *E-mail:* greenwood. enquiries@harcourteducation.co.uk
Returns: Greenwood Publishing Group/Libraries Unlimited, 300 Exchange Dr, Suite B, Crystal Lake, FL 60014
Warehouse: Greenwood Publishing Group/Libraries Unlimited, 300 Exchange Dr, Suite B, Crystal Lake, FL 60014

Teachers & Writers Collaborative
5 Union Sq W, New York, NY 10003-3306
Tel: 212-691-6590 *Toll Free Tel:* 888-266-5789
Fax: 212-675-0171
E-mail: info@twc.org
Web Site: www.twc.org
Key Personnel
Publns Dir: Christopher Edgar *E-mail:* cedgar@twc.org
Ed: Christina Davis *E-mail:* cdavis@twc.org
Dist Mgr: Dierdra Colzie *E-mail:* dcolzie@twc.org
Founded: 1967
Book & magazine publication & distribution.
ISBN Prefix(es): 0-915924
Number of titles published annually: 3 Print
Total Titles: 55 Print; 1 Audio
Shipping Address: 21 E 15 St, New York, NY 10003-3306

§Teachers College Press
Affiliate of Teachers College, Columbia University
1234 Amsterdam Ave, New York, NY 10027
SAN: 213-263X
Tel: 212-678-3929 *Fax:* 212-678-4149
E-mail: tcpress@tc.columbia.edu
Web Site: www.teacherscollegepress.com
Key Personnel
Dir: Carole Saltz
Dir, Sales & Mktg: Leyli Shayegan
Exec Acqs Ed: Brian Ellerbeck
Sr Prod Ed: Karl Nyberg
Prod Ed: Lori Tate
Prod Mgr: Peter Sieger
Rts & Perms Mgr & Spec Sale Coord: Amy Kline
Founded: 1904
Professional books & textbooks in education; tests, classroom materials & reference works.
ISBN Prefix(es): 0-8077
Number of titles published annually: 60 Print; 1 CD-ROM
Total Titles: 1,123 Print; 1 CD-ROM
Foreign Rep(s): Baker & Taylor International (Australia, Africa, Asia, Latin America, Middle East, Orient, South America); Eurospan Ltd (UK, Europe); Guidance Center (Canada)
Returns: Returns Dept, 82 Wintersport Lane, Williston, VT 05495
Distribution Center: Teachers College Press, PO Box 20, Williston, VT 05495-2665
Membership(s): AAP; American Association of University Presses; BISG

§Teacher's Discovery
Division of American Eagle
2741 Paldan Dr, Auburn Hills, MI 48326
Tel: 248-340-7220 ext 207 *Toll Free Tel:* 800-521-3897 *Fax:* 248-340-7212
Toll Free Fax: 888-987-2436
Web Site: www.teachersdiscovery.com
Key Personnel
Buyer: Brenda Lemmert
Buyer & Prod Devt: Nina Linebaugh; Pat Nauf
Buyer: Julie Robinson
Prod Devt: Judy Iacofano
Founded: 1969
Distribute several proprietary items we create; also publish several works written by authors other than those employed by Teachers Discovery; social studies.
Number of titles published annually: 50 Print
Distributor for National Textbook Co

Teachers of English to Speakers of Other Languages Inc (TESOL)
700 S Washington St, Suite 200, Alexandria, VA 22314-4287
Tel: 703-836-0774 *Fax:* 703-836-7864
E-mail: info@tesol.org
Web Site: www.tesol.org
Key Personnel
Dir, Publg: Paul G Gibbs *Tel:* 703-518-2524 *Fax:* 703-836-6447 *E-mail:* pgibbs@tesol.org
Man Ed: Marilyn Kupetz *Tel:* 703-518-2525 *Fax:* 703-836-6447 *E-mail:* mkupetz@tesol.org
Exec Dir: Charles S Amorosino, Jr *E-mail:* camorosino@tesol.org
Founded: 1966
Professional Educator Association. Professional education related books.
ISBN Prefix(es): 0-939791
Number of titles published annually: 5 Print
Total Titles: 65 Print; 1 CD-ROM
Distributed by Alta Book Center; Delta Systems Inc; New Readers Press; Saddleback Educational
Distribution Center: Tesol Publications At Tasco, PO Box 753, Waldorf, MD 20604 *Toll Free Tel:* 888-891-0041 orders *E-mail:* tesolpubs@tasco1.com *Web Site:* www.tesol.org

Teaching & Learning Co
1204 Buchanan St, Carthage, IL 62321-0010
Mailing Address: PO Box 10, Carthage, IL 62321-0010
Tel: 217-357-2591 *Fax:* 217-357-6789
E-mail: customerservice@teachinglearning.com
Web Site: TeachingLearning.Com
Key Personnel
VP, Prodn: Jill Day *E-mail:* jday@teachinglearning.com
Founded: 1994
ISBN Prefix(es): 1-57310
Number of titles published annually: 45 Print
Total Titles: 300 Print

§Teaching Strategies
PO Box 42243, Washington, DC 20015
Tel: 202-362-7543 *Toll Free Tel:* 800-637-3652
Fax: 202-364-7273
E-mail: info@teachingstrategies.com
Web Site: www.teachingstrategies.com
Key Personnel
Dir, Mktg & Busn Devt: Larry Bram
E-mail: larry@teachingstrategies.com
Founded: 1988
Curriculum & training materials for early childhood education (birth-age 8) & parent's guides; web subscription service.
ISBN Prefix(es): 1-879537; 0-9602892
Number of titles published annually: 4 Print
Total Titles: 42 Print
Distributor for Gryphon House

Technical Association of the Pulp & Paper Industry (TAPPI)
15 Technology Pkwy S, Norcross, GA 30092
Mailing Address: PO Box 105113, Atlanta, GA 30348-5113
Tel: 770-446-1400 *Toll Free Tel:* 800-332-8686
Fax: 770-446-6947
E-mail: webmaster@tappi.org
Web Site: www.tappi.org
Key Personnel
Corp Rel Dir: Clare Regan
Publg Dir: Mary Beth Cornell
Founded: 1915
Technical books published on pulp & paper manufacture & related topics.
ISBN Prefix(es): 0-89852
Number of titles published annually: 12 Print
Total Titles: 95 Print
Distributed by American Technical Publishers

Technical Books for the Layperson Inc
PO Box 391, Lake Grove, NY 11755
SAN: 297-7184
Tel: 540-877-1477 *Fax:* 540-877-1477
E-mail: tbl_inc@yahoo.com
Web Site: tblbooks.com
Key Personnel
Rep: Mary Lewis
Founded: 1992
General nonfiction. Reader-friendly paperback, non-technical reference books on technical topics. Frequently revised to stay current with technical changes in a given field.
ISBN Prefix(es): 1-881818
Number of titles published annually: 3 Print
Total Titles: 4 Print

§Technology Training Systems Inc (TTS)
3131 S Vaughn Way, Suite 300, Aurora, CO 80014-3503
Tel: 303-368-0300 *Toll Free Tel:* 800-676-8871
Fax: 303-368-0312
E-mail: info@myplantstraining.com
Web Site: www.myplantstraining.com
Key Personnel
Mgr & Dir, Lib Sales & MPT.com: Jay Pankoff *Tel:* 303-368-0300 ext 117 *E-mail:* jayp@ttseagle.com
Founded: 1983
Training textbooks, process plant training & safety, on-line training.
ISBN Prefix(es): 1-57431
Number of titles published annually: 175 Print; 1 CD-ROM; 30 Online
Total Titles: 175 Print; 65 CD-ROM; 39 Online

§Temple University Press
Division of Temple University-of the Commonwealth System of Higher Education
1601 N Broad St, 083-42, USB Room 306, Philadelphia, PA 19122-6099
SAN: 202-7666
Tel: 215-204-8787 *Toll Free Tel:* 800-447-1656
Fax: 215-204-4719
E-mail: tempress@temple.edu
Web Site: www.temple.edu/tempress *Cable:* TEMPRESS
Key Personnel
Dir: Alex Holzman *Tel:* 215-204-3436 *E-mail:* aholzman@temple.edu
Rts & Perms & Intl Rts: Matthew Kull *Tel:* 215-204-5707 *E-mail:* matthew.kull@temple.edu
Asst Dir & Ed-in-Chief: Janet Francendese *Tel:* 215-204-3437 *E-mail:* janet.francendese@temple.edu
Sr Ed: Micah Kleit *Tel:* 215-204-3439 *E-mail:* micah.kleit@temple.edu; Peter Wissoker *Tel:* 202-986-7379 *E-mail:* peter.wissoker@temple.edu
Asst Ed: William M Hammell *Tel:* 215-204-3782 *E-mail:* william.hammell@temple.edu

Asst Dir & Mktg Dir: Ann-Marie Anderson *Tel:* 215-204-1108 *E-mail:* ann-marie.anderson@temple.edu
Adv & Promo Mgr: Irene Imperio Kull *Tel:* 215-204-1099 *E-mail:* irene.imperio@temple.edu
Publg Mgr: Gary Kramer *Tel:* 215-204-3440 *E-mail:* gkramer@temple.edu
Fin Mgr: Barry Adams *Tel:* 215-204-3444 *E-mail:* barry.adams@temple.edu
Cust Serv Mgr: Karen Baker *Tel:* 215-204-8606 *E-mail:* karen.baker@temple.edu
Asst Dir, Prodn & Electronic Pub: Charles Ault *Tel:* 215-204-3389 *E-mail:* charles.ault@temple.edu
Founded: 1969
Scholarly books; all regional interests.
ISBN Prefix(es): 0-87722; 1-56639; 1-59213
Number of titles published annually: 55 Print
Total Titles: 1,250 Print
Online services available through netLibrary.
Distributor for Asian American Writers Workshop
Foreign Rep(s): Baker & Taylor Ltd (Asia, Pacific, Worldwide exc Canada); Eurospan (Europe); Lynn McClory (Canada); Royden Muranaka, East-West Export Books (Asia, Pacific)
Returns: Temple University Press Chicago Distribution Center, 11030 S Langley, Chicago, IL 60628 *Tel:* 773-702-7062 *Toll Free Tel:* 800-621-2736 *Fax:* 773-702-7208 *Toll Free Fax:* 800-621-8476
Warehouse: Temple University Press Chicago Distribution Center, 11030 S Langley, Chicago, IL 60628, Contact: Sue Tranchita *Tel:* 773-702-7014 *Toll Free Tel:* 800-621-2736 *Fax:* 773-702-7002 *Toll Free Fax:* 800-621-8476
Membership(s): Association of American University Presses; Society for Scholarly Publishing

Templegate Publishers
302 E Adams St, Springfield, IL 62701
SAN: 123-0115
Mailing Address: PO Box 5152, Springfield, IL 62705-5152
Tel: 217-522-3353 (edit & sales); 217-522-3354 (billing) *Toll Free Tel:* 800-367-4844 (orders only) *Fax:* 217-522-3362
E-mail: wisdom@templegate.com; orders@templegate.com (sales)
Web Site: www.templegate.com *Cable:* OBELISK
Key Personnel
Dir & Owner: Thomas M Garvey *E-mail:* tmg@templegate.com
Exec Ed, Rts & Perms & Publicity: John Fisher
Sales & Adv Mgr, ISBN & Lib Sales Dir: Elaine Garvey
Founded: 1947
Nonfiction.
ISBN Prefix(es): 0-87243
Number of titles published annually: 12 Print
Total Titles: 225 Print
Imprints: Octavo Press
Foreign Rep(s): Bayard Distributing (Canada); Gracewing (Europe); Rainbow Book Agencies (Australia)

Templeton Foundation Press
5 Radnor Corporate Ctr, Suite 120, 100 Matsonford Rd, Radnor, PA 19087
Tel: 610-971-2670 *Toll Free Tel:* 800-561-3367
Fax: 610-971-2672
E-mail: tfp@templetonpress.org
Web Site: www.templetonpress.org
Key Personnel
Dir, Pubns: Joanna V Hill *E-mail:* jhill@templetonpress.org
Acqs Ed: Laura G Barrett *E-mail:* lbarrett@templetonpress.org
Busn Mgr: Ruth Macauley Barrett *E-mail:* rbarrett@templetonpress.org
Founded: 1987
Focus on science & religion, spirituality & health, character development & business.
ISBN Prefix(es): 1-890151; 1-932031

Number of titles published annually: 12 Print; 4 E-Book
Total Titles: 60 Print; 16 E-Book
Foreign Rights: DeepBooks Ltd (UK, Ireland, Europe); Hushion House Publishing Ltd (Canada)
Advertising Agency: Denhard & Stewart, 240 Madison Ave, New York, NY 10016, Contact: Jeff Stewart *Tel:* 212-481-3200 *Fax:* 212-689-9749 *E-mail:* jstewart22@aol.com
Billing Address: Chicago Distribution Ctr, 11030 S Langley, Chicago, IL 60628 *Toll Free Tel:* 800-621-2736 *Toll Free Fax:* 800-621-8476
Membership(s): Network of Alternatives for Publishers, Retailers & Artists Inc; Publishers Marketing Association

Temporal Mechanical Press
Division of Enos Mills Cabin Museum & Gallery
6760 Hwy 7, Estes Park, CO 80517-6404
Tel: 970-586-4706
E-mail: enosmillscbn@earthlink.net
Web Site: www.geocities.com/soho/nook/7587
Key Personnel
Owner: Elizabeth Mills; Eryn Mills
ISBN Prefix(es): 1-928878
Total Titles: 22 Print

Ten Speed Press
PO Box 7123, Berkeley, CA 94707
SAN: 202-7674
Tel: 510-559-1600 *Toll Free Tel:* 800-841-Book
Fax: 510-559-1629; 510-524-1052 (general)
E-mail: order@tenspeed.com
Web Site: www.tenspeed.com
Key Personnel
Pres & Publr: Philip Wood
Man Ed: Lorena Jones
Man Ed, Celestial Arts: Veronica Randall
VP & Spec Sales Mgr: Joann Deck
Publicity Dir: Kristin Casemore
Cont: Rakhi Rao
Founded: 1971
Trade, paperbound, fine editions: Americana & regional, art, book trade, business, history, social sciences, cooking, gardening, sports, hobbies, recreation, health, meditation, philosophy, education, humor, children's books, animal/pet, self-help, how-to, travel, reference.
ISBN Prefix(es): 0-913668; 0-89815
Number of titles published annually: 100 Print
Total Titles: 587 Print
Imprints: Double Elephant Books; Tricycle Press
Subsidiaries: Audio Literature; Celestial Arts
Distributor for Audio Literature; Lanier Publishing International
Foreign Rep(s): Airlift Books (UK, Europe); Berkeley Books (Malaysia, Singapore); E J Dwyer (Australia); Real Books (South Africa); Tandem Press (New Zealand); Ten Speed Press/PGW Sales Office (Canada)
Foreign Rights: Writer's House
Advertising Agency: Fifth Street Design
Warehouse: 1303 Ninth St, Berkeley, CA 94710

Teora USA LLC
2 Wisconsin Circle, Suite 870, Chevy Chase, MD 20815
Tel: 301-986-6990 *Toll Free Tel:* 800-358-3754
Fax: 301-986-6992 *Toll Free Fax:* 800-358-3754
E-mail: info@teora.com
Web Site: www.teorausa.com
Key Personnel
Pres: Teodor Raducanu
VP: Maria Nedelcu
ISBN Prefix(es): 1-59496
Number of titles published annually: 20 Print
Imprints: Teora
Membership(s): Publishers Marketing Association

TESOL, see Teachers of English to Speakers of Other Languages Inc (TESOL)

Teton New Media

4125 S Hwy 89, Suite 1, Jackson, WY 83001
Mailing Address: PO Box 4833, Jackson, WY 83001
Tel: 307-732-0028 *Toll Free Tel:* 877-306-9793
Fax: 307-734-0841
Key Personnel
Mktg Dir: Sara Scartz *Tel:* 307-732-0028 ext 101
E-mail: sara@tetonnm.com
Founded: 1999 (By John Sphar & Carroll Cann)
Health science publisher that focuses on producing high quality, affordable veterinary text & reference books.
Number of titles published annually: 6 Print; 2 CD-ROM
Total Titles: 25 Print; 18 CD-ROM
Distributed by Blackwells; LifeLearn; Logan Brothers; Rittenhouse; Yankee
Distributor for Barnes & Noble; Borders; Life-Learn

Tetra Press

Division of Pfizer Inc
3001 Commerce St, Blacksburg, VA 24060
Tel: 540-951-5400 *Toll Free Tel:* 800-526-0650
Fax: 540-951-5415
E-mail: consumer@tetra-fish.com
Web Site: www.tetra-fish.com
Key Personnel
Prod Mgr: Wayne Martin
Fish, reptiles, amphibians & ponds.
ISBN Prefix(es): 1-56465
Number of titles published annually: 3 Print
Total Titles: 114 Print
Branch Office(s)
Speciality Book Marketing Inc, 443 Park Ave S, New York, NY 10016, Contact: William Corsa
Distributed by Voyageur Press

Texas A&M University Press

Division of Texas A&M University
John H Lindsey Bldg, Lewis St, 4354 TAMU, College Station, TX 77843-4354
SAN: 207-5237
Tel: 979-845-1436 *Toll Free Tel:* 800-826-8911 (orders) *Fax:* 979-847-8752 *Toll Free Fax:* 888-617-2421 (orders)
E-mail: fdl@tampress.tamu.edu
Web Site: www.tamu.edu/upress/
Key Personnel
Dir: Charles Backus
Ed-in-Chief & Man Ed: Mary Lenn Dixon
Design Mgr: Mary Ann Jacob
Prodn Mgr: Susan Pettey
Mgr Cust Rel: Sharon Mills
Fin Mgr: Dianna Sells
Mktg Mgr & Lib Sales Dir: Gayla Christiansen
Trade Sales: Steve Griffis
Rts & Perms & Asst to Dir: Linda Salitros
E-mail: lls@tampress.tamu.edu
Founded: 1974
Scholarly nonfiction, regional studies, economics, history, environmental history, natural history, presidential studies, anthropology; US-Mexican borderlands studies; women's studies; nautical archaeology; military studies; Eastern European studies; agriculture; Texas history, literature & archaeology.
ISBN Prefix(es): 0-89096
Number of titles published annually: 40 Print
Total Titles: 609 Print; 4 Audio
Distributor for Baylor University Press; McWhiney Foundation Press; Sam Houston State University; Southern Methodist University; Texas Almanac/Dallas Morning News; Texas Christian University Press; Texas Review Press; Texas State Historical Association; University of North Texas Press
Foreign Rep(s): J Trevor Brown (Europe); L D Clepper (Latin America); EWEB (Australia, Asia, UK, Ireland, Europe, Middle East, New Zealand, Pacific Islands); Kellington & Associates (Canada); Texas A&M University Press
Foreign Rights: Linda Salitros, Tamu Press

Texas Christian University Press

PO Box 298300, Fort Worth, TX 76129
SAN: 202-7690
Tel: 817-257-7822 *Toll Free Tel:* 800-826-8911
Fax: 817-257-5075 *Toll Free Fax:* 888-617-2421
Web Site: www.prs.tcu.edu/prs/
Key Personnel
Dir & Rts & Perms: Judy Alter *E-mail:* j.alter@tcu.edu
Acqs: James W Lee *Tel:* 817-257-6872 *E-mail:* j.lee@tcu.edu
Founded: 1966
Scholarly research & regional.
ISBN Prefix(es): 0-912646; 0-87565
Number of titles published annually: 6 Print
Total Titles: 208 Print; 1 E-Book; 1 Audio
Distributed by Texas A&M University Press
Foreign Rep(s): Texas A&M University Press
Shipping Address: Tamus 4354, College Station, TX 77843-4354
Warehouse: Tamus 4354, College Station, TX 77843 *Toll Free Tel:* 800-826-8911
Membership(s): Association of American University Presses

§University of Texas Press

Division of University of Texas
PO Box 7819, Austin, TX 78713-7819
SAN: 212-9876
Tel: 512-471-7233 *Fax:* 512-232-7178
E-mail: utpress@uts.cc.utexas.edu
Web Site: www.utexas.edu/utpress
Key Personnel
CFO: Joyce Lewandoski
Dir: Joanna Hitchcock
Ed-in-Chief: Theresa May
Acq Ed: Bill Bishell; Jim Burr
Mgr & Intl Rts Contact: Laura Bost
Mktg Mgr: Dave Hamrick
Asst Mktg Mgr: Nancy Bryan
Sales Mgr: Darrell Windham
Credit Mgr & Cust Serv: Shirley Stewart
Prodn Mgr: David Cavazos
Adv, Exhibits Mgr: Lauren Zachry-Reynolds
Founded: 1950
General scholarly nonfiction, Latin America, Middle Eastern studies, Southwest regional, social sciences, humanities & science, linguistics, architecture, classics, natural history, Latin American literature in translation.
ISBN Prefix(es): 0-292
Number of titles published annually: 90 Print
Total Titles: 1,000 Print; 1 CD-ROM; 1 Online
Distributor for Bat Conservation International; Institute for Mesoamerican Studies; Menil Foundation; Rothko Chapel; San Antonio Museum of Art; SUNY Albany; Texas Parks & Wildlife Department
Foreign Rep(s): Trevor Brown Associates (UK, Europe); Marketing Dept, University of Texas (Caribbean); Michael Romano (Australia, Canada, New Zealand); United Publishers Services (Japan)
Shipping Address: 2100 Comal, Austin, TX 78722
Membership(s): AAP; Association of American University Presses

Texas State Historical Association

Affiliate of Center for Studies in Texas History at the University of Texas at Austin
University Sta, DO-901, Austin, TX 78712
Tel: 512-471-1525 *Fax:* 512-471-1551
E-mail: comments@tsha.utexas.edu
Web Site: www.tsha.utexas.edu
Key Personnel
Dir: Ron Tyler

Asst Dir: George Ward
Founded: 1897
Books & articles related to Texas history.
ISBN Prefix(es): 0-87611
Number of titles published annually: 8 Print
Total Titles: 75 Print; 1 Online
Distributed by Texas A&M University Press

Texas Tech University Press

2903 Fourth St, Lubbock, TX 79412
Mailing Address: PO Box 41037, Lubbock, TX 79409-1037
Tel: 806-742-2982 *Toll Free Tel:* 800-832-4042
Fax: 806-742-2979
E-mail: ttup@ttu.edu
Web Site: www.ttup.ttu.edu
Key Personnel
Lit Ed & Intl Rts: Judith Keeling *Tel:* 800-832-4042 ext 305 *E-mail:* judith.keeling@ttu.edu
Busn Mgr: Joel J Nichols *Tel:* 800-832-4042 ext 302 *E-mail:* joel.nichols@ttu.edu
Prodn: Barbara Werden *Tel:* 800-832-4042 ext 310 *E-mail:* bwerden@ttu.edu
Mktg & Sales Mgr: Jeff Walters *Tel:* 800-832-4042 ext 315 *E-mail:* jeff.walters@ttu.edu
Warehouse Mgr: Ramon Luna *Tel:* 806-742-3337
Dir, Man Ed & Journals Mgr: Noel Parsons
E-mail: noel.parsons@ttu.edu
Founded: 1971
Scholarly books & journals: biological sciences, literary criticism, museum-related sciences, specialized regional, poetry, history, fiction.
ISBN Prefix(es): 0-89672
Number of titles published annually: 32 Print
Total Titles: 345 Print
Imprints: Double Mountain Books
Distributor for ICASALS
Foreign Rep(s): Trevor Brown Associates (UK, London, Western Europe)
Warehouse: Texas Tech University, Holden Hall Memorial Circle, Lubbock, TX 79409-1037

Texas Western Press

Affiliate of University of Texas at El Paso
c/o University of Texas at El Paso, 500 W University Ave, El Paso, TX 79968-0633
SAN: 202-7712
Tel: 915-747-5688 *Toll Free Tel:* 800-488-3789
Fax: 915-747-7515
E-mail: twpress@utep.edu
Web Site: www.utep.edu/~twp
Key Personnel
Dir: Jon Amastae *Tel:* 915-747-7895
E-mail: jamastae@utep.edu
Founded: 1952
Scholarly books on the history, art, photography & culture of the American Southwest.
ISBN Prefix(es): 0-87404
Number of titles published annually: 6 Print
Total Titles: 50 Print; 1 Audio
Imprints: Southwestern Studies
Distributed by University of Texas Press
Membership(s): American Association of University Presses

Texere

55 E 52 St, New York, NY 10055
Tel: 212-317-5511 *Fax:* 212-317-5178
E-mail: Firstname_Lastname@etexere.com
Web Site: www.etexere.com; www.etexere.co.uk
Key Personnel
CEO & Publr: Myles C Thompson
E-mail: Myles.Thompson@etexere.com
Exec VP & Dir, Mktg: Liana Thompson *Tel:* 212-317-5139 *E-mail:* Liana_Thompson@etexere.com
Founded: 2000
Specialize in serious nonfiction with strong emphasis on business including management, finance, investment, economics, strategy, leadership & interdisciplinary business.

ISBN Prefix(es): 0-75283; 1-58799; 0-75281; 0-75282; 1-84203
Number of titles published annually: 60 Print; 1 E-Book
Total Titles: 175 Print
Foreign Office(s): Texere Publishing Ltd, 71-77 Leadenhall St, London EC3A 3DE, United Kingdom *Tel:* (020) 7204 3644 *Fax:* (020) 7208 6701
Distributed by W W Norton & Co Inc; Penguin-Technology Group, A Division of Pearson Canada
Foreign Rep(s): APD Singapore Pte Ltd (Brunei, Cambodia, Indonesia, Singapore & Malaysia, Thailand, Vietnam); Asia Publisher Services (China & Taiwan, Hong Kong & Macao, Korea, Philippines); Jonathan Ball Publishers (South Africa); Andrew Durnell (Europe); Littlehampton Book Services Inc (UK, Worldwide); Maya Publishers PVT Ltd (Bangladesh, India, Sri Lanka); TEXERE Publishing (all other territories); Woodslane Pty Lyd (Australia)
Foreign Rights: Gail Blackhall
Advertising Agency: Bennett Book Advertising, 60 E 42 St, Suite 463, New York, NY 10165
Membership(s): AAP; ABA; BISG

TFH Publications Inc
Affiliate of Central Garden & Pet
61 Third Ave, Neptune City, NJ 07753
SAN: 202-7720
Mailing Address: PO Box 427, Neptune, NJ 07754
Tel: 732-988-8400 *Toll Free Tel:* 800-631-2188 *Fax:* 732-988-5466
E-mail: info@tfh.com
Web Site: www.tfh.com *Telex:* 13-2468 *Cable:* TFHBOOKS ASBURY PARK NJ
Key Personnel
Pres & CEO: Glen Axelrod
Dir, Mktg Admin: Vallerie Hersch
Founded: 1952
Reference books & specialty magazines.
ISBN Prefix(es): 0-87666; 0-86622; 0-7938
Number of titles published annually: 22 Print
Total Titles: 1,200 Print
Divisions: Nylabone Products
Foreign Rep(s): Brooklands Aquarium Ltd (New Zealand); H & L Pet Supplies Inc (Canada); Rolf C Hagen Ltd (Canada); Pet Care Dist (South Africa); TFH Pty Ltd (Australia); TFH Publications Ltd (England)

Thames & Hudson
500 Fifth Ave, New York, NY 10110
SAN: 202-5795
Tel: 212-354-3763 *Toll Free Tel:* 800-233-4830 *Fax:* 212-398-1252
E-mail: bookinfo@thames.wwnorton.com
Web Site: www.thamesandhudsonusa.com
Key Personnel
Pres: Peter Warner
VP, Subs Rts & Mktg: Susan Dwyer
Serial Rts & Publicity: Allyn Rippin
Perms: Lisa Ronga
Founded: 1977
Nonfiction trade, quality paperbacks & college texts on art, archaeology, architecture, crafts, history & photography.
ISBN Prefix(es): 0-500
Number of titles published annually: 100 Print
Total Titles: 1,000 Print
Distributed by W W Norton & Co Inc
Advertising Agency: Denhard & Stewart Inc
Shipping Address: National Book Co Inc, Keystone Industrial Park, Scranton, PA 18512
Membership(s): AAP; BISG

Theatre Communications Group Inc
520 Eighth Ave, New York, NY 10018
SAN: 210-9387

Tel: 212-609-5900 *Fax:* 212-609-5901
E-mail: tcg@tcg.org
Web Site: www.tcg.org
Key Personnel
VP, Pubns: Terence Nemeth
Edit Dir: Kathy Sova
Founded: 1961
Performing arts.
ISBN Prefix(es): 0-930452; 1-55936
Number of titles published annually: 16 Print
Total Titles: 210 Print
Distributor for Absolute Classics; Aurora Metro Publications; Nick Hern Books; Oberon Books; Padua Playwrights Press; PAJ Publications; Playwrights Canada Press; Martin E Segal Theatre Center Publications; Ubu Repertory Theatre Publications
Foreign Rep(s): Nick Hern Books (UK); Playwrights Canada Press (Canada)
Distribution Center: Consortium Book Sales & Distribution, 1045 Westgate Dr, St Paul, MN 55114 *Toll Free Tel:* 800-283-3572

Theosophical Publishing House/Quest Books
Division of The Theosophical Society in America
306 W Geneva Rd, Wheaton, IL 60187
SAN: 202-5698
Mailing Address: PO Box 270, Wheaton, IL 60189-0270
Tel: 630-665-0130 *Toll Free Tel:* 800-669-9425 *Fax:* 630-665-8791
E-mail: questbooks@theosmail.net
Web Site: www.questbooks.net
Key Personnel
Publg Mgr: Sharron Dorr
Rts & Perms: Karen Schweizer
Opers Mgr: Betty Shimp
Intl Rts: DeLacy Sarantos
Mktg Coord: Nicole Krier
E-mail: questmarketing@theosmail.net
Publicity: Andy Lauffer
Founded: 1965
Religion, philosophy, psychology, transpersonal psychology, metaphysics, holistic healing, astrology & yoga; trade cloth originals, trade paperback originals & reprints.
ISBN Prefix(es): 0-8356
Number of titles published annually: 12 Print
Total Titles: 20 Audio
Imprints: Quest Books
Foreign Rep(s): Airlift Book Company (UK, Europe); Alternative Books (South Africa); Aquamarin Verlag (Germany); Brumby Books (Australia); Theosofische Vereniging in Nederland (Netherlands); Theosophical Publishing House (India); Theosophical Publishing House Manila (Philippines); Theosophical Society in New Zealand (New Zealand)
Distribution Center: National Book Network, 15200 NBN Way, Blue Ridge Summit, PA 17214

§Theosophical University Press
Affiliate of Theosophical Society (Pasadena)
PO Box C, Pasadena, CA 91109-7107
SAN: 205-4299
Tel: 626-798-3378 *Fax:* 626-798-4749
E-mail: tupress@theosociety.org
Web Site: www.theosociety.org
Key Personnel
Mgr & Intl Rts: Will Thackara
Dir: Grace F Knoche
Cust Serv: Trudy Rugland
Founded: 1886
Quality theosophical literature.
ISBN Prefix(es): 0-911500; 1-55700
Number of titles published annually: 5 Print; 5 Online
Total Titles: 84 Print; 101 E-Book; 5 Audio
Imprints: Sunrise Library
Foreign Office(s): Theosophical University Press Agency, 664 Glenhuntly Rd, Caulfield South,

Victoria 3162, Australia, Contact: Lo Guest
E-mail: loli@netspace.net.au
Pasadena-Centrum, c/o Tor Wahrn, Gomstigen 4C, SF-02130 Esbo, Finland
Theosophischer Verlag GmbH, Brunnenstr II, 56414 Hundsangen, Germany, Contact: Jochen Hannappel *E-mail:* info@theosophischer-verlag. de *Web Site:* www.theosophischer-verlag.de
Theosophical University Press Agency, Daal en Bergselaan 68, 2565 AG The Hague, Netherlands *E-mail:* tupa@theosofie.net
Theosophical University Press Agency S African Agency, PO Box 504, Constantia 7848, South Africa, Contact: Dewald Bester *E-mail:* dewald_b@yahoo.com
Teosofiska Bokforlaget, Barnhusgatan 13, 411 11 Goteborg, Sweden, Contact: Herbert Edlund *E-mail:* teobok@goteborg.utfors.se
The Theosophical Society, PO Box 60, Exeter, Devon EX4 4YP, United Kingdom, Contact: Renee Hall *E-mail:* ts.pasadena@eclipse.co.uk
Warehouse: 2416 N Lake Ave, Altadena, CA 91001, Contact: Will Thackara *E-mail:* tupress@theosociety.org

§Theta Reports
Subsidiary of PJB Publications Ltd
1775 Broadway, Suite 511, New York, NY 10019
Tel: 212-262-8230 *Fax:* 212-262-8234
Web Site: www.thetareports.com
Key Personnel
Account Exec: Lisa Schacterle
E-mail: lschacterle@thetareports.com
Man Ed: Oliver Yun
Founded: 1970
Market research reports in healthcare, biotechnology & pharmaceutical; monthly newsletter & custom consulting services.
Number of titles published annually: 50 Print
Online services available through Dialog.

Thieme New York
Subsidiary of Georg Thieme Verlag
333 Seventh Ave, 5th fl, New York, NY 10001
SAN: 202-7399
Tel: 212-760-0888 *Toll Free Tel:* 800-782-3488 *Fax:* 212-947-1112
E-mail: customerservice@thieme.com
Web Site: www.thieme.com *Cable:* THIEMEMED NEWYORK
Key Personnel
Pres: Brian Scanlan *Tel:* 212-584-4707 *E-mail:* bscanlan@thieme.com
CFO & VP, Fin: Peter Van Woerden *Tel:* 212-584-4677 *E-mail:* pvanwoerden@thieme.com
Sales Dir: Ross Lumpkin *Tel:* 212-584-4666 *E-mail:* rlumpkin@thieme.com
Founded: 1953
Books, journals, textbooks in clinical medicine, dentistry, speech & hearing, allied health, audiology; videotapes in neurosurgery & head & neck surgery.
ISBN Prefix(es): 0-913258; 0-86577
Number of titles published annually: 50 Print; 3 CD-ROM
Total Titles: 505 Print
Foreign Office(s): Georg Thieme Verlag, Ruedigerstrasse 14, 70469 Stuttgart, Germany
Foreign Rep(s): Elsevier (Australia); Login Canada (Canada); Login International (Brazil)
Foreign Rights: Barbara Pfeifer (Worldwide)
Advertising Agency: Cunningham Associates *Tel:* 201-767-4170
Warehouse: Maple Press Fulfillment Ctr, York County Industrial Park, Box M-100, York, PA 17405

Thinkers' Press Inc
1101 W Fourth St, Davenport, IA 52802
SAN: 176-4632
Mailing Address: PO Box 3037, Davenport, IA 52802-3037

Tel: 563-323-7117 *Toll Free Tel:* 800-397-7117
  Fax: 563-323-0511
E-mail: tpi@chessco.com
Web Site: www.chessco.com
Key Personnel
CEO: Bob Long *E-mail:* blong@chessco.com
Founded: 1967
Publisher of mostly books on chess & some other
  related areas; software, online titles, videos,
  etc. having to do with the game of chess.
ISBN Prefix(es): 0-938650; 1-888710
Number of titles published annually: 4 Print; 100
  Online
Total Titles: 99 Print; 1,500 Online
Distributor for Chess Enterprises; Hypermodern
  Press; SIEditrice; Chess Stars

§Thinking Publications
Division of McKinley Co Inc
424 Galloway, Eau Claire, WI 54703
Mailing Address: PO Box 163, Eau Claire, WI
  54702-0163
Tel: 715-832-2488 *Toll Free Tel:* 800-225-4769
  Fax: 715-832-9082 *Toll Free Fax:* 800-828-
  8885
E-mail: custserv@thinkingpublications.com
Web Site: www.thinkingpublications.com
Key Personnel
Ed-in-Chief: Nancy McKinley *E-mail:* nancy@
  thinkingpublications.com
COO: Linda Schreiber *E-mail:* linda@
  thinkingpublications.com
Founded: 1982
Books, educational games & instructional cards,
  university textbooks & software. Subjects in-
  clude speech-language pathology & communi-
  cation disorders.
ISBN Prefix(es): 0-930599; 1-888222; 1-932054
Number of titles published annually: 20 Print; 3
  CD-ROM; 15 Online; 1 E-Book
Total Titles: 150 Print; 9 CD-ROM; 150 Online;
  1 E-Book

Third World Press
7822 S Dobson Ave, Chicago, IL 60619
Mailing Address: PO Box 19730, Chicago, IL
  60619
Tel: 773-651-0700 *Fax:* 773-651-7286
E-mail: twpress3@aol.com
Web Site: www.thirdworldpressinc.com
Key Personnel
Publr: Haki R Madhubuti
Ed: Gwendolyn Mitchell
Founded: 1967
Publishers of quality Black fiction, nonfiction, po-
  etry, drama, young adult & children literature;
  primarily adult literature.
ISBN Prefix(es): 0-88378
Number of titles published annually: 6 Print
Total Titles: 80 Print
Distributed by Frontline International; Partners
  Book Distributing; Red Sea Press

Thomas Brothers Maps
17731 Cowan, Irvine, CA 92614
Tel: 949-852-9189 *Fax:* 949-757-1564
E-mail: webmaster@thomas.com
Web Site: www.randmcnally.com
Key Personnel
VP & Gen Mgr: Jim Welch
Founded: 1915
Complete line of street guides, atlases & wall
  maps for the West Coast & East Coast.
ISBN Prefix(es): 0-88130
Number of titles published annually: 132 Print
Total Titles: 132 Print

Charles C Thomas Publisher Ltd
2600 S First St, Springfield, IL 62704
SAN: 201-9485
Tel: 217-789-8980 *Toll Free Tel:* 800-258-8980
  Fax: 217-789-9130

E-mail: books@ccthomas.com
Web Site: www.ccthomas.com
Key Personnel
Pres: Michael Payne Thomas
Adv Mgr: Claire Slagle
Treas: Darlene McCarty
Founded: 1927
Medicine, allied health sciences, science, tech-
  nology, education, public administration, law
  enforcement, behavioral & social sciences, spe-
  cial education.
ISBN Prefix(es): 0-398
Number of titles published annually: 60 Print
Total Titles: 800 Print
Advertising Agency: Thomas Advertising Agency

Thomas Geale Publications Inc
PO Box 370540, Montara, CA 94037-0540
Tel: 650-728-5219 *Toll Free Tel:* 800-554-5457
  Fax: 650-728-0918
Key Personnel
Pres: Sydney Tyler-Parker
Sec: Nancy L Geale
Founded: 1982
Curriculum for schools, preschool through grade
  8; general educational materials, reading &
  thinking.
Number of titles published annually: 20 Print
Total Titles: 19 Print
Imprints: Just Think®; Stretch Think®; Thing
  Quest®; Young Think®
Foreign Rights: Nederlands Corp (Japan)
Shipping Address: 583 Sixth St, Montara, CA
  94037

§Thomas Nelson Inc
501 Nelson Place, Nashville, TN 37214
SAN: 209-3820
Mailing Address: PO Box 141000, Nashville, TN
  37214-1000
Tel: 615-889-9000 *Toll Free Tel:* 800-251-4000
  Fax: 615-902-1610
E-mail: publicity@thomasnelson.com
Web Site: www.thomasnelson.com *Cable:*
  NELSONASH
Key Personnel
Chmn & CEO: Sam Moore
Pres: Michael Hyatt
Exec VP & Sec: Joe Powers
Exec VP: Philip Stoner
Sr VP, Opers: Vance Lawson
Sr VP & Publr, Gen Trade Publg Div: David
  Dunham
VP & Gen Counsel: Eric Heyden
VP, Mktg Servs: Jeff Gott
Exec Dir, Fin: Troy Edens
Sales Mgr: Jerry Park
Intl Sales: Dan Johnson
Cust Rel: Mike Mitchell
Founded: 1961
Bibles & Testaments, trade, Christian & inspira-
  tional books, stationery gift items.
ISBN Prefix(es): 0-8407
Number of titles published annually: 515 Print
Total Titles: 3,500 Print; 6 CD-ROM; 30 Audio
Imprints: Catholic Bible Press; Markings; Re-
  gency
Subsidiaries: Editorial Caribe Inc; C R Gibson;
  Word Inc
Divisions: The Varsity Co
Distributed by Winston-Derek
Distributor for Discovery House; Focus on the
  Family; Oliver-Nelson (Atlanta, GA); Janet
  Thoma Books (SC)
Foreign Rep(s): Angela Gottlieb; Yvette Lopez;
  Harley Rollins; Snapdragon Productions; Lew
  Ullian
Foreign Rights: Winford Bluth
Advertising Agency: The Admasters
Shipping Address: 506 Nelson Place, Nashville,
  TN 37214
See separate listing for:
Caribe Betania Editores

Tommy Nelson
W Publishing Group

Thomas Publications
3245 Fairfield Rd, Gettysburg, PA 17325
Mailing Address: PO Box 3031, Gettysburg, PA
  17325
Tel: 717-642-6600 *Toll Free Tel:* 800-840-6782
  Fax: 717-642-5555
E-mail: thomaspub@blazenet.net
Web Site: www.thomaspublications.com
Key Personnel
Owner: Dean S Thomas
Mktg Dir: Truman Eyler
Founded: 1986
Civil War, U Boats, historical, all nonfiction.
ISBN Prefix(es): 0-939631; 1-57747
Number of titles published annually: 10 Print
Total Titles: 135 Print

William A Thomas Braille Bookstore
Division of Braille International Inc
3290 SE Slater St, Stuart, FL 34997
Tel: 772-286-8366 *Toll Free Tel:* 888-336-3142
  Fax: 772-286-8909
Web Site: www.brailleintl.org
Key Personnel
Pres: Jamie Redditt
Founded: 1992
Literary braille publisher, children & adult, fiction
  & nonfiction, children series in braille/print for-
  mat.
ISBN Prefix(es): 1-56956
Number of titles published annually: 155 Print
Total Titles: 1,000 Print

§Thomson Delmar Learning
Formerly Delmar Learning
Division of The Thomson Corp
5 Maxwell Dr, Clifton Park, NY 12065-8007
SAN: 206-7544
Mailing Address: PO Box 8007, Clifton Park, NY
  12065-8007
Tel: 518-464-3500 *Toll Free Tel:* 800-347-7707
  (cust serv); 800-998-7498 *Fax:* 518-464-0393
  Toll Free Fax: 800-487-8488 (cust serv)
Web Site: www.thomson.com; www.
  delmarlearning.com *Telex:* 38-6411
Key Personnel
Pres: Greg Burnell
VP, Learning Solutions: Nancy K Roberson
CFO: Mark Goldstein
VP, Prodn: Frederick J Sharer
VP, Sales & Mktg: Steve Zlotnick
VP, HR: Mark Howe
VP & Chief Technol Officer: Dan Conrad
Founded: 1945
Textbooks, software & supplementary, multi-
  media, professional reference & custom pub-
  lishing & training materials for post-secondary
  & secondary schools in business, industry &
  government education, retail, education, elec-
  tronics, technology, nursing & allied health,
  education & child care, agriculture, mathematics & vocational studies, automotive, travel &
  tourism & hospitality, cosmetology, engineering, paralegal, CAD, building trades, multimedia, graphic arts, distance education.
ISBN Prefix(es): 0-8273; 1-56253; 0-7668; 1-
  4018
Number of titles published annually: 200 Print
Total Titles: 8,653 Print; 595 CD-ROM; 5 Online;
  8 E-Book; 1,681 Audio
Imprints: Autodesk Press; Chilton; Frontline; Mi-
  lady; NetLearning; ONWord; PDR; Singular;
  Skidmore-Roth; West (Legal Studies)
Branch Office(s)
Thomson Learning International Division, 290
  Harbor Dr, 2nd fl, Stamford, CT 06902-7477
  Tel: 203-969-8700 *Fax:* 203-969-8751
Distributor for Aspire; Autodata; BOCA/ICC;
  CDX Global; Chilton; Haynes; Holt Enter-
  prises; LearningExpress; Meredith; NFPA;

Prompt; Scott Jones Publishing; Seloc; Truck-load Carrier Assoc; Video Active Productions
Foreign Rep(s): Paraninfo (Spain & Portugal); Thomson Learning (Asia, UK, Latin America); Nelson Thomson Learning (Australia & New Zealand, Canada)
Foreign Rights: Paraninfo (Spain); Thomson Learning (Asia, UK, Latin America)
Warehouse: Thomson Distribution Center, 10650 Toebben Dr, Independence, KY 41051

§Thomson Financial Publishing
Subsidiary of The Thomson Corp
4709 W Golf Rd, Suite 600, Skokie, IL 60076-1253
Tel: 847-676-9600; 847-677-8037
   Toll Free Tel: 800-321-3373 *Fax:* 847-676-9616
E-mail: custservice@tfp.com
Web Site: www.tfp.com; www.tgbr.com
Key Personnel
Man Dir: Glenn Gottfried
VP, Prodn: Terry Shark *Tel:* 770-381-2511 ext 202
HR: Patty Pickett
Founded: 1876
Leading worldwide provider of information on depository financial institutions throughout the world; specialize in Internet references/directories; software; databases.
ISBN Prefix(es): 1-56310
Number of titles published annually: 30 Print; 1 CD-ROM; 2 E-Book
Total Titles: 30 Print; 4 CD-ROM; 3 E-Book
Foreign Office(s): Level 7, 34 Hunter St, Sydney NSW 2000, Australia, Gen Mgr: Omer Soker *Tel:* (02) 9233-4855 *Fax:* (02) 9223-5275
Aldgate House, 33 Aldgate High St, London ECSN 1DL, United Kingdom, Gen Mgr: Malcolm Taylor *Tel:* (020) 7369 7750 *Fax:* (020) 7369 7751

§Thomson Gale
Unit of The Thomson Corp
27500 Drake Rd, Farmington Hills, MI 48331-3535
SAN: 213-4373
Tel: 248-699-4253 *Toll Free Tel:* 800-347-4253
   Fax: 248-699-8070 *Toll Free Fax:* 800-414-5043
E-mail: galeord@gale.com
Web Site: www.gale.com
Key Personnel
Pres: Allen W Paschal
Exec VP & CFO: Dennis Stepaniak
Exec VP, Edit & Prodn: Dennis Poupard
Exec VP, Opers: Edward W Pastorius
Exec VP, Global Mkt & Cust/Mkt Servs: Dedria Bryfonski
Exec VP, K-12 Mkt: Ben Mondloch
Exec VP, Pub/Academic Libs: Rich Foley
Exec VP, HR: Karla Kretzschmer
Founded: 1954
Electronic reference, research publishing & reference books.
ISBN Prefix(es): 0-8103; 0-7876; 3-598; 0-02-865; 0-684-806
Number of titles published annually: 50 Print
Imprints: Blackbirch Press; Charles Scribner's Sons; Five Star; Graham & Whiteside; Greenhaven Press; G K Hall & Co; K G Saur; Kidhaven Press; Lucent Books Inc; Macmillan Reference USA; Primary Source Media; St James Press; Schirmer Reference; Sleeping Bear Press; The Taft Group; Thorndike Press; Twayne Publishers; U X L; Wheeler Publishing
Advertising Agency: Sawyer, Finn & Thatcher
Distribution Center: 7625 Empire Dr, Florence, KY 41042
See separate listing for:
Greenhaven Press®
Lucent Books Inc
Sleeping Bear Press™
Thorndike Press

§Thomson Learning Inc
Division of The Thomson Corp
200 First Stamford Place, Suite 400, Stamford, CT 06902
Tel: 203-539-8000 *Fax:* 203-539-7581
E-mail: communications@thomsonlearning.com
Web Site: www.thomson.com/learning
Key Personnel
Pres & CEO: Ronald H Schlosser
Pres & CEO, Lifelong Learning Group: Eric Shuman
Pres & CEO, Academic & International Group: Ronald G Dunn
CFO: Dennis Beckingham
Sr VP & Chief Technol Officer: Carl Urbania
Sr VP, Corp Mktg: Dana Prestigiacomo
Sr VP, Strategic Planning & Busn Devt: Richard Benson-Armer
Sr VP, Opers: Charles Siegel
Sr VP, HR: Steve Mower
The Thomson Corp (www.thomson.com), with 2003 revenues from continuing operations of $7.44 billion, is a global leader in providing integrated information solutions to business & professional customers. Thomson provides value-added information, software tools & applications to more than 20 million users in the fields of law, tax, accounting, financial services, higher education, reference information, corporate training & assessment, scientific research & healthcare. With operational headquarters in Stamford, CT. Thomson has approximately 38,000 employees & provides services in approximately 130 countries. The Corporation's common shares are listed on the NY & Toronto stock exchanges (NYSE; TOC; TSX; TOC). Its learning businesses & brands serve the needs of individuals, learning institutions, corporations & government agencies with products & services for both traditional & distributed learning.
Subsidiaries: Thomson Course Technology (www.course.com); Thomson Custom Publishing (www.thomsoncustom.com); Thomson Delmar Learning (www.delmarlearning.com); Thomson Education Direct (www.educationdirect.com); Thomson Gale (www.gale.com); Thomson Heinle (www.heinle.com); Thomson Higher Education (www.thomson.com/learning); Thomson Learning Asia (www.thomsonlearningasia.com); Thomson Learning Australia (www.thomsonlearning.com.au); Thomson Learning EMEA (www.thomsonlearning.co.uk); Thomson Learning Iberoamerica (www.thomsonlearning.com.mx); Thomson Nelson in Canada (www.nelson.com); Thomson NETg (www.netg.com); Thomson Paraninfo (www.paraninfo.es); Thomson Peterson's (www.petersons.com); Thomson Prometric (www.prometric.com); Thomson South-Western (www.swlearning.com); Thomson Wadsworth (www.wadsworth.com)
Billing Address: Thomson Learning Distribution Center, 10650 Toebben Dr, Independence, KY 41051 *Toll Free Tel:* 877-201-3962 *Toll Free Fax:* 800-248-4724
Orders to: Thomson Learning Distribution Center, 10650 Toebben Dr, Independence, KY 41051
Returns: Thomson Learning Distribution Center, 10650 Toebben Dr, Independence, KY 41051 *Tel:* 859-525-2230 *Toll Free Fax:* 800-248-4724
Warehouse: Thomson Learning Distribution Center, 10650 Toebben Dr, Independence, KY 41051
Distribution Center: Thomson Learning Distribution Center, 10650 Toebben Dr, Independence, KY 41051 *Tel:* 859-525-2230 *Toll Free Fax:* 800-248-4724 *E-mail:* esales@thomsonlearning.com
Membership(s): AAP
See separate listing for:
Thomson Delmar Learning
Wadsworth Publishing

§Thomson Peterson's
Division of Thomson Learning Inc
2000 Lenox Dr, Lawrenceville, NJ 08648
SAN: 282-1591
Mailing Address: PO Box 67005, Lawrenceville, NJ 08648
Tel: 609-896-1800 *Toll Free Tel:* 800-338-3282
   Toll Free Fax: 800-772-2465
E-mail: sales@petersons.com
Web Site: www.petersons.com
Key Personnel
VP, Busn Devt & Mktg: Michael Fleischner
Founded: 1966
Education, career books, software & CD-ROM, data licensing, test preparation, financial aid & adult education.
ISBN Prefix(es): 1-56079; 0-7689
Number of titles published annually: 150 Print
Total Titles: 300 Print
Imprints: Peterson's/Pacesetter Books
Foreign Rep(s): Time-Warner
Foreign Rights: Ann-Christine Daniellsson Agency (Scandinavia); Frederique Parretta Agency (France, French Canada); International Editors (Latin America, Spain); Pikarski (Israel); Tuttle-Mori Agency (Japan, Thailand)
Warehouse: Thomson Distribution Center, 7625 Empire Dr, Florence, KY 41042
Membership(s): BISG

Thorndike Press
Imprint of Thomson Gale
295 Kennedy Memorial Dr, Waterville, ME 04901-4517
Tel: 207-859-1026 *Toll Free Tel:* 800-233-1244
   Fax: 207-859-1009 *Toll Free Fax:* 800-558-4676 (orders)
E-mail: printorders@thomson.com; international@thomson.com (orders for customers outside US & CA)
Web Site: www.gale.com/thorndike
Key Personnel
Publr & Gen Mgr: Jill Lectka
Mktg Mgr: Debbie Ludden
Assoc Publr: Jamie Knobloch
Man Ed: Mary P Smith
Promos Assoc: Barb Littlefield
Founded: 1977
Large print titles for the public library market.
ISBN Prefix(es): 0-7862; 1-4104; 1-58724; 1-59414; 1-59413; 1-59415
Number of titles published annually: 1,400 Print
Total Titles: 6,000 Print
Imprints: Five Star; Large Print Press; Walker Large Print; Wheeler Publishing
Distributor for Harlequin; HarperCollins; Mills & Boone; Simon & Schuster; Warner

ThorsonsElement US
Division of HarperCollins UK
Subsidiary of ThorsonElement UK
535 Albany St, 5th fl, Boston, MA 02118
Tel: 617-451-1533 *Fax:* 617-451-0971
Web Site: www.thorsons.com
Key Personnel
VP: Steve Fischer *Tel:* 617-451-8984
   E-mail: steve.fischer@harpercollins.co.uk
Dir, Mktg & Publicity: Chris Ahearn *Tel:* 617-451-8988
Founded: 1930
Publisher of mind, body, spirit books.
ISBN Prefix(es): 0-7225; 0-00; 1-8620; 1-8523; 1-85583
Number of titles published annually: 50 Print; 2 Audio
Total Titles: 150 Print
Foreign Office(s): HarperCollins Publishers, 77-85 Fullham Palace Rd, Hammersmith, London W68JB, United Kingdom *Tel:* (020) 8307 4788 *Web Site:* www.thorsons.com
Distributed by HarperCollins

Orders to: HarperCollins Order Dept, 1000 Keystone Park, Scranton, PA 18512
Returns: HarperCollins Returns Center, 2205 E Lincoln Way, Door 1, La Porte, IL 46350
Distribution Center: HarperCollins Publishers, 1000 Keystone Park, Scranton, PA 182512-4621 *Toll Free Tel:* 800-242-7737 *Toll Free Fax:* 800-822-4090
Membership(s): NEBA

Through the Bible Publishers
Subsidiary of Treasure Learning Systems
2643 Midpoint Dr, Fort Collins, CO 80524-3216
Tel: 970-484-8483 *Toll Free Tel:* 800-284-0158
Fax: 970-495-6700
E-mail: discipleland@throughthebible.com
Web Site: www.throughthebible.com
Key Personnel
Pres: Mark Steiner
VP, Commns: Ron Forseth
Founded: 1935
ISBN Prefix(es): 0-86606
Number of titles published annually: 20 Print
Total Titles: 55 Print; 30 E-Book
Foreign Rep(s): Angus Hudson Ltd

Thunder's Mouth Press
Imprint of Avalon Publishing Group - New York
245 W 17 St, 11th fl, New York, NY 10011-5300
SAN: 216-4663
Tel: 646-375-2570 *Fax:* 646-375-2571
Web Site: www.thundersmouth.com
Key Personnel
Sr VP & Publg Dir: Michele Martin
VP & Publr: John Oakes
Ed: Jofie Ferrari-Adler
Founded: 1980
Thunder's Mouth Press, an imprint of the Avalon Publishing Group, focuses on books about current affairs, popular culture, music & photography.
ISBN Prefix(es): 0-938410; 1-56025

Tia Chucha Press
12737 Glen Oaks Blvd, Suite 22, Sylmar, CA 91342
Tel: 818-362-7060 *Fax:* 818-362-7102
E-mail: info@tiachucha.com
Web Site: www.tiachucha.com
Key Personnel
Pres & Dir: Luis Rodriguiz
Founded: 1989
Poetry.
ISBN Prefix(es): 0-9624287; 1-882688
Number of titles published annually: 4 Print
Total Titles: 32 Print; 1 Audio
Shipping Address: Northwestern University Press, c/o Chicago Distribution Center, 11030 S Langley Ave, Chicago, IL 60628

Tiare Publications
PO Box 493, Lake Geneva, WI 53147-0493
SAN: 699-7066
Tel: 262-248-4845 *Toll Free Tel:* 800-420-0579
Fax: 262-249-0299
E-mail: info@tiare.com
Web Site: www.tiare.com
Key Personnel
Pres: Gerry L Dexter
Founded: 1986
Radio communication hobby books; general nonfiction; jazz/big bands.
ISBN Prefix(es): 0-936653
Number of titles published annually: 3 Print
Total Titles: 20 Print
Imprints: Balboa Books; Limelight Books; Tiare Publications
Shipping Address: 213 Forest St, Lake Geneva, WI 53147

Tide-mark Press
179 Broad St, Windsor, CT 06095

Mailing Address: PO Box 20, Windsor, CT 06095-0020
Tel: 860-683-4499 *Toll Free Tel:* 800-338-2508
Fax: 860-683-4055
E-mail: customerservice@tide-mark.com
Web Site: www.tidemarkpress.com
Key Personnel
Publr: Scott Kaeser *Tel:* 860-683-4499 ext 108
E-mail: scott@tide-mark.com
Publish illustrated books & calendars.
ISBN Prefix(es): 1-55949
Number of titles published annually: 6 Print
Total Titles: 16 Print
Foreign Rep(s): Gazelle (Europe)

Tidewater Publishers
Imprint of Cornell Maritime Press Inc
101 Water Way, Centreville, MD 21617
SAN: 202-0459
Mailing Address: PO Box 456, Centreville, MD 21617-0456
Tel: 410-758-1075 *Toll Free Tel:* 800-638-7641
Fax: 410-758-6849
E-mail: editor@cornellmaritimepress.com
Web Site: www.tidewaterpublishrs.com
Key Personnel
Pres: Joseph Johns
Man Ed & Intl Rts: Charlotte A Kurst
Founded: 1955
Regional books relating to Chesapeake Bay, the Delmarva Peninsula & Maryland in general.
ISBN Prefix(es): 0-87033
Number of titles published annually: 6 Print
Total Titles: 89 Print
Distributor for Chesapeake Bay Maritime Museum; Maryland Historical Trust Press; Maryland Sea Grant Program; Maryland State Archives Publications; Literary House Press
Foreign Rep(s): Baker & Taylor International (Australia, Indonesia, Malaysia)
Shipping Address: Cornell Maritime Press
Membership(s): AAP; ABA; Midatlantic Publishers Association; NAIPR; Small Publishers Association of North America

Tilbury House Publishers
Subsidiary of Harpswell Press Inc
2 Mechanic St, No 3, Gardiner, ME 04345
Tel: 207-582-1899 *Toll Free Tel:* 800-582-1899 (orders) *Fax:* 207-582-8229
E-mail: tilbury@tilburyhouse.com
Web Site: www.tilburyhouse.com
Key Personnel
Publr: Jennifer Bunting *Fax:* 207-582-8227
Trade Sales: Sue Beach
Mktg & Publicity: Beryl-Ann Johnson
E-mail: bajohnson@tilburyhouse.com
Children's Books: Audrey Maynard
Founded: 1990
ISBN Prefix(es): 0-88448
Number of titles published annually: 10 Print
Total Titles: 60 Print
Membership(s): ABA; Publishers Marketing Association

Timber Press Inc
133 SW Second Ave, Suite 450, Portland, OR 97204
SAN: 216-082X
Tel: 503-227-2878 *Toll Free Tel:* 800-327-5680
Fax: 503-227-3070
E-mail: mail@timberpress.com
Web Site: www.timberpress.com
Key Personnel
Pres & CEO: Robert B Conklin
E-mail: bconklin@timberpress.com
Publr & Intl Rts/Rts & Perms: Jane Connor
E-mail: jconnor@timberpress.com
Edit Dir: Eve Goodman *E-mail:* egoodman@timberpress.com
Sales Mgr: Jackie Thompson
E-mail: jthompson@timberpress.com

Exec Ed: Neal J Maillet *E-mail:* nmaillet@timberpress.com
Botanical Ed: Dale E Johnson *E-mail:* djohnson@timberpress.com
Founded: 1976
Gardening, horticulture, botany, natural history, Pacific Northwest regional.
ISBN Prefix(es): 0-917304; 0-88192; 0-931146
Number of titles published annually: 40 Print
Total Titles: 440 Print; 5 Audio
Imprints: Timber Press
Foreign Office(s): 2 Station Rd, Swavesey, Cambridge CB4 5QJ, United Kingdom, Contact: Carole Green *Tel:* (01954) 232959 *Fax:* (01954) 206040 *E-mail:* timberpressuk@btinternet.com

Time Being Books
Imprint of Time Being Press
10411 Clayton Rd, Suites 201-203, St Louis, MO 63131
Tel: 314-432-1771 *Toll Free Tel:* 866-840-4334
Fax: 314-432-7939 *Toll Free Fax:* 888-301-9121
E-mail: tbbooks@sbcglobal.net
Web Site: www.timebeing.com
Key Personnel
Sales Mgr: Trilogy Brodsky
Man Ed: Jerry Call
Founded: 1988
ISBN Prefix(es): 1-877770; 1-56809
Number of titles published annually: 5 Print; 5 Online
Total Titles: 77 Print; 77 Online; 5 E-Book; 21 Audio
Distributed by Amazon.com; BarnesandNoble.com

Time Warner Audio Books
Subsidiary of Time Warner Book Group
Sports Illustrated Bldg, 135 W 50 St, New York, NY 10020
Tel: 212-522-7334 *Fax:* 212-522-7994
Web Site: www.twbookmark.com/audiobooks
Key Personnel
VP & Publr (CA Office): Maja Thomas
Sr Producer (CA Office): Linda Ross
Mktg Dir (NY Office): Anthony Goff
Sr Prodn & Opers Mgr (NY Office): Kim Sayle
Mgr, Digital Tech & Design (NY Office): Karen Cera
Publicity (NY Office): Jessica Cardillo
ISBN Prefix(es): 1-58621; 1-57042; 1-59483
Total Titles: 160 Audio
Branch Office(s)
11766 Wilshire Blvd, Suite 1700, Los Angeles, CA 90025-6537 *Tel:* 310-268-7378 *Fax:* 310-268-7620

Time Warner Book Group
1271 Avenue of the Americas, New York, NY 10020
Tel: 212-522-7200 *Fax:* 212-522-7991
Web Site: www.twbookmark.com
Key Personnel
Chmn & CEO: Laurence J Kirshbaum
Pres & COO: Maureen Mahon Egen
Pres, Dist & Opers (Boston Office): William R Hall
Exec VP, Sales: Christine Barba
Exec VP & CFO: Thomas Maciag
Exec VP & Gen Counsel: Carol Fein Ross
Sr VP, Mfg & Prodn: Milton Batalion
Sr VP, Adv & Promo: Martha Otis
VP, Cust Fin Servs (Boston Office): Dennis Balog
VP, Fulfillment (Boston Office): Richard Coe
VP, Dist (Indiana Office): Gerry Cummings
VP, Opers (Boston Office): Lawrence Feldman
VP, Spec Mkts & Publg Dir, Ansel Adams: Jean Griffin
VP & Exec Man Ed: Harvey-Jane Kowal
VP & Natl Acct Dir: Peter Mauceri
VP, Intl Sales: Bob Michel

VP & Natl Acct Dir: Bruce Paonessa
VP, HR: Andrea Weinzimer
VP, Natl Accts/Client Servs & Children: Anne
  Zafian
Dir, Contracts, Copyrights & Perms: Andrea
  Shallcross
ISBN Prefix(es): 0-446
Imprints: Aspect; Bulfinch Press; Little, Brown
  and Company; Little, Brown and Company
  Books for Young Readers; Mysterious Press;
  Time Warner Audio Books; Warner Books
Distributor for Arcade Publishing; DC Comics;
  Disney Publishing Worldwide; Harry N
  Abrams, Inc; Hyperion; Kensington Book Co
  (Intl only); Microsoft Learning; Phaidon Press;
  Time Inc Home Entertainment
Shipping Address: Time Warner Book Group
  Distribution Center, 121 N Enterprise Blvd,
  Lebanon, IN 46052 *Tel:* 765-483-9900
  Fax: 765-483-0706
Distribution Center: H B Fenn & Co Ltd, 34
  Nixon Rd, Bolton, ON L7E 1W2, Canada
  Tel: 905-951-6600
See separate listing for:
Bulfinch Press
Little, Brown and Company Adult Trade Division
Little, Brown and Company Books for Young Readers
Time Warner Audio Books
Warner Books
Warner Faith (Christian Book Division of Time Warner Book Group)

Times Change Press
8453 Blackney Rd, Sebastopol, CA 95472
Tel: 707-824-9456
Key Personnel
Publr: Michael Sherick *E-mail:* mjsbook@neteze.
  com
Founded: 1970
Ethics & ecology.
ISBN Prefix(es): 0-87810
Number of titles published annually: 3 Print
Total Titles: 34 Print
Imprints: Table-Talk Press

TLC, see The Learning Connection (TLC)

Toad Hall Inc
RR 2, Box 2090, Laceyville, PA 18623
Tel: 570-869-2942 *Fax:* 570-869-1031
E-mail: toadhallco@aol.com
Web Site: www.laceyville.com/Toad-Hall
Key Personnel
Pres: Sharon Jarvis
Media Consultant: Anne P Pinzow
Founded: 1996
ISBN Prefix(es): 0-9637498
Number of titles published annually: 3 Print
Total Titles: 13 Print
Imprints: Belfry Books; The Bradford Press;
  Hands & Heart Books; Toad Hall Press
Distributor for Eye Scry Publications; Puppy
  Paws Press; St James Publishing
Foreign Rights: Rights Unlimited

The Toby Press LLC
2 Great Pasture Rd, Danbury, CT 06810
Mailing Address: PO Box 8531, New Milford,
  CT 06776-8531 SAN: 253-9985
Tel: 203-830-8508 *Fax:* 203-830-8512
E-mail: toby@tobypress.com
Web Site: www.tobypress.com
Key Personnel
Publr: Matthew Miller
Sales Dir: Stuart Schnee *Tel:* 203-830-8500
  Fax: 203-860-8516
Founded: 1999
Publish fiction, essays & literature.
ISBN Prefix(es): 1-902881
Number of titles published annually: 40 Print

Total Titles: 100 Print
Foreign Office(s): PO Box 2455, W1A 5WY London,
  United Kingdom *Tel:* (020) 7580 5440
  Fax: (020) 7580 5442 *E-mail:* toby@tobypress.
  com
Shipping Address: c/o Focus Mailing, 2 Great
  Pasture Rd, Danbury, CT 06810
Warehouse: c/o Focus Mailing, 2 Great Pasture
  Rd, Danbury, CT 06810 *Tel:* 203-830-8500
  Fax: 203-830-2516
Distribution Center: c/o Focus Mailing, 2 Great
  Pasture Rd, Danbury, CT 06810 *Tel:* 203-830-
  8500 *Fax:* 203-830-2516

§Todd Publications
PO Box 635, Nyack, NY 10960-0635
Tel: 845-358-6213 *Fax:* 845-358-6213
E-mail: toddpub@aol.com
Web Site: www.toddpublications.com
Key Personnel
Owner, Pres & Sr Ed: Barry Klein
Founded: 1973
Directories & reference books to the trade.
ISBN Prefix(es): 0-915344
Number of titles published annually: 10 Print; 2
  CD-ROM; 1 Online; 1 E-Book
Total Titles: 15 Print; 2 CD-ROM; 1 Online; 1 E-
  Book

Todd Publishing Inc
1224 N Nokomis NE, Alexandria, MN 56308
Tel: 320-763-5190 *Fax:* 320-763-9290
Key Personnel
Pres & Exec Dir: Robert G Johnson
Founded: 1962
Real estate, general business books; nonfiction &
  fiction.
ISBN Prefix(es): 0-935988
Number of titles published annually: 14 Print
Total Titles: 23 Print
Membership(s): AAP

TODTRI Book Publishers
4049 Broadway, Suite 153, New York, NY 10032
Tel: 212-695-6622 ext 10 *Toll Free Tel:* 800-696-
  7299 *Fax:* 212-695-6988 *Toll Free Fax:* 800-
  696-7482
E-mail: todtri@mindspring.com
Web Site: TODTRI.com
Key Personnel
Pres & Intl Rts: Robert Tod
Founded: 1989
Illustrated nonfiction.
ISBN Prefix(es): 1-880908; 1-57717
Number of titles published annually: 50 Print
Total Titles: 315 Print
Imprints: Todtri
Foreign Rep(s): Grange Books Plc (Asia, Europe,
  Middle East, South Africa); Universal International
  (Australia & New Zealand)
Warehouse: Mercedes Distribution Center Inc,
  Brooklyn Navy Yard, Bldg 3, Brooklyn, NY
  11205 *Tel:* 718-522-7111 *Fax:* 718-935-9647

Tommy Nelson
Division of Thomas Nelson Inc
PO Box 141000, Nashville, TN 37214-1000
Tel: 615-889-9000 *Toll Free Tel:* 800-251-4000
  Fax: 615-902-3330
Web Site: www.tommynelson.com
Key Personnel
Chmn & CEO: Sam Moore
Sr VP & Publr: Dan Lynch
Dir, Mktg, Adv & Publicity: Brian Mitchell
  Tel: 615-902-2226
Publicist: Jennifer Willingham
Founded: 1984
Inspirational children's books for evangelical &
  secular marketplace & other products.
ISBN Prefix(es): 0-8499; 1-4003

Number of titles published annually: 75 Print; 10
  Audio
Total Titles: 200 Print; 8 E-Book; 50 Audio

§Top of the Mountain Publishing
Division of Powell Productions
PO Box 2244, Pinellas Park, FL 33780-2244
SAN: 287-590X
Tel: 727-391-3958 *Fax:* 727-391-4598
E-mail: tag@abcinfo.com
Web Site: abcinfo.com; www.topofthemountain.
  com
Key Personnel
Dir: Judith Powell *E-mail:* judi@abcinfo.com;
  Tag Powell
PR: Lance Wilson
Intl Rts & Lib Sales Dir: Sharon Boulder
Founded: 1979
Exhibits at international, national bookfairs, BFA,
  Frankfurt Book Fairs; no unsol mss.
ISBN Prefix(es): 0-914295; 1-56087
Number of titles published annually: 6 Print; 100
  Audio
Total Titles: 23 Print; 12 CD-ROM
Imprints: W Farthingale Publishing
Distributed by Ingram Book Co; New Leaf Distributing
  Co; Walden Books
Advertising Agency: Powell Productions
Shipping Address: 4837 62 St N, Kenneth City,
  FL 33709

Tor Books, see Tom Doherty Associates, LLC

Torah Aura Productions
4423 Fruitland Ave, Los Angeles, CA 90058
Tel: 323-585-7312 *Toll Free Tel:* 800-238-6724
  Fax: 323-585-0327
E-mail: misrad@torahaura.com
Web Site: www.torahaura.com
Key Personnel
Pres: Alan Rowe *E-mail:* alan@torahaura.com
Founded: 1982
Textbooks, Judaica.
ISBN Prefix(es): 0-933873
Number of titles published annually: 15 Print
Total Titles: 400 Print
Distributor for Free Spirit (selected titles)

Torah Umesorah Publications
Division of Torah Umesorah-National Society for
  Hebrew Day Schools
5723 18 Ave, Brooklyn, NY 11204
Tel: 718-259-1223 *Fax:* 718-259-1795
E-mail: mail@tupublications.com; publications@
  tupublications.com
Key Personnel
Dir, Pubns: Yaakov Fruchter
Founded: 1946
Text teaching aids & visual aids for Yeshiva-day
  schools & Hebrew schools, students & teachers;
  posters & workbooks.
ISBN Prefix(es): 0-914131
Number of titles published annually: 3 Print
Total Titles: 82 Print
Foreign Rep(s): Chaim Turkel Volume Distributors
  (UK)

Tortuga Press
3919 Mayette Ave, Santa Rosa, CA 95405
SAN: 299-1756
Mailing Address: 2777 Yulupa Ave, PMB 181,
  Santa Rosa, CA 95405
Tel: 707-544-4720 *Fax:* 707-544-5609
E-mail: info@tortugapress.com
Web Site: www.tortugapress.com
Key Personnel
Publr: Matthew Gollub *E-mail:* mg@tortugapress.
  com
Mktg Mgr: Lane Wong
Founded: 1997

Creator of award-winning children's literature & multi-media products to delight & open young people's minds.
ISBN Prefix(es): 1-889910
Number of titles published annually: 4 Print; 2 Audio
Total Titles: 15 Print; 7 Audio
Foreign Rights: International Titles (Germany)
Warehouse: Anchor Mini Storage, 220 Business Park Dr, Rohnert Park, CA 94928, Contact: Stan Case *Tel:* 707-544-9424 *Fax:* 707-544-9424 *E-mail:* info@tortugapress.com *Web Site:* tortugapress.com
Membership(s): Publishers Marketing Association

Total Power Publishing
4274 Bay View Dr, Fernandina Beach, FL 32035
Tel: 904-321-1169 *Fax:* 904-321-2872
E-mail: stinger20007399@aol.com
Key Personnel
Pres: Joe Hill
VP: Chip Hill *Tel:* 770-982-6104
Founded: 1998
Specialize in biographical books on well known people.
ISBN Prefix(es): 1-890262
Number of titles published annually: 3 Print; 1 Audio
Total Titles: 2 Print; 1 Audio

Totline Publications
Affiliate of Frank Schaffer Publications
3195 Wilson Dr NW, Grand Rapids, MI 49544
Mailing Address: PO Box 141487, Grand Rapids, MI 49514-1487
Toll Free Tel: 800-417-3261 *Toll Free Fax:* 888-203-9361
Web Site: www.teacherspecialty.com
Founded: 1979
ISBN Prefix(es): 0-911019; 1-57029
Number of titles published annually: 18 Print
Total Titles: 40 Print
Distributed by Frank Schaffer Publications

§Tower Publishing Co
588 Saco Rd, Standish, ME 04084
Tel: 207-642-5400 *Toll Free Tel:* 800-969-8693
Fax: 207-642-5463
E-mail: info@towerpub.com
Web Site: www.towerpub.com
Key Personnel
Pres: Michael Lyons
Man Ed: Mary Anne Hildreth
Business & manufacturing directories, law publications, business databases.
ISBN Prefix(es): 0-89442
Number of titles published annually: 20 Print

TowleHouse Publishing
394 W Main St, Suite B-9, Hendersonville, TN 37075
SAN: 299-7797
Tel: 615-822-6405 *Fax:* 615-822-5535
E-mail: vermonte@aol.com
Web Site: www.towlehouse.com
Key Personnel
Pres & Publr: Mike Towle
Asst Publr: Holley Towle
Founded: 1998
Focus on two series: 'Potent Quotables' & 'Good Golf!'. "Insta-books" on contemporary issues, events, people & milestones.
ISBN Prefix(es): 0-9668774; 1-931249
Number of titles published annually: 10 Print
Total Titles: 30 Print
Distributed by National Book Network
Foreign Rep(s): Rights & Distribution, Inc (Worldwide)

§Traders Press Inc
703 Laurens Rd, Greenville, SC 29607-1912

Mailing Address: PO Box 6206, Greenville, SC 29606-6206
Tel: 864-298-0222 *Toll Free Tel:* 800-927-8222
Fax: 864-298-0221
Web Site: www.traderspress.com
Key Personnel
Pres & Intl Rts: Edward D Dobson
E-mail: eddobson@traderspress.com
Off Mgr: Cathy Rubert *E-mail:* cathy@traderspress.com
Founded: 1975
Books & courses on technical analysis, stock, option & commodity trading.
ISBN Prefix(es): 0-934380
Number of titles published annually: 8 Print
Total Titles: 75 Print
Distributor for McGraw-Hill; Penguin-Putnam; John Wiley & Sons Inc

Trafalgar Square
Howe Hill Rd, North Pomfret, VT 05053
SAN: 213-8859
Mailing Address: PO Box 257, North Pomfret, VT 05053-0257
Tel: 802-457-1911 *Toll Free Tel:* 800-423-4525
Fax: 802-457-1913
E-mail: tsquare@sover.net
Web Site: www.trafalgarsquarebooks.com
Key Personnel
Pres: Caroline Robbins
Man Dir: Paul Feldstein *E-mail:* pfeldstn@sover.net
Dir, Publicity: Constance Creed
Dir, Mktg & Promo: Deborah Sloan
Man Ed: Martha Cook
Founded: 1973
Publisher & US distributor for British publishers.
ISBN Prefix(es): 0-943955; 1-57076
Number of titles published annually: 25 Print
Total Titles: 250 Print; 2 Audio
Distributor for AA Publishing; The Akadine Press; Aurum Press; Duncan Baird; BBC Books; John Blake; Bloomsbury UK; Carroll & Brown; Kyle Cathie; Cico Books; Compass Equestrian; The Crowood Press; Andre Deutsch Ltd; DLM-Giles de la Mare; Edition Olms; Egmont; Evans Brothers Ltd; Granta UK; Robert Hale/J A Allen; HarperCollins UK; Haus Publishing; Hesperus Press; Hodder-Headline Ltd; Lion Publishing; Little Books; Macmillan UK; Mainstream Publishing; Metro Publications; John Murray Ltd; Oldcastle Books; Orion Publishing; Pallas Athene; Pavilion Books Ltd; Prion; Profile Books; Random House UK; Reynolds & Hearn; Scriptum Editions; Short Books; Sinclair-Stevenson; The Sportsman's Press; Tempus Publishing; Time Warner Books UK; Transworld Publishers; The Women's Press

§Trafton Publishing
109 Barcliff Terr, Cary, NC 27511
SAN: 298-5454
Tel: 919-363-0999
Web Site: www.rogbates.com
Key Personnel
Exec Dir: Rick Singer
Intl Rts Contact & Lib Sales Dir: Roger Bateman
E-mail: rogbates12@aol.com
Founded: 1993
How-to, self-help humor & health oriented books. Also seminars & workshops on using effective humor.
ISBN Prefix(es): 0-9642324
Number of titles published annually: 5 Print
Total Titles: 3 E-Book; 10 Audio

Trails Books
Division of Trails Media Group Inc
PO Box 317, Black Earth, WI 53515-0317
Tel: 608-767-8000 *Toll Free Tel:* 800-236-8088
Fax: 608-767-5444

E-mail: books@wistrails.com
Web Site: www.trailsbooks.com
Key Personnel
CEO: Scott Klug
VP: Anita Matcha
Dir: Eva Solcova
Founded: 1970
Regional trade books-Wisconsin & Upper Great Lakes, travel guide books.
ISBN Prefix(es): 1-879483; 1-931599; 0-915024
Number of titles published annually: 15 Print
Total Titles: 110 Print
Imprints: Acorn Guides; Prairie Classics; Prairie Oak Press; Trails Books Guide

§Trails Illustrated, Division of National Geographic Maps
Division of National Geographic Ventures
PO Box 4357, Evergreen, CO 80437-4357
Mailing Address: 210 Beaver Brook Canyon Rd, Evergreen, CO 80439
Tel: 303-670-3457 *Toll Free Tel:* 800-962-1643
Fax: 303-670-3644 *Toll Free Fax:* 800-626-8676
E-mail: topomaps@aol.com
Web Site: www.nationalgeographics.com
Key Personnel
Gen Mgr: Steven D Lownds
Sales Mgr: Tammy Buckenstose
Founded: 1977
Up-to-date topographic recreation maps, wallmaps, worldwide adventure maps & digital mapping products.
ISBN Prefix(es): 0-925873; 1-56695
Total Titles: 99 Print
Distributed by Bright Horizons; Canyonlands Publications; Map Link; Many Feathers Books & Maps; Peregrine Outfitters
Distributor for National Geographic Maps

Training Resource Network Inc (T R N)
PO Box 439, St Augustine, FL 32085-0439
Tel: 904-823-9800 (cust serv); 904-824-7121 (edit off) *Toll Free Tel:* 800-280-7010 (orders) *Fax:* 904-823-3554
E-mail: customerservice@trninc.com
Web Site: www.trninc.com
Key Personnel
Pres: Dale DiLeo
VP: Dawn Langton *E-mail:* dawnl@trninc.com
Founded: 1990
ISBN Prefix(es): 1-883302
Number of titles published annually: 4 Print
Total Titles: 44 Print
Distributed by Job Quest; The New Careers Center
Distributor for Attainment
Returns: 88 Riberia St, Suite 150, St Augustine, FL 32084

Trakker Maps Inc
Division of Langenscheidt Publishers Inc
8350 Parkline Blvd, Suite 360, Orlando, FL 32809
Tel: 407-447-6485 *Toll Free Tel:* 800-327-3108
Fax: 407-447-6488
E-mail: sales@trakkermaps.com
Web Site: www.trakkermaps.com
Key Personnel
Pres: Karl Langenscheidt
Sr VP: Andreas Langenscheidt
Exec VP: Stuart Dolgins
Founded: 1976
Maps, atlases & street guides.
ISBN Prefix(es): 1-877651
Total Titles: 10 Print
Imprints: American Map Corp
Distributor for Alexandria Drafting Co; Arrow Maps Inc; Creative Sales Corp; Hagstrom Map Co; Langenscheidt Publishers Inc

Trans-Atlantic Publications Inc
311 Bainbridge St, Philadelphia, PA 19147
SAN: 694-0234
Tel: 215-925-5083 *Fax:* 215-925-1912
E-mail: order@transatlanticpub.com
Web Site: www.transatlanticpub.com; www.
businesstitles.com
Key Personnel
Pres & Intl Rts: Ronald Smolin
Mgr: Jeff Goldstein
Founded: 1984
Popular culture.
ISBN Prefix(es): 0-13; 0-330; 1-85479; 0-333;
0-283; 0-7487; 0-85950; 1-85776; 1-87403;
1-85486; 0-7522; 1-891696; 0-273; 0-174; 0-
85242
Number of titles published annually: 50 Print
Total Titles: 300 Print
Imprints: BainBridgeBooks
Distributor for Book Guild; Financial Times Publishing; Longman; Pan MacMillan; Nexus Special Interests; Stanley Thornes

Trans Tech Publications
Division of Enfield Publishers
c/o Enfield Distribution Co, 234 May St, Enfield,
NH 03748
Mailing Address: PO Box 699, Enfield, NH
03748-0699
Tel: 603-632-7377 *Fax:* 603-632-5611
E-mail: usa-ttp@ttp.net; info@enfiedbooks.com
Web Site: www.ttp.net
Key Personnel
Dir: Linda Jones *E-mail:* usa-ttp@ttp.net
Intl Rts: Fred Woehlbier *E-mail:* f.woehlbier@ttp.net
ISBN Prefix(es): 0-87849; 3-908450
Number of titles published annually: 50 Print
Imprints: Scitec Publications
Foreign Office(s): Brandrain 6, 8707 Zuerich-uetikon, Switzerland

Transaction Publishers
Rutgers University, 35 Berrue Circle, Piscataway,
NJ 08854
SAN: 202-7941
Tel: 732-445-2280 *Toll Free Tel:* 888-999-6778
Fax: 732-445-3138
E-mail: trans@transactionpub.com
Web Site: www.transactionpub.com
Key Personnel
Chmn of the Bd & Edit Dir: Irving Louis
Horowitz *E-mail:* ihorowitz@transactionpub.com
Pres: Mary E Curtis *E-mail:* mcurtis@transactionpub.com
Pres, Express Book Freight: Scott B Bramson
Ed & ISBN Contact: Laurence Mintz
Rts & Perms: Marlena Davidian
Mktg Dir & Lib Sales Dir: Karen B Ornstein
Tel: 732-445-2280 ext 102 *E-mail:* kornstein@transactionpub.com
Cust Rel & Fulfillment: Nancy Conine
Founded: 1962
Social sciences, text, reference books & journals.
Child welfare, marriage & family, political science, criminology, urban studies, policy analysis.
ISBN Prefix(es): 1-56000; 0-87855; 0-88738; 0-7658; 1-4128
Number of titles published annually: 120 Print
Total Titles: 4,500 Print; 100 E-Book
Imprints: Advances in Criminological Theory;
African-American Studies; American Studies;
Anthropology; Asian Studies; Classics in Economics; Clinical & Social Psychology; Communication & Culture; Comparative Policy
Analysis; Comparative Politics; Evaluation &
Development; Foundations of Higher Education; History of Ideas & Ethics; International
Social Security; Judaica & Hebraica; Latin
American Studies; Library of Conservative
Thought; Library of Liberal Thought; Mar-

riage & Family Studies; The National Interest;
Organization & Management; Philosophy of
Science; Political Economy; Population Studies; Psychiatry & Psychology; Social Policy &
Social Theory; Social Science Classics; Sociology of Religion; Studies of Economic Culture;
Studies in Ethnicity; Transaction Large Print
Subsidiaries: Transaction Publishers (UK)
Divisions: Express Book Freight; Transaction
Distribution Services; Transaction/ISIS Large
Print; Transaction Periodicals Consortium
Foreign Office(s): Transaction Publishers, c/o Eurospan, 3 Henrietta St, Covent Garden, London
WC2 8LU, United Kingdom *Tel:* (020) 7240
0856 *Fax:* (020) 7379 0609
Distributor for Aksant Academic Publishers (The
Netherlands); Haan Publishing; IKO (International Communication Organization) (Germany); IWGIA (International Workgroup for
Indigenous Affairs) (Denmark); Lit Verlag
(Germany); Mets & Schilt (The Netherlands);
Noidic Africa Institute (Sweden); RAND
Corporation (United States); Shama Books
(Ethiopia); Social Philosophy & Policy Center-Bowling Green University (United States);
Transcript Verlag (Germany); Witwatersrand
University Press (South Africa)
Foreign Rep(s): Cariad Ltd (Canada); Footprint Books Pty Ltd (Australia); Maruzen Co
(Japan); Taylor & Francis (Asia & the Pacific,
China, Korea, Taiwan, Southeast Asia); Transaction Publishers (Middle East, UK & Europe);
Viva Books Private Ltd (Bangladesh, India,
Pakistan)
Foreign Rights: Akcali Copyright Agency
(Turkey); The Asano Agency (Japan); Eliane
Banisti Agent Litteraire (France); Big Apple-Tuttle Mori Agency (People's Republic of
China); International Editors Co (Brazil, Latin
America, Spain); Korea Copyright Agency (Korea); Prava I Prevodi (Bulgaria, Greece, Poland,
Romania, Russia, Serbia and Montenegro); Studio NABU (Italy)
Billing Address: Transaction Publishers Distribution, 390 Campus Dr, Somerset, NJ 08873
Orders to: Transaction Publishers Distribution,
390 Campus Dr, Somerset, NJ 08873, Contact: Nancy Lonine *Tel:* 732-445-1245 *Toll
Free Tel:* 888-999-6778 *Fax:* 732-445-9801
E-mail: orders@transactionpub.com
Returns: Transaction Publishers Distribution, 390
Campus Dr, Somerset, NJ 08873
Warehouse: Transaction Publishers Distribution,
390 Campus Dr, Somerset, NJ 08873, Contact:
Scott B Bramson *Tel:* 732-445-1245 *Toll Free
Tel:* 888-999-6778 *Fax:* 732-748-9801
Distribution Center: Transaction Publishers Distribution, 390 Campus Dr, Somerset, NJ 08873

Transatlantic Arts Inc
PO Box 6086, Albuquerque, NM 87197-6086
SAN: 202-7968
Tel: 505-898-2289 *Fax:* 505-898-2289
E-mail: books@transatlantic.com
Web Site: www.transatlantic.com/direct
Key Personnel
Pres: S A Vayna
Sec & Treas: L K Vayna
Founded: 1939
Reference, dictionaries, art, literature, nonfiction,
technical, scientific, sports, cookbooks, language books, textbooks for schools & colleges,
paperbacks.
ISBN Prefix(es): 0-693
Number of titles published annually: 10 Print
Total Titles: 96 Print

Transcontinental Music Publications
Division of Union of American Hebrew Congregations
633 Third Ave, New York, NY 10017
Tel: 212-650-4101 *Toll Free Tel:* 800-455-5223
Fax: 212-650-4109

E-mail: tmp@uahc.org
Web Site: www.transcontinentalmusic.com
Key Personnel
Publr: Kenneth Gesser *E-mail:* jeglash@uahc.org
Busn Mgr: Joel Eglash
Founded: 1938
Publishers of Jewish music.
ISBN Prefix(es): 1-8074
Number of titles published annually: 65 Print; 5
Audio
Total Titles: 900 Print; 75 Audio
Imprints: Cantors Assembly; Hazamir; Sacred
Music Press; Theophilis
Membership(s): Magazine Publishers of America;
NMPA

Transnational Publishers Inc
410 Saw Mill River Rd, Suite 2045, Ardsley, NY
10502
Tel: 914-693-5100 *Toll Free Tel:* 800-914-8186
(orders only) *Fax:* 914-693-4430
E-mail: info@transnationalpubs.com
Web Site: www.transnationalpubs.com
Key Personnel
Pres & Publr: Heike Fenton
Man Ed: Maria Angelini
Admin Asst: Virginia Aguirre *E-mail:* vaguirre@transnationalpubs.com
Founded: 1980
Publishers of law, including legal research, international environmental, international finance,
business & trade, international criminal & comparative law, dispute resolution, legal research
& terrorism.
ISBN Prefix(es): 0-941320; 1-57105
Number of titles published annually: 25 Print
Total Titles: 250 Print
Distributor for Intersentia

§Transportation Research Board
Division of National Academies
500 Fifth St NW, Washington, DC 20001
Mailing Address: Lock Box 289, Washington, DC
20055
Tel: 202-334-3213 *Fax:* 202-334-2519
E-mail: trbsales@nas.edu
Web Site: trb.org
Key Personnel
Mgr, Publg Sales & Affilliate Serv: Andrea Breeskin
Founded: 1920
Research results, bibliographies & abstracts on
books pertaining to civil engineering, public
transit, aviation, freight, transportation administration & economics & transportation law.
ISBN Prefix(es): 0-309
Number of titles published annually: 130 Print;
15 CD-ROM; 90 Online
Total Titles: 1,800 Print; 40 CD-ROM; 1,000 Online
Imprints: National Cooperative Highway Research
Program; Transit Cooperative Research Program; Transportation Research Information Service

§Transportation Technical Service Inc
500 Lafayette Blvd, Suite 230, Fredericksburg,
VA 22401
Tel: 540-899-9872 *Toll Free Tel:* 888-ONLY-TTS
(665-9887) *Fax:* 540-899-1948
E-mail: truckinfo@ttstrucks.com
Web Site: www.ttstrucks.com
Key Personnel
Exec VP: Thomas R Fugee
Founded: 1980
Books relating to data in the trucking industry;
directories online.
ISBN Prefix(es): 1-880701
Number of titles published annually: 5 Online
Total Titles: 2 Print; 6 CD-ROM; 5 Online

Travel Keys
PO Box 160691, Sacramento, CA 95816-0691

SAN: 682-2452
Tel: 916-452-5200 *Fax:* 916-452-5200
Key Personnel
Publr & Intl Rts: Peter B Manston
Ed: Robert C Bynum
Founded: 1984
How-to travel books & antique guides; travel books worldwide; newsletter about travel books.
ISBN Prefix(es): 0-931367
Number of titles published annually: 4 Print
Total Titles: 15 Print
Advertising Agency: 2510 "S" St, Sacramento, CA 95816-7307
Shipping Address: 2510 "S" St, Sacramento, CA 95816-7307

Travelers' Tales Inc
330 Townsend St, Suite 208, San Francisco, CA 94107
Tel: 415-227-8600 *Fax:* 415-227-8605
E-mail: ttales@travelerstales.com
Web Site: www.travelerstales.com
Key Personnel
Publr: James O'Reilly
Exec Ed: Larry Habegger
Dir, Prodn: Susan Brady *E-mail:* susan@travelerstales.com
Dir, Mktg & PR: Krista Holmstrom
Founded: 1992
ISBN Prefix(es): 1-885211; 1-932361
Number of titles published annually: 15 Print; 2 E-Book; 1 Audio
Total Titles: 80 Print; 2 E-Book; 1 Audio
Imprints: Travelers' Tales Guides; Footsteps
Sales Office(s): 1700 Fourth St, Berkeley, CA 94710
Orders to: Publishers Group West
Returns: Publishers Group West
Shipping Address: Publishers Group West
Warehouse: Publishers Group West
Distribution Center: Publishers Group West

Treasure Bay Inc
17 Parkgrove Dr, South San Francisco, CA 94080
Tel: 650-589-7980 *Fax:* 650-589-7927
E-mail: webothread@comcast.net
Key Personnel
Pres: Don Panec *E-mail:* donpanec@attbi.com
Founded: 1997
ISBN Prefix(es): 1-891327
Number of titles published annually: 4 Print
Total Titles: 25 Print

Treehaus Communications Inc
906 W Loveland Ave, Loveland, OH 45140
Mailing Address: PO Box 249, Loveland, OH 45140-0249
Tel: 513-683-5716 *Toll Free Tel:* 800-638-4287 (orders) *Fax:* 513-683-2882 (orders)
E-mail: treehaus@treehaus1.com
Web Site: www.treehaus1.com
Key Personnel
Pres: Gerard A Pottebaum
Founded: 1973
Children's books, liturgical & catechetical material for children & adults.
ISBN Prefix(es): 0-929496; 1-886510
Number of titles published annually: 6 Print
Total Titles: 44 Print

Triad Publishing Co
Imprint of Triad Communications
PO Drawer 13355, Gainesville, FL 32604
Tel: 352-373-5800 *Fax:* 352-373-1488
Toll Free Fax: 800-854-4947
Web Site: www.triadpublishing.com
Key Personnel
Chmn of the Bd & Publr: Lorna Rubin
E-mail: lorna@triadpublishing.com
Treas: Melvin L Rubin

Order Dept & Cust Rel: Donna L Hamon
E-mail: donna@triadpublishing.com
Founded: 1978
Consumer health & medical education for professionals.
ISBN Prefix(es): 0-937404
Number of titles published annually: 3 Print; 1 CD-ROM
Total Titles: 25 Print; 2 CD-ROM
Returns: IFM Services, 2302 Kanawha Terrace, St Albans, WV 25177-3212
Shipping Address: IFM Services, 2302 Kanawha Terr, St Albans, WV 25177-3212
Membership(s): National Association of Science Writers; Publishers Marketing Association; Small Publishers Association of North America

Trident Inc
885 Pierce Butler Rte, St Paul, MN 55104
Tel: 651-638-0077 *Fax:* 651-638-0084
E-mail: info@atlas-games.com
Web Site: www.atlas-games.com
Key Personnel
Intl Rts: John Nephew
Founded: 1990
Role-playing games, card games.
ISBN Prefix(es): 1-887801
Number of titles published annually: 20 Print
Total Titles: 120 Print
Imprints: Atlas Games

§Trident Media Inc
801 N Pitt St, Suite 123, Alexandria, VA 22314
SAN: 253-9802
Tel: 703-684-6895 *Fax:* 703-684-0639
E-mail: info@samhost.net
Web Site: www.edenplaza.com
Key Personnel
Pres: Samuel Asinugo
Contact: Elizabeth Irwin; Joseph Scott
Founded: 1992
Fiction, nonfiction, romance, western, science fiction, the family, young adult, travel, etc.
ISBN Prefix(es): 0-9707954
Number of titles published annually: 150 Print; 150 Online
Total Titles: 620 Print; 820 Online
Imprints: Mandrill; Washington House
Foreign Rep(s): Tate & Bywater (Canada, England)

Trident Press International
Subsidiary of Trident Promotional Corp
801 12 Ave S, Suite 400, Naples, FL 34102
Tel: 239-649-7077 *Toll Free Tel:* 800-593-3662 *Fax:* 239-649-5832 *Toll Free Fax:* 800-494-4226
E-mail: tridentpress@worldnet.att.net
Web Site: www.trident-international.com
Key Personnel
Pres: Simon Bailey
Intl Sales & Orders Contact: Elaine Evans
Founded: 1994
Reference sets, military & historical reprints, children's activity books.
ISBN Prefix(es): 1-888777; 1-58279; 1-86091
Total Titles: 182 Print
Warehouse: 395 W Mayes St, Jackson, MS 39213, Warehouse Mgr: Craig Fletcher
Tel: 601-936-3053 *Fax:* 601-936-6909
E-mail: tridentwhse@worldnet.att.net

Trigram Music Inc, see Wimbledon Music Inc & Trigram Music Inc

Trimarket Co
2264 Bowdoin St, Palo Alto, CA 94306
Tel: 650-494-1406 *Fax:* 650-494-1413
E-mail: info@trimarket.com
Web Site: www.trimarket.com

Key Personnel
Pres: Tony Svensson *E-mail:* tonyb@trimarket.com
Founded: 1985
ISBN Prefix(es): 0-9634568; 1-887565
Number of titles published annually: 3 Print
Total Titles: 12 Print

The Trinity Foundation
PO Box 68, Unicoi, TN 37692-0068
Tel: 423-743-0199 *Fax:* 423-743-2005
Web Site: www.trinityfoundation.org
Key Personnel
Pres & Dir: Dr John Robbins *E-mail:* jrob1517@aol.com
Founded: 1977
Scholarly Christian books.
ISBN Prefix(es): 0-940931; 1-891777
Number of titles published annually: 5 Print
Total Titles: 65 Print

Trinity Press International, see T & T Clark International

Trinity University Press
Unit of Trinity University
One Trinity Place, San Antonio, TX 78212-7200
Tel: 210-999-8884 *Fax:* 210-999-8838
E-mail: books@trinity.edu
Web Site: www.trinity.edu/tupress
Key Personnel
Dir: Barbara Ras
Mktg Mgr: Lynn Gosnell
Asst to the Dir: Sarah Nawrocki
Founded: 2002
Trinity University Press was revived in 2002 after 14 years of inoperation. The press publishes 6 to 8 titles a year for the general trade & academic markets. Titles are distributed by Publishers Group West.
ISBN Prefix(es): 1-59534; 0-911536
Number of titles published annually: 8 Print
Total Titles: 6 Print
Distribution Center: Publishers Group West, 1700 Fourth St, Berkeley, CA 94710 (booksellers & libraries) *Toll Free Tel:* 800-788-3123 *Fax:* 510-528-5511

TripBuilder Inc
15 Oak St, Westport, CT 06880
SAN: 297-7893
Tel: 203-227-1255 *Toll Free Tel:* 800-525-9745 *Fax:* 203-227-1257
E-mail: info@tripbuilder.com
Web Site: www.tripbuilder.com
Key Personnel
Pres: Nancy Judson *E-mail:* njudson@tripbuilder.com
Exec VP: Steven Tanzer
Founded: 1988
Travel guides.
ISBN Prefix(es): 1-56621
Number of titles published annually: 20 Print

TriQuarterly Books
Imprint of Northwestern University Press
2020 Ridge Ave, Evanston, IL 60208-4302
Tel: 847-491-3490 *Toll Free Tel:* 800-621-2736 (orders only) *Fax:* 847-467-2096
E-mail: nupress@northwestern.edu
Web Site: www.nupress.northwestern.edu
Key Personnel
Man Ed: Ian Morriss *Tel:* 847-467-7351
E-mail: i-morris@northwestern.edu
Founded: 1989
Special attention to new writing talent, the noncommercial work of established writers & writing in translation. Special emphasis on poetry.
ISBN Prefix(es): 0-8101
Number of titles published annually: 10 Print

Total Titles: 75 Print
Warehouse: Northwestern University Press, Chicago Distribution Ctr, 11030 S Langley Ave, Chicago, IL 60628

TriQuarterly Books, see Northwestern University Press

Tristan Publishing
Formerly Waldman House Press Inc
2300 Louisiana Ave, Suite B, Golden Valley, MN 55427
SAN: 295-0243
Tel: 763-545-1383 *Toll Free Tel:* 866-545-1383 *Fax:* 763-545-1387
E-mail: info@tristanpublishing.com
Web Site: www.tristanpublishing.com
Key Personnel
Owner: Brett Waldman *E-mail:* bwaldman@ tristanpublishing.com
Founded: 1978
Quality publishers of regional & national titles including children's books & gift books. Unique books of excellence with wide appeal.
ISBN Prefix(es): 0-931674
Number of titles published annually: 5 Print
Total Titles: 24 Print; 2 Audio

Triumph Books
601 S LaSalle St, Suite 500, Chicago, IL 60605
Tel: 312-939-3330 *Toll Free Tel:* 800-335-5323 *Fax:* 312-663-3557
E-mail: orders@triumphbooks.com
Web Site: www.triumphbooks.com
Key Personnel
Publr: Mitch Rogatz *E-mail:* M_Rogatz@ triumphbooks.com
Edit Dir: Tom Bast
Sales & Mktg Gen Mgr: Fred Walski
Dir, Opers: Bill Swanson
Dir, Sales: Phil Springstead
PR Mgr: Scott Rowan
Founded: 1990
Leading publisher of sports titles & official rule books of NFL, NHL, MLB, NCAA, among others.
ISBN Prefix(es): 1-880141; 1-57243; 1-892049
Number of titles published annually: 50 Print
Total Titles: 350 Print
Imprints: Benchmark Press
Foreign Rep(s): Monarch Books of Canada (Canada); Peribo Pty Ltd (Australia, New Zealand)
Warehouse: Kaplan Dearborn Logistics, 940 Enterprise St, Aurora, IL 60504

§Triumph Learning
Subsidiary of Haights Cross Communications Inc
333 E 38 St, 8th fl, New York, NY 10016
Tel: 212-652-0200 *Fax:* 212-652-0203
Web Site: www.triumphlearning.com
Key Personnel
Pres: Kevin McAliley *Tel:* 212-652-0222 *E-mail:* kmcaliley@triumphlearning.com
Exec VP, COO & CFO: Jay Shah *Tel:* 212-652-0252 *E-mail:* jshah@triumphlearning.com
Exec VP & Publr: Steven J Zweig *Tel:* 212-652-0299 *E-mail:* szweig@triumphlearning.com
Exec VP, Sales & Mktg: Ken Butkus *Tel:* 212-652-0234 *E-mail:* kbutkus@triumphlearning.com
Founded: 1964 (acquired 1999 by Haights Cross Communications)
Provides educational solutions for districts, schools & teachers looking to meet the demands of today's high-stakes testing &/or prepare their students to meet their state educational standards. Publishes test preparation materials for national tests grades K-12; publishes supplemental reading, mathematics, writing & social studies student texts for grades K-12 & provides materials for remedial reading &

math, life skills, & school-to-work transition for grades K-12.
ISBN Prefix(es): 0-87694; 1-58620
Number of titles published annually: 150 Print; 40 CD-ROM
Total Titles: 1,000 Print; 40 CD-ROM
Imprints: Sniffen Court; Tuman Publishing
Warehouse: One Beeman Rd, Northborough, MA 01532
Membership(s): AAP

Tropical Press Inc
PO Box 161174, Miami, FL 33116-1174
Tel: 305-971-1887 *Fax:* 305-378-1595
E-mail: tropicbook@aol.com
Web Site: www.tropicalpress.com
Key Personnel
Pres: G Witherspoon
VP: Susan Diez
Assoc Ed: Eva Maria Smith; Lynn Riggle
Founded: 1998
Number of titles published annually: 3 Print
Total Titles: 12 Print

Truman State University Press
Unit of Truman State University
100 E Normal St, Kirksville, MO 63501-4221
Tel: 660-785-7336 *Toll Free Tel:* 800-916-6802 *Fax:* 660-785-4480
E-mail: tsup@truman.edu
Web Site: tsup.truman.edu
Key Personnel
Dir & Ed-in-Chief: Nancy Rediger *Tel:* 660-785-7199 *E-mail:* nancyr@truman.edu
Founded: 1986
Specialize in University Press, scholarly, regional & general titles; 16th century essays & studies series & T S Eliot Prize for Poetry (New Odyssey Series).
ISBN Prefix(es): 0-940474; 0-943549; 1-931112
Number of titles published annually: 10 Print
Total Titles: 100 Print
Foreign Rep(s): Falcon House (Europe); Gazelle Book Services (Europe); Lancaster UK (Europe); Queen Square (Europe)

TSG Foundation, see TSG Publishing Foundation Inc

§TSG Publishing Foundation Inc
28641 N 63 Place, Cave Creek, AZ 85331
SAN: 250-6726
Mailing Address: PO Box 7068, Cave Creek, AZ 85237-7068
Tel: 480-502-1909 *Fax:* 480-502-0713
E-mail: info@tsgfoundation.org
Web Site: www.tsgfoundation.org
Key Personnel
Pres & Intl Rts: Gita Saraydarian
Founded: 1987
Publish & sell books by Torkom Saraydarian, spiritual training center.
ISBN Prefix(es): 0-929874; 0-911794; 0-9656203
Number of titles published annually: 5 Print
Total Titles: 47 Print; 1 CD-ROM
Distributed by Amazon.com; BarnesandNoble.com; Distribution Orion; New Leaf Distributors
Foreign Rep(s): TSG (UK) Ltd (UK & Europe)

Tundra Books of Northern New York
PO Box 1030, Plattsburgh, NY 12901
SAN: 202-8085
Tel: 416-598-4786 *Fax:* 416-598-0247
E-mail: tundra@mcclelland.com
Web Site: www.tundrabooks.com
Key Personnel
US Sales Mgr: Michael Januska
Intl Rts & Spec Sales: Catherine Mitchell
Publicity: Alison Morgan
Founded: 1971

Trade & juvenile.
ISBN Prefix(es): 0-88776
Number of titles published annually: 50 Print
Total Titles: 350 Print
Branch Office(s)
Tundra Books, 481 University Ave, Suite 900, Toronto, ON M5G 2E9, Canada
Distributed by Random House Inc
Foreign Rep(s): Edicones Samara (Mexico); Everybody's Books (South Africa); Forrester Books NZ Ltd (New Zealand); El Hombre Mancha (Costa Rica, Panama); El Hormiguero (Guatemala)
Returns: Random House Inc, 2002 Bethel Rd, Finksburg, MD 21048
Shipping Address: Random House Inc Distribution Center, 400 Hahn Rd, 28445 Highland Rd, Westminster, MD 21157 *Toll Free Tel:* 800-726-0600 *Toll Free Fax:* 800-659-2436

Turtle Books Inc
866 United Nations Plaza, Suite 525, New York, NY 10017
Tel: **212-644-2020** *Fax:* **212-223-4387**
E-mail: **turtlebook@aol.com**
Web Site: **www.turtlebooks.com**
Key Personnel
Publr: John R Whitman
Pres: Morris A Kirchoff
VP: Ronald P Zollshan
Founded: 1996
Publisher of illustrated children's trade picture books in English & Spanish editions. Turtle Media, a division of Turtle Books Inc, creates CD-ROMs & electronic software for the children's market.
ISBN Prefix(es): 1-890515
Number of titles published annually: 6 Print
Total Titles: 32 Print
Imprints: Turtle Books; Turtle Media
Branch Office(s)
Turtle Media, 897 Boston Post Rd, Madison, CT 06443
Foreign Rights: John R Whitman
Orders to: **c/o Publishers Group West, 1700 Fourth St, Berkeley, CA 94710** *Toll Free Tel:* **800-788-3123** *Fax:* **510-528-3444**
Returns: **c/o Publishers Group West, 1700 Fourth St, Berkeley, CA 94710** *Toll Free Tel:* **800-788-3123** *Fax:* **510-528-3444**
Distribution Center: **c/o Publishers Group West, 1700 Fourth St, Berkeley, CA 94710** *Toll Free Tel:* **800-788-3123** *Fax:* **510-528-3444**
Membership(s): AAP; ALA; International Reading Association

Turtle Point Press
233 Broadway, Rm 946, New York, NY 10279
Tel: 212-285-1019 *Fax:* 212-285-1019
E-mail: countomega@aol.com
Web Site: www.turtlepoint.com
Key Personnel
Pres & Intl Rts Contact: Jonathan D Rabinowitz
Founded: 1991
Lost literary fiction, contemporary fiction, art history, art criticism, poetry, biography.
ISBN Prefix(es): 0-9627987; 1-885983
Number of titles published annually: 10 Print
Total Titles: 60 Print
Imprints: Books and Co/Turtle Point; Helen Marx/Turtle Point; Turtle Point
Distributed by DAP Distributed Art Publishers
Distributor for Books & Co; Helen Marx

Foreign Rep(s): Tower Books (Australia); Turnaround (UK); Kate Walker & Co Ltd (Canada)
Shipping Address: c/o DAP Book Distribution, 575 Prospect St, Lakewood, NJ 08701

Tuttle Publishing
Member of Periplus Publishing Group
Airport Business Park, 364 Innovation Dr, North Clarendon, VT 05759-9436
SAN: 213-2621
Mailing Address: 153 Milk St, 4th fl, Boston, MA 02109 SAN: 213-2621
Tel: 617-951-4080 (edit); 802-773-8930 *Toll Free Tel:* 800-526-2778 *Fax:* 617-951-4045 (edit); 802-773-6993 *Toll Free Fax:* 800-FAX-TUTL
E-mail: info@tuttlepublishing.com
Web Site: www.tuttlepublishing.com
Key Personnel
Chmn of the Bd: Reiko Chiba Tuttle
CEO & Pres: Eric Oey
Sr VP & Gen Mgr: Michael Sargent
Publicity Mgr: Rod Hansen
Publg Dir: Ed Walters
Founded: 1948 (by Charles E Tuttle in Tokyo)
Books to span the East & West, publisher of high quality books & book kits on a wide range of topics including Asian culture, cooking, martial arts, spirituality, philosophy, travel, language, art, architecture & design.
ISBN Prefix(es): 0-8048 (Tuttle Publishing); 4-333 (Kosei Publishing Co); 1-85391 (Merehurst LTD); 0-460 (Everyman Paperbacks); 4-07 (Shufunotomo Co); 4-900737 (Tuttle Publishing); 962-593 (Periplus Editions); 0-945971 (Periplus Editions); 0-935621 (Healing Tao Books); 0-933756 (Paperweight Press); 0-7946 (Periplus Editions); 0-970171 (Kotan); 1-840590 (Milet); 9-799589 (Equinox)
Number of titles published annually: 220 Print
Total Titles: 1,300 Print; 20 Audio
Imprints: Equinox Publishing Pte Ltd; Everyman's Classic Library in Paperback; Healing Tao Books; Journey Editions; Kosei Publishing Co; Kotan Publishing Inc; Merehurst Ltd; Milet Publishing Ltd; Paperweight Press; Periplus Editions; Tuttle Publishing
Foreign Office(s): Tuttle Publishing, 5-4-12 Os-aki Shinagawa-ku, 141-0032 Tokyo, Japan *Tel:* (03) 5437 0171 *Fax:* (03) 5437 0755 *E-mail:* tuttle-sales@gol.com
Periplus Publishing Group, Olivine Bldg No 06-01/03, 130 Joo Seng Rd, Singapore 368357, Singapore *Tel:* 6280 3320 *Fax:* 6280 6290 *E-mail:* inquiries@periplus.com.sg *Web Site:* www.periplus.com
Distributor for Equinox Publishing Pte Ltd; Healing Tao Books; Kosei Publishing Co; Kotan Publishing Inc; Milet Publishing Ltd; Paperweight Press; Periplus Editions; Shufunotomo Co; Tai Chi Foundation; Zen Studies Society Press
Foreign Rep(s): Humphrys Roberts Assoc (Caribbean, Central/South America, Mexico); Ray Potts (Middle East)

Twayne Publishers
Imprint of Thomson Gale
27500 Drake Rd, Famington Hills, MI 48331-3535
Tel: 248-699-4253 *Toll Free Tel:* 800-877-4253
Web Site: www.galegroup.com/twayne
Key Personnel
VP, Mktg: Mary Mercantante
Adv Mgr: Vera Kelley
Founded: 1949
Critical biographies & studies on literature authors from around the world.
ISBN Prefix(es): 0-8057
Number of titles published annually: 3 Print

Twenty-First Century King James Bible Publishers
Division of Deuel Enterprises
215 Main Ave, Gary, SD 57237
Tel: 605-272-5575 *Toll Free Tel:* 800-225-5521 *Fax:* 605-272-5306
E-mail: kj21@kj21.com
Web Site: www.kj21.com
Key Personnel
Opers Mgr: Julene Kaiser
Bible publisher updating traditional King James Bible.
ISBN Prefix(es): 0-9630512; 1-891028

§Twenty-Third Publications
Division of Bayard Inc
185 Willow St, Mystic, CT 06355
Tel: 860-536-2611 *Toll Free Tel:* 800-321-0411 (orders) *Fax:* 860-536-5674 (edit) *Toll Free Fax:* 800-572-0788
Key Personnel
Pres: Pascal Ruffenach
Publr: Gwen Costello
Edit Dir & Rts & Perms: Mary Carol Kendzia *E-mail:* mckendzia@bayard-inc.com
Mktg Dir: Dan Smart
Compt: Valerie Westrate
Prodn Mgr: Andrea Carey
Cust Serv: Jane Silva
Founded: 1966
ISBN Prefix(es): 0-89622; 1-58595
Number of titles published annually: 45 Print; 6 CD-ROM
Total Titles: 450 Print; 24 CD-ROM
Distributed by Columba (UK); John Garrett (Australia); Novalis (Canada)
Distributor for Novalis (Canada)
Advertising Agency: Holub & Associates
Membership(s): Catholic Book Publishers Association; Catholic Press Association

§Twilight Times Books
PO Box 3340, Kingsport, TN 37664-0340
Tel: 423-323-0183 *Fax:* 423-323-0183
E-mail: publisher@twilighttimes.com
Web Site: www.twilighttimesbooks.com
Key Personnel
Publr: Lida E Quillen
Man Ed: Ardy M Scott
Ed: Julia Charpentier
Tech Support: Michael D Bobbitt
Founded: 1999
Royalty paying, non-subsidy electronic publisher of speculative fiction & New Age works. Our mission is to promote excellence in writing & great literature. Currently publishing electronic books CD-ROM & as downloads in various formats.
ISBN Prefix(es): 1-931201
Number of titles published annually: 12 Print; 6 CD-ROM; 12 E-Book
Total Titles: 6 CD-ROM; 27 Online; 27 E-Book
Imprints: Twilight Visions
Distributed by eBooksonthe.net; eBookHome.com
Foreign Rep(s): eBookAd.com (Canada); Editura Eminescu (Romania); Writer's Exchange (Australia)
Advertising Agency: Lady of the Net Productions, PO Box 3178, Kingsport, TN 37664-0178
Membership(s): Electronic Publishers Coalition; Electronically Published Internet Connection

Twin Peaks Press
PO Box 129, Vancouver, WA 98666-0129
Tel: 360-694-2462 *Fax:* 360-696-3210
E-mail: twinpeak@pacifier.com
Web Site: www.pacifier.com/~twinpeak
Key Personnel
Pres: Helen Hecker
Founded: 1982
ISBN Prefix(es): 0-933261

Number of titles published annually: 8 Print
Total Titles: 10 Print

Two Thousand Three Associates
4180 Saxon Dr, New Smyrna Beach, FL 32169
Tel: 386-427-7876 *Fax:* 386-423-7523
E-mail: ttta@worldnet.att.net
Key Personnel
Dir, Mktg: Hank Hankshaw
Publicity Dir: Barbara Brent
Intl Rts & Lib Sales Dir: Alicia Blanco
Asst to Pres: Samantha Kimberly
Founded: 1995
Nonfiction including humor, sports & travel.
ISBN Prefix(es): 0-9639905; 1-892285
Number of titles published annually: 4 Print
Total Titles: 18 Print

Tyndale House Publishers Inc
351 Executive Dr, Carol Stream, IL 60188
SAN: 206-7749
Mailing Address: PO Box 80, Wheaton, IL 60189-0080
Tel: 630-668-8303 *Toll Free Tel:* 800-323-9400
Web Site: www.tyndale.com
Key Personnel
CEO: Mark Taylor
COO: Jeff Johnson
VP, Group Publr: Ron Beers; Cliff Johnson; Douglas Knox
VP, Prodn: Joan Major
Cust Serv: Drew Shields
Rts & Perms, Books & Bibles: Michelle Alm; Dan Balow
Intl Accts Mgr: James Elwell
Natl Accts Mgr: Mark DiCicco
District Sales Mgr: Ev O'Bryan
Founded: 1962
Religion: hardcover & paperback originals & reprints; Bibles, DVDs, reference & calendars.
ISBN Prefix(es): 0-8423; 1-4143
Number of titles published annually: 125 Print
Total Titles: 1,000 Print
Imprints: HeartQuest (romance); Living Books (mass paperback); Salt River Books (deeper Christian thought); Thirsty (teen)
Foreign Rep(s): Dan Balow
Advertising Agency: Design Promotion

§Type & Archetype Press
Imprint of Type & Temperament Inc
PO Box 14285, Charleston, SC 29422-4285
Tel: 843-406-9113 *Toll Free Tel:* 800-447-8973 *Fax:* 843-406-9118
E-mail: info@typetemperament.com
Web Site: www.typearchetype.com
Key Personnel
Pres: William D G Murray *E-mail:* wdgmurray@aol.com
Founded: 1974
Books, materials, seminar kits, audio & video tapes for people interested in personality styles & practical applications of psychological type & archetypes, the Myers Briggs Type Indicator & the Pearson-Marr Archetype Indicator.
ISBN Prefix(es): 1-878287
Number of titles published annually: 3 Print
Total Titles: 23 Print; 7 CD-ROM; 24 Audio

§Tzipora Publications Inc
175 E 96 St, Suite 10-O, New York, NY 10128
Tel: 212-427-5399 *Fax:* 413-638-9158
E-mail: tziporapub@msn.com
Web Site: www.tziporapub.com
Key Personnel
Publr: Dina Grossman
Founded: 2002
Founded as a creative non fiction publishing house by a publisher with an art background.
ISBN Prefix(es): 0-9722595
Number of titles published annually: 3 Print
Total Titles: 3 Print

UAHC Press, see URJ Press

UCLA Fowler Museum of Cultural History
1586 Fowler, Los Angeles, CA 90095-1549
Mailing Address: PO Box 951549, Los Angeles,
CA 90095-1549
Tel: 310-825-9672 *Fax:* 310-206-7007
Web Site: www.fmch.ucla.edu
Key Personnel
Man Ed & Intl Rts Contact: Lynne Kostman
Tel: 310-794-9582 *E-mail:* lkostman@arts.ucla.
edu
Founded: 1963
ISBN Prefix(es): 0-930741; 0-9748729
Number of titles published annually: 5 Print
Total Titles: 71 Print
Distributed by University of Washington Press
Shipping Address: 308 Charles Young Dr, Los
Angeles, CA 90095-1549

UCLA Latin American Center Publications
UCLA Latin American Ctr, 10343 Bunche Hall,
Los Angeles, CA 90095
Mailing Address: PO Box 951447, Los Angeles,
CA 90095-1447
Tel: 310-825-6634 *Fax:* 310-206-6859
E-mail: lacpubs@international.ucla.edu
Web Site: www.international.ucla.edu/lac
Key Personnel
Pubns Dir: Colleen Trujillo *Tel:* 310-825-7547
E-mail: ctrujill@international.ucla.edu
Founded: 1959
Scholarly books & journals in Latin American
studies.
ISBN Prefix(es): 0-87903
Number of titles published annually: 6 Print; 1
CD-ROM; 1 Online
Total Titles: 124 Print; 1 CD-ROM; 1 Online

Ugly Duckling Presse
106 Ferris St, 2nd fl, Brooklyn, NY 11231
Tel: 718-852-5529
E-mail: udp_mailbox@yahoo.com
Web Site: www.uglyducklingpresse.org
Key Personnel
Pres: Matvei Yankelevich
Man Ed: Anna Moschovakis
Ed: Gregory L Ford; Ryan Haley; Julien Puirier
Artist Book Ed: Ellie Ga
Founded: 1993
A non-profit arts & publishing collective.
ISBN Prefix(es): 0-9727684
Number of titles published annually: 8 Print; 2
Audio
Total Titles: 20 Print
Imprints: Emergency Gazette; Knock-off Books;
New York Nights; 6 x 6 Magazine
Distributor for United Artists
Membership(s): Council of Literary Magazines &
Presses

UglyTown
2148 1/2 W Sunset Blvd, Suite 204, Los Angeles,
CA 90026-3148
Tel: 213-484-8334 *Fax:* 213-484-8333
E-mail: mayorsoffice@uglytown.com
Web Site: www.uglytown.com
Key Personnel
Publr: Tom Fassbender *E-mail:* uglytom@
uglytown.com; Jim Pascoe *E-mail:* uglyjim@
uglytown.com
Founded: 1996
An independent publisher of literary crime fiction.
ISBN Prefix(es): 0-9663473; 0-9724412
Number of titles published annually: 6 Print
Total Titles: 14 Print
Distributed by Words Distributing Co
Orders to: Words Distributing Co, 7900 Edge-
water Dr, Oakland, CA 94621 *Tel:* 510-553-
9673 *Fax:* 510-553-0729 *E-mail:* words@
wordsdistributing.com

Returns: Words Distributing Co, 7900 Edgewater Dr, Oakland, CA 94621 *Tel:* 510-553-
9673 *Fax:* 510-553-0729 *E-mail:* words@
wordsdistributing.com
Warehouse: Words Distributing Co, 7900 Edgewater Dr, Oakland, CA 94621 *Tel:* 510-553-
9673 *Fax:* 510-553-0729 *E-mail:* words@
wordsdistributing.com
Distribution Center: Words Distributing Co, 7900
Edgewater Dr, Oakland, CA 94621 *Tel:* 510-
553-9673 *Fax:* 510-553-0729 *E-mail:* words@
wordsdistributing.com

ULI-The Urban Land Institute
1025 Thomas Jefferson St NW, Suite 500 W,
Washington, DC 20007-5201
Tel: 202-624-7000 *Toll Free Tel:* 800-321-5011
Fax: 202-624-7140; 410-626-7147 (orders
only) *Toll Free Fax:* 800-248-4585
E-mail: bookstore@uli.org
Web Site: www.uli.org
Key Personnel
Sr VP, Policy & Practice: Rachelle Levitt
Tel: 202-624-7126 *E-mail:* rlevitt@uli.org
Foreign Rts Agent: Joanne Wang *Tel:* 718-721-
4945 *E-mail:* joannew@newyorknet.net
Founded: 1936
Books related to land use & development; real
estate.
ISBN Prefix(es): 0-87420
Number of titles published annually: 15 Print; 1
CD-ROM; 1 Online
Total Titles: 100 Print
Returns: 810 Cromwell Park Dr, Suite D, Glen
Burnie, MD 21061
Warehouse: 810 Cromwell Park Dr, Suite D, Glen
Burnie, MD 21061

Ultramarine Publishing Co Inc
12 Washington Ave, Hastings-on-Hudson, NY
10706
Mailing Address: PO Box 303, Hastings-on-
Hudson, NY 10706-0303
Tel: 914-478-1339
E-mail: washbook@sprynet.com
Key Personnel
Sales Mgr: Christopher P Stephens
Founded: 1970
ISBN Prefix(es): 0-89366
Number of titles published annually: 12 Print
Total Titles: 250 Print

Ulysses Press
PO Box 3440, Berkeley, CA 94703-0440
Tel: 510-601-8301 *Toll Free Tel:* 800-377-2542
Fax: 510-601-8307
E-mail: ulysses@ulyssespress.com
Web Site: www.ulyssespress.com
Key Personnel
Publr: Ray Riegert *E-mail:* rayriegert@
ulyssespress.com
Lib Sales Dir: Bryce Willett
E-mail: brycewillett@ulyssespress.com
Founded: 1983
Travel guides, health books, mind, body & spirit,
lifestyle & sexuality titles.
ISBN Prefix(es): 0-915233; 1-56975
Number of titles published annually: 50 Print
Total Titles: 150 Print
Imprints: Hidden Travel Series; Seastone
Distributed by Publishers Group West
Foreign Rep(s): Hi Marketing (UK, Central &
South America, Continental Europe, Far East,
South Africa); Raincoast Book Distribution Ltd
(Canada)
Foreign Rights: InterLicense
Shipping Address: 3286 Adeline St, Suite 1,
Berkeley, CA 94703 *Toll Free Tel:* 800-377-
2542
Membership(s): Publishers Marketing Associa-
tion; SATW

UMI, see Pro Quest Information & Learning

Unarius Academy of Science Publications
Division of Unarius Educational Foundation
145 S Magnolia Ave, El Cajon, CA 92020-4522
SAN: 168-9614
Tel: 619-444-7062 *Toll Free Tel:* 800-475-7062
Fax: 619-447-9637
E-mail: uriel@unarius.org
Web Site: www.unarius.org
Key Personnel
Busn Mgr: Franklin L Garlock
Admin Coord: Carol M Robinson
Founded: 1954
Books on the new science of life, past life, ther-
apy, extraterrestrial civilizations, the prehis-
tory of earth. Study courses, The Psychology
of Consciousness. A course in self mastery.
Principles & practice of past life therapy. Also
journals & mail order books.
ISBN Prefix(es): 0-932642; 0-935097
Number of titles published annually: 3 Print
Total Titles: 85 Print; 2 CD-ROM; 120 Audio
Imprints: Unarius Academy of Science Publica-
tions
Divisions: Audio Books; Greeting Cards; Inspira-
tional Art; Public Access Broadcasting; Unarius
Video Productions
Foreign Rights: Celeste

Underwood Books Inc
PO Box 1609, Grass Valley, CA 95945-1609
Fax: 530-274-7179
Web Site: www.underwoodbooks.com
Key Personnel
Pres: Tim Underwood *E-mail:* timunderwood@cs.
com
Intl Rts: Candace Groskreutz
Founded: 1976
ISBN Prefix(es): 1-887424; 0-88733; 0-934438
Number of titles published annually: 12 Print
Total Titles: 49 Print
Imprints: Greenway
Foreign Rights: Candace Groskreutz
Advertising Agency: Publishers Group West
Shipping Address: 13038 Squirrel Creek Rd,
Grass Valley, CA 95945

Unicor Medical Inc
4160 Carmichael Rd, Suite 101, Montgomery, AL
36106
Tel: 334-260-8150 *Toll Free Tel:* 800-825-7421
Fax: 334-272-1046 *Toll Free Fax:* 800-305-
8030
E-mail: sales@unicormed.com
Web Site: www.unicormed.com
Key Personnel
Pres: Dr Paul K Tanaka
CFO: Wanda K Hamm
Dir, Mktg: Nikki Vrocher
Medical books, medical ICD-9 coding books &
coding software.
ISBN Prefix(es): 1-56781
Number of titles published annually: 13 Print
Total Titles: 13 Print

Union Square Publishing
Imprint of Cardoza Publishing
857 Broadway, 3rd fl, New York, NY 10003
Tel: 212-255-6661 *Fax:* 212-255-6671
E-mail: cardozapub@aol.com
Web Site: www.cardozapub.com
Key Personnel
Pres: Avery Cardoza
Ed: Alixandra Gould; Brian Saliba
Admin: Mary Grimes
Founded: 2002
An independent publisher. Specialize in word
books, biographies, books on language & gen-
eral nonfiction titles.
ISBN Prefix(es): 1-58042
Number of titles published annually: 7 Print

Total Titles: 6 Print
Distributed by Simon & Schuster
Orders to: Simon & Schuster, 100 Front St, Riverside, NJ 08075, Order Processing Dept *Toll Free Tel:* 800-223-2336 *Toll Free Fax:* 800-943-9831 *E-mail:* order_desk@distican.com

Unique Publications Books & Videos
Subsidiary of CFW Enterprises Inc
4201 W Vanowen Place, Burbank, CA 91505
SAN: 214-3313
Tel: 818-845-2656 *Toll Free Tel:* 800-332-3330 *Fax:* 818-845-7761
E-mail: info@cfwenterprises.com
Web Site: www.cfwenterprises.com
Key Personnel
CEO: Curtis F Wong
Pres: Michael James
Sales Mgr: Beatrice Wong
Founded: 1973
Alternative health, paperbacks, periodicals & videos on martial arts, instructional & how-to.
ISBN Prefix(es): 0-86568
Number of titles published annually: 15 Print
Total Titles: 125 Print

The United Educators Inc
900 N Shore Dr, Suite 140, Lake Bluff, IL 60044
SAN: 204-8795
Tel: 847-234-3700 *Fax:* 847-234-8705
E-mail: arslms@aol.com *Cable:* AMEDEN
Key Personnel
Pres: Remo D Piazzi
VP: Anthony R Sacramento
Sec: Diane W Jones
Treas: Peter Ewing
Direct Mail: Diane Pracht
Founded: 1993
Encyclopedias & subscription books.
ISBN Prefix(es): 0-87566
Subsidiaries: Standard Educational Corp

§United Hospital Fund
350 Fifth Ave, 23rd fl, New York, NY 10118-2399
Tel: 212-494-0700 *Fax:* 212-494-0800
E-mail: info@uhfnyc.org
Web Site: www.uhfnyc.org
Key Personnel
Pres: James R Tallon, Jr
VP & Dir, Communs: Phyllis Brooks *Tel:* 212-494-0734
Founded: 1879
Publish research reports, policy briefs & statistical compilations, all relating to health care & hospital services.
ISBN Prefix(es): 0-934459; 1-881277
Number of titles published annually: 12 Print
Total Titles: 30 Print; 3 E-Book

§United Nations Publications
Subsidiary of United Nations
2 United Nations Plaza, Rm DC2-0853, New York, NY 10017
SAN: 206-6718
Tel: 212-963-8302 *Toll Free Tel:* 800-253-9646 *Fax:* 212-963-3489
E-mail: publications@un.org
Web Site: www.un.org/publications
Key Personnel
Chief, UN Pubns: Christopher Woodthorpe
Chief, External Publns: Renata Morteo
Deputy Chief: Gundega Trumkalne
Chief of Unit, Geneva, Europe, Middle East & Africa: Patrice Piguet
Adv & Promos Rep: Marta Cecilia Aviles
Trade Sales: Mohamed Faiz
Founded: 1946
Trade & textbooks published by United Nations, International Court of Justice, UNEP, INSTRAW, UNIDO, UNDP, UNU & UNITAR

on world & national economy, international trade, disarmament, social questions, human rights, international law, questions of international importance.
ISBN Prefix(es): 92-1
Number of titles published annually: 700 Print; 6 Online
Total Titles: 4,000 Print; 35 CD-ROM; 4 E-Book
Imprints: ICJ; INSTRAW; UNICEF; UNIDIR; UNIDO; UNITAR; UNU; UNDP; UNCITRAL; UNEP
Foreign Office(s): Section des Ventes et Commercialisation, Bureau E-4, 1211 Geneva 10, Switzerland, Contact: Patrice Piguet *Tel:* (022) 917-2614 *Fax:* (022) 917-0027
Distributor for ICJ; INSTRAW; IOM; UNFPA; UNICEF; UNICRI; UNU; UNDP; UNIDIR; UNIDO; UNITAR; UNCITRAL
Shipping Address: United Nations, NL-210, New York, NY 10017, Contact: Mohamed Faiz *Tel:* 212-963-8302 *Toll Free Tel:* 800-253-9646 *Fax:* 212-963-3489 *E-mail:* publications@un.org

§United States Holocaust Memorial Museum
100 Raoul Wallenberg Place SW, Washington, DC 20024-2126
Tel: 202-488-6115; 202-488-6144 (orders) *Toll Free Tel:* 800-259-9998 (orders) *Fax:* 202-488-2684; 202-488-0438 (orders)
Web Site: www.ushmm.org/
Key Personnel
Dir, Academic Pubns, Center for Advanced Holocaust Studies: Benton M Arnovitz *Tel:* 202-488-6117 *E-mail:* barnovitz@ushmm.org
Dir, Div Publg (Prodn): Mel Hecker
Mgr, Museum Bookstore & Holocaust Libr Sales Opers: Jerry Rehm
Edit Coord, Academic Pubns, Center for Advanced Holocaust Studies: Aleisa Fishman *Tel:* 202-488-6116 *E-mail:* afishman@ushmm.org
Exhibitions Projects: Ted Phillips
Perms: Karen Coe
Founded: 1993
Co-publish original monographs, translations, classic reprints, testimonial materials & a scholarly journal; publish memoirs & related titles of Holocaust Publications' Holocaust Library imprint (assets acquired in 1993), as well as occasional papers, exhibition catalogues & related works.
ISBN Prefix(es): 0-89604
Number of titles published annually: 12 Print
Total Titles: 115 Print; 2 CD-ROM; 1 E-Book
Imprints: Holocaust Library
Foreign Rights: Goldfarb & Associates (selected titles)

United States Institute of Peace Press
1200 17 St NW, Suite 200, Washington, DC 20036-3011
Tel: 202-457-1700 (edit); 703-661-1590 (cust serv) *Toll Free Tel:* 800-868-8064 (cust serv) *Fax:* 703-661-1501 (cust serv)
Web Site: www.usip.org
Key Personnel
Sales & Mktg Mgr: Kay Hechler *Tel:* 202-429-3816 *E-mail:* khechler@usip.org
Ed: Peter Pavilionis *Tel:* 202-429-3812
Prodn Mgr: Marie Marr *Tel:* 202-429-3815
Founded: 1989
Area of international peacebuilding, policy analysis & conflict resolution. Primarily publish research results from grants, fellowship & commissioned research.
ISBN Prefix(es): 1-878379; 1-929223
Number of titles published annually: 10 Print
Total Titles: 90 Print
Foreign Rep(s): University Presses Marketing (UK, Ireland, Europe, Greece, India, Israel, Scandinavia)

Billing Address: PO Box 605, Herndon, VA 20172-0605 SAN: 254-6965
Orders to: PO Box 605, Herndon, VA 20172-0605 SAN: 254-6965
Shipping Address: 22883 Quicksilver Dr, Dulles, VA 20166

United States Pharmacopeia
12601 Twinbrook Pkwy, Rockville, MD 20852
Tel: 301-881-0666 *Toll Free Tel:* 800-227-8772 *Fax:* 301-816-8148; 301-816-8236 (mktg)
E-mail: marketing@usp.org
Web Site: www.usp.org
Key Personnel
CEO: Dr Roger L Williams *Tel:* 301-881-0666 ext 8300
Mgr, Library Servs: Florence Hogan *Tel:* 301-881-0666 ext 8352
Founded: 1820
Reference books & directories; Databases in print & electronic formats.
ISBN Prefix(es): 0-913595
Number of titles published annually: 3 Print
Total Titles: 25 Print; 2 CD-ROM
Distributed by Consumer Reports; Login Brothers Book Company; Login Publishing Consortium; Matthews Book Co; Rittenhouse Book Distributors, Inc; National Technical Information Service; Promachem LLC
Foreign Rep(s): Deutscher Apotheker Verlag (Austria, Germany, Switzerland); Ernesto Reichmann Distribuidora de Lirros Ltda (Brazil); Login Brothers Canada (Canada); Maruzen Company Ltd (Japan); Pharmaceutical Society of Australia (Australia); Pharmasystems (Canada)

United States Tennis Association
70 W Red Oak Lane, White Plains, NY 10604
Tel: 914-696-7000 *Fax:* 914-696-7027
Web Site: www.usta.com
Key Personnel
Dir, Publg: Rick Rennert *E-mail:* rennert@usta.com
Sr Ed: Edna Gabler *E-mail:* gabler@usta.com
Edit Dir: Mark Preston *E-mail:* preston@usta.com
Founded: 1881
Tennis materials; books, magazines & souvenir programs.
ISBN Prefix(es): 0-938822
Number of titles published annually: 5 Print
Total Titles: 25 Print
Distributed by Universe Publishing; H O Zimman Inc

United Synagogue Book Service
Division of United Synagogue of Conservative Judaism
155 Fifth Ave, New York, NY 10010
SAN: 203-0551
Tel: 212-533-7800 (ext 2003) *Toll Free Tel:* 800-594-5617 (warehouse only) *Fax:* 212-253-5422
E-mail: booksvc@uscj.org
Web Site: www.uscj.org/booksvc
Key Personnel
Dir: Joseph B Sandler
Educ Dir & Ed, Burning Bush Press: Robert Abramson
Asst to the Dir: Elaine Bieber
Adv & Mktg Dir: Ceil Skydell
Founded: 1913
Religion (Jewish); textbooks, juveniles; history, music, Hebrew language instruction, AV materials, liturgical, adult books & prayer books.
ISBN Prefix(es): 0-8381
Number of titles published annually: 5 Print
Total Titles: 230 Print
Imprints: Burning Bush Press; National Academy for Adult Jewish Studies; United Synagogue Commission on Jewish Education; United Synagogue of Conservative Judaism

Distributor for Rabbinical Assembly of America
Shipping Address: Mercedes Book Distributors, Brooklyn Navy Yard, Bldg 3, Brooklyn, NY 11205

Unity House
Division of Unity School of Christianity
1901 NW Blue Pkwy, Unity Village, MO 64065-0001
Tel: 816-524-3550 (ext 3300); 816-251-3571 (sales) *Fax:* 816-251-3557
E-mail: unity@unityworldhq.org
Web Site: www.unityonline.org
Key Personnel
Prodn Mgr: Adrianne Ford
Founded: 1889
Books, cassettes & CDs, pamphlets.
ISBN Prefix(es): 0-87159
Number of titles published annually: 3 Print
Total Titles: 120 Print; 30 Audio
Membership(s): Network of Alternatives for Publishers, Retailers & Artists Inc; Publishers Marketing Association

Univelt Inc
PO Box 28130, San Diego, CA 92198-0130
Tel: 760-746-4005 *Fax:* 760-746-3139
E-mail: 76121.1532@compuserve.com
Web Site: www.univelt.com
Key Personnel
Pres & Publr: Robert H Jacobs
Off Mgr: Madeleine Bera
Founded: 1970
Publisher for American Astronautical Society & International Academy of Astronautics; Lunar & Planetary Society, National Space Society. Specialize in astronautics & aerospace engineering.
ISBN Prefix(es): 0-912183; 0-87703
Number of titles published annually: 10 Print
Total Titles: 343 Print
Imprints: American Astronautical Society
Distributor for Astronautical Society of Western Australia; US Space Foundation
Warehouse: 740 Metcalf St, Suite 13, Escondido, CA 92025-1671

Universe Publishing
Division of Rizzoli International Publications Inc
300 Park Ave S, 3rd fl, New York, NY 10010
Tel: 212-387-3400 *Fax:* 212-387-3535
Key Personnel
VP & Publr: Charles Miers
Publicity Dir: Pam Sommers
Sales Mgr: John Deen
Man Ed: Ellen Nidy
Founded: 1956
Architecture, fine art, photography, illustrated gift books, fashion, culinary, popular culture, children's, design, style & calendars.
ISBN Prefix(es): 0-7893
Number of titles published annually: 60 Print
Imprints: Universe; Universe Calendars
Distributed by Random House
Foreign Rep(s): Bill Bailey (Northern Europe); Bookport Associates (Southern Europe); H Marketing (UK); Marston Book Services Ltd (Europe); Random House (Canada)

University Council for Educational Administration
Univ of Missouri, 205 Hill Hall, Columbia, MO 65211-2185
Tel: 573-884-8300 *Fax:* 573-884-8302
E-mail: ucea@missouri.edu
Web Site: www.ucea.org
Key Personnel
Exec Dir: Michelle D Young
Founded: 1934
Books, journals, monographs, newsletters.
ISBN Prefix(es): 1-55996

Number of titles published annually: 5 Print
Total Titles: 23 Print

The University of Akron Press
374-B Bierce Library, Akron, OH 44325-1703
Tel: 330-972-5342 (ext 1703) *Toll Free Tel:* 877-827-7377 *Fax:* 330-972-8364
E-mail: uapress@uakron.edu
Web Site: www.uakron.edu/uapress
Key Personnel
Dir: Michael Carley *Tel:* 330-972-6896
  E-mail: mjcarley@uakron.edu
Mktg Rep: Marsha Cole *Tel:* 330-972-2795
Founded: 1988
Publish books on technology & the environment, poetry, Ohio history & culture, international political & economic history (series), law, politics & society.
ISBN Prefix(es): 1-884836; 0-9622628
Number of titles published annually: 12 Print; 1 CD-ROM
Total Titles: 60 Print
Distributor for Principia Press

University of Alabama Press
Box 870380, Tuscaloosa, AL 35487-0380
Tel: 205-348-5180; 773-702-7000 (orders) *Fax:* 205-348-9201
Web Site: www.uapress.ua.edu *Cable:* UNIPRESS TUSCALOOSA
Key Personnel
Dir: Daniel Ross *E-mail:* danross@uapress.ua.edu
Man Ed: Suzette Griffith
Prodn Mgr: W Richard Cook
Mktg Man: Elizabeth Motherwell
  E-mail: emother@uapress.ua.edu
Busn Mgr: Jill Kramer
Rts & Perms: Kathleen Domino
Founded: 1945
American & Latin American history & culture, religious & ethnohistory, rhetoric & communications, African American & Native American studies, Judaic studies, Southern regional studies, theatre & regional trade titles.
ISBN Prefix(es): 0-8173
Number of titles published annually: 90 Print
Total Titles: 593 Print
Foreign Rep(s): East-West Export Books (Asia); Eurospan (Europe); Scholarly Book Services (Canada)
Distribution Center: Chicago Distribution Center, 11030 S Langley, Chicago, IL 60628 (orders) *Tel:* 773-568-1550 *Toll Free Tel:* 800-621-2736 (orders only) *Fax:* 773-702-7212 SAN: 630-6047

University of Alaska Press
Eielson Bldg, Rm 104, Fairbanks, AK 99775-6240
SAN: 203-3011
Mailing Address: PO Box 756240, Fairbanks, AK 99775-6240
Tel: 907-474-5831 *Toll Free Tel:* 888-252-6657 (US only) *Fax:* 907-474-5502
E-mail: fypress@uaf.edu
Web Site: www.uaf.edu/uapress
Key Personnel
Exec Ed: Jennifer R Collier
Gen Mgr: Warren Fraser
Founded: 1967
Emphasis on scholarly & nonfiction works related to Alaska, the circumpolar regions & the North Pacific rim.
ISBN Prefix(es): 0-912006; 1-889963
Number of titles published annually: 12 Print
Total Titles: 105 Print
Imprints: Classic Reprint Series; LanternLight Library; Oral Biography Series; Rasmuson Library Historical Translation Series
Distributor for Geophysical Institute; Limestone Press; Spirit Mountain Press; UA Museum; White Mammoth

Membership(s): Alaska History Association; Alaska Library Association; Association of American University Presses; Publishers Marketing Association

The University of Arizona Press
355 S Euclid Ave, Suite 103, Tucson, AZ 85719-6654
SAN: 205-468X
Tel: 520-621-1441 *Toll Free Tel:* 800-426-3797 (orders) *Fax:* 520-621-8899 *Toll Free Fax:* 800-426-3797
E-mail: uapress@uapress.arizona.edu
Web Site: www.uapress.arizona.edu
Key Personnel
Ed-in-Chief & Dir: Christine Szuter
Mktg Dir: Kathryn Conrad *E-mail:* kconrad@uapress.arizona.edu
Design & Prodn Mgr: Anne Keyl
Busn Mgr & Electronic Publg: Elizabeth Swain
Publicity: Jennifer Pinkerton
Acquiring Ed: Patti Hartmann
Film Rts Contact, Paul Kohner Agency Inc: Gary Salt
Founded: 1959
Scholarly works related to the strengths of the University & regional nonfiction about Arizona, the American West & Mexico, Latino Studies & Native American studies.
ISBN Prefix(es): 0-8165
Number of titles published annually: 50 Print
Total Titles: 598 Print
Distributor for Amon Carter Museum; Arizona State Museum; Crow Canyon Archaeological Center; Ironwood Press; OSU Press; University of Arizona Mexican American Studies & Research Center; Statistical Research Inc
Foreign Rep(s): East-West Export Books (Asia, Pacific); University of British Columbia Press (Canada); William Gills (Africa, Europe, Middle East)
Shipping Address: 330 S Toole Ave, Tucson, AZ 85701

The University of Arkansas Press
Division of The University of Arkansas
McIlroy House, 201 Ozark Ave, Fayetteville, AR 72701
Tel: 479-575-3246 *Toll Free Tel:* 800-626-0090 *Fax:* 479-575-6044
E-mail: uapress@uark.edu
Web Site: www.uapress.com
Key Personnel
Dir: Lawrence Malley *Tel:* 479-575-3096
  E-mail: lmalley@uark.edu
Mktg Dir: Thomas Lavoie *Tel:* 479-575-6657
  E-mail: tlavoie@uark.edu
Dir, Editing, Design & Prodn: Brian King
  Tel: 479-575-6780 *E-mail:* brking@uark.edu
Founded: 1980
General humanities: popular culture, Middle East studies, Civil War & civil rights studies.
ISBN Prefix(es): 0-938626; 1-55728
Number of titles published annually: 25 Print
Total Titles: 560 Print; 560 Online
Distributor for Phoenix International
Foreign Rep(s): EWEB (Australia, Far East, Hawaii); PMRA (Caribbean, Latin America)
Advertising Agency: Ad Lib *Fax:* 479-575-6044
Membership(s): American Association of University Presses

University of California, ANR Publications, see ANR Publications University of California

§University of California Institute on Global Conflict & Cooperation
Subsidiary of University of California
9500 Gilman Dr, La Jolla, CA 92093-0518
Tel: 858-534-1979 *Fax:* 858-534-7655
Web Site: www.igcc.ucsd.edu *Cable:* 188929 UC WWD SIO SDG

Key Personnel
Man Ed: Lynne Bush *E-mail:* lbush@ucsd.edu
Founded: 1983
IGCC News Wired (policy briefs & newsletters),
IGCC Review (policy papers) & books au-
thored by members of the University of Cali-
fornia faculty & other participants in sponsored
research programs.
ISBN Prefix(es): 0-934637
Number of titles published annually: 6 Print
Total Titles: 74 Print; 60 E-Book
Distributed by Amazon.com; BarnesandNo-
ble.com; Brookings Institution Press; Columbia
International Affairs Online (CIAO); Cornell
University Press; Garland Publishers; Lynn-
Reinner Publishing; Penn State University
Press; Princeton University Press; Transaction
Publishers; University of Michigan Press; West-
view Press

§University of California Press
2120 Berkeley Way, Berkeley, CA 94720
Tel: 510-642-4247 *Toll Free Tel:* 800-777-4726
Fax: 510-643-7127 *Toll Free Fax:* 800-999-
1958
E-mail: askucp@ucpress.edu
Web Site: www.ucpress.edu *Cable:* CALPRESS
Key Personnel
Dir: Lynne Withey
CFO: Anna Weidman
Asst Dir: Sheila Levine
Ed: Laura Cerruti; Chuck Crumly; Blake Edgar;
Mary Francis; Stanley Holwitz; Deborah Kirsh-
man; Doris Kretschmer; Reed Malcolm; Naomi
Schneider; Kate Toll
Direct Mail Mgr: Shira Weisbach
Adv Mgr: Marta Gasoi
Publicity Mgr: Alexandra Dahne
Rts: Dan Dixon
Prod Mgr: Anthony Crouch
Man Ed: Marilyn Schwartz
Sales Dir: Anna Bullard
Sales Mgr: Amy-Lynn Fischer
UK Sales Mgr: Andrew Brewer
Mktg Dir: Julie Christianson
Journals Mgr: Rebecca Simon
ISBN Contact: Sierra Filucci
Perms: Rose Robinson
Founded: 1893
Trade nonfiction, scholarly & scientific nonfiction,
translations & journals; paperbacks, limited fic-
tion (reprints).
ISBN Prefix(es): 0-520
Number of titles published annually: 260 Print;
10 Online; 10 E-Book
Total Titles: 4,200 Print; 60 Online; 60 E-Book
Imprints: Philip E Lilienthal Asian Studies
Foreign Office(s): University Presses of Califor-
nia, Columbia & Princeton, One Oldlands Way,
Bognor Regis, West Sussex P022 9SA, United
Kingdom
Distributor for art-SITES; British Film Institute;
Huntington Library; Sierra Club Books (Adult
trade)
Foreign Rep(s): Thomas V Cassidy (China);
Adrian Greenwood (Europe & UK); Andrew
& Atsuko Ishigami (Japan); David Stimpson
(Australia, Canada)
Advertising Agency: Fiat Lux
Warehouse: California-Princeton Fulfillment
Services, Inc, 1445 Lower Ferry Rd, Ew-
ing, NJ 08618 *Tel:* 609-883-1759 *Toll Free
Tel:* 800-777-4726 *Fax:* 609-883-7413 *Toll Free
Fax:* 800-999-1958 *E-mail:* orders@cpfsinc.
com *Web Site:* www.ucpress.edu
Membership(s): AAP

University of Chicago Press, see Association of
American University Presses

University of Delaware Press
Affiliate of Associated University Presses

Associated University Presses, 2010 Eastpark
Blvd, Cranbury, NJ 08512
Tel: 609-655-4770 *Fax:* 609-655-8366
E-mail: aup440@aol.com
Key Personnel
Dir: Donald Mell
ISBN Contact: Julien Yoseloff
Founded: 1922
Shakespearean studies; 18th century literature;
naval, military & diplomatic history.
ISBN Prefix(es): 0-87413
Number of titles published annually: 35 Print
Total Titles: 400 Print
Distributed by Associated University Presses
Foreign Rep(s): Eurospan (Europe & UK); Schol-
arly Book Services (Canada); United Publishers
Services (Japan)

**University of Denver Center for Teaching
International Relations Publications**
Subsidiary of University of Denver
University of Denver, CTIR/GSIS, 2201 S Gay-
lord St, Denver, CO 80208
Tel: 303-871-3106 *Toll Free Tel:* 800-967-2847
Fax: 303-871-2456
Web Site: www.du.edu/ctir
Key Personnel
Ctr Dir: Mark Montgomery *Tel:* 303-871-2402
E-mail: mmontgom@du.edu
Founded: 1968
Educational press for primary & secondary teach-
ing materials, supplementary teaching material,
international & intercultural awareness, K-12 &
undergrad curriculum.
ISBN Prefix(es): 0-943804
Number of titles published annually: 8 Print
Total Titles: 26 Print

University of Georgia Press
330 Research Dr, Athens, GA 30602-4901
SAN: 203-3054
Tel: 706-369-6130 *Toll Free Tel:* 800-266-5842
(orders only) *Fax:* 706-369-6131
E-mail: books@ugapress.uga.edu
Web Site: www.ugapress.org
Key Personnel
Dir: Nicole Mitchell
Assoc Dir & Ed-in-Chief: Nancy Grayson
E-mail: ngrayson@ugapress.uga.edu
Design & Prodn: Sandra Hudson
Busn Mgr: Phyllis Wells
Man Ed, Ms Edit: Jennifer Reichlin
Cust Serv Mgr: Brenda Adams
Asst to Dir: Jane Kobres
Founded: 1938
Scholarly nonfiction: poetry, short fiction, regional
studies & natural history.
ISBN Prefix(es): 0-8203
Number of titles published annually: 80 Print
Total Titles: 900 Print
Foreign Office(s): Eurospan, 3 Henrietta St,
Covent Garden, London WC2E 8LU, United
Kingdom
Foreign Rep(s): Cariad Services to Publishers (In-
ternational); East-West Export Books (Asia, Far
East); Eurospan Group (Africa, Europe, Middle
East); Scholarly Book Services Inc (Canada)
See separate listing for:
Carl Vinson Institute of Government

University of Hawaii Press
2840 Kolowalu St, Honolulu, HI 96822
SAN: 202-5353
Tel: 808-956-8255 *Toll Free Tel:* 888-847-7377
Fax: 808-988-6052 *Toll Free Fax:* 800-650-
7811
E-mail: uhpbooks@hawaii.edu
Web Site: www.uhpress.hawaii.edu
Key Personnel
Dir & Intl Rts: William Hamilton
Exec Ed: Patricia Crosby
Ed: Masako Ikeda; Pam Kelley; Keith Leber

Sales Mgr, East-West Export Books Mgr: Royden
Muranaka
Mktg Mgr: Colins Kawai
Busn Mgr: Rosalyn Carr
Prod Mgr, Asian Studies: Steve Hirashima
Journals Mgr: Joel Bradshaw
Promo Mgr, Hawaii & Pacific Studies: Carol Abe
Prodn & Design Mgr: JoAnne Tenorio
Catalogs & E-Mail Mktg Mgr: Stephanie Chun
Electronic Publg: Wanda C China
Founded: 1947
Scholarly & general books & monographs, par-
ticularly those dealing with the Pacific & Asia;
regional books; journals.
ISBN Prefix(es): 0-8248; 0-87022
Number of titles published annually: 100 Print
Total Titles: 1,050 Print
Imprints: Kolowalu Books; Latitude 20
Subsidiaries: East-West Export Books
Distributor for Ateneo De Manila University
Press; Faculty of Asian Studies, Australian
National University; Global Oriental; Katy-
did Books; Nordic Insititute of Asian Studies;
Pasifika Press; Singapore University Press; Uni-
versity of the Phillippines Press
Foreign Rep(s): East-West Export Books (Aus-
tralia, Asia, New Zealand); The Eurospan
Group (Africa, UK, Continental Europe, Mid-
dle East); Scholarly Book Services (Canada)
Advertising Agency: Manini Promotions
Warehouse: 99-1422 Koaha Place, Aiea, HI
96701
Membership(s): American Association of Univer-
sity Presses

University of Healing Press
Division of God Unlimited/University of Healing
1101 Far Valley Rd, Campo, CA 91906-3213
Tel: 619-478-5111; 619-478-2506
Toll Free Tel: 888-463-8654 *Fax:* 619-478-5013
E-mail: unihealing@goduni.org
Web Site: www.university-of-healing.edu
Key Personnel
Pres, CEO & Chmn: Dr Ellen Jermini
Founded: 1975
Textbooks on positive philosophy & spiritual
healing for metaphysical & non-academic uni-
versities & schools around the world; daily
broadcasting (Thought for Today - Instant In-
spiration 10-15 minimuts on website).
ISBN Prefix(es): 0-940480
Number of titles published annually: 3 Print
Total Titles: 23 Print; 700 Audio
Imprints: University of Healing Logo
Foreign Rep(s): European Center for University
of Healing
Membership(s): Better Business Bureau

**§University of Illinois Graduate School of
Library & Information Science**
501 E Daniel St, Champaign, IL 61820-6211
SAN: 277-4917
Tel: 217-333-1359 *Fax:* 217-244-7329
E-mail: puboff@alexia.lis.uiuc.edu
Web Site: www.lis.uiuc.edu/puboff/
Key Personnel
Asst Dean, Pubns & Communs: Marlo Welshons
Tel: 217-244-4643 *E-mail:* welshons@uiuc.edu
Founded: 1949
Journal, conference proceedings, monographs.
ISBN Prefix(es): 0-87845
Number of titles published annually: 3 Print
Total Titles: 55 Print

§University of Illinois Press
Unit of University of Illinois
1325 S Oak, Champaign, IL 61820-6903
SAN: 202-5310
Tel: 217-333-0950; 212-577-5487 *Fax:* 217-244-
8082; 410-516-6969 (orders)
E-mail: uipress@uillinois.edu; journals@uillinois.
edu
Web Site: www.press.uillinois.edu

Key Personnel
Dir: Willis G Regier *Tel:* 217-244-0728
  E-mail: wregier@uillinois.edu
Assoc Dir & Ed-in-Chief: Joan Catapano
Journals Mgr & Asst Dir: Ann Lowry
Prodn Mgr: Kristine Ding
Mktg Dir: Pat Hoefling
Art Dir: Copenhaver Cumpston
Asst to Dir: Mary Wolfe
Man Ed: Rebecca Crist
Publicity Mgr: Danielle Wilberg
Direct Mail Mgr: Barbara Horne
Exhibits Mgr: Margo Chaney
Founded: 1918
Working-class & ethnic studies, religion architecture, Judaica, Mormon Studies, political science, folklore, Chicago, food studies, immigration studies, American history, women's history, music history.
ISBN Prefix(es): 0-252
Number of titles published annually: 140 Print; 3 CD-ROM; 25 E-Book
Total Titles: 1,500 Print; 4 CD-ROM; 10 Online; 35 E-Book; 10 Audio
Branch Office(s)
Chicago, IL
Foreign Rights: Cassidy & Assoc (China); East-West Export Books (Australia, Asia, Hawaii, New Zealand, Pacific); Scholarly Book Services Inc (Canada); University Presses Marketing (UK, Continental Europe)
Advertising Agency: Prairie State Agency
Orders to: c/o Hopkins Fulfillment Center, PO Box 50370, Baltimore, MD 21203 *Tel:* 410-516-6956
Returns: c/o Maple Press Co, Lebanon Distribution Center, 704 Legionaire Dr, Fredericksburg, PA 17026
Warehouse: c/o Maple Press Co, Lebanon Distribution Center, 704 Legionaire Dr, Fredricksburg, PA 17026
Membership(s): AAP; Association of American University Presses

University of Iowa Press
University of Iowa, 100 Kuhl House, Iowa City, IA 52242-1000
SAN: 282-4868
Tel: 319-335-2000 *Toll Free Tel:* 800-621-2736 (orders only) *Fax:* 319-335-2055
  Toll Free Fax: 800-621-8476 (orders only)
E-mail: uipress@uiowa.edu
Web Site: www.uiowapress.org
Key Personnel
Dir: Holly Carver *Tel:* 319-335-2013
  E-mail: holly-carver@uiowa.edu
Mktg Mgr: Megan Scott *Tel:* 319-335-2008
  E-mail: megan-scott@uiowa.edu
Prodn Ed: Karen Copp *Tel:* 319-335-2014
Founded: 1969
Creative fiction, nonfiction, poetry, regional studies, theatre history & literary criticism.
ISBN Prefix(es): 0-87745; 1-58729
Number of titles published annually: 35 Print
Total Titles: 400 Print
Online services available through netLibrary.
Foreign Rep(s): Eurospan (Europe & UK); EWEB (Asia & the Pacific, Australia & New Zealand)
Orders to: Chicago Distribution Center, 11030 S Langley Ave, Chicago, IL 60628
Returns: Chicago Distribution Center, 11030 S Langley Ave, Chicago, IL 60628
Distribution Center: Chicago Distribution Center, 11030 S Langley Ave, Chicago, IL 60628 *Toll Free Tel:* 800-621-2736 *Toll Free Fax:* 800-621-8476
Membership(s): American Association of University Presses

University of Louisiana at Lafayette, Center for Louisiana Studies
PO Box 40831, UL, Lafayette, LA 70504-0831

Tel: 337-482-6027 *Fax:* 337-482-6028
E-mail: ann@louisiana.edu
Web Site: www.cls.louisiana.edu
Key Personnel
Dir: Dr Carl Brasseaux
Asst Dir: James Wilson
Sales & Dist Mgr: Rebecca Watson
Res Assoc: Jennifer Cooper
Founded: 1973
State, history & culture books.
ISBN Prefix(es): 0-940984; 1-887366
Number of titles published annually: 10 Print
Total Titles: 100 Print
Shipping Address: 302 E St Mary Blvd, Lafayette, LA 70504

University of Massachusetts Press
PO Box 429, Amherst, MA 01004-0429
SAN: 203-3089
Tel: 413-545-2217 *Toll Free Tel:* 800-537-5487
  Fax: 413-545-1226; 410-516-6998 (fulfillment)
E-mail: info@umpress.umass.edu; hfcustserv@mail.press.jhu.edu
Web Site: www.umass.edu/umpress *Telex:* Mass Press
Key Personnel
Dir: Bruce Wilcox *Tel:* 413-545-4990
  E-mail: wilcox@umpress.umass.edu
Sr Ed: Clark Dougan *Tel:* 413-545-4989
  E-mail: cdougan@umpress.umass.edu
Boston Ed: Paul Wright *Tel:* 617-287-5710
  E-mail: paul.wright@umb.edu
Design & Prodn Mgr: Jack Harrison *Tel:* 413-545-4998 *E-mail:* harrison@umpress.umass.edu
Mktg, ISBN & Intl Rts: Bruce Wilcox *Tel:* 413-545-4990 *E-mail:* wilcox@umpress.umass.edu
Busn Mgr: Richard Lozier *Tel:* 413-545-4994
  E-mail: rlozier@umpress.umass.edu
Assoc Prodn Mgr: Sally Nichols
Founded: 1964
Scholarly works & books of general interest, including African-American studies, American studies, architecture & environmental design, biography, cultural criticism, history, literary criticism, poetry, policy studies, New England studies, women's & gender studies.
ISBN Prefix(es): 0-87023; 1-55849
Number of titles published annually: 40 Print
Total Titles: 940 Print
Online services available through netLibrary.
Branch Office(s)
University of Massachusetts at Boston Harbor Campus, Boston, MA 02125-3393, Contact: Paul Wright *Tel:* 617-287-5710 *E-mail:* paul.wright@umb.edu
Foreign Rep(s): East-West Export Books (Asia); Eurospan (Africa, Europe, Middle East); Scholarly Book Services (Canada)
Shipping Address: Hopkins Fulfillment Services, PO Box 50370, Baltimore, MD 21211-4370
Membership(s): American Association of University Presses

University of Michigan Center for Japanese Studies
Unit of University of Michigan
1085 Frieze Bldg, 1055 S State St, Ann Arbor, MI 48109-1285
Tel: 734-647-8885 *Fax:* 734-647-8886
E-mail: cjspubs@umich.edu
Web Site: www.umich.edu/~iinet/cjs/
Key Personnel
Exec Ed: Bruce E Willoughby *E-mail:* bew@umich.edu
Founded: 1947
ISBN Prefix(es): 0-939512; 1-929280
Number of titles published annually: 8 Print
Total Titles: 90 Print

University of Michigan Press
Unit of University of Michigan
839 Greene St, Ann Arbor, MI 48104-3209

SAN: 202-5329
Tel: 734-764-4388 *Fax:* 734-615-1540
E-mail: um.press@umich.edu
Web Site: www.press.umich.edu
Key Personnel
Dir: Phil M Pochoda
Asst Dir: Mary Erwin *E-mail:* merwin@umich.edu
Sales Mgr: Michael Kehoe *Tel:* 734-936-0388
  E-mail: mkehoe@umich.edu
Sr Exec Ed: LeAnn Fields *Tel:* 734-936-0451
  E-mail: lfields@umich.edu
Man Ed: Christina Milton *E-mail:* cmilton@umich.edu
Prodn Mgr: John Grucelski *E-mail:* jgrucel@umich.edu
ESL Mgr: Kelly Sippell *E-mail:* ksippell@umich.edu
Mktg Dir: Peter Sickman-Garner
  E-mail: pgarner@umich.edu
Direct Mail: Margaret Haas *Tel:* 734-936-0389
  E-mail: mhaas@umich.edu
Publicist: Mary Bisbee-Beek *E-mail:* bisbeeb@umich.edu
Founded: 1930
Aims for diversity in its books & in its audiences.
ISBN Prefix(es): 0-472
Number of titles published annually: 150 Print; 1 E-Book; 2 Audio
Total Titles: 2,342 Print; 5 CD-ROM; 2 Online; 2 E-Book; 24 Audio
Imprints: Ann Arbor Paperbacks
Distributed by Plymbridge Distributors Ltd (Territory restricted to Europe, Israel & UK; Telex: 45635)
Distributor for Center for Chinese Studies, University of Michigan; Center for South & Southeast Asian Studies, University of Michigan; K G Saur (Teubner titles only)
Foreign Rep(s): APAC Publishers Services (Asia & the Pacific); Tom Cassidy (Hong Kong, People's Republic of China, Taiwan); Harry Howell (Australia, New Zealand); UBC Press (Canada); United Publishers Servs Ltd (Japan); University Presses Marketing (UK, Israel); Wolfgang Wingerter (Europe)
Returns: Chicago Distribution Center, 11030 S Langley Ave, Chicago, IL 60628 *Toll Free Tel:* 800-621-2736 *Toll Free Fax:* 800-621-8476
  E-mail: custserv@press.uchicago.edu
Distribution Center: Chicago Distribution Center, 11030 S Langley Ave, Chicago, IL 60628 *Toll Free Tel:* 800-621-2736 *Toll Free Fax:* 800-621-8476 *E-mail:* custserv@press.uchicago.edu

University of Minnesota Press
111 Third Ave S, Suite 290, Minneapolis, MN 55401-2520
SAN: 213-2648
Tel: 612-627-1970 *Fax:* 612-627-1980
E-mail: ump@tc.umn.edu
Web Site: www.upress.umn.edu
Key Personnel
Dir: Doug Armato
Mgr MMPI: Beverly Kaemmer
Acqs Ed: Richard Morrison; Carrie Mullen; Todd Orjala
Prodn Mgr: Adam Grafa
Publicity & Adv Mgr: Patricia McFadden
Copyediting Mgr: Laura Westlund
Sales Coord: Katie Hoolihan
Intl Rts Contact: Jeff Moen
Direct Mail: Stacy Zellmann
Founded: 1927
University press, scholarly, professional, reference, textbooks; regional nonfiction; cultural theory, media studies, literary theory, gay & lesbian studies, sociology, art, political science, geography, anthropology.
ISBN Prefix(es): 0-8166
Number of titles published annually: 110 Print
Total Titles: 900 Print

Foreign Rep(s): Harry Howell (Australia, New Zealand); Lexa Publishers (Canada); United Publishers Services Ltd (Japan); University Presses Marketing (UK, Israel); Wolfgang Wingerter (Europe)
Returns: Chicago Distribution Center, 11030 S Langley Ave, Chicago, IL 60628
Shipping Address: Chicago Distribution Center, 11030 S Langley Ave, Chicago, IL 60628
Tel: 773-568-1550 *Toll Free Tel:* 800-621-2736 (orders only) *Toll Free Fax:* 800-621-8476 (orders only)
Membership(s): Association of American University Presses

University of Missouri Press
2910 Le Mone Blvd, Columbia, MO 65201
SAN: 203-3143
Tel: 573-882-7641 *Toll Free Tel:* 800-828-1894 (orders) *Fax:* 573-884-4498
Web Site: www.umsystem.edu/upress
Key Personnel
Dir: Beverly Jarrett
Mktg Mgr: Karen D Renner
Rts Mgr: Linda H Frech
Perms: Susan King
Publicity & Sales Asst: Laura Endicott
Founded: 1958
Scholarly books, general trade, art, regional, intellectual thought, short fiction, history, literary criticism, essays, African-American, journalism, political science.
ISBN Prefix(es): 0-8262
Number of titles published annually: 66 Print
Total Titles: 600 Print
Distributor for Missouri Historical Society Press
Foreign Rep(s): East-West Export Books (Asia, New Zealand, Pacific Islands); Eurospan (Africa, UK, Continental Europe, Middle East); Scholarly Book Services (Canada)

University of Nebraska at Omaha Center for Public Affairs Research
6001 Dodge St, Omaha, NE 68182
SAN: 665-4339
Tel: 402-554-2134 *Fax:* 402-554-4946
Web Site: www.cpara.unomaha.edu/
Key Personnel
Dir: Jerry Deichert *E-mail:* jdeicher@mail. unomaha.edu
Professional books.
ISBN Prefix(es): 1-55719
Number of titles published annually: 6 Print
Total Titles: 130 Print

University of Nebraska Press
Division of University of Nebraska, Lincoln
233 N Eighth St, Lincoln, NE 68588-0255
SAN: 202-5337
Tel: 402-472-3581 *Toll Free Tel:* 800-755-1105 (orders) *Fax:* 402-472-0308 *Toll Free Fax:* 800-526-2617
E-mail: press@un1.edu
Web Site: www.nebraskapress.unl.edu; www. bisonbooks.com *Telex:* 48-4340
Key Personnel
Dir: Paul Royster
Asst Mgr & Prodn Mgr: Debra Turner
Acting Dir: Gary Dunham *Tel:* 402-472-4452 *E-mail:* gdunham1@unl.edu
Rts & Perms, Intl Rts: Elaine Maruhn
Man Ed: Beth Ina
Mktg Mgr: Sandra Johnson
Cont: Kandra Hahn
Artist/Designer: Richard Eckersley
Publicity Mgr: Erika Kuebler Rippeteau *Tel:* 402-472-5938 *E-mail:* erippeteau1@unl.edu
Founded: 1941
General scholarly nonfiction, including agriculture & natural resources, anthropology, history, literature & criticism, musicology, philosophy, psychology, wildlife & reference works; em-

phasis on literature & the history of the Trans-Mississippi West. Trade paperbacks, including fiction & science fiction.
ISBN Prefix(es): 0-8032
Total Titles: 1,600 Print; 2 CD-ROM
Imprints: Bison Books; Landmark Editions
Distributor for Buros Institute; Creighton University Press; Dalkey Archive Press; Gordian Knot Books; Reedy Press; Society for American Baseball Research; Zoo Press
Foreign Rep(s): Combined Academic Publishers Ltd (Europe); East-West Export Books (EWEB) (Australia, Asia, New Zealand, Pacific); Lexa Publisher's Representatives (Canada)
Advertising Agency: Scholarly Press Advertising Services
Warehouse: 401 N Ninth St, Lincoln, NE 68588-0484
Membership(s): American Association of University Presses

University of Nevada Press
MS 166, Reno, NV 89557-0076
SAN: 203-316X
Tel: 775-784-6573 *Toll Free Tel:* 800-682-6657 *Fax:* 775-784-6200 *Toll Free Fax:* 877-682-6657
Web Site: www.nvbooks.nevada.edu
Key Personnel
Ed-in-Chief & Dir: Joanne O'Hare *Tel:* 775-784-6573 ext 228 *E-mail:* johare@unr.edu
Ed: Michelle Filippini *Tel:* 775-784-6573 ext 234 *E-mail:* filippin@unr.edu
Busn Mgr: Sheryl Laguna *E-mail:* sll@scs.unr. edu
Man Ed: Sara Velez Mallea *E-mail:* velez@unr. edu
Mktg Mgr: Vicki Davies *Tel:* 775-784-6573 ext 232 *E-mail:* vickid@unr.nevada.edu
Design & Prodn Mgr: Carrie Nelson House *E-mail:* chouse@unr.edu
Warehouse Mgr: Michael Jackson *Tel:* 775-972-2654 *E-mail:* jackson@scs.unr.edu
Off Mgr: Charlotte Heatherly *Tel:* 775-784-6573 ext 222 *E-mail:* ceh@unr.edu
Founded: 1961
ISBN Prefix(es): 0-87417
Number of titles published annually: 50 Print
Total Titles: 315 Print
Distributed by Companion Press
Distributor for Institute for the Study of Gambling & Commercial Gaming; Nevada Humanities Committee
Foreign Rep(s): Eurospan University Press Group (world exc USA & Canada); Scholarly Book Service (Canada)
Warehouse: University of Nevada Press, 5625 Fox Ave, Rm 120, Stead, NV 89506 *E-mail:* jackson@scs.unr.edu

University of New Mexico Press
1720 Lomas Blvd NE, MSC01 1200, Albuquerque, NM 87131-0001
SAN: 213-9588
Tel: 505-277-2346; 505-277-4810 (order dept) *Toll Free Tel:* 800-249-7737 (orders only) *Fax:* 505-277-3350 *Toll Free Fax:* 800-622-8667
E-mail: unmpress@unm.edu; custserv@upress. unm.edu (order dept)
Web Site: unmpress.com
Key Personnel
Dir: Luther Wilson
Busn Mgr: Richard Schuetz
Art & Prodn Mgr: Melissa Tandish *E-mail:* melissat@unm.edu
Assoc Dir & Ed: David V Holtby
Sales & Mktg Mgr: Glenda Madden *Tel:* 505-277-7553 *E-mail:* gmadden@unm.edu
Founded: 1929
General, young adult, scholarly & regional books.
ISBN Prefix(es): 0-8263

Number of titles published annually: 82 Print
Total Titles: 2,000 Print
Branch Office(s)
3721 Spirit Dr SE, Albuquerque, NM 87106 *Tel:* 505-277-4810 *Fax:* 505-277-3350
Distributed by University of British Columbia Press (territory restricted to Canada)
Distributor for La Alameda Press; Ancient City Press; Museum of New Mexico Press
Foreign Rep(s): Astra Agency (Israel); Berj Jamkojian Associates (Africa & Mideast exc South Africa & Israel); Codasat (Canada); EWEB (Australia, Asia); Gazelle Book Distribution (UK, Europe)
Membership(s): Association of American University Presses

University of New Orleans Press
Division of University of New Orleans Foundation
c/o UNO Foundation, 6601 Franklin Ave, New Orleans, LA 70122
Mailing Address: 2000 Lakeshore Dr, ADC 2, New Orleans, LA 70148
Tel: 504-280-1375 *Fax:* 504-280-7339
Web Site: www.uno.edu
Key Personnel
VP, Advancement UNO Foundation: Sharon Gruber *E-mail:* swgruber@uno.edu
Ed, UNO Press: Gabrielle Gautreaux *E-mail:* gabrielle.gautreaux@uno.edu
Edit Asst: Jessica Emerson; Amanda Pederson
Founded: 2000
University Publishing House.
ISBN Prefix(es): 0-9728143
Number of titles published annually: 3 Print
Total Titles: 4 Print
Distributed by Biblio
Membership(s): Publishers Association of the South; Publishers Marketing Association

§The University of North Carolina Press
116 S Boundary St, Chapel Hill, NC 27514-3808
SAN: 203-3151
Tel: 919-966-3561 *Toll Free Tel:* 800-848-6224 (orders only) *Fax:* 919-966-3829 *Toll Free Fax:* 800-272-6817 (orders)
E-mail: uncpress@unc.edu
Web Site: www.uncpress.unc.edu
Key Personnel
Dir: Kate D Torrey
Assoc Dir & Design Prodn Mgr: Richard Hendel
Mktg Mgr: Kathleen Ketterman
Sales Mgr: Johanna Grimes
Ed-in-Chief: David Perry
Sr Ed: Charles Grench
Man Ed: Ron Maner
Rts & Perms & Intl Rts: Vicky Wells
ISBN Contact & Publicity Mgr: Regina M Mahalek
Electronic Projs Coord: Marjorie L Fowler
Adv & Dir, Mktg: Chris L Egan
Founded: 1922
General, scholarly, regional.
ISBN Prefix(es): 0-8078
Number of titles published annually: 100 Print
Total Titles: 1 E-Book
Distributor for Museum of Early Southern Decorative Arts (selected); North Carolina Museum of Art (selected); Southeastern Center for Contemporary Art (selected); Valentine Museum (selected)
Foreign Rep(s): East-West Export Books (Australia, Asia, New Zealand, Pacific); EDIREP (Caribbean, Central America, Mexico, South America); Eurospan University Press Group (Africa, UK, Continental Europe, Middle East); Scholarly Book Services (Canada)
Advertising Agency: Brimley Agency
Warehouse: 925 Branch St, Chapel Hill, NC 27516
Membership(s): AAP; BISG

University of North Texas Press
1820 Highland St, Bain Hall 101, Denton, TX 76201
SAN: 249-4280
Mailing Address: PO Box 311336, Denton, TX 76203-1336
Tel: 940-565-2142 *Fax:* 940-565-4590
Web Site: www.unt.edu/untpress
Key Personnel
Dir: Ronald Chrisman *E-mail:* rchrisman@unt.edu
Man Ed: Karen DeVinney *E-mail:* kdevinney@unt.edu
Founded: 1987
Texana, Mexican-American studies, folklore.
ISBN Prefix(es): 0-929398; 1-57441
Number of titles published annually: 16 Print; 5 Online
Total Titles: 247 Print; 75 Online
Online services available through netLibrary.
Distributed by Texas A&M University Press
Foreign Rep(s): Cariad Ltd (Canada); East-West Export Books (Australia, Asia, Hawaii, New Zealand, Pacific Islands); Eurospan Group (Europe); US Pub Rep Inc (Latin America)
Distribution Center: University Consortium, John H Lindsey Bldg, Lewis St, 4354 Tamu, College Station, TX 77843-4354 *Toll Free Tel:* 800-826-8911 *Toll Free Fax:* 888-617-2421

University of Notre Dame Press
310 Flanner Hall, Notre Dame, IN 46556
SAN: 203-3178
Tel: 574-631-6346 *Toll Free Tel:* 800-621-2736 (orders) *Fax:* 574-631-8148 *Toll Free Fax:* 800-621-8476 (orders)
E-mail: nd.undpress.1@nd.edu
Web Site: www.undpress.nd.edu *Telex:* 95-3008 *Cable:* DULAC
Key Personnel
Dir: Barbara Hanrahan
Ed: Rebecca De Boer
Busn Mgr: Diane Schaut *Tel:* 574-631-4904
Intl Rts: Lowell Francis
Prodn Ed & ISBN Contact: Wendy McMillen
Secy: Gina Bixler
Founded: 1949
Academic books, hardcover & paperback; philosophy, Irish studies, literature, theology, international relations, sociology & general interest.
ISBN Prefix(es): 0-268
Number of titles published annually: 50 Print
Total Titles: 700 Print
Foreign Rep(s): Eurospan; EWEB
Returns: Chicago Distribution Center, 11030 S Langley, Chicago, IL 60628
Distribution Center: Chicago Distribution Center, 11030 S Langley Ave, Chicago, IL 60628 *Toll Free Tel:* 800-621-2736 (orders) *Toll Free Fax:* 800-621-8476 (orders)
Membership(s): American Association of University Presses

University of Oklahoma Press
4100 28 Ave NW, Norman, OK 73069-8218
Mailing Address: 2800 Venture Dr, Norman, OK 73069-8218 SAN: 203-3194
Tel: 405-325-2000 *Toll Free Tel:* 800-627-7377 (orders) *Fax:* 405-364-5798 (orders) *Toll Free Fax:* 800-735-0476 (orders)
E-mail: oupress@ou.edu
Web Site: www.oupress.com
Key Personnel
Dir & Acq Ed: John Drayton
CFO: Diane Cotts
Ed-in-Chief & Acq Ed: Charles Rankin
Man Ed: Alice Stanton
Acq Ed: Karen Wieder
Ms Ed: Jennifer Cunningham; Julie Shilling; Marian Stewart
Prod Mgr: Patsy Willcox
Sales & Mktg Dir: Dale Bennie *Tel:* 405-325-3207

Publicity Mgr: Caroline Dwyer
Promo Mgr: Joy Warren
Design: Tony Roberts
Exhibits Mgr: Jo Ann Reece
Contracts, Rts & Perms: Angelika Tietz
Founded: 1928
General scholarly nonfiction, Americana, regional, American Indian studies, natural history, anthropology, archaeology, history, literature, classical studies, women's studies, political science, western history.
ISBN Prefix(es): 0-8061
Number of titles published annually: 80 Print
Total Titles: 1,050 Print; 1 CD-ROM
Distributor for Vanderbilt University Press; University Press of Colorado; University Press of the West Indies
Warehouse: University of Oklahoma Press
Membership(s): AAP; American Association of University Presses

§The University of Pennsylvania Museum of Archaeology & Anthropology
Division of University of Pennsylvania
3260 South St, Philadelphia, PA 19104-6324
Tel: 215-898-5723 *Fax:* 215-573-2497
E-mail: publications@museum.upenn.edu
Web Site: www.museum.upenn.edu/publications
Key Personnel
Dir, Museum Pubns: Walda Metcalf
E-mail: metcalfw@sas.upenn.edu
Founded: 1889
ISBN Prefix(es): 0-686; 0-934718; 0-924171; 1-873415; 1-931707
Number of titles published annually: 14 Print
Total Titles: 210 Print; 6 CD-ROM
Imprints: University of Pennsylvania Museum of Archaeology & Anthropology
Billing Address: Hopkins Fulfillment Service, PO Box 50370, Baltimore, MD 21211-4370 *Toll Free Tel:* 800-537-5487 *Fax:* 410-516-6998
Orders to: Hopkins Fulfillment Service, PO Box 50370, Baltimore, MD 21211-4370 *Toll Free Tel:* 800-537-5487 *Fax:* 410-516-6998
Returns: Hopkins Fulfillment Service, PO Box 50370, Baltimore, MD 21211-4370 *Toll Free Tel:* 800-537-5487 *Fax:* 410-516-6998
Shipping Address: Hopkins Fulfillment Service, PO Box 50370, Baltimore, MD 21211-4370 *Toll Free Tel:* 800-537-5487 *Fax:* 410-516-6998

University of Pennsylvania Press
4200 Pine St, Philadelphia, PA 19104-4011
SAN: 202-5345
Tel: 215-898-6261 *Toll Free Tel:* 800-445-9880 (orders & cust serv only) *Fax:* 215-898-0404; 410-516-6998 (orders)
E-mail: custserv@pobox.upenn.edu
Web Site: www.upenn.edu/pennpress
Key Personnel
Dir: Eric Halpern *Tel:* 215-848-6263
E-mail: ehalpern@pobox.upenn.edu
Mktg Dir: Laura Waldron *Tel:* 215-898-1673
E-mail: lwaldron@pobox.upenn.edu
Busn Mgr: Julie Schilling *Tel:* 215-898-1670
E-mail: juliesch@pobox.upenn.edu
Editing & Prodn Mgr: George Lang *Tel:* 215-898-1675 *E-mail:* gwlang@pobox.upenn.edu
Publicity & PR Mgr: Jessica M Pigza *Tel:* 215-898-1674 *E-mail:* jpigza@pobox.upenn.edu
Direct Mail & Adv Mgr: Laura Lindquist *Tel:* 215-898-9184 *E-mail:* laurajl@pobox.upenn.edu
Man Ed: Alison Anderson *Tel:* 215-898-1678 *E-mail:* anderaa@pobox.upenn.edu
Art & Architecture Ed: Jo Joslyn *Tel:* 215-898-5754 *E-mail:* joslyn@pobox.upenn.edu
Humanities Ed: Jerome E Singerman *Tel:* 215-898-1681 *E-mail:* singerma@pobox.upenn.edu
History Ed: Robert Lockhart *Tel:* 215-898-1677 *E-mail:* rlochhar@pobox.upenn.edu
Social Sciences Ed: Peter A Agree *Tel:* 215-573-3816 *E-mail:* agree@pobox.upenn.edu

Team Leader, Order Processing: Melinda Kelly
Tel: 410-516-6948 *E-mail:* mkelly@mail.press.jhu.edu
Founded: 1890
Scholarly & semipopular nonfiction, especially in art & architecture, history, literature & criticism, social sciences, human rights, mid-Atlantic regional studies.
ISBN Prefix(es): 0-8122
Number of titles published annually: 75 Print
Total Titles: 900 Print; 370 Online
Online services available through netLibrary.
Imprints: Pine Street Books
Foreign Rights: East-West Export Books Inc (SE Asia); Scholarly Book Services (Canada); University Presses Marketing (UK, Europe, Middle East)
Orders to: Penn Press, Hopkins Fulfillment Services, PO Box 50370, Hampden Sta, Baltimore, MD 21211
Returns: Penn Press, c/o Maple Press Co, Lebanon Distribution Ctr, 704 Legionaire Dr, Fredericksburg, PA 17026
Membership(s): American Association of University Presses

University of Pittsburgh Press
3400 Forbes Ave, 5th fl, Pittsburgh, PA 15260
SAN: 203-3216
Tel: 412-383-2456 *Fax:* 412-383-2466
E-mail: press@pitt.edu
Web Site: www.pitt.edu/~press
Key Personnel
Dir: Cynthia Miller *E-mail:* cymiller@pitt.edu
Mktg Dir: Dennis Lloyd *Tel:* 412-383-2495
E-mail: dlloyd@pitt.edu
Busn Mgr: Cindy Wessels *E-mail:* caw1@pitt.edu
Rts & Perms: Margie K Bachman
E-mail: mkbachma@pitt.edu
Acquisitions Ed: Nathan MacBrien
E-mail: macbrien@pitt.edu
Founded: 1936
Scholarly nonfiction; poetry, regional books, short fiction; Russian & East European studies; composition & rhetoric, Latin American studies, environmental history, philosophy of science, political science.
ISBN Prefix(es): 0-8229
Number of titles published annually: 55 Print
Total Titles: 600 Print; 35 E-Book
Imprints: Golden Triangle Books (historical fiction for young readers)
Sales Office(s): Chicago Distribution Ctr, 11030 S Langley, Chicago, IL 60628-3893
Distributed by University of Chicago Press Distribution Ctr
Foreign Rep(s): East-West Export Books (Asia, Oceania); Eurospan (UK, Europe); Scholarly Book Services (Canada)
Billing Address: Chicago Distribution Ctr, 11030 S Langley, Chicago, IL 60628-3893
Returns: Chicago Distribution Ctr, 11030 S Langley, Chicago, IL 60628-3893
Warehouse: Chicago Distribution Ctr, 11030 S Langley, Chicago, IL 60628-3893 *Tel:* 773-702-7000 *Toll Free Tel:* 800-621-2736 *Fax:* 773-702-7212 *Toll Free Fax:* 800-621-8476
Distribution Center: Chicago Distribution Ctr, 11030 S Langley, Chicago, IL 60628-3893

University of Puerto Rico Press
Subsidiary of University of Puerto Rico
Edificio EDUPR/Dialogo, Carr No 1, KM 12-0, Piso 2, Jardin Bota'nico Area Norte, San Juan, PR 00931
Mailing Address: PO Box 23322, Rio Piedras, PR 00931-3322 SAN: 208-1245
Tel: 787-758-6932; 787-758-8345 (sales); 787-250-0046; 787-250-0000 *Fax:* 787-753-9116; 787-751-8785 (sales dept)
Key Personnel
Dir: Manuel G Sandoval
Busn Mgr: Sr Carlos Gonzalez Luna

Prod Coord: Marta Aponte Alsina
Sales Dir: Jose A Burgos
Mktg Dir: Rosa Henche
Billing Contact: Myrna Lee Colon
Founded: 1932
General fiction & nonfiction, reference books, college texts; Latin America.
ISBN Prefix(es): 0-8477
Number of titles published annually: 30 Print
Total Titles: 792 Print
Imprints: Coleccion Aquiy Ahora; Coleccion Caribena; Coleccion Cultura Basica; Coleccion Infantil; Coleccion Mente y Palabra; Coleccion Puertorriquena; Coleccion San Pedrito; Coleccion Uprex
Foreign Rep(s): Lectorum Publications (USA); Libreria La Trinitaria (Dominican Republic); Libros Sin Fronteras (USA)
Warehouse: Planta Piloto de Ron, Rd No 1, KM-12-0, UPR Botanical Garden, San Juan, PR 00931 (Directories on road from Piedras to Caguas)
Membership(s): American Association of University Presses

University of Rochester Press
Affiliate of Boydell & Brewer
668 Mt Hope Ave, Rochester, NY 14620
Tel: 585-275-0419 *Fax:* 585-271-8778
E-mail: boydell@boydellusa.net
Web Site: boydellandbrewer.com
Key Personnel
Dir, Sales & Mktg: Susan Dykstra-Poel *E-mail:* dykstrapoel@boydellusa.net
Ed: Timothy Madigan *E-mail:* madigan@uofrochesterpress.net
Accts Mgr: Eloise Puls *E-mail:* puls@boydellusa.net
Founded: 1989
Specializing in philosophy, music & African studies titles.
ISBN Prefix(es): 1-878822; 1-58046
Number of titles published annually: 25 Print
Total Titles: 132 Print
Foreign Office(s): PO Box 9, Woodbridge Suffolk IP12 3DF, United Kingdom
Foreign Rep(s): Boydell & Brewer (Europe, Japan)
Warehouse: Publishers Shipping & Storage, 231 Industrial Park, 46 Development Rd, Fitchburg, MA 01420-6019, Contact: John Salvey *Tel:* 978-345-2121 *Fax:* 978-348-1233

University of Scranton Press
Division of University of Scranton
445 Madison Ave, Scranton, PA 18510
Tel: 570-941-4228 *Toll Free Tel:* 800-941-3081 *Fax:* 570-941-6256 *Toll Free Fax:* 800-941-8804
Web Site: www.scrantonpress.com (Catalog)
Key Personnel
Dir: Richard W Rousseau, S J *Tel:* 570-941-7449 *E-mail:* richard.rousseau@scranton.edu
Prodn: Patricia Mecadon *E-mail:* mecadonp1@scranton.edu
Founded: 1988
Specialize in religious studies & philosophy of religion & culture of Northeast PA.
ISBN Prefix(es): 0-940866; 1-58966
Number of titles published annually: 10 Print; 5 Online; 5 E-Book
Total Titles: 80 Print; 38 Online; 26 E-Book
Imprints: Ridge Row Books
Subsidiaries: Ridge Row Press
Advertising Agency: Trinka Ravaioli Pettinato Grapevine Design, 1641 Sanderson Ave, Scranton, PA 18509 *Tel:* 570-558-0203 *Fax:* 570-558-0204 *E-mail:* grapevine_design@yahoo.com

Distribution Center: Offset Paperback, Wilkes Barre, PA 18705 *Tel:* 570-675-5261 *Fax:* 570-675-8572
Membership(s): American Association of University Presses; Association of Jesuit University Presses

§University of South Carolina Press
Affiliate of University of South Carolina
1600 Hampton St, 5th fl, Columbia, SC 29208
SAN: 203-3224
Tel: 803-777-5243 *Toll Free Tel:* 800-768-2500 (orders) *Fax:* 803-777-0160 *Toll Free Fax:* 800-868-0740 (orders)
Web Site: www.sc.edu/uscpress/
Key Personnel
Dir: Curtis L Clark *Tel:* 803-777-5245
Design & Prodn Mgr: Pat Callahan *Tel:* 803-777-2449 *E-mail:* mpcallah@sc.edu
Asst Dir & Mktg Mgr: Linda Fogle *Tel:* 803-777-4848 *E-mail:* lfogle@sc.edu
Busn Mgr & Perms: Dianne Smith *Tel:* 803-777-1773 *E-mail:* dismith@sc.edu
Credit Mgr: Vicki Sewell *Tel:* 803-777-7754 *E-mail:* sewellv@sc.edu
Man Ed: William Adams *Tel:* 803-777-5075 *E-mail:* adamswb@sc.edu
Asst to Dir: Karen Riddle *Tel:* 803-777-5245 *E-mail:* riddlek@sc.edu
Founded: 1944
American history/studies, Southern studies, military history, maritime history, literary studies including Contemporary American & British literature & modern world literature, religious studies, speech/communication, social work.
ISBN Prefix(es): 0-87249; 1-57003
Number of titles published annually: 45 Print
Total Titles: 700 Print; 2 CD-ROM; 2 Audio
Distributor for McKissick Museum; SC Historical Society; Saraland Press; South Carolina Bar Association
Foreign Rep(s): East-West Export Books; Eurospan University Press Group (UK, Europe); Scholary Book Services (Canada)
Advertising Agency: Palmetto In-House Advertising Agency, Contact: Lynne Parker *Tel:* 803-777-5231 *E-mail:* parker11@sc.edu *Web Site:* www.sc.edu/uscpress
Warehouse: University of South Carolina Press, 718 Devine St, Columbia, SC 29208, Contact: Libby Mack *Tel:* 803-777-1108 *Toll Free Tel:* 800-768-2500 *Fax:* 803-777-0026 *Toll Free Fax:* 800-868-0740
Membership(s): American Association of University Presses; Publishers Association of the South; Southeast Booksellers Association

University of Tennessee Press
110 Conference Center Bldg, Knoxville, TN 37996-4108
SAN: 212-9930
Tel: 865-974-3321 *Toll Free Tel:* 800-621-2736 (ordering) *Fax:* 865-974-3724
E-mail: custserv@utpress.org
Web Site: www.utpress.org
Key Personnel
Dir: Jennifer Siler
Man Ed: Stan Ivester
Acqs Ed: Scott Danforth
Mktg Mgr: Cheryl Carson
Publicity Mgr: Tom Post *E-mail:* tpost@utk.edu
Busn Mgr: Tammy Berry
Founded: 1940
Scholarly & regional nonfiction.
ISBN Prefix(es): 0-87049; 1-57233
Number of titles published annually: 40 Print
Total Titles: 650 Print; 1 Online
Foreign Rep(s): East-West Export Books Inc (Asia & the Pacific)
Orders to: Toll Free Tel: 800-621-2736

Distribution Center: Chicago Distribution Center, 11030 S Langley, Chicago, IL 60628
Membership(s): AAP; Association of American University Presses

University of Texas at Arlington School of Urban & Public Affairs
University Hall, 5th fl, 601 S Naderman Dr, Arlington, TX 76010
Mailing Address: PO Box 19588, Arlington, TX 76019
Tel: 817-272-3071 *Fax:* 817-272-5008
E-mail: supapubs@uta.edu
Web Site: www.uta.edu/supa
Key Personnel
Dean: Richard L Cole
Commus Dir: Victoria Gillette
Newsletter, working papers, books, reports on community revitalization, population projection, charter school evaluation, strategic planning, land use planning, transportation planning, social welfare policy, urban politics, social planning, urban public finance, consensus, building & dispute resolution, group facilitation, urban management, environmental planning & analysis.
ISBN Prefix(es): 0-936440
Number of titles published annually: 15 Print
Total Titles: 40 Print

§The University of Utah Press
Subsidiary of University of Utah
1795 E South Campus Dr, Rm 101, Salt Lake City, UT 84112-9402
SAN: 220-0023
Tel: 801-581-6671 *Toll Free Tel:* 800-773-6672 *Fax:* 801-581-3365
E-mail: info@upress.utah.edu
Web Site: www.uofupress.com
Key Personnel
Prodn Mgr: Virginia Fontana
Dir: Jeff Grathwohl
Busn Mgr: Sharon Day
Mktg & Sales Mgr: Marcelyn Ritchie *Tel:* 801-585-9786 *E-mail:* mritchie@upress.utah.edu
Founded: 1949
Scholarly books, regional studies, anthropology, archaeology, linguistics, Mesoamerican studies, natural history, western history, outdoor recreation.
ISBN Prefix(es): 0-87480
Number of titles published annually: 30 Print
Total Titles: 275 Print; 1 CD-ROM
Distributor for BYU Museum of Peoples & Cultures; Utah Museum of Natural History
Foreign Rep(s): East-West Export Books (Australia, Asia, Hawaii, New Zealand, Oceania); Scholarly Book Services Inc (Canada)

The University of Virginia Press
Affiliate of University of Virginia
PO Box 400318, Charlottesville, VA 22904-4318
Tel: 434-924-3468 (cust serv); 434-924-3469 (cust serv) *Toll Free Tel:* 800-831-3406 (cust serv) *Fax:* 434-982-2655 *Toll Free Fax:* 877-288-6400
E-mail: upressvirginia@virginia.edu
Web Site: www.upressvirginia.edu
Key Personnel
Dir: Penelope J Kaiserlian
Dir, Mktg: Mark Saunders *Tel:* 434-924-6064 *E-mail:* mhs5u@virginia.edu
Mktg Mgr: Nancy J Mills *Tel:* 434-924-6070
Prod & Design: Martha Farlow
Rts & Perms & Asst to Dir: Mary MacNeil
Acqs Ed, Humanities: Cathie Brettschneider
Acqs Ed, Social Science & History: Richard Holway
Acqs Ed, Regional & Reprints: Boyd Zenner
Cust Serv: Brenda Fitzgerald
Busn Mgr: David Garrett
Publicist: Emily Grandstaff

Founded: 1963
General scholarly nonfiction with emphasis on history, literature & regional books.
ISBN Prefix(es): 0-8139
Number of titles published annually: 55 Print
Total Titles: 1,250 Print; 2 E-Book
Distributor for Colonial Society of Massachusetts; Mount Vernon Ladies Association
Foreign Rep(s): East-West Export Books (Pacific); Eurospan (Europe)
Shipping Address: 500 Edgemont, Charlottesville, VA 22903
Membership(s): American Association of University Presses

§University of Washington Press
1326 Fifth Ave, Suite 555, Seattle, WA 98101-2604
Mailing Address: PO Box 50096, Seattle, WA 98145-5096 SAN: 212-2502
Tel: 206-543-4050; 206-543-8870
   Toll Free Tel: 800-441-4115 (orders) *Fax:* 206-543-3932 *Toll Free Fax:* 800-669-7993 (orders)
E-mail: uwpord@u.washington.edu
Web Site: www.washington.edu/uwpress/
Key Personnel
Dir: Pat Soden
Exec Ed: Michael Duckworth
Ed-at-Large: Naomi B Pascal
Man Ed: Marilyn Trueblood
Prodn Mgr: John Stevenson *Tel:* 206-221-5893
   E-mail: jasbooks@u.washington.edu
Mktg Mgr: Alice Herbig
Rts & Perms & Intl Rts: Denise Clark *Tel:* 206-543-4057 *E-mail:* ddclark@u.washington.edu
Art Dir: Audrey Meyer
Gen Mgr: Mary Andersen
Asst Man Ed: Mary Ribesky
Sales Mgr: Marcy Garrard
Publicist: Gigi Lamm
Adv Mgr: Alice Schroeter
Founded: 1920
General scholarly nonfiction, reprints, imports.
ISBN Prefix(es): 0-295
Number of titles published annually: 50 Print
Total Titles: 1,375 Print; 1 CD-ROM
Foreign Rep(s): Combined Academic Publisher Ltd (UK); Douglas & McIntyre (Canada); University of British Columbia Press (Canada)
Warehouse: 1126 N 98 St, Seattle, WA 98103

University of Wisconsin Press
1930 Monroe St, 3rd fl, Madison, WI 53711
SAN: 501-0039
Tel: 608-263-1110 *Toll Free Tel:* 800-621-2736 (Orders) *Fax:* 608-263-1120
   Toll Free Fax: 800-621-8476 (Orders)
E-mail: uwiscpress@uwpress.wisc.edu (Main Office)
Web Site: www.wisc.edu/wisconsinpress/
Key Personnel
Dir: Robert Mandel *Tel:* 608-263-1101
   E-mail: ramandel@wisc.edu
Acqs Ed: Raphael Kadushin *Tel:* 608-263-1062
   E-mail: kadushin@wisc.edu
Rts & Perms: Margaret A Walsh *Tel:* 608-263-1131 *E-mail:* mawalsh1@wisc.edu
Assoc Dir: Steve Salemson *Tel:* 608-263-0263
   E-mail: salemson@wisc.edu
Asst Dir, Busn: Rod Knutson *Tel:* 608-263-0165
   Fax: 608-263-1120 *E-mail:* rpknutso@wisc.edu
Outreach Dir: Sheila M Leary *Tel:* 608-263-0795
   E-mail: smleary@wisc.edu
Mktg & Sales Mgr: Andrea Christofferson
   Tel: 608-263-0814 *E-mail:* aschrist@wisc.edu
Prodn Mgr & ISBN Contact: Terry Emmrich
   Tel: 608-263-0731 *E-mail:* temmrich@wisc.edu
Journals Mgr: John Delaine *Tel:* 608-263-0667
   Fax: 608-263-1173 *E-mail:* jkdelaine@wisc.edu
Publicity Mgr: Bensen Gardner
   E-mail: publicity@uwpress.wisc.edu
Founded: 1937

Academic Press, including Regional Midwest titles & trade titles.
ISBN Prefix(es): 0-87972; 0-299; 1-928755; 0-87020; 0-9671787; 1-931; 8-158; 0-9682722; 0-924119; 0-9655464; 0-9718963; 0-9624369; 0-932900; 1-931569
Number of titles published annually: 80 Print; 1 CD-ROM; 1 Audio
Total Titles: 1,385 Print; 8 CD-ROM; 3 Audio
Imprints: Popular Press; Terrace Books
Foreign Office(s): East-West Export Books, Univ Hawaii Press, 2840 Kolowalu St, Honolulu, HI 96822 (Asia, the Pacific, Australia & New Zealand) *Tel:* 808-956-8830 *Fax:* 808-988-6052 *E-mail:* eweb@hawaii.edu
Eurospan Ltd, 3 Henrietta St, Covent Garden, London WC2E 8LU, United Kingdom (Africa, Europe, Middle East & UK) *Tel:* (020) 7240 0856 *Fax:* (020) 7379 0609 *E-mail:* info@eurospan.co.uk
Distributor for The Center for the Study of Upper Midwestern Culture; Dryad Press; Elvehjem Museum of Art; International Brecht Society; Max Kade Institute for German-American Studies; Spring Freshet Press; Wisconsin Academy of Sciences, Arts & Letters; Wisconsin Historical Society Press; Wisconsin Veterans Museum
Foreign Rights: East-West Export Books Inc (Asia & the Pacific, Australia & New Zealand); Eurospan Ltd (Africa, UK, Continental Europe, Ireland, Iceland, Middle East)
Advertising Agency: Ad Vantage, Anne Herger
Orders to: Chicago Distribution Center, 11030 S Langley Ave, Chicago, IL 60628-3892 SAN: 202-5280
Returns: Chicago Distribution Center, 11030 S Langley Ave, Chicago, IL 60628-3892 SAN: 202-5280
Shipping Address: Chicago Distribution Center, 11030 S Langley Ave, Chicago, IL 60628-3892 SAN: 202-5280
Warehouse: Chicago Distribution Center, 11030 S Langley Ave, Chicago, IL 60628-3892 SAN: 202-5280
Distribution Center: Chicago Distribution Center, 11030 S Langley Ave, Chicago, IL 60628-3892 *Tel:* 773-568-1550 *Toll Free Tel:* 800-621-2736 *Fax:* 773-660-2235 *Toll Free Fax:* 800-621-8476 SAN: 202-5280
Membership(s): Association of American University Presses; Upper Midwest Booksellers Association; Wisconsin Library Association

University of Wisconsin-Milwaukee Center for Architecture & Urban Planning Research
PO Box 413, Milwaukee, WI 53201-0413
Tel: 414-229-2878 *Fax:* 414-229-6976
E-mail: caupr@uwm.edu
Web Site: www.uwm.edu/SARUP
Key Personnel
Dir: Susan Weistrop *E-mail:* susatrop@uwm.edu
Pubns Secy: Barb Garncarz
Specialize in architecture, design & urban planning.
ISBN Prefix(es): 0-938744
Number of titles published annually: 3 Print
Total Titles: 50 Print

University Press of America Inc
Member of Rowman & Littlefield Publishing Group
4501 Forbes Blvd, Suite 200, Lanham, MD 20706
SAN: 200-2256
Tel: 301-459-3366 *Toll Free Tel:* 800-462-6420
   Fax: 301-429-5748 *Toll Free Fax:* 800-338-4550
Web Site: www.univpress.com
Key Personnel
Chmn: Stanley D Plotnick
Pres & Publr: James E Lyons
VP & Dir: Judith L Rothman

CFO: George Franzak
Exec VP & COO: Irv Myers
VP & Mfg: Joyce Culley
VP, Mktg: Nora Kisch
Ed & ISBN Contact: Beverly Baum
Mgr, Rts & Perms & Intl Rts Contact: Kelly L Rogers
Edit Admin: MacDuff Stewart
Founded: 1974
Scholarly monographs, college texts, conference proceedings, professional books & reprints in the social sciences & the humanities.
ISBN Prefix(es): 0-8191; 0-7618
Number of titles published annually: 275 Print
Total Titles: 10,000 Print; 15 Online
Imprints: Hamilton Books
Divisions: UPA Co-Publishing; UPA Publishers' Reprints
Branch Office(s)
67 Mowat Ave, Suite 241, Toronto, ON M6K 3E3, Canada, Contact: Les Petriw *Tel:* 416-534-1660 *Fax:* 416-534-3699
Foreign Office(s): Oxford Publicity Partnership, 12 Hid's Copse Rd, Summer Hill, Oxford OX2 9JJ, United Kingdom, Contact: Gary Hall *Tel:* 1865-865-466 *Fax:* 1865-862-763
Distributor for Atlantic Council; Center for National Policy Press; Harvard Center for International Affairs; International Law Institute; Joint Center for Political & Economic Studies Press; Society of the Cincinnati; White Burkett Miller Center
Foreign Rep(s): NBN Plymbridge (Europe & UK); United Publishers Services
Foreign Rights: United Publishers Service (Japan)
Advertising Agency: ABC Marketing
Shipping Address: 15200 NBN Way, Blue Ridge Summit, PA 17214 *Toll Free Tel:* 800-462-6420 *Fax:* 717-794-3812 *Toll Free Fax:* 800-338-4550
Membership(s): AAP

University Press of Colorado
5589 Arapahoe Ave, Suite 206-C, Boulder, CO 80303
SAN: 202-1749
Tel: 720-406-8849 *Toll Free Tel:* 800-627-7377
   Fax: 720-406-3443
Web Site: www.upcolorado.com
Key Personnel
Dir & Ed: Darrin Pratt *E-mail:* darrin@upcolorado.com
Prodn Mgr: Laura Furney
Founded: 1969
Scholarly & regional nonfiction.
ISBN Prefix(es): 0-87081
Number of titles published annually: 30 Print; 10 E-Book
Total Titles: 259 Print; 290 E-Book
Distributor for Center for Literary Publishing; Colorado Historical Society
Foreign Rep(s): East-West Export Books Inc (Asia, Middle East, Near East, Pacific); Gazelle Book Services (UK, Ireland, Europe)
Advertising Agency: Center for Literary Publishing
Returns: University of Oklahoma Press, 4100 20 Ave NW, Norman, OK 73069
Distribution Center: University of Oklahoma Press, 4100 20 Ave NW, Norman, OK 73069
Membership(s): Association of American University Presses

University Press of Florida
Affiliate of State University System of Florida
15 NW 15 St, Gainesville, FL 32611-2079
SAN: 207-9275
Tel: 352-392-1351 *Toll Free Tel:* 800-226-3822 (orders only) *Fax:* 352-392-7302
   Toll Free Fax: 800-680-1955 (orders only)
E-mail: info@upf.com
Web Site: www.upf.com

Key Personnel
Dir: Kenneth J Scott *E-mail:* ks@upf.com
Assoc Dir & Ed-in-Chief: John Byram
    E-mail: john@upf.com
Sr Ed: Meredith Morris-Babb *E-mail:* mb@upf.
    com
Asst Dir & Man Ed: Deidre Bryan *E-mail:* db@
    upf.com
Assoc Dir & Mktg Mgr: James Denton
    E-mail: jd@upf.com
Assoc Dir & CFO: Benny Layfield *E-mail:* bl@
    upf.com
Assoc Dir & Prepress Mgr: Lynn Werts
    E-mail: lw@upf.com
Assoc Dir & Sales Mgr: Andrea Dzavik
    E-mail: ad@upf.com
Founded: 1945
Scholarly & regional nonfiction.
ISBN Prefix(es): 0-8130
Number of titles published annually: 96 Print
Total Titles: 820 Print
Membership(s): American Association of University Presses

§University Press of Kansas
2501 W 15 St, Lawrence, KS 66049-3905
SAN: 203-3267
Tel: 785-864-4154; 785-864-4155 (orders)
    Fax: 785-864-4586
E-mail: upress@ku.edu
Web Site: www.kansaspress.ku.edu
Key Personnel
Ed-in-Chief: Michael Briggs *Tel:* 785-864-9162
    E-mail: mbriggs@ku.edu
Dir: Fred M Woodward *Tel:* 785-864-4667
    E-mail: fwoodward@ku.edu
Asst Dir, Mktg Mgr & Intl Rts: Susan Schott
    Tel: 785-864-9165 *E-mail:* sschott@ku.edu
Acctg Mgr: Robert Racy *Tel:* 785-864-9159
    E-mail: rracy@ku.edu
Publicity Mgr: Ranjit Arab *Tel:* 785-864-9170
    E-mail: rarab@ku.edu
Exhibits & Direct Mail Mgr: Debra Diehl
    Tel: 785-864-9166 *E-mail:* ddieh1@ku.edu
Adv Coord & Mktg Designer: Karl Janssen
    Tel: 785-864-9164 *E-mail:* kjanssen@ku.edu
Founded: 1946
General scholarly nonfiction: American & western history, government & political science, military history, legal history, regional, women's studies, cultural studies, presidential studies.
ISBN Prefix(es): 0-7006
Number of titles published annually: 55 Print
Total Titles: 650 Print; 1 CD-ROM
Distributor for KU Natural History Museum
Foreign Rep(s): East-West Export Books (Asia, Pacific); Eurospan Ltd (Africa, UK, Europe, Middle East)
Warehouse: University Press of Kansas Warehouse, 2425-B W 15 St, Lawrence, KS 66049
Membership(s): Association of American University Presses

§The University Press of Kentucky
663 S Limestone St, Lexington, KY 40508-4008
SAN: 203-3275
Tel: 859-257-8761; 859-257-8442 (mktg)
    Toll Free Tel: 800-839-6855 (orders) *Fax:* 859-323-1873
Web Site: www.kentuckypress.com *Telex:* 20-4009
Key Personnel
Dir: Stephen M Wrinn *Tel:* 859-257-8432
    E-mail: smwrin@uky.edu
Ed-in-Chief: Joyce Harrison *Tel:* 859-257-8434
    Fax: 859-257-2984 *E-mail:* jharr@uky.edu
Asst Dir & Busn Mgr: Craig Wilkie *Tel:* 859-257-8436 *E-mail:* crwilk00@uky.edu
Mktg Mgr: Leila Salisbury *Tel:* 859-257-8442
    Fax: 859-323-4981 *E-mail:* leilas@uky.edu
Prodn & Edit Dir: Lin Wirkus *Tel:* 859-257-8438
    Fax: 859-257-2984 *E-mail:* mwirk2@uky.edu

Warehouse & Dist Mgr: Teresa Collins *Tel:* 859-257-8405 *Fax:* 859-257-8481 *E-mail:* twell1@uky.edu
Asst to Dir: Anne Dean Watkins
    E-mail: adwatk@uky.edu
Founded: 1943
ISBN Prefix(es): 0-8131
Number of titles published annually: 50 Print
Total Titles: 845 Print; 1 Audio
Warehouse: 2100 Capstone, Suite 101, Lexington, KY 40511, Contact: Teresa Collins
    Tel: 859-257-8405 *Toll Free Tel:* 800-839-6855 *Fax:* 859-257-8481 *E-mail:* twell1@uky.edu
SAN: 203-3275
Membership(s): AAP; American Association of University Presses

University Press of Mississippi
3825 Ridgewood Rd, Jackson, MS 39211-6492
SAN: 203-1914
Tel: 601-432-6205 *Toll Free Tel:* 800-737-7788
    Fax: 601-432-6217
E-mail: press@ihl.state.ms.us
Web Site: www.upress.state.ms.us
Key Personnel
Dir: Seetha Srinivasan *E-mail:* seetha@ihl.state.ms.us
Assoc Dir & Busn Mgr: Isabel Metz
    E-mail: isabel@ihl.state.ms.us
Ed-in-Chief: Craig Gill *E-mail:* gill@ihl.state.ms.us
Adv & Mktg Servs Mgr: Kathy Burgess
    E-mail: kerr@ihl.state.ms.us
Asst Mktg Mgr: Ginger Tucker *E-mail:* ginger@ihl.state.ms.us
Art Dir: John Langston *E-mail:* john@ihl.state.ms.us
Mktg Mgr: Steve Yates *E-mail:* syates@ihl.state.ms.us
Founded: 1970
Publisher of trade & scholarly books, nonfiction, fiction & regional.
ISBN Prefix(es): 0-87805; 1-57806
Number of titles published annually: 60 Print
Total Titles: 800 Print; 1 Audio
Imprints: Margaret Walker Alexander Series in African American Studies; American Made Music Series; Author & Artist Series; Banner Books; Center for the Study of Southern Culture Series; Chancellor Porter L Fortune Symposium in Southern History Series; Conversations with Comic Artists Series; Conversations with Filmmakers Series; Conservations with Public Intellectuals Series; Faulkner & Yoknapatawpha Series; Folk Art & Artists Series; Folklife in the South Series; Literary Conversations Series; Willie Morris Books in Memoir & Biography; Muscadine Books; Performance Studies Series; Studies in Popular Culture Series; Understanding Health & Sickness Series
Distributor for Northcote House
Foreign Rep(s): Bill Bailey Publishers' Representatives (Europe); East-West Export Books (Australia, Asia, Pacific); Roundhouse Publishing Group (Africa, UK, Ireland, India, Middle East); Scholarly Book Services Inc (Canada)
Foreign Rights: c/o University Press of Mississippi
Advertising Agency: P M Productions, 203 Summer Hill Rd, Madison, MS 39110, Contact: Patti Mitchell *Fax:* 601-853-2591
    E-mail: pattipmpro@aol.com
Returns: Attention: Returns, 931 Hwy 80 W, Dock 34, Jackson, MS 39204, Contact: Tammy Priest *Tel:* 601-354-7533
Warehouse: 931 Hwy 80 W, Dock 34, Jackson, MS 39204, Contact: Tammy Priest *Tel:* 601-354-7533
Membership(s): American Association of University Presses

University Press of New England
One Court St, Lebanon, NH 03766

SAN: 203-3283
Tel: 603-448-1533 *Toll Free Tel:* 800-421-1561
    (orders only) *Fax:* 603-448-7006; 603-643-1540
E-mail: university.press@dartmouth.edu
Web Site: www.upne.com
Key Personnel
Dir: Richard M Abel
Assoc Dir, Oper & Cust Serv Mgr: Thomas Johnson *Tel:* 603-643-5585
Dir, Design & Prod: Michael Burton
Exec Ed: Phyllis Deutsch
Acqs Ed: John Landrigan *Tel:* 603-448-1533;
    Ellen Wicklum
Man Ed: Mary Crittendon
Dir, Sales & Mktg: Sarah L Welsch
Publicity & Rts Mgr: Barbara L Briggs
Mktg & Adv Assoc: Johanna Hollway
Sales & Trade Exhibits Mgr: Sherri Strickland
    Tel: 603-643-5585
Founded: 1970
Scholarly, nonfiction, regional, New England fiction.
ISBN Prefix(es): 0-87451; 1-58465
Number of titles published annually: 80 Print
Total Titles: 825 Print; 300 E-Book
Imprints: Brandeis University Press; Dartmouth College Press; Hardscrabble Books; Tufts University Press; University of New Hampshire Press; University of Vermont Press
Distributor for Bibliopola Press; Chipstone Foundation; Fence Books; Four Way Books; Isabella Stewart Gardner Museum; National Poetry Foundation; Nicolin Fields Publishing; Peter E Randall Publisher; The Sheep Meadow Press; Wesleyan University Press; Winterthur Museum Garden & Library
Foreign Rep(s): East-West Export Books (Australia & New Zealand, Pacific); Eurospan University Press Group (Europe & UK, Middle East); University of British Columbia Press (Canada)
Advertising Agency: New England Imprints, One Court St, Lebanon, NH 03766, Sara J Carpenter *Tel:* 603-448-1533 ext 231 *Fax:* 603-448-7006
Billing Address: 37 Lafayette St, Lebanon, NH 03766 *E-mail:* university.press@dartmouth.edu
    Web Site: www.upne.com
Orders to: 37 Lafayette St, Lebanon, NH 03766
    Toll Free Tel: 800-421-1561 *Fax:* 603-643-1540
    E-mail: university.press@dartmouth.edu
Shipping Address: 37 Lafayette St, Lebanon, NH 03766
Warehouse: 37 Lafayette St, Lebanon, NH 03766
Membership(s): Association of American University Presses; NEBA

University Publishing Co
1134-A 28 St, Richmond, CA 94804
E-mail: unipub@earthlink.net
Key Personnel
Publr & Intl Rts: Robert Allred
Founded: 1996
Novels, anthologies, nonfiction.
ISBN Prefix(es): 1-57502
Number of titles published annually: 4 Print
Total Titles: 4 Print

University Publishing Group
138 W Washington St, Suites 403-405, Hagerstown, MD 21740
Tel: 240-420-0036 *Toll Free Tel:* 800-654-8188
    Fax: 240-420-0037
E-mail: editorial@upgbooks.com; orders@upgbooks.com
Web Site: www.upgbooks.com
Key Personnel
Pres: Leslie Le Blanc
Publr: Norman Quist *E-mail:* quist@upgbooks.com
Cust Serv: Wanda Koontz
Founded: 1985

Publish books, journals & newsletters in medicine, social sciences, philosophy & law.
ISBN Prefix(es): 1-55572
Number of titles published annually: 6 Print
Total Titles: 35 Print
Distributor for The Journal of Clinical Ethics; Organizational Ethics: Healthcare, Business & Policy

University Publishing House
PO Box 1664, Mannford, OK 74044
Tel: 918-865-4726 *Fax:* 918-865-4726
E-mail: upub2@juno.com
Web Site: www.universitypublishinghouse.com
Key Personnel
Pres: Randell Nyborg
Off Mgr & Intl Rts: Bruce Robertson
Founded: 1987
Industrial & automotive, classic fiction reprints, mail order books & industrial processes.
ISBN Prefix(es): 1-877767; 1-57002
Number of titles published annually: 5 Print
Total Titles: 140 Print

University Science Books
55-D Gate Five Rd, Sausalito, CA 94965
SAN: 213-8085
Tel: 415-332-5390 *Fax:* 415-332-5393
E-mail: univscibks@igc.org
Web Site: www.uscibooks.com
Key Personnel
Pres: Bruce Armbruster
VP & Intl Rts Contact: Kathy Armbruster
Founded: 1978
Intermediate level college textbooks & monographs in astronomy, chemistry, biochemistry & physics, environmental science, technical writing, biology; reference books.
ISBN Prefix(es): 0-935702; 1-891389
Number of titles published annually: 8 Print
Total Titles: 120 Print; 1 CD-ROM
Foreign Rep(s): W H Freeman (Europe)
Orders to: PO Box 605, Herndon, VA 20172 (Must receive permission prior to returning fax 415-332-5390 for instructions; 10% restocking fee), Contact: Todd Riggleman *Tel:* 703-661-1572 *Fax:* 703-661-1501
Distribution Center: Books International, 22841 Quicksilver Dr, Dulles, VA 20166 (10% discount on all web orders) *Tel:* 703-661-1572 *E-mail:* univscibks@igc.org *Web Site:* www.uscibooks.com

UnKnownTruths.com Publishing Co
8815 Conroy Windermere Rd, Suite 190, Orlando, FL 32835
SAN: 255-6375
Tel: 407-929-9207 *Fax:* 407-876-3933
E-mail: info@unknowntruths.com
Web Site: unknowntruths.com
Key Personnel
Pres: Walter Parks *E-mail:* wparks@unknowntruths.com
CFO: Lynda Cassidy *Tel:* 407-876-7737 *E-mail:* info@unknowntruths.com
Prodn: Dan Diehl *Tel:* 407-977-2105 *E-mail:* books@unknowntruths.com
PR: Cherie Carter *E-mail:* cherie@unknowntruths.com
Founded: 2002
Formed to publish true stories of the unusual or of the previously unexplained. Stories typically provide radically different views from those that have shaped the understandings of our natural world, our religions, our science, our history & even the foundations of our civilizations. Also include stories of the very important life-extending medical breakthroughs: stem cell therapies, genetic therapies, cloning & other emerging findings that promise to change the very meaning of life.
ISBN Prefix(es): 0-9745393

Number of titles published annually: 5 Print
Total Titles: 2 Print
Advertising Agency: James Brooke & Associates, 2660 Second St, Suite 1, Santa Monica, CA 90405, PR: Cherie Carter *Tel:* 310-396-8070 *Fax:* 310-396-8071 *E-mail:* cherie@unknowntruths.com
Distribution Center: Quality Books Inc
Membership(s): Publishers Marketing Association; Small Publishers Association of North America

Unlimited Publishing LLC
PO Box 3007, Bloomington, IN 47402
Toll Free Tel: 800-218-8877
E-mail: operations@unlimitedpublishing.com
Web Site: www.unlimitedpublishing.com
Founded: 2000
Republish out-of-print books.
ISBN Prefix(es): 1-58832
Number of titles published annually: 25 Print
Total Titles: 125 Print
Orders to: Ingram, La Vergne, TN
Returns: Ingram, La Vergne, TN
Warehouse: Ingram, La Vergne, TN
Membership(s): Publishers Marketing Association

W E Upjohn Institute for Employment Research
300 S Westnedge Ave, Kalamazoo, MI 49007-4686
Tel: 269-343-5541; 269-343-4330 (pubns) *Toll Free Tel:* 888-227-8569 *Fax:* 269-343-7310
E-mail: publications@upjohninstitute.org
Web Site: www.upjohninstitute.org
Key Personnel
Mgr, Publns: Richard Wyrwa *E-mail:* wyrwa@upjohninstitute.org
Founded: 1959
Labor economics & industrial relations.
ISBN Prefix(es): 0-88099
Number of titles published annually: 12 Print; 5 E-Book
Total Titles: 160 Print; 40 E-Book

§Upper Room Books
Division of The Upper Room
1908 Grand Ave, Nashville, TN 37212
SAN: 203-3364
Mailing Address: PO Box 340004, Nashville, TN 37203-0004
Toll Free Tel: 800-972-0433 *Fax:* 615-340-7266
Web Site: www.upperroom.org
Key Personnel
Exec Ed: JoAnn E Miller
Mktg Dir: John Brown
Dir, Intl Rts & Perms: Sarah Schaller-Linn
Prodn Mgr: Debbie Keller
Dir, Electronic Publg & Commun: Beth Richardson
Founded: 1935
Prayer & devotional life publications. No fiction or poetry accepted.
ISBN Prefix(es): 0-8358
Warehouse: PBD Inc, 1650 Bluegrass Pkwy, Alpharetta, GA 30201

Upstart Books™
Imprint of Highsmith Inc
W5527 State Rd 106, Fort Atkinson, WI 53538-8428
Mailing Address: PO Box 800, Fort Atkinson, WI 53538-0800
Tel: 920-563-9571 *Toll Free Tel:* 800-448-4887 *Fax:* 920-563-7395 *Toll Free Fax:* 800-448-5828
Web Site: www.highsmith.com
Key Personnel
CEO: Paul Moss
Publr: Matt Mulder *E-mail:* mmulder@highsmith.com
Man Ed: Michelle McCardell

Founded: 1990
Reading activities & library skills for teachers & children's librarians; storytelling activity books & internet resources.
ISBN Prefix(es): 0-917846; 0-913853; 1-57950; 1-932146
Number of titles published annually: 12 Print
Total Titles: 100 Print

Upublish.com
Division of Dissertation.com
23331 Water Circle, Boca Raton, FL 33486-8540
SAN: 299-3635
Tel: 561-750-4344 *Toll Free Tel:* 800-636-8329 *Fax:* 561-750-6797
E-mail: info4@upublish.com
Web Site: www.universal-publishers.com
Founded: 1997
Dictionaries, encyclopedias, textbooks-all, university presses. Scholarly books, reprints, professional books, paperbacks, directories & reference books.
ISBN Prefix(es): 1-58112
Number of titles published annually: 60 Print; 50 E-Book
Total Titles: 600 Print; 600 E-Book
Imprints: Universal Publishers
Distributed by Bertrams UK

The Urban Institute Press
2100 "M" St NW, Washington, DC 20037
SAN: 203-3380
Tel: 202-261-5687 *Toll Free Tel:* 877-UIPRESS (847-7377) *Fax:* 202-467-5775
E-mail: pubs@ui.urban.org
Web Site: www.uipress.org
Key Personnel
Acting Dir: Kathleen Courrier
Prod Supv: Scott Forrey *Tel:* 202-261-5647
Mktg Mgr: Glenn Popson *Tel:* 202-261-5744 *E-mail:* gpopson@ui.urban.org
Founded: 1968
Public policy, economics, government, social sciences.
ISBN Prefix(es): 0-87766
Number of titles published annually: 10 Print

§Urban Land Institute
1025 Thomas Jefferson St NW, Suite 500 W, Washington, DC 20007
Tel: 202-624-7000 *Toll Free Tel:* 800-321-5011 *Fax:* 410-626-7140
E-mail: Bookstore@uli.org
Web Site: www.bookstore.uli.org
Key Personnel
Exec VP & Publr: Rachelle Levitt
VP, Mktg: Lori Hatcher *E-mail:* lghatcher@uli.org
Accts Mgr & Cust Serv: Ruth Ayres *Tel:* 202-624-7088 *E-mail:* rayres@uli.org
Founded: 1936
International non-profit research & education institute concentrating on best practices in real estate development & responsible use of land.
ISBN Prefix(es): 0-87420
Number of titles published annually: 15 Print; 1 CD-ROM
Total Titles: 78 Print; 4 CD-ROM
Imprints: ULI
Foreign Rep(s): Joanne Wang (China)

Urim Publications
Division of Lambda Publishers Inc
3709 13 Ave, Brooklyn, NY 11218
Tel: 718-972-5449 *Fax:* 718-972-6307
E-mail: publisher@urimpublications.com
Web Site: www.urimpublications.com
Key Personnel
Pres & Publr: Tzvi Mauer
Children's Book Ed: Shari Dash Greenspan *E-mail:* children@urimpublications.com
Founded: 1997

Publisher & worldwide distributor of new & classic books with Jewish content.
ISBN Prefix(es): 965-7108
Number of titles published annually: 8 Print
Total Titles: 35 Print
Subsidiaries: Flashlight Press
Editorial Office(s): PO Box 52287, Jerusalem 91521, Israel *Tel:* (02) 679-7633 *Fax:* (02) 679-7634 *Web Site:* www.urimpublications.com

§URJ Press
Formerly UAHC Press
Division of Union for Reform Judaism
633 Third Ave, New York, NY 10017-6778
SAN: 203-3291
Tel: 212-650-4100 *Toll Free Tel:* 888-489-UAHC (489-8242) *Fax:* 212-650-4119
E-mail: press@urj.org
Web Site: www.urjpress.com
Key Personnel
Pres: Eric H Yoffie
Chmn, Exec Bd: Russell Silverman
Acqs, Media & Text: Hara Person
Publr: Kenneth Gesser
Mktg Mgr: Richard Abrams
Founded: 1873
Religion (Jewish), Reform Judaism; textbooks, juveniles & adult trade books, audiovisual materials, social action, history, biography, ceremonies.
ISBN Prefix(es): 0-8074
Number of titles published annually: 15 Print
Total Titles: 150 Print; 2 CD-ROM; 8 Online; 71 Audio
Distribution Center: Mercedes Distribution Center, Brooklyn Navy Yard, Bldg 3, Brooklyn, NY 11205
Membership(s): AAP

US Conference of Catholic Bishops
USCCB Publishing, 3211 Fourth St NE, Washington, DC 20017-1194
Tel: 202-541-3090 *Toll Free Tel:* 800-235-8722 (orders only) *Fax:* 202-541-3089
Web Site: www.usccb.org/publishing
Key Personnel
Exec Dir: Paul Henderson
Founded: 1938
The official publisher for the United States Catholic Bishop & Vatican documents; English & Spanish.
ISBN Prefix(es): 1-55586; 1-57455
Number of titles published annually: 39 Print
Total Titles: 735 Print
Returns: USCCB Returns, 3570 Blatensburg Rd, Brentwood, MD 20722
Membership(s): Catholic Book Publishers Association

US Games Systems Inc
179 Ludlow St, Stamford, CT 06902
SAN: 206-1368
Tel: 203-353-8400 *Toll Free Tel:* 800-544-2637 (800-54GAMES) *Fax:* 203-353-8431
E-mail: info@usgamesinc.com
Web Site: www.usgamesinc.com
Key Personnel
Chmn, Ed & Rts & Perms: Stuart R Kaplan
Treas: Alfonso Hector
Art Dir: Elizabeth Kerkstra *E-mail:* ekerkstra@usgamesinc.com
Founded: 1968
Popular & scholarly works in the field of tarot & the history of symbolism of playing cards; reprints of historical tarot decks & playing cards from the past five centuries.
ISBN Prefix(es): 0-913866; 0-88079; 1-57281
Number of titles published annually: 6 Print
Total Titles: 300 Print
Imprints: Cove Press
Distributor for Carta Mundi; A G Muller & Cie

Foreign Rep(s): Airlift Book Company (UK); Koppenhol Agenturen (Netherlands); Lion Playing Card Co (Israel); A G Muller & Cie (Switzerland); David Westnedge Ltd (UK)

§US Government Printing Office
Division of US Government Agency
Superintendent of Documents, Washington, DC 20401
Tel: 202-512-1707 *Toll Free Tel:* 888-293-6498 (cust serv); 866-512-1800 (orders) *Fax:* 202-512-1655 (bibliographic info); 202-512-2250 (orders & pricing) *Toll Free Fax:* 866-512-1800
E-mail: orders@gpo.gov
Web Site: bookstore.gpo.gov (sales); gpoaccess.gov
Key Personnel
Dir, Mktg: Jeffrey Turner
Chief, Biblio Systems Branch: Joseph McClane
Founded: 1861
Distributor & printer of federal government publications & public documents in various formats; military, space exploration, political science.
ISBN Prefix(es): 0-16
Number of titles published annually: 800 Print; 15 Online
Total Titles: 600 Print; 140 CD-ROM
Orders to: Superintendent of Documents, PO Box 371954, Pittsburgh, PA 15250-7954

Utah Geological Survey
Division of Utah Dept of Natural Resources
1594 W North Temple, Suite 3110, Salt Lake City, UT 84116
Mailing Address: PO Box 146100, Salt Lake City, UT 84114-6100
Tel: 801-537-3300 *Toll Free Tel:* 888-UTAH-MAP (882-4627 bookstore) *Fax:* 801-537-3400
E-mail: geostore@utah.gov
Web Site: geology.utah.gov
Key Personnel
Ed: James Stringfellow *Fax:* 801-537-3300
Founded: 1935
ISBN Prefix(es): 1-55791
Number of titles published annually: 30 Print; 7 CD-ROM; 5 Online
Total Titles: 702 Print; 30 CD-ROM; 38 Online

Utah State University Press
Division of Utah State University
7800 Old Main Hill, Logan, UT 84322-7800
Tel: 435-797-1362 *Toll Free Tel:* 800-239-9974 *Fax:* 435-797-0313
Web Site: www.usu.edu/usupress
Key Personnel
Dir: Michael Spooner *E-mail:* michael.spooner@usu.edu
Intl Rts: Cathy Tarbet
Mktg Mgr: Brooke Bigelow *E-mail:* brooke.bigelow@usu.edu
Founded: 1969
ISBN Prefix(es): 0-87421
Number of titles published annually: 18 Print
Total Titles: 120 Print
Membership(s): Association of American University Presses

VanDam Inc
11 W 20 St, 4th fl, New York, NY 10011-3704
Tel: 212-929-0416 *Toll Free Tel:* 800-UNFOLDS (863-6537) *Fax:* 212-929-0426
E-mail: info@vandam.com
Web Site: www.vandam.com
Key Personnel
Pres: Stephan C VanDam *E-mail:* stephan@vandam.com
Dir, Sales: Jesse Corda
Founded: 1984
Publisher of UNFOLDS® maps; licensor of patented folding technology used to produce UNFOLDS® products.
Number of titles published annually: 25 Print

Imprints: Eurostar; Smartmaps®; That VanDam Book; UNFOLDS®; @tlas®
Divisions: VanDam Advertising; VanDam Licensing; VanDam Publishing
Foreign Rep(s): LAC (Italy); RV Verlag (Germany)
Advertising Agency: Streetsmart®; Travelsmart®; VanDam Advertising

Vandamere Press
3580 Morris St N, Saint Petersburg, FL 33713
SAN: 657-3088
Mailing Address: PO Box 149, Saint Petersburg, FL 33711
Tel: 727-556-0950 *Toll Free Tel:* 800-551-7776 *Fax:* 727-556-2560
E-mail: orders@vandamere.com
Web Site: www.vandamere.com
Key Personnel
Publr & Ed-in-Chief: Arthur Brown *E-mail:* abrown@vandamere.com
Sr Book Ed: Pat Berger
Acq Ed: Jerry Frank
Dir, Spec Sales: Stephanie Brown
Wholesale Sales: John Cabin
Founded: 1984
Tradebook.
ISBN Prefix(es): 0-918339
Number of titles published annually: 10 Print
Total Titles: 40 Print
Distributor for ABI Professional Publications (non-exclusive); Quodlibetal Features; NRH Press (non-exclusive)
Membership(s): Publishers Association of the South
See separate listing for:
ABI Professional Publications

Vanderbilt University Press
Division of Vanderbilt University
201 University Plaza Bldg, 112 21 Ave S, Nashville, TN 37203
SAN: 202-9308
Tel: 615-322-3585 *Toll Free Tel:* 800-627-7377 (orders only) *Fax:* 615-343-8823
Toll Free Fax: 800-735-0476 (orders only)
E-mail: vupress@vanderbilt.edu
Web Site: www.vanderbilt.edu/vupress
Key Personnel
Dir: Michael Ames
Cust Rel, ISBN Contact & Rts & Perms: Martha Gerdeman
Mktg Mgr: Polly Rembert
Ed & Prodn Mgr: Daniel Mayer
Ed Coord: Betsy Phillips
Founded: 1940
Scholarly nonfiction, humanities, social sciences, literary criticism, history, regional studies, applied mathematics, philosophy.
ISBN Prefix(es): 0-8265
Number of titles published annually: 20 Print
Total Titles: 116 Print; 2 CD-ROM; 1 E-Book
Imprints: Country Music Foundation Press; Vanderbilt Library of American Philosophy
Distributed by University of Oklahoma Press
Distributor for Country Music Foundation Press
Foreign Rep(s): Royden Muranaka (Australia, China & Hong Kong, India, Japan, Korea, New Zealand, Pacific Islands, Pakistan, Philippines, SE Asia, Taiwan)

Vault.com Inc
150 W 22 St, 5th fl, New York, NY 10011
Tel: 212-366-4212 ext 384 *Fax:* 212-366-6117
E-mail: feedback@staff.vault.com
Web Site: www.vault.com
Key Personnel
PR: Kate Kaibni *E-mail:* kate@staff.vault.com
Founded: 1997
"Insider" career development for professionals.
ISBN Prefix(es): 1-58131

Number of titles published annually: 35 Print; 10 Online
Total Titles: 161 Print; 124 Online
Distribution Center: Client Distribution Services Inc, 193 Edwards Dr, Jackson, TN 38301, Pres: Gilbert Perlman *Toll Free Tel:* 800-343-4499 *Toll Free Fax:* 800-351-5073 *E-mail:* orderentry@cdsbooks.com SAN: 631-760X

Vedanta Press
Subsidiary of Vedanta Society of Southern California
1946 Vedanta Place, Hollywood, CA 90068
Tel: 323-960-1727 *Fax:* 323-465-9568
E-mail: info@vedanta.org
Web Site: www.vedanta.com
Founded: 1945
ISBN Prefix(es): 0-87481
Number of titles published annually: 13 CD-ROM; 13 Online; 14 Audio
Total Titles: 13 CD-ROM; 13 Online; 14 Audio
Distributor for Advaita; Ashrama; Ramakrishna Math
Membership(s): Publishers Marketing Association

The Vendome Press
1334 York Ave, 3rd fl, New York, NY 10021
Tel: 212-737-5297 *Fax:* 212-737-5340
E-mail: vendomepress@earthlink.net
Key Personnel
Publr & Intl Rts Contact: Alexis Gregory
Publr: Mark Magowan
Founded: 1981
Illustrated art, architecture & lifestyle books.
ISBN Prefix(es): 0-86565
Number of titles published annually: 12 Print
Distributed by Harry N Abrams

Venture Press, see Williams & Co Publishers

Venture Publishing Inc
1999 Cato Ave, State College, PA 16801
SAN: 240-897X
Tel: 814-234-4561 *Fax:* 814-234-1651
E-mail: vpublish@venturepublish.com
Web Site: www.venturepublish.com
Key Personnel
Gen Mgr: Kay Whiteside
Prodn Supv: Richard Yocum
Founded: 1979
Parks & recreation, social sciences & sociology, leisure studies, long term care, therapeutic recreation.
ISBN Prefix(es): 0-910251; 1-892132
Number of titles published annually: 8 Print
Total Titles: 86 Print; 75 E-Book
Foreign Rep(s): Canadian Parks & Recreation Assn (Canada); Creative & More Inc (Taiwan); Hepper, Marriot & Associates (Australia, New Zealand); Vigor Book Agents (South Africa)

Verbatim Books
Subsidiary of Laurence Urdang Inc
4 Laurel Heights, Old Lyme, CT 06371
SAN: 211-1047
Tel: 860-434-2104
Web Site: www.verbatimbooks.com
Key Personnel
Pres & Ed-in-Chief: Laurence Urdang
  E-mail: urdang@sbcglobal.net
Founded: 1974
Dictionaries, reference books, popular & scholarly books about language, especially English.
ISBN Prefix(es): 0-930454
Total Titles: 17 Print
Imprints: Laurence Urdang Reference Book; Verbatim Book
Foreign Office(s): PO Box 156, Chearsley, Aylesbury, Bucks HP18 0DQ, United Kingdom

Vermilion Inc, see Moon Lady Press

Verso
180 Varick St, 10th fl, New York, NY 10014-4606
Tel: 212-807-9680 *Fax:* 212-807-9152
E-mail: versony@versobooks.com
Web Site: www.versobooks.com *Telex:* 6801368 METHUENUW
Key Personnel
Gen Sales Mgr, US & Canada: Niels Hooper
Publicity, London: Fiona Price *Tel:* (020) 7437-3548 *Fax:* (020) 7734-0059
US Publicity Mgr: Rachel Guidera
US Ed: Amy Scholder
Founded: 1970
Nonfiction, progressive studies on politics, history, society & culture.
ISBN Prefix(es): 0-86091; 0-85984; 0-84467
Number of titles published annually: 40 Print
Total Titles: 486 Print
Foreign Office(s): 6 Meard St, London W1F OE6, United Kingdom
Distributed by Penguin (Canada); W W Norton (USA)
Foreign Rep(s): Verso (England)
Foreign Rights: Verso (World)
Shipping Address: Marston Book Services, Kemp Hall Bindery, Osney Mead, Oxford, United Kingdom
Warehouse: National Book Co Inc, 800 Keystone Industrial Park, Scranton, PA 18512

Victory in Grace Printing
Division of Quentin Road Ministries
60 Quentin Rd, Lake Zurich, IL 60047
Tel: 847-438-4494 *Toll Free Tel:* 800-784-7223
  Fax: 847-438-4232
Web Site: www.victoryingrace.org
Key Personnel
Dir: Neal Dearyan *Tel:* 847-438-4494 ext 1039
  E-mail: neal@victoryingrace.org
Ed: Julie Dearyan *Tel:* 847-438-4494 ext 1068
  E-mail: julie@victoryingrace.org; Daniel Darling *Tel:* 847-438-4494 ext 1055 *E-mail:* dan@victoryingrace.org
Publicist: Kristen Tanney *Tel:* 847-738-4232 ext 1065 *E-mail:* ktanney@qrbbc.org
Founded: 2000
Publish conservative evangelical books, audio series, magazines & tracts.
ISBN Prefix(es): 0-9679145; 0-9719262
Number of titles published annually: 3 Print; 4 E-Book; 3 Audio
Total Titles: 9 Print; 4 E-Book; 15 Audio

Viking
Imprint of Penguin Group (USA) Inc
375 Hudson St, New York, NY 10014
SAN: 282-5074
Tel: 212-366-2000
E-mail: online@penguinputnam.com
Web Site: www.penguin.com
Key Personnel
Pres: Clare Ferraro
VP, Viking Edit: Pamela Dorman
VP, Publicity, Assoc Publr, Viking & Sr Ed, Viking Penguin: Paul Slovak
VP & Dir, Mktg: Nancy Sheppard
Dir, Publicity: Carolyn Coleburn
Dir, Adv & Promo: Julie Shiroishi
Exec Man Ed: Tory Klose
Exec Ed, Penguin & Dir, Penguin Arkansas: Janet Goldstein
Exec Ed: Wendy Wolf; Rick Kot; Carolyn Carlson
Sr Ed: Ray Roberts; Molly Stern
Founded: 1925
ISBN Prefix(es): 0-670
Number of titles published annually: 146 Print
Total Titles: 407 Print

Imprints: Viking Compass
Advertising Agency: Spier NY

Viking Children's Books
Imprint of Penguin Group (USA) Inc
345 Hudson St, New York, NY 10014
SAN: 282-5074
Tel: 212-366-2000
E-mail: online@penguinputnam.com
Web Site: www.penguin.com
Key Personnel
Pres & Publr: Regina Hayes
Assoc Publr & Man Ed: Gerard Mancini
Art Dir: Denise Cronin
Exec Ed: Tracy Gates
Sr Ed: Joy Peskin; Jill Davis
Founded: 1925
ISBN Prefix(es): 0-670
Number of titles published annually: 83 Print
Total Titles: 638 Print
Membership(s): Children's Book Council

Viking Penguin
Division of Penguin Group (USA) Inc
375 Hudson St, New York, NY 10014
SAN: 282-5074
Tel: 212-366-2000
E-mail: online@penguinputnam.com
Web Site: www.penguin.com
Key Personnel
Chmn: Susan J Petersen Kennedy
Pres, Viking: Clare Ferraro
Pres, Penguin: Kathryn Court
VP & Ed-at-Large: Carole DeSanti
VP, Prodn: Pat Lyons
VP & Art Dir: Paul Buckley
Founded: 1975
ISBN Prefix(es): 0-14; 0-453; 0-670
Number of titles published annually: 407 Print
Total Titles: 4,893 Print; 339 Audio
Imprints: Stephen Greene Press; Allen Lane, The Penguin Press; Pelham; Penguin Audio Books; Penguin Books; Penguin Classics; Penguin Compass; The Penguin Press; Viking; Viking Compass; Viking Studio
Advertising Agency: Spier NY

Viking Studio
Imprint of Penguin Group (USA) Inc
375 Hudson St, New York, NY 10014
SAN: 282-5074
Tel: 212-366-2000
E-mail: online@penguinputnam.com
Web Site: www.penguin.com
Key Personnel
Publr & Ed-in-Chief: Megan Newman
VP & Dir, Mktg: Nancy Sheppard
VP, Publicity: Maureen Donnelly
Founded: 1988
ISBN Prefix(es): 0-14; 0-670
Number of titles published annually: 23 Print
Total Titles: 101 Print
Advertising Agency: Spier NY

Carl Vinson Institute of Government
University of Georgia, 201 N Milledge Ave, Athens, GA 30602
Tel: 706-542-2736 *Fax:* 706-542-6239
Web Site: www.cviog.uga.edu
Key Personnel
Dir: James Ledbetter
PR Coord: Ann Allen *Tel:* 706-542-6221
  E-mail: allen@cviog.uga.edu
Founded: 1927
Instruction, technical assistance, research & publications for state & local governments & communities.
ISBN Prefix(es): 0-89854
Number of titles published annually: 10 Print; 2 CD-ROM
Total Titles: 70 Print; 3 CD-ROM

Vintage & Anchor Books
Division of Random House Inc
1745 Broadway, New York, NY 10019
Tel: 212-751-2600 *Fax:* 212-572-6043
Key Personnel
Exec VP & Ed-in-Chief: Martin Asher
VP & Publr: Anne Messitte
VP, Exec Ed & Dir, Edit: Luann Walther
VP & Dir, Publicity, Vintage & Anchor: Russell
Perreault
Dir, Art & Design: John Gall
Dir, Adv & Promos: Irena Vukov-Kendes
Mgr, Adv, Promo & New Media: Paige Smith
Sr Mgr, Prodn: Quinn O'Neill
Dir, Academic Mktg: Keith Goldsmith
Man Ed: Steven McNabb
Mgr, Backlist: Barbara Richard
Sr Ed: Anjali Singh
Ed: Edward Kastenmeier; Alice van Straalen; An-
drew Miller
Founded: 1952
Random House Inc & its publishing entities are
not accepting unsol submissions, proposals,
mss, or submission queries via e-mail at this
time.
ISBN Prefix(es): 0-02; 0-679
Imprints: Vintage Contemporaries; Vintage
Crime/Black Lizard; Vintage Departures; Vin-
tage International
Foreign Rights: Arts & Licensing International
Inc (China); Caroline van Gelderen Agency
(Netherlands); DRT International (Korea);
Graal Ltd (Poland); JLM Literary Agency
(Greece); Katai & Bolza (Hungary); Licht &
Licht Agency (Scandinavia); Literarni Agentura
(Czech Republic); Michelle Lapautre Agency
(France); Roberto Santachiara (Italy); The En-
glish Agency (Japan)

Visible Ink Press
43311 Joy Rd, Suite 414, Canton, MI 48187-2075
Tel: 734-667-3211 *Fax:* 734-667-4311
E-mail: inquiries@visibleink.com
Web Site: www.visibleink.com
Key Personnel
Pres: Roger Janecke
Publr: Martin Connors
Founded: 1990
Popular reference publisher specializing in handy
answer books, spiritual phenomena, videohound
guides & encyclopedias.
ISBN Prefix(es): 0-8103; 0-7876; 1-57859
Number of titles published annually: 10 Print
Total Titles: 50 Print
Foreign Rep(s): Mint Publishers (North America)

Vision Works Publishing
Division of Visionary International Partnerships
47 Sheffield Rd, Suite A, Boxford, MA 01921
Mailing Address: PO Box 217, Boxford, MA
01921-0217
Tel: 978-887-3125 *Toll Free Tel:* 888-821-3135
Fax: 630-982-2134
E-mail: visionworksbooks@email.com
Key Personnel
CEO: Dr Joseph Rubino *E-mail:* drjrubino@
email.com
Mktg Dir: Janice Strekofsky
Pres, Visionary Intl Partnerships: Thomas Ven-
tullo
Founded: 1991
Produces paperback & hardcover books & audio-
cassette tapes on the subjects of business, per-
sonal development, leadership, self-help & in-
spirational topics.
ISBN Prefix(es): 0-9678529; 0-9728840
Number of titles published annually: 5 Print; 1
Audio
Total Titles: 10 Print; 2 Audio
Distributed by Hushion House - Canada

Foreign Rights: Janice Strekotsky
Membership(s): Publishers Marketing Associa-
tion; Small Publishers Association of North
America

Visions Communications
200 E Tenth St, Suite 714, New York, NY 10003
Tel: 212-529-4029 *Fax:* 212-529-4029
E-mail: bayvisions@aol.com; info@visionsbooks.
com
Key Personnel
Pres & Mktg Mgr: Beth Bay
Founded: 1994
Specialize in trade, business, self-help & how-to
books.
ISBN Prefix(es): 1-885750
Number of titles published annually: 3 Print
Total Titles: 7 Print
Distributed by Penwell Books

Vista Publishing Inc
151 Delaware Ave, Oakhurst, NJ 07755
E-mail: info@vistapubl.com; sales@vistapubl.
com
Web Site: www.vistapubl.com
Key Personnel
Pres & Intl Rts: Carolyn Zagury
E-mail: czagury@vistapubl.com
Sales Mgr & Lib Sales Dir: David Zagury
E-mail: dzagury@vistapubl.com
Founded: 1991
Specialize in fiction & nonfiction titles in nursing,
healthcare & women's issues.
ISBN Prefix(es): 1-880254
Number of titles published annually: 10 Print
Total Titles: 71 Print

§Visual Reference Publications Inc
302 Fifth Ave, New York, NY 10001
SAN: 213-1552
Tel: 212-279-7000 *Toll Free Tel:* 800-251-4545
Fax: 212-279-7014
Web Site: www.visualrefernce.com
Key Personnel
Publr: Larry Fuersich *Tel:* 212-279-7000 ext 14
E-mail: larry@visualreference.com
Founded: 1931
Architecture, interior & graphic design.
ISBN Prefix(es): 1-58471
Number of titles published annually: 15 Print
Total Titles: 115 Print; 75 Online
Imprints: Visual Reference Publication
Distributed by Watson-Guptill Publications (US &
Canada)
Foreign Rep(s): HarperCollins International (out-
side US & Canada)
Foreign Rights: Visual Refernce Publications Inc;
Joanne Wang

Vital Health Publishing
149 Old Branchville Rd, Ridgefield, CT 06877
Mailing Address: PO Box 152, Ridgefield, CT
06877
Tel: 203-894-1882 *Toll Free Tel:* 877-848-2665
(orders) *Fax:* 203-894-1866
E-mail: info@vitalhealthbooks.com
Web Site: www.vitalhealthbooks.com
Key Personnel
Publg Dir: David Richard
Off Mgr: Heather Flournoy
Founded: 1996
Publish books related to health through nutrition,
wholistic complimentary medicine, ecology &
creativity.
ISBN Prefix(es): 1-890612 (Vital Health Publish-
ing); 1-890995 (Enhancement Books)
Number of titles published annually: 12 Print; 1
E-Book
Total Titles: 35 Print
Imprints: Enhancement Books

Distributed by Brumby (Gemcraft) (Australia);
Deep Books (UK, Europe); New Horizon
(South Africa); Peaceful Living (New Zealand)
Warehouse: Now Foods, 395 S Glen Ellen Rd,
Bloomingdale, IL 60108
Distribution Center: Now Foods, 395 S Glen
Ellen Rd, Bloomingdale, IL 60108
Membership(s): Publishers Marketing Association

§Vocalis Ltd
100 Avalon Circle, Waterbury, CT 06710
Tel: 203-753-5244 *Fax:* 203-574-5433
E-mail: vocalis@sbcglobal.net; info@vocalisesl.
com
Web Site: www.vocalisesl.com; www.
vocalisfiction.com; www.vocalisltd.com
Key Personnel
Pres: Mary Gretchen *Tel:* 203-753-5244 ext 101
VP: Charles E Beyer *Tel:* 203-753-5244 ext 102
E-mail: cbeyer@vocalisesl.com
Edit Dir: Evelyn Martinez *Tel:* 203-753-5244 ext
110
ESL Coord: Ariel Selwyn Santiago *Tel:* 203-753-
5244 ext 104
Founded: 1998
Publisher of ESL (English as a second language)
multimedia; last year we started a division, Vo-
calis Fiction, to publish children's trade fiction
books.
ISBN Prefix(es): 0-9665743; 0-9709948; 1-
932653
Number of titles published annually: 4 Print; 2
CD-ROM; 3 Online; 4 E-Book; 1 Audio
Total Titles: 6 Print; 5 CD-ROM; 16 Online; 8 E-
Book; 3 Audio
Imprints: Vocalis ESL (English as a Second Lan-
guage multimedia products); Vocalis Fiction
(children's trade fiction)
Orders to: Baker & Taylor
Returns: Baker & Taylor
Shipping Address: Baker & Taylor
Warehouse: Greenleaf Book Group
Membership(s): Literacy Volunteers of America;
Publishers Marketing Association; Teachers of
English to Speakers of Other Languages

Volcano Press Inc
21496 National St, Volcano, CA 95689
Mailing Address: PO Box 270, Volcano, CA
95689-0270 SAN: 220-0015
Tel: 209-296-4991 *Toll Free Tel:* 800-879-9636
Fax: 209-296-4995
E-mail: sales@volcanopress.com
Web Site: www.volcanopress.com
Key Personnel
Pres & Publr: Ruth Gottstein *Tel:* 209-296-7989
E-mail: ruth@volcanopress.com
Assoc Publr: Adam Gottstein
Founded: 1969
General trade, professional books, Spanish lan-
guage books; medicine, health & nutrition,
psychology, social sciences, women's studies,
domestic violence.
ISBN Prefix(es): 0-912078; 1-884244
Number of titles published annually: 6 Print
Total Titles: 40 Print; 1 Audio
Imprints: Glide Publications; Kazan Books; Tufa
Productions

Voyageur Press
123 N Second St, Stillwater, MN 55082
Mailing Address: PO Box 338, Stillwater, MN
55082
Tel: 651-430-2210 *Toll Free Tel:* 800-888-9653
Fax: 651-430-2211
E-mail: books@voyageurpress.com
Web Site: www.voyageurpress.com
Key Personnel
Publr & CEO: Tom Lebovsky
Edit Dir: Michael Dregni
Mktg Dir: Dave Hohman

Promos Mgr: Tricia Theurer *E-mail:* ttheurer@
   voyageurpress.com
Sales Mgr: Dennis Tomfohrde
Publicist: Dorothy Molstad
Founded: 1972
Nature, wildlife, natural history, regional, Ameri-
   cana, travel.
ISBN Prefix(es): 0-89658
Number of titles published annually: 45 Print
Total Titles: 190 Print
Distributed by Raincoast Books
Distributor for Colin Baxter; Car Tech; Fountain
   Press; Hove; Specialty Press; Tetra Press
Returns: Voyageur Press Returns, c/o Ware-Pak,
   2427 Bond St, University Park, IL 60466

W Publishing Group
Division of Thomas Nelson Inc
PO Box 141000, Nashville, TN 37214-1000
Tel: 615-889-9000 *Fax:* 615-902-2112
Web Site: www.wpublishinggroup.com
Founded: 1951
Editing, marketing & distribution of Christian
   books, audio & video, Bibles.
ISBN Prefix(es): 0-8499
Number of titles published annually: 50 Print
Total Titles: 817 Print

Wadsworth, see Wadsworth Publishing

Wadsworth Group, see Wadsworth Publishing

§Wadsworth Publishing
Formerly Wadsworth Group
Division of Thomson Learning Inc
10 Davis Dr, Belmont, CA 94002-3002
SAN: 200-2213
Toll Free Tel: 800-357-0092 *Fax:* 650-592-3342
   Toll Free Fax: 800-522-4923
Web Site: www.wadsworth.com *Telex:* 34-8383
Key Personnel
Pres & CEO: Susan Badger
Pres, Soc Sci & Humanities Publg: Sean Wakely
Pres, Mathematics & Sci Publg: Michael Johnson
Pres, Busn & Prof Publg: Ed Mousa
Sr VP & CFO: Ty Field
Sr VP, Mktg: Jonathan Hulbert
Sr VP, Prodn & Mfg: Kathie Head
Sr VP & Chief Technol Officer: Pat Call
VP, HR: Paula Sari
Founded: 1956
A leading provider of higher education textbooks,
   software & Internet materials for the humani-
   ties, social sciences, behavioral sciences, math-
   ematics, science, statistics, business & profes-
   sional.
ISBN Prefix(es): 0-314; 0-312; 0-534; 0-8222;
   0-8384; 0-89582; 0-8304; 1-56593; 0-8125; 1-
   57259; 0-324; 0-922914; 0-028; 0-030; 0-126;
   0-155; 0-759; 0-766; 0-769; 0-827; 0-829; 0-
   8783; 0-882; 1-87910; 0-9997
Number of titles published annually: 700 Print
Total Titles: 3,350 Print; 125 CD-ROM; 170 E-
   Book; 325 Audio
Imprints: Brooks/Cole; Duxbury; Schirmer;
   Southwestern; Wadsworth; West
Distributed by Thomson Learning International
   Group; Thomson Learning; Nelson Thomas
   Learning
Foreign Rep(s): Nelson Thomson Learning
   (Canada); Thomas Nelson Australia-Thomson
   Learning (Australia, New Zealand); Thomson
   Learning Editories (Caribbean, Latin America);
   Thomson Learning International (Asia, Europe,
   France, Germany, Japan, Middle East, South
   Africa)
Foreign Rights: Thomson Learning, Foreign
   Rights Division (Worldwide)
Distribution Center: Thomson Learning Distribu-
   tion Center, 10650 Toebben Dr, Independence,
   KY 41051 *Toll Free Tel:* 800-347-7707
Membership(s): AAP

Wake Forest University Press
A5 Tribble Hall, Wake Forest University,
   Winston-Salem, NC 27109
Mailing Address: PO Box 7333, Winston-Salem,
   NC 27109
Tel: 336-758-5448 *Fax:* 336-758-5636
E-mail: wfupress@wfu.edu
Web Site: www.wfu.edu/wfupress
Key Personnel
Founder: Dillon Johnston
Edit Dir: Jefferson Holdridge
Mgr & Asst Dir: Candide Jones
   E-mail: jonescm@wfu.edu
Founded: 1975
Contemporary Irish poetry & bilingual editions of
   contemporary French poetry.
ISBN Prefix(es): 0-916390; 1-930630
Number of titles published annually: 5 Print
Total Titles: 58 Print

J Weston Walch Publisher
321 Valley St, Portland, ME 04104
SAN: 203-0268
Mailing Address: PO Box 658, Portland, ME
   04104
Tel: 207-772-2846 *Toll Free Tel:* 800-341-6094
   Fax: 207-772-3105 *Toll Free Fax:* 888-991-
   5755
E-mail: customerservice@mail.walch.com
Web Site: www.walch.com
Key Personnel
Chmn of the Bd: Peter S Walch
Pres: John Thoreson *E-mail:* jthoreson@walch.
   com
Ed-in-Chief: Susan Blair *E-mail:* sblair@walch.
   com
CFO: Don Poole *E-mail:* dpoole@walch.com
Dir, Sales & Mktg: Jeff Taplin *Tel:* 207-772-2846
   ext 239 *E-mail:* jtaplin@walch.com
Opers Dir: Chuck Thomas *E-mail:* cthomas@
   walch.com
Catalog Mgr: Glen Halliday *E-mail:* ghalliday@
   walch.com
Dealer Sales Mgr: Jeff Files *E-mail:* jfiles@
   walch.com
Cust Serv Mgr: Nathan Confer *E-mail:* nconfer@
   walch.com
Founded: 1927
Educational books & supplementary materials for
   middle school through adult.
ISBN Prefix(es): 0-8251
Number of titles published annually: 100 Print;
   75 Online
Total Titles: 1,500 Print; 850 Online
Membership(s): ASCD; International Reading As-
   sociation; National Council for the Social Stud-
   ies; National Council of Teachers of English;
   National Council of Teachers of Mathematics;
   National Science Teachers Association

Walch Publishing, see J Weston Walch Publisher

Waldman House Press Inc, see Tristan
   Publishing

Walker & Co
Division of Walker Publishing Co Inc
104 Fifth Ave, 7th fl, New York, NY 10011
SAN: 202-5213
Tel: 212-727-8300 *Toll Free Tel:* 800-289-2553
   Fax: 212-727-0984 *Toll Free Fax:* 800-218-
   9367
E-mail: firstinitiallastname@walkerbooks.com
Web Site: www.walkerbooks.com *Cable:*
   REKLAWSAM
Key Personnel
Chmn: Ramsey R Walker
Pres & Publr: George L Gibson
   E-mail: ggibson@walkerbooks.com
CFO: Theodore Rosenfeld *E-mail:* trosenfeld@
   walkerbooks.com

Dir, Edit Prod & Design & Art Dir, Children's
   Books: Marlene Tungseth *E-mail:* mtungseth@
   walkerbooks.com
Ed, Nonfiction: Jacqueline Johnson
   E-mail: jjohnson@walkerbooks.com
Mktg Mgr, Adult Nonfiction: Maya Baran
Publr, Juv Books: Emily Easton
   E-mail: eeaston@walkerbooks.com
Intl Rts: Eilenn Pagan *E-mail:* epagan@
   walkerbooks.com
Sales Dir: Josh Wood *E-mail:* jwood@
   walkerbooks.com
Mktg & Assoc Sales Mgr, Books for Young
   Readers: Beth Eller
Founded: 1959
Adult & juvenile fiction & nonfiction, paper &
   hardcover.
ISBN Prefix(es): 0-8027
Number of titles published annually: 70 Print
Total Titles: 1,070 Print
Foreign Rep(s): Fitzhenry and Whiteside, Publish-
   ers (Canada)
Foreign Rights: Omiros Ausamides (Greece); Er-
   ica Berla (Italy); Beatriz Coll (Portugal, Spain);
   Ann-Christine Danielsson (Scandinavia); Si-
   monia Kessler (Romania); Efrat Lev (Israel);
   Frederique Porretta (France); Natalia Sanina
   (Russia); Thomas Schluck (Germany); Caro-
   line Van Gelderen (Netherlands); Anke Vogel
   (Hungary); Eric Yang (Korea)
Warehouse: WA Book Service Inc, 10 Constance
   Ct, Hauppauge, NY 11788
Membership(s): Children's Book Council

§Russ Walter Publisher
196 Tiffany Lane, Manchester, NH 03104-4782
Tel: 603-666-6644 *Fax:* 603-666-6644
E-mail: russ@secretfun.com
Web Site: www.secretfun.com
Key Personnel
Publr: Russ Walter *E-mail:* russ@secretfun.com
Busn Mgr: Donna Walter *E-mail:* donna@
   secretfun.com
Founded: 1982
Publish the *Secret Guide to Computers*, an ency-
   clopedic tutorial that explains all computer top-
   ics & is updated annually; also publish *Tricky
   Living*, covers everything about life beyond
   computers.
ISBN Prefix(es): 0-939151
Number of titles published annually: 3 Print; 2
   CD-ROM; 2 Online; 2 E-Book
Total Titles: 6 Print; 1 CD-ROM; 2 Online; 2 E-
   Book

Wm K Walthers Inc
5601 W Florist Ave, Milwaukee, WI 53218
Mailing Address: PO Box 3039, Milwaukee, WI
   53201-3039
Tel: 414-527-0770 *Toll Free Tel:* 800-877-7171
   Fax: 414-527-4423
E-mail: comments@walthers.com
Web Site: www.walthers.com
Key Personnel
CEO: Phil Walthers
Founded: 1932
Model railroading, reference books.
ISBN Prefix(es): 0-941952
Number of titles published annually: 3 Print
Total Titles: 3 Print

Wanderlust Publications
2009 S Tenth St, McAllen, TX 78503-5405
Mailing Address: PO Box 310, McAllen, TX
   78505-0310
Tel: 956-686-3601 *Fax:* 956-686-0732
E-mail: info@sanbornsinsurance.com
Web Site: www.sanbornsinsurance.com
Key Personnel
Gen Mgr: Rocio Morales
Contact: Tete Castillo
Founded: 1994
Mexico travel & Mexico general.

ISBN Prefix(es): 1-878166
Number of titles published annually: 9 Print
Total Titles: 7 Print

WANT Publishing Co
420 Lexington Ave, Suite 300, New York, NY
10170
Tel: 212-687-3774 *Fax:* 212-687-3779
Web Site: www.courts.com
Key Personnel
Pres: Robert Want *E-mail:* rwant@courts.com
Founded: 1975
ISBN Prefix(es): 0-9701229
Total Titles: 2 Print; 1 Online

Frederick Warne
Imprint of Penguin Group (USA) Inc
345 Hudson St, New York, NY 10014
SAN: 282-5074
Tel: 212-366-2000
E-mail: online@penguinputnam.com
Web Site: www.penguin.com
Key Personnel
Assoc Publr, Viking & Warne: Elizabeth Law
Founded: 1865
ISBN Prefix(es): 0-7232
Number of titles published annually: 13 Print
Total Titles: 145 Print
Foreign Rep(s): Agenzia Letteraria Internazionale
(Italy); DRT International (Korea); I Pikarski
Ltd Literary Agency (Israel); International
Press Agency (South Africa); Japan UNI
(Japan); La Nouvelle Agence (France); Lit-
erari Agentura (Czech Republic); Mohrbooks
(Germany); ICBS (Netherlands, Scandinavia);
Bardon-Chinese (China)

Warner Books
Subsidiary of Time Warner Book Group
1271 Avenue of the Americas, New York, NY
10020
SAN: 282-5368
Tel: 212-522-7200 *Fax:* 212-522-7991
Web Site: www.twbookmark.com
Key Personnel
Sr VP & Publr: Jamie Raab
VP & Assoc Publr: Les Pockell
Assoc Publr: Ivan Held
VP, Publicity: Emi Battaglia
VP, Spec Mkts: Jean Griffin
VP, Creative Dir: Anne Twomey
VP, Dir of Mktg: Karen Torres
VP, Subs Rts: Nancy Wiese
Exec Dir, Fin & Planning: Mitchell Kinzer
Edit Dir, Mass Mkt: Beth de Guzman
VP, Edit Dir Trade Pbks, Exec Ed: Amy Einhorn
Dir of Inventory Mgmt & Analysis: Larry Wicker
Exec Art Dir: Diane Luger
Royalty Mgr: Rolande Joseph
Assoc Dir, Foreign Rts: Erika Riley
Publr, Walk Worthy Press: Denise Stinson
Founded: 1961
Hardcover, trade paperback & mass market pa-
perback, reprint & original, fiction & nonfic-
tion, audio books. Unsol/unagented mss not
accepted.
ISBN Prefix(es): 0-445; 0-446; 0-89296
Number of titles published annually: 270 Print
Total Titles: 3,600 Print
Imprints: Aspect; Mysterious Press; Walk Worthy;
Warner Business Books; Warner Faith; Warner
Forever; Warner Vision
Foreign Rights: Antonella Antonelli Agenzia Let-
teraria (Italy); Bardon Far Eastern Agents (Tai-
wan); Imprima Korea (Korea); Katai + Bolza
(Hungary); Simona Kessler (Romania); Maria
Starz-Kanska (Poland); La Nouvelle Agence
(France); Andrew Nurnberg Associates (Baltic
States, Bulgaria, Mainland China, Russia); O
A Agency (Greece); Kristin Olson (Czech Re-
public, Slovak Republic); Pikarski Agency (Is-
rael); RDC Agencia Literaria (Brazil, Latin

America, Spain); Thomas Schluck Literary &
Art Agency (Germany); Ulf Toregard Agency
(Denmark, Finland, Iceland, Norway, Sweden);
Zvonimir Majdak (Croatia, Slovenia)
Advertising Agency: Publishers Advertising
Shipping Address: TIme Warner Book Group
Distribution Center, 121 N Enterprise Blvd,
Lebanon, IN 46052 *Tel:* 765-483-9900
Fax: 765-483-0706
Membership(s): AAP; BISG

Warner Bros Publications Inc
15800 NW 48 Ave, Miami, FL 33014
Tel: 305-620-1500 *Toll Free Tel:* 800-327-7643
Fax: 305-621-4869
E-mail: wbpsales@warnerchappell.com
Web Site: www.warnerbrospublications.com
Key Personnel
CEO: Fred S Anton
Intl Rts: David Olsen
Lib Sales Dir: Vincent Martino
VP, Mktg: Andrea Nelson *Tel:* 305-521-1608
Specialize in printed music & instructional music
videos & DVDs.
ISBN Prefix(es): 0-7692; 1-57623; 0-89724
Number of titles published annually: 1,000 Print
Distributor for Belwin-Mills; Bradley Publica-
tions; Brimhall Music Publishing; Frances
Clark; Expressions Music Curriculum™;
Kalmus; Music Expressions™; Summy-
Birchard Inc; Suzuki; Warner Brothers
Membership(s): Book Tech West

§Warner Bros Worldwide Publishing
Division of Warner Bros Consumer Products
4000 Warner Blvd, Bldg 118, Burbank, CA
91522-1704
Tel: 818-954-5450 *Fax:* 818-954-5595
Web Site: www.warnerbros.com
Key Personnel
Dir: Isabelle Giggins *Tel:* 818-954-5572
E-mail: isabelle.giggins@warnerbros.com
VP, Publg: Paula K Allen *E-mail:* paula.allen@
warnerbros.com
Founded: 1993
Licensing Warner Bros film, TV & cartoon prop-
erties; comics & magazines.
Number of titles published annually: 400 Print;
20 CD-ROM; 2 Audio
Total Titles: 3,000 Print; 50 CD-ROM; 18 Audio
Sales Office(s): Worldwide Publishing, 4000
Warner Blvd, Burbank, CA 91522, VP: Paula
Allen *Tel:* 818-954-5450 *Fax:* 818-954-5595
E-mail: paula.allen@warnerbros.com

**Warner Faith (Christian Book Division of
Time Warner Book Group)**
Subsidiary of Time Warner Book Group
2 Creekside Crossing, 10 Cadillac Dr, Suite 220,
Brentwood, TN 37027
Tel: 615-221-0996 *Fax:* 615-221-0962
Web Site: www.twbookmark.com
Key Personnel
VP & Publr: Rolf Zettersten
Mktg Dir: Lori Quinn
Sales Dir: Robert Nealeigh
Mktg Mgr: Preston Cannon
Publicity Dir: Andrea Davis
Ed: Leslie Peterson; Stephen Wilburn
Founded: 2001
ISBN Prefix(es): 0-446
Number of titles published annually: 35 Print; 6
E-Book; 6 Audio
Total Titles: 150 Print; 12 E-Book; 12 Audio
Membership(s): CBA; Evangelical Christian Pub-
lishers Association

Warren Communications News
2115 Ward Ct NW, Washington, DC 20037-1209
Tel: 202-872-9200 *Fax:* 202-293-3435
E-mail: info@warren-news.com
Web Site: www.warren-news.com

Key Personnel
Chmn, Ed & Publr: Albert Warren
VChmn & Assoc Publr: Daniel Warren
Pres & Exec Publr: Paul Warren
Exec Ed: Dawson B Nail
Sr Ed: Jeff Berman
Man Ed: R Michael Feazel
Assoc Man Ed: Edith Herman; Patrick Ross
NY Bureau Chief: Paul Gluckman
Founded: 1945
Newsletters & directories.
ISBN Prefix(es): 0-911486
Number of titles published annually: 10 Print
Total Titles: 10 Print
Branch Office(s)
276 Fifth Ave, Suite 1111, New York, NY 10001,
Contact: Paul Gluckman *Toll Free Tel:* 800-
771-5410

Warren, Gorham & Lamont
Subsidiary of Research Institute of America Inc
395 Hudson St, New York, NY 10014
SAN: 202-9480
Tel: 212-367-6300 *Toll Free Tel:* 800-431-9025;
800-678-2185 (cust serv) *Fax:* 212-367-6305
Web Site: www.riahome.com
Key Personnel
Pres & CEO: Mark Schlageter
Dir, Mktg: Nicole Gagnon
Founded: 1846
References, treatises, manuals, reports, journals
& newsletters in the fields of financial services,
law, taxation, real estate, accounting, human
resource & management information systems.
ISBN Prefix(es): 0-88262; 0-88712
Number of titles published annually: 150 Print
Total Titles: 464 Print
Imprints: Auerbach Publications
Branch Office(s)
31 St James Place, Boston, MA 02116

Washington State University Press
Cooper Publications Bldg, Grimes Way, Pullman,
WA 99164-5910
SAN: 206-6688
Mailing Address: PO Box 645910, Pullman, WA
99164-5910
Tel: 509-335-3518 *Toll Free Tel:* 800-354-7360
Fax: 509-335-8568
E-mail: wsupress@wsu.edu
Web Site: wsupress.wsu.edu
Key Personnel
Ed-in-Chief: Glen Lindeman
Order Fulfillment Coord: Jennifer S Lynn
Tel: 509-335-7880 *E-mail:* jslynn@wsu.edu
Ed & Composition: Nancy Grunewald *Tel:* 509-
335-5817
Prodn Coord: Jean Taylor
Mktg & Promos: Caryn Lawton
Founded: 1928
Trade & scholarly books focusing on the history,
natural history, military history, culture & pol-
itics of the greater Pacific Northwest region
(Washington, Idaho, Oregon, Western Montana,
British Columbia & Alaska).
ISBN Prefix(es): 0-87422
Number of titles published annually: 10 Print
Total Titles: 160 Print; 2 Online; 65 E-Book
Divisions: Washington State University
Distributed by UBC Press (Canada)
Distributor for The Hutton Settlement; Museum
of Art; Oregon Writers Colony; Pacific Institute
(distribute only one title)
Shipping Address: UNIpresses, 34 Armstrong
Ave, Georgetown, ON L7G 4R9, Canada
Tel: 905-873-9781 *Toll Free Tel:* 877-864-8477
Fax: 905-873-6170 *Toll Free Fax:* 877-864-
4272 *E-mail:* orders@gtwcanada.com
Membership(s): Association of American Uni-
versity Presses; Pacific Northwest Booksellers
Association

Water Environment Federation
601 Wythe St, Alexandria, VA 22314-1994
Tel: 703-684-2400 *Toll Free Tel:* 800-666-0206
Fax: 703-684-2492
E-mail: csc@wef.org
Web Site: www.wef.org
Key Personnel
Publr & Mktg Dir: Jack Benson *Tel:* 703-684-2400 ext 2493
Founded: 1928
Scientific publisher of environmental titles. Seeks authors of sound, state-of-the-art environmental material.
ISBN Prefix(es): 0-943244; 1-881369
Number of titles published annually: 15 Print
Total Titles: 190 Print

§Water Resources Publications LLC
PO Box 260026, Highlands Ranch, CO 80163-0026
Tel: 720-873-0171 *Fax:* 720-873-0173
E-mail: info@wrpllc.com
Web Site: www.wrpllc.com
Key Personnel
Contact: Jennie Campbell
Founded: 1973
Publish & distribute books & computer programs on water resources & related fields.
ISBN Prefix(es): 0-918334; 1-887201
Number of titles published annually: 15 Print
Total Titles: 450 Print; 35 CD-ROM
Distributor for ASAE; ASCE

Water Row Press
Subsidiary of Water Row Books
PO Box 438, Sudbury, MA 01776
Tel: 508-485-8515 *Fax:* 508-229-0885
E-mail: contact@waterrowbooks.com
Web Site: www.waterrowbooks.com
Key Personnel
Pres: Jeffrey H Weinberg
Ed: Cisco Harland
Prodn Mgr: Betsy Kirschbaum
Founded: 1982
Publishers of modern literature, poetry, graphic novels; specialize in books by & about "Beat" writers; comic art.
ISBN Prefix(es): 0-934953
Number of titles published annually: 12 Print
Total Titles: 29 Print
Distributed by Water Row Books
Distributor for Water Row Books; Weinberg Books

WaterBrook Press
Division of Random House Inc
2375 Telstar Dr, Suite 160, Colorado Springs, CO 80920
Tel: 719-590-4999 *Toll Free Tel:* 800-603-7051 (orders) *Fax:* 719-590-8977 *Toll Free Fax:* 800-294-5686 (orders)
Web Site: www.waterbrookpress.com
Key Personnel
Pres & Publr: Steve Cobb
VP & Dir, Publg: Don Pape
VP & Dir, Sales: Brian McGinley
Edit Dir: Laura J Barker
Dir, Mktg & Publicity: Ginia Hairston
Fiction Ed: Dudley Delffs
Sr Ed: Ron Lee; Bruce Nygren
Founded: 1996
Offer a broad range of Christian nonfiction & fiction titles in hardcover & trade paperback for adult & young readers, as well as children's books.
Random House Inc & its publishing entities are not accepting unsol submissions, proposals, mss, or submission queries via e-mail at this time.
ISBN Prefix(es): 1-57856; 1-87788 (Shaw)
Number of titles published annually: 65 Print; 3 CD-ROM; 5 E-Book; 2 Audio

Total Titles: 510 Print; 3 CD-ROM; 11 Audio
Imprints: Shaw Books
Membership(s): Evangelical Christian Publishers Association

Waterfront Books
85 Crescent Rd, Burlington, VT 05401
SAN: 289-6923
Tel: 802-658-7477 *Toll Free Tel:* 800-639-6063 (orders) *Fax:* 802-860-1368
E-mail: helpkids@waterfrontbooks.com
Web Site: www.waterfrontbooks.com
Key Personnel
Pres & Publr: Sherrill N Musty
Founded: 1983
Quality paperbacks; adult & juvenile; trade, school & library; psychology, self-help, how-to, family, family guidance & social issues, parenting & special issues for children.
ISBN Prefix(es): 0-914525
Number of titles published annually: 3 Print
Total Titles: 35 Print
Advertising Agency: Nelson Advertising

WaterPlow Press™
Amherst Office Park, 441 West Street, Suite G, Amherst, MA 01002
Mailing Address: PO Box 2475, Amherst, MA 01004-2475
Tel: 413-253-1520 *Toll Free Tel:* 866-367-3300 (orders only) *Fax:* 413-253-1521
E-mail: sales@waterplowpress.com
Web Site: www.waterplowpress.com
Key Personnel
Publr: Amy Vickers *E-mail:* ava-inc@amyvickers.com
Founded: 2000
Publishes printed material, namely books, on a wide variety of topics including water use, conservation & water efficiency.
ISBN Prefix(es): 1-931579
Number of titles published annually: 3 Print
Total Titles: 1 Print
Distributed by American Water Works Association
Membership(s): Publishers Marketing Association

Watson-Guptill Publications
Division of VNU Business Media Inc
770 Broadway, New York, NY 10003
SAN: 200-2396
Tel: 646-654-5450 *Toll Free Tel:* 800-278-8477 (orders only) *Fax:* 646-654-5486; 646-654-5487
E-mail: info@watsonguptill.com
Web Site: www.watsonguptill.com
Key Personnel
Dir, Sales & Mktg: Charles Whang
Dir, Ed & Prodn: Sharon Kaplan
Sr Ed, Crafts: Joy Aquilino
Sr Ed, Amphoto & Lifestyle: Victoria Craven
Exec Ed, Billboard Bks: Bob Nirkind
Exec Ed, Art: Candace Raney
Publicist: Lee Wiggins
Gen Mgr: Bob Ferro
Intl Sales Mgr: Alison Smith
Rts, Co-edition & Bk Club Sales: Sheila Emery
Special Sales Assoc: Amy Alexander
  E-mail: aalexander@watsonguptill.com
Founded: 1937
Art instruction, graphic design, fine arts, photography, crafts, interior design, architecture, music, theatre, film & pop culture.
ISBN Prefix(es): 0-8230; 0-8174
Number of titles published annually: 200 Print
Total Titles: 1,000 Print
Imprints: Amphoto; Back Stage Books; Billboard Books; Radio Amateur Callbook; Watson-Guptill; The Whitney Library of Design
Distributor for Allworth Press; C & T Publishing
Foreign Rep(s): Bookwise International (Australia & New Zealand); Georgetown Publications

(Canada); Christopher Humphrys (Caribbean, Central America); Peter Hyde Associates (South Africa); International Publishers Representatives (Middle East, North Africa); Terry Roberts (South America); Windsor Books (UK & Europe)
Returns: 575 Prospect, Lakewood, NJ 08701-5040 *Toll Free Tel:* 800-451-1741
Shipping Address: 575 Prospect, Lakewood, NJ 08701-5040 *Toll Free Tel:* 800-451-1741
Warehouse: 575 Prospect, Lakewood, NJ 08701-5040 *Toll Free Tel:* 800-451-1741
Distribution Center: 575 Prospect, Lakewood, NJ 08701-5040 *Toll Free Tel:* 800-451-1741

Watson Publishing International
PO Box 1240, Sagamore Beach, MA 02562-1240
Tel: 508-888-9113 *Fax:* 508-888-3733
E-mail: orders@watsonpublishing.com
Web Site: www.watsonpublishing.com; www.shpusa.com
Key Personnel
Publr, CEO & Pres: Neale W Watson
  E-mail: nww@watsonpublishing.com
Founded: 1971
College textbooks & scholarly books on science & medicine.
ISBN Prefix(es): 0-88135
Number of titles published annually: 7 Print
Total Titles: 143 Print
Imprints: Prodist; Science History Publications USA; Neale Watson Academic Publications
Shipping Address: Publishers Storage, 46 Development Rd, Fitchburg, MA 01420-6020

Waveland Press Inc
4180 IL Rte 83, Suite 101, Long Grove, IL 60047-9580
SAN: 209-0961
Tel: 847-634-0081 *Fax:* 847-634-9501
E-mail: info@waveland.com
Web Site: www.waveland.com
Key Personnel
Pres & Publr: Neil Rowe
Ed: Carol Rowe
Mktg Mgr: Thomas Curtin
Prodn Mgr & Intl Rts: Don Rosso
Off Mgr: Bonnie Highsmith
Founded: 1975
College textbooks & supplements.
ISBN Prefix(es): 0-88133; 0-917974; 1-57766
Number of titles published annually: 25 Print
Total Titles: 553 Print
Subsidiaries: Sheffield Publishing Co
Distribution Center: Lakeland Storage Co, PO Box 359, 9009 Antioch Rd, Salem, WI 53168-0359
See separate listing for:
Sheffield Publishing Co

Wayne State University Press
Leonard N Simons Bldg, 4809 Woodward Ave, Detroit, MI 48201-1309
SAN: 202-5221
Tel: 313-577-4600 *Toll Free Tel:* 800-978-7323 *Fax:* 313-577-6131
Key Personnel
Chmn, Edit Bd: Renata Wasserman
Dir: Jane Hoehner
Acquiring Ed: Kathryn Wildfong
Sales Mgr: Renee Tambeau
Order Fulfillment: Theresa Martinelli
Busn Mgr: Theresa Mahoney
Man Ed: Kristin Harpster Lawrence
Founded: 1941
Scholarly & trade books in African American studies, film & television, German studies, childhood studies, women's studies, Jewish studies, literary criticism, speech & language pathology, folklore, regional studies, urban & labor studies.
ISBN Prefix(es): 0-8143

Number of titles published annually: 35 Print
Total Titles: 575 Print; 1 CD-ROM
Imprints: Great Lakes Books
Distributor for Cranbrook Institute of Science;
Detroit Institute of Arts; Hebrew Union College Press
Foreign Rights: Europsan (Africa, UK, Europe, Middle East); EWEB (Far East); Scholarly Book Services (Canada)
Warehouse: 40 W Hancock, Detroit, MI 48201

Wayside Publications
PO Box 318, Goreville, IL 62939
Tel: 618-995-1157
Web Site: www.waysidepublications.com
Key Personnel
Owner: Violet M Toler *E-mail:* violet@waysidepublications.com
Ed: N Nottingham
Founded: 2004
Publishes "Teacher Tips" books for religious teachers of children ages 4-11. Each book is a collection of ideas from several authors, featuring all aspects of children's worship (Bible lessons, puzzles, games, activities, crafts, puppets, songs, prayer, discipline & more).
Submissions must be original, unpublished material, written in a clear, concise manner. Artistic ability is not required, but rough sketches are encouraged, if necessary, to portray an idea.
We are looking for fresh, easy, fun activities & lessons that are not limited to a specific denomination. Now accepting teacher tips of no more than 350 words. E-mail submission preferred.
Payment is made in copies of the published book.
Number of titles published annually: 6 Print
Total Titles: 4 Print
Imprints: Churchmouse Tales Books

Wayside Publishing
11 Jan Sebastian Way, Suite 5, Sandwich, MA 02563
Tel: 508-833-5096 *Toll Free Tel:* 888-302-2519
Fax: 508-833-6284
E-mail: wayside@sprintmail.com
Web Site: www.waysidepublishing.com
Key Personnel
Owner & Publr: David Greuel
Mktg/Sales Mgr: Doc Kim
Founded: 1987
Humanities, English & foreign language textbooks & history.
ISBN Prefix(es): 1-877653
Number of titles published annually: 5 Print
Total Titles: 50 Print

Weatherhill Inc
Subsidiary of Tankosha (Japan)
41 Monroe Tpke, Trumbull, CT 06611
Tel: 203-459-5090 *Toll Free Tel:* 800-437-7840
Fax: 203-459-5095 *Toll Free Fax:* 800-557-5601
E-mail: weatherhill@weatherhill.com
Web Site: www.weatherhill.com
Key Personnel
COO: Martin Berke
VP, Sales & Mktg & Rts & Perms: Barbara Brackett
Edit Dir: Ray Furse
Founded: 1962
Publishers & distributors of fine books on Asia & the Pacific, flower arranging books, design, art, culture, language, travel, literature, Zen, photography & history. Also non-Asian books, art, photography, design, history, chess & other subjects.
ISBN Prefix(es): 0-8348
Number of titles published annually: 55 Print
Total Titles: 850 Print
Imprints: Weatherhill
Divisions: B H B International

Distributed by Canadian MANDA; InterBook Marketing; New Holland Publishers Ltd; Peribo; Marta Schooler; Yohan
Distributor for A R E Press; Gambit Publications; The Hoberman Connection; Hollym Corp; Luzac Orientals; New Holland; Serindia Publications; Shufunotomo Co Ltd; Wakefield Press; Windhorse Publications
Membership(s): AAP

Webb Research Group, Publishers
PO Box 314, Medford, OR 97501-0021
SAN: 222-1934
Tel: 541-664-5205 *Fax:* 541-664-9131
E-mail: pnwbooks@pnwbooks.com
Web Site: www.pnorthwestbooks.com
Key Personnel
Owner, Publr & Ed-in-Chief: Bert Webber
Dist Mgr & Lib Sales Dir: M J Webber
Founded: 1979
Books about the Pacific Northwest, Oregon Trail, selected WWII & other related subjects.
ISBN Prefix(es): 0-936738; 1-878815
Number of titles published annually: 5 Print
Total Titles: 66 Print; 66 E-Book
Imprints: Reflected Images Publishers
Distributed by Pacific Northwest Books Co

Weidner & Sons Publishing
Division of The Weidner Publishing Group
PO Box 2178 (Cinnaminson), Riverton, NJ 08077
Tel: 856-486-1755 *Fax:* 856-486-7583
E-mail: weidner@waterw.com
Web Site: www.arlhs.com/weidnerpublishing
Key Personnel
Pres & Man Dir: James H Weidner
Founded: 1985
Natural history, environmental science monographs & textbooks, medicine, education, law, development. No fiction or poetry.
ISBN Prefix(es): 0-85148; 0-938198
Number of titles published annually: 7 Print
Total Titles: 67 Print
Imprints: Bird-Sci Books; Delaware Estuary Press; Hazlaw Books; Lighthouse Publications; Medlaw Books; Pulse Publications; Tycooly Publishing USA
Divisions: Bird-Sci Books; Delaware Estuary Press; Delaware Museum Books; Pulse Publications; Tycooly Publishing USA
Distributor for Delaware Estuary Press; Delaware Museum of Natural History; Hazlaw Books; Lighthouse Publications; Pulse Publications; Medlaw Books; Tycooly Publishing USA
Distribution Center: Tycooly USA, 114 Woodbine Ave, Merchantville, NJ 08109

§Weil Publishing Co Inc
150 Capitol St, Augusta, ME 04330
Mailing Address: PO Box 1990, Augusta, ME 04332-1990
Tel: 207-621-0029 *Toll Free Tel:* 800-877-9345
Fax: 207-621-0069
E-mail: info@weilpublishing.com
Web Site: www.weilpublishing.com
Key Personnel
VP: James Blanchard
Founded: 1985
Administration rule & regulations - State of ME, VT, RI & government registers for same (all products updated monthly), Massachusetts: Index to CMR, Weil's Code of MA Regs, Wyoming Rules & Govt Register.
ISBN Prefix(es): 0-916812
Number of titles published annually: 22 Print
Total Titles: 167 Print

Weiss Ratings Inc
15430 Endeavor Dr, Jupiter, FL 33478
Tel: 561-627-3300 *Toll Free Tel:* 800-289-9222
Fax: 561-625-6685
E-mail: wr@weissinc.com

Web Site: www.weissratings.com
Publishing & book trade reference. The most accurate source available for evaluating the financial stability of banks, insurance companies, HMOs & securities brokers. Unlike the other major rating agencies, Weiss accepts no compensation from the companies being rated, making us the only source for totally independent, unbiased evaluations & solvency ratings.
Number of titles published annually: 8 Print

Welcome Books
Imprint of Welcome Enterprises
6 W 18 St, 3rd fl, New York, NY 10011
Tel: 212-989-3200 *Fax:* 212-989-3205
E-mail: info@welcomebooks.com
Web Site: www.welcomebooks.com
Key Personnel
Pres: Hiro Clark Wakabayashi *E-mail:* clark@welcomebooks.com
Publr: Lena Tabori *E-mail:* lena@welcomebooks.com
Project Dir: Katrina Fried *E-mail:* katrina@welcomebooks.com
Art Dir: Greg Wakabayashi *E-mail:* greg@welcomebooks.com
Founded: 1980
Illustrated books for adult trade & gift market.
ISBN Prefix(es): 0-941807
Number of titles published annually: 8 Print
Total Titles: 47 Print
Distributed by Andrews McMeel Publishing
Foreign Rights: John Wallace
Distribution Center: Simon & Schuster, 2207 Radcliffe St, Dock A, Bristol, PA 19007 *Toll Free Tel:* 800-851-8923 (sales & mktg); 800-943-9839 (cust serv & orders)
Membership(s): American Book Producers Association

Welcome Rain Publishers LLC
532 Laguardia Place, Suite 473, New York, NY 10012
Tel: 718-832-1607 *Fax:* 212-889-0869
E-mail: welcomrain@aol.com
Key Personnel
Publr: John Weber
Founded: 1997
General trade publisher.
ISBN Prefix(es): 1-56649
Number of titles published annually: 8 Print
Total Titles: 93 Print
Subsidiaries: Writers House
Distributed by National Book Network

Wellington Press
Division of BooksUPrint.com Inc
9601-30 Miccosukee Rd, Tallahassee, FL 32309
Tel: 850-878-6500
E-mail: booksuprint@aol.com; wellpress@aol.com
Web Site: www.booksuprint.com
Key Personnel
Pres & Intl Rts: David Felder *E-mail:* felderdave@aol.com
Founded: 1982
Books related to peace, philosophy, politics, textbooks in all desciplines & role play simulations of conflicts in both electronic & print format.
ISBN Prefix(es): 0-910959; 1-57501
Number of titles published annually: 10 Print; 10 E-Book
Total Titles: 85 Print; 90 Online; 100 E-Book

Wellness Institute Inc
1007 Whitney Ave, Gretna, LA 70056
Tel: 504-361-1845 *Fax:* 504-365-0114
Web Site: selfhelpbooks.com
Key Personnel
Owner & Dir: Harold Dawley *E-mail:* hdawley@bellsouth.net
Founded: 1974
Exclusively publisher of self-help books.

ISBN Prefix(es): 1-58741
Number of titles published annually: 30 Print; 30 E-Book
Total Titles: 100 Print; 70 E-Book
Imprints: Selfhelpbooks.com

Werbel Publishing Co Inc
686 Deer Park Ave, Dix Hills, NY 11746-6219
Tel: 631-243-0032 *Toll Free Tel:* 800-293-7235
Fax: 631-243-0069
E-mail: info@werbel.com
Web Site: www.werbel.com
Key Personnel
Pres: C Monteforte
Founded: 1938
Insurance & finance, pre-licensing text & exams.
ISBN Prefix(es): 1-884803
Number of titles published annually: 16 Print
Total Titles: 16 Print

Eliot Werner Publications Inc
31 Willow Lane, Clinton Corners, NY 12514
Mailing Address: PO Box 268, Clinton Corners, NY 12514
Tel: 845-266-4241 *Fax:* 845-266-3317
E-mail: ewerner@earthlink.net
Web Site: www.eliotwerner.com
Founded: 2001
Academic & scholarly books in anthropology, archaeology, psychology, sociology & related fields; writing, copy-editing & contract publishing.
ISBN Prefix(es): 0-9712427; 0-9719587; 0-9752738
Number of titles published annually: 8 Print
Total Titles: 24 Print
Imprints: Percheron Press

Wescott Cove Publishing Co
Subsidiary of NetPV Inc
PO Box 560989, Rockledge, FL 32956
Tel: 321-690-2224 *Fax:* 321-690-0853
E-mail: customerservice@wescottcovepublishing.com
Web Site: www.wescottcovepublishing.com
Key Personnel
Publr: Will Standley
Books on boating, cruising, yachting & the adventurous life.
ISBN Prefix(es): 0-918752
Number of titles published annually: 16 Print; 4 E-Book
Total Titles: 16 Online; 16 E-Book
Membership(s): Small Publishers Association of North America

Wesleyan Publishing House
Division of Wesleyan Church Corporation
13300 Olio Rd, Noblesville, IN 46060
Mailing Address: PO Box 50434, Indianapolis, IN 46250
Tel: 317-774-3853 *Toll Free Tel:* 800-493-7539
Fax: 317-774-3860 *Toll Free Fax:* 800-788-3535
E-mail: wph@wesleyan.org
Web Site: www.wesleyan.org/wph
Key Personnel
Gen Publr: Donald Cady
Man Ed: Larry Wilson
Founded: 1968
ISBN Prefix(es): 0-89827
Number of titles published annually: 10 Print
Total Titles: 60 Print
Membership(s): Christian Booksellers Association; Christian Holiness Partnership; Holiness Publisher's Association; Protestant Church-Owned Publishers Association

§Wesleyan University Press
215 Long Lane, Middletown, CT 06459-0433
Tel: 860-685-7711 *Fax:* 860-685-7712
Web Site: www.wesleyan.edu/wespress *Cable:* WESPRESS MIDDLETOWN
Key Personnel
Dir & Intl Rts: Thomas R Radko *Tel:* 860-685-7715 *E-mail:* tradko@wesleyan.edu
Ed-in-Chief: Suzanna L Tamminen *Tel:* 860-685-7727 *E-mail:* stamminen@wesleyan.edu
Mktg Mgr: Leslie Starr *Tel:* 860-685-7725 *E-mail:* lstarr@wesleyan.edu
Acqs Ed: Leonora Gibson *Tel:* 860-685-7730 *E-mail:* lgibson@wesleyan.edu
Mktg Asst & Exhibits/Adv Coord: Kim Radowiecki *Tel:* 860-685-7716 *E-mail:* kradowiecki@wesleyan.edu
Publicist: Stephanie Elliott *Tel:* 860-685-7723 *E-mail:* selliott@wesleyan.edu
Founded: 1957
Editorial Program which has been awarded six Pulitzer Prizes; Distinguished history of publishing scholarly & trade books that have influenced American poetry & critical thought over the last four decades.
ISBN Prefix(es): 0-8195
Number of titles published annually: 40 Print; 4 CD-ROM
Total Titles: 425 Print
Imprints: Disseminations: Psychoanalysis in Contexts; Early Classics of Science Fiction; Wesleyan Poetry
Foreign Rep(s): East-West Export Books (Asia & the Pacific, Australia & New Zealand); Eurospan University Press Group (Europe & Middle East); University of British Columbia Press (Canada); University of Presses Marketing (UK, Greece, Israel)
Shipping Address: UPNE, 37 Lafayette St, Lebanon, NH 03766-1446 *Toll Free Tel:* 800-421-1561 *Fax:* 603-643-1540
Distribution Center: University Press of New England, One Court St, Suite 250, Lebanon, NH 03766, Contact: Sarah L Welsch *Tel:* 603-448-1533 *Fax:* 603-643-1540 *E-mail:* sarah.l.welsch@dartmouth.edu
Membership(s): AAP; Association of American University Presses; NEBA

West, see Wadsworth Publishing

West, A Thomson Business
Formerly West Group
Division of The Thomson Corporation
610 Opperman Dr, Eagan, MN 55123
Tel: 651-687-7000 *Toll Free Tel:* 800-328-9352 (sales); 800-328-4880 (cust serv) *Fax:* 651-687-7302
Web Site: www.west.com
Key Personnel
CEO: Brian Hall
Founded: 1804
Publisher of state statutes, attorney general opinions & practice manuals for the US & international.
ISBN Prefix(es): 0-8322; 0-7620; 0-8366; 0-87632
Number of titles published annually: 4 Print
Branch Office(s)
6111 Oak Tree Blvd, Cleveland, OH 44131 *Tel:* 216-520-5600 *Fax:* 216-520-5655 SAN: 204-5370
Aqueduct Bldg, Rochester, NY 14694 *Tel:* 585-546-5530 *Toll Free Tel:* 800-527-0430 *Fax:* 585-327-6269
Distributor for Law Library Microform Consortium
Returns: 545 Wescott Rd, Eagan, MN 55123

West Group, see West, A Thomson Business

Westcliffe Publishers Inc
2650 S Zuni St, Englewood, CO 80110-1145
SAN: 239-7528
Mailing Address: PO Box 1261, Englewood, CO 80150-1261
Tel: 303-935-0900 *Toll Free Tel:* 800-523-3692 *Fax:* 303-935-0903
E-mail: sales@westcliffepublishers.com
Web Site: www.westcliffepublishers.com
Key Personnel
Pres & CEO: John Fielder *E-mail:* john@westcliffepublishers.com
Assoc Publr: Linda J Doyle *E-mail:* linda@westcliffepublishers.com
Sales Dir: Karen Woodward *E-mail:* karen@westcliffepublishers.com
Cont: Janet Heisz *E-mail:* janet@westcliffepublishers.com
Founded: 1981
Photographic publisher; specialize in landscape, nature & scenic subjects, trail guides.
ISBN Prefix(es): 0-942394; 0-929969; 1-56579
Number of titles published annually: 16 Print; 16 Online
Total Titles: 125 Print; 125 Online

Western National Parks Association
12880 N Vistoso Village Dr, Tucson, AZ 85737-8797
Tel: 520-622-1999 *Toll Free Tel:* 888-569-SPMA (orders only) *Fax:* 520-623-9519
E-mail: info@wnpa.org
Web Site: www.wnpa.org
Key Personnel
Dir, Pubns & Intl Rts: Derek Gallagher *E-mail:* dgallagher@wnpa.org
Lib Sales Dir: Roger Downey *Tel:* 520-219-9535 *Fax:* 520-297-2739
Founded: 1938
Site specific books-interpretive publications on natural history, archeology, history having to do with the 63 national parks we serve.
ISBN Prefix(es): 0-911408; 1-877856; 1-58369
Number of titles published annually: 5 Print
Total Titles: 186 Print; 2 Audio

Western New York Wares Inc
Affiliate of Meyer Enterprises
PO Box 733, Ellicott Sta, Buffalo, NY 14205
Mailing Address: PO Box 733, Buffalo, NY 14205
Tel: 716-832-6088
E-mail: buffalobooks@att.net
Web Site: www.buffalobooks.com
Key Personnel
Pres & Intl Rts: Brian Meyer
Founded: 1984
Publish, market & distribute books that focus on Western New York history, architecture & tourism.
ISBN Prefix(es): 1-879201; 0-9620314
Number of titles published annually: 4 Print
Total Titles: 50 Print; 1 Audio
Imprints: Meyer Enterprises
Distributor for Canisius College Press; DLR Imagery
Returns: 419 Parkside Ave, Buffalo, NY 14216, Tom Connolly *Tel:* 716-832-6088
Membership(s): Small Publishers Association of North America

Western Pennsylvania Genealogical Society
4400 Forbes Ave, Pittsburgh, PA 15213-4080
Tel: 412-687-6811 (answering machine)
E-mail: info@wpgs.org
Web Site: www.wpgs.org
Key Personnel
Ed: Jean S Morris
Founded: 1974
Number of titles published annually: 100 Print; 30 CD-ROM; 40 Online; 40 E-Book; 20 Audio
Total Titles: 40 Print; 1 CD-ROM; 1 Online; 1 E-Book; 2 Audio
Distributed by Mechling Associates

Western Reflections Publishing Co
219 Main St, Montrose, CO 81401
Tel: 970-249-7180 *Toll Free Tel:* 800-993-4490
 Fax: 970-249-7181
E-mail: westref@montrose.net
Web Site: www.westernreflectionspub.com
Key Personnel
Pres: P David Smith
Founded: 1996
Specialize in fine Colorado books.
ISBN Prefix(es): 1-890437; 1-932738
Number of titles published annually: 12 Print
Total Titles: 90 Print
Imprints: Peak Publishing
Membership(s): Colorado Independent Publishers
 Association; Publishers Marketing Association;
 Small Publishers Association of North America

Westernlore Press
PO Box 35305, Tucson, AZ 85740-5305
SAN: 202-9650
Tel: 520-297-5491 *Fax:* 520-297-1722
Key Personnel
Pres & Ed: Lynn R Bailey
Treas & ISBN Contact: Anne G Bailey
Founded: 1941
History & biography, anthropology, historic ar-
 chaeology & historic sites & ethnohistory per-
 taining to the greater American West.
ISBN Prefix(es): 0-87026
Number of titles published annually: 6 Print
Total Titles: 65 Print

§Westminster John Knox Press
Imprint of Presbyterian Publishing Corp
100 Witherspoon St, Louisville, KY 40202-1396
SAN: 202-9669
Tel: 502-569-5052 *Toll Free Tel:* 800-227-
 2872 (US only) *Fax:* 502-569-8308
 Toll Free Fax: 800-541-5113 (US only)
E-mail: wjk@wjkbooks.com
Web Site: www.wjkbooks.com
Key Personnel
Pres & Publr: Davis Perkins
Exec Ed: Stephanie Egnotovich
PR: Jennifer Cox
Trade & Academic Sales Dir: Chris Conver
 Tel: 502-569-5055 *E-mail:* cconver@presbypub.
 com
Dir, Sales & Mktg: Bill Falvey *E-mail:* bfalvey@
 presbypub.com
Gen Mgr: Marc Lewis
VP, Publg & Dir: Dr Jack A Keller, Jr
Events & Author Rel Mgr: Mary Bright
 E-mail: mbright@presbypub.com
Founded: 1838
With a publishing heritage that dates back more
 than 160 years, WJK Press publishes religious
 & theological books & resources for scholars,
 clergy, laity & general readers. The publisher
 employs the motto "Challenging the Mind,
 Nourishing the Soul".
ISBN Prefix(es): 0-664; 0-8042
Number of titles published annually: 80 Print
Total Titles: 1,100 Print; 2 CD-ROM; 2 Audio
Foreign Office(s): Marlborough House, 159 High
 St, Harrow Middlesex HA3 5DX, United King-
 dom, Contact: Jennifer Ellis *Tel:* (020) 8861
 5871 *Fax:* (020) 8861 5873 *E-mail:* wjkuk@
 globalnet.co.uk
Distributor for SCM
Foreign Rep(s): Academic Books for Seminaries
 (Taiwan); Africa Christian Textbooks (Nigeria);
 Baker & Taylor International Ltd (Worldwide);
 Claretian Communications Inc (Philippines);
 Cross Communications Ltd (Hong Kong);
 Import-Export & Wholesale Center (India);
 Korea Christian Book Service Inc (South Ko-
 rea); Marston Book Services (Europe & UK);
 Omega Distributors Ltd (New Zealand); Open-
 book Publishers (Australia); SKS Books Ware-
 house (Singapore); SPCK (European Union);
 Wood Lake Books (Canada)

Distribution Center: Presbyterian Publishing
 Corp, 341 Great Circle Rd, Nashville, TN
 37228 *Toll Free Tel:* 800-227-2872 *Toll Free
 Fax:* 800-541-5113 *Web Site:* www.ppcpub.com

Westview Press
Member of Perseus Books Group LLC
5500 Central Ave, Boulder, CO 80301
SAN: 219-970X
Tel: 303-444-3541 *Toll Free Tel:* 800-386-5656
 Fax: 720-406-7336
E-mail: westview.orders@perseusbooks.com
Web Site: www.perseusbooksgroup.com; www.
 westviewpress.com *Telex:* 23-9479 WVP UR
 Cable: WESTVIEW BDR
Key Personnel
Pres & CEO: Jack McKeown
Sr VP & CFO: Tom Kilkenny
VP & Group Dir, Fin & Opers: Robert Mancuso
VP & Group Dir, Mktg: Matthew Goldberg
VP & Group Dir, Rts: Carolyn Saravese
 E-mail: carolyn.saravese@perseusbooks.com
VP & Dir, Fin: Sharon Rupp-Rivers
VP & Dir, Prod: Tari Warwick
VP, Sales: John Whalen
Sr Ed: Steve Catalano; Jill Rothenberg; Sarah
 Warner *E-mail:* sarah.warner@perseusbooks.
 com; Karl Yambert *E-mail:* karly@
 perseusbooks.com
Dir, Mktg: Cathleen Tetro
Dir, Acad Mktg: Michelle Mallin
Founded: 1975
Quality nonfiction, general audience trade books
 & college textbooks in the following areas: his-
 tory, political science, international relations,
 military history, sociology, current affairs, crim-
 inology, women's studies, gender studies, jour-
 nalism, anthropology, archaeology, art & art
 history, philosphy, religion, physics, mathemat-
 ics, earth, planetary & space sciences.
ISBN Prefix(es): 0-8133
Number of titles published annually: 100 Print
Total Titles: 2,000 Print
Online services available through ebrary, Questia.
Sales Office(s): 387 Park Ave S, New York City,
 NY 10016
Foreign Office(s): Westview Press, Cumnor Hill,
 12 Hids Copse Rd, Oxford 0X2 9JJ, United
 Kingdom
Distributed by HarperCollins
Foreign Rep(s): Chris Ashdown (Middle East);
 Jonathon Ball Publishers (South Africa); James
 Benson (Northeast England); Thomas V Cas-
 sidy (People's Republic of China); Claire
 De Gruchy (Cyprus, Malta); Bernd Feldman
 (Austria, Germany, Switzerland); Colin Flint
 (Scandinavia); Charles Gibbs (Greece); Ben
 Greig (Scandinavia); HarperCollins Canada Ltd
 (Canada); HarperCollins International (Canada);
 Steven Haslemere (Scandinavia); Lazlo Hor-
 vath (Central & Eastern Europe); Natalie Jones
 (London); Kemper Conseil (Belgium, Nether-
 lands, Luxembourg); Ivan Kerr (Ireland, North-
 ern Ireland); Kinokuniya Co Ltd (Japan);
 Marston Book Services Distribution (UK,
 Ireland, Northern Ireland, Western Europe);
 Maruzen Co Ltd (Japan); Donald McDonald
 (Scotland); Palgrave Macmillan (Australia);
 Perseus Books Group (UK & Europe); David
 Pickering (Italy, Malta); Bruno Pojre (France,
 Italy); Ray Potts (Middle East); Sabrina Righi
 (France); Cristina De Lara Ruiz (Spain & Por-
 tugal); David Smith (England); Southern Pub-
 lishers Group Ltd (New Zealand); Taylor &
 Francis (Asia & the Pacific, Brunei, Cambo-
 dia, Hong Kong, Indonesia, Laos, Malaysia,
 Myanmar, Philippines, South Korea, Singapore,
 Taiwan, Thailand, Vietnam); United Publishers
 Services Ltd (Japan)
Foreign Rights: Perseus Books Group Subsidiary
 Rights
Advertising Agency: Bennett Books

Warehouse: HarperCollins Publishers, 1000 Keystone Industrial Park, Scranton, PA 18512 *Toll
 Free Tel:* 800-242-7737 *Toll Free Fax:* 800-
 822-4090
Distribution Center: HarperCollins Publishers,
 1000 Keystone Industrial Park, Scranton, PA
 18512 *Toll Free Tel:* 800-242-7737 *Toll Free
 Fax:* 800-822-4090
Membership(s): AAP

WH&O International
Division of Meristem Systems Corp
892 Worcester St, Suite 130, Wellesley, MA
 02482
Mailing Address: PO Box 812785, Wellesley, MA
 02482-0025
Tel: 781-239-0822 *Toll Free Tel:* 800-553-6678
 Fax: 781-239-0822
E-mail: whobooks@hotmail.com
Web Site: www.whobooks.com
Key Personnel
Pres: Dennis Hamilton
Founded: 1989
Technical books.
ISBN Prefix(es): 1-878960
Number of titles published annually: 6 Print
Total Titles: 12 Print
Foreign Rep(s): Generation Systems of UK

Wheatherstone Press
Subsidiary of Dickinson Consulting Group
10250 SW Greenburg Rd, No 125, Portland, OR
 97223
Tel: 503-244-8929 *Toll Free Tel:* 800-980-0077
 Fax: 503-244-9795
E-mail: relocntr@europa.com
Web Site: www.wheatherstonepress.com
Key Personnel
Pres & CEO: Jan Dickinson
Founded: 1983
Publishes handbooks & step-by-step guides cover-
 ing all phases of relocation, including interna-
 tionally.
ISBN Prefix(es): 0-9613011
Number of titles published annually: 37 Print
Total Titles: 37 Print

Whereabouts Press
1111 Eighth St, Suite D, Berkeley, CA 94710-
 1455
Tel: 510-527-8280 *Fax:* 510-527-8780
E-mail: mail@whereaboutspress.com
Web Site: www.whereaboutspress.com
Key Personnel
Publr: David Peattie
Founded: 1992
Publish literary travel companions.
ISBN Prefix(es): 1-883513
Number of titles published annually: 4 Print
Total Titles: 11 Print
Distributed by Consortuim Book Sales & Distri-
 bution (PUBNET)
Foreign Rep(s): Gazelle (Europe); Wakefield
 Press (Australia)

Whitaker House
30 Hunt Valley Circle, New Kensington, PA
 15068
Tel: 724-334-7000 *Toll Free Tel:* 877-793-9800
 Fax: 724-334-1200 *Toll Free Fax:* 800-765-
 1960
E-mail: sales@whitakerhouse.com
Key Personnel
VP: Robert Whitaker, Jr
Founded: 1970
ISBN Prefix(es): 0-88368
Number of titles published annually: 24 Print
Total Titles: 500 Print; 11 E-Book; 40 Audio
Foreign Rep(s): Donna Bonacoti
Foreign Rights: Saralinda Newbury
Membership(s): BEA; CBA; National Religious
 Broadcasters

White Cliffs Media Inc
PO Box 6083, Incline Village, NV 89450
SAN: 200-2965
Tel: 775-831-4899 *Toll Free Tel:* 800-345-6665
(orders only) *Fax:* 603-357-2073
E-mail: wcm@wcmedia.com
Web Site: www.wcmedia.com
Key Personnel
Ed & Pres: Lawrence Aynesmith
Founded: 1985
Performing arts & music.
ISBN Prefix(es): 0-941677
Number of titles published annually: 4 Print
Total Titles: 14 Print; 7 Audio
Foreign Rep(s): Japan Uni Agency (Japan)
Distribution Center: Mel Bay Publications Inc
(music trade), 4 Industrial Dr, Pacific, MO
63069-3611 (International distribution of
books to the music trade), Doug Wither-
spoon *Tel:* 636-257-3970 *Fax:* 636-257-5062
E-mail: email@melbay.com
Pathway Book Services, 4 Whitebrook Rd,
Gilsum, NH 03448 (Distribute to trade) *Toll
Free Tel:* 800-345-6665

White Cloud Press
PO Box 3400, Ashland, OR 97520
Tel: 541-488-6415 *Toll Free Tel:* 800-380-8286
Fax: 541-482-7708
Web Site: www.whitecloudpress.com
Key Personnel
Publr & Intl Rts: Steven Scholl *E-mail:* steven@
whitecloudpress.com
Founded: 1993
General trade, emphasis on religion & memoirs.
ISBN Prefix(es): 1-883991
Number of titles published annually: 8 Print
Total Titles: 60 Print
Distribution Center: SCB Distributors, 15608
S New Century Dr, Gardena, CA 90248
Tel: 310-532-9400 *Toll Free Tel:* 800-729-6432
Fax: 310-532-7001

White Mane Kids
Division of White Mane Publishing Co Inc
63 W Burd St, Shippensburg, PA 17257
Mailing Address: PO Box 708, Shippensburg, PA
17257-0708
Tel: 717-532-2237 *Toll Free Tel:* 888-WHT-
MANE (948-6263) *Fax:* 717-532-6110
E-mail: marketing@whitemane.com; editorial@
whitemane.com
Key Personnel
VP & Ed: Harold Collier
Founded: 1991
ISBN Prefix(es): 0-942597; 0-932751; 1-57249
Number of titles published annually: 15 Print
Total Titles: 25 Print

White Mane Publishing Co Inc
73 W Burd St, Shippensburg, PA 17257
SAN: 667-1934
Mailing Address: PO Box 708, Shippensburg, PA
17257-0708
Tel: 717-532-2237 *Toll Free Tel:* 888-948-6263
Fax: 717-532-6110
E-mail: marketing@whitemane.com; editorial@
whitemane.com
Key Personnel
VP & Ed: Harold E Collier
Founded: 1987
ISBN Prefix(es): 0-942597; 1-57249
Number of titles published annually: 48 Print
Total Titles: 270 Print
Imprints: White Mane Books
Divisions: Beidel Printing House; Burd Street
Press; Ragged Edge Press; White Mane Kids
Shipping Address: 63 W Burd St, Shippensburg,
PA 17257
Warehouse: 63 W Burd St, Shippensburg, PA
17257

See separate listing for:
Ragged Edge Press
White Mane Kids

White Pine Press
PO Box 236, Buffalo, NY 14201-0236
Tel: 716-627-4665 *Fax:* 716-627-4665
E-mail: wpine@whitepine.org
Web Site: www.whitepine.org
Key Personnel
Dir: Dennis Maloney *Tel:* 716-851-5013
E-mail: dennismaloney@yahoo.com
Man Dir: Elaine La Mattina
Founded: 1973
Specialize in poetry, essays, fiction, literature in
translation.
ISBN Prefix(es): 0-934834; 1-877727; 1-877800;
1-893996
Number of titles published annually: 10 Print
Total Titles: 120 Print
Subsidiaries: Springhouse Editions
Distributed by Consortium Book Sales
Distributor for Springhouse Editions

White Wolf Publishing Inc
1554 Litton Dr, Stone Mountain, GA 30083
Tel: 404-292-1819 *Toll Free Tel:* 800-454-9653
Fax: 678-382-3883
Web Site: www.white-wolf.com
Key Personnel
Pres: Michael Tinney
Fiction Ed: Philippe Boulle *E-mail:* prboulle@
white-wolf.com
Founded: 1986
Fiction & game books.
ISBN Prefix(es): 1-56504; 1-58846
Number of titles published annually: 60 Print
Total Titles: 280 Print
Imprints: Borealis; Exalted; Sword & Sorcery;
Two Wolf Press; World of Darkness

Whitehorse Press
107 E Conway Rd, Center Conway, NH 03813
Tel: 603-356-6556 *Toll Free Tel:* 800-531-1133
Fax: 603-356-6590
E-mail: customerservice@whitehorsepress.com
Web Site: www.whitehorsepress.com
Key Personnel
Pres: Daniel W Kennedy
Publr: Jack Savage
VP, Mktg & Fin: Judith M Kennedy
Founded: 1989
Books & directories; motorcycle touring, care &
maintenance, restoration.
ISBN Prefix(es): 0-9621834; 1-884313
Number of titles published annually: 8 Print
Total Titles: 40 Print
Imprints: Whirlaway Books
Distributed by Motorbooks International
Foreign Rep(s): Gazelle Books Ltd (UK); Wood-
slane (Australia)

Albert Whitman & Co
6340 Oakton St, Morton Grove, IL 60053-2723
SAN: 201-2049
Tel: 847-581-0033 *Toll Free Tel:* 800-255-7675
Fax: 847-581-0039
E-mail: mail@awhitmanco.com
Web Site: www.albertwhitman.com
Key Personnel
Pres, Prodn & Rts & Perms: Joseph Boyd
Ed-in-Chief: Kathleen Tucker
VP & Treas: Richard Gutrich
Adv & Promo Mgr: Denise Shanahan
Founded: 1919
Juveniles, language arts, fiction & nonfiction.
ISBN Prefix(es): 0-8075
Number of titles published annually: 35 Print
Total Titles: 400 Print
Imprints: Prairie Books

Whitston Publishing Co Inc
1717 Central Ave, Suite 201, Albany, NY 12205
SAN: 203-2120
Tel: 518-452-1900 *Toll Free Tel:* 877-571-1900
Fax: 518-452-1777
E-mail: whitston@capital.net
Web Site: www.whitston.com
Key Personnel
Pres & CEO: Michael O Laddin
E-mail: mladdin@whitston.com
Founded: 1969
Specialize in nonfiction & reference books. Also
scholarly books in the humanities with a par-
ticular emphasis on those pertaining to litera-
ture, scholarly, critical & creative anthologies
of modern letters; bibliographies, checklists &
indexes.
ISBN Prefix(es): 0-87875
Number of titles published annually: 15 Print; 2
Online
Total Titles: 400 Print; 2 Online
Online services available through EBSCOhost.
Membership(s): AAP; Publishers Marketing Asso-
ciation; Society for Scholarly Publishing

§Whittier Publications Inc
64 Alabama Ave, Island Park, NY 11558
Tel: 516-432-8120 *Toll Free Tel:* 800-897-TEXT
(897-8398) *Fax:* 516-889-0341
E-mail: info@whitbooks.com
Key Personnel
Pres: Judith Etra
Founded: 1990
Textbooks, trade, self-help, biology, history, math-
ematics, chemistry, sociology.
ISBN Prefix(es): 1-878045; 1-57604
Number of titles published annually: 200 Print
Imprints: Obelisk Books
Branch Office(s)
c/o Metro-pack Inc, 9 Jeanne Dr, Newburgh, NY
12550

§Whole Person Associates Inc
210 W Michigan St, Duluth, MN 55802-1908
Tel: 218-727-0500 *Toll Free Tel:* 800-247-6789
Fax: 218-727-0505
E-mail: books@wholeperson.com
Web Site: www.wholeperson.com
Key Personnel
Pres & Publr: Carlene Sippola
Edit Dir: Susan Gustafson
Founded: 1977
Stress management & wellness promotion.
ISBN Prefix(es): 0-938586; 1-57025
Number of titles published annually: 8 Print; 5
Audio
Total Titles: 60 Print; 29 CD-ROM; 38 Audio
Imprints: Whole Person Associates

§Wide World of Maps Inc
2626 W Indian School Rd, Phoenix, AZ 85017
Tel: 602-279-2323 *Toll Free Tel:* 800-279-7654
Fax: 602-279-2350
E-mail: sales@maps4u.com
Web Site: www.maps4u.com
Key Personnel
Pres: James L Willinger *Tel:* 602-433-0616
Fax: 602-433-0695 *E-mail:* james@maps4u.
com
Founded: 1976
Atlases, charts, guide books, maps.
ISBN Prefix(es): 0-938448; 1-887749
Number of titles published annually: 6 Print; 2
CD-ROM
Total Titles: 20 Print; 2 CD-ROM
Imprints: Yellow 1
Divisions: Desert Charts; Phoenix Mapping Ser-
vice
Distributed by Rand McNally
Distributor for Arizona Highways; Benchmark
Maps; DeLorme; Rand McNally

Wide World Publishing/Tetra
PO Box 476, San Carlos, CA 94070-0476
SAN: 211-1462
Tel: 650-593-2839 *Fax:* 650-595-0802
E-mail: wwpbl@aol.com
Web Site: wideworldpublishing.com
Key Personnel
Partner & Intl Rts: Elvira Monroe
Founded: 1976
Trade paperbacks, cookbooks, mathematics, calendars, travel books & guides, math books.
ISBN Prefix(es): 0-933174; 1-884550
Number of titles published annually: 6 Print
Total Titles: 22 Print
Imprints: Math Products Plus; Wide World Publishing
Distributed by The Islander Group Inc; Publishers Group West
Foreign Rep(s): Publishers Group West (Asia, Canada, Europe); Tarquin Publications (England)

Markus Wiener Publishers Inc
231 Nassau St, Princeton, NJ 08542
SAN: 282-5465
Tel: 609-921-1141; 609-921-7686 (orders)
    Fax: 609-921-1140; 609-279-0657 (orders)
E-mail: publisher@markuswiener.com; orders@
    markuswiener.com
Web Site: www.markuswiener.com
Key Personnel
Pres: Dr Markus Wiener
VP & Ed: Shelley Frisch
Ed: Susan Lorand
Mktg & Adv: Noah J Wiener
Prodn: Cheryl Mirkin
Strategic Planning: Aaron M Wiener
Bookkeeping/Ordering: Barbara Hagadorn
Founded: 1981
New titles in business administration, history & literature; Jewish & Third World studies, museum studies, Middle Eastern, Latin American & Caribbean studies, world history.
ISBN Prefix(es): 0-910129; 0-945179; 1-55876
Number of titles published annually: 25 Print
Total Titles: 199 Print
Imprints: Critical Accounting; Masterworks of Modern Jewish Writing; Rutgers Series in Accounting Research; Topics in World History
Foreign Rep(s): Eurospan (Europe); Levant (Beirut); Ian Randle (Caribbean, Jamaica)
Foreign Rights: Levant (Beirut); Ian Randle (Jamaica); Verlagsburo Welterstein (Germany)
Warehouse: 60 Clyde Rd, Somerset, NJ 08873

Michael Wiese Productions
11288 Ventura Blvd, Suite 621, Studio City, CA 91604
Tel: 818-379-8799 *Toll Free Tel:* 800-379-8808
    Fax: 818-986-3408
Web Site: www.mwp.com
Key Personnel
VP: Ken Lee *Tel:* 206-283-2948 *E-mail:* kenlee@
    mwp.com
Founded: 1981
ISBN Prefix(es): 0-941188
Number of titles published annually: 12 Print
Total Titles: 50 Print
Distributed by National Book Network

Wildcat Canyon Press
Division of Council Oak Books
2105 E 15 St, Suite B, Tulsa, OK 74104
Toll Free Tel: 800-247-8850
E-mail: order@counciloakbooks.com
Key Personnel
Assoc Publr: Ja'Lene Clark
Founded: 1993
Publisher of quality books on self-care, food, fashion, lifestyle, parenting & relationships.
ISBN Prefix(es): 1-885171
Number of titles published annually: 6 Print

Total Titles: 40 Print
Foreign Rep(s): Airlift Book Co (UK, Europe); Candace Groskreutz (World); Peaceful Living Publications (New Zealand); Raincoast Book Distribution Ltd (Canada); Specialist Book Distribution (Australia)
Foreign Rights: Paulette Millichap
Distribution Center: Council Oak Books Fulfillment Ctr, 1616 W Airport Rd, Stillwater, OK 74075

Wilde Publishing
Division of Wilde Oil
211 Cornell SE, Albuquerque, NM 87106
Mailing Address: PO Box 4581, Albuquerque, NM 87196
Tel: 505-255-6096 *Fax:* 419-715-1430
E-mail: wilde@unm.edu
Web Site: www.davidwilde.cx
Key Personnel
Pres: David Wilde
Founded: 1989
ISBN Prefix(es): 0-9625472; 1-882204
Number of titles published annually: 9 Print; 2 Online; 2 E-Book; 1 Audio
Total Titles: 52 Print; 52 Online; 9 E-Book; 1 Audio
Imprints: Snails Pace Press
Foreign Rep(s): Jackie Negus (UK)
Shipping Address: 19 Westfield Dr, Lboro, Leicestershire LE11, United Kingdom

Wilderness Adventures Press Inc
45 Buckskin Rd, Belgrade, MT 59714
Tel: 406-388-0112 *Toll Free Tel:* 800-925-3339
    Fax: 406-388-0120 *Toll Free Fax:* 800-390-7558
E-mail: books@wildadv.com
Web Site: www.wildadv.com
Key Personnel
Pres, Prodn Ed & Sales Mgr: Chuck Johnson
    E-mail: chuckj@wildadv.com
Secy & Treas: Blanche Johnson
Founded: 1994
Outdoor guidebooks, sporting books & cookbooks.
ISBN Prefix(es): 1-885106; 1-932098
Number of titles published annually: 8 Print
Total Titles: 60 Print
Distributed by Angler's Book Supply; Books West; Inter Sports; Partners Book Distributor; Partners West

§Wilderness Press
1200 Fifth St, Berkeley, CA 94710
SAN: 203-2139
Tel: 510-558-1666 *Toll Free Tel:* 800-443-7227
    Fax: 510-558-1696
E-mail: info@wildernesspress.com
Web Site: www.wildernesspress.com
Key Personnel
Publr: Caroline Winnett
Dir, Mktg & Opers: Laura Keresty
    E-mail: marketing@wildernesspress.com
Man Ed: Roz Bullas
Founded: 1967
Outdoor books & maps.
ISBN Prefix(es): 0-89997
Number of titles published annually: 20 Print
Total Titles: 150 Print; 1 CD-ROM

Wildlife Education Ltd
12233 Thatcher Ct, Poway, CA 92064-6880
Tel: 858-513-7600 *Toll Free Tel:* 800-992-5034
    (subns); 800-992-5034 (sales) *Fax:* 858-513-7660
E-mail: animals@zoobooks.com
Web Site: www.zoobooks.com
Key Personnel
Sales Mgr: Kurt Von Herthsenberg
Founded: 1980
Books on wildlife & animals.

ISBN Prefix(es): 0-937934; 1-888153
Number of titles published annually: 12 Print
Total Titles: 120 Print

Wildside Press
PO Box 301, Holicong, PA 18928-0301
Tel: 215-345-5645 *Fax:* 215-345-1814
E-mail: wildsidepress@yahoo.com
Web Site: www.wildsidepress.com
Key Personnel
Owner: John Betancourt
Founded: 1989
Reprints of classic science fiction, fantasy, mystery, reference & mainstream.
ISBN Prefix(es): 1-880448; 1-58715; 1-59224
Number of titles published annually: 700 Print; 100 E-Book
Total Titles: 3,000 Print; 300 E-Book
Imprints: Cosmos Books

§John Wiley & Sons Inc
111 River St, Hoboken, NJ 07030
SAN: 202-5183
Tel: 201-748-6000 *Toll Free Tel:* 800-225-5945
    (cust serv) *Fax:* 201-748-6088
E-mail: info@wiley.com
Web Site: www.wiley.com
Key Personnel
Chmn of the Bd: Peter Booth Wiley, II
Pres & CEO: William J Pesce
Exec VP, Prof/Trade Publg: Stephen A Kippur
Exec VP, CFO & COO: Ellis Cousens
Sr VP & Gen Mgr, Higher Educ: Bonnie Lieberman
Sr VP, Scientific, Tech, Med Publg: Eric A Swanson
Sr VP, Gen Counsel: Gary Rinck
Sr VP, Corp Communs: Deborah E Wiley
Sr VP, HR: William J Arlington
Sr VP, Planning & Devt: Timothy B King
VP, Corp Controller & CAO: Ed Melando
VP & Treas: Walter J Conklin
Corp Sec: Josephine A Bacchi
Dir, Contracts, Copyright & Perms: Peggy Garry
Founded: 1807
Global publisher of print & electronic products specializing in professional & consumer books & subscription services; scientific, technical, medical books & journals; textbooks & educational materials for undergraduate & graduate students as well as lifelong learners. Wiley has publishing, marketing & distribution centers in the United States, Canada, Europe, Asia & Australia.
ISBN Prefix(es): 0-470; 0-471; 0-442; 0-8436; 0-87055
Number of titles published annually: 1,500 Print
Total Titles: 15,000 Print
Imprints: Audel™; Betty Crocker®; Capstone; CliffsNotes™; Ernst & Sohn; For Dummies®; Frommer's™; Halsted Press; Howell Book House; John Wiley & Sons; Jossey-Bass; Pfeiffer; Scripta-Technica; Valusource; Visual™; Webster's New World™; Wiley; Wiley-Heyden; Wiley Interscience®; Wiley-Liss; Wiley-VCH; Wrox™
Shipping Address: John Wiley & Sons Inc, One Wiley Dr, Somerset, NJ 08875-1272 *Tel:* 732-469-4400 *Fax:* 732-302-2300
Membership(s): AAP
See separate listing for:
John Wiley & Sons Inc Education Publishing Group
John Wiley & Sons Inc Professional & Trade Group
John Wiley & Sons Inc Scientific/Technical/Medical Publishing

John Wiley & Sons Inc Education Publishing Group
Division of John Wiley & Sons Inc
111 River St, Hoboken, NJ 07030

Tel: 201-748-6000 *Fax:* 201-748-6088
E-mail: info@wiley.com
Web Site: www.wiley.com
Key Personnel
Sr VP, Higher Educ: Bonnie Lieberman
Publr, Engg, Math & Computer Sci: Bruce Spatz
VP & Exec Publr, Sciences: Kaye Pace
VP & Natl Sales Mgr: Patty Stark
VP, Prodn & Mfg, High School: Ann Berlin
VP, Prod & E-Busn Devt: Joe Heider
VP & Busn Publr: Susan Elbe
VP, Sales & Mktg: M J O'Leary
VP, Mktg: Frank Lyman
Dir, New Initiatives: Jon Stowe
Mktg & Sales Coord: Kathi Zhang
Total Titles: 615 Print

**John Wiley & Sons Inc Professional & Trade
   Group**
Division of John Wiley & Sons Inc
111 River St, Hoboken, NJ 07030
Tel: 201-748-6000 *Toll Free Tel:* 800-225-5945
   (cust serv) *Fax:* 201-748-6088
E-mail: info@wiley.com
Web Site: www.wiley.com
Key Personnel
VP, Trade Sales: Dean Karrel
VP, Prodn & Mfg, Prof & Trade Publg: Elizabeth
   Doble
VP & Dir P/T Sales: George Stanley
VP, Mktg: Marjorie Schustack
Exec VP P/T: Stephen A Kippur
VP & Dir, Mktg: Larry Olsen

**John Wiley & Sons Inc
   Scientific/Technical/Medical Publishing**
Division of John Wiley & Sons Inc
111 River St, Hoboken, NJ 07030
Tel: 201-748-6000 *Toll Free Tel:* 800-225-5945
   (cust serv) *Fax:* 201-748-8728
E-mail: info@wiley.com
Web Site: www.wiley.com
Key Personnel
Sr VP & Gen Mgr: Eric Swanson
VP, Opers: Craig Van Dyke
VP, Global Mktg: Reed Elfenbein
Dir, Fin: Andrew Phillips

§William Andrew Publishing
13 Eaton Ave, Norwich, NY 13815
SAN: 209-2840
Tel: 607-337-5000 *Toll Free Tel:* 800-932-7045
   Fax: 607-337-5090
E-mail: publishing@williamandrew.com
Web Site: www.williamandrew.com
Key Personnel
CEO: William Woishnis *E-mail:* billw@
   williamandrew.com
Dir, Mktg & Webmaster: Brent Beckley
   E-mail: bbeckley@williamandrew.com
Publr: Martin Scrivener *E-mail:* mscrivener@
   williamandrew.com
Sr Acqs Ed: Millicent Treloar *E-mail:* mtreloar@
   williamandrew.com
Mgr, Retail & Corp Sales: Polly Wirtz *Tel:* 303-
   322-9797 *E-mail:* pwirtz@williamandrew.com
Prod Mgr: Betty Leahy *E-mail:* bleahy@
   williamandrew.com
Cust Serv: Hope Crawford *E-mail:* hcrawford@
   williamandrew.com
Founded: 1959
Books on petroleum, environment, materials, tox-
   icology, energy, engineering, biology & elec-
   tronics.
ISBN Prefix(es): 0-8155; 1-891121; 1-884207
Number of titles published annually: 12 Print; 1
   CD-ROM; 5 Online; 5 E-Book
Total Titles: 385 Print; 3 CD-ROM; 3 Online; 3
   E-Book
Imprints: Noyes Publications; Plastics Design Li-
   brary; Sci-Tech Publishing

Branch Office(s)
Sales Resellers Corporate Government, 2370
   Cherry St, Denver, CO *Tel:* 303-322-9797
   Fax: 303-377-0770
Foreign Rep(s): American Technical Publishers
   (Europe); Cranbury International (South Amer-
   ica); D A Book Depot Pty Ltd (Australia); In-
   dia Book Distributors (India); Kay Kato Asso-
   ciates (Japan); Tony Poh (Asia)

§William K Bradford Publishing Co Inc
35 Forest Ridge Rd, Concord, MA 01742
SAN: 250-4456
Tel: 978-402-5300 *Toll Free Tel:* 800-421-2009
   Fax: 978-318-9500
E-mail: wkb@wkbradford.com
Web Site: www.wkbradford.com
Key Personnel
Pres & VP, Sales: Thomas M Haver
VP: Hal Wexler
VP, Design & Prodn: Jessica Holland
Founded: 1988
Educational software & copymasters supplemen-
   tary material, K-12 mathematics, testing &
   guide books (classmaster).
ISBN Prefix(es): 1-55930; 0-7898
Number of titles published annually: 12 Print; 15
   CD-ROM
Total Titles: 60 Print; 100 CD-ROM
Membership(s): AAP

§Williams & Co Publishers
Formerly Venture Press
1317 Pine Ridge Dr, Savannah, GA 31406
Tel: 912-352-0404
E-mail: bookpub@comcast.net
Web Site: www.pubmart.com
Key Personnel
Publr & Ed-in-Chief: Thomas A Williams
   E-mail: tom@pubmart.com
Founded: 1989
How-to books, literary fiction.
ISBN Prefix(es): 1-878853
Number of titles published annually: 10 Print; 10
   Online; 10 E-Book
Total Titles: 15 Print; 10 Online; 25 E-Book
Imprints: Venture Press; Williams & Co

Williamson Books
Imprint of Ideals Publications a Division of
   Guideposts Inc
535 Metroplex Dr, Suite 250, Nashville, TN
   37211
Tel: 802-425-2713 (edit) *Toll Free Tel:* 800-586-
   2572 (sales & orders) *Fax:* 802-425-2714 (edit)
Web Site: www.williamsonbooks.com
Key Personnel
Publr: Pat Pingry *Tel:* 615-781-1420
Dir: Martin Flanagan *Tel:* 615-781-1441
Edit Dir: Susan Williamson *E-mail:* susan@
   kidsbks.net
Spec Sales: Jack Williamson *E-mail:* jack@
   kidsbks.net
Founded: 1983
Kids active learning, science, history, crafts, arts
   & education, quality trade books for children
   ages 4 to 14.
ISBN Prefix(es): 0-8249; 0-913589; 1-885593
Number of titles published annually: 8 Print
Total Titles: 140 Print
Editorial Office(s): PO Box 185, Charlotte, VT
   05445
Warehouse: Ideals Returns Center, c/o Whitehurst
   & Clark, 1200 County Rd, Rte 523, Fleming-
   ton, NJ 08822

Willow Creek Press
9931 Hwy 70 W, Minocqua, WI 54548
Mailing Address: PO Box 147, Minocqua, WI
   54548
Tel: 715-358-7010 *Toll Free Tel:* 800-850-9453
   Fax: 715-358-2807

E-mail: info@willowcreekpress.com
Web Site: www.willowcreekpress.com
Key Personnel
Publr: Tom Petrie
Exec Sales Dir: Jeremy Petrie
Man Ed: Andrea Donner *E-mail:* andread@
   willowcreekpress.com
Founded: 1986
Willow Creek Press specializes in publishing high
   quality books most specifically related to na-
   ture, animals, wildlife, hunting, fishing & gar-
   dening. The company also offers a unique line
   of cookbooks & has established a niche in the
   pet book market. The company also publishes
   high quality nature, wild life, fishing, pet &
   sporting calendars.
ISBN Prefix(es): 1-57223
Number of titles published annually: 24 Print
Total Titles: 130 Print; 3 Audio
Membership(s): AAM; AAP

§Wilshire Book Co
12015 Sherman Rd, North Hollywood, CA 91605
SAN: 205-5368
Tel: 818-765-8579 *Fax:* 818-765-2922
Web Site: www.mpowers.com
Key Personnel
Pres & Rts & Perms: Melvin Powers
   E-mail: mpowers@mpowers.com
Founded: 1947
Mail order; advertising, psychological self-help
   books, calligraphy, sports & gambling; orig-
   inals & reprints, fables for adults; computer
   business book on Internet, horse books, joke
   books.
ISBN Prefix(es): 0-87980
Number of titles published annually: 25 Print
Total Titles: 400 Print
Foreign Rep(s): Baker & Taylor International
   (Worldwide exc Canada)

H W Wilson
950 University Ave, Bronx, NY 10452-4224
SAN: 203-2961
Tel: 718-588-8400 *Toll Free Tel:* 800-367-6770
   Fax: 718-590-1617 *Toll Free Fax:* 800-590-
   1617
E-mail: custserv@hwwilson.com
Web Site: www.hwwilson.com
Key Personnel
Pres & CEO: Harold Regan
VP, Edit Servs: Michael Schultze
Founded: 1898
An icon in the library community for more than
   100 years, H W Wilson is dedicated to providing the highest-quality references in the
   world. Via the WilsonWeb Internet Service,
   on WilsonDisc CD-ROM, & in print, more
   than 50 H W Wilson reference databases meet
   the research needs of customers around the
   globe. Wilson periodicals databases bring
   users full-text, page images, abstracts & indexing of thousands of leading magazines &
   journals. Acclaimed Wilson specialty library
   catalogs support collection development in
   children's, school & public libraries & Wilson print references consistently earn reviewers' praise. For more on H W Wilson visit
   www.hwwilson.com. Types of publications:
   reference databases (biography databases, periodicals databases: full text articles, abstracts,
   indexing) & reference books.
ISBN Prefix(es): 0-8242
Number of titles published annually: 13 Print
Total Titles: 200 Print; 50 CD-ROM; 80 Online

Wimbledon Music Inc & Trigram Music Inc
1801 Century Park E, Suite 2400, Los Angeles,
   CA 90067-2326
Tel: 310-556-9683 *Fax:* 310-277-1278
E-mail: webmaster@wimbtri.com
Web Site: www.wimbtri.com

Key Personnel
Dir, Pubns: Peter Dorfman
Founded: 1977
ISBN Prefix(es): 0-938170
Number of titles published annually: 35 Print

Wimmer Cookbooks
Subsidiary of Mercury Printing
4650 Shelby Air Dr, Memphis, TN 38118
Tel: 901-362-8900 *Toll Free Tel:* 800-548-2537
Toll Free Fax: 800-794-9806
E-mail: wimmer@wimmerco.com
Web Site: www.wimmerco.com
Key Personnel
VP: Ashley Schilhab *E-mail:* ashleys@wimmerco.
com
Founded: 1946
Development, publishing, manufacturing, marketing & distribution of community & self-published cookbooks.
ISBN Prefix(es): 1-879958
Number of titles published annually: 50 Print
Total Titles: 250 Print
Imprints: Tradery House

§Wind Canyon Books Inc
PO Box 511, Brawley, CA 92227
Tel: 760-344-5545 *Toll Free Tel:* 800-952-7007
Fax: 760-344-8841
E-mail: books@windcanyon.com
Web Site: www.windcanyon.com; www.aviation-heritage.com
Key Personnel
Pres: George Jaquith
Founded: 1996
Number of titles published annually: 5 Print
Total Titles: 70 Print

Windham Bay Press
PO Box 1198, Occidental, CA 95465
SAN: 214-4905
Tel: 707-823-7150 *Fax:* 707-823-7150
Key Personnel
Publr: Ellen Searby *E-mail:* ellnsearby@aol.com
Founded: 1979
Select authors for very limited number of titles; do not send mss.
ISBN Prefix(es): 0-942297
Number of titles published annually: 4 Print
Total Titles: 4 Print
Foreign Rep(s): International Travel Maps (World)
Shipping Address: 11850 Occidental Rd, Sebastopol, CA 95472

Windsor Books
Division of Windsor Marketing Corp
141 John St, Babylon, NY 11702
SAN: 203-2945
Mailing Address: PO Box 280, Brightwaters, NY 11718
Tel: 631-321-7830 *Toll Free Tel:* 800-321-5934
Fax: 631-321-1435
E-mail: windsor.books@att.net
Web Site: www.windsorpublishing.com
Key Personnel
Pres: Alfred Schmidt
Man Ed: Jeff Schmidt
Founded: 1968
Business, economics & investment.
ISBN Prefix(es): 0-930233
Number of titles published annually: 5 Print
Advertising Agency: A Schmidt Agency

§Windstorm Creative
PO Box 28, Port Orchard, WA 98366
Tel: 360-769-7174
E-mail: queries@windstormcreative.com
Web Site: www.windstormcreative.com
Key Personnel
COO & Sr Ed: Cris Di Marco

Founded: 1989
Historical fiction, science fiction, fantasy, erotica, children's books, games, mysteries & fiction. Writers must visit the website for guidelines.
ISBN Prefix(es): 1-886383; 1-883573; 1-59092
Number of titles published annually: 80 Print
Total Titles: 300 Print; 1 CD-ROM; 2 Audio
Imprints: Blue Works; Digital Leaf & E-Press; Dog Wing Media; Faith's Compass; House With Bee Art Books; Immortal Day Publishing; Lightening Rod Publishing; Little Blue Works; Mama's Cafe Press; Orchard Academy Press; Paper Frog Productions; Picture Imperfect; RAMPANT Gaming

Windswept House Publishers
584 Sound Dr, Mount Desert, ME 04660
SAN: 687-4363
Mailing Address: PO Box 159, Mount Desert, ME 04660-0159
Tel: 207-244-5027 *Fax:* 207-244-3369
E-mail: windswt@acadia.net
Web Site: www.booknotes.com/windswept/
Key Personnel
Publr: Caspar Weinberger, Jr
Ed-in-Chief: Mavis Weinberger
Founded: 1984
Juvenile & young adult & adult.
ISBN Prefix(es): 0-932433; 1-883650
Number of titles published annually: 4 Print
Total Titles: 100 Print
Imprints: Windswept, Too

§The Wine Appreciation Guild Ltd
360 Swift Ave, Unit 30-40, South San Francisco, CA 94080
Tel: 650-866-3020 *Toll Free Tel:* 800-231-9463
Fax: 650-866-3513
E-mail: shannon@wineappreciation.com; info@wineappreciation.com
Web Site: www.wineappreciation.com
Key Personnel
Pres: Donna Bottrell
Ed: Maurice Sullivan
Intl Rts: Elliott Mackey
Lib Sales Dir: Bryan Imelli
Founded: 1974
Publisher of books on the subject of wine.
ISBN Prefix(es): 0-932664; 1-891267
Number of titles published annually: 7 Print; 1 CD-ROM; 1 Audio
Total Titles: 65 Print; 3 CD-ROM; 5 Audio
Imprints: Forrest Hill Press; Vintage Image; Wine Advisory Board
Foreign Rep(s): Books for Europe (Continental Europe, Middle East); Eos Libros (Latin America); Horizon Books (Singapore & Malaysia); Peribo Books (Australia); Stephen Phillips Pty Ltd (South Africa); Vanwell Publishing (Canada); Vine House Distribution (UK)
Advertising Agency: Vintage Image, 360 Swift Ave, Suite 34, South San Francisco, CA 94080
Fax: 415-731-3928

Winner Enterprises
670 Nighthawk Circle, Winter Springs, FL 32708
Tel: 407-696-2103 *Fax:* 407-696-2103
Web Site: www.winnerenterprises.com
Key Personnel
Publr: Erv Lampert *E-mail:* erv@winnerenterprises.com
Founded: 1982
Wildlife, nature, outdoor activities, history & cookbooks; gardening, horticulture & educational coloring books; Florida.
ISBN Prefix(es): 0-932855
Total Titles: 73 Print
Imprints: Famous Florida Cookbooks; Pocket Library of Florida Gardening; Winner's Wildlife & Nature Series
Distributed by Florida Flair Books; Great Outdoors Publishing; Palm Island Press; Southern Book Service

Winters Publishing
705 E Washington St, Greensburg, IN 47240
SAN: 298-1645
Mailing Address: PO Box 501, Greensburg, IN 47240
Tel: 812-663-4948 *Toll Free Tel:* 800-457-3230
Fax: 812-663-4948 *Toll Free Fax:* 800-457-3230
Key Personnel
Publr: Tracy Winters *E-mail:* tmwinters@juno.com
Founded: 1988
Publish Christian books, bed & breakfast cookbooks, directories, other nonfiction & children's books.
ISBN Prefix(es): 0-9625329; 1-883651
Number of titles published annually: 6 Print
Total Titles: 40 Print
Distributor for Tattersall Press

Winterthur Museum, Garden & Library
Publications Division, Winterthur, DE 19735
Tel: 302-888-4613 *Toll Free Tel:* 800-448-3883
Fax: 302-888-4950
Web Site: www.winterthur.org
Key Personnel
Dir: Susan Randolph *E-mail:* srandolph@winterthur.org
ISBN Prefix(es): 0-912724
Number of titles published annually: 4 Print
Total Titles: 40 Print
Distributed by University Press of New England

§Wisconsin Dept of Public Instruction
125 S Webster St, Madison, WI 53702
Mailing Address: PO Box 7841, Madison, WI 53707-7841
Tel: 608-266-2188 *Toll Free Tel:* 800-243-8782
Fax: 608-267-9110
E-mail: pubsales@dpi.state.wi.us
Web Site: www.dpi.state.wi.us
Key Personnel
Pubns & Mktg Dir: Sandi McNamer *E-mail:* sandi.mcnamer@dpi.state.wi.us
Specialize in English, math, science & social studies, character education, driver education & traffic safety, career & technical education, world languages & teaching strategies.
ISBN Prefix(es): 1-57337
Number of titles published annually: 8 Print; 4 CD-ROM
Total Titles: 120 Print; 10 CD-ROM
Sales Office(s): Drawer 179, Milwaukee, WI 53293-0179, S

Wisdom Publications Inc
199 Elm St, Somerville, MA 02144
Tel: 617-776-7416 *Fax:* 617-776-7841
E-mail: info@wisdompubs.org
Web Site: www.wisdompubs.org
Key Personnel
Publr: Timothy McNeill *Tel:* 617-776-7416 ext 22
Promo: Rod Meade Sperry *Tel:* 617-776-7416 ext 29 *E-mail:* promotions@wisdompubs.org
Acqs Ed: Joshi Radin *Tel:* 617-776-7416 ext 25 *E-mail:* editorial@wisdompubs.org
Founded: 1976
Books on Buddhism published in various series encompassing theory & practice, biography, history, art & culture.
ISBN Prefix(es): 0-86171
Number of titles published annually: 20 Print
Total Titles: 158 Print
Imprints: Pali Text Society
Divisions: Wisdom Archive
Foreign Rep(s): Mandala Books (Australia); Wisdom Books (Europe)
Foreign Rights: ACER (Spain); Eliane Benisti (France); Chinese Connection Agency (China);

Fritz Literary Agency (Germany); Eric Yang Agency (Korea)
Orders to: National Book Network (NBN), 4720 Boston Way, Lanham, MD 20706 *Toll Free Tel:* 800-462-6420 *Toll Free Fax:* 800-338-4550

Wish Publishing
PO Box 10337, Terre Haute, IN 47801-0337
Tel: 812-299-5700 *Fax:* 928-447-1836
Web Site: www.wishpublishing.com
Key Personnel
Publr: Holly Kondras *E-mail:* holly@wishpublishing.com
Founded: 1999
Trade publishing focused exclusively on women's sports, health & fitness.
ISBN Prefix(es): 1-930546
Number of titles published annually: 8 Print
Total Titles: 28 Print
Imprints: Equilibrium Books
Distributed by Cardinal Publishers Group
Membership(s): Publishers Marketing Association

Wittenborn Art Books
1109 Geary Blvd, San Francisco, CA 94109
Tel: 415-292-6500 *Toll Free Tel:* 800-660-6403
Fax: 415-292-6594
E-mail: wittenborn@art-books.com
Web Site: art-books.com
Key Personnel
Ed: Alan Hyman
Opers Mgr: J Thrombly
Acqs: Lancelot Andrewes
Rts: Mark Hyman
Prodn: Duke Mantee
Founded: 1939
Publish deluxe edition art reference books & artist books. Subject specialties include art, bibliography & decorative arts.
ISBN Prefix(es): 0-8150
Number of titles published annually: 9 Print
Total Titles: 175 Print
Imprints: George Wittenborn
Billing Address: PO Box 2210, San Francisco, CA 94126

Wizards of the Coast Inc
Subsidiary of Hasbro Inc
PO Box 707, Renton, WA 98057-0707
Web Site: www.wizards.com/books
Key Personnel
CEO: Loren Greenwood
Dir: Peter Archer *Tel:* 425-254-2287 *Fax:* 425-204-5889 *E-mail:* peter.archer@wizards.com
VP, Publg: Mary Kirchoff
Founded: 1975
Publisher of fantasy, science fiction & horror novels. Young adult game material; role-playing games, trading card games, board games & books, makers of Dungeons & Dragons.
ISBN Prefix(es): 0-88038; 1-56076; 0-7869
Number of titles published annually: 60 Print
Total Titles: 300 Print
Distributed by Holtzbrink Publishing

WJ Fantasy Inc
955 Connecticut Ave, Bridgeport, CT 06607
Tel: 203-333-5212 *Toll Free Tel:* 800-222-7529 (orders) *Fax:* 203-366-3826 *Toll Free Fax:* 800-200-3000
E-mail: wjfantasy.inc@snet.net
Web Site: www.wjfantasy.com
Key Personnel
Pres: John H McGrath *E-mail:* mcgrath@wjfantasy.com
Founded: 1988
Specializes in children's books, toys & advent calendars.
ISBN Prefix(es): 1-56021
Number of titles published annually: 10 Print
Total Titles: 60 Print
Membership(s): ABA; Museum Store Association

Alan Wofsy Fine Arts
1109 Geary Blvd, San Francisco, CA 94109
SAN: 207-6438
Mailing Address: PO Box 2210, San Francisco, CA 94126-2210
Tel: 415-292-6500 *Fax:* 415-512-0130 (acctg); 415-292-6594 (off & cust serv)
E-mail: beauxarts@earthlink.net (cust serv); editeur@earthlink.net (edit); order@art-books.com (orders)
Web Site: art-books.com
Key Personnel
PR Mgr: Milton J Goldbaum
CEO: Alan Wofsy
Chmn of the Bd: Lord Cohen
Rts: Elizabeth Regina Snowden
Libn: Adios Butler
Art Dir: Zeke Greenberg
Mktg: Craig Pederson; Andy Redkin
Ed, German Books: Steve Connell
Ed, French Books: Robin Bodkin
Counsel: Judith Mazia
Founded: 1969
Art reference books, bibliographies, art books, prints, posters & notecards.
ISBN Prefix(es): 0-915346; 1-55660
Number of titles published annually: 20 Print
Total Titles: 310 Print
Imprints: Beauxarts; Collegium Graphicum; The Picasso Project
Branch Office(s)
401 China Basin St, San Francisco, CA 94107 (sales & cust serv)
Distributor for Bora; Brusberg (Berlin); Cramer (Geneva); Huber; Ides et Calendes; Kornfeld & Co; Welz; Wittenborn Art Books
See separate listing for:
Picasso Project

Wolf Den Books
5783 SW 40 St, Suite 221, Miami, FL 33155
Toll Free Tel: 877-667-9737 *Fax:* 305-667-7751
E-mail: info@wolfdenbooks.com
Web Site: www.wolfdenbooks.com
Key Personnel
Owner: Gail Shivel *E-mail:* shivel@wolfdenbooks.com
Founded: 2000
ISBN Prefix(es): 0-9708035
Number of titles published annually: 3 Print; 1 Online
Total Titles: 2 Print
Distributed by IPG/Paul & Co
Membership(s): Publishers Marketing Association

Wolters Kluwer US Corp
Subsidiary of Wolters Kluwer NV (The Netherlands)
2700 Lake Cook Rd, Riverwoods, IL 60015
Tel: 847-267-7000 *Fax:* 847-580-5192
Web Site: www.wolterskluwer.com
Key Personnel
Pres: Christopher Cartwright
Exec VP & CFO: Bruce Lenz *Tel:* 847-580-5020 *E-mail:* bruce_lenz@cch.com
Medical books & journals, law books, business & tax publications.
Total Titles: 5,000 Print
Imprints: Adis International; CCH INCORPORATED; CT Corporation; Aspen Publishers Inc; Lippincott Williams & Wilkins
Foreign Office(s): Apollollan 153, PO Box 75248, 1070 AE Amsterdam, Netherlands (headquarters) *Tel:* (020) 6070 400

Woodbine House
6510 Bells Mill Rd, Bethesda, MD 20817
SAN: 269-3445
Tel: 301-897-3570 *Toll Free Tel:* 800-843-7323
Fax: 301-897-5838
E-mail: info@woodbinehouse.com

Web Site: www.woodbinehouse.com *Telex:* 19-7617 *Cable:* SVECUT
Key Personnel
Publr & Perms: Irvin N Shapell
Prodn Mgr: Brenda A Ruby *E-mail:* bruby@woodbinehouse.com
Acqs Ed/Asst Ed: Nancy Gray Paul *E-mail:* ngpaul@woodbinehouse.com
Mktg Mgr: Fran M Marinaccio *E-mail:* fmarinaccio@woodbinehouse.com
Intl Rts & Lib Sales Dir: Sarah A Strickler *E-mail:* sstrickler@woodbinehouse.com
Ed: Susan S Stokes *E-mail:* sstokes@woodbinehouse.com
Founded: 1985
Trade nonfiction, hardcover & paperback.
ISBN Prefix(es): 0-933149; 1-890627
Number of titles published annually: 10 Print
Total Titles: 65 Print; 1 CD-ROM
Foreign Rep(s): Gazelle Book Service (Europe); Monarch Books (Canada); Silvereye Education Publications (Australia, Pacific Rim)
Foreign Rights: Writer's House
Returns: IFC, 3570 Bladensburg Rd, Brentwood, MD 20722 *Tel:* 301-779-4660
Warehouse: Woodbine House, c/o IFC, 3570 Bladensburg Rd, Brentwood, MD 20722

Woodland Publishing Inc
448 E 800 N, Orem, UT 84097
SAN: 219-3531
Tel: 801-434-8113 *Toll Free Tel:* 800-777-2665
Fax: 801-334-1913
Web Site: www.woodlandpublishing.com
Key Personnel
Pres: Calvin W Harper
Founded: 1974
General trade hardcovers & paperbacks, professional books; health & nutrition.
ISBN Prefix(es): 0-89557; 1-58054
Number of titles published annually: 15 Print
Total Titles: 200 Print
Distributed by Koen Book Distributors Inc; New Leaf; Nutri-Books; Summit Beacon
Warehouse: 500 N 1030 W, Lindon, UT 84042 *Toll Free Tel:* 800-777-2665 *Fax:* 801-785-8511

Ralph Woodrow Evangelistic Association Inc
PO Box 21, Palm Springs, CA 92263-0021
Tel: 760-323-9882 *Toll Free Tel:* 877-664-1549
Fax: 760-323-3982
E-mail: ralphwoodrow@earthlink.net
Web Site: www.ralphwoodrow.com
Key Personnel
Pres: Ralph Woodrow
Founded: 1961
Bible-related topics, many otherwise neglected or little-known.
ISBN Prefix(es): 0-916938
Number of titles published annually: 3 Print
Total Titles: 15 Print

The Woodrow Wilson Center Press
Division of The Woodrow Wilson International Center for Scholars
One Woodrow Wilson Plaza, 1300 Pennsylvania Ave NW, Washington, DC 20004-3027
Tel: 202-691-4000 *Fax:* 202-691-4001
E-mail: press@wwics.si.edu
Web Site: wilsoncenter.org
Key Personnel
Dir: Joseph F Brinley, Jr *Tel:* 202-691-4042 *E-mail:* brinleyj@wwic.si.edu
Ed: Yamile Kahn *Tel:* 202-691-4041 *E-mail:* kahnym@wwic.si.edu
Founded: 1988
Humanities & social sciences; policy studies.
ISBN Prefix(es): 0-943875; 1-930365
Number of titles published annually: 12 Print
Total Titles: 115 Print
Imprints: Wilson Center Press; Woodrow Wilson Center Press/Johns Hopkins University Press; Woodrow Wilson Center Press/Stan-

ford University Press; Woodrow Wilson Center Series/Cambridge University Press; Woodrow Wilson Center Special Studies
Distributed by Cambridge University Press; Columbia University Press; The Johns Hopkins University Press; Stanford University Press; University of California Press

§Word Wrangler Publishing Inc
332 Tobin Creek Rd, Livingston, MT 59047
Tel: 406-686-4230; 406-686-4417
Toll Free Tel: 866-896-2897 *Fax:* 406-686-4417
E-mail: wrdwranglr@aol.com
Web Site: www.wordwrangler.com
Key Personnel
Pres: Barbara Quanbeck
Founded: 1999
Home of personally recommended books.
ISBN Prefix(es): 1-58630
Number of titles published annually: 10 Print; 30 Online; 15 E-Book
Total Titles: 12 Print; 150 Online; 150 E-Book

Wordtree branching dictionary
10876 Bradshaw W102, Overland Park, KS 66210-1148
SAN: 214-1752
Tel: 913-469-1010
Web Site: www.wordtree.com
Key Personnel
Publr: Dr Henry G Burger *E-mail:* burger@cctr. umkc.edu
Founded: 1984
Compiles & markets add-on (skip-branching) dictionaries that bifurcate each verb; all parts are cross-referenced; reader looks up any goal, then branches back toward all its causes, or forward toward effects; research service (supplementing the dictionary); pay-per-clipping of the context of any listed word.
ISBN Prefix(es): 0-936312
Total Titles: 1 Print
Distributed by Amazon.com; Brodart
Membership(s): Dictionary Society of North America; European Association for Lexicography; International Association for Semiotic Studies

§Wordware Publishing Inc
2320 Los Rios Blvd, Suite 200, Plano, TX 75074
SAN: 291-4786
Tel: 972-423-0090 *Toll Free Tel:* 800-229-4949
Fax: 972-881-9147
E-mail: info@wordware.com
Web Site: www.wordware.com
Key Personnel
Pres & CEO: Russell A Stultz
COO & Publr: Tim McEvoy
Acqs Ed: Wes Beckwith
Founded: 1983
Technical books with special emphasis on advanced computers, books, regional books (Texas), computer game development, Delphi programming & other intermediate level computer programming topics.
ISBN Prefix(es): 0-915381; 1-55622
Number of titles published annually: 60 Print
Total Titles: 300 Print; 3 Audio
Imprints: Republic of Texas Press
Divisions: Educational Products
Distributor for Seaside Press
Foreign Rights: Dan Broze

Workers Compensation Research Institute
955 Massachusetts Ave, Cambridge, MA 02139
Tel: 617-661-9274 *Fax:* 617-661-9284
E-mail: wcri@wcinet.org
Web Site: www.wcrinet.org
Founded: 1983
Workers compensation public policy research.
ISBN Prefix(es): 0-935149

Number of titles published annually: 14 Print
Total Titles: 86 Print

§Workman Publishing Co Inc
708 Broadway, New York, NY 10003-9555
SAN: 203-2821
Tel: 212-254-5900 *Toll Free Tel:* 800-722-7202
Fax: 212-254-8098
E-mail: info@workman.com
Web Site: www.workman.com
Key Personnel
Pres & CEO: Peter Workman
COO: Walter Weintz
Assoc Publr: Katie Workman
Dir, Children's Publg: David Allender
Publicity Dir: Kim Hicks *Tel:* 212-614-7705
E-mail: kimc@workman.com
Licensing Dir: Pat Upton
Dir, Intl Mktg: Carolan R Workman
Creative Dir: Paul Gamarello; Paul Hanson
Art Dir: Lisa Hollander
Premium & Spec Sales Dir: Jenny Mandel
Prodn Mgr: Wayne Kirn
School & Lib Sales Mgr: Maribeth Casey
Cont: Richard Petry
Ed-in-Chief: Susan Bolotin
Exec Ed: Suzanne Rafer
Man Ed: Katherine Adzima *Tel:* 212-614-7720
E-mail: katherinea@workman.com
Sr Ed: Jennifer Griffin; Margot Herrera; Richard Rosen; Ruth Sullivan
Founded: 1967
General nonfiction, calendars.
ISBN Prefix(es): 0-89480; 1-56305; 0-7611
Number of titles published annually: 45 Print
Divisions: Algonquin Books of Chapel Hill; Artisan
Distributor for Black Dog & Leventhal; Greenwich Workshop Press; Storey Publishing
Foreign Rep(s): Thomas Allen & Son Ltd (Canada); Bookreps New Zealand (New Zealand); Hardie Grant Books (Australia); Melia Publishing Services (UK, Ireland)
Foreign Rights: Big Apple Tuttle-Mori Agency (China, Taiwan); Graal Ltd (Poland); Japan UNI Agency (Japan); JLM Literary Agency (Greece); KCC (Korea); Alexander Korahenevski Agency (Russia); Caroline van Gelderen (Netherlands); Julio F Yanez (Latin America, Portugal, Spain)
Shipping Address: George Banta Co, 677 Brighton Beach Rd, Menasha, WI 54952-2998
Membership(s): AAP

World Almanac Books
Division of World Almanac Education Group
512 Seventh Ave, 22nd fl, New York, NY 10018
SAN: 211-6944
Tel: 646-312-6800 *Fax:* 646-312-6839
E-mail: info@waegroup.com
Web Site: www.worldalmanac.com
Key Personnel
VP, Sales & Mktg: James R Keenley *Tel:* 646-312-6822 *E-mail:* jkeenley@waegroup.com
Edit Dir & Rts & Perms: William McGeveran *Tel:* 646-312-6866 *Fax:* 646-312-6838
E-mail: bmcgeveran@waegroup.com
Gen Mgr: Kenneth Park *Tel:* 212-896-4247
Fax: 646-312-6838 *E-mail:* kpark@facts.com
Founded: 1868
Annual juvenile & adult reference books.
ISBN Prefix(es): 0-88687
Number of titles published annually: 2 Print
Total Titles: 2 Print; 3 Online
Online services available through EBSCOhost, LexisNexis, NewsBank, OCLC.
Distributed by St Martin's Press Inc
Foreign Rep(s): Adnkronos Libri SRL (Italy)

§World Bank Publications
Member of The World Bank Group

Office of the Publisher, 1818 "H" St NW, U-11-1104, Washington, DC 20433
Tel: 202-473-0393 (sales mgr) *Toll Free Tel:* 800-645-7247 (cust serv) *Fax:* 202-522-2631
Fax on Demand: 703-661-1501
E-mail: books@worldbank.org; pubrights@ worldbank.org (foreign rts)
Web Site: www.worldbank.org/publications
Telex: WUI 69145 *Cable:* INTBAFRAD
Key Personnel
Publr: H Dirk Koehler
Sales Mgr: Jose de Buerba *E-mail:* jdebuerba@ worldbank.org
Foreign Rts Mgr: Valentina Kalk
E-mail: pubrights@worldbank.org
Founded: 1944
Publish over 200 new titles annually in support of the World Bank's mission to fight poverty & distributes them globally in both print & electronic formats; electronic online subscription database; international affairs.
ISBN Prefix(es): 0-8213
Number of titles published annually: 200 Print; 10 CD-ROM; 3 Online; 30 E-Book
Total Titles: 1,600 Print; 50 CD-ROM; 3 Online; 50 E-Book
Imprints: World Bank
Foreign Rep(s): International Publishing Services (Middle East, North Africa)
Billing Address: PO Box 960, Herndon, VA 20172-0960
Orders to: PO Box 960, Herndon, VA 20172-0960 *Toll Free Tel:* 800-645-7247
Returns: Returns Dept, 22883 Quicksilver Dr, Dulles, VA 20166
Shipping Address: Returns Dept, 22883 Quicksilver Dr, Dulles, VA 20166
Warehouse: c/o Books International, PO Box 960, Herndon, VA 20172-0960
Distribution Center: c/o Books International, PO Box 960, Herndon, VA 20172-0960
Membership(s): AAP

§World Book Inc
Subsidiary of The Scott Fetzer Co
233 N Michigan, Suite 2000, Chicago, IL 60601
SAN: 201-4815
Tel: 312-729-5800 *Toll Free Tel:* 800-967-5325 (consumer sales, US); 800-463-8845 (consumer sales, Canada); 800-975-3250 (school & library sales, US); 800-837-5365 (school & library sales, Canada); 866-866-5200 (web sales) *Fax:* 312-729-5600; 312-729-5606
Toll Free Fax: 800-433-9330 (school & library sales, US); 888-690-4002 (school library sales, Canada)
Web Site: www.worldbook.com
Key Personnel
VP, School/Library & Direct Sales: Robert R Hall
VP & CFO: Donald D Keller
VP, Edit: Dominic J Miccolis
VP, Intl Sales: S R Prabaharan
Ed-in-Chief, World Book Inc: Dale W Jacobs
Gen Man Ed: Paul Kobasa
Edit Administrator & Perms Ed: Janet T Peterson
Founded: 1917
Publisher of high-quality, award-winning, educational reference & nonfiction publications for the school & library market & home market, in print, CD-ROM & online formats.
ISBN Prefix(es): 0-7166
Number of titles published annually: 40 Print; 6 CD-ROM
Total Titles: 270 Print; 91 CD-ROM; 8 Online

World Citizens
Affiliate of Cinema Investments Co Inc
96 La Verne Ave, Mill Valley, CA 94941
Mailing Address: PO Box 131, Mill Valley, CA 94942-0131
Tel: 415-380-8020 *Toll Free Tel:* 800-247-6553 (orders only)
Web Site: soultosoulmedia.com; skateman.com

Key Personnel
Ed-in-Chief: Joan Ellen
Ed: John Ballard
Sales Mgr & Intl Rts: Steve Ames
Assoc Ed: Jack Henry
Founded: 1984
Cross cultural & multi-cultural novels & texts. Adult, educational, trade & young adult divisions.
ISBN Prefix(es): 0-932279
Number of titles published annually: 6 Print; 4 CD-ROM; 6 E-Book; 4 Audio
Total Titles: 18 Print; 2 CD-ROM; 10 Online; 10 E-Book; 8 Audio
Imprints: Classroom Classics; New Horizons Book Publishing Co; Skateman Publications
Distributed by Inland
Returns: Bookmasters Distribution Center, 30 Amberwood Pkwy, Ashland, OH 44805
Distribution Center: Bookmasters Distribution Center, PO Box 388, Ashland, OH 44805-0388 *Toll Free Tel:* 800-247-6553 *Fax:* 419-201-6883

World Eagle
Division of Independent Broadcasting Associates Inc
111 King St, Littleton, MA 01460-1527
Tel: 978-486-9180 *Toll Free Tel:* 800-854-8273 *Fax:* 978-486-9652
E-mail: iba@ibaradio.org
Web Site: www.worldeagle.com; www.ibaradio.org
Key Personnel
Pres & Ed: Martine L Crandall-Hollick
Founded: 1977
Resource materials for teachers, libraries & media centers; maps & atlases.
ISBN Prefix(es): 0-930141; 0-9608016
Number of titles published annually: 3 Print
Total Titles: 45 Print; 30 Audio

World Leisure Corp
177 Paris St, Boston, MA 02128
SAN: 289-4742
Mailing Address: PO Box 160, Hampstead, NH 03841-0160
Tel: 617-569-1966 *Toll Free Tel:* 877-863-1966
Web Site: www.worldleisure.com
Key Personnel
Pres, Publr & Intl Rts: Charles Leocha
E-mail: leocha@worldleisure.com
Founded: 1977
Travel books, self-help, gift books, sports, cross country & downhill skiing & snowboarding.
ISBN Prefix(es): 0-915009
Number of titles published annually: 4 Print
Total Titles: 15 Print
Foreign Rep(s): Hushion House (Canada); Portfolio Books (UK)
Distribution Center: Midpoint Trade Books, 1263 Southwest Blvd, Kansas City, KS 66103 *Tel:* 913-831-2233 *Fax:* 913-362-7401
Hushion House, 36 Northline Rd, Toronto, ON M4B 3E2, Canada *Tel:* 416-285-6100 *Fax:* 416-285-1777 *Web Site:* www.hushion.com

World Publishing
404 BNA Dr, Bldg 200, Suite 208, Nashville, TN 37217
Mailing Address: PO Box 145001, Nashville, TN 37214-5001
Tel: 615-902-2395 *Toll Free Tel:* 800-363-0308 *Fax:* 615-902-2397 *Toll Free Fax:* 800-822-4271 (orders)
E-mail: questions@worldpublishing.com; orders@worldpublishing.com
Web Site: www.worldpublishing.com
Key Personnel
VP & Ed-in-Chief: Frank Couch
VP & Publr: Terry Draughon
Founded: 1980

Bibles & Testaments & reference books.
ISBN Prefix(es): 0-529
Number of titles published annually: 30 Print
Total Titles: 850 Print
Distributor for Inspirational Press
Foreign Rep(s): John McElwee

§World Resources Institute
10 "G" St NE, Suite 800, Washington, DC 20002
Mailing Address: PO Box 4852, Hampton Sta, Baltimore, MD 21211
Tel: 202-729-7600 *Toll Free Tel:* 800-822-0504 *Fax:* 202-729-7707
E-mail: publications@wri.org
Web Site: www.wri.org/wri
Key Personnel
Dir, Pubns: Hyacinth Billings *Tel:* 202-729-7740
Founded: 1982
Professional, scholarly & general interest publications, including energy, the environment, agriculture, forestry, natural resources, economics, geography, climate, biotechnology & development. Some titles co-published with university presses & commercial publishers.
ISBN Prefix(es): 0-915825; 1-56973
Number of titles published annually: 20 Print
Total Titles: 395 Print; 2 CD-ROM
Foreign Rep(s): DA Information Services (Australia, New Zealand, Papua New Guinea); Earthscan Publications Ltd (UK); Renouf Publishing (Canada); Systematics Studies (Trinidad West Indies)

§World Scientific Publishing Co Inc
27 Warren St, Suite 401-402, Hackensack, NJ 07601
Tel: 201-487-9655 *Toll Free Tel:* 800-227-7562 *Fax:* 201-487-9656 *Toll Free Fax:* 888-977-2665
E-mail: wspc@wspc.com
Web Site: www.wspc.com
Key Personnel
Publisher: K K Phua
Contact: Calandra Braswell
Founded: 1980
Number of titles published annually: 400 Print
Total Titles: 5,000 Print
Subsidiaries: Imperial College Press
Warehouse: 51 Stiles Lane, Pine Brook, NJ 07058-9535

§World Trade Press
1450 Grant Ave, Suite 204, Novato, CA 94945
Tel: 415-898-1124 *Toll Free Tel:* 800-833-8586 *Fax:* 415-898-1080
E-mail: admin@worldtradepress.com
Web Site: www.worldtradepress.com
Key Personnel
Publr: Edward G Hinkelman
Man Ed: Sibylla M Putzi
Founded: 1990
Professional books for international trade & business travel.
ISBN Prefix(es): 0-9631864; 1-885073
Number of titles published annually: 5 Print; 2 CD-ROM; 2 Online; 2 E-Book
Total Titles: 70 Print; 3 CD-ROM; 2 E-Book
Distributed by Reference Press
Foreign Rep(s): Goodwill Bookstore (Philippines); Kirby Book Co Pty Ltd (Australia, New Zealand); Longman Singapore (PTE); McGraw Hill-Europe (UK, Europe); SBP Co (India); Turboglen (Gulf States)

§The Wright Group/McGraw-Hill, a Division of McGraw-Hill Learning Group
Division of McGraw-Hill Learning Group
One Prudential Plaza, 130 E Randolph, 4th fl, Chicago, IL 60601
Tel: 312-233-6520 *Toll Free Tel:* 800-537-4740 *Fax:* 312-233-6605
Web Site: www.wrightgroup.com

Key Personnel
Exec VP: James R McNeely
VP, Sales: John Atkocaitis
VP, Mktg: Janet Meyers
VP, Strategic Busn Devt: Jeanine Fukuda
Founded: 1975
Publish books for early childhood, elementary & middle school market. Specialize in reading, language arts & math for small group & whole group instruction; teacher guides & lessons, posters, professional training material; reading, language arts, mathematics & professional development; literacy. Develops & markets material for Breakthrough to Literacy & Contemporary Books (Adult Ed/ESL).
ISBN Prefix(es): 0-940156; 0-55624; 0-07; 0-7802; 0-322; 1-4045
Number of titles published annually: 200 Print; 8 CD-ROM; 8 E-Book; 10 Audio
Total Titles: 3,000 Print; 30 CD-ROM; 3 E-Book; 240 Audio
Imprints: Breakthrough; Contemporary Book; Creative Publications; DLM; Everyday Mathematics

Write Stuff Enterprises Inc
1001 S Andrew Ave, 2nd fl, Fort Lauderdale, FL 33316
Tel: 954-462-6657 *Toll Free Tel:* 800-900-2665 *Fax:* 954-463-2220
E-mail: legends@writestuffbooks.com
Web Site: www.writestuffbooks.com
Key Personnel
Pres & CEO: Jeffrey L Rodergen
Leading publisher of works on industry & technology.
ISBN Prefix(es): 0-945903
Number of titles published annually: 30 Print; 30 E-Book
Imprints: Write Stuff®
Foreign Office(s): Write-On Limited, 28 Old Brumpton Rd, Suite 532, South Kensington, London SWT355, United Kingdom
Membership(s): ABA; NBAA; Publishers Marketing Association

Writer's AudioShop
1316 Overland Stage Rd, Dripping Springs, TX 78620
Tel: 512-264-9210 *Toll Free Tel:* 800-88-WRITE (889-7483) *Fax:* 512-264-9210
E-mail: writersaudio@timberwdfinc.com; wrtaudshop@aol.com
Web Site: www.writersaudio.com
Key Personnel
Publr: Elaine Davenport
Founded: 1985
Audio Publisher.
ISBN Prefix(es): 1-880717
Number of titles published annually: 4 Print
Total Titles: 35 Print
Sales Office(s): Timberwolf Press (TWP), 202 N Allen Dr, Suite A, Allen, TX 75013 *Toll Free Tel:* 888-808-0912
Distributed by Timberwolf Press (TWP)
Billing Address: Timberwolf Press (TWP), 202 N Allen Dr, Suite A, Allen, TX 75013 *Toll Free Tel:* 888-808-0912
Orders to: Timberwolf Press (TWP), 202 N Allen Dr, Suite A, Allen, TX 75013 *Toll Free Tel:* 888-808-0912
Returns: Timberwolf Press (TWP), 202 N Allen Dr, Suite A, Allen, TX 75013 *Toll Free Tel:* 888-808-0912
Shipping Address: Timberwolf Press (TWP), 202 N Allen Dr, Suite A, Allen, TX 75013 *Toll Free Tel:* 888-808-0912
Warehouse: Timberwolf Press (TWP), 202 N Allen Dr, Suite A, Allen, TX 75013 *Toll Free Tel:* 888-808-0912

Distribution Center: Timberwolf Press (TWP), 202 N Allen Dr, Suite A, Allen, TX 75013 *Toll Free Tel:* 888-808-0912
Membership(s): Audio Publishers Association

The Writers' Collective
780 Reservoir Ave, Suite 243, Cranston, RI 02910
Tel: 401-537-9175
E-mail: info@writerscollective.org
Web Site: www.writerscollective.org
Key Personnel
Pres: Lisa Grant *E-mail:* lgrant@writerscollective.org
Admin: Colleen Martin *E-mail:* colleen@writerscollective.org
Founded: 2002
ISBN Prefix(es): 1-932133; 1-59411; 1-59590 (Books 2 Go)
Number of titles published annually: 40 Print
Total Titles: 120 Print
Imprints: Bear Manor Media; Chanting Press
Divisions: Books 2 Go
Distributor for Beef on Weck Press; Lucky Duck Press; Twilight Times Books; Twin Stars Unlimited
Orders to: Baker & Taylor
Distribution Center: Midpoint Trade Books *Web Site:* midpointtrade.com
Membership(s): National Writers Union; Small Publishers Association of North America

Writer's Digest Books
Imprint of F+W Publications Inc
4700 E Galbraith Rd, Cincinnati, OH 45236
SAN: 212-064X
Tel: 513-531-2690 *Toll Free Tel:* 800-289-0963
Fax: 513-891-7185
Web Site: www.writersdigest.com
Key Personnel
Pres & CEO: Stephen J Kent *E-mail:* Stephen.Kent@fwpubs.com
Pres, Book Clubs & Book Publg: William Budge Wallis, Jr *E-mail:* Budge.Wallis@fwpubs.com
Sr VP, New Prods: David Lewis *E-mail:* David.Lewis@fwpubs.com
Prodn Dir: Barbara Schmitz *E-mail:* Barbara.Schmitz@fwpubs.com
Sales Dir: Michael Murphy *Tel:* 800-666-0963 ext 1270 *E-mail:* michael.murphy@fwpubs.com
Book Club Dir: Peg Sousa *E-mail:* Peg.Sousa@fwpubs.com
Rts & Perms: Laura Smith *E-mail:* Laura.Smith@fwpubs.com
Founded: 1919
Top-quality instructional & reference books to help creative people find personal satisfaction & professional success. Topics covered include writing, photography, songwriting & poetry.
ISBN Prefix(es): 1-59233; 0-89879; 1-58297
Number of titles published annually: 160 Print
Total Titles: 150 Print; 1 CD-ROM
Distributor for Rockport Publishers
Foreign Rep(s): David Bateman Ltd (New Zealand); BookMovers Group (Canada); Capricorn Link (Australia); David & Charles Ltd (UK); Real Books (South Africa); Marta Schooler (Asia, Central America, Mexico, Middle East, South America)
Returns: Aero Fulfillment Services, 2800 Henkle Dr, Lebanon, OH 45036

§The Writings of Mary Baker Eddy/Publisher
Division of The First Church of Christ, Scientist
175 Huntington Ave, Suite A-16-10, Boston, MA 02115
Tel: 617-450-3514; 617-450-2000 (Christian Science Church Boston) *Toll Free Tel:* 800-288-7090 *Fax:* 617-450-7334
Web Site: www.spirituality.com
Key Personnel
Publr: Virginia S Harris

Man Publr & Gen Mgr: Carol Hohle
Mktg Mgr: Chuck Howes
Opers Mgr: Betty Carneal
Founded: 1879
Books on spirituality; major title: *Science & Health with Key to the Scriptures*; 16 languages & English braille.
ISBN Prefix(es): 0-87952
Number of titles published annually: 17 Print
Total Titles: 17 Print

Wyndham Hall Press
5050 Kerr Rd, Lima, OH 45806
SAN: 686-6743
Tel: 419-648-9124 *Toll Free Tel:* 866-895-0977
Fax: 419-648-9124; 413-208-2409
E-mail: whpbooks@wcoil.com
Web Site: www.wyndhamhallpress.com
Key Personnel
Man Ed: Mark S McCullough *E-mail:* mark@wyndhamhallpress.com
Founded: 1981
Scholarly monographs & text books.
ISBN Prefix(es): 1-55605; 0-932269
Number of titles published annually: 12 Print
Total Titles: 130 Print

Wyrick & Co
284-A Meeting St, Charleston, SC 29401
Mailing Address: PO Box 89, Charleston, SC 29402-0089
Tel: 843-722-0881 *Toll Free Tel:* 800-227-5898
Fax: 843-722-6771
E-mail: wyrickco@bellsouth.net
Key Personnel
Pres: Charles L Wyrick, Jr
Mktg & Sales Mgr: Connie H Wyrick
Busn Off: Kay L Overton
Orders: Laura Moses
Founded: 1986
Hardcover & trade paperback.
ISBN Prefix(es): 0-941711
Number of titles published annually: 8 Print
Total Titles: 70 Print; 8 E-Book; 2 Audio
Imprints: Tarboro Books
Sales Office(s): IPG/CRP Warehouse, 600 N Pulaski Rd, Chicago, IL 60624 *Toll Free Tel:* 800-888-4741
Foreign Office(s): Gazelle Book Services Ltd, Falcon House, Queen Sq, Lancaster LA1 1RN, United Kingdom
Foreign Rep(s): Gazelle Book Services Ltd (UK, Continental Europe)
Advertising Agency: Dixie Media Inc, PO Box 69, Charleston, SC 29402-0069
Orders to: Independent Publishers Group, 814 N Franklin St, Chicago, IL 60610 *Toll Free Tel:* 800-888-4741 *Fax:* 312-337-5985
Returns: IPG/CRP Warehouse, 600 N Pulaski Rd, Chicago, IL 60624 *Toll Free Tel:* 800-888-4741
Warehouse: IPG/CRP Warehouse, 600 N Pulaski Rd, Chicago, IL 60624 *Toll Free Tel:* 800-888-4741
Membership(s): ABA; Publishers Association of the South; Southeast Booksellers Association

§XC Publishing
931 E Avenida de las Flores, Thousand Oaks, CA 91360
Tel: 805-495-7768 *Fax:* 413-431-5515
E-mail: xuhl@xcpublishing.com
Web Site: www.xcpublishing.com
Key Personnel
Publr: Xina Marie Uhl *E-mail:* xinamarieuhl@earthlink.net
Publr & Ed: Cheryl Dyson *E-mail:* cdyson@xcpublishing.com
Founded: 1999
Electronic publisher of high-quality genre fiction & nonfiction.
ISBN Prefix(es): 1-930805
Number of titles published annually: 8 Print

Total Titles: 12 Print
Membership(s): SPAWN

§Xlibris Corp
436 Walnut St, 11th fl, The Independence Bldg, Philadelphia, PA 19106
Tel: 215-923-4686 *Toll Free Tel:* 888-795-4274
Fax: 215-923-4685
E-mail: info@xlibris.com
Web Site: www.xlibris.com
Key Personnel
CEO: John Feldcamp *E-mail:* john.feldcamp@xlibris.com
VP, Mktg & Sales: David Hisbrook *E-mail:* david.hisbrook@xlibris.com
Mgr, Publg Servs: Megan Gallagher *E-mail:* megan.gallagher@xlibris.com
Founded: 1997
ISBN Prefix(es): 0-7388
Number of titles published annually: 2,400 Print
Total Titles: 10,000 Print

Yale Center for British Art
1080 Chapel St, New Haven, CT 06520
Mailing Address: PO Box 208280, New Haven, CT 06510-2302
Tel: 203-432-2800; 203-432-2850 *Fax:* 203-432-4530
E-mail: bacinfo@yale.edu
Web Site: www.yale.edu/ycba
Key Personnel
Museum Shop Mgr: Lizbeth O'Connor *E-mail:* lizbeth.oconnor@yale.edu
Founded: 1977
Exhibition catalogues.
ISBN Prefix(es): 0-930606
Number of titles published annually: 3 Print
Total Titles: 61 Print
Foreign Office(s): Premier Book Marketing, One Gower St, London WC1E 6HA, United Kingdom
Foreign Rep(s): Premier Book Marketing (UK)

§Yale University Press
Division of Yale University
302 Temple St, New Haven, CT 06511
SAN: 203-2740
Mailing Address: PO Box 209040, New Haven, CT 06520-9040
Tel: 203-432-0960; 401-531-2800 (cust serv) *Toll Free Tel:* 800-405-1619 (cust serv) *Fax:* 203-432-0948; 401-531-2801 (cust serv) *Toll Free Fax:* 800-406-9145 (cust serv)
E-mail: customer.care@trilateral.org (cust serv)
Web Site: www.yale.edu/yup/
Key Personnel
Chmn of the Bd: Peter Workman
Dir: John Donatich
CFO: John D Rollins
Publg Dir: Tina C Weiner
Publicity Dir: Heather D'Auria
Edit Dir: Jonathan Brent
Promo Dir: Sarah F Clark
Prodn Dir: Christina Coffin
Adv Mgr: Peter Sims
Mgr, Design: Nancy Ovedovitz
Direct Mail Mgr: Debra Bozzi
ISBN Contact: Anne Richardson
Publr, Langs: Mary Jane Peluso
Publr, Art & Architecture: Patricia Fidler
Publr, History: Laura Heimert
Ed: John Kulka; Ed O'Malley; Jean E Thomson-Black
Founded: 1908
Scholarly.
ISBN Prefix(es): 0-300
Number of titles published annually: 330 Print; 2 CD-ROM
Total Titles: 3,600 Print; 4 CD-ROM; 3 Audio
Foreign Office(s): 47 Bedford Sq, London WC1B 3DP, United Kingdom

Foreign Rep(s): Rockbook (Japan, South Korea, Taiwan); David Stimpson (Australia, Canada, New Zealand)
Foreign Rights: Ann Bihan (England); Craig Falk (Latin America, Mexico, South America)
Shipping Address: TriLiteral, 100 Maple Ridge Dr, Cumberland, RI 02864-1769 *Tel:* 401-658-4226
Membership(s): AAP

Yard Dog Press
710 W Redbud Lane, Alma, AR 72921-7247
Tel: 479-632-4693 *Fax:* 479-632-4693
Web Site: www.yarddogpress.com
Key Personnel
Ed-in-Chief: Selina Rosen
Founded: 1996
Micro press specialiing in sci/fi, fantasy & horror.
ISBN Prefix(es): 1-893687
Number of titles published annually: 10 Print
Total Titles: 50 Print

Yardbird Books
601 Kennedy Rd, Airville, PA 17302
SAN: 248-0182
Mailing Address: PO Box 5333, Harrisburg, PA 17110-0333
Tel: 717-927-6377 *Toll Free Tel:* 800-622-6044 (Sales) *Fax:* 717-927-6377
E-mail: info@yardbird.com
Web Site: www.yardbird.com
Key Personnel
Publr: Charles McCarthy
Founded: 1988
Also wholesale & retail distributor.
ISBN Prefix(es): 1-882611; 0-9620251
Number of titles published annually: 10 Print
Total Titles: 25 Print
Imprints: Yardbird

YBK Publishers Inc
425 Broome St, New York, NY 10013
Tel: 212-219-0135 *Fax:* 212-219-0136
E-mail: info@ybkpublishers.com
Key Personnel
Pres: Otto Barz
Founded: 2001
Print-on-demand; general trade & nonfiction.
ISBN Prefix(es): 0-9703923
Number of titles published annually: 7 Print
Total Titles: 9 Print
Distribution Center: Lightning Source, 1246 Heil Quaker Blvd, La Vergne, TN 37086 *Tel:* 615-213-5815 *Fax:* 615-213-4426 *E-mail:* inquiry@ybkpublishers.com
Membership(s): Publishers Marketing Association; Small Press Center

Ye Galleon Press
107 E Main St, Fairfield, WA 99012
Mailing Address: PO Box 287, Fairfield, WA 99012-0287
Tel: 509-283-2422 *Toll Free Tel:* 800-829-5586 (orders only) *Fax:* 509-283-2422
Key Personnel
Binding Operator, Mgr: Garry Adams
Founded: 1937
Specialize in rare historical reprints.
ISBN Prefix(es): 0-87770
Number of titles published annually: 10 Print

Ye Olde Genealogie Shoppe
PO Box 39128, Indianapolis, IN 46239
Tel: 317-862-3330 *Toll Free Tel:* 800-419-0200 *Fax:* 317-862-2599
E-mail: yogs@iquest.net
Web Site: www.yogs.com
Key Personnel
Pres: Patricia Gooldy
Founded: 1974

Genealogy (local history records); books of instruction.
ISBN Prefix(es): 0-932924; 1-878311
Number of titles published annually: 20 Print
Total Titles: 500 Print
Imprints: Heritage House
Shipping Address: 9605 Vandergriff Rd, Indianapolis, IN 46239

Yeshiva University Press
500 W 185 St, New York, NY 10033-3201
Mailing Address: KTAV Publishing House Inc, 930 Newark Ave, Jersey City, NJ 07306
Tel: 212-960-5400 *Fax:* 212-960-0043
E-mail: yuadmit@yu.edu
Web Site: www.yu.edu *Telex:* 22-0883TAUR
Key Personnel
Pres: Richard Joel
Ed: Jeffrey Gurock
Admin: David Rosen
Pub Rel: Sam Hartstein
Founded: 1960
ISBN Prefix(es): 0-87068; 0-88125
Total Titles: 7 Print
Distributed by KTAV Publishing House Inc

YMAA Publication Center
Division of Yangs Oriental Arts Association
4354 Washington St, Roslindale, MA 02131
SAN: 665-2077
Tel: 617-323-7215 *Toll Free Tel:* 800-669-8892 *Fax:* 617-323-7417
E-mail: ymaa@aol.com
Web Site: www.ymaa.com
Key Personnel
Dir: David Ripianzi *E-mail:* davidr@ymaa.com
Founded: 1984
Publisher of indepth books & videos on martial arts & Asian health.
ISBN Prefix(es): 0-940871; 1-886969
Number of titles published annually: 10 Print
Total Titles: 54 Print; 4 Audio
Distributed by National Book Network; New Leaf
Distributor for Wind Records
Foreign Rep(s): CKK Ltd (Indonesia); Paul Crompton Ltd (Europe); NBN Canada (Canada); Zen Imports (Australia)
Foreign Rights: Daniel Doglioli (Italy); Julio F-Yanez (Spain); Matlock Agency (Russia); Andrew Nurnberg (Bulgaria)
Membership(s): ABA; NEBA; Publishers Marketing Association

York Press Inc
9540 Deereco Rd, Timonium, MD 21093
Mailing Address: PO Box 504, Timonium, MD 21094
Tel: 410-560-1557 *Toll Free Tel:* 800-962-2763 *Fax:* 410-560-6758
E-mail: york@abs.net
Web Site: www.yorkpress.com
Key Personnel
Pres: Elinor L Hartwig
Founded: 1972
ISBN Prefix(es): 0-912752
Number of titles published annually: 5 Print
Total Titles: 44 Print
Distributed by A G Bell Association for the Deaf; Educators Publishing Service

Young People's Press Inc (YPPI)
3033 Fifth Ave, Suite 200, San Diego, CA 92103
Tel: 619-688-9040 *Toll Free Tel:* 800-231-9774 *Fax:* 619-688-9044
E-mail: info@youngpeoplespress.com
Web Site: www.youngpeoplespress.com
Key Personnel
Chmn of the Bd: Robert J Saielli
Pres: Patricia A Pflum
Founded: 1994

Elementary curriculum in social skills & character building, language arts, literature & social sciences.
ISBN Prefix(es): 1-885658; 1-57279
Number of titles published annually: 10 Print
Total Titles: 245 Print; 24 Audio
Warehouse: 3535 Jefferson St, Stevens Point, WI 54481

YPPI, see Young People's Press Inc (YPPI)

Yucca Tree Press
Imprint of Barbed Wire Publishing
270 Avenida de Mesilla, Las Cruces, NM 88005
Tel: 505-525-9707 *Toll Free Tel:* 888-817-1990 *Fax:* 505-525-9711
E-mail: thefolks@barbed-wire.net
Web Site: www.barbed-wire.net
Key Personnel
Pres: Maria Schuster
Publr: George Stein *E-mail:* gstein@barbed-wire.net
Founded: 1998
Western & military history.
ISBN Prefix(es): 0-9622940; 1-881325
Number of titles published annually: 5 Print
Total Titles: 40 Print
Distributor for B & J Publications; Eakin Press; Filter Press; Gently Worded Books; Nita Stewart Haley Library; High Lonesome Books; KIVA Publications; Rimrock Press
Membership(s): Mountains & Plains Booksellers Association; New Mexico Book Association; Publishers Association of the West

YWAM Publishing
Division of Youth with a Mission
PO Box 55787, Seattle, WA 98155-0787
Tel: 425-771-1153 *Toll Free Tel:* 800-922-2143 *Fax:* 425-775-2383
E-mail: information@ywampublishing.com
Web Site: www.ywampublishing.com
Key Personnel
Intl Rts: Terry Bragg
Founded: 1987
Books on missions, evangelism & discipleship & also religious classics.
ISBN Prefix(es): 0-927545
Number of titles published annually: 10 Print
Total Titles: 160 Print; 1 CD-ROM; 5 Audio
Distributor for Emerald Books
Shipping Address: 7825 230 St SW, Edmonds, WA 98026
Warehouse: 7825 230 St SW, Edmonds, WA 98026

§Zagat Survey
4 Columbus Circle, New York, NY 10019
SAN: 289-4777
Tel: 212-977-6000 *Toll Free Tel:* 800-333-3421 (gen inquiries); 888-371-5440 (orders); 800-540-9609 (corp sales) *Fax:* 212-977-9760; 802-864-9846 (order related)
E-mail: corpsales@zagat.com; shop@zagat.com
Web Site: www.zagat.com
Key Personnel
Pres: Eugene H Zagat
Dir, Communs: Alexa Rudin
Contact: Nina S Zagat
Founded: 1982
ISBN Prefix(es): 1-57006
Number of titles published annually: 35 Print
Total Titles: 35 Print
Foreign Rep(s): Prentice-Hall (Canada)

Zaner-Bloser Inc
Subsidiary of Highlights for Children Inc
2200 W Fifth Ave, Columbus, OH 43215
Mailing Address: PO Box 16764, Columbus, OH 43216-6764

Tel: 614-486-0221 *Toll Free Tel:* 800-421-3018
Fax: 614-487-2699 *Toll Free Fax:* 800-992-
6087
E-mail: info@zaner-bloser.com
Web Site: www.zaner-bloser.com
Key Personnel
Pres: Robert Page
VP, Mktg: Richard Northup
Mktg: Jill Keasel
Founded: 1888
Elementary textbooks for critical thinking, whole
  language, substance abuse prevention, spelling
  & handwriting; modality (learning styles) kit,
  professional education books, storytelling kits
  & early childhood education.
ISBN Prefix(es): 0-88309; 0-88085
Number of titles published annually: 200 Print
Foreign Rep(s): Childrens Press
Advertising Agency: EDPUB
Warehouse: 4200 Parkway Ct, Hilliard, OH
  43026

Zebra Books, see Kensington Publishing Corp

Zeig, Tucker & Theisen Inc
3614 N 24 St, Phoenix, AZ 85016
Tel: 602-957-1270 *Toll Free Fax:* 800-688-2877
E-mail: zttorders@mindspring.com
Web Site: www.zeigtucker.com
Key Personnel
Dir: Jeffrey K Zeig *E-mail:* jeff@zeigtucker.com
Ed-in-Chief: Suzi Tucker *E-mail:* suzi@
  zeigtucker.com
Founded: 1998
ISBN Prefix(es): 1-891944; 1-932462
Number of titles published annually: 10 Print
Total Titles: 45 Print; 8 Audio
Editorial Office(s): 343 Newton Tpke, Redding,
  CT 06896, Contact: Suzi Tucker *Tel:* 203-938-
  7499 *Fax:* 203-938-1006 *E-mail:* tuckersuzi@
  aol.com
Billing Address: Cornell University Press Ser-
  vices, PO Box 6525, Ithaca, NY 14851
Orders to: Cornell University Press Services,
  PO Box 6525, Ithaca, NY 14851 *Tel:* 607-
  277-2211 *Toll Free Tel:* 800-666-2211
  E-mail: orderbook@cupserv.org
Returns: Cornell University Press Services,
  PO Box 6525, Ithaca, NY 14851 *Tel:* 607-
  277-2211 *Toll Free Tel:* 800-666-2211
  E-mail: orderbook@cupserv.org
Shipping Address: Cornell University Press Ser-
  vices, PO Box 6525, Ithaca, NY 14851

Warehouse: Cornell University Press Services, PO
  Box 6525, Ithaca, NY 14851
Distribution Center: Cornell University Press Ser-
  vices, PO Box 6525, Ithaca, NY 14851

Zephyr Press Catalog
814 N Franklin St, Chicago, IL 60610
Tel: 312-337-5985 *Toll Free Tel:* 800-232-2187
  Fax: 312-337-1651
E-mail: neways2learn@zephyrpress.com
Web Site: www.zephyrpress.com
Key Personnel
Publr: J Tanner
Sr Ed: Jerome Pohlen
Ed: Veronica Durie
Mktg: Betsy Gabler
Founded: 1979
Cutting-edge educational materials based on lat-
  est research on brain, brain-based learning &
  educational research.
ISBN Prefix(es): 0-913705; 1-56976
Number of titles published annually: 10 Print
Total Titles: 250 Print
Distributed by Opportunities for Learning Inc;
  Sundance Publishers & Distributors
Distributor for Dale Seymour Publications; B L
  Winch Associates
Foreign Rights: Hawker-Brownlow (Australia)
Membership(s): AAP; Publishers Marketing Asso-
  ciation

§Zondervan
Division of HarperCollins Publishers
5300 Patterson Ave SE, Grand Rapids, MI 49530
SAN: 203-2694
Tel: 616-698-6900 *Toll Free Tel:* 800-727-1309
  (cust serv) *Fax:* 616-698-3439; 616-698-3255
  (cust serv)
Web Site: www.zondervan.com *Telex:* 27-1839
Key Personnel
Pres & CEO: Bruce E Ryskamp *Tel:* 616-698-
  3494 *E-mail:* Bruce.Ryskamp@zondervan.com
Sr VP, Inspirio (The Gift Group of Zondervan):
  Caroline H Blauwkamp *Tel:* 616-698-3343
  E-mail: Caroline.Blauwkamp@zondervan.com
Exec VP & Publr: Scott W Bolinder *Tel:* 616-
  698-3444 *E-mail:* Scott.Bolinder@zondervan.
  com
Exec VP, Sales: Chris H Doornbos *Tel:* 616-698-
  3408 *E-mail:* Chris.Doornbos@zondervan.com
Exec VP & CFO: James G Schreiber *Tel:* 616-
  698-3269 *E-mail:* James.Schreiber@zondervan.
  com

Sr VP, Info Systems & Corp Communs: Sue-
  Anne J Boylan *Tel:* 616-698-3361 *E-mail:* Sue-
  Anne.Boylan@zondervan.com
Sr VP, Support Opers: Allen R Kerkstra *Tel:* 616-
  698-3409 *E-mail:* Al.Kerkstra@zondervan.com
Sr VP, HR: Nancy L Thole *Tel:* 616-698-3262
  E-mail: Nancy.Thole@zondervan.com
Founded: 1931
Religion (Christian); books, Bibles, ArMor (aca-
  demic & resource materials), ZonderKidz
  (children's books), New Media, Inspirio (gift
  group).
ISBN Prefix(es): 0-310
Total Titles: 3,291 Print
Imprints: Inspiro; Vida; ZonderKidz; Zondervan
Foreign Rep(s): Paul Van Duinen
Shipping Address: 5249 Corporate Grove Dr SE,
  Grand Rapids, MI 49512

Zone Books
Division of Urzone Inc
1226 Prospect Ave, Brooklyn, NY 11218
Tel: 718-686-0048 *Toll Free Tel:* 800-405-1619
  (orders & cust serv) *Fax:* 212-625-9772; 718-
  686-9045 *Toll Free Fax:* 800-406-9145 (orders)
E-mail: urzone@zonebooks.org; mitpress-orders@
  mit.edu (orders)
Key Personnel
Gen Mgr & Intl Rts: Gus Kiley
Man Ed: Meighan Gale
Ed: Jonathan Crary; Michel Feher; Ramona
  Naddaff
Founded: 1986
Also publishes a journal *Zone.*
ISBN Prefix(es): 0-942299; 1-890951
Number of titles published annually: 6 Print
Total Titles: 59 Print
Imprints: Swerve Editions
Foreign Office(s): John Wiley & Sons, South-
  ern Cross Trading Estate, One Oldlands Way,
  Bognor Regis, West Sussex PO22 9SA, United
  Kingdom *Tel:* (01243) 779777 *Fax:* (01243)
  820250 *E-mail:* cs-books@wiley.co.uk
Distributed by The MIT Press
Foreign Rights: Petra Eggers (Germany)
Warehouse: The Mit Press c/o Triliteral LLC, 100
  Maple Ridge Dr, Cumberland, RI 02864-1769
Distribution Center: The MIT Press, 5 Cambridge
  Ctr, Cambridge, MA 02142 *E-mail:* mitpress-
  orders@mit.edu

U.S. Publishers — Geographic Index

U.S. Publishers — Type of Publication Index

AV MATERIALS

CHILDREN'S BOOKS

DATABASES

DIRECTORIES, REFERENCE BOOKS

FINE EDITIONS, ILLUSTRATED BOOKS

JUVENILE & YOUNG ADULT BOOKS

PERIODICALS, JOURNALS

PROFESSIONAL BOOKS

SCHOLARLY BOOKS

TEXTBOOKS - ELEMENTARY

TEXTBOOKS - SECONDARY

TEXTBOOKS - COLLEGE

VIDEO CASSETTES

U.S. Publishers — Subject Index

AMERICANA, REGIONAL

ANIMALS, PETS

ANTHROPOLOGY

ART

ASIAN STUDIES

BIBLICAL STUDIES

BIOLOGICAL SCIENCES

BUSINESS

CAREER DEVELOPMENT

CHEMISTRY, CHEMICAL ENGINEERING

CHILD CARE & DEVELOPMENT

COOKERY

CRAFTS, GAMES, HOBBIES

CRIMINOLOGY

EARTH SCIENCES

ECONOMICS

EDUCATION

ELECTRONICS, ELECTRICAL ENGINEERING

ENERGY

ENGINEERING (GENERAL)

ENGLISH AS A SECOND LANGUAGE

ENVIRONMENTAL STUDIES

EROTICA

FILM, VIDEO

FINANCE

FOREIGN COUNTRIES

HEALTH, NUTRITION

HUMAN RELATIONS

LIBRARY & INFORMATION SCIENCES

LITERATURE, LITERARY CRITICISM, ESSAYS

MARITIME

MARKETING

MATHEMATICS

MECHANICAL ENGINEERING

MEDICINE, NURSING, DENTISTRY

MYSTERIES

MYTHOLOGY

NATIVE AMERICAN STUDIES

NATURAL HISTORY

NONFICTION (GENERAL)

OUTDOOR RECREATION

PHOTOGRAPHY

PHYSICAL SCIENCES

PHYSICS

POETRY

PSYCHOLOGY, PSYCHIATRY

PUBLIC ADMINISTRATION

PUBLISHING & BOOK TRADE REFERENCE

RADIO, TV

REAL ESTATE

REGIONAL INTERESTS

RELIGION - BUDDHIST

RELIGION - CATHOLIC

RELIGION - HINDU

RELIGION - OTHER

SCIENCE FICTION, FANTASY

SOCIAL SCIENCES, SOCIOLOGY

THEOLOGY

Imprints, Subsidiaries & Distributors

A & B Publishers Group, *subsidiary of* A & B Distributors, *distributor for* Random House Inc, Simon & Schuster, *distributed by* African World Press, D & J Books, Lushena Books

A Cappella Books, *imprint of* Chicago Review Press

A D D Warehouse, *subsidiary of* Specialty Press Inc, *distributor for* Bantam, Guilford Press, Plenum, Simon & Schuster, Slossen, Woodbine House, *distributed by* American Guidance Service, Boys Town Press, Child Play, Hawthorne Publications, MHS, Thinking Publications

A G Fiction™, *imprint of* Pleasant Company Publications

A K Peters Ltd, *distributor for* Association for Symbolic Logic, Canadian Human-Computer Communications Society

AK Press Distribution, *subsidiary of* AK Press Inc, AK Press Inc, *distributor for* AK Press, Crimethinc, Freedom Press, Payback Press, Phoenix Press, Rebel Inc, Rebel Press

A M C Nature Walks Series, *imprint of* Appalachian Mountain Club Books

A M C Quiet Water Guides, *imprint of* Appalachian Mountain Club Books

A M C River Guides, *imprint of* Appalachian Mountain Club Books

A M C Trail Guides, *imprint of* Appalachian Mountain Club Books

A Plus Discounted Materials, *division of* Golden Educational Center

A R E Press, *distributed by* Weatherhill Inc

A-R Editions Inc, *distributor for* AIM (American Institute of Musicology)

A R O Publishing Co, *distributed by* Barnes & Noble, Follett

A-To-Z Series, *imprint of* Incentive Publications Inc

A U A Language Center, *distributed by* Cornell University Southeast Asia Program Publications

AA Publishing, *distributed by* Paul & Company, Trafalgar Square

AAA Publishing, *distributed by* Simon & Schuster Inc

AAAI Press, *imprint of* American Association for Artificial Intelligence, *distributed by* The MIT Press

AANS-American Association of Neurological Surgeons, *distributor for* American Medical Association

AAPG (American Association of Petroleum Geologists), *distributor for* Geological Society of London, *distributed by* Affiliated East - West Press Private Limited, Canadian Society of Petroleum Geologists, Geological Society of London

AAPPL, *distributed by* Sterling Publishing Co Inc

Abaris Books, *division of* Opal Publishing

Abbeville, *imprint of* Abbeville Publishing Group, Artabras Inc

Abbeville Kids, *imprint of* Abbeville Publishing Group, Artabras Inc

Abbeville Press, *distributor for* American Federation of Arts

Abbeville Publishing Group, *distributor for* Art Institute of Chicago

Abbey of Saint Peter of Solesmes, *distributed by* Paraclete Press

Abbott, Langer & Associates, *distributor for* Aspen, McGraw-Hill, Prentice Hall, John Wiley

ABC-CLIO Ltd, *subsidiary of* ABC-CLIO

ABC Intl Group Inc, *distributed by* Kazi Publications Inc

Abdo & Daughters Publishing, *imprint of* Abdo Publishing

Abdo Publishing, *subsidiary of* Abdo Consulting Group Inc (ACGI), Abdo Consulting Group Inc (ACGI), *distributed by* Rockbottom Book Co

The Aberdeen Group, *distributor for* Craftsman Book Co

ABI Professional Publications, *imprint of* Vandamere Press, *distributor for* Vandamere Press (non-exclusive), *distributed by* Vandamere Press, Vandamere Press (non-exclusive)

Abiko Literary Press, *distributed by* Birch Brook Press

Abingdon Press, *division of* The United Methodist Publishing House, *imprint of* Abingdon Press, *distributor for* Chalice Press, Cokesbury, Dimensions for Living, Kingswood Books, Laughing Elephant, Presbyterian Publishing Corp, SPCK

Abjad Books, *imprint of* Kazi Publications Inc

Abradale, *imprint of* Harry N Abrams Inc

Abrams, *distributor for* National Gallery of Art, Nevraumont Publishing Co, *distributed by* Perfection Learning Corp

Abrams & University of Washington Press, *distributor for* Amon Carter Museum

Harry N Abrams, *distributor for* The Vendome Press

Harry N Abrams Inc, *subsidiary of* La Martiniere Groupe, *distributor for* American Federation of Arts, Art Institute of Chicago, The Colonial Williamsburg Foundation, *distributed by* Heimburger House Publishing Co

The ABS Group, *distributed by* American Academy of Environmental Engineers

Absolute Classics, *distributed by* Theatre Communications Group Inc

Ac-u-Kwik, *imprint of* PRIMEDIA Business Directories & Books

ACA, *imprint of* American Counseling Association

Academic Book Center, *distributor for* Investor Responsibility Research Center, Rocky River Publishers LLC

Academic Impressions, *distributor for* Primary Research Group

Academic Press, *imprint of* Elsevier, *distributor for* Harcourt Professional Publishing, The Psychological Corp, *distributed by* Food & Nutrition Press Inc (FNP)

Academy Chicago Publishers, *distributor for* Facets Multimedia, Wicker Park Press

Academy Health Services & Health Policy Research/Health Administration Press, *imprint of* Health Administration Press

Academy of Continuing Education, *division of* Success Advertising & Publishing

The Academy of Producer Insurance Studies Inc, *division of* The National Alliance for Insurance Education & Research

Acatos, *distributed by* Antique Collectors Club Ltd

Accent Publications, *subsidiary of* Cook Communications Ministries

Access, *imprint of* HarperCollins General Books Group, HarperCollins Publishers Sales

ACCT FOR KIDS, *distributor for* MAR*CO Products Inc

Ace, *imprint of* Penguin Group (USA) Inc

Ace Books, *imprint of* Berkley Books, Berkley Publishing Group, *distributed by* Perfection Learning Corp

ACE/Oryx, *imprint of* American Council on Education

Ace/Putnam, *imprint of* Penguin Group (USA) Inc, G P Putnam's Sons (Hardcover)

ACER, *distributor for* Psychological Assessment Resources Inc (PAR)

ACI Publishing, *distributed by* Dog-Eared Publications

ACM Press, *imprint of* Association for Computing Machinery

Acorn Guides, *imprint of* Trails Books

Acorn Media Publishing, *distributed by* Heimburger House Publishing Co

Acres USA, *division of* Acres USA Inc, Acres USA Inc

ACS Publications, *subsidiary of* ASTRO Communications Services Inc, *affiliate of* International Media Holdings (IMH), *distributor for* Whitford Press, *distributed by* Llewellyn, New Leaf Distributors

ACT Proficiency Examination Program, *imprint of* National Learning Corp

ACTA Publications, *distributor for* Grief Watch, Veritas

Action Publishing LLC, *distributor for* Bamboo Grove, The Unifont Co

ACU Press, *affiliate of* Abilene Christian University

Ad Fontes LLC, *distributed by* Alexander Street Press LLC

Ad Infinitum Books, *distributed by* Cross-Cultural Communications

AD Publishing, *distributed by* Krause Publications

ADC Map, *imprint of* Langenscheidt Publishers Inc

ADC the Map People, *subsidiary of* American Map Corp, Langenscheidt Publishers, Langenscheidt Publishing Group, *distributed by* Hagstrom Map Co Inc

Addison Wesley, *distributor for* Public Citizen

Addison Wesley Higher Education Group, *division of* Pearson Education

Adirondack Museum, *imprint of* Syracuse University Press

Adis International, *imprint of* Wolters Kluwer US Corp

Adlard Coles Nautical, *distributed by* Sheridan House Inc

Adler Planetarium & Astronomy, *distributed by* Antique Collectors Club Ltd

Admission Test Series, *imprint of* National Learning Corp

Adult Trade, *division of* Chronicle Books LLC

Advaita, *distributed by* Vedanta Press

Advances in Criminological Theory, *imprint of* Transaction Publishers

Advantage Publishers Group, *division of* Advanced Marketing Services Inc

Adventure Guides, *imprint of* Hunter Publishing Inc

Adventure Publications, *distributor for* Blacklock Nature Photography, Blue Sky Marketing Inc

Adventure Roads Travel, *imprint of* Ocean Tree Books

Adventures in Odyssey, *imprint of* Focus on the Family

Adventures Unlimited, *distributor for* Book World Inc/Blue Star Productions

Adventures Unlimited Press, *distributor for* EDFU Books

Advocate Books, *imprint of* Alyson Publications

The AEI Press, *division of* American Enterprise Institute for Public Policy Research, *distributed by* MIT (selected titles)

Aerial Fiction, *imprint of* Farrar, Straus & Giroux Books for Young Readers

Aerial Perspective Publishing, *distributed by* Stackpole Books

Aerie Books, *imprint of* Tom Doherty Associates, LLC

Aeronautical Publishers, *imprint of* Possibility Press

Aesop House, *imprint of* A & B Publishers Group

Affiliated East - West Press Private Limited, *distributor for* AAPG (American Association of Petroleum Geologists)

African-American Book Distributors Inc, *subsidiary of* Path Press Inc

African-American Studies, *imprint of* Transaction Publishers

African World Press, *distributor for* A & B Publishers Group

African Writers Series, *imprint of* Heinemann

Africana Publishing Co, *subsidiary of* Holmes & Meier Publishers Inc

Aftershocks Media, *division of* Epicenter Press Inc

Agape, *division of* Hope Publishing Co

Agathon Press, *imprint of* Algora Publishing

Ages Software, *distributed by* Pilgrim Publications

Agora Publications, *distributed by* Philosophy Documentation Center

AGP Publishing, *imprint of* Athletic Guide Publishing

Aguilar, *imprint of* Santillana USA Publishing Co Inc

AHA (American Hospital Association), *imprint of* Health Forum Inc

Aha Communications, *distributed by* Gryphon House Inc

AHA Press, *subsidiary of* Health Forum Inc, *imprint of* Health Forum Inc, *distributor for* American Society for Quality

Ahsahta Press, *distributed by* Small Press Distribution

AIM (American Institute of Musicology), *distributed by* A-R Editions Inc

Keith Ainsworth Pty Ltd, Australia, *distributor for* Interweave Press

AIPH - Association International de Producteurs de l'Horticulture, *distributed by* Ball Publishing

Aircraft of the Aces, *imprint of* Osprey Publishing Ltd

Airlife Books, *distributed by* Stackpole Books

Airlift, *distributor for* Media Associates

Airmont, *distributed by* Perfection Learning Corp

Airphoto International Ltd, *distributed by* W W Norton & Company Inc

AK Press, *distributed by* AK Press Distribution

AK Press Audio, *imprint of* AK Press Distribution

The Akadine Press, *distributed by* Trafalgar Square

Aksant Academic Publishers, *distributed by* Transaction Publishers

AKTRIN Furniture Information Centre, *distributor for* AMA Research, Business & Research Associates

Aladdin Books, *distributed by* Sundance Publishing

Aladdin Paperbacks, *imprint of* Simon & Schuster Children's Publishing

La Alameda Press, *distributed by* University of New Mexico Press

Alamo Square, *distributor for* Rising Tide Press

Alan Wofsy Fine Arts, *distributor for* Bora, Brusberg (Berlin), Cramer (Geneva), Huber, Ides et Calendes, Kornfeld & Co, Picasso Project, Welz, Wittenborn Art Books

Alaska Native Language Center, *division of* University of Alaska Fairbanks

Alaska Northwest Books®, *imprint of* Graphic Arts Center Publishing Co

Alba House, *division of* The Society of St Paul, The Society of St Paul

Albatross Publishing House, *distributed by* W W Norton & Company Inc

Albion Press, *imprint of* Moyer Bell Ltd

Alchemical Press, *imprint of* Holmes Publishing Group

Alemany Press, *imprint of* Pearson Higher Education Division

Alephoe Books/The Poetry Mission, *distributed by* Fordham University Press

The Alexander Graham Bell Association for the Deaf & Hard of Hearing, *distributor for* Delmar Thomson, Temple University Press, Woodbine Press, York Press

Margaret Walker Alexander Series in African American Studies, *imprint of* University Press of Mississippi

Alexander Street Press LLC, *distributor for* Ad Fontes LLC

Alexandria Drafting Co, *distributed by* Trakker Maps Inc

Alexandrian Press, *imprint of* Holmes Publishing Group

Vefa Alexiadou, *distributed by* Howell Press Inc

Alfaguara, *imprint of* Santillana USA Publishing Co Inc

Alfred Publishing Company Inc, *distributor for* Dover, Faber Music, Myklas Music Press, National Guitar Workshop

Algonquin Books of Chapel Hill, *division of* Workman Publishing Co Inc, *distributed by* Workman Publishing Co Inc

ALI-ABA Committee on Continuing Professional Education, *affiliate of* American Bar Association & American Law Institute, American Bar Association & American Law Institute

Alice James Books, *division of* Alice James Poetry Cooperative Inc

Alive Guides, *imprint of* Hunter Publishing Inc

All America Distributors Corp, *distributor for* Holloway House Publishing Co

All-in-One Books, *imprint of* Modern Publishing

Ian Allan, *distributed by* Casemate Publishers

Umberto Allemandi, *distributed by* Antique Collectors Club Ltd

Allen & Unwin, *distributed by* Paul & Company

Allen D Bragdon Publishers Inc, *distributed by* Walker & Co New York

Allen Lane The Penguin Press, *imprint of* Penguin Group (USA) Inc

Allied Health Publications, *division of* California College for Health Sciences

Allmaps, *subsidiary of* Rand McNally

Alloy Entertainment, *division of* Alloy Online, *distributed by* Avon Books, HarperCollins, Hyperion, Little, Brown and Co, Millbrook Press, MTV Books, Penguin Putnam Inc, Pocket Books, Puffin Books, Random House Inc, Scholastic Books, Simon & Schuster

Allworth Press, *distributed by* Brenner Information Group, Watson-Guptill Publications

Allyn & Bacon, *division of* Pearson Education, *imprint of* Pearson Higher Education Division, *distributor for* National Association of Broadcasters (NAB)

Alomega Press, *division of* Alomega Services Inc, Alomega Services Inc

Alpha Books, *imprint of* Penguin Group (USA) Inc

The Alpha Non-Lawyers A-B Trust Kit, *imprint of* ALPHA Publications of America Inc

The Alpha Non-Lawyers Arizona Corporation Kit, *imprint of* ALPHA Publications of America Inc

The Alpha Non-Lawyers Arizona Divorce Kit, *imprint of* ALPHA Publications of America Inc

The Alpha Non-Lawyers Arizona Limited Liability Company Kit, *imprint of* ALPHA Publications of America Inc

The Alpha Non-Lawyers California Divorce Kit, *imprint of* ALPHA Publications of America Inc

The Alpha Non-Lawyers Chapter 7 Bankruptcy Kit, *imprint of* ALPHA Publications of America Inc

The Alpha Non-Lawyers Chapter 13 Bankruptcy Kit, *imprint of* ALPHA Publications of America Inc

The Alpha Non-Lawyers Corporation Kit, *imprint of* ALPHA Publications of America Inc

The Alpha Non-Lawyers Home Sales Kit, *imprint of* ALPHA Publications of America Inc

The Alpha Non-Lawyers Last Will & Testament Kit, *imprint of* ALPHA Publications of America Inc

The Alpha Non-Lawyers Limited Liability Company Kit, *imprint of* ALPHA Publications of America Inc

The Alpha Non-Lawyers Living Trust Kit, *imprint of* ALPHA Publications of America Inc

The Alpha Non-Lawyers Living Will Kit, *imprint of* ALPHA Publications of America Inc

The Alpha Non-Lawyers New Mexico Divorce Kit, *imprint of* ALPHA Publications of America Inc

The Alpha Non-Lawyers Non-Profit Corporation Kit, *imprint of* ALPHA Publications of America Inc

The Alpha Non-Lawyers Partnership Kit, *imprint of* ALPHA Publications of America Inc

The Alpha Non-Lawyers Pre-Marriage Kit, *imprint of* ALPHA Publications of America Inc

ALPHA Publications of America Inc, *affiliate of* Alpha Legal Forms & More

AlphaKids® Guided Readers, *imprint of* Sundance Publishing

AlphaKids® Plus Guided Readers, *imprint of* Sundance Publishing

ALPS Publishing, *distributor for* Pieces of Learning

Alta Book Center, *distributor for* Teachers of English to Speakers of Other Languages Inc (TESOL)

AltaMira Press, *division of* Rowman & Littlefield Publishers Inc, *distributor for* American Association for State & Local History, *distributed by* National Book Network/University Press of America

Althos Publishing, *distributor for* John-Wiley, McGraw-Hill, *distributed by* TMC/Internet Telephony, USTA

Alva Press, *imprint of* Book Sales Inc

Alvin House, *imprint of* A & B Publishers Group

Alyson Books, *imprint of* Alyson Publications

Alyson Publications, *division of* LPI Media

Alyson Wonderland, *imprint of* Alyson Publications

Am Yisroel Chai Press, *distributed by* Philipp Feldheim Inc

AMA, *distributed by* Mel Bay Publications Inc

AMA Research, *distributed by* AKTRIN Furniture Information Centre

AMACOM Books, *division of* American Management Association, American Management Association (AMA), *distributed by* McGraw-Hill International

Amacom Division of American Management Division, *distributor for* J J Keller & Associates, Inc

Amacon, *distributed by* SAS Publishing

Amadeus Press, *distributed by* Hal Leonard Corp

Frank Amato Publications Inc, *distributed by* Anglers Book Supply, Intersports, Partners

Amazon.com, *distributor for* AVKO Dyslexia & Spelling Research Foundation Inc, Book World Inc/Blue Star Productions, Brenner Information Group, Center for East Asian Studies (CEAS), Educational Impressions Inc, Essence of Vermont, Excalibur Publications, G W Medical Publishing Inc, Investor Responsibility Research Center, Leadership Publishers Inc, Noble Publishing Corp, Paladin Press, Rising Tide Press, SynergEbooks, Time Being Books, TSG Publishing Foundation Inc, University of California Institute on Global Conflict & Cooperation, Wordtree branching dictionary

Ambassador Books, *distributor for* Primary Research Group

Ambassador-Emerald, *distributed by* Pilgrim Publications

Amber-Allen Publishing, *imprint of* New World Library

Amber Books, *distributed by* Casemate Publishers

Amber Heat, *imprint of* Amber Quill Press LLC

Amber Kisses, *imprint of* Amber Quill Press LLC

America House, *imprint of* PublishAmerica

America West Publishers, *subsidiary of* Global Insights Inc

American Academy for Park & Recreation Admin, *distributed by* Sagamore Publishing LLC

American Academy of Environmental Engineers, *distributor for* The ABS Group, CRC Press, McGraw-Hill, Pearson Education, Prentice Hall, John Wiley & Sons Inc

American Academy of Family Physicians, *distributor for* Medical Group Management Association

American Academy of Orthopaedic Surgeons, *distributed by* Jones & Bartlett Publishers

American Adventure, *imprint of* Barbour Publishing Inc

American Aeronautical Archives, *imprint of* Possibility Press

American Alpine Club Press, *distributed by* The Mountaineers Books

The American Alpine Club Press, *division of* The American Alpine Club, *distributed by* Mountaineers Books

American Antiquarian Society, *distributed by* Oak Knoll Press

American Association for State & Local History, *distributed by* AltaMira Press

American Association for Vocational Instructional Materials, *distributor for* Southeastern Cooperative Wildlife Disease Study

American Association of Blood Banks, *distributed by* Karger, Login Brothers

American Association of Community Colleges (AACC), *distributor for* ITC, Jossey-Bass Inc, Publishers, Oryx Press, Random House, RTS

American Astronautical Society, *imprint of* Univelt Inc

American Atheist Press, *affiliate of* Charles E Stevens American Atheist Library & Archives Inc, Charles E Stevens American Atheist Library & Archives Inc

American Biographical History Series, *imprint of* Harlan Davidson Inc/Forum Press Inc

American Biographical Institute, *division of* Historical Preservations of America Inc, Historical Preservations of America Inc

American Book Business Press, *imprint of* American Book Publishing

American Book Classics, *imprint of* American Book Publishing

American Ceramic Society (ACerS), *distributor for* American Society for Nondestructive Testing

The American Chemical Society, *distributor for* Royal Society of Chemistry, *distributed by* Oxford University Press, Oxford University Press, Inc

American College of Healthcare Executives Management Series, *imprint of* Health Administration Press

American College of Physician Executives, *distributor for* American Hospital Publishing Inc, Aspen Publishers, Jossey Bass, Boland Healthcare, Capitol Publications, Hatherleigh Co, Health Administration Press, *distributed by* American Hospital Publishing Inc, Jossey Bass, Health Administration Press

American College of Surgeons, *distributed by* Cine-Med, Inc, Scientific American Medicine

American Council for an Energy Efficient Economy (ACEEE), *distributed by* Chelsea Green Publishing Co

American Council on Education, *distributed by* Greenwood

American Counseling Association, *distributor for* American School Counseling Association, Association for Assessment in Counseling & Education, Association for Counselor Education & Supervision, Association for Spiritual, Ethical & Religious Values in Counseling, National Career Development Association, *distributed by* Book Clubs Inc (Behavioral Sciences), Counseling Outfitters, JIST Works Inc, Mental Health Resources, Paperbacks for Educators, Self-Esteem Shop, Social Sciences School Services

American Demographics, *distributed by* American Marketing Association

American Diabetes Association, *distributed by* McGraw-Hill

American Dust Publications Inc, *distributed by* Dustbooks

American Eagle Publications Inc, *distributor for* Lexington & Concord Partners Ltd, Panama

American Express, *distributed by* Sterling Publishing Co Inc

American Federation of Arts, *distributed by* Abbeville Press, Harry N Abrams Inc, Distributed Art Publishers, Hudson Hills Press Inc, Scala Publishers, University of Washington Press

American Foundation for the Blind (AFB Press), *distributed by* RNIB National Education Services

American Geological Institute (AGI), *distributed by* W H Freeman, It's About Time Inc, Prentice Hall

American Girl Library®, *imprint of* Pleasant Company Publications

The American Girls Collection®, *imprint of* Pleasant Company Publications

American Guidance Service, *distributor for* A D D Warehouse, *distributed by* Psychological Assessment Resources Inc (PAR), Random House Inc

American Guidance Service (AGS), *distributor for* Chronicle Guidance Publications Inc

American Health Publishing Co, *affiliate of* Learn®-The LifeStyle Co, Learn®-The Lifestyle Company

American Heritage Dictionary, *imprint of* Houghton Mifflin Trade & Reference Division

American History Press, *division of* Northwoods Press, *distributed by* Northwoods Press

American History Series, *imprint of* Harlan Davidson Inc/Forum Press Inc

American Hospital Publishing Inc, *distributor for* American College of Physician Executives, *distributed by* American College of Physician Executives

American Indian Studies Center Publications at UCLA, *division of* University of California, Los Angeles, *distributor for* Gale Research, *distributed by* Blackwell

American Institute of Certified Public Accountants, *distributed by* Practitioners Publishing Co

American Institute of Chemical Engineers (AICHE), *distributor for* ASM International (selected titles), Dechema (selected titles), Engineering Foundation, IchemE (selected titles), *distributed by* Dechema (selected titles)

American Institute of Physics, *distributed by* Springer-Verlag

American Institute of Physics (AIP), *distributor for* The Electrochemical Society Inc

American Journal of Economics & Sociology, *subsidiary of* Robert Schalkenbach Foundation

American Library Preview, *division of* Gareth Stevens Inc

American Made Music Series, *imprint of* University Press of Mississippi

American Map Corp, *division of* Langenscheidt Publishers Inc, *subsidiary of* Langenscheidt Publishers Inc, Langenscheidt Publishing Group, *imprint of* Trakker Maps Inc, *distributor for* DeLorme Atlas, Langenscheidt Publishers Inc, RV Guides, Stubs Magazine, *distributed by* Arrow Maps Inc, Creative Sales Corp, Hagstrom Map Co Inc

American Maritain Association, *distributed by* The Catholic University of America Press

American Maritime Library, *imprint of* Mystic Seaport

American Marketing Association, *division of* Health Services Marketing Div, *distributor for* American Demographics, CRC Press, The Free Press, Irwin Professional Publications, Jossey-Bass, McGraw-Hill, New Strategist, Kogan Page, Paramount Books, RACOM, Thomson Learning, John Wiley & Sons, *distributed by* NTC Business Books

American Mathematical Society, *distributor for* Annales de la faculte des sciences de Toulouse mathematiques, Bar-Ilan University, Brown University, European Mathematical Society, Hindustan Book Agency, Independent University of Moscow, International Press, Mathematica Josephina, Mathematical Society of Japan, Narosa Publishing House, Ramanujan Mathematical Society, Science Press New York & Science Press Beijing, Societe Mathematique de France, Tata Institute of Fundamental Research, Theta Foundation of Bucharest, University Press, Vieweg Verlag Publications

American Medical Association, *distributor for* G W Medical Publishing Inc, Ingenix Inc, *distributed by* AANS-American Association of Neurological Surgeons, Ingenix Inc, Random House Sales & Marketing

American Numismatic Society, *distributed by* David Brown Books, Sanford J Durst

American Nurserymen, *distributor for* Ball Publishing

American Phytopathological Society, *distributed by* Ball Publishing

American Poetry Review/Honickman, *distributed by* Copper Canyon Press

American Press, *subsidiary of* American Magazine

American Products Publishing Co, *division of* American Products Corp

American Psychiatric Association, *distributed by* American Psychiatric Publishing Inc

American Psychiatric Publishing Inc, *subsidiary of* American Psychiatric Association, *distributor for* American Psychiatric Association, Group for the Advancement of Psychiatry

American Psychology Press, *distributor for* Current Medicine

American Quilter's Society, *subsidiary of* Schroeder Publishing Co Inc, Schroeder Publishing Co Inc, *distributor for* C & T Publishing, Patchwork Place Publishers, Sterling Publishers

American Research Press, *division of* Erhus University Press, *subsidiary of* Xiquan Publishing House

American School Counseling Association, *distributed by* American Counseling Association

American School Publishers, *imprint of* McGraw-Hill Learning Group

The American Sciences Press Series in Mathematical & Management Sciences, *imprint of* American Sciences Press Inc

American Society for Mechanical Engineers (ASME), *distributor for* American Society for Nondestructive Testing

American Society for Metals (ASM), *distributor for* American Society for Nondestructive Testing

American Society for Nondestructive Testing, *distributed by* American Ceramic Society (ACerS), American Society for Mechanical Engineers (ASME), American Society for Metals (ASM), The American Welding Society (AWS), ASTM, Edison Welding Institute, Mean Free Path

American Society for Photogrammetry & Remote Sensing, *distributor for* International Geographic Information Foundation, Taylor & Francis, Thomasson Grant, University of Chicago Press, US Geological Survey, Van Nostrand Reinhold, Whittles Publishing, John Wiley & Sons Inc, *distributed by* RICS, Space Publication

American Society for Quality, *unit of* American Society for Quality (ASQ), American Society for Quality (ASQ), *distributed by* AHA Press,

GOAL/QPC, IEEE Computer Society Press, McGraw-Hill Professional Publishing, Productivity Press

American Society for Training & Development (ASTD), *distributor for* Jossey Bass, Berrett-Kohler, McGraw-Hill, Random House Inc

American Society of Association Executives, *distributor for* BoardSource

American Society of Civil Engineers (ASCE), *distributor for* Institution of Civil Engineers (UK), Thomas Telford (UK)

American Society of Mechanical Engineers (ASME), *distributor for* Professional Engineering Publishing

American String Teachers Association, *distributed by* MENC - The National Association for Music Education

American Studies, *imprint of* Transaction Publishers

American Technical Publishers, *distributor for* Craftsman Book Co, Society of Manufacturing Engineers, Technical Association of the Pulp & Paper Industry (TAPPI)

American Technical Publishers Inc, *distributor for* Craftsman Book Co

American Trust Publications, *affiliate of* North American Islamic Trust

American University & Colleges Press, *imprint of* American Book Publishing

American University of Beirut, *distributed by* Syracuse University Press

American Water Works Association, *distributor for* Fulcrum, McGraw-Hill, Prentice-Hall, Technomic, WaterPlow Press™, John Wiley & Sons

The American Welding Society (AWS), *distributor for* American Society for Nondestructive Testing

American West Books, *distributor for* Sierra Press

AmericanKids Preview, *division of* Gareth Stevens Inc

America's Best Comics, *imprint of* DC Comics

The Americas Review, *subsidiary of* Arte Publico Press

The Americas Society, *distributed by* St Joseph's University Press

Amerotica, *imprint of* NBM Publishing Inc

AMES (automotive), *distributed by* Graphic Arts Center Publishing Co

Amherst Media, *distributor for* Marathon Press

Amherst Media Inc, *distributor for* Firefly

Amirah Publishing, *affiliate of* IBTS, *distributed by* IBTS

Amistad, *imprint of* HarperCollins Children's Books Group, HarperCollins General Books Group, HarperCollins Publishers Sales

Amon Carter Museum, *distributed by* Abrams & University of Washington Press, The University of Arizona Press

Amphoto, *imprint of* Watson-Guptill Publications

AMS, *distributor for* International Press of Boston Inc

The Amwell Press, *subsidiary of* National Sporting Fraternity Ltd, National Sporting Fraternity Ltd

Anacus Press, *imprint of* Finney Co

The Analytic Press, *division of* Lawrence Erlbaum Associates Inc, Lawrence Erlbaum Associates Inc, *distributor for* Gestalt Institute of Cleveland Press, *distributed by* Lawrence Erlbaum Associates Inc

Ancestry Publishing, *imprint of* MyFamily.com Inc

Anchor Bay Entertainment, *distributor for* Bridge Publications Inc

The Anchor Bible, *imprint of* Doubleday Broadway Publishing Group

Anchor Bible Commentary, *imprint of* Random House Inc

Anchor Bible Dictionary, *imprint of* Random House Inc

Anchor Bible Reference Library, *imprint of* Random House Inc

Anchor Books, *imprint of* Doubleday Broadway Publishing Group, Random House Inc

Anchor Distributors, *distributor for* Bridge-Logos Publishers

Ancient City Press, *distributed by* University of New Mexico Press

And/Or Books, *imprint of* Ronin Publishing Inc

Anderson, *distributed by* Police Executive Research Forum

Anderson Northstar Editions, *imprint of* Lynx House Press

Andrews McMeel Publishing, *division of* Andrews McMeel Universal, *distributor for* Carlton Books, Diamond Select, Melcher Media, National Geographic Calendars, Michael O'Mara Books (North America only), Signatures Network, Sporting News, Universe Publishing Calendars, Welcome Books, *distributed by* Simon & Schuster Inc

Andrews University Press, *division of* Andrews University, *distributed by* Pacific Press Publishing, Review & Herald Publishing

Angel Books, *distributed by* Dufour Editions Inc

Angelus Press, *distributed by* Catholic Treasures, Fatima Crusader

Angler's Book Supply, *distributor for* Wilderness Adventures Press Inc

Anglers Book Supply, *distributor for* Frank Amato Publications Inc

Anglican Book Centre, *distributed by* Forward Movement Publications

Anhinga Press, *distributed by* Small Press Distribution

Ann Arbor Paperbacks, *imprint of* University of Michigan Press

Annales de la faculte des sciences de Toulouse mathematiques, *distributed by* American Mathematical Society

Anness Publishing Inc: Hermes House, Lorenz Books, *distributed by* Random House Inc

Annick Press, *distributed by* Perfection Learning Corp

Anthem Press, *distributed by* Stylus Publishing LLC

Anthropology, *imprint of* Transaction Publishers

Anthropos Publishers, *distributed by* Lake View Press

Antique Collectors Club, *distributor for* The Colonial Williamsburg Foundation

Antique Collector's Club (ACC), *distributor for* Philadelphia Museum of Art

Antique Collectors Club Ltd, *division of* Antique Collectors Club Ltd (England), Antique Collectors Club Ltd (England), *distributor for* Acatos, Adler Planetarium & Astronomy, Umberto Allemandi, Architectura & Natura, Arnoldsche, Arsenale Editrice, Art Price.com, Wadsworth Athenaeum, Bard Graduate Center, Barn Elms Publishing, Beagle Press, Chris Beetles Ltd, Benteli Verlag, Birmingham Museum of Art, Brioni Books, British Museum Press, Canal & Stamperia, Cartago, Colonial Williamsburg, Colophon, Colwood Press Ltd, The William G Congdon Foundation, Conran Octopus, Currier Publications, Alain De Gourcuff Editeur, M H De Young Memorial Museum, Richard Dennis, Detroit Institute of Arts, Editions Vasour, Editoriale Jaca Book, Edizione Press, Elvehjem Museum of Art, Gambero Rosso, Grayson Publishing, Hachette Livre, Robert Hale, Han-Shan Tang Books, Alan Hartman, High Museum of Art, Images Publications, India Book House Ltd, Frances Lincoln, Loft Publications, Lowry Press, Mapin, Marshall Editions, Merrick & Day, Museum of American Folk Art, National Galleries of Scotland, National Portrait Gallery, The National Trust, New Architecture Group Ltd, New Cavendish Books Ltd, Newark Museum, Packard Publishing, Peabody Essex Museum, Philadelphia Museum of Art, River Books Co Ltd, Michael Russell, Saigo Trust, Scala Publishers, Superbrands Ltd, Third Millenium Publishing, Ursus Books, Wallace Collection, Watermark Press, Websters International Publishers, Philip Wilson Publishers

Antique Collectors' Club Ltd, *distributor for* George Braziller Inc, *distributed by* Ball Publishing

Antique Trader Books, *division of* Krause Publications, *imprint of* Krause Publications, *distributed by* Krause Publications

Anvil Books (Dublin) & The Children's Press, *distributed by* Dufour Editions Inc

Anvil Series, *imprint of* Krieger Publishing Co

AOCS Press, *division of* American Oil Chemists' Society, *distributor for* The Oily Press

Aonian Press, *imprint of* James A Rock & Co Publishers

AP Natural World, *imprint of* Academic Press

Aperture, *distributed by* Farrar, Straus & Giroux, LLC, Graywolf Press

Aperture Books, *division of* Aperture Foundation Inc, *distributed by* Farrar, Straus & Giroux Inc

Aperture Monographs, *imprint of* Aperture Books

The Apex Press, *affiliate of* The Council on International & Public Affairs, *distributor for* Bootstrap Press (US), The Labor Institute, The Other India Press (India), Zed Books (London), *distributed by* Jon Carpenter Publishing (UK), IT Pubs (London), Zed Books (London)

Appalachian, *distributor for* College Press Publishing Co, Faith Library Publications

Appalachian Bible, *distributor for* Bridge-Logos Publishers

Appalachian Bible Co Inc, *distributor for* Bob Jones University Press

Appalachian Dist, *distributor for* Evangel Publishing House

Appalachian Distributors, *distributor for* Christian Liberty Press, NewLife Publications

Appalachian Mountain Club, *distributed by* The Globe Pequot Press

Appalachian Mountain Club Books, *division of* Appalachian Mountain Club, *distributed by* The Globe Pequot Press

Applause Theatre & Cinema Books, *distributed by* Hal Leonard Corp, Hal Leonard Corp

Appleseed Audio, *imprint of* Listen & Live Audio Inc

J Appleseed & Co, *distributed by* Swedenborg Foundation Publishers/Chrysalis Books

Appleton Davies, *imprint of* Davies Publishing Inc

Appleton Lange, *distributor for* Current Medicine

Applewood Books, *distributor for* Lost Classics Book Co

Appraisal Institute, *distributed by* Dearborn Trade

APS Press, *imprint of* American Phytopathological Society, The American Phytopathological Society

AQS, *imprint of* American Quilter's Society

Aqua Quest Publications Inc, *distributor for* J L Publications

Aquamarin, *imprint of* Amber Lotus

Arba Sicula, *distributed by* Cross-Cultural Communications

ARC (Magazine & Press), *imprint of* Cross-Cultural Communications

Arcade Publishing, *distributed by* Time Warner Book Group

Arcade Publishing Inc, *distributed by* Time Warner Book Group

Arcadia Enterprises Inc, *distributor for* Dogwood Ridge Books, Tapestry Press Ltd

Arcadia Publishing, *imprint of* Tempus Publishing Group

Arcana Publishing, *imprint of* Lotus Press

ArcheBooks Publishing, *division of* Gelinas & Wolf Inc

Archetype (UK), *distributed by* Fons Vitae

Archhunter Publications, *distributor for* Canyon Country Publications

Architectura & Natura, *distributed by* Antique Collectors Club Ltd

Archival, *distributed by* Donald M Grant Publisher Inc

Archival Publications International, *distributed by* Ross Publishing Inc

Archives Press, *imprint of* Media Associates

Archon Books, *imprint of* The Shoe String Press Inc

Archway, *distributed by* Perfection Learning Corp

Arco Iris Internacional, *division of* Rainbow Studies International

Ardent Media Inc, *distributor for* Cyrco Press, MSS Information Corp

ARE Press, *division of* The Association for Research & Enlightenment Inc (ARE), The Association for Research & Enlightenment Inc (ARE)

Ares Publishing Co, *distributed by* Sanford J Durst

Ariel Press, *subsidiary of* Light, *distributor for* Enthea, Kudzu House

The Arion Press, *division of* Lyra Corp, Lyra Corp

Arizona Highways, *distributed by* Wide World of Maps Inc

Arizona State Museum, *distributed by* The University of Arizona Press

Arkangel, *distributed by* Penguin Group (USA) Inc, Putnam Berkley Audio

Arkangel Complete Shakespeare, *distributed by* Penguin Audiobooks

Arkangel Shakespeare, *imprint of* Penguin Audiobooks

Arkive.com, *imprint of* Media Associates

Arkives Books, *imprint of* Media Associates

Armenian Genocide-Bibliography, *imprint of* Armenian Reference Books Co

Armenian Reference Books, *imprint of* Armenian Reference Books Co

Armenian Wisdom, *imprint of* Armenian Reference Books Co

Armenian Yellow Pages, *imprint of* Armenian Reference Books Co

The Armenians, *imprint of* Armenian Reference Books Co

Armenians & Iran, *imprint of* Armenian Reference Books Co

Eric Armin Inc Education Ctr, *distributor for* National Council of Teachers of Mathematics

Arms & Armour Press, *distributed by* Casemate Publishers

The Army War College Foundation Press, *distributed by* Stackpole Books

Arnica Publishing Inc, *distributor for* New Leaf

Arno Press, *imprint of* Ayer Company, Publishers Inc

Arnoldsche, *distributed by* Antique Collectors Club Ltd

ARO Publishing, *distributed by* Forest House Publishing Co Inc & HTS Books

Jason Aronson Inc, *imprint of* Rowman & Littlefield Publishing Group

Arris Publishing, *distributed by* Casemate Publishers

Arrow Map, *division of* Langenscheidt Publishers Inc, *imprint of* Langenscheidt Publishers Inc

Arrow Map Inc, *affiliate of* Langenscheidt Publishers Inc

Arrow Maps Inc, *subsidiary of* American Map Corp, *distributor for* American Map Corp, *distributed by* Hagstrom Map Co Inc, Trakker Maps Inc

Arroyo Books, *distributor for* Fondo de Cultura Economica USA Inc

Arsenale Editrice, *distributed by* Antique Collectors Club Ltd

Art Global, *distributed by* Howell Press Inc

Art Image Publications, *division of* GB Publishing Inc

Art Institute of Chicago, *distributed by* Abbeville Publishing Group, Harry N Abrams Inc, Bulfinch Press, Chronicle Books, Distributed Art Publishers (DAP), Ernst & Sohn, Editorial Gustavo Gili SA, Grupo Azabache, Hudson Hills Press Inc, Dorling Kindersley Ltd, LTI (Learn Technologies Interactive), Ars Nicolai (Great Britain Scandinavia & Europe, Prestel-Verlag, Princeton Univ Press, Rizzoli International Publications Inc, Thames & Hudson, Thames & Hudson (UK), University of Chicago Press, University of Indiana Press, University of Washington Press, Ernst Wasmuth Verlag

Art Media Resources Inc, *distributor for* Serindia Publications

Art Price.com, *distributed by* Antique Collectors Club Ltd

Art Sales Index, *distributed by* Dealer's Choice Books Inc

Art Scroll Series, *imprint of* Mesorah Publications Ltd

art-SITES, *distributed by* University of California Press

Art Treasures, *imprint of* Branden Publishing Co Inc

Artabras, *imprint of* Abbeville Publishing Group, Artabras Inc

Artabras Inc, *division of* Abbeville Publishing Group

Arte Publico Press, *affiliate of* University of Houston, *distributor for* Bilingual Review Press, Latin American Review Press, *distributed by* Empire Publishing Service

Artech House Inc, *subsidiary of* Horizon House Publications Inc, Horizon House Publications Inc

Arthur A Levine Books, *imprint of* Scholastic Trade Division

Artisan, *division of* Workman Publishing Co Inc, Workman Publishing Company Inc, *distributor for* Greenwich Workshop Press

Artistpro, *distributed by* Hal Leonard Corp

ArtPrice.com, *distributed by* Dealer's Choice Books Inc

Arts End Books, *distributor for* The Smith Publishers

ArtWorks, *imprint of* MFA Publications

ASAE, *distributed by* Water Resources Publications LLC

Francis Asbury Press, *imprint of* Evangel Publishing House

ASCA, *distributor for* MAR*CO Products Inc

ASCE, *distributed by* Water Resources Publications LLC

Ascension Press, *member of* Catholic Word

ASCP Press, *subsidiary of* American Society for Clinical Pathology

Ashgate, *imprint of* Ashgate Publishing Co, *distributed by* William S Hein & Co Inc

Ashgate Publishing Co, *subsidiary of* Ashgate Publishing Ltd, *distributor for* A A Balkema Publishers, Gower Publishing, Gregg, Lund Humphries, Pickering & Chatto, Swets & Zeitlinger Publishers, *distributed by* Synapse Information Resources Inc

Ashland Poetry Press, *affiliate of* Ashland University

Ashley Music, *distributed by* Hal Leonard Corp

Ashrama, *distributed by* Vedanta Press

Asian American Writers Workshop, *distributed by* Temple University Press

Asian Development Bank, *distributed by* Paul & Company

Asian Humanities Press, *imprint of* Jain Publishing Co

Asian Studies, *imprint of* Transaction Publishers

AsiaPac, *distributed by* China Books & Periodicals Inc

ASL, *distributed by* Copywriter's Council of America (CCA)

Aslan Publishing, *subsidiary of* Renaissance Book Services Corp

ASM International, *distributed by* NACE International

ASM International (selected titles), *distributed by* American Institute of Chemical Engineers (AICHE), Metal Powder Industries Federation

ASM Press, *division of* American Society for Microbiology

ASME, *distributor for* Society of Manufacturing Engineers

ASME Press, *imprint of* American Society of Mechanical Engineers (ASME)

Aspatore Business Reviews, *imprint of* Aspatore Books

Aspect, *imprint of* Time Warner Book Group, Warner Books

Aspen, *distributed by* Abbott, Langer & Associates, William S Hein & Co Inc

Aspen Institute, *distributed by* The Brookings Institution Press

Aspen Publishers, *distributed by* American College of Physician Executives, Medical Group Management Association

Aspen Publishers Inc, *imprint of* Wolters Kluwer US Corp

Asphodel Press, *imprint of* Moyer Bell Ltd, *distributed by* Moyer Bell Ltd

Aspire, *distributed by* Thomson Delmar Learning

Assembly of Western European Union, *distributed by* Manhattan Publishing Co

Associated Publisher's Group, *distributed by* Sundance Publishing

Associated Publishers Group, *distributor for* Celebrity Press, Ideals Publications Inc

Associated University Presses, *distributor for* Balch Institute Press, Bucknell University Press, Fairleigh Dickinson University Press, Herzl Press, Lehigh University Press, Susquehanna University Press, University of Delaware Press

Association for Assessment in Counseling & Education, *distributed by* American Counseling Association

Association for Counselor Education & Supervision, *distributed by* American Counseling Association

Association for Gravestone Studies, *distributed by* Center for Thanatology Research & Education Inc

Association for Spiritual, Ethical & Religious Values in Counseling, *distributed by* American Counseling Association

Association for Symbolic Logic, *distributed by* A K Peters Ltd

Association of American University Presses, *distributor for* Canadian Museum of Nature, Conservation International, National Bureau of Economic Research, National Gallery of Canada, National Society for the Study of Education, Oriental Institute

Association of College & Research Libraries, *division of* American Library Association, American Library Association (ALA)

ASTD Press, *imprint of* American Society for Training & Development (ASTD)

ASTM, *distributor for* American Society for Nondestructive Testing, *distributed by* NACE International

Astronautical Society of Western Australia, *distributed by* Univelt Inc

ASVP, *imprint of* Elsevier

At a Glance, *distributor for* Jim Henson Publishing/Muppet Press

Ateneo De Manila University Press, *distributed by* University of Hawaii Press

Athena Books Trade Paperbacks, *imprint of* Paragon House

Wadsworth Athenaeum, *distributed by* Antique Collectors Club Ltd

Atheneum, *distributed by* Perfection Learning Corp

Atheneum Books for Young Readers, *imprint of* Simon & Schuster Children's Publishing

Athletic Press, *imprint of* Golden West Books

Atlantic Boating Almanac, *imprint of* ProStar Publications Inc

Atlantic Council, *distributed by* University Press of America Inc

Atlantic Law Book Co, *division of* Peter Kelsey Publishing Inc, Peter Kelsey Publishing Inc

Atlantic Monthly Press, *imprint of* Grove/Atlantic Inc

Atlantic University, *division of* ARE Press

Atlantis Productions, *distributed by* Denlinger's Publishers Ltd

Atlas Games, *imprint of* Trident Inc

AtRandom.com, *imprint of* Random House Inc

Atria, *imprint of* Simon & Schuster Adult Publishing Group

Atria Books, *imprint of* Simon & Schuster

AttaGirl Press, *imprint of* Damron Co

Attainment, *distributed by* Training Resource Network Inc (T R N)

Attic/Atrium, *distributed by* Dufour Editions Inc

@tlas®, *imprint of* VanDam Inc

Auckland U Press, *distributed by* Paul & Company

Audel™, *imprint of* John Wiley & Sons Inc

Audio Adventures, *subsidiary of* Haights Cross Communications Inc, *imprint of* Haights Cross Communications Inc

Audio Books, *division of* Unarius Academy of Science Publications

Audio-Forum, *division of* Jeffrey Norton Publishers Inc, *imprint of* Jeffrey Norton Publishers Inc

Audio Literature, *subsidiary of* Ten Speed Press, *distributed by* Ten Speed Press

Audio Renaissance, *division of* Holtzbrinck Publishers Holdings LLC, Holtzbrinck Publishers Holdings LLC, *distributor for* Highroads Audio

Audio Renaissance Tapes, *distributed by* St Martin's Press LLC

AUDIOWORKS, *imprint of* Simon & Schuster Audio

Auerbach Publications, *imprint of* Warren, Gorham & Lamont

Augsburg Books, *imprint of* Augsburg Fortress Publishers, Publishing House of the Evangelical Lutheran Church in America

August House Audio, *imprint of* August House Publishers Inc

August House LittleFolk, *imprint of* August House Publishers Inc

August House Publishers Inc, *distributor for* High Windy Audio

AUPHA Press/Health Administration Press, *imprint of* Health Administration Press

Aura Imaging, *imprint of* Blue Dolphin Publishing Inc

Aurora Metro Publications, *distributed by* Theatre Communications Group Inc

Aurora Press, *distributed by* Paul & Company

Aurum Press, *distributed by* Trafalgar Square

Australasian Corrosion Association, *distributor for* NACE International

Australian Institute of Criminology, *distributed by* Criminal Justice Press

Author & Artist Series, *imprint of* University Press of Mississippi

Autodata, *distributed by* Thomson Delmar Learning

Autodesk Press, *imprint of* Thomson Delmar Learning

AVA Publishing, *distributed by* Sterling Publishing Co Inc

Avalon Books, *imprint of* Thomas Bouregy & Co Inc

Avalon Travel Publishing, *imprint of* Avalon Publishing Group - California, Avalon Publishing Group Inc

Avant-Guide, *imprint of* Empire Press Media/Avant-Guide

Avanti, *imprint of* Holloway House Publishing Co, *distributed by* Holloway House Publishing Co

Ave Maria Press, *distributor for* Christian Classics, Forest of Peace, Thomas More, Sorin Books, SunCreek Books

Avery, *imprint of* Penguin Group (USA) Inc, Penguin Group (USA) Inc, The Putnam Publishing Group

Avery Color Studios, *distributed by* Partners Book Distributing

Avesta Fiction Series, *imprint of* Concourse Press

Aviation Elite Units, *imprint of* Osprey Publishing Ltd

Avid Reader Press, *division of* VWI Corp

AVKO Dyslexia & Spelling Research Foundation Inc, *distributed by* Amazon.com, The Distributors

Avon, *imprint of* HarperCollins Children's Books Group, HarperCollins General Books Group, *distributed by* Sundance Publishing

Avon Books, *imprint of* HarperCollins Publishers Sales, *distributor for* Alloy Entertainment

AWS, *distributed by* NACE International

AWWA, *imprint of* American Water Works Association

AWWA Research Foundation, *imprint of* American Water Works Association

Azure Green, *distributor for* Original Publications

B & H Pub, *imprint of* Broadman & Holman Publishers

B & J Publications, *distributed by* Yucca Tree Press

B H B International, *division of* Weatherhill Inc

Back Bay Books, *imprint of* Little, Brown and Company Adult Trade Division

Back Stage Books, *imprint of* Watson-Guptill Publications

Back to Eden Books, *distributed by* Lotus Press

Backbeat Books, *division of* CMP Media LLC, *imprint of* United Entertainment Media, *distributed by* Hal Leonard Corp

Backcountry Guides, *imprint of* The Countryman Press

Backcountry Publications, *imprint of* W W Norton & Company Inc

BADM Books, *distributed by* Father & Son Publishing

Baedeker's Guides, *distributor for* Fodor's Travel Publications, *distributed by* Fodor's Travel Publications

Baen Books, *distributed by* Simon & Schuster Inc

Baen Publishing Enterprises, *distributed by* Simon & Schuster

Baha'i Distribution Service, *distributor for* Kalimat Press

Bahai Distribution Service, *distributor for* Naturegraph Publishers Inc

Baha'i Publishing, *imprint of* Baha'i Publishing Trust

Baha'i Publishing Trust, *subsidiary of* The National Spiritual Assembly of the Baha'is of the United States, *imprint of* Baha'i Publishing Trust

Bailliere-Tindall (UK), *distributed by* W B Saunders Ltd

BainBridgeBooks, *imprint of* Trans-Atlantic Publications Inc

Duncan Baird, *distributed by* Trafalgar Square

Baker & Taylor, *distributor for* Rising Tide Press

Baker & Taylor Books, *distributor for* Bancroft-Sage Publishing

Baker Books, *division of* Baker Publishing Group, *distributor for* Focus on the Family, *distributed by* Perfection Learning Corp

Baker Bytes, *imprint of* Baker Books

Baker's Plays, *division of* Samuel French Inc, *distributed by* Samuel French Inc

Balboa Books, *imprint of* Tiare Publications

Balch Institute Press, *distributed by* Associated University Presses

Balcony Press, *distributed by* Princeton Architectural Press

Baldar (computer programming books & electronic media), *imprint of* Ross Books

A A Balkema Publishers, *distributed by* Ashgate Publishing Co

Ball Publishing, *division of* Ball Horticultural Co, *distributor for* AIPH - Association International de Producteurs de l'Horticulture, American Phytopathological Society, Antique Collectors' Club Ltd, DK Publishing Inc, Paul Ecke Ranch, Erdiciones de Horticultura SL,

Flora Publications International Pty Ltd, Growers Press Inc, Harcourt Brace & Co and Subsidiaries, HortiTecnia, International Flower Bulb Centre, IPC Plant, ITP Educational Division - Intl Thomas Publishing, NSW Agriculture, Palmer Publications Inc, Pathfast Publishing, Prentice Hall, The Reference Publishing Co, Seven Hills Book Distributors, Smithmark Publishers, A Division of US Media Holding Inc, Stipes Publishing LLC, Thomson Publications, Timber Press Inc, Truett Software Development, University of Connecticut, John Wiley & Sons Inc, Woodbridge Press, *distributed by* American Nurserymen

Ballantine, *distributed by* Perfection Learning Corp

Ballantine Books, *imprint of* Random House Inc, Random House Publishing Group, *distributed by* Sundance Publishing

Ballantine Wellspring, *imprint of* Random House Inc

Ballinger Publishing Co, *distributor for* National Bureau of Economic Research Inc

Balsam Abrams, *distributed by* Mystic Seaport

The Baltimore Sun, *division of* The Tribune Co, Tribune Co

Bamboo Grove, *distributed by* Action Publishing LLC

Bancroft-Sage Publishing, *imprint of* The Finney Co, *distributed by* Baker & Taylor Books, Follett Library Resources

Bandanna Books, *division of* Sabine Design, *affiliate of* Sabine Design

Bandanna College classics, *imprint of* Bandanna Books

Bandit Books, *distributed by* John F Blair Publisher

Banks Channel Books, *distributed by* John F Blair Publisher

Banner Books, *imprint of* University Press of Mississippi

Bantam, *distributor for* Parachute Publishing LLC, *distributed by* A D D Warehouse, Perfection Learning Corp, Sundance Publishing

Bantam Books, *imprint of* Bantam Dell Publishing Group, Random House Inc

Bantam Classics, *imprint of* Bantam Dell Publishing Group

Bantam Dell Publishing Group, *division of* Random House Inc

Bantam Hardcover, *imprint of* Random House Inc

Bantam Mass Market, *imprint of* Random House Inc

Bantam Skylark, *imprint of* Random House Inc

Bantam Starfire, *imprint of* Random House Inc

Bantam Trade Paperback, *imprint of* Random House Inc

Banyan Tree, *distributor for* Rising Tide Press

Baptist Spanish Publishing House (d/b/a Casa Bautista de Publicaciones), *affiliate of* Southern Baptist Convention, *distributed by* LifeWay Christian Resources

Bar Ilan, *distributed by* Gefen Books

Bar-Ilan University, *distributed by* American Mathematical Society

Bar-Ilan University Press, *distributed by* Sepher-Hermon Press

Barba-Cue Specials, *imprint of* Harian Creative Books

Barbary Coast Books, *subsidiary of* Berkeley Slavic Specialties

Barbed Wire Publishing, *imprint of* Barbed Wire Publishing, *distributor for* Eakon Press, Kiva Publishers, Texas Technical University Press, Texas Western Press

Barbour Books, *imprint of* Barbour Publishing Inc

Barbour Publishing Inc, *distributor for* Discovery House Publishers

BAR/BRI Group, *division of* Harcourt Inc, Thomson Learning

Barcelona Publishers, *distributed by* General Music Store, MMB Music, West Music

Bard Graduate Center, *distributed by* Antique Collectors Club Ltd

Barefoot Books, *subsidiary of* The Barefoot Child

Barn Elms Publishing, *distributed by* Antique Collectors Club Ltd

Barnell-Loft, *imprint of* McGraw-Hill Learning Group

Barnes & Noble, *distributor for* A R O Publishing Co, Educational Impressions Inc, Epimetheus Books Inc, Excalibur Publications, G W Medical Publishing Inc, Leadership Publishers Inc, MAR*CO Products Inc, Paladin Press, SynergEbooks, *distributed by* Teton New Media

Barnes & Noble Books, *imprint of* Rowman & Littlefield Publishers Inc, *distributor for* Platinum Press Inc

Barnes & Noble Books (Imports & Reprints), *division of* Rowman & Littlefield Publishers Inc, *distributor for* Cooper Square, *distributed by* Rowman & Littlefield Publishers Inc, University Press of America Inc

BarnesandNoble.com, *distributor for* Noble Publishing Corp, Time Being Books, TSG Publishing Foundation Inc, University of California Institute on Global Conflict & Cooperation

Jean Barnes Books, *distributor for* MAR*CO Products Inc

Baronet Books, *imprint of* Playmore Inc, Publishers

Barricade Books, *imprint of* Barricade Books Inc

Barrons, *distributed by* Perfection Learning Corp

Barron's Educational Publishers, *distributed by* Sundance Publishing

Bartleby Press, *subsidiary of* Jackson Westgate Inc, *distributor for* BJE Press

Baseball America, *distributed by* Simon & Schuster Inc

Basic Books, *member of* The Perseus Books Group, *imprint of* The Perseus Books Group, *distributed by* HarperCollins, HarperCollins Publishers

Basic Civitas, *imprint of* Basic Books

Basic Civitas Books, *imprint of* The Perseus Books Group

Basic Health Guides, *imprint of* Basic Health Publications Inc

Basic Health Publications, *imprint of* Basic Health Publications Inc

Basic/Not Boring K-8 Grades, *imprint of* Incentive Publications Inc

Jossey Bass, *distributor for* American College of Physician Executives, *distributed by* American College of Physician Executives, American Society for Training & Development (ASTD), Medical Group Management Association

Bat Conservation International, *distributed by* University of Texas Press

Batsford, *distributed by* Sterling Publishing Co Inc

Battelle Press, *division of* Battelle

Battery Classics, *imprint of* Battery Press Inc

Battle Orders, *imprint of* Osprey Publishing Ltd

Battlebridge Publications, *distributed by* Paul & Company

Batwing Press, *imprint of* Harbor House

Colin Baxter, *distributed by* Voyageur Press

Bay Books, *imprint of* Bay/SOMA Publishing Inc

Bay/SOMA Publishing Inc, *subsidiary of* Windmere Durable Holdings Inc, *distributed by* Publishers Group West

Bayard, *distributor for* GemStone Press

Baylor University Press, *distributed by* Texas A&M University Press

BBC Audiobooks America, *subsidiary of* BBC Audiobooks, BBC AudioBooks Ltd

BBC Books, *distributed by* Trafalgar Square

BBC (selected titles), *distributed by* Jeffrey Norton Publishers Inc

BBT, *distributor for* Bhaktivedanta Book Publishing Inc

BDD Audio Publishing, *imprint of* Random House Inc

Be Puzzled, *division of* University Games

Be Somebody Be Yourself Institute, *distributed by* Center For Self Sufficiency

Beacham Publishing Corp, *distributed by* The Gale Group

BeachHouse Books, *imprint of* Science & Humanities Press

Beacon Hill Press of Kansas City, *subsidiary of* Nazarene Publishing House

Beacon Music, *distributed by* Hal Leonard Corp

Beacon Press, *distributed by* Houghton Mifflin, Houghton Mifflin Co, Houghton Mifflin Trade & Reference Division

Beagle Press, *distributed by* Antique Collectors Club Ltd

Bear & Co, *imprint of* Bear & Co Inc, Inner Traditions International Ltd

Bear & Co Inc, *subsidiary of* Inner Traditions International Ltd

Bear Cub Books, *imprint of* Bear & Co Inc, Inner Traditions International Ltd

Bear Manor Media, *imprint of* The Writers' Collective

Bear Meadows Research Group, *imprint of* Crumb Elbow Publishing

Bear Print, *distributed by* Mountain Press Publishing Co

Bearly Cooking, *imprint of* Mountain n' Air Books

Beaux Arts Editions, *imprint of* Hugh Lauter Levin Associates Inc

Beauxarts, *imprint of* Alan Wofsy Fine Arts

Mitchell Beazley, *distributed by* Phaidon Press Inc

Bebop Books, *imprint of* Lee & Low Books Inc

Marcelo D Beccaceci, *distributed by* Pangaea Publications

Becket Publications, *distributed by* Random House Inc

BEDE Productions, *division of* Stemmer House Publishers Inc, *imprint of* Stemmer House Publishers Inc

Bedford/St Martin's, *division of* Holtzbrinck Publishers Holdings LLC, Holtzbrinck Publishers Holdings LLC

Bedside Books, *imprint of* American Book Publishing

Beech Seal Press, *imprint of* Images from the Past Inc

Beech Tree Books, *imprint of* HarperCollins Publishers

Beef on Weck Press, *distributed by* The Writers' Collective

Beekman Publishers Inc, *distributor for* CIPO Chartered Institute for Personnel Development, C W Daniel, Gomer Press, Music Sales Corp, Kogan Page

Beeler Large Print, *imprint of* Thomas T Beeler Publisher

Chris Beetles Ltd, *distributed by* Antique Collectors Club Ltd

Begell-Atom LLC, *subsidiary of* Begell House Inc Publishers

Beginner Books, *imprint of* Random House Children's Books

Behrman House Inc, *distributor for* Rossel Books

Beidel Printing House, *division of* White Mane Publishing Co Inc

Belair Books, *imprint of* Incentive Publications Inc

Belair Publications Ltd, *distributed by* Incentive Publications Inc

Belfry Books, *imprint of* Toad Hall Inc

Belknap Press, *imprint of* Harvard University Press

A G Bell Association for the Deaf, *distributor for* York Press Inc

Bell Books, *imprint of* Boyds Mills Press

Bell Pond Books, *imprint of* Steiner Books, *distributed by* Steiner Books

Bell Tower, *imprint of* Crown Publishing Group, Random House Inc

Bellemore Books, *imprint of* Greenwich Publishing Group Inc

Bellwood Press, *imprint of* Baha'i Publishing Trust

Belwin-Mills, *distributed by* Warner Bros Publications Inc

BenBella Books, *distributed by* IPG Returns Dept

Benchmark Books, *imprint of* Marshall Cavendish Corp

Benchmark Maps, *distributed by* Wide World of Maps Inc

Benchmark Press, *imprint of* Triumph Books

Matthew Bender & Co Inc, *member of* The LexisNexis Group

Benjamin & Matthew Book Co, *distributor for* Maval Publishing Inc

Benjamin Cummings, *member of* Addison Wesley Higher Education Group

John Benjamins Publishing Co, *subsidiary of* John Benjamins BV, John Benjamins BV (Netherlands)

Benteli Verlag, *distributed by* Antique Collectors Club Ltd

Bentley Publishers, *division of* Robert Bentley Inc

Benziger, *imprint of* Macmillan/McGraw-Hill

Berg Publishers, *distributed by* St Martin's Press LLC

Berghahn Book Ltd (UK), *division of* Berghahn Books

Berghahn Books, *affiliate of* Berghahn Books Ltd, Berghahn Books Ltd (UK), *distributor for* Yad Vashem

Bergquist, *distributor for* Penfield Books

Berklee Press, *imprint of* Hal Leonard Corp, *distributed by* Hal Leonard Corp

Berkley, *distributed by* Perfection Learning Corp, Sundance Publishing

Berkley Books, *imprint of* Berkley Publishing Group, Penguin Group (USA) Inc, Penguin Group (USA) Inc

Berkley Publishing Group, *division of* Penguin Group (USA) Inc, Penguin Group (USA) Inc

Berkshire House, *imprint of* The Countryman Press

Berlitz Publishing, *imprint of* Langenscheidt Publishers Inc

Bernan, *division of* Kraus Organization Ltd, The Kraus Organization Ltd, *distributor for* Bureau of the Census, Food & Agriculture Organization, Government Printing Office, International Atomic Energy Agency (IAEA), International Monetary Fund (IMF), Library of Congress, National Technical Information Service (NTIS), Office for Official Publications of the European Communities (EC), Pan American Health Organization (Stationary Off-UK), (Represent) Bernan Press, UNESCO, United Nations (UN), World Bank, World Tourism Organization (WTO), World Trade Organization (WTO)

Berrett-Koehler Publishers Inc, *distributed by* Publishers Group West

Berrett-Kohler, *distributed by* American Society for Training & Development (ASTD)

Bertelsmann Foundation Publishers, *distributed by* The Brookings Institution Press

Bertrams, *distributor for* Paraview Publishing, Protea Publishing

Bertrams UK, *distributor for* Dissertation.com, Upublish.com

Bess Press, *distributor for* Kamehameha Schools Press

A Bessie Book, *imprint of* Counterpoint Press

Best Books International, *subsidiary of* Empire Publishing Service

Best Business Books, *imprint of* The Haworth Press Inc

Best Places® Guidebooks Series, *imprint of* Sasquatch Books

Bethany Fellowship, *distributed by* Christian Literature Crusade Inc

Bethany House Publishers/Baker Bookhouse, *division of* Baker Bookhouse

Bethel Publishing, *distributed by* Evangel Publishing House

Bethlehem Books, *affiliate of* Bethlehem Community, *distributed by* Ignatius Press

Betterway Books, *imprint of* David & Charles Ltd, F & W Publications, *distributor for* Rockport Publishers

Betty Crocker®, *imprint of* John Wiley & Sons Inc

Between-the-Lines, *distributed by* Dufour Editions Inc

Beverly Foundation, *distributed by* Hartman Publishing Inc

Beyda Associates Inc, *distributor for* Dog-Eared Publications

Beyond Words Publishing Inc, *distributed by* Publishers Group West

BFL, *imprint of* Ayer Company, Publishers Inc

Bhaktivedanta Book Publishing Inc, *distributed by* BBT

BHB International, *distributor for* Guild Publishing

Bibli O'Phile, *distributed by* Penguin Group (USA) Inc

Biblical Institute Press, *distributed by* Loyola Press

Biblio, *distributor for* Moo Press Inc, University of New Orleans Press, *distributed by* Bloch Publishing Co

Biblio Press, *distributed by* Cross-Cultural Communications, Holmes & Meier Publishers Inc

Bibligraghical Society of University of Virginia, *distributed by* Oak Knoll Press

Bibliographical Society of America, *distributed by* Oak Knoll Press

The Bibliographical Society (UK), *distributed by* Oak Knoll Press

Bibliopola Press, *distributed by* University Press of New England

Biblioteca Quinto Centenario, *distributed by* Latin American Literary Review Press

Bibliotheca Persica (Co-Publishers), *distributed by* Mazda Publishers Inc

Bibliotheca Persica Press, *affiliate of* Persian Heritage Foundation

Biblo, *imprint of* Biblo & Tannen Booksellers & Publishers Inc

Biblo & Tannen Booksellers & Publishers Inc, *subsidiary of* Biblo-Moser

Biblo Distribution, *distributor for* Rattapallax Press

Biblo-Moser, *imprint of* Biblo & Tannen Booksellers & Publishers Inc

Biblo-Tannen, *imprint of* Biblo & Tannen Booksellers & Publishers Inc

Big Meteor, *distributed by* Omnibus Press

Big Meteor Publishing, *distributed by* Schirmer Trade Books

Big Tree Books, *imprint of* Easy Money Press

Bigwig Briefs, *imprint of* Aspatore Books

Bilingual Press/Editorial Bilingue, *distributor for* Dos Pasos Editores, Lalo Press, Latin American Literary Review Press, Maize Press, Trinity University Press, Waterfront Press (selected titles from all)

Bilingual Publications Co, *distributor for* Fondo de Cultura Economica USA Inc

Bilingual Review Press, *distributor for* Latin American Literary Review Press, *distributed by* Arte Publico Press

Billboard Books, *imprint of* Watson-Guptill Publications

Binational Press, *imprint of* San Diego State University Press

Bindu Books, *imprint of* Inner Traditions International Ltd

Biographical Publishing Co, *distributor for* Eagles Landing Publishing, Spyglass Books LLC

Biological Diversity Handbook Series, *distributed by* Smithsonian Institution Press

Biological Sciences Press, *imprint of* Cooper Publishing Group

BioTechniques Books, *division of* Eaton Publishing

Birch Brook Impressions, *subsidiary of* Birch Brook Press

Birch Brook Press, *imprint of* Birch Brook Press, *distributor for* Abiko Literary Press, Natural Heritage Press, Persephone Press

Bird-Sci Books, *division of* Weidner & Sons Publishing, *imprint of* Weidner & Sons Publishing

Birkhauser Boston, *division of* Springer-Verlag New York Inc, *imprint of* Springer-Verlag New York Inc, *distributed by* Springer-Verlag New York Inc

Birkhauser Verlag, *distributed by* Princeton Architectural Press

Birlinn Ltd UK, *distributed by* Interlink Publishing Group Inc

Birlinn Publishing, *distributed by* Casemate Publishers

Birmingham Museum of Art, *distributed by* Antique Collectors Club Ltd

Bisk CPA Review, *imprint of* Bisk Education

Bisk CPE, *imprint of* Bisk Education

Bisk Education, *distributed by* Bisk Publishing Co

Bisk Publishing Co, *distributor for* Bisk Education

Bisk-Totaltape, *imprint of* Bisk Education

Bison Books, *imprint of* University of Nebraska Press

BizBest Media Features, *division of* BizBest Media Corp

BizBest100.com, *subsidiary of* BizBest Media Corp

BJE Press, *distributed by* Bartleby Press

BKMK Press of the University of Missouri-Kansas City, *division of* University of Missouri-Kansas City

Black & White Publishing, *imprint of* Neo-Tech Publishing

Black & White Publishing UK, *distributed by* Interlink Publishing Group Inc

Black Classic Press, *distributed by* Publishers Group West

Black Dagger Mysteries, *imprint of* BBC Audiobooks America

Black Dog & Leventhal, *imprint of* Black Dog & Leventhal Publishers Inc, *distributed by* Heimburger House Publishing Co, Workman Publishing Co Inc

Black Dog & Leventhal Publishers Inc, *distributed by* Workman Publishing

Black Dog Paperbacks, *imprint of* Black Dog & Leventhal Publishers Inc

Black Ice Books, *imprint of* Fiction Collective Two Inc

Black Iron Cookin' Co, *imprint of* Quixote Press

Black Iron Cooking Co, *imprint of* Hearts & Tummies Cookbook Co

Black River Books, *imprint of* Creative Arts Book Co

Black Shadow Books, *imprint of* Creative Arts Book Co

Black Sparrow Books, *distributed by* David R Godine Publisher Inc

Black Squirrel Books, *imprint of* Kent State University Press

Blackbirch Picturebooks, *imprint of* Blackbirch Press®

Blackbirch Press, *imprint of* Thomson Gale

Blackbirch Press®, *imprint of* Gale

Blackhall Publishing, *distributed by* Paul & Company

Blacklock Nature Photography, *distributed by* Adventure Publications

Blackstaff Press Ltd, *distributed by* Dufour Editions Inc

Blackwell, *distributor for* American Indian Studies Center Publications at UCLA

Blackwell Northamerica Inc, *distributor for* Investor Responsibility Research Center

Blackwell Publishers, *subsidiary of* Blackwell Publishers Ltd (UK), Blackwell Publishers Ltd (England)

Blackwell Publishing/Futura, *imprint of* Blackwell Publishing, *distributed by* Blackwell Science

Blackwell Publishing Ltd, *distributor for* Blackwell Publishing Professional

Blackwell Publishing Professional, *subsidiary of* Blackwell Publishing, *distributor for* Blackwell Science Ltd, British Small Animal Veterinary Association, Manson Publishing Ltd, *distributed by* Blackwell Publishing Ltd

Blackwell Science, *distributor for* Blackwell Publishing/Futura, Current Medicine, Humana Press

Blackwell Science Ltd, *distributed by* Blackwell Publishing Professional

Blackwells, *distributor for* Teton New Media

John F Blair Publisher, *distributor for* Bandit Books, Banks Channel Books, Down Home Press, NewSouth Books, Novello Festival Press, Pennywell Press, Walkabout Press, *distributed by* The Overmountain Press

Blake Books, *distributed by* Perfection Learning Corp

John Blake, *distributed by* Trafalgar Square

Blandford Press Ltd, *distributed by* Sterling Publishing Co Inc

Bloch Publishing Co, *distributor for* Biblio, Menorah, Scarf Press, Sephardic House, Soncino

Benjamin Blom, *imprint of* Ayer Company, Publishers Inc

Bloodaxe Books Ltd, *distributed by* Dufour Editions Inc

Bloom Literary Criticism, *imprint of* Chelsea House Publishers LLC, Haights Cross Communications Inc

Bloomberg Personal Bookshelf, *imprint of* Bloomberg Press

Bloomberg Press, *subsidiary of* Bloomberg LP, *imprint of* Bloomberg Press, *distributed by* W W Norton, W W Norton & Company Inc

Bloomberg Professional Library, *imprint of* Bloomberg Press

Bloomsbury Publishing, *distributed by* Holtzbrink Publishers

Bloomsbury UK, *distributed by* Trafalgar Square

Bloomsbury USA, *distributed by* St Martin's Press LLC

Blue & Grey, *imprint of* Book Sales Inc

Blue Book, *distributed by* Omnibus Press

Blue Dove Press, *distributor for* Motilal Banarsidass (Authorized American Distributor for Motilal Banarsidas & other publishers of India)

Blue Hen Putnam, *imprint of* G P Putnam's Sons (Hardcover)

Blue Jeans Poetry, *imprint of* Coda Publications

Blue Moon Books, *imprint of* Avalon Publishing Group Inc, Avalon Publishing Group - New York

Blue Mountain Press®, *imprint of* Blue Mountain Arts Inc

Blue Note, *imprint of* Blue Note Publications

Blue Note Books, *imprint of* Blue Note Publications

Blue Note Music Manuscript Books, *imprint of* Blue Note Publications

Blue Note Publications, *division of* Blue Note Publications Inc

Blue Poppy Herbs, *division of* Blue Poppy Press

Blue Poppy Press, *division of* Blue Poppy Enterprises Inc, *distributed by* New Leaf Books, Redwing Book Co

Blue Poppy Seminars, *subsidiary of* Blue Poppy Press

Blue Ribbon Books, *imprint of* Alpine Publications Inc

Blue Sky Marketing Inc, *distributor for* Lakeland Color Press, *distributed by* Adventure Publications

The Blue Sky Press, *imprint of* Scholastic Trade Division

Blue Star Productions, *imprint of* Book World Inc/Blue Star Productions

Blue Unicorn Press Inc, *distributed by* XLIBRIS

Blue Works, *imprint of* Windstorm Creative

BlueHen, *imprint of* The Putnam Publishing Group

Bluestreak, *imprint of* Beacon Press

Bluewood Books, *imprint of* The Siyeh Group Inc, The Siyeh Group Inc, *distributed by* SCB Distributors

Blushing Rose Publishing, *distributed by* Cogan Books, Folens Ltd (UK), Ingram Books

BMC Publications, *distributed by* Stackpole Books

BNA Books, *division of* The Bureau of National Affairs Inc, The Bureau of National Affairs Inc

BoardSource, *distributed by* American Society of Association Executives

BOCA/ICC, *distributed by* Thomson Delmar Learning

Fred Bock Music Company, *distributed by* Hal Leonard Corp

Boheme Press, *distributed by* Paul & Company

Boland Healthcare, *distributed by* American College of Physician Executives

Bolchazy-Carducci Publishers Inc, *distributor for* Georg Olms Verlag

Bold Strummer, *distributed by* Paul & Company

Bollingen Series, *imprint of* Princeton University Press

Bonus Books Inc, *distributor for* Precept Press

Book Clubs Inc, *distributor for* American Counseling Association

The Book Co Publishing Pty Ltd, *distributed by* Penton Overseas Inc

Book Design, *subsidiary of* Homestead Publishing

Book East, *distributor for* The Hokuseido Press, Kaibunsha

Book Guild, *distributed by* Trans-Atlantic Publications Inc

The Book House, *distributor for* Investor Responsibility Research Center, Primary Research Group

Book Marketing Plus, *distributor for* Penfield Books

Book Marketing Works, *subsidiary of* Book Marketing Works LLC

Book Peddlers, *distributed by* Gryphon House Inc, PGW

Book People, *distributor for* Dine College Press, Original Publications

Book Publishing Co, *distributor for* Cherokee Publications, Crazy Crow, CRCS Publications, Critical Path, Gentle World, Magni Co, Sproutman Publications

Book Sales Inc, *division of* The Quarto Group Inc, *distributed by* Heimburger House Publishing Co

Book World Inc/Blue Star Productions, *distributed by* Adventures Unlimited, Amazon.com, New Leaf

Book World Services Inc, *distributor for* One Planet Publishing House

Bookbooters, *distributor for* SynergEbooks

Bookcraft, *imprint of* Deseret Book Co

Bookhaus, *distributor for* Bookhaven Press LLC

Bookhaven Press LLC, *distributed by* Bookhaus, Planning Communications

The Bookies, *distributor for* MAR*CO Products Inc

Booklines Hawaii, *distributor for* Centerstream Publishing LLC, Dog-Eared Publications

The Bookman Inc, *distributor for* One Planet Publishing House

Bookmasters, *distributor for* The Linick Group Inc

Bookpeople, *distributor for* Larson Publications

Bookplate Society, *distributed by* Oak Knoll Press

BookProcessor, *imprint of* Media Associates

Books Americana, *imprint of* Krause Publications, *distributed by* Krause Publications

Books & Co, *distributed by* Turtle Point Press

Books and Co/Turtle Point, *imprint of* Turtle Point Press

Books & Libros, *division of* Gareth Stevens Inc

Books for Independent Minds, *imprint of* Ronin Publishing Inc

Books for Young Readers, *imprint of* Henry Holt and Company, LLC

Books in Motion, *division of* Classic Ventures, Ltd, Classic Ventures, Ltd

Books on Disk & CD-ROM, *subsidiary of* Gallopade International Inc

Books on Tape®, *division of* Random House Inc, *distributor for* Listening Library®

Books on Wings, *distributor for* Fondo de Cultura Economica USA Inc

Books 2 Go, *division of* The Writers' Collective

Books West, *distributor for* Wilderness Adventures Press Inc

Books West LLC, *distributor for* Ocean Tree Books

Booksails Press, *imprint of* LangMarc Publishing

Booksource, *distributor for* Fondo de Cultura Economica USA Inc

Booksurge, *distributor for* Six Gallery Press

BookWorld, *distributor for* Independent Information Publications

Bookworld Services Inc, *distributor for* Outcomes Unlimited Press Inc

Boone & Crockett Club, *distributed by* The Globe Pequot Press

Boosey & Hawkes, *distributed by* Hal Leonard Corp

Bootstrap Press (US), *distributed by* The Apex Press

Bora, *distributed by* Alan Wofsy Fine Arts

Borders, *distributor for* Paladin Press, *distributed by* Teton New Media

Borders Books, *distributor for* Excalibur Publications

Borealis, *imprint of* White Wolf Publishing Inc

Borealis Books, *imprint of* Minnesota Historical Society Press

Boson Books, *imprint of* C & M Online Media Inc

Boson Romances, *imprint of* C & M Online Media Inc

Boston Globe Puzzle Books, *imprint of* Random House Reference

The Boswell Institute, *affiliate of* Credit Card Users of America

Botanica Press, *imprint of* Book Publishing Co

Bottom Dog Press, *distributor for* Collinwood Media, The Firelands Writing Center

Boulden, *distributed by* MAR*CO Products Inc

Boulden Publishing, *distributor for* MAR*CO Products Inc

Boulevard, *imprint of* Berkley Publishing Group, Penguin Group (USA) Inc

Boulevard Books, *imprint of* Berkley Books

BoundSound™, *imprint of* Callaway Editions Inc

Bowers & Merena Galleries Inc, *distributed by* Sanford J Durst

R R Bowker, *distributed by* Hollywood Film Archive

R R Bowker LLC, *subsidiary of* Cambridge Information Group Inc

BowTie Press, *division of* BowTie Inc

Boydell & Brewer Inc, *affiliate of* Boydell & Brewer Ltd, Boydell & Brewer Ltd (UK)

Boydell Press, *imprint of* Boydell & Brewer Inc

Boyds Mill Press, *distributed by* Sundance Publishing

Boyds Mills Press, *subsidiary of* Highlights for Children Inc

Boye Knives Press, *distributed by* Chelsea Green Publishing Co

Boynton/Cook, *imprint of* Heinemann

Boys Town Press, *division of* Father Flanagan's Boy's Home, Father Flanagan's Boys' Home, *distributor for* A D D Warehouse, Character Counts Coalition, *distributed by* Deep Books (UK), Footprint Books, Australia, Quality Books

Boys Town (selected titles), *distributed by* Butte Publications Inc

Boze Books, *distributed by* Gem Guides Book Co

BPI Records, *imprint of* Bridge Publications Inc

Bradford Books, *imprint of* The MIT Press

The Bradford Press, *imprint of* Toad Hall Inc

Bradley Publications, *distributed by* Warner Bros Publications Inc

Henry Bradshaw Society, *imprint of* Boydell & Brewer Inc

Brady, *imprint of* Pearson Higher Education Division, *distributed by* Fire Engineering Books & Videos

BradyGAMES Publishing, *division of* Pearson Technology Group

Brainstormers, *imprint of* Aspatore Books

Brainwaves Books, *imprint of* Allen D Bragdon Publishers Inc

Brandeis University Press, *imprint of* University Press of New England

Branden Publishing Co, *distributor for* Dante University of America Press Inc

Branden Publishing Co Inc, *unit of* Branden Books, *distributor for* Dante University of America Press Inc

Brashear Music Co, *imprint of* Branden Publishing Co Inc

Brassey's Inc, *subsidiary of* Books International, Books International Inc

Brassey's Sports, *imprint of* Brassey's Inc

Brassey's UK, *distributed by* Casemate Publishers

Brava, *imprint of* Kensington Publishing Corp

George Braziller Inc, *distributed by* Antique Collectors' Club Ltd, W W Norton, W W Norton & Company Inc

Karen & Michael Braziller Books, *imprint of* Persea Books Inc

Breakfast Communications, *distributed by* SAS Publishing

Breakout Productions Inc, *distributed by* Loompanics Unlimited, Loompanics Unlimited Ingram

Breakthrough, *imprint of* The Wright Group/McGraw-Hill, a Division of McGraw-Hill Learning Group

Breakthrough Publications, *imprint of* Breakthrough Publications Inc

Nicholas Brealey Publishing, *distributed by* Intercultural Press Inc

Brenner Information Group, *division of* Brenner Microcomputing Inc, *distributor for* Allworth Press, *distributed by* Amazon.com, Publishing Perfection

Breslov Research Institute, *distributed by* Moznaim Publishing Corp

Brethren Press, *division of* Church of the Brethren General Board, *distributor for* LifeQuest, *distributed by* Spring Arbor

D S Brewer, *imprint of* Boydell & Brewer Inc

Brewers Publications, *division of* Association of Brewers, *distributed by* National Book Network

Brick Tower Press, *subsidiary of* J T Colby & Co Inc

BrickHouse Books Inc, *distributor for* Salmon Publishing, *distributed by* Salmon Publishing

Bridge, *imprint of* Bridge-Logos Publishers

Bridge Audio, *imprint of* Bridge Publications Inc

Bridge-Logos Publishers, *distributed by* Anchor Distributors, Appalachian Bible, Ingram, MPH Distributors, Riverside Distributors, SSS Distributors

Bridge Publications Inc, *distributed by* Anchor Bay Entertainment, CyberRead, Libronauta

Bridge Works Publishing, *imprint of* Rowman & Littlefield Publishing Group, *distributed by* National Book Network

Bridgepoint, *imprint of* Baker Books

Bridgestone, *imprint of* Capstone Press

Brief Books, *imprint of* Birch Brook Press

Briefings Publishing Group, *division of* Wicks Business Info @ LLC, Wicks Business Information LLC Co

Bright Horizons, *distributor for* Trails Illustrated, Division of National Geographic Maps

Bright Ring Publishing, *distributed by* Gryphon House Inc

Brill Academic Publishers Inc, *subsidiary of* Koninklijke Brill N V

Brimhall Music Publishing, *distributed by* Warner Bros Publications Inc

Brio Girls, *imprint of* Focus on the Family

Brioni Books, *distributed by* Antique Collectors Club Ltd

Bristol, *imprint of* Bristol Publishing Enterprises

Bristol Fashion Publications Inc, *distributed by* Lightning Source

British Film Institute, *distributed by* University of California Press

British Museum Press, *distributed by* Antique Collectors Club Ltd

British Small Animal Veterinary Association, *distributed by* Blackwell Publishing Professional

Broadman & Holman Publishers, *distributor for* National Publishing Co

Brodart, *distributor for* The Info Devel Press, Rocky River Publishers LLC, Standard Educational Corp, Wordtree branching dictionary

Brodart Co, *distributor for* Do-It-Yourself Legal Publishers

The Bronx County Historical Society, *distributor for* College of Mount St Vincent Press, *distributed by* Crown, Grolier, New York University Press

Brook Street Press LLC, *distributed by* Midpoint Trade Books

Paul H Brookes Publishing Co, *distributed by* Elsevier Australia (New Zealand & Australia), The Eurospan Group (Europe & UK), Unifacmanu Trading Co Ltd (Taiwan)

Brookings Institution Press, *distributor for* Council on Foreign Relations Press, University of California Institute on Global Conflict & Cooperation

The Brookings Institution Press, *division of* Brookings Institution, *distributor for* Aspen Institute, Bertelsmann Foundation Publishers, Carnegie Endowment for International Peace, Centre for Economic Policy Research, The Century Foundation, Council on Foreign Relations, Economica, Hudson Institute, International Labor Offices, Japan Center for International Exchange, OECD, Royal Institute of International Affairs, The Trilateral Commission, United Nations University Press, Washington Institute for Near East Policy

Brooklands Books Ltd, *distributed by* CarTech Inc

Brookline Books, *distributed by* Pathway Book Service

Brooklyn Botanic Garden, *distributed by* Sterling Publishing Co Inc

Brooklyn Botanic Garden All-Region Guides, *imprint of* Brooklyn Botanic Garden

Brooks (selected titles), *distributed by* Council for Exceptional Children

Brooks/Cole, *imprint of* Wadsworth Publishing

449

Brotherhood of St Herman of Alaska, *imprint of* St Herman Press

Gustav Broukal Press, *imprint of* American Atheist Press

Brown Barn Books, *division of* Pictures of Record Inc

David Brown Books, *distributor for* American Numismatic Society

John Carter Brown Library, *distributed by* Oak Knoll Press

Brown Judaic Studies, *distributed by* Society of Biblical Literature

Karen Brown, *distributed by* Random House Sales & Marketing

Karen Brown Guides, *distributor for* Fodor's Travel Publications, *distributed by* Fodor's Travel Publications, Random House Inc

Karen Brown's Guides Inc, *distributed by* Random House

Brown University, *distributed by* American Mathematical Society

Brown Walker Press, *subsidiary of* Dissertation.com, *imprint of* Dissertation.com

Brumby (Gemcraft), *distributor for* Vital Health Publishing

Brunner/Routledge, *subsidiary of* Taylor & Francis Inc, *distributed by* Taylor & Francis Inc

Brunner-Routledge, *member of* Taylor & Francis Group, *imprint of* Taylor & Francis

Brusberg (Berlin), *distributed by* Alan Wofsy Fine Arts

Bryn Mawr Commentaries, *distributed by* Hackett Publishing Co Inc

Brynmorgen Press, *distributed by* Gem Guides Book Co

Bubble Books, *imprint of* Modern Publishing

Bucknell University Press, *affiliate of* Associated University Presses, *distributed by* Associated University Presses

Buddy Books, *imprint of* Abdo Publishing

Buena Vista DVDs, *distributed by* Recorded Books LLC

Bufflehead Books, *imprint of* Down The Shore Publishing Corp

Bugling-The Complete Bugler Series, *imprint of* R S V Products

BuilderBooks.com, *division of* National Association of Home Builders, *distributor for* National Association of Home Builders

Building Blocks, *distributed by* Gryphon House Inc

Building Excellence, *imprint of* Mel Bay Publications Inc

Building News, *division of* B N I Publications Inc, BNI Publications Inc, *distributed by* Macmillan

Building News Inc, *distributed by* Craftsman Book Co

Bulfinch/Little, *distributor for* National Gallery of Art

Bulfinch Press, *subsidiary of* Time Warner Book Group, *imprint of* Time Warner Book Group, *distributor for* Art Institute of Chicago

Bulgarian-American Cultural Society ALEKO, *subsidiary of* Cross-Cultural Communications

Burd Street Press, *division of* White Mane Publishing Co Inc

The Bureau For At-Risk Youth, *subsidiary of* The Guidance Channel

Bureau of Economic Geology, University of Texas at Austin, *division of* University of Texas at Austin, *distributor for* Gulf Coast Association of Geological Societies

Bureau of the Census, *distributed by* Bernan

Burford Books, *distributed by* National Book Network

Burnell books, *distributor for* MAR*CO Products Inc

Burning Bush Press, *imprint of* United Synagogue Book Service

Buros Institute, *distributed by* University of Nebraska Press

Business & Research Associates, *distributed by* AKTRIN Furniture Information Centre

Business Development, *division of* Scholastic Education

Business Research Services Inc, *distributor for* PanOptic, Riley & Johnson, *distributed by* Gale Research Inc

Business Success Series, *imprint of* PREP Publishing

Business/Technology Information Services (B/T Info), *imprint of* Business/Technology Books (B/T Books)

Business Travel Bible, *imprint of* Aspatore Books

Butte Publications Inc, *distributor for* Boys Town (selected titles), Gallaudet University Press (selected titles), Infant Hearing Resources (selected titles), Pro Ed (selected titles)

Butterworth-Heinemann, *distributor for* Current Medicine, *distributed by* Metal Powder Industries Federation, NACE International

Butterworth (Law in Context series), *distributed by* Northwestern University Press

Butterworths, *distributed by* William S Hein & Co Inc

BWI, *distributor for* Raven Tree Press LLC

By Design Press, *imprint of* Quite Specific Media Group Ltd

BYU Museum of Peoples & Cultures, *distributed by* The University of Utah Press

C & T Publishing, *distributed by* American Quilter's Society, Watson-Guptill Publications

C & T Publishing Inc, *distributor for* Rowan UK, *distributed by* Watson-Guptill Publications

C E P Inc, *imprint of* Paladin Press

CABI, *distributed by* Oxford University Press, Inc

Cache River Press, *imprint of* Quick Publishing

Cademon, *imprint of* HarperCollins Publishers Sales

Cadence Jazz Books, *division of* Cadnor Ltd, Cadnor Ltd, *distributed by* North Country Distributors

Cadogan Guides, *imprint of* The Globe Pequot Press, *distributed by* The Globe Pequot Press

Caedmon, *imprint of* HarperCollins General Books Group

Caissa Editions, *affiliate of* Dale A Brandreth Books

Cal-Earth, *distributed by* Chelsea Green Publishing Co

California From The Air, *imprint of* Squarebooks Inc

California Journal Press, *division of* Information for Public Affairs Inc

California Legacy Books, *imprint of* Heyday Books

Calkius Creek Books, *imprint of* Boyds Mills Press

Calvary Hospital, *distributed by* Center for Thanatology Research & Education Inc

Calyx, *imprint of* Calyx Books

Calyx Books, *division of* Calyx Inc

Cambridge, *imprint of* Pearson Higher Education Division

Cambridge Educational, *division of* Films for the Humanities & Sciences, *subsidiary of* Films for the Humanities & Sciences, *distributor for* Chronicle Guidance Publications Inc

Cambridge University Press, *division of* Department of Cambridge University, *distributor for* The Mathematical Association of America, National Gallery of Art, The Woodrow Wilson Center Press, *distributed by* Dominie Press Inc, NACE International, Jeffrey Norton Publishers Inc

Camden House, *imprint of* Boydell & Brewer Inc

Campaign, *imprint of* Osprey Publishing Ltd

Campanile Press, *imprint of* San Diego State University Press

Canadian Caboose Press, *distributed by* Heimburger House Publishing Co

Canadian Centre for Architecture, *distributed by* The MIT Press

Canadian Human-Computer Communications Society, *distributed by* A K Peters Ltd

Canadian MANDA, *distributor for* Weatherhill Inc

Canadian Museum of Nature, *distributed by* Association of American University Presses

Canadian Society of Petroleum Geologists, *distributor for* AAPG (American Association of Petroleum Geologists)

Canal & Stamperia, *distributed by* Antique Collectors Club Ltd

Canal Press, *imprint of* Schiffer Publishing Ltd

Candle Books, *distributed by* Kregel Publications

Candlewick Press, *subsidiary of* Walker Books Ltd, Walker Books Ltd (London), *distributed by* Penguin Group (USA) Inc, Penguin Group (USA) Inc, Perfection Learning Corp, Sundance Publishing

Canisius College Press, *distributed by* Western New York Wares Inc

Canongate US, *imprint of* Grove/Atlantic Inc

Canterbury & York Society, *imprint of* Boydell & Brewer Inc

Canterbury Press Norwich (UK), *distributed by* Morehouse Publishing Co

Gloriae Dei Cantores, *distributed by* Paraclete Press

Cantors Assembly, *imprint of* Transcontinental Music Publications

Canyon Country Distribution, *distributor for* Canyon Country Publications

Canyon Country Publications, *distributed by* Archhunter Publications, Canyon Country Distribution

Canyonlands Publications, *distributor for* Sierra Press, Trails Illustrated, Division of National Geographic Maps

CAP, *imprint of* C A P Publishing & Literary Co LLC

Capital Enquiry Inc, *distributor for* Center for Investigative Reporting

Capital Press, *imprint of* Eagle Publishing Inc

Capitol Preservation Committee, *distributed by* Stackpole Books

Capitol Publications, *distributed by* American College of Physician Executives

Capra Press, *distributed by* Gem Guides Book Co (selected titles)

Capstone, *imprint of* John Wiley & Sons Inc

Car Tech, *distributed by* Voyageur Press

Aristide D Caratzas, *imprint of* Aristide D Caratzas, Publisher

Aristide D Caratzas, Publisher, *affiliate of* Melissa International Publications Ltd, Melissa International Publications Ltd

Caravan Books, *subsidiary of* Academic Resources Corp, Academic Resources Corp

Carcanet, *distributed by* The Sheep Meadow Press

Carcanet Press, *distributed by* Paul & Company

Cardinal Publishers Group, *distributor for* Wish Publishing

Cardinal Van Thuan Series, *imprint of* Pauline Books & Media

Cardoza, *distributed by* Simon & Schuster Inc

Cardoza Publishing, *distributed by* Simon & Schuster

Care Spring, *imprint of* Hartman Publishing Inc

Career Examination Series, *imprint of* National Learning Corp

Career Kids FYI, *distributor for* MAR*CO Products Inc

CareerJournal, *imprint of* Aspatore Books

Caribbean Writers Series, *imprint of* Heinemann

Caribe Betania Editores, *division of* Thomas Nelson Inc, Thomas Nelson Inc

Carisch SPA, *distributed by* Summy-Birchard Inc

Carlton Books, *distributed by* Andrews McMeel Publishing

Carmania Press, London, *distributed by* Purple Mountain Press Ltd

Carnegie Endowment for International Peace, *distributed by* The Brookings Institution Press

Caroline House, *imprint of* Boyds Mills Press

Carolrhoda Books Inc, *division of* Lerner Publishing Group, *imprint of* Lerner Publishing Group

Jon Carpenter, *distributed by* Paul & Company

Jon Carpenter Publishing (UK), *distributor for* The Apex Press

Carr Peer Resources, *distributor for* MAR*CO Products Inc

Carroll & Brown, *distributed by* Trafalgar Square

Carroll & Graf Publishers, *imprint of* Avalon Publishing Group Inc, Avalon Publishing Group - New York

Carson-Dellosa Publishing Co Inc, *subsidiary of* Cinar Films, *distributor for* Kelley Wingate Publications, Mark Twain Media, The Wild Goose Co

Carson Enterprises, *imprint of* Carson Enterprises Inc

Carstens Hobby Books, *imprint of* Carstens Publications Inc

Carta Mundi, *distributed by* US Games Systems Inc

Cartago, *distributed by* Antique Collectors Club Ltd

CarTech Inc, *distributor for* Brooklands Books Ltd, SA Design, *distributed by* Voyageur Press

Amon Carter Museum, *distributed by* Abrams & University of Washington Press, The University of Arizona Press

Carthage Reprints, *imprint of* St Augustine's Press Inc

Cartwheel Books, *imprint of* Scholastic Trade Division

Carysfort Press, *distributed by* Dufour Editions Inc

Casa Bautista, *distributed by* Editorial Bautista Independiente

Casa Creation (International Publishing Group), *imprint of* Charisma House

Cascade Expeditions, *imprint of* Crumb Elbow Publishing

Cascade Geographic Society, *imprint of* Crumb Elbow Publishing

Casemate, *distributed by* Casemate Publishers

Casemate Publishers, *distributor for* Ian Allan (UK), Amber Books (UK), Arms & Armour Press (UK), Arris Publishing (UK), Birlinn Publishing (UK), Brassey's UK, Casemate (USA), Cassell (UK, military titles only), Compendium Publishing (UK), CondeNast/Johansens (UK), Conway Maritime Press (UK), D-Day Publishing (Belgium), DACO Publications (Belgium), De Krijger (Belgium), Earthbound Publications (South Africa), Editions Charles Herissey (France), Editions Heimdal, Emperor's Press (USA), Formac Publishing (Canada), Front Street Press (USA), Grub Street (UK), Helion & Co Ltd (UK), Histoire & Collections (France), Historical Indexes (USA), Indo Editions (France), Ironclad Publishing (USA), National Maritime Museum (UK), Pen & Sword Books Lrd (UK), Public Record Office (UK), Riebel-Roque, RZM Publishing (USA), Salamander (USA), Savas Beatie (USA), Spellmount Publishers (UK), Travel Publishing Ltd (UK), Vanwell Publishing (Canada), Vegetarian Guides (UK), Weidenfeld & Nicolson (UK, military titles only)

Cassell, *distributed by* Casemate Publishers, Sterling Publishing Co Inc

Cassell Illustrated, *distributed by* Sterling Publishing Co Inc

Cassidy Video (Little Explorers), *distributed by* Penton Overseas Inc

CASTI Publishing, *distributed by* NACE International

Castle Books, *imprint of* Book Sales Inc

Castle Keep Books, *imprint of* James A Rock & Co Publishers

Catalpa Press, *distributed by* Oak Knoll Press

Catechesis of the Good Shepherd Publications, *imprint of* Liturgy Training Publications

Cathedral Music Press, *division of* Mel Bay Publications Inc, *imprint of* Mel Bay Publications Inc

The Catherine Collective Corp (Canada only), *distributed by* Mint Publishers Group

Kyle Cathie, *distributed by* Trafalgar Square

Catholic Bible Press, *imprint of* Thomas Nelson Inc

Catholic Dossier, *subsidiary of* Ignatius Press

Catholic Faith, *subsidiary of* Ignatius Press

Catholic Treasures, *distributor for* Angelus Press

The Catholic University of America Press, *distributor for* American Maritain Association

The Catholic World Report, *subsidiary of* Ignatius Press

Cave Books, *affiliate of* Cave Research Foundation, *distributor for* Zephyrus Press

Caxton Press, *division of* The Caxton Printers Ltd, The Caxton Printers Ltd, *distributor for* University of Idaho Press

Edgar Cayce Foundation, *division of* ARE Press

Cayce-Reilly School of Massotherapy, *division of* ARE Press

CBD, *distributor for* College Press Publishing Co

CBP/EMH, *imprint of* Baptist Spanish Publishing House (d/b/a Casa Bautista de Publicaciones)

CCA, *imprint of* Copywriter's Council of America (CCA), The Linick Group Inc

CCH Inc, *subsidiary of* Wolters Kluwer

CCH INCORPORATED, *imprint of* Wolters Kluwer US Corp

CCH Peterson, *subsidiary of* CCH Inc

CCH Riverwoods, *subsidiary of* CCH Inc

CCH St Petersburg, *subsidiary of* CCH Inc

CCH Tax Compliance, *subsidiary of* CCH Inc

CCH Washington DC, *subsidiary of* CCH Inc

CDL Press, *imprint of* CDL Press

CDX Global, *distributed by* Thomson Delmar Learning

Cedco Publishing Co, *distributed by* Heimburger House Publishing Co

CEF Press, *subsidiary of* Child Evangelism Fellowship Inc, Child Evangelism Fellowship Inc

Celebrity Press, *division of* Hambleton Hill Publishing Inc, *imprint of* Hambleton-Hill Publishing, *distributed by* Associated Publishers Group

Celestial Arts, *subsidiary of* Ten Speed Press

Celestial Arts Publishing Co, *subsidiary of* Ten Speed Press, *imprint of* Ten Speed Press

Center for Chinese Studies, University of Michigan, *distributed by* University of Michigan Press

Center for Contemporary Judaica, *imprint of* Prayer Book Press Inc

Center for Creative Leadership, *distributor for* Free Press, Harvard Business School Press, Jossey Bass/Wiley, Lominger Inc, *distributed by* Jossey Bass/Wiley

Center for East Asian Studies (CEAS), *subsidiary of* Western Washington University, *distributed by* Amazon.com

Center for Global Development, *distributed by* Institute for International Economics

Center for International Studies, *distributed by* Ohio University Press

Center for International Training & Education/CITE, *imprint of* The Apex Press

Center for Investigative Reporting, *distributed by* Capital Enquiry Inc

Center for Literary Publishing, *distributed by* University Press of Colorado

The Center for Migration Studies, *distributed by* Jerome S Ozer Publisher Inc

Center for National Policy Press, *distributed by* University Press of America Inc

Center for Self-Governance, *imprint of* ICS Press

Center For Self Sufficiency, *distributor for* Be Somebody Be Yourself Institute, Center For Self Sufficiency Library

Center For Self Sufficiency Library, *distributed by* Center For Self Sufficiency

Center for South & Southeast Asian Studies, University of Michigan, *distributed by* University of Michigan Press

Center for Spirituality & Healing, *imprint of* Fairview Press

Center for Study of American Constitution, *distributed by* Madison House Publishers

Center for Thanatology Research & Education Inc, *distributor for* Association for Gravestone Studies, Calvary Hospital, Greenwood Cemetery

Center For The Child Care Workforce, *distributed by* Gryphon House Inc

Center for the Study of Southern Culture Series, *imprint of* University Press of Mississippi

The Center for the Study of Upper Midwestern Culture, *distributed by* University of Wisconsin Press

Center for Urban Policy Research, *affiliate of* Rutgers University

Center for Youth Issues Stars, *distributed by* MAR*CO Products Inc

Center of Emigrants from Serbia, *distributed by* Cross-Cultural Communications

Centerbrook Publishing, *subsidiary of* Centerstream Publishing LLC

Centering Corp, *distributor for* Doug Smith

Centerstream Publications, *imprint of* Hal Leonard Corp, *distributed by* Hal Leonard Corp

Centerstream Publishing LLC, *distributed by* Booklines Hawaii, Hal Leonard Corp

Central European University Press, *distributor for* International Debate Education Association, Local Government & Public Service Reform Initiative

Centre for Economic Policy Research, *distributed by* The Brookings Institution Press

The Century Foundation, *distributed by* The Brookings Institution Press

The Century Foundation Press, *division of* The Century Foundation Inc, The Century Foundation Inc

Century Press, *distributed by* Dan River Press, Kalimat Press, Northwoods Press

Certification Press, *imprint of* McGraw-Hill/Osborne, McGraw-Hill Professional

Certified Nurse Series (CN), *imprint of* National Learning Corp

CeShore Publishing Co, *imprint of* SterlingHouse Publisher Inc

CFKR Career, *distributor for* MAR*CO Products Inc

Chain Store Guide, *subsidiary of* Lebhar-Friedman Inc, Lebhar-Friedman Inc

Chalcombe Publications (UK), *distributed by* Scholium International Inc

Chalice Press, *division of* Christian Board of Publications, *distributed by* Abingdon Press

Chancellor Porter L Fortune Symposium in Southern History Series, *imprint of* University Press of Mississippi

Chancellor Press, *distributed by* Sterling Publishing Co Inc

Chanterelle, *distributed by* Mel Bay Publications Inc

Chanting Press, *imprint of* The Writers' Collective

Chapin Library, *distributed by* Oak Knoll Press

Paul Chapman Publishing, *distributed by* Corwin Press

Chapter by Chapter®, *imprint of* Haights Cross Communications Inc, Sundance Publishing

Character Counts Coalition, *distributed by* Boys Town Press

Charisma House, *imprint of* Strang Communications Co, *distributed by* Creation House

Charisma Life, *distributed by* CharismaLife Publishers

CharismaLife Publishers, *division of* Strang Communications Co, Strang Communications Co, *distributor for* Charisma Life, Cross Training, KIDS Church

CharismaLife (Sunday School Curriculum Group), *imprint of* Charisma House

Charismatic Renewal Services, *distributor for* St Bede's Publications

Charles E Tuttle Shokai, *distributor for* High/Coo Press

Charles McCann, *distributed by* Sundance Publishing

The Charles Press, Publishers, *subsidiary of* Oxbridge Corp, Oxbridge Corp

Charles River Media, *division of* Books International, Books International Inc

Charles Scribner's Sons, *unit of* Macmillan Library Reference USA, Thomson Gale, *imprint of* Thomson Gale

Charlesbridge Press, *distributed by* Perfection Learning Corp

Charlesbridge Publishing, *distributed by* Sundance Publishing

Charming Small Hotel Guides, *imprint of* Hunter Publishing Inc

Chartwell Books, *imprint of* Book Sales Inc

Chatelaine Press, *subsidiary of* Log Research Ltd, Log Research Ltd, *distributor for* Law Quest

Chatterbox Press, *distributed by* Gryphon House Inc

The Checkerboard Library, *imprint of* Abdo Publishing

Checkmark Books, *imprint of* Facts on File Inc

Chelsea Clubhouse, *imprint of* Chelsea House Publishers LLC, Haights Cross Communications Inc

Chelsea Green Publishing Co, *distributor for* American Council for an Energy Efficient Economy (ACEEE), Boye Knives Press, Cal-Earth, Deep Stream Press, Earth Justice, Ecological Design Press, Good Earth, Goosefoot Acres, Greenleaf, Jenkins Publishing, Moonsmile Press, Morning Sun Press, Natural Heritage Books, Ottographics, Out on Bale, Peregrinzilla, Polyface, Radical Weeds, Solar Design Association, Spring Wheat, Sussex, Sustainability Press, Trust for Public Land, Watershed Media

Chelsea House, *subsidiary of* Haights Cross Communications Inc, *imprint of* Haights Cross Communications Inc, *distributed by* Perfection Learning Corp

Chelsea House Publishers LLC, *division of* Haights Cross Communications Inc

Chelsea Publishing Co Inc, *imprint of* American Mathematical Society

Chemical Education Resources Inc, *division of* Thomson Learning, Thomson Learning Custom Publishing

Cheng & Tsui Co Inc, *distributor for* China International Book Trading Co (Beijing, selected titles only), Commercial Press (Hong Kong), Renditions Paperbacks, Wellsweep Press

Cherokee Publications, *distributed by* Book Publishing Co

Cherry Lane Music Co, *imprint of* Hal Leonard Corp, *distributed by* Hal Leonard Corp, Hal Leonard Corp

Chesapeake Bay Maritime Museum, *distributed by* Cornell Maritime Press Inc, Tidewater Publishers

Chesnut Hills Press, *subsidiary of* BrickHouse Books Inc, *imprint of* BrickHouse Books Inc

Chess Digest Inc, *distributor for* Trends

Chess Enterprises, *distributed by* Thinkers' Press, Thinkers' Press Inc

Chess Information & Research Center, *distributed by* W W Norton & Company Inc

Chess Stars, *distributed by* Thinkers' Press Inc

Chicago Review Press, *affiliate of* Independent Publishers Group, *distributed by* Gryphon House Inc

Chicago Spectrum Press, *subsidiary of* Evanston Publishing Inc, *distributed by* Evanston Publishing Inc

Chicago Tribune Crosswords, *imprint of* Random House Reference

The Chicken House, *imprint of* Scholastic Trade Division

Child Play, *distributor for* A D D Warehouse

Child's Play, *affiliate of* Child's Play (International) Ltd, Child's Play International, Ltd, *distributed by* Heimburger House Publishing Co

Children's Book Press, *distributed by* Publishers Group West (trade market), Sundance Publishing

Children's Classics, *imprint of* Random House Inc, Random House Value Publishing

Children's Media, *imprint of* Random House Inc

Children's Press, *division of* Scholastic Library Publishing, *distributed by* Perfection Learning Corp, Sundance Publishing

Children's Resources International, *distributed by* Gryphon House Inc

Child's Play, *affiliate of* Child's Play (International) Ltd, Child's Play International, Ltd, *distributed by* Heimburger House Publishing Co

The Child's World Inc, *distributor for* Tradition Books

Childswork/Childsplay LLC, *subsidiary of* Guidance Channel, The Guidance Channel

Chilton, *imprint of* Thomson Delmar Learning, *distributed by* Thomson Delmar Learning

Chilton Book Co, *distributed by* J J Keller & Associates, Inc

Chilton Books, *imprint of* Krause Publications

China Books & Periodicals Inc, *division of* C & C Joint Printing Co (HK) Ltd under Sino United Publishing (Holdings) Ltd, Sino United Publications (Holdings) Ltd, *distributor for* AsiaPac, CIBTC, Commercial Press, Foreign Languages Press, Joint Publishers, New World Press, Panda Books, Peace Books, Red Mansions Publishing

China International Book Trading Co, *distributed by* Cheng & Tsui Co Inc

Chinese University Press, *distributed by* Columbia University Press

Chipstone Foundation, *distributed by* University Press of New England

Chiron Publications, *distributed by* Steiner Books

Chivers Audio Books, *imprint of* BBC Audiobooks America

Chivers Children's Audio Books, *imprint of* BBC Audiobooks America

Chosen Books, *division of* Baker Book House Co, Baker Book House Co

Chosen People Ministries, *distributed by* Lederer Books, Messianic Jewish Publishers

Christian Classics, *imprint of* Ave Maria Press, *distributed by* Ave Maria Press

Christian Community, *imprint of* LifeQuest

Christian Fellowship, *distributed by* Christian Literature Crusade Inc

Christian Focus, *distributed by* Pilgrim Publications

Christian Liberty Press, *distributed by* Appalachian Distributors

The Christian Library, *imprint of* Barbour Publishing Inc

Christian Literature Crusade Inc, *distributor for* Bethany Fellowship, Christian Fellowship, Christian Publications, Lutterworth

Christian Living Books Inc, *imprint of* Pneuma Life Publishing, Pneuma Life Publishing Inc, *distributed by* Pneuma Life Publishing

Christian Publications, *distributed by* Christian Literature Crusade Inc

Christopher Publishing House, *member of* A T I Group

Chronicle, *distributor for* Country Music Foundation Press

Chronicle Books, *distributor for* Art Institute of Chicago, Front Street Inc, Handprint Books Inc, innovative Kids™, Princeton Architectural Press, Quirk Books, Ragged Bears, *distributed by* Perfection Learning Corp, Sundance Publishing

Chronicle Books for Children, *division of* Chronicle Books LLC

Chronicle Books LLC, *distributor for* Handprint, Innovative Kids, North/South, Princeton Architectural Press, Ragged Bears

Chronicle Gift, *division of* Chronicle Books LLC

Chronicle Guidance Publications Inc, *distributed by* American Guidance Service (AGS), Cambridge Educational, Communication Skills Inc, Ebsco Subscription Services, EdITS, Educational & Psychological Services International (EPSI), JIST Works Inc, Meridian Education Corp, Nimco Inc, Psychological Assessment Resources Inc (PAR), Southern Media Systems Inc

Chrysalis Books, *imprint of* Swedenborg Foundation Publishers/Chrysalis Books

Chrysalis Reader, *imprint of* Swedenborg Foundation Publishers/Chrysalis Books

Church Growth Institute, *subsidiary of* Ephesians Four Ministries

Churchmouse Tales Books, *imprint of* Wayside Publications

CIBTC, *distributed by* China Books & Periodicals Inc

Cico Books, *distributed by* Trafalgar Square

Cigar Aficionado, *distributed by* Running Press Book Publishers

Cinco Puntos Press, *distributor for* Mariposa Publishing, Trails West Publishing

Cine-Med, Inc, *distributor for* American College of Surgeons

Cinema Book Society, *subsidiary of* Hollywood Film Archive

Cinema Books, *distributed by* Hal Leonard Corp

Cinnamon Tree, *imprint of* Deseret Book Co

CIPO Chartered Institute for Personnel Development, *distributed by* Beekman Publishers Inc

Circle Time Publishers, *distributed by* Gryphon House Inc

Circlet Press Inc, *distributed by* SCB Distributors

Circumflex, *imprint of* Circlet Press Inc

CIS Publishers & Distributors, *division of* CIS Communications

Cistercian Publications, *distributor for* St Bede's Publications

Cistercian Publications Inc, Editorial Office, *distributor for* Fairacres Press, Peregrina Press

Citadel, *imprint of* Kensington Publishing Corp

Citebook, *imprint of* Starlite Inc

Citrus Publishing, *distributor for* John Milton Society for the Blind

Ciudad Nueva (Spain/Argentina), *distributed by* New City Press

Civitas, *distributed by* HarperCollins Publishers

Clairview Books, *distributed by* Steiner Books

Clara House Books, *imprint of* The Oliver Press Inc

Arnold Clarendon, *distributed by* Oxford University Press, Inc

Clarendon Press, *imprint of* Oxford University Press, Inc

Claridge Press, *distributed by* Paul & Company

Clarion Books, *division of* Houghton Mifflin Co, *subsidiary of* Houghton Mifflin Co, *imprint of* Houghton Mifflin Trade & Reference Division, *distributed by* Houghton Mifflin Co

Clarity Press Inc, *member of* ACLU Society for Scholarly Publishing

Clarity Sound & Light, *imprint of* Crystal Clarity Publishers

Frances Clark, *distributed by* Warner Bros Publications Inc

Clarkson Potter, *imprint of* Clarkson Potter Publishers, Crown Publishing Group, Random House Inc, *distributor for* The Colonial Williamsburg Foundation

Clarkson Potter Publishers, *division of* Random House Inc, *subsidiary of* Crown Publishing Group, *distributed by* Random House

Classic Publishers, *distributed by* Harmony House Publishers - Louisville

Classic Reprint Series, *imprint of* University of Alaska Press

Classics in Economics, *imprint of* Transaction Publishers

Classics With a Twist, *imprint of* Empire Publishing Service

Classroom Classics, *imprint of* World Citizens

Clear Creek Publishing, *distributed by* Gem Guides Book Co

Clear Horizon Books, *imprint of* Macalester Park Publishing Co

Clear Light Books, *distributed by* Kiva Publishing Inc

Clear Light Distribution, *distributor for* Ocean Tree Books

Clearfield, *distributed by* Ericson Books

Clearfield Co Inc, *subsidiary of* Genealogical Publishing Co Inc

Cleartype American Map Corp, *imprint of* American Map Corp

Clearwater, *imprint of* LexisNexis Academic & Library Solutions

Sydney Gurewitz Clemens, *distributed by* Gryphon House Inc

Clerc Books, *imprint of* Gallaudet University Press

Clever Kids, *imprint of* Modern Publishing

CLIE, *distributed by* Editorial Bautista Independiente

Client Distribution Services, *distributor for* Harvard Business School Press

Cliffhanger, *imprint of* DC Comics

Cliffs Notes, *distributed by* Penton Overseas Inc

CliffsNotes™, *imprint of* John Wiley & Sons Inc

Clinamen Press, *distributed by* Paul & Company

Clinical Advances, *imprint of* Oakstone Medical Publishing

Clinical & Social Psychology, *imprint of* Transaction Publishers

The Clinician's Toolbox, *imprint of* The Guilford Press

Clipper Audio, *imprint of* Haights Cross Communications Inc

Clipper Audio (UK), *imprint of* Haights Cross Communications Inc, Recorded Books LLC

Clo Iar-Chonnachta, *distributed by* Dufour Editions Inc

Cloister Recordings (audio & video tapes), *distributed by* Gateways Books & Tapes

Close Up Publishing, *division of* Close Up Foundation

Closson Press, *distributed by* Hearthstone Books, Heritage/Willowbend, Masthof Press

Clovernook Printing House for the Blind, *division of* The Clovernook Center for the Blind

Clymer ProSeries, *imprint of* PRIMEDIA Business Directories & Books

Clymer Publications, *imprint of* PRIMEDIA Business Directories & Books

CMP Books, *division of* CMP Media LLC, *imprint of* United Business Media

Coastal Living Books, *imprint of* Oxmoor House Inc

Coastal New England Publications, *imprint of* Harvest Hill Press

Cobblestone Publishing Co, *division of* The Cricket Magazine Group

Cobra Institute, *imprint of* DIANE Publishing Co

Coda Publications, *imprint of* Coda Publications

Codhill Press, *distributed by* Steiner Books

Cogan Books, *distributor for* Blushing Rose Publishing

Cogito Books, *imprint of* Medical Physics Publishing Corp

Cognitive Concepts Inc, *subsidiary of* Houghton Mifflin Co

Cokesbury, *imprint of* Abingdon Press, *distributed by* Abingdon Press

Cold Spring Harbor Laboratory Press, *division of* Cold Spring Harbor Laboratory

Cold Spring Press, *imprint of* Open Road Publishing

Coleccion Aquiy Ahora, *imprint of* University of Puerto Rico Press

Coleccion Caribena, *imprint of* University of Puerto Rico Press

Coleccion Cultura Basica, *imprint of* University of Puerto Rico Press

Coleccion Infantil, *imprint of* University of Puerto Rico Press

Coleccion Mente y Palabra, *imprint of* University of Puerto Rico Press

Coleccion Puertorriquena, *imprint of* University of Puerto Rico Press

Coleccion San Pedrito, *imprint of* University of Puerto Rico Press

Coleccion Uprex, *imprint of* University of Puerto Rico Press

Colgate University Press, *distributed by* Syracuse University Press

Armand Colin, *distributed by* Lacis Publications

Colleagues Books, *imprint of* Michigan State University Press (MSU Press), *distributed by* Michigan State University Press (MSU Press)

Collectors Press Inc, *distributed by* Ten Speed Press

The College Board, *distributed by* Henry Holt, Henry Holt and Company, LLC

College Days Press, *imprint of* R J Berg/Destinations Press Ltd

College Level Examination Series, *imprint of* National Learning Corp

College of Mount St Vincent Press, *distributed by* The Bronx County Historical Society

College Press Publishing Co, *distributor for* David C Cook Publishing, Gospel Light, *distributed by* Appalachian, CBD, Midwest Library Service, Riverside, Spring Arbor

College Proficiency Examination Series, *imprint of* National Learning Corp

Collegiate Memories Press, *imprint of* R J Berg/ Destinations Press Ltd

Collegium Graphicum, *imprint of* Alan Wofsy Fine Arts

Collins & Brown, *distributed by* Sterling Publishing Co Inc

Collins Press, *distributed by* Dufour Editions Inc

Collinwood Media, *distributed by* Bottom Dog Press

Colonial Society of Massachusetts, *distributed by* The University of Virginia Press

Colonial Williamsburg, *imprint of* The Colonial Williamsburg Foundation, *distributed by* Antique Collectors Club Ltd

The Colonial Williamsburg Foundation, *distributed by* Harry N Abrams Inc, Antique Collectors Club, Ohio University Press, Clarkson Potter, Quite Specific Media Ltd, Random House Children's Books, Scholastic, Stackpole, University Press of New England, Yale University Press

Colophon, *distributed by* Antique Collectors Club Ltd

Colorado Geological Survey, *division of* Department of Natural Resources State of Colorado

Colorado Historical Society, *distributed by* University Press of Colorado

Colorado Mountain Club Press, *distributed by* The Mountaineers Books

Colorado Railroad Museum, *subsidiary of* Colorado Railroad Historical Foundation

Colorprint American Map Corp, *imprint of* American Map Corp

Columba, *distributor for* Twenty-Third Publications

The Columba Press, *distributed by* Dufour Editions Inc

Columbia International Affairs Online (CIAO), *distributor for* University of California Institute on Global Conflict & Cooperation

Columbia University Press, *distributor for* Chinese University Press, East European Monographs, Edinburgh University Press, Kegan Paul, National Bureau of Economic Research Inc, University of Tokyo Press, Wallflower Press, The Woodrow Wilson Center Press

Colwood Press Ltd, *distributed by* Antique Collectors Club Ltd

Combat Aircraft, *imprint of* Osprey Publishing Ltd

Combined Publishing, *imprint of* The Perseus Books Group

ComicsLit, *imprint of* NBM Publishing Inc

Commercial Press, *distributed by* China Books & Periodicals Inc

Commercial Press (Hong Kong), *distributed by* Cheng & Tsui Co Inc

Commodity Trend Service, *division of* Dearborn Trade Publishing

Common Courage Press, *distributor for* Odonian Press, Real Story Series

Common Ground Distributors, *distributor for* Dog-Eared Publications

Commons House Journal, *imprint of* South Carolina Dept of Archives & History

Commonwealth Book Co, *imprint of* McClanahan Publishing House Inc

Commonwealth Editions, *imprint of* Memoirs Unlimited Inc

The Commonwealth Secretariat, *distributed by* Stylus Publishing LLC

Communication & Culture, *imprint of* Transaction Publishers

Communication Skills Inc, *distributor for* Chronicle Guidance Publications Inc

Community Intervention, *distributor for* MAR*CO Products Inc

Community Music Videos, *distributed by* Hal Leonard Corp

Companion Press, *distributor for* University of Nevada Press

Comparative Policy Analysis, *imprint of* Transaction Publishers

Comparative Politics, *imprint of* Transaction Publishers

Compass American Guides, *division of* Fodors Travel Publications /Random House, Fodors Travel Publications/Random House Inc, *imprint of* Fodor's Travel Publications, *distributed by* Random House Inc (Contact Fodor's)

Compass Equestrian, *distributed by* Trafalgar Square

Compass Point Mysteries, *imprint of* Quincannon Publishing Group

Compass Press, *distributed by* Paul & Company

The Compass Press, *imprint of* Howells House

Compass Publications, *distributed by* NACE International

Compendium Publishing, *distributed by* Casemate Publishers

Compu-Tek, *distributed by* Copywriter's Council of America (CCA)

CompuMaster, *division of* SkillPath Publications

Computer Connections, *imprint of* The Learning Connection (TLC)

Comstock Publishing Associates, *imprint of* Cornell University Press

Conari Press, *distributed by* Gryphon House Inc

Conation Press, *imprint of* Greenleaf Book Group LLC

Conciliar Press, *affiliate of* Antiochian Archdiocese, *distributor for* Light & Life, *distributed by* Light & Life, St Vladimir's

Concord Library, *imprint of* Beacon Press

Concordia Academic Press, *division of* Concordia Publishing House

Concourse Poetry Series, *imprint of* Concourse Press

Concourse Press, *subsidiary of* East-West Fine Arts Corp, East-West Fine Arts Corp, *distributor for* Hafezieh Publications (Germany)

CondeNast/Johansens, *distributed by* Casemate Publishers

The William G Congdon Foundation, *distributed by* Antique Collectors Club Ltd

Congress Watch, *division of* Public Citizen

Congressional Information Service, *imprint of* LexisNexis Academic & Library Solutions

Congressional Quarterly Press, *division of* Congressional Quarterly Inc, Congressional Quarterly Inc

The Connectcut Law Tribune, *imprint of* Law Tribune Books

Conner Prairie Press, *imprint of* Emmis Books

Conran, *distributed by* Sterling Publishing Co Inc

Conran Octopus, *distributed by* Antique Collectors Club Ltd

Consciousness Classics, *imprint of* Gateways Books & Tapes

Conservation International, *distributed by* Association of American University Presses

Conservations with Public Intellectuals Series, *imprint of* University Press of Mississippi

Consortium Book Sales, *distributor for* Gryphon House Inc, White Pine Press

Consortium Book Sales & Distribution, *distributor for* Leapfrog Press, Redleaf Press, Stone Bridge Press LLC

Consortium Book Sales & Distribution Inc, *distributor for* Ocean Press

Consortuim Book Sales & Distribution (PUB-NET), *distributor for* Whereabouts Press

Consultants News, *imprint of* Kennedy Information

Consulting Magazine, *imprint of* Kennedy Information

Consumer Guide/PIL, *distributed by* Penguin Group (USA) Inc

Consumer Reports, *distributor for* United States Pharmacopeia, *distributed by* St Martin's Press LLC

Consumer Software, *division of* Rand McNally

Consumertronics, *affiliate of* Top Secret Consumertronics Global (TSC-Global)

Contemporary Book, *imprint of* The Wright Group/McGraw-Hill, a Division of McGraw-Hill Learning Group

Contemporary Books, *distributor for* Creative Publishing International Inc

Contemporary Classics by Women, *imprint of* The Feminist Press at The City University of New York

Contemporary Drama Service, *subsidiary of* Meriwether Publishing Ltd/Contemporary Drama Service, *imprint of* Meriwether Publishing Ltd/Contemporary Drama Service

Continental Afrikan Publishers, *division of* Afrikamawu Miracle Mission AMI, Afrikamawu Miracle Mission, AMI Inc

Continental Atlantic (US only), *distributed by* Mint Publishers Group

Continental Book Co, *distributor for* Fondo de Cultura Economica USA Inc

Continuing Education Press, *affiliate of* Portland State University Extended Studies

Continuum International Publishing, *distributor for* Paragon House

The Continuum International Publishing Group, *distributor for* Continuum London, Medio Media, Morehouse, Paragon House, Spring Publications, *distributed by* Continuum London

Continuum London, *distributor for* The Continuum International Publishing Group, *distributed by* The Continuum International Publishing Group

Contra/Thought, *imprint of* Holmes Publishing Group

Conversations with Comic Artists Series, *imprint of* University Press of Mississippi

Conversations with Filmmakers Series, *imprint of* University Press of Mississippi

Conway Maritime Press, *distributed by* Casemate Publishers

Cook Communications, *distributor for* Focus on the Family

Cook Communications Ministries, *division of* Cook Communications Ministries, *distributor for* Lion Publishing

David C Cook Publishing, *distributed by* College Press Publishing Co

Thomas Cook Publishing, *distributed by* The Globe Pequot Press

Cooking for the Rushed (US & Canada), *distributed by* Mint Publishers Group

Cooking Light Books, *imprint of* Oxmoor House Inc

Cookworks, *distributed by* Sterling Publishing Co Inc

Cooper Square, *distributed by* Barnes & Noble Books (Imports & Reprints)

Cooper Square Press, *member of* Rowman & Littlefield Publishing Group

Coordinating Research Council Inc, *distributed by* SAE (Society of Automotive Engineers International)

Copernicus, *imprint of* Springer-Verlag New York Inc, *distributed by* Springer-Verlag New York Inc

Copley Custom Publishing Group, *imprint of* Copley Publishing Group

Copley Editions, *imprint of* Copley Publishing Group

Copley Publishing Group, *imprint of* Copley Publishing Group, ProQuest Information & Learning, ProQuest Information & Learning Co

Copper Beech, *imprint of* The Millbrook Press Inc

Copper Canyon Press, *distributor for* American Poetry Review/Honickman

Coptales, *imprint of* Oak Tree Publishing

Copywriter's Council of America (CCA), *division of* The Linick Group Inc, *distributor for* ASL, Compu-Tek, NAPS, Picture Profits

CorelPRESS, *imprint of* McGraw-Hill/Osborne

Cork University Press, *distributed by* Stylus Publishing LLC

Cormorant Books, *imprint of* Down The Shore Publishing Corp

Cormorant Calendars, *imprint of* Down The Shore Publishing Corp

Cornell Maritime Press Inc, *distributor for* Chesapeake Bay Maritime Museum, Literary House Press, Maryland Historical Trust Press, Maryland Sea Grant Program, Maryland State Archives Publications

Cornell University Press, *division of* Cornell University, *distributor for* University of California Institute on Global Conflict & Cooperation

Cornell University Press Services, *distributor for* Oberlin College Press

Cornell University Southeast Asia Program Publications, *unit of* Cornell University, *distributor for* A U A Language Center

Cornerstone Books, *imprint of* Monthly Review Press

Cornerstone Productions Inc, *division of* Reggae Legends of Trench-Town Jamaica

Cornwal Books, *distributor for* Herzl Press

Coronet Books & Publications, *distributor for* Coronet Books & Publications, *distributed by* Coronet Books & Publications

Cortina Institute of Language, Instituto Linguistico Cortina, *division of* Cortina Learning International Inc

Cortina Learning International Inc, *distributor for* Linguaphone Institute Ltd, *distributed by* Henry Holt and Company Inc, Henry Holt and Company, LLC

Corwin Press, *subsidiary of* Sage Publications, *distributor for* Paul Chapman Publishing, Sage Ltd, Sage Publications

Corwin Press Inc, *subsidiary of* Sage Publications

Cosmic-World Publishing, *imprint of* Neo-Tech Publishing

Cosmos Books, *imprint of* Wildside Press

Cost Annuals, *division of* R S Means Co Inc

Costume & Fashion Press, *imprint of* Quite Specific Media Group Ltd

Joanna Cotler Books, *imprint of* HarperCollins Children's Books Group

Cottonwood Press Inc, *distributed by* Elder Song Publications Inc, Lakeshore Learning, NASCO, PCI, Social Studies School Services, Teacher Discovery

Cottonwood Publishing, *distributed by* Mountain Press Publishing Co

Council for Exceptional Children, *distributor for* Brooks (selected titles), Longman, Love Publishing, Pearson, Pro Ed, Sopris West, *distributed by* Free Spirit Publishing Inc, LMD Inc (selected titles), Orchard House Inc

The Council for Research in Values & Philosophy, *imprint of* Council for Research in Values & Philosophy (RVP)

Council Oak Books, *distributor for* Crane Hill Publishers, *distributed by* Gryphon House Inc

Council of Europe, *distributed by* Manhattan Publishing Co

Council on Foreign Relations, *distributed by* The Brookings Institution Press

Council on Foreign Relations Press, *division of* Council on Foreign Relations, *distributed by* Brookings Institution Press

Counseling Outfitters, *distributor for* American Counseling Association

Counterpoint, *distributed by* HarperCollins Publishers

Counterpoint Press, *member of* Perseus Books Group, The Perseus Books Group, *imprint of* The Perseus Books Group, *distributed by* HarperCollins

The Country Cottage, *distributed by* Moon Lady Press

Country Music Foundation Press, *division of* Country Music Hall of Fame® & Museum, COUNTRY MUSIC HALL OF FAME® MUSEUM, *imprint of* Vanderbilt University Press, *distributed by* Chronicle, Oxford University Press Inc, Providence Publishing, Universe, Vanderbilt University Press

Countryman Press, *imprint of* W W Norton & Company Inc

The Countryman Press, *division of* W W Norton & Co Inc, *imprint of* W W Norton & Company Inc, *distributor for* Mountain Pond Publishing Corp, *distributed by* W W Norton & Co Inc, Penguin Books (Canada only)

Countrysport Press, *imprint of* Down East Books

Courage Books, *imprint of* The Perseus Books Group, Running Press Book Publishers

Course Technology, *subsidiary of* International Thomson Publishing, International Thomson Publishing (ITP), *distributed by* South-Western Publishing

Court Street Press, *imprint of* NewSouth Inc

Coutts Library Service, *distributor for* Investor Responsibility Research Center, Primary Research Group

Cove Press, *imprint of* US Games Systems Inc

Cover Craft, *imprint of* Perfection Learning Corp

Cover-to-Cover, *imprint of* Perfection Learning Corp

Franklin Covey, *distributed by* SkillPath Publications

Coward-McCann, *imprint of* The Putnam Publishing Group

Cowboy Artists of America, *distributed by* Johnson Books

Cowley Publications, *division of* Society of St John the Evangelist

Coyote Press, *affiliate of* Archaeological Consulting

CQ Inc, *imprint of* Congressional Quarterly Press

CQ Press, *subsidiary of* Congressional Quarterly Inc, Congressional Quarterly Inc, *imprint of* Congressional Quarterly Press

Crabtree Publishing, *distributed by* Perfection Learning Corp

Crabtree Publishing Canada, *subsidiary of* Crabtree Publishing Co

Crabtree Publishing UK, *subsidiary of* Crabtree Publishing Co

Craftsman Book Co, *distributor for* Building News Inc, Home Builders Press, *distributed by* The Aberdeen Group, American Technical Publishers, American Technical Publishers Inc, Quality Books

Robert L Crager & Co, *imprint of* Pelican Publishing Co Inc

Cramer (Geneva), *distributed by* Alan Wofsy Fine Arts

Cramer (Switzerland), *distributed by* Picasso Project

Cranbrook Institute of Science, *distributed by* Wayne State University Press

Crane Hill Publishers, *distributed by* Council Oak Books

Cranky Nell Books, *imprint of* Kane/Miller Book Publishers

Craven Street Books, *imprint of* Linden Publishing Company Inc

Crazy Crow, *distributed by* Book Publishing Co

Crazy Games, *imprint of* Price Stern Sloan

CRC Press, *distributor for* The Fairmont Press Inc, *distributed by* American Academy of Environmental Engineers, American Marketing Association, NACE International, SAS Publishing

CRC Press LLC, *subsidiary of* Taylor & Frances Book Inc, Taylor & Frances

CRCS Publications, *distributed by* Book Publishing Co

Creation House, *distributor for* Charisma House

Creation House Press (Co-Publishing Group), *imprint of* Charisma House

Creative Arts & Crafts, *imprint of* Creative Homeowner

Creative Arts Book Co, *distributor for* ZYZZYVA First Titles

Creative Arts Communications, *division of* Creative Arts Book Co, *imprint of* Creative Arts Book Co

Creative Arts Life & Health Books, *imprint of* Creative Arts Book Co

Creative Child Press, *imprint of* Playmore Inc, Publishers

Creative Concepts, *distributed by* Hal Leonard Corp

Creative Editions, *imprint of* The Creative Co

Creative Education, *imprint of* The Creative Co

Creative Homeowner, *division of* Federal Marketing Corp, Federal Marketing Corp, *distributor for* Publishing Solutions

Creative Homeowner Press, *distributor for* Home Planners LLC

Creative House (US & Canada), *distributed by* Mint Publishers Group

Creative Keyboard, *imprint of* Mel Bay Publications Inc

Creative Keyboard Publications, *division of* Mel Bay Publications Inc

Creative Map, *imprint of* Langenscheidt Publishers Inc

Creative Nell Books, *imprint of* Kane/Miller Book Publishers

Creative Outdoors, *imprint of* Creative Homeowner

Creative Publications, *imprint of* The Wright Group/McGraw-Hill, a Division of McGraw-Hill Learning Group

Creative Publishing International Inc, *distributed by* Contemporary Books

Creative Sales, *division of* Langenscheidt Publishers Inc

Creative Sales Corp, *subsidiary of* American Map Corp, *distributor for* American Map Corp, *distributed by* Hagstrom Map Co Inc, Trakker Maps Inc

Credit Card Users of America Press, *imprint of* The Boswell Institute

Creighton University Press, *distributed by* Fordham University Press, University of Nebraska Press

Crescendo, *imprint of* Taplinger Publishing Co Inc

Crescent, *imprint of* Random House Value Publishing

Crescent Books, *imprint of* Random House Inc

Cress Productions Co, *distributor for* MAR*CO Products Inc

Cricket Books, *division of* Carus Publishing, Carus Publishing Co

Crimeline, *imprint of* Random House Inc

Crimethinc, *distributed by* AK Press Distribution

Criminal Justice Press, *division of* Willow Tree Press Inc, *distributor for* Australian Institute of Criminology, European Institute for Crime Prevention & Control, *distributed by* Federation Press, Police Executive Research Forum

Crisp Books, *distributed by* Michigan Municipal League

Critical Accounting, *imprint of* Markus Wiener Publishers Inc

Critical Mass Energy Project, *division of* Public Citizen

Critical Path, *distributed by* Book Publishing Co

Croatian Musicological Society, *distributed by* Pendragon Press

Crocodile Books, *imprint of* Interlink Publishing Group Inc

Crofts Classics Series, *imprint of* Harlan Davidson Inc/Forum Press Inc

Cross-Cultural Communications, *subsidiary of* Cross-Cultural Communications Publications Corp, Cross-Cultural Communications Publications Corporation, *affiliate of* Cross-Cultural Literary Editions Inc, *distributor for* Ad Infinitum Books (United States), Arba Sicula (Magazine), Biblio Press (United States), Center of Emigrants from Serbia (Serbia), Decalogue Books (United States), Greenfield Review Press (United States), Hochelaga (Canada), Legas (Publishers, United States), Lips (Magazine & Press), Pholiota Press Inc (England), Shabdaguchha (Magazine & Press) (United States), Sicilia Parra (Magazine, United States), Word & Quill Press (United States), *distributed by* Hochelaga (Canada)

Cross-Cultural Memoir Series, *imprint of* The Feminist Press at The City University of New York

Cross-Cultural Prototypes, *imprint of* Cross-Cultural Communications

Cross Roads Books, *division of* Cross Cultural Publications Inc, *imprint of* Cross Cultural Publications Inc

Cross Training, *distributed by* CharismaLife Publishers

Cross Training (Youth Group-Curriculm Group), *imprint of* Charisma House

The Crossing Press, *imprint of* Ten-Speed Press

Crossquarter Breeze, *imprint of* Crossquarter Publishing Group

Crossroad, *imprint of* The Crossroad Publishing Company

CrossTIME, *imprint of* Crossquarter Publishing Group

Crossway Books, *division of* Good News Publishers

Crow Canyon Archaeological Center, *distributed by* The University of Arizona Press

Crown, *imprint of* Crown Publishing Group, *distributor for* The Bronx County Historical Society, *distributed by* Perfection Learning Corp

Crown Books for Young Readers, *imprint of* Random House Children's Books, Random House Inc

Crown Business, *imprint of* Crown Publishing Group

Crown Forum, *imprint of* Crown Publishing Group

Crown House Publishing, *unit of* Crown House Publishing Ltd

Crown Publishers, *distributed by* Sundance Publishing

Crown Publishers Inc, *imprint of* Random House Inc

Crown Publishing Group, *division of* Random House Inc, Random House Inc, *distributor for* Nevraumont Publishing Co

The Crowood Press, *distributed by* Trafalgar Square

Cruise & Resorts Press, *imprint of* R J Berg/Destinations Press Ltd

Cruise Concepts Inc (Licensor) Cruise Control, *distributed by* Penton Overseas Inc

Crystal Fountain Publications, *division of* Crystal Fountain Ministries Inc, Crystal Fountain Ministries Inc, *distributor for* Judson Press, *distributed by* Spring Arbor

Crystal Sea Books, *imprint of* Beacon Hill Press of Kansas City

Crystal Star/Jones Products, *distributor for* Healthy Healing Publications

CSI Publications, *imprint of* Christian Schools International

CSLI Publications, *distributed by* University of Chicago Press

CT Corporation, *imprint of* Wolters Kluwer US Corp

CTB/McGraw-Hill, *division of* McGraw-Hill Education, The McGraw-Hill Companies, *imprint of* McGraw-Hill Education

CTW Publishing, *imprint of* Random House Inc

Cumberland House-Hearthside Books, *imprint of* Cumberland House Publishing Inc

Curious Little Critters Series, *imprint of* Stemmer House Publishers Inc

Curious Nell Books, *imprint of* Kane/Miller Book Publishers

Currency, *imprint of* Doubleday Broadway Publishing Group, Random House Inc

Current Medicine, *division of* Current Science Group, *distributed by* American Psychology Press, Appleton Lange, Blackwell Science, Butterworth-Heinemann, W B Saunders, Springer Verlag, Thieme, Williams & Wilkins

Current Science Inc, *imprint of* Current Medicine

Currier Publications, *distributed by* Antique Collectors Club Ltd

CyberAge Books, *imprint of* Information Today, Inc

CyberRead, *distributor for* Bridge Publications Inc, SynergEbooks

Cycle Publishing, *distributed by* Chris Lloyd

Cynthia Publishing Co, *distributor for* HarperCollins Publishers

Cyrco Press, *distributed by* Ardent Media Inc

D A P, *distributor for* MFA Publications, Robert Miller Gallery

D & J Books, *distributor for* A & B Publishers Group

D-Day Publishing, *distributed by* Casemate Publishers

Da Capo Press, *imprint of* The Perseus Books Group

Da Capo Press Inc, *member of* Perseus Books Group, The Perseus Books Group, *distributed by* HarperCollins

Da Fina, *imprint of* Kensington Publishing Corp

DA Information Services, *distributor for* Institute for International Economics

DACO Publications, *distributed by* Casemate Publishers

Dakini Books, *distributed by* powerHouse Books

Dakota West Books, *distributor for* Naturegraph Publishers Inc

Dalkey Archive Press, *distributed by* University of Nebraska Press

Dame Publications Inc, *imprint of* South-Western, A Thomson Business

Dan River Press, *division of* Conservatory of American Letters, *distributor for* Century Press, Northwoods Press

Dan River Press (textbook div), *distributed by* Northwoods Press

Dance Books Ltd, *distributed by* Princeton Book Co Publishers

Dance Horizons, *imprint of* Princeton Book Co Publishers

Dance Horizons Video, *division of* Princeton Book Co Publishers, *imprint of* Princeton Book Co Publishers

Dance Notation Bureau, *distributed by* Princeton Book Co Publishers

Dandy Lion Press, *distributor for* Great Potential Press

C W Daniel, *distributed by* Beekman Publishers Inc

John Daniel & Co, Publishers, *division of* Daniel & Daniel, Publishers Inc, Daniel & Daniel, Publishers Inc, *distributor for* Fithian Press, Perserverance Press

Dante Series, *imprint of* National Learning Corp

Dante University of America Press Inc, *distributed by* Branden Publishing Co, Branden Publishing Co Inc

DAP Distributed Art Publishers, *distributor for* MIT List Visual Arts Center, Turtle Point Press

Darby Creek, *distributed by* Lerner Publishing Group

Dark Horse Books, *imprint of* Dark Horse Comics

Dark Horse Comics, *imprint of* Dark Horse Comics, *affiliate of* Dark Horse Entertainment, *distributed by* LPC Group Inc

Dark Oak Mysteries, *imprint of* Oak Tree Publishing

Darling & Co, *imprint of* Laughing Elephant

Dartmouth College Press, *imprint of* University Press of New England

Dartmouth Publishing, *imprint of* Ashgate Publishing Co

Dartnell, *distributed by* Professional Publishing

The Dartnell Corp, *subsidiary of* LRP Publications

Darton Longman & Todd Ltd (selected titles), *distributed by* Pickwick Publications

Darwin® Books, *imprint of* The Darwin Press Inc

The Darwin Press Inc, *imprint of* Darwin® Books

David Publishing, *distributor for* Fire Engineering Books & Videos

Davies-Black Publishing, *division of* Consulting Psychologists Press Inc, CPP Inc, *distributed by* National Book Network

Davies Direct Booksellers, *division of* Davies Publishing Inc

Davis, *distributed by* Sterling Publishing Co Inc

DAW, *imprint of* Penguin Group (USA) Inc

DAW Books Inc, *affiliate of* Penguin Group (USA) Inc, *distributed by* Penguin Group (USA) Inc, Penguin Group (USA) Inc

DAW/Fantasy, *imprint of* DAW Books Inc

DAW/Fiction, *imprint of* DAW Books Inc

DAW/Science Fiction, *imprint of* DAW Books Inc

The Dawn Horse Press, *division of* Avataric Pan-Communion of Adidam, *distributed by* De Vorss, Dempsey & Deep Books, Ingram Books, New Leaf Distributing

Dawn Sign Press, *distributed by* Gryphon House Inc

DawnSignPress, *distributor for* Gallaudet University Press, MIT Press, Random House Inc, *distributed by* Gryphon House

Dawson France, *distributor for* Investor Responsibility Research Center

Dawson UK Ltd, *distributor for* Investor Responsibility Research Center

Dawsons Book Shop, *distributed by* Sunbelt Publications Inc

Day Hikes Books Inc, *distributed by* The Globe Pequot Press

The Day That Was Different, *imprint of* Gallopade International Inc

Moshe Dayan Center for Middle Eastern & African Studies, *distributed by* Syracuse University Press

DBI Books, *division of* Krause Publications, Krause Publications Inc, *imprint of* Krause Publications, *distributed by* Krause Publications

dbS Productions, *distributed by* ERI Bookstore, NASAR Bookstore, Oklahoma State University

DC Comics, *division of* Warner Bros, A Time Warner Entertainment Co, Warner Bros, A Time Warner Entertainment Co, *distributed by* Time Warner Book Group, Time Warner Trade Publishing

DC Press, *division of* Diogenes Consortium

DC Publications, *distributed by* Hal Leonard Corp

DD Equestrian Library, *imprint of* Doubleday Broadway Publishing Group

Alain De Gourcuff Editeur, *distributed by* Antique Collectors Club Ltd

Mouton de Gruyter, *division of* Walter de Gruyter, Inc, Walter de Gruyter GmbH & Co KG, *distributed by* Walter de Gruyter Inc

Walter de Gruyter Inc, *distributor for* Mouton de Gruyter

Walter de Gruyter, Inc, *division of* Walter de Gruyter GmbH & Co KG, Walter de Gruyter GmbH & Co KG

De Krijger, *distributed by* Casemate Publishers

De Vorss & Co, *distributor for* Science of Mind Publications, White Eagle Publishing Trust (England)

De Vorss, Dempsey & Deep Books, *distributor for* The Dawn Horse Press

M H De Young Memorial Museum, *distributed by* Antique Collectors Club Ltd

Dealer's Choice Books Inc, *distributor for* Art Sales Index, ArtPrice.com, E Benezit Librairie

Dearborn, *imprint of* Dearborn Trade Publishing

Dearborn Financial Institute Inc, *subsidiary of* Dearborn Trade Publishing

Dearborn Trade, *division of* Dearborn Trade Publishing, *distributor for* Appraisal Institute

Dearborn Trade Publishing, *division of* Dearborn Publishing Group Inc, *distributor for* National Education Standards

Decalogue Books, *distributed by* Cross-Cultural Communications

Dechema (selected titles), *distributor for* American Institute of Chemical Engineers (AICHE), *distributed by* American Institute of Chemical Engineers (AICHE)

Dechema Series, *distributed by* Scholium International Inc

B C Decker, *imprint of* Elsevier

Dedalus Press, *distributed by* Dufour Editions Inc

Ivan R Dee Publisher, *member of* Rowman & Littlefield Publishing Group

Deep Books, *distributor for* Vital Health Publishing

Deep Books (UK), *distributor for* Boys Town Press

Deep Stream Press, *distributed by* Chelsea Green Publishing Co

DeFiance Audio, *imprint of* Listen & Live Audio Inc

Marcel Dekker Inc, *distributor for* The Electrochemical Society Inc, *distributed by* NACE International

Del Rey, *imprint of* Random House Inc, Random House Publishing Group

Del Rey Books, *imprint of* Random House Publishing Group

Delacorte Books for Young Readers, *imprint of* Random House Children's Books

Delacorte Press, *imprint of* Bantam Dell Publishing Group, Random House Inc

Delaney Books Inc, *subsidiary of* National Learning Corp

Delaware Estuary Press, *division of* Weidner & Sons Publishing, *imprint of* Weidner & Sons Publishing, *distributed by* Weidner & Sons Publishing

Delaware Museum Books, *division of* Weidner & Sons Publishing

Delaware Museum of Natural History, *distributed by* Weidner & Sons Publishing

Dell, *imprint of* Random House Inc

Dell Books, *imprint of* Bantam Dell Publishing Group

Dell Laurel Leaf, *imprint of* Random House Inc

Dell Yearling, *imprint of* Random House Inc

Delmar, *distributor for* LearningExpress LLC

Delmar Publishers Inc, *distributed by* Gryphon House Inc

Delmar Thomson, *distributed by* The Alexander Graham Bell Association for the Deaf & Hard of Hearing

DeLorme, *distributed by* Wide World of Maps Inc

DeLorme Atlas, *distributed by* American Map Corp, Hagstrom Map Co Inc

Delorme Maps, *distributed by* Langenscheidt Publishers Inc

Delta, *imprint of* Random House Inc

Delta Books, *imprint of* Bantam Dell Publishing Group

Delta Education, *distributor for* National Council of Teachers of Mathematics

Delta Systems Inc, *distributor for* Teachers of English to Speakers of Other Languages Inc (TESOL)

The Denali Press, *distributor for* Libris, Meridian Books

Denlinger's Publishers Ltd, *distributor for* Atlantis Productions

Richard Dennis, *distributed by* Antique Collectors Club Ltd

Deo, *distributed by* Presbyterian Publishing Corp

Derrydale, *imprint of* Random House Inc

Desert Charts, *division of* Wide World of Maps Inc

Design Books, *distributed by* The Lyons Press

Deskmap Systems, *distributed by* Heimburger House Publishing Co

Destiny Books, *imprint of* Inner Traditions International Ltd

Destiny Image, *distributor for* Mercy Place

Destiny Image Fiction, *imprint of* Destiny Image

Destiny Recordings, *imprint of* Inner Traditions International Ltd

Detect-A-Word, *imprint of* Modern Publishing

Detroit Institute of Arts, *distributed by* Antique Collectors Club Ltd, Wayne State University Press

Andre Deutsch Ltd, *distributed by* Trafalgar Square

Devine Entertainment Corp, *distributed by* Hal Leonard Corp

Devora Publishing, *imprint of* Pitspopany Press

Devores, *distributor for* SOM Publishing

Deya Brashears, *distributed by* Gryphon House Inc

DGM Informationsgesellschaft (selected titles), *distributed by* Metal Powder Industries Federation

Dharma Publishing, *imprint of* Windhorse Books

Diablo Press Inc, *affiliate of* Kensington Book Co, Kensington Book Co

Dial Books for Young Readers, *imprint of* Penguin Group (USA) Inc, Penguin Group (USA) Inc, Penguin Young Readers Group

Dial Press, *imprint of* Bantam Dell Publishing Group

The Dial Press, *imprint of* Random House Inc

Dialogue Foundation, *distributed by* Signature Books Publishing LLC

Diamond Books, *imprint of* Berkley Books, Berkley Publishing Group

Diamond Farm Book Publishers, *division of* Yesteryear Toys & Books Inc, Yesteryear Toys & Books Inc, *distributor for* Farming Press, Whittet

Diamond Select, *distributed by* Andrews McMeel Publishing

Didax Educational Resources, *distributor for* National Council of Teachers of Mathematics

Dietz Press, *distributed by* Ericson Books

Digital-I Books, *imprint of* Purdue University Press

Digital Leaf & E-Press, *imprint of* Windstorm Creative

Dimensions for Living, *imprint of* Abingdon Press, *distributed by* Abingdon Press

Dine College Press, *division of* Navajo Nation, *affiliate of* Navajo Nation, *distributed by* Book People, Five Star Publications Inc, Territory Titles

Dipti, *imprint of* Lotus Press, *distributed by* Lotus Press

Direct-Mail Division, *division of* Bobley Harmann Corp

Discipleship Publications International (DPI), *division of* Boston Church of Christ

Discoveries, *imprint of* Latin American Literary Review Press

Discovery Books, *imprint of* Random House Inc

Discovery Enterprises Ltd, *distributor for* National Archives

Discovery House, *distributed by* Thomas Nelson Inc

Discovery House Publishers, *distributed by* Barbour Publishing Inc

Discovery Links, *imprint of* Haights Cross Communications Inc

Disney Children's Book Group, *division of* Disney Publishing Worldwide

Disney Press, *division of* The Walt Disney Co, The Walt Disney Co, *distributed by* Perfection Learning Corp, Time Warner Publishing

Disney Publishing Worldwide, *subsidiary of* The Walt Disney Co, Walt Disney Co, *distributed by* Time Warner Book Group

Disseminations: Psychoanalysis in Contexts, *imprint of* Wesleyan University Press

Dissertation, *imprint of* Dissertation.com

Dissertation.com, *distributed by* Bertrams UK

Distri Books, *distributed by* Perfection Learning Corp

Distributed Art Publishers, *distributor for* American Federation of Arts

Distributed Art Publishers (DAP), *distributor for* Art Institute of Chicago, The Museum of Modern Art, Philadelphia Museum of Art

Distribution Orion, *distributor for* TSG Publishing Foundation Inc

The Distributors, *distributor for* AVKO Dyslexia & Spelling Research Foundation Inc

Dixie Press, *imprint of* Pelican Publishing Co Inc

Djoef Publishing, *distributed by* Enfield Publishing & Distribution Co

DK Publishing, *distributed by* Perfection Learning Corp

DK Publishing Inc, *subsidiary of* Pearson plc, *distributed by* Ball Publishing

DLM, *imprint of* The Wright Group/McGraw-Hill, a Division of McGraw-Hill Learning Group

DLM-Giles de la Mare, *distributed by* Trafalgar Square

DLR Imagery, *distributed by* Western New York Wares Inc

DNA Press, *distributed by* Paul & Company

Do-It-Yourself Legal Publishers, *affiliate of* Self-helper Law Press of America, *distributed by* Brodart Co, Midwest Library Service, Quality Books, Unique Books

The DO-NOT PRESS, *distributed by* Dufour Editions Inc

Documentext, *imprint of* McPherson & Co

The Documents of Colorado Art, *imprint of* Ocean View Books

Dog-Eared Publications, *distributor for* ACI Publishing, Earth Heart, Nichols Garden Nursery Press, *distributed by* Beyda Associates Inc, Booklines Hawaii, Common Ground Distributors, Interstate Periodicals, Lone Pine Publishing, Partners Book Distributing, Partners West

Dog Wing Media, *imprint of* Windstorm Creative

Doggone Days, *imprint of* Modern Publishing

Dogwood Ridge Books, *distributed by* Arcadia Enterprises Inc

Tom Doherty Associates, LLC, *subsidiary of* Holtzbrinck Publishers Holdings LLC, *distributor for* Wizards of the Coast, *distributed by* Holtzbrinck Publishers, Warner Publishers Services

Dolmen Press Ltd, *distributed by* Dufour Editions Inc

Domain, *imprint of* Random House Inc

Dominie Press Inc, *distributor for* Cambridge University Press (limited number of titles)

Domus Latina Publishing, *distributed by* Focus Publishing/R Pullins Co Inc

The Donning Co, *distributed by* Schiffer Publishing Ltd

The Donning Co/Publishers, *subsidiary of* Walsworth Publishing Co, Walsworth Publishing Co Inc

Doodle Art, *imprint of* Price Stern Sloan

Dorchester Publishing Co Inc, *division of* Dorchester Publishing Co Inc

Dordt College Press, *affiliate of* Dordt College

Dorland Biomedical, *imprint of* Dorland Healthcare Information

Dorland Healthcare Information, *imprint of* Dorland Healthcare Information, *affiliate of* Dorland Data Network, Dorland Data Networks, *distributor for* Health Leaders

Dos Pasos Editores, *distributed by* Bilingual Press/Editorial Bilingue

dot dot dot, *distributed by* Princeton Architectural Press

Double Decker Press, *distributed by* Sierra Press

Double Dutch Press, *imprint of* Blade Publishing

Double Elephant Books, *imprint of* Ten Speed Press

Double Mountain Books, *imprint of* Texas Tech University Press

Doubleday, *imprint of* Random House Inc, *distributed by* Perfection Learning Corp

Doubleday Bible Commentary, *imprint of* Random House Inc

Doubleday Books for Young Readers, *imprint of* Random House Children's Books

Doubleday Broadway Publishing Group, *division of* Random House Inc

Doubleday/Galilee, *imprint of* Random House Inc

Doubleday/Image, *imprint of* Random House Inc

Douglas & McIntyre Ltd, *distributed by* Heimburger House Publishing Co

Dover, *distributed by* Alfred Publishing Company Inc

Dover Publications, *distributed by* Prestwick House Inc

Dover Publications Inc, *division of* Courier Corp

Down East Books, *division of* Down East Enterprise Inc, Down East Enterprise Inc, *distributor for* Nimbus Publishing Ltd (selected titles) (Canadian sales only)

Down Home Press, *distributed by* John F Blair Publisher

Down There Press, *division of* Open Enterprises Cooperative Inc, Open Enterprises Cooperative Inc, *distributor for* Red Alder Books

Downtown Press, *imprint of* Pocket Books, Simon & Schuster Adult Publishing Group

Dragonfly, *imprint of* Random House Children's Books

Dragonfly Books, *imprint of* Random House Inc

Drama Publishers, *imprint of* Quite Specific Media Group Ltd

Dramaline® Publications, *distributed by* Ingram Book Co

Dramatic Lines, *distributed by* Empire Publishing Service

Dream Works, *distributed by* Penguin Group (USA) Inc

Drummond Children's Books, *imprint of* The Drummond Publishing Group

Drummond Creative, *imprint of* The Drummond Publishing Group

Dry Bones, *imprint of* Dry Bones Press Inc

Dry Bones Press Inc, *distributor for* Simplex Publications, Straight From The Heart Press, *distributed by* PublishingOnline.com

Dryad Press, *distributed by* University of Wisconsin Press

DTP, *imprint of* Random House Inc

Ducks Unlimited, *distributed by* The Globe Pequot Press

W M Duforcelf, *imprint of* Black Classic Press

Dufour Editions' Distributed Presses, *imprint of* Dufour Editions Inc

Dufour Editions Inc, *distributor for* Angel Books, Anvil Books (Dublin) & The Children's Press, Attic/Atrium, Between-the-Lines, Blackstaff Press Ltd, Bloodaxe Books Ltd, Carysfort Press, Clo Iar-Chonnachta, Collins Press, The Columba Press, Dedalus Press, The DO-NOT PRESS, Dolmen Press Ltd, Eland Books/Sickle Moon, Enitharmon Press, Forest Books, Gallery Books, Goblinshead, Institute of Irish Studies, Iynx, The Liffey Press, Lilliput Press Ltd, Mare's Nest, New Island Books, Norvik Press, Peter Owen Ltd, Parthian, Salmon Poetry, Colin Smythe Ltd, Tindal Street Press, University College Dublin Press, The Waywiser Press

Duke University Press, *imprint of* Combined Academic Publishers, *distributor for* Forest History Society

Dumb Ox Books, *distributed by* St Augustine's Press Inc

Dumbarton Oaks, *distributed by* Harvard University Press

Dunhill Publishing, *division of* Warwick Associates

Thomas Dunne Books, *imprint of* St Martin's Press LLC

Dunwoody Press, *division of* McNeil Technologies Inc

Sanford J Durst, *distributor for* American Numismatic Society, Ares Publishing Co, Bowers & Merena Galleries Inc, Krause Publications, Obol International, Seabys Ltd, Spink & Son Ltd, Stanton Books Numismatics International, Whitman Publishing Co

Dustbooks, *affiliate of* Associated Writing Programs, Association of Writers & Writing Programs (AWP), *distributor for* American Dust Publications Inc, *distributed by* Pushcart Press, Seventh-Wing Publications

Dutton, *division of* Penguin Group (USA) Inc, Penguin Group (USA) Inc, *imprint of* Dutton, Dutton Children's Books, Penguin Group (USA) Inc, *distributed by* Perfection Learning Corp, Sundance Publishing

Dutton Children's Books, *imprint of* Penguin Group (USA) Inc, Penguin Group (USA) Inc, Penguin Young Readers Group

Dutton Interactive, *imprint of* Penguin Young Readers Group

Duxbury, *imprint of* Wadsworth Publishing, *distributed by* SAS Publishing

E B P Latin America Group Inc, *subsidiary of* Editorial Barsa Planeta Inc, Editorial Barsa Planetta Inc

E Benezit Librairie, *distributed by* Dealer's Choice Books Inc

e-Scholastic, *division of* Scholastic Inc, Scholastic Inc

Eagan Press, *imprint of* American Association of Cereal Chemists

Eagle Book Clubs Inc, *subsidiary of* Eagle Publishing Inc

Eagle Gate, *imprint of* Deseret Book Co

Eagle List Division, *division of* Eagle Publishing Inc

Eagle (UK, music audio), *distributed by* Morehouse Publishing Co

Eagles Landing Publishing, *distributed by* Biographical Publishing Co

Eagle's View Publishing, *subsidiary of* Westwind Inc, Westwind Inc

Eakin Press, *division of* Sunbelt Media Inc, *distributor for* German Texan Heritage Society, San Antonio Express-News, Ellen Temple Publishing, *distributed by* Yucca Tree Press

Eakon Press, *distributed by* Barbed Wire Publishing

E&FN Spon, *distributed by* NACE International

Early Classics of Science Fiction, *imprint of* Wesleyan University Press

Early Editions Books, *imprint of* Science & Humanities Press

Early Educator's Press, *distributed by* Gryphon House Inc

Early Learners, *imprint of* Modern Publishing

Early Math, *imprint of* Haights Cross Communications Inc, Newbridge Educational Publishing

Early Science, *imprint of* Haights Cross Communications Inc, Newbridge Educational Publishing

Early Social Studies, *imprint of* Haights Cross Communications Inc, Newbridge Educational Publishing

The Early Years, *imprint of* Stylewriter Inc

Earth Heart, *distributed by* Dog-Eared Publications

Earth Justice, *distributed by* Chelsea Green Publishing Co

Earth Love Publishing, *distributed by* Gem Guides Book Co

Earthbound Publications, *distributed by* Casemate Publishers

Earthbound Sports, *distributed by* The Globe Pequot Press

Earthling Press, *subsidiary of* Awe-Struck E-Books Inc

Earthpress, *imprint of* Nova Publishing Co

Earthscan, *distributed by* Stylus Publishing LLC

The Earthsong Collection, *imprint of* Beyond Words Publishing Inc

East Asian Legal Studies Program, *affiliate of* University of Maryland School of Law

East Asian Research Aids & Translations, Studies on East Asia, *imprint of* Center for East Asian Studies (CEAS)

East European Monographs, *distributed by* Columbia University Press

East Gate Books, *imprint of* M E Sharpe Inc

East-West Export Books, *subsidiary of* University of Hawaii Press

East-West Film, Theatre & Art Institute, *subsidiary of* Concourse Press

East-West Review of Literature & The Arts, *subsidiary of* Concourse Press

East-West Translation Institute, *subsidiary of* Concourse Press

Eastern Book Co, *distributor for* Investor Responsibility Research Center

Eastland Press, *imprint of* Terence Dalton Ltd, *distributor for* Journal of Chinese Medicine Publications, *distributed by* Elsevier (Great Britain) (2 titles)

Ebon Research Systems Publishing LLC, *distributed by* Quality Books Inc

eBookHome.com, *distributor for* Twilight Times Books

eBooksonthe.net, *distributor for* Twilight Times Books

Ebsco Subscription Services, *distributor for* Chronicle Guidance Publications Inc, Investor Responsibility Research Center

EC&M Books, *imprint of* PRIMEDIA Business Directories & Books

Ecco, *imprint of* HarperCollins General Books Group, HarperCollins Publishers Sales

ECI, *distributed by* Phoenix Learning Resources

Eckankar, *distributed by* Hushion House Publishing, Inc

Paul Ecke Ranch, *distributed by* Ball Publishing

Eclipse Press, *subsidiary of* The Blood-Horse Publications Inc, *imprint of* Eclipse Press, *distributed by* National Book Network

Ecological Design Press, *distributed by* Chelsea Green Publishing Co

Economica, *distributed by* The Brookings Institution Press

Ecosystem Research Group, *imprint of* Crumb Elbow Publishing

ECS Publishing, *distributor for* Wayne Leupold Editions

EDC Publishing, *division of* Educational Development Corp, Educational Development Corp, *distributor for* Usborne Publishing

EDC/Usborne, *imprint of* EDC Publishing

EDFU Books, *distributed by* Adventures Unlimited Press

Edge Books, *imprint of* Capstone Press

Edgewise Press, *distributor for* Editions d'Afrique du Nord

Edimat Libros sa, *distributed by* Soundprints

Edinburgh Bibliographical Society, *distributed by* Oak Knoll Press

Edinburgh University Press, *distributed by* Columbia University Press

Edison Welding Institute, *distributor for* American Society for Nondestructive Testing

Edition Olms, *distributed by* Trafalgar Square

Editions Charles Herissey, *distributed by* Casemate Publishers

Editions Classicae, *imprint of* Mel Bay Publications Inc

Editions d'Afrique du Nord, *distributed by* Edgewise Press

Editions de la Maison Francaise, *imprint of* French & European Publications Inc

Editions Durand, *distributed by* Hal Leonard Corp

Editions Flammarion, *distributed by* Rizzoli International Publications Inc

Editions France, *distributor for* Media Associates

Editions Heimdal, *distributed by* Casemate Publishers

Editions Max Eschig, *distributed by* Hal Leonard Corp

Editions Orphee Inc, *distributed by* Theodore Presser Co

Editions Salabert, *distributed by* Hal Leonard Corp

Editions Technip, *distributed by* Enfield Publishing & Distribution Co

Editions Vasour, *distributed by* Antique Collectors Club Ltd

Editorial Bautista Independiente, *division of* Baptist Mid-Missions, Baptist Mid-Missions, *distributor for* Casa Bautista, CLIE, Portavoz

Editorial Caribe Inc, *subsidiary of* Thomas Nelson Inc

Editorial Concordia, *division of* Concordia Publishing House

Editorial Forum, *imprint of* GEM Publications

Editorial Portavoz, *division of* Kregel Publications, *imprint of* Kregel Publications

Editorial Unilit, *division of* Spanish House

Editoriale Jaca Book, *distributed by* Antique Collectors Club Ltd

EdITS, *distributor for* Chronicle Guidance Publications Inc

Edizione Press, *distributed by* Antique Collectors Club Ltd

Edizioni Quasar, *distributed by* Getty Publications

Edmunds, *distributed by* St Martin's Press LLC

The Education Digest, *imprint of* Prakken Publications Inc

Education Equity Concepts, *distributed by* Gryphon House Inc

Educational & Psychological Services International (EPSI), *distributor for* Chronicle Guidance Publications Inc

Educational Esteem, *distributor for* MAR*CO Products Inc

Educational Impressions Inc, *distributed by* Amazon.com, Barnes & Noble, Newbridge Communications Inc, Scholastic Inc, Scholastic-Tab Publications

Educational Media, *distributor for* MAR*CO Products Inc, *distributed by* MAR*CO Products Inc

Educational Packets 1-7, *imprint of* South Carolina Dept of Archives & History

Educational Products, *division of* Wordware Publishing Inc

Educational Publishing, *division of* Rand McNally

Educators for Social Responsibility, *distributed by* Gryphon House Inc

Educators Outlet, *distributor for* National Council of Teachers of Mathematics

Educators Publishing Service, *distributor for* York Press Inc

Educators Publishing Service Inc, *subsidiary of* Delta Education LLC

Edusoft, *subsidiary of* Houghton Mifflin Co

Eerdmans Books for Young Readers, *imprint of* Wm B Eerdmans Publishing Co

Egmont, *distributed by* Trafalgar Square

Eight Street Alano, *distributor for* MAR*CO Products Inc

Eland Books/Sickle Moon, *distributed by* Dufour Editions Inc

Elbow Books, *imprint of* Crumb Elbow Publishing

Elder Song Publications Inc, *distributor for* Cottonwood Press Inc

Elderberry Press LLC, *distributor for* Poison Vine Books, Red Anvil Press, *distributed by* Quality Book Co Inc

Electa, *distributed by* Phaidon Press Inc

Electric Strawberry Press, *imprint of* Radix Press

Electric Vehicle Information Services (EVINFO), *imprint of* Business/Technology Books (B/T Books)

The Electric Wigwam, *subsidiary of* Sweetgrass Press LLC

Electrical Wholesaling, *imprint of* PRIMEDIA Business Directories & Books

The Electrochemical Society Inc, *distributed by* American Institute of Physics (AIP) (journals), Marcel Dekker Inc (monographs), John Wiley & Sons (monographs)

The Electronics Source Book, *imprint of* PRIMEDIA Business Directories & Books

Element Books, *imprint of* HarperCollins Publishers, *distributed by* National Book Network

Elephant Paperbacks, *imprint of* Ivan R Dee Publisher

Elephant's Eye, *imprint of* The Overlook Press

Edward Elgar Publishing Inc, *distributor for* Financial Executives Research Foundation Inc

Elite, *imprint of* Osprey Publishing Ltd

Elite Books, *division of* Author's Publishing Cooperative (APC)

Elliott & Clark Publishing, *imprint of* River City Publishing, LLC

Donald S Ellis, *imprint of* Creative Arts Book Co

Ellora's Cave Publishing Inc, *distributed by* Ingrams

Eloka.com, *distributor for* SynergEbooks

Elsevier, *division of* Reed Elsevier Inc, *subsidiary of* Reed Elsevier, *imprint of* Butterworth-Heinemann, *distributor for* G W Medical Publisher, *distributed by* Illuminating Engineering Society of North America

Elsevier Australia, *distributor for* Paul H Brookes Publishing Co, Health Professions Press

Elsevier Engineering Information Inc (Ei), *subsidiary of* Elsevier Science Inc

Elsevier (Great Britain), *distributor for* Eastland Press

Elsevier Science, *distributor for* G W Medical Publishing Inc

Elsevier Science Inc, *subsidiary of* Reed Elsevier US Holdings Inc, *distributor for* Pergamon Press

Elsevier Science Publishers, *distributed by* NACE International

Elvehjem Museum of Art, *distributed by* Antique Collectors Club Ltd, University of Wisconsin Press

Elysian Editions, *division of* Princeton Book Co Publishers, *imprint of* Princeton Book Co Publishers

EM Books, *distributed by* Hal Leonard Corp

Embiid Publishing, *division of* Embiid Inc, *distributor for* Meisha Merlin

EMC/Paradigm Publishing, *division of* EMC Corporation, *distributor for* Sybex Inc

Emerald Books, *division of* The Emerald Book Co, The Emerald Book Company, *distributed by* Ywam Publishing

Emergency Gazette, *imprint of* Ugly Duckling Presse

Emery Pratt Co, *distributor for* Investor Responsibility Research Center

EMI Christian, *distributed by* Hal Leonard Corp

Emmaus Road Publishing Inc, *division of* Catholics United for the Faith

EMP, *imprint of* Easy Money Press

Emperor's Press, *distributed by* Casemate Publishers

Empire Press Media/Avant-Guide, *unit of* Empire Press Media Inc, *distributed by* Publishers Group West

Empire Publishing Service, *distributor for* Arte Publico Press (world), Dramatic Lines (USA & Canada), Ian Henry Publications (world), ISH Group (world exc Australia), Picadilly Books (world)

Empty Bowl Press, *distributed by* Pleasure Boat Studio: A Literary Press

Enchanted Lion, *distributed by* Farrar, Straus & Giroux, LLC

Enchanted Lion Books, *distributed by* Farrar, Straus & Giroux

Encore, *imprint of* Simon & Schuster Audio

Encore Editions, *imprint of* Star Publishing Co

Encounter the Saints Series, *imprint of* Pauline Books & Media

Encyclopaedia Africana, *division of* Reference Publications Inc, *imprint of* Reference Publications Inc

Energy Information Administration, EI-30 National Energy Information Center, *distributed by* EPO, NTIS

Enfield Publishing & Distribution Co, *distributor for* Djoef Publishing, Editions Technip, Faculty Ridge Books, Gadsden Publishing, Glad Day Books, Gold Charm Press, Green Lion Press, Hill Winds Press, Letterland International Ltd, Lightning Up Press, Moose Country Press, Publishing Works, Safe Harbor Books, Science Publisher Inc, Secret Passage Press, Star Festival, Trans Tech Publishing, Vermont Schoolhouse Press, Writers Publishing Co-op

Engineering Foundation, *distributed by* American Institute of Chemical Engineers (AICHE)

Engineering Press, *distributed by* Oxford University Press, Inc

The English Spanish Foundation Series, *imprint of* me+mi publishing inc

Enhancement Books, *imprint of* Vital Health Publishing

Enitharmon Press, *distributed by* Dufour Editions Inc

EntertainmentPro, *imprint of* Quite Specific Media Group Ltd

Enthea, *imprint of* Ariel Press, *distributed by* Ariel Press

Environmental Ethics Books, *division of* Center for Environmental Philosophy

Eos, *imprint of* HarperCollins Children's Books Group, HarperCollins General Books Group, HarperCollins Publishers Sales

Eothen Press, *distributed by* Paul & Company

Epicenter Press (Alaskan history & travel), *distributed by* Graphic Arts Center Publishing Co

Epicenter Press Inc, *distributed by* Graphic Arts Center Publishing Co

Epimetheus Books Inc, *distributed by* Barnes & Noble

EPM, *imprint of* Howell Press Inc

EPO, *distributor for* Energy Information Administration, EI-30 National Energy Information Center

Epoch Press, *imprint of* Warren H Green Inc

Epona Books, *imprint of* Media Associates

Epworth, *distributed by* Presbyterian Publishing Corp

Equestrian Distribution, *distributor for* Media Associates

Equilibrium Books, *imprint of* Wish Publishing

Equinox Publishing Pte Ltd, *imprint of* Tuttle Publishing, *distributed by* Tuttle Publishing

Equipment Watch, *imprint of* PRIMEDIA Business Directories & Books

Erdiciones de Horticultura SL, *distributed by* Ball Publishing

ERI Bookstore, *distributor for* dbS Productions

Ericson Books, *distributor for* Clearfield, Dietz Press, GPC Southern History Press, *distributed by* Mountain Press, Byron Sistler

Lawrence Erlbaum Assoc, *distributor for* National Association of Broadcasters (NAB)

Lawrence Erlbaum Associates Inc, *distributor for* The Analytic Press, Hermagoras Press, Lea Software & Alternative Media Inc, Learning Inc

Ernst & Sohn, *imprint of* John Wiley & Sons Inc, *distributor for* Art Institute of Chicago

Ernst Publishing Company LLC, *affiliate of* Legal Publications, Legal Publications LLC

Eros Books, *distributed by* Ex Libris

Eros Comix, *imprint of* Fantagraphics Books

Eschat Press, *imprint of* Loft Press Inc

eSchool News, *imprint of* eSchool News

Eshel Books, *imprint of* Bartleby Press

ESPN Books, *distributed by* Hyperion

Essence of Vermont, *distributed by* Amazon.com

Essential Histories, *imprint of* Osprey Publishing Ltd

ETA Cuisenaire, *distributor for* National Council of Teachers of Mathematics

Ethnic Cuisines: A Comprehensive Biblio, *imprint of* Armenian Reference Books Co

Etruscan Press (US & Canada), *distributed by* Mint Publishers Group

European Conference of Ministries of Transport, *distributed by* Organization for Economic Cooperation & Development

European Court of Human Rights, *distributed by* Manhattan Publishing Co

European Institute for Crime Prevention & Control, *distributed by* Criminal Justice Press

European Mathematical Society, *distributed by* American Mathematical Society

The Eurospan Group, *distributor for* Paul H Brookes Publishing Co, Health Professions Press, Institute for International Economics

Eurostar, *imprint of* VanDam Inc

Eurotica, *imprint of* NBM Publishing Inc

Evaluation & Development, *imprint of* Transaction Publishers

Evangel Publishing House, *division of* Brethren in Christ Board for Media Ministries Inc, *distributor for* Bethel Publishing, *distributed by* Appalachian Dist, Ingram/Spring Arbor

Evangelical Press, *distributed by* P & R Publishing Co

Evangelisches Verlagswerk, *imprint of* Walter de Gruyter, Inc

Evans Brothers Ltd, *distributed by* Trafalgar Square

Evanston Publishing Inc, *distributor for* Chicago Spectrum Press

Evergreen, *imprint of* Taschen America

Evergreen Pacific Publishing, *imprint of* Evergreen Pacific Publishing Ltd

Evergreen Press, *distributed by* Heimburger House Publishing Co

Everyday Mathematics, *imprint of* The Wright Group/McGraw-Hill, a Division of McGraw-Hill Learning Group

Everyman Chess, *distributed by* The Globe Pequot Press

Everyman's Classic Library in Paperback, *imprint of* Tuttle Publishing

Everyman's Library, *imprint of* Alfred A Knopf, Random House Inc

Ex Libris, *distributor for* Eros Books

Exalted, *imprint of* White Wolf Publishing Inc

Excalibur Publications, *distributed by* Amazon.com, Barnes & Noble, Borders Books

Excelsior Cee Publishing, *distributor for* Great Thought Books, Heirloom Lifestories

Exclusive: Anue Productions, *distributed by* Metamorphous Press

ExecRecs, *imprint of* Aspatore Books

Executive Essentials, *imprint of* Health Administration Press

Executive Recruiter News, *imprint of* Kennedy Information

Helen Exley Giftbooks, *subsidiary of* Helen Exley Giftbooks, Exley Publications Ltd

Expert, *distributed by* Sterling Publishing Co Inc

Explorations, *imprint of* Latin American Literary Review Press

Exploring Community History Series, *imprint of* Krieger Publishing Co

Expose Press, *imprint of* Stylewriter Inc

Express Book Freight, *division of* Transaction Publishers

Expressions Music Curriculum™, *distributed by* Warner Bros Publications Inc

Expressive Editions, *imprint of* Cross-Cultural Communications

Extending Horizons Books, *imprint of* Porter Sargent Publishers Inc

Eye Scry Publications, *distributed by* Toad Hall Inc

F & W Publications, *distributor for* Guild Publishing, Rockport Publishers

F&W Publications, *distributed by* Perfection Learning Corp

Faber & Faber, *imprint of* Farrar, Straus & Giroux, LLC

Faber & Faber Inc, *affiliate of* Farrar, Straus & Giroux LLC, Farrar, Straus & Giroux, LLC

Faber Music, *distributed by* Alfred Publishing Company Inc

Faber Music Ltd, *distributed by* Hal Leonard Corp

Face to Face Books, *imprint of* Midwest Traditions Inc

Facet, *distributed by* Neal-Schuman Publishers Inc

Facets Multimedia, *distributed by* Academy Chicago Publishers

Fact Finders, *imprint of* Capstone Press

Fact Meets Fiction, *imprint of* Haights Cross Communications Inc, Sundance Publishing

Fact Publishers, *imprint of* Cross-Cultural Communications

Facticity, *distributed by* Metamorphous Press

Factor Press, *distributed by* Gazelle, Marginal

Faculty of Asian Studies, Australian National University, *distributed by* University of Hawaii Press

Faculty Ridge Books, *distributed by* Enfield Publishing & Distribution Co

Fair Winds Press, *imprint of* Rockport Publications Inc, Rockport Publishers

Fairacres Press, *distributed by* Cistercian Publications Inc, Editorial Office

Fairchild Books, *division of* Fairchild Publications Inc, Fairchild Publications Inc

Fairfield Press, *distributor for* Maharishi University of Management Press

Fairleigh Dickinson University Press, *affiliate of* Associated University Presses, *distributed by* Associated University Presses

The Fairmont Press Inc, *distributed by* CRC Press

Fairmount Press, *imprint of* Pearson Higher Education Division

Fairview Press, *division of* Fairview Health System

Fairview Publications, *imprint of* Fairview Press

Faith Alive, *imprint of* CRC Publications

Faith & Culture, *imprint of* Pauline Books & Media

Faith & Fellowship Press, *subsidiary of* Church of the Lutheran Brethren

Faith & Life Resources, *division of* Mennonite Publishing Network, *distributed by* Herald Press

Faith Communications, *imprint of* Health Communications Inc

Faith Kids, *imprint of* Cook Communications Ministries

Faith Library Publications, *subsidiary of* RHEMA Bible Church, *distributed by* Appalachian, Harrison House, Spring Arbor, Whitaker

Faith Marriage, *imprint of* Cook Communications Ministries

Faith Parenting, *imprint of* Cook Communications Ministries

Faith Weaver Bible Curriculum™, *imprint of* Group Publishing Inc

Faithful Woman, *imprint of* Cook Communications Ministries

faithQuest, *imprint of* Brethren Press

Faith's Compass, *imprint of* Windstorm Creative

FaithWorks/NBN, *distributor for* Gazelle Publications

Falcon®, *imprint of* The Globe Pequot Press

Falcon Press, *imprint of* New Falcon Publications/ Falcon

FalconGuide®, *imprint of* The Globe Pequot Press

Falling Leaf, *imprint of* Scarecrow Press Inc

Falmer Press, *distributed by* Taylor & Francis Inc

Family Album, *imprint of* Pearson Higher Education Division

Family Center of Nova University, *distributed by* Gryphon House Inc

Family Films, *division of* Concordia Publishing House

Family of Man Press, *imprint of* G F Hutchison Press

Family Process Institute Inc, *division of* Family Process Inc, Family Process Inc

Family Tree Books, *imprint of* Betterway Books

Famous Artists School, *division of* Cortina Learning International Inc

Famous Florida Cookbooks, *imprint of* Winner Enterprises

Famous Writers School, *division of* Cortina Learning International Inc

Fanfare, *imprint of* Random House Inc

Fantagraphics Books, *distributed by* W W Norton & Company Inc

Far Muse Press, *imprint of* Loft Press Inc

Far West Publishing Co, *subsidiary of* Sun Books - Sun Publishing, *distributed by* Sun Books - Sun Publishing

Farming Press, *distributed by* Diamond Farm Book Publishers

Farrar Straus & Giroux, *distributed by* Sundance Publishing

Farrar, Straus & Giroux, *distributor for* Enchanted Lion Books, Graywolf Press

Farrar, Straus & Giroux Books for Young Readers, *imprint of* Farrar, Straus & Giroux, LLC

Farrar, Straus & Giroux Inc, *distributor for* Aperture Books, *distributed by* Perfection Learning Corp

Farrar, Straus & Giroux, LLC, *distributor for* Aperture, Enchanted Lion, Greywolf, R & S Books

W Farthingale Publishing, *imprint of* Top of the Mountain Publishing

Father & Son Publishing, *affiliate of* Father & Son Associates Inc, *distributor for* BADM Books

Fatima Crusader, *distributor for* Angelus Press

Faulkner & Yoknapatawpha Series, *imprint of* University Press of Mississippi

Fawcett, *imprint of* Random House Inc, *distributed by* Perfection Learning Corp

Fawcett Books, *distributed by* Sundance Publishing

Faxon Canada, *distributor for* Investor Responsibility Research Center

The Faxon Co Inc, *distributor for* Investor Responsibility Research Center

FC&A Publishing, *distributed by* NBN

FC2/Black Ice Books, *distributed by* Northwestern University Press

Fearon Teacher, *imprint of* American Society for Quality

Feather Books (Canada only), *distributed by* Mint Publishers Group

Federal Jobs Digest, *imprint of* Breakthrough Publications Inc

Federal Street Press, *division of* Merriam-Webster Inc, Merriam-Webster Inc, *imprint of* Merriam-Webster Inc

Federation Press, *distributor for* Criminal Justice Press

FedEx Trade Networks, *division of* FedEx Corp

Philipp Feldheim Inc, *distributor for* Am Yisroel Chai Press, Targum Press

Feldheim Publishers, *imprint of* Philipp Feldheim Inc

Jean Feldman, *distributed by* Gryphon House Inc

Fence Books, *distributed by* University Press of New England

H B Fenn, *distributor for* Soundprints

H B Fenn & Co, *distributor for* Home Planners LLC

Fenris Brothers, *imprint of* Crossquarter Publishing Group

Fiber Studio Press, *imprint of* Martingale & Co

David Fickling Books for Young Readers, *imprint of* Random House Children's Books

Fiction Collective Two Inc, *distributed by* Northwestern University Press

Fiction International (Journal), *imprint of* San Diego State University Press

Fictionwise, *distributor for* SynergEbooks

The Film Movement DVDs, *distributed by* Recorded Books LLC

Film Review Publications, *imprint of* Jerome S Ozer Publisher Inc

Filter Press, *distributed by* Yucca Tree Press

The Final Edition, *imprint of* Crumb Elbow Publishing

Finance & Operations, *division of* Scholastic Education

Financial Executives Research Foundation Inc, *affiliate of* Financial Executives Institute, *distributed by* Edward Elgar Publishing Inc

Financial Times/Prentice Hall, *imprint of* Prentice Hall PTR

Financial Times Publishing, *distributed by* Trans-Atlantic Publications Inc

Findhorn Press, *distributed by* Lantern Books, Steiner Books

Finding Out Books, *imprint of* Enslow Publishers Inc

Fine Communications, *division of* Fine Creative Media, Fine Creative Media Inc

FineEdge.com, *distributed by* Heritage House, Sunbelt Publications Inc

Fire Engineering Books & Videos, *division of* PennWell Publishing, PennWell Publishing Co, *distributor for* Brady, IDEA Bank, IFSTA, Mosby, *distributed by* David Publishing, Fire Protection Publications

Fire Protection Publications, *distributor for* Fire Engineering Books & Videos

Firefly, *distributed by* Amherst Media Inc, Perfection Learning Corp

Firefly Books, *distributed by* Heimburger House Publishing Co

Firefly Ltd, *distributed by* Sundance Publishing

The Firelands Writing Center, *distributed by* Bottom Dog Press

Fireside, *imprint of* Fireside & Touchstone, Simon & Schuster Adult Publishing Group

Fireside & Touchstone, *imprint of* Simon & Schuster Adult Publishing Group

First Avenue, *distributed by* Perfection Learning Corp

First Avenue Editions, *imprint of* Lerner Publishing Group

First Choice, *imprint of* Sunbelt Publications Inc

First Choice Chapter Books, *imprint of* Random House Inc

First Facts, *imprint of* Capstone Press

First Fruits of Zion, *distributed by* Lederer Books, Messianic Jewish Publishers

Fischer Productions, *imprint of* St Anthony Messenger Press

Fisher Books, *imprint of* The Perseus Books Group

Fithian Press, *distributed by* John Daniel & Co, Publishers

5 Continents, *distributed by* Paul & Company

Five Star, *imprint of* Thomson Gale, Thorndike Press

Five Star Publications Inc, *distributor for* Dine College Press

Flashlight Press, *subsidiary of* Urim Publications

Fleur de Luce Books, *imprint of* The Invisible College Press LLC

Flexographic Technical Association, *distributor for* Jelmar Publishing Co Inc

Flip N Fun, *imprint of* Modern Publishing

Flora & Fauna Books, *division of* Scientific Publishers Inc

Flora Publications International Pty Ltd, *distributed by* Ball Publishing

Florida Academic Press, *division of* F A P Books, FAP Books, *distributor for* Worsley Press

Florida Flair Books, *distributor for* Winner Enterprises

Florida Funding Publications Inc, *subsidiary of* John L Adams & Co Inc, John L Adams & Co Inc

Florida Literary Foundation Press (FLF), *imprint of* Starbooks Press

Floris Books, *distributor for* Lindisfarne Books, *distributed by* Gryphon House Inc, Steiner Books

Flying Frog Publishing, *division of* Allied Publishing Group

Flying Machines Press, *imprint of* Paladin Press

FMP, *imprint of* Forward Movement Publications

FNP Military Division, *imprint of* Food & Nutrition Press Inc (FNP)

Focal Press, *distributor for* National Association of Broadcasters (NAB), *distributed by* Silver Pixel Press

Focus Classical Library, *imprint of* Focus Publishing/R Pullins Co Inc

Focus on Performance, *imprint of* Focus Publishing/R Pullins Co Inc

Focus on the Family, *imprint of* Focus on the Family, *distributed by* Baker Books, Cook Communications, Harvest House, Moody Press, Tommy Nelson, Standard Publishing Co, Thomas Nelson Inc, Tyndale House Publishers, Zondervan

Focus Philosophical Library, *imprint of* Focus Publishing/R Pullins Co Inc

Focus Publishing/R Pullins Co Inc, *subsidiary of* R Pullins Co, R Pullins Co, *distributor for* Domus Latina Publishing, *distributed by* The Peoples Publishing Group

Fodor's, *imprint of* Fodor's Travel Publications, Random House Inc

Fodor's Travel Publications, *division of* Random House Inc, *subsidiary of* Random House Inc, *distributor for* Baedeker's Guides, Karen Brown Guides, *distributed by* Baedeker's Guides, Karen Brown Guides

Phyllis Fogelman Books, *imprint of* Penguin Young Readers Group

Folens Ltd (UK), *distributor for* Blushing Rose Publishing

Foleor Editions, *distributed by* Ross Publishing Inc

Folger, *distributed by* Sundance Publishing

Folk Art & Artists Series, *imprint of* University Press of Mississippi

Folklife in the South Series, *imprint of* University Press of Mississippi

Follett, *distributor for* A R O Publishing Co, Raven Tree Press LLC, Teach Me Tapes Inc

Follett Audiovisual Resources, *distributor for* In Audio

Follett Library Resources, *distributor for* Bancroft-Sage Publishing, Rocky River Publishers LLC

Fondo de Cultura Economica USA Inc, *subsidiary of* Fondo de Cultura Economica (Mexico), *distributed by* Arroyo Books, Bilingual Publications Co, Books on Wings, Booksource, Continental Book Co, Girol Books Inc, Hispanic Books Distributors, Mariuccia Iaconi Book Imports, Ideal Foreign Books, Latin Trading Corp, Lectorum Publications Inc, Libreria Martinez, Libros Sin Fronteras, Los Andes Publishing

Fons Vitae, *distributor for* Archetype (UK), The Foundation for Traditional Studies (US), Golganooza (UK), Islamic Texts Society (UK), Pir Press (NY), Quilliam Press (UK), Quinta Essentia (UK), Tradigital (Germany), Turab (Jordan), World Wisdom (US)

Food & Agriculture Organization, *distributed by* Bernan

Food & Nutrition Press Inc (FNP), *distributor for* Academic Press

Food Chemical News, *imprint of* CRC Press LLC

The Food Paper, *division of* Gault Millau Inc/Gayot Publications

Food Products Press, *imprint of* The Haworth Press Inc

Footprint Books, Australia, *distributor for* Boys Town Press

Footprint Publishing, *distributed by* Heimburger House Publishing Co

Footsteps, *imprint of* Travelers' Tales Inc

For Dummies®, *imprint of* John Wiley & Sons Inc

Fordham University Press, *distributor for* Alephoe Books/The Poetry Mission, Creighton University Press, IASTA Press, Little Room Press, M & M Maschietto & Ditore, The Reconstructionist Press, Rockhurst University Press, St Bede's, St Louis University Press, Sleepy Hollow Press, Something More Publications, University of San Francisco, YMCA of Greater New York, *distributed by* Heimburger House Publishing Co

Foreign Affairs Information Service, *imprint of* George Kurian Reference Books

Foreign Languages Press, *distributed by* China Books & Periodicals Inc

Forerunner Books, *division of* College Press Publishing Co

Forest Books, *distributed by* Dufour Editions Inc

Forest History Society, *distributed by* Duke University Press

Forest House®, *imprint of* Forest House Publishing Co Inc & HTS Books

Forest House Publishing Co Inc & HTS Books, *distributor for* ARO Publishing

Forest of Peace, *imprint of* Ave Maria Press, *distributed by* Ave Maria Press

Forge Books, *imprint of* Tom Doherty Associates, LLC, *distributed by* St Martin's Press LLC

Foris Publications, *imprint of* Walter de Gruyter, Inc, Mouton de Gruyter

Formac, *distributed by* Orca Book Publishers

Formac Publishing, *distributed by* Casemate Publishers

Forrest Hill Press, *imprint of* The Wine Appreciation Guild Ltd

Fort Ross Inc, *distributor for* MIR (Russia), Yuridicheskaya Literatura (Russia), *distributed by* Hippocrene Books Inc

Fort Ross Inc International Rights, *division of* Fort Ross Inc

Fort Ross Inc Russian-American Publishing Projects, *division of* Fort Ross Inc

Fort Ross International Representation for Artists, *division of* Fort Ross Inc

Fortress, *imprint of* Osprey Publishing Ltd

Fortress Press, *imprint of* Augsburg Fortress Publishers, Publishing House of the Evangelical Lutheran Church in America

Forum Books, *imprint of* Franciscan Press

Forward Movement Publications, *distributor for* Anglican Book Centre

Frances Foster Books, *imprint of* Farrar, Straus & Giroux Books for Young Readers

Walter Foster, *distributor for* Jim Henson Publishing/Muppet Press

Walter Foster Publishing Inc, *member of* The Quarto Group Inc

Foul Play Press, *imprint of* W W Norton & Company Inc

G T Foulis, *distributed by* Haynes Manuals Inc

Foundation Book & Periodical Division, *imprint of* Center for Thanatology Research & Education Inc

Foundation for Traditional Studies, *distributed by* Kazi Publications Inc

The Foundation for Traditional Studies (US), *distributed by* Fons Vitae

Foundation of Thanatology & Periodical Div, *imprint of* Center for Thanatology Research & Education Inc

Foundation Press Inc, *division of* Thompson Co

Foundations of Higher Education, *imprint of* Transaction Publishers

The Fountain, *imprint of* The Light Inc, The Light Inc

Fountain Press, *distributed by* Voyageur Press

Four Seas, *imprint of* Branden Publishing Co Inc

Four Walls Eight Windows, *subsidiary of* Avalon Publishing Group, Avalon Publishing Group Inc

Four Way Books, *distributed by* University Press of New England

Fourth Estate, *imprint of* HarperCollins General Books Group, HarperCollins Publishers Sales

Fox Chapel Publishing Co Inc, *distributor for* Reader's Digest, Taunton Sterling Dover

Fox River Press, *distributed by* Pilgrim Publications

Francis-Joseph Publications, *distributed by* Krause Publications

Franciscan Communications, *imprint of* St Anthony Messenger Press

Franciscan Communications (books & videos), *distributed by* St Anthony Messenger Press

Franciscan Press, *subsidiary of* Quincy University

Franciscan Press Books, *imprint of* Franciscan Press

Franklin Book Co Inc, *distributor for* Investor Responsibility Research Center

Burt Franklin, *imprint of* Ayer Company, Publishers Inc

Franklin Covey Audiobooks, *distributed by* Simon & Schuster Audio

Franklin Watts, *division of* Scholastic Library Publishing

Fraser Direct (Jaguar), *distributor for* R D R Books

Frederick Fell Publishers Inc, *distributed by* Kensington Publishing Corp

Frederick Warne, *subsidiary of* Penguin Group (USA) Inc, *imprint of* Penguin Group (USA) Inc, Penguin Group (USA) Inc, Penguin Young Readers Group, *distributed by* Perfection Learning Corp

Free Presbyterian Publications, *distributed by* P & R Publishing Co

Free Press, *imprint of* Simon & Schuster Adult Publishing Group, *distributed by* Center for Creative Leadership

The Free Press, *distributed by* American Marketing Association

Free Press Division of MacMillan, *distributed by* Society of Manufacturing Engineers

Free Spirit, *distributed by* Perfection Learning Corp, Peytral Publications Inc

Free Spirit Publishing Inc, *distributor for* Council for Exceptional Children

Free Spirit (selected titles), *distributed by* Torah Aura Productions

Freedom Press, *distributed by* AK Press Distribution

Freedom Press (London), *distributor for* See Sharp Press

W H Freeman, *distributor for* American Geological Institute (AGI)

W H Freeman and Co, *subsidiary of* Holtzbrinck Publishers

Freestone, *imprint of* Peachtree Publishers Ltd

The French & Spanish Book Corp, *imprint of* French & European Publications Inc

Samuel French Inc, *distributor for* Baker's Plays, Samuel French Ltd, *distributed by* Samuel French Ltd

Samuel French Ltd, *distributor for* Samuel French Inc, *distributed by* Samuel French Inc

Fresh Bread, *imprint of* Destiny Image

Frieda Carrol Communications, *distributor for* Gumbo Media (www.gumbomedia.com), *distributed by* Sey Yes Marketing (www.seyyesmarketing.com)

Friedman/Fairfax, *distributed by* Heimburger House Publishing Co

Friends United Press, *subsidiary of* Friends United Meeting

Friendship Bible Studies, *imprint of* CRC Publications

Frog Books, *imprint of* Kumarian Press Inc

Frog Ltd, *imprint of* North Atlantic Books, *distributed by* North Atlantic Books

From Here to Fame, *distributed by* powerHouse Books

Frommer's™, *imprint of* John Wiley & Sons Inc

Front Street, *imprint of* Front Street Inc

Front Street Inc, *distributed by* Chronicle Books

Front Street/Lemniscant, *imprint of* Front Street Inc

Front Street Press, *distributed by* Casemate Publishers

The Frontier Press Co (selected titles), *distributor for* Standard Educational Corp

Frontline, *imprint of* Thomson Delmar Learning

Frontline International, *distributor for* Third World Press

FTA, *distributed by* Jelmar Publishing Co Inc

Fulcrum, *distributed by* American Water Works Association, Perfection Learning Corp

Fulcrum Resources, *imprint of* Fulcrum Publishing Inc

Fun Pads, *imprint of* Playmore Inc, Publishers

Fun with the Family, *imprint of* The Globe Pequot Press

Funny Farm Books, *imprint of* Coda Publications

FW Friends™, *imprint of* Group Publishing Inc

The G A T Abouts, *imprint of* Modern Publishing

G K Hall & Co, *imprint of* Thomson Gale

G Q Publishing, *imprint of* Great Quotations Inc

G W Medical Publisher, *distributed by* Elsevier

G W Medical Publishing Inc, *distributed by* Amazon.com, American Medical Association, Barnes & Noble, Elsevier Science (London, Australia, Asia, Philadelphia, New York, St Louis)

Gadsden Publishing, *distributed by* Enfield Publishing & Distribution Co

Gail's Guides, *distributed by* The News Group, Partners West

Galahad Books, *distributed by* Sterling Publishing Co Inc

Galaxy Large Print Books, *imprint of* BBC Audiobooks America

Galaxy Music Corp, *division of* ECS Publishing, *imprint of* ECS Publishing

The Gale Group, *distributor for* Beacham Publishing Corp

Gale Research, *distributed by* American Indian Studies Center Publications at UCLA

Gale Research Inc, *distributor for* Business Research Services Inc

Galilee Books, *imprint of* Doubleday Broadway Publishing Group

Gallaudet University Press, *distributor for* Signum Verlag, *distributed by* DawnSignPress

Gallaudet University Press (selected titles), *distributed by* Butte Publications Inc

Gallery Books, *distributed by* Dufour Editions Inc

Gallery Six (US & Canada), *distributed by* Mint Publishers Group

Galt Press, *division of* Galt International Inc, Galt International Inc, *distributor for* Sphinx Publishing

Galvin Publications, *distributed by* Phoenix Learning Resources

Gambero Rosso, *distributed by* Antique Collectors Club Ltd

Gambit Books, *imprint of* The Harvard Common Press

Gambit Publications, *distributed by* Weatherhill Inc

Games Workshop, *distributed by* Simon & Schuster Inc

Garden Art Press, *imprint of* Antique Collectors Club Ltd

Gardener's Bookshelf, *imprint of* Fulcrum Publishing Inc

Isabella Stewart Gardner Museum, *distributed by* University Press of New England

Gardners, *distributor for* Protea Publishing

Gareth Stevens Inc, *division of* World Almanac Education Group Inc, *subsidiary of* WRC Media Inc

Garland-Clark Editors, *distributed by* Players Press Inc

Garland Publishers, *distributor for* University of California Institute on Global Conflict & Cooperation

Garland Science Publishing, *member of* Taylor & Francis Books Inc

Garlinghouse Inc, *subsidiary of* Sabot Publishing Inc

John Garrett, *distributor for* Twenty-Third Publications

Garrigue Books, *imprint of* Catbird Press

Gaslight Publications, *imprint of* Empire Publishing Service

Gateway, *imprint of* Eagle Publishing Inc

Gateway Editions, *imprint of* Regnery Publishing Inc

Gateways Books & Tapes, *division of* Institute for the Development of the Harmonious Human Being Inc, Institute for the Development of the Harmonious Human Being Inc, *distributor for* Cloister Recordings (audio & video tapes)

Gateways Retro SF, *imprint of* Gateways Books & Tapes

GATF (Graphic Arts Technical Foundation), *distributor for* Jelmar Publishing Co Inc

Gato Negro Books, *division of* Creative Arts Book Co

Gault Millau Inc/Gayot Publications, *distributed by* Publishers Group West

Gaultmillau, *imprint of* Gault Millau Inc/Gayot Publications

GAYOT, *imprint of* Gault Millau Inc/Gayot Publications

Gazelle, *distributor for* Factor Press

Gazelle Publications, *distributed by* FaithWorks/NBN

Gefen Books, *distributor for* Bar Ilan, Magnes Press

Gefen Publishing Ltd, *imprint of* Gefen Books

Gem Guides, *distributor for* Sierra Press

Gem Guides Book Co, *distributor for* Boze Books, Brynmorgen Press, Clear Creek Publishing, Earth Love Publishing, Geoscience Press, Golden Hands Press, Grand Canyon Association, Historical Society of Southern California, Cy Johnson & Son, KC Publications Inc, Natureagraph, Natureagraph Publishers Inc, Nevada Publications, Old El Toro Press, Pinyon Publishing, Primer Publications, Ram Publishing, L R Ream Publishing, Recreation Sales, Sierra Press, La Siesta Press, To the Point Press, Treasure Chest, Trees Company, Weseanne Publications, Western Trails Publications, *distributed by* Nevada Publications

Gem Guides Book Co (selected titles), *distributor for* Capra Press

Gembooks, *imprint of* Gem Guides Book Co

GemStone Press, *division of* Longhill Partners Inc, Longhill Partners Inc, *distributed by* Bayard (Canada), Pleroma (New Zealand), Rainbow Book Agencies (Australia)

Genealogical Publishing Co, *distributed by* Higginson Book Co

Genealogical Publishing Co Inc, *subsidiary of* Chodak Inc, Chodak Inc

General Music Store, *distributor for* Barcelona Publishers

Genesis Book I, *distributor for* MAR*CO Products Inc

Genetic Engineering News, *division of* Mary Ann Liebert Inc

Geneva Press, *imprint of* Presbyterian Publishing Corp

Gentle World, *distributed by* Book Publishing Co

Gently Worded Books, *distributed by* Yucca Tree Press

Geological Society of London, *distributor for* AAPG (American Association of Petroleum Geologists), *distributed by* AAPG (American Association of Petroleum Geologists)

Geology Underfoot Series, *imprint of* Mountain Press Publishing Co

Geophysical Institute, *distributed by* University of Alaska Press

George Wittenborn, *imprint of* Wittenborn Art Books

Georgetown Publications Inc (Canada), *distributor for* Kane/Miller Book Publishers

Geoscience Press, *distributed by* Gem Guides Book Co

Laura Geringer Books, *imprint of* HarperCollins Children's Books Group, HarperCollins Publishers

German Texan Heritage Society, *distributed by* Eakin Press

Gestalt Institute of Cleveland Press, *distributed by* The Analytic Press

Gestalt Journal Press, *division of* The Center for Gestalt Development Inc, The Center For Gestalt Development Inc

Die Gestalten Verlag (DGV), *distributed by* Prestel Publishing

getfitnow.com Books, *imprint of* Hatherleigh Press

Getty, *distributed by* Oxford University Press, Inc

Getty Conservation Institute, *imprint of* Getty Publications

J Paul Getty Museum, *imprint of* Getty Publications

Getty Publications, *distributor for* Edizioni Quasar, Visions SrL, *distributed by* Oxford University Press Inc (US only)

Getty Research Institute, *imprint of* Getty Publications

C R Gibson, *subsidiary of* Thomas Nelson Inc

Gift of Time (US & Canada), *distributed by* Mint Publishers Group

Editorial Gustavo Gili SA, *distributor for* Art Institute of Chicago

The Gillemajigs, *imprint of* Modern Publishing

Girol Books Inc, *distributor for* Fondo de Cultura Economica USA Inc

Glad Day Books, *distributed by* Enfield Publishing & Distribution Co

Glas, *distributed by* Northwestern University Press

Michael Glazier Books, *imprint of* Liturgical Press

GLB, *imprint of* GLB Publishers

Glencannon, *distributed by* Mystic Seaport

Glencoe/McGraw-Hill, *division of* McGraw-Hill Education, *imprint of* McGraw-Hill Education, *distributed by* SkillPath Publications

Peter Glenn Publications, *division of* Blount Communications

Glide Publications, *imprint of* Volcano Press Inc

Glimmer Train Press Inc, *distributor for* Glimmer Train Stories

Glimmer Train Stories, *distributed by* Glimmer Train Press Inc

Glitterati Inc, *distributed by* powerHouse Books

Global IT Services, *imprint of* Kennedy Information

Global Oriental, *distributed by* University of Hawaii Press

Global Research Inc, *distributor for* Primary Research Group

Global Trade Watch, *division of* Public Citizen

Globe Fearon, *imprint of* Pearson Learning, Pearson Learning Group

Globe Pequot Press, *distributor for* Montana Historical Society Press

The Globe Pequot Press, *division of* Morris Book Publishing LLC, *distributor for* Appalachian Mountain Club, Appalachian Mountain Club Books, Boone & Crockett Club, Cadogan Guides, Thomas Cook Publishing, Day Hikes Books Inc, Ducks Unlimited, Earthbound Sports, Everyman Chess, Menasha Ridge Press, Menasha Ridge Press Inc, Mobil Travel Guide, Montana Historical Society Press, New Holland Publishers Ltd, Oval Books, Alastair Sawday Publishing, Trailblazer Publications, Vacation Work Publications, Waterford Press, Western Horseman, Woodall Publications, *distributed by* Heimburger House Publishing Co

Go Facts Guided Writing, *imprint of* Haights Cross Communications Inc

GOAL/QPC, *distributor for* American Society for Quality

Goals Unlimited Press, *distributed by* Mountain Press Publishing Co

Goblinshead, *distributed by* Dufour Editions Inc

David R Godine Publisher Inc, *distributor for* Black Sparrow Books

GoFacts Guided Writing, *imprint of* Newbridge Educational Publishing

Gold Charm Press, *distributed by* Enfield Publishing & Distribution Co

Golden Books, *imprint of* Random House Children's Books, *distributor for* Parachute Publishing LLC, *distributed by* Perfection Learning Corp

Golden Books Family Entertainment, *distributor for* Jim Henson Publishing/Muppet Press

Golden Dawn Publications, *imprint of* New Falcon Publications/Falcon

Golden Hands Press, *distributed by* Gem Guides Book Co

Golden Hill Press, *distributed by* Heimburger House Publishing Co

Golden Triangle Books, *imprint of* University of Pittsburgh Press

Golden West Books, *division of* Pacific Railroad Publications Inc

Goldentree Bibliographies, *imprint of* Harlan Davidson Inc/Forum Press Inc

Golganooza (UK), *distributed by* Fons Vitae

Gollancz, *distributed by* Sterling Publishing Co Inc

Gollehon Books, *imprint of* Gollehon Press Inc

Gomer Press, *distributed by* Beekman Publishers Inc

Gomer Press (selected titles), *distributed by* Pickwick Publications

Gonca, *distributed by* The Light Inc

Good Apple, *imprint of* American Society for Quality

Good Books, *subsidiary of* Good Enterprises Ltd, Good Enterprises Ltd

Good Earth, *distributed by* Chelsea Green Publishing Co

Good Life Center Books, *imprint of* Chelsea Green Publishing Co

Goosefoot Acres, *distributed by* Chelsea Green Publishing Co

Gordian Knot Books, *distributed by* University of Nebraska Press

Gordian Press, *distributor for* Phaeton Press

Gorse, *distributed by* Lacis Publications

Gospel Light, *distributed by* College Press Publishing Co

Gospel Publishing House, *division of* General Council of the Assemblies of God, *distributed by* Spring Arbor

Gotham, *imprint of* Penguin Group (USA) Inc

Government Institutes, *imprint of* Scarecrow Press Inc

Government Jobs Series, *imprint of* PREP Publishing

Government Printing Office, *distributed by* Bernan

Gower, *imprint of* Ashgate Publishing Co, Elsevier

Gower Publishing, *distributed by* Ashgate Publishing Co

GP Subscription Publications, *imprint of* Greenwood Publishing Group Inc

GPC/Gollehon, *imprint of* Gollehon Press Inc

GPC Southern History Press, *distributed by* Ericson Books

Grace Publications, *imprint of* American Society for Quality

Graceland Press, *imprint of* Herald Publishing House

Gracewing (UK), *distributed by* Morehouse Publishing Co

Grade Finders Inc, *distributed by* Graphic Arts Association, National Paper Trade Assoc

Graduate Record Examination Series, *imprint of* National Learning Corp

Grafco Rock Books, *imprint of* Grafco Productions Inc

Graham & Whiteside, *imprint of* Thomson Gale

Gramercy, *imprint of* Random House Value Publishing

Gramercy Books, *imprint of* Random House Inc

Grammar with a Grin, *imprint of* Haights Cross Communications Inc, Sundance Publishing

Gramophone, *distributed by* Omnibus Press

Grand Canyon Association, *distributed by* Gem Guides Book Co

Donald M Grant Publisher Inc, *distributor for* Archival, Oswald Train

Granta, *distributed by* Penguin Group (USA) Inc

Granta UK, *distributed by* Trafalgar Square

Graphic Arts Association, *distributor for* Grade Finders Inc

Graphic Arts Books, *imprint of* Graphic Arts Center Publishing Co

Graphic Arts Center Publishing Co, *distributor for* AMES (automotive), Epicenter Press (Alaskan history & travel), Epicenter Press Inc, Harbour Publishing, Roundup Press (aviation), Stoecklein Publishing, Whitecap Books (cookbooks), Wolf Creek Books

Graphic Learning, *division of* Abrams & Co Publishers Inc

Grasshopper Books, *distributed by* Orca Book Publishers

Grave Issues, *imprint of* Spinsters Ink

Grayson Publishing, *distributed by* Antique Collectors Club Ltd

Graywolf Press, *distributor for* Aperture, *distributed by* Farrar, Straus & Giroux

Great Architectural Replica Series, *imprint of* Stemmer House Publishers Inc

Great Books of the Islamic World, *distributed by* Kazi Publications Inc

Great Destinations, *imprint of* Berkshire House

Great Lakes Books, *imprint of* Wayne State University Press

Great Outdoors Publishing, *distributor for* Winner Enterprises

Great Potential Press, *division of* Anodyne Inc, Anodyne Inc, *distributed by* Dandy Lion Press, KIDPROV, Zephyr Press Inc

Great Source Education Group, *subsidiary of* Houghton Mifflin Co, Houghton Mifflin Co

Great Thought Books, *distributed by* Excelsior Cee Publishing

Great Valley Books, *imprint of* Heyday Books

Greatdream Publications, *distributed by* Sweetgrass Press LLC

The Greeley Co, *subsidiary of* HCPro

Kendall Green Publications, *imprint of* Gallaudet University Press

Green Light Readers, *imprint of* Harcourt Trade Publishers

Green Lion Press, *distributed by* Enfield Publishing & Distribution Co

Green Tiger Press, *imprint of* Laughing Elephant

Greenart Books, *imprint of* Warren H Green Inc

Greenberg Books, *imprint of* Kalmbach Publishing Co

Greene Bark Press Inc, *distributor for* Pumpkin Patch Publishing

Greene Bark Press Music Co, *division of* Greene Bark Press Inc

Stephen Greene Press, *imprint of* Viking Penguin

T J Greene Associates, *division of* Greene Bark Press Inc

Greenfield Review Press, *distributed by* Cross-Cultural Communications

Greenhaven Press, *imprint of* Thomson Gale

Greenhaven Press®, *imprint of* Thomson Gale

Greenhaven Press Inc, *distributor for* Lucent Books Inc, *distributed by* Lucent Books Inc, Perfection Learning Corp

Greenhill Books, *distributed by* Stackpole Books

Greenleaf, *distributed by* Chelsea Green Publishing Co

Greenleaf Book Group LLC, *division of* Greenleaf Enterprises Inc

Greenleaf Enterprises Inc, *imprint of* Greenleaf Book Group LLC

Greenway, *imprint of* Underwood Books Inc

Greenwich Medical Media, *distributed by* Oxford University Press, Inc

Greenwich Workshop Press, *distributed by* Artisan, Workman Publishing Co Inc

Greenwillow Books, *imprint of* HarperCollins Children's Books Group, HarperCollins Publishers

Greenwood, *distributor for* American Council on Education

Greenwood Cemetery, *distributed by* Center for Thanatology Research & Education Inc

Greenwood Electronic Media, *imprint of* Greenwood Publishing Group Inc

Greenwood Press, *imprint of* Greenwood Publishing Group Inc

Greenwood Publishing Group Inc, *division of* Reed Elsevier, Reed-Elsevier

Greenwood Research, *imprint of* Greenwood Research Books & Software, *distributor for* Greenwood Research Books & Software

Greenwood Research Books & Software, *division of* Greenwood Research, *distributed by* Greenwood Research, Midwest Library Service

Greeting Cards, *division of* Unarius Academy of Science Publications

Gregg, *imprint of* Glencoe/McGraw-Hill, *distributed by* Ashgate Publishing Co

Gregg Revivals, *imprint of* Ashgate Publishing Co

Gregorian University Press, *distributed by* Loyola Press

Grey House, *imprint of* Grey House Publishing Inc

Greywolf, *distributed by* Farrar, Straus & Giroux, LLC

Grief Watch, *distributed by* ACTA Publications

Griffin, *imprint of* St Martin's Press LLC

Grinder & Associates, *imprint of* Metamorphous Press

M Grinder & Associates, *distributed by* Metamorphous Press

Griot Audio, *imprint of* Haights Cross Communications Inc, Recorded Books LLC

Grolier, *distributor for* The Bronx County Historical Society, Jim Henson Publishing/Muppet Press

Grolier Educational, *division of* Scholastic Library Publishing

Grolier Online, *division of* Scholastic Library Publishing

Grosset, *distributor for* Parachute Publishing LLC

Grosset & Dunlap, *subsidiary of* Penguin Group (USA) Inc, *imprint of* Penguin Group (USA) Inc, Penguin Group (USA) Inc, Penguin Young Readers Group

Grosset/Putnam, *imprint of* Penguin Group (USA) Inc, G P Putnam's Sons (Hardcover)

Groundwood, *distributed by* Sundance Publishing

Group for the Advancement of Psychiatry, *distributed by* American Psychiatric Publishing Inc

Group for the Advancement of Psychology, *imprint of* American Psychiatric Publishing Inc

Group Publishing, *distributed by* Saint Mary's Press

Group Workcamps™, *imprint of* Group Publishing Inc

Group's Hands-On Bible Curriculum™, *imprint of* Group Publishing Inc

Grove/Atlantic Inc, *distributor for* Open City Books, *distributed by* Publishers Group West

Grove Dictionaries, *distributed by* Oxford University Press, Inc

Grove Press, *imprint of* Grove/Atlantic Inc

Growers Press Inc, *distributed by* Ball Publishing

Grownup's Guides (US & Canada), *distributed by* Mint Publishers Group

Grub Street, *distributed by* Casemate Publishers

B R Gruener Publishing Co, *imprint of* John Benjamins Publishing Co

Grupo Azabache, *distributor for* Art Institute of Chicago

Gryphon Books, *distributor for* PPC, Zeon

Gryphon Crime Series, *imprint of* Gryphon Books

Gryphon Doubles, *imprint of* Gryphon Books

Gryphon Gangster Series, *imprint of* Gryphon Books

Gryphon House, *distributor for* DawnSignPress, Redleaf Press, *distributed by* Teaching Strategies

Gryphon House Inc, *distributor for* Aha Communications, Book Peddlers, Bright Ring Publishing, Building Blocks, Center For The Child Care Workforce, Chatterbox Press, Chicago Review Press, Children's Resources International, Circle Time Publishers, Sydney Gurewitz Clemens, Conari Press, Council Oak Books, Dawn Sign Press, Delmar Publishers Inc, Deya Brashears, Early Educator's Press, Education Equity Concepts, Educators for Social Responsibility, Family Center of Nova University, Jean Feldman, Floris Books, Hawthorne Press, Highscope, Hunter House Publishers, Independent Publishers Group, Kaplan Press, Loving Guidance Inc, Miss Jackie Inc, Monjeu Press, National Association for the Education of Young Children, National Center Early Childhood Workforce, New England AEYC, New Horizons, Nova Southeastern University, Pademelon Press, Partner Press, Pollyanna Productions, Redleaf Press, Robins Lane Press, School Age Notes, School Renaissance, Southern Early Childhood Association, Steam Press, Syracuse University Press, Teaching Strategies, Telshare Publishing, *distributed by* Consortium Book Sales (Gryphon House & Robins Lane press titles only)

Gryphon SF Rediscovery Series, *imprint of* Gryphon Books

GT Publishing, *distributed by* HarperCollins Publishers

Guernica Editions, *distributed by* Paul & Company

Guild Bindery Press, *distributed by* Providence Publishing Corp

Guild of Mastercraftsman, *distributed by* Sterling Publishing Co Inc

Guild Publishing, *affiliate of* Guild Inc, Guild Inc, *distributed by* BHB International, F & W Publications

Guilford Press, *distributed by* A D D Warehouse

The Guilford Press, *division of* Guilford Publications Inc

Guitar One, *distributed by* Hal Leonard Corp

Guitar World, *distributed by* Hal Leonard Corp

Gulf Coast Association of Geological Societies, *distributed by* Bureau of Economic Geology, University of Texas at Austin

Gulf Publishing, *distributed by* NACE International

Gulliver Books, *imprint of* Harcourt Trade Publishers

Gumbo Media, *distributed by* Frieda Carrol Communications

Gumdrop, *distributor for* Ozark Publishing Inc

Gunsmoke Westerns, *imprint of* BBC Audiobooks America

Haan Publishing, *distributed by* Transaction Publishers

Haase House, *imprint of* Easy Money Press

Hachai Publications Inc, *distributor for* Kerem

Hachette Livre, *distributed by* Antique Collectors Club Ltd

Hackett Publishing Co Inc, *distributor for* Bryn Mawr Commentaries

Hafezieh Publications (Germany), *distributed by* Concourse Press

Hagstrom Map, *imprint of* Langenscheidt Publishers Inc

Hagstrom Map Co, *distributed by* Trakker Maps Inc

Hagstrom Map Co Inc, *subsidiary of* American Map Corp, *distributor for* ADC The Map People, American Map Corp, Arrow Maps Inc, Creative Sales Corp, DeLorme Atlas, Hammond World Atlas Corporation, Langenscheidt, RV International Maps & Atlases, Stubs Guides, Trakker Maps Inc

Hal Leonard Corp, *distributor for* Amadeus Press, Applause Theatre & Cinema Books, Artistpro, Ashley Music, Backbeat Books, Beacon Music, Berklee Press, Fred Bock Music Company, Boosey & Hawkes, Centerstream Publications, Centerstream Publishing LLC, Cherry Lane Music Co, Cinema Books, Community Music Videos, Creative Concepts, DC Publications, Devine Entertainment Corp, Editions Durand, Editions Max Eschig, Editions Salabert, EM Books, EMI Christian, Faber Music Ltd, Guitar One, Guitar World, Home Recording, Homespun Tapes, Houston Publications, Hudson Music, iSong CD-ROMs, Kenyon Publications, Limelight Editions, Ashley Mark Publishing Co, Edward B Marks Music, Meredith Music, Modern Drummer Publications, Musicians Institute Press, Musikverlage Han Sikorski, Christopher Parkening, Reader's Digest, Record Research, Ricordi, Lee Roberts Publications, Rubank Publications, G Schirmer Inc (Associated Music Publishers), Second Floor Music, Sing Out Corporation, Star Licks Videos, Bernard Stein Music Co, String Letter Press, Tara Publications, Transcontinental Music, 21st Century Publications, Vintage Guitar, Word Music, Writer's Digest

Halcyon House, *imprint of* National Book Co

Halcyon House Publishers, *imprint of* Acres USA

Robert Hale, *distributed by* Antique Collectors Club Ltd

Robert Hale & Co, *distributor for* Paradise Cay Publications Inc

Robert Hale/J A Allen, *distributed by* Trafalgar Square

Nita Stewart Haley Library, *distributed by* Yucca Tree Press

Half Halt Press Inc, *distributor for* The Kenilworth Press Ltd

Halsted Press, *imprint of* John Wiley & Sons Inc

Hambledon, *distributed by* St Martin's Press LLC

Hamewith, *imprint of* Baker Books

Hamilton Books, *imprint of* University Press of America, University Press of America Inc

Hamlyn, *distributed by* Sterling Publishing Co Inc

Hammond Pub, *distributed by* Perfection Learning Corp

Hammond World Atlas Corp, *division of* Langenscheidt Publishing Group, *subsidiary of* American Map Corp, *distributor for* HarperCollins Cartographic

Hammond World Atlas Corporation, *distributed by* Hagstrom Map Co Inc

Hampshire Books, *imprint of* Bethany House Publishers/Baker Bookhouse

Hampton Press, *imprint of* Hampton Press Inc

Han-Shan Tang Books, *distributed by* Antique Collectors Club Ltd

Handbook of North American Indians, *distributed by* Smithsonian Institution Press

Handbook Series, *imprint of* Porter Sargent Publishers Inc

Handprint, *distributed by* Chronicle Books LLC

Handprint Books Inc, *distributed by* Chronicle Books

Hands & Heart Books, *imprint of* Toad Hall Inc

Handsel Books, *imprint of* Other Press LLC

Hanley & Belfus, *imprint of* Elsevier Health Sciences

Hanley-Wood LLC, *division of* Hanley-Wood Inc, Hanley-Wood Inc

Hanser Gardner Publications, *affiliate of* Gardner Publications Inc & Carl Hanser Verlag, Gardner Publications Inc & Carl Hanser Verlag

Happy Cat Books, *distributed by* Star Bright Books

Happy Day Books, *imprint of* Standard Publishing Co

Harbor Hill Books, *division of* Purple Mountain Press Ltd

Harbor House, *distributed by* National Book Network

Harbor Lights Press (HLP), *affiliate of* Harbor Lights Navigation

Harbor Press, *imprint of* Harbor Press Inc

Harbor Press Inc, *distributed by* National Book Network (NBN)

Harbour Publishing, *distributed by* Graphic Arts Center Publishing Co, Heimburger House Publishing Co

Harcourt, *distributed by* Learning Links Inc, SAS Publishing

Harcourt Achieve, *division of* Harcourt Education, *subsidiary of* Harcourt Inc

Harcourt Assessment, *subsidiary of* Harcourt Inc

Harcourt Assessment Inc, *division of* Reed Elsevier Group, plc, *subsidiary of* Harcourt Inc

Harcourt Brace & Co, *distributed by* Perfection Learning Corp, Sundance Publishing

Harcourt Brace & Co and Subsidiaries, *distributed by* Ball Publishing

Harcourt Canada (Toronto & Montreal), *subsidiary of* Harcourt Inc

Harcourt Children's Books, *imprint of* Harcourt Trade Publishers

Harcourt Paperbacks, *imprint of* Harcourt Trade Publishers

Harcourt Professional Publishing, *distributed by* Academic Press

Harcourt School Publishers, *division of* Harcourt Inc

Harcourt Trade Publishers, *division of* Harcourt Inc, Harcourt Inc

Harcourt Yours Classics, *imprint of* Harcourt Trade Publishers

Hardie Press, *distributed by* Mel Bay Publications Inc

Hardscrabble Books, *imprint of* University Press of New England

Harian Creative Associates, *subsidiary of* Harian Creative Books

Harian Creative Books, *division of* Harian Creative Enterprises

Harian Creative Enterprises, *subsidiary of* Harian Creative Books

The Harian Press, *imprint of* Harian Creative Books

Harlequin, *imprint of* Harlequin Enterprises Ltd, *distributed by* Simon & Schuster Inc, Thorndike Press

Harlequin Enterprises Ltd, *subsidiary of* Torstar Corp, *imprint of* Harlequin Enterprises Ltd, *distributed by* Simon & Schuster Mass Merchandise Sales Co

Harmony Books, *imprint of* Crown Publishing Group, Random House Inc

Harmony House Publishers - Louisville, *distributor for* Classic Publishers

The Bill Harp Professional Teacher's Library, *imprint of* Christopher-Gordon Publishers Inc

Harper Entertainment, *distributor for* Parachute Publishing LLC

HarperAudio, *imprint of* HarperCollins General Books Group, HarperCollins Publishers Sales

HarperBusiness, *imprint of* HarperCollins General Books Group, HarperCollins Publishers Sales

HarperCollins, *imprint of* HarperCollins General Books Group, HarperCollins Publishers, HarperCollins Publishers Sales, *distributor for* Alloy Entertainment, Basic Books, Counterpoint Press, Da Capo Press Inc, Parachute Publishing LLC, PublicAffairs, ThorsonsElement US, Westview Press, *distributed by* Heimburger House Publishing Co, Learning Links Inc, MAR*CO Products Inc, Sundance Publishing, Thorndike Press

HarperCollins Cartographic, *distributed by* Hammond World Atlas Corp

HarperCollins Children's Books, *imprint of* HarperCollins Children's Books Group

HarperCollins Children's Books Group, *division of* HarperCollins

HarperCollins General Books Group, *division of* HarperCollins Publishers

HarperCollins Publishers, *subsidiary of* News Corporation, *distributor for* Basic Books, Civitas, Counterpoint, GT Publishing, Perseus (Addison Wesley Trade), The Perseus Books Group, Public Affairs, TV Books, *distributed by* Cynthia Publishing Co

HarperCollins Publishers Sales, *division of* HarperCollins Publishers

HarperCollins UK, *distributed by* Trafalgar Square

HarperDesign, *imprint of* HarperCollins General Books Group, HarperCollins Publishers Sales

HarperEntertainment, *imprint of* HarperCollins General Books Group, HarperCollins Publishers Sales

HarperFestival, *imprint of* HarperCollins Children's Books Group

HarperKids Entertainment, *imprint of* HarperCollins Children's Books Group

HarperLarge Print, *imprint of* HarperCollins Publishers Sales

HarperLargePrint, *imprint of* HarperCollins General Books Group

HarperResource, *imprint of* HarperCollins General Books Group, HarperCollins Publishers Sales

Harper's Magazine Foundation, *division of* Franklin Square Press

HarperSanFrancisco, *imprint of* HarperCollins General Books Group, HarperCollins Publishers Sales

HarperTempest, *imprint of* HarperCollins Children's Books Group

HarperTorch, *imprint of* HarperCollins General Books Group, HarperCollins Publishers Sales

HarperTrophy, *imprint of* HarperCollins Children's Books Group

Harrington Park Press, *imprint of* The Haworth Press Inc

Harrison House, *distributor for* Faith Library Publications

Tom Harrison Cartography, *distributed by* Mountain n' Air Books

Harry N Abrams, Inc, *distributed by* Time Warner Book Group

Alan Hartman, *distributed by* Antique Collectors Club Ltd

Hartman Publishing Inc, *distributor for* Beverly Foundation

Hartmore House Inc, *affiliate of* Media Judaica Inc, Media Judaica Inc

Harvard Business Reference, *imprint of* Harvard Business School Press

Harvard Business School Press, *division of* Harvard Business School Publishing, *distributed by* Center for Creative Leadership, Client Distribution Services, SAS Publishing

Harvard Center for International Affairs, *distributed by* University Press of America Inc

Harvard Center for Middle Eastern Studies, *distributed by* Harvard University Press

Harvard Center for Population Studies, *distributed by* Harvard University Press

Harvard Center for the Study of World Religions, *distributed by* Harvard University Press

Harvard College Library, *distributed by* Harvard University Press

Harvard Department of Sanskrit & Indian Studies, *distributed by* Harvard University Press

Harvard Department of The Classics, *distributed by* Harvard University Press

Harvard Education Letter, *imprint of* Harvard Education Publishing Group

Harvard Education Press, *imprint of* Harvard Education Publishing Group

Harvard Education Publishing Group, *division of* Harvard University

Harvard Educational Review Reprint Series, *imprint of* Harvard Education Publishing Group

Harvard Ukrainian Research Institute, *subsidiary of* Harvard University, *distributed by* Harvard University Press

Harvard University Art Museums, *distributed by* Arthur Schwartz & Co Inc

Harvard University Asia Center, *distributed by* Harvard University Press

Harvard University David Rockefeller Center for Latin American Studies, *distributed by* Harvard University Press

Harvard University Press, *distributor for* Dumbarton Oaks, Harvard Center for Middle Eastern Studies, Harvard Center for Population Studies, Harvard Center for the Study of World Religions, Harvard College Library (Including Houghton Library Judaica Division), Harvard Department of Sanskrit & Indian Studies, Harvard Department of The Classics, Harvard Ukrainian Research Institute, Harvard University Asia Center, Harvard University David Rockefeller Center for Latin American Studies, Harvard-Yenching Institute, Peabody Museum of Archaeology & Ethnology

Harvard-Yenching Institute, *distributed by* Harvard University Press

Harvest Books, *imprint of* Harcourt Trade Publishers

Harvest House, *distributor for* Focus on the Family

Hastings House/Daytrips Publishers, *subsidiary of* Lini LLC

Hatherleigh Co, *distributed by* American College of Physician Executives

The Hatherleigh Company Ltd, *distributed by* W W Norton & Company Inc

Hatherleigh Press, *subsidiary of* Hatherleigh Co Ltd, Hatherleigh Co Ltd, *distributed by* W W Norton & Company Inc

Haus Publishing, *distributed by* Trafalgar Square

Haven, *imprint of* Bridge-Logos Publishers

The Haworth Clinical Practice Press, *imprint of* The Haworth Press Inc

Haworth Customized Textbook Service, *division of* The Haworth Press Inc

Haworth Document Delivery Service, *division of* The Haworth Press Inc

The Haworth Herbal Press, *imprint of* The Haworth Press Inc

The Haworth Hispanic/Latino Press, *imprint of* The Haworth Press Inc

The Haworth Hospitality Press, *imprint of* The Haworth Press Inc

The Haworth Information Press, *imprint of* The Haworth Press Inc

The Haworth Integrative Healing Press, *imprint of* The Haworth Press Inc

The Haworth Judaica Practice Press, *imprint of* The Haworth Press Inc

The Haworth Medical Press, *imprint of* The Haworth Press Inc

The Haworth Pastoral Press, *imprint of* The Haworth Press Inc

The Haworth Political Press, *imprint of* The Haworth Press Inc

The Haworth Reference Press, *imprint of* The Haworth Press Inc

The Haworth Trauma & Maltreatment Press, *imprint of* The Haworth Press Inc

Hawthorn Press, *distributed by* Steiner Books

Hawthorne, *subsidiary of* Emmis Books

Hawthorne Press, *distributed by* Gryphon House Inc

Hawthorne Publications, *distributor for* A D D Warehouse

Hayden Publishing (US & Canada), *distributed by* Mint Publishers Group

Hayes, *distributed by* Perfection Learning Corp

Haynes, *distributed by* Thomson Delmar Learning

Haynes Manuals Inc, *division of* The Haynes Publishing Group, *distributor for* G T Foulis, Haynes Owners Workshop Manuals, Oxford Illustrated Press, *distributed by* Motorbooks International

Haynes Owners Workshop Manuals, *distributed by* Haynes Manuals Inc

Nicolas Hays Inc, *distributed by* Red Wheel/Weiser/Conari

Hazamir, *imprint of* Transcontinental Music Publications

Hazelden Books, *distributed by* Health Communications Inc

Hazelden/Johnson Institute, *imprint of* Hazelden Publishing & Educational Services

Hazelden/Keep Coming Back, *imprint of* Hazelden Publishing & Educational Services

Hazelden-Pittman Archives Press, *imprint of* Hazelden Publishing & Educational Services

Hazelden Publishing & Educational Services, *division of* Hazelden Foundation, *distributor for* Obsessive Anonymous, *distributed by* Health Communications Inc (trade)

Hazlaw Books, *imprint of* Weidner & Sons Publishing, *distributed by* Weidner & Sons Publishing

HCI Books, *imprint of* Health Communications Inc

HCI Espanol, *imprint of* Health Communications Inc

HCI Teens, *imprint of* Health Communications Inc

Healing Arts Press, *imprint of* Inner Traditions International Ltd

Healing Tao Books, *imprint of* Tuttle Publishing, *distributed by* Tuttle Publishing

Health Administration Press, *division of* Foundation of the American College of Healthcare Executives, *distributor for* American College of Physician Executives, *distributed by* American College of Physician Executives

Health Books, *imprint of* Oxmoor House Inc

Health Communications Inc, *distributor for* Hazelden Books, Hazelden Publishing & Educational Services

Health Forum Inc, *subsidiary of* American Hospital Association

Health Information Press (HIP), *imprint of* Practice Management Information Corp (PMIC)

Health Leaders, *distributed by* Dorland Healthcare Information

Health Press Intl, *imprint of* American Psychiatric Publishing Inc

Health Professions Press, *division of* Paul H Brookes Publishing Co, *subsidiary of* Paul H Brookes Publishing Co, *distributed by* Elsevier Australia, The Eurospan Group, Login Brothers, Unifacmanu Trading Co Ltd

Health Research GP Buyers UP, *division of* Public Citizen

Healthwatch, *imprint of* Players Press Inc

Healthy Healing Publications, *distributed by* Crystal Star/Jones Products, Words Distributors

Healthy Living, *imprint of* Book Publishing Co

Healthy Living Books, *imprint of* Hatherleigh Press

Hearst Books, *imprint of* HarperCollins Publishers, Sterling Publishing Co Inc

Hearthstone Books, *distributor for* Closson Press

Heartline Romances, *imprint of* Holloway House Publishing Co

HeartQuest, *imprint of* Tyndale House Publishers Inc

Hearts & Tummies Cookbook Co, *division of* Quixote Press, *imprint of* Quixote Press

Heartsong Presents, *imprint of* Barbour Publishing Inc

Hebrew Union College Press, *division of* Hebrew Union College, *distributed by* Wayne State University Press

Heimburger House Publishing Co, *distributor for* Harry N Abrams Inc, Acorn Media Publishing, Black Dog & Leventhal, Book Sales Inc, Canadian Caboose Press, Cedco Publishing Co, Child's Play, Deskmap Systems, Douglas & McIntyre Ltd, Evergreen Press, Firefly Books, Footprint Publishing, Fordham University Press, Friedman/Fairfax, The Globe Pequot Press, Golden Hill Press, Harbour Publishing, HarperCollins, Highland Station Inc, Hot Box Press, Howling at the Moon Press, Iconografix Inc, Indiana University Press, Johns Hopkins University Press, Judson Press, Kansas City Star Books, Krause Publications, Motorbooks Intl, Omega Innovative Marketing, Penquin Putman Inc, Pictorial Histories, Publishers Group West, Running Press, Smithmark Publishers, Sono Nis Press, Stackpoole Books, Sterling Publishing, Syracuse University Press, Thunder Bay Press, Voyageur Press, Walker & Co, Westcliffe Publishing, John Wiley & Sons

William S Hein & Co Inc, *distributor for* Ashgate, Aspen, Butterworths, Investor Responsibility Research Center, Sweet & Maxwell, John Wiley & Sons Inc

Heinemann, *division of* Greenwood Publishing Group Inc

Heinemann/Boynton Cook Publishers Inc, *division of* Greenwood Publishing Group Inc, Heinemann

Heirloom Lifestories, *distributed by* Excelsior Cee Publishing

Helgate Press, *distributed by* Midpoint Trade Books

Helion & Co Ltd, *distributed by* Casemate Publishers

Helios Press, *imprint of* Allworth Press

Hellgate Press, *imprint of* Hellgate Press, PSI Research, *distributed by* Midpoint Trade Books

Hemisphere Pub Corp, *imprint of* Taylor & Francis Editorial, Production & Manufacturing Division

Hendrick-Long Publishing Co, *distributor for* NES, The Official Tasp Study Guide

Henry Holt, *distributor for* The College Board, Nevraumont Publishing Co, *distributed by* Sundance Publishing

Ian Henry Publications, *distributed by* Empire Publishing Service

Joseph Henry Press, *imprint of* National Academies Press

Jim Henson's Muppets, *distributed by* Running Press Book Publishers

Hera, *imprint of* Soho Press Inc

Herald Books, *imprint of* Franciscan Press

Herald Press, *subsidiary of* Mennonite Publishing House Inc, *distributor for* Faith & Life Resources

Herald Publishing House, *division of* Community of Christ, *imprint of* Herald Publishing House

Herder & Herder, *imprint of* The Crossroad Publishing Company

Here & Now: Things Kids Want to Learn About Today!, *imprint of* Gallopade International Inc

Heritage Builders, *imprint of* Focus on the Family

Heritage House, *imprint of* Ye Olde Genealogie Shoppe, *distributor for* FineEdge.com

Heritage Pittston Realty Company Inc, *subsidiary of* Penguin Group (USA) Inc

Heritage/Willowbend, *distributor for* Closson Press

Hermagoras Press, *distributed by* Lawrence Erlbaum Associates Inc

Hermon Press Books, *imprint of* Sepher-Hermon Press

Nick Hern Books, *distributed by* Theatre Communications Group Inc

Heroes & Helpers: Those Who Help Us in Times of Crises-& Everyday!, *imprint of* Gallopade International Inc

Heroes of the Faith, *imprint of* Barbour Publishing Inc

Herzl Press, *subsidiary of* W Z O, *distributed by* Associated University Presses, Cornwal Books

Hesperus Press, *distributed by* Trafalgar Square

Hess Publications, *distributed by* Pilgrim Publications

Heuristic Books, *imprint of* Science & Humanities Press

Hewitt Homeschooling Resources, *division of* Hewitt Research Foundation

Heyden & Son, *distributor for* Investor Responsibility Research Center

Hi Marketing, *distributor for* National Geographic Books

Hi Willow Research & Publishing, *distributed by* LMC Source

Hidden Travel Series, *imprint of* Ulysses Press

HiddenSpring, *imprint of* Paulist Press

Higganum Hill Books, *distributed by* Paul & Company

Higginson Book Co, *distributor for* Genealogical Publishing Co

High/Coo Press, *affiliate of* Brooks Books, *distributed by* Charles E Tuttle Shokai

High Lonesome Books, *distributed by* Yucca Tree Press

High Lonesome Press, *distributed by* Johnson Books

High Museum of Art, *distributed by* Antique Collectors Club Ltd

High Sierra Books, *distributed by* Paul & Company

High Windy Audio, *distributed by* August House Publishers Inc

Highborn Lady Press, *imprint of* Kalimat Press

Highbridge Audio, *distributed by* Penguin Audiobooks, Penguin Group (USA) Inc

Highland Books, *imprint of* Cumberland House Publishing Inc

Highland Station Inc, *distributed by* Heimburger House Publishing Co

Highroads Audio, *distributed by* Audio Renaissance

Highscope, *distributed by* Gryphon House Inc

Adam Hilger (selected titles), *distributed by* Metal Powder Industries Federation

Hill & Wang, *division of* Farrar, Straus & Giroux LLC, Farrar, Straus & Giroux, LLC

Hill Street Books, *imprint of* Hill Street Press LLC

Hill Street Classics, *imprint of* Hill Street Press LLC

Hill Winds Press, *distributed by* Enfield Publishing & Distribution Co

Hillenbrand Books, *imprint of* Liturgy Training Publications

Hillsboro Press, *imprint of* Providence Publishing Corp

Hillsdale College Press, *division of* Hillsdale College

Himalayan Institute Press, *division of* Himalayan International Institute of Yoga Science and Philosophy

Hindustan Book Agency, *distributed by* American Mathematical Society

Hinkler Books Pty Ltd, *distributed by* Penton Overseas Inc

Hippocrene Books Inc, *distributor for* Fort Ross Inc

Hispanic Books Distributors, *distributor for* Fondo de Cultura Economica USA Inc

Histoire & Collections, *distributed by* Casemate Publishers

Historical Images, *imprint of* Bright Mountain Books Inc

Historical Indexes, *distributed by* Casemate Publishers

Historical Society of Southern California, *distributed by* Gem Guides Book Co

History Mysteries®, *imprint of* Pleasant Company Publications

History Mystery, *imprint of* Gallopade International Inc

History of Ideas & Ethics, *imprint of* Transaction Publishers

Hoard's Dairyman, *imprint of* W D Hoard & Sons Co

Hobby House Press, *distributor for* Hobby House Press Inc

Hobby House Press Inc, *distributed by* Hobby House Press

The Hoberman Connection, *distributed by* Weatherhill Inc

Hochelaga, *distributor for* Cross-Cultural Communications

Hochelaga (Canada), *distributed by* Cross-Cultural Communications

Hodder-Headline Ltd, *distributed by* Trafalgar Square

Hodder Headline USA, *distributed by* Simon & Schuster Inc

Hoffman Press Division, *imprint of* Rayve Productions Inc

Hogrefe & Huber Publishers, *distributor for* Hogrefe Verlag fur Psychologie (Germany), Hans Huber AG (Switzerland)

Hogrefe Verlag fur Psychologie, *distributed by* Hogrefe & Huber Publishers

Hohm Press, *subsidiary of* HSM LLC

The Hokuseido Press, *distributed by* Book East

Holiday Bazaar Guide-OR, *imprint of* Gail's Guides

Holiday Bazaar Guide-WA, *imprint of* Gail's Guides

Holiday House, *distributed by* Sundance Publishing

Holloway House Publishing Co, *distributor for* Avanti, Mankind, Melrose Square, Premiere, *distributed by* All America Distributors Corp

Hollym Corp, *distributed by* Weatherhill Inc

Hollywood Creative Directory, *affiliate of* Lone Eagle Publishing

Hollywood Film Archive, *distributor for* R R Bowker

Holmes & Meier Publishers Inc, *distributor for* Biblio Press

Holocaust Library, *imprint of* United States Holocaust Memorial Museum

Holt Concepts, *distributed by* Penton Overseas Inc

Holt Enterprises, *distributed by* Thomson Delmar Learning

Henry Holt, *distributor for* The College Board, Nevraumont Publishing Co, *distributed by* Sundance Publishing

Henry Holt & Co Inc, *distributor for* Institute for Language Study

Henry Holt and Company Inc, *distributor for* Cortina Learning International Inc

Henry Holt and Company, LLC, *unit of* Holtzbrinck Publishers Holdings LLC, Holtzbrinck Publishing Holdings, *distributor for* The College Board, Cortina Learning International Inc, Slack Inc, Viceroy Press

Holt, Rinehart and Winston, *division of* Harcourt Inc

Holtzbrinck, *distributor for* Rizzoli International Publications Inc

Holtzbrinck Publishers, *subsidiary of* Verlagsgruppe Georg von Holtzbrinck GmbH, Verlagsgruppe Georg von Holtzbrinck GmbH, *distributor for* Tom Doherty Associates, LLC

Holtzbrink Publishers, *distributor for* Bloomsbury Publishing

Holtzbrink Publishing, *distributor for* Wizards of the Coast Inc

Holy Cross Orthodox Press, *division of* Hellenic College Inc, Hellenic College Inc

Homage, *imprint of* DC Comics

Home Builders Press, *distributed by* Craftsman Book Co

Home Planners LLC, *subsidiary of* Hanley-Wood Inc, Hanley-Wood Inc, *distributed by* Creative Homeowner Press, H B Fenn & Co

Home Recording, *distributed by* Hal Leonard Corp

Homemade Books, *imprint of* Media Associates

Homespun Tapes, *distributed by* Hal Leonard Corp

Homestead Book Co, *distributor for* Ronin Publishing Inc

Homestead Publishing, *affiliate of* Book Design

Homestore Plans & Publications, *division of* Homestore Inc, *distributed by* HomeStyles Only

HomeStyles Only, *distributor for* Homestore Plans & Publications

Homiletic & Pastoral Review, *subsidiary of* Ignatius Press

Honey Bear Books, *imprint of* Modern Publishing

Honey Bear Video, *imprint of* Modern Publishing

Honor Books, *imprint of* Cook Communications Ministries

Alan C Hood & Co Inc, *distributed by* Maryland Historical Society

Hoover Institution Press, *subsidiary of* Hoover Institution on War, Revolution & Peace, Hoover Institution on War, Revolution & Peace

Hoover's Business Press, *imprint of* Hoover's, Inc

Hoover's Handbooks, *imprint of* Hoover's, Inc

Hope Publishing House, *distributed by* Pelican Publishing Co Inc

Hops Press, *distributed by* Mountain Press Publishing Co

Horizon Publishers & Distributors Inc, *imprint of* Cedar Fort Inc

The Horse Health Care Library, *imprint of* Eclipse Press

Horse Latitudes Press, *imprint of* Crumb Elbow Publishing

Horticulture Books, *imprint of* Betterway Books

HortiTecnia, *distributed by* Ball Publishing

Horwitz Martin Education, *distributed by* Richard C Owen Publishers Inc

Ellis Horwood, *imprint of* Pearson Higher Education Division

Horwood Publishing, *distributed by* Paul & Company

Hospital & Healthcare Compensation Service, *subsidiary of* John R Zabka Associates Inc, John R Zabka Associates Inc

Hot Box Press, *distributed by* Heimburger House Publishing Co

Hot Cross Books, *imprint of* Hill Street Press LLC

Hotei Publishing, *distributed by* Stylus Publishing LLC

Houghton Mifflin, *imprint of* Houghton Mifflin Trade & Reference Division, *distributor for* Beacon Press, *distributed by* Learning Links Inc

Houghton Mifflin Books for Children, *imprint of* Houghton Mifflin Trade & Reference Division

Houghton Mifflin College Division, *division of* Houghton Mifflin Co, Houghton Mifflin Co

Houghton Mifflin Co, *distributor for* Beacon Press, Clarion Books, *distributed by* Sundance Publishing

Houghton Mifflin School Division, *division of* Houghton Mifflin Co, Houghton Mifflin Co

Houghton Mifflin Trade & Reference Division, *division of* Houghton Mifflin Co, Houghton Mifflin Co, *distributor for* Beacon Press, Larausse, Old Farmers Almanac

Hourglass, *imprint of* Baker Books

House of Anansi, *distributed by* Paul & Company

House of Collectibles, *imprint of* Random House Inc, Random House Information Group, Random House Reference

House to House Publications, *division of* DOVE Christian Fellowship International

House With Bee Art Books, *imprint of* Windstorm Creative

Houston Publications, *distributed by* Hal Leonard Corp

Hove, *distributed by* Voyageur Press

HOW Design Books, *imprint of* North Light Books

How to Get Money, Now!, *imprint of* Gallopade International Inc

How to Make a Million, *imprint of* Gallopade International Inc

Howell Book House, *imprint of* John Wiley & Sons Inc

Howell Press Inc, *distributor for* Vefa Alexiadou, Art Global, Top Ten Publishing, Vanwell Publishing, *distributed by* Spellmount Publishers (UK), Vanwell Publishing (Canada)

Howling at the Moon Press, *distributed by* Heimburger House Publishing Co

HPBooks, *imprint of* Berkley Publishing Group, Penguin Group (USA) Inc, Penguin Group (USA) Inc

HQN Books, *imprint of* Harlequin Enterprises Ltd

HRW School, *division of* Harcourt Inc

HTS Books™, *imprint of* Forest House Publishing Co Inc & HTS Books

Huber, *distributed by* Alan Wofsy Fine Arts

Hans Huber AG, *distributed by* Hogrefe & Huber Publishers

Hudson Hills, *distributor for* National Gallery of Art

Hudson Hills Press Inc, *distributor for* American Federation of Arts, Art Institute of Chicago

Hudson Hills Press LLC, *distributed by* National Book Network

Hudson Institute, *distributed by* The Brookings Institution Press

Hudson Music, *distributed by* Hal Leonard Corp

Hudson Park Press, *distributed by* Publishers Group West

Hudson Street Press, *imprint of* Penguin Group (USA) Inc

Hugh Lauter Levin Assoc, Inc, *distributed by* Hugh Lauter Levin Associates Inc

Hugh Lauter Levin Associates Inc, *distributor for* Hugh Lauter Levin Assoc, Inc, *distributed by* Publishers Group West

Human Events Publishing LLC, *subsidiary of* Eagle Publishing Inc

Human Kinetics Australia, *subsidiary of* Human Kinetics Inc

Human Kinetics Canada, *subsidiary of* Human Kinetics Inc

Human Kinetics Europe, *subsidiary of* Human Kinetics Inc

Human Kinetics New Zealand, *subsidiary of* Human Kinetics Inc

Human Rights Watch Books, *imprint of* Human Rights Watch

Humana Press, *distributed by* Blackwell Science

Humanics, *imprint of* Humanics Publishing Group

Humanics Audio, *imprint of* Humanics Publishing Group

Humanics Learning, *imprint of* Humanics Publishing Group

Humanics New Age, *imprint of* Humanics Publishing Group

Humanics Psychological Test Corp, *imprint of* Humanics Publishing Group

Humanics Publishing Group, *distributed by* New Leaf, Emery Pratt

Humanics Trade Paperback, *imprint of* Humanics Publishing Group

Humanics Training Institute, *division of* Humanics Publishing Group

Humanity Books, *imprint of* Prometheus Books

Bruce Humphries, *imprint of* Branden Publishing Co Inc

Lund Humphries, *imprint of* Ashgate Publishing Co, *distributed by* Ashgate Publishing Co

Hunter House Publishers, *distributed by* Gryphon House Inc

Susan Hunter Publishing, *subsidiary of* Cherokee Publishing Co

Huntington House Publishers, *distributor for* Vital Issues Press

Huntington House Publishers Vital Issues Press, *imprint of* Huntington House Publishers

Huntington Library, *distributed by* University of California Press

Huntington Library Press, *division of* Huntington Library Art Collections & Botanical Gardens, *distributed by* University of California Press

Huron River Press, *imprint of* Clock Tower Press

Hushion House - Canada, *distributor for* Vision Works Publishing

Hushion House Publishing, Inc, *distributor for* Eckankar

Hushion House Publishing Ltd, *distributor for* Penmarin Books Inc

The Hutton Settlement, *distributed by* Washington State University Press

Hydra Books, *imprint of* Northwestern University Press

Hyperion, *division of* ABC Inc, *distributor for* Alloy Entertainment, ESPN Books, Wenner Books, *distributed by* Sundance Publishing, Time Warner Book Group

Hyperion Books for Children, *division of* Disney Publishing Worldwide Inc

Hypermedia Inc, *imprint of* Frederic C Beil Publisher Inc

Hypermodern Press, *distributed by* Thinkers' Press Inc

Hyphen Press, *distributed by* Princeton Architectural Press

I&T Shop Service, *imprint of* PRIMEDIA Business Directories & Books

I N K Books, *imprint of* Book Peddlers

Mariuccia Iaconi Book Imports, *distributor for* Fondo de Cultura Economica USA Inc

IASTA Press, *distributed by* Fordham University Press

IBEX Press, *imprint of* Ibex Publishers

Ibex Publishers, *distributor for* Iranian Oral History Project at Harvard University

IBFD Publications USA Inc (International Bureau of Fiscal Documentation), *subsidiary of* IBFD Publications B V

ibooks, *distributed by* Simon & Schuster Inc

ibooks Inc, *affiliate of* Byron Preiss Visual Publications Inc, *distributed by* Simon & Schuster

IBTS, *distributor for* Amirah Publishing

ICARUS, *division of* The Rosen Publishing Group Inc

ICASALS, *distributed by* Texas Tech University Press

ICC Publishing Inc, *subsidiary of* International Chamber of Commerce (ICC)

ICCT, *imprint of* JMW Group Inc

IchemE (selected titles), *distributed by* American Institute of Chemical Engineers (AICHE)

Ichor Business Books, *imprint of* Purdue University Press

Ichus Guides, *imprint of* Avocet Press Inc

ICJ, *imprint of* United Nations Publications, *distributed by* United Nations Publications

ICLE, *imprint of* Institute of Continuing Legal Education

Iconografix Inc, *distributed by* Heimburger House Publishing Co, Motorbooks International

ICS Press, *division of* Institute for Comtemporary Studies (ICS), Institute for Contemporary Studies (ICS)

Idaho Center for the Book, *affiliate of* Library of Congress

IDC, *division of* Harris InfoSource

Ide House Inc, *affiliate of* Publisher's Associates, Publisher's Associates, *distributed by* Publisher's Associates

IDEA Bank, *distributed by* Fire Engineering Books & Videos

IdeaJournal, *imprint of* Aspatore Books

Ideal Foreign Books, *distributor for* Fondo de Cultura Economica USA Inc

Ideals Gift Books, *distributed by* Ideals Publications Inc

Ideals Magazine, *distributed by* Ideals Publications Inc

Ideals Publications Inc, *distributor for* Ideals Gift Books, Ideals Magazine, Smart Squares Games Sets, *distributed by* Associated Publishers Group

Ideas in Conflicts, *imprint of* GEM Publications

Ides et Calendes, *distributed by* Alan Wofsy Fine Arts

IDRC, *distributed by* Stylus Publishing LLC

IEE, *imprint of* IEE

IEEE Computer Society Press, *distributor for* American Society for Quality

IEEE Press, *division of* Institute of Electrical & Electronics Engineers (IEEE), Institute of Electrical & Electronics Engineers Inc, *distributed by* John Wiley & Sons Inc

IFES, *imprint of* International Foundation for Election Systems

IFSTA, *distributed by* Fire Engineering Books & Videos

Ignatius, *imprint of* Ignatius Press

Ignatius Press, *division of* Guadalupe Associates Inc, Guadalupe Associates Inc, *distributor for* Bethlehem Books, Veritas

IHS Press, *distributed by* Paul & Company

IIP Consumers Series, *imprint of* Independent Information Publications

IKO (International Communication Organization), *distributed by* Transaction Publishers

Ikonographics, *imprint of* St Anthony Messenger Press

Ikonographics (videos), *distributed by* St Anthony Messenger Press

Illinois State Museum Society, *affiliate of* Illinois State Museum

Illuminating Engineering Society of North America, *distributor for* Elsevier, McGraw-Hill, John Wiley & Sons Inc, *distributed by* Thompson/Delmar Learning

Illumination, *imprint of* Stylewriter Inc

The Illustrated Bartsch, *imprint of* Abaris Books

Illustrated Living History Series, *imprint of* The Globe Pequot Press

ILR Press, *imprint of* Cornell University Press

Image Books, *imprint of* Doubleday Broadway Publishing Group

Images Publications, *distributed by* Antique Collectors Club Ltd

Imagine, *imprint of* Stylewriter Inc

Imago Mundi, *imprint of* David R Godine Publisher Inc

ImaJinn Books, *division of* ImaJinn

IMM, *imprint of* Institute of Mediaeval Music

Immortal Day Publishing, *imprint of* Windstorm Creative

IMP, *distributed by* Summy-Birchard Inc

Impact, *imprint of* North Light Books

Impact Alliance Press, *imprint of* Pact Publications

Impact Publications, *division of* Development Concepts Inc, Development Concepts Inc, *distributed by* National Book Network

Impact Publishers, *distributed by* SkillPath Publications

Imperial College Press, *subsidiary of* World Scientific Publishing Co Inc

Imperium Proviso Publishing, *distributed by* IPP

Imprint Academic, *distributed by* Philosophy Documentation Center

Impromptu Journaling Books, *imprint of* Stone Bridge Press LLC

In Audio, *imprint of* Sound Room Publishers, Sound Room Publishers Inc, *distributed by* Follett Audiovisual Resources

Incentive Plus, *distributor for* MAR*CO Products Inc

Incentive Publications Inc, *distributor for* Belair Publications Ltd

Independence Press, *imprint of* Herald Publishing House

Independent Information Publications, *division of* Computing, Computing!, *distributed by* BookWorld

Independent Institute, *distributed by* Paul & Company

Independent Music Press, *distributed by* Schirmer Trade Books

Independent Publishers Group, *distributor for* Interweave Press, Marlor Press Inc, Palm Island Press, *distributed by* Gryphon House Inc

Independent Publishers Group (IPG), *distributor for* Plexus Publishing Inc

Independent University of Moscow, *distributed by* American Mathematical Society

India Book House Ltd, *distributed by* Antique Collectors Club Ltd

India Research Press, *distributed by* Paul & Company

Indian Culture Series, *imprint of* Council for American Indian Education

Indiana University Press, *imprint of* Combined Academic Publishers, *distributed by* Heimburger House Publishing Co

INDIGO, *imprint of* Genesis Press Inc

Indo Editions, *distributed by* Casemate Publishers

Industrial Press, *distributed by* NACE International, Society of Manufacturing Engineers

Infant Hearing Resources (selected titles), *distributed by* Butte Publications Inc

The Info Devel Press, *division of* The Info Devels Inc, The Info Devels Inc, *distributed by* Brodart, Motorbooks International, Zenith Books

The Info Devel Press/Book Premium Division, *division of* The Info Devel Press

Information & Media Services, *division of* The McGraw-Hill Companies Inc

Infosential Press, *distributed by* netLibrary

Infosource Publications Inc, *imprint of* Art Direction Book Co Inc

Ingenix Inc, *distributor for* American Medical Association, Medical Economics, Mosby, *distributed by* American Medical Association, Mosby

Ingram, *distributor for* Bridge-Logos Publishers, PublishAmerica

Ingram Book Co, *distributor for* Dramaline® Publications, Top of the Mountain Publishing

Ingram Books, *distributor for* Blushing Rose Publishing, The Dawn Horse Press

Ingram Periodicals, *distributor for* Rattapallax Press

Ingram/Spring Arbor, *distributor for* Evangel Publishing House

Ingrams, *distributor for* Ellora's Cave Publishing Inc

Inland, *distributor for* Media Associates, World Citizens

Inner Traditions, *imprint of* Inner Traditions International Ltd

Inner Traditions en espanol, *imprint of* Inner Traditions International Ltd

Inner Traditions India, *imprint of* Inner Traditions International Ltd

Inner Worlds Music, *distributed by* Lotus Press

Innerchoice Publishing, *imprint of* Jalmar Press

Innovative Kids, *distributed by* Chronicle Books LLC

innovative Kids™, *division of* Innovative USA, Inc, Innovative USA® Inc, *distributed by* Chronicle Books

Inservice Reviews, *imprint of* Oakstone Medical Publishing

Inside the Minds, *imprint of* Aspatore Books

Insiders' Guides®, *imprint of* The Globe Pequot Press

Insight Travel Guides, *imprint of* Langenscheidt Publishers Inc, *distributed by* Jeffrey Norton Publishers Inc

Inspec, *imprint of* IEE

Inspirational Art, *division of* Unarius Academy of Science Publications

Inspirational Library, *imprint of* Barbour Publishing Inc

Inspirational Press, *distributed by* World Publishing

Inspire Books, *imprint of* Peter Pauper Press Inc

Inspiro, *imprint of* Zondervan

Institute for International Economics, *distributor for* Center for Global Development, *distributed by* DA Information Services (Handles Australia, New Zealand & Papua New Guinea), The Eurospan Group (Handles Western & Eastern Europe, Russia, Turkey, Israel & Iran), Renouf Bookstore (Handles Canada), Taylor & Francis Asia Pacific (Covers Singapore, Thailand, China, Taiwan, Philippines, Malaysia, Indonesia, Canbodia & Vietnam), United Publishers Services Ltd (Japan & the Republic of Korea), Viva Books PVT (India, Bangladesh, Nepal & Sri Lanka)

Institute for Language Study, *affiliate of* Cortina Learning International Inc, *distributed by* Henry Holt & Co Inc

Institute for Language Study Inc, *subsidiary of* Cortina Learning International Inc

Institute for Mesoamerican Studies, *distributed by* University of Texas Press

Institute for Regional Studies of the Californias, *distributed by* San Diego State University Press

Institute for Research Information, *division of* PJD Publications Ltd

Institute for the Study of Gambling & Commercial Gaming, *distributed by* University of Nevada Press

Institute of East Asian Studies, University of California, *unit of* University of California

Institute of Governmental Studies, *subsidiary of* University of California, Berkeley

Institute of Irish Studies, *distributed by* Dufour Editions Inc

Institute of Materials, *distributed by* NACE International

Institute of Materials (selected titles), *distributed by* Metal Powder Industries Federation

Institute of Packaging Professionals, *distributor for* Jelmar Publishing Co Inc

Institute of Police Technology & Management, *division of* University of North Florida

Institution of Civil Engineers (UK), *distributed by* American Society of Civil Engineers (ASCE)

INSTRAW, *imprint of* United Nations Publications, *distributed by* United Nations Publications

Instructional Fair Group, *affiliate of* Frank Schaffer Publications

Insurance Institute of America Inc, *affiliate of* American Institute for CPCU, American Institute for CPCU & Insurance Institute of America

INT Press, *distributor for* Soundprints

Integrating Instruction Series, *imprint of* Incentive Publications Inc

InteLex Corp, *distributed by* Philosophy Documentation Center

Inter-American Development Bank, *division of* Multilateral Development Bank, *distributed by* Johns Hopkins University Press

The Inter-American Development Bank, *distributed by* The Johns Hopkins University Press

Inter American Press Books, *imprint of* R J Berg/Destinations Press Ltd

Inter Esse, *imprint of* Cross-Cultural Communications

Inter Sports, *distributor for* Wilderness Adventures Press Inc

Inter-University Consortium for Political & Social Research, *affiliate of* University of Michigan Institute for Social Research

InterBook Marketing, *distributor for* Weatherhill Inc

Intercultural Press Inc, *division of* Nicholas Brealey Publishing, *distributor for* Nicholas Brealey Publishing

Interlingua, *imprint of* Interlingua Publishing

Interlink Books, *imprint of* Interlink Publishing Group Inc

Interlink Publishing Group Inc, *distributor for* Birlinn Ltd UK, Black & White Publishing UK, Macmillan Caribbean (UK), Mercat Press (UK), Neal Wilson Publishing (UK), Polygon (UK), Quartet Books (UK), Rudisack Readers (UK), Serif Publishing Ltd (UK), Sheldrake Press (UK), Stacey International (UK), Wolfhound Press (Ireland)

ITDG Publishing, *distributed by* Stylus Publishing LLC

International Air Transport Association, *distributed by* J J Keller & Associates, Inc

International Atomic Energy Agency (IAEA), *distributed by* Bernan

International Book Centre Inc, *distributor for* Library du Liban (Lebanon), Stacey Intl Ltd (London), University of Michigan

International Books, *distributed by* Paul & Company

International Brecht Society, *distributed by* University of Wisconsin Press

International Business Press, *imprint of* The Haworth Press Inc

International Conferences on the Unity of the Sciences, *distributed by* Paragon House

International Country Risk Guide, *imprint of* The PRS Group Inc

International Debate Education Association, *distributed by* Central European University Press

International Design Library, *imprint of* Stemmer House Publishers Inc

International Directory of Design, *imprint of* Penrose Press

International Ediemme Rome, *distributed by* Scholium International Inc

International Energy Agency, *distributed by* Organization for Economic Cooperation & Development

International Evangelism Crusades Inc, *distributed by* Universe Publishing

International Flower Bulb Centre, *distributed by* Ball Publishing

International Food Policy Research Institute, *member of* Consultative Group on International Agricultural Research (CGIAR), Consultative Group on International Agricultural Research (CGIAR), *distributed by* Johns Hopkins University Press

International Geographic Information Foundation, *distributed by* American Society for Photogrammetry & Remote Sensing

International IDEA, *distributed by* Paul & Company

International Intertrade Index, *division of* Printing Consultants Publishers, *subsidiary of* Russia China Travel News

International Labor Offices, *distributed by* The Brookings Institution Press

International Law Institute, *distributed by* University Press of America Inc

International Marine Publishing, *division of* McGraw-Hill Education, *imprint of* McGraw-Hill Professional

International Monetary Fund (IMF), *division of* International Org (IGO), International Org (IGO), *distributed by* Bernan

International Pocket Library, *imprint of* Branden Publishing Co Inc

International Press, *distributed by* American Mathematical Society

International Press of Boston Inc, *distributed by* AMS

International Print Edition, *distributor for* Mel Bay Publications Inc

International Social Security, *imprint of* Transaction Publishers

International Universities Press Inc, *distributor for* Psychosocial Press, Sphinx Press

Internet Practice Press, *imprint of* The Haworth Press Inc

Interpharm Press, *imprint of* CRC Press LLC

Intersentia, *distributed by* Transnational Publishers Inc

Intersports, *distributor for* Frank Amato Publications Inc

Interstate Periodicals, *distributor for* Dog-Eared Publications

InterVarsity Press, *division of* InterVarsity Christian Fellowship of the USA

Interweave Press, *distributed by* Keith Ainsworth Pty Ltd, Australia, Independent Publishers Group, Search Press, UK

The Intrepid Traveler, *distributed by* National Book Network Inc (NBN)

Investor Relations Newsletter, *imprint of* Kennedy Information

Investor Responsibility Research Center, *distributed by* Academic Book Center, Amazon.com, Blackwell Northamerica Inc, The Book House, Coutts Library Service, Dawson France, Dawson UK Ltd, Eastern Book Co, Ebsco Subscription Services, Emery Pratt Co, Faxon Canada, The Faxon Co Inc, Franklin Book Co Inc, William S Hein & Co Inc, Heyden & Son, Midwest Library Serv, Readmore, Rowe Com, Swets & Zeitlinger, Swets Subscription Serv, Yankee Book Peddler

IOM, *distributed by* United Nations Publications

IPC Plant, *distributed by* Ball Publishing

IPG, *distributor for* Manning Publications Co

IPG/Paul & Co, *distributor for* Wolf Den Books

IPG Returns Dept, *distributor for* BenBella Books

IPP, *imprint of* Imperium Proviso Publishing, *distributor for* Imperium Proviso Publishing

iPublish, *distributor for* Paraview Publishing

Iranbooks Press, *imprint of* Ibex Publishers

Iranian Oral History Project at Harvard University, *distributed by* Ibex Publishers

IRF Books, *imprint of* Paragon House

IRL, *distributed by* Oxford University Press, Inc

Ironclad Publishing, *distributed by* Casemate Publishers

Ironwood Press, *distributed by* The University of Arizona Press

Irwin Professional, *imprint of* McGraw-Hill Professional

Irwin Professional Publications, *distributed by* American Marketing Association

ISA Services Inc, *subsidiary of* ISA

ISH Group, *distributed by* Empire Publishing Service

ISH Institut des Sciences de l'Homme, *distributed by* Paul & Company

ISI Books, *imprint of* Intercollegiate Studies Institute Inc

ISIK, *distributed by* The Light Inc

Islamic Texts Society (UK), *distributed by* Fons Vitae

Island, *imprint of* Random House Inc

Island Press, *subsidiary of* Center for Resource Economics, *distributor for* IUCN

The Islander Group Inc, *distributor for* Wide World Publishing/Tetra

ISO, *distributed by* NACE International

iSong CD-ROMs, *distributed by* Hal Leonard Corp

IsraBook, *subsidiary of* Gefen Books

Isshin-Ryu Productions, *imprint of* The Linick Group Inc

Issues Press, *imprint of* Idyll Arbor Inc

IT Pubs (London), *distributor for* The Apex Press

ITC, *distributed by* American Association of Community Colleges (AACC)

ITP Educational Division - Intl Thomas Publishing, *distributed by* Ball Publishing

It's About Time Inc, *distributor for* American Geological Institute (AGI)

Itsy-Bitsy Story Books, *imprint of* Modern Publishing

IUCN, *distributed by* Island Press

iUniverse, *imprint of* Harlem Writers Guild Press

Ivy, *imprint of* Random House Inc

IWGIA (International Workgroup for Indigenous Affairs), *distributed by* Transaction Publishers

Iynx, *distributed by* Dufour Editions Inc

J L Publications, *distributed by* Aqua Quest Publications Inc

JA Majors, *distributor for* MedBooks

Jackson Square Press, *imprint of* Pelican Publishing Co Inc

Jade Rabbit, *imprint of* Quite Specific Media Group Ltd

Jalmar Press, *subsidiary of* The B L Winch Group Inc

Jam, *imprint of* Berkley Books, Berkley Publishing Group

James & James (Science) Ltd, *distributed by* Stylus Publishing LLC

Jane's Information Group, *subsidiary of* Jane's Information Group (England)

Jannes Art Press, *distributed by* Northwestern University Press

Janus Library, *imprint of* Abaris Books

Janus Publishing, *distributed by* Paul & Company

Japan Center for International Exchange, *distributed by* The Brookings Institution Press

Japan Publications Inc, *distributed by* Kodansha America Inc

Japan Publications Trading Co Inc, *distributed by* Kodansha America Inc

JayJo Books, *subsidiary of* Guidance Channel

Jefferson Editions, *imprint of* Mage Publishers Inc

Jelmar Publishing Co Inc, *distributor for* FTA, TAPPI (Technical Association of the Pulp & Paper Industry), *distributed by* Flexographic Technical Association, GATF (Graphic Arts Technical Foundation), Institute of Packaging Professionals, NAPLL (National Association of Printing Leadership), TAPPI (Technical Association of the Pulp & Paper Industry)

Jems, *imprint of* Elsevier

Jenkins Publishing, *distributed by* Chelsea Green Publishing Co

Jersey Yarns, *imprint of* Quincannon Publishing Group

Jerusalem Bible, *imprint of* Doubleday Broadway Publishing Group

Jesuit Historical Institute, *distributed by* Loyola Press

Jesuit Way, *imprint of* Loyola Press

Jewish Lights Publishing, *division of* Longhill Partners Inc, Longhill Partners Inc, *distributor for* Jewish Thought Series/Israel Mod Books

Jewish New Testament Publications, *distributed by* Lederer Books, Messianic Jewish Publishers

Jewish New Testament Publications Inc, *distributed by* Messianic Jewish Resources

Jewish Reader Press, *imprint of* Hachai Publications Inc

Jewish Thought Series/Israel Mod Books, *distributed by* Jewish Lights Publishing

JHPIEGO, *affiliate of* Johns Hopkins University

Jim Henson Publishing/Muppet Press, *affiliate of* The Jim Henson Co, The Jim Henson Company, *distributed by* At a Glance, Walter Foster, Golden Books Family Entertainment, Grolier, KidsBooks, Penguin Putnam, PK, Random House, Readers Digest/Childrens Press, Running Press, Simon & Schuster

Jist, *distributor for* MAR*CO Products Inc

JIST Life, *imprint of* JIST Publishing Inc

JIST Works, *imprint of* JIST Publishing Inc

JIST Works Inc, *distributor for* American Counseling Association, Chronicle Guidance Publications Inc

Job Quest, *distributor for* Training Resource Network Inc (T R N)

John Deere Publishing, *division of* Deere & Co

John Macrae Books, *imprint of* Henry Holt and Company, LLC

John Milton Society for the Blind, *distributed by* Citrus Publishing, Magnetix Corp, National Braille Press

John-Wiley, *distributed by* Althos Publishing

John Wiley & Sons, *imprint of* John Wiley & Sons Inc, *distributor for* The Electrochemical Society Inc, MDRT Center for Productivity, *distributed by* American Marketing Association, American Water Works Association, Heimburger House Publishing Co

The Johns Hopkins Press Ltd (London), *subsidiary of* The Johns Hopkins University Press

Johns Hopkins University Press, *distributor for* Inter-American Development Bank, International Food Policy Research Institute, *distributed by* Heimburger House Publishing Co

The Johns Hopkins University Press, *affiliate of* The Johns Hopkins University, The Johns Hopkins University, *distributor for* The Inter-American Development Bank, Performing Arts Publications, Resources for the Future, Resources for the Future Inc, The Woodrow Wilson Center Press, The Woodrow Wilson Center Press

Johnson Books, *division of* Johnson Printing Co, Johnson Publishing Co, *distributor for* Cowboy Artists of America, High Lonesome Press, Woodlands Press

Cy Johnson & Son, *distributed by* Gem Guides Book Co

Joint Center for Political & Economic Studies Press, *distributed by* University Press of America Inc

Joint Publishers, *distributed by* China Books & Periodicals Inc

Jones & Bartlett Publishers, *distributor for* American Academy of Orthopaedic Surgeons

Bob Jones University Press, *unit of* Bob Jones University, *distributed by* Appalachian Bible Co Inc, Spring Arbor Distributors

Proctor Jones, *distributed by* Stackpole Books

Jordan Publishing, *imprint of* Evangel Publishing House

Jossey-Bass, *imprint of* John Wiley & Sons Inc, Jossey-Bass, John Wiley & Sons Inc, *distributed by* American Marketing Association

Jossey-Bass Inc, Publishers, *distributed by* American Association of Community Colleges (AACC)

Jossey Bass/Wiley, *distributor for* Center for Creative Leadership, *distributed by* Center for Creative Leadership

Journal of Chinese Medicine Publications, *distributed by* Eastland Press

The Journal of Clinical Ethics, *distributed by* University Publishing Group

Journal of Feminist Studies in Religion, *distributed by* Society of Biblical Literature

The Journal of Regional Criticism, *subsidiary of* Arjuna Library Press

Journal Publishing, *division of* Slack Incorporated

Journalbytes, *imprint of* Oakstone Medical Publishing

Journey Books, *division of* Bob Jones University Press

Journey Editions, *division of* Periplus Editions, *imprint of* Tuttle Publishing, *distributed by* Charles E Tuttle Co Inc

Jove, *imprint of* Berkley Books, Berkley Publishing Group, Penguin Group (USA) Inc

Joy Publishing, *division of* California Clock Co

Joyce Media Inc, *imprint of* Joyce Media Inc

Judaica & Hebraica, *imprint of* Transaction Publishers

Judeo Christian Ethics Series, *imprint of* PREP Publishing

Judson Press, *division of* American Baptist Churches in the USA, *subsidiary of* National Ministries, *distributed by* Crystal Fountain Publications, Heimburger House Publishing Co

Judy Instructo, *imprint of* American Society for Quality

Jump at the Sun, *imprint of* Hyperion Books for Children

Junebug Books, *imprint of* NewSouth Inc

Juno Books, *distributed by* powerHouse Books

Jury Verdict Research; LRP Magazine Group, *division of* LRP Publications

Just Think®, *imprint of* Thomas Geale Publications Inc

Juta Academic & Cape Town University Press, *distributed by* Paul & Company

K G Saur, *imprint of* Thomson Gale, *distributed by* University of Michigan Press

Max Kade Institute for German-American Studies, *distributed by* University of Wisconsin Press

Kaeden Books, *imprint of* Kaeden Corp

KAGEAN BOOKS, *imprint of* Copper Canyon Press

Kahn & Averill Publishers, *distributed by* Paul & Company

Kaibunsha, *distributed by* Book East

Kaiser-Barlow, *imprint of* Schiffer Publishing Ltd

Kales Press, *distributed by* W W Norton & Company Inc

Kalimat Press, *distributor for* Century Press, Oneworld, George Ronald, *distributed by* Baha'i Distribution Service

Kalmbach Books, *imprint of* Kalmbach Publishing Co

Kalmbach Publishing Co, *division of* The Writer Inc

Kalmus, *distributed by* Warner Bros Publications Inc

Kamehameha Schools, *imprint of* Kamehameha Schools Press

Kamehameha Schools Bishop Estate, *imprint of* Kamehameha Schools Press

Kamehameha Schools Press, *division of* Kamehameha Schools, *imprint of* Kamehameha Schools Press, *distributed by* Bess Press, University of Hawaii Press

Kane Miller, *distributed by* Sundance Publishing

Kane/Miller Book Publishers, *distributed by* Georgetown Publications Inc (Canada)

Kane Publishing, *distributed by* Phoenix Learning Resources

Kansas City Star Books, *distributed by* Heimburger House Publishing Co

Kaplan, *imprint of* Simon & Schuster Adult Publishing Group

Kaplan Press, *distributed by* Gryphon House Inc

Kaplan Publishing, *affiliate of* Simon & Schuster Adult Publishing Group, Simon & Schuster Adult Publishing Group

Kar-Ben Publishing, *division of* Lerner Publishing Group

Karen Brown Guides, *distributor for* Fodor's Travel Publications, *distributed by* Fodor's Travel Publications, Random House Inc

Karger, *distributor for* American Association of Blood Banks

Karnac Books, *distributed by* Stylus Publishing LLC

Karnak House, *imprint of* Red Sea Press Inc, *distributed by* Paul & Company

Kate's Mystery Books, *imprint of* Justin, Charles & Co, Publishers

Katydid Books, *distributed by* University of Hawaii Press

KAV Books, *distributed by* Royal Fireworks Press

Kayak Press, *distributed by* Story Line Press

Kaynak, *distributed by* The Light Inc

Kazan Books, *imprint of* Volcano Press Inc

Kazi Publications Inc, *distributor for* ABC Intl Group Inc, Foundation for Traditional Studies, Great Books of the Islamic World, QIBLAH Books, Zero Productions

KC Publications Inc, *distributed by* Gem Guides Book Co

KCP Technologies Inc, *subsidiary of* Key Curriculum Press

Kegan Paul, *distributed by* Columbia University Press

J J Keller & Associates, Inc, *distributor for* Chilton Book Co, International Air Transport Association, National Archives & Records Administration, National Institute of Occupational Safety & Health, Office of the Federal Register, Research & Special Programs Administration of the US Department of Transportation, John Wiley & Sons Inc, *distributed by* Amacom Division of American Management Division

Kelley Wingate Publications, *distributed by* Carson-Dellosa Publishing Co Inc

Miles Kelly Publishing (Canada only), *distributed by* Mint Publishers Group

Kendall Hunt Publishing, *distributor for* Seedling Publications Inc

Kendall/Hunt Publishing Co, *subsidiary of* Westmark Enterprises Inc, Westmark Enterprises Inc

The Kenilworth Press Ltd, *distributed by* Half Halt Press Inc

Kennedy Information, *division of* Kennedy Information LLC

Kensington, *imprint of* Diablo Press Inc

Kensington Book Co, *distributed by* Time Warner Book Group

Kensington Books, *imprint of* Kensington Publishing Corp

Kensington Publishing Corp, *distributor for* Frederick Fell Publishers Inc, *distributed by* New Horizon Press, Penguin Group (USA) Inc

Kenyon Publications, *distributed by* Hal Leonard Corp

Kerem, *distributed by* Hachai Publications Inc

Key College Publishing, *division of* Key Curriculum Press, *imprint of* Key Curriculum Press, *distributed by* Key Curriculum Press

Key Curriculum Press, *affiliate of* Springer Science & Business Media, *distributor for* Key College Publishing

Keystone Books, *imprint of* The Pennsylvania State University Press

Kid Genesis, *imprint of* Genesis Press Inc

Kid-to-Kid Books, *imprint of* Haights Cross Communications Inc, Sundance Publishing

Kidhaven, *distributed by* Lucent Books Inc

Kidhaven Press, *imprint of* Thomson Gale

KIDPROV, *distributor for* Great Potential Press

Kids Books By Kids, *imprint of* Beyond Words Publishing Inc

Kids Can Press Ltd, *subsidiary of* Corus Entertainment

KIDS Church, *distributed by* CharismaLife Publishers

KIDS Church (Children's Church Curriculum Group), *imprint of* Charisma House

Kids Corner, *imprint of* Haights Cross Communications Inc, Sundance Publishing

Kids Creative Classics, *distributed by* Penton Overseas Inc

Kids Own Worship™, *imprint of* Group Publishing Inc

Kids' Stuff, *imprint of* Incentive Publications Inc

KidsBooks, *distributor for* Jim Henson Publishing/Muppet Press

Kidsrights, *imprint of* JIST Publishing Inc

Kidzup Entertainment, *distributed by* Penton Overseas Inc

KinderMed Press, *imprint of* Iron Gate Publishing

Dorling Kindersley Ltd, *distributor for* Art Institute of Chicago

Kingfisher Publications, *imprint of* Houghton Mifflin Trade & Reference Division

Kingswood Books, *imprint of* Abingdon Press, *distributed by* Abingdon Press

KIVA Publications, *distributed by* Yucca Tree Press

Kiva Publishers, *distributed by* Barbed Wire Publishing

Kiva Publishing Inc, *distributor for* Clear Light Books, Petrified Forest Museum Association, San Diego Museum of Man

Klutz, *division of* Scholastic Corp

Kluwer Academic/Plenum Publishers, *imprint of* Kluwer Academic Publishers

Kluwer Academic/Plenum Publishers/New York, *division of* Kluwer Academic Publishers, *imprint of* Kluwer Academic Publishers

Kluwer Academic Publishers/Boston, *division of* Kluwer Academic Publishers

Kluwer Academic Publishers/Dordrecht, *division of* Kluwer Academic Publishers

Knickerbocker Press, *imprint of* Book Sales Inc

Nasha Kniga, *subsidiary of* Cross-Cultural Communications

Knock-off Books, *imprint of* Ugly Duckling Presse

Alfred A Knopf, *subsidiary of* Random House Inc, Random House Inc

Alfred A Knopf Books for Young Readers, *imprint of* Random House Children's Books

Alfred A Knopf Inc, *imprint of* Random House Inc

Knopf Books for Young Readers, *imprint of* Random House Inc

Knopf Delacorte Dell Young Readers Group, *division of* Random House Children's Books

Knopf Paperbacks, *imprint of* Random House Inc

Knopf Travel Guides, *imprint of* Alfred A Knopf

Kodak, *distributed by* Sterling Publishing Co Inc

Kodak Books, *imprint of* Silver Pixel Press

Kodansha, *distributed by* Oxford University Press, Inc

Kodansha America Inc, *affiliate of* Kodansha Ltd (Japan), Kodansha Ltd (Japapn), *distributor for* Japan Publications Inc, Japan Publications Trading Co Inc, Nihon/Vogue, *distributed by* Oxford University Press

Kodansha Globe, *imprint of* Kodansha America Inc

Koen Book Distributors Inc, *distributor for* Woodland Publishing Inc

Kogan Page Ltd, *distributed by* Stylus Publishing LLC

Kolowalu Books, *imprint of* University of Hawaii Press

Konecky & Konecky, *imprint of* William S Konecky Associates Inc

Konemann, *distributed by* Mel Bay Publications Inc

Kornfeld & Co, *distributed by* Alan Wofsy Fine Arts

Kornfeld (Switzerland), *distributed by* Picasso Project

Kosei Publishing Co, *imprint of* Tuttle Publishing, *distributed by* Tuttle Publishing

Kotan Publishing Inc, *imprint of* Tuttle Publishing, *distributed by* Tuttle Publishing

KQED Books & Tapes™, *imprint of* Bay/SOMA Publishing Inc

H J Kramer, *division of* New World Library

Krause Publications, *distributor for* AD Publishing, Antique Trader Books, Books Americana, DBI Books, Francis-Joseph Publications, Wallace-Homestead, Warman's, *distributed by* Sanford J Durst, Heimburger House Publishing Co

Kregel Academic & Professional, *imprint of* Kregel Publications

Kregel Classics, *imprint of* Kregel Publications

Kregel Kidzone, *imprint of* Kregel Publications

Kregel Publications, *division of* Kregel Inc, Kregel Inc, *distributor for* Candle Books, Monarch Books

Kresge Art Museum, *distributed by* Michigan State University Press (MSU Press)

Kroshka Books, *imprint of* Nova Science Publishers Inc

Melanie Kroupa Books, *imprint of* Farrar, Straus & Giroux Books for Young Readers

KTAV Holiday Products Inc, *division of* KTAV Publishing House Inc

KTAV Publishing House Inc, *distributor for* Yeshiva University Press

KU Natural History Museum, *distributed by* University Press of Kansas

Kudzu House, *imprint of* Ariel Press, *distributed by* Ariel Press

Kumarian Press, *distributor for* Management Sciences for Health

Kwela Books, *distributed by* Paul & Company

The Labor Institute, *distributed by* The Apex Press

Lacis Publications, *distributor for* Armand Colin, Gorse, Little Hills, Mani di Fata, *distributed by* Unicorn

Lady Fern Press, *imprint of* Crumb Elbow Publishing

Lake View Press, *distributor for* Anthropos Publishers, Ravenswood Books

Lakeland Color Press, *distributed by* Blue Sky Marketing Inc

Lakeshore Learning, *distributor for* Cottonwood Press Inc

Lakeshore Learning Materials, *distributor for* National Council of Teachers of Mathematics

Lalo Press, *distributed by* Bilingual Press/Editorial Bilingue

LALRP, *distributed by* Latin American Literary Review Press

LAMA Books, *subsidiary of* Leo A Meyer Associates

Landauer Books, *distributor for* Debbie Mumm® Inc

Landmark Audio, *imprint of* Haights Cross Communications Inc

Landmark Editions, *imprint of* University of Nebraska Press

Allen Lane, The Penguin Press, *imprint of* Viking Penguin

Peter Lang Publishing Inc, *subsidiary of* Verlag Peter Lang AG (Switzerland), Verlag Peter Lang AG (Switzerland)

Lange Medical Books, *imprint of* McGraw-Hill Professional

Langenscheidt, *distributed by* Hagstrom Map Co Inc

Langenscheidt Dictionary, *imprint of* Langenscheidt Publishers Inc

Langenscheidt Publishers Inc, *distributor for* Delorme Maps, *distributed by* American Map Corp, Trakker Maps Inc

LangMarc, *distributor for* LangMarc Publishing

Langmarc & North Sea Press, *distributed by* LangMarc Publishing

LangMarc Publishing, *subsidiary of* North Sea Press, *distributor for* Langmarc & North Sea Press, *distributed by* LangMarc

Language Literacy Lessons, *imprint of* Incentive Publications Inc

Lanier Publishing International, *distributed by* Ten Speed Press

Lantern Books, *distributor for* Findhorn Press, *distributed by* Steiner Books

LanternLight Library, *imprint of* University of Alaska Press

Larausse, *distributed by* Houghton Mifflin Trade & Reference Division

Laredo Publishing Company Inc, *distributed by* McGraw-Hill SRA

Large Print, *division of* Lutheran Braille Workers, Lutheran Braille Workers Inc

Large Print Press, *imprint of* Thorndike Press

Lark Books, *division of* Sterling Publishing Co Inc, *imprint of* Sterling Publishing Co Inc

Larlin Corp, *subsidiary of* Cherokee Publishing Co

Larson Publications, *distributed by* Bookpeople, National Book Network, New Leaf, Reo Wheel/Weiser

Las Brisas Research Press, *imprint of* Macalester Park Publishing Co

Latin American Literary Review Press, *distributor for* Biblioteca Quinto Centenario, LALRP, *distributed by* Bilingual Press/Editorial Bilingue, Bilingual Review Press, Small Press Distribution

Latin American Review Press, *distributed by* Arte Publico Press

Latin American Studies, *imprint of* Transaction Publishers

Latin Trading Corp, *distributor for* Fondo de Cultura Economica USA Inc

Latitude 20, *imprint of* University of Hawaii Press

Laughing Elephant, *distributed by* Abingdon Press

Laura Geringer Books, *imprint of* HarperCollins Children's Books Group, HarperCollins Publishers

Laurel Creek Press, *imprint of* Blue Dove Press

Laurel Glen Publishing, *imprint of* Advantage Publishers Group

Laurel-Leaf, *imprint of* Random House Children's Books

Law for Laypersons, *imprint of* Lawells Publishing

Law Library Microform Consortium, *distributed by* West, A Thomson Business

Law Quest, *distributed by* Chatelaine Press

Law Tribune Books, *division of* American Lawyer Media

Law Tribune Newspapers, *imprint of* Law Tribune Books

Lawrence & Wishart, *distributed by* Paul & Company

Lawrence Hill Books, *imprint of* Chicago Review Press

Merloyd Lawrence Inc, *distributed by* Perseus Books Groups

Lea Software & Alternative Media Inc, *distributed by* Lawrence Erlbaum Associates Inc

Leadership Directories, *imprint of* Leadership Directories Inc

Leadership Publishers Inc, *distributed by* Amazon.com, Barnes & Noble

Leading Edge Reports, *affiliate of* Business Trend Analysts Inc, Business Trend Analysts Inc

League of Hard of Hearing, *distributed by* Sterling Publishing Co Inc

LEAP® (Literature Enrichment Activities for Paperbacks), *imprint of* Haights Cross Communications Inc, Sundance Publishing

Leapfrog Press, *distributed by* Consortium Book Sales & Distribution

The Learn Education Center; The Learn Institute, The Lifestyle Company, *division of* American Health Publishing Co

Learning & Coloring Books, *imprint of* Quincannon Publishing Group

Learning Express, *distributed by* Random House Inc

Learning Fun, *imprint of* Incentive Publications Inc

Learning Inc, *distributed by* Lawrence Erlbaum Associates Inc

Learning Links Inc, *distributor for* Harcourt, HarperCollins, Houghton Mifflin, Little Brown, Penguin Putnam, Random House Inc, Scholastic, Simon & Schuster

LearningExpress, *distributed by* Thomson Delmar Learning

LearningExpress LLC, *distributed by* Delmar (a division of Thomson Learning)

Lectorum Publications Inc, *division of* Scholastic Education, *subsidiary of* Scholastic Inc, *distributor for* Fondo de Cultura Economica USA Inc

Lederer Books, *division of* Messianic Jewish Publishers, *distributor for* Chosen People Ministries, First Fruits of Zion, Jewish New Testament Publications

Lee & Low Books, *distributed by* Sundance Publishing

Legacy Press, *imprint of* Rainbow Publishers

Legal Education Publishing, *division of* State Bar of Wisconsin

Legas, *distributed by* Cross-Cultural Communications

Legend Books, College Division, *division of* Legend Books

Legendary Books, *imprint of* Modern Publishing

Lehigh University Press, *affiliate of* Associated University Presses, *distributed by* Associated University Presses

Leisure Arts Inc, *distributor for* Oxmoor House Inc, Sunset Books/Sunset Publishing Corp

Lemma Publishers, *distributed by* Purdue University Press

Hal Leonard Corp, *distributor for* Amadeus Press, Applause Theatre & Cinema Books, Artistpro, Ashley Music, Backbeat Books, Beacon Music, Berklee Press, Fred Bock Music Company, Boosey & Hawkes, Centerstream Publications, Centerstream Publishing LLC, Cherry Lane Music Co, Cinema Books, Community Music Videos, Creative Concepts, DC Publications, Devine Entertainment Corp, Editions Durand, Editions Max Eschig, Editions Salabert, EM Books, EMI Christian, Faber Music Ltd, Guitar One, Guitar World, Home Recording, Homespun Tapes, Houston Publications, Hudson Music, iSong CD-ROMs, Kenyon Publications, Limelight Editions, Ashley Mark Publishing Co, Edward B Marks Music, Meredith Music, Modern Drummer Publications, Musicians Institute Press, Musikverlage Han Sikorski, Christopher Parkening, Reader's Digest, Record Research, Ricordi, Lee Roberts Publications, Rubank Publications, G Schirmer Inc (Associated Music Publishers), Second Floor Music, Sing Out Corporation, Star Licks Videos, Bernard Stein Music Co, String Letter Press, Tara Publications, Transcontinental Music, 21st Century Publications, Vintage Guitar, Word Music, Writer's Digest

Lerner Publications, *division of* Lerner Publishing Group, *imprint of* Lerner Publishing Group

Lerner Publishing Group, *distributor for* Darby Creek

LernerClassroom, *imprint of* Lerner Publishing Group

LernerSports, *imprint of* Lerner Publishing Group

Les Editions E T C, *distributed by* Lotus Press

The Letter People®, *division of* Abrams & Co Publishers Inc

Letterland International Ltd, *distributed by* Enfield Publishing & Distribution Co

Wayne Leupold Editions, *distributed by* ECS Publishing

Lewis Publishers, *imprint of* CRC Press LLC

Lexington & Concord Partners Ltd, Panama, *distributed by* American Eagle Publications Inc

Lexington Books, *member of* Rowman & Littlefield Publishing Group

LexisNexis, *distributor for* Standard Publishing Corp

LexisNexis®, *member of* Reed Elsevier Group plc, Reed Elsevier plc

LexisNexis Academic & Library Solutions, *member of* The LexisNexis family, The LexisNexis Group

Liberty Literary Works, *distributed by* Ocean Tree Books

Librairie de France, *imprint of* French & European Publications Inc

Libraries Unlimited, *division of* Greenwood Publishing, *member of* Greenwood Publishing Group, *imprint of* Greenwood Publishing Group Inc

Library du Liban (Lebanon), *distributed by* International Book Centre Inc

The Library of America, *distributed by* Penguin Group (USA) Inc, Penguin Putnam Inc

Library of Congress, *distributor for* National Braille Press, *distributed by* Bernan

Library of Conservative Thought, *imprint of* Transaction Publishers

Library of Contemporary Thought, *imprint of* Random House Inc

Library of Islam, *imprint of* Kazi Publications Inc

Library of Liberal Thought, *imprint of* Transaction Publishers

Library of Professional Picture Framing, *imprint of* Columba Publishing Co Inc

Library One Direct, *division of* Gareth Stevens Inc

Libreria Martinez, *distributor for* Fondo de Cultura Economica USA Inc

Libris, *distributed by* The Denali Press, Paul & Company

Libronauta, *distributor for* Bridge Publications Inc

Libros Desafio, *imprint of* CRC Publications

Libros en Espanol, *imprint of* Fireside & Touchstone

Libros Liguori, *imprint of* Liguori Publications

Libros Para Ninos, *imprint of* Simon & Schuster Children's Publishing

Libros Sin Fronteras, *distributor for* Fondo de Cultura Economica USA Inc

Libros Viajeros, *imprint of* Harcourt Trade Publishers

Life Cycle Books, *division of* Life Cycle Books Ltd (Canada), Life Cycle Books Ltd (Canada)

Life on the Edge, *imprint of* Focus on the Family

LifeGuide Bible Studies, *imprint of* InterVarsity Press

LifeLearn, *distributor for* Teton New Media, *distributed by* Teton New Media

LifeLine Press, *imprint of* Eagle Publishing Inc

LifeQuest, *distributor for* New Life Ministries, *distributed by* Brethren Press

LifeSounds Audio Library, *imprint of* NewLife Publications

Lifestyles, *imprint of* Hay House Inc

The Lifetime Series, *imprint of* JMW Group Inc

LifeTimes, *imprint of* Rayve Productions Inc

LifeWay Christian Resources, *distributor for* Baptist Spanish Publishing House (d/b/a Casa Bautista de Publicaciones)

Lifewrite, *imprint of* Gallopade International Inc

The Liffey Press, *distributed by* Dufour Editions Inc

Lift Every Voice, *imprint of* Moody Press

LIFT® (Literature is for Thinking), *imprint of* Haights Cross Communications Inc, Sundance Publishing

Light & Life, *distributor for* Conciliar Press, *distributed by* Conciliar Press

Light & Life Publishing Co, *distributor for* St Herman Press

The Light Inc, *distributor for* Gonca, ISIK, Kaynak, Nil, Selt, Zambak

Lightening Rod Publishing, *imprint of* Windstorm Creative

Lighthouse Press, *imprint of* ProStar Publications Inc

Lighthouse Publications, *imprint of* Weidner & Sons Publishing, *distributed by* Weidner & Sons Publishing

Lightning Source, *distributor for* Bristol Fashion Publications Inc

Lightning Source Inc, *distributor for* Protea Publishing, Ravenhawk™ Books

Lightning Up Press, *distributed by* Enfield Publishing & Distribution Co

Liguori Publications, *distributor for* Redemptorist Publications

Liguori/Triumph, *imprint of* Liguori Publications

Philip E Lilienthal Asian Studies, *imprint of* University of California Press

Lillenas Publishing Co, *imprint of* Beacon Hill Press of Kansas City

Lilliput Press Ltd, *distributed by* Dufour Editions Inc

LIM Editrice SRL (Italy), *distributor for* Pendragon Press

Limelight Books, *imprint of* Tiare Publications

Limelight Editions, *subsidiary of* Proscenium Publishers Inc, *distributed by* Hal Leonard Corp

Limestone Press, *distributed by* University of Alaska Press

The Linacre Centre, *distributed by* St Augustine's Press Inc

Frances Lincoln, *distributed by* Antique Collectors Club Ltd

Lincoln Record Society, *imprint of* Boydell & Brewer Inc

Lindisfarne Books, *imprint of* Anthroposophic Press, Steiner Books, *distributed by* Floris Books

John Liner Organization, *subsidiary of* Standard Publishing Corp

Lingua Forum, *distributed by* Paul & Company

Linguaphone Institute Ltd, *distributed by* Cortina Learning International Inc

The Linick Group Inc, *distributor for* Linick International, LKA Inc, NAPS, *distributed by* Bookmasters, New World Press

Linick International, *distributed by* The Linick Group Inc

Linick International Programs, *subsidiary of* Copywriter's Council of America (CCA)

Linnet Books, *imprint of* The Shoe String Press Inc

Linnet Professional Publications, *imprint of* The Shoe String Press Inc

Linns Stamp News-Ancillary Division, *division of* AMOS Hobby Publishing

Linux Journal Press, *imprint of* No Starch Press Inc, Specialized Systems Consultants Inc

Linworth Learning, *imprint of* Linworth Publishing Inc

Lion, *imprint of* Cook Communications Ministries

Lion Books Publisher, *division of* Sayre Publishing Inc, Sayre Publishing Inc

Lion Publishing, *distributed by* Cook Communications Ministries, Trafalgar Square

Lion's Paw Books, *imprint of* Coronet Books & Publications

Lippincott Williams & Wilkins, *subsidiary of* Wolters Kluwer Health, *imprint of* Wolters Kluwer US Corp

Lippincott, Williams & Wilkins, *distributor for* Rayve Productions Inc

Lips (Magazine & Press), *distributed by* Cross-Cultural Communications

LIS (Legal Information Services), *subsidiary of* CCH Inc

Lisa Drew Books, *imprint of* Scribner, Simon & Schuster Adult Publishing Group

Listening Library®, *division of* Books on Tape®, *imprint of* Books on Tape®, *distributed by* Books on Tape®

Lit Verlag, *distributed by* Transaction Publishers

Literacy Institute for Education (LIFE) Inc, *subsidiary of* B K Nelson Inc, B K Nelson Inc

Literary Conversations Series, *imprint of* University Press of Mississippi

Literary House Press, *distributed by* Cornell Maritime Press Inc, Tidewater Publishers

Literature & Thought, *imprint of* Perfection Learning Corp

Litigation GP, *division of* Public Citizen

Little America Publishing Co, *imprint of* Beautiful America Publishing Co

Little Blue Readers, *imprint of* Haights Cross Communications Inc, Sundance Publishing

Little Blue Works, *imprint of* Windstorm Creative

Little Books, *distributed by* Trafalgar Square

Little Brown, *distributed by* Learning Links Inc

Little Brown & Co, *distributed by* Sundance Publishing

Little, Brown & Co, *distributed by* Silver Pixel Press

Little, Brown and Co, *distributor for* Alloy Entertainment

Little, Brown and Company, *imprint of* Time Warner Book Group

Little, Brown and Company Adult Trade Division, *subsidiary of* Time Warner Book Group

Little, Brown and Company Books for Young Readers, *subsidiary of* Time Warner Book Group, *imprint of* Time Warner Book Group

Little Green Readers, *imprint of* Haights Cross Communications Inc, Sundance Publishing

Little Hills, *distributed by* Lacis Publications

Little Imp Books, *imprint of* Impact Publishers Inc

Little Lucy & Friends™, *imprint of* Playhouse Publishing

Little Red Readers, *imprint of* Haights Cross Communications Inc, Sundance Publishing

Little Room Press, *distributed by* Fordham University Press

Little Simon, *imprint of* Simon & Schuster Children's Publishing

Little Simon Inspirations, *imprint of* Simon & Schuster Children's Publishing

Little Soundprints, *imprint of* Soundprints

Littlefield, Adams Quality Paperbacks, *imprint of* Rowman & Littlefield Publishers Inc

Liturgical Press, *division of* The Order of St Benedict Inc, The Order of St Benedict Inc

Liturgical Press Books, *imprint of* Liturgical Press

Liturgy Training Publications, *subsidiary of* Archdiocese of Chicago, *distributor for* United States Catholic Conference Publications, *distributed by* Oregon Catholic Press

Liveright Publishing Corp, *subsidiary of* W W Norton & Company Inc

Living Aboard, *division of* Acres USA

Living Books, *imprint of* Tyndale House Publishers Inc

Living Language, *division of* Random House, *imprint of* Random House Inc

Livingston Press, *division of* University of West Alabama, *distributor for* Swallow's Tale Press

LKA Inc, *imprint of* The Linick Group Inc, *distributed by* The Linick Group Inc

Llewellyn, *distributor for* ACS Publications

Llewellyn Publications, *division of* Llewellyn Worldwide Ltd

Chris Lloyd, *distributor for* Cycle Publishing

LMC Source, *distributor for* Hi Willow Research & Publishing

LMD Inc (selected titles), *distributor for* Council for Exceptional Children

Local Government & Public Service Reform Initiative, *distributed by* Central European University Press

Locks Art Publications/Locks Gallery, *division of* Locks Gallery

Loft Publications, *distributed by* Antique Collectors Club Ltd

Logan Brothers, *distributor for* Teton New Media

Login Brothers, *distributor for* American Association of Blood Banks, Health Professions Press, Maval Publishing Inc

Login Brothers Book Company, *distributor for* United States Pharmacopeia

Login Publishing Consortium, *distributor for* United States Pharmacopeia

Logion Press, *imprint of* Gospel Publishing House

Logos, *imprint of* Bridge-Logos Publishers

Logos Bookstore, *distributor for* MAR*CO Products Inc

Lominger Inc, *distributed by* Center for Creative Leadership

Lone Eagle Publishing, *affiliate of* Hollywood Creative Directory

Lone Pine Publishing, *distributor for* Dog-Eared Publications

Lone Star Audio, *imprint of* Haights Cross Communications Inc, Recorded Books LLC

Longman, *distributed by* Council for Exceptional Children, Trans-Atlantic Publications Inc

Longman Publishers, *division of* Pearson Education

Longwood, *imprint of* Pearson Higher Education Division

Looking Glass Preschool Board Books, *imprint of* Modern Publishing

Loompanics Unlimited, *division of* Loompanics Enterprises Inc, Loompanics Enterprises Inc, *distributor for* Breakout Productions Inc

Loompanics Unlimited Ingram, *distributor for* Breakout Productions Inc

Looseleaf Law Publications Inc, *division of* Wardean Corp, Warodean Corp

James Lorimer & Co, *distributed by* Orca Book Publishers

Los Andes Publishing, *distributor for* Fondo de Cultura Economica USA Inc

Los Angeles Times Crosswords, *imprint of* Random House Reference

Lost & Found Times, *subsidiary of* Luna Bisonte Prods

Lost Classics Book Co, *distributed by* Applewood Books

Lothian Books, *distributed by* Star Bright Books

Lothrop, Lee & Shepard Books, *imprint of* HarperCollins Publishers

Lotus Press, *division of* Lotus Brands Inc, Lotus Brands Inc, *distributor for* Back to Eden Books, Dipti, Inner Worlds Music, Les Editions E T C, November Moon, S A B D A, Sadhana Publications, Samata Books, Sri Aurobindo Ashram, Star Sounds, *distributed by* Michigan State University Press (MSU Press)

Louisiana Book Distributors, *imprint of* Pelican Publishing Co Inc

Love Publishing, *distributed by* Council for Exceptional Children

Love Spectrum, *imprint of* Genesis Press Inc

Love Spell, *imprint of* Dorchester Publishing Co Inc

Loving Guidance Inc, *distributed by* Gryphon House Inc

Lowry Press, *distributed by* Antique Collectors Club Ltd

Loyola Press, *distributor for* Biblical Institute Press, Gregorian University Press, Jesuit Historical Institute, Oriental Institute Press

LPC Group Inc, *distributor for* Dark Horse Comics

LRP Magazine Group, *subsidiary of* LRP Publications

LRS, *division of* Library Reproduction Service

LTE Classics, *imprint of* JMW Group Inc

LTI (Learn Technologies Interactive), *distributor for* Art Institute of Chicago

Lucent, *distributor for* Lucent Books Inc, *distributed by* Lucent Books Inc

Lucent Books Inc, *imprint of* The Gale Group, Thomson Gale, *distributor for* Greenhaven Press Inc, Kidhaven, Lucent, Sleeping Bear Press, Thorndike (Young Adult), *distributed by* Greenhaven Press Inc, Lucent

Lucky Duck Press, *distributed by* The Writers' Collective

Lullabies, *imprint of* Modern Publishing

Lumen, *imprint of* Brookline Books

Luna Books, *imprint of* Harlequin Enterprises Ltd

Lund Humphries/Ashgate, *distributor for* National Gallery of Art

Lushena Books, *distributor for* A & B Publishers Group

Lutterworth, *distributed by* Christian Literature Crusade Inc

Luzac Orientals, *distributed by* Weatherhill Inc

Lynn-Reinner Publishing, *distributor for* University of California Institute on Global Conflict & Cooperation

Lynx House Press, *distributed by* Michigan State University Press, Small Press Distribution

The Lyons Press, *imprint of* The Globe Pequot Press, *distributor for* Design Books

M & B Distributors, *distributor for* MAR*CO Products Inc

M & H Type, *division of* The Arion Press

M & M Maschietto & Ditore, *distributed by* Fordham University Press

M R T S, *imprint of* ACMRS

M S G-Haskell House Publishers Ltd, *subsidiary of* M S G

MacAdam/Cage Publishing Children's, *imprint of* MacAdam/Cage Publishing Inc

Macalester Park Publishing Co, *division of* Beard Communications, *distributor for* Priority Multimedia

Mackinad Historic Parks, *distributed by* Michigan State University Press (MSU Press)

Macmillan, *distributor for* Building News

Macmillan Caribbean (UK), *distributed by* Interlink Publishing Group Inc

Macmillan Education (UK), *distributed by* Players Press Inc

Macmillan/McGraw-Hill, *division of* McGraw-Hill Education, *imprint of* McGraw-Hill Education

Macmillan of Canada (Toronto), *distributor for* Professional Publishing

Pan MacMillan, *distributed by* Trans-Atlantic Publications Inc

Macmillan Press Ltd (selected titles), *distributed by* Pickwick Publications

Macmillan Publishing Co, *distributor for* National Association of Broadcasters (NAB)

Macmillan Reference USA, *imprint of* Thomson Gale

Macmillan Reference USA™, *unit of* Pearson Technology Group (PTG), *imprint of* Thomson Gale

Macmillan (UK), *distributed by* Scholium International Inc

Macmillan UK, *distributed by* Trafalgar Square

MacroPrintBooks, *imprint of* Science & Humanities Press

'MAD' Books, *imprint of* DC Comics

Made Simple Books, *imprint of* Doubleday Broadway Publishing Group

Madison Books, *imprint of* Cooper Square Press

Madison House Publishers, *member of* Rowman & Littlefield Publishing Group, *distributor for* Center for Study of American Constitution

Mage Publishers Inc, *distributed by* University of Toronto Press

Magic Carpet Books, *imprint of* Harcourt Trade Publishers

Magill's Choice, *imprint of* Salem Press Inc

Magnes Press, *distributed by* Gefen Books

Magnet Books, *imprint of* Bristol Publishing Enterprises

Magnetix Corp, *distributor for* John Milton Society for the Blind

Magni Co, *distributed by* Book Publishing Co

The Magni Co, *subsidiary of* The Magni Group Inc

Magnum Books, *imprint of* Playmore Inc, Publishers

Maharishi University of Management Press, *subsidiary of* Maharishi University of Management, *distributed by* Fairfield Press, Penguin Group (USA) Inc

Main Street/Back List, *imprint of* Doubleday Broadway Publishing Group

Main Street Books, *imprint of* Random House Inc

Mainstream Publishing, *distributed by* Trafalgar Square

Maisonneuve Press, *division of* Institute for Advanced Cultural Studies, *distributed by* Merlin Press (London, England), Paul & Company

Maize Press, *distributed by* Bilingual Press/Editorial Bilingue

J A Majors, *distributor for* Tarascon Publishing

Malley's, *distributed by* Mel Bay Publications Inc

Mama's Cafe Press, *imprint of* Windstorm Creative

Management Consultant International, *imprint of* Kennedy Information

Management Sciences for Health, *distributed by* Kumarian Press

Manatee Publishing, *subsidiary of* Four Seasons Publishers

Manchester University Press, *distributed by* St Martin's Press LLC

Mandala Publishing, *affiliate of* Palace Press International, *distributed by* Ten Speed Press

Mandarin, *imprint of* Heinemann

Mandate Press, *imprint of* William Carey Library

Mandrill, *imprint of* Trident Media Inc

Mango Publishing, *distributed by* Paul & Company

Manhattan Publishing Co, *division of* US & Europe Books Inc, *distributor for* Assembly of Western European Union, Council of Europe, European Court of Human Rights

Mani di Fata, *distributed by* Lacis Publications

Manic D Press, *distributed by* Publishers Group West

Mankind, *imprint of* Holloway House Publishing Co, *distributed by* Holloway House Publishing Co

Manning Publications Co, *distributed by* IPG, Pearson Education, Prentice Hall, TransQuest Publishers Pte Ltd, Woodslane Pty Ltd

Manson Publishing Ltd, *distributed by* Blackwell Publishing Professional

Many Feathers Books & Maps, *distributor for* Trails Illustrated, Division of National Geographic Maps

Manzanila Books.com, *distributor for* Park Place Publications

Map & Atlas Publishing, *division of* Rand McNally

Map Link, *distributor for* Trails Illustrated, Division of National Geographic Maps

Mapin, *distributed by* Antique Collectors Club Ltd

MAR*CO Products Inc, *distributor for* Boulden, Center for Youth Issues Stars, Educational Media, HarperCollins, *distributed by* ACCT FOR KIDS, ASCA, Barnes & Noble, Jean Barnes Books, The Bookies, Boulden Publishing, Burnell books, Career Kids FYI, Carr Peer Resources, CFKR Career, Community Intervention, Cress Productions Co, Educational Esteem, Educational Media, Eight Street Alano, Genesis Book I, Incentive Plus, Jist, Logos Bookstore, M & B Distributors, Mental Health Resources, National Professional Resources, National Resource Center Youth Services, NIMCO Bookstore, Pale House Publishers, Paperbacks for Educators, PCI, R & K Bookstore, SourceResource, STARS, Teachers Gear, UMICOM Education, US Book Distributor, YOUTHLIGHT

Marathon Press, *division of* Sanford J Durst, *imprint of* Sanford J Durst, *distributed by* Amherst Media

MARC Publications, *subsidiary of* World Vision International

Mare's Nest, *distributed by* Dufour Editions Inc

Marginal, *distributor for* Factor Press

Marian Wood Books, *imprint of* Penguin Group (USA) Inc, The Putnam Publishing Group, G P Putnam's Sons (Hardcover)

Marine Survey Press, *imprint of* Marine Education Textbooks Inc

Mariner Books, *imprint of* Houghton Mifflin Trade & Reference Division

Mariposa Publishing, *distributed by* Cinco Puntos Press

Ashley Mark Publishing Co, *imprint of* Hal Leonard Corp, *distributed by* Hal Leonard Corp

Market Data Retrieval, *division of* The Dun & Bradstreet Corp, Dunn & Bradstreet Corp

Market House Books, *imprint of* EduCare Press

Marketing Smarter, *imprint of* OneOnOne Computer Training

MarketResearch.com, *distributor for* Primary Research Group

Markham Press Fund, *imprint of* Baylor University Press

Markings, *imprint of* Thomas Nelson Inc

Edward B Marks Music, *distributed by* Hal Leonard Corp

The Marlboro Press, *imprint of* Northwestern University Press

Marlor Press Inc, *distributed by* Independent Publishers Group

Marlowe & Co, *imprint of* Avalon Publishing Group Inc

Marlowe & Company, *imprint of* Avalon Publishing Group Inc, Avalon Publishing Group - New York

Marmac Publishing Co, *distributed by* Pelican Publishing Co Inc

Marriage & Family Studies, *imprint of* Transaction Publishers

Carole Marsh Books, *subsidiary of* Gallopade International Inc, *imprint of* Gallopade International Inc

Carole Marsh Family CD-ROM & Interactive Multimedia, *imprint of* Gallopade International Inc

Carole Marsh Family Interactive Multimedia, *subsidiary of* Gallopade International Inc

Marshall & Swift, *distributed by* McGraw-Hill Book Co

Marshall Cavendish Children's Books, *imprint of* Marshall Cavendish Corp

Marshall Cavendish Corp, *member of* Times International Publishing, Times Publishing Group, *distributed by* Peter Pal Library Supplier

Marshall Cavendish Online, *imprint of* Marshall Cavendish Corp

Marshall Cavendish Reference, *imprint of* Marshall Cavendish Corp

Marshall Editions, *distributed by* Antique Collectors Club Ltd

Martindale-Hubbell, *division of* Reed Business Information, *member of* The Reed Elsevier Group

Martingale & Co, *distributor for* That Patchwork Place

Martino Fine Books, *distributed by* Oak Knoll Press

Helen Marx, *distributed by* Turtle Point Press

Helen Marx/Turtle Point, *imprint of* Turtle Point Press

Maryland Historical Society, *distributor for* Alan C Hood & Co Inc

Maryland Historical Trust Press, *distributed by* Cornell Maritime Press Inc, Tidewater Publishers

Maryland Sea Grant Program, *distributed by* Cornell Maritime Press Inc, Tidewater Publishers

Maryland State Archives Publications, *distributed by* Cornell Maritime Press Inc, Tidewater Publishers

Massachusetts Historical Society, *distributed by* Northeastern University Press

Master Books, *subsidiary of* New Leaf Press

Masters of Photography, *imprint of* Aperture Books

Masterwork Books, *imprint of* Kidsbooks Inc

Masterworks of Modern Jewish Writing, *imprint of* Markus Wiener Publishers Inc

Masthof Press, *distributor for* Closson Press

Math Products Plus, *imprint of* Wide World Publishing/Tetra

Mathematica Josephina, *distributed by* American Mathematical Society

The Mathematical Association of America, *distributed by* Cambridge University Press

Mathematical Society of Japan, *distributed by* American Mathematical Society

Matthews Book Co, *distributor for* United States Pharmacopeia

Matthews Medical, *distributor for* Tarascon Publishing

Maui Media LLC, *distributed by* Penton Overseas Inc

Maval Publishing Inc, *subsidiary of* Editora Maval Ltda, *distributed by* Benjamin & Matthew Book Co, Login Brothers, Rittenhouse Book Distributors

Maverick, *distributor for* Naturegraph Publishers Inc

Maverick Distributors, *subsidiary of* Maverick Publications Inc

Kevin Mayhew Ltd, *distributed by* Mel Bay Publications Inc

Mazda Publishers Inc, *distributor for* Bibliotheca Persica (Co-Publishers)

McDougal Littell, *subsidiary of* Houghton Mifflin Co, Houghton Mifflin Co

Margaret K McElderry Books, *imprint of* Simon & Schuster Children's Publishing

McFarland & Co Ltd, Publishers (London, UK), *subsidiary of* McFarland & Co Inc Publishers

McGraw-Hill, *imprint of* McGraw-Hill Learning Group, McGraw-Hill Science, Engineering, Mathematics, *distributor for* American Diabetes Association, Phoenix Learning Resources, Society of Manufacturing Engineers, The Sporting News Publishing Co, A Vulcan Sports Media Company, *distributed by* Abbott, Langer & Associates, Althos Publishing, American Academy of Environmental Engineers, American Marketing Association, American Society for Training & Development (ASTD), American Water Works Association, Illuminating Engineering Society of North America, NACE International, Police Executive Research Forum, SAS Publishing, Society of Manufacturing Engineers, Traders Press Inc

McGraw-Hill Education - Australia, New Zealand and South Africa, *imprint of* McGraw-Hill Education

McGraw-Hill Book Co, *distributor for* Marshall & Swift

McGraw-Hill Custom Publishing, *imprint of* McGraw-Hill Education, McGraw-Hill Higher Education

McGraw-Hill Digital Learning, *imprint of* McGraw-Hill Education

McGraw-Hill/Dushkin, *division of* The McGraw-Hill Companies Inc, *imprint of* McGraw-Hill Education, McGraw-Hill Higher Education

McGraw-Hill Education, *division of* The McGraw-Hill Companies Inc, The McGraw-Hill Companies

McGraw-Hill Education Europe, Middle East and Africa, *imprint of* McGraw-Hill Education

McGraw-Hill Education Latin America, *imprint of* McGraw-Hill Education

McGraw-Hill Education - Spain, *imprint of* McGraw-Hill Education

McGraw-Hill Higher Education, *division of* McGraw-Hill/Dushkin, McGraw-Hill Education, *subsidiary of* McGraw-Hill Education

McGraw-Hill Humanities, Social Sciences and World Languages, *imprint of* McGraw-Hill Education

McGraw-Hill Humanities, Social Sciences, Languages, *division of* McGraw-Hill Higher Education, *imprint of* McGraw-Hill Higher Education

McGraw-Hill International, *distributor for* AMACOM Books

McGraw-Hill International Publishing Group, *division of* McGraw-Hill Education

McGraw-Hill/Irwin, *division of* McGraw-Hill Higher Education, *imprint of* McGraw-Hill Education, McGraw-Hill Higher Education

McGraw-Hill Learning Group, *division of* McGraw-Hill Education

McGraw-Hill Osborne, *imprint of* McGraw-Hill Education

McGraw-Hill/Osborne, *division of* McGraw-Hill Education

McGraw-Hill Primis Custom Publishing, *division of* McGraw-Hill Higher Education

McGraw-Hill Professional, *division of* McGraw-Hill Education, McGraw-Hill Education, *imprint of* McGraw-Hill Education

McGraw-Hill Professional Publishing, *imprint of* Professional Publishing, *distributor for* American Society for Quality

McGraw-Hill Ryerson, *imprint of* McGraw-Hill Education

McGraw-Hill Science, Engineering, Mathematics, *division of* McGraw-Hill Higher Education, *imprint of* McGraw-Hill Education, McGraw-Hill Higher Education

McGraw-Hill Science, Technical & Medical, *imprint of* McGraw-Hill Education

McGraw-Hill SRA, *distributor for* Laredo Publishing Company Inc

McGraw-Hill Trade, *division of* McGraw-Hill Education, *imprint of* McGraw-Hill Education

McGraw-Hill Professional Development, *imprint of* McGraw-Hill Education

McGrawHill, *distributed by* Medical Group Management Association

McIntosh & Otis, *subsidiary of* Louisiana State University Press

McKay Chess Library, *imprint of* Random House Reference

Anne McKinney Career Series, *imprint of* PREP Publishing

McKissick Museum, *distributed by* University of South Carolina Press

Andrews McMeel Publishing, *division of* Andrews McMeel Universal, *distributor for* Carlton Books, Diamond Select, Melcher Media, National Geographic Calendars, Michael O'Mara Books (North America only), Signatures Network, Sporting News, Universe Publishing Calendars, Welcome Books, *distributed by* Simon & Schuster Inc

McPherson & Co, *imprint of* McPherson & Co, *distributor for* Raymond Saroff Editions

John McQuarrie Books, *distributed by* Mountain Press Publishing Co

McWhiney Foundation Press, *distributed by* Texas A&M University Press

Md Books, *imprint of* May Davenport Publishers

MDRT Center for Productivity, *division of* Million Dollar Round Table, *distributed by* Nightingale-Conant, John Wiley & Sons

Meadow Creek Press, *imprint of* Crumb Elbow Publishing

Meadowbrook Press, *distributed by* Simon & Schuster (book trade only), Simon & Schuster Inc

Mean Free Path, *distributor for* American Society for Nondestructive Testing

R S Means Co Inc, *subsidiary of* Construction Market Data Group

Mechling Associates, *distributor for* Western Pennsylvania Genealogical Society

Medals of America Press, *division of* Medals of America Ltd

MedBooks, *division of* Professional Education Workshops & Seminars, *distributed by* JA Majors

Medford Press, *imprint of* Plexus Publishing Inc

Media Action International, *distributed by* Paul & Company

Media & Methods, *subsidiary of* American Society of Educators

Media Associates, *subsidiary of* Archives Publications, *distributed by* Airlift, Editions France, Equestrian Distribution, Inland, New Leaf, Samuel Weiser

Medical Economics, *distributed by* Ingenix Inc

Medical Group Management Association, *distributor for* Aspen Publishers, Jossey Bass, McGrawHill, *distributed by* American Academy of Family Physicians

Medical Publishing (Gefen), *division of* Gefen Books

Medieval Institute Publications, *division of* Medieval Institute of Western Michigan University

Medio Media, *distributed by* The Continuum International Publishing Group

Medlaw Books, *imprint of* Weidner & Sons Publishing, *distributed by* Weidner & Sons Publishing

Megan Tingley Books, *imprint of* Little, Brown and Company Books for Young Readers

Mel Bay Publications Inc, *distributor for* AMA, Chanterelle, Hardie Press, Konemann, Malley's, Kevin Mayhew Ltd, Voggenreiter Publishers, Walton's, *distributed by* International Print Edition

Melbourne University Press, *distributed by* Paul & Company

Melcher Media, *distributed by* Andrews McMeel Publishing

Melissa Media Associates Inc, *division of* Aristide D Caratzas, Publisher, *imprint of* Aristide D Caratzas, Publisher

Edwin Mellen, (Canada, UK), *division of* The Edwin Mellen Press

Mellen Poetry Press, *imprint of* The Edwin Mellen Press

Melrose Square, *imprint of* Holloway House Publishing Co, *distributed by* Holloway House Publishing Co

Memento Mori Mysteries, *imprint of* Avocet Press Inc

Memoirs, *imprint of* American Philosophical Society

Memories Press, *imprint of* R J Berg/Destinations Press Ltd

Men at Arms, *imprint of* Osprey Publishing Ltd

Menasha Ridge Press, *distributed by* The Globe Pequot Press

Menasha Ridge Press Inc, *distributed by* The Globe Pequot Press

MENC - The National Association for Music Education, *distributor for* American String Teachers Association

Menil Foundation, *distributed by* University of Texas Press

Menorah, *distributed by* Bloch Publishing Co

Mental Health Resources, *distributor for* American Counseling Association, MAR*CO Products Inc

Mentor, *imprint of* NAL, Penguin Group (USA) Inc

MEP Publications, *division of* Marxist Educational Press

Mercat Press (UK), *distributed by* Interlink Publishing Group Inc

Mercy Place, *distributed by* Destiny Image

Meredith, *distributed by* Thomson Delmar Learning

Meredith Music, *distributed by* Hal Leonard Corp

Merehurst Ltd, *imprint of* Tuttle Publishing

Meridian, *imprint of* NAL, Penguin Group (USA) Inc

Meridian Books, *distributed by* The Denali Press

Meridian Education Corp, *distributor for* Chronicle Guidance Publications Inc

Merit Publishing International Inc, *affiliate of* Merit Publishing International

Meisha Merlin, *distributed by* Embiid Publishing

Merlin Press, *distributed by* Paul & Company

Merlin Press (London, England), *distributor for* Maisonneuve Press

Merriam-Webster, *distributed by* Sundance Publishing

Merriam-Webster Inc, *subsidiary of* Encyclopaedia Britannica, Encyclopaedia Britannica Inc

Merrick & Day, *distributed by* Antique Collectors Club Ltd

Robert G Merrick Editions, *imprint of* The Johns Hopkins University Press

Merrill, *imprint of* Glencoe/McGraw-Hill, McGraw-Hill Learning Group, Pearson Higher Education Division

Frank Merriwell Inc, *subsidiary of* National Learning Corp

Merry Muse Press, *imprint of* Loft Press Inc

Mesorah Publications Ltd, *distributor for* Mesorah Publications Ltd, NCSY Publications, *distributed by* Mesorah Publications Ltd

Messianic Jewish Publishers, *division of* Messianic Jewish Communications, *distributor for* Chosen People Ministries, First Fruits of Zion, Jewish New Testament Publications

Messianic Jewish Resources, *distributor for* Jewish New Testament Publications Inc

Metal Bulletin Books, *imprint of* Metal Bulletin Inc

Metal Bulletin Inc, *subsidiary of* Metal Bulletin PLC (UK)

Metal Powder Industries Federation, *distributor for* ASM International (selected titles), Butterworth-Heinemann, DGM Informationsgesellschaft (selected titles), Adam Hilger (selected titles), Institute of Materials (selected titles), MPR Publishing (selected titles), Plenum Publishing Corp (selected titles), Prentice Hall (selected titles), TMS (selected titles), Verlag Schmid (selected titles)

Metamorphous Advanced Product Services, *division of* Metamorphous Press

Metamorphous Press, *division of* Metamorphous Press Inc, Metamorphous Press Inc, *distributor for* Exclusive: Anue Productions, Facticity, M Grinder & Associates

Metascience, *imprint of* Ariel Press

Methuen Drama, *imprint of* Heinemann

Metro Publications, *distributed by* Trafalgar Square

Metropolitan Books, *imprint of* Henry Holt and Company, LLC

The Metropolitan Museum of Art, *distributed by* Yale University Press

Mets & Schilt, *distributed by* Transaction Publishers

David Meyer Magic Books, *imprint of* Meyerbooks Publisher

Meyer Enterprises, *imprint of* Western New York Wares Inc

MFA Publications, *division of* Museum of Fine Arts Boston, *distributed by* D A P

MHS, *distributor for* A D D Warehouse

Micelle Press, *distributed by* Scholium International Inc

Michael di Capua Books, *imprint of* Hyperion Books for Children

Michelin Travel Publications, *division of* Michelin North America Inc

Michi Japanese Arts and Ways, *imprint of* Stone Bridge Press LLC

Michie, *imprint of* LexisNexis®

Michigan Municipal League, *affiliate of* National League of Cities, *distributor for* Crisp Books

Michigan State University Press, *distributor for* Lynx House Press

Michigan State University Press (MSU Press), *division of* Michigan State University, *distributor for* Colleagues Books, Kresge Art Museum, Lotus Press, Mackinad Historic Parks, MSU Museum, National Museum of Science & Industry UK, University of Calgary Press, *distributed by* Raincoast, UBC Press, Canada

MicroMash, *subsidiary of* Thomson

Microsoft Learning, *distributed by* Time Warner Book Group

Microsoft Press, *division of* Microsoft Corp

Microsoft Press France, *subsidiary of* Microsoft Press

Microsoft Press Germany, *subsidiary of* Microsoft Press

Midmarch Arts Press, *distributor for* N Paradoxa

Midnight Editions, *imprint of* Cleis Press

Midpoint, *distributor for* Mosaic Press

Midpoint Trade Books, *distributor for* Brook Street Press LLC, Helgate Press, Hellgate Press, Penmarin Books Inc, Possibility Press

Midrashic Editions, *imprint of* Cross-Cultural Communications

Midwest Library Serv, *distributor for* Investor Responsibility Research Center

Midwest Library Service, *distributor for* College Press Publishing Co, Do-It-Yourself Legal Publishers, Greenwood Research Books & Software, Primary Research Group

MidWest Plan Service, *affiliate of* Iowa State University, *distributor for* Natural Resource Agriculture & Engineering Service, *distributed by* Natural Resource Agriculture & Engineering Service

Milady, *imprint of* Thomson Delmar Learning

Milady Publishing, *division of* Thomson Learning, Thomson Learning Japan, *subsidiary of* Delmar Learning

Milet Publishing Ltd, *imprint of* Tuttle Publishing, *distributed by* Tuttle Publishing

Military Living Publications, *division of* Military Marketing Services Inc, Military Marketing Services Inc

Military Model Distributors, *distributor for* Monogram Aviation Publications

Millbrook Press, *distributor for* Alloy Entertainment, *distributed by* Sundance Publishing

Millennial Mind Publishing, *imprint of* American Book Publishing

Robert Miller Gallery, *distributed by* D A P

Mills & Boone, *distributed by* Thorndike Press

Sally Milner, *distributed by* Sterling Publishing Co Inc

Mind Your Own Business, *imprint of* Gallopade International Inc

Mindbranch, *distributor for* Primary Research Group

The Minerals, Metals & Materials Society (TMS), *affiliate of* AIME

Minerva, *imprint of* Heinemann

Minimed Series, *imprint of* Rayve Productions Inc

Minnesota Historical Society Press, *division of* Minnesota Historical Society

Minority Rights Group, *distributed by* Paul & Company

Minotaur, *imprint of* St Martin's Press LLC

Mint Publishers Group, *distributor for* The Catherine Collective Corp (Canada only), Continental Atlantic (US only), Cooking for the Rushed (US & Canada), Creative House (US & Canada), Etruscan Press (US & Canada), Feather Books (Canada only), Gallery Six (US & Canada), Gift of Time (US & Canada), Grownup's Guides (US & Canada), Hayden Publishing (US & Canada), Miles Kelly Publishing (Canada only), Open Door Publishing (US & Canada), Patron's Pick (US only), Ripley Entertainment Inc (US & Canada), Top That! Publishing (Canada only), Visible Ink Press (US & Canada)

MIR (Russia), *distributed by* Fort Ross Inc

MIRA Books, *imprint of* Harlequin Enterprises Ltd

Miranda Press Trade Division, *imprint of* Cognizant Communication Corp

Mirasol, *imprint of* Farrar, Straus & Giroux Books for Young Readers

MIRASOL Libros Juveniles, *imprint of* Farrar, Straus & Giroux, LLC

Miss Jackie Inc, *distributed by* Gryphon House Inc

Miss Spider™, *imprint of* Callaway Editions Inc

Missouri Historical Society Press, *division of* Missouri Historical Society, *distributed by* University of Missouri Press, University of New Mexico Press, University of Southern Illinois, Wayne State University Press

MIT List Visual Arts Center, *distributed by* DAP Distributed Art Publishers

MIT Press, *distributor for* National Bureau of Economic Research Inc, *distributed by* DawnSignPress

The MIT Press, *distributor for* AAAI Press, Canadian Centre for Architecture, Zone Books

MIT (selected titles), *distributor for* The AEI Press

MJF BOOKS, *imprint of* Fine Communications

MKSAP Audio Companion, *imprint of* Oakstone Medical Publishing

MMB Music, *distributor for* Barcelona Publishers

Mobil Travel Guide, *distributed by* The Globe Pequot Press

Mobile Post Office Society, *affiliate of* American Philatelic Society

Mobipocket, *distributor for* SynergEbooks

Moby Books, *imprint of* Playmore Inc, Publishers

Modelling Musterclass, *imprint of* Osprey Publishing Ltd

Modern Curriculum Press, *division of* Pearson Learning, *imprint of* Pearson Learning Group

Modern Drummer Publications, *distributed by* Hal Leonard Corp

Modern Library, *imprint of* Random House Inc, Random House Publishing Group

Modern Masters, *imprint of* Abbeville Publishing Group, Artabras Inc

Modern Pictures, *imprint of* Modern Publishing

Modern Publishing, *division of* Unisystems Inc, Unisystems Inc

Moment Point Press Inc, *distributed by* Red Wheel/Weiser

Mom's Guide to Sports, *division of* Moms-Guide.com Inc, *imprint of* MomsGuide.com Inc

The Monacelli Press, *distributed by* Penguin Group (USA) Inc, Penguin Putnam

Monarch Books, *distributed by* Kregel Publications

Monarch Books of Canada, *distributor for* Redleaf Press

Mondadori Spanish Language, *distributed by* Random House Sales & Marketing

Mondo, *imprint of* Mondo Publishing

Money Market Directories, *unit of* Standard & Poor's

The Monist (An International Philosophical Quarterly), *distributed by* Sherwood Sugden & Co

Monjeu Press, *distributed by* Gryphon House Inc

Monogram Aviation Publications, *distributed by* Military Model Distributors, Motorbooks International

Montana Historical Society Press, *distributed by* Globe Pequot Press, The Globe Pequot Press

Monthly Review Press, *division of* Monthly Review Foundation Inc, Monthly Review Foundation Inc, *distributed by* New York University Press

Moo Press Inc, *distributed by* Biblio, NBN

Moody Press, *affiliate of* Ministry of Moody Bible Institute, *distributor for* Focus on the Family

Moon Lady Press, *distributor for* The Country Cottage

Moonsmile Press, *distributed by* Chelsea Green Publishing Co

Moose Country Press, *distributed by* Enfield Publishing & Distribution Co

Thomas More, *imprint of* Ave Maria Press, *distributed by* Ave Maria Press

Morehouse, *distributed by* The Continuum International Publishing Group

Morehouse Publishing Co, *distributor for* Canterbury Press Norwich (UK), Eagle (UK, music audio), Gracewing (UK), Pendle Hill (US)

Morgan Kaufmann Publishers, *division of* Academic Press, *imprint of* Academic Press, Elsevier

Mormon History Association, *distributed by* Signature Books Publishing LLC

Morning Sun Press, *distributed by* Chelsea Green Publishing Co

Morningside Bookshop, *division of* Morningside House Inc, Morningside House Inc

Morningside House Inc, *imprint of* Morningside Bookshop

Morningside Press, *imprint of* Morningside Bookshop

Willie Morris Books in Memoir & Biography, *imprint of* University Press of Mississippi

Morrow, *distributed by* Sundance Publishing

Morrow Junior Books, *imprint of* HarperCollins Publishers

William Morrow, *imprint of* HarperCollins General Books Group, HarperCollins Publishers Sales, *distributor for* Nightingale-Conant

Mosaic Press, *distributed by* Midpoint, Round House Group, SCB Distributors, Wakefield Press

Mosby, *distributor for* Ingenix Inc, *distributed by* Fire Engineering Books & Videos, Ingenix Inc

Mosby Journal Division, *division of* Elsevier, Mosby

Moser, *imprint of* Biblo & Tannen Booksellers & Publishers Inc

Motilal Banarsidass, *distributed by* Blue Dove Press

Motorbooks International, *distributor for* Haynes Manuals Inc, Iconografix Inc, The Info Devel Press, Monogram Aviation Publications, Osprey Publishing Ltd, Whitehorse Press

Motorbooks Intl, *distributor for* Possibility Press, *distributed by* Heimburger House Publishing Co

Mount Olive College Press, *affiliate of* Mount Olive College

Mount Vernon Ladies Association, *distributed by* The University of Virginia Press

Mountain Air Books, *imprint of* Mountain n' Air Books

Mountain Biking Press/FineEdge.com, *imprint of* FineEdge.com

Mountain n' Air Books, *distributor for* Tom Harrison Cartography

Mountain Pond Publishing Corp, *distributed by* The Countryman Press

Mountain Press, *distributor for* Ericson Books

Mountain Press Publishing Co, *distributor for* Bear Print, Cottonwood Publishing, Goals Unlimited Press, Hops Press, John McQuarrie Books, Western Edge Press

Mountain Sports Press, *imprint of* Mountain Press Publishing Co

Mountain View Press, *division of* Epsilon Lyra Corp

Mountaineers Books, *distributor for* The American Alpine Club Press

The Mountaineers Books, *subsidiary of* The Mountaineers, *distributor for* American Alpine Club Press, Colorado Mountain Club Press

Mouton de Gruyter, *division of* Walter de Gruyter, Inc, Walter de Gruyter GmbH & Co KG, *distributed by* Walter de Gruyter Inc

Moyer Bell Ltd, *distributor for* Asphodel Press

Moznaim Publishing Corp, *distributor for* Breslov Research Institute, Red Wheel-Weiser Inc

MPH Distributors, *distributor for* Bridge-Logos Publishers

MPR Publishing (selected titles), *distributed by* Metal Powder Industries Federation

MSS Information Corp, *distributed by* Ardent Media Inc

MSU Museum, *distributed by* Michigan State University Press (MSU Press)

MTI, *distributed by* NACE International

MTV Books, *imprint of* Pocket Books, Simon & Schuster Adult Publishing Group, *distributor for* Alloy Entertainment

Mulberry Books, *imprint of* HarperCollins Publishers

A G Muller & Cie, *distributed by* US Games Systems Inc

MultiMedia Reviews, *imprint of* Oakstone Medical Publishing

Multnomah Books, *imprint of* Multnomah Publishers Inc

Multnomah Gift, *subsidiary of* Multnomah Publishers Inc

Debbie Mumm® Inc, *distributed by* Landauer Books

Mundania Press, *imprint of* Mundania Press LLC

Muppet Press, *imprint of* Jim Henson Publishing/Muppet Press

John Murray Ltd, *distributed by* Trafalgar Square

Muscadine Books, *imprint of* University Press of Mississippi

Museum of American Folk Art, *distributed by* Antique Collectors Club Ltd

Museum of Art, *distributed by* Washington State University Press

Museum of Early Southern Decorative Arts (selected), *distributed by* The University of North Carolina Press

The Museum of Modern Art, *affiliate of* Circulating Film & Video Library, *distributed by* Distributed Art Publishers (DAP)

Museum of New Mexico Press, *unit of* New Mexico State Office of Cultural Affairs, *distributed by* University of New Mexico Press

Museum Products, *distributor for* Naturegraph Publishers Inc

Music Expressions™, *distributed by* Warner Bros Publications Inc

Music Sales Corp, *distributor for* Six Strings Music Publishing, *distributed by* Beekman Publishers Inc

The Musical Linguist, *distributed by* Penton Overseas Inc

Musicians Institute Press, *imprint of* Hal Leonard Corp, *distributed by* Hal Leonard Corp

Musikverlage Han Sikorski, *distributed by* Hal Leonard Corp

Muska & Lipman Publishing, *division of* Thomson Course Technology

My Chaotic Life, *imprint of* Walter Foster Publishing Inc

My Chaotic Life™, *division of* Walter Foster Publishing Inc, *distributor for* Quarto

Mycroft & Moran, *imprint of* Arkham House Publishers Inc

Myklas Music Press, *distributed by* Alfred Publishing Company Inc

MyReportLinks.com Books, *imprint of* Enslow Publishers Inc

Mysterious Press, *imprint of* Time Warner Book Group, Warner Books

Mystic Ridge Books, *subsidiary of* Mystic Ridge Productions Inc

Mystic Seaport, *distributor for* Balsam Abrams, Glencannon, Ten Pound Island Books

N & A, *imprint of* The Nautical & Aviation Publishing Co of America Inc

NACE International, *distributor for* ASM International, ASTM, AWS, Butterworth-Heinemann, Cambridge University Press, CASTI Publishing, Compass Publications, CRC Press, Marcel Dekker Inc, E&FN Spon, Elsevier Science Publishers, Gulf Publishing, Industrial Press, Institute of Materials, ISO, McGraw-Hill, MTI, Prentice Hall, Professional Publications, SSPC, Swedish Corrosion Institute, John Wiley & Sons Inc, *distributed by* Australasian Corrosion Association

Naked Gourmet, *imprint of* Gallopade International Inc

NAL, *division of* Penguin Group (USA) Inc, Penguin Group (USA) Inc

NAPLL (National Association of Printing Leadership), *distributor for* Jelmar Publishing Co Inc

NAPS, *imprint of* Copywriter's Council of America (CCA), The Linick Group Inc, *distributed by* Copywriter's Council of America (CCA), The Linick Group Inc

Narosa Publishing House, *distributed by* American Mathematical Society

The Narrative Press, *distributed by* Stackpole Publishing

NASAR Bookstore, *distributor for* dbS Productions

NASCO, *distributor for* Cottonwood Press Inc, National Council of Teachers of Mathematics

NASSP, *imprint of* National Association of Secondary School Principals

Nataraj, *imprint of* New World Library

Nation Books, *imprint of* Avalon Publishing Group Inc, Avalon Publishing Group - New York

National Academies Press, *division of* National Academy of Sciences

National Academy for Adult Jewish Studies, *imprint of* United Synagogue Book Service

National Archives, *distributed by* Discovery Enterprises Ltd

National Archives & Records Administration, *distributed by* J J Keller & Associates, Inc

National Association for the Education of Young Children, *distributed by* Gryphon House Inc

National Association of Broadcasters (NAB), *distributed by* Allyn & Bacon, Lawrence Erlbaum Assoc, Focal Press, Macmillan Publishing Co, Tab Books, Wadsworth Inc

National Association of Home Builders, *distributed by* BuilderBooks.com

National Audubon Guides, *imprint of* Alfred A Knopf

National Book Co, *division of* Educational Research Associates

National Book Network, *distributor for* Brewers Publications, Bridge Works Publishing, Burford Books, Davies-Black Publishing, Eclipse Press, Element Books, Harbor House, Hudson Hills Press LLC, Impact Publications, Larson Publications, Open Horizons Publishing Co, Snow Lion Publications Inc, TowleHouse Publishing, Welcome Rain Publishers LLC, Michael Wiese Productions, YMAA Publication Center

National Book Network Inc (NBN), *distributor for* The Intrepid Traveler

National Book Network (NBN), *distributor for* Harbor Press Inc

National Book Network/University Press of America, *distributor for* AltaMira Press

National Braille Press, *distributor for* John Milton Society for the Blind, *distributed by* Library of Congress

National Bureau of Economic Research, *distributed by* Association of American University Presses

National Bureau of Economic Research Inc, *distributed by* Ballinger Publishing Co, Columbia University Press, MIT Press, Princeton University Press, University Microfilms International, University of Chicago Press

National Career Development Association, *distributed by* American Counseling Association

National Center Early Childhood Workforce, *distributed by* Gryphon House Inc

National Center for Children in Poverty, *division of* Columbia University School of Public Health

National Cooperative Highway Research Program, *imprint of* Transportation Research Board

National Council of Teachers of Mathematics, *distributed by* Eric Armin Inc Education Ctr, Delta Education, Didax Educational Resources, Educators Outlet, ETA Cuisenaire, Lakeshore Learning Materials, NASCO, Spectrum

National Doll Society of America, *division of* Success Advertising & Publishing

National Education Standards, *distributed by* Dearborn Trade Publishing

National Galleries of Scotland, *distributed by* Antique Collectors Club Ltd

National Gallery of Art, *distributed by* Abrams, Bulfinch/Little, Cambridge University Press, Hudson Hills, Lund Humphries/Ashgate, OAP, Princeton University Press, Thames & Hudson, Yale University Press

National Gallery of Canada, *distributed by* Association of American University Presses

National Geographic Adventure Classics, *imprint of* National Geographic Books

National Geographic Adventure Press, *imprint of* National Geographic Books

National Geographic Books, *division of* National Geographic Society, *imprint of* National Geographic Books, *distributed by* Hi Marketing (UK), Simon & Schuster (adult & children's titles, US & other markets)

National Geographic Calendars, *distributed by* Andrews McMeel Publishing

National Geographic Children's Books, *imprint of* National Geographic Books

National Geographic Directions, *imprint of* National Geographic Books

National Geographic Maps, *distributed by* Trails Illustrated, Division of National Geographic Maps

National Geographic Society, *distributed by* Simon & Schuster, Simon & Schuster Inc

National Guitar Workshop, *distributed by* Alfred Publishing Company Inc

National Information Standards Organization, *distributor for* Niso Press

National Institute for Trial Advocacy, *affiliate of* Notre Dame Law School

National Institute of Occupational Safety & Health, *distributed by* J J Keller & Associates, Inc

The National Interest, *imprint of* Transaction Publishers

National Library of Ireland, *distributed by* Syracuse University Press

National Maritime Museum, *distributed by* Casemate Publishers

National Museum of Science & Industry UK, *distributed by* Michigan State University Press (MSU Press)

The National Museum of Women in the Arts, *distributed by* Northeastern University Press, St Joseph's University Press, University of Washington Press

National Paper Trade Assoc, *distributor for* Grade Finders Inc

National Park Service Media Production, *subsidiary of* US Department of the Interior

National Poetry Foundation, *distributed by* University Press of New England

National Portrait Gallery, *distributed by* Antique Collectors Club Ltd

National Professional Resources, *distributor for* MAR*CO Products Inc

National Publishing Co, *subsidiary of* Courier Corp, *distributed by* Broadman & Holman Publishers

National Resource Center for Youth Services (NRCYS), *division of* University of Oklahoma-Outreach

National Resource Center Youth Services, *distributor for* MAR*CO Products Inc

National Society for the Study of Education, *distributed by* Association of American University Presses

National Sporting Fraternity Ltd, *imprint of* The Amwell Press

National Teacher Examination Series, *imprint of* National Learning Corp

National Technical Information Service, *distributor for* United States Pharmacopeia

National Technical Information Service (NTIS), *distributed by* Bernan

National Textbook Co, *imprint of* McGraw-Hill Learning Group, *distributed by* Teacher's Discovery

The National Trust, *distributed by* Antique Collectors Club Ltd

Native Voices, *imprint of* Book Publishing Co

Natural Heritage Books, *distributed by* Chelsea Green Publishing Co

Natural Heritage Press, *distributed by* Birch Brook Press

Natural Resource Agriculture & Engineering Service, *distributor for* MidWest Plan Service, *distributed by* MidWest Plan Service

Naturegraph, *distributed by* Gem Guides Book Co

Naturegraph Publishers Inc, *distributed by* Bahai Distribution Service, Dakota West Books, Gem Guides Book Co, Maverick, Museum Products, New Leaf, Partners West, Sunbelt, Treasure Chest Books

NaturEncyclopedia Series, *imprint of* Stemmer House Publishers Inc

Nature's Neighborhood, *subsidiary of* R S V Products

Naval Institute Press, *division of* US Naval Institute

NavPress, *imprint of* NavPress Publishing Group

NavPress Publishing Group, *division of* The Navigators

Nazarene Publishing House, *imprint of* Beacon Hill Press of Kansas City

NBM Publishing Inc, *distributor for* Plymptoon Books

NBN, *distributor for* FC&A Publishing, Moo Press Inc

NCP, *imprint of* New City Press

NCSY Publications, *distributed by* Mesorah Publications Ltd

NEA Professional Library, *imprint of* National Education Association (NEA)

Neal-Schuman Publishers Inc, *distributor for* Facet

Neal Wilson Publishing (UK), *distributed by* Interlink Publishing Group Inc

Near Eastern Press, *imprint of* Holmes Publishing Group

E T Nedder Publishing, *subsidiary of* Kan Distributing

Neibauer Press, *division of* Louis Neibauer Co Inc, Louis Neibauer Co Inc

Nelles Guides, *imprint of* Hunter Publishing Inc

Nelson Educational Publishing, *distributor for* Phoenix Learning Resources

Nelson Information, *division of* Thomson Financial Publishing

Nelson Thomas Learning, *distributor for* Wadsworth Publishing

Tommy Nelson, *division of* Thomas Nelson Inc, *distributor for* Focus on the Family

Neo-Tech Publishing, *affiliate of* Neo-Tech International, Neo-Tech International

NES, The Official Tasp Study Guide, *distributed by* Hendrick-Long Publishing Co

Neshui, *imprint of* Neshui Publishing

Net Biblio, *distributed by* Paul & Company

NetLearning, *imprint of* Thomson Delmar Learning

netLibrary, *distributor for* Infosential Press

Nevada Humanities Committee, *distributed by* University of Nevada Press

Nevada Publications, *distributor for* Gem Guides Book Co, *distributed by* Gem Guides Book Co

Nevraumont Publishing Co, *distributed by* Abrams, Crown Publishing Group, Henry Holt, W W Norton & Co, Princeton University Press, University of California Press, John Wiley, Yale University Press

New America Foundation (NAF Basic), *imprint of* Basic Books

New American Fiction Series, *imprint of* Sun & Moon Press

New American Library, *imprint of* NAL, *distributed by* Sundance Publishing

New American Poetry Series, *imprint of* Sun & Moon Press

New Amsterdam Books, *imprint of* Ivan R Dee Publisher

New Architecture Group Ltd, *distributed by* Antique Collectors Club Ltd

The New Careers Center, *distributor for* Training Resource Network Inc (T R N)

New Cavendish Books Ltd, *distributed by* Antique Collectors Club Ltd

New City (Great Britain), *distributed by* New City Press

New City Press, *division of* Focolare Movement, *distributor for* Ciudad Nueva (Spain/Argentina), New City (Great Britain), *distributed by* Riverside Distributors, Spring Arbor Distributors

New Clarion Press, *distributed by* Paul & Company

New Dawn Press, *distributed by* Paul & Company

New Directions, *distributed by* Sundance Publishing

New Directions Publishing Corp, *distributed by* W W Norton & Company Inc, W W Norton Co

New England AEYC, *distributed by* Gryphon House Inc

The New England University Press, *distributor for* The Sheep Meadow Press

New Falcon Publications, *imprint of* New Falcon Publications/Falcon

New Falcon Publications/Falcon, *subsidiary of* J W Brown Inc, J W Brown Inc, *distributed by* New Leaf Distributing Co

New Feminist Library, *imprint of* Monthly Review Press

New Holland, *distributed by* Sterling Publishing Co Inc, Weatherhill Inc

New Holland Publishers Ltd, *distributor for* Weatherhill Inc, *distributed by* The Globe Pequot Press

New Horizon, *distributor for* Vital Health Publishing

New Horizon Press, *distributor for* Kensington Publishing Corp

New Horizons, *distributed by* Gryphon House Inc

New Horizons Book Publishing Co, *imprint of* World Citizens

New In Chess, *imprint of* Chess Combination Inc

New Island Books, *distributed by* Dufour Editions Inc

New Jerusalem Bible, *imprint of* Doubleday Broadway Publishing Group

The New Jerusalem Bible, *imprint of* Random House Inc

New Leaf, *distributor for* Book World Inc/Blue Star Productions, Humanics Publishing Group, Larson Publications, Media Associates, Naturegraph Publishers Inc, Ocean Tree Books, Original Publications, Ronin Publishing Inc, Summit University Press, Woodland Publishing Inc, YMAA Publication Center, *distributed by* Arnica Publishing Inc

New Leaf Books, *distributor for* Blue Poppy Press

New Leaf Distributing, *distributor for* The Dawn Horse Press, SOM Publishing

New Leaf Distributing Co, *distributor for* New Falcon Publications/Falcon, Top of the Mountain Publishing

New Leaf Distributors, *distributor for* ACS Publications, TSG Publishing Foundation Inc

New Life Ministries, *distributed by* LifeQuest

New Marketplace, *imprint of* Oaklea Press

New Mexico Books, *imprint of* Coda Publications

New Page Books, *imprint of* The Career Press Inc

New Poets Series, *subsidiary of* BrickHouse Books Inc, *imprint of* BrickHouse Books Inc

The New Press, *division of* W W Norton & Co Inc, W W Norton & Company Inc, *distributed by* W W Norton & Co Inc, W W Norton & Company Inc

New Readers Press, *division of* Pro Literacy Worldwide, *distributor for* Teachers of English to Speakers of Other Languages Inc (TESOL), *distributed by* People's Publishing Group

New Republic Books, *imprint of* Basic Books

New School University Graduate Program in Global Affairs, *distributed by* Paul & Company

The New South Company, *imprint of* C & M Online Media Inc

New Strategist, *distributed by* American Marketing Association

New Vanguard, *imprint of* Osprey Publishing Ltd

New World Library, *division of* Whatever Publishing Inc, Whatever Publishing Inc

New World Paperbacks, *imprint of* International Publishers Co Inc

New World Press, *imprint of* Copywriter's Council of America (CCA), *distributor for* The Linick Group Inc, *distributed by* China Books & Periodicals Inc

New World Press (NWP), *imprint of* The Linick Group Inc

The New York Botanical Garden Press, *division of* New York Botanical Garden, The New York Botanical Garden

New York Nights, *imprint of* Ugly Duckling Presse

New York University Press, *distributor for* The Bronx County Historical Society, Monthly Review Press

New Yorker Desk Diary, *distributed by* Per Annum Inc

Newark Museum, *distributed by* Antique Collectors Club Ltd

Newbridge, *imprint of* Haights Cross Communications Inc

Newbridge Communications Inc, *distributor for* Educational Impressions Inc

Newbridge Discovery Links, *imprint of* Newbridge Educational Publishing

Newbridge Educational Publishing, *division of* Haights Cross Communications Inc

Newbridge Publishing, *subsidiary of* Haights Cross Communications Inc

Newbury Street Press, *imprint of* New England Historic Genealogical Society

Newletter Division, *division of* Eagle Publishing Inc

NewLife Publications, *affiliate of* A Ministry of Campus Crusade for Christ, *distributed by* Appalachian Distributors

The Newman Press, *imprint of* Paulist Press

Newmarket Medallion, *imprint of* Newmarket Publishing & Communications

Newmarket Press, *distributed by* W W Norton & Company Inc, Sundance Publishing

Newmarket Publishing & Communications, *division of* Newmarket Publishing & Communications Co, Newmarket Publishing & Communications Co, *distributed by* W W Norton

The News Group, *distributor for* Gail's Guides

NewSouth Books, *imprint of* NewSouth Inc, *distributed by* John F Blair Publisher

Nexus Press, *division of* Atlanta Contemporary Art Center

Nexus Special Interests, *distributed by* Trans-Atlantic Publications Inc

NFPA, *distributed by* Thomson Delmar Learning

Nibble Me Books™, *imprint of* Playhouse Publishing

Nice Books, *imprint of* Modern Publishing

Nichols Garden Nursery Press, *distributed by* Dog-Eared Publications

Ars Nicolai (Great Britain Scandinavia & Europe, *distributor for* Art Institute of Chicago

Nicolin Fields Publishing, *distributed by* University Press of New England

Nightingale-Conant, *distributor for* MDRT Center for Productivity, *distributed by* William Morrow, Simon & Schuster

Nightingale-Conant (UK), *subsidiary of* Nightingale-Conant

Nightingale Editions, *imprint of* Cross-Cultural Communications

Nihon/Vogue, *distributed by* Kodansha America Inc

Nil, *distributed by* The Light Inc

Nilgiri Press, *division of* Blue Mountain Center of Meditation

Nimbus Publishing Ltd (selected titles), *distributed by* Down East Books

NIMCO Bookstore, *distributor for* MAR*CO Products Inc

Nimco Inc, *distributor for* Chronicle Guidance Publications Inc

Niso Press, *distributed by* National Information Standards Organization

Nitty Gritty Cookbooks, *imprint of* Bristol Publishing Enterprises

No Exit Press, *imprint of* Four Walls Eight Windows

Noble Porter Press, *imprint of* Dramaline® Publications

Noble Publishing Corp, *division of* Eagle Ware Corp, *distributed by* Amazon.com, BarnesandNoble.com, RFCafe.com, Yankee Book Peddlers

Noidic Africa Institute, *distributed by* Transaction Publishers

Nonpareil Books, *imprint of* David R Godine Publisher Inc

The Noontide Press, *imprint of* Legion for the Survival of Freedom

Nordic Africa Institute, *distributed by* Stylus Publishing LLC

Nordic Insititue of Asian Studies, *distributed by* University of Hawaii Press

Norman Publishing, *division of* Jeremy Norman & Co Inc, Jeremy Norman & Co Inc

Nortex Press, *imprint of* Eakin Press

North Atlantic Books, *division of* Society for the Study of Native Arts & Sciences, Society for the Study of Native Arts & Sciences, *distributor for* Frog Ltd

North Carolina Museum of Art (selected), *distributed by* The University of North Carolina Press

North Country Books, *imprint of* North Country Books Inc

North Country Classics, *imprint of* North Country Books Inc

North Country Distributors, *distributor for* Cadence Jazz Books

North Country Press, *division of* Maine Fulfillment Corp, Maine Fulfillment Corp

North Light Books, *imprint of* F & W Publications, *distributor for* Rockport Publishers

North Point Press, *division of* Farrar, Straus & Giroux LLC, Farrar, Straus & Giroux, LLC, *imprint of* Farrar, Straus & Giroux, LLC

North/South, *distributed by* Chronicle Books LLC

North South Books, *distributed by* Sundance Publishing

North-South Center Press, *distributed by* Lynne Rienner Publishers Inc

North-South Center Press at the University of Miami, *division of* The Dante B Fascell North-South Center at the University of Miami, The Dante B Fascell North-South Center at the University of Miami

Northcote House, *distributed by* University Press of Mississippi

Northeast Midwest Institute, *affiliate of* Northeast Midwest Congressional & Senate Coalitions, Northeast Midwest Congressional & State Coalitions

Northeastern Music Publications Inc, *distributor for* Roncorp Inc

Northeastern University Press, *distributor for* Massachusetts Historical Society, The National Museum of Women in the Arts

Northfield Publishing, *imprint of* Moody Press

NorthSea Press, *imprint of* LangMarc Publishing

Northstone Publishing, *distributed by* The Pilgrim Press/United Church Press

Northwestern University Press, *distributor for* Butterworth (Law in Context series), FC2/Black Ice Books, Fiction Collective Two Inc, Glas, Jannes Art Press, Paper Mirror Press, Tia Chucha Press

Northwoods Press, *division of* Conservatory of American Letters, *distributor for* American History Press, Century Press, Dan River Press (textbook div), *distributed by* Dan River Press

NorthWord Press, *imprint of* Creative Publishing International Inc

Jeffrey Norton Publishers Inc, *distributor for* BBC (selected titles), Cambridge University Press, Insight Travel Guides

W W Norton, *distributor for* Bloomberg Press, George Braziller Inc, Newmarket Publishing & Communications, Verso

W W Norton & Co, *distributor for* Nevraumont Publishing Co, Peace Hill Press, Persea Books Inc

W W Norton & Co Inc, *distributor for* The Countryman Press, The New Press, Pushcart Press, Texere, Thames & Hudson

W W Norton & Company Inc, *distributor for* Airphoto International Ltd, Albatross Publishing House, Bloomberg Press, George Braziller Inc, Chess Information & Research Center, Fantagraphics Books, The Hatherleigh Company Ltd, Hatherleigh Press, Kales Press, New Directions Publishing Corp, The New Press, Newmarket Press, Ontario Review, Peace Hill Press, Persea Books Inc, Pushcart Press, Quantuck Lane Press, Rio Nuevo, Smithsonian Books, Thames & Hudson, Verso

W W Norton Co, *distributor for* New Directions Publishing Corp

Norvik Press, *distributed by* Dufour Editions Inc

Nota Bell Books, *imprint of* Purdue University Press

Nova Science Books, *imprint of* Nova Science Publishers Inc

Nova Social Science Books, *imprint of* Nova Science Publishers Inc

Nova Southeastern University, *distributed by* Gryphon House Inc

Novalis, *distributor for* Twenty-Third Publications, *distributed by* Twenty-Third Publications

Novel Ideas Plus, *imprint of* Haights Cross Communications Inc, Sundance Publishing

Novel Ideas Skills, *imprint of* Haights Cross Communications Inc, Sundance Publishing

Novel-Ties Study Guides, *imprint of* Learning Links Inc

Novello Festival Press, *distributed by* John F Blair Publisher

November Moon, *distributed by* Lotus Press

Noyes Publications, *imprint of* William Andrew Publishing

NPR, *distributed by* Peytral Publications Inc

NRH Press, *distributed by* Vandamere Press

NSW Agriculture, *distributed by* Ball Publishing

NTC Business Books, *distributor for* American Marketing Association

NTC Contemporary Books, *imprint of* McGraw-Hill Professional

NTIS, *distributor for* Energy Information Administration, EI-30 National Energy Information Center

Nuclear Energy Agency, *distributed by* Organization for Economic Cooperation & Development

nursesbooks.org, The Publishing Program of ANA, *division of* American Nurses Association

Nutri-Books, *distributor for* Woodland Publishing Inc

NY Review of Books, *distributed by* Random House Inc

Nylabone Products, *division of* TFH Publications Inc

Nystrom, *division of* Herff Jones

Oak Knoll Press, *distributor for* American Antiquarian Society, Bibliograghical Society of University of Virginia, Bibliographical Society of America, The Bibliographical Society (UK), Bookplate Society, John Carter Brown Library, Catalpa Press, Chapin Library, Edinburgh Bibliographical Society, Martino Fine Books, Private Libraries Association, St Paul's Bibliographies, Typophiles, University of Pittsburgh Press (Pittsburgh Biblio Series)

Oaklea Press, *unit of* S H Martin LLC, *imprint of* Oaklea Press

Oakstone Medical, *imprint of* Haights Cross Communications Inc

Oakstone Medical Publishing, *division of* Oakstone Publishing, Oakstone Publishing, A Haights Cross Co, *subsidiary of* Haights Cross Communications Inc

Oakstone Publishing, *imprint of* Haights Cross Communications Inc

Oakstone Wellness, *imprint of* Haights Cross Communications Inc

Oaktree Books, *imprint of* Oak Tree Publishing

OAP, *distributor for* National Gallery of Art

Obelisk Books, *imprint of* Whittier Publications Inc

Oberlin College Press, *subsidiary of* Oberlin College, *distributed by* Cornell University Press Services

Oberon Books, *distributed by* Theatre Communications Group Inc

Obol International, *division of* Sanford J Durst, *imprint of* Sanford J Durst, *distributed by* Sanford J Durst

Obsessive Anonymous, *distributed by* Hazelden Publishing & Educational Services

Occupational Competency Examination Series, *imprint of* National Learning Corp

Ocean Press, *distributed by* Consortium Book Sales & Distribution Inc

Ocean Publishing, *division of* The Gromling Group Inc

Ocean Tree Books, *distributor for* Liberty Literary Works, Sunlit Hills Press, *distributed by* Books West LLC, Clear Light Distribution, New Leaf, Treasure Chest Books

The Ocean View Doubles, *imprint of* Ocean View Books

Octameron Press, *imprint of* Octameron Associates

Octavo Press, *imprint of* Templegate Publishers

Odonian Press, *distributed by* Common Courage Press

Odonian Press (The Real Story Series), *distributed by* South End Press

Odyssey Classics, *imprint of* Harcourt Trade Publishers

OECD, *distributed by* The Brookings Institution Press

Off The Beaten Path®, *imprint of* The Globe Pequot Press

Office & Print Technologies, *division of* PJD Publications Ltd

Office for Official Publications of the European Communities (EC), *distributed by* Bernan

Office of the Federal Register, *distributed by* J J Keller & Associates, Inc

Ohio State University Foreign Language Publications, *division of* Foreign Language Center

Ohio State University Press, *division of* Foreign Language Center, *distributor for* Western Reserve Historical Society

Ohio University Press, *imprint of* Swallow Press, *distributor for* Center for International Studies, The Colonial Williamsburg Foundation, Swallow Press

The Oily Press, *distributed by* AOCS Press

Oklahoma State University, *distributor for* dbS Productions

Old Barn Publishing, *imprint of* Old Barn Enterprises Inc

Old El Toro Press, *distributed by* Gem Guides Book Co

Old Farmers Almanac, *distributed by* Houghton Mifflin Trade & Reference Division, Random House Sales & Marketing

Old Kings Road Press, *imprint of* Athletic Guide Publishing

Oldcastle Books, *distributed by* Trafalgar Square

Olive Branch Press, *imprint of* Interlink Publishing Group Inc

Olive Press, *distributed by* Paul & Company

Oliver-Nelson (Atlanta, GA), *distributed by* Thomas Nelson Inc

Georg Olms Verlag, *distributed by* Bolchazy-Carducci Publishers Inc

Olmstead Press, *imprint of* Moyer Bell Ltd

Michael O'Mara Books, *distributed by* Andrews McMeel Publishing

Omega Innovative Marketing, *distributed by* Heimburger House Publishing Co

Omnibus Press, *division of* Music Sales Corp, Music Sales Corp, *distributor for* Big Meteor, Blue Book, Gramophone

Omnidawn Publishing, *imprint of* Omnidawn Corp, *distributed by* Small Press Distribution

Omohundro Institute of Early American History & Culture, *distributed by* The University of North Carolina Press

On My Mind Series, *imprint of* The Globe Pequot Press

One Caring Place, *imprint of* Abbey Press

One Planet Publishing House, *distributed by* Book World Services Inc (Australia, Canada, Europe, New Zealand & US), The Bookman Inc, STD Distributors Pte Ltd (Brunei, Singapore/Malaysia)

One World, *imprint of* Random House Inc, Random House Publishing Group

OneOnOne Computer Training, *division of* Mosaic Media Inc, Mosaic Media Inc

Oneworld, *distributed by* Kalimat Press

Ontario Review, *distributed by* W W Norton & Company Inc

Ontario Review Press, *distributed by* Persea Books Inc

ONWord, *imprint of* Thomson Delmar Learning

Onyx, *imprint of* NAL, Penguin Group (USA) Inc

Open City Books, *distributed by* Grove/Atlantic Inc

Open Court, *imprint of* McGraw-Hill Learning Group

Open Court Publishing Co, *distributor for* Sherwood Sugden & Co

Open Door Books, *imprint of* CRC Publications

Open Door Publishing (US & Canada), *distributed by* Mint Publishers Group

Open Forum, *imprint of* Krieger Publishing Co

Open Gate Press, *distributed by* Paul & Company

Open Horizons Publishing Co, *distributed by* National Book Network

Open Road, *distributed by* Simon & Schuster Inc

Open Road Publishing, *distributed by* Quality Books, Simon & Schuster

Open Scroll, *imprint of* Bridge-Logos Publishers

OPIS/STALSBY Directories & Databases, *division of* United Communications Group

Opportunities for Learning Inc, *distributor for* Zephyr Press Catalog

Optical Data Co, *imprint of* McGraw-Hill Learning Group

Opus Communications, *imprint of* HCPro

Oracle Press, *imprint of* McGraw-Hill Professional

Oracle Press™, *imprint of* McGraw-Hill/Osborne

Oral Biography Series, *imprint of* University of Alaska Press

Orb Books, *imprint of* Tom Doherty Associates, LLC

Orbis Books, *division of* Maryknoll Fathers & Brothers, Maryknoll Fathers & Brothers

Orbit Series, *imprint of* Krieger Publishing Co

Orca Book Publishers, *distributor for* Formac, Grasshopper Books, James Lorimer & Co, Polestar Calendars, Roussand Press, Second Story Press, Sono Nis Pres, Sygnet Publications, Theytus Books, Walrus Publications, *distributed by* Sundance Publishing

Orchard Academy Press, *imprint of* Windstorm Creative

Orchard Books, *imprint of* Scholastic Trade Division, *distributed by* Sundance Publishing

Orchard House Inc, *distributor for* Council for Exceptional Children

Orchard Publications, *distributed by* Paul & Company

Oreade, *imprint of* Amber Lotus

Oregon Catholic Press, *distributor for* Liturgy Training Publications, *distributed by* Spring Arbor

Oregon Events Guide, *imprint of* Gail's Guides

Oregon Fever Books, *imprint of* Crumb Elbow Publishing

Oregon Historical Society Press, *affiliate of* Oregon Historical Society, *distributed by* University of Washington Press

Oregon River Watch, *imprint of* Crumb Elbow Publishing

Oregon State University Press, *distributed by* University of Arizona Press

Oregon Writers Colony, *distributed by* Washington State University Press

O'Reilly & Associates Inc, *subsidiary of* Patient-Centered Guides

Organica, *distributed by* Players Press Inc

Organization & Management, *imprint of* Transaction Publishers

Organization for Economic Cooperation & Development, *division of* Organization for Economic Cooperation & Development (France), *distributor for* European Conference of Ministries of Transport (Imprint), International Energy Agency (Imprint), Nuclear Energy Agency (Imprint)

Organizational Ethics: Healthcare, Business & Policy, *distributed by* University Publishing Group

Oriental Institute, *distributed by* Association of American University Presses

Oriental Institute Press, *distributed by* Loyola Press

Oriental Institute Publications Sales, *division of* University of Chicago

Original Publications, *distributed by* Azure Green, Book People, New Leaf

Orion, *distributed by* Sterling Publishing Co Inc

Orion Publishing, *distributed by* Trafalgar Square

Oronoko Books, *subsidiary of* Andrews University Press

Oryx Press, *distributed by* American Association of Community Colleges (AACC)

OSB Publishers, *distributed by* Paul & Company

Osborne, *imprint of* McGraw-Hill Professional

Osprey Modelling, *imprint of* Osprey Publishing Ltd

Osprey Publishing Ltd, *affiliate of* Osprey Publishing Ltd UK, *distributed by* Motorbooks International

Ostrich Editions, *imprint of* Cross-Cultural Communications

OSU Press, *distributed by* The University of Arizona Press

OTB Legacy Editions, *imprint of* Ocean Tree Books

The Other India Press (India), *distributed by* The Apex Press

Other Press LLC, *subsidiary of* Karnac Books Ltd

Ottographics, *distributed by* Chelsea Green Publishing Co

Our Orchids, *imprint of* Green Nature Books

Our Sunday Visitor Publishing, *division of* Our Sunday Visitor Inc

Out on Bale, *distributed by* Chelsea Green Publishing Co

Outcomes Unlimited Press Inc, *distributed by* Bookworld Services Inc

Outdoor Bible Series, *imprint of* Doubleday Broadway Publishing Group

Outdoor Books & Maps, *imprint of* Swagman Publishing Inc

Outdoor Publications, *division of* Outdoor Empire Publishing Inc

Outside America, *imprint of* The Globe Pequot Press

Oval Books, *distributed by* The Globe Pequot Press

The Overlook Press, *subsidiary of* Peter Mayer Publishers Inc, Peter Mayer Publishers Inc, *distributed by* Penguin Group (USA) Inc, Penguin Putnam Inc

The Overmountain Press, *division of* Sabre Industries Inc, Sabre Industries Inc, *distributor for* John F Blair Publisher

Peter Owen Ltd, *distributed by* Dufour Editions Inc

Richard C Owen Publishers Inc, *distributor for* Horwitz Martin Education

Owl Books, *imprint of* Henry Holt and Company, LLC, *distributed by* Sundance Publishing

Oxfam Publishing, *distributed by* Stylus Publishing LLC

Oxford, *distributed by* SAS Publishing

Oxford Illustrated Press, *distributed by* Haynes Manuals Inc

Oxford University Press, *distributor for* The American Chemical Society, Kodansha America Inc, *distributed by* Sundance Publishing

Oxford University Press Inc, *distributor for* Country Music Foundation Press, Getty Publications

Oxford University Press, Inc, *division of* University of Oxford, *distributor for* The American Chemical Society, CABI, Arnold Clarendon, Engineering Press, Getty, Greenwich Medical Media, Grove Dictionaries, IRL, Kodansha

Oxmoor House, *distributor for* Primedia Consumer Magazine & Internet Group

Oxmoor House Inc, *subsidiary of* Southern Progress Corp, *distributed by* Leisure Arts Inc

Ozark Publishing Inc, *distributed by* Gumdrop

Jerome S Ozer Publisher Inc, *distributor for* The Center for Migration Studies

P&R Publishing, *imprint of* P & R Publishing Co

P & R Publishing Co, *distributor for* Evangelical Press, Free Presbyterian Publications

Pace University Press, *unit of* Pace University

Pacific Boating Almanac, *imprint of* ProStar Publications Inc

Pacific Institute, *distributed by* Washington State University Press

Pacific Northwest Books Co, *distributor for* Webb Research Group, Publishers

Pacific Press Publishing, *distributor for* Andrews University Press

Packaging Division, *division of* Allen D Bragdon Publishers Inc

Packard Publishing, *distributed by* Antique Collectors Club Ltd

Pact Publications, *division of* Pack Inc, Pact Inc, *distributor for* VITA

Pademelon Press, *distributed by* Gryphon House Inc

Padua Playwrights Press, *distributed by* Theatre Communications Group Inc

Kogan Page, *distributed by* American Marketing Association, Beekman Publishers Inc

PAJ Publications, *distributed by* Theatre Communications Group Inc

Pajama Party Gang, *imprint of* Modern Publishing

PAKS-Parents & Kids, *imprint of* The Learning Connection (TLC)

Paladin Press, *division of* Paladin Enterprises, Paladin Enterprises Inc, *distributed by* Amazon.com, Barnes & Noble, Borders

Pale House Publishers, *distributor for* MAR*CO Products Inc

Palgrave Macmillan, *division of* St Martin's Press LLC, St Martin's Press LLC, *distributed by* St Martin's Press LLC

Palgrave Macmillan Academic, *distributed by* Paul & Company

Pali Text Society, *imprint of* Wisdom Publications Inc

Palladian Books Ltd, *distributed by* Scholium International Inc

Pallas Athene, *distributed by* Trafalgar Square

Palm Books, *imprint of* Pangaea Publications

Palm Island Press, *distributor for* Winner Enterprises, *distributed by* Independent Publishers Group

Palmer Publications Inc, *distributed by* Ball Publishing

Pan American Health Organization (Stationary Off-UK), *distributed by* Bernan

Panda Books, *distributed by* China Books & Periodicals Inc

Panel Publishers, *imprint of* Aspen Publishers, A Wolters Kluwer Company

Pangaea Publications, *distributor for* Marcelo D Beccaceci

PanOptic, *distributed by* Business Research Services Inc

Pantheon Books, *imprint of* Random House Inc

Pantheon Books/Schocken Books, *division of* Random House Inc, Random House Inc

Paper Frog Productions, *imprint of* Windstorm Creative

Paper Mirror Press, *distributed by* Northwestern University Press

Paper Tiger, *distributed by* Sterling Publishing Co Inc

Paperback Parade Collector Specials, *imprint of* Gryphon Books

Paperbacks for Educators, *distributor for* American Counseling Association, MAR*CO Products Inc

PaperStar, *imprint of* Penguin Group (USA) Inc, Penguin Young Readers Group, G P Putnam's Sons (Children's)

Paperweight Press, *imprint of* Tuttle Publishing, *distributed by* Tuttle Publishing

Papier-Mache Press, *imprint of* Moyer Bell Ltd

Papillion Publishing, *imprint of* Blue Dolphin Publishing Inc

Para Publishing, *member of* Publishers Marketing Association (PMA)

Para Publishing Seminars, *division of* Para Publishing

Para Research, *imprint of* Schiffer Publishing Ltd

Parabola Books, *subsidiary of* Society for the Study of Myth & Tradition, Society for the Study of Myth & Tradition

Parabola Storytime Series, *imprint of* Parabola Books

Parachute Entertainment LLC, *division of* Parachute Properties

Parachute Publishing LLC, *division of* Parachute Properties, *distributed by* Bantam, Golden Books, Grosset, Harper Entertainment, HarperCollins, Pocket, Scholastic

Parachuting Publications, *imprint of* Para Publishing

Paraclete Press, *division of* Creative Joys Inc, Creative Joys Inc, *distributor for* Abbey of Saint Peter of Solesmes, Gloriae Dei Cantores

Paradigm Publications, *division of* Redwing Book Co

Paradigm Publishing Inc, *subsidiary of* EMC/ Paradigm Publishing

Paradise Cay Publications Inc, *distributor for* Pardey Publications, *distributed by* Robert Hale & Co

Paradox Press, *imprint of* DC Comics

N Paradoxa, *distributed by* Midmarch Arts Press

Paragon Asia Co Ltd, *distributor for* Serindia Publications

Paragon House, *distributor for* International Conferences on the Unity of the Sciences, Professors World Peace Academy, *distributed by* Continuum International Publishing, The Continuum International Publishing Group

Paragon House Hardcovers, *imprint of* Paragon House

Paralists, *division of* Para Publishing

Parallax Press, *division of* Unified Buddhist Church

Paramount Books, *distributed by* American Marketing Association

Paraview Publishing, *distributed by* Bertrams (UK), iPublish (ebooks)

Pardey Publications, *imprint of* Paradise Cay Publications Inc, *distributed by* Paradise Cay Publications Inc

Parenting Press Inc, *distributor for* Raefield-Roberts, Publishers

Park Avenue Productions, *imprint of* JIST Publishing Inc

Park Place Publications, *distributed by* Manzanila Books.com

Park Street Press, *imprint of* Inner Traditions International Ltd

Christopher Parkening, *distributed by* Hal Leonard Corp

Parkwest Publications Inc, *distributor for* Taplinger Publishing Co Inc

Parthian, *distributed by* Dufour Editions Inc

Partner Press, *distributed by* Gryphon House Inc

Partners, *distributor for* Frank Amato Publications Inc, Penfield Books

Partners Book Distributing, *distributor for* Avery Color Studios, Dog-Eared Publications, Third World Press

Partners Book Distributor, *distributor for* Wilderness Adventures Press Inc

Partners Publishers Group, *distributor for* SterlingHouse Publisher Inc

Partners West, *distributor for* Dog-Eared Publications, Gail's Guides, Naturegraph Publishers Inc, Wilderness Adventures Press Inc

Pasifika Press, *distributed by* University of Hawaii Press

Passages, *imprint of* Perfection Learning Corp

Passbooks, *imprint of* National Learning Corp

Passion Press, *imprint of* Down There Press

Passport, *imprint of* International Broadcasting Services Ltd

Passport Press Inc, *imprint of* Travel Line Press

Passport to World Band Radio, *imprint of* International Broadcasting Services Ltd

Pastimes, *imprint of* Martingale & Co

Pastoral Press, *imprint of* OCP Publications Inc, OCP Publications Inc

Patchwork Place Publishers, *distributed by* American Quilter's Society

Pathfast Publishing, *distributed by* Ball Publishing

Pathfinder Press, *subsidiary of* Anchor Foundation

Pathway Book Service, *distributor for* Brookline Books

Patient-Centered Guides, *subsidiary of* O'Reilly & Associates Inc

Patron's Pick (US only), *distributed by* Mint Publishers Group

Paul & Company, *division of* Independent Publishers Group, *distributor for* AA Publishing, Allen & Unwin, Asian Development Bank, Auckland U Press, Aurora Press, Battlebridge Publications, Blackhall Publishing, Boheme Press, Bold Strummer, Carcanet Press, Jon Carpenter, Claridge Press, Clinamen Press, Compass Press, DNA Press, Eothen Press, 5 Continents, Guernica Editions, Higganum Hill Books, High Sierra Books, Horwood Publishing, House of Anansi, IHS Press, Independent Institute, India Research Press, International Books, International IDEA, ISH Institut des Sciences de l'Homme, Janus Publishing, Juta Academic & Cape Town University Press, Kahn & Averill Publishers, Karnak House, Kwela Books, Lawrence & Wishart, Libris, Lingua Forum, Maisonneuve Press, Mango Publishing, Media Action International, Melbourne University Press, Merlin Press, Minority Rights Group, Net Biblio, New Clarion Press, New Dawn Press, New School University Graduate Program in Global Affairs, Olive Press, Open Gate Press, Orchard Publications, OSB Publishers, Palgrave Macmillan Academic, Peepal Tree Press, Rivers-Oram Press/Pandora, Saxe Coburg Publications, Scribe Publications, Seren, Shepheard-Walwyn Publishers, Soar Dime, Society for Human Resource Management, Sun Tree, Temenos Press, Toccata Press, Tuckwell Press Ltd, University of Hertfordshire Press, University of Luton Press, University of Wales Press, Victoria University Press, VU University Press, VUB University Press, White Cockade Publishing, White Horse Press, Whiting & Birch, Who's Who in Italy, Bridget Williams Books, Wolf Den Books, Jerome Wycoff

Pauline Books & Media, *division of* Daughters of Saint Paul, Daughters of St Paul

Pauline Comics Series, *imprint of* Pauline Books & Media

Paulist Press, *distributor for* St Bede's Publications

Pavilion Books Ltd, *distributed by* Trafalgar Square

Paws IV, *imprint of* Sasquatch Books

Payback Press, *distributed by* AK Press Distribution

PCI, *distributor for* Cottonwood Press Inc, MAR*CO Products Inc

PDR, *imprint of* Thomson Delmar Learning

Peabody Essex Museum, *distributed by* Antique Collectors Club Ltd

Peabody Museum of Archaeology & Ethnology, *unit of* Harvard Univ, Harvard University, *distributed by* Harvard University Press

Peace Books, *distributed by* China Books & Periodicals Inc

Peace Hill Press, *distributed by* W W Norton & Co, W W Norton & Company Inc

Peaceful Living, *distributor for* Vital Health Publishing

Peacewatch Editions, *imprint of* Ocean Tree Books

Peachpit Press, *division of* Pearson Technology Group, *distributed by* Silver Pixel Press

Peachtree Jr, *imprint of* Peachtree Publishers Ltd

Peachtree Publishers, *distributed by* Sundance Publishing

Peak Publishing, *imprint of* Western Reflections Publishing Co

Pearson, *member of* Pearson Technology Group, *distributed by* Council for Exceptional Children

Pearson Custom Publishing, *unit of* Pearson Higher Education Division

Pearson Education, *division of* Addison Wesley Longman, *distributor for* Manning Publications Co, *distributed by* American Academy of Environmental Engineers

Pearson Education - Elementary Group, *division of* Pearson Education School Group

Pearson Education/ELT, *division of* Pearson Education

Pearson Higher Education Division, *division of* Pearson Education

Pearson Professional Development, *division of* Pearson Education Inc, Pearson Education (PENZ)

Pearson Technology, *distributed by* SkillPath Publications

Pearson Technology Group (PTG), *division of* Pearson Education

Pearson Technology Group Canada, *distributed by* Penguin Books

Pebble, *imprint of* Capstone Press

Pebble Plus, *imprint of* Capstone Press

Peepal Tree Press, *distributed by* Paul & Company

Pelham, *imprint of* Viking Penguin

Pelican International Corp, *subsidiary of* Pelican Publishing Co Inc

Pelican Pond Publishing, *imprint of* Blue Dolphin Publishing Inc

Pelican Publishing Co Inc, *distributor for* Hope Publishing House, Marmac Publishing Co

Pelion Press, *imprint of* The Rosen Publishing Group Inc

A W Peller & Associates, *distributor for* Pieces of Learning

Pembroke Publishers, *distributed by* Stenhouse Publishers

Pen & Ink, *imprint of* Genesis Press Inc

Pen & Sword Books Lrd, *distributed by* Casemate Publishers

The Pen Pals, *imprint of* Modern Publishing

Pendle Hill (US), *distributed by* Morehouse Publishing Co

Pendragon Press, *subsidiary of* Camelot Publishing Co Inc, Camelot Publishing Co Inc, *distributor for* Croatian Musicological Society, *distributed by* LIM Editrice SRL (Italy), G Ricordi

Penfield Books, *distributed by* Bergquist, Book Marketing Plus, Partners

Penguin, *imprint of* Penguin Books, Penguin Group (USA) Inc, *distributor for* Verso

Penguin Audio Books, *imprint of* Viking Penguin

Penguin Audiobooks, *imprint of* Penguin Group (USA) Inc, Penguin Group (USA) Inc, *distributor for* Arkangel Complete Shakespeare, Highbridge Audio

Penguin Books, *imprint of* Penguin Group (USA) Inc, Penguin Group (USA) Inc, Viking Penguin, *distributor for* Pearson Technology Group Canada, *distributed by* Sundance Publishing

Penguin Books (Canada only), *distributor for* The Countryman Press

Penguin Classics, *imprint of* Penguin Books, Penguin Group (USA) Inc, Viking Penguin

Penguin Compass, *imprint of* Penguin Books, Penguin Group (USA) Inc, Viking Penguin

Penguin Group (USA) Inc, *subsidiary of* Pearson plc, *distributor for* Arkangel, Bibli O'Phile, Candlewick Press, Consumer Guide/PIL, DAW Books Inc, Dream Works, Granta, HighBridge Audio, Kensington Publishing Corp, The Library of America, Maharishi University of Management Press, The Monacelli Press, The Overlook Press, Reader's Digest

Penguin Group USA, *distributor for* Rough Guides

Penguin Group (USA) Inc, *subsidiary of* Pearson plc, *distributor for* Arkangel, Bibli O'Phile, Candlewick Press, Consumer Guide/PIL, DAW

Books Inc, Dream Works, Granta, HighBridge Audio, Kensington Publishing Corp, The Library of America, Maharishi University of Management Press, The Monacelli Press, The Overlook Press, Reader's Digest

Penguin Press, *imprint of* Penguin Group (USA) Inc

The Penguin Press, *imprint of* Viking Penguin

Penguin Putnam, *distributor for* Jim Henson Publishing/Muppet Press, The Monacelli Press, *distributed by* Learning Links Inc

Penguin-Putnam, *distributed by* Traders Press Inc

Penguin Putnam Inc, *distributor for* Alloy Entertainment, The Library of America, The Overlook Press, Reader's Digest Trade Books

Penguin-Technology Group, A Division of Pearson Canada, *distributor for* Texere

Penguin 20th Century Classics, *imprint of* Penguin Books

Penguin Young Readers Group, *division of* Penguin Group (USA) Inc, Penguin Group (USA) Inc

Penguin*HighBridge Audio, *imprint of* Penguin Audiobooks

Penmarin Books Inc, *distributed by* Hushion House Publishing Ltd, Midpoint Trade Books

Penn State Press, *distributor for* Philadelphia Museum of Art

Penn State University Press, *distributor for* University of California Institute on Global Conflict & Cooperation

Pennsylvania Historical & Museum Commission, *subsidiary of* The Commonwealth of Pennsylvania

Pennsylvania State Data Center, *subsidiary of* Institute of State & Regional Affairs

The Pennsylvania State University Press, *division of* The Pennsylvania State University

PennWell Books & More, *division of* PennWell

Pennywell Press, *distributed by* John F Blair Publisher

Penobscot Press, *imprint of* Picton Press

PenPoint Press, *imprint of* Eakin Press

PenQuill Press, *imprint of* Jonathan David Publishers Inc

Penquin Putman Inc, *distributed by* Heimburger House Publishing Co

Pentecostal Publishing House, *subsidiary of* United Pentecostal Church International, *distributed by* Spring Arbor

Penton Kids Press™, *imprint of* Penton Overseas Inc

Penton Overseas Inc, *imprint of* Penton Overseas Inc, *distributor for* The Book Co Publishing Pty Ltd, Cassidy Video (Little Explorers), Cliffs Notes, Cruise Concepts Inc (Licensor) Cruise Control, Hinkler Books Pty Ltd, Holt Concepts, Kids Creative Classics, Kidzup Entertainment, Maui Media LLC, The Musical Linguist, Production Associates, Relax...Intuit, Rivertree Production, Sound Beginnings, Teach Me Tapes Inc, John Wiley & Sons (Wiley Audio)

Penwell Books, *distributor for* Visions Communications

People's Publishing Group, *distributor for* New Readers Press

The Peoples Publishing Group, *distributor for* Focus Publishing/R Pullins Co Inc

Per Annum Inc, *distributor for* New Yorker Desk Diary

Peradam Press, *subsidiary of* The Center for Cultural & Naturalist Studies

Percheron Press, *imprint of* Eliot Werner Publications Inc

Peregrina Press, *distributed by* Cistercian Publications Inc, Editorial Office

Peregrine Outfitters, *distributor for* Trails Illustrated, Division of National Geographic Maps

Peter Peregrinus Ltd, *imprint of* IEE

Peregrinzilla, *distributed by* Chelsea Green Publishing Co

Perennial, *imprint of* HarperCollins General Books Group, HarperCollins Publishers Sales

Perennial Currents, *imprint of* HarperCollins Publishers Sales

Perennial Dark Alley, *imprint of* HarperCollins Publishers Sales

PerfectBound, *imprint of* HarperCollins General Books Group, HarperCollins Publishers Sales

Perfection Learning Corp, *distributor for* Abrams, Ace Books, Airmont, Annick Press, Archway, Atheneum, Baker Books, Ballantine, Bantam, Barrons, Berkley, Blake Books, Candlewick Press, Charlesbridge Press, Chelsea House, Children's Press, Chronicle Books, Crabtree Publishing, Crown, Disney Press, Distri Books, DK Publishing, Doubleday, Dutton, F&W Publications, Farrar, Straus & Giroux Inc, Fawcett, Firefly, First Avenue, Free Spirit, Fulcrum, Golden Books, Greenhaven Press Inc, Hammond Pub, Harcourt Brace & Co, Hayes, Gareth Stevens, Frederick Warne

Performance Studies Series, *imprint of* University Press of Mississippi

Performing Arts Publications, *distributed by* The Johns Hopkins University Press

Pergamon Press, *distributed by* Elsevier Science Inc

Peribo, *distributor for* Weatherhill Inc

Perigee, *imprint of* Berkley Publishing Group, Penguin Group (USA) Inc

Perigee Books, *imprint of* Penguin Group (USA) Inc, Penguin Group (USA) Inc

Periplus Editions, *imprint of* Tuttle Publishing, *distributed by* Tuttle Publishing

Perrenial Currents, *imprint of* HarperCollins General Books Group

Perrenial Dark Alley, *imprint of* HarperCollins General Books Group

Persea, *distributed by* Sundance Publishing

Persea Books Inc, *distributor for* Ontario Review Press, *distributed by* W W Norton & Co, W W Norton & Company Inc

Persephone Press, *imprint of* Birch Brook Press, *distributed by* Birch Brook Press

Perserverance Press, *distributed by* John Daniel & Co, Publishers

Perseus (Addison Wesley Trade), *distributed by* HarperCollins Publishers

The Perseus Books Group, *distributed by* HarperCollins Publishers

Perseus Books Groups, *distributor for* Merloyd Lawrence Inc

Perseus Running Press, *imprint of* The Perseus Books Group

Personhood Press, *imprint of* Jalmar Press

Peter Pal Library Supplier, *distributor for* Marshall Cavendish Corp

Gerald Peters Gallery, *division of* The Peters Corp, The Peters Corp

Peterson Publishing Co, *distributed by* Safari Press

Peterson's/Pacesetter Books, *imprint of* Thomson Peterson's

Petrified Forest Museum Association, *distributed by* Kiva Publishing Inc

Petroleum Extension Service (PETEX), *division of* University of Texas at Austin - Petroleum Extension Service, University of Texas, Petroleum Extension Service

Peytral Publications Inc, *distributor for* Free Spirit, NPR, Woodbine

Pfeiffer, *imprint of* Jossey-Bass, John Wiley & Sons Inc

Pflaum Publishing Group, *imprint of* Peter Li Education Group, Peter Li Education Group

PGW, *distributor for* Book Peddlers

Phaeton Press, *imprint of* Gordian Press, *distributed by* Gordian Press

Phaidon Press, *distributed by* Time Warner Book Group

Phaidon Press Inc, *subsidiary of* Phaidon Press Ltd, *distributor for* Mitchell Beazley, Electa

Phantom Publications, *imprint of* Empire Publishing Service

Pharmaceutical Products Press, *imprint of* The Haworth Press Inc

Pharmasoft, *distributor for* Platypus Media LLC

Phi Delta Kappa International, *division of* Phi Delta Kappa International Inc

Philadelphia Museum of Art, *distributed by* Antique Collector's Club (ACC), Antique Collectors Club Ltd, Distributed Art Publishers (DAP), Penn State Press, Yale University Press

Philomel, *imprint of* Penguin Young Readers Group

Philomel Books, *imprint of* Penguin Group (USA) Inc

Philosophy Documentation Center, *distributor for* Agora Publications, Imprint Academic, InteLex Corp, Routledge, KG Saur Verlag

Philosophy of Science, *imprint of* Transaction Publishers

Phobos Books, *imprint of* Phobos Entertainment Holdings Inc

Phoenix Illustrated, *distributed by* Sterling Publishing Co Inc

Phoenix International, *distributed by* The University of Arkansas Press

Phoenix Learning Resources, *division of* The Phoenix Learning Group, *distributor for* ECI, Galvin Publications, Kane Publishing, Sterling, *distributed by* McGraw-Hill, Nelson Educational Publishing

Phoenix Mapping Service, *division of* Wide World of Maps Inc

Phoenix Press, *distributed by* AK Press Distribution, Sterling Publishing Co Inc

Pholiota Press Inc, *distributed by* Cross-Cultural Communications

PIA/GATF (Graphic Arts Technical Foundation), *affiliate of* Printing Industries of America (PIA), *distributor for* Printing Industries of America

Picadilly Books, *distributed by* Empire Publishing Service

Picador, *subsidiary of* Holtzbrinck Publishers Holdings LLC, *distributed by* St Martin's Press LLC

Picasso Project, *division of* Alan Wofsy Fine Arts, Alan Wofsy Fine Arts, *distributor for* Cramer (Switzerland), Kornfeld (Switzerland), Ramie (France), *distributed by* Alan Wofsy Fine Arts

The Picasso Project, *imprint of* Alan Wofsy Fine Arts

Piccin Nuova Libraria SPA, *distributed by* Scholium International Inc

Pickering & Chatto, *distributed by* Ashgate Publishing Co

Pickwick Publications, *distributor for* Darton Longman & Todd Ltd (selected titles), Gomer Press (selected titles), Macmillan Press Ltd (selected titles), SPCK (selected titles)

Picton Press, *imprint of* Countyvise Ltd

Pictorial Histories, *distributed by* Heimburger House Publishing Co

Picture Imperfect, *imprint of* Windstorm Creative

Picture Me Books™, *imprint of* Playhouse Publishing

Picture, Play & Tote™, *imprint of* Playhouse Publishing

Picture Profits, *distributed by* Copywriter's Council of America (CCA)

Picture Yearling, *imprint of* Random House Inc

Pieces of Learning, *division of* Creative Learning Consultants Inc, *distributed by* ALPS Publishing, A W Peller & Associates, Professional Associate Publishing, Prufrock Press Inc

The Pilgrim Press/United Church Press, *distributor for* Northstone Publishing, SPCK, Wood Lake Books

Pilgrim Publications, *distributor for* Ages Software, Ambassador-Emerald, Christian Focus, Fox River Press, Hess Publications, Soli Deo Gloria Publications

Pimsleur, *imprint of* Simon & Schuster Audio

Pinata Books, *imprint of* Arte Publico Press

Pine Barrens Press, *division of* Barnegat Light Press

Pine Forge Press, *subsidiary of* Sage Publications, SAGE Publications Inc, SAGE Publications Ltd

Pine Street Books, *imprint of* University of Pennsylvania Press

Pine Winds, *imprint of* Idyll Arbor Inc

Pinnacle Books, *imprint of* Kensington Publishing Corp

Pinon Press, *imprint of* NavPress Publishing Group

Pinyon Publishing, *distributed by* Gem Guides Book Co

Pir Press, *imprint of* Pir Publications Inc

Pir Press (NY), *distributed by* Fons Vitae

Pitspopany Press, *distributor for* Simcha Publishing

PJD Electronic Publishing, *division of* PJD Publications Ltd

PK, *distributor for* Jim Henson Publishing/Muppet Press

Planet Dexter, *imprint of* Grosset & Dunlap, Penguin Group (USA) Inc, Penguin Young Readers Group, Price Stern Sloan

Planners Press, *division of* American Planning Association, *distributed by* University of Chicago Press

Planning Communications, *distributor for* Bookhaven Press LLC

Planning/Communications, *distributed by* SCB Distributors (paperback editions only)

Plastics Design Library, *imprint of* William Andrew Publishing

Platinum Press Inc, *subsidiary of* Bobley Harmann Corp, *distributed by* Barnes & Noble Books

Platt & Munk, *imprint of* Grosset & Dunlap, Penguin Young Readers Group

Platypus Media LLC, *distributed by* Pharmasoft

Player Press A/Z Ltd, *division of* Players Press Inc

Player Press Ltd (UK), *division of* Players Press Inc

Players Press, *imprint of* Players Press Inc

Players Press (Canada), *division of* Players Press Inc

Players Press Inc, *distributor for* Garland-Clark Editors, Macmillan Education (UK), Organica, Preston Editions

Playhouse Publishing, *imprint of* Nibble Me Books, Playhouse Publishing

Playskool, *imprint of* Penguin Young Readers Group

Playwrights Canada Press, *distributed by* Theatre Communications Group Inc

Pleasant Company Publications, *subsidiary of* Mattel

Pleasure Boat Studio: A Literary Press, *distributor for* Empty Bowl Press

Plenum, *distributed by* A D D Warehouse

Plenum Publishing Corp (selected titles), *distributed by* Metal Powder Industries Federation

Pleroma, *distributor for* GemStone Press

Plexus Publishing Inc, *distributed by* Independent Publishers Group (IPG)

PLI, *imprint of* Practising Law Institute, *distributor for* Practising Law Institute

The Plough Publishing House, *subsidiary of* The Bruderhof Foundation Inc, The Bruderhof Foundation Inc

Ploughshares, *subsidiary of* Ploughshares Inc, Ploughshares Inc

Plume, *division of* Penguin Group (USA) Inc, *imprint of* Penguin Group (USA) Inc

Plymbridge Distributors Ltd, *distributor for* University of Michigan Press

Plymptoon Books, *distributed by* NBM Publishing Inc

Pneuma Life Publishing, *distributor for* Christian Living Books Inc

Pocket, *distributor for* Parachute Publishing LLC

Pocket Books, *division of* Simon & Schuster Adult Publishing Group, *imprint of* Simon & Schuster Adult Publishing Group, *distributor for* Alloy Entertainment, *distributed by* Sundance Publishing

Pocket Books Trade Paperback, *imprint of* Pocket Books

Pocket Library of Florida Gardening, *imprint of* Winner Enterprises

Pocket Paragon, *imprint of* David R Godine Publisher Inc

Pocket Star, *imprint of* Pocket Books, Simon & Schuster Adult Publishing Group

Poetry as Prayer Series, *imprint of* Pauline Books & Media

Pogo Press Inc, *distributed by* SCB Distributors

Poison Vine Books, *imprint of* Elderberry Press LLC, *distributed by* Elderberry Press LLC

Poisoned Pen Press Inc, *distributor for* Sibling Press

Polestar Calendars, *distributed by* Orca Book Publishers

Police Executive Research Forum, *distributor for* Anderson, Criminal Justice Press, McGraw-Hill, Sage Publications

Policy Studies Associates, *imprint of* The Apex Press

Political Economy, *imprint of* Transaction Publishers

Political Risk Services, *imprint of* The PRS Group Inc

Polity Press, *imprint of* Blackwell Publishers

Pollyanna Productions, *distributed by* Gryphon House Inc

Polyface, *distributed by* Chelsea Green Publishing Co

Polygon (UK), *distributed by* Interlink Publishing Group Inc

Pond Frog Editions, *imprint of* Red Moon Press

Poplar Books, *imprint of* Book Sales Inc

Popular Press, *imprint of* University of Wisconsin Press

Popular Technology, *imprint of* Branden Publishing Co Inc

Popular Woodworking Books, *imprint of* Betterway Books

Population Studies, *imprint of* Transaction Publishers

Portable Press, *imprint of* Advantage Publishers Group

Portavoz, *distributed by* Editorial Bautista Independiente

Portfolio, *imprint of* Penguin Group (USA) Inc

Portraits of America, *imprint of* The Donning Co/Publishers

Possibility Press, *imprint of* Markowski International Publishers, Possibility Press, *distributed by* Midpoint Trade Books, Motorbooks Intl

Clarkson Potter, *imprint of* Clarkson Potter Publishers, Crown Publishing Group, Random House Inc, *distributor for* The Colonial Williamsburg Foundation

Potter Style, *imprint of* Clarkson Potter Publishers

powerHouse Books, *division of* powerHouse Cultural Entertainment Inc, *distributor for* Dakini Books, From Here to Fame, Glitterati Inc, Juno Books, 6x6.com, Testify Books, True Agency, Umbrage Editions

Poynter Consulting, *division of* Para Publishing

PPC, *distributed by* Gryphon Books

Practical Reviews, *imprint of* Oakstone Medical Publishing

Practising Law Institute, *distributed by* PLI

Practitioners Publishing Co, *distributor for* American Institute of Certified Public Accountants

Prairie Books, *imprint of* Albert Whitman & Co

Prairie Classics, *imprint of* Trails Books

Prairie Oak Press, *imprint of* Trails Books

Emery Pratt, *distributor for* Humanics Publishing Group

Prayer Book Press Inc, *subsidiary of* Media Judaica Inc, Media Judaica Inc

PRC Publishing, *distributed by* Sterling Publishing Co Inc

Pre School Press, *imprint of* Playmore Inc, Publishers

Precept Press, *division of* Bonus Books Inc, *distributed by* Bonus Books Inc

Premier Novels, *imprint of* Center Press

Premiere, *imprint of* Holloway House Publishing Co, *distributed by* Holloway House Publishing Co

Prentice Hall, *imprint of* Pearson Higher Education Division, *distributor for* American Geological Institute (AGI), Manning Publications Co, *distributed by* Abbott, Langer & Associates, American Academy of Environmental Engineers, Ball Publishing, NACE International, Prestwick House Inc, Society of Manufacturing Engineers

Prentice Hall (selected titles), *distributed by* Metal Powder Industries Federation

Prentice-Hall, *distributed by* American Water Works Association, SAS Publishing

Prentice Hall Business Publishing, *unit of* Pearson Higher Education Division

Prentice Hall Canada, *imprint of* Pearson Higher Education Division

Prentice Hall Career & Technology, *imprint of* Pearson Higher Education Division

Prentice Hall Career, Health, Education & Technology, *division of* Pearson Education

Prentice Hall Engineering/Science & Math, *unit of* Pearson Higher Education Division

Prentice Hall Humanities & Social Sciences, *unit of* Pearson Higher Education Division

Prentice Hall Press, *division of* Penguin Group (USA) Inc

Prentice Hall Regents, *imprint of* Pearson Higher Education Division

Prentice Hall School, *unit of* Pearson Education

PREP Publishing, *subsidiary of* PREP Inc, PREP Inc

Presbyterian Publishing Corp, *distributor for* Deo, Epworth, SCM, *distributed by* Abingdon Press, Spring Arbor Distributors

Preservation Press, *distributed by* Sundance Publishing

Presidio Press, *imprint of* Random House Publishing Group

The Press at California State University, Fresno, *unit of* California State University, Fresno, California State University, Fresno, *distributed by* Southern Illinois University Press

Press of Morningside Bookshop, *imprint of* Morningside Bookshop

Theodore Presser Co, *distributor for* Editions Orphee Inc

Prestel Publishing, *distributor for* Die Gestalten Verlag (DGV), Schirmer/Mosel

Prestel-Verlag, *distributor for* Art Institute of Chicago

Preston Editions, *distributed by* Players Press Inc

Prestwick House Inc, *distributor for* Dover Publications, Prentice Hall, Westin Walch

Price Stern Sloan, *imprint of* Penguin Group (USA) Inc, Penguin Group (USA) Inc, Penguin Young Readers Group

Price Stern Sloan Inc, *imprint of* Penguin Group (USA) Inc

Priddy Books, *imprint of* St Martin's Press LLC

Prima Games, *imprint of* Random House Information Group

Primary Publishing, *division of* Scholastic Education

Primary Research Group, *distributed by* Academic Impressions, Ambassador Books, The Book House, Coutts Library Service, Global Research Inc, MarketResearch.com, Midwest Library Service, Mindbranch, Research & Markets, Yankee Book Peddler

Primary Source Media, *imprint of* Thomson Gale

Prime Crime, *imprint of* Berkley Books, Berkley Publishing Group, Penguin Group (USA) Inc

PRIMEDIA Business Directories & Books, *division of* Primedia Inc

Primedia Business Magazine & Media, *division of* Primedia Inc

Primedia Consumer Magazine & Internet Group, *division of* Primedia History Group, Primedia Inc, *distributed by* Oxmoor House, Sterling

Primedia Price Digests, *imprint of* PRIMEDIA Business Directories & Books

Primer Publications, *distributed by* Gem Guides Book Co

Prince Press, *imprint of* Hendrickson Publishers Inc

Princeton Architectural Press, *distributor for* Balcony Verlag, Birkhauser Verlag, dot dot dot, Hyphen Press, Springer Vienna, *distributed by* Chronicle Books, Chronicle Books LLC

Princeton Book Co Publishers, *distributor for* Dance Books Ltd, Dance Notation Bureau

Princeton Review, *distributed by* Random House Inc

The Princeton Review, *imprint of* Random House Inc, Random House Information Group

Princeton Univ Press, *distributor for* Art Institute of Chicago

Princeton University Press, *distributor for* National Bureau of Economic Research Inc, National Gallery of Art, Nevraumont Publishing Co, University of California Institute on Global Conflict & Cooperation

Principia Press, *distributed by* The University of Akron Press

Printing Industries of America, *imprint of* PIA/GATF (Graphic Arts Technical Foundation), *distributed by* PIA/GATF (Graphic Arts Technical Foundation)

Printlink Publishers Inc, *distributed by* Tyndale House Publishers, World Wide Features

Prion, *distributed by* Trafalgar Square

Priority Multimedia, *distributed by* Macalester Park Publishing Co

Private Libraries Association, *distributed by* Oak Knoll Press

Pro Ed, *distributed by* Council for Exceptional Children

Pro-Ed, *distributor for* Psychological Assessment Resources Inc (PAR), *distributed by* Psychological Assessment Resources Inc (PAR)

Pro Ed (selected titles), *distributed by* Butte Publications Inc

Pro Quest Information & Learning, *division of* Pro Quest Co

Proceedings, *imprint of* American Philosophical Society

Munson Williams Proctor Institute, *distributed by* Syracuse University Press

Prodist, *imprint of* Watson Publishing International

Production Associates, *distributed by* Penton Overseas Inc

Productivity Press, *distributor for* American Society for Quality

Productivity Press Spanish Imprint, *imprint of* Productivity Press

Professional Associate Publishing, *distributor for* Pieces of Learning

Professional Book Publishing, *division of* Slack Incorporated

Professional Development, *division of* Scholastic Education

Professional Engineering Publishing, *distributed by* American Society of Mechanical Engineers (ASME)

Professional Practices, *imprint of* Krieger Publishing Co

Professional Publications, *distributed by* NACE International

Professional Publishing, *division of* Professional Book Group of McGraw-Hill, *distributor for* Dartnell, *distributed by* Macmillan of Canada (Toronto)

Professional Resource Press, *imprint of* Professional Resource Exchange Inc

Professional Training Association, *imprint of* OneOnOne Computer Training

Professors World Peace Academy, *distributed by* Paragon House

Profile Books, *distributed by* Trafalgar Square

Promachem LLC, *distributor for* United States Pharmacopeia

Promise Press, *imprint of* Barbour Publishing Inc

Promissor Inc, *subsidiary of* Houghton Mifflin Co

Promontory Press, *distributed by* Sterling Publishing Co Inc

Prompt, *distributed by* Thomson Delmar Learning

Protea Publishing, *distributed by* Bertrams, Gardners, Lightning Source Inc, Replica Books

Providence House Publishers, *imprint of* Providence Publishing Corp

Providence Press, *division of* Hope Publishing Co

Providence Publishing, *distributor for* Country Music Foundation Press

Providence Publishing Corp, *distributor for* Guild Bindery Press

Provincetown Arts Inc, *affiliate of* Provincetown Arts Press Inc, Provincetown Arts Press Inc

Pruett Publishing Co, *division of* Pruett Inc

Prufrock Press Inc, *distributor for* Pieces of Learning

PS Press, *imprint of* The Psychology Society

PS&E Publications, *imprint of* Bartleby Press

PSG, *imprint of* Elsevier

PSS, *imprint of* Grosset & Dunlap, Penguin Young Readers Group

Psychiatry & Psychology, *imprint of* Transaction Publishers

Psychological Assessment Resources Inc (PAR), *distributor for* American Guidance Service, Chronicle Guidance Publications Inc, Pro-Ed, The Psychological Corp, Riverside Publishing Co, Rorschach Workshops, *distributed by* ACER, Pro-Ed, The Psychological Corp, Riverside Publishing, Western Psychological Service

The Psychological Corp, *distributor for* Psychological Assessment Resources Inc (PAR), *distributed by* Academic Press, Psychological Assessment Resources Inc (PAR)

Psychology Press, *division of* Taylor & Francis Publishers Inc, *imprint of* Taylor & Francis Inc, *distributed by* Taylor & Francis Inc

Psychosocial Press, *imprint of* International Universities Press Inc, *distributed by* International Universities Press Inc

PTG Software, *member of* Pearson Technology Group

Public Access Broadcasting, *division of* Unarius Academy of Science Publications

Public Affairs, *distributed by* HarperCollins Publishers

Public Citizen, *distributed by* Addison Wesley, Simon & Schuster Pocket Books

Public History, *imprint of* Krieger Publishing Co

Public Record Office, *distributed by* Casemate Publishers

PublicAffairs, *member of* Perseus Books Group, The Perseus Books Group, *imprint of* The Perseus Books Group, *distributed by* HarperCollins

PublishAmerica, *distributed by* Ingram

Publisher's Associates, *distributor for* Ide House Inc

Publishers Group West, *distributor for* Bay/SOMA Publishing Inc, Berrett-Koehler Publishers Inc, Beyond Words Publishing Inc, Black Classic Press, Empire Press Media/Avant-Guide, Gault Millau Inc/Gayot Publications, Grove/Atlantic Inc, Hudson Park Press, Hugh Lauter Levin Associates Inc, Manic D Press, Surrey Books, The Taunton Press Inc, Ulysses Press, Wide World Publishing/Tetra, *distributed by* Heimburger House Publishing Co

Publishers Group West (trade market), *distributor for* Children's Book Press

Publishers Trade Secrets Library, *imprint of* Copywriter's Council of America (CCA)

PublishingOnline.com, *distributor for* Dry Bones Press Inc

Publishing Perfection, *distributor for* Brenner Information Group

Publishing Poynters Newsletter, *division of* Para Publishing

Publishing Services, *division of* Scholastic Education

Publishing Solutions, *distributed by* Creative Homeowner

Publishing Works, *distributed by* Enfield Publishing & Distribution Co

Publr Group West, *distributor for* Ronin Publishing Inc

Pudding House Publications, *affiliate of* Pudding House Innovative Writers Programs

Pueblo Books, *imprint of* Liturgical Press

Puffin, *imprint of* Penguin Group (USA) Inc

Puffin Books, *imprint of* Penguin Group (USA) Inc, Penguin Group (USA) Inc, Penguin Young Readers Group, *distributor for* Alloy Entertainment

Pulgas Ridge Press, *distributed by* Stackpole Books

Pulse Books, *division of* Barrytown/Station Hill Press

Pulse Publications, *division of* Weidner & Sons Publishing, *imprint of* Weidner & Sons Publishing, *distributed by* Weidner & Sons Publishing

Pumpkin Patch Publishing, *distributed by* Greene Bark Press Inc

Punch Press, *imprint of* Loft Press Inc

PUP Books, *imprint of* Purdue University Press

Puppy Paws Press, *distributed by* Toad Hall Inc

Purdue University Press, *distributor for* Lemma Publishers, Rosenberg/Thela Thesis, Wageningen Pers

Purple Mountain Press Ltd, *distributor for* Carmania Press, London (North America only)

Purple Pomegranate Productions, *division of* Jews for Jesus

Pushcart Press, *distributor for* Dustbooks, *distributed by* W W Norton & Co Inc, W W Norton & Company Inc

Pussywillow, *imprint of* Bandanna Books

Putnam, *imprint of* Penguin Group (USA) Inc, G P Putnam's Sons (Hardcover)

Putnam Berkley Audio, *imprint of* Penguin Group (USA) Inc, Penguin Group (USA) Inc, The Putnam Publishing Group, G P Putnam's Sons (Hardcover), *distributor for* Arkangel

Putnam Publishing Co, *distributed by* Sundance Publishing

The Putnam Publishing Group, *division of* Penguin Group (USA) Inc, Penguin Group (USA) Inc

G P Putnam's Sons, *imprint of* Penguin Group (USA) Inc, Penguin Young Readers Group, The Putnam Publishing Group

G P Putnam's Sons (Children's), *member of* Penguin Young Readers Group

G P Putnam's Sons (Hardcover), *imprint of* Penguin Group (USA) Inc, Penguin Group (USA) Inc

PWPA Books, *imprint of* Paragon House

PYO (Publish Your Own) Co, *imprint of* Hearts & Tummies Cookbook Co

QIBLAH Books, *distributed by* Kazi Publications Inc

QMP, *imprint of* Quality Medical Publishing Inc

Qoool Press, *imprint of* Galt Press

Quail Ridge Press, *affiliate of* Quail Ridge Inc

Quality Book Co Inc, *distributor for* Elderberry Press LLC

Quality Books, *distributor for* Boys Town Press, Craftsman Book Co, Do-It-Yourself Legal Publishers, Open Road Publishing, Raven Tree Press LLC

Quality Books Inc, *distributor for* Ebon Research Systems Publishing LLC

Quality Education Data, Inc, *subsidiary of* Scholastic Inc

Quantuck Lane Press, *distributed by* W W Norton & Company Inc

Quantum Leap SLC Publications, *affiliate of* Anasazi Foundation for Indigenous Americans

Quarry Books, *imprint of* Rockport Publishers

Quarry Books (Regional imprint for Midwest), *imprint of* Indiana University Press

Quartet Books (UK), *distributed by* Interlink Publishing Group Inc

Quarto, *imprint of* Krause Publications, *distributed by* My Chaotic Life™

Quest Books, *imprint of* Theosophical Publishing House/Quest Books

Quest (Youth Group-Curriculum Group), *imprint of* Charisma House

Quick & Painless, *imprint of* Off the Page Press

Quicken Press, *imprint of* McGraw-Hill/Osborne

QuickScan Reviews, *imprint of* Oakstone Medical Publishing

Quill Trade Paperbacks, *imprint of* HarperCollins Publishers

Quiller, *distributed by* Safari Press

Quiller Press Ltd, *distributed by* Stackpole Books

Quilliam Press (UK), *distributed by* Fons Vitae

Quinta Essentia (UK), *distributed by* Fons Vitae

Quintessence Books, *imprint of* Quintessence Publishing Co Inc

Quintessence Editora Ltda (Brazil), *subsidiary of* Quintessence Publishing Co Inc

Quintessence of Dental Technology, *imprint of* Quintessence Publishing Co Inc

Quintessence Pockets, *imprint of* Quintessence Publishing Co Inc

Quintessence Publishing Co Inc, *distributor for* Quintessence Publishing Co Ltd (Japan), Quintessence Publishing Ltd (London), Quintessence Verlags GmbH

Quintessence Publishing Co Ltd (Japan), *distributed by* Quintessence Publishing Co Inc

Quintessence Publishing Ltd (London), *distributed by* Quintessence Publishing Co Inc

Quintessence Verlags GmbH, *distributed by* Quintessence Publishing Co Inc

Quirk Books, *distributed by* Chronicle Books

Quite Specific Media Ltd, *distributor for* The Colonial Williamsburg Foundation

Quixote Press, *imprint of* Hearts & Tummies Cookbook Co

Quodlibetal Features, *distributed by* Vandamere Press

R & K Bookstore, *distributor for* MAR*CO Products Inc

R & S Books, *distributed by* Farrar, Straus & Giroux, LLC

R D R Books, *distributor for* Wakefield Press Australia, *distributed by* Fraser Direct (Jaguar)

Rabbinical Assembly of America, *distributed by* United Synagogue Book Service

Rabbit's Foot Press™, *imprint of* Blue Mountain Arts Inc

RACOM, *distributed by* American Marketing Association

Radiant Books, *imprint of* Gospel Publishing House

Radiant Life Curricular, *imprint of* Gospel Publishing House

Radical Weeds, *distributed by* Chelsea Green Publishing Co

Radio Amateur Callbook, *imprint of* Watson-Guptill Publications

Radio Database International, *imprint of* International Broadcasting Services Ltd

Radio Theatre, *imprint of* Focus on the Family

Radix Press, *subsidiary of* UGF/OR

Raefield-Roberts, Publishers, *distributed by* Parenting Press Inc

Ragged Bears, *division of* Ragged Bears Publishing Ltd, Ragged Bears Publishing Ltd (UK), *distributed by* Chronicle Books, Chronicle Books LLC

Ragged Edge Press, *division of* White Mane Publishing Co Inc

Ragged Mountain Press, *division of* The McGraw-Hill Companies Inc, McGraw-Hill Education, *imprint of* McGraw-Hill Professional

Rainbow Book Agencies, *distributor for* Gem-Stone Press

Rainbow Publishers, *imprint of* Rainbow Publishers

RainbowSoft, *division of* Rainbow Studies International

Raincoast, *distributor for* Michigan State University Press (MSU Press)

Raincoast Books, *distributor for* Voyageur Press

Ram Publishing, *distributed by* Gem Guides Book Co

Ramakrishna Math, *distributed by* Vedanta Press

Ramanujan Mathematical Society, *distributed by* American Mathematical Society

Ramie (France), *distributed by* Picasso Project

RAMPANT Gaming, *imprint of* Windstorm Creative

Ramsey Chair of Private Enterprise (Georgia State University), *distributed by* St Johann Press

RAND Corporation, *distributed by* Transaction Publishers

Rand McNally, *distributor for* Wide World of Maps Inc, *distributed by* Sundance Publishing, Wide World of Maps Inc

Rand McNally for Kids, *imprint of* Rand McNally

Peter E Randall Publisher, *distributed by* University Press of New England

Random House, *imprint of* McGraw-Hill Learning Group, Random House Inc, Random House Publishing Group, *distributor for* Karen Brown's Guides Inc, Clarkson Potter Publishers, Jim Henson Publishing/Muppet Press, Universe Publishing, *distributed by* American Association of Community Colleges (AACC), Sundance Publishing

Random House Audio Publishing Group, *subsidiary of* Random House Inc

Random House Books for Young Readers, *imprint of* Random House Children's Books

Random House Children's Books, *division of* Random House Inc, *distributor for* The Colonial Williamsburg Foundation

Random House Children's Publishing, *imprint of* Random House Inc

Random House Direct Inc, *affiliate of* Random House Inc, Random House Inc

Random House/Golden Books Young Readers Group, *division of* Random House Children's Books

Random House Inc, *division of* Bertelsmann AG, *distributor for* Alloy Entertainment, American Guidance Service, Anness Publishing Inc: Hermes House, Lorenz Books, Becket Publications, Compass American Guides, Karen Brown Guides, Learning Express, NY Review of Books, Princeton Review, Rebus, Shambhala Publications Inc, Sierra Club Books, Storey Books, Tundra Books of Northern New York, *distributed by* A & B Publishers Group, American Society for Training & Development (ASTD), DawnSignPress, Learning Links Inc

Random House International, *division of* Random House Inc

Random House Large Print, *division of* Random House Inc

Random House Large Print Publishing, *imprint of* Random House Inc

Random House New Media Division, *unit of* Random House Inc

Random House Publishing Group, *division of* Random House Inc

Random House Reference, *imprint of* Random House Inc, Random House Information Group

Random House Reference & Information Publishing, *imprint of* Random House Inc

Random House Sales & Marketing, *division of* Random House Inc, *distributor for* American Medical Association, Karen Brown, Mondadori

Spanish Language, Old Farmers Almanac, Real V, Rizzoli, Rugged Land, Shambhala, Steerforth Press

Random House Trade Paperbacks, *imprint of* Random House Publishing Group

Random House UK, *distributed by* Trafalgar Square

Random House Value Publishing, *affiliate of* Random House Inc

Random House Websters, *imprint of* Random House Reference

R&R Newkirk, *imprint of* Dearborn Trade Publishing

Ranger Rick Science Program, *imprint of* Haights Cross Communications Inc, Newbridge Educational Publishing

Rank & File, *distributed by* Stackpole Books

Rapids Christian Press Inc, *division of* Gunderson Publications

Rasmuson Library Historical Translation Series, *imprint of* University of Alaska Press

Rattapallax Press, *distributed by* Biblo Distribution, Ingram Periodicals

Raven Tree Press LLC, *distributed by* BWI, Follett, Quality Books

Shannon Ravenel Books, *imprint of* Algonquin Books of Chapel Hill

Ravenhawk AudioBooks, *imprint of* Ravenhawk™ Books

Ravenhawk™ Books, *division of* The 6DOF Group, 6DOF, *distributed by* Lightning Source Inc

Ravenhawk VideoBooks, *imprint of* Ravenhawk™ Books

RavenhawkCD/DVD, *imprint of* Ravenhawk™ Books

Ravenswood Books, *distributed by* Lake View Press

Rayo, *imprint of* HarperCollins Children's Books Group, HarperCollins General Books Group, HarperCollins Publishers Sales

Rayve Fulfillment, *division of* Rayve Productions Inc

Rayve Productions Inc, *distributed by* Lippincott, Williams & Wilkins

Razorbill, *imprint of* Penguin Group (USA) Inc

RBL, *imprint of* McGraw-Hill Learning Group

RCL Resources for Christian Living, *division of* RCL Enterprises, RCL Enterprises, Inc

RDV Books, *imprint of* Akashic Books

ReAct, *imprint of* Haights Cross Communications Inc, Sundance Publishing

Read Only Productions, *division of* Ropes LLC

Reader's Digest, *distributed by* Fox Chapel Publishing Co Inc, Hal Leonard Corp, Penguin Group (USA) Inc

Reader's Digest Children's Books, *subsidiary of* Reader's Digest USA, *distributed by* Simon & Schuster Inc

Readers Digest/Childrens Press, *distributor for* Jim Henson Publishing/Muppet Press

Reader's Digest General Books, *division of* Reader's Digest Association Inc, Reader's Digest Association Inc

Reader's Digest Trade Books, *division of* Reader's Digest Association Inc, Reader's Digest Association Inc, *distributed by* Penguin Putnam Inc

Reader's Digest USA Select Editions, *division of* Reader's Digest Association Inc, Reader's Digest Association Inc

Reading Power Works™, *imprint of* Haights Cross Communications Inc

Reading PowerWorks™, *imprint of* Sundance Publishing

Reading Research, *division of* A R O Publishing Co

Readmore, *distributor for* Investor Responsibility Research Center

Read'n Run Books, *imprint of* Crumb Elbow Publishing

Ready Reader Storybooks, *imprint of* Modern Publishing

Ready Set Go, *imprint of* Modern Publishing

Ready Teddy, *imprint of* Modern Publishing

Ready to Learn, *imprint of* Incentive Publications Inc

The Real Deal, *imprint of* Haights Cross Communications Inc, Sundance Publishing

Real Estate Education Co, *imprint of* Dearborn Trade Publishing

Real Story Series, *distributed by* Common Courage Press

Real V, *distributed by* Random House Sales & Marketing

L R Ream Publishing, *distributed by* Gem Guides Book Co

Rebel Inc, *distributed by* AK Press Distribution

Rebel Press, *distributed by* AK Press Distribution

Rebus, *distributed by* Random House Inc

Recommended Country Inns®, *imprint of* The Globe Pequot Press

The Reconstructionist Press, *distributed by* Fordham University Press

Record Research, *distributed by* Hal Leonard Corp

Record Research Inc, *affiliate of* Billboard Magazine

Recorded Books, *subsidiary of* Haights Cross Communications Inc, *imprint of* Haights Cross Communications Inc

Recorded Books Audiolibros, *imprint of* Haights Cross Communications Inc, Recorded Books LLC

Recorded Books Development, *imprint of* Haights Cross Communications Inc, Recorded Books LLC

Recorded Books Inspirational, *imprint of* Haights Cross Communications Inc, Recorded Books LLC

Recorded Books Large Print, *imprint of* Haights Cross Communications Inc, Recorded Books LLC

Recorded Books LLC, *division of* Haights Cross Communications Inc, *distributor for* Buena Vista DVDs, The Film Movement DVDs

Recorded Books Publishing, *imprint of* Haights Cross Communications Inc, Recorded Books LLC

Recovered Classics, *imprint of* McPherson & Co

Recreation Sales, *distributed by* Gem Guides Book Co

Recruiting Trends, *imprint of* Kennedy Information

Red Alder Books, *distributed by* Down There Press

Red Anvil Press, *imprint of* Elderberry Press LLC, *distributed by* Elderberry Press LLC

Red Cedar Classics, *imprint of* Michigan State University Press (MSU Press)

Red Dress Ink, *imprint of* Harlequin Enterprises Ltd

Red Hen Press, *distributed by* Small Press Distribution

Red Mansions Publishing, *distributed by* China Books & Periodicals Inc

Red Moon Press, *distributed by* John Weatherhill Inc

Red River Press, *imprint of* Archival Services Inc

Red Sea Press, *distributor for* Third World Press

Red Slipper, *imprint of* Genesis Press Inc

Red Wagon Books, *imprint of* Harcourt Trade Publishers

Red Wheel/Weiser, *distributor for* Moment Point Press Inc

Red Wheel/Weiser/Conari, *distributor for* Nicolas Hays Inc

Red Wheel-Weiser Inc, *distributed by* Moznaim Publishing Corp

Charles Redd Center, *distributed by* Signature Books Publishing LLC

Redemptorist Publications, *distributed by* Liguori Publications

Redleaf Press, *division of* Resources for Child Caring Inc, Resources for Child Caring Inc, *distributed by* Consortium Book Sales & Distribution (Trade Market), Gryphon House (Education Market), Gryphon House Inc, Monarch Books of Canada (Canadian Market)

Redwing Book Co, *distributor for* Blue Poppy Press

Reedy Press, *distributed by* University of Nebraska Press

Referee Books, *imprint of* Referee Enterprises Inc

Reference Press, *distributor for* World Trade Press

The Reference Publishing Co, *distributed by* Ball Publishing

Reflected Images Publishers, *imprint of* Webb Research Group, Publishers

Regal Books, *division of* Gospel Light

Regan Books, *imprint of* HarperCollins Publishers Sales

ReganBooks, *imprint of* HarperCollins General Books Group

Regency, *imprint of* Literacy Institute for Education (LIFE) Inc, Thomas Nelson Inc

Regents External Degree Series, *imprint of* National Learning Corp

Reggae Book of Light (Matshafa Berhan), *division of* Cornerstone Productions Inc

Regis External MBA Program, *imprint of* Bisk Education

Regnery, *imprint of* Eagle Publishing Inc

Regnery Publishing Inc, *subsidiary of* Eagle Publishing, Eagle Publishing Inc

Regular Baptist Press, *division of* General Association of Regular Baptist Churches

Rei America Inc, *affiliate of* Grupo Anaya (Spain)

Relax...Intuit, *distributed by* Penton Overseas Inc

The Relaxation Co, *distributed by* Simon & Schuster Audio

Renaissance House, *imprint of* Laredo Publishing Co, Laredo Publishing Company Inc, *distributed by* SRA/McGraw-Hill

Renditions Paperbacks, *distributed by* Cheng & Tsui Co Inc

Renewing the Heart, *imprint of* Focus on the Family

Renouf Bookstore, *distributor for* Institute for International Economics

Reo Wheel/Weiser, *distributor for* Larson Publications

Replenishment, *imprint of* Six Gallery Press

Replica Books, *distributor for* Protea Publishing

(Represent) Bernan Press, *distributed by* Bernan

Republic of Texas Press, *imprint of* Wordware Publishing Inc

Research & Markets, *distributor for* Primary Research Group

Research & Special Programs Administration of the US Department of Transportation, *distributed by* J J Keller & Associates, Inc

Research Centrex, *imprint of* Crumb Elbow Publishing

Resources for the Future, *distributed by* The Johns Hopkins University Press

Resources for the Future Inc, *distributed by* The Johns Hopkins University Press

Retail, *division of* Rand McNally

The Retention Solutions Group, *division of* Dorland Healthcare Information

Retold Classics, *imprint of* Perfection Learning Corp

Reunion Solutions Press, *imprint of* Iron Gate Publishing

Fleming H Revell, *division of* Baker Book House Co, Baker Book House Co

Review & Herald Publishing, *distributor for* Andrews University Press

Revival Press, *imprint of* Destiny Image

Reynolds & Hearn, *distributed by* Trafalgar Square

RFCafe.com, *distributor for* Noble Publishing Corp

RFF Press, *imprint of* Resources for the Future

The RGU Group, *distributed by* Sunbelt

Ribbits, *imprint of* Focus on the Family

Ricordi, *distributed by* Hal Leonard Corp

G Ricordi, *distributor for* Pendragon Press

RICS, *distributor for* American Society for Photogrammetry & Remote Sensing

Ridge Row Books, *imprint of* University of Scranton Press

Ridge Row Press, *subsidiary of* University of Scranton Press

Riebel-Roque, *distributed by* Casemate Publishers

Lynne Rienner Publishers Inc, *distributor for* North-South Center Press

Rigby, *imprint of* Harcourt Achieve

Riley & Johnson, *distributed by* Business Research Services Inc

Rimrock Press, *distributed by* Yucca Tree Press

Rio Nuevo, *distributed by* W W Norton & Company Inc

Ripley Entertainment Inc (US & Canada), *distributed by* Mint Publishers Group

Rising Moon (children's books), *imprint of* Northland Publishing Co

Rising Tide Press, *distributed by* Alamo Square, Amazon.com, Baker & Taylor, Banyan Tree, Turnaround (London)

Rittenhouse, *distributor for* Tarascon Publishing, Teton New Media

Rittenhouse Book Distributors, *distributor for* Maval Publishing Inc

Rittenhouse Book Distributors, Inc, *distributor for* United States Pharmacopeia

River Books Co Ltd, *distributed by* Antique Collectors Club Ltd

River City Kids, *imprint of* River City Publishing, LLC

Riverhead Books, *imprint of* Penguin Group (USA) Inc, The Putnam Publishing Group

Riverhead Books (Hardcover), *imprint of* Penguin Group (USA) Inc, Penguin Group (USA) Inc

Riverhead Books (Paperback), *imprint of* Berkley Publishing Group

Riverhead Books (Trade Paperback), *imprint of* Penguin Group (USA) Inc, Penguin Group (USA) Inc

RiverOak Publishing, *imprint of* Cook Communications Ministries, Honor Books

Rivers-Oram Press/Pandora, *distributed by* Paul & Company

Riverside, *distributor for* College Press Publishing Co

Riverside Distributors, *distributor for* Bridge-Logos Publishers, New City Press

Riverside Publishing, *distributor for* Psychological Assessment Resources Inc (PAR)

Riverside Publishing Co, *distributed by* Psychological Assessment Resources Inc (PAR)

The Riverside Publishing Co, *subsidiary of* Houghton Mifflin Co, Houghton Mifflin Co

Rivertree Production, *distributed by* Penton Overseas Inc

Rizzoli, *distributed by* Random House Sales & Marketing

Rizzoli International Publications Inc, *subsidiary of* R C S Rizzoli Corp New York, *distributor for* Art Institute of Chicago, Editions Flammarion, Skira Editore, Villegas Editores, White Star, *distributed by* Holtzbrinck

Rizzoli, New York, *imprint of* Rizzoli International Publications Inc

RKT Trade Publishing, *distributed by* Stackpole Books

RNIB National Education Services, *distributor for* American Foundation for the Blind (AFB Press)

Roadside Geology Series, *imprint of* Mountain Press Publishing Co

Roadside History Series, *imprint of* Mountain Press Publishing Co

Lee Roberts Publications, *distributed by* Hal Leonard Corp

Robins Lane Press, *imprint of* Gryphon House Inc, *distributed by* Gryphon House Inc

Roc, *imprint of* NAL, Penguin Group (USA) Inc

Rock A Bye Preschool Board Book, *imprint of* Modern Publishing

The Rock Spring Collection of Japanese Literature, *imprint of* Stone Bridge Press LLC

Rockbottom Book Co, *distributor for* Abdo Publishing

Rockbridge Publishing, *imprint of* Howell Press Inc

Rockefeller Institute Press, *distributed by* State University of New York Press

Rockefeller University Press, *unit of* Rockefeller University

Rockhurst University Press, *distributed by* Fordham University Press

Rockport, *imprint of* Rockport Publishers

Rockport Publishers, *distributed by* Betterway Books, F & W Publications, North Light Books, Writer's Digest Books

Rocky River Publishers LLC, *distributed by* Academic Book Center, Brodart, Follett Library Resources

Rodale Books, *subsidiary of* Rodale Inc, *distributed by* St Martin's Press

Rodale Inc, *distributed by* St Martin's Press Inc

Rodale Press, *distributed by* St Martin's Press LLC

Roman Catholic Books, *division of* Catholic Media Apostolate

Romantic Sounds Audio, *imprint of* Haights Cross Communications Inc, Recorded Books LLC

Rompa Ltd, *distributor for* The Speech Bin Inc

George Ronald, *distributed by* Kalimat Press

Roncorp Inc, *distributed by* Northeastern Music Publications Inc (exclusive)

Roncorp Publications, *imprint of* Roncorp Inc

Ronin Publishing Inc, *distributed by* Homestead Book Co, New Leaf, Publr Group West

Rorschach Workshops, *distributed by* Psychological Assessment Resources Inc (PAR)

Fr Seraphim Rose Foundation, *imprint of* St Herman Press

Rose Hill Books, *imprint of* Fordham University Press

Rosenberg/Thela Thesis, *distributed by* Purdue University Press

Ross Books, *imprint of* Baldar

Ross Publishing Inc, *distributor for* Archival Publications International, Foleor Editions

Rossel Books, *distributed by* Behrman House Inc

Rothko Chapel, *distributed by* University of Texas Press

Fred B Rothman Publications, *imprint of* William S Hein & Co Inc

RotoVision, *imprint of* Rockport Publishers

Rough Guides, *subsidiary of* Pearson PLC, *distributed by* Penguin Group USA

The Rough Notes Co Inc, *subsidiary of* Insurance Publishing Plus Corp, Insurance Publishing Plus Corp

Round House Group, *distributor for* Mosaic Press

Roundup Press (aviation), *distributed by* Graphic Arts Center Publishing Co

Roussand Press, *distributed by* Orca Book Publishers

Routledge, *subsidiary of* Taylor & Frances Book Inc, Taylor & Francis Book Inc, *distributed by* Philosophy Documentation Center

Rowan UK, *distributed by* C & T Publishing Inc

Rowe Com, *distributor for* Investor Responsibility Research Center

Rowman & Littlefield Publishers Inc, *subsidiary of* Rowman & Littlefield Publishing Group, *distributor for* Barnes & Noble Books (Imports & Reprints)

Rowman & Littlefield Publishing Group, *subsidiary of* Bridge Works Publishing

Royal Fireworks Press, *distributor for* KAV Books, Silk Label Books, Trillium Press

Royal Historical Society, *imprint of* Boydell & Brewer Inc

Royal Institute of International Affairs, *distributed by* The Brookings Institution Press

Royal Society of Chemistry, *distributed by* The American Chemical Society

Royal Society of London, *distributed by* Scholium International Inc

Royalton Press, *division of* The Drummond Publishing Group

RSA PRESS, *imprint of* McGraw-Hill/Osborne

RSG Publishing, *subsidiary of* Robert's Service Group

RSV Publishing, *imprint of* R S V Products

RTP Publishing Group, *subsidiary of* Rocky Top Books

RTS, *distributed by* American Association of Community Colleges (AACC)

Rubank Publications, *distributed by* Hal Leonard Corp

Rudisack Readers (UK), *distributed by* Interlink Publishing Group Inc

Rudra, *distributed by* Sterling Publishing Co Inc

Rugged Land, *distributed by* Random House Sales & Marketing

Rune-Tales, *imprint of* Quincannon Publishing Group

Runestone Press, *imprint of* Lerner Publishing Group

Running Press, *distributor for* Jim Henson Publishing/Muppet Press, *distributed by* Heimburger House Publishing Co

Running Press Book Publishers, *member of* The Perseus Books Group, *distributor for* Cigar Aficionado, Jim Henson's Muppets, Star Wars, Wine Spectator Press

Running Press Kids, *imprint of* Running Press Book Publishers

Running Press-Kids, *imprint of* The Perseus Books Group

Running Press Miniature Editions, *imprint of* Running Press Book Publishers

Running Press-Miniature Editions, *imprint of* The Perseus Books Group

Crane Russak, *imprint of* Taylor & Francis Editorial, Production & Manufacturing Division

Michael Russell, *distributed by* Antique Collectors Club Ltd

Rutgers Series in Accounting Research, *imprint of* Markus Wiener Publishers Inc

Rutgers University Press, *division of* Rutgers, The State University

Rutledge Hill Press, *division of* Thomas Nelson Publishers

RV Guides, *distributed by* American Map Corp

RV International Maps & Atlases, *distributed by* Hagstrom Map Co Inc

RZM Publishing, *distributed by* Casemate Publishers

S A B D A, *distributed by* Lotus Press

S-A Design Books, *imprint of* CarTech Inc

S&S - Libros en Espanol, *imprint of* Simon & Schuster Adult Publishing Group

SA Design, *distributed by* CarTech Inc

SAB Konrad Suszczynski, *imprint of* Cross-Cultural Communications

Sacred Music Press, *imprint of* Transcontinental Music Publications

Saddleback Educational, *distributor for* Teachers of English to Speakers of Other Languages Inc (TESOL)

Sadhana Publications, *distributed by* Lotus Press

Sadlier, *division of* William H Sadlier Inc

Sadlier-Oxford, *division of* William H Sadlier Inc

SAE (Society of Automotive Engineers International), *distributor for* Coordinating Research Council Inc

Safari Press, *distributor for* Peterson Publishing Co, Quiller, Sportsman's Press

Safe Harbor Books, *distributed by* Enfield Publishing & Distribution Co

Saga, *imprint of* Stylewriter Inc

Sagamore Publishing LLC, *distributor for* American Academy for Park & Recreation Admin

Sage Hill Resources, *imprint of* Providence Publishing Corp

Sage Ltd, *distributed by* Corwin Press

Sage Publications, *division of* Sage Publications, *distributed by* Corwin Press, Police Executive Research Forum

Saigo Trust, *distributed by* Antique Collectors Club Ltd

Saint Andrews College Press, *subsidiary of* Saint Andrews Presbyterian College

St Anthony Messenger Press, *distributor for* Franciscan Communications (books & videos), Ikonographics (videos)

St Augustine's Press Inc, *distributor for* Dumb Ox Books, The Linacre Centre, St Michael's Abbey Press, Sapientia Pres, *distributed by* University of Chicago Press

St Bede's, *distributed by* Fordham University Press

St Bede's Publications, *distributed by* Charismatic Renewal Services, Cistercian Publications, Paulist Press

St Herman Press, *subsidiary of* Brotherhood of St Herman of Alaska, Brotherhood of St Herman of Alaska, *imprint of* St Herman Press, *distributed by* Light & Life Publishing Co

St James Press, *division of* Gale, *imprint of* Thomson Gale

St James Publishing, *distributed by* Toad Hall Inc

St Johann Press, *distributor for* Ramsey Chair of Private Enterprise (Georgia State University)

St Joseph Editions, *imprint of* Catholic Book Publishing Corp

St Joseph's University Press, *distributor for* The Americas Society, The National Museum of Women in the Arts

St Lawrence University, *distributed by* Syracuse University Press

St Louis University Press, *distributed by* Fordham University Press

St Lucie Press, *imprint of* CRC Press LLC

St Martin's Press, *distributor for* Rodale Books

St Martin's Press Inc, *distributor for* Rodale Inc, World Almanac Books

St Martin's Press LLC, *subsidiary of* Holtzbrinck Publishers Holdings LLC, *distributor for* Audio Renaissance Tapes, Berg Publishers, Bloomsbury USA, Consumer Reports, Edmunds, Forge Books, Hambledon, Manchester University Press, Palgrave Macmillan, Picador, Rodale Press, I B Tauris, Tor Books, World Almanac Books, Zed Books

St Martin's Press Paperback and Reference Group, *division of* St Martin's Press LLC, St Martin's Press LLC

St Martin's Press Trade Division, *division of* St Martin's Press LLC, St Martin's Press LLC

Saint Mary's Press, *subsidiary of* Christian Brothers Publications, *distributor for* Group Publishing

St Michael's Abbey Press, *distributed by* St Augustine's Press Inc

St Paisius Abbey, *imprint of* St Herman Press

St Paisius Missionary School, *imprint of* St Herman Press

St Paul's Bibliographies, *distributed by* Oak Knoll Press

St Vladimir's, *distributor for* Conciliar Press

St Xenia Skete, *imprint of* St Herman Press

The Saints Series, *imprint of* Pauline Books & Media

Salamander, *distributed by* Casemate Publishers

Sales & Marketing, *division of* Scholastic Education

The Salesman's Guide, *imprint of* Douglas Publications Inc

Salmon Poetry, *distributed by* Dufour Editions Inc

Salmon Publishing, *distributor for* BrickHouse Books Inc, *distributed by* BrickHouse Books Inc

Salt Creek Press, *imprint of* J & L Lee Co

Salt River Books, *imprint of* Tyndale House Publishers Inc

Sam Houston State University, *distributed by* Texas A&M University Press

Samata Books, *distributed by* Lotus Press

San Antonio Express-News, *distributed by* Eakin Press

San Antonio Museum of Art, *distributed by* University of Texas Press

San Diego Museum of Man, *distributed by* Kiva Publishing Inc

San Diego State College Press, *imprint of* San Diego State University Press

San Diego State University Press, *division of* San Diego State University Foundation, *distributor for* Institute for Regional Studies of the Californias, *distributed by* UPA (selected titles only)

Sandcastle, *imprint of* Abdo Publishing

J S Sanders Books, *imprint of* Ivan R Dee Publisher

Sandstone, *imprint of* Ohio State University Press

The Sandstone Press, *imprint of* Frederic C Beil Publisher Inc

Santillana, *imprint of* Santillana USA Publishing Co Inc

Santillana USA Publishing Co Inc, *imprint of* The Richmond Publishing Co Inc, The Richmond Publishing Co Ltd

Sapientia Pres, *distributed by* St Augustine's Press Inc

Saraland Press, *distributed by* University of South Carolina Press

Raymond Saroff Editions, *distributed by* McPherson & Co

SAS Publishing, *distributor for* Amacon, Breakfast Communications, CRC Press, Duxbury, Harcourt, Harvard Business School Press, McGraw-Hill, Oxford, Prentice-Hall, John Wiley & Sons Inc, *distributed by* John Wiley & Sons Inc

Saturday Night Specials, *imprint of* Creative Arts Book Co

Saunders College Publishing, *imprint of* Harcourt College Publishers, Thomson Learning

W B Saunders, *distributor for* Current Medicine

W B Saunders Ltd, *imprint of* Elsevier Health Sciences, *distributor for* Bailliere-Tindall (UK)

KG Saur Verlag, *distributed by* Philosophy Documentation Center

K G Saur, *imprint of* Thomson Gale, *distributed by* University of Michigan Press

Savas Beatie, *distributed by* Casemate Publishers

Alastair Sawday Publishing, *distributed by* The Globe Pequot Press

Saxe Coburg Publications, *distributed by* Paul & Company

Saxon, *imprint of* Harcourt Achieve

Sayre Ross Co, *imprint of* Lion Books Publisher

SC Historical Society, *distributed by* University of South Carolina Press

Scala Publishers, *distributor for* American Federation of Arts, *distributed by* Antique Collectors Club Ltd

Scarecrow Press/Government Institutes Div, *division of* Rowman & Littlefield

Scarecrow Press Inc, *member of* The Rowman & Littlefield Publishing Group Inc

Scarecrow Trade, *imprint of* Scarecrow Press Inc

Scarf Press, *distributed by* Bloch Publishing Co

SCB Distributors, *distributor for* Bluewood Books, Circlet Press Inc, Mosaic Press, Planning/Communications, Pogo Press Inc, Silver Lake Publishing

Frank Schaffer Publications, *distributor for* Totline Publications

Schaum, *imprint of* McGraw-Hill Professional

Helen Rose Scheuer Jewish Women's Series, *imprint of* The Feminist Press at The City University of New York

Schiffer Publishing Ltd, *distributor for* The Donning Co

Schirmer, *imprint of* Wadsworth Publishing

E C Schirmer Music Co, *division of* ECS Publishing, *imprint of* ECS Publishing

G Schirmer Inc (Associated Music Publishers), *distributed by* Hal Leonard Corp

Schirmer/Mosel, *distributed by* Prestel Publishing

Schirmer Reference, *imprint of* Thomson Gale

Schirmer Trade Books, *imprint of* Music Sales Corp, *distributor for* Big Meteor Publishing, Independent Music Press

Schocken Books, *imprint of* Pantheon Books/Schocken Books, Random House Inc

Scholars' Facsimiles & Reprints, *subsidiary of* Academic Resources Corp

Scholastic, *distributor for* The Colonial Williamsburg Foundation, Parachute Publishing LLC, *distributed by* Learning Links Inc

Scholastic Argentina SA, *subsidiary of* Scholastic International

Scholastic Australia Pty Ltd, *subsidiary of* Scholastic International

Scholastic Books, *distributor for* Alloy Entertainment, *distributed by* Sundance Publishing

Scholastic Canada Ltd, *subsidiary of* Scholastic International

Scholastic Education, *division of* Scholastic Inc, Scholastic Inc

Scholastic Education Curriculum Publishing, *division of* Scholastic Inc, Scholastic Inc

Scholastic Entertainment Inc, *division of* Scholastic Inc, Scholastic Inc

Scholastic Hong Kong Ltd, *subsidiary of* Scholastic International

Scholastic Inc, *distributor for* Educational Impressions Inc

Scholastic India Private Ltd, *subsidiary of* Scholastic International

Scholastic International, *division of* Scholastic Inc

Scholastic Library Publishing, *division of* Scholastic Inc

Scholastic Mexico SA, *subsidiary of* Scholastic International

Scholastic New Zealand Ltd, *subsidiary of* Scholastic International

Scholastic Non-Fiction, *imprint of* Scholastic Trade Division

Scholastic Paperbacks, *imprint of* Scholastic Trade Division

Scholastic Paperbacks, Teaching Resources & Reading Counts, *division of* Scholastic Inc

Scholastic Press, *imprint of* Scholastic Trade Division

Scholastic Publications Ltd (UK), *subsidiary of* Scholastic International

Scholastic Reference, *imprint of* Scholastic Trade Division

Scholastic-Tab Publications, *distributor for* Educational Impressions Inc

Scholastic Trade Division, *division of* Scholastic Inc, Scholastic Inc

Scholium International Inc, *distributor for* Chalcombe Publications (UK), Dechema Series, International Ediemme Rome, Macmillan (UK), Micelle Press, Palladian Books Ltd, Piccin Nuova Libraria SPA (Padua Italy), Royal Society of London, Sita Technology (UK), Viewpoint, Zuckschwerdt Verlag (Munich, Germany)

School Age Notes, *distributed by* Gryphon House Inc

School Guide Publications, *division of* Catholic News Publishing Co Inc

School of Government, *division of* The University of NC at Chapel Hill, The University of NC at Chapel Hill

School Renaissance, *distributed by* Gryphon House Inc

School Technology Alert, *imprint of* eSchool News

School Technology Best Practices, *imprint of* eSchool News

School Technology Funding Directory, *imprint of* eSchool News

School Technology One Book, *imprint of* eSchool News

Marta Schooler, *distributor for* Weatherhill Inc

Arthur Schwartz & Co Inc, *distributor for* Harvard University Art Museums

Sci-Tech Publishing, *imprint of* William Andrew Publishing

Science History Publications USA, *imprint of* Watson Publishing International

Science of Mind Publications, *distributed by* De Vorss & Co

Science Press New York & Science Press Beijing, *distributed by* American Mathematical Society

Science Publisher Inc, *distributed by* Enfield Publishing & Distribution Co

Scientific American Medicine, *distributor for* American College of Surgeons

Scitec Publications, *imprint of* Trans Tech Publications

SciVision, *division of* Academic Press, *imprint of* Academic Press

SCM, *distributed by* Presbyterian Publishing Corp, Westminster John Knox Press

Scolar, *imprint of* Ashgate Publishing Co

Scolari, *division of* Sage Publications, *subsidiary of* Sage Publications

Scots Plaid Press, *imprint of* Old Barn Enterprises Inc

Scott Foresman, *division of* Addison Wesley Longman

Scott Jones Publishing, *distributed by* Thomson Delmar Learning

Scott Publishing Co, *division of* AMOS Press, Amos Press Inc

Scribe Publications, *distributed by* Paul & Company

Scribner, *imprint of* Simon & Schuster Adult Publishing Group

Scribner Classics, *imprint of* Scribner, Simon & Schuster Adult Publishing Group

Scribner Paperback Fiction, *imprint of* Simon & Schuster Adult Publishing Group

Scribner Poetry, *imprint of* Scribner, Simon & Schuster Adult Publishing Group

Scripta Humanistica Publishing International, *subsidiary of* Brumar Communications

Scripta-Technica, *imprint of* John Wiley & Sons Inc

Scriptum Editions, *distributed by* Trafalgar Square

Scriptural Research & Publishing Co Inc, *distributed by* Scriptural Research Center

Scriptural Research Center, *distributor for* Scriptural Research & Publishing Co Inc, Truth Center

Scroll Saw Workshop Magazine, *imprint of* Fox Chapel Publishing Co Inc

Scythian Books, *imprint of* Berkeley Slavic Specialties

Seabys Ltd, *distributed by* Sanford J Durst

Seafarer Books, *distributed by* Sheridan House Inc

Seal Press, *imprint of* Avalon Publishing Group - California, Avalon Publishing Group Inc

Sealife Research Alliance, *imprint of* Crumb Elbow Publishing

Search Press, UK, *distributor for* Interweave Press

Seaside Press, *distributed by* Wordware Publishing Inc

Seastone, *imprint of* Ulysses Press

Second Chance Press, *imprint of* The Permanent Press, The Permanent Press

Second Chance Reading®, *imprint of* Haights Cross Communications Inc, Sundance Publishing

Second Floor Music, *distributed by* Hal Leonard Corp

Second Story Press, *distributed by* Orca Book Publishers

Secret Language Press, *imprint of* Lawells Publishing

Secret Passage Press, *distributed by* Enfield Publishing & Distribution Co, Sundance Publishing

Sedgwick Press, *imprint of* Grey House Publishing Inc

See Sharp Press, *distributed by* Freedom Press (London)

Seedling Publications Inc, *distributed by* Kendall Hunt Publishing

The SeedSowers, *subsidiary of* Christian Books Publishing House

Martin E Segal Theatre Center Publications, *distributed by* Theatre Communications Group Inc

Select, *imprint of* Oakstone Medical Publishing

Self-Counsel Press Inc, *subsidiary of* International Self-Counsel Press Ltd, International Self-Counsel Press Ltd

Self-Counsel Series, *imprint of* Self-Counsel Press Inc

Self-Esteem Shop, *distributor for* American Counseling Association

Selfhelpbooks.com, *imprint of* Wellness Institute Inc

The Selfhelper Law Press of America, *imprint of* Do-It-Yourself Legal Publishers

Selling Space, *imprint of* Interlingua Publishing

Seloc, *distributed by* Thomson Delmar Learning

Selt, *distributed by* The Light Inc

Sense of Wonder Press, *imprint of* James A Rock & Co Publishers

Sephardic House, *distributed by* Bloch Publishing Co

Sepher-Hermon Press, *distributor for* Bar-Ilan University Press, Vallentine, Mitchell & Co Ltd

Seren, *distributed by* Paul & Company

Serendipity, *imprint of* Price Stern Sloan

Serif Publishing Ltd (UK), *distributed by* Interlink Publishing Group Inc

Serindia Publications, *distributed by* Art Media Resources Inc, Paragon Asia Co Ltd (Thailand, Singapore & Southeast Asia), Thames & Hudson (Europe & United Kingdom), Weatherhill Inc, Wisdom Books (Backlist titles)

Servant Books, *imprint of* St Anthony Messenger Press

SESAP Audio Companion, *imprint of* Oakstone Medical Publishing

SETAC Press, *imprint of* Society of Environmental Toxicology & Chemistry

Seven Dials, *distributed by* Sterling Publishing Co Inc

Seven Hills Book Distributors, *distributed by* Ball Publishing

Seventh-Wing Publications, *distributor for* Dustbooks

Severn House, *imprint of* Severn House Publishers Inc

Severn House Publishers Inc, *subsidiary of* Severn House Publishers Inc, Severn House Publishers Ltd

Sex Stuff for Kids, *imprint of* Gallopade International Inc

Sey Yes Marketing, *distributor for* Frieda Carrol Communications

Dale Seymour Publications, *distributed by* Zephyr Press Catalog

Shaar Press, *imprint of* Mesorah Publications Ltd

Shabdaguchha (Magazine & Press), *distributed by* Cross-Cultural Communications

Shadow Mountain, *imprint of* Deseret Book Co

Shama Books, *distributed by* Transaction Publishers

Shambhala, *distributed by* Random House Sales & Marketing

Shambhala Publications Inc, *distributed by* Random House Inc

Shangri-La, *imprint of* Lotus Press

Sharon's Books, *imprint of* New Century Books

Sharpe Reference, *imprint of* M E Sharpe Inc

Shaw Books, *imprint of* WaterBrook Press

Shaye Areheart Books, *imprint of* Crown Publishing Group, Random House Inc

Shearwater Books, *imprint of* Island Press

The Sheep Meadow Press, *distributor for* Carcanet, *distributed by* The New England University Press, University Press of New England

Sheffield Publishing Co, *subsidiary of* Waveland Press Inc

Sheldrake Press (UK), *distributed by* Interlink Publishing Group Inc

Shengold Books, *imprint of* Schreiber Publishing Inc

Shepheard-Walwyn Publishers, *distributed by* Paul & Company

Sheridan House Inc, *distributor for* Adlard Coles Nautical, Seafarer Books

Shining Star, *imprint of* American Society for Quality

G Shirmer, *imprint of* Hal Leonard Corp

Shoemaker & Hoard, *imprint of* Avalon Publishing Group Inc

Shoemaker & Hoard, Publishers, *division of* Avalon Publishing Group Inc, Avalon Publishing Group, Inc

Short Books, *distributed by* Trafalgar Square

Show What You Know® Publishing, *division of* Englefield & Associates Inc

Showcase, *imprint of* Players Press Inc

ShowForth Videos, *division of* Bob Jones University Press

Shufunotomo Co, *distributed by* Tuttle Publishing

Shufunotomo Co Ltd, *distributed by* Weatherhill Inc

Sibling Press, *distributed by* Poisoned Pen Press Inc

Sicilia Parra, *distributed by* Cross-Cultural Communications

A Siddha Yoga Publication, *imprint of* Siddha Yoga Publications

Siddha Yoga Publications, *unit of* Syda Foundation

SIEditrice, *distributed by* Thinkers' Press Inc

Sierra Club Adult Books, *imprint of* Random House Inc

Sierra Club Books, *distributed by* Random House Inc, University of California Press

Sierra Club Books Adult Trade Division, *division of* Sierra Club Books, Sierra Club Books, *distributed by* University of California Press

Sierra Press, *subsidiary of* Panorama International Productions, Panorama International Productions Inc, *distributor for* Double Decker Press, *distributed by* American West Books, Canyonlands Publications, Gem Guides, Gem Guides Book Co

La Siesta Press, *distributed by* Gem Guides Book Co

Signature Books Publishing LLC, *distributor for* Dialogue Foundation, Mormon History Association, Charles Redd Center, Sunstone Foundation, Tanner Trust

Signatures Network, *distributed by* Andrews McMeel Publishing

Signet, *imprint of* NAL, Penguin Group (USA) Inc

Signet Classics, *imprint of* NAL, Penguin Group (USA) Inc

Signum Verlag, *distributed by* Gallaudet University Press

Siles Press, *division of* Silman-James Press

Silhouette, *imprint of* Harlequin Enterprises Ltd, Stylewriter Inc

Silhouette Imprints, *imprint of* Crumb Elbow Publishing

Silk Label Books, *distributed by* Royal Fireworks Press

Siloam Press (Health Publishing Group), *imprint of* Charisma House

Silver Burdett Ginn Religion, *imprint of* Pearson Education - Elementary Group

Silver Burdett Press, *imprint of* Modern Curriculum Press

Silver Dagger Mysteries, *imprint of* The Overmountain Press

Silver Dolphin Books, *imprint of* Advantage Publishers Group

Silver Lake Publishing, *distributed by* SCB Distributors

Silver Lining, *distributed by* Sterling Publishing Co Inc

Silver Pixel Press, *division of* The Tiffen Co, The Tiffen Company, *distributor for* Focal Press, Little, Brown & Co, Peachpit Press, Sterling Publishing Co Inc, *distributed by* Sterling Publishing Co Inc

Silver Press, *distributed by* Sundance Publishing

Silver Spur Westerns, *imprint of* Creative Arts Book Co

Silver Whistle Books, *imprint of* Harcourt Trade Publishers

Silverplume, *distributor for* Standard Publishing Corp

Simba Information, *unit of* R R Bowker LLC

Simcha Press, *imprint of* Health Communications Inc

Simcha Publishing, *distributed by* Pitspopany Press

Simon & Schuster, *imprint of* Simon & Schuster Adult Publishing Group, *distributor for* Alloy Entertainment, Baen Publishing Enterprises, Cardoza Publishing, ibooks Inc, Jim Henson Publishing/Muppet Press, Meadowbrook Press, National Geographic Books, National Geographic Society, Nightingale-Conant, Open Road Publishing, Union Square Publishing, *distributed by* A & B Publishers Group, A D D Warehouse, Learning Links Inc, SkillPath Publications, Sundance Publishing, Thorndike Press

Simon & Schuster Adult Publishing Group, *division of* Simon & Schuster Inc

Simon & Schuster Audio, *distributor for* Franklin Covey Audiobooks, The Relaxation Co

Simon & Schuster Audioworks, *imprint of* Simon & Schuster Audio

Simon & Schuster Books for Young Readers, *imprint of* Simon & Schuster Children's Publishing

Simon & Schuster Children's Publishing, *division of* Simon & Schuster Inc

Simon & Schuster Classic Editions, *imprint of* Simon & Schuster Adult Publishing Group

Simon & Schuster Inc, *division of* Viacom, *distributor for* AAA Publishing, Andrews McMeel Publishing (fulfillment & billing), Baen Books, Baseball America, Cardoza, Games Workshop, Harlequin (billing only), Hodder Headline USA, ibooks, Meadowbrook Press, National Geographic Society, Open Road, Reader's Digest Children's Books, VIZ (fulfillment & billing)

Simon & Schuster Mass Merchandise Sales Co, *distributor for* Harlequin Enterprises Ltd, Steeple Hill Books

Simon & Schuster Online, *division of* Simon & Schuster Inc

Simon & Schuster Pocket Books, *distributor for* Public Citizen

Simon & Schuster Sales & Distribution, *division of* Simon & Schuster Inc

Simon & Schuster Sound Ideas, *imprint of* Simon & Schuster Audio

Simon & Schuster Source, *imprint of* Simon & Schuster Adult Publishing Group

Simon Pulse, *imprint of* Simon & Schuster Children's Publishing

Simon Spotlight, *imprint of* Simon & Schuster Children's Publishing

Simon Spotlight Entertainment, *imprint of* Simon & Schuster Children's Publishing

SimonSays.com, *imprint of* Simon & Schuster Online

Simplex Publications, *distributed by* Dry Bones Press Inc

Sinclair-Stevenson, *distributed by* Trafalgar Square

Sing-Along Series, *imprint of* R S V Products

Sing Out Corporation, *distributed by* Hal Leonard Corp

Singapore University Press, *distributed by* University of Hawaii Press

Singular, *imprint of* Thomson Delmar Learning

Siris Books, *imprint of* Brewers Publications

Byron Sistler, *distributor for* Ericson Books

Sita Technology (UK), *distributed by* Scholium International Inc

6x6.com, *distributed by* powerHouse Books

6 x 6 Magazine, *imprint of* Ugly Duckling Presse

Six Gallery Press, *distributed by* Booksurge

Six House, *subsidiary of* Gallopade International Inc

Six Strings Music Publishing, *distributed by* Music Sales Corp

Sixth & Spring, *distributed by* Sterling Publishing Co Inc

Skateman Publications, *imprint of* World Citizens

Skidmore-Roth, *imprint of* Thomson Delmar Learning

SkillPath Publications, *division of* The Graceland College Center for Professional Development & Lifelong Learning Inc, The Graceland College Center for Professional Development & Lifelong Learning Inc, *distributor for* Franklin Covey, Glencoe/McGraw-Hill, Impact Publishers, Pearson Technology, Simon & Schuster, Thomson Publishing, John Wiley

Skinner House Books, *division of* Unitarian Universalist Association

Skira Editore, *distributed by* Rizzoli International Publications Inc

SkyLight Paths Publishing, *division of* Longhill Partners Inc, LongHill Partners Inc

Slack Inc, *distributed by* Henry Holt and Company, LLC

Sleeping Bear Press, *imprint of* Thomson Gale, *distributed by* Lucent Books Inc

Sleeping Bear Press™, *imprint of* Thomson Gale

Sleepy Dog, *imprint of* Lucky Press LLC

Sleepy Hollow Press, *distributed by* Fordham University Press

Slossen, *distributed by* A D D Warehouse

Small Business Weekly, *subsidiary of* BizBest Media Corp

Small Horizons, *imprint of* New Horizon Press

Small Press Distribution, *distributor for* Ahsahta Press, Anhinga Press, Latin American Literary Review Press, Lynx House Press, Omnidawn Publishing, Red Hen Press

Smart Kids™, *imprint of* Penton Overseas Inc

Smart Squares Games Sets, *distributed by* Ideals Publications Inc

Smartmaps®, *imprint of* VanDam Inc

Smiley Books, *imprint of* Hay House Inc

Smith & Kraus Books For Kids, *imprint of* Smith & Kraus Inc Publishers

Smith & Kraus Global, *subsidiary of* Smith & Kraus Inc Publishers

Smith & Kraus Inc, *distributed by* Smith & Kraus Inc Publishers

Smith & Kraus Inc Publishers, *distributor for* Smith & Kraus Inc

Doug Smith, *distributed by* Centering Corp

The Smith Publishers, *subsidiary of* The Generalist Association Inc, The Generalist Association Inc, *distributed by* Arts End Books

Smith Research Associates, *imprint of* Signature Books Publishing LLC

W H Smith UK, *distributor for* SynergEbooks

Smithmark Publishers, *distributed by* Heimburger House Publishing Co

Smithmark Publishers, A Division of US Media Holding Inc, *distributed by* Ball Publishing

Smithsonian Books, *imprint of* Smithsonian Institution Press, *distributed by* W W Norton & Company Inc

Smithsonian College Lecture Series, *imprint of* Haights Cross Communications Inc, Recorded Books LLC

Smithsonian Federal Series Section, *division of* Smithsonian Books

Smithsonian Institution Press, *division of* Smithsonian Institution, *distributor for* Biological Diversity Handbook Series, Handbook of North American Indians, Smithsonian Library of the Solar System, Smithsonian Series in Archaeological Inquiry, Smithsonian Series in Comparative Evolutionary Biology, Smithsonian Series in Ethnographic Inquiry

Smithsonian Library of the Solar System, *distributed by* Smithsonian Institution Press

Smithsonian Series in Archaeological Inquiry, *distributed by* Smithsonian Institution Press

Smithsonian Series in Comparative Evolutionary Biology, *distributed by* Smithsonian Institution Press

Smithsonian Series in Ethnographic Inquiry, *distributed by* Smithsonian Institution Press

Smooch, *imprint of* Dorchester Publishing Co Inc

Colin Smythe Ltd, *distributed by* Dufour Editions Inc

Snails Pace Press, *imprint of* Wilde Publishing

Sniffen Court, *imprint of* Haights Cross Communications Inc, Triumph Learning

Snow Lion, *imprint of* Snow Lion Publications Inc

Snow Lion Publications Inc, *distributed by* National Book Network

Tom Snyder Productions, *subsidiary of* Scholastic Inc

Soar Dime, *distributed by* Paul & Company

Social Ecology Press, *subsidiary of* Dog-Eared Publications

Social Philosophy & Policy Center-Bowling Green University, *distributed by* Transaction Publishers

Social Policy & Social Theory, *imprint of* Transaction Publishers

Social Science Classics, *imprint of* Transaction Publishers

Social Sciences School Services, *distributor for* American Counseling Association

Social Studies School Services, *distributor for* Cottonwood Press Inc

The Social Work Practice Press, *imprint of* The Haworth Press Inc

Societe Mathematique de France, *distributed by* American Mathematical Society

Society for American Baseball Research, *distributed by* University of Nebraska Press

Society for Human Resource Management, *distributed by* Paul & Company

Society of Biblical Literature, *distributor for* Brown Judaic Studies, Journal of Feminist Studies in Religion

Society of Manufacturing Engineers, *distributor for* Free Press Division of MacMillan, Industrial Press, McGraw-Hill, Prentice Hall, John Wiley & Sons Inc, *distributed by* American Technical Publishers, ASME, McGraw-Hill

Society of the Cincinnati, *distributed by* University Press of America Inc

Sociology of Religion, *imprint of* Transaction Publishers

Soffietto Editions, *imprint of* Red Moon Press

Software Engineering Press, *imprint of* The Systemsware Corp

Soho Crime, *imprint of* Soho Press Inc

Solar Design Association, *distributed by* Chelsea Green Publishing Co

Solar Energy Information Services (SEIS), *imprint of* Business/Technology Books (B/T Books)

Soli Deo Gloria Publications, *subsidiary of* Soli Deo Gloria Ministries Inc, Soli Deo Gloria Ministries Inc, *distributed by* Pilgrim Publications

SOM Publishing, *division of* School of Metaphysics, *subsidiary of* School of Metaphysics, *distributed by* Devores, New Leaf Distributing

SOMA Books, *imprint of* Bay/SOMA Publishing Inc

Somerset Press, *division of* Hope Publishing Co

Somerville House USA, *imprint of* Grosset & Dunlap

Something More Publications, *distributed by* Fordham University Press

Soncino, *distributed by* Bloch Publishing Co

Mark Sonnenfeld, *member of* Marymark Press

Sono Nis Pres, *distributed by* Orca Book Publishers

Sono Nis Press, *distributed by* Heimburger House Publishing Co

Sopris West, *distributed by* Council for Exceptional Children

Sopris West Educational Services, *imprint of* Cambium Learning

Sorin Books, *imprint of* Ave Maria Press, *distributed by* Ave Maria Press

Sound Beginnings, *distributed by* Penton Overseas Inc

Sound Ideas, *imprint of* Simon & Schuster Audio

Sound Library Audiobooks, *imprint of* BBC Audiobooks America

Sound Seminars, *imprint of* Jeffrey Norton Publishers Inc

SoundForth Music, *division of* Bob Jones University Press

Soundprints, *division of* Trudy Corp, Trudy Corp, *distributor for* Edimat Libros sa, *distributed by* H B Fenn, INT Press (Australia & New Zealand)

Sounds of SterlingHouse, *imprint of* SterlingHouse Publisher Inc

Sourcebooks Casablanca, *imprint of* Sourcebooks Inc

Sourcebooks Hysteria, *imprint of* Sourcebooks Inc

Sourcebooks Landmark, *imprint of* Sourcebooks Inc

Sourcebooks MediaFusion, *imprint of* Sourcebooks Inc

SourceResource, *distributor for* MAR*CO Products Inc

South Bay Entertainment, *imprint of* Listen & Live Audio Inc

South Carolina Bar Association, *distributed by* University of South Carolina Press

South End Press, *affiliate of* Institute for Social & Cultural Change, Institute for Social & Cultural Change, *distributor for* Odonian Press (The Real Story Series)

South-Western, A Thomson Business, *division of* Thomson

South-Western Publishing, *distributor for* Course Technology

Southeastern Center for Contemporary Art (selected), *distributed by* The University of North Carolina Press

Southeastern Cooperative Wildlife Disease Study, *distributed by* American Association for Vocational Instructional Materials

Southern Book Service, *distributor for* Winner Enterprises

Southern Early Childhood Association, *distributed by* Gryphon House Inc

Southern Illinois University Press, *division of* Southern Illinois University, *distributor for* The Press at California State University, Fresno

Southern Lights, *division of* Crane Hill Publishers, *imprint of* Crane Hill Publishers

Southern Living Books, *imprint of* Oxmoor House Inc

Southern Media Systems Inc, *distributor for* Chronicle Guidance Publications Inc

Southern Methodist University, *distributed by* Texas A&M University Press

Southern Methodist University Press, *distributed by* Texas A&M University Press

Southern Voices, *imprint of* Haights Cross Communications Inc, Recorded Books LLC

Southfarm Press, Publisher, *division of* Haan Graphic Publishing Services Ltd

Southwestern, *imprint of* Wadsworth Publishing

Southwestern Studies, *imprint of* Texas Western Press

Space Publication, *distributor for* American Society for Photogrammetry & Remote Sensing

Sparkle Shapes, *imprint of* Playhouse Publishing

Sparklers, *imprint of* Haights Cross Communications Inc, Sundance Publishing

SPCK, *distributed by* Abingdon Press, The Pilgrim Press/United Church Press

SPCK (selected titles), *distributed by* Pickwick Publications

Special Education Series, *imprint of* Porter Sargent Publishers Inc

Special Products Division, *division of* Eagle Publishing Inc

Special Promotions, *division of* Bobley Harmann Corp

Specialized Software, *imprint of* Lotus Press

Specialty Press, *distributed by* Voyageur Press

Speck Press, *imprint of* Corvus Publishing Group

Spectra, *imprint of* Random House Inc

Spectrum, *distributor for* National Council of Teachers of Mathematics

The Speech Bin Inc, *distributed by* Rompa Ltd (UK)

Spellmount Publishers, *distributor for* Howell Press Inc, *distributed by* Casemate Publishers

Sphinx Press, *distributed by* International Universities Press Inc

Sphinx Press Inc, *subsidiary of* International Universities Press Inc

Sphinx Publishing, *division of* Sourcebooks Inc, Sourcebooks Inc, *imprint of* Sourcebooks Inc, *distributed by* Galt Press

SPIE Press, *imprint of* SPIE, International Society for Optical Engineering

Spink & Son Ltd, *distributed by* Sanford J Durst

Spinsters Ink, *division of* Spinsters Ink Publishing Co

SPIRAL Books, *division of* SPIRAL Communications Inc, SPIRAL Communications Inc

The Spiral Group, *division of* SPIRAL Books

Spire Books, *imprint of* Fleming H Revell

Spirit Mountain Press, *distributed by* University of Alaska Press

Sporting News, *distributed by* Andrews McMeel Publishing

The Sporting News Publishing Co, A Vulcan Sports Media Company, *distributed by* McGraw-Hill

Sports Athletics, *imprint of* Idyll Arbor Inc

Sportsman's Press, *distributed by* Safari Press

The Sportsman's Press, *distributed by* Trafalgar Square

Spotlight Books, *imprint of* Empire Publishing Service

Jack Spratt Choral Music, *imprint of* Empire Publishing Service

Spring Arbor, *distributor for* Brethren Press, College Press Publishing Co, Crystal Fountain Publications, Faith Library Publications, Gospel Publishing House, Oregon Catholic Press, Pentecostal Publishing House

Spring Arbor Distributors, *distributor for* Bob Jones University Press, New City Press, Presbyterian Publishing Corp

Spring Creek Press, *imprint of* Johnson Books

Spring Freshet Press, *distributed by* University of Wisconsin Press

Spring Publications, *distributed by* The Continuum International Publishing Group

Spring Wheat, *distributed by* Chelsea Green Publishing Co

Springer Veriag New York Inc, *subsidiary of* Birkhauser Boston

Springer Verlag, *distributor for* Current Medicine

Springer-Verlag, *distributor for* American Institute of Physics

Springer-Verlag GmbH & Co KG, *distributed by* Springer-Verlag New York Inc

Springer-Verlag New York Inc, *subsidiary of* Springer Science+Business Media GmbH & Co KG, Springer-Verlag GmbH & Co KG, *distributor for* Birkhauser Boston, Copernicus, Springer-Verlag GmbH & Co KG, TELOS

Springer Vienna, *distributed by* Princeton Architectural Press

Springhouse Editions, *subsidiary of* White Pine Press, *distributed by* White Pine Press

Sproutman Publications, *distributed by* Book Publishing Co

SPSS, *imprint of* Pearson Higher Education Division

Spyglass Books LLC, *distributed by* Biographical Publishing Co

SRA, *imprint of* McGraw-Hill Learning Group

SRA/McGraw-Hill, *imprint of* McGraw-Hill Education, *distributor for* Renaissance House

SRA/McGraw-Hill, a Division of McGraw-Hill Learning Group, *division of* McGraw-Hill Learning Group

Sri Aurobindo Ashram, *distributed by* Lotus Press

SSPC, *distributed by* NACE International

SSS Distributors, *distributor for* Bridge-Logos Publishers

ST Publications Book Division, *division of* ST Publications Inc, ST Publications Inc

Stacey Intl Ltd (London), *distributed by* International Book Centre Inc

Stacey International (UK), *distributed by* Interlink Publishing Group Inc

Stackpole, *distributor for* The Colonial Williamsburg Foundation

Stackpole Books, *distributor for* Aerial Perspective Publishing, Airlife Books, The Army War College Foundation Press, BMC Publications, Capitol Preservation Committee, Greenhill Books, Proctor Jones, Pulgas Ridge Press, Quiller Press Ltd, Rank & File, RKT Trade Publishing, Swan Hill

Stackpole Publishing, *distributor for* The Narrative Press

Stackpoole Books, *distributed by* Heimburger House Publishing Co

Standard & Poor's, *division of* The McGraw-Hill Companies Inc

Standard Educational Corp, *subsidiary of* The United Educators Inc, *distributed by* Brodart, The Frontier Press Co (selected titles)

Standard Publishing Co, *division of* Standex International, *distributor for* Focus on the Family

Standard Publishing Corp, *distributed by* Lexis-Nexis, Silverplume

Stanford University Press, *distributor for* The Woodrow Wilson Center Press

Stanton Books Numismatics International, *distributed by* Sanford J Durst

Star Bright Books, *distributor for* Happy Cat Books, Lothian Books

Star Festival, *distributed by* Enfield Publishing & Distribution Co

Star Licks Videos, *distributed by* Hal Leonard Corp

Star Publishing Co, *division of* Star Business Group Inc, Star Business Group Inc

Star Sounds, *distributed by* Lotus Press

Star Trek®, *imprint of* Pocket Books, Simon & Schuster Adult Publishing Group

Star Wars, *distributed by* Running Press Book Publishers

Starbooks, *imprint of* Starbooks Press

Starbooks Press, *affiliate of* Florida Literary Foundation

Starbound Publishing, *division of* Collectors Press Inc

Starlite Inc, *subsidiary of* Viva Ltd

Starrhill Press, *imprint of* River City Publishing, LLC

STARS, *distributor for* MAR*CO Products Inc

Starscape, *imprint of* Tom Doherty Associates, LLC

Starseed Press, *imprint of* H J Kramer Inc

State Experience!, *imprint of* Gallopade International Inc

State Facts & Factivities, *imprint of* Gallopade International Inc

State Net, *division of* California Journal Press

State Stuff, *imprint of* Gallopade International Inc

State University of New York Press, *distributor for* Rockefeller Institute Press

Statistical Research Inc, *distributed by* The University of Arizona Press

STD Distributors Pte Ltd, *distributor for* One Planet Publishing House

Steam Press, *distributed by* Gryphon House Inc

Steck-Vaughn, *division of* Steck-Vaughn Co, *imprint of* Harcourt Achieve, *distributed by* Sundance Publishing

Steeple Hill, *imprint of* Harlequin Enterprises Ltd

Steeple Hill Books, *imprint of* Harlequin Enterprises, *distributed by* Simon & Schuster Mass Merchandise Sales Co

Steeple Hill Love Inspired, *imprint of* Steeple Hill Books

Steeple Hill Women's Fiction, *imprint of* Steeple Hill Books

Steerforth Italia, *imprint of* Steerforth Press

Steerforth Press, *distributed by* Random House Sales & Marketing

Bernard Stein Music Co, *distributed by* Hal Leonard Corp

Steiner Books, *distributor for* Bell Pond Books, Chiron Publications, Clairview Books, Codhill Press, Findhorn Press, Floris Books, Hawthorn Press, Lantern Books, Swedenborg Foundation, Swedenborg Foundation Publishers/Chrysalis Books, Temple Lodge Publishing, *distributed by* Rudolf Steiner Press UK

Rudolf Steiner Press UK, *distributor for* Steiner Books

Stenhouse Publishers, *subsidiary of* Teacher's Publishing Group, Teachers Publishing Group, *distributor for* Pembroke Publishers

Sterling, *distributor for* Primedia Consumer Magazine & Internet Group, *distributed by* Phoenix Learning Resources

Sterling Audio Books, *imprint of* BBC Audiobooks America

Sterling/Balloon, *imprint of* Sterling Publishing Co Inc

Sterling/Chapelle, *imprint of* Sterling Publishing Co Inc

Sterling/Pinwheel, *imprint of* Sterling Publishing Co Inc

Sterling Publishers, *distributed by* American Quilter's Society

Sterling Publishing, *distributed by* Heimburger House Publishing Co

Sterling Publishing Co Inc, *distributor for* AAPPL, American Express (selected titles), AVA Publishing (selected titles), Batsford (selected titles), Blandford Press Ltd (selected titles), Brooklyn Botanic Garden, Brooklyn Botanic Garden (selected titles), Cassell (selected titles), Cassell Illustrated (selected titles), Chancellor Press (selected titles), Collins & Brown (selected titles), Conran (selected titles), Cookworks (selected titles), Davis (selected titles), Expert (selected titles), Galahad Books (selected books), Gollancz (selected titles), Guild of Mastercraftsman (selected titles), Hamlyn (selected titles), Kodak (selected titles), League of Hard of Hearing (selected titles), Sally Milner (selected titles), New Holland (selected titles), Orion (selected titles), Paper Tiger (selected titles), Phoenix Illustrated (selected titles), Phoenix Press (selected titles), PRC Publishing (selected titles), Promontory Press (selected titles), Rudra (selected titles), Seven Dials (selected titles), Silver Lining (selected titles), Silver Pixel Press, Sixth & Spring (selected titles), Studio Vista (selected titles), Sun Designs (selected titles), Vega (selected titles), Ward Lock (selected titles), Weidenfeld & Nicolson (selected titles), *distributed by* Silver Pixel Press

Sterling/Tamos, *imprint of* Sterling Publishing Co Inc

Sterling/Zambezi, *imprint of* Sterling Publishing Co Inc

SterlingHouse Publisher Inc, *division of* Cynto-Media Corp, *distributed by* Partners Publishers Group

Gareth Stevens, *distributed by* Perfection Learning Corp

Stewart, Tabori & Chang, *division of* La Martiniere Groupe, La Martiniere Groupe

Stimulus Books, *imprint of* Paulist Press

Stipes Publishing LLC, *distributed by* Ball Publishing

Stoddart, *distributed by* Sundance Publishing

Stoecklein Publishing, *distributed by* Graphic Arts Center Publishing Co

Stoeger Publishing Co, *subsidiary of* Stoeger Industries

Stone Bridge Press LLC, *distributed by* Consortium Book Sales & Distribution

Stonewall, *subsidiary of* BrickHouse Books Inc, *imprint of* BrickHouse Books Inc

Storey Books, *division of* Storey Communications Inc, *distributed by* Random House Inc, Workman Publishing Co Inc

Storey Kids, *imprint of* Storey Books

Storey Publishing, *distributed by* Workman Publishing Co Inc

Story Line Press, *distributor for* Kayak Press

Story Time Stories That Rhyme, *distributor for* Story Time Stories Without Rhyme, Tapestry Collage Lesson Plans

Story Time Stories Without Rhyme, *distributed by* Story Time Stories That Rhyme

Straight From The Heart Press, *distributed by* Dry Bones Press Inc

Stretch Think®, *imprint of* Thomas Geale Publications Inc

String Letter Press, *distributed by* Hal Leonard Corp

Strong Books, *imprint of* Book Marketing Works LLC

STS Service Technicians Society, *imprint of* SAE (Society of Automotive Engineers International)

Lyle Stuart, *imprint of* Kensington Publishing Corp

Stubs Guides, *distributed by* Hagstrom Map Co Inc

Stubs Magazine, *distributed by* American Map Corp

Studies in Ethnicity, *imprint of* Transaction Publishers

Studies in Popular Culture Series, *imprint of* University Press of Mississippi

Studies of Economic Culture, *imprint of* Transaction Publishers

Studio Mouse LLC, *subsidiary of* Soundprints

Studio Vista, *distributed by* Sterling Publishing Co Inc

Stylus Publishing LLC, *distributor for* Anthem Press, The Commonwealth Secretariat, Cork University Press, Earthscan, Hotei Publishing, IDRC, ITDG Publishing, James & James (Sci-

ence) Ltd, Karnac Books, Kogan Page Ltd, Nordic Africa Institute, Oxfam Publishing, Trentham Books Ltd, Women, Law & Development International (WLDI)

Success, *imprint of* Simon & Schuster Audio

Success Advertising, *division of* Success Advertising & Publishing

Success Advertising & Publishing, *division of* The Success Group, The Success Group

Suffolk Records Society, *imprint of* Boydell & Brewer Inc

Sufi Books, *subsidiary of* Pir Publications Inc

Sufi Publishing, *imprint of* Hunter House Publishers

Sherwood Sugden & Co, *distributor for* The Monist (An International Philosophical Quarterly), *distributed by* Open Court Publishing Co

Summit Beacon, *distributor for* Woodland Publishing Inc

Summit Books, *imprint of* Perfection Learning Corp

Summit Publications, *division of* Ye Olde Genealogie Shoppe

Summit University Press, *distributed by* New Leaf

Summy-Birchard Inc, *division of* Warner/Chappell Inc, *distributor for* Carisch SPA, IMP, *distributed by* Warner Bros Publications Inc, Warner Bros Publications

Sun & Moon Classics, *imprint of* Sun & Moon Press

Sun & Moon Press, *affiliate of* Contemporary Arts Educational Project Inc, Contemporary Arts Educational Project Inc

Sun Books, *division of* Sun Books - Sun Publishing, *imprint of* Sun Books - Sun Publishing, *distributed by* Sun Books - Sun Publishing

Sun Books - Sun Publishing, *division of* The Sun Companies, *distributor for* Far West Publishing Co, Sun Books

Sun Cards, *division of* Sun Books - Sun Publishing

Sun Designs, *distributed by* Sterling Publishing Co Inc

Sun Tree, *distributed by* Paul & Company

Sunbelt, *distributor for* Naturegraph Publishers Inc, The RGU Group

Sunbelt Publications Inc, *distributor for* Dawsons Book Shop, FineEdge.com

Sunburst Books, *imprint of* Farrar, Straus & Giroux, LLC

Sunburst Paperbacks, *imprint of* Farrar, Straus & Giroux Books for Young Readers

SunCreek Books, *imprint of* Ave Maria Press, *distributed by* Ave Maria Press

Sundance, *imprint of* Haights Cross Communications Inc

Sundance Phonics Readers, *imprint of* Haights Cross Communications Inc, Sundance Publishing

Sundance Publishers & Distributors, *distributor for* Zephyr Press Catalog

Sundance Publishing, *division of* Haights Cross Communications Inc, *subsidiary of* Haights Cross Communications Inc, *distributor for* Aladdin Books, Associated Publisher's Group, Avon, Ballantine Books, Bantam, Barron's Educational Publishers, Berkley, Boyds Mill Press, Candlewick Press, Charles McCann, Charlesbridge Publishing, Children's Book Press, Children's Press, Chronicle Books, Crown Publishers, Dutton, Farrar Straus & Giroux, Fawcett Books, Firefly Ltd, Folger, Groundwood, Harcourt Brace & Co, HarperCollins, Henry Holt, Holiday House, Houghton Mifflin Co, Hyperion, Kane Miller, Lee & Low Books, Little Brown & Co, Merriam-Webster, Millbrook Press, Morrow, New American Library, New Directions, Newmarket Press, North South Books, Orca Book Publishers, Orchard Books, Owl Books, Oxford University Press, Peachtree Publishers, Penguin Books, Persea, Pocket Books, Preservation Press, Putnam Publishing Co, Rand McNally, Random House, Scholastic Books, Secret Passage Press, Silver Press, Simon & Schuster, Steck-Vaughn, Stoddart, TOR Books, Troll Books, University of Nebraska, Usborne, Walker Publishers, Warner Paperback Library, Washington Square Press

Sundial Books, *imprint of* Sunstone Press

Sundial Editions, *imprint of* Bobley Harmann Corp

SunLit Fluency Readers, *imprint of* Haights Cross Communications Inc, Sundance Publishing

Sunlit Hills Press, *distributed by* Ocean Tree Books

Sunny Books, *imprint of* JB Communications Inc

Sunrise Library, *imprint of* Theosophical University Press

Sunset Books/Sunset Publishing Corp, *distributed by* Leisure Arts Inc

Sunshine, *imprint of* Modern Publishing

Sunstone Foundation, *distributed by* Signature Books Publishing LLC

Sunstone Press, *subsidiary of* Sunstone Corp, Sunstone Corp

SUNY Albany, *distributed by* University of Texas Press

Supa Doopers, *imprint of* Haights Cross Communications Inc, Sundance Publishing

Supa Doopers Plus, *imprint of* Haights Cross Communications Inc, Sundance Publishing

Superbrands Ltd, *distributed by* Antique Collectors Club Ltd

Sure Fire Press, *imprint of* Holmes Publishing Group

Surrey Books, *distributed by* Publishers Group West (contact customer service)

Susquehanna University Press, *affiliate of* Associated University Presses, *distributed by* Associated University Presses

Sussex, *distributed by* Chelsea Green Publishing Co

Sustainability Press, *distributed by* Chelsea Green Publishing Co

Suzuki, *distributed by* Warner Bros Publications Inc

Suzuki Method International, *division of* Summy-Birchard Inc

Swallow Press, *imprint of* Ohio University Press, *distributed by* Ohio University Press

Swallow's Tale Press, *subsidiary of* Livingston Press, *distributed by* Livingston Press

Swan Books, *division of* Learning Links Inc

Swan Hill, *distributed by* Stackpole Books

Swan Isle Press, *distributed by* University of Chicago Press

Swedenborg Association, *division of* The Lord's New Church, *distributed by* Swedenborg Foundation

Swedenborg Foundation, *distributor for* Swedenborg Association, *distributed by* Steiner Books

Swedenborg Foundation Publishers/Chrysalis Books, *distributor for* J Appleseed & Co, Swedenborg Scientific Assoc, Swedenborg Society, *distributed by* Steiner Books

Swedenborg Scientific Assoc, *distributed by* Swedenborg Foundation Publishers/Chrysalis Books

Swedenborg Society, *distributed by* Swedenborg Foundation Publishers/Chrysalis Books

Swedish Corrosion Institute, *distributed by* NACE International

Sweet & Maxwell, *distributed by* William S Hein & Co Inc

Sweetgrass Fiction, *imprint of* Sweetgrass Press LLC

Sweetgrass Press LLC, *distributor for* Greatdream Publications

Swerve Editions, *imprint of* Zone Books

Swets & Zeitlinger, *distributor for* Investor Responsibility Research Center

Swets & Zeitlinger Publishers, *distributed by* Ashgate Publishing Co

Swets Subscription Serv, *distributor for* Investor Responsibility Research Center

Sword & Sorcery, *imprint of* White Wolf Publishing Inc

Sybex Inc, *distributed by* EMC/Paradigm Publishing

Sycamore Island Books, *imprint of* Paladin Press

Sygnet Publications, *distributed by* Orca Book Publishers

Symbol of Excellence Publishers Inc, *subsidiary of* Primedia Consumer Magazine & Internet Group

Symposium Publishing, *imprint of* Blue Dolphin Publishing Inc

Synapse Information Resources Inc, *distributor for* Ashgate Publishing Co

SynergEbooks, *distributed by* Amazon.com, Barnes & Noble, Bookbooters, CyberRead, Eloka.com, Fictionwise, Mobipocket, W H Smith UK

Synergy, *imprint of* Bridge-Logos Publishers

Syracuse University Lightworks, *distributed by* Syracuse University Press

Syracuse University Press, *distributor for* American University of Beirut, Colgate University Press, Moshe Dayan Center for Middle Eastern & African Studies, National Library of Ireland, Munson Williams Proctor Institute, St Lawrence University, Syracuse University Lightworks, *distributed by* Gryphon House Inc, Heimburger House Publishing Co

T & AD Poyser, *imprint of* Academic Press

T & T Clark International, *division of* Continuum

Tab Books, *distributor for* National Association of Broadcasters (NAB)

Tabard Press, *imprint of* William S Konecky Associates Inc

Tabernacle Publishing, *division of* Hope Publishing Co

Table-Talk Press, *imprint of* Times Change Press

Table Top Series, *imprint of* Incentive Publications Inc

Tafarinri Publishings, *imprint of* Cornerstone Productions Inc

Tafnews Press, *division of* Track & Field News

The Taft Group, *imprint of* Thomson Gale

Tai Chi Foundation, *distributed by* Tuttle Publishing

Tale Blazers, *imprint of* Perfection Learning Corp

Nan A Talese, *imprint of* Random House Inc

Nan A Talese Books, *imprint of* Doubleday Broadway Publishing Group

Truman Talley Books, *imprint of* St Martin's Press LLC

Tamar Books, *imprint of* Mesorah Publications Ltd

Tamesis, *imprint of* Boydell & Brewer Inc

Tampco, *imprint of* Scriptural Research Center

Tango 2, *imprint of* Genesis Press Inc

Tanner Trust, *distributed by* Signature Books Publishing LLC

Tapestry Collage Lesson Plans, *distributed by* Story Time Stories That Rhyme

Tapestry Press, *imprint of* Tapestry Press Ltd

Tapestry Press Ltd, *distributed by* Arcadia Enterprises Inc

Taplinger Publishing Co Inc, *distributed by* Parkwest Publications Inc

TAPPI (Technical Association of the Pulp & Paper Industry), *distributor for* Jelmar Publishing Co Inc, *distributed by* Jelmar Publishing Co Inc

Tara Publications, *distributed by* Hal Leonard Corp

Tarascon Publishing, *distributed by* J A Majors, Matthews Medical, Rittenhouse

Tarboro Books, *imprint of* Wyrick & Co

Jeremy P Tarcher, *imprint of* Penguin Group (USA) Inc, Penguin Group (USA) Inc, The Putnam Publishing Group

Tarcher/Penguin, *imprint of* The Putnam Publishing Group

Targum Press, *distributed by* Philipp Feldheim Inc

Taschen, *imprint of* Taschen America

Taschen GMBH, *subsidiary of* Taschen America

Tastes Newsletter, *subsidiary of* Gault Millau Inc/ Gayot Publications

Tata Institute of Fundamental Research, *distributed by* American Mathematical Society

Tata/McGraw-Hill, *imprint of* McGraw-Hill Education

Tattersall Press, *distributed by* Winters Publishing

The Taunton Press Inc, *distributed by* Publishers Group West

Taunton Sterling Dover, *distributed by* Fox Chapel Publishing Co Inc

I B Tauris, *distributed by* St Martin's Press LLC

Taurus, *imprint of* Santillana USA Publishing Co Inc

Taylor & Francis, *distributed by* American Society for Photogrammetry & Remote Sensing

Taylor & Francis Asia Pacific, *distributor for* Institute for International Economics

Taylor & Francis Editorial, Production & Manufacturing Division, *division of* Taylor & Francis Inc

Taylor & Francis Inc, *subsidiary of* Taylor & Francis Ltd, *distributor for* Brunner/Routledge, Falmer Press, Psychology Press

Teach Me Tapes Inc, *distributed by* Follett, Penton Overseas Inc

Teacher Discovery, *distributor for* Cottonwood Press Inc

Teacher Ideas Press, *division of* Greenwood Publishing Group, Libraries Unlimited

Teachers College Press, *affiliate of* Teachers College, Columbia University

Teacher's Discovery, *division of* American Eagle, *distributor for* National Textbook Co

Teachers Gear, *distributor for* MAR*CO Products Inc

Teachers License Examination Series, *imprint of* National Learning Corp

Teachers of English to Speakers of Other Languages Inc (TESOL), *distributed by* Alta Book Center, Delta Systems Inc, New Readers Press, Saddleback Educational

Teaching Resources, *division of* Scholastic Education

Teaching Strategies, *distributor for* Gryphon House, *distributed by* Gryphon House Inc

Tech Directions, *imprint of* Prakken Publications Inc

Tech Directions Books & Media, *imprint of* Prakken Publications Inc

Technical Association of the Pulp & Paper Industry (TAPPI), *distributed by* American Technical Publishers

Technology, *division of* Scholastic Education

Technomic, *distributed by* American Water Works Association

Katherine Tegen Books, *imprint of* HarperCollins Children's Books Group

Thomas Telford (UK), *distributed by* American Society of Civil Engineers (ASCE)

TELOS, *distributed by* Springer-Verlag New York Inc

TELOS (The Electronic Library of Science), *imprint of* Springer-Verlag New York Inc

Telshare Publishing, *distributed by* Gryphon House Inc

Temenos Press, *distributed by* Paul & Company

Ellen Temple Publishing, *distributed by* Eakin Press

Temple Lodge Publishing, *distributed by* Steiner Books

Temple University Press, *division of* Temple University-of the Commonwealth System of Higher Education, *distributor for* Asian American Writers Workshop, *distributed by* The Alexander Graham Bell Association for the Deaf & Hard of Hearing

Temporal Mechanical Press, *division of* Enos Mills Cabin Museum & Gallery

Tempus Publishing, *distributed by* Trafalgar Square

Ten Pound Island Books, *distributed by* Mystic Seaport

Ten Speed Press, *distributor for* Audio Literature, Collectors Press Inc, Lanier Publishing International, Mandala Publishing

Teora, *imprint of* Teora USA LLC

Terrace Books, *imprint of* University of Wisconsin Press

Terrapin Greetings, *imprint of* Down The Shore Publishing Corp

Territory Titles, *distributor for* Dine College Press

Tess Press, *imprint of* Black Dog & Leventhal Publishers Inc

Test Your Knowledge Books, *imprint of* National Learning Corp

Testament, *imprint of* Random House Value Publishing

Testament Books, *imprint of* Random House Inc

Testify Books, *distributed by* powerHouse Books

Teton New Media, *distributor for* Barnes & Noble, Borders, LifeLearn, *distributed by* Blackwells, LifeLearn, Logan Brothers, Rittenhouse, Yankee

Tetra Press, *division of* Pfizer Inc, *distributed by* Voyageur Press

Texas A&M University Press, *division of* Texas A&M University, Texas A&M Unversity, *distributor for* Baylor University Press, McWhiney Foundation Press, Sam Houston State University, Southern Methodist University, Southern Methodist University Press, Texas Almanac/Dallas Morning News, Texas Christian University Press, Texas Review Press, Texas State Historical Association, University of North Texas Press

Texas Almanac/Dallas Morning News, *distributed by* Texas A&M University Press

Texas Christian University Press, *distributed by* Texas A&M University Press, Texas A&M University Press

Texas Parks & Wildlife Department, *distributed by* University of Texas Press

University of Texas Press, *division of* University of Texas, *distributor for* Bat Conservation International, Institute for Mesoamerican Studies, Menil Foundation, Rothko Chapel, San Antonio Museum of Art, SUNY Albany, Texas Parks & Wildlife Department, Texas Western Press

Texas Review Press, *distributed by* Texas A&M University Press

Texas State Historical Association, *affiliate of* Center for Studies in Texas History at the University of Texas at Austin, Center for Studies in Texas History at the Unversity of Texas at Austin, *distributed by* Texas A&M University Press, Texas A&M University Press

Texas Tech University Press, *distributor for* ICASALS

Texas Technical University Press, *distributed by* Barbed Wire Publishing

Texas Western Press, *affiliate of* University of Texas at El Paso, University of Texas, El Paso, *distributed by* Barbed Wire Publishing, University of Texas Press

Texere, *distributed by* W W Norton & Co Inc, Penguin-Technology Group, A Division of Pearson Canada

Textbooks for Christian Schools, *imprint of* Bob Jones University Press

TFH Publications Inc, *affiliate of* Central Garden & Pet

Thames & Hudson, *distributor for* Art Institute of Chicago, National Gallery of Art, Serindia Publications, *distributed by* W W Norton & Co Inc, W W Norton & Company Inc

Thames & Hudson (UK), *distributor for* Art Institute of Chicago

That Patchwork Place, *distributed by* Martingale & Co

That the World May Know, *imprint of* Focus on the Family

That VanDam Book, *imprint of* VanDam Inc

Theatre Arts Books, *imprint of* Routledge

Theatre Communications Group Inc, *distributor for* Absolute Classics, Aurora Metro Publications, Nick Hern Books, Oberon Books, Padua Playwrights Press, PAJ Publications, Playwrights Canada Press, Martin E Segal Theatre Center Publications, Ubu Repertory Theatre Publications

Theophilis, *imprint of* Transcontinental Music Publications

Theosophical Publishing House/Quest Books, *division of* The Theosophical Society in America

Theosophical University Press, *affiliate of* Theosophical Society (Pasadena)

Theta Books, *imprint of* Bridge Publications Inc

Theta Foundation of Bucharest, *distributed by* American Mathematical Society

Theta Reports, *subsidiary of* P J B Publications Ltd, PJB Publications Ltd

Theytus Books, *distributed by* Orca Book Publishers

Thieme, *distributor for* Current Medicine

Thieme New York, *subsidiary of* Georg Thieme Verlag, Georg Thieme Verlag KG

Thing Quest®, *imprint of* Thomas Geale Publications Inc

Thinkers' Press, *distributor for* Chess Enterprises

Thinkers' Press Inc, *distributor for* Chess Enterprises, Chess Stars, Hypermodern Press, SIEditrice

Thinking Like a Scientist, *imprint of* Haights Cross Communications Inc, Newbridge Educational Publishing

Thinking Publications, *division of* McKinley Co Inc, McKinley Co Inc, *distributor for* A D D Warehouse

Third Millenium Publishing, *distributed by* Antique Collectors Club Ltd

Third World Press, *distributed by* Frontline International, Partners Book Distributing, Red Sea Press

Thirsty, *imprint of* Tyndale House Publishers Inc

Janet Thoma Books (SC), *distributed by* Thomas Nelson Inc

Thomas Nelson Inc, *distributor for* Discovery House, Focus on the Family, Oliver-Nelson (Atlanta, GA), Janet Thoma Books (SC), *distributed by* Winston-Derek

William A Thomas Braille Bookstore, *division of* Braille International Inc

Thomasson Grant, *distributed by* American Society for Photogrammetry & Remote Sensing

Thompson/Delmar Learning, *distributor for* Illuminating Engineering Society of North America

Thomson Course Technology, *subsidiary of* Thomson Learning Inc

Thomson Custom Publishing, *subsidiary of* Thomson Learning Inc

Thomson Delmar Learning, *division of* The Thomson Corp, *subsidiary of* Thomson Learning Inc, *distributor for* Aspire, Autodata, BOCA/ICC, CDX Global, Chilton, Haynes, Holt Enterprises, LearningExpress, Meredith, NFPA, Prompt, Scott Jones Publishing, Seloc, Truckload Carrier Assoc, Video Active Productions

Thomson Education Direct, *subsidiary of* Thomson Learning Inc

Thomson Financial Publishing, *subsidiary of* The Thomson Corp, Thomson Corporation

Thomson Gale, *unit of* The Thomson Corp, *subsidiary of* Thomson Learning Inc

Thomson Heinle, *subsidiary of* Thomson Learning Inc

Thomson Higher Education, *subsidiary of* Thomson Learning Inc

Thomson Learning, *distributor for* Wadsworth Publishing, *distributed by* American Marketing Association

Thomson Learning Asia, *subsidiary of* Thomson Learning Inc

Thomson Learning Australia, *subsidiary of* Thomson Learning Inc

Thomson Learning EMEA, *subsidiary of* Thomson Learning Inc

Thomson Learning Iberoamerica, *subsidiary of* Thomson Learning Inc

Thomson Learning Inc, *division of* The Thomson Corp, Thomson Corporation

Thomson Learning International Group, *distributor for* Wadsworth Publishing

Thomson Nelson in Canada, *subsidiary of* Thomson Learning Inc

Thomson NETg, *subsidiary of* Thomson Learning Inc

Thomson Paraninfo, *subsidiary of* Thomson Learning Inc

Thomson Peterson's, *division of* Thomson Learning Inc, Thomson Learning Japan, *subsidiary of* Thomson Learning Inc

Thomson Prometric, *subsidiary of* Thomson Learning Inc

Thomson Publications, *distributed by* Ball Publishing

Thomson Publishing, *distributed by* SkillPath Publications

Thomson South-Western, *subsidiary of* Thomson Learning Inc

Thomson Wadsworth, *subsidiary of* Thomson Learning Inc

Thorndike Press, *imprint of* Thomson Gale, *distributor for* Harlequin, HarperCollins, Mills & Boone, Simon & Schuster, Warner

Thorndike (Young Adult), *distributed by* Lucent Books Inc

Stanley Thornes, *distributed by* Trans-Atlantic Publications Inc

ThorsonsElement US, *division of* HarperCollins UK, *subsidiary of* ThorsonElement UK, *distributed by* HarperCollins

Three Rivers Press, *imprint of* Crown Publishing Group, Random House Inc

ThreeForks, *imprint of* The Globe Pequot Press

Thriller, *imprint of* Dorchester Publishing Co Inc

Thrillogy, *imprint of* Haights Cross Communications Inc, Sundance Publishing

Through the Bible Publishers, *subsidiary of* Treasure Learning Systems

Thunder Bay Press, *imprint of* Advantage Publishers Group, *distributed by* Heimburger House Publishing Co

Thunder's Mouth Press, *imprint of* Avalon Publishing Group Inc, Avalon Publishing Group - New York

Tia Chucha Press, *distributed by* Northwestern University Press

Tiare Publications, *imprint of* Tiare Publications

Tidewater Publishers, *imprint of* Cornell Maritime Press Inc, *distributor for* Chesapeake Bay Maritime Museum, Literary House Press, Maryland Historical Trust Press, Maryland Sea Grant Program, Maryland State Archives Publications

Tiger Books, *imprint of* Kidsbooks Inc

Tilbury House Publishers, *subsidiary of* Harpswell Press Inc

Timber Press, *imprint of* Timber Press Inc

Timber Press Inc, *distributed by* Ball Publishing

Timerberline Productions, *imprint of* Crumb Elbow Publishing

Timberwolf Press (TWP), *distributor for* Writer's AudioShop

Time Being Books, *imprint of* Time Being Press, *distributed by* Amazon.com, BarnesandNoble.com

Time Inc Home Entertainment, *distributed by* Time Warner Book Group

Time Warner Audio Books, *subsidiary of* Time Warner Book Group, *imprint of* Time Warner Book Group

Time Warner Book Group, *distributor for* Arcade Publishing, Arcade Publishing Inc, DC Comics, Disney Publishing Worldwide, Harry N Abrams, Inc, Hyperion, Kensington Book Co (Intl only), Microsoft Learning, Phaidon Press, Time Inc Home Entertainment

Time Warner Books UK, *distributed by* Trafalgar Square

Time Warner Publishing, *distributor for* Disney Press

Time Warner Trade Publishing, *distributor for* DC Comics

Timeless Love, *imprint of* Oak Tree Publishing

Times Books, *imprint of* Henry Holt and Company, LLC, Random House Inc

TIMS (Textbooks in Mathematical Sciences), *imprint of* Springer-Verlag New York Inc

Tindal Street Press, *distributed by* Dufour Editions Inc

TMC/Internet Telephony, *distributor for* Althos Publishing

TMS (selected titles), *distributed by* Metal Powder Industries Federation

To the Point Press, *distributed by* Gem Guides Book Co

Toad Hall Inc, *distributor for* Eye Scry Publications, Puppy Paws Press, St James Publishing

Toad Hall Press, *imprint of* Toad Hall Inc

Toccata Press, *distributed by* Paul & Company

Todtri, *imprint of* TODTRI Book Publishers

Tommy Nelson, *division of* Thomas Nelson Inc, *distributor for* Focus on the Family

Top of the Mountain Publishing, *division of* Powell Productions, *distributed by* Ingram Book Co, New Leaf Distributing Co, Walden Books

Top Ten Publishing, *distributed by* Howell Press Inc

Top That! Publishing (Canada only), *distributed by* Mint Publishers Group

Topaz, *imprint of* NAL, Penguin Group (USA) Inc

Topic Series, *imprint of* Oakstone Medical Publishing

Topics in World History, *imprint of* Markus Wiener Publishers Inc

Tor, *imprint of* Tom Doherty Associates, LLC

Tor Books, *distributed by* St Martin's Press LLC, Sundance Publishing

Tor Teen, *imprint of* Tom Doherty Associates, LLC

Torah Aura Productions, *distributor for* Free Spirit (selected titles)

Torah Umesorah Publications, *division of* Torah Umesorah-National Society for Hebrew Day Schools, Torah Umesorah-National Society for Hebrew Day Schools

ToryCorner Editions, *imprint of* Quincannon Publishing Group

Tot Shots, *imprint of* Modern Publishing

Totline Publications, *imprint of* American Society for Quality, *affiliate of* Frank Schaffer Publications, *distributed by* Frank Schaffer Publications

Toucan Tales, *imprint of* Rayve Productions Inc

Touchstone, *imprint of* Fireside & Touchstone, Simon & Schuster Adult Publishing Group

Tourism Dynamic, *imprint of* Cognizant Communication Corp

TowleHouse Publishing, *distributed by* National Book Network

Trade Book Publishing, *division of* Slack Incorporated

Traders Press Inc, *distributor for* McGraw-Hill, Penguin-Putnam, John Wiley & Sons Inc

Tradery House, *imprint of* Wimmer Cookbooks

Tradigital (Germany), *distributed by* Fons Vitae

Tradition Books, *imprint of* The Child's World Inc, *distributed by* The Child's World Inc

Trafalgar Square, *distributor for* AA Publishing, The Akadine Press, Aurum Press, Duncan Baird, BBC Books, John Blake, Bloomsbury UK, Carroll & Brown, Kyle Cathie, Cico Books, Compass Equestrian, The Crowood Press, Andre Deutsch Ltd, DLM-Giles de la Mare, Edition Olms, Egmont, Evans Brothers Ltd, Granta UK, Robert Hale/J A Allen, HarperCollins UK, Haus Publishing, Hesperus Press, Hodder-Headline Ltd, Lion Publishing, Little Books, Macmillan UK, Mainstream Publishing, Metro Publications, John Murray Ltd, Oldcastle Books, Orion Publishing, Pallas Athene, Pavilion Books Ltd, Prion, Profile Books, Random House UK, Reynolds & Hearn, Scriptum Editions, Short Books, Sinclair-Stevenson, The Sportsman's Press, Tempus Publishing, Time Warner Books UK, Transworld Publishers, The Women's Press

Trailblazer Publications, *distributed by* The Globe Pequot Press

Trails Books, *division of* Trails Media Group Inc

Trails Books Guide, *imprint of* Trails Books

Trails Illustrated, Division of National Geographic Maps, *division of* National Geographic Ventures, *distributor for* National Geographic Maps, *distributed by* Bright Horizons, Canyonlands Publications, Many Feathers Books & Maps, Map Link, Peregrine Outfitters

Trails West Publishing, *distributed by* Cinco Puntos Press

Oswald Train, *distributed by* Donald M Grant Publisher Inc

Training Resource Network Inc (T R N), *distributor for* Attainment, *distributed by* Job Quest, The New Careers Center

Trakker Maps Inc, *division of* Langenscheidt Publishers Inc, *subsidiary of* American Map Corp, *distributor for* Alexandria Drafting Co, Arrow Maps Inc, Creative Sales Corp, Hagstrom Map Co, Langenscheidt Publishers Inc, *distributed by* Hagstrom Map Co Inc

Trans-Atlantic Publications Inc, *distributor for* Book Guild, Financial Times Publishing, Longman, Pan MacMillan, Nexus Special Interests, Stanley Thornes

Trans Tech Publications, *division of* Enfield Publishers

Trans Tech Publishing, *distributed by* Enfield Publishing & Distribution Co

Transaction Distribution Services, *division of* Transaction Publishers

Transaction/ISIS Large Print, *division of* Transaction Publishers

Transaction Large Print, *imprint of* Transaction Publishers

Transaction Periodicals Consortium, *division of* Transaction Publishers

Transaction Publishers, *division of* Transaction Periodicals Consortium, *distributor for* Aksant Academic Publishers (The Netherlands), Haan Publishing, IKO (International Communication Organization) (Germany), IWGIA (International Workgroup for Indigenous Affairs) (Denmark), Lit Verlag (Germany), Mets & Schilt (The Netherlands), Noidic Africa Institute (Sweden), RAND Corporation (United States), Shama Books (Ethiopia), Social Philosophy & Policy Center-Bowling Green University (United States), Transcript Verlag (Germany), University of California Institute on Global Conflict & Cooperation, Witwatersrand University Press (South Africa)

Transaction Publishers (UK), *subsidiary of* Transaction Publishers

Transactions, *imprint of* American Philosophical Society

Transcontinental Music, *distributed by* Hal Leonard Corp

Transcontinental Music Publications, *division of* Union of American Hebrew Congregations

Transcript Verlag, *distributed by* Transaction Publishers

Transit Cooperative Research Program, *imprint of* Transportation Research Board

Transnational Publishers Inc, *distributor for* Intersentia

Transporation Research Information Service, *imprint of* Transportation Research Board

Transportation Data Management (TDM), *division of* Rand McNally

Transportation Research Board, *division of* National Academies, National Academy of Sciences/National Research Council

TransQuest Publishers Pte Ltd, *distributor for* Manning Publications Co

Transworld Publishers, *distributed by* Trafalgar Square

Travel & Entertainment, *division of* Bobley Harmann Corp

Travel Memories Press, *imprint of* R J Berg/Destinations Press Ltd

Travel Publishing Ltd, *distributed by* Casemate Publishers

Travelers Companion, *imprint of* The Globe Pequot Press

Travelers' Tales Guides, *imprint of* Travelers' Tales Inc

Treacle Press, *imprint of* McPherson & Co

Treasure Chest, *distributed by* Gem Guides Book Co

Treasure Chest Books, *distributor for* Naturegraph Publishers Inc, Ocean Tree Books

Treasure House, *imprint of* Destiny Image

tree frog publications, *imprint of* rada press inc

Trees Company, *distributed by* Gem Guides Book Co

Trends, *distributed by* Chess Digest Inc

Trentham Books Ltd, *distributed by* Stylus Publishing LLC

Tres Duendes, *imprint of* Munchweiler Press

Triad Publishing Co, *imprint of* Triad Communications, Triad Communications Ltd

Tricycle Press, *imprint of* Ten Speed Press

Trident Press International, *subsidiary of* Trident Promotional Corp

The Trilateral Commission, *distributed by* The Brookings Institution Press

Trillium Press, *distributed by* Royal Fireworks Press

Trillium Productions, *imprint of* Crumb Elbow Publishing

Trinity University Press, *unit of* Trinity University, *distributed by* Bilingual Press/Editorial Bilingue

Triple Play, *imprint of* Haights Cross Communications Inc, Sundance Publishing

TriQuarterly Books, *imprint of* Northwestern University Press

Triumph Learning, *subsidiary of* Haights Cross Communications Inc, *imprint of* Haights Cross Communications Inc

Triviagrams, *imprint of* Modern Publishing

Troitsa Books, *imprint of* Nova Science Publishers Inc

Troll Books, *distributed by* Sundance Publishing

Troubador Press, *imprint of* Price Stern Sloan

Truckload Carrier Assoc, *distributed by* Thomson Delmar Learning

True Agency, *distributed by* powerHouse Books

Truett Software Development, *distributed by* Ball Publishing

Truman State University Press, *unit of* Truman State University

Trust for Public Land, *distributed by* Chelsea Green Publishing Co

Truth Center, *imprint of* Scriptural Research Center, *distributed by* Scriptural Research Center

TSG Publishing Foundation Inc, *distributed by* Amazon.com, BarnesandNoble.com, Distribution Orion, New Leaf Distributors

Tuckwell Press Ltd, *distributed by* Paul & Company

Tufa Productions, *imprint of* Volcano Press Inc

Tufts University Press, *imprint of* University Press of New England

Tuman Publishing, *imprint of* Triumph Learning

Tumbleweed Series, *imprint of* Mountain Press Publishing Co

Tundra Books of Northern New York, *distributed by* Random House Inc

Turab (Jordan), *distributed by* Fons Vitae

Turman Publishing, *imprint of* Haights Cross Communications Inc

Turnaround (London), *distributor for* Rising Tide Press

Turtle Books, *imprint of* Turtle Books Inc

Turtle Media, *imprint of* Turtle Books Inc

Turtle Point, *imprint of* Turtle Point Press

Turtle Point Press, *distributor for* Books & Co, Helen Marx, *distributed by* DAP Distributed Art Publishers

Tusk Paperbacks, *imprint of* The Overlook Press

Charles E Tuttle Co Inc, *distributor for* Journey Editions

Tuttle Publishing, *member of* Periplus Publishing Group, *imprint of* Tuttle Publishing, *distributor for* Equinox Publishing Pte Ltd, Healing Tao Books, Kosei Publishing Co, Kotan Publishing Inc, Milet Publishing Ltd, Paperweight Press, Periplus Editions, Shufunotomo Co, Tai Chi Foundation, Zen Studies Society Press

TV Books, *distributed by* HarperCollins Publishers

Mark Twain Media, *distributed by* Carson-Dellosa Publishing Co Inc

Twayne Publishers, *unit of* Macmillan Library Reference USA, *imprint of* Thomson Gale

Twenty-First Century Books, *division of* The Millbrook Press Inc

Twenty-First Century King James Bible Publishers, *division of* Deuel Enterprises, Duel Enterprises

21st Century Publications, *distributed by* Hal Leonard Corp

Twenty-Third Publications, *division of* Bayard Inc, Bayard USA, *distributor for* Novalis (Canada), *distributed by* Columba (UK), John Garrett (Australia), Novalis (Canada)

Twilight Times Books, *distributed by* eBookHome.com, eBooksonthe.net, The Writers' Collective

Twilight Visions, *imprint of* Twilight Times Books

Twin Stars Unlimited, *distributed by* The Writers' Collective

Twin Texts™, *imprint of* Haights Cross Communications Inc

Twin Texts®, *imprint of* Sundance Publishing

Two Lane Press, *imprint of* Pig Out Publications Inc

Two Wolf Press, *imprint of* White Wolf Publishing Inc

TwoDot®, *imprint of* The Globe Pequot Press

Tycooly Publishing USA, *division of* Weidner & Sons Publishing, *imprint of* Weidner & Sons Publishing, *distributed by* Weidner & Sons Publishing

Tyee Press, *imprint of* Crumb Elbow Publishing

Tyndale House Publishers, *distributor for* Focus on the Family, Printlink Publishers Inc

Type & Archetype Press, *imprint of* Type & Temperament Inc

Typophiles, *distributed by* Oak Knoll Press

U X L, *imprint of* Thomson Gale

UA Museum, *distributed by* University of Alaska Press

UBC Press (Canada), *distributor for* Washington State University Press

UBC Press, Canada, *distributor for* Michigan State University Press (MSU Press)

Ubu Repertory Theatre Publications, *distributed by* Theatre Communications Group Inc

UCLA Fowler Museum of Cultural History, *distributed by* University of Washington Press

Ugly Duckling Presse, *distributor for* United Artists

UglyTown, *distributed by* Words Distributing Co

ULI, *imprint of* Urban Land Institute

The Ultra Violet Library, *imprint of* Circlet Press Inc

Ulysses Press, *distributed by* Publishers Group West

Umbrage Editions, *distributed by* powerHouse Books

UMICOM Education, *distributor for* MAR*CO Products Inc

Unarius Academy of Science Publications, *division of* Unarius Educational Foundation, *imprint of* Unarius Academy of Science Publications

Unarius Video Productions, *division of* Unarius Academy of Science Publications

UNCITRAL, *imprint of* United Nations Publications, *distributed by* United Nations Publications

Undergraduate Program Field Test Series, *imprint of* National Learning Corp

Understanding Health & Sickness Series, *imprint of* University Press of Mississippi

UNDP, *imprint of* United Nations Publications, *distributed by* United Nations Publications

UNEP, *imprint of* United Nations Publications

UNESCO, *distributed by* Bernan

UNFOLDS®, *imprint of* VanDam Inc

UNFPA, *distributed by* United Nations Publications

UNICEF, *imprint of* United Nations Publications, *distributed by* United Nations Publications

Unicorn, *distributor for* Lacis Publications

UNICRI, *distributed by* United Nations Publications

UNIDIR, *imprint of* United Nations Publications, *distributed by* United Nations Publications

UNIDO, *imprint of* United Nations Publications, *distributed by* United Nations Publications

Unifacmanu Trading Co Ltd, *distributor for* Paul H Brookes Publishing Co, Health Professions Press

The Unifont Co, *distributed by* Action Publishing LLC

Union Square Publishing, *imprint of* Cardoza Publishing, *distributed by* Simon & Schuster

Unique Books, *distributor for* Do-It-Yourself Legal Publishers

Unique Publications Books & Videos, *subsidiary of* CFW Enterprises Inc, CFW Enterprises Inc

UNITAR, *imprint of* United Nations Publications, *distributed by* United Nations Publications

United Artists, *distributed by* Ugly Duckling Presse

The United Educators Inc, *subsidiary of* Standard Educational Corp

The United Methodist Publishing House, *imprint of* Abingdon Press

United Nations Publications, *subsidiary of* United Nations, *distributor for* ICJ, INSTRAW, IOM, UNCITRAL, UNDP, UNFPA, UNICEF, UNICRI, UNIDIR, UNIDO, UNITAR, UNU

United Nations (UN), *distributed by* Bernan

United Nations University Press, *distributed by* The Brookings Institution Press

United Publishers Services Ltd, *distributor for* Institute for International Economics

United States Catholic Conference Publications, *distributed by* Liturgy Training Publications

United States Holocaust Memorial Museum, *affiliate of* United States Holocaust Memorial Council

United States Pharmacopeia, *distributed by* Consumer Reports, Login Brothers Book Company, Login Publishing Consortium, Matthews Book Co, National Technical Information Service, Promachem LLC, Rittenhouse Book Distributors, Inc

United States Tennis Association, *distributed by* Universe Publishing, H O Zimman Inc

United Synagogue Book Service, *division of* United Synagogue of Conservative Judaism, *distributor for* Rabbinical Assembly of America

United Synagogue Commission on Jewish Education, *imprint of* United Synagogue Book Service

United Synagogue of Conservative Judaism, *imprint of* United Synagogue Book Service

Unity House, *division of* Unity School of Christianity

Univelt Inc, *distributor for* Astronautical Society of Western Australia, US Space Foundation

Universal Publishers, *imprint of* Dissertation.com, Upublish.com

Universal Reference, *imprint of* Grey House Publishing Inc

Universe, *imprint of* Rizzoli International Publications Inc, Universe Publishing, *distributor for* Country Music Foundation Press

Universe Calendars, *imprint of* Universe Publishing

Universe Publishing, *division of* Rizzoli International Publications Inc, *distributor for* International Evangelism Crusades Inc, United States Tennis Association, *distributed by* Random House

Universe Publishing Calendars, *distributed by* Andrews McMeel Publishing

University College Dublin Press, *distributed by* Dufour Editions Inc

University Microfilms International, *distributor for* National Bureau of Economic Research Inc

The University of Akron Press, *distributor for* Principia Press

University of Alaska Press, *distributor for* Geophysical Institute, Limestone Press, Spirit Mountain Press, UA Museum, White Mammoth

University of Arizona Mexican American Studies & Research Center, *distributed by* The University of Arizona Press

The University of Arizona Press, *distributor for* Amon Carter Museum, Arizona State Museum, Crow Canyon Archaeological Center,

Ironwood Press, OSU Press, Statistical Research Inc, University of Arizona Mexican American Studies & Research Center

University of Arizona Press, *distributor for* Oregon State University Press

The University of Arkansas Press, *division of* The University of Arkansas, *distributor for* Phoenix International

University of British Columbia Press, *distributor for* University of New Mexico Press

University of Calgary Press, *distributed by* Michigan State University Press (MSU Press)

University of California Institute on Global Conflict & Cooperation, *subsidiary of* University of California, *distributed by* Amazon.com, BarnesandNoble.com, Brookings Institution Press, Columbia International Affairs Online (CIAO), Cornell University Press, Garland Publishers, Lynn-Reinner Publishing, Penn State University Press, Princeton University Press, Transaction Publishers, University of Michigan Press, Westview Press

University of California Press, *distributor for* artSITES, British Film Institute, Huntington Library, Huntington Library Press, Nevraumont Publishing Co, Sierra Club Books, Sierra Club Books (Adult trade), Sierra Club Books Adult Trade Division, The Woodrow Wilson Center Press

University of Chicago Press, *distributor for* Art Institute of Chicago, CSLI Publications, National Bureau of Economic Research Inc, Planners Press, St Augustine's Press Inc, Swan Isle Press, *distributed by* American Society for Photogrammetry & Remote Sensing

University of Chicago Press Distribution Ctr, *distributor for* University of Pittsburgh Press

University of Connecticut, *distributed by* Ball Publishing

University of Delaware Press, *affiliate of* Associated University Presses, *distributed by* Associated University Presses

University of Denver Center for Teaching International Relations Publications, *subsidiary of* University of Denver

University of Hawaii Press, *distributor for* Ateneo De Manila University Press, Faculty of Asian Studies, Australian National University, Global Oriental, Kamehameha Schools Press, Katydid Books, Nordic Insititute of Asian Studies, Pasifika Press, Singapore University Press, University of the Phillippines Press

University of Healing Logo, *imprint of* University of Healing Press

University of Healing Press, *division of* God Unlimited/University of Healing, God Unlimited/University of Healing

University of Hertfordshire Press, *distributed by* Paul & Company

University of Idaho Press, *distributed by* Caxton Press

University of Illinois Press, *unit of* University of Illinois

University of Indiana Press, *distributor for* Art Institute of Chicago

University of Luton Press, *distributed by* Paul & Company

University of Miami Music Press, *imprint of* Empire Publishing Service

University of Michigan, *distributed by* International Book Centre Inc

University of Michigan Center for Japanese Studies, *unit of* University of Michigan

University of Michigan Press, *unit of* University of Michigan, *distributor for* Center for Chinese Studies, University of Michigan, Center for South & Southeast Asian Studies, University of Michigan, K G Saur (Teubner titles only), University of California Institute on Global Conflict & Cooperation, *distributed by* Plymbridge Distributors Ltd (Territory restricted to Europe, Israel & UK; Telex: 45635)

University of Missouri Press, *distributor for* Missouri Historical Society Press

University of Nebraska, *distributed by* Sundance Publishing

University of Nebraska Press, *division of* University of Nebraska, Lincoln, *imprint of* Combined Academic Publishers, *distributor for* Buros Institute, Creighton University Press, Dalkey Archive Press, Gordian Knot Books, Reedy Press, Society for American Baseball Research, Zoo Press

University of Nevada Press, *distributor for* Institute for the Study of Gambling & Commercial Gaming, Nevada Humanities Committee, *distributed by* Companion Press

University of New Hampshire Press, *imprint of* University Press of New England

University of New Mexico Press, *distributor for* La Alameda Press, Ancient City Press, Missouri Historical Society Press, Museum of New Mexico Press, *distributed by* University of British Columbia Press (territory restricted to Canada)

University of New Orleans Press, *division of* University of New Orleans Foundation, *distributed by* Biblio

The University of North Carolina Press, *distributor for* Museum of Early Southern Decorative Arts (selected), North Carolina Museum of Art (selected), Omohundro Institute of Early American History & Culture, Southeastern Center for Contemporary Art (selected), Valentine Museum (selected)

University of North Texas Press, *distributed by* Texas A&M University Press, Texas A&M University Press

University of Oklahoma Press, *distributor for* University Press of Colorado, University Press of the West Indies, Vanderbilt University Press

The University of Pennsylvania Museum of Archaeology & Anthropology, *division of* University of Pennsylvania

University of Pennsylvania Museum of Archaeology & Anthropology, *imprint of* The University of Pennsylvania Museum of Archaeology & Anthropology

University of Pittsburgh Press, *distributed by* University of Chicago Press Distribution Ctr

University of Pittsburgh Press (Pittsburgh Biblio Series), *distributed by* Oak Knoll Press

University of Puerto Rico Press, *subsidiary of* University of Puerto Rico

University of Rochester Press, *imprint of* Boydell & Brewer Inc, *affiliate of* Boydell & Brewer, Boydell & Brewer Inc

University of San Francisco, *distributed by* Fordham University Press

University of Scranton Press, *division of* University of Scranton

University of South Carolina Press, *affiliate of* University of South Carolina, *distributor for* McKissick Museum, Saraland Press, SC Historical Society, South Carolina Bar Association

University of Southern Illinois, *distributor for* Missouri Historical Society Press

University of Texas Press, *division of* University of Texas, *distributor for* Bat Conservation International, Institute for Mesoamerican Studies, Menil Foundation, Rothko Chapel, San Antonio Museum of Art, SUNY Albany, Texas Parks & Wildlife Department, Texas Western Press

University of the Phillippines Press, *distributed by* University of Hawaii Press

University of Tokyo Press, *distributed by* Columbia University Press

University of Toronto Press, *distributor for* Mage Publishers Inc

The University of Utah Press, *subsidiary of* University of Utah, *distributor for* BYU Museum of Peoples & Cultures, Utah Museum of Natural History

University of Vermont Press, *imprint of* University Press of New England

The University of Virginia Press, *affiliate of* University of Virginia, *distributor for* Colonial Society of Massachusetts, Mount Vernon Ladies Association

University of Wales Press, *distributed by* Paul & Company

University of Washington Press, *imprint of* Combined Academic Publishers, *distributor for* American Federation of Arts, Art Institute of Chicago, The National Museum of Women in the Arts, Oregon Historical Society Press, UCLA Fowler Museum of Cultural History

University of Wisconsin Press, *distributor for* The Center for the Study of Upper Midwestern Culture, Dryad Press, Elvehjem Museum of Art, International Brecht Society, Max Kade Institute for German-American Studies, Spring Freshet Press, Wisconsin Academy of Sciences, Arts & Letters, Wisconsin Historical Society Press, Wisconsin Veterans Museum

University Press, *division of* Dan River Press, *distributed by* American Mathematical Society

University Press of America Inc, *member of* Rowman & Littlefield Publishing Group, Rowman & Littlefield Publishing Group, *distributor for* Atlantic Council, Barnes & Noble Books (Imports & Reprints), Center for National Policy Press, Harvard Center for International Affairs, International Law Institute, Joint Center for Political & Economic Studies Press, Society of the Cincinnati, White Burkett Miller Center

University Press of Colorado, *distributor for* Center for Literary Publishing, Colorado Historical Society, *distributed by* University of Oklahoma Press

University Press of Florida, *affiliate of* State University System of Florida

University Press of Kansas, *distributor for* KU Natural History Museum

University Press of Maryland, *imprint of* CDL Press

University Press of Mississippi, *distributor for* Northcote House

University Press of New England, *distributor for* Bibliopola Press, Chipstone Foundation, The Colonial Williamsburg Foundation, Fence Books, Four Way Books, Isabella Stewart Gardner Museum, National Poetry Foundation, Nicolin Fields Publishing, Peter E Randall Publisher, The Sheep Meadow Press, Wesleyan University Press, Winterthur Museum Garden & Library, Winterthur Museum, Garden & Library

University Press of the West Indies, *distributed by* University of Oklahoma Press

University Press of Washington, DC, *subsidiary of* Cherokee Publishing Co

University Publications of America, *imprint of* LexisNexis Academic & Library Solutions

University Publishing Group, *distributor for* The Journal of Clinical Ethics, Organizational Ethics: Healthcare, Business & Policy

University Science Books, *division of* University Books Inc

UNU, *imprint of* United Nations Publications, *distributed by* United Nations Publications

Unusual Publications, *imprint of* Bob Jones University Press

UPA, *distributor for* San Diego State University Press

UPA Co-Publishing, *division of* University Press of America Inc

UPA Publishers' Reprints, *division of* University Press of America Inc

Upper Elementary/Secondary & Magazines Publishing, *division of* Scholastic Education

Upper Room Books, *division of* The Upper Room

Upstart Books™, *imprint of* Highsmith Inc

Upstream, *imprint of* A & B Publishers Group

Upublish.com, *division of* Dissertation.com, *imprint of* Dissertation.com, *distributed by* Bertrams UK

Laurence Urdang Reference Book, *imprint of* Verbatim Books

Urim Publications, *division of* Lambda Publishers Inc

URJ Press, *division of* Union for Reform Judaism

Ursus Books, *distributed by* Antique Collectors Club Ltd

US Book Distributor, *distributor for* MAR*CO Products Inc

US Coast Pilot, *imprint of* ProStar Publications Inc

US Directory Service, *imprint of* Douglas Publications Inc

US Games Systems Inc, *distributor for* Carta Mundi, A G Muller & Cie

US Geological Survey, *distributed by* American Society for Photogrammetry & Remote Sensing

US Government Printing Office, *division of* US Government Agency

US Space Foundation, *distributed by* Univelt Inc

Usborne, *distributed by* Sundance Publishing

Usborne Publishing, *distributed by* EDC Publishing

User's Guides to Nutritional Supplements, *imprint of* Basic Health Publications Inc

USTA, *distributor for* Althos Publishing

Utah Geological Survey, *division of* Utah Dept of Natural Resources, Utah Dept of Natural Resources

Utah Museum of Natural History, *distributed by* The University of Utah Press

Utah State University Press, *division of* Utah State University

Vacation Memories Press, *imprint of* R J Berg/Destinations Press Ltd

Vacation Work Publications, *distributed by* The Globe Pequot Press

Vademecum, *imprint of* Landes Bioscience

Valaam Society of America, *imprint of* St Herman Press

Valentine Museum (selected), *distributed by* The University of North Carolina Press

Vallentine, Mitchell & Co Ltd, *distributed by* Sepher-Hermon Press

Valuation Press, *imprint of* Marshall & Swift

Valusource, *imprint of* John Wiley & Sons Inc

Van Nostrand Reinhold, *distributed by* American Society for Photogrammetry & Remote Sensing

VanDam Advertising, *division of* VanDam Inc

VanDam Licensing, *division of* VanDam Inc

VanDam Publishing, *division of* VanDam Inc

Vandamere Press, *distributor for* ABI Professional Publications, ABI Professional Publications (non-exclusive), NRH Press (non-exclusive), Quodlibetal Features, *distributed by* ABI Professional Publications

Vanderbilt Library of American Philosophy, *imprint of* Vanderbilt University Press

Vanderbilt University Press, *division of* Vanderbilt University, *distributor for* Country Music Foundation Press, *distributed by* University of Oklahoma Press

Vanwell Publishing, *distributor for* Howell Press Inc, *distributed by* Casemate Publishers, Howell Press Inc

Variorum, *imprint of* Ashgate Publishing Co

Varlik, *subsidiary of* Cross-Cultural Communications

The Varsity Co, *division of* Thomas Nelson Inc

Yad Vashem, *distributed by* Berghahn Books

Junius Vaughn Press Inc, *imprint of* Saint Aedan's Press & Book Distributors Inc

Vedanta Press, *subsidiary of* Vedanta Society of Southern California, *distributor for* Advaita, Ashrama, Ramakrishna Math

Vega, *distributed by* Sterling Publishing Co Inc

Vegetarian Guides, *distributed by* Casemate Publishers

The Vendome Press, *distributed by* Harry N Abrams

Venture Marketing, *imprint of* Juice Gallery Multimedia

Venture Press, *imprint of* Williams & Co Publishers

Verba Mundi, *imprint of* David R Godine Publisher Inc

Verbatim Book, *imprint of* Verbatim Books

Verbatim Books, *subsidiary of* Laurence Urdang Inc, Laurence Urdang Inc

Veritas, *distributed by* ACTA Publications, Ignatius Press

Verlag Schmid (selected titles), *distributed by* Metal Powder Industries Federation

Vermont Schoolhouse Press, *distributed by* Enfield Publishing & Distribution Co

Verso, *distributed by* W W Norton (USA), W W Norton & Company Inc, Penguin (Canada)

Vertigo, *imprint of* DC Comics

VH-1, *imprint of* Pocket Books, Simon & Schuster Adult Publishing Group

Viceroy Press, *distributed by* Henry Holt and Company, LLC

Victor, *imprint of* Cook Communications Ministries

Victoria University Press, *distributed by* Paul & Company

Victory in Grace Printing, *division of* Quentin Road Ministries

Vida, *imprint of* Zondervan

Video Active Productions, *distributed by* Thomson Delmar Learning

Video-Forum, *imprint of* Jeffrey Norton Publishers Inc

Vieweg Verlag Publications, *distributed by* American Mathematical Society

Viewpoint, *distributed by* Scholium International Inc

Viking, *imprint of* Penguin Group (USA) Inc, Penguin Group (USA) Inc, Viking Penguin

Viking Children's Books, *imprint of* Penguin Group (USA) Inc, Penguin Group (USA) Inc, Penguin Young Readers Group

Viking Compass, *imprint of* Penguin Group (USA) Inc, Viking, Viking Penguin

Viking Penguin, *division of* Penguin Group (USA) Inc, Penguin Group (USA) Inc

Viking Studio, *imprint of* Penguin Group (USA) Inc, Penguin Group (USA) Inc, Viking Penguin

Villard, *imprint of* Random House Publishing Group

Villard Books, *imprint of* Random House Inc

Villegas Editores, *distributed by* Rizzoli International Publications Inc

Carl Vinson Institute of Government, *unit of* University of Georgia Press

Vintage & Anchor Books, *division of* Random House Inc

Vintage Books, *imprint of* Random House Inc

Vintage Contemporaries, *imprint of* Vintage & Anchor Books

Vintage Crime/Black Lizard, *imprint of* Vintage & Anchor Books

Vintage Departures, *imprint of* Vintage & Anchor Books

Vintage Guitar, *imprint of* Hal Leonard Corp, *distributed by* Hal Leonard Corp

Vintage Image, *imprint of* The Wine Appreciation Guild Ltd

Vintage International, *imprint of* Vintage & Anchor Books

Visible Ink Press (US & Canada), *distributed by* Mint Publishers Group

Vision Works Publishing, *division of* Visionary International Partnerships, *distributed by* Hushion House - Canada

Visions Communications, *distributed by* Penwell Books

Visions SrL, *distributed by* Getty Publications

Visitor's Guides, *imprint of* Hunter Publishing Inc

Visual™, *imprint of* John Wiley & Sons Inc

Visual Reference Publication, *imprint of* Visual Reference Publications Inc

Visual Reference Publications Inc, *distributed by* Watson-Guptill Publications (US & Canada)

VITA, *distributed by* Pact Publications

Vital Health Publishing, *distributed by* Brumby (Gemcraft) (Australia), Deep Books (UK, Europe), New Horizon (South Africa), Peaceful Living (New Zealand)

Vital Issues Press, *distributed by* Huntington House Publishers

Viva Books PVT, *distributor for* Institute for International Economics

VIZ, *distributed by* Simon & Schuster Inc

Vocalis ESL, *imprint of* Vocalis Ltd

Vocalis Fiction, *imprint of* Vocalis Ltd

Voggenreiter Publishers, *distributed by* Mel Bay Publications Inc

Voices of Resistance, *imprint of* Monthly Review Press

Volo, *imprint of* Hyperion Books for Children

Vox Humana, *imprint of* Humana Press

VOYA (Voice of Youth Advocates) Magazine, *division of* Scarecrow Press Inc

Voyager Books, *imprint of* The Globe Pequot Press, Harcourt Trade Publishers

Voyageur Press, *distributor for* Colin Baxter, Car Tech, CarTech Inc, Fountain Press, Hove, Specialty Press, Tetra Press, *distributed by* Heimburger House Publishing Co, Raincoast Books

VU University Press, *distributed by* Paul & Company

VUB University Press, *distributed by* Paul & Company

W Publishing Group, *division of* Thomas Nelson Inc

Wadsworth, *imprint of* Wadsworth Publishing

Wadsworth Inc, *distributor for* National Association of Broadcasters (NAB)

Wadsworth Publishing, *division of* Thomson Learning Inc, *distributed by* Nelson Thomas Learning, Thomson Learning, Thomson Learning International Group

Wageningen Pers, *distributed by* Purdue University Press

Wakefield Press, *distributor for* Mosaic Press, *distributed by* Weatherhill Inc

Wakefield Press Australia, *distributed by* R D R Books

Walden Books, *distributor for* Top of the Mountain Publishing

Walk Worthy, *imprint of* Warner Books

Walkabout Press, *distributed by* John F Blair Publisher

Walker & Co, *division of* Walker Publishing Co Inc, Walker Publishing Co Inc, *distributed by* Heimburger House Publishing Co

Walker & Co New York, *distributor for* Allen D Bragdon Publishers Inc

Walker Large Print, *imprint of* Thorndike Press

Walker Publishers, *distributed by* Sundance Publishing

Wall Street Journal Books, *imprint of* Simon & Schuster Adult Publishing Group

Wallace Collection, *distributed by* Antique Collectors Club Ltd

Wallace-Homestead, *distributed by* Krause Publications

Wallflower Press, *distributed by* Columbia University Press

Walrus Publications, *distributed by* Orca Book Publishers

The Walt Disney Co, *division of* Jump at the Sun

Walter Lorraine Books, *imprint of* Houghton Mifflin Trade & Reference Division

Waltham Street Press, *imprint of* Meyerbooks Publisher

Walton's, *distributed by* Mel Bay Publications Inc

Ward Lock, *distributed by* Sterling Publishing Co Inc

Warman's, *imprint of* Krause Publications, *distributed by* Krause Publications

Frederick Warne, *subsidiary of* Penguin Group (USA) Inc, *imprint of* Penguin Group (USA) Inc, Penguin Group (USA) Inc, Penguin Young Readers Group, *distributed by* Perfection Learning Corp

Warner, *distributed by* Thorndike Press

Warner Books, *subsidiary of* Time Warner Book Group, *imprint of* Time Warner Book Group

Warner Bros Publications Inc, *distributor for* Belwin-Mills, Bradley Publications, Brimhall Music Publishing, Frances Clark, Expressions Music Curriculum™, Kalmus, Music Expressions™, Summy-Birchard Inc, Suzuki, Warner Brothers

Warner Bros Worldwide Publishing, *division of* Warner Bros Consumer Products

Warner Brothers, *distributed by* Warner Bros Publications Inc

Warner Bros Publications, *distributor for* Summy-Birchard Inc

Warner Business Books, *imprint of* Warner Books

Warner Faith, *imprint of* Warner Books

Warner Faith (Christian Book Division of Time Warner Book Group), *subsidiary of* Time Warner Book Group

Warner Forever, *imprint of* Warner Books

Warner Paperback Library, *distributed by* Sundance Publishing

Warner Publishers Services, *distributor for* Tom Doherty Associates, LLC

Warner Vision, *imprint of* Warner Books

Warren, Gorham & Lamont, *subsidiary of* Research Institute of America Inc

Warrior, *imprint of* Osprey Publishing Ltd

Washington Events Guide, *imprint of* Gail's Guides

Washington House, *imprint of* Trident Media Inc

Washington Institute for Near East Policy, *distributed by* The Brookings Institution Press

Washington Post Crosswords, *imprint of* Random House Reference

Washington Service Bureau, *subsidiary of* CCH Inc

Washington Square Press, *distributed by* Sundance Publishing

Washington State University, *division of* Washington State University Press

Washington State University Press, *division of* Washington State University, *distributor for* The Hutton Settlement, Museum of Art, Oregon Writers Colony, Pacific Institute (distribute only one title), *distributed by* UBC Press (Canada)

Ernst Wasmuth Verlag, *distributor for* Art Institute of Chicago

Water Resources Publications LLC, *distributor for* ASAE, ASCE

Water Row Books, *distributor for* Water Row Press, *distributed by* Water Row Press

Water Row Press, *subsidiary of* Water Row Books, *distributor for* Water Row Books, Weinberg Books, *distributed by* Water Row Books

WaterBrook Press, *division of* Random House Inc

Waterford Press, *distributed by* The Globe Pequot Press

Waterfront Press (selected titles from all), *distributed by* Bilingual Press/Editorial Bilingue

Watermark Press, *distributed by* Antique Collectors Club Ltd

WaterPlow Press™, *distributed by* American Water Works Association

Watershed Media, *distributed by* Chelsea Green Publishing Co

Watersport Books, *imprint of* Aqua Quest Publications Inc

Watson-Guptill, *imprint of* Watson-Guptill Publications

Watson-Guptill Publications, *division of* VNU Business Media Inc, *distributor for* Allworth Press, C & T Publishing, C & T Publishing Inc, Visual Reference Publications Inc

Neale Watson Academic Publications, *imprint of* Watson Publishing International

Wayne State University Press, *distributor for* Cranbrook Institute of Science, Detroit Institute of Arts, Hebrew Union College Press, Missouri Historical Society Press

The Waywiser Press, *distributed by* Dufour Editions Inc

Weatherhill, *imprint of* Weatherhill Inc

Weatherhill Inc, *subsidiary of* Tankosha, Tankosha (Japan), *distributor for* A R E Press, Gambit Publications, The Hoberman Connection, Hollym Corp, Luzac Orientals, New Holland, Serindia Publications, Shufunotomo Co Ltd, Wakefield Press, Windhorse Publications, *distributed by* Canadian MANDA, InterBook Marketing, New Holland Publishers Ltd, Peribo, Marta Schooler, Yohan

John Weatherhill Inc, *distributor for* Red Moon Press

Weaver Books, *imprint of* Pauline Books & Media

Webb Research Group, Publishers, *distributed by* Pacific Northwest Books Co

Websters International Publishers, *distributed by* Antique Collectors Club Ltd

Webster's New World™, *imprint of* John Wiley & Sons Inc

Wee Sing, *imprint of* Penguin Group (USA) Inc, Price Stern Sloan

Weidenfeld & Nicolson, *distributed by* Casemate Publishers, Sterling Publishing Co Inc

Weidner & Sons Publishing, *division of* The Weidner Publishing Group, *distributor for* Delaware Estuary Press, Delaware Museum of Natural History, Hazlaw Books, Lighthouse Publications, Medlaw Books, Pulse Publications, Tycooly Publishing USA

Weinberg Books, *distributed by* Water Row Press

Samuel Weiser, *distributor for* Media Associates

Welcome Books, *imprint of* Welcome Enterprises, *distributed by* Andrews McMeel Publishing, Andrews McMeel Publishing

Welcome Rain Publishers LLC, *distributed by* National Book Network

Wellfleet Press, *imprint of* Book Sales Inc

Wellington Press, *division of* BooksUPrint.com Inc

Wellsweep Press, *distributed by* Cheng & Tsui Co Inc

Welz, *distributed by* Alan Wofsy Fine Arts

Wendy Lamb Books, *imprint of* Random House Children's Books

Wenner Books, *distributed by* Hyperion

Wescott Cove Publishing Co, *subsidiary of* NetPV Inc

Weseanne Publications, *distributed by* Gem Guides Book Co

Wesleyan Poetry, *imprint of* Wesleyan University Press

Wesleyan Publishing House, *division of* Wesleyan Church Corporation

Wesleyan University Press, *distributed by* University Press of New England

West, *imprint of* Thomson Delmar Learning, Wadsworth Publishing

West, A Thomson Business, *division of* The Thomson Corporation, Thomson Corporation, *distributor for* Law Library Microform Consortium

West Music, *distributor for* Barcelona Publishers

West/Thomson Learning, *imprint of* South-Western, A Thomson Business

Westcliffe Publishing, *distributed by* Heimburger House Publishing Co

Western Edge Press, *distributed by* Mountain Press Publishing Co

Western Horseman, *distributed by* The Globe Pequot Press

Western New York Wares Inc, *affiliate of* Meyer Enterprises, *distributor for* Canisius College Press, DLR Imagery

Western Pennsylvania Genealogical Society, *distributed by* Mechling Associates

Western Psychological Service, *distributor for* Psychological Assessment Resources Inc (PAR)

Western Reserve Historical Society, *distributed by* Ohio State University Press

Western Trails Publications, *distributed by* Gem Guides Book Co

Westin Walch, *distributed by* Prestwick House Inc

Westminster John Knox Press, *division of* Presbyterian Publishing Corp, *imprint of* Presbyterian Publishing Corp, *distributor for* SCM

Westview Press, *member of* The Perseus Books Group, Perseus Books Group LLC, *imprint of* The Perseus Books Group, *distributor for* University of California Institute on Global Conflict & Cooperation, *distributed by* Harper-Collins

WestWinds Press®, *imprint of* Graphic Arts Center Publishing Co

Whalesback Books, *imprint of* Howells House

WH&O International, *division of* Meristem Systems Corp, Meristem Systems Corp

What Do You Know About Books, *imprint of* National Learning Corp

What Ifs, *imprint of* Aspatore Books

What's Cooking In...?, *imprint of* Harian Creative Books

Wheatherstone Press, *subsidiary of* Dickinson Consulting Group

Wheeler Publishing, *imprint of* Thomson Gale, Thorndike Press

Whereabouts Press, *distributed by* Consortuim Book Sales & Distribution (PUBNET)

Whirlaway Books, *imprint of* Whitehorse Press

Whitaker, *distributor for* Faith Library Publications

White Burkett Miller Center, *distributed by* University Press of America Inc

White Cockade Publishing, *distributed by* Paul & Company

White Eagle Publishing Trust (England), *distributed by* De Vorss & Co

White Horse Press, *distributed by* Paul & Company

White Mammoth, *distributed by* University of Alaska Press

White Mane Books, *imprint of* White Mane Publishing Co Inc

White Mane Kids, *division of* White Mane Publishing Co Inc

White Pine Press, *distributor for* Springhouse Editions, *distributed by* Consortium Book Sales

White Star, *distributed by* Rizzoli International Publications Inc

Whitecap Books (cookbooks), *distributed by* Graphic Arts Center Publishing Co

Whitehorse Press, *distributed by* Motorbooks International

Whitford Press, *division of* Schiffer Publishing Ltd, *imprint of* Schiffer Publishing Ltd, *distributed by* ACS Publications

Whiting & Birch, *distributed by* Paul & Company

Whitman Publishing Co, *distributed by* Sanford J Durst

The Whitney Library of Design, *imprint of* Watson-Guptill Publications

Whittet, *distributed by* Diamond Farm Book Publishers

Whittles Publishing, *distributed by* American Society for Photogrammetry & Remote Sensing

Whodunits, *imprint of* Modern Publishing

Whole Person Associates, *imprint of* Whole Person Associates Inc

Who's Who in Italy, *distributed by* Paul & Company

Who's Who Preschool Board Book, *imprint of* Modern Publishing

Wicker Park Press, *distributed by* Academy Chicago Publishers

Wide World of Maps Inc, *distributor for* Arizona Highways, Benchmark Maps, DeLorme, Rand McNally, *distributed by* Rand McNally

Wide World Publishing, *imprint of* Wide World Publishing/Tetra

Wide World Publishing/Tetra, *distributed by* The Islander Group Inc, Publishers Group West

Michael Wiese Productions, *distributed by* National Book Network

Wild Canyon Press, *imprint of* Council Oak Books LLC

The Wild Goose Co, *distributed by* Carson-Dellosa Publishing Co Inc

Wild Mountain Press, *imprint of* Crumb Elbow Publishing

Wildcat Canyon Press, *division of* Circulus Publishing Group Inc, Council Oak Books

Wilde Publishing, *division of* Wilde Oil

Wilderness Adventures Press Inc, *distributed by* Angler's Book Supply, Books West, Inter Sports, Partners Book Distributor, Partners West

Wildlife Research Group, *imprint of* Crumb Elbow Publishing

Wildstorm, *imprint of* DC Comics

Wiley, *imprint of* John Wiley & Sons Inc

Wiley-IEEE Press, *imprint of* IEEE Press, Institute of Electrical & Electronics Engineers Inc

Wiley Audio ™, *imprint of* Penton Overseas Inc

Wiley-Heyden, *imprint of* John Wiley & Sons Inc

Wiley-IEEE Press, *imprint of* IEEE Press, Institute of Electrical & Electronics Engineers Inc

Wiley Interscience®, *imprint of* John Wiley & Sons Inc

John Wiley, *distributor for* Nevraumont Publishing Co, *distributed by* Abbott, Langer & Associates, SkillPath Publications

John Wiley & Sons, *imprint of* John Wiley & Sons Inc, *distributor for* The Electrochemical Society Inc, MDRT Center for Productivity, *distributed by* American Marketing Association, American Water Works Association, Heimburger House Publishing Co

John Wiley & Sons Inc, *distributor for* IEEE Press, SAS Publishing, *distributed by* American Academy of Environmental Engineers, American Society for Photogrammetry & Remote Sensing, Ball Publishing, William S Hein & Co Inc, Illuminating Engineering Society of North America, J J Keller & Associates, Inc, NACE International, SAS Publishing, Society of Manufacturing Engineers, Traders Press Inc

John Wiley & Sons Inc Education Publishing Group, *division of* John Wiley & Sons Inc, John Wiley & Sons Inc

John Wiley & Sons Inc Professional & Trade Group, *division of* John Wiley & Sons Inc, John Wiley & Sons Inc

John Wiley & Sons Inc Scientific/Technical/Medical Publishing, *division of* John Wiley & Sons Inc

John Wiley & Sons (Wiley Audio), *distributed by* Penton Overseas Inc

Wiley-Liss, *imprint of* John Wiley & Sons Inc

Wiley-VCH, *imprint of* John Wiley & Sons Inc

William, James & Co, *imprint of* Franklin, Beedle & Associates Inc

William Morrow, *imprint of* HarperCollins General Books Group, HarperCollins Publishers Sales, *distributor for* Nightingale-Conant

William Morrow Cookbooks, *imprint of* HarperCollins General Books Group, HarperCollins Publishers Sales

William of Moerbeke Translation Services, *imprint of* St Augustine's Press Inc

Williams & Co, *imprint of* Williams & Co Publishers

Williams & Wilkins, *distributor for* Current Medicine

Bridget Williams Books, *distributed by* Paul & Company

Williamson Books, *imprint of* Ideals Publications, Ideals Publications a Division of Guideposts Inc

Wilson Center Press, *imprint of* The Woodrow Wilson Center Press

Philip Wilson Publishers, *distributed by* Antique Collectors Club Ltd

The Woodrow Wilson Center Press, *division of* The Woodrow Wilson International Center for Scholars, Woodrow Wilson International Center for Scholars, *distributed by* Cambridge University Press, Columbia University Press, The Johns Hopkins University Press, Stanford University Press, University of California Press

Wimmer Cookbooks, *subsidiary of* Mercury Printing

B L Winch & Associates, *imprint of* Jalmar Press

B L Winch Associates, *distributed by* Zephyr Press Catalog

Winchester Press, *imprint of* New Win Publishing Inc

Wind Records, *distributed by* YMAA Publication Center

Windflower Press, *imprint of* Crumb Elbow Publishing

Windhorse Publications, *distributed by* Weatherhill Inc

Windsor Books, *division of* Windsor Marketing Corp

Windswept, Too, *imprint of* Windswept House Publishers

Wine Advisory Board, *imprint of* The Wine Appreciation Guild Ltd

Wine Spectator Press, *distributed by* Running Press Book Publishers

Wings, *imprint of* Random House Value Publishing

Wings Books, *imprint of* Random House Inc

Winner Enterprises, *distributed by* Florida Flair Books, Great Outdoors Publishing, Palm Island Press, Southern Book Service

Winner's Wildlife & Nature Series, *imprint of* Winner Enterprises

Winston-Derek, *distributor for* Thomas Nelson Inc

Wintergreen/Orchard House Inc, *imprint of* The Riverside Publishing Co

Winters Publishing, *distributor for* Tattersall Press

Winterthur Museum Garden & Library, *distributed by* University Press of New England

Winterthur Museum, Garden & Library, *distributed by* University Press of New England

Wisconsin Academy of Sciences, Arts & Letters, *distributed by* University of Wisconsin Press

Wisconsin Historical Society Press, *distributed by* University of Wisconsin Press

Wisconsin Veterans Museum, *distributed by* University of Wisconsin Press

Wisdom Archive, *division of* Wisdom Publications Inc

Wisdom Books, *distributor for* Serindia Publications

Wish Publishing, *distributed by* Cardinal Publishers Group

Wittenborn Art Books, *distributed by* Alan Wofsy Fine Arts

Witwatersrand University Press, *distributed by* Transaction Publishers

Wizards of the Coast, *distributed by* Tom Doherty Associates, LLC

Wizards of the Coast Inc, *subsidiary of* Hasbro Inc, Hasbro Inc, *distributed by* Holtzbrink Publishing

Alan Wofsy Fine Arts, *distributor for* Bora, Brusberg (Berlin), Cramer (Geneva), Huber, Ides et Calendes, Kornfeld & Co, Picasso Project, Welz, Wittenborn Art Books

Wolf Creek Books, *distributed by* Graphic Arts Center Publishing Co

Wolf Den Books, *distributed by* IPG/Paul & Co, Paul & Company

Wolfe, *imprint of* Elsevier

Wolfhound Press (Ireland), *distributed by* Interlink Publishing Group Inc

Wolters Kluwer US Corp, *subsidiary of* Wolters Kluwer NV (The Netherlands)

Women Artists News Book Review, *subsidiary of* Midmarch Arts Press

Women Changing the World Series, *imprint of* The Feminist Press at The City University of New York

Women In Nontraditional Careers, *imprint of* Her Own Words

Women, Law & Development International (WLDI), *distributed by* Stylus Publishing LLC

Women Writers of the Middle East, *imprint of* The Feminist Press at The City University of New York

Women Writing Africa Series, *imprint of* The Feminist Press at The City University of New York

The Women's Press, *distributed by* Trafalgar Square

Women's Publications, *imprint of* Consumer Press

The Women's Stories Project, *imprint of* The Feminist Press at The City University of New York

Women's Studies Quarterly, *imprint of* The Feminist Press at The City University of New York

Wood Lake Books, *distributed by* The Pilgrim Press/United Church Press

Marian Wood Books, *imprint of* Penguin Group (USA) Inc, The Putnam Publishing Group, G P Putnam's Sons (Hardcover)

Woodall Publications, *distributed by* The Globe Pequot Press

Woodbine, *distributed by* Peytral Publications Inc

Woodbine House, *distributed by* A D D Warehouse

Woodbine Press, *distributed by* The Alexander Graham Bell Association for the Deaf & Hard of Hearing

Woodbridge Group, *imprint of* Moment Point Press Inc

Woodbridge Press, *distributed by* Ball Publishing

Woodcarvers Favorite Pattern Series, *imprint of* Fox Chapel Publishing Co Inc

Woodcarving Illustrated Magazine, *imprint of* Fox Chapel Publishing Co Inc

Woodland Publishing Inc, *distributed by* Koen Book Distributors Inc, New Leaf, Nutri-Books, Summit Beacon

Woodlands Press, *distributed by* Johnson Books

The Woodrow Wilson Center Press, *division of* The Woodrow Wilson International Center for Scholars, Woodrow Wilson International Center for Scholars, *distributed by* Cambridge University Press, Columbia University Press, The Johns Hopkins University Press, Stanford University Press, University of California Press

Woodrow Wilson Center Press/Johns Hopkins University Press, *imprint of* The Woodrow Wilson Center Press

Woodrow Wilson Center Press/Stanford University Press, *imprint of* The Woodrow Wilson Center Press

Woodrow Wilson Center Series/Cambridge University Press, *imprint of* The Woodrow Wilson Center Press

Woodrow Wilson Center Special Studies, *imprint of* The Woodrow Wilson Center Press

Woodslane Pty Ltd, *distributor for* Manning Publications Co

Word Aflame Press, *subsidiary of* Pentecostal Publishing House, *imprint of* Pentecostal Publishing House

Word & Quill Press, *distributed by* Cross-Cultural Communications

Word Inc, *subsidiary of* Thomas Nelson Inc

Word Music, *distributed by* Hal Leonard Corp

Words Distributing Co, *distributor for* UglyTown

Words Distributors, *distributor for* Healthy Healing Publications

Wordsong, *imprint of* Boyds Mills Press

Wordtree branching dictionary, *distributed by* Amazon.com, Brodart

Wordware Publishing Inc, *distributor for* Seaside Press

Working Smarter, *imprint of* OneOnOne Computer Training

Workman Publishing, *distributor for* Black Dog & Leventhal Publishers Inc

Workman Publishing Co Inc, *distributor for* Algonquin Books of Chapel Hill, Black Dog & Leventhal, Greenwich Workshop Press, Storey Books, Storey Publishing

World Almanac Books, *division of* World Almanac Education Group, *distributed by* St Martin's Press Inc, St Martin's Press LLC

World Bank, *imprint of* World Bank Publications, *distributed by* Bernan

World Bank Publications, *member of* The World Bank Group

World Book Inc, *subsidiary of* The Scott Fetzer Co

World Citizens, *affiliate of* Cinema Investments Co Inc, Cinema Investments Co Inc, *distributed by* Inland

World Eagle, *division of* Independent Broadcasting Associates Inc, Independent Broadcasting Associates Inc

World Literature Ministries, *imprint of* CRC Publications

World of Darkness, *imprint of* White Wolf Publishing Inc

World of Knowledges, *imprint of* Modern Publishing

World of Wildlife, *imprint of* Modern Publishing

World Publishing, *distributor for* Inspirational Press

World Reference Resources, *division of* Gareth Stevens Inc

World Tourism Organization (WTO), *distributed by* Bernan

World Trade Organization (WTO), *distributed by* Bernan

World Trade Press, *distributed by* Reference Press

WW II Journal, *imprint of* Merriam Press

WW II Memoirs, *imprint of* Merriam Press

World War II Monographs, *imprint of* Merriam Press

World Wide Features, *distributor for* Printlink Publishers Inc

World Wisdom (US), *distributed by* Fons Vitae

World Wrestling Entertainment, *imprint of* Pocket Books

The World's Largest Publishing Co, *subsidiary of* Gallopade International Inc

Worsley Press, *distributed by* Florida Academic Press

The Wright Group/McGraw-Hill, *imprint of* McGraw-Hill Education

The Wright Group/McGraw-Hill, a Division of McGraw-Hill Learning Group, *division of* McGraw-Hill Learning Group

Write Stuff®, *imprint of* Write Stuff Enterprises Inc

Write to Print, *imprint of* Sweetgrass Press LLC

Writers & Artists on Photography Series, *imprint of* Aperture Books

Writer's AudioShop, *distributed by* Timberwolf Press (TWP)

The Writers' Collective, *distributor for* Beef on Weck Press, Lucky Duck Press, Twilight Times Books, Twin Stars Unlimited

Writer's Digest, *distributed by* Hal Leonard Corp

Writer's Digest Books, *imprint of* F+W Publications Inc, F+W Publications Inc, *distributor for* Rockport Publishers

Writers House, *subsidiary of* Welcome Rain Publishers LLC

Writers Publishing Co-op, *distributed by* Enfield Publishing & Distribution Co

The Writings of Mary Baker Eddy/Publisher, *division of* First Church of Christ, Scientist, The First Church of Christ, Scientist

Wrox™, *imprint of* John Wiley & Sons Inc

WWE Books, *imprint of* Simon & Schuster Adult Publishing Group

Jerome Wycoff, *distributed by* Paul & Company

X Press, *imprint of* Media Associates

Xemplar, *imprint of* Crossquarter Publishing Group

XLIBRIS, *distributor for* Blue Unicorn Press Inc

Yale University Press, *division of* Yale University, *distributor for* The Colonial Williamsburg Foundation, The Metropolitan Museum of Art, National Gallery of Art, Nevraumont Publishing Co, Philadelphia Museum of Art

Yankee, *distributor for* Teton New Media

Yankee Book Peddler, *distributor for* Investor Responsibility Research Center, Primary Research Group

Yankee Book Peddlers, *distributor for* Noble Publishing Corp

Yardbird, *imprint of* Yardbird Books

Year Book, *imprint of* Elsevier

Yearling, *imprint of* Random House Children's Books

Yellow Book Directories, *imprint of* Leadership Directories Inc

Yellow 1, *imprint of* Wide World of Maps Inc

Yes Press, *imprint of* Down There Press

Yeshiva University Press, *distributed by* KTAV Publishing House Inc

YMAA Publication Center, *division of* Yangs Oriental Arts Association, *distributor for* Wind Records, *distributed by* National Book Network, New Leaf

YMCA of Greater New York, *distributed by* Fordham University Press

YMCA of the USA, *imprint of* Human Kinetics Inc

Yoga International, *imprint of* Himalayan Institute Press

Yohan, *distributor for* Weatherhill Inc

York Medieval Press, *imprint of* Boydell & Brewer Inc

York Press, *distributed by* The Alexander Graham Bell Association for the Deaf & Hard of Hearing

York Press Inc, *distributed by* A G Bell Association for the Deaf, Educators Publishing Service

You Can Teach Yourself, *imprint of* Mel Bay Publications Inc

Young Adult Resources, *division of* Gareth Stevens Inc

Young Hearts, *imprint of* J & L Lee Co

Noel Young Books, *imprint of* Capra Press

Young Reader's Christian Library, *imprint of* Barbour Publishing Inc

Young Think®, *imprint of* Thomas Geale Publications Inc

Your Domain Publishing, *imprint of* JIST Publishing Inc

Yourdon Press, *imprint of* Pearson Higher Education Division

YOUTHLIGHT, *distributor for* MAR*CO Products Inc

Yucca Tree Press, *imprint of* Barbed Wire Publishing, *distributor for* B & J Publications, Eakin Press, Filter Press, Gently Worded Books, Nita Stewart Haley Library, High Lonesome Books, KIVA Publications, Rimrock Press

Yuridicheskaya Literatura (Russia), *distributed by* Fort Ross Inc

Ywam Publishing, *division of* Youth with a Mission, *distributor for* Emerald Books

Zahava Publications, *imprint of* Judaica Press Inc

Zambak, *distributed by* The Light Inc

Zaner-Bloser Inc, *subsidiary of* Highlights for Children Inc

Zanzibar Press, *imprint of* Health Resources Press Inc

Zebra Books, *imprint of* Kensington Publishing Corp

Zed Books, *distributed by* St Martin's Press LLC

Zed Books (London), *distributor for* The Apex Press, *distributed by* The Apex Press

Zen Studies Society Press, *distributed by* Tuttle Publishing

Zenith Books, *distributor for* The Info Devel Press

Zeon, *distributed by* Gryphon Books

Zephyr Press Catalog, *distributor for* Dale Seymour Publications, B L Winch Associates, *distributed by* Opportunities for Learning Inc, Sundance Publishers & Distributors

Zephyr Press Inc, *distributor for* Great Potential Press

Zephyrus Press, *distributed by* Cave Books

Zero Productions, *distributed by* Kazi Publications Inc

H O Zimman Inc, *distributor for* United States Tennis Association

Zoland Books, *imprint of* Steerforth Press

Zon Association, *imprint of* Neo-Tech Publishing

ZonderKidz, *imprint of* Zondervan

Zondervan, *division of* HarperCollins Publishers, *imprint of* Zondervan, *distributor for* Focus on the Family

Zone Books, *division of* Urzone Inc, Urzone Inc, *distributed by* The MIT Press

Zoo Press, *distributed by* University of Nebraska Press

Zuckschwerdt Verlag (Munich, Germany), *distributed by* Scholium International Inc

ZYZZYVA First Titles, *distributed by* Creative Arts Book Co

Canadian Publishers

Listed in alphabetical order are those Canadian publishers that have reported to *LMP* that they produce an average of three or more books annually. Publishers that have appeared in a previous edition of *LMP*, but whose output currently does not meet our defined rate of activity, will be reinstated when their annual production reaches the required level. It should be noted that this rule of publishing activity does not apply to publishers of dictionaries, encyclopedias, atlases and braille books or to university presses.

The definition of a book is that used for *Books in Print* (R.R. Bowker LLC, 630 Central Avenue, New Providence, NJ 07974, USA) and excludes charts, pamphlets, folding maps, sheet music and material with stapled bindings. Publishers that make their titles available only in electronic or audio format are included if they meet the stated criteria. In the case of packages, the book must be of equal or greater importance than the accompanying piece. With few exceptions, new publishers are not listed prior to having published at least three titles within a year.

§ before the company name indicates those publishers involved in electronic publishing.

Academic Printing & Publishing
9-3151 Lakeshore Rd, Suite 403, Kelowna, BC
   V1W 3S9
Tel: 250-764-6427 *Fax:* 250-464-6428
E-mail: app@silk.net
Web Site: www.academicprintingandpublishing.
   com
Key Personnel
Proprietor: Roger Shiner
Busn Mgr: Sharon Pfenning
Publisher of books & journals.
Publishes in English, French.
ISBN Prefix(es): 0-920980
Number of titles published annually: 3 Print
Total Titles: 24 Print

ACTA Press/IASTED
4500 16 Ave NW, No 80, Calgary, AB T3B 0M6
Mailing Address: 1811 W Katella Ave, Suite 101,
   Anaheim, CA 92814, United States
Tel: 403-288-1195 *Fax:* 403-247-6851
E-mail: comments@actapress.com
Web Site: www.actapress.com
Key Personnel
Pres: Dr M H Hamza *E-mail:* hamza@iasted.com
Founded: 1971
Scientific & technical conference proceedings &
   journals; Computers, control & power systems,
   information technology, robotics, signal & im-
   age processing.
Publishes in English.
ISBN Prefix(es): 0-88986
Number of titles published annually: 30 Print; 3
   CD-ROM
Total Titles: 350 Print; 3 CD-ROM
U.S. Rep(s): ACTA Press

Actualisation
300 Leo-Pariseau, Suite 2200, Montreal, PQ H2X
   4B3
Tel: 514-284-2622 *Fax:* 514-284-2625
Web Site: www.actualisation.com
Key Personnel
Pres & Intl Rts: Jacques Lalanne
   E-mail: jlalanne@actualisation.com
Founded: 1980
Management training; human resources.
Publishes in French.
ISBN Prefix(es): 2-921547
Number of titles published annually: 4 Print
Total Titles: 146 Print
Foreign Rep(s): Geodif (France)
Membership(s): ANEL

The Althouse Press
Unit of University of Western Ontario
University of Western Ontario, 1137 Western Rd,
   London, ON N6G 1G7
SAN: 115-1142
Tel: 519-661-2096 *Fax:* 519-661-3833
E-mail: press@uwo.ca
Web Site: www.edu.uwo.ca/althousepress

Key Personnel
Intl Rts: Greg Dickinson *E-mail:* gdickins@uwo.
   ca
Edit Asst: Katherine Butson *E-mail:* kbutson@
   uwo.ca
Founded: 1977
Education, scholarly books, videotapes.
Publishes in English.
ISBN Prefix(es): 0-920354
Number of titles published annually: 3 Print
Total Titles: 53 Print
Distributed by SUNY Press; University of
   Chicago Press
Distributor for Lorimer; SUNY Press; Teachers
   College Press; University of Chicago Press

Altitude Publishing Canada Ltd
1500 Railway Ave, Canmore, AB T1W 1P6
SAN: 115-0049
Tel: 403-678-6888 *Toll Free Tel:* 800-957-6888
   Fax: 403-678-6951 *Toll Free Fax:* 800-957-
   1477
E-mail: orderdesk@altitudepublishing.com;
   sales@altitudepublishing.com (ordering)
Web Site: www.altitudepublishing.com
Key Personnel
Pres & Publr: Stephen Hutchings
VP, Fin & Opers: Laurie Smith
Sr Acct Mgr: John Walls
Commun Coord & Orders: Sue Anderson
   E-mail: sanderson@altitudepublishing.com
Billing Contact: Michelle Naffin
Warehouse, Shipping & Returns Contact: Kaila
   Mosa
Founded: 1978
Publish pictorial & guide books, postcards,
   posters & calendars related to the Canadian
   Rockies & Western Canada & Colorado, as
   well as historical books on these same regions.
   Also includes Canadian biography & amazing
   stories.
Publishes in English, French.
ISBN Prefix(es): 0-919381; 1-55153; 1-55265; 1-
   55149
Number of titles published annually: 40 Print
Total Titles: 150 Print
Editorial Office(s): Campana Place, Suite 402,
   609 14 St NW, Calgary, AB T2N 2A1
Membership(s): Canadian Booksellers Associa-
   tion; Pacific Northwest Booksellers Association

The Anglican Book Centre
80 Hayden St, Toronto, ON M4Y 3G2
Tel: 416-924-1332 *Toll Free Tel:* 800-268-1168
   (Canada only) *Fax:* 416-924-2760
E-mail: abc@nationalanglican.com
Web Site: www.anglicanbookcentre.com
Key Personnel
Publr: Robert Maclennan
Founded: 1920
Liturgical texts, religious trade books.
Publishes in English.

ISBN Prefix(es): 0-921846; 0-919030; 1-55126
Number of titles published annually: 13 Print
Total Titles: 100 Print
Distributed by SCM-Canterbury Press Norwich;
   Forward Movement

Annick Press Ltd
15 Patricia Ave, Toronto, ON M2M 1H9
SAN: 115-0065
Tel: 416-221-4802 *Fax:* 416-221-8400
E-mail: annick@annickpress.com
Web Site: www.annickpress.com
Key Personnel
Ed: Colleen MacMillan *Fax:* 604-879-5467
   E-mail: colleenm@annickpress.com; Rick
   Wilks
Sales & Rts Mgr: Susan Shipton *E-mail:* susans@
   annickpress.com
Lib Sales Dir, Firefly Books: Ann Quinn
Mktg Mgr: Libbie Lightstone *E-mail:* libbiel@
   annickpress.com
Founded: 1975
Children's books.
Publishes in English, French.
ISBN Prefix(es): 0-920236; 0-920303; 1-55037
Number of titles published annually: 25 Print
Total Titles: 425 Print
Branch Office(s)
288 W Eighth Ave, Suite 212, Vancouver, BC
   V5Y 1N5, Assoc Publr: Colleen MacMillan
   Tel: 604-718-1888 *Fax:* 604-879-5467
Distributed by Firefly Books Ltd
U.S. Rep(s): Nicholas H Altwerger; Lesley An-
   derson; Elizabeth Biernacki; Ian Booth; Bob
   Ditter; Lindsay Emberley; Paul G Emberley;
   Rachel Ginsburg; Debbie Johnson-Houstoni;
   Paul Lockwood; Ted Lucia; Thomas Martin;
   Thomas J McFadden Assoc; Glen McHaney;
   Bonnie McKenney; McLemore/Hollern & As-
   soc Inc; Kevin T Monahan; Doug Paton; Ann
   Quinn; Jim Sena; Ann Swanson; William Tier-
   ney; Beth Ann Walck; Dennis Walker; Karen
   Winters; Susan Zevnik
Foreign Rights: Sandra Homer
Membership(s): Association of Canadian Publish-
   ers; Canadian Booksellers Association; CCI;
   Ontario Book Publishers Organization

Anvilpress Inc
Formerly Blue Lake Books
PO Box 3008, Vancouver, BC V6B 3X5
Tel: 604-876-8710 *Toll Free Tel:* 800-565-9523
   (ordering) *Fax:* 604-879-2667
E-mail: info@anvilpress.com
Web Site: www.anvilpress.com
Key Personnel
Publr: Brian Kaufman
Founded: 1988
Literary, all genres; theater & modern contempo-
   rary literature. Canadian authored titles only.
Publishes in English.
ISBN Prefix(es): 1-895636

Number of titles published annually: 10 Print
Total Titles: 49 Print
Distribution Center: University of Toronto Press
Membership(s): Association of Book Publishers
of British Columbia; Association of Canadian
Publishers; Literary Press Group

Aquila Communications Inc
2642 Diab St, St Laurent, PQ H4S 1E8
Tel: 514-338-1065 *Toll Free Tel:* 800-667-7071
Fax: 514-338-1948 *Toll Free Fax:* 866-338-
1948
E-mail: aquila@aquilacommunications.com
Web Site: www.aquilacommunications.com
Key Personnel
Pres: Sami Kelada
Founded: 1970
High-interest/low-vocabulary readers for learn-
ers of French as a second language, grades 3
through college. Also, short humorous situa-
tional dialogues (1,200 words) in comic book
format for kids & teens. Funny episodes of
daily life of North American kids & teens
(home & school).
Publishes in English, French.
ISBN Prefix(es): 0-88510
Number of titles published annually: 15 Print
Total Titles: 15 Print
Distributed by Aquila Communications Ltd

Arsenal Pulp Press Book Publishers Ltd
1014 Homer St, Suite 103, Vancouver, BC V6B
2W9
Tel: 604-687-4233 *Toll Free Tel:* 888-600-PULP
(600-7857) *Fax:* 604-687-4283
E-mail: contact@arsenalpulp.com
Web Site: www.arsenalpulp.com
Key Personnel
Publr: Brian Lam
Man Ed: Blaine Kyllo
Sales Dir: Robert Ballantyne
Founded: 1982
Literary.
Publishes in English.
ISBN Prefix(es): 0-88978; 1-55152
Number of titles published annually: 24 Print
Total Titles: 130 Print
Imprints: Advance Editions; Pulp Press; Tillacum
Library
Subsidiaries: Pulp Press
U.S. Rep(s): Consortium Book Sales & Distribu-
tion
Distribution Center: Consortium Book Sales &
Distribution

**Association pour l'Avancement des Sciences et
des Techniques de la Documentation**
3414 Avenue du Parc, Bureau 202, Montreal, PQ
H2X 2H5
Tel: 514-281-5012 *Fax:* 514-281-8219
E-mail: info@asted.org
Web Site: www.asted.org
Key Personnel
Dir-Gen: Louis Cabral *E-mail:* lcabral@asted.org
Founded: 1974
Publishes in French.
ISBN Prefix(es): 2-921548
Number of titles published annually: 3 Print

B & B Publishing
4823 Sherbrooke St W, Office 275, Westmount,
PQ H3Z 1G7
Tel: 514-932-9466 *Fax:* 514-932-5929
E-mail: editions@ebbp.ca
Key Personnel
Publr: Paul Beullac
Founded: 1996
Publisher of educational materials; books & wall
maps for schools across Canada.
Publishes in English, French.
ISBN Prefix(es): 2-7615
Number of titles published annually: 7 Print

Total Titles: 381 Print
Distributed by Brault & Bouthillier Ltee; Brault
& Bouthillier School Supplies
Foreign Rep(s): ASCO (France); Bricolux (Bel-
gium); Leisure Fun (Australia); Siskel (Bel-
gium); Wesco (France)
Foreign Rights: World Trans Tech Corp (Taiwan)
Distribution Center: 700, ave Beaumont, Mon-
treal, PQ H3N 1V5 *Tel:* 514-273-9186
Fax: 514-273-8627

Banff Centre Press
107 Tunnel Mountain Dr, Box 1020, Banff, AB
T1L 1H5
Tel: 403-762-7532 *Fax:* 403-762-6699
E-mail: press@banffcentre.ca
Web Site: www.banffcentre.ca/press
Key Personnel
Man Ed: Jennifer Nault
Founded: 1995
Publisher of books on contemporary art & cul-
ture.
Publishes in English, French.
ISBN Prefix(es): 0-920159; 1-894773
Number of titles published annually: 5 Print
Total Titles: 37 Print; 2 CD-ROM
Orders to: ListDistCo, 100 Armstrong Ave,
Georgetown, ON L7G 5S4
Returns: ListDistCo, 100 Armstrong Ave,
Georgetown, ON L7G 5S4
Warehouse: ListDistCo, 100 Armstrong Ave,
Georgetown, ON L7G 5S4
Distribution Center: ListDistCo, 100 Armstrong
Ave, Georgetown, ON L7G 5S4
Membership(s): Book Publishers Association of
Alberta; Literary Press Group

Beach Holme Publishing
409 Granville St, Suite 1010, Vancouver, BC V6C
1T2
SAN: 115-0812
Tel: 604-733-4868 *Toll Free Tel:* 888-551-6655
(orders) *Fax:* 604-733-4860
E-mail: bhp@beachholme.bc.ca
Web Site: www.beachholme.bc.ca
Key Personnel
Chmn of the Bd: Ellen Godfrey
Pres: Dave Godfrey
Publr: Michael Carroll
Publicity & Mktg Coord: Sarah Warren
Prod Mgr: Jen Hamilton
Founded: 1971
Publish works by Canadian authors exclusively.
Publishes in English.
ISBN Prefix(es): 0-88878
Number of titles published annually: 11 Print
Total Titles: 60 Print
Imprints: Porcepic Books; Prospect Books; Sand-
castle Books

Beaconhill Books Catalogue
9972 Third St, Suite 10, Sidney, BC V8L 3B2
Tel: 250-656-0537 *Fax:* 250-656-0537
Web Site: www.beaconhillbooks.net
Key Personnel
Publr & Owner: Toni Graeme
Founded: 2003
North American book catalogue for self published
authors.
Publishes in English.
Number of titles published annually: 40 Print
Total Titles: 55 Print

Groupe Beauchemin, Editeur Ltee
(Beuchemin Group Limited)
3281 ave Jean Beraud, Laval, PQ H7T 2L2
Tel: 514-334-5912 *Toll Free Tel:* 800-361-2598
(US & Canada); 800-361-4504 (Canada Only)
Fax: 450-688-6269
E-mail: promotion@beauchemin.qc.ca
Web Site: www.beaucheminediteur.com

Key Personnel
CEO: Guy Frenette
VP: Michel C Perron
Mktg Dir: Nadine Naoum
Founded: 1842
Pre-K to college school books; arts reproduction
& musical.
Publishes in English, French.
ISBN Prefix(es): 2-7616
Number of titles published annually: 40 Print
Total Titles: 800 Print
U.S. Publishers Represented: G B Publishing Inc
Art Education
U.S. Rep(s): Rachel Ross

Between the Lines
720 Bathurst St, No 404, Toronto, ON M5S 2R4
SAN: 115-0189
Tel: 416-535-9914 *Toll Free Tel:* 800-718-7201
Fax: 416-535-1484
E-mail: btlbooks@web.ca
Web Site: www.btlbooks.com
Key Personnel
Edit Coord: Paul Eprile
Sales & Mktg Coord: Peter Steven
Founded: 1977
Nonfiction, social, economic & political works
dealing with international development issues
& Canadian social issues.
Publishes in English.
ISBN Prefix(es): 0-919946; 0-921284; 1-896357
Number of titles published annually: 12 Print
Total Titles: 110 Print
U.S. Rep(s): S C B Distributors
Warehouse: University of Toronto Press, 5201
Dufferin St, Downsview, ON M3H 5T8 *Toll
Free Fax:* 800-221-9985
Distribution Center: S C B Distributors, 15608 S
New Century Dr, Gardena, CA 90248, United
States (USA dist) *Tel:* 310-532-7001 *Toll Free
Tel:* 800-729-6423

Black Rose Books Ltd
CP 1258 Succ Place de Parc, Montreal, PQ H2X
4A7
SAN: 115-2653
Tel: 514-844-4076 *Toll Free Tel:* 800-565-9523
Fax: 514-849-4797 *Toll Free Fax:* 800-221-
9985
E-mail: blackrose@web.net
Web Site: www.web.net/blackrosebooks
Key Personnel
Publr & Intl Rts: Jacques Roux
Intl Rts Contact: Alexandre Negri
Mktg Promo: Linda Barton *E-mail:* linda@web.
net
Founded: 1969
Specialize in politics, book & journal publishing
in the social sciences & humanities.
Publishes in English.
ISBN Prefix(es): 0-919618; 0-919619; 0-920057;
0-921689; 1-55164
Number of titles published annually: 21 Print; 12
Online; 10 E-Book
Total Titles: 498 Print; 12 E-Book
Branch Office(s)
Black Rose Books Ltd c/o University of Toronto
Press, 2250 Military Rd, Tonawanda, NY
14150, United States *Tel:* 716-683-4547
Fax: 716-685-6895
Foreign Office(s): Black Rose Books Ltd, c/o
Central Books, 99 Wallis Rd, London E9
5LN, United Kingdom *Tel:* (020) 8986 4854
Fax: (020) 8533 5821 *E-mail:* orders@
centralbooks.com
Distributed by University of Toronto Press
U.S. Rep(s): Abraham Associates; The Karel/Dut-
ton Group; Palmer Associates; Roghaar Asso-
ciates Southeast; Rovers Inc
Advertising Agency: Turnaround c/o Central
Books, 99 Wallis Rd, London E9 5LN, United
Kingdom *Tel:* (020) 8986 4854 *Fax:* (020)
8533 5821 *E-mail:* orders@centralbooks.com

Orders to: Consortium Book Sales & Distribution, 1045 Westgate Dr, St Paul, MN 55114-1065, United States, Sales Mgr: Julie Schaper *Toll Free Tel:* 800-283-3572 *Fax:* 651-917-6406 *E-mail:* consortium@cbsd.com
Returns: Consortium Book Sales & Distribution, 1045 Westgate Dr, St Paul, MN 55114-1065, United States, Sales Mgr: Julie Schaper *Toll Free Tel:* 800-283-3572 *Fax:* 651-917-6406 *E-mail:* consortium@cbsd.com
Shipping Address: Consortium Book Sales & Distribution, 1045 Westgate Dr, St Paul, MN 55114-1065, United States, Sales Mgr: Julie Schaper *Toll Free Tel:* 800-283-3572 *Fax:* 651-917-6406 *E-mail:* consortium@cbsd.com
Distribution Center: Consortium Book Sales & Distribution, 1045 Westgate Dr, St Paul, MN 55114-1065, United States, Sales Mgr: Julie Schaper *Toll Free Tel:* 800-283-3572 *Fax:* 651-917-6406 *E-mail:* consortium@cbsd.com

Blue Lake Books, see Anvilpress Inc

Editions du Bois-de-Coulonge
1140 Demontigny, Sillery, PQ G1S 3T7
Tel: 418-683-6332 *Fax:* 418-683-6332
Web Site: www.ebc.qc.ca
Key Personnel
Owner & Pres: Richard Leclerc, PhD
Founded: 1995
Publish & distribute books about music, multimedia, television & movies.
Publishes in French.
ISBN Prefix(es): 2-9801397
Number of titles published annually: 1 Print
Total Titles: 7 Print
Membership(s): Association for the Export of Canadian Books

Books Collective
214-21 10405 Jasper Ave, Edmonton, AB T5J 3S2
Tel: 780-448-0590 *Fax:* 780-448-0640
E-mail: river@bookscollective.com
Web Site: www.bookscollective.com
Key Personnel
Man Ed: Candas Jane Dorsey
Founded: 1992
Canadian authors & artists only. Dinosaur Soup imprint is children's books, River/Slipstream Books imprints are poetry, essays & books that challenge the mainstream.
Publishes in English.
ISBN Prefix(es): 0-88878; 1-895836
Number of titles published annually: 3 Print; 1 Audio
Total Titles: 50 Print; 1 Audio
Imprints: Dinosaur Soup; River Books; Tesseract Books
Distributed by Coteau Books; Red Deer Press
U.S. Rep(s): General Distribution Services
Membership(s): Book Publishers Association of Alberta

Borealis Press Ltd
110 Bloomingdale St, Ottawa, ON K2C 4A4
Tel: 613-798-9299 *Fax:* 613-798-9747
E-mail: borealis@istar.ca
Web Site: www.borealispress.com
Key Personnel
Pres & Lib Sales Dir: Frank Tierney
VP & Sr Ed: Glenn Clever
Founded: 1971
Canadian-oriented general titles of most types.
Publishes in English, French.
ISBN Prefix(es): 0-88887; 1-896133
Number of titles published annually: 20 Print
Total Titles: 350 Print
Subsidiaries: Tecumseh Press
U.S. Rep(s): Baker & Taylor; Blackwell; Dawson; Ebsco; Ex Libris; Hein; Swets

Orders to: 57 Horner Dr, Ottawa, ON K2H 5G1
Shipping Address: 8 Mohawk Crescent, Ottawa, ON K2H 7G6 *Tel:* 613-829-0150 *Fax:* 613-829-7783

The Boston Mills Press
Division of Firefly Books Ltd
132 Main St, Erin, ON N0B 1T0
Tel: 519-833-2407 *Fax:* 519-833-2195
E-mail: books@bostonmillspress.com
Web Site: www.bostonmillspress.com
Key Personnel
Pres & Publr: John Denison
Intl Rts Contact: Sandra Homer *Tel:* 416-499-8412 *Fax:* 416-499-8313
Founded: 1974
Canadian & American history, guide books, large format colour photograph books.
Publishes in English.
ISBN Prefix(es): 0-919822; 0-919783; 1-55046
Number of titles published annually: 20 Print
Total Titles: 150 Print

Breakwater Books Ltd
100 Water St, St Johns, NF A1C 6E6
Mailing Address: PO Box 2188, St Johns, NF A1C 6E6
Tel: 709-722-6680 *Toll Free Tel:* 800-563-3333 *Fax:* 709-753-0708
E-mail: info@breakwater.nf.net
Web Site: www.breakwater.nf.net; www.breakwaterbooks.com
Key Personnel
Pres: Clyde Rose
Gen Mgr: Wade Foote
Founded: 1973
Books primarily about education & trade books.
Publishes in English, French.
ISBN Prefix(es): 0-919519; 0-919948; 0-920911; 1-55081
Number of titles published annually: 7 Print
Total Titles: 265 Print

Broadview Press
280 Perry St, Unit 5, Peterborough, ON K9J 2A8
SAN: 115-6772
Mailing Address: PO Box 1243, Peterborough, ON K9J 7H5
Tel: 705-743-8990 *Fax:* 705-743-8353
E-mail: customerservice@broadviewpress.com
Web Site: www.broadviewpress.com
Key Personnel
Pres: Don Le Pan *Tel:* 403-232-1443 *Fax:* 403-233-0001 *E-mail:* don.lepan@broadviewpress.com
VP: Michael Harrison *Tel:* 519-837-0915 *Fax:* 519-767-1643 *E-mail:* mharrison@broadviewpress.com
Prodn: Barbara Conolly *Tel:* 705-743-7581 ext 30 *E-mail:* bconolly@broadviewpress.com
Dist & Promo Coord: Lisa Gray *E-mail:* lgray@broadviewpress.com
Cont: Carol Richardson *E-mail:* crichardson@broadviewpress.com
Sr Accts Officer: LeeAnna Dykstra *E-mail:* ldykstra@broadviewpress.com
Founded: 1985
Textbooks & nonfiction, arts & social sciences.
Publishes in English.
ISBN Prefix(es): 0-921149; 1-55111
Number of titles published annually: 80 Print
Total Titles: 240 Print
Branch Office(s)
3576 California Rd, Orchard Park, NY 14127, United States
414-815 First St SW, Calgary, AB T2P 1N3
Tel: 403-232-6863 *Fax:* 403-233-0001
E-mail: broadview@broadviewpress.com
54 Glasgow St N, Guelph, ON N1H 4V7
Tel: 519-837-1257 *Fax:* 519-767-1643
Distributed by St Clair (Australia); Thomas Lyster, Ltd

U.S. Publishers Represented: Island Press
U.S. Rep(s): Hill/Martin Associates; John & Nancy Lovejoy; Miller Trade Book Marketing; Lois Shearer Associates

Broken Jaw Press Inc
5-2004 York St, Fredericton, NB E3B 5A6
SAN: 117-1437
Mailing Address: Box 596, Sta A, Fredericton, NB E3B 5A6
Tel: 506-454-5127 *Fax:* 506-454-5127
Web Site: www.brokenjaw.com
Key Personnel
Pres & Publr: Joe Blades *E-mail:* jblades@brokenjaw.com
Founded: 1985
Publish mostly literary books: poetry, fiction, drama & creative nonfiction.
Publishes in English, French.
ISBN Prefix(es): 0-921411; 1-896647; 1-55391
Number of titles published annually: 11 Print; 1 Audio
Total Titles: 91 Print; 40 E-Book; 2 Audio
Imprints: Book Rat; Broken Jaw Press; Broken Jaw Press eBooks; Cauldron Books; Dead Sea Physh Products; Maritimes Arts Projects Productions; SpareTime Editions; Velvet Touch; Your MAPP
Sales Office(s): Literary Press Group of Canada, 501-192 Spadina Ave, Toronto, ON M5T 2C2 *Tel:* 416-483-1321 *Fax:* 416-483-2510 *E-mail:* info@lpg.ca *Web Site:* www.lpg.ca
Distributor for White Dwarf Editions
U.S. Rep(s): Literary Press Group of Canada, 501-192 Spadina Ave, Toronto, ON M5T 2C2
Orders to: LitDistCo, 100 Armstrong Ave, Georgetown, ON L7G 5S4 *Tel:* 905-877-4411 *Toll Free Tel:* 800-591-6250 *Fax:* 905-877-4410 *Toll Free Fax:* 800-591-6251 *E-mail:* orders@litdistco.ca
Returns: LitDistCo, 100 Armstrong Ave, Georgetown, ON L7G 5S4 *Tel:* 905-877-4411 *Toll Free Tel:* 800-591-6250 *Fax:* 905-877-4410 *Toll Free Fax:* 800-591-6251 *E-mail:* orders@litdistco.ca
Shipping Address: LitDistCo, 100 Armstrong Ave, Georgetown, ON L7G 5S4 *Tel:* 905-877-4411 *Toll Free Tel:* 800-591-6250 *Fax:* 905-877-4410 *Toll Free Fax:* 800-591-6251 *E-mail:* orders@litdistco.ca
Warehouse: LitDistCo, 100 Armstrong Ave, Georgetown, ON L7G 5S4 *Tel:* 905-877-4411 *Toll Free Tel:* 800-591-6250 *Fax:* 905-877-4410 *Toll Free Fax:* 800-591-6251 *E-mail:* orders@litdistco.ca
Distribution Center: LitDistCo, 100 Armstrong Ave, Georgetown, ON L7G 5S4 *Tel:* 905-877-4411 *Toll Free Tel:* 800-591-6250 *Fax:* 905-877-4410 *Toll Free Fax:* 800-591-6251 *E-mail:* orders@litdistco.ca
Membership(s): Association of Canadian Publishers; Atlantic Publishers Marketing Association; Literary Press Group

Broquet Inc
97B Montee des Bouleaux, St Constant, PQ J5A 1A9
Tel: 450-638-3338 *Fax:* 450-638-4338
E-mail: info@broquet.qc.ca
Web Site: www.broquet.qc.ca
Key Personnel
Pres: Antoine Broquet
Founded: 1979
Nature books & astronomy.
Publishes in English, French.
ISBN Prefix(es): 2-89000
Number of titles published annually: 20 Print; 1 CD-ROM
Total Titles: 530 Print; 1 CD-ROM
Distributed by Diffusion Prologue

Callawind Publications Inc
3539 Saint Charles Blvd, Suite 179, Kirkland, PQ
H9H 3C4
Mailing Address: PMB 355, 2083 Hempstead
Tpke, East Meadow, NY 11554-1711, United
States
Tel: 514-685-9109 *Fax:* 514-685-7952
E-mail: info@callawind.com
Web Site: www.callawind.com
Key Personnel
Mktg: Pamela Carmen *E-mail:* pamela@
callawind.com
Founded: 1995
Book publisher & book packager, specializing in
cookbooks.
Publishes in English.
ISBN Prefix(es): 1-896511
Number of titles published annually: 3 Print
Total Titles: 11 Print
U.S. Rep(s): Biblio Distribution (division of
NBN)
Membership(s): Publishers Marketing Associa-
tion; Small Publishers Association of North
America

§Canada Law Book Inc
Subsidiary of Cartwright Omni Corp
240 Edward St, Aurora, ON L4G 3S9
Tel: 905-841-6472 *Toll Free Tel:* 800-263-2037
Fax: 905-841-5085
Web Site: www.canadalawbook.ca
Key Personnel
Dir, Mktg & Sales: Brian Loney *Tel:* 905-841-
6472 ext 151 *E-mail:* bloney@canadalawbook.
ca
Founded: 1855
Law books.
Publishes in English.
ISBN Prefix(es): 0-88804
Number of titles published annually: 50 Print; 3
CD-ROM; 3 E-Book
Total Titles: 480 Print; 19 CD-ROM; 10 Online;
9 E-Book
Online services available through LexisNexis,
QuickLaw.
Imprints: Aurora Professional Press; Western Le-
gal Publications (1982) Ltd
Subsidiaries: Canadian Lawyer Magazine; Law
Times
Branch Office(s)
c/o Western Legal Publications, Box 5, 501-595
Howe St, Vancouver, BC V6C 2T5 *Tel:* 604-
844-7855 *Fax:* 604-844-7813

Canadian Bible Society
10 Carnforth Rd, Toronto, ON M4A 2S4
SAN: 112-5559
Tel: 416-757-4171 *Toll Free Tel:* 800-465-2425
Fax: 416-757-3376
E-mail: custserv@biblesociety.ca
Web Site: www.biblescanada.com
Founded: 1804
Bibles, new testaments, scripture portions, selec-
tions; scriptures in foreign languages.
Publishes in English, French.
ISBN Prefix(es): 0-88834
Number of titles published annually: 20 Print; 3
CD-ROM; 10 Online; 5 Audio
Total Titles: 2,500 Print; 10 CD-ROM; 120 Audio
Foreign Rep(s): United Bible Societies Around
the World

Canadian Circumpolar Institute (CCI) Press
Unit of Canadian Circumpolar Institue
University of Alberta, Campus Tower, Suite 308,
8625 112 St, Edmonton, AB T6H 0H1
Tel: 780-492-4512 *Fax:* 780-492-1153
E-mail: ccinst@gpu.srv.ualberta.ca
Web Site: www.ualberta.ca/~ccinst/
Key Personnel
Man Ed: Elaine Maloney *E-mail:* elaine.
maloney@ualberta.ca

Dist: Cindy Mason
Founded: 1960
Polar research.
Publishes in English.
ISBN Prefix(es): 1-896445; 0-919058
Number of titles published annually: 5 Print; 1
CD-ROM
Total Titles: 76 Print; 1 CD-ROM
Membership(s): Book Publishers Association of
Alberta

Canadian Committee On Labour History
Faculty of Arts Publications, fm 2005, Memo-
rial University of Newfoundland, St John's, NF
A1C 5S7
Tel: 709-737-2144 *Fax:* 709-737-4342
E-mail: cclh@mun.ca
Web Site: www.mun.ca/cclh/
Founded: 1976
Journals & books on labour & working class his-
tory.
Publishes in English, French.
ISBN Prefix(es): 1-894000; 0-9695835; 0-
9692060
Number of titles published annually: 20 Print
Total Titles: 21 Print

The Canadian Council on Social Development
309 Cooper St, 5th fl, Ottawa, ON K2P 0G5
Tel: 613-236-8977 *Fax:* 613-236-2750
E-mail: council@ccsd.ca
Web Site: www.ccsd.ca
Key Personnel
Exec Dir: Marcel Lauziere
Commus Coord: Nancy Perkins
Founded: 1920
Social policy, poverty, retirement, income secu-
rity, economics, sustainable development self-
help & aboriginal peoples.
Publishes in English, French.
ISBN Prefix(es): 0-88810
Number of titles published annually: 12 Print
Total Titles: 5 Print
Distributed by Renouf Publishing Ltd

**Canadian Education Association/Association
canadienne d'education**
317 Adelaide St W, Suite 300, Toronto, ON M5V
1P9
Tel: 416-591-6300 *Fax:* 416-591-5345
E-mail: info@cea.ace.ca
Web Site: www.cea-ace.ca
Key Personnel
CEO: Penny Milton *Tel:* 416-591-6300 ext 236
E-mail: pmilton@acea.ca
Res Officer: Valerie Pierre-Pierre
Founded: 1891
Educational newsletters & reports; magazine &
directories.
Publishes in English, French.
ISBN Prefix(es): 0-920315; 0-919078; 1-896660
Number of titles published annually: 6 Print
Total Titles: 21 Print

Canadian Energy Research Institute
3512 33 St NW, Suite 150, Calgary, AB T2L 2A6
Tel: 403-282-1231 *Fax:* 403-284-4181
E-mail: ceri@ceri.ca
Web Site: www.ceri.ca
Key Personnel
Pres & CEO: Dr Phil Prince *Tel:* 403-220-2390
E-mail: pprince@ceri.ca
Admin Coord: Megan Murphy
E-mail: mmurphy@ceri.ca
Founded: 1975
Energy research books, conferences, training
courses.
Publishes in English.
ISBN Prefix(es): 0-920522; 1-896091
Number of titles published annually: 5 Print
Total Titles: 150 Print

Canadian Institute of Chartered Accountants
277 Wellington St W, Toronto, ON M5V 3H2
Tel: 416-977-3222 *Toll Free Tel:* 800-268-3793
(Canadian orders) *Fax:* 416-977-8585
E-mail: orders@cica.ca
Web Site: www.cica.ca
Key Personnel
Dir: Peter J Hoult *Tel:* 416-204-3330 *Fax:* 416-
204-3415 *E-mail:* peter.hoult@cica.ca
Founded: 1917
Taxation, accounting, auditing, financial.
Publishes in English, French.
ISBN Prefix(es): 0-88800
Number of titles published annually: 15 Print
Total Titles: 200 Print; 40 CD-ROM; 2 E-Book

Canadian Institute of Resources Law
University of Calgary, Murray Fraser Hall, Rm
3330, 2500 University Dr NW, Calgary, AB
T2N 1N4
Tel: 403-220-3200 *Fax:* 403-282-6182
E-mail: cirl@ucalgary.ca
Web Site: www.cirl.ca
Key Personnel
Info Resources Officer: Sue Parsons
Leading national centre of expertise on legal &
policy issues relating to Canada's natural re-
sources.
Publishes in English.
ISBN Prefix(es): 0-919269
Number of titles published annually: 2 Print; 4
Online
Total Titles: 51 Print

Canadian Institute of Ukrainian Studies Press
Division of Canadian Institute of Ukrainian Stud-
ies
University of Toronto, One Spadina Crescent, Rm
109, Toronto, ON M5S 2J5
Tel: 416-978-6934 *Fax:* 416-978-2672
E-mail: cius@chass.utoronto.ca (edit off)
Web Site: www.utoronto.ca/cius
Key Personnel
Dir, Publg: Roman Senkus *E-mail:* rsenkus@
toronto.ca
Man Dir: Marko R Stech *Tel:* 416-946-7326
E-mail: mstech@utoronto.ca
Founded: 1976
Publisher of scholarly works in Ukranian studies
& Ukranian Canadian studies.
Publishes in English.
ISBN Prefix(es): 0-920862; 1-895571; 1-894865
Number of titles published annually: 5 Print
Total Titles: 140 Print
Distributed by Libraries Unlimited
U.S. Rep(s): Baker & Taylor Books
Orders to: CIUS Press, 450 Athabasca Hall,
University of Alberta, Edmonton, AB T6G
2E8 *Tel:* 780-492-2973 *Fax:* 780-492-4967
E-mail: cius@ualberta.ca
Returns: CIUS Press, 450 Athabasca Hall,
University of Alberta, Edmonton, AB T6G
2E8 *Tel:* 780-492-2973 *Fax:* 780-492-4967
E-mail: cius@ualberta.ca
Distribution Center: CIUS Press, 450 Athabasca
Hall, University of Alberta, Edmonton, AB
T6G 2E8, Contact: Iryna Pak *Tel:* 780-492-
2973 *Fax:* 780-492-4967 *E-mail:* cius@
ualberta.ca

§Canadian Museum of Civilization
100 Laurier St, Hull, PQ J8X 4H2
Mailing Address: Box 3100, Sta B, Hull, PQ J8X
4H2
Tel: 819-776-8387 *Toll Free Tel:* 800-555-5621
(North America only) *Fax:* 819-776-8300
E-mail: publications@civilization.ca (mail order)
Web Site: www.civilization.ca
Key Personnel
Acting VP, Pub Rel & Publg: Mark O'Neill
Tel: 819-776-8499 *E-mail:* mark.oneill@
civilization.ca

Promo & Mktg: Pam Coulas *Tel:* 819-776-8394
E-mail: pam.coulas@civilization.ca
Prod Officer: Deborah Brownrigg *Tel:* 819-776-8389 *E-mail:* deborah.brownrigg@civilization.ca
Museology, anthropology, archaeology, ethnology, folk culture, history, contemporary Native & Inuit art.
Publishes in English, French.
ISBN Prefix(es): 0-660
Number of titles published annually: 10 Print; 1 CD-ROM
Total Titles: 100 Print; 8 CD-ROM
Distributed by University of British Columbia Press; University of Wales Press, Cardiff (UK)
U.S. Rep(s): University of Washington Press
Distribution Center: Raincoast Distribution Services, 8680 Cambie St, Vancouver, BC V6P 6M9 *Toll Free Tel:* 800-663-5714 *Toll Free Fax:* 800-565-3770 *E-mail:* custserv@raincoast.com
Membership(s): Association for the Export of Canadian Books; Association of Canadian Publishers

Canadian Plains Research Center
University of Regina, Regina, SK S4S 0A2
SAN: 115-0278
Tel: 306-585-4758; 306-585-4759 *Fax:* 306-585-4699
Web Site: www.cprc.uregina.ca
Key Personnel
Exec Dir: David Gauthier
Pubns Mgr & Intl Rts: Brian Mlazgar
E-mail: brianmlazgar@uregina.ca
Founded: 1973
Scholarly paperbacks & hardcovers on cultural & economic development & history of Canadian Plains & western Canada.
Publishes in English, French.
ISBN Prefix(es): 0-88977
Number of titles published annually: 10 Print
Total Titles: 100 Print; 1 CD-ROM

Canadian Poetry Press
Dept of English, University of Western Ontario, London, ON N6A 3K7
Tel: 519-673-1164; 519-661-2111 (ext 85834)
Fax: 519-661-3776
Web Site: www.canadianpoetry.ca
Key Personnel
Gen Ed: D M R Bentley
Founded: 1986
ISBN Prefix(es): 0-921243
Number of titles published annually: 3 Print; 4 Online
Total Titles: 30 Print; 40 Online

Canadian Scholars' Press Inc
Imprint of CSPI/Women's Press
180 Bloor St W, Suite 801, Toronto, ON M5S 2V6
SAN: 118-9484
Tel: 416-929-2774 *Fax:* 416-929-1926
E-mail: info@cspi.org
Web Site: www.cspi.org; www.womenspress.ca
Key Personnel
Pres & Publr: Jack Wayne
Gen Mgr: C Dick Yu *E-mail:* dickyu@cspi.org
Man Ed: Althea Prince
Prodn Mgr: Drew Hawkins
Acad Mktg Mgr: Renee Knapp
Founded: 1987
Scholarly books & texts for post-secondary education. Trade books-feminist orientation.
Publishes in English, French.
ISBN Prefix(es): 0-921627; 1-55130; 0-921881; 0-88961; 1-89418
Number of titles published annually: 24 Print
Total Titles: 357 Print
Orders to: GTW (Georgetown Terminal Warehouse Ltd), 34 Armstrong Ave, George-

town, ON L7G 4R9, Contact: Lesley Hillier
Tel: 905-873-2750 *Toll Free Tel:* 866-870-2774
Fax: 905-873-6170 *E-mail:* orders@gtwcanada.com *Web Site:* www.gtwcanada.com
Returns: GTW (Georgetown Terminal Warehouses Ltd), 15 Lawrence Bell Dr, Amherst, NY 14221, United States
Warehouse: GTW (Georgetown Terminal Warehouse Ltd), 34 Armstrong Ave, Georgetown, ON L7G 4R9, Contact: Lesley Hillier
Tel: 905-873-2750 *Toll Free Tel:* 866-870-2774
Fax: 905-873-6170 *E-mail:* orders@gtwcanada.com *Web Site:* www.gtwcanada.com

Captus Press Inc
1600 Steeles Ave W, Units 14-15, Concord, ON L4K 4M2
Tel: 416-736-5537 *Fax:* 416-736-5793
E-mail: info@captus.com
Web Site: www.captus.com
Key Personnel
Pres: Randy Hoffman *E-mail:* randy@captus.com
Mgr: Pauline Lai *E-mail:* pauline@captus.com
Accts Admin & Intl Rts: Lily Chu *E-mail:* lily@captus.com
Founded: 1987
Publication of textbooks, scholarly books, professional books, nonfiction trade books & multimedia Internet courses; also publishes in Spanish.
Publishes in English, French.
ISBN Prefix(es): 0-921801; 1-896691; 1-895712; 1-55322
Number of titles published annually: 14 Print; 5 Online
Total Titles: 144 Print; 5 Online; 1 E-Book
Imprints: Captus Press; Captus University Publications
Distributor for Fisher Hospitality; Iguana
U.S. Rep(s): Empire Publishing Services (for drama games, using drama to bring language to life only)

Carswell
Division of Thomson Professional Publishing
One Corporate Plaza, 2075 Kennedy Rd, Toronto, ON M1T 3V4
Tel: 416-609-8000 *Toll Free Tel:* 800-387-5164 (Canada & US) *Fax:* 416-298-5094 (Toronto); 403-233-8159 (Calgary); 604-685-5343 (Vancouver); 514-985-6605 *Toll Free Fax:* 877-750-9041
E-mail: comments@carswell.com
Web Site: www.carswell.com
Key Personnel
Pres & CEO: Don VanMeer
VP, Publg: Robert Freeman
VP, Sales & Cust Rels: Eric Sleigh
CFO: Stewart Katz
VP, Chief Info Officer: Paul McDowell
Corp Cont: R Leduc
VP Mgmt & Prodn: J Edmiston
VP, HR: H Oosterholt-Arnill
Corp Mktg Communs Supv: Dale Clarry
Tel: 416-298-5053 *E-mail:* dale.clarry@carswell.com
Founded: 1991
Specialize in being the knowledge source relied on by thousands of legal, tax, accounting & human resources professionals in Canada: CD-ROMs, online, diskettes, books, supplemental services, reports, digests, encyclopedias, journals & newsletters.
Publishes in English, French.
ISBN Prefix(es): 0-459; 0-88820
Number of titles published annually: 85 Print
Total Titles: 1,113 Print
Imprints: Carswell; Richard De Boo
Divisions: Carswell Custom Printing
Branch Office(s)
311 Sixth Ave, SW, Suite 1200, Calgary, AB T2P 3H2 *Tel:* 403-233-9300 *Toll Free Tel:* 800-561-0657 *Fax:* 403-233-8159

815 W Hastings St, Suite 710, Vancouver, BC V6C 1B4 *Tel:* 604-685-8171 *Toll Free Tel:* 800-663-1946 *Fax:* 604-685-5343
430 rue St Pierre, Montreal, PQ H2Y 2M5 *Tel:* 514-985-0824 *Fax:* 514-985-6605
Distributor for Australian Tax Practice; Brookers; Canada Communications Group; Canadian Council of International Law; Federal & State Government Printers; W Green & Son Ltd (Edinburgh); Incorporated Council (London); LBC Information Services; McGill University Air & Space Institute (Montreal); Native Law Center University of Saskatchewan; Professional Publishing (London); Provincial Government Printers; Research Institute of America; The Stationary Office (London); Sweet & Maxwell (London); Thomson Tax Ltd (London); UBC Press; University of Toronto Press; West Group; World Trade Press
U.S. Publishers Represented: American Arbitration Association; Research Institute of America; West Group; World Trade Press

§CASTI Publishing Inc
10544 106 St, Suite 210, Edmonton, AB T5H 2X6
Tel: 780-424-2552 *Fax:* 780-421-1308
E-mail: casti@casti.ca
Web Site: casti.ca
Publishes in English.
ISBN Prefix(es): 1-894038
Number of titles published annually: 12 Print
Total Titles: 12 Print; 8 E-Book
Distributed by ASM International (USA); ATP (UK)
Membership(s): American Society for Testing Materials

§CCH Canadian Limited, A Wolters Kluwer Company
Subsidiary of Wolters Kluwer NV
90 Sheppard Ave E, Suite 300, Toronto, ON M2N 6X1
Tel: 416-224-2224 *Toll Free Tel:* 800-268-4522 (Canada & US cust serv) *Fax:* 416-224-2243
Toll Free Fax: 800-461-4131
E-mail: cservice@cch.ca (cust serv)
Web Site: www.cch.ca
Key Personnel
Pres & CEO: Ian Rhind
VP, Fin & Admin: Allan Orr
VP, Technol: Rick Lewis
VP, Legal & Busn Mkts: Steve Monk
VP, Publications, CCH Ltee: Michel Masse
VP, Acctg, Tax & Fin Planning: Doug Finley
Founded: 1946
Produce information products that help its customers take command of complex regulatory issues in tax, financial planning, business & law. One of Canada's largest & most respected professional information providers, producing leading-edge research materials & application software in both English & French. Products are available via the internet as well as in CD-ROM & print formats. The company's longstanding success is based on technological innovation, information management expertise & a commitment to industry leadership. Works closely with experts from a variety of disciplines to provide insight & professional commentary that advances our customers' knowledge & productivity.
Publishes in English, French.
ISBN Prefix(es): 0-89366; 1-55141
Number of titles published annually: 50 Print
Total Titles: 3,000 Print
Branch Office(s)
CCH Quebec, 7005 boul Taschereau bur 190, Brossard, PQ J4Z 1A7 *Tel:* 450-678-4443

Tax Compliance Group, 1120 rue Cherbourg, CP 2300, Sherbrooke, PQ J1H 5N7 *Tel:* 819-566-2000
U.S. Publishers Represented: Aspen Publishers; CCH US

Centennial College Press
Affiliate of Centennial College
c/o Centennial College, PO Box 631, Sta A, Scarborough, ON M1K 5E9
Tel: 416-289-5000 (ext 8606) *Fax:* 416-289-5106
E-mail: ccpress@centennialcollege.ca
Web Site: www.centennialcollege.ca
Key Personnel
Mgr: Alison Maclean
Founded: 1974
Technical books for industry & college level.
Publishes in English.
ISBN Prefix(es): 0-919852
Number of titles published annually: 3 Print
Total Titles: 30 Print

Centre Franco-Ontarien de Ressources en Alphabetisation
432 Ave Westmount, Unit H, Sudbury, ON P3A 5Z8
Tel: 705-524-3672 *Toll Free Tel:* 888-814-4422 (orders, Canada only) *Fax:* 705-524-8535
E-mail: info@centrefora.on.ca
Web Site: www.centrefora.on.ca
Key Personnel
Dir: Yolande Clement
Admin Sec: Monique Lafontaine
  E-mail: mqlafontaine@centrefora.on.ca
Founded: 1989 (nonprofit organization)
Learning materials for adult literacy & distribute education materials for all ages.
Publishes in French.
ISBN Prefix(es): 2-921706
Number of titles published annually: 20 Print
Total Titles: 130 Print

CHA (Canadian Healthcare Association) Press
17 York St, Suite 100, Ottawa, ON K1N 9J6
Tel: 613-241-8005 (ext 264) *Fax:* 613-241-5055
E-mail: chapress@cha.ca
Web Site: www.cha.ca
Key Personnel
Dir, Publg & Intl Rts: Eleanor Sawyer
  E-mail: eleanor.sawyer@cha.ca
Pres: Sharon Sholzberg-Gray
Founded: 1989
Direct mail specialty publisher.
Publishes in English, French.
ISBN Prefix(es): 0-919100; 1-896151
Number of titles published annually: 5 Print; 1 CD-ROM
Total Titles: 80 Print; 1 CD-ROM
Imprints: CHA Press

The Charlton Press
Division of Charlton International Inc
PO Box 820, Sta Willowdale B, North York, ON M2K 2R1
Tel: 416-488-1418 *Toll Free Tel:* 800-442-6042 *Fax:* 416-488-4656 *Toll Free Fax:* 800-442-1542
E-mail: chpress@charltonpress.com
Web Site: www.charltonpress.com
Key Personnel
CEO: William K Cross
Founded: 1952
Specialize in Royal Doulton, Royal Worcester etc. Collectibles & antiques, 20th century numismatics, sports cards, ceramics.
Publishes in English.
ISBN Prefix(es): 0-88968
Number of titles published annually: 20 Print
Total Titles: 35 Print; 2 CD-ROM
Membership(s): Publishers Marketing Association

ChemTec Publishing
38 Earswick Dr, Scarborough, ON M1E 1C6
Tel: 416-265-2603 *Fax:* 416-265-1399
E-mail: info@chemtec.org; orderdesk@chemtec.org
Web Site: www.chemtec.org
Key Personnel
CEO: Anna Wypych
Circ Mgr: Anna Fox
Founded: 1988
Additives, blends, polymers, recycling & rheology.
Publishes in English.
ISBN Prefix(es): 1-895198
Number of titles published annually: 5 Print
Total Titles: 15 Print; 2 CD-ROM
Subsidiaries: ChemTec Laboratories Inc

Cheneliere/McGraw-Hill
7001 Saint Laurent Blvd, Montreal, PQ H2S 3E3
Tel: 514-273-1066 *Fax:* 514-276-0324
E-mail: chene@dlcmcgrawhill.ca
Web Site: www.dlcmcgrawhill.ca
Key Personnel
Pres: Michel de la Cheneliere
VP, Sales & Admin: Salvatore D'Urso
Publr & Intl Rts: Robert Pare
Sales & Mktg Mgr, School Div: Carole Girard
Sales Mgr & Lib Sales Dir, College & University Div: Jean Bouchard
Founded: 1971
School, college & university textbooks; vocational; French Immersion; teaching skills & book packaging (French & English languages).
Publishes in French.
ISBN Prefix(es): 0-07; 2-89310; 2-89461
Number of titles published annually: 100 Print
Total Titles: 500 Print
Imprints: Les Editions Cheneliere; McGraw-Hill
U.S. Publishers Represented: McGraw-Hill Inc
Warehouse: McGraw-Hill Ryerson Ltd, 300 Water St, Whitby, ON L1N 9B6

Chouette Publishing
4710 St Ambroise, Bureau 225, Montreal, PQ H4C 2C7
Tel: 514-925-3325 *Toll Free Tel:* 877-926-3325 *Fax:* 514-925-3323
E-mail: info@editions-chouette.com
Web Site: www.chouettepublishing.com
Key Personnel
Pres: Christine L'Heureux
Founded: 1987
Produce children's books adapted to a stage of childs development, from birth to age six.
Publishes in English, French.
ISBN Prefix(es): 2-921198; 2-89450
Number of titles published annually: 35 Print
Total Titles: 110 Print
U.S. Rep(s): Client Distribution Services
Foreign Rep(s): Lucie Rochette
Warehouse: Heritage, 300 rue Arran, St-Lambert, PQ J4R 1K5
Distribution Center: H B Fenn & Co, 34 Nixon Rd, Bolton, ON L7E 1W2 *Tel:* 905-951-6600 *Toll Free Tel:* 800-267-3366 *Fax:* 905-951-6601 *Toll Free Fax:* 800-465-3422 *E-mail:* sales@hbfenn.com

Christian History Project
10333 178 St, Edmonton, AB T5N 2H7
Tel: 780-443-4775 *Toll Free Tel:* 800-853-5402 *Fax:* 780-454-9298
E-mail: orders@christianhistoryproject.com
Web Site: www.christianhistoryproject.com
Key Personnel
Pres & CEO: Robert W Doull
Gen Mgr & VChmn: Ted Byfield
VP, Sales: Kathy Therrien
Market Devt Mgr: Leanne Nash
Acct Mgr: Terry White
Founded: 1999

Incorporated for the purpose of researching, writing, producing & distributing a 12-volume series on the history of Christianity from 30 AD to present day.
Publishes in English.
ISBN Prefix(es): 0-9689873
Number of titles published annually: 4 Print
Total Titles: 5 Print
Foreign Rep(s): Riggins International Rights Services
Shipping Address: Friesens Corp, One Printers Way, Altona, MB R0G 0B0
Warehouse: Friesens Corp, One Printers Way, Altona, MB R0G 0B0
Distribution Center: Friesens Corp, One Printers Way, Altona, MB R0G 0B0
Membership(s): Christian Booksellers Association

Clements Publishing
6021 Younge St, Suite 213, Toronto, ON M2M 3W2
Tel: 416-558-9439 *Fax:* 416-352-5997
E-mail: info@clementspublishing.com
Web Site: www.clementspublishing.com
Key Personnel
Dir: Rob Clements
Founded: 2000
Christian publisher.
Publishes in English.
ISBN Prefix(es): 1-894667
Number of titles published annually: 10 Print
Total Titles: 30 Print; 7 Audio
Orders to: Ingram

CNIB Library for the Blind
1929 Bayview Ave, Toronto, ON M4G 3E8
Tel: 416-480-7520 *Fax:* 416-480-7700
E-mail: sales@cnib.ca
Web Site: www.cnib.ca/library
Founded: 1906
Library for the blind.
Publishes in English, French.
Number of titles published annually: 50 Print
U.S. Publishers Represented: Blackstone Audiobooks; CBC Audio; Recorded Books
Membership(s): Canadian Library Association; International Federation of Library Associations & Institutions; Ontario Library Association

Coach House Books
401 Huron St, Rear, Toronto, ON M5S 2G5
Tel: 416-979-2217 *Toll Free Tel:* 800-367-6360 *Fax:* 416-977-1158
E-mail: mail@chbooks.com
Web Site: www.chbooks.com
Key Personnel
Ed: Alana Wilcox
Man Ed: Jason McBride
Literary small press specializing in experimental fiction & poetry.
Publishes in English.
ISBN Prefix(es): 1-55245
Number of titles published annually: 16 Print; 5 Online
Total Titles: 80 Print; 60 Online
Orders to: Literary Press Group
Membership(s): Association of Canadian Publishers; Literary Press Group

Coffragants & Pocketaudio
Subsidiary of Editions Alexandre Stanke
5400 rue Louis-Badaillac, Carignan, PQ J3L 4A7
Tel: 450-447-6114 *Fax:* 450-658-1377
E-mail: coffragants@videotron.ca
Web Site: www.coffragants.com
Key Personnel
Dir: Gaila Stanke
Founded: 1995
Children's audio books in English & in French, adult audio in French only; classic tales & psychology.
Publishes in English, French.

ISBN Prefix(es): 2-921997; 2-89558; 2-89517; 1-894980
Number of titles published annually: 36 Print
Total Titles: 200 Audio
Distributed by AdA Inc; Penton Overseas Inc

Collector Grade Publications Inc
PO Box 1046, Cobourg, ON K9A 4W5
Tel: 905-342-3434 *Fax:* 905-342-3688
E-mail: info@collectorgrade.com
Web Site: www.collectorgrade.com
Key Personnel
Pres: R Blake Stevens
Founded: 1979
Accurate, in-depth studies of modern small arms.
Publishes in English.
ISBN Prefix(es): 0-88935
Number of titles published annually: 4 Print
Total Titles: 30 Print

The Communication Project, see TCP Press

Company's Coming Publishing Ltd
2311 96 St, Edmonton, AB T6N 1G3
Tel: 780-450-6223 *Toll Free Tel:* 800-875-7108
(US & Canada) *Fax:* 780-450-1857
E-mail: info@companyscoming.com
Web Site: www.companyscoming.com
Key Personnel
Pres: Grant Lovig
VP, Mktg & Dist: Gail Lovig
Founded: 1981
Publish cookbooks.
Publishes in English, French.
ISBN Prefix(es): 0-9690695; 0-9693322; 1-895455; 1-896891
Number of titles published annually: 7 Print
Total Titles: 75 Print; 75 Online

The Continuing Legal Education Society of British Columbia
845 Cambie, Suite 300, Vancouver, BC V6B 5T2
Tel: 604-669-3544 *Toll Free Tel:* 800-663-0437
Fax: 604-669-9260
Web Site: www.cle.bc.ca
Key Personnel
Exec Dir: Jack Huberman *E-mail:* huberman@cle.bc.ca
Sales & Mktg Liaison: Karen Kerfoot *Tel:* 604-893-2110 *E-mail:* kkerfoot@cle.bc.ca
Dir, Pubns: Susan Munro *E-mail:* smunro@cle.bc.ca
Founded: 1976
Publish course materials, practice manuals & case digests.
Publishes in English.
ISBN Prefix(es): 0-86504; 1-55258
Number of titles published annually: 55 Print
Total Titles: 250 Print; 1 CD-ROM
Imprints: CLE

Cormorant Books Inc
215 Spadina Ave, Studio 230, Toronto, ON M5T 2C7
SAN: 115-4176
Tel: 416-929-4957
E-mail: cormorantbooksinc@bellnet.ca
Web Site: www.cormorantbooks.com
Key Personnel
Publr & Pres: Marc Cote
Founded: 1986
Literary fiction & some literary nonfiction.
Publishes in English.
ISBN Prefix(es): 0-920953; 1-896951; 1-896332
Number of titles published annually: 18 Print
Total Titles: 100 Print; 1 Audio
Distribution Center: University of Toronto Press, 5201 Defferin St, Toronto, ON M3H 5T8

Tel: 416-667-7791 *Toll Free Tel:* 800-565-9523
E-mail: utpbooks@utpress.utoronto.ca
2250 Military Rd, Tonawanda, NY 14150, United States *Toll Free Tel:* 800-565-9523
E-mail: utpbooks@utpress.utoronto.ca

Coteau Books
Division of Thunder Creek Publishing Co-operative
401-2206 Dewdney Ave, Regina, SK S4R 1H3
SAN: 115-1037
Tel: 306-777-0170 *Toll Free Tel:* 800-440-4471 (Canada Only) *Fax:* 306-522-5152
E-mail: coteau@coteaubooks.com
Web Site: www.coteaubooks.com
Key Personnel
Publr & Intl Rts: Geoffrey Ursell
Fulfillment-Accts: Karen Steadman
Man Ed: Nik Burton
Mktg Mgr: Deborah Rush *E-mail:* marketing@coteaubooks.com
Founded: 1975
Only publish Canadian authors.
Publishes in English.
ISBN Prefix(es): 0-919926; 1-55050
Number of titles published annually: 20 Print
Total Titles: 170 Print; 1 Audio
Distributed by Fitzhenry & Whiteside
Distributor for Books Collective; Edge Books

La Courte Echelle
5243 Saint Laurent Blvd, Montreal, PQ H2T 1S4
Tel: 514-274-2004 *Toll Free Tel:* 800-387-6192 (orders only) *Fax:* 514-270-4160
Toll Free Fax: 800-450-0391 (orders only)
E-mail: info@courteechelle.com
Key Personnel
Pres: Helene Derome
VP, Devt & Communs & Foreign Rts: Louise Mongeau
VP, Fin: Martine Benard
Founded: 1978
Children's, young adult & adult fiction. No unsol mss accepted.
Publishes in French.
ISBN Prefix(es): 2-89021
Number of titles published annually: 50 Print
Total Titles: 550 Print
U.S. Rep(s): Firefly Books
Warehouse: Firefly Books/Frontier, c/o CACHE, Tonawanda Commerce Center, 2221 Kenmore Ave, Tonawanda, NY 14207, United States *Fax:* 416-499-8313 *E-mail:* fireflybooks@globalserve.net
Distribution Center: Firefly Books Ltd

Crabtree Publishing Co Ltd
Subsidiary of Crabtree Publishing Co (USA)
612 Welland Ave, St Catharines, ON L2M 5V6
Tel: 905-682-5221 *Toll Free Tel:* 800-387-7650 *Fax:* 905-682-7166 *Toll Free Fax:* 800-355-7166
E-mail: custserv@crabtreebooks.com; sales@crabtreebooks.com; orders@crabtreebooks.com
Web Site: www.crabtreebooks.com
Key Personnel
Pres: Peter A Crabtree
Publr: Bobbie Kalman
Gen Man: John Siemens *E-mail:* jsiemens@crabtreebooks.com
Prodn Dir: Craig Culliford *E-mail:* ccraig@crabtreebooks.com
Mktg Dir & Intl Rts: Kathy Middleton *E-mail:* kathy@crabtreebooks.com
Natl Acct Mgr: Lisa Antonsen *E-mail:* antonsen@crabtreebooks.com
Sales Mgr: Andrea Crabtree *E-mail:* andrea@crabtreebooks.com
Art Dir: Rob MacGregor *E-mail:* robertmc@crabtreebooks.com
Founded: 1978

Specialize in children's nonfiction, library binding & paperback for school & trade.
Publishes in English.
ISBN Prefix(es): 0-86505; 0-7787
Number of titles published annually: 106 Print; 5 E-Book
Total Titles: 884 Print; 2 CD-ROM; 17 E-Book
Branch Office(s)
PMB 16A, 350 Fifth Ave, Suite 3308, New York, NY 10118, United States *Tel:* 212-496-5040 *Toll Free Tel:* 800-387-7650 *Toll Free Fax:* 800-355-7166
Foreign Rep(s): Electra Media (Asia); Int Press (Australia); Lavis Marketing (UK); South Pacific Books (New Zealand)
Membership(s): ABA; ALA; American Marketing Association; Canadian Booksellers Association; EPA; International Reading Association; Ontario Library Association

Creative Book Publishing
36 Austin St, St Johns, NF A1B 3T7
Mailing Address: PO Box 8660 Sta A, St Johns, NF A1B 3T7
Tel: 709-722-8500 *Toll Free Tel:* 877-722-1722 (Canada only) *Fax:* 709-579-7745
E-mail: nlbooks@transcontinental.ca
Web Site: www.nfbooks.com
Key Personnel
Gen Mgr: Angela Pitcher
Sales Mgr & Mktg Coord: Donna Francis *E-mail:* donna.francis@transcontinental.ca
Publr: Dwayne LaFitte
Founded: 1961
Literary, poetry, fiction, history & biography.
Publishes in English, French.
ISBN Prefix(es): 0-920021; 1-895387; 1-894294
Number of titles published annually: 15 Print
Total Titles: 100 Print
Imprints: Creative Publishers; Killick Press; Tuckamore Books
Membership(s): Association of Canadian Publishers; Atlantic Publishers Marketing Association; Literary Press Group; NLPA

Creative Bound International Inc
151 Tansley Dr, Carp, ON K0A 1L0
SAN: 116-7413
Mailing Address: PO Box 424, Carp, ON K0A 1L0
Tel: 613-831-3641 *Toll Free Tel:* 800-287-8610 (N America) *Fax:* 613-831-3643
E-mail: editor@creativebound.com
Web Site: www.creativebound.com
Key Personnel
Pres: Gail Baird
Dir, Mktg: Lindsay Pike *E-mail:* marketing@creativebound.com
Dir, Trade & Specialty Sales: Jill Grassie
Founded: 1986
Books that are resources for helping experts get their message out in the fields of personal growth, self-help, enhanced performance & motivation. We have a speakers bureau as well.
Publishes in English.
ISBN Prefix(es): 0-921165; 1-894439
Number of titles published annually: 12 Print
Total Titles: 105 Print; 5 Audio
U.S. Rep(s): Baker & Taylor; Creative Bound Inc; Ingram
Membership(s): Association of Canadian Publishers; Publishers Marketing Association

Daisy Books
991 King St W, Hamilton, ON L8S 4R5
Mailing Address: PO Box 89094, Hamilton, ON L8S 4R5
Tel: 905-526-0451 *Fax:* 905-526-0451
E-mail: admin@daisybooks.com
Web Site: www.daisybooks.com
Key Personnel
Sales & Event Coord: Roxanne Grainger

Submissions: Luke Fillion
Founded: 2002
Small press with submission guidelines posted at www.daisybooks.com.
Publishes in English.
ISBN Prefix(es): 0-9730639
Number of titles published annually: 3 Print
Total Titles: 11 Print
Distributed by Hushion House Publishing Ltd
Orders to: Hushion House Publishing Ltd, c/o Georgetown Terminal Warehouses, 34 Armstrong Ave, Georgetown, ON L7G 4R9 *Toll Free Tel:* 866-485-5556 *Toll Free Fax:* 866-485-6665
Warehouse: Hushion House Publishing Ltd, c/o Georgetown Terminal Warehouses, 34 Armstrong Ave, Georgetown, ON L7G 4R9 *Toll Free Tel:* 866-485-5556 *Toll Free Fax:* 866-485-6665

§Database Directories
588 Dufferin Ave, London, ON N6B 2A4
Tel: 519-433-1666 *Fax:* 519-430-1131
E-mail: info@databasedirectory.com; lclassic@databasedirectory.com
Web Site: www.databasedirectory.com
Key Personnel
CEO & Ed: Lesley Classic
Pres & Ed: Robert Kasher
Founded: 1995
Directories & e-files on libraries, schools, media outlets, retailers & municipalities.
Publishes in English.
ISBN Prefix(es): 1-896537
Number of titles published annually: 4 Print; 4 CD-ROM; 4 Online
Total Titles: 10 Print; 10 CD-ROM; 4 Online

Decarie, Editeur Inc
233 Ave Dunbar, Ville Mont-Royal, PQ H3P 2H4
Tel: 514-342-8500 *Fax:* 514-342-3982
E-mail: info@decarieediteur.com
Web Site: www.decarieediteur.com
Key Personnel
Pres, Gen Mgr & Intl Rts: Andre Decarie
Mktg Mgr: Micheline Groleau
Founded: 1979
Specialize in medicine, French, languages.
Publishes in French.
ISBN Prefix(es): 2-89137
Number of titles published annually: 10 Print
Total Titles: 100 Print; 1 CD-ROM
Foreign Rep(s): Vigot Maloine, Paris (Europe)

B C Decker Inc
20 Hughson St S, 10th fl, Hamilton, ON L8N 2A1
Mailing Address: PO Box 620, LCD 1, Hamilton, ON L8N 3K7
Tel: 905-522-7017 *Toll Free Tel:* 800-568-7281 *Fax:* 905-522-7839
E-mail: info@bcdecker.com
Web Site: www.bcdecker.com
Key Personnel
CEO: Brian C Decker *E-mail:* bcd@bcdecker.com
Exec VP & COO: John Hirst *E-mail:* jhirst@bcdecker.com
Cont: Philip Cook *E-mail:* pcook@bcdecker.com
HR Mgr: Marie Moore
Founded: 1981
Publishes textbooks & journals in all areas of medical & dental.
Publishes in English.
ISBN Prefix(es): 1-55009
Number of titles published annually: 55 Print
Total Titles: 150 Print; 1 Online
Divisions: Decker Electronic Publishing; Empowering Press
Distributed by Harcourt UK

Detselig Enterprises Ltd
210, 1220 Kensington Rd NW, Calgary, AB T2N 3P5
SAN: 115-0324
Tel: 403-283-0900 *Fax:* 403-283-6947
E-mail: temeron@telusplanet.net
Web Site: www.temerondetselig.com
Key Personnel
Pres & Intl Rts: T E Giles
Founded: 1975
Social sciences, humanities, educational academic books, Western Canada history, aboriginal studies, womens studies & police dog training.
Publishes in English.
ISBN Prefix(es): 0-920490; 1-55059
Number of titles published annually: 17 Print
Total Titles: 240 Print
U.S. Rep(s): Temeron Books Inc
Shipping Address: Temeron Books Inc, PO Box 896, Bellingham, WA 98227, United States *Fax:* 360-738-4016

§Double Dragon Publishing Inc
1-5762 Hwy 7 E, Markham, ON L3P 7Y4
Mailing Address: PO Box 54016, Markham, ON L3P 7Y4
Tel: 416-994-4514
E-mail: info@double-dragon-ebooks.com
Web Site: www.double-dragon-ebooks.com
Key Personnel
Publr: Deron Douglas *E-mail:* publisher@double-dragon-ebooks.com
Founded: 2001
Publishes e-books & trade paperbacks in the fantasy, science fiction, speculative fiction, horror & suspense genres. Established with the goal of building a Canadian based publishing venue for the growing number of good but unpublished fiction writers around the world. Dedicated to publishing quality works of fiction & nonfiction & will continue to publish works in various genres in both the e-book & traditional paper book formats. Make special efforts to publish a specific number of works written by North American Aboriginal authors each year.
Publishes in English.
ISBN Prefix(es): 1-894841; 1-55404
Number of titles published annually: 40 Print; 100 E-Book
Total Titles: 40 Print; 125 E-Book
Imprints: DDP Literary Press; Double Dragon eBooks; Double Dragon Press

Doubleday Canada
Division of Random House of Canada Ltd
One Toronto St, Suite 300, Toronto, ON M5C 2V6
SAN: 115-0340
Tel: 416-364-4449 *Fax:* 416-957-1587
Web Site: www.randomhouse.ca
Key Personnel
Chmn: John Neale
Exec VP & Publr, Doubleday Canada: Maya Mavjee
Exec VP & COO: Douglas Foot *Tel:* 905-624-0672
Exec VP & Dir, Sales & Mktg: Brad Martin
VP, Sales: Brian Cassin *Tel:* 905-624-0672
VP & Dir, Sales: Duncan Shields *Tel:* 905-624-0672
VP, Prodn: Janine Laporte
VP & Dir, Rts & Contracts: Jennifer Shepherd
VP, Online Mktg & Sales Dir: Lisa Charters
VP & Dir, Mktg & Communs: Tracey Turriff
VP & Dir, Media Rel: Scott Sellers
Dir, Mktg: Linda Scott *Tel:* 905-624-0672
Adv Dir: Mark Veldhuizen
Asst Prodn Mgr: Carla Kean
Man Ed, Seal & Mgr, Doubleday: Christine Innes
Exec Ed, Doubleday: Martha Kanya-Forstner
Asst Ed, Doubleday Canada: Nicholas Massey-Garrison
Busn Mgr: Ralph Burrows

Founded: 1937
General trade nonfiction (current affairs, politics, business, sports); fiction, children's illustrated.
Random House Inc & its publishing entities are not accepting unsol submissions, proposals, mss, or submission queries via e-mail at this time.
Publishes in English.
ISBN Prefix(es): 0-385; 0-7704
Total Titles: 45 Print
Imprints: Doubleday Canada; Seal Books; Vintage Canada
Subsidiaries: Anchor Canada
U.S. Publishers Represented: Anchor Press; BDD Audio; Bantam; Broadway; Byr; Delacorte Press; Dell Publishing; Doubleday; Image Books
U.S. Rep(s): Bantam Doubleday Dell Publishing Group Inc
Membership(s): Canadian Booksellers Association; Canadian Library Association; Canadian Publishers' Council

Douglas & McIntyre Publishing Group
2323 Quebec St, Suite 201, Vancouver, BC V5T 4S7
SAN: 115-1886
Tel: 604-254-7191 *Toll Free Tel:* 800-565-9523 (orders in Canada) *Fax:* 604-254-9099 *Toll Free Fax:* 800-221-9985 (orders in Canada)
E-mail: dm@douglas-mcintyre.com
Web Site: www.douglas-mcintyre.com
Key Personnel
Pres & Publr: Scott McIntyre *E-mail:* scott.mcintyre@douglas-mcintyre.com
Greystone Publr: Rob Sanders *E-mail:* rob.sanders@greystonebooks.com
Groundwood Publr: Patsy Aldana *Tel:* 416-537-2501 *Fax:* 416-537-4647 *E-mail:* 102461.475@compuserve.com
VP & Natl Sales & Mktg Mgr: Susan McIntosh *E-mail:* susanm@groundwood-dm.com
Mktg Dir: Liza Algar *E-mail:* liza.algar@douglas-mcintyre.com
Intl Rts & Perms: Lisa Nave *E-mail:* lisan@groundwood-dm.com
Founded: 1971
The Douglas & McIntyre Publishing group is structured in three publishing divisions. Douglas & McIntyre focuses on biographies, native art & history, architecture, literary fiction & cookbooks. The Greystone imprint is export-driven & publishes titles in the subject areas of popular culture, environmental issues, natural history & sports, for both adult & children. Groundwood Books produces award-winning children's & young adult titles; both fiction & nonfiction.
Publishes in English.
ISBN Prefix(es): 0-88894; 0-88899; 1-55044; 1-55365
Number of titles published annually: 80 Print
Total Titles: 1,500 Print
Imprints: Greystone Books; Groundwood Books
Divisions: Greystone Books; Groundwood Books
Distributor for Farrar Straus & Giroux
U.S. Publishers Represented: Farrar Straus & Giroux
U.S. Rep(s): Publishers Group West
Distribution Center: HarperCollins Canada Inc, 1995 Markham Rd, Scarborough, ON M1B 5M8 (order dept) *Tel:* 800-387-0117 *Fax:* 416-321-3033 *Toll Free Fax:* 800-668-5788 *E-mail:* hcorder@harpercollins.com SAN: 115-026X

Dovehouse Editions Inc
1890 Fairmeadow Crescent, Ottawa, ON K1H 7B9
Tel: 613-731-7601 *Fax:* 613-731-7601
Web Site: www.dovehouse.ca

Key Personnel
CEO & Dir: Donald Beecher
    E-mail: donald_beecher@carleton.ca
Founded: 1978
Academic books: Italian, Spanish, Renaissance
    plays in translation, Elizabethan fiction.
Publishes in English.
ISBN Prefix(es): 0-919473; 1-895537
Number of titles published annually: 9 Print
Total Titles: 100 Print
Editorial Office(s): Riche Series & Carleton Re-
    naissance Plays c/o Dept of English, Carleton
    University, 1125 Colonel By Dr, Ottawa, ON
    K1S 5B6

Dragon Moon Press
PO Box 64312, Calgary, AB T2K 6J7
Tel: 403-277-2140 *Fax:* 403-277-3679
E-mail: publisher@dragonmoonpress.com
Web Site: www.dragonmoonpress.com
Key Personnel
Publr: Gwen Gades
Contact: Thomas Anderson *E-mail:* tmanderson@
    dragonmoonpress.com
Founded: 1994
Traditional small press.
Publishes in English.
ISBN Prefix(es): 1-896944
Number of titles published annually: 4 Print; 4 E-
    Book
Total Titles: 8 Print; 12 Online; 4 E-Book
Distributed by Edge Science Fiction & Fantasy
    (Canada)
Orders to: Baker & Taylor, 2550 W Tyvola Rd,
    Suite 300, Charlotte, NC 28217, United States
    Tel: 704-998-3100 *Toll Free Tel:* 800-775-3700;
    800-775-1800 *E-mail:* btinfo@btol.com
Returns: Baker & Taylor, 2550 W Tyvola Rd,
    Suite 300, Charlotte, NC 28217, United States
    Tel: 704-998-3100 *Toll Free Tel:* 800-775-3700;
    800-775-1800 *E-mail:* btinfo@btol.com
Distribution Center: Baker & Taylor, 2550
    W Tyvola Rd, Suite 300, Charlotte, NC
    28217, United States *Tel:* 704-998-3100
    Toll Free Tel: 800-775-3700; 800-775-1800
    E-mail: btinfo@btol.com

Dundurn Press Ltd
8 Market St, 2nd fl, Toronto, ON M5E 1M6
SAN: 115-0359
Tel: 416-214-5544 *Fax:* 416-214-5556
E-mail: info@dundurn.com
Web Site: www.dundurn.com
Key Personnel
Pres: Kirk Howard *E-mail:* jkh@dundurn.com
Founded: 1973
Specialize in Canadian history, social sciences,
    some biography & art, fiction, mysteries.
Publishes in English, French.
ISBN Prefix(es): 0-919670; 1-55002; 0-88924; 0-
    88882
Number of titles published annually: 75 Print
Imprints: Boardwalk Books; Castle Street Myster-
    ies; Dundurn; Hounslow (popular nonfiction);
    Simon & Pierre (fiction)
Subsidiaries: Boardwalk Books; Hounslow Press;
    Simon & Pierre (fiction)
Branch Office(s)
Dundurn Distribution, c/o Lavis Marketing, 73
    Lime Walk, Headington, Oxford 0X3 7AD,
    United Kingdom
Membership(s): Association of Canadian Publish-
    ers

E-Z Publications
1932 Ambassador Dr, Windsor, ON N9C 3R5
Tel: 519-250-5138; 519-972-3962 *Fax:* 519-972-
    5256; 519-250-6588
E-mail: ezpublications@hotmail.com
Web Site: www.ezpublications.com
Key Personnel
CEO: Saeed Khan

Founded: 1993
Publishers & Distributors.
Number of titles published annually: 6 Print
Total Titles: 6 Print
Divisions: ICS (International Consulting Services)

EcceNova Editions
15-1594 Fairfield Rd, Victoria, BC V8S 1G1
Mailing Address: PO Box 50001, Victoria, BC
    V8S 5L8
Tel: 250-595-8401 *Fax:* 250-595-8401
E-mail: info@eccenova.com
Web Site: www.eccenova.com
Key Personnel
Owner & Ed: Janet Tyson *E-mail:* editor@
    eccenova.com
Founded: 2003
Interests include art history, philosophy, archae-
    ology. Specialize in nonfiction works in the
    humanities & sciences. Have a keen interest in
    religion (all religions plus biblical studies) but
    will consider nonfiction in most science sub-
    jects & the occult.
Publishes in English.
ISBN Prefix(es): 0-9731648; 0-9735341
Number of titles published annually: 4 Print
Total Titles: 4 Print
Distribution Center: B & T
Bertrams
Gardners
NACSCORP
Quality Books Inc

Ecrits des Forges
1497 La Violette, CP 335, Trois Rivieres, PQ
    G9A 1W5
Tel: 819-379-9813 *Fax:* 819-376-0774
E-mail: ecrits.desforges@tr.cgocable.ca
Key Personnel
Pres: Gaston Bellamare *E-mail:* gbellma@tr.
    cgocable.ca
Founded: 1971
Publishes in French.
ISBN Prefix(es): 2-89046
Number of titles published annually: 50 Print
Total Titles: 650 Print
Distributed by DCR

ECW Press
2120 Queen St E, Suite 200, Toronto, ON M4E
    1E2
SAN: 115-1274
Tel: 416-694-3348 *Fax:* 416-698-9906
E-mail: info@ecwpress.com
Web Site: www.ecwpress.com
Key Personnel
Publr: Jack David
Man Ed: Tracey Millen
Founded: 1974
Publishes in English.
ISBN Prefix(es): 0-920763; 1-55022; 0-920802
Number of titles published annually: 50 Print
Total Titles: 450 Print
Imprints: misFit
Foreign Rights: Bill Hanna (world exc USA &
    Canada)
Membership(s): Association of Canadian Publish-
    ers; Literary Press Group

EDGE Science Fiction & Fantasy Publishing
Imprint of Hades Publications Inc
PO Box 1714, Sta M, Calgary, AB T2P 2L7
Tel: 403-254-0160 *Toll Free Tel:* 877-254-0115
    Fax: 403-254-0456
E-mail: publisher@hadespublications.com
Web Site: www.edgewebsite.com
Key Personnel
Publr & Gen Mgr: Brian Hades
Edit Mgr: Kimberly Gammon
Founded: 1996
Encourage, produce & promote thought-provoking
    & fun-to-read science fiction & fantasy & hor-

ror literature by "bringing the magic alive-one
    world at a time" with each new book released.
    Independent publisher of science fiction & fan-
    tasy novels in hard cover or trade paperback
    format. Produce high-quality books with lots of
    attention to detail & lots of marketing effort.
Publishes in English.
ISBN Prefix(es): 1-894063
Number of titles published annually: 5 Print
Total Titles: 5 Print
Imprints: Alien Vistas; EDGE Fantasy; EDGE
    Science Fiction
U.S. Rep(s): Baker & Taylor; Fitzhenry & White-
    side
Membership(s): Book Publishers Association of
    Alberta; IPAC; Publishers Marketing Associa-
    tion

Edimag
CP 325, Succ Rosemont, Montreal, PQ H1X 3B8
Tel: 514-522-2244 *Fax:* 514-522-6301
Web Site: www.edimag.com
Key Personnel
Pres & Ed: Pierre Nadeau *E-mail:* pnadeau@
    edimag.com
Founded: 1988
Practical books; humor, sexuality, medicine, cui-
    sine, biographies & religion.
Publishes in French.
ISBN Prefix(es): 2-921207; 2-921735
Number of titles published annually: 25 Print
Total Titles: 300 Print
Distributed by ADP

Editions Anne Sigier Inc
1073 Blvd of Rene Levesque W, Sillery, PQ G1S
    4R5
Tel: 418-687-6086 *Toll Free Tel:* 800-463-6846
    (Canada only) *Fax:* 418-687-3565
E-mail: sigier@annesigier.qc.ca
Web Site: www.annesigier.qc.ca
Key Personnel
Contact: Jacques Sigier
Founded: 1975
Religious & photographic books.
Publishes in French.
ISBN Prefix(es): 2-89129
Number of titles published annually: 20 Print
Total Titles: 300 Print
Distributor for Edition Anne-Sigier France

Les Editions Brault et Bouthillier
Division of B & B School Supplies
4823, rue Sherbrooke Ouest, bureau 275, West-
    mount, PQ H3Z 1G7
Tel: 514-932-9466 *Toll Free Tel:* 800-668-1108
    Fax: 514-932-5929
E-mail: editions@ebbp.ca
Key Personnel
Pres: Jean Brault *Tel:* 514-273-9186
Founded: 1945
Pedagogical & scientific.
Publishes in English, French.
ISBN Prefix(es): 0-88537; 2-7615
Number of titles published annually: 100 Print
Distributed by DPLU Inc (Montreal); B B Jocus
    (Toronto)
Warehouse: 700 Beaumont Ave, Montreal, PQ
    H3N 1V5

editions CERES Ltd/Le Moyen Francais
CP 1657 Succ B, 1250 University, Montreal, PQ
    H3B 3L3
Tel: 514-937-7138 *Fax:* 514-937-9875
Web Site: www.editionsceres.ca
Key Personnel
Pres & Ed: G DiStefano
Secy, Treas & Ed: R M Bidler
Founded: 1979
Erudite volumes on 14th & 15th centuries French
    language, literature & Philology Romane. Our
    authors are international from US, Europe, Tu-
    nis, UK, Australia, Japan & Canada. It is open

to everyone who specializes in this discipline. University specialists & research.
Publishes in English, French.
ISBN Prefix(es): 0-919089
Number of titles published annually: 5 Print
Total Titles: 78 Print

Editions de l'Hexagone
Division of Le Groupe Ville Marie Litterature
1010, rue de la Gauchetiere Est, Montreal, PQ H2L 2N5
Tel: 514-523-1182 *Fax:* 514-282-7530
E-mail: vml@sogides.com
Web Site: www.edhexagone.com
Key Personnel
Pres & Lit Dir, Poetry: Pierre Graveline
Lit Dir, Fiction: Jean Yves Soucy
Lit Dir, Essays: Robert La Liberte
Prodn: Marie-Clark Barriere; Sabine Schir
Communs: Simon Saurer
Asst to the Ed: Josipp Lewis
Founded: 1953
General fiction, poetry, novels, stories & essays.
Publishes in French.
ISBN Prefix(es): 2-89006
Number of titles published annually: 30 Print
Total Titles: 35 Print
Distributed by Messageries ADP
Warehouse: 1761 Richardson, Montreal, PQ DH3K 1G6

Editions de Mortagne
BP 116, Boucherville, PQ J4B 5E6
Tel: 450-641-2387 *Fax:* 450-655-6092
E-mail: edm@editionsdemortagne.qc.ca
Key Personnel
Pres & Intl Rts: Max Permingeat
Founded: 1978
Novels.
Publishes in French.
ISBN Prefix(es): 2-89074
Number of titles published annually: 15 Print
Total Titles: 15 Print

Editions Marcel Didier Inc
Division of Editions Hurtubise HMH Ltee
1815 Ave de Lorimier, Montreal, PQ H2K 3W6
Tel: 514-523-1523 *Toll Free Tel:* 800-361-1664 (Canada) *Fax:* 514-523-9969
E-mail: hurtubisehmh@hurtubisehmh.com
Web Site: www.hurtubisehmh.com
Key Personnel
Pres & Intl Rts: Herve Foulon
Lib Sales Dir: Christian Reeves
Founded: 1964
Literary essays, novels.
Publishes in English, French.
ISBN Prefix(es): 2-89144
Number of titles published annually: 36 Print
Total Titles: 200 Print
Distributed by Editions Hurtubise HMH
U.S. Rep(s): Sosnowski Associates

Les Editions du Ble
340 Provencher Blvd, St Boniface, MB R2H 0G7
Mailing Address: PO Box 31, St Boniface, MB R2H 3B4
Tel: 204-237-8200 *Fax:* 204-233-8182
E-mail: trigo@mb.sympatico.ca
Key Personnel
Admin Dir: Lucien Chaput
Founded: 1974
Publish books in French (novels, essays, poetry) pertaining mainly to the Canadian West (but not exclusively).
Publishes in French.
ISBN Prefix(es): 2-921347
Number of titles published annually: 6 Print
Total Titles: 100 Print
Distribution Center: Diffusion Prologue, 1650 boul Lionel-Bertrand, Boisbriand, PQ J7E 4H4
Tel: 450-434-0306 *Fax:* 450-434-2627

Editions du Boreal Express
4447 rue St Denis, Montreal, PQ H2J 2L2
Tel: 514-287-7401 *Fax:* 514-287-7664
E-mail: boreal@editionsboreal.qc.ca
Web Site: www.editionsboreal.qc.ca
Key Personnel
Exec Dir: Pascal Assathiany
Founded: 1963
General literature, essays, history, translations, children's & philosophy.
Publishes in French.
ISBN Prefix(es): 2-89052; 2-7646
Number of titles published annually: 70 Print
Total Titles: 2,035 Print
Distributed by Editions Du Seuil (Europe)
Foreign Rep(s): Agence AMV (Spain); Brigitte Axter (Germany); Niki Doye (Greece); Heyum Agency (Scandinavia); Imorie & Dervis (UK); Japon Uni Agency (Japan)
Distribution Center: Export Livres, CP 307, St Lambert, PQ J4P 3P8
128 rue d'Alsace, Saint-Lambert, PQ J4S 1M7
Membership(s): Association Nationale des Editeurs de Livres

Editions du Meridien
Division of SIAP Inc
1980 Sherbrooke Ouest, No 540, Montreal, PQ H3H 1E8
Tel: 514-935-0464 *Fax:* 514-935-0458
E-mail: info@editionsdumeridien.com
Web Site: www.editionsdumeridien.com
Key Personnel
Pres & Intl Rts Contact: Francois Martin
Lib Sales Dir: Stephanie Evans
Founded: 1982
Additional subjects include: health science, politics, sexology, society, social work & sociology.
Publishes in English, French.
ISBN Prefix(es): 2-89415
Number of titles published annually: 30 Print
Total Titles: 400 Print

Editions du Noroit Ltee
PO Box 156, Succersale de Lorimier, Montreal, PQ H2H 2N6
Tel: 514-727-0005 *Fax:* 514-723-6660
E-mail: lenoroit@lenoroit.com
Web Site: www.lenoroit.com
Key Personnel
Lit Dir: Paul Belanger
Founded: 1971
Poetry.
Publishes in French.
ISBN Prefix(es): 2-89018
Number of titles published annually: 20 Print
Total Titles: 500 Print; 10 Audio
Billing Address: 4609 Rue D'Iberville, Local 202, Montreal, PQ H2H 2L9
Distribution Center: Fides, 165 Rue DesLauriers, Saint-Laurent, PQ H4N 2S4 *Tel:* 514-745-4290 *Toll Free Tel:* 800-363-1451 *Fax:* 514-745-4299 *Toll Free Fax:* 800-363-1452

Editions du Phare Inc
105 rue de Martigny Ouest, St Jerome, PQ J7Y 2G2
Tel: 450-438-8479 *Toll Free Tel:* 800-561-2371 (Canada) *Fax:* 450-432-3892
E-mail: info@mondiaduphare.net
Key Personnel
Pres & Dir Gen: Jean Canac-Marquis
Mktg Dir: Pierre David
Founded: 1983
French school textbooks K-6; laminated posters.
Publishes in French.
ISBN Prefix(es): 2-921084
Number of titles published annually: 14 Print
Warehouse: 765 rue Nobel, portes 105-106, St Antoine-des-Laurentides, PQ J7Z 7A3

Les Editions du Remue-Menage Inc
110, Ste-Therese, Bureau 501, Montreal, PQ H2Y 1E6
Tel: 514-876-0097 *Fax:* 514-876-7951
E-mail: info@editions-remuemenage.qc.ca
Key Personnel
Pres: Helene Larachauz
Founded: 1976
Specialize in feminist books.
Publishes in English, French.
ISBN Prefix(es): 2-89091
Number of titles published annually: 15 Print
Total Titles: 150 Print
Foreign Rep(s): Export Livre (Europe, USA); Librarie du Quebec (France)
Membership(s): Association Nationale des Editeurs de Livres

Editions du renouveau Pedagogique Inc
5757 rue Cypihot, St-Laurent, PQ H4S 1R3
Tel: 514-334-2690 *Toll Free Tel:* 800-263-3678 *Fax:* 514-334-4720 *Toll Free Fax:* 800-643-4720
E-mail: erpidlm@erpi.com
Web Site: www.erpi.com
Key Personnel
Pres & Intl Rts: Normand Cleroux *Fax:* 514-334-8809 *E-mail:* clerouxn@erpi.com
VP, Fin: Luc Garneau *Fax:* 514-334-5942 *E-mail:* garneaul@erpi.com
Prodn Mgr: Helene Cousineau *Fax:* 514-334-9188 *E-mail:* helene.cousineau@erpi.com
Intl Rts: Lise Barras *Fax:* 514-334-8809 ext 245 *E-mail:* lise.barras@erpi.com
Founded: 1965
Textbooks.
Publishes in English, French.
ISBN Prefix(es): 2-7613
Number of titles published annually: 15 Print; 12 CD-ROM; 10 Online
Total Titles: 850 Print; 15 CD-ROM; 10 Online
Imprints: ERPI
Divisions: Diffusion du Livre Mirabel
Distributed by De Boeck; Pearson Education France; Penguin Readers; Village Mondial
Distributor for Addison-Wesley, Pearson Education (English as a second language series); Campus Press France; Duculot; Prentice-Hall; Simon & Schuster
Membership(s): ANEL

Les Editions du Roseau
Subsidiary of Librairie Raffin Inc
6521 rue Louis-Hemon, Montreal, PQ H2G 2L1
Tel: 514-725-7772 *Fax:* 514-725-5889
E-mail: editions@roseau.ca
Web Site: www.roseau.ca
Key Personnel
Dir: Normand Gagne
Founded: 1984
Health, New Age, spirituality.
Publishes in French.
ISBN Prefix(es): 2-920083; 2-89466
Total Titles: 125 Print; 1 CD-ROM; 3 Audio
Foreign Rep(s): Dangles (France); Transat (Switzerland); Vander (Belgium)
Warehouse: Diffusion Raffin, 29 Royal, Le Gardeur, PQ J5Z 4Z3 *Tel:* 450-585-9909 *Toll Free Tel:* 800-361-4293
Membership(s): Association Nationale des Editeurs de Livres

Editions du Septentrion
1300 ave Maguire, Sillery, PQ G1T 1Z3
Tel: 418-688-3556 *Fax:* 418-527-4978
E-mail: sept@septentrion.qc.ca
Web Site: www.septentrion.qc.ca
Key Personnel
Mktg Coord: Manon Perron
Founded: 1988
Full service publisher.
Publishes in English, French.

ISBN Prefix(es): 2-89448
Number of titles published annually: 30 Print
Total Titles: 330 Print
Distribution Center: Dimedia, 539 boul Lebeau,
Saint-Laurent, PQ H4N 1S2

Editions du Trecarre
Subsidiary of Quebecor Media
7 chemin Bates, Outremont, PQ H2V 4V7
Tel: 514-270-6860 *Fax:* 514-276-2533
E-mail: edition@trecarre.com
Web Site: www.total-publishing.com
Key Personnel
Pres: Marc Laberge
Dir, Sales & Mktg Coord: Stephan Labbe
 Tel: 514-490-2715 *E-mail:* labbe.stephan@
 total-publishing.com
Founded: 1982
Coffee-table books, nature books, cookbooks,
 practical books.
Publishes in French.
ISBN Prefix(es): 2-89249; 2-89568
Number of titles published annually: 100 Print
Total Titles: 700 Print
Warehouse: 2185 Autoroute des Laurentides,
 Laval, PQ H7S 1Z6

Les Editions du Vermillon
305 rue Saint-Patrick, Ottawa, ON K1N 5K4
Tel: 613-241-4032 *Fax:* 613-241-3109
E-mail: leseditionsduvermillon@rogers.com
Web Site: www.primatech.ca/vermillon/index.
 html; vermillon.info.ca
Key Personnel
Pres: Jacques Flamand
Dir: Monique Bertoli
Founded: 1982
Poetry, novels, children's books, textbooks, es-
 says.
Publishes in English, French.
ISBN Prefix(es): 0-919925; 1-895873; 1-894547
Number of titles published annually: 15 Print
Total Titles: 260 Print
Distributed by Prologue
Foreign Rep(s): Diffusion Albert-le-Grand
 (Switzerland); Librairie du Quebec (France)
Foreign Rights: Montreal Contacts (World)

Editions Fides
165 rue Deslauriers, St-Laurent, PQ H4N 2S4
Tel: 514-745-4290 *Toll Free Tel:* 800-363-1451
 Fax: 514-745-4299
E-mail: editions@fides.qc.ca
Web Site: www.editionsfides.com
Key Personnel
Dir, Gen Editions: Antoine Del Busso
Sales Dir: Gilda Routy
Founded: 1937
Religion, philosophy, education, Canadian litera-
 ture & history, dictionaries.
Publishes in French.
ISBN Prefix(es): 0-7755; 2-7621; 2-87374; 2-
 89007
Number of titles published annually: 85 Print
Total Titles: 305 Print
Distributed by Carteblanche
Distributor for Arfuyen; Bibliotheque Quebecoise;
 La Difference; Editions Bellarmim; Editions
 Cerf; Editions Desdee de Brouwer; Editions
 du Noroit; Labor & Fides; Lettres Vives; Oie
 de Cravan; De la Pasteque; Point de Fuite;
 Presses de l'Universite de Montreal; Presses
 de l'Universite d'Ottawa; Rogers Media; Rudel
 Medias
Returns: Lessius

Les Editions Ganesha Inc
CP 484 Succursale Youville, Montreal, PQ H2P
 2W1
Tel: 450-641-2395 *Fax:* 450-641-2989
E-mail: courriel@editions-ganesha.qc.ca
Web Site: editions-ganesha.qc.ca

Key Personnel
Pres & Dir Gen: Andre Beaudoin
Lib Sales Dir: Lucie Cournoyer
Founded: 1978
Publishes in French.
ISBN Prefix(es): 2-89145
Number of titles published annually: 4 Print
Total Titles: 56 Print

Les Editions Heritage Inc
300 Rue D'Arran, St-Lambert, PQ J4R 1K5
Tel: 450-672-6710 *Fax:* 450-672-1481
Key Personnel
Pres: Luc Payette
CEO & Pres of the Council: Jacques Payette
Founded: 1968
Juvenile & adult.
Publishes in French.
ISBN Prefix(es): 0-7773; 2-7625
Number of titles published annually: 250 Print
Total Titles: 2,000 Print
Membership(s): Association for Canadian Pub-
 lishers in the US

Editions Hurtubise HMH Ltee
1815 De Lorimier, Montreal, PQ H2K 3W6
Tel: 514-523-1523 *Toll Free Tel:* 800-361-1664
 (Canada only) *Fax:* 514-523-9969; 514-523-
 5955 (edit)
E-mail: hurtubisehmh@hurtubisehmh.com
Web Site: www.hurtubisehmh.com
Key Personnel
Pres & Intl Rts: Herve Foulon
Asst Gen Mgr: Francois Gibeault
VP, Publg & Literary Publg Mgr: Jacques Allard
VP, Publg: Arnaud Fowler
School Books Publr: Pierre-Marie Paquin
Lib Sales Dir: Christian Reeves
Dir, Childrens Pubns: Dominique Thuillot
Founded: 1960
Textbooks, research, literary novels, children's.
Publishes in French.
ISBN Prefix(es): 2-89045; 2-89428
Number of titles published annually: 50 Print
Total Titles: 950 Print
Imprints: Bibliotheque Quebecoise (BQ)
Distributor for Marcel Didier Inc; Hurtubise
 HMH Ltee
U.S. Rep(s): Sosnowski Associates
See separate listing for:
Editions Marcel Didier Inc

Les Editions JCL
930 rue Jacques Cartier est, Chicoutimi, PQ G7H
 7K9
Tel: 418-696-0536 *Fax:* 418-696-3132
E-mail: jcl@jcl.qc.ca
Web Site: www.jcl.qc.ca
Key Personnel
Pres & Intl Rts: Jean-Claude Larouche
Founded: 1977
Novels, nonfiction.
Publishes in French.
ISBN Prefix(es): 2-920176; 2-89431
Number of titles published annually: 24 Print
Total Titles: 300 Print
Distributed by Histoire et Documents; Transat
Distribution Center: ADP, 955 rue Amherst,
 Montreal, PQ H2L 3K4, Contact: Jean-Pierre
 Elias *Toll Free Tel:* 800-771-3022 *Toll Free
 Fax:* 800-465-1237
Membership(s): ANEL

Editions Marie-France
9900 avenue des Laurentides, Montreal-Nord, PQ
 H1H 4V1
Tel: 514-329-3700 *Toll Free Tel:* 800-563-6644
 Fax: 514-329-0630
E-mail: editions@marie-france.qc.ca
Web Site: www.marie-france.qc.ca
Key Personnel
Pres: Jean Lachapelle

Lib Sales Dir: Joanne Lacombe
Founded: 1977
School, kindergarten, elementary & secondary in
 French, natural sciences, human sciences, En-
 glish, French, music, economic education &
 science physics.
Publishes in English, French.
ISBN Prefix(es): 2-89168
Number of titles published annually: 25 Print
Total Titles: 638 Print
Membership(s): Association Nationale des Edi-
 teurs de Livres

Les Editions Phidal Inc
5740 rue Ferrier, Montreal, PQ H4P 1M7
Tel: 514-738-0202 *Toll Free Tel:* 800-738-7349
 Fax: 514-738-5102
E-mail: info@phidal.com
Web Site: www.phidal.com
Key Personnel
Publr: Lionel Soussan
Founded: 1979
Full service publisher.
Publishes in English, French.
ISBN Prefix(es): 2-89393; 2-7643
Number of titles published annually: 35 Print
Total Titles: 450 Print
Divisions: Edilivre Inc

Editions Saint-Martin
5000, rue Iberville, bureau 203, Montreal, PQ
 H2H 2M2
Tel: 514-529-0920 *Fax:* 514-529-8384
E-mail: st-martin@gc.airle.com
Key Personnel
Pres & Intl Rts: Richard Vezina
Founded: 1974
Essays; communication, health, graphic arts, ani-
 mal care, sociology, political science, psychol-
 ogy, philosophy, history, economy, education,
 professional training, social science.
Publishes in French.
ISBN Prefix(es): 2-89035
Number of titles published annually: 10 Print
Total Titles: 512 Print
Imprints: Les Editions Saint-Martin
Distributed by One Prologue Inc; R V Diffusion
 Inc

Editions Sciences & Culture Inc
5090 rue de Bellechasse, Montreal, PQ H1T 2A2
Tel: 514-253-0403 *Fax:* 514-256-5078
E-mail: admin@sciences-culture.qc.ca
Web Site: www.sciences-culture.qc.ca
Key Personnel
Pres: Mathieu Beliveau
Founded: 1975
Specialize in recovery, geopolitics, medicine, tax-
 ation & motivation.
Publishes in French.
ISBN Prefix(es): 2-89092
Number of titles published annually: 20 Print
Total Titles: 200 Print
Distributed by Iris Diffusion
Foreign Rights: Casteilla (France); Transat
 (Switzerland); Vander (Belgium)

Editions Total Publishing
7 Bates Rd, Outremont, PQ H2V 4A7
Tel: 514-276-2520 *Fax:* 514-276-2533
Web Site: www.total-publishing.com
Key Personnel
Dir, Sales & Mktg: Stephane Labbe
 E-mail: labbe.stephane@total-publishing.com
Founded: 1999
Specialize in cookbooks, self-help, youth, coffee-
 table books.
ISBN Prefix(es): 2-89535
Number of titles published annually: 100 Print
Foreign Rights: Daniel Doglioli (Italy)

Editions Trois
4882 Cherrier, Laval, PQ H7T 2Y9
Tel: 450-978-5245 *Fax:* 450-978-0899
E-mail: ed3ama@videotron.ca
Key Personnel
Intl Rts Contact: Anne-Marie Alonzo
Founded: 1985
Literary, history of arts, human sciences.
Publishes in English, French.
ISBN Prefix(es): 2-920887
Number of titles published annually: 15 Print
Total Titles: 180 Print
Warehouse: Diffusion Prologue, 1650 Boul
 Lionel-Bertrand, Boisbriand, PQ J7E 4H4
 Tel: 450-434-0306 *Fax:* 450-434-2627
Membership(s): ANEL

Les Editions Un Monde Different
3925 Grande Allee, St-Hubert, PQ J4T 2V8
Tel: 450-656-2660 *Fax:* 450-445-9098
Web Site: www.umd.ca
Key Personnel
Pres: Andre Blanchard
Ed: Michel Ferron
Founded: 1977
Motivational & inspirational books.
Publishes in French.
ISBN Prefix(es): 2-89225
Number of titles published annually: 25 Print
Total Titles: 600 Print

Editions Vents d'Ouest
185 rue Eddy, Hull, PQ J8X 2X2
Tel: 819-770-6377 *Fax:* 819-770-0559
E-mail: info@ventsdouest.ca
Key Personnel
Pres: Bernard Guimdom
Dir: Colette Michaud
Founded: 1993
Novels, short stories, history.
Publishes in French.
ISBN Prefix(es): 2-921603; 2-89537
Number of titles published annually: 18 Print
Total Titles: 145 Print

Editions Yvon Blais
137 John, CP 180, Cowansville, PQ J2K 1W9
Tel: 450-266-1086 *Fax:* 450-263-9256
E-mail: commandes@editionsyvonblais.qc.ca
Web Site: www.editionsyvonblais.qc.ca
Key Personnel
Dir, Publg & Intl Rts: Louis Busse
Gen Mgr: Charmian Harvey
Mktg Mgr: Marie-Claude Vallee
Founded: 1978
Law books.
Publishes in French.
ISBN Prefix(es): 2-89073; 2-89451
Number of titles published annually: 30 Print
Total Titles: 500 Print
Branch Office(s)
430 St-Pierre, Montreal, PQ H2Y 2M5

Emond Montgomery Publications Ltd
Division of Cartwright Group of Cos
60 Shaftesbury Ave, Toronto, ON M4T 1A3
Tel: 416-975-3925 *Toll Free Tel:* 888-837-0815
 Fax: 416-975-3924
E-mail: info@emp.ca; orders@emp.ca
Web Site: www.emp.ca
Key Personnel
Pres: D Paul Emond
VP, Publg: James Black *E-mail:* jblack@emp.ca
VP, School Publg: Tim Johnston
 E-mail: tjohnston@emp.ca
Mktg & Prodn Coord: David Stokaluk
 E-mail: stokaluk@emp.ca
Founded: 1978
Legal academic publisher.
Publishes in English.
ISBN Prefix(es): 0-920722; 1-55239

Number of titles published annually: 15 Print; 1
 CD-ROM
Total Titles: 100 Print; 1 CD-ROM
Distributor for Canada Law Books Inc
Returns: Emond Montgomery Publications, c/o
 Canada Law Book, 240 Edward St, Aurora,
 ON L4G 3S9
Warehouse: 240 Edward St, Aurora, ON L4G 3S9

English Literary Studies (Monograph Series)
University of Victoria, Dept of English, Victoria,
 BC V8W 3W1
Mailing Address: University of Victoria, PO Box
 3070, MS 7236, Victoria, BC V8W 3W1
Tel: 250-721-7237 *Fax:* 250-721-6498
E-mail: english@uvic.ca
Web Site: www.engl.uvic.ca
Key Personnel
Busn Mgr: Hedy Thompson *Tel:* 250-721-7236
Scholarly monographs related to English litera-
 ture.
Publishes in English.
ISBN Prefix(es): 0-9691436; 0-920604
Number of titles published annually: 3 Print
Total Titles: 89 Print

ERPI, see Editions du renouveau Pedagogique
 Inc

Essence Publishing
20 Hanna Ct, Belleville, ON K8P 5J2
Tel: 613-962-2360 *Toll Free Tel:* 800-238-6376
 Fax: 613-962-3055
E-mail: info@essencegroup.com
Web Site: www.essence.on.ca

Fairwinds Press
Subsidiary of John Izzo Consulting Inc
200 Isleview Place, Lions Bay, BC V0N 2E0
Mailing Address: PO Box 668, Lions Bay, BC
 V0N 2E0
Tel: 604-913-0649 *Fax:* 604-913-0648
E-mail: info@izzoconsultants.com
Web Site: www.izzoconsultants.com
Key Personnel
Publr & Intl Rts: Leslie Nolin *E-mail:* leslie@
 izzoconsultants.com
Founded: 1997
Publishes in English.
ISBN Prefix(es): 0-9682149
Total Titles: 6 Print
Foreign Rep(s): Waterside Productions (Brazil)
Distribution Center: National Book Network,
 4720 Boston Way, Lanham, MD 20706,
 United States, Contact: Miriam Bass *Toll Free
 Tel:* 800-462-6420

Fenn Publishing Co Ltd
Division of H B Fenn & Co Ltd
34 Nixon Rd, Bolton, ON L7E 1W2
Tel: 905-951-6600 *Toll Free Tel:* 800-267-
 3366 (Canada only) *Fax:* 905-951-6601
 Toll Free Fax: 800-465-3422 (Canada Only)
E-mail: sales@hbfenn.com
Web Site: www.hbfenn.com
Key Personnel
Pres: Harold B Fenn
VP, Opers: Bradley Fenn
VP, Inventory: Michael Fenn
VP, Sales & Mktg: Marnie Ferguson
Dir, Publg & Intl Rts Contact: Jordan Fenn
 E-mail: jordan.fenn@hbfenn.com
Publicity: Heidi Winter
Mktg Mgr: Melissa Cameron
Founded: 1977
Fiction, nonfiction paperback, hardcover, chil-
 dren's books.
Publishes in English.
ISBN Prefix(es): 0-919768; 1-55168
Number of titles published annually: 6 Print
Total Titles: 125 Print

Distributed by H B Fenn & Company Ltd
Distributor for Creative Publishing; Griffin; Henry
 Holt; Lets Go; MacMillian UK; Palgrave; Pan;
 Picador; Piggy Toes Press; Renaissance; Riz-
 zoli; Rodale; School Zone; St Martins Press;
 TOR; Warner; Wizard of the Coast

Fernwood Publishing Co Ltd
32 Ocean Vista Lane, Black Point, NS B0J 1B0
Tel: 902-857-1388 *Fax:* 902-857-1328
E-mail: info@fernwoodbooks.ca
Web Site: www.fernwoodbooks.ca
Key Personnel
Publr: Errol Sharpe *E-mail:* errol@
 fernwoodbooks.ca
Founded: 1991
Social sciences & humanities, emphasizing labour
 studies, women's studies, gender studies, criti-
 cal theory & research, political economy, cul-
 tural studies & social work for use in under-
 graduate courses in colleges & universities.
Publishes in English.
ISBN Prefix(es): 1-895686; 1-55266
Number of titles published annually: 17 Print
Total Titles: 200 Print
Branch Office(s)
324 Clare Ave, Manitoba, ON R3L 1S3, Contact:
 Wayne Antony *Tel:* 204-474-2958 *Fax:* 204-
 475-2813 *E-mail:* wayne@fernwoodbooks.ca
U.S. Publishers Represented: APEX Press; Clarity
 Press; Monthly Review Press
U.S. Rep(s): Eiron Inc
Foreign Rep(s): Merlin Press (UK & Ireland)
Shipping Address: Fernwood Books Ltd, PO Box
 406, STNC, Toronto, ON M6J 3P5, Contact:
 Lindsay Sharpe *Tel:* 416-595-1085 *Fax:* 416-
 399-1140 *E-mail:* lindsay@fernwoodbooks.ca
Distribution Center: TTS Distributing, 45 Tyler,
 Aurora, ON L4G 3L5 *Tel:* 905-841-3898
 Fax: 905-841-3026

Fifth House Publishers
Division of Fitzhenry & Whiteside
1511 1800 Fourth St SW, Calgary, AB T2S 2S5
Tel: 403-571-5230 *Toll Free Tel:* 800-387-9776
 Fax: 403-571-5235 *Toll Free Fax:* 800-260-
 9777
Web Site: www.fitzhenry.ca/fifthhouse.htm
Key Personnel
Publr: Charlene Dobmeier
Sr Ed: Liesbeth Leatherbarrow
Promos Dir: Simone Lee *Tel:* 403-571-5233
 E-mail: simone@hillsboro.ca
Cust Serv Rep: Kathy Bogusky
Founded: 1982
Trade publisher focusing on Western Canadian
 interest books; aviation, gardening.
Publishes in English.
ISBN Prefix(es): 0-920079; 1-895618; 1-894004;
 1-894856
Number of titles published annually: 18 Print
Total Titles: 140 Print; 1 CD-ROM; 1 Audio
Distributed by Fitzhenry & Whiteside
Distributor for Glenbow Museum
Distribution Center: Fitzhenry & Whiteside, 1954
 Allstate Parkway, Markham, ON L3R 4T8 *Toll
 Free Tel:* 800-387-9776 *Toll Free Fax:* 800-
 260-9777 *E-mail:* godwit@fitzhenry.ca *Web
 Site:* www.fitzhenry.ca
Membership(s): Book Publishers Association of
 Alberta

Firefly Books Ltd
66 Leek Crescent, Richmond Hill, ON L4B 1H1
Tel: 416-499-8412 *Toll Free Tel:* 800-387-5085
 Fax: 416-499-1142 *Toll Free Fax:* 800-565-
 6034
E-mail: service@fireflybooks.com
Web Site: www.fireflybooks.com
Key Personnel
Pres: Lionel Koffler *E-mail:* lionel@fireflybooks.
 com

VP: Leon Gouzoules
Lib Sales Dir: Ann Quinn
Publicity Mgr: Valerie Hatton
Founded: 1976
Calendars, books.
Publishes in English.
ISBN Prefix(es): 0-920668; 1-895565; 1-896284; 1-55209
Number of titles published annually: 80 Print
Total Titles: 350 Print
Branch Office(s)
230 Fifth Ave, Suite 1600, New York, NY 10001, United States
Distributor for Annick Press; Black Moss Press; Key Porter; Mikaya Press; Owl; Robert Rose; Sound & Vision
U.S. Publishers Represented: Black Sparrow; Sybex
U.S. Rep(s): Nicholas H Altwerger; Boston Mills Press; Kevin T Monahan; Doug Paton; Joyce Ruff-Abdill; Stuart Associates; Jeffrey D Stuart; Beth Ann Walck
See separate listing for:
The Boston Mills Press

Fitzhenry & Whiteside Limited
195 Allstate Pkwy, Markham, ON L3R 4T8
SAN: 115-1444
Tel: 905-477-9700 *Toll Free Tel:* 800-387-9776 *Fax:* 905-477-9179 *Toll Free Fax:* 800-260-9777
E-mail: godwit@fitzhenry.ca
Web Site: www.fitzhenry.ca
Key Personnel
Pres: Sharon Fitzhenry
Pres, Trade Group: Nelson Doucet
Publicity & Promos: Tracey Dettman *Tel:* 905-477-9700 ext 212 *E-mail:* tdettman@fitzhenry.ca
Publr, Children's Books: Gail Winskill
Dir, Dist: Sonya Gilliss
CFO: Peter Stubbs
Compt: Jennifer Walters
Dir, Accts Receivable: Jill Stewart
Dir, Cust Serv: Judy Ghoura
Founded: 1966
Trade, reference & children's books, educational material for elementary, high school & college.
Publishes in English.
ISBN Prefix(es): 0-88902; 1-55005; 1-55041; 1-894004; 1-894856
Number of titles published annually: 70 Print
Total Titles: 1,100 Print
Imprints: Fifth House; Trifolium Books
Distributor for Kodansha
U.S. Publishers Represented: The Beacon Press; Kodansha International; Hal Leonard; Peachtree Publishing; Stackpole Books; Walker & Company; Albert Whitman

Flammarion Quebec
375 Ave Laurier ouest, Montreal, PQ H2V 2K3
Tel: 514-277-8807 *Fax:* 514-278-2085
E-mail: info@flammarion.qc.ca
Web Site: www.flammarion.qc.ca
Key Personnel
Pres: Jean-Michel Sivry
Publr: Louise Loiselle *E-mail:* lloiselle@flammarion.qc.ca
Gen Dir, Dist: Guy Gougeon
Founded: 1974
Best sellers, translations, Quebec literature.
Publishes in French.
ISBN Prefix(es): 2-89077
Number of titles published annually: 20 Print
Total Titles: 180 Print
Imprints: Advenir; Bis (Pocket Book); Super Sellers
Distributor for Acatos; Al Dante; Analogie; APCE; Arcane Institut; Arthaud; Association D'Economie Financiere; Assouline; Aubier; Beaux-Arts Hors Serie; Bipede; Casterman; CEA; Centre Georges Pompidou; Chasse

Au Snark; Competence Micro (Know Ware); CTBA; Delagrave Jeunesse; Michel de Maule; Le Dilettante; Dis Voir; Drole D'Epoque; Duculot; Eclair de Lune; ECM (Editions Comptables Maleshesrbes); EDF; Editions 84; Elenbi; EMS (Editions Management & Societe); Envie de Creer; Eyrolles; Farrago; Filipson; Fluide Glacial; Geresco; Grand Caractere; Grand Miroir; Viviane Hamy; Hoebeke; Homard; Horay; Horizon Illimite; Horlieu; Inedite; Institute De L'Image; J'ai Lu; JNF; Journal des Finances; Jury des Marques; Librio; Lignes/Manifestes; Ludion; Mae Erti; Maison Rustique; Medieco; Melville; Moulinsart; Musicrun; Neopol; OEM organisation; Organisation; Paquet; Part De L'Oeil; Pere Castor Flammarion; Petit Fute; Petit Musc; Picaron; Platypus Sante; Le Pli; Plume; La Presse; Presses des Ponts et Chaussees; Presqu'ile; Publibook; Publitronic; Pygmalion; Revue Cinema; Revue Fiduciaire; Revue Fusees; Revue Lignes & Manifestes; Revue L'Image Le Monde; Revue Transeuropeennes; Leo Scheer; SEBTP; Septembre; Sulliver; Super Sellers; Tabary; Une de Plus; Universalis; VDB; Via Valeriano; Vie & Cie; VM; Yellow Now; Zulma
Warehouse: 420 Stinson, St-Laurent, PQ H4N 2E9

Folklore Publishing
8025 102 St, Edmonton, AB T6E 4A2
Tel: 780-910-6216 *Fax:* 780-433-9646
Web Site: www.folklorepublishing.com
Key Personnel
Publr: Faye Boer *E-mail:* fboer@folklorepublishing.com
Founded: 2001
Publisher of popular history of western North America & celebrity biographies.
Publishes in English.
ISBN Prefix(es): 1-894864
Number of titles published annually: 5 Print
Total Titles: 15 Print
Membership(s): Book Publishers Association of Alberta

Food and Beverage Consultants
39 Burnview Crescent, Toronto, ON M1H 1B4
Tel: 416-431-2015 *Fax:* 416-431-2015
E-mail: h1rayr@netscape.com
Key Personnel
Pres & Intl Rts: Hrayr Berberoglu *E-mail:* hberbero@ryerson.ca
Founded: 1972
Specialize in reference books. Highly specialized company involved in publishing & hospitality consulting where everything is done centrally & efficiently. Specialize in hotel, restaurant & hospitality, tourism management textbooks; also publishes recipe books.
Publishes in English.
ISBN Prefix(es): 1-899861
Total Titles: 41 Print

The Fraser Institute
1770 Burrard St, 4th fl, Vancouver, BC V6J 3G7
Tel: 604-688-0221 *Toll Free Tel:* 800-665-3558 *Fax:* 604-688-8539
E-mail: sales@fraserinstitute.ca
Web Site: www.fraserinstitute.ca
Key Personnel
Dir, Devt: Sherry Stein *E-mail:* sherrys@fraserinstitute.ca
Dir, Communs: Suzanne Walters *Tel:* 604-714-4582 *E-mail:* suzannew@fraserinstitute.ca
Dir, Pubns: Kristin McCahon *E-mail:* kristinm@fraserinstitute.ca
Founded: 1974
Publish regulatory studies, health policy, social affairs, taxation, environmental studies, law & markets. Publish monthly magazine *Fraser Fo-*

rum. Also, publish current research in the form of books, critical issues bulletin & public policy sources.
Publishes in English, French.
ISBN Prefix(es): 0-88975
Number of titles published annually: 12 Print
Total Titles: 280 Print; 100 Online

Gaetan Morin Editeur Ltee
7001 Blvd Sainte-Laurent, Montreal, PQ H2S 3E3
Tel: 514-273-1066 *Fax:* 514-276-0324
E-mail: achat@groupemorin.com
Web Site: groupemorin.com
Key Personnel
Sales Mgr: Manon Thiffeault *E-mail:* manon.thiffeault@groupemorin.com
Founded: 1977
Textbooks, college, university & professional Books.
Publishes in French.
ISBN Prefix(es): 2-89105
Number of titles published annually: 20 Print; 1 CD-ROM
Total Titles: 300 Print; 2 CD-ROM

Gage Learning Corp
Division of Thomson Nelson
1120 Birchmount Rd, Scarborough, ON M1K 5G4
SAN: 115-0375
Tel: 416-752-9448 *Toll Free Tel:* 800-430-4445 *Fax:* 416-752-8101 *Toll Free Fax:* 800-430-4445
E-mail: inquire@nelson.com
Web Site: www.nelson.com
Founded: 1844
Educational, K-12.
Publishes in English.
ISBN Prefix(es): 0-7715; 0-7705
Number of titles published annually: 70 Print
Imprints: Dancing Sun; Gage; MacMillan; Methuen
Distributed by Dominie Press Inc
Distributor for Clare Development Inc (Canada); Earthscan Publications (UK); Editions MDI (France); Edustar; Jessica Kingsley (UK); Kogan Page (UK); MacMillan (Australia); Methuen (Canada); Nectar (Canada); Neufeld (Canada)
U.S. Publishers Represented: American Technical Publishers; Aspen Publishers; Belson/Hanwright Video; Dominie Press; Edunetics; Edustar; Janson Publications; Phoenix Learning Resources; Productivity Press; Science Works; Skillsbank; Sourcebooks Trade
U.S. Rep(s): Dominie Press Inc

Garamond Press Ltd
63 Mahogany Ct, Aurora, ON L4G 6M8
Tel: 905-841-1460 *Toll Free Tel:* 800-898-9535 *Fax:* 905-841-3031
E-mail: garamond@web.ca
Web Site: www.garamond.ca
Key Personnel
Pres, Publr & Exec VP, Edit: Peter Saunders
Mktg & Promos: Rita Surman
Founded: 1981
Social science monographs & texts, post-secondary level.
Publishes in English.
ISBN Prefix(es): 0-920059; 1-55193
Number of titles published annually: 8 Print
Total Titles: 70 Print; 1 CD-ROM
Foreign Rep(s): Global Book Marketing (UK & Europe)
Membership(s): Association of Canadian Publishers; Ontario Book Publishers' Association

General Store Publishing House
Division of Custom Printers of Renfrew Ltd
499 O'Brien Rd, Renfrew, ON K7V 4A6

Mailing Address: Box 415, Refrew, ON K7V 4A6
Tel: 613-432-7697 *Toll Free Tel:* 800-465-6072 *Fax:* 613-432-7184
Web Site: www.gsph.com
Key Personnel
Publr: Tim Gordon *E-mail:* timgordon@gsph.com
Founded: 1982
Local history, sport books, senior fitness, military. Publishes in English.
ISBN Prefix(es): 0-919431; 1-896182; 1-894263; 1-897113
Number of titles published annually: 25 Print
Total Titles: 400 Print

Gold Eagle
Division of Harlequin Enterprises Ltd
225 Duncan Mill Rd, Don Mills, ON M3B 3K9
Tel: 416-445-5860 *Fax:* 416-445-8655; 416-445-8736 *Telex:* 06966697
Key Personnel
Sr Ed: Feroze Mohammed *Tel:* 416-445-5860 ext 628 *E-mail:* feroze_mohammed@harlequin.ca
Founded: 1982
Mass market fiction, science fiction, action & adventure.
Publishes in English.
ISBN Prefix(es): 0-373
Number of titles published annually: 36 Print
Warehouse: 3010 Walden Ave, Depew, NY 14043, United States

Golden Meteorite Press
Subsidiary of Golden Meteorite Press Ltd
PO Box 1223 Main Post Office, Edmonton, AB T5J 2M4
Tel: 780-378-0063
Key Personnel
Ed & Lib Sales Dir: Stephanie N L Liu
Intl Rts: M Pretty
Founded: 1989
Preferred submission is outline. Canadian SASE or IRC is required or else material is recycled. Accept fiction & nonfiction mss in all categories & genres. Submit to editor. Response in 12 weeks on all complete ms submissions. No phone calls please.
Publishes in English.
ISBN Prefix(es): 1-895385
Number of titles published annually: 3 Print
Total Titles: 16 Print
Imprints: Golden Meteorite Press; RTAJ Fry Press; Shoestring Press

Goose Lane Editions
469 King St, Fredericton, NB E3B 1E5
SAN: 115-3420
Tel: 506-450-4251 *Toll Free Tel:* 888-926-8377 *Fax:* 506-459-4991
E-mail: gooselane@gooselane.com
Web Site: www.gooselane.com
Key Personnel
Publr: Susanne Alexander
Edit Dir & Foreign Rts: Laurel Boone
Accts Mgr: Patrick O'Donnell
Prodn Mgr: Julie Scriver
Founded: 1954
Primarily deal with Canadian authors. Submissions not accepted from outside of Canada.
Publishes in English.
ISBN Prefix(es): 0-920110; 0-919197; 0-86492
Number of titles published annually: 20 Print; 10 Audio
Total Titles: 200 Print; 50 Audio
Imprints: Between the Covers Classics (Audio); Between the Covers Collection (Audio); BTC Audiobooks; Fiddlehead Poetry Books; GLE Library; Goose Lane Editions
Sales Office(s): General Distribution Services Inc, 4500 Witmer Industrial Estates, PMB 128, Niagara Falls, NY 14305-1386, United States *Toll*

Free Tel: 800-805-1083 *Toll Free Fax:* 800-481-6207
Distributed by University of Toronto Press
Distributor for Acadiensis Press; Acorn Press; Beaverbrook Art Gallery; Confederation Centre of the Arts; Institute of Island Studies; LM Montgomery Institute of UPEI; New Brunswick Museum
Foreign Rep(s): James Bryner (USA); Jacqueline Davis (USA); Carolyn Gillis (New England); Don Gorman (USA); Susan Wallace (USA)
Shipping Address: 5201 Dufferin St, North York, ON M9W 5T8 *Toll Free Tel:* 800-565-9523 *Fax:* 416-667-7791
Membership(s): Association of Canadian Publishers; Atlantic Publishers Marketing Association; Literary Press Group

Greystone Books
Division of Douglas & McIntyre Publishing Group
2323 Quebec St, Suite 201, Vancouver, BC V5T 4S7
Tel: 604-254-7191 *Toll Free Tel:* 800-667-6902 *Fax:* 604-254-9099
Key Personnel
Publr: Rob Sanders *E-mail:* rob.sanders@greystonebooks.com
VP & Natl Sales & Mktg Mgr: Susan McIntosh
Founded: 1993
Publishes in English.
ISBN Prefix(es): 0-88894; 1-55054; 1-55365; 0-88833
Number of titles published annually: 30 Audio
Total Titles: 320 Audio
Distributor for Farrar Straus & Giroux
U.S. Publishers Represented: Farrar Straus & Giroux
U.S. Rep(s): Publishers Group West

Les Editions Griffon D'Argile, see
Modulo-Griffon Inc

Groundwood Books
Affiliate of Douglas & McIntyre Ltd
720 Bathurst St, Suite 500, Toronto, ON M5S 2R4
Tel: 416-537-2501 *Fax:* 416-537-4647
E-mail: genmail@groundwood-dm.com
Web Site: www.groundwoodbooks.com
Key Personnel
Pres & Publr: Patricia Aldana
VP, Sales & Mktg Douglas & McIntyre/Groundwood Books: Susan McIntosh *Tel:* 416-537-2501 ext 223 *E-mail:* susanm@groundwood-dm.com
Dir, US Sales & Natl Accts, Douglas & McIntyre Ltd/Groundwood Books: Molly Helferty *Tel:* 416-537-2501 ext 228 *E-mail:* mollyh@groundwood-dm.com
Dir, Regl Sales & Natl Accts Dir: Harry Kirchner *Tel:* 800-788-3123 ext 307 *E-mail:* harry.kirchner@pgw.com
Mktg Mgr: Debbie Brown *Tel:* 416-537-2501 ext 231 *E-mail:* dbrown@groundwood-dm.com
Rts Assoc: Sarah Quinn *Tel:* 416-537-2501 ext 229 *E-mail:* squinn@groundwood-dm.com
Founded: 1978
Publish children's books, picture books, novels, nonfiction & folktales; also publish in Spanish.
Publishes in English.
ISBN Prefix(es): 0-88899
Number of titles published annually: 25 Print
Total Titles: 435 Print
Branch Office(s)
841 Broadway, 4th fl, New York, NY 10003, United States *Tel:* 212-614-7888 *Fax:* 212-614-7866
Sales Office(s): Douglas & McIntrye Ltd, 2323 Quebec St, Suite 201, Vancouver, BC V5T 4S7 (Vancouver & lower mainland trade & lib accts), Contact: Richard Nadeau *Tel:* 604-

254-7191 *Fax:* 604-254-9099 *E-mail:* richard.nadeau@douglas-mcintyre.com
Hornblower Books Ltd, 1657 Barrington St, Suite 409, Halifax, NS B3J 2A1 (Atlantic Canada), Contact: Terrilee Bulger *Tel:* 902-423-9714 *Fax:* 902-422-2869 *E-mail:* tbulger@hornblowerbooks.com
Hornblower Books Ltd, 4001, rue Berri, Suite 201, Montreal, PQ H2L 4H2 (Quebec), Contact: Debra Schram *Tel:* 514-843-7410 *Fax:* 514-843-7798 *E-mail:* dschram@hornblowerbooks.com
Hornblower Books Ltd, 880 Wellington St, Suite 614, Ottawa, ON K1R 6K7 (Ottawa/Kingston), Contact: Bridget Barber *Tel:* 613-234-4665 *Fax:* 613-234-5484 *E-mail:* bbarber@hornblowerbooks.com
Hornblower Books Ltd, 270 Carlaw Ave, Suite 101, Toronto, ON M4M 3L1 (Southern ON & Metro Toronto), Contact: Jane Tarassoff *Tel:* 416-461-7973 *Fax:* 416-461-0365
Kate Walker & Co Ltd, 2523 Charlebois Dr NW, Calgary, AB T2L 0T5 (Southern AB trade & lib accts), Contact: Anthony Cooney *Tel:* 403-245-1585 *Fax:* 403-245-5377 *E-mail:* acooney@agt.net
Kate Walker & Co Ltd, 4819-111A St, Edmonton, AB T6H 3G4 (Northern AB & NT trade & lib accts), Contact: Sara Gavinchuk *Tel:* 780-434-3116 *E-mail:* saragavinchuk@yahoo.ca
Kate Walker & Co Ltd, 9050 Shaughnessy St, Vancouver, BC V6P 6E5 (BC trade & lib accts), Contact: Kate Walker *Tel:* 604-323-7111 *Fax:* 604-323-7118 *E-mail:* katew@katewalker.com
Kate Walker & Co Ltd, 1333 Fairfield Rd, Victoria, BC Y8S 1E4 (Vancouver Island trade & lib accts), Contact: Lorna MacDonald *Tel:* 250-382-1058 *Fax:* 250-383-0697 *E-mail:* lornam@katewalker.com
Kate Walker & Co Ltd, 737 Montrose St, Winnipeg, MB R3M 3M5 (MB/Lakehead SK trade & lib accts), Contact: Rorie Bruce *Tel:* 204-488-9481 *Fax:* 204-487-3993 *E-mail:* rorbruce@mts.net
Distributor for Farrar Straus Giroux
Foreign Rights: Bardon Media Agency (China); The Choicemaker Agency (Korea); The English Agency; Agence Litteraire Lora Fountain & Associates (France); Japan Uni Agency Inc (Japan); Karen Schindler Agency (Brazil)
Returns: HarperCollins Canada, 1995 Markham Rd, Scarborough, ON M1B 5M8 *Tel:* 416-321-2241 *Toll Free Tel:* 800-387-0117 *Fax:* 416-321-3033 *Toll Free Fax:* 800-668-5788
Distribution Center: HarperCollins Distribution & Fulfillment, 1995 Markham Rd, Scarborough, ON M1B 5M8 *Tel:* 416-321-2241 *Toll Free Tel:* 800-387-0117 *Fax:* 416-321-3033 *Toll Free Fax:* 800-668-5788
Publishers Group West, 1700 Fourth St, Berkeley, CA 94710, United States *Tel:* 510-528-1444 *Toll Free Tel:* 800-788-3123 *Fax:* 510-528-5511 (sales dept)
Membership(s): Association of Canadian Publishers; International Board on Books for Young People; Ontario Book Publishers Organization

Groupe Educalivres Inc
955, rue Bergar, Laval, PQ H7L 4Z6
Tel: 514-334-8466 *Toll Free Tel:* 800-567-3671 (Info Service) *Fax:* 514-334-8387
E-mail: commentaires@educalivres.com
Web Site: www.educalivres.com
Key Personnel
Pres & Owner: Jean-Guy Blanchette
Pres: Louis Martin
Exec VP, Fin & Admin: Joe Cristofaro
Founded: 1992
School, college, university & professional textbooks.
Publishes in French.

ISBN Prefix(es): 2-7607; 0-03; 0-88586
Divisions: COBA Management Software; Editions Etudes Vivantes (college); Editions HRW (school)

Guerin Editeur Ltee
4501 rue Drolet, Montreal, PQ H2T 2G2
Tel: 514-842-3481 *Toll Free Tel:* 800-398-8337
  Fax: 514-842-4923
Web Site: www.guerin-editeur.qc.ca
Key Personnel
Pres: Marc-Aime Guerin
VP: France Larochelle *E-mail:* france.larochelle@
  guerin-editeur.qc.ca
Prodn Mgr: Janick Salvaille
Lib Sales Dir: Lorraine Auger
Founded: 1970
Publishers of books for schools from kindergarten
  to university.
Publishes in English, French.
ISBN Prefix(es): 2-7601
Number of titles published annually: 80 Print; 2
  Audio
Total Titles: 2,081 Print; 43 Audio
Distributed by ADG

Guernica Editions Inc
PO Box 117, Sta P, Toronto, ON M5S 2S6
Tel: 416-658-9888 *Toll Free Tel:* 800-565-9523
  (orders) *Fax:* 416-657-8885 *Toll Free Fax:* 800-
  221-9985 (orders)
E-mail: guernicaeditions@cs.com
Web Site: guernicaeditions.com
Key Personnel
Pres & Publr: Antonio D'Alfonso
Lib Sales Dir: Halli Villegas
Founded: 1978
Literary Press specializing in translation into
  English, including literary criticism & ethnic
  history. Foreign language & bilingual books,
  art, drama, theater, ethnic, fiction, film, video,
  gay & lesbian, general nonfiction, poetry &
  women's studies.
Publishes in English.
ISBN Prefix(es): 0-919349; 0-920717; 2-89135;
  1-55071
Number of titles published annually: 28 Print
Total Titles: 320 Print
U.S. Rep(s): Independent Publishers Group, 814
  N Franklin St, Chicago, IL 60610, United
  States *Toll Free Tel:* 800-888-4741 *Fax:* 212-
  337-5987
Shipping Address: University of Toronto Press,
  5201 Dufferin St, Downsview, ON M3H 5T8
  Tel: 416-667-7846 *Toll Free Tel:* 800-565-9523
  Fax: 416-667-7832
Distribution Center: Independent Publishers
  Group, 814 N Franklin St, Chicago, IL 60610,
  United States *Toll Free Tel:* 800-888-4741
  Fax: 212-337-5987

Hancock House Publishers Ltd
19313 Zero Ave, Surrey, BC V3S 9R9
Mailing Address: 1431 Harrison Ave, Blaine, WA
  98230-5005, United States
Tel: 604-538-1114 *Toll Free Tel:* 800-938-1114
  Fax: 604-538-2262 *Toll Free Fax:* 800-983-
  2262
E-mail: promo@hancockwildlife.org; sales@
  hancockhouse.com
Web Site: www.hancockhouse.com
Key Personnel
Pres: David Hancock
Sales Mgr: George Wilson
Ed: Ingrid Lufers
Founded: 1975
Biographical nature guide books.
Publishes in English.
ISBN Prefix(es): 0-88839; 0-919654
Number of titles published annually: 20 Print; 20
  CD-ROM

Total Titles: 365 Print; 250 CD-ROM
Foreign Rep(s): Gazelle Book Services (UK)

Harbour Publishing Co Ltd
4437 Rondeview Rd, Madeira Park, BC V0N 2H0
Mailing Address: Box 219, Madeira Park, BC
  V0N 2H0
Tel: 604-883-2730 *Toll Free Tel:* 800-667-
  2988; 800-667-2988 *Fax:* 604-883-9451
  Toll Free Fax: 877-604-9449
E-mail: info@harbourpublishing.com
Web Site: www.harbourpublishing.com
Key Personnel
Publr: Howard White
Sales Mgr: Brian Lee
Prodn Mgr: Vicki Johnstone
Mktg Mgr: Alicia Miller
Founded: 1972
History & culture of British Columbia & West
  Coast, including fiction & poetry by Canadian
  authors.
Publishes in English.
ISBN Prefix(es): 0-920080; 1-55017
Number of titles published annually: 30 Print; 1
  CD-ROM; 1 Audio
Total Titles: 300 Print; 1 CD-ROM; 5 Audio
Distributor for Caitlin Press; Nightwood Editions
U.S. Rep(s): Graphic Arts Center Publishing Co;
  Robert Hale & Co; Ingram Book Co; Partners
  West
Foreign Rep(s): Gazelle Book Services Ltd (UK,
  Eastern Europe, Ireland, Western Europe)
Orders to: Harbour Publishing, Lagoon
  Rd, Madeira Park, BC V0N 2H0 *Toll
  Free Tel:* 800-667-2988 *E-mail:* orders@
  harbourpublishing.com
Distribution Center: Harbour Publishing, Lagoon
  Rd, Madeira Park, BC V0N 2H0

Harcourt Canada Ltd
Subsidiary of Harcourt Inc
55 Horner Ave, Toronto, ON M8Z 4X6
Tel: 416-255-4491; 416-255-0177 (Voice Mail)
  Toll Free Tel: 800-387-7278 (North Amer-
  ica); 800-387-7305 (North America) *Fax:* 416-
  255-6708 *Toll Free Fax:* 800-665-7307 (North
  America)
E-mail: firstname_lastname@harcourt.com
Web Site: www.harcourtcanada.com
Key Personnel
Pres: Wendy Cochran
VP, Fin: Sheilagh Fillion
VP, HR: Linda Cowan
VP, Fin - Elsevier Canada: Jewell Kennedy
Gen Sales Mgr - Harcourt Assessment: Scott
  Pawson
Founded: 1922
K-12, health sciences, testing & assessment.
Publishes in English.
ISBN Prefix(es): 0-399; 0-7747; 0-392; 0-9205;
  0-7796
Imprints: Butterworth Heinemann; Churchill Liv-
  ingstone; Harcourt; Harcourt Assessment; Har-
  vest Paperbacks; Holt, Rinehart and Winston
U.S. Publishers Represented: Harcourt Assess-
  ment; Harcourt Inc; Harcourt Religion; Holt,
  Rinehart and Winston; Steck-Vaughn

Harlequin Enterprises Ltd
Subsidiary of Torstar Corp
225 Duncan Mill Rd, Don Mills, ON M3B 3K9
Tel: 416-445-5860 *Fax:* 416-445-8655
Web Site: www.eharlequin.com; www.luna-books.
  com; www.mirabooks.com; www.reddressink.
  com; www.steeplehill.com
Key Personnel
Publr & CEO: Donna Hayes
Exec VP, Global Publg & Strategy: Loriana
  Sacilotto
Exec VP, Overseas: Steven Miles
Exec VP, Direct to Consumer: Mark Mailman
Exec VP, Retail Mktg: Craig Swinwood

Sr VP, Fin: David Holland
Sr VP, Oper: Jim Robinson
VP, PR: Katherine Orr
VP, Retail Sales: Alex Osuszek
VP, Info Systems: Ralph Stone
VP, Author & Asset Devt: Isabel Swift
Founded: 1949
Publishes in 27 languages.
Publishes in English, French.
ISBN Prefix(es): 0-373
Number of titles published annually: 1,200 Print
Imprints: Gold Eagle Books; Harlequin; HQN
  Books; Luna Books; MIRA Books; Red Dress
  Ink; Silhouette; Steeple Hill; Worldwide Li-
  brary
Branch Office(s)
233 Broadway, Suite 1001, New York, NY
  10279, United States *Tel:* 212-553-4200
  Fax: 212-227-8969
Foreign Office(s): Harlequin Mills & Boon,
  18-24 Paradise Rd, Richmond, Surrey TW9
  1SR, United Kingdom *Tel:* (0208) 288 2800
  Fax: (0208) 288 2899
Advertising Agency: Vickers & Benson-Direct
Distribution Center: 3010 Walden Ave, Depew,
  NY 14043, United States
Membership(s): AAP; Association of Canadian
  Publishers; BISG
See separate listing for:
Gold Eagle
Worldwide Library

HarperCollins Publishers Canada
Division of HarperCollins Publishers
2 Bloor St E, 20th fl, Toronto, ON M4W 1A8
Tel: 416-975-9334 *Fax:* 416-975-9884 (publish-
  ing); 416-975-5223 (sales)
E-mail: hccanada@harpercollins.com
Web Site: www.harpercanada.com
Key Personnel
Pres & CEO: David Kent *Tel:* 416-321-2241,ext
  212 *E-mail:* David.Kent@harpercollins.com
VP, Publr & Ed-in-Chief: Iris Tupholme *Tel:* 416-
  975-9334, ext 123 *E-mail:* Iris.Tupholme@
  harpercollins.com
VP, Admin & Opers: Jeff Shannon *Tel:* 416-
  321-2241 ext 280 *E-mail:* Jeff.Shannon@
  harpercollins.com
VP, Fin: Wayne Playter *Tel:* 416-321-2241, ext
  207 *E-mail:* Wayne.Playter@harpercollins.com
VP, Mktg & Sales: Kevin Hanson *Tel:* 416-
  975-9334, ext 122 *E-mail:* Kevin.Hanson@
  harpercollins.com
VP, Opers: Olive Khan *Tel:* 416-321-2241, ext
  204 *E-mail:* Olive.Kahn@harpercollins.com
Acting Dir, Publicity: Rob Firing *Tel:* 416-
  975-9334 ext 141 *E-mail:* Rob.Firing@
  harpercollins.com
Founded: 1989
Trade, mass market paperbacks, children's books,
  inspirational & religious books.
Publishes in English.
ISBN Prefix(es): 0-00
Total Titles: 500 Print
Imprints: HarperFlamingoCanada; Perennial-
  Canada
Distributor for HarperCollins Children's Books
  Group; HarperCollins General Books Group;
  HarperCollins Publishers; HarperCollins Pub-
  lishers Sales; Perseus Books Group; Zondervan
Warehouse: 1995 Markham Rd, Scarborough, ON
  M1B 5M8 *Tel:* 416-321-2241 (orders only)
  Fax: 416-321-3033

Hartley & Marks Publishers Ltd
3661 W Broadway, Vancouver, BC V6R 2B8
Tel: 604-739-1771 *Toll Free Tel:* 800-277-5887
  Fax: 604-738-1913 *Toll Free Fax:* 800-707-
  5887
E-mail: pbdesk@hartleyandmarks.com
Web Site: www.hartleyandmarks.com
Key Personnel
Pres & Publr: Vic Marks

Founded: 1973
Publishes in English.
ISBN Prefix(es): 0-88179
Number of titles published annually: 3 Print
Total Titles: 70 Print
Distributed by Raincoast Books
U.S. Rep(s): Publishers Group West, 1700 Fourth
St, Berkeley, CA 94710, United States

Herald Press
Division of Mennonite Publishing House Inc
490 Dutton Dr, Unit C-8, Waterloo, ON N2L 6H7
Tel: 519-747-5722 *Toll Free Tel:* 800-245-7894
(Canada & US) *Fax:* 519-747-5721
E-mail: hp@mph.org
Web Site: www.heraldpress.com
Key Personnel
Mktg Mgr & ISBN Contact: Patricia Weaver
Tel: 724-887-8500 ext 225 *E-mail:* patricia@
mph.org
Intl Rts: Levi Miller *Tel:* 724-887-8500 ext 280
E-mail: levi@mph.org
Founded: 1908
Christian books.
Publishes in English.
ISBN Prefix(es): 0-8361
Number of titles published annually: 20 Print
Total Titles: 450 Print
Shipping Address: 616 Walnut Ave, Scottdale, PA
15683, United States
Membership(s): Canadian Booksellers Associa-
tion; Christian Booksellers Association (Cana-
dian Chapter)

Heritage House Publishing Co Ltd
17665 66 "A" Ave, No 108, Surrey, BC V3S 2A7
Tel: 604-574-7067 *Toll Free Tel:* 800-665-3302
Fax: 604-574-9942 *Toll Free Fax:* 800-566-
3336
E-mail: publisher@heritagehouse.ca; editorial@
heritagehouse.ca; distribution@heritagehouse.ca
Web Site: www.heritagehouse.ca
Key Personnel
Publr: Rodger Touchie
Off Mgr: Diane Komorowski
Intl Rts Contact: Pat Touchie
Founded: 1967
Publishes in English.
ISBN Prefix(es): 1-895811
Number of titles published annually: 16 Print
Total Titles: 165 Print
Editorial Office(s): 301-3555 Outrigger Rd,
Nanoose Bay, BC V9P 9K1 *Tel:* 250-468-5328
Fax: 250-468-5318
Distributor for Frank Amato; Bellerophon; Fine
Edge Productions; Horsdal & Schubart; Sun-
fire; Whitecap

Highway Book Shop
RR 1, Cobalt, ON P0J 1C0
Tel: 705-679-8375 *Fax:* 705-679-8511
E-mail: bookshop@nt.net
Web Site: www.abebooks.com/home/
highwaybooks
Key Personnel
Owner & Mgr: Dr Douglas Pollard
Founded: 1957
Booksellers & publishers.
Publishes in English.
ISBN Prefix(es): 0-88954
Number of titles published annually: 5 Print
Total Titles: 200 Print
Membership(s): Association of Canadian Publish-
ers; Ontario Book Publishers Organization

Hounslow Press
Imprint of Dundurn Group
8 Market St, 2nd fl, Toronto, ON M5E 1M6
SAN: 115-1223
Tel: 416-214-5544 *Fax:* 416-214-5556
E-mail: info@dundurn.com
Web Site: www.dundurn.com

Key Personnel
Dir, Publg: Anthony Hawke
Founded: 1972
General trade on all subjects; popular nonfiction.
Publishes in English.
ISBN Prefix(es): 1-55002; 0-88882
Number of titles published annually: 15 Print
Total Titles: 150 Print
Distribution Center: University of Toronto Press

House of Anansi Press Ltd
110 Spadina Ave, Suite 801, Toronto, ON M5V
2K4
Tel: 416-363-4343 *Fax:* 416-363-1017
E-mail: info@anansi.ca
Web Site: www.anansi.ca
Key Personnel
Publr: Martha Sharpe
Founded: 1968
Literary publishing; fiction, poetry, criticism &
belles lettres.
Publishes in English.
ISBN Prefix(es): 0-88784
Number of titles published annually: 15 Print
Total Titles: 200 Print
Distribution Center: General Distribution Ser-
vices Ltd, 325 Humber College Rd, Toronto,
ON M9W 7L3 *Tel:* 416-213-1919 ext 199
Fax: 416-213-1917 *E-mail:* cservice@genpub.
com

C D Howe Institute
125 Adelaide St E, Toronto, ON M5C 1L7
Tel: 416-865-1904 *Fax:* 416-865-1866
E-mail: cdhowe@cdhowe.org
Web Site: www.cdhowe.org
Key Personnel
CEO & Pres: Jack Mintz
Ed: Kevin Doyle
Founded: 1973
Economics & social policy studies.
Publishes in English, French.
ISBN Prefix(es): 0-88806
Number of titles published annually: 4 Print
Total Titles: 150 Print
Distributed by McGraw-Hill Ryerson Ltd (trade
market); Renouf Publishing Co

Humanitas
990 Picard, Ville de Brossard, PQ J4W 1S5
Tel: 450-466-9737 *Fax:* 450-466-9737
E-mail: humanitas@cyberglobe.net
Key Personnel
Pres & Dir Gen: Constantin Stoiciu
Founded: 1983
General literature.
Publishes in French.
ISBN Prefix(es): 2-89396
Number of titles published annually: 15 Print
Total Titles: 305 Print
Distributed by Quebec Livres/Humanitas
Membership(s): Association Nationale des Edi-
teurs de Livres

Hybrid Publishing Co-op Ltd
860 Mountain Ave, Winnipeg, MB R2X 1C3
Tel: 204-589-4257 *Fax:* 204-589-4257
E-mail: mail@hybrid-publishing.ca
Web Site: www.hybrid-publishing.ca
Key Personnel
Man Ed: Catharine Johannson
Founded: 2001
Publishes in English.
ISBN Prefix(es): 0-9689709
Number of titles published annually: 6 Print
Total Titles: 10 Print

Hyperion Press Ltd
300 Wales Ave, Winnipeg, MB R2M 2S9
SAN: 115-124X
Tel: 204-256-9204 *Fax:* 204-255-7845

E-mail: tamos@mts.ca
Key Personnel
Pres: Dr Marvis Tutiah
Founded: 1978
How-to & children's picture books.
Publishes in English.
ISBN Prefix(es): 0-920534; 1-895340
Number of titles published annually: 10 Print
Total Titles: 68 Print
Divisions: Tamos Books Inc
Distributed by Sterling Publishing Inc
Warehouse: Premier Printing, One Begin Ave,
Winnipeg, MB R2J 3X5
See separate listing for:
Tamos Books Inc

§IDRC Books/Les Editions du CRDI
PO Box 8500, Ottawa, ON K1G 3H9
Tel: 613-236-6163 *Fax:* 613-563-2476
E-mail: pub@idrc.ca
Web Site: www.idrc.ca
Key Personnel
Man Ed: Bill Carman *E-mail:* bcarman@idrc.ca
Founded: 1971
Publishes in English, French.
ISBN Prefix(es): 0-88936; 1-55250
Number of titles published annually: 30 Print; 4
CD-ROM; 15 Online
Total Titles: 300 Print; 2 CD-ROM; 100 Online
Distributed by Renouf Publishing Co Ltd
U.S. Rep(s): Stylus Publishing Inc, 22883 Quick-
sliver Dr, Sterling, VA 20166-2012, United
States *Tel:* 703-661-1581 *Fax:* 703-661-1501
E-mail: styluspub@aol.com
Foreign Rep(s): Bookwell (South Asia); Gustro
Ltd (Eastern Africa); ITDG Publishing (Eu-
rope); Legacy Books & Distribution (Eastern
Africa); Publishers Marketing Services Pte Ltd
(Southeast Asia); Stylus Publishing Inc (Latin
America, USA)
Returns: Renouf Publishing Co Ltd, 5369
Canotek Rd, Unit 1, Ottawa, ON K1J 9J3
Tel: 613-745-2665 *Toll Free Tel:* 888-551-
7470 *Fax:* 613-745-7660 *E-mail:* order.dept@
renoufbooks.com
Shipping Address: DLS St Joseph Ottawa-Hull,
45 Sarce-Cover Blvd, Hull, PQ K1A 0S7
Warehouse: DLS St Joseph Ottawa-Hull, 45
Sarce-Cover Blvd, Hull, PQ K1A 0S7
Distribution Center: DLS St Joseph Ottawa-Hull,
45 Sarce-Cover Blvd, Hull, PQ K1A 0S7

Inclusion Press International
24 Thome Crescent, Toronto, ON M6H 2S5
Tel: 416-658-5363 *Fax:* 416-658-5067
E-mail: info@inclusion.com
Web Site: www.inclusion.com
Key Personnel
Pres: Jack Pearpoint
Founded: 1989
Inclusion, change, diversity & community.
Publishes in English.
ISBN Prefix(es): 1-895418
Number of titles published annually: 3 Print; 2
CD-ROM
Total Titles: 26 Print; 4 CD-ROM

Inner City Books
PO Box 1271 Sta Q, Toronto, ON M4T 2P4
SAN: 115-3870
Tel: 416-927-0355 *Fax:* 416-924-1814
E-mail: sales@innercitybooks.net
Web Site: www.innercitybooks.net
Key Personnel
Pres & Publr: Daryl Sharp *E-mail:* daryl@
innercitybooks.net
Founded: 1980
Studies in Jungian psychology by Jungian ana-
lysts.
Publishes in English.
ISBN Prefix(es): 0-919123; 1-894574
Number of titles published annually: 5 Print
Total Titles: 106 Print

Imprints: Inner City Books
U.S. Rep(s): Bookworld

Insomniac Press
192 Spadina Ave, Suite 403, Toronto, ON M5T
2C2
Tel: 416-504-6270 *Fax:* 416-504-9313
E-mail: mike@insomniacpress.com
Web Site: www.insomniacpress.com
Key Personnel
Prop & Publr: Mike O'Connor
Founded: 1992
General trade publisher, fiction & nonfiction.
Publishes in English.
ISBN Prefix(es): 1-895837; 1-894663
Number of titles published annually: 23 Print
Total Titles: 112 Print
Shipping Address: National Book Network, 15200
NBN Way, Blue Ridge Summit, PA 17214,
United States *Toll Free Tel:* 800-462-6420
Toll Free Fax: 800-338-4550 *Web Site:* www.
nbnbooks.com
Warehouse: PGC, 250-A Carlton St, Toronto, ON
M5A 2L1 *Toll Free Tel:* 800-663-5714 *Toll
Free Fax:* 800-565-3770
National Book Network, 15200 NBN Way, Blue
Ridge Summit, PA 17214, United States *Toll
Free Tel:* 800-462-6420 *Toll Free Fax:* 800-
338-4550 *Web Site:* www.nbnbooks.com

The Institute for Research on Public Policy
1470 Peel, Suite 200, Montreal, PQ H3A 1T1
Tel: 514-985-2461 *Fax:* 514-985-2559
E-mail: irpp@irpp.org
Web Site: www.irpp.org
Key Personnel
VP, Opers: Suzanne Osteguy McIntyre
Founded: 1972
Governability, social policy, small business
(French), social issues, books, monograms &
proceeding on public policy.
Publishes in English, French.
ISBN Prefix(es): 0-88645
Number of titles published annually: 5 Print
Total Titles: 500 Print
U.S. Rep(s): Gower Publishing

Institute of Intergovernmental Relations
Queen's University, Rm 301, Policy Studies Bldg,
Kingston, ON K7L 3N6
Tel: 613-533-2080 *Fax:* 613-533-6868
E-mail: iigr@iigr.ca
Web Site: www.iigr.ca
Key Personnel
Dir: Harvey Lazar
Pubns Sec: Mary Kennedy
Founded: 1965
Publish research & other scholarly work on Cana-
dian federalism & intergovernmental relations;
ethnicity, government & political science.
Publishes in English, French.
ISBN Prefix(es): 0-88911
Number of titles published annually: 4 Print
Total Titles: 90 Print
Distribution Center: McGill-Queen's University
Press, Georgetown Terminal Warehouses, 34
Armstrong Ave, Georgetown, ON L7G 4R9
Tel: 905-873-2750 *Fax:* 905-873-6170

Institute of Psychological Research, Inc.
34 Fleury St W, Montreal, PQ H3L 1S9
Tel: 514-382-3000 *Toll Free Tel:* 800-363-7800
Fax: 514-382-3007 *Toll Free Fax:* 888-382-
3007
E-mail: info@i-p-r.ca
Web Site: www.i-p-r.ca *Cable:* IRPSYCHO
Key Personnel
Pres: Robert Chevrier
Exec VP: Madeleine Bourassa-Chevrier
Computer Test Scoring: Pierre Poirier
Publicity, ISBN Contact & Asst Dir: Malko von
Osten *Tel:* 514-382-3003

Founded: 1958 (Incorporated in 1963)
Specialize in counseling guides, textbooks. Psy-
chological tests & materials, science.
Publishes in English, French.
ISBN Prefix(es): 0-88509; 2-89109
Number of titles published annually: 10 Print
Imprints: IPR; IRP
Distributed by Editions Editest (Belgium); Li-
brairie du Quebec a Paris (France)
Distributor for Hans Huber (Rorschach only)
U.S. Publishers Represented: Academic Ther-
apy Publications; American Orthopsychiatric;
Behavior Sciences Systems; Martin M Bruce;
Cardall Associates; Center for Psychological
Services; Clinical Psychology Publishing; Nigel
Cox; Educational & Clinical Publications; Edu-
cational Industrial Testing Service; Educational
Performance Associate; Educators Publishing
Services; Guidance Associates of Delaware;
Harvard University Press; Industrial Psychol-
ogy; Institute for Personality & Ability Testing;
International Tests; Language Research Asso-
ciates; National Foundation for Educational Re-
search; Pacific Book; Psychological Assessment
Resources; Psychological Test Specialists; Psy-
chologists & Educators; Sheridan Psychological
Services; Western Psychological Services

Institute of Public Administration of Canada
1075 Bay St, Suite 401, Toronto, ON M5S 2B1
Tel: 416-924-8787 *Fax:* 416-924-4992
E-mail: ntl@ipac.ca; ntl@iapc.ca
Web Site: www.ipac.ca; www.iapc.ca
Key Personnel
Exec Dir: Joseph Galimberti
E-mail: jgalimberti@ipac.ca
Founded: 1949
National bilingual English/French non-profit orga-
nization, concerned with the theory & practice
of public management, with 20 regional groups
across Canada. Provide networks & forums
regionally, nationally & internationally. Spe-
cialize in political science, Canadian history &
Canadian law.
Publishes in English, French.
ISBN Prefix(es): 0-919400; 0-920715; 0-919696;
1-55061
Number of titles published annually: 10 Print; 10
E-Book
Total Titles: 500 Print; 30 Online; 5 E-Book; 5
Audio

International Development Research Centre
250 Albert St, Ottawa, ON K1P 6M1
Mailing Address: PO Box 8500, Ottawa, ON
K1G 3H9
Tel: 613-236-6163 *Fax:* 613-238-7230
E-mail: pub@idrc.ca
Web Site: www.idrc.ca/booktique
Key Personnel
Chief Ed: Andrea Puppo
Ed: Bill Carman
Founded: 1971
Publishes research results & scholarly studies on
global & regional issues related to sustainable
& equitable development.
Publishes in English, French.
ISBN Prefix(es): 0-88936; 1-55250
Number of titles published annually: 30 Print; 20
Online
U.S. Rep(s): Stylus Publishing Inc

Irwin Law Inc
347 Bay St, Suite 501, Toronto, ON M5H 2R7
Tel: 416-862-7690 *Toll Free Tel:* 888-314-9014
Fax: 416-862-9236
Web Site: www.irwinlaw.com
Key Personnel
Publr: Jeffrey Miller *E-mail:* jmiller@irwinlaw.
com
Founded: 1996

Publisher of books & other material for lawyers
& law students.
Publishes in English.
ISBN Prefix(es): 1-55221
Number of titles published annually: 15 Print
Total Titles: 75 Print
Distributed by Gaunt Inc
Foreign Rep(s): Federation Press (Australia &
New Zealand)
Membership(s): Ontario Book Publishers Organi-
zation

Ivey Publishing, see Richard Ivey School of
Business

Richard Ivey School of Business
Division of Ivey Management Services
University of Western Ontario, London, ON N6A
3K7
Tel: 519-661-3208 *Toll Free Tel:* 800-649-6355
Fax: 519-661-3882
E-mail: cases@ivey.uwo.ca
Web Site: www.ivey.uwo.ca/cases
Key Personnel
Gen Mgr: Sheryl Gregson *Tel:* 519-661-3524
E-mail: sgregson@ivey.uwo.ca
Founded: 1923
Publish business case studies for university busi-
ness courses.
Publishes in English.
Number of titles published annually: 150 Print
Total Titles: 2,000 Print
Distributed by McGraw-Hill; Pearson Custom
Publishing; Xan Edu
Distributor for Harvard Business School Publish-
ing
U.S. Rep(s): Harvard Business School Publishing
Foreign Rep(s): European Case Clearing House
(Europe)

Jesperson Publishing
100 Water St, 3rd fl, St John's, NF A1C 6E6
Mailing Address: PO Box 2188, St John's, NF
A1C 6E6
Tel: 709-757-2216 *Fax:* 709-757-0708
E-mail: info@jespersonpublishing.nf.net
Web Site: www.jespersonpublishing.nf.net
Key Personnel
Pres: Debbie Hanlon
VP: Rebecca Rose
Natl Sales & Mktg: Karla Hayward
Intl Mktg: David Bowering
Founded: 1974
Educational & trade books; hard & soft cover.
Publishes in English.
ISBN Prefix(es): 0-920502; 0-921692
Number of titles published annually: 5 Print
Total Titles: 140 Print
Distributed by General Publishing; Irwin Publish-
ing (educ)

Key Porter Books Ltd
Division of Key Publishers
70 The Esplanade, 3rd fl, Toronto, ON M5E 1R2
SAN: 115-0561
Tel: 416-862-7777 *Fax:* 416-862-2304
E-mail: info@keyporter.com
Web Site: www.keyporter.com
Key Personnel
Pres: Diane Davy
VP & CFO: Allan Ibarra
Publr & CEO: Anna Porter
VP & Ed-in-Chief: Clare McKeon
Sales & Mktg: Brad Kalbfleish
Mgr, Rts: Jose Darrell *Tel:* 416-862-7777 ext 260
Founded: 1981
Publishes in English.
ISBN Prefix(es): 0-919493; 0-88619; 1-55013; 1-
55263
Number of titles published annually: 100 Print
Total Titles: 300 Print

Imprints: Key Porter Kids; L & OD; Lester &
Orpen Dennys Ltd; Sarasota Press
Distributed by Firefly Books
U.S. Rep(s): Firefly Books
Warehouse: H B Fenn & Co Ltd, 34 Nixon Rd,
Bolton, ON L7E 1W2 *Toll Free Tel:* 800-
267-3366 *Toll Free Fax:* 800-465-3422
E-mail: sales@hbfenn.com *Web Site:* www.
hbfenn.com

Kids Can Press Ltd
Division of Corus Entertainment
29 Birch Ave, Toronto, ON M4V 1E2
Tel: 416-925-5437 *Toll Free Tel:* 800-265-0884
Fax: 416-960-5437
E-mail: info@kidscan.com
Web Site: kidscanpress.com
Key Personnel
Publr: Valerie Hussey
Ed-in-Chief: Sheila Barry *E-mail:* sbarry@
kidscan.com
Assoc Publr: Karen Boersma
VP, Rts & Licensing: Barbara Howson
VP, Fin & Opers: Norma Goodger
E-mail: ngoodger@kidscan.com
Dir, Sales: Rick Walker *E-mail:* rwalker@kidscan.
com
Dir, Mktg: Fred Horler *E-mail:* fhorler@kidscan.
com
Founded: 1973
Books for children exclusively.
Publishes in English.
ISBN Prefix(es): 0-919964; 1-55074; 1-55337
Total Titles: 350 Print; 19 Audio
Imprints: Franklin; Kids Can Do It; Little Kids
Branch Office(s)
2250 Military Rd, Tonawanda, NY 14150, United
States (U.S. returns to this address also)
Distributed by University of Toronto Press
Orders to: University of Toronto Press, 5201 Duf-
ferin St, Downsview, ON M3H 5T8
Returns: University of Toronto Press, 5201 Duf-
ferin St, Downsview, ON M3H 5T8
Shipping Address: University of Toronto Press,
5201 Dufferin St, Downsview, ON M3H 5T8
Membership(s): Children's Book Council

Kindred Productions
Division of Mennonite Brethren Church of
Canada
4-169 Riverton Ave, Winnipeg, MB R2L 2E5
Tel: 204-669-6575 *Toll Free Tel:* 800-545-7322
Fax: 204-654-1865
E-mail: kindred@mbconf.ca
Web Site: www.kindredproductions.com
Key Personnel
Dir & Mgr: Marilyn E Hudson *Tel:* 204-654-5765
E-mail: mhudson@mbconf.ca
Founded: 1982
Denominational material, Low German Bible,
trade books.
Publishes in English.
ISBN Prefix(es): 0-919797; 0-921788; 1-894791
Number of titles published annually: 4 Print
Total Titles: 100 Print; 1 Audio
Branch Office(s)
315 S Lincoln, Hillsboro, KS 67063, United
States *Toll Free Tel:* 800-545-7322 *Fax:* 620-
947-3266
U.S. Publishers Represented: Kindred Productions

A J Kirby Co
301 Oxford St W, Box 24107, London, ON N6A
3Y6
Tel: 519-671-0124 *Fax:* 519-438-7935
E-mail: ajkirbyco@pobox.com
Web Site: www.ajkirbyco.com
Publishes in English.

Knopf Canada
Division of Random House of Canada Ltd

One Toronto St, Suite 300, Toronto, ON M5C
2V6
SAN: 201-3975
Tel: 416-364-4449 *Toll Free Tel:* 800-668-4247
(order desk) *Fax:* 416-364-0462
Web Site: www.randomhouse.ca
Key Personnel
Chmn: John Neale *Tel:* 905-624-0672
Chairwoman of Group Publg Bd, Exec VP &
Exec Publr, Knopf Canada: Louise Dennys
Exec VP & CAO: Doug Foot *Tel:* 905-624-0672
VP & Publr: Diane Martin
VP & Dir, Rts & Contracts: Jennifer Shepherd
VP & Dir, Production: Janine Laporte
Man Ed: Deidre Molina
Assoc Publr, Vintage Canada: Marion Garner
Sr Ed: Michael Schellenberg
Exec Asst to Chairwoman of Group Publg Bd,
Exec VP & Exec Publr Publr: Nina Ber-
Donkor
Prodn Mgr: Carla Kean
Asst Prodn Mgr: Lindsay Jones
Rts Mgr: Ron Eckel
Exec VP & Dir, Sales & Mktg: Brad Martin
Tel: 905-624-0672
VP & Dir, Sales: Brian Cassin *Tel:* 905-624-
0672; Duncan Shields *Tel:* 905-624-0672
VP & Dir, Online Sales & Mktg: Lisa Charters
Tel: 905-624-0672
VP & Dir, Mktg & Communs: Tracey Turriff
Dir, Mktg: Linda Scott *Tel:* 905-624-0672
Dir, Adv: Mark Veldhuizen
Creative Dir: Scott Richardson
Dir, Media Rel: Scott Sellers
Assoc Dir, Publicity: Sharon Klein
Publicist, Canadian Imprints: Adrienne Phillips
Edit Asst: Angelika Glover
Founded: 1991
Random House Inc & its publishing entities are
not accepting unsol submissions, proposals,
mss, or submission queries via e-mail at this
time.
ISBN Prefix(es): 0-02; 0-676
Number of titles published annually: 55 Print
Imprints: Seal Books; Vintage Canada
Distributed by Random House of Canada Ltd
Orders to: Random House of Canada Ltd
Shipping Address: 2775 Matheson Blvd East,
Mississauga, ON L4W 4P7
Membership(s): Canadian Booksellers Associa-
tion; Canadian Publishers' Council

Laurier Books Ltd
PO Box 2694, Sta D, Ottawa, ON K1P 5W6
SAN: 168-2806
Tel: 613-738-2163 *Fax:* 613-247-0256
E-mail: educa@travel-net.com
Web Site: www.travel-net.com/~educa/main.htm
Key Personnel
Pres: L Marthe
Lib Sales Dir: R Lalwani
Founded: 1975
All foreign language dictionaries, Native Ameri-
can publications, annuals, bibliographic prod-
ucts, business directories, distribution, publish-
ing, mail orders.
Publishes in English.
ISBN Prefix(es): 1-895959; 1-55394
Number of titles published annually: 15 Print
Total Titles: 15 Print
U.S. Rep(s): IBD Ltd

§LexisNexis Canada
Unit of LexisNexis Group
123 Commerce Valley Dr E, Suite 700, Markham,
ON L3T 7W8
Tel: 905-479-2665 *Toll Free Tel:* 800-668-6481
Fax: 905-479-2826 *Toll Free Fax:* 800-461-
3275
E-mail: orders@lexisnexis.ca
Web Site: www.lexisnexis.ca

Key Personnel
Direct Mktg Mgr: Susan Sanders *Tel:* 905-415-
5811 *E-mail:* ssanders@lexisnexis.ca
Founded: 1912
Books, looseleaf services, newsletters, journals,
legal publishing & online services.
Publishes in English.
ISBN Prefix(es): 0-409; 0-433
Number of titles published annually: 35 Print; 11
CD-ROM
Total Titles: 300 Print; 9 CD-ROM
Online services available through LexisNexis.
Distributor for Butterworths
Foreign Rep(s): Butterworths Affiliates (Australia,
Asia, UK, India, New Zealand, South Africa)

Lidec Inc
4350 Ave de l'Hotel-de-Ville, Montreal, PQ H2W
2H5
Mailing Address: CP 5000, Succursale "C", Mon-
treal, PQ H2X 3M1
Tel: 514-843-5991 *Toll Free Tel:* 800-350-5991
(Canada Only) *Fax:* 514-843-5252
E-mail: lidec@lidec.qc.ca
Web Site: www.lidec.qc.ca
Key Personnel
Gen Mgr & ISBN Contact: Claude Legault
Founded: 1965
Publisher of school books.
Publishes in French.
ISBN Prefix(es): 2-7608
Number of titles published annually: 50 Print
Total Titles: 1,500 Print

Life Cycle Books Ltd
421 Nugget Ave, Unit 8, Toronto, ON M1S 4L8
SAN: 110-8417
Tel: 416-690-5860 *Toll Free Tel:* 866-880-5860
Fax: 416-690-8532 *Toll Free Fax:* 866-690-
8532
E-mail: orders@lifecyclebooks.com
Web Site: www.lifecyclebooks.com
Key Personnel
Gen Mgr: Paul Broughton
Founded: 1973
Human life issues.
Publishes in English.
ISBN Prefix(es): 0-919225
Number of titles published annually: 6 Print
Total Titles: 32 Print
Branch Office(s)
PO Box 420, Lewiston, NY 14092-0420, United
States

Lilmur Publishing
147 Brooke Ave, Toronto, ON M5M 2K3
Tel: 416-486-0145 *Fax:* 416-486-5380
Key Personnel
Promos & Sales: Madhu Nanavati
Founded: 1984
The promotion of East Indian fairy tales & litera-
ture to schools & libraries.
Publishes in English.
ISBN Prefix(es): 0-9692729
Number of titles published annually: 3 Print
Total Titles: 3 Print
Distributed by Master Communications
U.S. Rep(s): Master Communications Inc, 4480
Lake Forest Dr, Suite 302, Cincinnati, OH
45242, United States

Lone Pine Publishing
10145 81 Ave, Edmonton, AB T6E 1W9
SAN: 115-4125
Tel: 780-433-9333 *Toll Free Tel:* 800-661-9017
Fax: 780-433-9646 *Toll Free Fax:* 800-424-
7173
E-mail: info@lonepinepublishing.com
Web Site: www.lonepinepublishing.com
Key Personnel
Pres: Grant Kennedy
Dir, Mktg: Ken Davis

Gen Mgr: Shane Kennedy
Sales Mgr & Intl Rts - Canada: David Cleary
Sr Ed: Nancy Foulds
Founded: 1980
Natural history, travel, recreation, popular history, bird guides & gardening.
Publishes in English.
ISBN Prefix(es): 1-55105; 1-894877 (Ghost House Imprint)
Number of titles published annually: 30 Print
Total Titles: 325 Print
Imprints: Pine Bough; Pine Candle; Pine Cone
Branch Office(s)
1808 "B" St NW, Suite 140, Auburn, WA 98001, United States, Sales Mgr: Helen Ibach *Toll Free Tel:* 800-518-3541 *Toll Free Fax:* 800-548-1169 *E-mail:* hibach@lonepinepublishing.com
Distributor for Coteau Books; Folklore Publishing; Fulcrum Publishing; InForum; Johnson & Gorman; Mountain Press; Proof Positive; Red Deer College Press
U.S. Publishers Represented: Fulcrum Publishing; Mountain Press
U.S. Rep(s): Baker & Taylor; Benjamin News; Book People; Ingram Book Co; Koen Book Distributors; Partners; Partners/West; Sunbelt

James Lorimer & Co Ltd, Publishers
35 Britain St, 3rd fl, Toronto, ON M5A 1R7
SAN: 115-1134
Tel: 416-362-4762 *Fax:* 416-362-3939
E-mail: info@lorimer.ca
Web Site: www.lorimer.ca
Key Personnel
Pres: James Lorimer
Founded: 1970
Hardcover & paperback trade; business, economics, finance, history, politics; children's books; social sciences & sociology; cookbooks.
Publishes in English.
ISBN Prefix(es): 1-55028; 0-88862
Number of titles published annually: 20 Print
Total Titles: 500 Print
Warehouse: Formac Publishing, 5502 Atlantic St, Halifax, NS B3H 1G4 *Tel:* 902-421-7022 *Fax:* 902-425-0166 *E-mail:* formac@ns.sympatico.ca

Le Loup de Gouttiere Inc
347 rue Sainte Paul, Quebec City, PQ G1K 3X1
Tel: 418-694-2224 *Fax:* 418-694-2225
E-mail: loupgout@videotron.ca
Key Personnel
Pres: Francine Vernac
Founded: 1989
Poesie & litterateur jeunesse.
Publishes in French.
ISBN Prefix(es): 2-921310; 2-89529
Number of titles published annually: 20 Print
Total Titles: 200 Print
Distributed by Raffin
Membership(s): ANEL; Reseau des femmes d'affaires du Quebec

§LTDBooks
200 N Service Rd W, Unit 1, Suite 301, Oakville, ON L6M 2Y1
Tel: 905-847-6060 *Fax:* 905-847-6060
E-mail: publisher@ltdbooks.com
Web Site: www.ltdbooks.com
Key Personnel
Publr: Laura Adlam
Man Dir, Opers: Christine Nowicki
Publisher of original fiction in electronic format. Selected titles available in trade paperback. Home to many critically acclaimed & award-winning titles in every genre, from romance to horror, historical to fantasy, mystery to humor & everthing in between.
Publishes in English.
ISBN Prefix(es): 1-55316

Number of titles published annually: 10 Print; 30 E-Book
Total Titles: 60 Print; 130 E-Book
Orders to: Baker & Taylor (paperbacks); Lightning Source (e-books)

Lugus Publications
Division of Lugus Productions Ltd
48 Falcon St, Toronto, ON M4S 2P5
Tel: 416-322-5113 *Fax:* 416-484-9512
E-mail: cymro43@hotmail.com
Key Personnel
Pres: Gethin James
Secy: Jacqueline James
Founded: 1981
Educational & trade publishing.
Publishes in English, French.
ISBN Prefix(es): 0-921633
Number of titles published annually: 6 Print
Total Titles: 206 Print
U.S. Publishers Represented: Spring Publications Inc
U.S. Rep(s): Baker & Taylor Books

Madison Press Books
1000 Yonge St, Toronto, ON M4W 2K2
Tel: 416-923-5027 *Fax:* 416-923-9708
E-mail: info@madisonpressbooks.com
Web Site: www.madisonpressbooks.com
Key Personnel
Chmn: A E Cummings
Pres & CEO: Brian Soye
Publr: Oliver Salzmann
VP, Busn Aff: Susan Barrable *E-mail:* sbarrable@madisonpressbooks.com
Edit Dir: Wanda Nowakowska
Founded: 1979
Illustrated nonfiction & calendars.
Publishes in English.
ISBN Prefix(es): 1-895892
Number of titles published annually: 10 Print
Total Titles: 15 Print

Maple Tree Press Inc
Subsidiary of Key Publishers Ltd
51 Front St E, Suite 200, Toronto, ON M5E 1B3
Tel: 416-304-0702 *Fax:* 416-304-0525
E-mail: info@mapletreepress.com
Web Site: www.mapletreepress.com
Key Personnel
Pres & Publr: Sheba Meland
Promos & Sales Coord: Erin Gault
Founded: 1975
Paperback & trade; specialize in nature & science & creative information books for juveniles.
Publishes in English.
ISBN Prefix(es): 0-920775; 1-895688; 1-894379; 1-897066
Number of titles published annually: 10 Print
Imprints: OWL Books
Distributed by Firefly Books (backlist); PGW (US); Raincoat Books (Canada)
U.S. Rep(s): Firefly Books (backlist only)

§Master Point Press
331 Douglas Ave, Toronto, ON M5M 1H2
Tel: 416-781-0351 *Fax:* 416-781-1831
E-mail: info@masterpointpress.com
Web Site: www.masterpointpress.com
Key Personnel
Publr: Ray Lee
Founded: 1994
Books on games, especially contract bridge.
Publishes in English.
ISBN Prefix(es): 0-9698461; 1-894154; 1-897106
Number of titles published annually: 15 Print; 1 CD-ROM
Total Titles: 100 Print; 4 CD-ROM
Distributor for Better Bridge Now; Panacea Press
U.S. Rep(s): Strauss Consultants, 45 Main St, Brooklyn, NY 11201, United States

Foreign Rep(s): Orca Books (Worldwide exc North America)
Orders to: Georgetown Terminal Warehouse, 34 Armstrong Ave, Georgetown, ON L7G 4R9
Shipping Address: Georgetown Terminal Warehouse, 34 Armstrong Ave, Georgetown, ON L7G 4R9
Warehouse: Georgetown Terminal Warehouse, 34 Armstrong Ave, Georgetown, ON L7G 4R9
Distribution Center: Georgetown Terminal Warehouse, 34 Armstrong Ave, Georgetown, ON L7G 4R9
Membership(s): Association of Canadian Publishers

McClelland & Stewart Ltd
481 University Ave, Suite 900, Toronto, ON M5G 2E9
SAN: 115-4192
Tel: 416-598-1114 *Fax:* 416-598-7764
E-mail: mail@mcclelland.com
Web Site: www.mcclelland.com
Key Personnel
Chmn: Avie Bennett
Pres & Publr: Douglas Pepper
VP & Gen Mgr: Krystyna Ross
Intl Rts: Marilyn Biderman
Founded: 1906
Publishes in English.
ISBN Prefix(es): 0-7710
Number of titles published annually: 70 Print
Total Titles: 2,000 Print
Imprints: Douglas Gibson Books
Shipping Address: Random House of Canada, 2775 Matheson Blvd E, Mississauga, ON L4W 4P7 *Toll Free Tel:* 800-668-4247

McGill-Queen's University Press
3430 McTavish St, Montreal, PQ H3A 1X9
Tel: 514-398-3750 *Fax:* 514-398-4333
E-mail: mqup@mqup.ca
Web Site: www.mqup.mcgill.ca *Telex:* 05268510
Cable: MCGILL UNIV MTL
Key Personnel
Exec Dir & Sr Ed: Philip Cercone
Sr Ed: Donald H Akenson *Tel:* 613-533-2155
Mktg Mgr: Roy Ward *Tel:* 514-398-6306 *Fax:* 514-398-5443
Busn Mgr: Arden Ford *Tel:* 514-398-8390 *Fax:* 514-398-4333
Prodn & Design Mgr: Susanne McAdam *Tel:* 514-398-6996 *Fax:* 514-398-4333
Founded: 1970
Original peer-reviewed, high-quality books in all areas of social sciences & humanities. While our emphasis is on providing an outlet for Canadian authors & scholarship, the authors come from across Canada & throughout the world. We are able to bring scholars together to create a mutually beneficial community of knowledge & expertise. Our marketing & sales department develops imaginative advertising & promotion campaigns for print, radio & TV as well as specialized journals & direct mail to reach both the general & scholarly markets.
Publishes in English, French.
ISBN Prefix(es): 0-88629; 0-7735
Number of titles published annually: 140 Print; 3 Audio
Total Titles: 2,400 Print; 2 CD-ROM
Branch Office(s)
Queen's University, Kingston, ON, Roger Martin *Tel:* 613-533-2155 *Fax:* 613-533-6822 *E-mail:* mqup@post.queensu.ca
Distributed by Institute for Research on Public Policy
Distributor for Queen's Policy Studies
U.S. Rep(s): CUP Services, PO Box 6525, Ithaca, NY 14851-6525, United States (United States distribution) *Toll Free Tel:* 800-666-2211 *Toll Free Fax:* 800-688-2877 *E-mail:* orderbook@cupserv.org

CANADIAN PUBLISHERS

Foreign Rep(s): Marston Book Services Ltd (Ireland, Middle East, North Africa, UK & Europe); UNIREPS (Australia & New Zealand); United Publishers Services Ltd (Japan)
Distribution Center: Georgetown Terminal Warehouses, 34 Armstrong Ave, Georgetown, ON L7G 4R9 (Canada distribution) *Tel:* 905-873-9781 *Toll Free Tel:* 877-864-8477 *Fax:* 905-873-6170 *Toll Free Fax:* 877-864-4272 *E-mail:* orders@gtwcanada.ca
CUP Services, PO Box 6525, Ithaca, NY 14851-6525, United States (United States distribution)
Marston Book Services Ltd, PO Box 269, Abingdon, Oxfordshire OX14 4YN, United Kingdom (UK distribution) *Tel:* (0) 1235 465500 *Fax:* (0) 1235 465556 *E-mail:* direct.order@marston.co.uk
Membership(s): American Association of University Presses; Association of Canadian Publishers

McGraw-Hill Ryerson Ltd
Division of McGraw-Hill Education
300 Water St, Whitby, ON L1N 9B6
SAN: 115-060X
Tel: 905-430-5000 *Toll Free Tel:* 800-565-5758 (cust serv) *Fax:* 905-430-5020
E-mail: johnd@mcgrawhill.ca
Web Site: www.mcgrawhill.ca
Key Personnel
Pres & CEO: John Dill
Pres, Higher Educ Div: Petra Cooper
Pres, School Div: Nancy Gerrish
Pres, Trade, Prof & Medical Div: Julia Woods
CFO: Gord Dyer
Founded: 1944
Publishes & distributes educational & professional products in both print & non-print media.
Publishes in English.
ISBN Prefix(es): 0-07
Number of titles published annually: 271 Print; 40 CD-ROM; 28 Online; 10 Audio
Total Titles: 114 Print; 17 CD-ROM; 5 Online; 10 E-Book
Imprints: McGraw-Hill Ryerson
Distributed by McGraw-Hill Publishing Cos
Distributor for Business Week Books; Glencoe/McGraw-Hill; Harvard Business School Press; International Marine; Irwin/McGraw-Hill; Jamestown Education; McGraw-Hill; MedMaster Inc; Open Court; Osborne; Ragged Mountain Press; Schaum's; SRA; Wright Group
U.S. Publishers Represented: The McGraw-Hill Companies
U.S. Rep(s): The McGraw-Hill Companies
Membership(s): Canadian Publishers' Council

McTavish & Nunn
517 River Rd, Canmore, AB T1W 2E4
Tel: 403-678-5859 *Fax:* 403-609-4072
Key Personnel
Exec: Carol McTavish
Publr & Author: Lori Nunn *E-mail:* nunn@agt.net
Founded: 2001
Publishes in English.
ISBN Prefix(es): 0-9688957
Number of titles published annually: 3 Print
Total Titles: 3 Print
Membership(s): Book Publishers Association of Alberta

P D Meany Publishers
71 Fermanagh Ave, Toronto, ON M6R 1M1
Tel: 416-516-2903 *Fax:* 416-516-7632
E-mail: info@pdmeany.com
Web Site: www.pdmeany.com
Key Personnel
Pres & Intl Rts: Pierre L'Abbe
Founded: 1976

Publish scholarly books.
Publishes in English.
ISBN Prefix(es): 0-88835
Number of titles published annually: 4 Print
Total Titles: 30 Print

Michelin Travel Publications
Subsidiary of Michelin North America (Canada) Ltd
2540 Daniel Johnson, Suite 510, Laval, PQ H7T 2T9
SAN: 115-0618
Tel: 450-978-4700 *Toll Free Tel:* 800-361-8236 (Canada) *Fax:* 450-978-1305 *Toll Free Fax:* 800-361-6937 (Canada)
E-mail: michelin.travel-publications-canada@ca.michelin.com
Web Site: www.michelin-travel.com
Key Personnel
Pres: Tom Bennett
Founded: 1900
Travel guides to Europe, North America, Asia, maps, atlases & globes in English, French, Spanish & Italian.
Publishes in English, French.
ISBN Prefix(es): 2-06
Number of titles published annually: 450 Print
Total Titles: 650 Print
Distributor for Cognoscenti Travel Guides; Perly's Inc
U.S. Publishers Represented: Michelin Travel Publications
Advertising Agency: Edelman, 214 King St W, Suite 600, Toronto, ON M5H 3S6, Contact: Peggy McMahan *Tel:* 416-979-1120 *Fax:* 416-979-0176 *E-mail:* peggy.mcmahan@edelman.com
Orders to: Michelin Travel Publications, 2000 Halpern, Ville St Laurent, PQ H4S 1N7, Contact: Sabrina Sale *Toll Free Tel:* 800-361-8236 *Toll Free Fax:* 800-361-6937
Returns: Michelin Travel Publications, 2000 Halpern, Ville St Laurent, PQ H4S 1N7, Contact: Sabrina Sale *Toll Free Tel:* 800-361-8236 *Toll Free Fax:* 800-361-6937
Distribution Center: Michelin Travel Publications, 2000 Halpern, Ville St Laurent, PQ H4S 1N7, Contact: Sabrina Sale *Toll Free Tel:* 800-361-8236 *Toll Free Fax:* 800-361-6937

§Micromedia ProQuest
20 Victoria St, Toronto, ON M5C 2N8
Tel: 416-362-5211 *Toll Free Tel:* 800-387-2689 *Fax:* 416-362-6161
E-mail: info@micromedia.ca
Web Site: www.micromedia.ca
Key Personnel
Cont: Brent Routledge
Dir, Sales: Mike Baida
Mktg Mgr: Peter Asselstine
Info Technol Mgr: Kevin Self
Founded: 1972
News & current affairs, indexing, business & economics, reference, government documents, Canadian patents, directories, technical documents; engineering, military specifications, international standards, regulatory information.
Publishes in English.
ISBN Prefix(es): 0-88892
Number of titles published annually: 10 Print; 50 CD-ROM; 40 Online; 10 E-Book
Online services available through Dialog, Infomart, LexisNexis.
U.S. Publishers Represented: H W Wilson

Mi'kmaq-Maliseet Institute
University of New Brunswick, PO Box 4400, Fredriction, NB E3B 6E3
Tel: 506-453-4840 *Fax:* 506-453-4784
E-mail: micmac@unb.ca
Web Site: www.unb.ca

Key Personnel
Dir: Robert M Leavitt *E-mail:* rleavitt@unb.ca
Coord: Lynda A Doige *E-mail:* ladoige@unb.ca
Admin Asst: Laura Bailey
Aboriginal studies, languages & history; offers programs for Aboriginal students at UNB, research, curriculum development, First Nations Business Administration Certificate Program.
Number of titles published annually: 1 Print; 1 Online
Total Titles: 12 Print; 2 Online
Distributed by Micmac Books

Modulo Editeur Inc
Member of Groupe Modulo
233 Ave Dunbar, Rm 300, Mont Royal, PQ H3P 2H4
Tel: 514-738-9818 *Toll Free Tel:* 888-738-9818 *Fax:* 514-738-5838 *Toll Free Fax:* 888-273-5247
Web Site: www.moduloediteur.com *Telex:* 05-2534 MOD
Key Personnel
Pers & Gen Dir: Roger Turcotte
VP, Fin & Admin: Jean-Bernard Lague
VP, Mktg & Sales: Michelle Paradis
Translation: Dominique Lefort
Founded: 1975
School books, dictionaries, children's books, professional & technical textbooks.
Publishes in English, French.
ISBN Prefix(es): 2-89113
Number of titles published annually: 50 Print
Distributed by Modulo
Distributor for Editions du Triangle D'Or

Modulo-Griffon Inc
Formerly Les Editions Griffon D'Argile
Member of Group Modulo
233 Dunbar Ave, Suite 300, Mont Royal, PQ H3P 2H4
Tel: 514-738-9818 *Toll Free Tel:* 888-738-9818 *Fax:* 514-738-5838 *Toll Free Fax:* 888-273-5247
Web Site: www.moduloediteur.com
Key Personnel
Pres & Dir Gen: Roger Turcotte
VP, Fin & Admin: Jean-Bernard Lague
VP, Mktg & Sales: Michelle Paradis
Translation: Dominique Lefort
Founded: 1970
School books, first level university.
Publishes in French.
ISBN Prefix(es): 2-920922; 2-89443
Number of titles published annually: 15 Print
Total Titles: 200 Print

Modus Vivendi Inc and Adventure Press
5150 Saint Laurent, 2nd fl, Montreal, PQ H2T 1R8
Tel: 514-272-0433 *Fax:* 514-272-7234
E-mail: enfo@modusadventure.com
Key Personnel
CEO: Marc Alain
Founded: 1991
General trade publishing.
Publishes in French.
ISBN Prefix(es): 2-921556; 2-922148
Number of titles published annually: 85 Print
Distributed by Les Messageries ADP
U.S. Publishers Represented: Hushion Press *Tel:* 416-285-6100
Distribution Center: Les Messageries ADP, 955 Amherst St, Montreal, PQ H2L 3K4

Mondia Editeurs Inc
105 de Martigny Ouest, St-Jerome, PQ J7Y 2G2
Tel: 450-438-8479 *Toll Free Tel:* 800-561-2371 (Canada) *Fax:* 450-432-3892
E-mail: info@mondiaduphare.net
Key Personnel
Pres & Dir Gen: Jean Canac-Marquis

Mktg Dir: Pierre David
Founded: 1981
Kindergarten-university school books; adult education; "On My Own" (English collection).
Publishes in English, French.
ISBN Prefix(es): 2-89114
Number of titles published annually: 18 Print
Total Titles: 5 Print
Distributed by Mondia

Editions Multimondes
930 rue Pouliot, Sainte-Foy, PQ G1V 3N9
Tel: 418-651-3885 *Toll Free Tel:* 800-840-3029
Fax: 418-651-6822 *Toll Free Fax:* 888-303-5931
E-mail: multimondes@multim.com
Web Site: www.multimondes.qc.ca
Key Personnel
Pres: Jean-Marc Gagnon
Founded: 1988
Books on science & the environment.
Publishes in English, French.
ISBN Prefix(es): 2-921146; 2-89544
Number of titles published annually: 20 Print
Total Titles: 150 Print

Napoleon Publishing/Rendezvous Press
Division of Transmedia Enterprises Inc
178 Willowdale Ave, Suite 201, Toronto, ON M2N 4Y8
SAN: 115-074X
Tel: 416-730-9052 *Toll Free Tel:* 877-730-9052
Fax: 416-730-8096
E-mail: napoleonpublishing@transmedia95.com
Web Site: www.transmedia95.com
Key Personnel
Publr: Sylvia McConnell *E-mail:* sylvia@transmedia95.com
Ed: Allister Thompson
Founded: 1989
Children's books, young adolescent fiction & junior novels, teacher resource materials, adult fiction.
Publishes in English.
ISBN Prefix(es): 0-929141; 1-894917
Number of titles published annually: 10 Print; 1 E-Book
Total Titles: 70 Print; 5 E-Book; 5 Audio
Imprints: Editions Napoleon; Rendezvous Press
Sales Office(s): Penguin Books, 10 Alcorn Ave, Suite 300, Toronto, ON M4V 3B2
Distributed by Penguin Canada, Toronto
U.S. Rep(s): Atlas Books
Foreign Rights: Lora Fountain (France)
Billing Address: Canbook Distribution Services, 195 Harry Walker Pkwy, Newmarket, ON L3Y 7B4 *Toll Free Tel:* 800-399-6858 *Toll Free Fax:* 800-363-2665
Orders to: Canbook Distribution Services, 195 Harry Walker Pkwy, Newmarket, ON L3Y 7B4 *Toll Free Tel:* 800-399-6858 *Toll Free Fax:* 800-363-2665
Returns: Canbook Distribution Services, 195 Harry Walker Pkwy, Newmarket, ON L3Y 7B4 *Toll Free Tel:* 800-399-6858 *Toll Free Fax:* 800-363-2665
Shipping Address: Canbook Distribution Services, 1220 Nicholson Rd, Newmarkt, ON L3Y 7V1
Distribution Center: Canbook Distribution Services, 195 Harry Walker Pkwy, Newmarket, ON L3Y 7B4 *Toll Free Tel:* 800-399-6858 *Toll Free Fax:* 800-363-2665
Membership(s): Association of Canadian Publishers; Ontario Book Publishers Organization

Narada Press
160 Columbia St W, Suite 147, Waterloo, ON N2L 3L3
Tel: 519-886-1969
Key Personnel
Pres: Diep Nguyen
Founded: 1993

General books on economic modeling & Vietnamese studies, including politics, arts & literature. Directories, reference books, foreign language & bilingual books, reprints, scholarly books, college textbooks, translations, Asian studies, developing countries, history, library & information sciences. Publishes in Vietnamese also.
Publishes in English.
ISBN Prefix(es): 1-895938
Number of titles published annually: 5 Print

National Gallery of Canada, The Bookstore
380 Sussex Dr, Ottawa, ON K1N 9N4
Mailing Address: PO Box 427 Sta A, Ottawa, ON K1N 9N4
Tel: 613-990-0962 (mail order sales) *Fax:* 613-990-1972
E-mail: ngcbook@gallery.ca
Web Site: www.national.gallery.ca
Key Personnel
Mktg, Admin Asst & Mail Order Sales: Robert Pelchat
Mgr, Opers: Patrick Aubin
Founded: 1980
Exhibition catalogues, monographs, permanent collection series, books on photography, exhibition handouts, videos & posters.
Publishes in English, French.
ISBN Prefix(es): 0-88884
Number of titles published annually: 4 Print
Total Titles: 38 Print; 38 E-Book
U.S. Rep(s): University of Chicago Press
Membership(s): ABA; Canadian Booksellers Association; Canadian Museums Association; Museum Store Association

Natural Heritage Books
PO Box 95, Sta O, Toronto, ON M4A 2M8
Tel: 416-694-7907 *Toll Free Tel:* 800-725-9982 (orders only) *Fax:* 416-690-0819
E-mail: info@naturalheritagebooks.com
Web Site: www.naturalheritagebooks.com
Key Personnel
Publr & Intl Rts: Barry L Penhale
Contact: Jane Gibson
Founded: 1983
Canadiana books & largely nonfiction books.
Publishes in English.
ISBN Prefix(es): 0-920474; 1-896219; 1-897045
Number of titles published annually: 12 Print
Total Titles: 200 Print
Imprints: Amethyst; Natural Heritage
Distributor for Atmosphere; Cornwall Editions; House of Lochar; Laurel Cottage Ltd; Petherwin Heritage; Three Dimensional Publishing; Tuckwell Press; Umbrella Press; Whittles Publishing
U.S. Rep(s): Cardinal Publishers Group; Three Dimensional Publishing
Returns: TTS Distributing Inc, 45 Tyler St, Aurora, ON L4G 2N1 *Tel:* 905-841-3893 *Fax:* 905-841-3026
Shipping Address: TTS Distributing Inc, 45 Tyler St, Aurora, ON L4G 2N1 *Tel:* 905-841-3898 *Fax:* 905-841-3026
Warehouse: TTS Distributing Inc, 45 Tyler St, Aurora, ON L4G 2N1 *Tel:* 905-841-3898 *Fax:* 905-841-3026

§NDE Publishing
15-30 Wertheim Ct, Richmond Hill, ON L4B 1B9
Tel: 905-731-1288 *Toll Free Tel:* 800-675-1263
Fax: 905-731-5744
E-mail: info@ndepublishing.com
Web Site: www.ndepublishing.com
Key Personnel
VP: Elena Mazour
Founded: 1998
Book & multimedia publishing.
Publishes in English.
ISBN Prefix(es): 1-55321; 1-55375

Number of titles published annually: 10 Print; 1 CD-ROM
Total Titles: 37 Print; 1 CD-ROM
Membership(s): Canadian Booksellers Association

Nelson
Division of Thomson Canada Ltd
1120 Birchmount Rd, Scarborough, ON M1K 5G4
Tel: 416-752-9448 *Toll Free Tel:* 800-268-2222 (cust serv); 800-430-4445 *Fax:* 416-752-8101
E-mail: inquire@nelson.com
Web Site: www.nelson.com
Key Personnel
Pres: George Bergquist
VP, Opers: Ed Berman
Sr VP, Media Servs: Susan Cline
Sr VP, Higher Educ: Lesley Gouldie
Sr VP, HR: Marlene Nyilassy
Sr VP, School: Greg Pilon
Acting CFO: Ron Reed
Exec Admin: Jeannie Falkner
Founded: 1914
School, college, test, professional & reference.
Publishes in English.
ISBN Prefix(es): 0-17
Number of titles published annually: 250 Print
Total Titles: 6,771 Print; 30 CD-ROM; 30 E-Book; 100 Audio
U.S. Publishers Represented: Act Educational Tech Centre; Alliance; Arco; Arden; Aseba; Autodesk; Brooks Cole; Chilton; Course Technology; Crisp Learning; Customer Publishing; D C Heath; Dame Publishing; Delmar Publishers Inc; Delmar School; Douglas & McIntyre; Duxbury Press; Enter Here; Global Elt; Harcourt Brace (Canada); Heinle & Heinle; Houghton Mifflin; International Thomson Business Press; Irwin; ITP France; Kogan Page; Language Teaching Publications; Learning Media Ltd; Milady Publishing Co; Muska & Lipman/Premier-Trade; Nelson Business Education; Nelson Canada (El-Hi); Nelson College; Nelson Price Milburn; Nelson/Houghton; Newbury House; Ontario Institute for Studies in Education; Onword Press (Acquired Titles); Peterson's Guides; Prompt; PWS Publishing; Scoring Services; Shelly/Cashman; Singular Publishing; Skidmore-Roth; South-Western; Texere; Thomas Learning; Thomas Nelson & Sons Ltd; Thomas Nelson Australia; Van Nostrand Reinhold; Wadsworth Publishing; Wave Tech; West Publishing; Wiley
Membership(s): Canadian Educational Resources Council; Canadian Publishers' Council

New Star Books Ltd
107-3477 Commercial St, Vancouver, BC V5N 4E8
SAN: 115-1908
Tel: 604-738-9429 *Fax:* 604-738-9332
E-mail: info@newstarbooks.com; orders@newstarbooks.com
Web Site: www.newstarbooks.com
Key Personnel
Pres: Rolf Maurer
Man Ed: Melua McLean
Founded: 1974
Social issues & current affairs, fiction, literary, history, international politics, labor, feminist & gay/lesbian studies.
Publishes in English.
ISBN Prefix(es): 0-919888; 0-919573; 0-921586; 1-55420
Number of titles published annually: 10 Print
Total Titles: 74 Print
Imprints: Transmontanus
Membership(s): Literary Press Group

§New World Publishing
PO Box 36075, Halifax, NS B3J 3S9
Toll Free Tel: 877-211-3334 *Fax:* 902-576-2095

E-mail: nwp1@eastlink.ca
Web Site: www.newworldpublishing.com
Key Personnel
Owner & Man Ed: Francis Mitchell
Publishes in English.
ISBN Prefix(es): 1-895814
Number of titles published annually: 3 Print; 1 CD-ROM; 1 Audio
Total Titles: 20 Print; 3 CD-ROM; 3 Audio
Subsidiaries: Artistic Ventures Atlantic (music production)
Membership(s): Atlantic Publishers Marketing Association; Canadian Booksellers Association

NeWest Press
8540 109 St, No 201, Edmonton, AB T6G 1E6
Tel: 780-432-9427 *Toll Free Tel:* 866-796-5433
Fax: 780-433-3179
E-mail: info@newestpress.com
Web Site: www.newestpress.com
Key Personnel
Gen Mgr: Ruth Linka *E-mail:* ruth@newestpress.com
Intl Rts: Bill Hanna *Tel:* 416-484-8356 *Fax:* 416-484-8356
Founded: 1977
Trade paperback books.
Publishes in English.
ISBN Prefix(es): 0-920316; 0-920897; 1-896300
Number of titles published annually: 13 Print; 4 E-Book
Total Titles: 118 Print; 9 E-Book
Sales Office(s): Literary Press Group, 501-192 Spadina Ave, Toronto, ON T6G 1E6 *Tel:* 416-483-1321 *Fax:* 416-483-2510 *E-mail:* jdavis@lpg.ca
Foreign Rep(s): Acacia House Publishing Services Ltd; Bill & Frances Hanna
Foreign Rights: Bill & Frances Hanna
Distribution Center: LitDist Co, 100 Armstrong Ave, Georgetown, ON L7G 5S4 *Toll Free Tel:* 800-591-6250 *Toll Free Fax:* 800-591-6251 *E-mail:* orders@litdistco.ca

Nimbus Publishing Ltd
3731 Mackintosh St, Halifax, NS B3K 5A5
SAN: 115-0685
Mailing Address: PO Box 9166, Halifax, NS B3K 5M8
Tel: 902-455-5304 *Toll Free Tel:* 800-646-2879
Fax: 902-455-5440
E-mail: customerservice@nimbus.ns.ca
Web Site: www.nimbus.ns.ca
Key Personnel
Man Ed: Sandra McIntyre
Mgr: Dan Soucoup
Founded: 1978
Regional nonfiction books, relevant to the Atlantic-Canadian experience, social & natural history, children's books, cookbooks, travel, biography, photography & nautical.
Publishes in English.
ISBN Prefix(es): 0-920852; 0-919380; 0-921054; 0-921128; 1-55109
Number of titles published annually: 30 Print
Total Titles: 500 Print
Imprints: Nimbus
Distributor for Breton Books; Pottersfield Press
U.S. Publishers Represented: Breton Books; Down East Books; Alan C Hood & Co Inc; Mystic Seaport Museum Inc; Norwood Publishing; Nova Scotia Museum; Pottersfield Press; Sheridan House; Tiller Publications; Wooden Boat
U.S. Rep(s): Downeast Books
Warehouse: 6377 Lady Hammond Rd, Halifax, NS B3K 2J4
Distribution Center: 6377 Lady Hammond Rd, Halifax, NS B3K 2J4

§North-South Institute/Institut Nord-Sud
55 Murray St, Suite 200, Ottawa, ON K1N 5M3

Tel: 613-241-3535 *Fax:* 613-241-7435
E-mail: nsi@nsi-ins.ca
Web Site: www.nsi-ins.ca
Key Personnel
CEO & Pres: Roy Culpeper
Coord Communs & Publns: Lois Ross *Tel:* 613-241-3535 ext 235 *E-mail:* lross@nsi-ins.ca
Lib Officer: Dina Shadid
Founded: 1976
North-South relations & foreign aid, economics & trade, with emphasis on Canada & developing countries, foreign policy & multilateral cooperation, gender & development, human rights, civil society, conflict & human security, markets & social responsibility. Also publishes newsletters.
Publishes in English, French.
ISBN Prefix(es): 0-921942; 1-896770
Number of titles published annually: 6 Print; 5 Online
Total Titles: 9 Print; 3 CD-ROM
Distributed by Renouf Publishing Co Ltd

Northern Canada Mission Distributors
Division of Northern Canada Evangelical Mission
PO Box 3030, Prince Albert, SK S6V 7V4
Tel: 306-764-3388 *Fax:* 306-764-3390
E-mail: missiondist@ncem.ca
Web Site: www.ncem.ca
Key Personnel
Mgr: Bill Dyck
Founded: 1967
Publish books, pamphlets, tracts, Bibles, audio CDs & audio cassettes. Subject specialty is native North American literature; also publishes in Spanish language.
Publishes in English, French.
ISBN Prefix(es): 1-920731; 1-896968
Number of titles published annually: 3 Print
Total Titles: 111 Print; 9 CD-ROM; 29 Audio
Membership(s): Christian Booksellers Association

Northstone Publishing
Imprint of Wood Lake Books Inc
9025 Jim Bailey Rd, Kelowna, BC V4V 1R2
SAN: 117-7346
Tel: 250-766-2778 *Toll Free Tel:* 800-299-2926
Fax: 250-766-2736
Web Site: www.joinhands.com
Key Personnel
Publr & Intl Rts Contact: Bonnie Schlosser
Mktg, Promos & Lib Sales Dir: Cheryl Perry
Ed: Mike Schwartzentruber
Promo Coord: Cassandra Redding
Founded: 1996
Books, spiritual speaking.
Publishes in English.
ISBN Prefix(es): 1-55145
Number of titles published annually: 12 Print
Total Titles: 117 Print
Distributed by The Pilgrim Press
Distributor for Geneva Press; The Pilgrim Press; Westminster Johnknox Press
U.S. Publishers Represented: John Knox Press; Logos; Westminster Johknox Press
U.S. Rep(s): Geneva Press; Words Distributing

Novalis Publishing
Division of Bayard Canada
49 Front St E, 2nd fl, Toronto, ON M5E 1B3
Tel: 416-363-3303 *Toll Free Tel:* 800-387-7164
Fax: 416-363-9409 *Toll Free Fax:* 800-204-4140
E-mail: novalis@interlog.com
Web Site: www.novalis.ca
Key Personnel
Dir: Ronald Albert
Dir, Periodical Mkt: Lauretta Santarossa
Dir, Book Mktg: Brian MacLean *Tel:* 416-363-3303 ext 240
Founded: 1935

Religious children's books, periodicals & religious books (Catholic).
Publishes in English, French.
ISBN Prefix(es): 2-89088; 2-89507
Number of titles published annually: 30 Print
Total Titles: 200 Print
Distributor for Bible Reading Fellowship; Canterbury Press; Church House Publishing; Cowley Publications; Crossroad Publishing; Darton Longman & Todd; Doubleday/Image Books; Editions du Signe; Gracewing; Loyola Press; Morehouse Publishing; Printery House; SCM Press; SPCK/Sheldon Press; St Paul Multimedia (UK); St Vladimir Seminary Press; Templegate Publishers; Trinity Press International; Twenty Third Publications
U.S. Publishers Represented: Cistercian Publications; William B Eerdmans; New City; Orbis; Paulist Press; Plough
Shipping Address: 6255 Hutchison, Montreal, PQ H2V 4C7

Oberon Press
Division of Michael Hardy Ltd
350 Sparks St, Suite 400, Ottawa, ON K1R 7S8
SAN: 115-0723
Tel: 613-238-3275 *Fax:* 613-238-3275
E-mail: oberon@sympatico.ca
Web Site: www3.sympatico.ca/oberon
Key Personnel
Pres: Michael Macklem
VP & Gen Mgr: Nicholas Macklem
Sec & Treas: Dilshad Engineer
Founded: 1966
Canadiana, fiction, history, biography, poetry & travel.
Publishes in English.
ISBN Prefix(es): 0-88750; 0-7780
Number of titles published annually: 12 Print
Total Titles: 603 Print

One Act Play Depot
132 Memorial Dr, Spiritwood, SK S0J 2M0
E-mail: plays@oneactplays.net; orders@oneactplays.net
Web Site: oneactplays.net
Key Personnel
Ed: K Balvenie
Man Ed: Fraser MacFarlane
Founded: 2002
Publication, sale & distribution of one-act plays. Accept approximately 1 out of every 100 submissions. Orders ship within 24 hours. Accept submissions only in February of each year.
Publishes in English.
ISBN Prefix(es): 1-894910
Number of titles published annually: 10 Print
Total Titles: 47 Print

Oolichan Books
Box 10, Lantzville, BC V0R 2H0
SAN: 115-4680
Tel: 250-390-4839 *Fax:* 250-390-4839
E-mail: oolichan@island.net
Web Site: www.oolichan.com
Key Personnel
Publr: Ronald Smith
Prodn Mgr: Jay Connolly
Publicist: Linda Martin
Ed: Hiro Boga
Founded: 1974
Publishers of literary nonfiction.
Publishes in English.
ISBN Prefix(es): 0-88982
Number of titles published annually: 8 Print
Total Titles: 120 Print
Shipping Address: 7190 Lantzville Rd, Lantzville, BC V0R 2H0
Distribution Center: The Heritage Group, 108-17665 66A Ave, Surrey, BC V3S 2A7 *Toll*

Free Tel: 800-665-3302 E-mail: distribution@heritagehouse.ca
Membership(s): Association of Book Publishers of British Columbia

Oxford University Press Canada
Subsidiary of Oxford University Press
70 Wynford Dr, Don Mills, ON M3C 1J9
Tel: 416-441-2941 Toll Free Tel: 800-387-8020
Fax: 416-444-0427 Toll Free Fax: 800-665-1771
E-mail: custserv@oupcan.com
Web Site: www.oup.com/ca
Key Personnel
Pres: Joanna Gertler
Dir, Trade & Ref: Leslie Anne Connell
Fin Dir: Geoff Forguson
Man Ed, Trade & Coll: Phyllis Wilson
Edit & Perm Asst: Jessica Coffey
Founded: 1904
School & college textbooks, reference, atlases, biography, poetry anthologies, literature, politics, economics, history.
Publishes in English, French.
Number of titles published annually: 50 Print
Total Titles: 650 Print
Imprints: Oxford University Press
Distributed by Oxford University Press (worldwide)
U.S. Publishers Represented: Scott/Jones Inc
Foreign Rep(s): Arnold (UK)

Pacific Educational Press
Faculty of Education, University of British Columbia, 6365 Biological Sciences Rd, Vancouver, BC V6T 1Z4
SAN: 115-1266
Tel: 604-822-5385 Fax: 604-822-6603
Web Site: www.pep.educ.ubc.ca
Key Personnel
Dir: Catherine Edwards Tel: 604-822-6561 E-mail: cedwards@interchange.ubc.ca
Founded: 1971
Textbooks for teacher education programs, education materials, materials which are generally used in classrooms or educational institutes, books on education topics & issues for a general readership.
Publishes in English.
ISBN Prefix(es): 0-88865; 1-895766
Number of titles published annually: 6 Print
Total Titles: 94 Print
Distributed by Georgetown Terminal Warehouse (order desk)
Distributor for Critical Thinking Consortium (TC 2); Moody's Lookout Press
Membership(s): Association of Book Publishers of British Columbia; Association of Canadian Publishers

Parachute
4060 Blvd St-Laurent, Bureau 501, Montreal, PQ H2W 1Y9
Tel: 514-842-9805 Fax: 514-842-9319
E-mail: info@parachute.ca
Web Site: www.parachute.ca
Key Personnel
Ed: Chantal Pontbriand
Dir, Dist & Adv: Monica Gyorkos
Founded: 1975
Contemporary art magazine & art books.
Publishes in English, French.
ISBN Prefix(es): 2-920284
Number of titles published annually: 4 Print
Total Titles: 114 Print

Paulines
5610 rue Beaubien est, Montreal, PQ H1T 1X5
Tel: 514-253-5610 Fax: 514-253-1907
E-mail: paulines.editions@videotron.ca
Key Personnel
Dir & Intl Rts Contact: Vanda Salvador

Lib Sales Dir: Lucille Paradis
Founded: 1955
Religious books.
Publishes in English, French.
ISBN Prefix(es): 2-920912
Number of titles published annually: 5 Print
Total Titles: 49 Print
Distributed by Mediaspaul (Montreal)

Pearson Education Canada Inc
Division of Pearson plc
26 Prince Andrew Place, Don Mills, ON M3C 2T8
SAN: 115-0022
Mailing Address: PO Box 580, Don Mills, ON M3C 2T8
Tel: 416-447-5101 Toll Free Tel: 800-567-3800; 800-387-8028 Fax: 416-443-0948 Toll Free Fax: 800-263-7733; 888-465-0536
E-mail: firstname.lastname@pearsoned.com
Web Site: www.pearsoned.com
Key Personnel
CEO & Pres: Allan Reynolds
Pres, School Div: Marty Keast
Pres, Penguin Books: Ed Carson
COO: Dan Lee
Higher Ed Div: Steve O'Hearn
Founded: 1966
Educational textbooks, trade, reference.
Publishes in English, French.
ISBN Prefix(es): 0-201
Total Titles: 5,700 Print
Imprints: Addison Wesley; Allyn & Bacon; Benjamin Cummings; Copp Clark; Ginn; Longman; Prentice Hall
Orders to: Pearson Education Operations Centre, 195 Harry Walker Pkwy N, Newmarket, ON L3Y 7B4 Toll Free Tel: 800-567-3800 (higher educ & PTR); 800-361-6128 (school) Toll Free Fax: 800-236-7733 (higher educ & PTR); 800-563-9196 (school)
Returns: Pearson Education Operations Centre, 195 Harry Walker Pkwy N, Newmarket, ON L3Y 7B4 Toll Free Tel: 800-567-3800 (higher educ & PTR); 800-361-6128 (school) Toll Free Fax: 800-263-7733 (higher educ & PTR); 800-563-9196 (school)
Distribution Center: 195 Harry Walker Pkwy N, Newmarket, ON L3Y 7B4 Tel: 905-853-7888

Pembroke Publishers Ltd
538 Hood Rd, Markham, ON L3R 3K9
Tel: 905-477-0650 Fax: 905-477-3691
Web Site: www.pembrokepublishers.com
Key Personnel
Pres & Intl Rts: Mary Macchiusi E-mail: mary@pembrokepublishers.com
Man Dir: Claudia Connolly
Founded: 1985
Educational, children's books.
Publishes in English.
ISBN Prefix(es): 0-921217; 1-55138
Number of titles published annually: 15 Print
Total Titles: 230 Print
Distributor for Stenhouse Publishers
U.S. Publishers Represented: Stenhouse Publishers, 477 Congress St, Suite 4B, Portland, ME 04101-3417, United States
U.S. Rep(s): Stenhouse Publishers, 477 Congress St, Suite 4B, Portland, ME 04101-3417, United States
Foreign Rep(s): BRNO (UK); Int Press (Australia); PMS (Singapore); Stenhouse Publishers (USA)
Membership(s): Canadian Educational Resources Council; Ontario Book Publishers' Association; Ontario Book Publishers Organization

Pemmican Publications Inc
150 Henry Ave, Winnipeg, MB R3B 0J7
SAN: 115-1657
Tel: 204-589-6346 Fax: 204-589-2063

E-mail: pemmicanpublications@hotmail.com
Web Site: www.pemmican.mb.ca
Key Personnel
Man Ed: Diane Ramsey
Founded: 1980
Books of native concern, juvenile & young adult books, trade paperbacks, scholarly books.
Publishes in English, French.
ISBN Prefix(es): 0-919143; 0-921827
Number of titles published annually: 5 Print
Distributor for Ancient Echoes; McClelland & Stewart Inc
U.S. Rep(s): Oyate
Advertising Agency: Quill & Quire

Penguin Books Canada Limited, see Penguin Group (Canada)

Penguin Group (Canada)
Division of Pearson Penguin Canada Inc
10 Alcorn Ave, Suite 300, Toronto, ON M4V 3B2
SAN: 115-074X
Tel: 416-925-2249 Fax: 416-925-0068
Web Site: www.penguin.ca
Key Personnel
Pres, Penguin Group Canada: Ed Carson
VP, Fin: Helena Hung
Pres & Publr, Penguin Publg Div: David Davidar
Dir, Publg Opers: Trudy Ledsham
Dir, Prodn: Kathrine Pummell
Dir, Sales: Petra Morin
Mgr: Brad Francis
Dir, HR: Ann Wood
Founded: 1974
General trade & paperback books, hardcover & classics, audio cassettes.
Publishes in English.
ISBN Prefix(es): 0-14; 0-452; 0-451; 0-453; 0-7214; 0-216
Number of titles published annually: 16 Print
Total Titles: 68 Print
Imprints: Arkana; Canada Wire; Granta; Ladybird; Penguin Canada; Puffin Canada; Viking Canada; Viking US Arkana
Distributor for Disney Audio; Element Books; Faber & Faber; Frederick Warne; Icon Books; Ladybird; Microsoft Press; Monacelli Press; New Directions; Overlook Press; Pushcart Press; Spot the Puppy; Thames & Hudson; W W Norton
Distribution Center: Canbook Distribution Services, 1220 Nicholson Rd, Newmarket, ON L3Y 7V1 Tel: 905-713-3852 Toll Free Tel: 800-399-6858 Toll Free Fax: 800-363-2665

Pippin Publishing Corp
170 The Donway W, Toronto, ON M3C 2G3
Tel: 416-510-2918 Toll Free Tel: 888-889-0001 Fax: 416-510-3359
Web Site: www.pippinpub.com
Key Personnel
Pres & Edit Dir: Jonathan Lovat Dickson E-mail: jld@pippinpub.com
Busn Mgr: Fiona Chow
Admin Dir: Cynthia Chen E-mail: cynthia@pippinpub.com
Founded: 1995
Educational books: English as a foreign language; English language teaching, books for teachers & students. Also trade military memoirs.
Publishes in English.
ISBN Prefix(es): 0-88751
Number of titles published annually: 6 Print
Total Titles: 77 Print
Imprints: Dominie Press (restricted to CN)
Distributed by Heinemann (US)
Foreign Rep(s): Heinemann
Warehouse: University of Toronto Press, 5201 Dufferin St, Toronto North York, ON M3H 5T8, Carol Trainor Tel: 416-667-7791 Toll Free Tel: 800-565-9523 Fax: 416-667-7832 Toll Free

Fax: 800-221-9985 *E-mail:* utpbooks@utpress.
utoronto.ca
University of Toronto Press, 2250 Military Rd,
Tonawanda, NY 14150, United States
Membership(s): Independent Publisher's Guild

Playwrights Canada Press
Subsidiary of Playwrights Guild of Canada
215 Spadina Ave, Sutie 230, Toronto, ON M5T
2C7
Tel: 416-703-0013 *Fax:* 416-408-3402
E-mail: orders@playwrightscanada.com
Web Site: www.playwrightscanada.com
Key Personnel
Publr: Angela Rebeiro *E-mail:* publisher@
playwrightscanada.com
Founded: 1971
Single scripts, anthologies & collections of Cana-
dian plays.
Publishes in English.
ISBN Prefix(es): 0-88754
Number of titles published annually: 21 Print
Total Titles: 130 Print
Distributed by Nick Hern Books; Theatre Com-
munications Group
Distributor for Nick Hern Books; Theatre Com-
munications Group
U.S. Publishers Represented: Theatre Communi-
cations Group
Foreign Rep(s): Nick Hern Books (UK); Theatre
Communications USA

Polestar Book Publishers
Imprint of Raincoast Books
9050 Shaughnessy St, Vancouver, BC V6P 6E5
Tel: 604-323-7100 *Toll Free Tel:* 800-663-5714
Fax: 604-323-2600 *Toll Free Fax:* 800-565-
3770
E-mail: info@raincoast.com
Web Site: www.raincoast.com
Key Personnel
CEO & Pres: Allan MacDougall
VP, Busn Devt: Kevin Williams
VP, Dist: Paddy Laidley
VP & Busn Mgr: John Sawyer
Rts & Contracts Mgr: Jesse Finkelstein
E-mail: jesse@raincoast.com
Mktg Dir: Jamie Broadhurst
Publr: Michelle Benjamin
Ed: Lynn Henry
Founded: 1984
Fiction, poetry, teen fiction, sports & general non-
fiction.
Publishes in English.
ISBN Prefix(es): 0-919591; 1-896095; 1-55192
Number of titles published annually: 60 Print
Total Titles: 80 Print
Distributed by Publishers Group West
Membership(s): Association of Book Publishers
of British Columbia; Association of Canadian
Publishers

Polyscience Publications Inc
PO Box 1606, Sta St-Martin, Laval, PQ H7V 3P8
Tel: 450-688-8484 *Fax:* 450-688-1930
E-mail: info@polysciencepublications.com
Web Site: www.polysciencepublications.com
Key Personnel
Pres: Albert H Du Fresne
Founded: 1986
Scientific books, proceedings of technical & sci-
entific meetings.
ISBN Prefix(es): 0-921317
Number of titles published annually: 5 Print; 2
CD-ROM
Total Titles: 93 Print; 2 CD-ROM

**Pontifical Institute of Mediaeval Studies, Dept
of Publications**
59 Queens Park Crescent E, Toronto, ON M5S
2C4
SAN: 115-0804

Tel: 416-926-7142 *Fax:* 416-926-7292
E-mail: pontifex@chass.utoronto.ca
Web Site: www.pims.ca
Key Personnel
Dir, Pubn: Ron B Thomson *Tel:* 416-926-7143
E-mail: thomson@chass.utoronto.ca
Ed: Jean Hoff; Fred Unwalla
Founded: 1936
Scholarly material on the Middle Ages.
Publishes in English, French.
ISBN Prefix(es): 0-88844
Number of titles published annually: 5 Print
Total Titles: 250 Print

Porcupine's Quill Inc
68 Main St, Erin, ON N0B 1T0
Tel: 519-833-9158 *Fax:* 519-833-9845
E-mail: pql@sentex.net
Web Site: www.sentex.net/~pql
Key Personnel
Publr: Tim Inkster
Founded: 1974
Modern Canadian literature, poetry & art.
Publishes in English.
ISBN Prefix(es): 0-88984
Number of titles published annually: 12 Print
Total Titles: 100 Print
U.S. Rep(s): University of Toronto Press
Membership(s): Association of Canadian Publish-
ers; Literary Press Group

Portage & Main Press
318 McDermot, Suite 100, Winnipeg, MB R3A
0A2
Tel: 204-987-3500 *Toll Free Tel:* 800-667-9673
Fax: 204-947-0080 *Toll Free Fax:* 866-734-
8477
E-mail: books@portageandmainpress.com
Web Site: www.portageandmainpress.com
Key Personnel
Owner & Publr: Mary Dixon
Dir: Catherine Gerbasi
Founded: 1967
Educational resource (K-8), interior design.
Publishes in English.
ISBN Prefix(es): 0-919566; 0-920541; 1-895411;
1-875327; 1-894110; 1-55379; 0-96996; 0-
9699032
Number of titles published annually: 14 Print
Total Titles: 150 Print
Imprints: Peguis Publishers

Potlatch Publications Ltd
30 Berry Hill, Waterdown, ON L0R 2H4
Tel: 905-689-2104 *Fax:* 905-689-1632
Web Site: www.angelfire.com/on3/potlatch
Key Personnel
Pres & Intl Rts: Robert F Nielsen
E-mail: robtnielsen@aol.com
Founded: 1972
Publisher of general trade books for the world
market.
Publishes in English.
ISBN Prefix(es): 0-919676
Number of titles published annually: 4 Print
Total Titles: 36 Print

Pottersfield Press
83 Leslie Rd, East Lawrencetown, NS B2Z 1P8
SAN: 115-0790
Toll Free Tel: 800-NIMBUS9 (646-2879-orders
only) *Toll Free Fax:* 888-253-3133
Web Site: www.pottersfieldpress.com
Key Personnel
Pres & Publr: Lesley Choyce
Founded: 1979
Fiction, books about the sea, science fiction,
books of Atlantic & Canada, nonfiction, literary
travel.
Publishes in English.
ISBN Prefix(es): 0-919001; 1-895900
Number of titles published annually: 6 Print

Total Titles: 86 Print; 2 CD-ROM; 4 Audio
Imprints: Atlantic Classics Series
Distributed by Nimbus Publishing
U.S. Rep(s): Nimbus Publishing
Shipping Address: c/o Nimbus Publishing, Box
9166, Halifax, NS B3K 5M8

Prairie View Press
PR 205, Rosenort, MB R0G 1W0
Mailing Address: PO Box 160, Rosenort, MB
R0G 1W0
Tel: 204-746-2375 *Toll Free Tel:* 800-477-7377
Fax: 204-746-2667
Key Personnel
Pres: Chester Goossen
VP: Dalen Goossen
Bookkeeper: Darleen Loewen
Founded: 1968
Quality, moral books; music.
Publishes in English.
ISBN Prefix(es): 0-920035; 1-896199; 1-897080
Number of titles published annually: 5 Print
Total Titles: 28 Print
Branch Office(s)
Box 88, 539 E Fifth St, Neche, ND 58265,
United States (US mailing address)
Distributed by Gospel Publishers

Les Presses de l'Universite du Quebec
Division of Universite Du Quebec
2875 Boul Laurier, Bureau 450, Ste-Foy, PQ G1V
2M2
Tel: 418-657-4399 *Fax:* 418-657-2096
E-mail: secretariat@puq.uquebec.ca; puq@puq.
uquebec.ca
Web Site: www.puq.ca *Telex:* 05131623
Key Personnel
Dir Gen & Intl Rts: Angele Tremblay
Founded: 1969
University press.
Publishes in French.
ISBN Prefix(es): 2-7605; 0-7770; 2-920073
Number of titles published annually: 60 Print
Total Titles: 900 Print
Subsidiaries: Distribution De Livres Univers
(senc)
Branch Office(s)
Distribution de Livres Univers (senc), 845 Marie-
Victorin, St Nicolas, PQ G0S 3L0
Distributor for CPAQ et Picador; CPVQ; Gea-
gri; Les editions Saint-Yves Inc; Teleuniversite;
UQAM (Dep Philosophie)
Distribution Center: Distribution De Livres
Univers (senc), 845 Marie-Victorin, St Nico-
las, PQ G0S 3L0

Les Presses De L'Universite Laval
Maurice-Pollack House, Office 3103, University
City, Sainte-Foy, PQ G1K 7P4
Tel: 418-656-2803 *Fax:* 418-656-3305
E-mail: presses@pul.ulaval.ca
Web Site: www.ulaval.ca/pul
Key Personnel
Gen Ed: Denis Dion; Leo Jacques
Founded: 1950
Books in the humanities & social sciences with
an emphasis on subjects of interest in Quebec
& Canada, administration, economy.
Publishes in French.
ISBN Prefix(es): 2-7637
Number of titles published annually: 1,000 Print
Distribution Center: Distribution University, 845
rue Marie-Victorin, St-Nicolas, PQ G0S 3L0
Tel: 418-831-7474 *Fax:* 418-831-4021

Prise de Parole Inc
C P 550, Sudbury, ON P3E 4R2
Tel: 705-675-6491 *Fax:* 705-673-1817
E-mail: prisedeparole@bellnet.ca
Key Personnel
Gen Mgr: Denise Truax
Admin Dir: Alain Mayotte
Founded: 1973

Poetry, novels, drama, textbooks, essays.
Publishes in French.
ISBN Prefix(es): 0-920814; 0-921573; 2-89423
Number of titles published annually: 15 Print
Total Titles: 15 Print
Shipping Address: 109 Elm St, Suite 205, Sudbury, ON P3C 1T4
Distribution Center: Diffusion Prologue, 1650 boul Lionel-Bertrand, Boisbriand, PQ J7H 1N7
Tel: 450-434-0306

Productive Publications
1930 Younge St, 1210, Toronto, ON M4S 1G9
SAN: 117-1712
Mailing Address: PO Box 7200, Sta A, Toronto, ON M5W 1X8
Tel: 416-483-0634 *Fax:* 416-322-7434
Web Site: www.productivepublications.com
Key Personnel
Owner, Pres & Intl Rts: Iain Williamson
Founded: 1985
Paperback books-trade; business, finance, communications, computers, management, marketing, taxation, personal finance, entrepreneurship, self-help.
Publishes in English.
ISBN Prefix(es): 0-920847; 1-896210; 1-55270
Number of titles published annually: 29 Print
Total Titles: 114 Print
Membership(s): Book Publishers Professional Association

Les Publications du Quebec
1500 rue Jean-Talon Nord, 1 etage, Ste Foy, PQ G1N 2E5
Tel: 418-644-1342 *Toll Free Tel:* 800-463-2100 (Quebec province only) *Fax:* 418-644-7813
E-mail: service.clientele@mrci.gouv.qc.ca
Web Site: www.publicationsduquebec.gouv.qc.ca
Key Personnel
Intl Rts: Sophie Gravel
Gen Dir: Marielle Seguin
Dir: Marie Claude Lanoue
Mktg Mgr: Eric Labbe
Founded: 1982
Government publications.
Publishes in French.
ISBN Prefix(es): 2-550; 2-551
Number of titles published annually: 200 Print
Total Titles: 4,300 Print
Warehouse: 2575 rue Watt, Ste Foy, PQ G1P 3T2, Pierre Otis

Les Publications Graficor 1989 Inc
Subsidiary of Groupe Morin
7001 boul Saint-Laurent, Montreal, PQ H2S 3E3
Tel: 514-273-1066 *Toll Free Tel:* 800-565-5531 *Fax:* 514-276-0324 *Toll Free Fax:* 800-814-0324
E-mail: graficor@gmorin.qc.ca
Web Site: www.graficor.qc.ca
Key Personnel
Commercialisation & Lib Sales Dir: Danielle Poitras
Founded: 1978
Tutorial material for grades K-6.
Publishes in French.
ISBN Prefix(es): 2-89242
Number of titles published annually: 200 Print

Purich Publishing Ltd
PO Box 23032, Market Mall Postal Outlet, Saskatoon, SK S7J 5H3
Tel: 306-373-5311 *Fax:* 306-373-5315
E-mail: purich@sasktel.net
Web Site: www.purichpublishing.com
Key Personnel
Publr: Karen Bolstad; Donald Purich
Founded: 1992
Books specializing in law, Aboriginal & Western Canada issues.
Publishes in English.

ISBN Prefix(es): 1-895830
Number of titles published annually: 3 Print
Total Titles: 25 Print
Returns: c/o Direct Distribution, 3030 Cleveland Ave, Saskatoon, SK S7K 8B5
Warehouse: c/o Direct Distribution, 3030 Cleveland Ave, Saskatoon, SK S7K 8B5
Membership(s): Association of Canadian Publishers; Saskatchewan Publishers Group

Quebec Dans Le Monde
CP 8503, Quebec, PQ G1V 4N5
SAN: 116-8657
Tel: 418-659-5540 *Fax:* 418-659-4143
E-mail: info@quebecmonde.com
Web Site: www.quebecmonde.com
Key Personnel
Dir Gen: Denis Turcotte
Founded: 1983
Specializes in reference books on Quebec.
Publishes in French.
ISBN Prefix(es): 2-9801130; 2-921309; 2-89525
Total Titles: 20 Print; 5 E-Book
Distributed by Librairie Du Quebec A Paris

Editions Michel Quintin
PO Box 340, Waterloo, PQ J0E 2N0
SAN: 116-5356
Tel: 450-539-3774 *Fax:* 450-539-4905
E-mail: info@michelquintin.ca
Key Personnel
Pres: Michel Quintin
Founded: 1981
Nonfiction on fauna, nature, environment.
Publishes in French.
ISBN Prefix(es): 2-920438; 2-89435
Number of titles published annually: 30 Print
Total Titles: 200 Print
Distributed by Les Messageries ADP
Foreign Rep(s): Bacon & Hughes (Canada); Le Colporeur Diffusion (France); Multi Livres Diffusion (France); Servidis SA (Belgium)

Raincoast Publishing
Division of Raincoast Book Distribution Ltd
9050 Shaughnessy St, Vancouver, BC V6P 6E5
SAN: 115-0871
Tel: 604-323-7100 *Toll Free Tel:* 800-663-5714 (Canada only) *Fax:* 604-323-2600 *Toll Free Fax:* 800-565-3700
E-mail: info@raincoast.com
Web Site: www.raincoast.com
Key Personnel
Pres & CEO: Allan MacDougall
Exec VP & Publr: Kevin Williams
VP, Dist & Dir, Sales: Paddy Laidley
Publr: Michelle Benjamin
Mktg Dir: Jamie Broadhurst
Rts & Contracts Mgr: Jesse Finkelstein
Founded: 1979
Book publishing & co-editions.
Publishes in English.
ISBN Prefix(es): 0-920417; 1-895714; 1-55192
Total Titles: 286 Print
Distributed by Publishers Group West (USA)

Random House of Canada Ltd
One Toronto St, Unit 300, Toronto, ON M5C 2V6
Tel: 416-364-4449 *Fax:* 416-364-6863 (edit & publicity); 416-364-6653 (subs rts)
Web Site: www.randomhouse.ca
Key Personnel
Chmn: John Neale
Exec VP & COO: Douglas Foot *Tel:* 905-624-0672
Exec VP & Dir, Sales & Mktg: Brad Martin
VP & Dir, Sales: Brian Cassin *Tel:* 905-624-0672; Duncan Shields *Tel:* 905-624-0672
VP, Prodn: Janine Laporte
VP & Dir, Rts & Contracts: Jennifer Shepherd
VP, Online Mktg & Sales Dir: Lisa Charters

VP & Dir, Mktg & Communs: Tracey Turriff
VP, Media Rel: Scott Sellers
Dir, Mktg: Linda Scott *Tel:* 905-624-0672
Adv Dir: Mark Veldhuizen
Asst Prodn Mgr: Carla Kean
Busn Mgr: Ralph Burrows
Founded: 1944
Random House of Canada Ltd & its publishing entities are not accepting unsol submissions, proposals, mss, or submission queries via e-mail at this time.
Publishes in English.
ISBN Prefix(es): 0-02; 0-679; 0-553; 0-385; 0-7704; 0-345; 0-449; 0-676
Imprints: Anchor Canada; Doubleday Canada; Knopf Canada; Random House Canada; Seal Books
Branch Office(s)
2775 Matheson Blvd E, Mississauga, ON L4W 4P7 (sales & opers) *Tel:* 905-624-0672 *Fax:* 905-624-6217 SAN: 115-088X
Membership(s): Canadian Booksellers Association; Canadian Library Association; Canadian Publishers' Council
See separate listing for:
Doubleday Canada
Knopf Canada
Seal Books

Reader's Digest Association (Canada) Ltd/Selection du Reader's Digest (Canada) Ltee
1100 Rene Levesque Blvd W, Montreal, PQ H3B 5H5
Tel: 514-940-0751 *Toll Free Tel:* 800-465-0780 *Fax:* 514-940-3637 (admin)
E-mail: customer.service@readersdigest.ca
Web Site: www.readersdigest.ca
Key Personnel
Chmn, Pres & CEO: Pierre Dion
VP, Books & Home Entertainment Publg: Andrea Martin
Founded: 1943
Mail order & retail books on cookery, crafts, games & hobbies, money management, gardening, geography & geology, health & nutrition, history, house & home, how-to, law, general medicine, nature & science, travel; dictionaries, atlases, encyclopedias; fiction & general nonfiction in condensed form.
Publishes in English, French.
ISBN Prefix(es): 0-88850
Number of titles published annually: 125 Print
Total Titles: 450 Print
Warehouse: 300 Orenda Rd, Brampton, ON L6T 1G2

The Resource Centre
Box 190, Waterloo, ON N2J 3Z9
SAN: 118-0061
Tel: 519-885-0826 *Toll Free Tel:* 800-923-0330 *Fax:* 519-747-5629
E-mail: resourcecentre@sympatico.ca
Web Site: www.theresourcecentre.com
Key Personnel
Pres: Neal Gridgeman
Founded: 1981
School books.
Publishes in English, French.
ISBN Prefix(es): 0-920701
Number of titles published annually: 9 Print
Total Titles: 48 Print
Distributor for Eli; Hodder & Stoughton Educational; Macmillan - Heinemann ELT; Nelson Thornes
U.S. Publishers Represented: Alta Book Center Publishers; Delta Publishing Co; Dominic Press Inc; Pro Lingua Associates
Warehouse: 105 Randall Dr, Unit 6, Waterloo, ON N2V 1C5

Rocky Mountain Books Ltd
406-13 Ave NE, Calgary, AB T2E 1C2

Tel: 403-249-9490 *Fax:* 403-249-2968
Web Site: www.rmbooks.com
Key Personnel
CEO: Gillean Daffern
Publr: Tony Daffern
Assoc Publr: David Finch *E-mail:* finch@
heritagehouse.ca
Founded: 1976
Regional publisher of books on outdoor activities.
Publishes in English.
ISBN Prefix(es): 0-9690038; 0-921102; 1-894765
Number of titles published annually: 6 Print
Total Titles: 62 Print
Sales Office(s): Heritage House Publishing,
17665 66A Ave, No 108, Surrey, BC V3S 2A7
Tel: 604-574-7067 *Toll Free Tel:* 800-665-3302
Fax: 604-574-9942
Distributed by AlpenBooks; Cordee (UK) Books;
Heritage House Publishing
Billing Address: Heritage House Publishing,
17665 66A Ave, No 108, Surrey, BC V3S 2A7
Tel: 604-574-7067 *Toll Free Tel:* 800-665-3302
Fax: 604-574-9942
Orders to: Heritage House Publishing, 17665
66A Ave, No 108, Surrey, BC V3S 2A7
Tel: 604-574-7067 *Toll Free Tel:* 800-665-3302
Fax: 604-574-9942
Returns: Heritage House Publishing, 17665
66A Ave, No 108, Surrey, BC V3S 2A7
Tel: 604-574-7067 *Toll Free Tel:* 800-665-3302
Fax: 604-574-9942
Shipping Address: Heritage House Publishing,
17665 66A Ave, No 108, Surrey, BC V3S 2A7
Tel: 604-574-7067 *Toll Free Tel:* 800-665-3302
Fax: 604-574-9942
Warehouse: Heritage House Publishing,
66A Ave, No 108, Surrey, BC V3S 2A7
Tel: 604-574-7067 *Toll Free Tel:* 800-665-3302
Fax: 604-574-9942
Distribution Center: Heritage House Publishing,
17665 66A Ave, No 108, Surrey, BC V3S 2A7
Tel: 604-574-7067 *Toll Free Tel:* 800-665-3302
Fax: 604-574-9942
Membership(s): Book Publishers Association of
Alberta

The Roeher Institute
York University, Kinsmen Bldg, 4700 Keele St,
North York, ON M3J 1P3
Tel: 416-661-9611 *Fax:* 416-661-5701
E-mail: info@roeher.ca
Web Site: www.roeher.ca
Key Personnel
Pres: Cam Crawford *E-mail:* cameronc@roeher.ca
Founded: 1970
Promote the equality, participation & self-
determination of people with intellectual &
other disabilities, by examining the causes of
marginalization & by providing research, infor-
mation & social development opportunities.
Publishes in English, French.
ISBN Prefix(es): 1-55766; 0-920121; 0-919648;
1-895070; 1-896989
Number of titles published annually: 5 Print
Total Titles: 190 Print

Ronsdale Press
3350 W 21 Ave, Vancouver, BC V6S 1G7
SAN: 116-2454
Tel: 604-738-4688 *Toll Free Tel:* 888-879-0919
Fax: 604-731-4548
E-mail: ronsdale@shaw.ca
Web Site: ronsdalepress.com
Key Personnel
Dir & Intl Rts: Ronald Hatch
Lib Sales Dir: Veronica Hatch
Founded: 1988
Literary press, children's, history, literary & re-
gional; specializing in Canadian authors.
Publishes in English.
ISBN Prefix(es): 0-921870; 1-55380
Number of titles published annually: 10 Print
Total Titles: 120 Print

U.S. Rep(s): Lit DistCo
Foreign Rep(s): James Bryner (USA); Jacqui
Davis (USA); Carolyn Gillis (New England,
USA); Don Gorman (USA); Susan Wallace
(USA)
Shipping Address: Lit DistCo (Literary Dis-
tribution Collective), 100 Armstrong Ave,
Georgetown, ON L7G 5S4 *Toll Free Tel:* 800-
591-6250 *Toll Free Fax:* 800-591-6251
E-mail: orders@litdistco.ca
Membership(s): Association of Book Publishers
of British Columbia; Association of Canadian
Publishers; Literary Press Group

Royal Ontario Museum Publications
100 Queen's Park, Toronto, ON M5S 2C6
Tel: 416-586-5581 *Fax:* 416-586-5887
E-mail: info@rom.on.ca
Web Site: www.rom.on.ca
Key Personnel
Dept Head & Intl Rts Contact: Glen Ellis
Tel: 416-586-5582 *E-mail:* glene@rom.on.ca
Founded: 1975
Scholarly & general books on art, archaeology &
sciences.
Publishes in English, French.
ISBN Prefix(es): 0-88854
Number of titles published annually: 8 Print
Total Titles: 200 Print
U.S. Rep(s): University of Toronto Press (NY)
Warehouse: 5201 Dufferin St, Downsview, ON
M3H 5T8, Contact: Carol Trainor *Toll Free
Tel:* 800-565-9523
Distribution Center: University of Toronto Press,
5201 Dufferin St, Downsview, ON M3H 5T8

Guy Saint-Jean editeur Inc
3154 Blvd Industriel, Laval, PQ H7L 4P7
Tel: 450-663-1777 *Fax:* 450-663-6666
E-mail: saint-jean.editeur@qc.aira.com
Web Site: www.saint-jeanediteur.com
Key Personnel
Pres: Guy Saint-Jean
Publr: Nicole Saint-Jean
PR Mgr: Marie-Claire Saint-Jean
Rts: Jacques Frechette
Founded: 1981
Publishes in English, French.
ISBN Prefix(es): 2-920340; 2-89455
Number of titles published annually: 20 Print
Total Titles: 195 Print
Imprints: Green Frog Publishing
Foreign Office(s): Saint-Jean Editeur (France), 48
rue des Ponts, 78290 Croissy-sur-Seine, France,
Contact: Christian Richard *Tel:* (01) 39-76-99-
43 *Fax:* (01) 39-76-21-78 *E-mail:* gsj.editeur@
free.fr
U.S. Publishers Represented: CDS, New York,
NY, United States (US)
Foreign Rep(s): Int Press (Australia & New
Zealand); Christian Richard (Europe)
Foreign Rights: Elizabeth Brayne (Europe)
Membership(s): ANEL

Sara Jordan Publishing
Division of Jordan Music Productions Inc
Sta "M", Box 160, Toronto, ON M6S 4T3
Tel: 905-938-5050 *Toll Free Tel:* 800-567-7733
Fax: 905-938-9970 *Toll Free Fax:* 800-229-
3855
Web Site: www.sara-jordan.com
Founded: 1990
Publish educational resources.
Publishes in English, French.
ISBN Prefix(es): 1-895523; 1-894262
Number of titles published annually: 6 Print
Total Titles: 40 Print; 40 Audio
Membership(s): Association of Canadian Publish-
ers

Scholastic Canada Ltd
Subsidiary of Scholastic Inc

175 Hillmount Rd, Markham, ON L6C 1Z7
SAN: 115-5164
Tel: 905-887-7323 *Toll Free Tel:* 800-
268-3848 (Canada) *Fax:* 905-887-1131
Toll Free Fax: 800-387-4944; 866-346-1288
Web Site: www.scholastic.ca
Key Personnel
Co-Pres: Iole Lucchese *Fax:* 905-887-3643
E-mail: ilucchese@scholastic.ca
Dir, Publg: Diane Kerner *Fax:* 905-887-3643
E-mail: dkerner@scholastic.ca
Dir, Mktg: Nancy Pearson *Fax:* 905-887-3643
E-mail: npearson@scholastic.ca
Art Dir: Yuksel Hassan *Fax:* 905-887-3643
E-mail: yhassan@scholastic.ca
Dir, French Mktg & Publg: Chantale LaLonde
Fax: 905-887-3643 *E-mail:* clalonde@
scholastic.ca
Dir, Educ: Wendy Graham *Fax:* 905-887-3642
E-mail: wgraham@scholastic.ca
Dir, Book Fairs: Jill Briers *Fax:* 905-887-3643
E-mail: jbriers@scholastic.ca
Gen Mgr, Trade Div: Kathy Goncharenko
Fax: 905-887-3643 *E-mail:* kgoncharenko@
scholastic.ca
Mgr, Trade Mktg: Denise Anderson *Fax:* 905-
887-3643 *E-mail:* danderson@scholastic.ca
Mgr, Natl Trade Sales: Marla Krisko *Fax:* 905-
887-3643 *E-mail:* mkrisko@scholastic.ca
Intl Rts: Diane Vanderkooy *Fax:* 905-887-3643
E-mail: dvanderkooy@scholastic.ca
Founded: 1957
Children's & juvenile trade books, educational
materials.
Publishes in English, French.
ISBN Prefix(es): 0-590; 0-439; 0-7791; 1-55268
Total Titles: 880 Print
Imprints: The Chicken House; Children's Press;
Franklin Watts (US); Grolier; Klutz; North
Winds Press; Orchard; Les editions Scholas-
tic
Divisions: Scholastic Book Fairs Canada Inc
U.S. Publishers Represented: Scholastic Inc
U.S. Rep(s): Scholastic Inc

Seal Books
Imprint of Random House of Canada Ltd
One Toronto St, Suite 300, Toronto, ON M5C
2V6
SAN: 201-3975
Tel: 416-364-4449 *Toll Free Tel:* 888-523-9292
(order desk) *Fax:* 416-957-1587
Web Site: www.randomhouse.ca
Key Personnel
Chmn & CEO: John Neale *Tel:* 905-624-0672
Exec VP & Chief Admin Officer: Doug Foot
Tel: 905-624-0672
Exec VP & Publr: Maya Mavjee
VP & Dir, Rts & Contracts: Jennifer Shepherd
VP & Dir, Prodn: Janine Laporte
Busn Analyst: Ralph Burrows
Sr Man Ed: Christine Innes
Prodn Mgr: Carla Kean
Rts Coord: Gloria Goodman
Exec VP, COO & Dir, Sales & Mktg: Brad Mar-
tin *Tel:* 905-624-0672
VP & Dir, Sales: Brian Cassin *Tel:* 905-624-0672
Exec VP & Dir, Sales: Duncan Shields *Tel:* 905-
624-0672
VP & Dir, Online Sales & Mktg: Lisa Charters
Tel: 905-624-0672
VP, Dir of Mktg & Dir of Corp Communs:
Tracey Turriff
Dir of Mktg: Linda Scott *Tel:* 905-624-0672
Adv Dir: Mark Veldhuizen
VP & Dir, Media Rel: Scott Sellers
Publicity Mgr: Stephanie Gowan
Founded: 1977
No unsol mss; prefer queries in advance from po-
tential authors.
Publishes in English.
ISBN Prefix(es): 0-7704
Number of titles published annually: 18 Print

Branch Office(s)
2775 Matheson Blvd E, Mississauga, ON L4W
4P7
Orders to: Random House of Canada Limited
Membership(s): Canadian Booksellers Association; Canadian Library Association; Canadian Publishers' Council

Second Story Feminist Press
720 Bathurst St, Suite 301, Toronto, ON M5S
2R4
Tel: 416-537-7850 *Fax:* 416-537-0588
E-mail: info@secondstorypress.ca
Web Site: www.secondstorypress.on.ca
Key Personnel
Publr: Margie Wolfe
Edit Coord: Laura McCurdy
Promo & Mktg Coord: Corina Eberle
Founded: 1988
Paperback & cloth books for juveniles & young adults, adult fiction & nonfiction.
Publishes in English.
ISBN Prefix(es): 0-925005; 1-896764
Number of titles published annually: 14 Print
Total Titles: 108 Print
Imprints: Amanita
Distributed by University of Toronto Press
Distributor for Book Publishing Co
U.S. Rep(s): Orca Books (children's books)
Orders to: University of Toronto Press, 5201 Dufferin St, Downsview, ON M3H 5T8
Shipping Address: University of Toronto Press, 5201 Dufferin St, Downsview, ON M3H 5T8
Distribution Center: University of Toronto Press, 5201 Dufferin St, Downsview, ON M3H 5T8

Second Story Press, see Second Story Feminist Press

Self-Counsel Press Inc
1481 Charlotte Rd, North Vancouver, BC V7J
1H1
SAN: 115-0545
Tel: 604-986-3366 *Toll Free Tel:* 800-663-3007
Fax: 604-986-3947
E-mail: service@self-counsel.com
Web Site: www.self-counsel.com
Key Personnel
Pres & Foreign Rts & Mktg Coord: Diana Douglas *E-mail:* drdouglas@self-counsel.com
Man Ed & ISBN Contact: Richard Day
Publicist: Roger Kettyls
Founded: 1977
Legal, business & reference.
Publishes in English.
ISBN Prefix(es): 0-88908; 1-55180
Number of titles published annually: 15 Print
Total Titles: 251 Print; 17 CD-ROM
Imprints: Self-Counsel Series
Branch Office(s)
4 Bram Ct, Brampton, ON L6W 3R6
1704 N State St, Bellingham, WA 98225, United States *Tel:* 360-676-4530 *Toll Free Tel:* 877-877-6490 *Fax:* 360-676-4549
Membership(s): Association for Canadian Publishers in the US; Association for the Export of Canadian Books; Association of Book Publishers of British Columbia

Services Documentaires Multimedia Inc (SDM Inc)
5650 Rue D'Iberville, Bureau 620, Montreal, PQ
H2G 2B3
Mailing Address: 75 Portroyal E, Suite 300, Montreal, PQ H3L 3T1
Tel: 514-382-0895 *Fax:* 514-384-9139
E-mail: info@sdm.qc.ca
Web Site: www.sdm.qc.ca
Key Personnel
CEO: Denis Brunet
Asst Mkt Dir: Reine Bertrand Guerin *Tel:* 514-382-0895 ext 322

Founded: 1964
Producer/provider of documentary databases.
Publishes in French.
ISBN Prefix(es): 2-89059
Total Titles: 16 Print

§J Gordon Shillingford Publishing
RPO Corydon Ave, Winnipeg, MB R3M 3S3
Mailing Address: PO Box 86, Winnipeg, MB R3M 3S3
Tel: 204-779-6967 *Fax:* 204-779-6970
Web Site: www.jgshillingford.com
Key Personnel
Publr: Gordon Shillingford *E-mail:* jgshill@allstream.net
Founded: 1992
Primarily a literary publisher (drama & poetry), but also 3-4 nonfiction titles per year.
Publishes in English.
ISBN Prefix(es): 0-9689709; 0-920486; 1-896239; 0-9697261
Number of titles published annually: 15 Print; 1 Audio
Total Titles: 160 Print; 3 Audio
Distributor for Aivilo Publishing; Galli Publishing; Hybrid Publishing Co-op
Membership(s): Association of Canadian Publishers; Association of Manitoba Book Publishers; Literary Press Group

Shoreline
23 Sainte Anne, Ste Anne de Bellevue, PQ H9X
1L1
SAN: 116-9564
Tel: 514-457-5733 *Fax:* 514-457-5733
E-mail: shoreline@sympatico.ca
Web Site: www.shorelinepress.ca
Key Personnel
Ed: Judith Isherwood
Founded: 1991
Publishes in English, French.
ISBN Prefix(es): 0-9695180; 0-9698752; 1-896754
Number of titles published annually: 5 Print
Total Titles: 50 Print
Membership(s): Association of Canadian Publishers; Association of English Language Publishers of Quebec; Quebeq Writer's Federation

Simon & Pierre Publishing Co Ltd
Imprint of The Dundurn Group
8 Market St, 2nd fl, Toronto, ON M5E 1M6
Tel: 416-214-5544 *Toll Free Tel:* 800-565-9523 (orders: Canada & US) *Fax:* 416-214-5556
Toll Free Fax: 800-221-9985 (orders)
E-mail: info@dundurn.com
Web Site: www.dundurn.com
Key Personnel
Pres & Publr: J Kirk Howard *E-mail:* jkh@dundurn.com
Founded: 1972
Fiction & nonfiction, drama.
Publishes in English.
ISBN Prefix(es): 1-55002; 0-88924
Number of titles published annually: 6 Print
Total Titles: 133 Print
Distributed by Dundurn Press

Skysong Press
35 Peter St S, Orillia, ON L3V 5A8
E-mail: skysong@bconnex.net
Web Site: www.bconnex.net/~skysong/index.html
Key Personnel
Publr: Steve Stanton
Founded: 1988
Publishes in English.
ISBN Prefix(es): 0-9680502
Number of titles published annually: 3 Print
Total Titles: 35 Print
Membership(s): EPA

Smallwood Center for Newfoundland Studies
Memorial University of Newfoundland, St John's,
NF A1C 5S7
Tel: 709-737-7474 *Fax:* 709-737-7560
E-mail: iser@mun.ca
Web Site: www.mun.ca/smallwood
Key Personnel
Busn Mgr: Al Potter *Tel:* 709-737-8343
E-mail: apotter@mun.ca
Founded: 1982
Encyclopedias, scholarly publications.
Publishes in English.
ISBN Prefix(es): 0-919666; 0-9693422
Number of titles published annually: 3 Print
Total Titles: 95 Print
Imprints: Encyclopedia of Newfoundland & Labrador
Membership(s): Association of Canadian Publishers; Association of Canadian University Presses

Sogides Ltee
955 rue Amherst, Montreal, PQ H2L 3K4
Tel: 514-523-1182 *Toll Free Tel:* 800-361-4806
Fax: 514-597-0370
Web Site: www.sogides.com; www.edhomme.com
Key Personnel
Pres: Pierre Lesperance
Exec VP: Celine Massiscotte
Publr: Pierre Bourdon
Dir, Sales: Stephane Masquida
Publr for France: Huguette Laurent
Rts & Perms: Erwan Leseul *E-mail:* eleseul@sogides.com
Founded: 1967
Practical books, cookbooks, biographies, general interest books, popular psychology, art books, poetry, diaries, art calendars & stationery, novels, drama.
Publishes in French.
ISBN Prefix(es): 2-7619; 0-7760; 2-89026; 2-89194
Number of titles published annually: 150 Print
Total Titles: 2,000 Print
Imprints: Les Editions de l'Homme; Le Jour Editeur; Utilis
Subsidiaries: Le Groupe Ville-Marie Litterature; L'Hexagone; Messageries ADP; Quinze
Divisions: VLB Editeur
Branch Office(s)
Editions de l'Homme, Le Jour Editeur, Immeuble Paryseine, 3 Allee de la Seine, 94854 Ivry Cedex, France
Distributed by Distribution OLS-SA; Viverdi Universal Publishing
Distributor for Actif; Atlas; Berlitz Fixot; Chouette; Claire Vigne; Le Cri; De L'Homme; Du Rocher; Edimag; Editions Modus Vivendi; Fleuve Noir; Gault & Millau; Heritage; Hors Collection; JCL; Julliard; Robert Laffont; Langues pour tous; Albin Michel; Albin Michel Education; Albin Michel Jeunesse; Nathan; Nathan Education; Option Sante; Olivier Orban; Perrin; Plon; Pocket; La Presse; Presses Libres; Presses de la Cite (Poche); Presses de la Cite Litterature; Michel Quintin; Quinze; Rouge & Or; Seghers; Selection du Reader's Digest; Solar; Time-Life; Trapeze; Usborne; VLB; XYZ (Typo Seulement)
U.S. Publishers Represented: Reader's Digest; Time-Life Books
Warehouse: 1751 Richardson, Pointe St-Charles, Montreal, PQ H3K 1G6

Gordon Soules Book Publishers Ltd
1359 Ambleside Lane, West Vancouver, BC V7T
2Y9
SAN: 115-0987
Tel: 604-922-6588; 604-688-5466 *Fax:* 604-688-5442
E-mail: books@gordonsoules.com
Web Site: www.gordonsoules.com
Key Personnel
Pres: Gordon Soules

Founded: 1965
Publishers & distributors of high quality trade books.
Publishes in English.
ISBN Prefix(es): 0-919574; 1-894661
Number of titles published annually: 4 Print
Total Titles: 65 Print
Distributor for Aerie Publishing; AEW Services; Aldo Intrieri; Apple Communications; Arcadian Productions; The Ardent Angler Group; Artadvisory; John Baldwin; David Bates; Battle Street Books; Bilkin Enterprises Ltd; Blackbird Naturgraphics Inc; Blue Poppy Press; Christine Boehringer; Bradt Publications (England); British Columbia Waterfowl Society; Brian Burt; C-Van Productions; Children's Studio Books; Chrismar Mapping Services Inc; Community Arts Council of Vancouver; Crazyhorse Press; Cream Books; Creative Classics Publications Inc; Creative Solutions Inc; Crompton Books; Crossroads Press; Patty-Anne Cumpstone; Dewaal Media Productions; Dragon Fly Publications Inc; The Drawing-Room Graphics Services Ltd; Duo Consultants; Eaglet Publishing; Environment Canada; Federation of Mountain Clubs of BC; Fforbez Publications; Fjelltur Books; The Flag Shop; Fore Shore Publishing; Francis; Giesbrecht & Associates; Goodwin; Gordon Soules Book Publishers Ltd; Gregson Communications Ltd; Grove Cottage Press; Lesley Hasselfield; Heartwood Books; Hillpointe Publishing; Hillside Publishing; The Hip List Inc; Hockering Press; Impressions in Print; Innovative Publishing; Intelligent Patient Guide; ITMB Publishing; G M Johnson & Associates Inc; Joy Dee Marketing; Just Muffins Ltd; Kachina Press; KMB Publishing; The Laurier Institution; Liahona Press; Maps Unlimited; Marine Tapestry Publications; Meridian House; Mighton House Publishing & Distribution; Moody's Lookout Press; Morning Dawn Publishing Co; Mussio Ventures Ltd; N C Publishing; Naikoon Marine; New Century Books; Norman Hacking Publishers; North Shore Family Services Society; Okanagan Mountain Biking; Omega Press; Outdoor Recreation Council of BC; The Pacific Salmon Commission; Panorama Publications; Paper Works; Paradox Publishing; Carmen Patrick; Physicians for the Prevention of Nuclear War; Quadra Island Child Care Society; Qualy Publishing; Rainbow's End Company; Raser Enterprises; Raxas Books; Rychkun Recreation Publications; Sunporch Publishing; Syntax Books; Paul Tawrell; Tenisall Inc; Treeline Publishing; Tricouni Press; Vancouver Natural History Society; Varsity Outdoor Club; Walbourne Enterprises; Waterwheel Press; West Indies Trading Co; Sandra Wong Publishing; Bruce Woodsworth; World Wide Books & Maps; Yan's Variety; Yellow Hat Press
U.S. Publishers Represented: Berndtson & Berndtson; Lilac Press; Living Overseas Books; Orthopedic Physical Therapy Products; San Juan Enterprises Inc; US Games Systems Inc; The Vegetarian Resource Group

Sound & Vision
359 Riverdale Ave, Toronto, ON M4J 1A4
Tel: 416-465-2828 *Fax:* 416-465-0755
Web Site: www.soundandvision.com
Key Personnel
Publr: Geoffrey Savage *E-mail:* geoff@soundandvision.com
Founded: 1983
Music genres of all types with a humorous slant. We also publish quotation books.
Publishes in English.
ISBN Prefix(es): 0-920151
Number of titles published annually: 3 Print; 12 Online
Total Titles: 26 Print; 12 Online; 12 E-Book
Online services available through netLibrary.

Distributed by Firefly Books
Orders to: Firefly Books, 3680 Victoria Park Ave, Willowdale, ON M2H 3K1 *Tel:* 416-499-8412 *Toll Free Tel:* 800-387-5085 *Toll Free Fax:* 800-565-6034 *E-mail:* service@fireflybooks.com *Web Site:* www.fireflybooks.com
Returns: Firefly Books/Frontier, c/o Cache, Tonawanda Commerce Ctr, 2221 Kenmore Ave, Tonawanda, NY 14207, United States

Sports Books Publisher Inc
278 Robert St, Toronto, ON M5S 2K8
Tel: 416-922-0860 *Fax:* 416-966-9022
E-mail: sbp@sportsbookpub.com
Web Site: www.sportsbookspub.com
Key Personnel
Pres: Peter Klavora *E-mail:* peter.klavora@utoronto.ca
Exec Dir: Tania Klavora
Founded: 1983
Activity books, sports books & videos; subjects include physical education & kinesiology.
Publishes in English.
ISBN Prefix(es): 0-920905
Number of titles published annually: 3 Print
Total Titles: 42 Print
Foreign Office(s): Cankarjeva c, 15b, Bled, Slovenia

Statistics Canada
Subsidiary of Canadian Government
R H Coats Bldg, Lobby, Holland Ave, Ottawa, ON K1A 0T6
Tel: 613-951-8116 *Toll Free Tel:* 800-700-1033 (Canada & US); 800-267-6677 (orders) *Fax:* 613-951-1584 (local); 613-951-7277 (orders); 613-951-0581 (requests) *Toll Free Fax:* 800-889-9734; 877-287-4369 (orders)
E-mail: order@statcan.ca; infostats@statcan.ca
Web Site: www.statcan.ca
Key Personnel
Circ Mgr, CSSS: Ken McSheffrey
Founded: 1919
Federal government's principal data collection agency in Canada. Collects, analyzes & publishes statistical information on Canada's population, labor force, economy, education, housing, transportation & social cultural life. One of Canada's largest publishers, producing over 300 books a year.
Publishes in English, French.
ISBN Prefix(es): 0-660
Number of titles published annually: 60 Print
Total Titles: 300 Print; 1,013 CD-ROM; 1,764 Online
Returns: R H Coats Bldg, 9th fl, Section K, Ottawa, ON K1A 0T6

Sumach Press
1415 Bathurst St, Suite 302, Toronto, ON M5R 3H5
Tel: 416-531-6250 *Fax:* 416-531-3892
E-mail: sumachpress@on.aibn.com
Web Site: www.sumachpress.com
Key Personnel
Fin & Mktg: Lois Pike
Man Ed: Rhea Tregebov
Design & Prodn: Elizabeth Martin
Founded: 2000
Feminist book publisher.
Number of titles published annually: 10 Print
Total Titles: 78 Print
Editorial Office(s): Sumach Press, 1415 Bathurst St, Suite 202, Toronto, ON M5R 3H8
Sales Office(s): Orca Book Publishers, PO Box 458, Custer, WA 98240-0468, United States
University of Toronto Press, 5201 Dufferin St, North York, ON M3H 5T8

Distributed by Orca Book Publishers (young adult titles in US); University of Toronto Press (all titles in Canada, adult titles in US)
Foreign Rights: Andreas Brunner Literary Agency (German lang rts)
Billing Address: Orca Book Publishers, PO Box 458, Custer, WA 98240-0468, United States; University of Toronto Press, 5201 Dufferin St, North York, ON M3H 5T8
Orders to: Orca Book Publishers, PO Box 458, Custer, WA 98240-0468, United States; University of Toronto Press, 5201 Dufferin St, North York, ON M3H 5T8
Returns: Orca Book Publishers, PO Box 458, Custer, WA 98240-0468, United States; University of Toronto Press, 5201 Dufferin St, North York, ON M3H 5T8
Shipping Address: Orca Book Publishers, PO Box 458, Custer, WA 98240-0468, United States; University of Toronto Press, 5201 Dufferin St, North York, ON M3H 5T8
Warehouse: Orca Book Publishers, PO Box 458, Custer, WA 98240-0468, United States
University of Toronto Press, 5201 Dufferin St, North York, ON M3H 5T8
Distribution Center: Orca Book Publishers, PO Box 458, Custer, WA 98240-0468, United States
University of Toronto Press, 5201 Dufferin St, North York, ON M3H 5T8
Membership(s): Association of Canadian Publishers; Ontario Book Publishers Organization

Synaxis Press
37323 Hawkins Pickle Rd, Dewdney, BC V0M 1H0
Tel: 604-826-9336 *Fax:* 604-820-9758
E-mail: synaxis@new-ostrog.org
Web Site: www.new-ostrog.org/synaxis
Key Personnel
Illus: Vasili Novakshonoff
Ed (retired Archbishop): Lazar Puhalo
Founded: 1972
Theology for the orthodox church & children's books.
Publishes in English.
ISBN Prefix(es): 0-919672
Number of titles published annually: 40 Print
Total Titles: 32 Print
Distributed by Light & Life Publishing Co

Tamos Books Inc
Division of Hyperion Press Ltd
300 Wales Ave, Winnipeg, MB R2M 2S9
Tel: 204-256-9204 *Fax:* 204-255-7845
E-mail: tamos@mts.net
Web Site: www.escape.ca/~tamos
Key Personnel
Pres: Marvis Tutiah
Mgr: Suzanne Fraser
Founded: 1991
Detailed instructions & how-to books.
ISBN Prefix(es): 1-895569
Number of titles published annually: 10 Print
Total Titles: 10 Print
Distributed by Canadian Manda Group
Warehouse: One Begin Ave, Winnipeg, MB R2J 3X5

TCP Press
Formerly The Communication Project
Imprint of The Communication Project
9 Lobraico Lane, Whitchurch-Stouffville, ON L4A 7X5
Tel: 905-640-8914 *Toll Free Tel:* 800-772-7765 *Fax:* 905-640-2922
E-mail: tcp@tcpnow.com
Web Site: www.tcppress.com
Key Personnel
Dir, Publg: Brian Puppa
Founded: 1984

Trade & educational books for both children &
adults.
Publishes in English, French.
ISBN Prefix(es): 1-896232
Number of titles published annually: 5 Print; 1
Audio
Total Titles: 21 Print

Theytus Books Ltd
Subsidiary of Okanagan Indian Educational Re-
sources Society
Lot 45, Green Mountain Rd, RR No 2, Site 50,
Comp 8, Penticton, BC V2A 6J7
SAN: 115-1517
Tel: 250-493-7181 *Fax:* 250-493-5302
E-mail: theytusbooks@vip.net
Web Site: www.theytusbooks.ca
Key Personnel
Publg Mgr: Anita Large
Off Opers Mgr: Leanne Flett Kruger
Founded: 1980
Native Indian history, culture, politics & educa-
tion & literature; Aboriginal literature.
Publishes in English.
ISBN Prefix(es): 0-919441
Number of titles published annually: 7 Print
Total Titles: 65 Print
U.S. Rep(s): Orca Books
Advertising Agency: Sandhill Marketing, 1270 El-
lis Suite, Ste 99, Kelowna, BC, Contact: Nancy
Wise *Tel:* 250-763-1406 *Fax:* 250-763-4051
E-mail: sandhill@wkpowerlink.com
Membership(s): Canadian Booksellers Associa-
tion; Literary Press Group

Thistledown Press Ltd
633 Main St, Saskatoon, SK S7H 0J8
SAN: 115-1061
Tel: 306-244-1722 *Fax:* 306-244-1762
E-mail: marketing@thistledown.sk.ca
Web Site: www.thistledown.sk.ca
Key Personnel
VP: Patrick O'Rourke
Publg Coord & Intl Rts: Jackie Forrie
Mktg Dir: Kathy Painchaud
Founded: 1975
Poetry, fiction & nonfiction by Canadian authors;
Irish poetry; fiction for young adults.
Publishes in English.
ISBN Prefix(es): 0-920066; 0-920633; 1-895449
Number of titles published annually: 14 Print
Total Titles: 160 Print
U.S. Rep(s): Amazon.Com; Baker & Taylor; Lit
Distco
Distribution Center: Lit Distco

Thompson Educational Publishing Inc
6 Ripley Ave, Suite 200, Toronto, ON M6S 3N9
Tel: 416-766-2763 (admin & orders) *Fax:* 416-
766-0398 (admin & orders)
E-mail: publisher@thompsonbooks.com
Web Site: www.thompsonbooks.com
Key Personnel
Pres: Keith Thompson
Founded: 1989
High school, college & university textbooks.
Publishes in English.
ISBN Prefix(es): 1-55077; 0-921332
Number of titles published annually: 5 Print
Total Titles: 90 Print
Branch Office(s)
General Distribution Services, 4500 Witmer In-
dustrial Estates, PMB 128, Niagara Falls, NY
14305-1386, United States *Toll Free Tel:* 800-
805-1083 *Toll Free Fax:* 800-841-6207
Distribution Center: General Distribution Ser-
vices, 325 Humber College Blvd, Toronto,
ON M9W 7C3 *Toll Free Tel:* 800 805-1083
Fax: 416-213-1917 *Toll Free Fax:* 800-841-
6207
Membership(s): Association of Canadian Publish-
ers; Ontario Book Publishers' Association

Editions Pierre Tisseyre
5757 Cypihot, St-Laurent, PQ H4S 1R3
Tel: 514-334-2690 *Toll Free Tel:* 800-263-3678
Fax: 514-334-8395 *Toll Free Fax:* 800-643-
4720 (Canada only)
E-mail: ed.tisseyre@erpi.com *Cable:* ROMAN
CERCLE
Key Personnel
Pres: Charles Tisseyre
Dir & ISBN Contact: Angel Delanois
Founded: 1947
French Canadian literature; adult & children's
books.
Publishes in French.
ISBN Prefix(es): 2-7613; 2-89051
Number of titles published annually: 30 Print
Distributed by Diffusion du Livre Mirabel

Tormont/Brimar Publication Inc
338 St Antoine E, 3rd fl, Montreal, PQ H2Y 1A3
Tel: 514-954-1441 *Fax:* 514-954-1443
E-mail: info@tormont.ca
Key Personnel
Pres: Guy Briere
VP, Mktg: Patrick Hudson
Sales: Wendy Sarrazin
Founded: 1984
Full-color, practical how-to books, cookbooks,
children's books & dictionaries, play & learn
books, children's educational, games books.
Publishes in English, French.
ISBN Prefix(es): 2-921171; 2-920845
Total Titles: 200 Print
Imprints: Brimar; Ovale; Tormont
Subsidiaries: Pacific Publications; Reliure BBB;
Tormont; Tormont Europe
Divisions: Product & Technology International
Distributed by Dami Editore; Five Mile Press;
Penguin Group (USA) Inc; Random House
U.S. Rep(s): Pete Mauer; Gordon Walsh
Shipping Address: 200 Christine, Joseph de
Beauce, PQ G0S 2V0

Townson Publishing Co Ltd
Affiliate of Lyric Productions Inc
PO Box 1404, Bentall Centre, Vancouver, BC
V6C 2P7
Tel: 604-263-0014 *Fax:* 604-263-0014
E-mail: info@townson.ca
Web Site: www.townson.ca
Key Personnel
Publr: Donald Townson
Ed: Jackson House
Founded: 1960
Reference, technical & trade books, literature in
translation.
Publishes in English, French.
Number of titles published annually: 6 Print
Total Titles: 12 Print
Imprints: ABZ; Arctic; General Publishing; Polar;
Townson
Subsidiaries: Associated Merchandisers Inc
(USA)
Branch Office(s)
Box 909, Blaine, WA 98231-0909, United States

Tradewind Books
1809 Maritime Mews, Vancouver, BC V6H 3W7
Tel: 604-662-4405 *Fax:* 604-730-0154
E-mail: tradewindbooks@eudoramail.com
Web Site: www.tradewindbooks.com
Key Personnel
Publr: Michael Katz
Founded: 1994
Children's books & young adults novels.
Publishes in English.
ISBN Prefix(es): 1-896580
Number of titles published annually: 5 Print
Total Titles: 22 Print
Branch Office(s)
46 Crosby St, Northampton, MA 01060-1804,

United States *Tel:* 413-582-7054 *Toll Free*
Tel: 800-238-LINK *Fax:* 413-582-7057
Foreign Office(s): Turnaround, Unit 3,
Olympia Trading Estate, Coburg Rd, Wood
Green, London N22 6TZ, United Kingdom
Tel: (020) 8829-3000 *Fax:* (020) 8881-5088
E-mail: orders@turnaround-uk.com *Web*
Site: www.turnaround-uk.com
U.S. Rep(s): Interlink Publishers Group
Foreign Rep(s): Hushion House (Canada);
Michael Reynolds Associates (Canada)
Distribution Center: Georgetown Terminal Ware-
houses Ltd, 34 Armstrong Ave, Georgetown,
ON L7G 4R9 *Tel:* 905-873-1994 *Toll Free*
Tel: 866-485-5556 *Fax:* 905-873-6170 *Toll Free*
Fax: 866-485-6665 *E-mail:* orders@gtwcanada.
com *Web Site:* www.gtwcanada.com
John Reed Book Distribution, Winbourne Estate,
Unit 4-F, 9 Winbourne Rd, Brookvale, NSW
2100, Australia *Tel:* (02) 9939 3041 *Fax:* (02)
9453 4545 *E-mail:* johnmreed@johnreedbooks.
com
Membership(s): Association of Book Publishers
of British Columbia; Association of Canadian
Publishers

Tralco Lingo Fun
1030 Upper James St, Suite 101, Hamilton, ON
L9C 6X6
Tel: 905-575-5717 *Toll Free Tel:* 888-487-2526
Fax: 905-575-1783 *Toll Free Fax:* 866-487-
2527
E-mail: sales@tralco.com
Web Site: www.tralco.com
Key Personnel
Owner & Pres: Karen Traynor *E-mail:* karen@
tralco.com
Founded: 1984
Publisher & distributor of second language educa-
tional materials.
Publishes in English, French.
ISBN Prefix(es): 0-921376
Number of titles published annually: 100 Print
Total Titles: 100 Print
Distributor for Gessler; Langenscheidt; J Weston
Walch
U.S. Publishers Represented: J Weston Walch
Foreign Rep(s): Langenscheidt

TSAR Publications
PO Box 6996, Sta A, Toronto, ON M5W 1X7
Tel: 416-483-7191 *Fax:* 416-486-0706
E-mail: treview@total.net
Web Site: www.tsarbooks.com
Key Personnel
Publr & Intl Rts: Ms Nurjehan Aziz
E-mail: naziz@tsarbooks.com
Founded: 1981
Canadian literature, multicultural & international
literature.
Publishes in English.
ISBN Prefix(es): 0-920661; 1-894770
Number of titles published annually: 8 Print
Total Titles: 95 Print
Imprints: TSAR
U.S. Rep(s): Small Press Distribution Inc, 1341
Seventh St, Berkeley, CA 94710, United States
Distribution Center: Small Press Distribution Inc,
1341 Seventh St, Berkeley, CA 94710, United
States *Tel:* 510-524-1668
LitDistCo, 100 Armstrong Ave, Georgetown, ON
L7G 5S4 *Tel:* 905-877-4411 *Fax:* 905-877-
4410 *E-mail:* orders@lpg.ca
Membership(s): Literary Press Group

Tundra Books
481 University Ave, Suite 900, Toronto, ON M5G
2E9
SAN: 115-5415
Tel: 416-598-4786 *Fax:* 416-598-0247
E-mail: tundra@mcclelland.com
Web Site: www.tundrabooks.com

Publicist: Alison Morgan *Tel:* 416-598-4786 ext 268 *E-mail:* amorgan@mcclelland.com
Publr: Kathy Lowinger
Foreign Rts & Export Sales: Catherine Mitchell
Founded: 1967
Children's books.
Publishes in English, French.
ISBN Prefix(es): 0-88776
Number of titles published annually: 40 Print
Total Titles: 250 Print
Branch Office(s)
Tundra Books of Northern New York, PO Box 1030, Plattsburgh, NY 12901, United States
U.S. Publishers Represented: Tundra Books of Northern New York
U.S. Rep(s): Consolino & Watson; Jack Eichkorn & Associates Inc; Ryen, Re & Associates; Southern Territory Associates Inc; Stuart Associates
Returns: Random House Inc, 2002 Bethell Rd, Finksburg, MD 21048, United States
Warehouse: Random House Inc, Distribution Center, 400 Hahn Rd, Westminster, MD 21157, United States
Membership(s): ABA; ALA; Association of Booksellers for Children; International Board on Books for Young People

Turnstone Press
607-100 Arthur St, Winnipeg, MB R3B 1H3
SAN: 115-1096
Tel: 204-947-1555 *Toll Free Tel:* 800-982-6472 *Fax:* 204-942-1555
E-mail: editor@turnstonepress.com; mktg@turnstonepress.com
Web Site: www.turnstonepress.com
Key Personnel
Man Ed & Intl Rts: Todd Besant
Ed, Acqs & Prodn: Sharon Caseburg *E-mail:* production@turnstonepress.mb.ca
Mgr, Mktg & Publicity: Kelly Stifora *Tel:* 204-947-1556
Founded: 1976
Literary press including fiction, nonfiction, poetry, literary criticism, biography, travel fiction & adventure all with a strong Canadian focus.
Publishes in English.
ISBN Prefix(es): 0-88801
Number of titles published annually: 10 Print
Total Titles: 162 Print
Imprints: Ravenstone
Distribution Center: Lit Dist Co, 100 Armstrong Ave, Georgetown, ON L7G 5S4 *Tel:* 905-877-4411 (USA) *Toll Free Tel:* 800-591-6250 (Canada) *Fax:* 905-877-4410 (USA) *Toll Free Fax:* 800-591-6251 (Canada) *E-mail:* orders@lpg.ca

UBC Press, see University of British Columbia Press

UCCB Press, see University College of Cape Breton Press Inc

Ulysses Travel Guides
4176 Saint Denis, Montreal, PQ H2W 2M5
Tel: 514-843-9447 *Fax:* 514-843-9448
E-mail: info@ulysses.ca
Web Site: www.ulyssesguides.com
Key Personnel
Pres: Daniel Desjardins *E-mail:* daniel@ulysses.ca
VP, Sales & Mktg: Claude Morneau *E-mail:* claude@ulysses.ca
Founded: 1980
Travel books.
Publishes in English.
ISBN Prefix(es): 2-921444; 2-89464
Number of titles published annually: 40 Print
Total Titles: 175 Print
Imprints: Editions Ulysses

Distributor for A A Publications; Canadian Geographic; Dakota; Editions Syvain Harvey; Fivedit; Footprint Handbooks; Hunter Publishing; ITMB Maps; Odyssey Publications; PassPorter Travel Press; Rother Walking Guides; Trans Canada Trail Foundation; Vacation Works Publications
U.S. Rep(s): Hunter Publishing

University College of Cape Breton Press Inc
1250 Grand Lake Rd, Sydney, NS B1P 6L2
Mailing Address: PO Box 5300, Sydney, NS B1P 6L2
Tel: 902-563-1604; 902-563-1421 *Fax:* 902-563-1177
E-mail: uucb_press@uccb.ca
Web Site: www.uccbpress.ca
Key Personnel
Ed-in-Chief: Mike R Hunter *E-mail:* mike_hunter@uccb.ca
Founded: 1975
Nonfiction regional books; fiction, short stories, poetry, community economic development.
Publishes in English.
ISBN Prefix(es): 0-920336; 1-897009
Number of titles published annually: 4 Print
Total Titles: 101 Print
Membership(s): APMA; Association of Canadian Publishers

University Extension Press
Division of University of Saskatchewan
117 Science Place, Saskatoon, SK S7N 5C8
Tel: 306-966-5558 *Fax:* 306-966-5567
E-mail: uep.books@usask.ca
Web Site: www.uep.usask.ca
Key Personnel
Man Ed: Perry Millar *E-mail:* perry.millar@usask.ca
Founded: 1993
Educational titles.
Publishes in English.
ISBN Prefix(es): 0-88880
Number of titles published annually: 3 Print
Total Titles: 24 Print; 3 CD-ROM
Distributed by Lone Pine Press
Distributor for Canadian Phytopathological Society; Centre for the Study of Co-Operatives University of Saskatchewan; University of Alberta Faculty of Extension
Membership(s): Saskatchewan Publishers Group

University of Alberta Press
Ring House 2, Edmonton, AB T6G 2E1
SAN: 115-110X
Tel: 780-492-3662 *Fax:* 780-492-0719
E-mail: uap@ualberta.ca
Web Site: www.uap.ualberta.ca
Key Personnel
Ed: Mary Mahoney-Robson
Dir: Linda Cameron
Acq Ed: Michael Luski *Tel:* 780-492-4945 *E-mail:* michael.luski@ualberta.com
Sales & Mktg Mgr: Cathie Crooks *Tel:* 780-492-5820 *E-mail:* ccrooks@ualberta.ca
Founded: 1969
Since 1969, the University of Alberta Press has published award-winning scholarly works & fine books for general audiences. The Press publishes books that explore important scholarly, cultural, literary, historical & political aspects of Canada & has also gained a reputation for publishing excellent reference books. Our program is particularly strong in the areas of biography, history, language, literature, natural history & books of regional interest.
Publishes in English.
ISBN Prefix(es): 0-88864
Number of titles published annually: 25 Print
Total Titles: 150 Print; 2 Audio
Imprints: Pica Pica Press
U.S. Rep(s): Michigan State University Press

Foreign Rep(s): Gazelle Book Services (Europe & UK)
Orders to: Georgetown Terminal Warehouses, 34 Armstrong Ave, Georgetown, ON L7G 4R9 *Tel:* 905-873-9781 *Toll Free Tel:* 877-864-8477 *Fax:* 905-873-6170 *Toll Free Fax:* 877-864-4272 *E-mail:* orders@gtwcanada.com *Web Site:* gtwcanada.com
Returns: Georgetown Terminal Warehouses, 34 Armstrong Ave, Georgetown, ON L7G 4R9 *Tel:* 905-873-9781 *Toll Free Tel:* 877-864-8477 *Fax:* 905-873-6170 *Toll Free Fax:* 877-864-4272 *E-mail:* orders@gtwcanada.com *Web Site:* gtwcanada.com
Shipping Address: Georgetown Terminal Warehouses, 34 Armstrong Ave, Georgetown, ON L7G 4R9 *Tel:* 905-873-9781 *Toll Free Tel:* 877-864-8477 *Fax:* 905-873-6170 *Toll Free Fax:* 877-864-4272 *E-mail:* orders@gtwcanada.com *Web Site:* gtwcanada.com
Warehouse: Georgetown Terminal Warehouses, 34 Armstrong Ave, Georgetown, ON L7G 4R9 *Tel:* 905-873-9781 *Toll Free Tel:* 877-864-8477 *Fax:* 905-873-6170 *Toll Free Fax:* 877-864-4272 *E-mail:* orders@gtwcanada.com *Web Site:* gtwcanada.com
Distribution Center: Georgetown Terminal Warehouses, 34 Armstrong Ave, Georgetown, ON L7G 4R9 *Tel:* 905-873-9781 *Toll Free Tel:* 877-864-8477 *Fax:* 905-873-6170 *Toll Free Fax:* 877-864-4272 *E-mail:* orders@gtwcanada.com *Web Site:* gtwcanada.com
Membership(s): Association of American University Presses; Association of Canadian Publishers; Association of Canadian University Presses; Book Publishers Association of Alberta

University of British Columbia Press
2029 West Mall, Vancouver, BC V6T 1Z2
SAN: 115-1118
Tel: 604-822-5959 *Toll Free Tel:* 877-377-9378 *Fax:* 604-822-6083 *Toll Free Fax:* 800-668-0821
E-mail: info@ubcpress.ca
Web Site: www.ubcpress.ca
Key Personnel
Dir: Peter Milroy
Sr Ed & Assoc Dir, Edit: Jean Wilson *Tel:* 604-822-6376 *E-mail:* wilson@ubcpress.ca
Asst Dir, Fin: Elizabeth Hu *Tel:* 604-822-8938 *E-mail:* hu@ubcpress.ca
Mgr, Adv & Promo: Andrea Kwan *Tel:* 416-538-8043 *E-mail:* kwan@ubcpress.ca
Assoc Dir, Mktg & Prodn: George Maddison *Tel:* 604-822-2053 *E-mail:* maddison@ubcpress.ca
Mgr, Acad Mktg: Liz Whitton *Tel:* 604-822-8226 *E-mail:* whitton@ubcpress.ca
Mgr, Inventory: Shari Martin *Tel:* 604-822-1221
Mgr, Awards & Exhibits: Kerri Kilmartin *Tel:* 604-822-8244
Asst Dir, Prodn & Edit Servs: Holly Kollar *Tel:* 604-822-4545
Founded: 1971
Academic & scholarly publications; film studies, law & society, military history, Northern studies, sexuality & political science.
Publishes in English.
ISBN Prefix(es): 0-7748
Number of titles published annually: 60 Print
Total Titles: 900 Print; 2 CD-ROM; 1 E-Book
Branch Office(s)
587 Markham St, 2nd fl, Toronto, ON M6G 2L7 *Fax:* 416-535-9677
Distributed by University of Washington Press (US)
Distributor for Canadian Forest Service (worldwide); Canadian Museum of Civilization; Canadian Wildlife Service (worldwide); Cavendish Publishing (UK); Edinboro University Press; Environmental Training Center; Hong Kong University Press; Jessica Kingsley

Publishers (UK); Manchester University Press; Oregon State University Press; Pluto Press; Royal BC Museum (worldwide); University of Arizona Press; University of Washington Press; Washington State University Press; Western Geographical Press (worldwide)
U.S. Publishers Represented: Brookings Institution; Michigan State University Press; Oregon State University Press; University of Arizona Press; University of Michigan; University of Washington Press; University Press of New England; Washington State University Press
U.S. Rep(s): University of Washington Press (trade)
Foreign Rep(s): Asia Publishers Services (Hong Kong, Singapore, Taiwan); East-West Export (Asia, Australia & New Zealand, Japan); Eurospan (Africa, UK, Europe, Middle East)
Shipping Address: UNI Press, 34 Armstrong Ave, Georgetown, ON L7G 4R9 *Tel:* 905-873-9781 *Toll Free Tel:* 877-864-8477 *Fax:* 905-873-6170 *Toll Free Fax:* 877-864-4272 *E-mail:* orders@gtwcanada.com

University of Calgary Press
2500 University Dr NW, Calgary, AB T2N 1N4
Tel: 403-220-7578 *Fax:* 403-282-0085
E-mail: whildebr@ucalgary.ca
Web Site: www.uofcpress.com
Key Personnel
Acqs Ed & Dir, Press & Intl Rts: Walter Hildebrandt *Tel:* 403-220-3511 *E-mail:* whildebr@ucalgary.ca
Journals Mgr: Judy Powell *Tel:* 403-220-3512 *E-mail:* powell@ucalgary.ca
Mktg Mgr: Barb Murray *Tel:* 403-220-5284 *E-mail:* bmurray@ucalgary.ca
Prodn Ed: John King *Tel:* 403-220-4208 *E-mail:* jking@ucalgary.ca
Founded: 1981
Scholarly press specializing in books about the "heartland of the continent," with series that include western history, parks & Latin America; northern studies, cultural studies, Holocaust, post-colonial, Latin American studies.
Publishes in English, French.
ISBN Prefix(es): 0-919813; 1-895176; 1-55238
Number of titles published annually: 25 Print; 2 CD-ROM
Total Titles: 246 Print; 5 CD-ROM
Online services available through netLibrary, Questia.
Sales Office(s): Canada uniPRESSES, c/o Georgetown Terminal Warehouses, 34 Armstrong Ave, Georgetown, ON L7G 4R9 (World exc UK & Europe)
Foreign Office(s): Gazelle Book Services, White Cross Mills, High Town, Lancaster LA1 4XS, United Kingdom *Tel:* (020) 1524 68765 *Fax:* (020) 1524 63232
Distributor for Michigan State University Press
U.S. Rep(s): Michigan State University Press, 25 Manly Miles Bldg, 1405 S Harrison Rd, East Lansing, MI 48823-5202, United States *Tel:* 517-355-9543 *Fax:* 517-432-2611 *Toll Free Fax:* 800-678-2120 *E-mail:* msupress@msu.edu
Foreign Rep(s): Gazelle (UK, Europe)
Foreign Rights: Roli Books (New Delhi)
Billing Address: Canada uniPRESSES, c/o Georgetown Terminal Warehouses, 34 Armstrong Ave, Georgetown, ON L7G 4R9 (World exc UK & Europe)
Orders to: Canada uniPRESSES, c/o Georgetown Terminal Warehouses, 34 Armstrong Ave, Georgetown, ON L7G 4R9 (World exc UK & Europe) *Toll Free Tel:* 877-864-8477 *Toll Free Fax:* 877-864-4272 *E-mail:* orders@gtwcanada.com
Returns: Canada uniPRESSES, c/o Georgetown Terminal Warehouses, 34 Armstrong Ave, Georgetown, ON L7G 4R9 (World exc UK & Europe) *Toll Free Tel:* 877-864-8477 *Toll Free Fax:* 877-864-4272

Distribution Center: Canada uniPRESSES, c/o Georgetown Terminal Warehouses, 34 Armstrong Ave, Georgetown, ON L7G 4R9 (World exc UK & Europe) *Tel:* 905-873-2750 *Toll Free Tel:* 877-864-8477 *Toll Free Fax:* 877-864-4272 *E-mail:* orders@gtwcanada.com
Membership(s): Association for Canadian Publishers in the US; Association of Canadian Publishers; Book Publishers Association of Alberta

University of Manitoba Press
St Johns College, Winnipeg, MB R3T 2N2
SAN: 115-5474
Tel: 204-474-9495 *Fax:* 204-474-7566
Web Site: www.umanitoba.ca/uofmpress
Key Personnel
Dir: David Carr *E-mail:* carr@ccumanitoba.ca
Man Ed: Pat Sanders
Ed Asst: Sharon Caseburg
Founded: 1967
Scholarly & general titles in humanities & social sciences; western Canadian history & native studies.
Publishes in English.
ISBN Prefix(es): 0-88755
Number of titles published annually: 6 Print
Total Titles: 60 Print; 1 Audio
Branch Office(s)
2250 Military Rd, Tonawanada, NY 14150, United States *Tel:* 716-693-2768
Distributed by University of Toronto Press
Shipping Address: University of Toronto Press, 5201 Dufferin St, Downsview, ON M3H 5T8 *Tel:* 416-667-7791 *Toll Free Tel:* 800-565-9523 *Fax:* 416-667-7832

University of Ottawa Press/Les Presses de l'Universite d'Ottawa
Affiliate of University of Ottawa
542 King Edward Ave, Ottawa, ON K1N 6N5
Tel: 613-562-5246 *Fax:* 613-562-5247
E-mail: press@uottawa.ca
Web Site: www.uopress.uottawa.ca
Key Personnel
Dir: Ruth Bradley
Founded: 1936
Scholarly & professional books; text & trade books.
Publishes in English, French.
ISBN Prefix(es): 0-7766; 2-7603
Number of titles published annually: 21 Print
Total Titles: 500 Print
Foreign Rep(s): FIDES (North America); University of Toronto Press (English, North America)
Distribution Center: Fides, 165 Rue Deslauriers, Saint Laurent, PQ H4N 2S4 (French titles) *Tel:* 514-745-4290 *Fax:* 514-745-4299 *E-mail:* editions@fides.qc.ca
University of Toronto Press - UTP, 5201 Dufferin St, North York, ON M3M 5T8 (English titles) *Tel:* 416-667-7791 *Toll Free Tel:* 800-565-9523 *Fax:* 416-667-7832 *Toll Free Fax:* 800-221-9985 *E-mail:* utpbooks@utpress.utoronto.ca *Web Site:* www.utpress.utoronto.ca
Membership(s): ANEL; Association of Canadian University Presses

University of Toronto Press Inc
10 St Mary St, Suite 700, Toronto, ON M4Y 2W8
SAN: 115-1134
Tel: 416-978-2239 (admin) *Fax:* 416-978-4738 (admin)
Web Site: www.utpress.utoronto.ca *Cable:* TORPRESS
Key Personnel
Pres & Publr: John Yates
Sr VP, Admin: Kathryn Bennett
Sr VP, Scholarly Publg: Bill Harnum
VP, Info Systems: Hamish Cameron

VP, Journals & Creative Servs: Anne Marie Corrigan
Founded: 1901
Scholarly books, scholarly journals.
Publishes in English.
ISBN Prefix(es): 0-8020
Number of titles published annually: 140 Print; 2 CD-ROM
Total Titles: 1,600 Print
Branch Office(s)
2250 Military Rd, Tonawanda, NY 14150, United States *Tel:* 716-693-2768 *Fax:* 716-692-7479
Distributor for Anvil Press; Applause Books; Ashlar/Pearson; Aspasia Books; Baltray Books; Between the Lines; Black Rose Books; The British Library; Canadian Museum of Nature; CAW/TCA Canada; Central European University Press KFT; Codasat Canada Ltd; Cormorant Books; Cornucopia Books; Dance Collection Danse; Diamond Mind Enterprises; Dundurn Group; Faculty of Applied Science & Engineering; G7 Report Inc; Goose Lane Editions; J Gordon Shillingford Publishing Inc; Great Plains Publications Ltd; Guernica Editions; Guidance Centre; HELP...We've Got Kids; ISSI; Kapable Kidz Inc; Edgar Kent; Kids Can Press; Lassonde Institute; Lobster Press Ltd; Mage Publishers; McDonald & Woodward Books; McGilligan Books; Ministry of Transportation, Ontario; La Montagne Secrete; Multicultural History Society of Canada; Multilingual Matters; National Museum of Science & Technology; The New Press; NYC Nonprofits Project; OISE Press; Penn State University Press; Pippin Publishing Corp; Porcupine's Quill; Quill Driver Books/Word Dancer Press Inc; RDR Books; RREES INC; Royal Ontario Museum; Saqi Books; Second Story Press; Elysa Schwartzman; Seraphim Editions; Sister Vision Press; Subway Books Ltd; Sumach Press; Talonbooks; Theytus Books; Thompson Educational Publishing; Twin Guinep Lt; University of Manitoba Press; University of Ottawa Press; University of Toronto Centre for Public Management
U.S. Rep(s): Luis Borella (North West coast); Savant Books (Canada & US college representative); Roger Sauls, Book Traveler (South East); Ben Schrager (North East); Trim Associates (Mid-West)
Foreign Rep(s): Ethan Atkin (Central & South America, Pakistan); James Bennett Pty Ltd (Australia & New Zealand); Cassidy & Associates Inc (China & Hong Kong, Taiwan); Justin Kok (Malaysia & Singapore); Danuta Pawlowska (Europe); Segment Book Distributors (South Asia); United Publishers Service (Japan); University Press Group (Australia & New Zealand, Canada); Wolfgang Wingerter (Europe); Yale University Press (UK)
Orders to: 5201 Dufferin, Toronto, ON M3H 5T8
Returns: 5201 Dufferin, Toronto, ON M3H 5T8
Warehouse: 2250 Military Rd, Tonawanda, NY 14150, United States
5201 Dufferin, Toronto, ON M3H 5T8
Distribution Center: 5201 Dufferin, Toronto, ON M3H 5T8

Vanwell Publishing Ltd
One Northrup Cres, St Catharines, ON L2R 7S2
Tel: 905-937-3100 *Toll Free Tel:* 800-661-6136 *Fax:* 905-937-1760
E-mail: sales@vanwell.com
Key Personnel
Pres: Ben Kooter *Tel:* 905-937-3100 ext 829 *E-mail:* ben.kooter@vanwell.com
VP, Opers: Diane Kooter *Tel:* 905-937-3100 ext 824 *E-mail:* diane.kooter@vanwell.com
Intl Rts Contact: Simon Kooter *Tel:* 905-937-3100 ext 800 *E-mail:* simon.kooter@vanwell.com
Sales Dir: Wendy Horhota *Tel:* 905-937-3100 ext 827 *E-mail:* wendy.horhota@vanwell.com
Founded: 1983

Publish books for children & books related to military history.
Publishes in English, French.
ISBN Prefix(es): 0-920277; 1-55068; 1-55125
Number of titles published annually: 10 Print
Total Titles: 120 Print
Branch Office(s)
Box 1207, Lewiston, NY 14092, United States
Editorial Office(s): PO Box 2131, St Catharines, ON L2R 7S2
Distributed by Casemate Publishers (USA); Helion & Co (UK)
U.S. Publishers Represented: Aberjona Books; Aerofax Publications; After the Battle Magazine; After the Battle Publications; Air Research Publications; AirData Publications; Airlife Publishing; Airplan Flight Equipment; Ian Allan Ltd; American Flight Manuals; American Society for Quality Control (ASQC); Arcadia Publishing; Art Global Editions; August House; Birlinn Ltd; Bonechi Books; Brassey's Inc (USA); Brassey's Publishers (UK); Bright Star Books; Caltrop Press; Canadian Institute of Strategic Studies Canadian Peacekeeping Press; Canav Books (selected titles); Candy Cane Press; Capital Books; Casemate Distribution; Cerberus Publishing; Chatham House; Cherry-tree Books; Chivers Audio Books; Classic Publications; Classic Warship Publications; Compendium Publishing; Allan T Condle; Connect Trading; Conway Maritime Press; CPG Books; Crecy Publishing; Crowood Books; Daco Publishing; D Day Publishing; De Krijger; P G De Lotz; John Donald; Earthbound Books; Emperor's Press; Europa Militaria; 4 Plus Publications; Flight Recorder; Front Street Press; Geddes & Grosset; GoodAll Paperbacks; Greenhill Books; Greenwood Guides; Grub Street; Guideposts; Happy Cat; Happy Landings; Heimdal Editions; Helion & Co; Charles Herissey Editions; Hikoki Publications; Histoire & Collections; Historic Aviation; Historic Indexes; Howell Press; Idea Shelf Publishing; Ideals Publishing; Independent Books; Indo Editions; Johnson Books; Laurier Centre for Military Strategic Disarmament Studies; Lewis International Inc; Little Hills Press; Lothian Books; Marhav Editions; MBI Publications; Midland Publishing; Monday Morning Books; Moonlight Publishing; National Archives; National Army Museum Publications; National Maritime Museum Publications; Naval Institute Press; North-South Books; OPC; Osprey Books; PC Publishing; Pen & Sword Books; Plymouth Press; Polygon Press; Priory Publications; Putnam Aeronautical Books; Red Kite; Reynolds & Hearn Books; Riebel-Roque; Roli Books; Roundup Press; Ryton Publications; RZM Imports; Salamander Books (selected titles); Scoval Books; Service Publications; Spellmount Publishers; Star Bright Books; Sunflower University Press; Teacher Created Material; Tempus Books; Ken Trotman Ltd; Uplands Books; Walka Books; Wheels & Tracks Magazine; Williamson Publishing; Wine Appreciation Guild; Wings & Wheels Publications; WR Press
Billing Address: PO Box 2131, St Catharines, ON L2R 7S2
Warehouse: PO Box 2131, St Catharines, ON L2R 7S2
Membership(s): Canadian Booksellers Association

Vehicle Press
125 Place du Parc Sta, Montreal, PQ H2X 4A3
SAN: 115-1150
Mailing Address: PO Box 125, Montreal, PQ H2X 4A3
Tel: 514-844-6073 *Fax:* 514-844-7543
E-mail: vp@vehiculepress.com
Web Site: www.vehiculepress.com
Key Personnel
Publr & Gen Ed: Simon Dardick; Nancy Marrelli

Man Ed: Vicki Marcok
Poetry Ed, Signal Editions: Carmine Starnino
Mktg & Promos: Scott McRae
Founded: 1973
Paperback trade; fiction, jazz, biography, literature, poetry. English-French bilingual editions.
Publishes in English, French.
ISBN Prefix(es): 0-919890; 1-55065
Number of titles published annually: 14 Print
Total Titles: 230 Print
Imprints: Esplanade Books (fiction); Signal Editions (poetry)
U.S. Rep(s): IPG (Independent Publishers Group)
Returns: LitDistCo, 100 Armstrong Ave, Georgetown, ON L7G 5S4 *Tel:* 905-877-4411 *Toll Free Tel:* 800-591-6250 *Fax:* 905-877-4410 *Toll Free Fax:* 800-591-6251
Shipping Address: LitDistCo, 100 Armstrong Ave, Georgetown, ON L7G 5S4 *Tel:* 905-877-4411 *Toll Free Tel:* 800-591-6250 *Fax:* 905-877-4410 *Toll Free Fax:* 800-591-6251
Distribution Center: LitDistCo, 100 Armstrong Ave, Georgetown, ON L7G 5S4 *Tel:* 905-877-4411 *Toll Free Tel:* 800-591-6250 *Fax:* 905-877-4410 *Toll Free Fax:* 800-591-6251
Membership(s): Association of Canadian Publishers; Literary Press Group

VLB Editeur Inc
Division of Le Groupe Ville-Marie Litterature
955 Amherst St, Montreal, PQ H2L 3K4
Tel: 514-523-1182 *Fax:* 514-282-7530
E-mail: vml@sogides.com
Web Site: www.edvlb.com
Key Personnel
Pres: Pierre Lesperance
Ed, VP, Publg & Literary Dir for Poetry: Pierre Graveline
Literary Dir for Fiction: Jean-Yves Soucy
Literary Dir for Essays: Robert Laliberte
Asst Ed: Josee Lewis
Founded: 1976
Publishes in French.
ISBN Prefix(es): 2-89005
Number of titles published annually: 30 Print
Total Titles: 600 Print
Distribution Center: Les Messageries ADP, 1751 Richardson, Montreal, PQ H3K 1G6

Wall & Emerson Inc
6 O'Connor Dr, Toronto, ON M4K 2K1
SAN: 116-0486
Tel: 416-467-8685 *Toll Free Tel:* 877-409-4601 *Fax:* 416-352-5368
E-mail: wall@wallbooks.com
Web Site: www.wallbooks.com
Key Personnel
Publr: Byron E Wall
VP & Ed: Martha Wall
Founded: 1987
Publishers of college, university texts & reference works for North America.
Publishes in English.
ISBN Prefix(es): 0-921332; 1-895131
Number of titles published annually: 3 Print
Total Titles: 50 Print
Imprints: Wall & Emerson
Branch Office(s)
1376 Arrow Sheath Dr, Dayton, OH 45449, United States

Warwick Publishing Inc
Division of Warwick Communications Inc
161 Frederick St, Toronto, ON M5A 4P3
Tel: 416-596-1555 *Fax:* 416-596-1520
Web Site: www.warwickgp.com
Key Personnel
Pres: James Williamson *E-mail:* jim@warwickgp.com
Publr: Nick Pitt *E-mail:* nick@warwickgp.com
Founded: 1981

Sports, business, lifestyle cooking, nonfiction, art & true crime.
Publishes in English.
ISBN Prefix(es): 1-895629; 1-894020
Number of titles published annually: 15 Print
Total Titles: 150 Print
U.S. Rep(s): Continental Sales Inc, 213 W Main St, Barrington, IL 60010, United States *Toll Free Tel:* 888-327-8537 *Toll Free Fax:* 800-582-9724
Shipping Address: Canadian Book Network, 34 Armstrong Ave, Georgetown, ON L7G 4R9 *Toll Free Tel:* 866-444-4930 *Toll Free Fax:* 866-444-4931 *Web Site:* www.canadianbooknetwork.com

Waterloo Music Co Ltd
3 Regina St N, Waterloo, ON N2J 4A5
Tel: 519-886-4990 *Toll Free Tel:* 800-563-9683 (Canada & US) *Fax:* 519-886-4999
E-mail: info@waterloomusic.com
Web Site: www.waterloomusic.com
Key Personnel
Pres & Owner: Andy Coffin
Educ Mgr: Tammy Stinson
Founded: 1922
Music theory, piano performance & school educational.
Publishes in English.
ISBN Prefix(es): 0-88909
Number of titles published annually: 3 Print
Total Titles: 30 Print
Distributed by Aukland Music; Guitar Solo; Mel Bay Inc; Music Exchange; Preissler; SEMI

Weigl Educational Publishers Ltd
6325 Tenth St SE, Calgary, AB T2H 2Z9
SAN: 115-1312
Tel: 403-233-7747 *Toll Free Tel:* 800-668-0766 *Fax:* 403-233-7769
E-mail: info@weigl.com
Web Site: www.weigl.com
Key Personnel
Publr: Linda Weigl
Founded: 1979
School library resources & textbooks for grades K-12 in English & French. Emphasis on: Canadian history, social studies & public affairs; science; multiculturalism; career/vocational/life management; distance education; books & guides for teachers.
Publishes in English, French.
ISBN Prefix(es): 0-919879; 1-896990; 1-55388
Number of titles published annually: 40 Print
Total Titles: 200 Print
Distributed by The Creative Co (United States); The Independent Publishers Group (IPG) (United States); Saunders Book Co (Canada); Smart Apple Media (United States)
Distributor for Able Publishing; Ampersand; Children's Book Press; CIS Educational; Gabriel Dumont; Milliken; Pacific View Press; Stanley Wilson Publishing; Y'inka Dene Institute
U.S. Publishers Represented: Able Publishing; Ampersand Press; Childrens Book Press; Educational Insights; Milliken; Pacific View Press; Vandameer Press
U.S. Rep(s): Dominie Press

White Knight Publications
Division of Bill Belfontaine Ltd
One Benvenuto Place, Suite 103, Toronto, ON M4V 2L1
Tel: 416-925-6458 *Fax:* 416-925-4165
E-mail: whitekn@istar.ca
Web Site: www.whiteknightpub.com
Founded: 2002
Publishes in English.
ISBN Prefix(es): 0-9497430; 0-9494816
Number of titles published annually: 8 Print
Total Titles: 15 Print
Foreign Rep(s): Hushion House (USA)
Orders to: Hushion House Publishing

Membership(s): Association of Canadian Publishers; Book Publishers Professional Association; CAA; CBA; Ontario Book Publishers Organization

Whitecap Books Ltd
351 Lynn Ave, North Vancouver, BC V7J 2C4
Tel: 604-980-9852 *Toll Free Tel:* 888-870-3442 ext 239 & 241 (cust serv) *Fax:* 604-980-8197 *Toll Free Fax:* 888-661-6630 (orders only)
E-mail: whitecap@whitecap.ca
Web Site: www.whitecap.ca
Key Personnel
Pres: Michael E Burch
VP: Nick Rundall
Publr: Robert McCullough
Dist Mgr: Barbara Faurot
Founded: 1977
Trade books, photography, cookery, regional, gardening, outdoor guide books, natural history, juvenile nonfiction & illustrated children's books, juvenile fiction.
Publishes in English.
ISBN Prefix(es): 1-55110; 1-55285
Number of titles published annually: 85 Print
Total Titles: 480 Print
Branch Office(s)
2 170 Shields Ct, Markham, ON L3R 9T5
Tel: 905-470-8484 *Fax:* 905-470-6787
E-mail: whitecap@globalserve.net
Distributor for Australian Women's Weekly
U.S. Rep(s): Graphic Arts

John Wiley & Sons Canada Ltd
Subsidiary of John Wiley & Sons Inc (USA)
6045 Fremont Blvd, Mississauga, ON L5R 4J3
Tel: 416-236-4433 *Toll Free Tel:* 800-467-4797 (orders only) *Fax:* 416-236-4447; 416-236-8743 (cust serv) *Toll Free Fax:* 800-565-6802 (orders)
E-mail: canada@wiley.com
Web Site: www.wiley.ca
Key Personnel
COO: Bill Zerter
Founded: 1968
Textbooks for colleges & universities; trade, professional & reference.
Publishes in English.
ISBN Prefix(es): 0-470; 0-471
Number of titles published annually: 40 Print
Total Titles: 300 Print
Distributor for John Wiley & Sons Inc

Wilfrid Laurier University Press
Subsidiary of Wilfrid Laurier University
75 University Ave W, Waterloo, ON N2L 3C5
SAN: 115-1525
Tel: 519-884-0710 (ext 6124) *Fax:* 519-725-1399
E-mail: press@wlu.ca
Web Site: www.press.wlu.ca
Key Personnel
Dir & Intl Rts: Brian Henderson *E-mail:* brian@press.wlu.ca
Mktg Mgr & Lib Sales Dir: Penelope Grows *E-mail:* pgrows@press.wlu.ca
Mktg Coord: Leslie Macredie *E-mail:* leslie@press.wlu.ca
Founded: 1974
Publishes in English.
ISBN Prefix(es): 0-88920
Number of titles published annually: 24 Print
Total Titles: 204 Print; 30 E-Book
Distributor for Cinematheque/Toronto International Film International (Canada only)
U.S. Rep(s): Martin Grandfield, United States; Hill/Martin Associates; Roger Sauls; Ben

Schrager, 735 Pelham Pkwy N, Bronx, NY 10467, United States
Foreign Rep(s): Gazelle Books
Distribution Center: Gazelle Books
Membership(s): American Association of University Presses; Association of Canadian Publishers; Association of Canadian University Presses

Wood Lake Books Inc
9025 Jim Bailey Rd, Kelowna, BC V4V 1R2
Tel: 250-766-2778 *Toll Free Tel:* 800-663-2775 (orders) *Fax:* 250-766-2736 *Toll Free Fax:* 888-841-9991 (orders)
E-mail: info@woodlake.com
Web Site: www.woodlakebooks.com
Key Personnel
Publr & Pres: Bonnie Schlosser
Assoc Publr: Lois Huey-Heck
Mktg, Promos & Lib Sales Dir: Karen Kranabetter
Ed: Mike Schwartzentruber
Opers Mgr & HR: Lynne Chilton
Mktg Promos, Northstone Publg: Cassandra Redding
Founded: 1982
Books, church curriculum & periodicals.
Publishes in English.
ISBN Prefix(es): 1-55145; 0-919599; 0-929032
Number of titles published annually: 5 Print
Total Titles: 117 Print
Distributed by Anglican Book Center; Canterbury Press; Logos; Mediacom; Presbyterian Church of Canada; Resource Publications; United Church Publishing House
Distributor for Geneva Press; Northstone; The Pilgrim Press; The United Church Press; Westminster John Knox Press
U.S. Publishers Represented: Geneva Press; Pilgrim Press; Westminster John Knox Press
U.S. Rep(s): Logos Productions; Words Distributing Co, Oakland, CA, United States
See separate listing for:
Northstone Publishing

Worldwide Library
Division of Harlequin Enterprises Ltd
225 Duncan Mill Rd, Don Mills, ON M3B 3K9
Tel: 416-445-5860 *Fax:* 416-445-8655; 416-445-8736
Web Site: www.eharlequin.com
Key Personnel
Exec VP, Global Publg & Strategy: Loriana Sacilotto
VP, Author & Asset Devt: Isabel Swift
Dir, Global Single Title Ed: Dianne Moggy
Edit Dir, Global Series: Randall Toye *E-mail:* randall_toye@harlequin.com
Exec Ed: Feroze Mohammed
Intl Rts: Jan Grammick
Founded: 1982
Mass market fiction.
Publishes in English.
ISBN Prefix(es): 0-373
Number of titles published annually: 72 Print
Imprints: Gold Eagle Books; Worldwide Mystery
Foreign Rights: Booklink (Europe)
Warehouse: 3010 Walden Ave, Depew, NY 14043, United States

XYZ Editeur
1781 rue Saint-Hubert, Montreal, PQ H2L 3Z1
Tel: 514-525-2170 *Fax:* 514-525-7537
Key Personnel
Pres: Gaetan Levesque *Tel:* 514-525-2170 ext 26
Ed-in-Chief: Andre Vanasse *Tel:* 514-525-2170 ext 25
Founded: 1985

Novels, short stories & essays on literature.
Publishes in French.
ISBN Prefix(es): 2-89261
Number of titles published annually: 40 Print
Total Titles: 30 Print
Distribution Center: Diffusion Dimedia, 539 blvd Le Beau Zille, Saint-Laurent, PQ H4N 1S2

XYZ Publishing
1781 Saint Hubert St, Montreal, PQ H2L 3Z1
Tel: 514-252-2170 *Fax:* 514-525-7537
E-mail: info@xyzedit.qc.ca
Web Site: www.xyzedit.qc.ca
Key Personnel
Pres: Gaetan Levesque
Edit Dir, English: Rhonda Bailey
Edit Dir, French: Andre Vanasse
ISBN Prefix(es): 0-9683601; 0-9688166; 1-894852
Billing Address: Fitzhenry & Whiteside, 195 Allstate Pky, Markham, ON L3R 4T8
Orders to: Fitzhenry & Whiteside, 195 Allstate Pky, Markham, ON L3R 4T8
Returns: Fitzhenry & Whiteside, 195 Allstate Pky, Markham, ON L3R 4T8
Distribution Center: Fitzhenry & Whiteside, 195 Allstate Pky, Markham, ON L3R 4T8
Membership(s): Association of Canadian Publishers; Literary Press Group

York Press Ltd
152 Boardwalk Dr, Toronto, ON M4L 3X4
Tel: 416-690-3788 *Fax:* 416-690-3797
E-mail: yorkpress@sympatico.ca
Web Site: www3.sympatico.ca/yorkpress
Key Personnel
Man Ed: Dr S Elkhadem
Founded: 1975
Scholarly studies in world literature: criticism, biography, translation & creative writing of an experimental nature.
Publishes in English.
ISBN Prefix(es): 0-919966; 1-896761
Number of titles published annually: 10 Print
Total Titles: 100 Print

§Zumaya Publications
Imprint of eXtasy Books
403-366 Howard Ave, Burnaby, BC V5B 4Y2
Mailing Address: PO Box 44062, Burnaby, BC V5B 4Y2
Tel: 604-299-8417
E-mail: editorial@zumayapublications.com
Web Site: www.zumayapublications.com
Key Personnel
Pres: Gerda Haveman *E-mail:* t_haveman@zumayapublications.com
VP: Diana Kemp-Jones *E-mail:* zumayapr@aol.com
Exec Ed (Austin, TX): Elizabeth K Burton *E-mail:* eburton@zumayapublications.com
Founded: 2001
Trade paperback & e-book formats offering full-length works of fiction.
Publishes in English.
ISBN Prefix(es): 1-894896; 1-894942
Number of titles published annually: 48 Print; 48 E-Book
Total Titles: 69 Print; 69 E-Book
Editorial Office(s): 1105 Nueces St, Suite 3, Austin, TX 78701-2129, United States
Tel: 512-477-6259 *E-mail:* editorial@zumayapublications.com
Orders to: BookSurge, 6341 Dorchester Rd, Suite 16, Charleston, SC 29418, United States *Toll Free Tel:* 866-308-7493 ext 20 *E-mail:* sales@digitz.net
Membership(s): Publishers Marketing Association

Small Presses

Listed here, in alphabetical order, are U.S. & Canadian publishers who were not eligible to be listed in the sections covering U.S. Publishers or Canadian Publishers. Many of these publishers are new or offer distinctive titles they wish to make known to the users of *Literary Market Place*. Entries in this section are paid listings.

Publishers interested in participating in this section in future editions of LMP are invited to contact **Chuck Fiorello, Advertising Sales** by e-mail at cfiorello@infotoday.com, by phone at 212-689-2855, by fax at 270-738-4305 or by mail at Information Today, Inc., 630 Central Avenue, New Providence, NJ 07974.

A & M Books
PO Box 283, Rehoboth Beach, DE 19971
Toll Free Tel: 800-489-7662
Key Personnel
Ed: Anyda Marchant
Founded: 1995
We publish books for a lesbian-feminist reader-ship but in fact have a wide audience. We are prepared to provide some financial assistance to authors whose work meets our criteria of feminist outlook & literary quality.
Titles include *Amantha*; *As I Lay Frying*; *Nina in the Wilderness*; *O Mistress Mine*
ISBN Prefix(es): 0-9646648
Membership(s): Publishers Marketing Association; Small Press Center

ACROPOLIS BOOKS, INC.

Acropolis Books Inc
8601 Dunwoody Place, Suite 303, Atlanta, GA 30350
Tel: 770-643-1118 *Toll Free Tel:* 800-773-9923
Fax: 770-643-1170
E-mail: acropolisbooks@mindspring.com
Web Site: www.acropolisbooks.com
Key Personnel
CEO: Michael R Krupp
VP, Sales & Opers: Christine Lindsey
Founded: 1958
Acropolis Books: your source for classical & contemporary works on mysticism & the spiritual life. For almost five decades, Acropolis Books has been a respected publisher of nonfiction books. In 1995, Acropolis reintroduced out-of-print classical mystical literature & began publishing works of the 20th Century mystic, Joel S. Goldsmith, whose teachings have helped hundreds of thousands of people around the world grasp the eternal principles of spiritual living. The knowledge of higher consciousness embodied in his inspired writings, gives readers the understanding & confidence they need to build a fulfilling & rewarding life.
Please bookmark our web site (www.acropolisbooks.com). For those exploring their own path to higher consciousness, we feel the pages of our web site offer you a life-changing resource - you are sure to find books here that are not available anywhere else. Thank you for stopping by. If you can see or think of ways we can better serve you, please let us know.
Titles include *God Formed Us For His Glory*; *The Journey Back to The Father's House*; *The Only Freedom*; *Showing Forth the Presence of God*
ISBN Prefix(es): 1-889051

Imprints: Acropolis Books; I Level
Distributed by Amazon.com; Baker & Taylor; Barnes & Noble; Borders; DeVorss; Ingram Book Group; New Leaf Distributing Co

Aliform Publishing
117 Warwick St SE, Minneapolis, MN 55414
Tel: 612-379-7639 *Fax:* 612-379-7639
E-mail: information@aliformgroup.com
Web Site: www.aliformgroup.com
Key Personnel
Dir: Jay Miskowiec *E-mail:* editor@aliformgroup.com
Graphic Designer: Carolyn Fox *E-mail:* foxcm@parknicollet.com
Founded: 2001
We specialize in Latin American & world literature in translation. We also distribute books for Mexican publisher Praxis & Argentine publishers Interzona & Adriana Hidalgo Editor.
Titles include *Jail*; *Mariana*; *My World Is Not of This Kingdom*
ISBN Prefix(es): 0-9707652
Distributed by Baker & Taylor; Brodart; The Distributors
Membership(s): ABA; Publishers Marketing Association

American Fantasy Press
Imprint of Garcia Publishing Services
919 Tappan St, Woodstock, IL 60098
Tel: 815-338-5512 *Fax:* 815-338-5512
E-mail: garpubserv@aol.com
Web Site: www.american-fantasy.com
Key Personnel
Owner: Robert T Garcia
Founded: 1991
Small press of contemporary fantasy, science fiction & horror, specializing in illustrated editions & art books.
Titles include *A Walking Tour of the Shambles*; *The Broecker Sampler*
ISBN Prefix(es): 0-9610352
Distributed by Diamond
Membership(s): Chicago Book Clinic

American Literary Press/Noble House
Subsidiary of American Literary Press Inc
8019 Belair Rd, Suite 10, Baltimore, MD 21236
Tel: 410-882-7700 *Fax:* 410-882-7703
E-mail: amerlit@americanliterarypress.com
Web Site: www.americanliterarypress.com
Key Personnel
Man Ed: Alan C Reese
Dir, Publg: Julia M Cuccarese
Pubns Mgr: Donna B Wessel
Founded: 1991
Complete in-house publishing services, including copy-editing, proofreading, typesetting, text design, illustrating, cover design, copyright service, supervising production, procuring ISBN, securing barcode, storage, distribution, advertising & promotional packaging - national & international levels. New authors welcome, all literary types considered.
Titles include *Greek Generations: A Medley of Ethnic Recipes, Folklore, and Village Tradi-*

tions; *Growing Camellias in Cold Climates*; *Pelican Games*; *The Road to Debt Freedom*; *Still the Target*
ISBN Prefix(es): 1-56167
Distributed by Baker & Taylor; Ingram; Quality Books

Amrita Foundation Inc
PO Box 190978, Dallas, TX 75219-0978
Tel: 214-522-7533 *Fax:* 214-522-6184
E-mail: prisi@amrita.com
Web Site: www.amrita.com
Key Personnel
Pres: Priscilla Alden Walker
Founded: 1976
Teachings & publications on the Kriyayoga of Paramhansa (Swami) Yogananda, Swami Dhirananda (aka Dr Basu Kumar Bagchi), Sri Nerode & the Kriyayoga of Lahiri Mahashay thru Shibendu Lahiri.
Titles include *Dhiranandaji's A Resume of Patanjali*; *Divine Perception*; *Divine Power and The Master in You*; *Glimpses of Light*; *How to Pray to Have Your Prayers Answered*; *Light-Star Correspondence Courses of Raja Yoga*; *Philosophic Insight*; *Praecepta Book*; *Praecepta Lessons*; *The Second Coming of Christ (vols 1, 2 & 3)*; *Think Like a God*
ISBN Prefix(es): 0-937134
Distributed by Amazon.com; Baker & Taylor; Barnes & Noble; Borders; New Leaf Distribution Co

Anti-Aging Press
4185 Pamona Ave, Miami, FL 33133
Mailing Address: PO Box 141489, Coral Gables, FL 33114
Tel: 305-661-2802; 305-662-3928
Toll Free Tel: 800-SO-YOUNG *Fax:* 305-661-4123
Key Personnel
Pres: Julia Busch *E-mail:* julia2@gate.net
Founded: 1992
Committed to anti-aging on every level - mental, physical, emotional & spiritual. Publish books, cassettes, special reports & the newsletter, *So Young* on holistic health & rejuvenation techniques, plus illustrated gift books. New age concepts are released under Kosmic Kurrents Imprint. Jewelry Sideline is released under the registered trademark Julia.
Julia Busch is the editor of the *So Young* newsletter & a contributing editor to Wednesday on the Web, Arizona Networking News & The New Mexico Light.
For your free Anti-Aging Infopac, contact Julia Busch by e-mail or phone.

Titles include *Facelift Naturally*; *My Secret Life with An Angel*; *Positively Young!*; *Power Color!*; *Powerful Prayer Secrets!*; *Treat Your Face Like A Salad!*; *Youth & Skin Secrets Revealed*
ISBN Prefix(es): 0-9632907; 1-886369
Distributed by New Leaf; Baker & Taylor; Brodart; Midwest Library Service
Foreign Rights: Gaia Media (Switzerland); Dieter Hagenbach

Barnard Co
2402 Third St, Suite 206, Santa Monica, CA 90405
Tel: 310-314-7727
E-mail: seyahllib@aol.com
Key Personnel
Pres: William Smith
Founded: 2004
Publishes fiction & nonfiction.

Blue Book Publications Inc.

Blue Book Publications Inc
8009 34 Ave S, Suite 175, Minneapolis, MN 55425
Tel: 952-854-5229 *Toll Free Tel:* 800-877-4867 *Fax:* 952-853-1486
E-mail: bluebook@bluebookinc.com
Web Site: www.bluebookinc.com
Key Personnel
Author & Publr: S P Fjestad
Exec Asst Ed: Cassandra J Faulkner
Assoc Ed: John Allen
Art Dir: Clint Schmidt
Opers Mgr: Beth Marthaler
CFO: Tom Stock
Founded: 1989
Publishes Blue Books & CD-ROMs on firearms, airguns, black powder arms, guitars, amplifiers & pool cues. Most titles also available for e-commerce download on web site.
Titles include *Blue Book of Acoustic Guitars*; *Blue Book of Airguns*; *Blue Book of Electric Guitars*; *Blue Book of Guitar Amplifiers*; *Blue Book of Guitars CD-ROM*; *Blue Book of Gun Values*; *Blue Book of Modern Black Powder Arms*; *Blue Book of Pool Cues*; *Colt Blackpowder Reproductions & Replicas*; *The Nethercutt Collection - The Cars of San Sylmar*; *Parker Gun Identification & Serialization*
ISBN Prefix(es): 0-9625943; 1-886768
Distributed by Baker & Taylor; Ingram

Blue Raven Press
Division of Blue Diamond Enterprises
219 SE Main St, Suite 506, Minneapolis, MN 55414
Tel: 612-331-8039 *Fax:* 612-331-8115
Web Site: www.blueravenpress.com
Key Personnel
Publr: Barbara J Gislason
E-mail: barbarajgislason@blueravenpress.com
Founded: 2002

Blue Raven Press publishes adult nonfiction & fiction about "other animals." Blue Raven Press books must express ideas & tell stories powerful enough to change people's views about animals, without overt sentimentality. All of our writers communicate effectively & compellingly about animals. Our nonfiction authors may be formally trained in animal subjects &/or may write from life experience. Our fiction authors enable readers to suspend disbelief through compelling characterizations, skillfully revealing what lies beneath the surface & competent word building. Our first two books will be *The Raven Zone*, John Rezmerski & *New Animal Stories*, David Brendan Hopes.
ISBN Prefix(es): 0-9743446
Membership(s): Midwest Independent Publishers Association; Minnesota Book Publishers Roundtable; Minnesota Intellectual Property Lawyers Association; Minnesota State Bar Association; Publishers Marketing Association

Books by W John Koch Publishing
11666-72 Ave, Edmonton, AB T6G 0C1, Canada
Tel: 780-436-0581 *Fax:* 780-430-1672
E-mail: wjohnkoch@wjkochpublishing.com
Web Site: www.wjkochpublishing.com
Key Personnel
Proprietor: W John Koch
Founded: 2002
Recently created small press specializing in 19/20th century biographies under its own imprint; also offers similar type of literature under other imprints.
Titles include *Daisy Princess of Pless: A Discovery*; *No Escape: My Young Years Under Hitler's Shadow*
ISBN Prefix(es): 0-9731579
Distributed by Baker & Taylor (US & Canada); Gardner's Books (UK)

Doug Butler Enterprises Inc
PO Box 1390, LaPorte, CO 80535
Tel: 970-221-0516 *Toll Free Tel:* 800-728-3826 (press 1) *Fax:* 970-482-8621
Key Personnel
Pres: Karl D Butler, Jr
Publr: Doug Butler
VP: Marsha Butler
Founded: 1974
Publish farrier science & horse foot care books, videos & other educational materials.
Titles include *Farrier Science: Study Guide & Workbook*; *Horse Foot Care*; *The Principles of Horseshoeing II*; *The Principles of Horseshoeing 3*; *Shoeing In Your Right Mind*; *Six-Figure Shoeing*
ISBN Prefix(es): 0-916992

Caughman Associates
Affiliate of Infinity Publishing
1094 New DeHaven St, Suite 100, West Conshohocken, PA 19428-2713

Mailing Address: PO Box 92, Gradyville, PA 19039
Tel: 610-558-3734 *Toll Free Tel:* 877-BUY BOOK *Fax:* 610-558-5001; 610-941-9999
Key Personnel
Owner: Joyce Caughman Morris
E-mail: jcmorris96@comcast.net
Promo Dir: Carol Dunn *E-mail:* carold@olg.com
Founded: 2003
Author owned outlet for fiction. Owner Joyce Caughman is also the author of nonfiction title *Real Estate Prospecting* published by Dearborn Publishing, Chicago.
Titles include *The End of Arrogance*
ISBN Prefix(es): 0-7414
Distributed by Amazon.com; Baker & Taylor; Dearborn Publishing; Infinity Publishing
Membership(s): Publishers Marketing Association

Definition Press
141 Greene St, New York, NY 10012
SAN: 201-310X
Tel: 212-777-4490 *Fax:* 212-777-4426
E-mail: mc@definitionpress.org
Web Site: www.definitionpress.org
Key Personnel
Ed-in-Chief: Ellen Reiss
Assoc Ed: Dorothy Koppelman; Margot Carpenter
Cust Serv Mgr: Nancy Huntting
Founded: 1955
Publisher of books about Aesthetic Realism, the education founded in 1941 by the American poet & philosopher Eli Siegel; includes ethics, art, education, poetry, economics, criticism, children, the self.
Titles include *Aesthetic Realism: We Have Been There - Six Artists on the Siegel Theory of Opposites*; *Children's Guide to Parents & Other Matters*; *Hail, American Development (poems)*; *Hot Afternoons Have Been in Montana: Poems (with a letter by William Carlos Williams)*; *James and the Children: A Consideration of Henry James's "The Turn of the Screw"*; *Modern Quarterly Beginnings of Aesthetic Realism (including "The Equality of Man" & "The Scientific Criticism")*; *Self and World: An Explanation of Aesthetic Realism*
ISBN Prefix(es): 0-910492
Distributed by Amazon.com; Baker & Taylor; Barnes & Noble
Membership(s): Small Press Center

Demery Publishing
20600 Eureka, Suite 900, Taylor, MI 48180
Tel: 734-671-1275 *Fax:* 734-671-0107
Web Site: www.demerypub.com
Key Personnel
Pres: Julie Calligaro *E-mail:* jcalligaro@msn.com
Founded: 1996
Publications about estate planning, personal finance, bereavement & family.
Titles include *Estate Planning in a Nutshell for Married Couples*
ISBN Prefix(es): 1-890117

Diamond Publishers
29260 Franklin Rd, Southfield, MI 48034
Tel: 248-353-2900 *Toll Free Tel:* 888-386-9688
    Fax: 248-357-0102
E-mail: info@goinglikelynn.com
Web Site: www.goinglikelynn.com
Key Personnel
Pres: Lynn Portnoy
Founded: 1999
Self-published travel writer of a series of liberat-
    ing travel guides for women called Going Like
    Lynn.
Titles include *Going Like Lynn - Florence*; *Going
    Like Lynn - New York*; *Going Like Lynn - Paris*
ISBN Prefix(es): 0-9670099
Distributed by Baker & Taylor; Bookpeople; In-
    gram

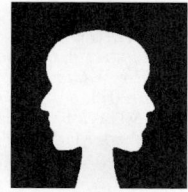

Disilgold Publishing Inc
Unit of Disilgold
2739 Mickle Ave, Bronx, NY 10469
Mailing Address: PO Box 652, Baychester Sta,
    Bronx, NY 10469
Tel: 917-757-1658 *Fax:* 718-547-0499
E-mail: disilgold@aol.com
Web Site: www.disilgold.com
Key Personnel
Publr: Heather Covington
Founded: 2001
Disilgold is the home of the DLNA, Younity Re-
    viewers Bookclub, Disilgold SOUL Literary
    Review & DNLA Awards Newsletter. We pub-
    lish articles, anthologies, books; provide re-
    views, awards & literary services. Also pub-
    lishes under the imprint Persoulnalities.
Titles include *Persoulnalities: Poems For Every
    Kind of Woman Series (Parts 1, 2 & 3)*
ISBN Prefix(es): 1-932055
Membership(s): Disilgold Literary Network Asso-
    ciation

Dynapress
PO Box 150217, Altamonte Springs, FL 32715-
    0217
SAN: 240-3234
Tel: 407-331-5550 *Fax:* 407-331-5550 (call first)
E-mail: itsdifferent@dynapress.com
Web Site: www.dynapress.com
Key Personnel
Publr: Karl Roebling
Founded: 1976
Self publishes my own books if larger compa-
    nies decline. Developing my own "Millennium
    Series" (12 religious/spiritual, Christian, nonde-
    nominational, Bible-based books) "outside the
    box" but not "far out".
Titles include *A Thinking Citizen*; *The Age of In-
    dividuality - America's Kinship with the Brook-
    lyn Bridge*; *Great Myths of WWII*; *Is There A
    Bible Science?*; *New York Blast*; *Not Jesus'
    Death - His Overcoming of Death*; *The Search
    for the Promised Land*; *The Seven Seals of
    Revelation*; *La Sorciere (by Michelet, reprint)*;
    Zap the Bottom!

ISBN Prefix(es): 0-942910
Distributed by Amazon.com; Baker & Taylor;
    Barnes & Noble; Ingram

FourWinds Press LLC
4157 Crossgate Dr, Cincinnati, OH 47025
Tel: 513-891-0415 *Fax:* 513-891-1648
Web Site: www.fourwindspress.com
Key Personnel
Pres: Vivien Schapera *E-mail:* viv@
    fourwindspress.com
Mktg Dir: Stephanie Tyler *E-mail:* stephanie@
    fourwindspress.com
Busn Dir: Drew Logan *E-mail:* drew@
    fourwindspress.com
Opers Dir: Nancy Dawley
Design Dir: Kathleen Noble *E-mail:* noblejak@
    fuse.net
Founded: 2003
FourWinds Press LLC is a small press, dedicated
    to publishing works that will educate, motivate
    & empower readers.
In addition to publishing books, FourWinds Press
    LLC offers mentoring & editing services to
    aspiring writers, committed to publishing, via
    workshops, seminars & coaching.
Titles include *How to Lose Weight and Gain
    Money: A Program for Putting Your Life in
    Order*
ISBN Prefix(es): 0-9709809
Distributed by Amazon.com; Baker & Taylor;
    BarnesandNoble.com; Greenleaf; New Leaf;
    Quality Books
Membership(s): Publishers Marketing Association

Global Travel Publishers Inc
5353 N Federal Hwy, Suite 300, Fort Lauderdale,
    FL 33308
Tel: 954-491-8877 *Toll Free Tel:* 800-882-9453
    Fax: 954-491-9060
E-mail: noltingaac@aol.com
Web Site: www.africanadventure.com
Key Personnel
Publr: Mark Nolting
Edit Coord: Kathy Berry
Founded: 1986
Publish travel guides & journals on Africa.
Titles include *African Safari Journal, 4th ed*;
    Africa's Top Wildlife Countries, 6th ed
ISBN Prefix(es): 0-939895
Distributed by Baker & Taylor; Ingram; Publish-
    ers Group West
Membership(s): ABA; Florida Publishers Group;
    National Association of Independent Publishers

Guru Beant Press
Division of You Can Do It! Productions
1505 Apakin Nene, Tallahassee, FL 32301
Tel: 850-878-6642
E-mail: infinipede@juno.com
Web Site: www.infinipede.com
Key Personnel
Owner: Bridget Kamke *Tel:* 850-284-7136
Founded: 2003
Guru Beant Press provides books that educate,
    uplift & inspire. We print children's books,
    health books, yoga books & poetry.
Titles include *The Raw Foods Bible*; *The Story of
    the Infinipede*
ISBN Prefix(es): 0-9744306
Distributed by Amazon.com; You Can Do It! Pro-
    ductions
Membership(s): Society of Children's Book Writ-
    ers & Illustrators

Harbor Island Books
1214 W Boston Post Rd, No 245, Mamaroneck,
    NY 10543
SAN: 255-9137
Tel: 914-420-9782 *Fax:* 914-835-7897
E-mail: publisher@lyingawake.net
Web Site: www.lyingawake.net
Key Personnel
Pres: Helen Furbush *E-mail:* hfurbush@earthlink.
    net
Founded: 2002
Independent publisher for titles in the educational
    children's picture book market.
Titles include *Lying Awake*
ISBN Prefix(es): 0-9741787
Distributed by Baker & Taylor; Greenleaf Book
    Group; Robert Hale & Co Inc; Hushion House
    Publishing (Canada); Ingram; Partners West
Membership(s): Publishers Marketing Associa-
    tion; Small Publishers Association of North
    America; Society of Children's Book Writers &
    Illustrators

Hickory Tales Publishing LLC
841 Newberry St, Bowling Green, KY 42103
Tel: 270-791-3242
Key Personnel
Ed & Publr: Andrew Donelson *E-mail:* jadonel@
    aol.com
Founded: 2001
Interests include history, historical fiction, young
    adult & children's books & religious books.
    Royalty 10-15% of net profit. Reply within 2-3
    months. Send complete work & SASE suffi-
    cient to return work & indicate whether return
    of work, not accepted, is desired. Accepted ti-
    tle published within 3-6 months. We look for
    heartfelt stories with a message, a lesson or a
    good feeling at conclusion, stories told in the
    manner you would speak to a close friend.
Titles include *Andrew Jackson Donelson: Jack-
    son's Confidant and Political Heir*; *BearClaw*;
    *Chalmette: The Battle for New Orleans and
    How the British Nearly Stole the Louisiana
    Territory*; *Hoot Owl Shares the Dawn*; *The
    Promise*; *Quicksilver Deep*
ISBN Prefix(es): 0-9709104
Distributed by Academic Book Center; Ama-
    zon.com; American Wholesale Books; Baker
    & Taylor; BarnesandNoble.com; Books a Mil-
    lion; Brodart; Partners West

Howie Publishing Inc
1695 Quigley Rd, Columbus, OH 43227
Toll Free Tel: 888-933-9314 *Fax:* 614-237-2157
Key Personnel
Pres: Carole J Weaver *E-mail:* pageleaf@aol.com
Founded: 1990
Publishes books to entertain, inform, enrich. Sub-
    jects of interest include multicultural, women's
    health, spiritual, New Age, Biblical fiction &
    dinosaurs.
Titles include *Daughters of Deborah*; *Hem, The
    Duckbill Dinosaur*; *Pyramid Discourses*; *Sis-
    tahs & Folks of the Neighborhood*; *Women's
    Health: Tomatoes, Your Best Friend*
ISBN Prefix(es): 1-885275
Distributed by Baker & Taylor; Brodart
Membership(s): AAP; Publishers Marketing As-
    sociation; Small Press Center; Small Publishers
    Association of North America

Humane Society Press
Imprint of The Humane Society of the United States
2100 L St NW, Washington, DC 20037
Tel: 202-452-1100 *Fax:* 301-258-3082
Web Site: www.hsus.org
Key Personnel
Dir: Deborah Salem *Tel:* 301-258-3020
  E-mail: dsalem@hsus.org
Founded: 2000
HSP publishes scholarly/professional titles for the animal care field (veterinarians, humane societies, etc) & the academic community.
Titles include *The Humane Society of the United States Euthanasia Training Manual*; *Protecting All Animals: A Fifty-Year History of the Humane Society of the United States*; *The State of the Animals II: 2003*
ISBN Prefix(es): 0-9658942

Ivy House Publishing Group
Imprint of Pentland Press Inc
5122 Bur Oak Circle, Raleigh, NC 27612
SAN: 298-5063
Tel: 919-782-0281 *Toll Free Tel:* 800-948-2786
  Fax: 919-781-9042
E-mail: thepublisher@ivyhousebooks.com
Web Site: www.ivyhousebooks.com
Key Personnel
Pres: Janet Evans *E-mail:* janetevans@ivyhousebooks.com
Acqs Ed: Benjamin Kay *E-mail:* bkay@ivyhousebooks.com
Asst to Pres: Anna Howland *E-mail:* ahowland@ivyhousebooks.com
Founded: 1993
Ivy House in an independent publisher who offers various levels of publishing services for authors. This includes digital printing to traditional offset printing. Depending on the service the author wants, Ivy House is able to do editing, proofing, book design, cover design, printing & binding, marketing, warehousing & distribution. Mss of all genres are accepted for review, but not all mss are accepted for publication. Genres include fiction, nonfiction, poetry, children's books, self-help, spiritual, memoirs, biographies & more. Inquiries should be made to the above address or to the e-mail address. Mss must be complete, Represented by Midpoint Trade.
This publisher has indicated that 95% of their product line is author subsidized.
Titles include *A Diminished President: FDR in 1944*; *The Alphabet of Sheep*; *Blood Mountain Covenant*; *Chronicle I: Matilda of Argyll*; *Daughters of Juno*; *Reach to the Wounded Healer*
ISBN Prefix(es): 1-57197
Distributed by Baker & Taylor; Ingram; Midpoint Trade Books
Membership(s): National Association of Independent Publishers; Publishers Association of the South; Publishers Marketing Association; Small Publishers Association of North America

Ladan Reserve Press
PO Box 881239, Steamboat Plaza, CO 80488-1239
Tel: 970-723-4916 *Fax:* 970-723-4918
E-mail: ladan@sprynet.com
Key Personnel
Pres: Jeffrey A Hayden
Founded: 1990
Publish fine quality, out of print or neglected books, written within the traditions of great literature. Literary fiction, verse, philosophy, essay. Publish no new work except occasional art/photography, or unusual children's. Bias for subjects historical (ancient/medieval), myth, spiritual philosophy (not religion) & the feminine.

Titles include *Growing Pains*; *The Judas Compound*; *Lares*; *Noter Damus*
ISBN Prefix(es): 0-9629287
Distributed by Biblio Distribution

LeveePressTwo
c/o Bolding, 330 Ft Pickens Rd, No 11A, Pensacola Beach, FL 32561
Tel: 850-934-1357 *Fax:* 850-932-1588
E-mail: HBOLD@worldnet.att.net
Web Site: www.LeveeFiction.com
Key Personnel
Owner: Sally Bolding
The name LeveePressTwo memorializes Greenville, Mississippi's Levee Press, publisher of Faulkner, Welty & William Alexander Percy, adoptive father of Walker Percy. Bolding's *Cyclops Window* aims at readers of Carson McCullars. Her short stories, *Riverbottom Decades*, will be available late 2004.
ForeWard Magazine review (Kunkel's) says "William Faulkner might be pleased to see his work carried on faithfully in this novel, or he might cringe that the author nailed such a dead-on depiction of small-town Mississippi life.".
Titles include *The Cyclops Window: A View into Southern Life*
ISBN Prefix(es): 0-9741709
Distributed by Baker & Taylor (hardcase); Ingram (softcover)

Magick Mirror Communications
511 Avenue of the Americas, PMB 173, New York, NY 10011-8436
Tel: 212-727-0002; 212-208-2951 (voice mail)
  Toll Free Tel: 800-356-6796 *Fax:* 212-208-2951
E-mail: MagickMirr@aol.com; Magickorders@aol.com
Web Site: magickmirror.com
Key Personnel
Artistic Dir: Eugenia Macer-Story
Founded: 1990
Publish poetry, playscripts & interdimensional journalism on supernatural & occult events.
Titles include *Carrying Thunder (poetry)*; *Crossing Jungle River (poetry)*; *The Dark Frontier (nonfiction occult)*; *Doing Business in the Adirondacks (nonfiction supernatural)*; *The Merry Piper's Hollow Hills (poetry)*; *Struck by Green Lightning aka Project Midas (novel)*; *Troll & Other Interdimensinal Invasions (short stories)*; *Vanishing Questions (poetry)*
ISBN Prefix(es): 1-879980
Distributed by Amazon.com; Barnes & Noble Online; New Leaf

MBA Publishing
Subsidiary of Macduff/Bunt Associates
925 E St, Walla Walla, WA 99362
Tel: 509-529-0244 *Fax:* 509-529-8865
E-mail: mba@bmi.net
Web Site: www.bmi.net/mba/
Key Personnel
Pres: Nancy Macduff
Founded: 1983
Specializes in books on the management & administration of volunteers & the programs in which they work. Books are practical & designed to help those who work with volunteers.
Titles include *Building Effective Volunteer Committees*; *Episodic Volunteering*; *Volunteer Recruiting & Retention: A Marketing Approach*
ISBN Prefix(es): 0-945795
Distributed by Point of Light Foundation Volunteer Readership (retail only)

Moonstone Press LLC
7820 Oracle Place, Potomac, MD 20854
Tel: 301-765-1081 *Fax:* 301-765-0510
E-mail: mazeprod@erols.com
Web Site: www.moonstonepress.net

Key Personnel
Publr: Stephanie Maze *E-mail:* mazeprod@erols.com
Art Dir: Alexandra Littlehales
Founded: 2001
Publishes high-quality photographic books for children ages 2-14 in English & Spanish.
Titles include *Momentos en el Reino Animal (Spanish series)*; *Moments in the Wild (English series)*
ISBN Prefix(es): 0-9707768
Distributed by Baker & Taylor; Book Network International; Gryphon House; Independent Publishers Group; Ingram
Membership(s): National Association for the Education of Young Children; Publishers Marketing Association; White House Press Photogaphers Association

M2 Pathways Inc
PO Box 733, Bozeman, MT 59771
Tel: 406-582-1009 *Fax:* 406-994-0496
E-mail: comments@m2pathways.com
Web Site: www.m2pathways.com
Key Personnel
Publr: Martha Joh Reeder-Kearns
Founded: 2003
Small press publisher.
Titles include *Ready, Set, Go! Take Control of Your Professional Future: A How-to Guide That Ignites Your Fire Within*
ISBN Prefix(es): 0-9742071
Distributed by Baker & Taylor
Membership(s): Publishers Marketing Association

Muse Imagery LLC
9811 W Charleston Blvd, Suite 2390, Las Vegas, NV 89117-7519
SAN: 256-1697
Tel: 702-233-5910 *Fax:* 702-233-1762
E-mail: publisher@museimagery.com
Web Site: www.museimagery.com
Key Personnel
CEO/Publr: Shirley Hildreth
Founded: 2003
Muse Imagery is a cutting-edge innovatively structured publishing company that has been formed to expedite the book publishing process in the most cost effective manner while maintaining a standard of quality equal to that of the major publishing companies.
This publisher has indicated that 90% of their product line is author subsidized.
Titles include *SETS Teaching Children How To Connect With God*
ISBN Prefix(es): 0-9740500
Imprints: Muse Imagery™
Distributed by Ingram Book Group; Spring Arbor Distributors
Membership(s): AAP; Publishers Marketing Association

Nightengale Press
1579 Nightengale Circle, Lindenhurst, IL 60046
Mailing Address: PO Box 574, Lake Villa, IL 60046
Tel: 847-507-0274 *Fax:* 847-245-4167
Web Site: www.nightengalepress.com
Key Personnel
Owner/Publr: Valerie Connelly
  E-mail: vconnelly@nightengalepress.com
Founded: 2003

We put authors first with publishing information, marketing training, one-on-one product development of their books, most of the profit from their work, to teach them how to produce a publishing ready ms, design a great cover, protect their work & develop a marketing plan.
Titles include *Crumpet Strumpet*; *How We See The World*; *Sacred Night*; *Sidetracks*; *What's Holding you Back?*
ISBN Prefix(es): 0-9743348
Distributed by Amazon.com; Baker & Taylor; BarnesandNoble.com; Borders.com; Ingram
Membership(s): Publishers Marketing Association

Noble House, see American Literary Press/Noble House

Other Press LLC
307 Seventh Ave, Suite 1807, New York, NY 10001
Tel: 212-414-0054 *Toll Free Tel:* 877-THE-OTHER *Fax:* 212-414-0939
E-mail: orders@otherpress.com
Web Site: www.otherpress.com
Key Personnel
Publr: Judith Feher-Gurewich
CEO: Ellen Vanook
CFO: Bill Foo
Exec Ed: Rosemary Ahern
Edit Dir, Handsel Books: Harry Thomas
Mktg Dir: Juliet Barnes
Publicity Dir: Sarah Russo
Founded: 1998
Other Press explores the ideas & concepts that shape our understanding of human subjectivity. We offer an interdisciplinary & multicultural space where authors can explore how psychic, cultural, historical & literary shifts come about & how they inform our vision of the world & or each other. We are committed to a dialectical exchange between disciplines & publish essays & novels as well as scholarly texts.
Titles include *Affect Regulation, Mentalization, and the Development of the Self*; *Dante's Cure*; *The Perfect American*; *San Remo Drive*
ISBN Prefix(es): 1-892746; 1-59051
Imprints: Handsel Books
Distributed by Eurospan (Europe); Footprint (Australia)

Pavior Publishing
2910 Camino Diablo, No 110, Walnut Creek, CA 94597
SAN: 299-4036
Tel: 925-295-0786 *Fax:* 925-935-7408
E-mail: editor@pavior.com
Web Site: www.pavior.com
Key Personnel
Pres: Ernest F Pecci, MD *E-mail:* pecci@pavior.com
Mktg Dir: Marguerite Kelley *E-mail:* margkel@pacbell.net
Founded: 1997

Pavior Publishing offers something of unique value for readers of every level of seeking, in a way that will bring them to a new understanding of their essential selves, their personal relationships & their spiritual connection. Pavior's books offer new approaches to conventional & unconventional, scientific, psychological & spiritual thinking in a format that is practical, approachable & easy to apply to daily life.
Titles include *Conscious Acts of Creation*; *Guidance From Within*
ISBN Prefix(es): 0-929331
Distributed by Baker & Taylor
Membership(s): Publishers Marketing Association; Small Publishers Association of North America

Platinum One Publishing
Division of Platinum One Group LLC
21W551 North Ave, Suite 132, Lombard, IL 60148
SAN: 256-1581
Tel: 630-935-7323 *Fax:* 203-651-1825
E-mail: customerservice@platinumonepublishing.com
Web Site: www.platinumonepublishing.com
Key Personnel
Dir of Proj Devt: Katrina Taylor
  E-mail: ktaylor@platinumonepublishing.com
PR: Lora Coburn *Tel:* 312-342-6357
  E-mail: lcoburn@platinumonepublishing.com
Founded: 2002
Today, our mission is to publish acclaimed titles yearly. We believe in promoting each title to success. Focusing primarily on quality, not quantity. Dedicating skills & resources to fiction, nonfiction (self-help) & children's books. The goal is to segment the target market first then position the product (book(s)) to reach the audience. Partnering with the most innovative distributors & wholesalers in the industry. Our mission is simply to set each signed author up with their own personal platform. This includes marketing, promotional time line & publicity campaigns to increase author exposure & product sales.
This publisher has indicated that their product line is author subsidized.
Titles include *Emotional Deception*
ISBN Prefix(es): 0-9752702
Distributed by Baker & Taylor; Ingram
Membership(s): AAP; Publishers Marketing Association

The Press at California State University, Fresno
Unit of California State University, Fresno
2380 E Keats, MB99, Fresno, CA 93740-8024
Tel: 559-278-3056 *Fax:* 559-278-6758
E-mail: press@csufresno.edu
Key Personnel
Man Ed, Adv & Sales: Carla Millar
Founded: 1982

Scholarly books, architecture, drama, music, art, autobiography.
Titles include *California Light: The Watercolors of Rollin Pickford*; *Federico Fellini: Comments on Film*; *Flamenco, Body and Soul*; *Frank Lloyd Wright: His Living Voice*; *Frank Lloyd Wright: Letters to Apprentices, Architects & Clients*; *Surviving the Storms*; *William Saroyan: An Armenian Trilogy*; *William Saroyan: Warsaw Visitor/Tales from the Vienna Streets*; *William Saroyan: Where the Bones Go*
ISBN Prefix(es): 0-912201
Distributed by Amazon.com; Baker & Taylor; Barnes & Noble; Midwest Library Service; Southern Illinois University Press, Carbondale; Yankee Book Peddler

Rodnik Publishing Company
PO Box 46956, Seattle, WA 98146-0956
SAN: 253-2697
Tel: 206-937-5189 *Fax:* 206-937-3554
E-mail: rodnik2@comcast.net
Web Site: www.rodnikpublishing.com
Key Personnel
Dir: Bob Powers
Mktg Dir: Hugo Gomez *Tel:* (033) 38-25-72-79 (Guadalajara, MX) *E-mail:* hugojgomez@megared.net.mx
Founded: 1995
Rodnik Publishing Company originally published a Russian language newspaper, "Klyuch K Rossii," for students & teachers of Russian. In 2000, we began publishing foreign-language phrasebooks, which now constitute our specialty. We have two phrasebooks in print, four that will appear in 2005 & five others in progress.
This publisher has indicated that some of their product line author subsidized.
Titles include *English-Russian Dictionary-Phrasebook of Love*; *Making Friends in Mexico: A Spanish Phrasebook*
ISBN Prefix(es): 1-929482
Distributed by Baker & Taylor; Ingram Book Co; Quality Books
Membership(s): Book Publishers of the Northwest; Publishers Marketing Association

Safe Harbor Books
504 Main St, New London, NH 03527
Mailing Address: PO Box 2568, New London, NH 03257-2568
Fax: 603-526-3500
E-mail: safeharborbooks@aol.com
Key Personnel
Man Ed: A Y Smyth
Founded: 1998
We publish fiction & photography. We tend to develop projects that interest us. We do not accept submissions without a query letter first.
Titles include *On Nantucket*
ISBN Prefix(es): 0-9665798
Distributed by Baker & Taylor; Ingram
Membership(s): NEBA; Publishers Marketing Association; Small Press Center; Small Publishers Association of North America

Seascape Press Ltd
1010 Roble Lane, Santa Barbara, CA 93103-2046
SAN: 299-8285
Tel: 805-965-4646 *Toll Free Tel:* 800-929-2906
  Fax: 805-963-8188
E-mail: seapress@aol.com
Web Site: www.seascapepress.com
Key Personnel
Pres: Len Lamensdorf
VP: Erica Kauls *E-mail:* voncruella@aol.com
Sales: Laura Greg
Libraries: Cynthia Klein
Founded: 1998
Titles include *The Crouching Dragon*; *The Flying Dragon*; *Gino, the Countess & Chagall*; *The Raging Dragon*; *The Rivals*; *The Five Minute*

Family Game - Calmer Kids & Higher Test Scores - Without Drugs
ISBN Prefix(es): 0-9669741
Distributed by Baker & Taylor; Brodart; Follett; Ingram; Quality Books
Membership(s): AAP; Publishers Marketing Association

Seven Springs Press
11150 Sanders Rd, Tensed, ID 83870
Tel: 208-274-2470
E-mail: sevenspringscc@aol.com
Key Personnel
Publr: Christina Crawford
Founded: 1998
Titles include *Daughters of the Inquisition*; *Mommie Dearest (20th Anniversary Edition)*
ISBN Prefix(es): 0-9663369
Distributed by Amazon.com; Baker & Taylor

ShipShape Publishing Inc
12 Pine St, Chatham, NJ 07928
SAN: 256-2081
Tel: 973-635-3000 *Fax:* 973-635-4363
E-mail: ShipShapeBooks@aol.com
Web Site: www.ShipShapePublishing.com
Key Personnel
Pres: Patricia Byrne
VP, Licensing & Mktg: Barbara Hess
Sr VP, Acqs: Linda Pinkus
Art Dir: Nancy Jackson
Founded: 2004
Late Spring 2005, ShipShape Publishing Inc rolls out its Toe Truck series with a campaign to promote leisure reading & the idea "books are fun".
The Toe Truck with its ensemble cast & off-beat adventures will keep kids entertained & adults amused.
ShipShape Publishing Inc will simultaneously release *Little Rickey At The Zoo*, which explores the world through the eyes & imagination of a vertically challenged kid.
Titles to be published in 2005: *Little Rickey at the Zoo*; *Toe Trucks Duck Truck Trouble*; *Toe Trucks Football Adventure*; *Toe Trucks Gone Fishin'*; *Toe Trucks on Thin Ice*.
ISBN Prefix(es): 0-9761062
Distributed by Baker & Taylor

Smart Luck Publishers
PO Box 81770, Las Vegas, NV 89180-1770
Tel: 702-365-1818 *Toll Free Tel:* 800-945-4245
Fax: 850-937-6999 *Toll Free Fax:* 800-876-4245
E-mail: books@smartluck.com
Web Site: www.smartluck.com
Key Personnel
Mktg Dir: Gail Howard
Dir of Opers: Rita Hall *E-mail:* Rita@smartluck.com
Gen Mgr: Joe Hicks *E-mail:* sales@smartluck.com
Founded: 1983
Smart Luck, publisher of *Lottery Master Guide* & other lottery titles, produces quality books with scientific strategies & easy-to-use systems to help the reader bet smarter.
Titles include *Lottery Master Guide, 4th edition*; *Lotto Wheel Five to Win, 2nd edition revised*; *Lotto Winning Wheels for Powerball & Mega Millions*
ISBN Prefix(es): 0-945760

Distributed by Baker & Taylor
Membership(s): Publishers Marketing Association

Smokin' Donut Books
381 Seaside Dr, Jamestown, RI 02835
SAN: 255-8688
Mailing Address: PO Box 37, Jamestown, RI 02835
Tel: 401-423-2400 *Toll Free Tel:* 877-474-8738
Fax: 401-423-2700
E-mail: info@smokindonut.com
Web Site: www.smokindonut.com
Key Personnel
Publr: Kristin Zhivago *E-mail:* kz@smokindonut.com
Founded: 2004
Publisher of business & how-to books.
Titles include *Rivers of Revenue: What to do when the money stops flowing*
ISBN Prefix(es): 0-9749179
Membership(s): Publishers Marketing Association

T J Publishers Inc
817 Silver Spring Ave, Suite 206, Silver Spring, MD 20910-4617
Tel: 301-585-4440 *Toll Free Tel:* 800-999-1168
Fax: 301-585-5930
E-mail: TJPubinc@aol.com
Key Personnel
Chmn: T Patrick O'Rourke
Pres: Angela K Thames
VP: Jerald A Murphy
Founded: 1978
Publisher & distributor of quality books, videotapes & other materials related to sign language & deafness including several best sellers.
Titles include *A Basic Course in American Sign Language (2nd ed)*; *A Basic Course in ASL Vocabulary Videotape*; *A Basic Vocabulary: American Sign Language for Parents and Children*; *From Mime to Sign*
ISBN Prefix(es): 0-932666
Distributed by Baker & Taylor; Brodart

Violet Prose Publications
PO Box 245, Victor, NY 14654
Tel: 585-924-3063 *Fax:* 585-924-4118
E-mail: VioletProsePubs@aol.com
Web Site: www.VioletProsePubs.com
Key Personnel
Owner: Laura Turner
Founded: 2003
A fresh voice in the subjects of natural health, wellness, self-improvement & spirituality. Owner Laura Turner is the author of *Spiritual Fitness: The 7-Steps to Living Well*, published by BookSurge LLC.
Distributed by BookSurge LLC; Ingram
Membership(s): Publishers Marketing Association

Vision Books International
775 E Blithedale Ave, No 342, Mill Valley, CA 94941

Tel: 415-383-0962 *Fax:* 415-383-4521
E-mail: publisher@vbipublishing.com
Web Site: www.vbipublishing.com
Key Personnel
Publr: Sharon Jones *E-mail:* sharon@vbipublishing.com
Founded: 1997
Independent full-service subsidy publisher of nonfiction, memoirs & children's books. VBI is an established full publishing company for authors interested in self-publishing. Service includes ms advice & deep editing, book & cover design including work with original art or photography, printing, storage, a press release & marketing opportunities.
Titles include *Always Alex*; *And Man Created God...:A Case for Secular Humanism*; *The Art of Moderation: An Alternative to Alcoholism*; *Be Your Own Therapist: Recipes for Emotional Health*; *The Bearables of Bernie Bear: Bernie's Forest Adventure*; *Circus in the Night Sky*; *Fire Fighting*; *First A Dream: A Community Builds a Library*; *The First 80 Years: A Memoir*; *In Small Doses: A Memoir about Accepting and Living with Bipolar Disorder*; *The Life of Mary*; *The Merry Mariner*; *The Pleasure Was Ours: Personal Encounters with the Greats, the Near-Greats and the Ingrates*; *Trivia Cafe: 2000 Questions for Parties, Fundraisers, School Events & Travel*
ISBN Prefix(es): 1-56550
Distributed by Baker & Taylor; The Book House; Ingram; Quality Books
Membership(s): Bay Area Small Publishers' Association; Irish Literary & Historical Society; Northern California Book Publicity & Marketing Association; Publishers Marketing Association; Small Publishers Association of North America

Viveca Smith Publishing
PMB 131, 3001 S Hardin Blvd, Suite 110, McKinney, TX 75070-9028
Tel: 214-793-0089 *Fax:* 972-562-7559
E-mail: vsmithpublishing@aol.com
Web Site: www.vivecasmithpublishing.com
Key Personnel
Ed/Publr: Viveca Smith
Founded: 2002
The focus of our company is international children's literature. We publish new translations of classic stories as well as new authors from around the world.
ISBN Prefix(es): 0-9740551
Membership(s): Publishers Marketing Association; Small Publishers Association of North America

White Stone Books
1501 S Florida Ave, Lakeland, FL 33803
Mailing Address: PO Box 2835, Lakeland, FL 33806
Toll Free Tel: 866-253-8622 *Toll Free Fax:* 800-830-5688
E-mail: info@whitestonebooks.com
Web Site: www.whitestonebooks.com
Key Personnel
VP, Mktg & Prod Devt: Debbie Justus Collins *E-mail:* debbiec@whitestonebooks.com
Founded: 2003
Christian book publisher.

ISBN Prefix(es): 1-59379
Membership(s): Christian Booksellers Association; Evangelical Christian Publishers Association

Women's Source Books, see Demery Publishing

Editorial Services & Agents

Editorial Services — Activity Index

FACT CHECKING

MANUSCRIPT ANALYSIS

PERMISSIONS

PHOTO RESEARCH

SPECIAL ASSIGNMENT WRITING

Editorial Services

For information on other companies who provide services to the book industry, see **Consultants, Book Producers, Typing & Word Processing Services** and **Artists & Art Services**.

A Abacus Group
PO Box 35, Ridgecrest, CA 93556
Tel: 760-375-5243 *Fax:* 760-375-1140
E-mail: gtd007@ridgenet.net
Web Site: www.ridgenet.net/~gtd007
Key Personnel
Dir: G T Dawson
Founded: 1981
Complete writing, rewriting, ghost writing, copy editing, ms analysis, special assignment writing, technical manuals (government/civilian/commercial); all word processing, desktop publishing, in-depth research on any imaginable subject matter; interviewing; advertising & promotion copy writing/editing; bibliographies; condensations; line editing, proofreading; transcriptions. The ghost writing agency-of-choice for well-known Hollywood & sports celebrities. Call or e-mail for information.

A+ English/ManuscriptEditing.com
1830 Guinevere St, Arlington, TX 76014-2521
Tel: 817-467-7127
E-mail: editor@manuscriptediting.com
Web Site: www.manuscriptediting.com;
www.englishedit.com; www.queryletters.com; www.scifieditor.com; www.writingnetwork.com; www.book-editing.com; www.dissertationadvisors.com; www.thesisproofreader.com; www.statisticstutors.com; www.apawriting.com
Key Personnel
Owner & Sr Ed: Lynda Lotman *E-mail:* mseditor@comcast.net
Founded: 1976
Serving publishers, agents & writers (mainstream, genre, trade & academic) since 1976. References are provided on site. 100+ books in publication. Coordinator of an international network of editors & writers that also includes legal, medical, scientific & technical specialists. Services include copy-editing, developmental editing, proofreading, critques, query letters, book proposals, writing assistance, mentoring, ghostwriting, typesetting, book design, indexing & publicity/promotions.
Membership(s): Science Fiction & Fantasy Writers of America

A Westport Wordsmith
104 Roseville Rd, Westport, CT 06880
Tel: 203-226-7098
E-mail: pj104daily@aol.com
Key Personnel
Proprietor: Peggy Daily
Founded: 1999
Proofreading (nonfiction & fiction), copy-editing (nonfiction) & indexing of trade books. Americanization. Also offers disk & online copyediting & proofreading.
Membership(s): American Society of Indexers; Editorial Freelancers Association

AAA Photos
401 Ocean Dr, Miami Beach, FL 33139
Tel: 305-534-0804
Web Site: www.PhotosPhotos.net
Key Personnel
Pres: Jeff Greenberg *E-mail:* jeffgreenberg@juno.com

Provides photos to tourism bureau, book publishers, magazine publishers, newspapers, travel publications, websites, & by assignment & stock.

AAH Graphics Inc
Subsidiary of Loft Press Inc
187 Myra Lane, Fort Valley, VA 22652
Mailing Address: PO Box 150, Fort Valley, VA 22652
Tel: 540-933-6210 *Fax:* 540-933-6523
Web Site: www.aahgraphics.com
Key Personnel
Pres: Ann Hunter
Complete editorial through production serving publishers & individuals. Design of text, jackets & covers, composition & production management through manufacturing.

Aaron-Spear
PO Box 42, Harborside, ME 04642
Tel: 207-326-8764
Key Personnel
Prop: Jody Spear
Developmental editing & copy editing of scholarly mss in the humanities. Rewriting for style & sensibility as well as clarity, consistency & accuracy. Specialize in art history & environmental studies.

AA's & PE's
129 Third Ave, Benton, WI 53803-0072
Mailing Address: PO Box 72, Benton, WI 53803-0072
Tel: 608-759-3303
Key Personnel
Contact: Stephen Calvert *E-mail:* calvertstephen@hotmail.com
Copy & line editing, fact checking, ms analysis, proofreading, rewriting; general nonfiction, fiction, directories & reference books, foreign languages; art history, library & information sciences; microcomputers, music, psychology & theater.

About Books Inc
425 Cedar St, Buena Vista, CO 81211-1500
Mailing Address: PO Box 1500-ED, Buena Vista, CO 81211
Tel: 719-395-2459 *Fax:* 719-395-8374
E-mail: abi@about-books.com
Web Site: www.about-books.com
Key Personnel
Pres: Scott Flora *E-mail:* scott@about-books.com
Complete writing, editorial & book development services: creative editing, writing of business, corporate & promotional materials, newsletters, & magazine articles; creative development of ideas to completed ms. Specialize in nonfiction books on all subjects.
Membership(s): American Society of Journalists & Authors; Authors Guild; Small Publishers Association of North America

Access Editorial Services
1133 Broadway, Suite 528, New York, NY 10010
Tel: 212-255-7306 *Fax:* 212-255-7306
E-mail: wiseword@juno.com
Key Personnel
Dir: Louise Weiss

Founded: 1990
Services include travel writing.
Membership(s): Authors Guild; Editorial Freelancers Association; New York Travel Writers Association; SATW

Accurate Writing & More
PO Box 1164, Northampton, MA 01061-1164
Tel: 413-586-2388 *Toll Free Tel:* 800-683-9673
Fax: 617-249-0153
Web Site: www.accuratewriting.com
Key Personnel
Dir: Dina Friedman; Shel Horowitz
E-mail: shel@principledprofits.com
Founded: 1981
Advertising & promotion copy writing, ghost writing, interviewing, ms analysis, research, rewriting, special assignment writing.
Membership(s): National Writers Union; Publishers Marketing Association; Western New England Editorial Freelancers Association

J Adel Graphic Design
586 Ramapo Rd, Teaneck, NJ 07666
Tel: 201-836-2606
E-mail: jadelnj@aol.com
Key Personnel
Creative Dir: Judith Adel
Freelance copy, illustration & design services for publishers.

AEIOU Inc
894 Piermont Ave, Piermont, NY 10968
Tel: 845-680-5380 *Fax:* 845-680-5381
Key Personnel
Pres: Cynthia Crippen *E-mail:* ccrippen@worldnet.att.net
Founded: 1976
Membership(s): American Society of Indexers

AFS Wordstead
27 Belvedere St, St Julie, PQ J3E 3M4, Canada
Tel: 450-922-0172 *Toll Free Tel:* 866-864-5448
Web Site: www.wordstead.com
Key Personnel
Man: Anthony F Shaker, PhD *Fax:* 450-922-9547
E-mail: afshaker@aol.com
Ghost writing, rewriting & editing of works in fiction & nonfiction: novels, memoirs/autobiographies, biographies, articles, scripts, book-to-screen adaptations. Popular & specialized markets in the US, Canada & UK.

Ainsworth Editorial Services
43-01 12 St, Suite 339, Long Island City, NY 11101
Tel: 718-361-5254 *Fax:* 718-361-2837
E-mail: nycedit@aol.com
Key Personnel
Dir: Joanne S Ainsworth
Professional & scholarly studies, especially in health care, social sciences & economics.

Albert Editorial Services
565 Bellevue Ave, No 1704, Oakland, CA 94610
Tel: 510-839-1140
Key Personnel
Pres: Janice Albert *E-mail:* jmalbert2002@earthlink.net

Assistance to authors, textbook annotations in humanities & literature, literary research. Quick turnaround, competitive rates.
Membership(s): National Council of Teachers of English

Rodelinde Albrecht
PO Box 444, Lenox Dale, MA 01242-0444
Tel: 413-243-4350 *Fax:* 413-243-3066
E-mail: rodelinde@juno.com
Web Site: www.concernedsingles.com
Full editorial services; scanning; copy/line editing (hardcopy/electronic); rewriting; castoff, typemarking; proofreading; proof-checking & consulting.

Gary Aleksiewicz
9110 NW 219 Place, Alachua, FL 32615
Tel: 386-462-6142
E-mail: gsaleks@hotmail.com
Indexing.

AllWrite Advertising & Publishing
PO Box 2363, Atlanta, GA 30301
Tel: 404-723-8872 *Fax:* 404-420-2604
E-mail: editor@e-allwrite.com
Web Site: www.e-allwrite.com
Key Personnel
Contact: Annette R Johnson
Founded: 1996
Editorial service providing editing, proofreading, indexing & creative services for articles, books, manuals, journals, periodicals, reports, advertising & promotional documents, contracts, speeches & web sites. We provide copy-editing, checking grammar, clarity & style; substantive/line editing, making significant changes to a ms such as rewriting & reorganizing text; developmental editing, working with writers to formulate ideas & rework original concepts; production editing, guiding a ms through the production process & hiring, when necessary, an entire editorial staff such as typesetters, proofreaders & layout artists. We also offer both content proofreaders, which check only text & design proofreaders, which check layout specifications. While most of our writing services consist of rewriting, we do offer original feature & speechwriting. Using the latest publishing software, we create text & graphic presentations such as pamphlets. We even edit HTML documents. Get free quotes, submit work & pay for service online at www.e-allwrite.com.

Almada & Associates
627 W Roscoe, Unit 2-B, Chicago, IL 60657
Tel: 773-404-9350 *Fax:* 773-404-9278
Key Personnel
Pres: Jeanette Almada *E-mail:* jmalmada@aol.com
Full editorial/research services. Editing, writing, rewriting or co-authoring books. Research all areas. Conduct & manage special projects & studies on subjects or issues targeted to be subject of your book.

Valinda Almeida
Subsidiary of Almeida Business & Travel Writing
284 Sunlit Cove Dr NE, St Petersburg, FL 33702
Tel: 727-577-3525 *Fax:* 727-577-3525 (call first)
E-mail: almeida1@tampabay.rr.com
Founded: 1990
Travel & business writing. Proofreading, research, rewriting, special assignment writing, interviewing.
Membership(s): Freelance Editorial Association

American Editing
69 Lansing St, Auburn, NY 13021
Tel: 315-258-8012

Key Personnel
Pres: Joseph P Berry
Founded: 1999
Editing service to help both experienced & beginning writers in getting published. Particularly receptive to unpublished college professors. Offers ms critiques & line-by-line editing for fiction & nonfiction.

Joyce L Ananian
25 Forest Circle, Waltham, MA 02452-4719
Tel: 781-894-4330
E-mail: jlananian@hotmail.com
Copy editing, fact checking, indexing, proofreading & line editing.

Barbara S Anderson
706 W Davis, Ann Arbor, MI 48103-4855
Tel: 734-995-0125; 734-994-6182 *Fax:* 734-994-5207
Key Personnel
Owner: Barbara S Anderson
Admin Asst: Martin B Tittle
Rewriting, proofreading, ms analysis & line editing. For related services see listing in Artists & Art Services.

Denice A Anderson
210 E Church St, Clinton, MI 49236
Tel: 517-456-4990 *Fax:* 517-456-4990
Founded: 1984
Copy-editing, line editing & proofreading; fiction & nonfiction; art, history, medical, legal, business, newspapers, journals & directories.
Membership(s): Editorial Freelancers Association

Jim Anderson
77 S Second St, Brooklyn, NY 11211
Tel: 718-388-1083
E-mail: jim.and@worldnet.att.net
Special assignment writing, copywriting, interviewing, line editing, copy editing, rewriting, proofreading, research, fact checking & ghost writing.

Patricia Anderson
1489 Marine Dr, Suite 515, West Vancouver, BC V7T 1B8, Canada
Tel: 604-740-0805 *Fax:* 604-740-0805
E-mail: query@helpingyougetpublished.com
Web Site: www.helpingyougetpublished.com
Key Personnel
Literary Consultant: Patricia Anderson, PhD
Founded: 1998
Editorial services & mentoring for authors seeking agents & publishers.
Membership(s): Authors Guild of America; Editors' Association of Canada/Association canadienne de reviseurs; The Writers' Union of Canada

Elaine Andrews
10596 Twin Rivers Rd, Columbia, MD 21044
Tel: 410-997-5890
E-mail: eekandrews@aol.com
Educational materials & nonfiction, adult & juvenile. Specialize in history & social studies.

Angel Publications
123-3691 Albion Rd S, Gloucester, ON K1T 1P2, Canada
Tel: 613-526-2277
E-mail: angelpublications@canada.com
Web Site: members.rogers.com/angelpub
Key Personnel
Pres: Diana Thistle Tremblay
Children's writing & nonfiction editing.
Membership(s): Editors' Association of Canada/Association canadienne de reviseurs; Society of Children's Book Writers & Illustrators

Arnica Publishing Inc
3739 SE Eighth Ave, Portland, OR 97202
Tel: 503-225-9900 *Fax:* 503-225-9901
E-mail: info@arnicapublishing.com
Web Site: www.arnicapublishing.com
Key Personnel
CEO, Pres & Publr: Ross Hawkins
COO & Ed-in-Chief: Gloria Gonzalez
Founded: 2002
General interest subjects; provide substantive editing, project reorganization, ms transcription, idea development, print management, marketing, fulfillment, distribution & warehousing.

ASJA Writer Referral Service
Affiliate of American Society of Journalists & Authors Inc
1501 Broadway, Suite 302, New York, NY 10036
Tel: 212-398-1934 *Fax:* 212-768-7414
E-mail: writers@asja.org
Web Site: www.asja.org
Key Personnel
Dir: Jennie L Phipps
Provide access & referrals to freelance nonfiction writers for articles, books (trade & text), booklets, brochures, annual reports, speeches, TV & film scripts, advertising copy publicity campaigns, corporate communications & website.

Associated Authors
Subsidiary of Robert Tralins
2299 Indian Ave S, Bellair Bluffs, FL 33770
Tel: 727-518-6262
Key Personnel
Principal: Robert Tralins *E-mail:* roberttralins@verizon.net
Founded: 1972
Assignment writing novels, book development, research specialist of paranormal experiences. Author Robert Tralins' stories now featured on SciFi Channel's "Beyond Belief: Fact or Fiction" show currently in its seventh worldwide satellite season.

Associated Editors
27 W 96 St, New York, NY 10025
Tel: 212-662-9703 *Fax:* 212-662-0549
Key Personnel
Contact: Lynne Glasner *E-mail:* lyngla@earthlink.net; Maury Siegel
Copy editing, rewriting, proofreading, indexing, research & royalty consultation. Specialize in elementary & secondary textbooks.

Astor Indexers
PO Box 950, Kent, CT 06757
Tel: 860-927-3654 *Toll Free Tel:* 800-848-2328
Fax: 860-927-3654
Key Personnel
Owner: Jane Farnol *E-mail:* bjfarnol@snet.net
Founded: 1970
Indexing is our only business; 40 years experience. Our staff handles all subjects; hard copy, e-mail or disk. Quality, speed & accuracy are our trademarks.

Audrey Owen
494 Eaglecrest Dr, Gibsons, BC V0N 1V8, Canada
E-mail: editor@writershelper.com
Web Site: www.writershelper.com
Key Personnel
Owner: Audrey Owen
Founded: 2002
Besides the editing services offered by other agencies, I also specialize in educative editing that becomes a mini tutorial designed for, but is not restricted to, self-publishing writers.
Membership(s): Editors' Association of Canada/Association canadienne de reviseurs; Federation of British Columbia Writers; Society of Children's Book Writers & Illustrators

Sylvia Auerbach
2401 Pennsylvania Ave, Suite 12B24, Philadelphia, PA 19130
Tel: 215-235-0607
E-mail: auersylvia@aol.com
Writing assignments on relationships of parents & adult children, gerontology, financial planning for older adults, fall prevention. Book Editing. Consultant to colleges & universities on book publishing courses. Lecturer on book publishing at Philadelphia Writers' Conference.
Membership(s): Authors Guild of America; Society of Journalists & Authors

The Author's Friend
548 Ocean Blvd, No 12, Long Branch, NJ 07740
Tel: 732-571-8051 *Toll Free Tel:* 877-485-7689
  Toll Free Fax: 877-485-7689
E-mail: authfriend@yahoo.com
Key Personnel
Prop: Judith Stein
Founded: 1976
Copy & line editing, proofreading & transcription editing. Specialize in religion & spirituality, psychology, medicine, self-help, bibliographies & esoterica.
Membership(s): Editorial Freelancers Association

Author's Helper
515 E Eighth St, Unit D, Davis, CA 95616
Mailing Address: PO Box 392, Davis, CA 95617-0392
Tel: 530-759-2091
E-mail: info@authorshelper.com
Web Site: www.authorshelper.com
Key Personnel
Ed & Owner: Cathy Dean *E-mail:* catdean@aol.com
Founded: 2002
Provides editing, writing, publisher submission help & self-published marketing. Also provide indexing, technical editing & copywriting.
Membership(s): Chamber of Commerce

Jerome Axelrod
467 Wingate Rd, Huntington Valley, PA 19006-8421
Tel: 215-947-8426 *Fax:* 215-947-3140
K-12 educational writer & reading specialist.

Backman Writing & Communications
32 Hillview Ave, Rensselaer, NY 12144
Tel: 518-449-4985 *Fax:* 518-449-7273
Web Site: www.backwrite.com
Key Personnel
Principal: John Backman *E-mail:* johnb@backwrite.com
Advertising & promotion copywriting & special assignment writing. Specialties in financial, high technology, travel & tourism, business-to-business & retail.

Janet H Baker
550 Gaspar Dr, Placida, FL 33946
Tel: 941-697-3581
Trade fiction.
Branch Office(s)
100 Kendal Dr, Kennett Square, PA 19348
  Tel: 610-388-6192

Baldwin Literary Services
935 Hayes St, Baldwin, NY 11510-4834
Tel: 516-546-8338 *Fax:* 516-867-6850
Key Personnel
Pres: Marjorie Gillette Jones
Edit Dir: Pat Meglin
Founded: 1982

Creative writing courses. Specialize in novels, historical novels, autobiographies, medical, gardening & nature, spiritual.
Membership(s): International Women's Writing Guild

Kathleen Barnes
238 W Fourth St, Suite 3C, New York, NY 10014
Tel: 212-924-8084 *Fax:* 212-255-5033
E-mail: yobarnes@aol.com
Writing, rewriting, line editing, copy editing & proofreading.

Melinda Barrett
17110 Donmetz St, Granada Hills, CA 91344
Tel: 818-368-2129
E-mail: mbarrett@ladpw.org
Copy editing, proofreading, rewriting & special assignment writing.

Diana Barth
535 W 51 St, Suite 3-A, New York, NY 10019
Tel: 212-307-5465
E-mail: diabarth@juno.com
Founded: 1970
All subjects; specialize in performing arts, health, psychology, education & travel. Feature & ghost writer.

Mark E Battersby
PO Box 527, Ardmore, PA 19003
Tel: 610-789-2480 *Fax:* 610-924-9159
E-mail: mebatt12@earthlink.net
  Telex: 6505179983 *Cable:* CRICKTRADE

Mr Loris Battin
251 E 51 St, No 8F, New York, NY 10022
Tel: 212-688-7668
E-mail: lolus@msn.com

Beaver Wood Associates
655 Alstead Center Rd, Alstead, NH 03602
Mailing Address: PO Box 717, Alstead, NH 03602
Tel: 603-835-7900 *Fax:* 603-835-6279
Web Site: www.beaverwood.com
Key Personnel
Pres: Jeanne C Moody *E-mail:* jcmoody@beaverwood.com
Founded: 1985
Indexing, copy editing, thesaurus construction.
Membership(s): American Society of Indexers

Ellen Becker
PO Box 5851, Santa Fe, NM 87502
Tel: 505-989-7543 *Fax:* 505-988-3953
E-mail: ebecker3@aol.com
All fiction & nonfiction; specialize in health care, humanities, social sciences, medicine, law.

Beehive Production Services
3 Fairview St, East Stroudsburg, PA 18301-2501
Tel: 570-421-3076 *Fax:* 570-421-3076
E-mail: beehive@ptd.net
Key Personnel
Owner: Bernice Pettinato
Written communications management: activities range from research & development guidance to ms production through camera-ready copy or disk. Provide complete project management with author contact, book design, illustration, jacket design & typesetting.

Marlowe Bergendoff
277 Water St, Suite 219, Exeter, NH 03833
Tel: 603-778-6245 *Fax:* 603-778-6245
Founded: 1990
Copy editing.

Barbara Bergstrom, MA
13 Stockton Way, Howell, NJ 07731
Tel: 732-363-8372
Key Personnel
CEO: Barbara Bergstrom
Complete editorial services, production services, writing, copy editing, ms analysis, critique & development, proofreading, research, rewriting, condensations, ghost writing, indexing, newsletters, special assignment writing, speeches & transcription editing for authors, publishers, academics, professionals, public figures, organizations & business. Specialize in editing of humanities, social sciences, behavioral, medical, psychological, natural & alternative healing sciences, meditation, "how to" & self help mss. Special expertise in comparative literature, English, English as a second language, East Asian culture (China, Korea & Japan), psychology, history, Eastern philosophy, religions & women's issues. Will travel to meet with author to develop & edit ms. Custom designed workshops. Act as liaison or author's agent. Project management. ESL authors welcome. Also see listing under consultants.

Berlow Technical Communications Inc
9 Prairie Ave, Suffern, NY 10901
Tel: 845-357-8215
E-mail: bteccinc@yahoo.com
Key Personnel
Pres: Lawrence H Berlow
Special assignment writing, rewriting, line editing & research.

Jean Brodsky Bernard
4609 Chevy Chase Blvd, Chevy Chase, MD 20815-5343
Tel: 301-654-8914 *Fax:* 301-718-8972
E-mail: dranreb@starpower.net
Founded: 1982

Bestseller Consultants
PO Box 922, Wilsonville, OR 97070
Tel: 503-694-5381 *Fax:* 503-694-5046
Key Personnel
Pres: Ursula Bacon *E-mail:* u-bacon@comcast.net
Ed: Thorn Bacon
Founded: 1991
Book development, writing, rewriting, editing & ghost writing of selected nonfiction projects. Work with authors to develop effective book proposals, improve ms ideas & refer them to appropriate literary agents or publishers. Book packaging of special projects & development of marketing & distribution plans for books.

Beta Computer Indexing
61 S Kashong Dr, Geneva, NY 14456
Tel: 315-719-0486 *Fax:* 315-719-0487
Key Personnel
Owner: Kathleen Garcia *E-mail:* kathygarcia@betaindexing.com
Web-indexing, camera-ready copy of indexes, periodical indexing & back-of-the-book indexing.
Membership(s): American Society of Indexers

Daniel Bial & Associates
41 W 83 St, Suite 5-C, New York, NY 10024
Tel: 212-721-1786 *Fax:* 309-213-0230
E-mail: dbialagency@juno.com
Web Site: www.danielbialagency.com
Founded: 1991
Specialize in creating, designing & producing illustrated el-hi & adult books; emphasis on reference sports.

Bibliogenesis
152 Coddington Rd, Ithaca, NY 14850
Tel: 607-277-9660 *Fax:* 607-277-6661

Key Personnel
Owner: Marian Hartman Rogers
  E-mail: mrogers@lightlink.com
Founded: 1987
Full editorial services encompassing all aspects of ms development: analysis, writing, rewriting, content editing, copy-editing, line editing, proofreading, fact checking, research & special assignment writing. Specialize in development, writing & editing of el-hi texts, teacher's editions & ancillaries in language arts, social studies, careers & other subject areas; scholarly works (classical & medieval studies, European history & literature, anthropology & gender studies, Middle Eastern studies, geography & travel); languages (French, German, Greek, Latin).

Christopher Blackburn
16 Purple Sageway, Toronto, ON M2H 2Z5, Canada
Tel: 416-491-4857 *Fax:* 416-491-1142
E-mail: cblackburn@rogers.com
Indexing of books & periodicals. Also perform abstracting, copy-editing, fact checking, proofreading & special assignment writing.
Membership(s): Editors' Association of Canada/Association canadienne de reviseurs; Indexing & Abstracting Society of Canada

Sam Blate Associates, LLC
10331 Watkins Mill Dr, Montgomery Village, MD 20886-3950
Tel: 301-840-2248 *Fax:* 301-990-0707
E-mail: info@writephotopro.com
Web Site: www.writephotopro.com
Key Personnel
Pres: Sam Blate
Founded: 1978
Complete prepublication services: copy-editing, substantive editing, rewriting, script writing, special assignment writing, library & internet research, proofreading, ms analysis & critique, indexing, creative development, interviewing, publications consulting; illustration & commercial & advertising photography; ethical ghostwriting.
Membership(s): Mason-Dixon Outdoor Writers Association

Bloom Ink Publishing Professionals
122 S Ninth St, Lafayette, IN 47901-1652
Tel: 765-429-4888 *Fax:* 765-420-9597
Web Site: www.awbo.org/bloomink.htm
Key Personnel
Pres: Carol Bloom *E-mail:* carol@bloomink.com
Founded: 1995
Full range of editorial services for publishers, educational organizations, businesses & authors. Specializes in secondary social studies education, the social sciences & professional development materials for educators. Editing, developmental editing, rewriting, writing, copyediting & condensing/copyfitting. Expert in transforming academic to reader-friendly language. Assist prospective nonfiction authors with ms analysis, editing sample chapters, book proposals & author representation.
Membership(s): Association of Advertising & Marketing Professionals; Association of Women Business Owners; Chicago Women in Publishing; Professionals in Communication

Heidi Blough, Book Indexer
502 Tanager Rd, St Augustine, FL 32086
Tel: 904-797-6572 *Fax:* 904-797-7617
E-mail: indexing@heidiblough.com
Web Site: www.heidiblough.com
Key Personnel
Owner: Heidi Blough
Founded: 2001

Indexing diverse topics that include: biography; business; cooking & nutrition; general trade subjects; health & hospital administration; history, government, & politics; how-to; maritime & transportation subjects.
Membership(s): American Society of Indexers

Blue & Ude Writers' Services
PO Box 145, Clinton, WA 98236
Tel: 360-341-1630
E-mail: blueyude@whidbey.com
Web Site: www.blueudewritersservices.com
Key Personnel
Partner: Marian Blue; Wayne Ude
Founded: 1991
Provides all aspects of creative & technical writing & editing, including critiques, revisions & promotional copy, as well as grant writing.

Rhoda Blumberg
1305 Baptist Church Rd, Yorktown Heights, NY 10598
Tel: 914-962-7700 *Fax:* 914-962-9800
E-mail: rbwrite@aol.com
Special assignment writing & research; picture research.

Book Builders LLC
425 Madison Ave, 19th fl, New York, NY 10017
Tel: 212-371-1110 *Fax:* 212-893-8680
E-mail: mail@bookbuildersllc.com
Web Site: www.bookbuildersllc.com
Key Personnel
Pres: Lauren Fedorko
Man Ed: Beverly Teague
General, full-service, book & ancillary development in school, college, library & general reference publishing. Editorial services include: proposals, consulting, hiring of freelance staffs, writing, research, editing, copy editing, proofreading, indexing, fact checking, translating, bibliographies, special assignment writing, typemarking.
Membership(s): AAP; American Book Producers Association

Book Developers Inc
930 Forest Ave, Palo Alto, CA 94301
Tel: 650-322-4595; 650-322-4379 *Fax:* 650-322-4379
E-mail: customerservice@bookdevelopers.com
Web Site: www.bookdevelopers.com
Key Personnel
Owner: Hector Pereyra-Suarez *E-mail:* hector@bookdevelopers.com
Foreign language editorial services; editing, translating, typesetting, proofreading, indexing, copy editing, ms analysis, research, rewriting, production & manufacturing.

BookCrafters LLC
Box C, Convent Station, NJ 07961
Tel: 973-984-7880
Web Site: bookcraftersllc.com
Key Personnel
Ed: Elizabeth Zack *E-mail:* ezack@bookcraftersllc.com
Founded: 2003
A professional editorial services firm specializing in book proposal & ms development. The company offers a variety of services for published authors, literary agents & first-time writers from creating a saleable book proposal to fine-tuning a ms. Its editor has over 16 years of experience in book publishing.

The Bookmill
22000 Mt Eden Rd, Saratoga, CA 95070-9729
Tel: 408-867-9450 *Fax:* 408-867-9450
E-mail: bookmill@ix.netcom.com
Web Site: www.marinacci.com/Bookmill

Key Personnel
Ed: Barbara Marinacci
Graphics: Rudy Marinacci
Founded: 1982
Book preparation; proposal writing; word processing; contacts with agents, editors & publishers.

BooksCraft Inc
4909 Eastbourne Dr, Indianapolis, IN 46226
Tel: 317-542-8327 *Fax:* 317-591-9809
E-mail: bookscraft@comcast.net
Web Site: www.bookscraft.com
Key Personnel
Pres: Donald S MacLaren
Man Ed: Ruth Frick
Founded: 1985
Complete editorial services, ms through bound books; digital page layout; digital illustration & image editing.

Booktec
2825 SE 67, Portland, OR 97206
Tel: 503-772-9177 *Fax:* 503-339-9908
Key Personnel
Contact: Robin Romer *E-mail:* robin@booktec.com
Providing development & production of academic, technical & other nonfiction writing for book publishers.

The Boston Word Works
PO Box 56419, Sherman Oaks, CA 91413-1419
Tel: 818-904-9088 *Fax:* 818-787-1431
Key Personnel
Owner: Leslie Paul Boston
  E-mail: bostonlespaul@adelphia.net
Founded: 1985
General fiction & nonfiction. Writing & editing. Evaluation, preparation of book proposals & sample chapters. Consultation on ideas, approaches & development.
Membership(s): Independent Writers of Southern California; National Writers Union

Brady Literary Management
Town Farm Hill, PO Box 164, Hartland Four Corners, VT 05049
Tel: 802-436-2455 *Fax:* 802-436-2466
Key Personnel
Owner: Sally R Brady; Upton B Brady
Ms analysis, conceptual, developmental & line editing, book doctoring, rewriting; trade fiction & nonfiction; contacts with agents, editors & publishers. Work on a fee &/or percentage basis.

Donna Lee Braunstein Your Personal Researcher
22848 Mesa Way, Lake Forest, CA 92630
Tel: 949-472-8538
E-mail: dlbraunstein@prodigy.net
Key Personnel
Res Specialist & Owner: Donna Lee Braunstein
Book, article & script researcher of technical, current nonfiction, literary authenticity, biography, true crime & government policy. Researcher of library & city/county archives, facts, data, papers, documents, articles & photographs on a broad range of topics worldwide & fact checking. Bibliographical verification & development, copyright permissions. Specialize in obtaining obscure documents & information with unknown source, incomplete title, etc. Additional research services include survey & geographic statistical compilation for tables & graphs. Writer of government policy & business trends for trade newsletters & reports.
Membership(s): Association of Independent Information Professionals; Los Angeles Public Library Researchers List

Norman Brown & Associates
50 Blackstone Blvd, Providence, RI 02906
Tel: 401-751-2641 *Fax:* 401-331-4612
E-mail: nhbrown@msn.com
Web Site: www.indexme.net
Key Personnel
Pres: Norman Brown
VP, Mktg: Freda Brown
VP, European Oper: Amy Brown
Founded: 1973
Production & revision; travel, health & personal finance.
Branch Office(s)
Fogelsunda 18695, Vallentuna, Sweden, Contact: Amy Brown *Tel:* (08) 512 30307 *Fax:* (08) 512 30308

Brown Publishing Network Inc
95 Sawyer Rd, Waltham, MA 02453
Tel: 781-237-7567 *Fax:* 781-237-8874
Web Site: www.brownpubnet.com
Key Personnel
Pres & CEO: Marie Brown *E-mail:* mbrown@brownpubnet.com
VP & COO: Anthony G Fisher
VP & CFO: Mark Brown *E-mail:* mark@brownpubnet.com
VP, Art & Design: Trelawney N Godell
VP, Prodn: Joseph A Hinckley
VP, Edit: Elinor Y Chamas
Exec Dir, NY Off: Alice Dickstein
Educational publishing & all subject areas for K-12 grades, college & trade materials. Provides a full range of publishing services including writing, editing, art, design, production, market research & fact checking. Includes pupil texts, workbooks, teacher's editions, test & other ancillary materials from creation of ms through bound book, or just one phase of the project, depending on the needs of the publisher. Distributes to publishers annual complimentary copies of *Brown's Who's Who in Educational Publishing* & *Brown's What's What in Education*.
Branch Office(s)
122 E 42 St, New York, NY 10168 *Tel:* 212-682-3330 *Fax:* 212-682-8530
Membership(s): AAP; Association of Educational Publishers

Gordon Brumm
1515 Saint Charles Ave, Lakewood, OH 44107
Tel: 216-226-6105 *Fax:* 216-226-1964
E-mail: brummg@cox.net
Quality Indexing.

Hilary R Burke
59 Sparks St, Ottawa, ON K1P 6C3, Canada
Tel: 613-237-4658
E-mail: pointtopoint@canada.com; hilary.burke@pointtopointbooks.com
Web Site: www.pointtopointbooks.com
Promotional writing of fiction & nonfiction.

BZ/Rights & Permissions Inc
121 W 27 St, Suite 901, New York, NY 10001
Tel: 212-924-3000 *Fax:* 212-924-2525
E-mail: info@bzrights.com
Web Site: www.bzrights.com
Key Personnel
Pres: Barbara Zimmerman *Tel:* 212-924-3000 ext 105 *E-mail:* bz@bzrights.com
Founded: 1980
Clear rights & permissions for literary material, music, photographs, art, TV & film clips; specialize in clearing copyrighted material for multimedia/electronic publishing, video & spoken word recordings.
Membership(s): Association of Independent Music Publishers; Copyright Society of the USA; Media Communications Association; Publishers Marketing Association

Camden House
Imprint of Boydell & Brewer Inc
668 Mount Hope Ave, Rochester, NY 14620
Tel: 585-273-5709; 585-275-0419 *Fax:* 585-271-8778
E-mail: boydell@boydellusa.net
Web Site: www.boydell.co.uk/camdenfr.htm; www.camden-house.com
Key Personnel
Ed-in-Chief & Acqs Ed: James Hardin
Man Ed: James Walker *E-mail:* walker@camdenhouse.net
Founded: 1978
Publish scholarly books in field of literature & criticism. Emphasis on German & American literature.
Imprints: Boydell & Brewer Ltd

Cariad Ltd
180 Bloor St, Suite 801, Toronto, ON M5S 2V6, Canada
Tel: 416-929-2774 *Fax:* 416-929-1926
E-mail: cariadreps@hotmail.com
Key Personnel
Man Dir: Rex J Williams
VP: Penny Williams-Sackman
Sales & marketing representation.
Branch Office(s)
389 Danforth Ave, Ottawa, ON K2A 0E1, Canada
Foreign Office(s): Ferrybank House, 6 Park Rd, Dun Laoghaire, Dublin, Ireland

Carlisle Communications Ltd
4242 Chavenelle Dr, Dubuque, IA 52002-2650
Tel: 563-557-1500 *Fax:* 563-557-1376
E-mail: carlisle@carcomm.com
Web Site: www.carcomm.com
Key Personnel
Pres & CEO: Rich Runde *E-mail:* rrunde@carcomm.com
Chmn of the Bd: John B Carlisle
VP, Opers: Tony Carlisle
Sales & Mktg Mgr: Julie A Carlisle *E-mail:* jucarlisle@carcomm.com
Mgr: Sandra Hahn
Offer experienced state-of-the-art book production, fulfilling all of your prepress needs including; complete project management, copyediting, rewriting, photo research, indexing, cover & internal design, technical & creative illustrations, high level scanning, electronic composition & disk or film to printer utilizing the eight-page imposed Linotron SignaSetter. Carlisle Communications Ltd is a fully electronic 4-color, full-service supplier dedicated to serving your needs from college, el-hi, journals, catalogs to commercial projects. For on-time, top of the line quality, call us.

Carlsbad Publications
3242 McKinley St, Carlsbad, CA 92008
Tel: 760-729-9543 *Fax:* 760-729-9543
E-mail: bunkobabe9@aol.com
Key Personnel
Mgr: Sue C Bosio
Specialize in technical material & editorial consultation on difficult mss.
Membership(s): Freelance Editorial Association

Charles Carmony
250 W 105 St, Suite 2A, New York, NY 10025
Tel: 212-749-1835
Indexing.

R E Carsch, MS-Consultant
1453 Rhode Island St, San Francisco, CA 94107-3248
Tel: 415-641-1095 *Fax:* 415-641-1095
E-mail: recarsch@mzinfo.com
Key Personnel
Consultant: R E Carsch

Founded: 1973
Full range editorial services including fact checking, interviewing, ms analysis, proofreading, research & industry overviews.
Membership(s): Art Libraries Society

Anne Carson Associates
3323 Nebraska Ave NW, Washington, DC 20016
Tel: 202-244-6679
Key Personnel
Ed-in-Chief: Anne Conover Carson *E-mail:* anne_conover@hotmail.com
Founded: 1976
Proofreading, research, rewriting, special assignment writing, indexing, ms analysis; specialize in Latin America, biography.
Membership(s): American Academy of Poets; Authors Guild; National Coalition of Independent Scholars; Washington Independent Writers

Claudia Caruana
PO Box 654, Murray Hill Sta, New York, NY 10016
Tel: 516-488-5815
E-mail: ccaruana29@hotmail.com
Copy editing, ms analysis, rights & permissions, picture search, proofreading, research, rewriting, special assignment writing, magazine photography.

Angela M Casey
331 S Wall St, Kingston, NY 12401
Tel: 845-340-8601
E-mail: angelamcasey@verizon.net
Specializing in holistic health, diet, exercise & inspirational titles.

Catalyst Communication Arts
94 Chuparr OsA, San Luis Obispo, CA 93401
Tel: 805-543-7250 *Fax:* 805-543-7250
Key Personnel
Owner: Sonsie Carbonara Conroy *E-mail:* sconroy@slonet.org
Editorial services with emphasis on line editing & rewriting. Specialize in indexing.

CATALYST Creative Services
619 Marion Plaza, Palo Alto, CA 94301-4251
Tel: 650-325-1500
Key Personnel
Owner & Chief Catalyst: Dennis Alan *E-mail:* dennis@catalyst96.com
Founded: 1975
Our clients get published & earn profits. We brainstorm & develop creative, direct ways to move your target audience. Our clients appear in trade books, magazines, journal articles & websites that inform, persuade & amuse. We accept both fees & royalty deals.
Membership(s): Graphic Arts Association; National Writers Union

Jeanne Cavelos Editorial Services
20 Levesque Lane, Mont Vernon, NH 03057
Tel: 603-673-6234 *Fax:* 603-673-6234
E-mail: jcavelos@sff.net
Web Site: www.sff.net/people/jcavelos
Key Personnel
Owner: Jeanne Cavelos
Founded: 1994
Published writer & former senior editor at major publishing house. Full editorial services for publishers, book packagers, businesses, agents & authors. From line edit to thorough edit to heavy edit. Detailed reader's reports. Book proposal doctoring. Editorial consulting, creative development. Newsletters, magazine articles, novelizations. Handle the full range of fiction & nonfiction. Specialize in thrillers, literary

fiction, fantasy, science fiction, horror, popular culture, self-help, health.

Membership(s): Horror Writers Association; Science Fiction & Fantasy Writers of America

Cebulash Associates

10245 E Via Linda Ave, Suite 221, Scottsdale, AZ 85258

Tel: 480-451-8400 *Fax:* 480-451-0848

E-mail: cebulash@att.net

Key Personnel

Pres: Dolly Cebulash

VP: Mel Cebulash

Man Ed: Kerry Rieth

Founded: 1980

Specialize in developing & writing ancillary materials, supplementary texts & special assignment fiction for el-hi publishers. Emphasis on reading, special reading & language arts materials; package fiction in series for school & library trade publishers; ms to complete production services available; nonfiction sports for juveniles & movie novelizations.

CeciBooks Editorial & Publishing Consultation

7057 26 Ave NW, Seattle, WA 98127

Mailing Address: PO Box 17229, Seattle, WA 98127

Tel: 206-706-9565

Web Site: www.cecibooks.com

Key Personnel

Owner: Ceci Miller

Founded: 1988

CeciBooks offers a professional orientation to the world of publishing, as well as effective & respectful promotional writing & coaching. We develop publishing & marketing strategies that express our clients' best intentions. Whether an author or publisher wants advice on how best to position a book in the current market, seeks developmental or substantive editing, or needs a fresh marketing strategy, CeciBooks offers expert advice that is both reliable & affordable.

Membership(s): Northwest Independent Editors Guild; Pacific Northwest Writers Association; Society of Children's Book Writers & Illustrators; Women's Business Exchange

Celo Book Production Service

160 Ohle Rd, Burnsville, NC 28714

Tel: 828-675-5918

Key Personnel

Prod Mgr: D Donovan

Copy editing, rewriting.

Membership(s): Editorial Freelancers Association; The Writers' Workshop

Margaret Cheasebro

246 Rd 2900, Aztec, NM 87410

Tel: 505-334-2869 *Fax:* 505-334-6434

E-mail: mcheasebro@fisi.net

Freelance writer. Specialize in people, places & issues of the Four Corners area, short plays, personality profiles, children's books, drama in real life stories & puzzle activities.

Ruth Chernia

81 Withrow Ave, Toronto, ON M4K 1C8, Canada

Tel: 416-466-0164 *Fax:* 416-466-3835

E-mail: rchernia@editors.ca; rchernia@sympatico.ca

Provides professional editorial & publishing consultation to companies & individuals. Branch office in Toronto.

Membership(s): Editors' Association of Canada/ Association canadienne de reviseurs

The Chestnut House Group Inc

2121 Saint Johns Ave, Highland Park, IL 60035

Tel: 847-432-3273 *Fax:* 847-432-3229

E-mail: info@chestnuthousegroup.com

Web Site: www.chestnuthousegroup.com

Key Personnel

Pres: Miles Zimmerman *E-mail:* milesz@ chestnuthousegroup.com

Founded: 1968

Complete editorial, design & production services. All editorial & product development services including ms development, rewrite, substantive editing, copy-editing, fact checking, proofreading, indexing & field-testing. All design & production services including book & program design, print & collateral materials design, art direction & acquisition, photo research & acquisition, page layout & desktop publishing. All prepress through final film or CTP-ready files in native format, PDF, or PostScript form on Macintosh & Windows platforms. Curricular specialties are reading, language arts, spelling, history, humanities, science & psychology. Experience with magazines, encyclopedias, print ads & campaigns, catalogs, brochures, poetry & fiction. Complete project management. For educational & trade publishers, small presses & selected authors.

Chrysalis Publishing Group Inc

34 Main St, Natick, MA 01760

Tel: 508-647-3730 *Toll Free Tel:* 877-922-1822 *Fax:* 508-653-3448

E-mail: info@chrysalispublishing.com

Web Site: www.chrysalispublishing.com

Key Personnel

Pres: Lucille Nava *E-mail:* lucillenava@ chrysalispublishing.com

Ed-in-Chief: Cynthia Tripp *E-mail:* cindytripp@ chrysalispublishing.com

Off Mgr: Gale DiRusso *E-mail:* galedirusso@ chrysalispublishing.com

Founded: 1999

Provide editorial, design & production services to educational publishers. Expertise in all content areas: reading/language arts, mathematics, science/health & social studies/history. Creative process includes conceptualizing, prototyping & developing print, web & electronic products. Services include writing; content-, line- & copy-editing; proofreading; indexing; researching & fact checking; developing correlations. Products include student & teacher materials; CD-ROMs; assessment & test preparation components; supplemental materials, state customizations; professional development materials.

Membership(s): International Reading Association; National Council for the Social Studies; National Council of Teachers of English; National Council of Teachers of Mathematics; National Science Teachers Association

Clear Concepts

1329 Federal Ave, Suite 6, Los Angeles, CA 90025

Tel: 310-473-5453

Key Personnel

Owner: Karen Kleiner

Founded: 1986

Provides substantive editing, copywriting & research. Specializes in business, technology, holistic health textbooks & children's books. Owner holds BA from UCLA in communication studies.

Membership(s): Society for Technical Communication

Clerical Plus

273 Derby Ave, Unit 214, Derby, CT 06418

Tel: 203-732-3843 *Fax:* 203-732-3843

E-mail: clericalplus@aol.com

Key Personnel

Pres: Rose E Brown

Coastside Editorial

1111 Date St, Montara, CA 94037

Mailing Address: PO Box 370953, Montara, CA 94037

Tel: 650-728-0902 *Fax:* 650-728-0905

Key Personnel

Contact: Beverly McGuire *E-mail:* bevjoe@ pacific.net

Copy editing, proofreading.

Robert L Cohen

182-12 Horace Harding Expressway, Suite 2M, Fresh Meadows, NY 11365

Tel: 617-254-0254; 718-595-2082 (NYC)

Toll Free Tel: 866-EDITING

E-mail: wordsmith@sterlingmp.com

Web Site: www.sterlingmp.com

Copy, line, & substantive/developmental editing of trade & academic/reference books; editing & rewriting of public policy books/reports/newsletters/monographs; lexicography; radio & AV scriptwriting; speechwriting. Specialize in urban affairs, public policy, public health, international relations, social sciences, psychology, education, Judaica, & music. Also: writing coach for businesses & nonprofits.

Branch Office(s)

Sterling Media Productions LLC, 182-12 Horace Harding Expressway, Suite 2M, Fresh Meadows, NY 11365 *Tel:* 718-595-2082 *Toll Free Tel:* 866-NYC-EDIT *Web Site:* www. sterlingmp.com

Membership(s): American Society for Jewish Music; Cambridge Academic Editors Network; Editorial Freelancers Association

E Calvin Coish

99 Lincoln Rd, Grand Falls, NF A2A 2T2, Canada

Tel: 709-489-6796 *Fax:* 709-489-6796

E-mail: c.coish@nf.sympatico.ca

Writing, publishing, editing, proofreading, fact checking, indexing, interviewing & research.

Zipporah W Collins

768 Peralta Ave, Berkeley, CA 94707-1842

Tel: 510-527-2140 *Fax:* 510-527-4155

E-mail: zipcol@aol.com

Complete ms-to-bound-book editorial & project management services since 1960, freelance since 1970. Text (humanities, social sciences, music, French, computer manuals, dance, women's studies, law, education, medicine) & trade (fiction, cookbooks, gardening, how-to, children's books, computer user guides, art, ecology, film, photography, biography). Mac-based electronic editing.

Membership(s): Bay Area Editors' Forum; Book-builders West; Editcetera; Women's National Book Association

Colophon Group

1306 Rousseau Cres, Greely, ON K4P 1B3, Canada

Tel: 613-821-0066 *Fax:* 613-821-9987

E-mail: colophongroup@rogers.com

Key Personnel

Pres: Ed Matheson

Book publishing consultants for publishers, business, government & individuals with publishing problems; also supplies Canadian book industry related mailing lists. Specialize in project management, general book design & production.

Connelly Editorial Services

1630 Main St, Suite 41, Coventry, CT 06238

Tel: 860-742-5279 *Fax:* 860-742-5279

E-mail: angelsus@aol.com

Key Personnel

Pres: Claire Connelly

Founded: 1969

MS or disk: Medical, law, psychology, science & computers, metaphysics, textbooks, fiction & nonfiction.
Membership(s): American Association of Marriage & Family Therapists; Society for Technical Communication

Martin Cook Associates Ltd
353 Strawtown Rd, New City, NY 10956
Tel: 845-639-5316 *Fax:* 845-639-5318
E-mail: mcanewcity@aol.com
Web Site: www.mcabooks.com
Key Personnel
Pres: Martin Cook
Full-service production source serving publishers, packagers & others. Design of text, illustration inserts, jackets & covers; composition; color separations; printing; binding; brokering for trade, reference, educational & art books.
Membership(s): Bookbinders Guild of New York

The Copy Shoppe
Subsidiary of CataLogistics Inc
PO Box 304, Mendham, NJ 07945
Tel: 973-543-2679 *Fax:* 973-543-9090
E-mail: catalogistics@juno.com
Key Personnel
Pres & Copy Chief: Jack Schrier
Founded: 1972
Specialize in direct response mailings, circulation & subscription promos, brochures, space ads, catalogs, sales letters, radio spots & publicity for book & magazine publishers, continuity programs & clubs.

Copywriter's Council of America (CCA)
Division of The Linick Group Inc
CCA Bldg, 7 Putter Lane, Middle Island, NY 11953-0102
Mailing Address: PO Box 102, Dept LMP 04, Middle Island, NY 11953-0102
Tel: 631-924-8555 *Fax:* 631-924-3890
E-mail: cca4dmcopy@att.net
Web Site: www.lgroup.addr.com/CCA.htm
Key Personnel
Chmn, Consulting Group: Andrew S Linick, PhD
   E-mail: linickgrp@att.net
VP: Roger Dextor
Dir, Spec Proj: Barbara Deal
Over 25,000 freelance advertising copywriters, editors, communication specialists & journalists; covering direct response/direct mail field for health, physical fitness, gourmet, how-to, martial arts, self improvement, travel & tourism, photography, sports & recreation, business communications & high tech for books, magazines, manuals, newsletters, in-house organs & courses. Marketing, research, rewriting, special assignment writing, copy-editing, indexing, proofreading, ms analysis; video production, audio-video news releases; interviews & profiles; rights & permissions. Also offer annual seminars, workshops & trade show to writers/editors who would like to increase their income. Phone consultation available. Provide comprehensive graphic re-design/new web site content development, interactive services with website marketing makeover advice for first-time authors, self-publishers, professionals & entrepreneurs. Specializes in flash, animation, merchant accounts, on-line advertising/PR, links to top search engines, consulting on a 100% satisfaction guarantee. Free site evaluation for LMP readers.

Corbett Gordon Co
6 Fort Rachel Place, Mystic, CT 06355
Tel: 860-536-4108 *Fax:* 860-536-3732
Key Personnel
Owner: Rose Corbett Gordon
   E-mail: rcgordonX@aol.com

Creative research for books, book covers & exhibits. Fine art & historical research; experience includes wide range of subject areas, such as government, politics, social science & biological sciences. Also, art direction/commissioning of assignment photography.

Corrington Indexing Services
2638 E Kenwood, Mesa, AZ 85213
Tel: 480-827-8904 *Fax:* 480-827-1182
Key Personnel
Owner: Paul Corrington *E-mail:* paulcorri@aol.com
Founded: 1997
Provide quality indexes for publishers, professional organizations & authors specializing in back-of-the-book & journal publications.

Cottage Communications Inc
128 Rte 6A, Sandwich, MA 02563
Tel: 508-833-1300 *Fax:* 508-833-6319
Key Personnel
Pres: Phil Le Faivre *E-mail:* p.lefaivre@verizon.net
Founded: 1989
Writing, editing, consulting, production & project management services for elementary & secondary textbook publishers. Specialize in reading, spelling, language arts & related areas.
Membership(s): International Reading Association; National Council of Teachers of English

Course Crafters Inc
44 Merrimac St, Newburyport, MA 01950
Tel: 978-465-2040 *Fax:* 978-465-5027
E-mail: info@coursecrafters.com
Web Site: www.coursecrafters.com
Key Personnel
CEO & Pres: Lise B Ragan *E-mail:* lragan@coursecrafters.com
Full-service development house & packager of educational materials, K-adult, with a unique focus in the growing English Language Learner Market (ELL). Specialize in English as a second language (ESL), bilingual education & literacy material for English language learners, their teachers & parents. Provide services to publishers in market research, consulting, conceptualizing, writing/editing, production, translation & developing marketing/sales plans. Also can develop customized materials for schools. Print, audio, video & multimedia in ESL & Spanish; professional development, instructional materials & assessment.

Mark Crawford
5101 Violet Lane, Madison, WI 53714
Tel: 608-240-4959 *Fax:* 608-245-9309
E-mail: giltedge@chorus.net
Founded: 1995
Servicing all audiences including academic, technical, science, corporate & public relations. Additional services include: substantive editing, promotional writing & writing of corporate histories.

Vallaurie Crawford
PO Box 668, Volcano, HI 96785
Tel: 808-985-8512 *Fax:* 808-967-7648
E-mail: crawford@hawaii.rr.com
Full range of services for publishers, authors, businesses & scholarly institutions: rewriting & revision, copy-editing, outlining, compilation, abstracting & condensation, proofreading, book reviewing, ms development & interviewing. Specialize in rewriting or polishing rough translations. Experience includes scholarly texts & journals, newsletters, proposals, newspapers, magazines, seminars & multi-author works. Deliver on disk or hard copy.

Creative Freelancers Inc
99 Park Ave, No 210-A, New York, NY 10016
Tel: 203-532-2924 *Toll Free Tel:* 800-398-9544; 888-398-9500 *Fax:* 203-532-2927
E-mail: cfonline@freelancers.com
Web Site: www.freelancers.com
Key Personnel
Pres: Marilyn Howard
Freelance copy & art services for publishing & advertising. Designers, artists, copy editors, all creative areas, translations.

Cross Pond Editing Group
333 Hook Rd, Katonah, NY 10536
Tel: 914-232-8687 *Fax:* 914-232-1258
Key Personnel
Ed: Susan Allport
Contact: Barbara Mayer
Line editing & ms evaluation of literary, commercial & scholarly works.

Ruth C Cross
51 Linden St, No 101, Brattleboro, VT 05301
Tel: 802-257-1456

Crystalline Sphere Publishing
47 Bridgeport Rd E, Waterloo, ON N2J 2J4, Canada
E-mail: csp@golden.net
Web Site: crystallinesphere.com
Key Personnel
Ed: David M Switzer
Founded: 1995
Provides copy-editing & ms analysis. Also publishes the science fiction & fantasy magazine *Challenging Destiny*.

CS International Literary Agency
43 W 39 St, New York, NY 10018
Tel: 212-921-1610
E-mail: csliterary@verizon.net
Key Personnel
Agent: Cynthia Neesemann
Ms analysis, evaluation & agent representation available for nonfiction, fiction & screenplays. Research, interviewing, permissions & some editing also available. We are particularly responsive to helping beginning writers to improve their writing skills & style with suggestions for better plotting, characterization, dialogue & structure. Fees very reasonable. Interests extend to full range of topics whether fact or fantasy, including international, occult, ethnic, political, historical & religious subjects, mysteries & comedies. Please query with short synopsis of project.

Cultural Studies & Analysis
1123 Montrose St, Philadelphia, PA 19147
Tel: 215-592-8544 *Fax:* 215-413-9041
E-mail: cultureking@comcast.net
Web Site: www.culturalanalysis.com
Key Personnel
Dir: Margaret J King, PhD
Specialize in cultural analysis; identify consumer values & decision making. We do not provide novel writing.

Culture Concepts Books
69 Ashmount Crescent, Toronto, ON M9R 1C9, Canada
Tel: 416-245-8119 *Fax:* 416-245-3383
E-mail: cultureconcepts@sympatico.ca
Web Site: www.cultureconcepts.ca
Key Personnel
Pres: Thelma Barer-Stein, PhD
Founded: 1980
Provides professional editorial services, literary agency (especially for nonfiction), book production for publishers. Also ms evaluation, developmental & project editing, substantive editing, rewriting, line & copy-editing.

Membership(s): Association of Canadian Publishers; Editors' Association of Canada/Association canadienne de reviseurs; The Writers' Union of Canada

Pat Cusick & Associates
370 Park St, Suite 9-B, Moraga, CA 94556
Tel: 925-376-4457 *Fax:* 925-376-4859
E-mail: pcusick@pacbell.net
Founded: 1988
Specializes in designing & producing educational materials. The company has the expertise to take the following or similar projects from concept development to final film: pupil texts, teacher's editions, activity books, workbooks, big books, posters, ancillary packages & testing instruments. Provides product concept, market data, writing, editing, design, art & production. Subject areas include reading, spelling, language arts, literature, math, science & social studies.

Custom Editorial Productions Inc (CEP)
546 W Liberty St, Cincinnati, OH 45214
Tel: 513-723-1100 Fax: 513-723-1103
E-mail: cep@customeditorial.com
Web Site: www.customeditorial.com
Key Personnel
Pres: Mary Lou Motl E-mail: mlmotl@customeditorial.com
Gen Mgr: Marvin Good E-mail: mcgood@customeditorial.com
Fin Mgr: Robert C Himmler
E-mail: rob_himmler@customeditorial.com
Founded: 1982
Since 1982, CEP has provided reliable high-quality prepress publishing services & met demanding schedules. Today our activities include writing, developmental editing, correlating educational materials to state standards, copy-editing, proofreading, indexing, page makeup, XML tagging, preparing illustrations, & project management. Our typical clients are publishers & professional organizations whose products are educational materials, both printed & electronic. We integrate our services into the established internal processes of our clients.

Cypress House
Affiliate of QED Press
155 Cypress St, Fort Bragg, CA 95437
Tel: 707-964-9520 *Toll Free Tel:* 800-773-7782
Fax: 707-964-7531
E-mail: publishing@cypresshouse.com
Web Site: www.cypresshouse.com
Key Personnel
Pres: Cynthia Frank *E-mail:* cynthia@cypresshouse.com
Sr Ed: Joe Shaw
Prodn Mgr: Michael Brechner
Complete editorial, design, production, marketing & promotion services to independent publishers. Editorial services include ms evaluation, editing, rewriting, copymarking & proofing. Production services include book, cover & page design & make-up to camera-ready. Marketing & promotion services for selected titles.
Membership(s): ABA; Bay Area Independent Publishers Association; Northern California Independent Booksellers Association; Pacific Northwest Booksellers Association; Publishers Marketing Association

Steven P d'Adolf
17852 Saint Andrews Dr, Poway, CA 92064
Tel: 858-451-2130 *Fax:* 858-451-2130
E-mail: sdadolf@san.rr.com
Ms analysis for technical subjects, technical research, book reviewing & development of user manuals.

DanaRae Pomeroy
139 Turner Circle, Greenville, SC 29609
Tel: 864-834-7549
E-mail: danarae@charter.net
Ms critique; contact before sending mss for critique or editing.
Membership(s): National League of American Pen Women; Romance Writers of America

Darla Bruno, Editor
80 Ports Harbor Rd, Addison, ME 04606
Tel: 207-229-5114
E-mail: editor@darlabruno.com
Web Site: www.darlabruno.com
Provide editorial service both in print & on the web: proofreading, copy-editing & substantive editing. Specializing in fiction & nonfiction; other subjects include literature, food, marketing, nonfiction. Co-authoring services offered.

Suzanne B Davidson
8084 N 44 St, Brown Deer, WI 53223
Tel: 414-355-6640
E-mail: davidson@execpc.com
Founded: 1984
Specialize in scholarly books, college texts, law, business, politics, gen nonfiction.

Winifred M Davis
1700 York Ave, Suite 9-L, New York, NY 10128
Tel: 212-534-0034
Scholarly, college, professional, general nonfiction. Specialize in literature, medical, architecture & art history.

Scottie Dayton
1112 Division St, Manitowoc, WI 54220-5733
Tel: 920-684-5228 *Fax:* 920-686-0820 (call first)
E-mail: sdayton@lakefield.net

Mari Lynch Dehmler, see Fine Wordworking

Devonshire House Books
4435 Holly Lane NW, Gig Harbor, WA 98335
Tel: 253-851-9896 *Fax:* 253-851-9897
Web Site: critiquemaster.com
Key Personnel
Pres: Hank Searls *E-mail:* hanksearls@harbornet.com
Founded: 1986
Author's workshop.

May Dikeman
70 Irving Place, New York, NY 10003
Tel: 212-475-4533
Comprehensive literary services.
Membership(s): PEN American Center

Christina DiMartino Literary Services
59 W 119 St, Suite 2, New York City, NY 10026
Tel: 212-996-9086; 917-972-6012
E-mail: writealot@earthlink.net
Key Personnel
Owner: Christina DiMartino
Full book line services, collaboration of book projects, freelance writing for national magazines, & teaching of writing.

DK Research Inc
14 Mohegan Lane, Commack, NY 11725
Tel: 631-543-5537 *Fax:* 631-543-5549
Key Personnel
Pres: Diane Kraut *E-mail:* dianekraut@att.net
Obtain copyright clearance for text material; research & edit photos for use in textbooks; negotiate photo & text permission fees.

Double Play
PO Box 22481, Kansas City, MO 64113

Tel: 816-651-7118 *Fax:* 816-822-2521
Key Personnel
Pres: Lloyd Johnson *E-mail:* lloydj@msn.com
VP: Connie Johnson
Writing & research about baseball; sports, baseball museum consultant, exhibits; working on database of professional baseball.
Membership(s): Pro Football Researchers Association; Society for American Baseball Research

Drennan Communications
6 Robin Lane, East Kingston, NH 03827
Tel: 603-642-8002 *Fax:* 603-642-8002
Key Personnel
Pres & Edit Dir: William D Drennan
VP & Sr Ed: Christina L Drennan
Founded: 1980
Line editing, copy editing, ms analysis, proofreading, rewriting, ghost writing, special assignment writing, condensations, typemarking, abstracting, fact checking, interviewing, research, advertising & promotion copywriting.

Drummond Books
2111 Cleveland St, Evanston, IL 60202
Tel: 847-869-5305
Key Personnel
Owner: Siobhan Drummond
Editorial services in book production including project editing & management of manufacturing (typesetting & printing including prepress), typesetting & projects by task; copy-editing, substantive editing & indexing.

Mary Duerson
5234 Texas Circle, Ames, IA 50014
Tel: 515-292-5918
E-mail: mduerson@mail.isunet.net
Copy editing, line editing, proofreading, ms analysis. Fiction & nonfiction, textbooks & teaching manuals, consumer health books; on-disk editing.

Moira Duggan Editorial Services
113A The Hook Rd, Bedford, NY 10506-1110
Tel: 914-234-7937 *Fax:* 914-234-7937
E-mail: mduggan@bestweb.net
Web Site: www.consulting-editors.com
Key Personnel
Contact: Moira Duggan *E-mail:* mduggan@bestweb.net
For authors, agents, editors, corporate departments. Offering critique & solutions in all phases of adult nonfiction book development: concept, presentation, writing style, factual correctness. Special-assignment writing; working to deadline. Network to book producers, agents, publishers, illustrators, picture researchers. Bio at www.consulting-editors.com.
Membership(s): Consulting Editors Alliance

E & J Proofreading
162 W Washington St, Hagerstown, MD 21740
Tel: 240-313-9250 *Fax:* 240-313-9250
E-mail: ejproofreading@yahoo.com
Key Personnel
Owner: Darrell Hull
Founded: 1987
Proofreading, refolio indexes, notes & references, verify mechanicals.

Earth Edit
PO Box 114, Maiden Rock, WI 54750
Tel: 715-448-3009
Key Personnel
Contact: George Dyke *E-mail:* georgedy@cannon.net
Copy editing & proofreading of earth science & geography texts.

East End Publishing Services Inc
916 Sound Shore Rd, Riverhead, NY 11901
Tel: 631-722-3921 *Fax:* 631-722-3921
Key Personnel
Pres: Edie Riker *E-mail:* edieriker@aol.com
Founded: 1984
Full-service book/long document production:
Project management including copy-editing, design, composition & art services, proofreading & indexing. Manage projects from author ms submission through checking blues from your printer. Deadline & cost conscious. Textbooks & trade books our specialty.

East Mountain Editing Services
Formerly Spanishindexing.com
PO Box 1895, Tijeras, NM 87059
Tel: 505-281-8422 *Fax:* 505-281-8422
Web Site: www.spanishindexing.com
Key Personnel
Mgr: Francine Cronshaw *E-mail:* cronshaw@nmia.com
Indexing in Spanish or English. Additional services include: translation & consulting on bilingual or Spanish-language editions; editing of translations.
Membership(s): American Society of Indexers; New Mexico Translators & Interpreters Association

Edelsack Editorial Service
201 Evergreen St, Vestal, NY 13850-2796
Mailing Address: PO Box 497, Vestal, NY 13851-0497
Tel: 607-797-1840 *Fax:* 607-729-1977
E-mail: pedelsack@aol.com
Key Personnel
Contact: Paula Edelsack
Project management (journals/books) copy editing, proofreading, typemarking.

EditAndPublishYourBook.com
PO Box 2965, Nantucket, MA 02584-2965
E-mail: michaeltheauthor@yahoo.com
Web Site: www.editandpublishyourbook.com
Key Personnel
Principal: Michael Wells Glueck
Founded: 2002
Services offered include abstracting, condensations, copy-editing, interviewing, line editing, ms analysis, proofreading, rewriting, special assignment writing & transcription editing. I can also submit your work to a reasonably priced subsidy publisher, shepherd it through the publication process & monitor online booksellers' websites to make sure that it remains available for purchase, that they list it correctly & that the listing includes a front-cover photograph & other features. I can also suggest unorthodox but effective marketing techniques & if you wish, I can write & submit reviews to online booksellers' websites. Recent projects include editing Flatlands, a novel written by Susan Sims Moody of Tennessee & published in November 2003 by iUniverse.com & both writing & editing reviews for the Fictional Rome website linked to the Richard Stockton College of New Jersey.

Edit Etc
321 Hollywood Ave, Ho-Ho-Kus, NJ 07423
Tel: 201-251-4796 *Fax:* 201-251-4797
E-mail: atkedit@cs.com
Web Site: anntkeene.com
Key Personnel
Pres: Ann T Keene
Founded: 1985
Editing, writing, copywriting, research, photo research.

EditAmerica
115 Jacobs Creek Rd, Ewing, NJ 08628
Tel: 609-882-5852 *Fax:* 609-882-5851
E-mail: editamerica@usa.com
Web Site: www.editamerica.com
Key Personnel
Principal: Paula Plantier *E-mail:* paulaplantier@rock.com
Founded: 1979
Experience consists of 25 years of expert, accurate & exacting professional copy-editing & proofreading of academic & scholarly material, advertising copy, bibliographies, biographies, brochures, bulletins, business & marketing communications material, college & graduate school application essays, college viewbooks, company annual reports & form 10-Ks, computer literature, cookbooks, cover letters, curricula vitae, directories, elementary school & high school textbooks, engineering books, finance & accounting literature, formal invitations, form letters, french, general nonfiction, graduate school theses, Internet site material, legal notices, mathematics books, medical books, medical journals, newsletters, news releases, peer-reviewed professional magazines, periodicals, press releases, professional trade publications, reference books, religious treatises, resumes, Spanish, user's manuals & web site content.

editcetera
2034 Blake St, Suite 5, Berkeley, CA 94704
Tel: 510-849-1110 *Fax:* 510-848-1448
E-mail: info@editcetera.com
Web Site: www.editcetera.com
Key Personnel
Dir: Barbara Fuller
Founded: 1971
Association & clearinghouse for editing & writing professionals. Clients include authors, packagers, trade publishers, el-hi & college textbook publishers, self-publishers, computer companies (software & hardware), corporations. Services available include production management from mss through bound books as well as writing, rewriting, developmental editing, copy-editing, coaching of writers, proofreading, indexing, web editing, web page design, book design & word processing. Stringent membership requirements.

Editing International LLC
2123 Marlow Lane, Suite 21, Eugene, OR 97401-6431
Tel: 541-344-9118
E-mail: info@4-edit.com
Web Site: www.4-edit.com
Key Personnel
Pres: Elizabeth Lyon *E-mail:* elyon123@comcast.net
VP: Candy Davis *Tel:* 541-942-8329
E-mail: cdavis@willamette.net; Carol L Craig *Tel:* 541-342-7300 *E-mail:* carollcraig@juno.com
Founded: 2002
Combining over 30 years of book editing, the three partners specialize in substantive/developmental editing & line/copy-editing to writers of novels, memoirs, nonfiction books & proposals. We assist our clients with marketing & are proud of the nearly 30 client publications with large & small presses. We maintian close relationships with literary agents. In addition, we edit query letters, synopses, short stories & articles, & subcontract to specialist editors of academic writings such as theses, comps & journals, & to editors of business reports, proposals & contracts. One of the partners is a successful screenplay writer, another has written four books on writing published by Perigee, & a third partner is co-writing the memoir of a well-known Native American chief.

Membership(s): American Society of Journalists & Authors; The Authors Guild Inc; Oregon Writers Colony; Williamette Writers Association; Women Writing the West

The Editorial Bag
3635 Pamela Dr, Columbus, OH 43230-1829
Tel: 614-939-9707 *Fax:* 614-939-9707
Key Personnel
Owner: Clare Wulker *E-mail:* cwulker@att.net

Editorial Consultants Inc (WA)
3639 36 Ave S, Seattle, WA 98118
Tel: 206-323-1039 *Fax:* 206-229-3448
E-mail: meowmixz@aol.com
Key Personnel
Principal: Sharon Tighe
Complete publications management services: copy-editing, development editing, production editing, writing, rewriting, indexing, proofreading; production supervision/coordination; supervising design, typesetting & printing; ms analysis & critique; writing, rewriting & editing printed documents for web publication; research; special assignment writing & technical editing. Specialize in nonfiction books, instructional/procedures manuals, user documentation manuals, technical manuals, reports & publications, educational workbooks, business publications & promotional materials; indexing; technical editing.
Membership(s): American Society of Indexers; Society for Technical Communication

The Editorial Department, LLC
1710 S Olympic Club Dr, Tucson, AZ 85710
Tel: 520-546-9992 *Toll Free Tel:* 866-360-6996
Fax: 520-546-9993
E-mail: admin@editorialdepartment.net
Web Site: www.editorialdepartment.net
Key Personnel
Pres: Ross Browne *E-mail:* rsb@editorialdepartment.net
Man Partner: Renni Browne
Founded: 1980
Ms editing, rewriting, cutting, ms analysis, screenplay analysis, ghost writing, novelizations & adaptations, book proposals, agent referral service seminars & workshops.

Editorial Options Inc
353 Lexington Ave, New York, NY 10016
Tel: 212-986-2888 *Fax:* 212-986-1194
Web Site: www.edop.com
Key Personnel
Pres: Shirley Petersen *Tel:* 212-986-2888, ext 32 *E-mail:* shirley.petersen@edop.com
VP: Gari Fairweather *Tel:* 212-986-2888, ext 24 *E-mail:* gari.fairweather@edop.com
Ed-in-Chief: Barbara Ryan
Design/Prodn Dir: Karen Donica
Complete publishing services for educational markets. Conceptualize, write & edit texts & multimedia materials in all curriculum areas, from early childhood through adult education, in both English & Spanish. Full range of art, design & production services.

Editorial Services Group Inc
2990 Heidelberg Dr, Boulder, CO 80305
Tel: 303-494-4197
E-mail: editor@boulder.net
Web Site: www.emsotw.com

Key Personnel
Founder & Pres: Jon Howard
Desktop editing, training & consulting, custom
templates & software licensing.

**Editorial Temps & Hot Bear - De Bella
Productions**
303 E 83 St, Suite 25-D, New York, NY 10028
Tel: 212-988-8189 *Fax:* 212-988-8189
Web Site: www.editorialtemps.com
Key Personnel
Pres & Copywriter: Rosalynd Carol Friedman
Founded: 1985
Published author. We will write & help you write
books, brochures, conference proceedings, employee manuals, direct response mail, advertising. All editorial & design services. Artist
manager, copywriting, writing, reporting, reviewing, editing & proofreading. Personalized
ms treatment or analysis & generation of ideas;
special assignment writing.
Membership(s): National Writers Union

EdiType
84 Ashley Ave, Charleston, SC 29401
Tel: 843-853-2214 *Fax:* 843-853-2214
Key Personnel
Dir: W Hank Schlau *E-mail:* whs@awod.com
Complete editorial & production services, including disk conversion & scanning, through
postscript disks or camera-ready copy. Specialize in theology, religious studies, literary
criticism & history. Rewriting, copy editing,
line editing, proofreading, indexing, design,
typesetting, project management.

Educational Media Co/TMA
18740 Paseo Nuevo Dr, Tarzana, CA 91356
Tel: 818-708-0962 *Fax:* 818-345-2980
Web Site: educationalmediacompany.com
Key Personnel
Pres: Susan Lee Meisel *E-mail:* susan@
educationalmediacompany.com
Founded: 1981
Writing/editorial services.

J M B Edwards, Writer & Editor
2432 California St, Berkeley, CA 94703
Tel: 510-644-8287
Key Personnel
Pres & CEO: J M B Edwards
Founded: 1971
Specialize in scholarly & technical works, general
nonfiction, computer books.

EEI Communications
66 Canal Center Plaza, Suite 200, Alexandria, VA
22314-5507
Tel: 703-683-0683 *Fax:* 703-683-4915
E-mail: info@eeicommunications.com
Web Site: www.eeicommunications.com
Key Personnel
Pres: Claire Kincaid
VP, Pubns: Robin Cormier *E-mail:* rcormier@
eeicom.com
Proj Mgr: Jayne Sutton *E-mail:* jsutton@eeicom.
com
Substantive editing, writing, transcription, design,
graphics, keyboarding, publications management, training in software & editorial skills;
specialize in books & reports, government,
technical/defense, management, communications & public health.
Branch Office(s)
8403 Colesville Rd, Suite 320, Silver Spring, MD
20910 *Tel:* 301-495-9800

Diane Eickhoff
3808 Genessee St, Kansas City, MO 64111
Tel: 816-561-6693
E-mail: diane@tvbarn.com

Founded: 2000
Membership(s): Society of Children's Book Writers & Illustrators

**Elizabeth Shaw Editorial & Publishing
Services**
3938 E Grant, Suite 502, Tucson, AZ 85712-2559
Tel: 520-325-0463 *Fax:* 520-323-7382
Key Personnel
Owner & Dir: Elizabeth Shaw
Editing scholarly & other serious nonfiction
books, at all levels from development to copy-
editing. Indexing & proofreading. Complete
packaging available, as needed, for projects we
are editing. Helping authors find appropriate
publishers & prepare effective book proposals.
Bilingual services: Spanish/English.

Elm Street Publishing Services Inc
828 N Elm St, Hinsdale, IL 60521
Tel: 630-789-2102 *Fax:* 630-789-2105
E-mail: esps@elmst.com
Web Site: www.elmst.com
Key Personnel
Pres: Jane Perkins *E-mail:* jane.perkins@elmst.
com
VP: Cate Rzasa
Gen Mgr: Tim Frelick
Devt Dir: Karen Hill
Tech Mgr: Jack Semens
Man Ed: Ingrid Mount
Design Mgr: Emily Friel
Art Mgr: Melissa Morgan
Project management, development & production
support for book publishers. Full range of ed-
itorial & production services from ms through
camera-ready copy, files or film. Services in-
clude text & art development, writing, copy-
editing, proofreading, indexing, photo research,
permissions, design, art & electronic composition, using QuarkXPress, Illustrator, Photoshop,
Autopage & PowerMath. Specialty areas are
business & economics, computer science, mathematics, science, history, English, medical &
education texts.

Irene Elmer
2806 Cherry, Berkeley, CA 94705-2310
Tel: 510-841-0466 *Fax:* 510-883-1265
E-mail: ielmer@earthlink.net
Founded: 1969
Trade nonfiction, textbooks & scholarly works.
Specialize in difficult rewrites. Special assignment writing of adult texts; trade nonfiction;
high-interest, low-readability el-hi texts (fiction,
drama, nonfiction). Specialize in dialogue &
lively presentation of difficult material.

Catherine C Elverston
4026 NW 17 Terr, Gainesville, FL 32605-1973
Tel: 352-372-6571
E-mail: elverston@hotmail.com
All aspects of editing, preparing mss for publica-
tion.
Membership(s): American Medical Writers Asso-
ciation; Board of Editors in the Life Sciences

Ruth Elwell
48 S Chestnut St, New Paltz, NY 12561
Tel: 845-255-4223
E-mail: ruth.elwell@att.net
Founded: 1975
Indexing.

Rohn Engh
Division of PhotoSource International
Pine Lake Farm, 1910 35 Rd, Osceola, WI 54020
Tel: 715-248-3800 (ext 21) *Toll Free Tel:* 800-
624-0266 (ext 21) *Fax:* 715-248-7394
Toll Free Fax: 800-photofax
E-mail: psi2@photosource.com

Web Site: www.photosource.com
Key Personnel
Man Dir: H T White
Publisher, *The Photoletter*, *Photo Stock Notes*,
Photodaily, market letter broadcasting photo
needs of photo buyers to photographers, picto-
rial statistics.
Branch Office(s)
16765 Armstead St, Granada Hills, CA 91344-
2702, On-line Ed: Bill Hopkins
PSI Midwest Office, PO Box 927, Wilber, NE
68465-0927, Edit Servs: Mike Karlsson

Enough Said
414 NW 36 Ave, Gainesville, FL 32607
Tel: 352-371-2935; 352-262-2971
Web Site: www.navi.net/~heathlynn
Key Personnel
Owner & Ed: Heath Lynn Silberfeld
E-mail: heathlynn@navi.net
Founded: 1984
Full range of hard-copy & electronic editorial
services for educational nonfiction trade, mass
market & self-publishing projects.

Ensemble Productions Inc
230 Central Park W, New York, NY 10024
Tel: 212-877-3848 *Fax:* 212-877-9363
Key Personnel
Pres: Martha Lattimore
Copy editing, proofreading, research, rewriting &
special assignment writing. Specialize in music,
social sciences & humanities for K-8 educational material.

Pearl Eppy
201 E 79 St, New York, NY 10021
Tel: 212-737-0354
Key Personnel
Pres: Pearl Eppy
Copy editing, ms analysis, proofreading, research,
rewriting. Medicine, psychiatry, humanities, social sciences, education & the arts, economics,
investments & communications, anthropology,
biography, drama, theatre, self-help.

Jack Ewing Concepts & Copy
PO Box 571, Boise, ID 83701
Tel: 208-345-1782 *Fax:* 208-345-1782 (call first)
E-mail: citzenew@aol.com
Key Personnel
Pres: Jack Ewing
Founded: 1970

Far Beyond Words
29 MacEwan Ridge Circle NW, Calgary, AB T3K
3W3, Canada
Tel: 403-516-3312 *Fax:* 403-516-3312
E-mail: beyondwords@shaw.ca
Key Personnel
Owner: Patsy Price
Founded: 1987
Support services for people & projects that make
a difference in our world. Editing, design, type-
setting, consultation, coaching.
Membership(s): Editors' Association of Canada/
Association canadienne de reviseurs

Stephanie Faul
4110 Jenifer St NW, Washington, DC 20015
Tel: 202-363-1449 *Fax:* 202-537-6851
E-mail: steph@faul.com
Publications consultants: writing, rewriting, special assignment writing, ms analysis, research,
editing. Complete editorial services on all types
of material.

Karyn L Feiden Editorial Services
392 Central Park W, Suite 10-P, New York, NY
10025
Tel: 212-663-4942

Key Personnel
Edit Consultant: Karyn Feiden
Projects managed from ms to publication. Specialize in nonfiction adult trade for major publishers & packagers. Particular expertise in public health & medicine.

Feik Indexers
1623 Third Ave, Suite 29-K, New York, NY 10128-3638
Tel: 212-369-3480 *Fax:* 212-410-0927
E-mail: indexer@earthlink.net
Key Personnel
Owner & Mgr: William R Feik
Founded: 1984
Indexing.

Lillian Mermin Feinsilver
510 McCartney St, Easton, PA 18042
Tel: 610-252-7005
Membership(s): Authors Guild

Betsy Feist Resources
140 E 81 St, New York, NY 10028-1875
Tel: 212-861-2014 *Fax:* 212-861-8304
E-mail: bfresources@rcn.com
Key Personnel
Pres: Betsy Feist
Complete editorial services, including development, writing, project management & editorial/production coordination. Specialize in instructional & informational materials.

Jerry Felsen
3960 NW 196 St, Miami, FL 33055
Tel: 305-625-5012
E-mail: jfelsen@hotmail.com
Computer science, artificial intelligence, information systems & computer applications in business & investing; professional papers & business reports.

Janet Fenn Editorial Services
1508 Jaeger Dr, Lyndhurst, OH 44124
Tel: 440-461-6902
E-mail: janetfenn@usa.net
Copy editing, proofreading & indexing.

Fine Wordworking
PO Box 3041, Monterey, CA 93942-3041
Tel: 831-375-6278
Key Personnel
Owner: Mari Lynch Dehmler
Founded: 1981
Assist individuals, publishers, small businesses & others. Provide special assignment writing, rewriting, editing, proofreading & more. Areas of nonfiction expertise include: child development, community, ecology, elders, family life/sex education, gardening, health & wellness, homebased education/homeschooling, interpersonal communication & relationships, mind/body medicine, Native Americans, nutrition, parenting, personal finance, religion/spirituality, small business, sustainable agriculture, Waldorf education, women's issues. References.

First Folio Resource Group Inc
10 King St E, Suite 801, Toronto, ON M5C 1C3, Canada
Tel: 416-368-7668 *Fax:* 416-368-9363
E-mail: mail@firstfolio.com
Web Site: www.firstfolio.com
Key Personnel
Proj Coord: Pauline Beggs; Fran Cohen; David Hamilton *E-mail:* dhamilton@firstfolio.com
Electronic Publg Coord: Tom Dart
Complete editorial & production services: research, conceptual development, substantive editing, writing & rewriting, copy editing, design & page layout, follow-up consultation & seminars.

Mary Bucher Fisher Editor
100 Glenmont Ave, Columbus, OH 43214-3255
Tel: 614-262-5628
Edit, proofread, typemark hard copy (mainly college textbooks or journals) in technical/general vocabularies such as education, engineering, geology or R&D. Serve publisher as link to author (phoning, corresponding, transferring query responses).
Membership(s): Association for Women in Communications; National League of American Pen Women; Society for Technical Communication

Karen Flemister
Subsidiary of Mikare Enterprises, PLC
3145 E Chandler Blvd, Suite 110-527, Phoenix, AZ 85048
Tel: 480-759-4840 *Fax:* 509-757-5006
E-mail: karen@mikare.com
Web Site: www.mikare.com
Specialize in copy-editing, proofreading page proofs & mss, advertising & promotion copywriting & researching.

Richard A Flom, see Lynn C Kronzek & Richard A Flom

Focus Strategic Communications Inc
535 Tipperton, Oakville, ON L6L 5E1, Canada
Tel: 905-825-8757 *Toll Free Tel:* 866-263-6287
Fax: 905-825-5724 *Toll Free Fax:* 866-613-6287
E-mail: info@focussc.com
Web Site: www.focussc.com
Key Personnel
Dir: Adrianna Edwards *E-mail:* aedwards@focussc.com; Ron Edwards *E-mail:* redwards@focussc.com
Founded: 1988
Provide complete book production from concept development to finished book. Innovative in assembling tailored & creative teams of experts to develop, write, edit, design & produce superior products. Specialty is general nonfiction, ranging from education to trade. Focus on various areas such as history, biography, how-to, business, reference & teachers resource guides. Produce publisher-initiated titles, as well as original books & will also work with other packagers to co-produce books.

Foster Travel Publishing
PO Box 5715, Berkeley, CA 94705-0715
Tel: 510-549-2202 *Fax:* 510-549-1131
E-mail: lee@fostertravel.com
Web Site: www.fostertravel.com
Key Personnel
Owner & Pres: Lee Foster *E-mail:* lee@fostertravel.com
Picture search, research, writing; travel (emphasizing locations, history, wine, nature). Specialize in Northern California, the West, Mexico-Baja, Europe, the Orient. Writing & photography available on website (www.fostertravel.com). Provides travel writing/photography services for print & web editorial markets.
Membership(s): American Society of Media Photographers; Bay Area Travel Writers; SATW

Sandi Frank
8 Fieldcrest Ct, Cortlandt Manor, NY 10567
Tel: 914-739-7088 *Fax:* 914-739-7058
E-mail: sfrankmail@aol.com
Specialize in dictionaries, bibliographies, medical texts & journals, social sciences, scholarly material & cookbooks.

Norman Frankel
Division of Frankel & Associates
5120 Wright Terr, Skokie, IL 60077-2142
Tel: 847-674-8417
E-mail: nfrankel@mindspring.com
Development of publishing projects, author recruitment, supervision of proposal & ms preparation. Special assignment writing & research; specialize in international relations, conflict studies, political terrorism, Arab politics, Israeli politics & Turkish politics; copyright, publishing, fantasy, publishing management & analysis.

Freelance Express Inc
111 E 85 St, New York, NY 10028
Tel: 212-427-0331
Indexing of all subjects: legal, medical, technical & general; proofreading, copy-editing, ms analysis & development, picture search, research, rewriting; complete editorial services (also in Spanish).

Sheila Freeman
3392 Old 3 "L" Hwy, Falmouth, KY 41040
Tel: 859-654-3132
E-mail: sheilafreeman@cs.com
Founded: 1987
Editorial services.

Frisbie/Communications
445 W Erie St, No 104, Chicago, IL 60610
Tel: 312-397-0992 *Fax:* 312-255-9865
Web Site: www.richardfrisbie.net
Key Personnel
Pres: Richard Frisbie *E-mail:* richfris@interaccess.com
VP: Margery Frisbie
Creative direction & editorial work.
Branch Office(s)
631 N Dunton Ave, Arlington Heights, IL 60004
Tel: 847-253-4377

Fromer Editorial Services
1606 Noyes Dr, Silver Spring, MD 20910-2224
Tel: 301-585-8827 *Fax:* 301-585-1369
E-mail: margotfromer@erols.com
Key Personnel
Pres: Margot J Fromer
Founded: 1980
Writing, rewriting & consultation in all aspects of health care & medicine; ms analysis, special assignment writing.
Membership(s): American Medical Writers Association; Science Writers' Association

G & S Editors
Division of G & S Typesetters Inc
410 Baylor, Austin, TX 78703-5312
Tel: 512-478-5341 *Fax:* 512-476-4756
Web Site: www.gstype.com
Key Personnel
Pres: Bill M Grosskopf *E-mail:* billg@gstype.com
Proj Ed: Fran Anderson *E-mail:* fran@gstype.com; Carolyn Brown *E-mail:* cbrown@gstype.com; Jessie Hunnicutt *E-mail:* jhunnicut@gstype.com; Alison A Rainey *E-mail:* arainey@gstype.com
Prepares project material for copy-editor, supervises the copy-editing, serves as liaison with the author, reviews the final ms & makes sure that all elements of the project are complete & ready to be turned over to a designer. Ensures that file conversions, coding & cleanup properly prepare book material for each stage in the process.

Diane Gallo
9 Hilton St, Gilbertsville, NY 13776
Mailing Address: PO Box 106, Gilbertsville, NY 13776

Tel: 607-783-2386 *Fax:* 607-783-2386
E-mail: gallod@norwich.net
Web Site: www.dianegallo.com
Interviewing, slide/tape & video scripts.
Membership(s): Association of Teaching Artists

The Gary-Paul Agency
1549 Main St, Stratford, CT 00615
Tel: 203-375-2636 *Fax:* 203-375-2636
Web Site: www.thegarypaulagency.com
Key Personnel
Owner, WGAE Signatory: Garret C Maynard
   E-mail: maynard@optonline.net
Founded: 1989
WGAe signatory Literary Agency that repre-
sents & promoted screenwriters & screenplays.
Agency specializes in ms editing & offers on-
line courses in screenwriting.
Branch Office(s)
27 Horseshoe Dr, Fayston, VT 05660 *Tel:* 802-
583-3251
Membership(s): Writers Guild of America East

Fred Gebhart
2346 25 Ave, San Francisco, CA 94116-2337
Tel: 415-681-3018 *Fax:* 415-681-0350
E-mail: fgebhart@pobox.com
Web Site: www.fredgebhart.com
Editorial & advertorial writing. Specialize in busi-
ness, consumer education, food & nutrition,
travel, healthcare, foreign countries, medicine,
science, transportation, wine & spirits.
Membership(s): American Medical Writers As-
sociation; American Society of Journalists
& Authors; International Society of Travel
Medicine; National Association of Science
Writers; SATW

Gelles-Cole Literary Enterprises
PO Box 341, Woodstock, NY 12498-0341
Tel: 845-247-8111
Web Site: www.consulting-editors.com
Key Personnel
Pres & Founder: Sandi Gelles-Cole
   E-mail: gellescole@yahoo.com
Founded: 1983
Editorial consultant to authors, publishers & literary agents, collaboration services & ghostwriter, specializing in commercial fiction &
nonfiction. Book deconstruction & reconstruction, plot development, character development.
Work one on one, page by page, focusing on
development projects of concept, characterization, & nonfiction structure; helping experts
& other authors develop their material for the
general public. Also work as writing coach for
writers at all levels from best sellers to first
time authors. Favorite soft spot: working with
first novels & watching authors grow.
Membership(s): Consulting Editors Alliance

Susan M Gerstein
620 E Valerio St, Santa Barbara, CA 93103
Tel: 805-569-2415
E-mail: gerstein@cox.net
College mathematics textbook copy editing, developmental editing, problem checking; rewriting & line editing.
Membership(s): Association of Women in Mathematics

GGP Publishing Inc
138 Chatsworth Ave, Suite 3-5, Larchmont, NY
   10538
Tel: 914-834-8896 *Fax:* 914-834-7566
Web Site: www.ggppublishing.com
Key Personnel
Pres: Generosa Gina Protano *E-mail:* ggprotano@
ggppublishing.com
Founded: 1991

Packager for trade & educational publishers: all
editorial, art & design, production & printing
services—from concept to bound books or any
segment of the publishing process. Trade (fiction & nonfiction) & children's books; textbooks (el-hi, college & adult education); professional, reference & how-to books; cookbooks; audiotapes & videotapes, CDs & CD-
ROMs. Specialize in the development of materials for the study of world languages—such
as English, French, German, Italian, Japanese,
Latin, Portuguese, Russian & Spanish—English
as a Second Language & language arts, as well
as for bilingual education. Also translate complete or partial programs from any of these
world languages to any other(s) & edit the
translation(s) for publication.
Membership(s): American Book Producers Association

Cathe Giffuni, see Research Research

Sheri Gilbert
123 Van Voorhis Ave, Rochester, NY 14617
Tel: 585-342-0331 *Fax:* 585-323-1828
E-mail: shergilb@aol.com
Reviews mss for permissions identification;
preparing permissions reports; obtaining permissions for text, art, photographs & song
lyrics. Creating credit lines & source notes.

Liane Gilmour-Pomfret
9330 Wandsworth Dr, Spring, TX 77379
Tel: 281-251-5917
E-mail: lpomfret@houston.rr.com
Provide a wide range of editorial services from
proofreading to final production editing. Specialize in telecommunications engineering &
associated sciences.

Michael Wells Glueck, see
EditAndPublishYourBook.com

Hadassah Gold
222 W 83 St, Rm 15-D, New York, NY 10024
Tel: 212-787-5668 *Fax:* 212-787-5668
E-mail: dasgold@aol.com

Donald Goldstein
1500 E 17 St, Brooklyn, NY 11230
Tel: 718-375-9346 *Fax:* 718-623-4676
E-mail: dgoldsbkyn@aol.com
Sports, sociology, American politics, the labor
movement, Israel, Jewish related subjects; research, interviewing, copy-editing, rewriting,
special assignment writing & proofreading.

Robert M Goodman
140 West End Ave, New York, NY 10023
Tel: 212-721-7725
E-mail: bgoodman@rcn.com
Membership(s): Editorial Freelancers Association

P M Gordon Associates Inc
2115 Wallace St, Philadelphia, PA 19130
Tel: 215-769-2525 *Fax:* 215-769-5354
E-mail: pmga@pond.com
Key Personnel
Pres: Peggy M Gordon
VP: Douglas C Gordon
Founded: 1982
Developmental editing, rewriting & copy editing
for trade, text & corporate books; indexing.
Complete design & production services.

C+S Gottfried
619 Cricklewood Dr, State College, PA 16803
Tel: 631-563-2841
E-mail: cs@lookoutnow.com
Web Site: www.lookoutnow.com/dtp

Key Personnel
Owner & Mktg Dir: Chet Gottfried
Mgr: Susan Gottfried
Founded: 1988
From electronic or paper ms to camera copy, as
well as printing-binding supervision.

Sherry Gottlieb
4900 Dunes St, Oxnard, CA 93035
Tel: 805-382-3425 *Fax:* 805-658-8601
E-mail: writer@wordservices.com
Web Site: www.wordservices.com
Key Personnel
Contact: Sherry Gottlieb
Specialize in fiction & screenplays.

Grace Associates
945 Fourth Ave, Suite 200-A, Huntington, WV
   25701
Tel: 304-697-3236 *Fax:* 304-697-3399
E-mail: publish@cloh.net
Web Site: www.booksbygrace.com
Key Personnel
Dir: John Patrick Grace
Mktg Mgr: Amanda Ballard
Founded: 1993
Collaborative writing, editing, book design & pro-
duction for experts in business, behavioral &
health sciences, health care & human resources.
Concept to finished book. Agenting for client
group. Example: "Brilliance Marketing Man-
agement: Let Your Strengths Build Your Busi-
ness" (Facts on Demand Press, '03) by Celia
Rocks.
Membership(s): American Book Producers Asso-
ciation; Publishers Marketing Association

Graphic World Publishing Services
Division of Graphic World Inc
11687 Adie Rd, Maryland Heights, MO 63043
Tel: 314-567-9854 *Fax:* 314-567-0360
Key Personnel
Pres: Kevin P Arrow
VP, Publg Servs: Michael J Loomis *E-mail:* mike.
loomis@gwps.com
Sales: Dean Grantham; Joe Hasenmueller; Ron
Swanberg
Complete editorial & project management ser-
vices from ms through final film or files, in-
cluding interior & cover design, composition
services, electronic publishing services & art
rendering.
Branch Office(s)
370 Seventh Ave, Suite 305, New York, NY
   10001

Tony Greenberg MD
Member of Harbor UCLA Medical Center
1000 W Carson St, Torrance, CA 90502
Mailing Address: Box 450, Torrance, CA 90502
Tel: 310-457-9398 (home); 310-222-2168 (office)
E-mail: tgreenberg@dhs.co.la.ca.us
Indexing, proofreading & rewriting of medical &
scientific books.

Cheryll Y Greene Editorial Services
158-18 Riverside Dr W, Suite 6E, New York, NY
   10032
Tel: 212-740-6003 *Fax:* 212-740-6003
E-mail: editorseye@mindspring.com
Key Personnel
Pres: Cheryll Y Greene
Founded: 1991
Extensive experience with literary, women's,
scholarly, cultural & African American
projects. Educational new-media development.
Editorial project management, book develop-
ment & ms consultation. Published editor.
Membership(s): PEN American Center

Paul Greenland Editorial Services
608 Dawson Ave, Rockford, IL 61107
Tel: 815-519-2588
E-mail: paul@paulgreenland.com
Key Personnel
Owner: Paul R Greenland
Services include writing, ghostwriting & collaboration, research, editing & proofreading. Published nonfiction author, marketing/communications professional & former senior editor of national business magazine. Contributor to many leading reference books (Gale Group, University of Chicago Press, St. James Press). Interview subjects include celebrities, athletes & leading business executives. Specializing in reference, business, biography & history. References available upon request.

Nancy J Gregg
1217 W Washington, Suite 5, Springfield, IL 62702
Tel: 217-793-2517

Rosemary F Gretton
660 Blueridge Ave, North Vancouver, BC V7R 2J3, Canada
Tel: 604-904-0223; 604-836-0610 (cell)
Fax on Demand: 604-904-0223
E-mail: rgretton@lyricism.ca
Web Site: www.lyricism.ca
Founded: 2003
Writing, editing & research services for publishers, government, business, nonprofit organizations & individuals. Specializes in advertising & promotion copywriting, copy-editing, fact checking, line editing, proofreading, research & rewriting.
Membership(s): Editors' Association of Canada/Association canadienne de reviseurs

Joan K Griffitts Indexing
3909 W 71 St, Indianapolis, IN 46268
Tel: 317-297-7312 *Fax:* 317-299-7717
E-mail: j.griffitts@sbcglobal.net
Founded: 1989
Indexing of textbooks, tradebooks, reference books, technical documentation, catalogs & newspapers by former librarian. Most subjects; specialize in business, science, sports, gardening, computer science, library science, education, taxation & social science. Various computer formats & e-mail delivery.
Membership(s): American Society of Indexers

Georgia Griggs
2636 Kansas Ave, Santa Monica, CA 90404
Tel: 310-828-4948
E-mail: ghgriggs@earthlink.net

Gerald Gross Associates LLC
63 Grand St, Croton-on-Hudson, NY 10520-2518
Tel: 914-271-8705 *Fax:* 914-271-1239
E-mail: grosassoc@aol.com
Web Site: www.bookdocs.com/jgross.html
Key Personnel
Pres: Jerry Gross
VP: Arlene C Gross
Founded: 1987
Developmental editing, book proposal development, revising, restructuring, fiction & nonfiction.
Membership(s): Independent Editors Group; National Writers Union; PEN American Center

Judith S Grossman
715 Cherry Circle, Wynnewood, PA 19096
Tel: 610-642-0906
E-mail: stogiz@aol.com
Founded: 1973
Editing, ms evaluation & analysis, proofreading, rewriting; fiction, humanities, social sciences.

GSC Communications
1761 S Columbia Ave, Tulsa, OK 74104-5820
Tel: 918-749-2360 *Fax:* 918-749-2360
E-mail: swwriter@juno.com
Key Personnel
Owner: Gretchen Collins
Founded: 1992
Writing, editing, promotions & marketing. More than 835 published credits. Work may be read at urbantulsa.com. Founder of Southwest Literacy Council.
Membership(s): Society of Professional Journalists

Hal Hager & Associates
15 N Richards Ave, Somerville, NJ 08876-2717
Tel: 908-231-9407 *Fax:* 908-725-0979
E-mail: halhager@verizon.net
Key Personnel
Pres: Hal Hager
Founded: 1994
Budget-conscious, experience & effective copywriting, copy & style editing, design & production of: printed marketing & communication materials; author & book print promotions—catalogs, reader's guides, brochures, pamphlets & newsletters; author interviews; all aspects of publications management; web site design & content management; related editorial & marketing consulting.

Hall Editorial Services
571 Carlton Ave, Brooklyn, NY 11238-3408
Tel: 718-789-4420 *Fax:* 718-857-4639
Key Personnel
Owner: David R Hall *E-mail:* davidrhall@earthlink.net
Founded: 1985
One-stop editorial services to corporate communications & nonfiction publishers, including overnight.
Membership(s): Editorial Freelancers Association

James E Hartman
1304 Water Oak Way N, Bradenton, FL 34209
Tel: 941-792-5654
E-mail: delt@tampabay.rr.com
Specialize in mathematics, science, technical material.

Anne Hebenstreit
20 Tip Top Way, Berkeley Heights, NJ 07922
Tel: 908-665-0536
Copy-editing & proofreading of el-hi & college texts & trade books.

Helm Editorial Services
707 SW Eighth Way, Fort Lauderdale, FL 33315
Tel: 954-525-5626 *Fax:* 954-525-5626 (call first)
E-mail: helmls@aol.com
Key Personnel
Owner: James Helm; Lynne Helm
Freelance writing, line editing & publishing for executives & authors.

Bryan Henry
1850 S Treasure Dr, No 1, Miami, FL 33141
Tel: 561-575-4254
E-mail: bryanhenry33140@yahoo.com
Web Site: www.envirobx.com/maritime.htm
Founded: 1985
Proofreader & trivia writer for book publishers & magazines. Twenty years of experience.

Herr's Indexing Service
1325 Poor Farm Rd, Washington, VT 05675
Tel: 802-883-5415 *Fax:* 802-883-5415
E-mail: index@together.net
Web Site: www.herrsindexing.com
Key Personnel
Contact: Linda Herr Hallinger *E-mail:* linda@herrsindexing.com
Founded: 1944
All types of indexing, including medical books.
Membership(s): American Society of Indexers

Diane Casella Hines
2366 Live Oak Meadow Rd, Malibu, CA 90265
Tel: 310-456-3220 *Fax:* 310-456-0549
E-mail: dchines@ispwest.com
Ms analysis, how-to interviewing, ghost writing, rewriting, special assignment writing. Specialize in art history, visual arts, craft instruction, family & child development.

L Anne Hirschel, DDS
20120 Ledgestone Dr, Southfield, MI 48076
Tel: 248-357-2165
E-mail: ahirschel154242mi@comcast.net
Medicine & dentistry, consumer/patient information.
Membership(s): American Dental Association; Medical Writers Association

Burnham Holmes
182 Lakeview Hill Rd, Poultney, VT 05764-9179
Tel: 802-287-9707 *Fax:* 802-287-9707 (Computer fax/modem)
E-mail: burnham.holmes@castleton.edu
Write textbooks, fiction & general nonfiction, juvenile, young adult & children's books.
Membership(s): Authors Guild; League of Vermont Writers

Henry Holmes Literary Agent/Book Publicist
PO Box 433, Swansea, MA 02777
Tel: 508-672-2258
Key Personnel
Pres, Literary Agent & Book Publicist: Henry Holmes
Founded: 1997
Specialize in nonfiction: biography, business, education, law, health, history etc. Exclusive literary agent/book publicist for authors. Authors must present complete book proposal with SASE when submitting. Impeccable presentation is a must. Prefer books targeted at general audiences rather than an exclusive or limited market. Send letter with a good hook. Send list of publishers you have contacted in the past. Do not send any spiral bound proposals; word count must be stated. Include past publicity & endorsement(s). Fees charged: commission, 15%. Contract must be signed, with initial payment, to establish a professional working relationship once author's work has been accepted by agent. Upon receipt of signed contract & payment, author will be sent a media portfolio with marketing data, tip sheet & full compliment of media contact listings. In addition to editorial services, other services offered for a fee: talk show contact listing (geographically or 50 states), professional consultation related to all media, freelance assignments, interviewing celebrities, professional athletes, musicians, political figures & other famous people.

Hot Bear - De Bella Productions & Editorial Temps, see Editorial Temps & Hot Bear - De Bella Productions

Hungry Samurai
Grand Central Sta, PO Box 824, New York, NY 10163-0824
Tel: 212-865-7786 *Fax:* 212-865-7786
E-mail: mail@hungrysamurai.com
Web Site: hungrysamurai.com
Key Personnel
Owner: Valerie Eads
Founded: 1980
Editorial services by staff of small publisher.

Imagefinders Inc
6101 Utah Ave NW, Washington, DC 20015
Tel: 202-244-4456 *Fax:* 202-244-3237
Key Personnel
Pres: Elisabeth M Hartjens *E-mail:* hartjens@
erols.com
Founded: 1985
Photo & illustration research & editing; fact
checking, information research. Specialize in
Washington public domain sources.

Impressions Book & Journal Services Inc
2016 Winnebago St, Madison, WI 53704
Tel: 608-244-6218 *Fax:* 608-244-7050
E-mail: info@impressions.com
Web Site: www.impressions.com
Key Personnel
Pres: William E Kasdorf *E-mail:* bkasdorf@aa.
impressions.com
Prodn Mgr: Russell Schwalbe
Electronic Publg Mgr: David Nelson
Systems & Facilities Mgr: Randy Otis
Edit Servs Mgr: Paul Schellinger
Cust Serv Mgr: Katie Gustafson
Admin & HR Mgr: Kathy Hendricks
Founded: 1925
Full-service composition, editorial services, type-
setting, book design & production management
& electronic publishing services for tradebooks,
textbooks, professional, scholarly & technical
books, journals. Proficient at SGML, XML &
PDF. Design, copy editing, composition, film-
work, artwork, proofreading, indexing.
Branch Office(s)
214 S Main St, Suite 207, Ann Arbor, MI 48104
Tel: 734-332-4220 *Fax:* 734-332-4225

Independent Publisher Online E-ZINE, see
Jenkins Group Inc

Information Diva
31 Jane St, New York, NY 10014
Tel: 212-229-1591 *Fax:* 413-778-3815
Web Site: www.informationdiva.com
Key Personnel
Pres & Principal Researcher: Donna Slawsky
E-mail: donna@informationdiva.com
Founded: 2001
Provides research on any subject including pic-
ture research, historical, biographical, cur-
rent events, business & news topics. Donna
Slawsky, principal researcher, has 15 years of
experience as a librarian. Information Diva also
provides Internet search training & designs re-
search portals.
Membership(s): Association for Independent In-
formation Professionals; SLA

InfoWorks Development Group
2801 Cook Creek Dr, Ann Arbor, MI 48103-8962
Tel: 734-327-9669 *Fax:* 734-327-9686
Key Personnel
Partner: David E Salamie *E-mail:* desalamie@aol.
com; Amy L Unterburger *E-mail:* aunterburg@
aol.com
Founded: 1995
Full range of editorial services, including project
management/editing, copy-editing, proofreading, SGML coding & bibliographies. Specialize
in reference & general nonfiction projects.

InstEdit
1440 Franklin St, Denver, CO 80218
Tel: 303-329-6446 *Fax:* 303-329-6446
Key Personnel
Ed: Scott Vickers *E-mail:* markwscottv@msn.com
Founded: 1992
Full editorial services.
Membership(s): RMBPA; Rocky Mountain Pub-
lishing Professionals Guild

Rose Jacobowitz
351 W 24 St, New York, NY 10011
Tel: 212-243-2074
Founded: 1982
Copy editing & book design, typemarking, production, especially scientific, technical & professional books.

Dorri Jacobs/Consulting & Editorial Services
784 Columbus Ave, Suite 1C, New York, NY
10025
Tel: 212-222-4606
E-mail: dorrija@aol.com
Web Site: members.aol.com/dorrija/yourwriter.
htm; members.aol.com/domediate; endespair.
com
Key Personnel
Owner & Dir: Dr Dorri Jacobs
Internationally published journalist, writer, editor, successful grant writer, visionary makes
vague, disorganized, technical content, clear,
concise, interesting, maintains the integrity of
your "voice," message. Special assignments,
projects, consultations from concept to completion, books, articles, reports, training manuals,
newsletters, brochures, advertorials, corporate
communication, profiles, proposals, interviews,
research, documentation, design, desktop publishing, Websites, e-magazines, resumes, new
author ms review, self-publishing strategy, design. Professional, reliable, flexible, personal
services for your aims, budget, deadline. Human resources, managing, psychology, self-
help, how-to, downsizing, stress, work issues,
careers, conflict resolution.
Membership(s): Editorial Freelancers Association;
National Writers Union

Cyrisse Jaffee
8 Hallron Rd, Newton, MA 02462
Tel: 617-965-7114
Adult & children's trade books as well as evaluating & preparing book proposals.

A Heath Jarrett
Bath Beach Sta, Brooklyn, NY 11214-0184
Mailing Address: Bath Beach Sta, PO Box 184,
Brooklyn, NY 11214-0184
Tel: 718-680-4084
Publicist, promotion & advertising. Use US mail
only.

Jenkins Group Inc
400 W Front St, Suite 4-A, Traverse City, MI
49684
Tel: 231-933-0445 *Toll Free Tel:* 800-706-4636
Fax: 231-933-0448
E-mail: info@bookpublishing.com
Web Site: www.bookpublishing.com
Key Personnel
CEO: Jerrold R Jenkins *E-mail:* jrj@
bookpublishing.com
Pres: James Kalajian *Tel:* 231-933-0445 ext 1006
E-mail: jjk@bookpublishing.com
Book Prodn Mgr: Nikki Stahl *E-mail:* nikki@
bookpublishing.com
Independent Publr, Online E-ZINE Man Ed: Jim
Barnes *E-mail:* jimb@bookpublishing.com
Dir, Cons Servs: Kim Hornyak
E-mail: khornyak@bookpublishing.com
Founded: 1990
Full-service custom book publishing services for
independent authors, organizations & small
press publishers. Services include registrations,
typesetting, cover design, color separations,
illustration & photo placement, galley prepara-
tion & print management.

JFE Editorial Services
PO Box 122417, Fort Worth, TX 76121-2417
Tel: 817-560-7018

E-mail: jford@jfe-editorial.com
Key Personnel
Pres & Owner: June Ford *E-mail:* jford@jfe-
editorial.com
Founded: 1987
Founded by Ms Ford - a nationally published author, ghostwriter, project manager, editor &
proofreader. Focus includes: writing, ghostwriting, rewriting, special assignment writing;
developmental, copy, line, style & content editing; proofreading; ms analysis; permissions,
interviewing; fact checking; database research,
coding, editing. Published in genres ranging
from children's, trade & true crime to scholastic, self-help & sports books; also a variety of
magazine articles. Coordinator of many high-
dollar projects & extremely successful at transforming complex material into easily under-
stood information. Ms Ford is a speaker for
grades 3-12, universities & conferences.

JL Communications
10205 Green Holly Terr, Silver Spring, MD
20902
Tel: 301-593-0640
E-mail: jlcomm@erols.com
Key Personnel
Writer-Ed: Joyce Latham
Founded: 1996
Membership(s): Washington Independent Writers

JMH Creative Solutions
PO Box 2443, Lewiston, ME 04241-2443
Tel: 207-784-9138
E-mail: poemwriter@midmaine.com;
poemwriter1@yahoo.com
Web Site: www.jmhcreativesolutions.com
Key Personnel
Ed & Owner: Jennifer Hollowell *E-mail:* editor@
jmhcreativesolutions.com
Founded: 1998
Copy-edit mss, anthology edit, proofread mss,
critique mss, market finished work, ghostwrite
(as told to & no credit), collaborate, represent
(both published & unpublished), write nonfiction proposals, write novel synopsis for fiction,
research (both fiction & nonfiction), rewrite
(both fiction & nonfiction), review published &
unpublished mss & design or redesign author
sites.

Cliff Johnson & Associates
10867 Fruitland Dr, Studio City, CA 91604
Tel: 818-761-5665 *Fax:* 818-761-9501
E-mail: quest@pacificnet.net
Key Personnel
Pres: Cliff Johnson
Founded: 1976
Nonfiction specialists (primarily medical, psy-
chology, religious, self-help & philosophical
books).

Curt Johnson
1097 Sandwick Ct, Highland Park, IL 60035
Tel: 847-940-4122
Copy editing, direct mail, revision, rewriting, production work; English, anthropology, education,
law, sociology, science & fiction.

K H Marketing Communications
16205 NE Sixth St, Bellevue, WA 98008
Tel: 425-562-0417 *Fax:* 425-746-4406
Key Personnel
Owner & Pres: Kathy D Hoggan *Tel:* 425-269-
7411 (cell) *E-mail:* kdhoggan@aol.com
Founded: 1991
Writer of compelling promo copy, including back
cover copy, catalog copy, press releases & display advertising. Ghost write articles for trade
& general publications, technical, educational,
home arts, children's; gift, educational, how-to
& business books.

Boche Kaplan
166 W Waukena Ave, Oceanside, NY 11572
Tel: 516-764-9828
Key Personnel
Owner: Roz Abisch
Owner & Staff Artist: Boche Kaplan
Complete research & ms preparation for children's books; editorial, copy-editing, proofreading & pictorial presentations; specialize in juvenile trade & mass market books & development of early learning concept materials, teaching aids & teachers' manuals, illustration, book design, spot drawings, art editing.

Sharon Kapnick
185 West End Ave, New York, NY 10023-5547
Tel: 212-787-7231
Specialize in writing food & wine articles for magazines & newspapers.

Ann T Keene, see Edit Etc

Keim Publishing
301 E 61 St, New York, NY 10021
Tel: 212-753-4404
Key Personnel
Pres: Betty Keim *E-mail:* blkeim@earthlink.net
Founded: 1985
Books & art catalogs, newsletters, brochures, promotional items, reference books, production & design, line editing, copy editing, indexing, permissions, photo research, proofreading, reference assignments, research, rewriting, typemarking, special assignment writing. All subjects; specialize in art, broadcasting, history, literature, science, mathematics & music.

Kessler Communications
280 W 86 St, New York, NY 10024
Tel: 212-724-8610
E-mail: lmp@etk.mailshell.com
Web Site: www.kesslercommunications.com
Key Personnel
Pres: Ellen Terry Kessler
Founded: 1986
Advertising & promotional copy, all types of editing & rewriting, brochures, catalogs, newsletters, book jackets, manuals, direct mail, advertorials, press releases, sales letters, special assignments, articles, interviewing, ghost writing.
Membership(s): Editorial Freelancers Association; National Writers Union

Jascha Kessler
218 16 St, Santa Monica, CA 90402-2216
Tel: 310-393-4648 *Fax:* 530-684-5120
E-mail: jkessler@ucla.edu
Freelance reviews of poetry, fiction, history, philosophy, current affairs. Criticism as well as "cultural commentary" on the arts, theater & dance.
Membership(s): ASCAP; Association of Literary Scholars & Critics

Frances Kianka Editorial Services
1624 Greenbriar Ct, Reston, VA 20190-4417
Tel: 703-481-6372 *Fax:* 703-481-6117
Founded: 1992
Copy editing, proofreading; history, art, archaeology, scholarly, French & Italian.

Judy King Editorial Services
PO Box 35038, Houston, TX 77235-5038
Tel: 713-721-3003 *Fax:* 713-721-7272
E-mail: judyking@pdq.net
Web Site: www.judykingedit.com
Key Personnel
Exec Ed: Judy King *E-mail:* judyking@pdq.net
Founded: 1994

Free sample editing & estimates gladly provided. 25 years of helping publishers & authors (published & unpublished) produce professional publications. Specialties: nonfiction books (how-to, family issues, genealogy, history, Christian topics, children's, etc.). I am thorough & honor deadlines.

KIRCHOFF/WOHLBERG

Kirchoff/Wohlberg Inc
866 United Nations Plaza, Suite 525, New York, NY 10017
Tel: 212-644-2020 *Fax:* 212-223-4387
E-mail: kirchwohl@aol.com
Web Site: www.kirchoffwohlberg.com
Key Personnel
Pres: Morris A Kirchoff
Dir, Opers: John R Whitman
VP, Edit: Mary Jane Martin
Artists' Rep: Elizabeth J Ford
Ed: Cynthia Rothman
Children's Trade Books Ms Rep: Liza Pulitzer-Voges
Photo Editing & Res Mgr: Jose Ramos
Founded: 1930
Ms development, copy editing, adapting, proofreading, production supervision; elementary & secondary textbooks & ancillaries; supplementary school & library books; juvenile & young adult books; general trade books (hardcover), dictionaries & encyclopedias; continuity book programs; CD-ROM, electronic books, development of both individual titles & complete series.
Branch Office(s)
897 Boston Post Rd, Madison, CT 06443
Tel: 203-245-7308
Membership(s): AAP; AIGA; ALA; ASPP; International Reading Association; National Council of Teachers of English; National Council of Teachers of Social Studies; Society of Illustrators
See Ad in this Section and in Book Producers section(s)

Theodore Knight
89 Johnson Rd, Foster, RI 02825
Tel: 401-397-9235
E-mail: tknight11@earthlink.net
Educational, young adult, nonfiction & reference.

Bill Koehnlein
236 E Fifth St, New York, NY 10003-8545
Tel: 212-674-9145
E-mail: bkoehnlein@nyc.rr.com
Indexing; all subjects, especially current affairs, social science, American labor & radical history, radical political movements & theory: socialism, Marxism, anarchism; no racist, sexist, or homophobic materials accepted.

Barry R Koffler
Featherside, 14 Ginger Rd, High Falls, NY 12440
Tel: 845-687-9851 *Fax:* 415-534-2200
E-mail: barkof@ulster.net
Web Site: www.feathersite.com
Founded: 1979
Writing all subjects (including encyclopedia); specialize in popular & scientific works on animals & natural history.

KOK Edit
15 Hare Lane, East Setauket, NY 11733-3606
Tel: 631-474-1170 *Fax:* 631-474-9849

E-mail: editor@kokedit.com
Web Site: www.kokedit.com
Key Personnel
Proprietor: Katharine O'Moore-Klopf
Founded: 1995
Provides copy-editing, substantive editing &
fact checking to publishers & packagers of
novels, college textbooks, professional books
(medicine, psychology, psychiatry, allied health,
music therapy) & nonfiction mass market
books (mainstream health care, alternative
health care, child care, human sexuality, psychology, women's issues).
Membership(s): Editorial Freelancers Association

Kraft & Kraft
100 Fourth Ave S, Suite 201, St Petersburg, FL
33701
Tel: 727-821-1627
Web Site: www.erickraft.com/kraftkraft
Key Personnel
Owner & Edit Dir: Eric Kraft *E-mail:* eric@
erickraft.com
Contact: Madeline Kraft
Founded: 1975
Design & development of educational materials.

Eileen Kramer
336 Great Rd, Stow, MA 01775
Tel: 978-897-4121
E-mail: kramer@tiac.com
Web Site: www.ekramer.com
Founded: 1985
Technical copy editor/proofreader. Specialties in-
clude web, science, math, statistics, technical
books, academic journals & textbooks.

Kenneth Kronenberg
51 Maple Ave, Cambridge, MA 02139
Tel: 617-868-8070
E-mail: mail@kfkronenberg.com
Web Site: www.kfkronenberg.com
Academic & substantive editing, argument & con-
tent structuring; humanities & social sciences.
Translation from German into English.
Membership(s): Cambridge Academic Editors
Network; New England Translators Association

Lynn C Kronzek & Richard A Flom
145 S Glenoaks Blvd, Suite 240, Burbank, CA
91502
Tel: 818-843-2625
E-mail: lckronzek@earthlink.net
Key Personnel
Principal: Lynn C Kronzek
Founded: 1989
Nonfiction writing & editorial services, with par-
ticular expertise in history, law, religion, biog-
raphy, government/public affairs & Judaic &
multicultural studies.

Polly Kummel
10111 46 Ave W, Bradenton, FL 34210
Tel: 941-795-2779
E-mail: pollyk1@msn.com
Nonfiction (all subjects): copy-editing, line editing, coaching, substantive & developmental
editing. Specialize in journalism, history, political science, memoir, equestrian subjects. Hard
copy & computer editing. More than 30 years
of experience.

Lachina Publishing Services Inc
3793 S Green Rd, Beachwood, OH 44122
Tel: 216-292-7959 *Fax:* 216-292-3639
Web Site: www.lachina.com
Key Personnel
Pres: Jeffrey A Lachina

Project management, editorial development, copy
editing, indexing, page composition, book &
jacket design, illustration, proofreading, spot
drawings & technical illustration.

Lynne Lackenbach Editorial Services
31 Pillsbury Rd, East Hampstead, NH 03826
Tel: 603-329-8133
E-mail: lynne@lackey.mv.com
Full line of editorial services to college & professional publishers. Specialize in scientific &
technical material.

Barbara Lagowski
237 Lenox Ave, Long Branch, NJ 07740
Tel: 732-571-9215 *Fax:* 732-571-9215
E-mail: blagowski@aol.com
Adaptations & novelizations, advertising & promotions copywriting, ghost writing, line editing, rewriting, special assignment writing.

Russ Lake
3903 Crail Rd, Champaign, IL 61822
Tel: 217-356-2021
E-mail: rlake@parkland.edu
Specialize in editing mss involved with sports,
computers & education; fiction & nonfiction;
special assignment writing; technical & trade
publications & college textbooks.

Land on Demand
20 Long Crescent Dr, Bristol, VA 24201
Tel: 276-642-1007; 423-366-0513 *Fax:* 760-437-
4511
E-mail: landondemand@cs.com
Key Personnel
Ed: Robert D Land
Editing, indexing, proofreading.

LaurelTech Integrated Publishing Solutions
1750 Elm St, Suite 201, Manchester, NH 03104
Tel: 603-606-5800 *Fax:* 603-606-5838
E-mail: sales@laureltech.com
Web Site: www.laureltech.com
Key Personnel
Pres: Michael Hodges *E-mail:* m_hodges@
laureltech.com
Acct Mgr: Amy Boilard *E-mail:* a_boilard@
laureltech.com
Founded: 1990
We specialize in meeting your educational publishing needs. Our full-service development &
project management experience includes editorial, production, art & prepress services for
textbooks & ancillaries. From developing, writing & editing mss to our state-of-the-art page
production, art rendering & prepress capabilities. Our in-house staff is experienced with all
phases & disciplines of K-17.

Anne Leach
78240 Bonanza Dr, Palm Desert, CA 92211
Tel: 760-360-1432 *Fax:* 760-360-1432
E-mail: aleach@dc.rr.com
Indexing; specialize in history, computers, avia-
tion, finance & accounting.

The Learning Source Ltd
644 Tenth St, Brooklyn, NY 11215
Tel: 718-768-0231 *Fax:* 718-369-3467
E-mail: info@learningsourceltd.com
Web Site: www.learningsourceltd.com
Key Personnel
Dir: Gary Davis; Wendy Davis
Provides a full range of editorial & book-
producing services from concept through ms &
design to film & bound book. Specialty areas
include children's fiction & nonfiction, adult
reference & nonfiction series, & classroom materials. Sister company to Ivy Gate Books.

Freda Leinwand
463 West St, Studio 229G, New York, NY 10014
Tel: 212-691-0997
Photo editing & picture research for editorial
& corporate clients. Photo program management & development including budgets, writing specs, acquisitions & permissions. Thorough knowledge of contemporary & historical
sources. Specialize in psychology, sociology,
history, fine art, science & foreign language.

Debra Lemonds
468 E Providencia Ave, Suite A, Burbank, CA
91501-2475
Tel: 818-563-2928 *Fax:* 818-563-1680
E-mail: dlemonds@earthlink.net
Founded: 1984
Photography, art & illustration, research & editing
services.
Membership(s): ASPP

Elizabeth J Leppman
2466 Imperial Dr, St Cloud, MN 56301
Tel: 320-203-9894 *Fax:* 320-308-1660
E-mail: ejleppman@stcloudstate.edu
Published author & experienced book/journal editor will perform developmental, content & copy
editing, ms reviewing, writing. Specialize in
geography & map editing.

Lexical Content, see Reference Wordsmith

LightSpeed Communications
1240 Kroucher Dr, Bartonsville, PA 18321
Mailing Address: PO Box 109, Bartonsville, PA
18321
Tel: 570-629-3495 *Fax:* 570-629-6252
Key Personnel
Owner: Jeff Widmer *E-mail:* jwid@ptd.net
Writing.
Membership(s): American Society of Journalists
& Authors; Authors Guild; International Asso-
ciation of Business Communicators; National
Writers Union

Andrew S Linick PhD, The Copyologist®
Subsidiary of The Linick Group Inc
Linick Bldg, 7 Putter Lane, Middle Island, NY
11953
Mailing Address: PO Box 102, Dept LMP 04,
Middle Island, NY 11953-0102
Tel: 631-924-8555 *Fax:* 631-924-3890
E-mail: linickgrp@att.net
Web Site: www.lgroup.addr.com
Key Personnel
CEO & Creative Dir: Andrew S Linick, PhD
VP: Roger Dextor
Complete editorial & copywriting services: copy
analysis & line editing, research, rewriting for
direct response, direct mail, mail order, sales
promotions; specialize in newsletters, newspapers, magazines, house organs & seminars;
catalog writing, business & consumer launch
packages & in-house seminars on how to sell
what you write; articles, nonfiction books &
manuals. Phone consultation available; consumer, trade, business to business, all markets,
media & subjects; ms analysis & development, proofreading, special assignment writing, ghostwriting, e-mail marketing campaigns
for publishers. Provide comprehensive graphic
re-design/new web site content development,
interactive services with website marketing
makeover advice for first-time authors, self-
publishers, professionals & entrepreneurs. Specializes in flash, animation, merchant accounts,
on-line advertising/PR, links to top search engines, consulting on a 100% satisfaction guarantee. Free site evaluation for LMP readers.

Elliot Linzer
43-05 Crommelin St, Flushing, NY 11355
Tel: 718-353-1261 *Fax:* 208-279-5936
E-mail: elinzer@juno.com
Founded: 1971
Indexing (computer-assisted) of trade books, text-
books, reference books & scholarly books.
Subject matter covered includes social sciences,
computers.
Membership(s): American Society of Indexers;
Editorial Freelancers Association

E Trina Lipton
60 E Eighth St, No 15F, New York, NY 10003
Tel: 212-674-5558 (call first, messages); 212-674-
3523 *Fax:* 212-674-3523
E-mail: trinalipton@hotmail.com
Thirty-five years experience of picture research
& picture editing: historical & contemporary
still photos & film footage, art illustrations.
Photography: stock photos (B&W & color, all
subjects). Also editorial research, fact checking
& permissions interviewing.
Membership(s): ASPP; NPPA; UFT

Eli & Gail Liss
41 Viking Lane, Woodstock, NY 12498
Tel: 845-679-7173
E-mail: lissindex@aol.com
Key Personnel
Contact: Eli Liss; Gail Liss
Founded: 1975
Indexing.

Literary Consultants LLC
7542 Bear Canyon Rd NE, Albuquerque, NM
87109
Tel: 505-797-9397
Key Personnel
Pres: Arthur Orrmont
VP: Leonie Rosenstiel *E-mail:* rosensti@
concentric.net
Liaison with literary agents.
Membership(s): ALSC; New Mexico Book Asso-
ciation

Little Chicago Editorial Services
154 Natural Tpke, Ripton, VT 05766
Mailing Address: PO Box 185, Ripton, VT 05766
Tel: 802-388-9782 *Fax:* 802-388-6525
Key Personnel
Ed: Andrea Chesman *E-mail:* folkfood@sover.net
Editorial Services.

Barbara S Littlewood
5109 Coney Weston Place, Madison, WI 53711
Tel: 608-273-1631 *Fax:* 608-273-9478
E-mail: barb_littlewood@compuserve.com
Founded: 1983
Indexing of scientific publications.

Auralie Phillips Logan
42 Rocky Ridge, Cortlandt Manor, NY 10567-
6530
Tel: 914-739-3469 *Fax:* 914-739-3469
E-mail: aplfgcnys@aol.com

LokiWorks
813-633 Bay St, Toronto, ON M5G 2G4, Canada
Tel: 416-599-4303 *Fax:* 416-599-4308
E-mail: editor@lokiworks.com
Web Site: www.lokiworks.com
Key Personnel
Contact: Jim MacLachlan
Designer: Beverley Gray
Founded: 1991
Consultants on form & content in publishing &
theatre, specializing in editing & costumes.
Membership(s): Editors' Association of Canada/
Association canadienne de reviseurs; The Writ-
ers' Union of Canada

Mari Lynch, see Fine Wordworking

Donald MacLaren & Associates
2021 46 St, Astoria, NY 11105
Tel: 718-932-7720 *Fax:* 718-932-7720
Key Personnel
Owner: Donald MacLaren
Ghost writing, ms analysis, proofreading &
rewriting.

Makeready Inc
233 W 77 St, New York, NY 10024
Tel: 212-595-5083
Key Personnel
Corp Sec: Beth Greenfeld *E-mail:* lgg233@aol.
com
Ed: Margaret Madigan; Susan Saunders
Founded: 1983
Ms preparation through bound book or periodical. Rewriting, ghost writing, condensations,
research, line editing, fact checking, special assignment writing, transcript editing, copy editing, proofreading, design. Specialize in general
fiction & nonfiction, business, social science,
illustrated books & juveniles.

Phyllis Manner
17 Springdale Rd, New Rochelle, NY 10804
Tel: 914-834-4707 *Fax:* 914-834-4707
E-mail: pmanner@aol.com
Specialize in medicine & biochemistry.
Membership(s): American Society of Indexers

Danny Marcus Word Worker
Division of D M Enterprises
62 Washington St, Suite 2, Marblehead, MA
01945-3553
Tel: 781-631-3886 *Fax:* 781-631-3886
E-mail: danny@thecia.net
Founded: 1984
Proofreading, line editing & copy editing. Spe-
cialize in politics, income taxes, government,
history, current events, all kinds of fiction &
general nonfiction.
Membership(s): Cambridge Academic Editors
Network

Frances Martin
154 W 73 St, New York, NY 10023
Tel: 212-877-8160
Proofreading, copy editing, rewriting, research;
general subjects as well as corporate magazines, travel brochures, annual reports, medical
advertising, investment, taxation, insurance,
classical music & opera.
Branch Office(s)
1030 E Rock Springs Rd NE, Atlanta, GA 30306
Tel: 404-872-3224

Math-Check
3 Herbert St, Baldwin, NY 11510
Tel: 516-623-6898
Key Personnel
Principal: Phillip A Angelillo
E-mail: pangeli850@aol.com
Founded: 1997
Accuracy checking of quantitative college textbooks & supplements for mathematical & computational accuracy; correctness of mathematical notation, charts, graphs, tables & art; proper
integration of mathematical concepts with text
discussion. Specialize in fields of mathematics,
engineering, quantitative business/economics.

Joy Matkowski
773 Lee Lane, Enola, PA 17025
Tel: 717-732-8767
E-mail: jmatkowski1@comcast.net
Copy editing & proofreading.

Peter Mayeux
Division of College of Journalism & Mass Com-
munications
RFD 1, Box 242 A3, Crete, NE 68333
Tel: 402-472-3046 *Fax:* 402-472-8403; 402-472-
8597
E-mail: pmayeux1@unl.edu
Broadcast dramatic & commercial writing, text-
books.

MBH Book Services
99 Willowbrook Blvd, Lewisburg, PA 17837
Tel: 570-523-8081
Key Personnel
Contact: Peggy Hoover *E-mail:* pbhoover@ptd.net
Copy editing, electronic publishing, word process-
ing & text editing: nonfiction.

James H McCallum Jr
29 Fletcher Rd, Monsey, NY 10952
Tel: 845-425-0882
Line editing, fact checking, rewriting, proofreading.

Kenya McCullum
31 Wellington Ave, 2nd fl, Albany, NY 12203
Tel: 518-435-1307
E-mail: kmccullum@mindspring.com
Founded: 1996
Copywriting press releases, newsletters,
brochures, articles, annual reports, sales letters,
direct mail pieces, web site content, multimedia
content, etc for corporations, advertising agencies, public relations firms, associations, nonprofit organizations, government agencies, etc;
ghostwriting; rewriting; proofreading books,
periodicals, newsletters, etc.

Pamela Dittmer McKuen
87 Tanglewood Dr, Glen Ellyn, IL 60137
Tel: 630-545-0867 *Fax:* 630-545-0868
E-mail: pmckuen@aol.com
Advertising & promotion copywriting, condensations, copy editing, ghost writing, interviewing,
research, special assignment writing, editorial
& commercial writing & rewriting for books,
periodicals & corporate projects.
Membership(s): Association of Health Care Journalists; National Association of Real Estate
Editors

Patricia A McLaughlin
29331 Clear View Lane, Highland, CA 92346
Tel: 909-864-5491
Services to writers are available through the mail.
Published author & specialist in general fiction
& nonfiction for both adults & children; also,
religious & inspirational subjects.
Membership(s): Society of Children's Book Writers & Illustrators

Pat McNees
10643 Weymouth St, Suite 204, Bethesda, MD
20814
Tel: 301-897-8557
E-mail: pmcnees@nasw.org
Web Site: www.patmcnees.com
Articles, books & summaries. Specialize in business & economics, social policy, psychology,
family relations, food & consumer affairs, biographies & organizational histories.
Membership(s): American Society of Journalists
& Authors; Association of Health Care Journalists; Association of Personal Historians; Authors Guild; National Association of Science
Writers; PEN International; Society for Technical Communication

MedWrite Associates
31651 Auburn Dr, Beverly Hills, MI 48025

Tel: 248-646-2895 *Fax:* 248-647-7593
Key Personnel
Dir: Patricia L Cornett *E-mail:* patsee@comcast.
net
Founded: 1985
Medicine & health care.
Membership(s): American Medical Writers Association

Barbara A Mele
2525 Holland Ave, New York, NY 10467-8703
Tel: 718-654-8047 *Fax:* 718-654-8047
E-mail: bannmele@aol.com
Freelance permissions.

Tom Mellers Publishing Services (TMPS)
60 Second Ave, New York, NY 10003
Mailing Address: PO Box 150, New York, NY 10003
Tel: 212-254-4958 *Fax:* 607-798-9988
E-mail: tmellers@clarityconnect.com
Comprehensive rights & permissions administration, acquiring & granting rights for text of all kinds, photos, art, video, film, music, spoken word. Acquiring services range from consulting with rightseekers, to evaluating permissionable material, setting up projects, sending & tracking requests, negotiating fees, preparing acknowledgments, administering payment & righting contracts. Granting services include drafting contracts, negotiating & collecting fees & preparing records (edit-in). Copyright registration. Specialize in literary estates. All subjects & media. Extensive editing & editorial services, from author consultation to ms analysis, fact checking & rewriting to project supervision (including typemarking, book design, line editing, copy-editing, proofreading). Ghost writing & special assignment writing,

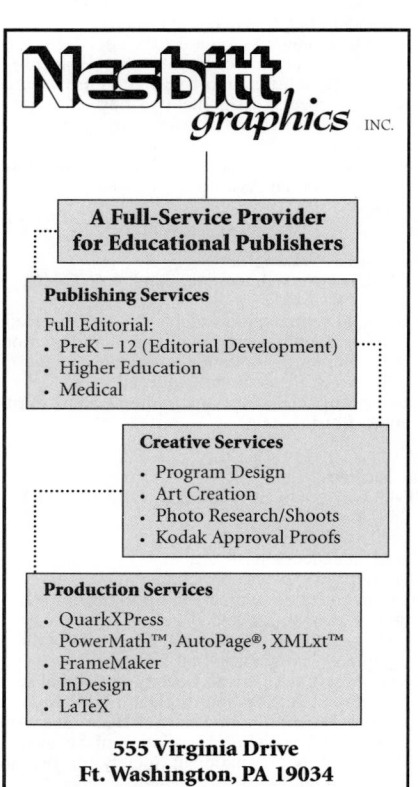

Nesbitt *graphics* INC.

A Full-Service Provider for Educational Publishers

Publishing Services
Full Editorial:
• PreK – 12 (Editorial Development)
• Higher Education
• Medical

Creative Services
• Program Design
• Art Creation
• Photo Research/Shoots
• Kodak Approval Proofs

Production Services
• QuarkXPress
PowerMath™, AutoPage®, XMLxt™
• FrameMaker
• InDesign
• LaTeX

555 Virginia Drive
Ft. Washington, PA 19034
www.Nesbittgraphics.com

215.591.9125   Fax 215.591.9093

author representation & photo research, drafting contracts, image research & international work with museums.
Branch Office(s)
4629 Vestal Pkwy E, Vestal, NY 13850 *Tel:* 607-798-7994

Fred C Mench, Professor of Classics
104 Iona Ave, Linwood, NJ 08221
Tel: 609-927-8430 *Fax:* 609-652-4550
E-mail: fmench@earthlink.net
Text editing, especially classical antiquity or English literature. Past projects included reading drafts of Roman historical novels for content & form, writing reviews of scholarly & fictional works (especially on ancient Rome). Book Review Editor of the journal Classical World for 15 years, involving extensive condensing of submitted texts. Special areas: Julius Caesar, Roman republic, Latin texts, the Bible, Greek mythology & G B Shaw. Also available for general editing.
Membership(s): American Philological Association; Association of Ancient Historians; Classical Association of the Atlantic States; Classical Humanities Society of South Jersey

Barbara Mary Merson
41 North St, Old Bridge, NJ 08857
Tel: 732-251-4604
E-mail: barbear28@aol.com
Founded: 1972
Writing, rewriting, editing, proofreading, literature search, line & copy editing. Specialize in children's literature & educational materials for el-hi & college: fiction & general nonfiction, language arts, reading, poetry. Also sports, humor, animals & animal rights, doll & teddy bear collecting, paralegal, teacher & education, Catholic subjects, pro-life, Conservative Republican, dolls, plush & toy retailing.
Membership(s): National Catholic Teachers Association; National Council of Teachers of English

Metropolitan Editorial & Writing Service
Subsidiary of Metropolitan Research Co
4455 Douglas Ave, Riverdale, NY 10471
Tel: 718-549-5518
Key Personnel
Pres: Chauncey G Olinger, Jr
Founded: 1982
Editing, ms analysis, rewriting & restyling of general, professional & scholarly writing, especially in economics, business, social sciences, humanities, medicine & pharmacy. Specialize in editorial collaboration with authors; oral history interviewing.

Susan T Middleton
366A Norton Hill Rd, Ashfield, MA 01330-9601
Tel: 413-628-4039
E-mail: smiddle@crocker.com
Collaboration, development & editing for trade & college markets in the sciences.

Robert J Milch
9 Millbrook Dr, Stony Brook, NY 11790-2914
Tel: 631-689-8546 *Fax:* 631-689-8546
E-mail: milchedit@aol.com

Stephen M Miller
15727 S Madison Dr, Olathe, KS 66062
Tel: 913-768-7997 *Fax:* 775-587-9195
E-mail: steve@miller-stephen.com
Web Site: www.miller-stephen.com
Writing, editing. Bible specialty. Health subspecialty. Former editor, books, magazines, newspaper. Seminary & journalism school gradu-

ate, Kansas City area. Clientele of top national book publishers & magazines.
Membership(s): EPA; Society of Bible Literature; Wesleyan Theological Society

Kathleen Mills Editorial & Production Services
PO Box 214, Chardon, OH 44024
Tel: 440-285-4347 *Fax:* 440-286-9213
E-mail: mills_edit@yahoo.com
Key Personnel
Edit Dir: Kathleen Mills
Founded: 1990
More than 25 years of publishing experience. Editing, indexing, writing, generation of electronic files, author liaison, project management. Technical, reference, medical, college, business, social sciences, arts & humanities, general nonfiction, Websites.

Sondra Mochson
18 Overlook Dr, Port Washington, NY 11050
Tel: 516-883-0984
All subjects, text & trade.

Mary Mueller
516 Bartram Rd, Moorestown, NJ 08057
Tel: 856-778-4769
E-mail: mamam49@aol.com
Abstracting, copy editing, ghost writing, indexing, proofreading & rewriting. Specialize in consumer education, gardening, health & nutrition, house & home, science, technology.

Nina Neimark Editorial Services
543 Third St, Brooklyn, NY 11215
Tel: 718-499-6804 *Fax on Demand:* 718-499-6804
E-mail: pneimark@hotmail.com
Key Personnel
Pres: Nina Neimark
Founded: 1965
Specializing in scholarly books & college texts on environmental issues, history, art, music, social sciences; also general nonfiction. Mss analysis & development, content & photo research, rewriting, copy editing, proofreading, production editing & complete book packaging services.

Nesbitt Graphics Inc
555 Virginia Dr, Fort Washington, PA 19034
Tel: **215-591-9125** *Fax:* **215-591-9093**
Web Site: **www.Nesbittgraphics.com**
Key Personnel
Pres: **Harry J Nesbitt, III** *E-mail:* **H_Nesbitt@ Nesbittgraphics.com**
VP, Technol: **Bruce Nesbitt**
E-mail: B_Nesbitt@Nesbittgraphics.com
VP, Prodn Servs: **Harry F Druding**
E-mail: H_Druding@Nesbittgraphics.com
VP, School Publg Servs: **Alison Abrohms**
E-mail: A_Abrohms@Nesbittgraphics.com
Founded: **1998**
Our school division offers complete Pre-K–12 educational publishing services including conceptual development, prototype development, research, writing, content editing, copy-editing, fact checking & production editing. Editorial expertise includes mathematics, science/health & reading/language arts. Extensive experience creating student & teacher's editions, alternative programs, supplemental materials, assessment, curriculum alignment, state customizations, correlations & professional developmental materials. Our higher education division provides expert full-service management for college, medical, nursing, allied health & scholarly publications. Production services for both school & higher education include instructional design, page layouts, art creation &

art services, photo research/shoots, electronic composition & prepress services.
Membership(s): **Bookbinders Guild of New York; Bookbuilders of Boston; Bookbuilders West; Chicago Book Clinic; National Association for the Education of Young Children; National Council of Supervisors of Mathematics; National Council of Teachers of Mathematics; National Science Teachers Association**
See Ad in this Section

Donald Nicholson-Smith
PO Box 272, Knickerbocker Sta, New York, NY 10002
Tel: 718-636-4732
E-mail: mnr.dns@verizon.net
French language proofreading.

Northeastern Graphic Inc
5 Emeline Dr, Hawthorne, NJ 07506
Tel: 973-221-0109 *Fax:* 973-221-0076
Web Site: www.northeasterngraphic.com
Key Personnel
Pres: Harvey Sussman *Tel:* 973-221-0109 ext 25
  E-mail: hsussman@northeasterngraphic.com
VP: Kate Scully *E-mail:* kscully@ northeasterngraphic.com
Founded: 1988
Copy-editing, fact checking, indexing, line editing, ms analysis, permissions, photo research, proofreading, rewriting & typemarking.

nSight Inc
One Van de Graaff Dr, Suite 202, Burlington, MA 01803
Tel: **781-273-6300** *Fax:* **781-273-6301**
E-mail: **projects@nsightworks.com; consulting@nsightworks.com**
Web Site: **www.nsightworks.com**
Key Personnel
Founder: Nan Fritz *E-mail:* nfritz@ nsightworks.com
Pres/CEO: Tom Le Blanc *E-mail:* tleblanc@ nsightworks.com
Dir, Mktg: Dan Cote *E-mail:* dcote@ nsightworks.com
Founded: 1982
Complete book & journal production services: writing, copy-editing, developmental editing, indexing, proofreading; project management; abstracting, advertising & promotion copywriting, bibliographies, fact checking, interviewing, line editing, ms analysis, rewriting, special assignment writing, statistics, transcription editing, typemarking; design, art rendering, photo research, covers & jackets; permissions; in-house composition as well as development of electronic publishing products, including HTML & SGML coding. supervising composition & printing. Online editing experts (visit EditExpress.com). Specialize in technical subject areas: college, medical & allied health, computer science, law, physical & life sciences & engineering.
Membership(s): **Bookbuilders of Boston**
See Ad in this Section

Veronica Oliva
26 Mizpah St, San Francisco, CA 94131
Tel: 415-469-0353 *Fax:* 415-469-0377
E-mail: olivasfca@aol.com
Permissions services: ms review; pursuit of permissions & releases. For print & electronic formats. Specializes in French & Spanish textbooks.
Membership(s): Bay Area Editors' Forum; Media Alliance

Orion Book Services
751 South St, West Brattleboro, VT 05301-4234

Tel: 802-254-2340 *Fax:* 802-254-2340
E-mail: gr8books@sover.net
Key Personnel
Pres: Orion M Barber
Complete book development services for trade; broker for manufacturing.
Membership(s): Bookbuilders of Boston; Vermont Book Professionals Association

Naomi Ornest
173 W 78 St, New York, NY 10024-6711
Tel: 212-873-9128

Oyster River Press
20 Riverview Rd, Durham, NH 03824-3313
Tel: 603-868-5006
E-mail: oysterriverpress@comcast.net
Web Site: oysterriverpress.com
Key Personnel
Publr & Gen Ed: Cicely Buckley
Ed: Tanya Gold
Interviewing, special assignment writing, translating services to/from French, Spanish, Russian, Polish.

Pacific Literary Services
1220 Club Ct, Richmond, CA 94803
Tel: 510-222-6555
Key Personnel
Ed-at-Large: Victor West
Critiques, ms analysis, adaptations to the screen, condensations, ghost writing, interviewing, editing, copy editing, line editing, proofreading, rewriting, novelizations, screenwriting, scriptwriting (film, audio-visual, television, radio), special assignment writing. Specialize in screenplays & scripts for film & television, fiction & nonfiction books. Broadcasting & agency experience; training at the American Film Institute.

Pacific Publishing Services
PO Box 1150, Capitola, CA 95010-1150
Tel: 831-476-8284 *Fax:* 831-476-8294
E-mail: pacpub@attglobal.net
Key Personnel
Pres: Albert Lee Strickland
Assoc: Lynne Ann De Spelder
Research, editorial & writing services for trade, text & corporate publications.

Robert J Palmer
209-14 Richland Ave, Oakland Gardens, NY 11364
Tel: 718-264-3021 *Fax:* 718-264-1824
E-mail: yanghao@okcom.net
Indexing all subjects by World War II combat veteran with special interest in Asia; over 3,000 indexing projects completed.
Membership(s): American Society of Indexers

Karen L Pangallo
27 Buffum St, Salem, MA 01970
Tel: 978-744-8796
E-mail: pangallo@noblenet.org
Abstracting; bibliographics; indexing; research.

Diane Patrick
140 Carver Loop, No 21A, Bronx, NY 10475-2954
Tel: 718-320-8251 *Fax:* 718-320-8251
E-mail: deepeedub@aol.com
Published author of biographies, researched or from interviews. Specialize in ghosting & cowriting biographies of African-American personages.
Membership(s): International Women's Writing Guild; New York Association of Black Journalists; Women's National Book Association

Sara Patton Book Production Services
160 River Rd, Wailuku, HI 96793
Tel: 808-242-7838 *Toll Free Tel:* 800-433-4804
  Fax: 808-242-6113
Key Personnel
Owner: Sara Patton
Transform your ms into a book that sells. Every project is a labor of love, receiving personalized attention & highest quality service. First-class interior design, page layout & overall project management/consultation. Also disk conversion & scanning. From typewritten ms or computer disk to camera-ready paper or film output. Specialize in 1- & 2-color nonfiction. 100% satisfaction guaranteed.

Beth Penney Editorial Services
PO Box 604, Pacific Grove, CA 93950-0604
Tel: 831-372-7625
Key Personnel
Pres: Beth Penney *E-mail:* beth@mbay.net
Founded: 1980
Membership(s): Editorial Freelancers Association; Society for Technical Communication

PeopleSpeak
25381G Alicia Pkwy, No 1, Laguna Hills, CA 92653
Tel: 949-581-6190 *Fax:* 949-581-4958
E-mail: pplspeak@norcov.com
Web Site: www.detailsplease.com/peoplespeak
Key Personnel
Sr Ed: Sharon Goldinger
An eye for details. Content editing; specialize in nonfiction mss, marketing materials, newsletters, directories.

Membership(s): Publishers Association of Los
Angeles; Publishers Marketing Association;
San Diego Professional Editors Network;
Women's National Book Association

Rebecca Pepper
434 NE Floral Place, Portland, OR 97232
Tel: 503-236-5802
E-mail: rpepper@rpepper.net
Membership(s): Editcetera; Northwest Independent Editors Guild

The Permissions Group
Division of CPG Ltd
1247 Milwaukee Ave, Suite 303, Glenview, IL
60025
Tel: 847-635-6550 *Fax:* 847-635-6968
E-mail: info@permissionsgroup.com
Web Site: www.permissionsgroup.com
Key Personnel
Dir: Cheryl Besenjak
Full-service copyright & permissions consulting
company. Specializing in ms review & analysis,
rights negotiation, individualized consulting,
seminars & training.

Philip A Perry, Freelance Editorial Services
1311 Wesley Ave, Evanston, IL 60201-4117
Tel: 847-733-1270
E-mail: philaperry@aol.com
Key Personnel
Owner & Ed: Philip A Perry
Founded: 1991
Freelance Editorial Services provides services
to the publishing community, including copy-
editing, developmental editing & proofreading.
Previous clients include authors, businesses,
scholars & academic & trade publishers in the
Chicago area & nationwide. Areas of special-
ization include business, journalistic nonfiction,
religion & history.
Membership(s): Independent Writers of Chicago;
National Writers Union; Society of Professional
Journalists

Elsa Peterson Ltd
41 East Ave, Norwalk, CT 06851
Tel: 203-846-8331 *Fax:* 203-846-8049
E-mail: epltd@earthlink.net
Key Personnel
Pres: John H Turner
Founded: 1984
Photo research & permissions.
Membership(s): ASPP; Editorial Freelancers Association

Evelyn Walters Pettit
PO Box 3073, Winter Park, FL 32790-3073
Tel: 407-629-9289; 407-644-1711 *Fax:* 407-644-
1099
E-mail: brandywine@floridabooksellers.com
Rewriting, copy & line editing, proofreading.
Specialize in college textbooks as well as professional & reference books & journals, but do
general subjects as well. Experience in wide
range of subjects from social & biological sciences to engineering & mathematics to business.

Janice M Phelps
Division of Lucky Press LLC
126 S Maple St, Lancaster, OH 43130
Tel: 740-689-2950 *Fax:* 740-689-2951
E-mail: jmp@janicephelps.com
Web Site: www.janicephelps.com
Founded: 1998
Editor for two Ben Franklin Award winners &
two finalists. Complete editorial & design ser-
vices for authors & publishers: cover design,
layout, illustrations, developmental & line edit-
ing, consulting services for project planning &

project management for fiction & nonfiction
book projects, also offers book design. Book
production services are one aspect of Lucky
Press, LLC, a trade publisher with 15 titles,
specializing in health, self-help, biography, military history & aviation.
Membership(s): Publishers Marketing Association

Meredith Phillips
Subsidiary of Perseverance Editorial Services
4127 Old Adobe Rd, Palo Alto, CA 94306
Tel: 650-857-9555 *Fax on Demand:* 650-857-
9555
E-mail: meredith.phillips@gte.net
Former author & award-nominated mystery publisher (Perseverance Press). Editing (developmental, line, copy), researching, fact checking,
proofreading of trade books (fiction or nonfiction).

PhotoEdit Inc
235 E Broadway, Suite 1020, Long Beach, CA
90802
Tel: 562-435-2722 *Toll Free Tel:* 800-860-2098
Fax: 562-435-7161 *Toll Free Fax:* 800-804-
3707
E-mail: sales@photoeditinc.com
Web Site: www.photoeditinc.com
Key Personnel
Pres: Leslye Borden *E-mail:* leslye.borden@
photoeditinc.com
VP: Liz Ely *E-mail:* liz.ely@photoeditinc.com
Founded: 1987
Photographers; large stock on hand.

Caroline Pincus Book Midwife
1237 Sixth Ave, San Francisco, CA 94122
Tel: 415-665-3200 *Fax:* 415-665-6502
E-mail: cpincus100@sbcglobal.net
Key Personnel
Book Ed: Caroline Pincus
Founded: 1998
Ms development & book doctoring for the gen-
eral trade, specializing in health, personal
growth, women's issues, narrative nonfiction.

Marilyn Pincus Inc
9645 E Holiday Way, Sun Lakes, AZ 85248
Tel: 408-883-1958
E-mail: MPscribe@aol.com
Key Personnel
Pres: Marilyn Pincus
Author, Ghostwriter & Consultant-to-
Management. Books published many languages. Works with clients on book development from A-Z. Ghostwrites some of all of
clients' books. Highly skilled interviewer & researcher. Also, updates & originates policies,
procedures, job descriptions & related documents.
Membership(s): International Association of Business Communicators; Toastmasters International; Women's Studies Advisory Council,
University of Arizona

Joann "JP" Pochron, Writer for Hire
830 Lake Orchid Circle, No 203, Vero Beach, FL
32962
Tel: 772-569-2967
E-mail: pageturn@bellsouth.net
Key Personnel
Writer: Joann "JP" Pochron
Advertising & promotion copywriting, interviewing, special assignment, writing, research, freelance writing, general commentary,
travel/resorts, fact-checking.

Wendy Polhemus-Annibell
4045 Bridge Lane, Cutchogue, NY 11935
Tel: 631-734-7239
E-mail: wannibel@suffolk.lib.ny.us

Founded: 1987
Freelance copy editing, line editing, development editing, proofreading, project management (ms
to prepress). Specializing in college textbooks
& fiction/nonfiction trade books, with an emphasis on editorial excellence.

Joan S Pollack
890 West End Ave, Suite 14B, New York, NY
10025
Tel: 212-663-8143 *Fax:* 212-666-4219
Editorial collaborations & consultations. Specialize in autobiography, biography, memoirs &
fiction.

Pre-Press Company Inc
362 N Bedford St, East Bridgewater, MA 02333
Tel: 508-378-1100 (plant); 508-378-1101 (sales)
Fax: 508-378-1105
Web Site: www.prepressco.com
Key Personnel
Pres: Rick A Vayo *E-mail:* r_vayo@prepressco.
com
CFO: Charlotte W Vayo
VP, Opers: Jack Mitchell
VP, Prod Devt: Margaret Saunders
Founded: 1974
Full-service development & packaging services including: project management, author-
ing, editorial research & development, design, copy-editing, photo research, permissions, indexing, proofreading, composition,
electronic/conventional art packages, scan-
ning/photo manipulation, XML tagging, file
conversions & re-purposing, preflight & PDF
preparation, content management & delivery
services. Complete development & packaging
services are available or any phase of development, editorial or electronic production is offered as an individual service. Areas of special-
ization include: el-hi, college & trade/reference
publishing across all subject matter including
math & foreign languages.

Procrustes/Sophia Editorial Services
241 Bonita Los Trancos Woods, Portola Valley,
CA 94028-8103
Tel: 650-851-1847 *Fax:* 650-210-9832
Key Personnel
Principal: Autumn Stanley
E-mail: autumn2_dave@compuserve.com
Contact: Kevin Simmons
Ideas, development, editing, cutting & co-writing.

The Professional Writer
PO Box 1631, Old Chelsea Sta, New York, NY
10113
Tel: 212-983-1951; 212-414-0188
E-mail: aprowrite@aol.com
Web Site: www.theprofessionalwriter.com
Key Personnel
Owner: Paul Wisenthal
Founded: 1989
Book networking to the industry, book
development-includes creative writing/editing,
writer's block, project preparation. Copywriting
for brochures, media kits, newsletters, business
& investment proposals & grants. Script writ-
ing, script doctor for TV/film/radio. Speech-
writing. Youth market specialists.
Membership(s): The Authors Guild Inc

Pronk&Associates Inc
200 Yorkland Ave, Suite 500, Toronto, ON M2J
5C1, Canada
Tel: 416-441-3760 *Fax:* 416-441-9991
E-mail: info@pronk.com
Web Site: www.pronk.com
Key Personnel
Pres: Gord Pronk
Founded: 1981

Complete book design & production; permissions pronto research; art direction; jacket design; layout; technical illustration; typesetting; complete prepress services; specializing in educational materials in print, CD-ROM & the internet.

Pro-Nouns Editorial Services Inc
10835-62 Ave, Edmonton, AB T6H 1M9, Canada
Tel: 780-436-0772 *Fax:* 780-438-7063
E-mail: info@pro-nouns.com
Web Site: www.pro-nouns.com
Key Personnel
Owner & Operator: Moira Calder *E-mail:* m.calder@shaw.ca
Founded: 1998 (purchased by Moira Calder in 2003)
Specializes in substantive editing, copy-editing & proofreading, indexing, library, archival & Internet research. The company's goal is to serve clients & their readers through thoughtful & creative work, attention to detail & commitment to meeting deadlines.
Membership(s): American Medical Writers Association; Editors' Association of Canada/Association canadienne de reviseurs; Indexing & Abstracting Society of Canada

Proof Positive/Farrowlyne Associates Inc
Subsidiary of The Black Dot Group
1620 Central St, Evanston, IL 60201
Tel: 847-866-9570 *Fax:* 847-866-9849
Key Personnel
VP & Gen Mgr: Carol K Karton *Tel:* 847-866-9570 ext 611 *E-mail:* ckarton@ppfainc.com
Edit Dir: Jamie West
Dir, Design & Prodn: Ann Lindstrom
Dir, Media: Kathleen Ermitage
Founded: 1983
Complete publishing services for school, college & corporate markets. Product development, research, writing & editing, design & production for print, video & DVD products. Expertise in all disciplines. Additional services: fact-checking, correlations & other quality assurance services, translation, competitive analysis, correlations & content reviews.
Membership(s): ASCD; International Reading Association; National Council for the Social Studies; National Council of Teachers of Mathematics; National Science Teachers Association

Generosa Gina Protano Publishing, see GGP Publishing Inc

Publicom Inc
60 Aberdeen Ave, Cambridge, MA 02138
Tel: 617-714-0300 *Fax:* 617-714-0268
E-mail: info@publicom1.com
Web Site: www.publicom1.com
Key Personnel
Pres: Meredith Rutter
VP, Edit, Design & Prodn: Neil Saunders
VP, Client Servs: Patricia White *E-mail:* pwhite@publicom1.com
Specializes in educational publishing for K-college, including student texts, teacher's editions, ancillary items, assessment materials, children's magazines, kit components & so on, from inception through production; English or Spanish full range of services - entire project or just one phase.

Resource is our middle name.

Publishers Resource Group
307 Camp Craft Rd, Austin, TX 78746
Tel: 512-328-7007 *Fax:* 512-328-9480
E-mail: info@prgaustin.com
Web Site: www.prgaustin.com
Key Personnel
VP & Gen Mgr: Ron Reed *E-mail:* rreed@prgaustin.com
VP, Prod Devt: David Lippman *E-mail:* dlippman@prgaustin.com
Founded: 1989
Complete K-12 educational publishing & accountability solutions to boost student achievement, specializing in curriculum alignment, assessment & customized product development in all subject areas. Experience extends to the development of teacher & student editions, ancillaries, teacher & professional development resources, supplementary programs, customized test prep, online assessments, CD-ROMs & more in print & electronic formats. Services provided include research & evaluation, product conceptualization & development, original writing, full-service editorial, assessment & item-writing, quality assurance checks, rights & permissions, art, design, production, correlations & project management. SMART™ (Standards Mapping & Assessment Resource Tool) system is available for licensing to streamline the development of standards-based curricula, assessments & correlations. Extensive experience creating cost-effective & efficient development plans to build customized, quality instructional programs for several markets simultaneously. Experts at implementing product development plans from start to finish for aligned, quality instructional programs that maximize speed to market.
Membership(s): AAP; American Council on the Teaching of Foreign Languages; American Educational Research Association; Association for Supervision & Curriculum Development; Association of Test Publishers; International Reading Association; International Society for Technology in Education; National Association for Bilingual Education; National Council for the Social Studies; National Council of Supervisors of Mathematics; National Council of Teachers of Mathematics; National Council on Measurement in Education; National Science Teachers Association; Teachers of English to Speakers of Other Languages; Texas State Reading Association

Publishers Workshop
63 Montague St, Brooklyn Heights, NY 11201-3350
Tel: 718-797-1157 *Fax:* 718-797-1157
Key Personnel
Exec Ed: Bert N Zelman
Founded: 1977
Specialize in editing & typemarking of sci-tech, biomedical, psychological, mathematical, historical & other scholarly publications.
Branch Office(s)
202 Berkshire "J", West Palm Beach, FL 33417-2162, Mgr: Nahum Zelman *Tel:* 561-686-9664

Publishing Resources Inc
PO Box 41307, San Juan, PR 00940-1307
Tel: 787-727-1800 *Fax:* 787-727-1823

E-mail: pri@chevako.net
Key Personnel
Pres: Ronald J Chevako
Edit Dir: Anne W Chevako
Founded: 1978
Complete services including ms development, research, writing, translation, indexing, content editing & line editing by US-trained professionals & full production services; books available on Puerto Rico include: 5 Centuries (history); Henry in the Caribbean (children); Ponce; Rebirth of a Valuable Heritage.

Publishing Services
525 E 86 St, Suite 10-E, New York, NY 10028
Tel: 212-628-9127 *Fax:* 212-628-9128
E-mail: pubserv525@aol.com
Key Personnel
Contact: Amy S Goldberger
Copy editing, fact checking, line editing, photo research, ms analysis, permissions, research & rewriting.
Membership(s): Editorial Freelancers Association; Women's National Book Association

Publishing Synthesis Ltd
425 Broome St, New York, NY 10013
Tel: 212-219-0135 *Fax:* 212-219-0136
E-mail: info@pubsyn.com
Web Site: www.pubsyn.com
Key Personnel
Pres: Otto H Barz *E-mail:* obarz@pubsyn.com
VP & Edit Dir: Ellen Small
Proj Mgr: George Ernsberger
Founded: 1975
Packager of college text & highly technical trade books.

The Quarasan Group Inc
405 W Superior St, Chicago, IL 60611
Tel: 312-981-2500 *Fax:* 312-981-2507
E-mail: info@quarasan.com
Web Site: www.quarasan.com
Key Personnel
Pres: Randi S Brill
Founded: 1982
Provide complete editorial, design & product development services including original writing, substantive & content editing, focus/field testing, fact checking, visual design, image procurement & all production related services for educational products. Top caliber project management. Specialize in el-hi products; all major disciplines including reading, language arts, science, math, social studies & standardized tests.
Membership(s): AAP; Association for Supervision & Curriculum Development; Association of Educational Publishers; International Reading Association; National Council for the Social Studies; National Council of Teachers of English; National Council of Teachers of Mathematics; National Science Teachers Association

Jane Rafal Editing Associates
325 Forest Ridge Dr, Scottsville, VA 24590
Tel: 434-286-6949 *Fax:* 434-286-6949
E-mail: janerafal@ntelos.net
Web Site: www.cstone.net/~jrafaled/
Key Personnel
Owner: Jane Rafal

Founded: 1993
Developmental editing, cutting & book proposal development. Specialize in general trade fiction & nonfiction.

Jerry Ralya
7909 Vermont Rte 14, Craftsbury Common, VT 05827
Tel: 802-586-2556 *Fax:* 802-586-2422
E-mail: ralya@earthlink.net
Editing, development & indexing of trade, technical, medical & reference books. Specialties include computers, behavioral sciences & the humanities. Twenty-five years of experience.
Membership(s): American Society of Indexers; Editorial Freelancers Association

The Reading Component
1827 Ximeno Ave, PMB 195, Long Beach, CA 90815-5801
Tel: 310-521-6457 *Fax:* 562-597-0462
Key Personnel
Owner: Helen M Winton *Tel:* 562-438-0666
  E-mail: hmwinton@hotmail.com
Founded: 1994

Reference Wordsmith
Formerly Lexical Content
29 Brooks Lane, Essex, CT 06426
Tel: 860-767-1551 *Fax:* 860-767-1288
Web Site: www.reference-wordsmith.com
Key Personnel
Pres: Barbara Ann Kipfer *E-mail:* bkipfer@earthlink.net
Revision & writing of dictionaries, thesauri & other reference books.

Donna Regen
Subsidiary of ProofMark Editorial Services
401 Orchard Lane, Allen, TX 75002
Tel: 214-495-8007 *Fax:* 214-495-9229
E-mail: donna@dallasrelo.com
Keymarking. Specialize in medical, health, college textbooks (math & science). Also compile & publish resource directories.

Reitt Editing Services
591 Coles Meadow Rd, Northampton, MA 01060
Tel: 413-584-8779 *Fax:* 413-584-8779
E-mail: redits@comcast.net
Key Personnel
Pres: Barbara B Reitt
Line editing, fact checking, ms analysis, research, rewriting. Expertise in life sciences & health sciences, especially geriatrics.
Membership(s): Board of Editors in the Life Sciences

Research Research
240 E 27 St, Suite 20-K, New York, NY 10016
Tel: 212-779-9540
Key Personnel
Principal: Cathe Giffuni
Membership(s): National Press Club; Small Press Center

Paula Reuben
291 W 22 St, Suite 103, San Pedro, CA 90731
Tel: 310-831-6057
E-mail: paulareuben@sbcglobal.net
Experienced, reliable editor, writer & consultant.

RGA Enterprises Inc
135 Marrus Dr, Columbus, OH 43230
Tel: 614-471-6385
E-mail: rgaenterprises@msn.com
Key Personnel
Rts & Perms Consultant: Joyce M Rosinger
Review mss for permissions necessary for publication; negotiate & secure permissions & provide complete acknowledgments; all disciplines. Can also grant permissions & follow-up on payments.

Linda L Rill Research
21 Wingate St, Unit 404, Haverhill, MA 01832
Tel: 978-374-0931 *Fax:* 978-374-1008
E-mail: llrill@bellatlantic.net
Text, graphics & photo research copyright clearance specialist. Field: textbooks; most disciplines. Photo Research specialty; social sciences, history & fine art. Experience with hard & soft sciences. Handle large projects. Extensive experience.
Membership(s): ASPP & PWP

Judith Riven Editorial Consultant
250 W 16 St, Suite 4F, New York, NY 10011
Tel: 212-255-1009 *Fax:* 212-255-8547
E-mail: rivenlit@att.net
Key Personnel
Pres & Edit Consultant: Judith Riven
  E-mail: rivenlit@att.net
Editorial consultation, developmental & structural editing, line editing, ms analysis.

The Roberts Group
1530 Thomas Lake Pointe Rd, No 119, Eagan, MN 55122
Tel: 651-330-1457 *Fax:* 651-330-0892
E-mail: info@editorialservice.com
Web Site: www.editorialservice.com
Key Personnel
Co-Owner: Sherry Roberts; Tony Roberts
Founded: 1990
Book design, production & editorial services. A one-stop creative resource for quality interior book design, typesetting, editing, proofread-

ing & indexing. Serving established presses & self-publishers. Competitive prices. Satisfaction guaranteed. We pay attention to details & will work to meet your deadlines. Visit our web site for a complete description of services.

Lillian R Rodberg & Associates
Subsidiary of Wainwright Press Inc
1600 Lehigh Pkwy E, Rm 9F, Allentown, PA 18103-3035
Tel: 610-740-0662
E-mail: wpressinc@aol.com
Key Personnel
Owner: Lillian R Rodberg *E-mail:* rodbergl@aol.com
Founded: 1988
Indexing: Professional texts. Subject areas: medicine, health professions, psychology & forensics.
Membership(s): American Society of Indexers; Board of Editors in the Life Sciences

Peter Rooney
332 Bleecker St, PMB X-6, New York, NY 10014-2980
Tel: 212-334-2042 *Fax:* 212-226-8047
E-mail: magnetix@ix.netcom.com
Web Site: www.magneticreports.com
Indexer, programmer/consultant for indexes, databases, directories, catalogues raisonnes. Large & small projects.

Dick Rowson
4701 Connecticut Ave NW, Suite 503, Washington, DC 20008
Tel: 202-244-8104 *Fax:* 202-244-8104
E-mail: rcrowson2@aol.com
Helps authors find good publishers & appraise mss.

Sachem Publishing Associates Inc
271 Lake Ave, Greenwich, CT 06831
Mailing Address: PO Box 4040, Greenwich, CT 06831
Tel: 203-661-3717 *Fax:* 203-661-0775
E-mail: sachempub@optonline.net
Key Personnel
Pres & Ed: Stephen P Elliott
Founded: 1974
Complete trade & mail order book preparation & packaging; editorial services, from concept to finished books. Specialize in consumer & educational reference books, including encyclopedias & dictionaries.

Barbara S Salz LLC Photo Research
127 Prospect Place, South Orange, NJ 07079
Tel: 973-762-6486 *Fax:* 973-762-3089
E-mail: b.salz@verizon.net
Photo research for books, magazines & advertising.
Membership(s): ASPP

Pat Samples
7152 Unity Ave N, Brooklyn Center, MN 55429
Tel: 763-560-5199 *Fax:* 763-560-5298
E-mail: patsamples@patsamples.com
Web Site: www.patsamples.com
Writing, research & editing for publishers, nonprofits & individuals.
Membership(s): Authors Guild

Paul Samuelson
117 Oak Drive, San Rafael, CA 94901
Tel: 415-459-5352 *Fax:* 415-459-5352
E-mail: paul@storywrangler.com
Web Site: www.storywrangler.com
Also consults on narrative material.

Joanne Sandstrom
1958 Manzanita Dr, Oakland, CA 94611
Tel: 510-643-6325; 510-339-1352 *Fax:* 510-643-7062
E-mail: joannes@socrates.berkeley.edu

Karen E Sardinas-Wyssling
6 Bradford Lane, Plainsboro, NJ 08536-2326
Tel: 609-275-9148
E-mail: starchild240@comcast.net
Psychology, psychiatry, medicine, children's literature, child care & development, fiction. Textbooks (all levels), professional books, reference books, medical books, journals, testing material. IBM PC: Word.

C J Scheiner Books
275 Linden Blvd, Suite B2, Brooklyn, NY 11226
Tel: 718-469-1089 *Fax:* 718-469-1089
Key Personnel
Owner: C J Scheiner
Literature searches, special assignment writing, fact checking, research, photo research illustrations provided, bibliographies & source lists, text & introduction writing. Specialize in erotica, curiosa & sexology.

Schroeder Indexing Services
2606 Old Mill Lane, Suite 1, Rolling Meadows, IL 60008
Tel: **847-303-0989** *Fax:* **847-303-1559**
E-mail: **sanindex@schroederindexing.com**
Web Site: **www.schroederindexing.com**
Key Personnel
Owner: Sandi Schroeder
Specialize in producing custom indexes using dedicated indexing software. Please visit www.schroederindexing.com for information on what we do & how we work. Available pages include current information on clients & titles indexed, information on planning your index, a downloadable Project Information Sheet & a request for an estimate.
Membership(s): American Society of Indexers
See Ad in this Section

Franklin L Schulaner
PO Box 507, Kealakekua, HI 96750-0507
Tel: 808-322-3785
E-mail: tankay@hgea.org
Special assignment writing.

Sherri Schultz Editorial Services
1508 Tenth Ave E, Suite 302, Seattle, WA 98102
Tel: 206-325-3523
E-mail: sherrischultz@earthlink.net
Copy-editing & proofreading of trade nonfiction, with special expertise in travel, the Northwest, the environment, women's studies & art.
Membership(s): Northwest Independent Editors Guild

Scribendi Inc
153 Harvey St, Chatham, ON N7M 1M6, Canada
Fax: 519-354-0192
E-mail: customerservice@scribendi.com
Web Site: www.scribendi.com
Key Personnel
Pres: Chandra Clarke
Sec: Terence Johnson *E-mail:* accounts@scribendi.com
Founded: 1997
Scribendi provides editorial & translation services on demand, through its website. The service is available 24 hours a day, there is no minimum or maximum word count for assignments & services are priced per word. Ordering online is instant & most short documents can be edited in less than 24 hours. We serve individual authors, students, academics, ESL speakers, business professionals & companies. We also provide outsourcing services to book & periodical publishers. Credit cards, e-checks & other payment methods accepted.
Membership(s): Association de l'Industrie de le Langue

Hank Searls
Division of Hank Searls Authors' Workshop
4435 Holly Lane NW, Gig Harbor, WA 98335
Tel: 253-851-9896 *Fax:* 253-851-9897
E-mail: hanksearls@harbornet.com
Web Site: www.critiquemaster.com
Founded: 1986
Ms consultation & analysis. Screenplays, marketing counsel for authors. Previous publications includes Jaws 2, Jaws: The Revenge (Universal Pictures), The New Breed (Creator), Overboard (Norton), Kataki (McGraw-Hill), Sounding (Random House), Blood Song (Villard Books), The Hero Ship (NAC World), Firewind (Doubleday), The Crowded Sky (Harper), The fugitive: Never Wave Goodbye.
Membership(s): Authors Guild; National Writers Union; Writers Guild of America

Richard Selman
14 Washington Place, New York, NY 10003
Tel: 212-477-1874 *Fax:* 212-473-1875
Multimedia & electronic desktop publishing, advertising & promotional copywriting; fact checking, line editing, permissions, research, photo research, proofreading, ms analysis, bibliographies, copy-editing, interviewing, rewriting, special assignment writing, transcript editing, indexing, audio/video text.

Alexa Selph
4300 McClatchey Circle, Atlanta, GA 30342
Tel: 404-256-3717
E-mail: Lexal01@aol.com

Laurie S Senz
2363 Deer Creek Trail, Deerfield Beach, FL 33442
Tel: 954-481-1930 *Fax:* 954-481-1939
E-mail: lsenz@aol.com
Specialize in special assignment writing, research & interviewing, copy-editing, line editing, ms analysis.

Seraphine Publishing
29 Queen St, Belleville, ON K8N 1T3, Canada
Tel: 613-921-7636 *Fax:* 613-771-1737
E-mail: info@seraphinepublishing.com
Web Site: www.seraphinepublishing.com
Key Personnel
Contact: Sherri Jackson
Founded: 1996
Editorial & production services. Branch offices in Toronto & Belleville.
Membership(s): Editors' Association of Canada/Association canadienne de reviseurs; Quinte Arts Council

Doris P Shalley
1093 General Sullivan Rd, Washington Crossing, PA 18977
Tel: 215-493-3521
Abstracting, copy & line editing, fact checking, indexing, ms analysis, research, rewriting.
Membership(s): SLA

Shane-Armstrong Information Systems
912 S Elmhurst Ave, Fayetteville, AR 72701
Mailing Address: PO Box 119, Fayetteville, AR 72702
Tel: 479-521-8657 *Fax:* 479-521-8657
Key Personnel
Contact: Lynn Armstrong *E-mail:* larmstro@uark.edu; C J Shane

Founded: 1982
Indexing.

Barry Sheinkopf
c/o The Writing Center, 601 Palisade Ave, Englewood Cliffs, NJ 07632
Tel: 201-567-4017 *Fax:* 201-567-7202
E-mail: 102100.1065@compuserve.com
Trade, scholarly & professional publications.

Monica Shoffman-Graves
70 Transylvania Ave, Key Largo, FL 33037
Tel: 305-451-1462 *Fax:* 305-451-1462
E-mail: Keysmobill@earthlink.net
Indexing, ms analysis, proofreading & research.

Esther T Silverman
443 Vermont Place, Columbus, OH 43201
Tel: 614-299-1034 *Fax:* 614-299-1034
E-mail: esilver@columbus.rr.com
Medical & textbook editorial services.
Membership(s): American Medical Writers Association

Roger W Smith
59-67 58 Rd, Maspeth, NY 11378-3211
Tel: 718-416-1334
E-mail: roger.smith106@verizon.net
Membership(s): Editorial Freelancers Association

Spanishindexing.com, see East Mountain Editing Services

Helen Spiroplaus
4916 Amberton Dr, Powder Springs, GA 30127
Tel: 770-419-8308 *Fax:* 770-419-9836
E-mail: spiro@bellsouth.net
Quick, accurate & professional turnaround. Mss, reports, screenplays, research papers, dissertations, resumes, theses, mailings, reports & articles. Experienced with literary, legal, medical & scholarly texts. Proofreading & laser printing, word processing & text editing. IBM compatible equipment & diskette storage. Coding mss onto disk for publishers & book compositors; editing (if authorized by client). Work from hard copy or your disk. Clients outside the immediate free pick-up & delivery area are accommodated through UPS or mail.

Spring Point Publishing Services
4 The Ledges, Hallowell, ME 04347
Tel: 207-622-3973 *Fax:* 207-622-3973
Key Personnel
Owner: Maggie Warren *E-mail:* maggiecw@adelphia.net
Copy editing, proofreading, typemarking, typesetting & transcription.

P Gregory Springer
Subsidiary of Springer/Petrie Inc
206 Wood St, Urbana, IL 61801
Tel: 217-239-4800 *Fax:* 775-459-4675
Web Site: 8am.com
Key Personnel
Pres & Ed: P G Springer *E-mail:* editor@8am.com
Internet editing & publishing, travel & entertainment writing, drama, theater & journalism.
Membership(s): American Theatre Critics Association

SSR Inc
116 Fourth St SE, Washington, DC 20003
Tel: 202-543-1800 *Fax:* 202-544-7432
E-mail: ssr@ssrinc.com
Key Personnel
Pres: Shirley Sirota Rosenberg
Writing, editing & design.

Stackler Editorial Agency
555 Lincoln Ave, Alameda, CA 94501
Tel: 510-814-9694 *Fax:* 510-814-9694
E-mail: stackler@aol.com
Web Site: www.fictioneditor.com
Key Personnel
Owner: Ed Stackler
Founded: 1996
Provide editorial services for authors of commercial fiction & nonfiction, including mysteries, thrillers & suspense.

Stanford Creative Services
7645 N Union Blvd, Suite 235, Colorado Springs, CO 80920
Tel: 719-599-7808 *Fax:* 719-590-7555
Web Site: www.stanfordcreative.com
Key Personnel
Owner: Eric Stanford *E-mail:* eric@stanfordcreative.com
Founded: 1998
A writing & editing services provider.

Nancy Steele
2210 Pine St, Philadelphia, PA 19103-6516
Tel: 215-732-5175
E-mail: NancyS1861@aol.com
Founded: 1999
Versatile, intuitive editor with more than 15 years of experience in editing nonfiction for all ages. Expertise includes American art & antiques, anthologies, biographies & memoirs/condensations, life science, psychology, general reference & illustrated books.
Membership(s): National Association of Science Writers

Brooke C Stoddard
101 N Columbus St, 4th fl, Alexandria, VA 22314
Tel: 703-838-1650 *Fax:* 703-836-3085
E-mail: brookecstoddard@cs.com
Magazine & book writing & editing. Can handle design & production.
Membership(s): American Society of Journalists & Authors

Jean Stoess
500 Ryland St, Suite 150, Reno, NV 89502
Tel: 775-322-5326 *Fax:* 775-322-8271
E-mail: jstoess@aol.com
Founded: 1977
Editorial services &/or collaboration on for publishers & authors, first to final draft. Collaborate on nonfiction & fiction. Audiotape transcription & editing (micro & regular cassettes). APA style is a specialty. Wordperfect 11.0 & Word 2003.

Jeri L Stolk
90 Bronson Terr, Springfield, MA 01108
Tel: 413-739-9585
E-mail: jeri.stolk@comcast.net
Ms development. Specialize in scholarly books & journals.

Straight Line Editorial Development Inc
3239 Sacramento St, San Francisco, CA 94115-2047
Tel: 415-864-2011 *Fax:* 415-864-2013
E-mail: sledinc@aol.com
Key Personnel
Pres & Man Ed: Peder Jones
VP & Exec Ed: Lana Costantini
Exec Ed: Noel Kaufman
Provide editorial services to el-hi publishers; new product development; writing, editing, content development for textbooks, magazines & interactive computer-based instruction systems, including CD-ROM & Internet; correlations &

marketing support. Subject areas: reading, language arts, social studies, mathematics, history, LEP support, Spanish reading & literature.

Stratford Publishing Services Inc
70 Landmark Hill Dr, Brattleboro, VT 05301
Mailing Address: PO Box 1338, Brattleboro, VT 05302
Tel: 802-254-6073 *Toll Free Tel:* 800-451-4328
 Fax: 802-254-5240
Web Site: www.stratfordpublishing.com
Key Personnel
Pres: James Bristol
VP, Sales: Wendy James *Tel:* 802-254-6073 ext 119 *E-mail:* wendyj@stratfordpublishing.com
Founded: 1997
Membership(s): Bookbinders Guild of New York; Bookbuilders of Boston

Barbara Cohen Stratyner
40 Lincoln Center Plaza, New York, NY 10023
Tel: 212-870-1830 *Fax:* 212-870-1870
Adaptations, bibliographies, fact checking, research, special assignment writing.

Elvira C Sylve—Editorial & Secretarial Services
PO Box 870602, New Orleans, LA 70187
Tel: 504-244-8357 *Fax:* 504-244-8357 (call first)
E-mail: elcsy58@aol.com
Key Personnel
Owner: Elvira C Sylve
Asst: Brenda Bailey, MLIS; Lillian Gail Laraque
Founded: 1989
Proofreading, editing, line editing, transcription editing of journals, newsletters, mss, proposals, magazines, articles, medical books, children's books, clinical articles, legal writing, research papers, etc. Specialize also in professional typing: reports, transcription, medical typing, grant proposals, academic & research papers, legal documents, court reports, articles & manuals. Other specialties: medical record analysis, medical coding using ICD-9-CM & CPT. Proofread & edit medical & non-medical documents.
Membership(s): American Health Information Management Association; Friends of the New Orleans Public Library

Carol Talpers
2738 Webster St, Berkeley, CA 94705
Tel: 510-549-9050
Ms analysis, rewriting, editing, research, indexing.

TechBooks Professional Publishing Group
11150 Main St, Suite 402, Fairfax, VA 22030
Tel: 703-352-0001 *Fax:* 703-352-8862
E-mail: info@techbooks.com
Web Site: www.techbooks.com
Key Personnel
Sr VP, Prodn Servs: Anita Gupta
Liaison for complete or any combination of production services, ranging from simple 1-color to complex 4-color projects & copy-editing.

Textbook Writers Associates Inc
12 Nathan Rd, Newton Centre, MA 02459
Tel: 617-630-8500 *Fax:* 617-630-8502
E-mail: info@textbookwriters.com
Web Site: www.textbookwriters.com
Key Personnel
Pres: Rose Sklare
Founded: 1993
Full service editorial/production company offering comprehensive scientific & professional book development & production. Provide extensive editorial work on medical journals; pharmaceutical writing of monographs, peer-reviewed articles & clinical trials. Services include project management, research, writing, on-line editing, design, art rendering, photo research, compo-

sition, proofreading, permissions, indexing. Specialize in medical, nursing & pharmaceutical sciences, as well as basic sciences, math & engineering.
Membership(s): American Medical Writers Association; Bookbuilders of Boston; Drug Information Association

Susan Thornton
5108 South St, Vermilion, OH 44089
Tel: 440-967-1757
E-mail: thornton@hbr.net
Key Personnel
Freelance Copy Ed: Allen Thornton; Susan Thornton
Medical, technical, mathematics, university press, college text, reference, trade nonfiction on hard copy & on disk.

Mary F Tomaselli
146-05 14 Ave, Whitestone, NY 11357
Tel: 718-767-3541
E-mail: indexer@aol.com
Web Site: members.aol.com/indexer/indexer.htm
Abstracting, indexing & index design; specialize in computer-assisted indexing in all fields.

Lynn Truppe
15980 W Marietta Dr, New Berlin, WI 53151
Tel: 262-782-7482
Educational writer/editor; specialize in educational materials for elementary, secondary & college level & business training materials. Services include writing, rewriting, copy-editing, fact-checking, line editing, proofreading, research, ms analysis & content & translation editing. Specialize in textbooks, instructor guides & workbooks in all academic areas, excluding math.

TSI Graphics
1300 S Raney, Effingham, IL 62401
Tel: 217-347-7733 *Fax:* 217-342-9611
Web Site: www.tsigraphics.com
Key Personnel
Pres: Richard Whitsitt
VP & Gen Mgr: David Nitsche
All aspects of editorial functions, from development through indexing.

Twin Oaks Indexing
Division of Twin Oaks Community
138 Twin Oaks Rd, Louisa, VA 23093
Tel: 540-894-5126 *Fax:* 540-894-4112
E-mail: indexing@twinoaks.org
Key Personnel
Mgr: Jake Kawatski *E-mail:* jake@twinoaks.org
Founded: 1982
Subsidiaries: Twin Oaks Industries Inc

Arlene S Uslander
1920 Chestnut Ave, Apt 105, Glenview, IL 60025
Tel: 847-729-7757 *Fax:* 847-729-8677
E-mail: auslander@theramp.net
Web Site: www.uslander.net
Founded: 1980
Editing services: whatever is necessary to prepare a ms to send to an agent or publisher, but no typing or ghost writing.

Samuel S Vaughan
23 Inness Rd, Tenafly, NJ 07670
Tel: 201-568-9485 *Fax:* 201-568-7527
E-mail: samuelsvaughan@aol.com

Visuals Unlimited
27 Meadow Dr, Hollis, NH 03049
Tel: 603-465-3340 *Fax:* 603-465-3360
E-mail: staff@visualsunlimited.com
Web Site: visualsunlimited.com
Key Personnel
Pres: John D Cunningham

Contact: Robert Folz; Shelly Folz *E-mail:* sfolz@
  visualsunlimited.com
Photo agent, photo research & stock agency.

Vocabula Communications Co
10 Grant Place, Lexington, MA 02420
Tel: 781-861-1515
E-mail: info@vocabula.com
Web Site: www.vocabula.com
Key Personnel
Pres: Robert Hartwell Fiske
Founded: 1986
Copy editing, developmental editing, technical
  editing & writing, copywriting, special as-
  signment writing, abstracting, interviewing,
  research, transcription editing, on-screen edit-
  ing, html coding & editing, website editing &
  proofreading & typemarking.

Dina von Zweck
80 Beekman St, No 6-K, New York, NY 10038
Tel: 212-732-1020
Complete editorial services for writers & book
  publishers. Ms development, writing, rewriting, copy-editing, proofreading, advertising,
  promotion & copywriting. Services for authors
  include ms evaluation, analysis & development
  of publishing proposals, ms editing & ghost
  writing.

Jayne Walker Literary Services
1406 Euclid Ave, Suite 1, Berkeley, CA 94708
Tel: 510-843-8265
Key Personnel
Owner: Jayne Walker
Editorial & marketing consultant. Specialize in
  active collaboration with authors: evaluation,
  developmental & line editing, copy-editing, research, rewriting & restyling of proposals &
  mss. Fiction & nonfiction; trade & academic
  books. Consulting on marketing, publicity &
  other publishing issues.

Dorothy Wall, Writing Consultant
3045 Telegraph Ave, Berkeley, CA 94705
Tel: 510-486-8008
Founded: 1984
Ms analysis, substantive editing, marketing assis-
  tance for fiction & nonfiction.

Wambtac Communications
17300 17 St, Suite J-276, Tustin, CA 92780
Tel: 714-954-0580 *Toll Free Tel:* 800-641-3936
  Fax: 714-954-0793
E-mail: wambtac@wambtac.com
Web Site: www.wambtac.com
Key Personnel
Owner, Writer & Ed: Claudia Suzanne
  E-mail: claudia@wambtac.com
Founded: 1995
Book writing & publishing.
Membership(s): Publishers Marketing Association

Andrea Warren
4908 W 71 St, Prairie Village, KS 66208
Tel: 913-722-2343 *Fax:* 913-722-4436
E-mail: awkansas@aol.com
Founded: 1982
Juvenile & young adult books.
Membership(s): American Society of Journalists
  & Authors

Washington Researchers Ltd
1655 N Fort Myer Dr, Suite 800, Arlington, VA
  22209
Tel: 703-312-2863 *Fax:* 703-527-4586
E-mail: research@researchers.com
Web Site: www.washingtonresearchers.com

Key Personnel
Mktg Mgr: Drustva Delgadillo
Customized research on any topic; publications &
  conferences on how to find information; company intelligence consulting.

Jesse A Weissman
10 Shore Blvd, Suite 1-L, Brooklyn, NY 11235-
  4022
Tel: 718-646-2118 *Fax:* 718-646-0520
E-mail: jesseaw1@earthlink.net
Founded: 1986
Proofreading of general fiction & nonfiction
  books, brochures, advertisements, press releases, proposals, reports & newsletters.
  Specialize in trade, romance, mysteries, ac-
  tion/adventure, humor, science fiction, children's, fantasy, horror & historical novels;
  reference books, how-to, self-help, New Age
  & biographies, statistical data, textbooks,
  newsletters, brochures, press releases & advertisements. Copy-editing of novels, nonfiction
  books & master's degree theses. Writing: promotional articles, press releases, advertisements
  & brochures. Honors: Who's Who in US Freelance Journalism & Lexington Who's Who of
  Professionals & Executives. Member of the
  Editorial Freelancers Association's Board of
  Governors. Business restricted to proofreading,
  copy-editing & writing; not a literary agent.
Membership(s): Editorial Freelancers Association

Anne Jones Weitzer
Subsidiary of Weitzer & Associates
60 Sutton Place S, Suite 9B South, New York,
  NY 10022-4168
Tel: 212-758-8149; 201-224-6931 *Fax:* 206-339-
  8149
E-mail: 47dehaven@msn.com; alas101@hotmail.
  com
Founded: 1989
Freelance writer & editor.
Branch Office(s)
5 Horizon Rd, Suite 808, Fort Lee, NJ 07024-
  6622 *Tel:* 201-224-6931 *Fax:* 206-339-8149
  E-mail: 47dehaven@msn.com
Membership(s): National Writers Union

Toby Wertheim
240 E 76 St, New York, NY 10021
Tel: 212-472-8587
E-mail: feb298@aol.com
Textbook picture search.

Rosemary Wetherold
4507 Cliffstone Cove, Austin, TX 78735
Tel: 512-892-1606
E-mail: roses@ix.netcom.com
Founded: 1985
Copy editing, substantitive editing, desktop pub-
  lishing. Varied subjects, including biological
  sciences & natural history.

Helen Rippier Wheeler
Subsidiary of Womanhood Media
1909 Cedar St, Suite 212, Berkeley, CA 94709-
  2037
Tel: 510-549-2970 *Fax:* 510-549-2970
E-mail: pen136@inreach.com
Consulting & professional development training.
Membership(s): Writer's Guild of Alberta

Barbara Mlotek Whelehan
7064 SE Cricket Ct, Stuart, FL 34997
Tel: 954-554-0765 (cell); 772-463-0818 (home)
E-mail: barbarawhelehan@bellsouth.net
More than 20 years of publishing experience. All
  subjects; specialize in personal finance, investments, mutual funds, business & consumer topics.

White Oak Editions
2000 Flat Run Rd, Seaman, OH 45679
Tel: 937-764-1303 *Fax:* 937-764-1303
Key Personnel
Pres & Ed-in-Chief: Carol Cartaino
  E-mail: cartaino@aol.com
Founded: 1986
Content, developmental & line editing; ms anal-
  ysis; rewriting & collaboration; development
  & packaging of book ideas & book programs.
  Nonfiction including how-to, self-help, refer-
  ence, humorous & highly illustrated books.
  Also expert assistance of all kinds for self-
  publishers & solutions for problem mss.

Whitehorse Productions
2417 W 35 Ave, Denver, CO 80211
Tel: 303-433-4400
Key Personnel
Owner: Michael Haldeman
  E-mail: michaelhaldeman@comcast.net
Founded: 1988
Indexing, publication design & production, self-
  publishing assistance.
Membership(s): Colorado Independent Publish-
  ers Association; Rocky Mountain Publishing
  Professionals Guild

Eleanor B Widdoes
417 W 120 St, New York, NY 10027
Tel: 212-870-3051; 212-222-6235
Line editing, indexing, proofreading, research,
  bibliographies & newsletters.

Jan Williams, Indexing & Editorial Services
300 Dartmouth College Hwy, Lyme, NH 03768
Tel: 603-795-4924 *Fax:* 603-795-9346
E-mail: jan.williams@valley.net
Key Personnel
Owner: Jan Williams
Founded: 1998
Back-of-book indexing for trade, scholarly &
  textbooks; Database/on-line indexing of med-
  ical journals. Proofreading & copy editing.
Membership(s): American Society of Indexers

Stephen Douglas Williford
7608 Poplar Pike, Germantown, TN 38138
Tel: 901-756-4661 *Fax:* 901-756-2429
E-mail: willifords@aol.com
Founded: 1980
Writing, co-writing & ghost writing biographies
  of CEOs, celebrities & corporations.

Windhaven Press Editorial Services
68 Hunting Rd, Auburn, NH 03032
Tel: 603-483-0929 *Fax:* 603-483-8022
E-mail: info@windhaven.com
Web Site: www.windhaven.com
Key Personnel
Dir & Exec Ed: Nancy C Hanger
  E-mail: nhanger@windhaven.com; director@
  windhaven.com
Assoc Ed: Andrew V Phillips
Founded: 1985
Consulting & developmental editing, line-editing,
  copy editing, proofreading.
Membership(s): Editorial Freelancers Association

Wings Press
627 E Guenther, San Antonio, TX 78210
Tel: 210-271-7805; 210-222-8449 *Fax:* 210-271-
  7805
Web Site: www.wingspress.com
Key Personnel
Publr & Ed: Bryce Milligan *E-mail:* milligan@
  wingspress.com
Founded: 1975
Literary publishing.

EDITORIAL SERVICES

Audur H Winnan
747 Tenth Ave, No 16-K, New York, NY 10019
Tel: 212-581-9766
Key Personnel
Contact: Audur H Winnan
Indexing; specialize in art books.

Roberta H Winston
15 Sabina Way, Belmont, MA 02478-2268
Tel: 617-489-4190
Freelance writing & editing services. Writing specialties include jacket copy; business & educational materials. Editing specialties include general nonfiction, business/careers, women's studies, Holocaust studies.

Winter Springs Editorial Services
2263 Turk Rd, Doylestown, PA 18901-2964
Tel: 215-340-9052 *Fax:* 215-340-9052
Key Personnel
CEO: Carol H Munson *E-mail:* chmunson@verizon.net
CFO: Lowell Munson
Founded: 1990
Editorial help from concept through ms to production. Book proposals & permissions. Book cover designs & images. Specialize in cookbooks, food, nutrition & health.

Nancy Wolff
125 Gates Ave, No 14, Montclair, NJ 07042
Tel: 973-746-7415
E-mail: wolffindex@aol.com
Indexing, most fields: biography (Leap of Faith/Queen Noor); cookbooks (Weight Watchers); Art (Modigliani/Jewish Museum/Yale University Press); books for young readers (Marian Anderson); current events (Madam Secretary/Madeleine Albright); business (Who Says Elephants Can't Dance?); health (The Perricone Prescription); natural history (H2O); travel (Adventure Guide to Panama). Professional; prompt.
Membership(s): American Society of Indexers

Wood & Wood Book Services
62 Great Ring Rd, Sandy Hook, CT 06482
Tel: 203-270-8206 *Fax:* 203-270-8362
Key Personnel
Founder: Marian Wood; Wally Wood
Business writers/editors bring extensive business background to trade & textbook assignments in business, marketing, sales, advertising, management, communications, banking, retailing & international business. Services include ms analysis, writing, rewriting, ghost writing, developmental & substantive editing, book proposal creation & refinement for business subjects only. Professional, dependable, conscious of budgets & deadlines; publisher references available.
Membership(s): American Marketing Association

WordCo Indexing Services
49 Church St, Norwich, CT 06360
Tel: 860-886-2532 *Toll Free Tel:* 877-967-3263
Fax: 860-886-1155
Web Site: www.wordco.com
Key Personnel
Owner: Stephen Ingle *E-mail:* sringle@wordco.com
Founded: 1988
Since 1988, WordCo has completed over 2000 indexes in many subject areas for dozens of publishers. Founder & owner Steve Ingle (BA, Yale 1979, Master's degrees in Russian & German) manages WordCo's in-house staff of six professionally trained indexers. We have the experience & capability to complete your indexing projects professionally & on time. Ask about our discount for first-time customers. Please visit our website or call for more information.
Membership(s): American Society of Indexers

WordCrafters Editorial Services Inc
22636 Glenn Dr, Suite 106, Sterling, VA 20164
Tel: 703-471-0160 *Fax:* 703-471-0693
E-mail: editors@wordcrafterseditorial.com
Key Personnel
Pres: Ann L Mohan *E-mail:* ann.mohan@wordcrafterseditorial.com
Founded: 1986
Full editorial, design & production services from ms through film or disk. Copy-editing, typemarking, proofreading, permissions, indexing, photo research, book interior & cover design, technical illustration, layout, total project management & scheduling, photocomposition, desktop publishing. Experienced in 2- & 4-color books. College textbooks & ancillaries, vo-tech, juvenile & trade books in all subjects.

WordForce Communications
206-264 Queen's Quay W, Toronto, ON M5J 1B5, Canada
Tel: 416-970-6733 *Fax:* 416-260-2229
E-mail: info@wordforce.ca
Web Site: www.wordforce.ca
Key Personnel
Pres: Maja Rehou *E-mail:* mrehou@wordforce.ca
Founded: 2003
WordForce Communications provides editing, writing & consulting services to help engineers, scientists, lawyers, web developers & business professionals improve the effectiveness & profitability of their technical documents & marketing materials.
Membership(s): Editors' Association of Canada/Association canadienne de reviseurs; Professional Services Marketing Association; Society of Technical Communicators; Women in Science & Engineering

WordMaster & Associates LLC
4317 W Farrand Rd, Clio, MI 48420
Tel: 810-686-2047 *Fax:* 810-564-9929
E-mail: wordmasterpub@comcast.net
Key Personnel
Owner & Consultant: Judith Karns
Copy-editing, line editing, proofreading. Mss: fiction, nonfiction, training manuals, how-tos. Rewriting, creative editing, concept development, desktop publishing, editorial consultation on marketing material.

Words into Print
200 W 86 St, Suite 14-1, New York, NY 10024
Tel: 212-877-3211 *Fax:* 212-873-3796
E-mail: sas22@ix.netcom.com
Web Site: www.wordsintoprint.org
Key Personnel
Ed: Janet Byrne *E-mail:* jbyrne18940@yahoo.com; Bonny V Fetterman *E-mail:* bvfetterman@aol.com; Penelope Franklin *E-mail:* penfrank@yahoo.com; Ruth Greenstein *E-mail:* ruthg@nyc.rr.com; Rob Kaplan *E-mail:* rkaplan@bestweb.net; Diane O'Connell *E-mail:* doconnell@nyc.rr.com; Susan A Schwartz *E-mail:* sas22@ix.netcom.com; Katharine Turok *E-mail:* kturok@mindspring.com; Daniel Zitin *E-mail:* d.zitin@worldnet.att.net
An alliance of top New York publishing professionals who offer a broad range of editorial services to authors, publishers, literary agents, book packagers & content providers from around the world; developmental editing & proposal writing.

Words That Work!
W7615 County Rd YY, Wautoma, WI 54982-8382

Tel: 920-787-2645 *Fax:* 920-787-2698
Key Personnel
Owner, Copyeditor & Proofreader: Amy J Schneider *E-mail:* ajschn@voyager.net
Founded: 1994
Freelance editorial services: fiction & nonfiction, textbooks, trade & professional books. Subjects include social science, education & mathematics. All subjects welcome.

Wordsworth Associates Editorial Services
9 Tappan Rd, Wellesley, MA 02482
Tel: 781-237-4761 *Fax:* 781-237-4758
Key Personnel
Pres & Man Ed: Grace Sheldrick *E-mail:* gsheldrick@comcast.net
Trade & text, all levels & subjects.

Wordsworth Communication
PO Box 9781, Alexandria, VA 22304-0468
Tel: 703-642-8775 *Fax:* 703-642-8775
Key Personnel
Pres: Franklin Wordsworth
Exec Dir: Paul Elliott
Founded: 1973
Special assignment & ghost writing, rewriting, copy & line editing, research, advertising & promotion copywriting, interviewing, condensations, abstracting, transcription editing.

The Wordwatcher
605-4854 Cote-des-Neiges, Montreal, PQ H3V 1G7, Canada
Tel: 514-739-9274; 514-398-1511
E-mail: wordwatcher@vif.com
Web Site: www.vif.com/users/wordwatcher/
Key Personnel
Contact: Paul Alan Nathanson

WordWitlox
642 Chiron Crescent, Pickering, ON L1V 4T4, Canada
Tel: 416-420-0669
Web Site: www.wordwitlox.com
Key Personnel
Ed/Writer: Cathy Witlox *E-mail:* cathy_witlox@editors.ca
Founded: 2004
Cathy Witlox has been writing & editing professionally since 1986, including 6-1/2 years full-time experience copy-editing for a large North American fiction publisher. Branch office in Toronto.
Membership(s): Editors' Association of Canada/Association canadienne de reviseurs

Working With Words
9720 SW Eagle Ct, Beaverton, OR 97008
Tel: 503-644-4317 *Fax:* 503-644-4317
E-mail: w3words@zzz.com
Key Personnel
Owner: Sue Mann
Founded: 1985
Freelance editorial services. General trade; nonfiction; scholarly journals; nonfiction subjects include cookbooks, spiritual, self-help. Substantive editing, online & hard copy.
Membership(s): Northwest Association of Book Publishers; Northwest Independent Editors Guild

The Write Watchman
Subsidiary of LRI Inc
9151 Yellowwood Dr, Cincinnati, OH 45251-1948
Tel: 603-643-6416 *Toll Free Tel:* 800-768-0829 ext 6416 *Fax:* 603-643-6416
E-mail: lmk42@earthlink.net
Key Personnel
Dir: L Kleinschmidt *E-mail:* linda.s.kleinschmidt@dartmouth.edu
Founded: 1988

614

Let the Write Watchman help you say what you want to say better. Experience in technical editing, copywriting, business & technical writing, scriptwriting/ghost writing, screenwriting, ms consultation, content editing, word processing, ms preparation; training, seminars, literary agenting & oral histories. Online editing & consulting for websites.

The Write Way
2449 Goddard Rd, Toledo, OH 43606
Tel: 419-531-9203 *Fax:* 419-531-9203
Key Personnel
Pres: Roberta Kane *E-mail:* robkane@
accesstoledo.com
Also handle advertising & marketing.

The Writer's Advocate/Literary Agenting & Editorial Services
1675 Larimer St, Suite 410, Denver, CO 80202
Tel: 303-297-1233 *Fax:* 303-297-3997
E-mail: thewritersadvocate@thelightningfactory.com
Web Site: www.thelightningfactory.com
Writing, co-authoring & ghostwriting; ms evaluation & editorial services; agenting services. Since 1991 handles regional as well as national writers & authors.

Writers Anonymous Inc
1302 E Coronado Rd, Phoenix, AZ 85006
Tel: 602-256-2830 *Fax:* 602-256-2830
Web Site: writersanonymousinc.com
Key Personnel
Pres: Jordan Richman *E-mail:* jrich9231@
wmconnect.com
Edit Dir: Vita Richman *E-mail:* vita4832@
wmconnect.com
Substantive editing, scholarly, education, humanities, social science, environment, philosophy, music, art, literature, health, general science, medical, legal.
Membership(s): American Society of Indexers; Editorial Freelancers Association

Writers: Free-Lance Inc
167 Bluff Rd, Strasburg, VA 22657
Tel: 540-635-4617
Key Personnel
Pres: Robert M Cullers
Founded: 1965
Over the past nearly 40 years we have been involved in the production of more than two

dozen books plus thousands of specific writing & editing assignments running the gamut of subjects.

The Writer's Lifeline Inc
Subsidiary of AEI (Atchity Editorial/Entertainment International Inc)
518 S Fairfax Ave, Los Angeles, CA 90036
Tel: **323-932-0905** *Fax:* **323-932-0321**
E-mail: **questions@thewriterslifeline.com;**
comments@thewriterslifeline.com
Web Site: **www.thewriterslifeline.com**
Key Personnel
Chmn: **Kenneth Atchity**
Pres: **Andrea McKeown** *E-mail:* **amc@**
thewriterslifeline.com
Founded: **1996**
A full-service editorial company, providing nonfiction book writers, novelists, business, professional, technical & screenwriters with assistance in storytelling, mentoring, perfecting their style & craft, style-structure-concept-line editing, publishing consulting, development, translation, advertising & promotion, printing & self-publishing, distribution & research.
Membership(s): **American Comparative Literature Association; Authors Guild; CAPE; Directors Guild of America; PEN American Center; Women in Film; Writers Guild of America**

Writer's Relief, Inc
245 Teaneck Rd, Ridgefield Park, NJ 07660
Tel: **201-641-3003** *Fax:* **201-641-1253**
Web Site: **www.wrelief.com**
Key Personnel
Pres: **Ronnie L Smith** *E-mail:* **ronnie@wrelief.com**
Highly recommended SUBMISSION SERVICE for all writers. Ms submissions, queries to agents or publishers, tracking, proofreading, professional ms preparation, submission consulting & reports for taxes, etc. Electronic submissions with personalized service. Submissions targeted to specific markets. Full service. Poetry, short stories, essays, book mss, children's market & others. Reasonable rates, references. Lists updated daily. Credit cards accepted. Request free brochure, call 201-641-3003, visit our web site at www.wrelief.com.

Donald Young
166 E 61 St, Suite 3-C, New York, NY 10021
Tel: 212-593-0010
E-mail: numiscribe@aol.com
Specialize in American history, current affairs & natural history (national parks, etc) for magazines, reference books, travel guides & trade nonfiction.
Membership(s): Editorial Freelancers Association

Jane Shapiro Zacek
104 Manning Blvd, Albany, NY 12203-1708
Tel: 518-489-7630; 518-388-6011 *Fax:* 518-388-6875
E-mail: zacekj@union.edu
Editing, abstracting, rewriting, proofreading, condensations, copy editing, interviewing, special assignment writing, transcription editing.

Zebra Communications
230 Deerchase Dr, Suite B, Woodstock, GA 30188
Tel: 770-924-0528 *Fax:* 770-592-7362
Web Site: www.zebraeditor.com
Key Personnel
Owner: Bobbie Christmas *E-mail:* bobbie@
zebraeditor.com
Founded: 1992
Membership(s): Better Business Bureau; Florida Writers Association; Georgia Writers Association; International Guild of Professional Business Consultants; South Carolina Writers Workshop; The Writers Network

Zeiders & Associates
PO Box 670, Lewisburg, PA 17837
Tel: 570-524-4315 *Fax:* 570-524-4315
Key Personnel
Contact: Barbara Zeiders
All editorial work & complete book production. Specialize in math & physical, natural, medical & technical sciences at college & professional levels.

Robert Zolnerzak
101 Clark St, Apt 20K, Brooklyn, NY 11201
Tel: 718-522-0591
Key Personnel
Indexer: Robert Zolnerzak
Computer-assisted indexing for medical, scientific & computer science textbooks & journals since 1973.

Literary Agents

The agents listed here are among the most active in the field. Prior to obtaining a listing in *LMP*, potential entrants are required to submit verifiable references from publishers with whom they have placed titles. Letters in parentheses following the agency name indicate fields of activity:

(L)–Literary Agent   (D)–Dramatic Agent   (L-D)–Literary & Dramatic Agent

Those individuals who are members of the Association of Authors' Representatives are identified by the presence of (AAR) after their name.

Authors seeking literary representation are advised that some agents request a nominal reading fee that may be applied to the agent's commission upon representation. Other agencies may charge substantially higher fees which may not be applicable to a future commission and which are not refundable. The recommended course is to first send a query letter with an outline, sample chapter, and a self-addressed stamped envelope (SASE). Should an agent express interest in handling the manuscript, full details of fees and commissions should be obtained in writing before the complete manuscript is sent. Should an agency require significant advance payment from an author, the author is cautioned to make a careful investigation to determine the agency's standing in the industry before entering an agreement. The author should always retain a copy of the manuscript in his or her possession.

A Abacus Group (L-D)
PO Box 35, Ridgecrest, CA 93556
Tel: 760-375-5243 *Fax:* 760-375-1140
E-mail: gtd007@ridgenet.net
Web Site: www.ridgenet.net/~gtd007
Key Personnel
Dir & Fiction/Nonfiction: G T Dawson
Deputy Dir & Fiction/Nonfiction: Susan Russell
Fiction: Kristy Quinn
Fiction/Nonfiction: Janet Evans; Michael Raines
Contract/Foreign Agent: William Charles
Founded: 1981
Adult fiction & nonfiction, including crime drama, romance, adventure, war, biographies, horror, political intrigue & sci-fi. Textbooks encouraged. Hardcopy, diskette or e-mail file attachment. Query letter not required. No fees. Hardcopy material not returned. No poetry, anthologies, or children's stories. Screenplays accepted. SASE. Complete mss only. Film & TV rights.
Member: Strathmore's, Who's Who In America; The National Directory, Who's Who in America; International Executives Guild; Fiction Writers of America (FWA). Former President, Greater Los Angeles Area Fiction Writers Association (LAFWA).
MENSA (since 1978).
Titles recently placed: *Killin' Time*, B Sadler; *Mr October*, T Randsberg; *My Mamy Lives*, C Ward Seitz; *Only the Lonely*, J B Orbison; *Opec Revisited*, F Laren Boyd; *Operation Flashpoint*, Christopher McKee; *The Day After*, R Dane Bradbury
Foreign Rep(s): William Charles (Canada, Europe)
Foreign Rights: William Charles (Canada, Europe)

AAA Books Unlimited (L)
88 Greenbrier E Dr, Deerfield, IL 60015
Tel: 847-945-0315 *Fax:* 847-444-1220
Web Site: www.aaabooksunlimited.com
Key Personnel
Principal: Nancy Rosenfeld *Tel:* 847-945-0315
E-mail: nancy@aaabooksunlimited.com
Founded: 1993
Full service literary agency to provide clients with first class service "over & above" what normally is handled by a literary agency. We offer content-copy-line editing services.
Titles recently placed: *Brainstorm*, Sheldon Cohen; *Charter Schools*, Frederick A Birkett, Janet Hale Tabin; *Family Lines*, Gwendoline Y Fortune; *Golden Medina*, Jack La Zebnik; *Growing Up Nigger Rich*, Gwendoline Y Fortune; *Healthy Anger: How to Help Children and Families Manage Their Anger*, Bernard Golden, PhD; *How to Stay Afloat Wearing Army Boots*, William T Melms; *Just As Much a Woman*, Nancy Rosenfeld, Dianna W Bolen,

PsyD; *Life! Ain't She a Hoot!!*, Shyam Amladi; *New Hope for Children & Teens with Bipolar Disorder*, Boris Birmaher, MD; *New Hope for People With Alzheimer's and Their Caregivers*, Porter Shimer; *New Hope for People With Bipolar Disorder*, Jan Fawcett, MD, Bernard Golden, PhD, Nancy Rosenfeld; *New Hope for People With Depression*, Marian Broida, RN; *New Hope for People With Diabetes*, Porter Shimer; *New Hope for People With Fibromyalgia*, Theresa Foy DiGeronimo; *New Hope for People With Lupus*, Sara J Henry, Theresa Foy DiGeronimo; *New Hope for People With Weight Problems*, Lawrence J Cheskin, MD, Ron Sauder; *Siren's Dance: Marriage to a Borderline*, Anthony Walker, MD; *The Ultimate Loss: Coping with the Loss of a Child*, Robert J Marx, PhD, Susan W Davidson, MA

The Aaland Agency (L)
PO Box 849, Inyokern, CA 93527-0849
Tel: 760-384-3910 *Fax:* 760-384-4435
Web Site: www.the-aaland-agency.com
Key Personnel
Dir & Fiction/nonfiction: Jo Ann Krueger
E-mail: anniejo@ridgenet.net
Fiction Crime Drama: Terrence Ross
Fiction: Richard Allan
Fiction Romance: Mitzi Rhone
Contracts: James Mason
Founded: 1991
Adult fiction & nonfiction. Queries not required. Author may submit in any format, e-mail file attachment, hardcopy or diskette (e-mail file attachment preferred). Crime drama, romance, children's stories, biographies & textbks gladly accepted. No fees. No partial submissions.
Titles recently placed: *Appointment at Dawn*, Dennis McBride; *Crazy Arms*, Melinda Jenkins; *Saving Your Soul*, L A Seitz; *Stir Fried-The Secret to Quick & Easy*, Mary Margaret Martin; *Take This Job and...*, J K Paycheck; *The Bismarck's Final Voyage*, John M Thompson
Foreign Rep(s): James Mason (Canada, Europe)

Carole Abel Literary Agent (L)
160 W 87 St, New York, NY 10024
Tel: 212-724-1168 *Fax:* 212-724-1384
E-mail: caroleabel@aol.com
Key Personnel
Agent: Carole Abel
Founded: 1980
Specialize in trade & mass market adult fiction & nonfiction books. Health (alternative & mainstream), parenting, relationship & pop reference. No screenplays, teleplays, children's books, science fiction, short stories, plays or poetry. No unsol mss, query first with SASE. Submit outline & sample chapters. No read-

ing fee. Fee for copies, overseas telephone & mailing. Agents in Hollywood & many foreign countries. Handle film & TV rights through representation in Hollywood.
Titles recently placed: *Complete Idiot's Guide to Organizing Your Life, 2nd Ed*, G Lockwood; *Debt-Free College–79 Secrets for Successful College Financing*, R Sparks, M Vaddi; *Instant Self-Hypnosis*, Forbes Robbins Blair; *The Woman's Heart Book*, C Libov, Dr F Pashkow; *Wordplay: Games for Children Who Learn Differently*, L Myers, L Goodman

Dominick Abel Literary Agency Inc (L)
146 W 82 St, Suite 1-B, New York, NY 10024
Tel: 212-877-0710 *Fax:* 212-595-3133
E-mail: agency@dalainc.com
Key Personnel
Contact: Dominick Abel (AAR)
Founded: 1975
Adult fiction & nonfiction. Handle film & TV rights. No unsol mss, query first with SASE; no reading fee. Representatives in Hollywood & all major foreign countries.
Foreign Rep(s): Luigi Bernabo (Italy); Big Apple Tuttle-Mori (Taiwan); The Buckman Agency (Scandinavia); The English Agency (Japan); David Grossman (UK); Korean Copyright Center (Korea); Lennart Sane (Central America, Netherlands, Portugal, South America, Spain); La Nouvelle Agence (France); I Pikarski (Israel); Prava I Prevodi (Czech Republic & Slovakia, Greece, Poland, Russia, Serbia and Montenegro); Thomas Schluck (Germany)

Abrams Artists Agency (L-D)
275 Seventh Ave, 26th fl, New York, NY 10001
Tel: 646-486-4600 *Fax:* 646-486-2358
Key Personnel
Literary Agent: Beth Blickers (AAR); Morgan Jenness; Maura Teitelbawn
Plays, screenplays, film & TV rights. No unsol mss, query first. Submit synopsis. No reading fee.

Acacia House Publishing Services Ltd (L)
51 Acacia Rd, Toronto, ON M4S 2K6, Canada
Tel: 416-484-8356; 416-484-1430 *Fax:* 416-484-8356
Key Personnel
Man Dir: Frances Hanna *E-mail:* fhanna.acacia@rogers.com
VP: Bill Hanna *E-mail:* bhanna.acacia@rogers.com
Founded: 1985
Specialize in adult fiction; no science fiction, occult, horror; most nonfiction. Handle film & TV rights. Handle foreign rights for nine client publishers. No unsol mss, query first; submit outline & first 50 pages. Only typed, dou-

ble spaced mss may be submitted with return postage. No reading fee. Fee charged for photocopying & postage or courier.

Foreign Rights: Agencia BMSR (Brazil); Akcali & Tuna (Turkey); Big Apple Tuttle-Mori (China); Carmen/Balcells Agencia Literaria SA (Spain); Anne Confuron (France); The English Agency (Japan); Graal Ltd (Poland); Hanserik Tonnheim (Scandinavia); Imprima Korea Agency (Korea); International Literatuur Bureau BV (Netherlands); International Press Agency (South Africa); JLM Agency (Greece); Katai & Bolza (Hungary); Simona Kessler (Romania); Alexander Korzhenevski (Russia); Daniela Micura Literary Services (Italy); Paul & Peter Fritz A G (Germany); Ilene Strickler Kreshka (Czech Republic, Slovak Republic & Slovenia); Tuttle-Mori (Japan)

AEI (Atchity Editorial/Entertainment International Inc) (L-D)
Affiliate of The Writer's Lifeline Inc
9601 Wilshire Blvd, No 1202, Beverly Hills, CA 90210
Tel: 323-932-0407 *Fax:* 323-932-0321
E-mail: submissions@aeionline.com
Web Site: www.aeionline.com
Key Personnel
Chair: Kenneth Atchity
Pres: Chi-Li Wong
VP, Devt: Brenna Lui
Off Mgr: Jennifer Pope
Creative Exec: Michael Kuciak
Asst Mgr, Books: Margaret O'Connor
Founded: 1996
Full-service literary management including PR, website & printing, etc. Specialize in commercial novels & self-published nonfiction & in book-film deals (ie a novel or true story that can be made into a highly dramatic TV or feature film). Query letter (by mail or e-mail only), include a 1-2 page synopsis & a SASE for a reply or return. Full ms & scripts only upon request. Handles book, film & TV rights. No fees are charged.
Titles recently placed: *Bedroom Games*, Mary Taylor; *Choking on the Silver Spoon*, Gary Buffone; *Danger Zone*, Shirley Palmer; *Dealing with PMS the Natural Way*, Nadine Taylor; *Do I Stand Alone?*, Governor Jesse Ventura; *Domain Resurrection Goliath*, Steve Alten; *Getting Loaded: How to Make a Million While You're Still Young Enough to Enjoy It*, Peter Bielagus; *Henry's List of Wrongs*, John Scott Shepherd; *I Ain't Got Time to Bleed*, Governor Jesse Ventura; *Moratorium*, April Christofferson; *Nano*, John Robert Marlow; *Ripley's Encyclopedia of the Bizarre*, Julie Mooney; *Sexual Archtypes*, Oona Mourier, Steve Herriot; *The Adjusters (series)*, Michael Walsh; *The Grangaard Strategy: Accumulating and Managing Wealth for Retirement*, Paul Grangaard; *The Myth of Tomorrow*, Gary Buffone; *The Trade*, Shirley Palmer
Foreign Rights: Baror International (outside US & Canada)
Membership(s): Authors Guild; Writers Guild of America

Agency Chicago (L-D)
28 E Jackson Blvd, 10th fl, Suite A-600, Chicago, IL 60604
Tel: 312-409-0205
Key Personnel
Owner: Ernest Santucci
Assoc: Shelly Chou
Professional writers only. No unsol mss; query letter first; handle film & TV rights; no reading fee. True crime, humor, politics, cross-over writers.

Agency For The Performing Arts Inc (L-D)
9200 Sunset Blvd, Suite 900, Los Angeles, CA 90069
Tel: 310-273-0744 *Fax:* 310-888-4242
Key Personnel
Exec VP, Literary Dept: Lee Dinstman
Handle film & TV rights. No unsol mss; query first. Submit outline & sample chapters & SASE. No reading fee; 10% commission.
Branch Office(s)
3017 Poston Ave, Nashville, TN 37203

Agent Research & Evaluation Inc (L-D)
25 Barrow St, New York, NY 10014
Tel: 212-924-9942 *Fax:* 212-924-1864
E-mail: info@agentresearch.com
Web Site: www.agentresearch.biz
Key Personnel
Pres: Bill Martin
Founded: 1996
Providing authors, editors & other professionals with data on clients & sales made by literary agents in the US, UK & Canada - (i.e., who sells what to whom for how much). Information is culled from the trade & general press & collection has been continuous since 1980. Individual reports on specific agents & various forms of ms-agent match-up services are available. Pricing can be found at the web site or send an SASE. In addition, "Talking Agents", the AR&E Newsletter, is published 10 times per year. There is also a free service at the web site offering agent verification: information on whether or not the database reflects that a given agent has created a public record of sales.

Agents Inc for Medical & Mental Health Professionals (L)
PO Box 4956, Fresno, CA 93744-4956
Tel: 559-438-1883 *Fax:* 559-438-1883
Key Personnel
Dir: Sydney H Harriet *Tel:* 559-438-8289
    E-mail: sh062@csufresno.edu
Founded: 1988
Health related nonfiction, business, cookbooks, sports, fiction, mystery, psychology, how-to, literary; no unsol mss-query first; send outline or sample chapters with a SASE; handle software. No reading fee.
Titles recently placed: *Infantry Soldier*, George Neil; *Senior Golfer's Answer Book*, Sol Grazi; *The Red Yeast Diet*, Maureen Keane

Ahearn Agency Inc (L-D)
2021 Pine St, New Orleans, LA 70118
Tel: 504-861-8395 *Fax:* 504-866-6434
Key Personnel
Pres: Pamela Ahearn *E-mail:* pahearn@aol.com
Founded: 1992
Specialize in general fiction, nonfiction, adult; no poetry, plays, young adult, articles or autobiographies. No unsol mss, query first. No reading fee.
Titles recently placed: *If She Should Die*, Carlene Thompson; *In the Prince's Bed*, Sabrina Jeffries; *The Performed Sleeve*, Laura Joh Rowland; *The Romanov Prophecy*, Steve Berry
Foreign Rights: Rights Unlimited; Thomas Schluek
Membership(s): Mystery Writers of America; Romance Writers of America

Akin & Randolph Agency for Representation for Authors, Artists & Athletes (Literary Division) (L-D)
One Gateway Ctr, Suite 2600, Newark, NJ 07102
Tel: 973-623-6834 *Toll Free Tel:* 888-870-0765
    Fax: 973-353-8417
Web Site: www.akinandrandolph.com

Key Personnel
Founding Agent: Wanda M Akin *E-mail:* wakin@akinandrandolph.com
Founded: 1996 (by Wanda M Akin & Carol Randolph)
Specialize in nonfiction & fiction. Public affairs & African American interest; query first with SASE; handle film & TV rights; submit fiction-synopsis & sample chapters; nonfiction send proposal & sample chapters; no reading fee. Sub rights agent for Random House in some foreign countries, Genesis Press & Africa World Press. Mail or fax queries, submissions, etc to New Jersey mailing address.
Titles recently placed: *Finding Mr Write*, Beverley East; *Private Lessons: Meditations For Teachers*, Joy Jones; *Richard Bruce Nugent, Jay Rebel of the Harlem Renaissance*, Tom Wirth; *Steppin' Out*, Carla Labat

Lee Allan Agency (L-D)
7464 N 107 St, Milwaukee, WI 53224-3706
Tel: 414-357-7708
Key Personnel
Owner & Agent: Lee A Matthias *E-mail:* lmatt@wi.rr.com
Assoc: Andrea Knickerbocker; Marc Reed
All genres & subjects except poetry, anthologies & textbooks. Genre fiction; science fiction, fantasy, mystery, horror, thrillers, men's adventure, historical, westerns & mainstream. No short stories. Specialize in screenplays, film & TV rights. No fax queries; no reading fees. 15% commission & required foreign rights & or sub-agent fees; commission & occasional special expenses reimbursement; copying, overseas calls & shipping charges. Signatory to writers guild - all entertainment rights commissions set by WGA. For unsol mss, query by phone or e-mail.

Linda Allen Literary Agency (L)
1949 Green St, Suite 5, San Francisco, CA 94123
Tel: 415-921-6437 *Fax:* 415-921-3733
Key Personnel
Owner & Dir: Linda Allen (AAR)
    E-mail: linda@lallenlitagency.com
Specialize in commercial & literary fiction, mysteries, thrillers, for adult market. Submit for fiction - first 20-40 pages & brief synopsis. No unsol mss, query first with SASE. No reading fee.

Allred & Allred Literary Agents (L-D)
7834 Alabama Ave, Canoga Park, CA 91304-4905
Tel: 818-346-4313 *Fax:* 818-346-4313
Key Personnel
Agent: Robert Allred; Kim Allred
Founded: 1992
Literary agency for both book mss & screenplays. For book mss, send the first 25 pages. For screenplays, send the entire script. For both, also send a 1- or 2-page synopsis covering the full length of the project, a cover letter & SASE for our reply. The ms must be printed in 10-point courier typeface with dark, clear printing. Do not send the original. If you wish the submission returned, your SASE must be large enough & include the proper postage on the envelope (no loose stamps in the envelope). Non-US submissions require the inclusion of enough International Postal Reply Coupons or US stamps. Response time varies; do not call. No fees charged. Allred & Allred receives 10% commission; term of the contract is one year.
Titles recently placed: *Biting Dogs Don't Bark*, Pat Smith; *From Main Street to the Mall*, Jack Jones; *The Yin and the Yang*, Brian Quan

Altair Literary Agency LLC (L)
PO Box 11656, Washington, DC 20008-0856

Tel: 202-237-8282
Web Site: www.altairliteraryagency.com
Key Personnel
Partner: Andrea Pedolsky (AAR)
  E-mail: apedolsky@altairliteraryagency.com;
  Nicholas Smith (AAR)
Founded: 1996
General nonfiction, including business, science, history, illustrated, art, biography, contemporary issues, gift books, museum & organization-branded books, novelty & activity, popular reference. Fiction: historical with pre-20th century settings only, mystery. No unsol mss; query first with letter &/or book proposal, or, for fiction, a full synopsis, with author's curriculum vitae with SASE. No reading fee. Fees for postage, copying, messengers & tape duplicating.
Foreign Rights: Lora Fountain (France); Thomas Schlueck (Germany)

Miriam Altshuler Literary Agency (L)
53 Old Post Rd N, Red Hook, NY 12571
Tel: 845-758-9408 *Fax:* 845-758-3118
Key Personnel
Pres: Miriam Altshuler (AAR)
Quality general fiction & nonfiction. No unsol mss, query first with SASE. No fax or e-mail queries. Submit outline & sample chapters if requested. No software. Handle film & TV rights. Reps in all major countries. No reading fee.
Foreign Rights: A M Heath & Co (England, Europe); Tuttle-Mori Agency (China, Japan, Korea)

Betsy Amster Literary Enterprises (L)
PO Box 27788, Los Angeles, CA 90027-0788
Tel: 323-662-1987 *Fax:* 323-660-4015
E-mail: amsterlit@compuserve.com
Key Personnel
Pres: Betsy Amster (AAR)
Literary fiction & adult nonfiction. Subject areas of interest: social issues, psychology, self-help, popular culture, narrative nonfiction, business, history, art & design, science & technology, health, parenting, cookbooks, gardening. No unsol mss, query first for fiction & enclose first three pages of ms. Submit proposal & sample chapter for nonfiction. No return of material without SASE. No phone, e-mail or fax queries. Handle film & TV rights for client book properties via sub-agents. No reading fee.

Marcia Amsterdam Agency (L)
41 W 82 St, New York, NY 10024-5613
Tel: 212-873-4945
Founded: 1970
Adult & young adult fiction; nonfiction, horror, science fiction, suspense, mainstream, historical romance & contemporary women's etc. Handle film & TV rights. No unsol mss, query with SASE. Submit outline & first three chapters. No reading fee. Other fees: standard agency fees.
Foreign Rights: Daniel Bial Agency
Membership(s): Other Agents' Group; Writers Guild of America

Anderson/Grinberg Literary Management Inc (L)
266 W 23 St, Suite 3, New York, NY 10011
Tel: 212-620-5883 *Fax:* 212-627-4725
E-mail: queries@andersongrinberg.com
Key Personnel
Partner: Kathleen Anderson *E-mail:* kathy@andersongrinberg.com; Jill Grinberg
  E-mail: jillgrin@aol.com
General fiction & nonfiction (adult & juvenile). Representation & management of literary properties for print, electronic, film & TV rights. Nonfiction: query letter, bio, detailed proposal.

Fiction: query, bio, synopsis & first 50 pages of completed novel. No reading fee or other fees; no unsol mss, query first with SASE. Do not send downloads.
Foreign Rep(s): Gillon Aitken Associates (translation)
Foreign Rights: Curtis Brown (Australia, UK); Gillon Aiken Associates (UK)
Membership(s): PEN American Center

Bart Andrews & Associates Inc (L)
7510 Sunset Blvd, Suite 100, Los Angeles, CA 90046-3418
Tel: 310-271-9916
Key Personnel
Pres: Bart Andrews
Founded: 1982
Trade & mass market nonfiction books. Specialize in show business titles. No unsol mss, query first with SASE. Submit outline. No reading fee. Fee for consultation. Handle film & TV rights.
Foreign Rep(s): Abner Stein (England); Elaine Benisti (France); Irina Reylander (Italy); Orley Pecker (Israel); Thomas Schluck (Germany)

Arcadia (L)
31 Lake Place N, Danbury, CT 06810
Tel: 203-797-0993 *Fax:* 203-730-2594
E-mail: arcadialit@att.net
Key Personnel
Pres: Victoria Gould Pryor (AAR)
Founded: 1986
Specialize in adult fiction & nonfiction. Handle film & TV rights with co-agents. Query letter & brief sample material plus SASE. No e-mail, fax or phone queries. No fees charged.
Foreign Rights: Barbara Levy Agency (UK); The Marsh Agency (translation); The Uni Agency (Japan)
Membership(s): Authors Guild

The Artists Agency (L-D)
1180 S Beverly Dr, Suite 400, Los Angeles, CA 90035
Tel: 310-277-7779 *Fax:* 310-785-9338
Key Personnel
Partner: Richard Shepherd
Off Mgr: Fredericka Miller
No unsol mss, query first. No reading fee. Represent screenplays for feature films & TV. Represent screenwriters & directors. Handle film & TV rights for authors. Work in conjunction with NY & British literary agencies.

Artists & Artisans Inc (L)
45 W 21 St, 3rd fl, New York, NY 10010
Tel: 212-924-9619 *Fax:* 212-242-1114
Web Site: www.artistsandartisans.com
Key Personnel
Literary Agent: Adam Chromy *E-mail:* adam@artistsandartisans.com
Founded: 2002
Full service literary agency representing writers of adult trade fiction & nonfiction.
After a stint at a renowned literary agency, Adam Chromy, went out on his own to represent a novel written by a close personal friend. The gamble paid off & the book was sold to a major publisher on a preemptive offer. Now, Adam & his Artists & Artisans Inc are well on their way representing quality projects being acquired by the industry's leading publishers.
No unsol mss, query first. Send query letter with description of project & brief author bio. Also handles film & TV rights.
Titles recently placed: *Life Without Ed: How One Woman Declared Independence From Her Eating Disorder & How You Can Too*, Jennifer Schaefer; *Man Out of Time*, Michael Hogan; *Metrosexual Guide to Style: A Hand-

book for the Modern Man*, Michael Flocker; *Pomegranate Soup: A Novel of Food, Love & Finding New Beginnings*, Marsha Mehran

The Artists Group Ltd (D)
10100 Santa Monica, Suite 2490, Los Angeles, CA 90067
Tel: 310-552-1100 *Fax:* 310-277-9513
Key Personnel
Pres: Robert Malcolm; Hal Stalmaster
Handle film & TV rights. No unsol mss; query first; no reading fee; commission on sales.

Authentic Creations Literary Agency (L-D)
Affiliate of Barnes & Noble Inc
875 Lawrenceville-Suwanee Rd, Suite 310-306, Lawrenceville, GA 30043
Tel: 770-339-3774 *Fax:* 770-339-7126
E-mail: ron@authenticcreations.com
Web Site: www.authenticcreations.com
Key Personnel
Agent: Mary Lee Laitsch; Ronald E Laitsch (AAR)
Founded: 1994
General fiction & nonfiction; all types of genre fiction, including romance (contemporary & historical), accepted. No poetry. Single sided, not bound. Affiliate handles TV & film rights; no unsol mss, query first with SASE; no reading fee; except for photocopying, format of submission to be discussed after query, charge for postage also.
Titles recently placed: *Hometown Killer*, Carol Rothgeb; *Sharing the Dream*, Dominic Pulera; *Siren Song*, Stephen Schwandt
Membership(s): Authors Guild; Romance Writers of America

Author Author Literary Agency Ltd (L)
Lougheed Mall RPO, 9855 Austin Ave, No 236, Burnaby, BC V3J 7W2, Canada
Mailing Address: PO Box 56534, Burnaby, BC V3J 7W2, Canada
Tel: 604-415-0056
Web Site: www.authorauthorliteraryagency.com
Key Personnel
Pres: Joan Rickard *E-mail:* joan@authorauthorliteraryagency.com
Asst: Eileen McGaughey
Founded: 1991
Handles book-length adult/children's fiction, nonfiction; no poetry, screenplays, short stories. Offers editing & ghostwriting services. Unpublished writers welcome. Written contract; no fee for authors book-published in same genres as current endeavors (excluding electronic &/or self-published books). For unpublished book writers: fully refundable entry evaluation fee $75 US per proposal. Evaluation fees are deducted from agency's commission on royalties when properties are placed with publishers. Long distance inquiries via phone/fax returned collect. E-mail contacts for submission inquiries only. Submit hard copy (paper) only; no disk, faxed or e-mailed submissions. Include synopsis & author's bio. Reports in approximately 8 weeks for submissions. For confirmation of proposal's arrival, must include e-mail location or SASE & pretyped form. Note: stamps are not valid beyond a country's borders. For response/ms returns, must send Canadian stamps, IRCs or adequate funds. Our 22-page booklet, "Crash Course" for Proposals to Book & Magazine Publishers: Business Letters, Basic Punctuation/Information Guidelines & Manuscript Formatting is available for $8.95 US (includes S&H). All funds by certified checks or international (if non-Canadian) money order only.
Titles recently placed: *If You are my Soul Mate, Why am I So Unhappy?*, Kelley Rosano; *National Nightmares*, William Rayner

The Author's Agency (L-D)
3355 N Five Mile Rd, Suite 332, Boise, ID 83713
Tel: 208-322-7239
E-mail: authoragency@aol.com
Key Personnel
Pres & Agent: Rhonda J Winchell
Founded: 1995 (Founded to support the endeavor of the artistic creation & expression of writers)
Full service agency. Nonfiction of a serious nature, popular culture, inspirational, religious, sports, cookbooks, business & finance, self-help of all kinds, fiction-both literary & commercial, screenplays, new media. Accept unsol, respond to query, partial mss (first three chapters). Film, TV & CD-ROM rights. Accept outline & three sample chapters with SASE. Also accept brief phone calls. Does not charge fees.
Titles recently placed: *American Dreamscape*, Carrol, Graf; *Beyond the Rhine*, Don Burqett; *The Dog Burglar*, Sharon Curry, Deliah Ahrendt; *The Pursuit of Happiness in Post War Suburbia*, Tom Mortinson
Membership(s): Writers Guild of America

Authors & Artists Group Inc (L)
41 E 11 St, 11th fl, New York, NY 10003
Tel: 212-944-9898 *Fax:* 212-944-6484
Key Personnel
Agent: Alfred Lowman
Nonfiction, commercial fiction, film & TV rights. Referrals only; no unsol mss; query by phone first; no fees charged.
Foreign Rights: B G Dilworth

Authors Marketing Services Ltd (L)
2336 Bloor St W, Box 84668, Toronto, ON M6S 4Z7, Canada
Tel: 416-763-8797 *Fax:* 416-763-1504
Key Personnel
Pres: Larry Hoffman *E-mail:* authorslhoffman@cs.com
VP: Antonia Hoffman
Dir: Sharon DeWynter
Founded: 1978
Full-length fiction, nonfiction & foreign rights. No children's. No unsol mss, query first with letter. Submit sample chapter & synopsis (plus annotated table of contents for nonfiction). Reading fee for unpublished writers. Handle software, TV & film rights when book is represented.
Titles recently placed: *Inside Canadian Intelligence*, Dwight Hamilton; *The Banks*, Les Whittinpton; *Tyranny of Niceness*, Dr Evelyn Sommers

Authorsbest.com, see Carol Susan Roth Literary & Creative

The Axelrod Agency (L)
55 Main St, Chatham, NY 12037
Mailing Address: PO Box 357, Chatham, NY 12037
Tel: 518-392-2100 *Fax:* 518-392-2944
E-mail: steve@axelrodagency.com
Key Personnel
Pres: Steven Axelrod (AAR) *E-mail:* steve@axelrodagency.com
Founded: 1983
Fiction & nonfiction, film & TV rights. No unsol mss, query first; no reading fee.

Elizabeth H Backman (L)
86 Johnnycake Hollow Rd, Pine Plains, NY 12567
Mailing Address: PO Box 762, Pine Plains, NY 12567-0762
Tel: 518-398-9344 *Fax:* 518-398-6368
E-mail: bethcountry@taconic.net
Key Personnel
Owner: Elizabeth H Backman

Adv Serv: Donn King Potter
Founded: 1981
Literary & commercial fiction; nonfiction; current events, politics, business, biography, the arts, cooking, diet, health, sports, gardening, history, science, self-help & psychology; audio & video cassettes. Author representatives, consulting editors, advertising & promotion copywriters. No unsol mss, query first with SASE; submit introduction, cover letter, chapter by chapter outline or table of contents, three sample chapters & authors bio or complete ms with cover letter & author's bio. Reading fees: $100 for proposals, $500 for complete mss; 15% agency fee plus expenses (phone, mail, photocopying, etc). Handle film & TV rights.
Titles recently placed: *Digital Hood and Other Stories*, Peter Rondinone; *Every Saint Has a Path, Every Sinner a Future*, Terry Cole-Whittaker
Foreign Rights: Lora Fountain (France); The International Editors (Central America, South America); Lennart Sane (Netherlands, Portugal, Scandinavia, Spain); Prava I Prevodi (Eastern Europe, Russia); Thomas Schluck (Germany); Lavinia Trevor (UK); Tuttle-Mori Agency Ltd (Japan)

Malaga Baldi Literary Agency (L-D)
233 W 99, Suite 19C, New York, NY 10025
Tel: 212-222-3213
E-mail: mbaldi@nyc.rr.com
Key Personnel
Pres: Malaga Baldi
Founded: 1986 (Independent literary agency)
Cultural history, nonfiction & literary-edgy fiction. No unsol mss, query first with SASE. No reading fee.
Titles recently placed: *All American Boy*, William Mann; *Boy Friend 101*, Jim Sullivan; *Creating Kate*, William Mann; *Crossing Bully Creek*, Margaret Erhart; *Edge of Midnite*, William Mann; *Grammatically Correct*, Anne Stilman; *Light Coming Back*, Ann Wadsworth; *Mermaids*, Patty Dann; *Ravenscliff Series*, William Mann; *Sweet & Craby*, Patty Dann; *The Black Swann*, Anne Batterson; *The Boys of the Brownstone*, Kevin Scott; *The Diary of Drag Queen*, Daniel Harris; *The First Time I Met Frank O'Hara*, Rick Whitaker; *The Tricky Part*, Martin Moran; *Whose Eye On Which Sparrow*, Robert Taylor
Foreign Rep(s): Abner Stein (UK)
Foreign Rights: Elaine Benisti (France); Marsh Agency (Europe); Owl Agency (Japan)

The Balkin Agency Inc (L)
PO Box 222, Amherst, MA 01004
Tel: 413-548-9835 *Fax:* 413-548-9836
Key Personnel
Pres: Richard A Balkin (AAR)
  E-mail: rick62838@crocker.com
Founded: 1972
Specialize in adult nonfiction, professional books & college textbooks. No fiction. No unsol mss, query first. Submit outline & one sample chapter. No reading fee, 15% agency commission; 20% foreign rights.
Foreign Rep(s): Bardon-Chinese Media (China & Taiwan); English Language Agency (Japan); Japan Uni (Japan)
Foreign Rights: Chandler Crawford (Europe)

A Richard Barber & Associates (L)
554 E 82 St, New York, NY 10028
Tel: 212-737-7266 *Fax:* 212-879-0183
E-mail: barberrich@aol.com
Key Personnel
Pres: A Richard Barber
Sr Assoc: Larry Gershel

Specialize in fiction & nonfiction. Handle software, film & TV rights. No fees. No fax or e-mail submissions accepted.
Branch Office(s)
PO Box 887, 80 N Main St, Kent, CT 06757
  Tel: 860-927-4911

Baror International Inc (L)
831 Mount Kisco Rd, Armonk, NY 10504
Mailing Address: PO Box 868, Armonk, NY 10504-0868
Tel: 914-273-9199 *Fax:* 914-273-5058
E-mail: barorint@aol.com
Key Personnel
Pres: Danny Baror
Foreign rights. Represent over 300 authors worldwide. Science fiction, fantasy, nonfiction, self-help, mystery, thrillers & general fiction. No unsol mss. No queries. No fee charged.

Loretta Barrett Books Inc (L)
101 Fifth Ave, New York, NY 10003
Tel: 212-242-3420 *Fax:* 212-807-9579
Key Personnel
Pres: Loretta A Barrett (AAR)
Agent & Rts Coord: Nick Mullendore (AAR)
Founded: 1990
Fiction & nonfiction. Handle film, TV & multimedia rights. No poetry, children's or young adult literature, no screenplays; no unsol mss; query first with SASE. Submit outlines, sample chapters, bio (nonfiction); synopsis, bio (fiction). No reading fee. Representatives on the West Coast & in all major foreign countries. No reading fee.

The Barry-Swayne Literary Agency (L-D)
Formerly The Swayne Agency Literary Management & Consulting
4 Manitou Rd, Garrison, NY 10524
Tel: 845-424-2448
E-mail: info@swayneagency.com
Web Site: www.swayneagency.com
Key Personnel
Pres: Susan Barry *E-mail:* sbarry@swayneagency.com
Founded: 1997
Specialize in technology-related nonfiction, e-commerce, science, investing, health & fitness, women's issues, business, narrative nonfiction & current events. Handle nonfiction only. No unsol mss, query first with one-page query letter & SASE via regular mail or e-mail (but cannot accept attachments or downloads). No reading fee. Handle film & TV rights, software, speaking & seminars for books represented. Agents in all major territories.
Titles recently placed: *Greenspan: The Man Behind the Money*, Justin Martin; *Netslaves: True Tales of Working the Web*, Bill Lessard, Steve Baldwin; *Slate Diaries*, Michael Kinsley

Bawn Publishers Inc (L-D)
8877 Meadowview Dr, West Chester, OH 45069-3545
Mailing Address: PO Box 1356, West Chester, OH 45071-1356
Tel: 513-759-6288 *Fax:* 513-759-6299
E-mail: bawn@one.net
Web Site: www.bawnagency.com
Key Personnel
Owner, Chmn & CEO: Willie Nason
Pres: Beverly Nason
VP: H A Townes
Founded: 1993
Electronic, literary & dramatic agents. No unsol mss. Novels & nonfiction books query first with sample chapters; screenplays query first for request. Handle film & TV rights. No reading fee.

Maximilian Becker, see Aleta M Daley/Maximilian Becker

Meredith G Bernstein (L)
2112 Broadway, Suite 503A, New York, NY 10023
Tel: 212-799-1007 *Fax:* 212-799-1145
Key Personnel
Contact: Meredith Bernstein (AAR)
Adult fiction (commercial & literary) & nonfiction; memoirs, current events, biography, health & fitness, women's issues, mysteries & special projects; crafts & creative endeavors. Welcome queries; no unsol mss. Outline & sample chapters upon request only. Handle film & TV rights only for books represented. Representatives in foreign countries & on the West Coast. Query first. No reading fees.
Membership(s): Authors Guild; Women's Media Group

Bethel Agency (L-D)
311 W 43 St, Suite 602, New York, NY 10036
Tel: 212-664-0455
Key Personnel
Pres: Lewis R Chambers
Founded: 1967
Books & articles, fiction & nonfiction; stage plays, motion picture & TV properties; foreign & domestic. Represent photographers. Handle film & TV rights. No unsol mss, query first; submit outline & sample chapters. No reading fee.

Daniel Bial Agency (L-D)
41 W 83 St, Suite 5-C, New York, NY 10024
Tel: 212-721-1786 *Fax:* 309-213-0230
E-mail: dbialagency@juno.com
Founded: 1991
Nonfiction: business, cookbooks, history, humor, languages, popular culture, psychology, reference, science, sports, travel; fiction: quality fiction. No juvenile, poetry, genre fiction, screenplays, textbooks. No unsol mss, query letter first with SASE or short e-mail. No reading fee.
Foreign Rights: Agence Hoffman (France); Agenzia Letteraria Internazionale (Italy); Alta Vista (UK); Book Publishers Association of Israel (Israel); Andrew Cribb (China); Anna Droumeva (Bulgaria); DRT International (Korea); Amina Marix Evans (Netherlands); Japan Uni (Japan); Simone Kessler (Romania); Ilene Strickler Kreshka (Czech Republic); Liepman (Germany); Ulla Lohren (Scandinavia); David Matlock (Russia); Jovan Milenkovic (Hungary); Karin Petrikova (Slovak Republic); Maria Strarz-Kanska (Poland); Julio F Yanez Agencia Literaria (Spain)

BigScore Productions (L-D)
PO Box 4575, Lancaster, PA 17604
Tel: 717-293-0247 *Fax:* 717-293-1945
E-mail: bigscore@bigscoreproductions.com
Web Site: www.bigscoreproductions.com
Key Personnel
Pres & Agent: David A Robie *E-mail:* drobie@bigscoreproductions.com
Agent: Sharon Hanby-Robie *E-mail:* srobie@bigscoreproductions.com
Founded: 1995
Fiction & nonfiction. Accept unsol queries by e-mail only. If interested, we will request more. Handle film & TV rights. No reading fee.
Titles recently placed: *Biggest Brother: The Life of Major Dick Winters*, Larry Alexander; *Scoring in the Red Zone*, Spencer Tillman

Vicky Bijur Literary Agency (L)
333 West End Ave, Suite 5-B, New York, NY 10023
Tel: 212-580-4108 *Fax:* 212-496-1572
E-mail: vbijur@aol.com
Key Personnel
Contact: Vicky Bijur (AAR)

Founded: 1988
Adult fiction & nonfiction. No unsol mss; query first with SASE. No e-mail queries. No reading fee. Agents in all principal foreign countries. Handle film & TV rights.

David Black Literary Agency (L-D)
Subsidiary of Black Inc
156 Fifth Ave, Suite 608, New York, NY 10010
Tel: 212-242-5080 *Fax:* 212-924-6609
Key Personnel
Contact: David Black (AAR); Leigh Ann Eliseo (AAR); Gary Morris (AAR); Susan Raihofer (AAR)
Agent: Linda Loewenthal; Joy E Tutela (AAR)
    E-mail: jtutela@dblackagency.com
Literary & commercial fiction & nonfiction, especially sports, politics, business, health, fitness, romance, parenting, psychology & social issues. No poetry. No unsol mss, query first with SASE. No reading fee. Agents in all principal foreign countries. Handle film & TV rights. No mysteries or thrillers.

Bleecker Street Associates Inc (L)
532 LaGuardia Place, No 617, New York, NY 10012
Tel: 212-677-4492 *Fax:* 212-388-0001
Key Personnel
Pres: Agnes Birnbaum (AAR)
Founded: 1984
No unsol mss, query first about book project & author with SASE (cannot respond nor return materials without SASE). Do not query via e-mail, phone or fax. Handle film & TV rights for clients' own work only. Fiction & nonfiction; no poetry, plays or screenplays; handle magazine articles by book clients only. No reading fee.
Foreign Rights: Agenzia Letteraria Internazionale (Italy); Bookman (Netherlands, Scandinavia); EAIS/Vera Le Marie (France); English Agency (Japan); International Editors (Portugal, South America, Spain); Thomas Schluck (Germany); Abner Stein (British Commonwealth)
Membership(s): Mystery Writers of America; Romance Writers of America

Judy Boals Inc & Jim Flynn Agency (L-D)
208 W 30 St, Suite 401, New York, NY 10001
Tel: 212-868-1068; 212-868-0924 *Fax:* 212-868-1052
Key Personnel
Contact: Judy Boals (AAR); Jim Flynn
Represent dramatic writing only for theater & film. No unsol mss, query first. Handle film & TV rights in regular clients' material. No reading fee.

Reid Boates Literary Agency (L-D)
69 Cooks Crossroad, Pittstown, NJ 08867-0328
Mailing Address: PO Box 328, Pittstown, NJ 08867-0328
Tel: 908-730-8523 *Fax:* 908-730-8931
E-mail: boatesliterary@att.net
Key Personnel
Prop: Reid Boates
Founded: 1985
Narrative &/or how-to nonfiction, health, spirituality, wellness, business & sports. Handle film & TV rights. No fiction. New clients by referral only. No reading fee. Agents in all major foreign markets.
Titles recently placed: *Anyone You Want Me To Be*, John Douglas, Steve Singular; *Catch This*, Terrell Owens, Stephen Singular; *Encyclopedia Neurotica*, Jon Winokur; *Ruling Your World*, Sakyong Mipham Rinpoche; *Rumi: The Drowned Book*, Coleman Barks

Foreign Rep(s): Elaine Benisti (France); English Agency (Japan); Michael Meller (UK, Eastern Europe, Germany); Raquel de la Concha (Spain)

Alison M Bond Ltd (L)
155 W 72 St, Suite 302, New York, NY 10023
Tel: 212-874-2850 *Fax:* 212-874-2892
E-mail: mail@bondlit.com
Key Personnel
Contact: Alison M Bond
Founded: 1982
Literary fiction & general nonfiction. No unsol mss, always query first with SASE; for nonfiction projects, brief proposal & sample chapters; for fiction, three chapters only plus author's background & writing credits; no reading fee. Agents in most European countries. No juvenile or genre categories.
Membership(s): Women's Media Guild

Bond Literary Agency (L)
1430 E Bates Ave, Englewood, CO 80113
Tel: 303-781-9305 *Fax:* 303-783-9166
Key Personnel
Owner: Sandra Bond *E-mail:* sbbond@aol.com
Founded: 1998
Specialize in adult commercial & literary fiction (no romance or science fiction); juvenile fiction; narrative nonfiction. No poetry. Talented, previously unpublished writers will be considered. Query with letter by mail first, no phone calls; please (must) include SASE. Ms submissions are to be made by request only. Will sell foreign & film/TV rights through subagents. No fees charged.

Book Deals Inc (L)
244 Fifth Ave, Suite 2164, New York, NY 10001-7604
Tel: 212-252-2701 *Fax:* 212-591-6211
E-mail: bookdeals@aol.com
Web Site: www.bookdealsinc.com
Key Personnel
Pres: Caroline Francis Carney (AAR)
Founded: 1997
Specialize in personality-driven commercial nonfiction & well-crafted narrative nonfiction & fiction. Mind, body, soul, money, ethnic, music, biography & women's issues-nonfiction; women's mainstream & high concept commercial & literary fiction. No unsol mss, query first with SASE, e-mail or fax. Submit proposals & sample mss via surface mail. Handle film & TV rights. No reading fee.
Titles recently placed: *Tales to Astonish: Two Men, Fifty Superheroes & the Transformation of American Pop Culture*, Ronim Ro; *The Personality-Type Diet*, Robert Kushner, MD, Nancy Kushner, RN; *Yet A Stranger: Why Black Americans Still Don't Feel At Home*, Deborah Mathis
Membership(s): Authors Guild

Book Smart Literary Agency & Consulting Group (L)
418 Farm Rd, Marlborough, MA 01752
Tel: 508-460-3499 *Fax:* 508-460-0285
E-mail: booksmart@comcast.net
Key Personnel
Pres: Richard L Wilcox
Founded: 1997
Projects submitted should be queried first, typed, double-spaced, one side only, loosely bound or clamped & should include an outline with no more than the first 50 pages of the work itself. Subjects include fiction, historical fiction, nonfiction, cookbooks, children's books, books on photography, mass-market medical books (health, nutrition, etc) & informational books for pet owners; no reading fees. No unsol submissions accepted.

BookEnds LLC (L)
136 Long Hill Rd, Gillette, NJ 07933
Tel: 908-604-2652
E-mail: editor@bookends-inc.com
Web Site: www.bookends-inc.com
Key Personnel
Founder: Jessica Faust; Jacky Sach
Assoc: Kim Lionetti
Founded: 1999
Submit strong query letter along with synopsis & first three chapters, but no more than 50 pages. No reading or evaluation fees charged.
Titles recently placed: *8 Weeks to Fabulous Foreplay*, Dr Patti Britton; *A Knitting Mystery Series*, Maggie Sefton; *A Poetic Death (mystery series)*, Diana Killian; *A Potter's Shed Mystery Series Starring Peggy Lee*, Joyce Lavene, Jim Lavene; *A Wine Lover's Mystery (series)*, Michele Scott; *Death of a Collector (mystery series)*, J B Stanley; *Expecting Twins, Triplets or More: A Doctor's Guide to a Healthy and Happy Multiple Pregnancy*, Rachel McClintock Franklin, MD; *HR Confidential*, Cynthia Shapiro; *Physical Attraction*, Michelle Celmer; *Picking Up the Pieces*, Barbara Gale; *Running on Empty*, Michelle Celmer; *Texas Cattlemen #4*, Michelle Celmer; *The Anxiety Answer Book*, Laurie Helgoe; *The Best Seller: Success Stories from Top Authors, Editors, Agents, and the Booksellers Behind Them*, Dee Powers, Brian Hill; *The Promise*, Michelle Celmer; *The Seduction Request*, Michelle Celmer
Membership(s): Mystery Writers of America; Romance Writers of America

Books & Such (L)
4788 Carissa Ave, Santa Rosa, CA 95405
Tel: 707-538-4184 *Fax:* 707-538-3937
E-mail: janet@janetgrant.com
Web Site: janetgrant.com
Key Personnel
Pres & Founder: Janet Kobobel Grant
Founded: 1997
Handles fiction & nonfiction for all ages. Submission by letter or e-mail (no attachments). No phone calls. Postage & photocopy fees charged.
Titles recently placed: *Gardenias for Breakfast*, Robin Jones Gunn; *Partly Cloudy with Scattered Worries*, Kathy Collard Miller; *The Penny Whistle*, B J Hoff
Membership(s): Advanced Writers & Speakers Association; American Christian Romance Writers; CBA

BookStop Literary Agency (L-D)
67 Meadow View Rd, Orinda, CA 94563
Web Site: www.bookstopliterary.com
Key Personnel
Owner & Literary Agent: Kendra Marcus
Founded: 1984
Juvenile & young adult mss only (fiction & nonfiction) & illustration for children's book, especially topics & mss for the Hispanic market in the US. Accept unsol mss. Submit full mss for fiction; sample chapters & outline with nonfiction. No reading fee. Mss evaluation services available.
Titles recently placed: *Becoming Naomi Leon*, Ryan; *Judy Moody Declares Independence*, McDonald; *You and Me and Home Sweet Home*, Lyon

Georges Borchardt Inc (L-D)
136 E 57 St, New York, NY 10022
Tel: 212-753-5785 *Fax:* 212-838-6518
E-mail: georges@gbagency.com
Key Personnel
Pres: Georges Borchardt (AAR)
Contact: Michelle Beaulieu; Anne Borchardt (AAR); Valerie Borchardt; DeAnna Heindel (AAR); Celine Little
Founded: 1967

Fiction & nonfiction. No unsol mss. Handle film & TV rights, software. No fees charged.
Titles recently placed: *Free World*, Timothy Garton Ash; *The Finishing School*, Muriel Spark; *The Inner Circle*, T Coraghessan Boyle; *Untitled Novel*, Ian McEwan

The Boston Literary Group Inc (L-D)
156 Mount Auburn St, Cambridge, MA 02138
Tel: 617-547-0800 *Fax:* 617-876-8474
Key Personnel
Dir & Pres: Kristen Wainwright
E-mail: wainwright@bostonliterary.com
Founded: 1995
Adult nonfiction: science, business reading, politics, health, biography, history. No e-mail queries. No unsol mss, no fees.

The Barbara Bova Literary Agency (L-D)
3951 Gulfshore Blvd, Suite PH1-B, Naples, FL 34103
Tel: 239-649-7237 *Fax:* 239-649-7263
E-mail: bovab4@aol.com
Web Site: barbarabovaliteraryagency.com
Key Personnel
Pres: Barbara Bova
Assoc: Marlene Stringer
Founded: 1974
Send all submissions & queries c/o Marlene Stringer, PO Box 770-365, Naples, FL 34107. No agency fees.
Titles recently placed: *Bouncing Off the Moon*, David Gerrold; *Crystal City*, Orson Scott Card; *First Meetings*, Orson Scott Card; *Precipice - Rock Rats*, Ben Bova; *Saturn*, Ben Bova; *The Cold Road*, Rick Wilber; *The Martian Child*, David Gerrold
Membership(s): Mystery Writers of America; Romance Writers of America

Brady Literary Management (L)
Town Farm Hill, PO Box 164, Hartland Four Corners, VT 05049
Tel: 802-436-2455 *Fax:* 802-436-2466
Key Personnel
Owner: Sally R Brady; Upton B Brady
Founded: 1988
Editorial service available. Represent literary & commercial fiction; general nonfiction. No unsol mss, query first with SASE. No telephone queries. Submit full mss for fiction, outline & two chapters for nonfiction. No reading fee for representation. Handle film & TV & foreign rights.

Brands-to-Books Inc (L-D)
155 W 72 St, Suite 302, New York, NY 10023
Tel: 212-362-6957 *Fax:* 212-874-2892
E-mail: agents@brandstobooks.com
Web Site: www.brandstobooks.com
Key Personnel
Principal: Robert Allen *Tel:* 212-362-7369 *E-mail:* rallen@brandstobooks.com; Kathleen Spinelli *E-mail:* kspinelli@brandstobooks.com
Founded: 2004
Full-service literary agency that focuses on the conception, development & selling of books that serve as a catalyst for brand marketing. Also provides consulting services. Concentrates on brand-name businesses, products & personalities whose platform, passion & appeal translate into successful publishing ventures. Categories include lifestyle, health, cooking, beauty, business, self-help, travel, reference, parenting, popular culture & sports. No unsol mss, query first including resume/company profile with SASE. Also handles Film & TV rights. No fees charged.
Titles recently placed: *The Travel Mom*, Emily Kaufman

Brandt & Hochman Literary Agents Inc (L)
1501 Broadway, Suite 2310, New York, NY 10036
Tel: 212-840-5760 *Fax:* 212-840-5776
Key Personnel
Pres: Carl Brandt (AAR); Gail Hochman (AAR)
Contact: Marianne Merola (AAR); Charles Schlessiger (AAR)
Fiction & nonfiction, film & TV rights; no original screenplays. No unsol mss, query first with letter. No reading fee. Agents in most foreign countries.
Foreign Rep(s): A M Heath & Co Ltd (UK)

The Joan Brandt Agency (L)
788 Wesley Dr NW, Atlanta, GA 30305
Tel: 404-351-8877 *Fax:* 404-351-0068
Key Personnel
Pres: Joan Brandt
Founded: 1990
Fiction & nonfiction (no science fiction, horror, fantasy or romance), film & TV rights. No unsol mss, query first with SASE; submit letter plus brief synopsis.
Foreign Rights: Agents in all principal countries

The Helen Brann Agency Inc (L)
94 Curtis Rd, Bridgewater, CT 06752
Tel: 860-354-9580 *Fax:* 860-355-2572
E-mail: helenbrannagency@earthlink.net
Key Personnel
Pres: Helen Brann (AAR)
Asst: Carol White
Founded: 1973
No unsol mss, query first. No reading fee.
Branch Office(s)
Flora Roberts Inc, 393 W 49 St, Suite 5G, New York, NY 10019 *Fax:* 212-246-7138
Foreign Rep(s): Carmen Balcells (Portugal, South America, Spain); Luigi Bernabo (Italy); Michelle Lapautre (France); Leonhardt (Scandinavia); Mohrbooks (Germany); Andrew Nurnberg (Eastern Europe); Tuttle-Mori (Japan)
Foreign Rights: Sara Menguc Association (UK)

Barbara Braun Associates Inc (L)
104 Fifth Ave, 7th fl, New York, NY 10011
Tel: 212-604-9023 *Fax:* 212-604-9041
E-mail: bba230@earthlink.net
Web Site: www.barbarabraunagency.com
Key Personnel
Pres: Barbara Braun (AAR)
Assoc: John F Baker; Danielle Winterton
Founded: 1994
Selective quality fiction, some children's & young adult. Nonfiction: art, design, biography, history, psychology, contemporary social, cultural & political issues. No poetry, science fiction or men's genre fiction. No unsol mss; query letter with SASE. For nonfiction submit proposal &/or chapter outline & sample chapter. For fiction, synopsis & sample chapters short bio, enclose SASE. No reading fee. Handle film & TV rights for clients only. Representation in Hollywood & all foreign countries.
Foreign Rights: Chandler Crawford (all territories)

M Courtney Briggs Esq, Authors Representative (L)
100 N Broadway Ave, 20th fl, Oklahoma City, OK 73102
Tel: 405-235-1900 *Fax:* 405-235-1995
Key Personnel
Author's Rep: M Courtney Briggs
Founded: 1994
Fiction & nonfiction, adult & juvenile with emphasis on children's books, including picture books, middle-grade & young adult books. Represent authors & illustrators of trade books of all types. Handle film & TV rights; no unsol mss, query first by regular mail with SASE,

include publishing history; published authors only; no reading fees.

Membership(s): Society of Children's Book Writers & Illustrators

Brockman Inc (L)
5 E 59 St, New York, NY 10022
Tel: 212-935-8900 *Fax:* 212-935-5535
E-mail: rights@brockman.com
Key Personnel
Chmn & CEO: John Brockman
Pres: Katinka Matson
Foreign Rts: Russell Weinberger
Literary & software agency. No unsol mss.
Foreign Rights: Deal direct in all foreign markets

Curtis Brown Canada Ltd, see The Cooke Agency Inc

Curtis Brown Ltd (L-D)
10 Astor Place, New York, NY 10003
Tel: 212-473-5400
Key Personnel
Chmn Emeritus: Perry H Knowlton
Pres: Peter L Ginsberg (AAR)
CEO: Timothy F Knowlton (AAR)
Book: Ellen Geiger (AAR); Elizabeth Harding (AAR); Emilie Jacobson (AAR); Ginger Knowlton (AAR); Laura Blake Peterson (AAR); Maureen Walters (AAR); Mitchell Waters (AAR)
Film & TV Rts: Edwin John Wintle (AAR)
Translation Rts: Dave Barbor (AAR)
Founded: 1914
Handle general trade fiction & nonfiction, juvenile. No unsol mss, query first with SASE. Submit outline or sample chapters. No reading fee. Other fees charged (for photocopies, express mail, etc). Handle software, film & TV rights & multimedia.
Branch Office(s)
1750 Montgomery St, San Francisco, CA 94111, Contact: Peter L Ginsberg *Tel:* 415-954-8566
Foreign Rep(s): In all major foreign countries

Marie Brown Associates (L)
412 W 154 St, New York, NY 10032
Tel: 212-939-9725 *Fax:* 212-939-9728
E-mail: mbrownlit@aol.com
Key Personnel
Owner & Pres: Marie D Brown
Founded: 1984
Adult & juvenile fiction & nonfiction. Handle film & TV rights through representatives in Hollywood. No unsol mss, query first; submit outline & sample chapters or full ms on request; send SASE, 12-point, double-spaced, one-sided only, typed, white paper & unbound.
Branch Office(s)
990 NE 82 Terr, Miami, FL 33138, Assoc: Janell Walden Agyeman *Tel:* 305-759-4849

Browne & Miller Literary Associates (L)
Formerly Multimedia Product Development Inc
410 S Michigan Ave, Suite 460, Chicago, IL 60605
Tel: 312-922-3063 *Fax:* 312-922-1905
E-mail: mail@browneandmiller.com
Web Site: www.browneandmiller.com
Key Personnel
Pres: Danielle Egan-Miller (AAR)
  E-mail: danielle@browneandmiller.com
Founded: 1971
General trade fiction & nonfiction. No poetry or plays. Handle film & TV rights. Also, agents in Hollywood & major foreign countries. No unsol mss, query first with SASE for submittal instructions. No reading fee. Fee charged for Xerox, foreign postage & foreign communication by fax or telephone.

Foreign Rep(s): A O Literary Agency (Greece); Eliane Benisti (France); Big Apple Tuttle-Mori Agency Inc (Taiwan); Book Publishers Association of Israel (Israel); Nicolas Costa (South America); The English Agency (Japan); Simona Kessler (Romania); Marsh Agency (Poland); Natoli, Stefan, Oliva (Italy); Andrew Nurnburg (Baltic States); Nurnburg Associates (Poland); Thomas Schluck (Germany); K Schumer (Brazil); Synopsis Agency (Russia); Tuttle-Mori (Japan); UNI (Japan); Julio Yanez (Spain); Eric Yang Agency (Korea, Mainland China)
Membership(s): Midwest Writers Association; Mystery Writers of America; Romance Writers of America

Don Buchwald & Associates Inc (L)
6500 Wilshire Blvd, Suite 2200, Los Angeles, CA 90048
Tel: 323-655-7400 *Fax:* 323-655-7470
Web Site: www.donbuchwald.com
Key Personnel
Pres (NY): Don Buchwald *Tel:* 212-867-1200
VP (NY): Richard Basch *Tel:* 212-867-1200; Rickie Olshan *Tel:* 212-867-1200
Agent (CA): Debbie Deuble *Tel:* 323-602-2345; Sheryl Petersen; Neil Stearns *Tel:* 323-602-2301; Max Stubblefield
Talent representatives & literary agency: TV, film, commercial, theatre & broadcasting. No unsol mss, query first. No reading fee.
Branch Office(s)
10 E 44 St, New York, NY 10017 *Tel:* 212-867-1200

Howard Buck Agency (L-D)
80 Eighth Ave, Suite 1107, New York, NY 10011
Tel: 212-924-9093
Key Personnel
Pres: Howard Buck
Contact: Mark Frisk
Founded: 1978
Fiction (no science fiction, fantasy, horror or screenplays) & nonfiction, adult; no juvenile or children's. No unsol mss, query first by letter with SASE. No original screenplays, teleplays or TV episodes. No reading fees; handle film rights.
Foreign Rep(s): A M Heath & Co Ltd (UK)

Judith Buckner Literary Agency (L-D)
12721 Hart St, North Hollywood, CA 91605
Tel: 818-982-8202 *Fax:* 818-764-6844
E-mail: jbuckner@pacbell.net
Key Personnel
Pres: Judith Buckner
Founded: 1970
Handle all literary & commercial fiction & nonfiction, film & TV scripts. Work closely with clients to polish & perfect their mss in order to place them with the best possible publishers & producers. No unsol mss; query first by letter or e-mail. Fiction: submit first 50 pages & brief synopsis of remainder. Nonfiction: submit proposal, outline or table of contents, sample chapters, author bio, overview of competition & reasons why your book is superior, marketing plan, if any. No reading fee. commission 15% domestic, 20% foreign. Handle film & TV rights. Clients include the literary estates of Isak Dinesen (Out of Africa, Babette's Feast) & Bess Streeter Aldrich (Miss Bishop, A Lantern in Her Hand).

The Bukowski Agency (L-D)
202-14 Prince Arthur Ave, Toronto, ON M5R 1A9, Canada
Tel: 416-928-6728 *Fax:* 416-963-9978
E-mail: assistant@thebukowskiagency.com
Web Site: www.thebukowskiagency.com

Key Personnel
Pres & Primary Agent: Denise Bukowski
Assoc Agent: Jackie Joiner
Adult trade except genre fiction by Canadian authors. No unsol mss, query first by regular mail. Submit proposal & sample for nonfiction; query & sample for fiction. No reading fees. Commission plus disbursements. Handle film & TV rights.
Foreign Rights: Big Apple Agency (China, Taiwan); Mary Clemmey Literary Agent (UK); Graal Ltd (Poland); Grandi (Italy); Harris-Elon Agency (Israel); Monica Heyum Agency (Scandinavia); International Copyright Agency Ltd (Romania); Japan UNI Agency Inc (Japan); JLM Literary Agency (Greece); Katia & Bolza (Hungary); Nurcihan Kesim Literary Agency (Turkey); Lijnkamp Literary Agents (Netherlands); Literarni Agentura (Czech Republic, Slovak Republic); Mohrbooks (Germany); La Nouvelle Agence (France); Andrew Nurnberg Associates; Lucia Riff (Brazil); Mrs Svetlana Stefanova Interrights (Bulgaria); Sterling Lord Literistic; Synopsis Literary Agency (Korea); Zvonimir Majdak (Croatia, Slovenia)

Knox Burger Associates Ltd (L)
Affiliate of Harold Ober Associates Inc
425 Madison Ave, New York, NY 10017
Tel: 212-759-8600 *Fax:* 212-759-9428
Key Personnel
Pres: Knox Burger (AAR)
Translation Rts Agent: Pamela Malpas (AAR)
Founded: 1970
Fiction & nonfiction. Handle film & TV rights. No unsol mss, query first with letter & SASE. No reading fee. Not taking on new clients.
Foreign Rep(s): Representatives in all major foreign countries

Sheree Bykofsky Associates Inc (L)
16 W 36 St, 13th fl, PMB 107, New York, NY 10018
Tel: 212-244-4144
E-mail: shereebee@aol.com
Web Site: www.shereebee.com
Key Personnel
Pres: Sheree Bykofsky (AAR)
Founded: 1991
Adult trade & mass market nonfiction & fiction. No unsol mss, submit one-page query with SASE, Handle film & TV rights through subagents. No fees.
Foreign Rights: Big Apple (China); International Editors Co (Spain); Alexander Korzhenevski (Russia); Piergiorgio Nicolazzini (Italy); Radoslav Trenev (Eastern Europe & Greece, Turkey); Tuttle Mori (Japan); Diana Voigt (Germany); Eric Yang (Korea)

Cambridge Literary Associates (L-D)
Division of Valentino Enterprises Inc
253 Low St, Newburyport, MA 01950
Tel: 978-499-0374 *Fax:* 978-499-9774
Web Site: cambridgeliterary.com
Key Personnel
Pres: Michael Valentino (AAR)
VP: Ralph Valentino (AAR)
Full literary agency. Fiction & nonfiction: action, mystery, romance, science fiction, screenplays. No unsol mss, query first with letter. No reading fee. Fee for editing.
Titles recently placed: *Broken Promises*, Joel Block; *Cutters Island*, Vincent Panella; *Do You Look Like Your Dog?*, Gini Graham Scott; *HarperCollins Encyclopedia of American Literature*, George Perkins; *Scream Black Murder*, Phillip McLaren; *The Global Negotiator*, Jeswald Salacuse

LITERARY AGENTS

Canadian Speakers & Writers' Service Ltd
(L-D)
44 Douglas Crescent, Toronto, ON M4W 2E7,
Canada
Tel: 416-921-4443 *Fax:* 416-922-9691
E-mail: pmmj@idirect.com
Key Personnel
Pres: Matie Molinaro
Sr Adviser: J A Molinaro
Off Mgr: Paul Molinaro
Founded: 1950 (Incorporated 1974)
Nonfiction, humor, cartoons; no essays or short
stories; handle film & TV rights. Ms sales, subsidiary rights, direct international placement for
nonfiction, plays, scripts, juveniles & transla-
tions. No unsol mss. Query first. Submit full
proposal & 10 sample pages. Evaluation fee for
total classification of mss including need for
changes to enhance marketing possibilities with
writer's approval; 15% commission. Evaluation
fee for unpublished writers based on length of
ms.
Titles recently placed: *Adding Spirituality to the
Healing Journey*, Dr Alastair Cunningham; *Association of Canadian Editorial Cartoonists*,
Guy Badeaux; *Biography-Marshall Miluhan*,
Terrence Gordon PhD; *Critical Edition*, Ter-
ence Gordon; *Education of a Canadian*, H
Gordon Skilling PhD; *Electric Crowd*, Eric
McLuhan; *Experiencing M McLuhan*, Marshall
McLuhan; *First Stage*, Tom Patterson, Allan
Gould; *Fortune & LaTour*, M A MacDonald;
Mechanical Bride, Marshall McLuhan; *Port-
foolio 18*, Guy Badeaux; *Portfoolio 19*, Guy
Badeaux; *Portfoolio 20*, Guy Badeaux; *Probes*,
Marshall McLuhan; *The Crest Theatre*, Paul El-
lidge; *The Essential McLuhan*, Eric McLuhan,
Frank Zingrone; *The Life of Jackson Piper*,
Ron Chudley; *The Mazovia Legacy*, Michael E
Rose; *Throw Your Heart Over the Fence*, Di-
ane Dupay; *Understanding Media*, Marshall
McLuhan; *You're Going To Do What?*, Kenneth
Walker MD

The Candace Lake Agency (L-D)
9200 Sunset Blvd, Suite 820, Los Angeles, CA
90069
Tel: 310-247-2115 *Fax:* 310-247-2116
E-mail: clagency@bwkliterary.com
Key Personnel
Pres & Agent: Candace Lake
Agent: Richard Ryba
Founded: 1980
Fiction, nonfiction. No unsol mss, query first; no
reading fee. Handle film & TV rights.
Membership(s): ATAS

Carlisle & Co LLC, see Inkwell Management

Maria Carvainis Agency Inc (L-D)
1350 Avenue of the Americas, Suite 2905, New
York, NY 10019
Tel: 212-245-6365 *Fax:* 212-245-7196
E-mail: mca@mariacarvainisagency.com
Key Personnel
Pres: Maria Carvainis (AAR)
Contracts Mgr: Anna Parrinello (AAR)
Literary Assoc: Moira Sullivan (AAR)
Literary Asst: David Harvey (AAR)
Founded: 1977
Literary & mainstream fiction: suspense/mystery,
thriller, historical, contemporary women's
fiction/romance, middle grade/young adult.
Nonfiction: business, biography, memoir, ad-
venture, women's issues, science, history,
health/medicine. Magazine rights handled for
clients who are book authors. No unsol mss,
query first with SASE, do not accept e-mailed
or faxed submissions. Submit outline & sample chapters or full ms only on request. Handle
film & TV rights. No reading fee. Signatory to
Writers Guild of America (WGA).

Foreign Rep(s): Representatives in Hollywood &
all major foreign markets
Membership(s): ABA; Authors Guild; Mystery Writers of America; Romance Writers of
America

Julie Castiglia Literary Agency (L)
1155 Camino Del Mar, Suite 510, Del Mar, CA
92014
Tel: 858-755-8761 *Fax:* 858-755-7063
E-mail: jaclagency@aol.com
Key Personnel
Pres & Agent: Julie Castiglia (AAR)
Assoc Agent: Winifred Golden
Founded: 1993
Specialize in ethnic, commercial & literary fic-
tion, science, biography, psychology, women's
issues, popular culture, health & niche books.
No unsol mss; submit query letter with bio &
one page writing sample of project, fiction or
nonfiction, including SASE. No phone queries.
Handle TV & film rights. Specialize in science,
health, biography, narrative nonfiction & liter-
ary fiction.
Titles recently placed: *Beyond the Bungalow*,
Paul Duchsharer; *Bride in Overdrive*, Jorie
Green Mark; *Classic Courtyard*, Douglas Keis-
ter; *Ecoterrorism*, Douglas Long; *Fat is Not
Your Fate*, Susan Mitchell, Catherine Christie;
George Orwell Critical Companion, Philip
Bader, Kent Rasmussen; *Historic English
Arts & Crafts Homes*, Brian Coleman; *Maya
Running*, Anjali Banfajee; *Orphanage*, Bob
Buettner; *Silver Palaces*, Douglas Keister; *The
Companion*, Shean Squires; *The New Vegan*,
Janet Hudson; *The Scalamandre Story*, Brian
Coleman; *Walt Whitman Critical Companion*,
Charles Oliver; *When Mommy Gets Sick*, Kris-
tine Breese
Foreign Rights: Representation in all major for-
eign countries
Membership(s): PEN American Center

The Catalog™ Literary Agency (L)
PO Box 2964, Vancouver, WA 98668-2964
Tel: 360-694-8531 *Fax:* 360-694-8531
Key Personnel
Literary Agent: Douglas Storey
Founded: 1986
Specialize in adult nonfiction & technical in al-
most all subjects, no fiction accepted. Submit
query letter & include a SASE. No reading fee
is charged. If the project is accepted there may,
or may not, be a $50 up front handling fee.
The agency commission rate is 15% on domes-
tic book royalties. The author is not charged
for photocopying, postage or phone calls made
by the agency, but will be asked to supply additional mss if needed.
Titles recently placed: *The Seven Story Tower*,
Curtiss Hoffman; *The Simplified Classroom
Aquarium*, Ed Stansbury

Jane Chelius Literary Agency, Inc (L)
548 Second St, Brooklyn, NY 11215
Tel: 718-499-0236 *Fax:* 718-832-7335
E-mail: queries@janechelius.com
Web Site: www.janechelius.com
Key Personnel
Pres: Jane Chelius (AAR)
Assoc: Mark Chelius
Adult fiction & nonfiction. No children's books;
no unsol mss, query first with SASE. No read-
ing fee; handle film & TV rights. Representa-
tion in all foreign markets.
Membership(s): International Association of
Crime Writers; Mystery Writers of America;
Women's Media Group

Linda Chester & Associates (L-D)
Rockefeller Ctr, 630 Fifth Ave, New York, NY
10111

EDITORIAL SERVICES

Tel: 212-218-3350 *Fax:* 212-218-3343
E-mail: lcassoc@mindspring.com
Web Site: www.lindachester.com
Key Personnel
Principal: Linda Chester (AAR)
West Coast Assoc: Laurie Fox
Off Mgr: Gary Jaffe *Tel:* 212-218-3345
E-mail: gjaffe@lindachester.com
Quality adult fiction & nonfiction. No unsol mss
or queries. Handle film & TV rights. No read-
ing fee.
Branch Office(s)
1678 Shattuck Ave, Suite 331, Berkeley, CA
94709, Contact: Laurie Fox *Tel:* 510-704-0971
Fax: 510-704-0972
Foreign Rep(s): Linda Michaels Ltd

Faith Childs Literary Agency Inc (L)
915 Broadway, Suite 1009, New York, NY 10010
Tel: 212-995-9600 *Fax:* 212-995-9709
E-mail: faith@faithchildsliteraryagencyinc.com
Key Personnel
Pres: Faith Hampton Childs (AAR)
Founded: 1990
Specialize in fiction & nonfiction film & TV
rights. No unsol mss, queries or unreferred
clients accepted. Agents in all principal coun-
tries.
Foreign Rep(s): Luigi Bernabo Associates S R L
(Italy); The English Agency (Japan); Lennart
Sane (Austria, Netherlands, France, Germany,
Scandinavia, Spain, Switzerland); Abner Stein
(England)

Chinese Connection Agency (L-D)
Division of The Yao Enterprises LLC
67 Banksville Rd, Armonk, NY 10504
Tel: 914-765-0296 *Fax:* 914-765-0297
E-mail: chinese@attglobal.net
Key Personnel
Pres: Mei C Yao
Founded: 1995
Specialize in translation rights sales of adult fic-
tion & nonfiction, professional/business man-
agement books, college books, personal de-
velopment, leisure books, etc. No unsol mss,
query first (e-mail queries welcome). No read-
ing fee. Handle software & film & TV rights.

William F Christopher Publication Services (L)
Unit of The Management Innovations Group
410 Sutcliffe Place, Walnut Creek, CA 94598-
3924
Tel: 925-943-5584 *Fax:* 925-943-5594
E-mail: billtmig@astound.net
Key Personnel
Pres: William F (Bill) Christopher
Founded: 2000
Provide consulting services, editorial services &
placement. Subject specialties include man-
agement, economics, productivity & quality,
technology & innovation, industrial psychology,
business best practices & socio-economic de-
velopment. No unsol mss, query first. Submit
book plan, sample text from mss & author bio.
Titles recently placed: *Downshifting: How to
Work Less and Enjoy Life More*, John D Drake;
*Lean Manufacturing Information Systems: Us-
ing IT for Continuous Improvement*, Steven
C Bell, CPIM; *Pathways to Discovery: Mak-
ing Innovation Happen*, Dr Wayne Bundy; *VA
Tear-Down: A New Value Analysis Process for
Product Improvement & Innovation*, Yoshihiko
Sato, J Jerry Kaufman
Membership(s): American Society for Quality;
National Association of Business Economists;
Society of Manufacturing Engineers; Society of
Plastics Engineers; World Academy of Produc-
tivity Science

Cine/Lit Representation (L-D)
PO Box 802918, Santa Clarita, CA 91380-2918
Tel: 661-513-0268 *Fax:* 661-513-0951

624

E-mail: cinelit@msn.com
Key Personnel
Partner: Anna Cottle; Mary Alice Kier (AAR)
Founded: 1991
Commercial & literary fiction & nonfiction.
    Emphasis in mainstream thrillers, sus-
    pense/mysteries, supernatural, horror & spec-
    ulative. Nonfiction interest in narrative envi-
    ronmental, adventure, travel & pop culture. No
    unsol mss, query first with author's bio & brief
    synopsis. No Reading Fee. Representatives in
    all major foreign markets. Handle film & TV
    rights.
Membership(s): British Academy of Film & Tele-
    vision Arts/Los Angeles; Independent Film
    Project/West; Mystery Writers of America;
    Women in Film

Wm Clark Associates (L)
355 W 22 St, 4th fl, New York, NY 10011
Tel: 212-675-2784 *Toll Free Tel:* 866-828-4252
E-mail: query@wmclark.com
Web Site: www.wmclark.com
Key Personnel
Pres: William Clark (AAR)
Founded: 1999
Represents mainstream & literary fiction & qual-
    ity nonfiction to the book publishing, motion
    picture, television & new media fields; e-mail
    queries only & should include a general de-
    scription of the work, a synopsis/outline, bi-
    ographical information & publishing history,
    if any. E-mails must be text only & e-mails
    with attachments will not be accepted. Unso-
    licited queries sent by any method other than
    e-mail to query@wmclark.com in the form de-
    scribed will be discarded unread. No reading
    fees; handle film & TV rights for books written
    by clients only; does not represent screenplays.
Titles recently placed: *Candy*, Mian Mian; *City
    on Fire: Burning Man & the Post-Millennial
    Search for Meaning (nonfiction)*, Brian Do-
    herty; *Fallingwater Rising: Frank Lloyd
    Wright, E. J. Kauffman & America's Most
    Extraordinary House*, Franklin Toker; *Fash-
    ion Victim: Our Love-Hate Relationship with
    Dressing, Shopping & the Cost of Style*,
    Michelle Lee; *Five Principles of Ageless Liv-
    ing: A Woman's Guide to Lifelong Health,
    Beauty & Well-being*, Dayle Haddon; *Hungry
    Ghost*, Keith Kachtick; *Nine Hills to Nam-
    bonkaha: Two Years in an African Town*, Sarah
    Erdman; *River Town*, Peter Hessler; *The Balt-
    hazar Cookbook*, Keith McNally, Riad Nasr,
    Lee Hanson; *The Bjork Book*, Bjork
Foreign Rep(s): All major foreign countries
Foreign Rights: Andrew Nurnberg Associates Ltd
    (outside UK); Ed Victor Ltd (UK)

Clausen Mays & Tahan Literary Agency LLC
    (L)
PO Box 1015, Cooper Sta, New York, NY
    10276-1015
Tel: 212-714-8181 *Fax:* 212-714-8282
E-mail: cmtassist@aol.com
Key Personnel
Agent & Principal: Stedman Mays
    E-mail: stedmays@aol.com; Mary M Tahan
    (AAR) *Tel:* 212-239-5246 *E-mail:* marytahan@
    aol.com
Founded: 1976
Nonfiction & fiction. In fiction: health, medical,
    nutrition, alternative medicine, relationships,
    women's issues, psychology, how-to, fash-
    ion/beauty, style, business/financial, men's is-
    sues, parenting, spirituality, religion, history,
    memoir, biography, autobiography, true sto-
    ries; handle rights for books optioned for TV
    movies & feature films. No unsol mss or faxed
    queries; a query letter (containing proposed
    book concept & author bio) or brief proposal
    (containing the following sections: concept,
    market analysis, competition, publicity, author's

credentials & outline), along with SASE for
    return of materials. In fiction: literary mystery,
    thriller, romance, women's literary & commer-
    cial fiction. Query letter with first chapter or
    first ten pages. Do not fax queries or proposals.
    Cannot respond to or return queries/samples re-
    ceived without SASE; (US stamps only-no me-
    ter tape, no international coupons, no checks,
    no cash), no reading fee.
Titles recently placed: *And If I Perish: Frontline
    US Army Nurses in WWII*, Evelyn M Mon-
    ahan, Rosemary Neidle-Greenlee; *Hormone
    Tightrope: A Lifelong Balancing Act*, Dr Robert
    A Greene, Leah Feldon; *In Search of Captain
    Zero: A Memoir*, Allan C Weisbecker; *Protect
    Your Pregnancy*, Bonnie C Campos, RN-C,
    MS, Jennifer Brown; *Stop Inflammation Now*,
    Richard Fleming MD, Tom Monte; *The Oki-
    nawa Program: How the World's Longest-Lived
    People Achieve Everlasting Health & How You
    Can Too*, Bradley Willcox MD, Craig Willcox
    PhD, Makoto Suzuki MD; *The Rules for On-
    line Dating*, Ellen Fein, Sherry Schneider; *The
    Secrets of Solace Glen: A Mystery*, Susan S
    James
Foreign Rights: ALI (Italy); Elaine Benisti
    (France); David Grossman (England); Inter-
    national Editions (Spain); Nurcihan Kesim
    (Turkey); Michaels & Licht (Scandinavia);
    Mohrbooks (Germany); Rogan Pikarski (Israel);
    Tuttle-Mori (China, Japan); Eric Yang (Korea)

Collier Associates (L)
37 Marina Gardens Dr, Palm Beach Gardens, FL
    33410
Mailing Address: PO Box 20149, West Palm
    Beach, FL 33416
Tel: 561-697-3541 *Fax:* 561-478-4316
Key Personnel
Mgr & Owner: Dianna Collier
Founded: 1976
Fiction & nonfiction adult books. Fiction: war
    novels, mysteries, true crime, romance, con-
    temporary & historical. Nonfiction: biographies
    & autobiographies of well-known people, pop-
    ular works of political subjects & history, ex-
    poses, popular works on medical & scientific
    subjects, finance, popular reference & how-
    to books, health, beauty & motherhood. Also
    handle film & TV rights for adult books only
    with co-agents. No unsol mss, query first with
    SASE; submit outline, sample chapters & bio;
    no reading fee for published authors of trade
    books, may charge fee for full length book mss
    for unpublished authors; charge cost of copy-
    ing ms; submission postage; books ordered for
    subsidiary rights. Co-agents on West Coast &
    in many foreign countries.
Foreign Rep(s): International Literature Bureau
    BV (Netherlands); Johnson & Alcock Ltd
    (British Commonwealth); Mohrbooks AG
    (Austria, Germany & Switzerland); Tuttle-
    Mori Agency (Japan, Taiwan); Julio F Yanez
    Agencia Literaria (Portugal & South America,
    Spain)
Foreign Rights: Agence Michelle La Pautre
    (France); Light & Burr (Denmark, Finland,
    Iceland, Norway & Sweden)
Membership(s): Mystery Writers of America

Frances Collin Literary Agent (L)
PO Box 33, Wayne, PA 19087-0033
Tel: 610-254-0555 *Fax:* 610-254-5029
Key Personnel
Owner: Frances Collin (AAR)
Asst: Marsha Kear
Founded: 1948
Trade fiction & nonfiction; no original screen-
    plays, No unsol mss, query with SASE only,
    please no fax queries. Handle software, film &
    TV rights through sub-agents; Representatives
    in all foreign markets. No fees.

Columbia Literary Associates Inc (L)
7902 Nottingham Way, Ellicott City, MD 21043
Tel: 410-465-1595 (call for fax)
Key Personnel
Pres: Linda Hayes
Not accepting any new projects.

Don Congdon Associates Inc (L)
156 Fifth Ave, Suite 625, New York, NY 10010-
    7002
Tel: 212-645-1229 *Fax:* 212-727-2688
E-mail: dca@doncongdon.com
Key Personnel
VP: Michael Congdon (AAR)
Contact: Cristina Concepcion (AAR); Don Cong-
    don (AAR); Susan Ramer (AAR)
Founded: 1983
Handle any & all trade books. Handle film &
    TV rights for regular clients. No unsol mss,
    query first with SASE. Almost never accept
    non-professional writers. No reading fee.
Foreign Rep(s): Big Apple (China); Michelle La-
    pautre (France); Lennart Sane Agency (Nether-
    lands, Scandinavia); Andrew Nurnberg As-
    sociates (Eastern Europe, Germany, Russia);
    Owl's Agency (Japan); Vicki Satlow (Italy);
    Abner Stein (UK); Tuttle-Mori Agency (Japan);
    Shin Won (Korea); Julio F Yanez (Spain &
    Portugal); Eric Yang (Korea)

The Connor Literary Agency (L)
2911 W 71 St, Minneapolis, MN 55423
Tel: 612-866-1486 *Fax:* 612-866-1486
E-mail: coolmkc@aol.com
Key Personnel
Agent & Owner: Marlene Connor Lynch
Asst: Deborah Coker
Mainstream fiction & nonfiction, multi-cultural
    fiction & nonfiction, political thought, pop cul-
    ture, crafts, current events, illustrated, business,
    spiritual, self-help, cookbooks. Handle film &
    TV rights for clients. No unsol mss, query first,
    include SASE; accept outline & brief sample
    (chapters upon request). Representatives in ma-
    jor foreign markets.

Contemporary Management, see Seventh
    Avenue Literary Agency

Molly Malone Cook Literary Agency (L)
535 Commercial St, Suite 1, Provincetown, MA
    02657-0016
Tel: 508-487-1931 *Fax:* 508-487-6461
E-mail: mmc338@aol.com
Founded: 1976
Fiction & nonfiction. No unsol mss, query first.
    No reading fee.

The Cooke Agency Inc (L-D)
Affiliate of Curtis Brown Ltd New York
278 Bloor St E, Suite 305, Toronto, ON M4W
    3M4, Canada
Tel: 416-406-3390 *Fax:* 416-406-3389
E-mail: agents@cookeagency.ca
Key Personnel
Pres: Dean Cooke
Dir, Subs Rts: Suzanne Brandreth
Literary fiction & nonfiction. Canadian represen-
    tative of Curtis Brown Ltd, New York. Primar-
    ily business, politics & social issues & popular
    culture. No unsol mss, query first with letter &
    info on book & author, include SASE or e-mail
    address for reply. No reading fees.
Titles recently placed: *Mme Proust & the Kosher
    Kitchen*, Kate Taylor; *The Last Crossing to
    Grove*, Guy Vanderhaeghe

The Doe Coover Agency (L)
PO Box 668, Winchester, MA 01890
Tel: 781-721-6000 *Fax:* 781-721-6727

Key Personnel
Pres: Doe Coover
Agent: Amanda Lewis; Colleen Mohyde
Nonfiction & fiction; specialize in literary & commercial fiction, social sciences, journalism, science, biography & cookbooks. Sample mss & SASE. Handle software, TV & film rights only on agency projects. No reading fee.
Foreign Rights: The English Agency (Japan); The Marsh Agency (Europe); Abner Stein (UK)

Crawford Literary Agency (L-D)
94 Evans Rd, Barnstead, NH 03218
Tel: 603-269-5851 *Fax:* 603-269-2533
E-mail: crawfordlit@att.net
Key Personnel
Pres: Susan Crawford
Assoc: Lorne Crawford; Kristen Hales; Scott Neister
Founded: 1988
Commercial fiction & nonfiction, thrillers, self-help/psychology, celebrity biographies, spirituality & social issues. Film & TV rights handled with co-agent Laurie Horowitz CAA. No unsol mss, query first with three sample chapters & SASE. No reading fee.
Titles recently placed: *Aristotle's Poetic's for Screenwriters*, Michael Tierno; *Elixir, Grey Matter*, Gary Braver; *EXCELSIOR! The Amazing Life of Stan Lee*, Stan Lee, George Main; *Handy At Home*, Richard Karn, George Main; *I Shook Up the World!*, Marium Ali; *Lore of the Dolphin*, Natalia Aponte; *Soul of a Butterfly*, Muhammad Ali, Hani Ali; *Twilight*, Billy Dee Williams, Elizabeth Atkins Bauman
Branch Office(s)
3920 Bayside Rd (winter off), Fort Myers Beach, FL 33931 *Tel:* 239-463-4651 *Fax:* 239-463-0125 *E-mail:* crawfordlit@worldnet.att.net
Foreign Rep(s): The Buckman Agency (Japan); Rosemarie Buckman (Europe); Laura Morris (UK); Prava I Prevodi (Eastern Europe)
Foreign Rights: Jessica Buckman (Japan); Rosemarie Buckman (Europe); Laura Morris (UK); Prava I Prevodi (Eastern Europe)

Creative Artists Agency (L-D)
9830 Wilshire Blvd, Beverly Hills, CA 90212-1825
Tel: 310-288-4545 *Fax:* 310-288-4800
Web Site: www.caa.com *Telex:* 68-8467 CREART LSA
Key Personnel
Agent: Robert Bookman; Richard Green; Brian Siberell; Shari Smiley; Matthew Snyder; Sally Willcox
Fiction & nonfiction; sale & packaging of all types of material in the TV & motion picture markets. No unsol mss.

The Creative Culture Inc (L)
72 Spring St, Suite 304, New York, NY 10012
Tel: 212-680-3510 *Fax:* 212-680-3509
Web Site: www.thecreativeculture.com
Key Personnel
Agent: Debra Goldstein (AAR); Mary Ann Naples (AAR)
Assoc Agent: Nicole Diamond Austin (AAR)
General nonfiction & selected literary fiction, check website for more details. No unsol mss, query first & include a few pages of ms & SASE. No reading fee. Handle film & TV rights through subagent.
Foreign Rights: Representatives in major foreign territories

Creative Media Agency Inc (L)
240 W 35 St, Suite 500, New York, NY 10001
Tel: 212-560-0909 *Fax:* 212-279-0927
E-mail: cmagency@yahoo.com
Web Site: www.paigewheeler.com; www.thecmagency.com

Key Personnel
Pres: Paige Wheeler
Assoc: Lisa Van Auken
Founded: 1997
No unsol mss, query first. Fiction: query letter, synopsis & SASE; nonfiction: query letter & SASE. Subject specialties for fiction include romances, mysteries, thrillers, suspense & espionage. Nonfiction specialties include travel, business, careers, women's fiction, lifestyle (decorating & gardening), popular reference, self-help & New Age. Representatives in foreign countries & in Hollywood.
Titles recently placed: *32AA*, Michelle Cunnah; *Adventures of a Salsa Goddess*, Joann Hornak; *AKA Goddess*, Evelyn Vaughn; *Cosmically Chic: Discovering Your Fashion Style through Astrology*, Greg Polkosnik; *Fear Itself*, Barret Schumacher; *Get Bunny Love*, Kathleen Long; *Guardian of the Grail*, Yvonne Jocks; *Made in America: The People Behind the Brand Names that Made America Great*, John Gove Berkley; *Man in a Kilt*, Sandy Blair; *On the Edge of the Woods*, Diane Tyrrel; *Sit Stay Slay*, Linda O Johnson; *Six Strokes Under*, Roberta Isleib; *Targeting the Job You Want*, Kate Wendleton; *The Brush Off*, Laura Bradley; *The Warrior's Game*, Denise Hampton; *To Marry the Duke*, Julianne MacLean
Membership(s): Romance Writers of America

CreativeWell Inc (L)
PO Box 3130, Memorial Sta, Upper Montclair, NJ 07043
Tel: 973-783-7575 *Fax:* 973-783-7530
E-mail: info@creativewell.com
Web Site: www.creativewell.com
Key Personnel
Pres: George M Greenfield *E-mail:* george@creativewell.com
Assoc: Beth Martin-Quittman
Fiction & nonfiction, film & TV rights. No unsol mss. No reading fee; other fees charged (for photocopies, express mail, etc). Representatives in principal foreign countries. Full-service lecture representation is also available.

Crichton & Associates (L)
6940 Carroll Ave, Takoma Park, MD 20912
Tel: 301-495-9663 *Fax:* 202-318-0050
E-mail: cricht1@aol.com
Web Site: www.crichton-associates.com
Key Personnel
Pres: Sha-Shana N L Crichton, Esq
Founded: 2002
For fiction, submit first three chapters with synopsis & bio. For nonfiction, submit proposal with bio. No fees charged.
Membership(s): Romance Writers of America

Bonnie R Crown International Literature & Arts Agency (L)
50 E Tenth St, New York, NY 10003
Tel: 212-475-1999
Founded: 1977
Adult fiction & nonfiction, international; specialize in works related to Asia & Asian arts, Asian American, cross-cultural, translations of literary works. No unsol mss, query first with SASE for submissions policy & instructions. Standard ms format, unbound. Consider completed mss only. No reading fee.

Richard Curtis Associates Inc (L)
171 E 74 St, Suite 2, New York, NY 10021
Tel: 212-772-7363 *Fax:* 212-772-7393
E-mail: rcurtis@curtisagency.com
Web Site: www.curtisagency.com
Key Personnel
Pres: Richard Curtis *E-mail:* rcurtis@curtisagency.com
Assoc: Amy Victoria Meo

Founded: 1979
All commercial fiction & nonfiction. Handle film & TV rights; no unsol mss, query first with SASE. Submit letter or three chapters via mail. No reading fee. See website for guidelines. Agents in Hollywood.
Foreign Rights: Baror International Inc

The Cypher Agency James R Cypher Author's Representative (L)
816 Wolcott Ave, Beacon, NY 12508-4261
Tel: 845-831-5677 *Fax:* 845-831-5677
Web Site: pages.prodigy.net/jimcypher
Key Personnel
Author's Rep: James R Cypher (AAR)
E-mail: jimcypher@prodigy.net
Founded: 1993
Nonfiction only. Most nonfiction except New Age, religious/spiritual, antiques, crafts, cookbooks, gardening & pets. No unsol mss, query first with SASE. Submit outline or proposal & two sample chapters for nonfiction. Online queries welcomed. No reading fee. Photocopying & postage fees.
Titles recently placed: *Killer With a Badge*, Charles Hurtmyre; *Lethal Guardian: A Twisted True Story of Sexual Obsession, Family Betrayal & Murder*, M William Phelps; *Murder 101: Homicide & Its Investigation*, Robert L Snow; *No Cleansing Fire*, Thomas Basinski; *Once Upon A Word: True Tales of Word Origins*, Rob Kyff; *September Sacrifice: The Girly Chew Hossencofft Story*, Mark A Horner; *The Super Bowl's Most Wanted: The Top 10 Book of Big Name Heroes, Pigskin Zeroes & Championship Oddities*, Walter Harvey; *True to the Roots*, Monte Dutton; *Witch*, Glenn Puit
Membership(s): Authors Guild

Aleta M Daley/Maximilian Becker (L)
444 E 82 St, New York, NY 10028
Tel: 212-744-1453 *Fax:* 212-249-2088
Key Personnel
Contact: Aleta Daley
Fiction & nonfiction books, films & TV rights; query first; submit outline & sample chapters; no reading fee. Handling fee for postage, long distance calls, etc. Agents in all principal foreign countries. If an in depth critique or editing service is requested by the writer, these are provided for a fee.
Foreign Rights: Agence Hoffman (France, Germany); Scott Ferris Assocs (England); Lennart Sane (Denmark, Netherlands, Finland, Italy, Norway); Prava I Prevodi (Czech Republic, Poland, Slovak Republic, Serbia and Montenegro)

Darhansoff, Verrill, Feldman Literary Agents (L)
236 W 26 St, Suite 802, New York, NY 10001-6736
Tel: 917-305-1300 *Fax:* 917-305-1400
Web Site: www.dvagency.com
Key Personnel
Agent: Liz Darhansoff; Leigh Feldman; Charles Verrill
Rts Dir: Kristin Lang
Founded: 1975
Fiction & nonfiction, literary fiction, history, science, biography, pop culture & current affairs. No unsol mss, query first with SASE. Film & TV rights handled by Los Angeles associates, Lynn Pleshette, Richard Green & UTA. Agents in many foreign countries. No fees charged.

Liza Dawson Associates (L)
240 W 35 St, Suite 500, New York, NY 10001
Tel: 212-465-9071
Key Personnel
Pres: Liza Dawson *E-mail:* ldawson@lizadawsonassociates.com
Assoc: Caitlin Blasdell *Tel:* 212-868-1365

Dawson: Fiction, both literary & commercial. Nonfiction: strong narratives, self-help, history, psychology, health, diet, memoirs & business books. No poetry, westerns or children's books.

Blasdell: science fiction, fantasy, romance, women's fiction & mysteries.

No unsol mss. Send query letter first with SASE. No reading fee. Agents in Hollywood & all foreign countries.

Titles recently placed: *48 Hours to a Stronger Marriage*, Bob Bonersox; *Blood Junction*, Caroline Carver; *Darjeeling*, Bharti Kirchner; *Festival of Fools*, Charles Stross; *Get Down*, John Callahan; *Hope*, Mary Ryan; *In Transit*, Olympia Dukakis; *Iron Sunrise*, Charles Stross; *Last Boy*, Robert H Lieberman; *Life or Debt*, Stacy Johnson; *My Mother's Island*, Marnie Muller; *Outremer*, Chaz Brenchley; *The Inappropriate Baby*, Jennifer Stinson; *The Little Book of Dirty Diet Secrets*, Carole Bodger; *The Summer of My Greek Taverna*, Tom Stone; *Wall Street is Not Your Friend*, Malcolm Berko; *What Do Women Really Want*, Donna L Barstow; *Wild Mothers*, Hope Ryden

The Lois de la Haba Agency Inc (L-D)
76-12 Grand Central Pkwy, Suite 4, New York, NY 11375
Tel: 718-544-2392 *Fax:* 718-544-2393
E-mail: habalit@aol.com
Key Personnel
Pres: Lois de la Haba
Accoc: Joseph Greco
Founded: 1978
General book-length adult & young adult fiction & nonfiction, art books, movies, biographies, books for TV & movies, mystery & suspense. No unsol mss, query first; submit outline & sample chapters; no reading fee; agents in all countries.
Foreign Rights: Representatives in all principal foreign countries

DeFiore & Co, Author Services (L)
72 Spring St, Suite 304, New York, NY 10012
Tel: 212-925-7744 *Fax:* 212-925-9803
E-mail: submissions@defioreandco.com
Web Site: defioreandco.com
Key Personnel
Pres: Brian DeFiore (AAR)
Agent: Laurie Abkemeier
Assoc Agent: Kate Garrick (AAR)
Founded: 1999
Handles mainstream fiction, suspense fiction, business, self-help, narrative nonfiction, cook books & memoirs.
Foreign Rep(s): Gillon Aitken Associates (UK); Andrew Nurnberg Associates

Joelle Delbourgo Associates, Inc Literary Management (L)
450 Seventh Ave, Suite 3004, New York, NY 10123
Tel: 212-279-9027 *Fax:* 212-279-8863
E-mail: info@delbourgo.com (queries)
Web Site: www.delbourgo.com/about.htm
Key Personnel
Pres & Agent: Joelle Delbourgo
Agent: Jennifer Greipo
Founded: 2000
Literary & consulting agency handling adult nonfiction & fiction. The fiction list ranges from literary fiction to commercial mainstream fiction. Represent a wide range of nonfiction including history, narrative nonfiction, psychology, business, science, religion & spirituality, health, self-help & parenting, sports, lifestyles, cookbooks. Check website for submission guidelines. Does not charge fees. No e-mail queries. Materials weighing more than one pound will not be returned.

Titles recently placed: *Ashley's Story: How I Was Lost in The Foster Care System & Found by a Family*, Ashley Marie Rhodes-Counter, Guy Counter; *Dr. Yoga: The Medical Benefits of Yoga*, Nirmala Heriza; *St Patrick: Murder, Mayhem & Slavery in Ancient Ireland*, Philip Mitchell Freeman; *The New Anti-Semitism: The Current Crisis & What We Must Do About It*, Phyllis Chesler
Foreign Rights: Duran Kim Agency (Korea); Jenny Meyer Literary Agency (Worldwide exc Asia); Andrew Nurnberg Associates Inc (China); Owl's Agency (Japan)
Membership(s): Women's Media Group

Ellen F Denison Literary Agent (L)
PO Box 129, Concord, MA 01742-0129
Tel: 978-371-1716 *Fax:* 978-371-2567
Founded: 1995
Specialize in adult literary fiction & nonfiction, including consumer reference, psychology, biography, history, contemporary social & family/parenting issues, cooking & gardening. Also young adult fiction & nonfiction, no poetry or science fiction. No unsol mss, query first with SASE; include outline & sample chapter with author bio & publication history. No reading fee.

Marilyn Dewey Literary Management (L)
Subsidiary of DewMar House Publishing
Dewey-Hannah House, 191 Packers Falls Rd, Durham, NH 03824
Tel: 603-659-5500 *Fax:* 603-659-4155
E-mail: dewmarh@aol.com
Key Personnel
Pres & CEO: Marilyn "MJ" Dewey
Founded: 1995
Query first, SASE; prefer e-mail. Free consultation. Not taking new clients.
Branch Office(s)
721 Fifth St N, St Petersburg, FL 33701

DH Literary Inc (L)
PO Box 990, Nyack, NY 10960
Tel: 212-753-7942
E-mail: dhendin@aol.com
Key Personnel
Pres: David Hendin (AAR)
Founded: 1993
We represent a small number of clients & we are not currently accepting new projects or queries.
Titles recently placed: *Miss Manners Guide to Excruciatingly Correct Behavior*, Judith Martin; *Murder Between the Covers*, Elaine Vets
Foreign Rep(s): Agents in all major foreign markets

DHS Literary Inc (L)
10711 Preston Rd, Suite 100, Dallas, TX 75230
Tel: 214-363-4422 *Fax:* 214-363-4423
E-mail: submissions@dhsliterary.com
Web Site: www.dhsliterary.com
Key Personnel
Pres: David Hale Smith *Tel:* 214-363-4422 ext 102
Founded: 1994
All adult commercial & literary book length fiction (especially thrillers, suspense & mysteries) & nonfiction for trade market. No children's, young adult, short stories or poetry. Considers queries & proposals by referral only. No unsol submissions accepted. Send queries to submissions@dhsliterary.com. Material not returned without SASE. No fees. Handle film & TV rights directly & via Hollywood co-agents.
Foreign Rights: Lennart Sane Agency (Sweden); Thomas Schluck (Germany); Abner Stein (UK)

Diamond Literary Agency Inc (L)
3063 S Kearney St, Denver, CO 80222

Tel: 303-753-6318
E-mail: diamondliteraryagency@yahoo.com
Key Personnel
Pres: Pat Dalton
Submissions: Jean Patrick
Founded: 1982
Specialize in fiction & nonfiction books. Particular interest in romance & women's fiction, thrillers, suspense/mystery; plus popular nonfiction, such as medical & self-help. Send SASE for agency info; do not otherwise query. Submit first 50 pages & synopsis with SASE & standard-sized cassette tape. Submission fee $15 for authors who have not sold the same type of project within the last five years. No telephone calls or e-mails from writers, except contracted clients. Co-agents with west coast & foreign representatives as warranted. Unable to consider authors without a published book credit before mid-2005.

Paula Diamond Agency (L)
60 Gramercy Park N, New York, NY 10010
Tel: 212-475-0549
E-mail: pdnyc2@aol.com
Not accepting new clients.

D4EO Literary Agency (L-D)
7 Indian Valley Rd, Weston, CT 06883
Tel: 203-544-7180; 203-545-7180 (cell phone)
 Fax: 203-544-7160
E-mail: d4eo@optionline.net
Web Site: www.publishersmarketplace.com/members/d4eo
Key Personnel
Principal: Robert G Diforio
Founded: 1991
Represent trade books of all types, fiction, nonfiction, business. No unsol mss, query first with SASE. Submit outline & sample chapters, if requested. No reading fee. Handle film & TV rights.
Titles recently placed: *Deep Fire Rising*, Jack Du Brul; *Fogbound*, Joseph T Klempner; *Heart of the Storm*, Colonel Edward Liam Fleming; *Hoax*, Robert K Tanenbaum; *Rift Zone*, Raelynn Hillhouse; *Sheila Kelley's S Factor, Strip Workouts for Every Woman*, Sheila Kelley; *Worry Free*, Robert Leahy, PhD
Foreign Rights: Baror International

Sandra Dijkstra Literary Agency (L)
1155 Camino del Mar, PMB 515, Del Mar, CA 92014-2605
Tel: 858-755-3115 *Fax:* 858-794-2822
E-mail: sdla@dijkstraagency.com
Key Personnel
Agent: Sandra Dijkstra (AAR)
Exec Asst: Elise Capron *Tel:* 858-755-3115 ext 18
Subs Rts: Babette Sparr *Tel:* 858-755-3115 ext 12
Acctg & Contracts: Elisabeth James *Tel:* 858-755-3115 ext 10
Submissions: Taryn Fagerness *Tel:* 858-755-3115 ext 20
Specialize in literary & commercial fiction & nonfiction, especially biography, business, health, history, psychology, popular culture, science, self-help. Fiction & nonfiction submissions must enclose SASE. Handle subsidiary rights; help new authors to become established. Require a query along with the first 50 pages for a work of fiction or a proposal for nonfiction. Double-spaced, single-sided, no computer disks, via mail with SASE (no e-mail submissions); handle electronic/software, film & TV rights but only as subsidiary rights in a book sale via subagents. No reading fee; clients billed for major postage, photocopies & other expenses.
Titles recently placed: *Double Shot*, Diane Mott Davidson; *Sorrows of Empire*, Chalmers John-

son; *The Devil's Highway*, Luis Urrea; *The Memory Prescription*, Gary Small; *The Perfect Sister*, Marcia Millman; *The Schopenhauer Cure*, Irvin Yalom
Foreign Rights: Agence Hoffman (Germany); Bernabo & Assocs (Italy); Mercedes Casanovas Agency (Spain); The English Agency - Japan (Japan); Van Gelderen Agency (Netherlands); Katai & Bolza (Hungary); La Nouvelle Agence (France); Licht & Licht (Scandinavia); Pikarski Agency (Israel); Abner Stein Agency (UK); Eric Yang Agency (Korea)

Diskant & Associates (L-D)
116 E De La Guerra St, Suite 9, Santa Barbara, CA 93101
Tel: 805-962-2961
Key Personnel
Pres: George E Diskant
Founded: 1970
Fiction & nonfiction, handle film & TV rights & software. No unsol mss or phone queries.

Diverse Talent Group (D)
1875 Century Park E, Suite 2250, Los Angeles, CA 90067
Tel: 310-201-6565 *Fax:* 310-201-6572
Key Personnel
Pres: Christopher Nassis; Susan Sussman
No unsol mss, query first; handle film & TV rights, no reading fee.

The Jonathan Dolger Agency (L)
49 E 96 St, Suite 9-B, New York, NY 10128
Tel: 212-427-1853 *Fax:* 212-369-7118
Key Personnel
Owner: Jonathan Dolger (AAR)
Contact: Herbert Erinmore
Adult fiction & nonfiction; illustrated books. Film & TV rights handled by Los Angeles associate. Agents in all principal foreign countries.

Donadio & Olson Inc Literary Representatives (L)
121 W 27 St, Suite 704, New York, NY 10001
Tel: 212-691-8077 *Fax:* 212-633-2837
E-mail: mail@donadio.com
Key Personnel
Assoc: Edward Hibbert; Neil Olson (AAR); Ira Silverberg (AAR)
Founded: 1968
Fiction & nonfiction, handle film & TV rights for clients.
Foreign Rights: Agence Eliane Benvemstri (France); Big Apple Tuttle Mori Agency (China & Taiwan); Efrat Lev (Israel); Licht & Burr (Scandinavia); Lijnkamp Literary Agents (Netherlands); Luigi Bernabo srl (Italy); MB Agencia Literaria (Spain); Andrew Nurmberg Associates (Bulgaria, Croatia, Czech Republic & Slovakia, Estonia, Hungary, Lithuania, Poland, Romania, Russia); Paul & Peter Fritz AG (Germany); Peake Assocs (UK)

Janis A Donnaud & Associates Inc (L-D)
525 Broadway, 2nd fl, New York, NY 10012
Tel: 212-431-2663 *Fax:* 212-431-2667
E-mail: JDonnaud@aol.com
Key Personnel
Pres: Janis A Donnaud (AAR) *Tel:* 212-431-2664
Founded: 1993
Nonfiction by experts in their fields: narrative nonfiction; healthcare & medicine; humour; cookbooks; women's issues; gardening; pop psychology, memoir; pop culture; Belle lettres & etymology. No unsol mss, query first; if requested, submit outline & sample chapters & curriculum vitae, with SASE with return postage, if return requested; paper copy required; No fiction. Handle film & TV rights. No phone calls. No reading fee.

Titles recently placed: *A Twist of the Wrist*, Nancy Silverton; *I am the Cat, Don't Forget That*, Ray Blount Jr, Val Shaft; *Paula Deen's The Lady & Friends Living It Up Southern Style*, Paula Deen; *The Triple Whammy Cure*, David Edelberg MD, Heidi Haugh; *Whole Pregnancy Handbook*, Joel Evans MD, Robin Bronson
Foreign Rep(s): Abner Stein (English, World)
Foreign Rights: Chandler Crawford (translation)
Membership(s): Authors Guild

Jim Donovan Literary (L)
4515 Prentice, Suite 109, Dallas, TX 75206
Tel: 214-696-9411 *Fax:* 214-696-9412
Key Personnel
Pres: Jim Donovan
Agent: Kathryn Lindsey
Founded: 1993
Literary & commercial fiction & nonfiction, especially biography, business, health, history, popular culture, self-help, sports. No poetry, short stories or children's. Accept unsol mss only with SASE. Prefer query first by letter. Submit outline & first two chapters (fiction) with synopsis & SASE. Handle film & TV rights. Agents in Hollywood & major foreign countries. No reading fee, 15% commission on monies earned.
Titles recently placed: *Given Up For Dead: America's Heroic Stand at Wake Island*, Bill Sloan; *Halfbreed*, David Halaas, Andrew Masich; *The Art of Client Service*, Robert Solomon; *Two Steps to a Perfect Swing*, Shawn Humphries, Brad Townsend

The Dorese Agency Ltd (L-D)
37965 Palo Verde Dr, Cathedral City, CA 92234
Tel: 760-321-1115 *Fax:* 760-321-1049
Web Site: www.doreseagency.com
Key Personnel
Pres: Alyss Dorese
Literary Agent: Don Meyer *Tel:* 760-773-2692
E-mail: don@dpmeyer.com
Founded: 1979
The genre of work represented includes fiction: horror, mysteries, romance, war, westerns, future & historical novels as well as nonfiction: tell all, how to, biographies, history, memoirs, instructional self-help, sports & true crime.
No unsol mss, query first. Submit outline & sample chapters (writings) with a SASE. Evaluation fee may be required for new, first time & unpublished writers. Please refer to web site for more details.

Doyen Literary Services Inc (L)
1931 660 St, Newell, IA 50568
Tel: 712-272-3300
Key Personnel
Pres: B J Doyen
Founded: 1988
Handles all types of trade nonfiction for adults plus a few novels. Specializes in business, health, fitness, how-to, psychology, self-improvement, cookbooks, spiritual/inspirational, biography & memoir & many more. No unsol mss, query first. Submissions should be print only. Electronic submission accepted from established clients only.
Titles recently placed: *An Egg on Three Sticks*, Jackie Fischer; *Birth Order Effect for Couples*, Cliff E Isaacson, Meg Schneider

Drennan Literary Agency (L)
6 Robin Lane, East Kingston, NH 03827
Tel: 603-642-8002 *Fax:* 603-642-8002
Key Personnel
Pres: William D Drennan
Contact: Christina L Drennan

Founded: 1980
Scholarly only. No unsol mss, query first with outline & SASE. No reading fee.

DSM Agency, see Doris S Michaels Literary Agency Inc

Dunham Literary Inc (L)
156 Fifth Ave, Suite 625, New York, NY 10010-7002
Tel: 212-929-0994 *Fax:* 212-929-0904
E-mail: dunhamlit@yahoo.com
Web Site: www.dunhamlit.com
Key Personnel
Pres: Jennie Dunham (AAR)
Founded: 2000
Specialize in literary fiction & nonfiction, alternative spirituality & children's book writers & illustrators. No plays or screenplays. Handle film & TV rights for books represented. No unsol mss; query letter first with SASE, no e-mail queries. No reading fee.
Foreign Rights: Big-Apple Tuttle-Mori (China); A M Heath (UK, Europe); Shin-Won (Korea); Tuttle-Mori (Japan)
Membership(s): Society of Children's Book Writers & Illustrators

Dunow & Carlson Literary Agency Inc (L)
27 W 20 St, Suite 1003, New York, NY 10011
Tel: 212-645-7606 *Fax:* 212-645-7614
E-mail: mail@dunowcarlson.com
Key Personnel
Literary Agent: Jennifer Carlson (AAR); Henry Dunow (AAR)
Query first, fiction & nonfiction. Handle film & TV rights. Agents in all foreign territories. Submit outlines & sample chapters with SASE. No reading fee.
Foreign Rep(s): David Higham (translation); Andrew Nurnberg Associates (UK)

Dupree, Miller & Associates Inc (L)
100 Highland Park Village, Suite 350, Dallas, TX 75205
Tel: 214-559-2665 *Fax:* 214-559-7243
E-mail: dmabook@aol.com
Key Personnel
Pres: Jan Miller
Exec Asst: Annabelle Baxter
Agent: Michael Broussard
Fiction & nonfiction. No children's, science fiction, fantasy, horror, short stories, poetry or screenplays. No unsol mss; accept query letter only, with SASE enclosed for reply. Market & promote own books both regionally & nationally.
Titles recently placed: *8 Minutes in the Morning*, Jorge Cruise; *businessThink*, Steve Smith, David Marcum, Mahan Khalsa; *The Wedding Workout*, Tracy Effinger, Suzanne Rowan

Dwyer & O'Grady Inc (L-D)
725 Third St, Cedar Key, FL 32625
Mailing Address: PO Box 790, Cedar Key, FL 32625-0790
Tel: 352-543-9307 *Fax:* 603-375-5373
Web Site: www.dwyerogrady.com
Key Personnel
Pres: Elizabeth O'Grady
Agent: Jeff Dwyer *Tel:* 603-863-9347
Founded: 1990
Not accepting new clients at this time. Specialize in children's fiction with emphasis on picture books & middle grade/young adult readers, nonfiction. Some adult fiction.
Branch Office(s)
PO Box 239, Lempster, NH 03605-0239 *Tel:* 603-863-9347
Membership(s): New Hampshire Writers Project; Society of Children's Book Writers & Illustrators; Society of Illustrators

Dystel & Goderich Literary Management
(L-D)
One Union Sq W, Suite 904, New York, NY
10003
Tel: 212-627-9100 *Fax:* 212-627-9313
Web Site: www.dystel.com
Key Personnel
Contact: Michael Bourret *E-mail:* mbourret@
dystel.com; Jane Dystel (AAR) *E-mail:* jane@
dystel.com; Stacey Glick *E-mail:* sglick@
dystel.com; Miriam Goderich *Tel:* 212-627-
9100 ext 16 *E-mail:* miriam@dystel.com; Jim
McCarthy *E-mail:* jmccarthy@dystel.com; Jes-
sica Papin *E-mail:* jpapin@dystel.com
Founded: 1994
General fiction & nonfiction, also cookbooks &
children's books. No unsol mss, query letter
with outline & first 50 pages. No reading fee.
Handle film & TV rights.
Titles recently placed: *Boy Gets Grill*, Bobby
Flay; *Journey West*, Richard Dreyfuss, Matthew
Kalash; *The Last Goodbye*, Reed Arvin;
Whiskey Sour, Joe Konrath
Foreign Rep(s): Ali (Italy); Elaine Benisti
(France); Big Apple Tuttle-Mori (China); In-
ternational Editors (Latin America, Spain);
Mohrbooks (Germany); Andrew Nurnberg
(Netherlands, Eastern Europe); I Pikarski (Is-
rael); Karin Schindler (Brazil); Abner Stein
(UK); Sane Toregard (Scandinavia); Tuttle-
Mori (Japan); Eric Yang Agency (Korea)

Anne Edelstein Literary Agency (L)
20 W 22 St, Suite 1603, New York, NY 10010
Tel: 212-414-4923 *Fax:* 212-414-2930
Web Site: www.aeliterary.com
Key Personnel
Contact: Anne Edelstein (AAR)
Founded: 1989
Fiction & nonfiction books; handle film & TV
rights; agents in all principal foreign countries.
No unsol mss or e-mail submissions, query first;
submit outline & sample chapters; SASE for
response &/or return of materials; no reading
fee.
Foreign Rights: Elaine Benisti (France); Luigi
Bernabo (Italy); Raquel de la Concha (Spain);
Petra Eggers (Germany); The Sayle Agency
(UK); Sane Toregard Agency (Scandinavia);
Caroline Van Gelderen (Netherlands)

Educational Design Services Inc (L)
7238 Treviso Lane, Boynton Beach, FL 33437-
7338
Tel: 561-739-9402
Key Personnel
Pres: Bertram L Linder *E-mail:* linder.eds@juno.
com
Contact: Bertram Linder
Founded: 1981
Materials for the el-hi educational market. Ac-
cept unsol mss with SASE, prefer query first.
Submit outline & sample chapter. No reading
fee.
Titles recently placed: *A New Teacher's Guide*,
Harvey Singer; *How to Solve Word Problems
in Mathematics*, Dr David Wayne; *Minority
Report*, Dr Harvey Gunn, Dr Jaswinder Sineh;
*Spreadsheets Made Simple: For Administrators,
Teachers & School Board Members*, Harvey
Singer

Ethan Ellenberg Literary Agency (L)
548 Broadway, Suite 5-E, New York, NY 10012
Tel: 212-431-4554 *Fax:* 212-941-4652
E-mail: agent@ethanellenberg.com
Web Site: www.ethanellenberg.com
Key Personnel
Pres & Agent: Ethan Ellenberg (AAR)
Founded: 1984
Commercial & literary fiction & nonfiction; fic-
tion: specialize in first novels, thrillers, ro-

mance & all women's fiction, children's books,
mysteries, science fiction, fantasy. Nonfiction:
specialize in health & spirituality, science, politics, cookbooks, pop culture & current affairs,
history, biography, true crime. Accepting new
clients, both published & unpublished. No
reading fees; accept unsol submissions with
SASE. E-mail submissions without attachments
accepted, but prefer submissions by mail. For
fiction: first three chapters, synopsis & SASE.
For nonfiction: proposal, including outline &
author bio, sample chapters, if available. Co-
agents in Hollywood & all principle foreign
countries.
Titles recently placed: *Baby Bat's Lullaby*, Julia Noonan; *Crimson Moon*, Rebecca York;
Crucible, Mel Odom; *Enemy Mine*, Lindsay McKenns; *Hunter's League*, Mel Odom;
Larabee, Kevin Luthhardt; *Love & Other Lies*,
Whitney Kelly Gaskell; *Mortal Sin*, Laurie Breton; *My Friend Rabbit*, Eric Rohmann; *Mystic & Ryder*, Sharon Shinn; *Philippa*, Bertrice
Small; *Punk's Fight*, Ward Carroll; *Silent As-
sault*, Ben Miller; *The Safe-Keeper's Secret*,
Sharon Shinn; *The Taste of the Season*, Di-
ane Worthington; *Undead & Unwed*, MaryJan-
ice Davidson; *Under Apache Skies*, Madeline
Baker; *War Plan Red*, Peter Sasgen
Foreign Rep(s): Agents in all major countries
Membership(s): International Association of Culinary Professionals; Mystery Writers of Amer-
ica; National Association of Science Writers;
Novelists Inc; Romance Writers of America;
Science Fiction & Fantasy Writers of America

Nicholas Ellison Inc (L)
Affiliate of Sanford J Greenburger Assoc
55 Fifth Ave, New York, NY 10003
Tel: 212-206-6050 *Fax:* 212-463-8718
Web Site: www.greenburger.com
Key Personnel
Pres: Nicholas Ellison
Agent & Dir, Foreign Rts: Jennifer Cayea
Assoc Agent: Abigail Koons
Fiction & narrative nonfiction (all subjects). No
children's or science fiction. No unsol mss,
query first. Submit sample chapters. Include a
cover letter & brief synopsis of first 20 pgs of
mss. Handle film & TV rights. Fees charged
for photocopying & books ordered. Agents in
principal foreign countries.

Ann Elmo Agency Inc (L-D)
60 E 42 St, New York, NY 10165
Tel: 212-661-2880; 212-661-2881 *Fax:* 212-661-
2883
Key Personnel
VP: Andree Abecassis (AAR)
Contact: Mari Cronin; Lettie Lee (AAR)
Handle books, plays, movie & TV rights. No un-
sol mss, must query first with letter & SASE.
No reading fee. 15% commission on everything
placed. Agents in all European countries.

Felicia Eth Literary Representation (L)
555 Bryant St, Suite 350, Palo Alto, CA 94301
Tel: 650-401-8891; 650-375-1276 *Fax:* 650-401-
8892
E-mail: feliciaeth@aol.com
Key Personnel
Pres: Felicia Eth (AAR)
Founded: 1989
Diverse nonfiction including narrative psychology,
health & popular science; including women's
issues, investigative journalism & biography.
Selective mainstream literary fiction. No unsol mss, query first for fiction, proposal for
nonfiction. No discs, no files by e-mail. Handle film & TV rights for clients books only
through sub-agents in LA. No reading fee, xeroxing costs & overseas mail, FedEx's charged
to client, commission is 15% domestic & 20%

foreign. Foreign rights agents & reps in all ma-
jor territories.
Titles recently placed: *Ancestral Mind*, Dr Gregg
Jacobs; *Breaking Trail*, Arlene Blum; *Jane
Austen In Boca*, Paula Marantz Cohen

Mary Evans Inc (L)
242 E Fifth St, New York, NY 10003
Tel: 212-979-0880 *Fax:* 212-979-5344
E-mail: merrylit@aol.com
Key Personnel
Pres: Mary Evans (AAR)
VP: Tanya McKinnon (AAR)
E-mail: tanyamckinnon@yahoo.com
Agent: Devin McIntyre *E-mail:* devinmci@yahoo.
com
Literary fiction, narrative nonfiction, commercial
fiction, self-help, science & history. Nonfiction
should be submitted in proposal form & fiction
with a query letter, a synopsis & three sample
chapters, SASE required. Accept unsol mss.
Handle film & TV rights, no reading fee.
Foreign Rights: Chandler Crawford Agency (Italy,
Latin America, Portugal & Spain, Scandinavia);
Michelle Lapautre Agency (France); Liepman
Agency (Germany); Lutyens-Rubinstein (UK);
The Owl Agency (Japan)

Charles Everitt Literary Agency Inc (L)
PO Box 1502, Manchester, MA 01944-0860
Tel: 978-526-4411 *Fax:* 978-526-4411
E-mail: cbela@msn.com
Founded: 1997
Fiction & nonfiction. No unsol mss, query first
with SASE. Stage two: if requested, send 30-
50 pages of mss, outline of the work & cover
letter about self. No reading fee.
Titles recently placed: *Faith: Stories*, C Michael
Curtis; *Private Guns, Public Health*, David
Hemenway; *Solovki: The Story of Russia*,
Roy R Robson; *The Boy Who Loved Win-
dows: Opening the Heart and Mind of a Child
Threatened with Autism*, Patricia Stacey; *The
Kemalist: History of Modern Turkey*, M Akey-
lan; *Thoreau Among the Trees*, Richard Higgins; *What the Numbers Say*, Derrick Nieder-
man, David Boyum

Executive Excellence Publishing (L)
1366 E 1120 S, Provo, UT 84606
Mailing Address: PO Box 50360, Provo, UT
84605-0360
Tel: 801-375-4060 *Toll Free Tel:* 800-304-9782
Fax: 801-377-5960
Web Site: www.eep.com
Key Personnel
Pres: Ken Shelton
Info Technol Mgr: Allan Jensen
Personal & professional development, business
management & leadership nonfiction trade
books; book packaging & self-publishing consulting services; accept unsol mss but prefer queries; send sample chapters & outline
overview on 8 1/2 x 11 with SASE; no reading fee; handle 3 1/2 inch disks in PC or Mac
formats.

Farber Literary Agency Inc (L-D)
14 E 75 St, New York, NY 10021
Tel: 212-861-7075 *Fax:* 212-861-7076
E-mail: farberlit@aol.com
Key Personnel
Pres: Ann Farber
Attorney: Donald C Farber *Tel:* 212-332-7735
E-mail: donaldc14@aol.com
Man Ed: Seth Farber
Founded: 1990
Fiction, nonfiction, plays. Accept unsol mss. Sub-
mit outline, three chapters with SASE. Handle
film & TV rights. No reading fee.
Titles recently placed: *Untitled Manuscript*, Kurt
Vonnegut

Farris Literary Agency Inc (L)
PO Box 570069, Dallas, TX 75357-0069
Tel: 972-203-8804
E-mail: farris1@airmail.net; agent@farrisliterary.com
Web Site: www.farrisliterary.com
Key Personnel
Pres: Mike Farris
Contact: Susan Morgan Farris
Founded: 2002
Handles fiction & nonfiction books, also occasional screenplay. Query first by e-mail or regular mail. If interested, we will request further submission. No fees charged.
Titles recently placed: *Balaam Gimble's Gumption*, Mike Nichols; *The I Don't Know How to Cook Book*, Mary-Lane Kamberg; *The Proud Bastards*, E Michael Helms; *Understanding Autism the Easy Way*, Alexander Durig

Feigen/Parrent Literary Management (L-D)
10158 Hollow Glen Circle, Bel Air, CA 90077
Tel: 310-271-4722 *Fax:* 310-274-0503
E-mail: feigenparrentlit@aol.com
Key Personnel
Pres: Brenda Feigen
VP: Joanne Parrent
Founded: 1995
Full service specializing in nonfiction books & literary fiction by published authors. Handle software, film & TV rights. Also represent & develop screenplays with production potential. No unsol mss, query by US mail only with two page synopsis (or description), author bio & SASE. No horror, science fiction, romance, religious or children's material. No poetry or short stories unless already published author. No reading fees. Feigen, a Harvard Law School graduate, acts as "lawyer-agent", charging fee for legal services when requested & appropriate. Parrent, a published author & produced film writer, provides editorial or co-writing services for a fee. Submissions of solicited material (after query has been answered) must include entire ms or for nonfiction, full ms or proposal with at least two sample chapters & outline. Send only requested (solicited) professionally formatted screenplays under 130 pages. All submissions must include 2-page full synopsis, author bio & SASE for returns.
Titles recently placed: *An Independent Woman: A Biography of Lee Harvey Hoover*, Anne Allen; *Come Rain or Come Shine: Friendships Between Women*, Linda Bucklin, Mary Keil; *Defy the Darkness: A Tale of Courage in the Shadow of Mengles*, Joe Rosenblum, David Kohn

Feigenbaum Publishing Consultants Inc (L)
61 Bounty Lane, Jericho, NY 11753
Tel: 516-647-8314 *Fax:* 516-681-9121
E-mail: readrover5@aol.com
Key Personnel
Pres: Laurie Feigenbaum
Founded: 1991
Contract negotiations & review, agenting, trademark & copyright registration, permissions clearance & general publishing advice. Expertise in book publishing & electronic publishing. No unsol mss, query first. Hourly fee or commission. Contracts negotiation, $75 per hour for contracts review, negotiation, trademark & copyright registration & permissions.

Robert L Fenton PC; Entertainment Attorney & Literary Agent (L-D)
Affiliate of Fenton Entertainment Group Inc
31800 Northwestern Hwy, Suite 204, Farmington Hills, MI 48334
Tel: 248-855-8780 *Fax:* 248-855-3302
E-mail: fenent@msn.com
Web Site: www.robertlfenton.com

Key Personnel
Pres: Robert L Fenton
Specialize in nonfiction, fiction, women's fiction, historical romances, action & suspense; limited poetry, children's or photographic books. Handle film & TV scripts. No unsol mss, preliminary letter or telephone call first. Submit outline & sample chapters. Reading fee ($350). Frequently charge an additional retainer along with a percentage if there is an agreement of representation. Extensive experience in all areas of publishing, film & TV. Producer at Universal Studios & 20th Century Fox; produced several feature films & Movies of the Week; published three best selling novels; Literary Guild, Doubleday Book-of-the-Month. Founded 1960. Writer's Workshop on Holland America Cruise Lines, Adjunct Professor, Creative Writing at Marygrove College, Detroit, MI; Writer's Digest Presents; The RLF Writer's Workshop on cruise lines, 2000; 1999 Guest Lecturer, Entertainment Law Seminar, University of MI Law School, April 1998. Mr Fenton prefers English but has limited working knowledge of French, Spanish, German & Russian. Will only represent seven or eight new writers each year. There is a waiting list.
Titles recently placed: *Dancing On A String*, Gloria Mallard Dunbar; *Dead Air*, Mike Brogan; *Deadline Murder*, Veronica White; *Freedom From the Press*, Miz Rahman; *McClellan Legacy*, LeeAnn M Doherty; *Red Moon Rising*, Wally Green; *The Ellerby Connection*, LeeAnn M Doherty; *The McKenna Dynasty*, Virgil Cross; *The Power Brokers*, Dipo Ola

James B Finn Literary Agency Inc (L)
PO Box 28227A, St Louis, MO 63132
Tel: 314-997-7133
Key Personnel
Pres: James B Finn
Fiction; no unsol mss, query first; outline & sample chapters. No reading fee.

The Firm (L-D)
9465 Wilshire Blvd, Beverly Hills, CA 90212
Tel: 310-860-8000 *Fax:* 310-860-8132
Key Personnel
Head, Dept: Alan Nevins *E-mail:* anevins@firmentertainment.net
Agent: Dominic Powall
Commercial fiction & nonfiction. Handle film & TV rights; novels; plays. No unsol mss. Query first. Handle highly recommended mss. Submit outlines & sample chapters. No reading fee, 15% commission.

First Books, see Rainmaker Literary Agency

Flaming Star Literary Enterprises (L)
320 Riverside Dr, Suite 12-D, New York, NY 10025
E-mail: flamingstarlit@aol.com
Key Personnel
Owner: Joseph B Vallely *Tel:* 212-222-0083
Contact: Janis C Vallely *Tel:* 212-666-1556 *Fax:* 212-864-3887
Upscale commercial nonfiction; handle film & TV rights through subagents. No unsol mss, query first with SASE. No phone calls. Submit outline & first three chapters (nonfiction). No reading fee. Representatives on the West Coast & in foreign countries.

Flannery Literary (L)
1155 S Washington St, Suite 202, Naperville, IL 60540
Tel: 630-428-2682 *Fax:* 630-428-2683
Key Personnel
Owner: Jennifer Flannery
Founded: 1992

Represents authors of books written for children & young adults. Query first with SASE. No fax or e-mail queries. No fees.
Membership(s): ABA; ALA; International Reading Association; National Council of Teachers of English; Society of Children's Book Writers & Illustrators

Peter Fleming Agency (L)
PO Box 458, Pacific Palisades, CA 90272
Tel: 310-454-1373
Key Personnel
Pres: Peter Fleming
Nonfiction: undiscovered truths, exposes with upside potential, popular works on medical science & health discoveries, populist, contrarian, suppressed information overlooked or avoided by mainstream media (ex: corporate & political crimes), biographies & autobiographies of well known people. Interested in authors with professional credibility with TV & talk radio, book tour & seminar potential. No unsol mss, query first with SASE. Submit outline. No reading fee. Clients billed for major postage, FedEx, foreign communication & other pre-approved expenses.
Titles recently placed: *Rulers Of Evil*, F Tupper Saussy; *Why Is It Always About You?*, Sandy Hotchkiss

Evan M Fogelman, Attorney & Counselor at Law, see The Fogelman Literary Agency

The Fogelman Literary Agency (L-D)
Division of Fogelman Publishing Interests Inc
7515 Greenville Ave, Suite 712, Dallas, TX 75231
Tel: 214-361-9956 *Fax:* 214-361-9553
E-mail: info@fogelman.com
Web Site: www.fogelman.com
Key Personnel
CEO: Evan M Fogelman (AAR)
Pres: Linda M Kruger (AAR)
E-mail: lindafoglit@aol.com
Founded: 1990
Romance & women's fiction & all types of nonfiction. No usol mss. Unpublished authors may query with SASE; published authors may call or query. Please submit a one- to two-page query with an SASE. We will respond in two to three business days. No reading fee. Handle film & TV rights.
Branch Office(s)
445 Park Ave, 9th fl, New York, NY 10022
Tel: 212-836-4803
Foreign Rep(s): Arianne Dubon (UK, France); Thos Schueck (Germany)
Foreign Rights: Konstattin Paltihikov (Baltic States, Belarus, Eastern Europe, Russia, Ukraine); Ulf Toregard (Denmark, Holland)
Membership(s): Romance Writers of America

Sheldon Fogelman Agency Inc (L-D)
10 E 40 St, Suite 3800, New York, NY 10016
Tel: 212-532-7250 *Fax:* 212-685-8939
E-mail: fogelman@worldnet.att.net; agency@sheldonfogelmanagency.com
Key Personnel
Pres & Literary Agent: Sheldon Fogelman
Literary Agent: Linda Pratt; Marcia Wernick
Trade books of all types, fiction & nonfiction, adult & juvenile, including all rights. Handle film, TV, film & software rights. No unsol mss, query first, include publishing history. No reading fee.

The Foley Agency (L)
34 E 38 St, New York, NY 10016
Tel: 212-686-6930
Key Personnel
Partner: Joan Foley; Joseph Foley
Founded: 1961

Fiction & nonfiction books. No unsol mss, query first with SASE & brief outline. No reading fee. 10% sales commission, 15% foreign rights fees. Rare but occasional fees for phone, mail or copying. Handle film & TV rights for own authors' published books. Agents in all major European countries.

Fort Ross Inc - International Rights (L)
Division of Fort Ross Inc
26 Arthur Place, Yonkers, NY 10701
Tel: 914-375-6448 *Fax:* 914-375-6439
E-mail: fort.ross@verizon.net
Web Site: www.fortross.net
Key Personnel
Exec Dir: Dr Vladimir P Kartsev
Founded: 1992
Fiction: romance, mysteries, science fiction, fantasy, adventure. Nonfiction: popular science, self-help & biography. Provide American publishers with books, mss & illustrations from Russia. Find European publishers for American book authors & illustrators. No unsol mss. Query first with brief synopsis, sample chapter & SASE; no fees.
Titles recently placed: *Fantasy World of Vladimir Kush*, Vladmir Kush; *Mastering Judo with Vladimir Putin*, Vladimir Putin; *Moses*, Howard Fast; *River's Dream*, Virginia Brown
Foreign Rep(s): Kristin Olson (Czech Republic, Slovak Republic); Konstantin Paltchikov (Baltic States, Belarus, Russia, Ukraine); Wicky Satlof (Western Europe); Rita Vivian (Italy)

Forthwrite Literary Agency & Speakers Bureau (L)
Subsidiary of Keller Media Inc
23852 W Pacific Coast Hwy, Suite 701, Malibu, CA 90265
Tel: 310-394-9840 *Toll Free Tel:* 866-62WRITE (629-7483) *Fax:* 310-394-9857
E-mail: agent@kellermedia.com
Web Site: www.KellerMedia.com
Key Personnel
Pres & Sr Agent: Wendy L Keller
    E-mail: wkeller@kellermedia.com
Founded: 1989
Exclusively nonfiction. Areas of expertise: business (sales, marketing, finance, management), self-help, pop psyche, inspiration, history, current affairs, science, metaphysical, parenting, how-to, computer & consumer reference on a variety of subjects, entrepreneurship, female empowerment, home-based business & alternative health, Americana, animals, art, biography, child guidance, journalism, cookbooks, crafts, gardening, health, nature, psychology, reference, women's issues. No unsol mss, query first with letter & SASE (e-mail queries preferred). Submit outline &/or proposal upon request. No reading fee.
Titles recently placed: *No More Cold Calling*, George Walther; *The Mom's Town Guide to Getting a Life*, Heather Reider, Mary Goulet; *The Retirement Revolutionary*, Patrick Astre
Foreign Rep(s): All Territories (Worldwide)
Membership(s): American Society of Training & Development; International Coach Federation; National Association for Female Executives; National Speakers Association; United States Women's Chamber of Commerce

The Fox Chase Agency Inc (L)
701 Lee Rd, Suite 102, Chesterbrook, PA 19087
Tel: 610-640-7560 *Fax:* 610-640-7562 *Cable:*
FOXQUILL
Key Personnel
Pres: A L Hart (AAR)
Contact: Jo C Hart (AAR)
Founded: 1972

No unsol mss, query first. No reading fee.
Foreign Rep(s): Campbell, Thomson & McLaughlin Ltd (UK)

Lynn C Franklin Associates Ltd (L-D)
1350 Broadway, Suite 2015, New York, NY 10018
Tel: 212-868-6311 *Fax:* 212-868-6312
E-mail: agency@fsainc.com
Key Personnel
Pres & Agent: Lynn C Franklin *E-mail:* lcf@fsainc.com
Rts Mgr: Claudia Nys
Adult commercial & literary fiction & general nonfiction with special interest in health, psychology, personal growth & biographies, as well as current international affairs. No unsol mss, query letter with SASE first. Submit outline & sample chapters with SASE. No reading fee. Representatives in Hollywood & in all major foreign countries. Handle film & TV rights.
Titles recently placed: *Biography of Alexander II*, Edvard Radzinsky; *God Has a Dream: A Vision of Hope for Our Time*, Desmond Tutu; *Meeting Faith: The Forest Journals of a Black Buddhist Nun in Thailand*, Faith Adiele; *Rabble Rouser For Peace: The Authorized Biography of Desmond Tutu*, John Allen
Foreign Rights: A C E R Agencia Literaria (Spain); Anthea Literary Agency (Bulgaria); Bardon-Chinese Media Agency (China & Taiwan); Bolza & Katai (Hungary); Book Publishers Association of Israel (Israel); Mary Clemmey (Australia, UK, New Zealand); The English Agency (Japan); Graal Ltd (Poland); Nurcihan Keslim Literary Agency Inc (Turkey); Simona Kessler International Copyright Agency (Romania); The Marsh Agency (Europe, Latin America); Kristin Olson (Czech Republic); Read n' Right Agency (Greece); Synopsis Literary Agency (Russia); Eric Yang Agency (Korea)

Jeanne Fredericks Literary Agency Inc (L)
221 Benedict Hill Rd, New Canaan, CT 06840
Tel: 203-972-3011 *Fax:* 203-972-3011
E-mail: jfredrks@optonline.net (no unsol attachments)
Key Personnel
Pres: Jeanne Fredericks (AAR) *E-mail:* jfredrks@optonline.net
Founded: 1997 (purchased assets of Susan P Urstadt Inc in May 1997)
Adult nonfiction only, especially practical popular reference, health & medical, gardening, business & finance, travel, practical how-to, biography, antiques & decorative arts, sports, natural history, cookbooks, women's issues, history. No unsol mss, query first with SASE. If requested, submit proposal, author biography (including previous publishing history), detailed outline & sample chapters with SASE. Do not require signature for delivery. Handle film & TV rights with co-agent. No reading fee.
Titles recently placed: *Cowboys & Dragons: Shattering Cultural Myths to Advance Chinese-American Business*, Charles Lec; *Creating Optimism: A Proven, Seven-Step Program for Overcoming Depression*, Bob Murray, PhD, Alicia Fortinberry, MS; *Fatal Waves: Survival & Heroism in America's Worst Tidal Wave*, Dennis Powers; *Homescaping*, Anne Halpin; *Lilias! Yoga Gets Better With Age*, Lilias Folan; *Perennials for All Seasons*, Douglas Green; *Stealing With Style*, Emyl Jenkins
Foreign Rights: Bardon-Chinese Media (China); Bookman Agency (Denmark); Elfriede Pexa, Living Agency (Italy); Eliane Benisti (France); Shin Won (Korea); Tuttle Mori (Japan); Ute Korner (Spain)
Membership(s): Authors Guild

Robert A Freedman Dramatic Agency Inc (D)
1501 Broadway, Suite 2310, New York, NY 10036
Tel: 212-840-5760 *Fax:* 212-840-5776
Key Personnel
Pres: Robert A Freedman (AAR)
    E-mail: rfreedmanagent@aol.com
Sr VP: Selma Luttinger (AAR)
VP & Agent (Motion Picture & TV Scripts): Robin Kaver (AAR) *Tel:* 212-840-5751
    E-mail: rkaver@bromasite.com
Agent: Marta Praeger (AAR)
Founded: 1928 (as Harold Freedman Brandt & Brandt Dramatic Department Inc, until 1981)
Dramatic scripts for stage, motion picture & TV. No unsol mss, query first. No reading fee. Agents in all European countries. Will co-agent with literary agents to handle film rights & books.

Samuel French Inc (D)
45 W 25 St, New York, NY 10010-2751
Tel: 212-206-8990 *Fax:* 212-206-1429
E-mail: samuelfrench@earthlink.net
Web Site: www.samuelfrench.com *Cable:*
THEATRICAL
Key Personnel
Pres & Man Dir: Charles R Van Nostrand (AAR)
Plays for publication & agency representation. Accept unsol mss, standard US play form. No reading fee. Handle film & TV rights for published works only. Send $4 for guidelines (recommended mss format).
ISBN Prefix(es): 0-573
Branch Office(s)
7623 Sunset Blvd, Hollywood, CA 90046, Contact: Leon Embry *Tel:* 323-876-0570 *Fax:* 323-876-6822
Samuel French Canada Ltd, 100 Lombard St, Lower Level, Toronto, ON M5C 1M3, Canada, Contact: Elizabeth Sperling *Tel:* 416-363-3536 *Fax:* 416-363-1108
Samuel French Ltd, 52 Fitzroy St, London W1P 6JR, United Kingdom, Contact: Vivian Goodwin *Tel:* (020) 7387 9373 *Fax:* (020) 7387 2161
Foreign Rep(s): Dominie Pty Ltd (Australia); Samuel French Ltd (UK, Canada)

Sarah Jane Freymann Literary Agency (L)
59 W 71 St, Suite 9B, New York, NY 10023
Tel: 212-362-9277 *Fax:* 212-501-8240
E-mail: sjfs@aol.com
Key Personnel
Owner & Agent: Sarah Jane Freymann
Assoc: Katharine Sands; Steven Schwartz
Founded: 1974
Represents book-length fiction & general nonfiction. Fiction: quality mainstream & literary fiction. Nonfiction: spiritual/inspirational, psychology, self-help; women's/men's issues; health (conventional & alternative); cookbooks; narrative nonfiction, natural science, nature, memoirs, biography; current events, multicultural issues, popular culture; illustrated books, lifestyle, garden, design & architecture. No unsol mss, query first with SASE. Handle film & TV rights with subagents. Representation in all foreign markets. No fees charged.
Titles recently placed: *Aroma: Food & Fragrance*, Daniel Patterson, Mandy Aftel; *Around the Bloc: Tales from Behind the Former Iron Curtain*, Stephanie Elizondo Griest; *Crossing the Boulevard: Strangers, Neighbors, Aliens in a New America*, Warren Lehrer, Judith Sloan; *Gay Dads: A Family Portrait*, David Strah, Susanna Margolis; *How to Share a Meal: How to Be Comfortable Having People Over*, Pam Anderson; *John Ash: Cooking One-on-One - Kitchen Secrets From a Master Teacher*, John Ash; *Serenity In Motion*, Nancy O'Hara; *Tarantula*, Sy Montgomery; *The Big Book of Small Gardens*, Melba Levick; *The Good Enough*

Teen, Brad Sachs PhD; *The Jewish Wedding*, Rita Milos Brownstein; *The Mother-Daughter Sacred Circle: Making Lifelong Connections with Your Teenager*, Celia Straus; *Vagabonding: An Uncommon Guide to the Art of Long-World Travel*, Rolf Potts; *Yoga Body Buddha Mind*, Cyndi Lee

Candice Fuhrman Literary Agency (L)
60 Greenwood Way, Mill Valley, CA 94941
Tel: 415-383-6081 *Fax:* 415-384-0739
E-mail: candicef@pacbell.net
Key Personnel
Pres: Candice Fuhrman (AAR)
Agent: Elsa Hurley *E-mail:* elsa100@pacbell.net
Nonfiction: memoir, psychology, women's issues, how-to & self-help; literary & commercial fiction. No unsol mss, query first with SASE. Submit outline, sample chapter, or complete ms; no reading fee.
Foreign Rights: Jenny Meyer Literary Agency

Marlene Gabriel Agency (L)
333 W 56 St, Suite 8-A, 8th fl, New York, NY 10019
Tel: 212-397-8322
E-mail: mgalit@aol.com
Key Personnel
Exec Dir: Ashala Gabriel
Asst: Jennifer Liberator
Founded: 1977
Nonfiction & mysteries. No unsol mss, no e-mail queries, only one-page inquiries with standard SASE will be responded to. One-time reading fee. MGA is not currently accepting new clients.
Foreign Rep(s): Marsh Agency (Europe, Far East, South America)
Foreign Rights: English Agency (Japan); The Marsh Agency (South America, Western Europe)

The Garamond Agency Inc (L)
12 Horton St, Newburyport, MA 01950
Tel: 978-462-5060 *Fax:* 978-462-6697
Web Site: www.garamondagency.com
Key Personnel
Dir: Lisa Adams; David Miller
Agent: Kerry Nugent-Wells
Adult nonfiction; all subjects. No unsol mss; query first. Submit cover letter, outline, synopsis, author bio & SASE. No reading fees. Handle TV & movie rights.
Foreign Rep(s): Angenzia Letteraria Internazionale (Italy); Bardon Chinese Media Agency (China, Taiwan); Ann Christine Danielsson Agency (Scandinavia); Raquel de la Concha Agencia Literaria (Spain & Portugal, Spanish languages); Harris/Elon Agency (Israel); Katai & Bolza (Hungary); Mohrbooks (Germany); Tuttle-Mori Agency (Japan); Caroline van Gelderen Agency (Netherlands); Eric Yang Agency (Korea)

Anthony Gardner Literary Agent (L)
2 Cornelia St, New York, NY 10014
Tel: 212-229-9407 *Fax:* 212-627-0511
E-mail: stylegal@aol.com
No unsol mss; query first, fiction & nonfiction. Query with synopsis & sample chapters including SASE. No reading fee. Handle motion picture & TV rights. Reps in all principal foreign countries.

Max Gartenberg Literary Agency (L)
12 Westminster Dr, Livingston, NJ 07039-1414
Tel: 973-994-4457 *Fax:* 973-994-4457
E-mail: gartenbook@att.net
Key Personnel
Owner/Agent: Max Gartenberg

Agent, Yardley, PA Office: Anne G Devlin
Tel: 800-760-1403 *Fax:* 215-295-9240
E-mail: agdevlin@aol.com; Will Devlin
E-mail: wad411@hotmail.com
Adult fiction & nonfiction books. No unsol mss, query first. Submit formal book proposal if nonfiction; outline & sample as requested if fiction. No reading fee. Handle film & TV rights. Agents in all principle foreign markets.
Titles recently placed: *The Dog & Other Stories*, Ruth Rudner; *Unorthodox Warfare*, Ralph D Sawyer
Branch Office(s)
912 N Pennsylvania Ave, Yardley, PA 19067

Gelfman Schneider Literary Agents Inc (L)
Affiliate of Incorporating John Farquharson Ltd
250 W 57 St, Suite 2515, New York, NY 10107
Tel: 212-245-1993 *Fax:* 212-245-8678
E-mail: mail@gelfmanschneider.com
Key Personnel
Contact: Jane Gelfman (AAR); Deborah Schneider (AAR)
General trade fiction & nonfiction. Queries by mail only. No unsol mss, query first with SASE. Submit sample chapters & outline. Handle film & TV rights. No reading fee.
Foreign Rights: Curtis Brown Ltd (UK, translation)
Membership(s): Authors Guild

GGP Publishing Inc (L)
138 Chatsworth Ave, Suite 3-5, Larchmont, NY 10538
Tel: 914-834-8896 *Fax:* 914-834-7566
Web Site: www.ggppublishing.com
Key Personnel
Pres: Generosa Gina Protano *E-mail:* ggprotano@ggppublishing.com
Founded: 1991
Fiction & nonfiction; educational materials, English & foreign languages. Handle film & TV rights. No unsol mss, query first. Reading fees on all submissions, refundable from commission; fee charged for photocopying & postage or courier. Editorial & translation services also available.
Membership(s): American Book Producers Association

Ghosts & Collaborators International (L)
Division of James Peter Associates Inc
PO Box 358, New Canaan, CT 06840
Tel: 203-972-1070 *Fax:* 203-972-1759
Key Personnel
Pres: Gene Brissie *E-mail:* gene_brissie@msn.com
Founded: 1971
Nonfiction books on a wide range of subjects. Provide ghostwriters & collaborators, mainly to publishers. No unsol mss, query first. Submit biographical information to be included in roster. No reading fee. Handle software, film & TV rights.

The Gislason Agency (L-D)
219 SE Main St, Suite 506, Minneapolis, MN 55414
Tel: 612-331-8033 *Fax:* 612-331-8115
E-mail: gislasonbj@aol.com
Web Site: www.TheGislasonAgency.com
Key Personnel
Attorney/Agent: Barbara J Gislason
Ed, Gen: Kevin Hedman; Trey Wodele
Ed, Fantasy/Science Fiction: Kellie Hultgren; Deborah Sweeney
Ed, Romance: Lisa Higgs
Ed, Mystery: Kris Olson
Ed, Nonfiction: Ellen Shriner
Fiction: mystery, suspense, thriller, science fiction, fantasy, visionary, romance, legal & westerns. No juvenile. Nonfiction: health, alterna-

tive medicine, science, spirituality, self-help, mind/body/spirit, New Age, animal behavior & communication, wildlife, popular psychology & sociology. Unpublished writers should send a cover letter, synopsis or outline, first three chapters & SASE. Published authors should send a cover letter, synopsis or outline, proposal or entire ms & SASE. Represent software, interactive media, audio, film & TV rights & electronic rights. No charge for editorial services. No fees; charge for expenses: mail, ms reproduction & international phone calls. Foreign rights: agents in principal foreign countries.
Titles recently placed: *Autumn World*, Joan Marie Verba et al; *Killing Gifts; Sins of a Shaker Summer*, Deborah Woodworth; *Silver Wind*, Linda Cook; *Skins*, Adrian Louis (film rights)

Gladden Unlimited (L)
3808 Georgia St, No 301, San Diego, CA 92103
Tel: 619-260-1544
Key Personnel
Owner: Carolan Gladden *E-mail:* carolan@cox.net
Founded: 1987
General interest book-length nonfiction & fiction. However, no children's, romance, fantasy, science fiction or Western. No unsol mss; query with SASE. Submit full ms on agency request only. No reading fee. If selected, we study entire ms & provide extensive written diagnostic marketability evaluation & "Be a Successful Writer" book; ($100-$200 refundable fee). Dedicated to helping new writers.

Susan Gleason (L)
325 Riverside Dr, New York, NY 10025
Tel: 212-662-3876 *Fax:* 212-864-3298
Adult trade & mass market, fiction & nonfiction. No unsol mss, query first with SASE
Handle film & TV rights. No fee reading.
Foreign Rights: The Marsh Agency (UK)

Goldfarb & Associates (L-D)
721 Gibbon St, Alexandria, VA 22314
Tel: 202-466-3030 *Fax:* 703-836-5644
E-mail: rglawlit@aol.com
Key Personnel
Owner: Ronald L Goldfarb
Literary Agent: Robbie Anna Hare
Founded: 1966
Only select new clients accepted. Fiction & nonfiction; no romance or science fiction. No unsol mss, query first with letter, outline or synopsis, sample of best chapter, bio & SASE. Handle software, foreign translations, film & TV rights. No reading fee.

Frances Goldin Literary Agency, Inc (L-D)
57 E 11 St, Suite 5B, New York, NY 10003
Tel: 212-777-0047 *Fax:* 212-228-1660
E-mail: agency@goldinlit.com
Web Site: www.goldinlit.com
Key Personnel
Agent & Off Mgr: David Csontos
Agent: Frances Goldin (AAR); Sydelle Kramer; Matt McGowan; Sam Stoloff (AAR)
Founded: 1975
No unsol mss or work previously submitted to publishers, query first with letter & SASE. No racist, sexist, agist, homophobic or pornographic material considered. Adult literary fiction & serious progressive nonfiction. Agents in Hollywood & all major foreign countries. No software. Handle film & TV rights. No reading fee.

Goodman-Andrew Agency Inc (L)
6680 Colgate Ave, Los Angeles, CA 90048
Tel: 310-387-0242 *Fax:* 323-653-3457

E-mail: ukseg@aol.com
Key Personnel
Owner: Sasha Goodman
Founded: 1992
Fiction (commercial & literary) & nonfiction, all areas. No unsol mss, query first. Submit outline & two sample chapters. No telephone queries, please. No reading fees. 15% agency commission.
Foreign Rights: Linda Michaels Agency (all territories)

Goodman Associates (L)
500 West End Ave, New York, NY 10024
Tel: 212-873-4806
Key Personnel
Pres: Arnold P Goodman (AAR)
VP: Elise Simon Goodman (AAR)
Founded: 1976
Adult book-length fiction & nonfiction. No plays, screenplays, poetry, textbooks, science fiction, children's books. No unsol mss, query first with SASE. No fees. Handle film & TV rights for clients' published materials. Representatives in Hollywood & major foreign markets. Accepting new clients by recommendation only.

Irene Goodman Literary Agency (L)
80 Fifth Ave, Suite 1101, New York, NY 10011
Tel: 212-604-0330 *Fax:* 212-675-1381
E-mail: igagency@aol.com
Key Personnel
Pres: Irene Goodman (AAR)
Busn Mgr: Alex Kamaroff
Founded: 1978
Popular fiction; especially women's fiction, romances, suspense, mysteries. Handle film & TV rights through Irene Webb, Infinity Management in Los Angeles. No unsol mss, query first with one chapter & synopsis with a SASE. No reading fee.
Foreign Rep(s): Danny Baror
Foreign Rights: Baror International Agency

The Thomas Grady Agency (L)
209 Bassett St, Petaluma, CA 94952-2668
Tel: 707-765-6229 *Fax:* 707-765-6810
Web Site: www.tgrady.com
Key Personnel
Owner: Tom O'Grady (AAR) *E-mail:* tom@tgrady.com
Founded: 1997
No unsol mss, query first by e-mail following the instructions posted on www.tgrady.com. Does not handle fiction, children's books, plays, screenplays, illustrated books or original poetry.
Titles recently placed: *A Seat at the Table*, Huston Smith, Phil Cousineau; *Gerard Manley Hopkins*, Paul Mariani; *Leaving Church*, Barbara Brown Taylor

Graham Agency (D)
311 W 43 St, New York, NY 10036
Tel: 212-489-7730
E-mail: grahamacynyc@aol.com
Key Personnel
Contact: Earl Graham
Founded: 1971
Full-length stage plays only. No unsol mss, query first. Submit brief description. No reading fee.

The Graybill & English Literary Agency LLC (L)
Subsidiary of Graybill & English LLC Law Offices
1875 Connecticut Ave, NW, Suite 712, Washington, DC 20009
Tel: 202-588-9798 *Fax:* 202-457-0662
Web Site: graybillandenglish.com

Key Personnel
Partner & Attorney/Agent: Elaine English (AAR)
  E-mail: elainengl@aol.com; Nina Graybill (AAR) *E-mail:* ninagraybill@aol.com
Attorney/Agent: Jeffrey Kleinman (AAR)
  E-mail: jmkagent@aol.com
Agent: Lynn Whittaker *E-mail:* lynnwhittaker@aol.com; Kristen Auclair *E-mail:* krisauc@aol.com
Founded: 1997
Adult literary & commercial fiction & general nonfiction. No poetry, children's, or science fiction. No unsol mss: Fiction: query, 2-3 chapters, synopsis, bio, SASE. Nonfiction: query, bio, proposal if available, SASE. Handle film, TV, foreign & other subrights. No reading fee. Charge for out-of-pocket submission expenses, including postage, photocopying, long distance, etc, for accepted clients only. Submission format: double-spaced hard copy with SASE, only upon invitation in response to query letter or e-mail. See website for appropriate agent.
Founded by Elaine English & Nina Graybill. In business since 1988 under other names including Goldfarb & Graybill.
Titles recently placed: *Fair Play*, Deirdre Martin; *Open My Eyes, Open My Soul*, Yolanda King; *The Ernesto "Che" Guevara School for Wayward Girls*, William F Gavin; *The Memory of Running*, Ron McLarty
Foreign Rep(s): Rachel Safier
Membership(s): Romance Writers of America; Washington Independent Writers; Writers Guild of America

Ashley Grayson Literary Agency (L)
1342 18 St, San Pedro, CA 90732
Tel: 310-548-4672 *Fax:* 310-514-1148
E-mail: graysonagent@earthlink.net
Key Personnel
Dir: Ashley Grayson (AAR); Carolyn Grayson (AAR) *E-mail:* carolyngrayson@earthlink.net
Agent: Dan Hooker *E-mail:* dan.graysonagent@earthlink.net
Founded: 1976
Literary & commercial fiction, nonfiction & young adult, no poetry or short stories. No unsol mss, query first with SASE. Submit outline & sample chapters after query with SASE. No reading fee; extraordinary fees will be charged to author with author's approval. Handle film & TV rights for books already represented, no original screenplays. Represent literary rights in all principal countries, also represent international publishers in US & UK.
Foreign Rights: Lora Fountain & Assoc (France)
Membership(s): Romance Writers of America; Science Fiction & Fantasy Writers of America

Sanford J Greenburger Associates Inc (L)
55 Fifth Ave, 15th fl, New York, NY 10003
Tel: 212-206-5600 *Fax:* 212-463-8718
Web Site: www.greenburger.com
Key Personnel
VP: Heide Lange (AAR) *Tel:* 212-206-5608
  E-mail: hlange@sjga.com
Contact: Julie Barer (AAR); Matthew Bialer; Elyse Cheney; Faith Hamlin (AAR); Theresa Park (AAR); Daniel Mandel (AAR)
Intl Rts Agent: Peter McGuigan
Fiction, nonfiction, handle film & TV rights. No unsol mss. Query first. Submit outline or synopsis & sample chapter. No reading fee. Copying fee. Agents in all principal foreign countries.

Blanche C Gregory Inc (L)
2 Tudor City Place, New York, NY 10017
Tel: 212-697-0828 *Fax:* 212-697-0828
E-mail: bcgliteraryagent@aol.com
Web Site: www.bcgliteraryagency.com

Key Personnel
Agent: Lynda C Gregory; Merry K (Gregory) Pantano (AAR)
Founded: 1936 (by Blanche C Gregory)
Fiction, nonfiction & children's. No unsol mss, query first with SASE. Handles film & TV rights of books placed by us. No reading fee.
Foreign Rights: ALI (Italy); Carmen Balcells (Brazil, Spain); Bardon-Chinese Media Agency; Michelle Lapautre (France); Lex Copyright & P & P (Eastern Europe); Lijnkamp Agency (Netherlands, Scandinavia); Sara Menguc (UK); Mohrbooks (Germany); Owl's Agency Inc (Japan); Shinwon Agency (Korea)

Maia Gregory Associates (L)
311 E 72 St, New York, NY 10021
Tel: 212-288-0310
Key Personnel
Contact: Maia Gregory
Fiction & nonfiction. No unsol mss, query first with SASE. By referral only. No reading fee.

Maxine Groffsky Literary Agency (L)
853 Broadway, Suite 708, New York, NY 10003
Tel: 212-979-1500 *Fax:* 212-979-1405
Key Personnel
Dir: Maxine Groffsky (AAR)
Founded: 1975
Fiction & nonfiction. No unsol queries or mss. Representatives in principal foreign countries.
Foreign Rep(s): Rogers, Coleridge & White Ltd (UK)

Jill Grosjean Literary Agency (L)
1390 Millstone Rd, Sag Harbor, NY 11963
Tel: 631-725-7419 *Fax:* 631-725-8632
E-mail: jill6981@aol.com
Key Personnel
Owner & Literary Agent: Jill Grosjean
Founded: 1999
Specialize in literary fiction, mystery/suspense, women's fiction, select nonfiction. No unsol mss, query first, e-mail queries preferred. No fees charged. Foreign rights in UK, France, Italy, Spain, Netherlands, South America.
Titles recently placed: *Cycling*, Greg Garrett; *East of the Sun*, Carole Bellacera; *Free Bird*, Greg Garrett; *I Love You Like a Tomato*, Marie Giordano; *Nectar*, David Fickett; *Sanctuary*, Greg Garrett; *Spectres in the Smoke*, Tony Broadbent; *The Smoke*, Tony Broadbent; *The View Above*, Marie Bostwick

Laura Gross Literary Agency Ltd (L)
75 Clinton Place, Newton Centre, MA 02459-1117
Tel: 617-964-2977 *Fax:* 617-964-3023
E-mail: lglitag@aol.com
Key Personnel
Pres: Laura Gross
VP: Charles Dellheim
Founded: 1988
No unsol mss. Query letter or e-mail first. Fiction, commercial & literary; nonfiction, serious topics, social, political, cultural issues & psychology. Include list of previous publications & bio. Send SASE with mss. Also handle TV, film & Internet. Agents in all major territories. Does not charge fees.

Deborah Grosvenor Literary Agency (L)
5510 Grosvenor Lane, Bethesda, MD 20814
Tel: 301-564-6231 *Fax:* 301-581-9401
E-mail: dcgrosveno@aol.com
Founded: 1995
General nonfiction & literary & commercial fiction. No unsol mss. Query first. Submit synopsis/outline, author bio & first three chapters plus SASE. Handle software, TV & film rights. No reading fee.

The Charlotte Gusay Literary Agency (L-D)
10532 Blythe Ave, Los Angeles, CA 90064
Tel: 310-559-0831 *Fax:* 310-559-2639
E-mail: gusay1@aol.com (for queries only)
Web Site: www.mediastudio.com/gusay
Founded: 1988
Fiction & nonfiction, screenplay, children & adult, humor, parenting; crossover literary/commercial fiction; gardening, women's & men's issues, feminism, psychology, memoir, biography, travel. Handle film & TV rights. Represent selected illustrators, especially children's. No unsol mss, query first with SASE; when agency requests, submit one page synopsis & first three chapters or first 50 pages (fiction); proposal (nonfiction). Include SASE. No reading fee. Once client is signed, expenses are shared.
Titles recently placed: *, said the shotgun to the head.*, Saul Williams; *A Place Called Waco*, David Thibodeau, Leon Whiteson; *Connemara Days*, Steve Mayhew; *Imperial Mongolian Cooking: Recipes From the Kingdoms of Genghis Khan*, Marc Cramer; *Love, Groucho: Letters from Groucho Marx to His Daughter Miriam*, Miriam Marx Allen; *Other Sorrows, Other Joys: The Marriage of Catherine and William Blake, A Novel*, Janet Warner; *RetroChic! The Ultimate Guide to Selected Resale & Vintage Shopping in North America & On-Line*, Diana Eden, Gloria Lintermans; *Rio LA: Tales from the Los Angeles River*, Patt Morrison; *Somebody's Child: Stories from the Private Files of an Adoption Attorney*, Randi G Barrow
Foreign Rep(s): Prava Prevod/Ana Milenkovic (Eastern Europe); Vincent Vichit Vadakan (Europe)
Membership(s): Authors Guild; PEN/West; Writers Guild of America West

Reece Halsey Agency/Reece Halsey North (L)
8733 Sunset Blvd, Suite 101, Los Angeles, CA 90069
Tel: 310-652-2409 *Fax:* 310-652-7595
Key Personnel
Pres: Dorris Halsey *E-mail:* gulyas911@aol.com
Literary Agent: Kimberley Cameron (AAR)
Tel: 415-789-9191 *Fax:* 415-789-9177
Founded: 1957
Fiction, nonfiction & literary fiction; quality writing in all fields. Handle film & TV rights. No unsol mss. Polite query invited with SASE, synopsis & first 10 pages. No reading fee. Does not charge fees. All new queries contact Tiburon office by mail with SASE.
Branch Office(s)
Reece Halsey North, 98 Main St, Suite 704, Tiburon, CA 94920, Literary Rep: Kimberley Cameron *Tel:* 415-789-9191 *Fax:* 415-789-9177 *E-mail:* info@reecehalseynorth.com *Web Site:* www.kimberleycameron.com
Membership(s): Sisters in Crime

The Mitchell J Hamilburg Agency (L-D)
11718 Barrington Ct, Suite 732, Los Angeles, CA 90049-2930
Tel: 310-471-4024 *Fax:* 310-471-9588
Key Personnel
Owner & Literary Agent: Michael Hamilburg
Fiction & nonfiction. Accept unsol mss or query first. Submit outline & two sample chapters, include SASE. Handle film & TV rights. No reading fee. No software.
Founded in the 1930's, literary agency since 1967.

Andrew Hamilton Literary Agency (L)
PO Box 604118, Cleveland, OH 44104-0118
Tel: 216-299-8809 *Fax:* 760-875-7292
E-mail: bkagent22@yahoo.com
Web Site: www.andrewhamiltonliterary.com

Key Personnel
CEO, Owner & Agent: Andrew Hamilton
Founded: 1991
Specialize in fiction & nonfiction. No unsol mss, query first. Submit complete mss in standard mss form (inkjet or laser printed, one side of page only). No reading fees. Query via mail or e-mail up to three sample chapters, synopsis & author's page. If we represent your work, a one time marketing fee of $350 is charged. The marketing fee is accessed to cover out-of-pocket expenses, mailings, phone calls, postage, etc.
Titles recently placed: *Diary of a Vampire*, Summer Royston; *Hallowed Ground*, Tanner Stewart; *Kid Twist*, Charles Mayo, Bob Freeman; *Tuffy's Heroes*, Joe Tofuri

Jeanne K Hanson Literary Agency (L)
6708 Cornelia Dr, Edina, MN 55435
Tel: 952-920-8819 *Fax:* 952-920-8819
Key Personnel
Pres: Jeanne K Hanson
Founded: 1984
Specialize in books by journalists. Agents for adult nonfiction books especially science, nature, history & biography, also some books for ages 8-12 with history, science or cultural backbone. No unsol mss, no unsol e-mail, query first with SASE & letter. Submit outline & sample chapter. No reading fee. Handle film & TV rights through sub-agent Joel Gotler.
Foreign Rights: Dan Bial

The Joy Harris Literary Agency (L)
156 Fifth Ave, Suite 617, New York, NY 10010
Tel: 212-924-6269 *Fax:* 212-924-6609
E-mail: gen.office@jhlitagent.com
Key Personnel
Pres: Joy Harris (AAR)
Assoc Agent: Leslie Daniels (AAR); Alexia Paul (AAR) *E-mail:* alexiapaul@jhlitagent.com
Foreign Rts Dir: Stephanie Abou (AAR) *E-mail:* stephanieabou@jhlitagent.com
Asst: Robin London
Young adult & adult fiction & nonfiction. No unsol mss; query first with SASE. Submit outline or sample chapters. No fees. Film & TV rights. Agents in all major territories.
Foreign Rights: Stephanie Abou

Harris Literary Agency (L)
PO Box 6023, San Diego, CA 92166
Tel: 619-697-0600 *Fax:* 619-697-0610
E-mail: hlit@adnc.com
Web Site: harrisliterary.com
Key Personnel
Pres: Barbara J Harris
VP: Norman Rudenberg
Contact: Barbara Harris
Founded: 1997
Fiction (mainstream, adventure, thrillers, mystery, science fiction, contemporary feminist & young adult) & nonfiction (general, biography, how-to, health/medicine, psychology, self-help). No unsol mss, query first. Submit one page description, genre, number of words & pages. No fees charged. However, prior unpublished authors are requested to provide submission materials plus postage. The agency can do so for $250 which is refundable upon publication.
Titles recently placed: *Don't Be Duped*, Larry Forness, PhD; *The Big Game: Strategies for Winning at Life*, Scott McMillan; *The Family Man*, Michael Patterson; *The Men's Club*, Bert Gottlieb, Thomas Mawn MD; *Undercurrents*, Laurel Mills; *Your Mind Power Unleashed*, Tom Foster

Hartnett Publishing Agency (L-D)
4301 S 36 St, Arlington, VA 22206
Tel: 703-998-0412 *Fax:* 801-730-2939

E-mail: hartnettinc@mindspring.com
Key Personnel
Contact: Teresa Hartnett
Founded: 1997
Publishing agency which selects up to six authors annually to develop for long-term success. Specializes in first-time book authors. Nonfiction subjects only in areas of faith, geopolitics & personal narrative. No unsol mss, query first. Projects must be submitted in hard copy, double spaced & as a word or comparable document file. Submissions should include one page summary, book outline, sample chapter or previously published materials. Handle all rights. No reading fee.

John Hawkins & Associates Inc (L)
71 W 23 St, Suite 1600, New York, NY 10010
Tel: 212-807-7040 *Fax:* 212-807-9555
Web Site: jhaliterary.com
Key Personnel
Pres & Entertainment Rts: John Hawkins (AAR)
VP: William Reiss (AAR) *E-mail:* reiss@jhaliterary.com
Assoc: J Warren Frazier (AAR) *E-mail:* frazier@jhaliterary.com; Anne Hawkins (AAR) *E-mail:* ahawkins@jhaliterary.com
Perms & Rts: Liz Free *E-mail:* jhafree@aol.com
No unsol mss, query first. Submit one-page bio & one- to three-page outline with SASE. No reading fee. Fees for other services. Handle film & TV rights, software.
Foreign Rep(s): Sara Menguc, Inc (UK)

The Jeff Herman Agency LLC (L)
9 South St, Stockbridge, MA 01262
Mailing Address: PO Box 1522, Stockbridge, MA 01262
Tel: 413-298-0077 *Fax:* 413-298-8188
Web Site: www.jeffherman.com
Key Personnel
Pres: Jeffrey H Herman *E-mail:* jeff@jeffherman.com
VP: Deborah Levine
Founded: 1985
Nonfiction, reference, health, self-help, how-to business, computers, spirituality & text books. No unsol mss, query first with letter & SASE. No reading fee. Handle software, film & TV rights. Agents in all principal foreign countries.
Titles recently placed: *A Man Named Dave*, Dave Pelzer; *Finding Your African Ancestors*, Tony Burroughs; *The Angry Child*, Tim Murphy
Foreign Rep(s): Asano (Japan); Bardon (China); De la Concha (Spain & Portugal)

Susan Herner Rights Agency Inc (L)
PO Box 57, Pound Ridge, NY 10576
Tel: 914-234-2864 *Fax:* 914-234-2866
E-mail: sherneragency@optonline.net
Key Personnel
Pres: Susan Herner
Founded: 1987
A full service literary agency representing a broad range of fiction & nonfiction authors. Especially looking for strong, mainstream women's fiction, thrillers & nonfiction works addressing women's issues, spirituality & popular science. No genre romance, fantasy/science fiction, poetry, or children's books. No unsol mss; query first with SASE. No reading fee. Also provide rights representation for publishers, packagers & authors.

Frederick Hill Bonnie Nadell Literary Agency (L)
1842 Union St, San Francisco, CA 94123
Tel: 415-921-2910 *Fax:* 415-921-2802
Key Personnel
Pres: Frederick Hill
VP: Bonnie Nadell
Assoc: Irene Moore
Founded: 1979

Specialize in adult fiction & nonfiction; film & TV rights only if handling the book. No unsol mss, query first with SASE. No reading fee, photocopying fee only. Agents in Hollywood & principal foreign countries.
Titles recently placed: *27 Bones*, Jonathan Nasaw; *Darwin's Wink*, Alison Anderson; *Enrique's Journey*, Sonic Nazario; *Hope in the Dark*, Rebecca Solnit; *Sentence of Death*, Richard North Patterson; *Sore Winners (And the Rest of Us) in George W Bush's America*, John Powers
Branch Office(s)
8899 Beverly Blvd, Suite 805, Los Angeles, CA 90048, Contact: Bonnie Nadell *Tel:* 310-860-9605 *Fax:* 310-860-9672
Foreign Rep(s): Mary Clemmey (UK)
Foreign Rights: Andrew Nurnberg

John L Hochmann Books (L)
320 E 58 St, New York, NY 10022
Tel: 212-319-0505
Key Personnel
Pres: John L Hochmann
Literary Consultant: Theodora Eagle
Founded: 1976
Primarily trade nonfiction, biographies, social history, current affairs & history, health, nutrition & food. Introductory & intermediate college textbooks. No unsol mss, query first. Submit detailed chapter outline (do not send jacket copy), one sample chapter, professional &/or academic qualifications, list of previously published books with SASE. No reading fee. We do not consider multiple submissions. Handle film & TV rights for published clients.
Titles recently placed: *Elaine & Bill: The Lives of Willem & Elaine de Kooning*, Lee Hall; *Manuel Puig & The Spider Woman: His Life & Fictions*, Suzanne Jill Levine
Membership(s): PEN American Center

The Barbara Hogenson Agency Inc (L-D)
165 West End Ave, Suite 19-C, New York, NY 10023
Tel: 212-874-8084 *Fax:* 212-362-3011
E-mail: bhogenson@aol.com
Key Personnel
Pres: Barbara Hogenson (AAR)
Founded: 1994
Query letters only. Literary fiction, nonfiction, full length plays, consider some illustrated books. No screenplays or teleplays. No fees.
Membership(s): Authors Guild; Society of Stage Directors & Choreographers; Writers Guild of America

Henry Holmes Literary Agent/Book Publicist
PO Box 433, Swansea, MA 02777
Tel: 508-672-2258
Key Personnel
Pres, Literary Agent & Book Publicist: Henry Holmes
Founded: 1997
Nonfiction, no unsol mss, query first. Send query letter with first three chapters, past publicity, books published & endorsements. Two book proposals should be sent along; send SASE. Specializes in marketing, media publicity & talk shows. Fees charged: talk show contact listings $100 per state or $600 covering entire US; 10 ms standard mailings each time $50/hr for time involvement; professional consultation, $100/hr; 15% commission; freelance assignments fee will be based on type of involvement & duration of project. Contact for additional agency fees.
Titles recently placed: *Leading by Heart*, Richard D Cheshire, PhD; *Molding Young Athletes*, Darrell Erickson; *Short Rage*, Deborah J Burris-Kitchen, PhD; *The Dear Betty Chronicles*, Morris B Rotman

Hornfischer Literary Management Inc (L)
PO Box 50544, Austin, TX 78763
Tel: 512-472-0011 *Fax:* 512-472-0077
E-mail: queries@hornfischerlit.com
Web Site: www.hornfischerlit.com
Key Personnel
Pres: Jim Hornfischer *E-mail:* jim@hornfischerlit.com
Founded: 2001
Quality narrative nonfiction, biography & autobiography, current events, US history, military history & world history, political & cultural subjects science, medicine/health, business/management/finance, academic writing & research that has a general-interest audience. No unsol mss; query first through e-mail, no longer accept queries through mail.
Titles recently placed: *A Good Forest for Dying*, Patrick Beach; *Flags of Our Fathers*, James Bradley, Ron Powers; *Grand Old Party*, Lewis Gould; *Kings of Texas*, Don Graham; *Lone Star Nation*, H W Brands; *My Life Had Stood a Loaded Gun*, Theo Padnor; *The First American: The Life & Times of Benjamin Franklin*, H W Brands; *The Man Who Flew the Memphis Belle*, Robert K Morgan, Ron Powers; *Tom & Huck Don't Live Here Anymore*, Ron Powers; *What to Do When Your Baby is Premature*, Joseph A Garcia-Prats MD, Sharon Simmons Hornfischer; *Why Things Break*, Mark Eberhart
Foreign Rights: Affiliated Agents (Worldwide)

IMG Literary (L)
825 Seventh Ave, 9th fl, New York, NY 10019
Tel: 212-774-6900 *Fax:* 212-246-1118
Web Site: www.imgworld.com
Key Personnel
Agent: Lisa Hyman *Tel:* 212-774-6754 *E-mail:* lhyman@imgworld.com; Lisa Queen *Tel:* 212-774-6759 *E-mail:* lqueen@imgworld.com
Handles celebrity books, sports-related books, commercial & literary fiction, nonfiction & how-to-business books. No theatre, children's books or poetry, cookbooks. No fees charged, open submission, submit by mail.
Branch Office(s)
IMG Literary UK, The Pier House, Strand on the Green, Chiswick, London W4 3NN, United Kingdom, Agent: Sarah Woolridge *Tel:* (020) 8233 5000 *Fax:* (020) 8233 5001
Foreign Rep(s): Lisa Queen

Independent Publishing Agency (L-D)
PO Box 176, Southport, CT 06890
Tel: 203-332-7629 *Fax:* 203-332-7629
Key Personnel
Owner & Agent: Henry Berry *E-mail:* henryberry@aol.com
Founded: 1990
Nonfiction & fiction in all areas. No unsol mss, query first. Submit outline, paper (hard copy-no disks only) synopsis, sample chapters & author background. Handle film & TV rights. Fees for mss critique & market evaluation, project development, editorial services based on length & complexity of work.

Inkwell Management (L)
521 Fifth Ave, 26th fl, New York, NY 10175
Tel: 212-922-3500 *Fax:* 212-922-0535
E-mail: contact@inkwellmanagement.com
Web Site: www.inkwellmanagement.com
Key Personnel
Pres & Agent: Michael Carlisle; Richard S Pine; Kim Witherspoon
Subs Rts Mgr: Lori Andiman
Agent: Maria Massie; George Lucas; Matthew Guma; David Forrer
Founded: 2004 (created through the merger of Arthur Pine Associates Inc, Carlisle & Co LLC & Witherspoon Associates Inc)

General nonfiction & fiction books. No screenplays, plays, poetry. Motion picture, TV & foreign rights. No unsol mss, query first with SASE; submissions must be on an exclusive basis. No fees.
Titles recently placed: *Relational Empowerment*, Terry Real; *The Crusades*, Thomas Asbridge; *The House of Mondavi*, Julia Flynn; *The Last Song of Dusk*, Siddharth Dhanvant Shanghvi; *The Skin Type Solution*, Dr Leslie Baumann; *Ya-Ya's in Bloom*, Rebecca Wells

The Insiders System for Writers (L-D)
1223 Wilshire Blvd, No 336, Santa Monica, CA 90403
Tel: 310-899-9775 *Toll Free Tel:* 800-397-2615 *Fax:* 310-899-9775
E-mail: insiderssystem@msn.com
Web Site: www.insiderssystem.com
Key Personnel
Owner & Operator: Natalie Lemberg Rothenberg
Founded: 1993
No unsol mss, query first. A 2-step system for new writers to break into the literary, film or TV business. In-depth, professional analysis of ms & exposure of work to industry insiders in quarterly *Showcase Magazine* & online. For writers serious about handling their work as professionals. Handle film & TV rights. Fees only for evaluation & exposure (fees-for-services company, no commissions).

InterLicense Ltd (L)
110 Country Club Dr, Suite A, Mill Valley, CA 94941
Tel: 415-381-9780 *Fax:* 415-381-6485
E-mail: ilicense@aol.com
Key Personnel
Exec Dir: Manfred Mroczkowski
Subsidiary rights with focus on foreign rights agency & management, sales, administrations & on domestic subsidiary rights such as film, reprint, TV & merchandising rights. No unsol mss, query first. Handle software. Submit synopsis & sample chapters. Nonfiction. No reading fee. Charge for consultations.

International Creative Management (L-D)
40 W 57 St, New York, NY 10019
Tel: 212-556-5600 *Fax:* 212-556-5665
Web Site: www.icmtalent.com
Key Personnel
Sr VP: Esther Newberg; Amanda Urban
Dir, Admin: Lara Klein
Foreign Rts: Betsy Robbins
Contact: Lisa Bankoff (AAR); Kristine Dahl; Mitch Douglas; Sloan Harris; Heather Schroder
Handle film & TV rights. No unsol mss, query first. No reading fee. Offices in New York, Los Angeles & London.

International Titles (L)
931 E 56 St, Austin, TX 78751-1724
Tel: 512-451-2221 *Fax:* 512-467-1330
Key Personnel
Dir: Loris Essary; Harry Smith
Represent all genres; primary emphasis on sales of foreign rights. No fees charged, no submission policy.

J de S Associates Inc (L)
9 Shagbark Rd, South Norwalk, CT 06854
Tel: 203-838-7571 *Fax:* 203-866-2713
Key Personnel
Pres: Jacques de Spoelberch *E-mail:* jdespoel@aol.com
Founded: 1975
Fiction & nonfiction. No unsol mss, query first. Send outline & two sample chapters; no reading fee. Agents & film representatives in major foreign countries.

Jabberwocky Literary Agency (L)
PO Box 4558, Sunnyside, NY 11104-0558
Tel: 718-392-5985 *Fax:* 718-392-5985
E-mail: jabagent@aol.com
Key Personnel
Prop: Joshua Bilmes
Founded: 1994
Full line of fiction & nonfiction trade books, particularly genre fiction (science fiction, fantasy, mystery, horror) & serious nonfiction (biography, science, history). No unsol mss, query first with biographical information & SASE. Will request mss after reviewing query if interested. Handle film & TV rights for regular clients. No reading fee. No fax or e-mail queries.
Titles recently placed: *Dead to the World*, Charlaine Harris; *Marque & Reprisal*, Elizabeth Moon
Foreign Rep(s): Agence Litteraire Lenclud (France); Big Apple Tuttle Mori (China); Bookman (Scandinavia); English Agency (Japan); Paul & Peter Fritz AG (Germany); GRAAL (Poland); Agnese Incisa (Italy); International Literatuur Bureau (Netherlands); Interrights (Bulgaria); Katai & Bolza (Hungary); Simona Kessler (Romania); Duran Kim (Korea); Alexander Korzhenevski (Russia); MBA Literary Agents (UK); Andrew Nurnberg (Baltic States); O A Agency (Greece); Kristin Olson (Czech Republic); Pikarski Agency (Israel); Tuttle-Mori Agency Inc (Japan); Julio F Yanez (Portugal, Spain)
Membership(s): Science Fiction & Fantasy Writers of America

Melanie Jackson Agency LLC (L-D)
41 W 72 St, No 3F, New York, NY 10023
Tel: 212-873-3373 *Fax:* 212-799-5063
No unsol mss, query first.
Foreign Rep(s): Eva Koralnik; Roberto Santochiara; Rogers, Coleridge & White

Janklow & Nesbit Associates (L)
445 Park Ave, New York, NY 10022
Tel: 212-421-1700 *Fax:* 212-980-3671
E-mail: postmaster@janklow.com *Cable:* JANKRAUM
Key Personnel
Sr Partner: Morton L Janklow
Partner: Lynn Nesbit
Sr VP: Anne Sibbald
VP: Tina Bennett; Eric Simonoff
VP & Dir, Foreign Rts: Cullen Stanley
Agent: Lucas W Janklow
Sub Rts: Amy Jameson; Richard Morris
Foreign Rts Agent: Cecile Barendsma; Dorothy Vincent
Rts & Perms: Eileen Godlis
Founded: 1989 (successor to Morton L Janklow Assoc Inc founded in 1975)
General fiction & nonfiction. No unsol mss; query first with outline & sample chapters; handle film & TV rights for book represented; no reading fee.
Foreign Office(s): Janklow & Nesbit (UK) Ltd, 29 Adam & Eve News, London W86UG, United Kingdom, Contact: Tifanny Loehnis *Tel:* (020) 7376 2733 *Fax:* (020) 7376 2915 *E-mail:* queries@janklow.co.uk

Janus Literary Agency (L)
Affiliate of AEI
PO Box 766, Ipswich, MA 01938
Tel: 978-312-1372
E-mail: ubklene@aol.com
Key Personnel
Owner: Lenny Cavallaro
Contact: Eva Wax
Founded: 1980
No unsol mss, query first, with or without SASE. Nonfiction: prospectus, outline, sample chapter; Fiction: synopsis. Will reply only if interested.

No reading fee. Handling fees if we represent the author. Provide ghost-writing services &/or rewrites for fee. Accept very few clients.

JCA Literary Agency Inc (L)
27 W 20 St, Suite 1103, New York, NY 10011
Tel: 212-807-0888 *Fax:* 212-807-0461
Web Site: www.jcalit.com
Key Personnel
VP: Jeff Gerecke (AAR) *E-mail:* jeff@jcalit.com
Contact: Tom Cushman; Tony Outhwaite (AAR)
Founded: 1978
General adult fiction & nonfiction. No unsol mss, query first; no children's books, no screenplays; no reading fees.

Jellinek & Murray Literary Agency (L-D)
Subsidiary of Clairemark Ltd
2024 Mauna Place, Honolulu, HI 96822
Tel: 808-521-4057 *Fax:* 808-521-4058
E-mail: jellinek@lava.net
Key Personnel
Pres: Roger Jellinek
VP: Eden-Lee Murray
Founded: 1995
General adult fiction & nonfiction. No genre fiction. No unsol mss, query first with letter or e-mail. Submit proposal, outline sample mss, two sample chapters, author bio & credentials by mail with SASE or e-mail. Proposals by e-mail accepted. No reading fees. Handle film & TV rights. Co-agents in all major markets.
Foreign Rep(s): Big Apple (China, Taiwan)

Carolyn Jenks Agency (L-D)
24 Concord Ave, Suite 412, Cambridge, MA 02138
Tel: 617-354-5099 *Fax:* 617-354-5099
E-mail: cbjenks@att.net
Founded: 1990
Quality fiction & nonfiction. Handle film & TV rights (WGA Signatory). No unsol mss. Query first by e-mail or letter of inquiry with description of project & brief author bio with SASE; no fees charged.
Membership(s): Writers Guild of America

JET Literary Associates Inc (L)
2570 Camino San Patricio, Santa Fe, NM 87505
Tel: 212-971-2494 (NY voice mail); 505-474-9139 *Fax:* 505-474-9139
E-mail: query@jetliterary.com
Web Site: www.jetliterary.com
Key Personnel
Pres (Austria Office): Jim Trupin
VP: Elizabeth Trupin-Pulli *E-mail:* etp@jetliterary.com
Founded: 1975
General book-length fiction & nonfiction. Specialize in adult fiction & commercial nonfiction. No unsol mss, query first. Submit outline & sample chapter (nonfiction). No reading fees. Telephone, mail & copying fee. Full representation in all foreign markets.
Branch Office(s)
Lerchengasse, 31/20, Vienna, Austria *Tel:* (01) 409 1455
Foreign Rep(s): Eliane Benisti (France); Big Apple Tuttle-Mori (China); Educational Materials Enterprises (Greece); Fritz Agency (Germany); Nurcihan Kesim (Turkey); Kohn (Netherlands); Lennart Sane (Sweden); Living Literary Agency (Italy); Tuttle-Mori (Japan); Julio F Yanez (Brazil, Spain)
Foreign Rights: Abner Stein (UK)

JLM Literary Agents (L)
5901 Warner Ave, Suite 61, Huntington Beach, CA 92649
Tel: 714-547-4870 *Fax:* 714-547-1807

Key Personnel
Owner & Rep: Judy Semler *E-mail:* jsemler168@aol.com
Women's nonfiction: health, fitness, any quirky interesting subjects considered, self-help & psychology. No unsol mss, query first. No e-mail queries. Submit proposal for nonfiction. No reading fee.
Foreign Rep(s): Michael Meller (UK, Netherlands, Germany, Italy, Scandinavia)

Jones Hutton Literary Associates (L-D)
160 N Compo Rd, Westport, CT 06880
Tel: 203-226-2588 *Fax:* 509-356-5190
Web Site: www.marquiswhoswho.net/huttonandhutton
Key Personnel
Man Ed: Caroline Du Bois Hutton *E-mail:* cdubh@optonline.net
Sr Ed, Womens Section: Enid Ford Jones
Ed, Nonfiction: Caroline T Chubet
Ed-at-Large: Virginia DuBois Hutton
Founded: 1994
Represents general & literary fiction & nonfiction by established & new authors & currently seeking new work. For nonfiction, please submit a proposal (outline is available by request from cdubh@optonline.net if needed). For fiction, please submit whole mss, with one to two page outline & author's bio. Fiction writing notes are available from cdubh@optonline.net. No reading fee; authors pay submission expenses to publishing houses. Authors choose how many submissions per month are sent out; editing as needed & agreed upon. Editing is available on an as needed basis for a fee which will be discussed on an individual case. No erotica, juvenile, sci-fi, or gay & lesbian. If you wish your work returned, please provide a large enough SASE. Electronic submissions are unacceptable; hard copy only.
Titles recently placed: *A Modern Approach to Graham & Dodd Investing*, Thomas P Au; *A Shift in the Wind*, Aminuddin Khan; *Last Summer*, Herbert Courser; *Lions in the City*, Jack Laflin; *Moment of Truth*, Herbert Coursen; *The Street Singer*, Arthur Tracy; *You Must Eat Meat*, Frank Murray
Membership(s): American Association of University Women

Lawrence Jordan Literary Agency (L-D)
Division of Morning Star Communications
345 W 121 St, New York, NY 10027
Tel: 212-662-7871 *Fax:* 212-662-8138
E-mail: ljlagency@aol.com
Key Personnel
Pres & Agent: Lawrence Jordan
VP & Dir, Mktg & Agent: Toni Banks *E-mail:* toniatljla@aol.com
Asst Agent: Melanie Okadigwe *E-mail:* melanieatljla@aol.com
Founded: 1978
General adult fiction & nonfiction: sports, travel, biography, autobiography, business, economics, health, medicine, memoirs, cookbooks, religious, inspirational, science, technology, self-improvement. Actively seeking spiritual & religious books, mystery novels, action suspense, thrillers, biographies, autobiographies, celebrity books. No poetry, movie scripts, stage plays, juvenile books or fantasy novels. Query with SASE, outline; e-mail queries accepted; responds in three weeks to queries, six weeks for mss. Agent receives 15% commission on domestic sales, 20% on foreign sales, 20% on dramatic rights sales. Most commissions are derived from commission on ms sales. Charge for long-distance calls, photocopying, foreign submissions cost, postage, cables & messengers.
Lawrence Jordan is the agent for mystery novels, sports, autobiographies, biographies & religion.

Toni Banks is the agent for religion, inspirational, women's studies, autobiography & memoirs.
Melanie Okadigwe is the agent for African American & Caribbean literature, speculative fiction, coming-of-age memoirs, women's studies, arts, travel, cookbooks & alternative health.
Titles recently placed: *Broken Silence: Opening Your Heart & Mind to Therapy—A Black Women's Recovery Guide*, Dr. D Kim Singleton; *The Godson*, Leo Tolstoy; *The Undiscovered Paul Robeson (vol 2)*, Paul Robeson Jr; *Walk in the Light, While There is Light*, Leo Tolstoy

The Karpfinger Agency (L)
357 W 20 St, New York, NY 10011-3379
Tel: 212-691-2690 *Fax:* 212-691-7129
Key Personnel
Owner: Barney M Karpfinger
Foreign Rts Dir: Agnes Krup
Contact: Inge De Taeye
Quality fiction & nonfiction. No unsol mss, query first; no reading fee. Agents in all foreign markets.

Herbert M Katz Inc (L-D)
151 E 83 St, New York, NY 10028
Tel: 212-861-5460
Key Personnel
Pres: Herbert M Katz
VP: Nancy B Katz
Founded: 1985
Commercial fiction & nonfiction, health, medicine, science, business, biography. Handle film & TV rights. No unsol mss; query first; with SASE. No fax or e-mail query. No reading fee. Agents worldwide. NO INQUIRIES FROM NEW CLIENTS ACCEPTED AT THIS TIME.
Titles recently placed: *AstroFit*, Dr William J Evans, Gerald S Couzens; *Brilliant Bodies For Women*, Peggy Brill; *Controlling Cholesterol the Nature Way*, Dr Kenneth H Cooper; *Fit Kids*, Dr Kenneth H Cooper; *Instant Relief*, Peggy Brill, Susan Suffes; *Tell Me Where It Hurts*, Peggy Brill; *The Politics of American Medicine*, Dr George Lundberg
Foreign Rep(s): Kyoshi Asano (Japan); Michael Meller (Eastern Europe); Tuttle Mori (Asia)
Foreign Rights: Kyoshi Asana (Japan); Michael Meller (Western Europe); Tuttle Mori (Asia)

The Kellock Co (L)
18811 Cypress Bend Ct, Boca Raton, FL 33498
Tel: 561-558-8603
E-mail: kellock@aol.com
Key Personnel
Owner: Alan C Kellock
Contact: Loren Kellock
Founded: 1990
Nonfiction only, all subjects; handle foreign rights & software; query first with SASE; no reading fees.

Natasha Kern Literary Agency Inc (L)
PO Box 2908, Portland, OR 97208-2908
Tel: 503-297-6190 *Fax:* 503-297-8241
E-mail: natasha@natashakern.com
Web Site: www.natashakern.com
Key Personnel
Pres: Natasha Kern
Edit Assoc: Krystin Hawkins *E-mail:* krystin@natashakern.com
Founded: 1986
We are a full service agency representing commercial adult fiction & nonfiction. We represent properties in the following nonfiction areas: investigative journalism, popular psychology & sociology, science, spirituality/inspiration, alternative health & general medicine, parenting, self-help, animals, controversial & women's issues, narrative nonfiction, trade nonfiction

by prominent authorities. In fiction, we are actively acquiring all women's fiction; historical contemporary paranormal & inspirational romances; medical, spiritual & historical thrillers; mysteries & psychological suspense. We DO NOT represent children's, horror, genre science fiction, fantasy, traditional westerns, short stores, poetry, sports, true crime, scholarly, coffee table books, educational, software or scripts. We handle film & TV rights. No reading fee, we charge for foreign submission expenses. Represented in all principle foreign countries, including Hollywood. No unsol mss. First look at website submission info. Send query with SASE; include for nonfiction a 2-3 page overview or for fiction a 3-5 page synopsis & the first 5 pages of ms.
Titles recently placed: *An Animated Death in Burbank*, Michael Joens; *Beautiful Ghost*, Eliot Pattison; *Beyond the Shadows*, Robin Lee Hatcher; *Biocosm*, James Gardner; *Bone Mountain*, Eliot Pattison; *Born To Love*, Leigh Greenwood; *Carnal Gift*, Pamela Clare; *Firstborn*, Robin Hatcher; *Kiss Me Once, Kiss Me Twice*, Kimberly Raye; *Master of Ecstasy*, Nina Bangs; *Midnight Embrace*, Nina Bangs; *Organizing For the Spirit*, Sunny Schlenger; *Running the Spiritual Path*, Roger Joslin; *Secret Life of God*, David Aaron; *Seduced By A Rogue*, Connie Mason; *Slatewiper*, Lewis Perdue; *Spirit Babies*, Walter Makichen; *Summer of Glorious Madness*, Christy Yorke; *Sweet As Sugar, Hot As Spice*, Kimberly Raye; *Sweet Release*, Pamela Clare; *The Davinci Legacy*, Lewis Perdue; *The Diamond Conspiracy*, Nickolas Kublicki; *The Independent Bride*, Leigh Greenwood; *The Last Rogue*, Connie Mason; *The Lincolns: An American Tragedy*, Jerry Packard; *The Power of Losing Control*, Joe Caruso; *The Secret Life of God*, Rabbi David Aaron; *The Unholy Deception*, Lynn Marzulli; *The Victory Club*, Robin Lee Hatcher; *The Waiting Child*, Cindy Champnella; *To Find You Again*, Maureen McKade
Foreign Rep(s): Agence Eliane Benisti (France); Luigi Bernabo (Italy); Phillip Chen (China, Taiwan); Ann Droumeva (Bulgaria); Gloria Gutierrez (Spain); Dieter Hagenbach (Germany); Angus Josts (Baltic States); Nelly Moukakou (Greece); Prava i Prevodi (Eastern Europe); Lucia Riff (Brazil); Junzo Sawa (Japan); Lorna Soifer (Israel); Hanserik Tonnheim (Iceland)

The Joyce Ketay Agency (L-D)
630 Ninth Ave, Suite 706, New York, NY 10036
Tel: 212-354-6825 *Fax:* 212-354-6732
Key Personnel
Agent: Joyce Ketay; Carl Mulert
Playwriting & screenwriting. No unsol mss, query first; submit outline; no reading fee unless accepted as client, then standard agent commission.

Louise B Ketz Agency (L)
1485 First Ave, Suite 4-B, New York, NY 10021
Tel: 212-535-9259 *Fax:* 212-249-3103
E-mail: ketzagency@aol.com
Key Personnel
Pres: Louise B Ketz
Founded: 1986
Nonfiction only: economics, science, reference, history. No unsol mss, query letter, chapter outline, table of contents, sample chapter, author biography. No reading fee.
Titles recently placed: *Blue Moons, Black Holes*, Melanie Knocke; *The Five Biggest Unsolved Problems in Science*, Charles Wynn, Arthur Wiggins, Sidney Harris

Virginia Kidd Agency Inc (L)
538 E Harford St, Milford, PA 18337

Mailing Address: PO Box 278, Milford, PA 18337
Tel: 570-296-6205 *Fax:* 570-296-7266
Web Site: vkagency.com *Telex:* CIS73107; CIS73311 *Cable:* ADVANCES
Key Personnel
Literary Agent: Nanci McCloskey
Contracts & Royalties: Vaughne Hansen
Foreign/Translation & Perms: Christine Cohen
Founded: 1965
Specialize in fiction; special interest in science fiction, fantasy, speculative fiction, mainstream fiction, women's fiction. No unsol mss, query first; submit two-page synopsis, first ten pages of mss with cover letter & SASE; no reading fee. Representative for dramatic rights: The William Morris Agency, Bill Contardi, New York contact. 15% commission; 15% higher commission on dramatic & foreign sales.
Titles recently placed: *Confidence Game*, Michelle M Welch; *Gifts*, Ursula K Le Guin; *Sliding Scales*, Alan Dean Foster; *The Anvil of the World*, Kage Baker; *The Knight: Book One of the Wizard Knight*, Gene Wolfe; *The Traveler, Book One*, Patty Briggs; *The Wave in the Mind*, Ursula K Le Guin
Foreign Rep(s): Agence Litteraire-Lenclud (France); Agenzia Letteraria Internazionale (Italy); Paul & Peter Fritz AG (Germany); International Editors Co (Portugal, South America, Spain); Alexander Korzhenevski (Russia); Lennart Sane (Netherlands, Scandinavia); Rogan Pikarski Agency (Israel); Prava I Prevodi (Eastern Europe, Greece, Turkey, Central Europe); Tuttle-Mori Agency Inc (Japan); Diana Tyler of MBA & Gerald Pollinger Ltd (UK)

Kirchoff/Wohlberg Inc (L-D)
866 United Nations Plaza, Suite 525, New York, NY 10017
Tel: 212-644-2020 *Fax:* 212-223-4387
E-mail: kirchwohl@aol.com
Web Site: www.kirchoffwohlberg.com
Key Personnel
Pres: Morris A Kirchoff
Dir, Opers: John R Whitman
Artists' Rep: Elizabeth J Ford
Authors' Rep: Liza Pulitzer-Voges (AAR)
Founded: 1930
Children & young adult fiction & nonfiction trade books only. Agency does not handle adult titles. No unsol mss, query first with outline, sample chapter & SASE. No reading fees or other fees. Handle film & TV rights.
Branch Office(s)
897 Boston Post Rd, Madison, CT 06443
Tel: 203-245-7308
Membership(s): AAP; AIGA; ALA; Authors Guild; International Reading Association; Society of Children's Book Writers & Illustrators; Society of Illustrators; Society of Photographers & Artists Representatives
See Ad in Book Producers, Editorial Services section(s)

Harvey Klinger Inc (L-D)
301 W 53 St, New York, NY 10019
Tel: 212-581-7068 *Fax:* 212-315-3823
E-mail: queries@harveyklinger.com
Key Personnel
Pres: Harvey Klinger (AAR) *E-mail:* harvey@harveyklinger.com
Contact: David Dunton; Wendy Silbert
Founded: 1977
Mainstream fiction & nonfiction. Handle film & TV rights. No unsol mss, faxes or e-mails. Do not phone or fax. No reading fee. Representatives in Hollywood & all principal foreign countries. New clients obtained by referrals.
Titles recently placed: *A Window Across the River*, Brian Morton; *Get Your Share*, Julie Stau; *The Sweet Potato Queens Guide to Life*, Jill Conner Browne; *The Valley of Light*, Terry

Kay; *What Women Want Men to Know*, Barbara De Angelis

Foreign Rights: Eliane Benisti (France); Luigi Bernabo (Italy); Big Apple Tuttle-Mori (Taiwan); David Grossman (UK); P & P (Eastern Europe, Russia); Lennart Sane (Latin America, Scandinavia, Spain); Thomas Schluck (Germany); Tuttle-Mori (Japan); Eric Yang (Korea)

Kneerim & Williams (L-D)
Subsidiary of Fish & Richardson PC
c/o Fish & Richardson PC, 225 Franklin St, Boston, MA 02110
Tel: 617-542-5070 *Fax:* 617-542-8906
Web Site: www.fr.com
Key Personnel
Dir: Jill Kneerim *Tel:* 617-521-7823
  E-mail: kneerim@fr.com; John Taylor Williams *Tel:* 617-521-7820 *E-mail:* jwilliams@fr.com
Subs Rts Dir: Elaine Rogers *Tel:* 617-521-7886
  E-mail: elaine.rogers@fr.com
Scout, Los Angeles: Rebecca Rickman
  E-mail: rrickman@sbcglobal.net
Attorney: Patricia Nelson *Tel:* 617-521-7862
  E-mail: nelson@fr.com
Agency Administrator: Hope Denekamp *Tel:* 617-521-7086 *E-mail:* denekamp@fr.com
Agent, NY: Brettne Bloom *Tel:* 212-641-2354
  E-mail: bloom@fr.com; Elisabeth Weed
  Tel: 212-641-2225 *E-mail:* weed@fr.com
Admin Asst: Seana McInerney *Tel:* 617-521-7084
  E-mail: mcinerney@fr.com
Founded: 1990
Handles books, screenplays & film & television rights. Does not handle poetry, children's literature, genre fiction; no romance, western, mystery, or science fiction & fantasy. No unsol mss, query first. Send query via US post. Query should contain a cover letter explaining your book & why you are qualified to write it, a two-page synopsis, a curriculum vitae or history of your publications & an SASE. Does not charge fees.
Titles recently placed: *2nd Untitled Novel*, Vyvyanne Loh; *52 Fights*, Jennifer Patterson Sameul; *A Job Like No Other*, Glen Stout, Charles Vitchers, Robert Gray; *A Life of Maimonides*, Joel Kraemer; *ADD That's Me*, Edward Hallowell, Catherine Corman; *All Deliberate Speed*, Charles Ogletree; *American Muse: The Life of Anne Bradstreet*, Charlotte Gordon; *At Risk*, Michael Patrick MacDonald; *Autobiography of a Poor Body*, Mary Childers; *Boiling Point*, Ross Gelbspan; *Boy Vey!*, Kristina Grish; *Boys of a Feather*, Meg Leder, Amy Helmes; *Breaking the Tongue*, Vyvyanne Loh; *Britain's Gulag: The End of Empire in Kenya*, Caroline Elkins; *Cheap Diamonds*, Norris Church Mailer; *Chinese Cinderella*, Adeline Yen Mah; *Descartes*, Amir Aczel; *Descartes's Notebook*, Amir Aczel; *Drawing & Imagination*, Bert Dodson; *Entrepreneurs*, Bo Burlingham; *Fairy Tales Can Come True: How a Driven Woman*, Rikki Klieman, Peter Knobler; *Fatal Equation*, Simon Winchester, Amir Aczel; *From Here to Maternity: The Education of a Rookie*, Beth Teitell; *George Washington*, Joseph J Ellis; *Getting Even*, Evelyn Murphy, E J Graff; *Grant & Sherman*, Charles Flood; *Great Occasions*, Scott-Martin Kosofsky, Jonathan Sarna; *House of Wits: The Private Life of the Very Public*, Paul Fisher; *How to Fall: Stories*, Edith Pearlman; *Indelible Stamp*, Edward O Wilson; *John Lennon Biography*, Tim Riley; *John Ono Lennon*, Tim Riley; *King David*, Robert Pinsky; *Leadership Legacy*, Robert Galford; *Lincoln's Men*, David Donald; *Made All Over*, Suzanne Berger; *Memoir*, Michael Patrick MacDonald; *Nightgales*, Gillian Gill; *Nuclear Terrorism*, Graham Allison; *Preventing a Nuclear 9/11*, Graham Allison; *Pullman Porters*, Larry Tye; *Rising from the Rails*, Larry Tye; *Rocks*, Tom Zoellner; *RX for a Planetary Fever*, Ross

Gelbspan; *Savage Mountain*, Jennifer Jordan; *Shock: ECT & the Battle Against Depression*, Kitty Dukakis, Larry Tye; *Sing Sing 475*, David Goewey; *Step-Child of the Revolution*, Joyce Malcolm; *Stop Suffering Now*, Arthur Barsky, Emily Deans; *Suburbia*, Bob Fogelson; *Taught by America Glenn Stout*, Sarah Sentilles; *The Book of Customs*, Scott Martin Kosofsky; *The Children's Blizzard*, David Laskin; *The Dodgers*, Glenn Stout, Richard Johnson; *The FBI Hero Hoover Destroyed*, Alston Purvis; *The Great Eagle*, Joel Kramer; *The Perfect Fit!*, Meghan Cleary; *The Perfect Manhattan*, Leanne Shear, Tracy Toomey; *The Secret Dragon Society*, Adeline Yen Mah; *The Short Bus Story*, Jonathan Mooney; *The Women of K2: A Book about the Women Who Climbed the World's Deadliest Mountain*, Jennifer Jordan; *The Zero Game*, Brad Meltzer; *Time Off Plan*, Rae Nelson, Karl Haigler; *Treat Well the Animals*, Douglas Whynott; *Untitled Novel*, Brad Meltzer; *Violin Dreams*, Arnold Steinhardt; *We Are Lincoln Men*, David Donald; *When Harry Met Hallie*, Susan Quinn; *Who We Are*, Arthur Kleinman
Branch Office(s)
45 Rockefeller Plaza, Suite 2800, New York, NY 10011 *Tel:* 212-765-5070 *Fax:* 212-258-2291
153 E 53 St, 52nd fl, New York, NY 10022
Foreign Rep(s): Baror International Inc
Foreign Rights: ACER Agencia Literaria (Spain); Agencia Literaria Balcells Mello (Brazil); Anthea Literary Agency (Bulgaria); Eliane Benisti Literary Agency (France); Bernabo & Associates (Italy); Big Apple Tuttle Mori Agency Inc (Taiwan); The English Agency (Japan); Japan Uni Agency (Japan); Licht & Burr Agency (Denmark); Judy Martin (UK); Mohrbooks (Germany); I Pikarski Ltd Inc (Israel); Prava Prevodi (Serbia and Montenegro); Shin Won Agency Co (Korea); Tuttle-Mori Agency (Japan); Deborah Taylor Williams (Netherlands)

The Knight Agency Inc (L-D)
577 S Main St, Madison, GA 30650
Mailing Address: PO Box 550648, Atlanta, GA 30355
Tel: 706-752-0096
E-mail: knightagency@msn.com; knightagent@aol.com (queries)
Web Site: www.knightagency.net
Key Personnel
Pres & Owner: Deidre Knight (AAR)
  E-mail: deidremk@aol.com
Assoc Agent & Subs Rights Dir: Pamela Harty (AAR) *E-mail:* pharty@hom.net
Busn Mgr & Ms Coord: Judson Knight
Founded: 1996
Fiction: romance, women's fiction, commercial fiction, literary & multicultural fiction. In nonfiction: business, self-help, finance, music/entertainment, media-related, pop culture, how-to, psychology, travel, health, inspirational/religious, reference & holiday books. No science fiction/fantasy, mysteries, action-adventure, horror, short story or poetry. No unsol mss, query first by sending a brief summary or proposal & author info by e-mail (no attachments). Allow a one to three week response time for queries. Upon request only submit the following: for fiction: first three chapters, synopsis or outline & copy of original query; nonfiction: proposal or outline, first one to three chapters, summary of author's qualifications, unique marketing opportunities & copy of original query. Allow 8-12 weeks for ms review. No reading fee. 15% commission on domestic sales, 10-25% on foreign. May use sub-agent for sale or film & foreign rights. Charge for copies, shipping/postage & overnight shipping.
Titles recently placed: *100 Careers in the Music Business*, Tanja Crouch; *A Beginner's*

Guide to Day Trading Online, Toni Turner; *A Beginnner's Guide to Short Term Investing*, Toni Turner; *A Change is Gonna Come*, Jacquelin Thomas; *Achieving Your Financial Potential*, Scott Kay; *Are Angels Real?*, Kathy Bostrom; *Arms of an Angel*, Adrianne Byrd; *Autumn's Awakening*, Irene Brand; *Beyond Success: The 15 Secrets to Effective Leadership & Life Based on Legendary Coach John Wooden's Pyramid of Success*, Brian Biro; *Beyond the Highland Mist*, Karen Moning; *Beyond World Class*, Alan M Ross, Cecil Murphey; *Candy Don't Come in Gray*, Roslyn Carrington; *Children of the Movement*, John Blake; *Dark Highlander*, Karen Moning; *Dream Wedding*, Alice Wootson; *Dressing Your Family on a Shoestring Budget*, Gwen Ellis, Jo Ann Janssen; *Encountering the Holy*, Cecil Murphey; *Futuring: Leading Your Church Into Tomorrow*, Dr Samuel Chand, Cecil Murphey; *God's Most Important Name*, Cecil Murphey; *How to be Your Own Publicist*, Jessica Hatchingan; *Kiss of the Highlander*, Karen Moning; *Love's Deception*, Adrianne Byrd; *O Solo Mia! The Hip Chick's Guide to Solo Fun*, Wendy Burt, Erin Kindberg; *Papa's Gift*, Kathleen Long Bostrom; *Record Time*, Beverly Brandt; *Room Service*, Beverly Brandt; *Serial Killers: The Method & Madness of Monsters*, Peter Vronski; *Simply Living*, Cecil Murphey; *Snowbound With Love*, Alice Wootson; *Soul's Desire*, Simona Taylor; *Strictly Forbidden*, Shelley Bradley; *Summer's Promise*, Irene Brand; *The Best Haunted Inns of the Southeast*, Sheila Turnage; *The Complete Cancer Cleanse*, Cherie Calbom; *The Devine None: African American Fraternities & Sororities 1906-2000*, Lawrence Ross; *The Healing Quilt*, Lauraine Snelling; *The Highlander's Touch*, Karen Moning; *The Power of a Partner*, Dr Richard Pimental-Habib; *The Prodigal Husband*, Jacquelin Thomas; *The Ways of Black Folks: A Year in the Life of a People*, Lawrence Ross; *To Tame a Highland Warrior*, Karen Moning; *True North*, Beverly Brandt; *Unconditional Excellence*, Alan M Ross, Cecil Murphey; *Undeniably Yours*, Jacquelin Thomas; *What About Heaven?*, Kathy Bostrom
Foreign Rights: Lennart Sane Agency (Netherlands, Portugal, Scandinavia, Spain); Ann Milenkovic/Prava I Prevodi (Eastern Europe); Schluck Literary Agency (Germany)
Membership(s): The Authors Guild Inc; Romance Writers of America

Paul Kohner Agency (L-D)
9300 Wilshire Blvd, Suite 555, Beverly Hills, CA 90212
Tel: 310-550-1060 *Fax:* 310-276-1083
Key Personnel
Pres: Pearl Wexler
Literary Agent: Brian Dreyfuss; Stephen Moore
Film & TV rights. No unsol mss, query first. No reading fee; fees for extensive copying or binding charges.

Linda Konner Literary Agency (L)
10 W 15 St, Suite 1918, New York, NY 10011
Tel: 212-691-3419 *Fax:* 212-691-0935
Key Personnel
Pres: Linda Konner (AAR) *E-mail:* ldkonner@cs.com
Founded: 1996
Health, nutrition, diet, relationships, sex, pop psychology, self-help, parenting, cookbooks & career/personal finance. No fiction or children's. No unsol mss, query first with one-page query & SASE. Submit outline & one to two sample chapters. No reading fee. 15% fee on US sales & 25% on foreign sales. One-time expense fee of $85, deducted from publisher's advance payment.

Titles recently placed: *Dating Mr Big: When You Love A Man Who Loves Himself*, W Keith Campbell PhD; *No More Type-2 Diabetic Kids!*, Sheri Colberg-Ochs PhD, Mary Friesz RD

Foreign Rights: Nancy Green Madia (Worldwide)

Elaine Koster Literary Agency LLC (L)
55 Central Park West, Suite 6, New York, NY 10023
Tel: 212-362-9488 *Fax:* 212-712-0164
E-mail: elainekost@aol.com
Key Personnel
Pres: Elaine Koster (AAR)
Assoc Agent: Stephanie Lehmann
Founded: 1998
Specialize in literary & quality commercial fiction, including medical, legal & international thrillers, suspense, psychological suspense, contemporary fiction & women's fiction. Diverse nonfiction: psychology, science, self-help, cookbooks, popular culture, business, spirituality & inspiration, women's issues & health. Submissions must be on an exclusive basis. No unsol mss, query first. Submit first 50 pages for fiction, or a proposal for nonfiction. Queries & submissions must include SASE. No reading fee. Handle film & TV rights. Representatives on the West Coast & in major foreign countries.
Titles recently placed: *Bitter in the Mouth*, Monique Truong; *The Best Kept Secret*, Kimberly Lawson Roby; *Trace Evidence*, Elizabeth Beoka
Membership(s): Authors Guild; Mystery Writers of America; Women's Media Group

Barbara S Kouts Literary Agency LLC (L)
PO Box 560, Bellport, NY 11713
Tel: 631-286-1278 *Fax:* 631-286-1538
E-mail: bkouts@aol.com
Key Personnel
Owner: Barbara S Kouts (AAR)
Founded: 1980
Specialize in children's fiction & nonfiction. No unsol mss, query first. Submit synopsis or outline & sample chapters. No reading fee, but copy fees would apply, no software. Handle film & TV rights from sale of books. Agents in all principal foreign countries.
Titles recently placed: *Dare To Be Scared*, Robert San Souci; *Pocahantas*, Joseph Bruchac; *When We Where Saints*, Han Nolan
Membership(s): Society of Children's Book Writers & Illustrators

Kraas Literary Agency (L)
13514 Winter Creek Ct, Houston, TX 77077
Tel: 281-870-9770 *Fax:* 281-870-9770
Web Site: www.kraasliterarygency.com
Key Personnel
Principal: Irene Kraas
Associate: Ashley Kraas
Founded: 1990
Dedicated to launching new authors & equally dedicated to our published authors. Submit first 50 pages of completed mss & SASE. No fees charged. Authors billed for copies & postage only.
Titles recently placed: *The Sword, The Shield & The Crown, a trilogy*, Hilari Bell
Branch Office(s)
507 NW 22 Ave, Suite 104, Portland, OR 97210, Contact: Ashley M Kraas *Tel:* 503-319-0900
Foreign Rights: Agence Hoffman (France); Kodansha (Japan); Alex Korzehevski Agency (Russia); Margara Onaf (Mexico); Thomas Schlueck (Germany)
Membership(s): Authors Guild

Edite Kroll Literary Agency Inc (L)
12 Grayhurst Park, Portland, ME 04102

Tel: 207-773-4922 *Fax:* 207-773-3936
Key Personnel
Pres: Edite Kroll
Founded: 1981
Adult feminist & humor; children's fiction & picture books. No unsol mss, query first. Submit outline, sample chapter or dummy & SASE. No reading fee. Legal & Xeroxing fees with authors' approval. Handle film & TV rights with West Coast agent.
Foreign Rep(s): ACER (Brazil, Portugal); Akcali (Turkey); Bookbank SA (Spain, Spanish Latin America); Ann-Christine Danielssen (adult books); ELST (Bulgaria); English Agency (Japan); Lora Fountain (France); David Grossman (UK); Ia Atterholm Agency (Scandinavia, childrens books); JLM Literary Agency (Greece); Living Literary Agency (Italy); Menno Kohn International Literatuur Bureau (Netherlands); I Pikarski (Israel); Schlueck Agency (Germany); Eric Yang Agency (Korea)
Foreign Rights: Bardon, Chinese Media & Big Apple Tuttle-Mori (China); Prava I Prevodi (Czech Republic, Estonia, Hungary, Poland, Serbia and Montenegro, Slovak Republic & Slovenia)

Lucy Kroll Agency, see The Barbara Hogenson Agency Inc

The LA Literary Agency, see The Maureen Lasher Agency/The LA Literary Agency

Peter Lampack Agency Inc (L)
551 Fifth Ave, Suite 1613, New York, NY 10176
Tel: 212-687-9106 *Fax:* 212-687-9109
E-mail: lampackag@verizon.net (other correspondence)
Key Personnel
Pres: Peter A Lampack
Agent/Foreign Rts (Italy, Germany & UK): Sandra Blanton *E-mail:* sandyblant@verizon.net(foreignrights)
Agent: Andrew M Lampack *E-mail:* alampack@verizon.net
Founded: 1977
Commercial & literary fiction; nonfiction by recognized experts in a given field (especially autobiography, biography, law, finance, politics, history). Handle motion picture & TV rights from book properties only. No original scripts or screenplays. No unsol mss; query letter which describes the nature of the ms plus the author's credentials if any, sample chapter, synopsis & SASE. No reading fee.
Titles recently placed: *A Night As Clear As Day*, R J Rosenblum; *Assassin*, Ted Bell; *Going Topless*, Megan McAndrew; *Lost City*, Clive Cussler; *Shades of Red*, Doris Mortman; *The Winds of Change*, Martha Grimes
Foreign Rep(s): Carmen Balcells Agencia Literaria (Portugal, South America, Spain); Nurcihan Kesim Literary Agency (Turkey); Michelle Lapautre (France); Jovan Milenkovic Agency (Eastern Europe, Greece, Russia); Pikarski Literary Agency (Israel); Lennart Sane (Netherlands & Scandinavia); Tuttle-Mori Agency (China, Japan, Thailand); Eric Yang Agency (Korea)

Michael Larsen/Elizabeth Pomada Literary Agents (L)
1029 Jones St, San Francisco, CA 94109
Tel: 415-673-0939
E-mail: larsenpoma@aol.com
Web Site: www.larsen-pomada.com
Key Personnel
Partner: Michael Larsen (AAR); Elizabeth Pomada (AAR)
Founded: 1972
General adult, book-length fiction & nonfiction. No unsol mss, query first. Nonfiction: after

reading Michael's "How to Write a Book Proposal," please see our website for submission instructions or send a No 10 SASE for free sixteen-page brochure "How to Make Yourself Irresistible to Any Agent or Editor." Fiction: send first ten pages & a two-page synopsis of a completed novel. Include SASE & daytime phone number with both. No reading fee. Representatives in major foreign countries & in Hollywood. Handle film & TV rights for clients. Fiction: literary, commercial, romance, mysteries, thrillers, historical, new voices. Nonfiction: business, psychology, biography, history, science, food, humor, how-to, reference, music, spirituality, futurism, technology, architecture, social issues, biographies, the arts, health, France, new ideas, memoirs.
Titles recently placed: *Ecstatic Goddess*, Francesca De Grandis; *Freedom, Passages in Independence & the Power of Choice*, Leonard Roy Frank; *Guerilla Marketing for Free*, Jay Conrad Levinson; *How to Sleep with a Movie Star*, Kristen Harmel; *Stooples*, Kevin Reifler; *The Runaway Duke*, Julie Ann Long
Foreign Rep(s): David Grossman (England)
Foreign Rights: Chandler Crawford (all territories)
Membership(s): American Society of Journalists & Authors; Authors Guild; National Speakers Association; National Writers Guild; PEN American Center; Women's National Book Association

The Maureen Lasher Agency/The LA Literary Agency (L-D)
PO Box 46370, Los Angeles, CA 90046
Tel: 323-654-5288 *Fax:* 323-654-5388
E-mail: laliteraryag@aol.com
Key Personnel
Pres: Maureen Lasher
Contact: Ann Cashman; Eric Lasher
Founded: 1980
Adult fiction & nonfiction books; handle film & TV rights. Query first with outline, sample pages (approximately 50), bio/resume & SASE. No fees charged.
Titles recently placed: *And the Walls Came Tumbling Down*, Michael Lief, H Mitchell Caldwell; *Antipasto*, Joyce Goldstein; *Teen Knitting Club*, Jennifer Wenger, Carol Abrams, Maureen Lasher; *The Framingham Heart Study*, Daniel Levy, MD, Susan Brink; *The New Wedding Cake Book*, Dede Wilson

The Lazear Agency Inc (L-D)
431 Second St, Suite 300, Hudson, WI 54016
Tel: 715-531-0012 *Fax:* 715-531-0016
Web Site: www.lazear.com
Key Personnel
Sr Agent: Christi Cardenas; Jonathon Lazear
Ed: Wendy Lazear
Assoc Ed: Anne Blackstone
Agent: Julie Mayo *E-mail:* jmayo@lazear.com
Founded: 1984
Full-service literary, motion picture & entertainment agency representing clients worldwide. Adult & select children's fiction & nonfiction, non-book related licensing, no poetry. No unsol mss, query first with number 10 SASE. Submit outline. No fees. Handle software, film & TV rights, syndication, book & non-book merchandising.
Titles recently placed: *All I Did Was Ask*, Terry Gross; *Bush On the Couch*, Justin A Frank MD; *Everything I Know About Cars*, Tom Lichtenheld; *Father Joe*, Tony Hendra; *Lies & the Lying Liars Who Tell Them*, Al Franken; *Living On The Edge*, Jeff Corwin; *The Ten Trusts*, Jane Goodall, Marc Bekoff; *We Got Fired & It Was The Best Thing That Ever Happened To Us*, Harvey MacKay; *You ain't Got No Easter Clothes*, Laura Love
Foreign Rights: Jenny Meyer

Sarah Lazin Books (L)
126 Fifth Ave, Suite 300, New York, NY 10011
Tel: 212-989-5757 *Fax:* 212-989-1393
Key Personnel
Pres: Sarah Lazin (AAR)
Assoc Agent: Paula Balzer (AAR)
General nonfiction, fiction & illustrated books. Handle film & TV rights. Domestic & foreign rights in all principal countries. No unsol mss, query first; no fees.
Foreign Rights: The English Agency (Japan); Graal Ltd (Poland); Katai & Bolza (Hungary); la Nouvelle Agence (France); Kristin Olson (Czech Republic); Owl Agency (Japan); I Pikarski (Israel); Vicki Satlow Agency (Italy); Thomas Schluck (Germany); Hanserik Tonnheim (Scandinavia); Tuttle-Mori (Japan); Caroline Van Gelderen (Netherlands); Lucas Alexander Whitley (Australia, UK); Julio F Yanez (Portugal & Spain); Eric Yang Agency (Korea)

Leap First Literary Agency (L)
1100 Melrose Ave, Elkins Park, PA 19027
Tel: 215-563-8050
E-mail: leapfirst@aol.com
Key Personnel
Pres: Lynn Rosen
Selected social issues, religion & spirituality; nonfiction in the areas of narrative journalism, popular culture, self-help, psychology & health. No fiction. Handle software, film & TV rights. No reading fee. Format of submissions is proposal & sample chapter. No unsol mss, query first.

The Ned Leavitt Agency (L)
70 Wooster St, Suite 4-F, New York, NY 10012
Tel: 212-334-0999
Key Personnel
Pres: Ned Leavitt (AAR)
Literary & commercial fiction & nonfiction, books on spirituality & psychology; handle film, TV & foreign rights. No unsol mss, query first with sample pages & SASE. Rejections not returned, no reading fee.

The Lee Shore Co Ltd (L-D)
Division of CyntoMedia Corp
7436 Washington Ave, Suite 100, Pittsburgh, PA 15218
Tel: **412-271-1100** *Toll Free Tel:* **800-898-7886**
Fax: **412-271-1900**
E-mail: **info@leeshoreagency.com**
Web Site: **www.leeshoreagency.com**
Key Personnel
CEO: C L Shore Sterling *E-mail:* csterling@ leeshoreagency.com
Rts Agent: Jennifer Piemme
E-mail: jpiemme@leeshoreagency.com
Founded: 1988
Nonfiction; self-help, genre, mass-market. No unsol mss, query first. Handles film & TV rights. Submit synopsis & ms for fiction; outline chapter by chapter for nonfiction. Evaluation fee $195 for unpublished authors & fees for postage, copies, etc. Also accepting no fee submissions.

The Adele Leone Agency Inc (L-D)
26 Nantucket Place, Scarsdale, NY 10583
Mailing Address: PO Box 2080, Cathedral Sta, New York, NY 10025
Fax: 212-866-0754 *Cable:* INLITBUR
Key Personnel
Pres: Richard Monaco *Tel:* 212-866-0271
VP: Adele Leone
Founded: 1978
Specialize in fiction & nonfiction. Accept unsol mss. Submit outline & sample chapters (double spaced) with SASE. No reading fee. Handle film & TV rights.

Foreign Rep(s): Andrew Nurnberg Associates (Netherlands); Copyright Hellas Publishing & Agency (Greece); Gerd Plessl Agency (Eastern Europe); International Editors Co (Latin America, Spain); Karin Schindler Rights Rep (Brazil); La Nouvelle Agence (France); Licht & Licht Agency (Scandinavia); Luigi Bernabo (Italy); Rogan Pikarski Agency (Israel); Thomas Schluck (Germany); Tuttle-Mori Agency (Japan)

The Lescher Agency Inc (L)
Affiliate of Lescher & Lescher
47 E 19 St, New York, NY 10003
Tel: 212-529-1790 *Fax:* 212-529-2716
Key Personnel
Pres & Agent: Susan Lescher (AAR)
E-mail: susanlescher@aol.com
Founded: 1994
Literary fiction, quality commercial fiction & nonfiction, cookbooks. No unsol mss. Query first with SASE. Submit double-spaced synopsis describing project at length & author bio. No fees charged.

Lescher & Lescher Ltd (L)
47 E 19 St, New York, NY 10003
Tel: 212-529-1790 *Fax:* 212-529-2716
Key Personnel
Pres & Agent: Robert Lescher (AAR)
E-mail: rl@lescherltd.com
Founded: 1964
Fiction (literary & commercial, including mystery & suspense; no sci-fi, fantasy or romance) & nonfiction (biography, contemporary issues & current affairs, memoir, law, popular culture & narrative history. No spiritual or self-help). Agents in all countries. Handle film & TV rights for clients only. No unsol mss. Query first with SASE. Submit double-spaced synopsis describing project at length & author bio. No fees charged.

Ellen Levine Literary Agency Inc, see Trident Media Group LLC

Levine-Greenberg Literary Agency Inc (L)
307 Seventh Ave, Suite 1906, New York, NY 10001
Tel: 212-337-0934 *Fax:* 212-337-0948
Web Site: www.levinegreenberg.com
Key Personnel
Principal: Daniel Greenberg; James Levine
Agent: Arielle Eckstut; Stephanie Rostan
Admin: Melynda Bissmeyer; Melissa Rowland
Narrative nonfiction, business, technology, psychology, parenting, health, humor, women's, men's, sexuality, education & social issues, popular culture, narrative nonfiction, fiction, cookbooks, sports; query first with resume, outline sample writing & SASE; identify market & competition. Prefer online submissions at www.jameslevine.com, where you have the opportunity to attach sample chapters or a proposal. Handle software, film & TV rights. No reading fee.
Foreign Rights: Agence Hoffman (Germany); Bardon-Chinese Media Agency (China); Elaine Benisti (France); International Editors (Argentina, Brazil); International Literatuur (Netherlands); KCC (Korea); Kiyoshi Asano (Japan); Suzanne Palme Literary Agency (Norway); Pikarski Literary Agency (Israel); Vicki Satlow (Italy); Abner Stein (UK)
Membership(s): ABA

Robert Lieberman Agency (L)
Subsidiary of Ithaca Film & Writing Works
400 Nelson Rd, Ithaca, NY 14850-9440
Tel: 607-273-8801
Web Site: www.people.cornell.edu/pages/RHL10/

Key Personnel
Pres: Robert Lieberman *E-mail:* rhl10@cornell.edu
Founded: 1994
Nonfiction only. Specialize in college level textbooks by established & recognized academics in all fields, as well as trade books in science, math, economics, engineering, medicine, psychology, computers & other academic areas that would be of general or popular interest. Represent producers of CD-ROM/multimedia/software, film & videos that fall into these categories. Submissions can be proposals &/or sample chapters, resume & table of contents. No unsol mss; query first (prefer e-mail query); will give quick response by e-mail but will accept mail query with SASE; handle software; no reading fee.
Titles recently placed: *Analytical Mechanics*, Louis N Hand, Janet D Finch; *College Physics (with CD-ROM)*, Betty Richardson, Alan Giambattista, Robert Richardson; *Conflict Theory*, Bartos, Wehr; *Electronics*, Thorne, Hagen; *Film, Form & Culture*, Robert P Kolker; *Modern Introductory Physics*, C H Holbrow, J N Lloyd, J C Amato; *Pre-Calculus CD-ROM Package*, Jere Confrey, Alan Maloney; *Quantun Mechanics*, Gottfried, Yan, Lepage; *Radio Frequency Electronics*, John B Hagen; *The Computer Wizard Series*, John Mason; *University Physics*, Alan Giambattista, Betty Richardson, Robert Richardson
Foreign Rep(s): East Communications (China)

Ray Lincoln Literary Agency (L)
Elkins Park House, Suite 107-B, 7900 Old York Rd, Elkins Park, PA 19027
Tel: 215-635-0827 *Fax:* 215-782-8019
Key Personnel
Owner: Mrs Ray Lincoln
Contact: Jerome A Lincoln
Founded: 1978
Adult, young adult & juvenile fiction & general nonfiction books; biography, science, nature, history, public affairs & how-to; handle film & TV rights. Handle software when book accepted by publisher. No unsol mss, query with SASE; on request submit outline with SASE in mss form, legible type, regulation-size paper; two sample chapters, no fee for sample. No reading fee but postage fee for full mss accepted for agency representation.

Wendy Lipkind Agency (L)
120 E 81 St, New York, NY 10028
Tel: 212-628-9653 *Fax:* 212-585-1306
E-mail: lipkindag@aol.com
Key Personnel
Contact: Wendy Lipkind (AAR)
No unsol mss; query first with SASE. Film & TV rights handled through co-agents in Hollywood. Agents in Hollywood & in major European countries; do not handle software.
British Agent: Lucas Alexander Whitley.

The Literary Agency Ltd (L)
Division of Bowman Inc
Subsidiary of State of the Art Ltd Publishing
4942 Morrison Rd, Denver, CO 80219
Tel: 303-936-1978 *Toll Free Tel:* 800-261-1797
Fax: 303-936-1770
E-mail: peci4942@aol.com
Web Site: www.peci.cc
Key Personnel
Owner: Harry M Fleenor, Jr
Editorial services, ghostwriting & writing assistance available. Handle software; query first. No unsol mss; query first with SASE. Submit synopsis & sample chapters. For list of services & rates, also send SASE.

Literary & Creative Artists Inc (L)
3543 Albemarle St NW, Washington, DC 20008-
4213
Tel: 202-362-4688 *Fax:* 202-362-8875
E-mail: query@lcadc.com (no attachments)
Web Site: www.lcadc.com
Key Personnel
Pres & Principal Contact: Muriel G Nellis (AAR)
VP: Jane F Roberts (AAR)
Ed: Stephen Ruwe
Founded: 1982
General nonfiction by credentialed authors; fiction, both literary & commercial. No unsol
mss, query first by mail or e-mail with synopsis & outline, author bio (including prior
publications & representation, if any) & SASE.
No fax. Require exclusive review period of two
to three weeks. Full-service agency; access to
collaborative writers/editors, promotion specialists & foreign film, TV & media representatives. Handle derivative rights for film, TV &
full range of multi-media. No reading fee. Visit
our web page for more information.
Membership(s): ABA; Authors Guild

Literary Artists Representatives (L)
575 West End Ave, Suite GRC, New York, NY
10024-2711
Tel: 212-787-3808 *Fax:* 212-595-2098
E-mail: litartists@aol.com
Key Personnel
Pres: Madeline Perrone
VP: Samuel Fleishman
Emphasizes adult trade, nonfiction, (narrative,
biography, memoir, current affairs, business, culture, history, how-to, film/TV, personal finance, sciences, sports, motivational
& mind/body/spirit) & selective quality fiction.
Handle film, TV electronic rights. Co-agents
in Hollywood & other selected cities. No unsol mss, query first with SASE, submit outline,
synopsis, sample chapters; complete mss only
on request. No fees.

The Literary Group International (L-D)
Division of Literary Agency East Inc
270 Lafayette St, Suite 1505, New York, NY
10012
Tel: 212-274-1616 *Fax:* 212-274-9876
Web Site: www.theliterarygroup.com
Key Personnel
Pres: Frank J Weimann *E-mail:* fweimann@
theliterarygroup.com
Agent: Ian Kleinert; Anita Diggs
Specialize in fiction, nonfiction. Accept unsol
mss. For fiction, submit overview & three
chapters. For nonfiction, submit proposal.
Handle film & TV rights. No reading fee. No
screenplays.
Titles recently placed: *Body By God*, Ben Lerner;
Don't Take Any Wooden Nickels, Mindy
Stearns-Clark; *I Heard You Paint Houses*,
Charles Brandt; *Keep It Simple*, Terry Brad-
shaw; *Russell Rules*, Bill Russell; *The Good
Guys*, Bill Bonanno, Joe Pistone; *What a Girl
Wants*, Kristin Billerbeck

Literary Management Group Inc (L)
4238 Morriswood Dr, Nashville, TN 37204
Tel: 615-832-7231 *Fax:* 615-832-7231
Web Site: www.literarymanagementgroup.com;
www.brucebarbour.com
Key Personnel
Pres & CEO: Bruce R Barbour *E-mail:* brb@
brucebarbour.com
Pres: Margaret Langstaff
Founded: 1995
Nonfiction: Christian, motivational & inspira-
tional. No unsol mss; query first with letter
prior to submission of ms for review. Submit
proposal, outline, sample chapters including

return postage. E-mail queries preferred to
brb@brucebarbour.com.
Shipping Address: 4870 Bethesda Rd, Thompson's Station, TN 37179
Membership(s): Christian Booksellers Association; Evangelical Christian Publishers Association

LitWest Group LLC
379 Burning Tree Ct, Half Moon Bay, CA 94019
Web Site: www.litwest.com
Key Personnel
Agent: Katherine Boyle; Linda Mead; Robert
Preskill
Founded: 1983
Nonfiction: business, personal finance, parenting,
women's issues, health & fitness, spiritual, religious, self-help, memoir, travel narrative. Commercial nonfiction; commercial & literary fiction, psychology, history, historicals, mysteries,
thriller. Send one-page cover letter & author
bio, proposal & sample chapter (nonfiction),
synopsis & three chapters (fiction); SASE for
return of materials or answer is a must. Before
submitting refer to website (www.litwest.com)
for individual agent information. No reading
fees.
Titles recently placed: *American Sideshow*, Marc
Hartzman; *Borderline Disorder Demystified*,
Robert Friedel, MD; *Forex Revolution*, Peter
Rosenstreich; *Free Burning*, Bayo Ojikutu;
Hedwig & Berti, Frieda Arkin; *Neoconomy*,
Daniel Altman; *Playing Sick*, Marc Feldman;
Small World, Brad Herzog; *Splendid Omens*,
Robley Wilson; *Successful Harvard Business
School Application Essays*, The Harbus; *The
Essential Nostradamus*, Richard Smoley; *The
Twins of Tribeca*, Rachel Pine
Foreign Rep(s): Sub-agents in Hollywood & all
major countries
Membership(s): The Authors Guild Inc; Women's
National Book Association

Los Angeles Literary Associates (L-D)
6324 Tahoe Dr, Los Angeles, CA 90068-1654
Tel: 323-464-6444 *Fax:* 323-464-6444
Key Personnel
Pres: Andrew Ettinger
Assoc: Heather Hewitt
Founded: 1991
General trade fiction & nonfiction: especially interested in highly commercial novels; popular
sociology & psychology; full range of popular culture topics; inspirational, motivational,
Christian, spiritual works; self-help & how-to
books; professional & business books; humor,
entertainment & personality books. No short
stories, poetry, science fiction, experimental
fiction, pornography, gay or lesbian materials
please. A query letter & outline/proposal required before sample chapters or ms consideration. Also include author background & SASE.
No reading fees. Standard commission of 10
to 15%, depending on author's credentials &
advance payment schedule. Ms development &
consulting fees based on hourly rate plus expenses. Our special agency network is utilized
for film/TV & international rights sales.

Nancy Love Literary Agency (L)
250 E 65 St, Suite 4A, New York, NY 10021
Tel: 212-980-3499 *Fax:* 212-308-6405
Key Personnel
Pres: Nancy Love (AAR)
Agent: Miriam Tager (AAR)
Founded: 1983
Adult fiction (mysteries & thrillers only) & nonfiction. Subjects include: health, medical, spirituality, pop culture, psychology, relationships
& parenting, foreign affairs, women's issues &
narrative nonfiction. No unsol mss, query first
by phone or mail, not fax. Submit proposal,

chapter outline & sample chapters for nonfic-
tion, synopsis & sample chapters for fiction.
No return without SASE. No fax or e-mail sub-
missions. Does not charge fees. Handle film &
TV rights to books, as well as foreign rights,
through sub-agents.
Titles recently placed: *Flat Crazy*, Ben Rehder;
Jack in the Pulpit, Cynthia Riggs; *Third in
Blanco Co, Texis, Mystery Series*, Ben Rehder;
Untitled Back Pain Book, Emile Hiesinger MD,
Marian Betancourt
Membership(s): American Society of Journalists
& Authors; Authors Guild

Lowenstein-Morel Associates Inc, see
Lowenstein-Yost Associates Inc

Lowenstein-Yost Associates Inc (L-D)
121 W 27 St, Suite 601, New York, NY 10001
Tel: 212-206-1630 *Fax:* 212-727-0280
Web Site: www.lowensteinyost.com
Key Personnel
Pres: Barbara Lowenstein (AAR)
Agent: Eileen Cope (AAR); Julie Culver; Dorian
Karchmar (AAR); Nancy K Yost (AAR)
Busn Aff: Norman Kurz
Founded: 1971 (as Lowenstein Associates)
Literary & commercial fiction, suspense/thriller,
women's fiction, historical novels, ethnic, short
story collection & gay & lesbian. Nonfiction
specialties include narrative nonfiction business,
relationships, current affairs, health & science,
biography & autobiography, ethnic, pop culture, psychology, women's studies, Buddhism,
Asian studies, history, contemporary social issues, sports, anthropology, the arts, film & self-
help. We do not represent children's, young
adult or science fiction. Commissions are 15%
domestic & 20% foreign; 20% dramatic. No
unsol mss, send query letter & SASE for fiction; query letter, curriculum vitae & SASE
for nonfiction. Reports within two weeks on
queries & one month on mss. No fees charged.

Lukeman Literary Management Ltd (L-D)
101 N Seventh St, Brooklyn, NY 11211
Tel: 718-599-8988
Web Site: www.lukeman.com
Key Personnel
Pres: Noah T Lukeman
Founded: 1996
No unsol mss, query first with one-page letter
(via e-mail or regular mail) & SASE. Repre-
sent literary & commercial fiction & nonfiction,
covering a wide range of subject matter. Han-
dle film & TV rights. No reading fee.
Titles recently placed: *American Terrorist: Tim-
othy McVeigh & the Oklahoma City Bombing*,
Lou Michel, Dan Herbeck; *Climbing Higher*,
Montel Williams, Larry Grobel; *Fire Point*,
John Smolens; *Justice for None*, Gene Hack-
man, Daniel Lenihan; *The Wisdom of Forgive-
ness*, Victor Chan; *You Remind Me of Me*, Dan
Chaon

Donald Maass Literary Agency (L)
160 W 95 St, Suite 1-B, New York, NY 10025
Tel: 212-866-8200 *Fax:* 212-866-8181
E-mail: dmla@mindspring.com
Key Personnel
Pres: Donald Maass (AAR)
Agent: Jennifer Jackson (AAR)
Rts Dir & Asst Agent: Rachel Vater (AAR)
 Tel: 212-866-8200 ext 11 *E-mail:* rvater@
maassagency.com
Asst Agent: Cameron McClure
Founded: 1980
Fiction only. No unsol mss, query first with one-
page letter, first five pages of novel & SASE.
Handle film & TV rights. No reading fee.
Titles recently placed: *Dragonsblood*, Todd Mc-
Caffrey; *No Graves As Yet*, Ann Perry; *Save*

One, Gregg Keizer; *The House of Gaian*, Anne Bishop; *The Salt Roads*, Nalo Hopkinson
Foreign Rights: Agence Hoffman (France); Agenzia Letteraria Internazionale (Italy); Alexandria Literary Agency (Russia); The English Agency, Owl's Agency (Japan); International Editors Co (South America, Spain); Lennart Sane Agency AB (Denmark, Netherlands, Finland, Norway, Sweden); MBA Literary Agents Ltd (UK); ONK Agency Ltd (Turkey); Prava I Prevodi (Czech Republic & Poland, Romania, Serbia and Montenegro); Rogan-Pikarski (Israel); Thomas Schluck (Germany); Eric Yang Agency (Korea)
Membership(s): Authors Guild; Mystery Writers of America; Romance Writers of America; Science Fiction & Fantasy Writers of America

Gina Maccoby Literary Agency (L)
PO Box 60, Chappaqua, NY 10514-0060
Tel: 914-238-5630 *Fax:* 914-238-5239
Key Personnel
Principal: Gina Maccoby (AAR)
Founded: 1986
Fiction & nonficton for adults & children. Handle film & TV rights. No unsol mss; query first with SASE. No reading fee, but may recover the costs of photocopying mss for submission, airmail shipping of books &/or mss overseas, overnight shipping domestically if requested by client & legal fees incurred with prior client approval. Agents in Hollywood & many foreign countries.
Foreign Rep(s): A M Heath & Co
Membership(s): The Authors Guild Inc

The Robert Madsen Literary Agency (L-D)
1331 E 34 St, Suite 1, Oakland, CA 94602
Tel: 510-223-2090
Key Personnel
Sr Ed: Liz Madsen
Fiction & nonfiction; science fiction/fantasy, action adventure/thriller, mystery, true crime, romance, men's western, humor, how-to, self-help, science, history, political, military, social & environmental. Accept unsol mss. Submit first 50 pages, double spaced, hand copy, synopsis, cover letter & SASE. No reading fees. Handle film & TV rights.
Titles recently placed: *The Art of War*, Sun Tzu

Carol Mann Agency (L)
55 Fifth Ave, New York, NY 10003
Tel: 212-206-5635 *Fax:* 212-675-4809
Key Personnel
Pres: Carol Mann (AAR)
Subs Rts: Kristy Mayer
Agent: Emily Nurkin (AAR) *Tel:* 212-206-5634
Founded: 1977
Literary & commercial fiction, no genre fiction, general nonfiction. Sub-agents in Los Angeles & for all foreign languages. No unsol mss, query first for submissions. Do not fax or e-mail query. No reading fee. Handle film & TV rights for book clients only. Fiction, synopsis & bio; nonfiction, outline, bio & sample chapters; always with SASE.

Freya Manston Associates Inc (L)
145 W 58 St, New York, NY 10019
Tel: 212-247-3075
Key Personnel
Pres: Freya Manston
Fiction & nonfiction. No unsol mss; not accepting new queries at this time. Agents in all principal countries.

Manus & Associates Literary Agency Inc (L)
445 Park Ave, New York, NY 10022
Mailing Address: 425 Sherman Ave, Suite 200, Palo Alto, CA 94306

Tel: 650-470-5151 (CA) *Fax:* 650-470-5159 (CA)
E-mail: manuslit@manuslit.com
Web Site: www.manuslit.com
Key Personnel
Chmn, New York Office: Janet Wilkens Manus (AAR) *E-mail:* manuslitny@aol.com
Pres, California Office: Jillian W Manus (AAR) *E-mail:* jillian@manuslit.com
Assoc, California Office: Stephanie Lee (AAR) *E-mail:* slee@manuslit.com; Jandy Nelson (AAR) *E-mail:* Jandy@ManusLit.com
General fiction & dramatic nonfiction books, TV & motion picture rights. No unsol mss. Fiction: query with synopsis & first 30 pages. Nonfiction: query letter & proposal. No reading fee. Offices in NY & CA; representatives in all major foreign countries. The New York office does NOT accept any unsol mss.
Foreign Rep(s): Danny Baror (World)
Foreign Rights: Baror International

March Tenth Inc (L)
4 Myrtle St, Haworth, NJ 07641
Tel: 201-387-6551 *Fax:* 201-387-6552
Key Personnel
Pres: Sandra Choron *E-mail:* schoron@aol.com
VP: Harry Choron *E-mail:* hchoron@aol.com
Founded: 1980
General nonfiction & fiction; specialize in popular culture. No unsol mss, query first with letter & SASE. Submit outline & sample chapter. No reading fee. Book production services available; 15% commission. Handle film & TV rights.
Titles recently placed: *Fourth of July, Asbury Park*, Daniel Wolff; *The 100 Simple Secrets of Happy Families*, David Niven

Denise Marcil Literary Agency Inc (L)
156 Fifth Ave, Suite 625, New York, NY 10010
Tel: 212-337-3402 *Fax:* 212-727-2688
Key Personnel
Pres & Agent: Denise Marcil (AAR)
Agent: Maura Kye
Founded: 1977
Commercial fiction especially contemporary women's fiction, thrillers, historical fiction & multicultural fiction. Nonfiction: intelligent self-help & how-to's including health, alternative health, parenting, business, business self-help (careers), psychology & relationships.
Titles recently placed: *A New Lu*, Laura Castoro; *No Way Home*, Peter Spiegelman; *The Baby Sleep Book*, Dr William Sears, Martha Sears, Dr Robert Sears, James Sears; *The Back Up Plan*, Sherryl Woods; *You Want Me to Work With Who*, Julie Jansen
Foreign Rights: Eliane Benisti (France); Kristin Oson (Czech Republic); Thomas Schluck (Germany); Abner Stein (England)

Elaine Markson Literary Agency Inc (L)
44 Greenwich Ave, New York, NY 10011
Tel: 212-243-8480 *Fax:* 212-691-9014
Key Personnel
Contact: Elaine Markson (AAR); Elizabeth Sheinkman; Geri Thoma (AAR)
Literary fiction & nonfiction. No unsol mss.
Foreign Rights: Liepman (Germany); MBagencia Literaria; La Nouvelle Agence (France); Vicki Satlow (Italy); Elizabeth Sheinkman

Mildred Marmur Associates Ltd (L)
2005 Palmer Ave, PMB 127, Larchmont, NY 10538
Tel: 914-834-1170 *Fax:* 914-834-2840
E-mail: marmur@westnet.com
Key Personnel
Pres: Mildred Marmur (AAR)

Fiction & nonfiction. No unsol mss; not accepting new queries at this time. Represented in Hollywood & foreign markets. Does not charge fees.

The Evan Marshall Agency (L)
6 Tristam Place, Pine Brook, NJ 07058-9445
Tel: 973-882-1122 *Fax:* 973-882-3099
Web Site: www.thenovelist.com
Key Personnel
Pres: Evan Marshall (AAR) *E-mail:* evanmarshall@thenovelist.com
Founded: 1987
Fiction. No unsol mss, query first with SASE. No reading fee. Representatives in Hollywood & foreign countries.
Membership(s): Mystery Writers of America

The Martell Agency (L-D)
545 Madison Ave, 7th fl, New York, NY 10022
Tel: 212-317-2672 *Fax:* 212-317-2676
Key Personnel
Contact: Stephanie Finman
Owner: Alice Fried Martell *E-mail:* afmartell@aol.com
Founded: 1985
Fiction & nonfiction. Handle film & TV rights. Submit query letters only, market analysis of nonfiction & author biography. Mss not returned. No reading fee. Represented in foreign markets.
Foreign Rep(s): Elaine Benisti (France); Bookbank SL (Spain); Jill Hughes Agent (Eastern Europe); Lennart Sane Agency (Sweden); Liepman Agency (Switzerland); Living Agency (Italy); Sara Menguc (UK); Tuttle Mori Agency (Japan)

Martin Literary Management (L)
17328 Ventura Blvd, Suite 138, Encino, CA 91316
Tel: 818-595-1130
Web Site: www.martinliterarymanagement.com
Key Personnel
Literary Mgr: Sharlene Martin *E-mail:* sharlene@martinliterarymanagement.com
Founded: 2003
Nonfiction books only. Online queries welcomed. No fees charged.
Titles recently placed: *Both Sides Now*, Dillon Khosla; *But You Knew That Already: What a Psychic Can Teach You About Life*, Dougall Fraser; *Champion-Success Within*, Lisa Nysocky; *Front of the Class*, Brad Cohen; *The Mommie Chronicles*, Sara Ellington, Stephanie Triplett
Foreign Rep(s): Danny Baror International (Worldwide)

Martin-McLean Literary Associates (L)
1602 S Cerritos Dr, Suite D, Palm Springs, CA 92264
Tel: 760-320-4552 *Fax:* 760-323-8792
E-mail: martinmcleanlit@aol.com
Web Site: www.martinmcleanlit.com; www.mcleanlit.com
Key Personnel
CEO & Agent: Lisa Ann Martin
Founded: 1986
Literary fiction, nonfiction, health issues, psychology, how-to, self-help, sports, new thought, critical thinking, scholarly, bio, memoirs, autobiographies & murder mystery. Requirements: send proposal with SASE, or call for agency brochure. Evaluation fee for 4 written pages is $250, which is refundable from standard 15% commission; work at $60/hr. New writers welcome.
Available: editing, proposal development, critique. Book development available. Ghost writers can be matched to author. Agents worldwide with Internet access.

Titles recently placed: *Age Reversal*, Skein; *Defensive Polo Handbook*, Kelly; *Hippies*, Jedick; *Lakota Conspiracy*, Garing; *Little Tricks for Dealing With Teenagers*, Hanks; *Reading to Heal*, Stanley; *The Spitting Image*, Lembcke; *Who Killed Public TV?*, Smith

Harold Matson Co Inc (L)
276 Fifth Ave, New York, NY 10001
Tel: 212-679-4490 *Fax:* 212-545-1224
E-mail: hmatsco@aol.com
Key Personnel
Agent: Ben Camardi (AAR); Jonathan Matson (AAR)
Founded: 1937
No unsol mss, query first with SASE. No reading fee. Handle film & TV rights. No screenplays.
Foreign Rep(s): Intercontinental Literary Agency (Europe); Abner Stein (UK)
Membership(s): Authors Guild

Jed Mattes Inc (L)
2095 Broadway, Suite 302, New York, NY 10023-2895
Tel: 212-595-5228 *Fax:* 212-595-5232
E-mail: general@jedmattes.com
Key Personnel
Pres: Fred Morris
Founded: 1989
Fiction & nonfiction. Handle film & TV rights. No unsol mss; query first. No reading fee. Agents in many foreign countries.
Foreign Rep(s): Greene & Heaton Ltd (UK); The Marsh Agency

MARGRET McBRIDE
L I T E R A R Y   A G E N C Y

Margret McBride Literary Agency (L)
7744 Fay Ave, Suite 201, La Jolla, CA 92037
Tel: **858-454-1550** *Fax:* **858-454-2156**
E-mail: **staff@mcbridelit.com**
Web Site: **www.mcbrideliterary.com**
Key Personnel
VP & Assoc Agent: Donna De Gutis
Agent: Margret McBride (AAR)
Founded: 1981
Specializes in fiction, nonfiction & business. No poetry, romance, children's or screenplays. No unsol mss, query first. Submit query & synopsis or outline with SASE. Send queries to the La Jolla office only. No e-mail or fax queries. No reading fee.
Foreign rights sub-agents in all major countries.
Membership(s): Writers Guild of America

E J McCarthy Agency (L)
21 Columbus Ave, Suite 210, San Francisco, CA 94111
Tel: 415-296-7706 *Fax:* 415-296-7706
E-mail: ejmagency@mac.com
Key Personnel
Owner: E J McCarthy
Founded: 2003
Independent literary agency. Subject specialties: history, military history, politics, sports, biography, media, memoir, thrillers, other nonfiction. Submissions should be double-spaced, single-sided, unbound pages. Use a standard serif typeface like Courier. Don't justify right margin. Type 25 lines of 60 characters or about 250 words per page. Number pages consecutively from beginning to end, not by chapter.

No reading fee. Query first by mail or regular mail. Phone calls okay.
Titles recently placed: *Hammer From Above*, Jay A Stout; *No Tearless Victory*, Nathaniel Fick; *The Sling & the Stone*, Thomas X Hammes
Foreign Rights: Baror International (World)

Gerard McCauley Agency Inc (L)
PO Box 844, Katonah, NY 10536-0844
Tel: 914-232-5700 *Fax:* 914-232-1506
Key Personnel
Pres: Gerard McCauley (AAR)
E-mail: gerrymccauley@earthlink.net
Founded: 1970
Nonfiction; educational materials. No unsol mss. Representatives in all major foreign countries. Not currently considering new mss. Does not charge fees.
Titles recently placed: *Heavens and the Earth*, William McDougall; *Jack Johnson*, Ken Burns; *Ruins of the Empire*, Ronald Spector; *Willow Temple*, Donald Hall

Anita D McClellan Associates (L-D)
50 Stearns St, Cambridge, MA 02138
Tel: 617-576-5960 *Fax:* 617-576-6950
Key Personnel
Agent: Anita McClellan (AAR) *Tel:* 781-283-2560 *E-mail:* amcclell@wellesley.edu
General fiction & nonfiction, including feminism. No unsol mss, mail queries only, no work previously submitted to publishers. Submit outline or synopsis & first chapter with SASE, no certified mail, no submissions returned. Handle film & TV rights. No software. No reading fees charged.

Helen McGrath & Associates (L)
1406 Idaho Ct, Concord, CA 94521
Tel: 925-672-6211 *Fax:* 925-672-6383
E-mail: hmcgrath_lit@yahoo.com
Key Personnel
Owner: Helen McGrath
Founded: 1977
Fiction & nonfiction books for general trade. Film & TV rights for books already sold. Do not accept unsol mss. Submit first three chapters & synopsis for fiction. Annotated table of contents, first 50 pages & resume for nonfiction. Charge 15% commission & expect author to supply photocopies & copies of books for foreign sales.
Foreign Rights: A S Bookman (Denmark); Agence Hoffman (France, Germany); Agenzia Letteraria Internazionale (Italy); Anthea Literary Agency (Bulgaria); Jane Conway-Gordon (UK); Raquel de la Concha (Spain); The English Agency (Japan); Imprima Korea (Korea); Lorna Soifer (Israel); Maria Strarz-Kanska Literary Agency (Poland)
Membership(s): Authors Guild; California Writers Club; Women's National Book Association

McHugh Literary Agency
1033 Lyon Rd, Moscow, ID 83843-9167
Tel: 208-882-0107 *Fax:* 847-628-0146
Key Personnel
Agent: Elisabet McHugh *E-mail:* elisabetmch@turbonet.com
Founded: 1994
Titles recently placed: *Clark Gable*, Chrys Spicer; *Crimson Sky: The Air Battle for Korea*, John R Bruning; *Deadly Intent*, Chris Walker; *Insignificant Murder*, Eric Peterson; *Jungle Ace: The Gerald Johnson Story*, John R Bruning; *Last Revenge*, Terry Anderson; *Never Again*, Sandra Walker; *Not For Love*, Jessica McIntyre; *Off the Hook: Reflections and Recipes From an Old Salt*, Roger Fitzgerald; *Summer Rain*, T R Evans; *Take His Heart*, Amanda S Long;

Voices From the Home Front: Women's Personal Recollections of WWII, Pauline Parker (editor)

McIntosh & Otis Inc (L)
353 Lexington Ave, Suite 1500, New York, NY 10016-0900
Tel: 212-687-7400 *Fax:* 212-687-6894
E-mail: info@mcintoshandotis.com
Key Personnel
Pres: Eugene H Winick (AAR)
Electronic, Multi-Media Rts & Agents Adult: Samuel L Pinkus (AAR)
Agent, Adult Fiction & Nonfiction, Subs Rts & Foreign Rts: Elizabeth Winick (AAR)
Assoc Agent & Mgr, Subs Rts: Henry Williams
Film, TV, Stage Rts: Evva Joan Pryor
Royalty Admin: Lorraine Stubits
Agent, Children & Juv: Edward Necarsulmer, IV (AAR)
Adult & juvenile literary fiction & nonfiction books. No unsol mss. Query first with SASE. Submit outline & sample chapters. No reading fee. Handle film & TV rights for represented clients only. Agents in most major foreign countries.
Foreign Rep(s): Bardon-Chinese Media (Mainland China, Taiwan); Luigi Bernabo (Italy); Bookman (Denmark, Scandinavia); Julio F-Yanez (Latin America, Portugal, Spain); Japan Uni (Japan); Nuricham Kesim (Turkey); La Novvelle Agence (France); Mohrbooks (Germany); Andrew Nurenburg (Eastern Europe); Prava I Prevodi Agency (Eastern Europe); Abner Stein (UK); Tuttle-Mori (Japan); Van Geldren (Netherlands)

McLean Literary Agency, see Nixon Agency

McLean Literary Associates, see Martin-McLean Literary Associates

Sally Hill McMillan & Associates Inc (L)
429 E Kingston Ave, Charlotte, NC 28203
Tel: 704-334-0897 *Fax:* 704-334-1897
E-mail: mcmagency@aol.com
Key Personnel
Pres: Sally McMillan (AAR)
Founded: 1990
Southern fiction & adult trade nonfiction; no unsol mss, query first with table of contents, sample chapter & overview. No reading fee. Handle film, TV, foreign & electronic rights through sub-agents.
Titles recently placed: *A Clean Kill*, Mike Stewart; *Fire in the Rock*, Joe Martin; *Forever Friends*, Lynne Hinton; *Home Across the Road*, Nancy Peacock; *Life a' la Mode*, Linda Lenhoff; *The Last Odd Day*, Lynne Hinton
Membership(s): Publishers Association of the South

Claudia Menza Literary Agency (L-D)
1170 Broadway, Suite 807, New York, NY 10001
Tel: 212-889-6850
E-mail: menzacmla@aol.com
Key Personnel
Owner & Pres: Claudia Menza (AAR)
Founded: 1983
Adult fiction & nonfiction & photographic books. Specializing in work by & about African-Americans. No romance, children's books or poetry. No unsol mss, query first. Submit cover letter, outline (for nonfiction), author bio, 25-page sample (for nonfiction or fiction). No reading fee; commission only. Handle limited TV & film rights. E-mail queries are not accepted.
Membership(s): PEN American Center

Scott Meredith Literary Agency LP (L)
200 W 57 St, Suite 904, New York, NY 10019
Tel: 646-274-1970 *Fax:* 212-977-5997
Web Site: www.writingtosell.com
Key Personnel
Pres: Arthur M Klebanoff
Dir, Subs Rts: Mary JoAnne Valko-Warner
Ed & Dir, Subs Rts: Barry Malzberg
Founded: 1946
More than 1,500 titles in print. Query first. Reading & critique fee of $450.
Titles recently placed: *Celebrate! Cookbook*, Sheila Lukins; *Guide to the Birds of the Eastern United States, 5th Edition*; *Janson History of Art, 6th Edition*, Roger Tory Peterson; *Mayo Clinic Family Health Book, 3rd Edition*; *Shut the Door*, Amanda Marquit; *Sullivan's Law*, Nancy Taylor Rosenberg; *The Value Factor*, Lars Nyberg, Mark Hurd; *True to Our Roots*, Paul Dolan

Mews Books Ltd (L)
20 Bluewater Hill, Westport, CT 06880
Tel: 203-227-1836 *Fax:* 203-227-1144
E-mail: mewsbooks@aol.com
Key Personnel
Pres: Sidney B Kramer
Asst: Fran Pollak
Founded: 1975
Adult fiction & nonfiction, specialize in young adult & juvenile, cookery, parenting, medical & scientific material both technical as well as for the layman, college texts. Also offer consultation with authors & publishers as to contractual, copyright & negotiation matters by attorney. International representation: all major markets by sub-agents. No unsol mss. Query first. Submit two sample chapters with descriptive summary presentable to publisher's editor by mail with SASE. Handle film & TV rights directly & by sub-agents. Handle electronic rights. Does not charge a reading fee. Charges for photocopying, postage expenses, telephone calls & other direct costs.

Helmut Meyer Literary Agency (L)
330 E 79 St, New York, NY 10021
Tel: 212-288-2421 *Cable:* MEYERBOOKS NEWYORK
Key Personnel
Owner: Helmut Meyer
Novel-length fiction; trade nonfiction & autobiographic material; foreign rights; motion picture & TV rights. No unsol mss, query first by telephone. Submit outline & sample chapters with SASE. No reading fee. Representatives & agents in all major foreign countries.

Jenny Meyer Literary Agency (L)
115 W 29 St, 10th fl, New York, NY 10001-5106
Tel: 212-564-9898 *Fax:* 212-564-6044
E-mail: jenny@meyerlit.com
Handle trade fiction & nonfiction, specializing in international properties. Represent agents, publishers, authors worldwide (excluding Asia) directly. No unsol mss; query first. Submit outline & sample chapters. No reading fee.

Doris S Michaels Literary Agency Inc (L)
1841 Broadway, Suite 903, New York, NY 10023
Tel: 212-265-9474 *Fax:* 212-265-9480
E-mail: info@dsmagency.com
Web Site: www.dsmagency.com
Key Personnel
Pres: Doris S Michaels (AAR)
Founded: 1994
Adult fiction: literary fiction that has a commercial appeal & strong screen potential & women's fiction. Adult nonfiction: business, current affairs, biography & memoirs, self-help, history, health, classical music, art, sports, women's issues, computers & pop culture. No

unsol mss, query first with e-mail according to the submission guidelines on our website at www.dsmagency.com. Read the home page carefully to determine the types of books we are interested in representing before sending query. No regular mail inquiries. No phone call inquiries. Handle film & TV rights through Hollywood co-agents. No reading fee.
Titles recently placed: *Healing Conversations: What to Say When You Don't Know What to Say*, Nance Guilmartin; *How to Make Big Money in Your Own Small Business*, Jeffrey J Fox; *Secrets of the Great Rainmakers*, Jeffrey J Fox
Foreign Rights: Agence Eliane Benisti (France); Bardon-Chinese Media Agency (China); Raquel de la Concha (Spain & Latin America); Ann-Christine Danielsson Agency (Scandinavia); Japan Uni (Japan); Simona Kessler International Copyright Agency (Romania); Lijnkamp Literary Agents (Netherlands); Literarni Agentura (Czech Republic); Piergiorgio Nicolazzini Literary Agency (Italy); OA Literary Agency (Greece); Pikarsky Literary Agency (Israel); Thomas Schlueck (Germany); Abner Stein (UK); Eric Yang Agency (Korea)

Linda Michaels Ltd International Literary Agents (L)
344 Main St, Lakeville, CT 06039-0567
Mailing Address: PO Box 567, Lakeville, CT 06039-0567
Tel: 860-435-1432 *Fax:* 860-435-1446
E-mail: lmlagency@aol.com
Key Personnel
Contact: Linda Michaels
International properties, both fiction & nonfiction to sell in US & abroad & in rights representation for agents, publishers & packagers worldwide. Fiction & nonfiction. No unsol mss.

Martha Millard Literary Agency (L-D)
50 W 67 St, Suite 1-G, New York, NY 10023
Tel: 212-787-7769 *Fax:* 212-787-7867
E-mail: marmillink@aol.com
Key Personnel
Prop: Martha Millard (AAR)
Founded: 1980
Handle film & TV rights. Handle software subsidiary to book deals. No unsol mss. Not currently reading queries. No e-mail or fax queries. No fees. Representatives in principal countries.
Titles recently placed: *A Shower Of Stars*, Nancy Herkness; *Backfire*, Peter Burrows; *Coyote Frontier*, Allen Steele
Foreign Rep(s): MBA Literary Agents Ltd (UK)
Foreign Rights: Agenzia Letteraria Internazionale (Italy); Paul & Peter Fritz AG (Germany); International Editors Co (Spain); Menno Kohn (Netherlands); Ulla Lohren (Scandinavia); Owl's Agency Inc (Japan); Prava I Prevodi (Eastern Europe); VVV Agency (France)
Membership(s): Science Fiction & Fantasy Writers of America

The Miller Agency Inc (L)
One Sheridan Sq 7B, No 32, New York, NY 10014
Tel: 212-206-0913 *Fax:* 212-206-1473
Web Site: milleragency.net
Key Personnel
Pres: Angela Miller *E-mail:* angela@milleragency.net
Admin: Joan Ward
Fiction & nonfiction. No unsol mss, query first with SASE, cover letter & outline. Handle software, film & TV rights. No reading fee. Sub-agents in all principle foreign countries.

Montreal-Contacts/The Rights Agency (L)
PO Box 596-C, Montreal, PQ H2L 4K4, Canada

Tel: 450-461-1575 *Fax:* 450-461-1505
Key Personnel
Partner: Claude Choquette *E-mail:* cchoquette@montreal-contacts.com; Luc Jutras *E-mail:* ljutras@montreal-contacts.com
Founded: 1981
Represents publishers &/or literary agents exclusively for foreign rights. No author representation. Does not handle original mss. Representation in all principal countries.
Branch Office(s)
Montreal-Contacts/The Rights Agency, 70 bd de Picpus, 75012 Paris, France *Tel:* (01) 43 40 06 10 *Fax:* (01) 43 40 02 12 *E-mail:* aconfuron@montreal-contacts.com
Foreign Rights: Agenzia Letteraria (Italy); Bardon-Chinese Media Agency (China, Taiwan); Bookman Agency (Denmark, Finland, Iceland, Norway, Sweden); Daniele Doglioli Agenzia Letteraria (Italy); Hagenbach & Bender GmbH (Austria, Germany, Switzerland); Inter-Ko Corp (Korea); International Editor's Co (Latin America); The International Press Agency (South Africa); Japan Uni Agency (Japan); Lex Copyright Office (Hungary); Ilidia da Fonseca Matos (Portugal); MBA Literary Agents (UK); Nurcihan Kesim Literary AGency (Turkey); O A Literary Agency (Greece); Permissions & Rights (Estonia, Latvia, Lithuania, Russia); I Pikarski Literary Agency (Israel); Prava i Prevodi (Bulgaria, Croatia, Czech Republic, Poland, Romania, Slovak Republic, Slovenia, Serbia and Montenegro); Silkroad Agency (Thailand); Julio F Yanez Agencia Literaria (Spain)

Moore Literary Agency (L)
10 State St, Suite 309, Newburyport, MA 01950
Tel: 978-465-9015 *Fax:* 978-465-8817
Key Personnel
Pres: Claudette Moore *E-mail:* cmoore@moorelit.com
Contact: Debbie McKenna *E-mail:* dmckenna@moorelit.com
Founded: 1989
High tech books & select nonfiction. No unsol mss, query first. Submit proposal or outline & sample chapter. No reading fee.
Titles recently placed: *Lessons Learned in Software Testing*, Cem Kanen, James Bach, Bret Pettichord; *Microsoft Windows XP Inside Out*, Ed Bott, Carl Siechert, Craig Stinson; *Programming Windows with C#*, Charles Petzold; *This Wired Home*, Alan Neibauer

Maureen Moran Agency (L)
PO Box 20191, Park West Sta, New York, NY 10025-1518
Tel: 212-222-3838 *Fax:* 212-531-3464
E-mail: maureenm@erols.com
Key Personnel
Owner: Maureen Moran
Book-length fiction for adult market. Specialize in women's fiction. Handle film & TV rights. No unpublished writers. No unsol mss, query first. Submit outline with SASE. No reading fee.

Howard Morhaim Literary Agency Inc (L)
11 John St, Suite 407, New York, NY 10038
Tel: 212-529-4433 *Fax:* 212-995-1112
Key Personnel
Pres: Howard Morhaim (AAR)
General adult, fiction & nonfiction. Accept unsol fiction mss. Submit sample chapters & outline with SASE. No unsol nonfiction mss, query first. No reading fee. Handle film & TV rights. Representatives in all principal foreign markets.
Foreign Rep(s): Baror International (Brazil, Netherlands, Eastern Europe, France & Germany, Greece, Israel, Italy, Japan, Russia, Scandinavia); RDC Agencia Literaria (Spain); Abner Stein (UK)

William Morris Agency (L-D)
1325 Avenue of the Americas, New York, NY
  10019
Tel: 212-586-5100 *Fax:* 212-903-1418
E-mail: wma@interport.net
Web Site: www.wma.com *Telex:* 62-0165 *Cable:*
  WILLMORRIS
Key Personnel
Worldwide Head of Lit Oper: Owen Laster
  (AAR)
Head, NY Lit Dept: Suzanne Gluck (AAR); Jen-
  nifer Rudolph Walsh (AAR)
Agent: Mel Berger (AAR)
Contact: Virginia Barber (AAR); Joni Evans
  (AAR); Tracy Fisher (AAR); Jay Mandel
  (AAR)
All subjects; handle software, film & TV rights.
  No unsol mss, query first; no reading fee.
Branch Office(s)
151 El Camino Dr, Beverly Hills, CA 90212
Tel: 310-859-4000
Foreign Office(s): Stratton House, One Strat-
  ton St, London W1X 6HB, United Kingdom
  Tel: (020) 7355 8500 *Fax:* (020) 7355 8600

Henry Morrison Inc (L)
PO Box 235, Bedford Hills, NY 10507-0235
Tel: 914-666-3500 *Fax:* 914-241-7846
Key Personnel
Pres: Henry Morrison
Founded: 1965
Fiction & nonfiction, screenplays. Handle film
  & TV rights. Accept unsol mss but must send
  query & outline first with SASE; no reading
  fee. Fee for ms copies, galleys, bound books
  for foreign & movie sales & ordering books for
  sub rights.
Titles recently placed: *Shadow Brook*, Beverly
  Swerling; *The Jewel House*, Christopher Hyde;
  The Motion of Light in Water, Samuel R De-
  lany; *The Tristan Betrayal*, Robert Ludlum;
  Truman on Leadership, Alan Axelrod

Multimedia Product Development Inc, see
  Browne & Miller Literary Associates

Mysterious Content (L)
Affiliate of Walking Bass Literary Agency
108 E 38 St, Suite 409, New York, NY 10016
Tel: 212-925-3721
E-mail: myscontent@aol.com
Key Personnel
Owner: Deborah Carter
Founded: 1998
An independent literary agency focusing on editorial development & the sale & administration
  of print, performance & foreign rights to literary works. Seeks storytellers from all walks
  of life with narrative voices that capture the
  reader. Those who submit should be receptive
  to editorial feedback & willing to revise. Writers should be aware of books like their own
  for sale in bookstores. Areas of interest: mysteries with literary merit, thrillers, suspense,
  espionage, crime fiction, action/adventure,
  military fiction; literary novels & short story
  collections; contemporary popular fiction (no
  romance, sci-fi or fantasy), children's fiction
  & nonfiction (mostly middle grade & young
  adult), narrative nonfiction: memoir, travel,
  sports, gardening, music & writing (please
  query other subjects). Standard 15% domestic
  & 20% subrights. All expenses pre-approved
  by the client (photocopying, postage). Prefers
  query by e-mail with no attachments. See web
  page at Publishers Marketplace for list of conferences.
Titles recently placed: *The Fund*, Wes De Mott

Bonnie Nadell Literary Agency, see Frederick
  Hill Bonnie Nadell Literary Agency

Jean V Naggar Literary Agency (L)
216 E 75 St, Suite 1-E, New York, NY 10021
Tel: 212-794-1082
Key Personnel
Subs Rts Dir & Agent, Children's Books: Jennifer
  Weltz (AAR)
Contact, Nonfiction only: Anne Engel
Contact: Jean Naggar (AAR); Alice Tasman
  (AAR); Mollie Glick
Founded: 1978
Trade & mass market fiction & nonfiction. Mo-
  tion picture, TV & foreign representation, film
  & TV rights for the books represented. No un-
  sol mss, query first with SASE; submit syn-
  opsis & sample chapter; no reading fee; com-
  missions: 15% domestic, 20% UK & foreign
  translation.
Titles recently placed: *A Hole in the Universe*,
  Mary McGarry Morris; *Ardor*, Lily Prior; *Be-
  neath Dark Water*, Nancy Connor; *Claire &
  Present Danger*, Gillian Roberts; *Dissolu-
  tion*, Christopher Sansom; *Fingersmith*, Sarah
  Waters; *Happily Married With Kids*, Carol
  Lindquist; *In the Salt Marsh*, Nancy Willard;
  Ironfire, David Ball; *Olivia Kidney*, Ellen Pot-
  ter; *Quantico Rules*, Gene Riehl; *The Average
  Human*, Ellen Toby-Potter; *The Hell Screen*,
  Ingrid Parker; *The Info Nesa*, Ed Regis; *The
  Snow Fox*, Susan Fromberg Schaeffer; *Ties
  That Bind*, Phillip Margolin; *Tiger Claws*, Joey
  Schauer; *Trust Me*, Judy Markey; *When the
  Messenger is Hot*, Elizabeth Crane
Foreign Rep(s): Ackali (Turkey); Luigi Bern-
  abo (Italy); Big Apple Tuttle-Mori Agency
  Inc (Japan, Mainland China, Taiwan); Peter
  Bolza (Hungary); Carol Heaton/Elaine Green
  Ltd (UK); Graal (Poland); Greene & Heaton
  (UK); ICA-Simona Kessler (Romania); Interna-
  tional Editors (Brazil & South America, Latin
  America, Portugal & Spain); JLM (Greece);
  Michelle Lapautre Literary Agency (France);
  Licht & Burr (Scandinavia); Ruth Liepman AG
  (Germany); Andrew Nurnberg (Baltic States,
  Bulgaria, Czech Republic, Netherlands, Rus-
  sia); PLIMA (Serbia and Montenegro); PT In-
  fozone (Indonesia); Rogan-Pikarski Agency
  (Israel); Silk Road (Thailand); Tuttle-Mori
  Agency Ltd (Japan); Eric Yang (Korea)

B K Nelson Inc Literary Agency (L-D)
Division of B K Nelson Inc
1565 Paseo Vida, Palm Springs, CA 92264
Tel: 760-778-8800 *Fax:* 914-778-0034
E-mail: bknelson4@cs.com
Web Site: www.bknelson.com
Key Personnel
Pres: Bonita K Nelson
VP, West Coast: Leonard Ashbach
Edit Dir, East Coast: John W Benson
CFO: Corp Reed

Off Mgr: Ellen Rosenfeld
Acctg Dept: Erwin Rosenfeld
Founded: 1980
Fiction & nonfiction, business, self-help, autobiography, political, modeling, fashions,
  cookbooks, trivia, stage plays, musicals,
  movies, TV, computer generated animated
  features, CD-ROM projects. Editorial services; reprints; Lecture Bureau. No unsol
  mss, query with SASE. Submit outline &
  sample chapters. Reading fee. Prompt service. Deals directly with foreign publishers.
  Handle software & film & TV rights.
Branch Office(s)
84 Woodland Rd, Pleasantville, NY 10570-1322
Tel: 914-741-1322 *Fax:* 914-741-1324
Foreign Rep(s): David Bolt Associates (England); McKee & Mouche (France, Germany); Tuttle-Mori Agency (Japan); Ulla
  Lohren Literary Agency (Scandinavia)
Foreign Rights: Alexandra Chapman
Membership(s): American Association of Uni-
  versity Women; Authors Guild; Dramatists
  Guild; NACA; National Association for Fe-
  male Executives
See Ad in this Section

Nelson Literary Agency LLC (L)
1020 15 St, Suite 26L, Denver, CO 80202
Tel: 303-463-5301 *Fax:* 720-384-0761
E-mail: query@nelsonagency.com
Web Site: nelsonagency.com
Key Personnel
Agent: Kristin Nelson
Literary Asst: Angie Hodapp
Founded: 2002
Accepts queries by e-mail only. Represents fiction
  & nonfiction. Does not acccept short story col-
  lection, mysteries, thrillers, Christian, horror,
  young adult, children's or screenplays. See web
  site for additional submission guidelines.
Titles recently placed: *An Accidental Goddess*,
  Linnea Sinclair; *Bachelorette #1*, Jennifer
  O'Connell; *Chair Shots and Other Obstacles:
  Winning Life's Wrestling Matches*, Bobby "the
  Brain" Heenan, Steve Anderson; *Dress Re-
  hearsal*, Jennifer O'Connell; *Finders Keepers*,
  Linnea Sinclair; *For Her Love*, Paula Reed;
  Gabriel's Ghost, Linnea Sinclair; *Into His
  Arms*, Paula Reed; *Leonard Wood and the
  Birth of the American Century*, Jack McCal-
  lum; *Magic, Spells & Illusions, Inc*, Shanna
  Swendson; *Nobody's Saint*, Paula Reed; *Siren*,
  Cheryl Sawyer; *The Chase*, Cheryl Sawyer
Foreign Rights: Nelson Agency (Whitney Lee)
  (Asia); Nelson Agency (Jenny Meyer) (World-
  wide exc Asia)
Membership(s): Romance Writers of America

New Age World Literary Services & Books (L)
6426 Valley View St, Space 49, Joshua Tree, CA
92252
Tel: 760-366-0117
E-mail: newagesphinx@yahoo.com
Web Site: www.joshuatreevillage.com
Key Personnel
Owner & Exec Dir: Victoria E Vandertuin
Tel: 760-366-0117
Founded: 1974
Book-length fiction & nonfiction; specialize in all
New Age themes & unpublished authors in astrology, self-help, mystical, unusual how-to's,
philosophy, inspirational, para-sciences, UFO,
occult, romance-fiction, poetry, metaphysics,
lost continents & contemporary fiction, theology & religion. Handle software. Accept unsol
mss or query first. Submit outline & two or
three sample chapters or complete mss with
SASE. Upon viewing submission, a fee &
method to represent a work is quoted. Reading, representation service & written critique,
available for fee (query first). Fee charges are
various, depending on amount of pages & work
in the ms to cover the costs to represent a ms.
Charges reading fee depending on ms. Charges
clients for expenses associated with ms representation & special expenses agreed to in
advance. Offers written agreement for one year.
Renewable by mutual consent. 60 day written
notice to terminate agreement.
Titles recently placed: *An Infinite Pathway*,
Joseph E Kelleher; *How the UFOs Used Pi
& Golden Section to Measure America & Ce-
lestial Worlds*, Kenneth L Larson; *Origins*,
Joseph Paige; *Roses on My Doorstep*, Coreen
Picconatto; *The Adventures of Meow Meow &
Friends*, Itsuko Tomonari; *The Fifth World*, A J
Ferrara; *The Golden Door*, A J Ferrare

New Age World Publishing (L)
**8345 NW 66 St, Suite 6344, Miami, FL 33166-
2626**
Tel: **305-735-8064** *Toll Free Fax:* **888-739-6129**
E-mail: **info@NAWPublishing.com**
Web Site: **www.NAWPublishing.com**
Key Personnel
Dir of Acqs: **Steve Silver, PhD**
Sr Exec Ed: **Benjamin Gold, PhD**
Founded: **1999**
General publishing: **fiction, nonfiction, reli-
gious, New Age; submission by disk pre-
ferred. Accept unsol ms; handle film rights.
See www.nawpublishing.com for submission
requirements. Also internet bookseller.**
Titles recently placed: *The Corporate Executive
Survival Guide*, **James R Doyle;** *To Live and
Die in L.A.*, **Gerald Petievich;** *Witchcraft: A
Concise Guide*, **Isaac Bonewits**
Branch Office(s)
New York
Membership(s): **AAP; ABA; Northern Califor-
nia Independent Booksellers Association**
**See Ad in this Section and in U.S. Publishers
section and on Book Publishers Tab Side(s)1**

New Brand Agency Group, LLC (L-D)
3389 Sheridan St, Suite 317, Hollywood, FL
33021
Tel: 954-579-8900 *Fax:* 443-241-2568

Web Site: www.literaryagent.net
Key Personnel
Pres & Man Partner: Mark D Ryan (AAR)
E-mail: mark@literaryagent.net
Management & publicity for authors of fiction &
nonfiction with bestseller or high commercial
potential. Nonfiction: gift books, novelty books,
humor, self-help, how-to, celebrity, autobi-
ography/biography, business, writing, dating,
marriage, relationships, parenting, religious,
spiritual, pets. Fiction: young adult, thrillers,
mysteries, horror, action-adventure, suspense,
historical.
Titles recently placed: *24/7*, Jim Brown; *Eat Or
Be Eaten*, Phil Porter; *Father to Son*, Harry
Harrison; *The Finnegan Zwake Mystery Series*, Michael Dahl; *The Hill*, Jim Brown; *The
Husband Book*, Harry Harrison; *The Marriage
Plan*, Aggie Jordan Ph D; *The Misfits Inc, Mystery Series*, Mark Delaney; *The She*, Carol
Plum-Ucci; *The Women's Guide to Legal Issues*, Phil Philcox, Nancy Jones; *What Hap-
pend to Lani Garver?*, Carol Plum-Ucci

New England Publishing Associates Inc (L)
PO Box 5, Chester, CT 06412-0005
Tel: 860-345-READ (345-7323) *Fax:* 860-345-
3660
E-mail: nepa@nepa.com
Web Site: www.nepa.com
Key Personnel
Pres: Elizabeth Frost-Knappman (AAR)
VP: Edward W Knappman (AAR)
Agent: Ron Formica *E-mail:* formica@nepa.com
Subs Rts Mgr: Kristine Schiavi *E-mail:* kris@
nepa.com
Res Ed: Victoria Harlow
Founded: 1983

Editorial guidance, representation & mss development for book projects. Handle general interest nonfiction & nonfiction for adult market, particularly health, Asian studies, literary criticism, reference, true crime, biography, women's issues, current events, history & politics. Accept unsol mss, query first. Submit outline & table of contents with one-paragraph descriptions, author's biography, sample chapters. See submission guidelines on our website. No reading fee. Commission only publishing consultants. Handle film & TV rights through Renaissance/AMG.
Titles recently placed: *A Patriot's History of America*, Larry Schweikart, Michael Allen; *Get Them on Your Side*, Samuel Bacharach; *Made for a Purpose*, Dandi Daley Mackell; *The Night Attila Died*, Michael Babcock; *The Story of French*, Jean-Benoit Nadeau, Julie Barlow; *Winning Habits*, Richard Lyles
Foreign Rights: Rachel Calder (UK)
Membership(s): American Society of Journalists & Authors; Authors Guild

Nine Muses & Apollo Inc (L-D)
525 Broadway, Rm 201, New York, NY 10012
Tel: 212-431-2665
Key Personnel
Pres: Ling Lucas *E-mail:* linglucas@aol.com
Founded: 1991
Primarily nonfiction; extremely selective with fiction; no children's. No unsol mss, query with letter & SASE only; provide bio showing expertise in subject area & comparison/competitive titles. Submit outline & two sample chapters. Do not fax or e-mail proposal. Handle film & TV rights. Representatives in major foreign countries; no materials returned without SASE. No reading fee.
Titles recently placed: *Journey Into Power*, Baron Baptiste; *Ruling Planets*, Christopher Renstrom

Nixon Agency
Formerly McLean Literary Agency
382 Audrey Dr, Suite 100, Loveland, CO 80537
Tel: 970-667-0920 *Fax:* 970-667-0920
E-mail: mcleanlit@aol.com
Web Site: donnanixonagency.com
Key Personnel
Owner: Donna McLean Nixon
Founded: 1986
New writers welcome. Please submit full ms with a synopsis or outline & your SASE if you want the ms returned. There is no charge for evaluation & we take most subjects: children, fiction, science fiction, fantasy, social commentary, biography, auto-biography & nonfiction. All work is completed & returned within 30 days. Markets include top publishers & many in Great Britain. Titles recently placed with top 25 publishers but we have many small publishers crying for new works.
Titles recently placed: *Gems of the 7 Color Rays*, Studer; *New Body*, Erser; *New Face*, Erser; *New Nose*, Erser; *Secret For Dealing With Teens*, Hanks; *Two Houses of Israel*, Johnson, Leffler

Regula Noetzli Literary Agent (L)
Affiliate of The Charlotte Sheedy Literary Agency Inc
2344 County Rte 83, Pine Plains, NY 12567
Tel: 518-398-6260 *Fax:* 518-398-6258
E-mail: regula@taconic.net
Adult fiction & nonfiction only, with special interest in mysteries, biographies, psychology, popular science, sociology & environmental issues. Query first with outline & sample chapter. Representatives in Hollywood & most major foreign countries. No reading fees, no software.
Foreign Rep(s): In all countries

The Betsy Nolan Literary Agency (L)
Division of The Nolan/Lehr Group Inc
224 W 29 St, 15th fl, New York, NY 10001
Tel: 212-967-8200 *Fax:* 212-967-7292
Key Personnel
Pres: Donald Lehr
Founding Partner: Betsy Nolan
Agent: Carla Glasser
Off Mgr: Jennifer Alperen
Nonfiction, popular culture, child care, psychology, cookbooks, how-to, biography, African-American & Judaica. No poetry. Film & TV rights. No unsol mss, query first; submit outline, no more than three sample chapters & author background; no reading fee; SASE.
Titles recently placed: *More From Magnolia*, Allysa Torey; *Pleasure*, Dr Hilda Hutcherson; *Tate's Bake Shop Cookbook*, Kathleen King

Harold Ober Associates Inc (L)
425 Madison Ave, New York, NY 10017
Tel: 212-759-8600 *Fax:* 212-759-9428
Key Personnel
Pres: Phyllis Westberg (AAR)
Agent: Knox Burger (AAR); Alex Smithline; Emma Sweeney (AAR)
Agent, Foreign Rts: Pamela Malpas (AAR)
Agent, Film Rts: Don Laventhall
Off Mgr: Craig Tenney (AAR) *Tel:* 212-759-8600 ext 216
Founded: 1929
General fiction & nonfiction. No e-mailed queries. No unsol mss, query first with letter & SASE. No reading fee.
Foreign Rep(s): David Higham Associates Ltd (UK)

Fifi Oscard Agency Inc (L-D)
110 W 40 St, New York, NY 10018
Tel: 212-764-1100 *Fax:* 212-840-5019
E-mail: agency@fifioscard.com
Web Site: www.fifioscard.com
Key Personnel
Pres: Fifi Oscard
VP: Carmen La Via; Peter Sawyer
Sr Agent: Carolyn French; Jerome Rudes; Kevin D McShane; Ivy Fischer Stone
Founded: 1955
General fiction & nonfiction, all areas; film & TV rights; scripts for stage, motion picture & TV. Have always represented talent as well. No fees charged. No unsol mss, query first; submit outline & sample chapter if requested. See website for more instruction.
Titles recently placed: *A Voice at the Borders of Silence*, Marielle Segal; *I'm Working On That*, William Shatner; *Perfect I'm Not*, David Wells; *Reagan & Gorbechev*, Jack Matlock; *To the Mountaintop*, Stewart Burns; *Will*, Grace Tiffany
Foreign Rep(s): Agenzia Letteraria Internazionale (Italy); Bardon-Chinese Media (China); Imprima Korea (Korea); Michelle Lapautre (France); Thomas Schlueck (Germany); Abner Stein (England); Transnet Contracts (Czech Republic, Poland); Caroline Van Gelderan (Netherlands); Julio F Yanez Agencia Literaria (Spain)

Paraview Literary Agency (L)
Division of Paraview Inc
40 Florence Circle, Bracey, VA 23919
Tel: 434-636-4138 *Fax:* 434-636-4138
Web Site: www.paraview.com
Key Personnel
Pres & Agent: Lisa Hagan *E-mail:* lhagan@paraview.com
Founded: 1985
Spiritual, paranormal, self-help, business & metaphysical. No unsol mss, query first with letter & proposal. Submit outline & sample chapters. Handle film & TV rights. No fee charged.

Titles recently placed: *A Night Without Armor*, Jewel; *Into The Buzzsaw*, Kristina Borjesson; *King Of The Cowboys*, Ty Murray; *Rule by Secrecy*, Jim Marrs; *Texas Cooking (Fiction)*, Lisa Wingate; *The Coming Global Superstorm*, Art Bell, Whitley Streiber; *The Seventh Sense*, Lyn Buchanan

The Richard Parks Agency (L)
138 E 16 St, Suite 5-B, New York, NY 10003
Tel: 212-254-9067 *Fax:* 212-228-1786
E-mail: rp@richardparksagency.com
Key Personnel
Contact: Richard Parks (AAR)
Founded: 1989
Fiction & nonfiction. No unsol mss, query first with SASE only, cannot respond to phone, fax or e-mail queries. No reading fee; fees for photocopies only at cost to us.
Foreign Rep(s): Barbara Levy Literary Agency (UK)
Foreign Rights: The Marsh Agency

Kathi J Paton Literary Agency (L)
19 W 55 St, New York, NY 10019-4907
Tel: 212-265-6586; 908-647-2117
E-mail: kjplitbiz@optonline.net
Key Personnel
Contact: Kathi J Paton
Founded: 1987
Book-length adult nonfiction & fiction; personal finance, self-health, psychology, humor, inspiration & mainstream fiction & short stories. Accept unsol mss. If requested, send proposal & sample chapters (nonfiction), or first 40 pages & plot summary (fiction); SASE; no reading fee. Agents in all major foreign markets.
Titles recently placed: *Future Wealth*, Francis McInerney, Sean White; *Unraveling the Mystery of Autism*, Karyn Seroussi

William Pell Agency (L-D)
22 Oak St, Southhampton, NY 11968
Tel: 631-204-0524 *Fax:* 631-287-4492
E-mail: wpellagency@hotmail.com
Key Personnel
Pres & Owner: William Pell
Founded: 1990
Fiction & nonfiction. Welcome new authors. No unsol mss, query first. Submit outline & first two chapters with SASE. Handle software, film & TV rights. Submission postage & photocopying fees. There is a $100 fee for reviewing a complete ms.
Titles recently placed: *Friendly Deception*, Stephen Murphy
Branch Office(s)
1416 Ricky Rd, Charlottesville, VA 22901, Contact: Derek Pell *Tel:* 434-923-0865

Rodney Pelter (L)
129 E 61 St, New York, NY 10021
Tel: 212-838-3432
Fiction; general & specialized nonfiction; no unsol mss, query first by letter with SASE; include resume, outline & first 50 pages. Handle film & TV rights.

Pema Browne Ltd, see Pema Browne Ltd

Pema Browne Ltd (L)
11 Tena Place, Valley Cottage, NY 10989
E-mail: ppbltd@optonline.net
Web Site: www.pemabrowneltd.com
Key Personnel
Pres: Pema Browne
VP & Treas: Perry J Browne
Founded: 1966
All subjects including all genre romance, mass market & trade; fiction, nonfiction, business, how-to, cookbooks, health, reference, inspirational. Children's picture books, novelty,

middle-grade, young adult, illustration. No unsol mss, query first (no fax, e-mail or phone queries). Submit cover letter, one page query with bio & SASE. Neat, wide margins, dark type, double-spaced, only one side of paper printed. We do NOT review mss that have previously been sent out to publishers. No reading fee; 15% commission, 20%. Work with foreign agents in major countries. Signatory to Writers Guild, Society of Children's Book Writers & Illustrators, Romance Writers of America.

Titles recently placed: *Fire & Smoke*, Susan Scott; *I Can Never Die*, Linda Cargill; *Magical Math Series*, Lynette Long; *Seducing Sybilla*, Madeline Conway; *Soul Echoes*, Thelma Freedman; *Sweet Potatoe Pie*, Kathleen Lindsey; *The Savior*, Faye Snowden

Membership(s): Romance Writers of America; Society of Children's Book Writers & Illustrators; Writers Guild of America

Dan Peragine Agency (L)
227 Beechwood Ave, Bogota, NJ 07603
Tel: 201-487-1296 *Fax:* 201-487-1433
E-mail: dpliterary@aol.com
Web Site: www.writers.net
Key Personnel
Pres: Dan Peragine
Exec VP: Karen A Peragine
Founded: 1991
Specialize in behavioral sciences, biography, environment, history, humor, nonfiction, self-help, computers, sports, photography, all hight school & college textbooks, advanced placement & testing; handle multimedia software, film & TV rights; no unsol mss, query first with a complete proposal, submit sample chapters single page, double spaced, or on disk (Do not send by e-mail if it needs to be downloaded.) No reading fees, fees charged for editorial development, re-writes, ghost writers, publishing consulting, full book packaging & book marketing.
Titles recently placed: *The Guggenheims*, John H Davis, Marilyn S Men, Jane Ellen Wayne
Membership(s): ABA; ASPP & PWP; NPPA

James Peter Associates Inc (L)
PO Box 358, New Canaan, CT 06840
Tel: 203-972-1070 *Fax:* 203-972-1759
Key Personnel
Pres: Gene Brissie *E-mail:* gene_brissie@msn.com
Founded: 1971
Nonfiction only, all subject areas. Handle software, film & TV rights through sub-agents in many foreign countries. No unsol mss, query first with SASE. Submit brief description of book, potential market, chapter outline, one sample chapter, competitive titles & author's credentials. No reading fee.

Stephen Pevner Inc (L-D)
382 Lafayette St, Suite 8, New York, NY 10003
Tel: 212-674-8403 *Fax:* 212-529-3692
Key Personnel
Pres: Stephen Pevner *E-mail:* spevner@aol.com
Devt Assoc: Doug Silbert
Founded: 1991
New fiction & general nonfiction, pop culture, humor, international film, TV & audio & electronic rights, plays, screenplays, independent producers & directors. No unsol mss or scripts, query first with SASE; submit outline & sample chapters or synopsis. No reading fees.

Phoenix Literary Agency (L-D)
216 S Yellowstone, Livingston, MT 59047
Tel: 902-232-2848; 520-404-4748 (cell)

Key Personnel
Pres: Robert Dattila
Book length fiction; query first. Handle film & TV rights, no fees.

Alison Picard Literary Agent (L-D)
PO Box 2000, Cotuit, MA 02635
Tel: 508-477-7192 *Fax:* 508-477-7192 (call first)
E-mail: ajpicard@aol.com
Founded: 1985
Representing fiction & nonfiction. Beginners welcome. No unsol mss, query first with letter & SASE; no phone or fax queries. Upon positive response, submit double-spaced complete ms. Does not charge fees.
Titles recently placed: *2030*, Any Zuckerman, James Daly; *And Years That Answer*, Sheila Wiliams; *Becoming Bobbie*, R J Stevens; *Between Girlfriends*, Elizabeth Dean; *Celebritrees*, Margi Preus; *Chasing Bliss*, Fiona Zedde; *Deadly Kin*, Tom Eslick; *Death in Dark Waters*, Patricia Hall; *Fashion Slave*, Louise de Teliga; *Gossip & Rumors*, Theresa Alan; *Hard Ticket Home*, David Housewright; *How to Protect Your 401(k)*, Elizabeth Opalka; *I'm Your Man*, Timothy James Beck; *Indigo Rose*, Susan Miller; *Mixed Up Doubles*, Elena Yates Eulo; *Spur of the Moment*, Theresa Alan; *Stanislawski The Great*, Mary Bartek; *Sting Like A Bee*, David Housewright; *The Deal*, Timothy Lambert, Becky Cochrane; *The Great Receiver*, Elena Yates Eulo; *The Lucky Stone*, Dina Friedman; *The Peace Bell*, Margi Preus; *Three Fortunes*, Timothy Lambert, Becky Cochrane; *Tranifesto*, Matthew Kailey; *Wearing Black to The White Party*, David Stukas; *Who You Know*, Theresa Alan
Foreign Rights: John Pawsey (Europe)

The Pimlico Agency Inc (L)
PO Box 20447, Cherokee Sta, New York, NY 10021
Tel: 212-628-9729 *Fax:* 212-535-7861
Key Personnel
Pres: Kay McCauley
Agent: Kirby McCauley
Busn Mgr: Christopher Shepard
Asst: Catherine Brooks
Founded: 1974
Adult fiction & nonfiction. Motion picture & TV rights from book properties only. No unsol mss. Projects by referral only. No reading fee. Agents in all principal foreign countries.
Foreign Office(s): PO Box 17377, London SW1 2PNE, United Kingdom

Pinder Lane & Garon-Brooke Associates Ltd (L-D)
159 W 53 St, Suite 14-E, New York, NY 10019
Tel: 212-489-0880 *Fax:* 212-489-7104
E-mail: pinderl@interport.net
Key Personnel
Owner & Agent: Dick Duane (AAR); Robert Thixton (AAR)
Fiction & nonfiction, film & TV rights. No unsol mss, query first. No reading fee. Submit short synopsis, double spaced & unbound. Representatives in Hollywood & all foreign markets.
Titles recently placed: *Jackie-The Clothes of Camelot*, Jay Mulvaney; *Nobody's Safe*, Richard Steinberg; *Savage Love*, Rosemary Rogers; *The 4 Phase Man*, Richard Steinberg; *The Invasion*, Eric Harry; *The Kill Boy, the Third Consequence*, Chris Stewart; *The Sixth Fleet*, David Meadows
Foreign Rep(s): Abner Stein (UK)
Foreign Rights: Rights Unltd

Arthur Pine Associates Inc, see Inkwell Management

Pippin Properties Inc (L)
155 E 38 St, Suite 2H, New York, NY 10016
Tel: 212-338-9310 *Fax:* 212-338-9579
E-mail: info@pippinproperties.com
Web Site: www.pippinproperties.com
Key Personnel
Owner: Holly M McGhee
Assoc: Emily van Beek *E-mail:* evanbeek@pippinproperties.com
Represent authors & artists for children's picture books, middle-grade novels, chapter books & young-adult novels. No unsol mss, query first with letter for lengthier submissions. For all submissions please include SASE. Handle film, TV & foreign rights.

PMA Literary & Film Management Inc (L-D)
Subsidiary of PMA
Affiliate of Millennium Lion Inc
PO Box 1817, Old Chelsea Sta, New York, NY 10011
Tel: 212-929-1222 *Fax:* 212-206-0238
E-mail: pmalitfilm@aol.com
Web Site: www.pmalitfilm.com
Key Personnel
Pres: Peter Miller *E-mail:* peter@pmalitfilm.com
Assoc: Scott Hoffman *E-mail:* scott@pmalitfilm.com; Lisa Silverman *E-mail:* lisa@pmalitfilm.com
Film & Television: Greg Takoudes
Edit: Betty Ferm
Commercial fiction, nonfiction, true crime & celebrity books. Handle film & TV rights. Represent literary & film properties internationally. No unsol mss, query first; submit one page synopsis or finished treatment & author bio. See website for additional submission guidelines. Co-agents in select foreign territories & deal directly with foreign publishers. Affiliate packages & produces feature films & TV. Does not charge fees. Visit website, www.pmalitfilm.com for submission guidelines.
Titles recently placed: *1906*, James Dalessandro; *A Travel Guide to Heaven*, Anthony De Stefano; *Look at the Stars: an Insider's Look at Coldplay*, Gary Spivack; *Mister: The Last Word on Frank Sinatra*, William Stadiem & George Jacobs, George Jacobs; *Taking Flight*, Lynne Kaufman; *Ten Prayers God Always Says Yes to*, Anthony De Stefano; *The Preservationist*, David Maine; *The Sinking of the Eastland: America's Forgotten Tragedy*, Jay Bonansinga; *The Sound of Blue*, Holly Payne; *Wild Women's Weekend*, Lynne Kaufman; *Zombies*, Walter Greatshell
Foreign Rep(s): Big Apple Tuttle Mori (China); Peter Bolza (Hungary); Tuttle-Mori Agency (Japan)

Poirot Literary Agency (L-D)
2685 Stephens Rd, Boulder, CO 80305
Tel: 303-494-0668 *Fax:* 303-494-9396
E-mail: poirotco@comcast.net
Key Personnel
Pres: Henry M Poirot
Founded: 1976
Fiction & nonfiction, no poetry. Handle film & TV rights. No unsol mss, query first. No reading fee.

Pom Inc (L-D)
611 Broadway, No 907-B, New York, NY 10012
Tel: 212-673-3835 *Fax:* 212-673-4653
E-mail: pom-inc@att.net
Key Personnel
Pres: Dan Green
VP: Simon Green
Founded: 1990
Specialize in fiction & general nonfiction. No unsol mss. Handle electronic, film & TV rights. No reading fee. Please do not fax or e-mail.

Titles recently placed: *America's Revolutionary Mothers*, Carl Berkin; *Bearwalking*, Frederik Reiken; *Bushwacked*, Molly Ivins, Lou Dubose; *Cronies*, Robert Bryce; *Eat My Words*, Mimi Sheraton; *Mountain Betty*, Hannah McCouch; *Pilates for Men*, Daniel Lyon; *Sow Bellies*, Monte Burke; *Talia*, Nate Blakeslee; *Who Let the Dogs Out*, Molly Ivins; *Woe is I*, Patricia O'Conner

Bella Pomer Agency Inc (L)
22 Shallmar Blvd, Penthouse 2, Toronto, ON M5N 2Z8, Canada
Tel: 416-781-8597 *Fax:* 416-782-4196
E-mail: belpom@sympatico.ca
Key Personnel
Pres: Bella Pomer
Founded: 1978
Full-length fiction (literary), mystery fiction & general interest narrative nonfiction. Film & TV rights handled for books already represented; no unsol screenplays. No unsol mss. Not accepting new clients. Representation or direct sale in all principal countries. No reading fee.
Titles recently placed: *Belonging*, Isabel Huggan; *Clean*, Katherine Ashenburg; *Critical Injuries*, Joan Barfoot; *Death at Lawyer's Bay*, Gail Bowen; *Draught For A Dead Man*, Caroline Roe; *Garbo Laughs*, Elizabeth Hay; *Lords of the Two Lands*, Pauline Gedge; *Luck*, Joan Barfoot; *Names of the Dead*, Diane Schoemperlen; *Red Plaid Shirt*, Diane Schoemperlen; *The Etruscan Chimera*, Lyn Hamilton; *The Hemingway Caper*, Eric Wright; *The Holding*, Merilyn Simonds; *The Magyar Venus*, Lyn Hamilton; *The Mourner's Dance*, Katherine Ashenburg; *Unless*, Carol Shields
Foreign Rights: Akcali & Tuna Copyright (Turkey); BMSR (Brazil); East Communications (China); Grandi & Associate (Italy); Ilana Pikarski Literary Agency (Israel); International Editors' Co (Portugal, South America, Spain); Japan Uni Agency (Japan); JLM Agency (Greece); Katai & Bolza (Hungary); Alexander Korschenevsky (Russia); Michelle Lapautre (France); Leonhardt & Hoier (Scandinavia); Liepman AG (Germany); Nurnberg (Netherlands); Prava & Prevoda (Bulgaria, Czech Republic, Poland, Romania, Slovak Republic)

Julie Popkin Literary Agency (L)
15340 Albright St, Suite 204, Pacific Palisades, CA 90272
Tel: 310-459-2834 *Fax:* 310-459-4128
Key Personnel
Literary Agent: Julie Popkin *E-mail:* j.popkin@verizon.net
Contact: Alyson Sena
Specialize in nonfiction: memoirs & fiction; social issues, mysteries, human rights, history, translations (especially Latin American). No unsol mss, query first with SASE. Submit two or three chapters of fiction only; author's brief biography with SASE. Nonfiction submit via snail mail, query letter & proposal & one chapter & outline. Minimal fee is $100, which partially covers photocopying, mailing & telephoning & faxing. Larger mss $150 annual fee; editorial services offered on graduated scale. Handle some film & TV rights for authors.
Titles recently placed: *Air in California*, David Carle; *America's Most Hated*, Ann Seaman, Madalyn O'Hair; *An Empty House*, Carlos Cerda; *Bodie's Boss Lawman*, Bill Merrell, David Carle; *Burning Questions*, David Carle; *Call Me Magdalena*, Alicia Steimberg; *From One Roots Many Flowers*, Virginia 21; *Introduction to Water in California*, David Carle; *Out of the Shadows. Twentieth Century Women Physicists*, Nina Byers, Gary Williams; *Quiet Street*, Zelda Popkin; *Reader's Trade*, Elizabeth

Burton; *Second Reef*, Jack Lopez; *Skeptical Philosophy for Everybody*, Richard H Popkin, Avrum Stroll; *Spinoza*, Richard H Popkin; *That Hell*, Monu Actis, Miriam Lewin, Christina Aldini, Lilianna Gardella; *The History of Scepticism from Savorarola to Bayle*, Richard H Popkin; *The Marrano Legacy*, Trudi Alexy; *The Rain Forest*, Alicia Steimberg; *The Red & The Black List*, Norma Barzman; *Truck of Fools*, Carlos Liscano; *Violation of The Love Story*, Psiche Hughes; *Water & the California Dream*, David Carle
Foreign Rights: Elizabeth Atkins (Spain); Andreas Brunner (Austria); Piergiorgio Nicolazzini (Continental Europe, Italy); Lennart Sane (Netherlands, Scandinavia); Abner Stein (UK)
Membership(s): PEN/West

The Poynor Group (L)
444 E 82 St, Suite 28C, New York, NY 10028
Tel: 212-734-5909 *Fax:* 212-734-5909
Key Personnel
Pres: Jay Poynor *E-mail:* jpoynor@fcc.net
VP/Acqs: Erica Orloff
Founded: 1985
Literary representation service & sales. Submit e-mail query first (mandatory). If agreeable, then send a synopsis & first three chapters. Commission: 15% of advance & royalties. No other fees.
Titles recently placed: *A Dose of Murder*, Lori Avocato

Helen F Pratt Inc Literary Agency (L)
1165 Fifth Ave, New York, NY 10029
Tel: 212-722-5081 *Fax:* 212-722-8569
E-mail: helenpratt@earthlink.net
Key Personnel
Owner & Pres: Helen F Pratt
Contact: Julia Benedict (AAR)
Quality fiction & nonfiction books. Illustrated books a specialty. No children's books. No unsol mss, query first with SASE. Submit outline & sample chapter. No fees.

Linn Prentis, Literary Agent (L)
155 E 116 St, No 2F-2R, New York City, NY 10029
Tel: 212-876-8557 *Fax:* 212-876-5565
E-mail: linnprentis@earthlink.net
Fine fiction, limited nonfiction: special interest in speculative fiction, science fiction & fantasy. Special interest in family saga. Also mainstream, women's, literary, young adult & middle-reader, men's, mystery, suspense, historical, non-category romance. Literary nonfiction. Film rights only as outgrowth of book sales through Bill Contardi, New York. No phone, fax or e-mail queries; no unsol mss; query by mail with SASE; Cover letter (credits, bio facts, word count, title & genre/target audience) 2-page synopsis, first 10 pages. Mss: double-spaced, unbound, one side of page, boxed with cover. No reading fee; 15% commission, 20% on dramatic & foreign sales. Founded as an affiliate of the Virginia Kidd Agency, now independent.
Titles recently placed: *A Brother's Price*, Wen Spencer; *Black Projects, White Knights*, Kage Baker; *Fifth Ring*, Mitchell Graham; *Gifts*, Ursula K Le Guin
Foreign Rep(s): ALI (Italy); International Editors (South America, Spain & Portugal); Korshenevski (Russia & former USSR); Lenclud (France); Lennart Sane (Scandinavia); LEX (Hungary); MBA (Meg Davis) (UK); P & P Fritz (Germany); PIP (Eastern Europe); Tuttle-Mori (Japan)
Membership(s): Science Fiction & Fantasy Writers of America

The Aaron M Priest Literary Agency Inc (L)
708 Third Ave, 23rd fl, New York, NY 10017
Tel: 212-818-0344 *Fax:* 212-573-9417
Key Personnel
Literary Agent: Lucy Childs (AAR); Paul Cirone (AAR); Molly Friedrich (AAR); Aaron M Priest (AAR); Lisa Erbach Vance (AAR)
Handle film & TV rights, fiction (literary & popular) & nonfiction. No screenplays, poetry, children or young adults literature. No unsol mss. SASE not required. If interested, will respond within two weeks of receipt of query. Will not respond if not interested. No reading fee. Copying, foreign postage fee. Agents in many foreign countries.

Generosa Gina Protano Publishing, see GGP Publishing Inc

Susan Ann Protter Literary Agent (L)
110 W 40 St, Suite 1408, New York, NY 10018
Tel: 212-840-0480
Key Personnel
Owner: Susan Ann Protter (AAR)
Founded: 1971
Fiction & nonfiction, health & medicine, how-to, mysteries, thrillers, science, science fiction or narrative nonfiction, biography, reference & self-help. No juveniles. No unsol mss. Query first with letter & SASE. No queries by phone or fax. No reading fee. Agents in Hollywood & all major foreign countries.
Foreign Rep(s): Abner Stein (UK)
Foreign Rights: Agenzia Letteraria Internazionale (Italy); Big Apple Tuttle-Mori (China); International Editors (Portugal, Spain); Alexander Korzhenevski (Russia); La Nouvelle Agence (France); Licht & Burr (Denmark, Finland, Norway, Sweden); Mohrbooks (Germany); Ilana Pikarski (Israel); Tuttle-Mori (Japan); Caroline Van Gelderen (Netherlands); Eric Yang (Korea)
Membership(s): Authors Guild

PSD Associates (L)
7392 Palm Ave, Sebastopol, CA 95472-6705
Key Personnel
Principal: John P van Gigch, PhD *E-mail:* vang@sonic.net
Specialize in perfecting academic, semi-academic & trade texts by critiquing & editing to reach publication. Management/business/economics, science/engineering/technology, education/psychology, marketing research, ethics in management, social sciences in general. Prefer proven & previously published authors. We actively promote the publication of mss on the web with copyright protection & royalties. No unsol mss, query first. E-mail inquiries accepted if short & concise, no attachments accepted or opened. No phone inquiries. Submit prospectus, sample text & credentials with SASE (required for reply & strictly enforced). No initial reading fee.

Publishing Services (L)
525 E 86 St, Suite 10-E, New York, NY 10028
Tel: 212-628-9127 *Fax:* 212-628-9128
E-mail: pubserv525@aol.com
Key Personnel
Contact: Amy S Goldberger
Upscale women's fiction & nonfiction. No unsol mss, query first with SASE. No phone calls. For fiction, send first 50 pages, for nonfiction, send outline & first three chapters. Handle film & TV rights. No reading fee.

Puddingstone Literary, Authors' Agents (L-D)
Subsidiary of SBC Enterprises Inc
11 Mabro Dr, Denville, NJ 07834-9607
Tel: 973-366-3622
Key Personnel
Dir: Alec Bernard

Contact: Eugenia Cohen
Founded: 1972
General trade & mass market fiction & nonfiction; motion picture scripts & teleplays. Handle film & TV rights. No unsol mss, query first with SASE. Submit outline & sample chapters. No reading fee. Representatives in Hollywood & foreign countries. Fee for ms copies, galleys & bound books for foreign & domestic submissions.

Liza Pulitzer Voges (L)
866 United Nations Plaza, New York, NY 10017
Tel: 212-644-2020 *Fax:* 212-223-4387
Founded: 1930
Represent authors & author/illustrators of children's books, picture books through young adult. Query letter with sample chapter for novel or long nonfiction. No reading fee.
Titles recently placed: *Leaf Man*, Lois Ehlert; *Miss Small if Off the Wall!*, Dan Gutman; *Moo Who?*, Keith Graves; *Mr Hynde is Out of His Mind!*, Dan Gutman; *Pie In The Sky*, Lois Ehlert; *Trembling Earth*, Kim Siegelson; *Wallace's Lists*, Barbara Bottner, Gerald Kruglik

Quicksilver Books Inc (L-D)
508 Central Park Ave, Suite 5101, Scarsdale, NY 10583
Tel: 914-722-4664 *Fax:* 914-722-4664
E-mail: quickbooks@optonline.net
Key Personnel
Pres: Bob Silverstein
Founded: 1973
Adult book-length trade & mass market fiction & nonfiction; including self-help, psychology, health, popular science, narrative nonfiction, reference, biography, nutrition, cookbooks, New Age & spirituality. Representation, packaging & editorial consultation. Handle film & TV rights. No unsol mss, query first with SASE. Submit proposal & sample chapters (nonfiction) & outline, sample chapters (fiction), author bio, or complete ms with SASE. All submissions must be typed & double-spaced. No reading fee.
Titles recently placed: *Callus On My Soul*, Dick Gregory; *Every Woman's Yoga*, Jaime Stover Schmitt; *Good Girls Don't Get the Corner Office*, Lois P Frankel, PhD; *Help Me to Heal*, Bernie S Siegel, MD, Yosaif August; *Jefferson's Great Gamble*, Charles Cerami; *Nature's Pharmacy For Kids*, Dr Lendon Smith, Lynne Paige Walker, Ellen H Brown; *Pictures From the Heart-A Tarot Dictionary*, Sandra Thomson; *The Look Great Naked Diet*, Brad Schoenfeld; *The Miracle Ball Method*, Elaine Petrone

Susan Rabiner Literary Agent (L)
240 W 35 St, Suite 500, New York, NY 10001-2506
Tel: 212-279-0316 *Fax:* 212-279-0932
E-mail: susan@rabiner.net
Key Personnel
Pres: Susan Rabiner
Agent: Susan Arellano *Tel:* 212-400-0772
  E-mail: susanarellao@yahoo.com
Founded: 1997
Serious nonfiction, narrative nonfiction, college texts; history, science, psychology, education, law, philosophy, gender studies, anthropology, archeology. Represent trade authors trying to place their mss with the major commercial publishing houses. Also represent a limited number of college text authors. Primarily academics, journalists, scientists & independent scholars; query first by e-mail, no faxes; no reading fees.
Titles recently placed: *Honor Killing*, David Stannard; *Icebound*, Gay Salisbury, Laney Salisbury; *Marriage: A History*, Stephanie Coontz; *The Chinese in America*, Iris Chang; *To the*

Tower of Babel, Charles Yang; *Trapped*, Elizabeth Warren, Amelia Tyagi
Foreign Rights: Agence Hoffmann (Germany); Agnese Incisa (Italy); The English Agency (Japan)

Raines & Raines (L-D)
103 Kenyon Rd, Medusa, NY 12120
Tel: 518-239-8311 *Fax:* 518-239-6029
Key Personnel
Partner: Joan Raines; Theron Raines (AAR)
Contact: Keith Korman
Founded: 1961
Handle film & TV rights. No unsol mss, query first; submit one page; no reading fee. Agents in all principal countries.
Foreign Rep(s): Agenzia Letteraria Internazionale; Balcells; Big Apple; Bookman; Campbell Thomson & McLaughlin; Fritz; Lapautre; Nurnberg; Tuttle-Mori

Rainmaker Literary Agency (L)
Formerly First Books
25 NW 23 Place, Suite 6, PMB 460, Portland, OR 97210-5599
Tel: 503-222-2249
E-mail: info@rainmakerliterary.com
Web Site: www.rainmakerliterary.com
Key Personnel
Pres: Jeremy Solomon
Agent: Ann W Frank
Founded: 1988
Fiction & nonfiction. No unsol mss, query first with letter & SASE. No reading fee. Reps in many foreign territories.
ISBN Prefix(es): 0-912301; 0-9719414; 1-59299
Titles recently placed: *Get Paid What You're Worth*, Robin Pinkley, Gregory Northcutt; *How Murray Saved Christmas*, Mike Reiss; *Mastering the Markets*, Ari Kiev; *One Hot Second*, Cathy Young; *Redeeming Eve*, Nicole Bokat; *Santa Claustrophobia*, Mike Reiss; *Senior Moments*, Joey Green, Alan Corcoran; *Sugars That Heal*, Emil Mondoa MD, Mindy Kitei; *The Book of InterHans*, Dianne Martin; *The Road to CEO*, Sharon Voros; *The Trouble With Normal*, Charise Mericle Harper
Membership(s): ABA

Diane Raintree (L-D)
360 W 21 St, New York, NY 10011
Tel: 212-242-2387
Founded: 1977
Fiction, adult, young adult novels, children's books, memoirs, nonfiction, poetry, plays, sitcoms, filmscripts. No unsol mss. Phone before sending anything. Submit complete mss or one to three consecutive chapters, beginning with the first, only after requested. Fiction, nonfiction & poetry double-spaced & unbound. Editing & critique available. Hourly rate charged for editing, amount adjusted to writer's circumstances.
Titles recently placed: *Too Tall*, Katherine Springfield

Charlotte Cecil Raymond, Literary Agent (L)
32 Bradlee Rd, Marblehead, MA 01945
Tel: 781-631-6722 *Fax:* 781-631-6722
E-mail: ccraymond@aol.com
Adult nonfiction & literary fiction; no juvenile, young adult, poetry, short stories, fantasy, science fiction or screenplays. No unsol mss; query first with SASE; submit outline & sample chapters. No reading fee.

The Erin Reel Literary Agency (ERLA) (L)
9006 Wilshire Blvd, Box 1, Beverly Hills, CA 90211
Tel: 818-706-3313 *Fax:* 818-706-3313
E-mail: erlaquery@sbcglobal.net

Web Site: www.erinreel.com
Key Personnel
Pres: Erin Reel *E-mail:* erin.reel@sbcglobal.net
CFO: Fletcher Reel
Founded: 2003
Focuses on a limited number of exceptional authors. Primarily interested in saleable fiction & nonfiction for the 18-35 market, though not exclusively. Send queries by mail or e-mail. Strongly discourages unsol materials.
Foreign Rights: Fielding Agency (Whitney Lee) (Worldwide)

Helen Rees Literary Agency (L)
376 North St, Boston, MA 02113-2103
Tel: 617-227-9014 *Fax:* 617-227-8762
Key Personnel
Contact: Helen Rees (AAR) *E-mail:* helen@reesagency.com
Assoc: Ann Collette *E-mail:* agent10702@aol.com; Larry Moulter
Contact: Lorin Rees *E-mail:* lorin@reesagency.com
Founded: 1982
Literary fiction, nonfiction, business, biography & health. No unsol mss, query first with synopsis, outline, sample chapters & 50 pages. Submit outline & three sample multiple or submissions or e-mail submissions. No reading fee. Handle film & TV rights.
Titles recently placed: *Giants of Enterprise: Seven Business Innovators & the Empires They Built*, Richard St Tedlow; *Video & DVD Guide (annual)*, Mick Martin, Marsha Porter; *Why Terrorism Works: Understanding the Threat, Responding to the Challenge*, Alan Dershowitz
Membership(s): PEN American Center

The Naomi Reichstein Literary Agency (L)
5031 Foothills Rd, Rm G, Lake Oswego, OR 97034
Tel: 503-636-7575 *Fax:* 503-636-3957
Key Personnel
Owner: Naomi Reichstein
General book-length fiction & nonfiction for adults, history, cultural issues, the arts, music, literary history, biography, science, the environment, psychology & how-to. No film/TV scripts, science fiction, fantasy, horror, technothrillers, paranormal books, poetry, individual short stories, articles plays or books for young adults. No unsol mss, query first by letter with SASE. Mss sent following a positive response to a query should be typed in 12-point font & double-spaced; no reading fee; queries by phone, fax or e-mail not accepted.

Jody Rein Books Inc (L)
7741 S Ash Ct, Centennial, CO 80122
Tel: 303-694-4430 *Fax:* 303-694-0687
Web Site: www.jodyreinbooks.com
Key Personnel
Pres: Jody Rein (AAR) *E-mail:* jodyrein@jodyreinbooks.com
Lit Assoc & Off Mgr: Johnna Hietala
  E-mail: jhietala@jodyreinbooks.com
Founded: 1994
Author representation; specialize in adult narrative & commercial nonfiction. Some commercial fiction. No unsol mss, mail a one to two page query letter with author bio first & SASE; no reading fee. Handle film & TV rights through agents. No e-mail queries.
Titles recently placed: *How to Remodel a Man*, Bruce Cameron; *Riding With the Queen*, Jennie Shortridge; *Skeletons on the Zahara*, Dean King; *The Big Year*, Mark Obmascik
Foreign Rights: Jenny Meyer Literary Agency

Marian Reiner (L)
71 Disbrow Lane, New Rochelle, NY 10804
Tel: 914-235-7808 *Fax:* 914-576-1432

E-mail: mreinerlit@aol.com
Founded: 1963
Handle only work for children; fiction, nonfiction. No unsol mss. No new clients. No reading fee. Charge for photocopying & overseas phone & mail. Handle film & TV rights only for books agency sold.
Titles recently placed: *Ancient Israelites & Their Neighbors*, Marian Broida; *Bedtime Poems*, Ralph Fletcher; *Black Earth, Gold Sun*, Patricia Hubbell; *Cold & Hot*, Jacqueline Sweeney; *Dynamic Earth*, Michelle O'Brien-Palmer; *Halloween*, Harry Behn; *Hello Harvest Moon*, Ralph Fletcher; *Honeybabe*, Barbara Brenner; *I Like Cats*, Patricia Hubbell; *I'm Small*, Lilian Moore; *Kids Express*, Jacqueline Sweeney; *Making History*, Marian Broida; *Marshfield Dreams*, Ralph Fletcher; *More Spice than Sugar*, Lillian Morrison; *Mural on Second Avenue (City Poems)*, Lilian Moore; *Rabbit Moon*, Patricia Hubbell; *Scary Poems*, Lilian Moore; *Sing of the Earth & Sky*, Aileen Fisher; *Splash*, Constance Levy; *The Circus Surprise*, Ralph Fletcher; *The Story of Red Rubber Ball*, Constance Levy; *Tommy Trouble and the Magic Marble*, Ralph Fletcher; *Trucks on the Long, Long Road*, Patricia Hubbell; *Uncle Daddy*, Ralph Fletcher; *Was It a Good Trade?*, Beatarice Schenk de Regniers; *Way To Go! Sports Poems*, Lillian Morrison; *What the Elephant Told*, Barbara Brenner; *You Don't Look Like Your Mother*, Aileen Fisher

The Amy Rennert Agency Inc (L)
98 Main St, Suite 302, Tiburon, CA 94920
Tel: 415-789-8955 *Fax:* 415-789-8944
E-mail: arennert@pacbell.net
Key Personnel
Pres: Amy Rennert
Assoc: Dena Fischer
Busn Mgr: Margie Perez
Founded: 1999
The agency represents books that matter, narrative nonfiction & literary & commercial fiction. For fiction, submit cover letter, 50-75 sample pages, synopsis & a brief expo; no reading fees. No submissions via e-mail or phone.
Titles recently placed: *A Mouthful of Air*, Amy Koppelman; *A Salty Piece of Land*, Jimmy Buffett; *Beyond the Outer Shores: A Cosmic Tale of Ecology, Myth & the Man Who Inspired John Steinbeck*, Eric Enno Tamm; *Birds of a Feather: A Maisie Dobbs Novel*, Jacqueline Winspear; *Black Heart*, Marilee Strong; *Dim Sum: The Art of Chinese Tea Lunch*, Ellen Blonder; *Following Our Bliss: How the Spiritual Ideals of the Sixities Shape Our Lives Today*, Don Lattin; *Hotel Secrets From The Travel Detective*, Peter Greenberg; *I Think There's a Terrorist in My Soup: How to Survive Personal & World Problems With Laughter-Seriously*, David Brenner; *Internal Bleeding: The Truth Behind America's Terrifying Epidemic of Medical Mistakes*, Dr Robert Wachter, Dr Kaveh Shojania; *Jann Wenner Biography*, David Weir; *Maisie Dobbs*, Jacqueline Winspear; *No Place to Hide: Technology, Surveillance & America's War on Terror*, Robert O'Harrow; *Offer of Proof*, Robert Heilbrun; *On Sanity*, Adam Phillips; *Prodigal Daughter: Charlotte Clarke & Her Times*, Kathryn Shevelow; *The BLT Cookbook*, Michele Anna Jordan; *The Madhouse Memoir of Mary Todd Lincoln: A Novel*, Janis Cooke Newman; *The Prize Winner of Defiance, Ohio: How My Mother Raised Ten Kids on Twenty-Five Words or Less*, Terry Ryan; *The Rabbi & The Hitman*, Arthur Magida; *The Transfat Solution*, Kim Severson; *The Unbridled Imagination*, Beth Kephart; *Untitled Autobiography*, Kris Kristofferson; *Where Inspiration Lives: Writers, Artists, & Their Creative Places*, John Miller, Aaron Kenedi; *Why I'm Like This*, Cynthia Kaplan

Foreign Rights: Chandler Crawford (Europe & Japan); Abner Stein (England)
Membership(s): Authors Guild

Jodie Rhodes Literary Agency (L)
8840 Villa La Jolla Dr, Suite 315, La Jolla, CA 92037
Key Personnel
Pres: Jodie Rhodes (AAR) *Tel:* 858-625-0544
E-mail: jrhodes1@san.rr.com
Fict Agent: Clark McCutcheon
Nonfict Agent: Robert McCarter
Movie & TV Agent: Irene Webb
Founded: 1998
Established to bring talented new writers to the attention of publishers & establish a successful long term career for all writers. Interested in literary fiction, memoirs, intelligent, sophisticated mysteries, suspense & thrillers with fresh original plots, women's books with a unique story, quirky coming-of-age books, African American & multicultural literature both fiction & nonfiction, politics, history, international affairs, science, medicine, health, fitness, women's issues, parenting. Send query, brief synopsis, first 30 to 50 pages, SASE with stamps—not metered slip. No fees charged; handles film & TV rights.
Titles recently placed: *A Writer's Paris*, Eric Maisel; *Anorexia Diaries*, Linda Rio, Tara Rio; *Antioxidents (short story collection)*, Terry Bennett; *Beijing, A Novel*, Phil Gambone; *Biography of Emily Dickinson*, Dr Sharon Leiter; *Biology for the New Century*, Dr Stanley Rice; *Butterflies On A Sea Breeze*, Ame Rudlow; *Changing Course*, Jeanne Lutz; *Combat Chaplain*, James Johnson; *Dictionary of Forensics*, Dr Suzanne Bell; *Down & Dirty Justice*, Gary Lowenthal; *Drugs, Poisons & Chemistry*, Suzanne Bell; *Encyclopedia of Evolution*, Dr Stanley Rice; *For Matrimonial Purposes*, Kavita Daswani; *Forensic Chemistry*, Suzanne Bell; *Ghostly Encounters*, Frances Kermeen; *Grasslands, A Novel*, Debra Seely; *Home Is East (a novel)*, Many Ly; *Inside the Crips*, Ann Pearlman; *Inside the Heart of Amazons*, Tom De Mott; *Inside Wall Street*, Susan Scherbel; *Intimate Partner Violence*, Dr Connie Mitchell; *Last of the Round-up Boys (a novel)*, Debra Seely; *Living In A Black & White World*, Ann Pearlman; *Post Adoption Blues*, Karen Foli; *Raising Healthy Eaters*, Dr Henry Joseph; *Ready To Learn*, Dr Stanley Goldburg; *Sapphire's Grave (a novel)*, Hilda Hurley Highgate; *Science of Circumstance*, Suzanne Bell; *Science vs Crime*, Max Houck; *Taming of the Chew*, Denise Lamothe; *The Brave: A Story of NYC Fire Fighters*, George Pickett; *The Chronology of Science*, Liza Rezenue; *The Darkest Clearing (thriller)*, Brian Railsback; *The Dwarf In Louis XIV's Court*, Paul Weidner; *The Myrtles (a memoir)*, Frances Kermeen; *The Village Bride In Beverly Hills*, Kavita Daswani; *The World of Physics*, Dr Kyle Kirkland
Foreign Rights: Vicki Satlow (World)

Rhodes Literary Agency (L-D)
PO Box 89133, Honolulu, HI 96830-7133
Tel: 808-947-4689 (let phone ring at least six times; then leave message)
Key Personnel
Pres, Dir & Agent: Fred C Pugarelli
Founded: 1971
Market fiction & nonfiction books & magazine mss; handle virtually all types of writing; motion picture scripts; stage plays, essays & poetry. No unsol mss, query first. Submit synopsis, author's bio & sample chapters or sample poems. Reading fee start at $165 for novels & nonfiction books, screenplays, plays & poetry - lengthy book mss over 65,000 words, $175. Lower rates for short stories, shorter children's

books. Reading fee & SASE. Handle film & TV rights; handle software when accompanied by a written copy of the ms on paper.
Membership(s): Writers Guild of America West

Richland Agency (D)
2828 Donald Douglas Loop N, Santa Monica, CA 90405
Tel: 310-392-1195 *Fax:* 310-392-0395
Key Personnel
Contact: Daniel Richland
Do not take mss, do take screenplays; handle film & TV writers, producers & directors.

Rights Unlimited Inc (L)
101 W 55 St, Suite 2D, New York, NY 10019
Tel: 212-246-0900 *Fax:* 212-246-2114
E-mail: faith@rightsunlimited.com
Web Site: rightsunlimited.com
Key Personnel
Pres: Raymond Kurman
VP: Francis Flannery; John Sansevere
Mgr of Rts: Betty-Anne Crawford
International rights.

John R Riina Literary Agency (L)
5905 Meadowood Rd, Baltimore, MD 21212
Tel: 410-433-2305
E-mail: jrriina@earthlink.net
Founded: 1972
Specialize in nonfiction books: science, health, medicine, textbooks & how-to. No unsol mss, query first with author's bio, one paragraph synopsis & outline. No return of material without SASE. No reading fee. No phone queries.
Titles recently placed: *Civil & Environmental Systems Engineering 2nd Ed*, C Revelle, E E Whitlatch Jr, J Wright; *Fabulous Floorcloths*, Caroline Kuchinsky; *It Shouldn't Be This Way: The Failure of Long Term Care*, R Kane, J West; *Managing Money in Outpatient Psychiatry*, C Mikalac; *Understanding Acid-Base*, Benjamin Abelow

The Angela Rinaldi Literary Agency (L)
PO Box 7877, Beverly Hills, CA 90212-7877
Tel: 310-842-7665 *Fax:* 310-837-8143
Key Personnel
Pres: Angela Rinaldi (AAR) *E-mail:* amr@rinaldiliterary.com
Founded: 1995
Commercial & literary fiction & nonfiction, no genre fiction; TV & motion picture rights for clients only. Brief e-mail inquiry okay. No attachments or downloads. Submit proposal or outline for nonfiction, first three chapters for fiction, include SASE for response in 4-6 weeks. No reading fee, fees for copying. Representation in foreign markets.
Titles recently placed: *Blood Orange*, Drusilla Campbell; *My First Crush*, Linda Kaplan; *Rescue Me*, Megan Clark; *Some Writers Deserve to Starve*, Elaura Niles

Ann Rittenberg Literary Agency Inc (L)
1201 Broadway, Suite 708, New York, NY 10001
Tel: 212-684-6936 *Fax:* 212-684-6929
Web Site: www.rittlit.com
Key Personnel
Pres: Ann Rittenberg (AAR)
Assoc: Ted Gideonse (AAR)
Founded: 1992
Specialize in literary fiction & nonfiction; no genre fiction. Foreign Reps all principal foreign countries. Query letter & first chapter with SASE. No reading fee. Brief one-page description & first two chapters with SASE, no e-mail queries.
Titles recently placed: *A Certain Slant of Light*, Laura Whitcomb; *Bad Cat*, Jim Edgar; *Busted*

Flush, Brad Smith; *Cities of Weather*, Matthew Fox; *The Book of Kehls*, Christine O'Hagen
Membership(s): Authors Guild; Publishing Triangle

Judith Riven Literary Agent/Editorial Consultant (L)
250 W 16 St, Suite 4F, New York, NY 10011
Tel: 212-255-1009 *Fax:* 212-255-8547
E-mail: rivenlit@att.net
Key Personnel
Owner & Pres: Judith Riven
Assoc: Linda Pennell
Fiction & nonfiction. No unsol mss; query first with SASE; must include SASE for return of material. Handle film & TV rights for book clients only. No reading fee.
Titles recently placed: *Bloodbath*, Gerald J Meyer; *Delaying the Real World*, Colleen Kinder; *Dreamworld*, Jonathan Leonard; *Gordito Doesn't Mean Healthy*, Lourdes Alcaniz, Claudia Gonzalez; *Happy Mealtimes*, Linda Piette; *Help! It's Broken*, Arianne Cohen; *Is Something Wrong With My Child*, Laurie Le Comer; *Letters from the Hive*, Stephen Buchmann, Banning Repplier; *One Cake One Hundred Desserts*, Gregory Case, Keri Fisher; *Pure Chocolate*, Fran Bigelow, Helene Siegal; *Ruth the Moabite*, Eva Etzioni-Halevy; *Shadows in the Vineyard*, Eva Etzioni-Halevy; *Tasting Eden*, Jenny Traunfeld; *The Passionate Olive*, Carol Firenze Anglin; *Wine for Women*, Leslie Sbrocco
Foreign Rights: Baror International

Riverside Literary Agency (L)
41 Simon Keets Rd, Leyden, MA 01337
Tel: 413-772-0067 *Fax:* 413-772-0969
E-mail: rivlit@sover.net
Key Personnel
Pres: Susan Lee Cohen
Founded: 1990
Adult fiction & nonfiction. No unsol mss, query first with SASE. No reading fees. Handle foreign film & TV rights with co-agents.
Titles recently placed: *Flame of Evil*, Mick Farren; *Letters to a Young Therapist*, Mary Pipher; *Letting Go Of The Person You Used To Be*, Lama Surya Das; *The Devil You Know: Immorality versus Conscience in Everyday Life*, Martha Stout; *The Macrobiotic Guide to Total Health*, Michio Kushi, Alex Jack

RLR Associates Ltd (L-D)
7 W 51 St, New York, NY 10019
Tel: 212-541-8641 *Fax:* 212-541-6052
Web Site: www.rlrassociates.net
Key Personnel
Pres: Robert L Rosen
VP: Jennifer Unter (AAR) *E-mail:* junter@rlrassociates.net
Literary Agent: Tara Mark *E-mail:* tmark@rlrassociates.net
Handle film rights. No unsol mss, query first. Submit outline & sample chapters. No reading fee. Agents in all principal foreign countries.
Titles recently placed: *Save Karyn*, Karen Bosnak; *Star Craving Mad*, Erise Miller

RMA (L)
612 Argyle Rd, Suite L5, Brooklyn, NY 11230
Tel: 718-434-1893 *Fax:* 718-434-2157
E-mail: ricia@ricia.com
Web Site: www.ricia.com
Key Personnel
Owner: Ricia Mainhardt
Popular fiction, especially science fiction, fantasy, mystery, thriller, romance; nonfiction, especially pop culture, history & science. Do not accept poetry or children's books. No unsol mss. Query with SASE. Submit first chapter

& synopsis. Handle software for client's books only. Affiliates handle film & TV rights for client's books. No reading fee.

B J Robbins Literary Agency (L)
5130 Bellaire Ave, North Hollywood, CA 91607
Tel: 818-760-6602 *Fax:* 818-760-6616
E-mail: robbinsliterary@aol.com
Key Personnel
Pres: B J Robbins (AAR)
Literary & commercial fiction, general nonfiction. Handle film & TV rights for agency clients. Submit first three chapters (fiction) or proposal (nonfiction) with SASE. No reading fee.
Titles recently placed: *Bird of Another Heaven*, James D Houston; *Bitten: True Medical Stories of Bites & Stings*, Pamela Nagami, MD; *Coffee & Kung Fu, Separation Anxiety*, Karen Brichoux; *Last Stand on the Little Bighorn*, James Donovan; *The Sex Lives of Cannibals*, J Maarten Troost
Foreign Rights: Paul Marsh Agency; Abner-Stein (UK)
Membership(s): PEN/West

Robbins Office Inc (L)
405 Park Ave, 9th fl, New York, NY 10022
Tel: 212-223-0720 *Fax:* 212-223-2535
Key Personnel
Pres: Kathy P Robbins
Agent: David Halpern; Teri Tobias
Assoc: Kate Rizzo *E-mail:* krizzo@robbinsoffice.com
Foreign Rights Assoc: Sandy Hodgman *E-mail:* shodgman@robbinsoffice.com
Founded: 1978
General fiction & nonfiction; TV & motion picture rights. No unsol mss, query first, by referral only; submit proposal or outline (nonfiction) or outline & sample chapters (fiction); no reading fee.
Foreign Rights: MB Agencia (Spain); Roberto Santachiara Agency (Italy); The English Agency (Japan); Caroline Van Gelderen Agency (Netherlands)

Rockmill & Company (L)
647 Warren St, Brooklyn, NY 11217
Tel: 718-638-3990
E-mail: agentrockmill@yahoo.com
Key Personnel
Pres: Jayne Rockmill
Founded: 1989
Represents artists, photographers & writers, specializing in illustrated books & licensing. For illustrated titles, submit a book summary, with sample text & illustrations along with author bio. For fiction & nonfiction book projects, submit a query letter with 3 sample chapters. Send SASE if anything needs to be returned.

Marie Rodell-Frances Collin Literary Agency, see Frances Collin Literary Agent

Linda Roghaar Literary Agency Inc (L)
133 High Point Dr, Amherst, MA 01002
Tel: 413-256-1921 *Fax:* 413-256-2636
E-mail: contact@lindaroghaar.com
Web Site: www.lindaroghaar.com
Key Personnel
Pres: Linda L Roghaar (AAR)
Founded: 1996
Full-service agency handling mainly nonfiction; women's issues, religion & spirituality, history, self-help, letters, diaries, personal accounts, memoir. Manage comprehensive rights. Query with SASE first. No reading fee. No unsol mss.

The Roistacher Literary Agency (L)
545 W 111 St, New York, NY 10025
Tel: 212-222-1405

Key Personnel
Pres: Robert E Roistacher *E-mail:* rer41@columbia.edu
Founded: 1978
General nonfiction, especially journalism, social science & public policy. Literary fiction only from published writers. No unsol mss, query first. Submit prospectus, curriculum vitae, two sample chapters, chapter outline & table of contents. No reading fee.

The Rosenberg Group (L)
23 Lincoln Ave, Marblehead, MA 01945
Tel: 781-990-1341 *Fax:* 781-990-1344
Web Site: www.rosenberggroup.com
Key Personnel
Agent: Barbara Collins Rosenberg (AAR)
Founded: 1998
No unsol mss, query first; handle film & TV rights on agency projects only; no phone calls or faxes; no electronic queries. No reading fee; other fees charged (photocopies, mailing international telephone calls, etc).
Foreign Rep(s): Representatives in all foreign markets
Membership(s): Authors Guild of America; Romance Writers of America

Rita Rosenkranz Literary Agency (L)
440 West End Ave, Suite 15D, New York, NY 10024-5358
Tel: 212-873-6333 *Fax:* 212-873-5225
Key Personnel
Agent: Rita Rosenkranz (AAR)
Founded: 1988
Specialize in nonfiction, adult; no unsol mss, query first with SASE. Submit outline & sample chapters. No fees.
Membership(s): Authors Guild; International Women's Writing Guild

Rosenstone/Wender (L-D)
38 E 29 St, 10th fl, New York, NY 10016
Tel: 212-725-9445 *Fax:* 212-725-9447
Key Personnel
Literary Agent: Susan Perlman Cohen; Sonia Pabley (AAR) *E-mail:* spabley@rosenstonewender.com; Phyllis Wender (AAR)
Fiction, nonfiction, adult & juvenile, film & TV rights. No unsol mss, query first. No reading fee.
Foreign Rights: The English Agency (Japan); La Nouvelle Agence (France); Licht & Burr (Scandinavia); Mohrbooks (Germany)

The Roth Agency (L)
138 Bay State Rd, Rehoboth, MA 02769
Tel: 508-252-5818
Key Personnel
Pres: Shelley Roth
Specialize in nonfiction including: psychology, social issues, women's issues, strong narratives, health, family/parenting, business/career, current affairs & cutting-edge issues, journalism, fiction (both literary & commercial). Handle film & TV rights. No phone queries. No unsol mss. For fiction query letter by mail with SASE. For nonfiction, send proposal, sample chapters, author bio & history of ms with SASE. No reading fee. Sub-agents in Hollywood for film & TV rights.
Foreign Rep(s): Agents in all principal foreign countries

Carol Susan Roth Literary & Creative (L)
PO Box 620337, Woodside, CA 94062
Tel: 650-323-3795
E-mail: carol@authorsbest.com
Founded: 1985
Previously Carol Susan Roth Presents! producing & promoting public events for best selling authors, including Scott Peck, Bernie Siegel & John Gray. Specialize in health, spirituality,

personal growth, business (nonfiction only). No unsol mss, query first with proposal & SASE. Submit proposal with two sample chapters & media kit, video & SASE. No fees charged.

Titles recently placed: *Baby Yoga*, Helen Garabedian; *Consumer Confidential*, Michael Finney; *DoJo Wisdom*, Jennifer Lawler; *Home Recording For Dummies*, Jeff Strong; *How Great Decisions Get Made*, Don Maruska; *Shifting Sands*, Steve Donohue; *The Highest Goal*, Michael Ray; *The Intenship Advantage*, Dario Bravo

Jane Rotrosen Agency LLC (L)
318 E 51 St, New York, NY 10022
Tel: 212-593-4330 *Fax:* 212-935-6985
Key Personnel
Contact: Jane Rotrosen Berkey (AAR) *E-mail:* jberkey@janerotrosen.com; Andrea Cirillo *E-mail:* acirillo@janerotrosen.com; Peggy Gordijn *E-mail:* pgordijn@janerotrosen.com; Annelise Robey *E-mail:* arobey@janerotrosen.com; Margaret Ruley *E-mail:* mruley@janerotrosen.com
Busn Aff: Donald Cleary *E-mail:* dcleary@janerotrosen.com
Founded: 1974
Fiction & nonfiction. No unsol mss or queries. Query by referral only. Handle film & TV rights. No reading fee. 15% commission in USA & Canada. Co-represented abroad & on the west coast.
Membership(s): Authors Guild

Damaris Rowland (L)
5 Peter Cooper Rd, No 13H, New York, NY 10010
Tel: 212-475-8942 *Fax:* 212-358-9411
Founded: 1994
Fiction & nonfiction. Handle film & TV rights. No unsol mss, query first with SASE. Submit outline & sample chapters.
Membership(s): AAR; Authors Guild; Mystery Writers of America; Romance Writers of America

Peter Rubie Literary Agency (L)
240 W 35 St, Suite 500, New York, NY 10001
Tel: 212-279-1776 *Fax:* 212-279-0927
E-mail: pralit@aol.com
Web Site: www.prlit.com
Key Personnel
Pres & Agent: Peter Rubie (AAR) *Tel:* 212-279-6214 *E-mail:* peterrubie@compuserve.com
Agent: June Clark *Tel:* 212-279-1776 *E-mail:* pralit@aol.com; Hanna Rubin *Tel:* 212-279-1282 *E-mail:* hanna.rubin@prlit.com
Founded: 2000
High quality fiction & nonfiction. Handle film, TV & foreign rights through sub-agents. No unsol mss. Query first. Submit outline & first two chapters with one page query letter & proposal. No reading fees. Photocopying fees. Some foreign mailing charges.
Titles recently placed: *Body Clock Advantage*, Mathew Edlund, MD; *Emperor & the Wolf*, Stewart Galbraith IV; *Heart So Hungry*, Randall Silvis; *History of American Prayer*, James P Moore, Jr; *No One Left Behind*, Amy Yarsinske; *On Night's shore*, Randall Silvis; *Soupy Sez*, Soupy Sales; *Telling the Story*, Peter Rubie; *The Child Goddess*, Louise Marley; *The Maquisarde*, Louise Marley; *Unfinished Business*, Harlan Ullman; *Walking Money*, James O Born
Foreign Rep(s): Big Apple Tuttle Mori (China); English Agency (Japan); David Grossman (UK); International Editors (Spain & Latin America); Lenclud Agency (France); Lennart Sane (Scandinavia); Literary Agency YRJ (Korea); Piergiorgio Nicolazzini (Italy); Prara I Prevodi (Eastern Europe); Thomas Schluck (Germany)

Russell & Volkening Inc (L)
50 W 29 St, Suite 7E, New York, NY 10001
Tel: 212-684-6050 *Fax:* 212-889-3026
Key Personnel
Pres: Timothy Seldes (AAR)
Founded: 1940
General fiction & nonfiction, film & TV rights, no screenplays; no romance or science fiction; submit outline & two sample chapters; no reading fee.
Foreign Rep(s): A M Heath & Co Ltd
Foreign Rights: Tuttle-Mori Agency (Japan)

Regina Ryan Publishing Enterprises Inc (L)
251 Central Park W, Suite 7D, New York, NY 10024
Tel: 212-787-5589
E-mail: queryreginaryanbooks@rcn.com
Founded: 1976
Book length adult nonfiction. Specialize in narrative nonfiction, psychology, popular culture, health, diet & fitness, self-help, parenting, nature, gardening, pets, art, architecture, design, memoirs, general history & biography, science, illustrated books, cookbooks, contemporary issues, especially women's issues. No poetry or science fiction; no unsol mss; query first, preferably by e-mail at queryreginaryanbooks@aol.com. If by mail, with SASE. No queries by fax or phone. Include resume, synopsis & sample, double-spaced; outline/table of contents, identify competition & market. No software, plays or movie scripts; no reading fee; handle film TV & foreign rights. Agents in major foreign countries.
Titles recently placed: *Autopsy of a Suicide*, Edwin Shneidman; *Beyond the Bake Sale: The Ultimate School Fund-Raising Book*, Jean Joachim; *Escape From Saigon*, Andrea Warren; *Ideas Triumphant: Women Building Movements That Change Society*, Lawrence Lader; *The Dowry*, Walter Keady; *Thomas Eakins (rev ed)*, William Innes Homer; *What Babies Say Before They Can Talk*, Paul Holinger MD
Membership(s): Women's Media Group

The Sagalyn Literary Agency (L)
7201 Wisconsin Ave, Suite 675, Bethesda, MD 20814
Tel: 301-718-6440 *Fax:* 301-718-6444
E-mail: agency@sagalyn.com
Web Site: www.sagalyn.com
Key Personnel
Agent: Jennifer Graham; Raphael Sagalyn (AAR)
Adult fiction & nonfiction. No unsol mss, query first with SASE. Handle film & TV rights. No reading fee.
Titles recently placed: *In the Company of Soldiers: A Chronicle of Combat in Iraq*, Rick Atkinson; *The Perfect Wife: The Life & Choices of Laura Bush*, Ann Gerhart; *The Priestly Sins*, Andrew M Greeley
Foreign Rights: Carmen Balcells (Spain); Bardon-Chinese Media (China); Graal (Poland); Greene & Heaton (UK); Korea Copyright Center (Korea); Michelle Lapautre (France); Licht & Burr (Scandinavia); Mohrbooks (Germany); Lucia Riff (Brazil); Caroline van Gelderen (Netherlands)

Victoria Sanders & Associates (L)
241 Avenue of the Americas, Suite 11H, New York, NY 10014
Tel: 212-633-8811 *Fax:* 212-633-0525
E-mail: queriesvsa@hotmail.com
Web Site: www.victoriasanders.com
Key Personnel
Partner: Diane Dickensheid; Victoria Sanders (AAR) *E-mail:* vsanders@victoriasanders.com
Founded: 1993
Fiction, both literary & commercial, African American, Asian & Latin; of special interest, women's, biography, history, autobiography, psychology, women's studies, gay studies, politics. No unsol mss, query first. E-mail queries only. Consult www.victoriasanders.com for address & further information. Handle film & TV rights.
Titles recently placed: *And the Shadows Took Him*, Daniel Chacon; *Asphalt*, Carl Hancock Rux; *Can't Stop, Won't Stop: Politics of the Hip-Hop Generation*, Jeff Chang; *Daughter*, asha bandele; *Earthbound & Heavenbent: Elizabeth Porter Phelps & Life at Forty Acres*, Elizabeth Porter Phelps; *Faithless*, Karin Slaughter; *Indelible*, Karin Slaughter; *Lemon City*, Elaine Brown; *Like A Charm*, Karin Slaughter; *My Jim*, Nancy Rawless; *Seasons of the Day*, Cecelie Berry; *The Spirit of Harlem*, Marberry & Cunningham
Foreign Rights: Chandler Crawford (all territories)

Sandum & Associates (L)
144 E 84 St, New York, NY 10028
Tel: 212-737-2011 *Fax:* 212-737-9296
Key Personnel
Man Dir: Howard E Sandum
Founded: 1987
Primarily nonfiction & literary fiction. No unsol mss, query first; submit one-page letter with brief author bio & several sample pages with SASE; no reading fee. New clients by referral only; handle film & TV rights.
Foreign Office(s): Scott Ferris Associates, London, United Kingdom
Foreign Rep(s): The English Agency (Japan); Scott Ferris Associates (UK); Lennart Sane Agency (Portugal, Scandinavia, Spain)

Jack Scagnetti Talent & Literary Agency (L-D)
5118 Vineland Ave, Suite 102, North Hollywood, CA 91601
Tel: 818-762-3871; 818-761-0580
Web Site: www.jackscagnetti.com
Key Personnel
Owner: Jack Scagnetti
Founded: 1974
Fiction & nonfiction books, sports, health & automobiles, how-to, no juveniles; screenplays, TV & film treatments. No unsol mss, query first. Submit synopsis, first chapter for books; paragraph or one-page synopsis for scripts. No reading fee, charge one-way postage for multiple submissions, 10% commission, 15% for books. Detailed critique & consultation services available for books on hourly basis. Signatory to Writer's Guild of America-West. Represented self in sale of 15 books which led to representing writer friends & others.
Membership(s): ATAS; Writers Guild of America West

Schiavone Literary Agency Inc (L-D)
236 Trails End, West Palm Beach, FL 33413-2135
Tel: 561-966-9294 *Fax:* 561-966-9294
E-mail: profschia@aol.com
Web Site: www.publishersmarketplace.com/members/profschia
Key Personnel
Pres: James Schiavone
Founded: 1996
Fiction & nonfiction, all genres: children's & young adult, scholarly books, textbooks, specialize in celebrity biography & autobiography & memoirs. No poetry. No unsol mss, query first with letter & SASE. No queries via phone

or fax. E-mail queries consisting of one page are acceptable (no attachments). No fees; commissions 15% domestic, 20% foreign. Representation in foreign markets.
Titles recently placed: *A Brother's Journey: Surviving a Childhood of Abuse*, Richard B Pelzer
Branch Office(s)
3671 Hudson Manor Terr, No 11H, Bronx, NY 10463-1139, Pres: James Schiavone *Tel:* 718-548-5332 (only June, July & Aug)
Foreign Rights: Iceberg Inc (Bulgaria, Eastern Europe); A Mediation Litteraire (France, Central Europe)
Membership(s): NEA

Wendy Schmalz Agency (L)
PO Box 831, Hudson, NY 12534-0831
Tel: 518-672-7697 *Fax:* 518-672-7662
E-mail: wendy@schmalzagency.com
Key Personnel
Owner: Wendy Schmalz (AAR)
Founded: 2002
Adult & children's fiction & nonfiction. Novel: complete ms; nonfiction: overview/sample chapters. No reading fees.
Foreign Rep(s): David Higham Associates (UK)

Harold Schmidt Literary Agency (L-D)
415 W 23 St, Suite 6F, New York, NY 10011
Tel: 212-727-7473
E-mail: hslanyc@aol.com
Key Personnel
Pres: Harold D Schmidt (AAR)
Specialize in fiction & nonfiction, film & TV rights, reprint rights for small presses & university presses. No unsol mss, query first with SASE; no reading fee. Representatives in Hollywood & in all principal foreign countries.
Foreign Rights: Agenzia Letteraria Internazionale (Italy); Lora Fountain (France); Japan UNI Agency (Japan); Lennart Sane Agency AB (Netherlands, Latin America, Scandinavia, Spain); Peake Associates (UK); Thomas Schluck Literary & Art Agency (Germany)

Susan Schulman, A Literary Agency (L-D)
454 W 44 St, New York, NY 10036
Tel: 212-713-1633 *Fax:* 212-581-8830
E-mail: schulman@aol.com
Web Site: www.susanschulman.com
Key Personnel
Owner: Susan Schulman (AAR)
Founded: 1980
Adult book-length genre & literary fiction & nonfiction especially women's studies, biography, psychology & the social sciences. No unsol mss. Query first with SASE or by e-mail. Submit outline & three sample chapters. No reading fee. Co-agent in all principal foreign countries. Handles film & TV rights for other agencies & individual titles.
Branch Office(s)
2 Bryan Plaza, Washington Depot, CT 06794
Tel: 860-868-3700 *Fax:* 860-868-3704
Foreign Rep(s): Elizabeth Atkins ACER (Portugal, South America, Spain); Big Apple Tuttle-Mori (China, Taiwan); Lora Fountain (France); Interrights Agency (Bulgaria); Korea Copyright Center (Korea); Leipman (Germany, Switzerland); Lennart Sane Agency (Scandinavia); Nurcihan Kesim (Turkey); Owl's Agency (Japan); Pikarski Literary Agency (Israel); Prava I Prevodi (Eastern Europe); The Rights Agency (French Canada); Synopsis Agency (Russia); Zevi Susanna Agency (Italy)
Membership(s): Authors Guild; The Dramatists Guild; Society of Children's Book Writers & Illustrators

A E Schwartz & Associates (L-D)
PO Box 79228, Waverley, MA 02479-0228
Tel: 617-926-9111 *Fax:* 617-926-0660

E-mail: pgbs@aeschwartz.com
Web Site: aeschwartz.com
Key Personnel
Pres: Andrew E Schwartz
Founded: 1985
Comprehensive organization, business, rights & permissions, publishing; specialize in human resource development, organizational development & related training topics, management, training & business how-to's. No unsol mss; query first. Submit outline & sample chapters. Handle software. Assist authors on all facets of contracting with publishers. Evaluation fee $175 (report).

Laurens R Schwartz, Esquire (L-D)
5 E 22 St, Suite 15-D, New York, NY 10010-5325
Tel: 212-228-2614
Founded: 1981
Full-service agency handling all media for all ages worldwide. No fees. Standard commissions; follow Guild requirements for Guild members. WGA Signatory. No unsol mss, CD-ROMs, transmissions, etc; query first with synopsis, resume, statement as to whether project has been shopped around or previously handled by an agent, & return mailer with prepaid postage. Only take on two to three new clients a year. Require four-week right of first refusal if request submission of work. Handle film & TV rights.
Membership(s): Writers Guild of America

S©ott Treimel NY (L)
434 Lafayette St, New York, NY 10003-6943
Tel: 212-505-8353 *Fax:* 212-505-0664
E-mail: st.ny@verizon.net
Key Personnel
Owner & Pres: Scott Treimel (AAR)
Founded: 1995
Represent children's book authors & illustrators: all categories from board & picture books through teen novels. No unsol mss (except for picture books, in which case send entire ms); requires 90-day exclusive for all submissions & queries. Submit outline & sample chapter for novels. Submissions received without proper SASE are recycled unread. Handle film & TV rights as subrights. No reading fee. Charges for messenger & photocopying.
Foreign Rep(s): Bardon (China); Donatella d'Ormesson (France); Annette Green (UK); Japan Uni (Japan); Michael Meller (Germany)
Membership(s): Authors Guild; Society of Children's Book Writers & Illustrators

Scovil Chichak Galen Literary Agency Inc (L)
381 Park Ave S, Suite 1020, New York, NY 10016
Tel: 212-679-8686 *Fax:* 212-679-6710
E-mail: mailroom@scglit.com
Web Site: www.scglit.com
Key Personnel
Pres: Russell Galen (AAR) *Tel:* 212-679-8686 ext 302 *E-mail:* rgalen@scglit.com
Man Dir: Jack Scovil *Tel:* 212-679-8686 ext 307 *E-mail:* jackscovil@scglit.com
Agent: Anna Ghosh (AAR) *Tel:* 212-679-8686 ext 301 *E-mail:* annaghosh@scglit.com
Founded: 1993
All types fiction & nonfiction, adult & juvenile. Handle film & TV rights. No unsol mss, query first. Submit outline & sample chapters. Does not charge fees.
Titles recently placed: *A Radical Line*, Thai Jones; *Lord John and the Private Matter*, Diana Gabaldon; *Testament*, Benson Bobrick
Foreign Rep(s): Baror International Inc (all other foreign rights)

Sebastian Agency (L)
557 W Seventh St, Suite 2, St Paul, MN 55102
Tel: 651-224-6670 *Fax:* 651-224-6895
Web Site: www.sebastianagency.com
Key Personnel
Owner & Agent: Laurie Harper (AAR)
E-mail: laurie@sebastianagency.com
Assoc Agent: Dawn Frederick *E-mail:* dawn@sebastianagency.com
Founded: 1985
Currently represent 40 plus authors of predominantly commercial nonfiction. No children's, poetry, scholarly material or original screenplays. Accepting few new clients, mainly by referral & generally for the following areas: history, science, biography (political, media-related, professional), business, psychology, health/nutrition, women's narratives, pop culture, social sciences, some women's fiction (approx. 1%). No unsol mss, query first (e-mail acceptable with no attachments). Submit outline or synopsis & sample chapters & SASE for fiction or proposal & SASE for nonfiction (hardcopies only - no electronic submissions). Do not send certified; use regular priority mail if proposal includes sample chapters. No reading fee. Commission is 15% domestic, 20% foreign. Handle subsidiary film & TV rights only from book sale not original scripts.
Titles recently placed: *Building Big Profits in Real Estate*, Wade Timmerson, Suzanne Caplan; *Forget Perfect!*, Lisa McLeod, JoAnn Swan Neely; *It Ends With You*, Tina Tessina; *Port in the Storm: How to Make a Medical Decision*, Cole Giller, MD; *The Art of the Advantage*, Kaihan Krippendorf; *The Warren Buffett Way, 2nd Ed*, Robert Hagstrom; *Untitled Betty Crocker Biography*, Susan Marks
Membership(s): Authors Guild

Lynn Seligman (L)
400 Highland Ave, Upper Montclair, NJ 07043
Tel: 973-783-3631
E-mail: seliglit@aol.com
Founded: 1986
Adult nonfiction & fiction. Handle film & TV rights through agents in Hollywood. Submit letter describing project with short sample. No unsol mss; query first with SASE. No reading fee.
Titles recently placed: *Family Inheritance*, Deborah Le Blanc; *My Father Before Me: How Fathers & Sons Influence Each Other Throughout Their Lives*, Dr Michael Diamond, Roberta Israeloff

Edythea Ginis Selman, Literary Agency Inc (L-D)
14 Washington Place, New York, NY 10003
Tel: 212-473-1874 *Fax:* 212-473-1875
Key Personnel
Pres & Agent: Edythea Ginis Selman (AAR)
Electronic Publg Dir: Richard Selman (AAR)
Literary commercial fiction & serious issue-oriented narrative nonfiction. Handle film & TV rights from novels, selected children's fiction/picture books (by referral only) in italics. No unsol mss, only upon request (with SASE). Submit author bio, two sample chapters or 50 pages (nonfiction) or complete ms (fiction). Must include SASE; fees for long distance phone & fax, mail, photocopy & consultation. Agent in Hollywood. Handle some children's multimedia interactive software.
Foreign Rights: Antonella Antonelli; Eliane Benisti (France); David Grossman (England); Ruth Liepman (Germany)
Membership(s): Authors Guild; International Copyright Society of America; National Writers Union; Society of Children's Book Writers & Illustrators; Women's National Book Association

Seventh Avenue Literary Agency (L-D)
Formerly Contemporary Management
Division of Contemporary Communications
1663 W Seventh Ave, Vancouver, BC V6J 1S4,
 Canada
Tel: 604-734-3663 *Fax:* 604-734-8906
Web Site: www.seventhavenuelit.com
Key Personnel
Dir: Robert Mackwood *E-mail:* rmackwood@
 seventhavenuelit.com
Literary Agent: Sally Harding *E-mail:* sharding@
 seventhavenuelit.com
Founded: 1974
Specialize in fiction & nonfiction. No unsol mss,
 query first. Expense fee of $200. Handle film
 & TV rights.

Mary Sue Seymour (L)
475 Miner Street Rd, Canton, NY 13617
Tel: 315-386-1831 *Fax:* 315-386-1037
E-mail: marysue@slic.com
Web Site: www.theseymouragency.com
Founded: 1992
Specialize in prescriptive nonfiction, women's
 fiction, Christian books, children's books, middle grade readers, young adult books. No short
 stories or poetry. No fees charged. Proposal &
 sample chapter 1 for nonfiction; query letter for
 fiction.
Titles recently placed: *2 untitled Harlequin Americans*, Penny McCusker; *250 Questions Home-
 buyers Ask*, Christie Craig; *Beloved Enemy*,
 Mary Schaller; *Everything Roberts Rules Book*,
 Barbara Cameron; *Tao of Bridge*, Brent Manley; *The Everything Sewing Book*, Sandra De-
 trixhe; *untitled Harlequin American*, Shelley
 Sabga Galloway
Membership(s): Authors Guild; Christian Booksellers Association; Romance Writers of America

Charlotte Sheedy Literary Agency Inc (L)
Affiliate of Sterling Lord Literistic
65 Bleecker St, 12th fl, New York, NY 10012
Tel: 212-780-9800 *Fax:* 212-780-0308
E-mail: sheedy@sll.com
Key Personnel
Owner: Charlotte Sheedy
Exec Asst: Carolyn Kim
Fiction & nonfiction film & TV rights. No unsol
 mss, query first (no screenplays); submit out-
 line & sample chapters; no reading fee. Agents
 in all principal countries.
Foreign Rep(s): The English Agency (Japan);
 Agnes Krup (Australia, Germany, Italy, Por-
 tugal, Switzerland); Lennart Sane (Netherlands,
 Scandinavia, Spain); Abner Stein (England)

The Shepard Agency (L)
73 Kingswood Dr, Bethel, CT 06801
Tel: 203-790-4230; 203-790-1780 *Fax:* 203-798-
 2924
E-mail: shepardagcy@mindspring.com
Web Site: home.mindspring.com/~shepardagcy
Key Personnel
Pres & Dir: Jean H Shepard
VP & Treas: Lance Hastings Shepard
Founded: 1986
Specialize in adult, children, general trade fiction
 & nonfiction, professional, reference & busi-
 ness. Handle film & TV rights. No unsol mss,
 e-mail queries only, include proposal & outline.
 No reading fee. Commission only on placed
 material (15%). Fee charged for long distance
 telephone calls, photocopying & postage.

The Robert E Shepard Agency (L)
1608 Dwight Way, Berkeley, CA 94703-1804
Tel: 510-849-3999
E-mail: query@shepardagency.com
Web Site: www.shepardagency.com

Key Personnel
Pres: Robert E Shepard
Founded: 1994
Nonfiction only, most subject areas, except memoir & spirituality. Specialize in narrative nonfiction, history, current affairs, pop culture,
 business, science for lay people, Judaica &
 gay/lesbian. No unsol mss, query first with
 SASE. Prefer queries by e-mail (no attach-
 ments) or regular mail. Do not phone or fax.
 Submit overview, annotated outline, curriculum
 vitae & two sample chapters. See website for
 guidelines. No reading fee. Handle film & TV
 rights.
Titles recently placed: *Gallant Harvest*, Donald
 Kladstrup, Petie Kladstrup; *Leave the Office
 Earlier*, Laura Stack; *The Root of Wild Mad-
 der*, Brian Murphy
Foreign Rep(s): The Chandler Crawford Agency
 (Europe)
Foreign Rights: The Chandler Crawford Agency
 (Europe)
Membership(s): Authors Guild

Ken Sherman & Associates (L-D)
9507 Santa Monica Blvd, Suite 211, Beverly
 Hills, CA 90210
Tel: 310-273-8840 *Fax:* 310-271-2875
E-mail: ksassociates@earthlink.net
Key Personnel
Pres: Ken Sherman
Founded: 1989
Fiction & nonfiction books plus screenplays, tele-
 plays, film & TV rights to books & life rights.
 No unsol mss. By referral only. Submit outline
 & minimun three sample chapters. No reading
 fee, ms copying charges if necessary.
Titles recently placed: *Backroads*, Tawni O'Dell;
 Henry, An Unlikely Hero, Kari Rene Hall;
 Prince of Persia, Jordan Mechner; *The Witches
 of Eastwick-The Musical*, John Updike; *Webs of
 Power*, Starhawk
Membership(s): American Film Institute Third
 Decade Council; ATAS; British Academy of
 Film & Television Arts/Los Angeles; PEN In-
 ternational

Wendy Sherman Associates Inc (L)
450 Seventh Ave, Suite 3004, New York, NY
 10123
Tel: 212-279-9027 *Fax:* 212-279-8863
Key Personnel
Pres: Wendy Sherman (AAR) *E-mail:* wendy@
 wsherman.com
Agent: Tracy Brown *E-mail:* tracy@wsherman.
 com
Founded: 1999
Represent a wide variety of fiction & nonfiction.
 Quality & commercial fiction, including sus-
 pense & upmarket women's fiction; nonfiction
 includes, narrative, practical & general nonfic-
 tion. No unsol mss. Query first, with SASE.
 Send synopsis & two sample chapters. No fees
 are charged. Go to www.wsherman.com for
 submission details, no longer accepting e-mail
 queries.
Titles recently placed: *Alvin Ailey: Dance Moves!*,
 Lise Friedman; *Breach of Trust*, D W Buffa;
 Chuch Close Portraits, Martin Friedman;
 Mating in Captivity, Esther Perel; *Past Due*,
 William Lashner; *Real Love*, Dr Greg Baer;
 Schopenhauer's Telescope, Gerard Donovan;
 Smarty Jones, Maggie Estep; *Southern Living*,
 Ad Hudler; *The Cloud Atlas*, Liam Callanan;
 The Holy Thief, Rabbi Mark Borovitz, Alan
 Eisenstock; *The Ice Chorus*, Sarah Stonich; *The
 Judas Field*, Howard Bahr; *The Kindergarten
 Wars*, Alan Eisenstock; *The Sea of Tears*, Nani
 Power; *When Dad Hurts Mom*, Lundy Bancroft
Foreign Rep(s): Jenny Meyer Literary Agency
 (UK, World, translation)
Foreign Rights: Jenny Meyer Literary Agency
Membership(s): Women's Media Group

Bobbe Siegel Literary Agency (L)
41 W 83 St, New York, NY 10024
Tel: 212-877-4985 *Fax:* 212-877-4985
E-mail: bobbesiegelagency@yahoo.com
Key Personnel
Owner: Bobbe Siegel
Assoc: Peter Siegel
Founded: 1973
Fiction & nonfiction originals; literary fiction,
 mysteries, suspense, fantasy, biography, true
 crime, New Age & sports. No juvenile, poetry,
 short stories, essays, humor, romance or cook-
 books. No unsol mss, query first with SASE.
 Submit plot outline & previous publications for
 fiction, description of project & author back-
 ground to show ability to handle subject for
 nonfiction. No reading fee. Fees for fax, pho-
 tocopies, overseas calls & packages. Handle
 foreign rights for literary agents, publishers &
 authors.
Titles recently placed: *Crofton's Fire*, Keith
 Coplin; *National Baseball Hall of Fame What
 Baseball Means to Me*, Carl Smith; *Storied
 Stadiums*, Curt Smith; *The Executioner's Mark*,
 Dick Cady
Foreign Rep(s): Agence Hoffman (France); Agen-
 zia Letteraria Internazionale (Italy); Amina
 Marix Evans (Netherlands); Bardon-Chinese
 Agency (China, Hong Kong, Malaysia, Tai-
 wan); Book Publisher Association of Israel
 (Israel); DRT International (Korea); Japan
 UNI (Japan); Simona Kessler (Romania);
 Ruth Liepman AG (Germany); Ulla Lohren
 (Scandinavia); David Matlock (Russia); John
 Pawsey (England); Prava I Prevoda (Eastern
 Block); Karin Schindler, Rts Rep (Brazil);
 Maria Starz-Kanska (Poland); Transnet Con-
 tracts Ltd (Czech Republic); Julio F Yanez
 Agencia Literaria (Spain)
Membership(s): Other Agents' Group

**Rosalie Siegel, International Literary Agent
 Inc** (L)
One Abey Dr, Pennington, NJ 08534
Tel: 609-737-1007 *Fax:* 609-737-3708
E-mail: rsiegel@ix.netcom.com
Key Personnel
President: Rosalie Siegel (AAR)
Adult fiction, nonfiction & foreign books, film &
 TV rights. No unsol mss; query first; no read-
 ing fee. Representatives in all major European
 countries & Asian countries. Not actively seek-
 ing new clients.

Evelyn Singer Agency Inc (L)
PO Box 594, White Plains, NY 10602-0594
Tel: 914-949-1147 *Fax:* 914-948-5565
Key Personnel
Pres: Evelyn Singer
Founded: 1951
Adult & juvenile (fourth grade to young adult
 reading level): nonfiction & fiction; biography,
 celebrity, career, contemporary culture, poli-
 tics, health, fitness, mature, ecology, personal
 finance, science, technology, suspense & literary. No romance or westerns. No original
 TV, motion picture or dramatic scripts; film
 & TV rights for published books already handled. No poetry. No unsol mss, query first with
 SASE. Submit outline plus two chapters, Curriculum vitae double spaced on 8 1/2" x 11"
 bond paper, printed or typed. No reading fee.
 Fees for long distance calls, ms postal charge,
 foreign mail & authorized legal & editorial services using non-agency personnel. Agents in all
 principal countries & on the West Coast. Must
 have earned $20,000 from free-lance writing.
 Handle film & TV rights of books represented
 by agency. Do not phone or fax; mail only; include SASE to return ms.
Titles recently placed: *Czech Republic*, Nakla-
 datelstvi; *Finland*, Paiva Osakeyhtio; *God's*

Smuggler, Brother Andrew; *Hiding Place*, Ten Boon; *The Return of Gabriel*, John Armistead
Foreign Rep(s): Laurence Pollinger Ltd (UK)

Irene Skolnick Literary Agency (L)
22 W 23 St, 5th fl, New York, NY 10010
Tel: 212-727-3648 *Fax:* 212-727-1024
E-mail: sirene35@aol.com
Key Personnel
CEO: Irene Skolnick (AAR)
Founded: 1994
Adult literary fiction & nonfiction, biography, memoir, current & contemporary affairs, gardening, travel; handle film & TV rights. No unsol mss, query first with SASE. Submit outline & sample chapter. No reading fee.
Titles recently placed: *Don't Get Too Comfortable*, David Rakoff; *Intuition*, Allegra Goodman; *Seven Lies*, James Lasdun; *The Verneys*, Adrian Tinniswood; *Two Lives*, Vikram Seth
Foreign Rights: Agents in Hollywood & principal foreign countries
Membership(s): PEN American Center; Women's Media Group

SLC Enterprises Inc (L-D)
6965 Oakbrook SE, Grand Rapids, MI 49546
Tel: 616-942-2665 (answering serv & voice mail) *Toll Free Tel:* 800-420-7222
Toll Free Fax: 800-420-7222
E-mail: candp5@comcast.net
Key Personnel
Pres: Stephen Cogil Casari
VP: Carole Golin
Founded: 1985
Fiction & nonfiction; specialize in first novelists. Children's books, women's issues, Judaica, sports, baseball. No unsol mss, query first. Submit proposal, outline &/or sample chapters. Reading fee ($150) per ms, refunded if sold. Evaluation & discussion of publishability. No additional fees. Handle film & TV rights.
Titles recently placed: *Baseball Was Then*, Vic Debs; *Full View*, Pegi Taylor; *The Raiders*, John Lomardo

Sligo Literary Agency LLC (L)
74-923 Hwy 111, Suite 173, Indian Wells, CA 92210
Tel: 760-340-6640 *Fax:* 760-340-4320
E-mail: ricsligo@aol.com
Key Personnel
Pres: Eric Bollinger
Agent: Kelly Myers
Founded: 1998
Represent authors to publishers. Work with co-agents for TV movie rights. E-mail a query first. No reading or evaluation fee.
Titles recently placed: *Golfing in the Zone, The Short Game*, Ron Di Zinno; *Golfing in the Zone: The Long Game*, Ron Di Zinno; *Master the Mental Game*, Dr Jim Thorness; *The Eagle Heist, A Beauford Sloan Mystery*, Raymond Austin
Foreign Rep(s): Thomas Schlueck (Germany); Japan Uni Agency; Several Foreign Reps in the UK

Beverley Slopen Literary Agency (L)
131 Bloor St W, Suite 711, Toronto, ON M5S 1S3, Canada
Tel: 416-964-9598 *Fax:* 416-921-7726
E-mail: beverley@slopenagency.ca
Web Site: www.slopenagency.on.ca
Founded: 1973
Serious fiction & nonfiction. No children's books, illustrated books, science fiction or fantasy. No software, no film or TV rights handled. Query letter & brief proposal sent by mail with Canadian postage if you want it returned; not taking on many new clients.

Titles recently placed: *Baroque-a-Nova*, Kevin Chong; *Downhill Chance*, Donna Morrissey; *Fatal Passage*, Ken McGoogan; *Marc Edwards Mystery Series*, Don Gutteridge; *Midnight Cab*, James W Nichol; *The Resue of Jerusalem*, Henry T Aubin
Foreign Rep(s): Agenzia Letteraria Internazionale (Italy); Paul & Peter Fritz (Germany); David Grossman (UK); Istanbul Literary Agency (Turkey); Alexander Korzhenevski (Russia); Michelle Lapautre (France); Licht & Burr Literary Agency (Scandinavia); Lucia Riff (Brazil); Tuttle-Mori (Japan); Julio F Yanez (Spain)

Smith/Skolnik Literary Management (L)
963 Belvidere, Plainfield, NJ 07060
Tel: 908-822-1870 *Fax:* 908-822-1871
Key Personnel
Pres: Nikki Smith
Adult fiction & nonfiction. No unsol mss, query first with SASE. No reading fee charged. Representatives in principal foreign countries.

Valerie Smith, Literary Agent (L)
1746 Rte 44-55, Modena, NY 12548
Tel: 845-883-5848
Key Personnel
Contact: Valerie Smith
Founded: 1978
Fiction & nonfiction; special interest in fantasy & science ficton. No unsol mss, query first; no reading fee. Representatives in Hollywood & all principal foreign countries. Outline & three sample chapters.
Titles recently placed: *Point of Honour*, Madeline Robins; *The Kings Peace*, Jo Walton

Michael Snell Literary Agency (L)
Subsidiary of H Michael Snell Inc
PO Box 1206, Truro, MA 02666-1206
Tel: 508-349-3718
Key Personnel
Pres: H Michael Snell
VP: Patricia Smith
Founded: 1979
Adult nonfiction; all levels of business & management from popular trade to professional reference; legal, medical, health, psychology, self-help & how-to books; animals & pets; women's issues in business, family & society; popular science & business; technical & scientific; professional & general computer books; parenting & relationships; project development & rewrite services. Welcome new authors. No unsol mss, query first. Submit outline, synopsis & up to 50 sample pages with SASE. Publication *How to Write a Book Proposal* available upon request with SASE, or consult Michael Shell's book, from *Book Idea to Bestseller* (Prima Publishing). Consider new clients on an exclusive basis.
Titles recently placed: *Conquering Consumer Space*, Michael Solomon; *Dreamcrafting*, Paul Levesque; *Fit & Fat*, Sally Edwards

Sobel Weber Associates Inc (L)
146 E 19 St, New York, NY 10003
Tel: 212-420-8585 *Fax:* 212-505-1017
E-mail: info@sobelweber.com
Web Site: www.sobelweber.com
Key Personnel
Contact: Nat Sobel; Judith Weber
General fiction & nonfiction. No unsol mss, query first with SASE, no electronic submissions. No reading fee. Handle film, TV & foreign rights; serialization & audio rights. Representatives on the West Coast & in all major foreign countries. Consult website for submission guidelines & client list.
Foreign Rights: Abner Stein (UK)

Southeast Literary Agency (L)
PO Box 910, Sharpes, FL 32959-0910
Tel: 321-632-5019
Key Personnel
Agent: Debbie Fine
Founded: 1996
Adult fiction & nonfiction, children's & young adult, poetry & short stories; represent new & previously published authors. Accept unsol mss. Submit complete ms, a one- to two-page synopsis for fiction, outline for nonfiction, marketing letter with SASE, standard double-space ms format. All editing should be complete. No reading fee.
Titles recently placed: *Gathering in the Garden*, Shelley Snow, Elaine Husband; *Self-Healing Reiki*, Barbara Emerson; *The Girl in the Red Cadillac*, Vernon Lichliter; *Your Turn in the Sun*, Edward Hammack Jr

Spectrum Literary Agency (L)
320 Central Park W, Suite 1-D, New York, NY 10025
Tel: 212-362-4323 *Fax:* 212-362-4562
Web Site: www.spectrumliteraryagency.com
Key Personnel
Pres & Agent: Eleanor Wood *E-mail:* eleanor@spectrumliteraryagency.com
Agent: Lucienne Diver (AAR) *E-mail:* varkat@attglobal.net
Founded: 1976
Commercial fiction & nonfiction. No unsol mss, query first. No reading fee. Agents in all principal foreign countries.
Titles recently placed: *For Us the Living*, Robert A Heinlein; *Paladin of Souls*, Lois McMaster Bujold; *Ringworld's Children*, Larry Niven; *Shield of the Sky*, Susan Krinard; *The Elder Gods*, David Eddings
Membership(s): Mystery Writers of America; Romance Writers of America; Science Fiction & Fantasy Writers of America

The Spieler Agency (L)
154 W 57 St, 13th fl, Rm 135, New York, NY 10019
Tel: 212-757-4439
Web Site: spieleragency.com
Key Personnel
Agent: Lisa M Ross; F Joseph Spieler; John F Thornton
Agent (Oakland, CA Office): Victoria Shoemaker
Assoc: Katya Balter *Tel:* 212-757-4439 ext 201
E-mail: katya@spieleragency.com
Agent: Deirdre Mullane
Nonfiction & literary fiction; children's books. Areas of interest include: environmental issues, business; women's issues; natural history & science for religious studies, psychology; health; history; biography. No unsol mss, query first with letter, prefer online submissions, no phone queries. Address all submissions attn: Katya Balter. Submit author background, description of work & sample chapter with SASE. Handle film & TV rights only for book clients. No reading fee.
Titles recently placed: *A Biography of Yassir Arafat*, Barry Rubin, Judith Colp Rubin; *A Needle to the Heart: Special Military Operations from the Heroic to the Nuclear Age*, Derek Leebaert; *Shark Chronicles*, Beverly MacMillan, Jack A Musick; *The Sudden Sea: The Great New England Hurricane of 1938*, R A Scotti
Branch Office(s)
Spieler Agency West, 4096 Piedmont Ave, Oakland, CA 94611, Contact: Victoria Shoemaker
Tel: 510-985-1422 *Fax:* 510-985-1323
Foreign Rights: Abner Stein Literary Agency (England); The Marsh Agency (Continental Europe)

Philip G Spitzer Literary Agency (L)
50 Talmage Farm Lane, East Hampton, NY 11937
Tel: 631-329-3650 *Fax:* 631-329-3651
E-mail: spitzer516@aol.com
Key Personnel
Contact: Philip Spitzer (AAR)
Literary fiction, suspense/thriller, general nonfiction, sports, politics, social issues, biography, film & TV rights. No unsol mss, query first with SASE, submit outline & sample chapters. No reading fee, photocopying fee. Foreign rights agents in all major markets.

Nancy Stauffer Associates (L-D)
PO Box 1203, Darien, CT 06820
Tel: 203-655-3717 *Fax:* 203-655-3704
E-mail: nanstauf@optonline.net
Key Personnel
Pres: Nancy Stauffer Cahoon
Founded: 1989
Literary fiction & literary, narrative nonfiction. No children's books or genre fiction. No unsol mss, query first with SASE (no e-mail queries). Handle film & TV rights for book clients only. Agents in all foreign markets.

Lyle Steele & Co Ltd Literary Agents (L)
511 E 73 St, Suite 6, New York, NY 10021
Tel: 212-288-2981
Key Personnel
Pres: Lyle Steele *E-mail:* lyol@aol.com
General fiction & nonfiction. Specialize in health, popular psychology, parenting, popular business, current events, biography, issue-oriented nonfiction. Handle film & TV rights. No unsol mss; query first; submit outline & sample chapters. No reading fee. Agents in Hollywood & many foreign countries.

Michael Steinberg Literary Agent (L)
PO Box 274, Glencoe, IL 60022-0274
Tel: 847-835-4000 *Fax:* 847-835-8881
E-mail: michael14steinberg@comcast.net
Key Personnel
Principal: Michael Steinberg
Founded: 1980
Book-length fiction (mystery, science fiction) & nonfiction (business topics). No unsol mss, query first. Submit outline & first three chapters (hardcopy). Will read only by personal reference from represented author or editor. $75 reading fee (waived for published authors) & other fees, including postage & phone. Rarely handle software occasionally & rarely handle TV & film rights.
Titles recently placed: *Be Ready This Time!*, Jake Bernstein; *Electronic Day Trader*, Jake Bernstein; *Euro Trading*, Jake Bernstein; *Guide to Investing*, Michael Steinberg; *How to Trade the New Stock Futures*, Jake Bernstein; *Stockmarket Electronic Day Trader*, Jake Bernstein; *Winning in the Futures Market*, Jake Bernstein

Sterling Lord Literistic Inc (L)
65 Bleecker St, New York, NY 10012
Tel: 212-780-6050 *Fax:* 212-780-6095
Key Personnel
Chmn: Sterling Lord
V Chmn: Peter Matson
Pres: Philippa Brophy
VP: Chris Calhoun; Laurie Liss (AAR)
Agent: Claudia Cross (AAR); Neeti Madan; George Nicholson; Jim Rutman; Charlotte Sheedy
Fiction & nonfiction; film & TV rights. No unsol mss, query first; submit outline & sample chapters with SASE; no reading fee. Affiliated agency: Charlotte Sheedy Agency.

Foreign Rep(s): Andrew Nurnberg Associates (& UK, world exc Japan)
Foreign Rights: The English Agency (Japan); Abner Stein (UK)

Gloria Stern (L-D)
12535 Chandler Blvd, Suite 3, North Hollywood, CA 91607
Tel: 818-508-6296 *Fax:* 818-508-6296
Web Site: www.geocities.com/athens/1980/writers.html
Founded: 1984
Specialize in long form fiction, screenplays & computer games/content design. Handle new media, software (CDs, DDS, DVDs & games), film & TV rights; genre & nonfiction. Gratuitous violence not accepted. No unsol mss, query first. Submit synopsis, author bio & resume with SASE. Double-spaced, one side only, one inch margins, numbered pages, unbound. $45 per hour reading fee or contractual. May require postage, photocopy & long distance telephone expenses. New authors may be charged screening fees for evaluation. A report is prepared with our findings & a printout is sent to the author. Consulting on electronic media.
Foreign Rep(s): Castilia Publishers, Sophia Vassileva (Bulgaria)

Gloria Stern Agency (L)
2929 Buffalo Speedway, Suite 2111, Houston, TX 77098
Tel: 713-963-8360 *Fax:* 713-963-8460
E-mail: dstern1391@earthlink.net
Key Personnel
Pres & Owner: Gloria Stern
Founded: 1976
Nonfiction, adult fiction, biography, history, politics, women's issues, self-help, health, science, education. No screenplays, poetry, science fiction & children's books. Handle film & TV rights for client's books. No unsol mss. Projects submitted only by recommendation from a known editor, client or author. No reading fee. Fee for copying, if requested. Representatives in all foreign countries.
Titles recently placed: *Faces of Feminism*, Sheila Tobias; *Republic of Dreams*, Ross Wetzsteon
Foreign Rep(s): A M Heath & Co Ltd (England & Europe); Longanesi & Co (Italy)
Foreign Rights: A M Heath & Co Ltd (UK); Lennart Sane Agency (Spain, Sweden); Michelle Lapautre (France); Mohrbooks (Germany, Switzerland); Eric Yang Agency (Korea)

Miriam Stern, Attorney-at-Law/Literary Agent (L-D)
303 E 83 St, 20th fl, New York, NY 10028
Tel: 212-794-1289
Fiction & nonfiction. No unsol mss, query first. Submit finished mss, treatments & proposals, outlines with sample chapters & artwork when applicable. Handle software, film & TV rights.

The Joan Stewart Agency (L)
800 Third Ave, 34th fl, New York, NY 10022
Tel: 212-418-7255 *Fax:* 212-486-6518
Key Personnel
Pres: Joan Stewart
Founded: 1983
Handle film & TV rights. No reading fee.

Stimola Literary Studio (L)
308 Chase Ct, Edgewater, NJ 07020
Tel: 201-945-9353 *Fax:* 201-945-9353
E-mail: LtryStudio@aol.com
Key Personnel
Pres: Rosemary B Stimola (AAR)
Founded: 1997

Literary agency specializing in fiction & nonfiction, preschool through young adult. Queries via e-mail or by mail. No unsol attachments. No fees.
Titles recently placed: *A Room on Lorelei St*, Mary Pearson; *Black & White*, Paul Volponi; *The Day the Dog Dressed Like Dad*, James Proimos, Tom Amico; *The History of Writing*, Denise Schmandt-Besserat
Foreign Rep(s): Schleuck Agency (Germany); Tuttle Mori (Japan)
Foreign Rights: Paul Marsh Agency (Worldwide exc Germany & Japan)
Membership(s): ALA; International Reading Association; Society of Children's Book Writers & Illustrators

Robin Straus Agency Inc (L)
229 E 79 St, New York, NY 10021
Tel: 212-472-3282 *Fax:* 212-472-3833
E-mail: springbird@aol.com
Key Personnel
Pres: Robin Straus (AAR)
Founded: 1983
High quality fiction & nonfiction. No screenplays, plays, romance, westerns, science fiction, fantasy, horror, children's or poetry. No unsol mss or downloaded submissions, query first by mail with outline or synopsis, short author biography & sample chapters. SASE for response & return of material must be included. No reading fee. Handle film & TV rights for represented clients' books. Foreign representatives in all major foreign countries.
Foreign Rights: Margaret Hanbury (UK); Deborah Harris (Israel); Andrew Nurnberg Assoc (Argentina, Brazil, China, Netherlands, Eastern Europe, France, Germany, Italy, Russia, Scandinavia, Spain, Taiwan); Tuttle-Mori (Japan); Eric Yang (Korea)

Marianne Strong Literary Agency (L-D)
65 E 96 St, New York, NY 10128
Tel: 212-249-1000 *Fax:* 212-831-3241
E-mail: stronglit@aol.com
Key Personnel
Pres: Marianne Strong
Assoc: Robert Hammond
Founded: 1978
Nonfiction, how-to books, biographies, gossip, society & entertainment, celebrity books, social history, life style, cookbooks, investigative biographies, mysteries, adventure, true crime fictionalized (or actual true crime), politics, self-help, inspirational, historic & memoirs. No unsol mss, query first. Submit outline & chapters with SASE. Proposals must include overview explaining storyline A to Z contents; table of contents, curriculum vitae of author, author's resume, thumbnail sketches of protagonist (optional), two to three consecutive chapters, SASE mandatory, books in similar genre. Handle film & TV rights. No stage or theatrical properties. We only accept these published by a mainstream publisher in the last five years or by a recognized expert in his or her field. We do have a critique service. Handle some fiction but will read & critique fiction for a fee. Representatives in many foreign countries. We use outside freelance editors for critiques - fee goes to them.
Titles recently placed: *Affirmed and Alydar*, Joe Durso; *Dead End*, Jeanne King; *Founding of the Guggenheim Museum*, Peter Lawson-Johnson; *Green Berets II*, Robin Moore; *Life of Joan Whitney Payson*, Lou Sabochi; *Papa's Table- A Moveable Friend*, Angela Hemingway; *Signature Sports*, Denise LeFrak Calecchio, Charles Patteson
Membership(s): Authors Guild

Barbara Ward Stuhlmann, Author's Representative (L)
PO Box 276, Becket, MA 01223-0276
Tel: 413-623-5170
Key Personnel
Dir: Barbara Ward Stuhlmann
Founded: 1954
Book-length material only. Literary fiction, biography, history & letters; no science fiction, romance, historical novels, children's books or detective. Handle film & TV rights on client properties only; no original scripts. No unsol mss, query first with SASE (submissions received without SASE, will not be answered); submit outline & sample chapter; no reading fee. Most foreign rights handled from main office. Select foreign reps for specific properties. Established in New York City but relocated to Becket in 1977. Inquiries to Main Office in Becket.

The Swayne Agency Literary Management & Consulting, see The Barry-Swayne Literary Agency

Carolyn Swayze Literary Agency Ltd (L)
15927 Pacific Place, White Rock, BC V4B 1S9, Canada
Mailing Address: WRPO Box 39588, White Rock, BC V4B 5L6, Canada
Tel: 604-538-3478 *Fax:* 604-531-3022
E-mail: cswayze@direct.ca
Web Site: www.swayzeagency.com
Founded: 1994
Representing emerging & established authors of literary fiction, commercial fiction, nonfiction & a few children's books. No science fiction. An inquiry must include an author bio, a short description of the available project & particulars of marketing efforts. No unsol mss; query first. No fees charged. Authors may consult website for current submission guidelines. Canadian authors only, please.
Titles recently placed: *A Complicated Kindness*, Miriam Toews; *Beauty Tips From Moose Jaw: Travels in Search of Canada*, Will Ferguson; *Cold, Dark Matter*, Alex Brett; *Flight Path*, Paul Grescoe; *From Tragedy to Triumph: The Honorary Michael Harcourt's Plan B*, John Lekich; *Hitching Rides with Buddha*, Will Ferguson; *Playing With My Food*, Pam Freir; *Sexual Spectrum*, Olive Skene Johnson; *She's No Lady*, Barb Daniel; *Sointula*, Bill Gaston; *Sweep Lotus*, Mark Zuehlke; *Sympathy*, Edyth Crane; *The Cure for Crushes*, Karen Rivers; *To Choose One's Own Way*, Sheila McDonald; *Unclutter Your Life*, Katherine Gibson; *Woodpeckers of North America*, Frances Backhouse
Foreign Rights: ALI (Italy); AMI (Spain); Chinese Connection Agency (China & Taiwan); Lora Fountain Agency (France); Mohr Books (Germany); I Pikorak Ltd (Israel); R T Copyright Ltd (Eastern Europe); Shirley Stewart Literary Agency (UK, Holland); Hanserik Tonnheim (Scandinavia); Tuttle Mori (Japan)

Robert E Tabian/Literary Agent (L)
31 E 32 St, Suite 300, New York, NY 10016
Tel: 212-481-8484 (ext 330) *Fax:* 212-481-9582
E-mail: retlit@mindspring.com
Key Personnel
Owner & Sole Proprietor: Robert E Tabian
    Tel: 212-481-8484 ext 330
Founded: 1992
Adult fiction & nonfiction; thrillers, mysteries, women's fiction, self-help, psychology, cookbooks, health & medicine, history, biography & popular culture & spirituality. No unsol mss, query first with SASE. Submit 100 pages (fiction) or outline & two sample chapters (nonfiction). Handle film & TV rights. Representatives in many foreign countries & Hollywood. No

reading fee. Clients are charged ms xeroxing & submission mailing charges.
Titles recently placed: *Global Braise*, Daniel Boulud; *The Southern Belle's Handbook*, Loraine Despres; *Touched & Untitled Novel #2*; *Untitled Novel*, Loraine Despres; *Untitled Teddy Weston Thriller*, Chris Gilson
Foreign Rights: Chandler Crawford Agency (World)

Roslyn Targ Literary Agency Inc (L)
105 W 13 St, Suite 15-E, New York, NY 10011
Tel: 212-206-9390 *Fax:* 212-989-6233
E-mail: roslyntarg@aol.com
Key Personnel
Pres: Roslyn Targ (AAR)
Founded: 1970
Fiction & nonfiction. No unsol mss. Query first. For fiction & nonfiction proposals, submit outline & two to three synopsis chapters with SASE. No fees. Agents in foreign countries. Handle film & TV rights only to clients whose books we have sold. No screenplays or plays, also submit background of writer.

Dawson Taylor Literary Agency (L)
4722 Holly Lake Dr, Lake Worth, FL 33463-5372
Tel: 561-965-4150 *Fax:* 561-641-9765
E-mail: dawsontaylo@aol.com
Key Personnel
Ed: Denise Taylor Martin; Christine Taylor Power
Founded: 1985
Fiction & nonfiction in all subjects, specialize in sports & true crime. No unsol mss, query first with letter plus outline, sample chapter, table of contents, description of author & SASE. No reading fee. Copy editing fees only $1, $1.50 & $2 a page depending on difficulty of editing. Handle software, film & TV rights.
Titles recently placed: *Life & Times of Jack Nicklaus*, Sid Matthew; *Picture Perfect Golf*, Gary Wren; *Playing Hurt, Pro Football Medicine Today*, Pierce E Stranton, MD; *Super-Power Golf*, Gary Wiren
Foreign Rights: Bobbe Siegel

Patricia Teal Literary Agency (L)
2036 Vista del Rosa, Fullerton, CA 92831
Tel: 714-738-8333 *Fax:* 714-738-8333
Key Personnel
Owner & Pres: Patricia Teal (AAR)
Founded: 1978
Handle full-length category fiction & nonfiction; specialize in romance literature & women's mainstream literature. Commercial self-help & how-to in nonfiction. No short stories, articles, poetry, scripts or syndicated material. No fees charged. No unsol mss; query first by mail. Not accepting new clients.
Titles recently placed: *Cowboy Country Club Series*, Marie Ferrarella; *Intimate Moments*, Margaret Watson; *Maitland Memorial Maternity Series*, Muriel Jensen; *The Boss's Baby Mistake Series*, Myrna McKensie
Membership(s): Authors Guild; Authors Guild of America; Romance Writers of America

3 Seas Literary Agency (L)
PO Box 8571, Madison, WI 53708
Tel: 608-221-4306
E-mail: threeseaslit@aol.com
Web Site: threeseaslit.com
Key Personnel
Literary Agent: Michelle Grajkowski
Founded: 2000
For submission of fiction, send three chapters with synopsis, bio & SASE. For nonfiction, send proposal with sample chapter(s). No fees charged.
Titles recently placed: *American Idle*, Alesia Holliday; *Chloe: Queen of Denial*, Naomi Nash; *E-mail to the Front*, Alesia Holliday; *Eye-*

liner of the Gods, Katie Maxwell; *Hard Days Knight*, Katie MacAlister; *Men in Kilts*, Katie MacAlister; *Out with the Old*, Nancy Robards Thompson; *Reinventing Olivia*, Nancy Robards Thompson; *Sarah's Legacy*, Brenda Mott; *Sex and the Single Vampire*, Katie MacAlister; *Stress in the City*, Stephanie Rowe; *The Corset Diaries*, Katie MacAlister; *The Secret Life of Walter Kitty*, Barbara Jean Hicks; *The Year My Life Went Down the Loo*, Katie Maxwell; *With This Ring*, Brenda Mott; *You are So Cursed*, Naomi Nash
Membership(s): Romance Writers of America

Toad Hall Inc (L-D)
RR 2, Box 2090, Laceyville, PA 18623
Tel: 570-869-2942 *Fax:* 570-869-1031
E-mail: toadhallco@aol.com
Web Site: www.laceyville.com/Toad-Hall
Key Personnel
Pres: Sharon Jarvis
Media Consultant: Anne P Pinzow
Asst: Peter Lybolt
Founded: 1983
Fiction & nonfiction, prefer nonfiction. No children's or young adult. No short material of any kind. Handle software, film & TV rights as outgrowth of book option. No unsol mss, query first with letter only. Submit letter, one-page synopsis or table of contents. No reading fee. Photocopy & legal fees. Affiliates Joel Gotler, Metropolitan, Rights Unlimited.
ISBN Prefix(es): 0-9637498
Titles recently placed: *Blood Moon*, Sharman Di Vono; *Collected Short Stories*, Vernor Vinge; *Shag Harbour Incident*, Ledger & Styles
Branch Office(s)
26 Cleveland St, Pearl River, NY 10965, Contact: A Phyllis Pinzow *Tel:* 845-735-3715
Foreign Rights: Rights Unlimited

The Tomasino Agency Inc (L)
70 Chestnut St, Dobbs Ferry, NY 10522
Tel: 914-674-9659 *Fax:* 914-693-0381
E-mail: BookNView@aol.com
Key Personnel
Pres: Christine K Tomasino
Founded: 1998
Commercial & literary fiction & nonfiction. Represent all subrights for book clients only. Specialize in conventional & mind/body health, women's issues, self-improvement, spirituality/esoterica, narrative nonfiction, lifestyle, adult illustrated & packaged books, sports. Translation of non-book content into book-related formats for corporate & non-profit organizational clients such as major web businesses & museums. No poetry, genre fiction, plays, science fiction or purely scholarly work. Foreign agents in all major markets. No unsol mss, query first.

Jeanne Toomey Associates (L)
95 Belden St, Rte 126, Falls Village, CT 06031
Mailing Address: PO Box 259, Falls Village, CT 06031-0259
Tel: 860-824-5469; 860-824-0831; 860-824-3020 *Fax:* 860-824-5460
Key Personnel
Pres & Dir: Jeanne Toomey
Nonfiction: animals & natural history, nature, psychiatry & true crimes. No unsol mss, query first. $100 reading fee for unpublished authors. Outline & three sample chapters.
Titles recently placed: *Backyard Birding in the Northeast US*, Elmer W Eriksson; *Beauty Within The Beast*, Steven F Stringham PhD; *Between the Bridges*, Beatrice Carton

Phyllis R Tornetta Literary Agency (L)
4 Kettle Lane, Mashpee, MA 02649
Tel: 508-539-8821
E-mail: phyl4@capecod.net

Key Personnel
Pres: Phyllis R Tornetta
Founded: 1982
Fiction & romance. No unsol mss, query first.
Submit outline & first three chapters. Reading
fees $150 for full mss; nothing for first three
chapters.
Titles recently placed: *Heart of the Hunter*,
Nancy Morse

Transatlantic Literary Agency Inc (L)
72 Glengowan Rd, Toronto, ON M4N 1G4,
Canada
Tel: 416-488-9214 *Fax:* 416-488-4531
E-mail: info@tla1.com
Web Site: www.tla1.com
Key Personnel
Chmn: David Bennett
VP: Lynn Bennett
Pres: Don Sedgwick *Tel:* 902-693-2026
E-mail: don@tla1.com
Agent: Marie Campbell *Tel:* 44 207 7433 3103
E-mail: marie@tla1.com; Andrea Cascardi
Tel: 516-255-9597 *Fax:* 516-255-9597
E-mail: andrea@tla1.com; Margaret Hart
Tel: 416-675-6622 ext 3442 *E-mail:* margaret@
tla1.com; Samantha Haywood *Tel:* 416-924-
4495 *E-mail:* samantha@tla1.com; Karen
Klockner *Tel:* 216-591-0041 *Fax:* 216-591-
9592 *E-mail:* karen@tla1.com; Leona Trainer
Tel: 416-287-3146 *Fax:* 416-287-0081
E-mail: leona@tla1.com
Founded: 1993
Children's, adult literary fiction & literary non-
fiction. Markets Canadian & American literary
properties to English language publishers in the
UK, USA & Canada & through sub-agents to
publishers around the world. Handles film &
TV rights for literary properties only: no film
scripts or tele-plays. No unsol mss; initial letter
of inquiry essential. No reading fees. See web
site for individual agent's submission details.
Titles recently placed: *A Poppy is to Remember*,
Ron Lightburn; *Barry Boyhound*, Andy Spear-
man; *Biography of Helen Keller*, Leslie Gar-
rett; *Bittersweet*, Carol Off; *Illusions*, Wallace
Edwards; *Miss Elva*, Stephens Gerard Mal-
one; *The Violent Friendship of Esther Johnson*,
Trudy Morgan-Cole
Foreign Rights: The Agency (Korea); Akcall
Copyright (Turkey); Ali (Italy); Bardon Chi-
nese Media Agency (Taiwan); ELST Liter-
ary Agent (Bulgaria); Lora Fountain (France,
Russia, Slovenia, Spain, Holland); Burkhard
Heiland (Germany); Katai & Bolza Literary
Agents (Hungary); Movit (China & Hong
Kong); Pikarski Ltd Literary Agency (Israel);
Tuttle-Mori (Japan)

Treimel, S©ott NY, see S©ott Treimel NY

Trident Media Group LLC (L)
Formerly Ellen Levine Literary Agency Inc
41 Madison Ave, 36th fl, New York, NY 10010
Tel: 212-262-4810 *Fax:* 212-725-4501
Web Site: www.tridentmediagroup.com
Key Personnel
Chmn: Robert Gottlieb
CEO: Daniel Strone
Pres: Sheldon Shultz
Sr VP: John Silbersack
Exec VP: Ellen Levine (AAR)
VP, Man Dir, Foreign Rts: Kimberly Whalen
Foreign Rts Agent: Sara Crowe
Literary Agent: Jenny Bent; Paul Fedorko;
Melissa Flashman; Alex Glass; Scott Miller
Consultant: Iazamir Gotta
Founded: 2001
General fiction & nonfiction. No unsol mss, query
first with SASE. Submit outline & sample
chapters if requested. No reading fee. Handle

film & TV rights for clients only. Representation in Hollywood.
Foreign Rights: Sara Crowe (Worldwide)

2M Communications Ltd (L)
121 W 27 St, Suite 601, New York, NY 10001
Tel: 212-741-1509 *Fax:* 212-691-4460
Web Site: www.2mcommunications.com
Key Personnel
Pres: Madeleine Morel *E-mail:* morel@
bookhaven.com
Founded: 1982
Nonfiction books only; specialize in contemporary
music, popular culture, cookbooks, pop psy-
chology, health, parenting, medical, spiritual,
humor, business African-American & multi-
cultural titles, women's issues & biographies.
No unsol mss, query first. Submit outline &
sample chapters double spaced with SASE.
Handle film & TV rights through sub-agents.
No reading fee.
Titles recently placed: *Are You Crazy?*, Andy
Williams; *Getting Good Loving*, Audrey Chap-
man; *Irish Pub Cookbook*, Margaret John-
son; *Net Carb Counter*, Maggie Greenwood-
Robinson; *Outkast*, Chris Nickson
Foreign Rights: The Asano Agency (Japan);
Raquel De La Concha (Spain); European
American Information Services Inc (France);
Elfriede Pexa (Italy); Thomas Schluck (Ger-
many); Abner Stein (UK)

United Talent Agency (L-D)
9560 Wilshire Blvd, Suite 500, Beverly Hills, CA
90212
Tel: 310-273-6700 *Fax:* 310-247-1111
Key Personnel
Owner: Gary C Cosay
Fiction, nonfiction. Handle film & TV rights. No
unsol mss, query first; reading fee.

United Tribes Media Inc (L)
240 W 35 St, Suite 500, New York, NY 10001
Tel: 212-244-4166; 212-534-7646
E-mail: janguerth@aol.com
Key Personnel
Pres & CEO: Jan-Erik Guerth
Founded: 1998
United Tribes Media Inc. is both a literary agency
& editorial consulting company. Standard agent
commission charged 15% domestic, 20% inter-
national. No other fees charged for agenting.
Query letter both by mail (SASE required) or
e-mail; response within 4 weeks. Nonfiction
only.

Ralph M Vicinanza Ltd (L)
303 W 18 St, New York, NY 10011
Tel: 212-924-7090 *Fax:* 212-691-9644
E-mail: ralphvic@aol.com
Key Personnel
Pres: Ralph M Vicinanza (AAR)
Agent: Sarah Goodman *E-mail:* sara.goodman@
vicinanzaltd.com; Christopher Lotts (AAR)
E-mail: chrislotts@aol.com; Christopher
Schelling *E-mail:* christopher.schelling@
vicinanzaltd.com; Eben Weiss *E-mail:* eben.
weiss@vicinanzaltd.com; Michelle Wolfson
E-mail: michelle.wolfson@vicinanzaltd.com
Literary fiction, women's fiction, multicultural
fiction, popular fiction (especially science fic-
tion, fantasy & thrillers), nonfiction (history,
business, science, biography, popular culture,
inspirational) & children's fiction. No unsol
mss. Handle film rights. No fees charged.
Branch Office(s)
Created By, Writer's Building, Rm No 9, 1041
N Formosa Ave, West Hollywood, CA 90046,
Contact: Vince Gerardis *E-mail:* createdby@
earthlink.net

The Vines Agency Inc (L-D)
648 Broadway, Suite 901, New York, NY 10012
Tel: 212-777-5522 *Fax:* 212-777-5978
Web Site: www.vinesagency.com
Key Personnel
Pres & Owner: James C Vines *E-mail:* jv@
vinesagency.com
Assoc: Alexis Caldwell
Founded: 1995
Fiction, nonfiction, celebrity books, screenplays,
thrillers, literary novels, mainstream, women's
novels, ethnic fiction, adventure nonfiction, prescriptive nonfiction, narrative nonfiction. CD-
ROM. No unsol mss, query first with SASE;
one-paragraph description of book if query is
sent by e-mail. Submit outline with first three
chapters & synopsis of the rest of the book
(double-spaced, single side of page), along with
the customary SASE. No reading fee. Agents
on the West Coast & in all principal foreign
countries. Handle software, film & TV rights.
Double-spaced, single side of each page, first
three chapters & synopsis.
Titles recently placed: *Bad Girlz*, Shannon
Holmes; *Camilla's Roses*, Bernice McFadden;
Ecstasy, Beth Saulnier; *Getting Our Breath
Back*, Shawne Johnson; *Out of the Deep I Cry*,
Julia Spencer-Fleming; *Spin State*, Chris Mo-
riarty; *Sunset & Sawdust*, Joe R Lansdale; *The
Coming Catholic Church*, David Gibson; *The
Power of the Dog*, Don Winslow; *The Power of
the Dog*, Don Winslow; *The Ring*, Koji Suzuki;
Things Will Get As Good As You Can Stand,
Laura Doyle; *Through Violet Eyes*, Stephen
Woodworth
Foreign Rep(s): Baror International (UK, transla-
tions)
Foreign Rights: Baror International (UK, transla-
tions)
Membership(s): Authors Guild; Writers Guild of
America

**Stephanie von Hirschberg Literary Agency
LLC** (L)
1290 Avenue of the Americas, 29th fl, New York,
NY 10104
Tel: 212-660-3000
Key Personnel
Owner: Stephanie von Hirschberg
Founded: 1999
Represents adult trade books. Specializes in non-
fiction, biography, cookbooks, health, nature
related books, psychology, self-help & spiritu-
ality. No unsol mss, query with SASE by mail;
no reading fee.
Titles recently placed: *Effortless Pain Relief: A
Guide to Self-Healing From Chronic Pain*,
Ingrid Bacci PhD; *Shakespeare By Another
Name: Biography of Edward DeVere, 17th Earl
of Oxford*, Mark A Anderson; *The Slow Air
of Ewan MacPherson, A Novel*, Thomas Fox
Averill
Branch Office(s)
1385 Baptist Church Rd, Yorktown Heights, NY
10598 *Tel:* 914-243-9250 *Fax:* 914-962-7285
Foreign Rights: Jean V Naggar Literary Agency
(World)

Mary Jack Wald Associates Inc (L-D)
111 E 14 St, New York, NY 10003
Tel: 212-254-7842 *Fax:* 212-254-7842
Key Personnel
Pres: Mary Jack Wald (AAR)
Assoc: Danis Sher; Alvin Wald (AAR)
Founded: 1985
Adult & juvenile fiction & nonfiction. Represent
all subsidiary rights for authors & publishers.
No unsol mss; query first with SASE. No soft-
ware submissions. No reading fee. Handle film
rights &TV rights (for agency clients only).
Titles recently placed: *All in a Day's Work*, Neil
Johnson; *Diadem (series of 7 books)*, John
Peel; *Firehouse Max*, Sara London; *The Secret

of Castle Cant, K P Bath; *The Unseen (series of 4 books, UK)*, Richie Trankensley Cusack; *The Unseen (series of 4 books, US)*, Richie Tankensley Cusack
Foreign Rep(s): Lynne Rabinoff Associates (Worldwide)
Membership(s): Authors Guild; Society of Children's Book Writers & Illustrators

Wales Literary Agency Inc (L)
PO Box 9428, Seattle, WA 98109-0428
Tel: 206-284-7114 *Fax:* 206-322-1033
E-mail: waleslit@waleslit.com
Web Site: www.waleslit.com
Key Personnel
Pres & Agent: Elizabeth Wales (AAR)
Foreign Rts: Adrienne Reed
Founded: 1990
Mainstream & literary fiction & nonfiction. No unsol mss, query first with writing sample & SASE. No reading fee. Handles film & TV rights & foreign rights for agency book projects. E-mail queries okay, please no attachments.
Titles recently placed: *Against Gravity*, Farnoosh Moshiri; *Breaking Ranks*, Norm Stamper; *The Last Flight of the Scarlet Macaw*, Bruce Barcott
Foreign Rights: Antonella Antonelli (Italy); Big Apple Tuttle-Mori Agency Inc (China); International Editor's Co (Latin America, Spain); Michelle La Pautre (France); Mohrbooks Literary Agency (Austria, Germany, Switzerland); Sane Toregard Agency (Scandinavia); Abner Stein (UK); Caroline Van Gelderen (Netherlands)

Wallace Literary Agency Inc (L)
177 E 70 St, New York, NY 10021
Tel: 212-570-9090 *Fax:* 212-772-8979
E-mail: walliter@aol.com
Key Personnel
Pres: Lois Wallace
CFO: Nicole Larson
Assoc: Cressida Connolly
Founded: 1988
Handle film & TV rights for agency clients only. No unsol mss, query first with SASE, no reading fee.
Foreign Rights: A M Heath (UK); Michelle Lapautre (France); Andrew Nurnberg Associates (Europe); Tuttle-Mori (Japan)

John A Ware Literary Agency (L)
392 Central Park W, New York, NY 10025
Tel: 212-866-4733 *Fax:* 212-866-4734
Key Personnel
Pres: John A Ware
Founded: 1978
Biography, history, current affairs & social commentary, investigative journalism, science, "bird's eye views" of phenomena, psychology, medicine & health (formal credentials required); sports, Americana: literary noncategory fiction, thrillers & mysteries. No personal memoirs. No unsol mss, query first with letter only (one- or two-page) & SASE. No reading fees; fees charged for photocopying & messenger service, if required. Handle film & TV rights. Agents in all principal foreign countries.
Titles recently placed: *Chain Lightning: The True Legend of Man O' War*, Dorothy Ours (St Martin's); *Sarah's Quilt*, Nancy Turner (Thomas Dunn Books); *The Butterfly Hunter: On Finding a Calling*, Chris Ballard; *The Family Business: The McIlhenny/Tabasco Story*, Jeff Rothfeder (Harper Collins)

Warwick Associates (L)
18340 Sonoma Hwy, Sonoma, CA 95476
Tel: 707-939-9212 *Fax:* 707-938-3515
E-mail: warwick@vom.com
Web Site: www.warwickassociates.net
Key Personnel
Pres: Simon Warwick-Smith
Founded: 1985
A "one-stop" agency handling any or all parts of literary agenting through publicity & sales, etc. Specialize in spirituality, metaphysics religion & psychology, celebrity memoirs, business, self-help, children's, pop culture. Literary agent for a number of celebrity spiritual authors. No reading fee. Accept unsol mss, query first; 2 chapters with SASE. No fiction, poetry.

Harriet Wasserman Literary Agency Inc (L)
137 E 36 St, New York, NY 10016
Tel: 212-689-3257 *Fax:* 212-689-3257
E-mail: hawlainc@aol.com
Key Personnel
Pres: Harriet Wasserman (AAR)
Contact: Michelle R Fields
Founded: 1981
Agents in all foreign countries. Film & TV rights for clients only. By referral only. No reading fee.

Waterside Productions Inc (L)
2187 Newcastle Ave, Suite 204, Cardiff, CA 92007
Tel: 760-632-9190 *Fax:* 760-632-9295
Web Site: www.waterside.com
Key Personnel
Pres: William Gladstone *E-mail:* bgladstone@waterside.com
Agent & VP: Carole McClendon *E-mail:* mcclend@dsp.net
VP & Agent: Matt Wagner *E-mail:* mwagner@waterside.com
Agent: William E Brown *E-mail:* webrown@waterside.com; David Fugate *E-mail:* david@waterside.com; Margot Hutchison *Tel:* 858-483-0426; Kimberly Valentini *E-mail:* kimberly@waterside.com; Craig Wiley *E-mail:* cwiley@waterside.com
Founded: 1982
How-to, technology, business, spiritual. Specialize in professional how-to (test prep), technical, educational & computer books & software, general nonfiction. No unsol mss, query first. Submit outline & two sample chapters with SASE or through website. No reading fee. Handle software, film & TV rights with co-agents. In-house international division. Affiliations with PR agencies for clients.
Foreign Rights: Neil Gudovitz (all territories)

Watkins Loomis Agency Inc (L)
133 E 35 St, Suite 1, New York, NY 10016
Tel: 212-532-0080 *Fax:* 212-889-0506 *Cable:* ANWAT NEWYORK
Key Personnel
Pres: Gloria Loomis
Agent: Katherine Fausset *E-mail:* watkloomis@aol.com
Literary fiction, political nonfiction. SASE required. For nonfiction, submit outline only. For fiction, submit letter & first three chapters (or approximate amount) of ms, hardcopies only; no faxes, e-mails or disks. No reading fee.
Foreign Rights: The Marsh Agency; Abner Stein (UK)

Sandra Watt & Associates (L-D)
1750 N Sierra Bonita St, Los Angeles, CA 90046
Tel: 323-874-0791
Key Personnel
Pres: Sandra Watt
Founded: 1978
Crime, category & women's fiction. Popular nonfiction: gardening, New Age, reference, spiritual, mystery, suspense, creativity, true crime, children's & young adults. Specialize books to film. No unsol mss, query first by letter, double

spaced with SASE. Fiction: submit first three chapters with synopsis. Nonfiction: table of contents plus chapter. Foreign agents in all major markets & no reading fee. Not taking new clients at this time.
Membership(s): Writers Guild of America West

Waxman Literary Agency (L)
80 Fifth Ave, Suite 1101, New York, NY 10011
Tel: 212-675-5556 *Fax:* 212-675-1381
E-mail: submit@waxmanagency.com
Web Site: www.waxmanagency.com
Key Personnel
Pres: Scott Waxman
Founded: 1997
Query first, fiction, nonfiction. No reading fee, charge for reproductions. Query via e-mail preferred.

Wecksler-Incomco (L)
170 West End Ave, New York, NY 10023
Tel: 212-787-2239 *Fax:* 212-496-7035
E-mail: jacinny@aol.com
Key Personnel
Pres: Sally Wecksler *E-mail:* jacinny@aol.com
Assoc: Joann Amparan-Close
Founded: 1973
Subsidiary & foreign rights. Literary fiction, nonfiction (biographies, performing arts), heavily illustrated books & reference, business, historical fiction, current events, art, photography, music (no rock books), children's, foreign & subsidiary rights. Query first with SASE; no reading fee, submit outline & three sample chapters & author's bio by mail, typewritten or word processed; commissions paid on sales income. No fax or e-mail submissions accepted.
Titles recently placed: *Charles Drew*, Linda Trice; *Don't Call Mommy at Work Today Unless the Sitter Runs Away*, Mary McBride; *Total Career Fitness*, William J Morin; *What Every Successful Woman Knows*, Janice Reals Ellig, William J Morin
Foreign Rep(s): Dai Nippon (Europe, Japan, USA)
Membership(s): Overseas Press Club; Women's National Book Association

The Wendy Weil Agency Inc (L-D)
232 Madison Ave, Suite 1300, New York, NY 10016
Tel: 212-685-0030 *Fax:* 212-685-0765
Key Personnel
Pres: Wendy Weil (AAR) *E-mail:* wweil@wendyweil.com
Agent: Emily Forland (AAR)
Assoc: Emma Patterson
Fiction & nonfiction. No unsol mss, query first. No reading fee. Handle film & TV rights.
Foreign Rights: Antonella Antonelli (Italy); Peter Fritz AG (Germany); David Higham Associates (England); Japan Uni Agency (Japan); La Nouvelle Agence (France); Andrew Nurnberg Associates (Netherlands, Latin America, Scandinavia, Spain)

Cherry Weiner Literary Agency (L)
28 Kipling Way, Manalapan, NJ 07726
Tel: 732-446-2096 *Fax:* 732-792-0506
E-mail: cherry8486@aol.com
Founded: 1977
Science fiction, general fiction & nonfiction. No unsol mss. Referred authors submit letter saying who referred. Submissions or recommendations only. No reading fee. Handle film & TV rights. Foreign representatives in England, Germany, Holland, Italy, Japan, Scandinavia, Russia, Spain, Eastern Europe & France.
Titles recently placed: *Hanging Valley*, Jack Ballas; *Murder on the Red Cliff*, Mandi Oakley Medawar; *Sequoyah*, Robert J Conley; *Sunset Rider*, Jory Sherman

The Weingel-Fidel Agency (L)
310 E 46 St, Suite 21-E, New York, NY 10017
Tel: 212-599-2959 *Fax:* 212-286-1986
E-mail: wfagy@aol.com
Key Personnel
Owner: Loretta Weingel-Fidel
Founded: 1989
General fiction & nonfiction. Provide services to book authors/writers. No unsol mss, query first, by referral only; no reading fee.
Foreign Rep(s): Fritz Agency (Germany); Japan UNI (Japan); Lennart Sane (Netherlands, Scandinavia, Spain); Luigi Bernabo (Italy); Mary Clemmey (UK); Michelle Lapautre (France)

Ted Weinstein Literary Management (L)
35 Stillman St, Suite 203, San Francisco, CA 94107
Web Site: www.twliterary.com
Key Personnel
Pres: Ted Weinstein (AAR)
Founded: 2001
A full-service literary agency, representing authors of intelligent, adult nonfiction. We are particularly interested in current affairs, politics, biography, history, business, science, technology, environment, pop culture, lifestyle, travel, self-help, health & medicine. We do not represent fiction, poetry, stage plays or screenplays, children's books or young adult books. Please visit our web site, which includes information about who we are & how to submit work to us, along with industry news & other resources to help writers understand & succeed in the publishing business.
No reading fee. No unsol mss, query or detailed proposal first. Send query letter or proposal by e-mail (preferred) or mail. E-mails must contain no attachments. Paper submission must include SASE for reply.
Titles recently placed: *American Nightingale*, Bob Welch; *Diva Julia: Public Romace & Private Agency of Julia Ward Howe (Trinity)*, Valarie Ziegler PhD; *Eczema Free*, Adnan Nasir MD PhD, Priscilla Burgess; *Human Pollution*, Nena Baker; *Kitty Bartholomew's ABC's*, Kitty Bartholomew; *Looking Forward to It*, Stephen Elliott; *More Than Human*, Ramez Naam; *Paris in Mind: Three Centuries of Americans in Paris (Vintage)*, Jennifer Y Lee (editor); *The Skeptic's Dictionary: An Encyclopedia of Strange Beliefs, Delusions and Deceptions (Wiley)*, Robert Carroll, PhD
Membership(s): American Historical Association; Authors Guild; Northern California Science Writers; Organization of American Historians

West Coast Literary Associates (L)
951 Old County Rd, No 140, Belmont, CA 94002
Tel: 650-557-0438
E-mail: wstlit@aol.com
Key Personnel
Agent & Owner: Richard Van Der Beets
Founded: 1986
Nonfiction books, novels in areas of biography/autobiography; current affairs; ethnic/cultural interests; government/politics/law; history; language/literature/criticism; music/dance/theater/film; nature/environment; psychology; true crime; women's issues/studies; action/adventure; contemporary issues; detective/police/crime; experimental; historical; mainstream. No unsol mss; query first. Submit two-page query letter to Acquisitions Editor. Handle film & TV rights. Refundable $75.00 marketing fee.
Titles recently placed: *Nine Dragons*, George Herman; *The Florentine Mourners*, George Herman; *The Toys of War*, George Herman
Membership(s): Authors Guild

The Westchester Literary Agency (L-D)
2533 Egret Lake Dr, West Palm Beach, FL 33413
Tel: 561-642-2908 *Fax:* 561-439-2228
Key Personnel
Pres: Dr Neil G McCluskey *E-mail:* neilagency@adelphia.net
Assoc: Diane Sheats; Elaine Jacobs
Founded: 1991
At the end of 2002, we officially closed down for new clients. However, we do continue to serve existing clients. Any correspondence should be addressed to Dr Neil G McCluskey.
Titles recently placed: *Killer 'Cane*, Robert Mykle; *Murder at the Panionic Games*, Michael B Edwards; *Piper*, John E Keegan

Westwood Creative Artists Ltd (L-D)
94 Harbord St, Toronto, ON M5S 1G6, Canada
Tel: 416-964-3302 *Fax:* 416-975-9209
Key Personnel
Pres: Bruce Westwood
Chmn: Michael Levine
Agent: Jackie Kaiser; Linda McKnight; Hilary McMahon; John Pearce
Film Agent: Ashton Westwood; Deborah Wood
Foreign Rts Agent: Nicole Winstanley *Tel:* 416-964-3302 ext 228 *E-mail:* nicole@wcaltd.com
General trade fiction & nonfiction for international marketplace; Canadian authors only. No unsol mss, query first. Handle film & TV rights. No reading fee.
Foreign Rep(s): AP Watt (UK); Akcali Copyright (Turkey); Antonella Antonelli (Italy); B & B Agents (Brazil, Latin America, Portugal, Spain); Big Apple-Tuttle Mori Agency (China); The English Agency (Japan); Graal (Poland); Japan Uni Agency (Japan); JLM Literary Agency (Greece); Katai & Bolza (Hungary); Simona Kessler (Romania); Michelle Lapautre (France); Liepman (Germany); Maja Mihic (Croatia); NiKa (Bulgaria); Andrew Nurnberg & Associates (Netherlands, Scandinavia); Kristin Olson (Czech Republic); I Pikarski (Israel); Shin Won Agency (Korea); Synopsis (Russia); Tuttle-Mori Agency (Japan, Thailand)
Foreign Rights: Andrew Nurnberg Baltic (Estonia, Latvia, Lithuania, Ukraine)

Rhoda Weyr Agency, see Dunham Literary Inc

Wieser & Elwell Inc (L-D)
80 Fifth Ave, Suite 1101, New York, NY 10011
Tel: 212-260-0860 *Fax:* 212-675-1381
E-mail: jetwell8@earthlink.net
Key Personnel
Pres: Jake Elwell (AAR)
Founded: 1976
Specialize in trade & mass market adult fiction & nonfiction books. Handle films & TV rights for represented authors. Foreign rights. No unsol mss, query first by mail. Submit outline & 100 pages with SASE. No reading fee. Fees for duplicating, foreign postage & faxes.
Foreign Rights: Eliane Benisti (France & Spain); Michael Meller (Germany); Nurnberg Associates (Eastern Europe); Lennart Sane (Scandinavia)

The Wilshire Literary Agency (L)
20 Barristers Walk, Dennis, MA 02638
Tel: 508-385-5200
Key Personnel
Contact: Hildegard Krische; Carol McCleary
Mainstream fiction & nonfiction in all genres. Query first with outline & sample chapters; no faxes; no reading fee. Representatives in Hollywood & all principal foreign countries.
Foreign Rep(s): Elaine Benisti (France); Big Apple Tuttle-Mori (Taiwan); David Grossman (UK); P&P (Eastern Europe); Lennart Sane (Latin America, Scandinavia, Spain); Roberto Santachiara (Italy); Thomas Schluck (Germany); Tuttle-Mori (Japan)

The Wilson Devereux Co (L)
5 Ledyard St, 2nd fl, Newport, RI 02840
Tel: 401-846-8081
E-mail: bdb4@wildev.com
Web Site: www.wildev.com
Key Personnel
Contact: B D Barker
Nonfiction trade science & "For Dummies" books. No fiction, religious or children's books please. Suggested query by e-mail. No reading fee.

Witherspoon Associates Inc, see Inkwell Management

Gary S Wohl Literary Agency (L)
400 Chambers St, Unit 28-H, New York, NY 10282-1019
Tel: 212-242-0125
E-mail: gwohl@earthlink.net
Founded: 1990
English as a second language & bilingual texts; school & college textbooks; nonfiction, how-to books, sports, business, self-help, personal improvement, true crime, investigative. No unsol mss, query first. Submit outline & three sample chapters. No reading fees. Handle software projects, film & TV rights, video gaming ideas. Agent receives 15% on domestic sales & 10 to 20% on foreign sales.
Titles recently placed: *Let's Speak Business English-Software*, Dr. Linda Cypress
Branch Office(s)
East Hampton, NY

Audrey R Wolf Literary Agency (L)
2510 Virginia Ave NW, Washington, DC 20037
Tel: 202-965-0405 *Fax:* 202-298-6966
E-mail: bigbad@earthlink.net
Key Personnel
Pres: Audrey R Wolf (AAR)
Founded: 1977
Fiction, nonfiction, health & medicine, psychology & self-help, film & TV rights. No unsol mss, no queries, by referral only, no reading fee. Agents in all principle foreign countries & Hollywood. Submit brief outline; three sample chapters. No children's books or screenplays. Must include SASE. No queries by e-mail, phone or fax.

Ann Wright Representatives (L-D)
165 W 46 St, Suite 1105, New York, NY 10036-2501
Tel: 212-764-6770 *Fax:* 212-764-5125
Key Personnel
Head, Literary Dept: Dan Wright
    E-mail: danwrightlit@aol.com
Specialize in fiction & themes with film potential. No unsol mss, query first with SASE. Handle film & TV rights. No fees except for postage, messenger & copies; accept work from international clients. Fee for postage, mailing & copy at time when a sale is made.
Foreign Rep(s): Agency Hamlet Jutis Biz
Membership(s): Writers Guild of America

The Writer's Advocate/Literary Agenting & Editorial Services (L)
1675 Larimer St, Suite 410, Denver, CO 80202
Tel: 303-297-1233 *Fax:* 303-297-3997
E-mail: thewritersadvocate@thelightningfactory.com
Web Site: www.thelightningfactory.com
Key Personnel
Ed Dir: Kendall Bohannon
Sr Ed: Wendy Du Bow
Specialize in trade & mass market fiction & nonfiction; accept unsol mss; offer editorial

& reading services to writer/clients for a fee; specialize in new &/or unpublished writers, as well as published writers; send complete mss.

Writers House LLC (L)
21 W 26 St, New York, NY 10010
Tel: 212-685-2400 *Fax:* 212-685-1781
Key Personnel
Chmn: Albert Zuckerman (AAR) *Tel:* 212-485-6550
Pres & CEO: Amy Berkower (AAR)
Exec VP, Fiction & Nonfiction: Merrilee Heifetz (AAR)
VP & Dir, Juv & Young Adults: Susan Cohen (AAR)
Treas: Ann Maurer
Assoc Dir, Foreign Rts: Jayna Maleri
Dir, Foreign Rts: Maja Nikolic
Mainstream Fiction & Nonfiction: Robin Rue (AAR)
Sr Agent: Susan Ginsburg; Jennifer Lyons (AAR)
Subs Rts & Agent: Michelle Rubin
Assoc, Royalty Acctg: Rose Acacia
Assoc: Ginger Clark; Kate Lastoria; Maya Rock; Rebecca Sherman; Emily Sylvan-Kim
Subs Rts Assoc: Nadia Grooms
Sr Agent: Simon Lipskar
Legal Aff & Young Adult Fiction: Jodi Reamer
Juv & Young Adult (San Diego): Steven Malk
Founded: 1974
Represent trade books of all types, fiction & nonfiction, including all rights. Handle film & TV rights. No screenplays, teleplays or software. No unsol mss, query first with an intelligent letter stating what's wonderful about the book, what it's about & what background & experience you, as an author, bring to it. No reading fee.
Titles recently placed: *American Gods*, Neal Gaiman; *Captain Underpants*, Dave Pilkey; *Eragon*, Christopher Paolini; *Incubus Dreams*, Laurel Hamilton; *Isle of Palms*, Dorothea Frank; *Junie B Jones*, Barbara Park; *Kiss Me While I Sleep*, Linda Howard; *Moneyball*, Michael Lewis; *Northern Lights*, Nora Roberts; *Rain Series*, VC Andrews; *Report From Ground Zero*, Dennis Smith; *See You Later, Gladiator*, Jon Scieszka; *Slow Cooker Cooking*, Lora Brody; *The Body of David Hayes*, Ridley Pearson; *The Book for People Who Do Too Much*, Bradley Trevor Greive, Joey Pigza, Jack Gantos; *The Complete Works of Isaac Babel*, Jon Scieszka; *The Morning After*, Lisa Jackson; *The Second Silence*, Eileen Goudge; *The Summer I Dared*, Barbara Delinsky; *The Universe in a Nutshell*, Stephen Hawking; *Tropic of Night*, Michael Gruber; *Whiteout*, Ken Follett
Branch Office(s)
3368 Governor Dr, San Diego, CA 92122, Dir: Steven Malk *Tel:* 858-678-8767 *Fax:* 858-678-8530
Foreign Rep(s): Dorie Simmonds, juvenile & young adults (UK)
Foreign Rights: Aleksandra Matuszak (Poland); Ia Atterholm (Scandinavia, childrens books, juv books); Bardon Agency (Taiwan); Eliane Benisti (France); Luigi Bernabo (Italy); Claude Choquette (French Canada); Raquel de la Concha (Portugal, Spain); DRT (Korea); Japan Uni (Japan, childrens books); JLM Literary Agency (Greece); Simona Kessler (Romania); Ulla Lohren (Scandinavia); Jovan Milenkovic (Croatia, Serbia and Montenegro); Andrew Nurnberg (Baltic States); Owl's Agency (Japan, adult books); Ilana Pikarski Ltd (Israel); Katalina Sabeva (Bulgaria); Karin Schindler (Brazil); Thomas Schlueck (Germany); Synopsis Literary Agency (Russia); Petra Tobiskova (Czech Republic); Caroline Van Gelderen (Netherlands)

Writers' Productions (L-D)
PO Box 630, Westport, CT 06881-0630
Tel: 203-227-8199
Key Personnel
Owner & Pres: David L Meth *E-mail:* dlm67@mac.com
Founded: 1977
Literary quality fiction & nonfiction. Handle film, TV & licensing rights. No unsol mss. No phone calls. No mss or samples by fax or e-mail.

Writers' Representatives LLC (L)
116 W 14 St, 11th fl, New York, NY 10011-7305
Tel: 212-620-9009 *Fax:* 212-620-0023
E-mail: transom@writersreps.com
Web Site: www.writersreps.com
Key Personnel
Contact: Lynn Chu; Glen Hartley *E-mail:* glen@writersreps.com
Founded: 1985
Represents authors of book-length works of nonfiction & literary fiction for adults. Once WRI agrees to represent an author, we give advice on how best to structure or edit an book proposal, discuss ideas for book projects & comment on finished ms material, with the goal of placing a book with the right publisher on the best possible terms for our author. We also discuss our authors' backgrounds & interests with publishers to promote upcoming projects or to find new ones. We sell to major publishers in the US & abroad.
Prefer to see ms material rather than synopses. Background about the authors' professional experience, particularly that which is relevant to the book, as well as a list of previously published works. We respond within two to five weeks on average. We require that all authors fully advise us as to whether any project has been previously submitted to a publisher & what the response was & if the project has been submitted to another agent. Submissions should be accompanied by SASE; no reading fees.
Titles recently placed: *Both: A Portrait in Two Parts*, Douglas Crase; *Bush Country*, John Podhoretz; *Call of The Mall*, Paco Underhill; *Of Paradise And Power*, Robert Kagan; *On Paradise Drive*, David Brooks; *Ripples of Battle*, Victor Davis Hanson; *The Language Police*, Diane Ravitch; *The Last Duel*, Eric Jager; *The Peloponnesian War*, Donald Kagan; *The Skeptic*, Terry Teachout; *To Rule the Waves*, Arthur Herman; *Where Shall Wisdom Be Found?*, Harold Bloom; *World on Fire*, Amy Chua

The Wylie Agency Inc (L)
250 W 57 St, Suite 2114, New York, NY 10107
Tel: 212-246-0069 *Fax:* 212-586-8953
E-mail: mail@wylieagency.com
Key Personnel
Pres: Andrew Wylie
Contact: Jin Auh; Sarah Chalfant; Lisa Halliday; Jeffrey Posternak
Founded: 1980
Literary fiction & nonfiction; query first with SASE; no unsol mss. Handle film & TV rights.
Foreign Office(s): The Wylie Agency (UK) Ltd, 17 Bedford Sq, London WC1B 3JA, United Kingdom *Tel:* (020) 7908-5900 *Fax:* (020) 7908-5901 *E-mail:* mail@wylieagency.co.uk
Foreign Rights: The Wylie Agency (UK) Ltd (UK)

Mary Yost Associates Inc (L)
59 E 54 St, Suite 73, New York, NY 10022
Tel: 212-980-4988 *Fax:* 212-935-3632
E-mail: yostbooks59@aol.com
Founded: 1958
Psychology, women's topics. No unsol mss, query first. Submit outline & sample chapters. Repre-

sentatives in many countries. Does not charge fees.
Titles recently placed: *Meaning of Anxiety; Power & Innocence*, Rollo May; *The Hemingway Women*, Bernice Kert; *The Retro Traveler*, Kevin Bagnato
Foreign Rep(s): Abner Stein (UK)
Foreign Rights: Lennart Sane (Scandinavia); Ruth Liepman (Germany)

The Young Agency (L)
156 Fifth Ave, Suite 617, New York, NY 10010
Tel: 212-229-2612 *Fax:* 212-924-6609
Key Personnel
Prop: Marian Young
Founded: 1986
Fiction & nonfiction. No unsol mss. Handle film & TV rights after book is sold.
Foreign Rep(s): Representatives in all major foreign countries

Zachary Shuster Harmsworth Agency (L-D)
1776 Broadway, New York, NY 10019
Tel: 212-765-6900 *Fax:* 212-765-6490
Web Site: www.zshliterary.com
Key Personnel
Partner: Jennifer Gates *E-mail:* jgates@zshliterary.com; Esmond Harmsworth *E-mail:* eharmsworth@zshliterary.com; Todd Shuster *E-mail:* tshuster@zshliterary.com; Lane Zachary *E-mail:* lzachary@zshliterary.com
Asst: Sandra Shagat *E-mail:* sshagat@zshliterary.com
Literary, commercial & genre fiction & nonfiction (except no science fiction or fantasy), mystery, thriller, non-category romance, biography, current affairs, business, psychology, memoir, science & history. No children's. No unsol mss: query letters, full plot; synopsis or detailed chapters summary plus three sample chapters up to 50 pages. No ms returned without SASE. No reading fee.
Titles recently placed: *A Mind At A Time*, Dr Mel Levine; *The Christmas Shoes*, Donna van Liere; *The Crazed*, Ha Jin; *The Darkest Jungle*, Todd Balf; *The Last Good Time*, Jonathan van Meter
Branch Office(s)
535 Boylston St, 11th fl, Boston, MA 02116
Tel: 617-262-2400 *Fax:* 617-262-2468
Foreign Rep(s): Esmond Harmsworth (UK)
Foreign Rights: Agence Hoffman (Germany); Big Apple Tuttle-Mori (China); Nurcihan Kesim Agency (Turkey); Lijnkamp Agency (Netherlands); Mercedes Casanovas Literary Agency (Spain); Michelle Lapautre (France); The English Agency (Japan); Tuttle-Mori (Japan); Tuttle-Mori Big Apple (Thailand); Eric Yang Agency (Korea)

The Zack Company Inc (L)
243 W 70 St, Suite 8-D, New York, NY 10023-4366
Tel: 212-712-2400 *Fax:* 212-712-9110
Web Site: www.zackcompany.com
Key Personnel
Pres: Andrew Zack (AAR)
Founded: 1996 (Originally The Andrew Zack Literary Agency)
Full service literary agency representing serious narrative nonfiction; history & oral history, particularly military history & intelligence services history; politics & current affairs works by established journalists & political insiders or pundits; science & technology & how they affect society, by established journalists, science writers or experts in their fields; biography/autobiography/memoir by or about newsworthy individuals, individuals whose stories can inspire millions, political & entertainment figures & individuals whose lives have made a contribution to the historical record; personal

finance & investing; parenting by established experts in their field; heath & medicine by doctors or established medical writers; business by nationally recognized business leaders or established business writers; relationship books by credentialed experts. Also, commercial fiction (but not "women's fiction"); thrillers in every shape & form-international, serial killer, medical, scientific, computer, psychological, military, legal; mysteries & crime novels; action novels; science fiction & fantasy, preferably hard science fiction or military science fiction & big, elaborate fantasies that take you to a new & established world; horror novels that take you on a roller-coaster ride; historical fiction (but not Westerns). 15-20% commission on domestic deals & 25% on UK & translation deals. Go to website: zackcompany.com for full guidelines on submission policy.
Membership(s): Authors Guild; Science Fiction & Fantasy Writers of America

Susan Zeckendorf Associates Inc (L)
171 W 57 St, Suite 11-B, New York, NY 10019
Tel: 212-245-2928
Key Personnel
Pres: Susan Zeckendorf (AAR)

Founded: 1979
Adult fiction & nonfiction, social history, commercial women's fiction, literary fiction, mystery, thrillers, health, music, science & child care. No unsol mss, query first with one page letter & SASE. No e-mail queries. No reading fee. Fee for photocopying. Agents in major foreign countries. Sub-agents for film & TV. No young adult, children's books or romances.
Titles recently placed: *How to Write a Darn Good Mystery*, James N Frey; *Something to Live For: The Biography of Susannah McCorkle*, North Eastern University Press; *The Hardscrabble Chronicles*, Laurie Morrow
Foreign Rights: Rosemarie Buckman (Europe, South America); Abner Stein (UK); Tuttle-Mori (China, Japan, Taiwan)

George Ziegler (L-D)
40 E Norwich Ave, Columbus, OH 43201
Tel: 614-299-2845
Founded: 1977
Not accepting new clients, except by referral.

Barbara J Zitwer Agency (L-D)
525 West End Ave, Apt 11H, New York, NY 10024

Tel: 212-501-8423 *Fax:* 212-501-8462
E-mail: bjzitwerag@aol.com
Founded: 1991
Fiction & popular nonfiction; memoir, pop culture, pop psychology. Look for ethnic authors, new voices of Black & Hispanic writers as well as writers from all over the world. No unsol mss. Submit letter & three sample chapters (typed & double-spaced on white, unbound, numbered pages - one-sided) with SASE through mail only. No electronic submissions read. Will look at ms on exclusive basis only. No reading fee. Handle software only in conjunction with ancillary rights of a book. Handle film & TV rights with co-agents in Hollywood.
Titles recently placed: *Beijing Doll*, Clun Sue; *Hot & Sweaty Rex*, Eric Garcia; *The Death You Deserve*, David Bowker; *The Rising*, Robert Frank
Foreign Rights: Peter Fraser & Dunlop (UK); Japan Uni (China, Japan); I Pikarski Agency (Israel); Prevodi & Prevoda (Eastern Europe); Vicki Satlow Literary Agency (Brazil, France, Germany, Italy, Latin America, Scandinavia, Spain, Holland)

Illustration Agents

Artists Associates
4416 La Jolla Dr, Bradenton, FL 34210-3927
Tel: 941-756-8445 *Fax:* 941-727-8840
Key Personnel
Dir: Bill Erlacher
Represents 9 artists.

Asciutto Art Representatives Inc
1712 E Butler Circle, Chandler, AZ 85225
Tel: 480-899-0600 *Fax:* 480-899-3636
E-mail: aartreps@cox.net
Key Personnel
Pres: Mary Anne Asciutto
Founded: 1980
Represent professional artists, supplying quality illustration for children's books. Provide a wide variety of illustration styles & techniques for publishers, design studios & packagers of children's materials.
Represents 12 artists.

Carol Bancroft & Friends
121 Dodgingtown Rd, Bethel, CT 06801
Mailing Address: PO Box 266, Bethel, CT 06801-0266
Tel: 203-748-4823 *Toll Free Tel:* 800-720-7020
Fax: 203-748-4581
E-mail: artists@carolbancroft.com
Web Site: www.carolbancroft.com
Key Personnel
Founder & Owner: Carol Bancroft
Founded: 1972
Represents many fine illustrators specializing in art for children of all ages. Servicing the publishing industry including, but not limited to: picture/mass market books & educational materials. We work with packagers, studios, toy companies & corporations in addition to licensing art to related products. Promotional packets sent upon request. A portfolio critiquing service is now offered to artists new to picture books. Unsol artwork not accepted.
Represents 40 artists.
Membership(s): Graphic Artists Guild; Society of Illustrators; Society of Photographers & Artists Representatives; SWCBI

Benoit & Associates
279 S Schuyler Ave, Kankakee, IL 60901
Tel: 815-932-2582 *Fax:* 815-932-2594
E-mail: benoitart@aol.com
Key Personnel
Pres: Michael J Benoit
Dir, Illustration: David Anderson
Photog: Peter Christie
Full-service design & advertising studio: specialize in technical & color airbrush illustration & computer generated art (Mac & IBM) design, art direction, in-house photography, elementary through college textbook cover & newsletters, brochures, letterheads & annual reports; high volume, high quality, quick turnaround & satisfaction guaranteed.

Berendsen & Associates Inc
2233 Kemper Lane, Cincinnati, OH 45206
Tel: 513-861-1400 *Fax:* 513-861-6420
Web Site: www.illustratorsrep.com; www.photographersrep.com; www.designersrep.com; www.stockartrep.com
Key Personnel
Pres: Robert Berendsen *E-mail:* bob@illustratorsrep.com

Represent artists, illustrators, photographers & graphic designers.
Represents 60 artists.

Bernstein & Andriulli Inc
58 W 40 St, 6th fl, New York, NY 10018
Tel: 212-682-1490 *Fax:* 212-286-1890
E-mail: info@ba-reps.com
Web Site: www.ba-reps.com
Key Personnel
Contact: Tony Andriulli
Commercial illustration & photography.
Represents 70 artists.

Bookmakers Ltd
40 Mouse House Rd, Taos, NM 87571
Mailing Address: 40 Mouse House Rd, Taos, NM 87571
Tel: 505-776-5435 *Fax:* 505-776-2762
E-mail: bookmakers@newmex.com
Web Site: www.bookmakersltd.com
Key Personnel
Owner & Pres: Gayle Crump McNeil
Founded: 1975
For 30 years Bookmakers has represented a group of the best children's book illustrators in the business. We also provide educational & trade publishers with a full range of production services, using Macintosh platform with Adobe Creative Suite capability.
Illustration
Photography
Design
Layout
Page Makeup
Packaging
Project Management
We've worked with most major publishers & design studios & look forward to helping create a success story with *your* next project.
Represents 20 artists.

Jan Collier Represents Inc
PO Box 470818, Mill Valley, CA 94941
Tel: 415-383-9026 *Fax:* 415-383-9037
E-mail: jan@jan-collier-represents.com
Web Site: www.jan-collier-represents.com
Key Personnel
Owner: Jan Collier
Represent commercial illustrators.
Represents 12 artists.

Cornell & McCarthy LLC
2-D Cross Hwy, Westport, CT 06880
Tel: 203-454-4210 *Fax:* 203-454-4258
Web Site: www.cornellandmccarthy.com
Key Personnel
Partner: Pat McCarthy; Merial Cornell
Founded: 1989
Professional illustrators, specializing in the children's book markets; educational, trade & mass market. Representing over 35 artists with a variety of styles & techniques.

Craven Design Studios Inc
234 Fifth Ave, 4th fl, New York, NY 10001
Tel: 212-696-4680 *Fax:* 212-532-2626
Web Site: www.cravendesignstudios.com
Key Personnel
Pres: Tema Siegel *E-mail:* ts@cravendesignstudios.com
Founded: 1981
Artist's representative: book illustration (text & trade), juvenile through adult; humorous, re-

alistic, decorative & technical; maps, charts, graphs.
Represents 35 artists.

Creative Arts of Ventura
PO Box 684, Ventura, CA 93002-0684
Tel: 805-643-4160; 805-659-0237
Key Personnel
Owner & Artist: Don Ulrich *E-mail:* ulrichxcal@aol.com; Lamia Ulrich
Founded: 1973 (Gallery/Studio)
Specialize in fine art, mixed media (from 2002-2005) wall sculptures curated by US State Department for the US Embassy in Riga Latvia. Listed in State Department Catalog 2002 at www.embassyrigaart.org. Published poetry online at www.poetry.com under Ulrich, Don. Painting & sculpture-abstract, lyric poetry, exhibitions & logos.
Represents 4 artists.

Dimension Creative
1500 McAndrews Rd W, Suite 217, Burnsville, MN 55337
Tel: 952-201-3981 *Fax:* 952-892-1722
Web Site: www.dimensioncreative.com
Key Personnel
Owner: Joanne Koltes *E-mail:* jkoltes@dimensioncreative.com
Founded: 1986
National network of professional illustrators & designers that have provided support services to the publishing industry for over 20 years. For complete information, see our website.

Dwyer & O'Grady Inc
725 Third St, Cedar Key, FL 32625
Mailing Address: PO Box 790, Cedar Key, FL 32625-0790
Tel: 352-543-9307 *Fax:* 603-375-5373
Web Site: www.dwyerogrady.com
Key Personnel
Pres: Elizabeth O'Grady
Agent: Jeff Dwyer *Tel:* 603-863-9347
Founded: 1990
Not accepting new clients. Represent illustrators as agents to publishers of children's picture books & young adult novels.
Represents 10 artists.
Branch Office(s)
PO Box 239, Lempster, NH 03605-0239 *Tel:* 603-863-9347
Membership(s): Authors Guild; Society of Children's Book Writers & Illustrators; Society of Illustrators

Fort Ross Inc - International Rights
Division of Fort Ross Inc
26 Arthur Place, Yonkers, NY 10701
Tel: 914-375-6448 *Fax:* 914-375-6439
E-mail: fort.ross@verizon.net
Web Site: www.fortross.net
Key Personnel
Exec Dir: Dr Vladimir P Kartsev
Founded: 1992
Foreign sales of subsidiary rights for illustrations, photographs & covers made by American & Canadian artists. Representation of Russian & East European artists & photographers in the USA & Canada.
Represents 80 artists.

Pat Foster Artist Representative
32 W 40 St, Suite 2 S, New York, NY 10018

Tel: 212-575-6887 *Fax:* 212-869-6871
E-mail: pfosterrep@aol.com
Web Site: www.patfosterartrep.com
Key Personnel
Owner: Pat Foster
Art representative.
Represents 7 artists.
Membership(s): Graphic Artists Guild; Society of
  Photographers & Artists Representatives

Foto Expression International (Toronto)
27 Saint Clair Ave E, Suite 1268, Toronto, ON
  M4T 2P4, Canada
Mailing Address: 266 Charlotte St, Suite 297,
  Peterborough, ON K9J 2V4, Canada
Tel: 705-745-5770 *Fax:* 705-745-9459
E-mail: operations@fotopressnews.org
Web Site: www.fotopressnews.org
Key Personnel
Opers Dir: John Milan Kubik

Gerald & Cullen Rapp Inc
420 Lexington Ave, Suite 3100, New York, NY
  10170
Tel: 212-889-3337 *Fax:* 212-889-3341
E-mail: gerald@rappart.com
Web Site: www.rappart.com
Key Personnel
Pres: Gerald Rapp *E-mail:* gerald@rappart.com
Rep: Nancy Moore *Tel:* 212-889-3337 ext 103
  E-mail: nancy@rappart.com
Founded: 1944
Represent leading commercial illustrators on an
  exclusive basis. Sell to magazine & book pub-
  lishers, ad agencies, design firms & major cor-
  porations.
Represents 50 artists.
Membership(s): Graphic Artists Guild; Society of
  Illustrators; Society of Photographers & Artists
  Representatives

Carol Guenzi Agents Inc
865 Delaware, Denver, CO 80204
Tel: 303-820-2599 *Toll Free Tel:* 800-417-5120
  Fax: 303-820-2598
E-mail: art@artagent.com
Web Site: www.artagent.com
Key Personnel
Off Mgr: Deborah Dennis *E-mail:* deborah@
  artagent.com
Contact: Carol Guenzi
Founded: 1984
A wide selection of talent in all areas of visual
  communications.
Represents 30 artists.

The Charlotte Gusay Literary Agency
10532 Blythe Ave, Los Angeles, CA 90064
Tel: 310-559-0831 *Fax:* 310-559-2639
E-mail: gusay1@aol.com (for queries only)
Web Site: www.mediastudio.com/gusay
Key Personnel
Pres & Founder: Charlotte Gusay
Founded: 1988
Represent children's book artists & illustrators.

Barb Hauser Another Girl Rep
PO Box 421443, San Francisco, CA 94142-1443
Tel: 415-647-5660 *Fax:* 415-546-4180
E-mail: barb@girlrep.com
Web Site: www.girlrep.com
Key Personnel
Contact: Barb Hauser
Founded: 1980
Represents 9 artists.

Herman Agency
350 Central Park W, New York, NY 10025
Tel: 212-749-4907 *Fax:* 212-662-5151
E-mail: hermanagen@aol.com
Web Site: www.hermanagencyinc.com

Key Personnel
Pres: Ronnie Ann Herman *Tel:* 518-794-7098
Founded: 1999
Represent illustrators, authors & au-
  thor/illustrators of children's books, trade &
  educational.
Represents 31 artists.
Branch Office(s)
PO Box 438, Canaan, NY 12029 (summer ad-
  dress) *Tel:* 518-794-7098 *Fax:* 518-794-0448
Membership(s): Society of Children's Book Writ-
  ers & Illustrators

HK Portfolio Inc
10 E 29 St, 40G, New York, NY 10016
Tel: 212-689-7830 *Fax:* 212-689-7829
Web Site: www.hkportfolio.com
Key Personnel
Agent: Mela Bolinao *E-mail:* mela@hkportfolio.
  com
Founded: 1986
Represents illustrators whose work is intended for
  juvenile market.
Represents 44 artists.
Membership(s): Graphic Artists Guild; Society of
  Illustrators; Society of Photographers & Artists
  Representatives

The Ivy League of Artists Inc
10 E 39 St, 7th fl, New York, NY 10016
Tel: 212-545-7766 *Fax:* 212-545-9437
E-mail: ilartists@aol.com
Key Personnel
Pres & Owner: Ivy Mindlin
Illustration, spot drawings, calligraphy, cartoons,
  comps, storyboards, design & mechanical art.
Represents 10 artists.

Kirchoff/Wohlberg Inc
866 United Nations Plaza, Suite 525, New York,
  NY 10017
Tel: 212-644-2020 *Fax:* 212-223-4387
E-mail: kirchwohl@aol.com
Web Site: www.kirchoffwohlberg.com
Key Personnel
Pres: Morris A Kirchoff
Dir, Opers: John R Whitman
Artists' Rep: Elizabeth J Ford
Founded: 1930
Specialize in children's trade books & both ele-
  mentary & secondary textbook illustration.
Represents 60 artists.
Branch Office(s)
897 Boston Post Rd, Madison, CT 06443
  Tel: 203-245-7308
Membership(s): AAP; AIGA; ALA; International
  Reading Association; Society of Children's
  Book Writers & Illustrators; Society of Illus-
  trators; Society of Photographers & Artists
  Representatives
See Ad in Book Producers, Editorial Services
  section(s)

Klimt Represents
15 W 72 St, Suite 7-U, New York, NY 10023
Tel: 212-799-2231 *Fax:* 212-799-2362
E-mail: klimt@nyc.rr.com
Web Site: klimtreps.com
Key Personnel
Contact: Bill Klimt; Maurine Klimt
Founded: 1979 (New name KLIMT represents as
  of 1996)
Illustrator's reps servicing publishing, advertising,
  entertainment industry.
Represents 11 artists.
Membership(s): Society of Illustrators

Lott Representatives
11 E 47 St, 6th fl, New York, NY 10017
Tel: 212-755-5737

Key Personnel
Pres: Peter Lott *E-mail:* peterlott@earthlink.net
Represent commercial illustrators.

Morgan Gaynin Inc
194 Third Ave, New York, NY 10003
Tel: 212-475-0440 *Fax:* 212-353-8538
E-mail: info@morgangaynin.com
Web Site: www.morgangaynin.com
Key Personnel
Rep: Gail Gaynin; Vicki Morgan
Illustrator's representative.
Represents 30 artists.

Pema Browne Ltd, see Pema Browne Ltd

Pema Browne Ltd
11 Tena Place, Valley Cottage, NY 10989
E-mail: info@pemabrowneltd.com
Web Site: www.pemabrowneltd.com
Key Personnel
Pres: Pema Browne
VP & Treas: Perry J Browne
Founded: 1966
Illustration: realistic, humorous, fantasy, decorative, all ages; for publishing. Also literary
  agents for fiction & nonfiction, children's picture books, middle grade, young adult; romance, all genre business, health, how-to,
  cookbooks, inspirational, reference; no fax,
  e-mail or telephone queries. A SASE must be
  included for reply; only accepting limited new
  clients at this time.
Represents 6 artists.
Membership(s): Romance Writers of America;
  Society of Children's Book Writers & Illustrators; Writers Guild of America

Portfolio Solutions
2419 Rte 82, Suite 208, Billings, NY 12510-0074
Mailing Address: PO Box 74, Billings, NY
  12510-0074
Tel: 845-226-8401 *Fax:* 845-226-8937
E-mail: PSJDC@frontiernet.net
Key Personnel
Owner: Janet De Carlo; Bernadette Szost
Founded: 1999
Agency representing illustrators of children's
  books & related materials.
Represents 36 artists.
Membership(s): Authors Guild; Society of Chil-
  dren's Book Writers & Illustrators

PortSort.com
Division of Woody Coleman Presents Inc
490 Rockside Rd, Cleveland, OH 44131
Tel: 216-661-4222 *Toll Free Tel:* 800-486-1248
  Fax: 216-661-2879
E-mail: woody@portsort.com
Web Site: www.portsort.com
Key Personnel
CEO: Laura Ray
International representative for selected commer-
  cial illustrators; operates online database of
  over 300 member illustrator's portfolios. Port-
  sort.com is a co-operative member controlled
  agency organization.
Represents 200 artists.

Publishers' Graphics Inc
231 Judd Rd, Easton, CT 06612-1025
Tel: 203-445-1511 *Fax:* 203-445-1411
E-mail: sales@publishersgraphics.com
Web Site: www.publishersgraphics.com
Key Personnel
Pres: Paige Gillies *E-mail:* paigeg@
  publishersgraphics.com
Founded: 1970
Representing fine children's book illustrators:
  Joann Adinolfi. R W Alley. Lynne Cravath,
  Benrei Huang, G Brian Karas, Lisa McCue,

Pam Paparone, R A Parker, S D Schindler, Teri Weidner.
Represents 14 artists.

Kerry Reilly: Representatives
1826 Asheville Place, Charlotte, NC 28203
Tel: 704-372-6007 *Fax:* 704-372-6007
E-mail: kerry@reillyreps.com
Web Site: www.reillyreps.com
Illustration & photography.
Represents 25 artists.

Renaissance House
Imprint of Laredo Publishing Co
9400 Lloydcrest Dr, Beverly Hills, CA 90210
Tel: 310-860-9930 *Toll Free Tel:* 800-547-5113
Fax: 310-860-9902
E-mail: laredo@renaissancehouse.net; info@
renaissancehouse.net
Web Site: renaissancehouse.net
Founded: 1991
Represents illustrators specializing in art for chil-
dren that provide a wide variety of styles &
techniques. Services the advertising & pub-
lishing industries, including children's books
& educational materials. Multicultural artists
are available. Promotional booklet sent upon
request.
ISBN Prefix(es): 1-56492
Represents 90 artists.

Roman Studios
814 Kaipii St, Kailua, HI 96734
Tel: 808-262-4708
Key Personnel
Principal & Illustrator: Barbara Roman
Founded: 1982
Children's books, young adult cover.
Represents 5 artists.

Rosenthal Represents
3850 Eddingham Ave, Calabasas, CA 91302
Tel: 818-222-5445 *Fax:* 818-222-5650
Key Personnel
Pres: Elise Rosenthal *E-mail:* eliselicenses@
hotmail.com
Founded: 1979
Illustrate book covers, children's & adult books.
Licensing agents.
Represents 35 artists.
Membership(s): LIMA; Society of Illustrators

Salzman International
Division of Richard W Salzman (License Div) d/
b/a Therapy Springs
824 Edwards St, Trinidad, CA 95570
Mailing Address: PO Box 41, Trinidad, CA
95570-0041
Tel: 212-997-0115; 707-677-0241 *Fax:* 707-677-
0242
Web Site: www.salzmaninternational.com
Key Personnel
Owner: Richard Salzman *E-mail:* richard@
salzmaninternational.com
Founded: 1982
Agents for visual artists for educational & trade
books specializing in art illustrators. Feature art
for magazines & periodicals. Editorial services
available.
Represents 25 artists.

Richard W Salzman Artist's Representative,
see Salzman International

The Schuna Group Inc
1503 Briarknoll Dr, Arden Hills, MN 55112
Tel: 651-631-8480 *Fax:* 651-631-8458
Web Site: www.schunagroup.com
Key Personnel
Pres: JoAnne Schuna
Represents 13 artists.

Freda Scott Inc
383 Missouri St, San Francisco, CA 94107-2819
Tel: 415-398-9121 *Fax:* 415-550-9120
E-mail: info@fredascott.com
Key Personnel
Owner: Freda Scott
Represent commercial illustrators & photogra-
phers.
Represents 30 artists.

SI International
43 E 19 St, New York, NY 10003
Tel: 212-254-4996 *Fax:* 212-995-0911
E-mail: info@si-i.com
Web Site: www.si-i.com *Cable:* SIART
Key Personnel
Dir: Herb Spiers *E-mail:* herb@si-i.com
Artists working in color & B&W available for
original commissions in all areas of commer-
cial illustration, especially children's, young
adult & educational text books; licensing work;
artists available for book covers, illustrated
novels, advertising, corporate, government, en-
tertainment & leisure. Stock art available; web
content provider & digital art.
Represents 45 artists.
Branch Office(s)
S I Artists, Rondee General Mitre, Suite 157,
Barcelona 08022, Spain

Tugeau 2 Inc
2132-A Central SE, Suite 196, Albuquerque, NM
87106
Tel: 505-842-0922
Web Site: www.tugeau2.com
Key Personnel
VP: Nicole Tugeau *E-mail:* nicole@tugeau2.com
Contact: Jeremy Tugeau *E-mail:* jeremy@
tugeau2.com
Founded: 2003
An artist's rep agency devoted to the representation of established & emerging artists interested in illustrating for the juvenile market.
From trade books & the mass market to periodicals & educational packagers & suppliers,
we work diligently at getting our wonderful
team of artists published while helping creative
directors & editors find what they are looking
for. We make several trips a year to personally
show the portfolios, publications & samples
of our team's work to potential clients in New
York City, Chicago & Boston.
Represents 23 artists.
Membership(s): Graphic Artists Guild; Society of
Children's Book Writers & Illustrators

Christina A Tugeau Artist Agent LLC
3009 Margaret Jones Lane, Williamsburg, VA
23185
Tel: 757-221-0666
E-mail: chris@catugeau.com
Web Site: www.CATugeau.com
Key Personnel
Owner & Agent: Chris Tugeau
Founded: 1994
Representing illustrators for children's publish-
ing: mass market & trade books, educational

(preschool through young adult). Agency effec-
tively closed to new artists.
Represents 40 artists.
Membership(s): Graphic Artists Guild; Society of
Children's Book Writers & Illustrators; Society
of Photographers & Artists Representatives

Melissa Turk & the Artist Network
9 Babbling Brook Lane, Suffern, NY 10901
Tel: 845-368-8606 *Fax:* 845-368-8608
E-mail: melissa@melissaturk.com
Web Site: www.melissaturk.com
Key Personnel
Contact: Dorothy Ziff
Founded: 1986
Represents professional artists supplying quality
illustration, calligraphy & cartography. Special-
ize in children's trade & educational illustration
as well as natural science illustration (wildlife,
botanical, medical, etc), publishing & interpre-
tive signage.
Represents 12 artists.

Wendy Lynn & Co
504 Wilson Rd, Annapolis, MD 21401
Tel: 410-224-2729; 410-507-1059 *Fax:* 410-224-
2183
Web Site: wendy-lynn.com
Key Personnel
Pres & Illustration Agent: Wendy Mays
E-mail: wendy@wendy-lynn.com
Illustration Agent: Janice Onken *E-mail:* janice@
wendy-lynn.com
Founded: 2002
Specialize in the children's publishing market.
Represent & promote our illustrators to pub-
lishing companies which produce work for
children & young adults.
Represents 18 artists.
Membership(s): Society of Children's Book Writ-
ers & Illustrators

Wilkinson Studios Inc
901 W Jackson Blvd, Suite 201, Chicago, IL
60607
Tel: 312-226-0007 *Fax:* 312-226-0404
Web Site: www.wilkinsonstudios.com
Key Personnel
Pres: Christine Wilkinson *E-mail:* chris@
wilkinsonstudios.com
VP: Lisa O'Hara
Founded: 1999
Specializing in representing illustrators & managing art programs for educational, trade book
& mass market publishing, children's magazines, games & related fields. Over 100 illustrators offering age appropriate artwork for pre-
K through college in a wide range of styles,
techniques & media, both conventional & electronic. Project management of large volume
blackline or color illustration programs by dedicated staff with art & design backgrounds,
working directly with the publisher or interfac-
ing with design & development house vendors.
Represents 100 artists.
Membership(s): Graphic Artists Guild; Society of
Children's Book Writers & Illustrators

Deborah Wolfe Ltd
731 N 24 St, Philadelphia, PA 19130
Tel: 215-232-6666 *Fax:* 215-232-6585
E-mail: info@illustrationonline.com
Web Site: www.illustrationonline.com
Founded: 1978
Commercial illustrators representative.
Represents 30 artists.

Lecture Agents

Listed below are some of the most active lecture agents who handle tours and single engagements for writers.

American Program Bureau Inc
36 Crafts St, Newton, MA 02458
Tel: 617-965-6600 *Toll Free Tel:* 800-225-4575
   Fax: 617-965-6610
E-mail: apb@apbspeakers.com
Web Site: www.apbspeakers.com
Key Personnel
VP: Jan Tavitian *Tel:* 617-614-1631
   E-mail: jtavitian@apbspeakers.com
Lecture representation/speakers bureau.

Authors Unlimited Inc
31 E 32 St, Suite 300, New York, NY 10016
Tel: 212-481-8484 (ext 336) *Fax:* 212-481-9582
Web Site: www.authorsunlimited.com
Key Personnel
Pres: Arlynn Greenbaum *E-mail:* arlynnj@cs.com
Founded: 1991
Speakers bureau representing over 400 authors of adult, trade books. Arrange speaking engagements with colleges, libraries, corporations, trade associations & the like.

Damon Brooks Associates Celebrity Coordination
1601 Holly Ave, Oxnard, CA 93036
Tel: 805-604-9017
E-mail: info@damonbrooks.com
Web Site: www.damonbrooks.com; www.disabilityspeakers.com
Key Personnel
Pres: Marc Goldman
Serves 2 functions: 1) Coordinator of celebrity involvement. 2) Speaker & entertainment bureau exclusively representing those who have a disability.

Burns Sports & Celebrities Inc
820 Davis St, Evanston, IL 60201
Tel: 847-866-9400 *Fax:* 847-491-9778
Web Site: www.burnssports.com
Key Personnel
Pres: Bob Williams
Sr VP: Doug Shabelman
Sports marketing, match corporations with sports celebrities for appearances, speeches & endorsements.

Capital Speakers Inc
2200 Wilson Blvd, Suite 850, Arlington, VA 22201
Tel: 703-894-0604 *Toll Free Tel:* 800-799-2629
   Fax: 703-894-0605
E-mail: ideas@capitalspeakers.com
Web Site: www.capitalspeakers.com
Key Personnel
Pres: Phyllis Corbett McKenzie
Founded: 1984
Since 1984, Capital Speakers Incorporated—the one and only Speaker Consultancy®—has provided creative ideas to events planners. Matching knowledge & experience with access to virtually any speaker or entertainer on earth, including those listed exclusively elsewhere, we offer customized & thoughtful recommendations designed to meet each client's special needs.

The Chelsea Forum Inc
377 Rector Place, No 12-I, New York, NY 10280
Tel: 212-945-3100 *Fax:* 212-945-3101

Web Site: www.chelseaforum.com
Key Personnel
Pres: Jane S Pasanen
Full service, customized lecture bureau. Specialize in conferences & individual bookings for colleges, libraries, organizations & businesses.

CreativeWell Inc
PO Box 3130, Memorial Sta, Upper Montclair, NJ 07043
Tel: 973-783-7575 *Fax:* 973-783-7530
E-mail: info@creativewell.com
Web Site: www.creativewell.com
Key Personnel
Pres: George M Greenfield *E-mail:* george@creativewell.com
Literary, lecture & arts management.

EKP Productions Inc
8484 Wilshire Blvd, Suite 205, Beverly Hills, CA 90211
Tel: 323-655-5696 *Fax:* 323-655-5173
E-mail: producedby@aol.com
Web Site: eddiekritzer.com
Key Personnel
Pres & CEO: Eddie Kritzer *Fax:* 310-451-1136
Founded: 1983
Produce corporate shows for conventions & meetings. "A Night At The Improv" will write, create & produce comedy shows & corporate videos. Produce shows worldwide, TV movies & specials. Accept submissions for mss, prefer nonfiction. Also produces movies. See website eddiekritzer.com for details.

Fass Speakers Bureau
26 W 17 St, Suite 802, New York, NY 10011
Tel: 212-691-9707 *Fax:* 212-691-5012
E-mail: fsb@fasspr.com
Web Site: www.fasspr.com
Key Personnel
Pres: Carol Fass
Founded: 2003
Features topnotch speakers from a variety of backgrounds & fields who can discuss topics of special interest to both mainstream & Jewish audiences.

The Fischer Ross Group Inc
249 E 48 St, 15th fl, New York, NY 10017
Tel: 212-355-5777 *Fax:* 212-355-7820
E-mail: frgstaff@earthlink.net
Key Personnel
Pres: Grada Fischer
Exclusive lecture agents for authors (fiction, nonfiction, trade) & journalists (print & broadcast), as well as nationally known celebrities & personalities. Arrange lecture tours & individual speaking engagements for the university, association & corporate markets.

Five Star Speakers & Trainers LLC
8685 W 96 St, Overland Park, KS 66212
Tel: 913-648-6480 *Fax:* 913-648-6484
E-mail: fivestar@fivestarspeakers.com
Web Site: www.fivestarspeakers.com
Key Personnel
Owner & VP: William Lauterbach *Tel:* 913-648-6480 ext 204 *E-mail:* wlauterbach@fivestarspeakers.com

Owner: Nancy Lauterbach *Tel:* 913-648-6480 ext 202
Founded: 1988
Helps organizations determine their speaking, celebrity, training & entertainment needs & find the best person or program to meet those needs. Represent business leaders, authors, sports personalities, politicians, economists & motivational speakers & trainers; audio & video training programs also available.
Membership(s): International Association of Speakers Bureaus

Frankel & Associates
5120 Wright Terr, Skokie, IL 60077
Tel: 847-674-8417
Key Personnel
Owner: Norman Frankel *E-mail:* nfrankel@mindspring.com
Compt: Bonnie Frankel
CTA: Ed Hirsch
Founded: 1982
International relations, strategic studies, Middle East studies, new media, electronic publishing, price modeling & self-help.

Richard Fulton Inc
66 Richfield St, Plainview, NY 11803
Tel: 516-349-0407 *Fax:* 516-349-0407
Key Personnel
Pres: Richard Fulton
VP, Sales Promo: Warren Quintin Braddock, II
Represent authors & famous personalities for speaking engagements at fraternal, charitable, religious, business organizations, colleges & universities.

Greater Talent Network Inc
437 Fifth Ave, New York, NY 10016
Tel: 212-645-4200 *Toll Free Tel:* 800-326-4211
   Fax: 212-627-1471
E-mail: gtn@greatertalent.com
Web Site: www.gtnspeakers.com
Key Personnel
Pres: Don R Epstein
Exclusive lecture & entertainment management. Represent authors, journalists & nationally & internationally known individuals. Arrange speaking engagements & tours for corporations, associations, colleges & universities, town halls, hospitals & other organizations, as well as literary, motion picture, television & radio representation.

ICM Lecture Division
Division of International Creative Management
40 W 57 St, New York, NY 10019
Tel: 212-556-5602 *Fax:* 212-556-6829
Web Site: www.icmtalent.com
Key Personnel
Dir: Carol Bruckner *E-mail:* cbruckner@icmtalent.com
Exclusively represents a long list of authors, entertainers & distinguished clients & celebrities from all fields for lectures & personal appearances.

International Entertainment Bureau
3612 N Washington Blvd, Indianapolis, IN 46205-3592
Tel: 317-926-7566

E-mail: ieb@prodigy.net
Key Personnel
Pres: David Leonards
Founded: 1972
Database, resource center & clearing house. Information on speakers, celebrities & entertainers available in marketplace. Planning, consulting, booking & producing.

Mark Sonder Productions
250 W 57 St, Suite 1830, New York, NY 10107
Tel: 212-262-4600 *Fax:* 212-246-0197
E-mail: msonder@marksonderproductions.com
Web Site: www.marksonderproductions.com
Key Personnel
Pres: Mark Sonder
Contact: Buddy Fox *E-mail:* bfox@marksonderproductions.com; Shelli Steinberg
Source for The Drifters, Coasters, Marvelettes, etc including production. Classical, jazz, big bands, dance bands & background music.

B K Nelson Inc Lecture Bureau
Subsidiary of B K Nelson Inc
84 Woodland Rd, Pleasantville, NY 10570
Tel: **914-741-1322; 212-889-0637** *Fax:* **914-741-1323**
E-mail: **bknelson4@cs.com**
Web Site: **www.bknelson.com**
Key Personnel
CEO & Pres: Bonita K Nelson *Tel:* **760-778-8800** *E-mail:* **bknelson4@cs.com**
CFO: **Corp Reed**
VP: **John W Benson**
Audio & Video: **Jennifer W Nelson**
Devt & Booker: **Chip Ashbach**
Founded: **1988**
Book authors & personalities, experts in diverse fields. Arrange seminars & keynote speaking engagements. Speech-writing/coaching. Publish B K Nelson's Speaker's Directory with photos each year. Online booking. Certification status granted by New York State Dept of Economic Development.**
Branch Office(s)
1565 Paseo Vida, Palm Springs, CA 92264, Booker & Contact: John Benson *Tel:* **760-778-8800** *E-mail:* **bknelson4@cs.com**
Membership(s): **ABA; American Association of University Women; Authors Guild of America; NACA; National Association for Female Executives; Writers Guild of America West**
See Ad in Literary Agents section(s)

Ramsey & Ramsey
PO Box 1045, Fort Belvoir, VA 22060
Tel: 703-721-3630
E-mail: yellowspeak@yahoo.com
Key Personnel
Contact: Donna E Ramsey *E-mail:* dramsey@dzn.com
Founded: 1993
Produce corporate shows for conventions & meetings; specialize in lecture & personal appearances at colleges, seminars; arrange seminars; represent authors & entertainers.

Royce Carlton Inc
866 United Nations Plaza, Suite 587, New York, NY 10017-1880
Tel: 212-355-7700 *Toll Free Tel:* 800-LECTURE (532-8873) *Fax:* 212-888-8659
E-mail: info@roycecarlton.com
Web Site: www.roycecarlton.com
Key Personnel
Pres: Carlton Sedgeley *Tel:* 212-355-7700 ext 5119 *E-mail:* carlton@roycecarlton.com
Exec VP: Lucy Lepage *Tel:* 212-355-7700 ext 5121 *E-mail:* lucy@roycecarlton.com

VP: Helen Churko *Tel:* 212-355-7700 ext 5123
E-mail: helen@roycecarlton.com
Founded: 1968
Agents, managers & brokers for speakers.

Speakers Guild
PO Box 1540, Sandwich, MA 02563-1540
Tel: 508-888-6702 *Fax:* 508-888-6771
E-mail: speakers@cape.com
Web Site: www.speakersguild.com
Key Personnel
Pres: Philip Frankio
Sec & Treas: Joy Orff
Lecture agent.

World Class Speakers & Entertainers
5200 Kanan Rd, Suite 210, Agoura Hills, CA 91301
Tel: 818-991-5400 *Fax:* 818-991-2226
E-mail: wcse@speak.com
Web Site: www.speak.com
Key Personnel
Pres: Joseph I Kessler *E-mail:* jkessler@speak.com
Founded: 1970
Represents world class speakers & entertainers. Database of 25,000 speakers & entertainers; directory/guide available.

Writers' League of Texas
1501 W Fifth St, Suite E-2, Austin, TX 78703
Tel: 512-499-8914 *Fax:* 512-499-0441
E-mail: wlt@writersleague.org
Web Site: www.writersleague.org
Key Personnel
Exec Dir: Helen Ginger
Off Administrator: Beverly Horne
E-mail: beverly@writersleague.org
Founded: 1981

Associations, Events, Courses & Awards

Book Trade & Allied Associations — Index

Book Trade & Allied Associations

Listed here are associations and organizations that are concerned with books, literacy, language and speech, media and communications as well as groups who provide services to the publishing community.

AAR, see Association of Authors' Representatives Inc (AAR)

The Academy of American Poets Inc
588 Broadway, Suite 604, New York, NY 10012
Tel: 212-274-0343 *Fax:* 212-274-9427
E-mail: academy@poets.org
Web Site: www.poets.org
Key Personnel
Exec Dir: Troy Swenson
Prog Dir: Ryan Murphy *Tel:* 212-274-0343 ext 17
   E-mail: rmurphy@poets.org
Founded: 1934
The country's largest nonprofit association devoted to poetry. Sponsors the James Laughlin Poetry Award, Walt Whitman Award, Harold Morton Landon Translation Award, Wallace Stevens Award, Lenore Marshall Poetry Prize & annual college poetry prizes; workshops for high school students; award fellowship to American poets for distinguished poetic achievement; presents an annual national series of poetry readings & symposia. Publishes biannual journal. Also administers the Greenwall Fund, National Poetry Month & the Online Poetry Classroom.
Number of Members: 10,000
Publication(s): *American Poet* (biannual)

Academy of Motion Picture Arts & Sciences (AMPAS)
1313 N Vine St, Hollywood, CA 90028
Tel: 310-247-3000 *Fax:* 310-859-9351
E-mail: ampas@oscars.org
Web Site: www.oscars.org
Key Personnel
Pres: Frank Pierson
Exec Dir: Bruce Davis
Fellowship Dir: Greg Beal
To advance the arts & sciences of motion pictures & to foster cooperation among the creative leadership of the motion picture industry for cultural, educational & technological progress. Confer annual awards of merit, serving as a constant incentive within the industry & focusing public attention upon the best in motion pictures.
Number of Members: 5,024
Publication(s): *Academy Players Directory, Annual Index to Motion Picture Credits, Nominations & Winners, List of Eligible Releases* (bulletin)

Academy of Television Arts & Sciences (ATAS)
5220 Lankershim Blvd, North Hollywood, CA 91601-3109
Tel: 818-754-2800 *Fax:* 818-761-2827
Web Site: www.emmys.tv
Key Personnel
CEO & Chmn of the Bd: Bryce Zabel
CFO: Frank Kohler
VP, Awards: John Leverence
Organization for those involved in national television; bestows Emmy awards for excellence in television; college television awards & college internship program; inducts deserving individuals in "Television Academy Hall of Fame".
Number of Members: 6,100
Meeting(s): Emmy Awards, End of Sept annually
Publication(s): *EMMY Magazine*

Access Copyright, The Canadian Copyright Licensing Agency
Member of International Federation of Reproductive Rights & Organizations IFRRO
One Yonge St, Suite 1900, Toronto, ON M5E 1E5, Canada
Tel: 416-868-1620 *Toll Free Tel:* 800-893-5777
   Fax: 416-868-1621
E-mail: info@accesscopyright.ca
Web Site: www.accesscopyright.ca
Key Personnel
Exec Dir: Maureen Cavan
Communs Mgr: Suzanne Bezuk *Tel:* 416-868-1620 ext 223 *E-mail:* sbezuk@accesscopyright.ca
Founded: 1988
Number of Members: 35
Publication(s): *CopyRight* (semiannual, newsletter, free); *Online Access* (10x/yr, newsletter, free)
Membership(s): Book & Periodical Council

Advertising Research Foundation
641 Lexington Ave, New York, NY 10022
Tel: 212-751-5656 *Fax:* 212-319-5265
E-mail: info@thearf.org
Web Site: www.thearf.org
Key Personnel
Pres: Bob Barocci *Tel:* 212-751-5656 ext 210
   E-mail: bb@thearf.org
Man Ed: Zena Pagan *Tel:* 212-751-5656, ext 216
   E-mail: zena@thearf.org
Founded: 1936
Advertising research service trade association.
Number of Members: 412
2005 Meeting(s): ARF Annual Convention, New York, NY, April 2005
Publication(s): *Journal of Advertising Research* (quarterly, $120/yr US & foreign;$275 nonmember US & foreign)

ALA, see American Library Association (ALA)

Alcuin Society
PO Box 3216, Vancouver, BC V6B 3X8, Canada
Tel: 604-937-3293
Web Site: www.alcuinsociety.com
Judges book design; publishes articles on book arts, collecting, typography, private presses, book collections, book binding.
Number of Members: 300
Publication(s): *Amphora* (quarterly, $40/yr includes membership for individuals, $60 for institutions)

American Academy of Arts & Sciences (AAAS)
Norton's Woods, 136 Irving St, Cambridge, MA 02138-1996
Tel: 617-576-5000 *Fax:* 617-576-5050
Web Site: www.amacad.org
Key Personnel
Pres: Patricia Meyer-Spacks *Tel:* 617-576-5000 ext 5010
Exec Officer: Leslie Berlowitz
Ed: James Miller *E-mail:* daedalus@amacad.org
Promote interchange of ideas through seminars & publications.
Number of Members: 17,000
Publication(s): *Daedalus*

American Academy of Political & Social Science
3814 Walnut St, Philadelphia, PA 19104
Tel: 215-746-6500 *Fax:* 215-898-1202
Web Site: www.aapss.org
Key Personnel
Exec Dir: Robert Pearson, PhD *Tel:* 215-746-7321 *E-mail:* rwpearso@sas.upenn.edu
Man Ed: Julie Odland *E-mail:* jodland@sas.upenn.edu
Founded: 1889
Education.
Number of Members: 2,100
New Election: Annually in June
2005 Meeting(s): Annual Symposium, Washington, DC, April 2005
Publication(s): *The Annals of American Academy of Political & Social Science* (bimonthly, $75/yr indiv, $490/yr instn)

American Antiquarian Society
185 Salisbury St, Worcester, MA 01609-1634
Tel: 508-755-5221 *Fax:* 508-754-9069
Web Site: www.americanantiquarian.org
Key Personnel
Pres: Ellen S Dunlap
VP, Collections & Progs: John B Hench
Dir, Scholarly Progs: Caroline F Sloat *Tel:* 508-471-2130 *E-mail:* csloat@mwa.org
Founded: 1812
Maintain research library in American history & culture through 1876.
Number of Members: 719
Publication(s): *Proceedings of the American Antiquarian Society* (semiannual, $45/yr)

American Association for the Advancement of Science
1200 New York Ave NW, Washington, DC 20005
Tel: 202-326-6400 *Fax:* 202-289-4021
E-mail: webmaster@aaas.org
Web Site: www.aaas.org
Key Personnel
Chmn: Floyd E Bloom
Exec Officer: Alan Leschner
Dir, Exec Office Aff: Gretchen Seiler
Mission is to further the work of scientists, to facilitate cooperation among them, foster scientific freedom & responsibility, improve effectiveness of science in the promotion of human welfare & to increase public understanding & appreciation of the importance & promise of the methods of science in human progress. There are many membership organizations & professional societies which have similar aims or have interest in supporting these objectives. For further information, contact the AAAS Office of News & Information at the above address. US regional divisions: Arctic; Caribbean; Pacific; Southwest & Rocky Mountains.
Number of Members: 140,000
2005 Meeting(s): Meeting, Washington, DC, Feb 2005
Publication(s): *Science* (weekly, $10/issue; $125/yr professional rate; $29.95 online)

American Association of Advertising Agencies (AAAA)
405 Lexington Ave, 18th fl, New York, NY 10174-1801
Tel: 212-682-2500 *Fax:* 212-682-8391

Web Site: www.aaaa.org
Key Personnel
Pres & CEO: O Burtch Drake *E-mail:* obd@aaaa.
 org
Pub Aff VP: Kipp Cheng *E-mail:* kipp@aaaa.org
National trade association for the advertising
 agency business.
Number of Members: 600
2005 Meeting(s): AAAA Media Conference &
 Trade Show, Hilton Riverside, New Orleans,
 LA, March 2-4, 2005; AAAA Management
 Conference, Fairmont Southampton, Southamp-
 ton, Bermuda, May 4-6, 2005
Publication(s): *Agency Magazine* (quarterly, free
 to members)
Branch Office(s)
130 Battery St, Suite 330, San Francisco, CA
 94111 *Tel:* 415-291-4999 *Fax:* 415-291-4995
1203 19 St NW, 4th fl, Washington, DC 20036
 Tel: 202-331-7345 *Toll Free Tel:* 800-536-7346
 Fax: 202-857-3675

**American Association of Sunday & Feature
 Editors**
College of Journalism, University of Maryland,
 Journalism Bldg, College Park, MD 20742-
 7111
Tel: 301-314-2631
E-mail: aasfe@jmail.umd.edu
Web Site: www.aasfe.org
Key Personnel
Exec Dir: Penny Bender Fuchs
Nonprofit trade association of Sunday & feature
 editors.
Number of Members: 250
2005 Meeting(s): Annual Convention, Denver,
 CO, Sept 28-Oct 1, 2005
Publication(s): *Style Magazine* (annual)

**American Auto Racing Writers &
 Broadcasters**
922 N Pass Ave, Burbank, CA 91505
Tel: 818-842-7005 *Fax:* 818-842-7020
E-mail: aarwba@compuserve.com
Web Site: www.aarwba.org
Key Personnel
Pres: Ms Dusty Brandel
Media people who cover auto racing.
Number of Members: 360
Publication(s): *Newsletter* (members only)

American Book Producers Association (ABPA)
160 Fifth Ave, Suite 622, New York, NY 10010
Tel: 212-645-2368 *Toll Free Tel:* 800-209-4575
 Fax: 212-242-6499
E-mail: office@abpaonline.org
Web Site: www.abpaonline.org
Key Personnel
Pres: Ellen Scordato; Dan Tucker
Bd of Dirs: Jim Buckley; John Glenn; Susan
 Knopf; Valerie Tomaselli
Admin: David Katz
An association of independent book producing
 companies in the US & Canada.
Number of Members: 60
Publication(s): *Booknews* (members only)

American Booksellers Association
828 S Broadway, Tarrytown, NY 10591
Tel: 914-591-2665 *Toll Free Tel:* 800-637-0037
 Fax: 914-591-2720
E-mail: editorial@booksense.com
Web Site: www.booksense.com *Cable:*
 AMBASSONEW NEW YORK
Key Personnel
CEO: Avin Mark Domnitz *Tel:* 914-591-2665 ext
 1205 *E-mail:* avin@bookweb.org
Founded: 1900
Trade organization representing booksellers.
Number of Members: 8,427

2005 Meeting(s): ABA Convention & Trade Ex-
 hibit, Jacob K Javits Convention Center, New
 York, NY, June 3-5, 2005
Publication(s): *Book Buyers Handbook*; *Book-
 selling This Week*
Membership(s): BISG

American Business Media
675 Third Ave, Suite 415, New York, NY 10017
Tel: 212-661-6360 *Fax:* 212-370-0736
E-mail: info@abmmail.com
Web Site: www.americanbusinessmedia.com
Key Personnel
Pres: Gordon T Hughes, II *E-mail:* hughes@
 abmmail.com
VP, Media Servs: John Holden
Mgr, Membership Devt: Carlese Westock
Founded: 1906
Nonprofit, global association for business-to-
 business information providers, including pro-
 ducers of magazines, Web site content/service
 providers, trade shows, newsletters, databases,
 custom publishers, as well as conventions, con-
 ferences, seminars & other ancillary media that
 build on the print medium. Call association for
 listing of events scheduled.
Number of Members: 224

American Christian Writers
PO Box 110390, Nashville, TN 37222
Tel: 615-834-0450 *Toll Free Tel:* 800-21-WRITE
 (219-7483) *Fax:* 615-834-7736
Web Site: www.acwriters.com
Key Personnel
Dir & Publr: Reg A Forder *E-mail:* regaforder@
 aol.com

American Civil Liberties Union
125 Broad St, 18th fl, New York, NY 10004
Tel: 212-549-2500 *Toll Free Tel:* 800-775-ACLU
 (orders)
E-mail: info@aclu.org
Web Site: www.aclu.org
Key Personnel
Pres: Nadine Strossen
Exec Dir: Anthony D Romero
Edit & Mktg Coord: Todd Drew *Tel:* 212-549-
 2564 *E-mail:* tdrew@aclu.org
Communs Dir: Emily Tynes
Protection of constitutional rights & civil liberties
 through litigation, legislative lobbying & public
 education; 250 branch offices.
Number of Members: 300,000
Publication(s): *Civil Liberties* (biannual, newslet-
 ter)

American Council on Education
One Dupont Circle NW, Washington, DC 20036
Tel: 202-939-9300 *Fax:* 202-939-9302
Web Site: www.acenet.edu
Key Personnel
Pres: David Ward
Dir, Pubns: Wendy Bressler
The nation's major coordinating body for postsec-
 ondary education. Professional books & guides
 in higher education (special studies & reports
 on higher education).
Number of Members: 1,850
2005 Meeting(s): ACE Annual Meeting, Feb,
 2005
Publication(s): *Higher Education & National Af-
 fairs*; *The Presidency* (3 times/yr, $32/yr); *Se-
 ries on Higher Education*

American Film Institute (AFI)
2021 N Western Ave, Los Angeles, CA 90027
Tel: 323-856-7600 *Toll Free Tel:* 800-774-4234
 (memberships) *Fax:* 323-467-4578
E-mail: info@afi.com
Web Site: www.afi.com

Key Personnel
CEO & Dir: Jean Picker Firstenberg
COO & Dir: James Hindmar
Dir, Corp Aff: Adrian Borneman
Exec Ed: Pat Hanson
A national trust dedicated to preserving the her-
 itage of film & TV; to identify, develop & train
 creative individuals; to present the moving im-
 age as an art form.
Number of Members: 5,000
Branch Office(s)
The John F Kennedy Center for the Performing
 Arts, Washington, DC 20566 *Tel:* 202-833-
 2348 *Fax:* 202-659-1970

American Forest & Paper Association
1111 19 St NW, Suite 800, Washington, DC
 20036
Tel: 202-463-2700 *Toll Free Tel:* 800-878-8878
 Fax: 202-463-4703
E-mail: info@afandpa.org
Web Site: www.afandpa.org
Key Personnel
Pres & CEO: W Henson Moore
Exec VP: Steve Lovett
Chief Counsel: Bob Kirshner
Dir, HR: Michael Hoagland
National trade association; complete listing of
 publications available on website.
Number of Members: 150

American Institute of Graphic Arts (AIGA)
164 Fifth Ave, New York, NY 10010
Tel: 212-807-1990 *Toll Free Tel:* 800-548-1634
 Fax: 212-807-1799
E-mail: aiga@aiga.org
Web Site: www.aiga.org
Key Personnel
Exec Dir: Richard Grefe
National nonprofit organization for graphic design
 profession. Organizes competitions, exhibitions,
 publications, educational activities & projects
 in the public interest to promote excellence in
 the graphic design industry.
Number of Members: 17,000
New Election: Annually in June
2005 Meeting(s): National Design Conference,
 Boston, MA, Sept 15-17, 2005
Publication(s): *365 AIGA Year in Review* (annual)

American Jewish Committee
Affiliate of Institute of Human Relations
165 E 56 St, New York, NY 10022
Tel: 212-751-4000 *Fax:* 212-891-1492
Web Site: www.ajc.org
Key Personnel
Exec Dir: David Harris
Ed: Lawrence Grossman *Tel:* 212-751-4000 ext
 308
Civic & religious rights of Jews in the USA &
 abroad; intergroup relations & human rights.
Number of Members: 43,000
2005 Meeting(s): American Jewish Committee
 Annual Meeting, Washington, DC, May 2005
Publication(s): *AJC Journal* (bimonthly, Free to
 members); *American Jewish Yearbook* ($30);
 Commentary ($4.50/issue)
Branch Office(s)
2027 Massachusetts Ave NW, Washington, DC
 20036

American Language Academy, see American
 Literacy Council

American Literacy Council
Affiliate of Simplified Spelling Society
148 W 117 St, New York, NY 10026
Tel: 212-663-4200 *Toll Free Tel:* 800-781-9985
E-mail: fyi@americanliteracy.com
Web Site: www.americanliteracy.com

Key Personnel
Pres: Alan Mole
Man Dir: Joseph Little
Founded: 1971
Produce & distribute literacy software & simpler
spelling materials.
Number of Members: 110
Publication(s): *Sound-Write Literacy Software*
($50)

American Literary Translators Association (ALTA)
Affiliate of University of Texas Dallas
PO Box 830688, Mail Sta MC 35, Richardson,
TX 75083-0688
Tel: 972-883-2093 *Fax:* 972-883-6303
Web Site: www.literarytranslators.org
Key Personnel
Dir: Rainer Schulte *E-mail:* schulte@utdallas.edu
Literary translation & translators.
Number of Members: 600
Publication(s): *Newsletter* (quarterly); *Transla-tion Review* (biannually, $30/yr US & Canada
individual, $60 renewal)

American Management Association
1601 Broadway, New York, NY 10019-7420
Tel: 212-586-8100 *Toll Free Tel:* 800-262-9699
Fax: 212-903-8168
Web Site: www.amanet.org
Key Personnel
CEO & Pres: Edward T Reilly
CFO & Treas: Vivianna Guzman
Sr VP, HR: Manny Avramidis
Sr VP, Gen Counsel & Corp Sec: Arthur Levy
Sr VP, USME Instruction Devt: Diane Laurenzo
Sr VP, Corp Learning Servs Div: Sam Davis
VP, Mktg Communs: Lawrence Geiger
VP & Events Mgr: Joan Castonguay
VP, Sales, Corp Learning Servs Div: Sam Davis
Pres & Publr, AMACOM: Hank Kennedy
Publish books, surveys & management briefings.
Produces videos, audio-cassette/workbook pro-
grams (self-study programs); Books On-line
in digital form (E-Books); CD-ROM; Corpo-
rate Learning Services; Operation Enterprise;
Library & Bookstores. Sponsor workshops &
awards. Publish practical solutions that are cru-
cial to business communications.
Number of Members: 700,000
New Election: Annually in March

American Marketing Association
311 S Wacker Dr, Suite 5800, Chicago, IL
60606-2266
Tel: 312-542-9000 *Toll Free Tel:* 800-262-1150
Fax: 312-542-9001
E-mail: info@ama.org
Web Site: www.marketingpower.com
Key Personnel
CEO: Dennis Dunlap
Mgr, Membership Mktg: Jennifer Kemper
Tel: 312-542-9089
A nonprofit, educational institution. Offers online
marketing info at www.marketingpower.com.
Sponsors seminars, conferences & student mar-
keting clubs & doctoral consortium. Publish
books, journals, magazines & proceedings of
conferences.
Number of Members: 38,000
Publication(s): *Journal of Marketing Research*
(quarterly, journal); *Journal of Public Policy
& Marketing* (semiannually, journal); *Mar-
keting Health Services* (quarterly); *Marketing
Management* (bimonthly); *Marketing News* (biweekly); *Marketing Research* (quarterly); *Proceedings of Conferences*

American Medical Association
515 N State St, Chicago, IL 60610
Tel: 312-464-5000 *Toll Free Tel:* 800-621-8335
Fax: 312-464-4184

Web Site: www.ama-assn.org
Key Personnel
Exec VP: Dr Michael Maves
Ed-in-Chief, Scientific Pubns & Multimedia: Dr
Catherine De Angelis, MD
Promotes the science & art of medicine & bet-
terment of public health. Association of physi-
cians.
Publication(s): *American Medical News* (weekly);
Archives of Dermatology (monthly); *Archives
of General Psychiatry* (monthly); *Archives of
Internal Medicine* (monthly); *Archives of Neu-
rology* (monthly); *Archives of Ophtholmology*
(monthly); *Archives of Otolaryngology-Head &
Neck Surgery* (monthly); *Archives of Pediatrics
& Adolescent Medicine* (monthly); *Archives of
Surgery* (monthly); *JAMA: The Journal of the
American Medical Association* (weekly)
Branch Office(s)
119 Cherry Hill Rd, Parsippany, NJ 07054

American Medical Publishers Association
14 Fort Hill Rd, Huntington, NY 11743
Tel: 631-423-0075 *Fax:* 631-423-0075
E-mail: info@ampaonline.org
Web Site: www.ampaonline.org
Key Personnel
COO: Ron McMillen
Dir, Digital Busn: Meg White
Exec Dir: Jill Rudansky *E-mail:* jillrudansky-
ampa@msn.com
Founded: 1960
Promote industry interests.
Number of Members: 75
Publication(s): *AMPA Newsletter* (quarterly,
newsletter, free to members)

American Medical Writers Association
40 W Gude Dr, Suite 101, Rockville, MD 20850-
1192
Tel: 301-294-5303 *Fax:* 301-294-9006
E-mail: info@amwa.org
Web Site: www.amwa.org
Key Personnel
Exec Dir: Donna Munari *E-mail:* dmunari@
amwa.org
Sponsor annual medical book awards & over 80
workshops at annual conference.
Number of Members: 4,700
2005 Meeting(s): Annual Conference, Pittsburgh,
PA, Sept 29-Oct 1, 2005
Publication(s): *AMWA Journal* (quarterly); *Free-
lance Directory Online*; *Membership Directory*
(annually)

American Political Science Association
1527 New Hampshire Ave NW, Washington, DC
20036
Tel: 202-483-2512 *Fax:* 202-483-2657
E-mail: apsa@apsanet.org
Web Site: www.apsanet.org
Key Personnel
Exec Dir: Michael Brintnall *E-mail:* brintnall@
apsanet.org
Deputy Dir: Robert Hauck *E-mail:* rhauck@
apsanet.org
Provide services to facilitate research, teaching &
professional development in political science,
including publications & services to assist college faculty, graduate students & researchers.
Number of Members: 16,500
2005 Meeting(s): Washington, DC, Sept 1-4,
2005
2006 Meeting(s): San Francisco, CA, Aug 31-
Sept 4, 2006
Publication(s): *American Political Science Review*
(quarterly); *Perspectives on Politics* (quarterly);
PS: Political Science & Politics (quarterly)

American Printing History Association
PO Box 4519, Grand Central Sta, New York, NY
10163-4519

Tel: 212-930-9220 *Fax:* 212-930-0079
Web Site: www.printinghistory.org
Key Personnel
Pres: Martin Antonetti
Exec Sec: Stephen G Crook *E-mail:* scrook@
nypl.org
Local chapters in New York City, New England,
Chesapeake, Southern & Northern California.
Number of Members: 750
New Election: Jan
Publication(s): *APHA Newsletter* (quarterly,
newsletter, free to members); *Printing History*
(semiannually, free to members)

American Psychological Association
750 First St NE, Washington, DC 20002-4242
Tel: 202-336-5500; 202-336-5540
Toll Free Tel: 800-374-2721 *Fax:* 202-336-5620
E-mail: order@apa.org
Web Site: www.apa.org
Key Personnel
CEO: Norman Anderson
Publish numerous periodicals & books in the field
of psychology.
Number of Members: 155,000
Publication(s): *American Psychologist* (monthly);
APA Membership Register (annually); *APA
Monitor* (monthly); *Directory of the APA* (1
issue/4 yrs)

American Public Human Services Association
810 First St NE, Suite 500, Washington, DC
20002
Tel: 202-682-0100 *Fax:* 202-289-6555
E-mail: pubs@aphsa.org
Web Site: www.aphsa.org
Key Personnel
Exec Dir: Jerry Friedman
Ed & Dir, Publns & Communs: Francis Solomon
Policy & Govt Aff Dept Exec Dir: Elaine M
Ryan
Leadership & Practice Devt Dept Exec Dir: Susan
Christie
Adv: Cherea Stoney
Fulfillment/Subscriptions Mgr: Demetrius
Williams
Founded: 1930
Membership organization of public human ser-
vices professionals.
Number of Members: 5,000
New Election: Annually in Dec
Publication(s): *Policy and Practice* (quarterly,
$75); *Public Human Services Directory* (annu-
ally, $95 members, $120 non-members); *This
Week In Washington* (45/yr, $110/yr APWA
members, $120/yr non-members); *W-Memo* (bi-
monthly, $90 members, $100 non-members)

American Society for Information Science & Technology (ASIS)
1320 Fenwick Lane, Suite 510, Silver Spring,
MD 20910
Tel: 301-495-0900 *Fax:* 301-495-0810
E-mail: asis@asis.org
Web Site: www.asis.org
Key Personnel
Exec Dir: Richard Hill *E-mail:* rhill@asis.org
To foster & lead the advancement of information
science & technology.
Number of Members: 4,000
Publication(s): *Annual Review of Information Sci-
ence & Technology*; *Bulletin*; *Journal*

American Society of Composers, Authors & Publishers (ASCAP)
One Lincoln Plaza, New York City, NY 10023
Tel: 212-621-6000 *Toll Free Tel:* 800-952-7227
Fax: 212-362-7328
E-mail: info@ascap.com
Web Site: www.ascap.com *Cable:* ASCAPNYK
Key Personnel
Chmn & Pres: Marilyn Bergman *E-mail:* pmb@
ascap.com

Founded: 1914
License nondramatic right of public performance of members' copyrighted musical compositions & distribute royalties to members on basis of performances. Members are composers, lyricists & music publishers.
Number of Members: 145,000

American Society of Indexers Inc (ASI)
10200 W 44 Ave, Suite 304, Wheat Ridge, CO 80033
Tel: 303-463-2887 *Fax:* 303-422-8894
E-mail: info@asindexing.org
Web Site: www.asindexing.org
Key Personnel
CEO: Jerry Bowman
Pres: Enid Zafran
Exec Dir: Francine Butler *E-mail:* fbutler@resourcecenter.com
Membership: Ruth Gleason
Educational programs for indexing field.
Number of Members: 950
New Election: May, 2005
2005 Meeting(s): Annual Meeting, Pasadena, CA, May 11-14, 2005

American Society of Journalists & Authors (ASJA)
1501 Broadway, Suite 302, New York, NY 10036
Tel: 212-997-0947 *Fax:* 212-768-7414
E-mail: staff@asja.org
Web Site: www.asja.org
Key Personnel
Pres: Lisa Collier Cool
Exec Dir: Ms Brett Harvey *E-mail:* execdir@asja.org
Founded: 1948
Service organization providing exchange of ideas, market information. Regular meetings with speakers from the industry, annual writers conference; medical plans available. Professional referral service, annual membership directory; first amendment advocacy group.
Number of Members: 1,100
Publication(s): *Annual Membership Directory* ($98); *ASJA Monthly* (11 times/yr, newsletter, members only)

American Society of Magazine Editors
810 Seventh Ave, 24th fl, New York, NY 10019
Tel: 212-872-3700 *Fax:* 212-906-0128
E-mail: asme@magazine.org
Web Site: www.asme.magazine.org
Key Personnel
Exec Dir: Marlene Kahan *E-mail:* mkahan@magazine.org
Founded: 1963
Professional society for senior magazine editors. Sponsor the National Magazine Awards & Magazine Internship Program; hold monthly luncheons for members & conduct periodic seminars.
Number of Members: 900
New Election: Annually in April

American Society of Media Photographers (ASMP)
150 N Second St, Philadelphia, PA 19106
Tel: 215-451-2767 *Fax:* 215-451-0880
E-mail: info@asmp.org
Web Site: www.asmp.org
Key Personnel
Exec Dir: Eugene Mopsik
Gen Mgr: Elena Goertz *E-mail:* goertz@asmp.org
Maintain & promote high professional standards & ethics in photography; cultivate mutual understanding among professional photographers; protect & promote interests of photographers whose work is for publication.
Number of Members: 5,500
Publication(s): *ASMP Professional Business Practices in Photography 5th Edition* ($23.95 plus

S&H); *The Business of Images Video* ($7 plus S&H); *Copyright Guide for Photographers* ($5.95 plus S&H); *Formalizing Agreements* ($12.00 plus S&H); *How to Shoot Stock Photos That Sell* ($15.95 plus S&H); *The Law (in Plain English) for Photographers* ($18.95 plus S&H); *Nature and Wildlife Photography* ($15.15 plus S&H); *On Buying Photography* (pkts of 20, $10.00 plus S&H); *The Photographer's Assistant* ($15.95 plus S&H); *The Photographer's Internet Handbook* ($15.15 plus S&H); *The Photography's Guide to Marketing and Self-Promotion* ($15.95 plus S&H); *Pricing Photography* ($19.95 plus S&H); *Rights & Value - In Traditional & Electronic Media* ($8.95 plus S&H); *Stock Photography Business Forms* ($15.15 plus S&H); *Travel Photography* ($18.35 plus S&H); *Valuation/Lost Damaged Transparencies* ($14.95 plus S&H)

American Sociological Association (ASA)
1307 New York Ave NW, Suite 700, Washington, DC 20005-4701
Tel: 202-383-9005 *Fax:* 202-638-0882
E-mail: executive.office@asanet.org
Web Site: www.asanet.org
Key Personnel
Pres: Troy Duster
Exec Officer: Sally T Hillsman
E-mail: hillsman@asanet.org
Pubn Dir: Karen Gray Edwards
E-mail: edwards@asanet.org
Founded: 1905
Nonprofit membership association dedicated to advancing sociology as a scientific discipline & profession serving the public good. Encompass sociologists who are faculty members at colleges & universities, researchers, practitioners & students.
Number of Members: 13,000
New Election: Annually in Aug
2005 Meeting(s): Annual Meeting, Marriott - Philadelphia, PA, Aug 13-16, 2005
Publication(s): *American Sociological Review* (bimonthly, $35 member, $80 non-member indiv, $160 non-member instn, $20 postage outside US); *Contemporary Sociology* (bimonthly, $35 member, $80 non-member indiv, $160 non-member instn, $20 postage outside US); *Employment Bulletin* (monthly, $10 member, $40 non-member indiv, $40 non-member instn, $15 postage outside US); *Footnotes* (monthly exc June & July, $40 non-member indiv, $40 non-member instn, $15 postage outside US); *Journal of Health & Social Behavior* (quarterly, $30 member, $70 non-member indiv, $140 non-member instn, $20 postage outside US); *Social Psychology Quarterly* (quarterly, $30 member, $70 non-member indiv, $140 non-member instn, $20 postage outside US); *Sociological Methodology* (annual, $45 member, $90 non-member indiv, $187 non-member instn, $20 postage outside US); *Sociological Theory* (semiannually, $30 member, $83 non-member indiv, $192 non-member instn, $20 postage outside US); *Sociology of Education* (quarterly, $30 member, $70 non-member indiv, $140 non-member instn, $20 postage outside US); *Teaching Sociology* (quarterly, $30 member, $70 non-member indiv, $140 non-member instn, $20 postage outside US)

American Speech-Language-Hearing Association (ASHA)
10801 Rockville Pike, Rockville, MD 20852
Tel: 301-897-5700 *Toll Free Tel:* 800-638-8255
Fax: 301-571-0457
Web Site: www.asha.org
Key Personnel
Dir, Pub: Joanne Jessen *E-mail:* jjessen@asha.org
Founded: 1925
Membership organization for 114,000 speech-language pathologists & audiologists. Pro-

vide consumers with information & referral on speech, language & hearing. Publish information brochures & packets.
Number of Members: 96,000
New Election: Annually in April
Publication(s): *American Journal of Audiology* (2 issues/yr, journal); *American Journal of Speech-Language Pathology* (4 issues/yr, journal); *The ASHA Leader* (2 times/mo, newspaper); *Journal of Speech, Language & Hearing Research* (bimonthly, journal); *Language, Speech & Hearing Services In The Schools* (quarterly, journal)

American Translators Association (ATA)
225 Reinekers Lane, Suite 590, Alexandria, VA 22314
Tel: 703-683-6100 *Fax:* 703-683-6122
E-mail: ata@atanet.org
Web Site: www.atanet.org
Key Personnel
Pres: Scott Brennan
Exec Dir: Walter Bacak *Tel:* 703-683-6100 ext 3006 *E-mail:* walter@atanet.org
Founded: 1959
Membership consists of those professionally engaged in translating, interpreting or closely allied work, as well as those who are interested in these fields. Membership: $120/yr individuals, $300/yr corporate.
Number of Members: 9,000
New Election: Nov 1
Publication(s): *ATA Chronicle* (11 issues/yr, $55)

Antiquarian Booksellers' Association of America
20 W 44 St, 4th fl, New York, NY 10036
Tel: 212-944-8291 *Fax:* 212-944-8293
E-mail: hq@abaa.org
Web Site: www.abaa.org
Key Personnel
Pres: John Crichton
Exec Dir: Liane Thomas Wade
Exec Dir & Admin: Susan Dixon
Treas: Rob Rulon-Miller
Chapters: Northern California, Southern California, Midwest, Middle Atlantic, New England, Southeast, Southwest & Pacific Northwest. Membership open to antiquarian booksellers only. ABAA sponsors three or four international book fairs per year in Los Angeles & San Francisco (alternately) in mid-winter; in New York in the spring; in Boston in late autumn.
Number of Members: 470
2005 Meeting(s): International Book Fair/San Francisco Book Fair, Concourse Exhibition Center, San Francisco, CA, Feb 2005
2006 Meeting(s): International Book Fair/Los Angeles Book Fair, Los Angeles, CA, Feb 2006
Publication(s): *Membership Directory* (annual, free with SASE + $1.26 postage)

Antiquarian Booksellers Association of Canada (ABAC)
Division of International League of Antiquarian Booksellers
824 Fort St, Victoria, BC V8W 1H8, Canada
Tel: 250-360-2929 *Fax:* 250-361-1812
E-mail: info@abac.org
Web Site: www.abac.org
Key Personnel
Pres: Bjarne Tokerud *E-mail:* bjarnetokerud@shaw.ca
Sec: Jeri Bass *E-mail:* jeri@wellsbooks.com
The Association's aim is to foster an interest in rare books & mss & to maintain high standards in the antiquarian book trades.
Number of Members: 70
Publication(s): *ABAC/ALAC National Directory* (free on request)

ASHA, see American Speech-Language-Hearing Association (ASHA)

Associated Business Writers of America Inc
Division of National Writers Association Inc
3140 S Peoria St, Suite 295, Aurora, CO 80014
Tel: 303-841-0246 *Fax:* 303-841-2607
Web Site: www.nationalwriters.com
Key Personnel
Exec Dir: Sandy Whelchel *E-mail:* sandywrter@aol.com
To help business writers & those seeking their services.
Number of Members: 150
Publication(s): *Professional Freelance Writers Directory* (available online for free)

Associated Press Broadcasters
1825 "K" St NW, Suite 800, Washington, DC 20006
Tel: 202-736-1100 *Fax:* 202-736-1199
Web Site: www.ap.org
Key Personnel
VP, Broadcast Servs: Jim Williams
Assignment Ed: Kate McKenna
Number of Members: 5,800
Publication(s): *AP Broadcast Handbook* ($24.95)

Association des Editeurs de Langue Anglaise du Quebec (AEAQ)
1200 Atwater Ave, Suite 3, Montreal, PQ H3Z 1X4, Canada
Tel: 514-932-5633 *Fax:* 514-932-5456
E-mail: aelaq@bellnet.ca
Key Personnel
Exec Dir: Margaret Goldik
Encourage publication, distribution & promotion of books published in English in Quebec.
Number of Members: 12

Association des Libraires du Quebec
1001, de Maisonneuve Est, Bureau 580, Montreal, PQ H2L 4P9, Canada
Tel: 514-526-3349 *Fax:* 514-526-3340
E-mail: info@alq.qc.ca
Web Site: www.alq.qc.ca
Key Personnel
Pres: Yvon Lachance
Quebec association of booksellers.
Number of Members: 125

Association for Information & Image Management International
1100 Wayne Ave, Suite 1100, Silver Spring, MD 20910
Tel: 301-587-8202 *Toll Free Tel:* 800-477-2446
Fax: 240-494-2661
E-mail: aiim@aiim.org
Web Site: www.aiim.org
Key Personnel
Ed: Bryant Duhon *Tel:* 301-916-7182
Mgr: Kristen Lewis
Web Spec: Lisa Morris
Global association bringing together the users of document technologies with the providers of that technology.
Number of Members: 9,197
Publication(s): *DOC.1* (weekly 50 weeks/yr, $15/yr members); *Edot Magazine* (magazine, Free)

Association for the Export of Canadian Books
One Nicholas, Suite 504, Ottawa, ON K1N 7B7, Canada
Tel: 613-562-2324 *Fax:* 613-562-2329
E-mail: aecb@aecb.org
Web Site: www.aecb.org
Key Personnel
Pres: Daniel Desjardins
Exec Dir: Suzanne Bosse
Intl Mktg Mgr: Catherine Montgomery
E-mail: cmontgomery@aecb.org
Intl Prog Mgr: Francois Charette
Pubns Mgr: Adam Becker
As the only national trade association that connects English & French language publishers across Canada, the Association for the Export of Canadian Books (AECB) has a mandate to foster Canadian publishers' export sales. The AECB coordinates Canadian publishers' presence at international book fairs, promotes Canadian titles abroad through its catalogues, exhibits & Web site, provides market intelligence & acts as a liaison between Canadian publishers & foreign buyers. The AECB also assists the industry by providing funding assistance for Canadian publishers' international marketing strategies & activities.
Publication(s): *Books on Canada Catalogue* (annual, free); *Rights Canada Catalogue* (semi-annually, free)

Association Nationale des Editeurs de Livres
2514 boul Rosemont, Montreal, PQ H1Y 1K4, Canada
Tel: 514-273-8130 *Fax:* 514-273-9657
E-mail: info@anel.org
Web Site: www.anel.org
Key Personnel
Dir: Jean-Louis Forpin
Professional association of French publishers in Canada.
Number of Members: 100
Publication(s): *Profession Editeur* (quarterly, free)

Association of American Editorial Cartoonists
1221 Stoneferry Lane, Raleigh, NC 27606
Tel: 919-859-5516 *Fax:* 919-859-3172
Key Personnel
Pres: Matt Davies
Gen Mgr: Wanda R Nicholson
E-mail: wnicholson@nc.rr.com
Founded: 1957
Trade Association.
Number of Members: 368
Publication(s): *Notebook* (quarterly)

Association of American Publishers (AAP)
71 Fifth Ave, 2nd fl, New York, NY 10003-3004
Tel: 212-255-0200 *Fax:* 212-255-7007
Web Site: www.publishers.org *Cable:* BOOKASSOC NEWYORK
Key Personnel
Pres & CEO: Patricia S Schroeder *Tel:* 202-347-3375 *Fax:* 202-347-3690
VP: Kathryn G Blough *Tel:* 212-255-0200 ext 263 *E-mail:* kblough@publishers.org
VP, Prof Scholarly Publg: Barbara J Meredith *Tel:* 212-255-0200 ext 223 *E-mail:* bmeredith@publishers.org
VP, Legal & Govt Aff: Allan R Adler *Tel:* 202-347-3375 *Fax:* 202-347-3690
VP, School Div: Steve Driesler *Tel:* 202-347-3375 *Fax:* 202-347-3690
Founded: 1970
Monitor & promote the USA publishing industry. Members: those actively engaged in the creation, publication & production of books, journals, electronic media, testing materials & a range of educational materials.
Number of Members: 300
Branch Office(s)
50 "F" St NW, Washington, DC 20001-1530, Dir, Communs & Pub Aff: Judith Platt *Tel:* 202-347-3375 *Fax:* 202-347-3690 *Web Site:* www.publsihers.org
Membership(s): BISG

Association of American University Presses (AAUP)
71 W 23 St, Suite 901, New York City, NY 10010
Tel: 212-989-1010 *Fax:* 212-989-0275; 212-989-0176
E-mail: info@aaupnet.org
Web Site: www.aaupnet.org
Key Personnel
Exec Dir: Peter J Givler
Admin Mgr: Linda McCall
Membership & affiliation consists of university presses in North America & abroad that function as the publishing arms of their respective universities, issuing some 9,000 titles annually. AAUP helps these presses do their work more economically, creatively & effectively through its own activities in professional development; fund raising; statistical research & analysis; promoting the value of university presses; community & institutional relations & through its marketing programs.
Number of Members: 120
Publication(s): *AAUP Book, Jacket, & Journal Show, Catalog* ($10); *Annual Directory* (annual, $23.00); *The Exchange, Newsletter* (quarterly, $15/yr; free to academia); *University Press Books for Public & Secondary School Libraries* (gratis)
Membership(s): BISG

Association of Authors' Representatives Inc (AAR)
PO Box 237201, Ansonia Sta, New York, NY 10023
E-mail: aarinc@mindspring.com
Web Site: www.aar-online.org
Key Personnel
Pres: Gail Hochman
VP, Literary: Wendy Weil
VP, Dramatic: Robin Kaver
Sec: Miriam Altshuler
Treas: Ann Rittenberg
Admin Sec: Joanne Brownstein *E-mail:* aarinc@mindspring.com
Founded: 1991
Voluntary & elective professional association of literary & play agents whose individual members subscribe to certain ethical practices. Members meet to discuss industry developments & problems of mutual interest.
Number of Members: 350
New Election: Annually in June

Association of Book Publishers of British Columbia
100 W Pender, Suite 107, Vancouver, BC V6B 1R8, Canada
Tel: 604-684-0228 *Fax:* 604-684-5788
E-mail: admin@books.bc.ca
Web Site: www.books.bc.ca
Key Personnel
Exec Dir: Margaret Reynolds
Number of Members: 55

Association of Canadian Publishers
161 Eglinton Ave, Suite 702, Toronto, ON M4P 1J5, Canada
Tel: 416-487-6116 *Fax:* 416-487-8815
Web Site: www.publishers.ca
Key Personnel
Exec Dir: John Pelletier *Tel:* 416-487-6116 ext 222
Association of English-language Canadian-owned book publishing companies in Canada. Sponsor professional development seminars for book publishers. Publish membership directories, studies & reports.
Number of Members: 140
Publication(s): *Directory of Members & Many Others*

Association of Canadian University Presses
10 St Mary St, Suite 700, Toronto, ON M4Y 2W8, Canada
Tel: 416-978-2239 ext 237 *Fax:* 416-978-4738
Key Personnel
Admin: Charley LaRose *E-mail:* clarose@utpress.utoronto.ca

Number of Members: 15
New Election: Annually in autumn
Publication(s): *Directory* (annual, free)

Association of College & University Printers
Penn State University, 101 Business Services
Bldg, University Park, PA 16802
Tel: 814-865-7544 *Fax:* 814-863-6376
Key Personnel
Dir: Michael Poorman
Mgr: Travis Long
Number of Members: 300

The Association of Educational Publishers (AEP)
510 Heron Dr, Suite 309, Logan Township, NJ
08085
Tel: 856-241-7772 *Fax:* 856-241-0709
E-mail: mail@edpress.org
Web Site: www.edpress.org
Key Personnel
Exec Dir: Charlene F Gaynor *E-mail:* cgaynor@
edpress.org
Opers Mgr: Jackie Schmenger
AEP supports educational publishing through its
programs & member services; The AEP logo
on member publications/products represents a
commitment to high quality publishing stan-
dards.
Number of Members: 400
Publication(s): *EdPress Membership Roster &
Freelance Directory* (annually, free to mem-
bers/not available to non-members); *Edpress
News* (monthly)

Association of Free Community Papers (AFCP)
1630 Miner St, Suite 204, Idaho Springs, CO
80452
Toll Free Tel: 877-203-2327 *Fax:* 781-459-7770
Web Site: www.afcp.org
Key Personnel
Dir: Craig McMullen
Organization of publishers serving the free-
circulation community newspaper & shopping
guide industry.
Number of Members: 200
2005 Meeting(s): Annual Conference, San Francisco, CA - Hyatt Regency Embarcadero, April
28-30, 2005
Publication(s): *Ink* (monthly, newsletter, free)

Association of Graphic Communications
Affiliate of Printing Industries of America/
Graphic Arts Technical Foundation
330 Seventh Ave, 9th fl, New York, NY 10001-
5010
Tel: 212-279-2100 *Fax:* 212-279-5381
Web Site: www.agcomm.org
Key Personnel
Pres: Susan G Greenwood *Tel:* 212-279-2115
E-mail: susie@agcomm.org
Founded: 1865
Continuing education/training, management semi-
nars, labor relations, technical & financial con-
sulting, employment referral, exhibitions, insur-
ance programs, credit & collection, government
affairs/environmental regulation compliance.
Number of Members: 630
Publication(s): *AGC World Newsletter* (quarterly);
Buyer Guide/Directory (annual)

Association of Jewish Book Publishers
c/o Jewish Lights Publishing Sunset Farm Offices,
PO Box 237, Woodstock, VT 05091
Tel: 802-457-4000 *Fax:* 802-457-4004
Web Site: www.jewishlights.com
Key Personnel
Pres: Stuart M Matlins *E-mail:* editorial@
jewishlights.com

Nonprofit organization which provides a forum to
discuss mutual interest of publishers, authors
& other individuals & institutions. Concerned
with Jewish books which span religion, history,
literature, children's books & cookbooks. The
association promotes the sale & use of Jewish
books through education, meetings, cooperative exhibits, promotional opportunities & the
exchange of information among members.
Number of Members: 45
Publication(s): *Combined Jewish Book Catalog*
(annual)

Association of Jewish Libraries (AJL)
15 E 26 St, New York, NY 10010-1579
Tel: 212-725-5359
E-mail: ajl@jewishbooks.org
Web Site: www.jewishlibraries.org
Key Personnel
Pres: Ronda Rose *E-mail:* frose@att.net
Corresponding Sec & Contact: Noreen Wachs
E-mail: noreen@ramaz.org
Member libraries in two divisions: Research &
Special Libraries & Synagogue, School & Cen-
ter Libraries. Promote librarianship, services &
standards in the field of Judaica.
Number of Members: 1,114
Publication(s): *AJL Newsletter* (quarterly); *Ju-
daica Librarianship* (irregular)

Association of Manitoba Book Publishers
100 Arthur St, Suite 404, Winnipeg, MB R3B
1H3, Canada
Tel: 204-947-3335 *Fax:* 204-956-4689
E-mail: assocpub@mb.sympatico.ca
Web Site: www.bookpublishers.mb.ca
Key Personnel
Exec Dir: Michelle Peters
Publishing industry association.
Number of Members: 11

Association of Medical Illustrators (AMI)
6660 Delmonico Dr, Suite D-107, Colorado
Springs, CO 80919
Tel: 719-598-8622
E-mail: hq@ami.org
Web Site: www.ami.org
Key Personnel
Chmn: John Martini
Pres: Marcia Hartsock
Exec Dir: Janet McAndless
Promote the use of high-quality artwork in medi-
cal publications to advance medical education.
Number of Members: 850
Publication(s): *AMI News* (bimonthly, newslet-
ter); *Directory* (annual); *Medical Illustration
Sourcebook* (semiannual)

Association of Writers & Writing Programs (AWP)
George Mason University, MS-1E3, Fairfax, VA
22030-4444
Tel: 703-993-4301 *Fax:* 703-993-4302
E-mail: awp@awpwriter.org
Web Site: www.awpwriter.org
Key Personnel
Exec Dir & Ed: D W Fenza
Dir, Conferences: Matt Scanlon
Pubns Mgr: Supriya Bhatnagar *Tel:* 703-993-4308
E-mail: supriya_b@awpwriter.org
Founded: 1967
Magazine, publications, directory, competitions
for awards (including publication), advocacy
for literature & education, annual meeting, job
placement.
Number of Members: 21,000
2005 Meeting(s): Associated Writing Programs
Annual Conference, Hyatt Regency & Fairmont
Hotel, Vancouver, BC, March 30-April 2, 2005

Publication(s): *AWP Official Guide to Writing
Programs* (biennially, $28.45 includes $3 shipping); *The Writer's Chronicle* (6 times/yr, free
to members)

Association pour l'Avancement des Sciences et des Techniques de la Documentation
3414 Avenue du Parc, Bureau 202, Montreal, PQ
H2X 2H5, Canada
Tel: 514-281-5012 *Fax:* 514-281-8219
E-mail: info@asted.org
Web Site: www.asted.org
Key Personnel
Pres: Pierre Tessier
Exec Dir: Louis Cabral
Treas: Diane Rochon
Sec: Marc Dion
Objective is the promotion of standards of excel-
lence in the services & personnel of libraries,
documentation & information centers.
Number of Members: 550
New Election: During Congress
Publication(s): *Documentation et Bibliotheques*
(quarterly, $47/yr Canada, $55/yr elsewhere)

Audit Bureau of Circulations (ABC)
900 N Meacham Rd, Schaumburg, IL 60173-4968
Tel: 847-605-0909 *Fax:* 847-605-0483
Web Site: www.accessabc.com
Key Personnel
Pres & Man Dir: Michael J Lavery
Cooperative association of advertisers, advertising
agencies & publishers of newspapers, magazines, farm & business publications. Audit &
report circulation & other data of newspaper &
periodical publisher members. Electronic publications.
Number of Members: 4,500
Branch Office(s)
405 Lexington Ave, 48th fl, New York, NY
10174-4805
151 Bloor St W, Suite 850, Toronto, ON M5S
1S4, Canada

Audit Bureau of Circulations (ABC), Canadian Office
151 Bloor St W, Suite 850, Toronto, ON M5S
1S4, Canada
Tel: 416-962-5840 *Fax:* 416-962-5844
Web Site: www.accessabc.com
Key Personnel
Sr VP: Robert White
Number of Members: 5,100

Authors Guild
31 E 28 St, New York, NY 10016
Tel: 212-563-5904 *Fax:* 212-564-8363; 212-564-
5363
E-mail: staff@authorsguild.org
Web Site: www.authorsguild.org
Key Personnel
Exec Dir: Paul Aiken
Pres: Nick Taylor
Founded: 1912
National membership organization for nonfiction
& fiction book authors & freelance journalists.
Deals with the business & professional inter-
ests of authors, in such fields as book contracts,
copyright, subsidiary rights, free expression,
taxes & others. Offer free contract reviews,
website development & hosting & health insur-
ance.
Number of Members: 8,400
Publication(s): *The Bulletin* (quarterly)

The Authors League Fund
31 E 28 St, New York, NY 10016
Tel: 212-268-1208 *Fax:* 212-564-5363
E-mail: authlgfund@aol.com
Web Site: www.authorsleaguefund.org

Key Personnel
Pres: Peter S Prescott
VP & Treas: George J W Goodman
VP: Sidney Offit
Admin: Sarah Heller
Sec: Madeleine L'Engle
Provide interest-free loans to professional authors during persnal hardship.
Number of Members: 935

The Authors League of America Inc
31 E 28 St, New York, NY 10016
Tel: 212-564-8350 *Fax:* 212-564-8363
E-mail: staff@authorsguild.com
Web Site: www.authorsguild.com
Key Personnel
Pres: Nick Taylor
Pres, The Dramatists Guild: John Weidman
    Tel: 212-398-9366
Exec Dir: Paul Aiken
Founded: 1912
National membership corporation to promote the professional interests of authors & dramatists, procure satisfactory copyright legislation & treaties, guard freedom of expression & support fair tax treatment for writers. Members of Authors Guild & Dramatists Guild are automatically enrolled.
Number of Members: 15,440

The Authors Registry Inc
31 E 28 St, 10th fl, New York, NY 10016
Tel: 212-563-6920 *Fax:* 212-564-5363
E-mail: staff@authorsregistry.org
Web Site: www.authorsregistry.org
Key Personnel
Man Dir: Paul Aiken
Opers Mgr: Terry King *E-mail:* tking@authorsregistry.org
A nonprofit corporation that provides an extensive contact directory of authors & a royalty collection & distribution service.
Number of Members: 30,000

The Baker Street Irregulars
7938 Mill Stream Circle, Indianapolis, IN 46278
Tel: 317-293-2212
Key Personnel
Wiggins, Chmn: Michael F Whelan
Literary society devoted to the study of Sherlock Holmes.
Number of Members: 300
2005 Meeting(s): Annual Dinner (by invitation only), New York, NY, USA, Jan 2005
Publication(s): *The Baker Street Journal* (quarterly, journal, $22.50/yr domestic, $25.00/yr foreign)

Banff Centre
Formerly Writer's Guild of Alberta
11759 Groat Rd, Edmonton, AB T5M 3K6, Canada
Tel: 780-422-8174 *Toll Free Tel:* 800-665-5354 (Alberta only) *Fax:* 780-422-2663
E-mail: mail@writersguild.ab.ca
Web Site: www.writersguild.ab.ca
Key Personnel
Exec Dir: Diane Walton
Founded: 1980
Promote writing, provide services to the literary arts community.
Number of Members: 750
Publication(s): *WestWord* (bimonthly)

Before Columbus Foundation
The Raymond House, 655 13 St, Suite 302, Oakland, CA 94612
SAN: 159-2955
Tel: 510-268-9775
Key Personnel
Exec Dir: Gundars Strads *Tel:* 510-642-7321
    E-mail: strads@haas.berkeley.edu

Provide information, research, consultation & promotional services for contemporary American multicultural writers & publishers. A nonprofit service organization that also sponsors classes, workshops, readings, public events & the annual American Book Awards.

Bibliographical Society of America
PO Box 1537, Lenox Hill Sta, New York, NY 10021-0043
Tel: 212-452-2710 *Fax:* 212-452-2710
E-mail: bsa@bibsocamer.org
Web Site: www.bibsocamer.org
Key Personnel
Pres, Morgan Lib: John Bidwell
VP: Irene Tichenor
Sec, Johns Hopkins University: Christine A Ruggere
Treas, Lazard Asset Mgt: R Dyke Benjamin
Exec Sec: Michele E Randall *Tel:* 212-734-2500
Sponsor short-term fellowships for bibliographic projects. Membership open to anyone interested in bibliographic projects & process.
Number of Members: 1,100
New Election: Annually in Jan
2005 Meeting(s): Annual Meeting of the Bibliographical Society of America, New York, NY, USA, Jan 28, 2005
Publication(s): *The Papers of the Bibliographical Society of America* (quarterly, $65 membership subscription fee, $20/yr for students providing proof of eligibility)

Bibliographical Society of the University of Virginia
c/o Alderman Library, University of Virginia, McCormick Rd, Charlottesville, VA 22904
Mailing Address: PO Box 400152, Charlottesville, VA 22904-4152
Tel: 434-924-7013 *Fax:* 434-924-1431
E-mail: bibsoc@virginia.edu
Web Site: etext.lib.virginia.edu/bsuva/
Key Personnel
Pres: G Thomas Tanselle
Exec Sec & Treas: Anne Ribble *E-mail:* ar3g@virginia.edu
Founded: 1947
Scholarly society promoting the study of books as physical objects, the history of the book & of printing & publishing.
Number of Members: 600
Publication(s): *Studies in Bibliography* (annual, $45)

Binding Industries Association (BIA)
Affiliate of Special Industry Group of Printing Industries of America
100 Daingerfield Rd, Alexandria, VA 22314
Tel: 703-519-8137 *Fax:* 703-548-3227
E-mail: bparrott@printing.org
Web Site: www.gain.net
Key Personnel
Exec Dir: Joanne Rock
Trade finishers & loose-leaf manufacturers united to conduct seminars, hold conventions, formulate & maintain industry standards. Bestow annual product of excellence awards.
Number of Members: 300
Publication(s): *The Binding Edge* (quarterly, magazine); *Membership Directory* (in print biennially, on-line, book, book)

BISG, see Book Industry Study Group Inc

BMI
320 W 57 St, New York, NY 10019
Tel: 212-586-2000 *Fax:* 212-246-2163
Web Site: www.bmi.com *Cable:* BROACASTMUS
Key Personnel
CEO & Pres: Frances Preston

Secure & license the performing rights of music on behalf of its creators. Established in 1940. Regional licensing offices in Hollywood, Atlanta, Miami, Los Angeles, Puerto Rico, UK.
Number of Members: 90,000
Publication(s): *BMI Music World* (quarterly)

Book & Periodical Council
192 Spadina Ave, Suite 107, Toronto, ON M5T 2C2, Canada
Tel: 416-975-9366 *Fax:* 416-975-1839
E-mail: bkper@interlog.com
Web Site: www.freedomtoread.ca
Key Personnel
Chmn: Mike Collinge
Exec Dir: Ann McCleland
Umbrella organization representing associations of authors, editors, publishers, book manufacturers, distributors, booksellers & librarians in the book & periodical industries in Canada.
Number of Members: 25
Publication(s): *Author & Editor: A Working Guide*; *Canadian Collections in Public Libraries*; *Dividends: The Value of Public Libraries in Canada* (free); *Freedom to Read Kit* (annual, free); *From Catalogue to Reader*; *Pathways: How to Access Electronic Information*; *Signposts: A Guide to Self-Publishing*; *When the Censor Comes* (shipping charge or SASE)

Book Industry Standards & Communications
Division of Book Industry Study Group Inc
19 W 21 St, Suite 905, New York, NY 10010
Tel: 646-336-7141 *Fax:* 646-336-6214
E-mail: info@bisg.org
Web Site: www.bisg.org
Key Personnel
Exec Dir: Jeff Abraham *E-mail:* jeff@bisg.org
Dir, Comm: Jessica Rossman *E-mail:* jessica@bisg.org
To improve the interchange of technical information pertaining to the ordering, handling & movement of published material.
Number of Members: 30
New Election: Annually in Sept
Publication(s): *Bisac X12 Manual* ($300); *Machine-Readable Guidelines for the Publishing Industry* (booklet, $7.50); *Minutes of Meetings* (bimonthly, $450/yr)

Book Industry Study Group Inc
19 W 21 St, Suite 905, New York, NY 10010
Tel: 646-336-7141 *Fax:* 646-336-6214
E-mail: info@bisg.org
Web Site: www.bisg.org
Key Personnel
Exec Dir: Jeff Abraham *E-mail:* jeff@bisg.org
Founded: 1975
Voluntary association of individuals & firms from the various sectors of the book industry: publishers, manufacturers, wholesalers, librarians, retailers, etc. Promote & support research in & about the industry.
Number of Members: 200
New Election: Annually in Sept
Publication(s): *Book Industry Trends* (annual, $750); *2002 Consumer Research Study on Book Purchasing* ($500)

Book Manufacturers' Institute Inc (BMI)
2 Armand Beach Dr, Suite 1B, Palm Coast, FL 32137
Tel: 386-986-4552 *Fax:* 386-986-4553
E-mail: info@bmibook.com
Web Site: www.bmibook.org
Key Personnel
Exec VP: Bruce W Smith
Founded: 1933
BMI recognition awards include Cased-In-Club-Award, Distinguished Master Bookman Award, Signature Award & Gutenberg Award.

"The Well Built Book: Art & Technology", a 28-minute video tape describing how a book is manufactured is available.
Number of Members: 90
2005 Meeting(s): BMI Management Conference, Sanibel Harbor Resort & Spa, Ft Myers, FL, May 1-3, 2005; BMI Annual Conference, Ritz Carlton Orlando Grande Lakes, Orlando, FL, Nov 6-9, 2005
Publication(s): *BMI Newsletter* (newsletter)
Membership(s): BISG

Book Publicists of Southern California
6464 Sunset Blvd, Rm 755, Hollywood, CA 90028
Tel: 323-461-3921 *Fax:* 323-461-0917
Key Personnel
Founder & Pres, Emeritus: Irwin Zucker
   E-mail: irwinzuckerpr@aol.com
Pres: Ernie Weckbaugh
VP: Patty Weckbaugh
Treas: Lynn Walford
Founded: 1976
Bimonthly meetings, varied, anything pertinent to promotion of books & authors.
Number of Members: 1,200
New Election: Annually in Nov
Publication(s): *Know Thy Shelf* (bimonthly, newsletter, free to members)

The Book Publisher's Association of Alberta
Affiliate of Association of Canadian Publishers (ACP)
10523 100 Ave, Edmonton, AB T5J 0A8, Canada
Tel: 780-424-5060 *Fax:* 780-424-7943
E-mail: info@bookpublishers.ab.ca
Web Site: www.bookpublishers.ab.ca
Key Personnel
Exec Dir: Katherine Shute
Project Coord: Duncan Turner
Sponsor Development Seminars Workshops & Alberta Book Industry Awards.
Number of Members: 34
Publication(s): *Best of the West* (annual, free); *Membership Directory* (annual, free)

The Bookbinders' Guild of New York
Dunn & Co, 110 Grand Ave, Ridgefield Park, NJ 07660
Tel: 201-229-1888 *Fax:* 201-229-1755
Web Site: www.bookbindersguild.org
Key Personnel
Pres: Tom Roche
VP: Michele Rothfarb
Treas: Irwin Wolfe
Fin & Membership: Eric Schwartz
Prog Co-Chmn: Tracy Cabanis
Recording Sec: Avery Fluck
For book publishing production, editorial, design & manufacturing people from the book community. Monthly dinner meetings, book show & educational seminars.
Number of Members: 800
New Election: Annually in April
Publication(s): *Newsletter* (bimonthly, free)

Bookbuilders of Boston
44 Highland Circle, Halifax, MA 02338
Tel: 781-293-8600 *Toll Free Fax:* 866-820-0469
E-mail: office@bbboston.org
Web Site: www.bbboston.org
Key Personnel
Pres: Victor Curran *Tel:* 978-970-1359 ext 337
   E-mail: vcurran@dsgraphics.com
Treas: Larry Bisso
Meetings, New England Book Show, seminars & scholarships; nonprofit organization.
New Election: Annually in April
Publication(s): *Directory* (annual, free)

Bookbuilders West
PO Box 7046, San Francisco, CA 94120-9727

Tel: 415-273-5790
Web Site: www.bookbuilders.org
Key Personnel
Pres: Michelle Bisson Savoy
VP: Amy Changar
Sec: Ramona Beville
Specialize in supporting the book publishing industry. Offers educational programs, seminars, scholarships. Produce an annual book show & have monthly dinner meetings.
Number of Members: 400
New Election: Annually in June
Publication(s): *Bookbuilders West Newsletter* (bimonthly, newsletter)

Books for Everybody
Division of St Joseph Media
70 The Esplanade, Suite 210, Toronto, ON M5E 1R2, Canada
Tel: 416-360-0044 *Fax:* 416-955-0794
E-mail: mail@booksforeverybody.com
Web Site: www.booksforeverybody.com
Key Personnel
Publr: Barbara Scott *E-mail:* bscott@ booksforeverybody.com
Assoc Publr: Attila Berki *E-mail:* aberki@ booksforeverybody.com
Founded: 1937
Publish consumer catalogues for independent book stores.
Publication(s): *Books for Everybody* (annually)
Membership(s): Canadian Booksellers Association

BPA International, see BPA Worldwide

BPA Worldwide
Formerly BPA International
2 Corporate Dr, Suite 900, Shelton, CT 06484
Tel: 203-447-2800 *Fax:* 203-447-2900
E-mail: info@bpaww.com
Web Site: www.bpaww.com
Key Personnel
Pres & CEO: Glenn Hansen *Tel:* 203-447-2801
   E-mail: ghansen@bpai.com
International, independent, not-for-profit organization whose membership consists of advertiser companies, advertising agencies & publications. Audit all-paid, all-controlled or any combination of paid & controlled circulation for 2600 business, technical, professional publications, consumer magazines, newspapers, web sites, e-mail, newsletters & face-to-face events-expos & shows.
Number of Members: 5,200
Foreign Office(s): 801 Stanhope House, 738 King's Rd, Hong Kong *Tel:* 852-2516-3411 *Fax:* 852-2516-9217
55-56 Russell Sq, London WC1B 4HP, United Kingdom *Tel:* (020) 7631-4809 *Fax:* (020) 7631-4810
Branch Office(s)
Pacific Gateway 2, Suite 350, 19191 S Vermont Ave, Torrance, CA 90502 *Tel:* 310-323-7220 *Fax:* 310-323-7231
10119 Maronda Dr, Riverview, FL 33569 *Tel:* 813-741-3142 *Fax:* 813-741-3162
29 N Wacker Dr, Suite 701, Chicago, IL 60606 *Tel:* 312-236-9070 *Fax:* 312-236-9075
90 Eglinton Ave E, Suite 980, Toronto, ON M4P 2X7, Canada *Tel:* 416-487-2418 *Fax:* 416-487-6405
1010 Rue Sherbrooke Ouest, Bureau 1800, Montreal, PQ H3A 2R7, Canada *Tel:* 514-845-0003 *Fax:* 514-845-0905

Broadcast Music Inc, see BMI

Broadcast Pioneers Library of American Broadcasting
Unit of University of Maryland Libraries

Hornbake Library, University of Maryland, College Park, MD 20742
Tel: 301-405-9160 *Fax:* 301-314-2634
E-mail: bp50@umail.umd.edu
Web Site: www.lib.umd.edu/LAB
Key Personnel
Curator: Chuck Howell
Founded: 1970
Library devoted to history of radio & television broadcasting. Contains 8,800 books; 320 vertical files of papers, documents & other print material; 25,000 photographs, 900 interviews & oral histories; 5,600 audiotapes; 5,000 discs; transcripts & scripts. Referral center to other sources of broadcast history.
Number of Members: 21
New Election: Annually in Nov
Publication(s): *Library American Broadcasting Transmitter*

Brooklyn Writers Club
PO Box 184, Bath Beach Sta, Brooklyn, NY 11214-0184
Tel: 718-680-4084
Key Personnel
Founder & Dir: A Dellarocco
Weekly meetings, various locations.
Number of Members: 50

Business Forms Management Association (BFMA)
319 SW Washington St, Suite 710, Portland, OR 97204
Tel: 503-227-3393 *Fax:* 503-274-7667
E-mail: bfma@bfma.org
Web Site: www.bfma.org
Key Personnel
Exec Dir: Andy Palatka *Tel:* 503-227-3393
   E-mail: andy@bfma.org
Founded: 1958
Sponsor professional training in all aspects of information resource management; classes are conducted in major cities in the United States & Canada. Bestow the association's highest award, the Jo Warner Award, to professionals in the information resources industry. Recipients do not have to be BFMA members.
Number of Members: 1,000
Publication(s): *Infocus* (6 issues/yr, $65/yr)

Business Marketing Association
400 N Michigan Ave, Suite 1510, Chicago, IL 60611
Tel: 312-822-0005 *Toll Free Tel:* 800-664-4262 *Fax:* 312-822-0054
E-mail: bma@marketing.org
Web Site: www.marketing.org
Key Personnel
Exec Dir: Rick Kean
Mgr Memb Servs: Michelle Coughlin
Provides information & resources to business-to-business marketers & marketing communicators.
Number of Members: 5,000
Publication(s): *The Business to Business Marketer* (6 issues/yr, magazine)

Canada Council for the Arts
350 Albert St, Ottawa, ON K1P 5V8, Canada
Mailing Address: PO Box 1047, Ottawa, ON K1P 5V8, Canada
Tel: 613-566-4414 *Toll Free Tel:* 800-263-5588 (Canada only) *Fax:* 613-566-4410
Web Site: www.canadacouncil.ca
Key Personnel
Head, Writing & Pubn Section: Melanuie Rutledge *E-mail:* melanie.rutledge@canadacouncil.ca
Admin Coord: Christian Mondor *Tel:* 613-566-4414 ext 4531 *E-mail:* christian.mondor@canadacouncil.com
Federal cultural granting agency for Canadian literature.

Canadian Authors Association (CAA)
320 S Shores Rd, Campbellford, ON K0L 1L0, Canada
Mailing Address: PO Box 419, Campbellford, ON K0L 1L0, Canada
Tel: 705-653-0323 *Toll Free Tel:* 866-216-6222 *Fax:* 705-653-0593
E-mail: info@canauthors.org
Web Site: www.CanAuthors.org
Key Personnel
Natl Pres: Isabel Moore
Admin: Alec McEachern
Encourage & develop a climate favorable to the literary arts in Canada. Assistance to professional & emerging writers. Represent the concerns & interests of members.
Number of Members: 600
Publication(s): *Canadian Writers Guide* (biennially, $30); *National Newsline* (quarterly, complementary)

Canadian Book Systems Advisory Committee
Subsidiary of Canadian Telebook Agency
110 Eglinton Ave W, Suite 401, Toronto, ON M4R 1A3, Canada
Tel: 416-545-1595 *Fax:* 416-545-1590
Key Personnel
Coord: Steven Tran

Canadian Bookbinders & Book Artists Guild (CBBAG)
60 Atlantic Ave, Suite 112, Toronto, ON M6K 1X9, Canada
Tel: 416-581-1071 *Fax:* 416-581-1053
E-mail: cbbag@web.net
Web Site: www.cbbag.ca
Key Personnel
Man Dir: Shelagh Smith
Founded: 1983
Presents workshops & courses on a wide variety of topics, including bookbinding, box making, paper making & decorating, letterpress printing, paper conservation & more. Also maintains a reference library & an audio-visual catalogue.
Number of Members: 540
Publication(s): *Newsletter* (quarterly)

Canadian Booksellers Association (CBA)
789 Don Mills Rd, Suite 700, Toronto, ON M3C 1T5, Canada
Tel: 416-467-7883 *Toll Free Tel:* 866-788-0790 *Fax:* 416-467-7886
E-mail: enquiries@cbabook.org
Web Site: www.cbabook.org
Key Personnel
Pres: Pat Joas
Exec Dir: Susan Dayus *Tel:* 416-467-7883 ext 225 *E-mail:* sdayus@cbabook.org
Founded: 1952
For firms or persons actively engaged in the retail sale of books & supplies.
Number of Members: 900
New Election: Annually in June
Publication(s): *Canadian Bookseller* (8 issues/yr, $24/yr)

Canadian Cataloguing in Publication Program
National Library of Canada, 395 Wellington St, Ottawa, ON K1A 0N4, Canada
Tel: 819-994-6881 *Fax:* 819-997-7517
E-mail: cip@nlc-bnc.ca
Web Site: www.nlc-bnc.ca
Key Personnel
CIP Coord: Luc Simard
Publication(s): *Livres a Paraitre/Forthcoming Books* (monthly, free)

Canadian Centre for Studies in Publishing
Simon Fraser University at Harbour Centre, 515 W Hastings St, Vancouver, BC V6B 5K3, Canada

Tel: 604-291-5242 *Fax:* 604-291-5239
E-mail: ccsp-info@sfu.ca
Web Site: www.harbour.sfu.ca/ccsp/
Key Personnel
Assoc Dir: Jo Anne Ray *E-mail:* joanne-ray@sfu.ca
Dir: Rowland Lorimer
Undergraduate, graduate & noncredit courses; research on publishing.
Publication(s): *Archival Gold: Managing & Preserving Publishers' Records* ($6.25)

The Canadian Children's Book Centre
40 Orchard View Blvd, Suite 101, Lower Level, Toronto, ON M4R 1B9, Canada
Tel: 416-975-0010 *Fax:* 416-975-8970
E-mail: ccbc@bookcentre.ca
Web Site: www.bookcentre.ca
Key Personnel
Exec Dir: Charlotte Teeple
Nonprofit promotion & information center concerned with Canadian children's books: library, information, promotion materials; sponsor Canadian Children's Book Week.
Number of Members: 1,300
Publication(s): *Children's Book News* (3 times/yr); *Our Choice catalog* (annually)

Canadian Copyright Institute
192 Spadina Ave, Suite 107, Toronto, ON M5T 2C2, Canada
Tel: 416-975-1756 *Fax:* 416-975-1839
E-mail: bkper@interlog.com
Key Personnel
Administrator: Anne McClelland
Corp Sec: Grace Westcott
Association of creators, producers & distributors of copyright works whose purpose is to give better understanding copyright law to engage in & foster research in copyright law.
Number of Members: 95
Publication(s): *Newsletter* (irregular, free)

Canadian Education Association/Association canadienne d'education
317 Adelaide St W, Suite 300, Toronto, ON M5V 1P9, Canada
Tel: 416-591-6300 *Fax:* 416-591-5345
E-mail: info@cea.ace.ca
Web Site: www.cea-ace.ca
Key Personnel
CEO: Penny Milton *Tel:* 416-591-6300 ext 236 *E-mail:* pmilton@acea.ca
Res Officer: Valerie Pierre-Pierre
Busn Mgr: Gilles Latour
Founded: 1891
A national bilingual, charitable organization that promotes improvement in education. The subscription prices are in Canadian dollars & include shipping.
Number of Members: 400
New Election: Annually in Sept or Oct
Publication(s): *Education Canada* (quarterly, magazine, Can $35.31/yr, US $53/yr, foreign $73/yr)

Canadian ISBN Agency
Affiliate of National Library of Canada, Acquisitions & Bibliographic Services Branch
National Library of Canada, 395 Wellington St, Ottawa, ON K1A 0N4, Canada
Tel: 819-994-6872 *Fax:* 819-997-7517
E-mail: isbn@nlc-bnc.ca
Web Site: www.nlc-bnc.ca *Telex:* 053-4311; 053-4312
Key Personnel
Rep & CIP Coord: Luc Simard

Canadian Library Association (CLA)
328 Frank St, Ottawa, ON K2P 0X8, Canada
Tel: 613-232-9625 *Fax:* 613-563-9895

E-mail: info@cla.ca
Web Site: www.cla.ca/
Key Personnel
Pres: Stephen Abram
Membership: Brenda Shields *Tel:* 613-232-9625 ext 318
National organization of personal & institutional members devoted to improving the quality of library & information service in Canada & developing higher standards of librarianship.
Number of Members: 3,000
Publication(s): *Feliciter* (bimonthly, free to members, $95/yr to non-members); *School Libraries in Canada* ($35/yr)

Canadian Magazine Publishers Association
425 Adelaide St W, Suite 700, Toronto, ON M5V 3C1, Canada
Tel: 416-504-0274 *Fax:* 416-504-0437
E-mail: cmpainfo@cmpa.ca
Web Site: www.cmpa.ca/; www.magomania.com
Key Personnel
Chpn: Al Zikovitz
Pres: Mark Jamison
Dist Mgr: Allen Pinkerton
Proj Coord: Tonya Stead
Distribution, promotion, professional development & lobbying for Canadian magazines.
Number of Members: 300
Publication(s): *Advertising Sales: A Handbook for Canadian Magazines* ($75 members); *Beginnings: The Basics of Publishing a Small-Circulation Magazine* ($85 non-members); *Circulation Promotion: A Handbook for Canadian Magazines* ($10 members); *Great Canadian Magazines* ($15 non-members); *Magazine Production: A Handbook for Canadian Magazines* ($75 members)

Canadian Newspaper Association
890 Yonge St, Suite 200, Toronto, ON M4W 3P4, Canada
Tel: 416-923-3567 *Fax:* 416-923-7206
Web Site: www.cna-acj.ca
Key Personnel
Pres & CEO: Anne Kothawala
Asst to the Pres: Adele Ritchie *Tel:* 416-923-3567 ext 235 *E-mail:* aritchie@cna-acj.ca
An organization providing service to its members in the area of marketing, member services & contesting legislation that is potentially harmful to newspapers & freedom of the press in general. The association brings the wisdom & dedication of all its members to foster & nurture a free press committed to providing the best possible service to its readers.
Number of Members: 99

Canadian Printing Industries Association
75 Albert St, Suite 906, Ottawa, ON K1P 5E7, Canada
Tel: 613-236-7208 *Fax:* 613-236-8169
Web Site: www.cpia-aci.ca
Key Personnel
Pres: Pierre Boucher
Canadian Book Manufacturers' Association & Canadian Business Documents & Systems Association.
Number of Members: 800
New Election: Annually in Sept every 2 years
Publication(s): *National Impressions* (newsletter)

Canadian Publishers' Council (CPC)
250 Merton St, Suite 203, Toronto, ON M4S 1B1, Canada
Tel: 416-322-7011 *Fax:* 416-322-6999
E-mail: pubadmin@pubcouncil.ca
Web Site: www.pubcouncil.ca
Key Personnel
Pres: Jim Allen
VP: William Zerter
Exec Dir: Jacqueline Hushion

Immediate Past-Pres: John Dill
Treas: Brian Robson
Dir, Canadian Educ Resources Council: Gerry McIntyre
Dir, Trade & Higher Educ Publrs Group: Colleen O'Neill
Off Admin: Lydia Pencarski *Tel:* 416-322-7011 ext 221
Founded: 1910
Promote professional development of the Canadian book industry.
Number of Members: 26
New Election: Annually in Feb
2005 Meeting(s): Feb 2005
Publication(s): *Publishing: A View from the Inside* ($2 plus GST); *Who Buys Books?* ($45 plus GST)

Canadian Society of Children's Authors Illustrators & Performers (CANSCAIP)
40 Orchard View Blvd, Suite 104, Toronto, ON M4R 1B9, Canada
Tel: 416-515-1559
E-mail: office@canscaip.org
Web Site: www.canscaip.org
Key Personnel
Pres: Sylvia McNicoll
Founded: 1977
A group of professionals in the field of children's culture with members from all parts of Canada. For over 20 years, CANSCAIP has been instrumental in the support & Promotion of children's literature through newsletters, workshops, meetings & other information programs for authors, parents, teachers, librarians, publishers & others. They have over 900 friends—teachers, librarians, parents & others—who are also interested in aspects of children's books, illustrations & performances.
Number of Members: 1,250
New Election: Oct 13, biennially
Publication(s): *Canscaip News* (quarterly, newsletter, $35/yr indiv, $75/yr inst)

CASW, see Council for the Advancement of Science Writing (CASW)

Catholic Book Publishers Association Inc
8404 Jamesport Dr, Rockford, IL 61108
Tel: 815-332-3245 *Fax:* 815-332-3476
E-mail: cbpa3@aol.com
Web Site: www.cbpa.org
Key Personnel
Pres: John D Wright
VP: Kay Weiss
Exec Dir: Terry Wessels
Sec: Jean Larkin
Treas: Therese Brown
Facilitate the sharing of professional information, networking, cooperation & friendship among those involved in Catholic book publishing in the US & abroad. Trade co-op catalog. Mailing list. Catholic bestsellers. Advertising insert program. Professional skills workshops.
Number of Members: 100
Publication(s): *Directory* (annual, $35)

Catholic Library Association
100 North St, Suite 224, Pittsfield, MA 01201-5109
Tel: 413-443-2252 *Fax:* 413-442-2252
E-mail: cla@cathla.org
Web Site: www.cathla.org
Key Personnel
Exec Dir: Jean R Bostley, SSJ
Founded: 1921
To promote literature & libraries of a Catholic nature & ecumenical spirit.
Number of Members: 1,000
Publication(s): *Catholic Library World* (4 issues/yr, $60 non-members US; $70/yr foreign

& $10 S&H); *The Catholic Periodical & Literature Index* (4 issues/yr, $400 unabridged; $100 abridged; foreign additional S&H fee)

Catholic Press Association of the US & Canada
3555 Veterans Memorial Hwy, Unit O, Ronkonkoma, NY 11779
Tel: 631-471-4730 *Fax:* 631-471-4804
E-mail: cathjourn@aol.com
Web Site: www.catholicpress.org
Key Personnel
Exec Dir: Owen P McGovern *E-mail:* omcg@aol.com
Writing, publishing, advertising; all facets of publishing.
Number of Members: 748
New Election: 2005
2005 Meeting(s): CPA Annual Convention, Orlando, FL, May, 2005
Publication(s): *The Catholic Journalist* (monthly); *Catholic Press Directory* (annually)

CCAB Inc
Division of BPA International
90 Eglinton Ave E, Suite 980, Toronto, ON M4P 2Y3, Canada
Tel: 416-487-2418 *Fax:* 416-487-6405
E-mail: info@bpai.com
Web Site: www.bpai.com
Key Personnel
Pres & CEO: Glenn Hansen
Sr VP: Peter Black; Patrick Monahan; Richard Murphy
Founded: 1937
Auditing of circulation.
Number of Members: 550

The Center for Book Arts
28 W 27 St, 3rd fl, New York, NY 10001
Tel: 212-481-0295 *Fax:* 212-481-9853 (call before faxing)
E-mail: info@centerforbookarts.org
Web Site: www.centerforbookarts.org
Key Personnel
Exec Dir: Alexander Canipos
Founded: 1974
Nonprofit, provides workspace, education, exhibitions & slide registry for book artists, hand papermakers & letter press printers; publication of fine art editions, lectures, Outreach Program.
Poetry Chapbook Competition 2006. Entries must be submitted by Dec 1, 2005.
Number of Members: 1,000
Publication(s): *Exhibition Catalogs*

The Center for Exhibition Industry Research
2301 S Lakeshore Dr, Suite E-1002, Chicago, IL 60616
Tel: 312-808-2347 *Fax:* 312-949-3472
E-mail: mceir@mpea.com
Web Site: www.ceir.org
Key Personnel
Pres & CEO: Douglas L Ducate
Communs & Res Coord: Tracy Nickless
Promote the exhibition industry by promoting the value & benefits of exhibitions in an integrated marketing program, through research, information & communications.
Number of Members: 600

The Center for the Book in the Library of Congress
The Library of Congress, 101 Independence Ave SE, Washington, DC 20540-4920
Tel: 202-707-5221 *Fax:* 202-707-0269
E-mail: cfbook@loc.gov
Web Site: www.loc.gov/cfbook
Key Personnel
Dir: John Y Cole *E-mail:* jcole@loc.gov

Prog Officer: Maurvene D Williams
E-mail: mawi@loc.gov
Established by law in 1977, the Center for the Book uses the influence & resources of the Library of Congress to stimulate public interest in books & reading & to encourage the study of books. Its program of symposia, projects, lectures, exhibitions & publications is supported by tax-deductible contributions from corporations & individuals. National reading promotion network includes more than 40 affiliated state centers & more than 90 educational & civic organizations.
Membership(s): BISG

Check Payment Systems Association
2025 "M" St, Suite 800, Washington, DC 20036
Tel: 202-857-1144 *Fax:* 202-223-4579
E-mail: info@cpsa-checks.org
Web Site: www.cpsa-checks.org
Key Personnel
Exec Dir: Wade Delk
Trade association representing the check & US payment system.
Number of Members: 55
Publication(s): *Directory*; *Newsletter* (quarterly)

Chicago Book Clinic
5443 N Broadway, Suite 101, Chicago, IL 60640
Tel: 773-561-4150 *Fax:* 773-561-1343
Web Site: www.chicagobookclinic.org
Key Personnel
Pres: Cheryl Horch
Exec Dir: Kevin G Boyer *E-mail:* kgboyer@ix.netcom.com
Founded: 1936
A nonprofit organization to promote high standards of craftsmanship in bookmaking & publishing & to provide a means through which those engaged in these enterprises can exchange ideas & experiences. Monthly meetings; seminars in book-publishing practices; Pubtech, a biennial trade show of publishing technologies; & an annual exhibit of award-winning book designs.
Number of Members: 1,100
Publication(s): *Annual Exhibit Catalogue* (free to members); *CBC News* (quarterly, free to members); *Membership Directory* (annual, free to members)

Chicago Women in Publishing
PO Box 268107, Chicago, IL 60626
Tel: 312-641-6311 *Fax:* 312-645-1078
E-mail: mail@cwip.org
Web Site: www.cwip.org
Key Personnel
Pres: Maureen Glasoe
VP: Karen Gaspers
VP, Strategic Planning: David Hayes
Jobline employment listing service, monthly newsletter, monthly program meetings, freelance directory, annual conference, annual membership awards, directory.
Number of Members: 500
Publication(s): *CWIP Clips* (monthly)

The Children's Book Council (CBC)
12 W 37 St, 2nd fl, New York, NY 10118-7480
Tel: 212-966-1990 *Toll Free Tel:* 800-999-2160 (orders only) *Fax:* 212-966-2073
Toll Free Fax: 888-807-9355 (orders only)
E-mail: info@cbcbooks.org
Web Site: www.cbcbooks.org
Key Personnel
Pres: Paula Quint
Founded: 1944
Nonprofit trade association of children's book publishers & related companies. Publish reading promotion display & informational materials. New electronic edition of Children's Books

Awards & Prizes; provides professional education & online member services.
Number of Members: 80
New Election: Annually, Sept
2005 Meeting(s): Young People's Poetry Week, April 11-17; Children's Book Week, Nov 14-20
Publication(s): *Awards & Prizes Online* (online database, $150 annually); *CBC Features* (semi-annual, $60 one-time charge)

Christian Booksellers Association (CBA)
9240 Explorer Dr, Colorado Springs, CO 80920
Tel: 719-265-9895 *Toll Free Tel:* 800-252-1950
  Fax: 719-272-3510
E-mail: info@cbaonline.org
Web Site: www.cbaonline.org
Key Personnel
Pres: Bill Anderson *E-mail:* banderson@cbonline.org
VP, Opers: Dorothy Gore *Tel:* 719-265-9895 ext 1102
Trade association serving Christian book selling industry. Associate members are publishers, music publishers & gift houses.
Number of Members: 3,200
New Election: Annually in July
Publication(s): *CBA Marketplace* (monthly)

Christian Booksellers Association of Canada
155 Suffolk St W, Suite 15, Guelph, ON N1H 2J7, Canada
Tel: 519-766-1683 *Fax:* 519-763-8184
E-mail: info@cbacanada.com
Web Site: www.cbacanada.com
Key Personnel
Exec Dir: Marlene Coghlin
Nonprofit trade association.
Number of Members: 300
Publication(s): *Canadian Suppliers Directory* (annual)

Jerry B Jenkins Christian Writers Guild
PO Box 88196, Black Forest, CO 80908
Toll Free Tel: 866-495-5177 *Fax:* 719-495-5181
E-mail: contactus@christianwritersguild.com
Web Site: www.christianwritersguild.com
Key Personnel
Owner: Jerry B Jenkins
Oper Dir: Rick Anderson *Tel:* 719-495-5179 ext 34 *E-mail:* rick@christianwritersguild.com
Founded: 1964
Offers annual Guild memberships, correspondence courses, contests, associated benefits (advocacy, critique service etc), workshops & conferences. Contact for a Free Starter Kit.
Number of Members: 2,000
2005 Meeting(s): Writing for the Soul, Broadmoor Hotel, Colorado Springs, Feb 17-20, 2005; Writing for the Soul, Billy Graham Training Ctr (The Cove, Asheville, NC, Aug 9-13, 2005
Publication(s): *The Word From the Forest* (Monthly, Free to members)

CiP Program, see Canadian Cataloguing in Publication Program

City & Regional Magazine Association
4929 Wilshire Blvd, Suite 428, Los Angeles, CA 90010
Tel: 323-937-5514 *Fax:* 323-937-0959
Web Site: www.citymag.org
Key Personnel
Exec Dir: C James Dowden *E-mail:* jdowden@prodigy.net
PR: Ken Alan *E-mail:* kalan@jonesagency.com
CRMA White Awards Competition, The City & Regional Magazine Award Program at the University of Missouri School of Journalism; city & regional magazine competition, annual conference.

Number of Members: 43
Publication(s): *Communicator* (quarterly, free)

Classroom Publishers Association (CPA)
c/o Highlights for Children, 1800 Watermark Dr, Columbus, OH 43216
Tel: 614-487-2601 *Fax:* 614-324-7946
Key Personnel
Chmn: Garry Myers
Disseminate information on postal affairs & appear in interventions before the Postal Rate Commission & deal with rate/cases & legislation.
Number of Members: 6

Coldset/Non-Heatset Web, see Web Printing Association

Committee On Scholarly Editions
Subsidiary of Modern Language Association
c/o Modern Language Association of America, 26 Broadway, 3rd fl, New York, NY 10004-1789
Tel: 646-576-5040 *Fax:* 646-458-0030
Web Site: www.mla.org
Key Personnel
Dir, MLA Book Pubns: David G Nicholls *E-mail:* dnicholls@mla.org
Founded: 1979
Assists editors & publishers in preparing reliable scholarly editions.
Number of Members: 7

Connecticut Authors & Publishers Association (CAPA)
PO Box 715, Avon, CT 06001-0715
Tel: 203-729-5335 *Fax:* 203-729-5335
E-mail: labriol200@aol.com
Web Site: www.aboutcapa.com
Key Personnel
Founder: Brian Jud *E-mail:* brianjud@msn.com
Founded: 1994
Number of Members: 150
New Election: 2005
Meeting(s): Monthly Meeting, Avon Community Center, Third Saturday of the month
Publication(s): *The Authority* (monthly, newsletter, Free with membership)

Copywriter's Council of America (CCA)
Division of The Linick Group, International
CCA Bldg, 7 Putter Lane, Middle Island, NY 11953
Mailing Address: PO Box 102, Middle Island, NY 11953-0102
Tel: 631-924-8555 *Fax:* 631-924-3890
E-mail: cca4dmcopy@att.net
Web Site: www.lgroup.addr.com/CCA.htm
Key Personnel
Chmn, Consulting Group: Andrew S Linick, PhD *E-mail:* linickgrp@att.net
Pres: Gaylen Andrews
VP: Roger Dextor
Dir, Spec Progs: Barbara Deal
Freelance direct response advertising copywriters, direct marketing consultants, PR & communication specialists & marketing researchers. Cover business-to-business, consumer & industrial markets. Creative services covering all media, all products & services A-Z, e-commerce, e-marketing, e-targeted public relations. Provide comprehensive graphic re-design/new web site content development, interactive services with marketing website makeover advice for first-time authors, self-publishers, professionals & entrepreneurs. Specialize in flash, animation, merchant accounts, on-line advertising/PR, links to top search engines, consulting on a 100% satisfaction guarantee. Free site evaluation for LMP readers.
Professional membership annual dues $125; associate annual membership $95.

Number of Members: 25,000
Publication(s): *The Digest* (quarterly, for members only)

Corp professionnelle des traducteurs et interpretes agrees du quebec
Affiliate of Conseil des traducteurs et interpretes du Canada
2021 Union Ave, Suite 1108, Montreal, PQ H3A 2S9, Canada
Tel: 514-845-4411 *Fax:* 514-845-9903
Key Personnel
Exec Dir: Diane McKay
Commun Agent: Alain Beauregard
Bring translators together to exchange information, send out offers of employment to members. Promote profession & protect public interest. Conferences, annual meeting, social activities, seminars, continuing education.
Number of Members: 1,957
Publication(s): *Circuit* (quarterly, $35 Canada, $40 outside Canada); *L'antenne* (monthly, members only)

Corporation for Public Broadcasting (CPB)
401 Ninth St NW, Washington, DC 20004-2037
Tel: 202-879-9600 *Fax:* 202-879-9700
E-mail: info@cpb.org
Web Site: www.cpb.org *Telex:* 44-0492
Key Personnel
Pres: Kathleen Cox
Dir, Press & PR: Jeannie Bunton
Through federally appropriated funds to support the nation's public TV & public radio industry, conduct support services & to stimulate the creation of programming on TV, radio & on-line.

Corporation of Professional Librarians of Quebec
353, rue Sainte Niclas, Suite 103, Montreal, PQ H2Y 2P1, Canada
Tel: 514-845-3327 *Fax:* 514-845-1618
E-mail: info@cbpq.qc.ca
Web Site: www.cbpq.qc.ca
Key Personnel
Exec Dir: Regine Horinstein
Founded: 1999
Publications, continuing education for information professionals.
Number of Members: 725
Publication(s): *Argus* (3 issues/yr, $42 US, $34 Canada)

Council for Advancement & Support of Education (CASE)
1307 New York Ave NW, Suite 1000, Washington, DC 20005
Tel: 202-328-5900 *Fax:* 202-387-4973
E-mail: info@case.org
Web Site: www.case.org
Key Personnel
Pres: John Lippincott
Membership comprised of colleges, universities & independent schools.
Number of Members: 23,500
Publication(s): *Currents* (monthly except August & December, $100/yr)

The Council for Exceptional Children
1110 N Glebe Rd, Arlington, VA 22201-5704
Tel: 703-620-3660 *Toll Free Tel:* 800-224-6830
  Fax: 703-264-9494
E-mail: service@cec.sped.org
Web Site: www.cec.sped.org
Key Personnel
Exec Dir: Drew Allbritten
AED/PS: Richard Mainer *Tel:* 703-264-9408 *E-mail:* richardm@cec.sped.org
Founded: 1922
Professional association, advocacy, conference, information dissemination, publications, technical assistance, training workshops.

Number of Members: 51,000
Publication(s): *CEC Today* (newsletter); *Exceptional Children*; *TEACHING Exceptional Children*

Council for the Advancement of Science Writing (CASW)
PO Box 910, Hedgesville, WV 25427
Tel: 304-754-5077 *Fax:* 304-754-5076
Web Site: www.casw.org
To advance science writing.

Council of Literary Magazines & Presses (CLMP)
154 Christopher St, Suite 3-C, New York, NY 10014-2839
Tel: 212-741-9110 *Fax:* 212-741-9112
E-mail: info@clmp.org
Web Site: www.clmp.org
Key Personnel
Exec Dir: Jeffrey Lependorf
Membership Mgr: Rob Casper *E-mail:* rcasper@clmp.org
Founded: 1967
A national nonprofit organization that provides services to noncommercial literary magazines & book publishers, including technical assistance, various publications, marketing workshops, an annual directory of literary magazines & granting programs for literary magazines & presses.
Number of Members: 429
Publication(s): *The Directory of Literary Magazines & Presses* (annual, $19 includes postage & handling)

Deadline Club
Division of Society of Professional Journalists
15 Gramercy Park S, New York, NY 10003
Tel: 212-353-9598 *Fax:* 212-468-6360
E-mail: deadline@spj.org
Web Site: www.pipeline.com/~deadline
Key Personnel
Pres: Frank Ucciardo
Monthly meetings.
Number of Members: 400
Publication(s): *Deadliner* (bimonthly, newsletter, $20/yr)

Digital Printing & Imaging Association
Affiliate of Screenprinting & Graphic Imaging Association Intl
10015 Main St, Fairfax, VA 22031-3489
Tel: 703-385-1339 *Toll Free Tel:* 888-385-3588
Fax: 703-273-0456
E-mail: dpi@dpia.org
Web Site: www.dpia.org
Key Personnel
Pres: Michael Robertson
Founded: 1992
Members are digital imaging producers, suppliers who sell to digital imagers & schools which teach digital imaging.
Number of Members: 900
Publication(s): *Kwikscan* (monthly); *RIP* (quarterly, book)

The Direct Marketing Association Inc (The DMA)
1120 Avenue of the Americas, New York, NY 10036-6700
Tel: 212-768-7277 *Fax:* 212-768-4547
E-mail: dma@the-dma.org *Telex:* 22-0560
Web Site: www.the-dma.org
Key Personnel
Pres & CEO: John Greco, Jr
Founded: 1917
A member organization representing the direct marketing business to legislators, regulators & the media, also offering educational & networking experiences for members.

Publication(s): *The DMA Bottom Line*; *The DMA News Digest*
Branch Office(s)
1111 19 St NW, Washington, DC 20036-3603
Tel: 202-955-5030 *Fax:* 202-955-0085

Dog Writers' Association of America Inc (DWAA)
173 Union Rd, Coatesville, PA 19320
Tel: 610-384-2436 *Fax:* 610-384-2471
E-mail: dwaa@dwaa.org
Web Site: www.dwaa.org
Key Personnel
Pres: Chris Walkowicz
Sec: Pat Santi
Founded: 1935
Provide information about dogs (sport, breeding & ownership) & assist writers in gaining access to exhibitions.
Number of Members: 545
New Election: 2005
2005 Meeting(s): 70th Annual Banquet, Southgate Hotel, Feb, 2005
Publication(s): *DWAA Newsletter* (monthly, newsletter, free to members)

Editorial Freelancers Association (EFA)
71 W 23 St, New York, NY 10010
Tel: 212-929-5400 *Fax:* 212-929-5439
E-mail: info@the-efa.org
Web Site: www.the-efa.org
Key Personnel
Exec: J P Partland; Martha Schueneman
A nonprofit, all-volunteer professional association of freelance editors, writers, copy editors, proofreaders, indexers, production specialists, researchers & translators. Provides job listing service, courses, dental & health insurance & related professional services. Monthly meetings from Sept to June.
Number of Members: 1,400
Publication(s): *EFA Directory* (on-line, free); *EFA Newsletter* (bimonthly, newsletter, $20 subscription)

Editors' Association of Canada/Association canadienne des reviseurs
27 Carlton St, Suite 502, Toronto, ON M5B 1L2, Canada
Tel: 416-975-1379 *Toll Free Tel:* 866-226-3348
Fax: 416-975-1637
E-mail: info@editors.ca
Web Site: www.editors.ca; www.reviseurs.ca
Key Personnel
Pres: Faith Gildenhuys
Exec Dir: Lynne Massey
Represents English & French editors working in many forms of print & electronic media: books, magazines, newsletters, corporate & government reports & advertising materials. Professional development seminars held several times a year across Canada.
Number of Members: 1,500
2005 Meeting(s): Toronto, June 17-19, 2005
Publication(s): *Active Voice* (bimonthly, newsletter); *EAC/ACR Directory of Members* (annual); *Editing Canadian English, 2nd ed* ($22.43 members, $29.99 non-members); *Meeting Editorial Standards* ($66 Canadian)

Education Writers Association
2122 "P" St NW, No 201, Washington, DC 20037
Tel: 202-452-9830 *Fax:* 202-452-9837
E-mail: ewa@ewa.org
Web Site: www.ewa.org
Key Personnel
Exec Dir: Lisa J Walker *E-mail:* lwalker@ewa.org
Conferences, seminars, newsletters, publications, employment services, freelance referral, workshops & national awards.
Number of Members: 850

Publication(s): *Covering the Education Beat* (2001, $60); *Education Reform* (6 issues/yr); *Education Reporter* (bimonthly, newsletter); *Money Matters: A Reporter's Guide to School Finance* (2003, $12); *New Networks Old Problems: Technology in Urban Schools* (2001, $10); *Standards for Education Reporters* (2002, $10); *Wolves at the Schoolhouse Door* ($10)

Educational Paperback Association (EPA)
PO Box 1399, East Hampton, NY 11937-0709
Tel: 631-329-3315
E-mail: edupaperback@aol.com
Web Site: www.edupaperback.org
Key Personnel
Exec Sec: Marilyn J Abel
Regular membership consists of educational paperback distributors; associate members are paperback publishers.
Number of Members: 90
New Election: 2006
2005 Meeting(s): Annual Meeting, Santa Fe, NM, Jan 26-29, 2005

ERIC Clearinghouse on Teaching & Teacher Education
1307 New York Ave NW, Suite 300, Washington, DC 20005
Tel: 202-293-2450 *Toll Free Tel:* 800-799-3742
Fax: 202-457-8095
Web Site: www.ericsp.org
Key Personnel
Dir: Mary E Dilworth
Abstract education-related books & documents for worldwide database. Sponsored by the Educational Resources Information Center (ERIC), Office of Educational Research & Improvement, US Department of Education under a contract with the American Association of Colleges for Teacher Education. Scope: the preparation & continuing development of elementary, secondary & collegiate level instructional personnel, their roles & functions & selected aspects of health, physical education, recreation & dance.
Publication(s): *Monographs & Digests*

Evangelical Christian Publishers Association
4816 S Ash Ave, Suite 101, Tempe, AZ 85282-7735
Tel: 480-966-3998 *Fax:* 480-966-1944
E-mail: info@ecpa.org
Web Site: www.ecpa.org
Key Personnel
Pres: Mark Kuyper *E-mail:* mkuyper@ecpa.org
Professional seminars, statistical studies & religious book awards.
Number of Members: 280
2005 Meeting(s): ECPA Spring Management Seminar, April 30-May 4, 2005; ECPA Publishing University, Nov 6-8, 2005
Publication(s): *Footprints* (monthly)
Membership(s): BISG

Evangelical Press Association (EPA)
PO Box 28129, Crystal, MN 55428-0129
Tel: 763-535-4793 *Fax:* 763-535-4794
E-mail: director@epassoc.org
Web Site: www.epassoc.org
Key Personnel
Exec Dir: Doug Trouten
Organization of Christian publications & original writers.
Number of Members: 400
2005 Meeting(s): Hyatt Regency Woodfield, Schaumburg, IL, April 24-27, 2005
Publication(s): *Liaison*

The Federation of British Columbia Writers
PO Box 3887, Sta Terminal, Vancouver, BC V6B 2Z3, Canada

Tel: 604-683-2057 *Fax:* 604-608-5522
E-mail: fedoffice@bcwriters.com
Web Site: www.bcwriters.com
Key Personnel
Exec Dir: Merrill Fearon
Pres: Margaret Thompson
Magazine, readings, workshop, literary competitions.
Number of Members: 800
New Election: Annually in April

Florida Freelance Writers Association
Affiliate of Cassell Network of Writers
Main St, North Stratford, NH 03590
Mailing Address: PO Box A, North Stratford, NH 03590
Tel: 603-922-8338 *Fax:* 603-922-8339
E-mail: FFWA@writers-editors.com
Web Site: www.writers-editors.com; www. ffwamembers.com
Key Personnel
Exec Dir: Dana K Cassell *E-mail:* dana@writers-editors.com
Network of freelance writers & editors, offering a job bank, Florida Markets directory, newsletter, etc.
Number of Members: 500
Publication(s): *Directory of Florida Markets for Writers* (included in newsletter & electronic formats, $35 or free with membership); *Freelance Writer's Report* (monthly, $49/yr or free with FFWA membership); *Guide to CNW/FFWA Writers* (continuously updated, free to qualified publishing companies & businesses)

The Florida Publishers Association Inc
PO Box 430, Highland City, FL 33846-0430
Tel: 863-647-5951 *Fax:* 863-647-5951
E-mail: fpabooks@aol.com
Web Site: www.flbookpub.org
Key Personnel
Pres: Sylvia Hemmerly
Assoc Exec: Betsy Wright-Lampe
Founded: 1979
Networking seminars, newsletter, publishing, book shows, catalog, workshops & consulting small presses, independents & self-publishers; authors annual award for best books published in Florida.
Number of Members: 125
Publication(s): *FPA Sell More Books! Newsletter* (electronically, monthly, newsletter, free to members, media, booksellers, libraries, reviewers)
Membership(s): AAP; Florida Library Association; Publishers Marketing Association; Small Publishers Association of North America; Southeast Booksellers Association

Foil Stamping & Embossing Association
2150 SW Westport Dr, Suite 101, Topeka, KS 66614
Tel: 785-271-5816 *Fax:* 785-271-6404
Web Site: www.fsea.com
Key Personnel
Exec Dir: Jeff Peterson *E-mail:* jeff@fsea.com
Founded: 1992
Trade association for graphics finishing industry.
Number of Members: 325
2005 Meeting(s): IADD/FSEA Odyssey, Atlanta, GA, June 15-17, 2005
Publication(s): *Inside Finishing Magazine* (quarterly)

Follett Higher Education Group
1818 Swift Dr, Oak Grove, IL 60523
Tel: 630-279-2330 *Toll Free Tel:* 800-323-4506
Fax: 630-279-2569
Web Site: www.fheg.follett.com

Key Personnel
Pres: Tom Christopher
College bookstore: used textbook distribution company.

FOLUSA, see Friends of Libraries USA

Clifford Ford Publications
120 Walnut Ct, Unit 15, Ottawa, ON K1R 7W2, Canada
Tel: 613-230-3666 *Fax:* 613-230-6725
E-mail: host@cliffordfordpublications.ca
Web Site: cliffordfordpublications.ca
Key Personnel
Prop: Clifford Ford
Founded: 2003

Foundation of American Women in Radio & Television
Subsidiary of American Women in Radio & Television
8405 Greensboro Dr, Suite 800, McLean, VA 22102
Tel: 703-506-3290 *Fax:* 703-506-3266
E-mail: info@awrt.org
Web Site: www.awrt.org
Key Personnel
Exec Dir: Maria Brennan
Mgr, Assoc Serv: Amy B Lotz *Tel:* 703-506-3260 *E-mail:* alotz@awrt.org
For members of the electronic & media industries.
Number of Members: 3,000
Publication(s): *Making Waves* (quarterly by mail, magazine); *News & Views* (monthly by email)

FPA, see The Florida Publishers Association Inc

Freedom of Information Center
Affiliate of Missouri School of Journalism
133 Neff Annex, Columbia, MO 65211-0012
Tel: 573-882-4856 *Fax:* 573-884-6204
E-mail: foi@missouri.edu
Web Site: foi.missouri.edu
Key Personnel
Exec Dir: Charles N Davis
Mgr: Kathleen Edwards
Web Ed: Kristin Birks
Founded: 1958
Maintain files which document actions by government, media & society affecting the movement & content of information. Dedicated to the people's right to know, this special library provides both reference & referral services. Publications issued by the FoI Center, 1959-85, are available for purchase. Specializing in research, instruction & advocacy on the public's right to accountability in government, the center offers current FOI topics on its web page, a biweekly electronic newsletter & historic files on the development of open meetings & open records laws. Member of the Freedom of Information Coalition.
Publication(s): *The FOI Advocate* (biweekly, free by e-mail subscription)

Friends of Libraries USA
1420 Walnut St, Suite 450, Philadelphia, PA 19102-4017
Tel: 215-790-1674 *Toll Free Tel:* 800-936-5872
Fax: 215-545-3821
E-mail: folusa@folusa.org
Web Site: www.folusa.org
Key Personnel
Exec Dir: Sally G Reed
Founded: 1979
Advocate for local Friends of Libraries & libraries/newsletter, fundraising, programs.
Number of Members: 2,000

New Election: ALA Annual Conference, Spring & Summer
Publication(s): *News Update* (bimonthly, free with membership)

GAMIS, see Graphic Arts Marketing Information Service (GAMIS)

Garden Writers Association of America
10210 Leatherleaf Ct, Manassas, VA 20111
Tel: 703-257-1032 *Fax:* 703-257-0213
E-mail: info@gwaa.org
Web Site: www.gwaa.org
Key Personnel
Exec Dir: Robert La Gasse
Founded: 1948
Professional association garden communicators working as staff or free-lance as newspaper columnists, magazine columnists, photographers & radio/TV hosts. Sponsor annual writer's contest & annual quill & trowel award program for published articles or books.
Number of Members: 1,700
2005 Meeting(s): Garden Writers Association of America Meeting & Symposium, Vancouver, BC, Canada, Sept, 2005
Publication(s): *Quill & Trowel* (bimonthly, newsletter)

Graphic Artists Guild Inc
90 John St, Rm 403, New York, NY 10038
Tel: 212-791-3400 *Fax:* 212-791-0333
E-mail: execdir@gag.org
Web Site: www.gag.org
Key Personnel
Chapter Administrator: Tricia McKiernan
Founded: 1967
Labor organization which advocates the advancement of artists' rights. Members are illustrators, graphic designers, surface & textile designers, computer graphics artists, cartoonists & others.
Number of Members: 3,000
Publication(s): *Pricing & Ethical Guidelines, 11th ed* (biannually, $34.95)

Graphic Arts Employers of America
Affiliate of Printing Industries of America
100 Daingerfield Rd, Alexandria, VA 22314
Tel: 703-519-8100; 703-519-8151 *Fax:* 703-548-3227
Web Site: www.gain.net
Key Personnel
Pres & CEO: Michael Makin
Mktg Mgr: Lisa Erdner *E-mail:* lerdner@gatf.org; Kim Lippincott *E-mail:* klippincott@printing.org
Represent commercial printers.
Number of Members: 4,000

Graphic Arts Marketing Information Service (GAMIS)
Division of Printing Industries of America
100 Daingerfield Rd, Alexandria, VA 22314
Tel: 703-519-8100; 703-519-8179
Toll Free Tel: 800-742-2666 *Fax:* 703-548-3227
E-mail: info@gamis.org
Web Site: www.gamis.org
Key Personnel
Exec Dir: Jacqueline Bland *E-mail:* jbland@printing.org
Research association of the graphic arts industry; provide data & research to printers, publishers & manufacturers of equipment & supplies for the printing/publishing industry.
Number of Members: 75
New Election: Annually in June
Publication(s): *Statistical Handbook for the Graphic Arts* (biennially, $495)

Graphic Arts Sales Foundation (GASF)
113 E Evans St, West Chester, PA 19380

Tel: 610-431-9780 *Fax:* 610-436-5238
E-mail: info@gasf.org
Web Site: www.gasf.org
Key Personnel
Pres: Richard Gorelick *Tel:* 610-436-9778
Administrator: Judy Warren
Provides management, sales, marketing & customer service training programs for graphic arts professionals. Monographs on industry burning issues.
Number of Members: 1,200

Graphic Arts Show Company
1899 Preston White Dr, Reston, VA 20191
Tel: 703-264-7200 *Fax:* 703-620-9187
E-mail: info@gasc.org
Web Site: www.gasc.org
Key Personnel
VP: Chris Thiel
Prodn Asst: Elaine Johnson
Tradeshow management for printing, publishing & graphic communications events.
2005 Meeting(s): Graphics Arts/The Charlotte Show, Charlotte Convention Center, Charlotte, NC, USA, March 17-19, 2005; Gutenberg Festival, Los Angeles Convention Center, Los Angeles, CA, April 28-30, 2005

Graphic Communications Council
1899 Preston White Dr, Reston, VA 20191-4367
Tel: 703-648-1768 *Fax:* 703-620-0994
E-mail: edcouncil@npes.org
Web Site: www.npes.org/edcouncil
Key Personnel
Admin: Carol Hurlburt *E-mail:* churlburt@npes.org
Coalition to promote careers & education.
Number of Members: 100
Publication(s): *Clearinghouse* (quarterly, free)

Gravure Association of America Inc
1200-A Scottsville Rd, Rochester, NY 14624
Tel: 585-436-2150 *Fax:* 585-436-7689
E-mail: gaa@gaa.org
Web Site: www.gaa.org
Key Personnel
Exec VP: Richard H Dunnington
Foster the advancement of gravure printing industry.
Number of Members: 200
2005 Meeting(s): GAA Expo 2005, Adams Mark Hotel, Philadelphia, PA, May 22-26, 2005
Publication(s): *Gravure Magazine* (bimonthly, $67/yr US)

Guild of Book Workers
521 Fifth Ave, 17th fl, New York, NY 10175
Tel: 212-292-4444
Web Site: www.palimpsest.stanford.ed
Key Personnel
Pres: Betsy Palmer Eldridge
Founded: 1906
A national nonprofit educational organization which fosters the hand book arts: binding, calligraphy, illumination, paper decorating. Sponsor exhibits, lectures, workshops.
Number of Members: 900
Publication(s): *Journal* ($60 members); *Newsletter* (bimonthly)

Horror Writers Association
PO Box 50577, Palo Alto, CA 94303
E-mail: hwa@horror.org
Web Site: www.horror.org/
Key Personnel
Pres: Joseph Nassise *E-mail:* president@horror.org
Membership Chmn: Nancy Etchemendy *Tel:* 650-322-4610 *E-mail:* membership@horror.org
Monthly newsletter, online information, Hardship Fund, Grievance Committee, Bram Stoker

Awards for Superior Achievement, a series of members-only anthologies, databases of agents, reviewers & book stores.
Number of Members: 777
2005 Meeting(s): Annual Gathering, New York, NY, Late Spring 2005
Publication(s): *Newsletter* (monthly)

The Ibsen Society of America
Dept of English, Long Island University, Brooklyn, NY 11201
Tel: 718-488-1050 *Fax:* 718-246-6302
Web Site: www.ibsensociety.liu.edu
Key Personnel
Pres: Joan Templeton *E-mail:* joan.templeton@liu.edu
Founded: 1978
A nonprofit corporation.
Number of Members: 250
Publication(s): *Ibsen News & Comment* (annual, newsletter, $15 libraries, free to members)

IDEAlliance
100 Daingerfield Rd, Alexandria, VA 22314
Tel: 703-837-1070 *Fax:* 703-837-1072
E-mail: info@gca.org
Web Site: www.idealliance.org
Key Personnel
Pres: David J Steinhardt
Represent printing, publishing, newspapers, suppliers, government organizations & advertising agencies. Seek productivity & technical improvement in creation & distribution of printed material.
Number of Members: 350
2005 Meeting(s): PRIMEX 2005 (Print Media Executive Summit), Biltmore Hotel, Coral Gables, FL, Feb 9-11, 2005; Spectrum 2005, El Conquistador, Tucson, AZ, Sept 24-27, 2005

Independent Writers of Chicago (IWOC)
5465 Grand Ave, Suite 100, PMB 119, Gurnee, IL 60031
Tel: 847-855-6670 *Fax:* 847-855-4502
E-mail: info@iwoc.org
Web Site: www.iwoc.org
Key Personnel
Pres: Jim Leman
Monthly meetings, workshops & seminars per year dealing with the business aspects of independent writing. Writers' line job referral. Speakers' Bureau.
Number of Members: 225
Publication(s): *Membership Directory* (annual, $10); *STET* (monthly, newsletter, $20/yr)

Inter American Press Association (IAPA)
1801 SW Third Ave, Miami, FL 33129
Tel: 305-634-2465 *Fax:* 305-635-2272
E-mail: info@sipiapa.org
Web Site: www.sipiapa.org
Key Personnel
Exec Dir: Julio E Munoz
To guard freedom of the press; to foster & protect the general & specific interests of the daily & periodical press of the Americas; to promote & maintain the dignity, rights & responsibilities of journalism; to encourage uniform standards of professional & business conduct; to exchange ideas & information which contribute to the cultural, material & technical development of the press; to foster a wider knowledge & greater interchange in support of the basic principles of a free society & individual liberty.
Number of Members: 1,138
Publication(s): *Hora de Cierre* (quarterly); *IAPA Annual Report* (annually); *IAPA News* (bimonthly); *Notisip* (quarterly)

International Association of Business Communicators (IABC)
One Hallidie Plaza, Suite 600, San Francisco, CA 94102
Tel: 415-544-4700 *Toll Free Tel:* 800-776-4222 *Fax:* 415-544-4747
E-mail: service_centre@iabc.com
Web Site: www.iabc.com
Key Personnel
Pres: Julie Freeman
PR Mgr: Heidi Upton
VP, Educ Info: Chris Grossgart
VP, Fin: Iqbal Parupia
Exec Asst: Grace Healey
Founded: 1970
Communication Association.
Number of Members: 13,000
2005 Meeting(s): International Conference, Washington, DC, June 2005
Publication(s): *Communication World* (bimonthly)

International Association of Crime Writers Inc, North American Branch
PO Box 8674, New York, NY 10116-8674
Tel: 212-243-8966 *Fax:* 815-361-1477
Key Personnel
Pres: Annette Meyers
Exec Dir: Mary A Frisque *E-mail:* mfrisque@igc.org
Sec-Treas: Jim Weikart
Sec: Johnny Temple
Founded: 1987
Promote communication among crime writers worldwide & enhance awareness & encourage translations of the genre in the USA & abroad.
Number of Members: 250
New Election: 2005
Publication(s): *Border Patrol* (quarterly, free to members)

International Council for Adult Education
UQAM Faculty of Education, PO Box 8888, Downtown Branch, Montreal, PQ H3C 3P8, Canada
Tel: 514-987-0029 *Fax:* 514-987-6753
E-mail: icae@er.uqam.ca
Web Site: www.icae.org.uy
Key Personnel
Info & Commune Coord: Jennifer Noriega
Founded: 1972
Adult education life long learning.
Number of Members: 107
Publication(s): *Convergence* (quarterly, journal, $51); *ICAE News* (quarterly, newsletter, free to members)

International Encyclopedia Society
PO Box 519, Baldwin Place, NY 10505-0519
Tel: 914-962-3287 *Fax:* 914-962-3287
Web Site: encyclopediasociety.com
Key Personnel
Pres: George Kurian *E-mail:* gtkurian@aol.com
Publication of books & journals; conferences; award of prizes.
Number of Members: 300
New Election: 2005
Publication(s): *Reference Desk Quarterly* ($29)

International Newspaper Financial Executives
21525 Ridgetop Circle, Suite 200, Sterling, VA 20166
Tel: 703-421-4060
Web Site: www.infe.org
Key Personnel
VP & Exec Dir: Robert J Kasabian
Founded: 1947
International association for newspaper financial management. Members representative of major newspaper publishing companies in North America.
Number of Members: 1,100
2005 Meeting(s): International Newspaper Financial Executives Annual Conference, Hilton in

the Walt Disney World Resort, Orlando, FL, June 25-29, 2005
Publication(s): *Newsletter-Online* (weekly, members only)

International Plate Printers', Die Stampers' & Engravers' Union of North America
3957 Smoke Rd, Doylestown, PA 18901
Tel: 215-340-2843
Key Personnel
Intl Secy-Treas: James Kopernick
Founded: 1893
Printers & engravers of all security documents.
Number of Members: 200

International Prepress Association
7200 France Ave S, Suite 223, Edina, MN 55435
Tel: 952-896-1908 *Fax:* 952-896-0181
E-mail: info@ipa.org
Web Site: www.ipa.org
Key Personnel
Pres: Steven Bonoff *E-mail:* steve@ipa.org
Trade association for color separation; seminars & conferences; bimonthly magazine, reports & surveys on the industry.
Number of Members: 375
Publication(s): *The Bulletin* (bimonthly, $20/yr); *Images* (monthly)
Branch Office(s)
552 W 167 St, South Holland, IL 60473 *Tel:* 708-596-5110 *Fax:* 708-596-5112

International Publishing Management Association (IPMA)
1205 W College St, Liberty, MO 64068-3733
Tel: 816-781-1111 *Fax:* 816-781-2790
E-mail: ipmainfo@ipma.org
Web Site: www.ipma.org
Key Personnel
Admin Dir: Cindy Pyles *E-mail:* cpyles@ipma.org
Ed: Jeff Langford *E-mail:* jlangford@ipma.org
Membership for plant & mailing managers. Annual conference & trade show in late spring. Write or call for information.
Number of Members: 1,800
Publication(s): *Perspectives* (monthly, $50/yr US, $75 intl)

International Reading Association
800 Barksdale Rd, Newark, DE 19714
Tel: 302-731-1600 *Fax:* 302-731-1057
Web Site: www.reading.org *Cable:* READING, NEWARK, DELAWARE
Key Personnel
Pres: MaryEllen Vogt
Exec Dir: Alan E Farstrup
Public Info Assoc: Beth Cady *Tel:* 302-731-1600 ext 293 *E-mail:* pubinfo@reading.org
Conferences; publications, research, membership services; publications on reading & related topics; professional journals.
Number of Members: 80,000
2005 Meeting(s): Annual Convention of the International Reading Association (50th), San Antonio, TX, May 1-5, 2005
2006 Meeting(s): Annual Convention of the International Reading Association (51st), Minneapolis, MN, April 30-May 4, 2006
2007 Meeting(s): Annual Convention of the International Reading Association (52nd), Chicago, IL, April 22-36, 2007
2008 Meeting(s): Annual Convention of the International Reading Association (53rd), Atlanta, GA, May 4-8, 2008

International Society of Copier Artists Ltd (ISCA)
759 President St, Suite 2H, Brooklyn, NY 11215
Tel: 718-638-3264
E-mail: isca4art2b@aol.com
Key Personnel
Dir: Louise Neaderland
Founded: 1981
Slide archive of xerographic prints & bookworks. Traveling exhibition ISCAGRAPHICS available. Lectures & slide shows also available. Sponsor workshops in using the copier as a creative tool-camera, darkroom & printing press, covering both printmaking & bookmaking. Original xerographic prints & artists' books. The ISCA quarterly assemblage project.
Number of Members: 135
Publication(s): *ISCA Biannual* ($90/yr US, $110/yr foreign)

International Society of Weekly Newspaper Editors
Missouri Southern State College, 3950 E Newman Rd, Joplin, MO 64501-1595
Tel: 417-625-9736 *Fax:* 417-659-4445
Web Site: www.mssc.edu/iswne
Key Personnel
Exec Dir: Dr Chad Stebbins *E-mail:* stebbins-c@mail.mssu.edu
Help those in weekly press to improve standards of editorial writing.
Number of Members: 300
Publication(s): *Grassroots Editor* (quarterly, $25/yr US & Canada)

International Standard Book Numbering (ISBN) US Agency, A Cambridge Information Group Co
Affiliate of R R Bowker LLC
630 Central Ave, New Providence, NJ 07974
Toll Free Tel: 877-310-7333 *Fax:* 908-219-0188
E-mail: ISBN-SAN@bowker.com
Web Site: www.isbn.org
Key Personnel
Sr Dir: Doreen Gravesande
Man Ed, ISBN: Paula Kurdi
Coordinate implementation of the ISBN, ISMN, SAN, DOI & ISTC standards.
Number of Members: 120,000

The International Women's Writing Guild (IWWG)
PO Box 810, Gracie Sta, New York, NY 10028-0082
Tel: 212-737-7536 *Fax:* 212-737-9469
E-mail: iwwg@iwwg.org
Web Site: www.iwwg.org
Key Personnel
Founder & Exec Dir: Hannelore Hahn *E-mail:* dirhahn@aol.com
Founded: 1976
Network for the empowerment of women through writing. Services include updated list of close to 35 literary agents, independent small presses, & other writing services. Ten writing conferences & events annually, subn to the bimonthly 32-page newsletter *Network*, regional clusters & opportunities for publications. IWWG is a supportive network open to any woman regardless of portfolio. As such, it has established a remarkable record of achievement in the publishing world as well as in circles where life-long learning & personal information are valued for their own sake.
Number of Members: 5,000
Publication(s): *Network* (bimonthly, 32 pgs, included in membership)

Internet Alliance (IA)
1111 19 St NW, Suite 1180, Washington, DC 20036
Tel: 202-955-8091; 202-861-2476 *Fax:* 202-955-8081
E-mail: ia@internetalliance.org
Web Site: www.internetalliance.org
Key Personnel
Exec Dir: Emily Hackett
State relations on Internet issues.

Investigative Reporters & Editors
138 Neff Annex, UMC School of Journalism, Columbia, MO 65211
Tel: 573-882-2042 *Fax:* 573-882-5431
E-mail: info@ire.org
Web Site: www.ire.org
Key Personnel
Exec Dir: Brant Houston
Help journalists write better stories.
Number of Members: 5,000
Publication(s): *The IRE Journal* (bimonthly, free with membership, $60/yr non-members, $70/yr institutions, $65/year foreign for electronic delivery, $75/yr foreign via regular mail)

ISCA Ltd, see International Society of Copier Artists Ltd (ISCA)

Jewish Book Council
15 E 26 St, 10th fl, New York, NY 10010-1579
Tel: 212-532-4949 (ext 297) *Fax:* 212-481-4174
E-mail: jbc@jewishbooks.org
Web Site: www.jewishbookcouncil.org
Key Personnel
Pres: Lawrence Krule
Exec Dir: Carolyn Starman Hessel *E-mail:* carolynhessel@jewishbooks.org
Sponsors programs based on its conviction that books of Jewish interest are an invaluable contribution to the welfare of the Jewish people. Works to promote the writing, publishing & reading of worthy books of Jewish content. Honors excellence in all fields of Jewish literary endeavor with awards to writers & citations to publishers. Serves as a resource providing guidance, program tools & publications; acts as a clearinghouse for information on all aspects of Jewish literature & publishing in North America.
2005 Meeting(s): Jewish Book Month, Nov 26-Dec 26, 2005
Publication(s): *Jewish Book Annual*; *Jewish Book Month Poster*; *Jewish Book World* (3 issues/yr)

James Joyce Society
26 Varick Ct, Rockville Centre, NY 11570
Tel: 516-764-3119 *Fax:* 516-255-9094
E-mail: info@joycesociety.org
Web Site: www.joycesociety.org
Key Personnel
Pres: A Nicholas Fargnoli
Quarterly meetings, devoted to the life, works & significance of the Irish Author.
Number of Members: 150
Publication(s): *Newsletter & Journal* (annual, $20/yr includes membership in the Society)

League of Canadian Poets
920 Yonge St, Suite 608, Toronto, ON M4W 3C7, Canada
Tel: 416-504-1657 *Fax:* 416-504-0096
E-mail: info@poets.ca
Web Site: www.poets.ca
Key Personnel
Exec Dir: Edita Page *E-mail:* page@poets.ca
Pres: Matt Robinson
Assoc Dir: Joanna Poblocka
Promote Canadian poetry & poets.
Number of Members: 600
New Election: Annually in May
Publication(s): *Poetry Markets for Canadians* (online only, $20/yr public, $100/yr schools or libraries); *Poets in the Classroom* ($12.95 + tax)

League of Vermont Writers
PO Box 172, Underhill Center, VT 05490

Tel: 802-253-9439
Web Site: www.leaguevtwriters.org
Key Personnel
Pres: Ida Washington *E-mail:* idahw@pshift.com
VP: Nancy Wolfe-Stead *E-mail:* nstead@twshift.
com
Membership: Mary Ann Dispirito
Treas: Phyllis Houle *E-mail:* writing@together.net
Four meetings per year (Jan, April, June, Sept),
reader & promotional services, newsletter four
times per year; occasional instructional semi-
nars & workshops, publication of anthologies
of members' work, writer's service.
Number of Members: 200
New Election: Annually in Jan
Publication(s): *Vermont Voices Jubilee, 75th An-*
niversary Edition; Vermont Voices III, An An-
thology ($17/issue)

League of Women Voters of the United States
1730 "M" St NW, 10th fl, Washington, DC 20036
Tel: 202-429-1965 *Fax:* 202-429-0854; 202-429-
4343
E-mail: lwv@lwv.org
Web Site: www.lwv.org
Key Personnel
Dir, Communs: Kelly Ceballos
Nonpartisan, grass roots political organization.
Publish information on public policy issues in
fields of natural resources, social policy, gov-
ernment, voter service & international relations.
Number of Members: 80,000
Publication(s): *A Citizen's Guide to Global Eco-*
nomic Policy Making; The National Voter (3x
year, magazine); *Safety on Tap: A Citizen's*
Drinking Water Guide; Thinking Globally,
Acting Locally: A Citizen's Guide to Commu-
nity Education on Global Issues; Understand-
ing Economic Policy: A Citizen's Handbook;
Women in Action: Rebels and Reformers 1920-
1980

Library & Archives Canada
Formerly National Library of Canada
395 Wellington St, Ottawa, ON K1A 0N4,
Canada
Tel: 613-995-7969 (Publications); 613-996-5115
(General Inquiries); 613-992-6969 (TTY)
Toll Free Tel: 866-578-7777 (Canada only);
866-299-1699 (Canada only) *Fax:* 613-991-
9871 (Publications); 613-996-5115 (General
Inquiries)
E-mail: distribution@lac-bac.gc.ca; reference@
lac-bac.gc.ca
Web Site: www.collectionscanada.ca
Key Personnel
Libn & Archivist Canada: Ian Wilson
Info Analyst: Peter Rochon *Tel:* 613-996-7498
Fax: 613-996-3573 *E-mail:* peter.rochon@lac-
bac.gc.ca
Founded: 2004
Library & Archives Canada (LAC) was created
when the Library & Archives Canada Act came
into force May 21, 2004. This new knowledge
institution for Canada replaces the former National Archives of Canada (established in 1872)
& National Library of Canada (established
1953). The Library & Archives Canada Act
introduces the concept of "Canada's documentary heritage" which includes publications &
records in all media to Canada, & sets out the
mandate of the new institution as: a) to acquire & preserve the documentary heritage; b)
to make the heritage known to Canadians & to
anyone with interest in Canada & to facilitate
access to it; c) to be the permanent repository
of publications of the government of Canada
& of government & ministerial records that are
of historical or archival value; d) to facilitate
the management of information by government
institutions; e) to coordinate the library services

of government institutions; & f) to support the
development of the library & archival communities.

Library Association of Alberta
80 Baker Crescent NW, Calgary, AB T2L 1R4,
Canada
Tel: 403-284-5818 *Toll Free Tel:* 877-522-5550
Fax: 403-282-6646
Web Site: www.laa.ab.ca
Key Personnel
Pres: Michael Perry
Exec Dir: Christine Sheppard *E-mail:* christine.
sheppard@show.ca
Number of Members: 625
2005 Meeting(s): Jasper Park Lodge, Jasper, AB,
Canada, April 2005
Publication(s): *Letter of the LAA* (5 issues/yr, for
members only)

Library Binding Institute
70 E Lake, Suite 300, Chicago, IL 60601
Tel: 312-704-5020 *Fax:* 312-704-5025
E-mail: info@lbibinders.org
Web Site: www.lbibinders.org
Key Personnel
Exec Dir: Joanne Rock *E-mail:* jrock@lbibinders.
org
Founded: 1935
Trade association for bookbinders. Hold annual
meetings & workshops; provide information
services, certification & technical review.
Number of Members: 85
Publication(s): *The New Library Scene* (quarterly,
$24/yr)

Linguistic Society of America
1325 18 St NW, Suite 211, Washington, DC
20036-6501
Tel: 202-835-1714 *Fax:* 202-835-1717
E-mail: lsa@lsadc.org
Web Site: www.lsadc.org
Key Personnel
Pres: Joan Bybee
Exec Dir: Margaret W Reynolds
Sec & Treas: Gregory Ward
Ed: Brian Joseph
Founded: 1924
Number of Members: 6,000
New Election: Annually in Dec
Publication(s): *Language* (quarterly, $135/yr org,
$75 reg, $30 students, add $10 for foreign ad-
dress); *LSA Bulletin* (quarterly, included in
price of Language); *LSA Meeting Handbook*
(annual, $10)

The Literary Press Group of Canada
192 Spadina Ave, Suite 501, Toronto, ON M5T
2C2, Canada
Tel: 416-483-1321 *Fax:* 416-483-2510
E-mail: info@lpg.ca
Web Site: www.lpg.ca
Key Personnel
Exec Dir: David Caron *E-mail:* dcaron@lpg.ca
Mktg Mgr: Rob Lidstone *E-mail:* rlidstone@lpg.
ca
National trade association providing cooperative
sales, marketing, advertising & publicity ser-
vices to members.
Number of Members: 40

Literary Translators' Association of Canada
Concordia University, SB 335, 1455 De Maison-
neuve West, Montreal, PQ H3G 1M8, Canada
Tel: 514-848-8702
E-mail: info@attlc-ltac.org
Web Site: www.attlc-ltac.org
Key Personnel
Pres: Phyllis Aronoff
Promote & protect interests of literary translators
in Canada; occasional meetings with local uni-

versities & occasional workshops, lobby for
funding, organize readings & other events.
Number of Members: 206
New Election: Annually in May
2005 Meeting(s): Annual general meeting, June,
2005
Publication(s): *Transmission* (3 issues/yr, free)

Livestock Publications Council
910 Currie St, Fort Worth, TX 76107
Tel: 817-336-1130 *Fax:* 817-232-4820
Web Site: www.livestockpublications.com
Key Personnel
Exec Dir: Diane Johnson *E-mail:* dianej@flash.
net
Association of livestock publications.
Number of Members: 195
New Election: Annually in July
2005 Meeting(s): Annual Meeting, Milwaukee,
WI, July, 2005
Publication(s): *Actiongram* (monthly, newsletter);
Membership Directory (annual)

Magazine Publishers of America
810 Seventh Ave, New York, NY 10019
Tel: 212-872-3700 *Fax:* 212-888-4217
E-mail: infocenter@magazine.org
Web Site: www.magazine.org
Key Personnel
Pres: Nina B Link
Dir, Info Ctr: Deborah Martin
Promote the value of magazines.
Number of Members: 242
2005 Meeting(s): Windham El Conquistador,
Puerto Rico, Oct 16-19
Branch Office(s)
1211 Connecticut Ave NW, Washington, DC
20036, Contact: James Cregan *Tel:* 202-296-
7277 *Fax:* 202-296-0343

Maine Writers & Publishers Alliance
1326 Washington St, Bath, ME 04530
Tel: 207-386-1400 *Fax:* 207-386-1401
Web Site: www.mainewriters.org
Key Personnel
Exec Dir: Shonna Humphrey *E-mail:* director@
mainewriters.org
Writing retreats, writing workshops, information
services.
Number of Members: 800
Publication(s): *Maine In Print* (bimonthly, $35/yr)

Manitoba Arts Council
525-93 Lombard Ave, Winnipeg, MB R3B 3B1,
Canada
Tel: 204-945-2237 *Toll Free Tel:* 866-994-2787
(in Manitoba) *Fax:* 204-945-5925
E-mail: info@artscouncil.mb.ca
Web Site: www.artscouncil.mb.ca
Key Personnel
Mgr, Communs: Dana Mohr *Tel:* 204-945-0646
E-mail: dmohr@artscouncil.mb.ca
Provincial arts council that funds professional
Manitoban artists & arts organizations.

Manitoba Library Association
600 100 Arthur St, Suite 416, Winnipeg, MB
R3B 1H3, Canada
Tel: 204-943-4567 *Fax:* 204-942-1555
E-mail: info@mla.mb.ca; mla@uwinnipeg.ca
Web Site: www.mla.mb.ca
Key Personnel
Pres: Theresa Lomas
Number of Members: 478
Publication(s): *Newsline: Newsletter Manitoba*
Library Association (monthly)

The Manitoba Writers' Guild Inc
206-100 Arthur St, Winnipeg, MB R3B 1H3,
Canada

Tel: 204-942-6134 *Toll Free Tel:* 888-637-5802
  Fax: 204-942-5754
E-mail: info@mbwriter.mb.ca
Web Site: www.mbwriter.mb.ca
Key Personnel
Exec Dir: Robyn Maharaj
Programming & Outreach Dir: Jamis Paulson
Founded: 1981
Membership $40/yr regular, $20/yr students or
  seniors on fixed income.
Number of Members: 450
Publication(s): *Word Wrap Newsletter* (bimonthly,
  newsletter, $40/yr, 550 circ); *The Writers'
  Handbook* ($6.95/yr & GST Canadian funds)

Media Alliance
942 Market St, Suite 503, San Francisco, CA
  94102
Tel: 415-546-6334; 415-546-6491 *Fax:* 415-546-
  6218
E-mail: info@media-alliance.org
Web Site: www.media-alliance.org
Key Personnel
Exec Dir: Jeffrey Perlstein
Educational programs in editing, writing & jour-
  nalism skills. Media relations & advocacy &
  hands-on computer skills. Job listings & re-
  sources, media watchdog activities.
Number of Members: 3,200
Publication(s): *Media How-to Guidebook* ($12);
  MediaFile (bimonthly, $35/yr); *People Behind
  the News* ($59)

Media Coalition Inc
139 Fulton St, Suite 302, New York, NY 10038
Tel: 212-587-4025 *Fax:* 212-587-2436
E-mail: mediacoalition@mediacoalition.org
Web Site: www.mediacoalition.org
Key Personnel
Exec Dir: David Horowitz
Trade association, defends first amendment
  rights to produce & distribute constitutionally-
  protected books, magazines, recordings &
  videos.
Number of Members: 12
Publication(s): *Censorship Update* (annual, $500);
  Obscenity Law Compilation ($500 w/annual
  update $50); *Shooting the Messenger, Why
  Censorship Won't Stop Violence* ($1); *The Van-
  ity of Bonfires* ($1.50)

Media Credit Association (MCA)
84 Broad St, Milford, CT 06460
Tel: 203-876-2182 *Fax:* 203-876-5091
Web Site: www.mediacreditassociation.com
Key Personnel
Exec Dir & VP: Vaughn P Benjamin
  E-mail: vbenjamin@mediacreditassociation.
  com
Credit guideline service for all members of the
  Media Credit Professionals. Exchange financial
  information on advertising agency, for members
  only.
Number of Members: 150

The Melville Society
University of Minnesota, 140 Appleby Hall, Min-
  neapolis, MN 55455
Fax: 612-625-0709
Key Personnel
Pres: Mary K Edwards
Ed, Subn: John Bryant
Treas, Membership & Subn: Dennis Berthold
Exec Sec: Prof Jill Barnum, PhD *Tel:* 612-625-
  0855 *E-mail:* gidma001@tc.umn.edu
Annual & special meetings & publications. Con-
  ferences in association with the Modern Lan-
  guage Association annual convention & Ameri-
  can Literature Association annual convention.
Number of Members: 760
New Election: Annually in the Spring

Publication(s): *Leviathan* (2 issues/yr, no extra
  charge); *Melville Society Extracts* (2 issues/yr,
  $15, $18 libraries)
Branch Office(s)
Hofstra University, c/o Ed, Extracts, Dept of English, Hempstead, NY 11550
Texas A&M University, c/o Treas, Dept of English, College Station, TX 77843-4227

The Mercantile Library
17 E 47 St, New York, NY 10017
Tel: 212-755-6710 *Fax:* 212-826-0831
E-mail: info@mercantilelibrary.org
Web Site: www.mercantilelibrary.org
Key Personnel
Chmn: Sharen Benenson
Dir: Harold Augenbraum
Founded: 1820
Circulating library of mainly fiction titles.
  Monthly programs, literary lectures & readings.
  Writers' studio. Inquiries invited.
Number of Members: 450
Publication(s): *The Literarian* (newsletter)

Metropolitan Lithographers Association Inc
950 Third Ave, 14th fl, New York, NY 10022
Tel: 212-644-1010 *Fax:* 212-644-1936
Key Personnel
Pres: Frank Stillo
Multi-employer lithographic trade association ac-
  tive in collective bargaining, labor relations,
  management educational programs & public
  relations.
Number of Members: 12
New Election: Annually in Jan

Midwest Travel Writers Association
PO Box 83542, Lincoln, NE 68501-3542
Tel: 402-438-2253 *Fax:* 402-438-2253
Web Site: www.mtwa.org
Key Personnel
Pres: Elizabeth Granger
Founded: 1951
To protect & upgrade travel writing as a profes-
  sion. Subjects addressed include: food, wine,
  music, dance, theater, photography, sports,
  recreation, travel & resorts.
Number of Members: 110
2005 Meeting(s): Annual Meeting/Awards Cere-
  mony, Cincinnati, OH, Spring
Publication(s): *MTWA Directory* (annual, $50/
  book, $65/CD); *Travel Times* (quarterly, for
  members only)

Miniature Book Society Inc
402 York Ave, Delaware, OH 43015
Web Site: www.mbs.org
Key Personnel
Pres: Neale Albert
VP: Jon Mayo
Sec: Patricia Pistner
Founded: 1983
Number of Members: 460
Publication(s): *Miniature Book Society Newsletter*
  (quarterly, newsletter, $40/yr)

Modern Language Association of America
  (MLA)
26 Broadway, 3rd fl, New York, NY 10004-1789
Tel: 646-576-5000 *Fax:* 646-458-0030
E-mail: convention@mla.org
Web Site: www.mla.org
Key Personnel
Dir, Conventions: Maribeth T Kraus
Exec Dir: Rosemary Feal
Dir, Book Publg & Intl Rts Contact: David
  Nicholls
Mktg Dir: Kathleen Hansen *Tel:* 646-576-5018
  E-mail: khansen@mla.org
Convention; employment information, profes-
  sional organization.

Number of Members: 31,500
2005 Meeting(s): MLA Annual Convention,
  Washington, DC, Dec 27-30, 2005
Publication(s): *MLA International Bibliography*
  (annual, inquire); *MLA Newsletter* (quarterly,
  free with membership); *PMLA* (6 issues/yr,
  inquire); *Profession* (annual, free with membership; $7.50 non member)

Motion Picture Association of America Inc
  (MPAA)
1600 "I" St NW, Washington, DC 20006
Tel: 202-293-1966 *Fax:* 202-293-7674
Web Site: www.mpaa.org
Key Personnel
CEO: Jack Valenti
VP, Pub Aff: Rich Taylor
Dir, Pub Aff: Phoung Yokitis
Trade association for the major motion picture
  producers & distributors. Administer motion
  picture industry's system of self-regulation &
  are spokespeople for production & distribution
  of motion pictures for theatrical, home video &
  TV use in the USA. Branch offices in Encino,
  CA & Washington, DC.
Number of Members: 60
Branch Office(s)
15503 Ventura Blvd, Encino, CA 91436 *Tel:* 818-
  995-6600 *Fax:* 818-382-1778

Music Publishers' Association of the United
  States
2435 Fifth Ave, Suite 236, New York, NY 10016
Tel: 212-327-4044 *Fax:* 212-327-4044
Web Site: host.mpa.org; www.mpa.org
Key Personnel
Pres: Beebe Bourne *E-mail:* bourne@
  bournemusic.com
VP: Fred Anton *E-mail:* Fred.Anton@
  WarnerChappell.com
2nd VP: Tom Broido *Fax:* tbroido@pesser.com
Sec: Robert Thompson *E-mail:* thompson@
  universaledition.com
Treas: Charles Slater *E-mail:* cslater@jwpepper.
  com
Founded: 1895
Foster trade & commerce in the interest of those
  in the music publishing business & encour-
  age understanding of & compliance with the
  copyright law to protect musical works against
  piracies & infringements.
Number of Members: 300
New Election: Annually in July

Mystery Writers of America
17 E 47 St, 6th fl, New York, NY 10017
Tel: 212-888-8171
E-mail: mwa@mysterywriters.org
Web Site: www.mysterywriters.org
Key Personnel
Off Mgr: Margery Flax
The premier organization for mystery writers &
  other professionals in the mystery field. MWA
  watches developments in legislation & tax
  laws, sponsors symposia & mystery confer-
  ences, presents the Edgar Awards & provides
  information for mystery writers. Membership
  open to published authors, editors, screenwrit-
  ers & other professionals in the field.
Number of Members: 2,900
Publication(s): *Mystery Writers Annual*; *The Third
  Degree* (10 issues/yr)

NAIP, see National Association of Independent
  Publishers (NAIP)

NAPL
75 W Century Rd, Paramus, NJ 07652
Tel: 201-634-9600 *Toll Free Tel:* 800-642-6275
  Fax: 201-634-0324
E-mail: membership@napl.org; orders@napl.org

Web Site: www.napl.org
Key Personnel
CEO & Pres: Joseph Truncale
Founded: 1933
Sponsor 35-40 seminars/workshops each year
throughout North America. Publish a variety
of print-specific periodicals & retail books for
the print community.
Number of Members: 3,600
Publication(s): *The Economic Edge* (quarterly);
*Journal of Graphics Communication Man-
agement* (quarterly); *On the Job* (quarterly);
Sheetfed Operations (quarterly); *Special Re-
ports* (8 issues/yr); *Tech Trends Reports* (quar-
terly)

NASW, see National Association of Science
Writers (NASW)

National Association for Printing Leadership,
see NAPL

**National Association of Black Journalists
(NABJ)**
c/o University of Maryland, 8701 Adelphi Rd,
Adelphi, MD 20783
Tel: 301-445-7100 *Fax:* 301-445-7101
E-mail: nabj@nabj.org
Web Site: www.nabj.org
Key Personnel
Pres: Herb Lowe
Exec Dir: Tangie Newborn *Tel:* 301-445-7100 ext
103
Founded: 1975
To strengthen the ties between Blacks in the
Black media & Blacks in the white media,
eliminate racism, expand Black coverage &
promote professionalism among Black journal-
ists.
Number of Members: 3,300
New Election: Biennially, odd yrs
Publication(s): *NABJ Journal* (quarterly, journal);
NABJ Update (6 issues/yr, newsletter)

National Association of Broadcasters (NAB)
1771 "N" St NW, Washington, DC 20036
Tel: 202-429-5300 *Toll Free Tel:* 800-368-5644
Fax: 202-429-3922
E-mail: nab@nab.org
Web Site: www.nab.org
Key Personnel
Convention Coord: Chris Brown
Trade association for radio & television stations.
Provide products, publications (over 130) &
other services related to broadcasting.
Number of Members: 9,000
2005 Meeting(s): NAB Annual Convention, Las
Vegas, NV, April 18-21, 2005

National Association of College Stores (NACS)
500 E Lorain St, Oberlin, OH 44074
Tel: 440-775-7777 *Toll Free Tel:* 800-622-7498
Fax: 440-775-4769
Web Site: www.nacs.org *Telex:* 98-0346; 98-0479
Key Personnel
Meetings & Expositions Coord: Linda Vargo
Tel: 440-775-7777 ext 2302
Trade association for college store industry.
Number of Members: 3,700
2005 Meeting(s): CAMEX, New Orleans, LA,
Feb 27-March 3, 2005
Publication(s): *Book Buyers' Manual* (annually);
Campus Marketplace (weekly); *The College
Store Journal* (bimonthly); *Directory of Col-
leges & College Stores* (annually); *List of
School Openings & Other Dates* (annually)
Membership(s): BISG

**National Association of Hispanic Publications
Inc (NAHP)**
National Press Bldg, 529 14 St, Suite 1085,
Washington, DC 20045
Tel: 202-662-7250 *Fax:* 202-662-7251
Key Personnel
Pres: Hernan Guaracao
Promote Hispanic media.
Number of Members: 165
Publication(s): *The Hispanic Press* (quarterly,
newsletter)

**National Association of Independent Publishers
(NAIP)**
Affiliate of Florida Publisher's Association Inc
PO Box 430, Highland City, FL 33846-0430
Tel: 863-648-4420 *Fax:* 863-647-5951
E-mail: naip@aol.com
Web Site: www.publishersreport.com
Key Personnel
Exec Dir: Betsy Lampe
Founded: 1979
A small private association that does the follow-
ing: networking seminars, newsletter, jacket
blurbs & consulting for small presses, indepen-
dents & self publishers.
Number of Members: 200
Publication(s): *Publishers' Report* (electronically
every month, $40 non-member, free with $75
membership)

**National Association of Independent Publishers
Representatives (NAIPR)**
Zeckendorf Towers, 111 E 14 St, PMB 157, New
York, NY 10003
Tel: 207-832-7744 *Toll Free Tel:* 888-624-7779
Fax: 207-832-6073 *Toll Free Fax:* 800-416-
2586
E-mail: naiprtwo@aol.com
Web Site: www.naipr.org
Key Personnel
Exec Dir: Mark Follstad
Information & promotion of commission selling
for book publishers.
Seasonal agreement with WordStock Inc to pre-
pare IBID & WordStock Frontlist-on-Floppy
(FROG) diskettes.
Number of Members: 1,108
New Election: 2006
Publication(s): *Marketing Advice for the Very
Small or Self-Publishers* (newsletter, free);
NAIPR News OnLine (monthly, newsletter,
free); *Selling on Commission* (free)

**National Association of Printing Ink
Manufacturers (NAPIM)**
581 Main St, Woodbridge, NJ 07095
Tel: 732-855-1525 *Fax:* 732-855-1838
E-mail: napim@napim.org
Web Site: www.napim.org
Key Personnel
Exec Dir: James E Coleman
Trade associations.
Number of Members: 136
2005 Meeting(s): Annual Convention, Hyatt Co-
conut Point, Bonita Springs, FL, April 7-11,
2005
Publication(s): *Commercial Printing Ink Manufac-
turers in the United States* ($100); *Printing Ink
Handbook* ($20)

National Association of Real Estate Editors
1003 NW Sixth Terr, Boca Raton, FL 33486-3455
Tel: 561-391-3599 *Fax:* 561-391-0099
Web Site: www.naree.org
Key Personnel
Exec Dir: Mary Doyle-Kimball
E-mail: madkimba@aol.com
Mgr: David Kimball *E-mail:* DaKimball@aol.com
Founded: 1929
Nonprofit professional association of writers Jour-
nalism Contest & seminars in winter, spring &

fall; $3,500 fellowship offered in fall; Mem-
berships active for journalists & associate for
communications professionals.
Number of Members: 650
Publication(s): *NAREE Network Roster* (annual,
free to members); *NAREE News* (quarterly, free
to members)

**National Association of Science Writers
(NASW)**
PO Box 890, Hedgesville, WV 25427
Tel: 304-754-5077 *Fax:* 304-754-5076
Web Site: www.nasw.org
Key Personnel
Exec Dir: Diane McGurgan *E-mail:* diane@nasw.
org
Founded: 1934
Local meetings in seven cities.
Number of Members: 2,400
2005 Meeting(s): National Association of Science
Writers Annual Meeting, Washington, DC, Feb
2005
Publication(s): *NASW* (quarterly, newsletter, free
with membership)

**National Cable Telecommunications
Association (NCTA)**
1724 Massachusetts Ave NW, Washington, DC
20036
Tel: 202-775-3550 *Fax:* 202-775-3676
Web Site: www.ncta.com
Key Personnel
Pres & CEO: Robert Sachs
Represent the cable television industry & its pro-
gram & equipment suppliers; inform leaders in
Congress, the Federal Communications Com-
mission & other federal agencies about industry
positions, problems & policies; represent the
complex interests of the cable television in-
dustry before courts of law & state regulatory
agencies & in dialogues with other industry
groups.
Publication(s): *A Cable Primer*; *Cable TV: All
TV Should Be*; *Legislative History of the Cable
Communications Policy Act*; *Producer's Source
Book*

National Cartoonists Society (NCS)
1133 W Morse Blvd, Suite 201, Winter Park, FL
32789
Tel: 407-647-8839 *Fax:* 407-629-2502
Web Site: www.reuben.org
Key Personnel
Pres: Steve McGarry
Fraternal Organization of Cartoonists.
Number of Members: 500
Publication(s): *The Cartoonist*

National Coalition Against Censorship (NCAC)
275 Seventh Ave, 9th fl, New York, NY 10001
Tel: 212-807-6222 *Fax:* 212-807-6245
E-mail: ncac@ncac.org
Web Site: www.ncac.org
Key Personnel
Exec Dir: Joan E Bertin
Prog Dir: Marvin Rich *E-mail:* rich@ncac.org
Dir, Educ & Pub Aff: Roz Udow
Off Mgr: Patricia Valencia
Promote & defend free speech, inquiry & expres-
sion; monitor & publicize censorship incidents;
sponsor public programs; assist in censorship
controversies through advice, materials, con-
tacts with local organizations & individuals.
Membership is comprised of national partici-
pating organizations; individuals may become
NCAC friends for $30 or more. Reprints & in-
formational materials available upon request.
Number of Members: 50
New Election: Annually in Dec
Publication(s): *Censorship News* (4 issues/yr,
$30/yr); *The Cyber-Library: Legal & Policy
Issues Facing Public Libraries in the High-*

Tech Era ($7.50); *Editorial Memorandum on Women, Censorship & "Pornography"* 1993 ($5); *Meese Commission Exposed: Proceedings of a NCAC Public Information Briefing on the Attorney General's Commission on Pornography, Including Kurt Vonnegut Jr, Betty Friedan & Colleen Dewhurst* ($6); *Public Education, Democracy, Free Speech: the Ideas that Define & Unite Us* ($2.50); *A Report on Book Censorship Litigation in Public Schools* (revised, $4); *The Sex Panic, a conference report* ($3.50)

National Coalition for Literacy
Affiliate of American Library Association
50 E Huron St, Chicago, IL 60611
Tel: 312-280-3275 *Toll Free Tel:* 800-228-8813
  Fax: 312-280-3256
E-mail: ncl@ala.org
Web Site: www.ala.org
Key Personnel
Chair: Robbin Sorensen
Pres: Dale Lipschultz
Founded: 1981
A coalition of national organizations concerned about adult functional illiteracy. The purpose is for an ongoing communication among national groups whose primary & continuing interest is literacy.
Number of Members: 44

National Communication Association
1765 North St NW, Washington, DC 20036
Tel: 202-464-4622 *Fax:* 202-464-4600
Web Site: www.natcom.org
Key Personnel
Assoc Dir: Sherry Morreale
Founded: 1914
To promote effective & ethical communication.
Number of Members: 7,000
New Election: Annually
2005 Meeting(s): National Communication Association-Annual Convention, Boston, MA, Nov, 2005
Publication(s): *Communication Education*; *Communication Monographs*; *Critical Studies in Mass Communication*; *Directory of Graduate Programs*; *The Quarterly Journal of Speech*; *Text & Performance Quarterly*

The National Conference for Community & Justice
475 Park Ave S, New York City, NY 10016
Tel: 212-545-1300 *Fax:* 212-545-8053
Web Site: www.nccj.org
Key Personnel
Pres: Sanford Cloud, Jr
Communs & Mktg Mgr: Christina Reyes
  Tel: 212-545-1300 ext 254 *E-mail:* creyes@nccj.org
A human relations organization dedicated to fighting bias, bigotry & racism in America by promoting respect & understanding among all races, religions & cultures through advocacy, conflict resolution & education.
Number of Members: 200,000
Publication(s): *Actions Speak Louder, Big, Big World & the People in It*; *Hate: A Concept Examined*; *Homework for Christians*; *Homework for Jews*; *Intergroup Relations in the United States: Programs & Organizations*; *Intergroup Relations in the United States: Research Perspectives*; *Intergroup Relations in the United States: Seven Promising Practices*

National Conference of Editorial Writers
3899 N Front St, Harrisburg, PA 17110
Tel: 717-703-3015 *Fax:* 717-703-3014
E-mail: ncew@pa-news.org
Web Site: www.ncew.org
Key Personnel
Dir, Membership: Sherid Virnig
Founded: 1947

Sponsor seminars, regional critique meetings & annual foreign tours for members; also cosponsors the Wells Award for exemplary leadership in offering minorities employment in journalism; outreach (critique) service to members & nonmembers; annual convention; Publishes *The Masthead* (professional journal), Circ 900.
Number of Members: 569
New Election: Annually in Sept
Publication(s): *The Masthead* (quarterly, $35/yr)

National Council of Teachers of English (NCTE)
1111 W Kenyon Rd, Urbana, IL 61801-1096
Tel: 217-328-3870 *Toll Free Tel:* 877-369-6283; 877-369-6283 (cust serv) *Fax:* 217-328-0977
E-mail: public_info@ncte.org
Web Site: www.ncte.org
Key Personnel
Exec Dir: Kent Williamson *Tel:* 217-278-3601
  Fax: 217-328-0977
Communs Specialist: Lori Bianchini
  Tel: 217-278-3644 *Fax:* 217-278-3761
  E-mail: lbianchini@ncte.org
Journal Mgr: Margaret Chambers *Tel:* 217-278-3623 *Fax:* 217-328-0977 *E-mail:* mchambers@ncte.org
Perms: Barbara Lamar *Tel:* 217-278-3621
  Fax: 217-278-0977 *E-mail:* blamear@ncte.org
Founded: 1911
Focus on the major concerns of teachers of English & the language arts; offer teaching aids, advice, direction & guidance for members. Publish educational books, journals, monographs, pamphlets, research reports, position papers & annotated booklists for all levels of the English teaching profession. Hold annual convention for members in November; sponsor conferences & workshops.
Number of Members: 60,000
2005 Meeting(s): Annual Convention of NCTE, Pittsburg, PA, Nov 17-22, 2005
2006 Meeting(s): Annual Convention of NCTE, Nashville, TN, Nov 16-21, 2006
Publication(s): *Classroom Notes Plus* (quarterly, $60/yr); *College Composition & Communication* (quarterly, journal, $65/yr); *College English* (6 times/yr, journal, $65/yr); *The Council Chronicle* (4 issues/yr, newspaper, $40/yr - included w/membership); *English Education* (quarterly, journal, $55/yr); *English Journal* (6 times/yr, journal, $65/yr); *English Leadership Quarterly* (quarterly, journal, $65/yr); *Language Arts* (6 times/yr, journal, $65/yr); *Research in the Teaching of English* (quarterly, journal, $60/yr); *School Talk* (quarterly, journal, $55/yr); *SLATE Newsletter & Starter Sheets* (3 issues/yr, newsletter, $15/yr); *Talking Points* (semiannual, journal, $70/yr); *Teaching English in the Two-year College* (quarterly, journal, $60/yr); *Voices from the Middle* (quarterly, journal, $60/yr)

National Education Association (NEA)
1201 16 St NW, Washington, DC 20036
Tel: 202-822-7200 *Fax:* 202-822-7206; 202-822-7292
Web Site: www.nea.org *Cable:* EDUCATION
Key Personnel
Pres: Reg Weaver
Exec Dir: John Wilson
Dir, PR: Andy Linebaugh
Professional association for over 2.7 million educators, with 14,000 local, 52 state & 6 regional affiliates.
Number of Members: 2,700,000
2005 Meeting(s): NEA Representative Assembly, Los Angeles, CA, July 1-6, 2005
2006 Meeting(s): NEA Representative Assembly, Orlando, FL, June 30-July 5, 2006

2007 Meeting(s): NEA Representative Assembly, Philadelphia, PA, June 30-July 5, 2007
Publication(s): *The NEA Almanac of Higher Education* (annual); *NEA Today* (9 issues/yr); *Thought & Action* (2 issues/yr)

National Federation of Abstracting & Information Services (NFAIS)
1518 Walnut St, Suite 1004, Philadelphia, PA 19102-3403
Tel: 215-893-1561 *Fax:* 215-893-1564
E-mail: nfais@nfais.org
Web Site: www.nfais.org
Key Personnel
Dir, Planning & Comm: Jill O'Neill
  E-mail: jilloneill@nfais.org
Sponsors research, carries out a comprehensive program of continuing education issues pertinent publications in all areas of documentation & information dissemination.
Number of Members: 55
Publication(s): *Beyond Boolean-New Approaches to Information Retrieval*; *Computer Support to Indexing*; *Guide to Database Distribution*; *Impacts of Changing Production Technologies*; *Membership Directory* (online only); *NFAIS E Notes* (online only); *NFAIS Newsletter* (online only, newsletter)

National Federation of Press Women Inc (NFPW)
PO Box 5556, Arlington, VA 22205-0056
Tel: 703-534-2500 *Toll Free Tel:* 800-780-2715
  Fax: 703-534-5751
E-mail: presswomen@aol.com
Web Site: www.nfpw.org
Key Personnel
Exec Dir: Carol Pierce
Founded: 1936
Conduct seminars & workshops to increase knowledge & develop professional skills of working media women; youth projects.
Number of Members: 2,000
2005 Meeting(s): NFPW Communication Conference, Seattle, WA, Sept 8-10, 2005
Publication(s): *Agenda* (quarterly)

National Information Standards Organization
4733 Bethesda Ave, Suite 300, Bethesda, MD 20814
Tel: 301-654-2512 *Fax:* 301-654-1721
E-mail: nisohq@niso.org
Web Site: www.niso.org
Key Personnel
Exec Dir: Patricia R Harris
Developing, maintaining & publishing technical standards used by libraries, information services & publishers. Accredited by the American National Standards Institute.
Number of Members: 85
Publication(s): *Information Standards Quarterly* (4 issues/yr, $85/yr US, $125/yr Canadian & foreign, free to voting members)

National League of American Pen Women
c/o National Pen Women-Scholarship, Pen Arts Bldg, 1300 17 St NW, Washington, DC 20036-1973
Web Site: www.americanpenwomen.org
Key Personnel
Pres: Anna Di Bella
Sec: Jean Elizabeth Holmes
Founded: 1897
Scholarships, letters, art & music workshops, awards & prizes. Must send SASE for information.
Number of Members: 5,000
Publication(s): *The Pen Woman* (6 issues/yr, $18/yr; free to members)

National Library of Canada, see Library & Archives Canada

National Mental Health Association
2001 N Beauregard St, 12th fl, Alexandria, VA 22311
Tel: 703-684-7722 *Toll Free Tel:* 800-969-6642 *Fax:* 703-684-5968
Web Site: www.nmha.org
Key Personnel
Pres & CEO: Michael Faenza
VP, Pub Educ: James Radack *Tel:* 703-838-7539 *E-mail:* jradack@nmha.org
Founded: 1909
Legislative advocacy, public education, healthcare reform, information & referral.
Number of Members: 1,000,000
Publication(s): *The Bell* (monthly); *Consumer Update* (monthly); *State Advocacy Update* (bimonthly)

National Music Publishers' Association (NMPA)
711 Third Ave, 8th fl, New York, NY 10017
Tel: 646-742-1651 *Fax:* 646-742-1779
Web Site: www.nmpa.org
Key Personnel
Pres: Edward P Murphy
Trade association of American Music Publishers.
Number of Members: 600

National Newspaper Association
University of Missouri, 127-129 Neff Annex, Columbia, MO 65211-1200
Mailing Address: PO Box 7540, Columbia, MO 65205-7540
Tel: 573-882-5800 *Toll Free Tel:* 800-829-4662 *Fax:* 703-884-5490
E-mail: info@nna.org
Web Site: www.nna.org
Key Personnel
Exec Dir: Brian Steffens
Asst Dir, Meetings: Cindy-Joy Rogers
Founded: 1885
Trade association.
Number of Members: 2,500
Publication(s): *Publishers Auxiliary* (monthly, $85/yr, $95/intl)

National Newspaper Publishers Assn (NNPA)
3200 13 St NW, Washington, DC 20010
Tel: 202-588-8764 *Fax:* 202-588-8960
E-mail: info@blackpressusa.com
Web Site: www.nnpa.org; www.blackpressusa.com
Key Personnel
Pres: Sonceria Messiah-Jiles

National Paper Trade Association, see NPTA Alliance

National Press Club (NPC)
529 14 St NW, 13th fl, Washington, DC 20045
Tel: 202-662-7500 *Fax:* 202-662-7569
E-mail: infocenter@npcpress.org
Web Site: www.press.org
Key Personnel
Club Pres: Sheila Cherry
Archivist: Christina Hostetter
Lib Dir: Tom Glad
Founded: 1908
Private professional organization for journalists. Sponsors workshops, rap sessions with authors, press forums, morning newsmakers, famous speaker luncheons; awards prizes for consumer journalism, environmental reporting; freedom of the press; diplomatic writing, Washington coverage & newsletters; book & art exhibits; computerized reference library; annual Book Fair & Authors' Night.
Number of Members: 4,000
Publication(s): *The Record* (weekly)

National Press Club of Canada
150 Wellington St, 2nd fl, Ottawa, ON K1P 5A4, Canada
Tel: 613-233-5641 *Fax:* 613-233-3511
E-mail: members@pressclub.on.ca
Web Site: www.pressclub.on.ca
Key Personnel
Pres: Tom MacGregor
Private club for reporters, journalists & media-related people; dining, bar & meeting facilities, catering for up to 150 people.
Number of Members: 600
2005 Meeting(s): Spring, 2005

The National Press Foundation
1211 Connecticut Ave NW, Suite 310, Washington, DC 20036
Tel: 202-530-5355 *Fax:* 202-530-2855
Web Site: www.nationalpress.org
Key Personnel
Pres: Bob Meyers
Prog Dir: Nolan Walters *Tel:* 202-663-7283
Provide grants, fellowships & seminars for journalists on topics fostering excellence in journalism.
2005 Meeting(s): National Press Foundation Annual Awards Dinner, Washington Hilton, Washington, DC, Feb 17, 2005

National Press Photographers Association Inc (NPPA)
3200 Croasdaile Dr, Suite 306, Durham, NC 27705
Tel: 919-383-7246 *Fax:* 919-383-7261
E-mail: info@nppa.org
Web Site: www.nppa.org
Key Personnel
Exec Dir: Greg Garneau *Tel:* 919-383-7246 ext 10 *E-mail:* director@nppa.org
Membership Dir: Jim Haverkamp *Tel:* 919-383-7246 ext 14 *E-mail:* members@nppa.org
Info Tech Mgr: Stephen Sample *Tel:* 919-383-7246 ext 15 *E-mail:* netgeek@nppa.org
Mail-order & e-Commerce Mgr: Eric Waters *Tel:* 919-383-7246 ext 16 *E-mail:* sales@nppa.org
Founded: 1946
Number of Members: 10,004
Publication(s): *News Photographer Magazine* (monthly, $28/yr with membership)

The National Society of Newspaper Columnists (NSNC)
Fillmore St, Suite 507, San Francisco, CA 94115
Tel: 415-541-5636
Web Site: www.columnists.com
Key Personnel
Exec Dir: Luenna H Kim *E-mail:* director@columnists.com
Pres: Mike Leonard *E-mail:* leonard@heraldt.com
VP: Suzette Stranding *E-mail:* suzmar@attbi.com
Sec: Dave Lieber *E-mail:* dlieber@star-telegram.com
Treas: Dave Glardon *E-mail:* dglardon@siscom.net
Newsletter Ed: Robert Haught *E-mail:* newseditor@columnists.com
Conference Chair: Sheila Stroup *E-mail:* sstroup@bellsouth.net
Contest Chair: Peter Rowe *E-mail:* PeteR2810@aol.com
Educ Chair: Joe Blundo *E-mail:* jblundo@dispatch.com
Annual conference.
Number of Members: 389
2005 Meeting(s): Annual Conference, Grapevine, TX, June 23-26, 2005
Publication(s): *The Columnist* (quarterly)

National State Publishing Association (NSPA)
207 Third Ave, Hattiesburg, MS 39401
Tel: 601-582-3330 *Fax:* 601-582-3354
E-mail: info@govpublishing.org
Web Site: www.govpublishing.org
Key Personnel
Pres, Ohio State Printing: Joe Tucker
Exec Dir: Lamar F Evans
Treas, State of Delaware General Assembly: Debby Messina
Central Reg Dir: Robert Gomez
Eastern Reg Dir: Scott Stovall
Southern Region Dir: Campbell King
Western Region Dir: Leona Olsen
NSPA quarterly newsletter sent to all members. Scholarship awarded to a college or university that has established a four-year program in printing & graphic arts. Information exchange central reference source & public arena for ongoing state publishing activities.
Number of Members: 100
New Election: Annually
2005 Meeting(s): Annual Conference, Biloxi, MS, Oct, 2005
Publication(s): *NSPA Newsletter* (quarterly, newsletter, free)

National Writers Association
3140 S Peoria, Suite 295, Aurora, CO 80014
Tel: 303-841-0246 *Fax:* 303-841-2607
Web Site: www.nationalwriters.com (magazine available on-line)
Key Personnel
Exec Dir: Sandy Whelchel *E-mail:* sandywrter@aol.com
Founded: 1937
Nonprofit representative organization of new & established writers, serving freelance writers throughout the world.
Number of Members: 3,000
Publication(s): *Authorship* (quarterly, $20/yr); *NWA Market Update* (quarterly); *NWA Newsletter* (monthly by e-mail only); *Professional Freelance Writers Directory* (available online only free)

National Writers Union
113 University Place, 6th fl, New York, NY 10003-4527
Tel: 212-254-0279 *Fax:* 212-254-0673
E-mail: nwu@nwu.org
Web Site: www.nwu.org/
Key Personnel
Pres: Gerard Colby
Organizing for better treatment of freelance writers by publishers; grievance procedures; negotiate union contracts with publishers; health insurance; conferences. Direct services include the Technical Writers Job Hotline & the Publication Rights Clearinghouse, a groundbreaking license fee collection system. National health insurance programs around the country; national grievance officers & contract advisors; agents database on-line for members; Authors Network, a Bed & Breakfast program for touring authors at over 160 sites throughout the country, including local reviewer's database, local press contacts & local bookstores/vendors.
Number of Members: 4,000
Publication(s): *American Writer* (quarterly); *local chapter newsletters*

NCTA, see Northern California Translators Association

Networking Alternatives for Publishers, Retailers & Artists Inc (NAPRA)
109 North Beach Rd, Eastsound, WA 98245
Mailing Address: PO Box 9, Eastsound, WA 98245-0009
Tel: 360-376-2702 *Toll Free Tel:* 800-367-1907 *Fax:* 360-376-2704
E-mail: napravision@napra.com
Web Site: www.napra.com

Key Personnel
Founder & Publr: Marilyn McGuire
Exec Dir: Suzanne Humes
Education, networking, bimonthly journal, trade show representation, membership gatherings. Marilyn McGuire is the publisher of NAPRA ReVive, circ 12,000.
Number of Members: 600
Publication(s): *NAPRA ReView* (bimonthly, $75/yr US; $125/yr outside of the US)
Membership(s): ASAE; Publishers Marketing Association

New England Booksellers Association Inc (NEBA)

1770 Massachusetts Ave, No 332, Cambridge, MA 02140
Mailing Address: PO Box 332, Cambridge, MA 02140
Tel: 617-576-3070 *Toll Free Tel:* 800-466-8711 *Fax:* 617-576-3091
Web Site: www.newenglandbooks.org
Key Personnel
Exec Dir: Wayne (Rusty) Drugan *E-mail:* rusty@neba.org
Trade association. Fall trade show annually in Sept or Oct; educational workshops, holiday gift catalog.
Number of Members: 650
Publication(s): *NEBA News* (quarterly, $20)

New England Poetry Club

2 Farrar St, Cambridge, MA 02138
Tel: 781-643-0029
Key Personnel
Pres: Diana Der Hovanessian
VP: Roseanna Warren
Sec: Diane Robitaille
Membership Chmn: Victor Howes
Info Officer: Virginia Thayer
Founded: 1915
Society for professional published poets. Sponsor various poetry contests & workshops. Workshops meet at the Yen Ching Institute (2 Divinity Ave Harvard Campus). Readings on first Monday, 7 pm at Cambridge Public Library; workshops third Mondays 7:30pm; monthly from Sept-May. Special programs at Longfellow House Sunday pm out of doors, $3,000 in prizes annually.
Number of Members: 500
Publication(s): *Best Published Poems of the Year* (free with annual dues); *Writ* (free with annual dues)

New Mexico Book Association (NMBA)

310 Read St, Santa Fe, NM 87504
Mailing Address: PO Box 1285, Santa Fe, NM 87504
Tel: 505-983-1412 *Fax:* 505-983-0899
E-mail: oceantree@earthlink.net
Web Site: www.nmbook.org
Key Personnel
Pres: Richard K Harris
VP: James Mafchir
Exec Dir: Richard Polese
Sec: Ruth Francis
Treas: Alexander MacGregor
Founded: 1994
Nonprofit association serving the interest of publishing & book professionals in New Mexico. Open to all involved in books &/or publishing. Need not be a resident of New Mexico.
Number of Members: 175
New Election: May 2005
2005 Meeting(s): Gala Banquet Luncheon, Santa Fe, NM, May 2005
Publication(s): *LIBRO Monthly* (monthly, newsletter, $62/yr with membership)
Membership(s): Publishers Association of the West; Publishers Marketing Association; Small Publishers Association of North America

New Orleans-Gulf South Booksellers Association

PO Box 750043, New Orleans, LA 70175-0043
Tel: 504-701-3417
E-mail: info@nogsba.com
Web Site: www.nogsba.com
Key Personnel
Chmn: Joseph Billingsley; Britton Trice
Founded: 1984
Information & consulting, promotions.
Number of Members: 50

Newsletter & Electronic Publishers Association

1501 Wilson Blvd, Suite 509, Arlington, VA 22209
Tel: 703-527-2333 *Toll Free Tel:* 800-356-9302 *Fax:* 703-841-0629
Web Site: www.newsletters.org
Key Personnel
Exec Dir: Patricia Wysocki
Dir, Membership: Barbara Lancaster
Members are subscription-based newsletter publishers representing small & large companies. Activities include postal matters, marketing, technical developments, copyright, business practices & editorial development.
Number of Members: 575
2005 Meeting(s): International Newsletter & Specialized News Conference, Mayflower Hotel, Washington, DC, June 2005
Publication(s): *Hotline* (biweekly, members only); *The Ultimate Guide to Newsletter Publishing* ($39.50 non-members/$20 members)

Newspaper Advertising Sales Association

411 W Fifth St, Los Angeles, CA 90013
Key Personnel
Pres: Carol Mintz *Tel:* 213-896-2230 *E-mail:* carol.mintz@laopinion.com
Chapters in Atlanta, Boston, Chicago, Dallas, Detroit, Los Angeles, Miami, New York & San Francisco.
Number of Members: 1,000

Newspaper Association of America (NAA)

1921 Gallows Rd, Suite 600, Vienna, VA 22182
Tel: 703-902-1600 *Fax:* 703-917-0636
Web Site: www.naa.org
Key Personnel
Pres: John F Sturm
Sr VP, Communs: Su-Lin Nichols
Exec Asst, Communs: Regina Woodson *Tel:* 703-902-1636 *E-mail:* woodr@naa.org
Serves newspapers & newspaper executives by working to advance the cause of a free press; to encourage the efficiency & economy of the newspaper publishing business in all departments & aspects; to engage in & promote research of use to newspapers; to gather & distribute among its member newspapers accurate, reliable & useful information about newspapers & their environment & to promote the highest standard of journalism.
Number of Members: 2,000
Publication(s): *Presstime* (monthly, journal)

The Newspaper Guild

501 Third St NW, Washington, DC 20001-2760
Tel: 202-434-7173 *Fax:* 202-434-1472
E-mail: guild@swa-union.org
Web Site: www.newsguild.org
Key Personnel
Pres: Linda K Foley
Ed: Andy Zipser
Labor union; AFL-CIO, CLC.
Number of Members: 34,000
Publication(s): *Guild Reporter* (monthly, $20 subscription rate non-members/free to members)

North American Agricultural Journalists

Texas A&M University, 201 Reed Macdonald, 2112 TAMU, College Station, TX 77843-2112
Tel: 979-845-2872 *Fax:* 979-845-2414
E-mail: ka-phillips@tamu.edu
Web Site: naaj.tamu.edu
Key Personnel
Exec Sec & Treas: Kathleen Phillips *E-mail:* ka-phillips@tamu.edu
Newsletter Ed: Duane Dailey
Self-improvement seminars; annual writing contest for members & non-members.
Number of Members: 140
2005 Meeting(s): North American Agricultural Journalists Spring Meeting, Washington, DC, April 2005
Publication(s): *NAAJ Newsletter* (8 issues/yr)
Branch Office(s)
University of Missouri-Columbia, Center for Agricultural Journalism, 3 Whitten Hall, Columbia, MO 65201

North American Bookdealers Exchange

PO Box 606, Cottage Grove, OR 97424-0026
Tel: 541-942-7455 *Fax:* 561-258-2625
E-mail: nabe@bookmarketingprofits.com
Web Site: www.bookmarketingprofits.com
Key Personnel
Exec Dir: Al Galasso
Promo Dir: Russ Von Hoelscher
Assoc Dir: Ingrid Crawford
Founded: 1980
International book marketing organization of independent publishers & mail order entrepreneurs. Activities include NABE Combined Book Exhibits at national & regional conventions serving the book, educational, gift & business trade. Publishers Preview Mail Order Program, National Press Release, Electronic Marketing plus complete publisher consultation services for printing, promoting & marketing books.
Number of Members: 1,000
Publication(s): *Book Dealers World* (quarterly, circ 10,000, $3/sample, $45/yr & $80/biennial US)

North American Graphic Arts Suppliers Association (NAGASA)

1604 New Hampshire Ave NW, Washington, DC 20009
Tel: 202-328-8441 *Fax:* 202-328-8513
E-mail: information@nagasa.org
Web Site: www.nagasa.org
Key Personnel
Pres: Greg Du Ross
Trade association committed to representing the distribution channel in the graphic arts, printing & imaging industry.
Number of Members: 200
Publication(s): *The Compass* (quarterly)

North American Snowsports Journalists Association

460 Sarsons Rd, Kelowna, BC V1W 1C2, Canada
Tel: 250-764-2143 *Fax:* 250-764-2145
E-mail: nasja@shaw.ca
Web Site: www.nasja.org
Key Personnel
Pres: Phil Johnson
Sec/Treas: Steven Threndyle
Founded: 1963 (first founded as the US Ski Writers Assn)
Professional group of writers, photographers, broadcasters, filmmakers, authors & editors who report ski & snowboard related news, info & features throughout the US, Canada & Mexico.
Number of Members: 298
New Election: Annually in March
2005 Meeting(s): Annual Meeting, Coeur d'Alene, ID, March 23-27, 2005

Northern California Independent Booksellers Association (NCIBA)
37 Graham St, San Francisco, CA 94129
Mailing Address: PO Box 29169, San Francisco, CA 94129-0169
Tel: 415-561-7686 *Fax:* 415-561-7685
E-mail: office@nciba.com
Web Site: www.nciba.com
Key Personnel
Pres: Alzada Knickerbocker *Tel:* 530-792-0710
Exec Dir: Hut Landon
Tradeshow, education seminars, collaborative advertising, regional holiday catalog.
Number of Members: 600
Publication(s): *The California Catalog, a holiday advertising sales tool*; *Membership Directory* (annually, members only); *Newsletter* (monthly, free with membership); *Sales Rep List & Access Guide* (annually, $10)
Membership(s): ABA

Northern California Translators Association
Affiliate of Chapter of the American Translators Association
PO Box 14015, Berkeley, CA 94712-5015
Tel: 510-845-8712 *Fax:* 510-883-1355
E-mail: ncta@ncta.org
Web Site: www.ncta.org
Key Personnel
Pres: Michael Metzger
Admin: Juliet Viola
Professional translators & interpreters association; an annual membership directory. Also a referral service.
Number of Members: 500
New Election: Annually in Feb
Publication(s): *A Practical Guide for Translators* ($10); *Professional Services Directory* ($25/yr); *The Translorial* (quarterly, newsletter, $25)

Northwest Association of Book Publishers
Affiliate of Publishers Marketing Association (PMA)
PO Box 3786, Wilsonville, OR 97070-3786
Tel: 503-223-9055
Key Personnel
Pres: Nancy Kelley *Tel:* 503-666-0150
E-mail: ncukell50@hotmail.com
Monthly meetings focusing on topics of interest to independent publishers; newsletter, special events.
Number of Members: 150
New Election: Annually in Oct
Publication(s): *Publishers Focus* (monthly, free with membership)

Northwest Territories Library Services
Unit of Information Networks Division
75 Woodland Dr, Hay River, NT X0E 1G1, Canada
Tel: 867-874-6531 *Toll Free Tel:* 866-297-0232
Fax: 867-874-3321
Web Site: www.nwtpls.gov.nt.ca
Key Personnel
Territorial Libn: Sandy MacDonald
E-mail: sandy_macdonald@gov.nt.ca

NPES The Association for Suppliers of Printing, Publishing & Converting Technologies
1899 Preston White Dr, Reston, VA 20191-4367
Tel: 703-264-7200 *Fax:* 703-620-0994
E-mail: npes@npes.org
Web Site: www.npes.org
Key Personnel
Pres: Regis J Delmontagne
Dir, Communs & Mktg: Carol J Hurlburt
E-mail: churlbur@npes.org
Represent manufacturers' & distributors' equipment, supplies, systems & software for printing, publishing & converting.
Number of Members: 420

Publication(s): *NPES Directory of International Suppliers of Printing, Publishing and Converting Technologies* (free); *NPES Pressroom Safety Manual*; *Safe Cleaning of Offset Sheetfed Presses*; *Safe Cleaning of Offset Webfed Presses*

NPTA Alliance
Formerly National Paper Trade Association
500 Bi-County Blvd, Suite 200E, Farmingdale, NY 11735
Tel: 631-777-2223 *Fax:* 631-777-2224
Web Site: www.gonpta.com
Key Personnel
Pres: William Frohlich
Number of Members: 2,600
New Election: Annually in Oct
Publication(s): *Distribution Sales & Management* (monthly)

Ontario Library Association
100 Lombard St, Suite 303, Toronto, ON M5C 1M3, Canada
Tel: 416-363-3388 *Toll Free Tel:* 866-873-9867
Fax: 416-941-9581 *Toll Free Fax:* 800-387-1181
Web Site: www.accessola.com
Key Personnel
Exec Dir: Larry Moore *E-mail:* lmoore@accessola.com
Founded: 1900
Number of Members: 4,200
2005 Meeting(s): Metro Toronto Convention Center, Toronto, ON, Canada, Feb 3-5, 2005
Publication(s): *Access* (quarterly); *The Teaching Librarian* (triannual)

Oregon Christian Writers
1647 SW Pheasant Dr, Aloha, OR 97006
Tel: 503-642-9844 *Fax:* 503-848-3658
E-mail: miholer@viser.net
Web Site: www.oregonchristianwriters.org
Key Personnel
Pres: Jennifer Anne Messing *Tel:* 503-775-6039
E-mail: mnjmessing@cs.com
Exec Ed: Sally Stuart *E-mail:* stuartcwmg@aol.com
Recording Sec: Tonya Johnson
E-mail: tonyaljohn@earthlink.net
Workshops & seminars for beginning & advanced writers; guest speakers & critiques by professional writers.
Number of Members: 350
2005 Meeting(s): Oregon Christian Writers Seminar, Salem, OR, Feb 2005; Oregon Christian Writers Seminar, Eugene, OR, May 2005; Oregon Christian Writers Coaching Conference, Canby Grove Conference Center, Canby, OR, Aug 2005; Oregon Christian Writers Seminar, Medford, OR, Sept 2005; Oregon Christian Writers Seminar, Portland, OR, Oct 2005
Publication(s): *Oregon Christian Writers Newletter* (3 times/yr, newsletter)

Organization of Book Publishers of Ontario
720 Bathurst St, Suite 301, Toronto, ON M5S 2R4, Canada
Tel: 416-536-7584 *Fax:* 416-536-7692
E-mail: obpo@interlog.com
Web Site: www.ontariobooks.ca
Key Personnel
Admin Dir: Julie Ford
Informational, professional development, group marketing & lobbying services for members.
Number of Members: 55

Overseas Press Club of America (OPC)
40 W 45 St, New York, NY 10036
Tel: 212-626-9220 *Fax:* 212-626-9210
Web Site: www.opcofamerica.org

Key Personnel
Pres: Alexis Gelber
Exec Dir: Sonya K Fry *E-mail:* sonya@opcofamerica.org
Founded: 1939
Maintain an international association of journalists, encourage professional skill & integrity of reportage, contribute to the freedom & independence of journalism & the press worldwide.
Number of Members: 640
2005 Meeting(s): OPC Annual Awards Dinner, April 2005
2006 Meeting(s): OPC Annual Awards Dinner, April 2006
Publication(s): *Bulletin*; *Dateline*; *Directory*

Pacific Northwest Booksellers Association
317 W Broadway, Suite 214, Eugene, OR 97401-2890
Tel: 541-683-4363 *Fax:* 541-683-3910
E-mail: info@pnba.org
Web Site: www.pnba.org
Key Personnel
Pres: Pat Rutledge
Exec Dir: Thom Chambliss *E-mail:* thom@pnba.org
Annual trade shows March & Sept, lists of publishing companies' sales reps, educational seminars; work with local literacy groups & anti-censorship organizations. Sponsor annual booksellers awards presented for books of exceptional quality by Northwest writers or publishers. Sponsor workshops & prizes. Rent mailing list of over 800 plus Northwest Bookstores.
Number of Members: 500
Publication(s): *Annual Rep List & Handbook*; *Footnotes* (monthly, newsletter, free to members)

Pacific Printing & Imaging Association
1400 SW Fifth Ave, Suite 815, Portland, OR 97201
Toll Free Tel: 877-762-7742 *Toll Free Fax:* 800-824-1911
E-mail: info@pacprinting.org
Web Site: www.pacprinting.org
Key Personnel
Exec Dir: Marcus Sassaman *E-mail:* marcus@pacprinting.com
Printing.

Pen American Center
Division of International PEN
588 Broadway, Suite 303, New York, NY 10012
Tel: 212-334-1660 *Fax:* 212-334-2181
E-mail: pen@pen.org
Web Site: www.pen.org
Key Personnel
Awards Dir: Peter Meyer *Tel:* 212-334-1660 ext 110 *E-mail:* awards@pen.org
Pres: Salman Rushdie
Intl Pres: Homero Aridjis
An international organization of writers, poets, playwrights, essayists, editors, novelists & translators, whose purpose is to bring about better understanding among writers of all nations.
Number of Members: 2,800
Publication(s): *Grants & Awards Available to American Writers* ($19.50); *Pamphlets*

PEN Canada
24 Ryerson Ave, Suite 214, Toronto, ON M5T 2P3, Canada
Tel: 416-703-8448 *Fax:* 416-703-3870
E-mail: pen@pencanada.ca
Web Site: www.pencanada.ca
Key Personnel
Pres: Reza Baraheni
Exec Dir: Isobel Harry
Number of Members: 500

PEN Center USA

Unit of International PEN
672 S Lafayette Park Place, Suite 42, Los Angeles, CA 90057
Tel: 213-365-8500 *Fax:* 213-365-9616
E-mail: pen@penusa.org
Web Site: www.penusa.org
Key Personnel
Pres: Carla Lazzareschi
VP, Progs: Geraldine Kennedy
Exec Dir: Adam Somers
Literary Progs Dir: Christina L Apeles
Sec & Treas: Celeste Fremon
Founded: 1981
National association of poets, playwrights, screenwriters, essayists, editors, novelists, historians, critics, journalists & translators whose purpose is to foster a sense of community among writers in the Western US & to advance the freedom to write throughout the world.
Number of Members: 1,300
Publication(s): *Author Access* (semiannual); *Electric PEN* (bimonthly); *Freedom to Write Publications*

Periodical & Book Association of America Inc

481 Eighth Ave, Suite 826, New York, NY 10001
Tel: 212-563-6502 *Fax:* 212-563-4098
Web Site: www.pbaa.net
Key Personnel
Pres: William Michalopoulous
Exec Dir: Lisa Scott
Trade organization for newsstand publishers.
Number of Members: 90
Publication(s): *Magazine* (annual, free to members)

The Periodical Publications Assn Inc (PPA)

PO Box 10669, Rockville, MD 20849-0669
Tel: 301-260-1646 *Fax:* 301-260-1647
E-mail: periodicalpubs@yahoo.com
Key Personnel
Exec Dir: Kimberly M Scott
To protect periodical mail rates & to represent periodical publishers before the Postal Service & Postal Rate Commission. To educate periodical mailers about critical postal issues.
Number of Members: 20

Periodical Writers' Association of Canada

215 Spadina Ave, Suite 123, Toronto, ON M5T 2C7, Canada
Tel: 416-504-1645 *Fax:* 416-913-2327
E-mail: pwac@web.net; info@pwac.ca
Web Site: www.pwac.ca; www.writers.ca
Key Personnel
Pres: Liz Warwick
Exec Dir: John Degan
Protect & promote the interests of periodical writers in Canada, develop & maintain professional standards in editor-writer relationships, lobby for higher standard fees for freelancers, sponsor professional development workshops & offset freelancers' isolation by circulating news, information & market data on the industry.
Number of Members: 525
2005 Meeting(s): Periodical Writers' Association of Canada Annual General Meeting, Hamilton, ON, May 2005
Publication(s): *PWAC Guide to Canadian Markets for Freelance Writers* (book, $15 per copy, available in pdf form only); *PWAC Guide to Editing as a Sideline for Freelance Writers* (book, $21.40 per copy, GST included); *PWAC Guide to Roughing in the Market* (book, $4.60 per copy, plus postage)

Photographic Society of America Inc (PSA)

3000 United Founders Blvd, Suite 103, Oklahoma City, OK 73112-3940
Tel: 405-843-1437 *Fax:* 405-843-1438
E-mail: psahg@theshop.net; hq@psa-photo.org
Web Site: www.psa-photo.org
Key Personnel
Ed: Diane Trout Harwood
Opers Mgr: Kara King
Sponsor workshops & awards for members.
Number of Members: 10,000
2005 Meeting(s): PSA International Conference of Photography, Sheraton City Centre Hotel, Salt Lake City, UT, Aug 29-Sept 3, 2005
Publication(s): *PSA Journal* (journal, $42/yr North America)

PIA/GATF (Graphic Arts Technical Foundation)

Affiliate of Printing Industries of America
200 Deer Run Rd, Sewickley, PA 15143-2600
Tel: 412-741-6860 *Toll Free Tel:* 800-910-4283
   Fax: 412-741-2311 *Fax on Demand:* 888-272-3329
E-mail: info@gain.net
Web Site: www.gain.net
Key Personnel
Pres: Michael Makin
COO: George Ryan
Mktg Mgr: Lisa Erdner
VP, Publg: Peter Oresick
Founded: 1924
Member organization providing research, educational & technical services to printing industry worldwide.
Number of Members: 14,000
Publication(s): *GATFWORLD Magazine* (bimonthly, $75/yr); *Publications Catalog* (free); *QC Catalog* (free); *Training Programs Catalog* (free)

Playwrights Guild of Canada

54 Wolseley St, 2nd fl, Toronto, ON M5T 1A5, Canada
Tel: 416-703-0201 *Fax:* 416-703-0059
E-mail: info@playwrightsguild.ca
Web Site: www.playwrightsguild.ca
Key Personnel
Exec Dir: Amela Simic
Founded: 1982
Contracts, amateur agent productions, script service, readings.
Number of Members: 475
Membership(s): Professional Association of Canadian Playwrights

Poetry Society of America (PSA)

15 Gramercy Park, New York, NY 10003
Tel: 212-254-9628 *Toll Free Tel:* 888-USA-POEM
   Fax: 212-673-2352
Web Site: www.poetrysociety.org
Key Personnel
Pres: William Louis Dreyfus
Exec Dir: Alice Quinn
Progs Dir: Brett Lauer
Founded: 1910
Contests, readings, lectures, symposia, seminars, weekly workshops for members.
Number of Members: 2,900
Publication(s): *Crossroads* (2 issues/yr, free to members)

Poets & Writers Inc

72 Spring St, Suite 301, New York, NY 10012
Tel: 212-226-3586 *Fax:* 212-226-3963
Web Site: www.pw.org
Key Personnel
Exec Dir: Elliot Figman
Founded: 1970
A nonprofit organization which offers information, support & exposure to writers at all stages in their careers. Founded to foster the development of poets & fiction writers & to promote communication throughout the literary community. It publishes the bimonthly *Poets & Writers Magazine*, which delivers to its readers profiles of noted authors & publishing professionals, practical how-to articles, a comprehensive listing of grants & awards for writers & special sections on subjects ranging from small presses to writers conferences. The Readings/Workshops Program supports public literary events through matching grants to community organizations.
Distributed by Small Press Distribution
Publication(s): *Poets & Writers Magazine* (bimonthly, $19.95/yr, $38/2 yrs, $4.95 single copy 1999 forward; prior to 1999 $3.95)

Print Buyers Association (Printing Industries of Northern Calif)

665 Third St, Suite 500, San Francisco, CA 94107
Tel: 415-495-8242 *Fax:* 415-543-7790
E-mail: info@pinc.org
Web Site: www.pinc.org
Key Personnel
Exec Dir: Dan Nelson *E-mail:* dan@pinc.org
Trade association.
Number of Members: 1,040

PrintImage International

70 E Lake St, Suite 333, Chicago, IL 60601
Tel: 312-726-8015 *Toll Free Tel:* 800-234-0040
   Fax: 312-726-8113
E-mail: info@printimage.org
Web Site: www.printimage.org
Key Personnel
Pres & CEO: Steven D Johnson
Chmn: Brian O'Day
Memb Devt Dir: Christina Vargas
   E-mail: cvargas@printimage.org
Founded: 1975
Formed in 1975 as NAQP, PrintImage International provides services to more than 1,600 quick printing, copying & small commercial printing members, located in the United States, Canada & several foreign countries. Members include both independent printers & franchise businesses with the focus of the organization on entrepreneurial printers & owner-operated businesses. Through working relationships with other graphics & print communication organizations, PrintImage International advances the interest of the industry domestically & internationally. The association produces the annual PrintImage tradeshow for the graphics & allied industries.
Number of Members: 1,600
2005 Meeting(s): The Quick Print Show, Orlando, FL, Feb 18-24, 2005
Publication(s): *PrintImage Network* (monthly, newsletter, free with membership)

Printing Association of Florida Inc

6275 Hazeltine National Dr, Orlando, FL 32822
Tel: 407-240-8009 *Fax:* 407-240-8333
Web Site: www.pafgraf.org
Key Personnel
Pres & CEO: Michael H Streibig
Sr Memb Serv Rep: Angela Regas
Trade association for the graphic arts industry.
Number of Members: 593
Publication(s): *Graphics Update* (monthly, free to members)

Printing Brokerage/Buyers Association

Subsidiary of PB/BA International Inc
PO Box 744, Palm Beach, FL 33480-0744
Tel: 561-586-9391 *Toll Free Tel:* 866-586-9391
   Fax: 561-845-7130
E-mail: info@pbbai.net
Web Site: www.pbbai.net
Key Personnel
Honorary Chmn: Vincent Mallardi
Pres & CFO: Merry Francen
Founded: 1985
Trade association for printing, sales brokerage & purchasing.
Number of Members: 785

Publication(s): *Brokerage* (5 times/yr, newsletter, free to members); *Hot Markets for Print* (annually, $675); *Law V: Printing* ($395); *PB/BA Sourcebook & Directory* (annually, free to members); *Reinvention of Print* ($195); *Why Use A Printing Independent* ($95)

Printing Industries of Maryland
2045 York Rd, 2nd fl, Timonium, MD 21093
Tel: 410-560-3300 *Toll Free Tel:* 800-560-3306
Fax: 410-560-3306
E-mail: pim@printmd.com
Web Site: www.printmd.com
Key Personnel
Pres: Arthur R Stowe
Number of Members: 380

Printing Industries of Wisconsin
Subsidiary of Printing Industries of America
13005 W Bluemount Rd, Brooksfield, WI 53005
Tel: 262-785-7040 *Fax:* 262-785-7043
E-mail: info@piw.org
Web Site: www.piw.org
Key Personnel
CEO & Pres: Niall Power
Number of Members: 150
Publication(s): *Monthly newsletter*

Printing Industry Association of the South
305 Plus Park Blvd, Nashville, TN 37217
Tel: 615-366-1094 *Toll Free Tel:* 800-821-3138
Fax: 615-366-4192
E-mail: info@pias.org
Web Site: www.pias.org
Key Personnel
Pres: Ed Chalifoux
Dir, PR: Whitney Pardue
Provide services & support to the printing industry.
Number of Members: 500
Publication(s): *Print South* (monthly, free with membership)

Protestant Church-Owned Publishers Association
748 Crabthicket Lane, St Louis, MO 63131
Tel: 314-505-7237 *Fax:* 314-505-7760
E-mail: pcpa@pcpanews.org
Web Site: www.pcpanews.org
Key Personnel
Exec Dir: Alan Meyer *E-mail:* meyerae@pcpanews.org
Number of Members: 36
Publication(s): *The Roundtable* (quarterly, newsletter)

Public Relations Society of America Inc
33 Maiden Lane, 11th fl, New York, NY 10038-5150
Tel: 212-460-1400 *Fax:* 212-995-0757
E-mail: hq@prsa.org
Web Site: www.prsa.org
Key Personnel
Exec Dir: Catherine Bolton
Association of public relations professionals dedicated to development & ethical practice of public relations.
Number of Members: 19,320
Publication(s): *Public Relations Tactics* (monthly, $44/yr); *The Strategist* (quarterly, $48/yr)

Publishers Association of the South (PAS)
4412 Fletcher St, Panama City, FL 32405-1017
Tel: 850-914-0766 *Fax:* 850-769-4348
E-mail: executive@pubsouth.org
Web Site: www.pubsouth.org
Key Personnel
Pres: Beth Wright
Assn Exec: Pat Sabiston
Founded: 1985
Trade association of Southern book publishers.

Number of Members: 130
New Election: Annually in Sept
Publication(s): *Manuscript Guidelines* ($20 PDF File, $35 in hardcopy, includes postage & handling); *PAS Newsletter* (Spring & Fall, free to members); *Southern Publishers Directory & New Book Announcements* (annually, free to members, $10 to all others)

Publishers Association of the West
PO Box 18157, Denver, CO 80218
Tel: 303-447-2320 *Fax:* 303-279-7111
E-mail: executivedirector@pubwest.org
Web Site: www.pubwest.org
Key Personnel
Exec Dir: Kalen Landow
Pres: Rick Rinehart
Founded: 1977
Members are small & medium-sized book publishers in the Western states & Canada. Supply marketing & technical information to members; conduct annual educational seminars; promote trade sales in the region. Trade show, including BEA, ALA, MPLA, MPBA, PNBA & Frankfurt.
Number of Members: 360
Publication(s): *The Endsheet* (quarterly, journal, free); *Publishers Association of the West Catalog & Directory* (annual, free)

Publishers Information Bureau (PIB)
810 Seventh Ave, 24th fl, New York, NY 10019
Tel: 212-872-3700 *Fax:* 212-888-4217
E-mail: pib@magazine.org
Web Site: www.magazine.org
Key Personnel
Pres: Wayne Eadie
Measure advertising linage & revenues in consumer magazines & newspaper supplements.
Number of Members: 250

Publishers Marketing Association (PMA)
627 Aviation Way, Manhattan Beach, CA 90266
Tel: 310-372-2732 *Fax:* 310-374-3342
E-mail: info@pma-online.org
Web Site: www.pma-online.org
Key Personnel
Exec Dir: Jan Nathan
Dir: Terry Nathan
A national nonprofit publishers' co-operative which coordinates discounted participation in major book & library exhibits & trade shows throughout the country, as well as ad placement in major publications & direct mail programs. Sponsor workshops, awards & prizes.
Number of Members: 4,000
New Election: Annually in May
Publication(s): *Membership & Service Directory*; *Newsletter & Sales Catalog of Members' Publications* (monthly)
Membership(s): ABA; ALA; BISG; Media Coalition

Quebec Writers' Federation
1200 Atwater Ave, Suite 3, Montreal, PQ H3Z 1X4, Canada
Tel: 514-933-0878
E-mail: admin@qwf.org
Web Site: www.qwf.org
Key Personnel
Admin Dir: Lori Schubert
Association of Quebec writers to promote English language writing in Quebec writing workshops & literary events.
Number of Members: 500
Publication(s): *QWrite* (quarterly, newsletter, free with membership)

Reference & User Services Association
Division of American Library Association
50 E Huron St, Chicago, IL 60611

Tel: 312-944-6780 *Toll Free Tel:* 800-545-2433
Fax: 312-280-3224
Web Site: www.ala.org
Key Personnel
Pres: Carol Brey-Casiano
Dir, Public Info: Mark Gould
Number of Members: 61,000
Publication(s): *American Libraries* (11 issues/yr, $6/issue, $60/yr, free to members)
Branch Office(s)
1301 Pennsylvania Ave NW, Suite 403, Washington, DC 20004

Reporters Committee for Freedom of the Press
1815 N Fort Myer Dr, Suite 900, Arlington, VA 22209-1817
Tel: 703-807-2100 *Toll Free Tel:* 800-336-4243
Fax: 703-807-2109
E-mail: rcfp@rcfp.org
Web Site: www.rcfp.org
Key Personnel
Exec Dir: Lucy Dalglish
Founded: 1970
Legal defense & research services for journalists & media lawyers.
Publication(s): *Access to Electronic Records* (handbook, $5); *Access to Places* ($3); *Agents of Discovery* (report, $3); *Can We Tape* ($3); *Confidential Sources & Information* ($3, handbook); *First Amendment Handbook* (handbook, $7.50); *FOI Guide Book* (handbook, $5); *The News Media & the Law* (quarterly, magazine, $30); *News Media Update* (biweekly, $60); *The Privacy Paradox* ($3); *Tapping Officials' Secrets: A State Open Government Compendium*

Research & Engineering Council of NAPL (National Association for Printing Leadership)
PO Box 1086, White Stone, VA 22578-1086
Tel: 804-436-9922 *Fax:* 804-436-9511
E-mail: recouncil@rivnet.net
Web Site: www.recouncil.org
Key Personnel
Man Dir: Ronald L Mihills
Nonprofit technical association.
Number of Members: 300
New Election: Annually in March
2005 Meeting(s): Binding, Finishing & Distribution Seminar, Marriott O'Hare, Chicago, IL, April 5-6, 2005
Publication(s): *Patents of Interest to the Graphic Arts Industry* (quarterly); *R & E Review* (quarterly)

Rocky Mountain Publishing Professionals Guild (RMPPG)
PO Box 17721, Boulder, CO 80308-7721
Tel: 303-447-0799
Web Site: RMPPG.org
Key Personnel
Pres: Alice Levine *Tel:* 303-447-0799
E-mail: alevineed@aol.com
Professional nonprofit freelancers association of editors, designers, indexers, researchers, writers, proofreaders & marketing & production specialists. Promotes the business & professional interests of its members through contact with publishers, clients & colleagues, enhancement of skills & standards & encouragement of professional ethics. Dues $35 annually.
Number of Members: 70
Publication(s): *Membership Directory* (Available upon request)

Romance Writers of America
16000 Stuebner Airline, Suite 140, Spring, TX 77379
Tel: 832-717-5200 *Fax:* 832-717-5201
E-mail: info@rwanational.org
Web Site: www.rwanational.org

Key Personnel
Exec Dir: Allison Kelley *E-mail:* akelley@rwanational.org
Promote recognition of the genre of romance writing as a serious book form. Conduct workshops, sponsor national & regional conferences & awards for members. Membership: $75/yr; $100/1st yr.
Number of Members: 9,000
2005 Meeting(s): RWA Conference, Reno Hilton Hotel, Reno, NV, July 27-30, 2005
2006 Meeting(s): RWA Conference, Atlanta Marriott Marquis, Atlanta, GA, July 26-29, 2006
Publication(s): *Bulletin Board* (monthly); *Romance Writers Report* (monthly, magazine)

SABEW, see Society of American Business Editors & Writers Inc

Saskatchewan Arts Board
2135 Broad St, Regina, SK S4P 3V7, Canada
Tel: 306-787-4056 *Toll Free Tel:* 800-667-7526 (Saskatchewan only) *Fax:* 306-787-4199
E-mail: sab@artsboard.sk.ca
Web Site: www.artsboard.sk.ca
Key Personnel
Exec Dir: Jeremy Morgan
Provide consultation, advice, grants, programs &/or services to individual artists, arts groups & organizations & members of the public. Programs support & encourage the development of artists, arts groups & organizations in the literary, performing, visual, media & multidisciplinary arts. Also develop & maintain a permanent collection of original works by Saskatchewan artists.

Science Fiction & Fantasy Writers of America Inc
PO Box 877, Chestertown, MD 21620
Toll Free Tel: 888-322-7392
E-mail: execdir@sfwa.org
Web Site: www.sfwa.org
Key Personnel
Pres: Jane Jewell
An organization of professional writers, editors, artists, agents & others in the science fiction & fantasy field.
Number of Members: 1,450
New Election: Annually in May
Publication(s): *Annual Membership Directory* ($60 non-members); *SFWA Bulletin* (quarterly, $18/yr non-members, $18.50 foreign)

Science Fiction Research Association Inc
6021 Grassmere, Corpus Christi, TX 78415
Tel: 512-855-9304
Key Personnel
Pres: Peter Brigg *E-mail:* pbrigg@uoguelph.ca
Professional study of science fiction & fantasy; annual scholar awards. Archives maintained at University of Kansas, Lawrence. Sponsor awards & prizes.
Number of Members: 350
Publication(s): *Annual Directory* (free to members); *SFRA Review* (6 issues/yr, free to members)

Screen Printing Technical Foundation
10015 Main St, Fairfax, VA 22031-3489
Tel: 703-385-1335 *Fax:* 703-273-0456
E-mail: sgia@sgia.org
Web Site: www.sgia.org
Key Personnel
Pres: Mike Robertson
Over 100 technical, managerial, educational, governmental, informational, safety, research services. Dozens of manuals on all aspects of screen printing & graphic imaging. Request a catalogue. Dozens of titles on technical, managerial, governmental, safety & education re-

lated to the screen printing industry; Educational/Technical Association.
Number of Members: 4,000
Publication(s): *Monthly Tabloid* (free to members); *SGIA Journal* (quarterly, free to members)

SF Canada
10438 86 Ave, Edmonton, AB T6E 2M5, Canada
Tel: 780-431-0562
Web Site: www.sfcanada.ca
Key Personnel
Pres: Candas Jane Dorsey
Founded: 1989
Number of Members: 110
Publication(s): *Communique* (quarterly, newsletter)

SHARP, see Society for the History of Authorship, Reading & Publishing Inc (SHARP)

The Bernard Shaw Society
Box 1159, Madison Square Sta, New York, NY 10159-1159
Tel: 212-989-7833; 212-982-9885
Key Personnel
Pres: Rhoda Nathan
VP & Ed: Daniel Leary; Sally Peters
Ed: Richard Nickson
Sec: Douglas Laurie
Founded: 1962
Sponsor monthly lectures & plays in New York City; publish journals on Shaw.
Number of Members: 400
Publication(s): *The Independent Shavian* (3 issues/yr, $20)

Short Mystery Fiction Society (SMFS)
1120 N 45 St, Waco, TX 76710
Web Site: groups.yahoo.com/group/shortmystery; www.shortmystery.net
Key Personnel
Pres: Michael Bracken *E-mail:* michael@crimefictionwriter.com
VP: Carol Kilgore
Founded: 1996
Online Yahoo group comprised of short story fiction writers. Current discussions on available market, sales & news related to the field of short story writing.
Number of Members: 500
New Election: June

Small Press Center
20 W 44 St, New York, NY 10036
Tel: 212-764-7021 *Fax:* 212-354-5365
E-mail: info@smallpress.org
Web Site: www.smallpress.org
Key Personnel
Exec Dir: Karin Taylor
National nonprofit association of independent publishers; exhibiting facility of small press books, hosting readings, publishing workshops, lectures & annual small press book fair. Published small press bibliographies of books for children, cookbooks & environmental books.
Number of Members: 1,000
Publication(s): *Book on Writing & Publishing: A Bibliography in Progress* ($39.95)

Small Publishers, Artists & Writers Network (SPAWN)
323 E Matilija St, Suite 110, PMB 123, Ojai, CA 93023
Tel: 818-886-4281 *Fax:* 818-886-3320
Web Site: www.spawn.org
Key Personnel
Pres: Patricia Fry *Tel:* 805-646-3045 *Fax:* 805-640-8213 *E-mail:* patricia@spawn.org

Tech Ed: Virginia Lawrence *E-mail:* virginia@spawn.org
Founded: 1996
Number of Members: 200

Small Publishers Association of North America (SPAN)
425 Cedar St, Buena Vista, CO 81211
Mailing Address: PO Box 1306, Buena Vista, CO 81211
Tel: 719-395-4790 *Fax:* 719-395-8374
E-mail: span@spannet.org
Web Site: www.spannet.org
Key Personnel
Exec Dir: Scott Flora *E-mail:* scott@spannet.org
Busn Mgr: Debi Flora
A trade association for independent presses, self-publishers & pro-active authors who want to sell more books.
Publication(s): *Span Connection* (monthly)

Social Sciences & Humanities Research Council of Canada (SSHRC)
350 Albert St, Ottawa, ON K1P 6G4, Canada
Mailing Address: PO Box 1610, Ottawa, ON K1P 6G4, Canada
Tel: 613-992-0691 *Fax:* 613-992-1787
E-mail: z-info@sshrc.ca
Web Site: www.sshrc.ca
Key Personnel
Pres: Marc Renaud *Tel:* 613-995-5488 *E-mail:* marc.renaud@sshrc.ca
Exec VP: Janet Halliwell *Tel:* 613-947-5265 *E-mail:* janet.halliwell@sshrc.ca
Exec Asst: Nicole Veillette *Tel:* 613-947-3275 *E-mail:* nicole.veillette@sshrc.ca
Founded: (SSHRC is a Federal Crown Corporation)
Offers two programs of support for scholarly publishing: Aid to scholarly publication program, aid to research & transfer journal program. Only Canadian citizens or permanent residents of Canada are eligible to apply under either program.
Number of Members: 22

Society for Scholarly Publishing
10200 W 44 Ave, Suite 304, Wheat Ridge, CO 80033-2840
Tel: 303-422-3914 *Fax:* 303-422-8894
E-mail: ssp@resourcecenter.com; info@sspnet.org
Web Site: www.sspnet.org
Key Personnel
Pres: Heather Joseph
Exec Dir: Francine Butler *E-mail:* fbutler@resourcecenter.com
Professional association for people in scholarly publishing industry; 12-16 seminars/workshops sponsored each year. Top Management Roundtable.
Number of Members: 800
2005 Meeting(s): Annual Meeting, Boston, MA, June 1-4, 2005
Publication(s): *Directory* (annually, only available to members)

Society for Technical Communication
901 N Stuart St, Suite 904, Arlington, VA 22203-1822
Tel: 703-522-4114 *Fax:* 703-522-2075
E-mail: stc@stc.org
Web Site: www.stc.org
Key Personnel
Exec Dir: Peter Herbst *Tel:* 703-522-4114 ext 250
Commun Dir: Maurice Martin *Tel:* 703-522-4114 ext 208
Professional society dedicated to the advancement of the theory & practice of technical communication in all media.
Number of Members: 25,000
Publication(s): *Intercom* (monthly, included in dues); *Technical Communication* (quarterly, free to members; $60/yr non-members)

Society for the History of Authorship, Reading & Publishing Inc (SHARP)
SHARP/University of South Carolina, PO Box 5816, Columbia, SC 29250
Tel: 803-777-5075 *Fax:* 803-782-0699
E-mail: membership@sharpweb.org
Web Site: www.sharpweb.org
Key Personnel
Pres: James L W West, III
Membership Sec: Barbara A Brannon *Tel:* 910-254-0308
Promotes the study of book history among academics & nonacademics.
Number of Members: 1,100
Publication(s): *Book History* (annual, journal, included with individual membership, $45/yr non-members & libraries); *SHARP Membership & Periodicals Directory* (annual, included with membership); *SHARP News* (quarterly, included with membership)

Society of American Business Editors & Writers Inc
Univ of Missouri, School of Journalism, 76 Gannett Hall, 134 Neff Annex, Columbia, MO 65211-1200
Tel: 573-882-7862 *Fax:* 573-884-1372
E-mail: sabew@missouri.edu
Web Site: www.sabew.org
Key Personnel
Pres: Rex Seline
Exec Dir: Carrie M Paden *E-mail:* padenc@missouri.edu
Founded: 1964
Professional development. Sponsor regional workshops. Specialize in business journalism.
Number of Members: 3,200
2005 Meeting(s): Society of American Business Editors & Writers Annual Convention & Exhibition, Red Lion Hotel, Seattle, WA, May 1-3, 2005
Publication(s): *The Business Journalist* (bimonthly, free to members, $65/yr non-members)

Society of American Travel Writers Foundation
1500 Sunday Dr, Suite 102, Raleigh, NC 27607
Tel: 919-861-5586 *Fax:* 919-787-4916
E-mail: satw@satw.org
Web Site: www.satw.org
Key Personnel
Pres: Milton Fullman
Membership Dir: Angela Battle
Number of Members: 1,250
Publication(s): *Directory of Members* ($195/yr print or diskette)

Society of Children's Book Writers & Illustrators (SCBWI)
8271 Beverly Blvd, Los Angeles, CA 90048
Tel: 323-782-1010 *Fax:* 323-782-1892
E-mail: membership@scbwi.org
Web Site: www.scbwi.org
Key Personnel
Pres: Steve Mooser
Exec Dir: Lin Oliver
Founded: 1968
An organization of children's writers & illustrators & others devoted to the interests of children's literature; annual workshops & conferences throughout the world.
Number of Members: 19,000
2005 Meeting(s): Winter Conference on Writing & Illustrating for Children, Hilton New York, Avenue of the Americas, New York, NY, Feb 5-6, 2005
Publication(s): *SCBWI Bulletin* (bimonthly, with membership)

Society of Illustrators (SI)
128 E 63 St, New York, NY 10021-7303

Tel: 212-838-2560 *Fax:* 212-838-2561
E-mail: info@societyillustrators.org
Web Site: www.societyillustrators.org
Key Personnel
Dir: Terrence Brown
Founded: 1901
Museum of American Illustration.
Number of Members: 950
New Election: Annually in June
Publication(s): *Annual of American Illustration* (annually, $49.95)

The Society of Midland Authors (SMA)
PO Box 10419, Chicago, IL 60610-0419
Tel: 773-506-7578 *Fax:* 773-784-5900
E-mail: info@midlandauthors.com
Web Site: www.midlandauthors.com
Key Personnel
Pres: R Craig Sautter *E-mail:* rcsautter@aol.com
Treas: Robert Remer
Corresponding Sec: Phyllis Ford Choyke
VP & Membership Sec: Tom Frisbie
   E-mail: tomfrisbie@aol.com
Newsletter Ed: Richard Frisbie
Recording Sec: Stella Pevsher
Webmaster: Mary Claire Hersh
   E-mail: maryclaire@prodigy.net
Founded: 1915
Monthly literary & professional programs, annual awards dinner, $300 & certificate, for best books of previous year in six categories: adult fiction & nonfiction, childrens fiction & nonfiction, poetry & biography.
Number of Members: 345
Publication(s): *Newsletter* (monthly)

Society of Motion Picture & Television Engineers (SMPTE)
595 W Hartsdale Ave, White Plains, NY 10607-1824
Tel: 914-761-1100 *Fax:* 914-761-3115
E-mail: smpte@smpte.org
Web Site: www.smpte.org
Key Personnel
Exec Dir: Frederick C Motts *Tel:* 914-761-1100 ext 106 *E-mail:* fmotts@smpte.org
Dir, Engg: Carlos V Girod, Jr *Tel:* 914-761-1100 ext 103
Dir, Pubns: David Juhren *Tel:* 914-761-1100 ext 107; David Juhren *Tel:* 914-761-1100 ext 107
To advance theory & practice of engineering in film, TV, motion imaging & allied arts & sciences; establishment of standards & practices.
Number of Members: 8,000
Publication(s): *SMPTE Journal* (monthly, journal)

Society of National Association Publications (SNAP)
8405 Greensboro Dr, No 800, McLean, VA 22102
Tel: 703-506-3285 *Fax:* 703-506-3266
E-mail: snapinfo@snaponline.org
Web Site: www.snaponline.org
Key Personnel
Exec Dir: Marilee Peterson *E-mail:* mpeterson@snaponline.org
SNAP is a non-profit professional society that serves the needs of association & society publications & their staff to represent, promote & advance the common interest of periodicals of voluntary associations & societies.
Number of Members: 625
2005 Meeting(s): SNAP Publications Management Conference, Washington, DC, June 2005; Publications Management Conference, Chicago, IL, Nov 2005
Publication(s): *Association Publishing* (bimonthly)

The Society of Professional Journalists
Eugene S Pulliam National Journalism Ctr, 3909 N Meridian St, Indianapolis, IN 46208
Tel: 317-927-8000 *Fax:* 317-920-4789

E-mail: spj@spj.org
Web Site: www.spj.org
Key Personnel
Exec Dir: Terrance G Harper *E-mail:* tharper@spj.org
Deputy Dir: Julie Grimes *E-mail:* jgrimes@spj.org
Promote professional development in journalism.
Number of Members: 10,000
2005 Meeting(s): National Convention, Las Vegas, NV, Autumn 2005
Publication(s): *Quill* (9 times/yr, $35/yr)

The Society of Southwestern Authors (SSA)
PO Box 30355, Tucson, AZ 85751-0355
Tel: 520-546-9382 *Fax:* 520-296-0409
E-mail: wporter202@aol.com
Web Site: www.azstarnet.com/nonprofit/ssa
Key Personnel
Pres: Mark Sneller, MD
Founded: 1972
Award one or more annual scholarships to promising new writers. Writers networking short story contest, 16 winning stories published in *The Story Teller* plus money prizes. Barnes & Noble $1,000, 3 first prizes for categories Short Fiction, Memoir, Poetry.
Number of Members: 600
2005 Meeting(s): Annual Writers' Workshop - Wrangling With Writing, Holiday Inn, Palo Verde, Tucson, AZ, USA, Jan 30, 31, 2005
Publication(s): *The Write Word* (bimonthly, newsletter, free to members)

Software & Information Industry Association (SIIA)
1090 Vermont Ave NW, 6th fl, Washington, DC 20005
Tel: 202-289-7442 *Fax:* 202-289-7097
E-mail: info@siia.net
Web Site: www.siia.net
Key Personnel
Pres: Ken Wasch
Dir, Mktg: Christina Stensvaag
Principal trade association of the software & information industry.
Number of Members: 850
Publication(s): *Membership Directory* (annual, free for members, $250 non-members); *Upgrade* (bimonthly, free for members, $79 non-members)

Southeast Booksellers Association (SEBA)
2611 Forest Dr, Suite 124, Columbia, SC 29204
Tel: 803-779-0118 *Toll Free Tel:* 800-331-9617 *Fax:* 803-779-0113
Web Site: www.sebaweb.org; arts.sebaweb.org (authors round the south); tradeshow.sebaweb.org (virtual trade show)
Key Personnel
Exec Dir: Wanda Jewell *E-mail:* wanda@sebaweb.org
The exclusive sponsor of the Spoken Word from Public Radio South. Book sense gift cerfiticates welcome at over 1,200 independent bookstores nationwide.
Number of Members: 500
2005 Meeting(s): Seba Trade Show, Adams Mark, Winston-Salem, NC, Sept 15-19, 2005
2006 Meeting(s): Seba Trade Show, Gaylord Palms Resort & Convention Center, Orlando, FL, Sept 8-10, 2006
Publication(s): *SEBA Holiday Catalog* (contact Ingram Book Co)

Spanish Evangelical Publishers Association (SEPA)/Asociacion de Editores Evangelicos Hispanos
1370 NW 88 Ave, Miami, FL 33172
Tel: 305-592-6136 *Fax:* 786-331-7720
E-mail: sepa@bmsi.com
Web Site: www.sepalit.org

Key Personnel
Pres: Esteban Fernandez
Exec Dir: David Ecklebarger
Treas: James L Cook
Evangelical books & Bibles. Service association to Evangelical publishers, distributors & suppliers.
Number of Members: 170
Publication(s): *Spanish Christian Books in Print*

Special Libraries Association (SLA)
313 S Patrick St, Alexandria, VA 22314
Tel: 703-647-4900 *Fax:* 703-647-4901
E-mail: sla@sla.org
Web Site: www.sla.org
Key Personnel
Deputy Dir: Lynn K Smith
Dir, PR: Anthony Blue *Tel:* 202-939-3633
Serial & nonserial publications; public relations; professional development; employment clearinghouse; resume referral service; computer-assisted, self-study programs; chapters, divisions, student groups & caucuses; government relations; fund development; scholarships; grants; honors & awards; annual conference & exhibit; winter meeting; information resources center.
Number of Members: 14,000

Tag & Label Manufacturers Institute Inc
40 Shuman Blvd, Suite 295, Naperville, IL 60563
Tel: 630-357-9222 *Fax:* 630-357-0192
E-mail: office@tlmi.com
Web Site: www.tlmi.com
Key Personnel
Exec Dir: Frank Sablone
Number of Members: 200
Publication(s): *Illuminator Newsletter* (bimonthly, $35/yr non-members)

Teachers & Writers Collaborative
5 Union Sq W, New York, NY 10003-3306
Tel: 212-691-6590 *Toll Free Tel:* 888-266-5789
Fax: 212-675-0171
E-mail: info@twc.org
Web Site: www.twc.org
Key Personnel
Publns Dir: Christopher Edgar *E-mail:* cedgar@twc.org
Ed: Christina Davis
Dist Mgr: Dierdra Colzie
Founded: 1967
Information source for those interested in teaching writing & literary arts; publish books & magazines about creative writing; distribute language arts books by various publishers; sponsor workshops. $35 per year for basic membership.
Publication(s): *Teachers & Writers* (5 issues/yr, $20/yr)

Technical Association of the Graphic Arts (TAGA)
68 Lomb Memorial Dr, Rochester, NY 14623-5604
Tel: 585-475-7470 *Fax:* 585-475-2250
E-mail: tagaofc@aol.com
Web Site: www.taga.org
Key Personnel
Pres: Bill Ray
Man Dir: Karen Lawrence
Annual conference; two focus group sessions held at conference (Color Issues; Ink, Paper & Press). Present TAGA Honors Awards, annually at each conference.
Number of Members: 800
2005 Meeting(s): TAGA 2005, Marriott Eaton Centre, Toronto, ON, Canada, April 17-20, 2005
Publication(s): *TAGA Proceedings* (annually)

Technical Association of the Pulp & Paper Industry (TAPPI)
15 Technology Pkwy S, Norcross, GA 30092
Tel: 770-446-1400 *Toll Free Tel:* 800-332-8686
Fax: 770-446-6947
E-mail: webmaster@tappi.org
Web Site: www.tappi.org
Key Personnel
Publg Dir: Mary Beth Cornell *E-mail:* mcornell@tappi.org
Corp Rel Dir: Clare Reagan *E-mail:* creagan@tappi.org
Corp Rel Coord: Kristi Ledbetter
Founded: 1915
Professional society of executives, operating managers, engineers, scientists & technologists serving the pulp, paper & allied industries.
Number of Members: 34,000
Publication(s): *TAPPI JOURNAL* (monthly); *TAPPI Membership Directory & Company Guide* (annual)

Texas Institute of Letters
3700 Mockingbird Lane, Dallas, TX 75205
Tel: 214-528-2655
Key Personnel
Pres: Mark Busby
VP: Joe Holley
Treas: Jim Hoggard
Sec: Fran Vick *E-mail:* franvick@aol.com
Sponsor awards for Texas-related books; cooperate in sponsorship of various writing fellowships.
Number of Members: 250
Publication(s): *Newsletter* (quarterly)

Text & Academic Authors Association Inc
PO Box 76477, St Petersburg, FL 33734-6477
Tel: 727-821-7277 *Fax:* 727-821-7271
E-mail: text@tampabay.rr.com
Web Site: www.taaonline.net
Key Personnel
Exec Dir: Ronald E Pynn *E-mail:* rpynn@tampabay.rr.com
Prog Asst: Janet Tucker
Founded: 1986
Number of Members: 1,100
Publication(s): *Academic Author* (monthly, $30/yr)

TNG Canada/CWA
Affiliate of The Newspaper Guild/CWA
7B-1050 Baxter Rd, Ottawa, ON K2C 3P1, Canada
Tel: 613-820-9777 *Toll Free Tel:* 877-486-4292
Fax: 613-820-8188
E-mail: info@tngcanada.org
Web Site: www.tngcanada.org
Key Personnel
Dir: Arnold Amber
Contact: Joanne Scheel
Union representing 8,972 members in Canada.
Number of Members: 8,972
Publication(s): *TNG Canada Today* (monthly)

Union des Ecrivaines et Ecrivains Quebecois
3492 avenue Laval, Montreal, PQ H2X 3C8, Canada
Tel: 514-849-8540 *Toll Free Tel:* 888-849-8540
Fax: 514-271-6239
E-mail: ecrivez@uneq.qc.ca
Web Site: www.uneq.qc.ca
Key Personnel
Pres: Bruno Roy
VP: Joel Des Rosiers
Dir, Commun: Ariane Bertouille
Founded: 1977
A writer's union.
Number of Members: 1,000

United Nations Association of the United States of America Inc
801 Second Ave, 2nd fl, New York, NY 10017
Tel: 212-907-1300 *Fax:* 212-682-9185
E-mail: unadc@unausa.org
Web Site: www.unausa.org *Cable:* UNASAMER
Key Personnel
Pres: William H Luers
Publications, non-profit information & educational services about international affairs & organizations.
Number of Members: 25,000

Upper Midwest Booksellers Association (UMBA)
3407 W 44 St, Minneapolis, MN 55410
Tel: 612-926-5868 *Toll Free Tel:* 800-784-7522
Fax: 612-926-6657
E-mail: umbaoffice@aol.com
Web Site: www.abookaday.com
Key Personnel
Exec Dir: Susan Walker
Asst Dir: Kati Gallagher *E-mail:* ktatumba@aol.com
Association of independent bookstores in Upper Midwest. Annual trade show & meeting. Readers book catalog for member stores to use with consumers. Educational programs for booksellers. Spring meeting.
Number of Members: 500
New Election: Annually in Sept
Publication(s): *Membership Directory* (annual); *Newsletter* (4 issues/yr, free to members); *Readers Catalog* (annual)

US Board on Books For Young People (USBBY)
Division of International Board on Books for Young People (IBBY)
c/o IRA, 800 Barksdale Rd, Newark, DE 19714
Mailing Address: PO Box 8139, Newark, DE 19714-8139
Tel: 302-731-1600 (ext 297) *Fax:* 302-731-1057
E-mail: usbby@reading.org
Web Site: www.usbby.org
Founded: 1953
Promotion of children's books & reading.
Number of Members: 500
2005 Meeting(s): 6th IBBY Regional Conference, Callaway Gardens, Pine Mountain, GA, Oct 28-30, 2005
Publication(s): *USBBY Newsletter* (semiannual, $25)

U.S.A. Books Abroad Inc®
46 Willow Dr, Briarcliff Manor, NY 10510
Tel: 914-762-2400 *Fax:* 914-762-2407
E-mail: booksabroad@optonline.net
Web Site: www.usabooksabroad.com
Key Personnel
Pres: Edward A Malinowski
Founded: 1983
Celebrating 70 years.....of bringing opportunities to Publishers & the Book Trade to make new profits from changing book markets in the US & abroad. U.S.A. Books Abroad, Inc® is certified by the US Department of Commerce under the Export Trading Act of 1982. Our focus is to assist The American Collective Stand, Inc® to make books affordable in all countries & enable Publishers & the Book Trade to buy & sell rights year round & develop strategic distribution alliances.

USBE: United States Book Exchange
2969 W 25 St, Cleveland, OH 44113
Tel: 216-241-6960 *Fax:* 216-241-6966
E-mail: usbe@usbe.com
Web Site: www.usbe.com
Key Personnel
Man Dir: John T Zubal; Marilyn Zubal

Redistribution of library materials to & from libraries.
Number of Members: 15,888

Veterans of Foreign Wars of the US
406 W 34 St, Kansas City, MO 64111
Tel: 816-756-3390 *Fax:* 816-968-1169
E-mail: info@vfw.org
Web Site: www.vfw.org
Key Personnel
Adjutant Gen: John Senk
Fraternal, patriotic, educational organization concentrating in service to veterans & their families & national security & foreign affairs & community service.
Number of Members: 1,800,000
Publication(s): *VFW Magazine* (10 issues/yr, free to members, $15 non-members)

Visual Artists & Galleries Association Inc (VAGA)
350 Fifth Ave, Suite 2820, New York City, NY 10118
Tel: 212-736-6666 *Fax:* 212-736-6767
E-mail: info@vagarights.com
Key Personnel
Exec Dir: Robert Panzer *E-mail:* rpanzer@vagarights.com
Licensing Exec: Andrea Mihavolic
Protects artists copyrights; provides art licensing & reproduction rights clearances & royalties collection for artists. Have archive of color transparencies & B&W images.
Number of Members: 18,000

Washington Independent Writers (WIW)
733 15 St NW, Suite 220, Washington, DC 20005
Tel: 202-737-9500 *Fax:* 202-638-7800
E-mail: info@washwriter.org
Web Site: www.washwriter.org
Key Personnel
Exec Dir: Donald O Graul, Jr *E-mail:* donald@washwriter.org
Founded: 1975
Established to promote the mutual interests of freelance writers & to provide a variety of services to members.
Number of Members: 1,500
Publication(s): *Directory of Members* (available online only to members); *The Washington Writer* (monthly, available online only)

Web Offset Association
200 Deer Run Rd, Sewickley, PA 15143
Tel: 412-741-6860 *Toll Free Tel:* 800-910-4283
Fax: 412-741-2311
Web Site: www.gain.net
Key Personnel
Exec Dir: Thomas Basore *E-mail:* tbasore@printing.org
Printing Trade Association members work in Web Offset, Heatset printing. Meetings, publications.
Number of Members: 7,500
New Election: Annually in May
2005 Meeting(s): Annual Web Offset Association Conference, Gaylord Texan Resort, Grapevine, TX, May 2-4, 2005
Publication(s): *Heatset Directory of Press Installations* (biennial-odd yrs); *Product Catalog of Heatset Companies* (biennial-even yrs)

Web Printing Association
Division of Printing Industries of America Inc
100 Daingerfield Rd, Alexandria, VA 22314
Tel: 703-519-8100 *Toll Free Tel:* 800-742-2666
Fax: 703-519-7109
Web Site: www.gain.net
Key Personnel
Exec Dir: Thomas B Basore *E-mail:* tbasore@printing.org

Printing Trade Association, members work in Coldset/Non-Heatset Web printing. Meetings, publications & awards competition.
Number of Members: 3,500
Publication(s): *Coldset/Non-Heatset Web* (biennial-odd yrs); *Product Catalog of Coldset/Non-Heat Web Companies* (biennial-even yrs)

West Coast Book People Association
27 McNear Dr, San Rafael, CA 94901-1545
Tel: 415-459-1227 *Fax:* 415-459-1227
Key Personnel
Sec: Frank Goodall *E-mail:* goodall@ucsbalom.com
Founded: 1936
Education & fellowship.
Number of Members: 200
Publication(s): *Newsletter* (irregular, free to members)

Western Writers of America Inc
1012 Fair St, Franklin, TN 37064
Tel: 615-791-1444 *Fax:* 615-791-1444
Web Site: www.westernwriters.org
Key Personnel
Pres: Rita Cleary *E-mail:* rmcleary@mindspring.com
VP: Cotton Smith
Sec & Treas: James A Crutchfield
  E-mail: tncrutch@aol.com
Founded: 1953
Nonprofit confederation of professional writers of fiction & nonfiction pertaining to, or inspired by tradition, legends, development & history of the American West.
Number of Members: 650
New Election: Feb 2005
2005 Meeting(s): Annual Conference, Spokane, WA, June 14-18, 2005
2006 Meeting(s): Annual Conference, Cody, WY, June 2006
Publication(s): *Roundup Magazine* (6 times/yr, $30/yr US, $50/yr foreign)

Willamette Writers
9045 SW Barbur Blvd, Suite 5-A, Portland, OR 97219
Tel: 503-452-1592 *Fax:* 503-452-0372
E-mail: wilwrite@willamettewriters.com
Web Site: www.willamettewriters.com
Key Personnel
Off Mgr: Bill Johnson
Monthly meeting (open to public); critique groups; writer referrals; monthly newsletter; annual literary contest, annual conference.
Number of Members: 900
Publication(s): *The Willamette Writer* (monthly, free to members)

Women In Production
276 Bowery, New York, NY 10012
Tel: 212-334-2106 *Fax:* 212-431-5786
E-mail: office@wip.org
Web Site: www.wip.org
Key Personnel
Exec Dir: Katerina Caterisano
600 men & women who are graphic arts professionals. Individuals from print, publishing & paper industries.
Number of Members: 600
New Election: Annually in June

Women Who Write
PO Box 652, Madison, NJ 07940
Tel: 908-232-1640 *Fax:* 908-317-8105
E-mail: info@womenwhowrite.org
Web Site: www.womenwhowrite.org
Key Personnel
Pres: Patrica Weissner

Contact: Lois Sarvetnick *E-mail:* lsarvetnick@aol.com
Writing groups, workshops, readings, literary events, a newsletter, a literary magazine.
Number of Members: 75
Publication(s): *Goldfinch: The Literary Magazine of Women Who Write* (annual); *Writer's Notes Newsletter* (quarterly)

Women's National Book Association Inc
c/o Susannah Greenberg Public Relations, 2166 Broadway, Suite 9-E, New York, NY 10024
Tel: 212-208-4629 *Fax:* 212-208-4629
E-mail: publicity@bookbuzz.com
Web Site: www.wnba-books.org
Key Personnel
Natl Pres: Jill A Tardiff
Natl Treas: Amy Barden
Increase opportunities for women & recognition of women in the world of books. Sponsor Women's National Book Association Award (formerly Constance Lindsay Skinner Award), Lucile Micheels Pannell Award & Ann Heidbreder Eastman Grant. Ten chapters: Atlanta, Binghamton, Boston, Dallas, Detroit, Los Angeles, Nashville, New York, San Francisco, Washington, DC.
Number of Members: 1,000
New Election: Biennially in May
Publication(s): *The Bookwoman* (3 issues/yr, free to members)

Writers' Alliance of Newfoundland & Labrador
Box 2681, St Johns, NF A1C 6K1, Canada
Tel: 709-739-5215 *Fax:* 709-739-5931
E-mail: wanl@nfld.com
Web Site: www.writersalliance.nf.ca
Founded: 1987
Not-for-profit organization established to create a supportive environment for writers & work towards the enhancement of literacy in our province.
Number of Members: 250
New Election: Oct

Writers' Alliance of Newfoundland & Labrador
155 Water St, Suite 102, St John's, NF A1C 6K1, Canada
Mailing Address: PO Box 2681, St John's, NF A1C 5M5, Canada
Tel: 709-739-5215 *Fax:* 709-739-5931
E-mail: wanl@nfld.com
Web Site: www.writersalliance.nf.ca
Key Personnel
Exec Dir: Libby Creelman
Founded: 1987
Organization of writers. Also publish literacy books for level 1 adult basic education, written by members, funded by federal grants.
Number of Members: 200

Writers Federation of Nova Scotia
1113 Marginal Rd, Halifax, NS B3H 4P7, Canada
Tel: 902-423-8116 *Fax:* 902-422-0881
E-mail: talk@writers.ns.ca
Web Site: www.writers.ns.ca
Key Personnel
Exec Dir: Jane Buss
Founded: 1975
Number of Members: 700

Writer's Guild of Alberta, see Banff Centre

Writers Guild of America East Inc (WGAE)
555 W 57 St, New York, NY 10019
Tel: 212-767-7800 *Fax:* 212-582-1909
E-mail: info@wgaeast.org
Web Site: www.wgaeast.org

Key Personnel
Pres: Herb Sargent
VP: Warren Leight
Exec Dir: Mona Mangan
Admin Dir: Uma Sarada
Sec-Treas: Gail Lee
Labor union representing professional writers in motion pictures, TV & radio. Membership available only through the sale of literary material or employment for writing services in one of these areas.
Number of Members: 4,200
Publication(s): *WGA East Newsletter* (quarterly, newsletter, $22/yr)

Writers Guild of America West Inc (WGAW)
7000 W Third St, Los Angeles, CA 90048
Tel: 323-951-4000 *Fax:* 323-782-4800
Web Site: www.wga.org
Key Personnel
Asst Exec Dir: Cheryl Rhoden
Labor union: collective bargaining representation for film, broadcast, interactive & new media writers. Awards dinner & seminars (sometimes for public).
Number of Members: 9,000
Publication(s): *Written By Magazine* (monthly exc Dec/Jan, $40/yr)

Writers' Haven Writers (WHW)
2244 Fourth Ave, San Diego, CA 92101
Tel: 619-696-0569
Key Personnel
Exec Dir: William H Martinez
Natl Co-Chmn: Jean Jenkins *E-mail:* bjinkss@aol.com; Michael Steven Gregory
State Dir, NY: Joe Renaldi
State Dir, OK: Joel Rizzo
State Dir, CO: John Stafford
Offers writers affiliation with a national organization; offer lifetime memberships & no dues. New members are nominated only by current WHWs in good standing. Workshops &/or informal gatherings of WHWs are sponsored by the WHWs involved, with the consent of their state director &/or the WHW headquarters in San Diego, whose officers gather weekly.
Number of Members: 200
Publication(s): *WHW Membership Directory* (members only, cost plus postage)

Writers-In-Exile Center, American Branch
42 Derby Ave, Orange, CT 06477
Tel: 203-397-1479 *Fax:* 203-785-4744; 203-397-5439
Key Personnel
Pres: Clara Gyorgyey *E-mail:* gyorgyey@aol.com
Helping imprisoned writers & their families; sponsor workshops, awards & prizes.
Number of Members: 104
Publication(s): *Newsletter* (quarterly)

Writers' League of Texas
1501 W Fifth St, Suite E-2, Austin, TX 78703
Tel: 512-499-8914 *Fax:* 512-499-0441
E-mail: wlt@writersleague.org
Web Site: www.writersleague.org
Key Personnel
Exec Dir: Helen Ginger *E-mail:* helen@writersleague.org
Workshops, seminars, classes, library resource center, technical assistance, audiotapes, newsletter, monthly programs, educational programs for young people. Memberships $50, $45 students & seniors, $70 family.
Number of Members: 1,600
New Election: Oct
Publication(s): *Scribe* (quarterly, free to members)

Writers' Union of Canada
90 Richmond St E, Suite 200, Toronto, ON M5C 1P1, Canada
Tel: 416-703-8982 *Fax:* 416-504-9090
E-mail: info@writersunion.ca
Web Site: www.writersunion.ca
Key Personnel
Exec Dir: Deborah Windsor
Project Coord: Allison Hrabluik
Assoc Dir: Siobhan O'Connor
Specialize in service for members & non-members including publications, newsletter, contract advice, competitions, ms evaluation & advocacy.
Number of Members: 1,400

Foundations

Listed below are foundations that are closely affiliated with the book trade.

Books for Asia
Division of The Asia Foundation
80 Elmira St, San Francisco, CA 94124
Tel: 415-656-8990 *Fax:* 415-468-8379
Web Site: www.asiafoundation.org
Key Personnel
Dir: Gavin Tritt
Founded: 1954
A program of the Asia Foundation that has distributed well over 36 million books, journals & non-print educational resources to libraries, schools, universities & research centers in over 40 nations throughout Asia since 1954. Averages over 500,000 books per year in all educational fields at all educational levels sent to Asia Foundation field offices located throughout the region. Books are distributed by Foundation staff to recipient institutions based on requests received by our staff from representatives of those needy organizations. The overwhelming majority of books distributed are donated new books to the Asia Foundation by American publishers. Publishers may receive a tax deduction of up to twice the manufacturing cost for each book donated to qualified 501©(3) nonprofit organizations, such as the Asia Foundation. Monetary donations welcomed.

Bridge to Asia
665 Grant Ave, San Francisco, CA 94108
Tel: 415-678-2990 *Fax:* 415-678-2996
E-mail: asianet@bridge.org
Web Site: www.bridge.org
Key Personnel
Pres: Jeffrey Smith *Tel:* 415-678-2994
  E-mail: jasmith@well.com
A nonprofit book-donation program, which provides donated books, journals & Internet based research services to developing countries in Asia. Primary book-donors include members of the National Association of College Stores, American Council of Learned Societies, the Nebraska Book Company, Follett Higher Education Group & several thousand individual book donors.
Membership(s): National Association of College Stores

The Canadian Writers' Foundation Inc/La fondation des ecrivains canadiens
PO Box 13281, Kanata Sta, Ottawa, ON K2K 1X4, Canada
Tel: 613-256-6937 *Fax:* 613-256-5457
Web Site: www.canauthors.org/cwf
Key Personnel
Exec Sec: Suzanne Williams *E-mail:* smw. enterprises@sympatico.ca
Founded: 1931
Benevolent trust. Raises money for needy yet distinguished Canadian writers.

The Century Foundation Press
41 E 70 St, New York, NY 10021
Tel: 212-535-4441 *Fax:* 212-535-7534
Web Site: www.tcf.org
Key Personnel
Pres: Richard C Leone

VP & Dir, Pubns: Beverly Goldberg
Engaged in research & public education on significant contemporary policy issues. Emphasis on international political affairs, national, economic & social questions, government & media issues. No grants to institutions or individuals, but foundation will review independent project proposals within program guidelines as well as soliciting its own.

Graphic Arts Education & Research Foundation (GAERF)
1899 Preston White Dr, Reston, VA 20191-4367
Tel: 703-264-7200 *Fax:* 703-620-3165
E-mail: gaerf@npes.org
Web Site: www.npes.org
Key Personnel
Pres: Regis J Delmontagne
Dir: Eileen D Cassidy
Financial support for educational projects & research designed to enhance the future of the graphic communications industry. Provide grants for improving the quality of teaching, attracting qualified teachers & students & solving manpower problems in graphic communications field. Also, environmental, educational & emerging technologies projects in graphic communications field. Grants are made to individuals, groups of individuals, schools or institutions.

John Simon Guggenheim Memorial Foundation
90 Park Ave, New York, NY 10016
Tel: 212-687-4470 *Fax:* 212-697-3248
E-mail: fellowships@gf.org
Web Site: www.gf.org
Key Personnel
Pres: Edward Hirsch
Sr VP & Sec: G Thomas Tanselle
VP & CFO: Coleen Higgins-Jacob
VP & Dir, Planning & Latin American Prog: Peter F Kardon
Dir, Devt & PR: Richard W Hatter
Founded: 1925
Provide fellowships to further the development of scholars & artists by assisting them to engage in research in any field of knowledge & creation in any of the arts; awarded to persons who have already demonstrated exceptional capacity for productive scholarship or exceptional creative ability in the arts.

Heldref Publications
Division of Helen Dwight Reid Educational Foundation
1319 18 St NW, Washington, DC 20036
Tel: 202-296-6267 *Toll Free Tel:* 800-365-9753
  Fax: 202-293-6130
E-mail: subscribe@heldref.org
Web Site: www.heldref.org
Key Personnel
Exec Dir: Douglas J Kirkpatrick
Promos Mgr: Jean Kline *E-mail:* jkline@heldref.org
Publisher of educational journals & magazines.

The Heritage Foundation
214 Massachusetts Ave NE, Washington, DC 20002-4999
Tel: 202-546-4400 *Fax:* 202-546-8328
Web Site: www.heritage.org *Telex:* 44-0235
  Cable: HERITAGE WASH DC
Key Personnel
Pres: Edwin J Feulner, Jr
Exec VP: Phil N Truluck
VP, Fin & Oper: Ted Schlenski
VP, PR: Rebecca Hagelin
VP, Govt Rel: Mike Franc
A tax exempt public policy research institute; complete publications list on request.

The National Endowment for the Arts
Nancy Hanks Ctr, 1100 Pennsylvania Ave NW, Room 720, Washington, DC 20506-0001
Tel: 202-682-5428 *Fax:* 202-682-5669
Web Site: www.arts.gov
Key Personnel
Dir, Lit: Cliff Becker
Lit Asst: James McNeel *Tel:* 202-682-5092
  E-mail: ncneelj@arts.gov
Grant-giving agency. Give grants to non-profit literary organizations. Guidelines available on website.

Sabre Foundation Inc
872 Massachusetts Ave, Suite 2-1, Cambridge, MA 02139
Tel: 617-868-3510 *Fax:* 617-868-7916
E-mail: sabre@sabre.org
Web Site: www.sabre.org
Key Personnel
Book Prog Mgr: Colin McCullough
  E-mail: colin@sabre.org
Book donation agency. Receives donated books & CD-ROMs from publishers & other donors & places them with libraries & educational institutions in Africa, Eastern Europe, the Former Soviet Union & selected countries in other regions of the world.

Western States Arts Federation
1743 Wazee St, Suite 300, Denver, CO 80202
Tel: 303-629-1166 *Fax:* 303-629-9717
E-mail: staff@westaf.org
Web Site: www.westaf.org
Key Personnel
Info Specialist: Valentine Sieferman
Fin: Adrianne Devereux
Performing, visual & folk arts programs in addition to literature program.

H W Wilson Foundation
950 University Ave, Bronx, NY 10452-4224
Tel: 718-588-8400 *Toll Free Tel:* 800-367-6770
  Fax: 718-538-2716 *Toll Free Fax:* 800-367-6770
E-mail: custserv@hwwilson.com
Web Site: www.hwwilson.com
Key Personnel
Pres & CEO: William Stanton
Scholarship program for American Library Association accredited library schools & grants for library-related research.

Calendar of Book Trade & Promotional Events— Alphabetical Index of Sponsors

Newsletter & Electronic Publishers Association
International Newsletter & Specialized - Information Conference
June 2005, pg 726
NEPA's Annual Fall Conference
Autumn 2005, pg 728

Newspaper Association of America (NAA)
Newspaper Association of America Annual Convention
April 2005, pg 723
April 2006, pg 734
May 2007, pg 737
NEXPO®
March 2005, pg 722
April 2006, pg 734
April 2007, pg 737

Nigeria International Book Fair
Nigeria International Book Fair
May 2005, pg 725

North American Agricultural Journalists
North American Agricultural Journalists Spring Meeting
April 2005, pg 723
April 2006, pg 734

Northern Arizona Book Festival
Northern Arizona Book Festival
April 2005, pg 723

NPES The Association for Suppliers of Printing, Publishing & Converting Technologies
NPES The Association for Suppliers of Printing, Publishing and Converting Technologies Annual Conference
October 2005, pg 731

Outdoor Writers Association of America
Outdoor Writers Association of America Annual Conference
June 2005, pg 727

Pacific Printing & Imaging Association
Print Buyers Conference
May 2005, pg 725

Packaging Machinery Manufacturers Institute
PACK EXPO International
October 2006, pg 735
PACK EXPO Las Vegas
September 2005, pg 730
October 2007, pg 738

Penton Media
Internet World North
June 2005, pg 727

Periodical Writers' Association of Canada
Periodical Writers' Association of Canada Annual General Meeting
May 2005, pg 725

Photographic Society of America Inc (PSA)
PSA International Conference of Photography
August 2005, pg 728
September 2006, pg 735
September 2007, pg 738

Post Newsweek Tech Media
FOSE
April 2005, pg 723

Poznan International Fair Ltd
Infosystem Fairs
April 2005, pg 723
Poligrafia
Spring 2005, pg 720

Primedia Business Exhibitions
The National Center for Database Marketing (NCDM)
Summer 2005, pg 726
Winter 2005, pg 732

PrintImage International
The Quick Print Show
February 2005, pg 720

Printing Association of Florida Inc
Graphics of the Americas
February 2005, pg 720

Printing Industries of America Inc
Print Sales & Marketing Executives Conference
June 2005, pg 727

Publishers Association of the South (PAS)
Publishers Association of the South Fall Conference & Annual Meeting
September 2005, pg 730
Publishers Winter Conclave
January 2005, pg 719

Rain Taxi Review of Books
Twin Cities Book Festival
Autumn 2005, pg 729

Reed Exhibitions
BookExpo America (BEA)
June 2005, pg 726

Reed Exhibitions Canada
BookExpo Canada
June 2005, pg 726

Reed Exhibitions Japan Ltd
DP: Digital Publishing Fair
July 2005, pg 727
TIBF: Tokyo International Book Fair
July 2005, pg 728

Reed Exhibitions (UK)
London Book Fair
March 2005, pg 721
Northprint
April 2005, pg 724

Reed Expositions France
Salon du Livre de Jeunesse (Childrens Book Fair)
November 2006, pg 736
Salon du Livre de Paris
March 2005, pg 722

Reed Messe Salzburg GmbH
Dataprint
April 2005, pg 723

Reed Midem
MILIA: World Interactive Content Forum
April 2005, pg 723

Reed Tradex Co Ltd
AsiaPack AsiaPrint
June 2005, pg 726

Research & Engineering Council of NAPL (National Association for Printing Leadership)
Binding, Finishing & Distribution Seminar
April 2005, pg 722

Romance Writers of America
RWA Annual National Conference
July 2005, pg 728
July 2006, pg 734
July 2007, pg 737
July 2008, pg 739
July 2009, pg 740

SABEW, see Society of American Business Editors & Writers Inc

Salon du Livre de Montreal
Salon du Livre de Montreal
November 2005, pg 732

The Dorothy L Sayers Society
The Dorothy L Sayers Society Annual Convention
August 2005, pg 728
Summer 2007, pg 737

School Library Association
School Library Association Annual Conference
June 2005, pg 727

Science Fiction Research Association Inc
Science Fiction Research Association Annual Meeting
June 2005, pg 727

Small Press Center
Small Press Book Fair
December 2005, pg 732

Small Publishers Association of North America (SPAN)
SPAN Conference
October 2005, pg 731

Society for Imaging Science & Technology (IS&T)
Color Imaging Conference - Color Science Systems & Applications
November 2005, pg 731
DPP 2005 - International Conference on Digital Production Printing
May 2005, pg 724
IS&T Archiving Conference
April 2005, pg 723
NIP 21: The 21st International Congress on Digital Printing Technologies
September 2005, pg 730

Society for Scholarly Publishing
Society for Scholarly Publishing Annual Meeting
June 2005, pg 727

Society of American Business Editors & Writers Inc
Society of American Business Editors & Writers Annual Convention & Exhibition
May 2005, pg 725

Society of Children's Book Writers & Illustrators (SCBWI)
Winter Conference on Writing & Illustrating for Children
February 2005, pg 720

The Society of Professional Journalists
Society of Professional Journalists National Convention
October 2005, pg 731

South African Booksellers Association
South African Booksellers Association Annual Conference
August 2005, pg 728
August 2006, pg 735

Southeast Booksellers Association (SEBA)
Southeast Booksellers Association Annual Meeting & Trade Show
September 2005, pg 730
September 2006, pg 735

Southern California Writers' Conference San Diego
Southern California Writers' Conference San Diego
February 2005, pg 720

Southern Kentucky Book Fest
Southern Kentucky Book Fest
April 2005, pg 724

Spanish Evangelical Publishers Association (SEPA)/Associacion de Editores Evangelicos and Editorial Unilit
EXPOLIT Exposicion de Literatura Cristiana Book Fair
May 2005, pg 725
May 2006, pg 734
May 2007, pg 737
May 2008, pg 738
May 2009, pg 739
May 2010, pg 740

Special Libraries Association (SLA)
Special Libraries Association Annual Conference
June 2005, pg 727
June 2006, pg 734
June 2007, pg 737
July 2008, pg 739
Special Libraries Association Leadership Summit
January 2005, pg 719

SPIE - The International Society for Optical Engineering
IS&T/SPIE Electronic Imaging Science & Technology
January 2005, pg 719

State Library of Louisiana
Louisiana Book Festival
October 2005, pg 730

Technical Association of the Pulp & Paper Industry (TAPPI)
AICC/TAPPI SuperCorrExpo® 2008
Autumn 2008, pg 739
Paper Expo
May 2005, pg 725
TAPPI Fall Technical Conference
August 2005, pg 728

Texas Book Festival
Texas Book Festival
October 2005, pg 731

Texas Graphic Arts Educational Foundation
Southwestern Graphics
May 2005, pg 725

Texas Outdoor Writers Association
Texas Outdoor Writers Association Annual Conference
March 2005, pg 722

Times Business Information Pte Ltd
World Book Fair
Spring 2005, pg 721

Tuyap Fuar ve Kongre Merkezi
Istanbul Book Fair
Autumn 2005, pg 728
Izmir Book Fair
Spring 2005, pg 720

UK Serials Group
UK Serials Group Annual Conference & Exhibition
April 2005, pg 724
April 2006, pg 734

Utah Humanities Council
Great Salt Lake Book Festival
September 2005, pg 729

Virginia Foundation for the Humanities
Virginia Festival of the Book
March 2005, pg 722
March 2006, pg 733
March 2007, pg 736
March 2008, pg 738
March 2009, pg 739

VNU Exhibitions Europe
Online Information & Content Management Europe
November 2005, pg 732

Vystaviste Flora Olomouc
Literary Festival
March 2005, pg 721

Web Offset Association
Annual Web Offset Association Conference
May 2005, pg 725
Spring 2006, pg 733

Weltverband der Lehrmittelfirmen, see Worlddidac

World Association of Publishers, Manufacturers & Distributors of Educational Materials, see Worlddidac

Worlddidac
China Didac/WORLDDIDAC
October 2005, pg 730
WORLDDIDAC Brazil 2005
November 2005, pg 732
WORLDDIDAC Mexico 2005
March 2005, pg 722

Writer's Summer School
SWANICK: The Writer's Summer School
August 2005, pg 728

Xplor International
Xplor Global Conference
November 2005, pg 732
November 2006, pg 736

Zimbabwe International Book Fair
Zimbabwe International Book Fair
August 2005, pg 728

Calendar of Book Trade & Promotional Events— Alphabetical Index of Events

Zimbabwe International Book Fair
August 2005, pg 728

Calendar of Book Trade & Promotional Events

Arranged chronologically by year and month, this section lists book trade events worldwide. Preceding to this section are two indexes: the Sponsor Index is an alphabetical list of event sponsors and includes the names and dates of the events they sponsor; the Event Index is an alphabetical list of events along with the dates on which they are held.

For more information on tradeshows, conferences and conventions that include exhibits in such areas as publishing, printing, art, photography, radio, TV and cable, see the current editions of the *Tradeshow Week Data Book* (Tradeshow Week, 5700 Wilshire Blvd., Suite 120, Los Angeles, CA 90036-5804).

2005

JANUARY

American Library Association Mid-Winter Meeting
Sponsored by American Library Association (ALA)
50 E Huron St, Chicago, IL 60611
Toll Free Tel: 800-545-2433 *Fax:* 312-944-6780
E-mail: ala@ala.org
Web Site: www.ala.org/events
Key Personnel
Public Info Dir: Mark Gould
Press Officer: Larra Clark
Location: Boston, MA, USA
Jan 14-19, 2005

Cairo International Book Fair
Sponsored by General Egyptian Book Organization
Corniche el-Nil - Ramlet Boulac, Cairo 11221, Egypt (Arab Republic of Egypt)
Tel: (02) 5799635; (02) 5775228; (02) 5775109; (02) 5775367; (02) 5775436; (02) 5775545; (02) 5775000 *Fax:* (02) 5765058; (02) 5799635
E-mail: info@egyptianbook.org
Web Site: www.cibf.org; www.egyptianbook.org
Cable: GEBO
Key Personnel
Chairman: Dr Mohamed Samir Sarhan
Location: Nasr City Fairground, Cairo, Egypt
Jan 26-Feb 8, 2005

CBA Advance
Formerly CBA Expo
Sponsored by CBA
9240 Explorer Dr, Colorado Springs, CO 80920-5001
Mailing Address: PO Box 62000, Colorado Springs, CO 80962-2000
Tel: 719-265-9895 *Toll Free Tel:* 800-252-1950
Fax: 719-272-3510
E-mail: info@cbaonline.org
Web Site: www.cbaonline.org
Key Personnel
Pres: William Anderson *E-mail:* banderson@cbaonline.org
VP & COO: Dorothy Gore
Convention & Expositions Mgr: Scott Graham
Location: Opryland Hotel, Nashville, TN, USA
Jan 31-Feb 4, 2005

ECPA Trade Show
Sponsored by Evangelical Christian Publishers Association
4816 S Ash Ave, Suite 101, Tempe, AZ 85282-7735
Tel: 480-966-3998 *Fax:* 480-966-3417
E-mail: TradeShows@ecpa.org
Web Site: www.ecpa.org
Key Personnel
Pres: Mark Kuyper *E-mail:* mkuyper@ecpa.org
Location: Greensboro, NC, USA
Jan 5-7, 2005
Location: Hershey, PA, USA

Jan 9-11, 2005
Location: Arlington, TX, USA
Jan 12-14, 2005
Location: Chicago, IL, USA
Jan 17-19, 2005
Location: Riverside, CA, USA
Jan 20-22, 2005

Football Writers Association of America Annual Meeting
Sponsored by Football Writers Association of America
18652 Vista Del Sol, Dallas, TX 75287
Tel: 972-713-6198 *Fax:* 972-713-6198
E-mail: tigerfwaa@aol.com
Web Site: www.fwaa.com; www.footballwriters.com
Key Personnel
Pres, New York Daily News: Dick Weiss
1st VP, Orlando Sentinel: Alan Schmadtke
2nd VP, CBS Sports Line: Dennis Dodd
Location: Miami, FL, USA
Jan 3-5, 2005

IS&T/SPIE Electronic Imaging Science & Technology
Sponsored by SPIE - The International Society for Optical Engineering
1000 20 St, Bellingham, WA 98225
Mailing Address: PO Box 10, Bellingham, WA 98227-0010
Tel: 360-676-3290 *Fax:* 360-647-1445
E-mail: info@imaging.org
Web Site: www.electronicimaging.org
Key Personnel
Symposium Chair: Thrasyvoulos N Pappas; Andrew J Woods
Exhibits Coord: Bonnie Peterson
Tech Coord: Jeanne Anderson
Location: San Jose, CA, USA
Jan 16-20, 2005

Macworld Conference & Expo
Sponsored by IDG World Expo
Unit of IDG
3 Speen St, Framingham, MA 01701
Tel: 508-879-6700 *Toll Free Tel:* 800-645-EXPO
Fax: 508-620-6668
Web Site: www.macworldexpo.com
Key Personnel
VP: Darrell Baker
Location: Moscone Convention Center, San Francisco, CA, USA
Jan 10-14, 2005

Publishers Winter Conclave
Sponsored by Publishers Association of the South (PAS)
4412 Fletcher St, Panama City, FL 32405-1017
Tel: 850-914-0766 *Fax:* 850-769-4348
E-mail: executive@pubsouth.org
Web Site: www.pubsouth.org
Key Personnel
Pres: Beth Wright
Assn Exec: Pat Sabiston

Location: Marriott Riverside, Charleston, SC, USA
Jan 28-30, 2005

Special Libraries Association Leadership Summit
Sponsored by Special Libraries Association (SLA)
313 S Patrick St, Alexandria, VA 22314
Tel: 703-647-4900 *Fax:* 703-647-4901
E-mail: sla@sla.org
Web Site: www.sla.org
Key Personnel
Exec Dir: Janice LaChance *E-mail:* janice@sla.org
Location: Tampa, FL, USA
Jan 26-29, 2005

Technology, Reading & Learning Difficulties (TRLD)
Sponsored by Don Johnson Inc
26799 W Commerce, Volo, IL 60073
Toll Free Tel: 888-594-1249 *Fax:* 847-740-7326
E-mail: info@trld.com
Web Site: www.trld.com
Key Personnel
Contact: Mary Krenz
TRLD is the only conference that integrates technology interventions with expert literacy strategies to ensure student success. The conference brings together educators, experienced literacy leaders & technology experts to share, discuss & work towards a solution to the nationwide concern of bringing literacy success to all students. Through quality speakers & relevant topics, TRLD gives educators ideas & strategies to immediately implement with students with high incidence disabilities.
Location: Grand Hyatt, Union Square, San Francisco, CA, USA
Jan 27-29, 2005

Westpack
Sponsored by Canon Communications
11444 W Olympic Blvd, Suite 900, Los Angeles, CA 90064
Tel: 310-445-4200 *Fax:* 310-996-9499
Web Site: www.cancom.com; www.canontradeshows.com
Location: Anaheim Convention Center, Anaheim, CA, USA
Jan 10-12, 2005

FEBRUARY

Antiques & Fine Arts Exhibition/Luxembourg Book Festival
Sponsored by LUXEXPO
10 circuit de la Foire Internationale, 1347 Luxembourg-Kirchberg, Luxembourg
Tel: 43991 *Fax:* 4399315
E-mail: info@luxexpo.lu
Web Site: www.luxexpo.lu

Location: LUXEXPO Luxembourg Conference &
Exhibition Center, Luxembourg, Luxembourg
Feb 17-20, 2005

Association of American Publishers Professional & Scholarly Publishing Divison Annual Meeting
Sponsored by Association of American Publishers
(AAP)
71 Fifth Ave, 2nd fl, New York, NY 10003-3004
Tel: 212-255-0200 *Fax:* 212-255-7007
Web Site: www.publishers.org
Key Personnel
Pres & CEO: Patricia S Schroeder *Tel:* 202-347-
3375 *Fax:* 202-347-3690
Location: Renaissance Mayflower Hotel, Wash-
ington, DC, USA
Feb 7-9, 2005

Association of American Publishers School Division Annual Meeting
Sponsored by Association of American Publishers
(AAP)
71 Fifth Ave, 2nd fl, New York, NY 10003-3004
Tel: 212-255-0200 *Fax:* 212-255-7007
Web Site: www.publishers.org
Key Personnel
Pres & CEO: Patricia S Schroeder *Tel:* 202-347-
3375 *Fax:* 202-347-3690
Location: Grand Hyatt Union Square, San Fran-
cisco, CA, USA
Feb 3-4, 2005

CAMEX
Sponsored by National Association of College
Stores (NACS)
500 E Lorain St, Oberlin, OH 44074
Tel: 440-775-7777 *Toll Free Tel:* 800-622-7498
Fax: 440-775-4769
E-mail: info@nacs.org
Web Site: www.nacs.org; www.camex.org
Key Personnel
CEO: Brian Cartier
PR Dir: Laura Nakoneczny *Tel:* 440-775-7777,
ext 2351 *E-mail:* lnakoneczny@nacs.org
Conference & tradeshow dedicated exclusively to
the more than $10 billion collegiate retailing
industry.
Location: New Orleans, LA, USA
Feb 27-March 3, 2005

Dog Writers' Association of America Annual Meeting
Sponsored by Dog Writers' Association of Amer-
ica Inc (DWAA)
173 Union Rd, Coatesville, PA 19320
Tel: 610-384-2436 *Fax:* 610-384-2471
E-mail: rhydowen@aol.com
Web Site: www.dwaa.org
Key Personnel
Pres: Chris Walkowicz
Sec: Pat Santi
Location: Southgate Hotel, New York, NY, USA
Feb 13, 2005

Graphics of the Americas
Sponsored by Printing Association of Florida Inc
6095 NW 167 St, Suite D7, Hialeah, FL 33015
Mailing Address: PO Box 170010, Hialeah, FL
33017-0010
Tel: 305-558-4855 *Toll Free Tel:* 800-749-4855
Fax: 305-823-8965
E-mail: goa@pafgraf.org
Web Site: www.graphicsoftheamericas.com
Key Personnel
VP, Trade Shows: Chris Price *Tel:* 305-558-4855,
ext 18 *E-mail:* cprice@pafgraf.org
Location: Miami Beach Convention Center, Mi-
ami Beach, FL, USA
Feb 4-6, 2005

International Book Fair/San Francisco Book Fair
Sponsored by Antiquarian Booksellers' Associa-
tion of America
20 W 44 St, 4th fl, New York, NY 10036
Tel: 212-944-8291 *Fax:* 212-944-8293
E-mail: hq@abaa.org
Web Site: www.abaa.org
Key Personnel
Dir: Liane Wade
Location: Concourse Exhibition Center, San Fran-
cisco, CA, USA
Feb 2005

Jerusalem International Book Fair
PO Box 775, Jerusalem 91007, Israel
Tel: (02) 6297922; (02) 6296412 *Fax:* (02)
6243144
E-mail: jerfairs@jerusalem.muni.il
Web Site: www.jerusalembookfair.com
Key Personnel
Chmn & Man Dir: Zev Birger
Location: Jerusalem International Convention
Center, Jerusalem, Israel
Feb 13-18, 2005

National Association of Science Writers Annual Meeting
Sponsored by National Association of Science
Writers (NASW)
PO Box 890, Hedgesville, WV 25427
Tel: 304-754-5077 *Fax:* 304-754-5076
Web Site: www.nasw.org
Key Personnel
Exec Dir: Diane McGurgan *E-mail:* diane@nasw.
org
Location: Washington, DC, USA
Feb 17-21, 2005

National Press Foundation Annual Awards Dinner
Sponsored by The National Press Foundation
1211 Connecticut Ave NW, Suite 310, Washing-
ton, DC 20036
Tel: 202-663-7280 *Fax:* 202-530-2855
E-mail: npf@nationalpress.org
Web Site: www.nationalpress.org
Key Personnel
Dir of Strategic Devt: Don Nunes
Location: Washington Hilton, Washington, DC,
USA
Feb 17, 2005

PRIMEX 2005 (Print Media Executive Summit)
Sponsored by IDEAlliance
100 Daingerfield Rd, Alexandria, VA 22314
Tel: 703-837-1070 *Fax:* 703-837-1072
E-mail: info@idealliance.org
Web Site: www.idealliance.org
Key Personnel
Dir, Exec Programs: Georgia Volakis *Tel:* 703-
837-1075 *E-mail:* gvolakis@idealliance.com
Location: Biltmore Hotel, Coral Gables, FL, USA
Feb 9-11, 2005

The Quick Print Show
Sponsored by PrintImage International
70 E Lake St, Suite 333, Chicago, IL 60601
Tel: 312-726-8015 *Toll Free Tel:* 800-234-0040
Fax: 312-726-8113
E-mail: conferences@printimage.org
Web Site: www.printimage.org
Key Personnel
Pres & CEO: Steven D Johnson
Memb Progs Mgr: Jessica Grindell
E-mail: jgrindell@printimage.org
Location: Orlando, FL, USA
Feb 18-24, 2005

Southern California Writers' Conference San Diego
Division of Random Cove, IE
1010 University Ave, Suite 54, San Diego, CA
92103
Tel: 619-233-4651 *Fax:* 619-233-4651
E-mail: wewrite@writersconference.com
Web Site: www.writersconference.com
Key Personnel
Exec Dir: Michael Gregory *E-mail:* msg@
writersconference.com
Location: San Diego, CA, USA
Feb 18-21, 2005

Winter Conference on Writing & Illustrating for Children
Formerly International Conference on Writing &
Illustrating for Children
Sponsored by Society of Children's Book Writers
& Illustrators (SCBWI)
8271 Beverly Blvd, Los Angeles, CA 90048
Tel: 323-782-1010 *Fax:* 323-782-1892
E-mail: conference@scbwi.org
Web Site: www.scbwi.org
Key Personnel
Pres: Steve Mooser
Location: Hilton New York, Avenue of the Amer-
icas, New York, NY, USA
Feb 5-6, 2005

SPRING

DGI Annual Meeting & Online Conference
Sponsored by Deutsche Gesellschaft fur Informa-
tionswissenschaft und informationspraxis eV
(German Society for Information Science &
Information Practice)
Ostbahnhofstr 13, 60314 Frankfurt am Main, Ger-
many
Tel: (069) 430313 *Fax:* (069) 4909096
E-mail: zentrale@dgi-info.de
Web Site: www.dgi-info.de
Location: Frankfurt Fairgrounds, Frankfurt, Ger-
many
Spring 2005

Izmir Book Fair
Sponsored by Tuyap Fuar ve Kongre Merkezi
E-S Karayolu Gurpinar Kavsagi, Beylikduzu/
Buyukcekmece, 34900 Istanbul, Turkey
Tel: (0212) 886 68 43 *Fax:* (0212) 886 62 43
E-mail: artlink@tuyap.com.tr
Web Site: www.tuyap.com.tr
Location: Izmir Culturepark Fair Venue, Izmir,
Turkey
Spring 2005

Poligrafia
Sponsored by Poznan International Fair Ltd
ul Glogowska 14, 60-734 Poznan, Poland
Tel: (061) 869 2599; (061) 869 2295 *Fax:* (061)
866 5827
E-mail: poligrafia@mtp.pl
Web Site: poligrafiamtp.pl
Key Personnel
Proj Mgr: Krzysztof Slatala *Tel:* (061) 869 2196
Fax: (061) 869 2661 *E-mail:* krzysztof.slatala@
mtp.pl
International fair of printing machines, materials
& services.
Location: Poznan, Poland
Spring 2005

Remainder & Promotional Book Fair
Sponsored by Ciana Ltd
24 Langroyd Rd, London SW17 7PL, United
Kingdom
Tel: (020) 8682 1969 *Fax:* (020) 8682 1997

E-mail: enquiries@ciana.co.uk
Web Site: www.ciana.co.uk
Location: Hilton Brighton Metropole Hotel,
King's Rd, Brighton, UK
Spring 2005

World Book Fair
Sponsored by Times Business Information Pte
Ltd
Division of Times Publishing Ltd
One New Industrial Rd, Times Centre, Singapore
536196, Singapore
Tel: 6213 9288 *Fax:* 6286 5754
E-mail: tceexh@tpl.com.sg
Web Site: www.bookfair.com.sg
Location: Suntec Singapore Convention & Exhibi-
tion, Singapore
Spring 2005

MARCH

AAAA Media Conference & Trade Show
Sponsored by American Association of Advertis-
ing Agencies (AAAA)
405 Lexington Ave, 18th fl, New York, NY
10174-1801
Tel: 212-682-2500 *Fax:* 212-573-8968
E-mail: aaaaconferences@aaaa.org
Web Site: www.aaaa.org
Key Personnel
Pres & CEO: O Burtch Drake *E-mail:* obd@aaaa.
org
Sr VP, Conferences & Special Events: Karen
Proctor *E-mail:* karen@aaaa.org
Conference Mgr: Michelle Montalto
E-mail: michelle@aaaa.org
Conference Coord: Michelle James
E-mail: mjames@aaaa.org
Location: Hilton Riverside, New Orleans, LA,
USA
March 2-4, 2005

Adelaide Bank Festival of Arts
Formerly Adelaide Writers' Week
Sponsored by Adelaide Festival Corp
105 Hindley St, Adelaide, SA 5000, Australia
Mailing Address: PO Box 8221, Station Arcade,
Adelaide, SA 5000, Australia
Tel: (08) 8216 4444 *Fax:* (08) 8216 4455
E-mail: afa@adelaidefestival.net.au
Web Site: www.adelaidefestival.com.au
Key Personnel
Artistic Dir: Brett Sheehy
Location: Pioneer Women's Memorial Gardens,
King William St, Adelaide, Australia
March 3-19, 2005

**Associated Writing Programs Annual
Conference & Bookfair**
Sponsored by Association of Writers & Writing
Programs (AWP)
George Mason University, MS-1E3, Fairfax, VA
22030-4444
Tel: 703-993-4301 *Fax:* 703-993-4302
E-mail: awp@awpwriter.org
Web Site: www.awpwriter.org
Key Personnel
Exec Dir: D W Fenza
Dir of Conferences: Matt Scanlon
Association of writers & writing programs.
Location: Hyatt Regency & Fairmont Hotel, Van-
couver, BC, Canada
March 30-April 2, 2005

**Association of American Publishers Annual
Meeting**
Sponsored by Association of American Publishers
(AAP)

71 Fifth Ave, 2nd fl, New York, NY 10003-3004
Tel: 212-255-0200 *Fax:* 212-255-7007
Web Site: www.publishers.org
Key Personnel
Pres & CEO: Patricia S Schroeder *Tel:* 202-347-
3375 *Fax:* 202-347-3690
Location: New York, NY, USA
March 3, 2005

**Association of American Publishers Annual
Meeting for Small & Independent Publishers**
Sponsored by Association of American Publishers
(AAP)
71 Fifth Ave, 2nd fl, New York, NY 10003-3004
Tel: 212-255-0200 *Fax:* 212-255-7007
Web Site: www.publishers.org
Key Personnel
Pres & CEO: Patricia S Schroeder *Tel:* 202-347-
3375 *Fax:* 202-347-3690
Location: New York, NY, USA
March 4, 2005

**Binding Industries Association International
Spring/Presidents Conference**
Sponsored by Binding Industries Association
(BIA)
Affiliate of Special Industry Group of Printing
Industries of America Inc
100 Daingerfield Rd, Alexandria, VA 22314
Tel: 703-519-8137 *Fax:* 703-548-3227
E-mail: bparrott@printing.org
Web Site: www.gain.net
Key Personnel
Exec Dir: Joanne Rock
Conference for top management held in conjunc-
tion with PIA/GATF Presidents Conference.
Specially designed educational events & nu-
merous networking activities for BIA members.
Location: The Ritz Carlton Golf Club, Naples,
FL, USA
March 1-4, 2005

BookTech Conference & Expo
Sponsored by BookTech
401 N Broad St, 5th Fl, Philadelphia, PA 19108
Toll Free Tel: 888-627-2630 *Fax:* 215-409-0100
E-mail: tradeshows@napco.com
Web Site: www.booktechexpo.com
BookTech incorporates the PrintMedia Confer-
ence & Expo & the In-Plant Graphics Confer-
ence plus a world-class expo on publishing &
printing solutions providers.
Location: Hilton New York, 1335 Avenue of the
Americas, New York, NY, USA
March 7-9, 2005

Buch-IBO
Sponsored by Boersenverein des Deutschen Buch-
handels, Landesverband Baden-Wuerttemberg
eV (Association of Publishers & Booksellers in
Baden-Wuerttemberg e V)
Division of Internationale Bodensee-Messe,
Friedrichshafen
Paulinenstr 53, 70178 Stuttgart, Germany
Tel: (0711) 619410 *Fax:* (0711) 6194144
E-mail: buchhorn@buchhandelsverband.de
Web Site: www.buchhandelsverband.de
Location: International Bodensee-Messe,
Friedrichshafen, Germany
March 12-20, 2005

Christian Booksellers Convention - UK
Sponsored by Christian Booksellers Convention
Ltd
Victoria House, Victoria Rd, Buckhurst Hill, Es-
sex IG9 5EX, United Kingdom
Tel: (020) 5592975; (020) 8559 1180 *Fax:* (020)
5029062
E-mail: 100067.1226@compuserve.com
Location: Doncaster Exhibition & Conference
Center, Doncaster, UK
March 7-9, 2005

**English Association Semiannual Teachers'
Conference**
Sponsored by The English Association
University of Leicester, University Rd, Leicester
LE1 7RH, United Kingdom
Tel: (0116) 252 3982 *Fax:* (0116) 252 2301
E-mail: engassoc@le.ac.uk
Key Personnel
Chief Exec: Helen Lucas
Conference Org: Louise Callen
Membership Coord: Jeremy Wiltshire
Location: Oxford, UK
March 2005

Graphic Arts/The Charlotte Show
Sponsored by Graphic Arts Show Company
1899 Preston White Dr, Reston, VA 20191-4367
Tel: 703-264-7200 *Fax:* 703-620-9187
E-mail: info@gasc.org
Web Site: www.gasc.org *Telex:* NPES MCLN
Key Personnel
Pres: Regis J Delmontagne
Biennial event featuring equipment, products &
services for graphic communications industry.
Location: Charlotte Convention Center, Charlotte,
NC, USA
March 17-19, 2005

**Inter American Press Association Mid-Year
Meeting**
Sponsored by Inter American Press Association
(IAPA)
Jules Dubois Bldg, 1801 SW Third Ave, Miami,
FL 33129
Tel: 305-634-2465 *Fax:* 305-635-2272
E-mail: info@sipiapa.org
Web Site: www.sipiapa.org
Key Personnel
Exec Dir: Julio E Munoz
Meeting Coord: Angeles Mase *E-mail:* amase@
sipiapa.org
Location: Panama City, Panama
March 11-14, 2005

Leipzig Book Fair
Sponsored by Leipziger Messe GmbH, Projekt-
team Buchmesse
Messe-Allee 1, 04356 Leipzig, Germany
Mailing Address: Postfach 100 720, 04007
Leipzig, Germany
Tel: (0341) 678 8240 *Fax:* (0341) 678 8242
E-mail: info@leipziger-buchmesse.de
Web Site: www.leipziger-buchmesse.de
Key Personnel
Exhibition Dir: Oliver Zille *Tel:* (0341) 678 8241
Held annually in conjunction with The Leipzig
Antiquarian Book Fair.
Location: Neues Messegelande, Leipzig, Germany
March 17-20, 2005

Literary Festival
Sponsored by Vystaviste Flora Olomouc
Wolkerova 17, 771 11 Olomouc, Czech Republic
Mailing Address: PO Box 46, 771 11 Olomouc,
Czech Republic
Tel: (0585) 726 111 *Fax:* (0585) 413 370
E-mail: info@flora-ol.cz
Web Site: www.flora-ol.cz
March 2005

London Book Fair
Sponsored by Reed Exhibitions (UK)
Division of Reed Business
Oriel House, 26 The Quadrant, Richmond, Surrey
TW9 1DL, United Kingdom
Tel: (020) 8910 7910 *Fax:* (020) 8940 2171
E-mail: lbfteam@reedexpo.co.uk
Web Site: www.lbf-virtual.com *Telex:* 8951389
ITFLONG

Key Personnel
Key Acct Mgr: Catriana Stemp *E-mail:* catriana.
stemp@reedexpo.co.uk
Sales Exec: Ruth Moses *E-mail:* ruth.moses@
reedexpo.co.uk
Sponsored by The Booksellers Association of the
United Kingdom & Ireland Limited. Spring
publishing event attended by publishers, booksellers, literary agents. librarians, authors, production & content managers & international
rights agents.
Location: Olympia Exhibition Centre, Hammersmith Rd, London, UK
March 13-15, 2005

**National Newspaper Association Annual
   Government Affairs Conference**
Sponsored by National Newspaper Association
PO Box 5737, Arlington, VA 22205-9998
Tel: 703-534-1278 *Fax:* 703-534-5751
E-mail: info@nna.org
Web Site: www.nna.org
Location: Wyndham Washington, Washington,
DC, USA
March 9-12, 2005

NEXPO®
Sponsored by Newspaper Association of America
(NAA)
1921 Gallows Rd, Suite 600, Vienna, VA 22182
Tel: 703-902-1600 *Fax:* 703-902-1843
E-mail: sarns@naa.org
Web Site: www.nexpo.com
Key Personnel
Dir of Exhibition Sales: Brad Smith
Annual technical exposition & conference for
newspapers.
Location: Dallas Convention Center, Dallas, TX,
USA
March 19-22, 2005

Plano Book Festival for Adult Literacy
Sponsored by Collin County Adult Literacy
Council
PO Box 941802, Plano, TX 75094
Tel: 972-633-9603
Web Site: www.ccalc.org
The purpose of the festival is to increase aware-
ness of & support for adults who do not have
the literacy skills necessary for everyday living.
Location: Downtown, Plano, TX, USA
March 6, 2005

Salon du Livre de Paris
Sponsored by Reed Expositions France
Subsidiary of Reed Exhibition Companies
11 rue du Colonel Pierre Avia, 75726 Paris Cedex
15, France
Tel: (01) 41 90 47 47 *Fax:* (01) 41 90 47 49
E-mail: salondulivre@reedexpo.fr; livre@
reedexpo.fr
Web Site: www.salondulivreparis.com
Key Personnel
Fair Mgr: Taya de Reynies
   E-mail: taya_reynies@reedexpo.fr
Annual international publishing event for publish-
ers, booksellers, teachers & librarians. Open to
the trade & the public. Guest of honor: Russia.
Location: Paris Expo, Hall 1, Porte de Versailles,
Paris, France
March 18-23, 2005

**Texas Outdoor Writers Association Annual
   Conference**
Sponsored by Texas Outdoor Writers Association
7503 Bayswater, Amarillo, TX 79119
Tel: 806-345-3280 *Fax:* 806-372-3717
Web Site: www.towa.org
Key Personnel
Pres: Jonette Childs *E-mail:* saltex@pyramid3.net

Exec Dir & Treas: Lee Leschper *E-mail:* l.
leschper@amarillonet.com
Location: Ramada Inn Bayfront Hotel, Corpus
Christi, TX, USA
March 3-5, 2005

Virginia Festival of the Book
Sponsored by Virginia Foundation for the Hu-
manities
145 Ednam Dr, Charlottesville, VA 22903
Tel: 434-924-6890 *Fax:* 434-296-4714
E-mail: vabook@virginia.edu
Web Site: www.vabook.org
Key Personnel
Program Dir: Nancy Damon *Tel:* 434-924-7548
   E-mail: ndamon@virginia.edu
Assoc Program Dir: Kevin McFadden
   E-mail: kmcfadden@virginia.edu
Annual free public festival for children & adults
featuring authors, illustrators, publishers, pub-
licists, agents & other book professionals in
panel discussions & readings for adults & chil-
dren of all ages.
Location: Charlottesville, VA, USA
March 16-20, 2005

WORLDDIDAC Mexico 2005
Sponsored by Worlddidac
Bollwerk 21, 3001 Bern, Switzerland
Mailing Address: PO Box 8866, 3001 Bern,
Switzerland
Tel: (031) 311 76 82 *Fax:* (031) 312 17 44
E-mail: info@worlddidac.org
Web Site: www.worlddidac.org
Key Personnel
Project Mgr: Esther Schindles *E-mail:* schindles@
worlddidac.org
International exhibition for educational materials,
professional training & e-learning.
Location: World Trade Center, Mexico City, Mex-
ico
March 2005

APRIL

**Advertising Research Foundation Annual
   Convention & Trade Show**
Sponsored by Advertising Research Foundation
641 Lexington Ave, New York, NY 10022
Tel: 212-751-5656 *Fax:* 212-319-5265
E-mail: info@thearf.org
Web Site: www.thearf.org
Key Personnel
Sr VP, Communs: Carol White *Tel:* 212-751-
5656, ext 227 *E-mail:* carol@thearf.org
VP, Conference Brands: Ajay Durani *Tel:* 212-
751-5656, ext 222 *E-mail:* ajay@thearf.org
Man Ed: Zena Pagan *Tel:* 212-751-5656, ext 216
   E-mail: zena@thearf.org
Location: New York, NY, USA
April 2005

African American Children's Book Festival
Sponsored by Kids Cultural Books
1081 Westover Rd, Stamford, CT 06902
Tel: 203-359-6925 *Fax:* 203-359-3226
E-mail: info@kidsculturalbooks.org
Web Site: www.kidsculturalbooks.org/festivals.
html
Location: Cathedral of St John the Divine, New
York, NY, USA
April 2005

Alberta Library Conference
Sponsored by Library Association of Alberta
80 Baker Crescent NW, Calgary, AB T2L 1R4,
Canada

Tel: 403-284-5818 *Toll Free Tel:* 877-522-5550
   Fax: 403-282-6646
E-mail: info@laa.ab.ca
Web Site: www.laa.ab.ca
Key Personnel
Pres: Pat Cavill
Exec Dir: Christine Sheppard *E-mail:* christine.
sheppard@show.ca
Location: Jasper Park Lodge, Jasper, AB, Canada
April 2005

Arizona Book Festival
Sponsored by Arizona Humanities Council
1242 N Central, Phoenix, AZ 85004
Tel: 602-257-0335
Web Site: www.azbookfestival.org/index.html
Location: Carnegie Center, Phoenix, AZ, USA
April 2, 2005

**Association of Directory Publishers Annual
   Meeting**
Sponsored by Association of Directory Publishers
116 Cass St, Traverse City, MI 49684-2505
Mailing Address: PO Box 1929, Traverse City,
MI 49685-1929
Toll Free Tel: 800-267-9002 *Fax:* 231-486-2182
E-mail: hq@adp.org
Web Site: www.adp.org
Key Personnel
Pres & CEO: R Lawrence Angove *E-mail:* larry.
angove@adp.org
Location: Worthington Renaissance Hotel, Ft
Worth, TX, USA
April 14-16, 2005

Binding, Finishing & Distribution Seminar
Sponsored by Research & Engineering Council
of NAPL (National Association for Printing
Leadership)
PO Box 1086, White Stone, VA 22578-1086
Tel: 804-436-9922 *Toll Free Tel:* 800-642-6275
(ext 1397) *Fax:* 804-436-9511
E-mail: recouncil@rivnet.net
Web Site: www.recouncil.org
Key Personnel
Man Dir: Ronald L Mihills
Seminar designed for bindery managers, manu-
facturing/operations executives & warehouse
supervisors.
Shipping Address: 816 Rappahannock Dr, White
Stone, VA 22578
Location: Marriott O'Hare, Chicago, IL, USA
April 5-6, 2005

Bologna Children's Book Fair
Sponsored by BolognaFiere
Via della Fiera, 20, 40128 Bologna, Italy
Tel: (051) 282 111 *Fax:* (051) 637 40 04
E-mail: dir.gen@bolognafiere.it; bookfair@
bolognafiere.it
Web Site: www.bookfair.bolognafiere.it
Location: Bologna Fiere Exhibition Centre,
Bologna, Italy
April 13-16, 2005

**Booksellers Association of the United Kingdom
   & Ireland Annual Conference**
Sponsored by Booksellers Association of the
United Kingdom & Ireland Ltd
Minster House, 272-274 Vauxhall Bridge Rd,
London SW1V 1BA, United Kingdom
Tel: (020) 7802 0802 *Fax:* (020) 7802 0803
E-mail: mail@booksellers.org.uk
Web Site: www.booksellers.org.uk
Key Personnel
Contact: Anna O'Kane *E-mail:* anna.okane@
booksellers.org.uk
Location: Glasgow, UK
April 10-12, 2005

Dataprint
Sponsored by Reed Messe Salzburg GmbH
Am Messezentrum 6, 5021 Salzburg, Austria
Mailing Address: Postfach 285, 5021 Salzburg,
 Austria
Tel: (0662) 44770 *Fax:* (0662) 4477161
E-mail: info@reedexpo.at; dataprint@reedexpo.at
Web Site: www.reedexpo.at; www.datapoint.at
Key Personnel
Dir: Johann Jungreithmair
Mgr: Max Poringer *E-mail:* max.poringer@
 reedexpo.at
Coord: Daniela Kogl-Egger *E-mail:* daniela.
 koegl@reedexpo.at
Trade fair for print media & digital production.
Location: Design Center, Linz, Austria
April 1, 2005

ECPA Management Seminar
Sponsored by Evangelical Christian Publishers
 Association
4816 S Ash Ave, Suite 101, Tempe, AZ 85282-
 7735
Tel: 480-966-3998 *Fax:* 480-966-1944
E-mail: info@ecpa.org
Web Site: www.ecpa.org
Key Personnel
Pres: Mark Kuyper *E-mail:* mkuyper@ecpa.org
April 30-May 4, 2005

Evangelical Press Association Annual Conference
Sponsored by Evangelical Press Association
 (EPA)
PO Box 28129, Crystal, MN 55428-0129
Tel: 763-535-4793 *Fax:* 763-535-4794
E-mail: director@epassoc.org
Web Site: www.epassoc.org
Key Personnel
Exec Dir: Doug Trouten
Location: Hyatt Regency Woodfield, Schaumburg,
 IL, USA
April 24-27, 2005

Federation of Children's Book Groups Annual Conference
Sponsored by Federation of Children's Book
 Groups
2 Bridge Wood View, Horsforth, Leeds, W Yorks
 LS18 5PE, United Kingdom
Tel: (0113) 2588910
E-mail: info@fcbg.org.uk
Web Site: www.fcbg.org.uk
Key Personnel
Contact: Jayne Truran
Theme "Windows on the World".
Location: The University of Hertfordshire, Hat-
 field, Herts, UK
April 1-3, 2005

FOSE
Sponsored by Post Newsweek Tech Media
10 G St NE, Suite 500, Washington, DC 20002-
 4228
Tel: 202-772-2500 *Toll Free Tel:* 866-447-6864
 Fax: 202-771-2511
E-mail: fose.exhibit@postnewsweektech.com
Web Site: www.fose.com; www.
 postnewsweektech.com
Key Personnel
VP, Trade Shows: Lorenz Hassenstein
 Tel: 202-772-5738 *E-mail:* lhassenstein@
 postnewsweektech.com
Dir: Gloria Lombardo *Tel:* 203-381-9245
 E-mail: glombardo@postnewsweektech.com
Trade Show Opers Mgr: Lauri Nichols *Tel:* 202-
 772-5750 *E-mail:* lnichols@postnewsweektech.
 com
Location: Washington Convention Center, Wash-
 ington, DC, USA
April 5-7, 2005

Gutenberg Festival
Sponsored by Graphic Arts Show Company
1899 Preston White Dr, Reston, VA 20191-4367
Tel: 703-264-7200 *Fax:* 703-620-9187
E-mail: info@gasc.org
Web Site: www.gasc.org
Key Personnel
Dir, Communs: David Poulos
Annual trade show for graphic design, digital pre-
 press, printing, publishing & converting.
Location: Long Beach Convention Center, Long
 Beach, CA, USA
April 28-30, 2005

Infosystem Fairs
Sponsored by Poznan International Fair Ltd
ul Glogowska 14, 60-734 Poznan, Poland
Tel: (061) 869 2000; (061) 869 2599; (061) 869
 2295 *Fax:* (061) 866 5827
E-mail: infosystem@mtp.pl
Web Site: www.mtp.pl; www.infosystem.pl
Telex: 413251
Key Personnel
Proj Mgr: Krzysztof Slatala *Tel:* (061) 869 2196
 Fax: (061) 869 2661 *E-mail:* krzysztof.slatala@
 mtp.pl
International fair of telecommunications, informa-
 tion technology & electronics.
Location: Poznan International Fairground, Poz-
 nan, Poland
April 19-22, 2005

International Children's Book Day
Sponsored by International Board on Books for
 Young People (IBBY)
Nonnenweg 12, 4003 Basel, Switzerland
Mailing Address: Nonnenweg 12, Postfach, Basel
 4003, Switzerland
Tel: (061) 272 29 17 *Fax:* (061) 272 27 57
E-mail: ibby@ibby.org
Web Site: www.ibby.org
On or around Hans Christian Andersen's birthday, April 2nd, International Children's Book
 day (ICBD) is celebrated to inspire a love of
 reading & to call attention to children's books.
 Each year a different national section has the
 opportunity to be the international sponsor. It
 decides upon a theme & invites a prominent
 author to write a message to the children of
 the world & a well-known illustrator to design
 a poster. These materials are used in different
 ways to promote books & reading around the
 world.
Location: India
April 2005

IS&T Archiving Conference
Sponsored by Society for Imaging Science &
 Technology (IS&T)
7003 Kilworth Lane, Springfield, VA 22151
Tel: 703-642-9090 *Fax:* 703-642-9094
E-mail: info@imaging.org
Web Site: www.imaging.org
Location: Radisson Hotel Old Town, Alexandria,
 VA, USA
April 26-29, 2005

Los Angeles Times Festival of Books
Sponsored by Los Angeles Times
Division of Tribune Co
202 W First St, 6th fl, Los Angeles, CA 90012
Tel: 213-237-5000 *Toll Free Tel:* 800-528-4637
 Fax: 213-237-2335
Web Site: www.latimes.com/events
Location: UCLA Campus, Los Angeles, CA,
 USA
April 23-24, 2005

MILIA: World Interactive Content Forum
Sponsored by Reed Midem
Subsidiary of Reed Exhibition Companies

11 rue du Colonnel Pierre Avia, 75015 Paris,
 France
Mailing Address: BP 572, 75726 Paris Cedex 15,
 France
Tel: (01) 41 90 44 00 *Fax:* (01) 41 90 44 70
E-mail: info@milia.com; milia.conferences@
 reedmidem.com
Web Site: www.milia.com
Key Personnel
Exec Dir: Laurine Garaude *E-mail:* laurine.
 garaude@reedmidem.com
Location: Palais des Festivals, Cannes, France
April 11-15, 2005

National Association of Printing Ink Manufacturers Annual Convention
Sponsored by National Association of Printing
 Ink Manufacturers (NAPIM)
581 Main St, Woodbridge, NJ 07095
Tel: 732-855-1525 *Fax:* 732-855-1838
E-mail: napim@napim.org
Web Site: www.napim.org
Key Personnel
Exec Dir: James E Coleman
Event Coord: Sue Coleman
Location: Hyatt Coconut Point, Bonita Springs,
 FL, USA
April 7-11, 2005

National Library Week
Sponsored by American Library Association
 (ALA)
50 E Huron St, Chicago, IL 60611
Tel: 312-944-6780 *Toll Free Tel:* 800-545-2433
 Fax: 312-944-8520
E-mail: pio@ala.org
Web Site: www.ala.org/events
Key Personnel
Public Info Dir: Mark Gould
Press Officer: Larra Clark *E-mail:* lclark@ala.org
Location: Nationwide throughout the USA
April 10-16, 2005

Newspaper Association of America Annual Convention
Sponsored by Newspaper Association of America
 (NAA)
1921 Gallows Rd, Suite 600, Vienna, VA 22182
Tel: 703-902-1600 *Fax:* 703-902-1790
E-mail: willa@naa.org
Web Site: www.naa.org
Key Personnel
Pres & CEO: John Sturm
Meetings Mgr: Annette Williams
Location: Fairmont San Francisco, San Francisco,
 CA, USA
April 17-20, 2005

North American Agricultural Journalists Spring Meeting
Sponsored by North American Agricultural Jour-
 nalists
Texas A&M University, 201 Reed Macdonald,
 2112 TAMU, College Station, TX 77843-2112
Mailing Address: 2604 Cumberland Ct, College
 Station, TX 77845
Tel: 979-845-2872 *Fax:* 979-845-2414
Web Site: naaj.tamu.edu
Key Personnel
Exec Sec, Treas: Kathleen Phillips *E-mail:* ka-
 phillips@tamu.edu
Location: Washington, DC, USA
April 2005

Northern Arizona Book Festival
PO Box 1871, Flagstaff, AZ 86002-1871
Tel: 928-607-2600
E-mail: bookfest@flagstaffcentral.com
Web Site: www.flagstaffcentral.com/bookfest/
Key Personnel
Exec Dir: Laura Rose Taylor

The Northern Arizona Book Festival offers a three day weekend of readings, workshops, panel discussions & other literary events for readers & writers of all ages. The festival is held at a variety of venues in historic Flagstaff, AZ.
Location: Flagstaff, AZ, USA
April 15-17, 2005

Northprint
Sponsored by Reed Exhibitions (UK)
Division of Reed Business
Oriel House, 26 The Quadrant, Richmond, Surrey TW9 1DL, United Kingdom
Tel: (020) 8910 7910 *Fax:* (020) 8940 2171
E-mail: northprint.helpline@reedexpo.co.uk
Web Site: www.northprintexpo.co.uk
    Telex: 8951389 ITFLONG
Key Personnel
Exhibition Dir: Andrew Furness *Tel:* (020) 8910 7836 *Fax:* (020) 8334 0704 *E-mail:* andrew. furness@reedexpo.co.uk
Exhibition Administrator: Hannah Tranfield *Tel:* (020) 8910 7817 *Fax:* (020) 8910 7848 *E-mail:* hannah.tranfield@reedexpo.co.uk
Location: Harrogate Exhibition Centre, Harrogate, UK
April 19-21, 2005

Paper Week
Sponsored by American Forest & Paper Association
1111 19 St NW, Suite 800, Washington, DC 20036
Tel: 202-463-2700 *Fax:* 202-463-4703
E-mail: info@afandpa.org
Web Site: www.afandpa.org; www.paperweek.org
Key Personnel
Pres & CEO: W Henson Moore
Location: Waldorf-Astoria Hotel & Towers, New York, NY, USA
April 10-13, 2005

The Quest for Excellence
Sponsored by American Society for Quality
600 N Plankinton Ave, Milwaukee, WI 53203
Mailing Address: PO Box 3005, Milwaukee, WI 53201-3005
Tel: 414-272-8575 *Toll Free Tel:* 800-248-1946
    Fax: 414-272-1734
E-mail: cs@asq.org
Web Site: www.asq.org *Telex:* 31-6567
Key Personnel
Exec Dir & Chief Strategic Officer: Paul Borawski
Events Mgmt Mgr: Shirley Krentz
Location: Marriott Wardman Park Hotel, Washington, DC, USA
April 10-13, 2005

Southern Kentucky Book Fest
106 Cravens Library, One Big Red Way, Bowling Green, KY 42101
Tel: 270-745-5016
Web Site: www.sokybookfest.org
Location: Sloan Convention Center, Bowling Green, KY, USA
April 15-16, 2005

SouthPack
Sponsored by Canon Communications
11444 W Olympic Blvd, Suite 900, Los Angeles, CA 90064
Tel: 310-445-4200 *Fax:* 310-996-9499
E-mail: feedback@devicelink.com
Web Site: www.cancom.com; www. canontradeshows.com
Biennial.
Location: Georgia World Congress Center, Atlanta, GA, USA
April 13-14, 2005

UK Serials Group Annual Conference & Exhibition
Sponsored by UK Serials Group
PO Box 5594, Newbury RG20 0YP, United Kingdom
Tel: (01635) 254292 *Fax:* (01635) 253826
E-mail: uksg.admin@dial.pipex.com
Web Site: www.uksg.org
Key Personnel
Busn Mgr: Alison Whitehorn
Location: Heriot-Watt University, Edinburgh, UK
April 11-13, 2005

Young People's Poetry Week
Sponsored by The Children's Book Council (CBC)
12 W 37 St, 2nd fl, New York, NY 10118-7480
Tel: 212-966-1990 *Toll Free Tel:* 800-999-2160 (orders only) *Fax:* 212-966-2073
    Toll Free Fax: 888-807-9355 (orders only)
Web Site: www.cbcbooks.org
Key Personnel
Pres: Paula Quint
Location: Nationwide throughout the USA
April 11-17, 2005

MAY

AAAA Management Conference
Sponsored by American Association of Advertising Agencies (AAAA)
405 Lexington Ave, 18th fl, New York, NY 10174-1801
Tel: 212-682-2500 *Fax:* 212-573-8968
E-mail: aaaaconferences@aaaa.org
Web Site: www.aaaa.org
Key Personnel
Pres & CEO: O Burtch Drake *E-mail:* obd@aaaa.org
Sr VP, Conferences & Special Events: Karen Proctor *E-mail:* karen@aaaa.org
Conference Mgr: Michelle Montalto *E-mail:* michelle@aaaa.org
Conference Coord: Michelle James *E-mail:* mjames@aaaa.org
Location: Fairmont Southampton, Southampton, Bermuda
May 4-6, 2005

AIIM 2005 Conference & Exposition
Sponsored by Advanstar Communications
70 Walnut St, Wellesley Hills, MA 02481
Tel: 781-239-7510 *Fax:* 781-239-7511
E-mail: aiim@aiim.org
Web Site: www.aiim.org
Key Personnel
Gen Mgr: Brian Randall *E-mail:* brandall@advanstar.com
Location: Pennsylvania Convention Center, Philadelphia, PA, USA
May 17-19, 2005

Amsterdam International Printing Allied Industries Trade Fair (Grafivak)
Sponsored by Amsterdam RAI
PO Box 77777, Amsterdam 1070-MS, Netherlands
Tel: (020) 5491212 *Fax:* (020) 5491843
E-mail: grafivak@rai.nl
Web Site: www.grafivak.nl
Key Personnel
Prod Mgr: Xander de Bruine *Tel:* (020) 549 22 44 *E-mail:* x.d.bruine@rai.nl
Location: Amsterdam RAI Exhibition Center, Amsterdam, Netherlands
May 10-13, 2005

ASQ World Conference on Quality & Improvement
Formerly Annual Quality Congress
Sponsored by American Society for Quality
600 N Plankinton Ave, Milwaukee, WI 53203
Tel: 414-272-8575 *Toll Free Tel:* 800-248-1946
    Fax: 414-272-1734
E-mail: cs@asq.org
Web Site: www.asq.org *Telex:* 31-6567
Key Personnel
Exec Dir & Chief Strategic Officer: Paul Borawski
Events Mgmt Mgr: Shirley Krentz
Location: Washington State Convention & Trade Center, Seattle, WA, USA
May 16-18, 2005

Beijing International Book Fair
Sponsored by BIBF Management Office, CNPIEC
16 Gongti E Rd, Chaoyang District, Beijing 100020, China
Tel: (010) 6506 3080 *Fax:* (010) 6506 3101; (010) 6508 9188
E-mail: bibffo@bibf.net
Web Site: www.bibf.net
Key Personnel
Dir: Mr Zhu Zhigang
Location: Beijing Exhibition Center, Beijing, China
May 2005

BMI Management Conference
Sponsored by Book Manufacturers' Institute Inc (BMI)
2 Armand Beach Dr, Suite 1B, Palm Coast, FL 32137
Tel: 386-986-4552 *Fax:* 386-986-4553
E-mail: info@bmibook.com
Web Site: www.bmibook.org
Key Personnel
Exec VP: Bruce W Smith
Location: Sanibel Harbor Resort & Spa, Ft Myers, FL, USA
May 1-3, 2005

Catholic Press Association of the US and Canada Annual Convention
Sponsored by Catholic Press Association of the US & Canada
3555 Veterans Memorial Hwy, Unit O, Ronkonkoma, NY 11779
Tel: 631-471-4730 *Fax:* 631-471-4804
E-mail: cathjourn@aol.com
Web Site: www.catholicpress.org
Key Personnel
Pres: Helen Osman *Tel:* 512-476-4888 *E-mail:* helen_osman@austindiocese.org
Exec Dir: Owen P McGovern *E-mail:* omcg@aol.com
Location: Orlando, FL, USA
May 2005

DPP 2005 - International Conference on Digital Production Printing
Sponsored by Society for Imaging Science & Technology (IS&T)
7003 Kilworth Lane, Springfield, VA 22151
Tel: 703-642-9090 *Fax:* 703-642-9094
E-mail: info@imaging.org
Web Site: www.imaging.org
Key Personnel
Conference Mgr: Pamela Forness
Location: Amsterdam RAI Europa Complex, Amsterdam, The Netherlands
May 9-13, 2005

Annual European Conference on Managing Directories
Formerly European Conference on Electronic Directories
Sponsored by European Association of Directory & Database Publishers (EADP)

127 Ave Franklin Roosevelt, 1050 Brussels, Belgium
Tel: (02) 6463060 *Fax:* (02) 6463637
E-mail: mailbox@eadp.org
Web Site: www.eadp.org
Key Personnel
Congress & Conference Officer: Paola Caruso
    E-mail: paolacaruso@eadp.org
Location: Rome, Italy
May 2005

EXPOLIT Exposicion de Literatura Cristiana Book Fair
Sponsored by Spanish Evangelical Publishers Association (SEPA)/Associacion de Editores Evangelicos and Editorial Unilit
1360 NW 88 Ave, Miami, FL 33172
Tel: 305-503-1191 *Toll Free Tel:* 800-767-7726
    Fax: 305-717-6886
E-mail: wendy@expolit.com
Web Site: www.expolit.com
Key Personnel
Pres, EXPOLIT: David Ecklebarger
Program Dir: Marie Tanayo
Spanish Christian Literature Convention.
Location: Radisson Mart Plaza Hotel & Convention Centre, Miami, FL, USA
May 19-24, 2005

GAA Expo 2005
Formerly Gravure Association of America Convention
Sponsored by Gravure Association of America Inc
1200-A Scottsville Rd, Rochester, NY 14624
Tel: 585-436-2150 *Fax:* 585-436-7689
E-mail: gaa@gaa.org
Web Site: www.gaa.org
Key Personnel
Meeting Planner: Pamela Schenk
Location: Adams Mark Hotel, Philadelphia, PA, USA
May 22-26, 2005

International Reading Association Annual Convention
Sponsored by International Reading Association
800 Barksdale Rd, Newark, DE 19714
Mailing Address: PO Box 8139, Newark, DE 19714-8139
Tel: 302-731-1600 *Fax:* 302-731-1057
E-mail: conferences@reading.org
Web Site: www.reading.org
Key Personnel
Pres: MaryEllen Vogt
Exec Dir: Alan E Farstrup
Location: San Antonio, TX, USA
May 1-5, 2005

Latino Book & Family Festival
Sponsored by Latino Literacy Now
2777 Jefferson St, Suite 200, Carlsbad, CA 92008
Tel: 760-434-4484
Web Site: www.latinobookfestival.com
Key Personnel
Mktg Dir: Jim Sullivan *Fax:* 760-434-7476
    E-mail: jim@lbff.us
Location: Southwestern College, San Diego, CA, USA
May 2005

Nigeria International Book Fair
Division of Nigerian Book Fair Trust
c/o Literamed Publications Ltd (Lantern House), Plot 45, Oregun Industrial Estate, Alausa Bus Stop, Ikeja, Lagos State, Nigeria
Mailing Address: PO Box 21068, Ikeja, Lagos State, Nigeria
Tel: (01) 4823402; (01) 3451208; (03) 4026971
    Fax: (01) 4935258
E-mail: info@nibf.org

Web Site: www.nbif.org
Key Personnel
Exec Secy: Kunle Oyediran
Location: Multi-Purpose Halls, University of Lagos, Lagos
May 10-14, 2005

ON DEMAND
Sponsored by Advanstar Communications
70 Walnut St, Wellesley Hills, MA 02481
Tel: 781-239-7510 *Fax:* 781-239-7511
E-mail: ondemand@advanstar.com
Web Site: www.ondemandexpo.com
Key Personnel
Conference Dir: Tom Bliss
Gen Mgr: Brian Randall *E-mail:* brandall@advanstar.com
Digital printing & publishing.
Location: Pennsylvania Convention Center, Philadelphia, PA, USA
May 17-19, 2005

Pacprint
Sponsored by Graphic Arts Merchants Association of Australia Inc (GAMMA)
PO Box 1051, Crows Nest, NSW 2065, Australia
Tel: (02) 9417 7433 *Fax:* (02) 9417 7433
E-mail: enquiry@gamma.net.au
Web Site: www.gamma.net.au; www.pacprint.com.au
Key Personnel
Chmn: Ron Patterson
Location: Melbourne Convention & Exhibition Centre, Melbourne, Australia
May 1, 2005

Paper Expo
Formerly Paper Summit & TAPPI Spring Technical Conference & Trade Fair
Sponsored by Technical Association of the Pulp & Paper Industry (TAPPI)
15 Technology Pkwy S, Norcross, GA 30092
Tel: 770-446-1400 *Toll Free Tel:* 800-332-8686
    Fax: 770-446-6947
Web Site: www.tappi.org
Key Personnel
Publg Dir: Mary Beth Cornell *E-mail:* mcornell@tappi.org
Corp Rel Dir: Clare Reagan *E-mail:* creagan@tappi.org
Adv Mgr: Vince Saputo *E-mail:* vsaputo@tappi.org
Location: Midwest Airlines Convention Center, Milwaukee, WI, USA
May 23-25, 2005

Periodical Writers' Association of Canada Annual General Meeting
Sponsored by Periodical Writers' Association of Canada
215 Spadina Ave, Suite 123, Toronto, ON M5T 2C7, Canada
Tel: 416-504-1645 *Fax:* 416-913-2327
E-mail: info@pwac.ca
Web Site: www.pwac.ca; www.writers.ca
Key Personnel
Exec Dir: John Degan
Location: Hamilton, ON, Canada
May 2005

Print Buyers Conference
Sponsored by Pacific Printing & Imaging Association
1400 SW Fifth Ave, Suite 815, Portland, OR 97201
Toll Free Tel: 877-762-7742 *Toll Free Fax:* 800-824-1911
E-mail: info@pacprinting.org
Web Site: www.pacprinting.org
Key Personnel
Exec Dir: Marcus Sassaman

Location: Portland, OR, USA
May 3, 2005
Location: Seattle, WA, USA
May 5, 2005

Society of American Business Editors & Writers Annual Convention & Exhibition
Sponsored by Society of American Business Editors & Writers Inc
University of Missouri, School of Journalism, 134 Neff Annex, Columbia, MO 65211-1200
Tel: 573-882-7862 *Fax:* 573-884-1372
E-mail: sabew@missouri.edu
Web Site: www.sabew.org
Key Personnel
Exec Dir: Carrie M Paden *E-mail:* padenc@missouri.edu
Exec Asst: Vicky Edwards
Location: Red Lion Hotel, Seattle, WA, USA
May 1-3, 2005

Southwestern Graphics
Sponsored by Texas Graphic Arts Educational Foundation
13410 Preston Rd, No 1-100, Dallas, TX 75240-5299
Tel: 940-763-8370 (Intl only) *Toll Free Tel:* 800-540-8280 *Fax:* 940-763-8395 (Intl Only)
    Toll Free Fax: 800-540-5019
E-mail: info@swgraphics.com
Web Site: www.swgraphics.com
Key Personnel
Asst Show Mgr: Laura Bates
Location: Arlington Convention Center, Dallas, TX, USA
May 19-21, 2005

Warsaw International Book Fair
Sponsored by Ars Polon SA - Warsaw International Book Fair Office
Office for Domestic & International Book Fairs, 7 Krakowskie Przedmiescie St, 00-068 Warsaw, Poland
Tel: (022) 826-92-56 *Fax:* (022) 826-92-56
E-mail: mtk@arspolona.com.pl
Web Site: www.bookfair.pl
Key Personnel
Sec Gen: Ms Joanna Aleksandrowicz
    Tel: (022) 826-97-12 *Fax:* (022) 826-97-12
    E-mail: joannaa@arspolona.com.pl
Location: Palace of Culture & Science, Warsaw, Poland
May 19-22, 2005

Annual Web Offset Association Conference
Sponsored by Web Offset Association
Division of PIA/GATF
200 Deer Run Rd, Sewickley, PA 15143
Tel: 412-741-6860 *Toll Free Tel:* 800-910-4283
    Fax: 412-741-2311
Web Site: www.gain.net
Key Personnel
Meetings Asst: Ricardo Vila-Roger
    E-mail: rvilaroger@gatf.org
Location: Gaylord Texan Resort, Grapevine, TX, USA
May 2-4, 2005

SUMMER

Buenos Aires International Children's Book Fair
Sponsored by Fundacion El Libro
Hipolito Yrigoyen 1628 - 5º piso, C1089AAF Buenos Aires, Argentina
Tel: (011) 4374 3288 *Fax:* (011) 4375 0268
E-mail: fundacion@el-libro.com.ar
Web Site: www.el-libro.com.ar

Key Personnel
Proj Mgr: Marta Diaz
Location: Centro de Exposiciones de la Ciudad
de Buenos Aires, Avdas Figueroa Alcorta y
Pueyrredón, Buenos Aires, Argentina
Summer 2005

The National Center for Database Marketing (NCDM)
Sponsored by Primedia Business Exhibitions
11 River Bend Dr S, Stamford, CT 06907
Mailing Address: PO Box 4254, Stamford, CT
06907-0254
Tel: 203-358-9900 *Toll Free Tel:* 800-927-5007
Fax: 203-358-5818
Web Site: www.primediabusiness.com; www.
ncdmsummer.com; www.ncdmwinter.com
Summer 2005

JUNE

ABA Convention & Trade Exhibit
Sponsored by American Booksellers Association
828 S Broadway, Tarrytown, NY 10591
Tel: 914-591-2665 *Toll Free Tel:* 800-637-0037
Fax: 914-591-2720
E-mail: info@bookweb.org
Web Site: www.bookweb.org
Key Personnel
Communs Mgr: Kristen Gilligan
Held in conjunction with BookExpo America.
Location: Jacob K Javits Convention Center, New
York, NY, USA
June 2-5, 2005

American Library Association Annual Conference
Sponsored by American Library Association
(ALA)
50 E Huron St, Chicago, IL 60611
Tel: 312-280-3200 *Toll Free Tel:* 800-545-2433
Fax: 312-944-7841
E-mail: ala@ala.org
Web Site: www.ala.org
Key Personnel
Public Info Dir: Mark Gould
Press Officer: Larra Clark
Dir, Intl Rel: Michael Dowling
Location: Chicago, IL, USA
June 23-29, 2005

AsiaPack AsiaPrint
Sponsored by Reed Tradex Co Ltd
32nd fl, Sathorn Nakorn Tower, 100/68-69, North
Sathorn Rd, Silom, Bangkok 10500, Thailand
Tel: (02) 636 7272 *Fax:* (02) 636 7282
E-mail: printpack@reedtradex.co.th
Web Site: www.asiapackasiaprint.com
Biennial international trade exhibition for print-
ing, packaging & processing machinery, equip-
ment materials, supplies & solutions. Co-
organized by the Thai Printing Association.
Location: Bangkok International Trade & Exhibi-
tion Centre, Bangkok, Thailand
June 2-5, 2005

Association of American University Presses Annual Meeting
Sponsored by Association of American University
Presses (AAUP)
71 W 23 St, Suite 901, New York, NY 10010
Tel: 212-989-1010 *Fax:* 212-989-0176; 212-989-
0275
E-mail: info@ aaupnet.org
Web Site: www.aaupnet.org
Key Personnel
Exec Dir: Peter J Givler
Asst Dir: Timothy Muench

Admin Mgr: Linda McCall
Location: Philadelphia, PA, USA
June 16-19, 2005

BookExpo America (BEA)
Sponsored by Reed Exhibitions
Affiliate of Reed Exhibition Companies
383 Main Ave, Norwalk, CT 06851
Tel: 203-840-5614 *Toll Free Tel:* 800-840-5614
Fax: 203-840-5580
E-mail: inquiry@bookexpo.america.com
Web Site: bookexpoamerica.com
Key Personnel
Sr VP: Tony Calanca
Industry VP & Show Mgr: Greg Topalian
E-mail: gtopalian@reedexpo.com
Mktg Dir: Tom Kobak *E-mail:* tkobak@reedexpo.
com
Sales Dir: Steven Rosato *E-mail:* srosato@
reedexpo.com
Produced & managed by Reed Exhibitions, BEA
is sponsored by American Booksellers Associa-
tion & Association of American Publishers.
Location: Jacob K Javits Convention Center, New
York, NY, USA
June 2-5, 2005

BookExpo Canada
Sponsored by Reed Exhibitions Canada
3761 Victoria Park Ave, Unit 1, Toronto, ON
M1W 3S2, Canada
Tel: 416-491-7565 (Toronto area); 514-845-1125
(Montreal area) *Toll Free Tel:* 888-322-7333
Fax: 416-491-7096 (Toronto area); 514-845-
8089 (Montreal area) *Toll Free Fax:* 888-633-
3376
Web Site: www.bookexpo.ca
Key Personnel
Show Mgr: Jennifer Sickinger *Tel:* 416-848-1692
E-mail: jsickinger@reedexpo.com
Canada's largest book industry event. Sponsored
by Canadian Booksellers Association.
Location: Metro Toronto Convention Centre,
Toronto, ON, Canada
June 17-20, 2005

British & Irish Association of Law Librarians Annual Conference
Sponsored by British & Irish Association of Law
Librarians
26 Myton Crescent, Warwick CV34 6QA, United
Kingdom
Tel: (01926) 491717 *Fax:* (01926) 491717
Key Personnel
BIALL Administer: Susan Frost
E-mail: susanfrost5@hotmail.com
Location: Harrogate, UK
June 10-12, 2005

The Bronte Society Annual General Meeting
Sponsored by The Bronte Society
The Bronte Parsonage Museum, Church St, Ha-
worth, Keighley, West Yorks BD22 8DR,
United Kingdom
Tel: (01535) 642323 *Fax:* (01535) 647131
E-mail: bronte@bronte.org.uk
Web Site: www.bronte.info
Key Personnel
Museum Mgr: Alan Bentley
Location: Haworth, UK
June 4, 2005

Canadian Library Association Annual Convention & Tradeshow
Sponsored by Canadian Library Association
(CLA)
328 Frank St, Ottawa, ON K2P 0X8, Canada
Tel: 613-232-9625 *Fax:* 613-563-9895
E-mail: info@cla.ca
Web Site: www.cla.ca

Key Personnel
Pres: Madeleine Lefebvre
Exec Dir: Don Butcher *E-mail:* dbutcher@cla.ca
Location: Calgary, AB, Canada
June 15-18, 2005

Eastpack: The Power of Packaging
Sponsored by Canon Communications
11444 W Olympic Blvd, Suite 900, Los Angeles,
CA 90064
Tel: 310-445-4200 *Fax:* 310-996-9499
Web Site: www.cancom.com; www.
canontradeshows.com
Location: Jacob K Javits Convention Center, New
York, NY, USA
June 13-15, 2005

Gutenberg Gesellschaft Annual General Meeting
Sponsored by Gutenberg-Gesellschaft eV (Guten-
berg Society)
Liebfrauenplatz 5, 55116 Mainz, Germany
Tel: (06131) 22 64 20 *Fax:* (06131) 23 35 30
E-mail: gutenberg-gesellschaft@freenet.de
Web Site: www.gutenberg-gesellschaft.uni-mainz.
de
Key Personnel
Sec Gen: Dr Cornelia Fischer
Location: Mainz, Germany
June 25, 2005

IEPRC Annual Conference
Sponsored by International Electronic Publishing
Research Centre Ltd (IEPRC)
c/o David Haywood, LCP, Elephant & Castle,
London SE1 6SB, United Kingdom
Tel: (020) 7514 6938 *Fax:* (020) 7514 6940
E-mail: admin@ieprc.org
Web Site: www.ieprc.org *Telex:* 929810
Location: Jonkoping University, Stockholm, Swe-
den
June 10-11, 2005

International Association of Business Communicators Conference
Sponsored by International Association of Busi-
ness Communicators (IABC)
One Hallidie Plaza, Suite 600, San Francisco, CA
94102
Tel: 415-544-4700 *Toll Free Tel:* 800-776-4222
Fax: 415-544-4747
E-mail: conf@iabc.com
Web Site: www.iabc.com
Key Personnel
Pres: Julie Freeman
Location: Washington, DC, USA
June 2005

International Newsletter & Specialized - Information Conference
Sponsored by Newsletter & Electronic Publishers
Association
1501 Wilson Blvd, Suite 509, Arlington, VA
22209
Tel: 703-527-2333 *Toll Free Tel:* 800-356-9302
Fax: 703-841-0629
E-mail: nepa@newsletters.org
Web Site: www.newsletters.org
Key Personnel
Exec Dir: Patti Wysocki
Location: Mayflower Hotel, Washington, DC,
USA
June 2005

International Newspaper Financial Executives Annual Conference
Sponsored by International Newspaper Financial
Executives
21525 Ridgetop Circle, Suite 200, Sterling, VA
20166
Tel: 703-421-4060
Web Site: www.infe.org

Key Personnel
VP & Exec Dir: Robert J Kasabian
Location: Hilton in the Walt Disney World Re-
sort, Orlando. FL, USA
June 25-29, 2005

International Plate Printers', Die Stampers' & Engravers' Union of North America Mini Meeting
Sponsored by International Plate Printers', Die
Stampers' & Engravers' Union of North Amer-
ica
3957 Smoke Rd, Doylestown, PA 18901
Tel: 215-340-2843
Key Personnel
Sec & Treas: James Kopernick
Location: Mont-Tremblant, Canada
June 2005

Internet World North
Sponsored by Penton Media
The Penton Media Bldg, 1300 E Ninth St, Cleve-
land, OH 44114
Tel: 216-696-7000 *Fax:* 216-696-1752
E-mail: information@penton.com
Web Site: www.internetworld.co.uk
Location: London, UK
June 2005

Outdoor Writers Association of America Annual Conference
Sponsored by Outdoor Writers Association of
America
158 Lower Georges Valley Rd, Spring Mills, PA
16875
Tel: 814-364-9557 *Fax:* 814-364-9558
E-mail: eking4owaa@cs.com
Web Site: www.owaa.org
Location: Madison, WI, USA
June 18-22, 2005

Print Sales & Marketing Executives Conference
Sponsored by Printing Industries of America Inc
200 Deer Run Rd, Sewickley, PA 15143
Tel: 703-519-8143 *Fax:* 412-741-2311
Web Site: www.gain.net
Location: Rancho Bernado Inn, San Diego, CA,
USA
June 26-29, 2005

School Library Association Annual Conference
Sponsored by School Library Association
Unit 2, Lotmead Business Village, Lotmead
Farm, Wanborough, Swindon, Wilts SN4 0UY,
United Kingdom
Tel: (01793) 791787 *Fax:* (01793) 791786
E-mail: info@sla.org.uk
Web Site: www.sla.org.uk
Key Personnel
Chief Executive: Kathy Lemaire *E-mail:* kathy@
sla.org.uk
Location: University of Guildford, Guildford, Sur-
rey, UK
June 17-19, 2005

Science Fiction Research Association Annual Meeting
Sponsored by Science Fiction Research Associa-
tion Inc
University of Guelph, Guelph, ON N1G 2W1,
Canada
Tel: 519-824-4120 (ext 53251)
Web Site: www.sfra.org
Key Personnel
Pres: Peter Brigg *E-mail:* pbrigg@uoguelph.ca
Organizer: Elizabeth Hull *E-mail:* ehull@
harpercollege.edu; Beverly Friend
E-mail: friend@oakton.edu

Location: Imperial Palace Hotel & Casino, Las
Vegas, NV, USA
June 23-26, 2005

Society for Scholarly Publishing Annual Meeting
Sponsored by Society for Scholarly Publishing
10200 W 44 Ave, Suite 304, Wheat Ridge, CO
80033-2840
Tel: 303-422-3914 *Fax:* 303-422-8894
E-mail: ssp@resourcenter.com; info@sspnet.org
Web Site: www.sspnet.org
Location: Westin Boston Copley, MA, USA
June 1-3, 2005

Special Libraries Association Annual Conference
Sponsored by Special Libraries Association
(SLA)
313 S Patrick St, Alexandria, VA 22314
Tel: 703-647-4900 *Fax:* 703-647-4901
E-mail: sla@sla.org
Web Site: www.sla.org
Key Personnel
Exec Dir: Janice LaChance *E-mail:* janice@sla.
org
Location: Toronto, ON, Canada
June 5-8, 2005

Umbrella 2005
Sponsored by Chartered Institute of Library &
Information Professionals (CILIP)
7 Ridgmount St, London WC1E 7AE, United
Kingdom
Tel: (020) 7255 0500 *Fax:* (020) 7255 0501
E-mail: umbrella@cilip.org.uk; conferences@
cilip.org.uk
Web Site: www.umbrella2005.org.uk
Key Personnel
Contact: Joan Thompson *Tel:* (020) 7255 0544
Location: UMIST, Manchester, UK
June 30-July 2, 2005

JULY

ARLIS/UK & Ireland Annual Conference
Sponsored by ARLIS/UK & Ireland Art Libraries
Society
The Courtauld Institute of Art, Somerset House,
The Strand, WC2R ORN London, United
Kingdom
Tel: (020) 7848 2703 *Fax:* (01527) 579298
Web Site: www.arlis.org.uk
Key Personnel
Administrator: Anna Mellows *E-mail:* arlis@
courtauld.ac.uk
Chair: Margaret Young
Location: Aston, Birmingham, UK
July 7-10, 2005

Bibliographical Society of Canada/La Societe bibliographique du Canada Annual Meeting
Sponsored by Bibliographical Society of Canada/
La Societe bibliographique du Canada
PO Box 575, Sta P, Toronto, ON M5S 2T1,
Canada
E-mail: mcgaughe@yorku.ca
Web Site: www.library.utoronto.ca/bsc
Key Personnel
Pres: Carl Spadoni
Conference Coord: Mary F Williamson
E-mail: mfw@yorku.ca; Joan Winearls
E-mail: joan.winearls@utoronto.ca
Location: Halifax, NS, Canada
July 2005

CBA International Convention
Sponsored by CBA

9240 Explorer Dr, Colorado Springs, CO 80920-
5001
Mailing Address: PO Box 62000, Colorado
Springs, CO 80962-2000
Tel: 719-265-9895 *Toll Free Tel:* 800-252-1950
Fax: 719-272-3510
E-mail: info@cbaonline.org
Web Site: www.cbaonline.org
Key Personnel
Pres: William Anderson *E-mail:* banderson@
cbaonline.org
VP & COO: Dorothy Gore
Convention & Expositions Mgr: Scott Graham
For almost 50 years, the annual CBA International Convention has been our industry's
single-most impacting week. During this week,
people of the industry from all over the world
meet face-to-face for buying & selling, educa-
tion, inspiration, fellowship & future planning.
Here individuals unite to further the mission of
seeing Christian product impact lives for God's
kingdom the world over. At this unique gathering, our industry's strength is most evident
& our goals are most clearly in focus. It is, in
short, the most important week in the ministry
of your business & of the industry as a whole.
Location: Colorado Convention Center, Denver,
CO, USA
July 9-14, 2005

Church & Synagogue Library Association Conference
Sponsored by Church & Synagogue Library As-
sociation
PO Box 19357, Portland, OR 97280-0357
Tel: 503-244-6919 *Toll Free Tel:* 800-542-2752
Fax: 503-977-3734
E-mail: csla@worldaccessnet.com
Web Site: www.worldaccessnet.com/~csla
Location: Embassy Suites Hotel, Portland, OR,
USA
July 24-26, 2005

DP: Digital Publishing Fair
Sponsored by Reed Exhibitions Japan Ltd
18F Shinjuku Nomura Bldg, 1-26-2 Nishi-
Shinjuku, Shinjuku-ku, Toyko 163-0570, Japan
Tel: (03) 3349 8507 *Fax:* (03) 3345 7929
E-mail: digi@reedexpo.co.jp
Web Site: www.reedexpo.co.jp/digi
Key Personnel
Deputy Show Dir: Keisuke Amano
Organized by Reed Exhibitions Japan Ltd, TIBF
Executive Committee.
Location: Tokyo Big Sight, Tokyo, Japan
July 6-9, 2005

Hong Kong Book Fair
Sponsored by Hong Kong Trade Development
Council
Unit 13, Expo Galleria, Hong Kong Convention
& Exhibition Centre, One Expo Dr, Wanchai,
Hong Kong
Tel: 2584-4333 *Fax:* 2824-0026; 2824-0249
E-mail: exhibitions@tdc.org.hk
Web Site: hkbookfair.tdc.org.hk
Key Personnel
Sales Adminstrator: Joyce P F Laing *Tel:* 2240-
4018
Location: Hong Kong Convention & Exhibition
Center, One Harbour Rd, Wanchai, Hong Kong
July 2005

International Association of Music Libraries, Archives & Documentation Centres Conference
Sponsored by International Association of Music
Libraries, Archives & Documentation Centres
National Library of New Zealand, Music Room,
PO Box 1467, Wellington 6001, New Zealand
Tel: (04) 474 3039 *Fax:* (04) 474 3035
Web Site: www.iaml.info

Key Personnel
Secretary General: Roger Flury *E-mail:* roger.
  flury@natlib.govt.nz
Location: Warsaw, Poland
July 10-15, 2005

RWA Annual National Conference
Sponsored by Romance Writers of America
16000 Stuebner Airline, Suite 140, Spring, TX
  77379
Tel: 832-717-5200 *Fax:* 832-717-5201
E-mail: info@rwanational.org
Web Site: www.rwanational.org
Key Personnel
Exec Dir: Allison Kelley *E-mail:* akelley@
  rwanational.org
Location: Reno Hilton Hotel, Reno, NV, USA
July 27-30, 2005

TIBF: Tokyo International Book Fair
Sponsored by Reed Exhibitions Japan Ltd
18F Shinjuku Nomura Bldg, 1-26-2 Nishi-
  Shinjuku, Shinjuku-ku, Toyko 163-0570, Japan
Tel: (03) 3349 8507 *Fax:* (03) 3345 7929
E-mail: tibf-eng@reedexpo.co.jp
Web Site: www.reedexpo.co.jp/tibf
Key Personnel
Deputy Show Dir: Keisuke Amano
Organized by Reed Exhibition Japan Ltd, TIBF
  executive committee.
Location: Tokyo Big Sight, Tokyo, Japan
July 6-9, 2005

AUGUST

**The Dorothy L Sayers Society Annual
  Convention**
Sponsored by The Dorothy L Sayers Society
Rose Cottage, Malthouse Lane, Hurstpierpoint,
  West Sussex BN6 9JY, United Kingdom
Tel: (01273) 833444 *Fax:* (01273) 835988
E-mail: info@sayers.org.uk
Web Site: www.sayers.org.uk
Key Personnel
Chairman: Christopher Dean
Location: Christ Church, Oxford, UK
Aug 12-15, 2005

Edinburgh International Book Festival
Scottish Book Centre, 137 Dundee St, Edinburgh
  EH11 1BG, United Kingdom
Tel: (0131) 228 5444 *Fax:* (0131) 228 4333
E-mail: admin@edbookfest.co.uk
Web Site: www.edbookfest.co.uk
Key Personnel
Dir: Catherine Lockerbie
PA to Dir: Lyn Trotter
The festival takes place in Charlotte Square Gar-
  dens (just off the West End of Princes St) over
  17 days each August. An extensive program
  showcases the work of the world's authors &
  thinkers for people of all ages.
Location: Charlotte Square Gardens, Edinburgh,
  UK
Aug 13-29, 2005

Graphic Arts
Sponsored by Business & Industrial Trade Fairs
  Ltd
Unit 103-105, New East Ocean Centre, 9 Science
  Museum Rd, Tsimshatsui East, Kowloon, Hong
  Kong
Tel: 2865 2633 *Fax:* 2866 1770; 2866 2076
E-mail: enquiry@bitf.com.hk
Key Personnel
Senior Manager: Louis Leung

Location: Hong Kong Convention & Exhibition
  Centre, Hong Kong
Aug 2005

Latino Book & Family Festival
Sponsored by Latino Literacy Now
2777 Jefferson St, Suite 200, Carlsbad, CA 92008
Tel: 760-434-4484
Web Site: www.latinobookfestival.com
Key Personnel
Mktg Dir: Jim Sullivan *Fax:* 760-434-7476
  E-mail: jim@lbff.us
Location: Phoenix Civic Plaza, Phoenix, AZ,
  USA
Aug 2005

Print & Pack Expo
Sponsored by Business & Industrial Trade Fairs
  Ltd
Unit 103-105, New East Ocean Centre, 9 Science
  Museum Rd, Tsimshatsui East, Kowloon, Hong
  Kong
Tel: 2865 2633 *Fax:* 2866 1770; 2866 2076
E-mail: enquiry@bitf.com.hk
Web Site: www.printpackexpo.com
Key Personnel
Senior Manager: Louis Leung
Location: Hong Kong Convention & Exhibition
  Centre, Hong Kong
Aug 2005

PSA International Conference of Photography
Sponsored by Photographic Society of America
  Inc (PSA)
3000 United Founders Blvd, Suite 103, Oklahoma
  City, OK 73112-3940
Tel: 405-843-1437 *Fax:* 405-843-1438
E-mail: psahg@theshop.net
Web Site: www.psa-photo.org
Key Personnel
VP, Conventions: Gerry Emmerich
Location: Sheraton City Centre Hotel, Salt Lake
  City, UT, USA
Aug 29-Sept 3, 2005

Seybold Seminars
Sponsored by MediaLive International
795 Folsom St, 6th fl, San Francisco, CA 94107-
  1243
Tel: 415-905-2300 *Fax:* 415-905-2329
Web Site: www.Seybold365.com
Key Personnel
VP & Gen Mgr: James Smith
Location: Moscone Convention Center, San Fran-
  cisco, CA, USA
Aug 29-31, 2005

**South African Booksellers Association Annual
  Conference**
Sponsored by South African Booksellers Associa-
  tion
PO Box 870, Bellville 7535, South Africa
Tel: (021) 945 1572 *Fax:* (021) 945 2169
E-mail: saba@sabooksellers.com
Web Site: sabooksellers.com
Location: Cape Town, South Africa
Aug 16-17, 2005

SWANICK: The Writer's Summer School
Sponsored by Writer's Summer School
10 Stag Rd, Lake Dandown, Isle of Wight PO36
  8PE, United Kingdom
Tel: (07050) 630949 *Fax:* (07050) 630949
E-mail: gxk@cs.nott.ac.uk
Web Site: www.wss.org.uk
Key Personnel
Sec: Jean Sutton *E-mail:* jean.sutton@lineone.net
A week-long summer school of informal talks
  & discussion groups, forums, panels, quizzes,
  competition & a lot of fun. Open to everyone,

from absolute beginners to published authors.
  Held annually in August.
Location: The Hayes Conference Centre, Swan-
  wick, Derbyshire, UK
Aug 2005

TAPPI Fall Technical Conference
Sponsored by Technical Association of the Pulp
  & Paper Industry (TAPPI)
15 Technology Pkwy S, Norcross, GA 30092
Tel: 770-446-1400 *Toll Free Tel:* 800-332-8686
  Fax: 770-446-6947
Web Site: www.tappi.org
Key Personnel
Publg Dir: Mary Beth Cornell *E-mail:* mcornell@
  tappi.org
Adv Mgr: Vince Saputo *E-mail:* vsaputo@tappi.
  org
Corp Rel Dir: Clare Reagan *E-mail:* creagan@
  tappi.org
Location: Philadelphia Marriott, Philadelphia, PA,
  USA
Aug 28-31, 2005

World Library & Information Congress
Sponsored by International Federation of Library
  Associations & Institutions (IFLA)
Postbus 95312, 2509 CH The Hague, Netherlands
Tel: (070) 3140884 *Fax:* (070) 3834827
E-mail: ifla@ifla.org
Web Site: www.ifla.org
Location: Oslo, Norway
Aug 2005

Zimbabwe International Book Fair
PO Box CY1179, Causeway, Harare, Zimbabwe
Tel: (04) 702104/8 *Fax:* (04) 702129
E-mail: information@zibf.org
Web Site: www.zibf.org
Location: Harare Sculpture Gardens, Harare, Zim-
  babwe
Aug 1-6, 2005

AUTUMN

Antwerp Book Fair
Sponsored by Boek.be
Hof ter Shrieklaan 17, 2600 Berchem/Antwerp,
  Belgium
Tel: (03) 2308923 *Fax:* (03) 2812240
E-mail: info@boek.be
Web Site: www.boek.be
Location: Bouwcentrum, Jan van Rijswijcklaan
  191, Antwerp, Belgium
Autumn 2005

Istanbul Book Fair
Sponsored by Tuyap Fuar ve Kongre Merkezi
E-S Karayolu Gurpinar Kavsagi, Beylikduzu/
  Buyukcekmece, 34900 Istanbul, Turkey
Tel: (0212) 886 68 43 *Fax:* (0212) 886 62 43
E-mail: artlink@tuyap.com.tr
Web Site: www.tuyap.com.tr
Location: Tuyap Fair Convention & Congress
  Center, Beylikduzu, Istanbul, Turkey
Autumn 2005

NEPA's Annual Fall Conference
Formerly Newsletter Marketing Conference
Sponsored by Newsletter & Electronic Publishers
  Association
1501 Wilson Blvd, Suite 509, Arlington, VA
  22209
Tel: 703-527-2333 *Toll Free Tel:* 800-356-9302
  Fax: 703-841-0629
E-mail: nepa@newsletters.org
Web Site: www.newsletters.org

Key Personnel
Exec Dir: Patti Wysocki
Autumn 2005

New York Is Book Country
c/o C2 Media, 423 W 55 St, 6th fl, New York, NY 10019
Tel: 646-557-6625 *Fax:* 646-557-6400
E-mail: nyibc@c2media.com
Web Site: www.nyisbookcountry.org
Key Personnel
Exec Dir: Ann Binkley
Annual five-day literary festival throughout the city, culminating in the Sunday, books-only street fair on Fifth Ave between 42nd & 57th Streets, New York, NY, USA.
Location: Fifth Ave, New York, NY, USA
Autumn 2005

Quod Libet/International Antiquarian Book Fair & Artists Books
Sponsored by Luckwaldt Messen
Bruechhorststr 34, 24641 Sievershuetten, Germany
Tel: (04) 194 8101 *Fax:* (04) 194 636
E-mail: frauke@luckwaldt.de
Web Site: www.quod-libet.com
Key Personnel
Organizer: Frauke Luckwaldt
Location: Hamburger Boerse, Adolphsplatz 1, Hamburg, Germany
Autumn 2005

Remainder & Promotional Book Fair
Sponsored by Ciana Ltd
24 Langroyd Rd, London SW17 7PL, United Kingdom
Tel: (020) 8682 1969 *Fax:* (020) 8682 1997
E-mail: enquiries@ciana.co.uk
Web Site: www.ciana.co.uk
Location: Business Design Centre, Islington, London, UK
Autumn 2005

Twin Cities Book Festival
Sponsored by Rain Taxi Review of Books
PO Box 3840, Minneapolis, MN 55403
Tel: 612-825-1528 *Fax:* 612-825-1528
E-mail: bookfest@raintaxi.com
Web Site: www.raintaxi.com
Key Personnel
Dir: Eric Lorberer
Gala celebration of books, featuring large exhibition, author readings & signings, book art activities, panel discussions, used book sale & children's events.
Location: Minneapolis, MN, USA
Autumn 2005

SEPTEMBER

American Medical Writers Association Annual Conference
Sponsored by American Medical Writers Association
40 W Gude Dr, Suite 101, Rockville, MD 20850-1192
Tel: 301-294-5303 *Fax:* 301-294-9006
E-mail: amwa@amwa.org
Web Site: www.amwa.org
Location: Pittsburgh, PA, USA
Sept 29-Oct 1, 2005

Beijing International Book Fair
Sponsored by BIBF Management Office, CNPIEC
16 Gongti E Rd, Chaoyang District, Beijing 100020, China

Tel: (010) 6506 3080 *Fax:* (010) 6506 3101; (010) 6508 9188
E-mail: bibffo@bibf.net
Web Site: www.bibf.net
Key Personnel
Dir: Mr Zhu Zhigang
Location: China International Exhibition Center, Beijing, China
Sept 2005

Distripress Annual Congress
Sponsored by Distripress
Beethovenstr 20, CH-8002 Zurich, Switzerland
Tel: (01) 2024121 *Fax:* (01) 2021025
E-mail: info@distripress.ch
Web Site: www.distripress.ch
Key Personnel
Managing Dir: Dr Peter Emod *E-mail:* peter.emod@distripress.ch
Non-profit association promoting the free international circulation of the press.
Location: Nice, France
Sept 25-29, 2005

European Association of Directory & Database Publishers Annual Congress
Sponsored by European Association of Directory & Database Publishers (EADP)
127 Ave Franklin Roosevelt, 1050 Brussels, Belgium
Tel: (02) 6463060 *Fax:* (02) 6463637
E-mail: mailbox@eadp.org
Web Site: www.eadp.org
Key Personnel
Congress & Conference Officer: Paola Caruso *E-mail:* paolacaruso@eadp.org
Location: Stockholm, Sweden
Sept 14-17, 2005

Garden Writers Association of America Meeting & Symposium
Sponsored by Garden Writers Association of America
10210 Leatherleaf Ct, Manassas, VA 20111
Tel: 703-257-1032 *Fax:* 703-257-0213
E-mail: info@gwaa.org
Web Site: www.gwaa.org
Key Personnel
Pres: Cathy Wilkerson Barash
Exec Dir: Robert LaGasse
Location: Vancouver, BC, Canada
Sept 2005

Goeteborg Book Fair
Sponsored by Bok & Bibliotek
SE-412 94 Goeteborg, Sweden
Tel: (031) 7088400 *Fax:* (031) 209103
E-mail: info@goteborg-bookfair.com
Web Site: www.goteborg-bookfair.com
Key Personnel
Man Dir: Anna Falck *E-mail:* af@goteborg-bookfair.com
Exhibition Mgr: Lisa Oden *E-mail:* lo@goteborg-bookfair.com
Location: Goeteborg, Sweden
Sept 29-Oct 5, 2005

Great Salt Lake Book Festival
Sponsored by Utah Humanities Council
202 W 300 N, Salt Lake City, UT 84103
Tel: 801-359-9670 *Fax:* 801-531-7869
Web Site: www.utahhumanities.org/bookfestival/bookfestival2003_01.php
Key Personnel
Asst Dir & Dir of Progs: Jean Cheney *Tel:* 801-359-9670
Free literary event featuring nationally known authors.
Location: Salt Lake City Library, Salt Lake City, UT, USA
Sept 17-18, 2005

Latino Book & Family Festival
Sponsored by Latino Literacy Now
2777 Jefferson St, Suite 200, Carlsbad, CA 92008
Tel: 760-434-4484
Web Site: www.latinobookfestival.com
Key Personnel
Mktg Dir: Jim Sullivan *Fax:* 760-434-7476
E-mail: jim@lbff.us
Location: California State University, Los Angeles, CA, USA
Sept 2005

Montana Festival of the Book
Sponsored by Montana Committee for the Humanities
311 Brantly Hall, University of Montana, Missoula, MT 59812-8214
Tel: 406-243-6022 *Toll Free Tel:* 800-624-6001 (MT only)
Web Site: www.bookfest-mt.org
Key Personnel
Coord: Kim Anderson
Two day celebration featuring over 70 authors & 50 events.
Location: Missoula, MT, USA
Sept 2005

Moscow International Book Fair
Sponsored by General Directorate of International Book Exhibitions & Fairs
16 Malaya Dmitrovka St, Moscow 127006, Russian Federation
Tel: (095) 2994034 *Fax:* (095) 9732132
E-mail: mibf@mibf.ru
Web Site: www.mibf.ru
Key Personnel
Gen Dir: Mr Nikolay Ph Ovsyannikov
Location: All Russian Exhibition Centre, Moscow, Russia
Sept 2005

National Design Conference
Sponsored by American Institute of Graphic Arts (AIGA)
164 Fifth Ave, New York, NY 10010
Tel: 212-807-1990 (ext 223) *Fax:* 212-807-1799
E-mail: aiga@aiga.org; programs@aiga.org
Web Site: www.aiga.org
Key Personnel
Exec Dir: Richard Grefe
Biennial event.
Location: Boston, MA, USA
Sept 15-17, 2005

National Federation of Press Women National Conference
Sponsored by National Federation of Press Women Inc (NFPW)
PO Box 5556, Arlington, VA 22205-0056
Tel: 703-534-2500 *Toll Free Tel:* 800-780-2715 *Fax:* 703-534-5751
E-mail: presswomen@aol.com
Web Site: www.nfpw.org
Key Personnel
Exec Dir: Carol Pierce
Location: Seattle, WA, USA
Sept 2005

National Newspaper Association Annual Convention & Trade Show
Sponsored by National Newspaper Association
PO Box 7540, Columbia, MO 65205-7540
Mailing Address: 127-129 Neff Annex, Columbia, MO 65211-1200
Tel: 573-882-5800 *Toll Free Tel:* 800-829-4662 *Fax:* 573-884-5490
E-mail: info@nna.org
Web Site: www.nna.org
Key Personnel
Exec Dir: Brian Steffens *E-mail:* briansteffens@nna.org

Meeting Planner: Cindy Joy-Rodgers
   E-mail: crodgers@nna.org
Location: Hyatt Regency, Milwaukee, WI, USA
Sept 28-30, 2005

NIP 21: The 21st International Congress on Digital Printing Technologies
Sponsored by Society for Imaging Science & Technology (IS&T)
7003 Kilworth Lane, Springfield, VA 22151
Tel: 703-642-9090 *Fax:* 703-642-9094
E-mail: info@imaging.org
Web Site: www.imaging.org
Location: Hyatt Regency & Sheridan, Baltimore, MD, USA
Sept 18-23, 2005

PACK EXPO Las Vegas
Sponsored by Packaging Machinery Manufacturers Institute
4350 N Fairfax Dr, Suite 600, Arlington, VA 22203
Tel: 703-243-8555 *Fax:* 703-243-3038
E-mail: expo@pmmi.org
Web Site: www.packexpo.com
Key Personnel
Exhibitor Servs Mgr: Kim Beaulieu
   E-mail: kim@pmmi.org
Location: Las Vegas Convention Center, Las Vegas, NV, USA
Sept 26-28, 2005

Publishers Association of the South Fall Conference & Annual Meeting
Sponsored by Publishers Association of the South (PAS)
4412 Fletcher St, Panama City, FL 32405-1017
Tel: 850-914-0766 *Fax:* 850-769-4348
E-mail: executive@pubsouth.org
Web Site: www.pubsouth.org
Key Personnel
Pres: Beth Wright
Assn Exec: Pat Sabiston
Location: Winston-Salem, NC, USA
Sept 15-16, 2005

Southeast Booksellers Association Annual Meeting & Trade Show
Sponsored by Southeast Booksellers Association (SEBA)
2611 Forest Dr, Suite 124, Columbia, SC 29204
Tel: 803-779-0118 *Fax:* 803-779-0113
E-mail: info@sebaweb.org
Web Site: www.sebaweb.org
Key Personnel
Exec Dir: Wanda Jewell *E-mail:* wanda@sebaweb.org
Location: Adam's Mark, Winston-Salem, NC, USA
Sept 15-19, 2005

Spectrum 2005
Sponsored by IDEAlliance
100 Daingerfield Rd, Alexandria, VA 22314
Tel: 703-837-1070 *Fax:* 703-837-1072
E-mail: info@idealliance.org
Web Site: www.idealliance.org
Key Personnel
Dir, Exec Programs: Georgia Volakis *Tel:* 703-837-1075 *E-mail:* gvolakis@idealliance.com
Location: El Conquistador, Tucson, AZ
Sept 24-27, 2005

OCTOBER

Belgrade International Book Fair
Sponsored by Association of Yugoslav Publishers & Booksellers

Kneza Milosa 25, 11000 Belgrade, Serbia and Montenegro
Tel: (011) 642-248; (011) 642-533 *Fax:* (011) 646-339
Web Site: www.beobookfair.co.yu
Key Personnel
General Dir: Mr Ognjen Lakicevic
   E-mail: ognjenl@eunet.yu
Location: Belgrade, Serbia and Montenegro
Oct 2005

Chicago Book Festival
Sponsored by Chicago Public Library
400 S State St, Chicago, IL 60605
Tel: 312-747-1194
E-mail: info@chicagopubliclibrary.org
Web Site: www.chicagopubliclibrary.org
Location: Chicago, IL, USA
Oct 2005

China Didac/WORLDDIDAC
Sponsored by Worlddidac
Bollwerk 21, 3001 Bern, Switzerland
Mailing Address: PO Box 8866, 3001 Bern, Switzerland
Tel: (031) 311 76 82 *Fax:* (031) 312 17 44
E-mail: info@worlddidac.org
Web Site: www.worlddidac.org
Key Personnel
Proj Mgr: Madeleine Kihm *E-mail:* kihm@worlddidac.org
International exhibition for educational materials, professional training & e-learning.
Location: China
Oct 2005

DMA Annual Conference & Exhibition
Sponsored by The Direct Marketing Association Inc (The DMA)
1120 Avenue of the Americas, New York, NY 10036-6700
Tel: 212-768-7277 *Fax:* 212-302-6714
E-mail: conference@the-dma.org
Web Site: www.dmaannual.org
Key Personnel
VP, Conference Opers: Tana Stellato
Location: Georgia World Congress Center, Atlanta, GA, USA
Oct 15-19, 2005

English Association Semiannual Teachers' Conference
Sponsored by The English Association
University of Leicester, University Rd, Leicester LE1 7RH, United Kingdom
Tel: (0116) 252 3982 *Fax:* (0116) 252 2301
E-mail: engassoc@le.ac.uk
Key Personnel
Chief Exec: Helen Lucas
Conference Org: Louise Callen
Membership Coord: Jeremy Wiltshire
Location: London, UK
October 2005

Frankfurt Book Fair
Sponsored by Ausstellungs-und Messe-GmbH des Borsenvereins des Deutschen Buchhandels
Reineckstr 3, 63013 Frankfurt am Main, Germany
Mailing Address: Postfach 100116, 60001 Frankfurt am Main, Germany
Tel: (069) 21020 *Fax:* (069) 2102 227
E-mail: info@book-fair.com
Web Site: www.frankfurt-book-fair.com *Cable:* BUCHMESSE
Key Personnel
CEO & Dir: Volker Neumann
Location: Frankfurt Fairgrounds, Frankfurt, Germany
Oct 19-24, 2005

Inter American Press Association General Assembly
Sponsored by Inter American Press Association (IAPA)
Jules Dubois Bldg, 1801 SW Third Ave, Miami, FL 33129
Tel: 305-634-2465 *Fax:* 305-635-2272
E-mail: info@sipiapa.org
Web Site: www.sipiapa.org
Key Personnel
Exec Dir: Julio E Munoz
Location: Westin Hotel, Indianapolis, IN, USA
Oct 7-11, 2005

Latino Book & Family Festival
Sponsored by Latino Literacy Now
2777 Jefferson St, Suite 200, Carlsbad, CA 92008
Tel: 760-434-4484
Web Site: www.latinobookfestival.com
Key Personnel
Mktg Dir: Jim Sullivan *Fax:* 760-434-7476
   E-mail: jim@lbff.us
Location: George R Brown Convention Center, Houston, TX, USA
Oct 2005

LIBER Feria Internacional del Libro
Sponsored by Federacion de Gremios de Editores de Espana (FGEE) (Spanish Publishers Association)
Cea Bermudez, 44-2° Dehe, Madrid 20003, Spain
Tel: (091) 5345195 *Fax:* (091) 5352625
E-mail: fgee@fge.es
Web Site: www.federacioneditores.org
Key Personnel
Executive Dir: Antonio Ma Avila
Location: Madrid, Spain
Oct 12-15, 2005

Louisiana Book Festival
Sponsored by State Library of Louisiana
701 N Fourth St, Baton Rouge, LA 70802
Toll Free Tel: 888-487-2700
Web Site: lbf.state.la.us
Location: Louisana State Capital & State Library, Baton Rouge, LA, USA
Oct 29, 2005

Monterrey International Book Fair
Sponsored by Instituto Tecnologico y de Estudios Superiores de Monterrey
Av Eugenio Garza Sada 2501, Col Tecnologico, 648497 Monterrey, Nuevo Leon, Mexico
Tel: (08) 328 43 28; (08) 328 42 82 *Fax:* (08) 359 96 23
E-mail: filmty@fil.mty.itesm.mx
Web Site: fil.mty.itesm.mx
Key Personnel
Opers Dir: Armando Ruiz
Oct 2005

National College Media Convention
Sponsored by Associated Collegiate Press (ACP)
Subsidiary of National Scholastic Press Assn
2221 University Ave SE, Suite 121, Minneapolis, MN 55414
Tel: 612-625-8335 *Fax:* 612-626-0720
E-mail: info@studentpress.org
Web Site: studentpress.org
Key Personnel
Assoc Dir: Ann Akers
Also sponsored by College Media Advisors.
Location: Hyatt Regency, New Orleans, LA, USA
Oct 27-30, 2005

New Atlantic Independent Booksellers Association Annual Trade Show
Sponsored by New Atlantic Independent Booksellers Association (NAIBA)
2667 Hyacinth St, Westbury, NY 11590
Tel: 516-333-0681 *Fax:* 516-333-0689
E-mail: info@naiba.com; readingent@aol.com

Web Site: www.naiba.com
Key Personnel
Exec Dir: Eileen Dengler
Location: Atlantic City, NJ, USA
Oct 23-24, 2005

NPES The Association for Suppliers of Printing, Publishing and Converting Technologies Annual Conference
Sponsored by NPES The Association for Suppliers of Printing, Publishing & Converting Technologies
1899 Preston White Dr, Reston, VA 20191-4367
Tel: 703-264-7200 *Fax:* 703-620-0994
E-mail: npes@npes.org
Web Site: www.npes.org
Key Personnel
Pres: Regis J Delmontagne
Dir, Communs & Mktg: Carol J Hurlburt
    E-mail: churlbur@npes.org
Trade Association representing companies which manufacture equipment, systems, software & supplies used in printing, publishing & converting.
Location: Key Biscayne, FL, USA
Oct 8-10, 2005

Society of Professional Journalists National Convention
Sponsored by The Society of Professional Journalists
Eugene S Pulliam National Journalism Ctr, 3909 N Meridian St, Indianapolis, IN 46208
Tel: 317-927-8000 *Fax:* 317-920-4789
E-mail: spj@spj.org
Web Site: www.spj.org
Key Personnel
Exec Dir: Terrance G Harper
Deputy Dir: Julie Grimes
Programs Coord: Carrie Copeland
Location: Las Vegas, NV, USA
Oct 23-25, 2005

SPAN Conference
Sponsored by Small Publishers Association of North America (SPAN)
425 Cedar St, Buena Vista, CO 81211
Mailing Address: PO Box 1306, Buena Vista, CO 81211-1306
Tel: 719-395-4790 *Fax:* 719-395-8374
E-mail: span@spannet.org
Web Site: www.spannet.org
Key Personnel
Exec Dir: Scott Flora *E-mail:* scott@spannet.org
Busn Mgr: Debi Flora
A meaty, in-depth college for independent presses, authors & self-publishers. Emphasis is on "can-do" marketing/PR strategies.
Location: Colorado, USA
Oct 2005

Texas Book Festival
610 Brazos St, Suite 200, Austin, TX 78701
Tel: 512-477-4055 *Fax:* 512-322-0722
E-mail: bookfest@texasbookfestival.org
Web Site: www.texasbookfestival.org
Key Personnel
Dir: Mary Herman *Tel:* 512-320-5451
    E-mail: maryherman@texasbookfestival.org
Prog Communs Mgr: Edward Nawotka *Tel:* 512-472-3808 *E-mail:* edward@texasbookfestival.org
Off Mgr: Andrea V Prestridge *E-mail:* andrea@texasbookfestival.org
The festival is a statewide program that promotes reading & literacy highlighted by a two-day festival featuring authors from Texas & across the country. Money raised from the festival is distributed as grants to public libraries throughout the state.
Location: State Capital Bldg, Austin, TX, USA
Oct 29-30, 2005

NOVEMBER

American Academy of Religion
Sponsored by American Schools of Oriental Research
825 Houston Mill Rd, Suite 201, Atlanta, GA 30329
Tel: 404-727-3049 *Fax:* 404-727-7959
E-mail: aar@aarweb.org
Web Site: www.aarweb.org
Key Personnel
Prog Dir: Aislinn Jones
Location: Philadelphia, PA, USA
Nov 19-22, 2005

American Translators Association Annual Conference
Sponsored by American Translators Association (ATA)
225 Reinekers Lane, Suite 590, Alexandria, VA 22314
Tel: 703-683-6100 *Fax:* 703-683-6122
E-mail: ata@atanet.org
Web Site: www.atanet.org
Key Personnel
Exec Dir: Walter Bacak *Tel:* 703-683-6100 ext 3006 *E-mail:* walter@atanet.org
Location: Seattle, WA, USA
Nov 9-12, 2005

BMI Annual Conference
Sponsored by Book Manufacturers' Institute Inc (BMI)
2 Armand Beach Dr, Suite 1B, Palm Coast, FL 32137
Tel: 386-986-4552 *Fax:* 386-986-4553
E-mail: info@bmibook.com
Web Site: www.bmibook.org
Key Personnel
Exec VP: Bruce W Smith
Location: Ritz Carlton Orlando Grande Lakes, Orlando, FL, USA
Nov 6-9, 2005

Cairo International Children's Book Fair
Sponsored by General Egyptian Book Organization
Corniche el-Nil - Ramlet Boulac, Cairo 11221, Egypt (Arab Republic of Egypt)
Tel: (02) 5799635; (02) 5775228; (02) 5775109; (02) 5775367; (02) 5775436; (02) 5775545; (02) 5775000 *Fax:* (02) 5765058; (02) 5799635
E-mail: info@egyptianbook.org
Web Site: www.cibf.org; www.egyptianbook.org
Location: Cairo, Egypt
Nov 2005

Children's Book Week
Sponsored by The Children's Book Council (CBC)
12 W 37 St, 2nd fl, New York, NY 10118-7480
Tel: 212-966-1990 *Toll Free Tel:* 800-999-2160 (orders only) *Fax:* 212-966-2073
    Toll Free Fax: 888-807-9355 (orders only)
Web Site: www.cbcbooks.org
Key Personnel
Pres: Paula Quint
Location: Nationwide across the USA
Nov 14-20, 2005

Color Imaging Conference - Color Science Systems & Applications
Sponsored by Society for Imaging Science & Technology (IS&T)
7003 Kilworth Lane, Springfield, VA 22151
Tel: 703-642-9090 *Fax:* 703-642-9094
E-mail: info@imaging.org
Web Site: www.imaging.org
Key Personnel
Gen Co-chair: Po-Chief Hung; Michael Brill

Location: SunBurst Hotel, Scottsdale, AZ, USA
Nov 8-11, 2005

ECPA Publishing University
Sponsored by Evangelical Christian Publishers Association
4816 S Ash Ave, Suite 101, Tempe, AZ 85282-7735
Tel: 480-966-3998 *Fax:* 480-966-1944
E-mail: info@ecpa.org
Web Site: www.ecpa.org
Key Personnel
Pres: Mark Kuyper *E-mail:* mkuyper@ecpa.org
Excellence in Christian publishing through professional instruction, interactive learning & practical training.
Nov 6-8, 2005

Feria Internacional del Libro
Sponsored by Feria Internacional del Libro Guadalajara
Av Alemania 1370, Colonia Moderna, 44190 Guadalajara Jalisco, Mexico
Tel: (033) 3810 0291; (033) 3810 0331
    Fax: (033) 3810 0379
E-mail: fil@fil.com.mx; filny@aol.com
Web Site: www.fil.com.mx
Key Personnel
Pres: Raul Padilla Lopez
Dir: Nubia Edith Macias Navarro *E-mail:* dirfil@fil.com.mx
Gen Coord, Events & Prizes: Laura Niembro Diaz *E-mail:* eventsof@fil.com.mx
Location: Guadalajara, Mexico
Nov 26-Dec 3, 2005

Hall of Fame Awards & Annual Convention
Sponsored by Copywriter's Council of America (CCA)
Division of The Linick Group Inc
CCA Bldg, 7 Putter Lane, Middle Island, NY 11953-0102
Mailing Address: PO Box 102, Middle Island, NY 11953-0102
Tel: 631-924-8555 (ext 203) *Fax:* 631-924-3890
Key Personnel
VP: Roger Dextor
Dir, Spec Proj: Barbara Deal
Location: Orlando, FL, USA
Nov 2005

Jewish Book Month
Sponsored by Jewish Book Council
15 E 26 St, New York, NY 10010-1579
Tel: 212-532-4949 (ext 297) *Fax:* 212-481-4174
E-mail: jbc@jewishbooks.org
Web Site: www.jewishbookcouncil.org
Key Personnel
Exec Dir: Carolyn Starman Hessel
    E-mail: carolynhessel@jewishbooks.org
Nov 26-Dec 26, 2005

Karlsruher Buecherschau
(Karlsruhe Book Exhibition)
Sponsored by Boersenverein des Deutschen Buchhandels, Landesverband Baden-Wuerttemberg eV (Association of Publishers & Booksellers in Baden-Wuerttemberg e V)
Paulinenstr 53, 70178 Stuttgart, Germany
Tel: (0711) 619410 *Fax:* (0711) 6194144
E-mail: post@buchhandelsverband.de
Web Site: www.buchhandelsverband.de
Key Personnel
Exhibition Mgr: Lisa Buchhorn *Tel:* (0711) 61941 26 *E-mail:* buchhorn@buchhandelsverband.de
Location: Landesgewerbeamt, Karl-Friedrich Str 17, Karlsruhe, Germany
Nov 11-Dec 4, 2005

Latino Book & Family Festival
Sponsored by Latino Literacy Now
2777 Jefferson St, Suite 200, Carlsbad, CA 92008
Tel: 760-434-4484
Web Site: www.latinobookfestival.com
Key Personnel
Mktg Dir: Jim Sullivan *Fax:* 760-434-7476
    E-mail: jim@lbff.us
Location: Unity School, Cicero, IL, USA
Nov 2005

Miami Book Fair International
300 NE Second Ave, Suite 3704, Miami, FL
    33132
Tel: 305-237-3258 *Fax:* 305-237-3003
E-mail: wbookfair@mdc.edu
Web Site: www.miamibookfair.com
Key Personnel
Exec Dir: Judy Schmelzer
Location: Miami-Dade Community College,
    Wolfson Campus, Miami FL, USA
Nov 2005

Multicultural Children's Book Festival
Sponsored by Kids Cultural Books
1081 Westover Rd, Stamford, CT 06902
Tel: 203-359-6925 *Fax:* 203-359-3226
E-mail: info@kidsculturalbooks.org
Web Site: www.kidsculturalbooks.org/festivals.
    html
Location: Kennedy Center, Washington, DC, USA
Nov 2005

**Online Information & Content Management
    Europe**
Formerly Online Information
Sponsored by VNU Exhibitions Europe
Subsidiary of VNU Business Media Europe
32-34 Broadwick St, London W1A 2HG, United
    Kingdom
Tel: (020) 7316 9539 *Fax:* (020) 7316 9598
E-mail: fiona.ashton@vnuexhibitions.co.uk
Web Site: www.online-information.co.uk; www.
    cme-expo.co.uk
Key Personnel
Event Dir: Vicky Bush *Tel:* (020) 7316 9585
    E-mail: victoria.bush@vnuexhibitions.co.uk
The show brings together hundreds of compa-
    nies exhibiting the worlds best information re-
    sources, together with solutions for information
    management, knowledge exchange, content
    management, intranets & extranets & epub-
    lishing. It attracts thousands of international
    information managers, knowledge managers,
    librarians, academics, publishers, information
    users & IT professionals.
Location: Olympia Grand Hall, London, UK
Nov 28-Dec 1, 2005

Salon du Livre de Montreal
(Montreal Book Show)
480 Boul St-Laurent, Suite 403, Montreal, PQ
    H2Y 3Y7, Canada
Tel: (514) 845-2365 *Fax:* (514) 845-7119
E-mail: slm.info@videotron.ca
Web Site: www.salondulivredemontreal.com
Key Personnel
Gen Mgr: Francine Bois
Location: La Place Bonaventure, Montreal, PQ,
    Canada
Nov 17-21, 2005

Stuttgarter Buchwochen (Stuttgart Bookweeks)
Sponsored by Boersenverein des Deutschen Buch-
    handels, Landesverband Baden-Wuerttemberg
    eV (Association of Publishers & Booksellers in
    Baden-Wuerttemberg e V)
Paulinenstr 53, 70178 Stuttgart, Germany
Tel: (0711) 619410 *Fax:* (0711) 6194144
E-mail: post@buchhandelsverband.de
Web Site: www.buchhandelsverband.de

Key Personnel
Contact: Maike Dreyer *Tel:* (0711) 619 41 28
    E-mail: dreyer@buchhandelsverband.de
Location: Haus der Wirtschaft, Stuttgart, Germany
Nov 10-Dec 4, 2005

WORLDDIDAC Brazil 2005
Sponsored by Worlddidac
Bollwerk 21, 3001 Bern, Switzerland
Mailing Address: PO Box 8866, 3001 Bern,
    Switzerland
Tel: (031) 311 76 82 *Fax:* (031) 312 17 44
E-mail: info@worlddidac.org
Web Site: www.worlddidac.org
International exhibition for educational materials,
    professional training & e-learning.
Location: Brazil
Nov 2005

Xplor Global Conference
Sponsored by Xplor International
24238 Hawthorne Blvd, Torrance, CA 90505-
    6505
Tel: 310-373-3633 *Toll Free Tel:* 800-669-7567
    (ext 521) *Fax:* 310-375-4240
E-mail: info@xplor.org
Web Site: www.xplor.org
Key Personnel
Dir Prod Devt & Opers: Ellen Dahlin
Location: Walt Disney World, Orlando, FL, USA
Nov 6-10, 2005

WINTER

**The National Center for Database Marketing
    (NCDM)**
Sponsored by Primedia Business Exhibitions
11 River Bend Dr S, Stamford, CT 06907
Mailing Address: PO Box 4254, Stamford, CT
    06907-0254
Tel: 203-358-9900 *Toll Free Tel:* 800-927-5007
    Fax: 203-358-5818
Web Site: www.primediabusiness.com; www.
    ncdmsummer.com; www.ncdmwinter.com
Winter 2005

DECEMBER

Latino Book & Family Festival
Sponsored by Latino Literacy Now
2777 Jefferson St, Suite 200, Carlsbad, CA 92008
Tel: 760-434-4484
Web Site: www.latinobookfestival.com
Key Personnel
Mktg Dir: Jim Sullivan *Fax:* 760-434-7476
    E-mail: jim@lbff.us
Location: Carousel Mall, San Bernardino, CA,
    USA
Dec 2005

**Modern Language Association of America
    Annual Convention**
Sponsored by Modern Language Association of
    America (MLA)
26 Broadway, 3rd fl, New York, NY 10004-1789
Tel: 646-576-5000 *Fax:* 646-576-9930
E-mail: convention@mla.org
Web Site: www.mla.org
Key Personnel
Dir, Conventions: Maribeth T Kraus
Assoc Dir, Conventions: Karin Bagnall
Location: Washington, DC, USA
Dec 27-30, 2005

Small Press Book Fair
Sponsored by Small Press Center
20 W 44 St, New York, NY 10036
Tel: 212-764-7021 *Fax:* 212-354-5365
E-mail: info@smallpress.org
Web Site: www.smallpress.org
Key Personnel
Dir: Karin Taylor
Location: Small Press Center, New York, NY,
    USA
Dec 4-5, 2005

Sofia International Book Fair
Sponsored by Bulgarian Book Publishers Associa-
    tion
11 Slaveikov Sq, 1000 Sofia, Bulgaria
Mailing Address: PO Box 1046, 1000 Sofia, Bul-
    garia
Tel: (02) 986 79 93; (02) 986 79 70 *Fax:* (02)
    986 79 93
E-mail: bba@otel.net; colibri@inet.bg
Web Site: www.bba-bg.org
Key Personnel
Dir: Raymond Wagenstein
Location: National Palace of Culture, Sofia, Bul-
    garia
Dec 2005

2006

JANUARY

**American Library Association Mid-Winter
    Meeting**
Sponsored by American Library Association
    (ALA)
50 E Huron St, Chicago, IL 60611
Toll Free Tel: 800-545-2433 *Fax:* 312-944-6780
E-mail: ala@ala.org
Web Site: www.ala.org/events
Key Personnel
Public Info Dir: Mark Gould
Press Officer: Larra Clark
Location: San Antonio, TX, USA
Jan 20-25, 2006

CBA Advance
Formerly CBA Expo
Sponsored by CBA
9240 Explorer Dr, Colorado Springs, CO 80920-
    5001
Mailing Address: PO Box 62000, Colorado
    Springs, CO 80962-2000
Tel: 719-265-9895 *Toll Free Tel:* 800-252-1950
    Fax: 719-272-3510
E-mail: info@cbaonline.org
Web Site: www.cbaonline.org
Key Personnel
Pres: William Anderson *E-mail:* banderson@
    cbaonline.org
VP & COO: Dorothy Gore
Convention & Expositions Mgr: Scott Graham
Location: Opryland Hotel, Nashville, TN, USA
Jan 23-27, 2006

**Technology, Reading & Learning Difficulties
    (TRLD)**
Sponsored by Don Johnson Inc
26799 W Commerce, Volo, IL 60073
Toll Free Tel: 888-594-1249 *Fax:* 847-740-7326
E-mail: info@trld.com
Web Site: www.trld.com
Key Personnel
Contact: Mary Krenz
TRLD is the only conference that integrates tech-
    nology interventions with expert literacy strate-
    gies to ensure student success. The conference
    brings together educators, experienced literacy

leaders & technology experts to share, discuss & work towards a solution to the nationwide concern of bringing literacy success to all students. Through quality speakers & relevant topics, TRLD gives educators ideas & strategies to immediately implement with students with high incidence disabilities.
Location: Hyatt Regency San Francisco, San Francisco, CA, USA
Jan 26-28, 2006

FEBRUARY

International Book Fair/Los Angeles Book Fair
Sponsored by Antiquarian Booksellers' Association of America
20 W 44 St, 4th fl, New York, NY 10036
Tel: 212-944-8291 *Fax:* 212-944-8293
E-mail: hq@abaa.org
Web Site: www.abaa.org
Key Personnel
Dir: Liane Wade
Location: Los Angeles, CA, USA
Feb 2006

National Association of Science Writers Annual Meeting
Sponsored by National Association of Science Writers (NASW)
PO Box 890, Hedgesville, WV 25427
Tel: 304-754-5077 *Fax:* 304-754-5076
Web Site: www.nasw.org
Key Personnel
Exec Dir: Diane McGurgan *E-mail:* diane@nasw.org
Location: St Louis, MO, USA
Feb 16-21, 2006

SPRING

Gutenberg Festival
Sponsored by Graphic Arts Show Company
1899 Preston White Dr, Reston, VA 20191-4367
Tel: 703-264-7200 *Fax:* 703-620-9187
E-mail: info@gasc.org
Web Site: www.gasc.org
Key Personnel
Dir, Commun: David Poulos
Annual trade show for graphic design, digital prepress, printing, publishing & converting.
Spring 2006

Annual Web Offset Association Conference
Sponsored by Web Offset Association
Division of PIA/GATF
200 Deer Run Rd, Sewickley, PA 15143
Tel: 412-741-6860 *Toll Free Tel:* 800-910-4283
Fax: 412-741-2311
Web Site: www.gain.net
Key Personnel
Meetings Asst: Ricardo Vila-Roger
E-mail: rvilaroger@gatf.org
Location: Orlando, FL, USA
Spring 2006

MARCH

BookTech Conference & Expo
Sponsored by BookTech
401 N Broad St, 5th Fl, Philadelphia, PA 19108
Toll Free Tel: 888-627-2630 *Fax:* 215-409-0100

E-mail: tradeshows@napco.com
Web Site: www.booktechexpo.com
BookTech incorporates the PrintMedia Conference & Expo & the In-Plant Graphics Conference plus a world-class expo on publishing & printing solutions providers.
Location: Hilton New York, 1335 Avenue of the Americas, New York, NY, USA
March 20-22, 2006

CAMEX
Sponsored by National Association of College Stores (NACS)
500 E Lorain St, Oberlin, OH 44074
Tel: 440-775-7777 *Toll Free Tel:* 800-622-7498
Fax: 440-775-4769
E-mail: info@nacs.org
Web Site: www.nacs.org; www.camex.org
Key Personnel
CEO: Brian Cartier
PR Dir: Laura Nakoneczny *Tel:* 440-775-7777, ext 2351 *E-mail:* lnakoneczny@nacs.org
Conference & tradeshow dedicated exclusively to the more than $10 billion collegiate retailing industry.
Location: Houston, TX, USA
March 3-7, 2006

Christian Booksellers Convention - UK
Sponsored by Christian Booksellers Convention Ltd
Victoria House, Victoria Rd, Buckhurst Hill, Essex 1G9 5EX, United Kingdom
Tel: (020) 5592975; (020) 8559 1180 *Fax:* (020) 5029062
E-mail: 100067.1226@compuserve.com
Location: Doncaster Exhibition & Conference Center, Doncaster, UK
March 6-8, 2006

Docugroup 2006
Sponsored by Docucorp International
5910 N Central Expressway, Suite 800, Dallas, TX 75206-5140
Tel: 214-891-6500 *Fax:* 214-987-8187
E-mail: info@docucorp.com
Web Site: www.docucorp.com
Key Personnel
Pres & CEO: Michael D Andereck
March 2006

Inter American Press Association Mid-Year Meeting
Sponsored by Inter American Press Association (IAPA)
Jules Dubois Bldg, 1801 SW Third Ave, Miami, FL 33129
Tel: 305-634-2465 *Fax:* 305-635-2272
E-mail: info@sipiapa.org
Web Site: www.sipiapa.org
Key Personnel
Exec Dir: Julio E Munoz
Meeting Coord: Angeles Mase *E-mail:* amase@sipiapa.org
Location: Quito, Ecuador
March 2006

Leipzig Book Fair
Sponsored by Leipziger Messe GmbH, Projektteam Buchmesse
Messe-Allee 1, 04356 Leipzig, Germany
Mailing Address: Postfach 100 720, 04007 Leipzig, Germany
Tel: (0341) 678 8240 *Fax:* (0341) 678 8242
E-mail: info@leipziger-buchmesse.de
Web Site: www.leipziger-buchmesse.de
Key Personnel
Exhibition Dir: Oliver Zille *Tel:* (0341) 678 8241
Held annually in conjunction with The Leipzig Antiquarian Book Fair.

Location: Neues Messegelande, Leipzig, Germany
March 16-19, 2006

Virginia Festival of the Book
Sponsored by Virginia Foundation for the Humanities
145 Ednam Dr, Charlottesville, VA 22903
Tel: 434-924-6890 *Fax:* 434-296-4714
E-mail: vabook@virginia.edu
Web Site: www.vabook.org
Key Personnel
Program Dir: Nancy Damon *Tel:* 434-924-7548
E-mail: ndamon@virginia.edu
Assoc Program Dir: Kevin McFadden
E-mail: kmcfadden@virginia.edu
Annual free public festival for children & adults featuring authors, illustrators, publishers, publicists, agents & other book professionals in panel discussions & readings for adults & children of all ages.
Location: Charlottesville, VA, USA
March 22-26, 2006

APRIL

African American Children's Book Festival
Sponsored by Kids Cultural Books
1081 Westover Rd, Stamford, CT 06902
Tel: 203-359-6925 *Fax:* 203-359-3226
E-mail: info@kidsculturalbooks.org
Web Site: www.kidsculturalbooks.org/festivals.html
Location: Cathedral of St John the Divine, New York, NY, USA
April 2006

International Children's Book Day
Sponsored by International Board on Books for Young People (IBBY)
Nonnenweg 12, 4003 Basel, Switzerland
Mailing Address: Nonnenweg 12, Postfach, Basel 4003, Switzerland
Tel: (061) 272 29 17 *Fax:* (061) 272 27 57
E-mail: ibby@ibby.org
Web Site: www.ibby.org
On or around Hans Christian Andersen's birthday, April 2nd, International Children's Book day (ICBD) is celebrated to inspire a love of reading & to call attention to children's books. Each year a different national section has the opportunity to be the international sponsor. It decides upon a theme & invites a prominent author to write a message to the children of the world & a well-known illustrator to design a poster. These materials are used in different ways to promote books & reading around the world.
Location: Slovakia
April 2006

Los Angeles Times Festival of Books
Sponsored by Los Angeles Times
Division of Tribune Co
202 W First St, 6th fl, Los Angeles, CA 90012
Tel: 213-237-5000 *Toll Free Tel:* 800-528-4637
Fax: 213-237-2335
Web Site: www.latimes.com/events
Location: UCLA Campus, Los Angeles, CA, USA
April 29-30, 2006

National Library Week
Sponsored by American Library Association (ALA)
50 E Huron St, Chicago, IL 60611
Tel: 312-944-6780 *Toll Free Tel:* 800-545-2433
Fax: 312-944-8520
E-mail: pio@ala.org
Web Site: www.ala.org/events

Key Personnel
Public Info Dir: Mark Gould
Press Officer: Larra Clark *E-mail:* lclark@ala.org
Location: Nationwide throughout the USA
April 2-8, 2006

Newspaper Association of America Annual Convention

Sponsored by Newspaper Association of America (NAA)
1921 Gallows Rd, Suite 600, Vienna, VA 22182
Tel: 703-902-1600 *Fax:* 703-902-1790
E-mail: willa@naa.org
Web Site: www.naa.org
Key Personnel
Pres & CEO: John Sturm
Meetings Mgr: Annette Williams
Location: Fairmont Chicago, Chicago, IL, USA
April 2-5, 2006

NEXPO®

Sponsored by Newspaper Association of America (NAA)
1921 Gallows Rd, Suite 600, Vienna, VA 22182
Tel: 703-902-1600 *Fax:* 703-902-1843
E-mail: sarns@naa.org
Web Site: www.nexpo.com
Key Personnel
Dir of Exhibition Sales: Brad Smith
Annual technical exposition & conference for newspapers.
Location: McCormick Place Conference, Chicago, IL, USA
April 1-4, 2006

North American Agricultural Journalists Spring Meeting

Sponsored by North American Agricultural Journalists
Texas A&M University, 201 Reed Macdonald, 2112 TAMU, College Station, TX 77843-2112
Mailing Address: 2604 Cumberland Ct, College Station, TX 77845
Tel: 979-845-2872 *Fax:* 979-845-2414
Web Site: naaj.tamu.edu
Key Personnel
Exec Sec, Treas: Kathleen Phillips *E-mail:* ka-phillips@tamu.edu
Location: Washington, DC, USA
April 2006

Paper Week

Sponsored by American Forest & Paper Association
1111 19 St NW, Suite 800, Washington, DC 20036
Tel: 202-463-2700 *Fax:* 202-463-4703
E-mail: info@afandpa.org
Web Site: www.afandpa.org; www.paperweek.org
Key Personnel
Pres & CEO: W Henson Moore
Location: Waldorf-Astoria Hotel & Towers, New York, NY, USA
April 9-12, 2006

UK Serials Group Annual Conference & Exhibition

Sponsored by UK Serials Group
PO Box 5594, Newbury RG20 0YP, United Kingdom
Tel: (01635) 254292 *Fax:* (01635) 253826
E-mail: uksg.admin@dial.pipex.com
Web Site: www.uksg.org
Key Personnel
Busn Mgr: Alison Whitehorn
Location: University of Warwick, Coventry, UK
April 3-5, 2006

Young People's Poetry Week

Sponsored by The Children's Book Council (CBC)

12 W 37 St, 2nd fl, New York, NY 10118-7480
Tel: 212-966-1990 *Toll Free Tel:* 800-999-2160 (orders only) *Fax:* 212-966-2073
Toll Free Fax: 888-807-9355 (orders only)
Web Site: www.cbcbooks.org
Key Personnel
Pres: Paula Quint
Location: Nationwide throughout the USA
April 10-16, 2006

MAY

ASQ World Conference on Quality & Improvement

Formerly Annual Quality Congress
Sponsored by American Society for Quality
600 N Plankinton Ave, Milwaukee, WI 53203
Tel: 414-272-8575 *Toll Free Tel:* 800-248-1946 *Fax:* 414-272-1734
E-mail: cs@asq.org
Web Site: www.asq.org *Telex:* 31-6567
Key Personnel
Exec Dir & Chief Strategic Officer: Paul Borawski
Events Mgmt Mgr: Shirley Krentz
Location: Midwest Airlines Center, Milwaukee, WI, USA
May 1-3, 2006

EXPOLIT Exposicion de Literatura Cristiana Book Fair

Sponsored by Spanish Evangelical Publishers Association (SEPA)/Associacion de Editores Evangelicos and Editorial Unilit
1360 NW 88 Ave, Miami, FL 33172
Tel: 305-503-1191 *Toll Free Tel:* 800-767-7726 *Fax:* 305-717-6886
E-mail: wendy@expolit.com
Web Site: www.expolit.com
Key Personnel
Pres, EXPOLIT: David Ecklebarger
Program Dir: Marie Tanayo
Spanish Christian Literature Convention.
Location: Radisson Mart Plaza Hotel & Convention Centre, Miami, FL, USA
May 18-23, 2006

JUNE

American Library Association Annual Conference

Sponsored by American Library Association (ALA)
50 E Huron St, Chicago, IL 60611
Tel: 312-280-3200 *Toll Free Tel:* 800-545-2433 *Fax:* 312-944-7841
E-mail: ala@ala.org
Web Site: www.ala.org
Key Personnel
Public Info Dir: Mark Gould
Press Officer: Larra Clark
Dir, Intl Rel: Michael Dowling
Location: New Orleans, LA, USA
June 22-28, 2006

Canadian Library Association Annual Convention & Tradeshow

Sponsored by Canadian Library Association (CLA)
328 Frank St, Ottawa, ON K2P 0X8, Canada
Tel: 613-232-9625 *Fax:* 613-563-9895
E-mail: info@cla.ca
Web Site: www.cla.ca
Key Personnel
Pres: Madeleine Lefebvre

Exec Dir: Don Butcher *E-mail:* dbutcher@cla.ca
Location: Ottawa, ON, Canada
June 14-17, 2006

International Plate Printers', Die Stampers' & Engravers' Union of North America Mini Meeting

Sponsored by International Plate Printers', Die Stampers' & Engravers' Union of North America
3957 Smoke Rd, Doylestown, PA 18901
Tel: 215-340-2843
Key Personnel
Sec & Treas: James Kopernick
Location: Washington, DC, USA
June 2006

Special Libraries Association Annual Conference

Sponsored by Special Libraries Association (SLA)
313 S Patrick St, Alexandria, VA 22314
Tel: 703-647-4900 *Fax:* 703-647-4901
E-mail: sla@sla.org
Web Site: www.sla.org
Key Personnel
Exec Dir: Janice LaChance *E-mail:* janice@sla.org
Location: Baltimore, MD, USA
June 10-15, 2006

JULY

CBA International Convention

Sponsored by CBA
9240 Explorer Dr, Colorado Springs, CO 80920-5001
Mailing Address: PO Box 62000, Colorado Springs, CO 80962-2000
Tel: 719-265-9895 *Toll Free Tel:* 800-252-1950 *Fax:* 719-272-3510
E-mail: info@cbaonline.org
Web Site: www.cbaonline.org
Key Personnel
Pres: William Anderson *E-mail:* banderson@cbaonline.org
VP & COO: Dorothy Gore
Convention & Expositions Mgr: Scott Graham
For almost 50 years, the annual CBA International Convention has been our industry's single-most impacting week. During this week, people of the industry from all over the world meet face-to-face for buying & selling, education, inspiration, fellowship & future planning. Here individuals unite to further the mission of seeing Christian product impact lives for God's kingdom the world over. At this unique gathering, our industry's strength is most evident & our goals are most clearly in focus. It is, in short, the most important week in the ministry of your business & of the industry as a whole.
Location: Colorado Convention Center, Denver, CO, USA
July 8-13, 2006

Church & Synagogue Library Association Conference

Sponsored by Church & Synagogue Library Association
PO Box 19357, Portland, OR 97280-0357
Tel: 503-244-6919 *Toll Free Tel:* 800-542-2752 *Fax:* 503-977-3734
E-mail: csla@worldaccessnet.com
Web Site: www.worldaccessnet.com/~csla
Location: Greensboro, NC, USA
July 2006

RWA Annual National Conference

Sponsored by Romance Writers of America

16000 Stuebner Airline, Suite 140, Spring, TX
77379
Tel: 832-717-5200 *Fax:* 832-717-5201
E-mail: info@rwanational.org
Web Site: www.rwanational.org
Key Personnel
Exec Dir: Allison Kelley *E-mail:* akelley@
rwanational.org
Location: Atlanta Marriott Marquis, Atlanta, GA,
USA
July 26-29, 2006

AUGUST

South African Booksellers Association Annual Conference
Sponsored by South African Booksellers Associa-
tion
PO Box 870, Bellville 7535, South Africa
Tel: (021) 945 1572 *Fax:* (021) 945 2169
E-mail: saba@sabooksellers.com
Web Site: sabooksellers.com
Location: Durban, South Africa
Aug 15-16, 2006

World Library & Information Congress
Sponsored by International Federation of Library
Associations & Institutions (IFLA)
Postbus 95312, 2509 CH The Hague, Netherlands
Tel: (070) 3140884 *Fax:* (070) 3834827
E-mail: ifla@ifla.org
Web Site: www.ifla.org
Location: Seoul, Korea
Aug 2006

AUTUMN

Business & Design Conference
Sponsored by American Institute of Graphic Arts
(AIGA)
164 Fifth Ave, New York, NY 10010
Tel: 212-807-1990 (ext 223) *Fax:* 212-807-1799
E-mail: aiga@aiga.org; programs@aiga.org
Web Site: www.aiga.org
Key Personnel
Exec Dir: Richard Grefe
Biennial event.
Autumn 2006

SEPTEMBER

Goeteborg Book Fair
Sponsored by Bok & Bibliotek
SE-412 94 Goeteborg, Sweden
Tel: (031) 7088400 *Fax:* (031) 209103
E-mail: info@goteborg-bookfair.com
Web Site: www.goteborg-bookfair.com
Key Personnel
Man Dir: Anna Falck *E-mail:* af@goteborg-
bookfair.com
Exhibition Mgr: Lisa Oden *E-mail:* lo@goteborg-
bookfair.com
Location: Goeteborg, Sweden
Sept 21-24, 2006

International Board on Books for Young People Biennial Congress
Sponsored by International Board on Books for
Young People (IBBY)
Nonnenweg 12, 4003 Basel, Switzerland

Mailing Address: Nonnenweg 12, Postfach, Basel
4003, Switzerland
Tel: (061) 272 29 17 *Fax:* (061) 272 27 57
E-mail: ibby@ibby.org
Web Site: www.ibby.org
IBBY's biennial congresses, hosted by different countries, are the most important meeting
points for IBBY members & other people involved in children's books & reading development. They are wonderful opportunities to
make contacts, exchange ideas & open horizons.
Location: Beijing, China
Sept 20-24, 2006

LIBER Feria Internacional del Libro
Sponsored by Federacion de Gremios de Editores
de Espana (FGEE) (Spanish Publishers Associ-
ation)
Cea Bermudez, 44-2° Dehe, Madrid 20003, Spain
Tel: (091) 5345195 *Fax:* (091) 5352625
E-mail: fgee@fge.es
Web Site: www.federacioneditores.org
Key Personnel
Executive Dir: Antonio Ma Avila
Location: Barcelona, Spain
Sept 27-30, 2006

PSA International Conference of Photography
Sponsored by Photographic Society of America
Inc (PSA)
3000 United Founders Blvd, Suite 103, Oklahoma
City, OK 73112-3940
Tel: 405-843-1437 *Fax:* 405-843-1438
E-mail: psahg@theshop.net
Web Site: www.psa-photo.org
Key Personnel
VP, Conventions: Gerry Emmerich
Location: Hunt Valley Inn, Baltimore, MD, USA
Sept 4-9, 2006

Southeast Booksellers Association Annual Meeting & Trade Show
Sponsored by Southeast Booksellers Association
(SEBA)
2611 Forest Dr, Suite 124, Columbia, SC 29204
Tel: 803-779-0118 *Fax:* 803-779-0113
E-mail: info@sebaweb.org
Web Site: www.sebaweb.org
Key Personnel
Exec Dir: Wanda Jewell *E-mail:* wanda@
sebaweb.org
Location: Gaylord Palms Resort & Convention
Center, Orlando, FL, USA
Sept 8-10, 2006

Spectrum 2006
Sponsored by IDEAlliance
100 Daingerfield Rd, Alexandria, VA 22314
Tel: 703-837-1070 *Fax:* 703-837-1072
E-mail: info@idealliance.org
Web Site: www.idealliance.org
Key Personnel
Dir, Exec Programs: Georgia Volakis *Tel:* 703-
837-1075 *E-mail:* gvolakis@idealliance.com
Location: Fairmont Princess Hotel, Scottsdale,
AZ, USA
Sept 16-19, 2006

OCTOBER

Distripress Annual Congress
Sponsored by Distripress
Beethovenstr 20, CH-8002 Zurich, Switzerland
Tel: (01) 2024121 *Fax:* (01) 2021025
E-mail: info@distripress.ch
Web Site: www.distripress.ch

Key Personnel
Managing Dir: Dr Peter Emod *E-mail:* peter.
emod@distripress.ch
Non-profit association promoting the free interna-
tional circulation of the press.
Location: Barcelona, Spain
Oct 15-19, 2006

Frankfurt Book Fair
Sponsored by Ausstellungs-und Messe-GmbH des
Borsenvereins des Deutschen Buchhandels
Reineckstr 3, 63013 Frankfurt am Main, Germany
Mailing Address: Postfach 100116, 60001 Frank-
furt am Main, Germany
Tel: (069) 21020 *Fax:* (069) 2102 227
E-mail: info@book-fair.com
Web Site: www.frankfurt-book-fair.com *Cable:*
BUCHMESSE
Key Personnel
CEO & Dir: Volker Neumann
Location: Frankfurt Fairgrounds, Frankfurt, Ger-
many
Oct 4-9, 2006

Inter American Press Association General Assembly
Sponsored by Inter American Press Association
(IAPA)
Jules Dubois Bldg, 1801 SW Third Ave, Miami,
FL 33129
Tel: 305-634-2465 *Fax:* 305-635-2272
E-mail: info@sipiapa.org
Web Site: www.sipiapa.org
Key Personnel
Exec Dir: Julio E Munoz
Location: Mexico City, Mexico
Oct 2006

PACK EXPO International
Sponsored by Packaging Machinery Manufactur-
ers Institute
4350 N Fairfax Dr, Suite 600, Arlington, VA
22203
Tel: 703-243-8555 *Fax:* 703-243-3038
E-mail: expo@pmmi.org
Web Site: www.packexpo.com
Key Personnel
Exhibitor Servs Mgr: Kim Beaulieu
E-mail: kim@pmmi.org
Location: McCormick Center, Chicago, IL, USA
Oct 29-Nov 2, 2006

NOVEMBER

American Academy of Religion
Sponsored by American Schools of Oriental Re-
search
825 Houston Mill Rd, Suite 201, Atlanta, GA
30329
Tel: 404-727-3049 *Fax:* 404-727-7959
E-mail: aar@aarweb.org
Web Site: www.aarweb.org
Key Personnel
Prog Dir: Aislinn Jones
Location: Washington, DC, USA
Nov 18-21, 2006

Children's Book Week
Sponsored by The Children's Book Council
(CBC)
12 W 37 St, 2nd fl, New York, NY 10118-7480
Tel: 212-966-1990 *Toll Free Tel:* 800-999-
2160 (orders only) *Fax:* 212-966-2073
Toll Free Fax: 888-807-9355 (orders only)
Web Site: www.cbcbooks.org
Key Personnel
Pres: Paula Quint
Location: Nationwide across the USA
Nov 13-19, 2006

Ghana International Book Fair
Sponsored by Ghana Trade Fair Co Ltd
Trade Fair Centre, Accra, Ghana
Mailing Address: PO Box TF 111, Accra, Ghana
Tel: (021) 776611; (021) 772376; (021) 776614;
  (024) 622891; (024) 513210 *Fax:* (021) 772012
E-mail: gtfa@ighmail.com
Web Site: www.ghanatradefair.com
Key Personnel
Acting Dir, Busn Devt: Gabriel K Kamasa
Location: Accra, Ghana
Nov 2006

Hall of Fame Awards & Annual Convention
Sponsored by Copywriter's Council of America
  (CCA)
Division of The Linick Group Inc
CCA Bldg, 7 Putter Lane, Middle Island, NY
  11953-0102
Mailing Address: PO Box 102, Middle Island,
  NY 11953-0102
Tel: 631-924-8555 (ext 203) *Fax:* 631-924-3890
Key Personnel
VP: Roger Dextor
Dir, Spec Proj: Barbara Deal
Location: Orlando, FL, USA
Nov 2006

Karlsruher Buecherschau
(Karlsruhe Book Exhibition)
Sponsored by Boersenverein des Deutschen Buch-
  handels, Landesverband Baden-Wuerttemberg
  eV (Association of Publishers & Booksellers in
  Baden-Wuerttemberg e V)
Paulinenstr 53, 70178 Stuttgart, Germany
Tel: (0711) 619410 *Fax:* (0711) 6194144
E-mail: post@buchhandelsverband.de
Web Site: www.buchhandelsverband.de
Key Personnel
Exhibition Mgr: Lisa Buchhorn *Tel:* (0711) 61941
  26 *E-mail:* buchhorn@buchhandelsverband.de
Location: Landesgewerbeamt, Karl-Friedrich Str
  17, Karlsruhe, Germany
Nov 17-Dec 10, 2006

National College Media Convention
Sponsored by Associated Collegiate Press (ACP)
Subsidiary of National Scholastic Press Assn
2221 University Ave SE, Suite 121, Minneapolis,
  MN 55414
Tel: 612-625-8335 *Fax:* 612-626-0720
E-mail: info@studentpress.org
Web Site: studentpress.org
Key Personnel
Assoc Dir: Ann Akers
Also sponsored by College Media Advisors.
Location: Adams Mark, St Louis, MO, USA
Nov 2-5, 2006

Salon du Livre de Jeunesse (Childrens Book Fair)
Sponsored by Reed Expositions France
Subsidiary of Reed Exhibition Companies
11 rue du Colonel Pierre Avia, 75726 Paris Cedex
  15, France
Tel: (01) 41 90 47 47 *Fax:* (01) 41 90 47 00
E-mail: cplj@ldg.tm.fr; infos@reedexpo.fr
Web Site: www.reed-expo.fr; www.ldj.tm.fr
Key Personnel
Contact: Denis-Luc Panthin *E-mail:* panthin@ldj.
  tm.fr
France's leading publishing event dedicated to
  children's books.
Location: Rue de Paris, Montreuil, France
Nov 23-19, 2006

Stuttgarter Buchwochen (Stuttgart Bookweeks)
Sponsored by Boersenverein des Deutschen Buchhandels, Landesverband Baden-Wuerttemberg
  eV (Association of Publishers & Booksellers in
  Baden-Wuerttemberg e V)

Paulinenstr 53, 70178 Stuttgart, Germany
Tel: (0711) 619410 *Fax:* (0711) 6194144
E-mail: post@buchhandelsverband.de
Web Site: www.buchhandelsverband.de
Key Personnel
Contact: Maike Dreyer *Tel:* (0711) 619 41 28
  E-mail: dreyer@buchhandelsverband.de
Location: Haus der Wirtschaft, Stuttgart, Germany
Nov 9-Dec 3, 2006

Xplor Global Conference
Sponsored by Xplor International
24238 Hawthorne Blvd, Torrance, CA 90505-
  6505
Tel: 310-373-3633 *Toll Free Tel:* 800-669-7567
  (ext 521) *Fax:* 310-375-4240
E-mail: info@xplor.org
Web Site: www.xplor.org
Key Personnel
Dir Prod Devt & Opers: Ellen Dahlin
Location: Walt Disney World, Orlando, FL, USA
Nov 5-9, 2006

2007

JANUARY

American Library Association Mid-Winter Meeting
Sponsored by American Library Association
  (ALA)
50 E Huron St, Chicago, IL 60611
Toll Free Tel: 800-545-2433 *Fax:* 312-944-6780
E-mail: ala@ala.org
Web Site: www.ala.org/events
Key Personnel
Public Info Dir: Mark Gould
Press Officer: Larra Clark
Location: Seattle, WA, USA
Jan 19-24, 2007

CBA Advance
Formerly CBA Expo
Sponsored by CBA
9240 Explorer Dr, Colorado Springs, CO 80920-
  5001
Mailing Address: PO Box 62000, Colorado
  Springs, CO 80962-2000
Tel: 719-265-9895 *Toll Free Tel:* 800-252-1950
  Fax: 719-272-3510
E-mail: info@cbaonline.org
Web Site: www.cbaonline.org
Key Personnel
Pres: William Anderson *E-mail:* banderson@
  cbaonline.org
VP & COO: Dorothy Gore
Convention & Expositions Mgr: Scott Graham
Location: Indiana Convention Center, Indianapo-
  lis, IN, USA
Jan 29-Feb 3, 2007

FEBRUARY

National Association of Science Writers Annual Meeting
Sponsored by National Association of Science
  Writers (NASW)
PO Box 890, Hedgesville, WV 25427
Tel: 304-754-5077 *Fax:* 304-754-5076
Web Site: www.nasw.org
Key Personnel
Exec Dir: Diane McGurgan *E-mail:* diane@nasw.
  org

Location: San Francisco, CA, USA
Feb 15-20, 2007

SPRING

Graphic Arts/The Charlotte Show
Sponsored by Graphic Arts Show Company
1899 Preston White Dr, Reston, VA 20191-4367
Tel: 703-264-7200 *Fax:* 703-620-9187
E-mail: info@gasc.org
Web Site: www.gasc.org *Telex:* NPES MCLN
Key Personnel
Pres: Regis J Delmontagne
Biennial event featuring equipment, products &
  services for graphic communications industry.
Location: Charlotte, NC, USA
Spring 2007

MARCH

CAMEX
Sponsored by National Association of College
  Stores (NACS)
500 E Lorain St, Oberlin, OH 44074
Tel: 440-775-7777 *Toll Free Tel:* 800-622-7498
  Fax: 440-775-4769
E-mail: info@nacs.org
Web Site: www.nacs.org; www.camex.org
Key Personnel
CEO: Brian Cartier
PR Dir: Laura Nakoneczny *Tel:* 440-775-7777,
  ext 2351 *E-mail:* lnakoneczny@nacs.org
Conference & tradeshow dedicated exclusively to
  the more than $10 billion collegiate retailing
  industry.
Location: Orlando, FL, USA
March 23-27, 2007

Inter American Press Association Mid-Year Meeting
Sponsored by Inter American Press Association
  (IAPA)
Jules Dubois Bldg, 1801 SW Third Ave, Miami,
  FL 33129
Tel: 305-634-2465 *Fax:* 305-635-2272
E-mail: info@sipiapa.org
Web Site: www.sipiapa.org
Key Personnel
Exec Dir: Julio E Munoz
Meeting Coord: Angeles Mase *E-mail:* amase@
  sipiapa.org
Location: Valencia, Venezuela
March 2007

Virginia Festival of the Book
Sponsored by Virginia Foundation for the Hu-
  manities
145 Ednam Dr, Charlottesville, VA 22903
Tel: 434-924-6890 *Fax:* 434-296-4714
E-mail: vabook@virginia.edu
Web Site: www.vabook.org
Key Personnel
Program Dir: Nancy Damon *Tel:* 434-924-7548
  E-mail: ndamon@virginia.edu
Assoc Program Dir: Kevin McFadden
  E-mail: kmcfadden@virginia.edu
Annual free public festival for children & adults
  featuring authors, illustrators, publishers, pub-
  licists, agents & other book professionals in
  panel discussions & readings for adults & chil-
  dren of all ages.
Location: Charlottesville, VA, USA
March 21-25, 2007

APRIL

Los Angeles Times Festival of Books
Sponsored by Los Angeles Times
Division of Tribune Co
202 W First St, 6th fl, Los Angeles, CA 90012
Tel: 213-237-5000 *Toll Free Tel:* 800-528-4637
   Fax: 213-237-2335
Web Site: www.latimes.com/events
Location: UCLA Campus, Los Angeles, CA,
   USA
April 28-29, 2007

National Library Week
Sponsored by American Library Association
   (ALA)
50 E Huron St, Chicago, IL 60611
Tel: 312-944-6780 *Toll Free Tel:* 800-545-2433
   Fax: 312-944-8520
E-mail: pio@ala.org
Web Site: www.ala.org/events
Key Personnel
Public Info Dir: Mark Gould
Press Officer: Larra Clark *E-mail:* lclark@ala.org
Location: Nationwide throughout the USA
April 15-21, 2007

NEXPO®
Sponsored by Newspaper Association of America
   (NAA)
1921 Gallows Rd, Suite 600, Vienna, VA 22182
Tel: 703-902-1600 *Fax:* 703-902-1843
E-mail: sarns@naa.org
Web Site: www.nexpo.com
Key Personnel
Dir of Exhibition Sales: Brad Smith
Annual technical exposition & conference for
   newspapers.
Location: Orange County Convention Center, Or-
   lando, FL, USA
April 21-24, 2007

Young People's Poetry Week
Sponsored by The Children's Book Council
   (CBC)
12 W 37 St, 2nd fl, New York, NY 10118-7480
Tel: 212-966-1990 *Toll Free Tel:* 800-999-
   2160 (orders only) *Fax:* 212-966-2073
   Toll Free Fax: 888-807-9355 (orders only)
Web Site: www.cbcbooks.org
Key Personnel
Pres: Paula Quint
Location: Nationwide throughout the USA
April 16-22, 2007

MAY

**EXPOLIT Exposicion de Literatura Cristiana
   Book Fair**
Sponsored by Spanish Evangelical Publishers
   Association (SEPA)/Associacion de Editores
   Evangelicos and Editorial Unilit
1360 NW 88 Ave, Miami, FL 33172
Tel: 305-503-1191 *Toll Free Tel:* 800-767-7726
   Fax: 305-717-6886
E-mail: wendy@expolit.com
Web Site: www.expolit.com
Key Personnel
Pres, EXPOLIT: David Ecklebarger
Program Dir: Marie Tanayo
Spanish Christian Literature Convention.
Location: Radisson Mart Plaza Hotel & Conven-
   tion Centre, Miami, FL, USA
May 17-22, 2007

**Newspaper Association of America Annual
   Convention**
Sponsored by Newspaper Association of America
   (NAA)
1921 Gallows Rd, Suite 600, Vienna, VA 22182
Tel: 703-902-1600 *Fax:* 703-902-1790
E-mail: willa@naa.org
Web Site: www.naa.org
Key Personnel
Pres & CEO: John Sturm
Meetings Mgr: Annette Williams
Location: New York Marriott Marquis, New York,
   NY, USA
May 6-9, 2007

PrintEx
Sponsored by Graphic Arts Merchants Associa-
   tion of Australia Inc (GAMMA)
PO Box 1051, Crows Nest, NSW 2065, Australia
Tel: (02) 9417 7433 *Fax:* (02) 9417 7433
E-mail: enquiry@gamma.net.au
Web Site: www.printex.net.au; www.gamma.net.au
PrintEx brings the latest printing & graphic com-
   munications technologies to the industry. Co-
   sponsored by The Printing Industries Associa-
   tion of Australia (PIAA).
Location: Sydney Convention & Exhibition Cen-
   tre, Darling Harbour, Sydney, NSW, Australia
May 2007

SUMMER

**The Dorothy L Sayers Society Annual
   Convention**
Sponsored by The Dorothy L Sayers Society
Rose Cottage, Malthouse Lane, Hurstpierpoint,
   West Sussex BN6 9JY, United Kingdom
Tel: (01273) 833444 *Fax:* (01273) 835988
E-mail: info@sayers.org.uk
Web Site: www.sayers.org.uk
Key Personnel
Chairman: Christopher Dean
Location: Wheaton College, Wheaton, IL, USA
Summer 2007

JUNE

**American Library Association Annual
   Conference**
Sponsored by American Library Association
   (ALA)
50 E Huron St, Chicago, IL 60611
Tel: 312-280-3200 *Toll Free Tel:* 800-545-2433
   Fax: 312-944-7841
E-mail: ala@ala.org
Web Site: www.ala.org
Key Personnel
Public Info Dir: Mark Gould
Press Officer: Larra Clark
Dir, Intl Rel: Michael Dowling
Location: Washington, DC, USA
June 21-27, 2007

**Special Libraries Association Annual
   Conference**
Sponsored by Special Libraries Association
   (SLA)
313 S Patrick St, Alexandria, VA 22314
Tel: 703-647-4900 *Fax:* 703-647-4901
E-mail: sla@sla.org
Web Site: www.sla.org
Key Personnel
Exec Dir: Janice LaChance *E-mail:* janice@sla.
   org

Location: Denver, CO, USA
June 2-7, 2007

JULY

CBA International Convention
Sponsored by CBA
9240 Explorer Dr, Colorado Springs, CO 80920-
   5001
Mailing Address: PO Box 62000, Colorado
   Springs, CO 80962-2000
Tel: 719-265-9895 *Toll Free Tel:* 800-252-1950
   Fax: 719-272-3510
E-mail: info@cbaonline.org
Web Site: www.cbaonline.org
Key Personnel
Pres: William Anderson *E-mail:* banderson@
   cbaonline.org
VP & COO: Dorothy Gore
Convention & Expositions Mgr: Scott Graham
For almost 50 years, the annual CBA International Convention has been our industry's
   single-most impacting week. During this week,
   people of the industry from all over the world
   meet face-to-face for buying & selling, education, inspiration, fellowship & future planning.
   Here individuals unite to further the mission of
   seeing Christian product impact lives for God's
   kingdom the world over. At this unique gathering, our industry's strength is most evident
   & our goals are most clearly in focus. It is, in
   short, the most important week in the ministry
   of your business & of the industry as a whole.
Location: Georgia World Congress, Atlanta, GA,
   USA
July 7-12, 2007

**Church & Synagogue Library Association
   Conference**
Sponsored by Church & Synagogue Library As-
   sociation
PO Box 19357, Portland, OR 97280-0357
Tel: 503-244-6919 *Toll Free Tel:* 800-542-2752
   Fax: 503-977-3734
E-mail: csla@worldaccessnet.com
Web Site: www.worldaccessnet.com/~csla
Location: Philadelphia, PA, USA
July 2007

RWA Annual National Conference
Sponsored by Romance Writers of America
16000 Stuebner Airline, Suite 140, Spring, TX
   77379
Tel: 832-717-5200 *Fax:* 832-717-5201
E-mail: info@rwanational.org
Web Site: www.rwanational.org
Key Personnel
Exec Dir: Allison Kelley *E-mail:* akelley@
   rwanational.org
Location: Hyatt Regency Dallas, Dallas, TX,
   USA
July 11-14, 2007

SEPTEMBER

Goeteborg Book Fair
Sponsored by Bok & Bibliotek
SE-412 94 Goeteborg, Sweden
Tel: (031) 7088400 *Fax:* (031) 209103
E-mail: info@goteborg-bookfair.com
Web Site: www.goteborg-bookfair.com
Key Personnel
Man Dir: Anna Falck *E-mail:* af@goteborg-
   bookfair.com

Exhibition Mgr: Lisa Oden *E-mail:* lo@goteborg-bookfair.com
Location: Goeteborg, Sweden
Sept 20-23, 2007

PSA International Conference of Photography
Sponsored by Photographic Society of America Inc (PSA)
3000 United Founders Blvd, Suite 103, Oklahoma City, OK 73112-3940
Tel: 405-843-1437 *Fax:* 405-843-1438
E-mail: psahg@theshop.net
Web Site: www.psa-photo.org
Key Personnel
VP, Conventions: Gerry Emmerich
Location: Starr Pass Marriott Resort & Spa, Tucson, AZ, USA
Sept 3-8, 2007

OCTOBER

Inter American Press Association General Assembly
Sponsored by Inter American Press Association (IAPA)
Jules Dubois Bldg, 1801 SW Third Ave, Miami, FL 33129
Tel: 305-634-2465 *Fax:* 305-635-2272
E-mail: info@sipiapa.org
Web Site: www.sipiapa.org
Key Personnel
Exec Dir: Julio E Munoz
Location: Miami, FL, USA
Oct 2007

National College Media Convention
Sponsored by Associated Collegiate Press (ACP)
Subsidiary of National Scholastic Press Assn
2221 University Ave SE, Suite 121, Minneapolis, MN 55414
Tel: 612-625-8335 *Fax:* 612-626-0720
E-mail: info@studentpress.org
Web Site: studentpress.org
Key Personnel
Assoc Dir: Ann Akers
Also sponsored by College Media Advisors.
Location: Washington Hilton, Washington, DC, USA
Oct 25-28, 2007

PACK EXPO Las Vegas
Sponsored by Packaging Machinery Manufacturers Institute
4350 N Fairfax Dr, Suite 600, Arlington, VA 22203
Tel: 703-243-8555 *Fax:* 703-243-3038
E-mail: expo@pmmi.org
Web Site: www.packexpo.com
Key Personnel
Exhibitor Servs Mgr: Kim Beaulieu
E-mail: kim@pmmi.org
Location: Las Vegas Convention Center, Las Vegas, NV, USA
Oct 15-18, 2007

NOVEMBER

American Academy of Religion
Sponsored by American Schools of Oriental Research
825 Houston Mill Rd, Suite 201, Atlanta, GA 30329
Tel: 404-727-3049 *Fax:* 404-727-7959
E-mail: aar@aarweb.org

Web Site: www.aarweb.org
Key Personnel
Prog Dir: Aislinn Jones
Location: San Diego, CA, USA
Nov 17-20, 2007

Children's Book Week
Sponsored by The Children's Book Council (CBC)
12 W 37 St, 2nd fl, New York, NY 10118-7480
Tel: 212-966-1990 *Toll Free Tel:* 800-999-2160 (orders only) *Fax:* 212-966-2073
Toll Free Fax: 888-807-9355 (orders only)
Web Site: www.cbcbooks.org
Key Personnel
Pres: Paula Quint
Location: Nationwide across the USA
Nov 12-18, 2007

Stuttgarter Buchwochen (Stuttgart Bookweeks)
Sponsored by Boersenverein des Deutschen Buchhandels, Landesverband Baden-Wuerttemberg eV (Association of Publishers & Booksellers in Baden-Wuerttemberg e V)
Paulinenstr 53, 70178 Stuttgart, Germany
Tel: (0711) 619410 *Fax:* (0711) 6194144
E-mail: post@buchhandelsverband.de
Web Site: www.buchhandelsverband.de
Key Personnel
Contact: Maike Dreyer *Tel:* (0711) 619 41 28
E-mail: dreyer@buchhandelsverband.de
Location: Haus der Wirtschaft, Stuttgart, Germany
Nov-Dec, 2007

2008
MARCH

Virginia Festival of the Book
Sponsored by Virginia Foundation for the Humanities
145 Ednam Dr, Charlottesville, VA 22903
Tel: 434-924-6890 *Fax:* 434-296-4714
E-mail: vabook@virginia.edu
Web Site: www.vabook.org
Key Personnel
Program Dir: Nancy Damon *Tel:* 434-924-7548
E-mail: ndamon@virginia.edu
Assoc Program Dir: Kevin McFadden
E-mail: kmcfadden@virginia.edu
Annual free public festival for children & adults featuring authors, illustrators, publishers, publicists, agents & other book professionals in panel discussions & readings for adults & children of all ages.
Location: Charlottesville, VA, USA
March 26-30, 2008

APRIL

National Library Week
Sponsored by American Library Association (ALA)
50 E Huron St, Chicago, IL 60611
Tel: 312-944-6780 *Toll Free Tel:* 800-545-2433
Fax: 312-944-8520
E-mail: pio@ala.org
Web Site: www.ala.org/events
Key Personnel
Public Info Dir: Mark Gould
Press Officer: Larra Clark *E-mail:* lclark@ala.org
Location: Nationwide throughout the USA
April 13-19, 2008

Young People's Poetry Week
Sponsored by The Children's Book Council (CBC)
12 W 37 St, 2nd fl, New York, NY 10118-7480
Tel: 212-966-1990 *Toll Free Tel:* 800-999-2160 (orders only) *Fax:* 212-966-2073
Toll Free Fax: 888-807-9355 (orders only)
Web Site: www.cbcbooks.org
Key Personnel
Pres: Paula Quint
Location: Nationwide throughout the USA
April 14-20, 2008

MAY

EXPOLIT Exposicion de Literatura Cristiana Book Fair
Sponsored by Spanish Evangelical Publishers Association (SEPA)/Associacion de Editores Evangelicos and Editorial Unilit
1360 NW 88 Ave, Miami, FL 33172
Tel: 305-503-1191 *Toll Free Tel:* 800-767-7726
Fax: 305-717-6886
E-mail: wendy@expolit.com
Web Site: www.expolit.com
Key Personnel
Pres, EXPOLIT: David Ecklebarger
Program Dir: Marie Tanayo
Spanish Christian Literature Convention.
Location: Radisson Mart Plaza Hotel & Convention Centre, Miami, FL, USA
May 15-20, 2008

JUNE

American Library Association Annual Conference
Sponsored by American Library Association (ALA)
50 E Huron St, Chicago, IL 60611
Tel: 312-280-3200 *Toll Free Tel:* 800-545-2433
Fax: 312-944-7841
E-mail: ala@ala.org
Web Site: www.ala.org
Key Personnel
Public Info Dir: Mark Gould
Press Officer: Larra Clark
Dir, Intl Rel: Michael Dowling
Location: Anaheim, CA, USA
June 26-July 2, 2008

IPA Congress
Sponsored by International Publishers Association
Av de Miremont 3, 1206 Geneva, Switzerland
Tel: (022) 3463018 *Fax:* (022) 3475717
E-mail: secretariat@ipa-uie.org
Web Site: www.ipa-uie.org
Key Personnel
Secretary General: Jens Bammel
Held every 4 years.
Location: Berlin, Germany
June 2008

JULY

CBA International Convention
Sponsored by CBA
9240 Explorer Dr, Colorado Springs, CO 80920-5001
Mailing Address: PO Box 62000, Colorado Springs, CO 80962-2000

Tel: 719-265-9895 *Toll Free Tel:* 800-252-1950
 Fax: 719-272-3510
E-mail: info@cbaonline.org
Web Site: www.cbaonline.org
Key Personnel
Pres: William Anderson *E-mail:* banderson@
cbaonline.org
VP & COO: Dorothy Gore
Convention & Expositions Mgr: Scott Graham
For almost 50 years, the annual CBA International Convention has been our industry's single-most impacting week. During this week, people of the industry from all over the world meet face-to-face for buying & selling, education, inspiration, fellowship & future planning. Here individuals unite to further the mission of seeing Christian product impact lives for God's kingdom the world over. At this unique gathering, our industry's strength is most evident & our goals are most clearly in focus. It is, in short, the most important week in the ministry of your business & of the industry as a whole.
Location: Orange County Convention Center, Orlando, FL, USA
July 12-17, 2008

RWA Annual National Conference
Sponsored by Romance Writers of America
16000 Stuebner Airline, Suite 140, Spring, TX 77379
Tel: 832-717-5200 *Fax:* 832-717-5201
E-mail: info@rwanational.org
Web Site: www.rwanational.org
Key Personnel
Exec Dir: Allison Kelley *E-mail:* akelley@
rwanational.org
Location: San Francisco Marriott, San Francisco, CA, USA
July 30-Aug 2, 2008

Special Libraries Association Annual Conference
Sponsored by Special Libraries Association (SLA)
313 S Patrick St, Alexandria, VA 22314
Tel: 703-647-4900 *Fax:* 703-647-4901
E-mail: sla@sla.org
Web Site: www.sla.org
Key Personnel
Exec Dir: Janice LaChance *E-mail:* janice@sla.org
Location: Seattle, WA, USA
July 26-31, 2008

AUTUMN

AICC/TAPPI SuperCorrExpo® 2008
Sponsored by Technical Association of the Pulp & Paper Industry (TAPPI)
15 Technology Pkwy S, Norcross, GA 30092
Tel: 770-446-1400 *Toll Free Tel:* 800-332-8686
 Fax: 770-446-6947
Web Site: www.tappi.org
Key Personnel
Publg Dir: Mary Beth Cornell *E-mail:* mcornell@tappi.org
Corp Rel Dir: Clare Reagan *E-mail:* creagan@tappi.org
Adv Mgr: Vince Saputo *E-mail:* vsaputo@tappi.org
Autumn 2008

SEPTEMBER

Goeteborg Book Fair
Sponsored by Bok & Bibliotek

SE-412 94 Goeteborg, Sweden
Tel: (031) 7088400 *Fax:* (031) 209103
E-mail: info@goteborg-bookfair.com
Web Site: www.goteborg-bookfair.com
Key Personnel
Man Dir: Anna Falck *E-mail:* af@goteborg-bookfair.com
Exhibition Mgr: Lisa Oden *E-mail:* lo@goteborg-bookfair.com
Location: Goeteborg, Sweden
Sept 25-28, 2008

International Board on Books for Young People Biennial Congress
Sponsored by International Board on Books for Young People (IBBY)
Nonnenweg 12, 4003 Basel, Switzerland
Mailing Address: Nonnenweg 12, Postfach, Basel 4003, Switzerland
Tel: (061) 272 29 17 *Fax:* (061) 272 27 57
E-mail: ibby@ibby.org
Web Site: www.ibby.org
IBBY's biennial congresses, hosted by different countries, are the most important meeting points for IBBY members & other people involved in children's books & reading development. They are wonderful opportunities to make contacts, exchange ideas & open horizons.
Location: Copenhagen, Denmark
Sept 7-11, 2008

OCTOBER

American Academy of Religion
Sponsored by American Schools of Oriental Research
825 Houston Mill Rd, Suite 201, Atlanta, GA 30329
Tel: 404-727-3049 *Fax:* 404-727-7959
E-mail: aar@aarweb.org
Web Site: www.aarweb.org
Key Personnel
Prog Dir: Aislinn Jones
Location: Chicago, IL, USA
Oct 25-28, 2008

2009
SPRING

Graphic Arts/The Charlotte Show
Sponsored by Graphic Arts Show Company
1899 Preston White Dr, Reston, VA 20191-4367
Tel: 703-264-7200 *Fax:* 703-620-9187
E-mail: info@gasc.org
Web Site: www.gasc.org *Telex:* NPES MCLN
Key Personnel
Pres: Regis J Delmontagne
Biennial event featuring equipment, products & services for graphic communications industry.
Location: Charlotte, NC, USA
Spring 2009

MARCH

Virginia Festival of the Book
Sponsored by Virginia Foundation for the Humanities
145 Ednam Dr, Charlottesville, VA 22903
Tel: 434-924-6890 *Fax:* 434-296-4714

E-mail: vabook@virginia.edu
Web Site: www.vabook.org
Key Personnel
Program Dir: Nancy Damon *Tel:* 434-924-7548
 E-mail: ndamon@virginia.edu
Assoc Program Dir: Kevin McFadden
 E-mail: kmcfadden@virginia.edu
Annual free public festival for children & adults featuring authors, illustrators, publishers, publicists, agents & other book professionals in panel discussions & readings for adults & children of all ages.
Location: Charlottesville, VA, USA
March 18-22, 2009

APRIL

National Library Week
Sponsored by American Library Association (ALA)
50 E Huron St, Chicago, IL 60611
Tel: 312-944-6780 *Toll Free Tel:* 800-545-2433
 Fax: 312-944-8520
E-mail: pio@ala.org
Web Site: www.ala.org/events
Key Personnel
Public Info Dir: Mark Gould
Press Officer: Larra Clark *E-mail:* lclark@ala.org
Location: Nationwide throughout the USA
April 12-18, 2009

Young People's Poetry Week
Sponsored by The Children's Book Council (CBC)
12 W 37 St, 2nd fl, New York, NY 10118-7480
Tel: 212-966-1990 *Toll Free Tel:* 800-999-2160 (orders only) *Fax:* 212-966-2073
 Toll Free Fax: 888-807-9355 (orders only)
Web Site: www.cbcbooks.org
Key Personnel
Pres: Paula Quint
Location: Nationwide throughout the USA
April 13-19, 2009

MAY

EXPOLIT Exposicion de Literatura Cristiana Book Fair
Sponsored by Spanish Evangelical Publishers Association (SEPA)/Associacion de Editores Evangelicos and Editorial Unilit
1360 NW 88 Ave, Miami, FL 33172
Tel: 305-503-1191 *Toll Free Tel:* 800-767-7726
 Fax: 305-717-6886
E-mail: wendy@expolit.com
Web Site: www.expolit.com
Key Personnel
Pres, EXPOLIT: David Ecklebarger
Program Dir: Marie Tanayo
Spanish Christian Literature Convention.
Location: Radisson Mart Plaza Hotel & Convention Centre, Miami, FL, USA
May 14-19, 2009

JULY

CBA International Convention
Sponsored by CBA
9240 Explorer Dr, Colorado Springs, CO 80920-5001

Mailing Address: PO Box 62000, Colorado Springs, CO 80962-2000
Tel: 719-265-9895 *Toll Free Tel:* 800-252-1950
Fax: 719-272-3510
E-mail: info@cbaonline.org
Web Site: www.cbaonline.org
Key Personnel
Pres: William Anderson *E-mail:* banderson@cbaonline.org
VP & COO: Dorothy Gore
Convention & Expositions Mgr: Scott Graham
For almost 50 years, the annual CBA International Convention has been our industry's single-most impacting week. During this week, people of the industry from all over the world meet face-to-face for buying & selling, education, inspiration, fellowship & future planning. Here individuals unite to further the mission of seeing Christian product impact lives for God's kingdom the world over. At this unique gathering, our industry's strength is most evident & our goals are most clearly in focus. It is, in short, the most important week in the ministry of your business & of the industry as a whole.
Location: Colorado Convention Center, Denver, CO, USA
July 11-16, 2009

RWA Annual National Conference
Sponsored by Romance Writers of America

16000 Stuebner Airline, Suite 140, Spring, TX 77379
Tel: 832-717-5200 *Fax:* 832-717-5201
E-mail: info@rwanational.org
Web Site: www.rwanational.org
Key Personnel
Exec Dir: Allison Kelley *E-mail:* akelley@rwanational.org
Location: Marriott Wardman Park Hotel, Washington, DC, USA
July 15-18, 2009

NOVEMBER

American Academy of Religion
Sponsored by American Schools of Oriental Research
825 Houston Mill Rd, Suite 201, Atlanta, GA 30329
Tel: 404-727-3049 *Fax:* 404-727-7959
E-mail: aar@aarweb.org
Web Site: www.aarweb.org
Key Personnel
Prog Dir: Aislinn Jones
Location: Montreal, PQ, Canada
Nov 7-10, 2009

2010

MAY

EXPOLIT Exposicion de Literatura Cristiana Book Fair
Sponsored by Spanish Evangelical Publishers Association (SEPA)/Associacion de Editores Evangelicos and Editorial Unilit
1360 NW 88 Ave, Miami, FL 33172
Tel: 305-503-1191 *Toll Free Tel:* 800-767-7726
Fax: 305-717-6886
E-mail: wendy@expolit.com
Web Site: www.expolit.com
Key Personnel
Pres, EXPOLIT: David Ecklebarger
Program Dir: Marie Tanayo
Spanish Christian Literature Convention.
Location: Radisson Mart Plaza Hotel & Convention Centre, Miami, FL, USA
May 13-18, 2010

Writers' Conferences & Workshops

The following lists workshops and seminars dealing with various aspects of the book trade. See **Courses for the Book Trade** for a list of college level programs and courses.

Alice B Acheson's Workshops for Writers, Illustrators & Photographers
Alice B Acheson
Unit of Acheson-Greub Inc
PO Box 735, Friday Harbor, WA 98250
Tel: 360-378-2815 *Fax:* 360-378-2841
E-mail: aliceba@aol.com
Key Personnel
Pres: Alice B Acheson
One- or two-day workshops on making a ms succeed in the market place. Writers utilize a pre-class assignment to determine techniques for finding & impressing an agent &/or publisher while class discussion includes discovering what's to come once the ms is under contract. Extensive written materials provided. Instructor shares 30 years of book publishing expertise in negotiating contracts, editing books & achieving award-winning book publicity.
Location: Book Passage, San Francisco, CA
Date: March 5-6, 2005

Advanced Sheetfed Press Operations
PIA/GATF (Graphic Arts Technical Foundation)
200 Deer Run Rd, Sewickley, PA 15143-2600
Tel: 412-741-6860 *Toll Free Tel:* 800-910-4283
  Fax: 412-741-2311
E-mail: info@gain.net
Web Site: www.gain.net
Key Personnel
Pres: Michael Makin
Mktg Mgr: Lisa Erdner
Training Mgr: Sara Hantz *Tel:* 412-741-6860 ext 113 *E-mail:* shantz@gatf.org

American Society of Journalists & Authors Writers Conference
American Society of Journalists & Authors (ASJA)
1501 Broadway, Suite 302, New York, NY 10036
Tel: 212-997-0947 *Fax:* 212-768-7414
E-mail: staff@asja.org
Web Site: www.asja.org
Key Personnel
Exec Dir: Ms Brett Harvey *E-mail:* execdir@asja.org
Don't miss out! Mark your calendars now for the event that attracts hundreds of freelance writers every year-the ASJA Writers Conference. You'll hear inside information from editors, agents & publishers, find inspiration & gain income-boosting ideas. Open to all, the ASJA Writers Conference features a Breaking into Print track, with topics for newer writers, & a Business of Writing track for more experienced pros. Other exciting, new panels & workshops will enrich you no matter where you are in your writing career. If you've attended before, we think you'll be pleased by the additions we've made to the program as well as by the new spins on popular subjects.
Location: Grand Hyatt Hotel, New York, NY
Date: April 16-17, 2005

AMWA Annual Conference
American Medical Writers Association
40 W Gude Dr, Suite 101, Rockville, MD 20850-1192
Tel: 301-294-5303 *Fax:* 301-294-9006
Web Site: www.amwa.org

Key Personnel
Exec Dir: Shari Lynn
Annual conference includes over 85 workshops.
Location: Pittsburgh, PA
Date: Sept 28-30, 2005

Antioch Writers' Workshop
Yellow Springs Writers' Workshop
PO Box 494, Yellow Springs, OH 45387-0494
Tel: 937-475-7357; 937-767-2700 (Board of Trustees)
E-mail: info@antiochwritersworkshop.com
Web Site: www.antiochwritersworkshop.com
Key Personnel
Pres: Priscilla Janney-Pace
VP: Janice Wilson
Dir: Laura Carlson
A week-long summer workshop featuring morning classes, midday presentations on writing profession, afternoon intensive seminars in a genre or type, evening faculty talks & readings & late evening ms feedback sessions.
Location: Antioch College, Yellow Springs, OH
Date: July 9-15, 2005

Arkansas Writers' Conference
Pioneer Branch of National League of American Pen Women/Arkansas Branch
6817 Gingerbread Lane, Little Rock, AR 72204
Tel: 501-565-8889 *Fax:* 501-565-7220
Key Personnel
Counselor & Contact: Peggy Vining
  E-mail: pvining@aristotle.net
Two-day annual conference; conference information available Feb 1. Thirty conference competitions are available. Please write for brochure at above address-enclose SASE.
Location: Holiday Inn Select, Little Rock, AR
Date: Always first full weekend in June, Fri & Sat

Aspen Summer Words Writing Retreat & Literary Festival
Aspen Writers' Foundation
110 E Hallam St, Suite 116, Aspen, CO 81611
Tel: 970-925-3122 *Fax:* 970-920-5700
E-mail: info@aspenwriters.org
Web Site: www.aspenwriters.org
Key Personnel
Dir: Lisa Consiglio
A four-day writing retreat with morning workshops in fiction, poetry, memoir & essay complimented by a five-day literary festival in the afternoons & evenings, featuring 17 events for readers as well as writers.

The Association for Women In Communications
The Association for Women in Communications
780 Richie Hwy, Suite 28-S, Severna Park, MD 21146
Tel: 410-544-7442 *Fax:* 410-544-4640
E-mail: info@womcom.org
Web Site: www.womcom.org
Key Personnel
Exec Dir: Patricia Troy
Membership Dir: Nancy Badertscher
Professional development workshops & exposition in various areas of the communications field.

Association pour l'Avancement des Sciences et des Techniques de la Documentation
3414 Avenue du Parc, Bureau 202, Montreal, PQ H2X 2H5, Canada
Tel: 514-281-5012 *Fax:* 514-281-8219
E-mail: info@asted.org
Web Site: www.asted.org

Atlantic Center for the Arts
Member of Alliance for Artists Communities
1414 Art Center Ave, New Smyrna Beach, FL 32168
Tel: 386-427-6975 *Toll Free Tel:* 800-393-6975
  Fax: 386-427-5669
E-mail: program@atlanticcenterforthearts.org
Web Site: www.atlantic-centerforthearts.org
Key Personnel
Exec Dir: Ann Brady
Progs: Jim Frost
Residency Mgr: Nicholas Conroy
Since 1982, Atlantic Center's residency program has provided artists from all artistic disciplines with spaces to live, work & collaborate during three-week residencies. Each residency session includes three master artists of different disciplines. The master artists each personally select a group of associates - talented, emerging artists - through an application process administered by ACA. During the residency, artists participate in informal sessions with their group, collaborate on projects & work independently on their own projects. The relaxed atmosphere & unstructured program provide considerable time for artistic regeneration & creation. The residency program is free to accepted artists.
Location: New Smyrna Beach, FL
Date: Feb 7-27, 2005
Location: New Smyrna Beach, FL
Date: March 7-27, 2005
Location: New Smyrna Beach, FL
Date: May 16-June 5
Location: New Smyrna Beach, FL
Date: June 27-July 17, 2005
Location: New Smyrna Beach, FL
Date: Sept 5-25, 2005
Location: New Smyna Beach, FL
Date: Oct 10-30, 2005

Autumn Authors' Affair
Love Designers Writers' Club
Affiliate of Chapter of RWA
1507 Burnham Ave, Calumet City, IL 60409
Tel: 708-862-9797
E-mail: exchbook@aol.com
Web Site: www.rendezvousreviews.com
Key Personnel
Pres: Nancy McCann
Corresponding Sec: Virginia A Deweese *Tel:* 219-931-2673 *E-mail:* vadew9340@aol.com
Publish *Rendezvous* (monthly review of women's contemporary & historical romances, fantasy, science fiction, mysteries & women's fiction).
Location: Hickory Ridge Conference Center, Lisle, IL
Date: Oct annually

Bard Society
1358 Tiber Ave, Jacksonville, FL 32207
Tel: 904-398-5352

Key Personnel
Dir: Frank Green *E-mail:* frankgrn@comcast.net
Fiction writing workshop. Schedule: one workshop a week, Tuesday evening, three hours.

Bennington Writing Seminars
Bennington College
One College Dr, Bennington, VT 05201
Tel: 802-440-4452 *Fax:* 802-440-4453
E-mail: writing@bennington.edu
Web Site: www.bennington.edu/graduateprogram
Key Personnel
Dir: Liam Rector
Asst Dir: Priscilla Hodgkins *E-mail:* phodgkin@bennington.edu
Graduate program in creative writing & literature: fiction, nonfiction, poetry.

Beyond the Book
Copyright Clearance Center (CCC)
222 Rosewood Dr, Danvers, MA 01923
Toll Free Tel: 800-928-3887 (ext 2420) *Fax:* 978-750-4250
E-mail: beyondthebook@copyright.com
Web Site: www.copyright.com
Key Personnel
Dir, Author & Creator Rels: Christopher Kenneally *Tel:* 978-646-2705 *E-mail:* chrisk@copyright.com
Our programs also include online seminars & telephone conference calls with distinguished experts. Created with authors in mind, Beyond the Book seeks to provide information on the latest business issues facing the creative professions - from initial research to final publication & beyond. Your connection to leading editors, publishing analysts & information technology experts, as well as innovative authors. For information on all programs & details about upcoming events visit our website or call the toll-free number.

Book Producing: Making Books Happen
American Book Producers Association (ABPA)
160 Fifth Ave, New York, NY 10010-7003
Tel: 212-645-2368 *Toll Free Tel:* 800-209-4575 *Fax:* 212-242-6799
E-mail: office@abpaonline.org
Web Site: www.abpaonline.org
Key Personnel
Pres: Ellen Scordato; Dan Tucker
Bd of Dirs: Jim Buckley; Katrina Fried; John Glenn; Susan Knopf; Valerie Tomaselli
Admin: David Katz

Bread Loaf Writers' Conference
Middlebury College
Kirk Alumni Center, Middlebury, VT 05753
Tel: 802-443-5286 *Fax:* 802-443-2087
E-mail: blwc@middlebury.edu
Web Site: www.middlebury.edu
Key Personnel
Dir: Michael Collier
Assoc Dir: Devon Jersild
Admin Mgr: Noreen Cargill
For writers of poetry, fiction & nonfiction. Eleven-day conference.
Date: Mid-to-late Aug

The Brockport Writers' Forum
SUNY College at Brockport, Dept of English
350 New Campus Dr, Brockport, NY 14420-2968
Tel: 585-395-5713 *Fax:* 585-395-2391
Web Site: www.acs.brockport.edu/~wforum/Main.html
Key Personnel
Dir: Stan Sanvel Rubin
Week-long workshop on fiction & poetry for writers & aspiring writers; journals, poetry, fiction, creative nonfiction, science fiction; plus occasionally mystery writing, children's literature.

College credit available. Scholarship available; call for information.
Location: Special Weekend Workshops: SUNY Brockport, Brockport, NY, USA
Date: Weekends in Jan
Location: Regular Workshop: SUNY Brockport, Brockport, NY, USA
Date: Last week in June

Brooklyn Writers Club
PO Box 184, Bath Beach Sta, Brooklyn, NY 11214-0184
Tel: 718-680-4084
Key Personnel
Founder & Dir: A Dellarocco
Weekly meetings, ms critique, editing, marketing information, workshops & contests at various locations.

Annual Cape Cod Writers' Conference
Cape Cod Writers' Center
PO Box 408, Osterville, MA 02655
Tel: 508-420-0200
E-mail: ccwc@capecod.net
Web Site: www.capecodwriterscenter.com
Key Personnel
Pres: Shirley Eastmen
Dir: Jacqueline M Loring
To hone skills as you learn from top professionals about your craft & the business of writing. In addition to classes in fiction, nonfiction, mystery, poetry, children's & other genres, the conference, set in a rustic setting overlooking Nantucket Sound, offers opportunities to meet with an editor-in-residence & agents-in-residence. Personal conferences & ms evaluations are available as well as a Young Writers Workshop. Many special events added for this year.
Location: Craigville Conference Center, Craigville, Cape Cod, MA

Caribbean Christian Writers Conference Cruise
American Christian Writers Association
PO Box 110390, Nashville, TN 37222
Tel: 615-834-0450 *Toll Free Tel:* 800-21-WRITE (219-7483)
Web Site: www.acwriters.com
Key Personnel
Dir: Reg Forder *E-mail:* regaforder@aol.com

Central Ohio Writers of Literature for Children
St Joseph Montessori School (SJMS) & Second Avenue Elementary School
c/o St Joseph Montessori School, 933 Hamlet St, Columbus, OH 43201-3595
Tel: 614-291-8644 *Fax:* 614-291-7411
E-mail: cowriters@mail.com
Web Site: www.sjms.net/conf
Key Personnel
Dir: Hari Ruiz *E-mail:* cowriters@mail.com
SJMS, Devt Dir: Jim Mengel
Programming Chair: Robert Miller
Fundraising Chair: Ernestine Jackson
Registrations Chair: Wendy Harper
School Visits Co-Chair: Nancy Addington; Marci Kipfer
Conference for teachers, parents, librarians, writers & illustrators. Provide breakout sessions in two interest tracks: teacher/parent/librarian & writer/illustrator, mss evaluations, illustration portfolio evaluations, writers' workshops, an illustrators workshop & two keynote speakers. Evaluations & workshops are provided at an additional cost. Certificates of Attendance are available for teachers for CEU credit.
Location: Fawcett Conference Center, 2400 Olentangy River Rd, Columbus, OH
Date: April 23, 2005

Chautauqua Writers' Workshop
The Writer's Center at Chautauqua
PO Box 28, Chautauqua, NY 14722-0408
Tel: 716-357-6200 *Toll Free Tel:* 800-836-ARTS (836-2787)
E-mail: cpaul@chautauquava-inst.com
Web Site: www.ciweb.org
Key Personnel
Pres: Thomas M Becker *Tel:* 716-357-6221
Writing workshop in poetry & prose at 130 year-old Chautauqua Institution, international center for the arts, education, religion & recreation.
Location: Chautauqua Institution, Chautauqua, NY
Date: Last week in June - end of August

Christian Writers' Conference
Mount Hermon Christian Conference Center
PO Box 413, Mount Hermon, CA 95041-0413
Tel: 831-335-4466 *Fax:* 831-335-9413
Web Site: www.mounthermon.org/writers
Key Personnel
Dir, Adult Ministries: David R Talbott *E-mail:* dtalbott@mhcamps.org
A working, five-day professional writing conference.
Location: Mount Hermon Christian Conference Center, Mount Hermon, CA
Date: March 18-22, 2005
Location: Mount Hermon Christian Conference Center, Mount Hermon, CA
Date: April 7-11, 2006

Christian Writers' Conference
American Christian Writers
Division of Christian Writers Institute
PO Box 110390, Nashville, TN 37222-0390
Tel: 615-834-0450 *Toll Free Tel:* 800-219-7483 *Fax:* 615-834-7736
E-mail: acwriters@aol.com
Web Site: www.acwriters.com
Key Personnel
Dir: Reg A Forder *E-mail:* regaforder@aol.com
Correspondence courses; 36 Christian Writers' conferences annually, approximately three per month in major cities throughout the US. Monthly magazine by subscription.
Location: Houston, TX
Date: Feb 12, 2005
Location: Dallas, TX
Date: Feb 18-19, 2005
Location: Oklahoma City, OK
Date: Feb 25-26, 2005
Location: Atlanta, GA
Date: March 18-19, 2005
Location: Charlotte, NC
Date: April 1-2, 2005
Location: Richmond, VA
Date: April 8-9, 2005
Location: Cleveland, OH
Date: April 15-16, 2005
Location: Fort Wayne, IN
Date: April 29-30, 2005
Location: Nashville, TN
Date: May 20-21, 2005
Location: Columbus, OH
Date: June 3-4, 2005
Location: Buffalo, NY
Date: June 10-11, 2005
Location: Grand Rapids, MI
Date: June 24-25, 2005
Location: Louisville, KY
Date: July 30, 2005
Location: Indianapolis, IN
Date: Aug 5-6, 2005
Location: Minneapolis, MN
Date: Aug 12-13, 2005
Location: Springfield, MO
Date: Aug 20, 2005
Location: Colorado Springs, CO
Date: Sept 9-10, 2005
Location: Boise, ID
Date: Sept 17, 2005

Location: Seattle, WA
Date: Sept 24, 2005
Location: Sacramento, CA
Date: Oct 15, 2005
Location: Anaheim, CA
Date: Oct 21-22, 2005
Location: Phoenix, AZ
Date: Oct 28-29, 2005
Location: Orlando, FL
Date: Nov 19, 2005
Location: Caribbean Cruise
Date: Nov 27-Dec 4, 2005

Clarion Workshop in Science Fiction & Fantasy Writing
Michigan State University, College of Arts & Letters
Michigan State University, 112 Olds Hall, East Lansing, MI 48824-1047
Tel: 517-355-9598 *Fax:* 517-353-4765
Web Site: www.msu.edu/~clarion
Key Personnel
Contact: Mary Sheridan *E-mail:* sherida3@msu.edu
Science fiction & fantasy writing workshop.
Date: June 12-July 22, 2005

Color Management for the Pressroom
PIA/GATF (Graphic Arts Technical Foundation)
200 Deer Run Rd, Sewickley, PA 15143-2600
Tel: 412-741-6860 *Toll Free Tel:* 800-910-4283
   Fax: 412-741-2311
E-mail: info@gain.net
Web Site: www.gain.net
Key Personnel
Pres: Michael Makin
Mktg Mgr: Lisa Erdner
Training Mgr: Sara Hantz *Tel:* 412-741-6860 ext 113 *E-mail:* shantz@gatf.org

Creative Writing Conference
Eastern Kentucky University
Case Annex 467, 512 Lancaster Ave, Richmond, KY 40475-3102
Tel: 859-622-5861 *Fax:* 859-622-3156
Web Site: www.english.eku.edu
Key Personnel
Contact: Christine Delea
Lectures/workshops in drama, poetry & fiction.
Location: Eastern Kentucky University, Richmond, KY
Date: Summer, 2005

Creative Writing Day & Workshops
Virginia Highland Festival
PO Box 801, Abingdon, VA 24212-0801
Tel: 276-623-5266 *Fax:* 276-623-5266
E-mail: vhf@eva.org
Web Site: www.vahighlandsfestival.org
Key Personnel
Coord: Erna Wilkin
Lectures, readings & workshops in creative writing with noteworthy authors.
Location: Abingdon, VA
Date: July 30-Aug 14, 2005

Desert Writers Workshop
Canyonlands Field Institute
PO Box 68, Moab, UT 84532
Tel: 435-259-7750 *Toll Free Tel:* 800-860-5262
   Fax: 435-259-2335
E-mail: info@canyonlandsfields.com
Web Site: www.canyonlandsfieldinst.com
Key Personnel
Exec Dir: Karla Vander Zanden
Workshop highlights a weeklong program. Oriented toward understanding the vital connection between human beings & the natural world. Participants work with instructors in small groups at a retreat lodge setting. The program includes faculty & student readings, individual consultations & optional naturalists-guided hikes.

Duke University Writers' Workshop
Duke University
PO Box 90700, Durham, NC 27708-0700
Tel: 919-684-6259 *Fax:* 919-681-8235
E-mail: learnmore@duke.edu
Web Site: www.learnmore.duke.edu
Key Personnel
Dir: Georgann Eubanks *E-mail:* geubanks@duke.edu
Poetry, nonfiction & variety of fiction workshops; individual conferences; readings & lectures; beach cookout.

Education Writers Association Workshops
Education Writers Association
2122 "P" St NW, No 201, Washington, DC 20037
Tel: 202-452-9830 *Fax:* 202-452-9837
E-mail: ewa@ewa.org
Web Site: www.ewa.org
Key Personnel
Exec Dir: Lisa J Walker *E-mail:* lwalker@ewa.org
National Seminar, regional meetings.
Location: Philadelphia, PA
Date: Feb, 2005

Emerson College Publishing Seminars
Emerson College
120 Boylston St, Boston, MA 02116-8750
Tel: 617-824-8280 *Fax:* 617-824-8158
E-mail: continuing@emerson.edu
Web Site: www.emerson.edu/ce
Key Personnel
Dir, Continuing Educ: Hank Zappala *Tel:* 617-824-8281
Chmn, Div of WLP: Daniel Tobin
Seminar Coord: Leslie Busler
Graduate level seminars in all aspects of book & magazine publishing, leading to a formal certificate. Two semester course on Tues & Thurs evenings.

Emory Summer Writers' Institute & Festival
Emory University, Summer School
c/o Creative Writing Program, Emory University, Rm N209, Callaway Center, Atlanta, GA 30322
Tel: 404-727-4683 *Fax:* 404-727-4672
Web Site: www.emory.edu/college/creativewriting
Key Personnel
Admin Asst: Paula Vitaris *E-mail:* pvitari@emory.edu
College credit workshops, free festival events with major author.

Feminist Women's Writing Workshops, Inc
Feminist Women's Writing Workshops Inc
PO Box 6583, Ithaca, NY 14851-6583
Tel: 607-274-3325
Key Personnel
Workshop Dir: Katharyn Howd Machan *E-mail:* machan@ithaca.edu
Annual summer writing workshop based in Ithaca.

Festival of Poetry
The Robert Frost Place
Ridge Rd, Franconia, NH 03580
Mailing Address: PO Box 74, Franconia, NH 03580
Tel: 603-823-5510
E-mail: rfrost@nci.net
Web Site: www.frostplace.org
Key Personnel
Dir: Donald Sheehan *E-mail:* donald.sheehan@dartmouth.edu

Asst Dir: Keisha Luce
Daily seminars, workshops & readings in a seven-day program.

Fine Tune Your CTP Installation
PIA/GATF (Graphic Arts Technical Foundation)
200 Deer Run Rd, Sewickley, PA 15143-2600
Tel: 412-741-6860 *Toll Free Tel:* 800-910-4283
   Fax: 412-741-2311
E-mail: info@gain.net
Web Site: www.gain.net
Key Personnel
Pres: Michael Makin
Mktg Mgr: Lisa Erdner
Training Mgr: Sara Hantz *Tel:* 412-741-6860 ext 113 *E-mail:* shantz@gatf.org

Florida Suncoast Writers' Conference
University of South Florida, Dept of English
4202 Fowler Ave, MHH 116, Tampa, FL 33620-6756
Tel: 813-974-1711 *Fax:* 813-974-1459
Web Site: english.cas.usf.edu/fswc/
Writing workshops, seminars, lectures & conferences.
Location: University of South Florida, St Petersburg, FL

Florida Writers Association Conference
Florida Writers Association Inc
10615 Limewood Dr, Jacksonville, FL 32257
Tel: 904-343-4188 *Toll Free Fax:* 800-536-5919
Web Site: www.floridawriters.net
Key Personnel
Chmn: Marcia Rankin *E-mail:* annmar11@msn.com
Date: Autumn 2005

Fun in the Sun 2005
Florida Romance Writers Inc
Affiliate of Romance Writers of America
PO Box 451356, Sunrise, FL 33345
Tel: 954-748-1707
Web Site: www.frwriters.org
Key Personnel
Pres: Ona Bustos *E-mail:* onabus6@aol.com
Highlights include a full series of workshops on the art, craft & business of writing that will appeal to writers in all genres. Exclusive Q&A with our keynote speaker, live & silent auction & raffle, on-site bookstore, author book signing event, editor/agent appointments & more. Registration fees from $145-$175. Workshop speakers entitled to discounted registration fee. Group rates available for groups of 5 or more; special hotel rates for conference attendees also available. Use the mailing address for all conference correspondence.

General Trade Publishing & Retailing
Evangelical Christian Publishers Association
4816 S Ash Ave, Suite 101, Tempe, AZ 85282-7735
Tel: 480-966-3998 *Fax:* 480-966-1944
Web Site: www.ecpa.org
Key Personnel
Pres: Mark Kuyper *E-mail:* mkuyper@ecpa.org

Harvard Summer Writing Program
Harvard University, Div of Continuing Education
51 Brattle St, Dept S760, Cambridge, MA 02138-3722
Tel: 617-495-4024 *Fax:* 617-495-9176
E-mail: summer@hudce.harvard.edu
Web Site: www.summer.harvard.edu
Key Personnel
Dir & Prog Contact: Dr Patricia Bellanca
Eight-week program starting at the end of June; full-semester college-credit workshop courses in creative, professional & expository writing. These include: beginning fiction, poetry, jour-

nalism, playwriting & screenwriting; advanced creative nonfiction; writing grant proposals, effective business communication, legal writing & principles of editing; cross-cultural expository writing, writing about social & ethical issues & writing about literature.

Haystack Writing Program
Affiliate of Portland State University, Summer Session
PO Box 1491, Portland, OR 97207-1491
Tel: 503-725-3276; 503-725-4186 *Fax:* 503-725-4840
Web Site: www.haystack.pdx.edu
Key Personnel
Coord: Elizabeth Snyder *E-mail:* snydere@pdx.edu
College credit (optional), workshops in fiction, nonfiction, poetry, music, art, gardening & screenwriting; one-week long, Mon-Fri 9-4; some weekend workshops.
Location: Cannon Beach, OR, USA

27th Annual Highland Summer Conference
Subsidiary of Radford University
PO Box 7014, Radford University, Radford, VA 24142-7014
Tel: 540-831-5366 *Fax:* 540-831-5951
Web Site: www.radford.edu/~arsc
Key Personnel
Dir: Grace Toney Edwards
Program based on Appalachian culture & writing; directed for two weeks by a fiction writer/poet/dramatist. Elective seminar-workshop combination offers the opportunity to study & practice creative & expository writing.
Location: Radford University, Radford, VA, USA

The Highlights Foundation Writers Workshop at Chautauqua
Highlights Foundation
Affiliate of Highlights for Children Inc
814 Court St, Dept CF, Honesdale, PA 18431
Tel: 570-253-1192 *Fax:* 570-253-0179
E-mail: contact@highlightsfoundation.org
Web Site: www.highlightsfoundation.org
Key Personnel
Exec Dir: Kent Brown
Intensive week-long retreat is designed for individuals interested in writing for children. Have the opportunity to work in individual & small-group sessions with some of the most accomplished & prominent authors, illustrators, editors & publishers in the world of children's literature.
Location: The Chautauqua Institute, Chautauqua, NY, USA
Date: July 16-23, 2005
Location: The Chautauqua Institute, Chautauqua, NY, USA
Date: July 15-22, 2006

How to be Published Workshops
PO Box 100031, Birmingham, AL 35210
Tel: 205-907-0140
Web Site: www.writing2sell.com
Key Personnel
Pres: Michael Garrett *E-mail:* mike@writing2sell.com
Workshops teaching all aspects of how to be successfully published.

The Hurston/Wright Writer's Week
The Zora Neal Hurston/Richard Wright Foundation
6525 Bellcrest Rd, Suite 531, Hyattsville, MD 20782
Tel: 301-683-2134 *Fax:* 301-277-1262
E-mail: info@hurston-wright.org
Web Site: www.hurston-wright.org

Key Personnel
CEO & Pres: Marita Golden
Exec Dir & CFO: Clyde McElvene

Implementing Color Management
PIA/GATF (Graphic Arts Technical Foundation)
200 Deer Run Rd, Sewickley, PA 15143-2600
Tel: 412-741-6860 *Toll Free Tel:* 800-910-4283
   Fax: 412-741-2311
E-mail: info@gain.net
Web Site: www.gain.net
Key Personnel
Pres: Michael Makin
Mktg Mgr: Lisa Erdner
Training Mgr: Sara Hantz *Tel:* 412-741-6860 ext 113 *E-mail:* shantz@gatf.org

Indiana University Writers' Conference
Indiana Universiy
Indiana University, Dept of English, 464 Ballantine Hall, Bloomington, IN 47405
Tel: 812-855-1877 *Fax:* 812-855-9535
E-mail: writecon@indiana.edu
Web Site: www.indiana.edu/~writecon/
Key Personnel
Dir: Amy Locklin
Asst Dir: Laura Otto
Week-long, annual conference for writers of poetry, fiction, nonfiction & script writing. Second oldest such conference in the US. Past staff includes Raymond Carver, Allen Tate & Katherine Anne Porter.

Introducing ECPA Publishing University
Evangelical Christian Publishers Association
4816 S Ash Ave, Suite 101, Tempe, AZ 85282-7735
Tel: 480-966-3998 *Fax:* 480-966-1944
Web Site: www.ecpa.org
Key Personnel
Pres: Mark Kuyper *E-mail:* mkuyper@ecpa.org
ECPA Publishing University.
Date: Nov 6-8, 2005

Iowa Summer Writing Festival
Division of University of Iowa Continuing Education
100 Oakdale Campus, Rm W310, Iowa City, IA 52242
Tel: 319-335-4160
E-mail: iswfestival@uiowa.edu
Web Site: www.uiowa.edu/~iswfest
Key Personnel
Dir: Amy Margolis *E-mail:* amy-margolis@uiowa.edu
Annual week-long & weekend non-credit, intensive writing workshops in all genres; non-exclusionary.

Kentucky Women Writers Conference
University of Kentucky
University of Kentucky, 113 Bowman Hall, Lexington, KY 40506-0059
Tel: 859-257-8734; 859-257-6420; 859-257-8451 *Fax:* 859-257-8737
E-mail: kywwc@hotmail.com
Web Site: www.uky.edu/conferences/kywwc
Key Personnel
Contact: Rebecca Howell *E-mail:* rghowe00@uky.edu; Evie Russell *E-mail:* egruss0@email.uky.edu
Oldest conference of its kind in the country featuring invited women writers offering workshops, reading & panel discussions.
Location: University of Kentucky, Downtown Campus, Lexington, KY, USA
Date: March 24-26, 2005

Key West Literary Seminar Inc
717 Love Lane, Key West, FL 33040
Toll Free Tel: 888-293-9291

E-mail: mail@keywestliteraryseminar.org
Web Site: www.keywestliteraryseminar.org
Key Personnel
Exec Dir: Miles Frieden
Literary conferences & workshops.

Ligonier Valley Writers Conference
PO Box B, Ligonier, PA 15658-1602
Tel: 724-537-3341 *Fax:* 724-537-0482
E-mail: sarshi@wpa.net
Key Personnel
PR Dir: Judith Gallagher
Conference Dir: Dr Kirk Weixel
Contact: Sally Shirey
Writer's Conference.
Date: Annually in July

Maritime Writers' Workshop
Affiliate of UNB College of Extended Learning
PO Box 4400, Fredericton, NB E3B 5A3, Canada
Tel: 506-474-1144 *Fax:* 506-474-1144 (call first)
E-mail: k4jc@unb.ca
Web Site: www.unb.ca/extend/writers
Key Personnel
Coord: Rhona Sawlor
Week-long workshop for fiction, poetry, nonfiction, & writing for children, screenwriting. Application deadline is June 7.
Location: Maritime Writers Workshop, Fredericton Campus of the University of New Brunswick, Fredericton, NB, Canada
Date: 2nd week of July

Mastering Color for Print Production
PIA/GATF (Graphic Arts Technical Foundation)
200 Deer Run Rd, Sewickley, PA 15143-2600
Tel: 412-741-6860 *Toll Free Tel:* 800-910-4283
   Fax: 412-741-2311
E-mail: info@gain.net
Web Site: www.gain.net
Key Personnel
Pres: Michael Makin
Mktg Mgr: Lisa Erdner
Training Mgr: Sara Hantz *Tel:* 412-741-6860 ext 113 *E-mail:* shantz@gatf.org
Managing color subjectivity, put into prospective the objective of the color reproduction process, how color reproduction works & other topics.

McHugh's Rights/Permissions Workshop™
John B McHugh Publishing Consultant
PO Box 170665, Milwaukee, WI 53217-8056
Tel: 414-351-3056 *Fax:* 414-351-0666
Web Site: www.johnbmchugh.com
Key Personnel
Principal: John B McHugh *E-mail:* j.b.mchugh@att.net
Provide on-site customized workshops in all aspects of publishing management.

Midland Writers' Conference
Grace A Dow Memorial Library
1710 W St Andrews, Midland, MI 48640
Tel: 989-837-3435 *Fax:* 989-837-3468
Key Personnel
Ref Libn: Ann Jarvis *E-mail:* ajarvis@midland-mi.org
Annual writers' conference.
Location: Grace A Dow Memorial Library, Midland, MI
Date: One-day seminar, usually 2nd Saturday in June

Mississippi River Writing Workshop
St Cloud State University, English Dept
720 Fourth Ave S, Riverview 101-D, St Cloud, MN 56301-4498
Tel: 320-308-3061; 320-308-4947 *Fax:* 320-308-5524
Key Personnel
Dir: Bill Meissner *E-mail:* wmeissner@stcloudstate.edu

Napa Valley Writers' Conference-Poetry & Fiction Sessions
Napa Valley College
Upper Valley Campus, 1088 College Ave, St Helena, CA 94574
Tel: 707-967-2900 (ext 1611) *Fax:* 707-967-2909
E-mail: writecon@napavalley.edu
Web Site: www.napavalley.edu/writersconf
Key Personnel
Man Dir: Anne Evans *Tel:* 707-253-8196
Prog Dir: John Leggett
Poetry & fiction sessions each year, offering small workshops, craft lectures & readings.

Napa Writing Retreats
PO Box 3214, Napa, CA 94558
Tel: 707-252-1030 *Toll Free Tel:* 866-848-2961
E-mail: info@napawritingretreats.com
Web Site: www.napawritingretreats.com
Key Personnel
Owner: Jill Winkelstein
Creative writing retreats that follow the Amherst Writers & Artists method.

The National Society of Newspaper Columnists (NSNC)
Courier-Journal Newspaper, 525 W Broadway, Louisville, KY 40201-7431
Mailing Address: PO Box 740031, Louisville, KY 40201-7431
Tel: 502-582-4011 *Fax:* 502-582-4665
Web Site: www.courierjournal.com
Key Personnel
Pres & Publr: Edward E Manassah *Tel:* 502-582-4101 *E-mail:* emanassa@louisvil.gannett.com
Treas & Metro Columnist: Bob Hill *Tel:* 502-582-4646 *E-mail:* bhill@courierjournal.com
Annual conference & contest, occasional newsletter & networking with staff & syndicated columnists & regular freelance columnists.
Location: Washington, DC
Date: Jan

The National Writer's Voice Project
Subsidiary of YMCA of the USA, Dept of Arts & Humanities
101 N Wacker Dr, Suite 1400, Chicago, IL 60606
Tel: 312-419-8658 *Toll Free Tel:* 800-USA-YMCA (800-872-9622) *Fax:* 312-977-4801
Web Site: www.ymca.net
Key Personnel
Founder & Exec Dir: Jason Shinder *E-mail:* jason.shinder@ymca.net
Network of YMCA-based literary arts centers with locations throughout the United States, offering courses in fiction, poetry & nonfiction writing workshops & seminars for adults; school-based creative writing workshops for high school students, community service programs; public event featuring literary artists.

New York State Writers Institute
State University of New York
University at Albany, New Library 320, Albany, NY 12222
Tel: 518-442-5620 *Fax:* 518-442-5621
E-mail: writers@uamail.albany.edu
Web Site: www.albany.edu/writers-inst/
Key Personnel
Exec Dir: William Kennedy
Dir: Donald Faulkner
Asst Dir: Suzanne Lance
Literary program organization featuring visiting writers, classic film, special literary events & conferences, writing courses & workshops.
Date: Year-round; write for dates & locations

North Carolina Writers' Network Annual Fall Conference
North Carolina Writers' Network
PO Box 954, Carrboro, NC 27510-0954
Tel: 919-967-9540 *Fax:* 919-929-0535
E-mail: mail@ncwriters.org
Web Site: www.ncwriters.org
Key Personnel
Prog Dir: Carol Henderson *E-mail:* carol@ncwriters.org
Workshops, readings, newsletter, conferences, critiquing service & round table discussions.
Date: Autumn 2005

Northeast Texas Community College Annual Writers Conference
Northeast Texas Community College
Continuing Education, PO Box 1307, Mount Pleasant, TX 75456-1307
Tel: 903-572-1911 *Fax:* 903-572-6712
E-mail: jbowers@ntcc.edu
Web Site: www.ntcc.edu
Key Personnel
Pres: Dr Charles Florio
Location: Northeast Texas Community College, Mount Pleasant, TX
Date: Annually in Spring; March or April

NWAF Annual Conference
The National Writers Association Foundation
3140 S Peoria St, PMB 295, Aurora, CO 80014
Tel: 303-841-0246 *Fax:* 303-841-2607
Web Site: www.nationalwriters.com
Key Personnel
Exec Dir: Sandy Whelchel *E-mail:* sandywrter@aol.com

Odyssey: The Summer Fantasy Writing Workshop
20 Levesque Lane, Mont Vernon, NH 03057
Tel: 603-673-6234 *Fax:* 603-673-6234
Web Site: www.sff.net/odyssey
Key Personnel
Dir: Jeanne Cavelos *E-mail:* jcavelos@sff.net
Intensive six-week workshop for writers of fantasy, science fiction & horror. Director Jeanne Cavelos is a former senior editor at Dell Publishing & winner of the World Fantasy Award. Guest lecturers include some of the top writers in the field. College credit available. Application deadline: April 15.
Location: Southern New Hampshire University, Manchester, NH
Date: June 13-July 22, 2005

Of Dark & Stormy Nights
Mystery Writers of America, Midwest Chapter
Subsidiary of Mystery Writers of America Inc
PO Box 6804, South Bend, IN 46660-6804
Tel: 212-888-8171 *Fax:* 212-888-8107
Web Site: www.mwamidwest.org
Key Personnel
Contact: Jeanne Dams *E-mail:* jdams@jeannedams.com
Mystery fiction & true crime writing.
Location: Of Dark & Stormy Nights

Oregon Christian Writers Coaching Conference
Oregon Christian Writers
1647 SW Pheasant Dr, Aloha, OR 97006
Tel: 503-642-9844 *Fax:* 503-848-3658
E-mail: miholer@viser.net
Web Site: www.oregonchristianwriters.org
Key Personnel
Exec Ed: Sally Stuart *E-mail:* stuartcwmg@aol.com
Summer Conference Dir: Sandy Cathcart *E-mail:* sandycathcart@compuserve.com
Seven hours of hands-on help from well-published professionals, many specialized workshops, consultations with editors & networking with successful writers.
Location: Canby Grove Conference Center, Canby, OR
Date: Aug 2005

Oregon Christian Writers Seminar
Oregon Christian Writers
1647 SW Pheasant Dr, Aloha, OR 97006
Tel: 503-642-9844 *Fax:* 503-848-3658
E-mail: miholer@viser.net
Web Site: www.oregonchristianwriters.org
Key Personnel
Pres: Jennifer Ann Messing *Tel:* 503-775-6039 *E-mail:* president@oregonchristianwriters.org
Writers' workshops.
Location: Salem, OR
Date: Feb 2005
Location: Eugene, OR
Date: May 2005
Location: Medford, OR
Date: Sept 2005
Location: Portland, OR
Date: Oct 2005

Orientation to the Graphic Arts
PIA/GATF (Graphic Arts Technical Foundation)
200 Deer Run Rd, Sewickley, PA 15143-2600
Tel: 412-741-6860 *Toll Free Tel:* 800-910-4283 *Fax:* 412-741-2311
E-mail: info@gain.net
Web Site: www.gain.net
Key Personnel
Pres: Michael Makin
Mktg Mgr: Lisa Erdner
Training Mgr: Sara Hantz *Tel:* 412-741-6860 ext 113 *E-mail:* shantz@gatf.org

Outdoor Writers Association of America Conference
Outdoor Writers Association of America
158 Lower Georges Valley Rd, Spring Mills, PA 16875
Tel: 814-364-9557 *Fax:* 814-364-9558
Web Site: www.owaa.org
Key Personnel
Meeting Planner: Eileen N King *E-mail:* eking4owaa@cs.com
Seminars & writing workshops; photography & controversial subjects.
Location: OWAA, Madison, WI
Date: June 18-22, 2005

Ozark Creative Writers Inc Annual Conference
Ozark Creative Writers Inc
1818 N Taylor, Little Rock, AR 72207-4637
E-mail: carlj@mail.uca.edu; ozarkcreativewriters@earthlink.net
Web Site: www.ozarkcreativewriters.org
Key Personnel
Counselor: W C Jameson
Writers' conference for beginners & professionals. Contest information in brochures available after May 1. Send No 10 SASE.

Pacific Northwest Children's Book Conference
University Haystack Summer Program in the Arts
1633 SW Park Ave, Portland, OR 97207
Mailing Address: PO Box 1491, Portland, OR 97207
Tel: 503-725-4186 *Toll Free Tel:* 800-547-8887 (ext 4186) *Fax:* 503-725-4840
E-mail: snydere@pdx.edu
Web Site: www.haystack.pdx.edu/children
Key Personnel
Dir: Elizabeth Snyder *E-mail:* snydere@pdx.edu
Focus on the craft of writing & illustrating for children & young people while working with an outstanding faculty of acclaimed editors, authors & illustrators. Housing & meals will be available on campus to allow more opportunities for networking & ongoing discussion with faculty & fellow students. Afternoon small-group, faculty-led workshops for writers & il-

lustrators. Indivdual mss & portfolio reviews available. Graduate credit available through Portland State University.

Pacific Northwest Writers Conference
Pacific Northwest Writers Association
23607 Hwy 99, Suite 2C, Edmonds, WA 98026
Tel: 425-673-2665
E-mail: staff@pnwa.org
Web Site: www.pnwa.org
Key Personnel
Pres: Sharyn Bolton
Rec Sec: Jenny Zappala
Location: Summer Conference, Hilton Seattle Airport & Conference Center, Seattle, WA
Date: July 15-18, 2005

Paris-American Academy Writing Workshop
Paris-American Academy
277 Rue St Jacques, 75005 Paris, France
Mailing Address: HC1, Box 102, Plainview, TX 79072-0102
Tel: 806-889-3533 *Fax:* 806-889-3533
Web Site: www.parisamericanacademy.edu; www.parisamericanacademy.fr
Key Personnel
Pres: Peter Carman
Dir: Bettye Givens *E-mail:* bettye@parisamericanacademy.edu
Fine arts & French language, art history, painting, fashion & design & literature classes offered. Send SASE. Year-round school, writer's workshops. Shared apartment included with fees.
Location: Paris American Academy, Paris, France
Date: Annually in July

PennWriters Conference
5576 Edwards Rd, Murrysville, PA 15568
Tel: 724-327-2725
Web Site: www.pennwriters.org
Key Personnel
Conference Coord: Carol A Silvis *E-mail:* snax@nb.net
Workshops, seminars with authors, agents & editors in romance, mystery, short story, nonfiction, poetry, read & critique sessions, hands-on workshops & contests, Agent/Editor appointments.
Location: The Write Connection, Penn Writers Conference, The Windham Hotel, Pittsburgh, PA
Date: May 12-14, 2005

Philadelphia Writers' Conference
PO Box 7171, Elkins Park, PA 19027-0171
Tel: 215-782-3288
E-mail: info@pwcwriters.org
Web Site: pwcwriters.org
Key Personnel
Trustee & Contact: Gloria Delamar *E-mail:* delamarg@juno.com
Educational conferences for writers, workshops, critiques, contests, featured speakers, agents, editors.
Location: Philadelphia, PA
Date: Yearly 3-day event; 2nd full weekend of June
Location: Philadelphia, PA
Date: One-day forum; 1st, 2nd or 3rd Sat of Oct

Pima Writers' Workshop
Pima College
Pima College West Campus, 2202 W Anklam Rd, Tucson, AZ 85709-0170
Tel: 520-206-6084 *Fax:* 520-206-6020
Key Personnel
Dir: Meg Files *E-mail:* mfiles@pima.edu
The three-day conference in May offers opportunities to meet with authors, editors & agents & to have mss critiqued.

Location: Tucson, AZ
Date: May 2005

Poetry Flash at Cody's
Poetry Flash & Cody's Books
1450 Fourth St, Suite 4, Berkeley, CA 94710
Tel: 510-525-5476 *Fax:* 510-525-6752
E-mail: editor@poetryflash.org
Key Personnel
Exec Dir: Joyce Jenkins
Publication; conducts a reading & poetry series in conjunction with Cody's Books. Poetry series takes place at Cody's Books 2454 Telegraph Ave, Berkely, every Sunday evening 7:30, except for Aug & Dec. It is sponsored/produced by Poetry Flash magazine & Cody's.

Port Townsend Writers' Conference
Centrum Foundation
PO Box 1158, Port Townsend, WA 98368-0958
Tel: 360-385-3102 *Toll Free Tel:* 800-733-3608 (ticket office) *Fax:* 360-385-2470
E-mail: centrum@centrum.org
Web Site: www.centrum.org
Key Personnel
Prog Dir: Sam Hamill
Workshops, lectures & readings.

Progress in the Pressroom Seminar
Research & Engineering Council of NAPL (National Association for Printing Leadership)
PO Box 1086, White Stone, VA 22578-1086
Tel: 804-436-9922 *Fax:* 804-436-9511
E-mail: recouncil@rivnet.net
Web Site: www.recouncil.org
Key Personnel
Man Dir: Ronald L Mihills
Annual event highlights technical growth & improvement in print press technology.

The Publishing Game
Peanut Butter & Jelly Press LLC
PO Box 590239, Newton, MA 02459-0002
SAN: 299-7444
Tel: 617-630-0945
E-mail: info@publishinggame.com
Web Site: www.publishinggame.com
Key Personnel
Mgr: Alyza Harris *E-mail:* alyza@publishinggame.com
All-day workshop covers how to find a literary agent, how to self-publish & how to successfully promote your book. Offered in 12 cities: New York, Boston, Philadelphia, DC, Boca Raton, Chicago, San Francisco, Los Angeles, Seattle, Phoenix, Dallas & several 'floating cities' each year. $195 includes workshop course binder. See www.publishinggame.com for latest locations, dates & details.

Robert Quackenbush's Children's Book Writing & Illustration Workshops
Robert Quackenbush Studios
460 E 79 St, New York, NY 10021
Tel: 212-744-3822 *Fax:* 212-861-2761
E-mail: rqstudios@aol.com
Web Site: www.rquackenbush.com
Annual workshops at author/artists' studio; focus on planning children's books from concept to completion. Special four-day intensive workshop second week in July, annually.
Location: New York, NY
Date: July 11-14, 2005

Remember the Magic Annual Summer Conference
The International Women's Writing Guild (IWWG)
PO Box 810, Gracie Sta, New York, NY 10028-0082
Tel: 212-737-7536 *Fax:* 212-737-9469

E-mail: iwwg@iwwg.org
Web Site: www.iwwg.org
Key Personnel
Founder & Exec Dir: Hannelore Hahn *E-mail:* dirhahn@aol.com
The Guild sponsors about ten writing events each year in various parts of the country. For one week in Aug the Guild brings together close to 500 women in a shared-interest writing community, offering some 70 workshops each & every day. For further information please call 212-737-7536.
Location: Saratoga Springs, NY
Date: Summer

Romance Writers of America National Conference
Romance Writers of America
16000 Stuebner Airline, Suite 140, Spring, TX 77379
Tel: 832-717-5200 *Fax:* 832-717-5201
E-mail: info@rwanational.org
Web Site: www.rwanational.org
Key Personnel
Exec Dir: Allison Kelley *E-mail:* akelley@rwanational.org
Promote recognition of the genre of romance writing as a serious book form. Conduct workshops, sponsor national & regional conferences & awards for members.
Date: July 27-30, 2005

San Diego Christian Writers' Guild Conference
San Diego CHRISTIAN Writers' Guild
PO Box 270403, San Diego, CA 92198
Tel: 619-221-8183 *Fax:* 619-255-1131
E-mail: info@sandiegocwg.org
Web Site: www.sandiegocwg.org
Key Personnel
Pres: Jennie Gillespie; Robert Gillespie
One day seminar & workshop; personal consultations with editors. Journalism, magazine writing, fiction. Seminar is always the third Saturday in Sept.

San Francisco Writers Conference 2005
1029 Jones St, San Francisco, CA 94109
Tel: 415-673-0939 *Toll Free Tel:* 866-862-7392 *Fax:* 415-673-0367
E-mail: sfwriterscon@aol.com
Web Site: www.sanfranciscowritersconference.com
Key Personnel
Founder: Michael Larsen; Elizabeth Pomada
A craft & market oriented writers conference covering fiction, nonfiction, film & poetry with name authors.
Date: President's Weekend, Feb 18-20, 2005

Sandhills Writers' Conference
Augusta State University
Languages, Literature & Communication, 2500 Walton Way, Augusta, GA 30904
Tel: 706-667-4437 *Fax:* 706-667-4770
Web Site: www.sandhills.aug.edu
Key Personnel
Dir: Tony Kellman *E-mail:* akellman@aug.edu
Fiction, nonfiction, songwriting, childrens literature, plays & poetry writing conferences & lectures; participants write in all genres for credit or awards. Enrollment limited. Ms deadline Feb 4, 2005.
Location: Augusta State University, Augusta, GA
Date: March 2005

Santa Barbara Book Promotion Workshop
Para Publishing
PO Box 8206-R, Santa Barbara, CA 93118-8206
SAN: 215-8981
Tel: 805-968-7277 *Toll Free Tel:* 800-727-2782 *Fax:* 805-968-1379
E-mail: orders@parapublishing.com
Web Site: www.parapublishing.com

Key Personnel
Owner & Publr: Dan Poynter
  E-mail: danpoynter@parapublishing.com
Book marketing, promoting & distributing; four workshops per year; Jan, Apr, July & Oct.
Location: Santa Barbara, CA
Date: Jan, Apr, July, Oct; Reservations required, attendance limited to 23

SDSU Writers' Conference
College of Extended Studies
5250 Campanile Dr, Rm 2503, San Diego, CA 92182-1920
Tel: 619-594-2517 *Fax:* 619-594-8566
E-mail: extended.std@sdsu.edu
Web Site: www.ces.sdsu.edu
Key Personnel
Coord, Noncredit Community Educ: Becky Ryan
  E-mail: rjryan@mail.sdsu.edu
Weekend annual writers' conference. Topics include screenwriting, fiction, nonfiction, genre novels & children's writing. Personal editor & agent appointments available.
Location: Doubletree Hotel, San Diego, CA
Date: Jan 21-23, 2005

Hank Searls Authors Workshop
4435 Holly Lane NW, Gig Harbor, WA 98335
Mailing Address: PO Box 1877, Gig Harbor, WA 98335
Tel: 253-851-9897 *Fax:* 253-851-9897
E-mail: hanksearls@harbornet.com
Web Site: critiquemaster.com
Key Personnel
Pres & CEO: Hank Searls *Tel:* 253-851-9896
  E-mail: hanksearls@harbornet.com
Novel & full-length fiction writing, teaching & critiquing full-length fiction & nonfiction.
Location: Gig Harbor, WA
Date: Year-round

Selling to Hollywood
American Screenwriters Association
269 S Beverly Dr, Suite 2600, Beverly Hills, CA 90212-3807
Toll Free Tel: 866-265-9091 *Toll Free Fax:* 866-265-9091
E-mail: asa@goasa.com
Web Site: www.goasa.com
Key Personnel
Exec Dir, American Screenwriters Association: John Johnson
Special guest speakers, seminars, panels, film agent & producer appointments, over 50 faculty of film & TV pros.
Date: Annually in July or Aug

7 Ways to Make a Scene Sizzle
Martha Alderson
708 Blossom Hill Rd, No 146, Los Gatos, CA 95032
Tel: 408-482-4678 *Fax:* 408-356-1798
Web Site: www.blockbusterplots.com
Key Personnel
Owner & Author: Martha Alderson
  E-mail: martha@blockbusterplots.com
Martha Alderson will help fiction, memoir & creative nonfiction writers maximize the scenes in their stories.
Location: Los Gatos, CA
Date: Feb 26, 2005
Location: Los Gatos, CA
Date: April 16, 2005
Location: Los Gatos, CA
Date: Aug 5, 2005
Location: Los Gatos, CA
Date: Oct 1, 2005

Sewanee Writers' Conference
310 St Lukes Hall, 735 University Ave, Sewanee, TN 37383-1000

Tel: 931-598-1141
Web Site: www.sewaneewriters.org
Key Personnel
Dir: Wyatt Prunty
Creative Writing Progs Mgr: Cheri Peters
  E-mail: cpeters@sewanee.edu
Workshops in poetry, fiction & playwriting.
Location: The University of the South, Sewanee, TN
Date: Last two weeks in July

Sheetfed Offset Press Operating
PIA/GATF (Graphic Arts Technical Foundation)
200 Deer Run Rd, Sewickley, PA 15143-2600
Tel: 412-741-6860 *Toll Free Tel:* 800-910-4283
  Fax: 412-741-2311
E-mail: info@gain.net
Web Site: www.gain.net
Key Personnel
Pres: Michael Makin
Mktg Mgr: Lisa Erdner
Training Mgr: Sara Hantz *Tel:* 412-741-6860 ext 113 *E-mail:* shantz@gatf.org

SLA Annual Conference
Special Libraries Association (SLA)
313 S Patrick St, Alexandria, VA 22314
Tel: 202-234-4700 *Fax:* 703-647-4901
E-mail: sla@sla.org
Web Site: www.sla.org
Key Personnel
Deputy Dir: Lynn K Smith
Dir, Conferences: Alicia Cronin-DiMaio
Trade show; publisher; contact SLA for current info.

SLA Workshops
Special Libraries Association (SLA)
313 S Patrick St, Alexandria, VA 22314
Tel: 703-647-4900 *Fax:* 703-647-4901
E-mail: sla@sla.org
Web Site: www.sla.org
Key Personnel
Deputy Dir: Lynn K Smith
Strategic Learning Catalyst: Shelba Suggs
  Tel: 202-939-3627 *E-mail:* shelba@sla.org
Professional development workshops; full-& half-day sessions. Contact SLA for current information.

Small Publishers Association of North America (SPAN)
425 Cedar St, Buena Vista, CO 81211
Tel: 719-395-4790 *Fax:* 719-395-8374
E-mail: span@spannet.org
Web Site: www.spannet.org
Key Personnel
VP: Cathy Bowman
VP, Mktg: Deb Ellis
Exec Dir: Scott Flora *E-mail:* scott@spannet.org
Busn Mgr: Debi Flora
Results oriented three-day annual college for independent publishers & serious book authors to master the art of selling more books.

Society for Technical Communication
901 N Stuart St, Suite 904, Arlington, VA 22203-1822
Tel: 703-522-4114 *Fax:* 703-522-2075
E-mail: stc@stc.org
Web Site: www.stc.org
Key Personnel
Exec Dir: Peter Herbst
Commun Dir: Maurice Martin *Tel:* 703-522-4114 ext 208
Educational conference for technical communicators.

Solid Gold Marketing Design Workshops
Creative Communications
Division of Sparkle Presentations

PO Box 2373, La Mesa, CA 91943-2373
Tel: 858-569-6555 *Toll Free Tel:* 800-932-0973
Fax: 858-569-5924
Web Site: www.sparklepresentations.com
Key Personnel
Owner & Creative Dir: Sheryl Roush
  E-mail: sheryl@sparklepresentations.com
Design sessions teach creativity, design tactics, feedback & fun. Specializing in newsletters, brochures, flyers & presentation materials. Keynote addresses on attitude, creating a positive workplace. See website for scheduled events.
Membership(s): PMA, National Speakers Association & Toastmasters International.

Southampton Writers' Conference
LIU/Southampton Campus
239 Montauk Hwy, Southampton, NY 11968
Tel: 631-287-8175 *Fax:* 631-287-8253
E-mail: summer@southampton.liu.edu
Web Site: www.southampton.liu.edu/summer
Key Personnel
Summer Dir: Carla Caglioti *E-mail:* carla.caglioti@liu.edu
Six workshops; one workshop in short fiction, one in poetry, one in long nonfiction, three rotating workshops; also ten evening readings.

Southern California Writers' Conference/Los Angeles/San Diego/Palm Springs
Division of Random Cove LLC
1010 University Ave, Suite 54, San Diego, CA 92103
Tel: 619-233-4651 *Fax:* 253-390-8577
E-mail: wewrite@writersconference.com
Web Site: www.writersconference.com
Key Personnel
Exec Dir: Michael Gregory *E-mail:* msg@writersconference.com
Assoc Dir: Wes Albers *E-mail:* wes@writersconference.com
Fiction, nonfiction & scriptwriting mss eligible for advance critique submission before the conference followed by one-on-one consultation; awards given. Major speakers; banquet; workshops in fiction, nonfiction, scriptwriting, poetry, short story; conference emphasis on fiction & nonfiction; one agent panel to read & critique.
Location: San Diego, CA
Date: Feb 18-21, 2005
Location: Palm Springs, CA
Date: May 27-30, 2005

SouthWest Writers Conference Series
SouthWest Writers
3721 Morris St NE, Suite A, Albuquerque, NM 87111-3611
Tel: 505-265-9485 *Fax:* 505-265-9483
E-mail: swriters@aol.com
Web Site: www.southwestwriters.org
Key Personnel
Pres: Robert Spiegel
Series of one-day conferences, annual writing contest (deadline June 1 yearly), twice-monthly programs.
Location: SWW Screenwriter's Conference
Date: November
Location: SWW Sci-Fi/Fantasy/Horror Conference
Date: Feb
Location: SWW Romance/Mainstream Conference
Date: May
Location: SWW Children's Literature Conference
Date: August
Location: Kris Rusch & Dean Wesley Smith
Date: November

Split Rock Arts Program
University of Minnesota

360 Coffey Hall, 1420 Eckles Ave, St Paul, MN 55108-6084
Tel: 612-625-8100 *Fax:* 612-624-6210
E-mail: srap@cce.umn.edu
Web Site: www.cce.umn.edu/splitrockarts
Key Personnel
Prog Assoc: Vivien Oja *Tel:* 612-624-4936
   E-mail: voja@cce.umn.edu
Week-long intensive writing workshops with renowned visiting writers. Fiction, poetry, nonfiction, multi-genre.
Location: University of Minnesota, St Paul, MN
Date: July 3-Aug 13, 2005

Squaw Valley Community of Writers Workshops
Member of Writer's Conferences & Centers/Associated Writing Programs
PO Box 1416, Nevada City, CA 95959
Tel: 530-470-8440
E-mail: brett@squawvalleywriters.org
Web Site: www.squawvalleywriters.org
Key Personnel
Gen Dir: Oakley Hall
Dir, Poetry: Robert Hass
Dir, Screenwriting: Diana Fuller
Dir, Fiction: Lisa Alvarez; Louis B Jones
Exec Dir: Ms Brett Hall Jones
Summer writing workshops; each workshop is one week.
Location: Poetry Workshop, Olympic Village Lodge, Squaw Valley, CA
Date: July 23-30, 2005
Location: Writers Workshop (Fiction, Nonfiction & Memoir) Olympic Village Lodge, Squaw Valley, CA
Date: Aug 6-13, 2005
Location: Screenwriting Workshop, Olympic Village Lodge, Squaw Valley, CA
Date: Aug 6-13, 2005

State of Maine Writers' Conference
Affiliate of Ocean Park Association
16 Foley Ave, Saco, ME 04072
Tel: 207-284-4119
Web Site: www.suiteonedesign.com
Key Personnel
Chpn: Jeff Belyea *E-mail:* jeff@suiteonedesign.com
An eclectic, economical & intensive annual conference for writers of both poetry & prose of varying abilities & accomplishments.

Summer Poetry in Idyllwild
Idyllwild Arts Academy
52500 Temecula Dr, Idyllwild, CA 92549
Mailing Address: PO Box 38, Idyllwild, CA 92549-0038
Tel: 909-659-2171 *Fax:* 909-659-4383
Web Site: www.idyllwildarts.org
Key Personnel
Dean, Admin & Fin Aid: Karen Porter
   Tel: 909-659-2171 ext 2343 *E-mail:* kporter@idyllwildarts.org
Week-long poetry festival with visiting poets. Includes workshops, discussions & readings.

Summer Writers' Workshops
Hofstra University
UCCE, 250 Hofstra University, Hempstead, NY 11549-2500
Tel: 516-463-7600 *Fax:* 516-463-4833
E-mail: uccelibarts@hofstra.edu
Web Site: www.hofstra.edu/writers
Key Personnel
Dir: Marion Flomenhaft *Tel:* 516-463-5737
   E-mail: marion.flomenhaft@hofstra.edu
Writers' workshops, readings, special guest speakers, banquets, dorm rooms available.
Location: Hempstead, Long Island, NY
Date: July 11-22, 2005

Take the Panic Out of Plot
Martha Alderson
708 Blossom Hill Rd, No 146, Los Gatos, CA 95032
Tel: 408-482-4678 *Fax:* 408-356-1798
Web Site: www.blockbusterplots.com
Key Personnel
Owner & Author: Martha Alderson
   E-mail: martha@blockbusterplots.com
Martha Alderson will provide simple techniques to help you grasp plot with ease & increase your chances of getting published. Whether you write novels, short stories or memoirs, now is the time to learn what separates a blockbuster hit from a book that falls flat.
Location: Los Gatos, CA
Date: March 12, 2005
Location: Los Gatos, CA
Date: May 14, 2005
Location: Los Gatos, CA
Date: Aug 13, 2005
Location: Los Gatos, CA
Date: Oct 8, 2005

Troubleshooting Sheetfed Offset Press Problems
PIA/GATF (Graphic Arts Technical Foundation)
200 Deer Run Rd, Sewickley, PA 15143-2600
Tel: 412-741-6860 *Toll Free Tel:* 800-910-4283
   Fax: 412-741-2311
E-mail: info@gain.net
Web Site: www.gain.net
Key Personnel
Pres: Michael Makin
Mktg Mgr: Lisa Erdner
Training Mgr: Sara Hantz *Tel:* 412-741-6860 ext 113 *E-mail:* shantz@gatf.org

28th Appalachian Writers' Workshop
Hindman Settlement School
PO Box 844, Hindman, KY 41822-0844
Tel: 606-785-5475 *Fax:* 606-785-3499
E-mail: hss@tgtel.com
Web Site: www.hindmansettlement.org
Key Personnel
Exec Dir: Mike Mullins
Poetry, nonfiction, short story, novel, dramatic writing & children's writing.
Location: Hindman Settlement School, Hindman, KY
Date: July 31-Aug 5, 2005

UCI Extension Writers' Program
University of California, Irvine Extension
PO Box 6050, Irvine, CA 92616
Tel: 949-824-5990 *Fax:* 949-824-3651
Web Site: www.unex.uci.edu
Key Personnel
Dir: Kirwan Rockefeller, PhD *E-mail:* krockefe@uci.edu
Fiction, nonfiction & screen writing. Check catalogue for dates.
Location: University of California, Irvine Extension, Irvine, CA
Date: Check catalogue

Vermont Studio Center
PO Box 613, Johnson, VT 05656
Tel: 802-635-2727 *Fax:* 802-635-2730
E-mail: info@vermontstudiocenter.org
Web Site: www.vermontstudiocenter.org
Key Personnel
Dir, Admissions: Kathy Black
Founder & Dir: Jon Gregg
Dir, Writing Prog: Gary Clark
Two through 12-week writer's residencies year round; visiting writers lecture series, two visitors per month. Full fellowship application deadline 3 times a year.

Victoria School of Writing
306-620 View St, Victoria, BC V8W 1J6, Canada

Tel: 250-595-3000
E-mail: info@victoriaschoolofwriting.org
Web Site: www.victoriaschoolofwriting.org
Key Personnel
Exec Dir: Jill Margo
Five-day writers' conference; workshops in fiction, poetry, screenwriting, children's literature, humor, nonfiction; literary trade fair.
Location: Literary Info-Fair
Date: May 7, 2005
Location: Victoria School of Writing, Victoria, BC, Canada
Date: July 17-22, 2005

Visiting Writers Series
University of Alaska Fairbanks
English Dept, PO Box 755720, Fairbanks, AK 99775
Tel: 907-474-7193 *Fax:* 907-474-5247
E-mail: faengl@uaf.edu
Web Site: www.uaf.edu/english/
Key Personnel
Workshop Coord: John Reinhard *Tel:* 907-474-5233 *E-mail:* ffjmr1@uaf.edu
Readings from & discussion of own writings; poetry, fiction, nonfiction.
Location: Fairbanks, AK
Date: Contact for schedule

Web Offset Press Operating
PIA/GATF (Graphic Arts Technical Foundation)
200 Deer Run Rd, Sewickley, PA 15143-2600
Tel: 412-741-6860 *Toll Free Tel:* 800-910-4283
   Fax: 412-741-2311
E-mail: info@gain.net
Web Site: www.gain.net
Key Personnel
Pres: Michael Makin
Mktg Mgr: Lisa Erdner
Training Mgr: Sara Hantz *Tel:* 412-741-6860 ext 113 *E-mail:* shantz@gatf.org

Wesleyan Writers Conference
Wesleyan University
c/o Wesleyan University, 279 Court St, Middletown, CT 06459
Tel: 860-685-3604 *Fax:* 860-685-2441
Web Site: www.wesleyan.edu/writers
Key Personnel
Dir: Anne Greene *E-mail:* agreene@wesleyan.edu
Seminars, readings & talks focused on novels, short stories, film, poetry & nonfiction; ms consultation; scholarships & fellowships. Participants are welcome to attend seminars in all genres; visits from editors & agents. Award-winning writers as faculty & guest speakers. This is the 48th year.
Location: Wesleyan University, Middletown, CT
Date: Annually during the third week in June

The "Why It's Great" Writing Workshop & Retreat
World Fellowship Center
Collioure Books, 21 Aviation Rd, Albany, NY 12205
Mailing Address: White Mountains, PO Box 2280, Conway, NH 03818
Tel: 518-453-0890 (regarding workshop); 603-447-2280 (World Fellowship Ctr)
   Toll Free Tel: 800-720-1170 (regarding workshop) *Fax:* 603-447-1820 (World Fellowship Ctr)
E-mail: workshop@whyitsgreat.com
Web Site: www.whyitsgreat.com
Key Personnel
Workshop Dir: David Vigoda
Writing workshop unites great technique with great heart with fiction & nonfiction being emphasized, but poets & playwrights will also benefit. All levels, non-competitive.
Location: Conway (White Mountains), NH
Date: Annually in July

Willamette Writers' Conference
Willamette Writers
Subsidiary of Willamette Writers
9045 SW Barbur Blvd, Suite 5-A, Portland, OR
  97219
Tel: 503-452-1592 *Fax:* 503-452-1592
E-mail: wilwrite@willamettewriters.com
Web Site: www.willamettewriters.com
Key Personnel
Pres: Cynthia Whitcomb
Off Mgr: Bill Johnson
Annual summer three-day conference: consul-
  tations with over 30 national agents/editors;
  workshops (fiction, nonfiction, children's,
  screen/TV, genres, craft of writing); editing
  room available. Year-round: monthly meetings,
  writing contest, workshops, newsletter.

Wisconsin Retreat
Society of Children's Book Writers & Illustrators
15255 Turnberry Dr, Brookfield, WI 53005
Tel: 262-783-4890
Web Site: www.scbwi.org
Key Personnel
Regional Advisor: Ann Angel *E-mail:* aangel@
  aol.com
Workshop on writing for children/ms critique.
  Guest faculty includes editors & award-winning
  writers. Faculty for 2005 include Michael
  Stearns, Houghton Misslin, Robbie Mayes &
  Farar, Strauss & Giriroux. Writers include Car-
  olyn Crimi & Mary Ann Rodman.
Location: Siena Center, Racine, WI
Date: Oct 7-9, 2005

Women's Writing Conferences & Retreats
The International Women's Writing Guild
  (IWWG)
PO Box 810, Gracie Sta, New York, NY 10028-
  0082
Tel: 212-737-7536 *Fax:* 212-737-9469
E-mail: iwwg@iwwg.org
Web Site: www.iwwg.org
Key Personnel
Founder & Exec Dir: Hannelore Hahn
  E-mail: dirhahn@aol.com
Network for the personal & professional empow-
  erment of women through writing. It engen-
  ders & supports the joyful camaraderie that
  comes from shared interests of a woman's writ-
  ing community. Open to any woman regardless
  of portfolio. Sponsors about ten writing events
  each year in various parts of the country. Big
  Apple Writing Workshop, held twice annually
  in New York, NY includes an open house to
  meet authors & agents.

Women's National Book Association/Los
  Angeles Chapter
PO Box 7034, Beverly Hills, CA 90212-0034
Tel: 310-474-9917 *Fax:* 310-474-6436
Key Personnel
Pres: Margaret Flanders
Speakers' forum for Excellence in Children's Lit-
  erature; writers network; newsletter; annual
  Judy Lopez Memorial Award.
Location: Beverly Hills Library, Beverly Hills,
  CA
Date: Third Tues of the month (except Dec, June,
  July & Aug)

Wrangling With Writing
Annual Writers' Conference
Affiliate of The Society of Southwestern Authors
  (SSA)
PO Box 30355, Tucson, AZ 85751-0355
Tel: 520-575-9063
Web Site: www.azstarnet.com/nonprofit/ssa
Key Personnel
Conference Dir: Al Petrillo *E-mail:* apetrillo@
  earthlink.net

Two days of 30 workshops, covering multiple
  genres including mystery, horror, adventure, romance, biography, suspense, scripts, children's
  books, articles, poetry & short stories. Cost including five meals: $325 (general admission),
  $250 (seniors over 65), $225 (SSA members).
Location: Holiday Inn, Palo Verde, Tucson, AZ
Date: Jan 28-29, 2005

Writers' League of Texas
1501 W Fifth St, Suite E-2, Austin, TX 78703
Tel: 512-499-8914 *Fax:* 512-499-0441
E-mail: wlt@writersleague.org
Web Site: www.writersleague.org
Key Personnel
Exec Dir: Helen Ginger *E-mail:* helen@
  writersleague.org
Conferences, workshops, seminars, classes, e-mail
  classes.
Location: Writer's League of Texas Resource
  Center/Library & other locations, ongoing pro-
  grams throughout Texas
Date: Ongoing throughout year

Writers Retreat Workshop (WRW)
5721 Magazine St, Suite 161, New Orleans, LA
  70115
Toll Free Tel: 800-642-2494
E-mail: wrw04@netscape.net
Web Site: www.writersretreatworkshop.com
Key Personnel
Dir: Jason Sitzes
WRW Author Mentor-in-Residence: Frank
  Strunk; Keith Wilson
WRW Masters Instructor: Elizabeth Lyon
WRW Ed-in-Residence: Lorin Oberweger
Agent-in-Residence w/Serendipity Literary
  Agency: Regina Brooks
Agent-in-Residence w/Donald Mass Literary
  Agency: Rachel Vater
Ten-day intensive workshop for writers of novels-
  in-progress, including private writing time &
  space, guest speakers & consultation with New
  York agent or editor, author instructor, as well
  as diagnostic sessions of participants' mss &
  daily assignments. Other retreats available, see
  website for details.
Location: Writers Retreat Workshop, Marydale
  Retreat Center, Erlanger, KY (near Cincinnati
  Airport)
Date: May 27-June 5, 2005

Writers Workshop in Children's Literature
Society of Children's Book Writers & Illustrators,
  Florida Chapter
10305 SW 127 Ct, Miami, FL 33186
Tel: 305-382-2677
Key Personnel
Workshop Dir, Florida SCBWL Reg Advisor:
  Linda Bernfeld *E-mail:* lrbjsb@bellsouth.net;
  Saundra Rubiera *E-mail:* s.rubiera@earthlink.
  net
Workshops in writing & illustrating picture
  books, juvenile & young adult fiction & nonfic-
  tion, children's magazines & marketing, given
  by published authors, illustrators & editors.
Location: SCBWI
Date: Jan 21-26, 2005

Writers Workshop in Science Fiction
University of Kansas Center for the Study of Sci-
  ence Fiction
University of Kansas English Dept, 3114 Wescoe
  Hall, Lawrence, KS 66045-2350
Tel: 785-864-3380 *Fax:* 785-864-1159
Key Personnel
Dir: James Gunn *E-mail:* jgunn@ku.edu
A noncredit, two-week intensive workshop of-
  fered in association with the Campbell Confer-
  ence on science fiction by the Center for the
  Study of Science Fiction.

Location: University of Kansas, Lawrence, KS
Date: June 27-July 10, 2005

The Writing Center
601 Palisade Ave, Englewood Cliffs, NJ 07632
Tel: 201-567-4017 *Fax:* 201-567-7202
E-mail: 102100.1065@compuserve.com
Key Personnel
Dir: Barry Sheinkopf
Writing seminars, editorial services & publishing
  services.
Location: 601 Palisade Ave, Englewood Cliffs, NJ
Date: Year-round, 13-week writing seminars; fall
  seminars begin Sept; 5-week summer session

The Writing for Children Founders Workshops
Highlights Foundation
Affiliate of Highlights for Children Inc
814 Court St, Dept CF, Honesdale, PA 18431
Tel: 570-253-1192 *Fax:* 570-253-0179
E-mail: contact@highlightsfoundation.org
Web Site: www.highlightsfoundation.org
Key Personnel
Exec Dir: Kent Brown
For professional children's writers & illustrators
  seeking to sharpen their focus. Helps to im-
  prove your craft with the help of a master,
  finding the time & space in which to work
  & marketing yourself & your books. Cost of
  workshops range from $495 & up which in-
  cludes tuition, meals, conference supplies &
  housing.
Location: Boyds Mills, PA
Date: Spring 2005 (March, April, May & June)
Location: Boyds Mills, PA
Date: Fall 2005 (Sept, Oct & Nov)

Writing Today
Birmingham-Southern College
PO Box 549003, Birmingham, AL 35282-9765
Tel: 205-226-4921 *Toll Free Tel:* 800-523-5793
  Fax: 205-226-4931
E-mail: dcwilson@bsc.edu
Web Site: www.bsc.edu
Key Personnel
Dir, Special Events & Conference Coord: Annie
  Green *E-mail:* agreen@bsc.edu
Two-day conference includes 24 workshops, four
  major lectures, two lunches & one reception.
Location: Birmingham Southern College, Birm-
  ingham, AL
Date: March 11-12, 2005

Writing Workshops
UC Davis Extension
Affiliate of University of California, Davis
1333 Research Park Dr, Davis, CA 95616
Tel: 530-754-5237 *Toll Free Tel:* 800-752-0881
  Fax: 530-754-5105
Web Site: www.extension.ucdavis.edu
Key Personnel
Continuing Educ Specialist: Gene Crumley
Workshops.
Location: University of California, Davis &
  Sacramento, CA
Date: Year-round, call for dates

Young Writer's Workshop
Cape Cod Writers' Center
PO Box 408, Osterville, MA 02655
Tel: 508-375-0516
E-mail: ccwc@capecod.net
Web Site: www.capecodwriterscenter.com
Key Personnel
Pres: Shirley Eastmen
Exec Dir: Jacqueline Loring
Location: Craigville, Cape Cod, MA

Courses for the Book Trade

Various courses covering different phases of the book trade are given each year. Detailed information on any of these courses can be obtained by writing directly to the sponsoring organization. For up-to-date information on book trade courses, workshops and seminars, consult the calendar section of *Publishers Weekly* (Reed Business Information, 360 Park Avenue South, New York, NY 10010). For related information see **Writers' Conferences & Workshops**.

Arizona State University, Creative Writing Program
Dept of English, Box 870302, Tempe, AZ 85287-0302
Tel: 480-965-7454; 480-965-3528 *Fax:* 480-965-3451
Web Site: www.asu.edu/clas/english/creativewriting
Key Personnel
Prog Coord: Karla Elling *E-mail:* karla.elling@asu.edu
Undergraduate & graduate courses in creative writing: workshops, theory & special topics.

Arkansas State University Printing Program
PO Box 1930, Dept of Journalism & Printing, State University, AR 72467-1930
Tel: 870-972-2072 *Fax:* 870-910-8001
Web Site: www.astate.edu
Key Personnel
Dir, Printing: David Maloch
Courses include Basic Printing Practices
Bindery-Finishing Methods
Desktop Publishing
Emphasis on Printing Management-Scheduling Estimating 1 & ll
Graphic Arts Film Procedures
Image Assembly for Platemaking
Management on Printing Productions-24 hours General Business
Paper & Ink
Small Offset Presses

Association of Graphic Communications, Graphic Arts Education Center
Affiliate of Printing Industries of America/Graphic Arts Technical Foundation
330 Seventh Ave, 9th fl, New York, NY 10001-5010
Tel: 212-279-2100 *Fax:* 212-279-5381
Key Personnel
Dir, Educ & Training: Diane Chavan *E-mail:* dchavan@agcomm.org
Full-day & half-day seminars & workshops.
Courses include Binding: Production, Techniques & Impositions
Color Litho Reproduction & Management Skills for Supervisors
Desktop Publishing
Desktop Publishing Certification Program
Direct Mail Production Techniques
Dynamics of Sales & Marketing
Estimating Printing
Fundamentals of Printing Production
Graphic Design on the Mac Intosh for the Graphic Arts
How to Buy Printing Advanced Printing Production
Illustrator Intro, Intermediate & Advanced
Innovations in Prepress Technology
Introduction to Desktop Publishing & Prepress for the Graphic Arts
QuarkXPress
Photoshop
Principles of Typography
Production for Designers
Proofreading & Copy Editing
Scanning
Understanding Color Separation
Web Design

Baylor University, Writing Program
Division of Dept of English
One Baylor Place, Waco, TX 76798
Mailing Address: PO Box 97404, Waco, TX 76798-7404
Tel: 254-710-1768 *Fax:* 254-710-3894
Web Site: www.baylor.edu
Key Personnel
Chmn: Maurice Hunt
Asst Professor of Eng: Robert Darden *E-mail:* robert_darden@baylor.edu
Comprehensive writing program.
Courses include Advanced Argumentative & Persuasive Writing
Advanced Creative Writing: Poetry
Advanced Creative Writing: Prose
Advanced Expository Writing
Advanced Writing for the Popular Market
Creative Writing: Poetry
Creative Writing: Prose
Internship in Professional Writing
Professional & Technical Writing
Screenplay & Scriptwriting
Special Topics in Writing
Thinking & Writing
Thinking, Writing & Research
Writing for the Popular Market
Writing for the Workplace

Binghamton University Writing Program
Division of State University of New York at Binghamton
c/o Dept of English, PO Box 6000, Binghamton, NY 13902-6000
Tel: 607-777-2168 *Fax:* 607-777-2408
Key Personnel
Distinguished Professor: John Vernon
Professor: Maria Gillan; Leslie Heywood; Liz Rosenberg
Professor Emerita: Ruth Stone
Asst Professor: Jaimee Wriston Colbert; Thomas Glave; Lisa Yun
Assoc Professor: Pamela Gay
Asst to Chmn, Eng: Ruth Stanek
Undergraduate & graduate courses.
Courses include Advanced Workshops in Creative Writing
Fiction Workshop
Fundamentals of Creative Writing
Independent Study in Creative Writing
Intermediate Creative Writing
Poetry Workshop
Senior Projects in Creative Writing
Studies for Writers

Boston University
236 Bay State Rd, Boston, MA 02215
Tel: 617-353-2510 *Fax:* 617-353-3653
Web Site: www.bu.edu/writing/
Key Personnel
Dir: Leslie Epstein *E-mail:* leslieep@bu.edu
Admin Coord: Barbara Checkoway *E-mail:* bcheckow@bu.edu
Contact: Prof Robert Pinsky; Prof Derek Walcott; Prof David Ferry; Prof Rosanna Warren; Prof Kate Snodgrass; Prof Richard Schotter
Workshops. Offer a one-year Master's degree in creative writing.
Courses include Fiction
Playwriting
Poetry

Bowling Green State University, Creative Writing Program
Affiliate of Dept of English
226 East Hall, Bowling Green, OH 43403
Tel: 419-372-8370 *Fax:* 419-372-6805
E-mail: mmcgowa@bgnet.bgsu.edu
Web Site: www.bgsu.edu/departments/creative-writing
Key Personnel
Dir: Dr Lawrence Coates *E-mail:* coatesl@bgnet.bgsu.edu
Secy: Mary McGowan
Providers of comprehensive & rigorous education in professional writing, editing & marketing of poetry & fiction, since 1967.
Courses include Advanced Fiction Writing Workshop
Advanced Poetry Writing Workshop
Assistant Editing, Mid-American Review
Graduate Writers' Workshop in Poetry, Fiction
Studies in Contemporary Poetry, Fiction
Techniques of Fiction
Techniques of Poetry

The Center for Book Arts
28 W 27 St, 3rd fl, New York, NY 10001
Tel: 212-481-0295 *Fax:* 212-481-9853 (call before faxing)
E-mail: info@centerforbookarts.org
Web Site: www.centerforbookarts.org
Key Personnel
Exec Dir: Alexander Campos
Offers classes & workshops during three semesters each year.
Courses include Hand Bookbinding
Hand Papermaking
Letterpress Printing

Chicago Book Clinic Seminars
5443 N Broadway, Suite 101, Chicago, IL 60640
Tel: 773-561-4150 *Fax:* 773-561-1343
Web Site: www.chicagobookclinic.org
Key Personnel
Pres: Cheryl Horch
Exec Dir: Kevin Boyer
Various seminars for publishers, manufacturers, freelancers & printers involved in all publishing markets.

College of General Studies Special Programs, University of Pennsylvania
3440 Market St, Suite 100, Philadelphia, PA 19104-3335
Tel: 215-898-7326 *Fax:* 215-573-2053
E-mail: cgs@sas.upenn.edu
Web Site: www.sas.upenn.edu/cgs
Key Personnel
Mgr, Serv Progs: Nadia Daniel *E-mail:* ndaniel@sas.upenn.edu
Writing courses, beginning through advanced, taught by published authors; non-residential; fees vary; program catalog available for writing courses Sept-July.

Columbia Publishing Course at Columbia University
2950 Broadway, MC 3801, New York, NY 10027
Tel: 212-854-1898 *Fax:* 212-854-7618
E-mail: publishing@jrn.columbia.edu
Web Site: www.jrn.columbia.edu/publishing

Key Personnel
Dir: Lindy Hess
Asst Dir: V Leslie Hendrickson
Provides an intensive introduction to book, magazine & electronic publishing. Students learn the entire publishing process from established publishing professionals & gain hands-on experience from evaluations of original mss to the sales & marketing of finished products.
Courses include Book, Magazine & Multi-Media Publishing

Columbia University School of the Arts, Writing Division
Division of Columbia University
415 Dodge Hall, School of the Arts, Columbia University, 2960 Broadway, New York, NY 10027
Tel: 212-854-4391 *Fax:* 212-854-7704
E-mail: writing@columbia.edu
Web Site: www.columbia.edu/cu/arts/writing
Key Personnel
Chmn: Alan Ziegler
Admin Coord: Anna Peterson *Tel:* 212-854-4392 *E-mail:* amd75@columbia.edu
The Writing Division offers a 60-point course of study.
Courses include Fiction
Nonfiction
Poetry

Dynamic Graphics Training
Division of Dynamic Graphics Inc
6000 N Forest Park Dr, Peoria, IL 61614-3556
Tel: 309-687-0141 *Fax:* 309-688-8515
Web Site: www.dgusa.com
Key Personnel
Admin: Sherry Rodgers *Tel:* 309-687-0137 *E-mail:* rodgers@dgusa.com
Professional workshops & seminars. Courses offered at varied levels in several locations throughout the US.
Courses include Art Direction Management
Creativity
Desktop Publishing
Multimedia
Print Production
Web Master
Writing & Typography

EEI Communications
66 Canal Center Plaza, Suite 200, Alexandria, VA 22314-5507
Tel: 703-683-7453 *Fax:* 703-683-7310
E-mail: train@eeicom.com
Web Site: www.eeicommunications.com
Key Personnel
Dir of Training: Joe Robinson *E-mail:* jrobinson@eeicom.com
Basic through advanced-level. Classes held in Alexandria, VA, Silver Spring, MD & Washington, DC & at client facilities. Visit our web site for schedule & fees.
Courses include Design
Desktop Publishing
Editing
Grammar
Graphics
Mac & PC Training
New Media
Photo Manipulation
Production
Proofreading
Publications Management & Newsletters
Web Site Development
Word Processing
Writing

Emerson College, Writing & Publishing Program
120 Boylston St, Boston, MA 02116-8750
Tel: 617-824-8750

Web Site: www.emerson.edu
Key Personnel
Dir, MA Prog in Publishing & Writing: Jeffrey Seglin *E-mail:* jeffrey_seglin@emerson.edu
Offers MA degree in publishing & writing.
Courses include The Art of Magazine Editing
Book Design & Production
Book Editing
Book Publicity
Book Publishing Overview
Column Writing
Copyediting
Desktop Publishing
Editorial Practices
Electronic Publishing
Ethics in Magazine Publishing
Literary Publishing
Magazine Design & Production
Magazine Publishing Overview
Writer-Editor Relationship

Fordham University, Graduate School of Business Administration
Dept of Communications & Media Management, 113 W 60 St, New York, NY 10023
Tel: 212-636-6199 *Fax:* 212-765-5573
Key Personnel
Chmn & Dir, Ctr for Commun: Everette P Dennis
Professor: Albert N Greco *E-mail:* angreco@aol.com
Assoc Professor: Paul P Baard; Sharon Livesey; Edmond H Weiss
Asst Professor: Philip Napoli
Dir, Busn Commun: Katherine A Combellick
Offers MBA degree with a major in Communications & Media Management. MBA Graduate courses & additional MBA course work.
Courses include Accounting
Marketing with Public Relations
The Book Publishing Industry
Broadcast & Cable Marketing & Advertising
Sales Business & Legal Aspects of Cable TV
Broadcast Management
Business & the Mass Media
Consumer Behavior
Coping with Global Corporate Crisis
Corporate Power & the Public
Direct Marketing
Economics
Executive Communications
Finance
Information & Communications Systems
International Marketing
Legal & Ethical Studies
Magazine Management
Managing Newspapers & Their Electronic Ventures
Marketing Management, Advertising & Media Planning
Mass Media in America
New Media & Mass Communications
Persuasion in Public Relations
Public Relations & Broadcasting
Public Relations as a Management Tool
Sales Management
Special Topics in Communications & Media Management: Book Publishing
The Press, the Law & the Corporation

Gaylord College of Journalism & Mass Communication, Professional Writing Program
c/o University of Oklahoma, 860 Van Vleet Oval, Rm 101, Norman, OK 73019-0270
Tel: 405-325-2721 *Fax:* 405-325-7565
Key Personnel
Professor: J Madison Davis *Tel:* 405-325-4171 *E-mail:* jmadisondavis@ou.edu
Coursework on writing for commercial markets.
Courses include Analyzing Category Fiction
Film Script Writing
Magazine Article Writing

Short Story Writing
Writing The Novel

Graphic Artists Guild Inc
90 John St, Rm 403, New York, NY 10038
Tel: 212-791-3400 *Fax:* 212-791-0333
E-mail: pr@gag.org
Web Site: www.gag.org
Key Personnel
Exec Dir: Staciellen Stevenson Heasley
Business workshops & seminars for professional artists. Publish Graphic Artists Guild Handbook: Pricing & Ethical Guidelines.

Graphic Arts Association
1100 Northbrook Dr, Suite 120, Trevose, PA 19053
Tel: 215-396-2300 *Fax:* 215-396-9890
E-mail: gaa@gaa1900.com
Web Site: www.gaa1900.com
Key Personnel
Pres: Marge Baumhauer
Educ Coord: Maria Allen
Courses include Computer Laptop Training
Estimating
Graphic Arts Fundamentals
Industrial Relations Training
Production
Sales & Management

Hamilton College, English/Creative Writing
Dept of English, 198 College Hill Rd, Clinton, NY 13323
Tel: 315-859-4370 *Fax:* 315-859-4390
Web Site: www.hamilton.edu
Key Personnel
Chmn: John O'Neill
Faculty: Naomi Guttman; Doran Larson
Academic program; students may concentrate on creative writing. Three faculty members who specialize in creative writing courses.

Hofstra University, English Dept
204 Calkins, Hempstead, NY 11549
Tel: 516-463-5454 *Fax:* 516-463-6395
E-mail: engpmu@hofstra.edu
Web Site: www.hofstra.edu
Key Personnel
Chmn, English Dept: Paula Uruburu, PhD
Dir, Creative Writing Progs: Julia Markus *Tel:* 516-463-6294
Dir, Publg & Lit: Alexander Burke
Undergraduate courses in all phases of publishing & creative writing, leading to a BA in English. MA in English Literature with concentration in creative writing.

Hollins University, Writing Program
Affiliate of Hollins University Dept of English
English Dept, Roanoke, VA 24020
Tel: 540-362-6317 *Fax:* 540-362-6097
E-mail: creative.writing@hollins.edu
Web Site: www.hollins.edu
Key Personnel
Dir: Pinckney Benedict
Master's degree in English & creative writing, all genres; nine-month residency. MFA in creative writing, 2 yr program in residency.

Louisiana State University, Writing Program
Dept of English, Baton Rouge, LA 70803
Tel: 225-578-3040 *Fax:* 225-578-4129
Web Site: www.lsu.edu
Key Personnel
Dir, First Year Writing: Dr Peckham
A graduate program leading to the degree of Master of Fine Arts in creative writing.

Massachusetts College of Art, Writing Children's Literature
Affiliate of Continuing Education Dept
621 Huntington Ave, Boston, MA 02115

Tel: 617-879-7200 *Fax:* 617-879-7171
E-mail: continuing_education@massart.edu
Web Site: www.massart.edu
Key Personnel
Acting Dean, Graduate & Continuing Education:
  George Creamer
Courses include Book Design
Computer Graphics
Design
Fine Arts
Illustrating Children's Books
Typography

McNeese State University, Writing Program
Affiliate of Dept of English
PO Box 92655, Lake Charles, LA 70609-0001
Tel: 337-475-5000; 337-475-5326
Web Site: www.mcneese.mfa.com
Key Personnel
Dir: John Wood *Tel:* 337-439-1614
  E-mail: jwood@mail.mcneese.edu
Poetry Workshop Dir: Morri Creech
Fiction Workshop Dir: Neil Connelly
MFA program in creative writing - 60 hour pro-
  gram.
Courses include Contemporary Fiction
Contemporary Poetry
Fiction Workshop
Form & Theory of Fiction
Form & Theory of Poetry
Poetry Workshop

**Mississippi Review/University of Southern
  Mississippi, Center for Writers**
Affiliate of Dept of English
Box 5144 USM, Hattiesburg, MS 39406
Tel: 601-266-5600 *Fax:* 601-266-5757
E-mail: rief@mississippireview.com
Web Site: www.mississippireview.com; www.
  centerforwriters.com
Key Personnel
Man Ed: Rie Fortenberry *E-mail:* alma.
  fortenberry@usm.edu
Ed: Frederick Barthelme *E-mail:* fbx@comcast.
  net
Edit Asst: Carrie Hoffman *E-mail:* product@
  netdoor.com
Graduate & undergraduate courses in fiction &
  poetry writing.
Mississippi Review.

Mystery Writers of America
17 E 47 St, 6th fl, New York, NY 10017
Tel: 212-888-8171
E-mail: mwa@mysterywriters.org
Web Site: www.mysterywriters.org
Key Personnel
Off Mgr: Margery Flax
Mystery writing workshops given at various times
  throughout the year by regional chapters.

New York City College of Technology
Division of City University of New York
300 Jay St, Brooklyn, NY 11201
Tel: 718-260-5822; 718-260-5000 *Fax:* 718-260-
  5198
E-mail: connect@citytech.cuny.edu
Key Personnel
Pres: Fred W Beaufait, PhD
Coord, Graphic Arts Dept: Lloyd Carr
Two year or four year degree in graphic arts, cer-
  tificates, associates or baccalaureate.
Courses include Advertising
Printing & Publishing

New York University, Center for Publishing
Affiliate of School of Continuing Education
11 W 42 St, Rm 400, New York, NY 10036
Tel: 212-992-3232 *Fax:* 212-992-3233
E-mail: pub.center@nyu.edu
Web Site: www.scps.nyu.edu/publishing

Key Personnel
Dir: Robert Baensch
Assoc Dir: Heidi Johnson
Offers a certificate in publishing, consisting of
  five courses. Individual courses may be taken.
  A total of 13 book, 14 magazine & 7 online
  publishing. Also offers a certificate in editing
  with 10 courses each year. The Summer Publishing Institute is an intensive residential program for recent college graduates, planning to
  enter the publishing industry. Consists of three
  week module in book publishing & three week
  module in magazine publishing, each including
  an overview of the industry, lectures, workshops, field trips & professional simulations,
  job fair & placement assistance. Application
  deadline; April 1 MS in publishing; contact Assoc Dir Heidi Johnson. Program consists of 38
  graduate credits chosen from a required core
  of courses in the functional areas of publishing & a concentration in either book or maga-
  zine publishing. Courses are all offered in the
  evening.
Courses include Advanced Copyediting
Advanced Magazine Editing
Advanced Special Project in Publishing
Advertising in Magazines
Advertising Sales & Integrated Marketing for
  Business-to-Business Publishers
The Basics of the Book Publishing Industry: To-
  day & Tomorrow
Book Design Strategies
Book Editing
Book Marketing
Book Packaging
Book Production & Manufacturing
Book Publicity, Promotion & Public Relations
Books from Writer to Reader: An Overview of
  the Publishing Process
Bookselling: From Publisher to Reader
The Business of Book Publishing: Financial Man-
  agement in a Creative Environment
The Business of Business-to-Business Publishing
The Business of Online Publishing
The Business of Publishing for US Hispanic Mar-
  kets
Children's Book Publishing
The Circulation Challenge: Newsstand, Retail &
  Speciality Outlets
Controlled Circulation
Cookbook Copyediting
Copyediting & Proofreading Fundamentals
Cross-Media Programs: The Future of Magazine
  Advertising Sales
Developmental Editing
Disk & Online Editing
E-mail Newsletters
The Economics of Magazine Publishing
Economics of Publishing
Editing Periodicals
Effective Marketing in Publishing Via the Digital
  Channels
Electronic Content Development
Electronic Publishing for Print & Online Part 1:
  Survey
Electronic Publishing for Print & Online Part II:
  Portfolio
The Evolving Business of Custom Publishing
Fact Checking
Financial Analysis I: Introduction to Financial
  Statement Analysis in Publishing
Financial Copyediting
Freelance Book Indexing
Fundamentals of Copyediting
Fundamentals of Proofreading
Globalization & the Web
Grammar for Publishing Professionals
How to Develop Your Career in Publishing
How to Market Your Freelance Editorial Services
How to Self-Publish Successfully & Profitably in
  Today's Market–An Intensive Two-Day Semi-
  nar
The Independent Publisher: How to Start, Sustain
  & Build a Small Press

Information Technology Management in Publish-
  ing
International Magazine Publishing
International Publishing
Internship
Journal Copyediting & Production
The Laws of Book Publishing: A Practical Guide
  to Contracts, Copyright & More
Legal Proofreading
Magazine Advertising Sales & Marketing
Magazine Branding & Franchise Development
Magazine Circulation
Magazine Copyediting
Magazine Editorial Planning & Management
Magazine Financial Management
Magazine Production & Manufacturing
Magazine Promotion, Events & Public Relations
Magazine Research: New Techniques to Acceler-
  ate Recovery Growth
Magazines from Mission to Magic & More: An
  Overview
Managing the Publishing Enterprise
Manuscript Editing
Marketing for Publishing
Media Ethics for Publishing Professionals
Mentored Academic Study
Multi-Channel Sales Promotion for Books
Multimedia Marketing & Product Development
ONIX: How Good Product Information Improves
  Sales
Online Publishing: Business, Technology & Strat-
  egy
Principles & Applications of Publishing on the
  Internet
Principles of Profitability in Book Publishing
Print Technology for Publishing
Production Editing
Professional Book & Information Publishing
Publishing: Books, Magazines & Multimedia
Publishing in Cyberspace: Legal & Practical
  Problems of Internet & Electronic Publishing
Publishing Law: Issues in Intellectual Property
Publishing On-Line
The Role of the Literary Agent in Book Publish-
  ing
Scientific, Technical & Medical Journal Copyedit-
  ing
Scientific, Technical & Medical Journal Copyedit-
  ing & Production
Scientific, Technical, Professional Publishing on
  the Internet
Secrets to Success in Magazine Freelance Writing
  & Editing
Special Sales, Licensing & Merchandising for
  Books
Starting a Small Book Publishing Co
Summer Institute in Book & Magazine Publishing
Trade & General Book Publishing
Usability: Information Architecture & the User
  Experience in Publishing
Web Marketing & E-Commerce
Web Page Development With HTML

**Ohio University, English Dept, Creative
  Writing Program**
Ohio University, English Dept, Ellis Hall, Athens,
  OH 45701
Tel: 740-593-2838 *Fax:* 740-593-2818
Web Site: www.english.ohio.edu/index.html
Key Personnel
Dir: Darrell Spencer *E-mail:* darrell.spencer.1@
  ohio.edu
Offer MA & PhD degrees with creative writing.
Courses include Essays
Fiction
Novels
Personal & Bibliophile
Plays
Poetry
Short Stories

Pace University, Master of Science in Publishing
Dept of Publishing, 551 Fifth Ave, Rm 805-E, New York, NY 10176
Tel: 212-346-1405 *Fax:* 212-661-8169
Web Site: www.pace.edu/dyson/mspub
Key Personnel
Chmn & Dir, Publg Progs: Sherman Raskin
  E-mail: sraskin@pace.edu
Program educates its students in all pertinent aspects of the publishing business. The program is offered in class & on-line.
Courses include Book Production & Design (PUB 606)
Childrens Book Publishing
Editorial Principles & Practices (PUB 624)
Electronic Publishing for Publishers (PUB 636)
Financial Aspects of Publishing (PUB 608)
Information Systems in Publishing (PUB 612)
Magazine Production & design (PUB 607)
Marketing Principles & Practices in Publishing (PUB 628)
Modern Technology in Publishing (PUB 620)
Subsidiary Rights, Acquisitions & the Function of the Literary Agent (PUB 610)

Parsons School of Design
Division of Continuing Education
66 Fifth Ave, New York, NY 10011
Tel: 212-229-8933 *Fax:* 212-229-5970
Web Site: www.parsons.edu/ce
Key Personnel
Dir: David Solomita
Comprehensive courses & advanced courses appropriate for book, magazine & advertising design.
Courses include Graphic & Advertising Design

PIA/GATF (Graphic Arts Technical Foundation)
200 Deer Run Rd, Sewickley, PA 15143-2600
Tel: 412-741-6860 *Toll Free Tel:* 800-910-4283
  Fax: 412-741-2311
Key Personnel
Pres: Michael Makin
Mktg Mgr: Lisa Erdner
Courses include Advanced Sheetfed Press Operations, 4 days
Color Management for the Pressroom, 5 days
Fine Tune Your CTP Installation, 3 days
Fundamentals of Estimating, 3 days
Implementing Color Management, 5 days
Mastering Color for Print Production, 4 days
Orientation to the Graphic Arts, 5 days
PDF/Digital Prepress Workflow, 3 days
Preflighting Files, 3 days
Print Production, 3 days
Process Controls Boot Camp, 2 days
Sheetfed Offset Press Operation, 5 days
Slashing Makeready-Sheetfed, 3 days
Supervising Print Production, 3 days
Troubleshooting Sheetfed Offset Press Problems, 3 days
Troubleshooting Web Offset Press Problems, 3 days
Web Offset Press Operating, 5 days

Publishing Certificate Program at City College
Division of Humanities NAC 5225, City College of New York, New York, NY 10031
Tel: 212-650-7925 *Fax:* 212-650-7912
E-mail: ccnypub@aol.com
Web Site: www.ccny.cuny.edu/
  publishing_certificate/index.html
Key Personnel
Dir: David Unger
Assoc Dir: Catherine McKinley
Program for undergraduates. Take four of 20 courses offered & then qualify for a paid internship in a publishing house of your interest.
Courses include Books for Young Readers
Copyediting & Proofreading, etc

The Editorial Process
Introduction to Publishing I & II

Rochester Institute of Technology, School of Print Media
69 Lomb Memorial Dr, Rochester, NY 14623-5603
Tel: 585-475-2727; 585-475-7223 *Fax:* 585-475-5336
E-mail: spmofc@rit.edu
Web Site: www.rit.edu/~spms
Key Personnel
Chmn, School of Printing: Pat Sorce
Classes in books & magazine production, typography, printing design, computer use, desktop prepress production, management, sales, finishing & bindery, quality control, marketing, finance & legal problems of publishing.
Courses include Book & Magazine Production
Computer Use
Desktop Prepress Production
Finance & Legal Problems of Publishing
Finishing & Bindery
Management
Marketing
Printing Design
Quality Control
Sales
Typography

Rosemont College
Dept of English, 1400 Montgomery Ave, Rosemont, PA 19010
Tel: 610-527-0200 (ext 2320) *Fax:* 610-526-2964
Web Site: www.rosemont.edu
Key Personnel
Dir: Ken Bingham *E-mail:* kbingham@rosemont.edu
Offers MA degree in English literature & publishing.
Courses include Design
Electronic Publishing
Legal Issues in Publishing
Literature
Manuscript Editing & Proofreading
Marketing
Production
Writing

School of Visual Arts
209 E 23 St, New York, NY 10010
Tel: 212-592-2100 *Fax:* 212-592-2116
Web Site: www.schoolofvisualarts.edu
Key Personnel
Dir, Admissions: Rick Longo
Non-degree programs beginning in Sept, Jan & June, including intensive two-week workshops.
Courses include Advertising & Graphic Design
Artists' Books'
BFA Programs in Film & Animation
Book Cover Design & Illustration Book Design
Book Illustration & Children's Book Writing & Illustration
Business Writing
Cartooning
Computer Art & Photography
Computer Graphics
Copywriting
Editorial Design
Fiction
Fine Arts
Illustration & Cartooning
Interior Design & Photography
MFA Programs in Fine Arts Illustration
Newspaper & Magazine Writing
Nonfiction
Photographic Printing Processes
Playwriting
Post-BFA in Art Education
Public Relations
Type & Design Agency Skills

Video Recording & Editing
Writing: Comedy

Small Publishers Association of North America (SPAN)
425 Cedar St, Buena Vista, CO 81211
Mailing Address: PO Box 1306, Buena Vista, CO 81211
Tel: 719-395-4790 *Fax:* 719-395-8374
E-mail: span@spannet.org
Web Site: www.spannet.org
Key Personnel
Exec Dir: Scott Flora *E-mail:* scott@spannet.org
Busn Mgr: Debi Flora
Results oriented three-day annual conference for independent publishers & serious book authors to master the art of selling more books.

Stanford Publishing Courses at Stanford University
Green Library, Rm 245-B, 557 Escondidio Mall, Stanford, CA 94305-6004
Tel: 650-725-5311 *Fax:* 650-736-1904
E-mail: publishing.courses@stanford.edu
Web Site: publishingcourses.stanford.edu
Key Personnel
Dir, Publg Courses: Holly Brady
Prog Coord: Melissa Vallejo *Tel:* 650-725-4301
  E-mail: mvallejo@leland.stanford.edu
Stanford University offers several courses on US book & magazine publishing for working professionals. Presented by leaders in the publishing & new media industries, the courses cover a broad range of topics, including strategic planning, editorial development, design, production, sales, marketing, promotion, finance, publishing lay, management issues & new technologies in publishing & printing.
Courses include Best Practices in Web Publishing for Nonprofits
Publishing on the Web Workshop
The Stanford Professional Publishing Course (SPPC)

Syracuse University Creative Writing Program
401 Hall of Languages, Syracuse, NY 13244-1170
Tel: 315-443-2174 *Fax:* 315-443-3660
Web Site: www.syr.edu
Key Personnel
Dir: Christopher Kennedy *Tel:* 315-443-3755
  E-mail: ckennedy@syr.edu
Courses include Eastern European Poetry/Translation
Fiction Workshop
Open Workshop - Fiction
Open Workshop - Poetry
Poetry Workshop
Prose Writing
The Essay
The Forms of Fiction
The Forms of Poetry
Writing of Fiction
Writing of Poetry
Writing the Novella

Syracuse University, SI Newhouse School of Public Communications
215 University Place, Syracuse, NY 13244-2100
Tel: 315-443-2301 *Fax:* 315-443-3946
E-mail: newhouse@syr.edu
Web Site: www.newhouse.syr.edu
Key Personnel
Dean: David M Rubin
Undergraduate degrees in advertising; broadcast, magazine, newspaper & journalism; public relations; television, radio, film; visual & interactive communications; Master's degrees in advertising; magazine; newspaper; media administration; visual & interactive communications; public relations; television-radio; PhD degrees in mass communications.

Courses include Advertising
Broadcast, Magazine & Newspaper Journalism
Film
Media Administration
Photography
Public Relations
Radio
Television

University of Alabama Program in Creative Writing
Affiliate of University of Alabama, Dept of English
PO Box 870244, Tuscaloosa, AL 35487-0244
Tel: 205-348-0766 *Fax:* 205-348-1388
E-mail: writeua@english.as.ua.edu
Web Site: www.as.ua.edu/english
Key Personnel
Poet & Professor: Robin Behn
Poet & Asst Professor: Joel Brouwer; Joyelle Mc-Sweeney
Fiction Writer & Professor: Michael Martone
Fiction Writer & Assoc Professor: Sandy Huss
Fiction Writer & Asst Professor: Wendy Rawlings
Three-year MFA degree program & creative writing course for undergraduates, minor in creative writing.

University of Baltimore - Yale Gordon College of Liberal Arts, Ampersand Institute for Words & Images
Division of Language Literature & Communications Design
1420 N Charles St, Baltimore, MD 21201-5779
Tel: 410-837-6022 *Fax:* 410-837-6029
Web Site: raven.ubalt.edu
Key Personnel
Dir: Edwin Gold *E-mail:* egold@ubalt.edu
Academic Prog Specialist: Jaye Crooks
Sponsors Fall & Spring lecture series, conducts advanced seminars, workshops, mini-courses & conferences on publishing topics including writing, design; also supports through the School of Communications Design, a Masters of Arts program in Publications Design an MFA in Integrated Design, an MFA in Creative Writing & Publishing Arts in a joint venture with The School of Information Arts & Technologies, a Doctoral program in Communications Design.

University of California Extension Professional Sequence in Copyediting & Courses in Publishing
1995 University Ave, Suite 200, Berkeley, CA 94720-7002
Tel: 510-642-6362 *Fax:* 510-643-0599
E-mail: letters@unx.berkeley.edu
Web Site: www.unex.berkeley.edu
Key Personnel
Prog Coord: Liz McDonough *Tel:* 510-643-1637
Certificate program in editing. Evening/weekend courses.
Courses include Editorial
Management
Marketing
Production & Design for Books & Magazines
Publishing

University of Chicago, Graham School of General Studies
Division of Professional Programs
1427 E 60 St, Chicago, IL 60637
Tel: 773-702-1682 *Fax:* 773-702-6814
Web Site: www.grahamschool.uchicago.edu
Key Personnel
Dir: Stephanie Medlock *E-mail:* s-medlock@uchicago.edu
Noncredit courses.
Courses include Advanced Novel Writing Workshop (Spring 2005)

Advanced Novel Writing Workshop (Winter 2005)
Basic Creative Writing (Spring 2005)
Basic Creative Writing (Winter 2005)
Intermediate Creative Nonfiction (Winter 2005)
Introduction to Freelance Journalism (Winter 2005)
Memoir Writing (Spring 2005)
Nuances of Grammar (Spring 2005)
Screenwriting Workshop: Writing the "Spec" Script (Spring 2005)
Screenwriting Workshop: Writing the "Spec" Script (Winter 2005)
Short Story Fiction (Spring 2005)
Writing for Educational Markets (Summer 2005)
Writing Novels for Children & Young Adults (Winter 2005)
Writing the Novel (Spring 2005)
Writing the Novel (Winter 2005)
Writing the Short Story 2 (Spring 2005)

The University of Connecticut, The Realities of Publishing
Dept of English, 337 Mansfield Rd, Rm 332, Storrs, CT 06269-1025
Mailing Address: PO Box U-1025, Storrs, CT 06269-1025
Tel: 860-486-2141 *Fax:* 203-486-1530
E-mail: halfyawk@aol.com (instructor)
Web Site: www.uconn.edu (for university); www.sp.uconn.edu/~en291isi/wecometopublishing.html
Key Personnel
Dept Head: Robert Tilton
Lecturer: Janice Trecker
This course provides a background for undergraduate students interested in professional careers in writing & publishing. Lectures by practitioners describe varied careers. Topics include: Consumer & Institutional Public Relations, Desktop Publishing, Journalism & Freelance Writing, Magazine & Book Publishing.

University of Denver Publishing Institute
2075 S University Blvd, D-114, Denver, CO 80210
Tel: 303-871-2570 *Fax:* 303-871-2501
Web Site: www.du.edu/pi
Key Personnel
Dir: Elizabeth A Geiser *Tel:* 212-752-8652
  Fax: 212-752-4658 *E-mail:* egeiser@worldnet.att.net
Assoc Dir: Jill N Smith *E-mail:* jsmith7@du.edu
Four-week graduate program in book publishing held July-Aug each year. Provides hands on workshops, lecture-teaching sessions on every phase of book publishing. Faculty consists of leading executives from publishing houses across the country. Emphasis on career counseling & job placement. Offers six quarter hours of graduate credit.
Courses include Children's Books
College Textbooks
E-Books
Economics of Publishing
Editing Workshop
Foreign Rights
Independent Presses
International Publishing
Marketing on the Internet
Marketing Workshop
Production & Design
Publicity & Promotion
Publishing & the Law
Reference Publishing in an Electronic World
Scholarly Books
Special Session on Magazine Publishing
Trade & Scholarly Books
University Presses

University of Hawaii
Affiliate of Manoa Writing Program

Bilger Hall, Rm 104, 2545 McCarthy Mall, Honolulu, HI 96822
Tel: 808-956-6660 *Fax:* 808-956-9170
E-mail: mwp@hawaii.edu
Web Site: www.hawaii.edu/mwp
Key Personnel
Dir: Thomas Hilgers
Supports the instructional mission of the University of Hawaii.

University of Houston Creative Writing Program
Affiliate of Dept of English
229 Roy Cullen Bldg, Houston, TX 77204-3015
Tel: 713-743-3015 *Fax:* 713-743-3697
E-mail: cwp@uh.edu
Web Site: www.uh.edu/cwp
Key Personnel
Off Coord: Shatera Dixon
Interim Dir: Jay Kastely
Offers MA, MFA & PhD in creative writing.

University of Illinois at Chicago, Program for Writers
Affiliate of Dept of English
601 S Morgan St, Chicago, IL 60607-7120
Tel: 312-413-2229; 312-413-2200 (English Dept)
  Fax: 312-413-1005
Key Personnel
Dir, Prog for Writers: Eugene Wildman
Asst to Dir: Lisa Stolley *Tel:* 312-413-2228
Graduate program for writers. Students in this program take literature classes as well as writing workshops. Offers MA & PhD in writing. Undergraduates seeking a BA in English may also specialize in writing.
Courses include Fiction
Nonfiction
Poetry

University of Illinois, Dept of Journalism
Unit of College of Communications/University of Illinois
Gregory Hall, Rm 120A, 810 S Wright St, Urbana, IL 61801
Tel: 217-333-0709 *Fax:* 217-333-7931
E-mail: journ@uiuc.edu
Web Site: www.uiuc.edu/spike/index.pl
Key Personnel
Interim Head: Walt Harrington
Courses include Graphics
Magazine Article Writing
Masters degree; Courses offered:
News Editing
Photojournalism
Reporting I & II

University of Iowa, Writers' Workshop, Graduate Creative Writing Program
102 Dey House, 507 N Clinton St, Iowa City, IA 52242-1000
Tel: 319-335-0416 *Toll Free Tel:* 800-553-4692 (ext 0416) *Fax:* 319-335-0420
Web Site: www.uiowa.edu/~iww/
Key Personnel
Dir: Frank Conroy
Graduate: fiction & poetry workshops & seminars. Undergraduate: creative, fiction & poetry writing.

University of Missouri-Kansas City, New Letters Weekend Writers Conference
College of Arts & Sciences, Continuing Education Div, 5300 Rockhill Rd, Kansas City, MO 64110
Tel: 816-235-2736 *Fax:* 816-235-5279
Web Site: www.umkc.edu
Key Personnel
Admin Assoc: Sharon Seaton *Tel:* 816-235-2717
  E-mail: seatons@umkc.edu

State University: a variety of credit & noncredit courses on creative writing including fiction, poetry, essays & short stories.
Courses include Essay
Fiction
Poetry
Short Story

University of Montana, Environmental Writing Institute
Subsidiary of Environmental Studies Program
Environmental Studies, University of Montana, Missoula, MT 59812
Tel: 406-243-2904 *Fax:* 406-243-6090
E-mail: evst@selway.umt.edu
Web Site: www.umt.edu/ewi
Key Personnel
Prog Mgr & Dir: Phil Condon *E-mail:* phil.condon@mso.umt.edu
Writing workshop for environmental & nature subjects held in May.

University of Southern California, Professional Writing Program
Waite Phillips Hall, Rm 404, Los Angeles, CA 90089-4034
Tel: 213-740-3252 *Fax:* 213-740-5775
E-mail: mpw@usc.edu
Web Site: www.usc.edu/dept/LAS/mpw
Key Personnel
Dir: James Ragan, PhD
Prog Asst: Diana Lopez
Multi-disciplinary Creative Writing Master's program & Master's of Arts degree in Professional Writing.
Courses include Creative Nonfiction
Fiction
Journalism
Playwriting
Poetry
Screenwriting
Technical Writing
TV Writing

University of Texas at Austin, Creative Writing Program
Dept of English, One University Sta, B5000, Austin, TX 78712-1164
Tel: 512-475-6356 *Fax:* 512-471-2898
Web Site: www.en.utexas.edu/grad/crwconc.html
Key Personnel
Professor, Fiction: Michael Adams; Laura Furman; Elizabeth Harris; Rolando Hinojosa-Smith; Peter La Salle; James Magnuson
Professor, Poetry: Zulfikar Ghose; Judith Kroll; Khaled Mattawa; David Wevill; Thomas Whitbread
Admissions Coord: Patricia Schaub
  E-mail: gradeng@uts.cc.utexas.edu
Graduate Coord: Kevin Carney *E-mail:* kcarney@mail.utexas.edu
A full range of poetry & fiction writing courses is offered, leading to the MA degree in English with concentration in creative writing.

University of Texas at El Paso, Dept Creative Writing, MFA with Bilingual Option
500 W University Ave, PMB 670, El Paso, TX 79968-9991

Tel: 915-747-5713 *Fax:* 915-747-5523
E-mail: mfadirector@utep.edu
Web Site: www.utep.edu/cw
Key Personnel
Dir, Bilingual MFA: Prof Johnny Payne
  E-mail: jpayne@utep.edu
Professor: Rosa Alcala; Daniel Chacon; Amy Perez; Luis Arturo Ramos; Benjamin Saenz; Lex Williford; Leslie Ullman
Monolingual & bilingual workshops in fiction, poetry, playwriting, screenwriting & nonfiction.

University of Virginia Publishing & Communications Institute
104 Midmont Lane, Charlottesville, VA 22904-4764
Tel: 434-982-5345 *Toll Free Tel:* 800-346-3882
  Fax: 434-982-5239
Key Personnel
Dir, Publg & Communs Institute, Univ of VA School of Continuing & Prof Studies: Beverly Jane Loo *E-mail:* beverlyloo@virginia.edu
Offers certificate programs in electronic publishing, editing & book publishing. Each certificate program consists of 12 courses (9 required core courses & 3 electives), which may also be taken individually without applying for a certificate.
Branch Office(s)
Northern Virginia Center, 7054 Haycock Rd, Falls Church, VA 22043-2311 *Tel:* 703-536-1100, 536-1105 *Toll Free Tel:* 800-676-4882
Courses include Book Publishing
Editing
Electronic Publishing

University of Wisconsin - Madison Liberal Studies & the Arts
621 Lowell Hall, 610 Langdon St, Madison, WI 53703-1195
Tel: 608-262-3982 *Fax:* 608-265-2475
Web Site: www.dcs.wisc.edu/lsa
Key Personnel
Prog Coord: Christine De Smet *Tel:* 608-262-3447
Full Professor: Marshall Cook
Writing book trade & online writing courses offered, in-person retreats & conferences.
Courses include Writers Institute Conference
Critique Services
How to Write Feature Articles Online Course
Newsletter Workshop
Script Writing Workshop
Writing Retreats

Vermont College, MFA in Writing Program
36 College St, Montpelier, VT 05602
Tel: 802-828-8840 *Fax:* 802-828-8649
Web Site: www.tui.edu/vermontcollege
Key Personnel
Admin Dir: Louise Crowley *E-mail:* louise.crowley@tui.edu
Degree work in poetry, fiction, creative nonfiction, writing for children & young adults. Intensive 12-day residencies & nonresident six-month writing projects.

Warren Wilson College, MFA Program for Writers
PO Box 9000, Asheville, NC 28815-9000
Tel: 828-771-3715 *Fax:* 828-771-7005
E-mail: mfa@warren-wilson.edu
Web Site: www.warren-wilson.edu/~mfa
Key Personnel
Dir, MFA Prog: Peter Turchi
Prog Asst: Amy Grimm *Tel:* 828-771-2000 ext 3715
Full-time 2 year program with winter & summer semesters. Ten-day residency of classes, workshops & lectures on campus. The six-month project that follows is supervised through correspondence, with detailed ms criticism by faculty who are both accomplished writers & committed teachers.
Courses include Fiction
Poetry

Writer's Digest School
Division of F+W Publications Inc
4700 E Galbraith Rd, Cincinnati, OH 45236
Tel: 513-531-2690 *Toll Free Tel:* 800-759-0963
  Fax: 513-531-0798
E-mail: wds@fwpubs.com
Web Site: www.fwpubs.com
Key Personnel
Dir: Lynn Beirl *E-mail:* lynn.beirl@fwpubs.com
Courses Workshops are taught by active, published writers in the appropriate area, such as fiction & nonfiction. Courses Students participate online, via the Internet. Workshops range in length from 4 to 28 weeks. Correspondence; student has up to 2 years to complete; tuition installment plans available for most courses.
Courses include Advanced Article Writers Workshop
Advanced Memoir/Nonfiction Book Writers Workshop
Advanced Novel Writers Workshop
Advanced Poetry Writing Workshop
Advanced Story Writers Workshop
Creating Dynamic Characters
Creativity & Expression
Elements of Effective Writing I: Grammar & Mechanics
Elements of Effective Writing II: Form & Composition
Essentials of Business Writing
Essentials of Romance Writing
Essentials of Scrapbook Journaling
Extended Getting Started in Writing Workshop
Extended Novel Writing Workshop
Focus on the Nonfiction Magazine Article
Focus on the Novel
Focus on the Personal/Family Memoir
Focus on the Short Story
Focus on Writing for Children
Fundamentals of Fiction Writing
Fundamentals of Life Stories Writing
Fundamentals of Nonfiction Writing
Fundamentals of Poetry Writing
Fundamentals of Writing for Children
Getting Started in Writing
Writing Effective Dialogue
Writing the Nonfiction Book Proposal
Writing the Novel Proposal

Awards, Prize Contests, Fellowships & Grants

Major awards given to books, authors and publishers by various organizations are, for the most part, not open for application. However, many prize contests may be applied for by writing to the sponsor (for prompt response, always include a self-addressed, stamped envelope). Also included in this section is information relating to fellowships and grants that are primarily available to authors and students who are pursuing publishing related studies.

For more complete information about scholarships, fellowships and grants-in-aid, see *The Annual Register of Grant Support* (Information Today, Inc., 630 Central Avenue, New Providence, NJ 07974).

AAUP Book, Jacket & Journal Design Show
Association of American University Presses (AAUP)
71 W 23 St, Suite 901, New York, NY 10010
Tel: 212-989-1010 *Fax:* 212-989-0275; 212-989-0176
E-mail: info@aaupnet.org
Web Site: www.aaupnet.org
Key Personnel
Exec Dir: Peter J Givler
Admin Mgr: Linda McCall
Excellence in design; competition limited to member presses in AAUP.
Award: Certificate, winning entries are displayed in a traveling exhibit

Academy of American Poets Fellowship
The Academy of American Poets Inc
588 Broadway, Suite 604, New York, NY 10012
Tel: 212-274-0343 *Fax:* 212-274-9427
E-mail: academy@poets.org
Web Site: www.poets.org
Key Personnel
Exec Dir: Troy Swenson
Prog Dir: Ryan Murphy *Tel:* 212-274-0343 ext 17
  E-mail: rmurphy@poets.org
Established: 1937
To an American poet for distinguished poetic achievement. Chosen by confidential ballot by a board of chancellors. May not be applied for.
Award: $20,000
Presented: Annually

Milton Acorn Poetry Award
Prince Edward Island Council of the Arts
115 Richmond St, Charlottetown, PE C1A 1H7, Canada
Tel: 902-368-4410 *Fax:* 902-368-4418
E-mail: peiarts@peiartscouncil.com
Web Site: www.peiartscouncil.com
Key Personnel
Exec Dir: Darrin White
Maximum of ten pages of poetry. May submit as many entries as they wish. The work must be original & unpublished. Typewritten & double-spaced on one side of the page only. There is an entry fee. Contest is for Prince Edward Island residents only. Must be resident for six of the 12 months prior to the contest deadline. For further information please call or e-mail.
Award: $500 (1st prize), $200 (2nd prize), $100 (3rd prize)
Closing Date: Call or e-mail
Presented: Call or e-mail

Herbert Baxter Adams Prize
American Historical Association
400 "A" St SE, Washington, DC 20003
Tel: 202-544-2422 *Fax:* 202-544-8307
E-mail: info@historians.org
Web Site: www.historians.org
Key Personnel
Prize Admin: Debbie Ann Doyle *Tel:* 202-544-2422 ext 104 *E-mail:* ddoyle@historians.org
Established: 1938
For a distinguished book by an American author in the field of European history. Books on 1815 through 20th century European history will be eligible; entry must be the author's first substantial book; must have been published between May 1, 2004 - April 30, 2005; must be citizen or permanent resident of the US or Canada. Submission of an entry may be made by an author or by a third party as well as by a publisher. Publishers may submit as many entries as they wish. No application form, applicants must simply mail a copy of their book to each of the prize committee members who will be posted on our web site as the prize deadline approaches. All updated info on web site.
Award: Cash prize
Closing Date: May 16, 2005

Jane Addams Children's Book Award
Jane Addams Peace Association
Subsidiary of Women's International League for Peace & Freedom (WILPF)
777 United Nations Plaza, New York, NY 10017
Tel: 212-682-8830 *Fax:* 212-682-8211
E-mail: japa@igc.org
Web Site: www.janeaddamspeace.org
Key Personnel
Award Comm Chpn: Donna Barkman
  E-mail: barkman@bestweb.net
Established: 1953
For a book that best combines literary merit with themes stressing peace, social justice, world community & the equality of the sexes & all races. Publishers applying must submit two copies of a book to the Award Committe Chairperson at One Reservoir Rd, Ossining, NY 10562.
Other Sponsor(s): Women's International League for Peace & Freedom (WILPF)
Award: Certificate; Cash
Closing Date: Dec 31
Presented: Annually, April 28 announced; ceremony in Oct

Advancement of Literacy Award
Public Library Association
Unit of American Library Association
50 E Huron St, Chicago, IL 60611
Toll Free Tel: 800-545-2433 (ext 5026)
E-mail: pla@ala.org
Web Site: www.pla.org
Key Personnel
Exec Dir: Greta Southard *Tel:* 312-280-5028
  E-mail: g.southar@ala.org
Established: 1984
Honors a publisher, bookseller, hardware &/or software dealer, foundation or similar group (ie, not an individual) that has made a significant contribution to the advancement of adult literacy.
Other Sponsor(s): Library Journal
Award: Plaque
Closing Date: Dec 1
Presented: PLA President's Reception, ALA Annual Conference, Chicago, IL, 2005

AFCP's Annual Awards
Association of Free Community Papers (AFCP)
1630 Miner St, Suite 204, Idaho Springs, CO 80452
Mailing Address: PO Box 1989, Idaho Springs, CO 80452-1989
Toll Free Tel: 877-203-2327 *Fax:* 781-459-7770
Web Site: www.afcp.org
Key Personnel
Dir: Craig McMullen
Established: 1970
Awards for excellence in 37 categories, revolving around the theme of free community press.
Award: 1st, 2nd & 3rd place plaques, honorable mention certificates
Closing Date: Jan 31
Presented: AFCP's Annual Meeting, Spring

Agatha Awards
Malice Domestic Ltd
PO Box 31137, Bethesda, MD 20824-1137
Tel: 703-751-4444
Web Site: www.malicedomestic.org
Key Personnel
Chair: Tom O'Day *E-mail:* malicechair@aol.com
Agatha Awards Comm Chair: Linda Rutledge
  E-mail: agathas@malicedomestic.org
Established: 1988
Awards for best traditional mysteries of the calendar year.
Award: Best Novel, Best First Novel, Best Non-fiction Work, Best Short Story, Best Children's/Young Adult Novel
Closing Date: Dec 31
Presented: Malice Domestic Conference, Agatha Awards Banquet, April/May

Aggiornamento Award
Catholic Library Association
100 North St, Suite 224, Pittsfield, MA 01201-5109
Tel: 413-443-2252 *Fax:* 413-442-2252
E-mail: cla@cathla.org
Web Site: www.cathla.org
Key Personnel
Exec Dir: Jean R Bostley, SSJ
Established: 1980
To recognize contributions made by an individual or an organization for the renewal of parish & community life in the spirit of Pope John XXIII.
Award: Plaque
Closing Date: None; in-house votes

AHA Prize in Atlantic History
American Historical Association
400 "A" St SE, Washington, DC 20003
Tel: 202-544-2422 *Fax:* 202-544-8307
E-mail: info@historians.org
Web Site: www.historians.org
Key Personnel
Prize Admin: Debbie Ann Doyle *Tel:* 202-544-2422 ext 104 *E-mail:* ddoyle@historians.org
Established: 2001
In recognition of outstanding historical writing that explores aspects of integration of Atlantic worlds before the 20th century. Only books of high scholarly & literary merit will be considered. Research accuracy & originality also will

be important factors in the evaluation of the books. Books published between May 1, 2004 & April 30, 2005. No application form, applicants must simply mail a copy of their book to each of the prize committee members who will be posted on our web site as the prize deadline approaches. All updated info on web site.
Award: Cash prize
Closing Date: May 16, 2005

Aid to Individual Artists
Ohio Arts Council
727 E Main St, Columbus, OH 43205-1796
Tel: 614-466-2613 *Fax:* 614-466-4494
Web Site: www.oac.state.oh.us
Key Personnel
Exec Dir: Wayne P Lawson
Lit Prog Coord: Bob Fox
Individual Art Prog: Ken Emerick *E-mail:* ken.emerick@oac.state.oh.us
Established: 1978
Fellowships to Ohio residents for creative writing (poetry, fiction, nonfiction), criticism, playwriting, visual arts, choreography, media arts, crafts, photography & music composition.
Award: $5,000 or $10,000 (determined by panel)
Closing Date: Sept 1
Presented: Annually

AIGA 50 Books/50 Covers
American Institute of Graphic Arts (AIGA)
164 Fifth Ave, New York, NY 10010
Tel: 212-807-1990 *Toll Free Tel:* 800-548-1634 *Fax:* 212-807-1799
E-mail: competitions@aiga.org
Web Site: www.aiga.org
Key Personnel
Dir, Competitions & Exhibitions: Gabriela Mirensky *Tel:* 212-807-1990 ext 231
Established: 1924
For excellence of design in book publishing (complete sets of all books selected since 1924 at Columbia University Library - Rare Book Dept).
Award: Certificate of excellence, publication in AIGA annual, exhibition in 5th Avenue Gallery
Closing Date: March annually
Presented: Annually in Sept at listed address

AIM Magazine Short Story Contest
Division of AIM Publishing Co
PO Box 1174, Maywood, IL 60153-8174
Tel: 708-344-4414 *Fax:* 206-543-2746 (WA)
Web Site: www.aimmagazine.org
Key Personnel
Publr: Myron Apilado
Assoc Ed: Ruth Apilado *E-mail:* ruthone@earthlink.net
Established: 1980
Well written stories with lasting social significance proving that people from different racial/ethnic backgrounds are more alike than they are different; request guidelines by SASE; no inquiries by fax. Winners notified by mail. Maximum length 4000 words.
Award: $100
Closing Date: Annually, Aug 15
Presented: Sept 1

AIP Science Writing Award
American Institute of Physics
One Physics Ellipse, College Park, MD 20740-3843
Tel: 301-209-3096 *Fax:* 301-209-0846
Web Site: www.aip.org/aip/awards *Telex:* 96-0983
Key Personnel
Dir: Alicia Torres
Prog Coord: Lalena Lancaster *E-mail:* lalancast@aip.org
Established: 1969
The purpose of the awards is to promote effective science communication in print &

broadcast media in order to improve the general public's appreciation of physics, astronomy & allied science fields. More info at www.aip.org/aip/awards.
Award: $3,000; Windsor chair & certificate
Closing Date: March 1 annually

AJL Bibliography Award
Association of Jewish Libraries (AJL)
15 E 26 St, Suite 1034, New York, NY 10010-1579
Tel: 212-725-5359 *Fax:* 212-678-8998
E-mail: ajl@jewishbooks.org
Web Site: www.jewishlibraries.org
Key Personnel
Pres: Ronda Rose *E-mail:* frose@att.net
Ref & Bibliography Awards Comm Chair: Peggy Pearlstein *E-mail:* ppea@loc.gov
For best Judaica bibliography book published in previous calendar year. Publishers may nominate books to Reference & Bibliography Awards Committee Chair, Peggy Pearlstein at ppea@loc.gov.
Award: $500
Closing Date: March
Presented: June

AJL Reference Book Award
Association of Jewish Libraries (AJL)
15 E 26 St, Suite 1034, New York, NY 10010-1579
Tel: 212-725-5359 *Fax:* 212-678-8998
E-mail: ajl@jewishbooks.org
Web Site: www.jewishlibraries.org
Key Personnel
Pres: Ronda Rose *E-mail:* frose@att.net
Ref & Bibliography Awards Comm Chair: Peggy Pearlstein *E-mail:* ppea@loc.gov
Established: 1985
For outstanding Judaica reference book published during previous calendar year. Publishers should bring submissions to the attention of the Chair of the Award Committee, Peggy Pearlstein at, ppea@loc.gov.
Award: $500
Closing Date: March
Presented: June

AJL Scholarship
Association of Jewish Libraries (AJL)
15 E 26 St, New York, NY 10010-1579
Tel: 212-725-5359 *Fax:* 212-481-4174
E-mail: ajl@jewishbooks.org
Web Site: www.jewishlibraries.org
Key Personnel
Lib Dir, Scholarship Chair: Debbie Stern *Tel:* 215-576-0800 ext 234 *Fax:* 215-576-6143 *E-mail:* dstern@rrc.edu
In order to encourage students to train for, & enter, the field of Judaica librarianship, the Association of Jewish Libraries awards a scholarship of $500 to a student attending or planning to attend a graduate school of library & information science. Prospective candidates should have an interest in, & demonstrate a potential for pursuing a career in Judaic librarianship. In addition, applicants must provide documentation showing participation in Judaic studies at an academic or less formal level &/or experience working in Judaic libraries.
Award: $500 stipend per academic year
Closing Date: April 1
Presented: June

Alabama Artists Fellowship Awards
Alabama State Council on the Arts
201 Monroe St, Suite 110, Montgomery, AL 36130-1800
Tel: 334-242-4076 *Fax:* 334-240-3269
Key Personnel
Exec Dir: Albert B Head

Lit Prog Mgr: Randy Shoults *Tel:* 334-242-4076 ext 224 *E-mail:* randy@arts.state.al.us
Awarded based on quality of work &/or career status, achievement & potential; two-year residency required.
Award: Cash; Two $5,000 fellowships
Closing Date: Mar 1
Presented: Annually, Oct 1

Alberta Book Awards
Book Publishers Association of Alberta
10523-100 Ave, Edmonton, AB T5J 0A8, Canada
Tel: 780-424-5060 *Fax:* 780-424-7943
E-mail: info@bookpublishers.ab.ca
Web Site: www.bookpublishers.ab.ca
Key Personnel
Exec Dir: Katherine Shute
Project Coord: Duncan Turner
Established: 1989
Excellence in writing & publishing within the province of Alberta.
Award: Sculpture, certificate
Closing Date: Jan
Presented: Annually, May

Alcuin Society Awards in Excellence in Book Design in Canada
Alcuin Society
PO Box 3216, Vancouver, BC V6B 3X8, Canada
Tel: 604-937-3293
Web Site: www.alcuinsociety.com
Established: 1981
Recognizes the work of Canadian book designers & publishers through the Alcuin Citations awarded for excellence in book design & production. Must fulfill at least one of the following criteria: titles published exclusively in Canada or titles co-published with a publisher in another country but representing a book by a Canadian book designer. Categories are: general trade books, limited editions, text & reference books & juveniles.
Award: Certificate
Closing Date: April 1
Presented: Awards ceremony, June

Nelson Algren Awards
Chicago Tribune
Tribune Tower, LL2, 435 N Michigan Ave, Chicago, IL 60611
Fax: 312-222-5816
Web Site: www.chicagotribune.com
Key Personnel
Events Producer: Aleksandra Kostovski
Established: 1982
Given for an outstanding unpublished short fiction, 2,500-10,000 words in length, by an American writer. No entry form or fee required. Entries will not be returned. Entries by mail only to Aleksandra Kostovski at the above address: include cover letter with address & e-mail, do not put name on the ms; no telephone or e-mail inquiries.
Award: $5,000 & three runners-up awards of $1,500 each, with publication of winning stories in The Chicago Tribune
Closing Date: Feb 28
Presented: Chicago, Annually in autumn

Gracie Allen Awards®
Foundation of American Women in Radio & Television
Subsidary of American Women in Radio & Television
8405 Greensboro Dr, Suite 800, McLean, VA 22102
Tel: 703-506-3290 *Fax:* 703-506-3266
E-mail: info@awrt.org
Web Site: www.awrt.org
Key Personnel
Exec Dir: Maria E Brennan *E-mail:* mbrennan@awrt.org

Dir, Resource Devt: Shaughna Giracca
 E-mail: sgiracca@awrt.org
Awarded for programming in all mediums which
 contributes to positive & realistic portrayals
 of women, addresses interests of concern to
 women, enhances women's image, position &
 welfare. For application information, contact
 Lesa Faris.
Award: Statue
Presented: New York, NY, June

ALSC BWI/Summer Reading Program Grant
Association for Library Service to Children
Division of American Library Association
50 E Huron St, Chicago, IL 60611-2795
Tel: 312-280-2163 *Toll Free Tel:* 800-545-2433
 Fax: 312-944-7671
E-mail: alsc@ala.org
Web Site: www.ala.org/alsc
Key Personnel
Prog Coord: Meredith Parets *Tel:* 312-280-2166
 E-mail: mparets@ala.org
Encourages reading programs for children in a
 public library. Applicant must plan & present
 an outline for a theme-based summer reading
 program in a public library.
Award: $3,000
Closing Date: Dec 1
Presented: ALA Midwinter Meeting

ALTA Literacy Award
Association for Library Trustees & Advocates
 (ALTA)
Division of American Library Association
50 E Huron St, Chicago, IL 60611
Tel: 312-280-2161 *Toll Free Tel:* 800-545-2433
 Fax: 312-280-3257
Web Site: www.ala.org/alta
Key Personnel
Exec Dir: Kerry Ward
For volunteer contribution toward fighting illiter-
 acy in the US.
Award: Citation & Plaque
Closing Date: March 1
Presented: ALTA Specialized Outreach Services
 Luncheon; ALA Annual Conference

**American Association of University Women
 Award for Juvenile Literature**
AAUW, North Carolina Division
Affiliate of North Carolina Literary & Historical
 Association
4610 Mail Service Center, Raleigh, NC 27699-
 4610
Tel: 919-807-7290 *Fax:* 919-733-8807
Key Personnel
Awards Coord: Michael Hill *E-mail:* michael.
 hill@ncmail.net
Established: 1953
For a published work of juvenile fiction or non-
 fiction by a legal or actual resident of North
 Carolina for at least three years prior to the end
 of the contest period.
Other Sponsor(s): AAUW
Award: Cup
Closing Date: Annually, July 15
Presented: Raleigh, NC, Annually, Nov

American Book Award
Before Columbus Foundation
The Raymond House, 655 13 St, Suite 302, Oak-
 land, CA 94612
SAN: 159-2955
Tel: 510-268-9775
Key Personnel
Contact: Gundars Strads *E-mail:* strads@haas.
 berkeley.edu
Established: 1978
To recognize outstanding literary achievement by
 contemporary American authors without restric-
 tion for race, sex, ethnic background, or genre.
 The purpose is to acknowledge the excellence

& multicultural diversity of American writing.
 The awards are nonprofit. There are no cate-
 gories & all winners are accorded equal status.
 Award is given for books published within the
 current year.
Award: Plaque
Closing Date: Dec 31
Presented: Oakland, CA, Sept 5

American Illustration/American Photography
Amilus Inc
126 Fifth Ave, Suite 14B, New York, NY 10011
Tel: 212-243-5262 *Fax:* 212-243-5201
E-mail: aiap@skyweb.net
Web Site: www.ai-ap.com
Key Personnel
Dir: Mark Heflin
Established: 1981
For the finest illustrative work by students & pro-
 fessionals. Categories include: editorial, adver-
 tising & books, as well as unpublished work.
 Work will be published in the American Illus-
 tration annual & will include the artist's name,
 address & telephone. Also, similar competi-
 tion & annual for photography called American
 Photography. Both books are published in Nov.
Closing Date: Feb 15, Illustration; Jan 15, Pho-
 tography

The American Legion Fourth Estate Award
American Legion National Headquarters
700 N Pennsylvania St, Indianapolis, IN 46204
Tel: 317-630-1253 *Fax:* 317-630-1368
E-mail: pr@legion.org
Web Site: www.legion.org
Key Personnel
Dir: Joe March
Established: 1958
Annual award for excellence in journalism (any
 media). Material must have been published be-
 tween Jan 1 & Dec 31.
Award: 15-inch pylon ($2,000 stipend to defray
 expenses). Must accept award at national con-
 vention
Closing Date: Jan 31
Presented: American Legion National Convention

American Printing History Association Award
American Printing History Association
PO Box 4519, Grand Central Sta, New York, NY
 10163-4519
Tel: 212-930-9220 *Fax:* 212-930-0079
Web Site: www.printinghistory.org
Key Personnel
Pres: Martin Antonetti
Exec Sec: Stephen G Crook *E-mail:* scrook@
 nypl.org
Established: 1976
For achievement in the printing world or in
 closely related fields.
Award: Two framed award certificates, one for an
 individual & one for an institution
Presented: APHA meeting, New York, NY, Annu-
 ally, Jan

AMWA Medical Book Awards
American Medical Writers Association
40 W Gude Dr, Suite 101, Rockville, MD 20850-
 1192
Tel: 301-294-5303 *Fax:* 301-294-9006
All medical books published in previous year are
 eligible for the current year's competition.
Award: Trophy
Closing Date: March 1

Amy Writing Awards
The Amy Foundation
PO Box 16091, Lansing, MI 48901-6091
Tel: 517-323-6233 *Fax:* 517-321-2572
E-mail: amyfoundtn@aol.com
Web Site: www.amyfound.org

Key Personnel
Pres: James Russell
Exec Secy: Mary Spagnuolo
Established: 1985
For writing that presents the Biblical position on
 issues affecting the world today. To be eligible, submitted articles must be published in a
 secular, non-religious publication & contain
 a scriptural quote. Must have been published
 during 2004.
Award: $10,000 (1st prize), $5,000 (2nd prize),
 $4,000 (3rd prize), $3,000 (4th prize), $2,000
 (5th prize), $1,000 (10 prizes)
Closing Date: Jan 31, 2005

Anhinga Prize for Poetry
Anhinga Press
PO Box 10595, Tallahassee, FL 32302-2595
Tel: 850-442-6323 *Fax:* 850-442-6323
E-mail: info@anhinga.org
Web Site: www.anhinga.org
Key Personnel
Dir: Rick Campbell
Established: 1983
Poetry book.
Award: $2,000 & publication
Closing Date: Feb 15-May 1
Presented: Tallahassee, FL

**The Anisfield Wolf Book Award in Human
 Relations**
The Cleveland Foundation
1422 Euclid Ave, Suite 1300, Cleveland, OH
 44115-2001
Tel: 216-861-3810 *Fax:* 216-861-2229
E-mail: contactus@clevefdn.org
Key Personnel
Communs & Mktg Admin: Marcia Bryant
Established: 1935
Recognizes books that have made important con-
 tributions to our understanding of racism or our
 appreciation of the diversity of human cultures.
Award: $20,000 divided among winners
Closing Date: January 31

**R Ross Annett Award for Children's
 Literature**
Banff Centre
11759 Groat Rd, Percy Page Center, Edmonton,
 AB T5M 3K6, Canada
Tel: 780-422-8174 *Toll Free Tel:* 800-665-5354
 Fax: 780-422-2663
E-mail: mail@writersguild.ab.ca
Web Site: www.writersguild.ab.ca
Key Personnel
Exec Dir: Diane Walton
Established: 1982
Alberta Literary Award, must be resident of Al-
 berta.
Award: $1,000 plus leather-bound copy of book
Closing Date: Dec 31
Presented: Calgary, AB

**The May Hill Arbuthnot Honor Lecture
 Award**
Association for Library Service to Children
Division of American Library Association
50 E Huron St, Chicago, IL 60611-2795
Tel: 312-280-2163 *Toll Free Tel:* 800-545-2433
 Fax: 312-944-7671
E-mail: alsc@ala.org
Web Site: www.ala.org/alsc
Person appointed prepares a paper of significant
 contribution to the field of children's litera-
 ture & delivers a lecture based on the paper in
 April. Libraries & other institutions apply to
 host the lecture. The paper is also published in
 the ALSC journal "Childrens & Libraries".
Presented: The ALA Midwinter Meeting, Annu-
 ally

Artist Fellowship Awards Program
Wisconsin Arts Board

759

101 E Wilson St, 1st fl, Madison, WI 53702
Tel: 608-266-0190 *Fax:* 608-267-0380
E-mail: artsboard@arts.state.wi.us
Web Site: www.arts.state.wi.us
Key Personnel
Exec Dir: George Tzougros
Grant Progs & Servs Specialist: Mark Fraire
    E-mail: mark.fraire@arts.state.wi.us
Established: 1973
Grants to Wisconsin residents in fiction, nonfic-
    tion, poetry & playwriting.
Award: $8,000; fellowships
Closing Date: Sept 15 (even years)

Artist Fellowships
Connecticut Commission on Culture & Tourism,
    Arts Division
One Financial Plaza, 755 Main St, Hartford, CT
    06103
Tel: 860-566-4770 *Fax:* 860-566-6462
E-mail: artsinfo@ctarts.org
Web Site: www.ctarts.org
Key Personnel
Sr Prog Specialist: Linda Dente *E-mail:* ldente@
    ctarts.org
Established: 1970
Individual fellowships are given biennially to
    writers for new work or work in progress in
    the fields of fiction, playwriting & poetry. Ap-
    plicants must have lived & written profession-
    ally in Connecticut for at least one year. Ap-
    plications accepted in even numbered years.
    Twenty to 35 awards given.
Award: $5,000 & $2,500
Closing Date: Sept 20
Presented: Biennially

Artist Fellowships in Literature
Colorado Council on the Arts
Division of Higher Education, State of CO
1380 Lawrence St, Suite 1200, Denver, CO 80204
Tel: 303-866-2723 *Fax:* 303-866-4266
E-mail: coloarts@state.co.us
Web Site: www.coloarts.state.co.us
Key Personnel
Acting Exec Dir: Renee Bovee *E-mail:* renee.
    bovee@state.co.us
Fellowship grant to acknowledge outstanding ac-
    complishment & encourage new work, Col-
    orado artist only. Creative nonfiction. Appli-
    cants must be 18 years old & a resident for one
    year prior to the application deadline.
Award: $5,000
Closing Date: Contact agency for deadline

Artist Grants
South Dakota Arts Council
Affiliate of Dept of Tourism & State Develop-
    ment
800 Governors Dr, Pierre, SD 57501-2294
Tel: 605-773-3131 *Fax:* 605-773-6962
E-mail: sdac@state.sd.us
Web Site: www.sdarts.org
Key Personnel
Exec Dir: Dennis Holub
Awards made to residents of South Dakota, based
    on the quality of art work.
Award: $1,000 &/or $3,000
Closing Date: March 1, annually

Artist Trust Fellowship
Artist Trust
1835 12 Ave, Seattle, WA 98122
Tel: 206-467-8734 *Fax:* 206-467-9633
E-mail: info@artisttrust.org
Web Site: www.artisttrust.org
Key Personnel
Exec Dir: Barbara Courtney
Dir, Grant Progs: Fionn Meade
Established: 1988
Unrestricted grant to generative artists in Wash-
    ington State. Fellowships will be awarded in

music, media, literature & craft in odd years.
Fellowships will be awarded in dance, design,
theatre & visual arts in even years. Applications will be available in April & due early
summer.

Artists' Fellowships
New York Foundation for the Arts
155 Avenue of the Americas, 14th fl, New York,
    NY 10013-1507
Tel: 212-366-6900 *Fax:* 212-366-1778
E-mail: nyainfo@nyfa.org
Web Site: www.nyfa.org
Key Personnel
Dir: Penelope Dannenberg
Prog Officer: Shawn Miller *Tel:* 212-366-6900 ext
    350 *E-mail:* smiller@nyfa.org
Fellowship, application limited to New York State
    residents. Applications in fiction & playwrit-
    ing/screenwriting; applications will be available
    July.
Award: $7,000 cash award
Closing Date: Oct 1
Presented: New York, NY

Arts Recognition & Talent Search (ARTS)
National Foundation for Advancement in the Arts
444 Brickell Ave, Suite P14, Miami, FL 33131
Tel: 305-377-1140 *Toll Free Tel:* 800-970-2787
    Fax: 305-377-1149
E-mail: nfaa@nfaa.org
Web Site: www.artsawards.org
Key Personnel
Pres: William H Banchs
Prog Officer: Christopher Schram
Dir, Admin & Devt: Maggie Carrerou
Communs Dir: Beth Czeskleba *Tel:* 305-377-1140
    ext 15 *E-mail:* beth@nfaa.org
Dir, Fin: Marisa Morgan
Established: 1981
Cash award scholarship opportunities to 17-18
    year old artists with demonstrated talent in
    dance, jazz, film/video, music (classical & pop-
    ular), photography, theater, visual arts, voice &
    writing.
Award: Up to $10,000 in individual awards with
    potential for Presidential Scholar in the Arts
    medallion
Closing Date: June 1, late deadline Oct 1
Presented: Miami, FL, Jan

Vincent Astor Memorial Leadership Essay Contest
291 Wood Rd, Annapolis, MD 21402-5034
Tel: 410-268-6110 *Toll Free Tel:* 800-233-8764
    Fax: 410-295-1049
E-mail: articlesubmission@navalinstitute.org
Web Site: www.navalinstitute.org
Key Personnel
Commun Mgr: Jon Youngdahl
Man Ed, Proceedings Magazine: Julie Olver
Established: 1974
Essay on naval leadership up to 3500 words.
Other Sponsor(s): Vincent Astor Foundation
Award: $1,500, a Naval Institute Gold Medal & a
    lifetime membership in the Naval Institute (1st
    prize), $1,000 & a Naval Institute Silver Medal
    & a one year membership in the Naval Institute
    (2nd prize), $500 & a Naval Institute Bronze
    Medal & a one year membership in the Naval
    Institute (two 3rd prizes)
Closing Date: Feb 15
Presented: Annapolis, MD, April; 1st prize pub-
    lished in June issue of *Proceedings Magazine*

Athenaeum of Philadelphia Literary Award
Athenaeum of Philadelphia
219 S Sixth St, Philadelphia, PA 19106
Tel: 215-925-2688 *Fax:* 215-925-3755
Web Site: www.philaathenaeum.org

Key Personnel
Circ Libn: Ellen L Rose *E-mail:* erose@
    PhilaAthenaeum.org
Established: 1950
In recognition & encouragement of outstanding
    literary achievement in Philadelphia & the
    vicinity.
Award: Citation
Presented: Annually in the Spring

Atlantic Poetry Prize
Writers Federation of Nova Scotia
1113 Marginal Rd, Halifax, NS B3H 4P7, Canada
Tel: 902-423-8116 *Fax:* 902-422-0881
E-mail: talk@writers.ns.ca
Web Site: www.writers.ns.ca
Key Personnel
Exec Dir: Jane Buss
Established: 2001
Presented to the best full-length book of poetry
    by an Atlantic Canadian in the previous calen-
    dar year.
Award: $1,000
Closing Date: First Friday in Dec
Presented: Halifax, NS, Canada, May each year

Award for Fiction
Canadian Authors Association (CAA)
320 S Shores Rd, Campbellford, ON K0L 1L0,
    Canada
Mailing Address: PO Box 419, Campbellford, ON
    K0L 1L0, Canada
Tel: 705-653-0323 *Toll Free Tel:* 866-216-6222
    Fax: 705-653-0593
E-mail: info@canauthors.org
Web Site: www.canauthors.org
Entries must be full-length English-language liter-
    ature for adults by Canadian authors. Reprints
    are not eligible, nor is self-published work or
    work which has been published at the author's
    expense.
Award: $2,500 & silver medal
Closing Date: Dec 15

AWP Award Series
Association of Writers & Writing Programs
    (AWP)
Affiliate of George Mason University
George Mason University, MS-1E3, Fairfax, VA
    22030-4444
Tel: 703-993-4301 *Fax:* 703-993-4302
E-mail: awp@awpwriter.org
Web Site: www.awpwriter.org
Key Personnel
Exec Dir: D W Fenza
Pubns Mgr: Supriya Bhatnagar *Tel:* 703-993-4308
    E-mail: supriya_b@awpwriter.org
Established: 1967
An open competition for book-length mss in four
    categories: poetry, short fiction, novel & cre-
    ative (nonfiction). Send business-size SASE
    after Nov 1 for submission guidelines. Mss ac-
    cepted postmark Jan 1-Feb 28.
Award: Publication by a major university press &
    an honorarium of $2,000, for short fiction, non-
    fiction & novel. Donald Hall Prize in poetry-
    honorarium $4,000. One winner in each cate-
    gory
Closing Date: Feb 28 (postmark)

Baker & Taylor Conference Grants
Young Adult Library Services Association
    (YALSA)
Unit of American Library Association
50 E Huron St, Chicago, IL 60611
Tel: 312-280-4390 (ext 4391) *Toll Free Tel:* 800-
    545-2433 (ext 4390) *Fax:* 312-664-7459
E-mail: yalsa@ala.org
Web Site: www.ala.org/yalsa/printz
Key Personnel
Prog Officer: Nichole Gilbert *E-mail:* ngilbert@
    ala.org

Established: 1983
To young adult librarians in public or school libraries to attend an ALA Annual Conference for the first time. Candidates must be members of YALSA & have one to ten years of library experience.
Award: $1,000, two given yearly
Closing Date: Dec 1
Presented: ALA's midwinter meeting

Emily Clark Balch Prizes in Creative American Writing

Virginia Quarterly Review
One West Range, Charlottesville, VA 22903
Mailing Address: PO Box 400223, Charlottesville, VA 22904-4223
Tel: 434-924-3124 *Fax:* 434-924-1397
E-mail: vqreview@virginia.edu
Web Site: www.virginia.edu/vqr
Key Personnel
Ed: Ted Genoways
Asst to Ed: Janna O Gies *E-mail:* jco7e@virginia.edu
For the best poem & short story published in the Virginia Quarterly Review during a calendar year.
Award: $1,000 each
Presented: Annually

Bancroft Prizes

Columbia University
517 Butler Library, 535 W 114 St, New York, NY 10027
Tel: 212-854-4746 *Fax:* 212-854-9099
Web Site: www.columbia.edu/cu/lweb/eguides/amerihist/bancroft.html
Key Personnel
Contact: Matt Hampel
Established: 1948
Two awards for distinguished books in the fields of American history (including biography) & diplomacy. Award confined to books originally published in English or those with a published English translation. Books published in year preceding that in which award is made are eligible. Submit four copies & nominating letter.
Award: $10,000 each
Closing Date: Nov 1, page-proof copy may be submitted after Nov 1, provided the work will be published after that date & before Dec 31
Presented: Columbia University

Banff Centre National Arts Award

Banff Centre
107 Tunnel Mountain Dr, Banff, AB T1L 1H5, Canada
Mailing Address: Box 1020, Banff, AB T1L 1H5, Canada
Tel: 403-762-6154 *Toll Free Tel:* 800-413-8368
Fax: 403-762-6158
E-mail: communications@banffcentre.ca
Web Site: www.banffcentre.ca
Key Personnel
Dir, Mktg & Communs: Melanie Busby
E-mail: melanie_busby@banffcentre.ca
Communs Coord: Jenny Legget *Tel:* 403-762-6157
Established: 1980
For Canadian citizens only. Awarded annually on a rotational basis through literary, visual & media arts, theatre & dance, music & opera & aboriginal arts, to recognize a distinguished & continuing contribution to the development of the arts in Canada.
Award: $5,000 & two-week complimentary residency at The Banff Centre
Closing Date: By nomination varying between March & April
Presented: The Banff Centre, Banff, AB, To be determined

Banta Literary Award

Wisconsin Library Association Inc
5250 E Terrace Dr, Suite A-1, Madison, WI 53718-8345
Tel: 608-245-3640 *Fax:* 608-245-3646
Web Site: www.wla.lib.wi.us
Key Personnel
Exec Dir: Lisa K Strand
Memb Servs Coord: Brigitte E Vacha
E-mail: vacha@scls.lib.wi.us
Established: 1974
To honor a work by a Wisconsin author for a book published in the preceding year that contributes to the world of literature & ideas.
Award: Trophy & $500
Closing Date: May of year following publication
Presented: Annually awarded at Fall conference, Oct

James P Barry Ohioana Award for Editorial Excellence

Ohioana Library Association
274 E First Ave, Suite 300, Columbus, OH 43201
Tel: 614-466-3831 *Fax:* 614-728-6974
E-mail: ohioana@sloma.state.oh.us
Web Site: www.oplin.lib.oh.us/ohioana
Key Personnel
Exec Dir: Carol Roddy
Established: 1979
Only Ohio-based serial (magazine, journal, newspaper, etc) that covers subjects of interest to the Ohioana Library, namely literature, history, culture, the arts or the general humanities.
Closing Date: Dec 31

Basile Festival of Emerging American Theatre (FEAT)

The Phoenix Theatre
749 N Park Ave, Indianapolis, IN 46202
Tel: 317-635-7529 *Fax:* 317-635-0010
E-mail: info@phoenixtheatre.org
Web Site: www.phoenixtheatre.org
Key Personnel
Producing Dir: Bryan Fonseca
Devt Dir: Tom Robertson
Established: 1984
Playwriting contest.
Other Sponsor(s): Frank M Basile
Award: $1,000 for full-length plays
Closing Date: Scripts accepted Dec 1 - Feb 28 by solicitation only
Presented: Phoenix Theatre, Indianapolis, IN

Miriam Bass Award for Creativity in Independent Publishing

Association of American Publishers Inc (AAP)
71 Fifth Ave, 2nd fl, New York, NY 10003-3004
Tel: 212-255-0200 *Fax:* 212-255-7007
Web Site: www.publishers.org
For creativity & innovation in publishing.
Other Sponsor(s): National Book Network; Rowman & Littlefield
Award: $5,000
Closing Date: Dec 1, 2004
Presented: New York, NY, March 4, 2005

The Mildred L Batchelder Award

Association for Library Service to Children
Division of American Library Association
50 E Huron St, Chicago, IL 60611-2795
Tel: 312-280-2163 *Toll Free Tel:* 800-545-2433
Fax: 312-944-7671
E-mail: alsc@ala.org
Web Site: www.ala.org/alsc
Established: 1966
Awarded to an American publisher for an outstanding book originally published in a foreign language in a foreign country & subsequently translated to English & published in the U.S. during the previous year.

Award: Citation
Presented: ALSC Awards Program at the ALA Annual Conference, Annually

Bay Area Book Reviewers Association Book Awards

Bay Area Book Reviewers Association (BABRA)
c/o Poetry Flash, 1450 Fourth St, Suite 4, Berkeley, CA 94710
Tel: 510-525-5476 *Fax:* 510-525-6752
E-mail: babra@poetryflash.org; editor@poetryflash.org
Web Site: www.poetryflash.org
Key Personnel
Exec Dir: Joyce Jenkins
Established: 1981
Award by category (fiction, poetry, nonfiction & children's literature) for best book in category by a Northern California writer. Publishers Award given occasionally for special achievement by a Northern California publisher. Also, award given on irregular basis for excellence in translation. Send 3 copies of book; no application or fee necessary.
Other Sponsor(s): Northern California Independent Booksellers Association; San Francisco Public Library
Award: Cash & certificate
Closing Date: Dec 1
Presented: Koret Auditorium, San Francisco Main Public Library, Spring annually

The BC Book Prizes

West Coast Book Prize Society
207 W Hastings St, Suite 902, Vancouver, BC V6B 1H7, Canada
Tel: 604-687-2405 *Fax:* 604-669-3701
E-mail: info@bcbookprizes.ca
Web Site: www.bcbookprizes.ca
Key Personnel
Exec Dir: Bryan Pike
The following BC Book Prizes are awarded to a resident of BC or one who has lived in BC for three of the past five years: to the author of the best work of fiction; best book written for children 16 years & younger; best original nonfiction literary work; author of the best work of poetry. The following BC Book Prizes are also offered: originating publisher of the best book judged in terms of public appeal, initiative, design, production & content (publisher must have their head office in BC); author of the book which contributes most to the appreciation & understanding of BC (published anywhere the author may reside outside BC); author & illustrator of the best picture book written for children (author/illustrator must be a BC/Yukon resident or have lived in BC or the Yukon for three of the past five years).
Other Sponsor(s): BC Teachers' Federation; British Columbia Booksellers Association; British Columbia Library Association; Duthie Books 4th Avenue; Friesens; Transcontinental Publishing; Webcom
Award: $2,000 & certificate
Closing Date: Annually, Dec 1, with exceptions made for books published in Dec
Presented: The British Columbia Book Prizes Banquet, Spring

George Louis Beer Prize

American Historical Association
400 "A" St SE, Washington, DC 20003
Tel: 202-544-2422 *Fax:* 202-544-8307
E-mail: info@historians.org
Web Site: www.historians.org
Key Personnel
Prize Admin: Debbie Ann Doyle *Tel:* 202-544-2422 ext 104 *E-mail:* ddoyle@historians.org
Established: 1930
Recognition of outstanding historical writing in European international history since 1895 that

is submitted by a scholar who is a US citizen. Books published between May 1, 2004 & April 30, 2005 are eligible. Only books of a high scholarly historical nature should be submitted. No application form, applicants must simply mail a copy of their book to each of the prize committee members who will be posted on our web site as the prize deadline approaches. All updated info on web site.
Award: Cash prize
Closing Date: May 16, 2005
Presented: San Francisco

The Pura Belpre Award
Association for Library Service to Children
Division of American Library Association
50 E Huron St, Chicago, IL 60611-2795
Tel: 312-280-2163 *Toll Free Tel:* 800-545-2433
  Fax: 312-944-7671
E-mail: alsc@ala.org
Web Site: www.ala.org/alsc
Established: 1996
Biennial award presented to a Latino/Latina writer & illustrator whose children's work best celebrates the Latino cultural experience.
Other Sponsor(s): National Association to Promote Library Services to Latinos & the Spanish Speaking (REFORMA)
Award: Medal
Presented: Biennially

Curtis Benjamin Award
Association of American Publishers (AAP)
50 "F" St NW, Washington, DC 20001-1530
Tel: 202-347-3375 *Fax:* 202-347-3690
Web Site: www.publishers.org
Key Personnel
Communs Staff: Stephanie Beer *Tel:* 202-220-4550 *E-mail:* sbeer@publishers.org
Contact: Judith Platt *Tel:* 202-220-4551
Established: 1975
Awarded to an outstanding individual within the US publishing industry who has shown exceptional innovation & creativity in the field of publishing as evidenced in his or her career. Originality, usefulness & difficulty of achievement of a project or body of work are among the criteria used to select the winner.
Award: Plaque
Closing Date: Sept 1
Presented: AAP General Annual Meeting, March 2

Benjamin Franklin Book Awards
Publishers Marketing Association (PMA)
627 Aviation Way, Manhattan Beach, CA 90266
Tel: 310-372-2732 *Fax:* 310-374-3342
E-mail: info@pma-online.org
Web Site: www.pma-online.org
Key Personnel
Exec Dir: Jan Nathan
Established: 1987
Excellence in independent publishing in specific genre & design (books, audio & video).
Award: Etched glass & wooden standing plaque
Closing Date: Dec 31, 2004
Presented: New York, NY, June 1, 2005

George Bennett Fellowship
Phillips Exeter Academy
20 Main St, Exeter, NH 03833-2460
Tel: 603-772-4311
Web Site: www.exeter.edu
Key Personnel
Coord, Selection Comm: Charles Pratt
Established: 1968
Established to provide support for one academic year for an individual contemplating or pursuing a career as a professional writer. Selection is based on the literary promise of the ms submitted. The committee favors applicants who have not yet published a book-length work

with a major publisher. Send SASE for application or obtain from the Academy web site. Telephone inquiries strongly discouraged.
Award: $10,000 & housing & board at the Academy for the academic year
Closing Date: Dec 1
Presented: Annually in March

Naomi Berber Memorial Award
PIA/GATF (Graphic Arts Technical Foundation)
200 Deer Run Rd, Sewickley, PA 15143-2600
Tel: 412-741-6860 *Toll Free Tel:* 800-910-4283
  Fax: 412-741-2311
E-mail: info@gain.net
Web Site: www.gain.net
Key Personnel
Pres: Michael Makin
Mktg Mgr: Lisa Erdner
Established: 1976
Honors a woman who has made a major contribution to the development of the printing industry. A nominee must have worked in the printing industry for ten years or more.
Award: Engraved pendant
Closing Date: Annually, May 31
Presented: PIA/GATF Administrative Meetings, Annually, Nov

Jessie Bernard Award
American Sociological Association (ASA)
1307 New York Ave NW, Suite 700, Washington, DC 20005
Tel: 202-383-9005 *Fax:* 202-638-0882
E-mail: governance@asanet.org
Web Site: www.asanet.org
Key Personnel
Dir, Governance: Michael Murphy *Tel:* 202-383-9005 ext 327
For scholarly contributions that enlarge the horizons of sociology to encompass fully the role of women in society. Winner announced through newsletter "Footnotes", an ASA publication. Please go to web site for future awards.
Award: Certificate
Closing Date: June 15
Presented: ASA Annual Meeting, Annually, Aug

Albert J Beveridge Award in American History
American Historical Association
400 "A" St SE, Washington, DC 20003
Tel: 202-544-2422 *Fax:* 202-544-8307
E-mail: info@historians.org
Web Site: www.historians.org
Key Personnel
Prize Admin: Debbie Ann Doyle *Tel:* 202-544-2422 ext 104 *E-mail:* ddoyle@historians.org
Established: 1939
To promote & honor outstanding historical writing. The award is given for a distinguished book in English on the history of the US, Latin America, or Canada, from 1492 to the present. Books that employ new methodological or conceptual tools or that constitute significant re-examinations of important interpretive problems will be given preference. Literary merit is also an important criterion. Biographies, monographs & works of synthesis & interpretation are eligible; translations, anthologies & collections of documents are not. Books published after May 1, 2004 & before April 30, 2005 are eligible for the award; limited to five titles from any one publisher & must be submitted by sending a copy to each member of the committee. No application form. All updated info on web site.
Award: Cash prize
Closing Date: May 16, 2005

Albert J Beveridge Grant for Research in the History of the Western Hemisphere
American Historical Association
400 "A" St SE, Washington, DC 20003

Tel: 202-544-2422 *Fax:* 202-544-8307
E-mail: info@historians.org
Web Site: www.historians.org
Key Personnel
Prize Admin: Debbie Ann Doyle *Tel:* 202-544-2422 ext 104 *E-mail:* ddoyle@historians.org
To support research in the history of the Western hemisphere (United States, Canada & Latin America). Only members of the Association are eligible. The grants are intended to further research in progress & may be used for travel to a library or archive, for microfilms, photographs or photocopying - a list of purposes that is meant to be merely illustrative not exhaustive. Preference will be given to those with specific research needs, such as the completion of a project or completion of a discrete segment thereof; preference will be given to PhD candidates & junior scholars. Application forms available on website. Applications must include application form with estimated budget, curriculum vita & statement of no more than 750 words. A one page bibliography of the most relevant, secondary works on the topic.
Award: Individual grants will not exceed $1,000; preference to PhD candidates & scholars
Closing Date: Feb 15, 2005

The Geoffrey Bilson Award for Historical Fiction
Canadian Children's Book Centre
40 Orchard View Blvd, Toronto, ON M4R 1B9, Canada
Tel: 416-975-0010 *Fax:* 416-975-8970
E-mail: info@bookcentre.ca
Web Site: www.bookcentre.ca
Key Personnel
Award Admin: Brenda Halliday
Established: 1988
Award: $1,000
Presented: April 2005

Birks Family Foundation Award for Canadian Biography
Canadian Authors Association (CAA)
320 S Shores Rd, Campbellford, ON K0L 1L0, Canada
Mailing Address: PO Box 419, Campbellford, ON K0L 1L0, Canada
Tel: 705-653-0323 *Toll Free Tel:* 866-216-6222
  Fax: 705-653-0593
E-mail: info@canauthors.org
Web Site: www.canauthors.org
A biographical work about a Canadian written by a Canadian. Entries must be full-length English-language literature for adults by Canadian authors. Reprints are not eligible nor is self-published work or work which has been published at the author's expense.
Award: $2,500 & silver medal
Closing Date: Dec 15

Irma S & James H Black Award
Bank Street College of Education
610 W 112 St, New York, NY 10025
Tel: 212-875-4400 *Fax:* 212-875-4558
Web Site: streetcat.bankstreet.edu/html/isb.html
Key Personnel
Dir, Libr Servs: Linda Greengrass *Tel:* 212-875-4450 *E-mail:* lindag@bankstreet.edu
Established: 1972
For unified excellence of story line, language & illustration in a work for young children published during the previous year.
Award: Scroll & Gold Seals
Closing Date: Dec 15
Presented: Annually in May

Black Warrior Review Literary Awards
Black Warrior Review
University of Alabama, Tuscaloosa, AL 35486-0027

Mailing Address: PO Box 862936, Tuscaloosa,
AL 35486-0027
Tel: 205-348-4518
E-mail: bwr@ua.edu
Web Site: www.webdelsol.com/bwr
Key Personnel
Ed: Aaron Welborn
Man Ed: Laura Hendrix
Poetry Ed: Kimberly Campanello
Fiction Ed: Cayenne Sullivan
Established: 1984
Awards given to best fiction & best poetry pub-
lished in previous volume of the Black Warrior
Review; winners presented in fall issue each
year.
Award: Two $500 awards

Susan Smith Blackburn Prize
3239 Avalon Place, Houston, TX 77019
Tel: 713-308-2842 *Fax:* 713-654-8184
Web Site: www.blackburnprize.org
Key Personnel
Pres & Founding Dir: Emilie S Kilgore
Established: 1978
To an English-speaking woman for outstanding
full-length play written in English, produced or
unproduced within the preceding 12 months.
Award: Winner-$10,000 & signed deKooning
print;special commendation (at Judges' discre-
tion) $2,000; $1,000 to each of the other 8-11
finalists
Closing Date: Sept 20
Presented: New York or London, Annually in Feb

Neltje Blanchan Memorial Award
Wyoming Arts Council
Division of Wyoming Department of Parks &
Cultural Resources
2320 Capitol Ave, Cheyenne, WY 82002
Tel: 307-777-7742 *Fax:* 307-777-5499
Web Site: www.wyoarts.state.wy.us
Key Personnel
Lit Prog Mgr: Michael Shay *Tel:* 307-777-5234
E-mail: mshay@state.wy.us
Established: 1988
Best writing in any genre inspired by a relation-
ship with nature. Open to Wyoming residents
only. Blind judges, single juror.
Other Sponsor(s): Neltje
Award: $1,000
Closing Date: Annually, Aug 1
Presented: ARTSPEAK Conference, Announced
Nov 1

The James Boatwright III Prize for Poetry
Shenandoah: The Washington & Lee Review
Washington & Lee University, Mattingly House, 2
Lee Ave, Lexington, VA 24450-0303
Tel: 540-458-8765 *Fax:* 540-458-8461
Web Site: www.shenandoah.wlu.edu
Key Personnel
Man Ed: Lynn Leech *E-mail:* lleech@wlu.edu
Award is for the best poem published in Shenan-
doah during a volume year.
Award: $1,000
Presented: Annually

Frederick Bock Prize
Poetry Magazine
1030 N Clark St, Suite 420, Chicago, IL 60610
Tel: 312-787-7070 *Fax:* 312-787-6650
E-mail: poetry@poetrymagazine.org
Web Site: www.poetrymagazine.org
Key Personnel
Busn Mgr: Helen Klaviter *E-mail:* hklaviter@
poetrymagazine.org
Established: 1981
For poetry published during the preceding two
volumes of Poetry. No application necessary.
Award: $500
Presented: Annually in Dec

George Bogin Memorial Award
Poetry Society of America (PSA)
15 Gramercy Park, New York, NY 10003
Tel: 212-254-9628 *Fax:* 212-673-2352
Web Site: www.poetrysociety.org
Key Personnel
Progs Dir: Eve Grubin *E-mail:* eve@
poetrysociety.org
Established by the family & friends of George
Bogin, for a selection of four or five poems
that reflects the encounter of the ordinary &
the extraordinary, uses language in an orig-
inal way & takes a stand against oppres-
sion in any of its forms. No line limit; send
No 10 SASE for more information, or visit
www.poetrysociety.org.
Award: $500
Closing Date: Dec 22

Bogle International Library Travel Fund
International Relations Committee
Unit of American Library Association
50 E Huron St, Chicago, IL 60611-2795
Tel: 312-280-3201 *Toll Free Tel:* 800-545-2433
(ext 3201) *Fax:* 312-280-4392
E-mail: intl@ala.org
Web Site: www.ala.org
Key Personnel
Staff Liaison: Michael Dowling
To librarians to travel abroad to study &/or attend
first international conferences.
Award: $1,000
Closing Date: Dec of each year
Presented: ALA Conference, Annually in June

Waldo M & Grace C Bonderman Prize
Formerly Playwriting Competition for Playwrights
for Young Audiences
Indiana University-Purdue University-Indianapolis
140 W Washington St, Indianapolis, IN 46204
Tel: 317-635-5277 *Fax:* 317-236-0767
E-mail: bonderman@iupui.edu
Web Site: www.indianarep.com/bonderman
Key Personnel
Founder & Dir: Prof Dorothy Webb *Tel:* 317-274-
2095 *E-mail:* dwebb@iupui.edu
Established: 1984
Playwriting.
Other Sponsor(s): Bonderman Family
Award: $1,000, development workshop & re-
hearsed reading (up to 4 winners); certificates
for semi-finalists
Closing Date: Sept 30
Presented: Indiana Repertory Theatre, April

Book-It Award
Reader Riter Poll
Affiliate of A World of Books
137 Pelton Center Way, San Leandro, CA 94577
Tel: 510-483-5587 *Fax:* 510-483-3832
E-mail: aworldofbooks@aol.com
Web Site: www.aworldofbooks
Key Personnel
Dir: Barbara L Keenan
Best book for that year, most popular authors,
best contemporary & best historical.
Award: Trophy &/or certificate
Closing Date: Annually, Oct 30
Presented: San Francisco, CA

Book-of-the-Year Award
Kappa Delta Pi
3707 Woodview Trace, Indianapolis, IN 46268-
1158
Tel: 317-871-4900 *Toll Free Tel:* 800-284-3167
Fax: 317-704-2323
Web Site: www.kdp.org
Key Personnel
Exec Dir: Michael P Wolfe *E-mail:* wolfe@kdp.
org
Established: 1980
International recognition.

Award: Certificate
Closing Date: June 30
Presented: Nov, uneven years

Book Sense Book of the Year Award
American Booksellers Association
828 S Broadway, Tarrytown, NY 10591
Tel: 914-591-2665 *Toll Free Tel:* 800-637-0037
Fax: 914-591-2720
Web Site: www.bookweb.org
Key Personnel
Exec Dir: Avin Mark Domnitz
Award Admin & Dir, Mktg: Jill Perlstein
Tel: 914-591-2665 ext 1283 *E-mail:* jill@
bookweb.org
Established: 1991
ABA member booksellers select the book they
most enjoyed handselling & four finalists.
Presented: BookExpo America & ABA Conven-
tion

Boston Globe-Horn Book Award
The Boston Globe & The Horn Book Inc
56 Roland St, Suite 200, Boston, MA 02129
Tel: 617-628-0225 *Toll Free Tel:* 800-325-1170
Fax: 617-628-0882
E-mail: info@hbook.com
Web Site: www.hbook.com
Key Personnel
Ed-in-Chief, Horn Book: Roger Sutton
Assoc Publr & Mktg Dir: Anne Quirk *Tel:* 617-
628-0225 ext 228 *E-mail:* aquirk@hbook.com
Established: 1967
Honors excellence in children's & young adult
literature in three categories: fiction, nonfiction
& picture books. Published books only, mss not
accepted.
Award: $500 each
Closing Date: May 1
Presented: Annually in autumn

Bound to Stay Bound Books Scholarship
Association for Library Service to Children
Division of American Library Association
50 E Huron St, Chicago, IL 60611-2795
Tel: 312-280-2163 *Toll Free Tel:* 800-545-2433
Fax: 312-944-7671
E-mail: alsc@ala.org
Web Site: www.ala.org/alsc/
Key Personnel
Exec Dir: Malore Brown
For study in field of library service to children to-
ward the MLS or beyond in an ALA-accredited
program.
Award: $6,000 - 4 scholarships per yr
Closing Date: April 1
Presented: ALA Annual Conference, June/July

**Louise Louis & Emily F Bourne Student
Poetry Award**
Poetry Society of America (PSA)
15 Gramercy Park, New York, NY 10003
Tel: 212-254-9628 *Fax:* 212-673-2352
Web Site: www.poetrysociety.org
Key Personnel
Exec Dir: Alice Quinn
Established: 1971
For an unpublished poem by an American high
school or preparatory school student. Send
No 10 SASE for further guidelines, or visit
www.poetrysociety.org. Opening date Oct 1-
Dec 22.
Award: $250
Closing Date: Dec 22
Presented: Annually in April

Bowling Writing Competition
American Bowler Magazine
Subsidiary of American Bowling Congress
5301 S 76 St, Greendale, WI 53129
Tel: 414-421-6400 *Fax:* 414-321-8356
Web Site: www.bowl.com

Key Personnel
Ed: Bill Vint *Tel:* 414-321-8310
Established: 1953
For nonfiction stories published during 2002 or
broadcast with written script regarding the
sport of American tenpin bowling or individu-
als associated with the sport. Awarded in News,
Editorial & Feature categories.
Award: $3,800 cash (ten for Feature, seven for
News & Editorial)
Closing Date: Dec 15

Rosalie Boyle/Norma Farber Award
New England Poetry Club
16 Cornell St, Arlington, MA 02474
Web Site: www.nepoetryclub.org
Key Personnel
Pres: Diana Der Hovanessian
Contest Chmn: Elizabeth Crowell
Established: 1980
Poem in traditional form. Mark name of con-
test on envelope. Send to Elizabeth Crowell at
above address. For members only. Send poem
in duplicate with name of writer on one only.
Award: $100
Closing Date: June 30
Presented: Library, Cambridge, MA, Annually,
Fall

Barbara Bradley Prize
New England Poetry Club
16 Cornell St, Arlington, MA 02474
Web Site: www.nepoetryclub.org
Key Personnel
Pres: Diana Der Hovanessian
Contest Chmn: Elizabeth Crowell
Established: 1988
Poem in lyric form, under 21 lines, written by
a woman. Mark name of contest on envelope.
Send to Elizabeth Crowell at address above.
Send poem in duplicate with name of writer on
one only.
Award: $200
Closing Date: June 30
Presented: Annually, Fall

Brazo Bookstore (Houston Award)
Texas Institute of Letters
3700 Mockingbird Lane, Dallas, TX 75205
Tel: 214-528-2655
Web Site: www.stedwards.edu/newc/marks/til/
awards_and_rules.htm
Key Personnel
VP: Joe Holley
Dir: Mark Busby *Tel:* 512-245-2428
E-mail: mb13@swt.edu
Treas: Jim Hoggard
Sec: Fran Vick *E-mail:* franvick@aol.com
For the best short story published during the pre-
ceding year by a Texan or about Texas.
Other Sponsor(s): Brazos Bookstore
Award: $750
Closing Date: Jan 7, 2005
Presented: March banquet, Ft Worth, TX, USA,
March 2005

Bread Loaf Writers' Conference of Middlebury College
Middlebury College, Middlebury, VT 05753
Tel: 802-443-5286 *Fax:* 802-443-2087
E-mail: blwc@middlebury.edu
Web Site: www.middlebury.edu/~blwc
Key Personnel
Admin Mgr: Noreen Cargill
Fellowship competition.
Award: Full tuition, room & board at 11-day ses-
sion of conference
Closing Date: March 1
Presented: Notification in early June; Conference
in August

James Henry Breasted Prize
American Historical Association
400 "A" St SE, Washington, DC 20003
Tel: 202-544-2422 *Fax:* 202-544-8307
E-mail: info@historians.org
Web Site: www.historians.org
Key Personnel
Prize Admin: Debbie Ann Doyle *Tel:* 202-544-
2422 ext 104 *E-mail:* ddoyle@historians.org
Established: 1985
Best book in English in any field of history prior
to 1000 AD. Different geographic area will be
eligible each year. Entries must have been pub-
lished between May 1, 2004 & April 30, 2005.
No application form, applicants must simply
mail a copy of their book to each of the prize
committee members who will be posted on our
web site as the prize deadline approaches. All
updated info on web site.
Award: Cash prize
Closing Date: May 16, 2005
Presented: San Francisco, Jan 3-6

British Council Prize in the Humanities
North American Conference on British Studies
University of Kentucky, History Dept, Lexington,
KY 40506-0027
Tel: 859-257-1246 *Fax:* 859-323-3885
Web Site: www.nacbs.org
Key Personnel
Exec Sec: Prof Philip Harling *Tel:* 859-257-1246
E-mail: harling@uky.edu
Best book by a North American scholar in
any field of British studies from 1800 to the
present, published in the previous calendar
year.
Award: $500
Closing Date: April
Presented: Annual meeting

Brittingham & Felix Pollak Prizes in Poetry
University of Wisconsin Press
c/o Ron Wallace, Series Editor, University of
Wisconsin, Dept of English, 600 N Park St,
Madison, WI 53706
Web Site: www.wisc.edu/wisconsinpress/
Key Personnel
Ed: Ronald Wallace
Pollak & Brittingham are two prizes from one
competition. For book-length mss of poetry.
Mss not accepted before Sept 1 or after Sept
30; $20 reading fee required, check made
payable to: University of Wisconsin Press. Mss
not returned; send business-size SASE for con-
test guidelines & outcome information or check
web site.
Award: $1,000 & publication in University of
Wisconsin Press Poetry Series for each book
Closing Date: Sept 30

The Heywood Broun Award
The Newspaper Guild
Unit of Communications Workers of America
501 Third St NW, Washington, DC 20001-2760
Tel: 202-434-7173 *Fax:* 202-434-1472
Web Site: www.newsguild.org
Key Personnel
Ed: Andy Zipser
Established: 1941
Journalism.
Award: $5,000
Closing Date: Last Friday in Jan
Presented: Washington, DC, May each year

John Nicholas Brown Prize
Medieval Academy of America
104 Mount Auburn St, 5th fl, Cambridge, MA
02138
Tel: 617-491-1622 *Fax:* 617-492-3303
E-mail: speculum@medievalacademy.org
Web Site: www.medievalacademy.org

Key Personnel
Exec Dir & Ed, Speculum: Richard K Emmerson
Established: 1978
For a first book published four years prior to
award date, in the field of medieval studies.
Award: $1,000
Closing Date: Oct 15
Presented: Annually in April

Bucknell Seminar for Younger Poets
Stadler Center for Poetry
Bucknell University, Lewisburg, PA 17837
Tel: 570-577-1853 *Fax:* 570-577-3760
E-mail: stadlercenter@bucknell.edu
Web Site: bucknell.edu/stadlercenter
Key Personnel
Dir: Paula Closson-Buck
Opers Mgr: Andrew Ciotola *E-mail:* ciotola@
bucknell.edu
Established: 1985
Four-week residence in writing for undergraduate
poets. Applications should include an academic
transcript, two supporting recommendations
(at least one from a poetry-writing instructor)
& a ten-12 page portfolio. A letter of self-
presentation (a brief autobiography stressing
commitment to poetry writing, experience &
any publications) should accompany the application. For return of portfolio enclose SASE.
Closing Date: Annually, Jan 3
Presented: Four weeks in June & July

Georges Bugnet Award for Fiction (Novel)
Banff Centre
11759 Groat Rd, Edmonton, AB T5M 3K6,
Canada
Tel: 780-422-8174 *Toll Free Tel:* 800-665-5354
(Alberta only) *Fax:* 780-422-2663
E-mail: mail@writersguild.ab.ca
Web Site: www.writersguild.ab.ca
Key Personnel
Exec Dir: Diane Walton
Established: 1982
Alberta Literary Award, must be resident of Al-
berta.
Award: $1,000 plus leather-bound copy of book
Closing Date: Dec 31
Presented: Alberta Book Awards Gala, Edmonton,
Spring

Bunting Fellowship
The Radcliffe Institute for Advanced Study
34 Concord Ave, Cambridge, MA 02138
Tel: 617-495-8212; 617-495-8237 (personnel con-
tact) *Fax:* 617-495-8136
Web Site: www.radcliffe.edu
Key Personnel
Fellowship Administrator: Marilyn Hamilton
Scholars in any field with the receipt of a doctor-
ate or appropriate terminal degree at least two
years prior to appointment.
Closing Date: Oct 1

Arleigh Burke Essay Contest
US Naval Institute
291 Wood Rd, Annapolis, MD 21402-5034
Tel: 410-268-6110 *Toll Free Tel:* 800-233-8764
Fax: 410-295-1049
E-mail: essays@navalinstitute.org
Web Site: www.navalinstitute.org
Key Personnel
Commun Mgr: Jon Youngdahl
Man Ed, Proceedings Magazine: Julie Olver
Established: 1878
Naval essay up to 3,500 words on any subject
relating to the goal of the Naval Institute.
Award: $3,000, a Gold Medal & a lifetime mem-
bership in the Naval Institute (1st prize);
$2,000 & a Silver Medal & 1 year member-
ship in the Naval Institute (2nd prize), $1,000
& a Bronze Medal & 1 year membership in the
Naval Institute (3rd prize)

Closing Date: Dec 1
Presented: Annapolis, MD, April; published in
  May issue of *Proceedings Magazine*

**The John Burroughs List of Nature Books for
  Young Readers**
John Burroughs Association Inc
15 W 77 St, New York, NY 10024
Tel: 212-769-5169 *Fax:* 212-313-7182
Web Site: research.amnh.org/burroughs
Key Personnel
Sec: Lisa Breslof *E-mail:* breslof@amnh.org
To recognize writers, artists & publishers who
  produce outstanding nature literature for chil-
  dren. Nonfiction subjects of natural history,
  ecology & environmental studies. Works may
  include poetry, travel, art, adventure, biography. No guide books to identification, science
  texts, or reference works. Submit five copies of
  each entry, addressed to: Secretary, The John
  Burroughs Association.
Award: John Burroughs Certificate of Recognition
  to authors, illustrators & publishers of each selected book
Closing Date: Annually, second Fri of Dec
Presented: American Museum of Natural History,
  1st Monday in April

John Burroughs Medal
John Burroughs Association Inc
15 W 77 St, New York, NY 10024
Tel: 212-769-5169 *Fax:* 212-313-7182
Web Site: research.amnh.org/burroughs
Key Personnel
Sec: Lisa Breslof *E-mail:* breslof@amnh.org
Established: 1926
For the year's best book in the field of natural
  history. The work of John Burroughs, a literary
  naturalist, is the standard for the general char-
  acter of the books eligible. They should com-
  bine literary quality with accuracy & should be
  based on originality of observation & conclu-
  sion. Award is not given for compilations of
  others' findings. Submit five copies of each entry addressed to Secretary, The John Burroughs
  Association.
Award: Bronze medal
Closing Date: Oct 1
Presented: American Museum of Natural History,
  New York, NY, 1st Monday in April at a luncheon

**John Burroughs Outstanding Published Nature
  Essay Award**
Formerly Periodical Natural History Essay Award
John Burroughs Association Inc
15 W 77 St, New York, NY 10024
Tel: 212-769-5169 *Fax:* 212-313-7182
Web Site: research.amnh.org/burroughs
Key Personnel
Sec: Lisa Breslof *E-mail:* breslof@amnh.org
To recognize current authors of outstanding es-
  says published in magazines emphasizing John
  Burroughs Literary works, contributions & skill
  as an outstanding nature essayist; Submit six
  copies of each entry addressed to "Secretary,
  The John Burroughs Association".
Award: Certificate of Recognition
Closing Date: Dec 31
Presented: 1st Monday in April at the annual
  meeting

Bush Artist Fellows Program
Bush Foundation of St Paul, Minnesota
332 Minnesota St, E-900, St Paul, MN 55101
Tel: 651-227-5222 *Toll Free Tel:* 800-605-7315
  Fax: 651-297-6485
Web Site: www.bushfoundation.org
Key Personnel
Prog Asst: Kathi Polley *Tel:* 651-227-0891
  E-mail: kpolley@bushfound.org
Established: 1976

Must be published & produced writers, Min-
  nesota, South Dakota, North Dakota or Western
  Wisconsin residents at least 25 years old (no
  students). First judged by a preliminary panel
  specific to their discipline & then by a final in-
  terdisciplinary panel of non-Minnesota, South
  Dakota, North Dakota & Wisconsin residents.
  Categories include fiction, poetry, creative non-
  fiction, playwriting & screenwriting.
Award: 15 fellowships awarded biennially of
  $44,000 for a 12 to 24-month period
Closing Date: Oct
Presented: April

ByLine Magazine & Press
ByLine
PO Box 5240, Edmond, OK 73083-5240
Tel: 405-348-5591
Web Site: www.bylinemag.com
Key Personnel
Exec Ed & Publr: Marcia Preston
  E-mail: mpreston@bylinemag.com
Established: 1981
Annual literary award in short story & poetry,
  open to subscribers only. Annual poetry chap-
  book competition & monthly contests open to
  anyone.
Award: $250 (annual prize short story), $250 (an-
  nual prize poetry); $200 plus publication & 50
  author's copies (annual poetry chapbook); $10
  to $75 (monthly contests)
Closing Date: Annual poetry & fiction, Nov 1;
  annual chapbook, March 1; continuous on
  monthly
Presented: Monthly winners listed in each issue,
  Annual winners announced in Feb issue; chapbook award announced in June

Witter Bynner Foundation for Poetry
PO Box 10169, Santa Fe, NM 87504
Tel: 505-988-3251 *Fax:* 505-986-8222
E-mail: bynnerfoundation@aol.com
Web Site: www.bynnerfoundation.org
Key Personnel
Exec Dir: Steven Schwartz
Established: 1972
To nonprofit organizations for poetry-related
  projects.
Award: $1,000-$15,000, 3-yr maximum
Closing Date: Feb 1, letters on Internet accepted
  Aug 1-Dec 1
Presented: Annually

Gerald Cable Book Award
Silverfish Review Press
PO Box 3541, Eugene, OR 97403
Tel: 541-344-5060
E-mail: sfrpress@earthlink.net
Web Site: www.silverfishreviewpress.com
Key Personnel
Ed & Publr: Rodger Moody
Established: 1995
Poetry Book; for author who has not yet pub-
  lished a collection. Selection by Feb.
Award: $1,000 & publication by Silverfish Re-
  view Press & 100 copies of the book
Closing Date: Submit by Oct 15

The Randolph Caldecott Medal
Association for Library Service to Children
Division of American Library Association
50 E Huron St, Chicago, IL 60611-2795
Tel: 312-280-2163 *Toll Free Tel:* 800-545-2433
  Fax: 312-944-7671
E-mail: alsc@ala.org
Web Site: www.ala.org/alsc
Established: 1937
Given to the artist who created the most distin-
  guished American picture book for children
  published in the U.S. during the previous year.
  The artist must be a citizen or resident of the
  United States.

Award: Medal
Closing Date: Dec 31
Presented: ALA Annual Conference, Varies

California Book Awards
Commonwealth Club of California
595 Market St, San Francisco, CA 94105
Tel: 415-597-6700 *Fax:* 415-597-6729
E-mail: bookawards@commonwealthclub.org
Web Site: www.commonwealthclub.org/
  bookawards
Key Personnel
Book Awards Dir: Barbara Lane *E-mail:* blane@
  commonwealthclub.org
Established: 1931
Honors the exceptional literary merit of California
  writers & publishers. Awards are presented in
  the categories of fiction, nonfiction, poetry, first
  work of fiction, juvenile literature (up to age
  10), adult literature (ages 11-16), Californiana,
  works in translation & notable contribution to
  publishing. To be eligible, author must be resident in California at the time of publication
  & books must be published under the year in
  consideration.
Award: $2,000 Gold Medalists, $300 Silver
  Medalists
Closing Date: Dec 31
Presented: Annually in spring

**Canadian Authors Association Awards for
  Poetry & Drama**
Canadian Authors Association (CAA)
320 S Shores Rd, Campbellford, ON K0L 1L0,
  Canada
Tel: 705-653-0323 *Toll Free Tel:* 866-216-6222
  Fax: 705-653-0593
E-mail: info@canauthors.org
Web Site: www.canauthors.org
Key Personnel
Admin: Alec McEachern
Established: 1975
Honors writing by Canadians that achieves lit-
  erary excellence without sacrificing popular
  appeal, in six categories. Entries must be full-
  length English-language literature for adults.
  Reprints, self-published work & work which
  has been published at the author's expense are
  not eligible.
Award: $2,500 & sterling silver medal
Closing Date: Annually Dec 15
Presented: CAA conference, Annually in July

**Canadian Booksellers Association Author of
  the Year Award**
Canadian Booksellers Association (CBA)
789 Don Mills Rd, Suite 700, Toronto, ON M3C
  1T5, Canada
Tel: 416-467-7883 *Fax:* 416-467-7886
E-mail: enquiries@cbabook.org
Web Site: www.cbabook.org
Key Personnel
Pres: Pat Joas
Exec Dir: Susan Dayus *Tel:* 416-467-7883 ext
  225 *E-mail:* sdayus@cbabook.org
Chosen by Canadian booksellers & presented by
  Board of Directors; nominations from members
  only.
Presented: Libris Awards Presentation, Toronto
  Convention Centre, June

**Canadian Booksellers Association Libris
  Awards**
Canadian Booksellers Association (CBA)
789 Don Mills Rd, Suite 700, Toronto, ON M3C
  1T5, Canada
Tel: 416-467-7883 *Fax:* 416-467-7886
E-mail: enquiries@cbabook.org
Web Site: www.cbabook.org
Key Personnel
Pres: Pat Joas
Exec Dir: Susan Dayus *Tel:* 416-467-7883 ext
  225 *E-mail:* sdayus@cbabook.org

Chosen by Canadian booksellers; awards recognize the best of the Canadian bookselling business including authors, publishers, editors & booksellers.
Award: Trophy
Presented: Awards Recipient Presentation, Toronto Convention Centre, June 17-20, 2005

The Carl Sandburg Literary Awards
The Chicago Public Library Foundation
20 N Michigan Ave, Suite 102, Chicago, IL 60602
Tel: 312-201-9830 *Fax:* 312-201-9833
Established: 2000
Honors a significant work or a body of work that has enhanced the public's awareness of the written word & reflects the Library's commitment to the freedom of all people to read, to learn & to discover.
Award: $10,000
Presented: Annually in Oct

The Thomas H Carter Award For The Essay
Shenandoah: The Washington & Lee Review
Washington & Lee University, Mattingly House, 2 Lee Ave, Lexington, VA 24450-0303
Tel: 540-458-8765 *Fax:* 540-458-8461
Web Site: www.shenandoah.wlu.edu
Key Personnel
Man Ed: Lynn Leech *E-mail:* lleech@wlu.edu
Award made for the best essay published in Shenandoah during a volume year.
Award: $500
Presented: Annually

Catholic Book Awards
Catholic Press Association of the US & Canada
3555 Veterans Memorial Hwy, Unit "O", Ronkonkoma, NY 11779
Tel: 631-471-4730 *Fax:* 631-471-4804
E-mail: cathjourn@aol.com
Web Site: www.catholicpress.org
Key Personnel
Exec Dir: Owen P McGovern *E-mail:* omcg@aol.com
Several awards for best Catholic books in different categories.
Award: Certificate
Closing Date: Jan
Presented: Annual convention, Orlando, FL, May 2005

Catholic Press Association of the US & Canada Journalism Awards
Catholic Press Association of the US & Canada
3555 Veterans Memorial Hwy, Unit "O", Ronkonkoma, NY 11779
Tel: 631-471-4730 *Fax:* 631-471-4804
E-mail: cathjourn@aol.com
Web Site: www.catholicpress.org
Key Personnel
Exec Dir: Owen P McGovern *E-mail:* omcg@aol.com
Journalism entries from member publications.
Award: Certificates
Closing Date: Jan
Presented: Annual convention, Orlando, FL, May 2005

Cavendish Tourist Association Creative Writing Award for Young People
Prince Edward Island Council of the Arts
115 Richmond St, Charlottetown, PE C1A 1H7, Canada
Tel: 902-368-4410 *Fax:* 902-368-4418
E-mail: peiarts@peiartscouncil.com
Web Site: www.peiartscouncil.com
Key Personnel
Exec Dir: Darrin White
Elementary, junior & high school students may write on the topic of their choice. A maximum

of five pages of poetry or short story will constitute an entry. No entry fee. Residents only. For more information contact PEI Council of the Arts at address above.
Award: $75 (1st prize), $50 (2nd prize), $25 (3rd prize)
Closing Date: Call or e-mail
Presented: Call or e-mail

Center for Publishing Fellowships
New York University, School of Continuing Education, Center for Publishing
11 W 42 St, Rm 400, New York, NY 10036
Tel: 212-992-3232 *Fax:* 212-992-3233
E-mail: pub.center@nyu.edu
Web Site: www.scps.nyu.edu/publishing
Key Personnel
Assoc Dir: Heidi Johnson *E-mail:* heidi.johnson@nyu.edu
Awarded to students who enrolled part-time or full-time in master of science in publishing program. Need excellent academic record with experience in the field preferred.
Award: $1,000 to $10,000
Presented: Each semester

G S Sharat Chandra Prize for Short Fiction
BkMk Press - University of Missouri-Kansas City
5101 Rockhill Rd, Kansas City, MO 64110
Tel: 816-235-2558 *Fax:* 816-235-2611
E-mail: bkmk@umkc.edu
Web Site: www.umkc.edu/bkmk/
Key Personnel
Exec Ed: Robert Stewart *Tel:* 816-235-1120
Man Ed: Ben Furnish
Assoc Ed: Michelle Boisseau *Tel:* 816-235-2561
Established: 2001
Presented for the best book-length ms of short fiction in English by a living author. Ms must be typed on standard-sized paper in English & should be 50,000 words minimum, 100,000 words maximum, double-spaced. Entries must include two title pages: one with author name, address & phone number & one with no author information. Any acknowledgments should appear on a separate piece of paper. Entries must include a table of contents. Author's name must not appear anywhere on the ms. Do not submit your ms by fax or e-mail. A SASE should be included, for notification only. Note: No mss will be returned. A reading fee of $25 in US funds (check payable to BkMk Press) must accompany each ms. Entrants will receive a copy of the winning book when published.
Award: $1,000 plus book publication of winning manuscript by BkMk Press
Closing Date: Dec 1
Presented: Annually, Spring

Harry Chapin Media Awards
World Hunger Year
505 Eighth Ave, 21st fl, New York, NY 10018
Tel: 212-629-8850 *Toll Free Tel:* 800-5-HUNGRY (548-6479) *Fax:* 212-465-9274
E-mail: media@worldhungeryear.org
Web Site: www.worldhungeryear.org
Key Personnel
Exec Dir: William Ayres
Commun Coord, Awards & Media: Lisa Ann Batitto *Tel:* 212-629-8850 ext 122 *E-mail:* lisa@worldhungeryear.org
Established: 1982
Cash prizes to media professionals to honor their outstanding coverage that positively impacts hunger, poverty & self-reliance. Awards are given in five categories: book, newspaper, periodical, photojournalism & broadcast (radio, TV, or film).
Award: $2,500 in each category
Closing Date: mid-Jan
Presented: New York, NY

The Charles Bernheimer Prize
American Comparative Literature Association
University of Texas, Program in Comparative Literature, One University Sta B5003, Austin, TX 78712-0196
Tel: 512-471-8020
E-mail: info@acla.org
Web Site: www.acla.org
Key Personnel
ACLA Admin Asst: Kevin Carney; Ryan Fisher
Secy: Elizabeth Richmond-Garza
An outstanding dissertation in comparative literature completed by July 1.
Closing Date: July 15
Presented: Annual Meeting, Following spring

Chicago Book Clinic Annual Book Show Awards
Chicago Book Clinic
5443 N Broadway, Suite 101, Chicago, IL 60640
Tel: 773-561-4150 *Fax:* 773-561-1343
Web Site: www.chicagobookclinic.org
Key Personnel
Pres: Cheryl Horch
Exec Dir: Kevin G Boyer
Established: 1949
Juried Show; 35-50 books selected each year.
Award: Certificates of Award, photo & listing in show catalog & plaques
Closing Date: Varies

Chicago Book Clinic Distinguished Service Award
Chicago Book Clinic
5443 N Broadway, Suite 101, Chicago, IL 60640
Tel: 773-561-4150 *Fax:* 773-561-1343
Web Site: www.chicagobookclinic.org
Key Personnel
Pres: Cheryl Horch
Exec Dir: Kevin G Boyer
Recognizes long-time service in publishing, as determined by the Board of Directors.
Award: Plaque
Presented: Every two years

Chicano Latino Literary Contest
University of California Irvine
Subsidiary of Dept of Spanish & Portuguese
University of California, Dept Spanish & Portuguese, Irvine, CA 92697-5275
Tel: 949-824-5443 *Fax:* 949-824-2803
E-mail: cllp@uci.edu
Web Site: www.humanities.uci.edu/spanishandportuguese/contest.html
Key Personnel
Contest Coord: Adriana Gallardo
Genre of award changes every year. Please check website for updates.
Award: $1,000 & publication of the collection if not under previous contract (1st prize), $500 (2nd prize), $250 (3rd prize)
Closing Date: June 1
Presented: University of California, Irvine, Nov

Children's Literature Association Book Award
Children's Literature Association
PO Box 138, Battle Creek, MI 49016-0138
Tel: 269-965-8180 *Fax:* 269-965-3568
Web Site: www.childlitassn.org
Key Personnel
Admin: Kathy Kiessling *E-mail:* kkiessling@childlitassn.org
Book awards given for best book on children's literature history, scholarship & criticism. Published as a book in a given year. See web site for application requirements.
Award: $500 plus award certificate
Closing Date: June 15 & Oct 15
Presented: CHLA Annual Conference, April

ChLA Article Award
Children's Literature Association
PO Box 138, Battle Creek, MI 49016-0138

Tel: 269-965-8180 *Fax:* 269-965-3568
Web Site: www.childlitassn.org
Key Personnel
Admin: Kathy Kiessling *E-mail:* kkiessling@
childlitassn.org
Award for best literary criticism article published
within a given year on the topic of children's
literature. See web site for application require-
ments.
Award: $250 plus award certificate
Closing Date: Feb 1
Presented: ChLA annual conference, June

**ChLA Beiter Scholarships for Graduate
Students**
Children's Literature Association
PO Box 138, Battle Creek, MI 49016-0138
Tel: 269-965-8180 *Fax:* 269-965-3568
Web Site: www.childlitassn.org
Key Personnel
Scholarship Chair: Lynne Vallone
Admin: Kathy Kiessling *E-mail:* kkiessling@
childlitassn.org
Awarded for proposals of original scholarship
with the expectation that the undertaking will
lead to publication or a conference presentation
& contribute to the field of children's literature
criticism. Winners must either be members of
the Children's Literature Association or join
the association before they receive any funds.
Applications & supporting materials should be
written in or translated into English. Fellowships & scholarships for proposals that deal
with critical or original work in the areas of
fantasy & science fiction for children & ado-
lescents. Encouraging new scholars to enter
the field, the scholarship is intended to enable
"entry level" scholars (graduate students, instructors or assistant professors) to bring to a
publishable level dissertations, theses or papers
that they have written.
Award: $250 - $1,000 (based on the number &
needs of the winning applicants)
Closing Date: Feb 1
Presented: April, ChLA annual conference, April

The Christopher Awards
Division of The Christophers
12 E 48 St, New York, NY 10017
Tel: 212-759-4050 *Fax:* 212-838-5073
Web Site: www.christophers.org
Key Personnel
Prog Mgr: Judith Trojan *Tel:* 212-759-4050 ext
229 *E-mail:* j.trojan@christophers.org
Established: 1949
For adult (nonfiction only) & juvenile fiction &
nonfiction published during the calendar year.
Themes must reflect "highest values of the hu-
man spirit" criteria.
Award: Bronze medallion
Closing Date: June 1 & Nov 1; books evaluated
throughout the calendar year
Presented: New York, NY, Annually in Feb

John Ciardi Prize for Poetry
BkMk Press - University of Missouri-Kansas City
5101 Rockhill Rd, Kansas City, MO 64110
Tel: 816-235-2558 *Fax:* 816-235-2611
E-mail: bkmk@umkc.edu
Web Site: www.umkc.edu/bkmk/
Key Personnel
Exec Ed: Robert Stewart *Tel:* 816-235-1120
Man Ed: Ben Furnish
Assoc Ed: Michelle Boisseau *Tel:* 816-235-2561
Established: 1998
Presented for the best full-length ms of poetry in
English by a living author. Mss must be typed
on standard-sized paper & should be approx-
imately 50 pages minimum, 110 pages maxi-
mum, single spaced. Entries must include two
title pages: one with author name, address &
phone & one with no author information. Any

acknowledgements should appear on a separate piece of paper. Entries must include a
table of contents. Author's name must not appear anywhere on the ms. Do not submit your
ms by fax or e-mail. A SASE should be included, for notification only. Note: No mss will
be returned. A reading fee of $25 in US funds
(check made payable to BkMk Press) must accompany each ms. Entrants will receive a copy
of the winning book when it is published.
Closing Date: Dec 1
Presented: Annually, Spring

Cintas Fellowship Program
US Student Programs
Subsidiary of Institute of International Education
809 United Nations Plaza, New York, NY 10017-
3580
Tel: 212-984-5565 *Fax:* 212-984-5325
E-mail: cintas@iie.org
Web Site: www.iie.org/cintas
Key Personnel
Prog Mgr: Jonathan Akeley
Established: 1963
Professional development of talented, creative
artists in the fields of architecture, literature,
music composition, visual arts & photography.
Limited to artists living outside Cuba, who are
of Cuban citizenship or direct lineage & who
have completed their academic & technical
training.
Award: $10,000
Closing Date: Feb 15

City of Toronto Book Award
City of Toronto
Subsidiary of City of Toronto (Municipality)
Protocol Office, 100 Queen St W, 10th fl, West
Tower, Toronto, ON M5H 2N2, Canada
Tel: 416-392-8191 *Fax:* 416-392-1247
Key Personnel
Protocol Consultant: Bev Kurmey
E-mail: bkurmey@toronto.ca
Established: 1974
To honor authors of books of literary or artistic
merit that are evocative of Toronto published in
preceding year.
Award: $15,000 annually, $1,000 to each short
listed book, usually four to six books remain-
der to winner
Closing Date: Last Friday in Feb
Presented: Toronto

CLA Book of the Year for Children Award
Canadian Association of Children's Librarians,
Canadian Library Association
Subsidiary of Canadian Association of Public Li-
braries
328 Frank St, Ottawa, ON K2P 0X8, Canada
Tel: 613-232-9625 *Fax:* 613-563-9895
Web Site: www.cla.ca/
Key Personnel
Memb Servs Coord: Brenda Shields *Tel:* 613-232-
9625 ext 318 *E-mail:* bshields@cla.ca
Established: 1947
Awarded to the author of an outstanding Cana-
dian children's book in English. Author must
be a citizen or a resident of Canada.
Other Sponsor(s): National Book Service
Award: Leather-bound copy of winning book with
award seal gold embossed on cover
Closing Date: Dec 31
Presented: CLA conference, annually

The Clarion Awards
The Association for Women in Communications
780 Ritchie Hwy, Suite 28-S, Severna Park, MD
21146
Tel: 410-544-7442 *Fax:* 410-544-4640
Web Site: www.womcom.org

Key Personnel
Exec Dir: Patricia H Troy *E-mail:* pat@womcom.
org
Established: 1973
Honors the achievements of outstanding communicators in more than 135 categories including
book publishing.
Award: Engraved crystal plaque, press releases,
recognition at national professional conference
& coverage in The Professional Communicator
Closing Date: April 15 (early bird); May 1 (general entry)

**Cleveland State University Poetry Center
Prizes**
Cleveland State University Poetry Center
2121 Euclid Ave, Cleveland, OH 44115-2214
Tel: 216-687-3986 *Toll Free Tel:* 888-278-6473
Fax: 216-687-6943
E-mail: poetrycenter@csuohio.edu
Web Site: www.csuohio.edu/poetrycenter
Telex: 810-421-8252
Key Personnel
Coord: Rita M Grabowski *E-mail:* r.grabowski@
csuohio.edu
Ed: Susan Grimm Dumbrys
Established: 1986
Poetry book mss, in two categories, First Book
or Open Competition. Minimum 40 pages of
poetry (one poem per page), SASE guidelines;
readers fee required; simultaneous submissions
permitted; mss not returned. (Open competition
is limited to poets who have published a full
length collection, 48+pp, 500+ copies).
Award: $1,000 & publication in the Cleveland
State University Poetry Center series
Closing Date: Feb 1 postmark deadline
Presented: July

David H Clift Scholarship
ALA Scholarship Clearinghouse
Unit of American Library Association
50 E Huron St, Chicago, IL 60611
Toll Free Tel: 800-545-2433 (ext 4277) *Fax:* 312-
280-3256
E-mail: scholarships@ala.org
Web Site: www.ala.org/hrdr/scholarship.html
Key Personnel
Prog Off: Maxine Moore *E-mail:* mmoore@ala.
org
Established: 1969
To worthy US or Canadian citizen or permanent
resident to begin an MLS degree in an ALA-
accredited program.
Award: $3,000
Closing Date: Annually, March 1; applications
available beginning in Sept
Presented: Annually

**CLTA/Stan Heath Achievement in Literacy
Award**
Canadian Library Association (CLA)
328 Frank St, Ottawa, ON K2P 0X8, Canada
Tel: 613-232-9625 *Fax:* 613-563-9895
Web Site: www.cla.ca/
Key Personnel
Memb Servs Coord: Brenda Shields *Tel:* 613-232-
9625 ext 318 *E-mail:* bshields@cla.ca
Awarded to public library boards in honor of spe-
cial achievement in promotions & delivery of
literacy programs & services.
Closing Date: March 1
Presented: CLA Conference, annually

Codie Awards
Software & Information Industry Association
1090 Vermont Ave NW, 6th fl, Washington, DC
20005
Tel: 202-289-7442 *Fax:* 202-289-7097
E-mail: codieawards@siia.net
Web Site: www.siia.net

Key Personnel
Pres: Kenneth Wasch
Dir, Mktg: Christina Stensvaag
Established: 1986
Honors excellence in the software & information industries.
Award: Trophy
Closing Date: Oct
Presented: 2005 SIIA Annual Conference, May 2005

Fred Cody Award
Bay Area Book Reviewers Association (BABRA)
c/o Poetry Flash, 1450 Fourth St, Suite 4, Berkeley, CA 94710
Tel: 510-525-5476 *Fax:* 510-525-6752
E-mail: babra@poetryflash.org; editor@poetryflash.org
Web Site: www.poetryflash.org
Key Personnel
Exec Dir: Joyce Jenkins
Established: 1984
Lifetime achievement award that cannot be applied for. This award is for lifetime literary excellence & community involvement by a Northern California writer.
Other Sponsor(s): Northern California Independent Booksellers Association; The San Francisco Public Library
Award: $1,000 cash & certificate
Presented: San Francisco Public Library, Koret Auditorium, March, April or May annually

Coe College Playwriting Festival
Coe College
1220 First Ave NE, Cedar Rapids, IA 52402
Tel: 319-399-8624 *Fax:* 319-399-8557
Web Site: www.coe.edu
Key Personnel
Prof, Theater Arts, Chpn: Susan Wolverton
E-mail: swolvert@coe.edu
Established: 1992
Playwriting.
Award: $325 & room, board, travel for one week residency
Closing Date: Nov 1
Presented: Coe College, April

Matt Cohen Prize: In Celebration of a Writing Life
The Writers' Trust of Canada
90 Richmond St W, Suite 200, Toronto, ON M5C 1P1, Canada
Tel: 416-504-8222 *Fax:* 416-504-9090
E-mail: info@writerstrust.com
Web Site: www.writerstrust.com
Key Personnel
Exec Dir: Lascelle Wingate *Tel:* 416-504-8222 ext 242
Established: 2001
Recognizes a lifetime of distinguished work by a Canadian writer, working in either poetry or prose, in either French or English. Generously sponsored by anonymous donors.
Award: $20,000
Presented: The Great Literary Awards, March

Morton N Cohen Award for a Distinguished Edition of Letters
Modern Language Association of America (MLA)
26 Broadway, 3rd fl, New York, NY 10004-1789
Tel: 646-576-5141 *Fax:* 646-458-0030
E-mail: awards@mla.org
Web Site: www.mla.org
Key Personnel
Coord, Book Prizes & Spec Projs: Annie Reiser
Established: 1989
For an outstanding edition of letters published in two years prior to competition. Editions may be in single or multiple volumes. Editors need not be members of the MLA.
Award: $1,000 & certificate

Closing Date: Four copies by May 1
Presented: MLA convention, Biennially (odd-numbered years), Dec 28

Shaughnessy Cohen Award for Political Writing
The Writers' Trust of Canada
90 Richmond St W, Suite 200, Toronto, ON M5C 1P1, Canada
Tel: 416-504-8222 *Fax:* 416-504-9090
E-mail: info@writerstrust.com
Web Site: www.writerstrust.com
Key Personnel
Exec Dir: Lascelle Wingate *Tel:* 416-504-8222 ext 242
Established: 2000
Awarded for a nonfiction work contributing to the greater understanding of contemporary Canadian political & social issues.
Other Sponsor(s): CTV
Award: $10,000
Presented: The Politics & the Pen, March

The Victor Cohn Prize for Excellence in Medical Science Reporting
Council for the Advancement of Science Writing (CASW)
PO Box 910, Hedgesville, WV 25427
Tel: 304-754-5077 *Fax:* 304-754-5076
Web Site: www.casw.org
Key Personnel
Exec Dir: Diane McGurgan *E-mail:* diane@nasw.org
Medical science writing for the mass media within the last five years.
Award: $3,000
Closing Date: July 31

Carr P Collins Award
Texas Institute of Letters
Center for the Study of the Southwest, Southwest Texas State University, San Marcos, TX 78666
Tel: 512-245-2232 *Fax:* 512-245-7462
Web Site: www.stedwards.edu/newc/marks/til/awards_and_rules.htm
Key Personnel
VP: Joe Holley
Dir: Mark Busby *Tel:* 512-245-2428
E-mail: mb13@swt.edu
Treas: Jim Hoggard
Sec: Fran Vick *E-mail:* franvick@aol.com
For the best nonfiction book by a Texan or about Texas.
Other Sponsor(s): Carr P Collins Foundation
Award: $5,000
Closing Date: Jan 2005
Presented: March banquet, Ft Worth, TX, USA, March 2005

Colorado Book Awards
Colorado Center for the Book
Affiliate of Library of Congress
2123 Downing St, Denver, CO 80205
Tel: 303-839-8320 *Fax:* 303-839-8319
Web Site: www.coloradobook.org
Key Personnel
Exec Dir: Christiane H Citron
Established: 1991
Cash prize to Colorado authors in fiction, nonfiction, young adult, children's, poetry, romance & additional categories vary from year to year.
Other Sponsor(s): Scientific & Cultural Facilities District of Denver
Award: $250 (cash)
Closing Date: Jan 15
Presented: Nov 18

Betsy Colquitt Award for Poetry
Texas Christian University
TCU Box 297700, Fort Worth, TX 76129
Tel: 817-257-7240 *Fax:* 817-257-7709

E-mail: descant@tcu.edu
Web Site: www.eng.tcu.edu/journals/descant/index.html
Key Personnel
Ed: Dave Kuhne *Tel:* 817-257-6537 *E-mail:* d.kuhne@tcu.edu
Established: 1996
Best poem or series of poems by a single author in a volume.
Award: $500
Presented: Announced in journal, Summer

Bernard F Conners Prize for Poetry
The Paris Review Foundation
541 E 72 St, New York, NY 10021
Tel: 212-861-0016 *Fax:* 212-861-4504
Web Site: www.theparisreview.org
Key Personnel
Poetry Ed: Richard Howard
Given for a poem published in the Paris Review of over 200 lines. Contest will be judged by the editors.
Award: $1,000
Closing Date: None
Presented: Announced in the winter

Miles Conrad Memorial Lecture
National Federation of Abstracting & Information Services (NFAIS)
1518 Walnut St, Suite 1004, Philadelphia, PA 19102-3403
Tel: 215-893-1561 *Fax:* 215-893-1564
E-mail: nfais@nfais.org
Web Site: www.nfais.org
Key Personnel
Dir, Planning & Comm: Jill O'Neill
E-mail: jilloneill@nfais.org
Established: 1968
Annually given to an outstanding member of the content community who then delivers the "Miles Conrad Memorial Lecture" at the annual NFAIS Conference.
Award: Plaque & honorarium
Presented: Philadelphia, PA, Feb, Annually

James Fenimore Cooper Prize
Society of American Historians (SAH)
Affiliate of American Historical Society
Columbia University, 603 Fayerweather Hall, MC 2538, New York, NY 10027
Key Personnel
Pres: Robert Dallek
Exec Sec: Mark Carnes *Tel:* 212-854-5943
E-mail: mc422@columbia.edu
Admin Sec: Ene Sirvet *Tel:* 212-222-4902
E-mail: es28@columbia.edu
Established: 1993
Best historical novel on an American theme, awarded biennially. Must be published & have a copyright for two years prior to prize year.
Award: $2,500 & consideration for adoption by History Book Club
Closing Date: Jan 31
Presented: New York, NY, May

Albert B Corey Prize
Canadian Historical Association-American Historical Association
395 Wellington St, Ottawa, ON K1A 0N3, Canada
Tel: 613-233-7885 *Fax:* 613-567-3110
E-mail: cha-shc@archives.ca
Web Site: www.theaha.org/prizes
Key Personnel
Admin Asst: Joanne Mineault *E-mail:* jmineault@archives.ca
Awarded every two years for the best book dealing with Canadian/American relations; awarded jointly with the American Historical Association. No application form, applicants must simply mail a copy of their book to each of the prize committee members who will be

posted on our web site as the prize deadline approaches. All updated info on web site.
Award: $1,000
Closing Date: Dec 2004
Presented: University of Toronto, May 2005

The Creative Crayon Award
This New World Publishing LLC (TNW)
13500 SW Pacific Hwy, Suite 129, Tigard, OR 97223
Tel: 503-670-1153 *Fax:* 503-213-5889
Web Site: www.thisnewworld.com
Key Personnel
Publr: Diana Luce *E-mail:* dianal@thisnewworld.com
Established: 2003
Semi-annual writing & illustrating contest for kids & adults in the USA. Topic: anything by or for children. Many different categories in which to win; every bona fide entrant gets a prize. For complete entry information & rules, go to www.CreativeCrayonAward.com or write to TNW Publishing.
Award: $500 cash, crystal bowl, statue
Closing Date: Feb 14 annually
Presented: March 31 annually

Creativity Fellowship
Northwood University
Alden B Dow Creativity Center, 4000 Whiting Dr, Midland, MI 48640-2398
Tel: 989-837-4478 *Fax:* 989-837-4468
E-mail: creativity@northwood.edu
Web Site: www.northwood.edu/abd
Key Personnel
Asst Dir: Liz Drake
Applications welcome from all disciplines & areas of interest which have potential for impact in their fields; must be creative & innovative; $10 application fee. Available to US citizens only.
Award: Stipend, travel expenses (within US), room & board paid
Closing Date: Dec 31, preceding summer fellowship

Cunningham Commission for Youth Theatre
The Theatre School, DePaul University
2135 N Kenmore, Chicago, IL 60614
Tel: 773-325-7938 *Fax:* 773-325-7920
Web Site: theatreschool.depaul.edu
Key Personnel
Dir, Mktg: Lara Goetsch *E-mail:* lgoetsch@depaul.edu
Established: 1991
Playwriting award, limited to writers whose primary residence is within 100 miles of Chicago's loop.
Award: up to $5,000
Closing Date: Annually Dec 1
Presented: Presentation TBA, Winner notified by May 1

Watson Davis & Helen Miles Davis Prize
History of Science Society
University of Florida, 3310 Turlington Hall, Gainesville, FL 32611
Mailing Address: PO Box 117360, Gainesville, FL 32611-7360
Tel: 352-392-1677
E-mail: info@hssonline.org
Web Site: www.hssonline.org
Key Personnel
Exec Dir: Robert J Malone
Established: 1985
For the best book on the history of science directed to a broad public published during the preceding three years.
Award: $1,000
Closing Date: April 1
Presented: Late Nov

Dayton Playhouse FutureFest Inc
The Dayton Playhouse
1301 E Siebenthaler Ave, Dayton, OH 45414
Tel: 937-333-7469 *Fax:* 937-333-2827
E-mail: futurefest@daytonplayhouse.com
Web Site: www.daytonplayhouse.com
Key Personnel
Exec Dir: David Seyer
Established: 1991
National Playwriting Competition; send SASE or see website for submission guidelines.
Award: $1,000 (1st place)
Closing Date: Oct 31
Presented: The Dayton Playhouse, Last weekend in July

The Angie Debo Prize
University of Oklahoma Press
1005 Asp Ave, Norman, OK 73019-6051
Tel: 405-325-2000 *Fax:* 405-325-4000
Web Site: www.oupress.com
Key Personnel
Dir: John N Drayton
Ed-in-Chief & Acq Ed: Charles Rankin
For the best book about the American Southwest published by the Press. Mss must be submitted for publication by the University of Oklahoma Press. Book-length biographies, monographs & works of synthesis & interpretation are eligible; fiction, translations, anthologies & collections of documents are not. The finished books will be judged on the quality of their research, analysis & writing & the significance of their contribution to the study of the Southwest. Send inquiries to the Angie Debo Prize Committee at the above address.
Award: $5,000
Closing Date: Every 2 years; for a work published in 2003-2004
Presented: Norman, Oklahoma, Spring 2005

Deep South Writers Festival
Deep South Writers Conference
University of Louisiana at Lafayette, 104 University Circle, Lafayette, LA 70504
Mailing Address: PO Box 44691, Lafayette, LA 70504-4691
Tel: 337-482-5478 (Direct)
Key Personnel
Dir: Dr Jerry McGuire *E-mail:* jlm8047@usl.edu
Established: 1960
Literary contest, with the following categories: short fiction, novel, nonfiction, poetry, drama & French poetry & prose, children's literature & young adult literature. Send SASE for contest rules & address queries to contest clerk.

Delacorte Dell Yearling Contest for a First Middle-Grade Novel
Delacorte Press Books for Young Readers
1745 Broadway, New York, NY 10019
Tel: 212-782-9000 *Fax:* 212-782-9452
Web Site: www.randomhouse.com/kids
Submissions should be a book-length fiction ms & summary, either contemporary or historical, suitable for readers ages nine to 12 years old. MSS must be between 96 & 160 double-spaced typed pages. If you would like the ms returned, send SASE; otherwise, mss cannot be returned. Contest is open to American & Canadian writers who have not previously published a novel for middle-grade readers; no foreign language ms or translations are eligible. Winner announced no later than Oct 31.
Award: $1,500 cash prize & $7,500 advance against royalties
Closing Date: Postmarked no earlier than April 1 & no later than June 30

Delacorte Press Prize for a First Young Adult Novel
Delacorte Press Books for Young Readers

1745 Broadway, 9th fl, New York, NY 10019
Tel: 212-782-9000 *Fax:* 212-782-9452
Web Site: www.randomhouse.com/kids
Established: 1982
Submissions should be book length mss with a contemporary setting suitable for readers ages 12-18; mss must be between 100-224 double-spaced typed pages & include a brief plot summary with covering letter. Send SASE large enough to accommodate mss. Contest is open to American & Canadian writers who have not previously published a young adult novel; no foreign language mss or translations are eligible.
Award: $1,500 prize & $7,500 advance against royalties
Closing Date: Postmarked Oct 1-Dec 31
Presented: Annually on April 30

Delaware Division of the Arts Individual Artist Fellowships
820 N French St, Wilmington, DE 19801
Tel: 302-577-8278 *Fax:* 302-577-6561
Web Site: www.artsdel.org
Key Personnel
Coord: Kristin Pleasanton
Individual Artist Fellowships will be awarded to beginning or established poets & other creative writers. Applicants must be Delaware residents.
Award: A Masters Fellowship of $10,000 & established Professional Fellowships of $5,000 each & Emerging Professional Fellowships of $2,000
Closing Date: Aug 15
Presented: Annually (Master's awarded every three years in literature); winners notified in Dec

Der-Hovanessian Translation Prize
New England Poetry Club
16 Cornell St, Arlington, MA 02474
Web Site: www.nepoetryclub.org
Key Personnel
Pres: Diana Der Hovanessian
Contest Chmn: Elizabeth Crowell
For translation from any language. Send a copy of original with the poem.
Award: $100
Closing Date: June 30
Presented: Cambridge, MA, Annually, Fall

Derringer Award
Short Mystery Fiction Society (SMFS)
1120 N 45 St, Waco, TX 76710
Web Site: groups.yahoo.com/group/shortmystery; www.shortmystery.net
Key Personnel
Pres: Michael Bracken *E-mail:* michael@crimefictionwriter.com
VP: Carol Kilgore
Established: 1997
The SMFA created the Derringer Award for excellence in the field of short stories. The name "Derringer," after the palm-sized handgun, was chosen as a metaphor for a crime short story - small but dangerous. The Derringer was created to fill a void in the arena of American mystery awards which tend to concentrate on novels.
Award: Certificate & statue
Closing Date: Feb
Presented: Pennwriters Annual Conference, May

J Franklin Dew Award
The Poetry Society of Virginia
100 N Berwick, Williamsburg, VA 23188
Tel: 757-258-5582
Web Site: www.poetrysocietyofvirginia.org
Key Personnel
Pres: Edward Lull
Contest Chair: Norma Richardson
Series of three or four Haiku in theme. Send SASE for rules in Sept.

Award: $50 (1st place); $30 (2nd place); $20 (3rd place); Honorable mention
Closing Date: Jan 19
Presented: PSV Awards Luncheon; Richmond, VA, Third Saturday in April

Alice Fay Di Castagnola Award
Poetry Society of America (PSA)
15 Gramercy Park, New York, NY 10003
Tel: 212-254-9628 *Fax:* 212-673-2352
Web Site: www.poetrysociety.org
Key Personnel
Exec Dir: Alice Quinn
Established: 1965
In honor of a friend & benefactor of the Society. For a work in progress (poetry, prose or verse drama). Preliminary submission not to exceed 300 lines of sample verse if poetry or a sample chapter if prose; a sample scene if verse drama. Open to Society members only. Send No 10 SASE for complete information, or visit www.poetrysociety.org.
Award: $1,000
Closing Date: Dec 22
Presented: Annually in April

Dickinson Emily Award, see Emily Dickinson Award

Gordon W Dillon/Richard C Peterson Memorial Essay Prize
American Orchid Society Inc
16700 AOS Lane, Delray Beach, FL 33446
Tel: 561-404-2043 *Fax:* 561-404-2045
E-mail: theaos@aos.org
Web Site: www.orchidweb.org
Key Personnel
Dir, Pubns: James Watson
Established: 1985
Essay contest (orchid topics only; new theme announced each year).
Award: Cash award & a certificate of recognition
Closing Date: Annually Nov 30
Presented: Winning essay published in *Orchids* magazine, May issue

Discovery Prize, see Plimpton Prize

Discovery/The Nation Poetry Contest
The Unterberg Poetry Center
Affiliate of The Tisch Center for the Arts
92 St YM-YWHA, 1395 Lexington Ave, New York, NY 10128
Tel: 212-415-5759
Web Site: www.92y.org
Key Personnel
Dir: David Yezzi
Established: 1974
For poets who have not published a book; for guidelines visit the above website.
Other Sponsor(s): The Nation
Award: Publication in The Nation, reading at The Poetry Center & $500
Closing Date: Jan 21, 2005

Distinguished Scholarly Publication Award
American Sociological Association (ASA)
1307 New York Ave NW, Suite 700, Washington, DC 20005
Tel: 202-383-9005 *Fax:* 202-638-0882
E-mail: governance@asanet.org
Web Site: www.asanet.org
Key Personnel
Dir, Governance: Michael Murphy *Tel:* 202-383-9005 ext 327
This award is given for a single book or monograph published in the three calendar years preceding the award year. The winner of this award will be offered a lectureship known as the Sorokin Lecture. Regional & state sociological associations/societies may apply to ASA to

receive this lecture at ASA's expense after the award recipient is announced. Two members of the association must submit letters in support of each nomination for the award. Nominations should include name of author, title of book, date of publication, publisher & brief statements from two (differently located) sources as to why the book should be considered. Send nominations to: ASA office at above address.
Award: Certificate
Closing Date: Annually, April 15
Presented: ASA Annual Meeting, Chicago, IL, Annually, April

Dixon Ryan Fox Manuscript Prize
New York State Historical Association
Lake Rd, Cooperstown, NY 13326
Tel: 607-547-1491 *Fax:* 607-547-1405
E-mail: hennessy10@hotmail.com
Key Personnel
Dir, Pubns: Daniel H Goodwin
   E-mail: goodwind@nysha.org
Established: 1974
Encourage original scholarship in the history of New York State. Award granted to the best unpublished ms on the history of New York State.
Award: $3,000
Closing Date: Jan 20 of each year
Presented: Dirs Meeting, Cooperstown, NY, July

Dobie-Paisano Fellowship Project
Texas Institute of Letters & University of Texas at Austin
702 E Dean Keeton St, Austin, TX 78705
Tel: 512-471-8542 *Fax:* 512-471-9997
Web Site: www.utexas.edu/ogs/Paisano
Key Personnel
Dir & Coord: Audrey Slate *E-mail:* aslate@mail.utexas.edu
Established: 1967
Annual six-month grants to Texas writers, including free residence & a living allowance of $2,000 a month at J Frank Dobie's ranch near Austin, Texas. Applicants must have resided in Texas at least three years at some time or be natives of Texas or writers whose previously published work has a Texas subject. Applications available in Oct or online at above web site; $10 fee.
Award: $12,000 living allowance
Closing Date: Jan 25, 2005

Doctoral Dissertation Fellowship
Association of College & Research Libraries
Division of American Library Association
50 E Huron St, Chicago, IL 60611
Tel: 312-280-2514 *Toll Free Tel:* 800-545-2433 (ext 2514) *Fax:* 312-280-2520
Web Site: www.ala.org/acrl
Key Personnel
Prog Coord: Megan Bielefield
   E-mail: mbielefeld@ala.org
Established: 1984
To doctoral students in the field of academic librarianship whose research indicates originality, creativity & interest in scholarship. Sponsored by Thomson Scientific.
Award: $1,500 & plaque
Closing Date: Annually, first Fri in Dec
Presented: ALA Annual Conference

Dog Writers' Association of America Inc (DWAA) Annual Awards
Dog Writers' Association of America Inc (DWAA)
173 Union Rd, Coatesville, PA 19320
Tel: 610-384-2436 *Fax:* 610-384-2471
E-mail: dwaa@dwaa.org; rhydowen@aol.com
Web Site: www.dwaa.org
Key Personnel
Pres: Chris Walkowicz
Sec: Pat Santi

Established: 1935
To give recognition to an individual, club or group which has done an outstanding job in the dog writing field in different categories.
Award: Over several thousand dollars in cash prizes; plaques & certificates
Closing Date: Sept 28
Presented: Annual meeting

John Dos Passos Prize for Literature
Longwood University
Dept of English & Modern Languages, 201 High St, Farmville, VA 23909
Tel: 434-395-2155 *Fax:* 434-395-2145
Key Personnel
Chpn, Dos Passos Comm: Dr Martha Cook
Dept Chpn: Dr Gordon Van Ness
Established: 1980
To honor an imaginative prose writer. Preference given to those not previously honored. Winners are nominated & selected by a jury. Applications not accepted.
Award: $2,000 & a medallion
Presented: Longwood University, Farmville, VA, During fall semester

Alden B Dow Creativity Center Fellowship Award
Northwood University
Alden B Dow Creativity Center, 4000 Whiting Dr, Midland, MI 48640-2398
Tel: 989-837-4478 *Fax:* 989-837-4468
E-mail: creativity@northwood.edu
Web Site: www.northwood.edu/abd
Key Personnel
Contact: Dr Grover B Proctor *E-mail:* grover@northwood.edu
Established: 1979
Ten-week summer residency fellowships given to individuals in any discipline with an innovative project that has the potential of making an impact in its field; $10 application fee.
Award: Room, board, private study, $750 stipend for personal expenses &/or project materials
Closing Date: Dec 31
Presented: Annually

Violet Downey Book Award
The National Chapter of Canada IODE
40 Orchard View Blvd, Suite 254, Toronto, ON M4R 1B9, Canada
Tel: 416-487-4416 *Fax:* 416-487-4417
E-mail: iode@bellnet.ca
Web Site: www.iode.ca
Key Personnel
Award Administrator: Sandra Connery
Natl Pres: Pamela Gallagher
Established: 1983
Annual children's book award; text in English, Canadian author, at least 500 words, printed in Canada during previous calendar year, suitable for children 13 years & under.
Award: Not to exceed $4,000 annually
Closing Date: Annually Dec 31
Presented: The National Annual Meeting, Late May

Drainie-Taylor Biography Prize
The Writers' Trust of Canada
90 Richmond St W, Suite 200, Toronto, ON M5C 1P1, Canada
Tel: 416-504-8222 *Fax:* 416-504-9090
E-mail: info@writerstrust.com
Web Site: www.writerstrust.com
Key Personnel
Exec Dir: Lascelle Wingate *Tel:* 416-504-8222 ext 242
Established: 1998
Awarded for outstanding biography, autobiography or memoirs.
Other Sponsor(s): Drainie-Taylor Family
Award: $10,000
Presented: The Great Literary Awards, March

Katharine Drexel Award
Catholic Library Association
100 North St, Suite 224, Pittsfield, MA 01201-5109
Tel: 413-443-2252 *Fax:* 413-442-2252
E-mail: cla@cathla.org
Web Site: www.cathla.org
Key Personnel
Exec Dir: Jean R Bostley, SSJ
Established: 1966
Recognizes an outstanding contribution to the growth of high school librarianship.
Award: Plaque
Closing Date: none; in-house votes
Presented: Boston, MA, April 15

Drury University One Act Play Competition
Drury University
900 N Benton Ave, Springfield, MO 65802-3344
Tel: 417-873-7430
Key Personnel
Asst Prof, Theatre: Dr Mick Sokol *Tel:* 417-873-6821 *E-mail:* msokol@drury.edu
Established: 1986
One-act plays; competition is open to all playwrights; scripts are to be original, unpublished & unproduced; staged readings or workshop productions will not disqualify a script; musicals, monologues, children's plays & adaptations will not be considered; only stage plays will be judged; preference will be given to small cast, one-set shows with running times of no less than 20 & no more than 45 minutes; no more than one script per author; all scripts are to be typewritten & firmly bound; scripts cannot be acknowledged or returned unless accompanied by a SASE.
Award: $300 plus consideration for production by Drury University & special recommendation to the Open Eye Theater (1st prize); two honorable mentions $150 each
Closing Date: Biennially; next deadline is Dec 1, 2004
Presented: By mail no later than April 1, 2005

Dubuque Fine Arts Players
1686 Lawndale St, Dubuque, IA 52001
Tel: 563-582-5502
Key Personnel
Pres, DFAP Contest: Gary Arms *E-mail:* gary.arms@clarke.edu
Established: 1977
25th Annual National One-Act Playwriting Contest, $10 entry fee, two copies of script. Send SASE for entry form/guidelines; previously published or produced works, musicals & children's plays not accepted.
Award: $600 (1st prize), $300 (2nd prize), $200 (3rd prize), production of first 3 plays unless production is beyond our capabilities
Closing Date: Jan 31
Presented: Loras College Theater, late Aug

John H Dunning Prize in American History
American Historical Association
400 "A" St SE, Washington, DC 20003
Tel: 202-544-2422 *Fax:* 202-544-8307
E-mail: info@historians.org
Web Site: www.historians.org
Key Personnel
Prize Admin: Debbie Ann Doyle *Tel:* 202-544-2422 ext 104 *E-mail:* ddoyle@historians.org
Established: 1927
In recognition of outstanding historical writing in US history. To be awarded to a young scholar for an outstanding monograph in ms or in print on any subject relating to US history. To be eligible for consideration, an entry must be of a scholarly historical nature. It must be the author's first or second book, published or completed after May 1, 2004 & before April 30, 2005. Research accuracy, originality & literary merit are important factors. No application form, applicants must simply mail a copy of their book to each of the prize committee members who will be posted on our web site as the prize deadline approaches. All updated info on web site.
Award: Cash prize
Closing Date: May 16, 2005

Eaton Literary Associates Literary Awards
Eaton Literary Agency Inc
PO Box 49795, Sarasota, FL 34230-6795
Tel: 941-366-6589 *Fax:* 941-365-4679
E-mail: eatonlit@aol.com
Web Site: www.eatonliterary.com
Key Personnel
Pres: Ralph A Eaton
VP: Richard Lawrence
Established: 1984
Two awards are given, one for a book-length ms & one for a short story or article. These entries should not have been previously published.
Award: $2,500 (book-length program), $500 (short story or article program)
Closing Date: Aug 31 (book-length program), March 31 (short story or article program)
Presented: Sept (book-length program), April (short story or article program)

Edelstein Prize
Society for the History of Technology
Iowa State University, 603 Ross Hall, History Dept, Ames, IA 50011
Tel: 515-294-8469 *Fax:* 515-294-6390
E-mail: shot@iastate.edu
Web Site: www.shot.jhu.edu
Key Personnel
Exec Sec: Amy Sue Bix
Established: 1968
For the best book published on the history of technology in the past three years.
Other Sponsor(s): Ruth Edelstein Barrish & Family in memory of Sidney Edelstein
Award: $3,500 & plaque
Closing Date: April 1
Presented: SHOT annual meeting, Oct

Edgar Allan Poe Awards®
Mystery Writers of America
17 E 47 St, 6th fl, New York, NY 10017
Tel: 212-888-8171
E-mail: mwa@mysterywriters.org
Web Site: www.mysterywriters.org
Key Personnel
Off Mgr: Margery Flax
Established: 1945
For the best mystery novel & best first novel by an American author. Also awards for best juvenile novel & young adult, motion picture, fact-crime writing, TV, feature & episode short story, paperback original, critical/biographical work & play.
Award: Ceramic bust of Poe
Closing Date: Nov 30
Presented: New York, NY, Annually in late Spring

Editorial & Graphics Awards Competition-EXCEL Awards
Society of National Association Publications (SNAP)
8405 Greensboro Dr, No 800, McLean, VA 22102
Tel: 703-506-3285 *Fax:* 703-506-3266
E-mail: info@snaponline.org
Web Site: www.snaponline.org
Key Personnel
Exec Dir: Marilee Peterson *E-mail:* mpeterson@snaponline.org
Service excellence awards program for editorial/graphic contents.
Award: Brass Statues, Gold Award (1st prize); Framed Certificate, Bronze & Silver (2nd & 3rd prizes)
Closing Date: March
Presented: SNAP Publications Management Conference, Washington, DC, June

Editors' Prize
The Missouri Review
1507 Hillcrest Hall, Columbia, MO 65211
Tel: 573-882-4474 *Toll Free Tel:* 800-949-2505 *Fax:* 573-884-4671
E-mail: mr@missouri.org
Web Site: www.missourireview.org
Key Personnel
Assoc Ed: Evelyn Somers *E-mail:* rogerses@missouri.edu
Established: 1991
Awarded annually in fiction & essay. The magazine also sponsors the Larry Levis Editors' Prize in Poetry. Winners in each category receive cash prizes & publication in the spring issue of the magazine. Entry fee of $15 entitles entrant to one-year subscription. Writers should send a SASE for guidelines.
Other Sponsor(s): Friends & family of Larry Levis co-sponsor the poetry prize
Award: $2,000 (short fiction), $2,000 (essay), $2,000 (poetry)
Closing Date: Oct 15, Annually
Presented: Spring

Education Awards of Excellence
PIA/GATF (Graphic Arts Technical Foundation)
200 Deer Run Rd, Sewickley, PA 15143-2600
Tel: 412-741-6860 *Toll Free Tel:* 800-910-4283 *Fax:* 412-741-2311
E-mail: info@gain.net
Web Site: www.gain.net
Key Personnel
Pres: Michael Makin
Mktg Mgr: Lisa Erdner
Established: 1984
Honors one industry representative & one graphic arts educator who have each made outstanding contributions to graphic arts education & or training.
Award: Engraved plaque
Closing Date: Annually, May 31
Presented: PIA/GATF Administrative Meetings, Annually, Nov

Educator's Award
Delta Kappa Gamma Society, International
PO Box 1589, Austin, TX 78767-1589
Tel: 512-478-5748 *Fax:* 512-478-3961
E-mail: societyexec@deltakappagamma.org
Web Site: www.deltakappagamma.org
Key Personnel
Exec Coord: Jill Foltz
Annual award to the woman author(s) of a book whose work may influence the direction of thought & action necessary to meet the needs of today's complex society. The content must be of more than local interest with relationship, direct or implied, to education everywhere. The author must be a woman from Canada, Costa Rica, El Salvador, Finland, Germany, Great Britain, Guatemala, Iceland, Mexico, Netherlands, Norway, Puerto Rico, Sweden or the US.
Award: $1,500
Closing Date: Feb 1
Presented: One of Five Regional Conferences depending on where author lives, Varies

Margaret A Edwards Award
Young Adult Library Services Association (YALSA)
Unit of American Library Association
50 E Huron St, Chicago, IL 60611
Tel: 312-280-4390 *Toll Free Tel:* 800-545-2433 (ext 4390) *Fax:* 312-664-7459

E-mail: yalsa@ala.org
Web Site: www.ala.org/yalsa/
Key Personnel
Prog Officer: Nichole Gilbert *E-mail:* ngilbert@ala.org
Given to an author for lifetime achievement in writing for teen-agers.
Other Sponsor(s): School Library Journal
Award: $2,000 & citation
Closing Date: Nominations close in Dec
Presented: Midwinter meeting luncheon in which winner speaks at ALA Annual

Wilfrid Eggleston Award for Nonfiction
Banff Centre
11759 Groat Rd, Edmonton, AB T5M 3K6, Canada
Tel: 780-422-8174 *Toll Free Tel:* 800-665-5354 (Alberta only) *Fax:* 780-422-2663
E-mail: mail@writersguild.ab.ca
Web Site: www.writersguild.ab.ca
Key Personnel
Exec Dir: Diane Walton
Established: 1982
Alberta Literary Award, must be resident of Alberta.
Award: $1,000 plus leather-bound copy of book
Closing Date: Dec 31

Elliott Prize
Medieval Academy of America
104 Mount Auburn St, 5th fl, Cambridge, MA 02138
Tel: 617-491-1622 *Fax:* 617-492-3303
E-mail: speculum@medievalacademy.org
Web Site: www.medievalacademy.org
Key Personnel
Exec Dir & Ed, Speculum: Richard K Emmerson
Established: 1971
For a first article published two years prior to award date, in the field of medieval studies.
Award: $500
Closing Date: Oct 15
Presented: Annually in April

Emerging Playwright Award
Urban Stages
17 E 47 St, New York, NY 10017
Tel: 212-421-1380 *Fax:* 212-421-1387
E-mail: urbanstage@aol.com
Web Site: www.urbanstages.org
Key Personnel
Artistic Dir & Founder: Frances Hill
Prod Dir: T L Reilly
Man Dir: Sonya Kozlova
Scripts not previously produced; scripts should have no more than eight characters; well-written, imaginative situations & dialog; multicultural scripts are given special attention.
Award: $500 & production of play
Closing Date: Year-round, $5 processing fee
Presented: New York, Spring/Fall

Ralph Waldo Emerson Award
Phi Beta Kappa
1606 New Hampshire Ave NW, Washington, DC 20009
Tel: 202-265-3808 *Fax:* 202-986-1601
Web Site: www.pbk.org
Key Personnel
Awards Coord: Sandra Beasley
    E-mail: sbeasley@pbk.org
Established: 1960
For scholarly studies that contribute to interpretations of the intellectual & cultural condition of humanity. To be eligible, must have been published in USA by American author between April 30 & May 1 of the previous year. Works in history, philosophy, religion & related fields such as social sciences & anthropology are eligible. Nomination must come from publisher.
Award: $2,500

Closing Date: April 30 annually
Presented: Washington, DC, Annually in Dec

Prix Emile-Nelligan
Union des Ecrivaines et Ecrivains Quebecois
261 avenue Bloomfield, Outremont, PQ H2V 3R6, Canada
Tel: 514-849-8540 *Fax:* 514-271-6239
E-mail: info@fondation-nelligan.org
Web Site: www.fondation-nelligan.org
Key Personnel
Dir, Commun: Ariane Bertouille
Established: 1979
Award: $5,000 & a bronze medal
Closing Date: Collection must be published between Jan 1-Dec 31 of the preceding year
Presented: May

Emily Dickinson Award
Poetry Society of America (PSA)
15 Gramercy Park, New York, NY 10003
Tel: 212-254-9628 *Fax:* 212-673-2352
Web Site: www.poetrysociety.org
Key Personnel
Exec Dir: Alice Quinn
Established: 1971
For a poem inspired by Dickinson (though not necessarily in her style), not to exceed 30 lines. Open to Society members only. Opening date Oct 1. Send No 10 SASE for guidelines, or visit www.poetrysociety.org.
Award: $250
Closing Date: Dec 22
Presented: Annually in April

Empire State Award for Excellence in Literature for Young People
New York Library Association
252 Hudson Ave, Albany, NY 12210
Tel: 518-432-6952 *Fax:* 518-427-1697
E-mail: info@nyla.org
Web Site: www.nyla.org
Key Personnel
Exec Dir: Michael Borges
Asst Dir: Kat McGrath *Tel:* 518-432-6952 ext 102 *E-mail:* events@nyla.org
Established: 1990
One-time award presented to a living author or illustrator currently residing in New York State. The award honors excellence in children's or young adult literature & a body of work that has made a significant contribution to literature for young people.
Award: Engraved medallion

Marian Engel Award
The Writer's Trust of Canada
90 Richmond St W, Suite 200, Toronto, ON M5C 1P1, Canada
Tel: 416-504-8222 *Fax:* 416-504-9090
E-mail: info@writerstrust.com
Web Site: www.writerstrust.com
Key Personnel
Exec Dir: Lascelle Wingate *Tel:* 416-504-8222 ext 242
Established: 1986
Presented to a female writer for an outstanding body of work & continued contribution to the literary arts in Canada. Sponsored by the Honourable Hilary M Weston.
Award: $15,000
Presented: The Great Literary Awards, March

Norma Epstein Foundation
University of Toronto - University College
15 King's College Circle, Toronto, ON M5S 3H7, Canada
Tel: 416-978-8083 *Fax:* 416-971-2027
Web Site: www.utoronto.ca
Key Personnel
Registrar: Glenn Loney

Contact: Eleanor Dennison *E-mail:* eleanor.dennison@utoronto.ca
Literary competition held every odd-numbered year.
Award: $1,000
Closing Date: May 15, every odd-numbered year
Presented: Toronto, Nov

David W & Beatrice C Evans Biography & Handcart Awards
Western Literature Association
Division of College of Humanities, Arts & Social Sciences
0735 Old Main Hill, Logan, UT 84322-0735
Tel: 435-797-3630 *Fax:* 435-797-3899
E-mail: mwc@cc.usu.edu
Web Site: www.usu.edu/mountainwest
Key Personnel
Prog Coord: Elaine Thatcher *E-mail:* elaine.thatcher@usu.edu
Off Mgr: Glenda Nesbit *E-mail:* nesbitg@hass.usu.edu
Established: 1983
For the best biography or history with a significant biographical content of an individual associated with "Mormon Country" (a geographical, not religious, concept).
Award: $10,000 (The Evans Biography Award); $1,000 (The Evans Handcart Award)
Closing Date: Dec 1 for current year's publication
Presented: Utah State University, March or April

John E Fagg Prize
American Historical Association
400 "A" St SE, Washington, DC 20003
Tel: 202-544-2422 *Fax:* 202-544-8307
E-mail: info@historians.org
Web Site: www.historians.org
Key Personnel
Prize Admin: Debbie Ann Doyle *Tel:* 202-544-2422 ext 104 *E-mail:* ddoyle@historians.org
Established: 2001
For the best publication in the history of Spain, Portugal or Latin America. The prize will be awarded annually for a period of ten years beginning in 2001. Books published after May 1, 2004 & before April 20, 2005 will be eligible for the prize. No application form, applicants must simply mail a copy of their book to each of the prize committee members who will be posted on our web site as the prize deadline approaches.
Award: Cash prize
Closing Date: May 16, 2005

John K Fairbank Prize in East Asian History
American Historical Association
400 "A" St SE, Washington, DC 20003
Tel: 202-544-2422 *Fax:* 202-544-8307
E-mail: info@historians.org
Web Site: www.historians.org
Key Personnel
Prize Admin: Debbie Ann Doyle *Tel:* 202-544-2422 ext 104 *E-mail:* ddoyle@historians.org
Established: 1968
Outstanding book on the history of China proper, Vietnam, Chinese Central Asia, Mongolia, Manchuria, Korea or Japan since 1800; books published after May 1, 2004 & before April 30, 2005 will be eligible; anthologies, edited works & pamphlets are ineligible for the competition. No application form, applicants must simply mail a copy of their book to each of the prize committee members who will be posted on our web site as the prize deadline approaches. All updated info on web site.
Award: Cash prize
Closing Date: May 16, 2005
Presented: San Francisco

Norma Farber First Book Award
Poetry Society of America (PSA)
15 Gramercy Park, New York, NY 10003

Tel: 212-254-9628 *Fax:* 212-673-2352
Web Site: www.poetrysociety.org
Key Personnel
Exec Dir: Alice Quinn
For a first book of original poetry written by an American poet; publishers only may submit with entry form. Opening date Oct 1-Dec 22.
Award: $500
Closing Date: Dec 22
Presented: Annually in April

Virginia Faulkner Award for Excellence in Writing

Prairie Schooner
University of Nebraska, 201 Andrews Hall, Lincoln, NE 68588
Mailing Address: PO Box 880334, Lincoln, NE 68588-0334
Tel: 402-472-0911
E-mail: kgrey2@unl.edu
Web Site: www.unl.edu/schooner/psmain.htm
Key Personnel
Ed: Hilda Raz
Established: 1987
Annual writing prize for work published in Prairie Schooner Magazine. Only work published in Prairie Schooner in the previous year is considered.
Other Sponsor(s): Friends & family of Virginia Faulkner
Award: $1,000
Presented: Prairie Schooner Magazine, Annually in the spring issue

Feature Article Award

Prince Edward Island Council of the Arts
115 Richmond St, Charlottetown, PE C1A 1H7, Canada
Tel: 902-368-4410 *Fax:* 902-368-4418
E-mail: peiarts@peiartscouncil.com
Web Site: www.peiartscouncil.com
Key Personnel
Exec Dir: Darrin White
One feature article (intended for print, not broadcast) that is unpublished or published within the last 12 months of the competition closing date. Entries will have no maximum or minimum length & participants may submit as many entries as they wish. Contest for Prince Edward Island residents only. Call for further information or contact by e-mail.
Award: $500 (1st prize), $200 (2nd prize), $100 (3rd prize)
Closing Date: Call or e-mail
Presented: Call or e-mail

Herbert Feis Award

American Historical Association
400 "A" St SE, Washington, DC 20003
Tel: 202-544-2422 *Fax:* 202-544-8307
E-mail: info@historians.org
Web Site: www.historians.org
Key Personnel
Prize Admin: Debbie Ann Doyle *Tel:* 202-544-2422 ext 104 *E-mail:* ddoyle@historians.org
Established: 1984
To recognize the scholarly interests of historians outside academe & the importance of the work of independent scholars in the US. Works submitted may take the form of a book, article or series of articles of seminal importance in any field or era of history; an in-house publication which is shown to have had a major impact on the policy of the employing & circulating organization or of the formation of policy generally. Eligibility extends to individuals outside academe for a minimum of three years prior to the award year. Those historians whose careers have been chiefly in academia are not eligible. Works published or issued in-house between May 1, 2004 & April 30, 2005 will be eligible for the 2005 award. No application form, applicants must simply mail a copy of their book to each of the prize committee members who will be posted on our web site as the prize deadline approaches. All updated info on web site.
Award: Cash prize
Closing Date: May 16, 2005

Fellowship & Scholarship Program for Writers

Bread Loaf Writers' Conference
Middlebury College, Middlebury, VT 05753
Tel: 802-443-5286 *Fax:* 802-443-2087
E-mail: blwc@middlebury.edu
Web Site: www.middlebury.edu/~blwc
Key Personnel
Dir: Michael Collier
Assoc Dir: Devon Jersild
Admin Mgr: Noreen Cargill
Work study scholarship.
Award: Fellowship provides tuition, room & board during 11 day conference; Scholarship provides tuition during conference
Closing Date: Annually, March 1
Presented: Early June; To be used during conference in August

Fellowship In Aerospace History

American Historical Association
400 "A" St SE, Washington, DC 20003
Tel: 202-544-2422 *Fax:* 202-544-8307
E-mail: info@historians.org
Web Site: www.historians.org
Key Personnel
Asst Dir, Pub & Info Systems & Research: Robert Townsend
To provide a Fellow with an opportunity to engage in significant & sustained advanced research in all aspects of the history of aerospace from the earliest human interest in flight to the present, including cultural & intellectual history, economic history, history of law & public policy & the history of science, engineering & management. Must be a US citizen, possess a doctorate degree in history or in a closely related field, or be enrolled as a student (having completed all coursework) in a doctoral degree program. No application form, applicants must simply mail a copy of their book to each of the prize committee members who will be posted on our web site as the prize deadline approaches. All updated information on web site.
Award: Funding of one Fellowship term for at least 6 months but not more than 1 yr; maximum $30,000; graduate students up to $21,000

Fellowship Program

Rhode Island State Council on the Arts
Affiliate of Dept of Rhode Island State Government
One Capital Hill, 3rd fl, Providence, RI 02908
Tel: 401-222-3880 *Fax:* 401-222-3018
Web Site: www.arts.ri.gov
Key Personnel
Dir, Individual Artists & Public Arts Progs: Christina M Di Chiera *E-mail:* christina@arts.ri.gov
Established: 1967
Applicants must be Rhode Island residents who are not undergraduate or graduate students. Finalists are selected by a panel of state or regional writers & the winner is chosen by an out-of-state judge. Categories include crafts, fiction, film & video, folk arts, photography, poetry, playwriting/screenwriting & 3D art (April 1 deadline); choreography, design, drawing & printmaking, music composition & new genre (Oct 1 deadline).
Award: $5,000 recipient; $1,000 runner-up
Closing Date: April 1 & Oct 1
Presented: Annually

Fellowships for Creative Writers

National Endowment for the Arts
Nancy Hanks Ctr, 1100 Pennsylvania Ave NW, Rm 720, Washington, DC 20506-0001
Tel: 202-682-5428; 202-682-5034 (Literature Fellowships hotline) *Fax:* 202-682-5669
Web Site: www.arts.gov
Key Personnel
Dir, Lit: Cliff Becker
Asst: James McNeel *Tel:* 202-682-5092
E-mail: mcneelj@arts.gov
Established: 1967
Given to published writers of poetry, fiction & creative nonfiction; variable number of fellowships, based on available program funds. Applications accepted by genre (2006 prose & 2007 poetry) in alternating years. Applicants are restricted to applying in one fellowship category only in the same year. Must submit 9 copies as part of the application package. Guidelines available on web site.
Award: $20,000
Presented: Notifications to be sent by mail late Dec

Fellowships for Playwrights

Pennsylvania Council on the Arts
216 Finance Bldg, Harrisburg, PA 17120
Tel: 717-787-6883 *Fax:* 717-783-2538
Web Site: www.pacouncilonthearts.org
Key Personnel
Prog Dir: Lori Frush
Fellowships for playwrights who create & perform their own work. Must be PA resident. Biennial award given in even numbered years.
Award: $5,000 or $10,000
Closing Date: Aug 1

Shubert Fendrich Memorial Playwriting Contest

Pioneer Drama Service Inc
PO Box 4267, Englewood, CO 80155-4267
Tel: 303-779-4035 *Toll Free Tel:* 800-333-7262 *Fax:* 303-779-4315
E-mail: playwrights@pioneerdrama.com
Web Site: www.pioneerdrama.com
Key Personnel
Publr: Steven Fendrich
Asst Ed: Lori Conary
Established: 1990
Presented for plays suitable for publication by Pioneer Drama Service Inc.
Award: $1,000 advance on royalties
Closing Date: Annually, March 1

The Field Poetry Prize

Oberlin College Press
50 N Professor St, Oberlin, OH 44074-1095
Tel: 440-775-8408 *Fax:* 440-775-8124
E-mail: oc.press@oberlin.edu
Web Site: www.oberlin.edu/ocpress
Key Personnel
Man Ed: Linda Slocum
Ed: Pamela Alexander; Martha Collins; David Walker; David Young
Established: 1996
Original poetry ms of 50 to 80 pages.
Award: $1,000 & publication in the Field Poetry Series
Closing Date: May 31
Presented: Summer

Timothy Findley Award

The Writers' Trust of Canada
90 Richmond St W, Suite 200, Toronto, ON M5C 1P1, Canada
Tel: 416-504-8222 *Fax:* 416-504-9090
E-mail: info@writerstrust.com
Web Site: www.writerstrust.com
Key Personnel
Exec Dir: Lascelle Wingate *Tel:* 416-504-8222 ext 242
Established: 2002

Awarded to a Canadian male writer, in recognition of a body of work comprised of no less than 3 works of literary merit which are predominantly fiction. No age restrictions apply.
Award: $15,000
Presented: The Great Literary Awards, March

Fine Arts Work Center in Provincetown
24 Pearl St, Provincetown, MA 02657
Tel: 508-487-9960 *Fax:* 508-487-8873
E-mail: general@fawc.org
Web Site: www.fawc.org
Key Personnel
Exec Dir: Hunter O'Hanian
Established: 1968
Offer seven-month fellowships to ten artists & ten writers, Oct 1-May 1. The Center aims to aid emerging artists & writers at a critical stage of their careers. For application & brochure, see web site above or send SASE.
Award: Monthly stipends of up to $650 plus free rent for writers living at the Center; same for artists. Families welcome; no pets
Closing Date: Dec 1, writers; Feb 1, visual arts

Firman Houghton Prize
New England Poetry Club
16 Cornell St, Arlington, MA 02474
Web Site: www.nepoetryclub.org
Key Personnel
Pres: Diana Der Hovanessian
Established: 1987
Lyric poem sent in duplicate; $10 for three contest entries per poem entry for non-member, free for members & students.
Award: $250. Other NEPC awards include Daniel Varoujan Prize, $1,000. Erika Mumford Prize, $250. Sheila Motton Award, $500. Der-Hovanessian translation prize, $100
Closing Date: June 30
Presented: Annually, Fall

Robert L Fish Memorial Award
Mystery Writers of America
17 E 47 St, 6th fl, New York, NY 10017
Tel: 212-888-8171
E-mail: mwa@mysterywriters.org
Web Site: www.mysterywriters.org
Key Personnel
Off Mgr: Margery Flax
For the best first-published mystery short story by an American author.
Award: $500 & plaque
Closing Date: Nov 30
Presented: Edgars®, New York, NY, Annually in late Spring

Dorothy Canfield Fisher Children's Book Award
Vermont Dept of Libraries
109 State St, Montpelier, VT 05609-0601
Tel: 802-828-6954 *Fax:* 802-828-2199
E-mail: cbec@dol.state.vt.us
Web Site: www.dcfaward.org; dol.state.vt.us
Key Personnel
Chpn: Sally Margolis
Children's Consultant: Grace Worcester Greene
E-mail: grace.greene@dol.state.vt.us
Established: 1956
For a book by a living American author published one year previous, chosen by the children of Vermont, grades 4-8, from a master list of 30 titles.
Other Sponsor(s): Vermont PTA
Award: Illuminated scroll
Closing Date: Dec 1
Presented: Annually in May

William Flanagan Memorial Creative Persons Center
Edward F Albee Foundation

14 Harrison St, New York, NY 10013
Tel: 212-226-2020
E-mail: info@albeefoundation.org
Web Site: www.albeefoundation.org
Key Personnel
Dir: Edward Albee
Foundation Secy: Jakob Holder
Residency program for writers & visual artists. The only requirements are talent & need.
Award: Room (Writers)/Room & Studio (Visual Artists)
Closing Date: Applications taken between Jan 1 through April 1 for summer season
Presented: The Barn, Montauk, LI, June-Sept annually, every writer or artist can choose one month of the four

Florida Individual Artist Fellowships
Florida Dept of State, Division of Cultural Affairs
1001 DeSoto Park Dr, Tallahassee, FL 32301
Tel: 850-245-6470 *Fax:* 850-245-6492
Web Site: www.florida-arts.org
Key Personnel
Dir: Linda Downey
Arts Admin: Adela Brown
Arts Consultant: Erin Long *E-mail:* elong@dos.state.fl.us
Established: 1976
Fellowship program supports the general artistic & career advancement of individual artists & recognizes the creation of new artworks by these artists.
Award: $5,000 fellowship
Closing Date: Every other year. Next deadline will be summer 2006. Check web site for exact dates

Florida State Writing Competition
Florida Freelance Writers Association
Affiliate of Cassell Network of Writers
Main St, North Stratford, NH 03590
Mailing Address: PO Box A, North Stratford, NH 03590
Tel: 603-922-8338 *Fax:* 603-922-8339
E-mail: contest@writers-editors.com
Web Site: www.writers-editors.com
Key Personnel
Exec Dir: Dana Cassell
Established: 1984
Fiction, nonfiction, juveniles & poetry.
Award: Cash
Closing Date: Annually, March 15
Presented: May 31

Fordham University, Graduate School of Business Administration
33 W 60 St, 4th fl, Off of Graduate Admissions, New York, NY 10023
Tel: 212-636-6200 *Fax:* 212-636-7076
Key Personnel
Larkin Prof, Area Chair, Communs & Media Mgmt: Everette E Denis *Tel:* 212-636-6144
Established: 1969
Offers MBA degree with a major in Communications & Media Management. Its mission is to educate business professionals who can manage effectively in a range of leadership roles & who are equipped for continuous growth in a changing global environment. A variety of assistantships, fellowships & scholarships are available to highly qualified MBA candidates, such as Graduate Assistantships; New York Times Foundation Scholarship; Hitachi Fellowship; Xerox Fellowship; National Black MBA Association Scholarships; Minority Business Students Alliance Scholarship & Alexis Welsh Memorial Scholarship.
Closing Date: Ongoing
Presented: Each trimester

Morris D Forkosch Prize
American Historical Association

400 "A" St SE, Washington, DC 20003
Tel: 202-544-2422 *Fax:* 202-544-8307
E-mail: info@historians.org
Web Site: www.historians.org
Key Personnel
Prize Admin: Debbie Ann Doyle *Tel:* 202-544-2422 ext 104 *E-mail:* ddoyle@historians.org
In recognition of the best in English in the field of British, British Imperial or British Commonwealth history since 1485. The prize rotates between British Imperial & Commonwealth history & British history. Submissions of books relating to the shared common law heritage of the English-speaking world are particularly encouraged. Books on British Imperial or Commonwealth history published between May 1, 2004 & April 30, 2005 are eligible for the competition. No application form, applicants must simply mail a copy of their book to each of the prize committee members who will be posted on our web site as the prize deadline approaches. All updated info on web site.
Closing Date: May 16, 2005

49th Parallel Poetry Award
The Bellingham Review
Mail Stop 9053, Western Washington University, Bellingham, WA 98225
Tel: 360-650-4863
E-mail: bhreview@cc.wwu.edu
Web Site: www.wwu.edu/~bhreview
Key Personnel
Ed-in-Chief: Brenda Miller
Edit Advisor: Bruce Beasley; Kathleen Halme; Robin Hemley; Suzanne Paola
Founding Ed: Knute Skinner
Established: 1983
$15 for the first entry (one nonfiction work, one short story, or up to 3 poems). Each additional entry, including each additional poem, is $10. Please make checks payable to: The Western Foundation/The Bellingham Review. All entries will receive a complimentary two-issue subscription.
Award: $1,000 & publication in Summer issue of the Bellingham Review (1st prize)
Closing Date: Between Dec 1, 2004 & March 15, 2005
Presented: by Aug 2005

Foster City Writers Contest
Foster City Arts & Culture Committee
650 Shell Blvd, Foster City, CA 94404
Tel: 650-286-3380
Web Site: www.fostercity.org
Key Personnel
Chmn: Larry Staley
For fiction, humor, children's story & poetry & personal essay, rhymed verse, blank verse. Entries must be original, previously unpublished & in English. Fiction must be no more than 3,000 words; children's story no more than 2,000 words; poetry not to exceed two double-spaced typed pages in length. Open to all writers, no age or geographic limit. Send SASE for contest flyer.
Award: $250 in each category (1st place); $125 honorable mention (2nd place): children's, nonfiction, fiction, humor, poetry
Closing Date: Oct 31

Soeurette Diehl Fraser Award
Texas Institute of Letters
3700 Mockingbird Lane, Dallas, TX 75205
Tel: 512-245-2232 *Fax:* 512-245-7462
Web Site: www.stedwards.edu/newc/marks/til/awards_and_rules.htm
Key Personnel
VP: Joe Holley
Dir: Mark Busby *Tel:* 512-245-2428
E-mail: mb13@swt.edu
Treas: Jim Hoggard

Sec: Fran Vick *E-mail:* franvick@aol.com
Established: 1990
Award given for the best book of translation by a Texan.
Other Sponsor(s): Babette Fraser
Award: $1,000
Closing Date: Jan 2005
Presented: March banquet, Ft Worth TX, USA, Every two years

George Freedley Memorial Award
Theatre Library Association
Division of Benjamin Rosenthal Library
Queens College, CUNY, Flushing, NY 11367
Tel: 718-997-3672 *Fax:* 718-997-3753
Web Site: tla.library.unt.edu
Key Personnel
Asst Prof, Libr Dept: Richard Wall
  E-mail: rlw$lib@qc1.qc.edu
Exec Secy, TLA: Joseph M Yranski *Tel:* 212-621-0538
Established: 1968
To the author of a book in the field of theater, published in the US, on the basis of scholarship, readability & general contribution to knowledge. Only books related to live performance (including vaudeville, puppetry, pantomime & circus) will be considered.
Award: $500 winner, $200 Special Jury Prize; Certificate
Closing Date: Feb 15 of year following publication
Presented: New York, NY, Late May or early June

The Don Freeman Memorial Grant-In-Aid
Society of Children's Book Writers & Illustrators (SCBWI)
8271 Beverly Blvd, Los Angeles, CA 90048
Tel: 323-782-1010 *Fax:* 323-782-1892
E-mail: membership@scbwi.org
Web Site: www.scbwi.org
Key Personnel
Pres: Steve Mooser
Exec Dir: Lin Oliver
Established: 1977
To enable picture-book artists to further their understanding, training &/or work in any aspect of the picture-book genre. Grant may be used for the purchase of necessary materials, enrollment in illustrators' or writers' workshops or conferences, courses in advanced illustrating or writing techniques & travel for research or to expose to publishers/art directors. Open to Society members only.
Award: $1,500 & $500 for runner-up
Closing Date: Feb 10
Presented: Aug 15

The French-American Foundation Translation Prize
28 W 44 St, Suite 1420, New York, NY 10036
Tel: 212-829-8800 *Fax:* 212-829-8810
E-mail: info@frenchamerican.org
Web Site: www.frenchamerican.org
Key Personnel
Dir, Public Events: Isabel Carrion
  E-mail: icarrion@frenchamerican.org
Established: 1986
For distinguished translations of prose works from French into English which have been published in the US. Translations must be submitted by the US publisher. Technical, scientific, reference works & children's literature are not accepted. Works must have been published between Jan 1 & Dec 31, 2003.
Award: Two awards of $7,500, one for fiction; one for nonfiction
Closing Date: Nov 15
Presented: New York, NY, Annually in the Spring

Friends of American Writers Award
Friends of American Writers
680 N Lake Shore Dr, Suite L208, Chicago, IL 60611
Tel: 312-664-5628
Key Personnel
Pres: Minnie Orfanos
Adult Literary Awards: Vivien Mortensen
Juv Awards Chmn: Karen Harrington
Established: 1922
To resident emerging author of Midwest America who has no more than three books published previously or for a book with a Midwest American setting published in the current year. No poetry or scholarly dissertations; no mss.
Closing Date: Dec 15
Presented: Union League Club, Chicago, IL, Annually in April

Friends of the Dallas Public Library Award
Texas Institute of Letters
Center for the Study of the Southwest, Southwest Texas State University, San Marcos, TX 78666
Tel: 512-245-2232 *Fax:* 512-245-7462
Web Site: www.stedwards.edu/newc/marks/til/awards_and_rules.htm
Key Personnel
VP: Joe Holley
Dir: Mark Busby *Tel:* 512-245-2428
  E-mail: mb13@swt.edu
Treas: Jim Hoggard
Sec: Fran Vick *E-mail:* franvick@aol.com
For the most useful & informative scholarly book contributing to general knowledge, by a Texan or about Texas.
Other Sponsor(s): Friends of the Dallas Public Library
Award: $1,000
Closing Date: Jan 2005
Presented: March banquet, Ft Worth, TX, USA, March 2005

Fulbright Scholar Program
Council for International Exchange of Scholars
Division of The Institute of International Education
3007 Tilden St NW, Suite 5-L, Washington, DC 20008-3009
Tel: 202-686-4000 *Fax:* 202-362-3442
E-mail: cieswebmaster@cies.iie.org
Web Site: www.cies.org
Key Personnel
Exec Dir: Patti McGill Peterson
Deputy Exec Dir: Ellen Barclay
Dir, External Rel: Nancy Santos-Gainer
Established: 1947
CIES cooperates with the US Dept of State, Bureau of Educational & Cultural Affairs, in the administration of the Fulbright scholar program, which offers approximately 800 grants annually to US faculty & professionals for university lecturing &/or advanced research in over 140 countries.
Award: Grant benefits, which vary by country, generally include a stipend & round-trip travel for the grantee & dependent
Closing Date: Aug 1 - lecturing & research awards worldwide

Gabriela Mistral Inter-American Culture Prize
Organization of American States
Division of Program of Culture
Unit of Social Development, Education & Culture, 1889 "F" St NW, Suite 771, Washington, DC 20006-4499
Tel: 202-458-3140 *Fax:* 202-458-6115
E-mail: culture@oas.org
Web Site: www.oas.org
Key Personnel
Coord: Sara Meneses, PhD *E-mail:* smeneses@oas.org
Established: 1951

Literature & philosophy.
Presented: Washington, DC

Lewis Galantiere Prize
American Translators Association (ATA)
225 Reinekers Lane, Suite 590, Alexandria, VA 22314
Tel: 703-683-6100 *Fax:* 703-683-6122
E-mail: ata@atanet.org
Web Site: www.atanet.org
Key Personnel
Pres: Scott Brennan
Exec Dir: Walter Bacak *Tel:* 703-683-6100 ext 3006 *E-mail:* walter@atanet.org
Awarded in even years for recent published work in literary translations from any language but German into English.
Award: $500, a certificate & $500 towards expenses to attend the ATA annual conference
Closing Date: May 1, 2006
Presented: Annual conference

Francois-Xavier Garneau Medal
Canadian Historical Association
395 Wellington St, Ottawa, ON K1A 0N3, Canada
Tel: 613-233-7885 *Fax:* 613-567-3110
E-mail: cha-shc@archives.ca
Web Site: www.cha-shc.ca
Key Personnel
Admin Asst: Joanne Mineault
Established: 1980
Awarded every 5 years; commemorates the first Canadian Historian. Applicant should be a Canadian citizen or a legal immigrant. Given for the most outstanding scholarly book in the field of Canadian history within the previous five years.
Award: Minted medal & $2,000
Closing Date: Sept
Presented: Every five years; 2005

John Gassner Memorial Playwriting Award
The New England Theatre Conference Inc
PMB 502, 198 Tremont St, Boston, MA 02116-4750
Tel: 617-851-8535
E-mail: mail@netconline.org
Web Site: www.netconline.org
Established: 1967
Playwriting contest for new full-length plays.
Award: $1,000 (1st prize), $500 (2nd prize)
Closing Date: Annually, April 15
Presented: NETC Annual Convention, Nov

The Christian Gauss Award
Phi Beta Kappa
1606 New Hampshire Ave NW, Washington, DC 20009
Tel: 202-265-3808 *Fax:* 202-986-1601
Web Site: www.pbk.org
Key Personnel
Awards Coord: Sandra Beasley
  E-mail: sbeasley@pbk.org
Established: 1950
For outstanding books in the field of literary scholarship or criticism published in the USA between May 1, 2004 & April 30, 2005.
Award: $2,500
Closing Date: April 30
Presented: Washington, DC, Annually in Dec

The Gaylactic Spectrum Awards
Gaylactic Spectrum Awards Foundation
c/o Lambda Sci-Fi, PO Box 656, Washington, DC 20044
Tel: 202-483-6369
E-mail: info@spectrumawards.org
Web Site: www.spectrumawards.org
Key Personnel
Dir: Rob Gates
Established: 1999

Presented to outstanding works of science fiction, fantasy or horror with significant gay, lesbian, bisexual or transgender content.
Award: Statuette & cash prize
Closing Date: Nominations usually open through March 31 for works released previous year
Presented: Varies - World Science Fiction Convention, Gaylaxicon or other, Fall

Lionel Gelber Prize
Lionel Gelber Foundation
University of Toronto, Munk Centre for International Studies, One Devonshire Place, Toronto, ON M5S 3K7, Canada
Tel: 416-946-8901 *Fax:* 416-946-8915
E-mail: gelberprize.munk@utoronto.ca
Web Site: www.utoronto.ca/mcis/gelber
Established: 1989
Given to the author of the year's most outstanding work of nonfiction in the field of international relations. Designed to encourage authors who write about international relations & to stimulate the audience for these books to grow. Open to authors of all nationalities. Six copies of each title must be submitted by the publisher. Books must be published betwen Sept 1 & Aug 31 in English or English translation.
Award: $50,000 (Canadian)
Closing Date: June 3
Presented: Short list announced Sept; prize award in spring

Leo Gershoy Award
American Historical Association
400 "A" St SE, Washington, DC 20003
Tel: 202-544-2422 *Fax:* 202-544-8307
E-mail: info@historians.org
Web Site: www.historians.org
Key Personnel
Prize Admin: Debbie Ann Doyle *Tel:* 202-544-2422 ext 104 *E-mail:* ddoyle@historians.org
Established: 1975
In recognition of outstanding historical writing in 17th & 18th century Western European history. Books published between May 1, 2004 & April 30, 2005 will be eligible for the 2005 award. No application form, applicants must simply mail a copy of their book to each of the prize committee members who will be posted on our web site as the prize deadline approaches. All updated info on web site.
Award: Cash prize
Closing Date: May 16, 2005

Charles M Getchell Award, see Southeastern Theatre Conference New Play Project (SETC)

John Glassco Translation Prize
Literary Translators' Association of Canada
Concordia University, SB 335, 1455 De Maisonneuve West, Montreal, PQ H3G 1M8, Canada
Tel: 514-848-8702
E-mail: info@attlc-ltac.org
Web Site: www.attlc-ltac.org
Key Personnel
Pres: Phyllis Aronoff
Established: 1980
For a first book length literary translation into French or English published in Canada during the previous year. Must be Canadian citizen or landed immigrant.
Award: $1,000
Closing Date: Annually, June 30
Presented: Annually, Sept 30

Alexander Gode Medal
American Translators Association (ATA)
225 Reinekers Lane, Suite 590, Alexandria, VA 22314
Tel: 703-683-6100 *Fax:* 703-683-6122
E-mail: ata@atanet.org

Web Site: www.atanet.org
Key Personnel
Pres: Scott Brennan
Exec Dir: Walter Bacak *Tel:* 703-683-6100 ext 3006 *E-mail:* walter@atanet.org
Established: 1964
For distinguished service to the cause of translation.
Award: Medal
Closing Date: Annually, June 1
Presented: Annual conference

Gold Medallion Book Awards
Evangelical Christian Publishers Association
4816 S Ash Ave, Suite 101, Tempe, AZ 85282-7735
Tel: 480-966-3998 *Fax:* 480-966-1944
Web Site: www.ecpa.org
Key Personnel
Pres: Mark Kuyper *E-mail:* mkuyper@ecpa.org
Established: 1977
To the publishers of the most outstanding religious books in the previous year in 20 categories: inspirational/devotional Christian living, biography/autobiography, fiction, reference works/commentaries, theology/doctrine, missions/evangelism, Christianity & society, Christian ministry, Christian education, youth books, marriage, family & parenting gift books/poetry, personal/group bible study, bibles, Spanish, preschool & elementary children's books.
Award: Medallion & seal
Closing Date: Annually
Presented: Annually in July

Golden Cylinder Awards
Gravure Association of America
1200-A Scottsville Rd, Rochester, NY 14624
Tel: 585-436-2150 *Fax:* 585-436-7689
E-mail: gaa@gaa.org
Web Site: www.gaa.org
Key Personnel
Tech Sec: Linda Zornow
Encourage highest quality gravure printing from design through production.
Award: Golden Cylinders on pedestals
Closing Date: Feb 6, 2005

Golden Kite Awards
Society of Children's Book Writers & Illustrators (SCBWI)
8271 Beverly Blvd, Los Angeles, CA 90048
Tel: 323-782-1010 *Fax:* 323-782-1892
E-mail: scbwi@scbwi.org
Web Site: www.scbwi.org
Key Personnel
Pres: Steve Mooser
Contact: Tanya Brown
Established: 1973
Four awards, one each for fiction, nonfiction, picture book text & picture illustration, awarded each year to the most outstanding children's books published during that year & written or illustrated by members of the Society of Children's Book Writers & Illustrators. An honor book plaque is awarded in each category.
Award: Statuettes & plaques
Closing Date: Dec 15
Presented: April 15

Golden Rose Award
New England Poetry Club
Affiliate of Oldest Reading Series in US
16 Cornell St, Arlington, MA 02474
Web Site: www.nepoetryclub.org
Key Personnel
Pres: Diana Der Hovanessian
Established: 1920
Given annually to poet who has done the most for poetry during previous year or in a lifetime. Chosen by board members.

Award: Medal
Presented: Longfellow Garden, Cambridge, MA, July 8

The Goodheart Prize For Fiction
Shenandoah: The Washington & Lee Review
Washington & Lee University, Mattingly House, 2 Lee Ave, Lexington, VA 24450-0303
Tel: 540-458-8765 *Fax:* 540-458-8461
Web Site: www.shenandoah.wlu.edu
Key Personnel
Man Ed: Lynn Leech *E-mail:* lleech@wlu.edu
Award made for the best story published in Shenandoah during a volume year.
Award: $1,000
Presented: Annually

Governor General's Literary Awards
Canada Council for the Arts
350 Albert St, Ottawa, ON K1P 5V8, Canada
Mailing Address: PO Box 1047, Ottawa, ON K1P 5V8, Canada
Tel: 613-566-4414 (ext 5576) *Toll Free Tel:* 800-263-5588 (ext 5576, Canada only) *Fax:* 613-566-4410
Web Site: www.canadacouncil.ca
Key Personnel
Prog Officer, Writing & Publishing Section: Joanne Larocque-Poirier *Tel:* 613-566-4414 ext 5576 *E-mail:* joanne.larocque-poirier@canadacouncil.ca
Established: 1936
Given annually to the best English-language & French-language work in each of the seven categories of fiction, nonfiction, poetry, drama, translation, children's literature (text) & children's literature (illustrations). Books must be first-edition trade books that have been written, translated or illustrated by Canadian citizens or permanent residents of Canada & published in Canada or abroad during the previous year. In the case of translation, the original work must also be a Canadian-authored title. Books must be submitted by publishers & accompanied by a Publisher's Submission Form, which is available from the Writing & Publishing Section. A sheet describing guidelines for publishers is also available. Separate awards for books published in English & French. For books published between Sept 1, 2002 & Sept 30, 2003.
Award: $15,000 each & leather bound copy of the winning book
Closing Date: Aug 7, 2005
Presented: Awards ceremony at Rideau Hall in Ottawa, List of finalists announced in mid-Oct before the announcement of the winners a few weeks later

Grants for Artist Projects
Artist Trust
1835 12 Ave, Seattle, WA 98122
Tel: 206-467-8734 *Fax:* 206-467-9633
E-mail: info@artisttrust.org
Web Site: www.artisttrust.org
Key Personnel
Exec Dir: Barbara Courtney
Dir, Grant Progs: Fionn Meade
Established: 1988
Project grant open to Washington State artists. Applications for the GAP will be available in winter. GAPs will be awarded in late spring in all artistic disciplines.
Award: Up to $1,400
Presented: Last Friday in Feb

The Annual Great American Tennis Writing Awards
Tennis Week
15 Elm Place, Rye, NY 10580
Tel: 914-967-4890 *Fax:* 914-967-8178
E-mail: tennisweek@tennisweek.com
Web Site: www.tennisweek.com

Key Personnel
Publr: Eugene L Scott
Man Ed: Andre Christopher
Tennis journalism.
Closing Date: No closing date, stories accepted
all year

The Green Rose Prize in Poetry
New Issues Poetry & Prose
Western Michigan University, Dept of English,
1903 W Michigan Ave, Kalamazoo, MI 49008-
5331
Tel: 269-387-8185 *Fax:* 269-387-2562
Web Site: www.wmich.edu/newissues/
greenroseprize.html
Key Personnel
Ed: Herbert Scott *E-mail:* herbert.scott@wmich.
edu
Poets writing in English who have published one
or more full-length collections of poetry. A $20
reading fee must accompany each ms; do not
bind ms. Include a brief bio & relevant publication information, cover page with name,
address, phone number, e-mail address & title
of ms; include table of contents; enclose SASE.
Other Sponsor(s): Western Michigan University
Award: $2,000, book publication
Closing Date: Sept 30

The Greensboro Review Literary Award in Fiction & Poetry
University North Carolina at Greensboro, English
Dept, McIver Bldg, Rm 134, Greensboro, NC
27402-6170
Tel: 336-334-5459
Web Site: www.uncg.edu/eng/mfa
Key Personnel
Ed: Jim Clark *E-mail:* jlclark@uncg.edu
Man Ed: Terry Kennedy *E-mail:* tlkenned@uncg.
edu
Prodn Ed: Brandon Rauch *E-mail:* abrauch@
uncg.edu
Established: 1984
Short story - poetry.
Award: $500
Closing Date: Sept 15

Guideposts Young Writers Contest
Guideposts Book & Inspirational Media Division
16 E 34 St, New York, NY 10016
Tel: 212-251-8100 *Toll Free Tel:* 800-932-2145
Fax: 212-684-0679
Web Site: www.guidepostsbooks.com
Key Personnel
Man Ed: Rick Hamlin
Contributing Ed & Contest Coord: Kathryn
Slattery *Tel:* 212-251-8106 (Thurs only)
E-mail: kslattery@guideposts.org
Youth writing, open to high school juniors & se-
niors. Winners notified by phone, confirmed by
letter, recognized in June.
Award: $10,000 (1st prize), $8,000 (2nd prize),
$6,000 (3rd prize), $4,000 (4th prize), $3,000
(5th prize), $1,000 (6th-10th prize), $250
(11th-20th), gift certificate for school supplies
Closing Date: Nov 24
Presented: June

Hackmatack Children's Choice Award
Nova Scotia Provincial Library
c/o Nova Scotia Provincial Library, 3770 Kempt
Rd, Halifax, NS B3K 4X8, Canada
Tel: 902-424-3774 *Fax:* 902-424-0633
E-mail: hackmatack@hackmatack.ca
Web Site: www.hackmatack.ca
Key Personnel
Proj Coord: Norene Smiley
Established: 1999
Atlantic Canadian Children's Choice Award for
grades 4 to 6. Three categories: English fiction,
English nonfiction & French.
Award: Plaques

Closing Date: Dec 31 annually
Presented: Award ceremony, Spring annually

Hackney Literary Awards
Writing Today
Birmingham-Southern College, Box 549003,
Birmingham, AL 35254
Tel: 205-226-4921 *Toll Free Tel:* 800-523-5793
Fax: 205-226-3072
E-mail: dcwilson@bsc.edu
Web Site: www.bsc.edu
Key Personnel
Dir, Spec Events: Annie Green
Established: 1968
Short story, poetry & novel awards.
Award: Cash $5,000 total for short story &
poetry-1st, 2nd, 3rd place natl & state; $5,000
(novel - 1st prize only). Entry fee: novel $25,
short story & poetry $10
Closing Date: Annually Dec 30 for short story
& poetry entries; Annually Sept 30 for novel
entries
Presented: Birmingham-Southern College, Birm-
ingham, AL

Sarah Josepha Hale Award
Trustees of the Richards Library
58 N Main, Newport, NH 03773
Tel: 603-863-3430 *Fax:* 603-863-3022
E-mail: rfl@newport.lib.nh.us
Web Site: www.newport.lib.nh.us
Key Personnel
Admin: Andrea Thorpe
Established: 1956
A distinguished literary figure in some way as-
sociated with New England. Nominations or
applications are not accepted.
Award: Bronze medal & $500
Presented: Newport, NH

Handy Andy Prize
The Poetry Society of Virginia
100 N Berwick, Williamsburg, VA 23188
Web Site: www.poetrysocietyofvirginia.org
Key Personnel
Contest Chair: Norma Richardson
For a limerick. See web site for rules.
Award: $25; $15; $10
Closing Date: Jan 19
Presented: Annual contest awards luncheon, TBA,
April

Jason A Hannah Medal
Royal Society of Canada
283 Sparks St, Ottawa, ON K1R 7X9, Canada
Tel: 613-991-6990 *Fax:* 613-991-6996
E-mail: adminrsc@rsc.ca
Web Site: www.rsc.ca
Key Personnel
Awards Coord: Genevieve Gouin
Established: 1976
Awarded for imperative Canadian publications in
the history of medicine.
Other Sponsor(s): Hannah Institute
Award: $1,500, Bronze medal
Closing Date: March 1
Presented: Ottawa

Hans Christian Andersen Prize
United States Board on Books for Young People
(USBBY)
Division of International Board on Books for
Young People
800 Barksdale Rd, Newark, DE 19714
Mailing Address: PO Box 8139, Newark, DE
19714
Tel: 302-731-1600 (ext 297)
E-mail: usbby@reading.org
Web Site: www.usbby.org
Established: 1956

Two medals are awarded biennially, one to an author & one to an illustrator, for their complete
oeuvre. An Honor List is established with the
books chosen by the National Sections of the
International Board on Books for Young People
(IBBY). Each section chooses three books from
among those published in the country during
the preceding biennium: for writing, illustrating
& translating.
Award: Medals & honor list
Presented: IBBY Congress, Biennially in even-
numbered years

Harian Creative Awards
Harian Creative Books
Division of Harian Creative Enterprises
Affiliate of Harian Creative Associates
47 Hyde Blvd, Ballston Spa, NY 12020-1607
Tel: 518-885-6699; 518-885-7397
Key Personnel
CEO & Publr: Harry Barba
Mktg Consultant: Mary Peyton
Established: 1967
Awards in the areas of fiction, nonfiction, poetry,
art, musical composition, sculpture, photogra-
phy & excellence in performances & services.
Other Sponsor(s): Harian Creative Associates;
The Workshop Under the Sky Conference
Award: $500-$200 (1st-4th prize), $100 merit
awards, $100 equivalency awards in copies of
awards anthology to semifinalists
Closing Date: Open

Clarence Haring Prize
American Historical Association
400 "A" St SE, Washington, DC 20003
Tel: 202-544-2422 *Fax:* 202-544-8307
E-mail: info@historians.org
Web Site: www.historians.org
Key Personnel
Prize Admin: Debbie Ann Doyle *Tel:* 202-544-
2422 ext 104 *E-mail:* ddoyle@historians.org
For work by a Latin American in Latin American
history during the preceding five years. Offered
quinquennially. No application form, applicants
must simply mail a copy of their book to each
of the prize committee members who will be
posted on our web site as the prize deadline
approaches. Books published between May 1,
2001 & April 30, 2006 will be considered. All
updated info on web site.
Award: Cash prize
Closing Date: May 15, 2006
Presented: 2007

Aurand Harris Memorial Playwriting Award
The New England Theatre Conference Inc
Subsidiary of New England Theatre Conference
PMB 502, 198 Tremont St, Boston, MA 02116-
4750
Tel: 617-851-8535
E-mail: mail@netconline.org
Web Site: www.netconline.org
Established: 1997
Competition for new plays for young audiences.
Scripts must be unpublished & unproduced.
For guidelines, send SASE. Open to NETC
members & New England residents. Play-
wrights outside of New England may submit
by joining NETC.
Award: $1,000 (1st prize), $500 (2nd prize)
Closing Date: Annually, May 1
Presented: NETC Annual Convention, Nov

Julie Harris Playwright Award Competition
The Beverly Hills Theatre Guild
PO Box 39729, Los Angeles, CA 90039-0729
Key Personnel
Pres: Janet Salter
Competition Coord: Dick Dotterer
Established: 1978

Playwright; entries accepted Aug 1-Nov 1, with
application & guidelines available upon request
with SASE; announcement June 30.
Award: $3,500, $2,500 & $1,500
Closing Date: Nov 1
Presented: Los Angeles, CA, June 30

Haskins Medal Award
Medieval Academy of America
104 Mount Auburn St, 5th fl, Cambridge, MA
02138
Tel: 617-491-1622
E-mail: speculum@medievalacademy.org
Web Site: www.medievalacademy.org
Key Personnel
Exec Dir & Ed, Speculum: Richard K Emmerson
Established: 1940
For a book of outstanding importance in the me-
dieval field published no earlier than six years
prior to award date.
Award: Gold medal
Closing Date: Oct 15
Presented: Annually in Spring

Hawaii Award for Literature
Hawaii State Foundation on Culture & the Arts
Division of Dept of Accounting & General Ser-
vices/State of Hawaii
250 S Hotel St, 2nd fl, Honolulu, HI 96813
Tel: 808-586-0769 *Fax:* 808-586-0308
E-mail: sfca@sfca.state.hi.us
Web Site: www.hawaii.gov/sfca
Key Personnel
Admin Servs Asst: Fay Ann Chun *E-mail:* fay.
ann.chun@hawaii.gov
Established: 1974
Nominations are made thru membership of
Hawaii Literary Arts Council.
Other Sponsor(s): Hawaii Literary Arts Council
Award: Certificate/Cash
Closing Date: Annually, Nov
Presented: State Capitol

**R R Hawkins & Professional/Scholarly
Publishing Division Annual Awards Program**
Association of American Publishers (AAP)
Affiliate of Professional & Scholarly Publishing
Div
71 Fifth Ave, 2nd fl, New York, NY 10003-3004
Tel: 212-255-0200 *Fax:* 212-255-7007
Web Site: www.publishers.org; www.pspcentral.
org
Key Personnel
VP, Prof Scholarly Publg: Barbara J Meredith
Tel: 212-255-0200 ext 223 *E-mail:* bmeredith@
publishers.org
Established: 1976
Open to AAP/PSP members only.
Award: Plaque
Closing Date: Nov
Presented: Washington, DC, Feb

**Headlands Center for the Arts Residency for
CA, NC, OH & NJ Writers**
North Carolina Arts Council/Ohio Arts Council
944 Fort Barry, Sausalito, CA 94965
Tel: 415-331-2787 *Fax:* 415-331-3857
Web Site: www.headlands.org
Key Personnel
Residency Mgr: Holly Blake *E-mail:* hblake@
headlands.org
Prog Dir: Linda Samuels
A three-month residency at Headlands is granted
each year to writers of the Artist in Residency
Program. Writers who have lived in NC for at
least one year prior to the application deadline are eligible. Ohio applicants must have
received individual data, OAC Fellowship in
the last five years; there are no length of residency requirements for CA or NJ writers. Call
or write the HCA for the deadline & other information.

Other Sponsor(s): California Arts Council; Geral-
dine R Dodge Foundation
Award: Two/three-month stay, $500/mo stipend,
round-trip travel paid; 5 nights/wk
Closing Date: June 1
Presented: 2005 residency season

Drue Heinz Literature Prize
University of Pittsburgh Press
3400 Forbes Ave, Pittsburgh, PA 15260
Tel: 412-383-2456 *Fax:* 412-383-2466
Web Site: www.pitt.edu/~press
Established: 1980
For a collection of short fiction 150-300 pages
in length. Open to all writers who have pub-
lished a book-length collection of short fiction
or who have had three short stories or novellas
published in commercial magazines or literary
journals of national distribution. Before submit-
ting, send a SASE for complete rules.
Other Sponsor(s): Drue Heinz & The Drue Heinz
Trust
Award: $15,000 & publication by the University
of Pittsburgh Press
Closing Date: Mss must be postmarked between
May 1 & June 30
Presented: Pittsburgh, PA, Nov

**Ernest Hemingway Foundation/PEN Award for
First Fiction**
Pen American Center
Unit of PEN New England
PO Box 400725, North Cambridge, MA 02140
Tel: 617-499-9550 *Fax:* 617-353-7134
E-mail: hemingway@pen-ne.org
Web Site: www.pen-ne.org
Key Personnel
Coord: Mary Walsh
Established: 1976
For the best first book of fiction by an American
writer published during the calendar year.
Award: $7,500 & residence at the Ucross Founda-
tion
Closing Date: Dec 15
Presented: JFK Library, Boston, MA, April

Cecil Hemley Memorial Award
Poetry Society of America (PSA)
15 Gramercy Park, New York, NY 10003
Tel: 212-254-9628 *Fax:* 212-673-2352
Web Site: www.poetrysociety.org
Key Personnel
Exec Dir: Alice Quinn
Established: 1969
For an unpublished lyric poem on a philosophical
theme, not to exceed 100 lines. Open to Soci-
ety members only. Send No 10 SASE for more
information, or visit www.poetrysociety.org.
Opening date Oct 1.
Award: $500
Closing Date: Dec 22
Presented: Annually in April

Frances Henne YALSA/VOYA Research Grant
Young Adult Library Services Association
(YALSA)
Unit of American Library Association
50 E Huron St, Chicago, IL 60611
Toll Free Tel: 800-545-2433 (ext 4391) *Fax:* 312-
664-7459
E-mail: yalsa@ala.org
Web Site: www.ala.org/yalsa/printz
Key Personnel
Prog Officer: Nichole Gilbert *E-mail:* ngilbert@
ala.org
To provide seed money to an individual, insti-
tution or group for a project to encourage re-
search in library service to young adults.
Award: $500
Closing Date: Dec 1
Presented: ALA Midwinter Mtg, Jan

Brodie Herndon Memorial
The Poetry Society of Virginia
100 N Berwick, Williamsburg, VA 23188
Tel: 757-258-5582
Web Site: www.poetrysocietyofvirginia.org
Key Personnel
Contest Chair: Norma Richardson; Norma
Richardson
Poems in any form about the sea; 48 line limit.
To receive rules, see web site.
Award: $50, $30, honorable mention
Closing Date: Annually Jan 19
Presented: Annual PSV awards luncheon, TBA

Carl Hertzog Book Design Award
Friends of the University Library
Subsidiary of University of Texas at El Paso
University of Texas at El Paso, University Li-
brary, El Paso, TX 79968-0582
Tel: 915-747-5683 *Fax:* 915-747-5345
E-mail: llimas@libr.utep.edu
Web Site: libraryweb.utep.edu
Key Personnel
Dir: Dr Patricia A Phillips *Tel:* 915-747-6710
E-mail: pphillip@libr.utep.edu
Award for excellence in book design.
Award: $1,000, bronze medallion, certificate
Closing Date: Oct 1, odd-numbered years. Next
contest 2005
Presented: University of Texas, El Paso, February
2006

Highlights for Children Fiction Contest
Highlights for Children Inc
803 Church St, Honesdale, PA 18431
Tel: 570-253-1080 *Fax:* 570-251-7847
E-mail: eds@highlights-corp.com
Web Site: www.highlights.com
Key Personnel
Sr Ed: Marileta Robinson *E-mail:* msrobinson@
highlights-corp.com
Established: 1980
Fiction for children, subject varies annually. Send
No 10 SASE for guidelines & information;
2005 subject: funny stories that have fewer
than 500 words. Indicate word count in up-
per right-hand corner on the first page of mss.
No crime, violence or derogatory humor.
Award: $1,000 each for 3 top entries
Closing Date: Must be postmarked between Jan 1
& Feb 28
Presented: Award mailed in June

Sidney Hillman Foundation Awards
The Sidney Hillman Foundation
275 Seventh Ave, New York, NY 10001
Tel: 212-265-7000 *Fax:* 212-582-3175
Web Site: www.hillmanfoundation.org
Established: 1950
For published nonfiction on race relations, civil
liberties, trade union development, world un-
derstanding, economic security & related is-
sues. Other awards are given for journalism,
radio, magazines & TV. May be submitted by
author, publisher or agent.
Award: $2,000
Closing Date: Jan 31
Presented: New York, NY, Annually in May

Bess Hokin Prize
Poetry Magazine
1030 N Clark St, Suite 420, Chicago, IL 60610
Tel: 312-787-7070 *Fax:* 312-787-6650
E-mail: poetry@poetrymagazine.org
Web Site: www.poetrymagazine.org
Key Personnel
Busn Mgr: Helen Klaviter *E-mail:* hklaviter@
poetrymagazine.org
Established: 1948
For poetry published in the preceding two vol-
umes of Poetry. No application necessary.

Award: $500
Presented: Annually in Dec

Amelia Frances Howard-Gibbon Illustrator's Award
Canadian Association of Children's Librarians, Canadian Library Association
328 Frank St, Ottawa, ON K2P 0X8, Canada
Tel: 613-232-9625 *Fax:* 613-563-9895
Web Site: www.cla.ca/
Key Personnel
Memb Servs Coord: Brenda Shields *Tel:* 613-232-9625 ext 318 *E-mail:* bshields@cla.ca
Established: 1971
For outstanding illustrations of children's books published in Canada. Illustrator must be a citizen or resident of Canada.
Other Sponsor(s): National Book Service
Award: Leather-bound copy of winning book with award seal gold embossed on cover
Closing Date: Dec 31
Presented: CLA Conference, annually

The J Howard & Barbara M J Wood Prize
Poetry Magazine
1030 N Clark St, Suite 420, Chicago, IL 60610
Tel: 312-787-7070 *Fax:* 312-787-6650
E-mail: poetry@poetrymagazine.org
Web Site: www.poetrymagazine.org
Key Personnel
Busn Mgr: Helen Klaviter *E-mail:* hklaviter@poetrymagazine.org
Established: 1994
For poetry published in the preceding two volumes of *Poetry*. No application necessary.
Award: $5,000
Presented: Annually in Dec

HTC One-Act Playwriting Competition
Henrico Recreation & Parks
PO Box 27032, Richmond, VA 23273-7032
Tel: 804-501-5138 *Fax:* 804-501-5284
Key Personnel
Cultural Arts Coord: Amy Perdue
E-mail: per22@co.henrico.va.us
Established: 1985
One act playwriting.
Award: $300 & possible production (1st prize), $200 & possible production (2nd & 3rd prize)
Closing Date: July 1
Presented: Feb

L Ron Hubbard's Writers of the Future Contest
PO Box 1630, Los Angeles, CA 90078
Tel: 323-466-3310 *Fax:* 323-466-6474
Web Site: www.writersofthefuture.com
Key Personnel
Coordinating Judge: K D Wentworth
Contest Admin: Rachel Deuk *E-mail:* contests@authorservicesinc.com
Established: 1984
Short stories & novelettes (under 17,000 words) of science fiction & fantasy for new & amateur writers. No entry fee required, entrants retain all publication rights.
Other Sponsor(s): Author Services Inc
Award: Quarterly: $1,000 (1st place), $750 (2nd place), $500 (3rd place), $4,000 (yearly grand prize winner)
Closing Date: Quarters: Dec 31, March 31, June 30, Sept 30
Presented: Hollywood, CA

The Hurston/Wright Award for College Writers
The Zora Neal Hurston/Richard Wright Foundation
6525 Bellcrest Rd, Suite 531, Hyattsville, MD 20782
Tel: 301-683-2134 *Fax:* 301-277-1262

E-mail: info@hurston-wright.org
Web Site: www.hurston-wright.org
Key Personnel
CEO & Pres: Marita Golden
Exec Dir & CFO: Clyde McElvene
Established: 1990
Literary award presented to African American college fiction writers.
Award: $1,000 & story published in literary journal (1st prize), $500 (awarded to 2 runners-up)
Presented: Oct 1

The Hurston/Wright Legacy Award
The Zora Neal Hurston/Richard Wright Foundation
6525 Bellcrest Rd, Suite 531, Hyattsville, MD 20782
Tel: 301-683-2134 *Fax:* 301-277-1262
E-mail: info@hurston-wright.org
Web Site: www.hurston-wright.org
Key Personnel
CEO & Pres: Marita Golden
Exec Dir & CFO: Clyde McElvene
Established: 2000
Annual national literary award for debut fiction, fiction & nonfiction for published black writers.
Other Sponsor(s): Borders Books
Award: $10,000 for winners in 3 categories; $5,000 for 6 runners-up (2 in each category)

IACP Cookbook Awards
International Association of Culinary Professionals (IACP)
304 W Liberty St, Suite 201, Louisville, KY 40202-3068
Tel: 502-581-9786 *Fax:* 502-589-3602
E-mail: iacp@hqtrs.com
Web Site: www.iacp.com
Key Personnel
Dir, Commums: Jennifer A Montgomery
Established: 1985
Open to any food or beverage book published in the English language. Allows publishers to enter books in the category of their choice. Through a strict, two-tier system of judging & balloting, the entries are narrowed to three nominees in each category.
Closing Date: Dec
Presented: Annual Conference, location varies, Varies every year, usually held in April

Idaho Fellowship
Idaho Commission on the Arts
Affiliate of State of Idaho
PO Box 83720, Boise, ID 83720-0008
Tel: 208-334-2119 *Toll Free Tel:* 800-ART-FUND (278-3863 within Idaho) *Fax:* 208-334-2488
Key Personnel
Lit Dir: Cort Conley *Tel:* 208-334-2119 ext 30
E-mail: cconley@ica.state.id.us
Five fellowships awarded for literary excellence.
Award: $3,500
Closing Date: Jan 29, 2007
Presented: Triennially

Idaho Writer in Residence
Idaho Commission on the Arts
PO Box 83720, Boise, ID 83720-0008
Tel: 208-334-2119 *Toll Free Tel:* 800-ART-FUND (278-3863 within Idaho) *Fax:* 208-334-2488
Key Personnel
Lit Dir: Cort Conley *Tel:* 208-334-2119 ext 30
E-mail: cconley@ica.state.id.us
Recipient tours state & does readings (4 sites yearly). Open only to residents of Idaho; must have resided in Idaho at least one year. Award for artistic excellence, three year appointment.
Award: $8,000 ($2,700 per year over three-year period)
Closing Date: Jan 29, 2007
Presented: Triennial

Illinois Arts Council Artists Fellowships
Illinois Arts Council
James R Thompson Ctr, 100 W Randolph, Suite 10-500, Chicago, IL 60601
Tel: 312-814-6750 *Toll Free Tel:* 800-237-6994 (IL only) *Fax:* 312-814-1471
E-mail: info@arts.state.il.us
Web Site: www.state.il.us/agency/iac
Key Personnel
Supervising Dir, Progs: Rose Parisi
Awards in odd years for choreography, crafts, ethnic & folk arts, media arts, prose, new performance, scriptworks. Awards in even years for interdisciplinary/computer arts, music comp, photography, poetry & visual arts. Will be given to artists who have lived in Illinois at least one year prior to the application deadline, degree credit students may not apply.
Award: $7,000, finalists awards $700
Closing Date: Sept 1
Presented: Jan

John Phillip Immroth Memorial Award for Intellectual Freedom
Intellectual Freedom Round Table
Unit of American Library Association
50 E Huron St, Chicago, IL 60611
Tel: 312-280-4223; 312-280-4220
Toll Free Tel: 800-545-2433 *Fax:* 312-280-4227
E-mail: oif@ala.org
Web Site: www.ala.org/ifrt
Key Personnel
Prog Coord: Nanette Perez
Established: 1976
For notable contribution to intellectual freedom.
Award: $500 & citation
Closing Date: Annually, Dec 1
Presented: ALA Annual Conference, June

The Independent Publisher Book Awards
Independent Publisher Magazine
Division of Jenkins Group Inc
400 W Front St, Suite 4-A, Traverse City, MI 49684
Tel: 231-933-0445 *Toll Free Tel:* 800-706-4636 *Fax:* 231-933-0448
Key Personnel
CEO: Jerrold R Jenkins
Pres: James Kalajian *Tel:* 800-706-4636 ext 1006
E-mail: jjk@bookpublishing.com
Man Ed: Jim Barnes *E-mail:* jimb@bookpublishing.com
Recognizes the works of independent publishers in 55 categories, for excellence in literary merit, design & production, published during previous calendar year. Audio books are welcome.
Award: Plaques & certificates; foil seals available; winners featured in *Independent Publisher Magazine Online*
Closing Date: April 15
Presented: Book Expo America, Annually

Individual Artist Awards
Maryland State Arts Council
Affiliate of Dept of Business & Economic
175 W Ostend St, Suite E, Baltimore, MD 21230
Tel: 410-767-6555 *Fax:* 410-333-1062
Web Site: www.msac.org
Key Personnel
Exec Dir: Theresa Colvin
Solely based on excellence of previous work. Must be a Maryland resident. Applications available. Award catagories changed annually. Check with council for individual availability.
Award: $6,000, $3,000 & $1,000
Closing Date: July

Individual Artist Fellowships
Maine Arts Commission
Division of State of Maine
25 SHS, 193 State St, Augusta, ME 04333-0025
Tel: 207-287-2726 *Fax:* 207-287-2725

Web Site: www.mainearts.com
Key Personnel
Public Art Assoc, Contemporary Arts: Donna McNeil
Established: 1987
Awarded annually to visually performing & literary artists.
Award: $13,000
Closing Date: Annually, June 1 - check web site
Presented: Fall

Individual Artists Fellowships

Nebraska Arts Council
3838 Davenport St, Omaha, NE 68131-2329
Tel: 402-595-2122 *Fax:* 402-595-2334
Web Site: www.nebraskaartscouncil.org
Key Personnel
Progs Mgr: Lisa Tubach *E-mail:* ltubach@nebraskaartscouncil.org
Established: 1991
Fellowship for Nebraska residents only; operates on a 3-yr cycle rotating with visual & performing arts.
Award: $1,000-$5,000
Closing Date: Nov 15, 2005

Individual Artist's Fellowships in Literature

South Carolina Arts Commission (SCAC)
Division of State of South Carolina
1800 Gervais St, Columbia, SC 29201
Tel: 803-734-8696 *Fax:* 803-734-8526
Web Site: www.southcarolinaarts.org
Key Personnel
Dir, Literary Arts: Sara June Goldstein
  E-mail: goldstsa@arts.state.sc.us
Non-matching funds for South Carolina residents only. Two fellowships, one in poetry & one in prose.
Award: $2,000

Innis-Gerin Medal

Royal Society of Canada
283 Sparks St, Ottawa, ON K1R 7X9, Canada
Tel: 613-991-6990 *Fax:* 613-991-6996
E-mail: adminrsc@rsc.ca
Web Site: www.rsc.ca
Key Personnel
Awards Coord: Genevieve Gouin
Established: 1966
Awarded for a distinguished & sustained contribution to literature in social science, human geography & social psychology.
Award: Bronze medal
Closing Date: Dec 1
Presented: Ottawa, alternate years, Nov 2005

Institute of Puerto Rican Culture

PO Box 9024184, San Juan, PR 00902-4184
Tel: 787-724-0700 *Fax:* 787-724-8393
E-mail: www@icp.gobierno.pr
Web Site: www.icp.gobierno.pr
Key Personnel
Dir: Teresa Tio
Grant awarded to individual artists.
Award: Cash
Closing Date: April

International Cook Book & Culinary Arts Awards

Cordon d'Or - Gold Ribbon Cuisine
7500 Sunshine Skyway Lane, Unit T8, St Petersburg, FL 33711
Mailing Address: PO Box 40660, St Petersburg, FL 33743
Tel: 727-347-2437
E-mail: cordondor@aol.com
Web Site: www.cordondorcuisine.com; www.goldribboncookery.com
Key Personnel
CEO: Noreen Kinney *E-mail:* nmekinney@aol.com

Established: 2003
Maximum 2 authors per book; the food stylist & photographer of the Illustrated Cookbook receive awards also. Presented to the publisher & agent of the two books chosen. Hardback & paperbck originals published in the English language in 2004 are eligible for entry into the contest. Other contests in the culinary arena include Magazine & Article of the Year. Full information is available on the web site. Application forms can be downloaded.
Award: Trophies & plaques
Closing Date: May 31, 2005
Presented: St Petersburg, FL, Oct 2005

International Playwrights Competition

Siena College Theatre Program
Division of Siena College
Subsidiary of Creative Arts Department
515 Loudon Rd, Loudonville, NY 12211-1462
Tel: 518-783-2384 *Fax:* 518-783-2381
Web Site: www.siena.edu/theatre
Key Personnel
Dir, Theatre Prog: Gary Maciag *E-mail:* maciag@siena.edu
Established: 1986
Playwrights.
Award: $2,000 (honorarium), $2,000 (expenses for 6-week residency), full production of winning play; open date Feb 1
Closing Date: Postmark between Feb 1 & June 30 even numbered years

International Reading Association Children's Book Award

International Reading Association
800 Barksdale Rd, Newark, DE 19714
Tel: 302-731-1600 *Fax:* 302-731-1057
Web Site: www.reading.org
Key Personnel
Sr Secy: Mary Cash
Public Info Assoc: Beth Cady *Tel:* 302-731-1600 ext 293 *E-mail:* pubinfo@reading.org
Established: 1975
Six book awards will be offered for an author's first or second published children's book. Awards will be given for fiction & nonfiction in 3 categories. This award is intended for newly published authors who show unusual promise in the children's book field. Books from any country & in any language copyrighted during the 2004 calendar year will be considered. Entries in a language other than English must include a one-page abstract in English & a translation into English of one chapter or similar selection that in the submitter's estimation is representative of the book. For guidelines, write to the executive office or e-mail: exec@reading.org.
Award: $500
Closing Date: Nov
Presented: Annual Convention, Spring

International Reading Association Print Media Award

International Reading Association
800 Barksdale Rd, Newark, DE 19714
Tel: 302-731-1600 *Fax:* 302-731-1057
E-mail: pubinfo@reading.org
Web Site: www.reading.org
Key Personnel
Public Info Assoc: Beth Cady *Tel:* 302-731-1600 ext 293
Established: 1965
Recognizes outstanding reporting in newspapers, magazines & wire services. Entries may include in-depth studies of reading instruction, discussion of research or ongoing coverage of reading programs in the community & must have appeared between Jan 1 & Dec 31, 2004. The contest is limited to professional journalists. Association members are invited to inform

their local newspapers of the contest & to encourage the authors of worthwhile articles to enter. For applications, write to Public Information Office. E-mail: pubinfo@reading.org.
Award: Certificate
Closing Date: Jan 15
Presented: Annual Convention, spring

InterTech Technology Award

PIA/GATF (Graphic Arts Technical Foundation)
200 Deer Run Rd, Sewickley, PA 15143-2600
Tel: 412-741-6860 *Toll Free Tel:* 800-910-4283
  Fax: 412-741-2311
E-mail: info@gain.net
Web Site: www.gain.net
Key Personnel
Pres: Michael Makin
Mktg Mgr: Lisa Erdner
Established: 1978
Honors innovative technology excellence for the graphic communications industries. The criteria for nomination stresses that the technology be recently developed, proved in industrial application, but not yet in widespread use.
Award: Lucite ™ Star
Closing Date: Annually, May 28
Presented: PIA/GATF Administrative Meeting, Annually, Fall

IODE Book Award

IODE Municipal Chapter of Toronto
Division of National Iode & Provincial Iode
40 St Clair Ave E, Suite 205, Toronto, ON M4T 1M9, Canada
Tel: 416-925-5078 *Fax:* 416-925-5127
Key Personnel
Pres: Karen Barker
Treas: Geraldine Turner
Established: 1974
Children's book (Toronto area author or illustrator).
Award: $1,000 & certificate
Closing Date: Annually in Nov
Presented: Annually, April 1

The Iowa Short Fiction Award

Writers' Workshop, The University of Iowa
102 Dey House, 507 N Clinton St, Iowa City, IA 52242
Tel: 319-335-0416 *Fax:* 319-335-0420
Key Personnel
Contact: Connie Brothers; Frank Conroy
Established: 1970
For a previously unpublished collection of short stories of at least 150 typewritten pages by a writer who has not previously published a volume of prose fiction. Stories previously published in periodicals are eligible for inclusion. Include SASE. Write for further information.
Other Sponsor(s): University of Iowa Press
Award: Publication by University of Iowa Press
Closing Date: Aug 1-Sept 30

Island Literary Awards

Prince Edward Island Council of the Arts
115 Richmond St, Charlottetown, PE C1A 1H7, Canada
Tel: 902-368-4410 *Fax:* 902-368-4418
E-mail: peiarts@peiartscouncil.com
Web Site: www.peiartscouncil.com
Key Personnel
Exec Dir: Darrin White
Contests for poetry, short adult fiction, children's literature, feature article & creative writing for young people; must be resident of Prince Edward Island.
Closing Date: Call or e-mail
Presented: Call or e-mail

Joseph Henry Jackson Literary Award

The San Francisco Foundation
225 Bush St, Suite 500, San Francisco, CA 94104-4224

Tel: 415-733-8500 *Fax:* 415-477-2783
Web Site: www.sff.org
Key Personnel
Arts & Culture Program Officer: John Killacky
  E-mail: jrk@sff.org
Established: 1957
For the author of a work-in-progress, a novel,
  short story, nonfiction or poetry. Applicants
  must have been residents of northern California
  or Nevada for three consecutive years immedi-
  ately prior to the closing date & must be 20-35
  years old.
Award: $2,000 & certificate
Closing Date: Jan
Presented: Annually

**J Franklin Jameson Fellowship in American
  History**
American Historical Association
400 "A" St SE, Washington, DC 20003
Tel: 202-544-2422 *Fax:* 202-544-8307
E-mail: info@historians.org
Web Site: www.historians.org
Key Personnel
Prize Admin: Debbie Ann Doyle *Tel:* 202-544-
  2422 ext 104 *E-mail:* ddoyle@historians.org
To support significant scholarly research for one
  semester in the collections of the Library of
  Congress by new historians. At the time of
  application, applicants must hold the PhD degree or equivalent; must have received this degree within the last 5 years & must not have
  published or had accepted for publication a
  book-length historical work. The fellowship
  will not be awarded to permit completion of a
  doctoral dissertation. The applicant's project in
  American history must be one for which the
  general & special collections of the Library of
  Congress offer unique research support. Applicants should include a statement substantiating
  this relationship. Residency for at least three
  months at Library of Congress is required. Application instructions & all updated info available on web site.
Award: Cash prize

Jamestown Prize
Omohundro Institute of Early American History
  & Culture
109 Cary St, Williamsburg, VA 23185
Mailing Address: PO Box 8781, Williamsburg,
  VA 23187-8781 SAN: 201-5161
Tel: 757-221-1114 *Fax:* 757-221-1047
E-mail: ieahc1@wm.edu
Web Site: www.wm.edu/oieahc
Key Personnel
Dir: Ronald Hoffman
Asst to Dir: Sally D Mason *Tel:* 757-221-1115
  E-mail: sdmaso@wm.edu
Sec to Dir: Beverly Smith
For an exceptional book length scholarly ms per-
  taining to the early history & culture of Anglo-
  America or to related developments in the
  British Isles, other North American colonial
  empires (& their home countries), West Africa
  or the Caribbean - in short, any subject encom-
  passing the Atlantic World circa 1450-1815
  that bears upon the history & culture of what
  would & did become the United States.
Other Sponsor(s): Jamestown-Yorktown Founda-
  tion; University of North Carolina Press
Award: $3,000 & publication
Closing Date: None
Presented: biennially

Jane Chambers Playwriting Award
Women & Theatre Program of Association for
  Theatre in Higher Education
Division of Theatre, Meadows School of the Arts
Southern Methodist University, PO Box 750356,
  Dallas, TX 75275-0356
Tel: 214-768-2937 *Fax:* 214-768-1136

Web Site: www.smu.edu
Key Personnel
Coord: Gretchen E Smith *E-mail:* gesmith@mail.
  smu.edu
Established: 1984
Award for play or performance text by a woman
  which reflects a feminist perspective & contains a majority of opportunities for women
  performers. Scripts may be produced or unproduced; encourage experimentation with dramatic form; send SASE for application & full
  information; two copies of script required &
  not returned.
Award: $250 for students & 1 yr membership in
  Women & Theatre/$1,000 for Jane Chambers
  Award winner
Closing Date: Feb 15

**Japan-US Friendship Commission Translation
  Prize**
Japan-US Friendship Commission
Affiliate of The Donald Keene Center of Japanese
  Culture
Columbia University, 507 Kent Hall, MC3920,
  New York, NY 10027
Tel: 212-854-5036 *Fax:* 212-854-4019
E-mail: donald-keene-center@columbia.edu
Web Site: www.columbia.edu/cu/ealac/dkc/
  translation
Key Personnel
Asst Dir: Becky Le Gette
Established: 1979
Prize is given for the best translation of a modern
  work of literature or for the best classical liter-
  ary translation, or the prize is divided between
  a classical & a modern work. Translators of
  any nationality are welcome to apply. To qualify, works must be book-length translations of
  Japanese literary works: novels, collections of
  short stories, literary essays, memoirs, drama,
  or poetry. Submissions will be judged on the
  literary merit of the translation & the accuracy
  with which it reflects the spirit of the Japanese
  original. Applications are accepted from translators or their publishers. Previous winners are
  ineligible.
Award: $5,000 (either to one translator or divided
  between classical & modern)
Closing Date: Feb 1
Presented: Columbia University, Spring

Jefferson Cup Award
Virginia Library Association
Subsidiary of Children's/Young Adult Round Ta-
  ble
PO Box 8277, Norfolk, VA 23503-0277
Tel: 757-583-0041 *Fax:* 757-583-5041
Web Site: www.vla.org
Key Personnel
Exec Dir: Linda Hahne *E-mail:* lhahne@costalnet.
  com
Established: 1988
Fields of history, biography & historical fiction
  written especially for young people.
Award: 500 & engraved silver Jefferson Cup
Closing Date: June
Presented: Annual Conference of VLA

Jerome Award
Catholic Library Association
100 North St, Suite 224, Pittsfield, MA 01201-
  5109
Tel: 413-443-2252 *Fax:* 413-442-2252
E-mail: cla@cathla.org
Web Site: www.cathla.org
Key Personnel
Exec Dir: Jean R Bostley, SSJ
Established: 1992
For outstanding work in Catholic scholarship; no
  unsol mss.
Award: Plaque

Closing Date: none; in house votes
Presented: Boston, MA

Jerome Playwright-in-Residence Fellowship
The Playwrights' Center
2301 Franklin Ave E, Minneapolis, MN 55406
Tel: 612-332-7481 *Fax:* 612-332-6037
E-mail: info@pwcenter.org
Web Site: www.pwcenter.org
Key Personnel
Dir, New Play Devt: Kristen Gandrow *Tel:* 612-
  332-7481 ext 21
Established: 1976
Fellowships awarded annually to emerging play-
  wrights. Provides playwrights with funds &
  services to aid them in the development of
  their craft. One year in residence required,
  July 1 - June 30. Contact above for ap-
  plication & guidelines, or download from
  www.pwcenter.org.
Award: $9,000
Closing Date: Sept 15

Jewel Box Theatre Playwriting Competition
3700 N Walker, Oklahoma City, OK 73118-7099
Tel: 405-521-1786
Key Personnel
Prodn Dir: Charles Tweed
Original playwriting competition.
Award: $500
Closing Date: Jan 15
Presented: Banquet in Oklahoma City, April

Anson Jones MD Award
Texas Medical Association
c/o Texas Medical Association, 401 W 15 St,
  Austin, TX 78701
Tel: 512-370-1300 *Fax:* 512-370-1629
Web Site: www.texmed.org
Key Personnel
Media Rel Mgr: Brent Annear
Established: 1957
Annual award in recognition of outstanding cov-
  erage of health & medical issues to the public
  by Texas Media.
Award: $1,000 cash award & plaque for winners;
  certificate & $250 for citation of merit
Closing Date: Jan 15

Jesse H Jones Award
Texas Institute of Letters
3700 Mockingbird Lane, Dallas, TX 75205
Tel: 214-528-2655 *Fax:* 512-245-7462
Web Site: www.stedwards.edu/newc/marks/til/
  awards_and_rules.htm
Key Personnel
VP: Joe Holley
Dir: Mark Busby *Tel:* 512-245-2428
  E-mail: mb13@swt.edu
Treas: Jim Hoggard
Sec: Fran Vick *E-mail:* franvick@aol.com
For the best book of fiction by a Texan or about
  Texas.
Other Sponsor(s): Houston Endowment Inc
Award: $6,000
Closing Date: Jan 2005
Presented: March banquet

Jubilee Award for Short Stories
Canadian Authors Association (CAA)
320 S Shores Rd, Campbellford, ON K0L 1L0,
  Canada
Tel: 705-653-0323 *Toll Free Tel:* 866-216-6222
  Fax: 705-653-0593
E-mail: info@canauthors.org
Web Site: www.canauthors.org
Established: 1997
Entries must be collections of short stories by a
  Canadian author. The stories must be English-
  language literature for adults (not "young

adults"). Translations are not eligible nor are rare books published at the author's expense.
Award: $2,500 & silver medal
Closing Date: Dec 15

Juniper Prize for Poetry
University of Massachusetts Press
Juniper Prize, University of Massachusetts Press, Amherst, MA 01003
Tel: 413-545-2217 *Fax:* 413-545-1226
E-mail: info@umpress.umass.edu
Web Site: www.umass.edu/umpress
Key Personnel
Web & Promo Mgr: Alice Maldonado
  E-mail: maldonado@umpress.umass.edu
Established: 1975
Awarded annually for an original ms of poems. In alternating years, the program is open to poets either with or without previously published books.
Award: $1,500 & publication
Closing Date: Aug 1-Sept 30
Presented: April/May 2005; publication by spring 2006

Juvenile Literary Awards/Young People's Literature Awards
Friends of American Writers
680 N Lake Shore Dr-L208, Chicago, IL 60611
Tel: 312-664-5628
Key Personnel
Pres: Minnie Orfanos
Adult Literary Awards: Vivien Mortensen
Juv Awards Chmn: Karen Harrington
Established: 1960
For books written for young people from toddler through high school age & published in the current year, can only be author's 1st, 2nd or 3rd book & the author must be from the Midwest &/or the book must be about the Midwest.
Award: Two awards; $1,000 each for 1st & 2nd place
Closing Date: Dec 15
Presented: Union League Club, Chicago, IL, Annually in April

Frederick D Kagy Education Award of Excellence
PIA/GATF (Graphic Arts Technical Foundation)
200 Deer Run Rd, Sewickley, PA 15143-2600
Tel: 412-741-6860 *Toll Free Tel:* 800-910-4283
  Fax: 412-741-2311
E-mail: info@gain.net
Web Site: www.gain.net
Key Personnel
Pres: Michael Makin
Mktg Mgr: Lisa Erdner
Established: 1993
Honors a superior graphic communications program at the junior high, high school or community college level. School must be staffed by PIA/GAFT teacher member (membership cost $45).
Award: Engraved lithographic stone
Closing Date: Annually, May 31
Presented: PIA/GATF Administrative Meetings, annually in Nov

Ezra Jack Keats Memorial Fellowship
Ezra Jack Keats Foundation
University of Minnesota, 113 Andersen Library, 222 21 Ave S, Minneapolis, MN 55455
Tel: 612-624-4576 *Fax:* 612-625-5525
E-mail: clrc@tc.umn.edu
Web Site: www.ezra-jack-keats.org; special.lib.umn.edu/clrc/
Key Personnel
Curator Kerlan Collection: Karen Hoyle
Awarded to a talented writer &/or illustrator of children's books who wish to use the Kerlan

Collection to further his or her artistic development.
Award: $1,500
Closing Date: May 1

Joan Kelly Memorial Prize in Women's History
American Historical Association
400 "A" St SE, Washington, DC 20003
Tel: 202-544-2422 *Fax:* 202-544-8307
E-mail: info@historians.org
Web Site: www.historians.org
Key Personnel
Prize Admin: Debbie Ann Doyle *Tel:* 202-544-2422 ext 104 *E-mail:* ddoyle@historians.org
Established: 1984
For the book in women's history &/or feminist theory that best reflects the high intellectual & scholarly ideals exemplified by the life & work of Joan Kelly. Submissions shall be books in any chronological period, any geographical location, or in any area of feminist theory that incorporates an historical perspective. Books should demonstrate originality of research, creativity of insight, graceful stylistic presentation, analytical skills & a recognition of the important role of sex & gender in the historical process. The inter-relationship between women & the historical process should be addressed. Books published between May 1, 2004 & April 30, 2005 are eligible for the 2005 award. One copy of each entry must be received by each of the five committee members. The Association will announce the recipients of prizes & awards at its annual meeting during the first week in Jan. No application form. All updated info on web site.
Award: Cash prize
Closing Date: May 16, 2005

Robert F Kennedy Book Awards
Subsidiary of Robert F Kennedy Memorial
1367 Connecticut Ave NW, Suite 200, Washington, DC 20036-1859
Tel: 202-463-7575
E-mail: info@rfkmemorial.org
Web Site: www.rfkmemorial.org
Key Personnel
Spec Progs & Events Coord: Courtney Stamm
Established: 1980
For a book of fiction or nonfiction that most faithfully & forcefully reflects Robert Kennedy's interests & concerns. By Jan 28 publishers or authors should send four copies of books published in the previous year along with a press release. Each entry must be accompanied by an entry form & a handling fee of $40 made payable to the Robert F Kennedy Memorial.
Award: $2,500 & bust of Robert Kennedy
Closing Date: Annually, Jan 28
Presented: May

Kentucky Arts Council Fellowships in Writing
Kentucky Arts Council
Old Capitol Annex, 300 W Broadway, Frankfort, KY 40601
Tel: 502-564-3757 *Toll Free Tel:* 888-833-2787
  Fax: 502-564-2839
Web Site: www.artscouncil.ky.gov
Key Personnel
Dir, Individual Artist Progs: Heather Lyons
  Tel: 888-833-2787 ext 4827 *E-mail:* heather.lyons@mail.state.ky.us
Established: 1983
To assist in development of art work; Kentucky residents only.
Award: $7,500 cash
Closing Date: Sept 15 (biennially in even-numbered years)

Donald Keyhoe Journalism Award
Fund for UFO Research
PO Box 277, Mount Rainier, MD 20712
Tel: 703-684-6032 *Fax:* 703-684-6032
Web Site: www.fufor.com
Key Personnel
Chmn: Don Berliner
Secy: Rob Swiatek
Established: 1989
Journalism award.
Award: $1,000 (1st & 2nd prize)
Closing Date: Feb 15 of each year

Aga Khan Prize for Fiction
The Paris Review Foundation
541 E 72 St, New York, NY 10021
Tel: 212-861-0016 *Fax:* 212-861-4504
Web Site: www.theparisreview.org
Key Personnel
Exec Ed: Brigid Hughes
Prize awarded to best short fiction published in the magazine the previous year. No application necessary.
Award: $1,000
Presented: Annually, Winter

Coretta Scott King Awards
Ethnic & Multicultural Information Exchange Round Table
Unit of American Library Association
ALA Office for Literacy & Outreach Services, 50 E Huron St, Chicago, IL 60611
Tel: 312-280-4295; 312-280-4294 *Fax:* 312-280-3256
E-mail: olos@ala.org
Web Site: www.ala.org/olos
Key Personnel
Chpn, Coretta Scott King Book Award Committee: Fran Ware
Staff Liaison: Satia Orange
Established: 1970
To encourage the artistic expressions of the African-American experiences via literature & the graphic arts. Award to author & illustrator.
Other Sponsor(s): Johnson Publications, Encyclopedia Britannica World Book
Award: Award plaque, $1,000 & set of encyclopedias to each awardee
Closing Date: Annually, Dec 1
Presented: Coretta Scott King Awards Breakfast at the ALA Annual Conference, June

The Kiriyama Pacific Rim Book Prize
The Kiriyama Pacific Rim Institute
650 Delancy St, Suite 101, San Francisco, CA 94107-2082
Tel: 415-777-1628 *Fax:* 415-777-1646
Web Site: www.kiriyamaprize.org
Key Personnel
Prize Mgr: Jeannine Cuevas *E-mail:* jeannine@kiriyamaprize.org
Established: 1996
Annual Literary Prize; Entries submitted by publishers anywhere in the world provided the books are in English, either originally or in translation & the books concern the Pacific Rim in a significant way.
Award: $30,000 US ($15,000 to author(s) of fiction & $15,000 to author(s) of nonfiction winner)
Presented: Annually in the spring

Marc A Klein Playwriting Award for Students
Case Western Reserve University
Division of Dept of Theater & Dance
Dept of Theater & Dance, Eldred Hall, 10900 Euclid Ave, Cleveland, OH 44106-7077
Tel: 216-368-4868 *Toll Free Tel:* 800-429-3681
  Fax: 216-368-5184
E-mail: ksg@case.edu
Web Site: www.case.edu/artsci/thtr

Key Personnel
Busn Mgr: Scarlett Grala
Established: 1975
Playwriting competition.
Other Sponsor(s): Dr & Mrs Harold Klein
Award: $1,000
Closing Date: Dec 1
Presented: Eldred Theater at Case Western Reserve University

Katherine Singer Kovacs Prize
Modern Language Association of America (MLA)
26 Broadway, 3rd fl, New York, NY 10004-1789
Tel: 646-576-5141 *Fax:* 646-458-0030
E-mail: awards@mla.org
Web Site: www.mla.org
Key Personnel
Coord, Book Prizes & Spec Projs: Annie Reiser
Established: 1990
For an outstanding book published in year prior to competition in English in the field of Latin American & Spanish literature & cultures. Authors need not be members of MLA.
Award: $1,000 & certificate
Closing Date: Six copies by May 1
Presented: MLA Convention, Annually, Dec 28

Michael Kraus Research Grant in History
American Historical Association
400 "A" St SE, Washington, DC 20003
Tel: 202-544-2422 *Fax:* 202-544-8307
E-mail: info@historians.org
Web Site: www.historians.org
Key Personnel
Prize Admin: Debbie Ann Doyle *Tel:* 202-544-2422 ext 104 *E-mail:* ddoyle@historians.org
Grant to recognize the most deserving proposal relating to works in progress on a research project in American colonial history, with particular reference to the intercultural aspects of American & European relations. Only members of the Association are eligible. The grants are intended to further research in progress & may be used for travel to a library or archive, for microfilms, photographs, or xeroxing, for coding & key punching. Preference will be given to those with specific research needs, such as the completion of a project or completion of a discrete segment thereof. Preference will be given to PhD candidates & junior scholars. Application forms & all updated info on web site. Applications must include application form with estimated budget, curriculum vita, statement of no more than 750 words & a one page bibliography of the most recent relevant, secondary works on the topic.
Award: Individual grants will not exceed $1,000; preference to PhD candidates & scholars
Closing Date: Feb 15, 2005

Henry Kreisel Award for Best First Book
Banff Centre
11759 Groat Rd, Edmonton, AB T5M 3K6, Canada
Tel: 780-422-8174 *Toll Free Tel:* 800-665-5354 (Alberta only) *Fax:* 780-422-2663
E-mail: mail@writersguild.ab.ca
Web Site: www.writersguild.ab.ca
Key Personnel
Exec Dir: Diane Walton
Established: 1982
Alberta Literary Award, must be resident of Alberta.
Award: $1,000 plus leather-bound copy of book
Closing Date: Dec 31
Presented: Alberta

Kumu Kahua/UHM Theatre Dept Playwriting Contest
Kumu Kahua/UHM Theatre Dept
46 Merchant St, Honolulu, HI 96813
Tel: 808-536-4222 *Fax:* 808-536-4226

E-mail: info@kumakahua.org
Web Site: www.kumukahua.org
Key Personnel
Man Dir, Kumu Kahua Theatre: Alissa Alcosiba
Artistic Dir: Harry Wong, III
Hawaii Prize: open to residents of Hawaii & non-residents; full length (50 pages or more); play must be set in Hawaii &/or deal with the Hawaii experience.
Pacific Rim Prize: open to residents of Hawaii & non-residents; full length (50 pages or more); play must be set in &/or dealing with the Pacific Islands, Pacific Rim, or the Pacific/Asian-American experience.
Resident Prize: only open to residents of Hawaii; full length (50 pages or more) or one-acts; play can be on any topic.
Award: $500 (Hawaii Prize), $400 (Pacific Rim Prize), $200 (Resident Prize)
Closing Date: Jan 2
Presented: May

Lambda Literary Awards (Lammys)
Lambda Literary Foundation
1217 11 St NW, Washington, DC 20001
Tel: 202-682-0952 *Fax:* 202-682-0955
E-mail: lbreditor@lambdalit.org
Web Site: www.lambdalit.org
Key Personnel
Publr: Jim Marks
Established: 1989
Recognizing excellence in gay & lesbian literature.
Award: Trophy
Closing Date: Dec 2004 (nominations information on the website)
Presented: New York City, June 2005

Gerald Lampert Memorial Award
League of Canadian Poets
920 Yonge St, Suite 608, Toronto, ON M4W 3C7, Canada
Tel: 416-504-1657 *Fax:* 416-504-0096
E-mail: info@poets.ca
Web Site: www.poets.ca
Key Personnel
Exec Dir: Edita Page *E-mail:* page@poets.ca
Intended to recognize the work of a Canadian writer early in his or her career. Awarded for a first book of poetry published in the preceding year.
Award: $1,000
Closing Date: Annually, Nov 1
Presented: Annually, May

Harold Morton Landon Translation Award
The Academy of American Poets Inc
588 Broadway, Suite 604, New York, NY 10012
Tel: 212-274-0343 *Fax:* 212-274-9427
E-mail: academy@poets.org
Web Site: www.poets.org
Key Personnel
Prog Dir: Ryan Murphy *Tel:* 212-274-0343 ext 17 *E-mail:* rmurphy@poets.org
Established: 1976
To an American for a published translation of poetry from any language into English. May be a book-length poem, a collection of poems or a drama translated into verse. Three copies of the book (no mss) should be submitted.
Award: $1,000
Closing Date: Dec 31
Presented: Annually in March

Larew Christian Memorial Scholarship in Library & Information Technology, see LITA/Christian Larew Memorial Scholarship in Library & Information Technology

James Laughlin Award
The Academy of American Poets Inc

588 Broadway, Suite 604, New York, NY 10012
Tel: 212-274-0343 *Fax:* 212-274-9427
E-mail: academy@poets.org
Web Site: www.poets.org
Key Personnel
Prog Dir: Ryan Murphy *Tel:* 212-274-0343 ext 17 *E-mail:* rmurphy@poets.org
Established: 1954
Given annually to support the publication of a second book of poetry in a standard edition. Mss should be submitted by publishers & must be under contract & scheduled for publication. Send four copies. A gift from the Drue Heinz Trust in honor of James Laughlin. Send SASE for entry form.
Award: $5,000 & Academy will buy & distribute copies
Closing Date: Jan 1-April 30
Presented: Annually in Aug

Lawrence Foundation Award
Prairie Schooner
University of Nebraska, 201 Andrews Hall, Lincoln, NE 68588
Mailing Address: PO Box 880334, Lincoln, NE 68588-0334
Tel: 402-472-0911
Web Site: www.unl.edu/schooner/psmain.htm
Key Personnel
Ed: Hilda Raz
Established: 1978
Annual writing prize for the best short story published in Prairie Schooner magazine; only work published in Prairie Schooner in the previous year will be considered.
Other Sponsor(s): The Lawrence Foundation of New York City
Award: $1,000
Presented: In the spring magazine, Annually

Frank Lawrence & Harriet Chappell Owsley Award
Southern Historical Association
University of Georgia, Dept of History, Athens, GA 30602-1602
Tel: 706-542-8848 *Fax:* 706-542-2455
Web Site: www.uga.edu/~sha
Key Personnel
Admin Asst: Gloria Davis *E-mail:* gsdavis@uga.edu
Established: 1985
Awarded for most distinguished book in Southern history published in even-numbered years. Awarded in odd-numbered years.
Award: Cash
Closing Date: March 1, 2005
Presented: Atlanta, GA, Nov 3, 2005

Samuel Lazerow Fellowship for Research in Collections or Technical Services in Academic & Research Libraries
Association of College & Research Libraries
Division of American Library Association
50 E Huron St, Chicago, IL 60611
Tel: 312-280-2514 *Toll Free Tel:* 800-545-2433 (ext 2514) *Fax:* 312-280-2520
Web Site: www.ala.org/acrl
Key Personnel
Prog Coord: Megan Bielefield *E-mail:* mbielefeld@ala.org
Established: 1983
Research, travel or writing on topic in collections or technical services. Sponsored by Thomson Scientific.
Award: $1,000 & plaque
Closing Date: Annually, first Fri in Dec
Presented: ALA Annual Conference

LDA Award for Excellence
LDA Publishers
42-46 209 St, Suite B-11, Bayside, NY 11361-2747

Tel: 718-224-9484 *Toll Free Tel:* 888-388-9887
  Fax: 718-224-9487
Web Site: www.lilrc.org/~ncla1/awards.html
Key Personnel
Publr: Andrew V Ippolito *E-mail:* andy.ippolito@
  verizon.net
Ed-in-Chief, Directory of Long Island Li-
  braries & Media Center: Arthur Friedman
  E-mail: friedman@sunynassau.edu
Established: 1978
Award for Excellence in Library Achievement.
Award: Plaque
Closing Date: April 1
Presented: Long Island Library Conference
  (LILC), 2nd Wed in May

Stephen Leacock Memorial Award for Humour
Stephen Leacock Association
Box 854, Orillia, ON L3V 6K8, Canada
Tel: 705-835-3218 *Fax:* 705-835-5171
E-mail: moonwood@simpatico.ca
Web Site: www.leacock.ca/awards.html
Key Personnel
Pres: Dr Richard Johnston
Chair, Award Comm: Judith Rapson
  E-mail: drapson@encode.com
Established: 1946
Humorous writing by Canadian authors. All en-
  tries must have been published in the previous
  year award given. Ten copies of each book to
  be submitted along with $75 fee, authors bio & b&w photograph to Ms
  Judith D Rapson, Chair, Award Comm, 4223
  Line 12 N, RR 2, Coldwater, ON L0K 1E0,
  Canada, e-mail: drapson@encode.com.
Award: $10,000 Toronto Dominion Financial
  Group cash award & silver medal
Closing Date: Annually, Dec 31
Presented: Orillia, ON, Early June

James Leitch Gold Medal Award
Society of Motion Picture & Television Engineers
  (SMPTE)
595 W Hartsdale Ave, White Plains, NY 10607
Tel: 914-761-1100 *Fax:* 914-761-3115
E-mail: smpte@smpte.org
Web Site: www.smpte.org
Key Personnel
Exec Dir: Frederick C Motts *Tel:* 914-761-1100
  ext 106 *E-mail:* fmotts@smpte.org
Established: 2001
To recognize outstanding contributions in the ap-
  plication of digital technology to the motion
  imaging arts & sciences. Developments in soft-
  ware, equipment, systems or the standardiza-
  tion of technology involved in the acquisition,
  processing or distribution of sound & images
  related to motion imaging.
Award: Gold Medal

Lela Common Award for Canadian History
Canadian Authors Association (CAA)
320 S Shores Rd, Campbellford, ON K0L 1L0,
  Canada
Tel: 705-653-0323 *Toll Free Tel:* 866-216-6222
  Fax: 705-653-0593
E-mail: info@canauthors.org
Web Site: www.canauthors.org
Established: 1997
All entries must be historical nonfiction, on Cana-
  dian topics by Canadian authors. The books
  must be English-Language literature for adults
  (not "young adults"). Translations are not eli-
  gible, nor are books published at the author's
  expense.
Award: $2,500 & silver medal
Closing Date: Annually, Dec 15

Waldo G Leland Prize
American Historical Association
400 "A" St SE, Washington, DC 20003
Tel: 202-544-2422 *Fax:* 202-544-8307

E-mail: info@historians.org
Web Site: www.historians.org
Key Personnel
Prize Admin: Debbie Ann Doyle *Tel:* 202-544-
  2422 ext 104 *E-mail:* ddoyle@historians.org
Established: 1981
Offered every five years for the most outstanding
  reference tool in the field of history. Reference
  tool encompasses bibliographies, indexes, encyclopedias & other scholarly apparatus. The
  award is honorific. Books published between
  May 1, 2001 & April 30, 2006, will be eligible
  for consideration. No application form, applicant must simply mail a copy of their book to
  each of the prize committee members who will
  be posted on our web site as the prize deadline
  approaches. All updated info on web site.
Award: Cash prize
Closing Date: May 15, 2006

**Fenia & Yaakov Leviant Memorial Prize in
  Yiddish Culture**
Modern Language Association of America (MLA)
26 Broadway, 3rd fl, New York, NY 10004-1789
SAN: 202-6422
Tel: 646-576-5141 *Fax:* 646-458-0030
E-mail: awards@mla.org
Web Site: www.mla.org
Key Personnel
Coord, Book Prizes & Spec Projs: Annie Reiser
Established: 2001
Awarded alternately to an outstanding translation
  or an outstanding scholarly work in the field
  of Yiddish. For the competition in 2008, it will
  be awarded to an outstanding scholarly work in
  the field of Yiddish published between 2004 &
  2007, including cultural studies, critical biogra-
  phies, or edited works in the field of Yiddish
  folklore or linguistic studies. In 2006, the prize
  will be awarded to an English translation of a
  Yiddish literary work published between 2002
  & 2005. Authors need not be members of the
  MLA.
Award: $500 & certificate
Closing Date: Four copies by May 1
Presented: MLA Convention, Biennially (even-
  numbered years), Dec 28

Harry Levin Prize
American Comparative Literature Association
University of Texas, Program in Comparative Lit-
  erature, One University Sta B5003, Austin, TX
  78712-0196
Tel: 512-471-8020
E-mail: info@acla.org
Web Site: www.acla.org
Key Personnel
Secy: Elizabeth Richmond-Garza
ACLA Admin Asst: Kevin Carney
Established: 1968
Most outstanding book in literary history. Award
  given in alternate years. See web site for nomi-
  nation process.
Award: Certificate
Closing Date: Dec 31
Presented: Annual meeting, following spring

Levinson Prize
Poetry Magazine
1030 N Clark St, Suite 420, Chicago, IL 60610
Tel: 312-787-7070 *Fax:* 312-787-6650
E-mail: poetry@poetrymagazine.org
Web Site: www.poetrymagazine.org
Key Personnel
Busn Mgr: Helen Klaviter *E-mail:* hklaviter@
  poetrymagazine.org
Established: 1914
For poetry published in the preceding two vol-
  umes of Poetry. No application necessary.
Award: $500
Presented: Annually in Dec

The Ruth Lilly Poetry Prize
The Poetry Foundation
1030 N Clark St, Suite 420, Chicago, IL 60610
Tel: 312-787-7070 *Fax:* 312-787-6650
E-mail: poetry@poetrymagazine.org
Web Site: www.poetrymagazine.org
Key Personnel
Busn Mgr: Helen Klaviter *E-mail:* hklaviter@
  poetrymagazine.org
Contact: Christian Wiman
Established: 1986
Awarded to a United States poet, to recognize
  extraordinary artistic accomplishment.
Award: $100,000
Presented: Annually, June

Joseph W Lippincott Award
American Library Association
50 E Huron, Chicago, IL 60611
Tel: 312-280-3247 *Toll Free Tel:* 800-545-2433
  (ext 3247) *Fax:* 312-944-3897
E-mail: awards@ala.org
Web Site: www.ala.org
Key Personnel
Prog Off: Cheryl M Malden *E-mail:* cmalden@
  ala.org
Established: 1938
To a librarian for distinguished service to the pro-
  fession of librarianship, such service to include
  outstanding participation in the activities of
  professional library association, notable pub-
  lished professional writing or other significant
  activity on behalf of the profession & its aims.
Other Sponsor(s): Joseph W Lippincott III
Award: $1,000 & citation
Closing Date: Annually, Dec 1
Presented: ALA Annual Conference, Annually in
  June

**LITA/Christian Larew Memorial Scholarship
  in Library & Information Technology**
Library & Information Technology Association
  (LITA)
Division of American Library Association (ALA)
c/o American Library Association, 50 E Huron
  St, Chicago, IL 60611
Tel: 312-280-4269 *Toll Free Tel:* 800-545-2433
  Fax: 312-280-3257
E-mail: lita@ala.org
Web Site: www.lita.org
Key Personnel
Prog Coord: Valerie Edmonds
  E-mail: vedmonds@ala.org
Established: 1999
Awarded jointly on an annual basis. The schol-
  arship is designed to encourage the entry of
  qualified persons into the library & information
  technology field, who plan to follow a career
  in that field & who demonstrate academic ex-
  cellence, leadership & a vision in pursuit of
  library & information technology. This scholar-
  ship is for study in an ALA Accredited Master
  of Library Science (MLS) program.
Other Sponsor(s): Informata.com
Award: $3,000
Closing Date: March 1
Presented: LITA President's program held at the
  Annual Conference of the American Library
  Association

**LITA/LSSI Minority Scholarship in Library &
  Information Technology**
Library & Information Technology Association
  (LITA)
Division of American Library Association (ALA)
c/o American Library Association, 50 E Huron
  St, Chicago, IL 60611-2795
Tel: 312-280-4269 *Toll Free Tel:* 800-545-2433
  Fax: 312-280-3257
E-mail: lita@ala.org
Web Site: www.lita.org

Key Personnel
Prog Coord: Valerie Edmonds
  E-mail: vedmonds@ala.org
Established: 1994
Scholarship is designed to encourage the entry of qualified minorities into the library & automation field who plan to follow a career in that field & who demonstrate potential in & have a strong commitment to the use of automated systems in libraries. Applicants must be qualified members of a principal minority group (American Indian or Alaskan native, Asian or Pacific Islander, African-American or Hispanic). The recipient must be a US or Canadian citizen. The scholarship is for study in an ALA Accredited Master of Library Science (MLS) program.
Other Sponsor(s): LSSI
Award: $2,500
Closing Date: Annually, March 1
Presented: LITA President's Program held at the Annual Conference of the American Library Association

LITA/OCLC Minority Scholarship in Library & Information Technology
Library & Information Technology Association (LITA)
Division of American Library Association (ALA)
c/o American Library Association, 50 E Huron St, Chicago, IL 60611-2795
Tel: 312-280-4269 *Toll Free Tel:* 800-545-2433
  Fax: 312-280-3257
E-mail: lita@ala.org
Web Site: www.lita.org
Key Personnel
Prog Coord: Valerie Edmonds
  E-mail: vedmonds@ala.org
Established: 1991
For qualified members of a minority group. Must be US or Canadian citizen. For applicants who plan to enter a career in the library & automation field.
Other Sponsor(s): OCLC Inc
Award: $3,000
Closing Date: Annually, March 1
Presented: LITA Presidents' Program at Annual Conference of the American Library Association

LITA/SIRSI Scholarship in Library & Information Technology
Library & Information Technology Association (LITA)
Division of American Library Association (ALA)
c/o American Library Association, 50 E Huron St, Chicago, IL 60611
Tel: 312-280-4269 *Toll Free Tel:* 800-545-2433
  Fax: 312-280-3257
E-mail: lita@ala.org
Web Site: www.lita.org
Key Personnel
Prog Coord: Valerie Edmonds *Tel:* 312-280-4268
  E-mail: vedmonds@ala.org
Established: 1985
For work toward MLS degree in an ALA-accredited program with emphasis on library automation. Awarded annually to encourage students to enter the field of library automation & who demonstrate potential leadership in & a strong commitment to the use of automated systems in libraries.
Other Sponsor(s): Sirsi Corp
Award: $2,500
Closing Date: March 1
Presented: LITA President's Program at the Annual Conference of the American Library Association

Literary Translation Projects
Formerly Translation Projects in Poetry, Fiction
National Endowment for the Arts

Nancy Hanks Ctr, 1100 Pennsylvania Ave NW, Rm 720, Washington, DC 20506-0001
Tel: 202-682-5428; 202-682-5034 (Literature Fellowships hotline)
Web Site: www.arts.gov
Key Personnel
Dir, Lit: Cliff Becker
Asst: James McNeel *Tel:* 202-682-5092
  E-mail: mcneelj@arts.gov
Fellowships for published translators: for translations of published literary material into English. Applications accepted by genre. Guidelines available by website.
Award: $10,000 or $20,000, depending on the artistic excellence & merit of the project
Closing Date: Feb 2, 2005
Presented: Notification by mail

Littleton-Griswold Prize in American Law & Society
American Historical Association
400 "A" St SE, Washington, DC 20003
Tel: 202-544-2422 *Fax:* 202-544-8307
E-mail: info@historians.org
Web Site: www.historians.org
Key Personnel
Prize Admin: Debbie Ann Doyle *Tel:* 202-544-2422 ext 104 *E-mail:* ddoyle@historians.org
Established: 1985
Best book in any subject on the history of American law & society. Books published between May 1, 2004 & April 30, 2005 will be eligible for consideration. No application form, applicants must simply mail a copy of their book to each of the prize committee members who will be posted on our web site as the prize deadline approaches. All updated info on web site.
Award: Cash prize
Closing Date: May 16, 2005

Littleton-Griswold Research Grants
American Historical Association
400 "A" St SE, Washington, DC 20003
Tel: 202-544-2422 *Fax:* 202-544-8307
E-mail: info@historians.org
Web Site: www.historians.org
Key Personnel
Prize Admin: Debbie Ann Doyle *Tel:* 202-544-2422 ext 104 *E-mail:* ddoyle@historians.org
For research in American legal history & the field of law & society. Only members of the Association are eligible. Applications must include application form with estimated budget, curriculum vita & statement of no more than 750 words & a one page bibliography of the most recent, relevant, secondary works on the topic. Application form & all updated info on web site. Preference will be given to junior scholars, PhD candidates & those without access to institutional funds.
Award: Individual grants will not exceed $1,000; preference given to PhD candidates & scholars
Closing Date: Feb 15, 2005

Local 7's Annual National Poetry Competition
Santa Cruz/Monterey Local Seven National Writers Union
Unit of National Writers Union
PO Box 2409, Aptos, CA 95001
Tel: 831-784-4960
E-mail: bonnie.thomas@att.net
Web Site: home.earthlinl.net/~nwu-local7/
Key Personnel
Local 7 Coord: Bonnie Thomas
Established: 1985
Nationally advertised poetry competition.
Award: $500 (1st prize), $300 (2nd prize), $200 (3rd prize)
Closing Date: Nov 30
Presented: Feb 2005

Locus Awards
Locus Magazine
Division of Locus Publications
PO Box 13305, Oakland, CA 94661-0305
Tel: 510-339-9196 *Fax:* 510-339-8144
E-mail: locus@locusmag.com
Web Site: www.locusmag.com
Key Personnel
Man Ed: Kirsten Gong-Wong
Contact: C N Brown
Established: 1971
Presented for the best science fiction novel, fantasy novel, first novel, best adult horror novel, best novella, best short fiction, science fiction anthology, best nonfiction, art & artist, editor, magazine, best publisher & collection of the year.
Award: Trophy & free subscription
Presented: WesterCon Convention, July 4th weekend

The Gerald Loeb Awards
Anderson School at UCLA
Mullin Management Commons, Suite F-321B, 110 Westwood Plaza, Los Angeles, CA 90095-1481
Tel: 310-206-1877 *Fax:* 310-825-4479
E-mail: loeb@anderson.ucla.edu
Web Site: www.loeb.anderson.ucla.edu
Key Personnel
Prog Mgr: Mary Ann Lowe
Established: 1957
Distinguished business & finance journalism in print & broadcast media.
Award: $2,000 winners; $500 honorable mention
Closing Date: last Monday in Jan
Presented: last week in June

Loft-Mentor Series in Poetry & Creative Prose
The Loft Literary Center
Open Book, Suite 200, 1011 Washington Ave S, Minneapolis, MN 55415
Tel: 612-215-2575 *Fax:* 612-215-2576
E-mail: loft@loft.org
Web Site: www.loft.org
Key Personnel
Prog Dir: Jerod Santek *Tel:* 612-215-2586
  E-mail: jsantek@loft.org
Established: 1980
For poetry & fiction mss. Must be Minnesota State resident. Send SASE for current guidelines. Six different residencies scheduled throughout the year. Winners announced in Sept issue of "A View From the Loft". Open to poets, fiction writers & nonfiction writers.
Award: Stipend to defray costs of participating in the program & opportunity to study with six nationally known writer-mentors in brief residence during the course of the year
Closing Date: mid Spring
Presented: The Loft, annually

Wesley Logan Prize in African Diaspora History
American Historical Association
400 "A" St SE, Washington, DC 20003
Tel: 202-544-2422 *Fax:* 202-544-8307
E-mail: info@historians.org
Web Site: www.historians.org
Key Personnel
Prize Admin: Debbie Ann Doyle *Tel:* 202-544-2422 ext 104 *E-mail:* ddoyle@historians.org
Established: 1992
For an outstanding book in African Diaspora history. The prize is offered on some aspect of the history of the dispersion, settlement & adjustment & or return of peoples originally from Africa. Eligible for consideration are books in any chronological period & any geological location. Only books of high scholarly & literary merit will be considered. No application form, applicants must simply mail a copy of their

book to each of the prize committee members who will be posted on our web site as the prize deadline approaches. All updated info on web site. Books published between May 1, 2004 & April 30, 2005 will be considered.
Other Sponsor(s): Association for the study of Afro-American Life & History
Award: Cash prize
Closing Date: May 16, 2005

Judy Lopez Memorial Award For Children's Literature
Women's National Book Association/Los Angeles Chapter
PO Box 7034, Beverly Hills, CA 90212-0034
Tel: 310-474-9917 *Fax:* 310-474-6436
Key Personnel
Pres, WNBA/LA: Margaret Flanders
Chair Selection Comm: Terrie Dorio
Established: 1986
For best books for young readers 9-12 years of age, submitted by publishers, written by US citizen/US resident in year that precedes the award.
Award: Bronze medal & cash award
Closing Date: Feb 1
Presented: Los Angeles, CA, second Sunday in June

Los Angeles Times Book Prizes
Los Angeles Times
Subsidiary of Tribune Co
202 W First St, 6th fl, Los Angeles, CA 90012
Tel: 213-237-5775 *Fax:* 213-346-3599
Web Site: www.latimes.com/bookprizes
Key Personnel
Publr & CEO: John P Puerner
Dir: Kenneth Turan
Administrator: Tom Crouch *E-mail:* tom.crouch@latimes.com
Established: 1980
Annual prizes to authors in the categories of fiction, first fiction, young adult fiction, mystery/thriller, biography, current interest, history, poetry, science & technology. No submissions accepted; nominations are done by committees of appointed judges.
Award: $1,000 & citation (in 9 different categories, plus 10th category, lifetime award - Distinguished Author)
Presented: Annually in April

Louisiana Literature Poetry Prize
Louisiana Literature Press
Division of Southeastern Louisiana University
Southeastern Louisiana University, SLU Box 10792, Hammond, LA 70402
Tel: 985-549-5022
E-mail: lalit@selu.edu
Web Site: www.louisianaliterature.org
Key Personnel
Ed: Jack Bedell
Edit Asst: Ann Dukes
Established: 1984
Poetry by US citizen; all entries must be unpublished. Submit to Louisiana Literature Poetry Contest at the above address. Check web site for award/contest updates.
Award: $400; all entries will be considered for publication in Louisiana Literature
Closing Date: April 15 postmark

Louisville Grawemeyer Award in Religion
Louisville Presbyterian Theological Seminary & University of Louisville
1044 Alta Vista Rd, Louisville, KY 40205-1798
Tel: 502-895-3411 *Toll Free Tel:* 800-264-1839
  Fax: 502-894-2286
E-mail: grawemeyer@lpts.edu
Web Site: www.grawemeyer.org
Key Personnel
Dir: Susan R Garrett *Tel:* 502-895-3411 ext 396

Faculty Sec: Melisa Scarlott
Established: 1990
Given for a work presented or published in the eight years preceding the year of the award. Nominations are invited from religious organizations, appropriate academic associations, religious leaders & scholars, presidents of universities or schools of religion & publishers & editors of scholarly journals. Personal nominations accepted, self-nominations not accepted.
Award: $40,000 per year for five years
Closing Date: Nominations by Dec 1 annually
Presented: Annually in the spring

Love Creek Annual Short Play Festival
Love Creek Productions
2144 45 Ave, Long Island City, NY 11101
Tel: 212-714-9686
E-mail: creekread@aol.com
Key Personnel
Lit Mgr: Cynthia Granville-Callahan
Man Dir: Le Wilhelm
Established: 1988
Annual one-act play festival for unpublished scripts unproduced in New York City in previous year. Send SASE for information/guidelines which must be followed exactly.
Award: Cash (1st prize), mini-showcase production (finalists)
Closing Date: Revolving (annual festival)
Presented: New York, NY, various midtown venues, ongoing

Love Creek Mini Festivals
Love Creek Productions
2144 45 Ave, Long Island City, NY 11101
Tel: 212-714-9686
E-mail: creekread@aol.com
Key Personnel
Lit Mgr: Cynthia Granville-Callahan
Established: 1991
Series of one-act play festivals for unpublished scripts unproduced in New York City in past year, dealing with specific themes. Send SASE for additional information (complete rules & entry requirements); all entry requirements must be followed exactly. Mini festivals may be presented separately or as part of short play festivals.
Award: Cash (1st prize), mini-showcase production (finalists)
Closing Date: Send SASE for themes & deadlines
Presented: New York, NY, various midtown venues

James Russell Lowell Prize
Modern Language Association of America (MLA)
26 Broadway, 3rd fl, New York, NY 10004-1789
Tel: 646-576-5141 *Fax:* 646-458-0030
E-mail: awards@mla.org
Web Site: www.mla.org
Key Personnel
Coord, Book Prizes & Spec Projs: Annie Reiser
Established: 1969
For an outstanding literary or linguistic study, or critical biography by an MLA member published in year prior to competition.
Award: $1,000 & certificate
Closing Date: Six copies by March 1
Presented: MLA Convention, Annually, Dec 28

Pat Lowther Memorial Award
League of Canadian Poets
920 Yonge St, Suite 608, Toronto, ON M4W 3C7, Canada
Tel: 416-504-1657 *Fax:* 416-504-0096
E-mail: info@poets.ca
Web Site: www.poets.ca
Key Personnel
Exec Dir: Edita Page *E-mail:* page@poets.ca
For the best book of poetry written by a Canadian woman & published in the preceding year.

Award: $1,000
Closing Date: Annually, Nov 1
Presented: Annually, May

Jeremiah Ludington Award
Educational Paperback Association (EPA)
PO Box 1399, East Hampton, NY 11937-0709
Tel: 631-329-3315
E-mail: edupaperback@aol.com
Key Personnel
Exec Sec: Marilyn J Abel
Established: 1979
Presented to a person for distinguished work with young people & paperback books; selected by EPA committee & board; no application required.
Award: Citation & contribution to a cause chosen by recipient
Presented: Annually at EPA meeting, Jan

Hugh J Luke Award
Prairie Schooner
University of Nebraska, 201 Andrews Hall, Lincoln, NE 68588
Mailing Address: PO Box 880334, Lincoln, NE 68588-0334
Tel: 402-472-0911
E-mail: kgrey2@unl.edu
Web Site: www.unl.edu/schooner/psmain.htm
Key Personnel
Ed: Hilda Raz
Established: 1989
Annual writing prize for best work published in the Prairie Schooner magazine in the previous year.
Other Sponsor(s): Friends & family of Hugh J Luke (in memoriam)
Award: $250
Presented: winner announced in the Spring

Western Literature Association: The Thomas J Lyon Book Award
Western Literature Association
3200 Old Main Hill, College of Humanities, Arts & Social Sciences, Utah State University, Logan, UT 84322-0735
Tel: 435-797-3855 *Fax:* 435-797-4099
Web Site: www.usu.edu/westlit/tjlyonbookaward.html
Established: 1997
Honors outstanding single-author scholarly book on the literature & culture of the American West published in the previous year. Must submit a statement of support & three copies of the book.
Award: Monetary prize

Lyric Poetry Award
Poetry Society of America (PSA)
15 Gramercy Park, New York, NY 10003
Tel: 212-254-9628 *Fax:* 212-673-2352
Web Site: www.poetrysociety.org
Key Personnel
Exec Dir: Alice Quinn
Established: 1972
For a lyric poem, not to exceed 50 lines. Open to Society members only. Send No 10 SASE for further information, or visit www.poetrysociety.org. Opening date Oct 1-Dec 22.
Award: $500
Closing Date: Dec 22
Presented: Annually in April

Lyric Poetry Prizes
The Lyric
65 Vermont, Rte 15, Jericho, VT 05465
Mailing Address: PO Box 110, Jericho, VT 05465
Tel: 802-899-3993 *Fax:* 802-899-3993
Key Personnel
Ed: Jean Mellichamp Milliken

Established: 1921
Quarterly & annual prizes; awarded for poems published in "The Lyric" magazine. Winners of annual awards announced in the winter issue each year. Quarterly prize of $50. Send SASE for guidelines. $3 for sample copy of "The Lyric" subn price $12/yr, $22/2 yrs, $30/3 yr, $2 extra per year for foreign & Canadian. The annual awards are $100 Lyric Memorial Prize, $100 Leslie Mellichamp Prize (formerly Hajek Prize), $100 Roberts Memorial Prize, $50 Margaret Hailey Carpenter Prize, $50 New England Prize, $50 Fluvanna Prize. Honorable mentions, 1 year subscription to "The Lyric" magazine.
Award: Prizes total $700 annually
Presented: Quarterly prizes awarded in the following issue, annual prizes in the winter issue annually. Checks mailed to recipients

Sir John A MacDonald Prize
Canadian Historical Association
395 Wellington St, Ottawa, ON K1A 0N3, Canada
Tel: 613-233-7885 *Fax:* 613-567-3110
E-mail: cha-shc@archives.ca
Web Site: www.cha-shc.ca
Key Personnel
Admin Asst: Joanne Mineault
Established: 1976
Awarded for the best book on Canadian history. See web site for application details.
Award: $1,000
Closing Date: Dec 1
Presented: Annual meeting, Canadian Historical Association, May

The MacDowell Colony
100 High St, Peterborough, NH 03458
Tel: 603-924-3886 *Fax:* 603-924-9142
E-mail: info@macdowellcolony.org
Web Site: www.macdowellcolony.org
Key Personnel
Exec Dir: Cheryl Young
Communs Dir: Brendan Tapley
For a career of outstanding contributions to the arts, including musical composition, visual arts or literature, architecture, film & video, interdisciplinary arts.
Award: The Edward MacDowell Medal
Presented: Peterborough, NH, Annually in Aug
Branch Office(s)
163 E 81 St, New York, NY 10028 *Tel:* 212-535-9690 *Fax:* 212-737-3803

Magazine Merit Awards
Society of Children's Book Writers & Illustrators (SCBWI)
8271 Beverly Blvd, Los Angeles, CA 90048
Tel: 323-782-1010 *Fax:* 323-782-1892
E-mail: membership@scbwi.org
Web Site: www.scbwi.org
Key Personnel
Pres: Steve Mooser
Dir: Dorothy Leon
Established: 1988
For outstanding original magazine work for young people published during the calendar year & having been written or illustrated by SCBWI members.
Award: Four plaques (fiction, nonfiction, illustration, poetry), four honor certificates
Closing Date: Dec 15
Presented: April

The Magazine of the Year Award
Society of Publication Designers Inc
The Lincoln Bldg, 60 E 42 St, Suite 721, New York, NY 10165
Tel: 212-983-8585 *Fax:* 212-983-2308
E-mail: mail@spd.org
Web Site: www.spd.org

Established: 1996
For continuing excellence in the field of publication design.
Closing Date: Jan
Presented: Annual Awards Gala, New York Public Library, May

J Russell Major Prize
American Historical Association
400 "A" St SE, Washington, DC 20003
Tel: 202-544-2422 *Fax:* 202-544-8307
E-mail: info@historians.org
Web Site: www.historians.org
Key Personnel
Prize Admin: Debbie Ann Doyle *Tel:* 202-544-2422 ext 104 *E-mail:* ddoyle@historians.org
Established: 2001
Awarded for the best work in English on any aspect of French history. Books published between May 1, 2004 & April 30, 2005. No application form, applicants must simply mail a copy of their book to each of the prize committee members who will be posted on our web site as the prize deadline approaches. All updated info on web site.
Award: Cash prize
Closing Date: May 16, 2005

Margaret Mann Citation
Reference & User Services Association
Division of American Library Association
50 E Huron St, Chicago, IL 60611
SAN: 201-0062
Tel: 312-280-5037 *Toll Free Tel:* 800-545-2433 *Fax:* 312-944-6131
Web Site: www.ala.org/alcts
Key Personnel
Pres: Carol Brey-Casiano
Established: 1951
Annual award for outstanding professional achievement in cataloging or classification in a significant publication or by participation in a professional organization. Candidates are nominated. Citation recipient selected by jury.
Other Sponsor(s): OCLC
Award: Citation & $2,000 scholarship to the US or Canadian library school of winning author's choice
Closing Date: Dec 1
Presented: ALA Annual Conference

Many Voices Residencies
The Playwrights' Center
2301 Franklin Ave E, Minneapolis, MN 55406
Tel: 612-332-7481 *Fax:* 612-332-6037
E-mail: info@pwcenter.org
Web Site: www.pwcenter.org
Key Personnel
Dir, New Play Devt: Kristen Gandrow *Tel:* 612-332-7481 ext 21
Stipend, full scholarship to a Playwrights Center class & twice monthly roundtable to develop playwriting skills in a supportive artists' community. Residencies are open to artists of color who are citizens or permanent residents of the US & legal residents of Minnesota.
Award: $1,250 stipend & full scholarship
Closing Date: Must be postmarked by July 30, 2005

Marian Library Medal
University of Dayton, Marian Library
300 College Park, Dayton, OH 45469-1390
Tel: 937-229-4214 *Fax:* 937-229-4258
Web Site: www.udayton.edu
Key Personnel
Contact: William Fackovec
Established: 1953
To scholars in any country for outstanding achievement in Marian research.
Award: Medal

The Marilyn Hall Award
The Beverly Hills Theatre Guild
PO Box 39729, Los Angeles, CA 90039-0729
Key Personnel
Pres: Janet Salter
Competition Coord: Dick Dotterer
Established: 1999
Playwright, children's theatre grade 6th-8th, 9th-12th grade.
Award: $500, $300 $200
Closing Date: Postmark Jan 15 through last day of Feb
Presented: Los Angeles, CA, June 30

Helen & Howard R Marraro Prize in Italian History
American Historical Association
400 "A" St SE, Washington, DC 20003
Tel: 202-544-2422 *Fax:* 202-544-8307
E-mail: info@historians.org
Web Site: www.historians.org
Key Personnel
Prize Admin: Debbie Ann Doyle *Tel:* 202-544-2422 ext 104 *E-mail:* ddoyle@historians.org
Established: 1973
Each award will be given for the book or article deemed best by the committee which treats Italian history in any epoch, Italian cultural history, or Italian-American relations. Each book must be published between May 1, 2004 & April 30, 2005. Entries must first have been published in English by a historian whose usual residence is North America. No application form, applicants must simply mail a copy of their book to each of the prize committee members who will be posted on our web site as the prize deadline approaches. All updated info on web site.
Other Sponsor(s): American Catholic Historical Association; Society of Italian Historical Studies
Award: Cash prize
Closing Date: May 16, 2005

Howard R Marraro Prize
Modern Language Association of America (MLA)
26 Broadway, 3rd fl, New York, NY 10004-1789
Tel: 646-576-5141 *Fax:* 646-458-0030
E-mail: awards@mla.org
Web Site: www.mla.org
Key Personnel
Coord, Book Prizes & Spec Projs: Annie Reiser
Established: 1973
For an outstanding study in Italian literature or comparative literature involving Italian by an MLA member; books or essays published in the previous biennium.
Award: $1,000 & certificate
Closing Date: Four copies by May 1
Presented: MLA Convention, biennially (even-numbered years), Dec 28

Lenore Marshall Poetry Prize
The Academy of American Poets Inc
588 Broadway, Suite 604, New York, NY 10012
Tel: 212-274-0343 *Fax:* 212-274-9427
E-mail: academy@poets.org
Web Site: www.poets.org
Key Personnel
Prog Dir: Ryan Murphy *Tel:* 212-274-0343 ext 17 *E-mail:* rmurphy@poets.org
Established: 1975
Given annually for a book of poetry published in the previous year in a standard edition by a living American poet. Please send four copies of each entry to the Academy of American Poets. The deadline for submissions June 15.
Other Sponsor(s): The Nation Magazine
Award: $25,000
Closing Date: April 1-June 15
Presented: Annually in Oct

Jack Mason Award
Bay Area Independent Publishers Association (BAIPA)
Baipa, PO Box E, Corte Madera, CA 94976
Toll Free Tel: 866-622-1325
E-mail: info@baipa.net
Web Site: www.baipa.net
Key Personnel
Treas: Val Sherer *E-mail:* valpub@worldnet.att.net
Contact: Pete Masterson
Established: 1983
Annual Award of Merit-outstanding contribution to BAIPA organization & field of small publishing.
Award: Perpetual plaque & individual certificate
Presented: Redwood High School, Larkspur, CA, 2nd Saturday in March

Massachusetts Book Awards
Massachusetts Center for the Book
Hampshire College MCB, 893 West St, Amherst, MA 01002
Mailing Address: Hampshire College Post Office/MCB, 893 West St, Amherst, MA 01002
Tel: 413-559-5678 *Fax:* 413-559-5629
E-mail: massbook@hampshire.edu
Web Site: www.massbook.org
Key Personnel
Exec Dir: Sharon Shaloo
Prog Officer: Rebecca Frank
Established: 2000
Recognize significant achievements by Massachusetts writers &/or illustrators in fiction, nonfiction, poetry & children's literature & also present special awards for creative publishing or lifetime achievement in the Massachusetts book community. Visit www.massbook.org for more details.
Other Sponsor(s): Boston Athenaeum; The Boston Public Library; Hampshire College; Massachusetts Board of Library Commissioners; Massachusetts Foundation for the Humanities; Simmons College

Masters Literary Awards
Titan Press
PO Box 17897, Encino, CA 91416-7897
Tel: 818-377-4006
E-mail: titan.press@sbcglobal.net
Web Site: www.titanpress.info
Key Personnel
Man Ed: Stepani Wilson
Established: 1981
Fiction, poetry & song lyrics & nonfiction. All quality published & unpublished mss are eligible, submitted from double-spaced photocopies or tearsheets. Guidelines available with No 10 SASE.
Award: $1,000 yearly Grand Prize, four quarterly prizes of Honorable Mention
Closing Date: Submissions received prior to any award date are eligible for the subsequent award
Presented: Titan Press, March 15, June 15, Aug 15, Dec 15

Mature Women Scholarship Grant - Art/Letters/Music
National League of American Pen Women
Subsidiary of National League of American Pen Women Inc
c/o National Pen Women-Scholarship, Pen Arts Bldg, 1300 17 St NW, Washington, DC 20036-1973
Tel: 202-785-1997
Web Site: www.americanpenwomen.org
Key Personnel
Pres: Anna Di Bella
Established: 1976
Awarded every 2 years on even numbered year. Judges in each category (Art, Letters, Music)

change for each award every two years. Must send SASE with inquiry for requirements. Include an $8 fee payable to NLAPW with entry.
Award: $1,000 each (art, music, letters)
Closing Date: Oct 1 of odd-numbered year
Presented: NLAPW biennially in April, Notified by mail, Mar 15 & awarded in April

Maxim Mazumdar New Play Competition
Alleyway Theatre
One Curtain Up Alley, Buffalo, NY 14202-1911
Tel: 716-852-2600 *Fax:* 716-852-2266
E-mail: email@alleyway.com
Web Site: alleyway.com
Key Personnel
Dir, PR: Joyce Stilson *E-mail:* jstilson@alleyway.com
Contest limited to one submission per category, per author, per year. Category 1: entry must be a previously unproduced full-length (not less than 90 minutes) play or musical of any style, requiring no more than 10 performers & able to be presented on a unit or simple set. Category 2: entry must be a previously unproduced one-act (less than 20 minutes) play or musical of any style, requiring no more than 6 performers & able to be presented on a unit or simple set. Entries will not be returned without SASE, $5 entry fee. Category 3: previously unproduced children's play or musical, not more than 60 minutes in length, no more than 4 performers.
Award: Cash & premiere production of entry at Alleyway Theatre
Closing Date: Annually, July 1

McClelland & Stewart Journey Prize
The Writers' Trust of Canada
90 Richmond St W, Suite 200, Toronto, ON M5C 1P1, Canada
Tel: 416-504-8222 *Fax:* 416-504-9090
E-mail: info@writerstrust.com
Web Site: www.writerstrust.com
Key Personnel
Exec Dir: Lascelle Wingate *Tel:* 416-504-8222 ext 242
Established: 1988
Awarded to a new & developing writer of distinction for a short story published in a Canadian literary publication.
Other Sponsor(s): James A Michner (donation of his Canadian royalty earnings)
Award: $10,000
Presented: The Great Literary Awards, March

John H McGinnis Memorial Award
Southwest Review
Affiliate of Southern Methodist University
307 Fondren Library W, 6404 Hilltop Lane, Dallas, TX 75275-0374
Mailing Address: PO Box 750374, Dallas, TX 75274-0374
Tel: 214-768-1037 *Fax:* 214-768-1408
E-mail: swr@mail.smu.edu
Web Site: www.southwestreview.org
Key Personnel
Ed-in-Chief: Willard Spiegelman
Sr Ed: Elizabeth Mills *Tel:* 214-768-1036
Established: 1960
For the best essay & story appearing in the Southwest Review during the preceding year.
Award: $500-$1000 each (2-4 awards)
Presented: Annually in Jan

Harold W McGraw Jr - Prize in Education
The McGraw-Hill Companies Inc
1221 Avenue of the Americas, 47th fl, New York, NY 10020
Tel: 212-512-2435 *Fax:* 212-512-3611
Web Site: www.mcgraw-hill.com

Key Personnel
Communs Consultant: Laura A Breitenbach, PhD
E-mail: laura_breitenbach@mcgraw-hill.com
Established: 1988
Honors three individuals whose accomplishments, programs & ideas can serve as effective models for the education of future generations.
Award: $25,000 & bronze sculpture award
Closing Date: Mid-Feb
Presented: Usually at New York Public Library, end of September

Jenny McKean Moore Writer in Creative Writing
English Dept, The George Washington University, Washington, DC 20052
Tel: 202-994-6180 *Fax:* 202-994-7915
Web Site: www.gwu.edu/~english
Key Personnel
Chpn: Faye Moscowitz
One-year teaching position, $50,000.
Closing Date: Nov 15

McKnight Advancement Grants
The Playwrights' Center
2301 Franklin Ave E, Minneapolis, MN 55406
Tel: 612-332-7481 *Fax:* 612-332-6037
E-mail: info@pwcenter.org
Web Site: www.pwcenter.org
Key Personnel
Dir, New Play Devt: Kristen Gandrow *Tel:* 612-332-7481 ext 21
Grants to recognize playwrights whose work demonstrates exceptional artistic merit & potential. Playwright's primary residence must be in the state of Minnesota. Applicant must have had a minimum of one work fully produced by a professional theater at the time of application.
Award: Grants of $25,000 each
Closing Date: Must be postmarked by Feb 4, 2005

McKnight Artist Fellowship for Writers
The Loft Literary Center
Open Book, Suite 200, 1011 Washington Ave S, Minneapolis, MN 55415
Tel: 612-215-2575 *Fax:* 612-215-2576
E-mail: loft@loft.org
Web Site: www.loft.org
Key Personnel
Prog Dir: Jerod Santek *Tel:* 612-215-2586
E-mail: jsantek@loft.org
Established: 1982
Contest for Minnesota residents only.
Award: four $25,000 awards which alternate annually between poetry & creative prose; One $25,000 award in children's literature which alternates annually between writing for children 8 & under & older children
Closing Date: Late Fall
Presented: The Loft, Spring

McKnight National Residency & Commission
The Playwrights' Center
2301 Franklin Ave E, Minneapolis, MN 55406
Tel: 612-332-7481 *Fax:* 612-332-6037
E-mail: info@pwcenter.org
Web Site: www.pwcenter.org
Key Personnel
Dir, New Play Devt: Kristen Gandrow *Tel:* 612-332-7481 ext 21
Producing Artistic Dir: Polly K Carl *Tel:* 612-332-7481 ext 22
Established: 1982
Playwrights whose work has made a significant impact on the contemporary theater. Applicant must be a US citizen or permanent resident & must have had a minimum of two different works fully produced by professional theaters. Call or check web site for application information & deadline guidelines. Minnesota-based playwrights are not eligible for the award. Pro-

posals for the Residency & Commission must be agent/professional only. Send writers resume, a two or three page proposal & a writing sample of up to twenty pages.
Award: One $12,500
Closing Date: August
Presented: Sept

McLaren Memorial Comedy Playwriting Competition
Midland Community Theatre
2000 W Wadley, Midland, TX 79705
Tel: 432-682-2544 *Fax:* 432-682-6136
Web Site: www.mctmidland.org
Key Personnel
McLaren Co-Chair: Alathea Blischke
  E-mail: alatheablischke@sbcglobal.net
Volunteer Coord: Tracy Alexander
Established: 1990
2005 McLaren Memorial Comedy Play Writing Competition is accepting unpublished, never professionally produced COMEDY plays. See www.mctmidland.org for guidelines & required entry form. $10 entry fee per script, $15 if play submitted is on disc.
Award: $400 Full-Length; $200 One-Act; possible performance in future MCT season
Closing Date: Jan 31, 2005
Presented: Midland Community Theatre, TBA

McLemore Prize
Mississippi Historical Society
Affiliate of Mississippi Dept of Archives & History
PO Box 571, Jackson, MS 39205-0571
Tel: 601-576-6850 *Fax:* 601-576-6975
E-mail: mhs@mdah.state.ms.us
Web Site: www.mdah.state.ms.us
Key Personnel
Pres: Donna Dye
VP: Martha Swain
Sec-Treas, Historical Society: Elbert Hilliard
Pub Info: Katie Blount *E-mail:* kblount@mdah.state.ms.us
Established: 1980
For distinguished scholarly book on a topic in Mississippi history or biography.
Award: $700
Closing Date: Oct 31
Presented: Varies, 1st weekend in March at annual meeting

Medal of Honor for Literature
National Arts Club
15 Gramercy Park S, New York, NY 10003
Key Personnel
Chair, Literary Comm: Marjory Bassett
Established: 1968
Presented for a body of work of literary excellence; nominations within the club only.
Award: Medal

Lucille Medwick Memorial Award
Poetry Society of America (PSA)
15 Gramercy Park, New York, NY 10003
Tel: 212-254-9628 *Fax:* 212-673-2352
Web Site: www.poetrysociety.org
Key Personnel
Exec Dir: Alice Quinn
Established: 1974
For an original poem in any form on a humanitarian theme, not to exceed 100 lines. Translations are ineligible. Open to Society members only. Opening date Oct 1. Send No 10 SASE for more information, or visit www.poetrysociety.org.
Award: $500
Closing Date: Dec 22
Presented: Annually in April

Melcher Book Award
Unitarian Universalist Association

25 Beacon St, Boston, MA 02108-2800
Tel: 617-742-2100 (ext 303) *Fax:* 617-367-3237
Web Site: www.uua.org
Key Personnel
Contact: Nancy Lawrence *E-mail:* nlawrence@uua.org
Established: 1964
Given to a book making significant contribution to Liberal religious thought.
Award: $2,000 & certificate
Closing Date: Dec 31
Presented: Boston, MA, Oct

Frederic G Melcher Scholarship
Association for Library Service to Children
Division of American Library Association
50 E Huron St, Chicago, IL 60611-2795
Tel: 312-280-2163 *Toll Free Tel:* 800-545-2433
  Fax: 312-944-7671
E-mail: alsc@ala.org
Web Site: www.ala.org/alsc/
Established: 1956
To students entering the field of library service for graduate work in an ALA-accredited program & majoring in library service to children.
Award: $6,000 - 2 scholarships per yr
Closing Date: March 1
Presented: ALA Annual Conference, June/July

Vicky Metcalf Award for Children's Literature
The Writers' Trust of Canada
90 Richmond St W, Suite 200, Toronto, ON M5C 1P1, Canada
Tel: 416-504-8222 *Fax:* 416-504-9090
E-mail: info@writerstrust.com
Web Site: www.writerstrust.com
Key Personnel
Exec Dir: Lascelle Wingate *Tel:* 416-504-8222 ext 242
Awarded to a Canadian writer of children's literature for a body of work.
Other Sponsor(s): George Cedric Metcalf Foundation
Award: $15,000
Presented: The Great Literary Awards, March

Mid-List Press First Series Award for Creative Nonfiction
Mid-List Press
4324 12 Ave S, Minneapolis, MN 55407-3218
Tel: 612-822-3733 *Fax:* 612-823-8387
E-mail: guide@midlist.org
Web Site: www.midlist.org
Key Personnel
Publr: Lane Stiles
Exec Dir: Marianne Nora
Established: 1995
Outstanding work of creative nonfiction (either a collection of essays or a single book-length work) by a writer who has never published a book of creative nonfiction.
Award: $1,000 advance & publication
Closing Date: July 1

Mid-List Press First Series Award for Poetry
Mid-List Press
4324 12 Ave S, Minneapolis, MN 55407-3218
Tel: 612-822-3733 *Fax:* 612-823-8387
E-mail: guide@midlist.org
Web Site: www.midlist.org
Key Personnel
Publr: Lane Stiles
Exec Dir: Marianne Nora
Established: 1990
Outstanding collection of poetry by a writer who has never published a book of poetry.
Award: $500 advance & publication
Closing Date: Feb 1

Mid-List Press First Series Award for Short Fiction
Mid-List Press

4324 12 Ave S, Minneapolis, MN 55407-3218
Tel: 612-822-3733 *Fax:* 612-823-8387
E-mail: guide@midlist.org
Web Site: www.midlist.org
Key Personnel
Publr: Lane Stiles
Exec Dir: Marianne Nora
Established: 1995
Outstanding collection of short fiction (short stories, novellas) by a writer who has never published a book-length collection of short fiction.
Award: $1,000 advance & publication
Closing Date: July 1

Mid-List Press First Series Award for the Novel
Mid-List Press
4324 12 Ave S, Minneapolis, MN 55407-3218
Tel: 612-822-3733 *Fax:* 612-823-8387
E-mail: guide@midlist.org
Web Site: www.midlist.org
Key Personnel
Publr: Lane Stiles
Exec Dir: Marianne Nora
Established: 1990
Outstanding novel by a writer who has never published a novel.
Award: $1,000 advance & publication
Closing Date: Feb 1

Kenneth W Mildenberger Prize
Modern Language Association of America (MLA)
26 Broadway, 3rd fl, New York, NY 10004-1789
Tel: 646-576-5141 *Fax:* 646-458-0030
E-mail: awards@mla.org
Web Site: www.mla.org
Key Personnel
Coord, Book Prizes & Spec Projs: Annie Reiser
Established: 1980
For a work in the field of language, culture, literacy or literature with strong application to the teaching of languages other than English. Authors need not be members of the MLA.
Award: $1,000, certificate & 1 yr membership in the MLA
Closing Date: Seven copies by May 1
Presented: MLA Convention, Annually, Dec 28

Milkweed National Fiction Prize
Milkweed Editions
1011 Washington Ave S, Suite 300, Minneapolis, MN 55415
Tel: 612-332-3192 *Toll Free Tel:* 800-520-6455
  Fax: 612-215-2550
E-mail: editor@milkweed.org
Web Site: www.milkweed.org
Key Personnel
Ed: Emerson Blake
Man Dir: Hillary Reeves
Man Ed: Laurie Buss
Established: 1988
For an unpublished novel or collection of short stories &/or one or more novellas. Awarded to the best work of fiction Milkweed accepts for publication during each calendar year by a writer not previously published by Milkweed Editions. Writers must request complete guidelines before submitting ms (send SASE or visit www. milkweed.org). Open year-round.
Award: $5,000 advance against royalties
Closing Date: Year-round

Mill Mountain Theatre
Center in the Square, 2nd fl, One Market Sq, Roanoke, VA 24011-1437
Tel: 540-342-5771 *Fax:* 540-342-5745
E-mail: outreach@millmountain.org
Web Site: www.millmountain.org
Key Personnel
Producing Artistic Dir: Jere Lee Hodgin
Artistic Assoc: Daryn J Warner
Established: 1964

Accepts unsol one-acts only, year-round, all styles. All other submissions for the Norfolk Southern Festival of New Works, mainstage, second stage & touring productions by invitation only. Response time, 6-12 months.
Award: $50 plus a staged reading
Closing Date: year-round
Presented: CenterPieces, Mill Mountain Theatre, Roanoke, VA

Milner Award
Friends of the Atlanta-Fulton Public Library
One Margaret Mitchell Sq NW, Atlanta, GA 30303
Tel: 404-730-1845 Fax: 404-730-1851
Key Personnel
Man Central Lib-Child Dept: Kellye Baugh
Established: 1982
For living American authors of children's books voted on by the children of Atlanta. No application process.
Award: $1,000 & a glass sculpture by Hans Frabel
Closing Date: Second week of Nov (Children's Book Week)
Presented: Atlanta, GA, The following year during Children's Book Week

Milton Dorfman Poetry Prize
Rome Art & Community Center
308 W Bloomfield St, Rome, NY 13440
Tel: 315-336-1040 Fax: 315-336-1090
E-mail: racc@borg.com
Key Personnel
Interim Exec Dir: Sally Musgari
Educ Coord: Jennifer A Millington
Poetry, reading fee $5 per entry.
Award: $500 (1st prize), $200 (2nd prize), $100 (3rd prize)
Closing Date: Entries accepted July 1 to Dec 30

W O Mitchell Literary Prize
The Writers' Trust of Canada
90 Richmond St W, Suite 200, Toronto, ON M5C 1P1, Canada
Tel: 416-504-8222 Fax: 416-504-9090
E-mail: info@writerstrust.com
Web Site: www.writerstrust.com
Key Personnel
Exec Dir: Lascelle Wingate Tel: 416-504-8222 ext 242
Established: 1998
Awarded to a French-Canadian author who has produced an outstanding body of work, has acted during his/her career as a "caring mentor" for writers & has published a work of fiction & had a new stage play produced during the 3 year period specified for each competition.
Award: $15,000
Presented: The Great Literary Awards, March (every third year)

MLA Prize for a Distinguished Bibliography
Modern Language Association of America (MLA)
26 Broadway, 3rd fl, New York, NY 10004-1789
Tel: 646-576-5141 Fax: 646-458-0030
E-mail: awards@mla.org
Web Site: www.mla.org
Key Personnel
Coord, Book Prizes & Spec Projs: Annie Reiser
Established: 1998
For enumerative & descriptive bibliographies, published in serial, monographic, book or electronic format in two years prior to competition. Criteria for determining excellence include evidence of analytical rigor, meticulous scholarship, intellectual creativity & subject range & depth, Editors need not be members of MLA.
Award: $1,000 & certificate

Closing Date: Four copies by May 1
Presented: MLA convention, Biennially (even-numbered yrs), Dec 28

MLA Prize for Independent Scholars
Modern Language Association of America (MLA)
26 Broadway, 3rd fl, New York, NY 10004-1789
Tel: 646-576-5141 Fax: 646-458-0030
E-mail: awards@mla.org
Web Site: www.mla.org
Key Personnel
Coord, Book Prizes & Spec Projs: Annie Reiser
Established: 1983
For a distinguished scholarly book in the field of English or another modern language written by an independent scholar published in year prior to competition. Author enrolled in a program leading to an academic degree or holding a tenured, tenure-accruing, or tenure-track position in post-secondary education at the time of publication is not eligible.
Award: $1,000, a certificate & one-year membership
Closing Date: Six copies & application form by May 1
Presented: MLA Convention, Annually, Dec 28

Modern Language Association Prize for a Distinguished Scholarly Edition
Modern Language Association of America (MLA)
26 Broadway, 3rd fl, New York, NY 10004-1789
Tel: 646-576-5141 Fax: 646-458-0030
E-mail: awards@mla.org
Web Site: www.mla.org
Key Personnel
Coord, Book Prizes & Spec Projs: Annie Reiser
Established: 1994
Committee solicits submissions of editions published in previous biennium. A multivolume edition is eligible if at least one volume has been published during that period. The editor need not be a member of the MLA. Edition should be based on an examination of all available relevant textual sources; text should be accompanied by appropriate textual & other historical contextual information; the edition should exhibit the highest standards of accuracy in the presentation of its text & apparatus & the text & apparatus should be presented as accessibly & elegantly as possible.
Award: $1,000, certificate
Closing Date: Four copies by May 1
Presented: MLA Annual Convention, Biennially (odd-numbered years), Dec 28

Modern Language Association Prize for a First Book
Modern Language Association of America (MLA)
26 Broadway, 3rd fl, New York, NY 10004-1789
Tel: 646-576-5141 Fax: 646-458-0030
E-mail: awards@mla.org
Web Site: www.mla.org
Key Personnel
Coord, Book Prizes & Spec Projs: Annie Reiser
For an outstanding scholarly work published in year prior to competition as the first book-length publication by a current member of the MLA.
Award: $1,000 check & certificate
Closing Date: Six copies by April 1
Presented: MLA Convention, Annually, Dec 28

Modern Language Association Prize in United States Latina & Latina & Latino & Chicana & Chicano Literary & Cultural Studies
Modern Language Association of America (MLA)
26 Broadway, 3rd fl, New York, NY 10004-1789
Tel: 646-576-5141 Fax: 646-458-0030
E-mail: awards@mla.org
Web Site: www.mla.org
Key Personnel
Coord, Book Prizes & Spec Projs: Annie Reiser

Established: 2002
For an outstanding scholarly work published in year prior to competition in the fields of Latina/Latino or Chicano/Chicano literary or cultural studies by a current member of the MLA.
Award: $1000 check & certificate
Closing Date: May 1
Presented: MLA Convention, Annually, Dec 28

Lucy Maud Montgomery Literature for Children Prize
Prince Edward Island Council of the Arts
115 Richmond St, Charlottetown, PE C1A 1H7, Canada
Tel: 902-368-4410 Fax: 902-368-4418
E-mail: peiarts@peiartscouncil.com
Web Site: www.peiartscouncil.com
Key Personnel
Exec Dir: Darrin White
The ms must be a story written for children five to 12 yrs of age. Maximum length sixty pages. May submit as many entries as they wish. The work must be original & unpublished. Entry shall be typewritten & double spaced on one side of page only. Illustration may be submitted with the story. Contest for Prince Edward Island residents only. Call or e-mail for further information.
Award: $500 (1st prize), $200 (2nd prize), $100 (3rd prize)
Closing Date: Call or e-mail
Presented: Call or e-mail

William Morris Society in the United States Fellowships
William Morris Society in the United States
PO Box 53263, Washington, DC 20009
Web Site: www.morrissociety.org
Key Personnel
Pres: Mark Samuels Lasner E-mail: us@morrissociety.org
VP: Florence Boos E-mail: vp@morrissociety.org
Sec & Treas: Hartley Spatt E-mail: secretary@morrissociety.org
Established: 1996
For scholarly or creative projects related to William Morris (1834-96); given to US citizens or permanent residents.
Award: Up to $1,000
Closing Date: Dec 1

Samuel French Morse Poetry Prize
Northeastern University, English Dept
406 Holmes, Boston, MA 02115
Tel: 617-373-4540
Web Site: www.casdn.neu.edu/~english
Key Personnel
Ed: Guy Rotella Tel: 617-373-4546
E-mail: grotella@neu.edu
Established: 1983
Annual prize awarded for poetry to first or second book by US poet (50-75 pages).
Award: publication of ms by Northeastern University Press & $1,000
Closing Date: Sept 15, single copy of ms & $15 reading fee, payable to NU English Dept
Presented: Annually, Jan

George L Mosse Prize
American Historical Association
400 "A" St SE, Washington, DC 20003
Tel: 202-544-2422 Fax: 202-544-8307
E-mail: info@historians.org
Web Site: www.historians.org
Key Personnel
Prize Admin: Debbie Ann Doyle Tel: 202-544-2422 ext 104 E-mail: ddoyle@historians.org
Established: 2001
For an outstanding major work of extraordinary scholarly distinction, creativity & originality in the intellectual & cultural history of Europe

since the Renaissance. Only books of a high scholarly distinction should be submitted. Research accuracy, originality & literary merit are important selection factors. Books published between May 1, 2004 & April 30, 2005 are eligible. No application form, applicants must simply mail a copy of their book to each of the prize committee members who will be posted on our web site as the prize deadline approaches. All updated info on web site.
Award: Cash prize
Closing Date: May 16, 2005

Frank Luther Mott-Kappa Tau Alpha Research Award
University of Missouri, School of Journalism, Columbia, MO 65211-1200
Tel: 573-882-7685 *Fax:* 573-884-1720
E-mail: umcjourkta@missouri.edu
Key Personnel
Exec Dir: Keith Sanders
Established: 1944
For the best research for books in journalism, exclusive of textbooks, published in the previous year. Awarded by Kappa Tau Alpha.
Award: $1,000 (1st prize); certificates to the top five entrants
Closing Date: Dec 7, 2004
Presented: Annually in Aug

Sheila Margaret Motton Prize
New England Poetry Club
16 Cornell St, Arlington, MA 02474
Web Site: www.nepoetryclub.org
Key Personnel
Pres: Diana Der Hovanessian
Contest Chmn: Elizabeth Crowell
For a book of poems published in the last 2 years. Send 2 copies of the book with $5 handling fee for non-members.
Award: $500
Closing Date: June 30
Presented: Cambridge, MA, Annually, Fall

MS Public Education Awards Program
National Multiple Sclerosis Society
733 Third Ave, New York, NY 10017
Tel: 212-476-0436 *Fax:* 212-986-7981
Web Site: www.nationalmssociety.org
Key Personnel
PR Dir: Arney Rosenblat
Established: 1974
To encourage editors, writers & broadcast program directors to report in depth on multiple sclerosis. Print, radio or TV stories in four categories: print/general lifestyle, print/medical science, broadcast/general lifestyle, broadcast/medical stories for broadcast stories aired during the previous year.
Award: Cash &/or plaques for winners
Closing Date: Feb 1
Presented: National Board Meeting, also chapters present awards locally, June

Erika Mumford Prize
New England Poetry Club
16 Cornell St, Arlington, MA 02474
Web Site: www.nepoetryclub.org
Key Personnel
Contest Chmn: Elizabeth Crowell
Pres: Diana Der Hovanessian
Established: 1988
Poem about foreign culture or travel. Mark name of contest on envelope. Send poem in duplicate, name of writer on one only. Send to Elizabeth Crowell at above address.
Award: $250
Closing Date: June 30
Presented: Annually, Fall

Mythopoeic Awards
Mythopoeic Society

PO Box 320486, San Francisco, CA 94132
E-mail: edith.crowe@sjsu.edu
Web Site: www.mythsoc.org
Key Personnel
Awards Admin: Eleanor M Farrell
  E-mail: emfarrell@earthlink.net
Established: 1967
The Scholarship Awards (two) honor scholarship in the Inklings (JRR Tolkien, CS Lewis, Charles Williams) & the general fields of myth & fantasy studies; each is given to the author of a book published in the previous three years. The Fantasy Awards (two) for adult & children's literature honor novels or single-author collections in the spirit of the Inklings; each is given to the author of a book published the previous year.
Award: Statuette
Closing Date: Members make nominations Jan-Feb, winners picked by late July (annually)
Presented: Society's Annual Conference, July or Aug

National Awards for Education Reporting
Education Writers Association
2122 "P" St NW, No 201, Washington, DC 20037
Tel: 202-452-9830 *Fax:* 202-452-9837
E-mail: ewa@ewa.org
Web Site: www.ewa.org
Key Personnel
Exec Dir: Lisa J Walker *E-mail:* lwalker@ewa.org
Established: 1960
Best education reporting in print & broadcast media.
Award: Grand prize, 1st prize, 2nd prize, special citation, in 20 categories; plaques & certificates
Closing Date: Jan 21
Presented: Annual Mtg/Banquet, April 2005

National Book Awards
National Book Foundation
95 Madison Ave, Suite 709, New York, NY 10016
Tel: 212-685-0261 *Fax:* 212-213-6570
E-mail: nationalbook@national.org
Web Site: www.nationalbook.org
Key Personnel
Exec Dir: Harold Augerbraun
Assoc Dir: Meg Kearney
Sr Prog Officer: Meredith Andrews; Maryann Jacob; Sherrie Young
Established: 1950
Living American authors for books in USA, for fiction, nonfiction, poetry; young people's literature.
Award: $10,000 cash & bronze sculpture for winner in each genre
Presented: New York City, NY, Nov

The National Business Book Award
PricewaterhouseCoopers
Royal Trust Tower, TD Centre, Suite 3000, 77 King St W, Toronto, ON M5K 1G8, Canada
Mailing Address: PO Box 82, Toronto, ON M5K 1G8, Canada
Tel: 416-941-8383 *Fax:* 416-941-8345
Web Site: www.pwcglobal.com
Key Personnel
Dir, Natl Mktg & Commun: Faye Mattachione
  Tel: 416-941-8344 *E-mail:* faye.mattachione@ca.pwcglobal.com
Established: 1985
Excellence in business writing.
Other Sponsor(s): Bank of Montreal; Canadian Business Magazine; Maclean's Magazine
Award: $10,000
Closing Date: Annually, Dec
Presented: April

National Endowment for the Humanities Fellowships & Folger Longterm & Short-term Fellowships & Andrew W Mellon Foundations
Folger Shakespeare Library
c/o Fellowship Committee, 201 E Capitol St SE, Washington, DC 20003
Tel: 202-544-4600 (ext 348) *Fax:* 202-544-4623
Web Site: www.folger.edu
Key Personnel
Dir: Gail Kern Paster
Fellowship Admin: Carol Brobeck
Residential fellowships awarded to advanced scholars who have made substantial contributions in their fields of research & who are pursuing research projects appropriate to the collections of the Folger. Application form supported by four copies (short-term fellowship) or seven copies (long-term fellowship) of the applicant's curriculum vitae, four copies (short-term fellowship) or eight copies (long-term fellowship) of a 1,000-word description of the research project & three letters of recommendation.
Other Sponsor(s): National Endowment for the Humanities
Award: $1,800 (short-term fellowship), up to $30,000 (stipend up to $40,000 NEH long-term fellowship), Mellon Foundations fellowships $50,000 & $35,000, short-term stipend fellowship $2,000/month
Closing Date: Nov 1, long-term fellowship; March 1, short-term fellowship

National Federation of State Poetry Societies Annual Poetry Contest
National Federation of State Poetry Societies (NFSPS)
13211 NW Holly Rd, Bremerton, WA 98312
Web Site: www.NFSPS.com
Key Personnel
Sec: Sharon Svendsen
Contest Chair: Kathleen Pederzani
  E-mail: pederzanik@aol.com
Membership: Sy Swann
Established: 1959
Fifty poetry contests, one for students only; rules & categories change, must have current rules provided on web site.
Other Sponsor(s): Individual states' poetry society as host society
Award: $10-$1,500
Closing Date: March 15 annually

National Jewish Book Award-Children's Literature
Jewish Book Council
15 E 26 St, 10th fl, New York, NY 10010-1579
Tel: 212-532-4949 (ext 297) *Fax:* 212-481-4174
E-mail: jbc@jewishbooks.org
Web Site: www.jewishbookcouncil.org
Key Personnel
Exec Dir: Carolyn Starman Hessel
  E-mail: carolynhessel@jewishbooks.org
Award: Citation & publicity
Closing Date: April 30
Presented: Center for Jewish History, Fall

National Jewish Book Award-Children's Picture Book
Jewish Book Council
15 E 26 St, 10th fl, New York, NY 10010-1579
Tel: 212-532-4949 (ext 297) *Fax:* 212-481-4174
E-mail: jbc@jewishbooks.org
Web Site: www.jewishbookcouncil.org
Key Personnel
Exec Dir: Carolyn Starman Hessel
  E-mail: carolynhessel@jewishbooks.org
Award: Citation & publicity
Closing Date: April 30
Presented: Center for Jewish History, Fall

National Jewish Book Award-Contemporary Jewish Life & Practices
Jewish Book Council
15 E 26 St, 10th fl, New York, NY 10010-1579
Tel: 212-532-4949 (ext 297) *Fax:* 212-481-4174
E-mail: jbc@jewishbooks.org
Web Site: www.jewishbookcouncil.org
Key Personnel
Exec Dir: Carolyn Starman Hessel
    E-mail: carolynhessel@jewishbooks.org
Award: Citation & publicity
Closing Date: April 30
Presented: Center for Jewish History, Fall

National Jewish Book Award-Contemporary Jewish Thought & Experience
Jewish Book Council
15 E 26 St, 10th fl, New York, NY 10010-1579
Tel: 212-532-4949 (ext 297) *Fax:* 212-481-4174
E-mail: jbc@jewishbooks.org
Web Site: www.jewishbookcouncil.org
Key Personnel
Exec Dir: Carolyn Starman Hessel
    E-mail: carolynhessel@jewishbooks.org
Award: Citation & publicity
Closing Date: April 30
Presented: Center for Jewish History, Fall

National Jewish Book Award-Jewish History
Jewish Book Council
15 E 26 St, 10th fl, New York, NY 10010-1579
Tel: 212-532-4949 (ext 297) *Fax:* 212-481-4174
E-mail: jbc@jewishbooks.org
Web Site: www.jewishbookcouncil.org
Key Personnel
Exec Dir: Carolyn Starman Hessel
    E-mail: carolynhessel@jewishbooks.org
Award: Citation & publicity
Closing Date: April 30
Presented: Center for Jewish History, Fall

National Jewish Book Award-Scholarship
Jewish Book Council
15 E 26 St, 10th fl, New York, NY 10010-1579
Tel: 212-532-4949 (ext 297) *Fax:* 212-481-4174
E-mail: jbc@jewishbooks.org
Web Site: www.jewishbookcouncil.org
Key Personnel
Exec Dir: Carolyn Starman Hessel
    E-mail: carolynhessel@jewishbooks.org
Award: Citation, 7 publicity
Closing Date: April 30
Presented: Center for Jewish History, Fall

National Jewish Book Awards
Jewish Book Council
15 E 26 St, New York, NY 10010-1579
Tel: 212-532-4949 (ext 297) *Fax:* 212-481-4174
E-mail: jbc@jewishbooks.org
Web Site: www.jewishbookcouncil.org
Key Personnel
Pres: Maurice Corson
Exec Dir: Carolyn Starman Hessel
    E-mail: carolynhessel@jewishbooks.org
Asst to Dir: Shauna Eisenberg *E-mail:* shauna@
    jewishbooks.org
Established: 1948
Fourteen awards to US, Canadian or Israeli authors & translators of books of outstanding scholarship & literary merit on Jewish themes for the general, no specialist reader. Categories: autobiography
Memoire (Sandra Brandt & Arik Weintraub Award)
Children's Literature
Holocaust (Leon Jolson Award)
Israel (Morris J Kaplun Memorial Award)
Jewish History (Gerrard & Ella Berman Award)
Jewish Thought (Dorot Foundation Donor)
Scholarship (Sarah H Kushner Memorial Award)
Sephardic Studies (Maurice Amado Foundation),
Jewish Education (Anonymous Donor)

General nonfiction, fiction & children's awards
Jewish-Christian relations (Revson Foundation Award)
Eastern European Studies (Estee Lauder Award)
Yiddish Language & Culture (The Workmen's Circle Award).
Award: Cash prize
Closing Date: April 30
Presented: Center for Jewish History, Fall

National Looking Glass Poetry Chapbook Competition, see Pudding House Poetry Chapbook Competition

National One-Act Playwriting Competition
Little Theatre of Alexandria
600 Wolfe St, Alexandria, VA 22314
Tel: 703-683-5778 *Fax:* 703-683-1378
E-mail: asklta@thelittletheatre.com
Web Site: www.thelittletheatre.com
Key Personnel
Chmn, One-Act: Mary Beth Smith-Toomey
Established: 1978
One-act playwriting; send to Chmn for guidelines. One-Act Playwriting Competition. No more than two plays. Entries must be unpublished & unproduced as of date of entry. Entry fee of $20.
Award: $350 (1st prize), $250 (2nd prize), $150 (3rd prize), usually production of top plays
Closing Date: May 31

National Outdoor Book Awards
NOBA Foundation & Association of Outdoor Recreation & Education, Idaho State University
1065 S Eighth Ave, Pocatello, ID 83209
Mailing Address: Idaho State Univ, Box 8128, Pocatello, ID 83209
Tel: 208-236-3912 *Fax:* 208-236-4600
Web Site: www.isu.edu/outdoor/books/
Key Personnel
Chmn: Ron Watters *E-mail:* wattron@isu.edu
Established: 1995
Annual award recognizing the work of outstanding writers & publishers of outdoor books. Categories include history/biography, outdoor literature, instructional texts, outdoor adventure guides, nature guides, children's books, design/artistic merit & nature & environment. Guidelines on the web site.
Closing Date: Aug
Presented: International Conference on Outdoor Recreation & Education (Depending on the year, held in different locations in the US & Canada), Early Nov

National Poetry Competition
Northwoods Journal
Affiliate of Conservatory of American Letters
PO Box 298, Thomaston, ME 04861
Tel: 207-354-0998
E-mail: cal@americanletters.org
Web Site: www.americanletters.org
Key Personnel
Pres: Robert W Olmsted
VP: Elaine B Olmsted
Established: 1995
Book-length work, no more than 10% may have been previously published. Prizes awarded each January prior to publication. Deadline Dec 31 each year. Submit with SASE & extras for any correspondence wanted or clear & simple instructions to discard ms, if not accepted. All mss will be judged within 72 hours of receipt. If your ms is "leading the pack" it will be retained until beaten by another. Judges will not be revealed until after the contest & then only upon request with SASE. Non-winning mss will not be commented on. Leaders for prize in publication will be posted on web site. Entrants may submit as often as wished. No subject or

length restrictions. See web site for more details.
Award: three prizes of $100 each plus publication by royalty contract (publication date in each fall)
Closing Date: Dec 31 & continuing

National Poetry Series Open Competition
National Poetry Society
57 Mountain Ave, Princeton, NJ 08540
Tel: 609-430-0999 *Fax:* 609-430-9933
Web Site: www.nationalpoetryseries.com
Established: 1978
For book-length typed ms of poetry, previously unpublished in book form; $25 entrance fee, payable to National Poetry Series; see website for guidelines.
Award: Five books to be published by trade publishers, small presses & university publishers. $1,000 cash award for each winner
Closing Date: Jan1-Feb 15 postmark
Presented: Summer

National Ten-Minute Play Contest
Actors Theatre of Louisville
316 W Main St, Louisville, KY 40202-4218
Tel: 502-584-1265
Web Site: www.actorstheatre.org
Key Personnel
Literary Mgr: Adrien-Alice Hansel
    E-mail: ahansel@actorstheatre.org
National Ten-Minute (ten-page) playwriting contest.
Award: $1,000 & possible production at Actors Theatre of Louisville
Closing Date: Dec 1, 2004
Presented: Fall

National Translation Award
American Literary Translator's Association
Box 830688, Mail Sta JO51, Richardson, TX 75083-0688
Tel: 972-883-2093 *Fax:* 972-883-6303
Web Site: www.literarytranslators.org
Key Personnel
Dir: Rainer Schulte, PhD *E-mail:* schulte@
utdallas.edu
Established: 1991
Publishers are invited to nominate one book in each category of contemporary fiction, contemporary poetry, contemporary nonfiction & literature of the past. Must be a full-length book or anthology translated from another language into English & must have been published in the previous year. Send four copies of each book.
Other Sponsor(s): University of Texas at Dallas
Award: National Translation Award, $2,500
Closing Date: March 31
Presented: ALTA Conference, Montreal, Canada, Nov 25

National Writers Association Novel Contest
National Writers Association
3140 S Peoria St, Suite 295, Aurora, CO 80014
Tel: 303-841-0246 *Fax:* 303-841-2607
Web Site: www.nationalwriters.com (magazine available on-line)
Key Personnel
Exec Dir: Sandy Whelchel *E-mail:* sandywrter@
aol.com
Established: 1937
Novel contest.
Award: $500 (1st prize), $300 (2nd prize), $100 (3rd prize)
Closing Date: April 1
Presented: NWAF Summer Conference, second weekend in June

Nautilus Award
Networking Alternatives for Publishers, Retailers & Artists Inc (NAPRA)
109 N Beach Rd, Eastsound, WA 98245

Mailing Address: PO Box 9, Eastsound, WA
   98245-0009
Tel: 360-376-2702 *Toll Free Tel:* 800-367-1907
   Fax: 360-376-2704
E-mail: napravision@napra.com
Web Site: www.napra.com
Key Personnel
Founder & Publr: Marilyn McGuire
Exec Dir: Suzanne Humes
Established: 2001
To recognize authors & titles that make a distin-
   guished literary contribution to spiritual growth,
   conscious living & positive social change.
Closing Date: Jan 15
Presented: July

The Nebraska Review Awards
The Nebraska Review Awards in Fiction, Poetry
   & Creative Nonfiction
Subsidiary of The Nebraska Review
University of Nebraska-Omaha, WFAB 212, Om-
   aha, NE 68182-0324
Tel: 402-554-3159 *Fax:* 402-614-2026
Web Site: www.zoopress.org/nebraskareview/
Key Personnel
Ed: Neil Azevedo
Poetry Ed: Mark Wunderlich
Fiction/Nonfiction Ed: Max Watman
Established: 1986
Send SASE for guidelines or see website. All en-
   tries must be previously unpublished works.
   The Nebraska Review is published in partner-
   ship with Zoo Press.
Award: $500 (fiction), $500 (poetry), $500 (es-
   say) & publication in the *Nebraska Review*
Closing Date: Annually, Sept 1 & Nov 30

Frank Nelson Doubleday Memorial Award
Wyoming Arts Council
Division of Wyoming Department of Parks &
   Cultural Resources
2320 Capitol Ave, Cheyenne, WY 82002
Tel: 307-777-7742 *Fax:* 307-777-5499
Web Site: www.wyoarts.state.wy.us
Key Personnel
Lit Prog Mgr: Michael Shay *Tel:* 307-777-5234
   E-mail: mshay@state.wy.us
Established: 1988
Best poetry, fiction, nonfiction or drama written
   by a woman author. Wyoming residents only.
   Blind judges & single juror.
Other Sponsor(s): Neltje
Award: $1,000
Closing Date: Annually Aug 1
Presented: Announced Nov 1

The Pablo Neruda Prize for Poetry
Nimrod, The University of Tulsa
Subsidiary of The Nimrod/Hardman Awards
Nimrod Intl Journal, University of Tulsa, 600 S
   College, Tulsa, OK 74104
Tel: 918-631-3080 *Fax:* 918-631-3033
E-mail: nimrod@utulsa.edu
Web Site: www.utulsa.edu/nimrod
Key Personnel
Ed: Francine Ringold, PhD
Man Ed: Eilis O'Neal
Established: 1978
No previously published works. Omit author's
   name on mss. Include a cover sheet contain-
   ing major title & subtitles of the work, author's
   name, address & phone. Mss will not be returned. Retain the rights to publish any contest submission. Works not accepted will be
   released. Winners & selected finalists will be
   published. Include SASE & a check for $20
   (includes a one-year subscription & processing).
Award: $2,000 (1st prize), $1,000 (2nd prize);
   published writers receive two copies of the
   journal; winners will be flown to Tulsa for a
   conference & banquet

Closing Date: Annually April 30
Presented: Univ of Tulsa, Annually in Oct

Neustadt International Prize for Literature
World Literature Today
Affiliate of The University of Oklahoma
630 Parrington Oval, Suite 110, Norman, OK
   73019-4033
Tel: 405-325-4531 *Toll Free Tel:* 800-523-7363
   Fax: 405-325-7495
Web Site: www.ou.edu/worldlit/
Key Personnel
Exec Dir: Robert Con Davis-Undiano
   E-mail: rcdavis@ou.edu
Established: 1970
To a living writer for outstanding literary achieve-
   ment; prize may honor a single major work
   or an entire oeuvre; writer's work must be
   available in a representative sample in En-
   glish, Spanish or French; writer must accept
   the award in person in ceremonies at the Uni-
   versity of Oklahoma; a special issue of *World
   Literature Today* is devoted to the laureate;
   Candidates must be nominated by a jury member.
Award: $50,000 & an eagle feather cast in silver
Presented: University of Oklahoma, Biennially
   (even-numbered years)

Allan Nevins Prize
Society of American Historians (SAH)
Affiliate of American Historical Society
Columbia University, 603 Fayerweather Hall, MC
   2538, New York, NY 10027
Key Personnel
Pres: Robert Dallek
Exec Dir: Mark Carnes *Tel:* 212-854-5943
   E-mail: mc422@columbia.edu
Admin Sec: Ene Sirvet *Tel:* 212-222-4902
   E-mail: es28@columbia.edu
Established: 1960
Annual prize for a PhD dissertation defended in
   the prior year in American history or biography
   that best combines sound scholarship & literary
   excellence.
Award: $1,000, a certificate & publication by a
   major commercial press & consideration for
   adoption by History Book Club
Closing Date: Jan 31
Presented: New York, NY, May

**New Brunswick Arts Board/Conseil des arts du
NB**
634 Queen St, Suite 300, Fredericton, NB E3B
   1C2, Canada
Tel: 506-444-4444 *Fax:* 506-444-5543
E-mail: nbabcanb@artsnb.ca
Web Site: www.artsnb.ca
Key Personnel
Exec Dir: Pauline Bourgue *E-mail:* pbourgue@
   artsnb.ca
Finance studies, provide subsistance allowance.
Award: $20,000 per year (arts award), up to
   $7,000 (creation grant)
Closing Date: Creation Grant Oct 1, Art Award
   Oct 1
Presented: Fredericton, NB

New England Book Awards
New England Booksellers Association Inc
   (NEBA)
1770 Massachusetts Ave, No 332, Cambridge,
   MA 02140
Mailing Address: PO Box 332, Cambridge, MA
   02140
Tel: 617-576-3070 *Toll Free Tel:* 800-466-8711
   Fax: 617-576-3091
Web Site: www.newenglandbooks.org
Key Personnel
Exec Dir: Wayne (Rusty) Drugan *E-mail:* rusty@
   neba.org
Established: 1990

Annual awards for fiction, nonfiction, children's
   & publishing are chosen by booksellers for
   the body of work of an under-recognized New
   England-based author or publisher.
Award: $500 donation to charity or literary group
   chosen by each author
Closing Date: May
Presented: Trade show, Sept/Oct

New Issues Poetry Prize
New Issues Poetry & Prose
Western Michigan University, Dept of English,
   1903 W Michigan Ave, Kalamazoo, MI 49008-
   5331
Tel: 269-387-8185 *Fax:* 269-387-2562
Web Site: www.wmich.edu/newissues
Key Personnel
Ed: Herbert Scott *E-mail:* herbert.scott@wmich.
   edu
US residents writing in English & US citizens
   living abroad who have not previously published a full-length collection (48 plus pages)
   of poems in an edition of 500 or more copies.
   Submit ms minimum 48 pages, typed on one
   side, single spaced; do not bind ms. Include
   brief bio & relevant publication information;
   cover page with name, address, phone & title
   of ms; include table of contents. A $15 reading
   fee for each ms; enclose SASE.
Other Sponsor(s): Western Michigan University
Award: $2,000; publication of poems
Closing Date: Nov 30

**New Jersey Council for the Humanities Book
Award**
New Jersey Council for the Humanities
28 W State St, 6th fl, Trenton, NJ 08608
Tel: 609-695-4838 *Fax:* 609-695-4929
E-mail: njch@njch.org
Web Site: www.njch.org
Key Personnel
Exec Dir: Jane Brailove Rutkoff
   E-mail: jrutkoff@njch.org
Established: 1988
Honors a nonfiction humanities book that bal-
   ances scholarship with general public appeal.
   The book establishes a connection to New Jer-
   sey either through its subject or the author's
   birth, residence, or occupation. Nominations
   must be submitted by the publisher accom-
   panied by six reading copies & a nomination
   form, which is available from the NJCH.
Award: $1,000 (Author); A gold seal imprinted
   with the award logo is available
Presented: Annual Awards Event, Oct

**New Jersey State Council on the Arts
Fellowship Program (NJSCA)**
New Jersey State Council on the Arts (NJSCA)
Division of NJ Dept of State
225 W State St, 4th fl, Trenton, NJ 08608
Mailing Address: PO Box 306, Trenton, NJ
   08625
Tel: 609-292-6130 *Fax:* 609-989-1440
Web Site: www.njartscouncil.org; www.
   midatlanticarts.org
Key Personnel
Prog Officer: Don Ehman *E-mail:* don@arts.sos.
   state.nj.us
Fellowships to individual artists. New Jersey res-
   idency required. Three writing categories: po-
   etry, prose & playwriting. Applicants apply
   even-numbered years, awarded odd-numbered
   years. Program is administered by the Mid At-
   lantic Arts Foundation (MAAF). Applications
   available online & should be sent to the Mid
   Atlantic Arts Foundation at 201 N Charles St,
   Suite 401, Baltimore, MD 21201.
Other Sponsor(s): Mid Atlantic Arts Foundation
   (MAAF)
Award: Varies ($5,000-$12,000)

Closing Date: Applications available in spring, deadline in July
Presented: Public meeting, Trenton, NJ, Announced by Feb 1

New Letters Literary Awards
New Letters Quarterly Magazine
5101 Rockhill Rd, Kansas City, MO 64110-2499
Tel: 816-235-1168 *Fax:* 816-235-2611
E-mail: newletters@umkc.edu
Web Site: www.newletters.org
Key Personnel
Awards Coord: Amy Lucas *E-mail:* lucasamy@umkc.edu
Established: 1986
Literary contest.
Award: Publication of winners & consideration of first runners-up in each category plus cash to winner: $1,000 (fiction), $1,000 (poetry), $1,000 (essay)
Closing Date: Annually around May 18

New Millennium Writings
Affiliate of New Messenger Books
PO Box 2463, Knoxville, TN 37901
Tel: 865-428-0389 *Fax:* 865-428-0389
Web Site: www.mach2.com
Key Personnel
Ed: Don Williams *E-mail:* donw@mach2.com
Established: 1996
Fiction, poetry & essay.
Award: $3,000 total, plus publication ($1,000 for fiction; $1,000 for poetry; $1,000 for nonfiction)
Closing Date: June 18 & Nov 18
Presented: Knoxville, Summer & Winter

New Play Development
Unicorn Theatre
3828 Main St, Kansas City, MO 64111
Tel: 816-531-7529 ext 15 *Fax:* 816-531-0421
Web Site: www.unicorntheatre.org
Key Personnel
Literary Asst: Herman Wilson
Original unpublished & professionally unproduced play in a contemporary setting with a cast limit of ten; no unsol scripts, query first with SASE or SASPC, submit synopsis & sample dialogue; scenes. All winners must agree to assign 2% subs rights of future productions of the scripts (in the US & Canada) to the Unicorn Theatre for a period of five years from the close of the production & all future productions must acknowledge the initial production by the Unicorn Theatre. We do not return scripts.
Award: $1,000 & production
Closing Date: No deadline; we accept scripts on an ongoing year-round basis

New Writer Awards
Great Lakes Colleges Association (GLCA)
535 W William, Suite 301, Ann Arbor, MI 48103
Tel: 734-761-4833 *Fax:* 734-761-3939
Web Site: www.glca.org
Established: 1969
For a first published work of fiction or a first book of poetry. Submissions may be made only by publishers; one entry each, poetry & fiction. Submit four copies of the work & an author's statement agreeing to the terms.
Award: Reading engagements at up to 12 colleges & universities of the GLCA
Closing Date: Feb 28

New York City Book Awards
New York Society Library
53 E 79 St, New York, NY 10021
Tel: 212-288-6900 (ext 230) *Fax:* 212-988-4071
E-mail: events@nysoclib.org
Web Site: www.nysoclib.org

Key Personnel
Events Coord: Sara Holliday
Established: 1995
Given to the authors of the best books about New York City. Must submit copy of nominated book the same year of publication.
Award: Plaque & varied monetary amount
Closing Date: Dec 1
Presented: The New York Society Library, early May, annually

The New York Public Library Helen Bernstein Book Award for Excellence in Journalism
The New York Public Library
Publications Office, Fifth Ave & 42 St, New York, NY 10018
Tel: 212-512-0202 *Fax:* 212-704-8620
E-mail: kvanwestering@nypl.org
Web Site: www.nypl.org
Key Personnel
PR, Assoc: Tina Hoerenz
Dir, Pubns: Karen Van Westering
Established: 1988
Requires overall journalistic excellence & a published book that stems from the author's reportage & exemplifies outstanding work; NOTE: nominations solicited only from publishers & editors-in-chief of major newspapers, news magazines & book publishers nationwide.
Award: $15,000
Closing Date: Annually, Oct 1 for books published in calendar year
Presented: The New York Public Library, April/May, annually

New York State Edith Wharton Citation of Merit for Fiction Writers
New York State Writers Institute
Subsidiary of University at Albany
University at Albany, LE 320, Albany, NY 12222
Tel: 518-442-5620 *Fax:* 518-442-5621
E-mail: writers@uamail.albany.edu
Web Site: www.albany.edu/writers-inst
Key Personnel
Dir: William Kennedy
Established: 1985
State author designation for a New York state fiction writer. Applications not accepted. Nominations by advisory panel only.
Award: $10,000
Presented: Albany, NY, biennially

New York State Walt Whitman Citation of Merit for Poets
New York State Writers Institute
Subsidiary of University at Albany
University at Albany, LE 320, Albany, NY 12222
Tel: 518-442-5620 *Fax:* 518-442-5621
E-mail: writers@uamail.albany.edu
Web Site: www.albany.edu/writers-inst
Key Personnel
Dir: William Kennedy
Asst Dir: Suzanne Lance *Tel:* 518-442-5624
E-mail: slance@uamail.albany.edu
Established: 1985
State author designation for New York state poet. Applications not accepted. Nominations by advisory panel only.
Award: $10,000
Presented: Albany, NY, biennially

John Newbery Medal
Association for Library Service to Children
Division of American Library Association
50 E Huron St, Chicago, IL 60611-2795
Tel: 312-280-2163 *Toll Free Tel:* 800-545-2433
Fax: 312-944-7671
E-mail: alsc@ala.org
Web Site: www.ala.org/alsc
Established: 1922
Awarded annually to the author of the most distinguished writing in a children's book pub-

lished during the preceding year. Restricted to authors who are citizens or residents of the US.
Award: Medal
Closing Date: Dec 31
Presented: ALA Annual Conference, Varies

Newcomen-Harvard Book Award
Harvard University
c/o Business History Review, Harvard Business School, Soldiers Field Rd, Boston, MA 02163
Tel: 617-495-1003 *Fax:* 617-495-0594
E-mail: bhr@hbs.edu
Web Site: www.newcomen.org
Key Personnel
Ed: Walter Friedman *E-mail:* wfriedman@hbs.edu; Thomas K McCraw
Established: 1964
Award given every three years for best book published in the US on the history of business. Selection by the editorial board of the Business History Review. Co-sponsored by the Newcomen Society of the US, located at 211 Welsh Pool Rd, Suite 240, Exton, PA 19341. Tel: 610-363-6600, Toll free tel: 800-466-7604, Fax: 610-363-0612, E-mail info@newcomen.org.
Other Sponsor(s): Newcomen Society of the US
Award: $4,000 & a certificate

Don & Gee Nicholl Fellowships in Screenwriting
Academy of Motion Picture Arts & Sciences (AMPAS)
1313 N Vine St, Hollywood, CA 90028
Tel: 310-247-3059; 310-247-3010 *Fax:* 310-247-3794
E-mail: nicholl@oscars.org
Web Site: www.oscars.org/nicholl
Key Personnel
Dir: Greg Beal
Established: 1986
Screenwriting, for information or application send SASE to AMPAS.
Award: Up to five awards of $30,000
Closing Date: Postmarked May 1
Presented: Beverly Hills, CA, Nov

Coutts Nijhoff International West European Specialist Study Grant
Association of College & Research Libraries
Division of American Library Association
50 E Huron St, Chicago, IL 60611
Tel: 312-280-2514 *Toll Free Tel:* 800-545-2433 (ext 2514) *Fax:* 312-280-2520
Web Site: www.ala.org/acrl
Key Personnel
Prog Coord: Megan Bielefield
E-mail: mbielefeld@ala.org
Established: 1986
Supports research pertaining to Western European studies, librarianship, or the book trade. Sponsored by Coutts Nijhoff International.
Award: Maximum 4,500 Euros
Closing Date: Annually first Fri in Dec
Presented: ALA Annual Conference

John Frederick Nims Memorial Prize
Poetry Magazine
1030 N Clark St, Suite 420, Chicago, IL 60610
Tel: 312-787-7070 *Fax:* 312-787-6650
E-mail: poetry@poetrymagazine.org
Web Site: www.poetrymagazine.org
Key Personnel
Busn Mgr: Helen Klaviter *E-mail:* hklaviter@poetrymagazine.org
Established: 1999
For poetry published in the preceding two volumes of poetry.
Award: $500
Closing Date: No application necessary
Presented: Annually in Dec

NMMA Discover Boating Director's Award
National Marine Manufacturers Association
200 E Randolph Dr, Suite 5100, Chicago, IL 60601
Tel: 312-946-6200 *Fax:* 312-946-0388
Web Site: nmma.org
Key Personnel
Contact: Dan Green *Tel:* 312-946-6269
  E-mail: dgreen@nmma.org
Established: 1957
The awards were designed to encourage journalists to communicate the joys of the boating lifestyle to the uninitiated. Categories include: newspapers with a circulation under 100,000, newspapers with a circulation over 100,000, magazine, broadcasts under 100,000 viewers & broadcasts over 100,000 viewers. Judges select winners based on the following criteria: a welcoming, positive or intriguing portrayal of boating reaching a non-boating audience; the ability to encourage the audience to try boating & originality & creativity.
Award: $1,000
Closing Date: Dec 31
Presented: Miami Intl Boat Show, FL, Feb

North American Indian Prose Award
University of Nebraska Press
233 N Eighth St, Lincoln, NE 68588-0255
Tel: 402-472-3581 *Fax:* 402-472-0308
E-mail: pressmail@unl.edu
Web Site: www.nebraskapress.unl.edu
Key Personnel
Ed-in-Chief: Elizabeth Demers
Acting Dir: Gary Dunham *Tel:* 402-472-4452
  E-mail: gdunham1@unl.edu
Established: 1990
Annual competition for complete mss in prose nonfiction; authors must be American Indians.
Other Sponsor(s): University of California (Berkeley)
Award: $1,000 advance against royalties
Closing Date: Annually, July 1
Presented: University of Nebraska

North Carolina Arts Council
Division of North Carolina State Government
Dept of Cultural Resources, Mail Service Ctr 4632, Raleigh, NC 27699-4632
Tel: 919-715-1519 *Fax:* 919-733-4834
Web Site: www.ncarts.org
Key Personnel
Lit Dir: Deborah McGill *E-mail:* debbie.mcgill@ncmail.net
Established: 1980
Eight fellowships are given every two years to poets & writers of fiction, literary nonfiction & literary translation & four are given every two years to playwrights & screenwriters. Writers who have lived in the state for at least one year as of application deadline are eligible.
Award: $8,000 for poets, fiction writers, literary nonfiction writers & literary translators. Also four $8,000 fellowships every two years for playwrights & screenwriters
Closing Date: Bi-annually, Nov of even-numbered years
Presented: Bi-annually, Summer of odd-numbered years

Notable Wisconsin Authors
Wisconsin Library Association Inc
5250 E Terrace Dr, Suite A-1, Madison, WI 53718-8345
Tel: 608-245-3640 *Fax:* 608-245-3646
Web Site: www.wla.lib.wi.us
Key Personnel
Exec Dir: Lisa K Strand
Memb Servs Coord: Brigitte E Vacha
  E-mail: vacha@scls.lib.wi.us
Established: 1973

Honors Wisconsin authors, past & present, for their literary contributions.
Award: Printed brochure with biographical information on the notable author, including a list of authors' works
Presented: WLA Annual Conference; usually late Oct, Annually at Fall

O Henry Award
Texas Institute of Letters
3700 Mockingbird Lane, Dallas, TX 75205
Tel: 512-245-2232 *Fax:* 512-245-7462
Web Site: www.stedwards.edu/newc/marks/til/awards_and_rules.htm
Key Personnel
VP: Joe Holley
Dir: Mark Busby *Tel:* 512-245-2428
  E-mail: mb13@swt.edu
Treas: Jim Hoggard
Sec: Fran Vick *E-mail:* franvick@aol.com
Award for best nonfiction writing appearing in a magazine, journal or other periodical or in a newspaper Sunday supplement. Only one story per entrant.
Other Sponsor(s): Sue Brandt & Frank McBee
Award: $1,000
Closing Date: Jan 7, 2005
Presented: March banquet, Ft Worth, TX

Eli M Oboler Memorial Award
Intellectual Freedom Round Table
Unit of American Library Association
50 E Huron St, Chicago, IL 60611
Tel: 312-280-4223; 312-280-4220
  Toll Free Tel: 800-545-2433 *Fax:* 312-280-4227
E-mail: oif@ala.org
Web Site: www.ala.org/ifrt
Key Personnel
Proj Coord: Nanette Perez
To an author of a published work in English, or an English translation dealing with issues, events, questions or controversies in the areas of intellectual freedom.
Award: $500 & citation
Closing Date: Dec 1, prior to ALA conference at which presented (biennial award)
Presented: ALA Annual Conference, location varies, June, every 2 yrs

The Flannery O'Connor Award for Short Fiction
University of Georgia Press
330 Research Dr, Athens, GA 30602-4901
Tel: 706-369-6130 (no phone queries accepted)
  Fax: 706-369-6131
Web Site: www.ugapress.org
Key Personnel
Assoc Dir & Ed-in-Chief: Nancy Grayson
  E-mail: ngrayson@ugapress.uga.edu
Asst Ed & Competition Coord: Andrew Berzanskis *E-mail:* andrewb@ugapress.uga.edu
Established: 1981
Collections of original short fiction. Ms should be 200-275 pages & should be accompanied by a $20 handling fee, ms will not be returned. Two volumes will be selected from ms submitted between April 1 & May 31. Open to both published & unpublished writers. Applicants should write The Press for guidelines. Must include SASE.
Award: $1,000 & publication by the University of Georgia Press under a standard publishing contract
Closing Date: May 31

O'Connor Prize for Fiction (Descant Publication)
Texas Christian University
TCU Box 297700, Fort Worth, TX 76129
Tel: 817-257-7240 *Fax:* 817-257-7709
E-mail: descant@tcu.edu

Web Site: www.eng.tcu.edu/journals/descant/index.html
Key Personnel
Ed: Dave Kuhne *Tel:* 817-257-6537 *E-mail:* d.kuhne@tcu.edu
Established: 1957
Best published fiction in each volume of Descant.
Award: $500
Presented: Announced in journal, Summer

Scott O'Dell Award for Historical Fiction
1100 E 57 St, S-109, Chicago, IL 60637
Tel: 773-702-4085 *Fax:* 773-702-0775
Key Personnel
Award Committee Chmn: Hazel Rochman
Libn: Anne Carlson
Established: 1982
Presented for a work of historical fiction published by a US publisher & set in the New World. Winner is selected by O'Dell Award Committee.
Award: $5,000
Closing Date: Dec 31

Annual Off-Off-Broadway Original Short Play Festival
Love Creek Productions
c/o Samuel Frenchz Inc, 45 W 25 St, New York, NY 10010
Tel: 212-206-8990 *Fax:* 212-206-1429
E-mail: samuelfrench@earthlink.net
Web Site: www.samuelfrench.com *Cable:* THEATRICAL NEW YORK
Key Personnel
Festival Coord: Kenneth Dingledine
Established: 1976
Selected plays are presented on the final day of the festival.
Award: Publication of top 5-6 plays
Closing Date: Variable, Jan-March
Presented: American Theater of Actors

Howard O'Hagan Award for Short Fiction
Banff Centre
11759 Groat Rd, Edmonton, AB T5M 3K6, Canada
Tel: 780-422-8174 *Toll Free Tel:* 800-665-5354 (Alberta only) *Fax:* 780-422-2663
E-mail: mail@writersguild.ab.ca
Web Site: www.writersguild.ab.ca
Key Personnel
Exec Dir: Diane Walton
Established: 1982
Alberta Literary Award, must be resident of Alberta.
Award: $1,000 plus leather-bound copy of book
Closing Date: Dec 31

Ohioana Award for Children's Literature
Ohioana Library Association
274 E First Ave, Suite 300, Columbus, OH 43201
Tel: 614-466-3831 *Fax:* 614-728-6974
E-mail: ohioana@sloma.state.oh.us
Web Site: www.oplin.lib.oh.us/ohioana
Key Personnel
Exec Dir: Carol Roddy
Established: 1990
Annually to an Ohio author of children's literature for a body of work or for a lifetime of contributions to children's literature.
Award: $1,000
Closing Date: Dec 31

Ohioana Book Awards
Ohioana Library Association
274 E First Ave, Suite 300, Columbus, OH 43201
Tel: 614-466-3831 *Fax:* 614-728-6974
E-mail: ohioana@sloma.state.oh.us
Web Site: www.oplin.lib.us/ohioana/
Key Personnel
Exec Dir: Carol Roddy

Ed, Ohioana Quarterly: Kate Templeton Fox
  E-mail: kfox@sloma.state.oh.us
Established: 1942
For the best books by Ohio authors in vari-
  ous fields of writing or books about Ohio or
  Ohioans. Submit two copies of a nominated
  book on or before its publication date.
Award: Citations & medals
Closing Date: Annually, Dec 31
Presented: Annually in Oct

Ohioana Career Award
Ohioana Library Association
274 E First Ave, Suite 300, Columbus, OH 43201
Tel: 614-466-3831 *Fax:* 614-728-6974
E-mail: ohioana@sloma.state.oh.us
Web Site: www.oplin.lib.oh.us/ohioana
Key Personnel
Exec Dir: Carol Roddy
Established: 1942
Awarded each year to a native born Ohioan who
  has had an outstanding career in the arts & hu-
  manities. The recipient is an honored guest at
  Ohioana Day & must be present to receive the
  award.
Closing Date: Dec 31
Presented: Ohioan Day

Ohioana Citations
Ohioana Library Association
274 E First Ave, Suite 300, Columbus, OH 43201
Tel: 614-466-3831 *Fax:* 614-728-6974
E-mail: ohioana@sloma.state.oh.us
Web Site: www.oplin.lib.oh.us/ohioana
Key Personnel
Exec Dir: Carol Roddy
For outstanding contributions & accomplishments
  in a specific field or area of the arts & human-
  ities. Four Ohioana Citations, generally given
  in four different fields, including the Ohioana
  Music Citation, may be given each year. The
  recipient must have been born in Ohio or lived
  in Ohio for a minimum of 5 years.
Closing Date: Dec 31

Ohioana Pegasus Award
Ohioana Library Association
274 E First Ave, Suite 300, Columbus, OH 43201
Tel: 614-466-3831 *Fax:* 614-728-6974
E-mail: ohioana@sloma.state.oh.us
Web Site: www.oplin.lib.oh.us/ohioana
Key Personnel
Exec Dir: Carol Roddy
Established: 1964
Given to recognize unique or outstanding contri-
  butions or achievements in the arts & human-
  ities. Given at the discretion of the trustees of
  the association. Must have been born in Ohio
  or resided in Ohio for a minimum of 5 years.
Closing Date: Dec 31

Ohioana Poetry Award
Ohioana Library Association
274 E First Ave, Suite 300, Columbus, OH 43201
Tel: 614-466-3831 *Fax:* 614-728-6974
E-mail: ohioana@sloma.state.oh.us
Web Site: www.oplin.lib.oh.us/ohioana
Key Personnel
Exec Dir: Carol Roddy
Established: 1984
Annual award to an Ohio poet for a body of pub-
  lished work that has made & continues to make
  a significant contribution to poetry & through
  whose work as a writer, teacher, administrator
  or in community service, interest in poetry has
  been developed.
Award: $1,000
Closing Date: Dec 31

Ohioana Walter Rumsey Marvin Grant
Ohioana Library Association

274 E First Ave, Suite 300, Columbus, OH 43201
Tel: 614-466-3831 *Fax:* 614-728-6974
E-mail: ohioana@sloma.state.oh.us
Web Site: www.oplin.lib.oh.us/ohioana
Key Personnel
Exec Dir: Carol Roddy
Established: 1982
Writing competition; awarded to young, (30 yrs
  of age or younger) unpublished Ohio authors
  who were born or have lived in Ohio five years
  or more.
Award: $1,000
Closing Date: Jan 31
Presented: Columbus, OH, October

Opie Prize
American Folklore Society/Children's Folklore
  Section
Mershon Ctr, Ohio State University, 1501 Neil
  Ave, Columbus, OH 43201-2602
Tel: 614-292-3375 *Fax:* 614-292-2407
Key Personnel
Exec Dir: Timothy Lloyd *E-mail:* lloyd.100@osu.
  edu
Awarded for an outstanding contribution to the
  understanding of the folklore & folklife of chil-
  dren. Edited volumes, collections of folklore
  & authored studies published in English dur-
  ing previous two years are eligible. Authors
  or publishers should submit two copies of the
  book.
Award: $200
Closing Date: Annually July 1
Presented: Oct

Natalie Ornish Poetry Award
Texas Institute of Letters
3700 Mockingbird Lane, Dallas, TX 75205
Tel: 512-245-2232 *Fax:* 512-245-7462
Web Site: www.stedwards.edu/newc/marks/til/
  awards_and_rules.htm
Key Personnel
VP: Joe Holley
Dir: Mark Busby *Tel:* 512-245-2428
  E-mail: mb13@swt.edu
Treas: Jim Hoggard
Sec: Fran Vick *E-mail:* franvick@aol.com
For the first best book of poetry by a poet with a
  Texas association.
Other Sponsor(s): Natalie Ornish
Award: $1,000
Closing Date: Jan 2005
Presented: March banquet, Ft Worth, TX, USA,
  March 2005

George Orwell Award
National Council of Teachers of English (NCTE)
1111 W Kenyon Rd, Urbana, IL 61801-1096
Tel: 217-328-3870 *Toll Free Tel:* 877-369-6283
  Fax: 217-328-0977
E-mail: public_info@ncte.org
Web Site: www.ncte.org
Key Personnel
Journal Mgr: Margaret Chambers *Tel:* 217-278-
  3623 *Fax:* 217-328-0977 *E-mail:* mchambers@
  ncte.org
Established: 1975
Recognizes individuals for distinguished contribu-
  tions to honesty & clarity in public language.
Other Sponsor(s): NCTE Committee on Public
  Doublespeak
Award: Certificate
Closing Date: Sept 30
Presented: NCTE Annual Convention, Pittsburgh,
  PA, Nov 20, 2005

Pacific Northwest Book Awards
Pacific Northwest Booksellers Association
317 W Broadway, Suite 214, Eugene, OR 97401-
  2890
Tel: 541-683-4363 *Fax:* 541-683-3910
E-mail: info@pnba.org

Web Site: www.pnba.org/awards.htm
Key Personnel
Comm Chair: Lynn Dixon *Tel:* 907-258-4544
  Fax: 907-258-4491 *E-mail:* pnbabookawards@
  pnba.org
Established: 1965
Closing Date: Oct 31
Presented: Spring Banquet, Mid March, annually

**Pacific Northwest Young Reader's Choice
Award**
Pacific Northwest Library Association (PLNA)
Affiliate of University of Washington/Graduate
  School of Library & Information Science
Mary Gates Hall, Suite 370, Seattle, WA 98195-
  2840
Tel: 208-232-1263 (ext 28) *Fax:* 208-232-9266
Web Site: www.pnla.org
Key Personnel
Chair YRCA: Carole Monlux *Tel:* 406-543-5358
  E-mail: monlux@montana.com
Established: 1940
Nominations taken only from children, teachers,
  parents & librarians of the Pacific Northwest
  (Washington, Oregon, Alaska, Idaho, Montana,
  British Columbia & Alberta). Nominated ti-
  tles were published three years previously in
  the US or Canada. Only 4th to 12th graders in
  the Pacific Northwest vote on a selected list of
  titles. Awarded to the author of a book most
  popular with children. Send SASE for information or contact through e-mail address.
Award: Silver Medal
Closing Date: March
Presented: Pacific Northwest Library Association's Annual Conference, Annually

Palma Julia de Burgos
Association for Puerto Rican-Hispanic Culture
c/o Peter Bloch, 83 Park Terr W, Suite 6-A, New
  York, NY 10034
Tel: 212-942-2338 *Fax:* 718-367-0780
Web Site: www.buscapique.com
Key Personnel
Pres: Peter Bloch
Established: 1969
For artistic or intellectual merit of Hispanic
  persons who have not yet received sufficient
  recognition for their achievements & have co-
  operated with the Association for Puerto Rican-
  Hispanic Culture. Selection by the Board of
  Directors.
Award: Trophy

**Lucile Micheels Pannell Award for Excellence
in Children's Bookselling**
Women's National Book Association
c/o Susannah Greenberg Public Relations, 2166
  Broadway, Suite 9E, New York, NY 10024
Mailing Address: 5200 S Sixth Place, Arlington,
  VA 22204
Tel: 212-208-4629 *Fax:* 212-208-4629
E-mail: publicity@bookbuzz.com
Web Site: www.wnba-books.org; www.wnba-
  books.org/awards
Key Personnel
Chmn: Eileen Hanning
Established: 1982
The Pannell Award recognizes retail bookstores
  that excel at creatively bringing books & children together & inspiring children's interest in
  books & reading. One general book store with
  a children's section & one children's speciality
  store are selected each year by a jury of five
  book industry professionals based on creativity,
  responsiveness to community needs, passion
  & understanding of children's books & young
  readers.
Award: $2,000 (two at $1,000 each) plus 1 piece
  of original art
Presented: BookExpo America

Mildred & Albert Panowski Playwriting Award

Northern Michigan University
Forest Roberts Theatre, Northern Michigan University, 1401 Presque Isle Ave, Marquette, MI 49855-5364
Tel: 906-227-2559 *Fax:* 906-227-2567
Web Site: www.nmu.edu/theatre
Key Personnel
Coord: David Hansen
Established: 1977
Provides students & faculty the unique opportunity to mount & produce an original work on the university stage. The playwright will benefit from seeing the work on its feet in front of an audience & from professional adjudication by guest critics. There is no restriction as to theme or genre; only one play per playwright may be entered.
Award: $2,000 cash, production in Nov & airline fare, room & board for the week of production
Closing Date: Friday Nov 19 (receipt not postmark)
Presented: Forest Roberts Theatre, Northern Michigan Univ

Francis Parkman Prize

Society of American Historians (SAH)
Affiliate of American Historical Society
Columbia University, 603 Fayerweather Hall, MC 2538, New York, NY 10027
Key Personnel
Pres: Robert Dallek
Exec Sec: Mark Carnes *Tel:* 212-854-5943
E-mail: mc422@columbia.edu
Admin Sec: Ene Sirvet *Tel:* 212-222-4902
E-mail: es28@columbia.edu
Established: 1956
Awarded annually for the best nonfiction book, including biography on any aspect of the history of what is now the United States. Entries must have prior year copyright.
Award: $2,500, engraved bronze medal & certificate & automatic adoption by the History Book Club
Closing Date: Jan 31
Presented: New York, NY, May

The Alicia Patterson Foundation Fellowship Program

The Alicia Patterson Foundation
1730 Pennsylvania Ave, Suite 850, Washington, DC 20006
Tel: 202-393-5995 *Fax:* 301-951-8512
E-mail: info@aliciapatterson.org
Web Site: www.aliciapatterson.org
Key Personnel
Exec Dir: Margaret Engel *E-mail:* engel@charm.net
Established: 1963
Yearly or 6 month stipend, not for academic study, for professional print journalist with five years experience & must be US citizen.
Award: $35,000 over 12 months; $17,500 over 6 months. Applicants choose whether they want 6 or 12 month grants
Closing Date: Annually, Oct 1
Presented: 1st week of Dec

Pearson Writers' Trust Non-Fiction Prize

The Writers' Trust of Canada
90 Richmond St W, Suite 200, Toronto, ON M5C 1P1, Canada
Tel: 416-504-8222 *Fax:* 416-504-9090
E-mail: info@writerstrust.com
Web Site: www.writerstrust.com
Key Personnel
Exec Dir: Lascelle Wingate *Tel:* 416-504-8222 ext 242
Established: 1997
Awarded for an outstanding work of nonfiction published in the previous year.

Other Sponsor(s): Pearson Canada
Award: $15,000
Presented: The Great Literary Awards, March

William Peden Prize in Fiction

The Missouri Review
1507 Hillcrest Hall, Columbia, MO 65211
Tel: 573-882-4474 *Toll Free Tel:* 800-949-2505
Fax: 573-884-4671
E-mail: tmr@moreview.com
Web Site: www.missourireview.com
Key Personnel
Assoc Ed: Evelyn Somers *Tel:* 573-884-7839
E-mail: rogerses@missouri.edu
Contact: Richard Sowienski
Awarded annually to the best story to appear in the magazine the previous volume year. Winner is selected by an outside judge. It is not a contest that writers can enter, since the winner is selected from stories already published in the magazine.
Other Sponsor(s): First National Bank
Award: $1,000
Presented: Columbia, MO, Annually in Oct

The PEN Award for Poetry in Translation

Pen American Center
588 Broadway, Suite 303, New York, NY 10012
Tel: 212-334-1660 *Fax:* 212-334-2181
E-mail: pen@pen.org
Web Site: www.pen.org
Key Personnel
Dir, Literary Awards: Peter Meyer *Tel:* 212-334-1660 ext 110 *E-mail:* awards@pen.org
Recognizes book-length translations of poetry from any language into English, published during the current calendar year & is judged by a single translator of poetry appointed by the PEN Translation Committee. All books must have been published in the US, although translators may be of any nationality (US residency or citizenship is not required). No application form. May be submitted by publishers, agents or the translators themselves.
Award: $3,000
Closing Date: Dec 15, 2004
Presented: May 2005

PEN Award for the Art of the Essay

Formerly PEN/Spielvogel Diamonstein Award
Pen American Center
588 Broadway, Suite 303, New York, NY 10012
Tel: 212-334-1660 *Fax:* 212-334-2181
E-mail: pen@pen.org
Web Site: www.pen.org
Key Personnel
Awards Dir: Peter Meyer *Tel:* 212-334-1660 ext 110 *E-mail:* awards@pen.org
Established: 1990
For a distinguished book of essays by an American writer published in the preceding calendar year.
Award: $5,000
Closing Date: Dec 15
Presented: May

PEN/Robert Bingham Fellowships for Writers

Pen American Center
588 Broadway, Suite 303, New York, NY 10012
Tel: 212-334-1660 *Fax:* 212-334-2181
E-mail: pen@pen.org
Web Site: www.pen.org
Key Personnel
Literary Awards Dir: Peter Meyer *Tel:* 212-334-1660 ext 110 *E-mail:* awards@pen.org
Honor exceptionally talented fiction writers whose debut work–a first novel or collection of short stories published in 2004 or 2005 – represents distinguished literary achievement & suggests great promise. Nominations are welcome from any source. To be eligible, a candidate's first novel or first collection of short fiction must

have been published by a US trade publisher between Jan 1, 2004 & Dec 31, 2005. Candidates must be US residents but American citizenship is not required.
Award: 3 fellowships: each $35,000/yr for 2 yrs & $10,000 annually to support each writer's project
Closing Date: Jan 15, 2006

PEN Book-of-the-Month Translation Prize

Pen American Center
588 Broadway, Suite 303, New York, NY 10012
Tel: 212-334-1660 *Fax:* 212-334-2181
E-mail: pen@pen.org
Web Site: www.pen.org
Key Personnel
Awards Dir: Peter Meyer *Tel:* 212-334-1660 ext 110 *E-mail:* awards@pen.org
Established: 1963
For the best book-length translation into English from any language published in the US during the previous year. Technical, scientific or reference works are not eligible.
Other Sponsor(s): Book-of-the-Month Clubs
Award: $3,000
Closing Date: Dec 15
Presented: New York, NY, May

PEN Center USA Literary Awards

PEN Center USA
Affiliate of Center of International PEN
672 S Lafayette Park Place, Suite 42, Los Angeles, CA 90057
Tel: 213-365-8500 *Fax:* 213-365-9616
E-mail: awards@penusa.org
Web Site: www.penusa.org
Key Personnel
Awards Coord: Teena Apeles
Established: 1979
Literary awards for: fiction, nonfiction, poetry, translation, children's literature, drama, screenplay, teleplay, journalism. Author must live west of Mississippi River.
Award: Cash awards $1,000
Closing Date: Book categories Dec 30, Non-book categories Jan 30, 2005
Presented: Los Angeles, CA, Fall

PEN/Faulkner Award for Fiction

PEN/Faulkner Foundation
Folger Shakespeare Library, 201 E Capitol St SE, Washington, DC 20003
Tel: 202-675-0345 *Fax:* 202-608-1719
Web Site: www.penfaulkner.org
Key Personnel
Exec Dir: Janice F Delaney *E-mail:* delaney@folger.edu
Established: 1980
For a distinguished work of fiction published by an American citizen writer (for published work only). Send four copies of each book or four bound gallies for those being published in Nov & Dec.
Award: $15,000 & $5,000 each to runners-up
Closing Date: Oct 31
Presented: Washington, DC, May

PEN/Jerard Fund Award

Pen American Center
588 Broadway, Suite 303, New York, NY 10012
Tel: 212-334-1660 *Fax:* 212-334-2181
E-mail: pen@pen.org
Web Site: www.pen.org
Key Personnel
Awards Dir: Peter Meyer *Tel:* 212-334-1660 ext 110 *E-mail:* awards@pen.org
Established: 1987
For an emerging woman writer of nonfiction with a book in progress; given in odd-numbered years.
Award: $5,500
Closing Date: Jan 6, 2005
Presented: New York, NY, May, 2005

PEN Martha Albrand Award for The Art of Memoir
Pen American Center
588 Broadway, Suite 303, New York, NY 10012
Tel: 212-334-1660 *Fax:* 212-334-2181
E-mail: pen@pen.org
Web Site: www.pen.org
Key Personnel
Awards Dir: Peter Meyer *Tel:* 212-334-1660 ext
110 *E-mail:* awards@pen.org
Established: 1988
There is no application form; send three copies
of each eligible book. Eligible books must
have been published in the current calendar year. Authors must be American citizens
or permanent residents; they can have published books in any other literary genre, but
the work submitted for this prize must be their
first memoir to be published. Books submitted
for this award may not be submitted for the
PEN/Martha Albrand Award for First Nonfiction. Each award is judged by a separate panel
of writers of nonfiction.
Award: $1,000
Closing Date: Dec 15
Presented: New York, NY, May

PEN/Phyllis Naylor Working Writer Fellowship
Pen American Center
588 Broadway, Suite 303, New York, NY 10012
Tel: 212-334-1660 *Fax:* 212-334-2181
E-mail: pen@pen.org
Web Site: www.pen.org
Key Personnel
Literary Awards Dir: Peter Meyer *Tel:* 212-334-
1660 ext 110 *E-mail:* awards@pen.org
Established: 2001
To an author of children's or young-adult fiction
in financial needs, who has published at least
two books but no more than three during the
past ten years. These books may have been
well received by literary critics, but which have
not generated sufficient income to support the
author. Must be nominated by an editor or fellow writer.
Award: $5,000
Closing Date: Annually, Jan 5
Presented: Annual PEN Literary Awards, May,
annually

The PEN/Ralph Manheim Medal for Translation
Pen American Center
588 Broadway, Suite 303, New York, NY 10012
Tel: 212-334-1660 *Fax:* 212-334-2181
E-mail: pen@pen.org
Web Site: www.pen.org
Key Personnel
Literary Awards Dir: Peter Meyer *Tel:* 212-334-
1660 ext 110 *E-mail:* awards@pen.org
Established: 1982
Given to a translator who has demonstrated ex-
ceptional commitment to excellence throughout
the body of his work. Candidates nominated by
the PEN Translation Committee.
Award: Medal
Closing Date: 2006 (given every 3 years)
Presented: New York, May

PEN/Spielvogel Diamonstein Award, see PEN
Award for the Art of the Essay

PEN Writers Fund
Pen American Center
Affiliate of International PEN
588 Broadway, Suite 303, New York, NY 10012
Tel: 212-334-1660 *Fax:* 212-334-2181
E-mail: pen@pen.org
Web Site: www.pen.org

Key Personnel
Coord: Stephen Motika *Tel:* 212-334-1660 ext
101 *E-mail:* motika@pen.org
Established: 1921
Grants for professional published writers & produced playwrights in financial emergencies due
to personal circumstances. These are not literary awards.
Award: Up to $2,500
Closing Date: Applications are accepted year-
round & reviewed approximately every 8 to 12
weeks

Pennsylvania Council on the Arts Literature Program
Pennsylvania Council on the Arts
216 Finance Bldg, Harrisburg, PA 17120
Tel: 717-787-6883 *Fax:* 717-783-2538
Web Site: www.pacouncilonthearts.org
Key Personnel
Prog Dir: Lori Frush
Awarded annually to poets & writers of fiction
& creative nonfiction, on the basis of artistic
quality. Categories alternate annually. In 2005,
poets are eligible. In 2004, fiction & creative
nonfiction writers are eligible. Applicants must
be Pennsylvania residents & nonstudents; call
for guidelines before June 1.
Award: $5,000 & $10,000
Closing Date: Aug 2

Periodical Natural History Essay Award, see
John Burroughs Outstanding Published Nature
Essay Award

Pfizer Award
History of Science Society
Affiliate of American Council of Learned Soci-
eties
University of Florida, 3310 Turlington Hall,
Gainesville, FL 32611
Mailing Address: PO Box 117360, Gainesville,
FL 32611-7360
Tel: 352-392-1677
E-mail: info@hssonline.org
Web Site: www.hssonline.org
Key Personnel
Exec Dir: Robert J Malone
Established: 1958
For an outstanding book in English, published
during the preceding three years, on a topic
related to the history of science.
Award: $2,500 & a medal
Closing Date: April 1
Presented: Late Nov

James D Phelan Literary Award
The San Francisco Foundation
225 Bush St, Suite 500, San Francisco, CA
94104-4224
Tel: 415-733-8500 *Fax:* 415-477-2783
Web Site: www.sff.org
Key Personnel
Arts & Culture Program Officer: John Killacky
E-mail: jrk@sff.org
Established: 1935
For the author of a work-in-progress, a novel,
short story, nonfiction, poetry or drama. Appli-
cants must be California-born & 20-35 years
old.
Award: $2,000 & certificate
Closing Date: Jan
Presented: Annually

Phi Beta Kappa Award in Science
Phi Beta Kappa
1606 New Hampshire Ave NW, Washington, DC
20009
Tel: 202-265-3808 *Fax:* 202-986-1601
Web Site: www.pbk.org

Key Personnel
Awards Coord: Sandra Beasley
E-mail: sbeasley@pbk.org
Established: 1959
For an outstanding interpretation of science writ-
ten by a scientist & published in the US during
the previous year. Works in the physical & bi-
ological sciences & mathematics are eligible
for the award. Highly technical works, mono-
graphs & reports on research are not eligible.
Nominations must come from publisher.
Award: $2,500
Closing Date: April 30 annually
Presented: Washington, DC, Annually in Dec

PIA/GATF/NAPL Sheetfed Executive of the Year
PIA/GATF (Graphic Arts Technical Foundation)
200 Deer Run Rd, Sewickley, PA 15143-2600
Tel: 412-741-6860 *Toll Free Tel:* 800-910-4283
Fax: 412-741-2311
E-mail: info@gain.net
Web Site: www.gain.net
Key Personnel
Pres: Michael Makin
Mktg Mgr: Lisa Erdner
Established: 1995
Acknowledges industry individual who has made
a major career contribution to technical & sci-
entific development of graphic/communication
industry. Honors a sheetfed industry leader who
has demonstrated exceptional service & com-
mitment to his or her community, company &
the sheetfed printing industry.
Other Sponsor(s): NAPL (National Association
for Printing Leadership)
Award: Sculpted eagle
Closing Date: Annually, March 1
Presented: PIA/GAFT/NAPL Sheetfed Pressroom
Conference, Annually, June

Robert J Pickering Award for Playwriting Excellence
Coldwater Community Theater
89 Division, Coldwater, MI 49036
Tel: 517-279-7963
Key Personnel
Comm Chmn: J Richard Colbeck
Established: 1984
Playwriting.
Other Sponsor(s): Hospice
Award: $300 & production (1st prize), $50 (2nd
prize), $25 (3rd prize)
Closing Date: Due by Dec 31 annually, entries
ongoing
Presented: Tibbits Opera House, Coldwater, MI,
Second weekend in Feb

Lorne Pierce Medal
Royal Society of Canada
283 Sparks St, Ottawa, ON K1R 7X9, Canada
Tel: 613-991-6990 *Fax:* 613-991-6996
E-mail: adminrsc@rsc.ca
Web Site: www.rsc.ca
Key Personnel
Awards Coord: Genevieve Gouin
Established: 1926
Awarded for an achievement of significance &
conspicuous merit in imaginative or critical lit-
erature.
Award: Medal
Closing Date: Dec 1
Presented: Ottawa, Alternate yrs in Nov; Next in
2006

Pilgrim Award & Pioneer Award
Science Fiction Research Association Inc
6021 Grassmere, Corpus Christi, TX 78415
Tel: 530-752-1699
E-mail: sands@uwm.edu
Web Site: www.sfra.org

Key Personnel
Pres: Peter Brigg *E-mail:* pbrigg@uoguelph.ca
VP: Janice Bogstad *E-mail:* bogstajm@uwec.edu
Established: 1970
Pilgrim: annual award for outstanding contributions to science fiction & fantasy scholarship; Pioneer: annual award for best scholarly article on science fiction & fantasy.
Award: Plaque
Closing Date: January
Presented: Annual conference, Mid Summer

Playboy College Fiction Contest
Playboy Enterprises Inc
730 Fifth Ave, New York, NY 10019
Tel: 212-261-5000 *Fax:* 212-957-2900
Web Site: www.playboy.com
Established: 1985
Short story contest for accredited college/university students.
Award: $3,000; publication in Oct (college) issue
Closing Date: Dec 31
Presented: Spring, by mail

Playhouse on the Square
Circuit Playhouse
51 S Cooper, Memphis, TN 38104
Tel: 901-725-0776 *Fax:* 901-272-7530
Key Personnel
Prod: Jackie Nichols
Established: 1980
Playwriting.
Award: $500
Closing Date: Annually, April 1
Presented: Circuit Playhouse

PlayLabs
The Playwrights' Center
2301 Franklin Ave E, Minneapolis, MN 55406
Tel: 612-332-7481 *Fax:* 612-332-6037
E-mail: info@pwcenter.org
Web Site: www.pwcenter.org
Key Personnel
Dir, New Play Devt: Kristen Gandrow *Tel:* 612-332-7481 ext 21
Established: 1982
Playwrights; applicants must be US citizens or permanent residents. Only unproduced, unpublished scripts are eligible. Participants are required to attend all of the conferences. Contact above for application form & guidelines or download from www.pwcenter.org.
Closing Date: Posted on website in the fall

Playwright Discovery Award
VSA arts
1300 Connecticut Ave NW, Suite 700, Washington, DC 20036
Tel: 202-628-2800 *Toll Free Tel:* 800-933-8721
Fax: 202-737-0725
Web Site: www.vsarts.org
Key Personnel
Dir, Performing Arts: Elena Widder
Established: 1984
Playwriting program for students with & without disabilities, grades 6-12. Script documents the experience of living with a disability.
Award: Attend performance of their script at JFK Center, scholarship funds
Presented: JFK Center for Performing Arts

Playwrights Project
450 "B" St, Suite 1020, San Diego, CA 92101-8093
Tel: 619-239-8222 *Fax:* 619-239-8225
E-mail: write@playwrightsproject.com
Web Site: www.playwrightsproject.com
Key Personnel
Exec Dir: Deborah Salzer
Los Angeles Coord: Kathryn Johnson-Schwartz
Devt Mgr: Laurel Withers

Established: 1985
Playwriting contest for Californians under 19 years of age.
Award: Professional production at the Old Globe Theatre in San Diego, royalty
Closing Date: June 1, 2005
Presented: San Diego, Jan 2006
Branch Office(s)
1612 Garden St, Glendale, CA 91201-2614
Tel: 818-242-3984

Playwriting Competition for Playwrights for Young Audiences, see Waldo M & Grace C Bonderman Prize

Plimpton Prize
Formerly Discovery Prize
The Paris Review Foundation
541 E 72 St, New York, NY 10021
Tel: 212-861-0016 *Fax:* 212-861-4504
Web Site: www.theparisreview.org
Awarded annually to the best work of fiction or poetry publishing in The Paris Review that year by an emerging or previously unpublished writer.
Award: $5,000
Presented: Annually, Winter

PMC Canadian Letters Award
Foundation for Advancement of Canadian Letters (FACL) & Periodical Marketers of Canada (PMC)
175 Bloor St E, South Tower, Suite 1007, Toronto, ON M4W 3R8, Canada
Tel: 416-968-7218 *Fax:* 416-968-6182
Key Personnel
Exec Dir: Ray Argyle *E-mail:* rargyle@periodical.ca
Established: 1976
To recognize an individual or an organization who has made an outstanding contribution to literacy & literature in Canada, either through writing, publishing, teaching or administration. Granted for recognition of achievement in either the French or English language. Through FACL, PMC maintains a selection committee to determine the recipient of the award for each year.
Award: Statuette & $5,000 (Canadian) donation to the charitable organization or educational institution of the winner's choice
Closing Date: Dec 31
Presented: April

PNWA Literary Competition
Pacific Northwest Writers Association
23607 Hwy 99, Suite 2C, Edmonds, WA 98026
Mailing Address: PO Box 2016, Edmonds, WA 98020-9516
Tel: 425-673-2665
E-mail: staff@pnwa.org
Web Site: www.pnwa.org
Key Personnel
Pres: Sharyn Bolton
Multiple categories by genre.
Presented: Annual summer conference

Poe Edgar Allan Awards, see Edgar Allan Poe Awards®

Poetry Center Book Award
Poetry Center & American Poetry Archives at San Francisco State University
1600 Holloway Ave, San Francisco, CA 94132
Tel: 415-338-2227 *Fax:* 415-338-0966
E-mail: poetry@sfsu.edu
Web Site: www.sfsu.edu/~poetry
Key Personnel
Busn Mgr: Elise Ficarra
Established: 1980

For an outstanding book of poetry published in the year of the award. Volumes by individual authors; anthologies & translations not accepted. Poets or publishers should send one copy of each book & a $10 fee. Include a cover letter noting author name, book title(s), name of person issuing check & check number.
Award: $500 & an invitation to read in the Poetry Center's series
Closing Date: Jan 31
Presented: Summer

Poetry In Print
PO Box 30981, Albuquerque, NM 87190-0981
Tel: 505-888-3937 *Fax:* 505-888-3937
Web Site: www.poets.com/RobertEnglish.html
Key Personnel
Owner & Dir: Robert G English
Established: 1991
National contest open to all age groups. Poetry 60 lines & no limit. $10 reading fee.
Award: $1,000
Closing Date: Annually in Aug
Presented: Albuquerque, NM, Annually in Aug

The George Polk Awards
Long Island University
The Brooklyn Campus, University Plaza, Brooklyn, NY 11201
Tel: 718-488-1115 *Fax:* 718-246-6302
Key Personnel
Curator: Sidney Offit
Chmn: Robert Donald Spector
Established: 1949
For outstanding discernment & reporting of a news or feature story on the Internet, in newspapers, radio or television. Entries originating from publication offices, newsrooms or individual reporters are considered. Submit two copies of stories or tapes. No entry fees or application forms; entries will not be returned.
Award: Plaque
Closing Date: January 8
Presented: Spring

Poor Richards Award
Small Press Center
20 W 44 St, New York, NY 10036
Tel: 212-764-7021 *Fax:* 212-354-5365
E-mail: info@smallpress.org
Web Site: www.smallpress.org
Key Personnel
Exec Dir: Karin Taylor
Established: 1991
An individual who has done much to advance the cause of small press publishing over a period of at least two decades. Winner selected by Executive Board of the Small Press Center.
Award: Statuette of Benjamin Franklin
Presented: Small Press Center, in conjunction with the annual Small Press Book Fair in New York, NY, end of March, annually

Katherine Anne Porter Prize for Fiction
Nimrod, The University of Tulsa
Subsidiary of The Nimrod/Hardman Awards
University of Tulsa, 600 S College, Tulsa, OK 74104
Tel: 918-631-3080 *Fax:* 918-631-3033
E-mail: nimrod@utulsa.edu
Web Site: www.utulsa.edu/nimrod
Key Personnel
Ed: Francine Ringold, PhD
Man Ed: Eilis O'Neal
Established: 1978
7500 words maximum. No previously published works or works accepted for publication elsewhere. Author's name must not appear on manuscript. Include a cover sheet containing major title & subtitles, author's name, address, phone number & e-mail address. "Contest Entry" must be on envelope. Manuscripts will not be returned. Nimrod retains the right to publish

any submission. Works not accepted will be released; SASE for results only.
Award: $2,000 (1st prize), $1,000 (2nd prize); plus each published writer receives two copies of the journal; winners are flown to Tulsa for a conference & banquet
Closing Date: April 30 Annually
Presented: Tulsa, OK, Annually in Oct

Prairie Schooner Readers' Choice Awards
University of Nebraska/Prairie Schooner
University of Nebraska, 201 Andrews Hall, Lincoln, NE 68588
Mailing Address: PO Box 880334, Lincoln, NE 68588-0334
Tel: 402-472-0911
E-mail: kgrey2@unl.edu
Web Site: www.unl.edu/schooner/psmain.htm
Key Personnel
Ed: Hilda Raz
Established: 1989
Annual writing prizes for best work published in the magazine. Only work published in Prairie Schooner in the previous year is considered.
Other Sponsor(s): Local & national donors to the magazine
Award: $250 cash
Presented: Winners announced in spring issue

Prairie Schooner Strousse Award
University of Nebraska/Prairie Schooner
University of Nebraska, 201 Andrews Hall, Lincoln, NE 68588
Mailing Address: PO Box 880334, Lincoln, NE 68588-0334
Tel: 402-472-0911 *Fax:* 402-472-9771
Web Site: www.unl.edu/schooner/psmain.htm
Key Personnel
Ed: Hilda Raz
Established: 1975
For best poetry published in the magazine each year.
Other Sponsor(s): Friends & family of Flora Strousse
Award: $500
Presented: Prairie Schooner, March

Derek Price/Rod Webster Prize Award
History of Science Society
Affiliate of American Council of Learned Societies
University of Florida, 3310 Turlington Hall, Gainesville, FL 32611
Mailing Address: PO Box 117360, Gainesville, FL 32611-7360
Tel: 352-392-1677
E-mail: info@hssonline.org
Web Site: www.hssonline.org
Key Personnel
Exec Dir: Robert J Malone
Established: 1978
For article appearing in Isis during the preceding three years.
Award: $1,000
Closing Date: April 1
Presented: Cambridge, MA, Late Oct or early Nov

Printing Industries of America Premier Print Award
Printing Industries of America Inc
200 Deer Run Rd, Sewickley, PA 15143
Tel: 412-741-6860 *Fax:* 412-741-2311
Web Site: www.gain.net
Key Personnel
Chmn of the Bd: Chuck Stay
CEO: Michael Makin
Pres: Ray Roper
Dir, Mktg: Nancy Shafranski-Campabello
Established: 1950
Awards competition for printed material.

Award: Plaques & certificates
Closing Date: May

Michael L Printz Award
Young Adult Library Services Association (YALSA)
Unit of American Library Association
50 E Huron St, Chicago, IL 60611
Tel: 312-280-4390 *Toll Free Tel:* 800-545-2433 (ext 4390) *Fax:* 312-664-7459
E-mail: yalsa@ala.org
Web Site: www.ala.org/yalsa/printz
Key Personnel
Prog Officer: Nichole Gilbert *E-mail:* ngilbert@ala.org
Established: 1999
Honors excellence in literature written for young adults. May be fiction, nonfiction, poetry or an anthology & must have been published during the preceding year & designated as young adult book or ages 12-18.
Closing Date: Dec 1
Presented: YALSA Printz Reception during ALA Annual Conference

Prism International Fiction Contest
Prism International
University of British Columbia, Buch E462, 1866 Main Mall, Vancouver, BC V6T 1Z1, Canada
Tel: 604-822-2514 *Fax:* 604-822-3616
E-mail: prism@interchange.ubc.ca
Web Site: prism.arts.ubc.ca
Key Personnel
Exec Ed: Brenda Leifso
Ed: Amanda LaMarche; Catharine Chen
Established: 1986
Short fiction.
Award: $2,000 (grand prize), $200 (5 runners-up prizes)
Closing Date: Annually on Jan 31

Prix Alvine-Belisle
ASTED
3414 Avenue Du Parc, Bureau 202, Montreal, PQ H2X 2H5, Canada
Tel: 514-281-5012 *Fax:* 514-281-8219
E-mail: info@asted.org
Web Site: www.asted.org
Key Personnel
Agent: Marie-Helene Parent
Dir Gen: Louis Cabral
To the best books for young people published in French in Canada during the previous year.
Award: $1,000
Closing Date: End of June
Presented: Salon Du Livre, Montreal, PQ

Prix Champlain
Le Conseil De La Vie Francaise En Amerique
Maison de la francophonie, 39, rue Dalhousie, Quebec, PQ G1K 8R8, Canada
Tel: 418-646-9117 *Fax:* 418-644-7670
E-mail: cvfa@cvfa.ca
Web Site: www.cvfa.ca
Key Personnel
Dir Gen: Guy Lefebure *E-mail:* guylef@cvfa.ca
Established: 1957
Award: $1,500 & certificat d'attestation
Closing Date: Dec 31
Presented: Quebec, April 29

Prize for the Translation of Japanese Literature, see Japan-US Friendship Commission Translation Prize

Prize Stories: The O Henry Awards
Anchor Books
Division of Random House Inc
Univ of Texas at Austin, One University Sta B 5000, Austin, TX 78712
Tel: 212-572-2016

Web Site: www.ohenryprizestories.com
Key Personnel
Ed: Laura Furman
Publicist: Sloane Crosley
Established: 1918
For the best English language short stories published in American & Canadian magazines & written by American or Canadian authors during the previous Jan 1 to Dec 31. No submissions; selections made by the editor from among more than 300 published in the approximately 260 magazines with print editions consulted for the series. Top three prizes chosen by a jury of writers. The Magazine Award is given to the magazine with the most stories selected for a given volume of O'Henry Awards.

Prometheus Awards
Libertarian Futurist Society
26 Partridge Hill, Honeye Falls, NY 14472
Tel: 585-582-1068
Web Site: www.lfs.org
Key Personnel
Dir: Victoria Varga *E-mail:* vvarga@rochester.rr.com
Asst Dir: Fran Van Cleave
Established: 1979
Prometheus Award - best published novel of previous year that dramatizes the value of freedom. Hall of Fame—classic libertarian fiction.
Award: Prometheus one ounce gold coin; Hall of Fame one-eighth ounce coin
Closing Date: March 1st of each year for previous year
Presented: World Science Fiction Convention or NASFIC, Labor Day weekend

Pudding House Poetry Chapbook Competition
Formerly National Looking Glass Poetry Chapbook Competition
Pudding House Publications
81 Shadymere Lane, Columbus, OH 43213
Tel: 614-986-1881
E-mail: info@puddinghouse.com
Web Site: www.puddinghouse.com
Key Personnel
Pres: Jennifer Bosveld
Established: 1980
Poetry chapbook. Send poems about any subject; any style. We often lean toward social concerns, human services, interpersonal relations, popular culture, justice issues. Enclose SASE. No postcards. $15 entry fee for 10-30 poems, themed or not.
Award: Minimum of $100 & 20 copies of published book; some special larger awards possible
Closing Date: Annually, Sept 30
Presented: Pudding House Publications, Columbus, OH, By Dec 1

Pulitzer Prizes
Columbia University
709 Journalism Bldg, New York, NY 10027
Tel: 212-854-3841 *Fax:* 212-854-3342
E-mail: pulitzer@pulitzer.org
Web Site: www.pulitzer.org
Key Personnel
Admin: Sig Gissler
Admin Asst: Joseph O Legaspi
Dept Admin: Edward Kliment
Established: 1917
Given to American authors for a distinguished book of fiction, performed play, history of the US, biography or autobiography, verse or general nonfiction, as well as journalism prizes for newspaper work in US dailies or weeklies, books must be first published in the calendar year.
Award: Gold medal for public service journalism category; $10,000 & certificate in all other categories

Closing Date: July 1 for books published Jan 1-
June 30, Nov 1 for books published July 1-Dec
31 literary prizes, Feb 1 (journalism), March 1
(drama) March 1 (music)
Presented: Annually in spring

Pushcart Prize: Best of the Small Presses
Pushcart Press
PO Box 380, Wainscott, NY 11975-0380
Tel: 631-324-9300
Key Personnel
Pres: Bill Henderson
Established: 1976
Awarded for works previously published by a
small press or literary journal.
Award: Copies of the book The Pushcart Prize:
Best of the Small Presses
Closing Date: Dec 1, annually
Presented: Annually in the spring

QPB/New Visions Award
Quality Paperback Book Club
Division of Bookspan
Time & Life Bldg, 1271 Avenue of the Americas,
New York, NY 10020
Tel: 212-522-4200 *Fax:* 212-467-0239
E-mail: pr@bookspan.com
Web Site: www.bookspan.com
Key Personnel
Ed-in-Chief: Vivan Kasha
Established: 1990
No submissions accepted for award. Presented to
the most distinctive & promising author of a
published work of nonfiction. Books are chosen
from club's titles from the previous year.
Award: $5,000
Presented: Annually in the winter

QPB/New Voices Award
Quality Paperback Book Club
Division of Bookspan
Time & Life Bldg, 1271 Avenue of the Americas,
New York, NY 10020
Tel: 212-522-4200 *Fax:* 212-467-0239
E-mail: pr@bookspan.com
Web Site: www.bookspan.com
Key Personnel
Ed-in-Chief: Vivan Kasha
Established: 1984
No submissions accepted. Presented to the most
distinctive & promising author of a published
work of fiction offered by the club during the
year.
Award: $5,000
Presented: Annually in winter

Quarterly Review of Literature International Poetry Book Competition
Quarterly Review of Literature
26 Haslet Ave, Princeton, NJ 08540
Fax: 609-258-2230
E-mail: qrl@princeton.edu
Web Site: www.princeton.edu/~qrl
Key Personnel
Man Ed: Renee Weiss
Established: 1978
International. Send SASE for important informa-
tion.
Award: Four to six awards of $1,000 each for
books of poetry, publication & 100 copies of
the volume

Quarterly West Novella Competition
University of Utah
255 S Central Campus Dr, Dept of English
LNCO3500, Salt Lake City, UT 84112-9109
Tel: 801-581-3938 *Fax:* 801-585-5167
E-mail: quarterlywest@utah.edu
Web Site: www.utah.edu/quarterlywest
Key Personnel
Ed: David C Hawkins

Established: 1981
Biennial Novella Competition; $25 entry fee.
Award: 2 winners $600 each & publication in
Quarterly West
Presented: Univ of Utah, Oct 2005

QWF Prizes
Quebec Writers' Federation (QWF)
1200 Atwater Ave, Suite 3, Montreal, PQ H3Z
1X4, Canada
Tel: 514-933-0878
E-mail: admin@qwf.org
Web Site: www.qwf.org
Key Personnel
Pres: Ian Ferrier
Sec: Derek Webster
Admin Dir: Lori Schubert
Established: 1988
Literary for Quebec, English language authors.
Award: A M Klein Prize (poetry): $2,000; Hugh
MacLennon Prize (fiction): $2,000; Mavis Gal-
lant Prize (nonfiction): $2,000; McAuslan First
Book Prize: $2,000; Translation Prize: $2,000
Closing Date: May 31 & Aug 1. Request details

Thomas Head Raddall Atlantic Fiction Award
Writers Federation of Nova Scotia
1113 Marginal Rd, Halifax, NS B3H 4P7, Canada
Tel: 902-423-8116 *Fax:* 902-422-0881
E-mail: talk@writers.ns.ca
Web Site: www.writers.ns.ca
Key Personnel
Exec Dir: Jane Buss
Presented to best fiction book, published by an
Atlantic Canadian writer in previous calendar
year.
Award: $10,000
Closing Date: First Friday in Dec
Presented: Halifax, NS, Canada, May of each
year

The Ragan Old North State Cup for Nonfiction
North Carolina Literary & Historical Association
Affiliate of North Carolina Literary & Historical
Association
4610 Mail Service Center, Raleigh, NC 27699-
4610
Tel: 919-807-7290 *Fax:* 919-733-8807
Key Personnel
Awards Coord: Michael Hill *E-mail:* michael.
hill@ncmail.net
Established: 2003
For published book of nonfiction, not technical or
scientific, by a legal or actual resident of North
Carolina for at least three years prior to end of
contest.
Award: Cup
Closing Date: July 15 annually
Presented: Raleigh, NC, Annually in Nov

Raiziss/de Palchi Fellowship
The Academy of American Poets Inc
588 Broadway, Suite 604, New York, NY 10012
Tel: 212-274-0343 *Fax:* 212-274-9427
E-mail: academy@poets.org
Web Site: www.poets.org
Key Personnel
Prog Dir: Ryan Murphy *Tel:* 212-274-0343 ext 17
E-mail: rmurphy@poets.org
Established: 1995
Given biennially to enable an American trans-
lator of 20th century Italian poetry to travel,
study, or otherwise advance a significant work-
in-progress. For guidelines & entry form, send
SASE in August of even-numbered years.
Award: $20,000 & residency at the American
Academy in Rome
Closing Date: Sept 1-Nov 1(even-numbered
years)
Presented: Jan

Raiziss/de Palchi Translation Award
The Academy of American Poets Inc
588 Broadway, Suite 604, New York, NY 10012
Tel: 212-274-0343 *Fax:* 212-274-9427
E-mail: academy@poets.org
Web Site: www.poets.org
Key Personnel
Prog Dir: Ryan Murphy *Tel:* 212-274-0343 ext 17
E-mail: rmurphy@poets.org
Established: 1995
Given biennially for a translation into English of
a significant work of modern Italian poetry by
a living American translator. Send SASE for
guidelines.
Award: $5,000 book prize (odd-numbered yrs);
$20,000 fellowship (even-numbered yrs)
Closing Date: Aug 1-Nov 1 (odd-numbered years)
Presented: Jan

Sir Walter Raleigh Award for Fiction
North Carolina Literary & Historical Association
Affiliate of North Carolina Literary & Historical
Association
4610 Mail Service Center, Raleigh, NC 27699-
4610
Tel: 919-807-7290 *Fax:* 919-733-8807
Key Personnel
Awards Coord: Michael Hill *E-mail:* michael.
hill@ncmail.net
Established: 1952
For the best book of fiction by an author who has
been a legal or actual resident of North Car-
olina for at least three years prior to the end of
the contest.
Other Sponsor(s): Historical Book Club of North
Carolina
Award: Statuette
Closing Date: July 15 annually
Presented: Raleigh, NC, Annually in Nov

The Rea Award for the Short Story
Dungannon Foundation
53 W Church Hill Rd, Washington, CT 06794
Web Site: reaaward.org
Key Personnel
Pres: Elizabeth R Rea
Established: 1986
Sponsored annually by the Dungannon Founda-
tion, the Rea Award was established in 1986
by Michael M Rea to honor a living US or
Canadian writer who has made a significant
contribution to the short story form. No sub-
missions accepted. The recipient is nominated
& selected by a jury.
Award: $30,000

Robert F Reed Technology Medal
PIA/GATF (Graphic Arts Technical Foundation)
200 Deer Run Rd, Sewickley, PA 15143-2600
Tel: 412-741-6860 *Toll Free Tel:* 800-910-4283
Fax: 412-741-2311
E-mail: info@gain.net
Web Site: www.gain.net
Key Personnel
Pres: Michael Makin
Mktg Mgr: Lisa Erdner
Established: 1974
Acknowledges industry individual who has made
a major career contribution to technical & sci-
entific development of graphic/communication
industry.
Award: Engraved medal

Regina Medal Award
Catholic Library Association
100 North St, Suite 224, Pittsfield, MA 01201-
5109
Tel: 413-443-2252 *Fax:* 413-442-2252
E-mail: cla@cathla.org
Web Site: www.cathla.org
Key Personnel
Exec Dir: Jean R Bostley, SSJ
Established: 1959

For continued distinguished lifetime contribution to children's literature; no unsol mss.
Award: Sterling silver medal
Closing Date: none; in-house votes

Residency
Millay Colony for the Arts
454 E Hill Rd, Austerlitz, NY 12017
Mailing Address: PO Box 3, Austerlitz, NY 12017-0003
Tel: 518-392-3103; 518-392-4144 *Fax:* 518-392-7664
E-mail: apply@millaycolony.org
Web Site: www.millaycolony.org
Key Personnel
Exec Dir: Drake Patten *E-mail:* director@millaycolony.org
Exec Asst: Nikki Hayes
Residencies for writers, composers & visual artists; send SASE to receive application & information; applications available by e-mail at address above.
Award: One-month residencies offered; no cash award
Closing Date: Oct 1

The Harold U Ribalow Prize
Hadassah Magazine
50 W 58 St, New York, NY 10019
Tel: 212-451-6289 *Fax:* 212-451-6257
E-mail: imarks@hadassah.org
Web Site: www.hadassah.org
Key Personnel
Exec Ed: Alan M Tigay
Established: 1983
An outstanding English-language work of fiction on a Jewish theme by an author deserving of recognition.
Other Sponsor(s): Harold U Ribalow family
Award: $2,000
Closing Date: April of the year following publication
Presented: Annually in autumn

Evelyn Richardson Memorial Literary Trust Award
Writers Federation of Nova Scotia
1113 Marginal Rd, Halifax, NS B3H 4P7, Canada
Tel: 902-423-8116 *Fax:* 902-422-0881
E-mail: talk@writers.ns.ca
Web Site: www.writers.ns.ca
Key Personnel
Exec Dir: Jane Buss
Established: 1978
Presented to the best nonfiction book, published by a native or resident Nova Scotian in the previous calendar year.
Award: $1,000
Closing Date: First Friday in Dec
Presented: Halifax, NS, Canada, May

Mary Roberts Rinehart Fund
George Mason Univ, English Dept, 4400 University Dr, Mail Stop Number 3E4, Fairfax, VA 22030-4444
Tel: 703-993-1185
Web Site: www.gmu.edu/depts/english
Key Personnel
Graduate Studies Coord: Barb Gomperts *E-mail:* bgompert@gmu.edu
Contact: William Miller
Established: 1983
For best nominated manuscript in fiction, nonfiction & poetry. Must be nominated by someone in the field. Candidates for grants in fiction & nonfiction should submit a freestanding entry. No entry should exceed 30 pages. Candidates in poetry should submit ten pages of individual or collected poems. Submit nominating letter, two copies of the mss & a brief autobiographical statement in one envelope. Those who wish

to receive a printed announcement should send a SASE.
Award: Three grants of $2,000 each (varies by year)
Closing Date: Nov 30
Presented: Spring

Gwen Pharis Ringwood Award for Drama
Banff Centre
11759 Groat Rd, Edmonton, AB T5M 3K6, Canada
Tel: 780-422-8174 *Toll Free Tel:* 800-665-5354 (Alberta only) *Fax:* 780-422-2663
E-mail: mail@writersguild.ab.ca
Web Site: www.writersguild.ab.ca
Key Personnel
Exec Dir: Diane Walton
Established: 1982
Alberta Literary Award, must be resident of Alberta.
Award: $1,000 plus leather-bound copy of book
Closing Date: Dec 31
Presented: Alberta

Rip Van Winkle Award
School Library Media Specialists of Southeastern New York
Division of New York Library Association
252 Hudson Ave, Albany, NY 12210
Tel: 518-432-6952 (NY Libr Assn)
Web Site: www.nyla.org
Key Personnel
SLMSSENY Pres: Ellen Rubin
Established: 1980
To an outstanding author of children's or young adult literature who resides in our seven-county Southeastern New York area.
Award: Crystal clock
Presented: March or April

River City Writing Awards
Hohenburg Foundation
c/o University of Memphis, Dept English, Memphis, TN 38152
Tel: 901-678-4591 *Fax:* 901-678-2226
E-mail: rivercity@memphis.edu
Web Site: www.people.memphis.edu/~rivercity/contests.html
Key Personnel
Ed-in-Chief: Mary Leader
Man Ed: Kathleen Bradley
Awarded annually to best poem & fiction.
Award: Fiction:1st prize $1,500, 2nd $350, 3rd $150; Poetry: 1st prize $1,000, 2nd & 3rd publication & 1 year subscription
Closing Date: March
Presented: June

River City Writing Awards in Fiction
Hohenburg Foundation
University of Memphis, Dept of English, Memphis, TN 38152
Tel: 901-678-4591 *Fax:* 901-678-2226
E-mail: rivercity@memphis.edu
Web Site: www.people.memphis.edu/~rivercity/contests.html
Key Personnel
Assoc Ed: Tom Carlson
Edit Bd: Gordon Osing
Poetry Ed: Liza Kirk
Established: 1987
Any previously unpublished short story of up to 7500 words is eligible. No novel chapters. Writers may enter one ms, typed, double-spaced & accompanied by a cover letter. The authors' name should NOT appear anywhere on the ms itself. Indicate Contest Entry on your outer envelope accompanied by a $12 entry fee. Indicate if you would like the fee to begin or extend a subscription to River City. River City will publish the prize-winning stories &

retains the right of first refusal to publish any contest entry. No mss will be returned.
Award: $1,500 (1st prize), $350 (2nd prize), $150 (3rd prize)
Closing Date: March 1
Presented: April

Roanoke-Chowan Award for Poetry
North Carolina Literary & Historical Association
Affiliate of North Carolina Literary & Historical Association
4610 Mail Service Center, Raleigh, NC 27699-4610
Tel: 919-807-7290 *Fax:* 919-733-8807
Key Personnel
Awards Coord: Michael Hill *E-mail:* michael.hill@ncmail.net
Established: 1953
For the best published book of poetry by a legal or actual resident of North Carolina for at least three years prior to the end of the contest period.
Other Sponsor(s): Roanoke-Chowan Group of Writers & Allied Artists
Award: Cup
Closing Date: Annually, July 15
Presented: Raleigh, Nov

Rocky Mountain Book Award
PO Box 42, Lethbridge, AB T1J 3Y3, Canada
Tel: 403-381-7164
E-mail: rockymountainbookaward@shaw.ca
Web Site: www.lethsd.ab.ca/lvbookaward
Key Personnel
Contact: Michelle Dimnik
Established: 2001
Grade 4-7 Children's Choice Book Award.
Closing Date: Jan 15, 2005
Presented: Lethbridge, AB, varies

Nicholas Roerich Poetry Prize
Story Line Press
2091 Suncrest Rd, Talent, OR 97540
Mailing Address: PO Box 1240, Ashland, OR 97520-0055
Tel: 541-512-8792 *Fax:* 541-512-8793
E-mail: mail@storylinepress.com
Web Site: www.storylinepress.com
Key Personnel
Publr & Ed: Robert McDowell *E-mail:* robert@storylinepress.com
Prodn: Sharon McCann
Established: 1987
First book contest for an unpublished ms of poetry.
Other Sponsor(s): Nicholas Roerich Museum
Award: $1,000 & reading at the Roerich Museum in NY on publication (1st prize)
Closing Date: Annually Oct 31

Rogers Writers' Trust Fiction Prize
The Writers' Trust of Canada
90 Richmond St W, Suite 200, Toronto, ON M5C 1P1, Canada
Tel: 416-504-8222 *Fax:* 416-504-9090
E-mail: info@writerstrust.com
Web Site: www.writerstrust.com
Key Personnel
Exec Dir: Lascelle Wingate *Tel:* 416-504-8222 ext 242
Established: 1997
Awarded for a work of fiction novel or collection of short stories published in the previous year.
Other Sponsor(s): Rogers Communications
Award: $15,000
Presented: The Great Literary Awards, March

Rolling Stone's Annual College Journalism Competition
Rolling Stone
Subsidiary of Wenner Media
1290 Avenue of the Americas, 2nd fl, New York, NY 10104

Tel: 212-484-1616; 212-484-1636 *Fax:* 212-484-3434
Web Site: www.rollingstone.com
Key Personnel
CJC Coord: Kerry Smith *E-mail:* kerry.smith@rollingstone.com
Journalism competition.
Award: $2,500 (3 cash prizes in 3 categories)
Closing Date: Announces in Fall, Nov 1
Presented: Fall

Romance Writers of America Awards
Romance Writers of America
16000 Stuebner Airline, Suite 140, Spring, TX 77379
Tel: 832-717-5200 *Fax:* 832-717-5201
E-mail: info@rwanational.org
Web Site: www.rwanational.org
Key Personnel
Exec Dir: Allison Kelley *E-mail:* akelley@rwanational.org
Established: 1981
Golden Heart: for unpublished romance novelist; RITA Award: best published romance novels for preceding year.
Award: Heart necklace for Golden Heart, Statue for RITA Award
Closing Date: Nov
Presented: Annual National Conference, Summer

Lois Roth Award for a Translation of a Literary Work
Modern Language Association of America (MLA)
26 Broadway, 3rd fl, New York, NY 10004-1789
Tel: 646-576-5141 *Fax:* 646-458-0030
E-mail: awards@mla.org
Web Site: www.mla.org
Key Personnel
Coord, Book Prizes & Spec Projs: Annie Reiser
Committee solicits submissions of translations of literary works. Translations published in year prior to competition are eligible. Translators need not be members of the association.
Award: $1,000 & certificate
Closing Date: Six copies & 12-15 pages of original text by April 1
Presented: MLA Convention, Biennially (even-numbered years) Dec 28

William B Ruggles Journalism Scholarship
National Institute for Labor Relations Research
5211 Port Royal Rd, Suite 510, Springfield, VA 22151
Tel: 703-321-9606 *Fax:* 703-321-7342
E-mail: research@nilrr.org
Web Site: www.nilrr.org
Key Personnel
Scholarship Coord: Cathy Jones
Established: 1974
Scholarship grant.
Award: $2,000
Closing Date: Dec 31

The Cornelius Ryan Award
Overseas Press Club of America (OPC)
40 W 45 St, New York, NY 10036
Tel: 212-626-9220 *Fax:* 212-626-9210
Web Site: www.opcofamerica.org
Key Personnel
Exec Dir: Sonya Fry
Awarded for best nonfiction book on international affairs.
Award: Scroll - Cash Award
Closing Date: Jan 31
Presented: New York City, Late April

Saint Louis Literary Award
Saint Louis University Library Associates
40 N Kingshighway Blvd, 10-J, St Louis, MO 63108
Tel: 314-361-1616 *Fax:* 314-361-0812

Key Personnel
Exec Sec: Bernice H Shepherd
Established: 1967
For body of author's work. No applications; awardee chosen by committee.
Award: Honorarium, Citation

The Ernest Sandeen & Richard Sullivan Prizes in Fiction & Poetry
University of Notre Dame Press
356 O'Shaughnessy Hall, Notre Dame, IN 46556
Tel: 574-631-7526
E-mail: english.righter.1@nd.edu
Web Site: www.nd.edu
Key Personnel
Dir: William O'Rourke
The Sandeen Prize in Poetry & the Sullivan Prize in Short Fiction are awarded to authors who have published at least one volume of short fiction or one volume of poetry. Please include a photocopy of the copyright & the title page of your previous volume. Vanity press publications do not fulfill this requirement. Please include a vita &/or a biographical statement which includes your publishing history. We will be glad to see a selection of reviews of the earlier collection. Please submit two copies of your ms & inform us if the ms is available on computer disk. Include an SASE for acknowledgment of receipt of your submission. If you would like your ms returned, send an SASE. A $15 administrative fee should accompany submissions.
Award: $1,000 prize, $500 award & $500 advance against royalties from the Notre Dame Press
Closing Date: May 1-Sept 1, 2006 (Richard Sullivan Prize); May 1-Sept 1, 2007 (Ernest Sandeen Prize)

Marie Sandoz Award
Nebraska Library Association
c/o Margaret Harding, PO Box 98, Crete, NE 68333-0098
Tel: 402-826-2636 *Fax:* 402-826-2636
E-mail: gh12521@alltel.net
Web Site: www.nebraskalibraries.org
Key Personnel
Exec Dir: Margaret Harding
Established: 1971
Given to a distinguished Nebraska author.
Award: Plaque
Closing Date: March 1
Presented: NLA Fall Convention, Oct

May Sarton Award
New England Poetry Club
16 Cornell St, Arlington, MA 02474
Web Site: www.nepoetryclub.org
Key Personnel
Contest Chmn: Elizabeth Crowell
Pres: Diana Der Hovanessian
Honorary awards for work that inspires other writers. Chosen by board members. Mark name of contest on envelope, send poem in duplicate with name of author on one only.
Closing Date: June 30
Presented: Cambridge Library, Annually, Spring

SATW Foundation Lowell Thomas Travel Journalism Competition
Society of American Travel Writers Foundation
1500 Sunday Dr, Suite 102, Raleigh, NC 27607
Tel: 919-861-5586; 713-532-6461 *Fax:* 919-787-4916
Web Site: www.satw.org
Key Personnel
Pres: Milton Fullman
Established: 1985
Premier awards for the best work in travel journalism. Competition is open to all North American journalists & is judged by the University

of Missouri School of Journalism. There are 27 categories, including individual & publication awards. Among them: Grand Award for Travel Journalist of the Year for a portfolio of work, Best Newspaper Travel sections (divided by circulation), Best Travel Magazine, Best Travel Coverage in Other Magazines, Best Guidebook, Best Travel Book, Best Travel Web Publication & 17 categories for writing & photography. For entry details & forms, visit www.satw.org (click on Lowell Thomas Awards). Check for deadline; new materials usually updated by Feb. 1 yearly.
Award: $19,850 total in prize money in 19 categories: $1,500 (top prize), $500 (1st place)
Closing Date: April 15 (subject to change)
Presented: Location varies

The Barbara Savage
The Mountaineers Books
1001 SW Klickitat Way, Suite 201, Seattle, WA 98134
Tel: 206-223-6303 *Fax:* 206-223-6306
E-mail: mbooks@mountaineers.org
Web Site: www.mountaineersbooks.org
Key Personnel
Rts Mgr: Mary Metz *Tel:* 206-223-6303 ext 119 *E-mail:* marym@mountaineersbooks.org
Established: 1990
Compelling nonfiction account of a personal outdoor adventure. Acceptable subjects include personal narratives involving hiking, mountain climbing, bicycling, paddle sports, skiing, snowshoeing, nature, conservation, ecology & adventure travel not based on motorized transport. Subjects not acceptable are fishing, hunting, horseback-riding & any motorized or competitive sports.
Award: $3,000 cash award, $12,000 advance against royalties & publication by The Mountaineers Books
Closing Date: March 1, 2004 (biannual award)
Presented: Publication of award-winning ms will occur within 18 months of completion of manuscript, March 1, 2005 (on or before) announcement of winning submission made by March 1, 2005

Aldo & Jeanne Scaglione Prize for a Translation of a Literary Work
Modern Language Association of America (MLA)
26 Broadway, 3rd fl, New York, NY 10004-1789
Tel: 646-576-5141 *Fax:* 646-458-0030
E-mail: awards@mla.org
Web Site: www.mla.org
Key Personnel
Coord, Book Prizes & Spec Projs: Annie Reiser
Established: 1994
Awarded each even-numbered year for an outstanding translation into English of a book-length literary work; books must have been published in year prior to competition. Translators need not be members of MLA.
Award: $2,000 & certificate
Closing Date: Six copies & 12-15 pages of original text by April 1
Presented: MLA Convention, Biennially (even-numbered yrs), Dec 28

Aldo & Jeanne Scaglione Prize for a Translation of a Scholarly Study of Literature
Modern Language Association of America (MLA)
26 Broadway, 3rd fl, New York, NY 10004-1789
SAN: 202-6422
Tel: 646-576-5141 *Fax:* 646-458-0030
E-mail: awards@mla.org
Web Site: www.mla.org
Key Personnel
Coord, Book Prizes & Spec Projs: Annie Reiser
For an outstanding translation into English of a book-length work of literary history, literary

criticism, philology or literary theory published in two years prior to competition.
Award: $2,000 & certificate
Closing Date: Four copies by May 1
Presented: MLA Convention, Biennially (odd-numbered yrs), Dec 28

Aldo & Jeanne Scaglione Prize for Comparative Literary Studies
Modern Language Association of America (MLA)
26 Broadway, 3rd fl, New York, NY 10004-1789
Tel: 646-576-5141 *Fax:* 646-458-0030
E-mail: awards@mla.org
Web Site: www.mla.org
Key Personnel
Coord, Book Prizes & Spec Projs: Annie Reiser
Established: 1992
For an outstanding scholarly work by a member of the MLA in the field of comparative literary studies involving at least two literatures, published in year prior to competition. Must be a member of the MLA.
Award: $2,000 & certificate
Closing Date: Four copies by May 1
Presented: MLA Convention, Annually, Dec 28

Aldo & Jeanne Scaglione Prize for French & Francophone Studies
Modern Language Association of America (MLA)
26 Broadway, 3rd fl, New York, NY 10004-1789
Tel: 646-576-5141 *Fax:* 646-458-0030
E-mail: awards@mla.org
Web Site: www.mla.org
Key Personnel
Coord, Book Prizes & Spec Projs: Annie Reiser
Established: 1992
For an outstanding scholarly work by a member of the MLA in the field of French or Francophone literary or linguistic studies published the previous year. Authors must be members of the MLA.
Award: $2,000 & certificate
Closing Date: Four copies by May 1
Presented: MLA Convention, Annually, Dec 28

Aldo & Jeanne Scaglione Prize for Italian Studies
Modern Language Association of America (MLA)
26 Broadway, 3rd fl, New York, NY 10004-1789
Tel: 646-576-5141 *Fax:* 646-458-0030
E-mail: awards@mla.org
Web Site: www.mla.org
Key Personnel
Coord, Book Prizes & Spec Projs: Annie Reiser
Established: 2000
For an outstanding study in Italian literature or comparative literature involving Italian by an MLA member for books published in the year prior to competition.
Award: $2,000 & certificate
Closing Date: Four copies by May 1
Presented: MLA Convention, Bienially (odd-numbered years), Dec 28

Aldo & Jeanne Scaglione Prize for Studies in Germanic Languages & Literature
Modern Language Association of America (MLA)
26 Broadway, 3rd fl, New York, NY 10004-1789
Tel: 646-576-5141 *Fax:* 646-458-0030
E-mail: awards@mla.org
Web Site: www.mla.org
Key Personnel
Coord, Book Prizes & Spec Projs: Annie Reiser
Open only to members of the Association for an outstanding scholarly work on the linguistics or literatures of the Germanic languages including Danish, Dutch, German, Icelandic, Norwegian, Swedish & Yiddish & published in the two years prior to competition.
Award: $2,000 & certificate

Closing Date: 4 copies by May 1
Presented: MLA Convention, Biennially (even-numbered years), Dec 28

Aldo & Jeanne Scaglione Prize for Studies in Slavic Languages & Literature
Modern Language Association of America (MLA)
26 Broadway, 3rd fl, New York, NY 10004-1789
Tel: 646-576-5141 *Fax:* 646-458-0030
E-mail: awards@mla.org
Web Site: www.mla.org
Key Personnel
Coord, Book Prizes & Spec Projs: Annie Reiser
For an outstanding scholarly work on the linguistics or literatures of the Slavic languages & published in the two years prior to the competition. Authors need not be members of the MLA.
Award: $2,000 & certificate
Closing Date: Four copies by May 1
Presented: MLA Convention, Biennially (odd-numbered yrs), Dec 28

Aldo & Jeanne Scaglione Publication Award for a Manuscript in Italian Literary Studies
Modern Language Association of America (MLA)
26 Broadway, 3rd fl, New York, NY 10004-1789
Tel: 646-576-5141 *Fax:* 646-458-0030
For an outstanding ms dealing with any aspect of the languages & literatures of Italy. Ms accepted for publication by a member of the AAUP before award deadline; authors must be current members of the MLA.
Award: $8,000, submission to the press, $2,000 & certificate to the author
Closing Date: Four copies by Aug 1
Presented: MLA Convention, Dec 28, annually

William Sanders Scarborough Prize
Modern Language Association of America (MLA)
26 Broadway, 3rd fl, New York, NY 10004-1789
SAN: 202-6422
Tel: 646-576-5141 *Fax:* 646-458-0030
E-mail: awards@mla.org
Web Site: www.mla.org
Key Personnel
Coord, Book Prizes & Spec Projs: Annie Reiser
Established: 2001
For an outstanding scholarly study of Black American literature or culture published the previous year. Author need not be a member of the MLA.
Award: $1,000 & certificate
Closing Date: Four copies by May 1
Presented: MLA Convention, Annually, Dec 28

SCBWI Work-In-Progress Grants
Society of Children's Book Writers & Illustrators (SCBWI)
8271 Beverly Blvd, Los Angeles, CA 90048
Tel: 323-782-1010 *Fax:* 323-782-1892
E-mail: membership@scbwi.org
Web Site: www.scbwi.org
Key Personnel
Pres: Steve Mooser
Exec Dir: Lin Oliver
Contact: Sue Burgess
Established: 1978
The General Work-In-Progress Grant, the Work-In-Progress Grant for Nonfiction Research, the Work-In-Progress Grant for a Contemporary Novel for Young People & the Grant for a Work by an Author Who Has Never Been Published have been established to assist children's book writers in the completion of a specific project. Must be SCBWI member to qualify.
Award: $1,500 each & $500 for one runner-up in each category
Closing Date: March 1
Presented: Sept

William D Schaeffer Environmental Award
PIA/GATF (Graphic Arts Technical Foundation)
200 Deer Run Rd, Sewickley, PA 15143-2600
Tel: 412-741-6860 Toll Free Tel: 800-910-4283
Fax: 412-741-2311
E-mail: info@gain.net
Web Site: www.gain.net
Key Personnel
Pres: Michael Makin
Mktg Mgr: Lisa Erdner
Honors significant contributions to environmental awareness by an individual in the printing industry.
Award: Engraved Plaque
Closing Date: May 30
Presented: PIA/GATF Administrative Meetings

Bernadotte E Schmitt Grants
American Historical Association
400 "A" St SE, Washington, DC 20003
Tel: 202-544-2422 *Fax:* 202-544-8307
E-mail: info@historians.org
Web Site: www.historians.org
Key Personnel
Prize Admin: Debbie Ann Doyle *Tel:* 202-544-2422 ext 104 *E-mail:* ddoyle@historians.org
Support research in the history of Europe, Africa & Asia. Only members of the Association are eligible. The grants are intended to further research in progress & may be used for travel to a library or archive, for microfilms, photographs, or xeroxing, for coding & key punching. Preference will be given to those with specific research needs, such as the completion of a project or completion of a discrete segment thereof. Preference will be given to junior scholars, PhD candidates & those without access to institutional funds. No application form, applicants must simply mail a copy of their book to each of the prize committee members who will be posted on our web site as the prize deadline approaches. All updated info on web site.
Award: Individual grants will not exceed $1,000; Preference to PhD candidates & scholars
Closing Date: Feb 15, 2005

Scholastic Library/Grolier National Library Week Grant
American Library Association (ALA)
50 E Huron St, Chicago, IL 60611
Tel: 312-280-4020 Toll Free Tel: 800-545-2433 (ext 4020) *Fax:* 312-944-8520
E-mail: pio@ala.org
Web Site: www.ala.org
Key Personnel
Coord, The Campaign for America's Libraries: Megan Humphrey *E-mail:* mhumphrey@ala.org
All types of libraries are encouraged to apply. The $5,000 award is presented annually to a single library to support its National Library Week Communications initiatives that use the "@your library" logo. See web site (www.ala.org/@yourlibrary) for more information & to download an application available annually, midsummer.
Award: $5,000
Closing Date: Annually in the Fall, call for specific date
Presented: Annually in Jan

Henry & Ida Schuman Prize
History of Science Society
Affiliate of American Council of Learned Societies
University of Florida, 3310 Turlington Hall, Gainesville, FL 32611
Mailing Address: PO Box 117360, Gainesville, FL 32611-7360
Tel: 352-392-1677
E-mail: info@hssonline.org
Web Site: www.hssonline.org

Key Personnel
Exec Dir: Robert J Malone
Established: 1955
For an original essay, not to exceed 8,000 words, in history of science & its cultural influences. Open to graduate students only. Must send in three copies of essay with a detachable author/title page.
Award: $500 (& up to $500 travel reimbursement)
Closing Date: April 1
Presented: Late Nov

Ruth Schwartz Children's Book Award
Ruth Schwartz Foundation
c/o Ontario Arts Council Literature Office, 151 Bloor St W, 5th fl, Toronto, ON M5S 1T6, Canada
Tel: 416-961-1660 (ext 7438) *Toll Free Tel:* 800-387-0058 (Canada) *Fax:* 416-961-7796
E-mail: info@arts.on.ca
Web Site: www.arts.on.ca
Key Personnel
Lit Officer: Lorraine Filyer
Established: 1975
For outstanding work of author/illustrator in Canadian children's literature. May not be applied for; by nomination only by Canadian children's booksellers. For Canadian writers & illustrators only.
Other Sponsor(s): Canadian Booksellers Association; Ontario Arts Council
Award: $3,000 (Canadian) picture book; $2,000 (Canadian) young adult/middle reader
Presented: Toronto, ON, Annually, spring

Science in Society Journalism Awards
National Association of Science Writers (NASW)
PO Box 890, Hedgesville, WV 25427
Web Site: www.nasw.org
Key Personnel
Exec Dir: Diane McGurgan *E-mail:* diane@nasw.org
Established: 1972
To provide recognition for investigative reporting about the sciences & their impact for good & bad, for material published or broadcast between the period of June 1 & May 31 prior to presentation. Awarded in six categories: newspapers, magazines, television, radio, website & books. Publishers & broadcasters will also receive certificates of recognition.
Award: $1,000, Certificate of Recognition in each category
Closing Date: Postmarked July 1, annually
Presented: February

Sentner Memorial Short Story Award
Prince Edward Island Council of the Arts
115 Richmond St, Charlottetown, PE C1A 1H7, Canada
Tel: 902-368-4410 *Fax:* 902-368-4418
E-mail: peiarts@peiartscouncil.com
Web Site: www.peiartscouncil.com
Key Personnel
Exec Dir: Darrin White
One short story constitutes an entry. May submit as many entries as they wish. Work must be original & unpublished. Contest for Prince Edward Island residents only. Call for further information or e-mail.
Award: $500 (1st prize), $200 (2nd prize), $100 (3rd prize)
Closing Date: Call or e-mail
Presented: Call or e-mail

Sequoyah Children's Book Award
Oklahoma Library Association
300 Hardy Dr, Edmond, OK 73013
Tel: 405-348-0506 *Fax:* 405-348-1629
Web Site: www.oklibs.org

Key Personnel
Exec Dir: Kay Boies *E-mail:* kboies@coxinet.net
Established: 1959
School children's choice of a book by a living US author from a selected list. Elementary grade students are eligible to participate.
Award: Plaque
Closing Date: Jan 31
Presented: OLA Spring Conference, April 2005

Sequoyah Young Adult Book Award
Oklahoma Library Association
300 Hardy Dr, Edmond, OK 73013
Tel: 405-348-0506 *Fax:* 405-348-1629
Web Site: www.oklibs.org
Key Personnel
Exec Dir: Kay Boies *E-mail:* kboies@coxinet.net
Established: 1988
For school children's choice of a book by a living US author from a selected list. Middle school/junior high students are eligible to participate.
Award: Plaque
Closing Date: Jan 31
Presented: OLA Spring Conf, April 2005

SFWA Nebula Awards
Science Fiction & Fantasy Writers of America Inc
PO Box 877, Chestertown, MD 21620
Toll Free Tel: 888-322-7392
E-mail: execdir@sfwa.org
Web Site: www.sfwa.org
Key Personnel
Pres: Jane Jewell
VP: Catherine Asaro
Sec: ElizaBeth Gilligan
Treas: Lawrence Evans
Established: 1966
Winners are selected by the members of the SFWA in the categories of novel, novella, novelette & short story.
Award: Lucite trophy

Mina P Shaughnessy Prize
Modern Language Association of America (MLA)
26 Broadway, 3rd fl, New York, NY 10004-1789
Tel: 646-576-5141 *Fax:* 646-458-0030
E-mail: awards@mla.org
Web Site: www.mla.org
Key Personnel
Coord, Book Prizes & Spec Projs: Annie Reiser
Established: 1980
For an outstanding publication in the field of language, culture, literacy, or literature with strong application to the teaching of English, published in year prior to competition. Authors need not be a member of the MLA.
Award: $1,000, certificate & one-year membership in the association
Closing Date: Seven copies by May 1
Presented: MLA Convention, Annually, Dec 28

Shenandoah International Playwrights Retreat
Shenandoah International Playwrights Inc
717 Quick's Mill Rd, Staunton, VA 24401
Tel: 540-248-4113 *Fax:* 540-248-4113 (call first)
E-mail: sip@ntelos.net
Key Personnel
Artistic Dir: Robert Graham Small *E-mail:* rgsmall@ntelos.net
Man Dir: Kathleen Tosco
Established: 1976
Retreats & residencies for American & international writers at Pennroyal farm in Shenandoah Valley; program geared to facilitate major rewrite or new draft of existing script; personal writing balanced by workshops & staged readings with professional company of dramaturgs, directors & actors. Full fellowships available.
Other Sponsor(s): Asian Cultural Council; Augusta Foundation; Dalmas Foundation; Hong

Kong Arts Development Corp; Joelson Foundation; National Foundation for Jewish culture; Stanley Foundation; The Jordon Society; Viet Nam Generations Inc; Virginia Commission for the Arts
Award: Fellowship
Closing Date: Feb 1 of each year

Short Story Award/Debut Author Award - The Blaggard Award
New Mystery Magazine
101 W 23 St, Penthouse No 1, New York, NY 10011
Tel: 212-353-3495
E-mail: editorial@newmystery.tv
Web Site: www.newmystery.tv
Key Personnel
Chmn: Charles A Raisch, III
Established: 1989
All new mystery, crime & suspense, short fiction, annual "Best First Mystery Story" for first-time authors short story.
Award: Publication of story plus prizes & party fete
Closing Date: Annually, Dec 31
Presented: Lock Museum Library, New York, NY, late April

Robert F Sibert Informational Book Award
Association for Library Service to Children
Division of American Library Association
50 E Huron St, Chicago, IL 60611-2795
Tel: 312-280-2163 *Toll Free Tel:* 800-545-2433 *Fax:* 312-944-7671
E-mail: alsc@ala.org
Web Site: www.ala.org/alsc
Presented to the author of the most distinguished informational book published during the previous year.
Other Sponsor(s): Bound to Stay Bound Books Inc
Award: Medal
Presented: ALSC Membership Meeting held during ALA, Annually

Dorothy Silver Playwriting Competition
Jewish Community Center of Cleveland
3505 Mayfield Rd, Cleveland Heights, OH 44118
Tel: 216-382-4000 (ext 215) *Fax:* 216-382-5401
E-mail: halletheatre@clevejcc.org
Web Site: www.clevejcc.org
Key Personnel
Competition Coord: Deborah Bobrow
Established: 1982
Original works not previously produced at time of submission; suitable for full-length presentation; directly concerned with the Jewish experience. A condition of the award is that the JCC Theatre will have permission to perform the first fully staged production of the winning script following the staged reading without payment of additional royalties.
Award: $1,000 plus staged reading
Closing Date: May 1
Presented: Jewish Community Center of Cleveland, Annually

Francis B Simkins Award
Southern Historical Association
University of Georgia, Dept of History, Athens, GA 30602-1602
Tel: 706-542-8848 *Fax:* 706-542-2455
Web Site: www.uga.edu/~sha
Key Personnel
Admin Asst: Gloria Davis *E-mail:* gsdavis@uga.edu
Established: 1977
Awarded for the most distinguished first book by an author in Southern history over a two-year period. Awarded in odd-numbered years for book published in two previous years.
Award: Cash

Closing Date: March 1, 2005
Presented: Atlanta, GA, Nov 3, 2005

The John Simmons Short Fiction Award
Writers' Workshop, The University of Iowa
Univ of Iowa, Writers Workshop, 102 Dey House,
   507 N Clinton St, Iowa City, IA 52242
Tel: 319-335-0416 *Toll Free Tel:* 800-553-4692
   (ext 0416) *Fax:* 319-335-0420
Any writer who has not previously published a
   volume of prose fiction is eligible to enter the
   competition for prizes. Revised mss which have
   been previously entered may be resubmitted.
   Writers who have published a volume of poetry
   are eligible. Mss must be a collection of short
   stories of at least 150 typewritten pages. Stories previously published in periodicals are eligible for inclusion. Xeroxed copies are acceptable. SASE return packaging must accompany
   the mss. Do not send cash, checks, or money
   orders. Not responsible for loss of mss in the
   mail or for the return of those not accompanied
   by a stamped envelope. We assume the author
   retains the original copy of the mss.
Award: Publication by University of Iowa Press
Closing Date: Aug 1-Sept 30
Presented: Annually in autumn

Charlie May Simon Award
Arkansas State Dept of Education
Division of School Improvement
Arkansas Dept of Education, Rm 401-B, No 4
   Capitol Mall, Little Rock, AR 72201
Tel: 501-682-4232 *Fax:* 501-682-4441
Web Site: arkedu.state.ar.us
Established: 1970
State of Arkansas upper elementary students
   read books selected by the award committee
   throughout the year & vote on favorite choice.
   Most popular book wins award (medallion) &
   second place award rewarded as Honor Book
   (plaque).
Award: CMS Medallion for first place, plaque for
   Honor Book
Closing Date: May 1, Annual vote
Presented: Little Rock, AR, Sept

Skipping Stones Honor Awards
Skipping Stones Inc
1309 Lincoln St, Eugene, OR 97401
Mailing Address: PO Box 3939, Eugene, OR
   97403
Tel: 541-342-4956 *Fax on Demand:* 541-342-
   4956
E-mail: info@skippingstones.org
Web Site: www.skippingstones.org
Key Personnel
Exec Ed: Arun N Toke *E-mail:* editor@
   skippingstones.org
Established: 1993
Honors exceptional multicultural & international
   awareness books, nature/ecology books, teaching resources & educational videos/DVDs. A
   panel of parents, teachers, librarians, students
   & editors of Skipping Stones select the winning entries.
Award: Honor award certificate, award seals, reviews, press releases, e-releases
Closing Date: Jan 20, annually
Presented: Eugene Multicultural Storytelling Con-
   cert, End of April, reviewed in May-Aug issue
   of Skipping Stones

Bernice Slote Award
Prairie Schooner
University of Nebraska, 201 Andrews Hall, Lin-
   coln, NE 68588
Mailing Address: PO Box 880334, Lincoln, NE
   68588-0334
Tel: 402-472-0911
E-mail: kgrey2@unl.edu
Web Site: www.unl.edu/schooner/psmain.htm

Key Personnel
Ed: Hilda Raz
Established: 1985
Annual writing prize for best work by a begin-
   ning writer published in Prairie Schooner in the
   previous year.
Award: $500
Presented: Prairie Schooner Magazine, Annually
   in the spring issue

Kay Snow Literary Contest
Willamette Writers
9045 SW Barbur Blvd, Suite 5-A, Portland, OR
   97219
Tel: 503-452-1592 *Fax:* 503-452-0372
E-mail: wilwrite@willamettewriters.com
Web Site: www.willamettewriters.com
Key Personnel
Off Mgr: Bill Johnson
Contest Coord: Marlene Moore
Established: 1971
Literary competition in six categories: fiction,
   nonfiction, juvenile, poetry, scriptwriting, stu-
   dent writer. Entry fee $10/$15. Free for stu-
   dents.
Award: $300 (1st prize), $150 (2nd prize), $50
   (3rd prize)

The Society of Midland Authors Awards
The Society of Midland Authors (SMA)
PO Box 10419, Chicago, IL 60610-0419
Tel: 773-506-7578 *Fax:* 773-784-5900
E-mail: info@midlandauthors.com
Web Site: www.midlandauthors.com
Key Personnel
Pres: R Craig Sautter *E-mail:* rcsautter@aol.com
Treas: Robert Remer
Corresponding Sec: Phyllis Ford Choyke
Recording Sec: Stella Pevsher
VP & Membership Sec: Tom Frisbie
   E-mail: tomfrisbie@aol.com
Webmaster: Mary Claire Hersh
   E-mail: maryclaire@prodigy.net
Established: 1915
For books published in the previous year in the
   following categories: adult & children's fiction
   & nonfiction, biography, poetry. Also lifetime
   achievement awards.
Award: Monetary award (varies, $300 minimum)
   & plaque
Closing Date: Feb 1
Presented: The Cliff Dwellers Club, 200 S Michi-
   gan Ave, Chicago, IL, Annually second Tues-
   day in May

The Society of Southwestern Authors (SSA)
PO Box 30355, Tucson, AZ 85751-0355
Tel: 520-546-9382 *Fax:* 520-296-0409
Web Site: www.azstarnet.com/nonprofit/ssa
Key Personnel
Pres & Conference Chmn: Penny Porter
   E-mail: wporter202@aol.com
Established: 1972
Awards for short fiction, 3,000 words max, per-
   sonal essays & memoirs 2,000 words & poetry
   40 lines.
Other Sponsor(s): Barnes & Noble, Tucson, AZ
Award: $300 (1st prize), $150 (2nd prize), $75
   (3rd prize)
Closing Date: Sept 30
Presented: Barnes & Noble, Tucson, AZ

Sophie Kerr Prize
Washington College
c/o College Relations Office, 300 Washington
   Ave, Chestertown, MD 21620
Tel: 410-778-2800 *Toll Free Tel:* 800-422-1782
   Fax: 410-810-7150
Web Site: www.washcoll.edu
Key Personnel
Assoc Dir, Coll Rel: Marcia Landskroener
   E-mail: mlandskroener2@washcoll.edu

Established: 1968
Literary award to graduating senior. Only open to
   undergraduates of Washington College.
Award: $56,000
Closing Date: April 15
Presented: Washington College Commencement,
   Chestertown, MD, May 22, 2005

**Southeastern Theatre Conference New Play
Project**
Southeastern Theatre Conference
1114 Whitehall Rd, Murfreesboro, TN 37130
Tel: 336-272-3645 *Fax:* 336-272-8810
E-mail: setc@sectonline.com
Web Site: www.setc.org
Key Personnel
Chair, New Play Project: Deborah Anderson
   Tel: 731-424-3520 ext 438
Membership Mgr: Hardy Koenig
New play contest.
Award: $1,000, travel & expenses, possible publi-
   cation
Closing Date: March-June
Presented: Southeastern Theatre Conference Con-
   vention, March 2005

Southern Books Competition
Southeastern Library Association
1438 W Peachtree St NW, Suite 200, Atlanta, GA
   30309-2955
Tel: 404-892-0943 *Fax:* 404-892-7879
Web Site: www.solinet.net
Established: 1952
Recognition for excellence in bookmaking. Win-
   ners are displayed at SELA Conference & in
   a traveling exhibit available to institutions &
   organizations. It has been borrowed throughout
   the South, Canada, Scandinavia, Soviet Union
   & South Africa.
Award: Published recognition list. Rotating &
   permanent display of winning books
Closing Date: Annually, date fluctuates

Southern Playwrights Competition
Dept of English/Jacksonville State University
700 Pelham Rd N, Jacksonville, AL 36265-1602
Tel: 256-782-5414 *Fax:* 256-782-5441
Web Site: www.jsu.edu/depart/english/southpla.
   htm
Key Personnel
Coord: J Maloney *E-mail:* sjmloney@jsucc.jsu.
   edu; Steven J Whitton *E-mail:* swhitton@jsucc.
   jsu.edu
Established: 1988
Drama.
Award: $1,000 honorarium & production of win-
   ning entry
Closing Date: Feb 15

**The Southern Review/LSU Short Fiction
Award**
Southern Review/Louisiana State University
Louisiana State University, 43 Allen Hall, Baton
   Rouge, LA 70803-5005
Tel: 225-578-5108 *Fax:* 225-578-5098
E-mail: bmacon@lsu.edu
Web Site: www.lsu.edu/thesouthernreview
Key Personnel
Contact: John Easterly
Best first collection of short stories published
   in previous year in US. Must be a US author.
   Winner will be invited to read at LSU.
Award: $500
Closing Date: Jan 31 of year following publica-
   tion
Presented: By letter, early summer

**Sovereign Award Outstanding Newspaper
Story, Outstanding Feature Story**
The Jockey Club of Canada
Woodbine Sales Pavilion, 555 Rexdale Blvd, Rex-
   dale, ON M9W 5L2, Canada

Mailing Address: PO Box 66, Sta B, Etobicoke, ON M9W 5K3, Canada
Tel: 416-675-7756 *Fax:* 416-675-6378
E-mail: jockeyclub@bellnet.ca
Web Site: www.jockeyclubcanada.com
Key Personnel
Exec Dir: Bridget Bimm
Established: 1975
Submissions must be of Canadian Thoroughbred Racing content.
Award: Bronze statue of
Closing Date: Oct 31
Presented: Wyndham Bristol Place, Toronto, ON, Dec

The Sow's Ear Poetry Prize & The Sow's Ear Chapbook Prize
The Sow's Ear Poetry Review
Division of The Word Process Inc
355 Mount Lebanon Rd, Donalds, SC 29638-9115
Tel: 864-379-8061
Key Personnel
Contest Dir & Man Ed: Errol Hess
 E-mail: errol@kitenet.net
Established: 1988
Single poem & chapbook.
Award: Poem: $1,000 (1st prize), $250 (2nd prize), $100 (3rd prize); Chapbook: $1,000 plus 25 copies (1st prize), $200 (2nd prize), $100 (3rd prize)
Closing Date: Accepted Sept & Oct (poem), Accepted March & April (chapbook)

SPUR Awards
Western Writers of America Inc
1012 Fair St, Franklin, TN 37064
Tel: 615-791-1444 *Fax:* 615-791-1444
Web Site: www.westernwriters.org
Key Personnel
Pres: Rita Cleary *E-mail:* rmcleary@mindspring.com; Paul Andrew Hutton *E-mail:* wha@unm.edu
VP: Cotton Smith
Sec & Treas: James A Crutchfield
 E-mail: tncrutch@aol.com
Established: 1953
Various categories (western fiction/nonfiction).
Award: Plaques & recognition
Closing Date: Dec 31 of current year for awards, presentation following June
Presented: Mequire, NV 2004; Spokane, WA 2005, June

The Edna Staebler Award for Creative Non-Fiction
Wilfrid Laurier University
75 University Ave W, Waterloo, ON N2L 3C5, Canada
Tel: 519-884-1970 (ext 3109) *Fax:* 519-884-8202
Key Personnel
Award Admin: Kathryn Wardropper
 E-mail: kwardrop@wlu.ca
Established: 1991
Literary, for a first or second published book of creative nonfiction. Open to Canadian residents only; to encourage new Canadian writers.
Award: $3,000
Closing Date: April 30 postmark, annually
Presented: Wilfrid Laurier University, Fall annually

Stanley Drama Award
Wagner College
One Campus Rd, Staten Island, NY 10301
Tel: 718-390-3157 *Fax:* 718-390-3323
Key Personnel
Asst Prof: Felicia J Ruff *E-mail:* fruff@wagner.edu
Established: 1957
Award given for original full-length play or musical which has not been professionally produced or received tradebook publication. Writers of musicals are urged to submit music on cassette tapes as well as books & lyrics. Consideration will also be given to a series of two or three thematically related one-act plays. Scripts must be accompanied by a SASE. Former winners are not eligible to compete. Applications are obtained by sending SASE.
Award: $2,000
Closing Date: Oct 1
Presented: Annually in April

Edward Stanley Award
Prairie Schooner
University of Nebraska, 201 Andrews Hall, Lincoln, NE 68588
Mailing Address: PO Box 880334, Lincoln, NE 68588-0334
Tel: 402-472-0911 *Fax:* 402-472-9771
E-mail: kgrey2@unl.edu
Web Site: www.unl.edu/schooner/psmain.htm
Key Personnel
Ed: Hilda Raz
Established: 1992
Annual writing prize for best poem or group of poems in the volume. Only contributors to the magazine are eligible.
Other Sponsor(s): Friends & family of Marion Edward Stanley (in memorium)
Award: $1,000
Presented: Prairie Schooner Magazine, Annually in the spring

Agnes Lynch Starrett Poetry Prize
University of Pittsburgh Press
3400 Forbes Ave, Pittsburgh, PA 15260
Tel: 412-383-2456 *Fax:* 412-383-2466
Web Site: www.pitt.edu/~press
Key Personnel
Asst to Dir: Sue Hasychak *Tel:* 412-383-2492
 E-mail: susief@pitt.edu
Established: 1981
Open to any poet who has not had a full-length book previously published. Submit typed 48-100 page poetry mss on white paper with SASE & check or money order of $20 for each ms submitted. Entries must be postmarked between March 1 & April 30.
Award: $5,000 cash & publication
Closing Date: April 30
Presented: Pittsburgh, PA, Fall

Stegner Fellowship
Stanford University
Stanford Creative Writing Program, Mail Code 2087, Stanford, CA 94305-2087
Tel: 650-723-2637 *Fax:* 650-723-3679
Web Site: www.stanford.edu/dept/english/cw/fellowship.html
Key Personnel
Prog Admin: Virginia Hess *E-mail:* vfhess@stanford.edu
Fellowship; residence required for two years at Stanford beginning autumn quarter each year.
Award: $22,000 & required tuition
Closing Date: Dec 1

Stephan G Stephannson Award for Poetry
Banff Centre
11759 Groat Rd, Edmonton, AB T5M 3K6, Canada
Tel: 780-422-8174 *Toll Free Tel:* 800-665-5354 (Alberta only) *Fax:* 780-422-2663
E-mail: mail@writersguild.ab.ca
Web Site: www.writersguild.ab.ca
Key Personnel
Exec Dir: Diane Walton
Established: 1982
Alberta Literary Award, must be resident of Alberta.
Award: $1,000 plus leather-bound copy of book
Closing Date: Dec 31

Elizabeth Matchett Stover Memorial Award
Southwest Review
Affiliate of Southern Methodist University
307 Fondren Library W, 6404 Hilltop Lane, Dallas, TX 75275-0374
Mailing Address: PO Box 750374, Dallas, TX 75274-0374
Tel: 214-768-1037 *Fax:* 214-768-1408
E-mail: swr@mail.smu.edu
Web Site: www.southwestreview.org
Key Personnel
Ed-in-Chief: Willard Spiegelman
Sr Ed: Elizabeth Mills *Tel:* 214-768-1036
Established: 1978
To the author of the best poem or group of poems published in the Southwest Review during the preceding year.
Award: $250
Presented: Annually

The Sugarman Family Award for Jewish Children's Literature
The District of Columbia Jewish Community Center
1529 16 St NW, Washington, DC 20036
Tel: 202-518-9400 *Fax:* 202-518-9420
Key Personnel
Dir, Literature, Music & Dance: Jessika Cirkus
 Tel: 202-777-3208 *E-mail:* jessika@dcjcc.org
Established: 1994
Award for the best Jewish children's book published in 2005. Submissions accepted starting July 1. Presented biennially; contact office for dates.
Award: $750 (cash)
Closing Date: Dec 2005
Presented: Jewish Literary Festival, Oct 2006

Joan G Sugarman Children's Book Award
Washington Independent Writers Legal & Educational Fund, Inc
1851 Columbia Rd NW, No 205, Washington, DC 20009
Mailing Address: PO Box 70437, Washington, DC 20024-0437
Tel: 202-466-1344
E-mail: sugarman@lefund.org
Web Site: www.washwriter.org
Key Personnel
Coord: Rob Anderson
Established: 1987
For books of fiction or nonfiction geared to children ages one to 15. The book must be written by a resident of Washington, DC, Virginia or Maryland.
Award: $1,000
Presented: Washington, DC, Biennial

Richard Sullivan Prizes in Fiction & Poetry, see The Ernest Sandeen & Richard Sullivan Prizes in Fiction & Poetry

May Swenson Poetry Award
Utah State University Press
7800 Old Main Hill, Logan, UT 84322-7800
Tel: 435-797-1362 *Fax:* 435-797-0313
Web Site: www.usu.edu/usupress
Key Personnel
Dir: Michael Spooner *E-mail:* michael.spooner@usu.edu
Exec Ed: John Alley *E-mail:* john.alley@usu.edu

Sydney Taylor Book Awards
Association of Jewish Libraries (AJL)
15 E 26 St, New York, NY 10010-1579
Tel: 212-725-5359 *Fax:* 212-481-4174
E-mail: ajl@jewishbooks.org
Web Site: www.jewishlibraries.org

Key Personnel
Chair: Sydney Taylor
Libn: Heidi Estrin *Tel:* 561-241-1482 ext 206
  E-mail: heidi@cbiboca.org
Established: 1968
Literary content for outstanding children's books
  in field of Jewish literature. Two categories:
  picture book for young children & older chil-
  dren's books.
Award: $2,000 (2-4 awards)
Closing Date: Dec 31
Presented: AJL Annual Convention, June

Sydney Taylor Manuscript Award
Association of Jewish Libraries (AJL)
15 E 26 St, New York, NY 10010-1579
Tel: 212-725-5359 *Fax:* 212-678-8998
E-mail: ajl@jewishbooks.org
Web Site: www.jewishlibraries.org
Key Personnel
Competition Coord: Rachel K Glasser
  E-mail: rkglasser@aol.com
To encourage outstanding new books written by
  an unpublished author with Jewish themes but
  with appeal to all children ages 8-11 & to help
  launch new children's writers in their careers.
Award: $1,000
Closing Date: Dec 31
Presented: annual convention, June

Charles S Sydnor Award
Southern Historical Association
University of Georgia, Dept of History, Athens,
  GA 30602-1602
Tel: 706-542-8848 *Fax:* 706-542-2455
Web Site: www.uga.edu/~sha
Key Personnel
Admin Asst: Gloria Davis *E-mail:* gsdavis@uga.
  edu
Established: 1956
Awarded for the most distinguished book in
  Southern history published in odd-numbered
  years. Awarded in even-numbered years.
Award: Cash
Closing Date: March 1
Presented: Memphis, TN, Nov

T S Eliot Prize for Poetry
Truman State University Press
100 E Normal St, Kirksville, MO 63501-4221
Tel: 660-785-7336 *Toll Free Tel:* 800-916-6802
  Fax: 660-785-4480
E-mail: tsup@truman.edu
Web Site: tsup.truman.edu
Key Personnel
Dir: Nancy Rediger
Established: 1997
Annual award for the best unpublished book-
  length collection of poetry in English.
Award: $2,000 & publication
Closing Date: Oct 31
Presented: Jan

**Rennie Taylor-Alton Blakeslee Fellowships in
Science Writing**
Council for the Advancement of Science Writing
  (CASW)
PO Box 910, Hedgesville, WV 25427
Tel: 304-754-5077 *Fax:* 304-754-5076
Web Site: www.casw.org
Key Personnel
Exec Dir: Ben Patrusky
Established: 1975
For tuition & books for graduate study only.
Award: $1,000 to $2,000
Closing Date: July 1

Teddy Award for Children's Books
Writers' League of Texas
1501 W Fifth St, Suite E-2, Austin, TX 78703
Tel: 512-499-8914 *Fax:* 512-499-0441

E-mail: wlt@writersleague.org
Web Site: www.writersleague.org
Key Personnel
Exec Dir: Helen Ginger *E-mail:* helen@
  writersleague.org
Established: 1995
Award for outstanding children's & young adult
  book published by Writers' League members.
  Membership fee may accompany entry.
Other Sponsor(s): Barnes & Noble
Award: $1,000 cash prize & a teddy bear trophy
Closing Date: May 31 for books published June-
  May
Presented: Barnes & Noble Bookstore Austin,
  TX, Annually in Sept

Tennessee Arts Commission Fellowships
Tennessee Arts Commission
401 Charlotte Ave, Nashville, TN 37243-0780
Tel: 615-741-1701 (voice & TDD) *Fax:* 615-741-
  8559
Web Site: www.arts.state.tn.us
Key Personnel
Dir, Literary Arts: Kim Leavitt *E-mail:* kim.
  leavitt@statet.tn.us
Literary fellowships given to Tennessee writers of
  every genre with special emphasis on emerging
  writers.
Award: $5,000
Closing Date: Jan 2005

The Texas Bluebonnet Award
Texas Library Association
3355 Bee Cave Rd, Suite 401, Austin, TX 78746
Tel: 512-328-1518 *Toll Free Tel:* 800-580-2852
  Fax: 512-328-8852
Web Site: www.txla.org
Key Personnel
Admin: Carolyn Reynolds *E-mail:* carolynr@txla.
  org
Established: 1979
Awarded to favorite title on annual list, voted on
  by 200,000 children, grades three through six.
Other Sponsor(s): Children's Round Table &
  Texas Association of School Librarians
Award: Medallion in desk mount
Closing Date: Aug 1
Presented: April

Texas Institute of Letters Awards
Texas Institute of Letters
3700 Mockingbird Lane, Dallas, TX 75205
Tel: 512-245-2232 *Fax:* 512-245-7462
Web Site: www.stedwards.edu/newc/marks/til/
  awards_and_rules.htm; www.english.swt.
  edu/css/til/rules.htm
Key Personnel
VP: Joe Holley
Dir: Mark Busby *Tel:* 512-245-2428
  E-mail: mb13@swt.edu
Treas: Jim Hoggard
Sec: Fran Vick *E-mail:* franvick@aol.com
Established: 1936
For books published by Texas residents or on
  Texas-related subjects. Write for instructions.
Award: Eleven cash awards, totalling $20,600
Closing Date: Jan 7, 2005
Presented: March banquet, Ft Worth, TX, USA,
  March 2005

The Theatre Library Association Award
The Theatre Library Association
Division of Benjamin Rosenthal Library
Queens College, CUNY, Flushing, NY 11367
Tel: 718-997-3762 *Fax:* 718-997-3753
Web Site: tla.library.unt.edu
Key Personnel
Chmn: Richard Wall *E-mail:* rlw$lib@qcl.qc.edu
Exec Secy, TLA: Joseph M Yranski *Tel:* 212-621-
  0538
Established: 1973

Honors books published in US in the field of
  recorded performance including motion picture,
  TV & radio. Ineligible books are: directories,
  collections from previously published sources
  & reprints.
Award: $500 winner, $200 Special Jury Prize;
  certificate
Closing Date: Feb 15 of year following publication
Presented: New York City, NY, late May or early
  June

Theatre-Scriptworks
Pennsylvania Council on the Arts
216 Finance Bldg, Harrisburg, PA 17120
Tel: 717-787-6883 *Fax:* 717-783-2538
Web Site: www.pacouncilonthearts.org
Key Personnel
Prog Dir: Lori Frush
Fellowships for playwrights who create & per-
  form their own work. Must be PA resident.
  Biennial award, odd-numbered years.
Award: $5,000 or $10,000
Closing Date: Aug 1

Three Day Novel Contest
Anvilpress Inc
3495 Cambie St, Suite 364, Vancouver, BC V5Z
  4R3, Canada
E-mail: 3day@bluelakebooks.com
Web Site: www.anvilpress.com
Established: 1977
International novel writing competition, $50
  Canadian, $40 US registration fee, postmarked
  up until one day before contest.
Other Sponsor(s): SubTerrain Magazine
Award: Off-publication, sales royalties
Closing Date: Registration
Presented: Annually on Labor Day weekend

The Three Oaks Prize in Fiction
Story Line Press
2091 Suncrest Rd, Talent, OR 97540
Mailing Address: PO Box 1240, Ashland, OR
  97520-0055
Tel: 541-512-8792 *Fax:* 541-512-8793
E-mail: mail@storylinepress.com
Web Site: www.storylinepress.com
Key Personnel
Publr & Ed: Robert McDowell *E-mail:* robert@
  storylinepress.com
Prodn Dir: Sharon McCann *E-mail:* sharon@
  storylinepress.com
Open to novels, short stories & novellas.
Award: $1,500 & publication
Closing Date: April 30, annually

Thurber Prize for American Humor
Thurber House
77 Jefferson Ave, Columbus, OH 43215
Tel: 614-464-1032 *Fax:* 614-280-3645
E-mail: thurberhouse@thurberhouse.org
Web Site: www.thurberhouse.org
Key Personnel
Exec Dir: Susanne Jaffe
Mgr, Mktg & Spec Events: Emily Swartzlander
Annual award for the most outstanding book of
  humor writing published in the United States.
  The award is presented by Thurber House, a
  non-profit literary center in Columbus, OH &
  the former home of American humorist, author
  & New Yorker cartoonist James Thurber.
Award: $5,000, commemorative plaque & a na-
  tionwide media campaign
Closing Date: April 1 (annually)
Presented: The Algonquin Hotel, New York City,
  Fall (annually)

Towngate Theatre Playwriting Contest
Oglebay Institute
Stifel Fine Arts Ctr, 1330 National Rd, Wheeling,
  WV 26003
Tel: 304-242-7700 *Fax:* 304-242-7747

Key Personnel
Dir, Performing Arts: Kate Crosbie
Established: 1976
National playwriting contest. All full-length non-musical plays that have never been professionally produced or published are eligible.
Award: $300 plus limited-run production
Closing Date: Dec 31
Presented: Oglebay Institute Towngate Theatre, Wheeling, WV

Towson University Prize for Literature
Towson University
English Dept, 8000 York Rd, Towson, MD 21252
Tel: 410-704-2847 *Fax:* 410-704-6392
Web Site: www.towson.edu
Key Personnel
Chpn: Prof Edwin Duncan *E-mail:* eduncan@towson.edu
Established: 1980
Awarded for a single book or book-length ms of fiction, poetry, drama or imaginative nonfiction by a young Maryland writer. Applicant must have resided in Maryland at least three years prior to applying & must be a Maryland resident when the prize is awarded.
Award: $1,000
Closing Date: June 15
Presented: Annually

Translation Prize
American-Scandinavian Foundation Publishing Division
58 Park Ave, New York, NY 10016
Tel: 212-879-9779 *Fax:* 212-686-2115
E-mail: info@amscan.org
Web Site: www.amscan.org
Key Personnel
Dir, Fellowships & Grants: Ellen McKey
Contact: Andrey Henkin *E-mail:* ahenkin@amscan.org
Established: 1980
For translations of contemporary poetry or fiction by Danish, Finnish, Icelandic, Norwegian or Swedish authors born after 1800. Write to ASF for full copy of rules.
Award: $2,000 (either poetry or fiction) & publication of excerpt in an issue of Scandinavian Review. $1,000 Inger Sjoberg Prize for runner-up
Closing Date: Annually, June 1
Presented: Varies

Translation Projects in Poetry, Fiction, see
Literary Translation Projects

Trillium Book Award/Prix Trillium
Ontario Media Development Corp (OMDC)
Division of Ontario Government
175 Bloor St E, Suite 501, South Tower, Toronto, ON M4W 3R8, Canada
Tel: 416-642-6698 *Fax:* 416-314-6876
Web Site: www.omdc.on.ca
Key Personnel
Coord: Janet Hawkins *E-mail:* jhawkins@omdc.on.ca
Established: 1987
Open to books in any genre; fiction, nonfiction, drama & children's books. There is no restrictions regarding the previous works of the author.
Award: $20,000 to winning authors in English & French; $2,500 to publishers of winning book in English & French
Closing Date: Jan 6
Presented: Toronto

Harry S Truman Book Award
Harry S Truman Library Institute for National & International Affairs

500 W US Hwy 24, Independence, MO 64050-1798
Tel: 816-268-8248 *Fax:* 816-268-8295
E-mail: truman.library@nara.gov
Web Site: www.trumanlibrary.org
Key Personnel
Off Mgr: Lisa Sullivan
Established: 1963
For the best book published during the previous two years on the presidency of Harry S Truman. The book must deal with some aspect of the political, economic or social development of the US, principally between April 12, 1945 & Jan 20, 1953 or with the public career of Truman. Submit five copies of the nominated book to Grants Administrator. Book must have been published between Jan 1, 2004 & Dec 31, 2005.
Award: $1,000
Closing Date: Jan 20, 2006

Trustus Playwrights' Festival
Trustus Theatre
520 Lady St, Columbia, SC 29201
Mailing Address: PO Box 11721, Columbia, SC 29211-1721
Tel: 803-254-9732 *Fax:* 803-771-9153
E-mail: trustus@trustus.org
Web Site: www.trustus.org
Key Personnel
Artistic Dir: Jim Thigpen
Man Dir: Kay Thigpen
Lit Mgr: Jon Tuttle *Tel:* 843-661-1521
   E-mail: jtuttle@fmarion.edu
Established: 1988
Experimental, hard-hitting, off-the-wall comedies or dramas suitable for open-minded audiences. No topic taboo, no musicals or plays for young audiences. Two copies of synopsis, resume & completed application. Send SASE for application & guidelines. Applications accepted between Dec 1, 2004-Feb 28, 2005.
Award: Selected play receives a public staged reading & $250, followed after a 1 year development period by full production, $500, plus travel/accommodations
Presented: Trustus, Aug, 2005 Reading; Aug 2006 Full Production

Kate Tufts Discovery Award
Claremont Graduate University
Subsidiary of Claremont Graduate University
160 E Tenth St, Harper East B7, Claremont, CA 91711
Tel: 909-621-8974
Web Site: www.cgu.edu/tufts
Key Personnel
Awards Admin: Betty Terrell
Established: 1993
Most worthy first book of poetry written between Sept 1, 2003 & Sept 1, 2004; Award presented for a first book by a poet of genuine promise.
Award: $10,000 cash
Closing Date: Sept 15
Presented: Claremont Graduate University, Annually

Kingsley Tufts Poetry Award
Claremont Graduate University
160 E Tenth St, Harper E B7, Claremont, CA 91711-6165
Tel: 909-621-8974
Web Site: www.cgu.edu/tufts
Key Personnel
Awards Admin: Betty Terrell
Established: 1992
Most worthy book of poetry written between Sept 15, 2002 & Sept 15, 2003. This award honors an emerging poet, one who is past the very beginning, but has not yet reached the acknowledged pinnacle of his or her career.
Award: $100,000 cash

Closing Date: Sept 15
Presented: Claremont Graduate University, Annually

Nancy Byrd Turner Memorial
The Poetry Society of Virginia
100 N Berwick, Williamsburg, VA 23188
Web Site: www.poetrysocietyofvirginia.org
Key Personnel
Contest Chair: Norma Richardson
Sonnet.
Award: $50; $30; $20; honorable mention
Closing Date: Annually, Jan 19
Presented: Annual PSV Awards Luncheon, April

The 25 Most "Censored" Stories of 2003
Project Censored - Sonoma State University
Sonoma State University, 1801 E Cotati Ave, Rohnert Park, CA 94928
Tel: 707-664-2500 *Fax:* 707-664-2108
E-mail: censored@sonoma.edu
Web Site: www.projectcensored.org
Key Personnel
Awards Dir: Peter Phillips *E-mail:* peter.phillips@sonoma.edu
Established: 1976
Investigative journalism.
Award: Plaque & certificate
Presented: Last week in Sept

Ucross Foundation Residency Program
30 Big Red Lane, Clearmont, WY 82835
Tel: 307-737-2291 *Fax:* 307-737-2322
E-mail: info@ucross.org
Web Site: www.ucrossfoundation.org
Key Personnel
Exec Dir: Sharon Dynak *E-mail:* sdynak@ucross.org
Established: 1983
Artist & writer residency program.
Award: Room, studio & board
Closing Date: March 1 & Oct 1

Undergraduate Paper Competition in Cryptology
Cryptologia
Division of Cryptologia
Dept Math Sciences, US Military Academy, West Point, NY 10996
Tel: 845-938-3200
Web Site: www.dean.usma.edu/math/pubs/cryptologia
Key Personnel
Ed: Brian J Winkel *E-mail:* brian-winkel@usma.edu
Established: 1979
Essay, paper, or research on cryptology by undergraduate.
Award: $300 (plus publication in Cryptology of winning essay)
Closing Date: Jan 1

Union League Civic & Arts Foundation Poetry Prize
Poetry Magazine
1030 N Clark St, Suite 420, Chicago, IL 60610
Tel: 312-787-7070 *Fax:* 312-787-6650
E-mail: poetry@poetrymagazine.org
Web Site: www.poetrymagazine.org
Key Personnel
Busn Mgr: Helen Klaviter *E-mail:* hklaviter@poetrymagazine.org
Established: 1993
For poetry published in the preceding two volumes of Poetry. No application necessary.
Award: $1,000
Presented: Annually in Dec

University of Iowa, Writer's Workshop
University of Iowa, Writers' Workshop, Graduate Creative Writing Program

102 Dey House, 507 N Clinton St, Iowa City, IA 52242
Tel: 319-335-0416 *Fax:* 319-335-0420
Key Personnel
Dir: Frank Conroy
The Iowa Short Fiction Award; The John Simmons Short Fiction Award. For guidelines & further information send SASE.
Other Sponsor(s): University of Iowa Press & The Iowa Arts Council
Award: Publication
Closing Date: Jan 3
Presented: First quarter

Utah Arts Council, Literature Progrram, see Utah Original Writers Competition

Utah Original Writers Competition
Formerly Utah Arts Council, Literature Progrram
Utah Arts Council, Literature Program
Subsidiary of Utah State Dept of Community & Economic Development
617 E South Temple, Salt Lake City, UT 84102-1177
Tel: 801-236-7553 *Fax:* 801-236-7556
Web Site: www.arts.utah.gov
Key Personnel
Lit Coord: Guy Lebeda *E-mail:* glebeda@utah.gov
Established: 1958
Applicants must be Utah residents.
Award: $8,450 in prizes in seven categories; $5,000 publication prize for winners from book-length categories
Closing Date: June (the last Friday)
Presented: Salt Lake City, UT, Annually in Oct

Daniel Varoujan Award
New England Poetry Club
16 Cornell St, Arlington, MA 02474
Web Site: www.nepoetryclub.org
Key Personnel
Contest Chmn: Elizabeth Crowell
Pres: Diana Der Hovanessian
Established: 1979
For an unpublished poem in English worthy of the Armenian poet executed by the Turks in 1915 at the onset of the genocide of the Armenian population; $10 for up to three entries for non-members. Send poem in duplicate, name of writer on one only.
Other Sponsor(s): Anthology of Armenian Poetry royalties
Award: $1,000
Closing Date: Annually, June 30
Presented: Harvard University, Cambridge, MA, Annually, Fall

Vermont Arts Council Grants
136 State St, Drawer 33, Montpelier, VT 05633-6001
Tel: 802-828-3291 *Fax:* 802-828-3363
E-mail: info@vermontartscouncil.org
Web Site: www.vermontartscouncil.org
Key Personnel
Dir, Artists Progs: Michele Bailey *Tel:* 802-828-3294 *E-mail:* mbailey@vermontartscouncil.org
Established: 1997
Individual grants (opportunity grants) are given to Vermont residents.
Award: $250-$5,000
Closing Date: 1-6 deadlines per year
Presented: Spring, summer, fall & winter

Vermont Studio Center Writer's Fellowships
Vermont Studio Center
PO Box 613, Johnson, VT 05656
Tel: 802-635-2727 *Fax:* 802-635-2730
E-mail: writing@vermontstudiocenter.org; info@vermontstudiocenter.org
Web Site: www.vermontstudiocenter.org

Key Personnel
Dir: Gary Clark
Writing Dir: Jill Osier
12 writers per month receive a four-week residency.
Award: 4 week residency
Closing Date: Feb 15, June 15, Oct 1, apply 6-9 months prior to residency date

Violet Crown Book Awards
Writers' League of Texas
1501 W Fifth St, Suite E-2, Austin, TX 78703
Tel: 512-499-8914 *Fax:* 512-499-0441
E-mail: wlt@writersleague.org
Web Site: www.writersleague.org
Key Personnel
Exec Dir: Helen Ginger
Established: 1991
Three awards for best books published June through May by Writers' League of Texas members. Membership fee may accompany entry.
Other Sponsor(s): Barnes & Noble Bookstore
Award: $1,000 each award
Closing Date: May 31 for books published June-May
Presented: Barnes & Noble Bookstore Austin, TX, Annually in Sept

Stanley Walker Journalism Award
Texas Institute of Letters
3700 Mockingbird Lane, Dallas, TX 75205
Tel: 512-245-2232 *Fax:* 512-245-7462
Key Personnel
Pres: Carolyn Osborn
VP: Joe Holley
Dir: Mark Busby *Tel:* 512-245-2428 *E-mail:* mb13@swt.edu
Treas: Jim Hoggard
Sec: Fran Vick *E-mail:* franvick@aol.com
For the best work of journalism in a daily newspaper by a Texan.
Other Sponsor(s): Sue Brant & Frank McBee
Award: $1,000
Closing Date: Jan 7, 2005
Presented: March banquet, Ft Worth, TX, USA, March 2005

Bronwen Wallace Memorial Award
The Writers' Trust of Canada
90 Richmond St W, Suite 200, Toronto, ON M5C 1P1, Canada
Tel: 416-504-8222 *Fax:* 416-504-9090
E-mail: info@writerstrust.com
Web Site: www.writerstrust.com
Key Personnel
Exec Dir: Lascelle Wingate *Tel:* 416-504-8222 ext 242
Established: 1994
Awarded to a young author, 35 years of age & under, who has not been previously published in book form. The award alternates each year between short fiction & poetry.
Other Sponsor(s): Friends of Bronwen Wallace
Award: $1,000
Presented: The Great Literary Awards, March

Edward Lewis Wallant Book Award
Dr & Mrs Irving Waltman
3 Brighton Rd, West Hartford, CT 06117
Tel: 860-232-1421
Key Personnel
Sponsor of Award: Fran Waltman; Irving Waltman
Established: 1963
For a creative work of fiction (novel or collection of short stories) significant to American Jews. The author must be American & the book must have been published during the current year.
Award: $500 & scroll
Closing Date: Dec 31
Presented: Annually

Theodore Ward Prize for Playwriting
Columbia College
Columbia College, Theater Dept, 72 E 11 St, Chicago, IL 60605
Tel: 312-344-6136 *Fax:* 312-344-8077
Key Personnel
Contact: Chuck Smith *E-mail:* chigochuck@aol.com
Established: 1986
Full-length plays, one completed script per African-American playwright.
Award: $2,000 & full production (1st prize), $500 & stage reading (2nd prize)
Closing Date: Annual submittals April 1 to July 1
Presented: Getz Theater, Columbia College, Chicago, IL

Rene Wellek Prize
American Comparative Literature Association
University of Texas, Program in Comparative Literature, One University Sta B5003, Austin, TX 78712-0196
Tel: 512-471-8020
E-mail: info@acla.org
Web Site: www.acla.org
Key Personnel
Secy: Elizabeth Richmond-Garza
ACLA Admin Asst: Kevin Carney
Established: 1968
Prize for best book of year in literary & cultural theory. Award given in alternate years. See web site for nomination process.
Award: Certificate
Closing Date: Dec 31
Presented: Annual meeting, following spring

West Coast Ensemble Full Play Competition
West Coast Ensemble
PO Box 38728, Los Angeles, CA 90038
Tel: 323-876-9337 *Fax:* 323-876-8916
Key Personnel
Artistic Dir: Les Hanson
Established: 1989
Play contests. Play should have no more than 12 characters; one submission per playwright; include SASE.
Award: $500 & production the following year
Closing Date: Dec 31 of each year

Western Heritage Awards (Wrangler Award)
National Cowboy & Western Heritage Museum
Member of American Museums Association
1700 NE 63 St, Oklahoma City, OK 73111
Tel: 405-478-2250 *Fax:* 405-478-4714
Web Site: www.nationalcowboymuseum.org
Key Personnel
Pubns Dir: M J Van Deventer
Established: 1961
Honors works which preserve the spirit of the American West.
Award: Bronze sculpture
Closing Date: Dec 31 (TV & Film), Nov 30 (Literary)
Presented: Banquet & Awards Ceremonies, National Cowboy & Western Heritage Museum, Third Sat in April

Western Magazine Awards Foundation
Main PO Box 2131, Vancouver, BC V6B 3T8, Canada
Tel: 604-669-3717 *Fax:* 604-204-9302
E-mail: wma@direct.ca
Web Site: www.westernmagazineawards.com
Key Personnel
Pres: Lila MacLellan
Exec Dir: Liesl Jauk; Bryan Pike
Established: 1983
Magazine awards honors editorial & artistic excellence in 26 categories; restricted to Western Canadian Publications.
Award: $500 Canadian

Closing Date: Annually in Feb
Presented: Vancouver, BC, Canada, June

Western US Book Design & Production Awards

Publishers Association of the West
501 S Cherry St, Suite 320, Denver, CO 80246
Mailing Address: PO Box 18157, Denver, CO 80218
Tel: 303-447-2320 *Fax:* 303-279-7111
E-mail: executivedirector@pubwest.org
Web Site: www.pubwest.org
Key Personnel
Exec Dir: Kalen Landow
Pres: Rick Rinehart
Established: 1982
First-place & runner-up awards are given in ten categories. Illustrated trade book, non-illustrated trade book, scholarly/technical book, guide/travel book, how-to book, children/young adult book, jacket/cover (three colors or less), jacket/cover (four colors or more), catalog & calendar.
Award: Certificates & plaques
Closing Date: Sept
Presented: Nov

White Bird Annual Playwriting Contest

White Bird Productions Inc
138 S Oxford St, Suite 3-A, Brooklyn, NY 11217
Tel: 718-398-3658 *Fax:* 718-398-3658
E-mail: info@whitebirdproductions.org
Web Site: www.whitebirdproductions.org
Key Personnel
Contact: Kathryn Dickinson
Established: 1989
Playwriting contest; awards best play that deals with an environmental issue, plot or theme.
Award: $200 honorarium & New York City reading
Closing Date: Annually, March 15

Jackie White Memorial National Children's Playwriting Contest

Columbia Entertainment Co
309 Parkade Blvd, Columbia, MO 65202
Tel: 573-874-5628
Web Site: cec.missouri.org
Key Personnel
Pres, Community Theatre: Mary Paulsell
Dir: Betsy Phillips
Established: 1988
Children's play; $10 entry fee, send SASE for complete rules & entry form.
Other Sponsor(s): City of Columbia, Office of Cultural Affairs
Award: $500 production (possible, not guaranteed) 1st place. We reserve the right to award the cash prize without production
Closing Date: June 1

William Allen White Children's Book Awards

Emporia State University, William Allen White Library
William Allen White Library, 1200 Commercial St, Emporia, KS 66801-5092
Mailing Address: Emporia State University - Box 4051, Emporia, KS 66801-5092
Tel: 620-341-5719 *Fax:* 620-341-6208
Web Site: waw.emporia.edu
Key Personnel
Exec Dir: Joyce N Davis *Tel:* 620-341-5208
E-mail: davisjoy@emporia.edu
Established: 1952
Two children's books are selected by the children of Kansas, grades 3-5 & 6-8, from two master lists of books chosen by a selection committee. When a student has read two books from either of the Master Lists, he or she is eligible to vote at their school (homeschooled vote at their local public library) for the annual White Award winners. Votes are recorded by each school

or district & submitted to the William Allen White Children Book Awards Program.
Other Sponsor(s): Trusler Foundation
Award: Two bronze medals, one for each grade level
Closing Date: Votes must be received by April 15 by the program
Presented: William L White Auditorium, Emporia KS, Announced late April & award presented in fall

Whiting Writers' Awards

Mrs Giles Whiting Foundation
1133 Avenue of the Americas, 22nd fl, New York, NY 10036
Tel: 212-336-2138
Key Personnel
Dir: Barbara K Bristol
Dir, Opers: Kellye Rosenheim
Established: 1985
For creative writing. Applications not accepted by the foundation; confidential nominators propose candidates for selection committee consideration.
Award: Ten awards of $35,000 each

Walt Whitman Award

The Academy of American Poets Inc
588 Broadway, Suite 604, New York, NY 10012
Tel: 212-274-0343 *Fax:* 212-274-9427
E-mail: academy@poets.org
Web Site: www.poets.org
Key Personnel
Prog Dir: Ryan Murphy *Tel:* 212-274-0343 ext 17
E-mail: rmurphy@poets.org
Established: 1975
For a book-length ms of poetry by a living American poet who has not published a book of poetry. Write with SASE for entry form in late Aug.
Award: $5,000 & publication by Louisiana State University Press & distribution of copies by the Academy & a one-month residency at the Vermont Studio Center
Closing Date: Sept 15-Nov 15
Presented: Annually in April

Carnegie-Whitney Award

ALA Publishing Committee
Unit of American Library Association (ALA)
50 E Huron St, Chicago, IL 60611
Tel: 312-280-5416 *Toll Free Tel:* 800-545-2433
Fax: 312-280-4380
Web Site: www.ala.org
Key Personnel
Prog Off: Cheryl Malden
For the preparation of bibliographic aids for research with scholarly intent & general applicability. Decisions made at Publishing Committee Meeting, each Jan. Completed proposals should be sent to Chair, ALA Publishing Committee at the above address.
Other Sponsor(s): James Gyman Whitney Fund, Andrew Carnegie Fund
Award: Up to $5,000 annually
Closing Date: Nov 10

Jon Whyte Essay Competition

Writers Guild of Alberta/Banff Centre for the Arts
11759 Groat Rd, Edmonton, AB T5M 3K6, Canada
Tel: 780-422-8174 *Toll Free Tel:* 800-665-5354 (Alberta only) *Fax:* 780-422-2663
E-mail: mail@writersguild.ab.ca
Web Site: www.writersguild.ab.ca
Key Personnel
Exec Dir: Diane Walton
Essay writing.
Award: $2,000 in all ($1,000 winner, $500 to two runner-ups) plus publications in major Alberta newspapers

Closing Date: Feb 28
Presented: Alberta Book Awards Gala

Wichita State University Playwriting Contest

Wichita State University Theatre (WSU)
Division of School of Performing Arts
1845 Fairmount St, Wichita, KS 67260-0153
Tel: 316-978-3368 *Fax:* 316-978-3202
Web Site: www.wichita.edu
Key Personnel
Chpn: Dr Steven Peters
Dir, Theater: Drew Tombrello *E-mail:* drew.tombrello@wichita.edu
Admin Specialist: Elnora E Watson
E-mail: elnora.watson@wichita.edu
For college students only (graduate or undergraduate).
Other Sponsor(s): Miller Trust
Award: Production of play, transportation & housing for playwright to attend performance
Closing Date: Feb 15
Presented: Annually in the fall

The Laura Ingalls Wilder Medal

Association for Library Service to Children
Division of American Library Association
50 E Huron St, Chicago, IL 60611-2795
Tel: 312-280-2163 *Toll Free Tel:* 800-545-2433
Fax: 312-944-7671
E-mail: alsc@ala.org
Web Site: www.ala.org/alsc
Established: 1954
Biennial award presented to an author or illustrator whose books have made a substantial & lasting contribution to children's literature. The books must have been published in the United States.
Award: Medal
Presented: ALA Annual Conference, Varies

Oscar Williams/Gene Derwood Award

NY Community Trust
2 Park Ave, New York, NY 10016
Tel: 212-686-0010 *Fax:* 212-532-8528
E-mail: info@nycommunitytrust.org
Web Site: www.nycommunitytrust.org
Key Personnel
Grants Admin: Liza Lagunoff *E-mail:* ll@nyct-cfi.org
Established: 1971
Intended to help needy or worthy poets & artists who have had long & distinguished careers. Nominations or applications are not accepted in any form.
Award: Cash varies in amount
Presented: Annually

William Carlos Williams Award

Poetry Society of America (PSA)
15 Gramercy Park, New York, NY 10003
Tel: 212-254-9628 *Fax:* 212-673-2352
Web Site: www.poetrysociety.org
Key Personnel
Exec Dir: Alice Quinn
For a book of poetry published by a small press or a nonprofit or university press. Submissions, accompanied by an entry form, from publishers only. Send SASE for complete guidelines.
Award: Purchase prize between $500 & $1,000
Closing Date: Dec 22
Presented: April

H W Wilson Co Indexing Award

American Society of Indexers Inc (ASI)
10200 W 44 Ave, Suite 304, Wheat Ridge, CO 80033
Tel: 303-463-2887 *Fax:* 303-422-8894
E-mail: info@asindexing.org
Web Site: www.asindexing.org
Key Personnel
Pres: Enid Zafran
CEO: Jerry Bowman

Exec Dir: Francine Butler *E-mail:* fbutler@resourcecenter.com
Established: 1972
Awarded to the indexer & the publisher of year's best monograph index.
Award: $1,000 & citation (indexer), citation (publisher)
Closing Date: April 1
Presented: annual meeting

The H W Wilson Library Staff Development Grant
ALA Awards Program
Affiliate of American Library Association
50 E Huron St, Chicago, IL 60611
Tel: 312-280-3247 *Toll Free Tel:* 800-545-2433 (ext 3247) *Fax:* 312-944-3897
E-mail: awards@ala.org
Web Site: www.ala.org
Key Personnel
Prog Off: Cheryl Malden *E-mail:* cmalden@ala.org
To a library organization for a program to further its staff development goals & objectives.
Award: $3,500 & 24k gold-framed citation
Closing Date: Annually on Dec 1
Presented: ALA Annual Conference, Annually in June

Laurence L Winship Book Award
Boston Globe & PEN New England
Emerson College, 120 Boylston St, Boston, MA 02116
Tel: 617-824-8820
E-mail: pen_ne@emerson.edu
Web Site: www.pen-ne.org
Key Personnel
Exec Coord: Valerie Duff-Strautmann
Established: 1975
For a US author who is of New England origin or whose work provides a New England theme or atmosphere. Awards for books published in calendar year 2003. Send inquiries to Mary Walsh.
Award: $3,000
Closing Date: Dec 15

Justin Winsor Essay Prize
The Library History Round Table of American Library Association
50 E Huron St, Chicago, IL 60611
Tel: 312-280-4273 *Toll Free Tel:* 800-545-2433 (ext 4273) *Fax:* 312-280-4392
Web Site: www.ala.org
Key Personnel
Dir: Denise Davis
To author of an outstanding essay embodying original historical research on a significant subject of library history.
Award: $500 & essay publication
Closing Date: Jan 28

Paul A Witty Short Story Award
International Reading Association
800 Barksdale Rd, Newark, DE 19714
Tel: 302-731-1600 *Fax:* 302-731-1057
E-mail: pubinfo@reading.org
Web Site: www.reading.org
Key Personnel
Admin Asst: Mary Cash
Established: 1986
For an original story published for the first time during the calendar year in a periodical for children. The short story should serve as a literary standard that encourages young readers to read periodicals.
Award: $1,000
Closing Date: Dec 1
Presented: Annual Convention, Spring

Thomas Wolfe Student Prize
Thomas Wolfe Society

809 Gardner St, Raleigh, NC 27607
Tel: 919-834-6983 *Fax:* 919-515-7856
Web Site: www.thomaswolfe.org
Key Personnel
Chair: James Clark
Established: 1981
All essays must be related to Thomas Wolfe & his work. Essays must be between 8-15 double-spaced typed pages in English. Documentation should follow the current Chicago Manual of Style. Essays are judged on originality, style, clarity, documentation & contribution to knowledge of Thomas Wolfe. Send mss to Dr James Clark, Chmn at above address.
Award: $500, delivery of winning essay at next meeting, publication in the Thomas Wolfe Review, one year membership in the Society
Closing Date: Jan 15
Presented: Cambridge, MA, March 15

Women's National Book Association Award
Women's National Book Association Inc
c/o Susannah Greenberg Public Relations, 2166 Broadway, Suite 9-E, New York, NY 10024
Tel: 212-208-4629 *Fax:* 212-208-4629
E-mail: publicity@bookbuzz.com
Web Site: www.wnba-books.org
Key Personnel
Natl Pres: Jill A Tardiff
Established: 1940
Presented to a living American woman for her outstanding contribution to the world of books as well as society (through books).
Award: Citation
Presented: Varies, Biennially in even-numbered years

Carter G Woodson Book Awards
National Council for the Social Studies
8555 16 St, Suite 500, Silver Spring, MD 20910
Tel: 301-588-1800 *Toll Free Tel:* 800-296-7840 *Fax:* 301-588-2049
E-mail: excellence@ncss.org
Web Site: www.socialstudies.org
Key Personnel
Exec Dir: Susan Griffin
Dir, Meetings: Ella McDowell
Dir, Pubns: Michael Simpson
Dir, Partnerships Prog Initiatives: Ana Post *Tel:* 301-588-1800 ext 114 *E-mail:* apost@ncss.org
Established: 1974
The Carter G Woodson Book Award was established by National Council for the Social Studies to recognize the most distinguished nonfiction books for young readers which depict ethnicity in the US. Eligible books deal with the experiences of one or more racial/ethnic minority groups in the US. Publisher must provide copy of each title for submission requirements.
Award: One elementary (K-6) & one middle level (5-8), one secondary (7-12) annual award, runner-up books designated Woodson Honor Books, seals are now available to publishers $.25 each for less than 1,000 & less for larger quantities
Closing Date: Feb annually
Presented: Annual Conference, Kansas City, MO, 2005

Word Works Washington Prize
The Word Works
7129 Alger Rd, Falls Church, VA 22042
Mailing Address: PO Box 42164, Washington, DC 20015-0764
Fax: 703-527-9384
E-mail: editor@wordworksdc.com
Web Site: www.wordworksdc.com
Key Personnel
Pres & Chpn of Bd Dir: Karren L Alenier
Washington Prize Dir: Ann Rayburn
Established: 1981

For an unpublished ms of poetry. Submission may be made by any living American writer except those connected with Word Works. Include one copy, title page with name, address, telephone number & signature. No entry form is required. Submissions should be 48-64 pages, in English; $20 entry fee, table of contents, acknowledgment page & brief bio. Business sized SASE mandatory with entry. Write for complete rules & include SASE. Address for prize entries changes every year.
Award: $1,500 & publication
Closing Date: March 1
Presented: Annually

World Book Inc Continuing Education Grant
Catholic Library Association
100 North St, Suite 224, Pittsfield, MA 01201-5109
Tel: 413-443-2252 *Fax:* 413-442-2252
E-mail: cla@cathla.org
Web Site: www.cathla.org
Key Personnel
Exec Dir: Jean R Bostley, SSJ
Established: 1973
For continuing education in school & children's librarianship for association members.
Award: $1,500
Closing Date: March 15
Presented: Boston, MA, April 15

World's Best Short-Short Story Contest
The Southeast Review
Dept of English, The Florida State University, Tallahassee, FL 32306-1036
Tel: 850-644-2773; 850-644-4230
E-mail: southeastreview@english.fsu.edu
Web Site: www.english.fsu.edu/southeastreview/default.htm
Established: 1986
Best 500 word (max) previously unpublished short story. Include a brief (100) word bio. All entries will be considered for publication. $10 entry fee for up to 3 stories.
Other Sponsor(s): FSU English Dept's Creative Writing Program
Award: $500 & a box of Florida oranges
Closing Date: Feb 1
Presented: Tallahassee, FL, April

The Writers Community
YMCA National Writer's Voice
Subsidiary of YMCA of the USA
101 N Wacker Dr, Chicago, IL 60606
Toll Free Tel: 800-USA-YMCA, Ext 6830 *Fax:* 312-977-1729
E-mail: jason.shinder@ymca.net
Web Site: www.ymca.net
Key Personnel
Dir: Jason Shinder
Semester-long teaching residencies at YMCA Writer's Voice Centers, awarded semiannually to mid-career writers by the YMCA National Writer's Voice on the basis of literary achievement & promise. Each center selects & nominates residents. Those nominated are judged by an advisory panel. Application procedures & deadlines vary from center to center. Send a SASE for a directory of centers.
Award: $6,000

Writer's Digest Writing Competition
Writer's Digest Magazine
Division of F+W Publications
4700 E Galbraith Rd, Cincinnati, OH 45236
Tel: 513-531-2690 (ext 580) *Fax:* 513-531-0798
E-mail: writing-competition@fwpubs.com
Web Site: www.writersdigest.com
Key Personnel
Contest Dir: Sandi Luppert
Cust Serv Rep: Terri Boes *Tel:* 513-531-2690 ext 1328
Established: 1931

Original, unpublished mss in 10 categories: genre
& mainstream, short stories, articles, rhyming
& non-rhyming poetry & scripts, TV/movie,
plays, personal essays & children's fiction.
Award: Expense-paid trip to New York to meet
with editors or agents (grand prize); cash, reference books, subscriptions & certificates
Closing Date: May 31
Presented: Oct

The Writer's Emergency Assistance Fund
The American Society of Journalists & Authors
Charitable Trust Inc (ASJA)
1501 Broadway, Suite 302, New York, NY 10036
Tel: 212-997-0947 *Fax:* 212-768-7414
E-mail: staff@asja.org
Web Site: asja.org
Key Personnel
Chmn of the Board: Patricia Schiff-Estess
Exec Dir: Ms Brett Harvey
Grants given to disabled or elderly professional
freelance writers of nonfiction or those writers
who are caught up in an extraordinary profes-
sional crisis.

Writers' Fellowships
Arizona Commission on the Arts
417 W Roosevelt Ave, Phoenix, AZ 85003
Tel: 602-255-5882 *Fax:* 602-256-0282
Key Personnel
Lit Dir: Paul Morris *Tel:* 602-229-8226
    E-mail: pmorris@arizonaarts.org
Arizona poets & fiction writers only.
Award: Cash $5,000 - $7,500
Closing Date: Mid Sept

Writers Guild of Alberta Annual Awards Program
Banff Centre
11759 Groat Rd, Edmonton, AB T5M 3K6,
    Canada
Tel: 780-422-8174 *Toll Free Tel:* 800-665-5354
    (Alberta only) *Fax:* 780-422-2663
E-mail: mail@writersguild.ab.ca
Web Site: www.writersguild.ab.ca
Key Personnel
Exec Dir: Diane Walton
Established: 1982
Alberta Literary Award, must be resident of Al-
berta.
Award: $500 (Canadian funds) & Leather Bound
    Volume
Closing Date: Dec 31

Writers Guild of America Awards
Writers Guild of America West Inc (WGAW)
7000 W Third St, Los Angeles, CA 90048
Tel: 323-951-4000 *Fax:* 323-782-4802
Web Site: www.wga.org
Key Personnel
Exec Dir: John McLean
PR: Cheryl Rhoden
Awards: Barbara Ditlow
Established: 1948
Annual, any eligible film exhibited for one week
    during calendar year; best adapted screenplay;
    best screenplay directly for screen. TV & radio
    awards. Only members can enter.
Award: Statuette
Closing Date: Nov 30

Writers' Journal Annual Fiction Contest
Val-Tech Media
PO Box 394, Perham, MN 56573
Tel: 218-346-7921 *Fax:* 218-346-7924
E-mail: writersjournal@lakesplus.com
Web Site: www.writersjournal.com
Key Personnel
Partner & Publr: John Ogroske
Partner & Ed: Leon Ogroske

Offered annually for unpublished works; length
not to exceed 2,000 words; mss must be typed,
double-spaced on 8 1/2 x 11 white paper. One
copy of each entry required. Writer's name
must not appear on submission. A separate
cover sheet must accompany each entry with
the following information: Name of contest,
title of submission, writer's name, address,
telephone number & e-mail (if available). Mss
will not be returned, photocopies accepted. For
those without Web access, a winners list can be
obtained by sending a No 10 SASE. $5 read-
ing fee per entry must be included (US funds
only). Requires only one-time publishing rights
to winning entries.
Award: $50 (1st prize), $25 (2nd prize), $15 (3rd
prize) plus selected honorable mentions in
Writer's Journal magazine
Closing Date: Jan 30 annually

Writers' Journal Annual Horror/Ghost Contest
Val-Tech Media
PO Box 394, Perham, MN 56573
Tel: 218-346-7921 *Fax:* 218-346-7924
E-mail: writersjournal@lakesplus.com
Web Site: www.writersjournal.com
Key Personnel
Partner & Publr: John Ogroske
Partner & Ed: Leon Ogroske
Offered annually for unpublished works; length
not to exceed 2,000 words; mss must be typed,
double-spaced on 8 1/2 x 11 white paper. One
copy of each entry required. Writer's name
must not appear on submission. A separate
coversheet must accompany each entry with the
following information: Name of contest, title of
submission, writer's name, address, telephone
number & e-mail (if available). Mss will not be
returned, photocopies accepted. For those without Web access, a winners list can be obtained
by sending a No 10 SASE. $5 reading fee per
entry must be included (US funds only). Requires only one-time publishing rights to winning entries.
Award: $50 (1st prize); $25 (2nd prize); $15
(3rd prize) plus selected honorable mentions
in *Writer's Journal* magazine
Closing Date: March 30 annually

Writers' Journal Annual Romance Contest
Val-Tech Media
PO Box 394, Perham, MN 56573
Tel: 218-346-7921 *Fax:* 218-346-7924
E-mail: writersjournal@lakesplus.com
Web Site: www.writersjournal.com
Key Personnel
Partner & Publr: John Ogroske
Partner & Ed: Leon Ogroske
Offered annually for unpublished works; length
not to exceed 2,000 words; ms must be typed,
double-spaced on 8 1/2 x 11 white paper. One
copy of each entry required. Writer's name
must not appear on submissions. A separate
cover sheet must accompany each entry with
the following information: name of contest,
title of submission, writer's name, address, telephone number & e-mail address (if available).
Mss will not be returned, photocopies accepted.
For those without Web access, a winners list
can be obtained by sending a No 10 SASE.
$5 reading fee per entry must be included (US
funds only). Requires only one-time publishing
rights to winning entries.
Award: $50 (1st prize); $25 (2nd prize); $15
(3rd prize) plus selected honorable mentions
in *Writer's Journal* magazine; winners will be
included in future issues
Closing Date: July 30 annually

Writers' Journal Annual Short Story Contest
Val-Tech Media

PO Box 394, Perham, MN 56573
Tel: 218-346-7921 *Fax:* 218-346-7924
E-mail: writersjournal@lakesplus.com
Web Site: www.writersjournal.com
Key Personnel
Partner & Publr: John Ogroske
Partner & Ed: Leon Ogroske
Offered annually for unpublished works; length
not to exceed 2,000 words; ms must be typed,
double-spaced on 8 1/2 x 11 white paper. One
copy of each entry required. Writer's name
must not appear on submission. A separate
cover sheet must accompany each entry with
the following information: name of contest,
title of submission, writer's name, address, telephone number & e-mail address (if available).
Mss will not be returned, photocopies accepted.
For those without Web access, a winners list
can be obtained by sending a No 10 SASE.
$7 reading fee per entry must be included (US
funds only). Requires only one-time publishing
rights to winning entries.
Award: $300 (1st prize), $100 (2nd prize), $50
(3rd prize) plus selected honorable mentions
in *Writer's Journal Magazine*; winners will be
included in future issues
Closing Date: May 30 annually

Writers' Journal Annual Travel Writing Contest
Val-Tech Media
PO Box 394, Perham, MN 56573
Tel: 218-346-7921 *Fax:* 218-346-7924
E-mail: writersjournal@lakesplus.com
Web Site: www.writersjournal.com
Key Personnel
Partner & Ed: Leon Ogroske
Compose a nonfiction travel story about vacation
travel. The story should not be written in the
first person. Offered annually for unpublished
works; length not to exceed 2,000 words; mss
must be typed, double-spaced on 8 1/2 x 11
white paper. One copy of each entry required.
Writer's name must not appear on submission.
A separate cover sheet must accompany each
entry with the following information: name of
contest, title of submission, writer's name, address, telephone number & e-mail address (if
available). Mss will not be returned, photocopies accepted. For those without Web access,
a winners list can be obtained by sending a
No 10 SASE. $5 reading fee per entry must be
included (US funds only). Requires only one-
time publishing rights to winning entries.
Award: $50 (1st prize); $25 (2nd prize); $15
(3rd prize) plus selected honorable mentions
in *Writer's Journal* magazine; winners will be
published in a future issue
Closing Date: Nov 30 annually

Writers' Journal Poetry Contest
Val-Tech Media
PO Box 394, Perham, MN 56573
Tel: 218-346-7921 *Fax:* 218-346-7924
E-mail: writersjournal@lakesplus.com
Web Site: www.writersjournal.com
Key Personnel
Partner & Publr: John Ogroske
Partner & Ed: Leon Ogroske
Contact: Esther M Leiper
Each poem may not be longer than 25 lines. En-
ter as often as you like. Original unpublished
works only; poems must be typed on 8 1/2 X
11 white paper. One copy of each entry required. Each entry must be submitted in duplicate. Name, address, telephone number & e-
mail address (if available) in upper left corner
of one sheet. No name or address on duplicate.
No staples please. Photocopies accepted-poems
will not be returned. For those without Web access, a winners list can be obtained by sending
a No 10 SASE. Only previously unpublished
poems accepted. Copyright to poems remain

with author. Writers Journal requires only one-
time rights to winning entries (US funds only).
Award: $50 (1st prize), $25 (2nd prize) & $15
(3rd prize), plus honorable mentions. Winners
will be published in *Writer's Journal Magazine*
Closing Date: Apr 30 annually- Aug 30 annually-
Dec 30 annually

Wyoming Arts Council Literature Fellowships
Wyoming Arts Council
Division of Wyoming Department of Parks &
    Cultural Resources
2320 Capitol Ave, Cheyenne, WY 82002
Tel: 307-777-7742 *Fax:* 307-777-5499
Web Site: www.wyoarts.state.wy.us
Key Personnel
Lit Prog Mgr: Michael Shay *Tel:* 307-777-5234
    E-mail: mshay@state.wy.us
Established: 1986
Most exciting new creative writing by Wyoming
    residents. Blind judges & one juror.
Award: $3,000 (three)
Closing Date: May 1
Presented: Casper College Literary Conference,
    Annually in the Fall

Yale Series of Younger Poets
Yale University Press
302 Temple St, New Haven, CT 06511
Mailing Address: PO Box 209040, New Haven,
    CT 06520-9040
Tel: 203-432-0900 *Fax:* 203-432-2394; 203-432-
0948
Web Site: www.yale.edu/yup/ *Cable:*
    YALEPRESS
Key Personnel
Acqs Ed: John Kulka *E-mail:* john.kulka@yale.
    edu
Established: 1919
For poetry mss, 48-64 pages, by American writ-
    ers under age 40 who have not previously had
    a volume of verse published. Submission fee
    $15. Send SASE for rules.
Award: Publication & royalties
Closing Date: Submissions for the competition
    must be postmarked no earlier than Oct 1 of
    each calendar year & no later than Nov 15
Presented: Annually

YES New Play Festival
Northern Kentucky University
205 FA Theatre Dept, Nunn Dr, Highland
    Heights, KY 41099-1007
Tel: 859-572-6362 *Fax:* 859-572-6057
Key Personnel
Proj Dir: Sandra Forman *Tel:* 859-572-6303
    E-mail: forman@nku.edu
Established: 1983
New play contest.
Award: $500 honoraria, travel & housing for three
    different playwrights
Closing Date: Plays accepted May 1-Oct 1
Presented: April 21-May 1, 2005

The Young Adult Canadian Book Award
Canadian Library Association (CLA)
328 Frank St, Ottawa, ON K2P 0X8, Canada
Tel: 613-232-9625 *Fax:* 613-563-9895
Web Site: www.cla.ca
Key Personnel
Award Admin: Brenda Shields *Tel:* 613-232-9625
    ext 318 *E-mail:* bshields@cla.ca
Established: 1980
Awarded to the author of Canadian children's
    books. Author must be citizen or resident of
    Canada.
Award: Leather-bound copy of winning book with
    award seal gold embossed on cover
Closing Date: Jan 1
Presented: CLA Annual Conference

Young Lions Fiction Award
New York Public Library
Office of Development, Rm 73, Fifth Ave & 42
    St, New York, NY 10018
Tel: 212-930-0887 *Fax:* 212-930-0983
E-mail: younglions@nypl.org
Web Site: www2.nypl.org
Established: 2001
Given annually to an American writer age 35 or
    younger for either a novel or collection of short
    stories.
Award: $10,000
Closing Date: Aug 9
Presented: The New York Public Library, March
    2005

**Phyllis Smart Young Poetry Prize & Chris
O'Malley Fiction Prize**
The Madison Review
University of Wisconsin - English Dept, 7193
    HCW, 600 N Park St, Madison, WI 53706
Tel: 608-263-0566
E-mail: madreview@mail.studentorg.wisc.edu
Web Site: mendota.english.wisc.edu/~MadRev/
    main.html
Key Personnel
Dir: Ronald Kuka
Chmn Dept: Thom Schaub
Submissions are limited to one short story (30 pg
    max) or three poems. All entries will be con-
    sidered as submissions to the Madison Review
    for publication.
Award: Cash $500 for fiction, $500 for poetry;
    winners published in the Madison Review
Closing Date: Entries accepted between Sept 1 &
    Sept 30
Presented: Announced in Dec

**Anna Zornio Memorial Children's Theatre
Playwriting Award**
University of New Hampshire Department of
    Theatre & Dance
Paul Creative Arts, 30 College Rd, D-22,
    Durham, NH 03824-3538
Tel: 603-862-3038 *Fax:* 603-862-0298
Key Personnel
Admin Mgr, Theatre & Dance: Michael Wood
    Tel: 603-862-3038 *E-mail:* mike.wood@unh.
    edu
Theatre Chair: Gay Nardone
Established: 1980
Well-written play or musical appropriate for
    young audiences, Pre-K to 12th grade.
Award: Cash award, up to $1,000 & play under-
    written & produced by the UNH Theatre De-
    partment
Closing Date: Sept 1
Presented: University of New Hampshire, 2005-
    2006 theatre season

Books & Magazines for the Trade

Reference Books for the Trade

AAP Industry Statistics 2003
Published by Association of American Publishers Inc (AAP)
71 Fifth Ave, 2nd fl, New York, NY 10003-3004
Tel: 212-255-0200 *Fax:* 212-255-7007
Web Site: www.publishers.org
Key Personnel
VP: Kathryn Blough *Tel:* 212-255-0200 ext 263
  E-mail: kblough@publishers.org
Contains sales data for consumer, el-hi, higher
  education & professional books & operating
  data for el-hi companies.
annual.
Free to members, $1,150 for non-members

ACEI Education Resource Catalogue
Published by Association for Childhood Educa-
  tion International
17904 Georgia Ave, Suite 215, Olney, MD 20832
Tel: 301-570-2111 *Toll Free Tel:* 800-423-3563
  Fax: 301-570-2212
E-mail: aceihq@aol.com; aceied@aol.com
Web Site: www.acei.org
Key Personnel
Dir, Pubns: Anne Bauer
Free resource catalog available.

Adweek Directory
Published by Adweek Directories
Division of VNU Business Media Inc
770 Broadway, New York, NY 10003
Tel: 646-654-5210 *Toll Free Tel:* 800-562-2706
  Fax: 646-654-5886
E-mail: info@adweek.com
Web Site: www.adweek.com/directories
Key Personnel
Ed: Adela Brito *E-mail:* abrito@adweek.com
Publg Dir: Mitch Tebo *Tel:* 646-654-5215
  E-mail: mtebo@adweek.com
Directory of addresses, telephone numbers, per-
  sonnel, billings & accounts for advertising
  agencies & related organizations.
Annual.
1,247 pp, $230 print, $399 online

All-in-One Directory
Published by Gebbie Press
PO Box 1000, New Paltz, NY 12561-0017
Tel: 845-255-7560 *Fax:* 845-256-1239
E-mail: gebbiepress@pipeline.com
Web Site: www.gebbieinc.com
Key Personnel
Pres: Mark Gebbie
Lists contact information for all US daily &
  weekly newspapers, including Black & Spanish
  language papers, radio & TV stations including
  Black & Spanish language stations & a compre-
  hensive listing of magazines available in
  print, software & text files-on-disk.

Annual.
33rd ed, 2004: 550 pp, $125 print, $550 software,
  $335 text files

Almanac of Famous People
Published by Thomson Gale
Unit of The Thomson Corp
27500 Drake Rd, Farmington Hills, MI 48331-
  3535
Tel: 248-699-4253 *Toll Free Tel:* 800-347-4253
  Fax: 248-699-8062 *Toll Free Fax:* 800-414-
  5043
E-mail: galeord@gale.com
Web Site: www.gale.com
Key Personnel
Ed: Jennifer Mossman
A guide to sources of biographical information on
  36,000 prominent persons, past & present, famous & infamous, who are of popular interest.
  Entries include basic personal data for quick
  identifications, plus citations to material appearing in biographical sources. Vol 2 indexes
  the entries chronologically by year & day of
  birth & death, geographically using places of
  birth & death, alphabetically by occupation.
8th ed, 2 vols, 2003: 2,964 pp, $145/set
ISBN(s): 0-7876-7535-0 (Ed 8)

American Book Prices Current
Published by Bancroft Parkman Inc
PO Box 1236, Washington, CT 06793-0236
Tel: 860-868-7408; 212-737-2715 *Fax:* 860-868-
  0080
E-mail: abpc@snet.net
Web Site: www.bookpricescurrent.com
Key Personnel
Exec Ed: Katharine Kyes Leab
Ed: Daniel J Leab *E-mail:* danleab@earthlink.net
Research price guide detailing prices realized at
  auction in the USA & abroad in the world
  of books, mss, autographs, maps, broadsides
  & charts. Also the proprietor of a series of
  databases dealing with the prices realized at
  auction of books recording missing books &
  mss.
Annual.
Vol 108, Jan 2002: 1,100 pp, $165
ISBN(s): 0-914022-38-5

American Book Publishing Record Cumulative
Published by R R Bowker LLC
Subsidiary of Cambridge Information Group Inc
630 Central Ave, New Providence, NJ 07974
SAN: 214-1191
Tel: 908-286-1090 *Toll Free Tel:* 888-BOWKER2
  Fax: 908-219-0185
E-mail: info@bowker.com
Web Site: www.bowker.com

Key Personnel
Sr Man Dir: Roy Crego
Comprehensive & convenient, ABPR 2003 brings
  you catalog records for the entire year of book
  publishing in one cost-effective volume. More
  than 87,680 cataloged entries for books published or distributed in the United States are
  arranged in Dewey sequence, with separate
  sections for Adult & Juvenile Fiction. Author,
  Title & Subject indexes conveniently refer you
  to main section entries.
Annual.
2003: 4,070 pp, $415.00/2 vol set
ISBN(s): 0-8352-4629-9 (2 vol set)

American Book Trade Directory
Published by Information Today, Inc
630 Central Ave, New Providence, NJ 07974
Toll Free Tel: 800-409-4929 *Fax:* 908-219-0192
E-mail: custserv@infotoday.com
Key Personnel
Man Ed: Beverley McDonough *Tel:* 908-219-
  0278 *E-mail:* bmcdonough@infotoday.com
Comprehensive directory of over 25,000 book-
  sellers & wholesalers in the USA & Canada,
  arranged by state/province & city; includes in-
  formation on sidelines, appraisers, auctioneers
  & dealers in foreign-language books.
Annual.
50th ed, 2004-2005: 1,861 pp, $289.00 cloth
ISBN(s): 1-57387-186-9

American Library Directory
Published by Information Today, Inc
630 Central Ave, New Providence, NJ 07974
Toll Free Tel: 800-300-9868 (cust serv); 800-409-
  4929 (ext 3015) *Fax:* 908-219-0192
E-mail: custserv@infotoday.com
Key Personnel
Man Ed: Beverley McDonough *Tel:* 908-219-
  0278 *E-mail:* bmcdonough@infotoday.com
Comprehensive directory of over 39,000 libraries
  throughout the United States & Canada. Also
  includes listings of library schools, networks,
  consortia, cooperative library organizations,
  state library agencies & US Armed Forces libraries overseas. Automation & database system vendor information, as well as e-mail addresses for libraries & library personnel included. Entries arranged geographically by
  state, province & city. Personnel Index section
  arranged alphabetically.
Annual.
57th ed, 2004-2005: 3,786 pp, $299.00/2 vol set
  cloth
ISBN(s): 1-57387-190-7

American Reference Books Annual
Published by Libraries Unlimited

Member of Greenwood Publishing Group
88 Post Rd W, Westport, CT 06881
Tel: 303-770-1220 *Toll Free Tel:* 800-225-5800
 Fax: 603-431-2214 (orders)
E-mail: arba@lu.com
Web Site: www.lu.com
Key Personnel
Co-Ed-in-Chief: Martin Dillon; Graff Hysell
The premier sources of information for the library
 & information community for more than three
 decades. Includes more than 1,800 descriptive
 & evaluative entries for recent reference publi-
 cations. Reviews by subject experts of materi-
 als from more than 300 publishers & in nearly
 500 subject areas. ARBA assists in answering
 everyday reference questions & in building a
 reference collection.
Annual.
Vol 35, 2004: 832 pp, $125
ISBN(s): 1-59158-167-2

American-Soviet Playwrights Directory
Published by O'Neill Theater Center
305 Great Neck Rd, Waterford, CT 06385
Tel: 860-443-5378 *Fax:* 860-443-9653
E-mail: localplaywrights@aol.com
Web Site: www.members.aol.com/
 localplaywrights/oneill.htm
Key Personnel
Ed: Phyllis Johnson Kaye; George C White
A landmark volume featuring 100 Soviet playwrights (in English) & 100 American playwrights (in Russian). Each entry contains
 photo, contacts, list of all entrants' plays &
 many synopses. Not available to the general
 public.
1st ed, 1988: 140 pp, $39 plus postage & han-
 dling $5
ISBN(s): 0-9605160-1-8

**An Author's Guide to Children's Book
 Promotion**
Published by Raab Associates
345 Millwood Rd, Chappaqua, NY 10514
Tel: 914-241-2117 *Fax:* 914-241-0050
E-mail: info@raabassociates.com
Web Site: www.raabassociates.com
Key Personnel
Partner: Susan Raab
Provides authors & illustrators with the tools they
 need to get their books into the hands of key
 decision-makers: teachers, librarians, book-
 sellers & reviewers. The book features a de-
 tailed directory of key associations, children's
 book information sources & trade & educa-
 tional publications.
Annual.
9th ed, 2003: 76 pp, $12.95
ISBN(s): 0-9621211-0-X

The Art & Science of Book Publishing
Published by Ohio University Press
Scott Quadrangle, Athens, OH 45701
Tel: 740-593-1155 *Fax:* 740-593-4536
Key Personnel
Dir & Rts & Perms: David Sanders
Cust Serv Mgr: Judy Wilson
Publicity Mgr: Richard Gilbert
Introduction to basics of book publishing.
1990 ed: 234 pp, $14.95 paper
ISBN(s): 0-8214-0970-0

Annual ASJA Directory of Writers
Published by American Society of Journalists &
 Authors (ASJA)
1501 Broadway, Suite 302, New York, NY 10036
Tel: 212-997-0947 *Fax:* 212-768-7414
E-mail: staff@asja.org
Web Site: www.asja.org
Key Personnel
Exec Dir: Ms Brett Harvey *E-mail:* execdir@asja.
 org

Exec Dir Asst: Zeleika Raboy
Lists more than 1,100 freelance writers, cross-
 indexed by geographic location, pseudonym,
 media expertise & over 100 subject specialties.
Annual.
2002: 110 pp, $98

**The Association of American University
 Presses Directory 2003-2004**
Published by Association of American University
 Presses
71 W 23 St, Suite 901, New York, NY 10010
Tel: 212-989-1010 *Toll Free Tel:* 800-621-2736
 (orders) *Fax:* 773-702-9756 (sales)
Key Personnel
Exec Dir: Peter Giuler
A detailed introduction to the structure & staff
 of the AAUP & to the publishing programs &
 personnel of member presses.
Annual.
2003-2004: 220 pp, $18 paper
ISBN(s): 0-945103-17-4

Authors Series, see World Authors Series

AV Market Place
Published by Information Today, Inc
630 Central Ave, New Providence, NJ 07974
Tel: 908-286-1090 *Toll Free Tel:* 800-409-4929;
 800-300-9868 (cust serv) *Fax:* 908-219-0192
E-mail: custserv@infotoday.com
Key Personnel
Man Ed: Karen Hallard *Tel:* 908-219-0277
 E-mail: khallard@infotoday.com
A comprehensive directory of the AV market, listing the activities of over 6,500 manufacturers,
 distributors & production service companies
 & over 1,250 products & services. Heavily indexed. Also contains information on related
 associations, state & local film & television
 commissions, awards & festivals, periodicals,
 reference books & AV-oriented conferences &
 exhibits. Covers all 50 states plus Canada.
Annual.
32nd ed, 2004: 1,702 pp, $195.00 paper
ISBN(s): 1-57387-187-7

**Banned in the USA: A Reference Guide to
 Book Censorship in Schools & Public
 Libraries Revised & Expanded Edition**
Published by Greenwood Press
Subsidiary of Greenwood Publishing Group Inc
88 Post Rd W, Westport, CT 06881
Tel: 203-226-3571 *Fax:* 203-222-1502
E-mail: bookinfo@greenwood.com
Web Site: www.greenwood.com
Key Personnel
Author: Herbert N Foerstel
VP, Mktg: Linda May *Tel:* 203-226-3571 ext
 3351
Foerstel's book is the perfect book to hand to stu-
 dents writing papers on censorship or anyone
 doing research on the subject.
2002: 328 pp, $54.95
ISBN(s): 0-313-31166-8

Be Your Own Literary Agent
Published by Ten Speed Press
PO Box 7123, Berkeley, CA 94710
Tel: 510-559-1600 *Fax:* 510-524-4588
E-mail: order@tenspeed.com
Web Site: www.tenspeed.com
The ultimate insider's guide to getting published.
3rd ed: 256 pp, $15.95
ISBN(s): 1-58008-338-2

Biography & Genealogy Master Index
Published by Thomson Gale
Unit of The Thomson Corp
27500 Drake Rd, Farmington Hills, MI 48331-
 3535

Tel: 248-699-4253 *Toll Free Tel:* 800-347-4253
 Fax: 248-699-8074 *Toll Free Fax:* 800-414-
 5043
E-mail: galeord@gale.com
Web Site: www.gale.com
Key Personnel
Ed: Jennifer Mossman
An eight-volume guide to 3.25 million entries
 in more than 350 current biographical works.
 Supersedes the first edition, published as *Bio-
 graphical Dictionaries Master Index.*
Twice a year updates add 600,000 citations &
 more than 900 pages; entries are cumulated
 every five years.
2004: 6,000 pp, $295; 5 yr cum $1,095
ISBN(s): 0-7876-4057-3 (Ed 2004, Vol 1); 0-
 7876-4058-1 (Ed 2004, Vol 2); 0-7876-4059-X
 (Ed 2005, Vol 1)

Book Blitz, Getting Your Book in the News
Published by Best Sellers
7456 Evergreen Dr, Goleta, CA 93117
Tel: 805-968-8567 *Fax:* 805-968-5747
E-mail: bgaughenmu@aol.com
Web Site: www.goodmorningworld.org
Key Personnel
Author: Barbara Gaughen *E-mail:* barbara@rain.
 org; Ernest Weckbaugh
A hands-on publicity guide for authors; 60 steps
 for instant book success.
1994: 268 pp, $12.95
ISBN(s): 1-881474-02-X

**Book Fairs: An Exhibiting Guide for
 Publishers**
Published by Para Publishing
PO Box 8206-R, Santa Barbara, CA 93118-8206
SAN: 215-8981
Tel: 805-968-7277 *Toll Free Tel:* 800-727-2782
 Fax: 805-968-1379
E-mail: orders@parapublishing.com
Web Site: www.parapublishing.com
Key Personnel
Owner & Publr: Dan Poynter
 E-mail: danpoynter@parapublishing.com
How to select, arrange & operate a booth at a
 book fair. Includes lists of fairs, exhibiting ser-
 vices, display materials & sources.
4th ed, 1986: 96 pp, $7.95 paper
ISBN(s): 0-915516-43-8

**Book Fulfillment: Order Entry, Picking,
 Packing & Shipping**
Published by Para Publishing
PO Box 8206-R, Santa Barbara, CA 93118-8206
SAN: 215-8981
Tel: 805-968-7277 *Toll Free Tel:* 800-727-2782
 Fax: 805-968-1379
E-mail: orders@parapublishing.com
Web Site: www.parapublishing.com
Key Personnel
Owner & Publr: Dan Poynter
 E-mail: danpoynter@parapublishing.com
How to set up your publishing company.
Biennially.
8th ed, 2002: 51 pp, $19.95 paper
ISBN(s): 0-56860-037-2

Book Industry Trends
Published by Book Industry Study Group Inc
19 W 21 St, Suite 905, New York, NY 10010
Tel: 646-336-7141 *Fax:* 646-336-6214
E-mail: info@bisg.org
Web Site: www.bisg.org
Key Personnel
Exec Dir: Jeff Abraham *E-mail:* jeff@bisg.org
Statistics of book sales by market.
Annual.
2003: 225 pp, $750 non members, $100 members
ISBN(s): 0-940016-81-8

Book Marketing: A New Approach
Published by Para Publishing
PO Box 8206-R, Santa Barbara, CA 93118-8206
SAN: 215-8981
Tel: 805-968-7277 *Toll Free Tel:* 800-727-2782
  Fax: 805-968-1379
E-mail: orders@parapublishing.com
Web Site: www.parapublishing.com
Key Personnel
Owner & Publr: Dan Poynter
  E-mail: danpoynter@parapublishing.com
How to sell books to bookstores, libraries & non-
  traditional markets.
Biennially.
10th ed, 2002: 76 pp, $14.95 paper
ISBN(s): 1-56860-029-1

Book Prices Used & Rare
Published by Spoon River Press
Division of BookQuote Inc
2319-C W Rohmann, Peoria, IL 61604
Mailing Address: PO Box 3635, Peoria, IL
  61612-3635
Tel: 309-672-2665 *Fax:* 309-672-7853
E-mail: srppress@aol.com
Key Personnel
Ed: Edward N Zempel
Annual.
7th ed, 1999: 798 pp, $73 cloth
ISBN(s): 0-930358-14-7

Book Review Index, 1985-1992 Master
  Cumulation
Published by Thomson Gale
Unit of The Thomson Corp
27500 Drake Rd, Farmington Hills, MI 48331-
  3535
Tel: 248-699-4253 *Toll Free Tel:* 800-347-4253
  Fax: 248-699-8074 *Toll Free Fax:* 800-414-
  5043
E-mail: galeord@gale.com
Web Site: www.gale.com
Key Personnel
Man Ed: Debra M Kirby
Ed: Dana Ferguson *Tel:* 248-699-4253 ext 1345
  E-mail: dana.ferguson@galegroup.com
Provides more than 1 million review citations to
  approximately 500,000 different books.
1992 ed: 8,500 pp, $1495
ISBN(s): 0-8103-9626-2

The Book Trade in Canada
Published by Quill & Quire
70 The Esplanade, Suite 210, Toronto, ON M5E
  1R2, Canada
Tel: 416-360-0044 *Fax:* 416-955-0794
E-mail: btic@idirect.ca
Web Site: www.quillandquire.com/html/btic.html
Key Personnel
Publr: Sharon McAuley
Ed: Scott Anderson *E-mail:* sanderson@
  quillandquire.com
Complete guide to the Canadian publishing mar-
  ketplace. Includes complete information on
  publishers, distributors, agency lines, industry
  organizations, booksellers, suppliers, book me-
  dia, awards & writing courses.
Annual in Jan.
2004: 500 pp, $175 US paper, $125 Canada
First published 1975

Bookbinding Materials & Techniques
  1700-1920
Published by Canadian Bookbinders & Book
  Artists Guild (CBBAG)
60 Atlantic Ave, Suite 112, Toronto, ON M6K
  1X9, Canada
Tel: 416-581-1071 *Fax:* 416-581-1053
E-mail: cbbag@web.net
Web Site: www.cbbag.ca
Key Personnel
Author: Margaret Lock

Bookman's Price Index
Published by Thomson Gale
Unit of The Thomson Corp
27500 Drake Rd, Farmington Hills, MI 48331-
  3535
Tel: 248-699-4253 *Toll Free Tel:* 800-347-4253
  Fax: 248-699-8075
E-mail: galeord@gale.com
Web Site: www.gale.com
Key Personnel
Ed: Michael Reade
A guide to the prices & availability of more than
  25,000 rare or out-of-print antiquarian books
  as offered for sale in the catalogs of nearly 200
  leading bookdealers in the US, UK & Canada.
  Each volume lists almost 15,000 titles. Volumes do not supersede previous volumes. Each
  volume covers catalogs from the previous 4-6
  months. Each entry includes title, author, edition, year published, physical description (size,
  binding, illustrations), condition of the book &
  price. Arranged alphabetically by author.
3-4 times/yr.
Vol 76-79, 2004; Vol 80-81, 2005: 1,300 pp,
  $415/vol
First published 1964
ISBN(s): 0-7876-6687-4 (Vol 76); 0-7876-7832-
  5 (Vol 77); 0-7876-7833-3 (Vol 78); 0-7876-
  7834-1 (Vol 79); 0-7876-7835-X (Vol 80); 0-
  7876-7836-8 (Vol 81)

Books for the Teen Age
Published by New York Public Library Office of
  Young Adult Services
455 Fifth Ave, 6th fl, New York, NY 10016-0109
Tel: 212-340-0909
Key Personnel
Ed: Sandra Payne *E-mail:* spayne@nypl.org
Retrospective & current list of quality books for
  ages 12-18.
Annual.
75th ed, 2004: 28 pp, $10 plus $1 mailing & han-
  dling
ISBN(s): 0-87104-763-2

Books in Print
Published by R R Bowker LLC
Subsidiary of Cambridge Information Group Inc
630 Central Ave, New Providence, NJ 07974
SAN: 214-1191
Tel: 908-286-1090 *Toll Free Tel:* 888-BOWKER2
  Fax: 908-219-0185
E-mail: info@bowker.com
Web Site: www.bowker.com; www.booksinprint.
  com
Key Personnel
Sr Man Dir: Roy Crego
Sr Dir: Constance Harbison *E-mail:* constance.
  harbison@bowker.com
In eight volumes of author, title & publisher indexes, this core reference guide delivers; entries for over 2.2 million active citations of all
  kinds—adult, juvenile, popular, scholarly &
  reprints—with more than 180,000 new titles
  added annually. The most complete & current
  bibliographic & ordering information for every
  title–updated by the publishers themselves–
  from pages, price & publisher to edition, binding & ISBN. Over a million price & entry
  revisions reflecting the rapid changes taking
  place in the publishing world today. A Publishers Index to more than 70,000 companies
  including 5,000 new publishers, wholesalers
  & distributors. In the ever-changing world of
  book publishing, nothing you can put on your
  shelf keeps your reference, acquisitions & collection development activities as organized &
  up to date as Books in Print 2004-2005. It's
  the one unfailing resource you can count on
  to stay on top of all book changes. Additional
  value added data, such as cover art, contributor biographies & review citations are available
  to customers who receive Books In Print in

specific electronic & through subscriptions to
  www.booksinprint.com.
Annual.
2004-2005: 23,088 pp, $799.00
ISBN(s): 0-8352-4642-6 (8 vol set)

Books in Print Supplement
Published by R R Bowker LLC
Subsidiary of Cambridge Information Group Inc
630 Central Ave, New Providence, NJ 07974
SAN: 214-1191
Tel: 908-286-1090 *Toll Free Tel:* 888-BOWKER2
  Fax: 908-219-0185
E-mail: info@bowker.com
Web Site: www.bowker.com
Key Personnel
Sr Man Dir: Roy Crego
Here's the sure way to keep your Books In Print
  fresh & current. This essential mid-year supplement brings you up to date with six full
  months of book publishing changes, to ensure top performances & service in your library
  or bookstore throughout the year. The supplement features separate Title, Author, Subject
  & Publisher indexes – so you'll handle the
  latest reference & ordering questions just as
  easily as with Books In Print. You'll find: Up
  to date bibliographic & ordering information
  for more than 106,000 new & forthcoming titles. More than 550,000 entries with major revisions. More than 132,000 titles & editions
  flagged out-of-print or out-of-stock. Another
  3,000 new publishers - & more than 15,000
  publishers' address changes & new toll-free
  numbers. Some 62,000 entries in the Subject
  Index. Use this information to answer patron
  queries, keep your collection current, verify
  prices, confirm availability & keep the latest
  book world information in your sights all year
  long.
Annual.
2003-2004: 9,000 pp, $425.00/3 vol set
ISBN(s): 0-8352-4618-3

Books Out Loud
Formerly Words on Cassette
Published by R R Bowker LLC
Subsidiary of Cambridge Information Group Inc
630 Central Ave, New Providence, NJ 07974
SAN: 214-1191
Tel: 908-286-1090 *Toll Free Tel:* 888-BOWKER2
  Fax: 908-219-0185
E-mail: info@bowker.com
Web Site: www.bowker.com
Key Personnel
Sr Man Dir: Roy Crego
With the increasing popularity of audiobooks,
  Books Out Loud: Bowker's Guide to Audiobooks (formerly "Words on Cassette") is now,
  more than ever, a must-have collection development & reference tool for your library or
  bookstore. This 19th edition contains bibliographic information on over 115,000 titles by
  more than 80,000 authors. Detailed listings include reader's name, price, running time, number of cassettes or CD's, content summary, release date, abridged or unabridged version &
  rental availability. This two-volume set features a unique Author/Reader/Performer Index,
  making locating your favorite audiobook contributor quick & easy. To help you choose the
  most popular audiobooks for your bookstore or
  library, a separate listing of best audio books
  & bestsellers from Publisher's Weekly & the
  Audio Publishers Association is included.
Annual.
19th ed, 2004: 4,992 pp, $255.00/2 vol set
ISBN(s): 0-8352-4611-6 (2 vol set)

Bowker Annual Library & Book Trade
  Almanac
Published by Information Today, Inc

630 Central Ave, New Providence, NJ 07974
Tel: 908-286-1090 *Toll Free Tel:* 800-409-4929;
  800-300-9868 (cust serv) *Fax:* 908-219-0192
E-mail: custserv@infotoday.com
Key Personnel
Ed: Dave Bogart *E-mail:* dbogart@ptd.net
Almanac of US library & book trade statistics,
  standards, programs & major events of the
  year, as well as international statistics & developments. Includes lists of library & literary awards & prizes, notable books, library
  schools, scholarship sources; directory of book
  trade & library associations at state, regional,
  national & international levels; employment
  sources; calendar of events.
Annual.
49th ed, 2004: 800 pp, $199.00 cloth
ISBN(s): 0-57387-193-1

The Bowker Buyer's Guide
Published by R R Bowker LLC
Subsidiary of Cambridge Information Group Inc
630 Central Ave, New Providence, NJ 07974
SAN: 214-1191
Tel: 908-286-1090 *Toll Free Tel:* 800-521-8110
E-mail: info@bowker.com
Web Site: www.bowker.com
Each issue contains top publishers' forthcoming
  selections along with helpful indexes, cover
  images & some current book industry highlights. The two main indexes are: Subjects &
  Publishers. The Subject Index contains the full
  bibliographic entry for each title & is arranged
  by general subject categories conforming to the
  industry standard BISAC list. A color-coded
  key is also used for various main subjects
  found on each page, as well as the table of
  contents page. The Publisher Index lists, alphabetically by name, all the publishers found in
  the Buyer's Guide. Each listing includes complete contact information.
3x/yr.
336 pp, $200.00

Bowker's Guide to Characters in Fiction
Published by R R Bowker LLC
Subsidiary of Cambridge Information Group Inc
630 Central Ave, New Providence, NJ 07974
SAN: 214-1191
Tel: 908-286-1090 *Toll Free Tel:* 800-521-8110
E-mail: info@bowker.com
Web Site: www.bowker.com
Reference tool covering all genres of fiction. One
  volume includes over 200,000 bibliographic
  listings of fiction titles for adults; the other volume includes over 80,000 bibliographic listings
  of fiction titles for children. Includes indices of
  over 4,000 recurring characters (3,800+ adults;
  500+ children's) & over 1,000 settings in fiction (both real & imaginary); indices on ethnic groups, historical events, occupations &
  relationships found in fictional works also provided.
Annually.
2003-2004, $225.00/2 vol set
First published 2003
ISBN(s): 0-8352-4608-6 (2 vol set)

Bowker's News Media Directory
Published by R R Bowker LLC
Subsidiary of Cambridge Information Group Inc
630 Central Ave, New Providence, NJ 07974
SAN: 214-1191
Tel: 908-286-1090 *Toll Free Tel:* 800-521-8110
  Fax: 908-219-0182
E-mail: nmd@bowker.com
Web Site: www.bowker.com
Key Personnel
Sr Ed: Valerie Mahon
A comprehensive directory of US newspapers,
  magazines & radio & TV stations with detailed
  profiles directed at advertisers, publicists, com-

munications professionals, researchers & freelance writers. Vol 1: *Newspaper Directory* (includes syndicates) Vol 2: *Magazine & Newsletter Directory* Vol 3: *TV & Radio Directory.*
Annual.
55th ed, Sept 2004: 2,200 pp, $560.00/3 vol set
ISBN(s): 0-8352-4662-0 (3 vol set)

Brand Week Directory
Published by Adweek Directories
Division of BPI Communications Inc
770 Broadway, New York, NY 10003
Tel: 646-654-5202 *Toll Free Tel:* 800-562-2706
  Fax: 646-654-5886
Web Site: www.adweek.com/directories
Key Personnel
Ed: Allen McCormack *E-mail:* amccormack@
  adweek.com
Publg Dir: Mitch Tebo *Tel:* 646-654-5215
  E-mail: mtebo@adweek.com
Directory of addresses, telephone numbers, per-
  sonnel & media expenditures for brands &
  brand marketers.
Annual.
1,065 pp, $230 print, $399 online

Breathing Life Into Your Characters
Published by Writer's Digest Books
4700 E Galbraith Rd, Cincinnati, OH 45236
Tel: 513-531-2690 *Fax:* 513-531-0798
Web Site: www.writersdigest.com
Learn techniques to help you tap your uncon-
  scious.
256 pp, $22.99

Broadcasting & Cable Yearbook
Published by Reed Business Information
Division of Reed Elsevier Inc
630 Central Ave, New Providence, NJ 07974
Tel: 908-286-1090 *Toll Free Tel:* 888-BOWKER2
  Fax: 908-219-0182
Web Site: www.bowker.com
A complete guide to the broadcasting & cable
  industries, including complete directories of
  radio, TV & cable, as well as all support indus-
  tries, government agencies, law & regulations,
  market statistics.
Annual.
2005: 1,500 pp, $199.95
ISBN(s): 1-56056-024-X

**Business & Legal Forms for Authors &
  Self-Publishers**
Published by Allworth Press
Subsidiary of Allworth Communications Inc
10 E 23 St, Suite 510, New York, NY 10010
Tel: 212-777-8395 *Toll Free Tel:* 800-491-2808
  Fax: 212-777-8261
E-mail: pub@allworth.com
Web Site: www.allworth.com
Key Personnel
Publr & Author: Tad Crawford
Assoc Publr: Bob Porter
Contains 24 ready-to-use forms, negotiation
  checklist, extra tear-out forms & forms on CD-
  ROM.
Annually, Jan.
3rd ed: 160 pp, $29.95 (includes CD-ROM)
ISBN(s): 1-58115-395-3

**Business Letters for Publishers: Creative
  Correspondence Outlines**
Published by Para Publishing
PO Box 8206-R, Santa Barbara, CA 93118-8206
SAN: 215-8981
Tel: 805-968-7277 *Toll Free Tel:* 800-727-2782
  Fax: 805-968-1379
E-mail: orders@parapublishing.com
Web Site: www.parapublishing.com
Key Personnel
Owner & Publr: Dan Poynter
  E-mail: danpoynter@parapublishing.com

A collection of form letters conforming to
  publishing-industry procedures, designed to
  save time in drafting letters for sales, promotion, collections & other daily problems on
  disk.
6th ed, 2001: 82 pp, $29.95 magnetic disk
ISBN(s): 0-915516-47-0

**Cabell's Directory of Publishing Opportunities
  in Accounting**
Published by Cabell Publishing Co
PO Box 5428, Tobe Hahn Sta, Beaumont, TX
  77726-5428
Tel: 409-898-0575 *Fax:* 409-866-9554
E-mail: publish@cabells.com
Web Site: www.cabells.com
Key Personnel
Pres & Ed: David W Cabell
Ed: Deborah L English
Information on over 160 journals in accounting.
Biennial.
9th ed, 2004-2005: 566 pp, $99.95 paper
ISBN(s): 0-911753-22-2

**Cabell's Directory of Publishing Opportunities
  in Economics & Finance**
Published by Cabell Publishing Co
PO Box 5428, Tobe Hahn Sta, Beaumont, TX
  77726-5428
Tel: 409-898-0575 *Fax:* 409-866-9554
E-mail: publish@cabells.com
Web Site: www.cabells.com
Key Personnel
Pres & Ed: David W Cabell
Ed: Deborah L English
Information on over 400 journals in economics &
  finance - 3 volumes.
Biennial.
9th ed, 2004-2005: 1,458 pp, $119.95
ISBN(s): 0-911759-23-0

**Cabell's Directory of Publishing Opportunities
  in Education, Curriculum & Methods**
Published by Cabell Publishing Co
PO Box 5428, Tobe Hahn Sta, Beaumont, TX
  77726-5428
Tel: 409-898-0575 *Fax:* 409-866-9554
E-mail: publish@cabells.com
Web Site: www.cabells.com
Key Personnel
Pres & Ed: David W Cabell
Ed: Deborah L English
Information on 350 journals listed in 2 vols.
6th ed, 2002-2003, $99.95
ISBN(s): 0-911753-18-4

**Cabell's Directory of Publishing Opportunities
  in Educational Psychology & Administration**
Published by Cabell Publishing Co
PO Box 5428, Tobe Hahn Sta, Beaumont, TX
  77726-5428
Tel: 409-898-0575 *Fax:* 409-866-9554
E-mail: publish@cabells.com
Web Site: www.cabells.com
Key Personnel
Pres & Ed: David W Cabell
Ed: Deborah L English
Information in 225 journals listed in 2 vols.
6th ed, 2002-2003
ISBN(s): 0-911752-19-2

**Cabell's Directory of Publishing Opportunities
  in Management**
Published by Cabell Publishing Co
PO Box 5428, Tobe Hahn Sta, Beaumont, TX
  77726-5428
Tel: 409-898-0575 *Fax:* 409-866-9554
E-mail: publish@cabells.com
Web Site: www.cabells.com
Key Personnel
Pres & Ed: David W Cabell
Ed: Deborah L English

Information on over 620 journals in management
- 4 volumes.
9th ed, 2004-2005: 2,511 pp, $174.95 paper
ISBN(s): 0-911753-24-9

**Cabell's Directory of Publishing Opportunities
in Marketing**
Published by Cabell Publishing Co
PO Box 5428, Tobe Hahn Sta, Beaumont, TX
77726-5428
Tel: 409-898-0575 *Fax:* 409-866-9554
E-mail: publish@cabells.com
Web Site: www.cabells.com
Key Personnel
Pres & Ed: David W Cabell
Ed: Deborah L English
Information on over 210 journals in marketing.
Biennially.
9th ed, 2004-2005: 874 pp, $99.95 paper
ISBN(s): 0-911753-25-7

Canadian Book Review Annual
44 Charles St W, Suite 3205, Toronto, ON M4Y
1R8, Canada
Tel: 416-961-8537 *Fax:* 416-961-1855
E-mail: cbra@interlog.com
Web Site: www.interlog.com/~cbra
Key Personnel
Ed-in-Chief & Publr: Joyce M Wilson
Ed Trade Ref: Sarah Robertson
Ed, Childrens Lit: Steve Pitt
Reviews of Canadian trade, scholarly, reference &
children's titles.
Annual.
29th ed, 2004: 680 pp, $129.95 cloth, US
ISBN(s): 0-9732301-1-8

**Canadian Books in Print: Author & Title
Index & Subject Index**
Published by University of Toronto Press Inc
10 Saint Mary St, Suite 700, Toronto, ON M4Y
2W8, Canada
Tel: 416-978-2239 (ext 230); 416-667-7791 (lo-
cal orders) *Toll Free Tel:* 800-565-9523 (or-
ders Canada & US) *Fax:* 416-978-4738 (edit)
Toll Free Fax: 800-221-9985
E-mail: utpbooks@utpress.utoronto.ca
Web Site: www.utpress.utoronto.ca
Key Personnel
Ed: Marian Butler *Tel:* 416-265-1631
Ed & Mgr, Ref Div: Elizabeth Lumley
Cloth: annual; microfiche: 3 times/yr.
2003: 2,518 pp, $175 cloth (author-title), $220
with quarterly microfiche service, $150 (subject
index)
ISBN(s): 0-8020-8888-0 (author & title index);
0-8020-8889-9 (subject index); 0-8020-8891-0
(quarterly service-author & title index & qauar-
terly microfiche)

Canadian Copyright Law
Published by McGraw-Hill Ryerson Ltd
Affiliate of McGraw-Hill Inc
300 Water St, Whitby, ON L1N 9B6, Canada
Tel: 905-430-5143 *Toll Free Tel:* 800-565-
5758 (cust serv) *Fax:* 905-430-5203
Toll Free Fax: 800-463-5885 (Canada)
Web Site: www.mcgrawhill.ca
Key Personnel
Author: Lesley Ellen Harris
Ed: Joan Homewood
3rd ed, July 2001: 332 pp
ISBN(s): 007-560369-1

Careers for Your Characters
Published by Writer's Digest Books
4700 E Galbraith Rd, Cincinnati, OH 45236
Tel: 513-531-2690 *Fax:* 513-531-0798
Web Site: www.writersdigest.com
User friendly, interactive reference. Useful & in-
valuable resource at any level of skill or expe-
rience.

352 pp, $18.99
ISBN(s): 1-58297-083-1

Catholic Press Directory
Published by Catholic Press Association of the
US & Canada
3555 Veterans Memorial Hwy, Unit O,
Ronkonkoma, NY 11779
Tel: 631-471-4730 *Fax:* 631-471-4804
E-mail: cathjourn@aol.com
Web Site: www.catholicpress.org/index.htm
Key Personnel
Exec Dir: Owen P McGovern *E-mail:* omcg@aol.
com
Complete listings of more than 600 Catholic
newspapers, magazines, newsletters & foreign
language publications in the USA & Canada.
Also includes Catholic Book & General Pub-
lishers; Diocesan Directories.
Annual.
232 pp, $48.85
ISBN(s): 0-686-3036-0

CCOD, see Consultants & Consulting
Organizations Directory

Celebrity Directory 2004-2005
Published by Axiom Information Resources
PO Box 8015, Ann Arbor, MI 48107
Tel: 734-761-4842
E-mail: axiom@celebritylocator.com
Web Site: www.celebritylocator.com
Key Personnel
Pres: Rob Ten-Tronck
Publr: Terry Robinson
Directory of over 9,000 celebrities from enter-
tainment to business who may be contacted for
testimonials for the book trade.
Annually.
2004-2005: 258 pp, $39.95 paper
ISBN(s): 0-943213-48-7

**Censorship of Expression in the 1980s: A
Statistical Survey**
Published by Greenwood Press
Subsidiary of Greenwood Publishing Group Inc
88 Post Rd W, Westport, CT 06881
Mailing Address: PO Box 5007, Westport, CT
06881
Tel: 203-226-3571 *Fax:* 203-222-1502
E-mail: bookinfo@greenwood.com
Web Site: www.greenwood.com
Key Personnel
Author: Steven R Harris; John B Harer
VP, Mktg: Linda May *Tel:* 203-226-3571 ext
3351
The study of censorship is important because this
conflict between opposing forces threatens the
foundation of society.
1994: 200 pp, $85
ISBN(s): 0-313-28746-5

**Checklists for Print Media Advertising
Planning & Buying**
Published by Richler & Co
754 Palermo Dr, Suite A, Santa Barbara, CA
93105
Tel: 805-569-1668 *Fax:* 805-569-2279
Key Personnel
VP, Sales & Mktg: Roy M Buckley
1st ed, 1997: 61 pp, $19.95
ISBN(s): 1-879299-14-3

**Chicago Guide to Preparing Electronic
Manuscripts**
Published by Association of American University
Presses
1427 E 60 St, Chicago, IL 60637-2954
Tel: 773-702-7700 *Toll Free Tel:* 800-621-2736
(orders) *Fax:* 773-702-9756 (sales) *Telex:* 28-
0206

Key Personnel
Dir: Paula Barker Duffy
Asst to Dir: Lauren Nathan *Tel:* 773-702-8879
E-mail: lnathan@press.uchicago.edu
A practical guide for authors & publishers who
use computer disks & tapes for typesetting.
1987: 144 pp, $30 cloth, $13 paper
ISBN(s): 0-226-10392-7 (cloth); 0-226-10393-5
(paper)

The Chicago Manual of Style
Published by Association of American University
Presses
1427 E 60 St, Chicago, IL 60637-2954
Tel: 773-702-7700 *Toll Free Tel:* 800-621-2736
(orders) *Fax:* 773-702-9756 (sales)
E-mail: cmosfaq@press.uchicago.edu
Web Site: www.press.uchicago.edu/Misc/Chicago/
cmosfaq.html
Key Personnel
Dir: Paula Barker Duffy
Style manual for authors, editors & copywriters.
Revised every 10 years.
15th ed, revised & expanded, 2003: 984 pp, $55
cloth; $95 cloth w/CD-ROM; $55 CD-ROM
ISBN(s): 0-226-10403-6 (cloth); 0-226-10404-4
(CD-ROM); 0-226-10405-2 (cloth w/CD-ROM)

**Children's Book Review Index Cumulative
2003**
Published by Thomson Gale
Unit of The Thomson Corp
27500 Drake Rd, Farmington Hills, MI 48331-
3535
Tel: 248-699-4253 *Toll Free Tel:* 800-347-4253
Fax: 248-699-8074 *Toll Free Fax:* 800-414-
5043
Web Site: www.gale.com
Key Personnel
Ed: Dana Ferguson *Tel:* 248-699-4253 ext 1345
E-mail: dana.ferguson@galegroup.com
Contains citations of all children's book reviews
in *Book Review Index*. Approximately 25,000
review citations of 10,000 books are cited each
year from 500 periodicals indexed. Includes
Title Index & Illustrator Index.
Annual.
2003: 675 pp, $175/vol cloth
ISBN(s): 0-7876-7134-7

Children's Books: Awards & Prizes
Published by The Children's Book Council
(CBC)
12 W 37 St, 2nd fl, New York, NY 10118-7480
Tel: 212-966-1990 *Toll Free Tel:* 800-999-
2160 (orders only) *Fax:* 212-966-2073
Toll Free Tel: 888-807-9355 (orders only)
E-mail: info@cbcbooks.org
Web Site: www.cbcbooks.org
Key Personnel
Pres: Paula Quint
Lists over 200 major US, British Commonwealth
& international children's & young adult book
awards; for teachers, librarians & universi-
ties with English, library or education schools
teaching children's literature or creative writing. Includes indices, appendix & a list of information resources. Next edition will be available electronically, spring 2003.
Irregular.
$150 online

Children's Books in Print
Published by R R Bowker LLC
Subsidiary of Cambridge Information Group Inc
630 Central Ave, New Providence, NJ 07974
SAN: 214-1191
Tel: 908-286-1090 *Toll Free Tel:* 888-BOWKER2
Fax: 908-219-0185
E-mail: info@bowker.com
Web Site: www.bowker.com

Key Personnel
Sr Man Dir: Roy Crego
"...the most complete list of currently available children's books published in the U.S."
– Booklist. No children's collection is complete without this practical resource standing front & center on the reference shelf. The 2004 edition of Children's Books In Print puts the entire world of children's books at your fingertips, arranging in print titles alphabetically by title, author & illustrator for fast, convenient access. Updated with 39,000 new entries & thousands of entry revisions, this comprehensive work helps you: Track down any children's books – even hard-to-find titles from small presses. Locate all works by favorite authors or illustrators. Cut ordering time & effort with current prices, ISBNs, publishers' telephone numbers & addresses. Offer patrons a definitive, easy-access guide to all available titles geared for young readers.
Annual.
35th ed, 2004: 2,900 pp, $325.00/2 vol set cloth
ISBN(s): 0-8352-4597-7 (2 vol set)

Children's Literature Review
Published by Thomson Gale
Unit of The Thomson Corp
27500 Drake Rd, Farmington Hills, MI 48331-3535
Tel: 248-699-4253 *Toll Free Tel:* 800-347-4253
Fax: 248-699-8054
E-mail: galeord@gale.com
Web Site: www.gale.com
Key Personnel
Ed: Thomas Burns
Provides full texts from criticism on authors & illustrators of books for children & young adults. Includes indexes to titles, authors & nationality. Illustrations & photographs are included. Also available as an e-book.
multiple vols/yr.
Vol 93-101, 2004; Vols 102-107, 2005, $185/vol

Children's Writer's Word Book
Published by Writer's Digest Books
4700 E Galbraith Rd, Cincinnati, OH 45236
Tel: 513-531-2690 *Fax:* 513-531-0798
Web Site: www.writersdigest.com
Handy reference book to be used along with your dictionary or thesaurus. Gives guidelines for sentence length, word usage & theme at each reading level.
325 pp, $16.99
ISBN(s): 0-89879-951-1

Christian Bookwriters Marketing Guide
Published by Joy Publishing
PO Box 9901, Fountain Valley, CA 92708
Tel: 714-545-4321 *Toll Free Tel:* 800-454-8228
Fax: 714-708-2099
Web Site: www.joypublishing.com
Key Personnel
Pres: Woody Young *E-mail:* woody@joypublishing.com
Info on publishers (books & periodicals).
Annual.
3/1994: 386 pp, $19.95
ISBN(s): 0-939513-94-3

The CLMP Directory of Literary Magazines & Presses, 21st ed
Published by Council of Literary Magazines & Presses (CLMP)
154 Christopher St, Suite 3-C, New York, NY 10014-2839
Tel: 212-741-9110 *Fax:* 212-741-9112
E-mail: info@clmp.org
Web Site: www.clmp.org
Key Personnel
Prog Admin: Jamie Schwartz

Descriptive directory of over 500 literary magazines & presses. Organized alphabetically by title, each entry includes address, editor(s), editorial philosophy, contributors, distributors frequency & materials published. Prepared for reference libraries, writers, publishers & advertisers.
Annual.
21: 247 pp, $15 paper ($19 with postage & handling)

Colorado Book Guide: A Directory of the Colorado Book Community
Published by The Bloomsbury Review
1553 Platte St, Suite 206, Denver, CO 80202
Tel: 303-455-3123 *Toll Free Tel:* 800-783-3338
Fax: 303-455-7039
E-mail: bloomsb@aol.com
Web Site: www.bloomsburyreview.com
Key Personnel
Publr & Ed-in-Chief: Marilyn Auer
Directory of Colorado Book Community (bookstores, libraries, etc).
Biennial.
5th ed, 2001-2002: 200 pp, $10.95 paper
ISBN(s): 0-9631589-7-X

Communicating Ideas: The Politics of Publishing in a Post-Industrial Society
Published by Transaction Publishers
Rutgers University, Bldg 4051, 35 Berrue Circle, Piscataway, NJ 08854
Mailing Address: 1247 State Rd, Princeton, NJ 08540
Tel: 732-445-2280 *Fax:* 732-445-3138
Key Personnel
Chmn & Author: Irving Louis Horowitz
E-mail: ihorowitz@transactionpub.com
View of publishing in America & abroad. Addresses the political implications of scholarly communication in the era of the new computerized technology.
2nd ed, 1991: 356 pp, $24.95 paper
ISBN(s): 0-88738-898-1

Complete Directory of Large Print Books & Serials
Published by R R Bowker LLC
Subsidiary of Cambridge Information Group Inc
630 Central Ave, New Providence, NJ 07974
SAN: 214-1191
Tel: 908-286-1090 *Toll Free Tel:* 888-BOWKER2
Fax: 908-219-0185
E-mail: info@bowker.com
Web Site: www.bowker.com
Key Personnel
Sr Man Dir: Roy Crego
If you're building or managing a large-print collection, this proven guide helps you to keep tabs on the fast-growing large-print field like no other resource available & the entire volume is printed in 14-point type to facilitate use by sight-impaired readers. You'll discover up-to-date bookfinding & ordering information on more than 25,000 titles – including over 3,900 new & forthcoming works – with full entries for each separate Subject (General, Children's & Textbook), Author & Titles indexes. Books from British publishers are also listed. Up-to-date subject headings cover the full range of fiction & nonfiction topics & there's an enlarged Serials index to some 115 large-print periodicals & newspapers. For all of your large-print information needs, there's no better helper than The Complete Directory of Large Print Books & Serials 2004.
Annual.
2004: 2,112 pp, $245.00
ISBN(s): 0-8352-4614-0

The Complete Guide to Book Marketing
Published by Allworth Press

Subsidiary of Allworth Communications Inc
10 E 23 St, Suite 510, New York, NY 10010
Tel: 212-777-8395 *Toll Free Tel:* 800-491-2808
Fax: 212-777-8261
E-mail: pub@allworth.com
Web Site: www.allworth.com
Key Personnel
Author: David Cole
Publr: Tad Crawford
Assoc Publr: Robert Porter
Mktg Dir: Cynthia Rivelli *Tel:* 212-777-8395 ext 3 *E-mail:* crivelli@allworth.com
Comprehensive resource book covering all aspects of book marketing.
revised ed, 2004: 256 pp, $19.95
ISBN(s): 1-58115-322-8

The Complete Guide to Book Publicity
Published by Allworth Press
Subsidiary of Allworth Communications Inc
10 E 23 St, Suite 510, New York, NY 10010
Tel: 212-777-8395 *Toll Free Tel:* 800-491-2808
Fax: 212-777-8395
E-mail: pub@allworth.com
Web Site: www.allworth.com
Key Personnel
Publr: Tad Crawford
Assoc Publr: Robert Porter
Author: Jodee Blanco
Mktg Dir: Cynthia Rivelli *Tel:* 212-777-8395 ext 3 *E-mail:* crivelli@allworth.com
A comprehensive resource book covering all aspects of book publicity.
2nd ed, 2004: 304 pp, $19.95
ISBN(s): 1-58115-349-X

The Complete Guide to Self-Publishing
Published by Writer's Digest Books
Division of F+W Publications Inc
4700 E Galbraith Rd, Cincinnati, OH 45236
Tel: 513-531-2690 *Toll Free Tel:* 800-666-0963
Fax: 513-891-7185 *Toll Free Fax:* 888-590-4082
Web Site: www.fwpublications.com
Key Personnel
Author: Marilyn Ross; Tom Ross
Sales Dir: Michael Murphy *Tel:* 800-666-0963 ext 1270 *E-mail:* michael.murphy@fwpubs.com
Everything you need to write, publish, promote & sell your book.
4th ed, 2001: 528 pp, $19.99 paper
First published 1991
ISBN(s): 1-58297-091-2

The Complete Guide to Successful Publishing
Published by Cardoza Publishing
857 Broadway, 3rd fl, New York, NY 10003
Tel: 212-255-6661 *Toll Free Tel:* 800-577-WINS (577-9467) *Fax:* 212-255-6671
E-mail: cardozapub@aol.com
Web Site: www.cardozapub.com
Key Personnel
Publr: Avery Cardoza
Off Mgr: Mary Grimes
This step-by-step guide shows beginning & established publishers how to successfully produce professional-looking books that not only look good, but sell in the open market; readers learn how to find & develop ideas; set up the business from the ground up; design & layout a book; find authors, work contracts & negotiate deals; get distribution; expand a publishing company into a large enterprise; & more.
Revised every 2 years.
2nd ed, Oct 1998: 416 pp, $19.95 paper
ISBN(s): 1-58042-097-4

The Complete Handbook of Novel Writing
Published by Writer's Digest Books
4700 E Galbraith Rd, Cincinnati, OH 45236
Tel: 513-531-2690 *Fax:* 513-531-0798
Web Site: www.writersdigest.com

Everything you need to know about creating &
selling your work.
400 pp, $17.99
ISBN(s): 1-58297-159-5

Concise Dictionary of American Literary Biography
Published by Thomson Gale
Unit of The Thomson Corp
27500 Drake Rd, Farmington Hills, MI 48331-3535
Tel: 248-699-4253 *Toll Free Tel:* 800-347-4253
  Fax: 248-699-8070 *Toll Free Fax:* 800-414-5043
E-mail: galeord@gale.com
Web Site: www.gale.com
Key Personnel
Mgr, Corp Communs: Kim Gabbert *Tel:* 248-699-8193 *E-mail:* kimberly.gabbert@thomson.com
Covers only the American authors most fre-
quently studied in high school & college litera-
ture courses, extracts & fully updates essays in
their entirety from the much larger Dictionary
of Literary Biography series.
Volumes include: *Colonization to the American
Renaissance, 1640-1865*
Realism, Naturalism & Local Color, 1865-1917
The Twenties, 1917-1929
The Age of Maturity, 1929-1941
The New Consciousness, 1941-1968
Broadening Views, 1968-1988
Supplement: Modern American Writers.
1987: 440 pp, $535/6 vol set
ISBN(s): 0-7876-1695-8 (Vol 7); 0-8103-1818-0
  (6-vol set); 0-8103-1819-9 (Vol 1); 0-8103-
  1820-2 (Vol 4); 0-8103-1821-0 (Vol 2); 0-8103-
  1822-9 (Vol 5); 0-8103-1823-7 (Vol 6); 0-8103-
  1824-5 (Vol 3)

Concise Dictionary of British Literary Biography
Published by Thomson Gale
Unit of The Thomson Corp
27500 Drake Rd, Farmington Hills, MI 48331-3535
Tel: 248-699-4253 *Toll Free Tel:* 800-347-4253
  Fax: 248-699-8070 *Toll Free Fax:* 800-414-5043
E-mail: galeord@gale.com
Web Site: www.gale.com
Key Personnel
Mgr, Corp Communs: Kim Gabbert *Tel:* 248-699-8193 *E-mail:* kimberly.gabbert@thomson.com
Illustrated set provides thorough coverage of ma-
jor British literary figures of all eras. Vol 1:
*Writers of the Middle Ages & Renaissance Be-
fore 1660*; Vol 2: *Writers of the Restoration &
18th Century 1660-1789*; Vol 3: *Writers of the
Romantic Period 1789-1832*; Vol 4: *Victorian
Writers, 1832-1890*; Vol 5: *Late Victorian &
Edwardian Writers, 1890-1914*; Vol 6: *Mod-
ern Writers, 1914-1945*; Vol 7: *Writers After
World War II, 1945-1960*; Vol 8: *Contemporary
Writers, 1960-Present.*
Vol 1-8, 1991: 24,000 pp, $715/8 vol set
ISBN(s): 0-8103-7980-5 (Vol set); 0-8103-7981-3
  (Vol 1); 0-8103-7982-1 (Vol 2); 0-8103-7983-X
  (Vol 3); 0-8103-7984-8 (Vol 4); 0-8103-7985-6
  (Vol 5); 0-8103-7986-4 (Vol 6); 0-8103-7987-2
  (Vol 7); 0-8103-7988-0 (Vol 8)

Consultants & Consulting Organizations Directory
Published by Thomson Gale
Unit of The Thomson Corp
27500 Drake Rd, Farmington Hills, MI 48331-3535
Tel: 248-699-4253 *Toll Free Tel:* 800-347-4253
  Fax: 248-699-8069
E-mail: galeord@gale.com
Web Site: www.gale.com

Key Personnel
Ed: Julie A Gough *E-mail:* julie.gough@thomson.com
Important details, including services offered, full
contact information, date founded & principal
business executives. More than 25,000 firms &
individuals listed are arranged alphabetically
under 14 general fields of consulting activity
ranging from agriculture to marketing. More
than 400 specialties are represented, including
finance, computers, fund raising & others.
Annual.
27th ed, 2004, $895
ISBN(s): 0-7876-5278-4 (24th ed); 0-7876-5877-
  4 (25th ed); 0-7876-6737-4 (26th ed); 0-7876-
  6741-2 (27th ed)

Contemporary Authors
Published by Thomson Gale
Unit of The Thomson Corp
27500 Drake Rd, Farmington Hills, MI 48331-3535
Tel: 248-699-4253 *Toll Free Tel:* 800-347-4253
  Fax: 248-699-8070 *Toll Free Fax:* 800-414-5043
E-mail: galeord@gale.com
Web Site: www.gale.com
Key Personnel
Mgr, Corp Communs: Kim Gabbert *Tel:* 248-699-8193 *E-mail:* kimberly.gabbert@thomson.com
Each volume includes biographical information
on approximately 300 modern writers in fic-
tion, general nonfiction, poetry, journalism,
drama, motion pictures & television.
10 vols/yr, original vols; 10 vols/yr, new revision
series.
Vols 221-230, 2004, $195/vol
ISBN(s): 0-7876-6701-3 (Vol 221); 0-7876-6702-
  1 (Vol 222); 0-7876-6703-4 (Vol 223); 0-7876-
  6704-8 (Vol 224); 0-7876-6705-6 (Vol 225);
  0-7876-6706-4 (Vol 226); 0-7876-6707-2 (Vol
  227); 0-7876-6708-0 (Vol 228); 0-7876-6709-9
  (Vol 229); 0-7876-6710-2 (Vol 230)

Contemporary Authors Autobiography Series
Published by Thomson Gale
Unit of The Thomson Corp
27500 Drake Rd, Farmington Hills, MI 48331-3535
Tel: 248-699-4253 *Toll Free Tel:* 800-347-4253
  Fax: 248-699-8070 *Toll Free Fax:* 800-414-5043
Web Site: www.gale.com
Key Personnel
Mgr, Corp Communs: Kim Gabbert *Tel:* 248-699-8193 *E-mail:* kimberly.gabbert@thomson.com
Each volume in this series contains approximately
20 autobiographical essays written especially
for this series. Each essay is illustrated with
candid photographs of the subject. Bibliographies included. 30 vols in print. Every volume
includes a cumulative index.
2 vols/yr.
1998, vol 30: 350 pp, $199/vol
ISBN(s): 0-7876-1975-2 (Vol 30)

Contemporary Literary Criticism
Published by Thomson Gale
Unit of The Thomson Corp
27500 Drake Rd, Farmington Hills, MI 48331-3535
Tel: 248-699-4253 *Toll Free Tel:* 800-347-4253
  Fax: 248-699-8054
E-mail: galeord@gale.com
Web Site: www.gale.com
Key Personnel
Ed: Jeffrey Hunter
Each series volume contains full texts from crit-
icism & evaluations of about 4-7 major mod-
ern authors. 197 vols in print covering over
3,000 authors. Vols 12, 17, 21, 26, 30 & 35 are
devoted to criticism of young adult authors;

vols 16 & 20 are devoted to film criticism;
vols 151-197 focus on today's novelists, poets, playrights, short story writers, scriptwriters
& other creative writers. *Cumulative Title Index*
is published annually.
multiple vols/yr.
Vols 181-194, 2004; Vols 195-207, 2005: 450 pp,
$195/vol

Copy Editing
Published by Cambridge University Press
40 W 20 St, New York, NY 10011-4211
Tel: 212-924-3900 *Toll Free Tel:* 800-872-7423
  (orders US & Canada) *Fax:* 914-937-4712 (orders US & Canada)
Web Site: www.cup.org
Key Personnel
Author: Judith Butcher
Pubns Info Coord: Rochelle Katz *Tel:* 212-924-
  3900 ext 5072 *E-mail:* rkatz@cup.org
Copy Editing covers all aspects of the editorial
process involved in converting an author's ms
to the printed page. It covers the basics from
how to mark a ms for the designer & typesetter, through the ground rules of house style &
consistency, to how to read & correct proofs.
3rd ed, 1992: 483 pp, $60 cloth
ISBN(s): 0-521-40074-0

Copyediting: A Practical Guide
Published by Crisp Publications Inc
10650 Toebben Dr, Independence, KY 41051
Toll Free Tel: 800-842-3636 (orders); 800-648-
  7450 *Fax:* 859-525-1543 (orders); 617-757-
  7936
Web Site: www.courseilt.com
Key Personnel
Field Rep: Nick Keefe *Tel:* 415-379-3980
  E-mail: nick.keefe@thomson.com
For authors, publishing personnel, writers, edi-
tors, journalists, teachers, desktop publishing &
computer software workers.
3rd ed, 2001: 328 pp, $24.95 (one ed)
ISBN(s): 0-156052-608-4

Corporate Scriptwriting Book
Published by Communicom Publishing Co
19300 NW Sauvie Island Rd, Portland, OR 97231
Tel: 503-621-3049
Key Personnel
Owner: Donna Matrazzo
A step-by-step guide to writing business films,
videotapes & slide shows.
2nd ed; revised ed, 1985: 210 pp, $16.95 paper
ISBN(s): 0-932617-07-7

The Creative Writer's Style Guide
Published by Writer's Digest Books
4700 E Galbraith Rd, Cincinnati, OH 45236
Tel: 513-531-2690 *Fax:* 513-531-0798
Web Site: www.writersdigest.com
Guide addresses issues of grammar, punctuation
& usage specifically in the context of writing
short stories, novels, poetry & screenplays.
240 pp, $22.99
ISBN(s): 1-884910-55-6

The Criminal Mind
Published by Writer's Digest Books
4700 E Galbraith Rd, Cincinnati, OH 45236
Tel: 513-531-2690 *Fax:* 513-531-0798
Web Site: www.writersdigest.com
Puts right the media driven misconceptions about
the nature of the criminal psyche in order to
help you create more believable, convincing
characters.
256 pp, $17.99
ISBN(s): 1-58297-079-3

Critical Survey of Long Fiction
Published by Salem Press Inc

2 University Plaza, Suite 121, Hackensack, NJ 07601
SAN: 208-838X
Tel: 201-968-9899 *Toll Free Tel:* 800-221-1592
Fax: 201-968-1411
E-mail: csr@salempress.com
Web Site: www.salempress.com
Key Personnel
Publicist & Sales & Mktg Mgr: Luisa Torres
E-mail: ltorres@salempress.com
463 essays arranged alphabetically by author providing in-depth overviews of major authors in long fiction, both English language & foreign language.
Every 4-7 yrs.
2nd rev: 4,392 pp, $499
ISBN(s): 0-89356-882-1

Critical Survey of Short Fiction
Published by Salem Press Inc
2 University Plaza, Suite 121, Hackensack, NJ 07601
SAN: 208-838X
Tel: 201-968-9899 *Toll Free Tel:* 800-221-1592
Fax: 201-968-1411
E-mail: csr@salempress.com
Web Site: www.salempress.com
515 essays arranged alphabetically by author providing in-depth overviews of short story writers.
Every 5-7 yrs.
2nd rev: 2,900 pp, $473
ISBN(s): 0-89365-006-5

Dictionary of Literary Biography
Published by Thomson Gale
Unit of The Thomson Corp
27500 Drake Rd, Farmington Hills, MI 48331-3535
Tel: 248-699-4253 *Toll Free Tel:* 800-347-4253
Fax: 248-699-8070 *Toll Free Fax:* 800-414-5043
Web Site: www.gale.com
Key Personnel
Mgr, Corp Communs: Kim Gabbert *Tel:* 248-699-8193 *E-mail:* kimberly.gabbert@thomson.com
Multi-volume series; each volume focuses on a specific literary movement or period. Series aims to encompass all who have contributed to literary history from the Elizabethan Era to 20th century English, American, Canadian, French & German literature, drama & history. Major biographical & critical essays are presented for the most important figures of each era. Each essay includes a career chronology, list of publications & a bibliography of works by & about the subject. Produced by Bruccoli Clark & Layman for Gale. Also available online.
Vols 291-307, 2004, $205/vol
ISBN(s): 0-7876-6828-1 (Vol 291); 0-7876-6829-4 (Vol 292); 0-7876-6830-3 (Vol 293); 0-7876-6831-1 (Vol 294); 0-7876-6832-4 (Vol 295); 0-7876-6833-8 (Vol 296); 0-7876-6834-6 (Vol 297); 0-7876-6835-4 (Vol 298); 0-7876-6836-2 (Vol 299); 0-7876-6837-0 (Vol 300); 0-7876-6838-9 (Vol 301); 0-7876-6839-7 (Vol 302); 0-7876-6840-0 (Vol 303); 0-7876-6841-9 (Vol 304); 0-7876-6842-7 (Vol 305); 0-7876-6843-5 (Vol 306); 0-7876-6844-3 (Vol 307)

Dictionary of Modern English Usage
Published by Oxford University Press, Inc
198 Madison Ave, New York, NY 10016
Tel: 212-726-6000 *Toll Free Tel:* 800-451-7556 (orders) *Fax:* 212-726-6440
Web Site: www.oup.com/us
Key Personnel
Author: Henry W Fowler; Robert Burchfield
Adv Mgr: Woody Gilmartin

3rd revised ed, 2000: 1,000 pp, $29.95 cloth, $14.95 paper
ISBN(s): 0-19-860263-4

Digital Design Business Practices, Third Edition
Published by Allworth Press
Subsidiary of Allworth Communications Inc
10 E 23 St, Suite 510, New York, NY 10010
Tel: 212-777-8395 *Toll Free Tel:* 800-491-2808
Fax: 212-777-8261
E-mail: pub@allworth.com
Web Site: www.allworth.com
Key Personnel
Mktg Dir: Cynthia Rivelli *Tel:* 212-777-8395 ext 3 *E-mail:* crivelli@allworth.com
Author: Liane Sebastian
Guidelines for print production: ethics, roles, responsibilities, ownership, communication, policies & procedures.
3rd ed, April 2001: 416 pp, $29.95
ISBN(s): 1-58115-086-5

Direct Marketing Market Place
Published by National Register Publishing
562 Central Ave, New Providence, NJ 07974
Tel: 908-673-1001 *Toll Free Tel:* 800-473-7020
Fax: 908-673-1179
Key Personnel
CEO: Gene McGovern
A comprehensive source of direct marketing, listing over 15,600 key personnel & 9,300 leading direct marketing companies, suppliers & creative sources. Includes e-mail & web site addresses.
Annual.
25th, 2005: 1,281 pp, $345.00 paper
ISBN(s): 0-87217-825-0

Directories in Print
Published by Thomson Gale
Unit of The Thomson Corp
27500 Drake Rd, Farmington Hills, MI 48331-3535
Tel: 248-699-4253 *Toll Free Tel:* 800-347-4253
Fax: 248-699-8074 *Toll Free Fax:* 800-414-5043
E-mail: galeord@gale.com
Web Site: www.gale.com
Key Personnel
Ed: Kristin Mallegg *Tel:* 248-649-4253 ext 1824 *E-mail:* kristin.mallegg@thomson.com
Annotated guide to approximately 16,000 directories, rosters, lists & guides of all kinds. Contains completely updated entries, plus many new entries, including principal business & institutional directories from more than 80 countries. *DIP*-supplement, approximately 775 new entries.
Annual, with interedition supplement.
23rd ed, 2-3 vols, $460/2-vol set (without supplement); $590/3-vol set
ISBN(s): 0-7876-6846-X (3 vol set); 0-7876-6853-2 (2 vol set)

A Directory of American Poets & Fiction Writers
Published by Poets & Writers Inc
72 Spring St, Suite 301, New York, NY 10012
Tel: 212-226-3586 *Fax:* 212-226-3963
Web Site: www.pw.org
Key Personnel
Dir, Info Svcs: Jessie Koester
Names, addresses, telephone numbers & E-mail addresses of over 7,400 contemporary American fiction writers & poets. Includes information on each author's publications, preferences about which community groups they'd like to work with & how they identify themselves culturally, politically or socially. Now available online only.
Free

Directory of Business Information Resources
Published by Grey House Publishing
185 Millerton Rd, Millerton, NY 12546
Mailing Address: PO Box 860, Millerton, NY 12546
Tel: 518-789-8700 *Toll Free Tel:* 800-562-2139
Fax: 518-789-0556
E-mail: books@greyhouse.com
Web Site: www.greyhouse.com
Key Personnel
Pres: Richard Gottlieb *Fax:* 518-789-0544
E-mail: rhg@greyhouse.com
Edit Dir: Laura Mars
Publr: Leslie Mackenzie
Mktg Dir: Jessica Moody
Source for contacts in over 98 business areas—from advertising & agriculture to utilities & wholesalers; the magazines & journals that are important to the trade, the conventions that are "must attends," databases, directories & industry web sites that provide access to must-have marketing resources. The 18,000 detailed, informative entries, include contact names, phone & fax numbers, web sites & e-mail address along with descriptions, membership information, ordering details & more.
Annual.
June 2004: 1,800 pp, $230 softcover; $385 online database
ISBN(s): 1-59237-050-0

Directory of Business to Business Catalogs
Published by Grey House Publishing Inc
185 Millerton Rd, Millerton, NY 12546
Mailing Address: PO Box 860, Millerton, NY 12546
Tel: 518-789-8700 *Toll Free Tel:* 800-562-2139
Fax: 518-789-0556
E-mail: books@greyhouse.com
Web Site: www.greyhouse.com
Key Personnel
Pres: Richard Gottlieb *Fax:* 518-789-0544
E-mail: rhg@greyhouse.com
Edit Dir: Laura Mars *E-mail:* lmars@greyhouse.com
Publr: Leslie Mackenzie *E-mail:* lmackenzie@greyhouse.com
Mktg Dir: Jessica Moody *E-mail:* jmoody@greyhouse.com
Complete listing of business-to-business mail order catalogs for special sales & marketing managers, libraries, printers & more.
Annual.
12th ed, Jan 2004: 900 pp, $165 paper
ISBN(s): 1-59237-028-4

Directory of College Stores
Published by Todd Publications
PO Box 635, Nyack, NY 10960-0635
Tel: 845-358-6213 *Fax:* 845-358-6213
E-mail: toddpub@aol.com
Web Site: www.toddpublications.com
Key Personnel
Owner, Pres & Sr Ed: Barry Klein
Lists 4400 college stores geographically, showing manager's name, types of merchandise sold, college name, number of students, whether men, women or both & whether the store is owned by the college or privately.
2002: 100 pp, $75 paper
ISBN(s): 0-87340-017-8

Directory of Mailing List Companies
Published by Todd Publications
PO Box 635, Nyack, NY 10960-0635
Tel: 845-358-6213 *Fax:* 845-358-6213
E-mail: toddpub@aol.com
Web Site: www.toddpublications.com
Key Personnel
Owner, Pres & Sr Ed: Barry Klein
Provides alphabetically, with addresses, phone numbers & zip codes, the names of more than 1000 list companies, specialists & brokers,

together with their managers' names & telephones & other pertinent information.
Biennial.
15th ed, 2003: 100 pp, $75 perfect bound
ISBN(s): 0-915344-76-9

Directory of Poetry Publishers
Published by Dustbooks
PO Box 100, Paradise, CA 95967-0222
Tel: 530-877-6110 *Toll Free Tel:* 800-477-6110
Fax: 530-877-0222
E-mail: publisher@dustbooks.com
Web Site: www.dustbooks.com
Key Personnel
Ed & Publr: Len Fulton
Publishers of poetry, books & magazines.
Annual.
19th ed, 2003-2004: 400 pp, $23.95 paper
ISBN(s): 0-916685-98-5

Directory of Small Press-Magazine Editors & Publishers
Published by Dustbooks
PO Box 100, Paradise, CA 95967-0222
Tel: 530-877-6110 *Toll Free Tel:* 800-477-6110
Fax: 530-877-0222
E-mail: publisher@dustbooks.com
Web Site: www.dustbooks.com
Key Personnel
Ed & Publr: Len Fulton
Names & numbers in small publishing industry.
Annual.
34th ed, 2003-2004: 400 pp, $23.95 paper
ISBN(s): 0-916685-99-3

Directory of Special Libraries & Information Centers
Published by Thomson Gale
Unit of The Thomson Corp
27500 Drake Rd, Farmington Hills, MI 48331-3535
Tel: 248-699-4253 *Toll Free Tel:* 800-347-4253
Fax: 248-699-8075
E-mail: dsl@gale.com
Web Site: www.gale.com
Key Personnel
Ed: Matthew Miskelly *Tel:* 248-699-4253 ext 1744
A key to the holdings, services, electronic resources & personnel of more than 34,500 special libraries & special collections, information centers, documentation centers & similar units.
Annual.
30th ed, 2005: 2,850 pp, $975 (3 vol set)
ISBN(s): 0-7876-6864-8

Do-It-Yourself Book Publicity Kit
Published by Open Horizons Publishing Co
PO Box 205, Fairfield, IA 52556-0205
Tel: 641-472-6130 *Toll Free Tel:* 800-796-6130
Fax: 641-472-1560
E-mail: info@bookmarket.com
Web Site: www.bookmarket.com
Key Personnel
Publr & Author: John Kremer
E-mail: johnkremer@bookmarket.com
How to write a news release, put together a media kit, get reviews, schedule interviews & get on-going national publicity.
1997: 256 pp, $30

Drama Criticism
Published by Thomson Gale
Unit of The Thomson Corp
27500 Drake Rd, Farmington Hills, MI 48331-3535
Tel: 248-699-4253 *Toll Free Tel:* 800-347-4253
Fax: 248-699-8070 *Toll Free Fax:* 800-414-5043
E-mail: galeord@thomson.com
Web Site: www.gale.com

Key Personnel
Mgr, Corp Communs: Kim Gabbert *Tel:* 248-699-8193 *E-mail:* kimberly.gabbert@thomson.com
Wide variety of critical, biographical & bibliographical information on major plays & playwrights from all time periods. Substantial excerpts from significant commentary on the more widely-studied dramatists.
Annual.
2004, Vol 22-24: 485 pp, $135/vol
ISBN(s): 0-7876-6812-5 (Vol 22); 0-7876-6813-3 (Vol 23); 0-7876-6814-1 (Vol 24)

Dramatists Sourcebook
Published by Theatre Communications Group Inc
520 Eighth Ave, 24th fl, New York, NY 10018-4156
Tel: 212-609-5900 *Fax:* 212-609-5901
E-mail: tcg@tcg.org
Web Site: www.tcg.org
Key Personnel
Ed: Kathy Sova
Edit Asst: Gretchen Van Lente
Complete opportunities for playwrights, translators, composers, lyricists & librettists.
Annual.
2002-2003: 400 pp, $21.95 paper
ISBN(s): 1-55936-217-0

Dynamic Characters
Published by Writer's Digest Books
4700 E Galbraith Rd, Cincinnati, OH 45236
Tel: 513-531-2690 *Fax:* 513-531-0798
Web Site: www.writersdigest.com
Explores the fundamental relationship between characterization & plot.
272 pp, $18.99
ISBN(s): 0-89879-815-9

Editor & Publisher Annual Directory of Syndicated Services
Published by VNU Business Media
770 Broadway, New York, NY 10003-9595
Tel: 646-654-5270 *Toll Free Tel:* 800-336-4380
Fax: 646-654-5886
Web Site: www.editorandpublisher.com
Key Personnel
VP & Publr: Chas McKeown
Circ Dir: Mary Barnes
Publg Dir: Mitch Tebo *Tel:* 646-654-5215
E-mail: mtebo@adweek.com
Ed: David Maddux *E-mail:* dmaddux@editorandpublisher.com
Listing of syndicates & services alphabetically by title, author, classification & syndicate.
Annual.
2003: 150 pp, $25 paper

Editor & Publisher International Year Book
Published by VNU Business Media
770 Broadway, New York, NY 10003-9595
Tel: 646-654-5270 *Toll Free Tel:* 800-336-4380
Fax: 646-654-5886
Web Site: www.editorandpublisher.com
Key Personnel
VP & Publr: Chas McKeown
Circ Dir: Mary Barnes
Publg Dir: Mitch Tebo *Tel:* 646-654-5215
E-mail: mtebo@adweek.com
Ed: David Maddux *E-mail:* dmaddux@editorandpublisher.com
Listings for all United States & Canadian daily newspapers, 10,000 weekly newspapers & selected international newspapers, including contact names, newspaper address, phone/fax numbers. E-mail & web sites, circulation, mechanical specifications, ad rates, commodity consumption, installed equipment & more. Foreign newspaper listings include circulation, address, ownership, staff & ad rates. Special sections list news & syndicate services; mechanical & interactive equipment, supplies & services.

Annual.
2004: 1,200 pp, $230 print, $695 online

Editor & Publisher Market Guide
Published by VNU Business Media
770 Broadway, New York, NY 10003-9595
Tel: 646-654-5270 *Toll Free Tel:* 800-336-4380
Fax: 646-654-4380
Web Site: www.editorandpublisher.com
Key Personnel
Publg Dir: Mitch Tebo *Tel:* 646-654-5215
E-mail: mtebo@adweek.com
Ed: Carlynn Chironna *E-mail:* cchironna@adweek.com
Circ Dir: Mary Barnes
Demographic information regarding all daily newspaper markets in the US & Canada, with maps & statistics.
Annual.
2004: 618 pp, $150 paper

EFA Directory
Published by Editorial Freelancers Association (EFA)
71 W 23 St, New York, NY 10010
Tel: 212-929-5400 *Fax:* 212-929-5439
E-mail: info@the-efa.org
Web Site: www.the-efa.org
Key Personnel
Exec: J P Partland; Martha Schueneman
Ed: Marsha Zager
National, nonprofit professional organization comprising editors, writers, indexers, proofreaders, researchers, translators & other self-employed workers in the publishing industry. Works to raise the professional status of its members & to make the freelance life more dynamic & rewarding. Online directory searchable by skills, subject matter, expertise & location.
150 pp, free (online)
ISBN(s): 1-880407-13-2

El-Hi Textbooks & Serials in Print
Published by R R Bowker LLC
Subsidiary of Cambridge Information Group Inc
630 Central Ave, New Providence, NJ 07974
SAN: 214-1191
Tel: 908-286-1090 *Toll Free Tel:* 888-BOWKER2
Fax: 908-219-0185
E-mail: info@bowker.com
Web Site: www.bowker.com
Key Personnel
Sr Man Dir: Roy Crego
This always useful "resource finder" lets you locate just about everything needed by elementary & high school teachers & librarians, including texts, text series, workbooks, periodicals, tests, programmed learning materials, teaching aids, maps, professional books, AV materials, posters & other often hard-to-find resources. The 2004 edition of El-Hi Textbooks & Serials in Print contains more than 152,300 active publications, including more than 72,000 entries in series. Twenty-one subject categories & 380 subcategories make it easy for librarians & educators to access 45,500 subject-classified entries. Locate & order valuable supplemental teaching resources & materials. Order extra copies or replacement copies of damaged books or classroom tools. Track down the full range of el-hi materials – all types, subjects & formats –with a single, convenient reference guide.
Annual.
2004: 3,392 pp, $265.00/2 vol set cloth
ISBN(s): 0-8352-4615-9 (2 vol set)

The Elements of Style With Index, Third Edition
Published by Allyn & Bacon
Division of Pearson Education
75 Arlington St, Suite 300, Boston, MA 02116
Tel: 617-848-6000

E-mail: AandBpub@aol.com
Web Site: www.ablongman.com
Key Personnel
Author: William Strunk; E B White
Style & usage manual. Indexed.
4th ed, 2000: 105 pp, $14.95 cloth, $7.95 paper
ISBN(s): 0-205-30902-X (paper); 0-205-31342-6
  (cloth)

Encyclopedia of Associations, National Organizations of the US
Published by Thomson Gale
Subsidiary of The Thomson Corp
27500 Drake Rd, Farmington Hills, MI 48331-
  3535
Tel: 248-699-4253 *Toll Free Tel:* 800-347-4253
  Fax: 248-699-8075
Web Site: www.gale.com
Key Personnel
Ed: Kimberly N Hunt *Tel:* 800-347-4253 ext
  1780 *E-mail:* kim.hunt@thomson.com
A guide to nearly 23,000 US nonprofit membership organizations of national scope; includes
  trade & professional associations, social welfare & public affairs organizations, religious
  organizations, sports & hobby groups with voluntary members. Detailed entries furnish association name & complete contact information.
  This information is not duplicated anywhere in
  Encyclopedia of Associations. Name & key-
  word indexes accompany each volume. *Geographic & Executive Indexes* are available as
  a separate volume. A supplement is published
  between volumes.
Annual.
41st ed, 2004: 3,800 pp, $650; $510 for Geo/
  Exec Indexes; $535 for supplement
ISBN(s): 0-7876-6871-0

Fiction Writer's Brainstormer
Published by Writer's Digest Books
4700 E Galbraith Rd, Cincinnati, OH 45236
Tel: 513-531-2690 *Fax:* 513-531-0798
Web Site: www.writersdigest.com
Learn how to stimulate your creative juices, en-
  abling you to start, finish & polish your work.
292 pp, $18.99
ISBN(s): 0-89879-943-0

Finding Your Voice
Published by Writer's Digest Books
4700 E Galbraith Rd, Cincinnati, OH 45236
Tel: 513-531-2690 *Fax:* 513-531-0798
Web Site: www.writersdigest.com
Dramatically improve your chance of getting no-
  ticed by editors & agents & therefore, of get-
  ting published.
240 pp, $16.99
ISBN(s): 1-58297-173-0

First Editions: A Guide to Identification, Statements of Selected North American, British Commonwealth & Irish Publishers on Their Methods of Designating First Editions
Published by Spoon River Press
Division of BookQuote Inc
PO Box 3635, Peoria, IL 61612-3635
Tel: 309-672-2665 *Fax:* 309-672-7853
E-mail: srppress@aol.com
Key Personnel
Ed: Linda A Verkler; Edward N Zempel
4th ed: 608 pp, $60 hardcover
ISBN(s): 0-930358-18-X

45 Master Characters
Published by Writer's Digest Books
4700 E Galbraith Rd, Cincinnati, OH 45236
Tel: 513-531-2690 *Fax:* 513-531-0798
Web Site: www.writersdigest.com

Gives all the information you need to develop
  believable characters that resonate with every
  reader.
256 pp, $19.99
ISBN(s): 1-58297-069-6

Freed's Guide to Student Contests & Publishing
Published by Fountainpen Press
218 W Fountain Ave, Delaware, OH 43015-1656
Tel: 740-369-4306
Key Personnel
Author & Publr: Judith Freed *E-mail:* jmfreed@
  midohio.net
Contests & publishing opportunities for students
  K-12.
5th ed, 1994: 128 pp, $13.95 & shipping $2
ISBN(s): 0-9621647-3-9

From Page to Screen
Published by Thomson Gale
Unit of The Thomson Corp
27500 Drake Rd, Farmington Hills, MI 48331-
  3535
Tel: 248-699-4253 *Toll Free Tel:* 800-347-4253
  Fax: 248-699-8074 *Toll Free Fax:* 800-414-
  5043
Web Site: www.gale.com
Key Personnel
Ed: Joyce Moss; George Wilson
Man Ed: Ann Evory
Tool for information & evaluation of more than
  1400 video, 12mm film & laser disc adapta-
  tions of over 750 books read by students in
  kindergarten through high school.
1992: 450 pp, $80
ISBN(s): 0-8103-7893-0

Gale Directory of Databases
Published by Thomson Gale
Unit of The Thomson Corp
27500 Drake Rd, Farmington Hills, MI 48331-
  3535
Tel: 248-699-4253 *Toll Free Tel:* 800-347-4253
  Fax: 248-699-8074 *Toll Free Fax:* 800-414-
  5043
E-mail: galeord@gale.com
Web Site: www.gale.com
Key Personnel
Ed: Erin Nagel *E-mail:* erin.nagel@gale.com
Electronic Database Coord: Kathleen Young Mar-
  caccio
Current information about more than 14,5000 on-
  line & portable databases from more than 3800
  producers & accessible through more than 2900
  online services worldwide.
Semiannual (Sept & March).
2003 ed: 2,800 pp, $465
ISBN(s): 0-7876-6203-8

Gale Directory of Publications & Broadcast Media
Published by Thomson Gale
Unit of The Thomson Corp
27500 Drake Rd, Farmington Hills, MI 48331-
  3535
Tel: 248-699-4253 *Toll Free Tel:* 800-347-4253
  Fax: 248-699-8075
E-mail: galeord@gale.com
Web Site: www.gale.com
Key Personnel
Ed: Kristin Mallegg *Tel:* 248-649-4253 ext 1824
  E-mail: kristin.mallegg@thomson.com
Entries are arranged by country, state & province
  & then by city. Brief demographics are given
  for each city. Periodical entries: entry number, periodical title, publisher's name, address,
  telephone & FAX numbers, editorial address,
  e-mail addresses & URL sites, date established,
  frequency, contacts, subscription price, advertising rates, circulation & special notes. Broadcast
  media entries: contact information, station call

letter & channel, Area of Dominant Influence
  (ADI), mailing address & telephone number,
  name of owner/operator, network & syndicator
  addresses, network affiliation, contacts, local
  programs with air times & contacts, advertising
  rates, FAX numbers, e-mail addresses & URL
  sites.
Annual.
139th ed, 2005: 6,150 pp, $865/5 vol set, cloth
  (price includes free update)
ISBN(s): 0-7876-6854-0

General Issues in Literacy/Illiteracy in the World: A Bibliography
Published by Greenwood Press
Subsidiary of Greenwood Publishing Group Inc
88 Post Rd W, Westport, CT 06881
Mailing Address: PO Box 5007, Westport, CT
  06881
Tel: 203-226-3571 *Fax:* 203-222-1502
E-mail: bookinfo@greenwood.com
Web Site: www.greenwood.com
Key Personnel
VP, Mktg: Linda May *Tel:* 203-226-3571 ext
  3351
Author: William Eller; John Hladczuk; Sharon
  Hladczuk
Literacy-illiteracy; bibliography.
1st ed, 1990: 435 pp, $87.95 cloth
ISBN(s): 0-313-27327-8

Getting Into Print: The Decision Making Process in Scholarly Publishing
Published by Association of American University
  Presses
1427 E 60 St, Chicago, IL 60637-2954
Tel: 773-702-7700 *Toll Free Tel:* 800-621-2736
  (orders) *Fax:* 773-702-9756 (sales)
Key Personnel
Dir: Paula Barker Duffy
Exploration of two scholarly publishing compa-
  nies & how editors select titles they sponsor.
1st ed, 1985: 260 pp, $21 paper; $27 cloth
ISBN(s): 0-226-67704-4 (cloth); 0-226-67705-2
  (paper)

Government Information on the Internet
Published by Bernan
Division of The Kraus Organization Ltd
4611-F Assembly Dr, Lanham, MD 20706-4391
Tel: 301-459-7666 (cust serv); 301-459-2555
  Toll Free Tel: 800-416-4385 *Fax:* 301-459-0056
  (cust serv) *Toll Free Fax:* 800-865-3450
E-mail: info@bernan.com
Web Site: www.bernan.com
Key Personnel
Man Dir: Donald H Hagen
Mgr, Cust Serv: Rhonda Spraggins
Dir, Mktg: Bruce Samuelson
International statistics on population, education,
  book production, newspapers & other period-
  icals, paper consumption, film, radio, televi-
  sion, culture expenditures, libraries & science
  & technology. Published by Bernan Press.
Annual.
7th ed, 2004: 917 pp, $75

Grammatically Correct
Published by Writer's Digest Books
4700 E Galbraith Rd, Cincinnati, OH 45236
Tel: 513-531-2690 *Fax:* 513-531-0798
Web Site: www.writersdigest.com
Easy to use, quick reference & most of all, com-
  prehensive.
352 pp, $19.99

Grants & Awards Available to American Writers
Published by Pen American Center
588 Broadway, Suite 303, New York, NY 10012
Tel: 212-334-1660 *Fax:* 212-334-2181
E-mail: pen@pen.org
Web Site: www.pen.org *Cable:* ACINTERPEN

Key Personnel
Awards Dir: Peter Meyer *Tel:* 212-334-1660 ext
  110 *E-mail:* awards@pen.org
Listings of over 1,000 American & international
  awards & grants for writers in all fields.
  Biennial.
22nd ed 2002-2003, $19.50, paper only
ISBN(s): 0-934638-20-9

Graphic Arts Blue Book
Published by Reed Business Information
360 Park Ave S, New York, NY 10010
Tel: 646-746-7398 *Fax:* 646-746-7434
E-mail: bluebook@reedbusiness.com
Web Site: www.gabb.com
Key Personnel
VP & Publg Dir: Steve Reiss
Publr: Marguerite van Stolk *E-mail:* mvanstolk@
  reedbusiness.com
Dir, Sales: Carl Sartori *E-mail:* csartori@
  reedbusiness.com
Lists operating printing plants & other graphic
  arts plants & suppliers. Includes personnel
  information, paper directory, "where-to-buy-
  it" directory & alphabetical index by com-
  pany name & eight geographical indexes.
  The eight editions are: Northeastern; Metro
  New York/New Jersey; Delaware Valley/Ohio;
  Southeastern; Midwestern; Texas/Central;
  Pacific Northwestern; Southern Califor-
  nia/Southwestern.
Annual.
850 pp, $95
First published 1910

Guerrilla Marketing for Writers: 100 Weapons for Selling Your Work
Published by Writer's Digest Books
4700 E Galbraith Rd, Cincinnati, OH 45236
Tel: 513-531-2690 *Fax:* 513-531-0798
Web Site: www.writersdigest.com
How to sell your work before & after it's been
  published.
292 pp, $14.99
ISBN(s): 0-89879-983-X

A Guide to Academic Writing
Published by Greenwood Press
Subsidiary of Greenwood Publishing Group Inc
88 Post Rd W, Westport, CT 06881
Mailing Address: PO Box 5007, Westport, CT
  06881
Tel: 203-226-3571 *Fax:* 203-222-1502
E-mail: bookinfo@greenwood.com
Web Site: www.greenwood.com
Key Personnel
Author: Jeffery A Cantor
VP, Mktg: Linda May *Tel:* 203-226-3571 ext
  3351
A comprehensive guide to academic writing &
  publishing.
1993: 200 pp, $20.95/paperback; $70.95/hard-
  cover
ISBN(s): 0-275-94660-6 (paperback); 0-313-
  29017-2 (hardback)

Guide to American & International Directories
Published by Todd Publications
PO Box 635, Nyack, NY 10960-0635
Tel: 845-358-6213 *Fax:* 845-358-6213
E-mail: toddpub@aol.com
Web Site: www.toddpublications.com
Key Personnel
Owner, Pres & Sr Ed: Barry Klein
Complete information on more than 12,000 di-
  rectories, covering more than 300 trade, educa-
  tional & professional categories. Index.
Annual.
16th ed, 2003: 520 pp, $150
ISBN(s): 0-915344-87-4

Guide to Literary Agents, 2005: Over 600 Agents Who Sell What You Write
Published by Writer's Digest Books
4700 E Galbraith Rd, Cincinnati, OH 45236
Tel: 513-531-2222
E-mail: literaryagent@fwpubs.com
Web Site: www.writersmarket.com
Key Personnel
Ed: Kathryn S Brogan
Annual.
$24.99
ISBN(s): 1-58297-328-8

The Guide to Writers Conferences
Published by ShawGuides Inc Educational Pub-
  lishers
10 W 66 St, No 30H, New York, NY 10023
Tel: 212-799-6464 *Fax:* 212-724-9287
E-mail: info@shawguides.com
Web Site: www.shawguides.com
Key Personnel
Pres: Dorlene V Kaplan
Directory of conferences, seminars, workshops &
  retreats. Includes information about dates, facilities, faculty, writing specialties, daily activities, tuition, accommodations, refund policies,
  handicapped accessibility, nearby attractions.
  Also includes a 12-month conference calendar
  & a section on organizations (dues, benefits,
  activities). Contents indexed by location (covers 50 states & 11 countries); specialties (nine
  genres); availability of college credit, continuing education credit & scholarships; writing
  contests, college writing programs. Available
  on-line only: writing.shawguides.com.
Updated online.

Guild Book Workers Supply Directory
Published by Guild of Book Workers Inc
521 Fifth Ave, 17th fl, New York, NY 10175-
  0003
Tel: 212-292-4444
Web Site: www.palimpsest.stanford.edu
Key Personnel
Ed: Susan Martin
Supplies for the book arts.
Irregular.
2001: 116 pp, $15 (free to members)

Hey Look - I Made a Book!
Published by Ten Speed Press
PO Box 7123, Berkeley, CA 94710
Tel: 510-559-1600 *Toll Free Tel:* 800-841-BOOK
  (841-2665) *Fax:* 510-559-1629
E-mail: info@tenspeed.com
Web Site: www.tenspeed.com; www.
  tenspeedpress.com
Key Personnel
Author: Betty Doty; Rebecca Meredith
Mktg Assoc: Cheryl Foreman *E-mail:* cheryl@
  tenspeed.com
Book contains bookbinding instructions.
2000: 128 pp, $7.95 paperback
ISBN(s): 0-89815-686-6

How a Book is Published
Published by Crabtree Publishing Co
350 Fifth Ave, Suite 3308, PMB 16A, New York,
  NY 10118
Tel: 212-496-5040 *Toll Free Fax:* 800-355-7166
E-mail: editor@crabtreebooks.com
Web Site: www.crabtreebooks.com
Key Personnel
Author & Ed: Bobbie Kalman
Prodn Coord: Rose Gowsell *Tel:* 212-496-5040
  ext 232
How books are published from concept to print-
  ing for children.
1st ed, 1995: 32 pp, $22.60/$5.95
ISBN(s): 0-86505-618-8 (cloth); 0-86505-718-4
  (paper)

How Fiction Works
Published by Writer's Digest Books
4700 E Galbraith Rd, Cincinnati, OH 45236
Tel: 513-531-2690 *Fax:* 513-531-0798
Web Site: www.writersdigest.com
Fiction examined & illuminated with insights as
  to how each element must interact so that you
  can create a truly distinctive story.
228 pp, $14.99

How to Choose a Winning Title: A Guide for Writers, Editors & Publishers
Published by Greenwood Press
Division of Greenwood Publishing Group Inc
88 Post Rd W, Westport, CT 06881
Tel: 203-226-3571 *Toll Free Tel:* 800-225-5800
  Fax: 203-222-1502
E-mail: sales@greenwood.com
Web Site: www.greenwood.com
Key Personnel
Author: Nat G Bodian
Sr Mktg Mgr: Alex Petri *E-mail:* alex.petri@
  greenwood.com
1989: 192 pp, $27.95 (6 x 9 paper)
ISBN(s): 0-89774-540-X

How to Get Your E-Book Published
Published by Writer's Digest Books
4700 E Galbraith Rd, Cincinnati, OH 45236
Tel: 513-531-2690 *Fax:* 513-531-0798
Web Site: www.writersdigest.com
Insider's authoritative, comprehensive guide to
  this new opportunity for you as a writer.
228 pp, $16.99
ISBN(s): 1-58297-095-5

How to Make Big Profits Publishing City & Regional Books
Published by Communication Creativity
209 Church St, Buena Vista, CO 81211
Mailing Address: PO Box 909-LMP, Buena Vista,
  CO 81211
Tel: 719-395-8659 *Fax:* 719-633-1526
Web Site: www.communicationcreativity.com
Key Personnel
Author/Ed: Marilyn Ross; Tom Ross
Sales & Adv Mgr: Ann Markham *E-mail:* ann@
  communicationcreativity.com
Market research techniques, editorial tips & pro-
  motional strategies for successfully publishing
  such regional titles as travel guides, local cook-
  books, directories, etc. Audiences are regional
  publishers & authors of such works.
1st ed, 1987: 224 pp, $14.95 paper
ISBN(s): 0-918880-12-2

How to Publish & Market Your Own Book as an Independent African Heritage Book Publisher
Published by ECA Associates Press
925 Main Creek Rd, Chesapeake, VA 23320
Mailing Address: PO Box 15004, Chesapeake,
  VA 23328-0004
Tel: 757-547-5542 *Fax:* 757-547-5542
E-mail: eca@blackwordsonline.com
Web Site: www.blackwordsonline.com
Key Personnel
Pres: Dr E Curtis Alexander
Ed: Dr Mwalimu I Mwadilifu
1st ed: 140 pp, $15.95
ISBN(s): 0-938818-09-0

How to Write a Book Proposal
Published by Writer's Digest Books
4700 E Galbraith Rd, Cincinnati, OH 45236
Tel: 513-531-2690 *Fax:* 513-531-0798
Web Site: www.writersdigest.com
Details how the industry works, where it's headed
  & how you can be part of it.
3rd: 288 pp, $16.99

How to Write Funny
Published by Writer's Digest Books
4700 E Galbraith Rd, Cincinnati, OH 45236
Tel: 513-531-2690 *Fax:* 513-531-0798
Web Site: www.writersdigest.com
Provides advice, insights & humor from more
then 20 writers.
240 pp, $18.99
ISBN(s): 1-58297-054-8

Howdunit
Published by Writer's Digest Books
4700 E Galbraith Rd, Cincinnati, OH 45236
Tel: 513-531-2690 *Fax:* 513-531-0798
Web Site: www.writersdigest.com
All-in-one writer's crime reference. Investigative
techniques, causes of death, interrogation, pro-
filing & more.
406 pp, $19.99
ISBN(s): 1-58297-015-7

**Hudson's Washington News Media Contacts
Directory**
Published by Howard Penn Hudson
44 W Market St, Rhinebeck, NY 12572
Mailing Address: PO Box 311, Rhinebeck, NY
12572
Tel: 845-876-2081 *Toll Free Tel:* 800-572-3451
Fax: 845-876-2561
E-mail: hudsonsdir@aol.com
Web Site: www.hudsonsdirectory.com
Key Personnel
Ed: Helene F Wingard
Comprehensive listing of Washington Press
Corps.
Annual.
2004: 436 pp, $269
ISBN(s): 1-891489-07-0

The Huenefeld Guide to Book Publishing
Published by Mills & Sanderson, Publishers
Division of The Huenefeld Co Inc
15 Putnam Rd, Bedford, MA 01730-1540
Tel: 781-275-1070 *Fax:* 781-275-1713
Key Personnel
Author & Publr: John Huenefeld
Off Mgr: Georgia Huenefeld
Guide to publishing for book publishing.
6th ed: 400 pp, $42
First published 2001
ISBN(s): 0-938179-40-3

Information Industry Directory
Published by Thomson Gale
Unit of The Thomson Corp
27500 Drake Rd, Farmington Hills, MI 48331-
3535
Tel: 248-699-4253 *Toll Free Tel:* 800-347-4253
Fax: 248-699-8069 *Toll Free Fax:* 800-347-
4253
E-mail: galeord@thomson.com
Web Site: www.gale.com
Key Personnel
Mgr, Corp Communs: Kim Gabbert *Tel:* 248-699-
8193 *E-mail:* kimberly.gabbert@thomson.com
Descriptions of US & international organizations
concerned with computerized information prod-
ucts & services; more than 12,000 entries.
Annually.
27th ed, 2004: 3,292 pp, $695/2-vol set
ISBN(s): 0-7876-6897-4

**International Book Publishing: An
Encyclopedia**
Published by Garland Science Publishing
Member of The Taylor & Francis Group
270 Madison Ave, 4th fl, New York, NY 10016
Tel: 212-216-7800; 917-351-7100
Toll Free Tel: 800-634-7064 (warehouse)
Fax: 212-564-7854
E-mail: info@routledge-ny.com

Web Site: www.routledge-ny.com
1996: 800 pp, $135
ISBN(s): 1-8849-6416-8

**International Directory of Children's
Literature**
Published by George Kurian Reference Books
PO Box 519, Baldwin Place, NY 10505-0519
Tel: 914-962-3287
Key Personnel
Pres: George Kurian *E-mail:* gtkurian@aol.com
Information on children's literature around the
world.
Triennial.
4th ed, 2001: 166 pp, $39.95 cloth
First published 1974
ISBN(s): 0-8160-1411-6

**International Directory of Little Magazines &
Small Presses**
Published by Dustbooks
PO Box 100, Paradise, CA 95967-0222
Tel: 530-877-6110 *Toll Free Tel:* 800-477-6110
Fax: 530-877-0222
E-mail: publisher@dustbooks.com
Web Site: www.dustbooks.com
Key Personnel
Author, Ed & Publr: Len Fulton
For libraries & writers; 6000 small publishers
with full data.
Annual.
39th ed, 2003-2004: 946 pp, $55 cloth, $35.95
paper
ISBN(s): 0-916685-96-9 (paper); 0-916685-97-7
(cloth)

International Literary Market Place
Published by Information Today, Inc
630 Central Ave, New Providence, NJ 07974
Tel: 908-286-1090 *Toll Free Tel:* 800-409-4929;
800-300-9868 (cust serv) *Fax:* 908-219-0192
E-mail: custserv@infotoday.com
Web Site: www.literarymarketplace.com
Key Personnel
Man Ed: Karen Hallard *Tel:* 908-219-0277
E-mail: khallard@infotoday.com
A comprehensive directory of current data on the
book trade in 180 countries outside the US &
Canada, with over 10,200 publishers & over
3,600 book organizations, including agents,
booksellers & library associations. Includes in-
formation basic to conducting business in each
country. The US & Canada are covered by Lit-
erary Market Place. Also available online.
Annual.
38th ed, 2005: 1,796 pp, $239.00 paper
ISBN(s): 0-57387-205-9

Is There a Book Inside You?
Published by Para Publishing
PO Box 8206-R, Santa Barbara, CA 93118-8206
SAN: 215-8981
Tel: 805-968-7277 *Toll Free Tel:* 800-727-2782
Fax: 805-968-1379
E-mail: orders@parapublishing.com
Web Site: www.parapublishing.com
Key Personnel
Owner & Publr: Dan Poynter
E-mail: danpoynter@parapublishing.com
Author: Mindy Bingham
A step-by-step formula for researching & writing
a book. How to find & work with collabora-
tors.
5th ed, 1999: 236 pp, $14.95 paper
ISBN(s): 0-56860-046-1

**Jeff Herman's Guide to Book Publishers,
Editors, and Literary Agents**
Published by Kalmbach Publishing Co
21027 Crossroads Circle, Waukesha, WI 53187

Tel: 262-796-8776 *Toll Free Tel:* 800-533-6644
Fax: 262-798-6468
Key Personnel
Author: Jeff Herman *Tel:* 413-298-0077 *Fax:* 413-
298-8188 *E-mail:* jeff@jeffherman.com
Acqs Ed: Philip Martin
Writing/reference book. Directory of publishers (U.S., university, Canada) & U.S. literary agents. Includes interviews with editors
& agents as well as additional information on
submitting material to the publishing industry.
Annual.
15th ed, 2005: 892 pp, $24.95 paperback

Jewish Book Annual
Published by Jewish Book Council
15 E 26 St, 10th fl, New York, NY 10010-1579
Tel: 212-532-4949 (ext 297) *Fax:* 212-481-4174
E-mail: jbc@jewishbooks.org
Web Site: www.jewishbookcouncil.org
Key Personnel
Pres: Maurice Corson
Exec Dir: Carolyn Starman Hessel
E-mail: carolynhessel@jewishbooks.org
Contact: Stephen Garrin
Academic publication of essays & annotations
written in English, Hebrew & Yiddish.
Annual.
57th ed & 58th ed (Combined volume), 2002-
2003: 348 pp, $35 hardcover

The Joy of Publishing!
Published by Open Horizons Publishing Co
PO Box 205, Fairfield, IA 52556-0205
SAN: 265-170X
Tel: 641-472-6130 *Toll Free Tel:* 800-796-6130
Fax: 641-472-1560
E-mail: info@bookmarket.com
Web Site: www.bookmarket.com
Key Personnel
Author: Nat G Bodian
Publr & Author: John Kremer
E-mail: johnkremer@bookmarket.com
Fascinating facts, anecdotes, curiosities & his-
toric origins about books & authors, editors &
publishers, bookmaking & bookselling.
256 pp, $19.95
First published 1996
ISBN(s): 0-912411-47-3

**Jump Start Your Book Sales: A
Money-Making Guide for Authors,
Independent Publishers and Small Presses**
Published by Communication Creativity
209 Church St, Buena Vista, CO 81211
Mailing Address: PO Box 909-LMP, Buena Vista,
CO 81211
Tel: 719-395-8659 *Toll Free Tel:* 800 331-8355
Fax: 719-633-1526
Web Site: www.communicationcreativity.com
Key Personnel
Author: Marilyn Ross; Tom Ross
Sales & Adv Mgr: Ann Markham *E-mail:* ann@
communicationcreativity.com
Creative & money-making marketing ideas for
authors & publishers.
1st ed, 1999: 348 pp, $19.95 paper
ISBN(s): 0-918880-41-6

**Just the Facts, Ma'am: A Writer's Guide to
Investigators & Investigative Techniques**
Published by Writer's Digest Books
4700 E Galbraith Rd, Cincinnati, OH 45236
Tel: 513-531-2690 *Fax:* 513-531-0798
Web Site: www.writersdigest.com
Reference book for anyone writing about detec-
tives, detective work & crime.
208 pp, $16.99

Keys to Great Writing
Published by Writer's Digest Books

4700 E Galbraith Rd, Cincinnati, OH 45236
Tel: 513-531-2690 *Fax:* 513-531-0798
Web Site: www.writersdigest.com
From grammer to revision strategies.
240 pp, $19.99
ISBN(s): 0-89879-932-5

Law Books & Serials in Print
Published by R R Bowker LLC
Subsidiary of Cambridge Information Group Inc
630 Central Ave, New Providence, NJ 07974
SAN: 214-1191
Tel: 908-286-1090 *Toll Free Tel:* 888-BOWKER2
Fax: 908-219-0185
E-mail: info@bowker.com
Web Site: www.bowker.com
Key Personnel
Sr Man Dir: Roy Crego
Intended for legal professionals, with more than
56,500 total entries, including some 3,500 new
titles & some 6,700 subject headings, this unmatched bibliography lists virtually every current legal resource – more than 62,000 books,
17,000 serial titles, 3,000 multimedia publications & some 3,300 publishers & their distributors. Focusing on core legal & related
titles, Law Books & Serials in Print 2004 includes descriptive annotations that provide expert guidance on selecting the right sources for
every research need.
Annual.
2004: 3,456 pp, $899.00/3 vol set cloth
ISBN(s): 0-8352-4638-8 (3 vol set)

Legal Periodicals in English
Published by Glanville Publishers Inc
Affiliate of Oceana Publications Inc
75 Main St, Dobbs Ferry, NY 10522-1601
Tel: 914-693-8100 *Toll Free Tel:* 800-831-0758
Fax: 914-693-0402
E-mail: glanville@oceanalaw.com
Web Site: www.oceanalaw.com
Key Personnel
Pres: Fay Cohen
Man Ed: JoAnn Mitchell
Ed: Daniel May
Sr VP, Prod Dev & Gen Counsel: M C Susan De-
Maio
Edit Asst: Alden W Domizio *Tel:* 914-693-8100
ext 325 *E-mail:* adomizio@oceanalaw.com
This successor to Morse's Checklist of Anglo-
American Legal Periodicals catalogs all le-
gal periodicals published in the English lan-
guage. This work is assembled in a convenient
loose-leaf format for updating. Each listing
appears on its own page & includes: An identification number; a reproduction of the Library of Congress catalog entry; information
on frequency with variations, prior titles &
cross-references; subject category; index information; reprint & microfilm locations; &
Shepard's citations. An Index volume provides
cross-references for each entry & is arranged
alphabetically, geographically & by subject.
Annual updates.
Latest release - 2003-1, Looseleaf $130/release,
$525/set (purchase of a 6 vol set includes the
latest release at no extra charge)
ISBN(s): 0-87802-054-3

Lessons From a Lifetime of Writing
Published by Writer's Digest Books
4700 E Galbraith Rd, Cincinnati, OH 45236
Tel: 513-531-2690 *Fax:* 513-531-0798
Web Site: www.writersdigest.com
Insider secrets to help you achieve the next level
of literary success.
256 pp, $22.99 hardcover; $15.99 paper (2003)
ISBN(s): 1-58297-143-9 (hardcover); 1-58297-
270-2 (paperback)

Literary Market Place
Published by Information Today, Inc
630 Central Ave, New Providence, NJ 07974
Tel: 908-286-1090 *Toll Free Tel:* 800-409-4929;
800-300-9868 (cust serv) *Fax:* 908-219-0192
E-mail: custserv@infotoday.com
Web Site: www.literarymarketplace.com
Key Personnel
Man Ed: Karen Hallard *Tel:* 908-219-0277
E-mail: khallard@infotoday.com
Directory of over 35,000 companies & individuals
in US & Canadian publishing. Areas covered
include book publishers; associations; book
trade events; courses, conferences & contests;
agents & agencies; services & suppliers; direct-
mail promotion; review, selection & reference;
radio & television; wholesale, export & import
& book manufacturing. A two-volume set, each
containing two alphabetical names & numbers
indexes, one for key companies listed & one
for individuals. The rest of the world is covered by International Literary Market Place.
Also available online.
Annual.
65th ed, 2005: 2,000 pp, $299.00/2 vol set paper
ISBN(s): 1-57387-203-2 (2 vol set)

Lockwood-Post's Directory - North America
Formerly Lockwood-Post's Directory of the Pulp,
Paper & Allied Trades
Published by Paperloop Inc
55 Hawthorne, Suite 510, San Francisco, CA
94105
Tel: 415-947-3600 *Fax:* 415-947-3711
E-mail: info@paperloop.com
Web Site: www.paperloop.com *Cable:*
MILFREEPUB NEW YORK
Key Personnel
CEO, Paperloop: Ian Johnston
CFO: Raymond Yue
Sr VP, Info Prods: Rod Young
VP, Edit: Kelly Ferguson
Comprehensive information regarding North
American pulp & paper producers, paper con-
verters & paper merchants; also vendors of
equipment & supplies. International directory
also available separately.
Annual.
March 2003: 1,000 pp, $399
ISBN(s): 0-9723793

Lockwood-Post's Directory of the Pulp, Paper
& Allied Trades, see Lockwood-Post's
Directory - North America

Magazines for Libraries
Published by R R Bowker LLC
Subsidiary of Cambridge Information Group Inc
630 Central Ave, New Providence, NJ 07974
SAN: 214-1191
Tel: 908-286-1090 *Toll Free Tel:* 800-521-8110
Fax: 908-219-0182
E-mail: info@bowker.com
Web Site: www.bowker.com
Key Personnel
Ed: Cheryl LaGuardia
Consultant: Bill Katz; Linda Sternberg Katz
A critically annotated guide to magazine selec-
tion for public, college, school & special li-
braries, with 7,000 periodicals evaluated under
158 subject areas. Includes journals—print &
electronic, abstracts, indexes, annuals & news-
papers, with ordering information.
Annual.
12th ed, 2003: 1,200 pp, $225 cloth
ISBN(s): 0-8352-4541-1

Magill's Literary Annual
Published by Salem Press Inc
2 University Plaza, Suite 121, Hackensack, NJ
07601
SAN: 208-838X

Tel: 201-968-9899 *Toll Free Tel:* 800-221-1592
Fax: 201-968-1411
E-mail: csr@salempress.com
Web Site: www.salempress.com
Key Personnel
Publicist & Sales & Mktg Mgr: Luisa Torres
E-mail: ltorres@salempress.com
Ed: John Wilson
Offers 200 major examples of serious literature
published during the previous year, covering
the best of the best in fiction, poetry & nonfic-
tion.
Annual.
2 vols, 2004: 1,064 pp, $84/set; $129 Canada
ISBN(s): 1-58765-158-0

Mail Order Business Directory
Published by Todd Publications
PO Box 635, Nyack, NY 10960-0635
Tel: 845-358-6213 *Fax:* 845-358-6213
E-mail: toddpub@aol.com
Web Site: www.toddpublications.com
Key Personnel
Owner, Pres & Sr Ed: Barry Klein
Contains the names of the 5000 most active mail
order catalogs, listed by 40 product categories
with Alphabetical Index & Merchandise Cate-
gory Index.
Biennial.
19th ed, 2003: 420 pp, $125 paper
ISBN(s): 0-915344-91-2

Major 20th-Century Writers, 2nd edition
Published by Thomson Gale
Unit of The Thomson Corp
27500 Drake Rd, Farmington Hills, MI 48331-
3535
Tel: 248-699-4253 *Toll Free Tel:* 800-347-4253
Fax: 248-699-8070 *Toll Free Fax:* 800-414-
5043
E-mail: galeord@gale.com
Web Site: www.gale.com
Key Personnel
Mgr, Corp Communs: Kim Gabbert *Tel:* 248-699-
8193 *E-mail:* kimberly.gabbert@thomson.com
Biographical & bibliographical information on
1000 20th century authors who are most often
studied in college & high school.
2nd ed, 2002: $425/5 vol set
ISBN(s): 0-8103-8450-7

Managing the Publishing Process: An
Annotated Bibliography
Published by Greenwood Press
Subsidiary of Greenwood Publishing Group Inc
88 Post Rd W, Westport, CT 06881
Mailing Address: PO Box 5007, Westport, CT
06881
Tel: 203-226-3571 *Fax:* 203-222-1502
E-mail: bookinfo@greenwood.com
Web Site: www.greenwood.com
Key Personnel
Author: Bruce Speck
VP, Mktg: Linda May *Tel:* 203-226-3571 ext
3351
Cites & annotates more than 1200 books & arti-
cles on how to manage the publishing process.
1995: 360 pp, $90.95 cloth
ISBN(s): 0-313-27956-X

Manufacturing Standards & Specifications for
(El-Hi) Textbooks (MSST)
Published by Advisory Commission on Textbook
Specifications (ACTS)
2 Armand Beach Dr, Suite 1B, Palm Coast, FL
32137
Tel: 386-986-4552 *Fax:* 386-986-4553
Key Personnel
Exec VP: Bruce W Smith
Tech Dir: Robert Duncan
Revised annually if necessary.
Aug 2002: 68 pp, $20 looseleaf bound

Mark My Words: Instruction & Practice in Proofreading
Published by EEI Communications
66 Canal Center Plaza, Suite 200, Alexandria, VA 22314-5507
Tel: 703-683-0683 *Toll Free Tel:* 800-683-8380
 Fax: 703-683-4915
E-mail: press@eeicom.com
Web Site: www.eeicommunications.com
Key Personnel
Author: Peggy Smith
VP, Pubns: Robin Cormier *E-mail:* rcormier@eeicom.com
Ed: Linda Jorgensen
Proj Mgr: Jayne Sutton *E-mail:* jsutton@eeicom.com
Comprehensive revised reference & self-study text that teaches professional proofreading. Provides step-by-step procedures & examples of how errors should be marked.
3rd ed, 1997: 482 pp, $35
ISBN(s): 0-935012-23-0

Marketer's Guide to Media
Published by Adweek Directories
770 Broadway, New York, NY 10003
Tel: 646-654-5215 *Toll Free Tel:* 800-562-2706
 Fax: 646-654-5886
Web Site: www.adweek.com/directories
Key Personnel
Ed & Publg Dir: Mitch Tebo *E-mail:* mtebo@adweek.com
Directory of demographics, trends, rates & audience figures for all major media.
Annual.
2004 ed, Feb 2004: 256 pp, $129/book
ISBN(s): 1-891204-37-8

Marketing Managers Handbook
Published by Dartnell Corp
360 Hiatt Dr, Palm Beach Gardens, FL 33418
Tel: 561-622-6520 *Toll Free Tel:* 800-621-5463
 Fax: 561-622-2423
Web Site: www.lrp.com
Key Personnel
Author: Richard S Hodgson
Ed: Sidney J Levy
3rd ed, 1994: 1,432 pp, $69.95 hardcover ($12 shipping)
ISBN(s): 0-85013-203-7

The Marshall Plan for Getting Your Novel Published
Published by Writer's Digest Books
4700 E Galbraith Rd, Cincinnati, OH 45236
Tel: 513-531-2690 *Fax:* 513-531-0798
Web Site: www.writersdigest.com
Focuses on making a good novel better & taking the next step of sending work to editors & agents all with an insider's knowledge.
240 pp, $21.99
ISBN(s): 1-58297-196-X

The Marshall Plan for Novel Writing
Published by Writer's Digest Books
4700 E Galbraith Rd, Cincinnati, OH 45236
Tel: 513-531-2690 *Fax:* 513-531-0798
Web Site: www.writersdigest.com
Learn how to find a hook, create a conflict, develop a protagonist & set things in motion.
240 pp, $15.99
ISBN(s): 0-89879-848-5

The Marshall Plan Workbook
Published by Writer's Digest Books
4700 E Galbraith Rd, Cincinnati, OH 45236
Tel: 513-531-2690 *Fax:* 513-531-0798
Web Site: www.writersdigest.com
The most direct, practical & hands-on guide to get your novel completed & pitched in the marketplace.

256 pp, $19.99
ISBN(s): 1-58297-059-9

Mastering Point of View
Published by Writer's Digest Books
4700 E Galbraith Rd, Cincinnati, OH 45236
Tel: 513-531-2690 *Fax:* 513-531-0798
Web Site: www.writersdigest.com
How to choose & use point of view to create the most potent, effective fiction possible.
192 pp, $16.99

Masterplots II
Published by Salem Press Inc
2 University Plaza, Suite 121, Hackensack, NJ 07601
SAN: 208-838X
Tel: 201-968-9899 *Fax:* 201-968-1411
E-mail: csr@salempress.com
Web Site: www.salempress.com
Key Personnel
Publicist & Sales & Mktg Mgr: Luisa Torres
 E-mail: ltorres@salempress.com
American Fiction Series (rev), (6 vols), 3072 pp, $446 US, $687 Canada.
British & Commonwealth Fiction Series, (4 vols), 2024 pp, $383 US, $590 Canada.
Drama Series, (4 vols), 1952 pp, $404 US, $622 Canada.
Juvenile & Young Adult Fiction Series, (4 vols), 1792 $383 US, $590 Canada. Supplement, (3 vols) 1536 pp, $289 US, $445 Canada.
Short Story Series (6 vols), 5300 pp, $499 US, $768 Canada.
Poetry Series (2nd rev ed), (8 vols), 4652 pp, $499 US, $768 Canada.
Nonfiction Series, (4 vols), 1810 pp, $383 US, $590 Canada.
Women's Literature Series, (6 vols), 2698 pp, $525 US, $809 Canada.
European Fiction, (3 vols), 1482 pp, $126 US, $194 Canada.
British Fiction, (3 vols), 1832 pp, $126 US, $194 Canada.
American Fiction, (3 vols), 1532 pp, $126 US, $194 Canada.
Masterpolts, Revised Second Edition, (12 vols), 7680 pp, $630 US, $970 Canada.
MasterplotsComplete CD-ROM 2000 Edition, $788 US, $1214 Canada.
ISBN(s): 0-89356-468-0; 0-89356-478-8; 0-89356-491-5; 0-89356-579-2; 0-89356-594-6; 0-89356-871-6; 0-89356-898-8; 0-89356-916-X; 1-58765-037-1; 1-58765-116-5; 1-58765-140-8

Media Analysis Tools
Published by Richler & Co
754 Palermo Dr, Suite A, Santa Barbara, CA 93105
Tel: 805-569-1668 *Fax:* 805-569-2279
E-mail: richlerandco@worldnet.att.net
Key Personnel
VP, Sales & Mktg: Roy M Buckley
1st ed, 1997: 63 pp, $34.95
ISBN(s): 1-879299-13-5

Medical & Health Care Books & Serials in Print
Published by R R Bowker LLC
Subsidiary of Cambridge Information Group Inc
630 Central Ave, New Providence, NJ 07974
SAN: 214-1191
Tel: 908-286-1090 *Toll Free Tel:* 888-BOWKER2
 Fax: 908-219-0185
E-mail: info@bowker.com
Web Site: www.bowker.com
Key Personnel
Sr Man Dir: Roy Crego
Health care publishing has never been more fast-paced & this focused two-volume set will help you keep track of all the rapidly changing book

& serial developments with its convenient, targeted access. Listings for more than 100,000 books, including more than 3,000 U.S. & foreign serials – under 8,000 medical & health subject areas – are fully cross-referenced to help you cover the full range of biomedical & health sciences, including medicine, dentistry, veterinary medicine, psychiatry, psychology, behavioral science & more. Full ordering & publisher information is included to facilitate acquisitions.
Annual.
2004: 4,928 pp, $385.00/2 vol set cloth
ISBN(s): 0-8352-4632-9 (2 vol set)

Metro California Media Directory
Published by Bacon's Information Inc
Division of Observer AB
332 S Michigan Ave, Suite 900, Chicago, IL 60604
Tel: 312-922-2400 *Toll Free Tel:* 800-621-0561
 Fax: 312-922-3127
Web Site: www.bacons.com
Key Personnel
Sr VP: Ruth McFarland
Contains 4,000 listings with 30,000 key personnel contacts at newspapers, services, magazines, radio, TV & other consumer media in the state of California.
Annual.
1,585 pp, $250
ISBN(s): 0889-2776

Missing Persons: A Writer's Guide to Finding the Lost, the Abducted & the Escaped
Published by Writer's Digest Books
4700 E Galbraith Rd, Cincinnati, OH 45236
Tel: 513-531-2690 *Fax:* 513-531-0798
Web Site: www.writersdigest.com
Goes beyond the basic search & details the process of looking for someone, typical clients & the reaction once the missing is found.
272 pp, $16.99
ISBN(s): 0-89879-790-X

MLRC 50-State Survey: Employment Libel & Privacy Law
Published by Media Law Resource Center Inc
80 Eighth Ave, Suite 200, New York, NY 10011-5126
Tel: 212-337-0200 *Fax:* 212-337-9893
E-mail: ldrc@ldrc.com
Web Site: www.medialaw.org
Key Personnel
Exec Dir: Sandra Baron
Updated & published annually, the MLRC 50-State Surveys are easy-to-use compendiums of the law in all US jurisdictions, state & federal, used by journalists, lawyers, judges & law schools nationwide. Each state's chapter, prepared by experts in that jurisdiction, is presented in a uniform outline format.
Annual, Jan.
1,150 pp, $175

MLRC 50-State Survey: Media Libel Law
Published by Media Law Resource Center Inc
80 Eighth Ave, Suite 200, New York, NY 10011-5126
Tel: 212-337-0200 *Fax:* 212-337-9893
E-mail: ldrc@ldrc.com
Web Site: www.medialaw.org
Key Personnel
Exec Dir: Sandra Baron
Updated & published annually, the MLRC 50-State Surveys are easy-to-use compendiums of the law in all US jurisdictions, state & federal, used by journalists, lawyers, judges & law schools nationwide. Each state's chapter, prepared by experts in that jurisdiction, is presented in a uniform outline format.
Annual, Nov.
1,150 pp, $175

MLRC 50-State Survey: Media Privacy & Related Law
Published by Media Law Resource Center Inc
80 Eighth Ave, Suite 200, New York, NY 10011-5126
Tel: 212-337-0200 *Fax:* 212-337-9893
E-mail: ldrc@ldrc.com
Web Site: www.medialaw.org
Key Personnel
Exec Dir: Sandra Baron
Updated & published annually, the MLRC 50-State Surveys are easy-to-use compendiums of the law in all US jurisdictions, state & federal, used by journalists, lawyers, judges & law schools nationwide. Each state's chapter, prepared by experts in that jurisdiction, is presented in a uniform outline format.
Annual, July.
1,500 pp, $175 vol

Modern American Usage: A Guide
Published by Hill & Wang
Division of Farrar, Straus & Giroux LLC
19 Union Sq W, New York, NY 10003
Tel: 212-741-6900 *Fax:* 212-633-9385
Key Personnel
Publr: Elisabeth Sifton
Author: Wilson Follett
1998: 360 pp, $25 & $3 shipping
ISBN(s): 0-8090-6951-2 (paper)

Multicultural Marketing in America
Published by Adweek Directories
770 Broadway, New York, NY 10003
Tel: 646-654-5215 *Toll Free Tel:* 800-562-2706
 Fax: 646-654-5886
Web Site: www.adweek.com/directories
Key Personnel
Ed & Publg Dir: Mitch Tebo *E-mail:* mtebo@adweek.com
Directory of advertising, marketing & media contacts for the African American, Asian American, Hispanic & GLBT marketing industry.
Annual.
396 pp, $249
ISBN(s): 1-891204-35-1

National Playwrights Directory
Published by O'Neill Theater Center
305 Great Neck Rd, Waterford, CT 06385
Tel: 860-443-5378 *Fax:* 860-443-9653
E-mail: localplaywrights@aol.com
Web Site: www.members.aol.com/localplaywrights/oneill.htm
Key Personnel
Ed: Phyllis Johnson Kaye
Contains biographical sketches of more than 500 living American playwrights & details on 3,000 plays. Nearly every entry is accompanied by a photographic portrait. Not available to the general public.
2nd ed, 1982: 507 pp, $35 cloth including postage & handling
ISBN(s): 0-9605160-0-X

National Trade & Professional Associations of the United States
Published by Columbia Books Inc
1825 Connecticut Ave NW, Suite 625, Washington, DC 20009
Mailing Address: PO Box 251, Annapolis Junction, MD 20701-0251
Tel: 202-898-0662; 202-464-1622 (cust serv)
 Toll Free Tel: 888-265-0600 *Fax:* 202-898-0775; 202-464-1775; 240-646-7020 (cust serv)
E-mail: info@columbiabooks.com
Web Site: www.columbiabooks.com
Key Personnel
Sr Ed: Buck Downs
Covers 7,600 trade associations, professional societies & labor unions with national memberships with such data as chief executive, size

of membership & staff, budget, telephone, facsimile number, e-mail address, publications, meeting data & historical background. Includes indexes by subject, geography, budget, acronym & chief executive officer. Also includes a directory of 400 association management companies & the associations they manage.
Annual.
38th ed, 2003: 1,000 pp, $159 paper

New York Publicity Outlets
Published by Bacon's Information Inc
332 S Michigan Ave, Suite 900, Chicago, IL 60604
Tel: 312-922-2400 *Toll Free Tel:* 800-621-0561
 Fax: 312-922-3127
Web Site: www.bacons.com
Key Personnel
Sr VP: Ruth McFarland
Contains 3000 listings with 8000 key personnel contacts at newspapers, services, magazines, radio, TV & other consumer media located in the New York metropolitan area.
Annually.
1,530 pp, $250
ISBN(s): 0077-9024

The New York Times Manual of Style & Usage
Published by Three Rivers Press
1745 Broadway, New York, NY 10019
Mailing Address: 299 Park Ave, New York, NY 10171
Tel: 212-782-9000 *Fax:* 212-940-7408
Key Personnel
Author: William G Connolly; Allan M Siegal
Revised Edition 2002, $15.95
ISBN(s): 0-8129-6389-X

Newsletters In Print
Published by Thomson Gale
Unit of The Thomson Corp
27500 Drake Rd, Farmington Hills, MI 48331-3535
Tel: 248-699-4253 *Toll Free Tel:* 800-347-4253
 Fax: 248-699-8070 *Toll Free Fax:* 800-414-5043
E-mail: galeord@thomson.com
Web Site: www.gale.com
Key Personnel
Mgr, Corp Communs: Kim Gabbert *Tel:* 248-699-8193 *E-mail:* kimberly.gabbert@thomson.com
With descriptions of more than 12,000 newsletters in 4,000 different subject areas, this comprehensive resource acts as an invaluable tool for business & personal interest.
18th ed, 2004: 1,400 pp, $315
ISBN(s): 0-7876-6934-2

Nineteenth-Century Literature Criticism
Published by Thomson Gale
Unit of The Thomson Corp
27500 Drake Rd, Farmington Hills, MI 48331-3535
Tel: 248-699-4253 *Toll Free Tel:* 800-347-4253
 Fax: 248-699-8054
E-mail: galeord@gale.com
Web Site: www.gale.com
Key Personnel
Ed: Russell Whitaker
Each volume in the series provides critical overviews of four to eight poets, novelists, short story writers, playwrights, philosophers, & other creative writers, who died between 1800 & 1899. Most critical essays are full text. Every fourth volume covers literary topics including major literary movements, trends & other topics related to 19th-century literature.
multiple vols/yr.
Vols 133-145, 2004; Vols 146-154, 2005, $195/vol

No More Rejections
Published by Writer's Digest Books
4700 E Galbraith Rd, Cincinnati, OH 45236
Tel: 513-531-2690 *Fax:* 513-531-0798
Web Site: www.writersdigest.com
Secrets to writing a ms that sells. Thinking up original ideas, moving your story forward, developing characters with character, etc.
272 pp, $22.99

The Novel Writer's Toolkit
Published by Writer's Digest Books
4700 E Galbraith Rd, Cincinnati, OH 45236
Tel: 513-531-2690 *Fax:* 513-531-0798
Web Site: www.writersdigest.com
Covering every aspect of the creative journey.
256 pp, $22.99
ISBN(s): 1-58297-261-3

Novelists Essential Guide to Crafting Scenes
Published by Writer's Digest Books
4700 E Galbraith Rd, Cincinnati, OH 45236
Tel: 513-531-2690 *Fax:* 513-531-0798
Web Site: www.writersdigest.com
Leads you through the creative process, examining all the elements that go into making scenes successful, cohesive & compelling.
208 pp, $14.99
ISBN(s): 0-89879-973-2

O'Dwyer's Directory of Public Relations Firms
Published by O'Dwyer Co
271 Madison Ave, Rm 600, New York, NY 10016
Tel: 212-679-2471 *Fax:* 212-683-2750
E-mail: sales@odwyerpr.com
Web Site: www.odwyerpr.com
Key Personnel
Pres & Publr: Jack O'Dwyer *E-mail:* jack@odwyerpr.com
A listing of more than 2,900 PR firms in the US & overseas.
Annual.
2004: 500 pp, $175
First published 1969
ISBN(s): 0-941424-62-6

100 Things Every Writer Needs to Know
Published by Perigee
Member of Penguin Group (USA) Inc
375 Hudson St, New York, NY 10014
Tel: 212-366-2000
Web Site: www.penguin.com
ISBN(s): 0-399525084

1001 Ways to Market Your Books
Published by Open Horizons Publishing Co
PO Box 205, Fairfield, IA 52556-0205
Tel: 641-472-6130 *Toll Free Tel:* 800-796-6130
 Fax: 641-472-1560
E-mail: info@bookmarket.com
Web Site: www.bookmarket.com
Key Personnel
Publr & Author: John Kremer
 E-mail: johnkremer@bookmarket.com
Outlines more than 1000 different ways to market books. Uses many real-life examples describing how other publishers market their books. Includes planning & design, advertising & distribution, subsidiary rights & spinoffs.
Biennial.
6th ed, 2004: 704 pp, $27.95 paper
ISBN(s): 0-912411-49-X (paper)

1818 Ways to Write Better & Get Published
Published by Writer's Digest Books
4700 E Galbraith Rd, Cincinnati, OH 45236
Tel: 513-531-2690 *Fax:* 513-531-0798
Web Site: www.writersdigest.com
Easy to search, fast reference format; find tips on good writing, information resources, attitude, business matters & more.

225 pp, $15.99
ISBN(s): 0-89879-778-0

Periodical Title Abbreviations
Published by Thomson Gale
Subsidiary of The Thomson Corp
27500 Drake Rd, Farmington Hills, MI 48331-
3535
Tel: 248-699-4253 *Toll Free Tel:* 800-347-4253
   Fax: 248-699-8070 *Toll Free Fax:* 800-414-
5043
Web Site: www.gale.com
Key Personnel
Comp & Ed: Leland G Alkire, Jr
Ed: Michael Reade *E-mail:* michael.reade@
thomson.com
Contains 212,000 alphabetically arranged abbreviations, with full titles of magazines, journals &
newspapers found in frequently used abstracting & indexing services. Vol 1 by abbreviations; vol 2 by title.
15th ed, 2005, $275 vol 1, $275 vol 2
ISBN(s): 0-7876-7451-6 (Vol 1 (1500 pp)); 0-
7876-7452-4 (Vol 2 (1500 pp))

Photographer's Market
Published by Writer's Digest Books
Division of F+W Publications Inc
4700 E Galbraith Rd, Cincinnati, OH 45236
Tel: 513-531-2690 *Toll Free Tel:* 800-289-0963
   Fax: 513-531-0798 *Toll Free Fax:* 888-590-
4082
Web Site: www.fwpublications.com
Key Personnel
Ed: Donna Poehner *Tel:* 513-531-2690 ext 1226
Sales Dir: Michael Murphy *Tel:* 800-666-0963 ext
1270 *E-mail:* michael.murphy@fwpubs.com
Sales Admin Coord: Marcia Jones *Tel:* 513-531-
2690 ext 1288 *E-mail:* marcia.jones@fwpubs.
com
More than 2000 listings of photo buyers with
complete contact information; for freelance &
stock photographers.
Annual.
2004 edition: 640 pp, $24.99 paper
ISBN(s): 1-58297-186-2

Play Index
Published by H W Wilson
950 University Ave, Bronx, NY 10452-4224
Tel: 718-588-8400 *Toll Free Tel:* 800-367-6770
   Fax: 718-590-1617 *Toll Free Fax:* 800-367-
6770
E-mail: custserv@hwwilson.com
Web Site: www.hwwilson.com
Key Personnel
Dir, Catalog Servs: Joseph Miller *Tel:* 718-588-
8400 ext 2279 *E-mail:* jmiller@hwwilson.com
Indexes plays by author, title, subject, type of cast
& number of actors required, 1949-1952 Vol;
comp by Dorothy H West & Dorothy M Peake;
indexes 2,616 plays; $70 US & Canada, 1953-
1960 Vol; ed by Estelle A Fidell & Dorothy M
Peake; indexes 4,592 plays; $70 US & Canada,
1961-1967 Vol; ed by Estelle A Fidell; indexes
4,793 plays; $70 US & Canada, 1968-1972
Vol; ed by Estelle A Fidell; indexes 3,848
plays; $70 US & Canada, 1973-1977 Vol; ed
by Estelle A Fidell; indexes 3,878 plays; $70
US & Canada, 1978-1982 Vol; ed by Juli-
ette Yaakov; indexes 3,429 plays; $70 US &
Canada, 1983-1987 Vol; ed by Juliette Yaakov
& John Greenfieldt; indexes 3,964 plays; $190
US & Canada, 1988-1992 Vol; ed by Juliette
Yaakov & John Greenfieldt; indexes 4,387
plays; $190 US & Canada 1993-1997 Play
Index, $190 US & Canada; 1998-2002 Play
Index, $215 US & Canada.
Every 5 yrs.
ISBN(s): 0554-3037

Pocket Guide to Color Reproduction
Published by Graphic Arts Publishing Co Inc
3100 Bronson Hill Rd, Livonia, NY 14487
Tel: 585-346-6978 *Toll Free Tel:* 800-724-9476
   Fax: 585-346-2276
Web Site: www.graphicartspublishing.com
Key Personnel
Pres: Miles F Southworth *E-mail:* mfsouth@aol.
com
Author: Donna Southworth
Answer book.
2nd ed, 1987: 109 pp, $17.95
ISBN(s): 0-933600-09-7

The Pocket Muse
Published by Writer's Digest Books
4700 E Galbraith Rd, Cincinnati, OH 45236
Tel: 513-531-2690 *Fax:* 513-531-0798
Web Site: www.writersdigest.com
Unique ideas for overcoming writer's block, cre-
ativity boosters, revision tips & more.
256 pp, $19.99 hardcover; $12.99 paper (2004)
ISBN(s): 1-58297-142-0

Poetry Criticism
Published by Thomson Gale
27500 Drake Rd, Farmington Hills, MI 48331-
3535
Tel: 248-699-4253 *Toll Free Tel:* 800-347-4253
   Fax: 248-699-8070 *Toll Free Fax:* 800-414-
5043
E-mail: galeord@thomson.com
Web Site: www.gale.com
Key Personnel
Mgr, Corp Communs: Kim Gabbert *Tel:* 248-699-
8193 *E-mail:* kimberly.gabbert@thomson.com
Covers poets most frequently discussed & studied in high school & undergraduate literature
courses. Provides criticism, illustration & author commentary, arranged for quick information access.
4-5 times/yr.
Vols 53-58, 2004; Vols 59-64, 2005: 480 pp,
$145/vol
ISBN(s): 0-7876-6955-5 (Vol 53); 0-7876-6956-
3 (Vol 54); 0-7876-7453-2 (Vol 55); 0-7876-
7454-0 (Vol 56); 0-7876-8691-3 (Vol 57); 0-
7876-8692-1 (Vol 58); 0-7876-8693-X (Vol
59); 0-7876-8694-8 (Vol 60); 0-7876-8695-
6 (Vol 61); 0-7876-8696-4 (Vol 62); 0-7876-
8697-2 (Vol 63); 0-7876-8698-0 (Vol 64)

Poets' Encyclopedia
Published by Unmuzzled Ox Books & Magazine
105 Hudson St, New York, NY 10013
Tel: 212-226-7170
Key Personnel
Ed: Michael Andre *E-mail:* mandreox@aol.com
Author: W H Auden; Dan Berrigan; John Cage;
Allen Ginsberg
World's basic knowledge transformed by 225 po-
ets, artists, musicians & novelists.
1st ed, 1979: 310 pp, $45 cloth, $25 paper
ISBN(s): 0-934450-02-1 (cloth); 0-934450-03-X
(paper)

Poet's Market
Published by Writer's Digest Books
Division of F+W Publications Inc
4700 E Galbraith Rd, Cincinnati, OH 45236
Tel: 513-531-2690 *Toll Free Tel:* 800-289-0963
   Fax: 513-531-4082 *Toll Free Fax:* 888-590-
4082
Web Site: www.fwpublications.com; www.
writersdigest.com
Key Personnel
Ed: Nancy Breen
Sales Dir: Michael Murphy *Tel:* 800-666-0963 ext
1270 *E-mail:* michael.murphy@fwpubs.com
Sales Admin Coord: Marcia Jones *Tel:* 513-531-
2690 ext 1288 *E-mail:* marcia.jones@fwpubs.
com

Where & how to get poetry published; 1,800 US
& international publisher listings, also includes
contests & awards, writing colonies, organizations, conferences, workshops & publications
useful to poets.
Annual.
2005: 572 pp, $24.99 paper
ISBN(s): 1-58297-275-3

The Print Media Planning Manual
Published by Richler & Co
754 Palermo Dr, Suite A, Santa Barbara, CA
93105
Tel: 805-569-1668 *Fax:* 805-569-2279
E-mail: richlerandco@worldnet.att.net
Key Personnel
VP, Sales & Mktg: Roy M Buckley
Author: R L Ehler
Publishes books on advertising & how to.
1st ed, 1991: 291 pp, $49.95 paper
ISBN(s): 1-879299-11-9

**Print Publishing for the School Market
2003-2004**
Published by Simba Information
Unit of R R Bowker LLC
60 Long Ridge Rd, Suite 300, Stamford, CT
06902
SAN: 210-2021
Tel: 203-325-8193 *Toll Free Tel:* 888-BOWKER2
(orders) *Fax:* 203-325-8915
E-mail: info@simbanet.com
Web Site: www.simbanet.com
Key Personnel
Edit Dir: Linda Kopp
Man Ed: Kathy Mickey
Up-to-date descriptions & statistics on enroll-
ments, demographic trends, in several cate-
gories; publishers' sales, forecasts, expenditures
& profiles of the leading publishers in the K-12
market place.
Biennial.
2003-2004: 175 pp, $2,295 print report format or
electronic; $4,590 print & electronic

Printing Production Management
Published by Graphic Arts Publishing Co Inc
3100 Bronson Hill Rd, Livonia, NY 14487-9716
Tel: 585-346-2776 *Toll Free Tel:* 800-724-9476
   Fax: 716-346-2276
E-mail: mfsouth@aol.com
Web Site: www.graphicartspublishing.com
Key Personnel
VP: Donna Southworth
Author: Gary G Field
How to manage & optimize every aspect of a
printing company in today's market to achieve
a profit. Includes which equipment & when
to buy, purchase or lease, replacement point,
layout, scheduling, job layout & planning, production control, inventory optimization, quality
control, management theories & scientific management. Index, present value tables & quality
assurance sampling plans.
1st ed, 1996: 300 pp, $34.95 cloth
ISBN(s): 0-933600-11-9

**Professional Writing: Processes, Strategies &
Tips for Publishing in Education Journals**
Published by Krieger Publishing Co
PO Box 9542, Melbourne, FL 32902-9542
Tel: 321-724-9542 *Toll Free Tel:* 800-724-0025
   Fax: 321-951-3671
E-mail: info@krieger-publishing.com
Web Site: www.krieger-publishing.com
Key Personnel
Author: Roger Hiemstra
Provides insights, tips, strategies & recommenda-
tions for publishing in educational periodicals.
1994: 152 pp, $21.50 cloth
First published 1993
ISBN(s): 0-89464-660-5

Publish, Don't Perish: The Scholar's Guide to Academic Writing & Publishing
Published by Greenwood Press
Subsidiary of Greenwood Publishing Group Inc
88 Post Rd W, Westport, CT 06881
Mailing Address: PO Box 5007, Westport, CT 06881
Tel: 203-226-3571 *Fax:* 203-222-1502
E-mail: bookinfo@greenwood.com
Web Site: www.greenwood.com
Key Personnel
Author: Joseph M Moxley
VP, Mktg: Linda May *Tel:* 203-226-3571 ext 3351
Expressing a strongly positive view of the value of academic publishing that reaches far beyond what is implied by the book title, Moxley offers informed suggestions to faculty members for conceiving, developing & publishing scholarly documents as books or journal articles.
1992, $21.95/paperback; $60.95/hardcover
ISBN(s): 0-275-94453-0 (paperback); 0-313-27735-4 (hardcover)

Publishers Directory
Published by Thomson Gale
Unit of The Thomson Corp
27500 Drake Rd, Farmington Hills, MI 48331-3535
Tel: 248-699-4253 *Toll Free Tel:* 800-347-4253
Fax: 248-699-8074
E-mail: galeord@gale.com
Web Site: www.gale.com
Key Personnel
Ed: Louise Gagne *E-mail:* louise.gagne@thomson.com
Contains over 20,000 new & established, private & special interest, avant garde & alternative, organization & association, government & institutional presses in US & Canada, including electronic & audio publishers. Separate section covers wholesalers & distributors. Includes publisher, subject & geographic indexes. Also covers small independent presses & virtual publishers.
Annual.
26th ed, 2003; 27th ed, 2004, $450
ISBN(s): 0-7876-5931-2 (26th ed); 0-7876-5932-0 (27th ed)

Publishers, Distributors & Wholesalers of the United States
Published by R R Bowker LLC
Subsidiary of Cambridge Information Group Inc
630 Central Ave, New Providence, NJ 07974
SAN: 214-1191
Tel: 908-286-1090 *Toll Free Tel:* 888-269-5372
Fax: 908-219-0098
E-mail: info@bowker.com; pad@bowker.com
Web Site: www.bowker.com
Key Personnel
Sr Man Dir: Roy Crego
A directory of some 110,000 active US publishers, distributors, associations & wholesalers, listing editorial & ordering addresses with an ISBN Publishers' Prefix Index. Includes small & independent presses; producers of software & audio cassettes; phone, fax & toll free telephone numbers including toll free fax & fax-on-demand numbers; e-mail & website addresses; inactive & out of business publishers; discount schedules & return policies; publishers by fields of activity & Geographic Index to Publishers, Distributors & Wholesalers.
Annual.
2004-2005: 3,600 pp, $349.00/2 vol set hardcover
ISBN(s): 0-8352-4671-X (2 vol set)

Publishers' International ISBN Directory
Published by K G Saur Verlag GmbH, A Gale/ Thomson Learning Company
Ortlerstr 8, 81373 Munich, Germany

Mailing Address: Postfach 70 16 20, 81316 Munich, Germany
Tel: (089) 76902-0 *Fax:* (089) 76902-150
E-mail: saur.info@thomson.com
Web Site: www.saur.de *Telex:* 5212067

Publishing Contracts, Sample Agreements for Book Publishers on Disk
Published by Para Publishing
PO Box 8206-R, Santa Barbara, CA 93118-8206
SAN: 215-8981
Tel: 805-968-7277 *Toll Free Tel:* 800-727-2782
Fax: 805-968-1379
E-mail: orders@parapublishing.com
Web Site: www.parapublishing.com
Key Personnel
Owner & Publr: Dan Poynter
E-mail: danpoynter@parapublishing.com
Author: Charles Kent, Esq
22 different contracts covering every aspect of book publishing on disk, ready for computer customizing & printout.
3rd ed, 1995: 127 pp, $29.95 disk
ISBN(s): 0-915516-46-2

Publishing in the Information Age: A New Management Framework for the Digital Era
Published by Greenwood Press
Subsidiary of Greenwood Publishing Group Inc
88 Post Rd W, Westport, CT 06881
Mailing Address: PO Box 5007, Westport, CT 06881
Tel: 203-226-3571 *Fax:* 203-222-1502
E-mail: bookinfo@greenwood.com
Web Site: www.greenwood.com
Key Personnel
Author: Douglas M Eisenhart
VP, Mktg: Linda May *Tel:* 203-226-3571 ext 3351
A comprehensive single-volume study of the transformations underway in the publishing industry attributable to the penetration of digital information technologies & how publishers can benefit from them.
1996, $30.95/paperback; $88.95/hardcover
ISBN(s): 0-275-95696-2 (paperback); 0-89930-847-3 (hardcover)

Publishing to Niche Markets
Published by Communication Unlimited
PO Box 6405, Santa Maria, CA 93456
Tel: 805-937-8711 *Toll Free Tel:* 800-563-1454
Fax: 805-937-3035
E-mail: sops@fix.net
Web Site: www.sops.com
Key Personnel
Pres, Author & Ed: Gordon Burgett
E-mail: gburgett@sops.com
How-to information, step-by-step process & detailed example of niche publishing.
1994: 200 pp, $14.95 paper
ISBN(s): 0-910167-27-3

Quality & Productivity in the Graphic Arts
Published by Graphic Arts Publishing Co Inc
3100 Bronson Hill Rd, Livonia, NY 14487
Tel: 585-346-6978 *Toll Free Tel:* 800-724-9476
Fax: 585-346-2276
Web Site: www.graphicartspublishing.com
Key Personnel
Pres: Miles F Southworth *E-mail:* mfsouth@aol.com
Author: Killmon Layne; Donna Southworth
Contributing Author: Marathe Eisner; Werner Rebsamen
For the graphic arts, the total quality approach, an overview of Deming methods, managing quality, SPC, process control, quality circles, assurance programs & task forces, process control targets, instrumentation & tests as well as sources of controls, equipment & information.

1st ed, 1989; 2nd printing 1990: 544 pp, $34.95 hardcover
ISBN(s): 0-933600-05-4

Real-World Newsletter to Meet Your Unreal Demands
Published by EEI Communications
Division of EEI Press
66 Canal Center Plaza, Suite 200, Alexandria, VA 22314-5507
Tel: 703-683-0683 *Fax:* 703-683-4915
E-mail: press@eeicommunications.com
Web Site: www.eeicommunications.com
Key Personnel
Press Mgr: Linda B Jorgensen
Proj Mgr: Jayne Sutton *E-mail:* jsutton@eeicom.com
Softcover book; comprehensive guide to editing & producing newsletters.
366 pp, $34.95
ISBN(s): 0935-01-224-9

Research Centers Directory
Published by Thomson Gale
Unit of The Thomson Corp
27500 Drake Rd, Farmington Hills, MI 48331-3535
Tel: 248-699-4253 *Toll Free Tel:* 800-347-4253
Fax: 248-699-8075
E-mail: galeord@gale.com
Web Site: www.gale.com
Key Personnel
Ed: Donna Wood *Tel:* 248-699-4253, ext 1466
E-mail: donna.wood@thomson.com
Directory describes almost 14,000 University affiliated, govt affiliated & other nonprofit research centers in the US & Canada. Indexes: subject, geographic, personal name & master, including sponsoring organization, research center name & keywords.
Annual.
32nd ed, 2004, $695/2 vol set
ISBN(s): 0-7876-7113-4 (2 vol set)

Science Fiction & Fantasy Literature, 1975-1991
Published by Thomson Gale
Unit of The Thomson Corp
27500 Drake Rd, Farmington Hills, MI 48331-3535
Tel: 248-699-4253 *Toll Free Tel:* 800-347-4253
Fax: 248-699-8070 *Toll Free Fax:* 800-414-5043
E-mail: galeord@thomson.com
Web Site: www.gale.com
Key Personnel
Mgr, Corp Communs: Kim Gabbert *Tel:* 248-699-8193 *E-mail:* kimberly.gabbert@thomson.com
This edition follows the Science Fiction & Fantasy Literature, 1700-1974 & includes bibliographic data on more than 20,000 science fiction, fantasy & horror books as well as nonfiction monographs. Also includes indexes for book titles, series, awards & "doubles" & is arranged alphabetically by author.
Irregular.
1992, $250
ISBN(s): 0-8103-1825-3

The Self-Publishing Manual: How to Write, Print & Sell Your Own Book
Published by Para Publishing
PO Box 8206-R, Santa Barbara, CA 93118-8206
SAN: 215-8981
Tel: 805-968-7277 *Toll Free Tel:* 800-727-2782
Fax: 805-968-1379
E-mail: orders@parapublishing.com
Web Site: www.parapublishing.com
Key Personnel
Owner & Publr: Dan Poynter
E-mail: danpoynter@parapublishing.com

How to write, publish & announce a book & get it listed. Emphasis on market targeting, advertising & distribution.
Biennial.
14th ed, 2004: 432 pp, $19.95 paper
ISBN(s): 1-56860-088-7

Setting
Published by Writer's Digest Books
4700 E Galbraith Rd, Cincinnati, OH 45236
Tel: 513-531-2690 *Fax:* 513-531-0798
Web Site: www.writersdigest.com
You'll learn how to use this often overlooked fictional element to help tell credible, interesting stories & to heighten dramatic & thematic effects.
176 pp, $12

Shakespearean Criticism
Published by Thomson Gale
Unit of The Thomson Corp
27500 Drake Rd, Farmington Hills, MI 48331-3535
Tel: 248-699-4253 *Toll Free Tel:* 800-347-4253
Fax: 248-699-8070 *Toll Free Fax:* 800-414-5043
E-mail: galeord@thomson.com
Web Site: www.gale.com
Key Personnel
Mgr, Corp Communs: Kim Gabbert *Tel:* 248-699-8193 *E-mail:* kimberly.gabbert@thomson.com
Thematically arranged essays from 1960 to the present of commentary on Shakespeare's plays & poems. Illustrated series provides support to students & teachers at high school & college levels. Beginning with Vol 60, presents topic entries that analyze various themes of Shakespeare's works. Each volume has a cumulative character index, a topic index & a topic index arranged by play title.
6 times/yr.
Vol 80-86, 2004: 420 pp, $195
ISBN(s): 0-7876-7010-3 (Vol 80); 0-7876-7011-1 (Vol 81); 0-7876-7012-X (Vol 82); 0-7876-7013-6 (Vol 83); 0-7876-7456-7 (Vol 84); 0-7876-8823-1 (Vol 85); 0-7876-8824-X (Vol 86)

Short Story Criticism
Published by Thomson Gale
Unit of The Thomson Corp
27500 Drake Rd, Farmington Hills, MI 48331-3535
Tel: 248-699-4253 *Toll Free Tel:* 800-347-4253
Fax: 248-699-8070 *Toll Free Fax:* 800-414-5043
Web Site: www.gale.com
Key Personnel
Mgr, Corp Communs: Kim Gabbert *Tel:* 248-699-8193 *E-mail:* kimberly.gabbert@thomson.com
Series presenting critical views on the most widely studied writers of short fiction. Each volume includes overview of four to eight short story writers & a chronological historical survey of the critical response to his or her work. Most critical essays are full text.
Vols 67-75, 2005, $145

Short Story Index
Published by H W Wilson
950 University Ave, Bronx, NY 10452-4224
Tel: 718-588-8400 *Toll Free Tel:* 800-367-6770
Fax: 718-590-1617 *Toll Free Fax:* 800-367-6770
E-mail: custserv@hwwilson.com
Web Site: www.hwwilson.com
Key Personnel
Dir, Catalog Servs: Joseph Miller *Tel:* 718-588-8400 ext 2279 *E-mail:* jmiller@hwwilson.com
Ed: John Greenfieldt
Indexes short stories by author, title & subject in one alphabet. Basic Vol; Indexes 60,000 stories in 4,320 collections published from 1900-1949,

$180. 5-yr Vol, 1950-1954: Indexes 9,575 stories in 549 collections, $65. 4-yr Vol, 1955-1958: Indexes 6,392 stories in 376 collections, $65. 5-yr Vol, 1959-1963: Indexes 9,068 stories in 582 collections, $65. 5-yr Vol, 1964-1968: Indexes 11,301 stories in 793 collections, $65. 5-yr Vol, 1969-1973: Indexes 11,561 stories in 805 collections, $65. 5-yr Vol, 1974-1978: Indexes 16,519 stories in 930 collections & 71 periodicals, $95. 5-yr Vol, 1979-1983: Indexes 16,633 stories in 904 collections & 67 periodicals, $105. 5-yr Vol, 1984-1988: Indexes 22,431 stories in 1,307 collections & periodicals, $135.
Annual, with five year cumulations.
$180 US, $215 foreign, available in electronic format
ISBN(s): 0360-9774

Software & Intellectual Property Protection: Copyright & Patent Issues for Computer & Legal Professionals
Published by Greenwood Press
Subsidiary of Greenwood Publishing Group Inc
88 Post Rd W, Westport, CT 06881
Mailing Address: PO Box 5007, Westport, CT 06881
Tel: 203-226-3571 *Fax:* 203-222-1502
E-mail: bookinfo@greenwood.com
Web Site: www.greenwood.com
Key Personnel
Author: Bernard A Galler
VP, Mktg: Linda May *Tel:* 203-226-3571 ext 3351
A succinct, readable survey of the critical issues & cases in copyright & patent law applied to computer software, intended for computer professionals, academics & lawyers.
1995: 224 pp, $88.95
ISBN(s): 0-89930-974-7

The Software Encyclopedia
Published by R R Bowker LLC
Subsidiary of Cambridge Information Group Inc
630 Central Ave, New Providence, NJ 07974
SAN: 214-1191
Tel: 908-286-1090 *Toll Free Tel:* 888-BOWKER2
Fax: 908-219-0185
E-mail: info@bowker.com
Web Site: www.bowker.com
Key Personnel
Sr Man Dir: Roy Crego
Help all your PC-using patrons identify, compare, & select the programs they need for any conceivable application with the Software Encyclopedia 2004. The unmatched guide provides fully annotated listings for more than 41,000 programs, including 5,000 new programs & makes it easy for patrons to locate software for virtually every imaginable need or application form astrology charting to commodities trading to desktop publishing. Covering every format, from disk to CD-ROM, the Software Encyclopedia indexes all entries by title & by compatible systems & applications. The 2004 edition includes more than 5,000 new programs & more than 18,000 updated entries.
Annual.
May 2004: 3,500 pp, $355.00/2 vol set paper
ISBN(s): 0-8352-4635-3 (2 vol set)

Something About the Author
Published by Thomson Gale
Unit of The Thomson Corp
27500 Drake Rd, Farmington Hills, MI 48331-3535
Tel: 248-699-4253 *Toll Free Tel:* 800-347-4253
Fax: 248-699-8070 *Toll Free Fax:* 800-414-5043
E-mail: galeord@gale.com
Web Site: www.gale.com

Key Personnel
Mgr, Corp Communs: Kim Gabbert *Tel:* 248-699-8193 *E-mail:* kimberly.gabbert@thomson.com
Heavily illustrated child-oriented reference tool. Each volume contains biographies on about 100-140 juvenile & young adult authors & illustrators. The series covers more than 7000 authors. Entries include personal & career data, literary sidelights, complete bibliographies, critical comments & author portraits & book illustrations.
9 vols/yr.
Vol 145-153, 2004, $135/vol
ISBN(s): 0-7876-6991-1 (Vol 145); 0-7876-6992-4 (Vol 146); 0-7876-6993-8 (Vol 147); 0-7876-6994-6 (Vol 148); 0-7876-6995-4 (Vol 149); 0-7876-6996-2 (Vol 150); 0-7876-6997-0 (Vol 151); 0-7876-6998-9 (Vol 152); 0-7876-6999-7 (Vol 153)

Standard Periodical Directory
Published by Oxbridge Communications Inc
186 Fifth Ave, 6th fl, New York, NY 10010
Tel: 212-741-0231 *Toll Free Tel:* 800-955-0231
Fax: 212-633-2938
E-mail: info@oxbridge.com; custserv@oxbridge.com
Web Site: www.mediafinder.com
Key Personnel
CEO: Louis Hagood
Pres: Patricia Hagood
Edit Dir: Deborah Striplin *E-mail:* dstriplin@oxbridge.com
63,000 US & Canadian periodicals arranged by subject matter into 262 classifications & indexed by title. Listings include publishing company, address, telephone number; names of editor, publisher, ad director; annotations; frequency, circulation, advertising & subscription rates; year established; trim size, print method, page count.
Annual.
27th Ed-2004: 2,022 pp, $1,395 hardcover & $1,495 CD-ROM
ISBN(s): 1-891783-23-8

Star Guide 2004-2005
Published by Axiom Information Resources
PO Box 8015, Ann Arbor, MI 48107
Tel: 734-761-4842
E-mail: axiom@celebritylocator.com
Web Site: www.celebritylocator.com
Key Personnel
Pres: Rob Ten-Tronck
Publr: Terry Robinson
A directory of over 3,200 celebrities, from entertainment to business, who may be contacted for testimonials for the book trade.
Annual.
2004: 208 pp, $14.95 paper
ISBN(s): 0-943213-49-5

The State of Literacy in San Antonio
Published by Intercultural Development Research Association (IDRA)
5835 Callaghan Rd, Suite 350, San Antonio, TX 78228
Tel: 210-444-1710 *Fax:* 210-444-1714
E-mail: contact@idra.org
Web Site: www.idra.org
Key Personnel
Exec Dir: Maria Robledo Montecel
Communs Mgr: Christie Goodman
Communs Specialist: Sherry Carr Deer
1st ed, 1994: 24 pp, $6 paper
ISBN(s): 1-878-550-50-0

Study Opportunities in Book Arts
Published by Guild of Book Workers Inc
521 Fifth Ave, 17th fl, New York, NY 10175-0003
Tel: 212-292-4444; 212-873-4315

Opportunities in binding & book related activities & listings of people who teach book arts. available online only.
2003: 40 pp, Free on request

Subject Guide to Books In Print
Published by R R Bowker LLC
Subsidiary of Cambridge Information Group Inc
630 Central Ave, New Providence, NJ 07974
SAN: 214-1191
Tel: 908-286-1090; 908-219-0170 (editorial)
 Toll Free Tel: 888-BOWKER2 *Fax:* 908-219-0185
E-mail: info@bowker.com
Web Site: www.bowker.com
Key Personnel
Sr Man Dir: Roy Crego
Sr Dir: Constance Harbison *E-mail:* constance.harbison@bowker.com
A six-volume index listing 1.8 million total in-print books of over 73,000 US publishers & exclusive distributors under 83,000 Library of Congress headings with 43,000 cross-references. Entries include full finding & ordering data. Includes a name & address directory of all publishers & distributors represented.
Annual.
48th ed, 2004-2005: 17,130 pp, $525.00/6 vol set
ISBN(s): 0-8352-4651-5 (6 vol set)

Subject Guide to Children's Books in Print
Published by R R Bowker LLC
Subsidiary of Cambridge Information Group Inc
630 Central Ave, New Providence, NJ 07974
SAN: 214-1191
Tel: 908-286-1090 *Toll Free Tel:* 888-BOWKER2
 Fax: 908-219-0185
E-mail: info@bowker.com
Web Site: www.bowker.com
Key Personnel
Sr Dir: Constance Harbison *E-mail:* constance.harbison@bowker.com
Especially useful for expanding collections to support new curriculum areas. Annual publication to aid your subject collection activities & to help young patrons research topics of interest. Here you'll discover 188,000 fiction & nonfiction children's books arranged under 4,512 subject headings. Subject Guide to Children's Books In Print is the easiest, most cost-effective way to track down children's books on every subject imaginable; locate titles on current topics capturing the interest of young readers; build, update & expand children's & young adult collections; assist parents, teachers & young readers with subject-related research. Develop niche areas in your bookstore. Reduce ordering time & effort with current prices, ISBNs, publishers' telephone numbers & addresses.
Annual.
34th ed, 2004: 1,500 pp, $225.00/2 vol set cloth
ISBN(s): 0-8352-4540-3 (2 vol set)

Substance & Style: Instruction & Practice in Copyediting
Published by EEI Communications
66 Canal Center Plaza, Suite 200, Alexandria, VA 22314-5507
Tel: 703-683-0683 *Toll Free Tel:* 800-683-8380
 Fax: 703-683-4915
E-mail: press@eeicommunications.com
Web Site: www.eeicom.com
Key Personnel
Ed: Linda Jorgensen
VP: Robin Cormier
Proj Mgr: Jayne Sutton *E-mail:* jsutton@eeicom.com
Comprehensive reference & self-study text that teaches the basics of professional copy-editing. Includes extensive exercises, answer keys, discussions & style comparisons.

2nd ed, 1996: 362 pp, $35
ISBN(s): 0-935012-18-4

The Great Grammar Challenge: Test Yourself on Punctuation, Usage, Grammar & More
Published by EEI Communications
66 Canal Center Plaza, Suite 200, Alexandria, VA 22314-5507
Tel: 703-683-0683 *Toll Free Tel:* 800-683-8380
 Fax: 703-683-4915
E-mail: press@eeicommunications.com
Web Site: www.eeicom.com
Key Personnel
Proj Mgr: Jayne Sutton *E-mail:* jsutton@eeicom.com
Press Mgr: Linda B Jorgensen
1st ed: 242 pp, $24.95
ISBN(s): 0935-012-21-4

The Publisher's Direct Mail Handbook
Published by Greenwood Press
Division of Greenwood Publishing Group Inc
88 Post Rd W, Westport, CT 06881
Tel: 203-226-3571 *Toll Free Tel:* 800-225-5800
 Fax: 203-222-1502
E-mail: sales@greenwood.com
Web Site: www.greenwood.com
Key Personnel
Author: Nat G Bodian
Sr Mktg Mgr: Alex Petri *E-mail:* alex.petri@greenwood.com
1988: 284 pp, $46.95 cloth
ISBN(s): 0-89495-079-7

Training Guide to Frontline Bookselling
Published by Paz & Associates
1417 Sadler Rd, PMB 274, Fernandina Beach, FL 32034
Tel: 904-277-2664 *Toll Free Tel:* 800-260-8605
 Fax: 904-261-6742
Web Site: www.pazbookbiz.com
Key Personnel
Contact: Donna Paz-Kaufman *E-mail:* dpaz@pazbookbiz.com
12 chapters on all aspects of bookstore operations, includes trainers outline.
2nd ed, Jan 2001: 125 pp, $158 plus $8.50 shipping

Travel Writer's Guide
Published by Communication Unlimited
PO Box 6405, Santa Maria, CA 93456
Tel: 805-937-8711 *Fax:* 805-937-3035
E-mail: sops@fix.net
Web Site: www.sops.com
Key Personnel
Pres: Gordon Burgett *E-mail:* gburgett@sops.com
Writing/reference.
3rd ed, revised & updated, 2002: 376 pp, $17.95 paper

Travel Writing
Published by Writer's Digest Books
4700 E Galbraith Rd, Cincinnati, OH 45236
Tel: 513-531-2690 *Fax:* 513-531-0798
Web Site: www.writersdigest.com
How to write engagingly about your travels, whether in journals for your own pleasure or articles for publications.
256 pp, $14.99
ISBN(s): 1-58297-000-9

TRUMATCH Colorfinder
Published by TRUMATCH Inc
71 Hill St, Southampton, NY 11968
Tel: 631-204-9100 *Toll Free Tel:* 800-TRU-9100 (878-9100 US & Canada)
E-mail: info@trumatch.com
Web Site: www.trumatch.com
Key Personnel
Pres: Steven J Abramson

VP: Jane E Nichols *E-mail:* janen@trumatch.com
Digital guides for 4-color printing.
Annually.
2004: 255 pp, $85 coated & uncoated paper ed

Twentieth-Century Literary Criticism
Published by Thomson Gale
Unit of The Thomson Corp
27500 Drake Rd, Farmington Hills, MI 48331-3535
Tel: 248-699-4253 *Toll Free Tel:* 800-347-4253
 Fax: 248-699-8054
E-mail: galeord@gale.com
Web Site: www.gale.com
Key Personnel
Ed: Linda Pavlovski
Each volume in the series presents overviews to 4-5 authors & furnishes full texts from representative criticism on the great novelists, poets & playwrights of the period 1900-1999. Every fourth volume covers literary topics including major literary movements, trends & other topics related to 20th century literature.
multiple vols/yr.
Vols 142-154, 2004; Vols 155-165, 2005, $195/vol

20 Master Plots
Published by Writer's Digest Books
4700 E Galbraith Rd, Cincinnati, OH 45236
Tel: 513-531-2690 *Fax:* 513-531-0798
Web Site: www.writersdigest.com
How to take timeless storytelling structures & make them immediate, now, for fiction that's universal in how it speaks to the reader's heart.
240 pp, $14.99
ISBN(s): 1-58297-239-7

2001 Survey of Compensation & Personnel Practices in the Publishing Industry
Published by Association of American Publishers (AAP)
71 Fifth Ave, 2nd fl, New York, NY 10003-3004
Tel: 212-255-0200 *Fax:* 212-255-7007
Web Site: www.publishers.org
Key Personnel
VP: Kathryn Blough *Tel:* 212-255-0200 ext 263
 E-mail: kblough@publishers.org
Survey report contains salary & personnel practices information for more than 120 benchmark jobs in the publishing industry.
Biennial.
220 pp, Varies based on participation, company site & AAP membership status

2003/2004 Audiobook Reference Guide
Published by AudioFile Publications Inc
37 Silver St, Portland, ME 04101
Tel: 207-774-7563 *Toll Free Tel:* 800-506-1212
 Fax: 207-775-3744
E-mail: info@audiofilemagazine.com
Key Personnel
Ed: Robin F Whitten
Reference guide for audiobook publishers, distributors, libraries & support services; complete information.
9th ed, 2002-2003: 84 pp
ISBN(s): 0-9645649-3-9

Ulrich's Periodicals Directory
Published by R R Bowker LLC
Subsidiary of Cambridge Information Group Inc
630 Central Ave, New Providence, NJ 07974
SAN: 214-1191
Tel: 908-286-1090; 908-219-0286 (Ulrich's hotline) *Toll Free Tel:* 800-521-8110; 800-346-6049 (Ulrich's hotline US only) *Fax:* 908-219-0812
E-mail: ulrichs@bowker.com
Web Site: www.bowker.com; www.ulrichsweb.com
Key Personnel
Edit Dir: Laurie Kaplan

Dir, Print Sales & Cust Training: Serge Sarkis
Four-volume set, arranged by subject classification, includes periodicals, newsletters, newspapers, annuals & irregular serials published worldwide. Also available on the Internet, CD-ROM, online & magnetic tape.
Annual.
43rd ed, 2005: 11,000 pp, $799.00
First published 1932
ISBN(s): 0-8352-4666-3 (4 vol set)

Urge to Kill
Published by Writer's Digest Books
4700 E Galbraith Rd, Cincinnati, OH 45236
Tel: 513-531-2690 *Fax:* 513-531-0798
Web Site: www.writersdigest.com
Explores this intriguing subject step by step, empowering writers to create engaging & believable scenarios.
192 pp

Used Book Lover's Guide Series
Published by Book Hunter Press
PO Box 193, Yorktown Heights, NY 10598
Tel: 914-245-6608 *Fax:* 914-245-2630
E-mail: bookhunterpress@verizon.net
Web Site: www.bookhunterpress.com
Key Personnel
Owner: Susan Siegel
Series of seven annotated guides to over 8,000 used, out-of-print, rare & antiquarian book dealers in the United Sates & Canada. All editions updated with annual supplements. Also available online by subscription.
New England (2nd Rev), 2000; Mid-Atlantic (Rev), 1997; South Atlantic (Rev), 1997; Midwest (Rev), 1999; Pacific Coast States (Rev),2000; Central States, 1996; Canada, 1999. Updated annually, $14.95-$19.95

Walden's Paper Catalog
Published by Walden-Mott Corp
225 N Franklin Tpke, Ramsey, NJ 07446-1600
Tel: 201-818-8630 *Toll Free Tel:* 888-292-5336
Fax: 201-818-8720
E-mail: walden@walden-mott.cc
Web Site: www.papercatalog.com
Key Personnel
Ed: Linda Cohen
Publr: Alfred Walden, Sr
National directory of fine printing & writing papers. Alphabetical listing of brand names, their characteristics along with merchants that carry those manufacturers' grades. Sections: "Brand Name Index," "Paper Distributors," "Mill Catalog," "Papers by Grade," & "How to Buy Paper." Yearly subscription is for two issues, spring & fall.
Annual.
2004-2005, $50/issue, $80/2 yr subscription

Walden's Paper Handbook
Published by Walden-Mott Corp
225 N Franklin Tpke, Ramsey, NJ 07446-1600
Tel: 201-818-8630 *Fax:* 201-818-8720
E-mail: walden@walden-mott.cc
Web Site: www.walden-mott.com
Pulp & paper industry pocket guide.
3rd: 277 pp, $25

Who's Who in African Heritage Book Publishing
Published by ECA Associates Press
925 Main Creek Rd, Chesapeake, VA 23320
Mailing Address: PO Box 15004, Chesapeake, VA 23328-0004
Tel: 757-547-5542 *Fax:* 757-547-5542
E-mail: eca@blackwordsonline.com
Web Site: www.blackwordsonline.com
Key Personnel
Pres: Dr E Curtis Alexander

Ed: Dr Mwalimu I Mwadilifu
The International African Heritage Literary Marketplace. $49.95 paper, $4.45 shipping & handling.
4,000 listees annually.
8th ed: 280 pp
ISBN(s): 0-938818-95-3

Word Painting
Published by Writer's Digest Books
4700 E Galbraith Rd, Cincinnati, OH 45236
Tel: 513-531-2690 *Fax:* 513-531-0798
Web Site: www.writersdigest.com
Combines direct instruction with intriguing word exercises to teach you how to "paint" evocative descriptions that capture the images of your mind's eye & improve your writing.
256 pp, $14.99
ISBN(s): 1-58297-025-4

Words on Cassette, see Books Out Loud

World Authors Series
Formerly Authors Series
Published by H W Wilson
950 University Ave, Bronx, NY 10452-4224
Tel: 718-588-8400 *Toll Free Tel:* 800-367-6770
Fax: 718-590-1617 *Toll Free Fax:* 800-367-6770
E-mail: custserv@hwwilson.com
Web Site: www.hwwilson.com
Key Personnel
Pres & CEO: Harold Regan
American Authors, 1600-1900, $115.
British Authors Before 1800, $100.
British Authors of the 19th Century, $105.
European Authors, 1000-1900, $115.
Junior Book of Authors, $65 (2nd ed rev).
More Junior Authors, $60.
Third Book of Junior Authors, $65;
Fourth Book 1978, $70;
Fifth Book 1983, $80;
Sixth Book 1989, $80;
Seventh Book 1996, $80.
Index to the Wilson Author Series 1997, $50 (rev).
World Authors 1900-1950 (4 vols), $590.
World Authors 1950-1970, $150; 1970-1975, $130; 1975-1980, $130; 1980-1985, $130;
800 BC-Present, (CD-ROM), $595;
1900-Present, (CD-ROM), $495;
1950-Present, (CD-ROM).
Spanish American Authors: The Twentieth Century 1992, $160.
Eighth Book of Junior Authors, 2000, $95.
World Authors, 1985-1990, $130.
World Authors, 1990-1995, $145.
World Authors, 1995-2000, $150.
All prices US & Canada, other countries higher.
ISBN(s): 0-8242-0001-2; 0-8242-0006-3; 0-8242-0007-1; 0-8242-0013-6; 0-8242-0028-4; 0-8242-0036-5; 0-8242-0050-0; 0-8242-0408-5; 0-8242-0419-9; 0-8242-0429-0; 0-8242-0568-5; 0-8242-0640-1; 0-8242-0641-X; 0-8242-0694-0; 0-8242-0715-7; 0-8242-0777-7; 0-8242-0797-1; 0-8242-0806-4; 0-8242-0874-9; 0-8242-0875-7; 0-8242-0899-4; 0-8242-0900-1; 0-8242-0956-7; 0-8242-0968-0; 0-8242-1032-8

World Encyclopedia of Library & Information Services
Published by American Library Association
50 E Huron St, Chicago, IL 60611
SAN: 201-0062
Tel: 312-280-2425; 312-280-3247
Toll Free Tel: 800-545-2433 *Fax:* 312-944-8085
Web Site: www.ala.org
Key Personnel
Exec Dir: Keith Fiels
Dir, Publg Technol: Troy Linker
A one-volume synthesis of library, information & archival services throughout the world. Includes

over 340 articles, 300 illustrations & 144 statistical tables. Includes the work of more than 300 contributors from 145 countries.
Irregular.
3rd ed, 1993: 905 pp, $200 cloth
First published 1980
ISBN(s): 0-8389-0690-7

World Literature Criticism: A Selection of Major Author's from Gale's Literary Criticism
Published by Thomson Gale
Unit of The Thomson Corp
27500 Drake Rd, Farmington Hills, MI 48331-3535
Tel: 248-699-4253 *Toll Free Tel:* 800-347-4253
Fax: 248-699-8070 *Toll Free Fax:* 800-414-5043
E-mail: galeord@thomson.com
Web Site: www.gale.com
Key Personnel
Mgr, Corp Communs: Kim Gabbert *Tel:* 248-699-8193 *E-mail:* kimberly.gabbert@thomson.com
Subset of Gale's classic *Literary Criticism Series*. Includes excerpts of critical commentary, author biography & portrait, major media adaptations, bibliography listing sources for further study & alphabetical index by author, nationality & title for the 6-vol set. Authors, poets, novelists, essayists & major dramatists included are those most frequently studied in high school & college curricula.
1st ed, 6 vols, 1992: 4,209 pp, $450/set; $150 supplement (961pp)
ISBN(s): 0-7876-1696-6 (supplement); 0-8103-8361-6 (6 vol set)

World Literature Criticism: A Selection of Major Authors from Gale's Literary Criticism - Supplement
Published by Thomson Gale
Unit of The Thomson Corp
27500 Drake Rd, Farmington Hills, MI 48331-3535
Tel: 248-699-4253 *Toll Free Tel:* 800-347-4253
Fax: 248-699-8070 *Toll Free Fax:* 800-414-5043
E-mail: galeord@thomson.com
Web Site: www.gale.com
Key Personnel
Mgr, Corp Communs: Kim Gabbert *Tel:* 248-699-8193 *E-mail:* kimberly.gabbert@thomson.com
961 pp, $150
ISBN(s): 0-7876-1696-6

Write Faster, Write Better
Published by Writer's Digest Books
4700 E Galbraith Rd, Cincinnati, OH 45236
Tel: 513-531-2690 *Fax:* 513-531-0798
Web Site: www.writersdigest.com
Time saving techniques for writing great fiction & nonfiction.
256 pp, $22.99
ISBN(s): 1-58297-286-9

The Writer's Complete Fantasy Reference
Published by Writer's Digest Books
4700 E Galbraith Rd, Cincinnati, OH 45236
Tel: 513-531-2690 *Fax:* 513-531-0798
Web Site: www.writersdigest.com
Reveals the facts behind the fantasy, giving you the details you need to make your fiction vibrant, captivating & original.
278 pp, $14.99
ISBN(s): 1-58297-026-2

The Writer's Digest Writing Clinic
Published by Writer's Digest Books
4700 E Galbraith Rd, Cincinnati, OH 45236
Tel: 513-531-2690 *Fax:* 513-531-0798
Web Site: www.writersdigest.com
Shows you exactly how to analyze & improve your mss.

240 pp, $21.99; $16.99 paper (2004)
ISBN(s): 1-58297-220-6; 1-58297-318-0 (paper)

The Writer's Guide to Character Traits
Published by Writer's Digest Books
4700 E Galbraith Rd, Cincinnati, OH 45236
Tel: 513-531-2690 *Fax:* 513-531-0798
Web Site: www.writersdigest.com
Profiles the mental, emotional & physical qualities of dozens of different personality types.
332 pp, $15.99

The Writer's Guide to Crafting Stories for Children
Published by Writer's Digest Books
4700 E Galbraith Rd, Cincinnati, OH 45236
Tel: 513-531-2690 *Fax:* 513-531-0798
Web Site: www.writersdigest.com
Insightful advice for mastering storytelling basics with dozens of examples that illustrate a variety of plot-building techniques.
192 pp, $16.99
ISBN(s): 1-58297-052-1

Writer's Guide to Places
Published by Writer's Digest Books
4700 E Galbraith Rd, Cincinnati, OH 45236
Tel: 513-531-2690 *Fax:* 513-531-0798
Web Site: www.writersdigest.com
Provides information on more than 100 cities in the US & Canada, including the facts you need to develop convincing characters & compelling narratives.
448 pp, $21.99
ISBN(s): 1-58297-169-2

The Writer's Handbook 2005
Published by Kalmbach Publishing Co
21027 Crossroads Circle, Waukesha, WI 53187
Tel: 262-796-8776 *Toll Free Tel:* 800-533-6644
Fax: 262-798-6468
E-mail: editor@writermag.com
Web Site: www.writermag.com
Key Personnel
Sr Ed: Ronald Kovach
Ed: Elfrieda Abbe
Acqs Ed: Philip Martin
Compilation of 50 plus articles on writing for publication, many by recognized authors & editors. List of 3,000 plus markets for the sale of mss (fiction, nonfiction, poetry, drama, greeting card), plus lists of American literary agents, writers' organizations, literary contests & writing conferences.
Annual.
67th ed, 2003: 1,008 pp, $29.95 paper
ISBN(s): 0-87116-196-6

The Writer's Idea Book
Published by Writer's Digest Books
4700 E Galbraith Rd, Cincinnati, OH 45236
Tel: 513-531-2690 *Fax:* 513-531-0798
Web Site: www.writersdigest.com
Helps you to jump start your creativity & develop original ideas.
272 pp, $14.99
ISBN(s): 1-58297-179-X

The Writer's Idea Workshop
Published by Writer's Digest Books
4700 E Galbraith Rd, Cincinnati, OH 45236
Tel: 513-531-2690 *Fax:* 513-531-0798
Web Site: www.writersdigest.com
Takes your ideas to the next step by accessing them & growing them into finished pieces.
256 pp, $15.99

Writer's Market
Published by Writer's Digest Books
Division of F+W Publications Inc
4700 E Galbraith Rd, Cincinnati, OH 45236

Tel: 513-531-2690 *Toll Free Tel:* 800-289-0963
Fax: 513-531-4082 *Toll Free Fax:* 888-590-4082
Web Site: www.fwpublications.com; www.writersmarket.com
Key Personnel
Ed: Robert Lee Brewer; Kathryn Struckel Brogan
Sales Dir: Michael Murphy *Tel:* 800-666-0963 ext 1270 *E-mail:* michael.murphy@fwpubs.com
Sales Admin Coord: Marcia Jones *Tel:* 513-531-2690 ext 1288 *E-mail:* marcia.jones@fwpubs.com
Lists more than 4,000 places where freelance writers can sell articles, books, novels, stories, fillers, scripts; also includes complete contact informatin for 50 top literary agents & contests.
Annual.
2005: 1,120 pp, $29.99 paper; $49.99 (CD-ROM)
ISBN(s): 1-58297-271-0 (paper); 1-58297-272-9 (CD)

The Writer's Market Companion
Published by Writer's Digest Books
4700 E Galbraith Rd, Cincinnati, OH 45236
Tel: 513-531-2690 *Fax:* 513-531-0798
Web Site: www.writersdigest.com
Sound information on professional writing issues, focusing on everything from contracts to creativity.
2nd: 352 pp, $19.99
First published 2004
ISBN(s): 1-58297-291-5

Writer's Market FAQs
Published by Writer's Digest Books
4700 E Galbraith Rd, Cincinnati, OH 45236
Tel: 513-531-2690 *Fax:* 513-531-0798
Web Site: www.writersdigest.com
Answers all of your most asked questions. Arms you with the knowledge you need to make publishers, editors & agents your allies in the quest to get your work published.
240 pp, $18.99
ISBN(s): 1-58297-071-8

Writer's Northwest Handbook
Published by Media Weavers
PO Box 86190, Portland, OR 97286-0190
Tel: 503-771-0428 *Fax:* 503-771-5166
Web Site: www.mediaweavers.com
Key Personnel
Ed: Joleen Colombo
Publr: Marlene Howard
Northwest markets, resources, articles, interviews, how-to.
Biennial.
7th ed, 2003: 224 pp, $22.95/vol ($2 S&H)
ISBN(s): 0-9647212-6-0

Writer's Online Marketplace
Published by Writer's Digest Books
4700 E Galbraith Rd, Cincinnati, OH 45236
Tel: 513-531-2690 *Fax:* 513-531-0798
Web Site: www.writersdigest.com
Gives you everything you need to know to start exploring the possiblilities & get published now.
260 pp, $17.99
ISBN(s): 1-58297-016-5

Writer's Yearbook
Published by F+W Publications Inc
4700 E Galbraith Rd, Cincinnati, OH 45236
Tel: 513-531-2690 *Fax:* 513-891-7183
Web Site: www.fwpublications.com
Key Personnel
Publr: Colleen Cannon
Ed: Kristin Godsey
Circ Mgr: Lynn Kruetzkamp *Tel:* 513-531-2690 ext 1334 *E-mail:* lynn.kruetzkamp@fwpubs.com

Includes lists of magazine article markets & how-to articles on writing & publishing.
Annual.
80 pp, $5.99 paper
First published 1990

Writing Articles from the Heart
Published by Writer's Digest Books
4700 E Galbraith Rd, Cincinnati, OH 45236
Tel: 513-531-2690 *Fax:* 513-531-0798
Web Site: www.writersdigest.com
Advice for drawing the universal from the specific & how to get your stories down on paper in a readable & publishable form.
176 pp, $12.99
ISBN(s): 0-89879-988-0

Writing Creative Nonfiction
Published by Writer's Digest Books
4700 E Galbraith Rd, Cincinnati, OH 45236
Tel: 513-531-2690 *Fax:* 513-531-0798
Web Site: www.writersdigest.com
More than thirty essays examining every key element of the craft, from researching ideas & structuring the story, to reportage & personal reflection.
400 pp, $18.99
ISBN(s): 1-884910-50-5

Writing Down the Bones: Freeing the Writer Within
Published by Shambhala Publications
PO Box 308, Boston, MA 02117
Tel: 617-424-0030 *Fax:* 617-236-1563
E-mail: editors@shambhala.com
Web Site: www.shambhala.com
Key Personnel
Mktg Asst: David Smydra
ISBN(s): 1-570624240

Writing from the Heart: Inspiration & Excercise for Women Who Want to Write
Published by The Crossing Press
Unit of Ten Speed Press
PO Box 7123, Berkeley, CA 94707
Tel: 510-559-1600 *Toll Free Tel:* 800-841-2665 (orders & cust serv) *Fax:* 510-524-1052; 510-559-1629 (orders & cust serv)
E-mail: order@crossingpress.com
Web Site: www.crossingpress.com
ISBN(s): 0-895946416

Writing Life Stories
Published by Writer's Digest Books
4700 E Galbraith Rd, Cincinnati, OH 45236
Tel: 513-531-2690 *Fax:* 513-531-0798
Web Site: www.writersdigest.com
How to capture your own experiences & turn them into personal essays & book-length memoirs.
224 pp, $14.99
ISBN(s): 1-884910-47-5

Writing Mysteries
Published by Writer's Digest Books
4700 E Galbraith Rd, Cincinnati, OH 45236
Tel: 513-531-2690 *Fax:* 513-531-0798
Web Site: www.writersdigest.com
How to piece a perfect mystery together & create realistic stories that are taut, immediate & tense.
2nd, $16.99
ISBN(s): 1-58297-102-1

Writing the Breakout Novel
Published by Writer's Digest Books
4700 E Galbraith Rd, Cincinnati, OH 45236
Tel: 513-531-2690 *Fax:* 513-531-0798
Web Site: www.writersdigest.com
How to take your prose to the next level & write a breakout novel.

256 pp, $16.99
ISBN(s): 1-58297-182-X

Yearbook of Experts, Authorities & Spokespersons
Published by Broadcast Interview Source
2233 Wisconsin Ave NW, Washington, DC 20007
Tel: 202-333-4904 *Toll Free Tel:* 800-932-7266
   Fax: 202-342-5411
E-mail: editor@yearbook.com
Web Site: www.yearbook.com
Key Personnel
Publr: Mitchell P Davis *E-mail:* davis@yearbook.com
Listings of contacts at publishers, trade associations & public interest groups that welcome

media contacts; for both print & broadcast journalist use.
Annual.
21st ed, 2003: 674 pp, $39.95 paper
ISBN(s): 0-934333-42-4

You Can Write a Romance
Published by Writer's Digest Books
4700 E Galbraith Rd, Cincinnati, OH 45236
Tel: 513-531-2690 *Fax:* 513-531-0798
Web Site: www.writersdigest.com
Shows you how to take your story from idea to completed ms to signed book deal even if you've never tried to write a novel before.
128 pp, $12.99
ISBN(s): 0-89879-862-0

You Can Write Children's Books Workbook
Published by Writer's Digest Books
4700 E Galbraith Rd, Cincinnati, OH 45236
Tel: 513-531-2690 *Fax:* 513-531-0798
Web Site: www.writersdigest.com
Provides hands on instruction for finishing a ms, preparing it for publication & getting it published.
160 pp, $14.99
First published 2004

Magazines for the Trade

The magazines listed have been selected because they are published specifically for the book trade industry (apart from book review and index journals, which are listed in **Book Review & Index Journals & Services** in volume 2) or because they are widely used in the industry for reference.

For a comprehensive international directory of periodicals, see *Ulrich's Periodicals Directory* (R.R. Bowker LLC, 630 Central Avenue, New Providence, NJ 07974), which lists magazines by subject and includes notations indicating those that carry book reviews. See also *The International Directory of Little Magazines & Small Presses* (Dustbooks, PO Box 100, Paradise, CA 95967).

Writer's Digest (F+W Publications, Inc., 4700 East Galbraith Road, Cincinnati, OH 45236) publishes detailed magazine lists in certain issues. *The Writer's Handbook* (Kalmbach Publishing Co., 21027 Crossroads Circle, Waukesha, WI 53187) and *Writer's Market* (F+W Publications, Inc.) both contain classified lists of writers' markets.

Advertising Age
Published by Crain Communications Inc
711 Third Ave, New York, NY 10017
Tel: 212-210-0100 *Fax:* 212-210-0200 (NY)
Web Site: www.adage.com
Key Personnel
VP, Publg: Jill Manee
Edit Dir: David Klein
Exec Ed: Jonah Bloom
Man Ed: Judann Pollack
Ed: Scott Donaton
Ed-in-Chief, New York: Rance Crain
Covers advertising in business, media, trade newspapers & magazines.
First published 1930
Book Use: TV Commercial Reviews
Frequency: Weekly
Circulation: 61,123
$3.50/issue, $119/yr

American Journalism Review
Published by The Phillip Merrill College of Journalism
Division of University of Maryland Foundation
1117 Journalism Bldg, University of Maryland, College Park, MD 20742
Tel: 301-405-8803 *Fax:* 301-405-8323
Web Site: www.ajr.org
Key Personnel
Pres: Thomas Kunkel
Asst Man Ed: Jill Rosen
Sr VP & Ed: Rem Rieder
Circ Dir: Kathy Darragh
Edited for & by people working in the media & communications industry. Critiques journalism in all forms; including newspapers, TV, magazines, radio, cable TV, public relations, advertising, First Amendment issues & government regulation. Features book reviews, profiles, columns & news stories; cover stories which often correspond with media conventions taking place that month.
First published 1977
Frequency: 10 issues/yr
Avg pages per issue: 72
Circulation: 25,000
$3.95/issue, $24/yr
ISSN: 1067-8654

American Poetry Review
117 S 17 St, Suite 910, Philadelphia, PA 19103
Tel: 215-496-0439 *Fax:* 215-569-0808
Web Site: aprweb.org
Key Personnel
Ed: Stephen Berg; David Bonanno
 E-mail: dbonanno@aprweb.org; Arthur Vogelsang
Busn Mgr: Michael Duffy
Poetry, general essays, fiction.
First published 1972
Book Use: Excerpts & serial rights, reviews
Frequency: Bimonthly
Avg pages per issue: 52

Circulation: 18,000
$3.95/issue; $18/yr
ISSN: 0360-3709
Ad Rates: full pg - $900
Ad Closing Date(s): 45 days prior

The American Spectator
1611 N Kent St, Suite 901, Arlington, VA 22209
Tel: 703-807-2011 *Toll Free Tel:* 800-524-3469 (subscriptions) *Fax:* 703-807-2013
E-mail: editor@spectator.org
Web Site: www.spectator.org
Key Personnel
Publr: Alfred Regnery
Exec Ed: Wladyslaw Pleszczynski
Offers a unique blend of news reporting technology trends, social & political comment, humor pieces & cultural essays on the issues of the day.
First published 1967
Book Use: Book review section
Frequency: Monthly
Circulation: 100,000
$5.95/issue, $49.95/yr
Trim Size: 8.375 x 10.5
Ad Closing Date(s): 15th of each month

ANQ: A Quarterly Journal of Short Articles, Notes & Reviews
Subsidiary of Heldref Publications
1319 18 St NW, Washington, DC 20036-1802
Tel: 202-296-6267 *Fax:* 202-293-6130
E-mail: anq@heldref.org
Web Site: www.heldref.org
Key Personnel
Dir: Douglas Kirkpatrick
Man Ed: Elizabeth Foxwell
English & American literature for an academic & library audience.
First published 1987
Book Use: Reviews
Frequency: Quarterly
Avg pages per issue: 64
Circulation: 500
$52 indiv, $96 instns
ISSN: 0895-769X
Trim Size: 6x9
Ad Rates: $155 full, $90 half page
Ad Closing Date(s): Winter Oct 1, Spring Jan 5, Summer April 1, Fall July 1

The Artist's Magazine
Published by F+W Publications Inc
4700 E Galbraith Rd, Cincinnati, OH 45236
Tel: 513-531-2690 *Fax:* 513-531-1843
E-mail: tamedit@fwpubs.com
Web Site: www.artistsmagazine.com
Key Personnel
Man Ed: Jo Moore
Ed: Sandra Carpenter
Art instruction & advice for the working artist.
First published 1984

Book Use: Occasional book reviews (art-related titles only)
Frequency: Monthly
Avg pages per issue: 100
Circulation: 225,000
$4.99/issue $7.99 Canada; $27/yr; $54/2 yrs (US only)
ISSN: 0741-3351
Trim Size: 7 3/4 x 10 3/4

Authorship
Published by National Writers Association
3140 S Peoria St, Suite 295, Aurora, CO 80014-3178
Tel: 303-841-0246 *Fax:* 303-841-2607
Web Site: www.nationalwriters.com (magazine available on-line)
Key Personnel
Ed & Exec Dir: Sandy Whelchel
 E-mail: sandywrter@aol.com
Only take submissions dealing with writing.
Book Use: Review books for writers (in-house staff)
Frequency: Quarterly
Avg pages per issue: 36
Circulation: 10,000
$20/yr

Book Dealers World
Published by North American Bookdealers Exchange
PO Box 606, Cottage Grove, OR 97424-0026
Tel: 541-942-7455 *Fax:* 561-258-2625
E-mail: bookdealersworld@bookmarketingprofits.com
Key Personnel
Exec Dir: Al Galasso
Book marketing, self publishing, mail order.
First published 1980
Book Use: From NABE members
Frequency: Quarterly
Avg pages per issue: 40
Circulation: 20,000
$45/yr; sample $5

Book News & Book Business Mart
Published by Premier Publishers Inc
PO Box 330309, Fort Worth, TX 76163-0309
Tel: 817-293-7030 *Fax:* 817-293-3410
E-mail: prempubl@aol.com
Key Personnel
Pres: Neal Michaels
Combined source book, advertising forum & wholesale catalog for book sellers & mail order distributors worldwide.
First published 1971
Book Use: Reviews, paid advertising, news & info pertinent to mail order book sales
Frequency: 3 times/yr (Feb, June, Oct)
Avg pages per issue: 80
Circulation: 50,000
$3

Ad Rates: $25/ col inch
Ad Closing Date(s): Jan 15, May 15, Sept 15

Book Publishing Report
Published by Simba Information
Unit of R R Bowker LLC
60 Long Ridge Rd, Suite 300, Stamford, CT
  06902
SAN: 210-2021
Tel: 203-325-8193 *Toll Free Tel:* 888-BOWKER2
  (orders) *Fax:* 203-325-8915
E-mail: info@simbanet.com
Web Site: www.simbanet.com
Key Personnel
Edit Dir: Linda Kopp
Ed: Michael Norris
Newsletter; every weekly issue monitors, analyzes
  & reports on trends & developments in book
  publishing & what they mean to you. It covers
  the deals, the financials, market data, legal developments, technological issues, distribution,
  people & more. Monitors book industry news
  from a strategic, product, financial & marketing perspective; particular attention to emerging
  book industry companies, especially those that
  are exploiting the trends & developments that
  shape entirely new products.
ISBN Prefix(es): 0-918110
Frequency: 50 weekly issues
$689/yr

BookPage
Published by ProMotion Inc
2143 Belcourt Ave, Nashville, TN 37212
Tel: 615-292-8926 *Toll Free Tel:* 800-726-4242
  Fax: 615-292-8249
Web Site: www.bookpage.com
Key Personnel
Pres & Publr: Michael Zibart
Subn Mgr: Elizabeth Herbert *E-mail:* elizabeth@
  bookpage.com
Book reviews, author interviews; focus on gen-
  eral interest new releases. Monthly publication.
  Columns on romance, children, business, au-
  dio, science fiction, plus individual reviews on
  books in all categories. Focus is completely on
  new releases; no backlist reviewed. HC & PB
  titles reviewed.
First published 1988
Book Use: Reviews
Frequency: Monthly
Avg pages per issue: 32
Circulation: 500,000

Bookselling This Week
Published by American Booksellers Association
828 S Broadway, Tarrytown, NY 10591
Tel: 914-591-2665 *Toll Free Tel:* 800-637-0037
  Fax: 914-591-2720
E-mail: info@booksense.com
Web Site: www.booksense.com; www.bookweb.
  org
Key Personnel
Ed: Dan Cullen *Tel:* 914-591-2665 ext 1250
  E-mail: dan@bookweb.org
Book industry news; author tours; author media
  appearances; ABA membership news. Available
  online only.
Frequency: Weekly
Avg pages per issue: 5
Circulation: 7,000

**The Bulletin of the Center for Children's
Books**
Published by The Graduate School of Library &
  Information Science, University of Illinois at
  Urbana-Champaign & The University of Illi-
  nois Press
501 E Daniel St, Champaign, IL 61820
Tel: 217-244-0324 *Fax:* 217-333-5603
E-mail: bccb@alexia.lis.uiuc.edu
Web Site: www.lis.uiuc.edu/puboff/bccb

Key Personnel
Ed: Deborah Stevenson *Tel:* 217-244-9305
For teachers, librarians, parents & booksellers.
First published 1947
Book Use: Reviews of children's & young adult
  books for teachers, librarians, parents & book-
  sellers
Frequency: Monthly (exc Aug)
Avg pages per issue: 40
Circulation: 6,500
$50/yr, $66/yr instns; $15/students
ISSN: 0008-9036

ByLine
PO Box 5240, Edmond, OK 73083-5240
Tel: 405-348-5591
Web Site: www.bylinemag.com
Key Personnel
Ed & Publr: Marcia Preston *E-mail:* mpreston@
  bylinemag.com
Articles & tips for freelance writers.
First published 1981
Frequency: 11 issues/yr
Avg pages per issue: 36
Circulation: 3,500
$5/issue, $24/yr
ISSN: 0744-4249

Canadian Printer
Published by Rogers Media
One Mount Pleasant Rd, Toronto, ON M4Y 2Y5,
  Canada
Tel: 416-764-1530 *Fax:* 416-764-1738
Web Site: www.canadianprinter.com
Key Personnel
Ed: Doug Picklyk *E-mail:* dpicklyk@
  rmpublishing.com
National business publication for printers.
First published 1892
Frequency: 8 times/yr
Avg pages per issue: 60
Circulation: 11,500
$64/yr Canada, $126 foreign, $10.50/single copy
ISSN: 0849-0767

Capells Circulation Report
Published by Capell & Assocs
2038 18 St NW, No 403, Washington, DC 20009
Tel: 202-332-6272 *Fax:* 202-332-7428
Key Personnel
Pres: E Daniel Capell *E-mail:* dan_capell@att.net
Newsletter of magazine circulation.
First published 1982
Frequency: 20 issues/yr
Avg pages per issue: 10
$395
ISSN: 0736-9077

Catalog Age
Published by Prime Media Business
249 W 17 St, New York, NY 10011
Mailing Address: PO Box 4242, Stamford, CT
  06907-0242
Tel: 212-462-3371 *Toll Free Tel:* 800-975-5536
  Fax: 203-358-5823
Web Site: www.catalogage.com
Key Personnel
Exec Ed: Melissa Dowling *Tel:* 203-358-4221
  E-mail: mdowling@primemediabusiness.com
Edit Dir: Sherry Chiger
News & articles for the executives in the catalog
  marketing firms.
Frequency: Monthly
Circulation: 14,000
$74/yr
ISSN: 0740-3119

Catholic Library World
Published by Catholic Library Association
100 North St, Suite 224, Pittsfield, MA 01201-
  5109

Tel: 413-443-2CLA (443-2252) *Fax:* 413-442-
  2CLA (442-2252)
E-mail: cla@cathla.org
Web Site: www.cathla.org
Key Personnel
Prodn Ed: Allen Gruenke
Gen Ed: Mary Elizabeth Gallagher, SSJ
Exec Dir: Jean R Bostley, SSJ
Articles, book & media reviews for library infor-
  mation professionals.
First published 1929
Book Use: Regularly publish reviews of books &
  other media
Frequency: Quarterly
Avg pages per issue: 60
Circulation: 1,100
$60/yr (domestic), $70/yr + $10 postage (foreign)
ISSN: 0008-820X
Ad Rates: Full page, $390; 2/3 page, $330; 1/2
  page $270; 1/3 page $210; 1/6 page $150; Pre-
  ferred Space also available
Ad Closing Date(s): March issue, Feb 1; June is-
  sue, April 1; Sept issue, July 1; Dec issue, Oct
  1

CBA Marketplace
Published by CBA Service Corp
9240 Explorer Dr, Colorado Springs, CO 80920
Mailing Address: PO Box 62000, Colorado
  Springs, CO 80920-2000
Tel: 719-265-9895 *Toll Free Tel:* 800-252-1950
  Fax: 719-272-3510
Web Site: www.cbaonline.org
Key Personnel
Dir & Publr: Dorothy Gore
Adv Mgr: Carlton Dunn
Trade publication for the Christian retail indus-
  try; official publication of Christian Booksellers
  Association.
First published 1968
Book Use: Reviews, "Book Briefs", bestseller
  lists
Frequency: Monthly
Circulation: 8,713
$9.50/issue, $59.95/yr, $49.95/yr members
ISSN: 0006-7563

Children's Book News
Published by Canadian Children's Book Centre
40 Orchard View Blvd, Toronto, ON M4R 1B9,
  Canada
Tel: 416-975-0010 *Fax:* 416-975-8970
E-mail: info@bookcentre.ca
Web Site: www.bookcentre.ca
Key Personnel
Ed: Gillian O'Reilly
Reviews & articles on Canadian children's books,
  authors, illustrators & on the Canadian chil-
  dren's book industry.
Frequency: 3 issues/yr
Avg pages per issue: 30
Circulation: 1,200
Available with membership to the Canadian Chil-
  dren's Book Centre; also available in bulk sub-
  scriptions
ISSN: 0705-0038

Christian Retailing
Published by Charisma House
600 Rinehart Rd, Lake Mary, FL 32746
Tel: 407-333-0600 (all imprints) *Fax:* 407-333-
  7133
E-mail: magcustsvc@strang.com
Web Site: www.christianretailing.com
Key Personnel
Edit Dir: Larry J Leech, II
VP, Adv & Sales: Bob Minotti
VP, Mktg & Circ: Larry Bregel
Book & music industry news, contains articles,
  new books & music on merchandising, display,
  finance, promotions & management; successful

bookstore business stories; marketing & industry trends.
ISBN Prefix(es): 0-88419
First published 1955
Book Use: News of New Releases
Frequency: 20 issues/yr
Avg pages per issue: 60
Circulation: 9,700 paid, 10,000 cont
$75/yr, free to qualified retailers
ISSN: 0-8920281

The Chronicle of Higher Education
1255 23 St NW, Washington, DC 20037
Tel: 202-466-1000 *Fax:* 202-452-1033
E-mail: editor@chronicle.com
Web Site: chronicle.com
Key Personnel
Ed: Edward Weidlein
Ed-in-Chief: Philip Semas
Weekly newspaper covering higher education, including scholarly & publishing news.
First published 1966
Book Use: Articles on books of interest to an academic audience & on academic aspects of the publishing industry. Lists new books on higher education & new scholarly books; short & medium length excerpts from books on academic & literary issues
Frequency: Weekly (except for 2 issues in Dec & 1 in Aug)
Avg pages per issue: 100
Circulation: 85,000
$3.75/issue, $82.50/yr
ISSN: 0009-5982

Chronicle: SF, Fantasy & Horror's Monthly Trade Journal
Formerly Science Fiction Chronicle
Published by DNA Publications Inc
PO Box 2988, Radford, VA 24143-2988
Tel: 540-639-4288; 212-927-0594 (edit) *Fax:* 540-639-4289; 212-927-0594 (edit)
E-mail: chronicle@dnapublications.com
Web Site: www.dnapublications.com
Key Personnel
Pres & Publr: Warren Lapine
Reviewer: Don D'Ammassa *Tel:* 401-438-3296
  E-mail: dammassa@ix.netcom.com
News Ed: John R Douglas *Tel:* 212-927-0594
Adv Mgr: Xavier Calfee *E-mail:* xavier@dnapublications.com
Film, TV & Media Reviews: Jeff Rovin
  E-mail: jrovin7985@aol.com
Book Reviewer: Michael M Jones *Tel:* 540-776-3202 *E-mail:* everbard@ix.netcom.com
News, reviews, book buyers guide, market reports, interviews, letters & columns for science fiction, fantasy & horror professionals, booksellers, readers.
First published 1979
Book Use: Reviews, Excerpts
Frequency: monthly
Avg pages per issue: 84
Circulation: 12,000
$45/yr, $80/2 yr, $56/yr Canada, $75/yr foreign
ISSN: 0195-5365
Trim Size: 8 1/2 x 10 1/2
Ad Rates: $600/page B&W

Collection Connection, see School Selection Guide

College & Research Libraries
Published by Association of College & Research Libraries
Division of American Library Association
50 E Huron St, Chicago, IL 60611
Tel: 312-280-2511 *Toll Free Tel:* 800-545-2433 (ext 2517) *Fax:* 312-280-2520
Web Site: www.ala.org/acrl

Key Personnel
Ed-in-Chief: Stephanie Orphan *E-mail:* sorphan@ala.org
Theory & research relevant to academic & research librarians.
ISBN Prefix(es): 0-8389
First published 1939
Book Use: Reviews
Frequency: Bimonthly
Avg pages per issue: 100
Circulation: 11,000
$60/yr non-members
ISSN: 0010-0870

College Store Executive
Published by Executive Business Media Inc
825 Old Country Rd, Westbury, NY 11590
Tel: 516-334-3030 *Fax:* 516-334-8958
E-mail: ebm-mail@ebmpubs.com
Web Site: www.ebmpubs.com
Key Personnel
Pres & Publr: Murry Greenwald
Ed: Ken Bagliano *E-mail:* ken-cse@ebmpubs4.com
Acct Exec: Tom Kelly
Covers the retail industry of the college bookstore market.
First published 1970
Book Use: Reviews periodically
Frequency: 8 issues/yr
Avg pages per issue: 40
Circulation: 9,000
$5/issue, $35/yr, $6.50/issue, $50/yr foreign, $95/airmail, $70/2 yrs

Columbia Journalism Review
Published by Columbia Graduate School of Journalism
Affiliate of Columbia University
Journalism Bldg, 2950 Broadway, New York, NY 10027
Tel: 212-854-1881 (edit); 212-854-2716 (busn) *Fax:* 212-854-8580
E-mail: cjr@columbia.edu
Web Site: www.cjr.org
Key Personnel
Exec Ed: Mike Hoyt
Man Ed: Brent Cunningham
Publr: Evan Cornog
Edit Assoc: Tom O'Neill
Monitors & assesses the performance of journalism in all forms.
First published 1961
Frequency: Bimonthly
Circulation: 30,000
$4.95/issue, $27.95/yr, $40/2 yrs
ISSN: 0010-194X

Congressional Digest
Published by Congressional Digest Corp
1525-B 29 St NW, Suite 100, Washington, DC 20007
Mailing Address: PO Box 240, Boyds, MD 20841-0240
Tel: 202-333-7332 *Fax:* 202-625-6670
E-mail: info@congressionaldigest.com
Web Site: www.congressionaldigest.com
Key Personnel
Pres & Publr: Griff Thomas *Tel:* 202-333-7332 ext 100
Ed: Sarah Orrick
Pro & con monthly for unbiased coverage of major issues debated in Congress. Invaluable to political scholars since 1921.
First published 1921
Frequency: 10 issues/yr
$59/yr

Contacts
Published by MerComm Inc
500 Executive Blvd, Ossining on Hudson, NY 10562

Tel: 914-923-9400 *Fax:* 914-923-9484
Key Personnel
Publr: Reni L Witt *E-mail:* rwitt@mercommawards.com
Ed: Nora Madonick
Media Placement Opportunities for Publicists & Public Relations Professionals.
First published 1970
Frequency: Weekly - 50 issues/yr
$454

Country Folk Magazine
Published by Salaki Publishing & Design
HC 77, Box 608, Pittsburg, MO 65724
Tel: 417-993-5944 *Fax:* 417-993-5944
E-mail: info@countryfolkmag.com
Web Site: www.countryfolkmag.com
Key Personnel
Publr: Susan Salaki
First published 1994
Book Use: Reviews
Frequency: Bimonthly
Avg pages per issue: 43
Circulation: 6,000
$3.25/issue, $19.50/yr
ISSN: 1077-8802

Current Canadian Book/Livres Canadiens Courants
Published by Coutts Library Services Ltd
6900 Kinsmen Ct, Niagara Falls, ON L2E 7E7, Canada
Mailing Address: PO Box 1000, Niagara Falls, ON L2E 7E7, Canada
Tel: 905-356-6382 *Toll Free Tel:* 800-263-1686 *Fax:* 905-356-5064 *Telex:* 061-5299
Key Personnel
Mktg Coord: Lori Vaughan *E-mail:* lvaughan@couttsinfo.com
First published 1972
Book Use: Subject listing of bibliographical citations
Frequency: Quarterly
Free

Digital Imaging
Published by Cygnus Business Media
Unit of Cygnus Imaging Group
445 Broadhollow Rd, Melville, NY 11747
Tel: 631-845-2700 *Toll Free Tel:* 800-547-7377 *Fax:* 631-845-7109
E-mail: editor@digitalimagingmag.com
Web Site: www.digitalimagingmag.com
Key Personnel
Group Publr: Kathy Schneider
News & information for digital photographers & graphic artists.
ISBN Prefix(es): 0-941845
First published 1993
Frequency: 9 issues/yr
Circulation: 35,000
Free to graphic designers within the US
ISSN: 1084-5119

DIRECT
Published by Prime Media Business
249 W 17 St, New York, NY 10011
Tel: 212-462-3371
Web Site: www.directmag.com
Key Personnel
Ed: Ray Schultz *Tel:* 212-462-3371
  E-mail: rschultz@primemediabusiness.com
News, analysis & service articles for the direct marketing executive.
First published 1988
Frequency: 16 issues/yr
Avg pages per issue: 92
Circulation: 45,000
$10/issue, $88/yr
ISSN: 1046-4174

Directory Marketplace
Published by Todd Publications
PO Box 635, Nyack, NY 10960-0635
Tel: 845-358-6213 *Fax:* 845-358-6213
E-mail: toddpub@aol.com
Web Site: www.toddpublications.com
Key Personnel
Owner, Pres & Sr Ed: Barry Klein
Newsletter-catalog offering over 250 directories for sale in all fields. Advertising accepted.
ISBN Prefix(es): 0-915344
First published 1987
Book Use: New directories included
Frequency: Quarterly
Avg pages per issue: 8
Circulation: 100,000
ISSN: 0894-346X

The Editorial Eye
Published by EEI Press
Division of EEI Communications
66 Canal Center Plaza, Suite 200, Alexandria, VA 22314-5507
Tel: 703-683-0683 *Toll Free Tel:* 800-683-8380
Fax: 703-683-4915
E-mail: eye@eeicom.com
Web Site: www.eeicom.com/press/
Key Personnel
Ed: Linda B Jorgensen
VP: Robin Cormier
Encourages high professional standards & practices for editors, writers & publications managers. Uses published examples to teach. Includes articles on trends, techniques & language. Regular Test Yourself! grammar quizzes, reviews of production & editorial resources, *Black Eyes*, *On the Job* (scenarios & solutions), *The Right Word*, *The Watchful Eye*, *Infernal English*. Will research readers' usage questions.
First published 1978
Book Use: 100-500 words; identify author & title
Frequency: Monthly with index in Jan, various inserts
Avg pages per issue: 12
Circulation: 2,000
$129/yr US; $139/yr Canadian, $149/foreign
ISSN: 0193-7383

Editors' Association of Canada - Directory of Editors
Published by Editors' Association of Canada/Association canadienne des reviseurs
27 Carlton St, Suite 502, Toronto, ON M5B 1L2, Canada
Tel: 416-975-1379 *Toll Free Tel:* 866-226-3348
Fax: 416-975-1637
E-mail: info@editors.ca
Web Site: www.editors.ca
Key Personnel
Exec Dir: Lynne Massey
Online directory of descriptive listings of current association members indexed by specialty.
ISSN: 0226-9031

Educational Marketer
Published by Simba Information
Unit of R R Bowker LLC
60 Long Ridge Rd, Suite 300, Stamford, CT 06902
SAN: 210-2021
Tel: 203-325-8193 *Toll Free Tel:* 888-BOWKER2 (orders) *Fax:* 203-325-8915
E-mail: info@simbanet.com
Web Site: www.simbanet.com
Key Personnel
Edit Dir: Linda Kopp
Man Ed: Kathy Mickey
Newsletter; reports on educational publishing field (el-hi, college & audiovisual): enrollments, demographics, funding, mergers & acquisitions, new product developments & personnel changes. For suppliers & dealers in the educational market.
ISBN Prefix(es): 0-918110
First published 1968
Frequency: 3 issues/month
Avg pages per issue: 8
$599/yr
ISSN: 0013-1806
Trim Size: 7
Ad Rates: 995 full pg B&W; 575 1/2 pg B&W
Ad Closing Date(s): 12 days before publication date

Electronic Education Report
Published by Simba Information
Unit of R R Bowker LLC
60 Long Ridge Rd, Suite 300, Stamford, CT 06902
SAN: 210-2021
Tel: 203-325-8193 *Toll Free Tel:* 888-BOWKER2 (orders) *Fax:* 203-325-8915
E-mail: info@simbanet.com
Web Site: www.simbanet.com
Key Personnel
Edit Dir: Linda Kopp
Asst Ed: Karen Meaney
Published twice each month to provide industry decision-makers with the problem-solving information they need to make prudent business decisions in a rapidly evolving, billion dollar market. Technologies covered include hardware, software, multimedia/CD-ROM, integrated learning systems, videodisc, distance learning, online services, educational videocassettes & developments on the Information Superhighway. News coverage includes sales & distribution trends, company rankings & financial profiles, trademark & rights issues, strategic alliances & mergers, textbook legislation, site licensing & networks, etc. Analyzes el-hi, higher education & consumer markets. Readers are upper & middle management textbook & software publishers, software distributors, online service providers, videodisc publishers & computer hardware manufacturers.
ISBN Prefix(es): 0-918110
Frequency: 24x/yr
$579/yr

Electronic Information Report
Published by Simba Information
Unit of R R Bowker LLC
60 Long Ridge Rd, Suite 300, Stamford, CT 06902
SAN: 210-2021
Tel: 203-325-8193 *Toll Free Tel:* 888-BOWKER2 (orders) *Fax:* 203-325-8915
E-mail: info@simbanet.com
Web Site: www.simbanet.com
Key Personnel
Edit Dir: Linda Kopp
Ed: Anthony Carrick
News statistics & analysis about online content for the business & professional industry.
ISBN Prefix(es): 0-918110
First published 1979
Book Use: Excerpts of statistical studies
Frequency: 46x/yr
Avg pages per issue: 8
$649/yr
ISSN: 0197-0178

Electronic Publishing
Published by PennWell Publishing Co
98 Spit Brook Rd, Nashua, NH 03062-5737
Tel: 603-891-0123 *Fax:* 603-891-0539
Web Site: www.electronic-publishing.com
Key Personnel
Publr: Charlie Shively
Ed: Keith Hevenor
Electronic publishing.
First published 1976

Book Use: Reviews & press releases
Frequency: 12 issues/yr
Avg pages per issue: 63
Circulation: 70,000
$4.95/issue, $45/yr

Event
Published by Douglas College
PO Box 2503, New Westminster, BC V3L 5B2, Canada
Tel: 604-527-5293 *Fax:* 604-527-5095
E-mail: event@douglas.bc.ca
Web Site: event.douglas.bc.ca
Key Personnel
Ed: Cathy Stonehouse
Man Ed: Ian Cockfield
Fiction Ed: Christine Dewar
Poetry Ed: Gillian Harding-Russell
Reviews Ed: Susan Wasserman
Literary journal. Occasionally publish unsol reviews but should query first. Publish mostly Canadian writers, but are open to anyone writing in English. Do not read mss in Jan, July, Aug & Dec. Buy fiction, poetry, creative nonfiction.
First published 1971
Frequency: 3 issues/yr
Avg pages per issue: 136
Circulation: 1,100
$8
ISSN: 0315-3770
Trim Size: 6 x 9
Ad Rates: Full page $200; 1/2 pg $100
Ad Closing Date(s): Feb 15, June 15, Oct 15

Facilities
Published by Bedrock Communications
650 First Ave, 7th fl, New York, NY 10016
Tel: 212-532-4150 *Fax:* 212-213-6382
Key Personnel
Man Ed: Michael Caffin
Monthly trade magazine chronicling the facility, event & convention marketplace.
First published 1991
Frequency: Monthly
Avg pages per issue: 48
Circulation: 30,303
$4.95/issue, $48/yr

Folio:
Published by Prime Media Business
249 W 17 St, New York, NY 10011
Mailing Address: PO Box 4272, Stamford, CT 06907
Tel: 212-462-3371 *Toll Free Tel:* 800-975-5536
Fax: 203-358-5812
Web Site: www.foliomag.com
Key Personnel
Publr: Jennifer Taylor *Tel:* 203-358-9900 ext 156
News & articles for the magazine publishing executive.
First published 1972
Book Use: Excerpts & condensations
Frequency: 17 issues/yr
Avg pages per issue: 108
Circulation: 15,800
$96/yr, $116/yr Canada & Mexico, $199 elsewhere
ISSN: 0046-4333

Forecast
Published by Baker & Taylor Inc
2550 W Tyvola Rd, Suite 300, Charlotte, NC 28217
Mailing Address: PO Box 6885, Bridgewater, NJ 08807
Tel: 704-998-3100 *Toll Free Tel:* 800-775-1800
Fax: 704-998-3319
E-mail: btinfo@btol.com
Web Site: www.btol.com
Key Personnel
Prodn Coord: Donna Heffner *Tel:* 908-541-7412

Prepublication announcements for booksellers & librarians containing bibliographic data & descriptions of forthcoming adult hardcover future bestsellers, noteworthy midlist titles, university & independent press releases.
First published 1969
Frequency: Monthly
Avg pages per issue: 48
Circulation: 46,000
Free

Geist
Published by The Geist Foundation
1014 Homer St, Suite 103, Vancouver, BC V6B 2W9, Canada
Tel: 604-681-9161 *Fax:* 604-669-8250
E-mail: geist@geist.com
Web Site: www.geist.com
Key Personnel
Ed-in-Chief: Stephen Osborne
Canadian ideas & culture. Must have Canadian angle (either content or author residency). No email submissions.
First published 1990
Frequency: Quarterly
Avg pages per issue: 86
Circulation: 7,000
$5.95
ISSN: 1181-6554
Ad Rates: Full page $880

Graphic Arts Monthly
Published by Reed Business Information
Division of Reed Elsevier Inc
2000 Clearwater Dr, Oakbrook, IL 60523
Tel: 630-288-8000; 630-288-8537
Web Site: www.gammag.com
Key Personnel
Publr: Phil Saran
Edit Dir: Roger Ynostroza *Tel:* 646-746-7326
E-mail: ynostroza@reedbusiness.com
Man Ed: Christopher Yeich
For management & production personnel in the commercial printing industry. Features articles on current techniques & equipment, industry meetings, personnel & new products.
First published 1929
Book Use: Reviews
Frequency: Monthly (plus annual Sourcebook)
Avg pages per issue: 140
Circulation: 75,000
$10/issue, $142.99/yr
ISSN: 1047-9325

Graphic Monthly
Published by North Island Publishing
1606 Sedlescomb Dr, Suite 8, Mississauga, ON L4X 1M6, Canada
Tel: 905-625-7070 *Fax:* 905-625-4856
Web Site: www.graphicmonthly.ca
Key Personnel
Ed: Filomena Tamburri
Assoc Publr: Andrew Luke
Graphic, printing info.
First published 1980
Frequency: Bimonthly
Avg pages per issue: 120
Circulation: 10,000
$29.96/yr
ISSN: 0227-2806

Guild of Book Workers Newsletter
Published by Guild of Book Workers Inc
521 Fifth Ave, 17th fl, New York, NY 10175-0003
Tel: 212-292-4444
Web Site: www.palimpsest.stanford.edu
Key Personnel
Ed: Jody Beenk
Sec: Catherine Burkhard *Tel:* 214-363-7946
Articles, calendar of activities related to the book arts.

Frequency: Bimonthly
Avg pages per issue: 15
Circulation: 900
$40/yr

High Volume Printing
Published by The Innes Publishing Co
PO Box 7280, Libertyville, IL 60048
Tel: 847-816-7900 *Fax:* 847-247-8855
E-mail: hvpmag@innespub.com
Web Site: www.innespub.com
Key Personnel
Pres & Publr: Mary Ellin Innes
E-mail: meinnes@innespub.com
Ed: Ray Roth *E-mail:* rayroth@innespub.com
High-tech magazine for graphic arts industry managers; for web & sheetfed press users & printers who employ 20 or more people.
First published 1924
Frequency: Bimonthly
Avg pages per issue: 104
Circulation: 40,921
$89/yr
ISSN: 0737-1020

The Horn Book Guide
Published by Horn Book Inc
56 Roland St, Suite 200, Boston, MA 02129
Tel: 617-628-0225 *Toll Free Tel:* 800-325-1170
Fax: 617-628-0882
E-mail: info@hbook.com
Web Site: www.hbook.com
Key Personnel
Exec Ed: Kitty Flynn
Ed-in-Chief: Roger Sutton
Assoc Publr: Anne Quirk *Tel:* 617-628-0225 ext 228 *E-mail:* aquirk@hbook.com
Designer & Prodn Mgr: Lolly Robinson
E-mail: lrobinson@hbook.com
Reviews nearly every hardcover trade children's & young adult book published in the United States.
First published 1990
Book Use: Subject, series, reissues, new editions, author/illustrator & title indexes
Frequency: Semiannual
Avg pages per issue: 288
Circulation: 5,500
$25/issue, $49/yr
ISSN: 1044-405X
Trim Size: 8 1/2 x 11
Ad Rates: Covers 2 & 3 $1,050/each, Color covers $1,581
Ad Closing Date(s): Feb 1 for Spring issue, Aug 1 for Fall issue

Horn Book Magazine
Published by Horn Book Inc
56 Roland St, Suite 200, Boston, MA 02129
Tel: 617-628-0225 *Toll Free Tel:* 800-325-1170
Fax: 617-628-0882
E-mail: info@hbook.com
Web Site: www.hbook.com
Key Personnel
Ed-in-Chief: Roger Sutton
Exec Ed: Martha Parravano
Sr Ed: Jennifer Brabander
Assoc Publr: Anne Quirk *Tel:* 617-628-0225 ext 228 *E-mail:* aquirk@hbook.com
Ad Circ: Lauren Raece
Designer & Prodn Mgr: Lolly Robinson
E-mail: lrobinson@hbook.com
Children's literature journal featuring reviews, articles, essays, columns, interviews with children's book authors & illustrators, current announcements.
First published 1924
Book Use: Reviews & occasional excerpts
Frequency: Bimonthly
Avg pages per issue: 128
Circulation: 18,000
$48/yr indiv; $58/yr instns

ISSN: 0018-5078
Trim Size: 6 x 9
Ad Rates: Covers 2,3 & 4 $1,876/each, color covers $2,718; full page interior ad $1,484; preferred positions & spec placements add $75/page; classified $2.50/word, 10 word minimum
Ad Closing Date(s): 2 months before pub date

In Plant Graphics
Published by North American Publishing Co
401 N Broad St, Philadelphia, PA 19108
Tel: 215-238-5321 *Fax:* 215-238-5457
Web Site: www.ipgonline.com
Key Personnel
Ed: Bob Neubauer *E-mail:* bobneubauer@napco.com
VP, Circ: Valerie Tickle
Management, printing & reprographic articles.
First published 1941
Frequency: monthly
Avg pages per issue: 60
Circulation: 24,600
$82/yr
ISSN: 1043-1942

In-Plant Printer
Published by Innes Publishing Co
PO Box 7280, Libertyville, IL 60048
Tel: 847-816-7900 *Fax:* 847-247-8855
E-mail: ippmag@innespub.com
Web Site: www.innespub.com
Key Personnel
Pres & Publr: Mary Ellin Innes
E-mail: meinnes@innespub.com
Ed: Jack Klasnic
Case studies, features (how-to's, problem solution, reportage) re: in-plant printing industry.
First published 1960
Book Use: Departmental, paper, environmental, industry news, personnel announcements, products & literature
Frequency: Bimonthly
Avg pages per issue: 75
Circulation: 34,000
$85/yr
ISSN: 0891-8996

Independent Publisher Online
Published by Jenkins Group Inc
400 W Front St, Suite 4-A, Traverse City, MI 49684
Tel: 231-933-0445 *Toll Free Tel:* 800-706-4636
Fax: 231-933-0448
Web Site: www.independentpublisher.com
Key Personnel
CEO: Jerrold R Jenkins *E-mail:* jrj@bookpublishing.com
Pres: James Kalajian *Tel:* 231-933-0445 ext 1006
E-mail: jjk@bookpublishing.com
Independent Publr, Online E-ZINE Man Ed: Jim Barnes *E-mail:* jimb@bookpublishing.com
Book Review Coord: Cory Briggs
E-mail: cbriggs@bookpublishing.com
Article topics relevant to the business of book publishing, including marketing, promotion & distribution.
First published 1983
Book Use: Featured reviews & individual reviews from independently published works of the current year
Frequency: monthly
Avg pages per issue: 80
Circulation: 30,000
Free on-line; monthly sent via e-mail
ISSN: 1098-5735
Avg reviews per issue: 40

Industrial Purchasing Agent
Published by Publications for Industry
Division of Panes Publications Inc
Subsidiary of Publications for Industry
21 Russell Woods Rd, Great Neck, NY 11021

Tel: 516-487-0990 *Fax:* 516-487-0809
Web Site: www.publicationsforindustry.com
Key Personnel
Pres & Publr: Jack S Panes
New product releases.
First published 1946
Frequency: 10/yr
Circulation: 25,000
$25/yr
Ad Rates: $2,087 full page

Information Today

Published by Information Today, Inc
143 Old Marlton Pike, Medford, NJ 08055-8750
Tel: 609-654-6266 *Toll Free Tel:* 800-300-9868
(cust serv) *Fax:* 609-654-4309
E-mail: custserv@infotoday.com
Web Site: www.infotoday.com
For users & producers of digital information ser-
vices.
ISBN Prefix(es): 0-938734; 0-904933; 1-57387;
0-910965
First published 1984
Frequency: 11 issues/yr
Avg pages per issue: 56
Circulation: 10,000
$69.95 USA, $93 Canada & Mexico, $102 out-
side North America

inPRINT

Published by New Jersey Press Association
840 Bear Tavern Rd, Suite 305, West Trenton, NJ
08628-1019
Tel: 609-406-0600 *Fax:* 609-406-0300
E-mail: njpress@njpa.org
Web Site: www.njpa.org
Key Personnel
Commns Mgr: Missy Flynn *Tel:* 609-406-0600
ext 17 *E-mail:* mflynn@njpa.org
News of the NJ newspaper industry.
First published 1990
Book Use: No columns or frequent articles about
books, no book review
Frequency: Monthly
Avg pages per issue: 12
Circulation: 1,500
$12/yr
ISSN: 1067-5132

International Journal of Instructional Media (IJIM)

Published by Westwood Press Inc
Subsidiary of CAL Industries
118 Five Mile River Rd, Darien, CT 06820
Tel: 203-656-8680
Web Site: www.adprima.com/ijim.htm
Key Personnel
Exec Ed: Dr Phillip J Sleeman *Tel:* 860-875-5484
E-mail: psleeman@aol.com
Articles about programs in computer technology;
computer mediated communications including
the Internet; distance education, including the
Internet, ITV, video & audio conferencing; in-
structional media & technology; telecommuni-
cations; interactive video, videodisc & software
applications; instructional media management;
instructional development & systems; media
research & evaluation; media research & communications.
First published 1970
Book Use: Media reviews
Frequency: Quarterly
Avg pages per issue: 110
Circulation: 1,325
$186/yr domestic (plus $10 shipping), $196/yr
foreign (plus $20 shipping) for Vol 30, Nos
1-4, 2004-2005
ISSN: 0092-1815

IPA Bulletin

Published by IPA, The Association of Graphic
Solutions Providers

552 W 167 St, South Holland, IL 60473
Tel: 708-596-5110 *Fax:* 708-596-5112
Web Site: www.ipa.org
Key Personnel
Ed: Bessie Halfacre *E-mail:* bessie@ipa.org
Management & technical information relating to
graphic communication prepress & professional
imaging segment of the graphic arts from cre-
ative & digital photography through digital &
traditional printing.
First published 1911
Book Use: Reviews & excerpts
Frequency: Bimonthly
Avg pages per issue: 64
Circulation: 1,700
$20/yr US, $25/yr foreign
ISSN: 8750-2224
Trim Size: 8.25 x 10.75

Joke Writers Guild Newsletter

Published by Robert Makinson
542 Atlantic Ave, Brooklyn, NY 11217
Mailing Address: PO Box 605, Times Plaza Sta,
Brooklyn, NY 11217-0605
Tel: 718-855-3351
Web Site: www.angelfire.com/biz7/rbmakinson/
index.html
Key Personnel
Founder, Publr & Ed: Robert B Makinson
E-mail: makinsonrobert@hotmail.com
Marketing material; survey of the field; applica-
tion free with SASE.
First published 1989
Frequency: Semiannual
Avg pages per issue: 6
$5/issue, $10/yr

Journal of Marketing

Published by American Marketing Association
311 S Wacker Dr, Suite 5800, Chicago, IL
60606-2266
Tel: 312-542-9000 *Toll Free Tel:* 800-262-1150
Fax: 312-542-9001
E-mail: info@ama.org
Web Site: www.marketingpower.com
Key Personnel
Man Ed: Francesca Van Corp Cooley
Ed: Ruth Bolton
Pubns Prodn Mgr: Sally Schmitz
A scholarly journal that bridges the gap between
marketing theory & application by covering
applied research studies.
ISBN Prefix(es): 0-87757
First published 1936
Book Use: Some reviews & excerpts
Frequency: Quarterly
Avg pages per issue: 125
Circulation: 8,200
$20/issue, $80/yr indiv, $200/yr corp & instns,
$45/yr membership
ISSN: 0022-2429

Journal of Marketing Research

Published by American Marketing Association
311 S Wacker Dr, Suite 5800, Chicago, IL
60606-2266
Tel: 312-542-9000 *Toll Free Tel:* 800-262-1150
Fax: 312-542-9001
E-mail: info@ama.org
Web Site: www.marketingpower.com
Key Personnel
Man Ed: Francesca Van Corp Cooley
Ed: Dick Wittink
Pubns Prodn Mgr: Sally Schmitz
Scholarly journal for the technically oriented pro-
fessional researcher or academician.
ISBN Prefix(es): 0-87757
First published 1963
Book Use: Some reviews
Frequency: Quarterly
Avg pages per issue: 80
Circulation: 6,800

$20/issue, $80/yr indiv, $200/yr corp & instns,
$45/yr membership
ISSN: 0022-2437

Journal of Scholarly Publishing

Division of University of Toronto Press Inc
5201 Dufferin St, North York, ON M3H 5T8,
Canada
Tel: 416-667-7810 *Toll Free Tel:* 800-221-9985
Fax: 416-667-7881
E-mail: journals@utpress.utoronto.ca
Web Site: www.utpjournals.com
Key Personnel
Ed: Tom Radko
VP, Journals, Univ of Toronto Press: Anne Marie
Corrigan
Mktg Coord: Audrey Greenwood *Tel:* 416-667-
7766
Articles on the writing, publication & use of se-
rious nonfiction addressed to scholars, authors,
publishers, reviewers, editors & librarians.
First published 1969
Book Use: Reviews of books relating to publish-
ing
Frequency: Quarterly
Avg pages per issue: 64
Circulation: 800
$80/yr, $20/yr students, $30/yr personal
ISSN: 0036-634X
Trim Size: 6 x 9
Ad Rates: Full page, $295; 1/2 pg $200; Inside
Back Cover $350

Journal of the Medical Library Association

Published by Medical Library Association (MLA)
65 E Wacker Place, Suite 1900, Chicago, IL
60601-7298
Tel: 312-419-9094 *Fax:* 312-419-8950
E-mail: info@mlahq.org
Web Site: www.mlanet.org/publications/jmla/
index.html
Key Personnel
Ed: T Scott Plutchak
Dir, Pubns: Lynanne Feilen *Tel:* 312-419-9094 ext
23 *E-mail:* mlacom1@mlahq.org
Assoc Ed: Nancy Clemmons
Book Review Ed: Janet M Coggan
The quarterly JMLA is the premier scholarly
journal for health information science pro-
fessionals. It contains research & articles on
health science librarianship, including operating
medical libraries.
First published 1911
Book Use: Book reviews & electronic resources
reviews
Frequency: Quarterly
Avg pages per issue: 100
Circulation: 5,000
$42.50/issue, $136/yr US, Canada & Mexico,
$174/yr foreign
ISSN: 1536-5050
Ad Rates: 4-C, full pg (1x), $2449; B&W, full pg
(1x), $1390

JQ: Journalism & Mass Communication Quarterly

Published by Association for Education in Jour-
nalism & Mass Communications
234 Outlet Pointe Blvd, Suite A, Columbia, SC
29210-5667
Tel: 803-798-0271 *Fax:* 803-772-3509
E-mail: aejmcmemsub@aol.com
Web Site: www.aejmc.org
Key Personnel
Ed: Dan Riffe
Subn Mgr: Pamella Price *Tel:* 803-772-3507
Research in journalism & mass communication.
First published 1924
Frequency: Quarterly
Avg pages per issue: 1,000
Circulation: 5,000

$70/yr US indiv, $120/yr US inst, $140/yr intl
inst, $30/issue, $75 air mail surcharge, $80/yr
intl indiv
ISSN: 1077-6990

The Kenyon Review
Subsidiary of Kenyon College
Kenyon College, 104 College Dr, Gambier, OH
43022-2693
Tel: 740-427-5208 *Fax:* 740-427-5417
E-mail: mail@kenyonreview.org
Web Site: www.kenyonreview.org
Key Personnel
Ed: David Lynn
Man Ed: Meg Galipault *Tel:* 740-427-5202
E-mail: galipaultm@kenyon.edu
Fiction, poetry, essays, book reviews, drama. See
website for details.
First published 1939
Book Use: Reviews of 12 books
Frequency: 4 issues/yr
Avg pages per issue: 185
Circulation: 6,000
$30/yr, $50/2 yrs, single copies $10
ISSN: 0163-075X
Trim Size: 7 x 10
Ad Rates: $375 for full page
Ad Closing Date(s): Oct 10, Jan 10, April 10,
July 10

Knowledge Quest
Published by American Association of School
Librarians
Division of American Library Association
50 E Huron St, Chicago, IL 60611
Tel: 312-280-4386 *Toll Free Tel:* 800-545-2433
Fax: 312-664-7459
E-mail: aasl@ala.org
Web Site: www.ala.org/aasl
Key Personnel
Ed: Debbie Abilock
Man Ed: Steven Hofmann
Devoted to offering substantive information to as-
sist in building-level library media specialists,
supervisors, library educators & other deci-
sion makers concerned with the development
of school library media programs & services.
Articles address the integration of theory &
practice in school librarianship & new develop-
ments in education, learning theory & relevant
disciplines.
First published 1997
Frequency: 5 times/yr
Avg pages per issue: 56
Circulation: 10,000
$12/issue, $40/yr US non-members, $50/yr for-
eign
ISSN: 1094-9046

Law Books in Print Online
Published by Glanville Publishers Inc
Affiliate of Oceana Publications Inc
75 Main St, Dobbs Ferry, NY 10522-1601
Tel: 914-693-8100 *Toll Free Tel:* 800-831-0758
Fax: 914-693-0402
E-mail: glanville@oceanalaw.com
Web Site: www.oceanalaw.com
Key Personnel
Pres: Fay Cohen
Ed: Merle Slyhoff
Edit Asst: Alden W Domizio *Tel:* 914-693-8100
ext 325 *E-mail:* adomizio@oceanalaw.com
Provides bibliographic information on English-
language law & peripheral books & other
formats which are in-print from publishers
throughout the world. Provides listings by Author, Title, Subject, Publisher Title List, Series
Title List. *Law Books Published* (print only,
supplement) two issues/yr, with cumulation for
that year in second issue. Bibliographic information is supplied on forms provided by the
publisher.

ISBN Prefix(es): 0-87802
Frequency: Semi-annual (Law Books Published)
Circulation: 250 (Law Books Published)
'Law Books Published': $160/yr paper; 'Law
Books in Print', Online $195/yr
ISSN: 0023-9240 (Law Books Published)
Trim Size: 8 1/2 x 11 (Law Books Published)

Library Journal
Published by Reed Business Information
Division of Reed Elsevier Inc
360 Park Ave S, New York, NY 10016
Tel: 646-746-6819 *Fax:* 646-746-6734
E-mail: ljinfo@reedbusiness.com
Web Site: www.libraryjournal.com
Key Personnel
VP & Group Publr: Joe Tessitore
Ed-in-Chief: John N Berry, III
Man Ed: Bette Lee Fox
Adv Sales Dir & Assoc Publr: Ron Shank
Circ Dir, NY Div: Robert W De Angelis
Classified Adv Mgr: Joseph Murray
Art Dir: Kevin Henegan
Sr Ed, News: Norman Oder
Ed, Book Review: Barbara Hoffert
Book Review Asst: Tania Barnes
Ed: Francine Fialkoff
Asst to the Dir: Ann Kim
Reviews are written & edited specifically to as-
sess the value of a book for the library col-
lection. Also, review videocassettes, audiocas-
settes, magazines, databases, websites & CD-
ROMs.
First published 1876
Book Use: Reviews, news
Frequency: Semimonthly (exc monthly Jan, July,
Aug & Dec)
Avg pages per issue: 150
Circulation: 25,000
$8.50/issue, $141/yr US, $163/yr Canada & Mex-
ico, $221/yr foreign
ISSN: 0363-0277

**Library Media Connection: The Magazine for
School Library Media & Technology
Specialists**
Published by Linworth Publishing Inc
480 E Wilson Bridge Rd, Suite L, Worthington,
OH 43085-2372
Tel: 614-436-7107 *Toll Free Tel:* 800-786-5017
Fax: 614-436-9490
E-mail: linworth@linworthpublishing.com
Web Site: www.linworth.com
Key Personnel
Pres & Publr: Marlene Woo-Lun
Man Ed: Wendy Medvetz
Ed: Carol Simpson
K-12 school librarians & educators. See website
for information regarding ad rates & ad closing
dates.
ISBN Prefix(es): 0-938865; 1-58683
First published 1982
Book Use: Reviews; articles written by school
librarians
Frequency: 7 issues/school yr
Avg pages per issue: 96
Circulation: 20,000
$69/yr
ISSN: 0731-4388

The Library Quarterly
Published by The University of Chicago Press
Division of Graduate School of Education & In-
formation Studies at UCLA
Florida State University, School of Informa-
tion Studies, 101 Shores Bldg, Tallahasee, FL
32306-2100
Tel: 850-644-8118 *Fax:* 310-267-0333
E-mail: lq@lis.fsu.edu
Web Site: www.journals.uchicago.edu

Key Personnel
Ed: John V Richardson, Jr *E-mail:* jrichard@ucla.
edu
Library & information science & related subjects.
First published 1931
Book Use: Reviews
Frequency: Quarterly
Avg pages per issue: 180
Circulation: 2,000
$27/instns or $13.25/indiv, $92/yr instns; $6.50/is-
sue, $37/yr indiv; $28/yr students
ISSN: 0024-2519

Licensing Letter
Published by EPM Communications
160 Mercer St, 3rd fl, New York, NY 10012
Tel: 212-941-0099 *Fax:* 212-941-1622
Web Site: epmcom.com
Key Personnel
Ed: Marty Brochstein *E-mail:* mbrochstein@
epmcom.com
COO: Riva Bennett
News, statistics, trend analysis for licensing com-
munity.
First published 1977
Frequency: 22 issues/yr
Avg pages per issue: 16
$447
ISSN: 8755-6235

**Locus: The Magazine of the Science Fiction &
Fantasy Field**
Published by Locus Magazine
PO Box 13305, Oakland, CA 94661-0305
Tel: 510-339-9196; 510-339-9198 *Fax:* 510-339-
8144
E-mail: locus@locusmag.com
Web Site: www.locusmag.com
Key Personnel
Publr: Charles N Brown
Edit Dir: Jennifer A Hall
Man Ed: Kirsten Gong-Wong
Includes news, awards, interviews & annual anal-
ysis of the science fiction field, monthly best-
seller list & a complete monthly listing of new
publications. Primarily a trade magazine for
science fiction professionals, booksellers & li-
braries.
First published 1968
Book Use: Reviews
Frequency: Monthly
Avg pages per issue: 84
Circulation: 9,000
$5.95/issue, $52/yr individual, $55/yr libraries
ISSN: 0047-4959
Trim Size: 8 3/8" x 10 7/8"
Ad Rates: $800 B&W full page

Le Maitre Imprimeur
Subsidiary of L'Association des Arts Graphiques
du Quebec Inc
644 Boulevard Cure-Poirier W, Suite 100,
Longueuil, PQ J4J 2H9, Canada
Tel: 450-670-9311 *Fax:* 450-670-8762
Web Site: www.aagq.ca
Key Personnel
Pres: Jules Lizotte
Management, technology, news concerning the
printing industry.
First published 1937
Frequency: Monthly (10/yr), June/July, Dec/Jan
Avg pages per issue: 44
Circulation: 3,800
$36/yr, $66/2 yrs US, $30/yr, $54/2 yrs Canada,
$96/2 yrs foreign
ISSN: 0025-0996

**Marketing Research: A Magazine of
Management & Applications**
Published by American Marketing Association
311 S Wacker Dr, Suite 5800, Chicago, IL
60606-2266

Tel: 312-542-9000 Toll Free Tel: 800-262-1150
  Fax: 312-542-9001
E-mail: info@ama.org
Web Site: www.marketingpower.com
Key Personnel
Man Ed: Mary Egan-Leader
Pubns Prodn Mgr: Sally Schmitz
A practical publication for marketing research.
  Explores methods, techniques, legal issues, eth-
  ical concerns & professional development.
ISBN Prefix(es): 0-87757
First published 1989
Book Use: Book & software reviews in each is-
  sue
Frequency: Quarterly
Avg pages per issue: 48
Circulation: 3,700
$20/single issue, $45/AMA annual members, $70/
  annual indiv, $120/corp & instns
ISSN: 1040-8460

The Masthead
Published by National Conference of Editorial
  Writers
3899 N Front St, Harrisburg, PA 17110
Tel: 717-703-3015 Fax: 717-703-3014
E-mail: ncew@pa-news.org
Web Site: www.ncew.org
Key Personnel
Ed: Frank Partsch
Dir, Membership: Sherid Virnig
All aspects of the work of professional opinion
  writers in all media, from determining editorial
  policy to writing, design & production.
First published 1948
Book Use: Reviews (select)
Frequency: Quarterly
Avg pages per issue: 36
Circulation: 1,000
$8.75/issue, $35/yr
ISSN: 0025-5122

Media & Methods
Published by American Society of Educators
1429 Walnut St, Philadelphia, PA 19102
Tel: 215-563-6005 Toll Free Tel: 800-555-5657
  Fax: 215-587-9706
E-mail: mmedit@mediamethods.com
Web Site: www.media-methods.com
Key Personnel
Publr & Edit Dir: Michele Sokoloff
  E-mail: michelesok@media-methods.com
Man Ed: Christine Weiser E-mail: chris1@media-
  methods.com
Articles feature practical, hands-on applications
  of educational technology in K-12 school dis-
  tricts & libraries. Effective uses of presentation
  equipment & the latest technology resources,
  hardware & software for education today.
First published 1964
Book Use: Contains Book Reviews
Frequency: 7 times/yr
Avg pages per issue: 76
Circulation: 60,000
$33.50/yr, back issues $8
ISSN: 0025-6897

Medical Reference Services Quarterly
Published by The Haworth Press Inc
10 Alice St, Binghamton, NY 13904-1580
Tel: 607-722-5857 Toll Free Tel: 800-429-6784
  Fax: 607-722-1424
E-mail: getinfo@haworthpress.com
Web Site: www.haworthpressinc.com
Key Personnel
Prodn Mgr, Journal Div: Zella Ondrey Tel: 570-
  459-5933 ext 302 Fax: 570-459-5934
  E-mail: zondrey@haworthpressinc.com
Working tool journal for medical & health sci-
  ences librarians. Regularly publishes practice-
  oriented articles relating to medical reference

services with an emphasis on online search ser-
  vices.
ISBN Prefix(es): 0-86656; 0-917724; 0-918393;
  1-56022; 1-56023; 1-56024; 0-7890
First published 1982
Book Use: Reviews
Frequency: Quarterly
Avg pages per issue: 108
Circulation: 896
$60/yr, $275 libs & instns
ISSN: 0276-3869

Mergers & Acquisitions
Published by Thomson Media
Center Sq, East Tower, 1500 Market St, 12th fl,
  Philadelphia, PA 19102
Tel: 215-246-3464 Toll Free Tel: 800-455-5844
  (circ & cust serv) Fax: 215-665-5763
Web Site: majournal.nvst.com
Key Personnel
Ed: Martin Sikora E-mail: martin.sikora@tfn.com
Man Ed: Joan Harrison
Professional journal; covers the latest trends &
  influences impacting the buying & selling of
  businesses. Articles cover how to make money,
  save money & avoid disaster in the constantly
  changing merger & acquisition environment.
First published 1965
Frequency: Monthly
Avg pages per issue: 100
Circulation: 3,000
$550/yr
ISSN: 0026-0010

MLA News
Published by Medical Library Association (MLA)
65 E Wacker Place, Suite 1900, Chicago, IL
  60601-7298
Tel: 312-419-9094 Fax: 312-419-8950
E-mail: info@mlahq.org
Web Site: www.mlanet.org/publications/mlanews/
Key Personnel
Dir, Pubns: Lynanne Feilen Tel: 312-419-9094 ext
  23 E-mail: mlacom1@mlahq.org
MLA News covers topics about the association,
  the industry, legislation & international events.
  Regular features include updates & reviews of
  new information technology, Internet resources,
  classified job ads & educational courses.
First published 1961
Frequency: 10 times/yr
Avg pages per issue: 24
Circulation: 5,000
$48.50/yr US, Canada & Mexico, $61.50/yr for-
  eign
ISSN: 0541-5489
Trim Size: 8.5x11.875
Ad Rates: 4-C, full pg (1x), $2931; B&W, full
  page(1x), $1873
Ad Closing Date(s): One month before publica-
  tion date

**MLQ (Modern Language Quarterly): A
  Journal of Literary History**
Published by Duke University Press
Dept of English, Univ of Washington, Box
  354330, Seattle, WA 98195
Tel: 206-543-6827 Fax: 206-685-2673
E-mail: mlq@u.washington.edu
Web Site: www.mlq.washington.edu; www.
  dukeupress.edu
Key Personnel
Ed: Marshall Brown
Scholarly articles on literary history.
ISBN Prefix(es): 0-8223
First published 1940
Book Use: Reviews
Frequency: 4-5 per issue
Avg pages per issue: 130
Circulation: 2,000

$136 instn; $122 e-only instn; $35 individuals;
  $18 students. Add $12 postage & 7% GST for
  Canada; $16 postage for outside US & Canada
ISSN: 0026-7929

Network
Published by The International Women's Writing
  Guild (IWWG)
PO Box 810, Gracie Sta, New York, NY 10028-
  0082
Tel: 212-737-7536 Fax: 212-737-9469
E-mail: iwwg@iwwg.org
Web Site: www.iwwg.org
Key Personnel
Ed: Elizabeth Julia Stoumen
  E-mail: elizabethjulia88@aol.com
Founder & Exec Dir: Hannelore Hahn
  E-mail: dirhahn@aol.com
Member News, Regional Clusters, Correspon-
  dence Corner, Letters to Editors, Environmental
  Pop, Special Offerings, Profile of Guild Mem-
  ber, several hundred opportunities for publica-
  tion & submission in every issue.
First published 1978
Frequency: Bimonthly
Avg pages per issue: 32
Circulation: 4,000

New England Printer & Publisher
Published by Printing Industries of New England
5 Crystal Pond Rd, Southborough, MA 01772-
  1758
Tel: 508-804-4170 Fax: 508-804-4119
Web Site: www.pine.org
Key Personnel
Ed: John Scibelli
Trade magazine for printing & graphic commu-
  nication companies in New England & upstate
  New York.
First published 1938
Book Use: Book reviews & excerpts
Frequency: Monthly
Avg pages per issue: 56
Circulation: 4,000
$4/issue, $20/yr
ISSN: 0162-8771
Trim Size: 8 1/2 x 11
Ad Closing Date(s): Tenth of the month preced-
  ing publication

Newspapers & Technology
Published by Conley Magazines LLC
1623 Blake St, Suite 250, Denver, CO 80202-
  1053
Tel: 303-575-9595 Fax: 303-575-9555
E-mail: letters@newsandtech.com
Web Site: www.newsandtech.com
Key Personnel
Publr: Mary Van Meter E-mail: mvanmeter@
  newsandtech.com
Ed-in-Chief: Chuck Moozakis
  E-mail: cmoozakis@newsandtech.com
Ed: Tara McMeekin E-mail: tmcmeekin@
  newsandtech.com
Prodn Mgr: Chere Martin E-mail: cmartin@
  newsandtech.com
Adv Sales Mgr: Michele Romriell
  E-mail: mromriell@newsandtech.com
Monthly trade publication for newspaper pub-
  lishers & department managers involved in ap-
  plying & integrating technology. Written by
  industry experts who provide regular coverage
  of the following departments: prepress, press,
  postpress & new media.
First published 1988
Frequency: Monthly
Avg pages per issue: 32
Circulation: 20,000
Free to qualified personnel
ISSN: 1052-5572

North Carolina Literary Review (NCLR)

East Carolina University, English Dept,
 Greenville, NC 27858-4353
Tel: 252-328-1537 *Fax:* 252-328-4889
Web Site: www.ecu.edu/nclr
Key Personnel
Ed: Margaret Bauer *E-mail:* bauerm@mail.ecu.
 edu
Sr Assoc Ed: Lorraine Robinson
Articles, essays, interviews, fiction/poetry by &
 about North Carolina writers & literature, cul-
 ture & history.
First published 1992
Book Use: Excerpts from forthcoming books;
 essay reviews only - 2 or more books treated
 thematically
Frequency: Annual
Avg pages per issue: 200
Circulation: 350 + bookstore sales
$12/issue, $20/2 issues, $20/ppd from publishers,
 $36/4 issues, $12/ppd back issues
ISSN: 1063-0724
Ad Rates: $200 full page, $125 half page, $75
 quarter page
Ad Closing Date(s): Feb 1

Ohio Writer

Published by Poets' & Writers' League of Greater
 Cleveland
1220 Fairhill Rd, Suite 3A, Cleveland, OH 44120
Tel: 216-421-0403 *Fax:* 216-791-1727
E-mail: pwlgc@yahoo.com
Web Site: www.pwlgc.com
Key Personnel
Exec Dir: Darlene Montonaro
 E-mail: poetsleague@yahoo.com
Ed: Mark Kuhar
Asst Ed: Linda Durnbaugh
Reviews, how-to, profiles, interviews & calendar.
First published 1987
Book Use: Reviews
Frequency: Bimonthly
Avg pages per issue: 16
Circulation: 1,000
$2.50/issue, $15/yr, $20 instns
ISSN: 0896-5730
Ad Rates: $35 2 3/8 x 2/ 3/8; $90 half column 4
 1/2 x 4 1/2; $130 half pg 7 1/2 x 4 1/2; $260
 full pg 7 1/2 x 8 7/8
Ad Closing Date(s): Dec 1, Feb 1, Apr 1, June 1,
 Aug 1, Oct 1

Once Upon A Time

553 Winston Ct, St Paul, MN 55118
Tel: 651-457-6223
Web Site: onceuponatimemag.com
Key Personnel
Ed & Publr: Audrey B Baird
 E-mail: audreyouat@comcast.net
32-page support magazine for writers & illus-
 trators of children's literature. Submit by mail
 with SASE; articles to 900 words, poetry to 30
 lines; all writing or illustrating related.
First published 1990
Book Use: No reviews
Frequency: Quarterly
Avg pages per issue: 32
Circulation: 1,000
$26/yr, $5 sample copy, free 4-page brochure
ISSN: 1071-2526
Ad Rates: $40 quarter page

Paper Clips

Published by Baker & Taylor Inc
2550 W Tyvola Rd, Suite 300, Charlotte, NC
 28217
Mailing Address: PO Box 6885, Bridgewater, NJ
 08807
Tel: 704-998-3100 *Toll Free Tel:* 800-775-1800
 Fax: 704-998-3319
E-mail: btinfo@btol.com
Web Site: www.btol.com

Key Personnel
Prodn Coord: Donna Heffner *Tel:* 908-541-7412
Prepublication announcements of forthcoming
 adult & children's paperbacks & mass market
 trade.
Frequency: Monthly
Avg pages per issue: 48
Circulation: 40,000
Free

Plant Engineering Magazine

Published by Reed Business Information
Division of Reed Elsevier Inc
2000 Clearwater Dr, Oakbrook, IL 60523
Tel: 630-288-8000 *Fax:* 630-288-8781
Web Site: www.plantengineering.com
Key Personnel
Publr: Jim Langhenry
Ed: Richard Dunn
Asst to Publr: Sylvia Lauer
Serves the needs of plant engineers, includes en-
 gineering information on specification, pur-
 chase, design, development, operation, use,
 maintenance & improvement of industrial
 plants, equipment, services, systems & facili-
 ties.
First published 1947
Book Use: Reviews
Frequency: 12 issues/yr
Avg pages per issue: 128
Circulation: 100,041 cont
$10/issue, $131.99/yr, $163.90 Canada, free to
 qualified subscribers
ISSN: 0032-082x

Poetics Today

Published by Duke University Press
Dept of English, Univ of Washington, Box
 354330, Seattle, WA 98195
Tel: 919-687-3636 *Toll Free Tel:* 888-387-5765
 Fax: 919-688-2615
E-mail: subscriptions@dukepress.com
Web Site: www.mlq.washington.edu
Key Personnel
Adv & Sales Coord: Mandy Berman
ISBN Prefix(es): 0-8223
Book Use: Book reviews
Frequency: Quarterly
Avg pages per issue: 200
Circulation: 1,000
$36/yr indiv, $18/yr students (with photocopy of
 ID) $145/yr institutions

Poetry

Published by The Poetry Foundation
1030 N Clark St, Suite 420, Chicago, IL 60610
Tel: 312-787-7070 *Fax:* 312-787-6650
E-mail: poetry@poetrymagazine.org
Web Site: www.poetrymagazine.org
Key Personnel
Ed: Christian Wiman
Busn Mgr: Helen Lothrop Klaviter
 E-mail: hklaviter@poetrymagazine.org
Poetry, essays & book reviews. Complete
 submission guidelines can be found at
 www.poetrymagazine.org.
First published 1912
Frequency: Monthly
Avg pages per issue: 64
Circulation: 12,000
US $3.75/issue, $35/yr indiv, $38/yr instns, for-
 eign: $46/yr indiv, $49/yr instns
ISSN: 0032-2032
Trim Size: 5 1/2 x 9
Ad Rates: Full page, $387; 1/2 pg, $238; 1/4 pg
 $160
Ad Closing Date(s): 30th of the 4th month before
 issue date

Poets & Writers Magazine

Published by Poets & Writers Inc
Division of Poet & Writers Inc

72 Spring St, Suite 301, New York, NY 10012
Tel: 212-226-3586 *Fax:* 212-226-3963
E-mail: editor@pw.org
Web Site: www.pw.org
Key Personnel
Ed: Therese Eiben
Deputy Ed: Mary Gannon
News for & about the contemporary literary com-
 munity in the US. Pertinent articles, grants &
 awards, publishing opportunities, essays, inter-
 views with writers.
First published 1973
Book Use: First serial, excerpts, author interviews
Frequency: Bimonthly
Avg pages per issue: 132
Circulation: 60,000
$4.95/issue, $19.95/yr
ISSN: 0891-6136

Press

Published by Pennsylvania Newspaper Associa-
 tion
3899 N Front St, Harrisburg, PA 17110
Tel: 717-703-3000 *Fax:* 717-703-3001
Web Site: www.pa-newspaper.org
Key Personnel
Publr: Timothy M Williams
Publns Dir: Eric Wise *Tel:* 717-703-3071
 E-mail: ericw@pa-news.org
Quarterly publication covering the newspaper in-
 dustry in Pennsylvania.
First published 1929
Frequency: quarterly
Avg pages per issue: 32
Circulation: 3,000
$22/yr
ISSN: 0030-8196
Ad Closing Date(s): Tenth of each month prior to
 publication

Print: America's Graphic Design Magazine

Published by R C Publications Inc
38 E 29 St, 3rd fl, New York, NY 10016
Tel: 212-447-1430 *Fax:* 212-447-5231
Web Site: www.printmag.com
Key Personnel
Ed: Martin Fox
Adv Dir: Elayne Recupero
Art Dir: Steven Brower
Graphic design & visual communication for the
 creators of this material.
First published 1940
Book Use: Reviews
Frequency: Bimonthly
Avg pages per issue: 160
Circulation: 50,000
$55/yr
ISSN: 0032-8510

Print & Graphics

Published by Spencer Cygnus Regional Print Net-
 work LLC
445 Broadhollow Rd, Suite 21, Melville, NY
 11747
Tel: 631-845-2700 *Fax:* 631-845-5774
E-mail: info@printandgraphicsmag.com
Web Site: www.printandgraphicsmag.com
Key Personnel
Pres & Publr: Jan Levesque
Ed-in-Chief: David Lindsay, Jr
Print & Graphics is part of a national network
 of four distinct regional trade journals deliv-
 ered to top executives of printing, prepress
 & binding/finishing businesses in the United
 States. Coverage emphasizes "how to" in pre-
 press, press room, post press, sales, marketing
 & management. Circulation is: Northeast: Print
 & Graphics, 17,420; Midwest: Printing Views,
 16,216; South: Southern Graphics, 13,816;
 West: Printing Journal, 12,613. Total circulation is 60,065.
First published 1980

Frequency: Monthly
Avg pages per issue: 60
Circulation: 17,420
$39
ISSN: 0273-9550
Trim Size: 10 3/4 x 13 1/2
Ad Rates: Tab Page (one time), B&W $2,205;
half page, $1,542; third page, $1542; quarter
page, $926; eighth page $463
Ad Closing Date(s): Friday, two months before
publication date

Print Media Magazine
Published by North American Publishing Co
401 N Broad St, Philadelphia, PA 19108
Tel: 215-238-5300 *Fax:* 215-238-5273
Web Site: www.printmediamag.com
Key Personnel
Man Ed: Warren Chiara *E-mail:* wchiara@napco.
com
For buyers of printing, prepress, paper & pub-
lishing systems for magazines, catalogs, books,
agency & corporate communications.
First published 1987
Frequency: Monthly
Avg pages per issue: 78
Circulation: 30,000
Free qualified/controlled circulation
ISSN: 1048-3055
Trim Size: Standard

Printing Journal
Published by Spencer Cygnus Regional Print Network LLC
445 Broadhollow Rd, Suite 21, Melville, NY
11747
Tel: 631-845-2700 *Fax:* 631-845-5774
E-mail: info@printandgraphicsmag.com
Web Site: www.printandgraphicsmag.com
Key Personnel
Pres & Publr: Jan Levesque
Ed-in-Chief: David Lindsay, Jr
Part of a national network of four distinct re-
gional trade journals delivered to top executives
of printing, prepress & binding/finishing busi-
ness in the US. Coverage emphasizes "how-to"
in prepress, press room, post press, sales, mar-
keting & management.
First published 1974
Frequency: Monthly
Avg pages per issue: 48
Circulation: 12,613
$39
ISSN: 0191-8273
Trim Size: 10 3/4 x 13 1/2

PRISM international
Published by University of British Columbia
Creative Writing Program UBC, Main Mall, Buch
E462, Vancouver, BC V6T 1Z1, Canada
Tel: 604-822-2514 *Fax:* 604-822-3616
E-mail: prism@interchange.ubc.ca
Web Site: prism.arts.ubc.ca
Key Personnel
Exec Ed: Brenda Leifso
First published 1959
Frequency: Quarterly
Avg pages per issue: 80
Circulation: 1,200
$7/newstand

Professional Photographer
Published by PPA Publications & Events Inc
229 Peachtree St NE, Suite 2200, Atlanta, GA
30303
Tel: 404-522-8600 *Fax:* 404-614-6406
Web Site: www.ppa.com
Key Personnel
Dir, Pubns: Cameron Bishopp
Illustrated feature articles about photographers,
business & photographic techniques & trends;
for practicing professional photographers (por-

trait, wedding, commercial, illustration, free-
lance, industrial, biomedical & scientific).
First published 1907
Frequency: Monthly
Avg pages per issue: 80
Circulation: 31,000 paid
$27/yr, $43/yr Canada, $63/yr foreign

Publisher's Report
Published by National Association of Independent
Publishers (NAIP)
Affiliate of Florida Publishers Association Inc
PO Box 430, Highland City, FL 33846-0430
Tel: 863-648-4420 *Fax:* 863-647-5951
E-mail: naip@aol.com
Web Site: www.publishersreport.com
Key Personnel
Ed & Publr: Betsy Lampe
Info for indy/small presses on production, mar-
keting, PR, sales, distribution, display events,
educational events, media & books of note.
First published 1984
Book Use: Reviews & excerpts
Frequency: Monthly
Avg pages per issue: 10
Circulation: 500
$40/yr subscription, $75/yr w/NAIP membership,
$100/yr w/NAIP & FPA membership; free sam-
ple issue
ISSN: 0884-3090

Publishers Weekly
Published by Reed Business Information
Division of Reed Elsevier Inc
360 Park Ave S, New York, NY 10016
Tel: 646-746-6400; 646-746-6758 (edit); 646-746-
6549 (adv) *Fax:* 646-746-6977; 212-463-6631
(edit); 646-746-6598 (adv)
E-mail: i.taylor@reedbusiness.com
Web Site: www.publishersweekly.com
Key Personnel
VP & Group Publr: Joe Tessitore
Ed-in-Chief: Nora Rawlinson
Edit Dir: John F Baker
Exec Ed: Daisy Maryles
Exec Ed, Bookselling: John Mutter
Man Ed: Robin Lenz
Sr Man Ed & PW Interviews Ed: Michael Coffey
News Ed: Calvin Reid
Technol, Busn & Fin Ed: Jim Milliot
Book News Ed: Charlotte Abbott
Bookselling Ed: Kevin Howell
Children's Books Sr Ed: Diane Roback
Children's Books Forecasts Ed: Jennifer M
Brown
Assoc Ed, Children's Books: Joy Bean
Religion Ed: Lynn Garrett
Sr Forecasts Ed, Nonfiction: Sarah Gold
Assoc Ed, Nonfiction: Lynn Andriani
Assoc Ed, Mass Mkt & Audio: Brianna Ya-
mashita
Forecasts Ed, Poetry: Michael Scharf
Mysteries, Science Fiction Sr Ed: Peter Cannon
Forecasts Ed-at-Large & Fiction Ed: Jeff Zaleski
Ed, Religion Books: Jana Reiss
Art Dir: Clive Chiu
Classified/Media Servs Mgr: Joseph Murray; Jody
Fenty
Circ Dir, NY Div: Jim Fischer
PW Daily Ed: Karen Holt
PW Daily Ed, News: Stephen Zeitchik
News for the book trade.
First published 1872
Book Use: Reviews, excerpts, news, features &
statistics
Frequency: Weekly
Avg pages per issue: 112
Circulation: 25,302
$8/issue, $12/announcement issue, $225/yr with
subn card, $367/yr foreign
ISSN: 0000-0019

Publishing Poynters
Published by Para Publishing
PO Box 8206-R, Santa Barbara, CA 93118-8206
SAN: 215-8981
Tel: 805-968-7277 *Toll Free Tel:* 800-727-2782
Fax: 805-968-1379
E-mail: orders@parapublishing.com
Web Site: www.parapublishing.com
Key Personnel
Owner & Publr: Dan Poynter
E-mail: danpoynter@parapublishing.com
Book & information marketing news & ideas.
ISBN Prefix(es): 0-915516; 1-56860
First published 1986
Book Use: Review copies on book publishing ac-
cepted
Frequency: Bimonthly
Avg pages per issue: 20
Circulation: 21,500
$9.95/2 yrs; e-mail/free
ISSN: 1530-5694

Publishing Research Quarterly
Published by Transaction Publishers
Division of Transaction Periodicals Consortium
Rutgers University, 35 Berrue Circle, Piscataway,
NJ 08854
Tel: 732-445-2280 *Toll Free Tel:* 888-999-6778
Fax: 732-445-3138
E-mail: trans@transactionpub.com
Web Site: www.transactionpub.com
Key Personnel
Chmn of the Bd & Edit Dir: Irving Louis
Horowitz *E-mail:* ihorowitz@transactionpub.
com
Pres: Mary E Curtis *E-mail:* mcurtis@
transactionpub.com
Ed: Robert E Baensch
Adv: Karen B Ornstein
Covers significant research & analysis on or
about the full range of the publishing envi-
ronment, the distribution & marketing of books
& journals & the social, political, economic &
technological conditions that shape the publish-
ing process, from editorial decision-making to
order processing.
ISBN Prefix(es): 1-56000; 0-87855; 0-88738; 0-
7658; 1-4128
First published 1986
Book Use: Reviews
Frequency: Quarterly
Avg pages per issue: 96
Circulation: 1,000
$68/yr indiv, $192/yr instns
ISSN: 0741-6148
Ad Rates: $300 per page
Ad Closing Date(s): Two months before issue delivery
Editorial Office(s): New York University, Center
for Publishing, c/o Robert E Baensch, 11 West
42 St, Rm 400, New York, NY 10036-8002

Quill & Quire
70 The Esplanade, Suite 210, Toronto, ON M5E
1R2, Canada
Tel: 416-360-0044 *Fax:* 416-955-0794
E-mail: info@quillandquire.com
Web Site: www.quillandquire.com
Key Personnel
Ed: Derek Weiler *E-mail:* dweiler@quillandquire.
com
Publr: Alison Jones
Articles & features on book selling, publishing
& Canadian libraries for writers, booksellers,
publishers & librarians. Includes section, *Books
for Young People*, with news & reviews of chil-
dren's books & authors.
First published 1935
Book Use: Reviews
Frequency: Monthly
Avg pages per issue: 56
Circulation: 7,000

$59.95/yr Canada, $95/yr Canada for foreign subs
ISSN: 0033-6491

Quill & Scroll
Published by Quill and Scroll Society
Univ of Iowa, School of Journalism, Iowa City,
IA 52242
Tel: 319-335-3457; 319-335-3321 *Fax:* 319-335-
3502
E-mail: quill-scroll@uiowa.edu
Web Site: www.uiowa.edu/~quill-sc
Key Personnel
Ed & Publr: Richard P Johns *E-mail:* richard-
johns@uiowa.edu
Circulation Mgr: Judy M Hauge
Scholastic journalism publishing, editing, writing,
design, legal descriptions.
First published 1926
Frequency: Bimonthly during the school year
Avg pages per issue: 24
Circulation: 12,000
$4.50/issue, $15/yr, $27/2 yr
ISSN: 0033-6505

Quill Magazine
Published by Society of Professional Journalists
3909 N Meridian St, Indianapolis, IN 46208
Tel: 317-927-8000 *Fax:* 317-920-4789
E-mail: spj@spjhq.org
Web Site: www.spj.org
Key Personnel
Deputy Exec Dir: Julie Grimes *Tel:* 317-927-8000
ext 216
Examines the issues, changes & trends that influ-
ence the journalism profession.
Book Use: Book reviews
Frequency: 10 times/yr
$39/yr

Radio-TV Interview Report
Published by Bradley Communications Corp
PO Box 1206, Lansdowne, PA 19050-8206
Tel: 610-259-1070 *Toll Free Tel:* 800-989-1400
(ext 408) *Fax:* 610-284-3704
Web Site: www.rtir.com
Key Personnel
Mktg Coord: Nick Summa *E-mail:* nicks@rtir.
com
Publr: Steve Harrison
Lists authors, experts, celebrities, entrepreneurs &
others available for radio & TV appearances.

Reference & Research Book News
Published by Book News Inc
5739 NE Sumner St, Portland, OR 97218
Tel: 503-281-9230 *Fax:* 503-287-4485
E-mail: booknews@booknews.com
Web Site: www.booknews.com
Key Personnel
Ed: Jane Erskine
Publr: Fred Gullette
Quarterly periodical reviewing approximately
18,000 new books per year. Book News li-
censes its database of book reviews & anno-
tations to Internet sites, CD-ROMs & OPAC's.
Current syndication includes: *Books in Print*
& it's various sub-licensees; Baker & Taylor's
Title Source; three online bookstores: Barnes
& Noble, Amazon, Powells, EBSCO; also li-
cense reviews to the Syndetic Solutions OPAC
enrichment program.
Frequency: 4 issues/yr (Feb, May, Aug, Nov)
Circulation: 1,200
$175/yr institutional US & CN, $225/yr institutional foreign (air) delivery, $130/yr individual
US & CN, $180/yr individual foreign
ISSN: 0887-3763

Reference Desk
Published by International Encyclopedia Society
PO Box 519, Baldwin Place, NY 10505-0519
Tel: 914-962-3287
Key Personnel
Ed: George Kurian *E-mail:* gtkurian@aol.com
Articles on reference book publishing; reviews;
quarterly record of reference books; publisher
profiles.
First published 1991
Book Use: Book reviews; Index of publications
Frequency: Quarterly
Avg pages per issue: 32
Circulation: 2,700
$29/yr
ISSN: 1055-4777
Trim Size: 8 1/2 x 11
Ad Rates: Full page, $300; 1/2 pg $175
Ad Closing Date(s): March 30, June 30, Sept 30,
Dec 30

Rosebud
Subsidiary of Rosebud Inc
N3310 Asje Rd, Cambridge, WI 53523
Tel: 608-423-9780 *Fax:* 608-423-9976
E-mail: letters@rsbd.net
Web Site: www.rsbd.net
Key Personnel
Publr: Roderick Clark *E-mail:* jrodclark@
smallbytes.net
Adv Mgr & Assoc Publr: John Lehman *Tel:* 608-
423-9609 *E-mail:* santerra@aol.com
Short story, poetry, articles & interviews.
First published 1993
Book Use: Excerpts
Frequency: Quarterly
Avg pages per issue: 136
Circulation: 8,000
$7.95/issue, $30/yr
ISSN: 1072-1681

RUSQ
Published by Reference & User Services Associa-
tion
Division of American Library Association
50 E Huron St, Chicago, IL 60611
SAN: 201-0062
Tel: 312-280-4395 *Toll Free Tel:* 800-545-2433
(ext 4398) *Fax:* 312-944-8085
Key Personnel
Exec Dir: Cathleen Bourdon
Prodn Mgr: Karen Sheets
Opers Mgr: Bob Hershman
Official journal of Reference & User Services
Association Div (RUSA), American Library
Association; material of interest to reference &
adult service librarians, bibliographers & others
interested in user-oriented library services.
ISBN Prefix(es): 0-8389
First published 1960
Frequency: Quarterly
Avg pages per issue: 160
Circulation: 6,474 paid
$15/issue, $60/yr US, $65/yr Canada, Mexico,
$70/yr foreign
ISSN: 1094-9054

St Louis Journalism Review
470 E Lockwood, Rm 414, St Louis, MO 63119
Tel: 314-968-5905 *Fax:* 314-963-6104
E-mail: review@webster.edu
Web Site: www.stljr.org
Key Personnel
Ed & Publr Emeritus: Charles L Klotzer
Ed: Ed Bishop
Media critic of press & broadcasting particu-
larly of St Louis region, but also nationally.
No taboos.
First published 1970
Book Use: Book review & excerpts
Frequency: 10/yr, (monthly except combined July/
Aug & Dec/Jan)
Avg pages per issue: 24
Circulation: 4,000
$38

ISSN: 0036-2972
Trim Size: 11 x 17
Ad Closing Date(s): 20th of each month

Sales & Marketing Management Magazine
Published by VNU Business Publications
770 Broadway, New York, NY 10003
Tel: 646-654-4500 *Fax:* 646-654-7616
E-mail: smmedit@salesandmarketing.com
Web Site: www.salesandmarketing.com
Key Personnel
Ed-in-Chief: Melinda Ligos
Information on major marketing, sales & manage-
ment trends.
First published 1918
Book Use: Reviews
Frequency: Monthly
Avg pages per issue: 100
Circulation: 60,000
$48/yr, $62/yr Canada
ISSN: 0163-7517

School Library Journal
Published by Reed Business Information
Division of Reed Elsevier Inc
360 Park Ave S, New York, NY 10010
Tel: 646-746-6759 *Fax:* 646-746-6689
Web Site: www.slj.com
Key Personnel
VP & Group Publr: Joe Tessitore
Ed-in-Chief: Evan St Lifer
Adv Sales Dir & Assoc Publr: Ron Shank
News & Feature Ed: Rick Margolis
Man Ed & Multimedia Review Ed: Phyllis L
Mandell
Book Review Ed: Trevelyn E Jones
Technol Ed: Kathy Ishizuka
Articles about library service to children & young
adults; reviews of new books & multimedia
products for children & young adults by school
& public librarians.
First published 1954
Book Use: Reviews
Frequency: 12 issues/yr
Avg pages per issue: 115
Circulation: 38,000
$11/issue newsstand, $124/yr US, $170/yr
Canada, $182/yr foreign
ISSN: 0362-8930

School Selection Guide
Formerly Collection Connection
Published by Baker & Taylor Inc
2550 W Tyvola Rd, Suite 300, Charlotte, NC
28217
Mailing Address: PO Box 6885, Bridgewater, NJ
08807
Tel: 704-998-3100 *Fax:* 704-998-3319
E-mail: btinfo@btol.com
Web Site: www.btol.com
Key Personnel
Prodn Coord: Donna Heffner *Tel:* 908-541-7412
Recommended & high-demand titles for school
libraries; available in print & on the web page.
Book Use: Selection for recommendation
Frequency: Annual
Circulation: 50,000
Free

Science & Technology Libraries
Published by Haworth Press Journals
Division of The Haworth Press Inc
10 Alice St, Binghamton, NY 13904-1580
Tel: 607-722-5857 *Toll Free Tel:* 800-429-6784
Fax: 607-722-8465
E-mail: getinfo@haworth.com
Web Site: www.haworthpressinc.com
Key Personnel
Prodn Mgr, Journal Div: Zella Ondrey
Tel: 570-459-5933 ext 302 *E-mail:* zondrey@
haworthpressinc.com
Ed: Julie Hurd

Topics relevant to management, operations, collections, services & staffing of specialized libraries in science & technology fields.
First published 1980
Book Use: Reviews
Frequency: Quarterly
Avg pages per issue: 125
Circulation: 691
$60/yr, $275/yr instns & libs
ISSN: 0194-262X

Science Fiction Chronicle, see Chronicle: SF, Fantasy & Horror's Monthly Trade Journal

SciTech Book News
Published by Book News Inc
Affiliate of Reference & Research Book News
5739 NE Sumner St, Portland, OR 97218
Tel: 503-281-9230 *Fax:* 503-287-4485
E-mail: booknews@booknews.com
Web Site: www.booknews.com
Key Personnel
Publr: Fred Gullette
Ed: Jane Erskine
This quarterly periodical presents concise, speedy reviews of new books in the physical & biological sciences, mathematics, engineering, technology, medicine & agriculture. Over 2000 books are reviewed in each issue. Reviews are currently syndicated to: *Books in Print* & its myriad sub-licensees; Baker & Taylor's *Title Source*; three online bookstores: Barnes & Noble, Amazon & Powells; & Syndetic OPAC enrichment program; other contracts are pending.
First published 1976
Frequency: 4 issues/yr (March, June, Sept, Dec
Avg pages per issue: 200
Circulation: 1,200
$175/yr institutional US & CN, $225/yr institutional foreign (air) delivery, $130/yr individual US & CN, $180/yr individual foreign
ISSN: 0196-6006

Second Impressions Magazine
Division of 344401 Alberta Inc
35 Mill Dr, St Albert, AB T8N 1J5, Canada
Tel: 780-458-9889 *Fax:* 780-458-9839
E-mail: secimp@telusplanet.net
Key Personnel
Contact: Loretta Puckrin
First published 1985
Frequency: Bimonthly
ISSN: 0834-9304

The Serials Librarian
Published by Haworth Press Journals
Division of The Haworth Press Inc
10 Alice St, Binghamton, NY 13904-1580
Tel: 607-722-5857 *Toll Free Tel:* 800-429-6784
Fax: 607-722-1424
E-mail: getinfo@haworth.com
Web Site: www.haworthpressinc.com
Key Personnel
Prodn Mgr, Journal Div: Zella Ondrey
Tel: 570-459-5933 ext 302 *E-mail:* zondrey@ haworthpressinc.com
Ed: Jim Cole
Serials librarianship in academic, public, medical, law & other special libraries.
First published 1976
Book Use: Reviews
Frequency: Quarterly
Avg pages per issue: 209
Circulation: 1,129
$60/yr, $290/yr instns & libs
ISSN: 0361-526X

The Small Press Book Review
Division of Greenfield Press
PO Box 176, Southport, CT 06890-0176

Tel: 203-332-7629 *Fax:* 203-332-7629
E-mail: henryberry@aol.com
Key Personnel
Publr & Ed: Henry Berry *E-mail:* henryberry@ aol.com
Book reviews for online users. Not copywrited, so can be downloaded by anyone. Finished books only; no galleys. Books in all categories, including university press books. Reviews of selected books appear 2-4 months after submission.
First published 1985
Book Use: Book reviews
Frequency: Quarterly
Avg pages per issue: 24
Circulation: Internet & America Online users
Free to online users
ISSN: 8756-7202

Small Press Review/Small Magazine Review
Published by Dustbooks
PO Box 100, Paradise, CA 95967-0100
Tel: 530-877-6110 *Toll Free Tel:* 800-477-6110
Fax: 530-877-0222
E-mail: publisher@dustbooks.com
Web Site: www.dustbooks.com
Key Personnel
Ed & Publr: Len Fulton
Reviews, editorial opinion, lists of new publishers.
ISBN Prefix(es): 0-913218; 0-916685
First published 1966
Book Use: Reviews of books & magazines published by small, independent presses
Frequency: Bimonthly
Avg pages per issue: 32
Circulation: 3,500
$31/yr
ISSN: 0037-7228

Solander
Published by Historical Novel Society
5239 N Commerce Ave, Moorpark, CA 93066
Mailing Address: 409 Colony Woods Dr, Chapel Hill, NC 27517
Tel: 217-581-7538 *Fax:* 217-581-7534
Web Site: www.historicalnovelsociety.org
Key Personnel
Editor: James Hawking *E-mail:* hawking@nc.rr. com
Publr: Richard Lee
US Membership Sec: Debra Tash *E-mail:* debra. tash@historicalnovelsociety.org
Literary magazine for historical fiction; articles, interviews & short fiction.
First published 1997
Frequency: Semiannual
Avg pages per issue: 38
Circulation: 900
$38 airmail; $30 surface
ISSN: 1471-7484

Speakeasy Magazine
Published by The Loft Literary Center
Open Book, Suite 200, 1011 Washington Ave S, Minneapolis, MN 55415
Tel: 612-215-2575 *Fax:* 612-215-2576
E-mail: loft@loft.org
Web Site: www.loft.org
Key Personnel
Ed: Bart Schneider
Theme-based essays poetry, fiction, book reviews.
First published 2002
Book Use: Reviews of literary poetry, fiction & nonfiction
Frequency: Quarterly
Avg pages per issue: 40
$5.95/issue, $24/yr in US, $35/yr Canada, $50 all other foreign subscriptions in US currency by credit card only
ISSN: 1540-9422
Trim Size: 7 7/8 x 10 1/2

Stony Hills: News & Reviews of the Small Press
Published by Stony Hills Productions
3 Saltmarsh, New Sharon, ME 04955
Tel: 207-778-4699
Key Personnel
Ed: Diane Kruchkow
Reviews & information about small press publishing.
First published 1977
Book Use: Reviews, interviews, commentary
Frequency: Quarterly
Avg pages per issue: 12
Circulation: 5,000
$15/4 issues of Stony Hills (tabloid) & 4 issues of Small Press News (newsletter)
ISSN: 0146-2067

Subtext
Published by Open Book Publishing Inc
90 Holmes Ave, Darien, CT 06820
Mailing Address: PO Box 2228, Darien, CT 06820
Tel: 203-316-8008 *Fax:* 203-975-8469
Web Site: www.subtext.net
Key Personnel
Owner & Publr: Stephanie Oda *E-mail:* odasan@ aol.com; Glenn Sanislo
News & analysis on the book publishing & selling business, domestic & international.
First published 1995
Frequency: Biweekly
Avg pages per issue: 12
$449/yr

Verse
Dept of English, University of Georgia, Athens, GA 30602
Fax: 706-542-1261
E-mail: verse@versemag.org
Web Site: www.versemag.org
Key Personnel
Ed: Brian Henry
Poetry, interviews, book reviews, primarily by American, UK & Australian poets. Some poetry in translation; special features (ie: the prose poem; younger Slovene poets; Scottish, Latino, & Australian poetry; Women Irish poets.
First published 1985
Book Use: Reviews
Frequency: 3 issues/yr
Avg pages per issue: 250
Circulation: 1,000
$8/issue, $18/yr indiv, $36/yr lib
ISSN: 0268-3830
Trim Size: 6x9
Ad Rates: $150/pg

The Wordsworth Circle
Published by New York University, Dept of English
19 University Place, New York, NY 10003
Tel: 212-998-8800 *Fax:* 212-995-4019
Key Personnel
Ed: Marilyn Gaull *Tel:* 212-998-8812
E-mail: mg49@nyu.edu
Peer reviewed essays on all areas of British Romanticism.
First published 1970
Frequency: Quarterly
Avg pages per issue: 64
Circulation: 2,200
$25
ISSN: 0043-8006

The World & I
Published by The World & I (magazine)
Subsidiary of News World Communications
3600 New York Ave NE, Washington, DC 20002-1947

Tel: 202-636-3334 *Toll Free Tel:* 866-211-6040
  Fax: 202-832-5780
E-mail: education@worldandi.com
Web Site: www.worldandi.com
Key Personnel
Busn Dir: Charles Kim
Educ Outreach Coord: Burt Leavitt
Each issue contains 40 articles under these sections: current issues, the arts, life, natural science, book world, currents in modern thought & culture.
Frequency: Monthly
Avg pages per issue: 350
$36/yr individual
ISSN: 0887-9346

World Literature Today
Published by University of Oklahoma
630 Parrington Oval, Suite 110, Norman, OK 73019-4033
Tel: 405-325-4531 *Fax:* 405-325-7495
Web Site: www.ou.edu/worldlit
Key Personnel
Executive Dir: Robert Con Davis-Undiano
First published 1927
Frequency: Quarterly
Avg pages per issue: 160
Circulation: 3,000
$5.50/issue, $20/yr indiv, $36/yr Canada, $44/yr international; $98 yr/institutions, $114/yr institutions Canada, $122/yr international

The Writer
Published by Kalmbach Publishing Co
Division of The Writer Inc
21027 Crossroads Circle, Waukesha, WI 53187
Tel: 262-796-8776 *Toll Free Tel:* 800-533-6644
  Fax: 262-796-1615 (sales & cust serv)
E-mail: editor@writermag.com
Web Site: www.writermag.com
Key Personnel
Ed: Elfrieda Abbe
Man Ed: Jeff Reich
Sr Ed: Ronald Kovach
Instructional articles on freelance writing, plus markets for ms sales. See guidelines on web site.
ISBN Prefix(es): 0-89024; 0-913135; 0-89778; 0-933168
First published 1887
Book Use: Occasional reviews
Frequency: Monthly
Avg pages per issue: 68
Circulation: 50,000

$4.95/issue, $29/yr, $4.95/sample or back issue
ISSN: 0043-9517

Writer's Digest
Published by F+W Publications Inc
4700 E Galbraith Rd, Cincinnati, OH 45236
Tel: 513-531-2690 *Fax:* 513-891-7183
Web Site: www.writersdigest.com
Key Personnel
Publr: Colleen Cannon
Ed: Kristin Godsey
Circ Mgr: Lynn Kruetzkamp *Tel:* 513-531-2690 ext 1334 *E-mail:* lynn.kruetzkamp@fwpubs.com
Circ Dir: David Hoguet
How-to instruction, market information & inspiration for freelance writers.
First published 1920
Book Use: Reviews, excerpts, profiles of authors, tips & techniques
Frequency: Monthly
Avg pages per issue: 80
Circulation: 150,000
$4.99/issue, $36/yr
ISSN: 0043-9525
Trim Size: 7 3/4 x 10 3/4

Writers' Journal
Published by Val-Tech Media
PO Box 394, Perham, MN 56573
Tel: 218-346-7921 *Fax:* 218-346-7924
E-mail: writersjournal@lakesplus.com
Web Site: www.writersjournal.com
Key Personnel
Partner & Publr: John Ogroske
Partner & Ed: Leon Ogroske
Read by thousands of aspiring writers whose love of writing has taken them to the next step: writing for money. We are an instructional manual giving writers the tools & info necessary to get their work published. Also prints works by authors who have won our writing contests. Accepts freelance article submissions concerning the art & skill of writing & how to sell what writers write.
First published 1980
Frequency: Bimonthly
Avg pages per issue: 64
Circulation: 25,000
$4.99/issue, $19.97/yr
ISSN: 0891-8759
Ad Rates: B& W (1x) $930 full page; $512 1/2 pg; $282 1/4 pg; $155 1/8 pg; Covers 2&3 full page $1032; 1/2 pg $568; Cover 4, $1135; Color rates add 50% to B&W rates

Writer's Northwest
Published by Media Weavers
PO Box 86190, Portland, OR 97286-0190
Tel: 503-771-0428 *Fax:* 503-771-5166
Web Site: www.mediaweavers.com
Key Personnel
Ed: Joleen Colombo
Publr: Marlene Howard
Articles on writing/publishing, markets, book reviews.
First published 1986
Book Use: Lists new releases from Northwest authors or books from NW presses; book reviews of same
Frequency: Quarterly
Avg pages per issue: 16
Circulation: 10,000
$10/yr; $12/yr Canada
ISSN: 0895-898X

Writer's Yearbook
Published by F+W Publications Inc
4700 E Galbraith Rd, Cincinnati, OH 45236
Tel: 513-531-2690 *Fax:* 513-531-1843
E-mail: writersdigest@fwpubs.com
Web Site: www.fwpublications.com
Key Personnel
Ed: Kristin Godsey
A collection of the years' 100 Best Magazine Markets on writing, as chosen by the editors of Writer's Digest; inspiration & advice from & for writers.
First published 1930
Book Use: Reviews, excerpts, profiles of authors
Avg pages per issue: 84
Circulation: 75,000
$5.99/issue, $8.99/issue Canada or foreign, single copy sales only

Writing That Works
Published by Communication Concepts Inc
7481 Huntsman Blvd, Suite 720, Springfield, VA 22153-1648
Tel: 703-643-2200
E-mail: concepts@writingthatworks.com
Web Site: www.apexawords.com
Key Personnel
Ed & Publr: John De Lellis
Contents include writing techniques, style matters, managing publications & on-line publishing.
Frequency: Monthly
$119/yr, $169/2 yr, $199/3 yr
ISSN: 1050-4788

NOTES

NOTES

NOTES

NOTES

NOTES

The *Tools* For Tomorrow...

Today!

KMWORLD

KMWorld serves the information needs of business executives and departmental directors who leverage the various forms of business content to improve their day-to-day business processes. Focusing on content, document, and business knowledge management, *KMWorld* provides actionable information through real-world case studies, advice from key practitioners, and best-practice advice from market leaders. Subscription in the U.S. is free to qualified corporate executives who complete an electronic online subscription application form at *www.kmworld.com/subscribe*. For corporate libraries and non-qualified recipients, the annual subscription price is $63.95 U.S., $86 Canada & Mexico, and $116 Outside N.A. in U.S. funds and prepaid upon application.

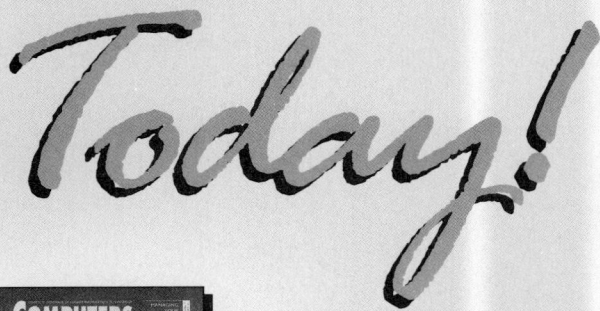

COMPUTERS IN LIBRARIES

Computers in Libraries provides the most complete coverage of library information technology. Every issue contains articles on library automation, online products and services, the Internet, CD-ROM/multimedia, document delivery, and much more! *Computers in Libraries* delivers clear, useful advice and ideas written by and for library professionals. 10 issues/yr. 1 yr. $99.95 U.S., $114 Canada & Mexico, $124 Outside N.A.

SEARCHER

Searcher: The Magazine for Database Professionals is a unique publication that explores and deliberates on a comprehensive range of issues important to the professional database searcher. *Searcher* contains evaluated online news, searching tips and techniques, reviews of search aid software and database documentation, and trenchant editorials, along with many topics of interest to the experienced database searcher. 10 issues/yr. 1 yr. $83.95 U.S., $107 Canada & Mexico, $113 Outside N.A.

ECONTENT

EContent magazine clearly identifies and explains emerging digital content trends, strategies, and resources to help professionals navigate the content maze and find a clear path to profits and business processes. *EContent* is the most reliable source for what matters in electronic content, the content infrastructure, and the business of digital content. 10 issues/yr. 1 yr. $112 U.S., $122 Canada & Mexico, $147 Outside N.A.

CRM

CRM magazine is the leading publication serving the field of customer relationship management. *CRM* is a business technology magazine written for senior level management in corporate, sales, marketing, service, and information technology and provides business leaders with the information they need to reach their strategic objectives through tactical implementation of CRM process and technology. *CRM* magazine is free to qualified subscribers who complete an electronic online subscription application at *www.destinationcrm.com*.

INFORMATION TODAY

Information Today is the newspaper for users and producers of electronic information services. *Information Today* provides complete coverage of online databases, the Internet, CD-ROM products, multimedia, library automation, electronic networking and publishing, and the essential hardware and software for delivery of electronic information. 11 issues/yr. 1 yr. $69.95 U.S., $93 Canada & Mexico, $102 Outside N.A.

Industry Yellow Pages — Company Index

Included in this index are the names, addresses, telecommunication numbers and electronic addresses of the organizations included in this volume of *LMP*. Entries also include the page number(s) on which the listings appear.

Sections not represented in this index are **Imprints, Subsidiaries & Distributors; Calendar of Book Trade & Promotional Events; Reference Books for the Trade** and **Magazines for the Trade.**

A Abacus Group, PO Box 35, Ridgecrest, CA 93556 *Tel:* 760-375-5243 *Fax:* 760-375-1140 *E-mail:* gtd007@ridgenet.net *Web Site:* www.ridgenet. net/~gtd007, pg 589, 617

A & B Publishers Group, 223 Duffield St, Brooklyn, NY 11201 *Tel:* 718-783-7808 *Fax:* 718-783-7267 *Web Site:* anbdonline.com, pg 1

A & M Books, PO Box 283, Rehoboth Beach, DE 19971 *Toll Free Tel:* 800-489-7662, pg 569

A D D Warehouse, 300 NW 70 Ave, Suite 102, Plantation, FL 33317 *Tel:* 954-792-8100 *Toll Free Tel:* 800-233-9273 *Fax:* 954-792-8545 *E-mail:* websales@addwarehouse.com *Web Site:* www. addwarehouse.com, pg 1

A K Peters Ltd, 888 Worcester St, Suite 230, Wellesley, MA 02482 *Tel:* 781-416-2888 *Fax:* 781-416-2889 *E-mail:* service@akpeters.com *Web Site:* www. akpeters.com, pg 1

AK Press Distribution, 674-A 23 St, Oakland, CA 94612 *Tel:* 510-208-1700 *Fax:* 510-208-1701 *Web Site:* www. akpress.org, pg 1

A+ English/ManuscriptEditing.com, 1830 Guinevere St, Arlington, TX 76014-2521 *Tel:* 817-467-7127 *E-mail:* editor@manuscriptediting.com *Web Site:* www.manuscriptediting.com; www. englishedit.com; www.queryletters.com; www. scifieditor.com; www.writingnetwork.com; www.book-editing.com; www.dissertationadvisors.com; www. thesisproofreader.com; www.statisticstutors.com; www. apawriting.com, pg 589

A-R Editions Inc, 8551 Research Way, Suite 180, Middleton, WI 53562 *Tel:* 608-836-9000 *Toll Free Tel:* 800-736-0070 (US book orders only) *Fax:* 608-831-8200 *E-mail:* info@areditions.com *Web Site:* www.areditions.com, pg 2

A R O Publishing Co, 398 S 1100 W, Provo, UT 84601 *Tel:* 801-377-8218 *Fax:* 801-818-0616 *E-mail:* aro@ yahoo.com *Web Site:* www.aropublishing.com, pg 2

A Westport Wordsmith, 104 Roseville Rd, Westport, CT 06880 *Tel:* 203-226-7098 *E-mail:* pj104daily@aol. com, pg 589

AAA Books Unlimited, 88 Greenbrier E Dr, Deerfield, IL 60015 *Tel:* 847-945-0315 *Fax:* 847-444-1220 *Web Site:* www.aaabooksunlimited.com, pg 617

AAA Photos, 401 Ocean Dr, Miami Beach, FL 33139 *Tel:* 305-534-0804 *Web Site:* www.PhotosPhotos.net, pg 589

AAAI Press, 445 Burgess Dr, Suite 100, Menlo Park, CA 94025-3496 *Tel:* 650-328-3123 *Fax:* 650-321-4457 *E-mail:* press@aaai.org *Web Site:* www.aaaipress.org, pg 2

AAH Graphics Inc, 187 Myra Lane, Fort Valley, VA 22652 *Tel:* 540-933-6210 *Fax:* 540-933-6523 *Web Site:* www.aahgraphics.com, pg 589

The Aaland Agency, PO Box 849, Inyokern, CA 93527-0849 *Tel:* 760-384-3910 *Fax:* 760-384-4435 *Web Site:* www.the-aaland-agency.com, pg 617

AANS-American Association of Neurological Surgeons, 5550 Meadow Brook Dr, Rolling Meadows, IL 60008 *Tel:* 847-378-0500 *Fax:* 847-378-0600 *E-mail:* info@ aans.org *Web Site:* www.neurosurgery.org, pg 2

AAPG (American Association of Petroleum Geologists), 1444 S Boulder Ave, Tulsa, OK 74119 *Tel:* 918-584-2555 *Toll Free Tel:* 800-364-AAPG (364-2274)

Fax: 918-560-2632 *Toll Free Fax:* 800-898-2274 *E-mail:* bookstore@aapg.org *Web Site:* www.aapg.org, pg 2

Aaron-Spear, PO Box 42, Harborside, ME 04642 *Tel:* 207-326-8764, pg 589

AA's & PE's, 129 Third Ave, Benton, WI 53803-0072 *Tel:* 608-759-3303, pg 589

AAUP Book, Jacket & Journal Design Show, 71 W 23 St, Suite 901, New York, NY 10010 *Tel:* 212-989-1010 *Fax:* 212-989-0275; 212-989-0176 *E-mail:* info@aaupnet.org *Web Site:* www.aaupnet.org, pg 757

Abacus, 5130 Patterson SE, Grand Rapids, MI 49512 *Tel:* 616-698-0330 *Toll Free Tel:* 800-451-4319 *Fax:* 616-698-0325 *E-mail:* info@abacuspub.com *Web Site:* www.abacuspub.com, pg 2

Abaris Books, 64 Wall St, Norwalk, CT 06850 *Tel:* 203-838-8402 *Fax:* 203-849-9181 *E-mail:* abarisbooks@ abarisbooks.com *Web Site:* abarisbooks.com, pg 2

Abbeville Publishing Group, 116 W 23 St, Suite 500, New York, NY 10011 *Tel:* 646-375-2039 *Toll Free Tel:* 800-ART-BOOK (278-2665) *Fax:* 646-375-2040 *E-mail:* abbeville@abbeville.com *Web Site:* www. abbeville.com, pg 2

Abbey Press, One Hill Dr, St Meinrad, IN 47577 *Tel:* 812-357-6611 *Toll Free Tel:* 800-962-4760 *Fax:* 812-357-8388 *E-mail:* dep@abbeypress.com *Web Site:* www.abbeypress.com, pg 2

Abbott, Langer & Associates, 548 First St, Crete, IL 60417 *Tel:* 708-672-4200 *Fax:* 708-672-4674 *E-mail:* sales@abbott-langer.com *Web Site:* www. abbott-langer.com, pg 2

ABC-CLIO, 130 Cremona Dr, Santa Barbara, CA 93117 *Tel:* 805-968-1911 *Toll Free Tel:* 800-368-6868 *Fax:* 805-685-9685 *E-mail:* sales@abc-clio.com *Web Site:* www.abc-clio.com, pg 2

Abdo Publishing, 4940 Viking Dr, Suite 622, Edina, MN 55435 *Tel:* 952-831-2120 (ext 223) *Toll Free Tel:* 800-800-1312 *Fax:* 952-831-1632 *E-mail:* info@abdopub. com *Web Site:* www.abdopub.com, pg 3

Carole Abel Literary Agent, 160 W 87 St, New York, NY 10024 *Tel:* 212-724-1168 *Fax:* 212-724-1384 *E-mail:* caroleabel@aol.com, pg 617

Dominick Abel Literary Agency Inc, 146 W 82 St, Suite 1-B, New York, NY 10024 *Tel:* 212-877-0710 *Fax:* 212-595-3133 *E-mail:* agency@dalainc.com, pg 617

ABELexpress, 601 Beechwood Ave, Carnegie, PA 15106 *Tel:* 412-279-0672 *Toll Free Tel:* 800-542-9001 *Fax:* 412-429-2911, pg 3

ABI Professional Publications, 3580 Morris St N, Saint Petersburg, FL 33713 *Tel:* 727-556-0950 *Toll Free Tel:* 800-551-7776 *Fax:* 727-556-2560 *E-mail:* abipropub@vandamere.com; orders@ vandamere.com *Web Site:* www.abipropub.com, pg 3

Abingdon Press, 201 Eighth Ave S, Nashville, TN 37203-3919 *Tel:* 615-749-6290 (publicist); 615-749-6000; 615-749-6451 (sales) *Toll Free Tel:* 800-251-3320 *Fax:* 615-749-6056 *Web Site:* www. abingdonpress.com, pg 3

About Books Inc, 425 Cedar St, Buena Vista, CO 81211-1500 *Tel:* 719-395-2459 *Fax:* 719-395-8374 *E-mail:* abi@about-books.com *Web Site:* www.about-books.com, pg 589

Abrams & Co Publishers Inc, 61 Mattatuck Heights Rd, Waterbury, CT 06705 *Tel:* 203-756-6562 *Toll Free Tel:* 800-227-9120 *Fax:* 203-756-2895 *Toll Free Fax:* 800-737-3322, pg 3

Abrams Artists Agency, 275 Seventh Ave, 26th fl, New York, NY 10001 *Tel:* 646-486-4600 *Fax:* 646-486-2358, pg 617

Harry N Abrams Inc, 100 Fifth Ave, New York, NY 10011 *Tel:* 212-206-7715 *Toll Free Tel:* 800-345-1359 *Fax:* 212-645-8437 *E-mail:* webmaster@abramsbooks. com *Web Site:* www.abramsbooks.com, pg 3

Absey & Co Inc, 23011 Northcrest Dr, Spring, TX 77389 *Tel:* 281-257-2340 *Toll Free Tel:* 888-412-2739 *Fax:* 281-251-4676 *E-mail:* abseyandco@aol.com *Web Site:* www.absey.com, pg 4

Acacia House Publishing Services Ltd, 51 Acacia Rd, Toronto, ON M4S 2K6, Canada *Tel:* 416-484-8356; 416-484-1430 *Fax:* 416-484-8356, pg 617

Academic International Press, PO Box 1111, Gulf Breeze, FL 32562-1111 *Tel:* 850-932-5478 *Fax:* 850-934-0953 *E-mail:* info@ai-press.com *Web Site:* www. ai-press.com, pg 4

Academic Press, 525 B St, Suite 1900, San Diego, CA 92101 *Tel:* 619-231-6616 *Toll Free Tel:* 800-321-5068 (cust serv) *Fax:* 619-699-6715 *E-mail:* firstinitiallastname@acad.com; firstinitial. lastname@elsevier.com *Web Site:* www.elsevier.com, pg 4

Academic Printing & Publishing, 9-3151 Lakeshore Rd, Suite 403, Kelowna, BC V1W 3S9, Canada *Tel:* 250-764-6427 *Fax:* 250-464-6428 *E-mail:* app@silk.net *Web Site:* www.academicprintingandpublishing.com, pg 535

Academy Chicago Publishers, 363 W Erie St, Chicago, IL 60610 *Tel:* 312-751-7300 *Toll Free Tel:* 800-248-7323 *Fax:* 312-751-7306 *E-mail:* info@ academychicago.com *Web Site:* www.academychicago. com, pg 4

Academy of American Poets Fellowship, 588 Broadway, Suite 604, New York, NY 10012 *Tel:* 212-274-0343 *Fax:* 212-274-9427 *E-mail:* academy@poets.org *Web Site:* www.poets.org, pg 757

The Academy of American Poets Inc, 588 Broadway, Suite 604, New York, NY 10012 *Tel:* 212-274-0343 *Fax:* 212-274-9427 *E-mail:* academy@poets.org *Web Site:* www.poets.org, pg 675

Academy of Motion Picture Arts & Sciences (AMPAS), 1313 N Vine St, Hollywood, CA 90028 *Tel:* 310-247-3000 *Fax:* 310-859-9351 *E-mail:* ampas@oscars.org *Web Site:* www.oscars.org, pg 675

The Academy of Producer Insurance Studies Inc, PO Box 27027, Austin, TX 78755-2027 *Tel:* 512-346-7050 *Toll Free Tel:* 800-526-2777 *Fax:* 512-343-2167 *E-mail:* alliance@scic.com *Web Site:* www. thenationalalliance.com, pg 4

Academy of Television Arts & Sciences (ATAS), 5220 Lankershim Blvd, North Hollywood, CA 91601-3109 *Tel:* 818-754-2800 *Fax:* 818-761-2827 *Web Site:* www. emmys.tv, pg 675

Accent Publications, 4050 Lee Vance View, Colorado Springs, CO 80918 *Tel:* 719-536-0100 *Toll Free Tel:* 800-708-5550; 800-535-2905 (cust serv) *Fax:* 719-535-2928 *Toll Free Fax:* 800-430-0726 *Web Site:* www.accentpublications.com, pg 4

Access Copyright, The Canadian Copyright Licensing Agency, One Yonge St, Suite 1900, Toronto, ON M5E 1E5, Canada *Tel:* 416-868-1620 *Toll Free Tel:* 800-893-5777 *Fax:* 416-868-1621 *E-mail:* info@ accesscopyright.ca *Web Site:* www.accesscopyright.ca, pg 675

Access Editorial Services, 1133 Broadway, Suite 528, New York, NY 10010 *Tel:* 212-255-7306 *Fax:* 212-255-7306 *E-mail:* wiseword@juno.com, pg 589

Accurate Writing & More, PO Box 1164, Northampton, MA 01061-1164 *Tel:* 413-586-2388 *Toll Free Tel:* 800-683-9673 *Fax:* 617-249-0153 *Web Site:* www.accuratewriting.com, pg 589

ACETO Bookmen, 5721 Antietam Dr, Sarasota, FL 34231-4903 *Tel:* 941-924-9170, pg 4

Alice B Acheson's Workshops for Writers, Illustrators & Photographers, PO Box 735, Friday Harbor, WA 98250 *Tel:* 360-378-2815 *Fax:* 360-378-2841 *E-mail:* aliceba@aol.com, pg 741

Milton Acorn Poetry Award, 115 Richmond St, Charlottetown, PE C1A 1H7, Canada *Tel:* 902-368-4410 *Fax:* 902-368-4418 *E-mail:* peiarts@ peiartscouncil.com *Web Site:* www.peiartscouncil.com, pg 757

Acres USA, PO Box 91299, Austin, TX 78709-1299 *Tel:* 512-892-4400 *Toll Free Tel:* 800-355-5313 *Fax:* 512-892-4448 *E-mail:* info@acresusa.com; editor@acresusa.com *Web Site:* www.acresusa.com, pg 4

Acrobat Books, PO Box 870, Venice, CA 90294-0870 *Tel:* 310-578-1055 *Fax:* 310-823-8447 *E-mail:* acrobooks@cs.com, pg 4

Acropolis Books Inc, 8601 Dunwoody Place, Suite 303, Atlanta, GA 30350 *Tel:* 770-643-1118 *Toll Free Tel:* 800-773-9923 *Fax:* 770-643-1170 *E-mail:* acropolisbooks@mindspring.com *Web Site:* www.acropolisbooks.com, pg 569

ACS Publications, 5521 Ruffin Rd, San Diego, CA 92123 *Tel:* 858-492-9919 *Toll Free Tel:* 800-888-9983 (orders only) *Fax:* 858-492-9917 (orders only) *E-mail:* sales@astrocom.com *Web Site:* www.astrocom.com, pg 4

ACTA Press/IASTED, 4500 16 Ave NW, No 80, Calgary, AB T3B 0M6, Canada *Tel:* 403-288-1195 *Fax:* 403-247-6851 *E-mail:* comments@actapress.com *Web Site:* www.actapress.com, pg 535

ACTA Publications, 4848 N Clark St, Chicago, IL 60640-4711 *Tel:* 773-271-1030 *Toll Free Tel:* 800-397-2282 *Fax:* 773-271-7399 *Toll Free Fax:* 800-397-0079 *E-mail:* actapublications@aol.com *Web Site:* www.actapublications.com, pg 4

Action Publishing LLC, PO Box 391, Glendale, CA 91209 *Tel:* 323-478-1667 *Toll Free Tel:* 800-705-7482 *Fax:* 323-478-1767 *E-mail:* info@actionpublishing.com *Web Site:* www.actionpublishing.com, pg 5

Actualisation, 300 Leo-Pariseau, Suite 2200, Montreal, PQ H2X 4B3, Canada *Tel:* 514-284-2622 *Fax:* 514-284-2625 *Web Site:* www.actualisation.com, pg 535

ACU Press, 1648 Campus Ct, Abilene, TX 79601 *Tel:* 325-674-2720 *Toll Free Tel:* 800-444-4228 *Fax:* 325-674-6471 *E-mail:* acupress@acu.edu *Web Site:* www.acu.edu/acupress, pg 5

Adams & Ambrose Publishing, PO Box 259684, Madison, WI 53725-9684 *Tel:* 608-257-5700 *Fax:* 608-257-5719 *E-mail:* info@adamsambrose.com, pg 5

Adams-Blake Publishing, 8041 Sierra St, Suite 102, Fair Oaks, CA 95628 *Tel:* 916-962-9296 *E-mail:* info@ adams-blake.com *Web Site:* www.adams-blake.com, pg 5

Herbert Baxter Adams Prize, 400 "A" St SE, Washington, DC 20003 *Tel:* 202-544-2422 *Fax:* 202-544-8307 *E-mail:* info@historians.org *Web Site:* www.historians.org, pg 757

Adams Media, An F+W Publications Co, 57 Littlefield St, 2nd fl, Avon, MA 02322 *Tel:* 508-427-7100 *Fax:* 508-427-6790 *Toll Free Fax:* 800-872-5628

E-mail: authors@adamsmedia.com; orders@ adamsmedia.com *Web Site:* www.adamsmedia.com, pg 5

ADASI Publishing Co, 6 Dover Point Rd, Suite B, Dover, NH 03820-4698 *Tel:* 727-488-7353 *E-mail:* info@adasi.com *Web Site:* www.adasi.com, pg 5

ADC The Map People, 6440 General Green Way, Alexandria, VA 22312 *Tel:* 703-750-0510 *Toll Free Tel:* 800-232-6277 *Fax:* 703-750-3092 *E-mail:* adc@ adcmap.com *Web Site:* www.adcmap.com, pg 5

Jane Addams Children's Book Award, 777 United Nations Plaza, New York, NY 10017 *Tel:* 212-682-8830 *Fax:* 212-682-8211 *E-mail:* japa@igc.org *Web Site:* www.janeaddamspeace.org, pg 757

Addicus Books Inc, PO Box 45327, Omaha, NE 68145 *Tel:* 402-330-7493 *Toll Free Tel:* 800-352-2873 (orders) *Fax:* 402-330-1707 *E-mail:* info@ addicusbooks.com; addicusbks@aol.com *Web Site:* www.addicusbooks.com, pg 5

Addison Wesley Higher Education Group, 75 Arlington St, Boston, MA 02116 *Tel:* 617-848-7500 *Fax:* 617-848-6016 *E-mail:* firstname.lastname@pearsoned.com *Web Site:* www.awl.com, pg 5

J Adel Graphic Design, 586 Ramapo Rd, Teaneck, NJ 07666 *Tel:* 201-836-2606 *E-mail:* jadelnj@aol.com, pg 589

Adenine Press Inc, 2066 Central Ave, Schenectady, NY 12304 *Tel:* 518-456-0784 *Fax:* 518-452-4955 *E-mail:* info@adeninepress.com *Web Site:* www.adeninepress.com, pg 5

Adirondack Mountain Club, 814 Goggins Rd, Lake George, NY 12845-4117 *Tel:* 518-668-4447 *Toll Free Tel:* 800-395-8080 *Fax:* 518-668-3746 *E-mail:* adkinfo@adk.org *Web Site:* www.adk.org, pg 5

Advance Publishing Inc, 6950 Fulton St, Houston, TX 77022 *Tel:* 713-695-0600 *Fax:* 713-695-8585 *E-mail:* ap@advancepublishing.com *Web Site:* www.advancepublishing.com, pg 5

Advanced Sheetfed Press Operations, 200 Deer Run Rd, Sewickley, PA 15143-2600 *Tel:* 412-741-6860 *Toll Free Tel:* 800-910-4283 *Fax:* 412-741-2311 *E-mail:* info@gain.net *Web Site:* www.gain.net, pg 741

Advancement of Literacy Award, 50 E Huron St, Chicago, IL 60611 *Toll Free Tel:* 800-545-2433 (ext 5026) *E-mail:* pla@ala.org *Web Site:* www.pla.org, pg 757

Advantage Publishers Group, 5880 Oberlin Dr, San Diego, CA 92121 *Tel:* 858-457-2500 *Toll Free Tel:* 800-284-3580 *Fax:* 858-812-6476 *Toll Free Fax:* 800-499-3822 *E-mail:* apgcuserv@advmkt.com *Web Site:* www.advantagebooksonline.com, pg 6

Adventure House, 914 Laredo Rd, Silver Spring, MD 20901 *Tel:* 301-754-1589 *Fax:* 978-215-7412 *Web Site:* www.adventurehouse.com, pg 6

Adventure Publications, 820 Cleveland St, Cambridge, MN 55008 *Tel:* 763-689-9800 *Toll Free Tel:* 800-678-7006 *Fax:* 763-689-9039, pg 6

Adventures Unlimited Press, One Adventure Place, Kempton, IL 60946 *Tel:* 815-253-6390 *Fax:* 815-253-6300 *E-mail:* auphq@frontiernet.net *Web Site:* www.adventuresunlimitedpress.com, pg 6

Advertising Research Foundation, 641 Lexington Ave, New York, NY 10022 *Tel:* 212-751-5656 *Fax:* 212-319-5265 *E-mail:* info@thearf.org *Web Site:* www.thearf.org, pg 675

Aegean Park Press, PO Box 2120, Walnut Creek, CA 94595 *Tel:* 925-947-2533 *Toll Free Tel:* 800-736-3587 (orders only) *Fax:* 925-947-2144 *E-mail:* books@ aegeanparkpress.com *Web Site:* www.aegeanparkpress.com, pg 6

AEI (Atchity Editorial/Entertainment International Inc), 9601 Wilshire Blvd, No 1202, Beverly Hills, CA 90210 *Tel:* 323-932-0407 *Fax:* 323-932-0321 *E-mail:* submissions@aeionline.com *Web Site:* www.aeionline.com, pg 618

The AEI Press, 1150 17 St NW, Washington, DC 20036 *Tel:* 202-862-5800 *Fax:* 202-862-7177 *Web Site:* www.aei.org, pg 6

AEIOU Inc, 894 Piermont Ave, Piermont, NY 10968 *Tel:* 845-680-5380 *Fax:* 845-680-5381, pg 589

Aerial Photography Services Inc, 2511 S Tryon St, Charlotte, NC 28203 *Tel:* 704-333-5143 *Fax:* 704-333-5148 *Toll Free Fax:* 800-204-4910 *E-mail:* aps@aps-1.com *Web Site:* www.aps-1.com, pg 6

AFCP's Annual Awards, 1630 Miner St, Suite 204, Idaho Springs, CO 80452 *Toll Free Tel:* 877-203-2327 *Fax:* 781-459-7770 *Web Site:* www.afcp.org, pg 757

Africa World Press Inc, 541 W Ingham Ave, Suite B, Trenton, NJ 08638 *Tel:* 609-695-3200 *Fax:* 609-695-6466 *E-mail:* awprsp@africanworld.com; awprsp@ intar.com *Web Site:* africanworld.com, pg 6

African American Images, 1909 W 95 St, Chicago, IL 60643 *Tel:* 773-445-0322 *Toll Free Tel:* 800-552-1991 *Fax:* 773-445-9844 *E-mail:* customer@africanamericanimages.com *Web Site:* africanamericanimages.com, pg 6

AFS Wordstead, 27 Belvedere St, St Julie, PQ J3E 3M4, Canada *Tel:* 450-922-0172 *Toll Free Tel:* 866-864-5448 *Web Site:* www.wordstead.com, pg 589

Agatha Awards, PO Box 31137, Bethesda, MD 20824-1137 *Tel:* 703-751-4444 *Web Site:* www.malicedomestic.org, pg 757

Agathon Press, 2741 Arlington Ave, Bronx, NY 10463-4806 *Tel:* 718-543-6207 (edit & busn); 908-788-5753 (fulfillment) *Toll Free Tel:* 800-488-8040 (orders only) *Fax:* 718-543-6211 (edit & busn); 908-237-2407 (fulfillment) *Web Site:* www.agathonpress.com, pg 6

Ageless Press, 3759 Collins St, Sarasota, FL 34232 *Tel:* 941-365-1367 *Fax:* 941-365-1367 *E-mail:* irishope@comcast.net *Web Site:* irisforrest.com, pg 6

Agency Chicago, 28 E Jackson Blvd, 10th fl, Suite A-600, Chicago, IL 60604 *Tel:* 312-409-0205, pg 618

Agency For The Performing Arts Inc, 9200 Sunset Blvd, Suite 900, Los Angeles, CA 90069 *Tel:* 310-273-0744 *Fax:* 310-888-4242, pg 618

Agent Research & Evaluation Inc, 25 Barrow St, New York, NY 10014 *Tel:* 212-924-9942 *Fax:* 212-924-1864 *E-mail:* info@agentresearch.com *Web Site:* www.agentresearch.biz, pg 618

Agents Inc for Medical & Mental Health Professionals, PO Box 4956, Fresno, CA 93744-4956 *Tel:* 559-438-1883 *Fax:* 559-438-1883, pg 618

Aggiornamento Award, 100 North St, Suite 224, Pittsfield, MA 01201-5109 *Tel:* 413-443-2252 *Fax:* 413-442-2252 *E-mail:* cla@cathla.org *Web Site:* www.cathla.org, pg 757

AGS Publishing, 4201 Woodland Rd, Circle Pines, MN 55014-1716 *Tel:* 651-287-7220 *Toll Free Tel:* 800-328-2560 *Toll Free Fax:* 800-471-8457 *E-mail:* agsmail@ agsnet.com *Web Site:* www.agsnet.com, pg 7

AHA Press, One N Franklin, Suite 2800, Chicago, IL 60606 *Tel:* 312-893-6800 *Fax:* 312-422-4500 *Web Site:* www.hospitalconnect.com; www.ahaonlinestore.com (orders), pg 7

AHA Prize in Atlantic History, 400 "A" St SE, Washington, DC 20003 *Tel:* 202-544-2422 *Fax:* 202-544-8307 *E-mail:* info@historians.org *Web Site:* www.historians.org, pg 757

Ahearn Agency Inc, 2021 Pine St, New Orleans, LA 70118 *Tel:* 504-861-8395 *Fax:* 504-866-6434, pg 618

Ahsahta Press, Boise State University, Dept of English, Boise, ID 83725 *Tel:* 208-426-2195 *Fax:* 208-426-4373, pg 7

Aid to Individual Artists, 727 E Main St, Columbus, OH 43205-1796 *Tel:* 614-466-2613 *Fax:* 614-466-4494 *Web Site:* www.oac.state.oh.us, pg 758

AIGA 50 Books/50 Covers, 164 Fifth Ave, New York, NY 10010 *Tel:* 212-807-1990 *Toll Free Tel:* 800-548-1634 *Fax:* 212-807-1799 *E-mail:* competitions@aiga.org *Web Site:* www.aiga.org, pg 758

AIM Magazine Short Story Contest, PO Box 1174, Maywood, IL 60153-8174 *Tel:* 708-344-4414 *Fax:* 206-543-2746 (WA) *Web Site:* www.aimmagazine.org, pg 758

AIMS Education Foundation, 1595 S Chestnut Ave, Fresno, CA 93702-4706 *Tel:* 559-255-4094 *Toll Free Tel:* 888-733-2467 *Fax:* 559-255-6396 *E-mail:* aimsed@aimsedu.org *Web Site:* www.aimsedu.org/, pg 7

Ainsworth Editorial Services, 43-01 12 St, Suite 339, Long Island City, NY 11101 *Tel:* 718-361-5254 *Fax:* 718-361-2837 *E-mail:* nycedit@aol.com, pg 589

Aio Publishing Co LLC, PO Box 30788, Charleston, SC 29417 *Tel:* 843-225-3698 *Toll Free Tel:* 888-287-9888 *Web Site:* www.aiopublishing.com, pg 7

AIP Science Writing Award, One Physics Ellipse, College Park, MD 20740-3843 *Tel:* 301-209-3096 *Fax:* 301-209-0846 *Web Site:* www.aip.org/aip/awards, pg 758

Airmont Publishing Co Inc, 160 Madison Ave, New York, NY 10016 *Tel:* 212-598-0222 *Fax:* 212-979-1862, pg 7

AJL Bibliography Award, 15 E 26 St, Suite 1034, New York, NY 10010-1579 *Tel:* 212-725-5359 *Fax:* 212-678-8998 *E-mail:* ajl@jewishbooks.org *Web Site:* www.jewishlibraries.org, pg 758

AJL Reference Book Award, 15 E 26 St, Suite 1034, New York, NY 10010-1579 *Tel:* 212-725-5359 *Fax:* 212-678-8998 *E-mail:* ajl@jewishbooks.org *Web Site:* www.jewishlibraries.org, pg 758

AJL Scholarship, 15 E 26 St, New York, NY 10010-1579 *Tel:* 212-725-5359 *Fax:* 212-481-4174 *E-mail:* ajl@jewishbooks.org *Web Site:* www.jewishlibraries.org, pg 758

Akashic Books, PO Box 1456, New York, NY 10009 *Tel:* 212-433-1875 *Fax:* 212-414-3199 *E-mail:* akashic7@aol.com *Web Site:* www.akashicbooks.com, pg 7

Akin & Randolph Agency for Representation for Authors, Artists & Athletes (Literary Division), One Gateway Ctr, Suite 2600, Newark, NJ 07102 *Tel:* 973-623-6834 *Toll Free Tel:* 888-870-0765 *Fax:* 973-353-8417 *Web Site:* www.akinandrandolph.com, pg 618

AKTRIN Furniture Information Centre, 164 S Main St, Suite 307, High Point, NC 27260 *Tel:* 336-841-8535 *Fax:* 336-841-5435 *E-mail:* aktrin@aktrin.com (Canada); aktrinusa@northstate.net (US) *Web Site:* www.aktrin.com, pg 7

Alabama Artists Fellowship Awards, 201 Monroe St, Suite 110, Montgomery, AL 36130-1800 *Tel:* 334-242-4076 *Fax:* 334-240-3269, pg 758

Alaska Native Language Center, PO Box 757680, Fairbanks, AK 99775-7680 *Tel:* 907-474-7874 *Fax:* 907-474-6586 *Web Site:* www.uaf.edu/anlc/, pg 7

Alba House, 2187 Victory Blvd, Staten Island, NY 10314 *Tel:* 718-761-0047 (edit & prodn); 718-698-2759 (mktg & billing) *Toll Free Tel:* 800-343-2522 *Fax:* 718-761-0057 *E-mail:* albabooks@aol.com *Web Site:* www.albahouse.org, pg 7

The Alban Institute Inc, 2121 Cooperative Way, Suite 100, Herndon, VA 20171 *Tel:* 703-964-2700 *Toll Free Tel:* 800-486-1318 *Fax:* 703-964-0370 *E-mail:* webmaster@alban.org *Web Site:* www.alban.org, pg 7

Albert Editorial Services, 565 Bellevue Ave, No 1704, Oakland, CA 94610 *Tel:* 510-839-1140, pg 589

Alberta Book Awards, 10523-100 Ave, Edmonton, AB T5J 0A8, Canada *Tel:* 780-424-5060 *Fax:* 780-424-7943 *E-mail:* info@bookpublishers.ab.ca *Web Site:* www.bookpublishers.ab.ca, pg 758

Rodelinde Albrecht, PO Box 444, Lenox Dale, MA 01242-0444 *Tel:* 413-243-4350 *Fax:* 413-243-3066 *E-mail:* rodelinde@juno.com *Web Site:* www.concernedsingles.com, pg 590

Alcuin Society, PO Box 3216, Vancouver, BC V6B 3X8, Canada *Tel:* 604-937-3293 *Web Site:* www.alcuinsociety.com, pg 675

Alcuin Society Awards in Excellence in Book Design in Canada, PO Box 3216, Vancouver, BC V6B 3X8, Canada *Tel:* 604-937-3293 *Web Site:* www.alcuinsociety.com, pg 758

Gary Aleksiewicz, 9110 NW 219 Place, Alachua, FL 32615 *Tel:* 386-462-6142 *E-mail:* gsaleks@hotmail.com, pg 590

The Alexander Graham Bell Association for the Deaf & Hard of Hearing, 3417 Volta Place NW, Washington, DC 20007-2778 *Tel:* 202-337-5220 *Fax:* 202-337-8314 *Web Site:* www.agbell.org, pg 8

Alexander Street Press LLC, 3212 Duke St, Alexandria, VA 22314 *Tel:* 703-212-8520 *Toll Free Tel:* 800-889-5937 *Fax:* 240-465-0561 *E-mail:* sales@alexanderstreet.com *Web Site:* www.alexanderstreet.com, pg 8

Alfred Publishing Company Inc, PO Box 10003, Van Nuys, CA 91410-0003 *Tel:* 818-891-5999 *Toll Free Tel:* 800-292-6122 (dealer sales) *Fax:* 818-892-9239 *Toll Free Fax:* 800-632-1928 (dealer sales) *E-mail:* customerservice@alfred.com *Web Site:* www.alfred.com, pg 8

Algonquin Books of Chapel Hill, 127 Kingston Dr, Suite 105, Chapel Hill, NC 27514 *Tel:* 919-967-0108 *Fax:* 919-933-0272 *E-mail:* dialogue@algonquin.com *Web Site:* www.algonquin.com, pg 8

Algora Publishing, 222 Riverside Dr, Suite 16-D, New York, NY 10025-6809 *Tel:* 212-678-0232 *Toll Free Tel:* 888-405-0689 *Fax:* 212-666-3682 *E-mail:* editors@algora.com *Web Site:* www.algora.com, pg 8

Nelson Algren Awards, Tribune Tower, LL2, 435 N Michigan Ave, Chicago, IL 60611 *Fax:* 312-222-5816 *Web Site:* www.chicagotribune.com, pg 758

ALI-ABA Committee on Continuing Professional Education, 4025 Chestnut St, Philadelphia, PA 19104 *Tel:* 215-243-1600 *Toll Free Tel:* 800-CLE-NEWS *Fax:* 215-243-1664; 215-243-1683 *Web Site:* www.ali-aba.org, pg 8

Alice James Books, 238 Main St, Farmington, ME 04938 *Tel:* 207-778-7071 *Fax:* 207-778-7071 *E-mail:* ajb@umf.maine.edu *Web Site:* www.alicejamesbooks.org, pg 8

Aliform Publishing, 117 Warwick St SE, Minneapolis, MN 55414 *Tel:* 612-379-7639 *Fax:* 612-379-7639 *E-mail:* information@aliformgroup.com *Web Site:* www.aliformgroup.com, pg 569

All About Kids Publishing, 117 Bernal Rd, No 70, PMB 405, San Jose, CA 95119 *Tel:* 408-846-1833 *Fax:* 408-846-1835 (ordering) *Web Site:* www.aakp.com, pg 8

All Wild-Up Productions, 303 Fourth Ave SE, Puyallup, WA 98372 *Tel:* 206-457-1949 *Fax:* 206-457-1949 *E-mail:* mail@allwildup.com *Web Site:* www.allwildup.com, pg 8

Lee Allan Agency, 7464 N 107 St, Milwaukee, WI 53224-3706 *Tel:* 414-357-7708, pg 618

Alleluia Press, 672 Franklin Tpke, Allendale, NJ 07401 *Tel:* 201-327-3513, pg 8

Allen D Bragdon Publishers Inc, 252 Great Western Rd, South Yarmouth, MA 02664-2210 *Tel:* 508-398-4440 *Toll Free Tel:* 877-8-SMARTS (876-2787) *Fax:* 508-760-2397 *E-mail:* admin@brainwaves.com *Web Site:* www.brainwaves.com, pg 9

Gracie Allen Awards®, 8405 Greensboro Dr, Suite 800, McLean, VA 22102 *Tel:* 703-506-3290 *Fax:* 703-506-3266 *E-mail:* info@awrt.org *Web Site:* www.awrt.org, pg 758

Linda Allen Literary Agency, 1949 Green St, Suite 5, San Francisco, CA 94123 *Tel:* 415-921-6437 *Fax:* 415-921-3733, pg 618

Allied Health Publications, 5295 S Commerce Dr, Salt Lake City, UT 84107 *Toll Free Tel:* 800-221-7374 (enrollment); 800-497-7157 *Fax:* 801-263-0345 *E-mail:* ahp@cchs.edu *Web Site:* www.cchs.edu, pg 9

Alloy Entertainment, 151 W 26 St, 11th fl, New York, NY 10001 *Tel:* 212-244-4307, pg 9

Allred & Allred Literary Agents, 7834 Alabama Ave, Canoga Park, CA 91304-4905 *Tel:* 818-346-4313 *Fax:* 818-346-4313, pg 618

Allworth Press, 10 E 23 St, Suite 510, New York, NY 10010 *Tel:* 212-777-8395 *Toll Free Tel:* 800-491-2808 *Fax:* 212-777-8261 *E-mail:* pub@allworth.com *Web Site:* www.allworth.com, pg 9

AllWrite Advertising & Publishing, PO Box 2363, Atlanta, GA 30301 *Tel:* 404-723-8872 *Fax:* 404-420-2604 *E-mail:* editor@e-allwrite.com *Web Site:* www.e-allwrite.com, pg 590

Allyn & Bacon, 75 Arlington St, Suite 300, Boston, MA 02116 *Tel:* 617-848-6000 *Fax:* 617-848-6016 *E-mail:* AandBpub@aol.com *Web Site:* www.ablongman.com, pg 9

Almada & Associates, 627 W Roscoe, Unit 2-B, Chicago, IL 60657 *Tel:* 773-404-9350 *Fax:* 773-404-9278, pg 590

Valinda Almeida, 284 Sunlit Cove Dr NE, St Petersburg, FL 33702 *Tel:* 727-577-3525 *Fax:* 727-577-3525 (call first) *E-mail:* almeida1@tampabay.rr.com, pg 590

Alms House Press, PO Box 218, Woodbourne, NY 12788-0218 *Tel:* 845-436-0070 *Fax:* 845-436-0099, pg 9

Alomega Press, 4601 N Cleveland Ave, Kansas City, MO 64117 *Tel:* 816-454-0980 *Fax:* 816-454-0980, pg 9

ALPHA Publications of America Inc, 4500 E Speedway Blvd, Suite 31, Tucson, AZ 85712-5325 *Tel:* 520-795-7100 *Toll Free Tel:* 800-528-3494 *Toll Free Fax:* 800-770-4329 *E-mail:* alphalegalkits@alphapublications.com *Web Site:* www.alphapublications.com, pg 9

Alpine Publications Inc, PO Box 7027, Loveland, CO 80537-0027 *Tel:* 970-667-2017 *Toll Free Tel:* 800-777-7257 (orders only) *Fax:* 970-667-9157 *E-mail:* alpinecsr@aol.com *Web Site:* www.alpinepub.com, pg 9

ALSC BWI/Summer Reading Program Grant, 50 E Huron St, Chicago, IL 60611-2795 *Tel:* 312-280-2163 *Toll Free Tel:* 800-545-2433 *Fax:* 312-944-7671 *E-mail:* alsc@ala.org *Web Site:* www.ala.org/alsc, pg 759

ALTA Literacy Award, 50 E Huron St, Chicago, IL 60611 *Tel:* 312-280-2161 *Toll Free Tel:* 800-545-2433 *Fax:* 312-280-3257 *Web Site:* www.ala.org/alta, pg 759

Altair Literary Agency LLC, PO Box 11656, Washington, DC 20008-0856 *Tel:* 202-237-8282 *Web Site:* www.altairliteraryagency.com, pg 618

AltaMira Press, 1630 N Main St, No 367, Walnut Creek, CA 94596 *Tel:* 925-938-7243 *Fax:* 925-933-9720 *E-mail:* explore@altamirapress.com *Web Site:* www.altamirapress.com, pg 9

Althos Publishing, 106 W Vance St, Fuquay-Varina, NC 27526 *Tel:* 919-557-2260 *Toll Free Tel:* 800-227-9681 *Fax:* 919-557-2261 *E-mail:* info@althos.com *Web Site:* www.althosbooks.com; www.telecomdefinitions.com, pg 10

The Althouse Press, University of Western Ontario, 1137 Western Rd, London, ON N6G 1G7, Canada *Tel:* 519-661-2096 *Fax:* 519-661-3833 *E-mail:* press@uwo.ca *Web Site:* www.edu.uwo.ca/althousepress, pg 535

Altitude Publishing Canada Ltd, 1500 Railway Ave, Canmore, AB T1W 1P6, Canada *Tel:* 403-678-6888 *Toll Free Tel:* 800-957-6888 *Fax:* 403-678-6951 *Toll Free Fax:* 800-957-1477 *E-mail:* orderdesk@altitudepublishing.com; sales@altitudepublishing.com (ordering) *Web Site:* www.altitudepublishing.com, pg 535

Miriam Altshuler Literary Agency, 53 Old Post Rd N, Red Hook, NY 12571 *Tel:* 845-758-9408 *Fax:* 845-758-3118, pg 619

Alyson Publications, 6922 Hollywood Blvd, Suite 1000, Los Angeles, CA 90028 *Tel:* 323-860-6065 *Fax:* 323-467-0152 *E-mail:* mail@alyson.com *Web Site:* www.alyson.com, pg 10

AMACOM Books, 1601 Broadway, New York, NY 10019-7406 *Tel:* 212-586-8100; 518-891-5510 (orders) *Toll Free Tel:* 800-262-9699 (cust serv) *Fax:* 212-903-8168; 518-891-2372 (orders) *Web Site:* www.amanet.org, pg 10

Amadeus Press, 512 Newark Pompton Tpke, Pompton Plains, NJ 07444 *Tel:* 973-835-6375 *Fax:* 973-835-6504 *Web Site:* www.amadeuspress.com, pg 10

Frank Amato Publications Inc, PO Box 82112, Portland, OR 97282 *Tel:* 503-653-8108 *Toll Free Tel:* 800-541-9498 *Fax:* 503-653-2766 *Web Site:* www.amatobooks.com, pg 10

Ambassador Books Inc, 91 Prescott St, Worcester, MA 01605 *Tel:* 508-756-2893 *Toll Free Tel:* 800-577-0909 *Fax:* 508-757-7055 *Web Site:* www.ambassadorbooks.com, pg 10

Amber Lotus, Strawberry Creek Design Ctr, 1250 Addison St, Studio 214, Berkeley, CA 94702 *Tel:* 510-225-0149 *Toll Free Tel:* 800-625-8378 (orders only) *Fax:* 510-665-6083 *E-mail:* info@amberlotus.com *Web Site:* www.amberlotus.com, pg 10

Amber Quill Press LLC, PO Box 265, Indian Hills, CO 80454 *E-mail:* customer_service@amberquillpress.com *Web Site:* amberquill.com, pg 10

Amboy Associates, 620 Venture St, Suite A, Escondido, CA 92029 *Toll Free Tel:* 800-448-4023 *Fax:* 760-546-0404 *Web Site:* www.oshastuff.com, pg 10

America West Publishers, PO Box 2208, Carson City, NV 89702-2208 *Tel:* 775-885-0700 *Toll Free Tel:* 800-729-4131 *Toll Free Fax:* 877-726-2632, pg 10

American Academy of Arts & Sciences (AAAS), Norton's Woods, 136 Irving St, Cambridge, MA 02138-1996 *Tel:* 617-576-5000 *Fax:* 617-576-5050 *Web Site:* www.amacad.org, pg 675

American Academy of Environmental Engineers, 130 Holiday Ct, Suite 100, Annapolis, MD 21401 *Tel:* 410-266-3311 *Fax:* 410-266-7653 *E-mail:* academy@aaee.net *Web Site:* www.aaee.net, pg 10

American Academy of Orthopaedic Surgeons, 6300 N River Rd, Rosemont, IL 60018-4262 *Tel:* 847-823-7186 *Toll Free Tel:* 800-346-2267 *Fax:* 847-823-8125 *Toll Free Fax:* 800-999-2939 *E-mail:* golembiewski@aaos.org *Web Site:* www.aaos.org, pg 11

American Academy of Pediatrics, 141 NW Point Blvd, Elk Grove Village, IL 60007-1098 *Tel:* 847-434-4000 *Toll Free Tel:* 888-227-1770 *Fax:* 847-228-1281 *E-mail:* pubs@aap.org *Web Site:* www.aap.org, pg 11

American Academy of Political & Social Science, 3814 Walnut St, Philadelphia, PA 19104 *Tel:* 215-746-6500 *Fax:* 215-898-1202 *Web Site:* www.aapss.org, pg 675

The American Alpine Club Press, 710 Tenth St, Suite 100, Golden, CO 80401 *Tel:* 303-384-0110 *Fax:* 303-384-0111 *E-mail:* aacpress@americanalpineclub.org *Web Site:* www.americanalpineclub.org, pg 11

American Anthropological Association, Publications Dept, 2200 Wilson Blvd, Suite 600, Arlington, VA 22201 *Tel:* 703-528-1902 ext 3014 *Fax:* 703-528-3546 *Web Site:* www.aaanet.org, pg 11

American Antiquarian Society, 185 Salisbury St, Worcester, MA 01609-1634 *Tel:* 508-755-5221 *Fax:* 508-754-9069 *Web Site:* www.americanantiquarian.org, pg 675

American Association for the Advancement of Science, 1200 New York Ave NW, Washington, DC 20005 *Tel:* 202-326-6400 *Fax:* 202-289-4021 *E-mail:* webmaster@aaas.org *Web Site:* www.aaas.org, pg 675

American Association for Vocational Instructional Materials, 220 Smithonia Rd, Winterville, GA 30683-9527 *Tel:* 706-742-5355 *Toll Free Tel:* 800-228-4689 *Fax:* 706-742-7005 *E-mail:* sales@aavim.com *Web Site:* www.aavim.com, pg 11

American Association of Advertising Agencies (AAAA), 405 Lexington Ave, 18th fl, New York, NY 10174-1801 *Tel:* 212-682-2500 *Fax:* 212-682-8391 *Web Site:* www.aaaa.org, pg 675

American Association of Blood Banks, 8101 Glenbrook Rd, Bethesda, MD 20814-2749 *Tel:* 301-907-6977 *Toll Free Tel:* 866-222-2498 (sales) *Fax:* 301-907-6895 *E-mail:* aabb@aabb.org; sales@aabb.org (ordering) *Web Site:* www.aabb.org, pg 11

American Association of Cereal Chemists, 3340 Pilot Knob Rd, St Paul, MN 55121-2097 *Tel:* 651-454-7250 *Toll Free Tel:* 800-328-7560 *Fax:* 651-454-0766 *E-mail:* aacc@scisoc.org *Web Site:* www.aaccnet.org, pg 11

American Association of Colleges for Teacher Education (AACTE), 1307 New York Ave NW, Suite 300, Washington, DC 20005-4701 *Tel:* 202-293-2450 *Fax:* 202-457-8095 *E-mail:* aacte@aacte.org *Web Site:* www.aacte.org, pg 11

American Association of Collegiate Registrars & Admissions Officers, One Dupont Circle NW, Suite 520, Washington, DC 20036-1135 *Tel:* 202-293-9161 *Toll Free Tel:* 877-338-3733 *Fax:* 202-872-8857 *E-mail:* info@aacrao.org *Web Site:* www.aacrao.org, pg 11

American Association of Community Colleges (AACC), One Dupont Circle NW, Suite 410, Washington, DC 20036 *Tel:* 202-728-0200; 301-490-8116 (orders) *Toll Free Tel:* 800-500-6557 *Fax:* 202-223-9390 (edit); 301-604-0158 (orders) *E-mail:* aaccpub@pmds.com (orders) *Web Site:* www.aacc.nche.edu, pg 11

American Association of Sunday & Feature Editors, College of Journalism, University of Maryland, Journalism Bldg, College Park, MD 20742-7111 *Tel:* 301-314-2631 *E-mail:* aasfe@jmail.umd.edu *Web Site:* www.aasfe.org, pg 676

American Association of University Women Award for Juvenile Literature, 4610 Mail Service Center, Raleigh, NC 27699-4610 *Tel:* 919-807-7290 *Fax:* 919-733-8807, pg 759

American Atheist Press, PO Box 5733, Parsippany, NJ 07054-6733 *Tel:* 908-276-7300 *Fax:* 908-276-7402 *E-mail:* info@atheists.org *Web Site:* www.atheists.org, pg 11

American Auto Racing Writers & Broadcasters, 922 N Pass Ave, Burbank, CA 91505 *Tel:* 818-842-7005 *Fax:* 818-842-7020 *E-mail:* aarwba@compuserve.com *Web Site:* www.aarwba.org, pg 676

American Bankers Association, 1120 Connecticut Ave NW, Washington, DC 20036 *Tel:* 202-663-5087 *Toll Free Tel:* 800-BANKERS (226-5377) *Fax:* 202-663-5087 (cust serv) *Web Site:* www.aba.com, pg 12

American Bar Association, 321 N Clark St, Suite LL-2, Chicago, IL 60610 *Tel:* 312-988-5000 *Toll Free Tel:* 800-285-2221 (orders) *Fax:* 312-988-6030 *E-mail:* askaba@abanet.org *Web Site:* www.abanet.org, pg 12

American Bible Society, 1865 Broadway, New York, NY 10023-7505 *Tel:* 212-408-1200 *Toll Free Tel:* 800-322-4253 (orders only) *Fax:* 212-408-1259 *E-mail:* info@americanbible.org *Web Site:* www.americanbible.org, pg 12

American Biographical Institute, 5126 Bur Oak Circle, Raleigh, NC 27612 *Tel:* 919-781-8710 *Fax:* 919-781-8712, pg 12

American Book Award, The Raymond House, 655 13 St, Suite 302, Oakland, CA 94612 *Tel:* 510-268-9775, pg 759

American Book Producers Association (ABPA), 160 Fifth Ave, Suite 622, New York, NY 10010 *Tel:* 212-645-2368 *Toll Free Tel:* 800-209-4575 *Fax:* 212-242-6499 *E-mail:* office@abpaonline.org *Web Site:* www.abpaonline.org, pg 676

American Book Publishing, 325 E 2400 S, Salt Lake City, UT 84115 *Tel:* 801-486-8639 *E-mail:* info@american-book.com *Web Site:* www.american-book.com, pg 12

American Booksellers Association, 828 S Broadway, Tarrytown, NY 10591 *Tel:* 914-591-2665 *Toll Free Tel:* 800-637-0037 *Fax:* 914-591-2720 *E-mail:* editorial@booksense.com *Web Site:* www.booksense.com, pg 676

American Business Media, 675 Third Ave, Suite 415, New York, NY 10017 *Tel:* 212-661-6360 *Fax:* 212-370-0736 *E-mail:* info@abmmail.com *Web Site:* www.americanbusinessmedia.com, pg 676

American Catholic Press, 16565 S State St, South Holland, IL 60473 *Tel:* 708-331-5845 *Fax:* 708-331-5484 *E-mail:* acp@acpress.org *Web Site:* www.acpress.org, pg 12

The American Ceramic Society, 735 Ceramic Place, Westerville, OH 43081-8720 *Tel:* 614-794-5890 *Fax:* 614-794-5892 *E-mail:* info@ceramics.org *Web Site:* www.ceramics.org, pg 12

The American Chemical Society, 1155 16 St NW, Washington, DC 20036 *Tel:* 202-872-4600 *Toll Free Tel:* 800-227-5558 *Fax:* 202-872-6067 *Web Site:* www.acs.org; pubs.acs.org, pg 12

American Christian Writers, PO Box 110390, Nashville, TN 37222 *Tel:* 615-834-0450 *Toll Free Tel:* 800-21-WRITE (219-7483) *Fax:* 615-834-7736 *Web Site:* www.acwriters.com, pg 676

American Civil Liberties Union, 125 Broad St, 18th fl, New York, NY 10004 *Tel:* 212-549-2500 *Toll Free Tel:* 800-775-ACLU (orders) *E-mail:* info@aclu.org *Web Site:* www.aclu.org, pg 676

American College, 270 S Bryn Mawr Ave, Bryn Mawr, PA 19010 *Tel:* 610-526-1000 *Fax:* 610-526-1310 *Web Site:* www.amercoll.edu, pg 12

American College of Physician Executives, 4890 W Kennedy Blvd, Suite 200, Tampa, FL 33609 *Tel:* 813-287-2000 *Toll Free Tel:* 800-562-8088 *Fax:* 813-287-8993 *E-mail:* acpe@acpe.org *Web Site:* www.acpe.org, pg 12

American College of Surgeons, 633 N Saint Clair St, Chicago, IL 60611-3211 *Tel:* 312-202-5000 *Toll Free Tel:* 800-621-4111 *Fax:* 312-202-5001 *E-mail:* postmaster@facs.org *Web Site:* www.facs.org, pg 13

American Correctional Association, 4380 Forbes Blvd, Lanham, MD 20706-4322 *Tel:* 301-918-1800 *Toll Free Tel:* 800-222-5646 *Fax:* 301-918-1886 *Web Site:* www.aca.org, pg 13

American Council on Education, One Dupont Circle NW, Washington, DC 20036 *Tel:* 202-939-9380; 202-939-9300 *Fax:* 202-939-9302 *Web Site:* www.acenet.edu, pg 13

American Council on Education, One Dupont Circle NW, Washington, DC 20036 *Tel:* 202-939-9300 *Fax:* 202-939-9302 *Web Site:* www.acenet.edu, pg 676

American Counseling Association, 5999 Stevenson Ave, Alexandria, VA 22304-3300 *Tel:* 703-823-9800 *Toll Free Tel:* 800-422-2648 (ext 222 - book orders only) *Fax:* 703-461-9260 *Toll Free Fax:* 800-473-2329 *Web Site:* www.counseling.org, pg 13

American Diabetes Association, 1701 N Beauregard St, Alexandria, VA 22311 *Tel:* 703-299-2046 *Toll Free Tel:* 800-232-6733 *Fax:* 908-806-2301 *Web Site:* www.diabetes.org, pg 13

American Dietetic Association, 120 S Riverside Plaza, Suite 2000, Chicago, IL 60606 *Tel:* 312-899-0040 *Fax:* 312-899-4757 *Web Site:* www.eatright.org, pg 13

American Eagle Publications Inc, 35610 Highway, Show Low, AZ 85901 *Tel:* 623-556-2925 *Toll Free Tel:* 866-764-2925 *Fax:* 623-556-2926 *E-mail:* custservice@ameaglepubs.com *Web Site:* www.ameaglepubs.com, pg 13

American Editing, 69 Lansing St, Auburn, NY 13021 *Tel:* 315-258-8012, pg 590

American Fantasy Press, 919 Tappan St, Woodstock, IL 60098 *Tel:* 815-338-5512 *Fax:* 815-338-5512 *E-mail:* garpubserv@aol.com *Web Site:* www.american-fantasy.com, pg 569

American Federation of Arts, 41 E 65 St, New York, NY 10021 *Tel:* 212-988-7700 *Toll Free Tel:* 800-232-0270 *Fax:* 212-861-2487 *E-mail:* publicat@afaweb.org *Web Site:* www.afaweb.org, pg 13

American Federation of Astrologers Inc, 6535 S Rural Rd, Tempe, AZ 85283-3746 *Tel:* 480-838-1751 *Toll Free Tel:* 888-301-7630 *Fax:* 480-838-8293 *E-mail:* afa@msn.com *Web Site:* www.astrologers.com, pg 13

American Film Institute (AFI), 2021 N Western Ave, Los Angeles, CA 90027 *Tel:* 323-856-7600 *Toll Free Tel:* 800-774-4234 (memberships) *Fax:* 323-467-4578 *E-mail:* info@afi.com *Web Site:* www.afi.com, pg 676

American Fisheries Society, 5410 Grosvenor Lane, Suite 110, Bethesda, MD 20814-2199 *Tel:* 301-897-8616 *Fax:* 301-897-8096 *E-mail:* main@fisheries.org *Web Site:* www.fisheries.org, pg 13

American Forest & Paper Association, 1111 19 St NW, Suite 800, Washington, DC 20036 *Tel:* 202-463-2700 *Toll Free Tel:* 800-878-8878 *Fax:* 202-463-4703 *E-mail:* info@afandpa.org *Web Site:* www.afandpa.org, pg 676

American Foundation for the Blind (AFB Press), 11 Penn Plaza, Suite 300, New York, NY 10001 *Tel:* 212-502-7600 *Toll Free Tel:* 800-232-3044 (orders) *Fax:* 212-502-7777 *E-mail:* afbinfo@afb.net *Web Site:* www.afb.org, pg 13

American Geological Institute (AGI), 4220 King St, Alexandria, VA 22302-1507 *Tel:* 703-379-2480 *Fax:* 703-379-7563 *E-mail:* pubs@agiweb.org *Web Site:* www.agiweb.org, pg 14

American Geophysical Union (AGU), 2000 Florida Ave NW, Washington, DC 20009 *Tel:* 202-462-6900 *Toll Free Tel:* 800-966-2481 (North America) *Fax:* 202-328-0566 *E-mail:* service@agu.org *Web Site:* www.agu.org, pg 14

American Health Publishing Co, Texas Star Pkwy, Suite 120, Euless, TX 76040 *Tel:* 817-545-4500 *Toll Free Tel:* 800-LEARN41 *Fax:* 817-545-2211 *E-mail:* contact@thelifestylecompany.com *Web Site:* www.thelifestylecompany.com, pg 14

American Historical Association, 400 "A" St SE, Washington, DC 20003 *Tel:* 202-544-2422 *Fax:* 202-544-8307 *E-mail:* aha@historians.org *Web Site:* www.historians.org, pg 14

American Historical Press, 10755 Sherman Way, Suite 2, Sun Valley, CA 91352 *Tel:* 818-503-0133 *Toll Free Tel:* 800-550-5750 *Fax:* 818-503-9081 *E-mail:* ahp@amhistpress.com *Web Site:* www.amhistpress.com, pg 14

American Illustration/American Photography, 126 Fifth Ave, Suite 14B, New York, NY 10011 *Tel:* 212-243-5262 *Fax:* 212-243-5201 *E-mail:* aiap@skyweb.net *Web Site:* www.ai-ap.com, pg 759

American Indian Studies Center Publications at UCLA, 3220 Campbell Hall, Los Angeles, CA 90095-1548 *Tel:* 310-825-7315; 310-206-7508 *Fax:* 310-206-7060 *E-mail:* aiscpubs@ucla.edu; aisc@ucla.edu *Web Site:* www.sscnet.ucla.edu, pg 14

American Industrial Hygiene Association, 2700 Prosperity Ave, Suite 250, Fairfax, VA 22031-4319 *Tel:* 703-849-8888 *Fax:* 703-207-3561 *E-mail:* infonet@aiha.org *Web Site:* www.aiha.org, pg 14

American Institute for CPCU & Insurance Institute of America, 720 Providence Rd, Malvern, PA 19355-0716 *Tel:* 610-644-2100 *Toll Free Tel:* 800-644-2101 *Fax:* 610-640-9576; 610-644-7629 *E-mail:* cserv@cpcuiia.org *Web Site:* www.aicpcu.org, pg 14

American Institute of Aeronautics & Astronautics, 1801 Alexander Bell Dr, Suite 500, Reston, VA 20191 *Tel:* 703-264-7500 *Toll Free Tel:* 800-639-2422 *Fax:* 703-264-7551 *E-mail:* custserv@aiaa.org *Web Site:* www.aiaa.org, pg 14

American Institute of Certified Public Accountants, Harborside Financial Ctr, 201 Plaza Three, Jersey City, NJ 07311-3881 *Tel:* 201-938-3000 *Toll Free Tel:* 888-777-7077 *Fax:* 201-938-3329 *Web Site:* www.aicpa.org, pg 15

American Institute of Chemical Engineers (AICHE), 3 Park Ave, New York, NY 10016-5991 *Tel:* 212-591-7338 *Toll Free Tel:* 800-242-4363 *Fax:* 212-591-8888 *E-mail:* xpress@aiche.org *Web Site:* www.aiche.org, pg 15

American Institute of Graphic Arts (AIGA), 164 Fifth Ave, New York, NY 10010 *Tel:* 212-807-1990 *Toll Free Tel:* 800-548-1634 *Fax:* 212-807-1799 *E-mail:* aiga@aiga.org *Web Site:* www.aiga.org, pg 676

American Institute of Physics, 2 Huntington Quadrangle, Suite 1NO1, Melville, NY 11747-4502 *Tel:* 516-576-2477 *Fax:* 516-576-2474 *E-mail:* proceedings-mgr@aip.org *Web Site:* www.aip.org, pg 15

American Institute of Ultrasound in Medicine, 14750 Sweitzer Lane, Suite 100, Laurel, MD 20707-5906 *Tel:* 301-498-4100 *Toll Free Tel:* 800-638-5352 *Fax:* 301-498-4450 *E-mail:* publications@aium.org *Web Site:* www.aium.org, pg 15

American Jewish Committee, 165 E 56 St, New York, NY 10022 *Tel:* 212-751-4000 *Fax:* 212-891-1492 *Web Site:* www.ajc.org, pg 676

American Judicature Society, 2700 University Ave, Des Moines, IA 50311 *Tel:* 515-271-2281 *Fax:* 515-279-3090 *Web Site:* www.ajs.org, pg 15

American Law Institute, 4025 Chestnut St, Philadelphia, PA 19104-3099 *Tel:* 215-243-1600 *Toll Free Tel:* 800-253-6397 *Fax:* 215-243-1664; 215-243-1683 *Web Site:* www.ali.org, pg 15

The American Legion Fourth Estate Award, 700 N Pennsylvania St, Indianapolis, IN 46204 *Tel:* 317-630-1253 *Fax:* 317-630-1368 *E-mail:* pr@legion.org *Web Site:* www.legion.org, pg 759

American Library Association (ALA), 50 E Huron St, Chicago, IL 60611 *Tel:* 312-944-6780 *Toll Free Tel:* 800-545-2433 *Fax:* 312-944-8741 *E-mail:* editionsmarketing@ala.org *Web Site:* www.ala.org, pg 15

American Library Publishing Co, PO Box 4272, Sedona, AZ 86340-4272 *Tel:* 928-282-4922 *E-mail:* grace@sedonaarizona.com, pg 15

American Literacy Council, 148 W 117 St, New York, NY 10026 *Tel:* 212-663-4200 *Toll Free Tel:* 800-781-9985 *E-mail:* fyi@americanliteracy.com *Web Site:* www.americanliteracy.com, pg 676

American Literary Press/Noble House, 8019 Belair Rd, Suite 10, Baltimore, MD 21236 *Tel:* 410-882-7700 *Fax:* 410-882-7703 *E-mail:* amerlit@americanliterarypress.com *Web Site:* www.americanliterarypress.com, pg 569

American Literary Translators Association (ALTA), PO Box 830688, Mail Sta MC 35, Richardson, TX 75083-0688 *Tel:* 972-883-2093 *Fax:* 972-883-6303 *Web Site:* www.literarytranslators.org, pg 677

American Management Association, 1601 Broadway, New York, NY 10019-7420 *Tel:* 212-586-8100 *Toll Free Tel:* 800-262-9699 *Fax:* 212-903-8168 *Web Site:* www.amanet.org, pg 677

American Map Corp, 46-35 54 Rd, Maspeth, NY 11378 *Tel:* 718-784-0055 *Toll Free Tel:* 800-432-MAPS *Fax:* 718-784-0640 (admin); 718-784-1216 (sales & orders), pg 15

American Marketing Association, 311 S Wacker Dr, Suite 5800, Chicago, IL 60606-2266 *Tel:* 312-542-9000 *Toll Free Tel:* 800-262-1150 *Fax:* 312-542-9001 *E-mail:* info@ama.org *Web Site:* www.marketingpower.com, pg 15, 677

American Mathematical Society, 201 Charles St, Providence, RI 02904-2294 *Tel:* 401-455-4000 *Toll Free Tel:* 800-321-4267 *Fax:* 401-331-3842; 401-455-4046 (cust serv) *E-mail:* ams@ams.org *Web Site:* www.ams.org, pg 16

American Medical Association, 515 N State St, Chicago, IL 60610 *Tel:* 312-464-5000 *Toll Free Tel:* 800-621-8335 (cust serv) *Fax:* 312-464-4184 *Web Site:* www.ama-assn.org, pg 16

American Medical Association, 515 N State St, Chicago, IL 60610 *Tel:* 312-464-5000 *Toll Free Tel:* 800-621-8335 *Fax:* 312-464-4184 *Web Site:* www.ama-assn.org, pg 677

American Medical Publishers Association, 14 Fort Hill Rd, Huntington, NY 11743 *Tel:* 631-423-0075 *Fax:* 631-423-0075 *E-mail:* info@ampaonline.org *Web Site:* www.ampaonline.org, pg 677

American Medical Writers Association, 40 W Gude Dr, Suite 101, Rockville, MD 20850-1192 *Tel:* 301-294-5303 *Fax:* 301-294-9006 *E-mail:* info@amwa.org *Web Site:* www.amwa.org, pg 677

American Numismatic Society, 26 Fulton St, New York, NY 10038 *Tel:* 212-571-4470 *Fax:* 212-571-4479 *E-mail:* info@amnumsoc.org; info@numismatics.org *Web Site:* www.amnumsoc.org; www.numismatics.org, pg 16

American Occupational Therapy Association Inc, 4720 Montgomery Lane, Bethesda, MD 20824 *Tel:* 301-652-2682 *Fax:* 301-652-7711 *Web Site:* www.aota.org, pg 16

American Philosophical Society, 104 S Fifth St, Philadelphia, PA 19106 *Tel:* 215-440-3425 *Fax:* 215-440-3450 *Web Site:* www.amphilsoc.org, pg 16

American Phytopathological Society, 3340 Pilot Knob Rd, St Paul, MN 55121-2097 *Tel:* 651-454-7250 *Toll Free Tel:* 800-328-7560 *Fax:* 651-454-0766 *E-mail:* aps@scisoc.org *Web Site:* www.apsnet.org, pg 16

American Political Science Association, 1527 New Hampshire Ave NW, Washington, DC 20036 *Tel:* 202-483-2512 *Fax:* 202-483-2657 *E-mail:* apsa@apsanet.org *Web Site:* www.apsanet.org, pg 677

American Press, 28 State St, Suite 1100, Boston, MA 02109 *Tel:* 617-247-0022 *Fax:* 617-247-0022 *E-mail:* ampress@flash.net *Web Site:* www.americanpressboston.com, pg 16

American Printing History Association, PO Box 4519, Grand Central Sta, New York, NY 10163-4519 *Tel:* 212-930-9220 *Fax:* 212-930-0079 *Web Site:* www.printinghistory.org, pg 677

American Printing History Association Award, PO Box 4519, Grand Central Sta, New York, NY 10163-4519 *Tel:* 212-930-9220 *Fax:* 212-930-0079 *Web Site:* www.printinghistory.org, pg 759

American Printing House for the Blind Inc, 1839 Frankfort Ave, Louisville, KY 40206 *Tel:* 502-895-2405 *Toll Free Tel:* 800-223-1839 (cust serv) *Fax:* 502-899-2274 *E-mail:* info@aph.org *Web Site:* www.aph.org, pg 16

American Products Publishing Co, 10950 SW Fifth St, Suite 155, Beaverton, OR 97005-4782 *Tel:* 503-672-7502 *Toll Free Tel:* 800-668-8181 *Fax:* 503-672-7104 *E-mail:* info@american-products.com *Web Site:* www.american-products.com, pg 16

American Program Bureau Inc, 36 Crafts St, Newton, MA 02458 *Tel:* 617-965-6600 *Toll Free Tel:* 800-225-4575 *Fax:* 617-965-6610 *E-mail:* apb@apbspeakers.com *Web Site:* www.apbspeakers.com, pg 669

American Psychiatric Publishing Inc, 1000 Wilson Blvd, Suite 1825, Arlington, VA 22209 *Tel:* 703-907-7322 *Toll Free Tel:* 800-368-5777 *Fax:* 703-907-1091 *E-mail:* appi@psych.org *Web Site:* www.appi.org, pg 16

American Psychological Association, 750 First St NE, Washington, DC 20002-4242 *Tel:* 202-336-5500 *Toll Free Tel:* 800-374-2721 *Fax:* 202-336-5620 *E-mail:* order@apa.org *Web Site:* www.apa.org/books, pg 17

American Psychological Association, 750 First St NE, Washington, DC 20002-4242 *Tel:* 202-336-5500; 202-336-5540 *Toll Free Tel:* 800-374-2721 *Fax:* 202-336-5620 *E-mail:* order@apa.org *Web Site:* www.apa.org, pg 677

American Public Human Services Association, 810 First St NE, Suite 500, Washington, DC 20002 *Tel:* 202-682-0100 *Fax:* 202-289-6555 *E-mail:* pubs@aphsa.org *Web Site:* www.aphsa.org, pg 677

American Public Works Association, 2345 Grand Blvd, Suite 500, Kansas City, MO 64108-2641 *Tel:* 816-472-6100 *Fax:* 816-472-1610 *E-mail:* apwa@apwa.net *Web Site:* www.apwa.net, pg 17

American Quilter's Society, 5801 Kentucky Dam Rd, Paducah, KY 42002 *Tel:* 270-898-7903 *Toll Free Tel:* 800-626-5420 (orders) *Fax:* 270-898-8890 *E-mail:* info@aqsquilt.com *Web Site:* www.aqsquilt.com, pg 17

American Research Press, PO Box 141, Rehoboth, NM 87322 *Web Site:* www.gallup.unm.edu/~smarandache, pg 17

American Sciences Press Inc, 20 Cross Rd, Syracuse, NY 13224-2104, pg 17

American Showcase Inc, 915 Broadway, New York, NY 10010 *Tel:* 212-673-6600 *Toll Free Tel:* 800-894-7469 *Fax:* 212-673-9795 *E-mail:* info@amshow.com *Web Site:* www.amshow.com, pg 17

American Society for Information Science & Technology (ASIS), 1320 Fenwick Lane, Suite 510, Silver Spring, MD 20910 *Tel:* 301-495-0900 *Fax:* 301-495-0810 *E-mail:* asis@asis.org *Web Site:* www.asis.org, pg 677

American Society for Nondestructive Testing, 1711 Arlingate Lane, Columbus, OH 43228-0518 *Tel:* 614-274-6003 *Toll Free Tel:* 800-222-2768 *Fax:* 614-274-6899 *E-mail:* webmaster@asnt.org *Web Site:* www.asnt.org, pg 17

American Society for Photogrammetry & Remote Sensing, 5410 Grosvenor Lane, Suite 210, Bethesda, MD 20814-2160 *Tel:* 301-493-0290 *Fax:* 301-493-0208 *E-mail:* asprs@asprs.org *Web Site:* www.asprs.org, pg 17

American Society for Quality, 600 N Plankinton Ave, Milwaukee, WI 53203 *Tel:* 414-272-8575 *Toll Free Tel:* 800-248-1946 *Fax:* 414-272-1734 *E-mail:* cs@asq.org *Web Site:* www.asq.org, pg 17

American Society for Training & Development (ASTD), 1640 King St, Alexandria, VA 22313-2043 *Tel:* 703-683-8100 *Toll Free Tel:* 800-628-2783 *Fax:* 703-683-1523 *E-mail:* publications@astd.org *Web Site:* www.astd.org, pg 17

American Society of Agricultural Engineers, 2950 Niles Rd, St Joseph, MI 49085-9659 *Tel:* 269-429-0300 *Fax:* 269-429-3852 *E-mail:* hq@asae.org *Web Site:* www.asae.org, pg 18

American Society of Agronomy, 677 S Segoe Rd, Madison, WI 53711-1086 *Tel:* 608-273-8080 *Fax:* 608-273-2021 *E-mail:* headquarters@agronomy.org *Web Site:* www.agronomy.org, pg 18

American Society of Civil Engineers (ASCE), 1801 Alexander Bell Dr, Reston, VA 20191-4400 *Tel:* 703-295-6200 *Toll Free Tel:* 800-548-2723 *Fax:* 703-295-6278 *E-mail:* marketing@asce.org *Web Site:* www.asce.org, pg 18

American Society of Composers, Authors & Publishers (ASCAP), One Lincoln Plaza, New York City, NY 10023 *Tel:* 212-621-6000 *Toll Free Tel:* 800-952-7227 *Fax:* 212-362-7328 *E-mail:* info@ascap.com *Web Site:* www.ascap.com, pg 677

American Society of Electroneurodiagnostic Technologists Inc, 426 W 42 St, Kansas City, KS 64111 *Tel:* 816-931-1120 *Fax:* 816-931-1145 *E-mail:* info@aset.org *Web Site:* www.aset.org, pg 18

American Society of Health-System Pharmacists, 7272 Wisconsin Ave, Bethesda, MD 20814 *Tel:* 301-657-3000 *Toll Free Tel:* 866-279-0681 (orders) *Fax:* 301-664-8867 *E-mail:* info@ashp.org *Web Site:* www.ashp.org, pg 18

American Society of Indexers Inc (ASI), 10200 W 44 Ave, Suite 304, Wheat Ridge, CO 80033 *Tel:* 303-463-2887 *Fax:* 303-422-8894 *E-mail:* info@asindexing.org *Web Site:* www.asindexing.org, pg 678

American Society of Journalists & Authors (ASJA), 1501 Broadway, Suite 302, New York, NY 10036 *Tel:* 212-997-0947 *Fax:* 212-768-7414 *E-mail:* staff@asja.org *Web Site:* www.asja.org, pg 678

American Society of Journalists & Authors Writers Conference, 1501 Broadway, Suite 302, New York, NY 10036 *Tel:* 212-997-0947 *Fax:* 212-768-7414 *E-mail:* staff@asja.org *Web Site:* www.asja.org, pg 741

American Society of Magazine Editors, 810 Seventh Ave, 24th fl, New York, NY 10019 *Tel:* 212-872-3700 *Fax:* 212-906-0128 *E-mail:* asme@magazine.org *Web Site:* www.asme.magazine.org, pg 678

American Society of Mechanical Engineers (ASME), 3 Park Ave, New York, NY 10016 *Tel:* 212-591-7000 *Toll Free Tel:* 800-843-2763 (cust serv) *Fax:* 212-591-7674; 973-882-1717 (cust serv) *E-mail:* infocentral@asme.org *Web Site:* www.asme.org, pg 18

American Society of Media Photographers (ASMP), 150 N Second St, Philadelphia, PA 19106 *Tel:* 215-451-2767 *Fax:* 215-451-0880 *E-mail:* info@asmp.org *Web Site:* www.asmp.org, pg 678

American Society of Plant Taxonomists, University of Michigan Herbarium, 3600 Varsity Dr, Ann Arbor, MI 48108-2287 *Tel:* 734-647-2812 *Fax:* 734-647-5719 *Web Site:* www.sysbot.org, pg 18

American Sociological Association (ASA), 1307 New York Ave NW, Suite 700, Washington, DC 20005-4701 *Tel:* 202-383-9005 *Fax:* 202-638-0882 *E-mail:* executive.office@asanet.org *Web Site:* www.asanet.org, pg 678

American Speech-Language-Hearing Association (ASHA), 10801 Rockville Pike, Rockville, MD 20852 *Tel:* 301-897-5700 *Toll Free Tel:* 800-638-8255 *Fax:* 301-571-0457 *Web Site:* www.asha.org, pg 678

American Technical Publishers Inc, 1155 W 175 St, Homewood, IL 60430-4600 *Tel:* 708-957-1100 *Toll Free Tel:* 800-323-3471 *Fax:* 708-957-1101 *E-mail:* service@americantech.net *Web Site:* www.go2atp.com, pg 18

American Translators Association (ATA), 225 Reinekers Lane, Suite 590, Alexandria, VA 22314 *Tel:* 703-683-6100 *Fax:* 703-683-6122 *E-mail:* ata@atanet.org *Web Site:* www.atanet.org, pg 678

American Trust Publications, 745 McClintock Dr, Suite 114, Burr Ridge, IL 60527 *Tel:* 630-789-9191 *Toll Free Tel:* 888-319-5858 *Fax:* 630-789-9455 *Web Site:* www.nait.net, pg 18

American Water Works Association, 6666 W Quincy Ave, Denver, CO 80235 *Tel:* 303-794-7711 *Toll Free Tel:* 800-926-7337 *Fax:* 303-347-0804 *Web Site:* www.awwa.org, pg 18

America's Health Insurance Plans (AHIP), South Bldg, 601 Pennsylvania Ave NW, Suite 500, Washington, DC 20004 *Tel:* 202-778-3200 *Fax:* 202-861-6354 *Web Site:* www.insuranceeducation.org, pg 18

Amherst Media Inc, 175 Rano St, Suite 200, Buffalo, NY 14207 *Tel:* 716-874-4450 *Fax:* 716-874-4508 *E-mail:* amherstmed@aol.com *Web Site:* www.amherstmedia.com, pg 18

Amirah Publishing, IBTS, 22-55 31 St, Long Island City, NY 11105 *Tel:* 718-721-4246 (IBTS) *Toll Free Tel:* 800-337-4287 (IBTS) *Fax:* 718-721-6108 (IBTS) *E-mail:* amirahpbco@aol.com; information@ibtsonline.com, pg 19

Amrita Foundation Inc, PO Box 190978, Dallas, TX 75219-0978 *Tel:* 214-522-7533 *Fax:* 214-522-6184 *E-mail:* prisi@amrita.com *Web Site:* www.amrita.com, pg 569

AMS Press Inc, Brooklyn Navy Yard, Bldg 292, Suite 417, 63 Flushing Ave, New York, NY 11205 *Tel:* 212-777-4700; 718-875-8100 *Fax:* 212-995-5413 *E-mail:* amserve@earthlink.net, pg 19

Amsco School Publications Inc, 315 Hudson St, New York, NY 10013-1085 *Tel:* 212-886-6500; 212-886-6565 *Toll Free Tel:* 800-969-8398 *Fax:* 212-675-7010 *E-mail:* info@amscopub.com *Web Site:* www.amscopub.com, pg 19

Betsy Amster Literary Enterprises, PO Box 27788, Los Angeles, CA 90027-0788 *Tel:* 323-662-1987 *Fax:* 323-660-4015 *E-mail:* amsterlit@compuserve.com, pg 619

Marcia Amsterdam Agency, 41 W 82 St, New York, NY 10024-5613 *Tel:* 212-873-4945, pg 619

AMWA Annual Conference, 40 W Gude Dr, Suite 101, Rockville, MD 20850-1192 *Tel:* 301-294-5303 *Fax:* 301-294-9006 *Web Site:* www.amwa.org, pg 741

AMWA Medical Book Awards, 40 W Gude Dr, Suite 101, Rockville, MD 20850-1192 *Tel:* 301-294-5303 *Fax:* 301-294-9006, pg 759

The Amwell Press, Ridge Plaza, 2004 Rte 31 & Cregar Rd, Clinton, NJ 08809 *Tel:* 908-638-9033 *Fax:* 908-638-4728, pg 19

Amy Writing Awards, PO Box 16091, Lansing, MI 48901-6091 *Tel:* 517-323-6233 *Fax:* 517-321-2572 *E-mail:* amyfoundtn@aol.com *Web Site:* www.amyfound.org, pg 759

Anacus Press, 3943 Meadowbrook Rd, Minneapolis, MN 55426-4505 *Tel:* 952-938-9330 *Toll Free Tel:* 800-846-7027 *Fax:* 952-938-7353 *E-mail:* feedback@finney-hobar.com *Web Site:* www.anacus.com, pg 19

The Analytic Press, 101 West St, Hillsdale, NJ 07642 *Tel:* 201-358-9477; 201-236-9500 *Toll Free Tel:* 800-926-6579 (orders only); 800-627-0629 (journal orders) *Fax:* 201-358-4700 (edit); 201-760-3735 (orders only) *E-mail:* tap@analyticpress.com *Web Site:* www.analyticpress.com, pg 19

Joyce L Ananian, 25 Forest Circle, Waltham, MA 02452-4719 *Tel:* 781-894-4330 *E-mail:* jlananian@hotmail.com, pg 590

Ancestry Publishing, 360 W 4800 N, Provo, UT 84064 *Tel:* 801-705-7305 *Toll Free Tel:* 800-262-3787 *Fax:* 801-426-3501 *E-mail:* editor@ancestry.com; dealersales@ancestry-inc.com *Web Site:* www.ancestry.com, pg 19

Anchor Publishing, Virginia, PO Box 9558, Virginia Beach, VA 23450-9558 *Tel:* 757-431-1366 *Web Site:* www.antion.com, pg 19

Anchorage Press Plays Inc, PO Box 2901, Louisville, KY 40201-2901 *Tel:* 502-583-2288 *E-mail:* applays@bellsouth.net *Web Site:* applays.com, pg 19

Barbara S Anderson, 706 W Davis, Ann Arbor, MI 48103-4855 *Tel:* 734-995-0125; 734-994-6182 *Fax:* 734-994-5207, pg 590

Denice A Anderson, 210 E Church St, Clinton, MI 49236 *Tel:* 517-456-4990 *Fax:* 517-456-4990, pg 590

Anderson/Grinberg Literary Management Inc, 266 W 23 St, Suite 3, New York, NY 10011 *Tel:* 212-620-5883 *Fax:* 212-627-4725 *E-mail:* queries@andersongrinberg.com, pg 619

Jim Anderson, 77 S Second St, Brooklyn, NY 11211 *Tel:* 718-388-1083 *E-mail:* jim.and@worldnet.att.net, pg 590

Patricia Anderson, 1489 Marine Dr, Suite 515, West Vancouver, BC V7T 1B8, Canada *Tel:* 604-740-0805 *Fax:* 604-740-0805 *E-mail:* query@helpingyougetpublished.com *Web Site:* www.helpingyougetpublished.com, pg 590

Bart Andrews & Associates Inc, 7510 Sunset Blvd, Suite 100, Los Angeles, CA 90046-3418 *Tel:* 310-271-9916, pg 619

Elaine Andrews, 10596 Twin Rivers Rd, Columbia, MD 21044 *Tel:* 410-997-5890 *E-mail:* eekandrews@aol.com, pg 590

Andrews University Press, Andrews University Press, 213 Information Services Bldg, Berrien Springs, MI 49104-1700 *Tel:* 269-471-6915 *Toll Free Tel:* 800-467-6369 (Visa & MC orders only) *Fax:* 269-471-6224 *E-mail:* aupress@andrews.edu *Web Site:* www.andrewsuniversitypress.com; www.ancrews.edu/universitypress, pg 19

Andujar Communication Technologies Inc, 7946 Ivanhoe Ave, Suite 314, La Jolla, CA 92037 *Tel:* 858-459-2673 *Fax:* 858-459-9768, pg 19

Angel City Press, 2118 Wilshire Blvd, No 880, Santa Monica, CA 90403 *Tel:* 310-395-9982 *Toll Free Tel:* 800-949-8039 *Fax:* 310-395-3353 *E-mail:* info@angelcitypress.com *Web Site:* www.angelcitypress.com, pg 20

Angel Publications, 123-3691 Albion Rd S, Gloucester, ON K1T 1P2, Canada *Tel:* 613-526-2277 *E-mail:* angelpublications@canada.com *Web Site:* members.rogers.com/angelpub, pg 590

Angelus Press, 2915 Forest Ave, Kansas City, MO 64109 *Tel:* 816-753-3150 *Toll Free Tel:* 800-966-7337 *Fax:* 816-753-3557 *Toll Free Fax:* 888-855-9022 *E-mail:* info@angeluspress.org *Web Site:* www.angeluspress.org, pg 20

The Anglican Book Centre, 80 Hayden St, Toronto, ON M4Y 3G2, Canada *Tel:* 416-924-1332 *Toll Free Tel:* 800-268-1168 (Canada only) *Fax:* 416-924-2760 *E-mail:* abc@nationalanglican.com *Web Site:* www.anglicanbookcentre.com, pg 535

Anhinga Press, PO Box 10595, Tallahassee, FL 32302-2595 *Tel:* 850-442-1408 *Fax:* 850-442-6323 *E-mail:* info@anhinga.org *Web Site:* www.anhinga.org, pg 20

Anhinga Prize for Poetry, PO Box 10595, Tallahassee, FL 32302-2595 *Tel:* 850-442-6323 *Fax:* 850-442-6323 *E-mail:* info@anhinga.org *Web Site:* www.anhinga.org, pg 759

The Anisfield Wolf Book Award in Human Relations, 1422 Euclid Ave, Suite 1300, Cleveland, OH 44115-2001 *Tel:* 216-861-3810 *Fax:* 216-861-2229 *E-mail:* contactus@clevefdn.org, pg 759

Anker Publishing Co Inc, 176 Ballville Rd, Bolton, MA 01740-1255 *Tel:* 978-779-6190 *Fax:* 978-779-6366 *E-mail:* info@ankerpub.com *Web Site:* www.ankerpub.com, pg 20

R Ross Annett Award for Children's Literature, 11759 Groat Rd, Percy Page Center, Edmonton, AB T5M 3K6, Canada *Tel:* 780-422-8174 *Toll Free Tel:* 800-665-5354 *Fax:* 780-422-2663 *E-mail:* mail@writersguild.ab.ca *Web Site:* www.writersguild.ab.ca, pg 759

Annick Press Ltd, 15 Patricia Ave, Toronto, ON M2M 1H9, Canada *Tel:* 416-221-4802 *Fax:* 416-221-8400 *E-mail:* annick@annickpress.com *Web Site:* www.annickpress.com, pg 535

Annual Reviews, 4139 El Camino Way, Palo Alto, CA 94306 *Tel:* 650-493-4400 *Toll Free Tel:* 800-523-8635 *Fax:* 650-855-9815 *E-mail:* service@annualreviews.org *Web Site:* www.annualreviews.org, pg 20

ANR Publications University of California, 6701 San Pablo Ave, 2nd fl, Oakland, CA 94608-1239 *Tel:* 510-642-2431 *Toll Free Tel:* 800-994-8849 *Fax:* 510-643-5470 *E-mail:* danrcs@ucdavis.edu *Web Site:* anrcatalog.ucdavis.edu, pg 20

Anti-Aging Press, 4185 Pamona Ave, Miami, FL 33133 *Tel:* 305-661-2802; 305-662-3928 *Toll Free Tel:* 800-SO-YOUNG *Fax:* 305-661-4123, pg 569

Antioch Writers' Workshop, PO Box 494, Yellow Springs, OH 45387-0494 *Tel:* 937-475-7357; 937-767-2700 (Board of Trustees) *E-mail:* info@antiochwritersworkshop.com *Web Site:* www.antiochwritersworkshop.com, pg 741

Antiquarian Booksellers' Association of America, 20 W 44 St, 4th fl, New York, NY 10036 *Tel:* 212-944-8291 *Fax:* 212-944-8293 *E-mail:* hq@abaa.org *Web Site:* www.abaa.org, pg 678

Antiquarian Booksellers Association of Canada (ABAC), 824 Fort St, Victoria, BC V8W 1H8, Canada *Tel:* 250-360-2929 *Fax:* 250-361-1812 *E-mail:* info@abac.org *Web Site:* www.abac.org, pg 678

Antique Collectors Club Ltd, 116 Pleasant St, East Hampton, MA 01027 *Tel:* 413-529-0861 *Toll Free Tel:* 800-252-5231 *Fax:* 413-297-0862 *E-mail:* info@antiquecc.com *Web Site:* www.antiquecc.com, pg 20

Antique Trader Books, c/o Krause Publications, 700 E State St, Iola, WI 54990-0001 *Tel:* 715-445-2214 *Toll Free Tel:* 888-457-2873 *Fax:* 715-445-4087 *Web Site:* www.krause.com, pg 20

Antrim House, 21 Goodrich Rd, Simsbury, CT 06070-1804 *Tel:* 860-217-0023 *Fax:* 860-217-0023 *E-mail:* eds@antrimhousebooks.com *Web Site:* www.antrimhousebooks.com, pg 20

Anvilpress Inc, PO Box 3008, Vancouver, BC V6B 3X5, Canada *Tel:* 604-876-8710 *Toll Free Tel:* 800-565-9523 (ordering) *Fax:* 604-879-2667 *E-mail:* info@anvilpress.com *Web Site:* www.anvilpress.com, pg 535

AOCS Press, 2211 W Bradley Ave, Champaign, IL 61821-1827 *Tel:* 217-359-2344 *Toll Free Tel:* 800-336-AOCS (336-2627) *Fax:* 217-351-8091 *E-mail:* publications@aocs.org; orders@aocs.org *Web Site:* www.aocs.org, pg 20

Aperture Books, 20 E 23 St, New York, NY 10010 *Tel:* 212-505-5555 *Toll Free Tel:* 800-929-2323 *Fax:* 212-598-4015 *E-mail:* info@aperture.org *Web Site:* www.aperture.org, pg 20

The Apex Press, 777 United Nations Plaza, Suite 3-C, New York, NY 10017 *Tel:* 914-271-6500 *Toll Free Tel:* 800-316-2739 *Fax:* 914-271-6500 *Toll Free Fax:* 800-316-2739 *E-mail:* cipany@igc.org *Web Site:* www.cipa-apex.org, pg 21

Apogee Press, 2308 Sixth St, Berkeley, CA 94710 *E-mail:* editors@agopeepress.com *Web Site:* www.agopeepress.com, pg 21

Apollo Managed Care Consultants, 860 Ladera Lane, Santa Barbara, CA 93108 *Tel:* 805-969-2606 *Fax:* 805-969-3749 *E-mail:* mail@apollomanagedcare.com *Web Site:* www.apollomanagedcare.com, pg 21

APPA: The Association of Higher Education Facilities Officers, 1643 Prince St, Alexandria, VA 22314-2818 *Tel:* 703-684-1446 *Fax:* 703-549-2772 *Web Site:* www.appa.org, pg 21

Appalachian Mountain Club Books, 5 Joy St, Boston, MA 02108 *Tel:* 617-523-0655 *Fax:* 617-523-0722 *Web Site:* www.outdoors.org, pg 21

Appalachian Trail Conference, PO Box 807, Harpers Ferry, WV 25425 *Tel:* 304-535-6331 *Toll Free Tel:* 888-287-8673 (for orders only) *Fax:* 304-535-2667 *E-mail:* info@atconf.org *Web Site:* www.appalachiantrail.org; www.atctrailstore.org, pg 21

Applause Theatre & Cinema Books, 151 W 46 St, New York, NY 10036 *Tel:* 212-575-9265 *Fax:* 646-562-5852 *E-mail:* info@applausepub.com *Web Site:* www.applausepub.com, pg 21

Applewood Books Inc, 128 The Great Rd, Bedford, MA 01730 *Tel:* 781-271-0055 *Fax:* 781-271-0056 *E-mail:* applewood@awb.com *Web Site:* www.awb.com, pg 21

Appraisal Institute, 550 W Van Buren St, Suite 1000, Chicago, IL 60607 *Tel:* 312-335-4100 *Fax:* 312-335-4400 *Web Site:* www.appraisalinstitute.org, pg 22

APS Press, 3340 Pilot Knob Rd, St Paul, MN 55121-2097 *Tel:* 651-454-7250 *Toll Free Tel:* 800-328-7560 *Fax:* 651-454-0766 *E-mail:* aps@scisoc.org *Web Site:* www.shopapspress.org, pg 22

Aqua Quest Publications Inc, 18 Garvies Point Rd, Glen Cove, NY 11542 *Tel:* 516-759-0476 *Toll Free Tel:* 800-933-8989 *Fax:* 516-759-4519 *E-mail:* info@aquaquest.com *Web Site:* www.aquaquest.com, pg 22

Aquila Communications Inc, 2642 Diab St, St Laurent, PQ H4S 1E8, Canada *Tel:* 514-338-1065 *Toll Free Tel:* 800-667-7071 *Fax:* 514-338-1948 *Toll Free Fax:* 866-338-1948 *E-mail:* aquila@aquilacommunications.com *Web Site:* www.aquilacommunications.com, pg 536

The May Hill Arbuthnot Honor Lecture Award, 50 E Huron St, Chicago, IL 60611-2795 *Tel:* 312-280-2163 *Toll Free Tel:* 800-545-2433 *Fax:* 312-944-7671 *E-mail:* alsc@ala.org *Web Site:* www.ala.org/alsc, pg 759

Arbutus Press, 2364 Pinehurst Trail, Traverse City, MI 49686 *Tel:* 231-946-7240 *Toll Free Tel:* 866-794-8793 *Fax:* 231-946-4196 *E-mail:* info@arbutuspress.com *Web Site:* www.arbutuspress.com, pg 22

Arcade Publishing Inc, 141 Fifth Ave, New York, NY 10010 *Tel:* 212-475-2633 *Fax:* 212-353-8148 *E-mail:* arcadeinfo@arcadepub.com *Web Site:* www.arcadepub.com, pg 22

Arcadia, 31 Lake Place N, Danbury, CT 06810 *Tel:* 203-797-0993 *Fax:* 203-730-2594 *E-mail:* arcadialit@att.net, pg 619

Arcadia Enterprises Inc, PO Box 206, Fruitland, MD 21826 *Tel:* 410-742-2682 *Toll Free Tel:* 877-742-2682 *Fax:* 410-742-2708 *Web Site:* www.buyarcadiabooks.com, pg 22

Arcadia Publishing, 420 Wando Park Blvd, Mount Pleasant, SC 29464 *Tel:* 843-853-2070 *Toll Free Tel:* 888-313-2665 (orders only) *Fax:* 843-853-0044 *E-mail:* sales@arcadiapublishing.com *Web Site:* www.arcadiapublishing.com, pg 22

ArcheBooks Publishing, 9101 W Sahara Ave, Suite 105-112, Las Vegas, NV 89117 *Tel:* 702-253-1338 *Toll Free Tel:* 800-358-8101 *Fax:* 561-868-2127 *E-mail:* publisher@archebooks.com *Web Site:* www.archebooks.com, pg 22

Archer Books, PO Box 1254, Santa Maria, CA 93456-1254 *Tel:* 805-934-9977 *Fax:* 805-934-9977 *E-mail:* info@archer-books.com *Web Site:* www.archer-books.com, pg 22

Arden Press Inc, PO Box 418, Denver, CO 80201-0418 *Tel:* 303-697-6766 *Fax:* 303-697-3443 *E-mail:* ardenpress@msn.com, pg 23

Ardent Media Inc, 522 E 82 St, Suite 1, New York, NY 10028 *Tel:* 212-861-1501 *Fax:* 212-861-0998 *E-mail:* ivyboxer@aol.com, pg 23

ARE Press, 215 67 St, Virginia Beach, VA 23451 *Tel:* 757-428-3588 *Toll Free Tel:* 800-333-4499 *Fax:* 757-491-0689 *E-mail:* are@edgarcayce.org *Web Site:* www.edgarcayce.org, pg 23

Ariadne Press, 270 Goins Ct, Riverside, CA 92507 *Tel:* 951-684-9202 *Fax:* 951-779-0449 *E-mail:* ariadnepress@aol.com *Web Site:* ariadnepress.com, pg 23

Ariel Press, 90 Steve Tate Hwy, Suite 201, Marble Hill, GA 30148 *Tel:* 770-894-4226 *Fax:* 706-579-1865 (orders), pg 23

Ariel Starr Productions Ltd, PO Box 17, Demarest, NJ 07627-0017 *Tel:* 201-784-9148 *Fax:* 201-541-8796 *E-mail:* darkbird@aol.com, pg 23

The Arion Press, The Presidio, 1802 Hays St, San Francisco, CA 94129 *Tel:* 415-561-2542 *Fax:* 415-561-2545 *E-mail:* arionpress@arionpress.com *Web Site:* www.arionpress.com, pg 23

Arizona State University, Creative Writing Program, Dept of English, Box 870302, Tempe, AZ 85287-0302 *Tel:* 480-965-7454; 480-965-3528 *Fax:* 480-965-3451 *Web Site:* www.asu.edu/clas/english/creativewriting, pg 751

Arjuna Library Press, 1025 Garner St D, Space 18, Colorado Springs, CO 80905-1774, pg 23

Arkansas Research Inc, PO Box 303, Conway, AR 72033-0303 *Tel:* 501-470-1120 *Fax:* 501-470-1120 *Web Site:* www.arkansasresearch.com, pg 23

Arkansas State University Printing Program, PO Box 1930, Dept of Journalism & Printing, State University, AR 72467-1930 *Tel:* 870-972-2072 *Fax:* 870-910-8001 *Web Site:* www.astate.edu, pg 751

Arkansas Writers' Conference, 6817 Gingerbread Lane, Little Rock, AR 72204 *Tel:* 501-565-8889 *Fax:* 501-565-7220, pg 741

Arkham House Publishers Inc, PO Box 546, Sauk City, WI 53583-0546 *Tel:* 608-643-4500 *Fax:* 608-643-5043 *E-mail:* sales@arkhamhouse.com *Web Site:* www.arkhamhouse.com, pg 23

Armenian Reference Books Co, PO Box 231, Glendale, CA 91209 *Tel:* 818-504-2550 *Toll Free Tel:* 877-504-2550 *Fax:* 818-504-9283 *E-mail:* info@vassiliansdepot.com *Web Site:* www.vassiliansdepot.com/arb, pg 23

Arnica Publishing Inc, 3739 SE Eighth Ave, Portland, OR 97202 *Tel:* 503-225-9900 *Fax:* 503-225-9901 *E-mail:* info@arnicapublishing.com *Web Site:* www.arnicapublishing.com, pg 23, 590

Jason Aronson Inc, 4501 Forbes Blvd, Lanham, MD 20706 *Toll Free Tel:* 800-462-6420 (orders) *Fax:* 201-767-4330; 201-767-1576 (orders) *Web Site:* www. aronson.com, pg 23

Arrow Map Inc, 58 Norfolk Ave, Unit 4, South Easton, MA 02375 *Tel:* 508-230-2112 *Toll Free Tel:* 800-343-7500 *Fax:* 508-230-8186 *E-mail:* amisales@arrowmap. com *Web Site:* www.arrowmap.com, pg 24

Arsenal Pulp Press Book Publishers Ltd, 1014 Homer St, Suite 103, Vancouver, BC V6B 2W9, Canada *Tel:* 604-687-4233 *Toll Free Tel:* 888-600-PULP (600-7857) *Fax:* 604-687-4283 *E-mail:* contact@ arsenalpulp.com *Web Site:* www.arsenalpulp.com, pg 536

Art Direction Book Co Inc, 456 Glenbrook Rd, Glenbrook, CT 06906 *Tel:* 203-353-1441 *Fax:* 203-353-1371, pg 24

Art from Latin America, Box 1948, Murray Hill Sta, New York, NY 10156-0612 *Tel:* 212-683-2136, pg 24

Art Image Publications, PO Box 160, Derby Line, VT 05830-0160 *Toll Free Tel:* 800-361-2598 *Toll Free Fax:* 800-559-2598 *E-mail:* info@ artimagepublications.com *Web Site:* www. artimagepublications.com, pg 24

Art Institute of Chicago, 111 S Michigan Ave, Chicago, IL 60603-6110 *Tel:* 312-443-3600; 312-443-3540 (pubns); 312-443-3533 (sales & orders) *Fax:* 312-443-0849; 312-443-1334 (pubns) *E-mail:* webmaster@ artic.edu *Web Site:* www.artic.edu, pg 24

Artabras Inc, 116 W 23 St, Suite 500, New York, NY 10011 *Tel:* 646-375-2039 *Toll Free Tel:* 800-ART-BOOK *Fax:* 646-375-2040 *E-mail:* abbeville@ abbeville.com *Web Site:* www.abbeville.com, pg 24

Arte Publico Press, University of Houston, 4800 Calhoun, Houston, TX 77204-2174 *Tel:* 713-743-2841 *Toll Free Tel:* 800-633-2783 *Fax:* 713-743-2847 *Web Site:* www.arte.uh.edu, pg 24

Artech House Inc, 685 Canton St, Norwood, MA 02062 *Tel:* 781-769-9750 *Toll Free Tel:* 800-225-9977 *Fax:* 781-769-6334 *E-mail:* artech@artechhouse.com *Web Site:* www.artechhouse.com, pg 24

Artisan, 708 Broadway, New York, NY 10003-9555 *Tel:* 212-254-5900 *Fax:* 212-254-8098 *E-mail:* artisaninfo@workman.com *Web Site:* www. artisanbooks.com, pg 25

Artist Fellowship Awards Program, 101 E Wilson St, 1st fl, Madison, WI 53702 *Tel:* 608-266-0190 *Fax:* 608-267-0380 *E-mail:* artsboard@arts.state.wi.us *Web Site:* www.arts.state.wi.us, pg 759

Artist Fellowships, One Financial Plaza, 755 Main St, Hartford, CT 06103 *Tel:* 860-566-4770 *Fax:* 860-566-6462 *E-mail:* artsinfo@ctarts.org *Web Site:* www. ctarts.org, pg 760

Artist Fellowships in Literature, 1380 Lawrence St, Suite 1200, Denver, CO 80204 *Tel:* 303-866-2723 *Fax:* 303-866-4266 *E-mail:* coloarts@state.co.us *Web Site:* www.coloarts.state.co.us, pg 760

Artist Grants, 800 Governors Dr, Pierre, SD 57501-2294 *Tel:* 605-773-3131 *Fax:* 605-773-6962 *E-mail:* sdac@ state.sd.us *Web Site:* www.sdarts.org, pg 760

Artist Trust Fellowship, 1835 12 Ave, Seattle, WA 98122 *Tel:* 206-467-8734 *Fax:* 206-467-9633 *E-mail:* info@ artisttrust.org *Web Site:* www.artisttrust.org, pg 760

The Artists Agency, 1180 S Beverly Dr, Suite 400, Los Angeles, CA 90035 *Tel:* 310-277-7779 *Fax:* 310-785-9338, pg 619

Artists & Artisans Inc, 45 W 21 St, 3rd fl, New York, NY 10010 *Tel:* 212-924-9619 *Fax:* 212-242-1114 *Web Site:* www.artistsandartisans.com, pg 619

Artists Associates, 4416 La Jolla Dr, Bradenton, FL 34210-3927 *Tel:* 941-756-8445 *Fax:* 941-727-8840, pg 665

Artists' Fellowships, 155 Avenue of the Americas, 14th fl, New York, NY 10013-1507 *Tel:* 212-366-6900 *Fax:* 212-366-1778 *E-mail:* nyainfo@nyfa.org *Web Site:* www.nyfa.org, pg 760

The Artists Group Ltd, 10100 Santa Monica, Suite 2490, Los Angeles, CA 90067 *Tel:* 310-552-1100 *Fax:* 310-277-9513, pg 619

Arts Recognition & Talent Search (ARTS), 444 Brickell Ave, Suite P14, Miami, FL 33131 *Tel:* 305-377-1140 *Toll Free Tel:* 800-970-2787 *Fax:* 305-377-1149 *E-mail:* nfaa@nfaa.org *Web Site:* www.artsawards.org, pg 760

Ascension Press, 20 Hagerty Blvd, Suite 3, West Chester, PA 19382 *Tel:* 610-696-7795 *Toll Free Tel:* 800-376-0520 (sales off) *Fax:* 610-696-7796; 608-565-2025 (sales off) *E-mail:* info@ascensionpress.com *Web Site:* www.ascensionpress.com, pg 25

Asciutto Art Representatives Inc, 1712 E Butler Circle, Chandler, AZ 85225 *Tel:* 480-899-0600 *Fax:* 480-899-3636 *E-mail:* aartreps@cox.net, pg 665

ASCP Press, 2100 W Harrison St, Chicago, IL 60612 *Tel:* 312-738-4866; 312-738-1336 *Toll Free Tel:* 800-621-4142 *Fax:* 312-738-1619 *Web Site:* www.ascp.org, pg 25

Ashgate Publishing Co, 101 Cherry St, Suite 420, Burlington, VT 05401-4405 *Tel:* 802-865-7641 *Fax:* 802-865-7847 *E-mail:* info@ashgate.com *Web Site:* www.ashgate.com, pg 25

Ashland Poetry Press, Ashland University, 401 College Ave, Ashland, OH 44805 *Tel:* 419-289-5110 *Fax:* 419-289-5638 *Web Site:* www.ashland.edu/aupoetry, pg 25

ASIS International, 1625 Prince St, Alexandria, VA 22314 *Tel:* 703-518-1475 *Fax:* 703-518-1517, pg 25

ASJA Writer Referral Service, 1501 Broadway, Suite 302, New York, NY 10036 *Tel:* 212-398-1934 *Fax:* 212-768-7414 *E-mail:* writers@asja.org *Web Site:* www.asja.org, pg 590

Aslan Publishing, 2490 Black Rock Tpke, Fairfield, CT 06432 *Tel:* 203-372-0300 *Toll Free Tel:* 800-786-5427 *Fax:* 203-374-4766 *E-mail:* info@aslanpublishing.com *Web Site:* www.aslanpublishing.com, pg 25

ASM International, 9639 Kinsman Rd, Materials Park, OH 44073-0002 *Tel:* 440-338-5151 *Toll Free Tel:* 800-336-5152; 800-368-9800 (Europe) *Fax:* 440-338-4634 *E-mail:* cust-srv@asminternational.org *Web Site:* www. asminternational.org, pg 25

ASM Press, 1752 "N" St NW, Washington, DC 20036-2904 *Tel:* 202-737-3600 *Toll Free Tel:* 800-546-2416 *Fax:* 202-942-9342 *E-mail:* books@asmusa.org *Web Site:* www.asmpress.org, pg 25

Aspatore Books, 264 Beacon St, 2nd fl, Boston, MA 02116 *Tel:* 617-369-7017 *Fax:* 617-249-1970 *E-mail:* info@aspatore.com *Web Site:* www.aspatore. com, pg 26

Aspen Publishers, A Wolters Kluwer Company, 1185 Avenue of the Americas, New York, NY 10036 *Tel:* 212-597-0200 *Toll Free Tel:* 800-234-1660 (cust serv); 800-447-1717 (orders); 800-950-5259 (legal educ); 800-LAW-PLGL (paralegal textbook); 800-317-3113 (bookstore sales); 800-364-2512 (Loislaw) *Web Site:* www.aspenpublishers.com, pg 26

Aspen Summer Words Writing Retreat & Literary Festival, 110 E Hallam St, Suite 116, Aspen, CO 81611 *Tel:* 970-925-3122 *Fax:* 970-920-5700 *E-mail:* info@aspenwriters.org *Web Site:* www. aspenwriters.org, pg 741

Associated Authors, 2299 Indian Ave S, Bellair Bluffs, FL 33770 *Tel:* 727-518-6262, pg 590

Associated Business Writers of America Inc, 3140 S Peoria St, Suite 295, Aurora, CO 80014 *Tel:* 303-841-0246 *Fax:* 303-841-2607 *Web Site:* www. nationalwriters.com, pg 679

Associated Editors, 27 W 96 St, New York, NY 10025 *Tel:* 212-662-9703 *Fax:* 212-662-0549, pg 590

Associated Press Broadcasters, 1825 "K" St NW, Suite 800, Washington, DC 20006 *Tel:* 202-736-1100 *Fax:* 202-736-1199 *Web Site:* www.ap.org, pg 679

Associated University Presses, 2010 Eastpark Blvd, Cranbury, NJ 08512 *Tel:* 609-655-4770 *Fax:* 609-655-8366 *E-mail:* AUP440@aol.com, pg 26

Association des Editeurs de Langue Anglaise du Quebec (AEAQ), 1200 Atwater Ave, Suite 3, Montreal, PQ H3Z 1X4, Canada *Tel:* 514-932-5633 *Fax:* 514-932-5456 *E-mail:* aelaq@bellnet.ca, pg 679

Association des Libraires du Quebec, 1001, de Maisoneuve Est, Bureau 580, Montreal, PQ H2L 4P9, Canada *Tel:* 514-526-3349 *Fax:* 514-526-3340 *E-mail:* info@alq.qc.ca *Web Site:* www.alq.qc.ca, pg 679

Association for Computing Machinery, 1515 Broadway, New York, NY 10036 *Tel:* 212-869-7440 *Toll Free Tel:* 800-342-6626 *Fax:* 212-869-0481 *E-mail:* acmhelp@acm.org *Web Site:* www.acm.org, pg 26

Association for Information & Image Management International, 1100 Wayne Ave, Suite 1100, Silver Spring, MD 20910 *Tel:* 301-587-8202 *Toll Free Tel:* 800-477-2446 *Fax:* 240-494-2661 *E-mail:* aiim@ aiim.org *Web Site:* www.aiim.org, pg 679

Association for Supervision & Curriculum Development (ASCD), 1703 N Beauregard St, Alexandria, VA 22311-1453 *Tel:* 703-578-9600 *Toll Free Tel:* 800-933-2723 *Fax:* 703-575-5400 *E-mail:* member@ascd.org *Web Site:* www.ascd.org, pg 26

Association for the Export of Canadian Books, One Nicholas, Suite 504, Ottawa, ON K1N 7B7, Canada *Tel:* 613-562-2324 *Fax:* 613-562-2329 *E-mail:* aecb@ aecb.org *Web Site:* www.aecb.org, pg 679

The Association for Women In Communications, 780 Richie Hwy, Suite 28-S, Severna Park, MD 21146 *Tel:* 410-544-7442 *Fax:* 410-544-4640 *E-mail:* info@ womcom.org *Web Site:* www.womcom.org, pg 741

Association Nationale des Editeurs de Livres, 2514 boul Rosemont, Montreal, PQ H1Y 1K4, Canada *Tel:* 514-273-8130 *Fax:* 514-273-9657 *E-mail:* info@anel.org *Web Site:* www.anel.org, pg 679

Association of American Editorial Cartoonists, 1221 Stoneferry Lane, Raleigh, NC 27606 *Tel:* 919-859-5516 *Fax:* 919-859-3172, pg 679

Association of American Publishers (AAP), 71 Fifth Ave, 2nd fl, New York, NY 10003-3004 *Tel:* 212-255-0200 *Fax:* 212-255-7007 *Web Site:* www.publishers. org, pg 679

Association of American University Presses, 1427 E 60 St, Chicago, IL 60637 *Tel:* 773-702-7700; 773-702-7600 *Toll Free Tel:* 800-621-2736 (orders) *Fax:* 773-702-9756 (sales); 773-660-2235 (orders); 773-702-2708 *E-mail:* general@press.uchicago.edu *Web Site:* www.press.uchicago.edu, pg 26

Association of American University Presses (AAUP), 71 W 23 St, Suite 901, New York City, NY 10010 *Tel:* 212-989-1010 *Fax:* 212-989-0275; 212-989-0176 *E-mail:* info@aaupnet.org *Web Site:* www.aaupnet.org, pg 679

Association of Authors' Representatives Inc (AAR), PO Box 237201, Ansonia Sta, New York, NY 10023 *E-mail:* aarinc@mindspring.com *Web Site:* www.aar-online.org, pg 679

Association of Book Publishers of British Columbia, 100 W Pender, Suite 107, Vancouver, BC V6B 1R8, Canada *Tel:* 604-684-0228 *Fax:* 604-684-5788 *E-mail:* admin@books.bc.ca *Web Site:* www.books.bc. ca, pg 679

Association of Canadian Publishers, 161 Eglinton Ave, Suite 702, Toronto, ON M4P 1J5, Canada *Tel:* 416-487-6116 *Fax:* 416-487-8815 *Web Site:* www. publishers.ca, pg 679

Association of Canadian University Presses, 10 St Mary St, Suite 700, Toronto, ON M4Y 2W8, Canada *Tel:* 416-978-2239 ext 237 *Fax:* 416-978-4738, pg 679

Association of College & Research Libraries, 50 E Huron St, Chicago, IL 60611 *Tel:* 312-280-2511 *Toll Free Tel:* 800-545-2433 (ext 2517) *Fax:* 312-280-2520 *E-mail:* acrl@ala.org *Web Site:* www.ala.org/acrl, pg 26

Avery, 375 Hudson St, New York, NY 10014 *Tel:* 212-366-2000 *Fax:* 212-366-2643 *E-mail:* online@ penguinputnam.com *Web Site:* www.penguinputnam. com, pg 29

Avery Color Studios, 511 "D" Ave, Gwinn, MI 49841 *Tel:* 906-346-3908 *Toll Free Tel:* 800-722-9925 *Fax:* 906-346-3015 *E-mail:* avery@portup.com, pg 29

Avid Reader Press, 6705 W Hwy 290, Suite 502-295, Austin, TX 78735 *Tel:* 512-288-5349 *Fax:* 512-288-0317 *E-mail:* info@avidreaderpress.com; orders@ avidreaderpress.com *Web Site:* www.avidreaderpress. com, pg 29

Avisson Press Inc, 3007 Taliaferro Rd, Greensboro, NC 27408 *Tel:* 336-288-6989 *Fax:* 336-288-6989 *E-mail:* avisson4@aol.com, pg 29

AVKO Dyslexia & Spelling Research Foundation Inc, 3084 W Willard Rd, Clio, MI 48420 *Tel:* 810-686-9283 *Toll Free Tel:* 866-285-6612 *Fax:* 810-686-1101 *E-mail:* avkoemail@aol.com *Web Site:* www.avko.org, pg 29

Avocet Press Inc, 19 Paul Ct, Pearl River, NY 10965-1539 *Tel:* 845-735-6807 *Toll Free Tel:* 877-428-6238, pg 29

Avotaynu Inc, 155 N Washington Ave, Bergenfield, NJ 07621 *Tel:* 201-387-7200 *Toll Free Tel:* 800-286-8296 *Fax:* 201-387-2855 *E-mail:* info@avotaynu.com *Web Site:* www.avotaynu.com, pg 29

Award for Fiction, 320 S Shores Rd, Campbellford, ON K0L 1L0, Canada *Tel:* 705-653-0323 *Toll Free Tel:* 866-216-6222 *Fax:* 705-653-0593 *E-mail:* info@ canauthors.org *Web Site:* www.canauthors.org, pg 760

Awe-Struck E-Books Inc, 2458 Cherry St, Dubuque, IA 52001-5749 *E-mail:* editor@awe-struckebooks.net; tech@awestruckebooks.net *Web Site:* www.awe-struck. net (ordering), pg 29

AWP Award Series, George Mason University, MS-1E3, Fairfax, VA 22030-4444 *Tel:* 703-993-4301 *Fax:* 703-993-4302 *E-mail:* awp@awpwriter.org *Web Site:* www. awpwriter.org, pg 760

The Axelrod Agency, 55 Main St, Chatham, NY 12037 *Tel:* 518-392-2100 *Fax:* 518-392-2944 *E-mail:* steve@ axelrodagency.com, pg 620

Jerome Axelrod, 467 Wingate Rd, Huntington Valley, PA 19006-8421 *Tel:* 215-947-8426 *Fax:* 215-947-3140, pg 591

Ayer Company, Publishers Inc, One Lower Mill Rd, North Stratford, NH 03590 *Tel:* 603-669-7032 *Fax:* 603-669-7945 *E-mail:* ayerpub@yahoo.com *Web Site:* www.ayerpub.com, pg 30

Aztex Corp, PO Box 50046, Tucson, AZ 85703-1046 *Tel:* 520-882-4656 *Fax:* 520-792-8501 *Web Site:* www. aztexcorp.com, pg 30

B & B Publishing, 4823 Sherbrooke St W, Office 275, Westmount, PQ H3Z 1G7, Canada *Tel:* 514-932-9466 *Fax:* 514-932-5929 *E-mail:* editions@ebbp.ca, pg 536

Babbage Press, 8740 Penfield Ave, Northbridge, CA 91324-3224 *Tel:* 818-341-3161 *E-mail:* books@ babbagepress.com *Web Site:* www.babbagepress.com, pg 30

Backbeat Books, 600 Harrison St, San Francisco, CA 94107 *Tel:* 415-947-6615 *Toll Free Tel:* 866-222-5232 (orders only) *Fax:* 415-947-6015; 408-848-8294 (orders only) *E-mail:* books@musicplayer.com; books@cmp.com *Web Site:* www.backbeatbooks.com, pg 30

Elizabeth H Backman, 86 Johnnycake Hollow Rd, Pine Plains, NY 12567 *Tel:* 518-398-9344 *Fax:* 518-398-6368 *E-mail:* bethcountry@taconic.net, pg 620

Backman Writing & Communications, 32 Hillview Ave, Rensselaer, NY 12144 *Tel:* 518-449-4985 *Fax:* 518-449-7273 *Web Site:* www.backwrite.com, pg 591

Baen Publishing Enterprises, PO Box 1403, Riverdale, NY 10471-0605 *Tel:* 919-570-1640 *Fax:* 919-570-1644 *Web Site:* baen.com, pg 30

Baha'i Publishing Trust, 415 Linden Ave, Wilmette, IL 60091 *Tel:* 847-425-7950 *Fax:* 847-425-7951 *E-mail:* bpt@usbnc.org, pg 30

BajonHouse Publishing, 609 Broad Ave, Belle Vernon, PA 15012 *Tel:* 724-929-5997 *Fax:* 724-929-5997, pg 30

Baker & Taylor Conference Grants, 50 E Huron St, Chicago, IL 60611 *Tel:* 312-280-4390 (ext 4391) *Toll Free Tel:* 800-545-2433 (ext 4390) *Fax:* 312-664-7459 *E-mail:* yalsa@ala.org *Web Site:* www.ala. org/yalsa/printz, pg 760

Baker Books, PO Box 6287, Grand Rapids, MI 49516-6287 *Tel:* 616-676-9185 *Toll Free Tel:* 800-877-2665; 800-679-1957 *Fax:* 616-676-9573 *Toll Free Fax:* 800-398-3110 *Web Site:* www.bakerpublishinggroup.com, pg 30

Janet H Baker, 550 Gaspar Dr, Placida, FL 33946 *Tel:* 941-697-3581, pg 591

The Baker Street Irregulars, 7938 Mill Stream Circle, Indianapolis, IN 46278 *Tel:* 317-293-2212, pg 681

Baker's Plays, PO Box 699222, Quincy, MA 02269-9222 *Tel:* 617-745-0805 *Fax:* 617-745-9891 *Web Site:* www. bakersplays.com, pg 30

Emily Clark Balch Prizes in Creative American Writing, One West Range, Charlottesville, VA 22903 *Tel:* 434-924-3124 *Fax:* 434-924-1397 *E-mail:* vqreview@ virginia.edu *Web Site:* www.virginia.edu/vqr, pg 761

Malaga Baldi Literary Agency, 233 W 99, Suite 19C, New York, NY 10025 *Tel:* 212-222-3213 *E-mail:* mbaldi@nyc.rr.com, pg 620

Baldwin Literary Services, 935 Hayes St, Baldwin, NY 11510-4834 *Tel:* 516-546-8338 *Fax:* 516-867-6850, pg 591

The Balkin Agency Inc, PO Box 222, Amherst, MA 01004 *Tel:* 413-548-9835 *Fax:* 413-548-9836, pg 620

Ball Publishing, 335 N River St, Batavia, IL 60510 *Tel:* 630-208-9080 *Fax:* 630-208-9350 *E-mail:* info@ ballpublishing.com *Web Site:* www.ballpublishing.com, pg 30

Ball-Stick-Bird Publications Inc, PO Box 429, Williamstown, MA 01267-0429 *Tel:* 413-664-0002 *Fax:* 413-664-0002 *E-mail:* info@ballstickbird.com *Web Site:* www.ballstickbird.com, pg 31

Ballinger Publishing, 41 N Jefferson St, Suite 300, Pensacola, FL 32501 *Tel:* 850-433-1166 *Fax:* 850-435-9174 *E-mail:* info@ballingerpublishing.com *Web Site:* www.ballingerpublishing.com, pg 31

The Baltimore Sun, 501 N Calvert St, Baltimore, MD 21278 *Tel:* 410-332-6000 *Toll Free Tel:* 800-829-8000 *Fax:* 410-332-6466 *E-mail:* sunsource@baltsun.com *Web Site:* www.baltimoresun.com, pg 31

Carol Bancroft & Friends, 121 Dodgingtown Rd, Bethel, CT 06801 *Tel:* 203-748-4823 *Toll Free Tel:* 800-720-7020 *Fax:* 203-748-4581 *E-mail:* artists@ carolbancroft.com *Web Site:* www.carolbancroft.com, pg 665

Bancroft Prizes, 517 Butler Library, 535 W 114 St, New York, NY 10027 *Tel:* 212-854-4746 *Fax:* 212-854-9099 *Web Site:* www.columbia.edu/cu/lweb/eguides/ amerihist/bancroft.html, pg 761

Bancroft-Sage Publishing, 3943 Meadowbrook Rd, Minneapolis, MN 55426 *Tel:* 952-938-9330 *Toll Free Tel:* 800-846-7027 *Fax:* 952-938-7353 *E-mail:* feedback@finney-hobar.com *Web Site:* www. finney-hobar.com, pg 31

Bandanna Books, 1212 Punta Gorda St, Suite 13, Santa Barbara, CA 93103 *Tel:* 805-899-2145 *Fax:* 805-899-2145 *E-mail:* bandanna@cox.net *Web Site:* www. beachcollege.net/bookstore, pg 31

Bandido Books, 9806 Heaton Ct, Orlando, FL 32817 *Tel:* 407-657-9707 *Toll Free Tel:* 877-814-6824 (pin 1174) *Fax:* 407-677-9796 *E-mail:* publish@ bandidobooks.com *Web Site:* www.bandidobooks.com, pg 31

Banff Centre, 11759 Groat Rd, Edmonton, AB T5M 3K6, Canada *Tel:* 780-422-8174 *Toll Free Tel:* 800-665-5354 (Alberta only) *Fax:* 780-422-2663 *E-mail:* mail@writersguild.ab.ca *Web Site:* www. writersguild.ab.ca, pg 681

Banff Centre National Arts Award, 107 Tunnel Mountain Dr, Banff, AB T1L 1H5, Canada *Tel:* 403-762-6154 *Toll Free Tel:* 800-413-8368 *Fax:* 403-762-6158 *E-mail:* communications@banffcentre.ca *Web Site:* www.banffcentre.ca, pg 761

Banff Centre Press, 107 Tunnel Mountain Dr, Box 1020, Banff, AB T1L 1H5, Canada *Tel:* 403-762-7532 *Fax:* 403-762-6699 *E-mail:* press@banffcentre.ca *Web Site:* www.banffcentre.ca/press, pg 536

Banner of Truth, PO Box 621, Carlisle, PA 17013 *Tel:* 717-249-5747 *Toll Free Tel:* 800-263-8085 (orders) *Fax:* 717-249-0604 *E-mail:* info@ banneroftruth.org *Web Site:* www.banneroftruth.co.uk, pg 31

Banta Literary Award, 5250 E Terrace Dr, Suite A-1, Madison, WI 53718-8345 *Tel:* 608-245-3640 *Fax:* 608-245-3646 *Web Site:* www.wla.lib.wi.us, pg 761

Bantam Dell Publishing Group, 1745 Broadway, New York, NY 10019 *Tel:* 212-782-9000 *Toll Free Tel:* 800-223-6834 *Fax:* 212-302-7985 *Web Site:* www. randomhouse.com/bantamdell, pg 31

Baptist Spanish Publishing House (d/b/a Casa Bautista de Publicaciones), 7000 Alabama St, El Paso, TX 79904 *Tel:* 915-566-9656 *Toll Free Tel:* 800-755-5958 (cust serv & orders); 800-985-9971 (Casa Bautista Miami) *Fax:* 915-562-6502; 915-565-9008 (orders) *E-mail:* cbpmail@casabautista.org *Web Site:* www. casabautista.org, pg 31

Barbed Wire Publishing, 270 Avenida de Mesilla, Las Cruces, NM 88005 *Tel:* 505-525-9707 *Toll Free Tel:* 888-817-1990 *Fax:* 505-525-9711 *E-mail:* thefolks@barbed-wire.net *Web Site:* www. barbed-wire.net, pg 32

A Richard Barber & Associates, 554 E 82 St, New York, NY 10028 *Tel:* 212-737-7266 *Fax:* 212-879-0183 *E-mail:* barberrich@aol.com, pg 620

Barbour Publishing Inc, 1810 Barbour Dr, Uhrichsville, OH 44683 *Tel:* 740-922-6045 *Fax:* 740-922-5948 *E-mail:* info@barbourbooks.com *Web Site:* www. barbourbooks.com, pg 32

BAR/BRI Group, 111 W Jackson Blvd, Chicago, IL 60604 *Tel:* 312-894-1688 *Toll Free Tel:* 800-328-9352 *Fax:* 312-360-1842 *Toll Free Fax:* 800-430-9378 (orders) *Web Site:* www.gilbertlaw.com, pg 32

Barcelona Publishers, Pathway Book Service, 4 White Brook Rd, Gilsum, NH 03448 *Tel:* 603-357-0236 *Toll Free Tel:* 800-345-6665 *Fax:* 603-357-2073 *E-mail:* pbs@pathwaybooks.com *Web Site:* barcelonapublishers.com, pg 32

Bard Society, 1358 Tiber Ave, Jacksonville, FL 32207 *Tel:* 904-398-5352, pg 741

Barefoot Books, 2067 Massachusetts Ave, 5th fl, Cambridge, MA 02140 *Tel:* 617-576-0660 *Fax:* 617-576-0049 *E-mail:* ussales@barefootbooks.com; help@ barefootbooks.com *Web Site:* www.barefootbooks.com, pg 32

Barnard Co, 2402 Third St, Suite 206, Santa Monica, CA 90405 *Tel:* 310-314-7727 *E-mail:* seyahllib@aol. com, pg 570

Barnes & Noble Books (Imports & Reprints), 4501 Forbes Blvd, Suite 200, Lanham, MD 20706 *Tel:* 301-459-3366 *Toll Free Tel:* 800-462-6420 (orders only) *Fax:* 301-429-5748 *Toll Free Fax:* 800-338-4550 (orders only) *Web Site:* www.rowmanlittlefield.com, pg 32

Kathleen Barnes, 238 W Fourth St, Suite 3C, New York, NY 10014 *Tel:* 212-924-8084 *Fax:* 212-255-5033 *E-mail:* yobarnes@aol.com, pg 591

Baror International Inc, 831 Mount Kisco Rd, Armonk, NY 10504 *Tel:* 914-273-9199 *Fax:* 914-273-5058 *E-mail:* barorint@aol.com, pg 620

Loretta Barrett Books Inc, 101 Fifth Ave, New York, NY 10003 *Tel:* 212-242-3420 *Fax:* 212-807-9579, pg 620

Melinda Barrett, 17110 Donmetz St, Granada Hills, CA 91344 *Tel:* 818-368-2129 *E-mail:* mbarrett@ladpw.org, pg 591

Barricade Books Inc, 185 Bridge Plaza N, Suite 308A, Fort Lee, NJ 07024 *Tel:* 201-944-7600 *Fax:* 201-944-6363 *E-mail:* customerservice@barricadebooks.com *Web Site:* www.barricadebooks.com, pg 32

Barron's Educational Series Inc, 250 Wireless Blvd, Hauppauge, NY 11788 *Tel:* 631-434-3311 *Toll Free Tel:* 800-645-3476 *Fax:* 631-434-3723 *E-mail:* info@barronseduc.com (Books can be purchased online), pg 32

James P Barry Ohioana Award for Editorial Excellence, 274 E First Ave, Suite 300, Columbus, OH 43201 *Tel:* 614-466-3831 *Fax:* 614-728-6974 *E-mail:* ohioana@sloma.state.oh.us *Web Site:* www.oplin.lib.oh.us/ohioana, pg 761

The Barry-Swayne Literary Agency, 4 Manitou Rd, Garrison, NY 10524 *Tel:* 845-424-2448 *E-mail:* info@swayneagency.com *Web Site:* www.swayneagency.com, pg 620

Barrytown/Station Hill Press, 120 Station Hill Rd, Barrytown, NY 12507 *Tel:* 845-758-5293 *E-mail:* publishers@stationhill.org *Web Site:* www.stationhill.org, pg 33

Diana Barth, 535 W 51 St, Suite 3-A, New York, NY 10019 *Tel:* 212-307-5465 *E-mail:* diabarth@juno.com, pg 591

Bartleby Press, 11141 Georgia Ave, Suite A-3, Silver Spring, MD 20902 *Tel:* 301-949-2443 *Fax:* 301-949-2205 *E-mail:* inquiries@bartlebythepublisher.com *Web Site:* www.bartlebythepublisher.com, pg 33

Basic Books, 387 Park Ave S, 12th fl, New York, NY 10016-8810 *Tel:* 212-340-8100 *Toll Free Tel:* 800-242-7737 (orders) *Fax:* 212-340-8135 *E-mail:* basic.books@perseusbooks.com *Web Site:* www.basicbooks.com, pg 33

Basic Health Publications Inc, 8200 Boulevard E, Suite 25-G, North Bergen, NJ 07047 *Tel:* 201-868-8336 *Toll Free Tel:* 800-575-8890 *Fax:* 201-868-8335, pg 33

Basile Festival of Emerging American Theatre (FEAT), 749 N Park Ave, Indianapolis, IN 46202 *Tel:* 317-635-7529 *Fax:* 317-635-0010 *E-mail:* info@phoenixtheatre.org *Web Site:* www.phoenixtheatre.org, pg 761

Miriam Bass Award for Creativity in Independent Publishing, 71 Fifth Ave, 2nd fl, New York, NY 10003-3004 *Tel:* 212-255-0200 *Fax:* 212-255-7007 *Web Site:* www.publishers.org, pg 761

The Mildred L Batchelder Award, 50 E Huron St, Chicago, IL 60611-2795 *Tel:* 312-280-2163 *Toll Free Tel:* 800-545-2433 *Fax:* 312-944-7671 *E-mail:* alsc@ala.org *Web Site:* www.ala.org/alsc, pg 761

Battelle Press, 505 King Ave, Columbus, OH 43201-2693 *Tel:* 614-424-6393 *Toll Free Tel:* 800-451-3543 *Fax:* 614-424-3819 *E-mail:* press@battelle.org *Web Site:* www.battelle.org/bookstore, pg 33

Mark E Battersby, PO Box 527, Ardmore, PA 19003 *Tel:* 610-789-2480 *Fax:* 610-924-9159 *E-mail:* mebatt12@earthlink.net, pg 591

Battery Press Inc, 1020 Fourth Ave S, Nashville, TN 37210 *Tel:* 615-298-1401 *Fax:* 615-298-1401 *E-mail:* batterybks@aol.com *Web Site:* www.batterypress.com, pg 33

Mr Loris Battin, 251 E 51 St, No 8F, New York, NY 10022 *Tel:* 212-688-7668 *E-mail:* lolus@msn.com, pg 591

Bawn Publishers Inc, 8877 Meadowview Dr, West Chester, OH 45069-3545 *Tel:* 513-759-6288 *Fax:* 513-759-6299 *E-mail:* bawn@one.net *Web Site:* www.bawnagency.com, pg 620

Bay Area Book Reviewers Association Book Awards, c/o Poetry Flash, 1450 Fourth St, Suite 4, Berkeley, CA 94710 *Tel:* 510-525-5476 *Fax:* 510-525-6752 *E-mail:* babra@poetryflash.org; editor@poetryflash.org *Web Site:* www.poetryflash.org, pg 761

Bay/SOMA Publishing Inc, 444 De Haro, Suite 130, San Francisco, CA 94107 *Tel:* 415-252-4350 *Fax:* 415-252-4352 *E-mail:* info@baybooks.com *Web Site:* www.baybooks.com, pg 33

Baylor University Press, Baylor University, Waco, TX 76798-7363 *Tel:* 254-710-3164 *Toll Free Tel:* 800-710-3217 *Fax:* 254-710-3440 *Web Site:* www.baylorpress.com, pg 33

Baylor University, Writing Program, One Baylor Place, Waco, TX 76798 *Tel:* 254-710-1768 *Fax:* 254-710-3894 *Web Site:* www.baylor.edu, pg 751

Baywood Publishing Co Inc, 26 Austin Ave, Amityville, NY 11701 *Tel:* 631-691-1270 *Toll Free Tel:* 800-638-7819 *Fax:* 631-691-1770 *E-mail:* baywood@baywood.com *Web Site:* www.baywood.com, pg 33

BBC Audiobooks America, One Lafayette Rd, Hampton, NH 03842 *Tel:* 603-926-8744 *Toll Free Tel:* 800-621-0182 *Fax:* 603-929-3890 *E-mail:* info@bbcaudiobooksamerica.com, pg 34

The BC Book Prizes, 207 W Hastings St, Suite 902, Vancouver, BC V6B 1H7, Canada *Tel:* 604-687-2405 *Fax:* 604-669-3701 *E-mail:* info@bcbookprizes.ca *Web Site:* www.bcbookprizes.ca, pg 761

Be Puzzled, 2030 Harrison St, San Francisco, CA 94110 *Tel:* 415-503-1600 *Toll Free Tel:* 800-347-4818 *Fax:* 415-503-0085 *E-mail:* orders@areyougame.com *Web Site:* www.areyougame.com, pg 34

Beach Holme Publishing, 409 Granville St, Suite 1010, Vancouver, BC V6C 1T2, Canada *Tel:* 604-733-4868 *Toll Free Tel:* 888-551-6655 (orders) *Fax:* 604-733-4860 *E-mail:* bhp@beachholme.bc.ca *Web Site:* www.beachholme.bc.ca, pg 536

Beacham Publishing Corp, PO Box 1810, Nokomis, FL 34274-1810 *Tel:* 941-480-9644 *Toll Free Tel:* 800-466-9644 *Fax:* 941-480-9644 *E-mail:* beachampub@aol.com *Web Site:* www.beachampublishing.com, pg 34

Beacon Hill Press of Kansas City, PO Box 419527, Kansas City, MO 64141-6527 *Tel:* 816-931-1900 *Toll Free Tel:* 800-877-0700 (retail order) *Fax:* 816-753-4071 *Toll Free Fax:* 800-849-9827 (order) *Web Site:* www.beaconhillbooks.com, pg 34

Beacon Press, 41 Mount Vernon St, Boston, MA 02108 *Tel:* 617-742-2110 *Toll Free Tel:* 800-225-3362 (orders only) *Fax:* 617-723-3097; 617-742-2290 *Web Site:* www.beacon.org, pg 34

Beaconhill Books Catalogue, 9972 Third St, Suite 10, Sidney, BC V8L 3B2, Canada *Tel:* 250-656-0537 *Fax:* 250-656-0537 *Web Site:* www.beaconhillbooks.net, pg 536

Bear & Co Inc, One Park St, Rochester, VT 05767 *Tel:* 802-767-3174 *Toll Free Tel:* 800-932-3277 *Fax:* 802-767-3726 *E-mail:* orders@InnerTraditions.com *Web Site:* InnerTraditions.com, pg 34

Beard Books Inc, 306 N Market St, Frederick, MD 21701-5337 *Tel:* 240-629-3300 *Toll Free Tel:* 888-563-4573 (book orders) *Fax:* 240-629-3360 *E-mail:* info@beardbooks.com; order@beardbooks.com *Web Site:* www.beardbooks.com, pg 34

Groupe Beauchemin, Editeur Ltee, 3281 ave Jean Beraud, Laval, PQ H7T 2L2, Canada *Tel:* 514-334-5912 *Toll Free Tel:* 800-361-2598 (US & Canada); 800-361-4504 (Canada Only) *Fax:* 450-688-6269 *E-mail:* promotion@beauchemin.qc.ca *Web Site:* www.beaucheminediteur.com, pg 536

Beautiful America Publishing Co, 2600 Progress Way, Woodburn, OR 97071 *Tel:* 503-982-4616 *Toll Free Tel:* 800-874-1233 *Fax:* 503-982-2825 *E-mail:* bapco@beautifulamericapub.com *Web Site:* www.beautifulamericapub.com, pg 34

Beaver Wood Associates, 655 Alstead Center Rd, Alstead, NH 03602 *Tel:* 603-835-7900 *Fax:* 603-835-6279 *Web Site:* www.beaverwood.com, pg 591

Ellen Becker, PO Box 5851, Santa Fe, NM 87502 *Tel:* 505-989-7543 *Fax:* 505-988-3953 *E-mail:* ebecker3@aol.com, pg 591

Bedford/St Martin's, 75 Arlington St, Boston, MA 02116 *Tel:* 617-399-4000 *Fax:* 617-426-8582 *Web Site:* www.bedfordstmartins.com, pg 35

Beehive Production Services, 3 Fairview St, East Stroudsburg, PA 18301-2501 *Tel:* 570-421-3076 *Fax:* 570-421-3076 *E-mail:* beehive@ptd.net, pg 591

Beekman Publishers Inc, 2626 Rte 212, Woodstock, NY 12498 *Tel:* 845-679-2300 *Toll Free Tel:* 888-BEEKMAN (orders) *Fax:* 845-679-2301 *E-mail:* beekman@beekmanpublishers.com *Web Site:* www.beekmanpublishers.com, pg 35

Thomas T Beeler Publisher, 710 Main St, Suite 300, Rollinsford, NH 03869 *Tel:* 603-749-0392 *Toll Free Tel:* 800-818-7574 *Fax:* 603-749-0395 *Toll Free Fax:* 888-222-3396 *E-mail:* cservice@beelerpub.com *Web Site:* www.beelerpub.com, pg 35

George Louis Beer Prize, 400 "A" St SE, Washington, DC 20003 *Tel:* 202-544-2422 *Fax:* 202-544-8307 *E-mail:* info@historians.org *Web Site:* www.historians.org, pg 761

Before Columbus Foundation, The Raymond House, 655 13 St, Suite 302, Oakland, CA 94612 *Tel:* 510-268-9775, pg 681

Begell House Inc Publishers, 145 Madison Ave, Suite 601, New York, NY 10016 *Tel:* 212-725-1999 *Fax:* 212-213-8368 *E-mail:* orders@begellhouse.com *Web Site:* www.begellhouse.com, pg 35

Behrman House Inc, 11 Edison Place, Springfield, NJ 07081 *Tel:* 973-379-7200 *Fax:* 973-379-7280 *Web Site:* www.behrmanhouse.com, pg 35

Frederic C Beil Publisher Inc, 609 Whitaker St, Savannah, GA 31401 *Tel:* 912-233-2446 *Fax:* 912-233-6456 *E-mail:* beilbook@beil.com *Web Site:* www.beil.com, pg 35

Bell Springs Publishing, PO Box 1240, Willits, CA 95490-1240 *Tel:* 707-459-6372 *Toll Free Tel:* 800-515-8050 *Fax:* 707-459-8614 *E-mail:* info@bellsprings.com *Web Site:* bellsprings.com, pg 35

Bellerophon Books, PO Box 21307, Santa Barbara, CA 93121-1307 *Tel:* 805-965-7034 *Toll Free Tel:* 800-253-9943 *Fax:* 805-965-8286 *E-mail:* sales@bellerophonbooks.com *Web Site:* www.bellerophonbooks.com, pg 35

The Pura Belpre Award, 50 E Huron St, Chicago, IL 60611-2795 *Tel:* 312-280-2163 *Toll Free Tel:* 800-545-2433 *Fax:* 312-944-7671 *E-mail:* alsc@ala.org *Web Site:* www.ala.org/alsc, pg 762

Benator Publishing LLC, 1240 Johnson Ferry Place, Suite C-5, Marietta, GA 30068 *Tel:* 770-977-5750 *Fax:* 770-977-8464 *E-mail:* benpubl2@bellsouth.net *Web Site:* www.benatorpublishing.com, pg 35

BenBella Books, 6440 N Central Expressway, Suite 617, Dallas, TX 75206 *Tel:* 214-750-3600 *Fax:* 214-750-3645 *E-mail:* editor@benbellabooks.com *Web Site:* www.benbellabooks.com, pg 35

Matthew Bender & Co Inc, 744 Broad St, 7th fl, Newark, NJ 07102 *Tel:* 973-820-2000 *Fax:* 973-820-2007 *Web Site:* www.bender.com, pg 35

R James Bender Publishing, PO Box 23456, San Jose, CA 95153-3456 *Tel:* 408-225-5777 *Fax:* 408-225-4739 *E-mail:* order@bender-publishing.com *Web Site:* www.bender-publishing.com, pg 36

The Benefactory, PO Box 128, Cohasset, MA 02025 *Tel:* 781-383-8027 *Toll Free Tel:* 800-729-7251 *Fax:* 781-383-8026 *E-mail:* thebenefactory@aol.com *Web Site:* www.readplay.com, pg 36

Benjamin Cummings, 1301 Sansome St, San Francisco, CA 94111 *Tel:* 415-402-2500 *Fax:* 415-402-2591 *E-mail:* question@aw.com *Web Site:* www.aw-bc.com, pg 36

Curtis Benjamin Award, 50 "F" St NW, Washington, DC 20001-1530 *Tel:* 202-347-3375 *Fax:* 202-347-3690 *Web Site:* www.publishers.org, pg 762

Benjamin Franklin Book Awards, 627 Aviation Way, Manhattan Beach, CA 90266 *Tel:* 310-372-2732 *Fax:* 310-374-3342 *E-mail:* info@pma-online.org *Web Site:* www.pma-online.org, pg 762

Benjamin Scott Publishing, 20 E Colorado Blvd, No 202, Pasadena, CA 91105 *Tel:* 626-449-1339 *Toll Free Tel:* 800-488-4959 *Fax:* 626-449-1389 *E-mail:* info@jobsourcenetwork.com *Web Site:* www. jobsourcenetwork.com, pg 36

John Benjamins Publishing Co, 821 Bethlehem Pike, Erdenheim, PA 19038 *Tel:* 215-836-1200 *Toll Free Tel:* 800-562-5666 *Fax:* 215-836-1204 *E-mail:* service@benjamins.com *Web Site:* www. benjamins.com, pg 36

George Bennett Fellowship, 20 Main St, Exeter, NH 03833-2460 *Tel:* 603-772-4311 *Web Site:* www.exeter. edu, pg 762

Bennington Writing Seminars, One College Dr, Bennington, VT 05201 *Tel:* 802-440-4452 *Fax:* 802-440-4453 *E-mail:* writing@bennington.edu *Web Site:* www.bennington.edu/graduateprogram, pg 742

Benoit & Associates, 279 S Schuyler Ave, Kankakee, IL 60901 *Tel:* 815-932-2582 *Fax:* 815-932-2594 *E-mail:* benoitart@aol.com, pg 665

Bentley Publishers, 1734 Massachusetts Ave, Cambridge, MA 02138 *Tel:* 617-547-4170 *Toll Free Tel:* 800-423-4595 *Fax:* 617-876-9235 *E-mail:* sales@bentleypublishers.com *Web Site:* www. bentleypublishers.com, pg 36

Naomi Berber Memorial Award, 200 Deer Run Rd, Sewickley, PA 15143-2600 *Tel:* 412-741-6860 *Toll Free Tel:* 800-910-4283 *Fax:* 412-741-2311 *E-mail:* info@gain.net *Web Site:* www.gain.net, pg 762

Berendsen & Associates Inc, 2233 Kemper Lane, Cincinnati, OH 45206 *Tel:* 513-861-1400 *Fax:* 513-861-6420 *Web Site:* www.illustratorsrep.com; www. photographersrep.com; www.designersrep.com; www. stockartrep.com, pg 665

R J Berg/Destinations Press Ltd, 450 E 96 St, Suite 500, Indianapolis, IN 46290 *Toll Free Tel:* 800-638-3909 *Fax:* 317-251-5901 *E-mail:* r. j.berg@destinationspressltd.com *Web Site:* www. destinationspressltd.com, pg 36

Marlowe Bergendoff, 277 Water St, Suite 219, Exeter, NH 03833 *Tel:* 603-778-6245 *Fax:* 603-778-6245, pg 591

Berghahn Books, 150 Broadway, Suite 812, New York, NY 10038 *Tel:* 212-222-6502 *Fax:* 212-222-5209 *E-mail:* info@berghahnbooks.com *Web Site:* www. berghahnbooks.com, pg 36

Barbara Bergstrom, MA, 13 Stockton Way, Howell, NJ 07731 *Tel:* 732-363-8372, pg 591

Berkeley Hills Books, 1435 Fourth St, Berkeley, CA 94710 *Tel:* 510-559-8650 *Fax:* 510-559-8670 *Web Site:* www.berkeleyhills.com, pg 36

Berkeley Slavic Specialties, PO Box 3034, Oakland, CA 94609-0034 *Tel:* 510-653-8048 *Fax:* 510-653-6313 *E-mail:* 71034.456@compuserve.com *Web Site:* www. berkslav.com, pg 36

Berkley Books, 375 Hudson St, New York, NY 10014 *Tel:* 212-366-2000 *Fax:* 212-366-2666 *E-mail:* online@penguinputnam.com *Web Site:* www. penguin.com, pg 36

Berkley Publishing Group, 375 Hudson St, New York, NY 10014 *Tel:* 212-366-2000 *E-mail:* online@ penguinputnam.com *Web Site:* www.penguin.com, pg 37

Berkshire House, 1206 Rte 12, Woodstock, VT 05091 *Tel:* 802-457-4826 *Toll Free Tel:* 800-245-4151 *Fax:* 802-457-1678 *Web Site:* www.countrymanpress. com, pg 37

Berlow Technical Communications Inc, 9 Prairie Ave, Suffern, NY 10901 *Tel:* 845-357-8215 *E-mail:* bteccinc@yahoo.com, pg 591

Bernan, 4611-F Assembly Dr, Lanham, MD 20706-4391 *Tel:* 301-459-2255; 301-459-7666 (cust serv) *Toll Free Tel:* 800-274-4447; 800-274-4888 (cust serv) *Fax:* 301-459-9235; 301-459-0056 (cust serv) *Toll Free Fax:* 800-865-3450 *E-mail:* info@bernan.com *Web Site:* www.bernan.com, pg 37

Jean Brodsky Bernard, 4609 Chevy Chase Blvd, Chevy Chase, MD 20815-5343 *Tel:* 301-654-8914 *Fax:* 301-718-8972 *E-mail:* dranreb@starpower.net, pg 591

Jessie Bernard Award, 1307 New York Ave NW, Suite 700, Washington, DC 20005 *Tel:* 202-383-9005 *Fax:* 202-638-0882 *E-mail:* governance@asanet.org *Web Site:* www.asanet.org, pg 762

Bernstein & Andriulli Inc, 58 W 40 St, 6th fl, New York, NY 10018 *Tel:* 212-682-1490 *Fax:* 212-286-1890 *E-mail:* info@ba-reps.com *Web Site:* www.ba-reps.com, pg 665

Meredith G Bernstein, 2112 Broadway, Suite 503A, New York, NY 10023 *Tel:* 212-799-1007 *Fax:* 212-799-1145, pg 621

Berrett-Koehler Publishers Inc, 235 Montgomery St, Suite 650, San Francisco, CA 94104 *Tel:* 415-288-0260 *Fax:* 415-362-2512 *E-mail:* bkpub@bkpub.com *Web Site:* www.bkconnection.com, pg 37

Bess Press, 3565 Harding Ave, Honolulu, HI 96816 *Tel:* 808-734-7159 *Toll Free Tel:* 800-910-2377 *Fax:* 808-732-3627 *E-mail:* sales@besspress.com *Web Site:* www.besspress.com, pg 37

A M Best Co, Ambest Rd, Oldwick, NJ 08858 *Tel:* 908-439-2200 *Fax:* 908-439-3385 *E-mail:* customerservice@ambest.com; sales@ambest. com *Web Site:* www.ambest.com, pg 37

Best Publishing Co, PO Box 30100, Flagstaff, AZ 86003-0100 *Tel:* 928-527-1055 *Toll Free Tel:* 800-468-1055 *Fax:* 928-526-0370 *E-mail:* divebooks@bestpub. com *Web Site:* www.bestpub.com, pg 37

Bestseller Consultants, PO Box 922, Wilsonville, OR 97070 *Tel:* 503-694-5381 *Fax:* 503-694-5046, pg 591

Beta Computer Indexing, 61 S Kashong Dr, Geneva, NY 14456 *Tel:* 315-719-0486 *Fax:* 315-719-0487, pg 591

Bethany House Publishers/Baker Bookhouse, PO Box 6287, Grand Rapids, MI 49516-6287 *Tel:* 616-676-9185 *Toll Free Tel:* 800-877-2665 *Web Site:* www. bethanyhouse.com; www.bakerpublishinggroup.com, pg 37

Bethel Agency, 311 W 43 St, Suite 602, New York, NY 10036 *Tel:* 212-664-0455, pg 621

Bethlehem Books, 10194 Garfield St S, Bathgate, ND 58216 *Tel:* 701-265-3725 *Toll Free Tel:* 800-757-6831 *Fax:* 701-265-3716 *E-mail:* help@bethlehembooks. com *Web Site:* www.bethlehembooks.com, pg 37

Betterway Books, 4700 E Galbraith Rd, Cincinnati, OH 45236 *Tel:* 513-531-2690 *Toll Free Tel:* 800-666-0963 *Fax:* 513-891-7185 *Toll Free Fax:* 888-590-4082 *Web Site:* www.fwpublications.com, pg 38

Between the Lines, 720 Bathurst St, No 404, Toronto, ON M5S 2R4, Canada *Tel:* 416-535-9914 *Toll Free Tel:* 800-718-7201 *Fax:* 416-535-1484 *E-mail:* btlbooks@web.ca *Web Site:* www.btlbooks. com, pg 536

Albert J Beveridge Award in American History, 400 "A" St SE, Washington, DC 20003 *Tel:* 202-544-2422 *Fax:* 202-544-8307 *E-mail:* info@historians.org *Web Site:* www.historians.org, pg 762

Albert J Beveridge Grant for Research in the History of the Western Hemisphere, 400 "A" St SE, Washington, DC 20003 *Tel:* 202-544-2422 *Fax:* 202-544-8307 *E-mail:* info@historians.org *Web Site:* www.historians. org, pg 762

Beyond the Book, 222 Rosewood Dr, Danvers, MA 01923 *Toll Free Tel:* 800-928-3887 (ext 2420) *Fax:* 978-750-4250 *E-mail:* beyondthebook@ copyright.com *Web Site:* www.copyright.com, pg 742

Beyond Words Publishing Inc, 20827 NW Cornell Rd, Suite 500, Hillsboro, OR 97124-9808 *Tel:* 503-531-8700 *Fax:* 503-531-8773 *Web Site:* www.beyondword. com, pg 38

Bhaktivedanta Book Publishing Inc, 9701 Vencie Blvd, Unit 3, Los Angeles, CA 90034 *Tel:* 310-559-4455 *Toll Free Tel:* 800-927-4152 *Fax:* 310-837-1056 *E-mail:* bbt2@webcom.com *Web Site:* www.krishna. com, pg 38

Daniel Bial Agency, 41 W 83 St, Suite 5-C, New York, NY 10024 *Tel:* 212-721-1786 *Fax:* 309-213-0230 *E-mail:* dbialagency@juno.com, pg 621

Daniel Bial & Associates, 41 W 83 St, Suite 5-C, New York, NY 10024 *Tel:* 212-721-1786 *Fax:* 309-213-0230 *E-mail:* dbialagency@juno.com *Web Site:* www. danielbialagency.com, pg 591

Bibliogenesis, 152 Coddington Rd, Ithaca, NY 14850 *Tel:* 607-277-9660 *Fax:* 607-277-6661, pg 591

Bibliographical Society of America, PO Box 1537, Lenox Hill Sta, New York, NY 10021-0043 *Tel:* 212-452-2710 *Fax:* 212-452-2710 *E-mail:* bsa@ bibsocamer.org *Web Site:* www.bibsocamer.org, pg 681

Bibliographical Society of the University of Virginia, c/o Alderman Library, University of Virginia, McCormick Rd, Charlottesville, VA 22904 *Tel:* 434-924-7013 *Fax:* 434-924-1431 *E-mail:* bibsoc@virginia.edu *Web Site:* etext.lib.virginia.edu/bsuva/, pg 681

Bibliotheca Persica Press, 450 Riverside Dr, Suite 4, New York, NY 10027 *Tel:* 212-851-5723 *Fax:* 212-749-9524, pg 38

Biblo & Tannen Booksellers & Publishers Inc, PO Box 302, Cheshire, CT 06410-0302 *Tel:* 203-250-1647 *Toll Free Tel:* 800-272-8778 *Fax:* 203-250-1647 *Toll Free Fax:* 800-272-8778 *E-mail:* biblo.moser@snet.net, pg 38

Bick Publishing House, 307 Neck Rd, Madison, CT 06443 *Tel:* 203-245-0073 *Fax:* 203-245-5990 *E-mail:* bickpubhse@aol.com *Web Site:* www. bickpubhouse.com, pg 38

Big Guy Books Inc, 7750 El Camino Real, Suite F, Carlsbad, CA 92009 *Tel:* 760-334-1222 *Toll Free Tel:* 866-210-5938 (Booksellers cust serv); 800-741-6493 (For parents, teachers, schools & libraries) *Fax:* 760-334-1225 *E-mail:* info@bigguybooks. com; orders@bigguybooks.com *Web Site:* www. bigguybooks.com, pg 38

BigScore Productions, PO Box 4575, Lancaster, PA 17604 *Tel:* 717-293-0247 *Fax:* 717-293-1945 *E-mail:* bigscore@bigscoreproductions.com *Web Site:* www.bigscoreproductions.com, pg 621

Vicky Bijur Literary Agency, 333 West End Ave, Suite 5-B, New York, NY 10023 *Tel:* 212-580-4108 *Fax:* 212-496-1572 *E-mail:* vbijur@aol.com, pg 621

Bilingual Press/Editorial Bilingue, Hispanic Research Ctr, Arizona State Univ, Tempe, AZ 85287-2702 *Tel:* 480-965-3867 *Fax:* 480-965-8309 *E-mail:* brp@ asu.edu *Web Site:* www.asu.edu/brp/brp, pg 38

The Geoffrey Bilson Award for Historical Fiction, 40 Orchard View Blvd, Toronto, ON M4R 1B9, Canada *Tel:* 416-975-0010 *Fax:* 416-975-8970 *E-mail:* info@ bookcentre.ca *Web Site:* www.bookcentre.ca, pg 762

Binding Industries Association (BIA), 100 Daingerfield Rd, Alexandria, VA 22314 *Tel:* 703-519-8137 *Fax:* 703-548-3227 *E-mail:* bparrott@printing.org *Web Site:* www.gain.net, pg 681

Binford & Mort Publishing Inc, 5245 NE Elam Young Pkwy, Suite C, Hillsboro, OR 97124 *Tel:* 503-844-4960 *Toll Free Tel:* 888-221-4514 *Fax:* 503-844-4959, pg 38

Binghamton University Writing Program, c/o Dept of English, PO Box 6000, Binghamton, NY 13902-6000 *Tel:* 607-777-2168 *Fax:* 607-777-2408, pg 751

Biographical Publishing Co, 35 Clark Hill Rd, Prospect, CT 06712-1011 *Tel:* 203-758-3661 *Fax:* 253-793-2618 *E-mail:* biopub@aol.com *Web Site:* members. aol.com/biopub, pg 39

BioTechniques Books, One Research Dr, Suite 400 A, Westborough, MA 01581 *Tel:* 508-614-1414 *Fax:* 508-616-2930 *Web Site:* www.biotechniques.com, pg 39

Birch Brook Press, PO Box 81, Delhi, NY 13753 *Tel:* 607-746-7453 (book sales & prodn) *Fax:* 607-746-7453 *E-mail:* birchbrook@usadatanet. net; birchbrkpr@yahoo.com *Web Site:* www. birchbrookpress.info, pg 39

Birkhauser Boston, 675 Massachusetts Ave, Cambridge, MA 02139 *Tel:* 617-876-2333 *Toll Free Tel:* 800-777-4643 (cust serv) *Fax:* 617-876-1272 *E-mail:* service@birkhauser.com *Web Site:* www.birkhauser.com, pg 39

Birks Family Foundation Award for Canadian Biography, 320 S Shores Rd, Campbellford, ON K0L 1L0, Canada *Tel:* 705-653-0323 *Toll Free Tel:* 866-216-6222 *Fax:* 705-653-0593 *E-mail:* info@canauthors.org *Web Site:* www.canauthors.org, pg 762

George T Bisel Co Inc, 710 S Washington Sq, Philadelphia, PA 19106 *Tel:* 215-922-5760 *Toll Free Tel:* 800-247-3526 *Fax:* 215-922-2235 *E-mail:* info@bisel.com *Web Site:* www.bisel.com, pg 39

Bisk Education, 9417 Princess Palm Ave, Suite 400, Tampa, FL 33619 *Tel:* 813-621-6200 *Toll Free Tel:* 800-874-7877 *Fax:* 813-621-0127 *Toll Free Fax:* 800-345-8273 *E-mail:* bisk@bisk.com *Web Site:* www.bisk.com, pg 39

BizBest Media Corp, 860 Via de la Paz, Suite D-4, Pacific Palisades, CA 90272 *Tel:* 310-230-6868 *Toll Free Tel:* 800-873-5205; 877-424-9237 *Fax:* 310-454-6130 *E-mail:* info@bizbest.com *Web Site:* www.bizbest.com, pg 39

BKMK Press of the University of Missouri-Kansas City, 5101 Rockhill Rd, Kansas City, MO 64110-2499 *Tel:* 816-235-2558 *Fax:* 816-235-2611 *E-mail:* bkmk@umkc.edu *Web Site:* www.umkc.edu/bkmk, pg 39

Black Classic Press, PO Box 13414, Baltimore, MD 21203 *Tel:* 410-358-0980 *Fax:* 410-358-0987 *E-mail:* bcp@charm.net *Web Site:* www.blackclassic.com, pg 39

David Black Literary Agency, 156 Fifth Ave, Suite 608, New York, NY 10010 *Tel:* 212-242-5080 *Fax:* 212-924-6609, pg 621

Black Diamond Book Publishing, PO Box 492299, Los Angeles, CA 90049-8299 *Tel:* 310-472-9833 *Toll Free Tel:* 800-962-7622 *Fax:* 310-472-9833 *Toll Free Fax:* 800-962-7622, pg 39

Black Dog & Leventhal Publishers Inc, 151 W 19 St, 12th fl, New York, NY 10011 *Tel:* 212-647-9336 *Fax:* 212-647-9332 *E-mail:* information@bdlev.com *Web Site:* www.bdlev.com, pg 39

Black Dome Press Corp, 1011 Rte 296, Hensonville, NY 12439 *Tel:* 518-734-6357 *Fax:* 518-734-5802 *E-mail:* blackdomep@aol.com *Web Site:* www.blackdomepress.com, pg 40

Black Heron Press, PO Box 95676, Seattle, WA 98145-2676 *Tel:* 206-363-5210 *Fax:* 206-363-5210 *Web Site:* www.blackheronpress.com, pg 40

Irma S & James H Black Award, 610 W 112 St, New York, NY 10025 *Tel:* 212-875-4400 *Fax:* 212-875-4558 *Web Site:* streetcat.bankstreet.edu/html/isb.html, pg 762

Black Rose Books Ltd, CP 1258 Succ Place de Parc, Montreal, PQ H2X 4A7, Canada *Tel:* 514-844-4076 *Toll Free Tel:* 800-565-9523 *Fax:* 514-849-4797 *Toll Free Fax:* 800-221-9985 *E-mail:* blackrose@web.net *Web Site:* www.web.net/blackrosebooks, pg 536

Black Warrior Review Literary Awards, University of Alabama, Tuscaloosa, AL 35486-0027 *Tel:* 205-348-4518 *E-mail:* bwr@ua.edu *Web Site:* www.webdelsol.com/bwr, pg 762

Blackbirch Press®, 27500 Drake Rd, Farmington Hills, MI 48311-3535 *Toll Free Tel:* 800-877-4253 *Toll Free Fax:* 800-414-5043 (orders) *E-mail:* galeord@gale.com; customerservice@gale.com *Web Site:* www.gale.com, pg 40

Christopher Blackburn, 16 Purple Sageway, Toronto, ON M2H 2Z5, Canada *Tel:* 416-491-4857 *Fax:* 416-491-1142 *E-mail:* cblackburn@rogers.com, pg 592

The Blackburn Press, PO Box 287, Caldwell, NJ 07006-0287 *Tel:* 973-228-7077 *Fax:* 973-228-7276 *Web Site:* www.blackburnpress.com, pg 40

Susan Smith Blackburn Prize, 3239 Avalon Place, Houston, TX 77019 *Tel:* 713-308-2842 *Fax:* 713-654-8184 *Web Site:* www.blackburnprize.org, pg 763

Blacksmith Corp, PO Box 280, North Hampton, OH 45349-0280 *Tel:* 937-969-8389 *Toll Free Tel:* 800-531-2665 *Fax:* 937-969-8399 *E-mail:* sales@blacksmithcorp.com *Web Site:* www.blacksmithcorp.com, pg 40

Blackwell Publishers, 350 Main St, Malden, MA 02148 *Tel:* 781-388-8200 *Fax:* 781-388-8210 *E-mail:* books@blackwellpublishing.com *Web Site:* www.blackwellpublishing.com, pg 40

Blackwell Publishing/Futura, 3 W Main St, Elmsford, NY 10523 *Tel:* 914-593-0731 *Toll Free Tel:* 800-759-6102 *Fax:* 914-593-0732 *E-mail:* jbellhouse@ny.blackwellpublishing.com *Web Site:* www.blackwellpublishing.com/futura; www.blackwellfutura.com, pg 40

Blackwell Publishing Professional, 2121 State Ave, Ames, IA 50014 *Tel:* 515-292-0140 *Toll Free Tel:* 800-862-6657 (orders only) *Fax:* 515-292-3348 *Web Site:* www.blackwellprofessional.com, pg 40

Blade Publishing, 4540 Kearny Villa Rd, Suite 103, San Diego, CA 92123 *Tel:* 619-440-2309 *Fax:* 619-334-7070 *E-mail:* bladeinternational@yahoo.com, pg 40

John F Blair Publisher, 1406 Plaza Dr, Winston-Salem, NC 27103 *Tel:* 336-768-1374 *Toll Free Tel:* 800-222-9796 *Fax:* 336-768-9194 *E-mail:* blairpub@blairpub.com *Web Site:* www.blairpub.com, pg 41

Neltje Blanchan Memorial Award, 2320 Capitol Ave, Cheyenne, WY 82002 *Tel:* 307-777-7742 *Fax:* 307-777-5499 *Web Site:* www.wyoarts.state.wy.us, pg 763

Sam Blate Associates, LLC, 10331 Watkins Mill Dr, Montgomery Village, MD 20886-3950 *Tel:* 301-840-2248 *Fax:* 301-990-0707 *E-mail:* info@writephotopro.com *Web Site:* www.writephotopro.com, pg 592

Bleecker Street Associates Inc, 532 LaGuardia Place, No 617, New York, NY 10012 *Tel:* 212-677-4492 *Fax:* 212-388-0001, pg 621

Bloch Publishing Co, 118 E 28 St, Suite 501-503, New York, NY 10016-8413 *Tel:* 212-532-3977 *Fax:* 212-779-9169 *E-mail:* blochpub@worldnet.att.net *Web Site:* www.blochpub.com, pg 41

Bloom Ink Publishing Professionals, 122 S Ninth St, Lafayette, IN 47901-1652 *Tel:* 765-429-4888 *Fax:* 765-420-9597 *Web Site:* www.awbo.org/bloomink.htm, pg 592

Bloomberg Press, PO Box 888, Princeton, NJ 08542-0888 *Tel:* 609-279-4600 *E-mail:* press@bloomberg.com *Web Site:* www.bloomberg.com/books, pg 41

Bloomsbury Publishing, 175 Fifth Ave, Suite 300, New York, NY 10010 *Tel:* 212-674-5151 *Toll Free Tel:* 800-221-7945 *Fax:* 212-780-0115 *Web Site:* www.bloomsbury.com/usa, pg 41

Heidi Blough, Book Indexer, 502 Tanager Rd, St Augustine, FL 32086 *Tel:* 904-797-6572 *Fax:* 904-797-7617 *E-mail:* indexing@heidiblough.com *Web Site:* www.heidiblough.com, pg 592

Blue & Ude Writers' Services, PO Box 145, Clinton, WA 98236 *Tel:* 360-341-1630 *E-mail:* blueyude@whidbey.com *Web Site:* www.blueudewritersservices.com, pg 592

Blue Book Publications Inc, 8009 34 Ave S, Suite 175, Minneapolis, MN 55425 *Tel:* 952-854-5229 *Toll Free Tel:* 800-877-4867 *Fax:* 952-853-1486 *E-mail:* bluebook@bluebookinc.com *Web Site:* www.bluebookinc.com, pg 570

Blue Crane Books, PO Box 380291, Cambridge, MA 02238 *Tel:* 617-926-8989 *Fax:* 617-926-0982 *E-mail:* bluecrane@arrow1.com, pg 41

Blue Dolphin Publishing Inc, 12428 Nevada City Hwy, Grass Valley, CA 95945 *Tel:* 530-265-6925 *Toll Free Tel:* 800-643-0765 *Fax:* 530-265-0787 *E-mail:* bdolphin@netshel.net *Web Site:* www.bluedolphinpublishing.com, pg 41

Blue Dove Press, 4204 Sorrento Valley Blvd, Suite K, San Diego, CA 92121 *Tel:* 858-623-3330 *Toll Free Tel:* 800-691-1008 (orders) *Fax:* 858-623-3325 *E-mail:* mail@bluedove.org *Web Site:* www.bluedove.org, pg 41

Blue Moon Books, 245 W 17 St, 11th fl, New York, NY 10011-5300 *Tel:* 212-981-9898 *Fax:* 646-375-2571, pg 41

Blue Mountain Arts Inc, PO Box 4549, Boulder, CO 80306 *Tel:* 303-449-0536 *Toll Free Tel:* 800-473-2082 *Fax:* 303-417-6496 *Toll Free Fax:* 800-256-1213 *E-mail:* booksbma@mindspring.com; ordersbma@mindspring.com *Web Site:* www.sps.com, pg 41

Blue Note Publications, 400 W Cocoa Beach Causeway, Suite 3, Cocoa Beach, FL 32931 *Tel:* 321-799-2583 *Toll Free Tel:* 800-624-0401 *Fax:* 321-799-1942 *E-mail:* order@bluenotebooks.com *Web Site:* www.bluenotebooks.com, pg 41

Blue Poppy Press, 5441 Western Ave, No 2, Boulder, CO 80301 *Tel:* 303-447-8372 *Toll Free Tel:* 800-487-9296 *Fax:* 303-245-8362 *E-mail:* info@bluepoppy.com *Web Site:* www.bluepoppy.com, pg 42

Blue Raven Press, 219 SE Main St, Suite 506, Minneapolis, MN 55414 *Tel:* 612-331-8039 *Fax:* 612-331-8115 *Web Site:* www.blueravenpress.com, pg 570

Blue Sky Marketing Inc, PO Box 21583, St Paul, MN 55121-0583 *Tel:* 651-687-9835 *Fax:* 651-687-9836, pg 42

Blue Unicorn Press Inc, 4153 SE 39 Ave, Suite 35, Portland, OR 97202-3176 *Tel:* 503-775-9322 *E-mail:* unicornpress404@aol.com, pg 42

Bluestocking Press, 3333 Gold Country Dr, El Dorado, CA 95623 *Tel:* 530-621-1123 *Toll Free Tel:* 800-959-8586 *Fax:* 530-642-9222 *E-mail:* customerservice@bluestockingpress.com *Web Site:* www.bluestockingpress.com, pg 42

Bluewood Books, 38 South "B" St, Suite 202, San Mateo, CA 94401 *Tel:* 650-548-0754 *Fax:* 650-548-0654 *E-mail:* bluewoodb@aol.com, pg 42

Rhoda Blumberg, 1305 Baptist Church Rd, Yorktown Heights, NY 10598 *Tel:* 914-962-7700 *Fax:* 914-962-9800 *E-mail:* rbwrite@aol.com, pg 592

Blushing Rose Publishing, 29 Katrina Rd, San Anselmo, CA 94960 *Tel:* 415-458-2090 *Toll Free Tel:* 800-898-2263 *Fax:* 415-458-2091 *E-mail:* info@blushingrose.com *Web Site:* www.blushingrose.com, pg 42

BMI, 320 W 57 St, New York, NY 10019 *Tel:* 212-586-2000 *Fax:* 212-246-2163 *Web Site:* www.bmi.com, pg 681

BNA Books, 1231 25 St NW, Washington, DC 20037 *Tel:* 202-452-4343 *Toll Free Tel:* 800-960-1220 *Fax:* 202-452-4997 (editorial off); 732-346-1624 (cust serv) *E-mail:* books@bna.com *Web Site:* www.bnabooks.com, pg 42

BNI Publications Inc, 1612 S Clementine St, Anaheim, CA 92802 *Tel:* 714-517-0970 *Toll Free Tel:* 800-873-6397 *Fax:* 714-535-8078 *Web Site:* www.bnibooks.com, pg 42

BOA Editions Ltd, 260 East Ave, Rochester, NY 14604 *Tel:* 585-546-3410 *Fax:* 585-546-3913 *Web Site:* www.boaeditions.org, pg 42

Judy Boals Inc & Jim Flynn Agency, 208 W 30 St, Suite 401, New York, NY 10001 *Tel:* 212-868-1068; 212-868-0924 *Fax:* 212-868-1052, pg 621

BoardSource, 1828 "L" St NW, Suite 900, Washington, DC 20036-5104 *Tel:* 202-452-6262 *Toll Free Tel:* 800-883-6262 *Fax:* 202-452-6299 *E-mail:* mail@boardsource.org *Web Site:* www.boardsource.org, pg 42

Reid Boates Literary Agency, 69 Cooks Crossroad, Pittstown, NJ 08867-0328 *Tel:* 908-730-8523 *Fax:* 908-730-8931 *E-mail:* boatesliterary@att.net, pg 621

The James Boatwright III Prize for Poetry, Washington & Lee University, Mattingly House, 2 Lee Ave, Lexington, VA 24450-0303 *Tel:* 540-458-8765 *Fax:* 540-458-8461 *Web Site:* www.shenandoah.wlu.edu, pg 763

Bobley Harmann Corp, 311 Crossways Park Dr, Woodbury, NY 11797 *Tel:* 516-364-1800 *Fax:* 516-364-1899 *E-mail:* info@bobley.com *Web Site:* www.bobley.com, pg 42

Frederick Bock Prize, 1030 N Clark St, Suite 420, Chicago, IL 60610 *Tel:* 312-787-7070 *Fax:* 312-787-6650 *E-mail:* poetry@poetrymagazine.org *Web Site:* www.poetrymagazine.org, pg 763

George Bogin Memorial Award, 15 Gramercy Park, New York, NY 10003 *Tel:* 212-254-9628 *Fax:* 212-673-2352 *Web Site:* www.poetrysociety.org, pg 763

Bogle International Library Travel Fund, 50 E Huron St, Chicago, IL 60611-2795 *Tel:* 312-280-3201 *Toll Free:* 800-545-2433 (ext 3201) *Fax:* 312-280-4392 *E-mail:* intl@ala.org *Web Site:* www.ala.org, pg 763

Editions du Bois-de-Coulonge, 1140 Demontigny, Sillery, PQ G1S 3T7, Canada *Tel:* 418-683-6332 *Fax:* 418-683-6332 *Web Site:* www.ebc.qc.ca, pg 537

Bolchazy-Carducci Publishers Inc, 1000 Brown St, Unit 101, Wauconda, IL 60084 *Tel:* 847-526-4344 *Fax:* 847-526-2867 *Web Site:* www.bolchazy.com, pg 43

Bollix Books, 1609 W Callender Ave, Peoria, IL 61606 *Tel:* 309-453-4903 *Fax:* 309-676-6558 *E-mail:* editor@bollixbooks.com *Web Site:* www.bollixbooks.com, pg 43

Alison M Bond Ltd, 155 W 72 St, Suite 302, New York, NY 10023 *Tel:* 212-874-2850 *Fax:* 212-874-2892 *E-mail:* mail@bondlit.com, pg 621

Bond Literary Agency, 1430 E Bates Ave, Englewood, CO 80113 *Tel:* 303-781-9305 *Fax:* 303-783-9166, pg 621

Waldo M & Grace C Bonderman Prize, 140 W Washington St, Indianapolis, IN 46204 *Tel:* 317-635-5277 *Fax:* 317-236-0767 *E-mail:* bonderman@iupui.edu *Web Site:* www.indianarep.com/bonderman, pg 763

Bonus Books Inc, 1452 Second St, Santa Monica, CA 90403 *Tel:* 310-260-9400 *Toll Free Tel:* 800-225-3775 *E-mail:* webmaster@bonusbooks.com *Web Site:* www.bonusbooks.com, pg 43

Book & Periodical Council, 192 Spadina Ave, Suite 107, Toronto, ON M5T 2C2, Canada *Tel:* 416-975-9366 *Fax:* 416-975-1839 *E-mail:* bkper@interlog.com *Web Site:* www.freedomtoread.ca, pg 681

Book Beat Ltd, 26010 Greenfield, Oak Park, MI 48237 *Tel:* 248-968-1190 *Fax:* 248-968-3102 *E-mail:* bookbeat@aol.com *Web Site:* www.thebookbeat.com, pg 43

Book Builders LLC, 425 Madison Ave, 19th fl, New York, NY 10017 *Tel:* 212-371-1110 *Fax:* 212-893-8680 *E-mail:* mail@bookbuildersllc.com *Web Site:* www.bookbuildersllc.com, pg 592

Book Deals Inc, 244 Fifth Ave, Suite 2164, New York, NY 10001-7604 *Tel:* 212-252-2701 *Fax:* 212-591-6211 *E-mail:* bookdeals@aol.com *Web Site:* www.bookdealsinc.com, pg 621

Book Developers Inc, 930 Forest Ave, Palo Alto, CA 94301 *Tel:* 650-322-4595; 650-322-4379 *Fax:* 650-322-4379 *E-mail:* customerservice@bookdevelopers.com *Web Site:* www.bookdevelopers.com, pg 592

Book East, 2330 NE 61 Ave, Portland, OR 97213 *Tel:* 503-287-0974 *Fax:* 503-281-3693, pg 43

Book Industry Standards & Communications, 19 W 21 St, Suite 905, New York, NY 10010 *Tel:* 646-336-7141 *Fax:* 646-336-6214 *E-mail:* info@bisg.org *Web Site:* www.bisg.org, pg 681

Book Industry Study Group Inc, 19 W 21 St, Suite 905, New York, NY 10010 *Tel:* 646-336-7141 *Fax:* 646-336-6214 *E-mail:* info@bisg.org *Web Site:* www.bisg.org, pg 681

Book-It Award, 137 Pelton Center Way, San Leandro, CA 94577 *Tel:* 510-483-5587 *Fax:* 510-483-3832 *E-mail:* aworldofbooks@aol.com *Web Site:* aworldofbooks, pg 763

Book Manufacturers' Institute Inc (BMI), 2 Armand Beach Dr, Suite 1B, Palm Coast, FL 32137 *Tel:* 386-986-4552 *Fax:* 386-986-4553 *E-mail:* info@bmibook.com *Web Site:* www.bmibook.org, pg 681

Book Marketing Works LLC, 50 Lovely St, Avon, CT 06001 *Tel:* 860-675-1344 *Toll Free Tel:* 800-562-4357 *Fax:* 203-729-5335 *Web Site:* www.bookmarketingworks.com, pg 43

Book-of-the-Year Award, 3707 Woodview Trace, Indianapolis, IN 46268-1158 *Tel:* 317-871-4900 *Toll Free Tel:* 800-284-3167 *Fax:* 317-704-2323 *Web Site:* www.kdp.org, pg 763

Book Peddlers, 15245 Minnetonka Blvd, Minnetonka, MN 55345-1510 *Tel:* 952-912-0036 *Toll Free Tel:* 800-255-3379 *Fax:* 952-912-0105 *Web Site:* www.bookpeddlers.com; www.practicalparenting.com, pg 43

Book Producing: Making Books Happen, 160 Fifth Ave, New York, NY 10010-7003 *Tel:* 212-645-2368 *Toll Free Tel:* 800-209-4575 *Fax:* 212-242-6799 *E-mail:* office@abpaonline.org *Web Site:* www.abpaonline.org, pg 742

Book Publicists of Southern California, 6464 Sunset Blvd, Rm 755, Hollywood, CA 90028 *Tel:* 323-461-3921 *Fax:* 323-461-0917, pg 682

The Book Publisher's Association of Alberta, 10523 100 Ave, Edmonton, AB T5J 0A8, Canada *Tel:* 780-424-5060 *Fax:* 780-424-7943 *E-mail:* info@bookpublishers.ab.ca *Web Site:* www.bookpublishers.ab.ca, pg 682

Book Publishing Co, 415 Farm Rd, Summertown, TN 38483 *Tel:* 931-964-3571 *Toll Free Tel:* 888-260-8458 *Fax:* 931-964-3518 *E-mail:* info@bookpubco.com *Web Site:* www.bookpubco.com, pg 43

Book Sales Inc, 114 Northfield Ave, Edison, NJ 08837 *Tel:* 732-225-0530 *Toll Free Tel:* 800-526-7257 *Fax:* 732-225-2257 *E-mail:* sales@booksalesusa.com; customerservice@booksalesusa.com *Web Site:* www.booksalesusa.com, pg 43

Book Sense Book of the Year Award, 828 S Broadway, Tarrytown, NY 10591 *Tel:* 914-591-2665 *Toll Free Tel:* 800-637-0037 *Fax:* 914-591-2720 *Web Site:* www.bookweb.org, pg 763

Book Smart Literary Agency & Consulting Group, 418 Farm Rd, Marlborough, MA 01752 *Tel:* 508-460-3499 *Fax:* 508-460-0285 *E-mail:* booksmart@comcast.net, pg 621

The Book Tree, PO Box 16476, San Diego, CA 92176 *Tel:* 619-280-1263 *Fax:* 619-280-1285 *E-mail:* booktree1@cs.com *Web Site:* www.thebooktree.com, pg 43

Book World Inc/Blue Star Productions, 9666 E Riggs Rd, No 194, Sun Lakes, AZ 85248 *Tel:* 480-895-7995 *Fax:* 480-895-6991 *E-mail:* bsp@bluestarproductions.net *Web Site:* www.bluestarproductions.net, pg 44

The Bookbinders' Guild of New York, Dunn & Co, 110 Grand Ave, Ridgefield Park, NJ 07660 *Tel:* 201-229-1888 *Fax:* 201-229-1755 *Web Site:* www.bookbindersguild.org, pg 682

Bookbuilders of Boston, 44 Highland Circle, Halifax, MA 02338 *Tel:* 781-293-8600 *Toll Free Fax:* 866-820-0469 *E-mail:* office@bbboston.org *Web Site:* bbboston.org, pg 682

Bookbuilders West, PO Box 7046, San Francisco, CA 94120-9727 *Tel:* 415-273-5790 *Web Site:* www.bookbuilders.org, pg 682

BookCrafters LLC, Box C, Convent Station, NJ 07961 *Tel:* 973-984-7880 *Web Site:* bookcraftersllc.com, pg 592

BookEnds LLC, 136 Long Hill Rd, Gillette, NJ 07933 *Tel:* 908-604-2652 *E-mail:* editor@bookends-inc.com *Web Site:* www.bookends-inc.com, pg 622

Bookhaven Press LLC, 249 Field Club Circle, McKees Rocks, PA 15136 *Tel:* 412-494-6926 *Toll Free Tel:* 800-782-7424 (orders only) *Fax:* 412-494-5749 *E-mail:* bookhaven@aol.com *Web Site:* members.aol.com/bookhaven, pg 44

Bookmakers Ltd, 40 Mouse House Rd, Taos, NM 87571 *Tel:* 505-776-5435 *Fax:* 505-776-2762 *E-mail:* bookmakers@newmex.com *Web Site:* www.bookmakersltd.com, pg 665

The Bookmill, 22000 Mt Eden Rd, Saratoga, CA 95070-9729 *Tel:* 408-867-9450 *Fax:* 408-867-9450 *E-mail:* bookmill@ix.netcom.com *Web Site:* www.marinacci.com/Bookmill, pg 592

Books & Such, 4788 Carissa Ave, Santa Rosa, CA 95405 *Tel:* 707-538-4184 *Fax:* 707-538-3937 *E-mail:* janet@janetgrant.com *Web Site:* janetgrant.com, pg 622

Books by W John Koch Publishing, 11666-72 Ave, Edmonton, AB T6G 0C1, Canada *Tel:* 780-436-0581 *Fax:* 780-430-1672 *E-mail:* wjohnkoch@wjkochpublishing.com *Web Site:* www.wjkochpublishing.com, pg 570

Books Collective, 214-21 10405 Jasper Ave, Edmonton, AB T5J 3S2, Canada *Tel:* 780-448-0590 *Fax:* 780-448-0640 *E-mail:* river@bookscollective.com *Web Site:* www.bookscollective.com, pg 537

Books for Asia, 80 Elmira St, San Francisco, CA 94124 *Tel:* 415-656-8990 *Fax:* 415-468-8379 *Web Site:* www.asiafoundation.org, pg 705

Books for Everybody, 70 The Esplanade, Suite 210, Toronto, ON M5E 1R2, Canada *Tel:* 416-360-0044 *Fax:* 416-955-0794 *E-mail:* mail@booksforeverybody.com *Web Site:* www.booksforeverybody.com, pg 682

Books in Motion, 9922 E Montgomery, Suite 31, Spokane, WA 99206 *Tel:* 509-922-1646 *Toll Free Tel:* 800-752-3199 *Fax:* 509-922-1445 *E-mail:* sales@booksinmotion.com *Web Site:* www.booksinmotion.com, pg 44

Books on Tape®, Customer Service, 400 Hahn Rd, Westminster, MD 21157 *Toll Free Tel:* 800-733-3000 *Toll Free Fax:* 800-659-2436 *E-mail:* botlib@booksontape.com *Web Site:* library.booksontape.com, pg 44

BooksCraft Inc, 4909 Eastbourne Dr, Indianapolis, IN 46226 *Tel:* 317-542-8327 *Fax:* 317-591-9809 *E-mail:* bookscraft@comcast.net *Web Site:* www.bookscraft.com, pg 592

BookStop Literary Agency, 67 Meadow View Rd, Orinda, CA 94563 *Web Site:* www.bookstopliterary.com, pg 622

Booktec, 2825 SE 67, Portland, OR 97206 *Tel:* 503-772-9177 *Fax:* 503-339-9908, pg 592

Georges Borchardt Inc, 136 E 57 St, New York, NY 10022 *Tel:* 212-753-5785 *Fax:* 212-838-6518 *E-mail:* georges@gbagency.com, pg 622

Borealis Press Ltd, 110 Bloomingdale St, Ottawa, ON K2C 4A4, Canada *Tel:* 613-798-9299 *Fax:* 613-798-9747 *E-mail:* borealis@istar.ca *Web Site:* www.borealispress.com, pg 537

Boson Books, 3905 Meadow Field Lane, Raleigh, NC 27606 *Tel:* 919-233-8164 *Fax:* 919-233-8578 *E-mail:* boson@bosonbooks.com *Web Site:* bosonbooks.com, pg 44

Boston America Corp, 125 Walnut St, Watertown, MA 02472 *Tel:* 617-923-1111 (ext 249) *Fax:* 617-923-8839 *E-mail:* info@bostonamerica.com *Web Site:* www.bostonamerica.com, pg 44

Boston Globe-Horn Book Award, 56 Roland St, Suite 200, Boston, MA 02129 *Tel:* 617-628-0225 *Toll Free Tel:* 800-325-1170 *Fax:* 617-628-0882 *E-mail:* info@hbook.com *Web Site:* www.hbook.com, pg 763

The Boston Literary Group Inc, 156 Mount Auburn St, Cambridge, MA 02138 *Tel:* 617-547-0800 *Fax:* 617-876-8474, pg 622

The Boston Mills Press, 132 Main St, Erin, ON N0B 1T0, Canada *Tel:* 519-833-2407 *Fax:* 519-833-2195 *E-mail:* books@bostonmillspress.com *Web Site:* bostonmillspress.com, pg 537

Boston University, 236 Bay State Rd, Boston, MA 02215 *Tel:* 617-353-2510 *Fax:* 617-353-3653 *Web Site:* www.bu.edu/writing/, pg 751

The Boston Word Works, PO Box 56419, Sherman Oaks, CA 91413-1419 *Tel:* 818-904-9088 *Fax:* 818-787-1431, pg 592

The Boswell Institute, PO Box 7100, Beverly Hills, CA 90212-7100 *Tel:* 818-343-4434, pg 44

Bottom Dog Press, c/o Firelands College of Bowling Green State University, PO Box 425, Huron, OH 44839-0425 *Tel:* 419-433-5560 *Fax:* 419-433-9696 *Web Site:* members.aol.com/lsmithdog/bottomdog, pg 44

Bound to Stay Bound Books Scholarship, 50 E Huron St, Chicago, IL 60611-2795 *Tel:* 312-280-2163 *Toll Free:* 800-545-2433 *Fax:* 312-944-7671 *E-mail:* alsc@ala.org *Web Site:* www.ala.org/alsc/, pg 763

Thomas Bouregy & Co Inc, 160 Madison Ave, New York, NY 10016 *Tel:* 212-598-0222 *Fax:* 212-979-1862 *E-mail:* customerservice@avalonbooks.com *Web Site:* avalonbooks.com, pg 44

Louise Louis & Emily F Bourne Student Poetry Award, 15 Gramercy Park, New York, NY 10003 *Tel:* 212-254-9628 *Fax:* 212-673-2352 *Web Site:* www.poetrysociety.org, pg 763

The Barbara Bova Literary Agency, 3951 Gulfshore Blvd, Suite PH1-B, Naples, FL 34103 *Tel:* 239-649-7237 *Fax:* 239-649-7263 *E-mail:* bovab4@aol.com *Web Site:* barbarabovaliteraryagency.com, pg 622

Eddie Bowers Publishing Inc, PO Box 130, Peosta, IA 52068-0130 *Tel:* 563-876-3119 *Toll Free Tel:* 800-747-2411 *Fax:* 563-876-3206 *E-mail:* eddiebowerspub@aol.com *Web Site:* www.eddiebowerspublishing.com, pg 44

R R Bowker LLC, 630 Central Ave, New Providence, NJ 07974 *Tel:* 908-286-1090 *Toll Free Tel:* 888-269-5372; 888-269-5372 (cust serv - press 2 for returns) *Fax:* 908-219-0098 *E-mail:* orderinfo@bowker.com *Web Site:* www.bowker.com, pg 44

Bowling Green State University, Creative Writing Program, 226 East Hall, Bowling Green, OH 43403 *Tel:* 419-372-8370 *Fax:* 419-372-6805 *E-mail:* mmcgowa@bgnet.bgsu.edu *Web Site:* www.bgsu.edu/departments/creative-writing, pg 751

Bowling Writing Competition, 5301 S 76 St, Greendale, WI 53129 *Tel:* 414-421-6400 *Fax:* 414-321-8356 *Web Site:* www.bowl.com, pg 763

BowTie Press, 3 Burroughs, Irvine, CA 92618 *Tel:* 949-855-8822 *Toll Free Tel:* 800-426-2516 *Fax:* 949-458-3856 *Web Site:* www.bowtiepress.com, pg 45

Marion Boyars Publishers Inc, c/o The Feminist, 365 Fifth Ave, Suite 5406, New York, NY 10016 *Tel:* 212-697-9676 *Fax:* 212-808-0664 *Web Site:* www.marionboyars.co.uk, pg 45

Boydell & Brewer Inc, 668 Mount Hope Ave, University of Rochester, Rochester, NY 14620 *Tel:* 585-275-0419 *Fax:* 585-271-8778 *Web Site:* www.boydellandbrewer.co.uk, pg 45

Boyds Mills Press, 815 Church St, Honesdale, PA 18431 *Tel:* 570-253-1164 *Toll Free Tel:* 877-512-8366 *Fax:* 570-253-0179 *Web Site:* www.boydsmillspress.com, pg 45

Rosalie Boyle/Norma Farber Award, 16 Cornell St, Arlington, MA 02474 *Web Site:* www.nepoetryclub.org, pg 764

Boys Town Press, 14100 Crawford St, Boys Town, NE 68010 *Tel:* 402-498-1320 *Toll Free Tel:* 800-282-6657 *Fax:* 402-498-1310 *E-mail:* btpress@boystown.org *Web Site:* www.boystownpress.org, pg 45

BPA Worldwide, 2 Corporate Dr, Suite 900, Shelton, CT 06484 *Tel:* 203-447-2800 *Fax:* 203-447-2900 *E-mail:* info@bpaww.com *Web Site:* www.bpaww.com, pg 682

Bradford Publishing Co, 1743 Wazee St, Denver, CO 80202 *Tel:* 303-292-2590 *Toll Free Tel:* 800-446-2831 *Fax:* 303-298-5014 *E-mail:* marketing@bradfordpublishing.com *Web Site:* www.bradfordpublishing.com, pg 45

Barbara Bradley Prize, 16 Cornell St, Arlington, MA 02474 *Web Site:* www.nepoetryclub.org, pg 764

Brady Literary Management, Town Farm Hill, PO Box 164, Hartland Four Corners, VT 05049 *Tel:* 802-436-2455 *Fax:* 802-436-2466, pg 592, 622

BradyGAMES Publishing, 800 E 96 St, 3rd fl, Indianapolis, IN 46240 *Tel:* 317-428-3000 *Toll Free Tel:* 800-545-5912; 800-571-5840 (cust serv) *E-mail:* bradyquestions@pearsoned.com *Web Site:* www.bradygames.com, pg 45

Braille Co Inc, 65-B Town Hall Sq, Falmouth, MA 02540-2754 *Tel:* 508-540-0800 *Fax:* 508-548-6116 *E-mail:* braillinc@capecod.net *Web Site:* home.capecod.net/~braillinc, pg 45

Branden Publishing Co Inc, PO Box 812094, Wellesley, MA 02482-0013 *Tel:* 781-235-3634 *Fax:* 781-790-1056 *E-mail:* branden@branden.com *Web Site:* www.branden.com, pg 45

Brands-to-Books Inc, 155 W 72 St, Suite 302, New York, NY 10023 *Tel:* 212-362-6957 *Fax:* 212-874-2892 *E-mail:* agents@brandstobooks.com *Web Site:* www.brandstobooks.com, pg 622

Brandt & Hochman Literary Agents Inc, 1501 Broadway, Suite 2310, New York, NY 10036 *Tel:* 212-840-5760 *Fax:* 212-840-5776, pg 622

The Joan Brandt Agency, 788 Wesley Dr NW, Atlanta, GA 30305 *Tel:* 404-351-8877 *Fax:* 404-351-0068, pg 622

Brandywine Press, 154 General Pulaski Walk, Naugatuck, CT 06770-2978 *Tel:* 203-729-7556 *Toll Free Tel:* 800-345-1776 *Fax:* 203-729-7567 *Web Site:* www.brandywinepress.com, pg 45

The Helen Brann Agency Inc, 94 Curtis Rd, Bridgewater, CT 06752 *Tel:* 860-354-9580 *Fax:* 860-355-2572 *E-mail:* helenbrannagency@earthlink.net, pg 622

Brassey's Inc, 22841 Quicksilver Dr, Dulles, VA 20166 *Tel:* 703-661-1548 *Toll Free Tel:* 800-775-2518 (orders only) *Fax:* 703-661-1547 *E-mail:* djacobs@booksintl.com *Web Site:* www.brasseysinc.com, pg 45

Barbara Braun Associates Inc, 104 Fifth Ave, 7th fl, New York, NY 10011 *Tel:* 212-604-9023 *Fax:* 212-604-9041 *E-mail:* bba230@earthlink.net *Web Site:* www.barbarabraunagency.com, pg 622

Donna Lee Braunstein Your Personal Researcher, 22848 Mesa Way, Lake Forest, CA 92630 *Tel:* 949-472-8538 *E-mail:* dlbraunstein@prodigy.net, pg 592

George Braziller Inc, 171 Madison Ave, Suite 1105, New York, NY 10016 *Tel:* 212-889-0909 *Fax:* 212-689-5405 *E-mail:* georgebraziller@earthlink.net *Web Site:* www.georgebraziller.com, pg 46

Brazo Bookstore (Houston Award), 3700 Mockingbird Lane, Dallas, TX 75205 *Tel:* 214-528-2655 *Web Site:* www.stedwards.edu/newc/marks/til/awards_and_rules.htm, pg 764

Bread Loaf Writers' Conference, Kirk Alumni Center, Middlebury, VT 05753 *Tel:* 802-443-5286 *Fax:* 802-443-2087 *E-mail:* blwc@middlebury.edu *Web Site:* www.middlebury.edu, pg 742

Bread Loaf Writers' Conference of Middlebury College, Middlebury College, Middlebury, VT 05753 *Tel:* 802-443-5286 *Fax:* 802-443-2087 *E-mail:* blwc@middlebury.edu *Web Site:* www.middlebury.edu/~blwc, pg 742

Breakaway Books, PO Box 24, Halcottsville, NY 12438-0024 *Tel:* 607-326-4805 *Toll Free Tel:* 800-548-4348 (voicemail) *Fax:* 212-898-0408 *E-mail:* mail@breakawaybooks.com; orders@breakawaybooks.com; info@breakawaybooks.com *Web Site:* www.breakawaybooks.com, pg 46

Breakout Productions Inc, PO Box 1643, Port Townsend St, WA 98368-0129 *Tel:* 360-379-1965 *Fax:* 360-379-3794, pg 46

Breakthrough Publications Inc, 326 Main St, Emmaus, PA 18049 *Tel:* 610-965-3200 *Toll Free Tel:* 800-824-5000 *Fax:* 610-965-5836 *Web Site:* www.booksonhorses.com, pg 46

Breakwater Books Ltd, 100 Water St, St Johns, NF A1C 6E6, Canada *Tel:* 709-722-6680 *Toll Free Tel:* 800-563-3333 *Fax:* 709-753-0708 *E-mail:* info@breakwater.nf.net *Web Site:* www.breakwater.nf.net; www.breakwaterbooks.com, pg 537

Nicholas Brealey Publishing, 3704 Beard Ave N, Minneapolis, MN 55422 *Tel:* 763-208-3169 *Toll Free Tel:* 888-BREALEY (273-2539) *Fax:* 763-208-3170 *E-mail:* booksmatter@earthlink.net *Web Site:* www.nbrealey-books.com, pg 46

James Henry Breasted Prize, 400 "A" St SE, Washington, DC 20003 *Tel:* 202-544-2422 *Fax:* 202-544-8307 *E-mail:* info@historians.org *Web Site:* www.historians.org, pg 764

Brenner Information Group, 9282 Samantha Ct, San Diego, CA 92129 *Tel:* 858-538-0093 *Toll Free Tel:* 800-811-4337 *Fax:* 858-484-2599 *E-mail:* info@brennerbooks.com; sales@brennerbooks.com (ordering) *Web Site:* www.brennerbooks.com, pg 46

Brentwood Christian Press, 4000 Beallwood Ave, Columbus, GA 31904 *Tel:* 706-576-5787 *Toll Free Tel:* 800-334-8861 *E-mail:* brentwood@aol.com *Web Site:* www.brentwoodbooks.com, pg 46

Brethren Press, 1451 Dundee Ave, Elgin, IL 60120-1694 *Tel:* 847-742-5100 *Toll Free Tel:* 800-323-8039 *Fax:* 847-742-1407 *Web Site:* www.brethrenpress.com, pg 46

Brewers Publications, 736 Pearl St, Boulder, CO 80302 *Tel:* 303-447-0816 *Toll Free Tel:* 888-822-6273 (Canada & US) *Fax:* 303-447-2825 *Web Site:* www.beertown.org, pg 46

Brick Tower Press, 1230 Park Ave, New York, NY 10128 *Tel:* 212-427-7139 *Toll Free Tel:* 800-68-BRICK (682-7425) *Fax:* 212-860-8852 *E-mail:* bricktower@aol.com *Web Site:* www.bricktowerpress.com, pg 47

BrickHouse Books Inc, 306 Suffolk Rd, Baltimore, MD 21218 *Tel:* 410-704-2869; 410-235-7690 *Fax:* 410-704-3999; 410-235-7690 *Web Site:* www.towson.edu; www.brickhousebooks.edu, pg 47

Bridge Learning Systems Inc, 351 Los Altos, American Canyon, CA 94589 *Tel:* 925-228-3177 *Toll Free Tel:* 800-487-9868 *Fax:* 925-372-6099 *E-mail:* bridge@blsinc.com *Web Site:* www.blsinc.com, pg 47

Bridge-Logos Publishers, 17310 NW 32 Ave, Newberry, FL 32669 *Tel:* 352-472-7900 *Toll Free Tel:* 800-631-5802 *Fax:* 352-472-7908 *Toll Free Fax:* 800-935-6467 *E-mail:* info@bridgelogos.com *Web Site:* www.bridgelogos.com, pg 47

Bridge Publications Inc, 4751 Fountain Ave, Los Angeles, CA 90029 *Tel:* 323-953-3320 *Toll Free Tel:* 800-722-1733; 800-843-7389 (CA) *Fax:* 323-953-3328 *E-mail:* info@bridgepub.com *Web Site:* www.bridgepub.com, pg 47

Bridge to Asia, 665 Grant Ave, San Francisco, CA 94108 *Tel:* 415-678-2990 *Fax:* 415-678-2996 *E-mail:* asianet@bridge.org *Web Site:* www.bridge.org, pg 705

Bridge Works Publishing, PO Box 1798, Bridgehampton, NY 11932-1798 *Tel:* 631-537-3418 *Fax:* 631-537-5092 *E-mail:* bap@hamptons.com, pg 47

Briefings Publishing Group, 1101 King St, Suite 110, Alexandria, VA 22314 *Tel:* 703-548-3800 *Toll Free Tel:* 800-888-2086 *Fax:* 703-684-2136 *E-mail:* customerservice@briefings.com *Web Site:* www.briefings.com, pg 47

M Courtney Briggs Esq, Authors Representative, 100 N Broadway Ave, 20th fl, Oklahoma City, OK 73102 *Tel:* 405-235-1900 *Fax:* 405-235-1995, pg 622

Bright Mountain Books Inc, 206 Riva Ridge Dr, Fairview, NC 28730 *Tel:* 828-628-1768 *Toll Free Tel:* 800-437-3959 *Fax:* 828-628-1755 *E-mail:* booksbmb@charter.net, pg 47

Brighton Publications, PO Box 120706, New Brighton, MN 55112-0022 *Tel:* 651-636-2220 *Toll Free Tel:* 800-536-2665 *Fax:* 651-636-2220, pg 47

Brill Academic Publishers Inc, 112 Water St, Suite 601, Boston, MA 02109 *Tel:* 617-263-2323 *Toll Free Tel:* 800-962-4406 *Fax:* 617-263-2324 *E-mail:* cs@brillusa.com *Web Site:* www.brill.nl, pg 47

Brilliance Audio, 1704 Eaton Dr, Grand Haven, MI 49417 *Tel:* 616-846-5256 *Toll Free Tel:* 800-648-2312 (orders only) *Fax:* 616-846-0630 *Web Site:* www.brillianceaudio.com, pg 47

Bristol Fashion Publications Inc, PO Box 4676, Harrisburg, PA 17111-0676 *Tel:* 772-559-1379 *Toll Free Tel:* 800-478-7147 *Fax:* 717-564-1711 *Toll Free Fax:* 800-543-9030 *E-mail:* orders@bfpbooks.com *Web Site:* www.bfpbooks.com, pg 48

Bristol Publishing Enterprises, 2714 McCone Ave, Hayward, CA 94545 *Tel:* 510-783-5472 *Toll Free Tel:* 800-346-4889 *Fax:* 510-783-5492 *Web Site:* www.bristolpublishing.com, pg 48

British Council Prize in the Humanities, University of Kentucky, History Dept, Lexington, KY 40506-0027 *Tel:* 859-257-1246 *Fax:* 859-323-3885 *Web Site:* www.nacbs.org, pg 764

Brittingham & Felix Pollak Prizes in Poetry, c/o Ron Wallace, Series Editor, University of Wisconsin, Dept of English, 600 N Park St, Madison, WI 53706 *Web Site:* www.wisc.edu/wisconsinpress/, pg 764

Broadcast Pioneers Library of American Broadcasting, Hornbake Library, University of Maryland, College Park, MD 20742 *Tel:* 301-405-9160 *Fax:* 301-314-2634 *E-mail:* bp50@umail.umd.edu *Web Site:* www.lib.umd.edu/LAB, pg 682

Broadman & Holman Publishers, 127 Ninth Ave N, Nashville, TN 37234-0114 *Tel:* 615-251-2520 *Fax:* 615-251-5004 *Web Site:* www.broadmanholman.com, pg 48

Broadview Press, 280 Perry St, Unit 5, Peterborough, ON K9J 2A8, Canada *Tel:* 705-743-8990 *Fax:* 705-743-8353 *E-mail:* customerservice@broadviewpress.com *Web Site:* www.broadviewpress.com, pg 537

Brockman Inc, 5 E 59 St, New York, NY 10022 *Tel:* 212-935-8900 *Fax:* 212-935-5535 *E-mail:* rights@brockman.com, pg 623

The Brockport Writers' Forum, 350 New Campus Dr, Brockport, NY 14420-2968 *Tel:* 585-395-5713 *Fax:* 585-395-2391 *Web Site:* www.acs.brockport.edu/~wforum/Main.html, pg 742

Broken Jaw Press Inc, 5-2004 York St, Fredericton, NB E3B 5A6, Canada *Tel:* 506-454-5127 *Fax:* 506-454-5127 *Web Site:* www.brokenjaw.com, pg 537

The Bronx County Historical Society, 3309 Bainbridge Ave, Bronx, NY 10467 *Tel:* 718-881-8900 *Fax:* 718-881-4827 *Web Site:* www.bronxhistoricalsociety.org, pg 48

Brooding Heron Press, 101 Bookmonger Rd, Waldron Island, WA 98297 *Tel:* 360-202-6621, pg 48

Brook Street Press LLC, 200 Plantation Chase, Saint Simons Island, GA 31522 *Tel:* 912-638-0264 *Fax:* 912-638-0265 *E-mail:* info@brookstreetpress.com *Web Site:* www.brookstreetpress.com, pg 48

Paul H Brookes Publishing Co, PO Box 10624, Baltimore, MD 21285-0624 *Tel:* 410-337-9580 *Toll Free Tel:* 800-638-3775 *Fax:* 410-337-8539 *E-mail:* custserv@brookespublishing.com *Web Site:* www.brookespublishing.com, pg 48

Brookhaven Press, PO Box 2287, La Crosse, WI 54602-2287 *Tel:* 608-781-0850 *Toll Free Tel:* 800-236-0850 *Fax:* 608-781-3883 *E-mail:* brookhaven@nmt.com *Web Site:* www.brookhavenpress.com, pg 48

The Brookings Institution Press, 1775 Massachusetts Ave NW, Washington, DC 20036-2188 *Tel:* 202-797-6000 *Toll Free Tel:* 800-275-1447 *Fax:* 202-797-6195 *E-mail:* bibooks@brook.edu *Web Site:* www.brookings.edu, pg 48

Brookline Books, PO Box 1209, Brookline, MA 02445 *Toll Free Tel:* 800-666-2665; 800-345-6665 (orders) *Fax:* 617-734-6772 *Web Site:* www.brooklinebooks.com, pg 49

Brooklyn Botanic Garden, 1000 Washington Ave, Brooklyn, NY 11225-1099 *Tel:* 718-623-7200 *Toll Free Tel:* 800-367-9692 (orders) *Fax:* 718-622-7839 *Toll Free Fax:* 800-542-7567 (orders) *E-mail:* publications@bbg.org *Web Site:* www.bbg.org, pg 49

Brooklyn Writers Club, PO Box 184, Bath Beach Sta, Brooklyn, NY 11214-0184 *Tel:* 718-680-4084, pg 682, 742

Damon Brooks Associates Celebrity Coordination, 1601 Holly Ave, Oxnard, CA 93036 *Tel:* 805-604-9017 *E-mail:* info@damonbrooks.com *Web Site:* www.damonbrooks.com; www.disabilityspeakers.com, pg 669

Broquet Inc, 97B Montee des Bouleaux, St Constant, PQ J5A 1A9, Canada *Tel:* 450-638-3338 *Fax:* 450-638-4338 *E-mail:* info@broquet.qc.ca *Web Site:* www.broquet.qc.ca, pg 537

The Heywood Broun Award, 501 Third St NW, Washington, DC 20001-2760 *Tel:* 202-434-7173 *Fax:* 202-434-1472 *Web Site:* www.newsguild.org, pg 764

Brown Barn Books, 119 Kettle Creek Rd, Weston, CT 06883 *Tel:* 203-227-3387 *Toll Free Tel:* 888-227-3308 *Fax:* 203-222-9673 *E-mail:* editorial@brownbarnbooks.com *Web Site:* www.brownbarnbooks.com, pg 49

Curtis Brown Ltd, 10 Astor Place, New York, NY 10003 *Tel:* 212-473-5400, pg 623

John Nicholas Brown Prize, 104 Mount Auburn St, 5th fl, Cambridge, MA 02138 *Tel:* 617-491-1622 *Fax:* 617-492-3303 *E-mail:* speculum@medievalacademy.org *Web Site:* www.medievalacademy.org, pg 764

Karen Brown's Guides Inc, PO Box 70, San Mateo, CA 94401-0070 *Tel:* 650-342-9117 *Fax:* 650-342-9153 *E-mail:* karen@karenbrown.com *Web Site:* www.karenbrown.com, pg 49

Marie Brown Associates, 412 W 154 St, New York, NY 10032 *Tel:* 212-939-9725 *Fax:* 212-939-9728 *E-mail:* mbrownlit@aol.com, pg 623

Norman Brown & Associates, 50 Blackstone Blvd, Providence, RI 02906 *Tel:* 401-751-2641 *Fax:* 401-331-4612 *E-mail:* nhbrown@msn.com *Web Site:* www.indexme.net, pg 593

Brown Publishing Network Inc, 95 Sawyer Rd, Waltham, MA 02453 *Tel:* 781-237-7567 *Fax:* 781-237-8874 *Web Site:* www.brownpubnet.com, pg 593

Browne & Miller Literary Associates, 410 S Michigan Ave, Suite 460, Chicago, IL 60605 *Tel:* 312-922-3063 *Fax:* 312-922-1905 *E-mail:* mail@browneandmiller.com *Web Site:* www.browneandmiller.com, pg 623

BrownTrout Publishers Inc, PO Box 280070, San Francisco, CA 94128-0070 *Tel:* 650-340-9800 *Toll Free Tel:* 800-777-7812 *Fax:* 310-316-1138 *E-mail:* sales@browntrout.com *Web Site:* www.browntrout.com, pg 49

Bruccoli Clark Layman Inc, 2006 Sumter St, Columbia, SC 29201 *Tel:* 803-771-4642 *Fax:* 803-799-6953, pg 49

Gordon Brumm, 1515 Saint Charles Ave, Lakewood, OH 44107 *Tel:* 216-226-6105 *Fax:* 216-226-1964 *E-mail:* brummg@cox.net, pg 593

Brunner-Routledge, 270 Madison Ave, New York, NY 10016 *Tel:* 212-216-7800 *Toll Free Tel:* 800-634-7064 (orders); 800-797-3803 *Fax:* 212-643-1430, pg 49

Brunswick Publishing Corp, 1386 Lawrenceville Plank Rd, Lawrenceville, VA 23868 *Tel:* 434-848-3865 *Fax:* 434-848-0607 *E-mail:* brunswickbooks@earthlink.net *Web Site:* www.brunswickbooks.com, pg 49

Don Buchwald & Associates Inc, 6500 Wilshire Blvd, Suite 2200, Los Angeles, CA 90048 *Tel:* 323-655-7400 *Fax:* 323-655-7470 *Web Site:* www.donbuchwald.com, pg 623

Howard Buck Agency, 80 Eighth Ave, Suite 1107, New York, NY 10011 *Tel:* 212-924-9093, pg 623

Bucknell Seminar for Younger Poets, Bucknell University, Lewisburg, PA 17837 *Tel:* 570-577-1853 *Fax:* 570-577-3760 *E-mail:* stadlercenter@bucknell.edu *Web Site:* bucknell.edu/stadlercenter, pg 764

Bucknell University Press, c/o Associated University Presses, 2010 Eastpark Blvd, Cranbury, NJ 08512 *Tel:* 609-655-4770 *Fax:* 609-655-8366 *E-mail:* aup440@aol.com, pg 49

Judith Buckner Literary Agency, 12721 Hart St, North Hollywood, CA 91605 *Tel:* 818-982-8202 *Fax:* 818-764-6844 *E-mail:* jbuckner@pacbell.net, pg 623

Georges Bugnet Award for Fiction (Novel), 11759 Groat Rd, Edmonton, AB T5M 3K6, Canada *Tel:* 780-422-8174 *Toll Free Tel:* 800-665-5354 (Alberta only) *Fax:* 780-422-2663 *E-mail:* mail@writersguild.ab.ca *Web Site:* www.writersguild.ab.ca, pg 764

BuilderBooks.com, 1201 15 St NW, Washington, DC 20005-2800 *Tel:* 202-822-0200; 202-266-8200 *Toll Free Tel:* 800-223-2665 (orders); 800-368-5242 ext 8368 (editorial) *Fax:* 202-266-8096 (edit); 202-266-5889 (edit) *Web Site:* www.builderbooks.com, pg 49

Building News, 502 Maple Ave W, Vienna, VA 22180 *Tel:* 703-319-0498 *Toll Free Tel:* 888-264-2665 *Fax:* 703-319-9158 *E-mail:* sales@bnibooks.com *Web Site:* www.bnibooks.com, pg 49

The Bukowski Agency, 202-14 Prince Arthur Ave, Toronto, ON M5R 1A9, Canada *Tel:* 416-928-6728 *Fax:* 416-963-9978 *E-mail:* assistant@thebukowskiagency.com *Web Site:* www.thebukowskiagency.com, pg 623

Bulfinch Press, 1271 Avenue of the Americas, New York, NY 10020 *Tel:* 212-522-8700 *Toll Free Tel:* 800-759-0190 *Fax:* 212-467-2886 *Web Site:* www.twbookmark.com, pg 50

Bull Publishing Co, PO Box 1377, Boulder, CO 80306-1377 *Tel:* 303-545-6350 *Toll Free Tel:* 800-676-2855 *Fax:* 303-545-6354 *E-mail:* bullpublishing@msn.com *Web Site:* www.bullpub.com, pg 50

Bunting Fellowship, 34 Concord Ave, Cambridge, MA 02138 *Tel:* 617-495-8212; 617-495-8237 (personnel contact) *Fax:* 617-495-8136 *Web Site:* www.radcliffe.edu, pg 764

The Bureau For At-Risk Youth, 135 Dupont St, Plainview, NY 11803-0760 *Tel:* 516-349-5520 *Fax:* 516-349-5521 *E-mail:* info@at-risk.com *Web Site:* www.at-risk.com, pg 50

Bureau of Economic Geology, University of Texas at Austin, 10100 Burnet Rd, Bldg 130, Austin, TX 78750 *Tel:* 512-471-7144 *Toll Free Tel:* 888-839-4365 *Fax:* 512-471-0140 *Toll Free Fax:* 888-839-6277 *E-mail:* pubsales@beg.utexas.edu *Web Site:* www.beg.utexas.edu, pg 50

Burford Books, 32 Morris Ave, Springfield, NJ 07081 *Tel:* 973-258-0960 *Fax:* 973-258-0113 *E-mail:* info@burfordbooks.com *Web Site:* www.burfordbooks.com, pg 50

Knox Burger Associates Ltd, 425 Madison Ave, New York, NY 10017 *Tel:* 212-759-8600 *Fax:* 212-759-9428, pg 623

Arleigh Burke Essay Contest, 291 Wood Rd, Annapolis, MD 21402-5034 *Tel:* 410-268-6110 *Toll Free Tel:* 800-233-8764 *Fax:* 410-295-1049 *E-mail:* essays@navalinstitute.org *Web Site:* www.navalinstitute.org, pg 764

Hilary R Burke, 59 Sparks St, Ottawa, ON K1P 6C3, Canada *Tel:* 613-237-4658 *E-mail:* pointtopoint@canada.com; hilary.burke@pointtopointbooks.com *Web Site:* www.pointtopointbooks.com, pg 593

Burns Sports & Celebrities Inc, 820 Davis St, Evanston, IL 60201 *Tel:* 847-866-9400 *Fax:* 847-491-9778 *Web Site:* www.burnssports.com, pg 669

Burrelle's Information Services, 75 E Northfield Rd, Livingston, NJ 07039 *Tel:* 973-992-6600 *Toll Free Tel:* 800-631-1160 *Fax:* 973-992-7675 *Toll Free Fax:* 800-898-6677 *E-mail:* directory@burrelles.com; directorysales@burrelles.com *Web Site:* www.burrellesluce.com, pg 50

The Canadian Council on Social Development, 309 Cooper St, 5th fl, Ottawa, ON K2P 0G5, Canada *Tel:* 613-236-8977 *Fax:* 613-236-2750 *E-mail:* council@ccsd.ca *Web Site:* www.ccsd.ca, pg 538

Canadian Education Association/Association canadienne d'education, 317 Adelaide St W, Suite 300, Toronto, ON M5V 1P9, Canada *Tel:* 416-591-6300 *Fax:* 416-591-5345 *E-mail:* info@cea.ace.ca *Web Site:* www. cea-ace.ca, pg 538, 683

Canadian Energy Research Institute, 3512 33 St NW, Suite 150, Calgary, AB T2L 2A6, Canada *Tel:* 403-282-1231 *Fax:* 403-284-4181 *E-mail:* ceri@ceri.ca *Web Site:* www.ceri.ca, pg 538

Canadian Institute of Chartered Accountants, 277 Wellington St W, Toronto, ON M5V 3H2, Canada *Tel:* 416-977-3222 *Toll Free Tel:* 800-268-3793 (Canadian orders) *Fax:* 416-977-8585 *E-mail:* orders@ cica.ca *Web Site:* www.cica.ca, pg 538

Canadian Institute of Resources Law, University of Calgary, Murray Fraser Hall, Rm 3330, 2500 University Dr NW, Calgary, AB T2N 1N4, Canada *Tel:* 403-220-3200 *Fax:* 403-282-6182 *E-mail:* cirl@ ucalgary.ca *Web Site:* www.cirl.ca, pg 538

Canadian Institute of Ukrainian Studies Press, University of Toronto, One Spadina Crescent, Rm 109, Toronto, ON M5S 2J5, Canada *Tel:* 416-978-6934 *Fax:* 416-978-2672 *E-mail:* cius@chass.utoronto.ca (edit off) *Web Site:* www.utoronto.ca/cius, pg 538

Canadian ISBN Agency, National Library of Canada, 395 Wellington St, Ottawa, ON K1A 0N4, Canada *Tel:* 819-994-6872 *Fax:* 819-997-7517 *E-mail:* isbn@ nlc-bnc.ca *Web Site:* www.nlc-bnc.ca, pg 683

Canadian Library Association (CLA), 328 Frank St, Ottawa, ON K2P 0X8, Canada *Tel:* 613-232-9625 *Fax:* 613-563-9895 *E-mail:* info@cla.ca *Web Site:* www.cla.ca/, pg 683

Canadian Magazine Publishers Association, 425 Adelaide St W, Suite 700, Toronto, ON M5V 3C1, Canada *Tel:* 416-504-0274 *Fax:* 416-504-0437 *E-mail:* cmpainfo@cmpa.ca *Web Site:* www.cmpa.ca/; www.magomania.com, pg 683

Canadian Museum of Civilization, 100 Laurier St, Hull, PQ J8X 4H2, Canada *Tel:* 819-776-8387 *Toll Free Tel:* 800-555-5621 (North America only) *Fax:* 819-776-8300 *E-mail:* publications@civilization.ca (mail order) *Web Site:* www.civilization.ca, pg 538

Canadian Newspaper Association, 890 Yonge St, Suite 200, Toronto, ON M4W 3P4, Canada *Tel:* 416-923-3567 *Fax:* 416-923-7206 *Web Site:* www.cna-acj.ca, pg 683

Canadian Plains Research Center, University of Regina, Regina, SK S4S 0A2, Canada *Tel:* 306-585-4758; 306-585-4759 *Fax:* 306-585-4699 *Web Site:* www.cprc. uregina.ca, pg 539

Canadian Poetry Press, Dept of English, University of Western Ontario, London, ON N6A 3K7, Canada *Tel:* 519-673-1164; 519-661-2111 (ext 85834) *Fax:* 519-661-3776 *Web Site:* www.canadianpoetry.ca, pg 539

Canadian Printing Industries Association, 75 Albert St, Suite 906, Ottawa, ON K1P 5E7, Canada *Tel:* 613-236-7208 *Fax:* 613-236-8169 *Web Site:* www.cpia-aci.ca, pg 683

Canadian Publishers' Council (CPC), 250 Merton St, Suite 203, Toronto, ON M4S 1B1, Canada *Tel:* 416-322-7011 *Fax:* 416-322-6999 *E-mail:* pubadmin@ pubcouncil.ca *Web Site:* www.pubcouncil.ca, pg 683

Canadian Scholars' Press Inc, 180 Bloor St W, Suite 801, Toronto, ON M5S 2V6, Canada *Tel:* 416-929-2774 *Fax:* 416-929-1926 *E-mail:* info@cspi.org *Web Site:* www.cspi.org; www.womenspress.ca, pg 539

Canadian Society of Children's Authors Illustrators & Performers (CANSCAIP), 40 Orchard View Blvd, Suite 104, Toronto, ON M4R 1B9, Canada *Tel:* 416-515-1559 *E-mail:* office@canscaip.org *Web Site:* www. canscaip.org, pg 684

Canadian Speakers & Writers' Service Ltd, 44 Douglas Crescent, Toronto, ON M4W 2E7, Canada *Tel:* 416-921-4443 *Fax:* 416-922-9691 *E-mail:* pmmj@idirect. com, pg 624

The Canadian Writers' Foundation Inc/La fondation des ecrivains canadiens, PO Box 13281, Kanata Sta, Ottawa, ON K2K 1X4, Canada *Tel:* 613-256-6937 *Fax:* 613-256-5457 *Web Site:* www.canauthors.org/cwf, pg 705

The Candace Lake Agency, 9200 Sunset Blvd, Suite 820, Los Angeles, CA 90069 *Tel:* 310-247-2115 *Fax:* 310-247-2116 *E-mail:* clagency@bwkliterary. com, pg 624

Candlewick Press, 2067 Massachusetts Ave, Cambridge, MA 02140 *Tel:* 617-661-3330 *Fax:* 617-661-0565 *E-mail:* bigbear@candlewick.com *Web Site:* www. candlewick.com, pg 52

Canon Law Society of America, 108 N Payne St, Suite C, Alexandria, VA 22314-2906 *Tel:* 703-739-2560 *Fax:* 703-739-2562 *E-mail:* coordinator@clsa.org *Web Site:* www.clsa.org, pg 52

Canyon Country Publications, PO Box 963, Moab, UT 84532-0963 *Tel:* 435-259-6700, pg 52

Annual Cape Cod Writers' Conference, PO Box 408, Osterville, MA 02655 *Tel:* 508-420-0200 *E-mail:* ccwc@capecod.net *Web Site:* www. capecodwriterscenter.com, pg 742

Capital Books Inc, 22841 Quicksilver Dr, Sterling, VA 20166 *Tel:* 703-661-1571 *Toll Free Tel:* 800-758-3756 *Fax:* 703-661-1547 *Web Site:* www.capital-books.com, pg 52

Capital Enquiry Inc, 1034 Emerald Bay Rd, No 435, South Lake Tahoe, CA 96150 *Tel:* 916-442-1434 *Fax:* 916-244-2704 *E-mail:* info@capenq.com *Web Site:* www.capenq.com, pg 52

Capital Speakers Inc, 2200 Wilson Blvd, Suite 850, Arlington, VA 22201 *Tel:* 703-894-0604 *Toll Free Tel:* 800-799-2629 *Fax:* 703-894-0605 *E-mail:* ideas@ capitalspeakers.com *Web Site:* www.capitalspeakers. com, pg 669

Capra Press, 155 Canon View Rd, Santa Barbara, CA 93108 *Tel:* 805-969-0203 *Fax:* 805-565-0724 *E-mail:* order@caprapress.com *Web Site:* www. caprapress.com, pg 52

Capstone Press, 151 Good Counsel Dr, Mankato, MN 56002 *Toll Free Tel:* 800-747-4992 *Toll Free Fax:* 888-262-0705 *Web Site:* www.capstonepress.com, pg 53

Captain Fiddle Publications, 4 Elm Ct, Newmarket, NH 03857 *Tel:* 603-659-2658 *E-mail:* cfiddle@tiac.net *Web Site:* www.captainfiddle.com, pg 53

Captus Press Inc, 1600 Steeles Ave W, Units 14-15, Concord, ON L4K 4M2, Canada *Tel:* 416-736-5537 *Fax:* 416-736-5793 *E-mail:* info@captus.com *Web Site:* www.captus.com, pg 539

Aristide D Caratzas, Publisher, PO Box 344-H, Scarsdale, NY 10583 *Tel:* 914-725-4847 *Toll Free Tel:* 800-204-2665 *Fax:* 914-725-4847 (call first) *E-mail:* info@caratzas.com *Web Site:* www.caratzas. com, pg 53

Caravan Books, PO Box 5934, Carefree, AZ 85377-5934 *Tel:* 480-575-9945 *Fax:* 480-575-9451 *E-mail:* maxinmin@umich.edu, pg 53

Cardoza Publishing, 857 Broadway, 3rd fl, New York, NY 10003 *Tel:* 212-255-6661 *Fax:* 212-255-6671 *E-mail:* cardozapub@aol.com *Web Site:* www. cardozapub.com, pg 53

Cardweb.com Inc, 10 N Jefferson St, Suite 301, Frederick, MD 21701 *Tel:* 301-631-9100 *Fax:* 301-631-9112 *E-mail:* cardservices@cardweb.com; cardstaff@cardweb.com *Web Site:* www.cardweb.com, pg 53

The Career Press Inc, 3 Tice Rd, Franklin Lakes, NJ 07417 *Tel:* 201-848-0310 *Toll Free Tel:* 800-CAREER-1 (227-3371) *Fax:* 201-848-1727 *Web Site:* www.careerpress.com, pg 53

William Carey Library, PO Box 40129, Pasadena, CA 91114-7129 *Tel:* 626-798-0819 *Toll Free Tel:* 866-732-6657 *E-mail:* publishing@wclbooks.com *Web Site:* www.wclbooks.com, pg 53

Cariad Ltd, 180 Bloor St, Suite 801, Toronto, ON M5S 2V6, Canada *Tel:* 416-929-2774 *Fax:* 416-929-1926 *E-mail:* cariadreps@hotmail.com, pg 593

Caribbean Christian Writers Conference Cruise, PO Box 110390, Nashville, TN 37222 *Tel:* 615-834-0450 *Toll Free Tel:* 800-21-WRITE (219-7483) *Web Site:* www. acwriters.com, pg 742

Caribe Betania Editores, 501 Nelson Place, Nashville, TN 37214 *Tel:* 615-391-3937 *Toll Free Tel:* 800-322-7426 *Fax:* 615-883-9376 *E-mail:* caribe@ editorecaribe.com *Web Site:* www.caribebetania.com, pg 53

The Carl Sandburg Literary Awards, 20 N Michigan Ave, Suite 102, Chicago, IL 60602 *Tel:* 312-201-9830 *Fax:* 312-201-9833, pg 766

Carlisle Communications Ltd, 4242 Chavenelle Dr, Dubuque, IA 52002-2650 *Tel:* 563-557-1500 *Fax:* 563-557-1376 *E-mail:* carlisle@carcomm.com *Web Site:* www.carcomm.com, pg 593

Carlisle Press - Walnut Creek, 2673 Township Rd 421, Sugarcreek, OH 44681 *Tel:* 330-852-1900 *Toll Free Tel:* 800-852-4482 *Fax:* 330-852-3285, pg 53

Carlsbad Publications, 3242 McKinley St, Carlsbad, CA 92008 *Tel:* 760-729-9543 *Fax:* 760-729-9543 *E-mail:* bunkobabe9@aol.com, pg 593

Charles Carmony, 250 W 105 St, Suite 2A, New York, NY 10025 *Tel:* 212-749-1835, pg 593

Carnegie Mellon University Press, 5032 Forbes Ave, Pittsburgh, PA 15289-1021 *Tel:* 412-268-2861 *Fax:* 412-268-8706 *Web Site:* www.cmu.edu/ universitypress, pg 53

Carnot USA Books, 22 W 19 St, 5th fl, New York, NY 10011 *Tel:* 212-255-6505 *Fax:* 212-807-8831 *E-mail:* sales@carnot.fr *Web Site:* www.carnotbooks. com, pg 53

Carolina Academic Press, 700 Kent St, Durham, NC 27701 *Tel:* 919-489-7486 *Toll Free Tel:* 800-489-7486 *Fax:* 919-493-5668 *E-mail:* cap@cap-press.com *Web Site:* www.cap-press.com; www.caplaw.com, pg 54

Carolrhoda Books Inc, 241 First Ave N, Minneapolis, MN 55401 *Tel:* 612-332-3344 *Toll Free Tel:* 800-328-4929 *Fax:* 612-332-7615 *Toll Free Fax:* 800-332-1132 *E-mail:* info@lernerbooks.com *Web Site:* www. lernerbooks.com, pg 54

Carousel Publications Ltd, 1304 Rte 42, Sparrowbush, NY 12780 *Tel:* 212-758-9399 *Fax:* 212-758-6453 *E-mail:* info@carousel-music.com *Web Site:* www. carousel-music.com, pg 54

Carroll & Graf Publishers, 245 W 17 St, 11th fl, New York, NY 10011-5300 *Tel:* 646-375-2570 *Fax:* 646-375-2571 *Web Site:* www.carrollandgraf.com, pg 54

Carroll Publishing, 4701 Sangamore Rd, Suite S-155, Bethesda, MD 20816 *Tel:* 301-263-9800 *Toll Free Tel:* 800-336-4240 *Fax:* 301-263-9801 *E-mail:* custsvc@carrollpub.com *Web Site:* www. carrollpub.com, pg 54

R E Carsch, MS-Consultant, 1453 Rhode Island St, San Francisco, CA 94107-3248 *Tel:* 415-641-1095 *Fax:* 415-641-1095 *E-mail:* recarsch@mzinfo.com, pg 593

Anne Carson Associates, 3323 Nebraska Ave NW, Washington, DC 20016 *Tel:* 202-244-6679, pg 593

Carson-Dellosa Publishing Co Inc, PO Box 35665, Greensboro, NC 27425-5665 *Tel:* 336-632-0084 *Fax:* 336-632-0087 *Web Site:* www.carsondellosa.com, pg 54

Carson Enterprises Inc, PO Box 716, Dona Ana, NM 88032-0716 *Tel:* 505-541-1732, pg 54

Carstens Publications Inc, 108 Phil Hardin Rd, Newton, NJ 07860 *Tel:* 973-383-3355 *Fax:* 973-383-4064 *E-mail:* hal@carstens-publications.com *Web Site:* www.carstens-publications.com, pg 54

Carswell, One Corporate Plaza, 2075 Kennedy Rd, Toronto, ON M1T 3V4, Canada *Tel:* 416-609-8000 *Toll Free Tel:* 800-387-5164 (Canada & US) *Fax:* 416-298-5094 (Toronto); 403-233-8159 (Calgary); 604-685-5343 (Vancouver); 514-985-6605 *Toll Free Fax:* 877-750-9041 *E-mail:* comments@carswell.com *Web Site:* www.carswell.com, pg 539

CarTech Inc, 39966 Grand Ave, North Branch, MN 55056 *Tel:* 651-277-1200 *Toll Free Tel:* 800-551-4754 *Fax:* 651-277-1203 *E-mail:* info@cartechbooks.com *Web Site:* www.cartechbooks.com, pg 54

Amon Carter Museum, 3501 Camp Bowie Blvd, Fort Worth, TX 76107-2631 *Tel:* 817-738-1933 (ext 625) *Toll Free Tel:* 800-573-1933 *Fax:* 817-336-1123 *Web Site:* www.cartermuseum.org, pg 54

The Thomas H Carter Award For The Essay, Washington & Lee University, Mattingly House, 2 Lee Ave, Lexington, VA 24450-0303 *Tel:* 540-458-8765 *Fax:* 540-458-8461 *Web Site:* www.shenandoah.wlu. edu, pg 766

Claudia Caruana, PO Box 654, Murray Hill Sta, New York, NY 10016 *Tel:* 516-488-5815 *E-mail:* ccaruana29@hotmail.com, pg 593

Maria Carvainis Agency Inc, 1350 Avenue of the Americas, Suite 2905, New York, NY 10019 *Tel:* 212-245-6365 *Fax:* 212-245-7196 *E-mail:* mca@ mariacarvainisagency.com, pg 624

Cascade Pass Inc, 4223 Glencoe Ave, Suite C-105, Marina Del Rey, CA 90292 *Tel:* 310-305-0210 *Toll Free Tel:* 888-837-0704 *Fax:* 310-305-7850 *Web Site:* www.cascadepass.com, pg 54

Casemate Publishers, 2114 Darby Rd, Havertown, PA 19083 *Tel:* 610-853-9131 *Fax:* 610-853-9146 *E-mail:* casemate@casematepublishing.com *Web Site:* www.casematepublishing.com, pg 54

Angela M Casey, 331 S Wall St, Kingston, NY 12401 *Tel:* 845-340-8601 *E-mail:* angelamcasey@verizon.net, pg 593

CASTI Publishing Inc, 10544 106 St, Suite 210, Edmonton, AB T5H 2X6, Canada *Tel:* 780-424-2552 *Fax:* 780-421-1308 *E-mail:* casti@casti.ca *Web Site:* casti.ca, pg 539

Julie Castiglia Literary Agency, 1155 Camino Del Mar, Suite 510, Del Mar, CA 92014 *Tel:* 858-755-8761 *Fax:* 858-755-7063 *E-mail:* jaclagency@aol.com, pg 624

The Catalog™ Literary Agency, PO Box 2964, Vancouver, WA 98668-2964 *Tel:* 360-694-8531 *Fax:* 360-694-8531, pg 624

Catalyst Communication Arts, 94 Chuparr OsA, San Luis Obispo, CA 93401 *Tel:* 805-543-7250 *Fax:* 805-543-7250, pg 593

CATALYST Creative Services, 619 Marion Plaza, Palo Alto, CA 94301-4251 *Tel:* 650-325-1500, pg 593

Catbird Press, 16 Windsor Rd, North Haven, CT 06473-3015 *Tel:* 203-230-2391 *Fax:* 203-286-1091 *E-mail:* info@catbirdpress.com *Web Site:* www. catbirdpress.com, pg 55

Catholic Book Awards, 3555 Veterans Memorial Hwy, Unit "O", Ronkonkoma, NY 11779 *Tel:* 631-471-4730 *Fax:* 631-471-4804 *E-mail:* cathjourn@aol.com *Web Site:* www.catholicpress.org, pg 766

Catholic Book Publishers Association Inc, 8404 Jamesport Dr, Rockford, IL 61108 *Tel:* 815-332-3245 *Fax:* 815-332-3476 *E-mail:* cbpa3@aol.com *Web Site:* www.cbpa.org, pg 684

Catholic Book Publishing Corp, 77 West End Ave, Totowa, NJ 07512 *Tel:* 973-890-2400 *Fax:* 973-890-2410 *E-mail:* cbpcl@bellatlantic.net, pg 55

The Catholic Health Association of the United States, 4455 Woodson Rd, St Louis, MO 63134-3797 *Tel:* 314-427-2500 *Fax:* 314-253-3540 *Web Site:* www. chausa.org, pg 55

Catholic Library Association, 100 North St, Suite 224, Pittsfield, MA 01201-5109 *Tel:* 413-443-2252 *Fax:* 413-442-2252 *E-mail:* cla@cathla.org *Web Site:* www.cathla.org, pg 684

Catholic News Publishing Co Inc, 210 North Ave, New Rochelle, NY 10801 *Tel:* 914-632-7771 *Toll Free Tel:* 800-433-7771 *Fax:* 914-632-3412 *Web Site:* www. graduateguide.com, pg 55

Catholic Press Association of the US & Canada, 3555 Veterans Memorial Hwy, Unit O, Ronkonkoma, NY 11779 *Tel:* 631-471-4730 *Fax:* 631-471-4804 *E-mail:* cathjourn@aol.com *Web Site:* www. catholicpress.org, pg 684

Catholic Press Association of the US & Canada Journalism Awards, 3555 Veterans Memorial Hwy, Unit "O", Ronkonkoma, NY 11779 *Tel:* 631-471-4730 *Fax:* 631-471-4804 *E-mail:* cathjourn@aol.com *Web Site:* www.catholicpress.org, pg 766

The Catholic University of America Press, 240 Leahy Hall, 620 Michigan Ave NE, Washington, DC 20064 *Tel:* 202-319-5052 *Fax:* 202-319-4985 *E-mail:* cua-press@cua.edu *Web Site:* cuapress.cua.edu, pg 55

Cato Institute, 1000 Massachusetts Ave NW, Washington, DC 20001-5403 *Tel:* 202-842-0200 *Toll Free Tel:* 800-767-1241 *Fax:* 202-842-3490 *E-mail:* books@cato.org *Web Site:* www.cato.org, pg 55

Caughman Associates, 1094 New DeHaven St, Suite 100, West Conshohocken, PA 19428-2713 *Tel:* 610-558-3734 *Toll Free Tel:* 877-BUY BOOK *Fax:* 610-558-5001; 610-941-9999, pg 570

Cave Books, 277 Clamer Rd, Trenton, NJ 08628 *Tel:* 609-490-6359 (ed); 937-233-3561 (publr); 937-233-3561 (edit) *Web Site:* www.cavebooks.com, pg 55

Jeanne Cavelos Editorial Services, 20 Levesque Lane, Mont Vernon, NH 03057 *Tel:* 603-673-6234 *Fax:* 603-673-6234 *E-mail:* jcavelos@sff.net *Web Site:* www.sff. net/people/jcavelos, pg 593

Cavendish Tourist Association Creative Writing Award for Young People, 115 Richmond St, Charlottetown, PE C1A 1H7, Canada *Tel:* 902-368-4410 *Fax:* 902-368-4418 *E-mail:* peiarts@peiartscouncil.com *Web Site:* www.peiartscouncil.com, pg 766

Caxton Press, 312 Main St, Caldwell, ID 83605-3299 *Tel:* 208-459-7421 *Toll Free Tel:* 800-657-6465 *Fax:* 208-459-7450 *E-mail:* publish@caxtonpress.com *Web Site:* www.caxtonpress.com, pg 55

CCAB Inc, 90 Eglinton Ave E, Suite 980, Toronto, ON M4P 2Y3, Canada *Tel:* 416-487-2418 *Fax:* 416-487-6405 *E-mail:* info@bpai.com *Web Site:* www.bpai. com, pg 684

CCC Publications LLC, 9725 Lurline Ave, Chatsworth, CA 91311 *Tel:* 818-718-0507 *Toll Free Tel:* 800-248-LAFF (248-5233) *Fax:* 818-718-0655 *Web Site:* www. whyleavethehouse.com, pg 55

CCH Canadian Limited, A Wolters Kluwer Company, 90 Sheppard Ave E, Suite 300, Toronto, ON M2N 6X1, Canada *Tel:* 416-224-2224 *Toll Free Tel:* 800-268-4522 (Canada & US cust serv) *Fax:* 416-224-2243 *Toll Free Fax:* 800-461-4131 *E-mail:* cservice@cch.ca (cust serv) *Web Site:* www.cch.ca, pg 539

CCH Inc, 2700 Lake Cook Rd, Riverwoods, IL 60015 *Tel:* 847-267-7000 *Toll Free Tel:* 888-224-7377 *Web Site:* www.cch.com, pg 55

CDL Press, PO Box 34454, Bethesda, MD 20854 *Tel:* 301-762-2066 *Fax:* 253-484-5542 *E-mail:* cdlpress@erols.com, pg 56

Cebulash Associates, 10245 E Via Linda Ave, Suite 221, Scottsdale, AZ 85258 *Tel:* 480-451-8400 *Fax:* 480-451-0848 *E-mail:* cebulash@att.net, pg 594

CeciBooks Editorial & Publishing Consultation, 7057 26 Ave NW, Seattle, WA 98127 *Tel:* 206-706-9565 *Web Site:* www.cecibooks.com, pg 594

Cedar Fort Inc, 925 N Main St, Springville, UT 84663 *Tel:* 801-489-4084 *Toll Free Tel:* 800-759-2665 *Fax:* 801-489-1097 *E-mail:* skybook@cedarfort.com *Web Site:* www.cedarfort.com, pg 56

Cedco Publishing Co, 100 Pelican Way, San Rafael, CA 94901 *Tel:* 415-451-3000 *Toll Free Tel:* 800-227-6162 *Fax:* 415-457-4839 *E-mail:* sales@cedco.com *Web Site:* www.cedco.com, pg 56

CEF Press, PO Box 348, Warrenton, MO 63383-0348 *Tel:* 636-456-4380 *Toll Free Tel:* 800-748-7710 *Fax:* 636-456-4321 *Web Site:* www.cefonline.com, pg 56

Celebrity Press, 1501 County Hospital Rd, Nashville, TN 37218 *Tel:* 615-254-2450 *Toll Free Tel:* 800-327-5113 *Fax:* 615-254-2408, pg 56

Celestial Arts Publishing Co, 999 Harrison St, Berkeley, CA 94710 *Tel:* 510-559-1600 *Toll Free Tel:* 800-841-BOOK *Fax:* 510-524-1052 *E-mail:* order@tenspeed. com *Web Site:* www.tenspeed.com, pg 56

Celo Book Production Service, 160 Ohle Rd, Burnsville, NC 28714 *Tel:* 828-675-5918, pg 594

Centennial College Press, c/o Centennial College, PO Box 631, Sta A, Scarborough, ON M1K 5E9, Canada *Tel:* 416-289-5000 (ext 8606) *Fax:* 416-289-5106 *E-mail:* ccpress@centennialcollege.ca *Web Site:* www. centennialcollege.ca, pg 540

The Center for Book Arts, 28 W 27 St, 3rd fl, New York, NY 10001 *Tel:* 212-481-0295 *Fax:* 212-481-9853 (call before faxing) *E-mail:* info@centerforbookarts.org *Web Site:* www. centerforbookarts.org, pg 684, 751

Center for Creative Leadership, One Leadership Place, Greensboro, NC 27438-6300 *Tel:* 336-288-7210 *Fax:* 336-288-3999 *Web Site:* www.ccl.org/ publications, pg 56

Center for East Asian Studies (CEAS), Western Washington University, Bellingham, WA 98225-9056 *Tel:* 360-650-3448 *Fax:* 360-650-7789 *Web Site:* www. ac.wwu.edu/~eas/publications.html, pg 56

The Center for Exhibition Industry Research, 2301 S Lakeshore Dr, Suite E-1002, Chicago, IL 60616 *Tel:* 312-808-2347 *Fax:* 312-949-3472 *E-mail:* mceir@ mpea.com *Web Site:* www.ceir.org, pg 684

Center for Futures Education Inc, 345 Erie St, Grove City, PA 16127 *Tel:* 724-458-5860 *Toll Free Tel:* 800-966-2554 *Fax:* 724-458-5962 *E-mail:* info@thectr.com *Web Site:* www.thectr.com, pg 56

The Center for Learning, 24600 Detroit Rd, Suite 201, Westlake, OH 44145 *Tel:* 440-250-9341 *Fax:* 440-250-9715 *Web Site:* www.centerforlearning.org, pg 56

Center for Migration Studies of New York Inc, 209 Flagg Place, Staten Island, NY 10304-1199 *Tel:* 718-351-8800 *Fax:* 718-667-4598 *E-mail:* cms@cmsny.org *Web Site:* www.cmsny.org, pg 56

Center for Publishing Fellowships, 11 W 42 St, Rm 400, New York, NY 10036 *Tel:* 212-992-3232 *Fax:* 212-992-3233 *E-mail:* pub.center@nyu.edu *Web Site:* www.scps.nyu.edu/publishing, pg 766

Center For Self Sufficiency, PO Box 416, Denver, CO 80201-0416 *Tel:* 303-575-5676 *Fax:* 303-575-1187 *E-mail:* mail@gumbomedia.com *Web Site:* www. centerforselfsufficiency.org, pg 57

Center for Strategic & International Studies, 1800 "K" St NW, Washington, DC 20006 *Tel:* 202-775-3119 *Fax:* 202-775-3199 *E-mail:* books@csis.org *Web Site:* www.csis.org, pg 57

Center for Thanatology Research & Education Inc, 391 Atlantic Ave, Brooklyn, NY 11217-1701 *Tel:* 718-858-3026 *Fax:* 718-852-1846 *Web Site:* www.thanatology. org, pg 57

The Center for the Book in the Library of Congress, The Library of Congress, 101 Independence Ave SE, Washington, DC 20540-4920 *Tel:* 202-707-5221 *Fax:* 202-707-0269 *E-mail:* cfbook@loc.gov *Web Site:* www.loc.gov/cfbook, pg 684

Center for Urban Policy Research, 33 Livingston Ave, Suite 400, New Brunswick, NJ 08901-1982 *Tel:* 732-932-3133 *Fax:* 732-932-2363 *Web Site:* www.policy. rutgers.edu/cupr, pg 57

Center for Women Policy Studies, 1211 Connecticut Ave NW, Suite 312, Washington, DC 20036 *Tel:* 202-872-1770 *Fax:* 202-296-8962 *E-mail:* cwps@ centerwomenpolicy.org *Web Site:* www. centerwomenpolicy.org, pg 57

Center Press, PO Box 6936, Thousand Oaks, CA 91360-6936 *Tel:* 818-889-7071 *Fax:* 818-889-7072 *Web Site:* centerbooks.com, pg 57

Centering Corp, 7230 Maple St, Omaha, NE 68134 *Tel:* 402-553-1200 *Fax:* 402-553-0507 *E-mail:* j1200@aol.com *Web Site:* www.centering.org, pg 57

Centerstream Publishing LLC, PO Box 17878, Anaheim Hills, CA 92817-7878 *Tel:* 714-779-9390 *Toll Free Tel:* 877-312-8687 *Fax:* 714-779-9390 *E-mail:* centerstrm@aol.com *Web Site:* www.centerstream-usa.com, pg 57

Central Conference of American Rabbis/CCAR Press, 355 Lexington Ave, 18th fl, New York, NY 10017 *Tel:* 212-972-3636 *Toll Free Tel:* 800-935-2227 *Fax:* 212-692-0819 *E-mail:* ccarpress@ccarnet.org *Web Site:* www.ccarpress.org, pg 57

Central European University Press, 400 W 59 St, New York, NY 10019 *Tel:* 212-547-6932 *Fax:* 646-557-2416 *Web Site:* www.ceupress.com, pg 57

Central Ohio Writers of Literature for Children, c/o St Joseph Montessori School, 933 Hamlet St, Columbus, OH 43201-3595 *Tel:* 614-291-8644 *Fax:* 614-291-7411 *E-mail:* cowriters@mail.com *Web Site:* www.sjms.net/conf, pg 742

Centre Franco-Ontarien de Ressources en Alphabetisation, 432 Ave Westmount, Unit H, Sudbury, ON P3A 5Z8, Canada *Tel:* 705-524-3672 *Toll Free Tel:* 888-814-4422 (orders, Canada only) *Fax:* 705-524-8535 *E-mail:* info@centrefora.on.ca *Web Site:* www.centrefora.on.ca, pg 540

The Century Foundation Press, 41 E 70 St, New York, NY 10021 *Tel:* 212-535-4441 *Fax:* 212-535-7534 *E-mail:* info@tcf.org *Web Site:* www.tcf.org, pg 58

The Century Foundation Press, 41 E 70 St, New York, NY 10021 *Tel:* 212-535-4441 *Fax:* 212-535-7534 *Web Site:* www.tcf.org, pg 705

CHA (Canadian Healthcare Association) Press, 17 York St, Suite 100, Ottawa, ON K1N 9J6, Canada *Tel:* 613-241-8005 (ext 264) *Fax:* 613-241-5055 *E-mail:* chapress@cha.ca *Web Site:* www.cha.ca, pg 540

Chain Store Guide, 3922 Coconut Palm Dr, Tampa, FL 33619 *Tel:* 813-627-6800 *Toll Free Tel:* 800-927-9292 *Fax:* 813-627-6882 *E-mail:* info@csgis.com *Web Site:* www.csgis.com, pg 58

Chalice Press, 1221 Locust St, Suite 1200, St Louis, MO 63103 *Tel:* 314-231-8500 *Toll Free Tel:* 800-366-3383 *Fax:* 314-231-8524 *E-mail:* chalicepress@cbp21.com *Web Site:* www.cbp21.com; www.chalicepress.com, pg 58

Champion Press Ltd, 4308 Blueberry Rd, Fredonia, WI 53021 *Tel:* 262-692-3897 *Toll Free Tel:* 877-250-3354 *Fax:* 262-692-3342 *E-mail:* info@championpress.com *Web Site:* www.championpress.com, pg 58

Chandler & Sharp Publishers Inc, 11 Commercial Blvd, Suite A, Novato, CA 94949 *Tel:* 415-883-2353 *Fax:* 415-440-5004 *Web Site:* www.chandlersharp.com, pg 58

G S Sharat Chandra Prize for Short Fiction, 5101 Rockhill Rd, Kansas City, MO 64110 *Tel:* 816-235-2558 *Fax:* 816-235-2611 *E-mail:* bkmk@umkc.edu *Web Site:* www.umkc.edu/bkmk/, pg 766

Harry Chapin Media Awards, 505 Eighth Ave, 21st fl, New York, NY 10018 *Tel:* 212-629-8850 *Toll Free Tel:* 800-5-HUNGRY (548-6479) *Fax:* 212-465-9274 *E-mail:* media@worldhungeryear.org *Web Site:* www.worldhungeryear.org, pg 766

Charisma House, 600 Rinehart Rd, Lake Mary, FL 32746 *Tel:* 407-333-0600 (all imprints) *Toll Free Tel:* 800-283-8494 (Charisma House, Siloam Press, Creation House Press); 800-665-1468 *Fax:* 407-333-7100 (all imprints) *E-mail:* webmaster@charismahouse.com; webmaster@creationhouse.com *Web Site:* www.charismamag.com; www.strang.com (all imprints), pg 58

CharismaLife Publishers, 600 Rinehart Rd, Lake Mary, FL 32746 *Tel:* 407-333-0600 *Toll Free Tel:* 800-451-4598 *Fax:* 407-333-7100 *E-mail:* charismalife@strang.com *Web Site:* www.charismamag.com, pg 58

The Charles Bernheimer Prize, University of Texas, Program in Comparative Literature, One University Sta B5003, Austin, TX 78712-0196 *Tel:* 512-471-8020 *E-mail:* info@acla.org *Web Site:* www.acla.org, pg 766

The Charles Press, Publishers, 117 S 17 St, Suite 310, Philadelphia, PA 19103 *Tel:* 215-496-9616; 215-496-9625 *Fax:* 215-496-9637 *E-mail:* mailbox@charlespresspub.com *Web Site:* www.charlespresspub.com, pg 58

Charles River Media, 10 Downer Ave, Hingham, MA 02043 *Tel:* 781-740-0400 (edit offices) *Toll Free Tel:* 800-382-8505 (orders) *Fax:* 781-740-8816; 703-996-1010 (orders) *E-mail:* info@charlesriver.com *Web Site:* www.charlesriver.com, pg 58

Charles Scribner's Sons, PO Box 9187, Farmington Hills, MI 48333-9187 *Toll Free Tel:* 800-877-4253 *Toll Free Fax:* 800-414-5043 *E-mail:* galeord@gale.com, pg 58

Charlesbridge Publishing Inc, 85 Main St, Watertown, MA 02472 *Tel:* 617-926-0329 *Toll Free Tel:* 800-225-3214 *Fax:* 617-926-5720 *E-mail:* books@charlesbridge.com *Web Site:* www.charlesbridge.com, pg 58

The Charlton Press, PO Box 820, Sta Willowdale B, North York, ON M2K 2R1, Canada *Tel:* 416-488-1418 *Toll Free Tel:* 800-442-6042 *Fax:* 416-488-4656 *Toll Free Fax:* 800-442-1542 *E-mail:* chpress@charltonpress.com *Web Site:* www.charltonpress.com, pg 540

Chatelaine Press, 6454 Honey Tree Ct, Burke, VA 22015 *Tel:* 703-569-2062 *Toll Free Tel:* 800-249-9527 *Fax:* 703-569-9610 *E-mail:* egm-help@enterprise-government.com *Web Site:* www.chatpress.com; www.enterprise-government.com, pg 59

Chatsworth Press, 9135 Alabama Ave, Suite B, Chatsworth, CA 91311 *Tel:* 818-341-3156 *Toll Free Tel:* 800-262-7367 (US); 800-272-7367 (CA) *Fax:* 818-341-3562 *E-mail:* info@pac-media.com *Web Site:* pac-media.com, pg 59

Chautauqua Writers' Workshop, PO Box 28, Chautauqua, NY 14722-0408 *Tel:* 716-357-6200 *Toll Free Tel:* 800-836-ARTS (836-2787) *E-mail:* cpaul@chautauquava-inst.com *Web Site:* www.ciweb.org, pg 742

Margaret Cheasebro, 246 Rd 2900, Aztec, NM 87410 *Tel:* 505-334-2869 *Fax:* 505-334-6434 *E-mail:* mcheasebro@fisi.net, pg 594

Check Payment Systems Association, 2025 "M" St, Suite 800, Washington, DC 20036 *Tel:* 202-857-1144 *Fax:* 202-223-4579 *E-mail:* info@cpsa-checks.org *Web Site:* www.cpsa-checks.org, pg 684

Jane Chelius Literary Agency, Inc, 548 Second St, Brooklyn, NY 11215 *Tel:* 718-499-0236 *Fax:* 718-832-7335 *E-mail:* queries@janechelius.com *Web Site:* www.janechelius.com, pg 624

The Chelsea Forum Inc, 377 Rector Place, No 12-I, New York, NY 10280 *Tel:* 212-945-3100 *Fax:* 212-945-3101 *Web Site:* www.chelseaforum.com, pg 669

Chelsea Green Publishing Co, PO Box 428, White River Junction, VT 05001-0428 *Tel:* 802-295-6300 *Toll Free Tel:* 800-639-4099 (cust serv & consumer orders); 800-807-6726 (trade & wholesale orders) *Fax:* 802-295-6444 *Web Site:* www.chelseagreen.com, pg 59

Chelsea House Publishers LLC, 2080 Cabot Blvd W, Suite 201, Langhorne, PA 19047-1813 *Tel:* 610-353-5166 *Toll Free Tel:* 800-848-BOOK (848-2665) *Fax:* 610-359-1439 *Toll Free Fax:* 877-780-7300 *E-mail:* sales@chelseahouse.com *Web Site:* www.chelseahouse.com, pg 59

Chemical Education Resources Inc, c/o Brooks/Cole, Thomson Learning, 3501 Market St, Philadelphia, PA 19104 *Toll Free Tel:* 800-523-1850 ext 3781 *Toll Free Fax:* 800-451-3661 *Web Site:* www.cerlabs.com, pg 59

Chemical Publishing Co Inc, 527 Third Ave, Suite 427, New York, NY 10016 *Tel:* 212-779-0090 *Toll Free Tel:* 800-786-3659 *Fax:* 212-889-1537 *E-mail:* chempub@aol.com *Web Site:* www.chemicalpublishing.com, pg 59

ChemTec Publishing, 38 Earswick Dr, Scarborough, ON M1E 1C6, Canada *Tel:* 416-265-2603 *Fax:* 416-265-1399 *E-mail:* info@chemtec.org; orderdesk@chemtec.org *Web Site:* www.chemtec.org, pg 540

Cheneliere/McGraw-Hill, 7001 Saint Laurent Blvd, Montreal, PQ H2S 3E3, Canada *Tel:* 514-273-1066 *Fax:* 514-276-0324 *E-mail:* chene@dlcmcgrawhill.ca *Web Site:* www.dlcmcgrawhill.ca, pg 540

Cheng & Tsui Co Inc, 25 West St, 5th fl, Boston, MA 02111-1213 *Tel:* 617-988-2401 *Toll Free Tel:* 800-554-1963 *Fax:* 617-426-3669 *E-mail:* service@cheng-tsui.com *Web Site:* www.cheng-tsui.com, pg 59

Ruth Chernia, 81 Withrow Ave, Toronto, ON M4K 1C8, Canada *Tel:* 416-466-0164 *Fax:* 416-466-3835 *E-mail:* rchernia@editors.ca; rchernia@sympatico.ca, pg 594

Cherokee Publishing Co, 1710 Defoor Ave, NW, Atlanta, GA 30318 *Tel:* 404-467-4189 *Toll Free Tel:* 800-653-3952 *Fax:* 404-237-1062 *E-mail:* cherokeepub@defoorcentre.com, pg 59

Cherry Lane Music Co, 6 E 32 St, 11th fl, New York, NY 10016 *Tel:* 212-561-3000 *Fax:* 212-679-8157 *E-mail:* publishing@cherrylane.com *Web Site:* www.cherrylane.com, pg 60

Chess Combination Inc, PO Box 2423, Noble Sta, Bridgeport, CT 06608-0423 *Tel:* 203-301-0791 *Toll Free Tel:* 800-354-4083 *Fax:* 203-301-0792 *Web Site:* chessNIC.com, pg 60

Chess Digest Inc, PO Box 609, Ardmore, TN 38449-0609 *Toll Free Tel:* 800-524-3527 (orders) *Fax:* 256-423-8345 *E-mail:* info@chessdigest.com *Web Site:* www.chessdigest.com, pg 60

Chess Enterprises, 107 Crosstree Rd, Coraopolis, PA 15108-2607 *Tel:* 412-262-2138, pg 60

Linda Chester & Associates, Rockefeller Ctr, 630 Fifth Ave, New York, NY 10111 *Tel:* 212-218-3350 *Fax:* 212-218-3343 *E-mail:* lcassoc@mindspring.com *Web Site:* www.lindachester.com, pg 624

The Chestnut House Group Inc, 2121 Saint Johns Ave, Highland Park, IL 60035 *Tel:* 847-432-3273 *Fax:* 847-432-3229 *E-mail:* info@chestnuthousegroup.com *Web Site:* www.chestnuthousegroup.com, pg 594

Chicago Book Clinic, 5443 N Broadway, Suite 101, Chicago, IL 60640 *Tel:* 773-561-4150 *Fax:* 773-561-1343 *Web Site:* www.chicagobookclinic.org, pg 684

Chicago Book Clinic Annual Book Show Awards, 5443 N Broadway, Suite 101, Chicago, IL 60640 *Tel:* 773-561-4150 *Fax:* 773-561-1343 *Web Site:* www.chicagobookclinic.org, pg 766

Chicago Book Clinic Distinguished Service Award, 5443 N Broadway, Suite 101, Chicago, IL 60640 *Tel:* 773-561-4150 *Fax:* 773-561-1343 *Web Site:* www.chicagobookclinic.org, pg 766

Chicago Book Clinic Seminars, 5443 N Broadway, Suite 101, Chicago, IL 60640 *Tel:* 773-561-4150 *Fax:* 773-561-1343 *Web Site:* www.chicagobookclinic.org, pg 751

Chicago Review Press, 814 N Franklin St, Chicago, IL 60610 *Tel:* 312-337-0747 *Toll Free Tel:* 800-888-4741 *Fax:* 312-337-5110 *E-mail:* editorial@ipgbook.com, pg 60

Chicago Spectrum Press, 4824 Brownsboro Center Arcade, Louisville, KY 40207 *Tel:* 502-899-1919 *Toll Free Tel:* 800-594-5190 *Fax:* 502-896-0246 *E-mail:* evanstonpublish@aol.com *Web Site:* www.evanstonpublishing.com, pg 60

Chicago Women in Publishing, PO Box 268107, Chicago, IL 60626 *Tel:* 312-641-6311 *Fax:* 312-645-1078 *E-mail:* mail@cwip.org *Web Site:* www.cwip.org, pg 684

Chicano Latino Literary Contest, University of California, Dept Spanish & Portuguese, Irvine, CA 92697-5275 *Tel:* 949-824-5443 *Fax:* 949-824-2803 *E-mail:* cllp@uci.edu *Web Site:* www.humanities.uci.edu/spanishandportuguese/contest.html, pg 766

The Children's Book Council (CBC), 12 W 37 St, 2nd fl, New York, NY 10118-7480 *Tel:* 212-966-1990 *Toll Free Tel:* 800-999-2160 (orders only) *Fax:* 212-966-2073 *Toll Free Fax:* 888-807-9355 (orders only) *E-mail:* info@cbcbooks.org *Web Site:* www.cbcbooks.org, pg 684

Children's Book Press, 2211 Mission St, San Francisco, CA 94110 *Tel:* 415-821-3080 *Fax:* 415-821-3081 *E-mail:* info@childrensbookpress.org *Web Site:* www.cbookpress.org, pg 60

Children's Literature Association Book Award, PO Box 138, Battle Creek, MI 49016-0138 *Tel:* 269-965-8180 *Fax:* 269-965-3568 *Web Site:* www.childlitassn.org, pg 766

Faith Childs Literary Agency Inc, 915 Broadway, Suite 1009, New York, NY 10010 *Tel:* 212-995-9600 *Fax:* 212-995-9709 *E-mail:* faith@faithchildsliteraryagencyinc.com, pg 624

Child's Play, 67 Minot Ave, Auburn, ME 04210 *Toll Free Tel:* 800-472-0099; 800-639-6404 *Toll Free Fax:* 800-854-6989 *E-mail:* cplay@earthlink.net *Web Site:* www.childs-play.com, pg 60

The Child's World Inc, PO Box 326, Chanhassen, MN 55317-0326 *Tel:* 952-906-3939 *Toll Free Tel:* 800-599-READ (599-7323) *Fax:* 952-906-3940 *E-mail:* info@childsworld.com *Web Site:* www.childsworld.com, pg 60

Childswork/Childsplay LLC, 135 Dupont St, Plainview, NY 11803 *Tel:* 516-349-5520 *Toll Free Tel:* 800-962-1141 (cust serv) *Fax:* 516-349-5521 *Toll Free Fax:* 800-262-1886 (orders) *E-mail:* info@childswork.com *Web Site:* www.childswork.com, pg 60

China Books & Periodicals Inc, 2929 24 St, San Francisco, CA 94110-4126 *Tel:* 415-282-2994 *Toll Free Tel:* 800-818-2017 *Fax:* 415-282-0994 *E-mail:* info@chinabooks.com *Web Site:* www.chinabooks.com, pg 60

Chinese Connection Agency, 67 Banksville Rd, Armonk, NY 10504 *Tel:* 914-765-0296 *Fax:* 914-765-0297 *E-mail:* chinese@attglobal.net, pg 624

Chitra Publications, 2 Public Ave, Montrose, PA 18801 *Tel:* 570-278-1984 *Toll Free Tel:* 800-628-8244 *Fax:* 570-278-2223 *E-mail:* chitra@epix.net *Web Site:* www.quilttownusa.com, pg 60

ChLA Article Award, PO Box 138, Battle Creek, MI 49016-0138 *Tel:* 269-965-8180 *Fax:* 269-965-3568 *Web Site:* www.childlitassn.org, pg 766

ChLA Beiter Scholarships for Graduate Students, PO Box 138, Battle Creek, MI 49016-0138 *Tel:* 269-965-8180 *Fax:* 269-965-3568 *Web Site:* www.childlitassn.org, pg 767

Chosen Books, PO Box 6287, Grand Rapids, MI 49516-6287 *Tel:* 616-676-9185 *Toll Free Tel:* 800-877-2665 *Fax:* 616-676-2315 *Web Site:* www.bakerpublishinggroup.com, pg 61

Chouette Publishing, 4710 St Ambroise, Bureau 225, Montreal, PQ H4C 2C7, Canada *Tel:* 514-925-3325 *Toll Free Tel:* 877-926-3325 *Fax:* 514-925-3323 *E-mail:* info@editions-chouette.com *Web Site:* www.chouettepublishing.com, pg 540

Christian Booksellers Association (CBA), 9240 Explorer Dr, Colorado Springs, CO 80920 *Tel:* 719-265-9895 *Toll Free Tel:* 800-252-1950 *Fax:* 719-272-3510 *E-mail:* info@cbaonline.org *Web Site:* www.cbaonline.org, pg 685

Christian Booksellers Association of Canada, 155 Suffolk St W, Suite 15, Guelph, ON N1H 2J7, Canada *Tel:* 519-766-1683 *Fax:* 519-763-8184 *E-mail:* info@cbacanada.com *Web Site:* www.cbacanada.com, pg 685

Christian Fellowship Ministries, 915 E Dunlap, Phoenix, AZ 85021 *Tel:* 602-678-1543 *Toll Free Tel:* 888-678-1543 *Fax:* 602-678-4196 *E-mail:* ministry@cfmin.net *Web Site:* www.cfmin.net, pg 61

Christian History Project, 10333 178 St, Edmonton, AB T5N 2H7, Canada *Tel:* 780-443-4775 *Toll Free Tel:* 800-853-5402 *Fax:* 780-454-9298 *E-mail:* orders@christianhistoryproject.com *Web Site:* www.christianhistoryproject.com, pg 540

Christian Liberty Press, 502 W Euclid Ave, Arlington Heights, IL 60004 *Tel:* 847-259-4444 *Fax:* 847-259-2941 *Web Site:* www.christianlibertypress.com, pg 61

Christian Light Publications Inc, 1066 Chicago Ave, Harrisonburg, VA 22802 *Tel:* 540-434-0768, pg 61

Christian Literature Crusade, 701 Pennsylvania Ave, Fort Washington, PA 19034-8449 *Tel:* 215-542-1242 *Toll Free Tel:* 800-659-1240 (orders) *Fax:* 215-542-7580 *E-mail:* clcbooks@safeplace.net *Web Site:* www.clcpublications.com, pg 61

Christian Living Books Inc, 12103 Woodwind Lane, Mitchellville, MD 20721 *Tel:* 301-218-9092 *Toll Free Tel:* 800-727-3218 (ordering) *Fax:* 301-218-4943 *E-mail:* info@christianlivingbooks.com *Web Site:* www.christianlivingbooks.com, pg 61

Christian Publications Inc, 3825 Hartzdale Dr, Camp Hill, PA 17011 *Tel:* 717-761-7044 *Toll Free Tel:* 800-233-4443 *Fax:* 717-761-7273 *E-mail:* editorial@christianpublications.com *Web Site:* www.christianpublications.com, pg 61

Christian Schools International, 3350 E Paris Ave SE, Grand Rapids, MI 49512-3054 *Tel:* 616-957-1070 *Toll Free Tel:* 800-635-8288 *Fax:* 616-957-5022 *E-mail:* info@csionline.org *Web Site:* www.csionline.org, pg 61

Christian Writers' Conference, PO Box 110390, Nashville, TN 37222-0390 *Tel:* 615-834-0450 *Toll Free Tel:* 800-219-7483 *Fax:* 615-834-7736 *E-mail:* acwriters@aol.com *Web Site:* www.acwriters.com, pg 742

Christian Writers' Conference, PO Box 413, Mount Hermon, CA 95041-0413 *Tel:* 831-335-4466 *Fax:* 831-335-9413 *Web Site:* www.mounthermon.org/writers, pg 742

Jerry B Jenkins Christian Writers Guild, PO Box 88196, Black Forest, CO 80908 *Toll Free Tel:* 866-495-5177 *Fax:* 719-495-5181 *E-mail:* contactus@christianwritersguild.com *Web Site:* www.christianwritersguild.com, pg 685

The Christopher Awards, 12 E 48 St, New York, NY 10017 *Tel:* 212-759-4050 *Fax:* 212-838-5073 *Web Site:* www.christophers.org, pg 767

Christopher-Gordon Publishers Inc, 1502 Providence Hwy, Suite 12, Norwood, MA 02062 *Tel:* 781-762-5577 *Toll Free Tel:* 800-934-8322 *Fax:* 781-762-2110 *Web Site:* www.christopher-gordon.com, pg 61

Christopher Publishing House, 24 Rockland St, Hanover, MA 02339 *Tel:* 781-826-7474; 781-826-5494 *Fax:* 781-826-5556 *E-mail:* cph@atigroupinc.com, pg 61

William F Christopher Publication Services, 410 Sutcliffe Place, Walnut Creek, CA 94598-3924 *Tel:* 925-943-5584 *Fax:* 925-943-5594 *E-mail:* billtmig@astound.net, pg 624

Chronicle Books LLC, 85 Second St, 6th fl, San Francisco, CA 94105 *Tel:* 415-537-4200 *Toll Free Tel:* 800-722-6657 (cust serv) *Fax:* 415-537-4460 *Toll Free Fax:* 800-858-7787 (orders) *E-mail:* frontdesk@chroniclebooks.com *Web Site:* www.chroniclebooks.com, pg 61

Chronicle Guidance Publications Inc, 66 Aurora St, Moravia, NY 13118 *Tel:* 315-497-0330 *Toll Free Tel:* 800-622-7284 *Fax:* 315-497-3359 *E-mail:* customerservice@chronicleguidance.com *Web Site:* www.chronicleguidance.com, pg 62

Chrysalis Publishing Group Inc, 34 Main St, Natick, MA 01760 *Tel:* 508-647-3730 *Toll Free Tel:* 877-922-1822 *Fax:* 508-653-3448 *E-mail:* info@chrysalispublishing.com *Web Site:* www.chrysalispublishing.com, pg 594

Church Growth Institute, PO Box 7, Elkton, MD 21922-0007 *Tel:* 434-525-0022 *Toll Free Tel:* 800-553-4769 (orders only) *Fax:* 434-525-0608 *Toll Free Fax:* 800-644-4729 (orders only) *E-mail:* cgimail@churchgrowth.org *Web Site:* www.churchgrowth.org, pg 62

John Ciardi Prize for Poetry, 5101 Rockhill Rd, Kansas City, MO 64110 *Tel:* 816-235-2558 *Fax:* 816-235-2611 *E-mail:* bkmk@umkc.edu *Web Site:* www.umkc.edu/bkmk/, pg 767

Cinco Puntos Press, 701 Texas Ave, El Paso, TX 79901 *Tel:* 915-838-1625 *Toll Free Tel:* 800-566-9072 *Fax:* 915-838-1635 *E-mail:* info@cincopuntos.com *Web Site:* www.cincopuntos.com, pg 62

Cine/Lit Representation, PO Box 802918, Santa Clarita, CA 91380-2918 *Tel:* 661-513-0268 *Fax:* 661-513-0951 *E-mail:* cinelit@msn.com, pg 624

Cintas Fellowship Program, 809 United Nations Plaza, New York, NY 10017-3580 *Tel:* 212-984-5565 *Fax:* 212-984-5325 *E-mail:* cintas@iie.org *Web Site:* www.iie.org/cintas, pg 767

Circlet Press Inc, 1770 Massachusetts Ave, Suite 278, Cambridge, MA 02140 *Tel:* 617-864-0492 *Toll Free Tel:* 800-729-6423 (orders) *Fax:* 617-864-0663 *E-mail:* info@circlet.com *Web Site:* www.circlet.com, pg 62

CIS Publishers & Distributors, 180 Park Ave S, Lakewood, NJ 08701 *Tel:* 732-905-3000 *Fax:* 732-367-6666, pg 62

Cistercian Publications Inc, Editorial Office, WMU, 1903 W Michigan Ave, Kalamazoo, MI 49008 *Tel:* 269-387-8920 *Fax:* 269-387-8390 *E-mail:* cistpub@wmich.edu *Web Site:* www.spencerabbey.org/cistpub, pg 62

City & Regional Magazine Association, 4929 Wilshire Blvd, Suite 428, Los Angeles, CA 90010 *Tel:* 323-937-5514 *Fax:* 323-937-0959 *Web Site:* www.citymag.org, pg 685

City Lights Books Inc, 261 Columbus Ave, San Francisco, CA 94133 *Tel:* 415-362-8193 *Fax:* 415-362-4921 *E-mail:* staff@citylights.com *Web Site:* www.citylights.com, pg 62

City of Toronto Book Award, Protocol Office, 100 Queen St W, 10th fl, West Tower, Toronto, ON M5H 2N2, Canada *Tel:* 416-392-8191 *Fax:* 416-392-1247, pg 767

CLA Book of the Year for Children Award, 328 Frank St, Ottawa, ON K2P 0X8, Canada *Tel:* 613-232-9625 *Fax:* 613-563-9895 *Web Site:* www.cla.ca/, pg 767

The Clarion Awards, 780 Ritchie Hwy, Suite 28-S, Severna Park, MD 21146 *Tel:* 410-544-7442 *Fax:* 410-544-4640 *Web Site:* www.womcom.org, pg 767

Clarion Books, 215 Park Ave S, New York, NY 10003 *Tel:* 212-420-5800 *Toll Free Tel:* 800-225-3362 (orders) *Fax:* 212-420-5855 *Web Site:* www.clarion.com, pg 62

Clarion Workshop in Science Fiction & Fantasy Writing, Michigan State University, 112 Olds Hall, East Lansing, MI 48824-1047 *Tel:* 517-355-9598 *Fax:* 517-353-4765 *Web Site:* www.msu.edu/~clarion, pg 743

Clarity Press Inc, 3277 Roswell Rd NE, Suite 469, Atlanta, GA 30305 *Toll Free Tel:* 800-729-6423 (orders); 877-613-1495 *Fax:* 404-231-3899 *Toll Free Fax:* 877-613-7868 *E-mail:* clarity@islandnet.com; claritypress@usa.net (editorial) *Web Site:* www.claritypress.com, pg 62

I E Clark Publications, PO Box 246, Schulenburg, TX 78956 *Tel:* 979-743-3232 *Fax:* 979-743-4765 *E-mail:* ieclark@cvtv.net *Web Site:* www.ieclark.com, pg 63

Clark Publishing Inc, 1000 N Second Ave, Logan, IA 51546 *Tel:* 712-644-2831 *Toll Free Tel:* 800-845-1916 *Fax:* 712-644-2392 *Toll Free Fax:* 800-543-2745 *E-mail:* orders@perfectionlearning.com *Web Site:* www.perfectionlearning.com, pg 63

Wm Clark Associates, 355 W 22 St, 4th fl, New York, NY 10011 *Tel:* 212-675-2784 *Toll Free Tel:* 866-828-4252 *E-mail:* query@wmclark.com *Web Site:* www.wmclark.com, pg 625

Clarkson Potter Publishers, 1745 Broadway, New York, NY 10019 *Tel:* 212-782-9000 *Toll Free Tel:* 888-264-1745 *Fax:* 212-572-6181 *Web Site:* www.clarksonpotter.com; www.randomhouse.com/crown/clarksonpotter, pg 63

Classic Books, PO Box 130, Murrieta, CA 92564-0130 *Toll Free Tel:* 888-265-3547 *Toll Free Fax:* 888-265-3550 *E-mail:* 4classic@gte.net, pg 63

Classroom Connect, 8000 Marina Blvd, Suite 400, Brisbane, CA 94005 *Tel:* 650-351-5100 *Toll Free Tel:* 800-638-1639 (cust support) *Fax:* 650-351-5300 *E-mail:* connect@classroom.com *Web Site:* www.classroom.com, pg 63

Classroom Publishers Association (CPA), c/o Highlights for Children, 1800 Watermark Dr, Columbus, OH 43216 *Tel:* 614-487-2601 *Fax:* 614-324-7946, pg 685

Clausen Mays & Tahan Literary Agency LLC, PO Box 1015, Cooper Sta, New York, NY 10276-1015 *Tel:* 212-714-8181 *Fax:* 212-714-8282 *E-mail:* cmtassist@aol.com, pg 625

Clear Concepts, 1329 Federal Ave, Suite 6, Los Angeles, CA 90025 *Tel:* 310-473-5453, pg 594

Clear Light Publishers, 823 Don Diego, Santa Fe, NM 87505 *Tel:* 505-989-9590 *Toll Free Tel:* 888-253-2747 (orders) *Fax:* 505-989-9519 *E-mail:* market@clearlightbooks.com *Web Site:* www.clearlightbooks.com, pg 63

Clear View Press, PO Box 11574, Marina del Rey, CA 90295 *Tel:* 310-902-0786 *Fax:* 310-821-9007 *E-mail:* editor@clearviewpress.com, pg 63

Cleis Press, PO Box 14684, San Francisco, CA 94114-0684 *Tel:* 415-575-4700 *Toll Free Tel:* 800-780-2279 (US) *Fax:* 415-575-4705 *E-mail:* cleis@cleispress.com *Web Site:* www.cleispress.com, pg 63

Clements Publishing, 6021 Younge St, Suite 213, Toronto, ON M2M 3W2, Canada *Tel:* 416-558-9439 *Fax:* 416-352-5997 *E-mail:* info@clementspublishing.com *Web Site:* www.clementspublishing.com, pg 540

Clerical Plus, 273 Derby Ave, Unit 214, Derby, CT 06418 *Tel:* 203-732-3843 *Fax:* 203-732-3843 *E-mail:* clericalplus@aol.com, pg 594

Cleveland State University Poetry Center Prizes, 2121 Euclid Ave, Cleveland, OH 44115-2214 *Tel:* 216-687-3986 *Toll Free Tel:* 888-278-6473 *Fax:* 216-687-6943 *E-mail:* poetrycenter@csuohio.edu *Web Site:* www.csuohio.edu/poetrycenter, pg 767

David H Clift Scholarship, 50 E Huron St, Chicago, IL 60611 *Toll Free Tel:* 800-545-2433 (ext 4277) *Fax:* 312-280-3256 *E-mail:* scholarships@ala.org *Web Site:* www.ala.org/hrdr/scholarship.html, pg 767

Clock Tower Press, 3622 W Liberty Rd, Ann Arbor, MI 48103 *Tel:* 734-769-5600 *Toll Free Tel:* 800-956-8999 *Fax:* 734-769-5607 *Web Site:* www.clocktowerpress.com; huronriverpress.com, pg 63

Close Up Publishing, 44 Canal Center Plaza, Alexandria, VA 22314 *Toll Free Tel:* 800-765-3131 *Fax:* 703-706-3564 *E-mail:* cup@closeup.org *Web Site:* closeup.org/publishing, pg 63

Closson Press, 1935 Sampson Dr, Apollo, PA 15613-9208 *Tel:* 724-337-4482 *Fax:* 724-337-9484 *E-mail:* clossonpress@comcast.net *Web Site:* www.clossonpress.com, pg 63

Clovernook Printing House for the Blind, 7000 Hamilton Ave, Cincinnati, OH 45231-5297 *Tel:* 513-522-3860 *Toll Free Tel:* 888-234-7156 *Fax:* 513-728-3946 (admin); 513-728-3950 (sales) *Web Site:* www.clovernook.org, pg 63

CLTA/Stan Heath Achievement in Literacy Award, 328 Frank St, Ottawa, ON K2P 0X8, Canada *Tel:* 613-232-9625 *Fax:* 613-563-9895 *Web Site:* www.cla.ca/, pg 767

CMP Books, 600 Harrison St, San Francisco, CA 94107 *Tel:* 415-947-6615; 408-848-3854 (orders) *Toll Free Tel:* 800-500-6875 (orders) *Fax:* 415-947-6015; 408-848-5784 (orders) *E-mail:* books@cmp.com *Web Site:* www.cmpbooks.com, pg 63

CNIB Library for the Blind, 1929 Bayview Ave, Toronto, ON M4G 3E8, Canada *Tel:* 416-480-7520 *Fax:* 416-480-7700 *E-mail:* sales@cnib.ca *Web Site:* www.cnib.ca/library, pg 540

Coach House Books, 401 Huron St, Rear, Toronto, ON M5S 2G5, Canada *Tel:* 416-979-2217 *Toll Free Tel:* 800-367-6360 *Fax:* 416-977-1158 *E-mail:* mail@chbooks.com *Web Site:* www.chbooks.com, pg 540

Coaches Choice, 4 Justin Ct, Monterey, CA 93940 *Toll Free Tel:* 888-229-5745 *Fax:* 831-372-6075 *E-mail:* info@coacheschoice.com *Web Site:* www.coacheschoice.com, pg 64

Coastside Editorial, 1111 Date St, Montara, CA 94037 *Tel:* 650-728-0902 *Fax:* 650-728-0905, pg 594

Cobblestone Publishing Co, 30 Grove St, Suite C, Peterborough, NH 03458 *Tel:* 603-924-7209 *Toll Free Tel:* 800-821-0115 *Fax:* 603-924-7380 *E-mail:* custsvc@cobblestone.mv.com *Web Site:* www.cobblestonepub.com, pg 64

Coda Publications, CR A-68, Bldg 92, Raton, NM 87740 *Tel:* 505-445-4455 *Fax:* 505-445-4455 *E-mail:* newmexicobooks@bacavalley.com; coda@bacavalley.com, pg 64

Codie Awards, 1090 Vermont Ave NW, 6th fl, Washington, DC 20005 *Tel:* 202-289-7442 *Fax:* 202-289-7097 *E-mail:* codieawards@siia.net *Web Site:* www.siia.net, pg 767

Fred Cody Award, c/o Poetry Flash, 1450 Fourth St, Suite 4, Berkeley, CA 94710 *Tel:* 510-525-5476 *Fax:* 510-525-6752 *E-mail:* babra@poetryflash.org; editor@poetryflash.org *Web Site:* www.poetryflash.org, pg 768

Coe College Playwriting Festival, 1220 First Ave NE, Cedar Rapids, IA 52402 *Tel:* 319-399-8624 *Fax:* 319-399-8557 *Web Site:* www.coe.edu, pg 768

Coffee House Press, 27 N Fourth St, Suite 400, Minneapolis, MN 55401 *Tel:* 612-338-0125 *Fax:* 612-338-4004 *Web Site:* www.coffeehousepress.org, pg 64

Coffragants & Pocketaudio, 5400 rue Louis-Badaillac, Carignan, PQ J3L 4A7, Canada *Tel:* 450-447-6114 *Fax:* 450-658-1377 *E-mail:* coffragants@videotron.ca *Web Site:* www.coffragants.com, pg 540

Cognizant Communication Corp, 3 Hartsdale Rd, Elmsford, NY 10523-3701 *Tel:* 914-592-7720 *Fax:* 914-592-8981 *E-mail:* cogcomm@aol.com *Web Site:* www.cognizantcommunication.com, pg 64

Matt Cohen Prize: In Celebration of a Writing Life, 90 Richmond St W, Suite 200, Toronto, ON M5C 1P1, Canada *Tel:* 416-504-8222 *Fax:* 416-504-9090 *E-mail:* info@writerstrust.com *Web Site:* www.writerstrust.com, pg 768

Morton N Cohen Award for a Distinguished Edition of Letters, 26 Broadway, 3rd fl, New York, NY 10004-1789 *Tel:* 646-576-5141 *Fax:* 646-458-0030 *E-mail:* awards@mla.org *Web Site:* www.mla.org, pg 768

Robert L Cohen, 182-12 Horace Harding Expressway, Suite 2M, Fresh Meadows, NY 11365 *Tel:* 617-254-0254; 718-595-2082 (NYC) *Toll Free Tel:* 866-EDITING *E-mail:* wordsmith@sterlingmp.com *Web Site:* www.sterlingmp.com, pg 594

Shaughnessy Cohen Award for Political Writing, 90 Richmond St W, Suite 200, Toronto, ON M5C 1P1, Canada *Tel:* 416-504-8222 *Fax:* 416-504-9090 *E-mail:* info@writerstrust.com *Web Site:* www.writerstrust.com, pg 768

The Victor Cohn Prize for Excellence in Medical Science Reporting, PO Box 910, Hedgesville, WV 25427 *Tel:* 304-754-5077 *Fax:* 304-754-5076 *Web Site:* www.casw.org, pg 768

E Calvin Coish, 99 Lincoln Rd, Grand Falls, NF A2A 2T2, Canada *Tel:* 709-489-6796 *Fax:* 709-489-6796 *E-mail:* c.coish@nf.sympatico.ca, pg 594

Cold Spring Harbor Laboratory Press, 500 Sunnyside Blvd, Woodbury, NY 11797-2924 *Tel:* 516-422-4100 *Toll Free Tel:* 800-843-4388 *Fax:* 516-422-4097 *E-mail:* cshpress@cshl.edu *Web Site:* www.cshlpress.com, pg 64

Collector Grade Publications Inc, PO Box 1046, Cobourg, ON K9A 4W5, Canada *Tel:* 905-342-3434 *Fax:* 905-342-3688 *E-mail:* info@collectorgrade.com *Web Site:* www.collectorgrade.com, pg 541

Collectors Press Inc, 15655 SW 74 Ave, Suite 200, Tigard, OR 97224 *Tel:* 503-684-3030 *Toll Free Tel:* 800-423-1848 *Fax:* 503-684-3777 *Web Site:* www.collectorspress.com, pg 64

College & University Professional Association for Human Resources, Tyson Place, 2607 Kingston Pike, Suite 250, Knoxville, TN 37919 *Tel:* 865-637-7673 *Fax:* 865-637-7674 *E-mail:* communications@cupahr.org *Web Site:* www.cupahr.org, pg 64

The College Board, 45 Columbus Ave, New York, NY 10023-6992 *Tel:* 212-713-8000 *Fax:* 212-713-8143 *Web Site:* www.collegeboard.com, pg 64

College of General Studies Special Programs, University of Pennsylvania, 3440 Market St, Suite 100, Philadelphia, PA 19104-3335 *Tel:* 215-898-7326 *Fax:* 215-573-2053 *E-mail:* cgs@sas.upenn.edu *Web Site:* www.sas.upenn.edu/cgs, pg 751

College Press Publishing Co, 223 W Third St, Joplin, MO 64801 *Tel:* 417-623-6280 *Toll Free Tel:* 800-289-3300 *Fax:* 417-623-8250 *E-mail:* books@collegepress.com *Web Site:* www.collegepress.com, pg 64

Collier Associates, 37 Marina Gardens Dr, Palm Beach Gardens, FL 33410 *Tel:* 561-697-3541 *Fax:* 561-478-4316, pg 625

Jan Collier Represents Inc, PO Box 470818, Mill Valley, CA 94941 *Tel:* 415-383-9026 *Fax:* 415-383-9037 *E-mail:* jan@jan-collier-represents.com *Web Site:* www.jan-collier-represents.com, pg 665

Frances Collin Literary Agent, PO Box 33, Wayne, PA 19087-0033 *Tel:* 610-254-0555 *Fax:* 610-254-5029, pg 625

Carr P Collins Award, Center for the Study of the Southwest, Southwest Texas State University, San Marcos, TX 78666 *Tel:* 512-245-2232 *Fax:* 512-245-7462 *Web Site:* www.stedwards.edu/newc/marks/til/awards_and_rules.htm, pg 768

Zipporah W Collins, 768 Peralta Ave, Berkeley, CA 94707-1842 *Tel:* 510-527-2140 *Fax:* 510-527-4155 *E-mail:* zipcol@aol.com, pg 594

The Colonial Williamsburg Foundation, PO Box 1776, Williamsburg, VA 23187-1776 *Tel:* 757-229-1000 *Toll Free Tel:* 800-HISTORY *Fax:* 757-220-7325 *Web Site:* www.colonialwilliamsburg.org/publications, pg 65

Colophon Group, 1306 Rousseau Cres, Greely, ON K4P 1B3, Canada *Tel:* 613-821-0066 *Fax:* 613-821-9987 *E-mail:* colophongroup@rogers.com, pg 594

Color Management for the Pressroom, 200 Deer Run Rd, Sewickley, PA 15143-2600 *Tel:* 412-741-6860 *Toll Free Tel:* 800-910-4283 *Fax:* 412-741-2311 *E-mail:* info@gain.net *Web Site:* www.gain.net, pg 743

Colorado Book Awards, 2123 Downing St, Denver, CO 80205 *Tel:* 303-839-8320 *Fax:* 303-839-8319 *Web Site:* www.coloradobook.org, pg 768

Colorado Geological Survey, 1313 Sherman St, Rm 715, Denver, CO 80203 *Tel:* 303-866-2611; 303-866-4762 (pubns) *Fax:* 303-866-2461 *E-mail:* cgspubs@state.co.us *Web Site:* www.geosurvey.state.co.us, pg 65

Colorado Railroad Museum, 17155 W 44 Ave, Golden, CO 80402 *Tel:* 303-279-4591 *Toll Free Tel:* 800-365-6263 *Fax:* 303-279-4229 *E-mail:* library@crrm.org *Web Site:* crrm.org, pg 65

Betsy Colquitt Award for Poetry, TCU Box 297700, Fort Worth, TX 76129 *Tel:* 817-257-7240 *Fax:* 817-257-7709 *E-mail:* descant@tcu.edu *Web Site:* www.eng.tcu.edu/journals/descant/index.html, pg 768

Columba Publishing Co Inc, 2003 W Market St, Akron, OH 44313 *Tel:* 330-836-2619 *Toll Free Tel:* 800-999-7491 *Fax:* 330-836-9659 *Web Site:* www.columbapublishing.com, pg 65

Columbia Books Inc, 1825 Connecticut Ave NW, Suite 625, Washington, DC 20009 *Tel:* 202-464-1662 *Toll Free Tel:* 888-265-0600 (cust serv) *Fax:* 202-464-1775; 240-646-7020 (cust serv) *E-mail:* info@columbiabooks.com *Web Site:* www.columbiabooks.com, pg 65

Coronet Books & Publications, PO Box 957, Eagle Point, OR 97524 Tel: 541-858-5585 Fax: 541-858-5595 E-mail: lionspaw@country.net, pg 69

Corp professionnelle des traducteurs et interpretes agrees du quebec, 2021 Union Ave, Suite 1108, Montreal, PQ H3A 2S9, Canada Tel: 514-845-4411 Fax: 514-845-9903, pg 685

Corporation for Public Broadcasting (CPB), 401 Ninth St NW, Washington, DC 20004-2037 Tel: 202-879-9600 Fax: 202-879-9700 E-mail: info@cpb.org Web Site: www.cpb.org, pg 685

Corporation of Professional Librarians of Quebec, 353, rue Sainte Niclas, Suite 103, Montreal, PQ H2Y 2P1, Canada Tel: 514-845-3327 Fax: 514-845-1618 E-mail: info@cbpq.qc.ca Web Site: www.cbpq.qc.ca, pg 685

Corrington Indexing Services, 2638 E Kenwood, Mesa, AZ 85213 Tel: 480-827-8904 Fax: 480-827-1182, pg 595

Cortina Learning International Inc, 7 Hollyhock Rd, Wilton, CT 06897-4414 Tel: 203-762-2510 Toll Free Tel: 800-245-2145 Fax: 203-762-2514 E-mail: info@cortina-languages.com; cortinainc@aol.com Web Site: www.cortina-languages.com (English language animation & sound); www.cursos-ingles-cortina.com (Spanish language animation & sound), pg 69

Corwin Press, 2455 Teller Rd, Thousand Oaks, CA 91320 Tel: 805-499-9734 Fax: 805-499-5323 Toll Free Fax: 800-417-2466 E-mail: info@corwinpress.com Web Site: www.corwinpress.com, pg 69

Coteau Books, 401-2206 Dewdney Ave, Regina, SK S4R 1H3, Canada Tel: 306-777-0170 Toll Free Tel: 800-440-4471 (Canada Only) Fax: 306-522-5152 E-mail: coteau@coteaubooks.com Web Site: www.coteaubooks.com, pg 541

Cotsen Institute of Archaeology at UCLA, PO Box 951510, Los Angeles, CA 90095-1510 Tel: 310-825-7411 Fax: 310-206-4723 E-mail: ioapubs@ucla.edu Web Site: www.sscnet.ucla.edu/ioa, pg 69

Cottage Communications Inc, 128 Rte 6A, Sandwich, MA 02563 Tel: 508-833-1300 Fax: 508-833-6319, pg 595

Cottonwood Press, University of Kansas, Kansas Union, Rm 400, 1301 Jayhawk Blvd, Lawrence, KS 66045 Tel: 785-864-3777, pg 69

Cottonwood Press Inc, 109-B Cameron Dr, Fort Collins, CO 80525 Tel: 970-204-0715 Toll Free Tel: 800-864-4297 Fax: 970-204-0761 E-mail: cottonwood@cottonwoodpress.com Web Site: www.cottonwoodpress.com, pg 69

Council for Advancement & Support of Education (CASE), 1307 New York Ave NW, Suite 1000, Washington, DC 20005 Tel: 202-328-5900 Fax: 202-387-4973 E-mail: info@case.org Web Site: www.case.org, pg 685

Council for American Indian Education, 1240 Burlington Ave, Billings, MT 59102-4224 Tel: 406-248-3465 (PM); 406-652-7598 (AM) Fax: 406-248-1297 E-mail: cie@cie-mt.org Web Site: www.cie-mt.org, pg 69

Council for Exceptional Children, 1110 N Glebe Rd, Suite 300, Arlington, VA 22201 Tel: 703-620-3660 Toll Free Tel: 888-232-7733 (cust serv) Fax: 703-264-9494 E-mail: service@cec.sped.org Web Site: www.cec.sped.org, pg 70

The Council for Exceptional Children, 1110 N Glebe Rd, Arlington, VA 22201-5704 Tel: 703-620-3660 Toll Free Tel: 800-224-6830 Fax: 703-264-9494 E-mail: service@cec.sped.org Web Site: www.cec.sped.org, pg 685

Council for Research in Values & Philosophy (RVP), Catholic University, Washington, DC 20064 Tel: 202-319-6089 Fax: 202-319-6089 Toll Free Tel: 800-659-9962 E-mail: cua-rvp@cua.edu Web Site: www.crvp.org, pg 70

Council for the Advancement of Science Writing (CASW), PO Box 910, Hedgesville, WV 25427 Tel: 304-754-5077 Fax: 304-754-5076 Web Site: www.casw.org, pg 686

Council Oak Books LLC, 2105 E 15 St, Suite B, Tulsa, OK 74104 Tel: 918-743-BOOK (743-2665) Toll Free Tel: 800-247-8850 Fax: 918-743-4288 E-mail: publicity@counciloakbooks.com; orders@counciloakbooks.com Web Site: www.counciloakbooks.com, pg 70

Council of Literary Magazines & Presses (CLMP), 154 Christopher St, Suite 3-C, New York, NY 10014-2839 Tel: 212-741-9110 Fax: 212-741-9112 E-mail: info@clmp.org Web Site: www.clmp.org, pg 686

Council of State Governments, 2760 Research Park Dr, Lexington, KY 40511 Tel: 859-244-8000 Toll Free Tel: 800-800-1910 Fax: 859-244-8001 Web Site: www.csg.org, pg 70

Council on Foreign Relations Press, 58 E 68 St, New York, NY 10021 Tel: 212-434-9400 Fax: 212-434-9859 E-mail: publications@cfr.org; communications@cfr.org Web Site: www.cfr.org, pg 70

Council on Social Work Education, 1725 Duke St, Suite 500, Alexandria, VA 22314-3457 Tel: 703-683-8080 Fax: 703-683-8099 E-mail: webmaster@cswe.org Web Site: www.cswe.org, pg 70

Counterpoint Press, 387 Park Ave S, New York, NY 10016 Tel: 212-340-8100 Fax: 212-340-8135 (edit); 212-340-8115 E-mail: counterpointpress@perseusbooks.com Web Site: www.counterpointpress.com, pg 70

Country Music Foundation Press, 222 Fifth Ave S, Nashville, TN 37203 Tel: 615-416-2001 Fax: 615-255-2245 Web Site: www.countrymusichalloffame.com, pg 70

The Countryman Press, 1206 Rte 12 N, Woodstock, VT 05091 Tel: 802-457-4826 Toll Free Tel: 800-245-4151 Fax: 802-457-1678 E-mail: countrymanpress@wwnorton.com Web Site: www.countrymanpress.com, pg 70

Course Crafters Inc, 44 Merrimac St, Newburyport, MA 01950 Tel: 978-465-2040 Fax: 978-465-5027 E-mail: info@coursecrafters.com Web Site: www.coursecrafters.com, pg 595

Course Technology, 25 Thomson Place, Boston, MA 02210 Tel: 617-757-7900 Toll Free Tel: 800-881-8922 Fax: 617-757-7969 Web Site: www.course.com, pg 71

La Courte Echelle, 5243 Saint Laurent Blvd, Montreal, PQ H2T 1S4, Canada Tel: 514-274-2004 Toll Free Tel: 800-387-6192 (orders only) Fax: 514-270-4160 Toll Free Fax: 800-450-0391 (orders only) E-mail: info@courteechelle.com, pg 541

Covenant Communications Inc, 920 E State Rd, Suite F, American Fork, UT 84003-0416 Tel: 801-756-9966 Toll Free Tel: 800-662-9545 Fax: 801-756-1049 E-mail: sales@covenant-lds.com Web Site: www.covenant-lds.com, pg 71

Cowley Publications, 4 Brattle St, Cambridge, MA 02138 Tel: 617-441-0300 Toll Free Tel: 800-225-1534 Fax: 617-441-0120 Toll Free Fax: 877-225-6675 E-mail: cowley@cowley.org Web Site: www.cowley.org, pg 71

Coyote Press, PO Box 3377, Salinas, CA 93912-3377 Tel: 831-422-4912 Fax: 831-422-4913 E-mail: coyote@coyotepress.com Web Site: www.coyotepress.com, pg 71

CQ Press, 1255 22 St NW, Suite 400, Washington, DC 20037 Tel: 202-729-1800 Toll Free Tel: 866-427-7737 Fax: 202-729-1923 Toll Free Fax: 800-380-3810 E-mail: customerservice@cqpress.com Web Site: www.cqpress.com, pg 71

Crabtree Publishing Co, 350 Fifth Ave, Suite 3308, PMB 16-A, New York, NY 10118 Tel: 212-496-5040 Toll Free Tel: 800-387-7650 Toll Free Fax: 800-355-7166 E-mail: letters@crabtreebooks.com Web Site: www.crabtreebooks.com, pg 71

Crabtree Publishing Co Ltd, 612 Welland Ave, St Catharines, ON L2M 5V6, Canada Tel: 905-682-5221 Toll Free Tel: 800-387-7650 Fax: 905-682-

7166 Toll Free Fax: 800-355-7166 E-mail: custserv@crabtreebooks.com; sales@crabtreebooks.com; orders@crabtreebooks.com Web Site: www.crabtreebooks.com, pg 541

Craftsman Book Co, 6058 Corte Del Cedro, Carlsbad, CA 92009 Tel: 760-438-7828 Toll Free Tel: 800-829-8123 Fax: 760-438-0398 Web Site: www.craftsman-book.com, pg 71

Crane Hill Publishers, 3608 Clairmont Ave, Birmingham, AL 35222 Tel: 205-714-3007 Toll Free Tel: 800-247-8850 Fax: 205-714-3008 E-mail: cranies@cranehill.com Web Site: www.cranehill.com, pg 71

Craven Design Studios Inc, 234 Fifth Ave, 4th fl, New York, NY 10001 Tel: 212-696-4680 Fax: 212-532-2626 Web Site: www.cravendesignstudios.com, pg 665

Crawford Literary Agency, 94 Evans Rd, Barnstead, NH 03218 Tel: 603-269-5851 Fax: 603-269-2533 E-mail: crawfordlit@att.net, pg 626

Mark Crawford, 5101 Violet Lane, Madison, WI 53714 Tel: 608-240-4959 Fax: 608-245-9309 E-mail: giltedge@chorus.net, pg 595

Vallaurie Crawford, PO Box 668, Volcano, HI 96785 Tel: 808-985-8512 Fax: 808-967-7648 E-mail: crawford@hawaii.rr.com, pg 595

CRC Press LLC, 2000 NW Corporate Blvd, Boca Raton, FL 33431 Tel: 561-994-0555 Toll Free Tel: 800-272-7737 Fax: 561-997-7249 (edit); 561-998-8491 (mfg); 561-361-6057 (acctg); 561-994-0313 Toll Free Fax: 800-643-9428 (sales); 800-374-3401 (orders) E-mail: orders@crcpress.com Web Site: www.crcpress.com, pg 71

CRC Publications, 2850 Kalamazoo Ave SE, Grand Rapids, MI 49560 Tel: 616-224-0819; 616-224-0728 Toll Free Tel: 800-333-8300 Fax: 616-224-0834 E-mail: sales@crcpublications.org Web Site: www.faithaliveresources.org, pg 72

Creating Keepsakes Books, 14901 S Heritagecrest Way, Bluffdale, UT 84065 Tel: 801-984-2070 Toll Free Tel: 800-815-3538 Fax: 801-984-2080 Web Site: www.creatingkeepsakes.com, pg 72

Creative Artists Agency, 9830 Wilshire Blvd, Beverly Hills, CA 90212-1825 Tel: 310-288-4545 Fax: 310-288-4800 Web Site: www.caa.com, pg 626

Creative Arts Book Co, 833 Bancroft Way, Berkeley, CA 94710 Tel: 510-848-4777 Fax: 510-848-4844 E-mail: staff@creativeartsbooks.com; capublisher@yahoo.com Web Site: www.creativeartsbooks.com, pg 72

Creative Arts of Ventura, PO Box 684, Ventura, CA 93002-0684 Tel: 805-643-4160; 805-659-0237, pg 665

Creative Book Publishing, 36 Austin St, St Johns, NF A1B 3T7, Canada Tel: 709-722-8500 Toll Free Tel: 877-722-1722 (Canada only) Fax: 709-579-7745 E-mail: nlbooks@transcontinental.ca Web Site: www.nfbooks.com, pg 541

Creative Bound International Inc, 151 Tansley Dr, Carp, ON K0A 1L0, Canada Tel: 613-831-3641 Toll Free Tel: 800-287-8610 (N America) Fax: 613-831-3643 E-mail: editor@creativebound.com Web Site: www.creativebound.com, pg 541

The Creative Co, 123 S Broad St, Mankato, MN 56001 Tel: 507-388-6273 Toll Free Tel: 800-445-6209 Fax: 507-388-2746 E-mail: creativeco@aol.com, pg 72

The Creative Crayon Award, 13500 SW Pacific Hwy, Suite 129, Tigard, OR 97223 Tel: 503-670-1153 Fax: 503-213-5889 Web Site: www.thisnewworld.com, pg 769

The Creative Culture Inc, 72 Spring St, Suite 304, New York, NY 10012 Tel: 212-680-3510 Fax: 212-680-3509 Web Site: www.thecreativeculture.com, pg 626

Creative Freelancers Inc, 99 Park Ave, No 210-A, New York, NY 10016 Tel: 203-532-2924 Toll Free Tel: 800-398-9544; 888-398-9500 Fax: 203-532-2927 E-mail: cfonline@freelancers.com Web Site: www.freelancers.com, pg 595

Creative Homeowner, 24 Park Way, Upper Saddle River, NJ 07458-9960 *Tel:* 201-934-7100 *Toll Free Tel:* 800-631-7795 *Fax:* 201-934-8971 *E-mail:* info@creativehomeowner.com *Web Site:* www.creativehomeowner.com, pg 72

Creative Media Agency Inc, 240 W 35 St, Suite 500, New York, NY 10001 *Tel:* 212-560-0909 *Fax:* 212-279-0927 *E-mail:* cmagency@yahoo.com *Web Site:* www.paigewheeler.com; www.thecmagency.com, pg 626

Creative Publishing International Inc, 18705 Lake Dr E, Chanhassen, MN 55317 *Tel:* 952-936-4700 *Toll Free Tel:* 800-328-0590 (sales) *Fax:* 952-933-1456 *Web Site:* www.creativepub.com, pg 72

Creative Sales Corp, 780 W Belden, Suite A, Addison, IL 60101 *Tel:* 630-458-1500 *Fax:* 630-458-1511 *Web Site:* www.americanmag-csc.com, pg 72

Creative Writing Conference, Case Annex 467, 512 Lancaster Ave, Richmond, KY 40475-3102 *Tel:* 859-622-5861 *Fax:* 859-622-3156 *Web Site:* www.english.eku.edu, pg 743

Creative Writing Day & Workshops, PO Box 801, Abingdon, VA 24212-0801 *Tel:* 276-623-5266 *Fax:* 276-623-5266 *E-mail:* vhf@eva.org *Web Site:* www.vahighlandsfestival.org, pg 743

CreativeWell Inc, PO Box 3130, Memorial Sta, Upper Montclair, NJ 07043 *Tel:* 973-783-7575 *Fax:* 973-783-7530 *E-mail:* info@creativewell.com *Web Site:* www.creativewell.com, pg 626, 669

Creativity Fellowship, Alden B Dow Creativity Center, 4000 Whiting Dr, Midland, MI 48640-2398 *Tel:* 989-837-4478 *Fax:* 989-837-4468 *E-mail:* creativity@northwood.edu *Web Site:* www.northwood.edu/abd, pg 769

Crichton & Associates, 6940 Carroll Ave, Takoma Park, MD 20912 *Tel:* 301-495-9663 *Fax:* 202-318-0050 *E-mail:* cricht1@aol.com *Web Site:* www.crichton-associates.com, pg 626

Cricket Books, 332 S Michigan Ave, Suite 1100, Chicago, IL 60604 *Tel:* 312-939-1500 *Fax:* 312-939-8150 *Web Site:* www.cricketmag.com, pg 72

Criminal Justice Press, PO Box 249, Monsey, NY 10952-0249 *Tel:* 845-354-9139 *Toll Free Tel:* 800-914-3379 *Web Site:* www.criminaljusticepress.com, pg 72

Crop Circle Books Press, 1123 N Las Posas Ct, Ridgecrest, CA 93555 *Tel:* 760-446-1938 *E-mail:* cropcircles@webtv.net *Web Site:* www.cropcirclebooks.com, pg 72

Cross-Cultural Communications, 239 Wynsum Ave, Merrick, NY 11566-4725 *Tel:* 516-868-5635 *Fax:* 516-379-1901 *E-mail:* cccpoetry@aol.com *Web Site:* www.cross-culturalcommunications.com, pg 73

Cross Cultural Publications Inc, 53310 Peggy Lane, South Bend, IN 46635 *Tel:* 574-273-6526 *Toll Free Tel:* 800-273-6526 *Fax:* 574-273-5973 *E-mail:* crosscult@aol.com *Web Site:* crossculturalpub.com, pg 73

Cross Pond Editing Group, 333 Hook Rd, Katonah, NY 10536 *Tel:* 914-232-8687 *Fax:* 914-232-1258, pg 595

Ruth C Cross, 51 Linden St, No 101, Brattleboro, VT 05301 *Tel:* 802-257-1456, pg 595

The Crossing Press, PO Box 7123, Berkeley, CA 94707 *Tel:* 510-559-1600 *Toll Free Tel:* 800-841-2665 (orders & cust serv) *Fax:* 510-524-1052 *E-mail:* publicity@tenspeed.com *Web Site:* www.tenspeed.com, pg 73

Crossquarter Publishing Group, 1910 Sombra Ct, Santa Fe, NM 87505 *Tel:* 505-438-9846 *Fax:* 505-438-9846 *E-mail:* sales@crossquarter.com; info@crossquarter.com *Web Site:* www.crossquarter.com, pg 73

The Crossroad Publishing Company, 16 Penn Plaza, Suite 1550, New York, NY 10001 *Tel:* 212-868-1801 *Toll Free Tel:* 800-395-0690 (orders) *Fax:* 212-868-2171 *Toll Free Tel:* 800-462-6420 (orders) *E-mail:* ask@crossroadpublishing.com *Web Site:* www.crossroadpublishing.com, pg 73

Crossway Books, 1300 Crescent St, Wheaton, IL 60187 *Tel:* 630-682-4300 *Fax:* 630-682-4785 *E-mail:* editorial@goodnews-crossway.org *Web Site:* www.crosswaybooks.org, pg 73

Bonnie R Crown International Literature & Arts Agency, 50 E Tenth St, New York, NY 10003 *Tel:* 212-475-1999, pg 626

Crown House Publishing, 4 Berkely St, Norwalk, CT 06850 *Tel:* 203-852-9504 *Toll Free Tel:* 877-925-1213 (orders) *Fax:* 203-852-9619 *Web Site:* www.chpus.com, pg 73

Crown Publishing Group, 1745 Broadway, New York, NY 10019 *Tel:* 212-782-9000 *Toll Free Tel:* 888-264-1745 *Fax:* 212-940-7408 *Web Site:* www.randomhouse.com/crown, pg 73

Crumb Elbow Publishing, PO Box 294, Rhododendron, OR 97049-0294 *Tel:* 503-622-4798, pg 74

Crystal Clarity Publishers, 14618 Tyler Foote Rd, Nevada City, CA 95959 *Tel:* 530-478-7600 *Toll Free Tel:* 800-424-1055 *Fax:* 530-478-7610 *E-mail:* clarity@crystalclarity.com *Web Site:* www.crystalclarity.com, pg 74

Crystal Fountain Publications, 500-A N Golden Springs Dr, Diamond Bar, CA 91765 *Tel:* 909-396-1201 *Fax:* 909-860-7803 *Web Site:* www.crystalfountain.org, pg 74

Crystal Productions, 1812 Johns Dr, Glenview, IL 60025 *Tel:* 847-657-8144 *Toll Free Tel:* 800-255-8629 *Fax:* 847-657-8149 *Toll Free Fax:* 800-657-8149 *E-mail:* custserv@crystalproductions.com *Web Site:* www.crystalproductions.com, pg 74

Crystal Publishers, 3460 Lost Hills Dr, Las Vegas, NV 89122 *Tel:* 702-434-3037 *Fax:* 702-434-3037 *Web Site:* www.crystalpub.com, pg 74

Crystalline Sphere Publishing, 47 Bridgeport Rd E, Waterloo, ON N2J 2J4, Canada *E-mail:* csp@golden.net *Web Site:* crystallinesphere.com, pg 595

CS International Literary Agency, 43 W 39 St, New York, NY 10018 *Tel:* 212-921-1610 *E-mail:* csliterary@verizon.net, pg 595

CSLI Publications, Stanford University, Ventura Hall, 220 Panama St, Stanford, CA 94305-4115 *Tel:* 650-723-1839 *Fax:* 650-725-2166 *E-mail:* pubs@csli.stanford.edu *Web Site:* cslipublications.stanford.edu, pg 74

CTB/McGraw-Hill, 20 Ryan Ranch Rd, Monterey, CA 93940-5703 *Tel:* 831-393-0700 *Toll Free Tel:* 800-538-9547 *Fax:* 831-393-7825 *Web Site:* www.ctb.com, pg 74

Cultural Studies & Analysis, 1123 Montrose St, Philadelphia, PA 19147 *Tel:* 215-592-8544 *Fax:* 215-413-9041 *E-mail:* cultureking@comcast.net *Web Site:* www.culturalanalysis.com, pg 595

Culture Concepts Books, 69 Ashmount Crescent, Toronto, ON M9R 1C9, Canada *Tel:* 416-245-8119 *Fax:* 416-245-3383 *E-mail:* cultureconcepts@sympatico.ca *Web Site:* www.cultureconcepts.ca, pg 595

Cumberland House Publishing Inc, 431 Harding Industrial Dr, Nashville, TN 37211 *Tel:* 615-832-1171 *Toll Free Tel:* 888-439-2665 *Fax:* 615-832-0633 *E-mail:* information@cumberlandhouse.com *Web Site:* www.cumberlandhouse.com, pg 74

Cummings & Hathaway Publishers, 395 Atlantic Ave, East Rockaway, NY 11518 *Tel:* 516-593-3607 *Fax:* 516-593-1401 *E-mail:* chpublish@aol.com, pg 74

Cunningham Commission for Youth Theatre, 2135 N Kenmore, Chicago, IL 60614 *Tel:* 773-325-7938 *Fax:* 773-325-7920 *Web Site:* theatreschool.depaul.edu, pg 769

Curbstone Press, 321 Jackson St, Willimantic, CT 06226 *Tel:* 860-423-5110 *Fax:* 860-423-9242 *E-mail:* info@curbstone.org *Web Site:* www.curbstone.org, pg 74

Current Clinical Strategies Publishing, 27071 Cabot Rd, Suite 126, Laguna Hills, CA 92653-7011 *Tel:* 949-348-8404 *Toll Free Tel:* 800-331-8227 *Fax:* 949-348-

8404 *Toll Free Fax:* 800-965-9420 *E-mail:* info@ccspublishing.com *Web Site:* www.ccspublishing.com, pg 75

Current Medicine, 400 Market St, Suite 700, Philadelphia, PA 19106 *Tel:* 215-574-2266 *Toll Free Tel:* 800-427-1796 *Fax:* 215-574-2270 *E-mail:* info@phl.cursci.com, pg 75

Richard Curtis Associates Inc, 171 E 74 St, Suite 2, New York, NY 10021 *Tel:* 212-772-7363 *Fax:* 212-772-7393 *E-mail:* rcurtis@curtisagency.com *Web Site:* www.curtisagency.com, pg 626

Pat Cusick & Associates, 370 Park St, Suite 9-B, Moraga, CA 94556 *Tel:* 925-376-4457 *Fax:* 925-376-4859 *E-mail:* pcusick@pacbell.net, pg 596

Custom Editorial Productions Inc (CEP), 546 W Liberty St, Cincinnati, OH 45214 *Tel:* 513-723-1100 *Fax:* 513-723-1103 *E-mail:* cep@customeditorial.com *Web Site:* www.customeditorial.com, pg 596

Cycle Publishing, 1282 Seventh Ave, San Francisco, CA 94122-2526 *Tel:* 415-665-8214 *Toll Free Tel:* 877-353-1207 *Fax:* 415-753-8572 *E-mail:* pubrel@cyclepublishing.com *Web Site:* www.cyclepublishing.com, pg 75

CyclopsMedia.com, 1076 Eagle Dr, Salinas, CA 93905 *Tel:* 831-776-9500 *Fax:* 831-422-5915 *E-mail:* custserv@cyclopsmedia.com *Web Site:* www.cyclopsmedia.com, pg 75

Cyclotour Guide Books, 160 Harvard St, Rochester, NY 14607 *Tel:* 585-244-6157 *Fax:* 585-244-6157 *E-mail:* cyclotour@cyclotour.com *Web Site:* www.cyclotour.com, pg 75

The Cypher Agency James R Cypher Author's Representative, 816 Wolcott Ave, Beacon, NY 12508-4261 *Tel:* 845-831-5677 *Fax:* 845-831-5677 *Web Site:* pages.prodigy.net/jimcypher, pg 626

Cypress House, 155 Cypress St, Fort Bragg, CA 95437 *Tel:* 707-964-9520 *Toll Free Tel:* 800-773-7782 *Fax:* 707-964-7531 *E-mail:* publishing@cypresshouse.com *Web Site:* www.cypresshouse.com, pg 596

Da Capo Press Inc, 11 Cambridge Center, Cambridge, MA 02142 *Tel:* 617-252-5200 *Toll Free Tel:* 800-242-7737 (orders) *Fax:* 617-252-5285 *E-mail:* custserve@lrp.com *Web Site:* www.dacapopress.com, pg 75

Steven P d'Adolf, 17852 Saint Andrews Dr, Poway, CA 92064 *Tel:* 858-451-2130 *Fax:* 858-451-2130 *E-mail:* sdadolf@san.rr.com, pg 596

Daisy Books, 991 King St W, Hamilton, ON L8S 4R5, Canada *Tel:* 905-526-0451 *Fax:* 905-526-0451 *E-mail:* admin@daisybooks.com *Web Site:* www.daisybooks.com, pg 541

Aleta M Daley/Maximilian Becker, 444 E 82 St, New York, NY 10028 *Tel:* 212-744-1453 *Fax:* 212-249-2088, pg 626

Dalkey Archive Press, Illinois State University 8905, Normal, IL 61790-8905 *Tel:* 309-438-7555 *Fax:* 309-438-7422 *E-mail:* contact@dalkeyarchive.com *Web Site:* www.dalkeyarchive.com, pg 75

Damron Co, PO Box 422458, San Francisco, CA 94142-2458 *Tel:* 415-255-0404 *Toll Free Tel:* 800-462-6654 *Fax:* 415-703-9049 *E-mail:* editor@damron.com *Web Site:* www.damron.com, pg 75

Dan River Press, PO Box 298, Thomaston, ME 04861 *Tel:* 207-354-0998 *E-mail:* cal@americanletter.org *Web Site:* www.americanletters.org, pg 75

DanaRae Pomeroy, 139 Turner Circle, Greenville, SC 29609 *Tel:* 864-834-7549 *E-mail:* danarae@charter.net, pg 596

Dandy Lion Publications, 3563 Sueldo, Suite L, San Luis Obispo, CA 93401 *Tel:* 805-543-3332 *Toll Free Tel:* 800-776-8032 *Fax:* 805-544-2823 *E-mail:* dandy@dandylionbooks.com *Web Site:* www.dandylionbooks.com, pg 75

John Daniel & Co, Publishers, PO Box 2790, McKinleyville, NY 95519 *Tel:* 707-839-3495 *Toll Free Tel:* 800-662-8351 *Fax:* 707-839-3242 *E-mail:* dandd@danielpublishing.com *Web Site:* www.danielpublishing.com, pg 75

Dante University of America Press Inc, PO Box 812158, Wellesley, MA 02482 *Tel:* 781-235-3634 *Fax:* 781-790-1056 *E-mail:* danteu@danteuniversity.org *Web Site:* www.danteuniversity.org, pg 76

Darhansoff, Verrill, Feldman Literary Agents, 236 W 26 St, Suite 802, New York, NY 10001-6736 *Tel:* 917-305-1300 *Fax:* 917-305-1400 *Web Site:* www.dvagency.com, pg 626

Dark Horse Comics, 10956 SE Main St, Milwaukie, OR 97222 *Tel:* 503-652-8815 *Fax:* 503-654-9440 *E-mail:* dhcomics@darkhorsecomics.com *Web Site:* www.darkhorse.com, pg 76

Darla Bruno, Editor, 80 Ports Harbor Rd, Addison, ME 04606 *Tel:* 207-229-5114 *E-mail:* editor@darlabruno.com *Web Site:* www.darlabruno.com, pg 596

The Dartnell Corp, 360 Hiatt Dr, Palm Beach Gardens, FL 33418 *Tel:* 561-622-6520 *Toll Free Tel:* 800-621-5463 *Fax:* 561-622-2423 *Web Site:* www.dartnellcorp.com, pg 76

The Darwin Press Inc, 280 N Main St, Pennington, NJ 08534 *Tel:* 609-737-1349 *Fax:* 609-737-0929 *E-mail:* books@darwinpress.com *Web Site:* www.darwinpress.com, pg 76

Data Trace Publishing Co, 110 West Rd, Suite 227, Towson, MD 21204-2316 *Tel:* 410-494-4994 *Toll Free Tel:* 800-342-0454 (orders only) *Fax:* 410-494-0515 *E-mail:* info@datatrace.com *Web Site:* www.datatrace.com, pg 76

Database Directories, 588 Dufferin Ave, London, ON N6B 2A4, Canada *Tel:* 519-433-1666 *Fax:* 519-430-1131 *E-mail:* info@databasedirectory.com; lclassic@databasedirectory.com *Web Site:* www.databasedirectory.com, pg 542

May Davenport Publishers, 26313 Purissima Rd, Los Altos Hills, CA 94022 *Tel:* 650-947-1275 *Fax:* 650-947-1373 *E-mail:* mdbooks@earthlink.net *Web Site:* www.maydavenportpublishers.com, pg 76

Suzanne B Davidson, 8084 N 44 St, Brown Deer, WI 53223 *Tel:* 414-355-6640 *E-mail:* davidson@execpc.com, pg 596

Davies-Black Publishing, 3803 E Bayshore Rd, Palo Alto, CA 94303 *Tel:* 650-969-8901 *Toll Free Tel:* 800-624-1765 *Fax:* 650-623-9271 *Web Site:* www.daviesblack.com, pg 76

The Davies Group Publishers, PO Box 440140, Aurora, CO 80044-0140 *Tel:* 303-750-8374 *Fax:* 303-337-0952 *E-mail:* daviesgroup@msn.com, pg 76

Davies Publishing Inc, 32 S Raymond Ave, Pasadena, CA 91105-1935 *Tel:* 626-792-3046 *Toll Free Tel:* 877-792-0005 *Fax:* 626-792-5308 *E-mail:* daviescorp@aol.com *Web Site:* www.daviespublishing.com, pg 76

F A Davis Co, 1915 Arch St, Philadelphia, PA 19103 *Tel:* 215-568-2270 *Toll Free Tel:* 800-523-4049 *Fax:* 215-568-5065 *E-mail:* info@fadavis.com *Web Site:* www.fadavis.com, pg 76

Watson Davis & Helen Miles Davis Prize, University of Florida, 3310 Turlington Hall, Gainesville, FL 32611 *Tel:* 352-392-1677 *E-mail:* info@hssonline.org *Web Site:* www.hssonline.org, pg 769

Winifred M Davis, 1700 York Ave, Suite 9-L, New York, NY 10128 *Tel:* 212-534-0034, pg 596

DAW Books Inc, 375 Hudson St, 3rd fl, New York, NY 10014 *Tel:* 212-366-2096 *Fax:* 212-366-2090 *E-mail:* daw@us.penguingroup.com *Web Site:* www.dawbooks.com, pg 77

Dawbert Press Inc, PO Box 67, Duxbury, MA 02331 *Tel:* 781-934-7202 *Toll Free Tel:* 800-933-2923 *Fax:* 781-934-2945 *E-mail:* info@dawbert.com *Web Site:* www.dawbert.com; www.familiesonthego.com; www.petsonthego.com, pg 77

The Dawn Horse Press, 12040 N Seigler Rd, Middletown, CA 95461 *Tel:* 707-928-6590 *Toll Free Tel:* 877-770-0772 *Fax:* 707-928-5068 *E-mail:* dhp@adidam.org *Web Site:* www.dawnhorsepress.com, pg 77

Dawn Publications Inc, 12402 Bitney Springs Rd, Nevada City, CA 95959 *Tel:* 530-274-7775 *Toll Free Tel:* 800-545-7475 *Fax:* 530-274-7778 *E-mail:* nature@dawnpub.com *Web Site:* www.dawnpub.com, pg 77

DawnSignPress, 6130 Nancy Ridge Dr, San Diego, CA 92121-3223 *Tel:* 858-625-0600 *Toll Free Tel:* 800-549-5350 *Fax:* 858-625-2336 *E-mail:* info@dawnsign.com *Web Site:* www.dawnsign.com, pg 77

Liza Dawson Associates, 240 W 35 St, Suite 500, New York, NY 10001 *Tel:* 212-465-9071, pg 626

Dayton Playhouse FutureFest Inc, 1301 E Siebenthaler Ave, Dayton, OH 45414 *Tel:* 937-333-7469 *Fax:* 937-333-2827 *E-mail:* futurefest@daytonplayhouse.com *Web Site:* www.daytonplayhouse.com, pg 769

Scottie Dayton, 1112 Division St, Manitowoc, WI 54220-5733 *Tel:* 920-684-5228 *Fax:* 920-686-0820 (call first) *E-mail:* sdayton@lakefield.net, pg 596

DBI Books, 700 E State St, Iola, WI 54990-0001 *Tel:* 715-445-2214 *Toll Free Tel:* 888-457-2873 *Fax:* 715-445-4087 *Web Site:* www.krause.com, pg 77

dbS Productions, University Sta, Charlottesville, VA 22903 *Tel:* 434-293-5502 *Toll Free Tel:* 800-745-1581 *Fax:* 434-293-5502 *E-mail:* info@dbs-sar.com *Web Site:* www.dbs-sar.com, pg 77

DC Comics, 1700 Broadway, New York, NY 10019 *Tel:* 212-636-5400 *Toll Free Tel:* 800-759-0190 (distribution) *Fax:* 212-636-5481 *Web Site:* www.dccomics.com; www.madmag.com, pg 77

DC Press, 2445 River Tree, Sanford, FL 32771 *Tel:* 407-688-1156 *Toll Free Tel:* 866-602-1476 *Fax:* 407-688-1135 *E-mail:* info@focusonethics.com *Web Site:* www.focusonethics.com, pg 77

Walter de Gruyter, Inc, 500 Executive Blvd, Ossining, NY 10562 *Tel:* 914-762-5866 *Fax:* 914-762-0371 *E-mail:* info@degruyterny.com *Web Site:* www.degruyter.com, pg 78

The Lois de la Haba Agency Inc, 76-12 Grand Central Pkwy, Suite 4, New York, NY 11375 *Tel:* 718-544-2392 *Fax:* 718-544-2393 *E-mail:* habalit@aol.com, pg 627

De Vorss & Co, 553 Constitution Ave, Camarillo, CA 93012-8510 *Tel:* 805-322-9010 *Toll Free Tel:* 800-843-5743 *Fax:* 805-322-9011 *E-mail:* service@devorss.com *Web Site:* www.devorss.com, pg 78

Deadline Club, 15 Gramercy Park S, New York, NY 10003 *Tel:* 212-353-9598 *Fax:* 212-468-6360 *E-mail:* deadline@spj.org *Web Site:* www.pipeline.com/~deadline, pg 686

Dealer's Choice Books Inc, PO Box 710, Land O'Lakes, FL 34639 *Tel:* 813-996-6599 *Fax:* 813-996-5226 *E-mail:* order@dealerschoicebooks.com *Web Site:* www.dealerschoicebooks.com, pg 78

Dearborn Trade Publishing, 30 S Wacker Dr, Chicago, IL 60606-1719 *Tel:* 312-836-4400 *Fax:* 312-836-1021 *E-mail:* contactus@dearborn.com *Web Site:* www.dearborn.com, pg 78

The Angie Debo Prize, 1005 Asp Ave, Norman, OK 73019-6051 *Tel:* 405-325-2000 *Fax:* 405-325-4000 *Web Site:* www.oupress.com, pg 769

Decarie, Editeur Inc, 233 Ave Dunbar, Ville Mont-Royal, PQ H3P 2H4, Canada *Tel:* 514-342-8500 *Fax:* 514-342-3982 *E-mail:* info@decarieediteur.com *Web Site:* www.decarieediteur.com, pg 542

B C Decker Inc, 20 Hughson St S, 10th fl, Hamilton, ON L8N 2A1, Canada *Tel:* 905-522-7017 *Toll Free Tel:* 800-568-7281 *Fax:* 905-522-7839 *E-mail:* info@bcdecker.com *Web Site:* www.bcdecker.com, pg 542

Ivan R Dee Publisher, 1332 N Halsted St, Chicago, IL 60622-2694 *Tel:* 312-787-6262 *Toll Free Tel:* 800-462-6420 (orders) *Fax:* 312-787-6269 *Toll Free Fax:* 800-338-4550 (orders) *E-mail:* elephant@ivanrdee.com *Web Site:* www.ivanrdee.com, pg 78

Deep South Writers Festival, University of Louisiana at Lafayette, 104 University Circle, Lafayette, LA 70504 *Tel:* 337-482-5478 (Direct), pg 769

Definition Press, 141 Greene St, New York, NY 10012 *Tel:* 212-777-4490 *Fax:* 212-777-4426 *E-mail:* mc@definitionpress.org *Web Site:* www.definitionpress.org, pg 570

DeFiore & Co, Author Services, 72 Spring St, Suite 304, New York, NY 10012 *Tel:* 212-925-7744 *Fax:* 212-925-9803 *E-mail:* submissions@defioreandco.com *Web Site:* defioreandco.com, pg 627

Marcel Dekker Inc, 270 Madison Ave, New York, NY 10016 *Tel:* 212-696-9000 *Toll Free Tel:* 800-228-1160 (outside NY) *Fax:* 212-685-4540 *Web Site:* www.dekker.com, pg 78

Del Rey Books, 1745 Broadway, New York, NY 10019 *E-mail:* delrey@randomhouse.com *Web Site:* www.randomhouse.com, pg 78

Delacorte Dell Yearling Contest for a First Middle-Grade Novel, 1745 Broadway, New York, NY 10019 *Tel:* 212-782-9000 *Fax:* 212-782-9452 *Web Site:* www.randomhouse.com/kids, pg 769

Delacorte Press Prize for a First Young Adult Novel, 1745 Broadway, 9th fl, New York, NY 10019 *Tel:* 212-782-9000 *Fax:* 212-782-9452 *Web Site:* www.randomhouse.com/kids, pg 769

Delaware Division of the Arts Individual Artist Fellowships, 820 N French St, Wilmington, DE 19801 *Tel:* 302-577-8278 *Fax:* 302-577-6561 *Web Site:* www.artsdel.org, pg 769

Joelle Delbourgo Associates, Inc Literary Management, 450 Seventh Ave, Suite 3004, New York, NY 10123 *Tel:* 212-279-9027 *Fax:* 212-279-8863 *E-mail:* info@delbourgo.com (queries) *Web Site:* www.delbourgo.com/about.htm, pg 627

Delirium Books, PO Box 338, North Webster, IN 46555 *Tel:* 574-594-3200 *Web Site:* www.deliriumbooks.com, pg 78

Delorme Publishing Co Inc, 2 Delorme Dr, Yarmouth, ME 04096 *Tel:* 207-846-7000 *Fax:* 207-846-7051 *E-mail:* reseller@delorme.com *Web Site:* www.delorme.com, pg 79

Delta Systems Co Inc, 1400 Miller Pkwy, McHenry, IL 60050-7030 *Tel:* 815-363-3582 *Toll Free Tel:* 800-323-8270 *Fax:* 815-363-2948 *Toll Free Fax:* 800-909-9901 *E-mail:* custsvc@delta-systems.com *Web Site:* www.delta-systems.com, pg 79

Demery Publishing, 20600 Eureka, Suite 900, Taylor, MI 48180 *Tel:* 734-671-1275 *Fax:* 734-671-0107 *Web Site:* www.demerypub.com, pg 570

Demos Medical Publishing LLC, 386 Park Ave S, Suite 201, New York, NY 10016 *Tel:* 212-683-0072 *Toll Free Tel:* 800-532-8663 *Fax:* 212-683-0118 *E-mail:* info@demospub.com *Web Site:* www.demosmedpub.com, pg 79

The Denali Press, PO Box 021535, Juneau, AK 99802-1535 *Tel:* 907-586-6014 *Fax:* 907-463-6780 *E-mail:* denalipress@alaska.com *Web Site:* www.denalipress.com, pg 79

Ellen F Denison Literary Agent, PO Box 129, Concord, MA 01742-0129 *Tel:* 978-371-1716 *Fax:* 978-371-2567, pg 627

Denlinger's Publishers Ltd, PO Box 1030, Edgewater, FL 32132-1030 *Tel:* 386-424-1737 *Toll Free Tel:* 800-362-1810 *Fax:* 386-428-3534 *Toll Free Fax:* 800-589-1191 *E-mail:* editor@thebookden.com *Web Site:* www.thebookden.com, pg 78

Der-Hovanessian Translation Prize, 16 Cornell St, Arlington, MA 02474 *Web Site:* www.nepoetryclub.org, pg 769

Derringer Award, 1120 N 45 St, Waco, TX 76710 *Web Site:* groups.yahoo.com/group/shortmystery; www.shortmystery.net, pg 769

Deseret Book Co, 40 E South Temple, Salt Lake City, UT 84111 *Tel:* 801-534-1515 *Toll Free Tel:* 800-453-3876 *Fax:* 801-517-3199 *E-mail:* wholesale@deseretbook.com *Web Site:* www.deseretbook.com, pg 79

Desert Writers Workshop, PO Box 68, Moab, UT 84532 *Tel:* 435-259-7750 *Toll Free Tel:* 800-860-5262 *Fax:* 435-259-2335 *E-mail:* info@canyonlandsfields. com *Web Site:* www.canyonlandsfieldinst.com, pg 743

Design Image Group, 231 S Frontage Rd, Suite 17, Burr Ridge, IL 60527 *Tel:* 630-789-8991 *Toll Free Tel:* 800-563-5455 *Fax:* 630-789-9013 *E-mail:* dig@designimagegroup.com *Web Site:* www. designimagegroup.com, pg 79

Destiny Image, 167 Walnut Bottom Rd, Shippensburg, PA 17257-0310 *Tel:* 717-532-3040 *Toll Free Tel:* 800-722-6774 (orders only) *Fax:* 717-532-9291 *E-mail:* gates@destinyimage.com *Web Site:* www. destinyimage.com, pg 79

Detselig Enterprises Ltd, 210, 1220 Kensington Rd NW, Calgary, AB T2N 3P5, Canada *Tel:* 403-283-0900 *Fax:* 403-283-6947 *E-mail:* temeron@telusplanet.net *Web Site:* www.temerondetselig.com, pg 542

Developmental Studies Center, 2000 Embarcadero, Suite 305, Oakland, CA 94606-5300 *Tel:* 510-533-0213 *Toll Free Tel:* 800-666-7270 *Fax:* 510-842-0348 *E-mail:* pubs@devstu.org *Web Site:* www.devstu.org, pg 79

Devonshire House Books, 4435 Holly Lane NW, Gig Harbor, WA 98335 *Tel:* 253-851-9896 *Fax:* 253-851-9897 *Web Site:* critiquemaster.com, pg 596

J Franklin Dew Award, 100 N Berwick, Williamsburg, VA 23188 *Tel:* 757-258-5582 *Web Site:* www. poetrysocietyofvirginia.org, pg 769

Marilyn Dewey Literary Management, Dewey-Hannah House, 191 Packers Falls Rd, Durham, NH 03824 *Tel:* 603-659-5500 *Fax:* 603-659-4155 *E-mail:* dewmarh@aol.com, pg 627

Dewey Publications Inc, 2009 N 14 St, Suite 705, Arlington, VA 22201 *Tel:* 703-524-1355 *Fax:* 703-524-1463 *E-mail:* info@deweypub.com *Web Site:* www. deweypub.com, pg 79

DH Literary Inc, PO Box 990, Nyack, NY 10960 *Tel:* 212-753-7942 *E-mail:* dhendin@aol.com, pg 627

Dharma Publishing, 2910 San Pablo Ave, Berkeley, CA 94702 *Tel:* 510-548-5407 *Toll Free Tel:* 800-873-4276 *Fax:* 510-548-2230 *E-mail:* info@dharmapublishing. com *Web Site:* www.dharmapublishing.com, pg 79

DHS Literary Inc, 10711 Preston Rd, Suite 100, Dallas, TX 75230 *Tel:* 214-363-4422 *Fax:* 214-363-4423 *E-mail:* submissions@dhsliterary.com *Web Site:* www. dhsliterary.com, pg 627

Alice Fay Di Castagnola Award, 15 Gramercy Park, New York, NY 10003 *Tel:* 212-254-9628 *Fax:* 212-673-2352 *Web Site:* www.poetrysociety.org, pg 770

Diablo Press Inc, 3381-A Vincent Rd, Pleasant Hill, CA 94523-4310 *Toll Free Tel:* 800-488-2665 (orders only) *Fax:* 510-653-5310 *E-mail:* info@diablopress.com; diablo1@concentric.net *Web Site:* www.diablopress. com, pg 80

Dial Books for Young Readers, 345 Hudson St, New York, NY 10014 *Tel:* 212-366-2000 *Fax:* 212-414-3396 *E-mail:* online@penguinputnam.com *Web Site:* www.penguinusa.com, pg 80

Diamond Farm Book Publishers, Bailey Settlement Rd, Alexandria Bay, NY 13607 *Tel:* 613-475-1771 *Toll Free Tel:* 800-481-1353 *Fax:* 613-475-3748 *Toll Free Fax:* 800-305-5138 *E-mail:* info@diamondfarm.com *Web Site:* www.diamondfarm.com, pg 80

Diamond Literary Agency Inc, 3063 S Kearney St, Denver, CO 80222 *Tel:* 303-753-6318 *E-mail:* diamondliteraryagency@yahoo.com, pg 627

Paula Diamond Agency, 60 Gramercy Park N, New York, NY 10010 *Tel:* 212-475-0549 *E-mail:* pdnyc2@ aol.com, pg 627

Diamond Publishers, 29260 Franklin Rd, Southfield, MI 48034 *Tel:* 248-353-2900 *Toll Free Tel:* 888-386-9688 *Fax:* 248-357-0102 *E-mail:* info@goinglikelynn.com *Web Site:* www.goinglikelynn.com, pg 571

DIANE Publishing Co, 330 Pusey Ave, Suite 3 rear, Collingdale, PA 19023 *Tel:* 610-461-6200 *Toll Free Tel:* 800-782-3833 *Fax:* 610-461-6130 *E-mail:* dianepub@comcast.net *Web Site:* www. dianepublishingcentral.com, pg 80

D4EO Literary Agency, 7 Indian Valley Rd, Weston, CT 06883 *Tel:* 203-544-7180; 203-545-7180 (cell phone) *Fax:* 203-544-7160 *E-mail:* d4eo@optionline.net *Web Site:* www.publishersmarketplace.com/members/ d4eo, pg 627

Digital Printing & Imaging Association, 10015 Main St, Fairfax, VA 22031-3489 *Tel:* 703-385-1339 *Toll Free Tel:* 888-385-3588 *Fax:* 703-273-0456 *E-mail:* dpi@ dpia.org *Web Site:* www.dpia.org, pg 686

Sandra Dijkstra Literary Agency, 1155 Camino del Mar, PMB 515, Del Mar, CA 92014-2605 *Tel:* 858-755-3115 *Fax:* 858-794-2822 *E-mail:* sdla@dijkstraagency. com, pg 627

May Dikeman, 70 Irving Place, New York, NY 10003 *Tel:* 212-475-4533, pg 596

Gordon W Dillon/Richard C Peterson Memorial Essay Prize, 16700 AOS Lane, Delray Beach, FL 33446 *Tel:* 561-404-2043 *Fax:* 561-404-2045 *E-mail:* theaos@aos.org *Web Site:* www.orchidweb. org, pg 770

Christina DiMartino Literary Services, 59 W 119 St, Suite 2, New York City, NY 10026 *Tel:* 212-996-9086; 917-972-6012 *E-mail:* writealot@earthlink.net, pg 596

Dimension Books Inc, PO Box 9, Starrucca, PA 18462 *Tel:* 570-727-2486 *Fax:* 570-727-2813, pg 80

Dimension Creative, 1500 McAndrews Rd W, Suite 217, Burnsville, MN 55337 *Tel:* 952-201-3981 *Fax:* 952-892-1722 *Web Site:* www.dimensioncreative.com, pg 665

Dine College Press, Dine College, Tsaile, AZ 86556 *Tel:* 928-724-6635 *Fax:* 928-724-6637 *Web Site:* www. dinecollege.edu, pg 80

The Direct Marketing Association Inc (The DMA), 1120 Avenue of the Americas, New York, NY 10036-6700 *Tel:* 212-768-7277 *Fax:* 212-768-4547 *E-mail:* dma@the-dma.org; customerservice@the-dma.org *Web Site:* www.the-dma.org, pg 80

The Direct Marketing Association Inc (The DMA), 1120 Avenue of the Americas, New York, NY 10036-6700 *Tel:* 212-768-7277 *Fax:* 212-768-4547 *E-mail:* dma@ the-dma.org *Web Site:* www.the-dma.org, pg 686

Discipleship Publications International (DPI), 2 Sterling Rd, Billerica, MA 01862-2595 *Tel:* 978-670-8840 *Toll Free Tel:* 888-DPI-Book *Fax:* 978-670-8485 *E-mail:* dpibooks@icoc.org *Web Site:* www.dpibooks. org, pg 80

DiscoverGuides, 631 N Stephanie St, No 138, Henderson, NV 89014 *Tel:* 702-407-8777 *Fax:* 209-532-2699 *E-mail:* discoverguides@earthlink.net, pg 80

Discovery Enterprises Ltd, 31 Laurelwood Dr, Carlisle, MA 01741 *Tel:* 978-287-5401 *Toll Free Tel:* 800-729-1720 *Fax:* 978-287-5402 *E-mail:* ushistorydocs@aol. com *Web Site:* www.ushistorydocs.com, pg 80

Discovery House Publishers, 3000 Kraft SE, Grand Rapids, MI 49512 *Tel:* 616-942-9218; 616-974-2210 (cust serv) *Toll Free Tel:* 800-653-8333 *Fax:* 616-957-5741 *E-mail:* dhp@rbc.org *Web Site:* www.gospelcom. net/rbc/dhp/; www.rbc.net, pg 80

Discovery/The Nation Poetry Contest, 92 St YM-YWHA, 1395 Lexington Ave, New York, NY 10128 *Tel:* 212-415-5759 *Web Site:* www.92y.org, pg 770

Disilgold Publishing Inc, 2739 Mickle Ave, Bronx, NY 10469 *Tel:* 917-757-1658 *Fax:* 718-547-0499 *E-mail:* disilgold@aol.com *Web Site:* www.disilgold. com, pg 571

Diskant & Associates, 116 E De La Guerra St, Suite 9, Santa Barbara, CA 93101 *Tel:* 805-962-2961, pg 628

Disney Press, 114 Fifth Ave, New York, NY 10011 *Tel:* 212-633-4400 *Fax:* 212-807-5432 *Web Site:* www. disney.go.com, pg 81

Disney Publishing Worldwide, 500 S Buena Vista, Burbank, CA 91521 *Tel:* 212-633-4400 *Fax:* 212-633-4833 *Web Site:* www.disney.go.com/disneybooks, pg 81

Dissertation.com, 23331 Water Circle, Boca Raton, FL 33486-8540 *Tel:* 561-750-4344 *Toll Free Tel:* 800-636-8329 *Fax:* 561-750-6797 *E-mail:* publisher4@ dissertation.com; orders4@dissertation.com *Web Site:* www.dissertation.com, pg 81

Distinguished Scholarly Publication Award, 1307 New York Ave NW, Suite 700, Washington, DC 20005 *Tel:* 202-383-9005 *Fax:* 202-638-0882 *E-mail:* governance@asanet.org *Web Site:* www.asanet. org, pg 770

Diverse Talent Group, 1875 Century Park E, Suite 2250, Los Angeles, CA 90067 *Tel:* 310-201-6565 *Fax:* 310-201-6572, pg 628

Dixon Price Publishing, 9105 Leprechaun Lane, Kingston, WA 98346 *Tel:* 360-297-8702 *Fax:* 360-297-1620 *E-mail:* info@dixonprice.com *Web Site:* www.dixonprice.com, pg 81

Dixon Ryan Fox Manuscript Prize, Lake Rd, Cooperstown, NY 13326 *Tel:* 607-547-1491 *Fax:* 607-547-1405 *E-mail:* hennessy10@hotmail.com, pg 770

DK Publishing Inc, 375 Hudson St, 2nd fl, New York, NY 10014-3672 *Tel:* 212-213-4800 *Toll Free Tel:* 877-342-5357 (cust serv) *Fax:* 212-213-5202 *Web Site:* www.dk.com, pg 81

DK Research Inc, 14 Mohegan Lane, Commack, NY 11725 *Tel:* 631-543-5537 *Fax:* 631-543-5549, pg 596

Do It Now Foundation, 2750 S Hardy Dr, Suite 2, Tempe, AZ 85282 *Tel:* 480-736-0599 *Fax:* 480-736-0771 *E-mail:* doitnow@quest.net *Web Site:* www. doitnow.org, pg 81

Do-It-Yourself Legal Publishers, 60 Park Place, Suite 1013, Newark, NJ 07102 *Tel:* 973-639-0400 *Fax:* 973-639-1801 *E-mail:* selfhelp1@yahoo.com, pg 81

Dobie-Paisano Fellowship Project, 702 E Dean Keeton St, Austin, TX 78705 *Tel:* 512-471-8542 *Fax:* 512-471-9997 *Web Site:* www.utexas.edu/ogs/Paisano, pg 770

Doctoral Dissertation Fellowship, 50 E Huron St, Chicago, IL 60611 *Tel:* 312-280-2514 *Toll Free Tel:* 800-545-2433 (ext 2514) *Fax:* 312-280-2520 *Web Site:* www.ala.org/acrl, pg 770

Dog-Eared Publications, PO Box 620863, Middleton, WI 53562-0863 *Tel:* 608-831-1410 *Toll Free Tel:* 888-364-3277 *Fax:* 608-831-1410 *Toll Free Fax:* 888-364-3277 *Web Site:* www.dog-eared.com, pg 81

Dog Writers' Association of America Inc (DWAA), 173 Union Rd, Coatesville, PA 19320 *Tel:* 610-384-2436 *Fax:* 610-384-2471 *E-mail:* dwaa@dwaa.org *Web Site:* www.dwaa.org, pg 686

Dog Writers' Association of America Inc (DWAA) Annual Awards, 173 Union Rd, Coatesville, PA 19320 *Tel:* 610-384-2436 *Fax:* 610-384-2471 *E-mail:* dwaa@ dwaa.org; rhydowen@aol.com *Web Site:* www.dwaa. org, pg 770

Dogwood Press, HC 53 Box 345, Hemphill, TX 75948-0345 *Tel:* 409-579-2184 *Fax:* 409-579-2184 *Web Site:* dogwoodpress.myriad.net/, pg 81

Tom Doherty Associates, LLC, 175 Fifth Ave, 14th fl, New York, NY 10010 *Tel:* 212-388-0100 *Toll Free Tel:* 800-455-0340 *Fax:* 212-388-0191 *E-mail:* firstname.lastname@tor.com *Web Site:* www. tor.com, pg 81

The Jonathan Dolger Agency, 49 E 96 St, Suite 9-B, New York, NY 10128 *Tel:* 212-427-1853 *Fax:* 212-369-7118, pg 628

Domhan Books, 9511 Shore Rd, Suite 514, Brooklyn, NY 11209 *Tel:* 718-680-4362 *Toll Free Fax:* 888-823-4770 *E-mail:* domhan@att.net *Web Site:* www. domhanbooks.com, pg 82

Dominie Press Inc, 1949 Kellogg Ave, Carlsbad, CA 92008 *Tel:* 760-431-8000 *Toll Free Tel:* 800-232-4570 *Fax:* 760-431-8777 *E-mail:* info@dominie.com *Web Site:* www.dominie.com, pg 82

Donadio & Olson Inc Literary Representatives, 121 W 27 St, Suite 704, New York, NY 10001 *Tel:* 212-691-8077 *Fax:* 212-633-2837 *E-mail:* mail@donadio.com, pg 628

Janis A Donnaud & Associates Inc, 525 Broadway, 2nd fl, New York, NY 10012 *Tel:* 212-431-2663 *Fax:* 212-431-2667 *E-mail:* JDonnaud@aol.com, pg 628

The Donning Co/Publishers, 184 Business Park Dr, Suite 206, Virginia Beach, VA 23462 *Tel:* 757-497-1789; 660-376-3543 (Missouri office) *Toll Free Tel:* 800-296-8572 *Fax:* 757-497-2542 *Web Site:* www.donning. com, pg 82

Jim Donovan Literary, 4515 Prentice, Suite 109, Dallas, TX 75206 *Tel:* 214-696-9411 *Fax:* 214-696-9412, pg 628

Dorchester Publishing Co Inc, 200 Madison Ave, Suite 2000, New York, NY 10016 *Tel:* 212-725-8811 *Toll Free Tel:* 800-481-9191 (order dept) *Fax:* 212-532-1054 *E-mail:* dorchedits@dorchesterpub.com *Web Site:* www.dorchesterpub.com, pg 82

Dordt College Press, 498 Fourth Ave NE, Sioux Center, IA 51250 *Tel:* 712-722-6420 *Fax:* 712-722-1185 *E-mail:* dordtpress@dordt.edu *Web Site:* www.dordt. edu/dordt_press, pg 82

The Dorese Agency Ltd, 37965 Palo Verde Dr, Cathedral City, CA 92234 *Tel:* 760-321-1115 *Fax:* 760-321-1049 *Web Site:* www.doreseagency.com, pg 628

Dorland Healthcare Information, 1500 Walnut St, Suite 1000, Philadelphia, PA 19102 *Tel:* 215-875-1212 *Toll Free Tel:* 800-784-2332 *Fax:* 215-735-3966 *E-mail:* info@dorlandhealth.com *Web Site:* www. dorlandhealth.com, pg 82

Dorset House Publishing Co Inc, 353 W 12 St, New York, NY 10014 *Tel:* 212-620-4053 *Toll Free Tel:* 800-DHBOOKS (342-6657 orders only) *Fax:* 212-727-1044 *E-mail:* info@dorsethouse.com; dhpubco@aol.com *Web Site:* www.dorsethouse.com, pg 82

John Dos Passos Prize for Literature, Dept of English & Modern Languages, 201 High St, Farmville, VA 23909 *Tel:* 434-395-2155 *Fax:* 434-395-2145, pg 770

Double Dragon Publishing Inc, 1-5762 Hwy 7 E, Markham, ON L3P 7Y4, Canada *Tel:* 905-994-4514 *E-mail:* info@double-dragon-ebooks.com *Web Site:* www.double-dragon-ebooks.com, pg 542

Double Play, PO Box 22481, Kansas City, MO 64113 *Tel:* 816-651-7118 *Fax:* 816-822-2521, pg 596

Doubleday Broadway Publishing Group, 1745 Broadway, New York, NY 10019 *Tel:* 212-782-9000 *Toll Free Tel:* 800-223-6834; 800-223-5780 (sales) *Fax:* 212-302-7985 (correspondence); 212-492-9862 (orders), pg 82

Doubleday Canada, One Toronto St, Suite 300, Toronto, ON M5C 2V6, Canada *Tel:* 416-364-4449 *Fax:* 416-957-1587 *Web Site:* www.randomhouse.ca, pg 542

Douglas & McIntyre Publishing Group, 2323 Quebec St, Suite 201, Vancouver, BC V5T 4S7, Canada *Tel:* 604-254-7191 *Toll Free Tel:* 800-565-9523 (orders in Canada) *Fax:* 604-254-9099 *Toll Free Fax:* 800-221-9985 (orders in Canada) *E-mail:* dm@douglas-mcintyre.com *Web Site:* www.douglas-mcintyre.com, pg 542

Douglas Publications Inc, 2807 N Parham Rd, Suite 200, Richmond, VA 23294 *Tel:* 804-762-4455 *Toll Free Tel:* 800-223-1797 *Fax:* 804-935-0271 *E-mail:* info@douglaspublications.com *Web Site:* www.douglaspublications.com, pg 83

Dovehouse Editions Inc, 1890 Fairmeadow Crescent, Ottawa, ON K1H 7B9, Canada *Tel:* 613-731-7601 *Fax:* 613-731-7601 *Web Site:* www.dovehouse.ca, pg 542

Dover Publications Inc, 31 E Second St, Mineola, NY 11501 *Tel:* 516-294-7000 *Toll Free Tel:* 800-223-3130 (orders) *Fax:* 516-742-6953; 516-742-5049 (orders) *Web Site:* www.doverpublications.com; www. doverdirect.com, pg 83

Alden B Dow Creativity Center Fellowship Award, Alden B Dow Creativity Center, 4000 Whiting Dr, Midland, MI 48640-2398 *Tel:* 989-837-4478 *Fax:* 989-837-4468 *E-mail:* creativity@northwood.edu *Web Site:* www.northwood.edu/abd, pg 770

Down East Books, PO Box 679, Camden, ME 04843 *Tel:* 207-594-9544 *Toll Free Tel:* 800-766-1670 (ME only) *Fax:* 207-594-7215 *Web Site:* www. downeastbooks.com, pg 83

Down The Shore Publishing Corp, 638 Teal St, Cedar Run, NJ 08092 *Tel:* 609-978-1233 *Fax:* 609-597-0422 *E-mail:* shore@att.net *Web Site:* www.down-the-shore. com, pg 83

Down There Press, 938 Howard St, Suite 101, San Francisco, CA 94103 *Tel:* 415-974-8985 *Fax:* 415-974-8989 *E-mail:* downtherepress@excite.com *Web Site:* www.goodvibes.com/dtp/dtp.html, pg 83

Violet Downey Book Award, 40 Orchard View Blvd, Suite 254, Toronto, ON M4R 1B9, Canada *Tel:* 416-487-4416 *Fax:* 416-487-4417 *E-mail:* iode@bellnet.ca *Web Site:* www.iode.ca, pg 770

Doyen Literary Services Inc, 1931 660 St, Newell, IA 50568 *Tel:* 712-272-3300, pg 628

Dragon Moon Press, PO Box 64312, Calgary, AB T2K 6J7, Canada *Tel:* 403-277-2140 *Fax:* 403-277-3679 *E-mail:* publisher@dragonmoonpress.com *Web Site:* www.dragonmoonpress.com, pg 543

Drainie-Taylor Biography Prize, 90 Richmond St W, Suite 200, Toronto, ON M5C 1P1, Canada *Tel:* 416-504-8222 *Fax:* 416-504-9090 *E-mail:* info@writerstrust.com *Web Site:* www.writerstrust.com, pg 770

Dramaline® Publications, 36-851 Palm View Rd, Rancho Mirage, CA 92270-2417 *Tel:* 760-770-6076 *Fax:* 760-770-4507 *E-mail:* drama.line@verizon.net *Web Site:* dramaline.com, pg 83

Dramatic Publishing Co, 311 Washington St, Woodstock, IL 60098 *Tel:* 815-338-7170 *Toll Free Tel:* 800-448-7469 *Fax:* 815-338-8981 *Toll Free Fax:* 800-334-5302 *E-mail:* plays@dramaticpublishing.com *Web Site:* www.dramaticpublishing.com, pg 83

Dramatists Play Service Inc, 440 Park Ave S, New York, NY 10016 *Tel:* 212-683-8960 *Fax:* 212-213-1539 *E-mail:* postmaster@dramatists.com *Web Site:* www. dramatists.com, pg 83

Drennan Communications, 6 Robin Lane, East Kingston, NH 03827 *Tel:* 603-642-8002 *Fax:* 603-642-8002, pg 596

Drennan Literary Agency, 6 Robin Lane, East Kingston, NH 03827 *Tel:* 603-642-8002 *Fax:* 603-642-8002, pg 628

Katharine Drexel Award, 100 North St, Suite 224, Pittsfield, MA 01201-5109 *Tel:* 413-443-2252 *Fax:* 413-442-2252 *E-mail:* cla@cathla.org *Web Site:* www.cathla.org, pg 771

Drummond Books, 2111 Cleveland St, Evanston, IL 60202 *Tel:* 847-869-5305, pg 596

The Drummond Publishing Group, 362 N Bedford St, East Bridgewater, MA 02333 *Tel:* 508-378-1110 *Fax:* 508-378-1105 *Web Site:* www.drummondpub. com, pg 84

Drury University One Act Play Competition, 900 N Benton Ave, Springfield, MO 65802-3344 *Tel:* 417-873-7430, pg 771

Dry Bones Press Inc, PO Box 597, Roseville, CA 95678 *Tel:* 916-435-8355 *Fax:* 916-435-8355 *E-mail:* drybones@drybones.com *Web Site:* www. drybones.com, pg 84

Paul Dry Books, 117 S 17 St, Suite 1102, Philadelphia, PA 19103 *Tel:* 215-231-9939 *Fax:* 215-231-9942 *E-mail:* editor@pauldrybooks.com *Web Site:* www. pauldrybooks.com, pg 84

Dubuque Fine Arts Players, 1686 Lawndale St, Dubuque, IA 52001 *Tel:* 563-582-5502, pg 771

Mary Duerson, 5234 Texas Circle, Ames, IA 50014 *Tel:* 515-292-5918 *E-mail:* mduerson@mail.isunet.net, pg 596

Dufour Editions Inc, PO Box 7, Chester Springs, PA 19425-0007 *Tel:* 610-458-5005 *Toll Free Tel:* 800-869-5677 *Fax:* 610-458-7103 *E-mail:* info@dufoureditions. com *Web Site:* www.dufoureditions.com, pg 84

Moira Duggan Editorial Services, 113A The Hook Rd, Bedford, NY 10506-1110 *Tel:* 914-234-7937 *Fax:* 914-234-7937 *E-mail:* mduggan@bestweb.net *Web Site:* www.consulting-editors.com, pg 596

Duke University Press, 905 W Main St, Suite 18-B, Durham, NC 27701 *Tel:* 919-687-3600 *Toll Free Tel:* 888-651-0122 (orders only) *Fax:* 919-688-4574 *Toll Free Fax:* 888-651-0124 *Web Site:* www. dukepress.edu, pg 84

Duke University Writers' Workshop, PO Box 90700, Durham, NC 27708-0700 *Tel:* 919-684-6259 *Fax:* 919-681-8235 *E-mail:* learnmore@duke.edu *Web Site:* www.learnmore.duke.edu, pg 743

Dumbarton Oaks, 1703 32 St NW, Washington, DC 20007 *Tel:* 202-777-0091 *Fax:* 202-339-6419 *E-mail:* publications@doaks.org *Web Site:* www.doaks. org, pg 84

Dun & Bradstreet, 103 JFK Pkwy, Short Hills, NJ 07078 *Tel:* 973-921-5500 *Toll Free Tel:* 800-526-0651 *E-mail:* custserv@dnb.com *Web Site:* www.dnb.com, pg 84

Dundurn Press Ltd, 8 Market St, 2nd fl, Toronto, ON M5E 1M6, Canada *Tel:* 416-214-5544 *Fax:* 416-214-5556 *E-mail:* info@dundurn.com *Web Site:* www. dundurn.com, pg 543

Dunham Literary Inc, 156 Fifth Ave, Suite 625, New York, NY 10010-7002 *Tel:* 212-929-0994 *Fax:* 212-929-0904 *E-mail:* dunhamlit@yahoo.com *Web Site:* www.dunhamlit.com, pg 628

Dunhill Publishing, 18340 Sonoma Hwy, Sonoma, CA 95476 *Tel:* 707-939-0562 *Fax:* 707-938-3515 *E-mail:* dunhill@vom.com *Web Site:* www. dunhillpublishing.net, pg 84

John H Dunning Prize in American History, 400 "A" St SE, Washington, DC 20003 *Tel:* 202-544-2422 *Fax:* 202-544-8307 *E-mail:* info@historians.org *Web Site:* www.historians.org, pg 771

Dunow & Carlson Literary Agency Inc, 27 W 20 St, Suite 1003, New York, NY 10011 *Tel:* 212-645-7606 *Fax:* 212-645-7614 *E-mail:* mail@dunowcarlson.com, pg 628

Dunwoody Press, 6564 Loisdale Ct, Suite 800, Springfield, VA 22150 *Tel:* 703-921-1600 *Fax:* 703-921-1610 *E-mail:* dpadmin@mcneiltech.com *Web Site:* www.dunwoodypress.com, pg 84

Dupree, Miller & Associates Inc, 100 Highland Park Village, Suite 350, Dallas, TX 75205 *Tel:* 214-559-2665 *Fax:* 214-559-7243 *E-mail:* dmabook@aol.com, pg 628

Duquesne University Press, 600 Forbes Ave, Pittsburgh, PA 15282 *Tel:* 412-396-6610 *Toll Free Tel:* 800-666-2211 *Fax:* 412-396-5984 *Web Site:* www.dupress.duq. edu, pg 84

Sanford J Durst, 11 Clinton Ave, Rockville Centre, NY 11570 *Tel:* 516-766-4444 *Fax:* 516-766-4520 *E-mail:* sanfordjdurst@aol.com, pg 85

Dustbooks, PO Box 100, Paradise, CA 95967-0222 *Tel:* 530-877-6110 *Toll Free Tel:* 800-477-6110 *Fax:* 530-877-0222 *E-mail:* publisher@dustbooks.com *Web Site:* www.dustbooks.com, pg 85

Dutton, 375 Hudson St, New York, NY 10014 *Tel:* 212-366-2000 *Fax:* 212-366-2262 *E-mail:* online@ penguinputnam.com *Web Site:* www.penguin.com, pg 85

Dutton Children's Books, 345 Hudson St, New York, NY 10014 *Tel:* 212-366-2000 *E-mail:* online@ penguinputnam.com *Web Site:* www.penguin.com, pg 85

Dwyer & O'Grady Inc, 725 Third St, Cedar Key, FL 32625 *Tel:* 352-543-9307 *Fax:* 603-375-5373 *Web Site:* www.dwyerogrady.com, pg 628, 665

Dynamic Graphics Training, 6000 N Forest Park Dr, Peoria, IL 61614-3556 *Tel:* 309-687-0141 *Fax:* 309-688-8515 *Web Site:* www.dgusa.com, pg 752

Dynapress, PO Box 150217, Altamonte Springs, FL 32715-0217 *Tel:* 407-331-5550 *Fax:* 407-331-5550 (call first) *E-mail:* itsdifferent@dynapress.com *Web Site:* www.dynapress.com, pg 571

Dystel & Goderich Literary Management, One Union Sq W, Suite 904, New York, NY 10003 *Tel:* 212-627-9100 *Fax:* 212-627-9313 *Web Site:* www.dystel.com, pg 629

E & J Proofreading, 162 W Washington St, Hagerstown, MD 21740 *Tel:* 240-313-9250 *Fax:* 240-313-9250 *E-mail:* ejproofreading@yahoo.com, pg 596

E B P Latin America Group Inc, 175 E Delaware Place, Suite 8806, Chicago, IL 60611 *Tel:* 312-397-9590 *Fax:* 312-397-9593 *Web Site:* www.barsa.com, pg 85

E-Digital Books LLC, 1155 S Havana St, Suite 11, PMB 364, Aurora, CO 80012 *Tel:* 303-745-4997 *Fax:* 303-745-4997 *E-mail:* edigital@edigitalbooks.com *Web Site:* www.edigitalbooks.com, pg 85

e-Scholastic, 568 Broadway, 9th fl, New York, NY 10012 *Tel:* 212-343-7100 *Fax:* 212-343-4949, pg 85

E-Z Publications, 1932 Ambassador Dr, Windsor, ON N9C 3R5, Canada *Tel:* 519-250-5138; 519-972-3962 *Fax:* 519-972-5256; 519-250-6588 *E-mail:* ezpublications@hotmail.com *Web Site:* www.ezpublications.com, pg 543

Eagan Press, 3340 Pilot Knob Rd, St Paul, MN 55121-2097 *Tel:* 651-454-7250 *Toll Free Tel:* 800-328-7560 *Fax:* 651-454-0766 *E-mail:* aacc@scisoc.org *Web Site:* www.aaccnet.org, pg 85

Eagle Publishing Inc, One Massachusetts Ave NW, Washington, DC 20001 *Tel:* 202-216-0600 *Fax:* 202-216-0612 *Web Site:* www.regnery.com, pg 85

Eagle's View Publishing, 168W 12 St, Ogden, UT 84404 *Tel:* 801-393-4555; 801-745-0905 (edit) *Toll Free Tel:* 800-547-3364 (orders over $100) *Fax:* 801-745-0903 *E-mail:* eglcrafts@aol.com *Web Site:* eaglefeathertradingpost.com, pg 85

Eakin Press, 8800 Tara Lane, Austin, TX 78737 *Tel:* 512-288-1771 *Toll Free Tel:* 800-880-8642 *Fax:* 512-288-1813 *Web Site:* www.eakinpress.com, pg 85

Earth Edit, PO Box 114, Maiden Rock, WI 54750 *Tel:* 715-448-3009, pg 596

East Asian Legal Studies Program, 500 W Baltimore St, Baltimore, MD 21201-1786 *Tel:* 410-706-3870 *Fax:* 410-706-1516 *E-mail:* eastasia@law.umaryland.edu, pg 85

East End Publishing Services Inc, 916 Sound Shore Rd, Riverhead, NY 11901 *Tel:* 631-722-3921 *Fax:* 631-722-3921, pg 597

East Mountain Editing Services, PO Box 1895, Tijeras, NM 87059 *Tel:* 505-281-8422 *Fax:* 505-281-8422 *Web Site:* www.spanishindexing.com, pg 597

Eastern Washington University Press, Eastern Washington University, 705 W First Ave, Spokane, WA 99201 *Tel:* 509-623-4286 *Toll Free Tel:* 800-508-9095 *Fax:* 509-623-4283 *E-mail:* ewupress@ewu.edu *Web Site:* ewupress.ewu.edu, pg 86

Eastland Press, 3257 16 Ave W, Suite 2, Seattle, WA 98119 *Tel:* 206-217-0204 *Toll Free Tel:* 800-453-3278 (orders only) *Fax:* 206-217-0205 *Toll Free Fax:* 800-241-3329 (orders) *E-mail:* info@eastlandpress.com; orders@eastlandpress.com (orders-credit cards only) *Web Site:* www.eastlandpress.com, pg 86

Easy Money Press, 5419 87 St, Lubbock, TX 79424 *Tel:* 806-543-5215 *E-mail:* easymoneypress@yahoo.com, pg 86

Eaton Literary Associates Literary Awards, PO Box 49795, Sarasota, FL 34230-6795 *Tel:* 941-366-6589 *Fax:* 941-365-4679 *E-mail:* eatonlit@aol.com *Web Site:* www.eatonliterary.com, pg 771

Ebon Research Systems Publishing LLC, 812 Sweetwater Club Blvd, Longwood, FL 32779 *Tel:* 407-786-9200 *Fax:* 407-682-2384 *E-mail:* ebonrs@prodigy.net *Web Site:* ebonresearchsystems.com, pg 86

EcceNova Editions, 15-1594 Fairfield Rd, Victoria, BC V8S 1G1, Canada *Tel:* 250-595-8401 *Fax:* 250-595-8401 *E-mail:* info@eccenova.com *Web Site:* www.eccenova.com, pg 543

Eckankar, PO Box 27300, Minneapolis, MN 55427 *Tel:* 952-380-2200 *Toll Free Tel:* 866-485-5556 (CN orders); 888-408-0301 (US orders) *Fax:* 952-380-2395 *Toll Free Fax:* 866-485-6665 (CN orders) *E-mail:* eckbooks@eckankar.org *Web Site:* www.eckankar.org, pg 86

Eclipse Press, 3101 Beaumont Centre Circle, Lexington, KY 40513 *Tel:* 859-278-2361 *Toll Free Tel:* 800-866-2361 *Fax:* 859-276-6868 *E-mail:* editorial@eclipsepress.com; marketing@eclipsepress.com *Web Site:* www.eclipsepress.com, pg 86

Ecrits des Forges, 1497 La Violette, CP 335, Trois Rivieres, PQ G9A 1W5, Canada *Tel:* 819-379-9813 *Fax:* 819-376-0774 *E-mail:* ecrits.desforges@tr.cgocable.ca, pg 543

ECS Publishing, 138 Ipswich St, Boston, MA 02215 *Tel:* 617-236-1935 *Toll Free Tel:* 800-777-1919 *Fax:* 617-236-0261 *E-mail:* office@ecspub.com *Web Site:* www.ecspub.com, pg 86

ECW Press, 2120 Queen St E, Suite 200, Toronto, ON M4E 1E2, Canada *Tel:* 416-694-3348 *Fax:* 416-698-9906 *E-mail:* info@ecwpress.com *Web Site:* www.ecwpress.com, pg 543

EDC Publishing, 10302 E 55 Place, Tulsa, OK 74146-6515 *Tel:* 918-622-4522 *Toll Free Tel:* 800-475-4522 *Fax:* 918-665-7919 *Toll Free Fax:* 800-747-4509 *E-mail:* edc@edcpub.com *Web Site:* www.edcpub.com, pg 86

EDCO Publishing Inc, 2648 Lapeer Rd, Auburn Hills, MI 48326 *Tel:* 248-475-4678 *Toll Free Tel:* 888-510-3326 *Fax:* 248-475-9122 *E-mail:* info@edcopublishing.com *Web Site:* www.edcopublishing.com, pg 87

Edelsack Editorial Service, 201 Evergreen St, Vestal, NY 13850-2796 *Tel:* 607-797-1840 *Fax:* 607-729-1977 *E-mail:* pedelsack@aol.com, pg 597

Anne Edelstein Literary Agency, 20 W 22 St, Suite 1603, New York, NY 10010 *Tel:* 212-414-4923 *Fax:* 212-414-2930 *Web Site:* www.aeliterary.com, pg 629

Edelstein Prize, Iowa State University, 603 Ross Hall, History Dept, Ames, IA 50011 *Tel:* 515-294-8469 *Fax:* 515-294-6390 *E-mail:* shot@iastate.edu *Web Site:* www.shot.jhu.edu, pg 771

Eden Publishing, PO Box 20176, Keizer, OR 97307-0176 *Tel:* 503-390-9013 *Fax:* 503-390-9013 *E-mail:* info@edenpublishing.com *Web Site:* www.edenpublishing.com, pg 87

Edgar Allan Poe Awards®, 17 E 47 St, 6th fl, New York, NY 10017 *Tel:* 212-888-8171 *E-mail:* mwa@mysterywriters.org *Web Site:* www.mysterywriters.org, pg 771

Nellie Edge Resources Inc, PO Box 12399, Salem, OR 97309-0399 *Tel:* 503-399-0040 *Toll Free Tel:* 800-523-4594 *Fax:* 503-399-0435 *E-mail:* info@nellieedge.com *Web Site:* www.nellieedge.com, pg 87

EDGE Science Fiction & Fantasy Publishing, PO Box 1714, Sta M, Calgary, AB T2P 2L7, Canada *Tel:* 403-254-0160 *Toll Free Tel:* 877-254-0115 *Fax:* 403-254-0456 *E-mail:* publisher@hadespublications.com *Web Site:* www.edgewebsite.com, pg 543

Edgewise Press, 24 Fifth Ave, Suite 224, New York, NY 10011 *Tel:* 212-982-4818 *Fax:* 212-982-1364 *E-mail:* epinc@mindspring.com *Web Site:* www.edgewisepress.com, pg 87

Ediciones Universal, 3090 SW Eighth St, Miami, FL 33135 *Tel:* 305-642-3355 *Fax:* 305-642-7978 *E-mail:* ediciones@ediciones.com *Web Site:* www.ediciones.com, pg 87

Edimag, CP 325, Succ Rosemont, Montreal, PQ H1X 3B8, Canada *Tel:* 514-522-2244 *Fax:* 514-522-6301 *Web Site:* www.edimag.com, pg 543

EditAndPublishYourBook.com, PO Box 2965, Nantucket, MA 02584-2965 *E-mail:* michaeltheauthor@yahoo.com *Web Site:* www.editandpublishyourbook.com, pg 597

Edit Etc, 321 Hollywood Ave, Ho-Ho-Kus, NJ 07423 *Tel:* 201-251-4796 *Fax:* 201-251-4797 *E-mail:* atkedit@cs.com *Web Site:* anntkeene.com, pg 597

EditAmerica, 115 Jacobs Creek Rd, Ewing, NJ 08628 *Tel:* 609-882-5852 *Fax:* 609-882-5851 *E-mail:* editamerica@usa.com *Web Site:* www.editamerica.com, pg 597

editcetera, 2034 Blake St, Suite 5, Berkeley, CA 94704 *Tel:* 510-849-1110 *Fax:* 510-848-1448 *E-mail:* info@editcetera.com *Web Site:* www.editcetera.com, pg 597

Editing International LLC, 2123 Marlow Lane, Suite 21, Eugene, OR 97401-6431 *Tel:* 541-344-9118 *E-mail:* info@4-edit.com *Web Site:* www.4-edit.com, pg 597

Editions Anne Sigier Inc, 1073 Blvd of Rene Levesque W, Sillery, PQ G1S 4R5, Canada *Tel:* 418-687-6086 *Toll Free Tel:* 800-463-6846 (Canada only) *Fax:* 418-687-3565 *E-mail:* sigier@annesigier.qc.ca *Web Site:* www.annesigier.qc.ca, pg 543

Les Editions Brault et Bouthillier, 4823, rue Sherbrooke Ouest, bureau 275, Westmount, PQ H3Z 1G7, Canada *Tel:* 514-932-9466 *Toll Free Tel:* 800-668-1108 *Fax:* 514-932-5929 *E-mail:* editions@ebbp.ca, pg 543

editions CERES Ltd/Le Moyen Francais, CP 1657 Succ B, 1250 University, Montreal, PQ H3B 3L3, Canada *Tel:* 514-937-7138 *Fax:* 514-937-9875 *Web Site:* www.editionsceres.ca, pg 543

Editions de l'Hexagone, 1010, rue de la Gauchetiere Est, Montreal, PQ H2L 2N5, Canada *Tel:* 514-523-1182 *Fax:* 514-282-7530 *E-mail:* vml@sogides.com *Web Site:* www.edhexagone.com, pg 544

Editions de Mortagne, BP 116, Boucherville, PQ J4B 5E6, Canada *Tel:* 450-641-2387 *Fax:* 450-655-6092 *E-mail:* edm@editionsdemortagne.qc.ca, pg 544

Editions Marcel Didier Inc, 1815 Ave de Lorimier, Montreal, PQ H2K 3W6, Canada *Tel:* 514-523-1523 *Toll Free Tel:* 800-361-1664 (Canada) *Fax:* 514-523-9969 *E-mail:* hurtubisehmh@hurtubisehmh.com *Web Site:* www.hurtubisehmh.com, pg 544

Les Editions du Ble, 340 Provencher Blvd, St Boniface, MB R2H 0G7, Canada *Tel:* 204-237-8200 *Fax:* 204-233-8182 *E-mail:* trigo@mb.sympatico.ca, pg 544

Editions du Boreal Express, 4447 rue St Denis, Montreal, PQ H2J 2L2, Canada *Tel:* 514-287-7401 *Fax:* 514-287-7664 *E-mail:* boreal@editionsboreal.qc.ca *Web Site:* www.editionsboreal.qc.ca, pg 544

Editions du Meridien, 1980 Sherbrooke Ouest, No 540, Montreal, PQ H3H 1E8, Canada *Tel:* 514-935-0464 *Fax:* 514-935-0458 *E-mail:* info@editionsdumeridien.com *Web Site:* www.editionsdumeridien.com, pg 544

Editions du Noroit Ltee, PO Box 156, Succursale de Lorimier, Montreal, PQ H2H 2N6, Canada *Tel:* 514-727-0005 *Fax:* 514-723-6660 *E-mail:* lenoroit@lenoroit.com *Web Site:* www.lenoroit.com, pg 544

Editions du Phare Inc, 105 rue de Martigny Ouest, St Jerome, PQ J7Y 2G2, Canada *Tel:* 450-438-8479 *Toll Free Tel:* 800-561-2371 (Canada) *Fax:* 450-432-3892 *E-mail:* info@mondiaduphare.net, pg 544

Les Editions du Remue-Menage Inc, 110, Ste-Therese, Bureau 501, Montreal, PQ H2Y 1E6, Canada *Tel:* 514-876-0097 *Fax:* 514-876-7951 *E-mail:* info@editions-remuemenage.qc.ca, pg 544

Editions du renouveau Pedagogique Inc, 5757 rue Cyphiot, St-Laurent, PQ H4S 1R3, Canada *Tel:* 514-334-2690 *Toll Free Tel:* 800-263-3678 *Fax:* 514-334-4720 *Toll Free Fax:* 800-643-4720 *E-mail:* erpidlm@erpi.com *Web Site:* www.erpi.com, pg 544

Les Editions du Roseau, 6521 rue Louis-Hemon, Montreal, PQ H2G 2L1, Canada *Tel:* 514-725-7772 *Fax:* 514-725-5889 *E-mail:* editions@roseau.ca *Web Site:* www.roseau.ca, pg 544

Editions du Septentrion, 1300 ave Maguire, Sillery, PQ G1T 1Z3, Canada *Tel:* 418-688-3556 *Fax:* 418-527-4978 *E-mail:* sept@septentrion.qc.ca *Web Site:* www.septentrion.qc.ca, pg 544

Editions du Trecarre, 7 chemin Bates, Outremont, PQ H2V 4V7, Canada *Tel:* 514-270-6860 *Fax:* 514-276-2533 *E-mail:* edition@trecarre.com *Web Site:* www.total-publishing.com, pg 545

Les Editions du Vermillon, 305 rue Saint-Patrick, Ottawa, ON K1N 5K4, Canada *Tel:* 613-241-4032 *Fax:* 613-241-3109 *E-mail:* leseditionsduvermillon@rogers.com *Web Site:* www.primatech.ca/vermillon/index.html; vermillon.info.ca, pg 545

Editions Fides, 165 rue Deslauriers, St-Laurent, PQ H4N 2S4, Canada *Tel:* 514-745-4290 *Toll Free Tel:* 800-363-1451 *Fax:* 514-745-4299 *E-mail:* editions@fides.qc.ca *Web Site:* www.editionsfides.com, pg 545

Les Editions Ganesha Inc, CP 484 Succursale Youville, Montreal, PQ H2P 2W1, Canada *Tel:* 450-641-2395 *Fax:* 450-641-2989 *E-mail:* courriel@editions-ganesha.qc.ca *Web Site:* editions-ganesha.qc.ca, pg 545

Les Editions Heritage Inc, 300 Rue D'Arran, St-Lambert, PQ J4R 1K5, Canada *Tel:* 450-672-6710 *Fax:* 450-672-1481, pg 545

Editions Hurtubise HMH Ltee, 1815 De Lorimier, Montreal, PQ H2K 3W6, Canada *Tel:* 514-523-1523 *Toll Free Tel:* 800-361-1664 (Canada only) *Fax:* 514-523-9969; 514-523-5955 (edit) *E-mail:* hurtubisehmh@hurtubisehmh.com *Web Site:* www.hurtubisehmh.com, pg 545

Les Editions JCL, 930 rue Jacques Cartier est, Chicoutimi, PQ G7H 7K9, Canada *Tel:* 418-696-0536 *Fax:* 418-696-3132 *E-mail:* jcl@jcl.qc.ca *Web Site:* www.jcl.qc.ca, pg 545

Editions Marie-France, 9900 avenue des Laurentides, Montreal-Nord, PQ H1H 4V1, Canada *Tel:* 514-329-3700 *Toll Free Tel:* 800-563-6644 *Fax:* 514-329-0630 *E-mail:* editions@marie-france.qc.ca *Web Site:* www.marie-france.qc.ca, pg 545

Editions Orphee Inc, 1240 Clubview Blvd N, Columbus, OH 43235 *Tel:* 614-846-9517 *Fax:* 614-846-9794 *Web Site:* www.orphee.com, pg 87

Les Editions Phidal Inc, 5740 rue Ferrier, Montreal, PQ H4P 1M7, Canada *Tel:* 514-738-0202 *Toll Free Tel:* 800-738-7349 *Fax:* 514-738-5102 *E-mail:* info@phidal.com *Web Site:* www.phidal.com, pg 545

Editions Saint-Martin, 5000, rue Iberville, bureau 203, Montreal, PQ H2H 2M2, Canada *Tel:* 514-529-0920 *Fax:* 514-529-8384 *E-mail:* st-martin@gc.airle.com, pg 545

Editions Sciences & Culture Inc, 5090 rue de Bellechasse, Montreal, PQ H1T 2A2, Canada *Tel:* 514-253-0403 *Fax:* 514-256-5078 *E-mail:* admin@sciences-culture.qc.ca *Web Site:* www.sciences-culture.qc.ca, pg 545

Editions Total Publishing, 7 Bates Rd, Outremont, PQ H2V 4A7, Canada *Tel:* 514-276-2520 *Fax:* 514-276-2533 *Web Site:* www.total-publishing.com, pg 545

Editions Trois, 4882 Cherrier, Laval, PQ H7T 2Y9, Canada *Tel:* 450-978-5245 *Fax:* 450-978-0899 *E-mail:* ed3ama@videotron.ca, pg 546

Les Editions Un Monde Different, 3925 Grande Allee, St-Hubert, PQ J4T 2V8, Canada *Tel:* 450-656-2660 *Fax:* 450-445-9098 *Web Site:* www.umd.ca, pg 546

Editions Vents d'Ouest, 185 rue Eddy, Hull, PQ J8X 2X2, Canada *Tel:* 819-770-6377 *Fax:* 819-770-0559 *E-mail:* info@ventsdouest.ca, pg 546

Editions Yvon Blais, 137 John, CP 180, Cowansville, PQ J2K 1W9, Canada *Tel:* 450-266-1086 *Fax:* 450-263-9256 *E-mail:* commandes@editionsyvonblais.qc.ca *Web Site:* www.editionsyvonblais.qc.ca, pg 546

Editorial & Graphics Awards Competition-EXCEL Awards, 8405 Greensboro Dr, No 800, McLean, VA 22102 *Tel:* 703-506-3285 *Fax:* 703-506-3266 *E-mail:* info@snaponline.org *Web Site:* www.snaponline.org, pg 771

The Editorial Bag, 3635 Pamela Dr, Columbus, OH 43230-1829 *Tel:* 614-939-9707 *Fax:* 614-939-9707, pg 597

Editorial Bautista Independiente, 3417 Kenilworth Blvd, Sebring, FL 33870 *Tel:* 863-382-6350 *Toll Free Tel:* 800-398-7187 *Fax:* 863-382-8650 *E-mail:* info@ebi-bmm.org *Web Site:* www.ebi-bmm.org, pg 87

Editorial Consultants Inc (WA), 3639 36 Ave S, Seattle, WA 98118 *Tel:* 206-323-1039 *Fax:* 206-229-3448 *E-mail:* meowmixz@aol.com, pg 597

The Editorial Department, LLC, 1710 S Olympic Club Dr, Tucson, AZ 85710 *Tel:* 520-546-9992 *Toll Free Tel:* 866-360-6996 *Fax:* 520-546-9993 *E-mail:* admin@editorialdepartment.net *Web Site:* www.editorialdepartment.net, pg 597

Editorial Freelancers Association (EFA), 71 W 23 St, New York, NY 10010 *Tel:* 212-929-5400 *Fax:* 212-929-5439 *E-mail:* info@the-efa.org *Web Site:* www.the-efa.org, pg 686

Editorial Options Inc, 353 Lexington Ave, New York, NY 10016 *Tel:* 212-986-2888 *Fax:* 212-986-1194 *Web Site:* www.edop.com, pg 597

Editorial Portavoz, 733 Wealthy St SE, Grand Rapids, MI 49503-5553 *Tel:* 616-451-4775 *Toll Free Tel:* 800-733-2607 *Fax:* 616-451-9330 *E-mail:* portavoz@portavoz.com *Web Site:* www.kregel.com; www.portavoz.com, pg 87

Editorial Services Group Inc, 2990 Heidelberg Dr, Boulder, CO 80305 *Tel:* 303-494-4197 *E-mail:* editor@boulder.net *Web Site:* www.emsotw.com, pg 597

Editorial Temps & Hot Bear - De Bella Productions, 303 E 83 St, Suite 25-D, New York, NY 10028 *Tel:* 212-988-8189 *Fax:* 212-988-8189 *Web Site:* www.editorialtemps.com, pg 598

Editorial Unilit, 1360 NW 88 Ave, Miami, FL 33172 *Tel:* 305-592-6136 *Toll Free Tel:* 800-767-7726 *Fax:* 305-592-0087 *Web Site:* www.editorialunilit.com, pg 87

Editors' Association of Canada/Association canadienne des reviseurs, 27 Carlton St, Suite 502, Toronto, ON M5B 1L2, Canada *Tel:* 416-975-1379 *Toll Free Tel:* 866-226-3348 *Fax:* 416-975-1637 *E-mail:* editors@editors.ca *Web Site:* www.editors.ca; www.reviseurs.ca, pg 686

Editors' Prize, 1507 Hillcrest Hall, Columbia, MO 65211 *Tel:* 573-882-4474 *Toll Free Tel:* 800-949-2505 *Fax:* 573-884-4671 *E-mail:* mr@missouri.org *Web Site:* www.missourireview.org, pg 771

EdiType, 84 Ashley Ave, Charleston, SC 29401 *Tel:* 843-853-2214 *Fax:* 843-853-2214, pg 598

EduCare Press, PO Box 17222, Seattle, WA 98127 *Tel:* 206-782-4797 *Fax:* 206-782-4802 *E-mail:* educarepress@hotmail.com *Web Site:* www.educarepress.com, pg 87

Education Awards of Excellence, 200 Deer Run Rd, Sewickley, PA 15143-2600 *Tel:* 412-741-6860 *Toll Free Tel:* 800-910-4283 *Fax:* 412-741-2311 *E-mail:* info@gain.net *Web Site:* www.gain.net, pg 771

Education Writers Association, 2122 "P" St NW, No 201, Washington, DC 20037 *Tel:* 202-452-9830 *Fax:* 202-452-9837 *E-mail:* ewa@ewa.org *Web Site:* www.ewa.org, pg 686

Education Writers Association Workshops, 2122 "P" St NW, No 201, Washington, DC 20037 *Tel:* 202-452-9830 *Fax:* 202-452-9837 *E-mail:* ewa@ewa.org *Web Site:* www.ewa.org, pg 743

Educational Communications Inc, 1701 Directors Blvd, Suite 920, Austin, TX 78744 *Tel:* 512-440-2705 *Fax:* 512-447-1687 *Web Site:* www.honoring.com, pg 87

Educational Design Services Inc, 7238 Treviso Lane, Boynton Beach, FL 33437-7338 *Tel:* 561-739-9402, pg 629

Educational Directories Inc, 1025 W Wise Rd, Suite 101, Schaumburg, IL 60193 *Tel:* 847-891-1250 *Toll Free Tel:* 800-357-6183 *Fax:* 847-891-0945 *E-mail:* info@ediusa.com *Web Site:* www.ediusa.com, pg 87

Educational Impressions Inc, 116 Washington Ave, Hawthorne, NJ 07507 *Tel:* 973-423-4666 *Toll Free Tel:* 800-451-7450 *Fax:* 973-423-5569 *Web Site:* www.edimpressions.com; www.awpeller.com, pg 87

Educational Insights Inc, 18730 S Wilmington Ave, Suite 100, Rancho Dominguez, CA 90220 *Tel:* 310-884-2000 *Toll Free Tel:* 800-933-3277 *Fax:* 310-884-2015 *E-mail:* service@edin.com *Web Site:* www.educationalinsights.com, pg 87

Educational Media Co/TMA, 18740 Paseo Nuevo Dr, Tarzana, CA 91356 *Tel:* 818-708-0962 *Fax:* 818-345-2980 *Web Site:* educationalmediacompany.com, pg 598

Educational Paperback Association (EPA), PO Box 1399, East Hampton, NY 11937-0709 *Tel:* 631-329-3315 *E-mail:* edupaperback@aol.com *Web Site:* www.edupaperback.org, pg 686

Educational Technology Publications, 700 Palisade Ave, Englewood Cliffs, NJ 07632-0564 *Tel:* 201-871-4007 *Toll Free Tel:* 800-952-2665 *Fax:* 201-871-4009 *E-mail:* edtecpubs@aol.com *Web Site:* www.bookstoread.com/etp, pg 88

Educator's Award, PO Box 1589, Austin, TX 78767-1589 *Tel:* 512-478-5748 *Fax:* 512-478-3961 *E-mail:* societyexec@deltakappagamma.org *Web Site:* www.deltakappagamma.org, pg 771

Educator's International Press, 18 Colleen Rd, Troy, NY 12180 *Tel:* 518-271-9886 *Fax:* 518-266-9422 *Web Site:* www.edint.com, pg 88

Educators Progress Service Inc, 214 Center St, Randolph, WI 53956 *Tel:* 920-326-3126 *Toll Free Tel:* 888-951-4469 *Fax:* 920-326-3127 *E-mail:* epsinc@centurytel.net, pg 88

Educators Publishing Service Inc, 625 Mount Auburn St, Cambridge, MA 02139-9031 *Tel:* 617-547-6706 *Toll Free Tel:* 800-225-5750 *Fax:* 617-547-0412 *Toll Free Fax:* 888-440-2665 *E-mail:* epsbooks@epsbooks.com *Web Site:* www.epsbooks.com, pg 88

Edupress Inc, 208 Avenida Fabricante, Suite 200, San Clemente, CA 92672-7538 *Tel:* 949-366-9499 *Toll Free Tel:* 800-835-7978 *Fax:* 949-366-9441 *E-mail:* info@edupressinc.com *Web Site:* www.edupressinc.com, pg 88

J M B Edwards, Writer & Editor, 2432 California St, Berkeley, CA 94703 *Tel:* 510-644-8287, pg 598

Margaret A Edwards Award, 50 E Huron St, Chicago, IL 60611 *Tel:* 312-280-4390 *Toll Free Tel:* 800-545-2433 (ext 4390) *Fax:* 312-664-7459 *E-mail:* yalsa@ala.org *Web Site:* www.ala.org/yalsa/, pg 771

EEI Communications, 66 Canal Center Plaza, Suite 200, Alexandria, VA 22314-5507 *Tel:* 703-683-0683 *Fax:* 703-683-4915 *E-mail:* info@eeicommunications.com *Web Site:* www.eeicommunications.com, pg 598

EEI Communications, 66 Canal Center Plaza, Suite 200, Alexandria, VA 22314-5507 *Tel:* 703-683-7453 *Fax:* 703-683-7310 *E-mail:* train@eeicom.com *Web Site:* www.eeicommunications.com, pg 752

Wm B Eerdmans Publishing Co, 255 Jefferson Ave SE, Grand Rapids, MI 49503 *Tel:* 616-459-4591 *Toll Free Tel:* 800-253-7521 *Fax:* 616-459-6540 *E-mail:* sales@eerdmans.com *Web Site:* www.eerdmans.com, pg 88

Effective Learning Systems, 805 Ocean Ave, Point Richmond, CA 94801-3735 *Tel:* 510-232-8218 *Fax:* 510-965-0134, pg 88

Wilfrid Eggleston Award for Nonfiction, 11759 Groat Rd, Edmonton, AB T5M 3K6, Canada *Tel:* 780-422-8174 *Toll Free Tel:* 800-665-5354 (Alberta only) *Fax:* 780-422-2663 *E-mail:* mail@writersguild.ab.ca *Web Site:* www.writersguild.ab.ca, pg 772

Diane Eickhoff, 3808 Genessee St, Kansas City, MO 64111 *Tel:* 816-561-6693 *E-mail:* diane@tvbarn.com, pg 598

Eisenbrauns Inc, PO Box 275, Winona Lake, IN 46590-0275 *Tel:* 574-269-2011 *Fax:* 574-269-6788 *E-mail:* publisher@eisenbrauns.com *Web Site:* www.eisenbrauns.com/, pg 88

EKP Productions Inc, 8484 Wilshire Blvd, Suite 205, Beverly Hills, CA 90211 *Tel:* 323-655-5696 *Fax:* 323-655-5173 *E-mail:* producedby@aol.com *Web Site:* eddiekritzer.com, pg 669

Elder Books, PO Box 490, Forest Knolls, CA 94933 *Tel:* 415-488-9002 *Toll Free Tel:* 800-909-2673 (orders) *Fax:* 415-354-3306 *E-mail:* info@elderbooks.com *Web Site:* www.elderbooks.com, pg 88

Elderberry Press LLC, 1393 Old Homestead Dr, 2nd fl, Oakland, OR 97462-9506 *Tel:* 541-459-6043 *Fax:* 541-459-6043 *Web Site:* www.elderberrypress.com, pg 88

The Electrochemical Society Inc, 65 S Main St, Pennington, NJ 08534-2839 *Tel:* 609-737-1902 *Fax:* 609-737-2743 *E-mail:* ecs@electrochem.org *Web Site:* www.electrochem.org, pg 88

Element Books, 535 Albany St, 5th fl, Boston, MA 02118 *Tel:* 617-451-8984 *Web Site:* www.thorsons.com, pg 89

Edward Elgar Publishing Inc, 136 West St, Suite 202, Northampton, MA 01060 *Tel:* 413-584-5551 *Toll Free Tel:* 800-390-3149 (orders) *Fax:* 413-584-9933 *Web Site:* www.e-elgar.com, pg 89

Elite Books, 10 Hop Ranch Ct, Santa Rosa, CA 95407 *Tel:* 707-525-9292 *Fax:* 360-362-3634 *Web Site:* elitebooks.org, pg 89

Elizabeth Shaw Editorial & Publishing Services, 3938 E Grant, Suite 502, Tucson, AZ 85712-2559 *Tel:* 520-325-0463 *Fax:* 520-323-7382, pg 598

Ethan Ellenberg Literary Agency, 548 Broadway, Suite 5-E, New York, NY 10012 *Tel:* 212-431-4554 *Fax:* 212-941-4652 *E-mail:* agent@ethanellenberg.com *Web Site:* www.ethanellenberg.com, pg 629

Elliot's Books, PO Box 6, Northford, CT 06472-0006 *Tel:* 203-484-2184 *Fax:* 203-484-7644 *E-mail:* outofprintbooks@mindspring.com, pg 89

Elliott Prize, 104 Mount Auburn St, 5th fl, Cambridge, MA 02138 *Tel:* 617-491-1622 *Fax:* 617-492-3303 *E-mail:* speculum@medievalacademy.org *Web Site:* www.medievalacademy.org, pg 772

Nicholas Ellison Inc, 55 Fifth Ave, New York, NY 10003 *Tel:* 212-206-6050 *Fax:* 212-463-8718 *Web Site:* www.greenburger.com, pg 629

Ellora's Cave Publishing Inc, 1337 Commerce Dr, Suite 13, Stow, OH 44224 *Tel:* 330-689-1118 *E-mail:* service@ellorascave.com *Web Site:* www.ellorascave.com, pg 89

Elm Street Publishing Services Inc, 828 N Elm St, Hinsdale, IL 60521 *Tel:* 630-789-2102 *Fax:* 630-789-2105 *E-mail:* esps@elmst.com *Web Site:* www.elmst.com, pg 598

Irene Elmer, 2806 Cherry, Berkeley, CA 94705-2310 *Tel:* 510-841-0466 *Fax:* 510-883-1265 *E-mail:* ielmer@earthlink.net, pg 598

Ann Elmo Agency Inc, 60 E 42 St, New York, NY 10165 *Tel:* 212-661-2880; 212-661-2881 *Fax:* 212-661-2883, pg 629

Elsevier, 11830 Westline Industrial Dr, St Louis, MO 63146 *Tel:* 314-872-8370 *Toll Free Tel:* 800-325-4177 *Fax:* 314-432-1380 *Web Site:* www.elsevier.com; www.elsevierhealth.com, pg 89

Elsevier, 200 Wheeler Rd, 6th fl, Burlington, MA 01803 *Tel:* 781-313-4700 *Toll Free Tel:* 800-545-2522 (cust serv) *Fax:* 781-313-4880 *Toll Free Fax:* 800-535-9935 (cust serv) *Web Site:* www.focalpress.com, pg 89

Elsevier Engineering Information Inc (Ei), One Castle Point Terr, Hoboken, NJ 07030 *Tel:* 201-356-6800 *Toll Free Tel:* 800-221-1044 *Fax:* 201-356-6801 *Web Site:* www.ei.org, pg 89

Elsevier Science Inc, 360 Park Ave S, New York, NY 10010 *Tel:* 212-989-5800 *Fax:* 212-633-3965; 212-633-3990 *Web Site:* www.elsevier.com, pg 89

Catherine C Elverston, 4026 NW 17 Terr, Gainesville, FL 32605-1973 *Tel:* 352-372-6571 *E-mail:* elverston@hotmail.com, pg 598

Ruth Elwell, 48 S Chestnut St, New Paltz, NY 12561 *Tel:* 845-255-4223 *E-mail:* ruth.elwell@att.net, pg 598

Embiid Publishing, 600 Fouts St, Upham, ND 58789 *E-mail:* info@embiid.net; us@embiid.net; submissions@embiid.net *Web Site:* www.embiid.net, pg 89

EMC/Paradigm Publishing, 875 Montreal Way, St Paul, MN 55102 *Tel:* 651-290-2800 (corp) *Toll Free Tel:* 800-328-1452 *Fax:* 651-290-2899 *Toll Free Fax:* 800-328-4564 *E-mail:* educate@emcp.com *Web Site:* www.emcp.com, pg 89

Emerald Books, PO Box 635, Lynnwood, WA 98046 *Tel:* 425-771-1153 *Toll Free Tel:* 800-922-2143 *Fax:* 425-775-2383 *E-mail:* emeraldbooks@seanet.com *Web Site:* www.ywampublishing.com, pg 90

Emerging Playwright Award, 17 E 47 St, New York, NY 10017 *Tel:* 212-421-1380 *Fax:* 212-421-1387 *E-mail:* urbanstage@aol.com *Web Site:* www.urbanstages.org, pg 772

Emerson College Publishing Seminars, 120 Boylston St, Boston, MA 02116-8750 *Tel:* 617-824-8280 *Fax:* 617-824-8158 *E-mail:* continuing@emerson.edu *Web Site:* www.emerson.edu/ce, pg 743

Emerson College, Writing & Publishing Program, 120 Boylston St, Boston, MA 02116-8750 *Tel:* 617-824-8750 *Web Site:* www.emerson.edu, pg 752

The Emerson Co, 12342 Northup Way, Bellevue, WA 98005 *Tel:* 425-869-0655 *Fax:* 425-869-0746 *Web Site:* www.emersoncompany.com, pg 90

Ralph Waldo Emerson Award, 1606 New Hampshire Ave NW, Washington, DC 20009 *Tel:* 202-265-3808 *Fax:* 202-986-1601 *Web Site:* www.pbk.org, pg 772

Prix Emile-Nelligan, 261 avenue Bloomfield, Outremont, PQ H2V 3R6, Canada *Tel:* 514-849-8540 *Fax:* 514-271-6239 *E-mail:* info@fondation-nelligan.org *Web Site:* www.fondation-nelligan.org, pg 772

Emily Dickinson Award, 15 Gramercy Park, New York, NY 10003 *Tel:* 212-254-9628 *Fax:* 212-673-2352 *Web Site:* www.poetrysociety.org, pg 772

Emmaus Road Publishing Inc, 827 N Fourth St, Steubenville, OH 43952 *Tel:* 740-283-2484 *Toll Free Tel:* 800-398-5470 *Fax:* 740-283-4011 *Web Site:* www.emmausroad.org, pg 90

Emmis Books, 1700 Madison Rd, 2nd fl, Cincinnati, OH 45206 *Tel:* 513-861-4045 *Toll Free Tel:* 800-913-9563 *Fax:* 513-861-4430 *E-mail:* info@emmis.com *Web Site:* www.emmisbooks.com, pg 90

Emond Montgomery Publications Ltd, 60 Shaftesbury Ave, Toronto, ON M4T 1A3, Canada *Tel:* 416-975-3925 *Toll Free Tel:* 888-837-0815 *Fax:* 416-975-3924 *E-mail:* info@emp.ca; orders@emp.ca *Web Site:* www.emp.ca, pg 546

Emory Summer Writers' Institute & Festival, c/o Creative Writing Program, Emory University, Rm N209, Callaway Center, Atlanta, GA 30322 *Tel:* 404-727-4683 *Fax:* 404-727-4672 *Web Site:* www.emory.edu/college/creativewriting, pg 743

Empire Press Media/Avant-Guide, 444 Madison Ave, 35th fl, New York, NY 10122 *Tel:* 212-563-1003 *Fax:* 212-536-2419 *E-mail:* info@avantguide.com; editor@avantguide.com *Web Site:* www.avantguide.com, pg 90

Empire Publishing Service, PO Box 1344, Studio City, CA 91614-0344 *Tel:* 818-784-8918, pg 90

Empire State Award for Excellence in Literature for Young People, 252 Hudson Ave, Albany, NY 12210 *Tel:* 518-432-6952 *Fax:* 518-427-1697 *E-mail:* info@nyla.org *Web Site:* www.nyla.org, pg 772

Enchanted Lion Books, 115 W 18 St, 6th fl, New York, NY 10011 *Tel:* 212-675-1959 *Fax:* 212-675-2142 *E-mail:* enchantedlionbooks@yahoo.com, pg 90

Encore Performance Publishing, 2181 W California Ave, Suite 250, Salt Lake City, UT 84104 *Tel:* 801-485-5012 *Fax:* 801-485-4365 *E-mail:* encoreplay@aol.com *Web Site:* www.encoreplay.com, pg 90

Encounter Books, 665 Third St, Suite 330, San Francisco, CA 94107-1951 *Tel:* 415-538-1460 *Toll Free Tel:* 800-786-3839 *Fax:* 415-538-1461 *Toll Free Fax:* 877-811-1461 *E-mail:* read@encounterbooks.com *Web Site:* www.encounterbooks.com, pg 90

Encyclopaedia Britannica Inc, 310 S Michigan Ave, Chicago, IL 60604 *Tel:* 312-347-7000 *Toll Free Tel:* 800-323-1229 *Fax:* 312-347-7399 *E-mail:* editor@eb.com *Web Site:* www.eb.com; www.britannica.com, pg 91

Energy Information Administration, EI-30 National Energy Information Center, Dept of Energy, 1000 Independence Ave SW, Washington, DC 20585 *Tel:* 202-586-8800 *Fax:* 202-586-0727 *E-mail:* infoctr@eia.doe.gov *Web Site:* www.eia.doe.gov, pg 91

Enfield Publishing & Distribution Co, 234 May St, Enfield, NH 03748 *Tel:* 603-632-7377 *Fax:* 603-632-5611 *E-mail:* info@enfieldbooks.com *Web Site:* www.enfielddistribution.com, pg 91

Marian Engel Award, 90 Richmond St W, Suite 200, Toronto, ON M5C 1P1, Canada *Tel:* 416-504-8222 *Fax:* 416-504-9090 *E-mail:* info@writerstrust.com *Web Site:* www.writerstrust.com, pg 772

Rohn Engh, Pine Lake Farm, 1910 35 Rd, Osceola, WI 54020 *Tel:* 715-248-3800 (ext 21) *Toll Free Tel:* 800-624-0266 (ext 21) *Fax:* 715-248-7394 *Toll Free Fax:* 800-photofax *E-mail:* psi2@photosource.com *Web Site:* www.photosource.com, pg 598

English Literary Studies (Monograph Series), University of Victoria, Dept of English, Victoria, BC V8W 3W1, Canada *Tel:* 250-721-7237 *Fax:* 250-721-6498 *E-mail:* english@uvic.ca *Web Site:* www.engl.uvic.ca, pg 546

Enough Said, 414 NW 36 Ave, Gainesville, FL 32607 *Tel:* 352-371-2935; 352-262-2971 *Web Site:* www.navi.net/~heathlynn, pg 598

Ensemble Productions Inc, 230 Central Park W, New York, NY 10024 *Tel:* 212-877-3848 *Fax:* 212-877-9363, pg 598

Enslow Publishers Inc, 40 Industrial Rd, Berkeley Heights, NJ 07922 *Tel:* 908-771-9400 *Toll Free Tel:* 800-398-2504 *Fax:* 908-771-0925 *Web Site:* www.myreportlinks.com; www.enslow.com, pg 91

Entomological Society of America, 9301 Annapolis Rd, Lanham, MD 20706-3115 *Tel:* 301-731-4535 *Fax:* 301-731-4538 *E-mail:* pubs@entsoc.org *Web Site:* www.entsoc.org, pg 91

Environmental Ethics Books, 1704 W Mulberry St, UNT, EESAT Bldg 370, Denton, TX 76201 *Tel:* 940-565-2727 *Toll Free Tel:* 800-264-9962 *Fax:* 940-565-4439 *Toll Free Fax:* 800-295-0536 *E-mail:* ee@unt.edu *Web Site:* www.cep.unt.edu, pg 91

Environmental Law Institute, 1616 "P" St NW, Suite 200, Washington, DC 20036 *Tel:* 202-939-3800 *Fax:* 202-939-3868 *E-mail:* law@eli.org *Web Site:* www.eli.org, pg 91

Epicenter Press Inc, PO Box 82368, Kenmore, WA 98028 *Tel:* 425-485-6822 *Fax:* 425-481-8253 *E-mail:* info@epicenterpress.com *Web Site:* www.epicenterpress.com, pg 91

Epimetheus Books Inc, 2711 Centerville Rd, Suite 120-5336, Wilmington, DE 19808-1643 *Tel:* 646-345-2030 *E-mail:* epimetheus@att.net *Web Site:* www.epimetheusbooks.com, pg 91

Pearl Eppy, 201 E 79 St, New York, NY 10021 *Tel:* 212-737-0354, pg 598

Norma Epstein Foundation, 15 King's College Circle, Toronto, ON M5S 3H7, Canada *Tel:* 416-978-8083 *Fax:* 416-971-2027 *Web Site:* www.utoronto.ca, pg 772

ERIC Clearinghouse on Teaching & Teacher Education, 1307 New York Ave NW, Suite 300, Washington, DC 20005 *Tel:* 202-293-2450 *Toll Free Tel:* 800-799-3742 *Fax:* 202-457-8095 *Web Site:* www.ericsp.org, pg 686

Ericson Books, 1614 Redbud St, Nacogdoches, TX 75965 *Tel:* 936-564-3625 *Fax:* 936-552-8999 *E-mail:* info@ericsonbooks.com *Web Site:* www. ericsonbooks.com, pg 91

Lawrence Erlbaum Associates Inc, 10 Industrial Ave, Mahwah, NJ 07430-2262 *Tel:* 201-236-2199 *Toll Free Tel:* 800-9-BOOKS-9 (926-6579) *Fax:* 201-760-3735 *E-mail:* orders@erlbaum.com *Web Site:* www.erlbaum. com, pg 91

Ernst Publishing Company LLC, 1937 Delaware Tpke, Clarksville, NY 12041 *Toll Free Tel:* 800-345-3822 *Toll Free Fax:* 800-252-0906 *Web Site:* www.ernst.cc, pg 92

Eros Books, 463 Barlow Ave, Staten Island, NY 10308 *Tel:* 718-317-7484 *Web Site:* www.geocities.com/ marynicholaou/classic_blue.html, pg 92

eSchool News, 7920 Norfolk Ave, Suite 900, Bethesda, MD 20814 *Tel:* 301-913-0115 *Toll Free Tel:* 800-394-0115 *Fax:* 301-913-0119 *Web Site:* www.eschoolnews. com, pg 92

Essence of Vermont, 860 Panton Rd, Panton, VT 05491 *Tel:* 802-475-2933 *Fax:* 802-475-2933 *E-mail:* info@essenceofvermont.com *Web Site:* www. essenceofvermont.com, pg 92

Essence Publishing, 20 Hanna Ct, Belleville, ON K8P 5J2, Canada *Tel:* 613-962-2360 *Toll Free Tel:* 800-238-6376 *Fax:* 613-962-3055 *E-mail:* info@ essencegroup.com *Web Site:* www.essence.on.ca, pg 546

ETC Publications, 700 E Vereda del Sur, Palm Springs, CA 92262 *Tel:* 760-325-5332 *Toll Free Tel:* 800-382-7869 *Fax:* 760-325-8841 *E-mail:* etcbooks@earthlink. net, pg 92

Felicia Eth Literary Representation, 555 Bryant St, Suite 350, Palo Alto, CA 94301 *Tel:* 650-401-8891; 650-375-1276 *Fax:* 650-401-8892 *E-mail:* feliciaeth@aol. com, pg 629

Etruscan Press, PO Box 9685, Silver Spring, MD 20916-9685 *Tel:* 301-946-6228 *Fax:* 301-946-5838 *E-mail:* info@etruscanpress.org *Web Site:* www. etruscanpress.com, pg 92

Evan-Moor Educational Publishers, 18 Lower Ragsdale Dr, Monterey, CA 93940 *Tel:* 831-649-5901 *Toll Free Tel:* 800-777-4362 *Fax:* 831-649-6256 *E-mail:* customerservice@evan-moor.com *Web Site:* www.evan-moor.com, pg 92

Evangel Publishing House, 2000 Evangel Way, Nappanee, IN 46550 *Tel:* 574-773-3164 *Toll Free Tel:* 800-253-9315 (orders) *Fax:* 574-773-5934 *E-mail:* sales@evangelpublishing.com *Web Site:* www. evangelpublishing.com, pg 92

Evangelical Christian Publishers Association, 4816 S Ash Ave, Suite 101, Tempe, AZ 85282-7735 *Tel:* 480-966-3998 *Fax:* 480-966-1944 *E-mail:* info@ecpa.org *Web Site:* www.ecpa.org, pg 686

Evangelical Press Association (EPA), PO Box 28129, Crystal, MN 55428-0129 *Tel:* 763-535-4793 *Fax:* 763-535-4794 *E-mail:* director@epassoc.org *Web Site:* www.epassoc.org, pg 686

David W & Beatrice C Evans Biography & Handcart Awards, 0735 Old Main Hill, Logan, UT 84322-0735 *Tel:* 435-797-3630 *Fax:* 435-797-3899 *E-mail:* mwc@ cc.usu.edu *Web Site:* www.usu.edu/mountainwest, pg 772

M Evans & Co Inc, 216 E 49 St, New York, NY 10017 *Tel:* 212-688-2810 *Fax:* 212-486-4544 *E-mail:* editorial@mevans.com *Web Site:* www. mevans.com, pg 92

Mary Evans Inc, 242 E Fifth St, New York, NY 10003 *Tel:* 212-979-0880 *Fax:* 212-979-5344 *E-mail:* merrylit@aol.com, pg 629

Evanston Publishing Inc, 4824 Brownsboro Ctr, Louisville, KY 40207 *Tel:* 502-899-1919 *Toll Free Tel:* 888BOOKS80 *Fax:* 502-896-0246 *E-mail:* evanstonpublish@aol.com *Web Site:* www. evanstonpublishing.com, pg 93

Evergreen Pacific Publishing Ltd, 18002 15 Ave NE, Suite B, Shoreline, WA 98155-3838 *Tel:* 206-368-8157 *Fax:* 206-368-7968 *Web Site:* www. evergreenpacific.com, pg 93

Charles Everitt Literary Agency Inc, PO Box 1502, Manchester, MA 01944-0860 *Tel:* 978-526-4411 *Fax:* 978-526-4411 *E-mail:* cbela@msn.com, pg 629

Everyday Wisdom Press, 11010 Northup Way, Bellevue, WA 98004 *Tel:* 425-822-1950; 425-827-7120 *Toll Free Tel:* 866-319-5900 *Fax:* 425-828-9659 *E-mail:* everydaywisdom@everydaywisdom.net *Web Site:* everydaywisdom.net, pg 93

Evolutionary Products, 1653 N Magnolia Ave, Tucson, AZ 85712-4103 *Tel:* 520-323-1190 *Toll Free Tel:* 800-777-4751 *E-mail:* info@evolutionaryproducts.com *Web Site:* www.newagemarket.com, pg 93

Jack Ewing Concepts & Copy, PO Box 571, Boise, ID 83701 *Tel:* 208-345-1782 *Fax:* 208-345-1782 (call first) *E-mail:* citzenew@aol.com, pg 598

Excalibur Publications, PO Box 89667, Tucson, AZ 85752-9667 *Tel:* 520-575-9057 *Fax:* 520-575-9068 *E-mail:* excalibureditor@earthlink.net, pg 93

Excelsior Cee Publishing, 1311 Cherry Stone, Norman, OK 73072 *Tel:* 405-329-3909 *Fax:* 405-329-6886 *E-mail:* ecp@oecadvantage.net *Web Site:* www. excelsiorcee.com, pg 93

Executive Excellence Publishing, 1366 E 1120 S, Provo, UT 84606 *Tel:* 801-375-4060 *Toll Free Tel:* 800-304-9782 *Fax:* 801-377-5960 *Web Site:* www.eep.com, pg 629

Helen Exley Giftbooks, 185 Main St, Spencer, MA 01562 *Toll Free Tel:* 877-395-3942 *Toll Free Fax:* 800-807-7363 *E-mail:* helen.exleygiftbooks@ verizon.net, pg 93

Explorers Guide Publishing, 4843 Apperson Dr, Rhinelander, WI 54501 *Tel:* 715-362-6029 *Toll Free Tel:* 800-487-6029 *E-mail:* comment@explorers-guide. com *Web Site:* www.explorers-guide.com, pg 93

Eye On Education, 6 Depot Way W, Larchmont, NY 10538 *Tel:* 914-833-0551 *Fax:* 914-833-0761 *Web Site:* www.eyeoneducation.com, pg 93

Faber & Faber Inc, 19 Union Sq W, New York, NY 10003 *Tel:* 212-741-6900 *Toll Free Tel:* 888-330-8477 *Fax:* 212-633-9385 *Web Site:* www.fsgbooks. com/faberandfaber.htm, pg 93

Factor Press, 5204 Dove Point Lane, Salisbury, MD 21801 *Tel:* 410-334-6111 *Toll Free Tel:* 888-334-6677 *Fax:* 410-334-6111 *E-mail:* factorpress@earthlink.net, pg 93

Facts on File Inc, 132 W 31 St, 17th fl, New York, NY 10001 *Tel:* 212-967-8800 *Toll Free Tel:* 800-322-8755 *Fax:* 212-967-9196 *Toll Free Fax:* 800-678-3633 *E-mail:* custserv@factsonfile.com *Web Site:* www. factsonfile.com, pg 93

John E Fagg Prize, 400 "A" St SE, Washington, DC 20003 *Tel:* 202-544-2422 *Fax:* 202-544-8307 *E-mail:* info@historians.org *Web Site:* www.historians. org, pg 772

Fair Winds Press, 33 Commercial St, Gloucester, MA 01930 *Tel:* 978-282-9590 *Fax:* 978-283-2742 *Web Site:* www.rockpub.com; www.fairwindspress. com, pg 94

John K Fairbank Prize in East Asian History, 400 "A" St SE, Washington, DC 20003 *Tel:* 202-544-2422 *Fax:* 202-544-8307 *E-mail:* info@historians.org *Web Site:* www.historians.org, pg 772

Fairchild Books, 7 W 34 St, New York, NY 10001 *Tel:* 212-630-3880 *Toll Free Tel:* 800-932-4724 *Fax:* 212-630-3868; 212-630-3898 *Web Site:* www. fairchildbooks.com, pg 94

Fairleigh Dickinson University Press, c/o Associated University Presses, 2010 Eastpark Blvd, Cranbury, NJ 08512 *Tel:* 609-655-4770 *Fax:* 609-655-8366 *E-mail:* aup440@aol.com, pg 94

The Fairmont Press Inc, 700 Indian Trail, Lilburn, GA 30047 *Tel:* 770-925-9388 *Fax:* 770-381-9865 *Web Site:* www.fairmontpress.com, pg 94

Fairview Press, 2450 Riverside Ave, Minneapolis, MN 55454 *Tel:* 612-672-4180 *Toll Free Tel:* 800-544-8207 *Fax:* 612-672-4980 *Web Site:* www.fairviewpress.org, pg 94

Fairwinds Press, 200 Isleview Place, Lions Bay, BC V0N 2E0, Canada *Tel:* 604-913-0649 *Fax:* 604-913-0648 *E-mail:* info@izzoconsultants.com *Web Site:* www. izzoconsultants.com, pg 546

Faith & Fellowship Press, 1020 Alcott Ave W, Fergus Falls, MN 56537 *Tel:* 218-736-7357 *Toll Free Tel:* 800-332-9232 *Fax:* 218-736-2200 *E-mail:* ffpress@clba.org *Web Site:* www. faithandfellowship.org, pg 94

Faith & Life Resources, 616 Walnut Ave, Scottdale, PA 15683-1999 *Tel:* 724-887-8500 *Toll Free Tel:* 800-245-7894 *Fax:* 724-887-3111 *E-mail:* info@mph.org *Web Site:* www.mph.org, pg 94

Faith Library Publications, 1025 W Kenosha St, Broken Arrow, OK 74012 *Tel:* 918-258-1588 (ext 2218) *Toll Free Tel:* 888-258-0999 (orders only) *Fax:* 918-251-8016 (orders) *Web Site:* www.rhema.org, pg 94

FaithWalk Publishing, 333 Jackson St, Grand Haven, MI 49417 *Tel:* 616-846-9360 *Toll Free Tel:* 800-335-7177 *Fax:* 616-846-0072 *E-mail:* customerservice@ faithwalkpub.com *Web Site:* www.faithwalkpub.com, pg 94

Falk Art Reference, 61 Beekman Place, Madison, CT 06443 *Tel:* 203-245-2246 *Web Site:* www.falkart.com, pg 94

Family Process Institute Inc, c/o Eldredge, Fox & Porretti, 180 Canal View Blvd, Suite 100, Rochester, NY 14623 *Tel:* 716-879-4900 (ext 153) *Fax:* 212-744-0206 *E-mail:* info@familyprocess.org *Web Site:* www. familyprocess.org, pg 94

Fantagraphics Books, 7563 Lake City Way NE, Seattle, WA 98115 *Tel:* 206-524-1967 *Toll Free Tel:* 800-657-1100 *Fax:* 206-524-2104 *E-mail:* ffbicomix@ fantagraphics.com *Web Site:* www.fantagraphics.com, pg 95

Far Beyond Words, 29 MacEwan Ridge Circle NW, Calgary, AB T3K 3W3, Canada *Tel:* 403-516-3312 *Fax:* 403-516-3312 *E-mail:* beyondwords@shaw.ca, pg 598

Farber Literary Agency Inc, 14 E 75 St, New York, NY 10021 *Tel:* 212-861-7075 *Fax:* 212-861-7076 *E-mail:* farberlit@aol.com, pg 629

Norma Farber First Book Award, 15 Gramercy Park, New York, NY 10003 *Tel:* 212-254-9628 *Fax:* 212-673-2352 *Web Site:* www.poetrysociety.org, pg 772

W D Farmer Residence Designer Inc, 2007 Montreal Rd, Tucker, GA 30084 *Tel:* 770-934-7380 *Toll Free Tel:* 800-225-7526; 800-221-7526 (GA) *Fax:* 770-934-1700 *E-mail:* wdfarmer@wdfarmerplans. com *Web Site:* www.wdfarmerplans.com; www. homeplansbyfarmer.com, pg 598

Farrar, Straus & Giroux Books for Young Readers, 19 Union Sq W, New York, NY 10003 *Tel:* 212-741-6900 *Fax:* 212-633-2427 *E-mail:* childrens.marketing@ fsgbooks.com; childrens.editorial@fsgbooks.com *Web Site:* www.fsgkidsbooks.com, pg 95

Farrar, Straus & Giroux, LLC, 19 Union Sq W, New York, NY 10003 *Tel:* 212-741-6900 *Fax:* 212-741-6973 *Web Site:* www.fsgbooks.com, pg 95

Farris Literary Agency Inc, PO Box 570069, Dallas, TX 75357-0069 *Tel:* 972-203-8804 *E-mail:* farris1@ airmail.net; agent@farrisliterary.com *Web Site:* www. farrisliterary.com, pg 630

Fass Speakers Bureau, 26 W 17 St, Suite 802, New York, NY 10011 *Tel:* 212-691-9707 *Fax:* 212-691-5012 *E-mail:* fsb@fasspr.com *Web Site:* www.fasspr. com, pg 669

Father & Son Publishing, 4909 N Monroe St, Tallahassee, FL 32303 *Tel:* 850-562-3927 *Toll Free Tel:* 800-741-2712 (orders only) *Fax:* 850-562-0916 *Web Site:* www.fatherson.com, pg 95

Stephanie Faul, 4110 Jenifer St NW, Washington, DC 20015 *Tel:* 202-363-1449 *Fax:* 202-537-6851 *E-mail:* steph@faul.com, pg 598

Virginia Faulkner Award for Excellence in Writing, University of Nebraska, 201 Andrews Hall, Lincoln, NE 68588 *Tel:* 402-472-0911 *E-mail:* kgrey2@unl.edu *Web Site:* www.unl.edu/schooner/psmain.htm, pg 773

FC&A Publishing, 103 Clover Green, Peachtree City, GA 30269 *Tel:* 770-487-6307 *Toll Free Tel:* 800-537-1275 *Fax:* 770-631-4357 *E-mail:* customer_service@fca.com *Web Site:* www.fca.com, pg 95

Feature Article Award, 115 Richmond St, Charlottetown, PE C1A 1H7, Canada *Tel:* 902-368-4410 *Fax:* 902-368-4418 *E-mail:* peiarts@peiartscouncil.com *Web Site:* www.peiartscouncil.com, pg 773

Federal Bar Association, 2215 "M" St NW, Washington, DC 20037 *Tel:* 202-785-1614 *Fax:* 202-785-1568 *E-mail:* fba@fedbar.org *Web Site:* www.fedbar.org, pg 95

Federal Buyers Guide Inc, 718-B State St, Santa Barbara, CA 93101 *Tel:* 805-963-7470 *Fax:* 805-963-7478 *Web Site:* www.gov-world.com, pg 95

Federal Street Press, 2513 Old Kings Hwy N, Darien, CT 06820 *Tel:* 203-852-1280 *Fax:* 203-852-1389, pg 95

The Federation of British Columbia Writers, PO Box 3887, Sta Terminal, Vancouver, BC V6B 2Z3, Canada *Tel:* 604-683-2057 *Fax:* 604-608-5522 *E-mail:* fedoffice@bcwriters.com *Web Site:* www.bcwriters.com, pg 686

FedEx Trade Networks, 220 Montgomery St, Suite 448, San Francisco, CA 94104-3410 *Tel:* 415-391-7501 *Toll Free Tel:* 800-556-9334 *Fax:* 415-391-7537 (Fax/Modem) *E-mail:* info@worldtariff.com *Web Site:* www.worldtariff.com, pg 95

Karyn L Feiden Editorial Services, 392 Central Park W, Suite 10-P, New York, NY 10025 *Tel:* 212-663-4942, pg 598

Feigen/Parrent Literary Management, 10158 Hollow Glen Circle, Bel Air, CA 90077 *Tel:* 310-271-4722 *Fax:* 310-274-0503 *E-mail:* feigenparrentlit@aol.com, pg 630

Feigenbaum Publishing Consultants Inc, 61 Bounty Lane, Jericho, NY 11753 *Tel:* 516-647-8314 *Fax:* 516-681-9121 *E-mail:* readrover5@aol.com, pg 630

Feik Indexers, 1623 Third Ave, Suite 29-K, New York, NY 10128-3638 *Tel:* 212-369-3480 *Fax:* 212-410-0927 *E-mail:* indexer@earthlink.net, pg 599

Lillian Mermin Feinsilver, 510 McCartney St, Easton, PA 18042 *Tel:* 610-252-7005, pg 599

Herbert Feis Award, 400 "A" St SE, Washington, DC 20003 *Tel:* 202-544-2422 *Fax:* 202-544-8307 *E-mail:* info@historians.org *Web Site:* www.historians.org, pg 773

Betsy Feist Resources, 140 E 81 St, New York, NY 10028-1875 *Tel:* 212-861-2014 *Fax:* 212-861-8304 *E-mail:* bfresources@rcn.com, pg 599

Philipp Feldheim Inc, 200 Airport Executive Park, Nanuet, NY 10954 *Tel:* 845-356-2282 *Toll Free Tel:* 800-237-7149 *Fax:* 845-425-1908 *E-mail:* sales@feldheim.com *Web Site:* www.feldheim.com, pg 95

Fellowship & Scholarship Program for Writers, Middlebury College, Middlebury, VT 05753 *Tel:* 802-443-5286 *Fax:* 802-443-2087 *E-mail:* blwc@middlebury.edu *Web Site:* www.middlebury.edu/~blwc, pg 773

Fellowship In Aerospace History, 400 "A" St SE, Washington, DC 20003 *Tel:* 202-544-2422 *Fax:* 202-544-8307 *E-mail:* info@historians.org *Web Site:* www.historians.org, pg 773

Fellowship Program, One Capital Hill, 3rd fl, Providence, RI 02908 *Tel:* 401-222-3880 *Fax:* 401-222-3018 *Web Site:* www.arts.ri.gov, pg 773

Fellowships for Creative Writers, Nancy Hanks Ctr, 1100 Pennsylvania Ave NW, Rm 720, Washington, DC 20506-0001 *Tel:* 202-682-5428; 202-682-5034 (Literature Fellowships hotline) *Fax:* 202-682-5669 *Web Site:* www.arts.gov, pg 773

Fellowships for Playwrights, 216 Finance Bldg, Harrisburg, PA 17120 *Tel:* 717-787-6883 *Fax:* 717-783-2538 *Web Site:* www.pacouncilonthearts.org, pg 773

Jerry Felsen, 3960 NW 196 St, Miami, FL 33055 *Tel:* 305-625-5012 *E-mail:* jfelsen@hotmail.com, pg 599

The Feminist Press at The City University of New York, 365 Fifth Ave, Suite 5406, New York, NY 10016 *Tel:* 212-817-7926 *Fax:* 212-817-1593 *Web Site:* www.feministpress.org, pg 96

Feminist Women's Writing Workshops, Inc, PO Box 6583, Ithaca, NY 14851-6583 *Tel:* 607-274-3325, pg 743

Shubert Fendrich Memorial Playwriting Contest, PO Box 4267, Englewood, CO 80155-4267 *Tel:* 303-779-4035 *Toll Free Tel:* 800-333-7262 *Fax:* 303-779-4315 *E-mail:* playwrights@pioneerdrama.com *Web Site:* www.pioneerdrama.com, pg 773

Janet Fenn Editorial Services, 1508 Jaeger Dr, Lyndhurst, OH 44124 *Tel:* 440-461-6902 *E-mail:* janetfenn@usa.net, pg 599

Fenn Publishing Co Ltd, 34 Nixon Rd, Bolton, ON L7E 1W2, Canada *Tel:* 905-951-6600 *Toll Free Tel:* 800-267-3366 (Canada only) *Fax:* 905-951-6601 *Toll Free Fax:* 800-465-3422 (Canada Only) *E-mail:* sales@hbfenn.com *Web Site:* www.hbfenn.com, pg 546

Robert L Fenton PC; Entertainment Attorney & Literary Agent, 31800 Northwestern Hwy, Suite 204, Farmington Hills, MI 48334 *Tel:* 248-855-8780 *Fax:* 248-855-3302 *E-mail:* fenent@msn.com *Web Site:* www.robertlfenton.com, pg 630

Feral House, PO Box 39910, Los Angeles, CA 90039 *Tel:* 323-666-3311 *Fax:* 323-666-3330 *E-mail:* info@feralhouse.com *Web Site:* www.feralhouse.com, pg 96

Fernwood Publishing Co Ltd, 32 Ocean Vista Lane, Black Point, NS B0J 1B0, Canada *Tel:* 902-857-1388 *Fax:* 902-857-1328 *E-mail:* info@fernwoodbooks.ca *Web Site:* www.fernwoodbooks.ca, pg 546

Howard Fertig Inc, Publisher, 80 E 11 St, New York, NY 10003 *Tel:* 212-982-7922 *Fax:* 212-982-1099, pg 96

Festival of Poetry, Ridge Rd, Franconia, NH 03580 *Tel:* 603-823-5510 *E-mail:* rfrost@nci.net *Web Site:* www.frostplace.org, pg 743

Fiction Collective Two Inc, Florida State University, FC2, Dept of English, Tallahassee, FL 32306-1580 *Tel:* 850-644-2260 *Fax:* 850-644-6808 *E-mail:* fc2@english.fsu.edu *Web Site:* fc2.org, pg 96

The Field Poetry Prize, 50 N Professor St, Oberlin, OH 44074-1095 *Tel:* 440-775-8408 *Fax:* 440-775-8124 *E-mail:* oc.press@oberlin.edu *Web Site:* www.oberlin.edu/ocpress, pg 773

Fifth House Publishers, 1511 1800 Fourth St SW, Calgary, AB T2S 2S5, Canada *Tel:* 403-571-5230 *Toll Free Tel:* 800-387-9776 *Fax:* 403-571-5235 *Toll Free Fax:* 800-260-9777 *Web Site:* www.fitzhenry.ca/fifthhouse.htm, pg 546

The Figures, 5 Castle Hill, Great Barrington, MA 01230 *Tel:* 413-528-2552 *Web Site:* www.geoffreyyoung.com, pg 96

Film-Video Publications/Circus Source Publications, 7944 Capistrano Ave, West Hills, CA 91304 *Tel:* 818-340-0175 *Fax:* 818-340-6770 *E-mail:* circussource@aol.com, pg 96

Filter Press LLC, PO Box 95, Palmer Lake, CO 80133 *Tel:* 719-481-2420 *Toll Free Tel:* 888-570-2663 *Fax:* 719-481-2420 *E-mail:* filter.press@prodigy.net *Web Site:* filterpressbooks.com, pg 96

Financial Executives Research Foundation Inc, 200 Campus Dr, Florham Park, NJ 07932 *Tel:* 973-765-1000 *Fax:* 973-765-1023 *Web Site:* www.ferf.org, pg 96

Financial Times/Prentice Hall, One Lake St, Upper Saddle River, NJ 07458 *Tel:* 201-236-7000 *Toll Free Tel:* 800-922-0579 (orders) *Web Site:* www.phptr.com, pg 96

Timothy Findley Award, 90 Richmond St W, Suite 200, Toronto, ON M5C 1P1, Canada *Tel:* 416-504-8222 *Fax:* 416-504-9090 *E-mail:* info@writerstrust.com *Web Site:* www.writerstrust.com, pg 773

Fine Arts Work Center in Provincetown, 24 Pearl St, Provincetown, MA 02657 *Tel:* 508-487-9960 *Fax:* 508-487-8873 *E-mail:* general@fawc.org *Web Site:* www.fawc.org, pg 774

Fine Communications, 322 Eighth Ave, 15th fl, New York, NY 10001 *Tel:* 212-595-3500 *Fax:* 212-595-3779, pg 96

Fine Tune Your CTP Installation, 200 Deer Run Rd, Sewickley, PA 15143-2600 *Tel:* 412-741-6860 *Toll Free Tel:* 800-910-4283 *Fax:* 412-741-2311 *E-mail:* info@gain.net *Web Site:* www.gain.net, pg 743

Fine Wordworking, PO Box 3041, Monterey, CA 93942-3041 *Tel:* 831-375-6278, pg 599

FineEdge.com, 14004 Biz Point Lane, Anacortes, WA 98221 *Tel:* 360-299-8500 *Fax:* 360-299-0535 *Web Site:* www.fineedge.com, pg 97

James B Finn Literary Agency Inc, PO Box 28227A, St Louis, MO 63132 *Tel:* 314-997-7133, pg 630

Fire Engineering Books & Videos, 1421 S Sheridan Rd, Tulsa, OK 74112 *Toll Free Tel:* 800-752-9768 *Fax:* 918-831-9555 *E-mail:* sales@penwell.com *Web Site:* www.fireengineeringbooks.com, pg 97

Firefly Books Ltd, 66 Leek Crescent, Richmond Hill, ON L4B 1H1, Canada *Tel:* 416-499-8412 *Toll Free Tel:* 800-387-5085 *Fax:* 416-499-1142 *Toll Free Fax:* 800-565-6034 *E-mail:* service@fireflybooks.com *Web Site:* www.fireflybooks.com, pg 546

Fireside & Touchstone, 1230 Avenue of the Americas, New York, NY 10020, pg 97

The Firm, 9465 Wilshire Blvd, Beverly Hills, CA 90212 *Tel:* 310-860-8000 *Fax:* 310-860-8132, pg 630

Firman Houghton Prize, 16 Cornell St, Arlington, MA 02474 *Web Site:* www.nepoetryclub.org, pg 774

First Avenue Editions, 241 First Ave N, Minneapolis, MN 55401 *Tel:* 612-332-3344 *Toll Free Tel:* 800-328-4929 *Fax:* 612-332-7615 *Toll Free Fax:* 800-332-1132 *E-mail:* info@lernerbooks.com *Web Site:* www.lernerbooks.com, pg 97

First Folio Resource Group Inc, 10 King St E, Suite 801, Toronto, ON M5C 1C3, Canada *Tel:* 416-368-7668 *Fax:* 416-368-9363 *E-mail:* mail@firstfolio.com *Web Site:* www.firstfolio.com, pg 599

The Fischer Ross Group Inc, 249 E 48 St, 15th fl, New York, NY 10017 *Tel:* 212-355-5777 *Fax:* 212-355-7820 *E-mail:* frgstaff@earthlink.net, pg 669

Robert L Fish Memorial Award, 17 E 47 St, 6th fl, New York, NY 10017 *Tel:* 212-888-8171 *E-mail:* mwa@mysterywriters.org *Web Site:* www.mysterywriters.org, pg 774

Dorothy Canfield Fisher Children's Book Award, 109 State St, Montpelier, VT 05609-0601 *Tel:* 802-828-6954 *Fax:* 802-828-2199 *E-mail:* dol@dol.state.vt.us *Web Site:* www.dcfaward.org; dol.state.vt.us, pg 774

Mary Bucher Fisher Editor, 100 Glenmont Ave, Columbus, OH 43214-3255 *Tel:* 614-262-5628, pg 599

The Fisherman Library, 1622 Beaver Dam Rd, Point Pleasant, NJ 08742 *Tel:* 732-295-8600 *Fax:* 732-295-4162, pg 97

Fitzhenry & Whiteside Limited, 195 Allstate Pkwy, Markham, ON L3R 4T8, Canada *Tel:* 905-477-9700 *Toll Free Tel:* 800-387-9776 *Fax:* 905-477-9179 *Toll Free Fax:* 800-260-9777 *E-mail:* godwit@fitzhenry.ca *Web Site:* www.fitzhenry.ca, pg 547

Five Star Publications Inc, 4696 W Tyson St, Dept LM, Chandler, AZ 85226 *Tel:* 480-940-8182 *Fax:* 480-940-8787 *E-mail:* info@fivestarpublications.com *Web Site:* www.fivestarpublications.com; www.authorsandexperts.com; www.youcanpublish.com; www.schoolbookings.com, pg 97

Five Star Speakers & Trainers LLC, 8685 W 96 St, Overland Park, KS 66212 *Tel:* 913-648-6480 *Fax:* 913-648-6484 *E-mail:* fivestar@fivestarspeakers.com *Web Site:* www.fivestarspeakers.com, pg 669

FJH Music Co Inc, 2525 Davie Rd, Suite 360, Fort Lauderdale, FL 33317 *Tel:* 954-382-6061 *Toll Free Tel:* 800-262-8744 *Fax:* 954-382-3073 *E-mail:* custserv@fjhmusic.com *Web Site:* www.fjhmusic.com, pg 97

Flaming Star Literary Enterprises, 320 Riverside Dr, Suite 12-D, New York, NY 10025 *E-mail:* flamingstarlit@aol.com, pg 630

Flammarion Quebec, 375 Ave Laurier ouest, Montreal, PQ H2V 2K3, Canada *Tel:* 514-277-8807 *Fax:* 514-278-2085 *E-mail:* info@flammarion.qc.ca *Web Site:* www.flammarion.qc.ca, pg 547

William Flanagan Memorial Creative Persons Center, 14 Harrison St, New York, NY 10013 *Tel:* 212-226-2020 *E-mail:* info@albeefoundation.org *Web Site:* www.albeefoundation.org, pg 774

Flannery Literary, 1155 S Washington St, Suite 202, Naperville, IL 60540 *Tel:* 630-428-2682 *Fax:* 630-428-2683, pg 630

Peter Fleming Agency, PO Box 458, Pacific Palisades, CA 90272 *Tel:* 310-454-1373, pg 630

Karen Flemister, 3145 E Chandler Blvd, Suite 110-527, Phoenix, AZ 85048 *Tel:* 480-759-4840 *Fax:* 509-757-5006 *E-mail:* karen@mikare.com *Web Site:* www.mikare.com, pg 599

Florida Academic Press, PO Box 540, Gainesville, FL 32602-0540 *Tel:* 352-332-5104 *Fax:* 352-331-6003 *E-mail:* fapress@worldnet.att.net, pg 97

Florida Freelance Writers Association, Main St, North Stratford, NH 03590 *Tel:* 603-922-8338 *Fax:* 603-922-8339 *E-mail:* FFWA@writers-editors.com *Web Site:* www.writers-editors.com; www.ffwamembers.com, pg 687

Florida Funding Publications Inc, PO Box 561565, Miami, FL 33256 *Tel:* 305-251-2203 *Fax:* 305-251-2773 *E-mail:* info@floridafunding.com *Web Site:* www.floridafunding.com, pg 97

Florida Individual Artist Fellowships, 1001 DeSoto Park Dr, Tallahassee, FL 32301 *Tel:* 850-245-6470 *Fax:* 850-245-6492 *Web Site:* www.florida-arts.org, pg 774

The Florida Publishers Association Inc, PO Box 430, Highland City, FL 33846-0430 *Tel:* 863-647-5951 *Fax:* 863-647-5951 *E-mail:* fpabooks@aol.com *Web Site:* www.flbookpub.org, pg 687

Florida State Writing Competition, Main St, North Stratford, NH 03590 *Tel:* 603-922-8338 *Fax:* 603-922-8339 *E-mail:* contest@writers-editors.com *Web Site:* www.writers-editors.com, pg 774

Florida Suncoast Writers' Conference, 4202 Fowler Ave, MHH 116, Tampa, FL 33620-6756 *Tel:* 813-974-1711 *Fax:* 813-974-1459 *Web Site:* english.cas.usf.edu/fswc/, pg 743

Florida Writers Association Conference, 10615 Limewood Dr, Jacksonville, FL 32257 *Tel:* 904-343-4188 *Toll Free Tel:* 800-536-5919 *Web Site:* www.floridawriters.net, pg 743

Flower Valley Press Inc, 7851-C Beechcraft Rd, Gaithersburg, MA 20809 *Tel:* 301-654-1996 *Toll Free Tel:* 800-735-5197 *Web Site:* www.flowervalleypress.com, pg 97

Flying Frog Publishing, 107 Nob Hill Park Dr, Reistertown, MD 21136 *Tel:* 410-833-6261 *Fax:* 410-833-6193 *E-mail:* allied@allpubmd.com, pg 97

Focus on the Family, 8605 Explorer Dr, Colorado Springs, CO 80920 *Tel:* 719-531-3400 *Fax:* 719-531-3484 *Web Site:* www.family.org, pg 97

Focus Publishing/R Pullins Co Inc, 311 Merrimac St, Newburyport, MA 01950 *Tel:* 978-462-7288 (edit) *Toll Free Tel:* 800-848-7236 (orders) *Fax:* 978-462-9035 (orders) *E-mail:* pullins@pullins.com *Web Site:* www.pullins.com, pg 98

Focus Strategic Communications Inc, 535 Tipperton, Oakville, ON L6L 5E1, Canada *Tel:* 905-825-8757 *Toll Free Tel:* 866-263-6287 *Fax:* 905-825-5724 *Toll Free Fax:* 866-613-6287 *E-mail:* info@focussc.com *Web Site:* www.focussc.com, pg 599

Fodor's Travel Publications, 1745 Broadway, New York, NY 10019 *Tel:* 212-572-8784 *Toll Free Tel:* 800-733-3000 *Fax:* 212-572-2248 *Web Site:* www.fodors.com, pg 98

FOG Publications, 413 Pennsylvania NE, Albuquerque, NM 87108 *Tel:* 505-255-3096, pg 98

The Fogelman Literary Agency, 7515 Greenville Ave, Suite 712, Dallas, TX 75231 *Tel:* 214-361-9956 *Fax:* 214-361-9553 *E-mail:* info@fogelman.com *Web Site:* www.fogelman.com, pg 630

Sheldon Fogelman Agency Inc, 10 E 40 St, Suite 3800, New York, NY 10016 *Tel:* 212-532-7250 *Fax:* 212-685-8939 *E-mail:* fogelman@worldnet.att.net; agency@sheldonfogelmanagency.com, pg 630

Foil Stamping & Embossing Association, 2150 SW Westport Dr, Suite 101, Topeka, KS 66614 *Tel:* 785-271-5816 *Fax:* 785-271-6404 *Web Site:* www.fsea.com, pg 687

The Foley Agency, 34 E 38 St, New York, NY 10016 *Tel:* 212-686-6930, pg 630

Folklore Publishing, 8025 102 St, Edmonton, AB T6E 4A2, Canada *Tel:* 780-910-6216 *Fax:* 780-433-9646 *Web Site:* www.folklorepublishing.com, pg 547

Follett Higher Education Group, 1818 Swift Dr, Oak Grove, IL 60523 *Tel:* 630-279-2330 *Toll Free Tel:* 800-323-4506 *Fax:* 630-279-2569 *Web Site:* www.fheg.follett.com, pg 687

Fondo de Cultura Economica USA Inc, 2293 Verus St, San Diego, CA 92154 *Tel:* 619-429-0455 *Toll Free Tel:* 800-532-3872 *Fax:* 619-429-0827 *E-mail:* sales@fceusa.com *Web Site:* www.fceusa.com, pg 98

Fons Vitae, 49 Mockingbird Valley Dr, Louisville, KY 40207-1366 *Tel:* 502-897-3641 *Fax:* 502-893-7373 *E-mail:* fonsvitaeky@aol.com *Web Site:* www.fonsvitae.com, pg 98

Food and Beverage Consultants, 39 Burnview Crescent, Toronto, ON M1H 1B4, Canada *Tel:* 416-431-2015 *Fax:* 416-431-2015 *E-mail:* h1rayr@netscape.com, pg 547

Food & Nutrition Press Inc (FNP), 6527 Main St, Trumbull, CT 06611 *Tel:* 203-261-8587 *Fax:* 203-261-9724 *E-mail:* foodpress@worldnet.att.net *Web Site:* www.foodscipress.com, pg 98

Clifford Ford Publications, 120 Walnut Ct, Unit 15, Ottawa, ON K1R 7W2, Canada *Tel:* 613-230-3666 *Fax:* 613-230-6725 *E-mail:* host@cliffordfordpublications.ca *Web Site:* cliffordfordpublications.ca, pg 687

Fordham University, Graduate School of Business Administration, Dept of Communications & Media Management, 113 W 60 St, New York, NY 10023 *Tel:* 212-636-6199 *Fax:* 212-765-5573, pg 752

Fordham University, Graduate School of Business Administration, 33 W 60 St, 4th fl, Off of Graduate Admissions, New York, NY 10023 *Tel:* 212-636-6200 *Fax:* 212-636-7076, pg 774

Fordham University Press, 2546 Belmont Ave, Bronx, NY 10458-5172 *Tel:* 718-817-4780 *Toll Free Tel:* 800-247-6553 (orders) *Fax:* 718-817-4785 *Web Site:* www.fordhampress.com, pg 98

Forest House Publishing Co Inc & HTS Books, PO Box 13350, Chandler, AZ 85248 *Tel:* 480-802-1955 *Toll Free Tel:* 800-394-READ (394-7323) *Fax:* 480-802-1957 *E-mail:* info@forest-house.com *Web Site:* www.forest-house.com, pg 98

Morris D Forkosch Prize, 400 "A" St SE, Washington, DC 20003 *Tel:* 202-544-2422 *Fax:* 202-544-8307 *E-mail:* info@historians.org *Web Site:* www.historians.org, pg 774

Fort Ross Inc, 26 Arthur Place, Yonkers, NY 10701 *Tel:* 914-375-6448 *Fax:* 914-375-6439 *E-mail:* fort.ross@verizon.net *Web Site:* www.fortross.net, pg 99

Fort Ross Inc - International Rights, 26 Arthur Place, Yonkers, NY 10701 *Tel:* 914-375-6448 *Fax:* 914-375-6439 *E-mail:* fort.ross@verizon.net *Web Site:* www.fortross.net, pg 631, 665

Forthwrite Literary Agency & Speakers Bureau, 23852 W Pacific Coast Hwy, Suite 701, Malibu, CA 90265 *Tel:* 310-394-9840 *Toll Free Tel:* 866-62WRITE (629-7483) *Fax:* 310-394-9857 *E-mail:* agent@kellermedia.com *Web Site:* www.KellerMedia.com, pg 631

49th Parallel Poetry Award, Mail Stop 9053, Western Washington University, Bellingham, WA 98225 *Tel:* 360-650-4863 *E-mail:* bhreview@cc.wwu.edu *Web Site:* www.wwu.edu/~bhreview, pg 774

Forum Publishing Co, 383 E Main St, Centerport, NY 11721 *Tel:* 631-754-5000 *Fax:* 631-754-0630 *Web Site:* www.forumbooks.com, pg 99

Forward Movement Publications, 300 W Fourth St, Cincinnati, OH 45202 *Tel:* 513-721-6659 *Toll Free Tel:* 800-543-1813 *Fax:* 513-721-0729 *E-mail:* orders@forwarddaybyday.com *Web Site:* www.forwardmovement.org, pg 99

Foster City Writers Contest, 650 Shell Blvd, Foster City, CA 94404 *Tel:* 650-286-3380 *Web Site:* www.fostercity.org, pg 774

Pat Foster Artist Representative, 32 W 40 St, Suite 2 S, New York, NY 10018 *Tel:* 212-575-6887 *Fax:* 212-869-6871 *E-mail:* pfosterrep@aol.com *Web Site:* www.patfosterartrep.com, pg 665

Foster Travel Publishing, PO Box 5715, Berkeley, CA 94705-0715 *Tel:* 510-549-2202 *Fax:* 510-549-1131 *E-mail:* lee@fostertravel.com *Web Site:* www.fostertravel.com, pg 599

Walter Foster Publishing Inc, 23062 La Cadena Dr, Laguna Hills, CA 92653 *Tel:* 949-380-7510 *Toll Free Tel:* 800-426-0099 *Fax:* 949-380-7575 *Web Site:* www.walterfoster.com, pg 99

Foto Expression International (Toronto), 27 Saint Clair Ave E, Suite 1268, Toronto, ON M4T 2P4, Canada *Tel:* 705-745-5770 *Fax:* 705-745-9459 *E-mail:* operations@fotopressnews.org *Web Site:* www.fotopressnews.org, pg 666

The Foundation Center, 79 Fifth Ave, New York, NY 10003-3076 *Tel:* 212-807-3690 *Toll Free Tel:* 800-424-9836 *Fax:* 212-807-3691 *Web Site:* www.fdncenter.org, pg 99

The Foundation for Economic Education Inc, 30 S Broadway, Irvington-on-Hudson, NY 10533 *Tel:* 914-591-7230 *Toll Free Tel:* 800-960-4FEE (960-4333) *Fax:* 914-591-8910 *E-mail:* fee@fee.org *Web Site:* www.fee.org, pg 99

Foundation of American Women in Radio & Television, 8405 Greensboro Dr, Suite 800, McLean, VA 22102 *Tel:* 703-506-3290 *Fax:* 703-506-3266 *E-mail:* info@awrt.org *Web Site:* www.awrt.org, pg 687

Foundation Press Inc, 395 Hudson St, New York, NY 10014 *Tel:* 212-367-6790 *Fax:* 212-367-6799 *Web Site:* www.foundation-press.com, pg 99

Foundation Publications, PO Box 6439, Anaheim, CA 92816 *Tel:* 714-879-2286 *Toll Free Tel:* 800-257-6272 *Fax:* 714-535-2164 *E-mail:* info@foundationpublications.com *Web Site:* www.foundationpublications.com, pg 99

The Fountain, 26 Worlds Fair Dr, Unit C, Somerset, NJ 08873 *Tel:* 732-808-0210 *Fax:* 732-808-0211 *E-mail:* contact@fountainmagazine.com *Web Site:* www.fountainmagazine.com, pg 99

Four Paws Press LLC, 2460 Garden Rd, Suite B, Monterey, CA 93940 *Tel:* 831-375-PAWS (375-7297) *Fax:* 831-649-8007 *Web Site:* www.fourpawspress.com, pg 99

Four Walls Eight Windows, 245 W 17 St, 11th fl, New York, NY 10011 *Tel:* 646-375-2570 *Fax:* 646-375-2571 *Web Site:* www.4w8w.com, pg 99

FourWinds Press LLC, 4157 Crossgate Dr, Cincinnati, OH 47025 *Tel:* 513-891-0415 *Fax:* 513-891-1648 *Web Site:* www.fourwindspress.com, pg 571

Fox Chapel Publishing Co Inc, 1970 Broad St, East Petersburg, PA 17520 *Tel:* 717-560-4703 *Toll Free Tel:* 800-457-9112 *Fax:* 717-560-4702 *E-mail:* custservice@foxchapelpublishing.com *Web Site:* www.foxchapelpublishing.com, pg 99

The Fox Chase Agency Inc, 701 Lee Rd, Suite 102, Chesterbrook, PA 19087 *Tel:* 610-640-7560 *Fax:* 610-640-7562, pg 631

Fox Song Books, 2315 Glendale Blvd, Unit B, Los Angeles, CA 90039 *Toll Free Tel:* 888-369-2769 *Toll Free Fax:* 888-309-5063 *E-mail:* fox@foxsongbooks.com *Web Site:* foxsongbooks.com, pg 100

FPMI Solutions Inc, 4901 University Sq, Suite 3, Huntsville, AL 35816 *Tel:* 256-539-1850 *Fax:* 256-539-0911 *E-mail:* books@fpmi.com *Web Site:* www.fpmisolutions.com, pg 100

Franciscan Press, 1800 College Ave, Quincy, IL 62301-2699 *Tel:* 217-228-5670 *Fax:* 217-228-5672 *Web Site:* www.franciscanpress.com, pg 100

Sandi Frank, 8 Fieldcrest Ct, Cortlandt Manor, NY 10567 *Tel:* 914-739-7088 *Fax:* 914-739-7058 *E-mail:* sfrankmail@aol.com, pg 599

Frankel & Associates, 5120 Wright Terr, Skokie, IL 60077 *Tel:* 847-674-8417, pg 669

Norman Frankel, 5120 Wright Terr, Skokie, IL 60077-2142 *Tel:* 847-674-8417 *E-mail:* nfrankel@mindspring.com, pg 599

Franklin, Beedle & Associates Inc, 8536 SW St Helens Dr, Suite D, Wilsonville, OR 97070 *Tel:* 503-682-7668 *Toll Free Tel:* 800-322-2665 *Fax:* 503-682-7638 *Web Site:* www.fbeedle.com, pg 100

Franklin Book Co Inc, 7804 Montgomery Ave, Elkins Park, PA 19027 *Tel:* 215-635-5252 *Fax:* 215-635-6155 *E-mail:* service@franklinbook.com *Web Site:* www.franklinbook.com, pg 100

Lynn C Franklin Associates Ltd, 1350 Broadway, Suite 2015, New York, NY 10018 *Tel:* 212-868-6311 *Fax:* 212-868-6312 *E-mail:* agency@fsainc.com, pg 631

The Fraser Institute, 1770 Burrard St, 4th fl, Vancouver, BC V6J 3G7, Canada *Tel:* 604-688-0221 *Toll Free Tel:* 800-665-3558 *Fax:* 604-688-8539 *E-mail:* sales@fraserinstitute.ca *Web Site:* www.fraserinstitute.ca, pg 547

Fraser Publishing Co, PO Box 217, Flint Hill, VA 22627 *Tel:* 540-675-9976 *Toll Free Tel:* 877-996-3336 *Fax:* 786-513-2807 *E-mail:* info@fraserpublishing.com *Web Site:* www.fraserpublishing.com, pg 100

Soeurette Diehl Fraser Award, 3700 Mockingbird Lane, Dallas, TX 75205 *Tel:* 512-245-2232 *Fax:* 512-245-7462 *Web Site:* www.stedwards.edu/newc/marks/til/awards_and_rules.htm, pg 774

Frederick Fell Publishers Inc, 2131 Hollywood Blvd, Suite 305, Hollywood, FL 33020 *Tel:* 954-925-5242 *Toll Free Tel:* 800-771-FELL (771-3355) *Fax:* 954-925-5244 *E-mail:* info@fellpub.com *Web Site:* www.fellpub.com, pg 100

Jeanne Fredericks Literary Agency Inc, 221 Benedict Hill Rd, New Canaan, CT 06840 *Tel:* 203-972-3011 *Fax:* 203-972-3011 *E-mail:* jfredrks@optonline.net (no unsol attachments), pg 631

Free Press, 1230 Avenue of the Americas, New York, NY 10020 *Tel:* 212-698-7000 *Toll Free Tel:* 800-223-2345 (cust serv); 800-223-2336 (orders); 888-866-6631 (fulfillment), pg 100

Free Spirit Publishing Inc, 217 Fifth Ave N, Suite 200, Minneapolis, MN 55401-1299 *Tel:* 612-338-2068 *Toll Free Tel:* 800-735-7323 *Fax:* 612-337-5050 *E-mail:* help4kids@freespirit.com *Web Site:* www.freespirit.com, pg 100

George Freedley Memorial Award, Queens College, CUNY, Flushing, NY 11367 *Tel:* 718-997-3672 *Fax:* 718-997-3753 *Web Site:* tla.library.unt.edu, pg 775

Robert A Freedman Dramatic Agency Inc, 1501 Broadway, Suite 2310, New York, NY 10036 *Tel:* 212-840-5760 *Fax:* 212-840-5776, pg 631

Freedom of Information Center, 133 Neff Annex, Columbia, MO 65211-0012 *Tel:* 573-882-4856 *Fax:* 573-884-6204 *E-mail:* foi@missouri.edu *Web Site:* foi.missouri.edu, pg 687

Freelance Express Inc, 111 E 85 St, New York, NY 10028 *Tel:* 212-427-0331, pg 599

The Don Freeman Memorial Grant-In-Aid, 8271 Beverly Blvd, Los Angeles, CA 90048 *Tel:* 323-782-1010 *Fax:* 323-782-1892 *E-mail:* membership@scbwi.org *Web Site:* www.scbwi.org, pg 775

Sheila Freeman, 3392 Old 3 "L" Hwy, Falmouth, KY 41040 *Tel:* 859-654-3132 *E-mail:* sheilafreeman@cs.com, pg 599

W H Freeman and Co, 41 Madison Ave, 37th fl, New York, NY 10010 *Tel:* 212-576-9400 *Fax:* 212-689-2383 *Web Site:* www.whfreeman.com, pg 100

The French-American Foundation Translation Prize, 28 W 44 St, Suite 1420, New York, NY 10036 *Tel:* 212-829-8800 *Fax:* 212-829-8810 *E-mail:* info@frenchamerican.org *Web Site:* www.frenchamerican.org, pg 775

French & European Publications Inc, Rockefeller Center Promenade, 610 Fifth Ave, New York, NY 10020-2497 *Tel:* 212-581-8810 *Fax:* 212-265-1094 *E-mail:* livresny@aol.com *Web Site:* www.frencheuropean.com, pg 101

Samuel French Inc, 45 W 25 St, New York, NY 10010-2751 *Tel:* 212-206-8990 *Fax:* 212-206-1429 *E-mail:* samuelfrench@earthlink.net *Web Site:* www.samuelfrench.com, pg 101, 631

Sarah Jane Freymann Literary Agency, 59 W 71 St, Suite 9B, New York, NY 10023 *Tel:* 212-362-9277 *Fax:* 212-501-8240 *E-mail:* sjfs@aol.com, pg 631

Frieda Carrol Communications, PO Box 416, Denver, CO 80201-0416 *Tel:* 303-575-5676 *Fax:* 303-575-1187 *E-mail:* mail@gumbomedia.com, pg 101

Friends of American Writers Award, 680 N Lake Shore Dr, Suite L208, Chicago, IL 60611 *Tel:* 312-664-5628, pg 775

Friends of Libraries USA, 1420 Walnut St, Suite 450, Philadelphia, PA 19102-4017 *Tel:* 215-790-1674 *Toll Free Tel:* 800-936-5872 *Fax:* 215-545-3821 *E-mail:* folusa@folusa.org *Web Site:* www.folusa.org, pg 687

Friends of the Dallas Public Library Award, Center for the Study of the Southwest, Southwest Texas State University, San Marcos, TX 78666 *Tel:* 512-245-2232 *Fax:* 512-245-7462 *Web Site:* www.stedwards.edu/newc/marks/til/awards_and_rules.htm, pg 775

Friends United Press, 101 Quaker Hill Dr, Richmond, IN 47374 *Tel:* 765-962-7573 *Toll Free Tel:* 800-537-8839 *Fax:* 765-966-1293 *E-mail:* friendspress@fum.org *Web Site:* www.fum.org, pg 101

Frisbie/Communications, 445 W Erie St, No 104, Chicago, IL 60610 *Tel:* 312-397-0992 *Fax:* 312-255-9865 *Web Site:* www.richardfrisbie.net, pg 599

Frog Ltd, 1435 Fourth St, Berkeley, CA 94710 *Tel:* 510-559-8277 *Toll Free Tel:* 800-337-2665 (book orders only) *Fax:* 510-559-8279 *E-mail:* orders@northatlanticbooks.com *Web Site:* www.northatlanticbooks.com, pg 101

Fromer Editorial Services, 1606 Noyes Dr, Silver Spring, MD 20910-2224 *Tel:* 301-585-8827 *Fax:* 301-585-1369 *E-mail:* margotfromer@erols.com, pg 599

Front Street Inc, 862 Haywood Rd, Asheville, NC 28806 *Tel:* 828-236-3097 *Fax:* 828-221-2112 *E-mail:* contactus@frontstreetbooks.com *Web Site:* www.frontstreetbooks.com, pg 101

Fugue State Press, PO Box 80, Cooper Sta, New York, NY 10276 *Tel:* 212-673-7922 *Fax:* 208-693-6152 *E-mail:* info@fuguestatepress.com *Web Site:* www.fuguestatepress.com, pg 101

Candice Fuhrman Literary Agency, 60 Greenwood Way, Mill Valley, CA 94941 *Tel:* 415-383-6081 *Fax:* 415-384-0739 *E-mail:* candicef@pacbell.net, pg 632

Fulbright Scholar Program, 3007 Tilden St NW, Suite 5-L, Washington, DC 20008-3009 *Tel:* 202-686-4000 *Fax:* 202-362-3442 *E-mail:* cieswebmaster@cies.iie.org *Web Site:* www.cies.org, pg 775

Fulcrum Publishing Inc, 16100 Table Mountain Pkwy, Suite 300, Golden, CO 80403 *Tel:* 303-277-1623 *Toll Free Tel:* 800-992-2908 *Fax:* 303-279-7111 *Toll Free Fax:* 800-726-7112 *E-mail:* fulcrum@fulcrum-books.com *Web Site:* www.fulcrum-books.com, pg 101

Richard Fulton Inc, 66 Richfield St, Plainview, NY 11803 *Tel:* 516-349-0407 *Fax:* 516-349-0407, pg 669

Fun in the Sun 2005, PO Box 451356, Sunrise, FL 33345 *Tel:* 954-748-1707 *Web Site:* www.frwriters.org, pg 743

Future Horizons Inc, 721 W Abram St, Arlington, TX 76013 *Tel:* 817-277-0727 *Toll Free Tel:* 800-489-0727 *Fax:* 817-277-2270 *E-mail:* info@futurehorizons-autism.com *Web Site:* www.futurehorizons-autism.com, pg 102

G & S Editors, 410 Baylor, Austin, TX 78703-5312 *Tel:* 512-478-5341 *Fax:* 512-476-4756 *Web Site:* www.gstype.com, pg 599

G W Medical Publishing Inc, 77 Westport Plaza, Suite 366, St Louis, MO 63146-3124 *Tel:* 314-542-4213 *Toll Free Tel:* 800-600-0330 *Fax:* 314-542-4239 *E-mail:* info@gwmedical.com *Web Site:* www.gwmedical.com, pg 102

Marlene Gabriel Agency, 333 W 56 St, Suite 8-A, 8th fl, New York, NY 10019 *Tel:* 212-397-8322 *E-mail:* mgalit@aol.com, pg 632

Gabriela Mistral Inter-American Culture Prize, Unit of Social Development, Education & Culture, 1889 "F" St NW, Suite 771, Washington, DC 20006-4499 *Tel:* 202-458-3140 *Fax:* 202-458-6115 *E-mail:* culture@oas.org *Web Site:* www.oas.org, pg 775

Gaetan Morin Editeur Ltee, 7001 Blvd Sainte-Laurent, Montreal, PQ H2S 3E3, Canada *Tel:* 514-273-1066 *Fax:* 514-276-0324 *E-mail:* achat@groupemorin.com *Web Site:* groupemorin.com, pg 547

Gage Learning Corp, 1120 Birchmount Rd, Scarborough, ON M1K 5G4, Canada *Tel:* 416-752-9448 *Toll Free Tel:* 800-430-4445 *Fax:* 416-752-8101 *Toll Free Fax:* 800-430-4445 *E-mail:* inquire@nelson.com *Web Site:* www.nelson.com, pg 547

Gagosian Gallery, 980 Madison Ave, New York, NY 10021 *Tel:* 212-744-2313 *Fax:* 212-772-8696 *E-mail:* info@gagosian.com *Web Site:* www.gagosian.com, pg 102

Gail's Guides, PO Box 70323, Bellevue, WA 98005 *Tel:* 425-917-0737 *E-mail:* guides@oz.net *Web Site:* www.gailsguides.com, pg 102

Lewis Galantiere Prize, 225 Reinekers Lane, Suite 590, Alexandria, VA 22314 *Tel:* 703-683-6100 *Fax:* 703-683-6122 *E-mail:* ata@atanet.org *Web Site:* www.atanet.org, pg 775

Gallaudet University Press, 800 Florida Ave NE, Washington, DC 20002-3695 *Tel:* 202-651-5488 *Fax:* 202-651-5489 *E-mail:* gupress@gallaudet.edu *Web Site:* gupress.gallaudet.edu, pg 102

Diane Gallo, 9 Hilton St, Gilbertsville, NY 13776 *Tel:* 607-783-2386 *Fax:* 607-783-2386 *E-mail:* gallod@norwich.net *Web Site:* www.dianegallo.com, pg 599

Gallopade International Inc, 665 Hwy 74 S, Suite 600, Peachtree City, GA 30269 *Tel:* 770-631-4222 *Toll Free Tel:* 800-536-2GET (536-2438) *Fax:* 770-631-4810 *Toll Free Fax:* 800-871-2979 *E-mail:* info@gallopade.com *Web Site:* www.gallopade.com, pg 102

Galt Press, 1725 Clearwater-Largo Rd S, Clearwater, FL 33756 *Tel:* 727-581-8685 *Fax:* 727-585-8423 *E-mail:* galt@warda.net *Web Site:* www.warda.net/ GaltPress.html; www.galtpress.com, pg 102

The Garamond Agency Inc, 12 Horton St, Newburyport, MA 01950 *Tel:* 978-462-5060 *Fax:* 978-462-6697 *Web Site:* www.garamondagency.com, pg 632

Garamond Press Ltd, 63 Mahogany Ct, Aurora, ON L4G 6M8, Canada *Tel:* 905-841-1460 *Toll Free Tel:* 800-898-9535 *Fax:* 905-841-3031 *E-mail:* garamond@web.ca *Web Site:* www.garamond.ca, pg 547

Garden Writers Association of America, 10210 Leatherleaf Ct, Manassas, VA 20111 *Tel:* 703-257-1032 *Fax:* 703-257-0213 *E-mail:* info@gwaa.org *Web Site:* www.gwaa.org, pg 687

Anthony Gardner Literary Agent, 2 Cornelia St, New York, NY 10014 *Tel:* 212-229-9407 *Fax:* 212-627-0511 *E-mail:* stylegal@aol.com, pg 632

Gareth Stevens Inc, 330 W Olive St, Suite 100, Milwaukee, WI 53212 *Tel:* 414-332-3520 *Toll Free Tel:* 800-542-2595 *Fax:* 414-332-3567 *E-mail:* info@gspub.com; info@worldalmanaclibrary. com *Web Site:* www.garethstevens.com; www. worldalmanaclibrary.com, pg 102

Garland Science Publishing, 270 Madison Ave, New York, NY 10016 *Tel:* 212-216-7800 *Fax:* 212-947-3027 *E-mail:* info@garland.com *Web Site:* www. garlandscience.com, pg 102

Garlinghouse Inc, 174 Oakwood Dr, Glastonbury, CT 06033 *Tel:* 860-659-5667 *Fax:* 860-659-5692 *E-mail:* info@garlinghouse.com *Web Site:* www. garlinghouse.com, pg 102

Francois-Xavier Garneau Medal, 395 Wellington St, Ottawa, ON K1A 0N3, Canada *Tel:* 613-233-7885 *Fax:* 613-567-3110 *E-mail:* cha-shc@archives.ca *Web Site:* www.cha-shc.ca, pg 775

Max Gartenberg Literary Agency, 12 Westminster Dr, Livingston, NJ 07039-1414 *Tel:* 973-994-4457 *Fax:* 973-994-4457 *E-mail:* gartenbook@att.net, pg 632

The Gary-Paul Agency, 1549 Main St, Stratford, CT 00615 *Tel:* 203-375-2636 *Fax:* 203-375-2636 *Web Site:* www.thegarypaulagency.com, pg 600

John Gassner Memorial Playwriting Award, PMB 502, 198 Tremont St, Boston, MA 02116-4750 *Tel:* 617-851-8535 *E-mail:* mail@netconline.org *Web Site:* www.netconline.org, pg 775

Gateways Books & Tapes, PO Box 370, Nevada City, CA 95959 *Tel:* 530-477-8101 *Toll Free Tel:* 800-869-0658 *Fax:* 530-272-0184 *E-mail:* info@ gatewaysbooksandtapes.com *Web Site:* www. gatewaysbooksandtapes.com; www.retrosf.com, pg 103

Gault Millau Inc/Gayot Publications, 4311 Wilshire Blvd, Suite 405, Los Angeles, CA 90010 *Tel:* 323-965-3529 *Toll Free Tel:* 800-LE BEST 1 *Fax:* 323-936-2883 *E-mail:* info@gayot.com *Web Site:* www. gayot.com, pg 103

Gauntlet Press, 5307 Arroyo St, Colorado Springs, CO 80922 *Tel:* 719-591-5566 *Fax:* 719-591-6676 *E-mail:* info@gauntletpress.com *Web Site:* www. gauntletpress.com, pg 103

The Christian Gauss Award, 1606 New Hampshire Ave NW, Washington, DC 20009 *Tel:* 202-265-3808 *Fax:* 202-986-1601 *Web Site:* www.pbk.org, pg 775

Gay Sunshine Press/Leyland Publications, PO Box 410690, San Francisco, CA 94141 *Tel:* 415-626-1935 *Fax:* 415-626-1802 *Web Site:* www.gaysunshine.com, pg 103

The Gaylactic Spectrum Awards, c/o Lambda Sci-Fi, PO Box 656, Washington, DC 20044 *Tel:* 202-483-6369 *E-mail:* info@spectrumawards.org *Web Site:* www. spectrumawards.org, pg 775

Gaylord College of Journalism & Mass Communication, Professional Writing Program, c/o University of Oklahoma, 860 Van Vleet Oval, Rm 101, Norman, OK 73019-0270 *Tel:* 405-325-2721 *Fax:* 405-325-7565, pg 752

Gazelle Publications, 11560 Red Bud Trail, Berrien Springs, MI 49103 *Tel:* 269-471-4717 *Toll Free Tel:* 800-650-5076 *E-mail:* info@gazellepublications. com *Web Site:* www.gazellepublications.com, pg 103

Fred Gebhart, 2346 25 Ave, San Francisco, CA 94116-2337 *Tel:* 415-681-3018 *Fax:* 415-681-0350 *E-mail:* fgebhart@pobox.com *Web Site:* www. fredgebhart.com, pg 600

Gefen Books, 600 Broadway, Lynbrook, NY 11563 *Tel:* 516-593-1234 *Toll Free Tel:* 800-477-5257 *Fax:* 516-295-2739 *E-mail:* gefenny@gefenpublishing. com *Web Site:* www.israelbooks.com, pg 103

Lionel Gelber Prize, University of Toronto, Munk Centre for International Studies, One Devonshire Place, Toronto, ON M5S 3K7, Canada *Tel:* 416-946-8901 *Fax:* 416-946-8915 *E-mail:* gelberprize.munk@ utoronto.ca *Web Site:* www.utoronto.ca/mcis/gelber, pg 776

Gelfman Schneider Literary Agents Inc, 250 W 57 St, Suite 2515, New York, NY 10107 *Tel:* 212-245-1993 *Fax:* 212-245-8678 *E-mail:* mail@gelfmanschneider. com, pg 632

Gelles-Cole Literary Enterprises, PO Box 341, Woodstock, NY 12498-0341 *Tel:* 845-247-8111 *Web Site:* www.consulting-editors.com, pg 600

Gem Guides Book Co, 315 Cloverleaf Dr, Suite F, Baldwin Park, CA 91706 *Tel:* 626-855-1611 *Fax:* 626-855-1610 *E-mail:* gembooks@aol.com, pg 103

GEM Publications, 411 Mallalieu Dr, Hudson, WI 54016 *Tel:* 715-386-7113 *Toll Free Tel:* 800-290-6128 *Fax:* 715-386-7113 *E-mail:* gem@spacestar.net *Web Site:* www.spacestar.com/users/gem, pg 103

GemStone Press, Sunset Farm Offices, Rte 4, Woodstock, VT 05091 *Tel:* 802-457-4000 *Toll Free Tel:* 800-962-4544 *Fax:* 802-457-4004 *E-mail:* sales@ gemstonepress.com *Web Site:* www.gemstonepress. com, pg 103

Genealogical Publishing Co Inc, 1001 N Calvert St, Baltimore, MD 21202 *Tel:* 410-837-8271 *Toll Free Tel:* 800-296-6687 *Fax:* 410-752-8492 *E-mail:* orders@genealogical.com *Web Site:* www. genealogical.com, pg 103

General Store Publishing House, 499 O'Brien Rd, Renfrew, ON K7V 4A6, Canada *Tel:* 613-432-7697 *Toll Free Tel:* 800-465-6072 *Fax:* 613-432-7184 *Web Site:* www.gsph.com, pg 547

General Trade Publishing & Retailing, 4816 S Ash Ave, Suite 101, Tempe, AZ 85282-7735 *Tel:* 480-966-3998 *Fax:* 480-966-1944 *Web Site:* www.ecpa.org, pg 743

Genesis Press Inc, PO Box 101, Columbus, MS 39703 *Tel:* 662-329-9927 *Toll Free Tel:* 888-463-4461 (orders only) *Fax:* 662-329-9399 *E-mail:* books@genesis-press.com *Web Site:* www.genesis-press.com, pg 103

Genesis Publishing Co Inc, 36 Steeple View Dr, Atkinson, NH 03811 *Tel:* 603-362-4121 *Fax:* 603-362-4121 *E-mail:* genesis@genesisbook.com *Web Site:* genesispc.com, pg 104

Geological Society of America (GSA), 3300 Penrose Place, Boulder, CO 80301 *Tel:* 303-447-2020 *Toll Free Tel:* 800-472-1988 *Fax:* 303-357-1070 *E-mail:* pubs@ geosociety.org *Web Site:* www.geosociety.org, pg 104

Geolytics Inc, PO Box 10, East Brunswick, NJ 08816 *Tel:* 732-651-2000 *Toll Free Tel:* 800-577-6717 *Fax:* 732-651-2721 *E-mail:* support@geolytics.com *Web Site:* www.geolytics.com, pg 104

Georgetown University Press, 3240 Prospect St NW, Washington, DC 20007 *Tel:* 202-687-6251 (acq); 202-687-5889 (busn); 202-687-5641 (mktg); 410-516-6956 (orders) *Toll Free Tel:* 800-537-5487 *Fax:* 202-687-6340 (edit); 410-516-6998 (orders) *E-mail:* gupress@ georgetown.edu *Web Site:* www.press.georgetown.edu, pg 104

Geoscience Press Inc, PO Box 42948, Tuscon, AZ 85733-2948 *Tel:* 520-529-1567 *Fax:* 520-529-1567 *E-mail:* geobook@ix.netcom.com, pg 104

Gerald & Cullen Rapp Inc, 420 Lexington Ave, Suite 3100, New York, NY 10170 *Tel:* 212-889-3337 *Fax:* 212-889-3341 *E-mail:* gerald@rappart.com *Web Site:* www.rappart.com, pg 666

Leo Gershoy Award, 400 "A" St SE, Washington, DC 20003 *Tel:* 202-544-2422 *Fax:* 202-544-8307 *E-mail:* info@historians.org *Web Site:* www.historians. org, pg 776

Susan M Gerstein, 620 E Valerio St, Santa Barbara, CA 93103 *Tel:* 805-569-2415 *E-mail:* gerstein@cox.net, pg 600

Gestalt Journal Press, PO Box 278, Gouldsboro, ME 04607-0278 *Tel:* 845-691-7192 *Fax:* 775-254-1855 *E-mail:* tgjournal@gestalt.org *Web Site:* www.gestalt. org, pg 104

Getty Publications, 1200 Getty Center Dr, Suite 500, Los Angeles, CA 90049-1682 *Tel:* 310-440-7365 *Fax:* 310-440-7758 *E-mail:* pubsinfo@getty.edu *Web Site:* www. getty.edu/bookstore, pg 104

GGP Publishing Inc, 138 Chatsworth Ave, Suite 3-5, Larchmont, NY 10538 *Tel:* 914-834-8896 *Fax:* 914-834-7566 *Web Site:* www.ggppublishing.com, pg 600, 632

Ghosts & Collaborators International, PO Box 358, New Canaan, CT 06840 *Tel:* 203-972-1070 *Fax:* 203-972-1759, pg 632

GIA Publications, Inc, 7404 S Mason Ave, Chicago, IL 60638 *Tel:* 708-496-3800 *Toll Free Tel:* 800-442-1358 *Fax:* 708-496-3828 *E-mail:* custserv@giamusic.com *Web Site:* www.giamusic.com, pg 104

Gibbs Smith Publisher, 1877 E Gentile, Layton, UT 84040 *Tel:* 801-544-9800 *Toll Free Tel:* 800-748-5439 (orders only) *Fax:* 801-544-5582 *Toll Free Fax:* 800-213-3023 (orders only) *E-mail:* info@gibbs-smith.com *Web Site:* www.gibbs-smith.com, pg 104

Gifted Education Press, 10201 Yuma Ct, Manassas, VA 20109 *Tel:* 703-369-5017 *Web Site:* www. giftededpress.com; www.giftedpress.com, pg 104

Sheri Gilbert, 123 Van Voorhis Ave, Rochester, NY 14617 *Tel:* 585-342-0331 *Fax:* 585-323-1828 *E-mail:* shergilb@aol.com, pg 600

Liane Gilmour-Pomfret, 9330 Wandsworth Dr, Spring, TX 77379 *Tel:* 281-251-5917 *E-mail:* lpomfret@ houston.rr.com, pg 600

Gingerbread House, 602 Montauk Hwy, Westhampton Beach, NY 11978-1806 *Tel:* 631-288-5119 *Fax:* 631-288-5179 *E-mail:* ghbooks@optonline.net *Web Site:* gingerbreadbooks.com, pg 105

Girl Scouts of the USA, 420 Fifth Ave, New York, NY 10018-2798 *Tel:* 212-852-8000 *Toll Free Tel:* 800-478-7248 *Fax:* 212-852-6511 *Web Site:* www.girlscouts. org, pg 105

The Gislason Agency, 219 SE Main St, Suite 506, Minneapolis, MN 55414 *Tel:* 612-331-8033 *Fax:* 612-331-8115 *E-mail:* gislasonbj@aol.com *Web Site:* www. TheGislasonAgency.com, pg 632

Gival Press LLC, PO Box 3812, Arlington, VA 22203 *Tel:* 703-351-0079 *Fax:* 703-351-0079 *E-mail:* givalpress@yahoo.com *Web Site:* www. givalpress.prodigybiz.com; www.givalpress.com, pg 105

Gladden Unlimited, 3808 Georgia St, No 301, San Diego, CA 92103 *Tel:* 619-260-1544, pg 632

John Glassco Translation Prize, Concordia University, SB 335, 1455 De Maisonneuve West, Montreal, PQ H3G 1M8, Canada *Tel:* 514-848-8702 *E-mail:* info@ attlc-ltac.org *Web Site:* www.attlc-ltac.org, pg 776

GLB Publishers, 1028 Howard St, No 503, San Francisco, CA 94103 *Tel:* 415-621-8307 *Toll Free Tel:* 800-452-6119 *E-mail:* glbpubs@mindspring.com *Web Site:* www.glbpubs.com, pg 105

Susan Gleason, 325 Riverside Dr, New York, NY 10025 *Tel:* 212-662-3876 *Fax:* 212-864-3298, pg 632

Glenbridge Publishing Ltd, 19923 E Long Ave, Centennial, CO 80016-1969 *Tel:* 720-870-8381 *Toll Free Tel:* 800-986-4135 (orders) *Fax:* 720-870-5598 *E-mail:* glenbr@eazy.net *Web Site:* www. glenbridgepublishing.com, pg 105

Glencoe/McGraw-Hill, 8787 Orion Place, Columbus, OH 43240 Tel: 614-430-4000 Toll Free Tel: 800-848-1567 Web Site: www.glencoe.com, pg 105

Peter Glenn Publications, 6040 NW 43 Terr, Boca Raton, FL 33496 Tel: 561-999-8930 Toll Free Tel: 888-332-6700 Fax: 561-999-8931 E-mail: lynn@pgdirect.com Web Site: www.pgdirect.com, pg 105

Glimmer Train Press Inc, 1211 NW Glisan St, No 207, Portland, OR 97209 Tel: 503-221-0836 Fax: 503-221-0837 E-mail: info@glimmertrain.com Web Site: www.glimmertrain.com, pg 105

Global Training Center Inc, 7801 N Dixie Dr, Dayton, OH 45414-2779 Tel: 937-454-5044 Toll Free Tel: 800-860-5030 Fax: 937-454-5099 E-mail: xportnow@aol.com Web Site: www.globaltrainingcenter.com, pg 105

Global Travel Publishers Inc, 5353 N Federal Hwy, Suite 300, Fort Lauderdale, FL 33308 Tel: 954-491-8877 Toll Free Tel: 800-882-9453 Fax: 954-491-9060 E-mail: noltingaac@aol.com Web Site: www.africanadventure.com, pg 571

Globe Fearon, 299 Jefferson Rd, Parsippany, NJ 07054 Tel: 973-739-8000, pg 105

The Globe Pequot Press, 246 Goose Lane, Guilford, CT 06437 Tel: 203-458-4500 Toll Free Tel: 800-243-0495 (cust serv) Fax: 203-458-4601 Toll Free Fax: 800-820-2329 (orders & cust serv) E-mail: info@globepequot.com Web Site: www.globepequot.com, pg 105

Glory Bound Books, 6642 Marlette St, Suite 101, Marlette, MI 48453 Tel: 989-635-7520 E-mail: info@gloryboundenterprises.com Web Site: www.thegloryboundbookcompany.com, pg 106

Alexander Gode Medal, 225 Reinekers Lane, Suite 590, Alexandria, VA 22314 Tel: 703-683-6100 Fax: 703-683-6122 E-mail: ata@atanet.org Web Site: www.atanet.org, pg 776

David R Godine Publisher Inc, 9 Hamilton Place, Boston, MA 02108 Tel: 617-451-9600 Fax: 617-350-0250 E-mail: info@godine.com Web Site: www.godine.com, pg 106

Gold Eagle, 225 Duncan Mill Rd, Don Mills, ON M3B 3K9, Canada Tel: 416-445-5860 Fax: 416-445-8655; 416-445-8736, pg 548

Hadassah Gold, 222 W 83 St, Rm 15-D, New York, NY 10024 Tel: 212-787-5668 Fax: 212-787-5668 E-mail: dasgold@aol.com, pg 600

Gold Medallion Book Awards, 4816 S Ash Ave, Suite 101, Tempe, AZ 85282-7735 Tel: 480-966-3998 Fax: 480-966-1944 Web Site: www.ecpa.org, pg 776

Golden Cylinder Awards, 1200-A Scottsville Rd, Rochester, NY 14624 Tel: 585-436-2150 Fax: 585-436-7689 E-mail: gaa@gaa.org Web Site: www.gaa.org, pg 776

Golden Educational Center, 857 Lake Blvd, Redding, CA 96003 Tel: 530-244-0101 Toll Free Tel: 800-800-1791 Fax: 530-244-5939 E-mail: info@goldened.com Web Site: goldened.com, pg 106

Golden Gryphon Press, 3002 Perkins Rd, Urbana, IL 61802 Tel: 217-840-0672 Fax: 217-384-4205; 217-352-9748 E-mail: gryphon@goldengryphon.com, pg 106

Golden Kite Awards, 8271 Beverly Blvd, Los Angeles, CA 90048 Tel: 323-782-1010 Fax: 323-782-1892 E-mail: scbwi@scbwi.org Web Site: www.scbwi.org, pg 776

Golden Meteorite Press, PO Box 1223 Main Post Office, Edmonton, AB T5J 2M4, Canada Tel: 780-378-0063, pg 548

Golden Rose Award, 16 Cornell St, Arlington, MA 02474 Web Site: www.nepoetryclub.org, pg 776

Golden West Books, 525 N Electric Ave, Alhambra, CA 91801 Tel: 626-458-8148 Fax: 626-458-8148, pg 106

Golden West Publishers, 4113 N Longview, Phoenix, AZ 85014 Tel: 602-265-4392 Toll Free Tel: 800-658-5830 Fax: 602-279-6901 Web Site: www.goldenwestpublishers.com, pg 106

Goldfarb & Associates, 721 Gibbon St, Alexandria, VA 22314 Tel: 202-466-3030 Fax: 703-836-5644 E-mail: rglawlit@aol.com, pg 632

Frances Goldin Literary Agency, Inc, 57 E 11 St, Suite 5B, New York, NY 10003 Tel: 212-777-0047 Fax: 212-228-1660 E-mail: agency@goldinlit.com Web Site: www.goldinlit.com, pg 632

Donald Goldstein, 1500 E 17 St, Brooklyn, NY 11230 Tel: 718-375-9346 Fax: 212-623-4676 E-mail: dgoldsbkyn@aol.com, pg 600

Gollehon Press Inc, 6157 28 St SE, Grand Rapids, MI 49546 Tel: 616-949-3515 Fax: 619-949-8674, pg 106

Good Books, 3510 Old Philadelphia Pike, Intercourse, PA 17534 Tel: 717-768-3008 Toll Free Tel: 800-762-7171 Fax: 717-768-3433 Toll Free Fax: 888-768-3433 E-mail: custserv@goodbks.com Web Site: www.goodbks.com, pg 106

The Goodheart Prize For Fiction, Washington & Lee University, Mattingly House, 2 Lee Ave, Lexington, VA 24450-0303 Tel: 540-458-8765 Fax: 540-458-8461 Web Site: www.shenandoah.wlu.edu, pg 776

Goodheart-Willcox Publisher, 18604 W Creek Dr, Tinley Park, IL 60477-6243 Tel: 708-687-5000 Toll Free Tel: 800-323-0440 Fax: 708-687-0315 Toll Free Fax: 888-409-3900 E-mail: custserv@g-w.com Web Site: www.g-w.com, pg 106

Goodman-Andrew Agency Inc, 6680 Colgate Ave, Los Angeles, CA 90048 Tel: 310-387-0242 Fax: 323-653-3457 E-mail: ukseg@aol.com, pg 632

Goodman Associates, 500 West End Ave, New York, NY 10024 Tel: 212-873-4806, pg 633

Irene Goodman Literary Agency, 80 Fifth Ave, Suite 1101, New York, NY 10011 Tel: 212-604-0330 Fax: 212-675-1381 E-mail: igagency@aol.com, pg 633

Robert M Goodman, 140 West End Ave, New York, NY 10023 Tel: 212-721-7725 E-mail: bgoodman@rcn.com, pg 600

GoodSAMARitan Press, PO Box 803282, Santa Clarita, CA 91380 Tel: 661-799-0694, pg 107

Goose Lane Editions, 469 King St, Fredericton, NB E3B 1E5, Canada Tel: 506-450-4251 Toll Free Tel: 888-926-8377 Fax: 506-459-4991 E-mail: gooselane@gooselane.com Web Site: www.gooselane.com, pg 548

Gordian Press, 37 Crescent Ave, Staten Island, NY 10301 Tel: 718-273-4700 Fax: 718-273-4700, pg 107

P M Gordon Associates Inc, 2115 Wallace St, Philadelphia, PA 19130 Tel: 215-769-2525 Fax: 215-769-5354 E-mail: pmga@pond.com, pg 600

Gospel Publishing House, 1445 Boonville Ave, Springfield, MO 65802-1894 Tel: 417-831-8000 Toll Free Tel: 800-641-4310 Fax: 417-863-1874; 417-862-7566 Web Site: www.gospelpublishing.com, pg 107

Gossamer Books LLC, 2112 Gossamer Ave, Redwood Shores, CA 94065 Tel: 650-257-4058 Fax: 650-257-4058 E-mail: info@gossamerbooks.com Web Site: www.gossamerbooks.com, pg 107

C+S Gottfried, 619 Cricklewood Dr, State College, PA 16803 Tel: 631-563-2841 E-mail: cs@lookoutnow.com Web Site: www.lookoutnow.com/dtp, pg 600

Sherry Gottlieb, 4900 Dunes St, Oxnard, CA 93035 Tel: 805-382-3425 Fax: 805-658-8601 E-mail: writer@wordservices.com Web Site: www.wordservices.com, pg 600

Gould Publications Inc, 1333 N US Hwy 17-92, Longwood, FL 32750-3724 Tel: 407-695-9500 Toll Free Tel: 800-717-7917 Fax: 407-695-2906 E-mail: info@gouldlaw.com Web Site: www.gouldlaw.com, pg 107

Governor General's Literary Awards, 350 Albert St, Ottawa, ON K1P 5V8, Canada Tel: 613-566-4414 (ext 5576) Toll Free Tel: 800-263-5588 (ext 5576, Canada only) Fax: 613-566-4410 Web Site: www.canadacouncil.ca, pg 776

Grace Associates, 945 Fourth Ave, Suite 200-A, Huntington, WV 25701 Tel: 304-697-3236 Fax: 304-697-3399 E-mail: publish@cloh.net Web Site: www.booksbygrace.com, pg 600

Grade Finders Inc, 662 Exton Commons, Exton, PA 19341 Tel: 610-524-7070 Fax: 610-524-8912 E-mail: info@gradefinders.com Web Site: www.gradefinders.com, pg 107

The Graduate Group/Booksellers, 86 Norwood Rd, West Hartford, CT 06117-2236 Tel: 860-233-2330 Toll Free Tel: 800-484-7280 ext 3579 Fax: 860-233-2330 E-mail: graduategroup@hotmail.com Web Site: www.graduategroup.com, pg 107

The Thomas Grady Agency, 209 Bassett St, Petaluma, CA 94952-2668 Tel: 707-765-6229 Fax: 707-765-6810 Web Site: www.tgrady.com, pg 633

Grafco Productions Inc, 291 Pat Mell Rd, Suite 101, Marietta, GA 30060 Tel: 770-436-1500 Toll Free Tel: 888-656-1500 Fax: 770-444-9357 E-mail: jabo@rightconnections.net Web Site: www.jackwboone.com, pg 107

Graham Agency, 311 W 43 St, New York, NY 10036 Tel: 212-489-7730 E-mail: grahamacynyc@aol.com, pg 633

Donald M Grant Publisher Inc, PO Box 187, Hampton Falls, NH 03844-0187 Tel: 603-778-7191 Fax: 603-778-7191 E-mail: grantbooks@aol.com Web Site: www.grantbooks.com, pg 107

Grants for Artist Projects, 1835 12 Ave, Seattle, WA 98122 Tel: 206-467-8734 Fax: 206-467-9633 E-mail: info@artisttrust.org Web Site: www.artisttrust.org, pg 776

Graphic Artists Guild Inc, 90 John St, Rm 403, New York, NY 10038 Tel: 212-791-3400 Fax: 212-791-0333 E-mail: execdir@gag.org Web Site: www.gag.org, pg 687

Graphic Artists Guild Inc, 90 John St, Rm 403, New York, NY 10038 Tel: 212-791-3400 Fax: 212-791-0333 E-mail: pr@gag.org Web Site: www.gag.org, pg 752

Graphic Arts Association, 1100 Northbrook Dr, Suite 120, Trevose, PA 19053 Tel: 215-396-2300 Fax: 215-396-9890 E-mail: gaa@gaa1900.com Web Site: www.gaa1900.com, pg 752

Graphic Arts Center Publishing Co, 3019 NW Yeon Ave, Portland, OR 97210 Tel: 503-226-2402 Toll Free Tel: 800-452-3032 Fax: 503-223-1410 Toll Free Fax: 800-355-9685 E-mail: editorial@gacpc.com; sales@gacpc.com Web Site: www.gacpc.com, pg 107

Graphic Arts Education & Research Foundation (GAERF), 1899 Preston White Dr, Reston, VA 20191-4367 Tel: 703-264-7200 Fax: 703-620-3165 E-mail: gaerf@npes.org Web Site: www.npes.org, pg 705

Graphic Arts Employers of America, 100 Daingerfield Rd, Alexandria, VA 22314 Tel: 703-519-8100; 703-519-8151 Fax: 703-548-3227 Web Site: www.gain.net, pg 687

Graphic Arts Marketing Information Service (GAMIS), 100 Daingerfield Rd, Alexandria, VA 22314 Tel: 703-519-8100; 703-519-8179 Toll Free Tel: 800-742-2666 Fax: 703-548-3227 E-mail: info@gamis.org Web Site: www.gamis.org, pg 687

Graphic Arts Publishing Inc, 3100 Bronson Hill Rd, Livonia, NY 14487-9716 Tel: 716-346-6978 Toll Free Tel: 800-724-9476 Fax: 716-346-2276, pg 107

Graphic Arts Sales Foundation (GASF), 113 E Evans St, West Chester, PA 19380 Tel: 610-431-9780 Fax: 610-436-5238 E-mail: info@gasf.org Web Site: www.gasf.org, pg 687

Graphic Arts Show Company, 1899 Preston White Dr, Reston, VA 20191 Tel: 703-264-7200 Fax: 703-620-9187 E-mail: info@gasc.org Web Site: www.gasc.org, pg 688

Graphic Communications Council, 1899 Preston White Dr, Reston, VA 20191-4367 Tel: 703-648-1768 Fax: 703-620-0994 E-mail: edcouncil@npes.org Web Site: www.npes.org/edcouncil, pg 688

Graphic Learning, 61 Mattatuck Heights Rd, Waterbury, CT 06705 Tel: 203-756-6562 Toll Free Tel: 800-874-0029; 800-227-9120 Fax: 203-756-2895 Toll Free Fax: 800-737-3322, pg 108

Graphic World Publishing Services, 11687 Adie Rd, Maryland Heights, MO 63043 Tel: 314-567-9854 Fax: 314-567-0360, pg 600

Gravure Association of America Inc, 1200-A Scottsville Rd, Rochester, NY 14624 Tel: 585-436-2150 Fax: 585-436-7689 E-mail: gaa@gaa.org Web Site: www.gaa.org, pg 688

Gray & Company Publishers, 1588 E 40 St, Cleveland, OH 44103 Tel: 216-431-2665 Toll Free Tel: 800-915-3609 E-mail: info@grayco.com Web Site: www. grayco.com, pg 108

The Graybill & English Literary Agency LLC, 1875 Connecticut Ave, NW, Suite 712, Washington, DC 20009 Tel: 202-588-9798 Fax: 202-457-0662 Web Site: graybillandenglish.com, pg 633

Ashley Grayson Literary Agency, 1342 18 St, San Pedro, CA 90732 Tel: 310-548-4672 Fax: 310-514-1148 E-mail: graysonagent@earthlink.net, pg 633

Graywolf Press, 2402 University Ave, Suite 203, St Paul, MN 55114 Tel: 651-641-0077 Fax: 651-641-0036 E-mail: wolves@graywolfpress.org Web Site: www. graywolfpress.org, pg 108

The Annual Great American Tennis Writing Awards, 15 Elm Place, Rye, NY 10580 Tel: 914-967-4890 Fax: 914-967-8178 E-mail: tennisweek@tennisweek. com Web Site: www.tennisweek.com, pg 776

Great Potential Press, PO Box 5057, Scottsdale, AZ 85261 Tel: 602-954-4200 Toll Free Tel: 877-954-4200 Fax: 602-954-0185 E-mail: info@giftedbooks.com Web Site: www.giftedbooks.com, pg 108

Great Quotations Inc, 8102 Lemont Rd, Suite 300, Woodridge, IL 60517 Tel: 630-390-3580 Toll Free Tel: 800-830-3020 Fax: 630-390-3585 E-mail: greatquotations@yahoo.com, pg 108

Great Source Education Group, 181 Ballardvale St, Wilmington, MA 01887 Tel: 978-661-1300 Toll Free Tel: 800-289-4490 (orders), pg 108

Greater Talent Network Inc, 437 Fifth Ave, New York, NY 10016 Tel: 212-645-4200 Toll Free Tel: 800-326-4211 Fax: 212-627-1471 E-mail: gtn@greatertalent. com Web Site: www.gtnspeakers.com, pg 669

Green Knight Publishing, 360 Chiquita Ave, No 4, Mountain View, CA 94041 Tel: 650-964-4276 Fax: 650-964-4276 E-mail: gawaine@greenknight.com Web Site: www.greenknight.com, pg 108

Green Nature Books, 5290 SE 11 Dr, Bushnell, FL 33585 Tel: 352-793-5496 E-mail: info@ greennaturebooks.com Web Site: www. greennaturebooks.com, pg 108

The Green Rose Prize in Poetry, Western Michigan University, Dept of English, 1903 W Michigan Ave, Kalamazoo, MI 49008-5331 Tel: 269-387-8185 Fax: 269-387-2562 Web Site: www.wmich. edu/newissues/greenroseprize.html, pg 777

Warren H Green Inc, 8356 Olive Blvd, St Louis, MO 63132 Tel: 314-991-1335 Toll Free Tel: 800-537-0655 Fax: 314-997-1788 E-mail: whgreen@inlink.com Web Site: www.whgreen.com, pg 108

Tony Greenberg MD, 1000 W Carson St, Torrance, CA 90502 Tel: 310-457-9398 (home); 310-222-2168 (office) E-mail: tgreenberg@dhs.co.la.ca.us, pg 600

Sanford J Greenburger Associates Inc, 55 Fifth Ave, 15th fl, New York, NY 10003 Tel: 212-206-5600 Fax: 212-463-8718 Web Site: www.greenburger.com, pg 633

Greene Bark Press Inc, PO Box 1108, Bridgeport, CT 06601-1108 Tel: 203-372-4861 Fax: 203-371-5856 E-mail: greenebark@aol.com Web Site: www. greenebarkpress.com, pg 108

Cheryll Y Greene Editorial Services, 158-18 Riverside Dr W, Suite 6E, New York, NY 10032 Tel: 212-740-6003 Fax: 212-740-6003 E-mail: editorseye@ mindspring.com, pg 600

Greenhaven Press®, 15822 Bernardo Center Dr, Suite C, San Diego, CA 92127 Tel: 858-485-7424 Toll Free Tel: 800-877-4253 (cust serv & orders) Fax: 858-485-9549; 248-699-8051 (cust serv) Toll Free Fax: 800-414-5043 (orders only) E-mail: customerservice@gale. com; galeord@gale.com (orders) Web Site: www.gale. com/greenhaven, pg 108

Delano Greenidge Editions, 14 Mount Morris Park W, Suite 7, New York, NY 10027-6317 Tel: 917-492-8014 Fax: 917-492-0966 E-mail: dge@thing.net, pg 109

Paul Greenland Editorial Services, 608 Dawson Ave, Rockford, IL 61107 Tel: 815-519-2588 E-mail: paul@ paulgreenland.com, pg 601

Greenleaf Book Group LLC, Longhorn Bldg, Suite 600, 3rd fl, 4425 Mopac S, Austin, TX 78735 Tel: 512-891-6100 Toll Free Tel: 800-932-5420 Fax: 512-891-6150 E-mail: email@greenleafbookgroup.com Web Site: www.greenleafbookgroup.com, pg 109

Greenleaf Press, 3761 Hwy 109 N, Unit D, Lebanon, TN 37087 Tel: 615-449-1617 Fax: 615-449-4018 E-mail: info@greenleafpress.com Web Site: www. greenleafpress.com, pg 109

The Greensboro Review Literary Award in Fiction & Poetry, University North Carolina at Greensboro, English Dept, McIver Bldg, Rm 134, Greensboro, NC 27402-6170 Tel: 336-334-5459 Web Site: www.uncg. edu/eng/mfa, pg 777

Greenwich Publishing Group Inc, 929 Boston Post Rd, Suite 9, Old Saybrook, CT 06475 Tel: 860-388-9941 E-mail: info@greenwichpublishing.com Web Site: www.greenwichpublishing.com, pg 109

Greenwood Publishing Group Inc, 88 Post Rd W, Westport, CT 06880-4208 Tel: 203-226-3571 Toll Free Tel: 800-225-5800 Fax: 203-222-1502 E-mail: bookinfo@greenwood.com (general); firstintial&fulllastname@greenwood.com (individuals) Web Site: www.greenwood.com, pg 109

Greenwood Research Books & Software, PO Box 12102, Wichita, KS 67277-2102 Tel: 316-214-5103 E-mail: grnwdrsch@hotmail.com Web Site: grnwd. tripod.com, pg 109

Nancy J Gregg, 1217 W Washington, Suite 5, Springfield, IL 62702 Tel: 217-793-2517, pg 601

Blanche C Gregory Inc, 2 Tudor City Place, New York, NY 10017 Tel: 212-697-0828 Fax: 212-697-0828 E-mail: bcgliteraryagent@aol.com Web Site: bcgliteraryagency.com, pg 633

Maia Gregory Associates, 311 E 72 St, New York, NY 10021 Tel: 212-288-0310, pg 633

Rosemary F Gretton, 660 Blueridge Ave, North Vancouver, BC V7R 2J3, Canada Tel: 604-904-0223; 604-836-0610 (cell) E-mail: rgretton@lyrcism.ca Web Site: www.lyricism.ca, pg 601

Grey House Publishing Inc, 185 Millerton Rd, Millerton, NY 12546 Tel: 518-789-8700 Toll Free Tel: 800-562-2139 Fax: 518-789-0556 E-mail: books@greyhouse. com Web Site: www.greyhouse.com, pg 109

Greystone Books, 2323 Quebec St, Suite 201, Vancouver, BC V5T 4S7, Canada Tel: 604-254-7191 Toll Free Tel: 800-667-6902 Fax: 604-254-9099, pg 548

Griffin Publishing Group, 18022 Cowan, Suite 202, Irvine, CA 92614 Tel: 949-263-3733 Toll Free Tel: 800-472-9741 Fax: 949-263-3734 Web Site: www. griffinpublishing.com, pg 109

Joan K Griffitts Indexing, 3909 W 71 St, Indianapolis, IN 46268 Tel: 317-297-7312 Fax: 317-299-7717 E-mail: j.griffitts@sbcglobal.net, pg 601

Georgia Griggs, 2636 Kansas Ave, Santa Monica, CA 90404 Tel: 310-828-4948 E-mail: ghgriggs@earthlink. net, pg 601

Maxine Groffsky Literary Agency, 853 Broadway, Suite 708, New York, NY 10003 Tel: 212-979-1500 Fax: 212-979-1405, pg 633

Jill Grosjean Literary Agency, 1390 Millstone Rd, Sag Harbor, NY 11963 Tel: 631-725-7419 Fax: 631-725-8632 E-mail: jill6981@aol.com, pg 633

Gerald Gross Associates LLC, 63 Grand St, Croton-on-Hudson, NY 10520-2518 Tel: 914-271-8705 Fax: 914-271-1239 E-mail: grosassoc@aol.com Web Site: www. bookdocs.com/jgross.html, pg 601

Laura Gross Literary Agency Ltd, 75 Clinton Place, Newton Centre, MA 02459-1117 Tel: 617-964-2977 Fax: 617-964-3023 E-mail: lglitag@aol.com, pg 633

Grosset & Dunlap, 345 Hudson St, New York, NY 10014 Tel: 212-366-2000 E-mail: online@ penguinputnam.com Web Site: www.penguin.com, pg 109

Judith S Grossman, 715 Cherry Circle, Wynnewood, PA 19096 Tel: 610-642-0906 E-mail: stogiz@aol.com, pg 601

Deborah Grosvenor Literary Agency, 5510 Grosvenor Lane, Bethesda, MD 20814 Tel: 301-564-6231 Fax: 301-581-9401 E-mail: dcgrosveno@aol.com, pg 633

Groundwood Books, 720 Bathurst St, Suite 500, Toronto, ON M5S 2R4, Canada Tel: 416-537-2501 Fax: 416-537-4647 E-mail: genmail@groundwood-dm.com Web Site: www.groundwoodbooks.com, pg 548

Group Publishing Inc, 1515 Cascade Ave, Loveland, CO 80538 Tel: 970-669-3836 Toll Free Tel: 800-447-1070 Fax: 970-678-4392 E-mail: innovatr@grouppublishing. com Web Site: www.grouppublishing.com, pg 110

Groupe Educalivres Inc, 955, rue Bergar, Laval, PQ H7L 4Z6, Canada Tel: 514-334-8466 Toll Free Tel: 800-567-3671 (Info Service) Fax: 514-334-8387 E-mail: commentaires@educalivres.com Web Site: www.educalivres.com, pg 548

Grove/Atlantic Inc, 841 Broadway, 4th fl, New York, NY 10003-4793 Tel: 212-614-7850 Toll Free Tel: 800-521-0178 Fax: 212-614-7886 Web Site: www.groveatlantic. com, pg 110

Gryphon Books, PO Box 209, Brooklyn, NY 11228 Web Site: www.gryphonbooks.com, pg 110

Gryphon Editions, 515 Madison Ave, Suite 3200, New York, NY 10022 Tel: 212-750-1048 Toll Free Tel: 800-633-8911 Fax: 212-644-6828 E-mail: gryphonnyc@aol.com Web Site: www. gryphoneditions.com, pg 110

Gryphon House Inc, 10726 Tucker St, Beltsville, MD 20704 Tel: 301-595-9500 Toll Free Tel: 800-638-0928 Fax: 301-595-0051 E-mail: info@ghbooks.com Web Site: www.gryphonhouse.com, pg 110

GSC Communications, 1761 S Columbia Ave, Tulsa, OK 74104-5820 Tel: 918-749-2360 Fax: 918-749-2360 E-mail: swwriter@juno.com, pg 601

Carol Guenzi Agents Inc, 865 Delaware, Denver, CO 80204 Tel: 303-820-2599 Toll Free Tel: 800-417-5120 Fax: 303-820-2598 E-mail: art@artagent.com Web Site: www.artagent.com, pg 666

Guerin Editeur Ltee, 4501 rue Drolet, Montreal, PQ H2T 2G2, Canada Tel: 514-842-3481 Toll Free Tel: 800-398-8337 Fax: 514-842-4923 Web Site: www.guerin-editeur.qc.ca, pg 549

Guernica Editions Inc, 2250 Military Dr, Tonawanda, NY 14150 Tel: 716-693-2768 Toll Free Tel: 800-565-9523 (orders) Fax: 716-692-7479 Toll Free Fax: 800-221-9985 (orders) E-mail: guernicaeditions@cs.com Web Site: www.guernicaeditions.com, pg 110

Guernica Editions Inc, PO Box 117, Sta P, Toronto, ON M5S 2S6, Canada Tel: 416-658-9888 Toll Free Tel: 800-565-9523 (orders) Fax: 416-657-8885 Toll Free Fax: 800-221-9985 (orders) E-mail: guernicaeditions@cs.com Web Site: guernicaeditions.com, pg 549

John Simon Guggenheim Memorial Foundation, 90 Park Ave, New York, NY 10016 Tel: 212-687-4470 Fax: 212-697-3248 E-mail: fellowships@gf.org Web Site: www.gf.org, pg 705

Guideposts Book & Inspirational Media Division, 16 E 34 St, New York, NY 10016 *Tel:* 212-251-8100 *Fax:* 212-684-0679 *Web Site:* www.guidepostsbooks. com, pg 110

Guideposts Young Writers Contest, 16 E 34 St, New York, NY 10016 *Tel:* 212-251-8100 *Toll Free Tel:* 800-932-2145 *Fax:* 212-684-0679 *Web Site:* www. guidepostsbooks.com, pg 777

Guild of Book Workers, 521 Fifth Ave, 17th fl, New York, NY 10175 *Tel:* 212-292-4444 *Web Site:* www. palimpsest.stanford.ed, pg 688

Guild Publishing, 931 E Main St, Madison, WI 53703-2955 *Tel:* 608-257-2590 *Toll Free Tel:* 800-930-1856 *Fax:* 608-257-2690 *E-mail:* artinfo@guild.com *Web Site:* www.guild.com, pg 111

The Guilford Press, 72 Spring St, New York, NY 10012 *Tel:* 212-431-9800 *Toll Free Tel:* 800-365-7006 (orders) *Fax:* 212-966-6708 *E-mail:* orders@guilford. com *Web Site:* www.guilford.com, pg 111

Guru Beant Press, 1505 Apakin Nene, Tallahassee, FL 32301 *Tel:* 850-878-6642 *E-mail:* infinipede@juno. com *Web Site:* www.infinipede.com, pg 571

The Charlotte Gusay Literary Agency, 10532 Blythe Ave, Los Angeles, CA 90064 *Tel:* 310-559-0831 *Fax:* 310-559-2639 *E-mail:* gusay1@aol.com (for queries only) *Web Site:* www.mediastudio.com/gusay, pg 634, 666

H & M Productions II Inc, 226-06 56 Ave, Bayside, NY 11361 *Tel:* 718-357-6707 *Fax:* 718-357-8920 *E-mail:* handm@mft.com, pg 111

H D I Publishers, 2424 Elmen St, Houston, TX 77019-6710 *Tel:* 713-526-6900 *Toll Free Tel:* 800-321-7037 *Fax:* 713-526-7787 *Web Site:* www.hdipub.com, pg 111

Hachai Publications Inc, 156 Chester Ave, Brooklyn, NY 11218 *Tel:* 718-633-0100 *Toll Free Tel:* 800-50-HACHAI (504-2424) *Fax:* 718-633-0103 *E-mail:* info@hachai.com *Web Site:* www.hachai.com, pg 111

Hackett Publishing Co Inc, PO Box 44937, Indianapolis, IN 46244-0937 *Tel:* 317-635-9250; 617-497-6306 *Fax:* 317-635-9292 *Toll Free Fax:* 800-783-9213 *E-mail:* customer@hackettpublishing.com *Web Site:* www.hackettpublishing.com, pg 111

Hackmatack Children's Choice Award, c/o Nova Scotia Provincial Library, 3770 Kempt Rd, Halifax, NS B3K 4X8, Canada *Tel:* 902-424-3774 *Fax:* 902-424-0633 *E-mail:* hackmatack@hackmatack.ca *Web Site:* www. hackmatack.ca, pg 777

Hackney Literary Awards, Birmingham-Southern College, Box 549003, Birmingham, AL 35254 *Tel:* 205-226-4921 *Toll Free Tel:* 800-523-5793 *Fax:* 205-226-3072 *E-mail:* dcwilson@bsc.edu *Web Site:* www.bsc.edu, pg 777

Hadronic Press Inc, 35246 US 19 N, No 215, Palm Harbor, FL 34684 *Tel:* 727-934-9593 *Fax:* 727-934-9275 *E-mail:* hadronic@tampabay.rr.com *Web Site:* www.hadronicpress.com, pg 111

Hal Hager & Associates, 15 N Richards Ave, Somerville, NJ 08876-2717 *Tel:* 908-231-9407 *Fax:* 908-725-0979 *E-mail:* halhager@verizon.net, pg 601

Hagstrom Map Co Inc, 46-35 54 Rd, Maspeth, NY 11378 *Tel:* 718-784-0055 *Toll Free Tel:* 800-432-MAPS (432-6277) *Fax:* 718-784-0640 (admin); 718-784-1216 (sales & orders) *Web Site:* www. americanmap.com, pg 111

Haights Cross Communications Inc, 10 New King St, White Plains, NY 10604 *Tel:* 914-289-9400 *Fax:* 914-289-9401 *E-mail:* info@haightscross.com *Web Site:* www.haightscross.com, pg 111

Hal Leonard Corp, 7777 W Bluemound Rd, Milwaukee, WI 53213 *Tel:* 414-774-3630 *Toll Free Tel:* 800-524-4425 *Fax:* 414-774-3259 *E-mail:* halinfo@halleonard. com *Web Site:* www.halleonard.com, pg 112

Sarah Josepha Hale Award, 58 N Main, Newport, NH 03773 *Tel:* 603-863-3430 *Fax:* 603-863-3022 *E-mail:* rfl@newport.lib.nh.us *Web Site:* www.newport. lib.nh.us, pg 777

Half Halt Press Inc, 20042 Benevola Church Rd, Boonsboro, MD 21713 *Tel:* 301-733-7119 *Toll Free Tel:* 800-822-9635 (orders only) *Fax:* 301-733-7408 *E-mail:* gem@halfhaltpress.com *Web Site:* www. halfhaltpress.com, pg 112

Hall Editorial Services, 571 Carlton Ave, Brooklyn, NY 11238-3408 *Tel:* 718-789-4420 *Fax:* 718-857-4639, pg 601

Reece Halsey Agency/Reece Halsey North, 8733 Sunset Blvd, Suite 101, Los Angeles, CA 90069 *Tel:* 310-652-2409 *Fax:* 310-652-7595, pg 634

The Mitchell J Hamilburg Agency, 11718 Barrington Ct, Suite 732, Los Angeles, CA 90049-2930 *Tel:* 310-471-4024 *Fax:* 310-471-9588, pg 634

Alexander Hamilton Institute, 70 Hilltop Rd, Ramsey, NJ 07446-1119 *Tel:* 201-825-3377 *Toll Free Tel:* 800-879-2441 *Fax:* 201-825-8696 *E-mail:* editorial@ahipubs. com *Web Site:* www.ahipubs.com, pg 112

Andrew Hamilton Literary Agency, PO Box 604118, Cleveland, OH 44104-0118 *Tel:* 216-299-8809 *Fax:* 760-875-7292 *E-mail:* bkagent22@yahoo.com *Web Site:* www.andrewhamiltonliterary.com, pg 634

Hamilton Books, 4501 Forbes Blvd, Suite 200, Lanham, MD 20706 *Tel:* 301-459-3366, pg 112

Hamilton College, English/Creative Writing, Dept of English, 198 College Hill Rd, Clinton, NY 13323 *Tel:* 315-859-4370 *Fax:* 315-859-4390 *Web Site:* www. hamilton.edu, pg 752

Hammond World Atlas Corp, 95 Progress St, Union, NJ 07083 *Tel:* 908-206-1300 *Toll Free Tel:* 800-526-4953 *Fax:* 908-206-1104 *E-mail:* customerservice@ hammondmap.com; feedback@hammondmap.com *Web Site:* www.hammondmap.com, pg 112

Hampton-Brown Co Inc, 26385 Carmel Rancho Blvd, Carmel, CA 93923 *Tel:* 831-625-3666 *Toll Free Tel:* 800-933-3510 *Fax:* 831-625-8619 *E-mail:* customerservice@hampton-brown.com *Web Site:* www.hampton-brown.com, pg 113

Hampton Press Inc, 23 Broadway, Cresskill, NJ 07626 *Tel:* 201-894-1686 *Toll Free Tel:* 800-894-8955 *Fax:* 201-894-8732 *E-mail:* hamptonpr1@aol.com *Web Site:* www.hamptonpress.com, pg 113

Hampton Roads Publishing Co Inc, 1125 Stoney Ridge Rd, Charlottesville, VA 22902 *Tel:* 434-296-2772 *Toll Free Tel:* 800-766-8009 (orders) *Fax:* 434-296-5096 *Toll Free Fax:* 800-766-9042 *E-mail:* hrpc@hrpub.com *Web Site:* www.hrpub.com, pg 113

Hancock House Publishers, 1431 Harrison Ave, Blaine, WA 98230-5005 *Tel:* 604-538-1114 *Toll Free Tel:* 800-938-1114 *Fax:* 604-538-2262 *Toll Free Fax:* 800-983-2262 *E-mail:* sales@hancockhouse.com *Web Site:* www.hancockhouse.com, pg 113

Hancock House Publishers Ltd, 19313 Zero Ave, Surrey, BC V3S 9R9, Canada *Tel:* 604-538-1114 *Toll Free Tel:* 800-938-1114 *Fax:* 604-538-2262 *Toll Free Fax:* 800-983-2262 *E-mail:* promo@hancockwildlife. org; sales@hancockhouse.com *Web Site:* www. hancockhouse.com, pg 549

Handprint Books Inc, 413 Sixth Ave, Brooklyn, NY 11215-3310 *Tel:* 718-768-3696 *Fax:* 718-369-0844 *E-mail:* publisher@handprintbooks.com *Web Site:* www.handprintbooks.com, pg 113

Handy Andy Prize, 100 N Berwick, Williamsburg, VA 23188 *Web Site:* www.poetrysocietyofvirginia.org, pg 777

Hanging Loose Press, 231 Wyckoff St, Brooklyn, NY 11217 *Tel:* 212-206-8465 *Fax:* 212-243-7499 *E-mail:* print225@aol.com *Web Site:* www. hangingloosepress.com, pg 113

Hanley & Belfus, 170 S Independence Mall W, Suite 300 E, Philadelphia, PA 19106-3399 *Tel:* 215-238-7800 *Toll Free Tel:* 800-545-2522 (orders) *Fax:* 215-238-7883 *Web Site:* www.elsevierhealth.com, pg 113

Hanley-Wood LLC, 426 S Westgate St, Addison, IL 60101 *Tel:* 630-543-0870 *Toll Free Tel:* 800-837-0870 *Fax:* 630-543-3112 *Web Site:* www.hanleywood.com, pg 113

Hannacroix Creek Books Inc, 1127 High Ridge Rd, PMB 110, Stamford, CT 06905-1203 *Tel:* 203-321-8674 *Fax:* 203-968-0193 *E-mail:* hannacroix@aol.com *Web Site:* www.hannacroixcreekbooks.com, pg 113

Jason A Hannah Medal, 283 Sparks St, Ottawa, ON K1R 7X9, Canada *Tel:* 613-991-6990 *Fax:* 613-991-6996 *E-mail:* adminrsc@rsc.ca *Web Site:* www.rsc.ca, pg 777

Hans Christian Andersen Prize, 800 Barksdale Rd, Newark, DE 19714 *Tel:* 302-731-1600 (ext 297) *E-mail:* usbby@reading.org *Web Site:* www.usbby.org, pg 777

Hanser Gardner Publications, 6915 Valley Ave, Cincinnati, OH 45244-3029 *Tel:* 513-527-8977 *Toll Free Tel:* 800-950-8977 *Fax:* 513-527-8801 *Toll Free Fax:* 800-527-8801 *E-mail:* hgfeedback@gardnerweb. com *Web Site:* www.hansergardner.com, pg 113

Jeanne K Hanson Literary Agency, 6708 Cornelia Dr, Edina, MN 55435 *Tel:* 952-920-8819 *Fax:* 952-920-8819, pg 634

Harbor House, 111 Tenth St, Augusta, GA 30901 *Tel:* 706-738-0354 *Fax:* 706-738-0354 *E-mail:* harborbook@knology.net *Web Site:* harborhousebooks.com, pg 114

Harbor Island Books, 1214 W Boston Post Rd, No 245, Mamaroneck, NY 10543 *Tel:* 914-420-9782 *Fax:* 914-835-7897 *E-mail:* publisher@lyingawake.net *Web Site:* www.lyingawake.net, pg 571

Harbor Lights Press (HLP), PO Box 505, Gloucester City, NJ 08030-0505 *Tel:* 856-742-5810 *E-mail:* harborlightspress@yahoo.com *Web Site:* www. harborlightspress.com, pg 114

Harbor Press Inc, 5713 Wollochet Dr NW, PO Box 1656, Gig Harbor, WA 98335 *Tel:* 253-851-5190 *Fax:* 253-851-5191 *E-mail:* info@harborpress.com *Web Site:* harborpress.com, pg 114

Harbour Publishing Co Ltd, 4437 Rondeview Rd, Madeira Park, BC V0N 2H0, Canada *Tel:* 604-883-2730 *Toll Free Tel:* 800-667-2988; 800-667-2988 *Fax:* 604-883-9451 *Toll Free Fax:* 877-604-9449 *E-mail:* info@harbourpublishing.com *Web Site:* www. harbourpublishing.com, pg 549

Harcourt Achieve, 10801 N MoPac Expressway, Austin, TX 78759 *Tel:* 512-343-8227 *Toll Free Tel:* 800-531-5015 *Toll Free Fax:* 800-699-9459 *E-mail:* ecare@ harcourt.com *Web Site:* www.harcourtachieve.com, pg 114

Harcourt Assessment Inc, 19500 Bulverde Rd, San Antonio, TX 78259 *Tel:* 210-339-5000 *Toll Free Tel:* 800-211-8378 *Web Site:* www.harcourtassessment. com, pg 114

Harcourt Canada Ltd, 55 Horner Ave, Toronto, ON M8Z 4X6, Canada *Tel:* 416-255-4491; 416-255-0177 (Voice Mail) *Toll Free Tel:* 800-387-7278 (North America); 800-387-7305 (North America) *Fax:* 416-255-6708 *Toll Free Fax:* 800-665-7307 (North America) *E-mail:* firstname_lastname@harcourt.com *Web Site:* www.harcourtcanada.com, pg 549

Harcourt Inc, 6277 Sea Harbor Dr, Orlando, FL 32887 *Tel:* 407-345-2000 *Toll Free Tel:* 800-225-5425 (cust serv) *Fax:* 407-352-3445 (cust serv), pg 114

Harcourt Interactive Technology, 99 Powerhouse Rd, Suite 106, Roslyn Heights, NY 11577 *Tel:* 516-625-6755 *Toll Free Tel:* 800-745-3276 *Fax:* 516-625-6789 *E-mail:* hit@harcourt.com *Web Site:* www.hit.iloli. com, pg 114

Harcourt School Publishers, 6277 Sea Harbor Dr, Orlando, FL 32887 *Tel:* 407-345-2000 *Toll Free Tel:* 800-225-5425 (cust serv) *Fax:* 407-352-3445 *Toll Free Fax:* 800-874-6418 *E-mail:* hbspcs@hbschool. com *Web Site:* www.harcourtschool.com, pg 114

Harcourt Trade Publishers, 525 "B" St, Suite 1900, San Diego, CA 92101 *Tel:* 619-231-6616 *Toll Free Tel:* 800-543-1918 (cust serv) *Toll Free Fax:* 800-235-0256 (cust serv) *Web Site:* www.harcourtbooks.com, pg 115

Harian Creative Awards, 47 Hyde Blvd, Ballston Spa, NY 12020-1607 *Tel:* 518-885-6699; 518-885-7397, pg 777

Harian Creative Books, 47 Hyde Blvd, Ballston Spa, NY 12020-1607 *Tel:* 518-885-6699; 518-885-7397, pg 115

Clarence Haring Prize, 400 "A" St SE, Washington, DC 20003 *Tel:* 202-544-2422 *Fax:* 202-544-8307 *E-mail:* info@historians.org *Web Site:* www.historians.org, pg 777

Harlan Davidson Inc/Forum Press Inc, 773 Glenn Ave, Wheeling, IL 60090-6000 *Tel:* 847-541-9720 *Fax:* 847-541-9830 *E-mail:* harlandavidson@harlandavidson.com *Web Site:* www.harlandavidson.com, pg 115

Harlequin Enterprises Ltd, 233 Broadway, Suite 1001, New York, NY 10279 *Tel:* 212-553-4200 *Fax:* 212-227-8969 *E-mail:* customer.ecare@harlequin.ca *Web Site:* www.eharlequin.com; www.luna-books.com; www.mirabooks.com; www.reddressink.com; www.steeplehill.com, pg 115

Harlequin Enterprises Ltd, 225 Duncan Mill Rd, Don Mills, ON M3B 3K9, Canada *Tel:* 416-445-5860 *Fax:* 416-445-8655 *Web Site:* www.eharlequin.com; www.luna-books.com; www.mirabooks.com; www.reddressink.com; www.steeplehill.com, pg 549

Harmonie Park Press, 23630 Pinewood, Warren, MI 48091 *Tel:* 586-755-3080 *Toll Free Tel:* 800-886-3080 *Fax:* 586-755-4213 *E-mail:* info@harmonieparkpress.com *Web Site:* harmonieparkpress.com, pg 115

Harmony House Publishers - Louisville, 1008 Kent Rd, Goshen, KY 40026 *Tel:* 502-228-2010; 502-228-4446 *Fax:* 502-228-2010 *E-mail:* harmonypub@aol.com, pg 115

HarperCollins Children's Books Group, 1350 Sixth Ave, New York, NY 10019 *Tel:* 212-261-6500 *Web Site:* www.harperchildrens.com, pg 115

HarperCollins General Books Group, 10 E 53 St, New York, NY 10022 *Tel:* 212-207-7000 *Fax:* 212-207-7633, pg 115

HarperCollins Publishers, 10 E 53 St, New York, NY 10022 *Tel:* 212-207-7000 *Fax:* 212-207-7145 *Web Site:* www.harpercollins.com, pg 115

HarperCollins Publishers Canada, 2 Bloor St E, 20th fl, Toronto, ON M4W 1A8, Canada *Tel:* 416-975-9334 *Fax:* 416-975-9884 (publishing); 416-975-5223 (sales) *E-mail:* hccanada@harpercollins.com *Web Site:* www.harpercanada.com, pg 549

HarperCollins Publishers Sales, 10 E 53 St, New York, NY 10022 *Fax:* 212-207-7826 *Web Site:* www.harpercollins.com, pg 116

Harper's Magazine Foundation, 666 Broadway, New York, NY 10012 *Tel:* 212-420-5720 *Fax:* 212-228-5889 *Web Site:* www.harpers.org, pg 116

Denis J Harrington Publishers, 6207 Fushsimi Ct, Burke, VA 22015-3451 *Tel:* 703-440-8920 *Fax:* 703-440-8929, pg 116

Aurand Harris Memorial Playwriting Award, PMB 502, 198 Tremont St, Boston, MA 02116-4750 *Tel:* 617-851-8535 *E-mail:* mail@netconline.org *Web Site:* www.netconline.org, pg 777

Harris InfoSource, 2057 E Aurora Rd, Twinsburg, OH 44087 *Tel:* 330-425-9000 *Toll Free Tel:* 800-888-5900 *Fax:* 330-425-7150 *Toll Free Fax:* 800-643-5997 *Web Site:* www.harrisinfo.com, pg 116

The Joy Harris Literary Agency, 156 Fifth Ave, Suite 617, New York, NY 10010 *Tel:* 212-924-6269 *Fax:* 212-924-6609 *E-mail:* gen.office@jhlitagent.com, pg 634

Julie Harris Playwright Award Competition, PO Box 39729, Los Angeles, CA 90039-0729, pg 777

Harris Literary Agency, PO Box 6023, San Diego, CA 92166 *Tel:* 619-697-0600 *Fax:* 619-697-0610 *E-mail:* hlit@adnc.com *Web Site:* harrisliterary.com, pg 634

Harrison House Publishers, 2448 E 81 St, Suite 4800, Tulsa, OK 74137-4256 *Tel:* 918-523-5700 *Toll Free Tel:* 800-888-4126 *Fax:* 918-494-5688 (sales) *Toll Free Fax:* 800-830-5688 *Web Site:* www.harrisonhouse.com, pg 116

Hartley & Marks Publishers Ltd, 3661 W Broadway, Vancouver, BC V6R 2B8, Canada *Tel:* 604-739-1771 *Toll Free Tel:* 800-277-5887 *Fax:* 604-738-1913 *Toll Free Fax:* 800-707-5887 *E-mail:* pbdesk@hartleyandmarks.com *Web Site:* www.hartleyandmarks.com, pg 549

James E Hartman, 1304 Water Oak Way N, Bradenton, FL 34209 *Tel:* 941-792-5654 *E-mail:* delt@tampabay.rr.com, pg 601

Hartman Publishing Inc, 8529 Indian School Rd NE, Albuquerque, NM 87112 *Tel:* 505-291-1274 *Toll Free Tel:* 800-999-9534 *Fax:* 505-291-1284 *Toll Free Fax:* 800-474-6106 *E-mail:* orders@hartmanonline.com *Web Site:* www.hartmanonline.com, pg 116

Hartmore House Inc, 304 E 49 St, New York, NY 10017 *Tel:* 203-384-2284; 212-319-6666 *Fax:* 203-579-9109, pg 116

Hartnett Publishing Agency, 4301 S 36 St, Arlington, VA 22206 *Tel:* 703-998-0412 *Fax:* 801-730-2939 *E-mail:* hartnettinc@mindspring.com, pg 634

Harvard Business School Press, 300 N Beacon St, Watertown, MA 02472 *Tel:* 617-783-7400 *Toll Free Tel:* 888-500-1016 *Fax:* 617-783-7664 *E-mail:* bookpublisher@mail1.hbsp.harvard.edu *Web Site:* www.hbsp.harvard.edu, pg 116

The Harvard Common Press, 535 Albany St, Boston, MA 02118 *Tel:* 617-423-5803 *Toll Free Tel:* 888-657-3755 *Fax:* 617-695-9794 *E-mail:* orders@harvardcommonpress.com *Web Site:* www.harvardcommonpress.com, pg 117

Harvard Education Publishing Group, 8 Story St, 1st fl, Cambridge, MA 02138 *Tel:* 617-495-3432 *Toll Free Tel:* 800-513-0763 *Fax:* 617-496-3584 *E-mail:* hepg@harvard.edu *Web Site:* gseweb.harvard.edu/hepg, pg 117

Harvard Summer Writing Program, 51 Brattle St, Dept S760, Cambridge, MA 02138-3722 *Tel:* 617-495-4024 *Fax:* 617-495-9176 *E-mail:* summer@hudce.harvard.edu *Web Site:* www.summer.harvard.edu, pg 743

Harvard Ukrainian Research Institute, 1583 Massachusetts Ave, Cambridge, MA 02138 *Tel:* 617-496-8768 *Fax:* 617-495-8097 *E-mail:* huri@fas.harvard.edu *Web Site:* www.huri.harvard.edu, pg 117

Harvard University Art Museums, 32 Quincy St, Cambridge, MA 02138 *Tel:* 617-495-8286 *Fax:* 617-495-9985 *Web Site:* www.artmuseums.harvard.edu, pg 117

Harvard University Press, 79 Garden St, Cambridge, MA 02138-1499 *Tel:* 617-495-2600; 401-531-2800 (international orders) *Toll Free Tel:* 800-405-1619 (orders) *Fax:* 617-495-5898 (general); 617-496-4677 (edit & rts); 401-531-2801 (international orders) *Toll Free Fax:* 800-406-9145 (orders) *E-mail:* firstname_lastname@harvard.edu *Web Site:* www.hup.harvard.edu, pg 117

Harvest Hill Press, PO Box 55, Salisbury Cove, ME 04672 *Tel:* 207-288-8900 *Toll Free Tel:* 888-288-8900 *Fax:* 207-288-3611, pg 117

Harvest House Publishers Inc, 990 Owen Loop N, Eugene, OR 97402 *Tel:* 541-343-0123 *Toll Free Tel:* 800-547-8979 *Fax:* 541-342-6410 *E-mail:* admin@harvesthousepublishers.com *Web Site:* www.harvesthousepublishers.com, pg 117

Haskins Medal Award, 104 Mount Auburn St, 5th fl, Cambridge, MA 02138 *Tel:* 617-491-1622 *E-mail:* speculum@medievalacademy.org *Web Site:* www.medievalacademy.org, pg 778

Hastings House/Daytrips Publishers, 2601 Wells Ave, Suite 161, Fern Park, FL 32730 *Tel:* 407-339-3600 *Toll Free Tel:* 800-206-7822 *Fax:* 407-339-5900 *E-mail:* hastings_daytrips@earthlink.net *Web Site:* www.hastingshousebooks.com; www.daytripsbooks.com, pg 117

Hatherleigh Press, 5-22 46 Ave, Suite 200, Long Island City, NY 11101 *Tel:* 718-786-5338 *Toll Free Tel:* 800-528-2550 *Fax:* 718-706-6087 *E-mail:* info@hatherleigh.com *Web Site:* www.getfitnow.com; www.hatherleighpress.com, pg 117

Barb Hauser Another Girl Rep, PO Box 421443, San Francisco, CA 94142-1443 *Tel:* 415-546-4180 *Fax:* 415-546-4180 *E-mail:* barb@girlrep.com *Web Site:* www.girlrep.com, pg 666

Hawaii Award for Literature, 250 S Hotel St, 2nd fl, Honolulu, HI 96813 *Tel:* 808-586-0769 *Fax:* 808-586-0308 *E-mail:* sfca@sfca.state.hi.us *Web Site:* www.hawaii.gov/sfca, pg 778

HAWK Publishing Group, 7107 S Yale Ave, Suite 345, Tulsa, OK 74136-6308 *Tel:* 918-492-3677 *Fax:* 918-492-2120 *E-mail:* hawkpub@cox.net *Web Site:* www.hawkpub.com, pg 118

John Hawkins & Associates Inc, 71 W 23 St, Suite 1600, New York, NY 10010 *Tel:* 212-807-7040 *Fax:* 212-807-9555 *Web Site:* jhaliterary.com, pg 634

R R Hawkins & Professional/Scholarly Publishing Division Annual Awards Program, 71 Fifth Ave, 2nd fl, New York, NY 10003-3004 *Tel:* 212-255-0200 *Fax:* 212-255-7007 *Web Site:* www.publishers.org; www.pspcentral.org, pg 778

The Haworth Press Inc, 10 Alice St, Binghamton, NY 13904-1580 *Tel:* 607-722-5857 *Toll Free Tel:* 800-429-6784 *Fax:* 607-722-1424 *Toll Free Fax:* 800-895-0582 *E-mail:* getinfo@haworthpressinc.com *Web Site:* www.haworthpress.com, pg 118

Hay House Inc, 2776 Loker Ave W, Carlsbad, CA 92008 *Tel:* 760-431-7695 *Toll Free Tel:* 800-650-5115; 800-654-5126 (orders) *Fax:* 760-431-6948 *E-mail:* info@hayhouse.com *Web Site:* www.hayhouse.com, pg 118

Haynes Manuals Inc, 861 Lawrence Dr, Newbury Park, CA 91320 *Tel:* 805-498-6703 *Toll Free Tel:* 800-442-9637 *Fax:* 805-498-2867 *E-mail:* info@haynes.com *Web Site:* www.haynes.com, pg 118

Haystack Writing Program, PO Box 1491, Portland, OR 97207-1491 *Tel:* 503-725-3276; 503-725-4186 *Fax:* 503-725-4840 *Web Site:* www.haystack.pdx.edu, pg 744

Hazelden Publishing & Educational Services, 15251 Pleasant Valley Rd, Center City, MN 55012-0176 *Tel:* 651-213-4470 *Toll Free Tel:* 800-328-9000 *Web Site:* www.hazelden.org, pg 118

HCPro, 200 Hoods Lane, Marblehead, MA 01945 *Tel:* 781-639-1872 *Toll Free Tel:* 800-650-6787 *Fax:* 781-639-2982 *Toll Free Fax:* 800-639-8511 *E-mail:* customer_service@hcpro.com *Web Site:* www.hcpro.com, pg 118

Headlands Center for the Arts Residency for CA, NC, OH & NJ Writers, 944 Fort Barry, Sausalito, CA 94965 *Tel:* 415-331-2787 *Fax:* 415-331-3857 *Web Site:* www.headlands.org, pg 778

Health Administration Press, One N Franklin St, Suite 1700, Chicago, IL 60606-3491 *Tel:* 312-424-2800 *Fax:* 312-424-0014 *E-mail:* hap@ache.org *Web Site:* www.ache.org, pg 119

Health Communications Inc, 3201 SW 15 St, Deerfield Beach, FL 33442-8190 *Tel:* 954-360-0909 *Toll Free Tel:* 800-851-9100 (cust serv); 800-441-5569 (order entry) *Fax:* 954-360-0034 *Web Site:* www.hcibooks.com, pg 119

Health Forum Inc, One N Franklin St, 28th fl, Chicago, IL 60606 *Tel:* 312-893-6884 *Toll Free Tel:* 800-242-2626 *Fax:* 312-422-4600 *Web Site:* www.ahaonlinestore.com, pg 119

Health InfoNet Inc, 231 Market Place, No 331, San Ramon, CA 94583 *Tel:* 925-358-4370 *Toll Free Tel:* 800-446-1947 *Fax:* 925-358-4377 *Web Site:* hinbooks.com, pg 119

Health Press NA Inc, 2920 Carlisle Blvd NE, Albuquerque, NM 87110 *Tel:* 505-888-1394 *Fax:* 505-888-1521 *E-mail:* goodbooks@healthpress.com *Web Site:* www.healthpress.com, pg 119

Health Professions Press, PO Box 10624, Baltimore, MD 21285-0624 *Tel:* 410-337-9585 *Toll Free Tel:* 888-337-8808 *Fax:* 410-337-8539 *E-mail:* custserv@healthpropress.com *Web Site:* www.healthpropress.com, pg 119

Health Research, 62 Seventh St, Pomeroy, WA 99347 *Tel:* 509-843-2385 *Toll Free Tel:* 888-844-2386 *Fax:* 509-843-2387 *E-mail:* publish@pomeroy-wa.com *Web Site:* www.healthresearchbooks.com, pg 119

Health Resources Press Inc, 8609 Second Ave, Suite 405B, Silver Spring, MD 20910 *Tel:* 301-565-2494 *Fax:* 301-565-2494 *Web Site:* www.healthresourcespress.com, pg 120

Healthy Healing Publications, PO Box 436, Carmel Valley, CA 93924 *Tel:* 831-659-8324 *Fax:* 831-659-4044 *E-mail:* customerservice@healthyhealing.com *Web Site:* www.healthyhealing.com, pg 120

Heart Math, 14700 W Park Ave, Boulder Creek, CA 95006 *Tel:* 831-338-2161 *Toll Free Tel:* 800-450-9111 *Fax:* 831-338-9861 *Web Site:* www.heartmath.com, pg 120

Hearts & Tummies Cookbook Co, 1854 345 Ave, Wever, IA 52658 *Tel:* 319-372-7480 *Toll Free Tel:* 800-571-BOOK *Fax:* 319-372-7485 *E-mail:* heartsntummies@hotmail.com, pg 120

Anne Hebenstreit, 20 Tip Top Way, Berkeley Heights, NJ 07922 *Tel:* 908-665-0536, pg 601

Hebrew Union College Press, 3101 Clifton Ave, Cincinnati, OH 45220 *Tel:* 513-221-1875 *Fax:* 513-221-0321 *E-mail:* hucpress@huc.edu *Web Site:* www.huc.edu, pg 120

Heian International Inc, 20655 S Western Ave, Suite 105, Torrance, CA 90501 *Tel:* 310-328-7200 *Fax:* 310-328-7676 *E-mail:* heianemail@earthlink.net *Web Site:* heian.com, pg 120

Heimburger House Publishing Co, 7236 W Madison St, Forest Park, IL 60130 *Tel:* 708-366-1973 *Fax:* 708-366-1973 *Web Site:* www.heimburgerhouse.com, pg 120

William S Hein & Co Inc, 1285 Main St, Buffalo, NY 14209-1987 *Tel:* 716-882-2600 *Toll Free Tel:* 800-828-7571 *Fax:* 716-883-8100 *E-mail:* mail@wshein.com *Web Site:* www.wshein.com, pg 120

Heinemann, 361 Hanover St, Portsmouth, NH 03801-3912 *Tel:* 603-431-7894 *Toll Free Tel:* 800-225-5800 *Fax:* 603-431-4971; 603-431-7840 *E-mail:* info@heinemann.com *Web Site:* www.heinemann.com, pg 120

Heinemann/Boynton Cook Publishers Inc, 361 Hanover St, Portsmouth, NH 03801-3912 *Tel:* 603-431-7894 *Toll Free Tel:* 800-541-2086 *Fax:* 603-431-7840 *E-mail:* custserv@heinemann.com *Web Site:* www.boyntoncook.com, pg 120

Drue Heinz Literature Prize, 3400 Forbes Ave, Pittsburgh, PA 15260 *Tel:* 412-383-2456 *Fax:* 412-383-2466 *Web Site:* www.pitt.edu/~press, pg 778

Heldref Publications, 1319 18 St NW, Washington, DC 20036 *Tel:* 202-296-6267 *Toll Free Tel:* 800-365-9753 *Fax:* 202-293-6130 *E-mail:* subscribe@heldref.org *Web Site:* www.heldref.org, pg 705

Helgate Press, PO Box 3727, Central Point, OR 97502 *Tel:* 541-855-5566 *Toll Free Tel:* 800-795-4059 *Fax:* 541-855-1360 *Web Site:* www.hellgatepress.com, pg 120

Hellgate Press, 1375 Upper River Rd, Gold Hill, OR 97525 *Tel:* 541-855-5566 *Toll Free Tel:* 800-795-4059 *Fax:* 541-855-1360 *E-mail:* info@psi-research.com *Web Site:* www.psi-research.com, pg 121

Helm Editorial Services, 707 SW Eighth Way, Fort Lauderdale, FL 33315 *Tel:* 954-525-5626 *Fax:* 954-525-5626 (call first) *E-mail:* helmls@aol.com, pg 601

Ernest Hemingway Foundation/PEN Award for First Fiction, PO Box 400725, North Cambridge, MA 02140 *Tel:* 617-499-9550 *Fax:* 617-353-7134 *E-mail:* hemingway@pen-ne.org *Web Site:* www.pen-ne.org, pg 778

Hemingway Western Studies Series, Boise State University, 1910 University Dr, Boise, ID 83725 *Tel:* 208-426-1999 *Toll Free Tel:* 800-992-TEXT (992-8398) *Fax:* 208-426-4373 *Web Site:* www.boisestate.edu/hemingway/series.htm, pg 121

Cecil Hemley Memorial Award, 15 Gramercy Park, New York, NY 10003 *Tel:* 212-254-9628 *Fax:* 212-673-2352 *Web Site:* www.poetrysociety.org, pg 778

Hendrick-Long Publishing Co, 10635 Tower Oaks, Suite D, Houston, TX 77070 *Tel:* 832-912-READ (912-7323) *Fax:* 832-912-7353 *E-mail:* hendrick-long@worldnet.att.net *Web Site:* www.hendricklongpublishing.com, pg 121

Hendrickson Publishers Inc, PO Box 3473, Peabody, MA 01961-3473 *Tel:* 978-532-6546 *Toll Free Tel:* 800-358-3111 *Fax:* 978-531-8146 *E-mail:* orders@hendrickson.com *Web Site:* www.hendrickson.com, pg 121

Frances Henne YALSA/VOYA Research Grant, 50 E Huron St, Chicago, IL 60611 *Toll Free Tel:* 800-545-2433 (ext 4391) *Fax:* 312-664-7459 *E-mail:* yalsa@ala.org *Web Site:* www.ala.org/yalsa/printz, pg 778

Bryan Henry, 1850 S Treasure Dr, No 1, Miami, FL 33141 *Tel:* 561-575-4254 *E-mail:* bryanhenry33140@yahoo.com *Web Site:* www.envirobx.com/maritime.htm, pg 601

Hensley Publishing, 6116 E 32 St, Tulsa, OK 74135 *Tel:* 918-664-8520 *Toll Free Tel:* 800-288-8520 (orders only) *Fax:* 918-664-8562 *E-mail:* customerservice@hensleypublishing.com *Web Site:* www.hensleypublishing.com, pg 121

Her Own Words, PO Box 5264, Madison, WI 53705-0264 *Tel:* 608-271-7083 *Fax:* 608-271-0209 *E-mail:* herownword@aol.com *Web Site:* www.herownwords.com, pg 121

Herald Press, 616 Walnut Ave, Scottdale, PA 15683-1999 *Tel:* 724-887-8500 *Toll Free Tel:* 800-245-7894 *Fax:* 724-887-3111 *E-mail:* hp@mph.org *Web Site:* www.heraldpress.com, pg 121

Herald Press, 490 Dutton Dr, Unit C-8, Waterloo, ON N2L 6H7, Canada *Tel:* 519-747-5722 *Toll Free Tel:* 800-245-7894 (Canada & US) *Fax:* 519-747-5721 *E-mail:* hp@mph.org *Web Site:* www.heraldpress.com, pg 550

Herald Publishing House, 1001 W Walnut, Independence, MO 64051 *Tel:* 816-521-3015 *Toll Free Tel:* 800-767-8181 *Fax:* 816-521-3066 *E-mail:* marketing@heraldhouse.org *Web Site:* www.heraldhouse.org, pg 121

Heritage Books Inc, 65 E Main St, Westminster, MD 21157 *Tel:* 410-876-0371 *Toll Free Tel:* 866-282-2689 *Fax:* 410-871-2674 *E-mail:* info@heritagebooks.com *Web Site:* www.heritagebooks.com, pg 121

The Heritage Foundation, 214 Massachusetts Ave NE, Washington, DC 20002-4999 *Tel:* 202-546-4400 *Toll Free Tel:* 800-544-4843 *Fax:* 202-543-9647 *E-mail:* pubs@heritage.org *Web Site:* www.heritage.org, pg 121

The Heritage Foundation, 214 Massachusetts Ave NE, Washington, DC 20002-4999 *Tel:* 202-546-4400 *Fax:* 202-546-8328 *Web Site:* www.heritage.org, pg 705

Heritage House Publishing Co Ltd, 17665 66 "A" Ave, No 108, Surrey, BC V3S 2A7, Canada *Tel:* 604-574-7067 *Toll Free Tel:* 800-665-3302 *Fax:* 604-574-9942 *Toll Free Fax:* 800-566-3336 *E-mail:* publisher@heritagehouse.ca; editorial@heritagehouse.ca; distribution@heritagehouse.ca *Web Site:* www.heritagehouse.ca, pg 550

Herman Agency, 350 Central Park W, New York, NY 10025 *Tel:* 212-749-4907 *Fax:* 212-662-5151 *E-mail:* hermanagen@aol.com *Web Site:* www.hermanagencyinc.com, pg 666

The Jeff Herman Agency LLC, 9 South St, Stockbridge, MA 01262 *Tel:* 413-298-0077 *Fax:* 413-298-8188 *Web Site:* www.jeffherman.com, pg 634

Hermitage Publishers, PO Box 310, Tenafly, NJ 07670-0310 *Tel:* 201-894-8247 *Fax:* 201-894-5591 *Web Site:* www.hermitagepublishers.com, pg 121

Brodie Herndon Memorial, 100 N Berwick, Williamsburg, VA 23188 *Tel:* 757-258-5582 *Web Site:* www.poetrysocietyofvirginia.org, pg 778

Susan Herner Rights Agency Inc, PO Box 57, Pound Ridge, NY 10576 *Tel:* 914-234-2864 *Fax:* 914-234-2866 *E-mail:* sherneragency@optonline.net, pg 634

Herr's Indexing Service, 1325 Poor Farm Rd, Washington, VT 05675 *Tel:* 802-883-5415 *Fax:* 802-883-5415 *E-mail:* index@together.net *Web Site:* www.herrsindexing.com, pg 601

Carl Hertzog Book Design Award, University of Texas at El Paso, University Library, El Paso, TX 79968-0582 *Tel:* 915-747-5683 *Fax:* 915-747-5345 *E-mail:* llimas@libr.utep.edu *Web Site:* libraryweb.utep.edu, pg 778

Herzl Press, 633 Third Ave, 21st fl, New York, NY 10017 *Tel:* 212-339-6020 *Fax:* 212-318-6176 *E-mail:* midstreamthf@aol.com *Web Site:* www.midstreamthf.com, pg 121

Heuer Publishing LLC, 211 First Ave SE, Cedar Rapids, IA 52401 *Tel:* 319-368-8008 *Toll Free Tel:* 800-950-7529 *Fax:* 319-364-1771 *E-mail:* editor@hitplays.com *Web Site:* www.hitplays.com, pg 122

Hewitt Homeschooling Resources, 2103 "B" St, Washougal, WA 98671 *Tel:* 360-835-8708 *Toll Free Tel:* 800-348-1750 *Fax:* 360-835-8697 *E-mail:* info@hewitthomeschooling.com *Web Site:* www.hewitthomeschooling.com, pg 122

Heyday Books, 2054 University Ave, Berkeley, CA 94704 *Tel:* 510-549-3564 *Fax:* 510-549-1889 *E-mail:* heyday@heydaybooks.com *Web Site:* www.heydaybooks.com, pg 122

Hi Willow Research & Publishing, 312 S 1000 East, Salt Lake City, UT 84102 *Toll Free Tel:* 800-873-3043 *Fax:* 936-271-4560 *E-mail:* sales@lmcsource.com *Web Site:* www.lmcsource.com, pg 122

Hickory Tales Publishing LLC, 841 Newberry St, Bowling Green, KY 42103 *Tel:* 270-791-3242, pg 571

Higginson Book Co, 148 Washington St, Salem, MA 01970 *Tel:* 978-745-7170 *Fax:* 978-745-8025 *E-mail:* orders@higginsonbooks.com; higginson@cove.com *Web Site:* www.higginsonbooks.com, pg 122

High/Coo Press, 3720 N Woodridge Dr, Decatur, IL 62526-1117 *Tel:* 217-877-2966 *E-mail:* brooksbooks@q-com.com *Web Site:* www.family-net.net/~brooksbooks, pg 122

High Country Publishers Ltd, 197 New Market Center, No 135, Boone, NC 28607 *Tel:* 828-964-0590 *Fax:* 828-262-1973 *E-mail:* editor@highcountrypublishers.com *Web Site:* www.highcountrypublishers.com, pg 122

High Plains Press, 539 Cassa Rd, Glendo, WY 82213 *Tel:* 307-735-4370 *Toll Free Tel:* 800-552-7819 *Fax:* 307-735-4590 *E-mail:* editor@highplainspress.com *Web Site:* www.highplainspress.com, pg 122

High Tide Press, 3650 W 183 St, Homewood, IL 60430 *Tel:* 708-206-2054 *Fax:* 708-206-2044 *Web Site:* www.hightidepress.com, pg 122

27th Annual Highland Summer Conference, PO Box 7014, Radford University, Radford, VA 24142-7014 *Tel:* 540-831-5366 *Fax:* 540-831-5951 *Web Site:* www.radford.edu/~arsc, pg 744

Highlights for Children Fiction Contest, 803 Church St, Honesdale, PA 18431 *Tel:* 570-253-1080 *Fax:* 570-251-7847 *E-mail:* eds@highlights-corp.com *Web Site:* www.highlights.com, pg 778

The Highlights Foundation Writers Workshop at Chautauqua, 814 Court St, Dept CF, Honesdale, PA 18431 *Tel:* 570-253-1192 *Fax:* 570-253-0179 *E-mail:* contact@highlightsfoundation.org *Web Site:* www.highlightsfoundation.org, pg 744

Highway Book Shop, RR 1, Cobalt, ON P0J 1C0, Canada *Tel:* 705-679-8375 *Fax:* 705-679-8511 *E-mail:* bookshop@nt.net *Web Site:* www.abebooks.com/home/highwaybooks, pg 550

Hill & Wang, 19 Union Sq W, New York, NY 10003 *Tel:* 212-741-6900 *Fax:* 212-206-5340 *E-mail:* fsg. publicity@fsgbooks.com *Web Site:* www.fsgbooks. com, pg 122

Frederick Hill Bonnie Nadell Literary Agency, 1842 Union St, San Francisco, CA 94123 *Tel:* 415-921-2910 *Fax:* 415-921-2802, pg 634

Hill Street Press LLC, 191 E Broad St, Suite 209, Athens, GA 30601-2848 *Tel:* 706-613-7200 *Fax:* 706-613-7204 *Web Site:* www.hillstreetpress.com, pg 122

Sidney Hillman Foundation Awards, 275 Seventh Ave, New York, NY 10001 *Tel:* 212-265-7000 *Fax:* 212-582-3175 *Web Site:* www.hillmanfoundation.org, pg 778

Hillsdale College Press, 33 E College St, Hillsdale, MI 49242 *Tel:* 517-437-7341 *Toll Free Tel:* 800-437-2268 *Fax:* 517-437-3923 *E-mail:* news@hillsdale.edu *Web Site:* www.hillsdale.edu, pg 123

Hillsdale Educational Publishers Inc, 39 North St, Hillsdale, MI 49242 *Tel:* 517-437-3179 *Fax:* 517-437-0531 *E-mail:* davestory@aol.com *Web Site:* hillsdalepublishers.com; michbooks.com, pg 123

Himalayan Institute Press, 952 Bethany Tpke, Honesdale, PA 18431-9706 *Tel:* 570-253-5551 *Toll Free Tel:* 800-822-4547 *Fax:* 570-253-9078 *E-mail:* hibooks@himalayaninstitute.org *Web Site:* www.himalayaninstitute.org, pg 123

Diane Casella Hines, 2366 Live Oak Meadow Rd, Malibu, CA 90265 *Tel:* 310-456-3220 *Fax:* 310-456-0549 *E-mail:* dchines@ispwest.com, pg 601

Hippocrene Books Inc, 171 Madison Ave, New York, NY 10016 *Tel:* 212-685-4371 (edit); 718-454-2366 (sales & cust serv) *Fax:* 718-454-1391 (cust serv); 212-779-9338 (edit) *Toll Free Fax:* 800-809-3855 (sales) *E-mail:* orders@hippocrenebooks.com *Web Site:* www.hippocrenebooks.com, pg 123

L Anne Hirschel, DDS, 20120 Ledgestone Dr, Southfield, MI 48076 *Tel:* 248-357-2165 *E-mail:* ahirschel154242mi@comcast.net, pg 601

The Historic New Orleans Collection, 533 Royal St, New Orleans, LA 70130 *Tel:* 504-523-4662 *Fax:* 504-598-7108 *E-mail:* hnocinfo@hnoc.org *Web Site:* www. hnoc.org, pg 123

HK Portfolio Inc, 10 E 29 St, 40G, New York, NY 10016 *Tel:* 212-689-7830 *Fax:* 212-689-7829 *Web Site:* www.hkportfolio.com, pg 666

W D Hoard & Sons Co, 28 W Milwaukee Ave, Fort Atkinson, WI 53538-0801 *Tel:* 920-563-5551 *Fax:* 920-563-7298 *E-mail:* hoards@hoards.com *Web Site:* www.hoards.com, pg 123

Hobby House Press Inc, One Corporate Dr, Grantsville, MD 21536 *Tel:* 301-895-3792 *Toll Free Tel:* 800-554-1447 *Fax:* 301-895-5029 *E-mail:* email@hobbyhouse. com *Web Site:* www.hobbyhouse.com, pg 123

John L Hochmann Books, 320 E 58 St, New York, NY 10022 *Tel:* 212-319-0505, pg 635

Hofstra University, English Dept, 204 Calkins, Hempstead, NY 11549 *Tel:* 516-463-5454 *Fax:* 516-463-6395 *E-mail:* engpmu@hofstra.edu *Web Site:* www.hofstra.edu, pg 752

The Barbara Hogenson Agency Inc, 165 West End Ave, Suite 19-C, New York, NY 10023 *Tel:* 212-874-8084 *Fax:* 212-362-3011 *E-mail:* bhogenson@aol.com, pg 635

Hogrefe & Huber Publishers, 875 Massachusetts Ave, 7th fl, Cambridge, MA 02139 *Toll Free Tel:* 800-228-3749; 866-823-4726 *Fax:* 617-354-6875 *E-mail:* hh@hhpub.com *Web Site:* www.hhpub.com, pg 123

Hohm Press, PO Box 2501, Prescott, AZ 86302 *Tel:* 928-778-9189 *Toll Free Tel:* 800-381-2700 *Fax:* 928-717-1779 *E-mail:* hppublisher@cableone.net *Web Site:* www.hohmpress.com, pg 123

Bess Hokin Prize, 1030 N Clark St, Suite 420, Chicago, IL 60610 *Tel:* 312-787-7070 *Fax:* 312-787-6650 *E-mail:* poetry@poetrymagazine.org *Web Site:* www. poetrymagazine.org, pg 778

Holiday House Inc, 425 Madison Ave, New York, NY 10017 *Tel:* 212-688-0085 *Fax:* 212-421-6134, pg 123

Hollins University, Writing Program, English Dept, Roanoke, VA 24020 *Tel:* 540-362-6317 *Fax:* 540-362-6097 *E-mail:* creative.writing@hollins.edu *Web Site:* www.hollins.edu, pg 752

Holloway House Publishing Co, 8060 Melrose Ave, Los Angeles, CA 90046-7082 *Tel:* 323-653-8060 *Fax:* 323-655-9452 *E-mail:* info@hollowayhousebooks.com *Web Site:* www.hollowayhousebooks.com, pg 124

Hollym International Corp, 18 Donald Place, Elizabeth, NJ 07208 *Tel:* 908-353-1655 *Fax:* 908-353-0255 *E-mail:* hollym2@optonline.net *Web Site:* www. hollym.com, pg 124

Hollywood Creative Directory, 1024 N Orange Dr, Hollywood, CA 90038 *Tel:* 323-308-3490 *Toll Free Tel:* 800-815-0503 *Fax:* 323-308-3493 *Web Site:* www. hcdonline.com, pg 124

Hollywood Film Archive, 8391 Beverly Blvd, PMB 321, Hollywood, CA 90048 *Tel:* 323-655-4968, pg 124

Holmes & Meier Publishers Inc, 160 Broadway, East Bldg, New York, NY 10038 *Tel:* 212-374-0100 *Fax:* 212-374-1313 *E-mail:* info@holmesandmeier.com *Web Site:* www.holmesandmeier.com, pg 124

Burnham Holmes, 182 Lakeview Hill Rd, Poultney, VT 05764-9179 *Tel:* 802-287-9707 *Fax:* 802-287-9707 (Computer fax/modem) *E-mail:* burnham.holmes@ castleton.edu, pg 601

Henry Holmes Literary Agent/Book Publicist, PO Box 433, Swansea, MA 02777 *Tel:* 508-672-2258, pg 601, 635

Holmes Publishing Group, PO Box 623, Edmonds, WA 98020-0623 *Tel:* 425-771-2701 *Fax:* 425-771-5651, pg 124

Henry Holt and Company, LLC, 115 W 18 St, New York, NY 10011 *Tel:* 212-886-9200 *Toll Free Tel:* 888-330-8477 (orders) *Fax:* 212-633-0748 *E-mail:* publicity@hholt.com *Web Site:* www. henryholt.com, pg 124

Holt, Rinehart and Winston, 10801 N MoPac Expy, Bldg 3, Austin, TX 78759 *Tel:* 512-721-7000 *Toll Free Tel:* 800-225-5425 (cust serv) *Fax:* 512-721-7833 (mktg); 512-721-7898 (edit) *Web Site:* www.hrw.com, pg 124

Holtzbrinck Publishers, 175 Fifth Ave, New York, NY 10010 *Tel:* 212-674-5151 *Fax:* 212-420-9314 *E-mail:* firstname.lastname@hbpub.com *Web Site:* www.holtzbrinck.com, pg 124

Holy Cow! Press, Mount Royal Sta, Duluth, MN 55803 *Tel:* 218-724-1653 *Fax:* 218-724-1653 *E-mail:* holycow@cpinternet.com *Web Site:* www. holycowpress.org, pg 125

Holy Cross Orthodox Press, 50 Goddard Ave, Brookline, MA 02445 *Tel:* 617-731-3500 *Fax:* 617-850-1460 *E-mail:* press@hchc.edu *Web Site:* www.hchc.edu, pg 125

Home Planners LLC, 3275 W Ina Rd, Suite 220, Tucson, AZ 85741 *Tel:* 520-297-8200 *Toll Free Tel:* 800-322-6797 *Fax:* 520-297-6219 *Toll Free Fax:* 800-531-2555 *E-mail:* customerservice@eplans. com *Web Site:* www.eplans.com, pg 125

Homestead Publishing, PO Box 193, Moose, WY 83012-0193 *Tel:* 307-733-6248 *Fax:* 307-733-6248 *Web Site:* www.homesteadpublishing.net, pg 125

Homestore Plans & Publications, 213 E Fourth St, Suite 400, St Paul, MN 55101 *Tel:* 651-602-5000 *Toll Free Tel:* 888-626-2026 *Fax:* 651-602-5001 *Web Site:* homeplans.com, pg 125

Honor Books, 4050 Lee Vance View, Colorado Springs, CO 80918 *Tel:* 719-536-0100 *Toll Free Tel:* 800-708-5550 *Web Site:* www.cookministries.com, pg 125

Hoover Institution Press, 424 Galvez Mall, Stanford, CA 94305-6010 *Tel:* 650-723-3373 *Toll Free Tel:* 800-935-2882 *Fax:* 650-723-8626 *E-mail:* digest@hoover. stanford.edu; hooverpress@hoover.stanford.edu *Web Site:* www.hoover.org, pg 125

Hoover's, Inc, 5800 Airport Blvd, Austin, TX 78752 *Tel:* 512-374-4500 *Toll Free Tel:* 800-486-8666 (orders only) *Fax:* 512-374-4538 *E-mail:* info@hoovers.com *Web Site:* www.hoovers.com, pg 125

Hope Publishing Co, 380 S Main Place, Carol Stream, IL 60188 *Tel:* 630-665-3200 *Toll Free Tel:* 800-323-1049 *Fax:* 630-665-2552 *E-mail:* hope@ hopepublishing.com *Web Site:* www.hopepublishing. com, pg 125

Horizon Publishers & Distributors Inc, 50 S 500 W, Bountiful, UT 84010 *Tel:* 801-295-9451 *Toll Free Tel:* 800-759-2665 *Fax:* 801-489-1096 *E-mail:* horizonp@burgoyne.com *Web Site:* www. horizonpublishersbooks.com, pg 125

Hornfischer Literary Management Inc, PO Box 50544, Austin, TX 78763 *Tel:* 512-472-0011 *Fax:* 512-472-0077 *E-mail:* queries@hornfischerlit.com *Web Site:* www.hornfischerlit.com, pg 635

Horror Writers Association, PO Box 50577, Palo Alto, CA 94303 *E-mail:* hwa@horror.org *Web Site:* www. horror.org/, pg 688

Hospital & Healthcare Compensation Service, PO Box 376, Oakland, NJ 07436 *Tel:* 201-405-0075 *Fax:* 201-405-2110 *E-mail:* allinfo@hhcsinc.com *Web Site:* www.hhcsinc.com, pg 126

Host Publications, 2717 Wooldridge Dr, Austin, TX 78703 *Tel:* 512-482-8229 *Fax:* 512-482-0580 *Web Site:* www.hostpublications.com, pg 126

Hot House Press, 760 Cushing Hwy, Cohasset, MA 02025 *Tel:* 781-383-8360 *Toll Free Tel:* 866-331-8360 *Fax:* 781-383-8346 *Web Site:* www.hothousepress.com, pg 126

Houghton Mifflin College Division, 222 Berkeley St, Boston, MA 02116-3764 *Tel:* 617-351-5000 *Toll Free Tel:* 800-225-1464 (orders) *Web Site:* www.college. hmco.com, pg 126

Houghton Mifflin Co, 222 Berkeley St, Boston, MA 02116-3764 *Tel:* 617-351-5000 *Toll Free Tel:* 800-225-3362 (trade books); 800-733-2828 (text books); 800-225-1464 (college texts) *Fax:* 617-351-1125 *Web Site:* www.hmco.com, pg 126

Houghton Mifflin School Division, 222 Berkeley St, Boston, MA 02116-3764, pg 126

Houghton Mifflin Trade & Reference Division, 222 Berkeley St, Boston, MA 02116-3764 *Tel:* 617-351-5000 *Toll Free Tel:* 800-225-3362 *Web Site:* www. houghtonmifflinbooks.com, pg 126

Hounslow Press, 8 Market St, 2nd fl, Toronto, ON M5E 1M6, Canada *Tel:* 416-214-5544 *Fax:* 416-214-5556 *E-mail:* info@dundurn.com *Web Site:* www.dundurn. com, pg 550

House of Anansi Press Ltd, 110 Spadina Ave, Suite 801, Toronto, ON M5V 2K4, Canada *Tel:* 416-363-4343 *Fax:* 416-363-1017 *E-mail:* info@anansi.ca *Web Site:* www.anansi.ca, pg 550

House of Collectibles, 1745 Broadway, New York, NY 10019 *Tel:* 212-782-9000 *Fax:* 212-572-4997 *E-mail:* houseofcollectibles@randomhouse.com *Web Site:* www.houseofcollectibles.com; www. randomhouse.com, pg 126

House to House Publications, 1924 W Main St, Ephrata, PA 17522 *Tel:* 717-738-3751 *Toll Free Tel:* 800-848-5892 *Fax:* 717-738-0656 *E-mail:* H2HP@dcfi.org *Web Site:* www.dcfi.org, pg 127

Housing Assistance Council, 1025 Vermont Ave NW, Suite 606, Washington, DC 20005 *Tel:* 202-842-8600 *Fax:* 202-347-3441 *E-mail:* hac@ruralhome.org *Web Site:* www.ruralhome.org, pg 127

How to be Published Workshops, PO Box 100031, Birmingham, AL 35210 *Tel:* 205-907-0140 *Web Site:* www.writing2sell.com, pg 744

Amelia Frances Howard-Gibbon Illustrator's Award, 328 Frank St, Ottawa, ON K2P 0X8, Canada *Tel:* 613-232-9625 *Fax:* 613-563-9895 *Web Site:* www.cla.ca/, pg 779

The J Howard & Barbara M J Wood Prize, 1030 N Clark St, Suite 420, Chicago, IL 60610 Tel: 312-787-7070 Fax: 312-787-6650 E-mail: poetry@poetrymagazine.org Web Site: www.poetrymagazine.org, pg 779

Howard Publishing, 3117 N Seventh St, West Monroe, LA 71291 Tel: 318-396-3122 Toll Free Tel: 800-858-4109 Fax: 318-397-1882 E-mail: info@howardpublishing.com Web Site: howardpublishing.com, pg 127

Howard University Press, 2225 Georgia Ave NW, Suite 718, Washington, DC 20059 Tel: 202-238-2570 Fax: 202-588-9849 E-mail: howardupress@howard.edu Web Site: www.hupress.howard.edu, pg 127

C D Howe Institute, 125 Adelaide St E, Toronto, ON M5C 1L7, Canada Tel: 416-865-1904 Fax: 416-865-1866 E-mail: cdhowe@cdhowe.org Web Site: www.cdhowe.org, pg 550

Howell Press Inc, 1713-2D Allied Lane, Charlottesville, VA 22903 Tel: 434-977-4006 Toll Free Tel: 800-868-4512 Fax: 434-971-7204 Toll Free Fax: 888-971-7204 E-mail: custserv@howellpress.com Web Site: www.howellpress.com, pg 127

Howells House, PO Box 9546, Washington, DC 20016-9546 Tel: 202-333-2182 Fax: 202-333-2184 E-mail: hhi@ix.netcom.com, pg 127

Howie Publishing Inc, 1695 Quigley Rd, Columbus, OH 43227 Toll Free Tel: 888-933-9314 Fax: 614-237-2157, pg 571

HPBooks, 375 Hudson St, New York, NY 10014 Tel: 212-366-2000 E-mail: online@penguinputnam.com Web Site: www.penguin.com, pg 127

HRD Press, 22 Amherst Rd, Amherst, MA 01002 Tel: 413-253-3488 Toll Free Tel: 800-822-2801 Fax: 413-253-3490 E-mail: info@hrdpress.com; orders@hrdpress.com Web Site: www.hrdpress.com, pg 127

HSC Publications, 360-A W Merrick Rd, Suite 40, Valley Stream, NY 11580 Tel: 516-256-0223 E-mail: hscpub@aol.com Web Site: www.hscpub.com, pg 127

HTC One-Act Playwriting Competition, PO Box 27032, Richmond, VA 23273-7032 Tel: 804-501-5138 Fax: 804-501-5284, pg 779

L Ron Hubbard's Writers of the Future Contest, PO Box 1630, Los Angeles, CA 90078 Tel: 323-466-3310 Fax: 323-466-6474 Web Site: www.writersofthefuture.com, pg 779

Hudson Hills Press LLC, 74-2 Union St, Manchester, VT 05254 Tel: 802-362-6450 Fax: 802-362-6459 E-mail: artbooks@hudsonhills.com Web Site: www.hudsonhills.com, pg 128

Hudson Institute, 1015 18 St NW, Suite 300, Washington, DC 20036 Tel: 202-223-7770 Fax: 202-223-8537 E-mail: info@hudson.org Web Site: www.hudson.org, pg 128

Hudson Park Press, Johnny Cake Hollow Rd, Pine Plains, NY 12567 Tel: 212-929-8898 Fax: 212-242-6137 E-mail: hudpark@aol.com Web Site: www.hudsonpark.com, pg 128

Hugh Lauter Levin Associates Inc, 9 Burr Rd, Westport, CT 06880 Tel: 203-227-6422 Fax: 203-227-6717 E-mail: inquiries@hlla.com Web Site: www.hlla.com, pg 128

Human Kinetics Inc, PO Box 5076, Champaign, IL 61825-5076 Tel: 217-351-5076 Toll Free Tel: 800-747-4457 Fax: 217-351-1549 (orders/cust serv) E-mail: info@hkusa.com Web Site: www.humankinetics.com, pg 128

Human Rights Watch, 350 Fifth Ave, 34th fl, New York, NY 10118 Tel: 212-290-4700 Fax: 212-736-1300 E-mail: hrwnyc@hrw.org Web Site: www.hrw.org, pg 128

Humana Press, 999 Riverview Dr, Suite 208, Totowa, NJ 07512 Tel: 973-256-1699 Fax: 973-256-8341 E-mail: humana@humanapr.com Web Site: humanapress.com, pg 128

Humane Society Press, 2100 L St NW, Washington, DC 20037 Tel: 202-452-1100 Fax: 301-258-3082 Web Site: www.hsus.org, pg 572

Humanics Publishing Group, 12 S Dixie Hwy, Suite 203, Lake Worth, FL 33460 Tel: 561-533-6231 Toll Free Tel: 800-874-8844 Toll Free Fax: 888-874-8844 E-mail: humanics@mindspring.com Web Site: humanicspub.com; humanicslearning.com; humanicsdealer.com, pg 128

Humanitas, 990 Picard, Ville de Brossard, PQ J4W 1S5, Canada Tel: 450-466-9737 Fax: 450-466-9737 E-mail: humanitas@cyberglobe.net, pg 550

Hungry Samurai, Grand Central Sta, PO Box 824, New York, NY 10163-0824 Tel: 212-865-7786 Fax: 212-865-7786 E-mail: mail@hungrysamurai.com Web Site: hungrysamurai.com, pg 601

Hunter House Publishers, 1515 1/2 Park St, Alameda, CA 94501 Tel: 510-865-5282 Toll Free Tel: 800-266-5592 Fax: 510-865-4295 E-mail: acquisitions@hunterhouse.com Web Site: www.hunterhouse.com/, pg 128

Hunter Publishing Inc, 130 Campus Dr, Edison, NJ 08818 Tel: 732-225-1900 (orders) Toll Free Tel: 800-255-0343 Fax: 732-417-1744 E-mail: comments@hunterpublishing.com Web Site: www.hunterpublishing.com, pg 129

Huntington House Publishers, 104 Row 2, Suite A-1 & A-2, Lafayette, LA 70508 Tel: 337-237-7049; 337-749-4009 (sales); 337-237-3082 (opers) Toll Free Tel: 800-749-4009 (sales) Fax: 337-237-7060 E-mail: admin@alphapublishingonline.com; sales@alphapublishingonline.com Web Site: www.alphapublishingonline.com, pg 129

Huntington Library Press, 1151 Oxford Rd, San Marino, CA 91108 Tel: 626-405-2138 Fax: 626-585-0794 E-mail: booksales@huntington.org Web Site: www.huntington.org/HLPress/HEHPubs.html, pg 129

Huntington Press Publishing, 3687 S Procyon Ave, Las Vegas, NV 89103 Tel: 702-252-0655 Toll Free Tel: 800-244-2224 Fax: 702-252-0675 E-mail: books@huntingtonpress.com Web Site: www.huntingtonpress.com, pg 129

The Hurston/Wright Award for College Writers, 6525 Bellcrest Rd, Suite 531, Hyattsville, MD 20782 Tel: 301-683-2134 Fax: 301-277-1262 E-mail: info@hurston-wright.org Web Site: www.hurston-wright.org, pg 779

The Hurston/Wright Legacy Award, 6525 Bellcrest Rd, Suite 531, Hyattsville, MD 20782 Tel: 301-683-2134 Fax: 301-277-1262 E-mail: info@hurston-wright.org Web Site: www.hurston-wright.org, pg 779

The Hurston/Wright Writer's Week, 6525 Bellcrest Rd, Suite 531, Hyattsville, MD 20782 Tel: 301-683-2134 Fax: 301-277-1262 E-mail: info@hurston-wright.org Web Site: www.hurston-wright.org, pg 744

G F Hutchison Press, 319 S Block Ave, Suite 17, Fayetteville, AR 72701 Tel: 479-587-1726 E-mail: drwriterguy@netscape.net Web Site: www.familypress.com, pg 129

Hybrid Publishing Co-op Ltd, 860 Mountain Ave, Winnipeg, MB R2X 1C3, Canada Tel: 204-589-4257 Fax: 204-589-4257 E-mail: mail@hybrid-publishing.ca Web Site: www.hybrid-publishing.ca, pg 550

Hyperion, 77 W 66 St, 11th fl, New York, NY 10023-6298 Tel: 212-456-0100 Toll Free Tel: 800-759-0190 (cust serv) Fax: 212-456-0157 Web Site: hyperionbooks.com, pg 129

Hyperion Books for Children, 114 Fifth Ave, New York, NY 10011 Tel: 212-633-4400 Fax: 212-807-5880 Web Site: www.hyperionbooksforchildren.com, pg 129

Hyperion Press Ltd, 300 Wales Ave, Winnipeg, MB R2M 2S9, Canada Tel: 204-256-9204 Fax: 204-255-7845 E-mail: tamos@mts.ca, pg 550

IACP Cookbook Awards, 304 W Liberty St, Suite 201, Louisville, KY 40202-3068 Tel: 502-581-9786 Fax: 502-589-3602 E-mail: iacp@hqtrs.com Web Site: www.iacp.com, pg 779

Ibex Publishers, 8014 Old Georgetown Rd, Bethesda, MD 20814 Tel: 301-718-8188 Toll Free Tel: 888-718-8188 Fax: 301-907-8707 E-mail: info@ibexpub.com Web Site: www.ibexpub.com, pg 129

IBFD Publications USA Inc (International Bureau of Fiscal Documentation), PO Box 805, Valatie, NY 12184 Tel: 518-758-2245 Fax: 518-784-2963 E-mail: info@ibfd.org Web Site: www.ibfd.org, pg 130

ibooks Inc, 24 W 25 St, 11th fl, New York, NY 10010 Tel: 212-645-9870 Fax: 212-645-9874 Web Site: www.bpvp.com; www.ibooks.net, pg 130

The Ibsen Society of America, Dept of English, Long Island University, Brooklyn, NY 11201 Tel: 718-488-1050 Fax: 718-246-6302 Web Site: www.ibsensociety.liu.edu, pg 688

ICC Publishing Inc, 156 Fifth Ave, Suite 417, New York, NY 10010 Tel: 212-206-1150 Fax: 212-633-6025 E-mail: info@iccpub.net Web Site: www.iccbooksusa.com, pg 130

ICM Lecture Division, 40 W 57 St, New York, NY 10019 Tel: 212-556-5602 Fax: 212-556-6829 Web Site: www.icmtalent.com, pg 669

Iconografix Inc, 1830-A Hanley Rd, Hudson, WI 54016 Tel: 715-381-9755 Toll Free Tel: 800-289-3504 (orders only) Fax: 715-381-9756 E-mail: iconogfx@spacestar.net, pg 130

ICS Press, 3100 Harrison St, Oakland, CA 94611 Tel: 510-238-5010 Toll Free Tel: 800-326-0263 Fax: 510-238-8440 E-mail: mail@icspress.com Web Site: www.icspress.com, pg 130

Idaho Center for the Book, 1910 University Dr, Boise, ID 83725 Tel: 208-426-1999 Toll Free Tel: 800-992-8398 Fax: 208-426-4373 Web Site: www.lili.org/icb, pg 130

Idaho Fellowship, PO Box 83720, Boise, ID 83720-0008 Tel: 208-334-2119 Toll Free Tel: 800-ART-FUND (278-3863 within Idaho) Fax: 208-334-2488, pg 779

Idaho Writer in Residence, PO Box 83720, Boise, ID 83720-0008 Tel: 208-334-2119 Toll Free Tel: 800-ART-FUND (278-3863 within Idaho) Fax: 208-334-2488, pg 779

Ide House Inc, c/o Publishers Associates, PO Box 408, Radcliffe, IA 50230-0408 Tel: 515-899-2300 Fax: 515-899-2315 E-mail: orders@publishers-associates.com Web Site: www.publishers-associates.com, pg 130

IDEAlliance, 100 Daingerfield Rd, Alexandria, VA 22314 Tel: 703-837-1070 Fax: 703-837-1072 E-mail: info@gca.org Web Site: www.idealliance.org, pg 688

Ideals Publications Inc, 535 Metroplex Dr, Suite 250, Nashville, TN 37211 Tel: 615-781-1427 Toll Free Tel: 800-558-4343 (customer service) Fax: 615-781-1447 Web Site: www.idealsbooks.com, pg 130

IDRC Books/Les Editions du CRDI, PO Box 8500, Ottawa, ON K1G 3H9, Canada Tel: 613-236-6163 Fax: 613-563-2476 E-mail: pub@idrc.ca Web Site: www.idrc.ca, pg 550

Idyll Arbor Inc, 25119 SE 262 St, Ravensdale, WA 98051 Tel: 425-432-3231 Fax: 425-432-3726 E-mail: sales@idyllarbor.com Web Site: www.idyllarbor.com, pg 130

IEE, c/o Inspec, 379 Thornall St, Edison, NJ 08837-2225 Tel: 732-321-5575 Fax: 732-321-5702 E-mail: iee@inspecinc.com Web Site: www.iee.org/publishing, pg 130

IEEE Computer Society, 10662 Los Vaqueros Circle, Los Alamitos, CA 90720-1314 Tel: 714-821-8380 Toll Free Tel: 800-272-6657 Fax: 714-821-4010 E-mail: csbooks@computer.org Web Site: www.computer.org, pg 130

IEEE Press, 445 Hoes Lane, Piscataway, NJ 08854 Tel: 732-981-3418 Fax: 732-981-8062 E-mail: ieeepress@ieee.org Web Site: www.ieee.org/pubs/press/, pg 131

Ignatius Press, 2515 McAllister St, San Francisco, CA 94118 *Tel:* 415-387-2324 *Toll Free Tel:* 877-320-9276 (book orders) *Fax:* 415-387-0896 *E-mail:* info@ignatius.com *Web Site:* www.ignatius.com, pg 131

Illinois Arts Council Artists Fellowships, James R Thompson Ctr, 100 W Randolph, Suite 10-500, Chicago, IL 60601 *Tel:* 312-814-6750 *Toll Free Tel:* 800-237-6994 (IL only) *Fax:* 312-814-1471 *E-mail:* info@arts.state.il.us *Web Site:* www.state.il.us/agency/iac, pg 779

Illinois State Museum Society, 502 S Spring St, Springfield, IL 62706-5000 *Tel:* 217-782-7387 *Fax:* 217-782-1254 *E-mail:* editor@museum.state.il.us *Web Site:* www.museum.state.il.us, pg 131

Illuminating Engineering Society of North America, 120 Wall St, 17th fl, New York, NY 10005-4001 *Tel:* 212-248-5000 *Fax:* 212-248-5017; 212-248-5018 *Web Site:* www.iesna.org, pg 131

Illumination Arts Publishing, 13256 Northup Way, Suite 9, Bellevue, WA 98005 *Tel:* 425-644-7185 *Toll Free Tel:* 888-210-8216 *Fax:* 425-644-9274 *E-mail:* liteinfo@illumin.com *Web Site:* www.illum.com, pg 131

Imagefinders Inc, 6101 Utah Ave NW, Washington, DC 20015 *Tel:* 202-244-4456 *Fax:* 202-244-3237, pg 602

Images from the Past Inc, 155 W Main St, Bennington, VT 05201-2105 *Tel:* 802-442-3204 *Toll Free Tel:* 888-442-3204 *Fax:* 802-442-3204 *E-mail:* info@imagesfromthepast.com; sales@imagesfromthepast.com *Web Site:* www.imagesfromthepast.com, pg 131

ImaJinn Books, PO Box 545, Canon City, CO 81215 *Tel:* 719-275-0060 *Toll Free Tel:* 877-625-3592 *Fax:* 719-276-0741 *E-mail:* orders@imajinnbooks.com *Web Site:* www.imajinnbooks.com, pg 131

IMG Literary, 825 Seventh Ave, 9th fl, New York, NY 10019 *Tel:* 212-774-6900 *Fax:* 212-246-1118 *Web Site:* www.imgworld.com, pg 635

John Phillip Immroth Memorial Award for Intellectual Freedom, 50 E Huron St, Chicago, IL 60611 *Tel:* 312-280-4223; 312-280-4220 *Toll Free Tel:* 800-545-2433 *Fax:* 312-280-4227 *E-mail:* oif@ala.org *Web Site:* www.ala.org/ifrt, pg 779

Impact Publications, 9104 Manassas Dr, Suite N, Manassas Park, VA 20111-5211 *Tel:* 703-361-7300 *Fax:* 703-335-9486 *E-mail:* info@impactpublications.com *Web Site:* www.impactpublications.com; www.ishoparoundtheworld.com, pg 131

Impact Publishers Inc, PO Box 6016, Atascadero, CA 93423-6016 *Tel:* 805-466-5917 (opers & admin); 805-461-5911 (edit) *Toll Free Tel:* 800-246-7228 (orders) *Fax:* 805-466-5919 (opers & admin offices); 805-461-0554 (edit offices) *E-mail:* info@impactpublishers.com *Web Site:* www.impactpublishers.com; www.bibliotherapy.com, pg 131

Imperium Proviso Publishing, 814 E Platte Ave, Colorado Springs, CO 80903 *Tel:* 719-473-2765 *E-mail:* imppropub@hotmail.com *Web Site:* www.imperiumproviso.com, pg 131

Implementing Color Management, 200 Deer Run Rd, Sewickley, PA 15143-2600 *Tel:* 412-741-6860 *Toll Free Tel:* 800-910-4283 *Fax:* 412-741-2311 *E-mail:* info@gain.net *Web Site:* www.gain.net, pg 744

Impressions Book & Journal Services Inc, 2016 Winnebago St, Madison, WI 53704 *Tel:* 608-244-6218 *Fax:* 608-244-7050 *E-mail:* info@impressions.com *Web Site:* www.impressions.com, pg 602

Imprint Publications Inc, 230 E Ohio St, Suite 300, Chicago, IL 60611-3705 *Tel:* 312-337-9268 *Fax:* 312-337-9622 *E-mail:* imppub@aol.com, pg 131

In Audio, PO Box 3168, Falls Church, VA 22043 *Tel:* 540-722-2535 *Toll Free Tel:* 800-643-0295 *Fax:* 540-722-0903 *E-mail:* commuterslib@worldnet.att.net *Web Site:* inaudio.biz, pg 132

IN-D Press, PO Box 642556, Los Angeles, CA 90064 *Tel:* 310-445-9326 *Fax:* 310-694-0222 *E-mail:* info@in-d.com *Web Site:* www.in-d.com, pg 132

Incentive Publications Inc, 3835 Cleghorn Ave, Nashville, TN 37215 *Tel:* 615-385-2934 *Toll Free Tel:* 800-421-2830 *Fax:* 615-385-2967 *E-mail:* comments@incentivepublications.com *Web Site:* www.incentivepublications.com, pg 132

Inclusion Press International, 24 Thome Crescent, Toronto, ON M6H 2S5, Canada *Tel:* 416-658-5363 *Fax:* 416-658-5067 *E-mail:* info@inclusion.com *Web Site:* www.inclusion.com, pg 550

Independent Information Publications, 3357 21 St, San Francisco, CA 94110 *Tel:* 415-643-8600 *Fax:* 415-643-6100 *E-mail:* orders@movedoc.com *Web Site:* www.movedoc.com, pg 132

The Independent Publisher Book Awards, 400 W Front St, Suite 4-A, Traverse City, MI 49684 *Tel:* 231-933-0445 *Toll Free Tel:* 800-706-4636 *Fax:* 231-933-0448, pg 779

Independent Publishing Agency, PO Box 176, Southport, CT 06890 *Tel:* 203-332-7629 *Fax:* 203-332-7629, pg 635

Independent Writers of Chicago (IWOC), 5465 Grand Ave, Suite 100, PMB 119, Gurnee, IL 60031 *Tel:* 847-855-6670 *Fax:* 847-855-4502 *E-mail:* info@iwoc.org *Web Site:* www.iwoc.org, pg 688

Indiana Historical Society Press, 450 W Ohio St, Indianapolis, IN 46202-3269 *Tel:* 317-233-9557 (sales); 317-234-2716 (editorial) *Toll Free Tel:* 800-447-1830 (orders only) *Fax:* 317-234-0562 (sales); 317-233-0857 (editorial) *E-mail:* ihspress@indianahistory.org; orders@indianahistory.org (orders) *Web Site:* www.indianahistory.org; shop.indianahistory.org (orders), pg 132

Indiana University African Studies Program, Indiana University, 221 Woodburn Hall, Bloomington, IN 47405 *Tel:* 812-855-8254 *Fax:* 812-855-6734 *E-mail:* afrist@indiana.edu *Web Site:* www.indiana.edu/~afrist, pg 132

Indiana University Press, 601 N Morton St, Bloomington, IN 47404-3797 *Tel:* 812-855-8817 *Toll Free Tel:* 800-842-6796 (orders only) *Fax:* 812-855-7931 (orders only); 812-855-8507 *E-mail:* iupress@indiana.edu; iuorder@indiana.edu (orders) *Web Site:* www.iupress.indiana.edu, pg 132

Indiana University Writers' Conference, Indiana University, Dept of English, 464 Ballantine Hall, Bloomington, IN 47405 *Tel:* 812-855-1877 *Fax:* 812-855-9535 *E-mail:* writecon@indiana.edu *Web Site:* www.indiana.edu/~writecon/, pg 744

Individual Artist Awards, 175 W Ostend St, Suite E, Baltimore, MD 21230 *Tel:* 410-767-6555 *Fax:* 410-333-1062 *Web Site:* www.msac.org, pg 779

Individual Artist Fellowships, 25 SHS, 193 State St, Augusta, ME 04333-0025 *Tel:* 207-287-2726 *Fax:* 207-287-2725 *Web Site:* www.mainearts.com, pg 779

Individual Artists Fellowships, 3838 Davenport St, Omaha, NE 68131-2329 *Tel:* 402-595-2122 *Fax:* 402-595-2334 *Web Site:* www.nebraskaartscouncil.org, pg 780

Individual Artist's Fellowships in Literature, 1800 Gervais St, Columbia, SC 29201 *Tel:* 803-734-8696 *Fax:* 803-734-8526 *Web Site:* www.southcarolinaarts.org, pg 780

Industrial Press Inc, 200 Madison Ave, 21st fl, New York, NY 10016-4078 *Tel:* 212-889-6330 *Toll Free Tel:* 888-528-7852 *Fax:* 212-545-8327 *E-mail:* info@industrialpress.com *Web Site:* www.industrialpress.com, pg 132

The Info Devel Press, 32 Reilly Rd, Lagrangeville, NY 12540 *Tel:* 845-223-3269, pg 133

InfoBooks, PO Box 1018, Santa Monica, CA 90406 *Tel:* 310-394-4102 *Toll Free Tel:* 800-669-0409 *Fax:* 310-394-2603, pg 133

INFORM Inc, 120 Wall St, 14th fl, New York, NY 10005-4001 *Tel:* 212-361-2400 *Fax:* 212-361-2412 *Web Site:* www.informinc.org, pg 133

Information Age Publishing Inc, 80 Mason St, Greenwich, CT 06830 *Tel:* 203-661-7602 *Fax:* 203-661-7952 *E-mail:* infoage@infoagepub.com *Web Site:* www.infoagepub.com, pg 133

Information Diva, 31 Jane St, New York, NY 10014 *Tel:* 212-229-1591 *Fax:* 413-778-3815 *Web Site:* www.informationdiva.com, pg 602

Information Gatekeepers Inc, 320 Washington St, Suite 302, Boston, MA 02135 *Tel:* 617-782-5033 *Toll Free Tel:* 800-323-1088 *Fax:* 617-782-5735 *E-mail:* info@igigroup.com *Web Site:* www.igigroup.com, pg 133

Information Publications, 3790 El Camino Real, PMB 162, Palo Alto, CA 94306 *Tel:* 650-851-4250 *Toll Free Tel:* 877-544-4636 *Fax:* 650-529-9980 *Toll Free Fax:* 877-544-4635 *E-mail:* info@informationpublications.com *Web Site:* www.informationpublications.com, pg 133

Information Today, Inc, 143 Old Marlton Pike, Medford, NJ 08055-8750 *Tel:* 609-654-6266 *Toll Free Tel:* 800-300-9868 (cust serv) *Fax:* 609-654-4309 *E-mail:* custserv@infotoday.com *Web Site:* www.infotoday.com, pg 133

Infosential Press, 1162 Dominion Dr W, Mobile, AL 36695 *Tel:* 251-776-5656 *Fax:* 251-460-7181 *Web Site:* www.infosentialpress.com, pg 133

InfoServices International Inc, 313 Main St, Huntington, NY 11743 *Tel:* 631-549-0064 *Fax:* 631-549-6663 *E-mail:* typ@infoservices.com *Web Site:* www.infoservices.com, pg 133

Infosources Publishing, 140 Norma Rd, Teaneck, NJ 07666 *Tel:* 201-836-7072 *Web Site:* www.infosourcespub.com, pg 133

InfoWorks Development Group, 2801 Cook Creek Dr, Ann Arbor, MI 48103-8962 *Tel:* 734-327-9669 *Fax:* 734-327-9686, pg 602

Ingenix Inc, 2525 Lake Park Blvd, Salt Lake City, UT 84120 *Tel:* 801-982-3000 *Toll Free Tel:* 800-765-6014 *Web Site:* www.ingenix.com, pg 133

Inkwell Management, 521 Fifth Ave, 26th fl, New York, NY 10175 *Tel:* 212-922-3500 *Fax:* 212-922-0535 *E-mail:* contact@inkwellmanagement.com *Web Site:* www.inkwellmanagement.com, pg 635

Inner City Books, PO Box 1271 Sta Q, Toronto, ON M4T 2P4, Canada *Tel:* 416-927-0355 *Fax:* 416-924-1814 *E-mail:* sales@innercitybooks.net *Web Site:* www.innercitybooks.net, pg 550

Inner Ocean Publishing Inc, 1037 Makawao Ave, Makawao, Maui, HI 96768-1239 *Tel:* 808-573-8000 *Toll Free Tel:* 800-863-1449 *Fax:* 808-573-0700 *Toll Free Fax:* 800-755-4118 *E-mail:* info@innerocean.com *Web Site:* www.innerocean.com, pg 134

Inner Traditions International Ltd, One Park St, Rochester, VT 05767 *Tel:* 802-767-3174 *Toll Free Tel:* 800-246-8648 *Fax:* 802-767-3726 *E-mail:* orders@InnerTraditions.com *Web Site:* www.InnerTraditions.com, pg 134

Innis-Gerin Medal, 283 Sparks St, Ottawa, ON K1R 7X9, Canada *Tel:* 613-991-6990 *Fax:* 613-991-6996 *E-mail:* adminrsc@rsc.ca *Web Site:* www.rsc.ca, pg 780

innovative Kids™, 18 Ann St, Norwalk, CT 06854 *Tel:* 203-838-6400 *Fax:* 203-855-5582 *E-mail:* info@innovativekids.com *Web Site:* www.innovativekids.com, pg 134

Inscape Publishing, 6465 Wayzata Blvd, Suite 800, St Louis Park, MN 55426 *Tel:* 763-765-2222 *Fax:* 763-765-2277 *Web Site:* www.inscapepublishing.com, pg 134

The Insiders System for Writers, 1223 Wilshire Blvd, No 336, Santa Monica, CA 90403 *Tel:* 310-899-9775 *Toll Free Tel:* 800-397-2615 *Fax:* 310-899-9775 *E-mail:* insiderssystem@msn.com *Web Site:* www.insiderssystem.com, pg 635

Insomniac Press, 192 Spadina Ave, Suite 403, Toronto, ON M5T 2C2, Canada *Tel:* 416-504-6270 *Fax:* 416-504-9313 *E-mail:* mike@insomniacpress.com *Web Site:* www.insomniacpress.com, pg 551

InstEdit, 1440 Franklin St, Denver, CO 80218 *Tel:* 303-329-6446 *Fax:* 303-329-6446, pg 602

Institute for Byzantine & Modern Greek Studies Inc, 115 Gilbert Rd, Belmont, MA 02478-2200 *Tel:* 617-484-6595 *Fax:* 617-876-3600, pg 134

Institute for International Economics, 1750 Massachusetts Ave NW, Washington, DC 20036 *Tel:* 202-328-9000 *Toll Free Tel:* 800-522-9139 *Fax:* 202-328-5432 *E-mail:* orders@iie.com *Web Site:* www.iie.com, pg 134

Institute for Language Study, 7 Hollyhock Rd, Wilton, CT 06897 *Tel:* 203-762-2510 *Toll Free Tel:* 800-245-2145 *Fax:* 203-762-2514 *E-mail:* cortinainc@aol.com *Web Site:* www.cortina-languages.com; members.aol.com/cortinainc, pg 134

The Institute for Research on Public Policy, 1470 Peel, Suite 200, Montreal, PQ H3A 1T1, Canada *Tel:* 514-985-2461 *Fax:* 514-985-2559 *E-mail:* irpp@irpp.org *Web Site:* www.irpp.org, pg 551

Institute for the Study of Man Inc, 1133 13 St NW, Suite C-2, Washington, DC 20005-4298 *Tel:* 202-371-2700 *Fax:* 202-371-1523 *E-mail:* iejournal@aol.com *Web Site:* www.jies.org, pg 135

Institute of Continuing Legal Education, 1020 Greene St, Ann Arbor, MI 48109-1444 *Tel:* 734-764-0533 *Toll Free Tel:* 877-229-4350 *Fax:* 734-763-2412 *Toll Free Fax:* 877-229-4351 *E-mail:* icle@umich.edu *Web Site:* www.icle.org/, pg 135

Institute of East Asian Studies, University of California, IEAS Publications, 2223 Fulton St, Berkeley, CA 94720-2318 *Tel:* 510-643-6325 *Fax:* 510-643-7062 *E-mail:* easia@uclink.berkeley.edu *Web Site:* ieas.berkeley.edu/publications, pg 135

Institute of Electrical & Electronics Engineers Inc, 445 Hoes Lane, Piscataway, NJ 08854 *Tel:* 732-981-0060 *Toll Free Tel:* 800-678-4333 *Fax:* 732-981-9334 *E-mail:* c.fadvska@ieee.org *Web Site:* www.ieee.org, pg 135

Institute of Environmental Sciences and Technology - IEST, 5005 Newport Dr, Suite 506, Rolling Meadows, IL 60008 *Tel:* 847-255-1561 *Fax:* 847-255-1699 *E-mail:* publicationsales@iest.org *Web Site:* iest.org, pg 135

Institute of Governmental Studies, 102 Moses Hall, Berkeley, CA 94720-2370 *Tel:* 510-642-1428 *Fax:* 510-642-5537 *E-mail:* igspress@uclink2.berkeley.edu *Web Site:* www.igs.berkeley.edu, pg 135

Institute of Intergovernmental Relations, Queen's University, Rm 301, Policy Studies Bldg, Kingston, ON K7L 3N6, Canada *Tel:* 613-533-2080 *Fax:* 613-533-6868 *E-mail:* iigr@iigr.ca *Web Site:* www.iigr.ca, pg 551

Institute of Jesuit Sources, 3601 Lindell Blvd, St Louis, MO 63108 *Tel:* 314-977-7257 *Fax:* 314-977-7263 *E-mail:* ijs@slu.edu *Web Site:* www.jesuitsources.com, pg 135

Institute of Mathematical Geography, 1964 Boulder Dr, Ann Arbor, MI 48104 *Tel:* 734-975-0246 *Web Site:* www.instituteofmathematicalgeography.org, pg 135

Institute of Mediaeval Music, PO Box 295, Henryville, PA 18332-0295 *Tel:* 570-629-1278 *Fax:* 613-225-9487 *Web Site:* members.rogers.com/mediaeval1, pg 135

Institute of Police Technology & Management, University Ctr, 12000 Alumni Dr, Jacksonville, FL 32224-2678 *Tel:* 904-620-4786 *Fax:* 904-620-2453, pg 135

Institute of Psychological Research, Inc., 34 Fleury St W, Montreal, PQ H3L 1S9, Canada *Tel:* 514-382-3000 *Toll Free Tel:* 800-363-7800 *Fax:* 514-382-3007 *Toll Free Fax:* 888-382-3007 *E-mail:* info@i-p-r.ca *Web Site:* www.i-p-r.ca, pg 551

Institute of Public Administration of Canada, 1075 Bay St, Suite 401, Toronto, ON M5S 2B1, Canada *Tel:* 416-924-8787 *Fax:* 416-924-4992 *E-mail:* ntl@ipac.ca; ntl@iapc.ca *Web Site:* www.ipac.ca; www.iapc.ca, pg 551

Institute of Puerto Rican Culture, PO Box 9024184, San Juan, PR 00902-4184 *Tel:* 787-724-0700 *Fax:* 787-724-8393 *E-mail:* www@icp.gobierno.pr *Web Site:* www.icp.gobierno.pr, pg 780

Instructional Fair Group, 3195 Wilson Dr NW, Grand Rapids, MI 49544 *Tel:* 616-802-3000 *Toll Free Tel:* 800-417-3261 *Fax:* 616-802-3007 *Toll Free Fax:* 888-203-9361 *Web Site:* elementary-educators.teacherspecialty.com/Instructional_Fair/, pg 135

Insurance Institute of America Inc, 720 Providence Rd, Malvern, PA 19355 *Tel:* 610-644-2100 *Toll Free Tel:* 800-644-2101 *Fax:* 610-640-9576 *E-mail:* cserv@cpcuiia.org *Web Site:* www.aicpcu.org, pg 135

Inter-American Development Bank, 1300 New York Ave NW, Washington, DC 20577 *Tel:* 202-623-1000 *Fax:* 202-623-3096 *E-mail:* idb-books@iadb.org; idbcc@iadb.org *Web Site:* www.iadb.org/pub, pg 135

Inter American Press Association (IAPA), 1801 SW Third Ave, Miami, FL 33129 *Tel:* 305-634-2465 *Fax:* 305-635-2272 *E-mail:* info@sipiapa.org *Web Site:* www.sipiapa.org, pg 688

Inter-University Consortium for Political & Social Research, PO Box 1248, Ann Arbor, MI 48106-1248 *Tel:* 734-647-5000 *Fax:* 734-647-8200 *E-mail:* netmail@icpsr.umich.edu *Web Site:* www.icpsr.umich.edu, pg 136

Interchange Inc, 14025 23 Ave N, Suite B, Plymouth, MN 55447 *Tel:* 763-694-7596 *Toll Free Tel:* 800-669-6208 *Fax:* 763-694-7117 *Toll Free Fax:* 800-729-0395 *E-mail:* sales@interchangeinc.com *Web Site:* www.interchangeinc.com, pg 136

Intercultural Development Research Association (IDRA), 5835 Callaghan Rd, Suite 350, San Antonio, TX 78228-1190 *Tel:* 210-444-1710 *Fax:* 210-444-1714 *E-mail:* contact@idra.org *Web Site:* www.idra.org, pg 136

Intercultural Press Inc, PO Box 700, 374 US Rte One, Yarmouth, ME 04096 *Tel:* 207-846-5168 *Toll Free Tel:* 866-372-2665 *Fax:* 207-846-5181 *E-mail:* books@interculturalpress.com *Web Site:* www.interculturalpress.com, pg 136

InterLicense Ltd, 110 Country Club Dr, Suite A, Mill Valley, CA 94941 *Tel:* 415-381-9780 *Fax:* 415-381-6485 *E-mail:* ilicense@aol.com, pg 635

Interlingua Publishing, 423 S Pacific Coast Hwy, No 208, Redondo Beach, CA 90277 *Tel:* 310-792-3636 *Fax:* 509-479-8935 *E-mail:* interlingua@aol.com, pg 136

Interlink Publishing Group Inc, 46 Crosby St, Northampton, MA 01060 *Tel:* 413-582-7054 *Toll Free Tel:* 800-238-LINK (238-5465) *Fax:* 413-582-7057 *E-mail:* info@interlinkbooks.com *Web Site:* www.interlinkbooks.com, pg 136

International Association of Business Communicators (IABC), One Hallidie Plaza, Suite 600, San Francisco, CA 94102 *Tel:* 415-544-4700 *Toll Free Tel:* 800-776-4222 *Fax:* 415-544-4747 *E-mail:* service_centre@iabc.com *Web Site:* www.iabc.com, pg 688

International Association of Crime Writers Inc, North American Branch, PO Box 8674, New York, NY 10116-8674 *Tel:* 212-243-8966 *Fax:* 815-361-1477, pg 688

International Book Centre Inc, 2391 Auburn Rd, Shelby Township, MI 48317 *Tel:* 248-879-8436; 586-254-7230 *Fax:* 586-254-7230; 248-879-8436 *E-mail:* ibc@ibcbooks.com *Web Site:* www.ibcbooks.com, pg 136

International Broadcasting Services Ltd, 825 Cherry Lane, Penns Park, PA 18943 *Tel:* 215-598-3298 *Fax:* 215-598-3794 *E-mail:* hq@passband.com; mktg@passband.com *Web Site:* www.passband.com, pg 136

International City/County Management Association, 777 N Capitol St NE, Suite 500, Washington, DC 20002 *Tel:* 202-289-4262 *Fax:* 202-962-3500 *E-mail:* pubs@icma.org *Web Site:* icma.org, pg 136

International Code Council Inc, 5360 Workman Mill Rd, Whittier, CA 90601-2298 *Tel:* 562-699-0541 *Toll Free Tel:* 800-423-6587 *Web Site:* www.iccsafe.org, pg 137

International Cook Book & Culinary Arts Awards, 7500 Sunshine Skyway Lane, Unit T8, St Petersburg, FL 33711 *Tel:* 727-347-2437 *E-mail:* cordondor@aol.com *Web Site:* www.cordondorcuisine.com; www.goldribboncookery.com, pg 780

International Council for Adult Education, UQAM Faculty of Education, PO Box 8888, Downtown Branch, Montreal, PQ H3C 3P8, Canada *Tel:* 514-987-0029 *Fax:* 514-987-6753 *E-mail:* icae@er.uqam.ca *Web Site:* www.icae.org.uy, pg 688

International Council of Shopping Centers, 1221 Avenue of the Americas, 41st fl, New York, NY 10020-1099 *Tel:* 646-728-3800 *Fax:* 646-728-3800; 212-588-5555 *Web Site:* www.icsc.org, pg 137

International Creative Management, 40 W 57 St, New York, NY 10019 *Tel:* 212-556-5600 *Fax:* 212-556-5665 *Web Site:* www.icmtalent.com, pg 635

International Development Research Centre, 250 Albert St, Ottawa, ON K1P 6M1, Canada *Tel:* 613-236-6163 *Fax:* 613-238-7230 *E-mail:* pub@idrc.ca *Web Site:* www.idrc.ca/booktique, pg 551

International Encyclopedia Society, PO Box 519, Baldwin Place, NY 10505-0519 *Tel:* 914-962-3287 *Fax:* 914-962-3287 *Web Site:* encyclopediasociety.com, pg 688

International Entertainment Bureau, 3612 N Washington Blvd, Indianapolis, IN 46205-3592 *Tel:* 317-926-7566 *E-mail:* ieb@prodigy.net, pg 669

International Evangelism Crusades Inc, 21601 Devonshire St, Suite 217, Chatsworth, CA 91311-8415 *Tel:* 818-882-0039 *Fax:* 818-989-2165, pg 137

International Food Policy Research Institute, 2033 "K" St NW, Washington, DC 20006-1002 *Tel:* 202-862-5600 *Fax:* 202-467-4439 *E-mail:* ifpri@cgiar.org *Web Site:* www.ifpri.org, pg 137

International Foundation for Election Systems, 1101 15 St NW, 3rd fl, Washington, DC 20005 *Tel:* 202-828-8507 *Fax:* 202-822-9744 *Web Site:* www.ifes.org, pg 137

International Foundation of Employee Benefit Plans, 18700 W Bluemound Rd, Brookfield, WI 53045 *Tel:* 262-786-6700 *Toll Free Tel:* 888-334-3327 *Fax:* 262-786-8780 *E-mail:* books@ifebp.org *Web Site:* www.ifebp.org, pg 137

The International Institute of Islamic Thought, 500 Grove St, Suite 200, Herndon, VA 20170 *Tel:* 703-471-1133 *Fax:* 703-471-3922 *E-mail:* iiit@iiit.org *Web Site:* www.iiit.org, pg 137

International Intertrade Index, 636 Buchanan St, Hillside, NJ 07205 *Tel:* 908-686-2382 *Fax:* 908-686-2382, pg 137

International Linguistics Corp, 12220 Blue Ridge Blvd, Suite G, Grandview, MO 64030 *Tel:* 816-765-8855 *Toll Free Tel:* 800-237-1830 *Fax:* 816-765-2855 *E-mail:* info@learnables.com *Web Site:* www.learnables.com, pg 137

International Marine Publishing, 485 Commercial St, Rockport, ME 04856 *Tel:* 207-236-4837 *Fax:* 207-236-6314 *Web Site:* www.internationalmarine.com/im, pg 137

International Medical Publishing Inc, 1313 Dolly Madison Blvd, Suite 302, McLean, VA 22101 *Tel:* 703-356-2037 *Toll Free Tel:* 800-530-3142 *Fax:* 703-734-8987 *E-mail:* contact@medicalpublishing.com *Web Site:* www.medicalpublishing.com, pg 137

International Monetary Fund (IMF), 700 19 St NW, Suite 12-607, Washington, DC 20431 *Tel:* 202-623-7430 *Fax:* 202-623-7201 *E-mail:* publications@imf.org *Web Site:* www.imf.org, pg 137

International Newspaper Financial Executives, 21525 Ridgetop Circle, Suite 200, Sterling, VA 20166 *Tel:* 703-421-4060 *Web Site:* www.infe.org, pg 688

International Plate Printers', Die Stampers' & Engravers' Union of North America, 3957 Smoke Rd, Doylestown, PA 18901 *Tel:* 215-340-2843, pg 689

International Playwrights Competition, 515 Loudon Rd, Loudonville, NY 12211-1462 *Tel:* 518-783-2384 *Fax:* 518-783-2381 *Web Site:* www.siena.edu/theatre, pg 780

International Prepress Association, 7200 France Ave S, Suite 223, Edina, MN 55435 *Tel:* 952-896-1908 *Fax:* 952-896-0181 *E-mail:* info@ipa.org *Web Site:* www.ipa.org, pg 689

International Press of Boston Inc, PO Box 43502, Somerville, MA 02143 *Tel:* 617-623-3016 *Fax:* 617-623-3101 *E-mail:* orders@intlpress.com; journals@intlpress.com *Web Site:* www.intlpress.com, pg 137

International Publishers Co Inc, 239 W 23 St, 5th fl, New York, NY 10011 *Tel:* 212-366-9816 *Fax:* 212-366-9820 *E-mail:* service@intpubnyc.com *Web Site:* www.intpubnyc.com, pg 138

International Publishing Management Association (IPMA), 1205 W College St, Liberty, MO 64068-3733 *Tel:* 816-781-1111 *Fax:* 816-781-2790 *E-mail:* ipmainfo@ipma.org *Web Site:* www.ipma.org, pg 689

International Reading Association, 800 Barksdale Rd, Newark, DE 19714 *Tel:* 302-731-1600 *Fax:* 302-731-1057 *E-mail:* books@reading.org *Web Site:* www.reading.org, pg 138

International Reading Association, 800 Barksdale Rd, Newark, DE 19714 *Tel:* 302-731-1600 *Fax:* 302-731-1057 *Web Site:* www.reading.org, pg 689

International Reading Association Children's Book Award, 800 Barksdale Rd, Newark, DE 19714 *Tel:* 302-731-1600 *Fax:* 302-731-1057 *Web Site:* www.reading.org, pg 780

International Reading Association Print Media Award, 800 Barksdale Rd, Newark, DE 19714 *Tel:* 302-731-1600 *Fax:* 302-731-1057 *E-mail:* pubinfo@reading.org *Web Site:* www.reading.org, pg 780

International Research Center for Energy & Economic Development, 850 Willowbrook Rd, Boulder, CO 80302 *Tel:* 303-442-4014 *Fax:* 303-442-5042 *E-mail:* iceed@colorado.edu *Web Site:* www.iceed.org, pg 138

International Risk Management Institute Inc, 12222 Merit Dr, Suite 1450, Dallas, TX 75251-2276 *Tel:* 972-960-7693 *Toll Free Tel:* 800-827-4242 *Fax:* 972-371-5120 *E-mail:* info@irmi.com *Web Site:* www.irmi.com, pg 138

International Society for Technology in Education, 480 Charnelton St, Eugene, OR 97401-2626 *Tel:* 541-302-3777 *Toll Free Tel:* 800-336-5191 (orders only) *Fax:* 541-302-3778 *E-mail:* iste@iste.org *Web Site:* www.iste.org, pg 138

International Society of Copier Artists Ltd (ISCA), 759 President St, Suite 2H, Brooklyn, NY 11215 *Tel:* 718-638-3264 *E-mail:* isca4art2b@aol.com, pg 689

International Society of Weekly Newspaper Editors, Missouri Southern State College, 3950 E Newman Rd, Joplin, MO 64501-1595 *Tel:* 417-625-9736 *Fax:* 417-659-4445 *Web Site:* www.mssc.edu/iswne, pg 689

International Standard Book Numbering (ISBN) US Agency, A Cambridge Information Group Co, 630 Central Ave, New Providence, NJ 07974 *Toll Free Tel:* 877-310-7333 *Fax:* 908-219-0188 *E-mail:* ISBN-SAN@bowker.com *Web Site:* www.isbn.org, pg 689

International Students Inc, 7222 Commerce Center Dr, Suite 200, Colorado Springs, CO 80919 *Tel:* 719-576-2700 *Toll Free Tel:* 800-474-4147 ext 111 (orders) *Fax:* 719-576-5363 *E-mail:* information@isionline.org *Web Site:* www.isionline.org, pg 138

International Titles, 931 E 56 St, Austin, TX 78751-1724 *Tel:* 512-451-2221 *Fax:* 512-467-1330, pg 635

International Universities Press Inc, 59 Boston Post Rd, Madison, CT 06443 *Tel:* 203-245-4000 *Toll Free Tel:* 800-835-3487 *Fax:* 203-245-0775 *E-mail:* orders@iup.com *Web Site:* www.iup.com, pg 138

International Wealth Success Inc, PO Box 186, Merrick, NY 11566-0186 *Tel:* 516-766-5850 *Toll Free Tel:* 800-323-0548 *Fax:* 516-766-5919 *E-mail:* admin@iwsmoney.com *Web Site:* www.iwsmoney.com, pg 138

The International Women's Writing Guild (IWWG), PO Box 810, Gracie Sta, New York, NY 10028-0082 *Tel:* 212-737-7536 *Fax:* 212-737-9469 *E-mail:* iwwg@iwwg.org *Web Site:* www.iwwg.org, pg 689

Internet Alliance (IA), 1111 19 St NW, Suite 1180, Washington, DC 20036 *Tel:* 202-955-8091; 202-861-2476 *Fax:* 202-955-8081 *E-mail:* ia@internetalliance.org *Web Site:* www.internetalliance.org, pg 689

InterTech Technology Award, 200 Deer Run Rd, Sewickley, PA 15143-2600 *Tel:* 412-741-6860 *Toll Free Tel:* 800-910-4283 *Fax:* 412-741-2311 *E-mail:* info@gain.net *Web Site:* www.gain.net, pg 780

InterVarsity Press, 430 E Plaza Dr, Westmont, IL 60559-1234 *Tel:* 630-734-4000 *Toll Free Tel:* 800-843-7225 *Fax:* 630-734-4200 *E-mail:* mail@ivpress.com *Web Site:* www.ivpress.com, pg 138

Interweave Press, 201 E Fourth St, Loveland, CO 80537 *Tel:* 970-669-7672 *Toll Free Tel:* 800-272-2193 *Fax:* 970-667-8317 *E-mail:* customerservice@interweave.com *Web Site:* www.interweave.com, pg 138

The Intrepid Traveler, 371 Walden Green Rd, Branford, CT 06405 *Tel:* 203-488-5341 *Fax:* 203-488-7677 *E-mail:* info@intrepidtraveler.com *Web Site:* www.intrepidtraveler.com, pg 138

Introducing ECPA Publishing University, 4816 S Ash Ave, Suite 101, Tempe, AZ 85282-7735 *Tel:* 480-966-3998 *Fax:* 480-966-1944 *Web Site:* www.ecpa.org, pg 744

Investigative Reporters & Editors, 138 Neff Annex, UMC School of Journalism, Columbia, MO 65211 *Tel:* 573-882-2042 *Fax:* 573-882-5431 *E-mail:* info@ire.org *Web Site:* www.ire.org, pg 689

Investor Responsibility Research Center, 1350 Connecticut Ave NW, Suite 700, Washington, DC 20036 *Tel:* 202-833-0700 *Fax:* 202-833-3555 *E-mail:* sales@irrc.com *Web Site:* www.irrc.com, pg 139

The Invisible College Press LLC, 3703 Del Mar Dr, Woodbridge, VA 22193-0209 *Tel:* 703-590-4005 *E-mail:* sales@invispress.com *Web Site:* www.invispress.com, pg 139

IODE Book Award, 40 St Clair Ave E, Suite 205, Toronto, ON M4T 1M9, Canada *Tel:* 416-925-5078 *Fax:* 416-925-5127, pg 780

The Iowa Short Fiction Award, 102 Dey House, 507 N Clinton St, Iowa City, IA 52242 *Tel:* 319-335-0416 *Fax:* 319-335-0420, pg 780

Iowa Summer Writing Festival, 100 Oakdale Campus, Rm W310, Iowa City, IA 52242 *Tel:* 319-335-4160 *E-mail:* iswfestival@uiowa.edu *Web Site:* www.uiowa.edu/~iswfest, pg 744

Iron Gate Publishing, PO Box 999, Niwot, CO 80544 *Tel:* 303-530-2551 *Fax:* 303-530-5273 *E-mail:* editor@irongate.com; booknews@reunionsolutions.com *Web Site:* www.irongate.com; www.reunionsolutions.com, pg 139

Irwin Law Inc, 347 Bay St, Suite 501, Toronto, ON M5H 2R7, Canada *Tel:* 416-862-7690 *Toll Free Tel:* 888-314-9014 *Fax:* 416-862-9236 *Web Site:* www.irwinlaw.com, pg 551

ISA, 67 Alexander Dr, Research Triangle Park, NC 27709 *Tel:* 919-549-8411 *Fax:* 919-549-8288 *E-mail:* info@isa.org *Web Site:* www.isa.org, pg 139

ISI Books, PO Box 4431, 3901 Centerville Rd, Wilmington, DE 19807 *Tel:* 302-652-4600 *Toll Free Tel:* 800-526-7022 *Fax:* 302-652-1760 *E-mail:* bookstore@isi.org *Web Site:* www.isibooks.org, pg 139

Island Literary Awards, 115 Richmond St, Charlottetown, PE C1A 1H7, Canada *Tel:* 902-368-4410 *Fax:* 902-368-4418 *E-mail:* peiarts@peiartscouncil.com *Web Site:* www.peiartscouncil.com, pg 780

Island Press, 1718 Connecticut Ave NW, Suite 300, Washington, DC 20009 *Tel:* 202-232-7933 *Toll Free Tel:* 800-828-1302 *Fax:* 202-234-1328; 707-983-6414 (orders only) *E-mail:* info@islandpress.org *Web Site:* www.islandpress.org, pg 139

ITA Institute, PO Box 281, Grand Blanc, MI 48439 *Tel:* 810-232-6482 *E-mail:* hq@itatkd.com *Web Site:* www.itatkd.com, pg 139

Italica Press, 595 Main St, Suite 605, New York, NY 10044 *Tel:* 212-935-4230 *Fax:* 212-838-7812 *E-mail:* inquiries@italicapress.com *Web Site:* www.italicapress.com, pg 139

iUniverse, 2021 Pine Lake Rd, Suite 100, Lincoln, NE 68512 *Tel:* 402-323-7800 *Toll Free Tel:* 877-288-4737 *Fax:* 402-323-7824 *E-mail:* firstname.lastname@iuniverse.com; general.inquiries@iuniverse.com *Web Site:* www.iuniverse.com, pg 139

Richard Ivey School of Business, University of Western Ontario, London, ON N6A 3K7, Canada *Tel:* 519-661-3208 *Toll Free Tel:* 800-649-6355 *Fax:* 519-661-3882 *E-mail:* cases@ivey.uwo.ca *Web Site:* www.ivey.uwo.ca/cases, pg 551

Ivy House Publishing Group, 5122 Bur Oak Circle, Raleigh, NC 27612 *Tel:* 919-782-0281 *Toll Free Tel:* 800-948-2786 *Fax:* 919-781-9042 *E-mail:* thepublisher@ivyhousebooks.com *Web Site:* www.ivyhousebooks.com, pg 572

The Ivy League of Artists Inc, 10 E 39 St, 7th fl, New York, NY 10016 *Tel:* 212-545-7766 *Fax:* 212-545-9437 *E-mail:* ilartists@aol.com, pg 666

J & S Publishing Co Inc, 1300 Bishop Lane, Alexandria, VA 22302 *Tel:* 703-823-9833 *Fax:* 703-823-9834 *E-mail:* jandspub@hotmail.com *Web Site:* www.jandspub.com, pg 140

J de S Associates Inc, 9 Shagbark Rd, South Norwalk, CT 06854 *Tel:* 203-838-7571 *Fax:* 203-866-2713, pg 635

Jabberwocky Literary Agency, PO Box 4558, Sunnyside, NY 11104-0558 *Tel:* 718-392-5985 *Fax:* 718-392-5985 *E-mail:* jabagent@aol.com, pg 636

Joseph Henry Jackson Literary Award, 225 Bush St, Suite 500, San Francisco, CA 94104-4224 *Tel:* 415-733-8500 *Fax:* 415-477-2783 *Web Site:* www.sff.org, pg 780

Melanie Jackson Agency LLC, 41 W 72 St, No 3F, New York, NY 10023 *Tel:* 212-873-3373 *Fax:* 212-799-5063, pg 636

Rose Jacobowitz, 351 W 24 St, New York, NY 10011 *Tel:* 212-243-2074, pg 602

Dorri Jacobs/Consulting & Editorial Services, 784 Columbus Ave, Suite 1C, New York, NY 10025 *Tel:* 212-222-4606 *E-mail:* dorrija@aol.com *Web Site:* members.aol.com/dorrija/yourwriter.htm; members.aol.com/domediate; endespair.com, pg 602

Lee Jacobs Productions, PO Box 362, Pomeroy, OH 45769-0362 *Tel:* 740-992-5208 *Fax:* 740-992-0616 *E-mail:* ljacobs@frognet.net *Web Site:* www.leejacobsproductions.com, pg 140

Cyrisse Jaffee, 8 Hallron Rd, Newton, MA 02462 *Tel:* 617-965-7114, pg 602

Jain Publishing Co, PO Box 3523, Fremont, CA 94539 *Tel:* 510-659-8272 *Fax:* 510-659-0501 *E-mail:* mail@jainpub.com *Web Site:* www.jainpub.com, pg 140

Jalmar Press, 1050 Canyon Rd, Fawnskin, CA 92333 *Tel:* 909-866-2912 *Fax:* 909-866-2961 *E-mail:* jalmarpress@att.net *Web Site:* www.jalmarpress.com, pg 140

J Franklin Jameson Fellowship in American History, 400 "A" St SE, Washington, DC 20003 *Tel:* 202-544-2422 *Fax:* 202-544-8307 *E-mail:* info@historians.org *Web Site:* www.historians.org, pg 781

Jamestown Prize, 109 Cary St, Williamsburg, VA 23185 *Tel:* 757-221-1114 *Fax:* 757-221-1047 *E-mail:* ieahc1@wm.edu *Web Site:* www.wm.edu/oieahc, pg 781

K H Marketing Communications, 16205 NE Sixth St, Bellevue, WA 98008 *Tel:* 425-562-0417 *Fax:* 425-746-4406, pg 602

Kabbalah Publishing, 155 E 48 St, New York, NY 10017 *Tel:* 212-644-0025 *Toll Free Tel:* 866-524-8723 *Fax:* 212-317-1264 *E-mail:* ny@kabbalah.com *Web Site:* www.kabbalah.com, pg 143

Kabel Publishers, 11225 Huntover Dr, Rockville, MD 20852 *Tel:* 301-468-6463 *Toll Free Tel:* 800-543-3167 *Fax:* 301-468-6463 *E-mail:* kabelcomp@erols.com *Web Site:* www.erols.com/kabelcomp/index2.html, pg 143

Kaeden Corp, PO Box 16190, Rocky River, OH 44116-0190 *Tel:* 440-617-1400 *Toll Free Tel:* 800-890-7323 *Fax:* 440-617-1403 *E-mail:* info@kaeden.com *Web Site:* www.kaeden.com, pg 143

Frederick D Kagy Education Award of Excellence, 200 Deer Run Rd, Sewickley, PA 15143-2600 *Tel:* 412-741-6860 *Toll Free Tel:* 800-910-4283 *Fax:* 412-741-2311 *E-mail:* info@gain.net *Web Site:* www.gain.net, pg 782

Kalimat Press, 1600 Sawtelle Blvd, Suite 310, Los Angeles, CA 90025 *Tel:* 310-479-5668 (edit) *Fax:* 310-477-2840 *E-mail:* kalimatp@aol.com *Web Site:* www.kalimat.com, pg 143

Kalmbach Publishing Co, 21027 Crossroads Circle, Waukesha, WI 53187 *Tel:* 262-796-8776 *Toll Free Tel:* 800-533-6644 *Fax:* 262-796-1615 (sales & cust serv) *Web Site:* www.kalmbach.com, pg 143

Kamehameha Schools Press, 1887 Makuakane St, Honolulu, HI 96817-1887 *Tel:* 808-842-8719 *Fax:* 808-842-8895 *E-mail:* kspress@ksbe.edu *Web Site:* kspress.ksbe.edu, pg 144

Kane/Miller Book Publishers, PO Box 8515, La Jolla, CA 92038-8515 *Tel:* 858-456-0540 *Toll Free Tel:* 800-968-1930 *Fax:* 858-456-9641 *E-mail:* info@kanemiller.com *Web Site:* www.kanemiller.com, pg 144

The Kane Press, 240 W 35 St, Suite 300, New York, NY 10001-2506 *Tel:* 212-268-1435 *Fax:* 212-268-2044 *Web Site:* www.kanepress.com, pg 144

Boche Kaplan, 166 W Waukena Ave, Oceanside, NY 11572 *Tel:* 516-764-9828, pg 603

Kaplan Publishing, 1230 Avenue of the Americas, New York, NY 10020 *Fax:* 212-632-4973 *Web Site:* www.simonsays.com, pg 144

Sharon Kapnick, 185 West End Ave, New York, NY 10023-5547 *Tel:* 212-787-7231, pg 603

Kar-Ben Publishing, 1251 Washington Ave N, Minneapolis, MN 55401 *Tel:* 612-332-3344 *Toll Free Tel:* 800-4-KARBEN (452-7236) *Toll Free Fax:* 800-332-1132 *E-mail:* kar-ben@lernerbooks.com *Web Site:* www.karben.com, pg 144

The Karpfinger Agency, 357 W 20 St, New York, NY 10011-3379 *Tel:* 212-691-2690 *Fax:* 212-691-7129, pg 637

Herbert M Katz Inc, 151 E 83 St, New York, NY 10028 *Tel:* 212-861-5460, pg 637

Kazi Publications Inc, 3023 W Belmont Ave, Chicago, IL 60618 *Tel:* 773-267-7001 *Fax:* 773-267-7002 *E-mail:* info@kazi.org *Web Site:* www.kazi.org/, pg 144

KC Publications Inc, PO Box 94558, Las Vegas, NV 89193-4558 *Tel:* 702-433-3415 *Toll Free Tel:* 800-626-9673 *Fax:* 702-433-3420 *E-mail:* kcp@kcpublications.com *Web Site:* www.kcpublications.com, pg 144

Ezra Jack Keats Memorial Fellowship, University of Minnesota, 113 Andersen Library, 222 21 Ave S, Minneapolis, MN 55455 *Tel:* 612-624-4576 *Fax:* 612-625-5525 *E-mail:* clrc@tc.umn.edu *Web Site:* www.ezra-jack-keats.org; special.lib.umn.edu/clrc/, pg 782

Keim Publishing, 301 E 61 St, New York, NY 10021 *Tel:* 212-753-4404, pg 603

J J Keller & Associates, Inc, 3003 W Breezewood Lane, Neenah, WI 54957 *Tel:* 920-722-2848 *Toll Free Tel:* 800-327-6868 *Toll Free Fax:* 800-727-7516 *E-mail:* sales@jjkeller.com *Web Site:* www.jjkeller.com/jjk, pg 144

The Kellock Co, 18811 Cypress Bend Ct, Boca Raton, FL 33498 *Tel:* 561-558-8603 *E-mail:* kellock@aol.com, pg 637

Joan Kelly Memorial Prize in Women's History, 400 "A" St SE, Washington, DC 20003 *Tel:* 202-544-2422 *Fax:* 202-544-8307 *E-mail:* info@historians.org *Web Site:* www.historians.org, pg 782

Kelsey Street Press, 50 Northgate, Berkeley, CA 94708 *Tel:* 510-845-2260 *Fax:* 510-548-9185 *E-mail:* info@kelseyst.com *Web Site:* www.kelseyst.com, pg 144

Kendall/Hunt Publishing Co, 4050 Westmark Dr, Dubuque, IA 52002 *Tel:* 563-589-1000 *Toll Free Tel:* 800-228-0810 (orders only) *Fax:* 563-589-1114 *Toll Free Fax:* 800-772-9165 *Web Site:* www.kendallhunt.com, pg 144

Kennedy Information, One Phoenix Mill Lane, 5th fl, Peterborough, NH 03458 *Tel:* 603-924-0900 *Toll Free Tel:* 800-531-0007 *Fax:* 603-924-4460 *E-mail:* office@kennedyinfo.com *Web Site:* www.kennedyinfo.com, pg 145

Robert F Kennedy Book Awards, 1367 Connecticut Ave NW, Suite 200, Washington, DC 20036-1859 *Tel:* 202-463-7575 *E-mail:* info@rfkmemorial.org *Web Site:* www.rfkmemorial.org, pg 782

Kensington Publishing Corp, 850 Third Ave, New York, NY 10022 *Tel:* 212-407-1500 *Toll Free Tel:* 800-221-2647 *Fax:* 212-935-0699 *Web Site:* www.kensingtonbooks.com, pg 145

Kent State University Press, PO Box 5190, Kent, OH 44242-0001 *Tel:* 330-672-7913; 330-672-8097 (sales office) *Toll Free Tel:* 800-247-6553 (orders) *Fax:* 330-672-3104 *Web Site:* www.kentstateuniversitypress.com, pg 145

Kentucky Arts Council Fellowships in Writing, Old Capitol Annex, 300 W Broadway, Frankfort, KY 40601 *Tel:* 502-564-3757 *Toll Free Tel:* 888-833-2787 *Fax:* 502-564-2839 *Web Site:* www.artscouncil.ky.gov, pg 782

Kentucky Women Writers Conference, University of Kentucky, 113 Bowman Hall, Lexington, KY 40506-0059 *Tel:* 859-257-8734; 859-257-6420; 859-257-8451 *Fax:* 859-257-8737 *E-mail:* kywwc@hotmail.com *Web Site:* www.uky.edu/conferences/kywwc, pg 744

Natasha Kern Literary Agency Inc, PO Box 2908, Portland, OR 97208-2908 *Tel:* 503-297-6190 *Fax:* 503-297-8241 *E-mail:* natasha@natashakern.com *Web Site:* www.natashakern.com, pg 637

Kessinger Publishing Co, PO Box 4587, Whitefish, MT 59937 *E-mail:* message@kessinger.net *Web Site:* www.kessinger.net, pg 145

Kessler Communications, 280 W 86 St, New York, NY 10024 *Tel:* 212-724-8610 *E-mail:* lmp@etk.mailshell.com *Web Site:* www.kesslercommunications.com, pg 603

Jascha Kessler, 218 16 St, Santa Monica, CA 90402-2216 *Tel:* 310-393-4648 *Fax:* 530-684-5120 *E-mail:* jkessler@ucla.edu, pg 603

The Joyce Ketay Agency, 630 Ninth Ave, Suite 706, New York, NY 10036 *Tel:* 212-354-6825 *Fax:* 212-354-6732, pg 637

Louise B Ketz Agency, 1485 First Ave, Suite 4-B, New York, NY 10021 *Tel:* 212-535-9259 *Fax:* 212-249-3103 *E-mail:* ketzagency@aol.com, pg 637

Key Curriculum Press, 1150 65 St, Emeryville, CA 94608 *Tel:* 510-595-7000 *Toll Free Tel:* 800-995-6284 *Fax:* 510-595-7040 *Toll Free Fax:* 800-541-2442 *E-mail:* customer.service@keypress.com *Web Site:* www.keypress.com, pg 145

Key Porter Books Ltd, 70 The Esplanade, 3rd fl, Toronto, ON M5E 1R2, Canada *Tel:* 416-862-7777 *Fax:* 416-862-2304 *E-mail:* info@keyporter.com *Web Site:* www.keyporter.com, pg 551

Key West Literary Seminar Inc, 717 Love Lane, Key West, FL 33040 *Toll Free Tel:* 888-293-9291 *E-mail:* mail@keywestliteraryseminar.org *Web Site:* www.keywestliteraryseminar.org, pg 744

Donald Keyhoe Journalism Award, PO Box 277, Mount Rainier, MD 20712 *Tel:* 703-684-6032 *Fax:* 703-684-6032 *Web Site:* www.fufor.com, pg 782

Aga Khan Prize for Fiction, 541 E 72 St, New York, NY 10021 *Tel:* 212-861-0016 *Fax:* 212-861-4504 *Web Site:* www.theparisreview.org, pg 782

Frances Kianka Editorial Services, 1624 Greenbriar Ct, Reston, VA 20190-4417 *Tel:* 703-481-6372 *Fax:* 703-481-6117, pg 603

Virginia Kidd Agency Inc, 538 E Harford St, Milford, PA 18337 *Tel:* 570-296-6205 *Fax:* 570-296-7266 *Web Site:* vkagency.com, pg 637

Kids Can Press Ltd, 2250 Military Rd, Tonawanda, NY 14150 *Tel:* 416-925-5437 (Toronto, ON, Canada) *Toll Free Tel:* 800-265-0884; 866-481-5827 (orders) *Fax:* 416-960-5437 (Toronto, ON, Canada) *E-mail:* info@kidscan.com; lfyman@kidscan.com (orders) *Web Site:* www.kidscanpress.com, pg 145

Kids Can Press Ltd, 29 Birch Ave, Toronto, ON M4V 1E2, Canada *Tel:* 416-925-5437 *Toll Free Tel:* 800-265-0884 *Fax:* 416-960-5437 *E-mail:* info@kidscan.com *Web Site:* kidscanpress.com, pg 552

Kidsbooks Inc, 230 Fifth Ave, Suite 1710, New York, NY 10001 *Tel:* 212-685-4444 *Fax:* 212-889-1122 *Web Site:* www.kidsbooks.com, pg 145

Kindred Productions, 4-169 Riverton Ave, Winnipeg, MB R2L 2E5, Canada *Tel:* 204-669-6575 *Toll Free Tel:* 800-545-7322 *Fax:* 204-654-1865 *E-mail:* kindred@mbconf.ca *Web Site:* www.kindredproductions.com, pg 552

Coretta Scott King Awards, ALA Office for Literacy & Outreach Services, 50 E Huron St, Chicago, IL 60611 *Tel:* 312-280-4295; 312-280-4294 *Fax:* 312-280-3256 *E-mail:* olos@ala.org *Web Site:* www.ala.org/olos, pg 782

Judy King Editorial Services, PO Box 35038, Houston, TX 77235-5038 *Tel:* 713-721-3003 *Fax:* 713-721-7272 *E-mail:* judyking@pdq.net *Web Site:* www.judykingedit.com, pg 603

Kinship Books, 781 Rte 308, Rhinebeck, NY 12572 *Tel:* 845-876-4200 (orders); 845-876-4592 *Toll Free Tel:* 800-249-1109 (orders) *E-mail:* kinshipbooks@cs.com *Web Site:* www.kinshipny.com, pg 145

A J Kirby Co, 301 Oxford St W, Box 24107, London, ON N6A 3Y6, Canada *Tel:* 519-671-0124 *Fax:* 519-438-7935 *E-mail:* ajkirbyco@pobox.com *Web Site:* www.ajkirbyco.com, pg 552

Kirchoff/Wohlberg Inc, 866 United Nations Plaza, Suite 525, New York, NY 10017 *Tel:* 212-644-2020 *Fax:* 212-223-4387 *E-mail:* kirchwohl@aol.com *Web Site:* www.kirchoffwohlberg.com, pg 603, 637, 666

The Kiriyama Pacific Rim Book Prize, 650 Delancy St, Suite 101, San Francisco, CA 94107-2082 *Tel:* 415-777-1628 *Fax:* 415-777-1646 *Web Site:* www.kiriyamaprize.org, pg 782

Kirkbride Bible Co Inc, 335 W Ninth St, Indianapolis, IN 46202 *Tel:* 317-633-1900 *Toll Free Tel:* 800-428-4385 *Fax:* 317-633-1444 *E-mail:* sales@kirkbride.com *Web Site:* www.kirkbride.com, pg 146

Kirkland's Press, 101 Mount Rock Rd, Newville, PA 17241 *Tel:* 717-776-4232 *Web Site:* www.kirklandspress.com, pg 146

Kitemaug Press, 229 Mohawk Dr, Spartanburg, SC 29301-2827 *Tel:* 864-576-3338 *E-mail:* kitemaugpresswhq@msn.com, pg 146

Kiva Publishing Inc, 21731 E Buckskin Dr, Walnut, CA 91789 *Tel:* 909-595-6833 *Toll Free Tel:* 800-634-5482 *Fax:* 909-860-5424 *E-mail:* kivapub@aol.com *Web Site:* www.kivapub.com, pg 146

B Klein Publications, 6037 W Atlantic Ave, Delray Beach, FL 33482 *Tel:* 561-496-3316 *Fax:* 561-496-5546, pg 146

Marc A Klein Playwriting Award for Students, Dept of Theater & Dance, Eldred Hall, 10900 Euclid Ave, Cleveland, OH 44106-7077 *Tel:* 216-368-4868 *Toll Free Tel:* 800-429-3681 *Fax:* 216-368-5184 *E-mail:* ksg@case.edu *Web Site:* www.case.edu/artsci/thtr, pg 782

Klimt Represents, 15 W 72 St, Suite 7-U, New York, NY 10023 *Tel:* 212-799-2231 *Fax:* 212-799-2362 *E-mail:* klimt@nyc.rr.com *Web Site:* klimtreps.com, pg 666

Harvey Klinger Inc, 301 W 53 St, New York, NY 10019 *Tel:* 212-581-7068 *Fax:* 212-315-3823 *E-mail:* queries@harveyklinger.com, pg 637

Klutz, 455 Portage Ave, Palo Alto, CA 94306 *Tel:* 650-857-0888 *Fax:* 650-857-9110 *Web Site:* www.klutz.com, pg 146

Kluwer Academic Publishers, 101 Philip Dr, Assinippi Park, Norwell, MA 02061 *Tel:* 781-871-6600 *Fax:* 781-871-6528; 781-681-9045 (cust serv) *E-mail:* kluwer@wkap.com *Web Site:* www.wkap.nl, pg 146

Kneerim & Williams, c/o Fish & Richardson PC, 225 Franklin St, Boston, MA 02110 *Tel:* 617-542-5070 *Fax:* 617-542-8906 *Web Site:* www.fr.com, pg 638

The Knight Agency Inc, 577 S Main St, Madison, GA 30650 *Tel:* 706-752-0096 *E-mail:* knightagency@msn.com; knightagent@aol.com (queries) *Web Site:* www.knightagency.net, pg 638

Theodore Knight, 89 Johnson Rd, Foster, RI 02825 *Tel:* 401-397-9235 *E-mail:* tknight11@earthlink.net, pg 603

Allen A Knoll Publishers, 200 W Victoria St, 2nd fl, Suite A, Santa Barbara, CA 93101-3627 *Tel:* 805-564-3377 *Toll Free Tel:* 800-777-7623 *Fax:* 805-966-6657 *E-mail:* bookinfo@knollpublishers.com *Web Site:* www.knollpublishers.com, pg 146

Alfred A Knopf, 1745 Broadway, New York, NY 10019 *Tel:* 212-751-2600 *Toll Free Tel:* 800-638-6460 *Fax:* 212-572-2593 *Web Site:* www.randomhouse.com/knopf, pg 146

Knopf Canada, One Toronto St, Suite 300, Toronto, ON M5C 2V6, Canada *Tel:* 416-364-4449 *Toll Free Tel:* 800-668-4247 (order desk) *Fax:* 416-364-0462 *Web Site:* www.randomhouse.ca, pg 552

Kodansha America Inc, 575 Lexington Ave, 23rd fl, New York, NY 10022 *Tel:* 917-322-6200 *Fax:* 212-935-6929 *E-mail:* info@kodanshaamerica.com *Web Site:* www.kodansha-intl.com, pg 146

Bill Koehnlein, 236 E Fifth St, New York, NY 10003-8545 *Tel:* 212-674-9145 *E-mail:* bkoehnlein@nyc.rr.com, pg 603

Barry R Koffler, Featherside, 14 Ginger Rd, High Falls, NY 12440 *Tel:* 845-687-9851 *Fax:* 415-534-2200 *E-mail:* barkof@ulster.net *Web Site:* www.feathersite.com, pg 603

Paul Kohner Agency, 9300 Wilshire Blvd, Suite 555, Beverly Hills, CA 90212 *Tel:* 310-550-1060 *Fax:* 310-276-1083, pg 638

KOK Edit, 15 Hare Lane, East Setauket, NY 11733-3606 *Tel:* 631-474-1170 *Fax:* 631-474-9849 *E-mail:* editor@kokedit.com *Web Site:* www.kokedit.com, pg 603

William S Konecky Associates Inc, 72 Ayers Pt Rd, Old Saybrook, CT 06475 *Tel:* 860-388-0878 *Fax:* 860-388-0273, pg 147

Linda Konner Literary Agency, 10 W 15 St, Suite 1918, New York, NY 10011 *Tel:* 212-691-3419 *Fax:* 212-691-0935, pg 638

Elaine Koster Literary Agency LLC, 55 Central Park West, Suite 6, New York, NY 10023 *Tel:* 212-362-9488 *Fax:* 212-712-0164 *E-mail:* elainekost@aol.com, pg 639

KotaPress, PO Box 514, Vashon Island, WA 98070-0514 *Tel:* 206-251-6706 *E-mail:* editor@kotapress.com *Web Site:* www.kotapress.com, pg 147

Barbara S Kouts Literary Agency LLC, PO Box 560, Bellport, NY 11713 *Tel:* 631-286-1278 *Fax:* 631-286-1538 *E-mail:* bkouts@aol.com, pg 639

Katherine Singer Kovacs Prize, 26 Broadway, 3rd fl, New York, NY 10004-1789 *Tel:* 646-576-5141 *Fax:* 646-458-0030 *E-mail:* awards@mla.org *Web Site:* www.mla.org, pg 783

Kraas Literary Agency, 13514 Winter Creek Ct, Houston, TX 77077 *Tel:* 281-870-9770 *Fax:* 281-870-9770 *Web Site:* www.kraasliterarygency.com, pg 639

Kraft & Kraft, 100 Fourth Ave S, Suite 201, St Petersburg, FL 33701 *Tel:* 727-821-1627 *Web Site:* www.erickraft.com/kraftkraft, pg 604

Eileen Kramer, 336 Great Rd, Stow, MA 01775 *Tel:* 978-897-4121 *E-mail:* kramer@tiac.com *Web Site:* www.ekramer.com, pg 604

H J Kramer Inc, PO Box 1082, Tiburon, CA 94920-7002 *Tel:* 415-435-5367 *Fax:* 415-435-5364 *E-mail:* hjkramer@jps.net *Web Site:* www.newworldlibrary.com, pg 147

Michael Kraus Research Grant in History, 400 "A" St SE, Washington, DC 20003 *Tel:* 202-544-2422 *Fax:* 202-544-8307 *E-mail:* info@historians.org *Web Site:* www.historians.org, pg 783

Krause Publications, 700 E State St, Iola, WI 54990 *Tel:* 715-445-4612 ext 365 *Toll Free Tel:* 800-258-0929; 888-457-2873 *Fax:* 715-445-4087 *Web Site:* www.krause.com, pg 147

Kregel Publications, 733 Wealthy St SE, Grand Rapids, MI 49503-5553 *Tel:* 616-451-4775 *Toll Free Tel:* 800-733-2607 *Fax:* 616-451-9330 *E-mail:* kregelbooks@kregel.com *Web Site:* www.kregelpublications.com, pg 147

Henry Kreisel Award for Best First Book, 11759 Groat Rd, Edmonton, AB T5M 3K6, Canada *Tel:* 780-422-8174 *Toll Free Tel:* 800-665-5354 (Alberta only) *Fax:* 780-422-2663 *E-mail:* mail@writersguild.ab.ca *Web Site:* www.writersguild.ab.ca, pg 783

Krieger Publishing Co, PO Box 9542, Melbourne, FL 32902-9542 *Tel:* 321-724-9542 *Toll Free Tel:* 800-724-0025 *Fax:* 321-951-3671 *E-mail:* info@krieger-publishing.com *Web Site:* www.krieger-publishing.com, pg 147

Edite Kroll Literary Agency Inc, 12 Grayhurst Park, Portland, ME 04102 *Tel:* 207-773-4922 *Fax:* 207-773-3936, pg 639

Kenneth Kronenberg, 51 Maple Ave, Cambridge, MA 02139 *Tel:* 617-868-8070 *E-mail:* mail@kfkronenberg.com *Web Site:* www.kfkronenberg.com, pg 604

Lynn C Kronzek & Richard A Flom, 145 S Glenoaks Blvd, Suite 240, Burbank, CA 91502 *Tel:* 818-843-2625 *E-mail:* lckronzek@earthlink.net, pg 604

KTAV Publishing House Inc, 930 Newark Ave, Jersey City, NJ 07306 *Tel:* 201-963-9524 *Fax:* 201-963-0102 *E-mail:* orders@ktav.com *Web Site:* www.ktav.com, pg 147

Kumarian Press Inc, 1294 Blue Hills Ave, Bloomfield, CT 06002 *Tel:* 860-243-2098 *Toll Free Tel:* 800-289-2664 (orders only) *Fax:* 860-243-2867 *E-mail:* kpbooks@kpbooks.com *Web Site:* www.kpbooks.com, pg 147

Polly Kummel, 10111 46 Ave W, Bradenton, FL 34210 *Tel:* 941-795-2779 *E-mail:* pollyk1@msn.com, pg 604

Kumu Kahua/UHM Theatre Dept Playwriting Contest, 46 Merchant St, Honolulu, HI 96813 *Tel:* 808-536-4222 *Fax:* 808-536-4226 *E-mail:* info@kumakahua.org *Web Site:* www.kumukahua.org, pg 783

George Kurian Reference Books, PO Box 519, Baldwin Place, NY 10505-0519 *Tel:* 914-962-3287 *Fax:* 914-962-3287 *Web Site:* www.encyclopediasociety.com, pg 148

Labyrinthos, 3064 Holline Ct, Lancaster, CA 93535-4910 *Tel:* 661-946-2726 *Fax:* 661-946-2726, pg 148

Lachina Publishing Services Inc, 3793 S Green Rd, Beachwood, OH 44122 *Tel:* 216-292-7959 *Fax:* 216-292-3639 *Web Site:* www.lachina.com, pg 604

Lacis Publications, 3163 Adeline St, Berkeley, CA 94703 *Tel:* 510-843-7178 *Fax:* 510-843-5018 *E-mail:* staff@lacis.com *Web Site:* www.lacis.com, pg 148

Lynne Lackenbach Editorial Services, 31 Pillsbury Rd, East Hampstead, NH 03826 *Tel:* 603-329-8133 *E-mail:* lynne@lackey.mv.com, pg 604

Ladan Reserve Press, PO Box 881239, Steamboat Plaza, CO 80488-1239 *Tel:* 970-723-4916 *Fax:* 970-723-4918 *E-mail:* ladan@sprynet.com, pg 572

LadybugPress, 16964 Columbia River Dr, Sonora, CA 95370 *Tel:* 209-694-8340 *Toll Free Tel:* 888-892-5000 *Fax:* 209-694-8916 *E-mail:* ladybugpress@ladybugbooks.com *Web Site:* www.ladybugbooks.com, pg 148

Barbara Lagowski, 237 Lenox Ave, Long Branch, NJ 07740 *Tel:* 732-571-9215 *Fax:* 732-571-9215 *E-mail:* blagowski@aol.com, pg 604

Lake Claremont Press, 4650 N Rockwell St, Chicago, IL 60625 *Tel:* 773-583-7800 *Fax:* 773-583-7877 *E-mail:* lcp@lakeclaremont.com *Web Site:* www.lakeclarmont.com, pg 148

Russ Lake, 3903 Crail Rd, Champaign, IL 61822 *Tel:* 217-356-2021 *E-mail:* rlake@parkland.edu, pg 604

Lake View Press, Box 578279, Chicago, IL 60657-8279 *Tel:* 773-935-2694 *Web Site:* www.lakeviewpress.com, pg 148

LAMA Books, 2381 Sleepy Hollow Ave, Hayward, CA 94545 *Tel:* 510-785-1091 *Toll Free Tel:* 888-452-6244 *Fax:* 510-785-1099 *E-mail:* lama@lamabooks.com *Web Site:* www.lamabooks.com, pg 148

Lambda Literary Awards (Lammys), 1217 11 St NW, Washington, DC 20001 *Tel:* 202-682-0952 *Fax:* 202-682-0955 *E-mail:* lbreditor@lambdalit.org *Web Site:* www.lambdalit.org, pg 783

Peter Lampack Agency Inc, 551 Fifth Ave, Suite 1613, New York, NY 10176 *Tel:* 212-687-9106 *Fax:* 212-687-9109 *E-mail:* lampackag@verizon.net (other correspondence), pg 639

Gerald Lampert Memorial Award, 920 Yonge St, Suite 608, Toronto, ON M4W 3C7, Canada *Tel:* 416-504-1657 *Fax:* 416-504-0096 *E-mail:* info@poets.ca *Web Site:* www.poets.ca, pg 783

Lanahan Publishers Inc, 324 Hawthorn Rd, Baltimore, MD 21210 *Tel:* 410-366-2434 *Toll Free Tel:* 866-354-1949 *Fax:* 410-366-8798 *Toll Free Fax:* 888-345-7257 *E-mail:* lanahan@aol.com *Web Site:* www.lanahanpublishers.com, pg 148

Land on Demand, 20 Long Crescent Dr, Bristol, VA 24201 *Tel:* 276-642-1007; 423-366-0513 *Fax:* 760-437-4511 *E-mail:* landondemand@cs.com, pg 604

Landauer Books, 12251 Maffitt Rd, Cumming, IA 50061 *Tel:* 515-287-2144 *Toll Free Tel:* 800-557-2144 *Fax:* 515-287-1530 *E-mail:* landaucor@aol.com, pg 148

Landes Bioscience, 810 S Church St, Georgetown, TX 78626 *Tel:* 512-863-7762 *Toll Free Tel:* 800-736-9948 *Fax:* 512-863-0081 *Web Site:* www.landesbioscience.com, pg 148

Landmark Editions Inc, 1402 Kansas Ave, Kansas City, MO 64127 *Tel:* 816-241-4919 *Fax:* 816-483-3755 *E-mail:* l_m_e@swbell.net *Web Site:* www.landmarkeditions.com, pg 148

Harold Morton Landon Translation Award, 588 Broadway, Suite 604, New York, NY 10012 *Tel:* 212-274-0343 *Fax:* 212-274-9427 *E-mail:* academy@poets.org *Web Site:* www.poets.org, pg 783

Peter Lang Publishing Inc, 275 Seventh Ave, 28th fl, New York, NY 10001-6708 *Tel:* 212-647-7700 *Toll Free Tel:* 800-770-5264 (cust serv) *Fax:* 212-647-7707 *Web Site:* www.peterlangusa.com, pg 148

Langdon Enterprises, 16902 N Hardesty, Colbert, WA 99005 *Tel:* 509-238-4745 *Fax:* 509-238-1181, pg 149

Langenscheidt Publishers Inc, 46-35 54 Rd, Maspeth, NY 11378 *Tel:* 718-784-0055 *Toll Free Tel:* 800-432-MAPS (732-6277) *Fax:* 718-784-0640 *Toll Free Fax:* 888-773-7979 *E-mail:* sales@langenscheidt.com *Web Site:* www.langenscheidt.com, pg 149

LangMarc Publishing, PO Box 90488, Austin, TX 78709-0488 *Tel:* 512-394-0989 *Toll Free Tel:* 800-864-1648 *Fax:* 512-394-0829 *E-mail:* langmarc@booksails. com *Web Site:* www.langmarc.com; www.booksails. com, pg 149

Lantern Books, One Union Square W, Suite 201, New York, NY 10003 *Tel:* 212-414-2275 *Toll Free Tel:* 800-856-8664 *Fax:* 212-414-2412 *E-mail:* editorial@lanternbooks.com *Web Site:* www. lanternbooks.com, pg 149

Laredo Publishing Company Inc, 9400 Lloydcrest Dr, Beverly Hills, CA 90210 *Tel:* 310-860-9930 *Toll Free Tel:* 800-547-5113 *Fax:* 310-860-9902 *E-mail:* info@ laredopublishing.com, pg 149

Large Print, PO Box 5000, Yucaipa, CA 92399-1450 *Tel:* 909-795-8977 *Fax:* 909-795-8970 *E-mail:* lbw@ lbwinc.org *Web Site:* www.lbwinc.org, pg 149

Lark Books, 67 Broadway, Asheville, NC 28801 *Tel:* 828-253-0467 *Toll Free Tel:* 800-284-3388 (cust serv) *Fax:* 828-253-7952 *E-mail:* info@larkbooks.com *Web Site:* www.larkbooks.com, pg 149

Michael Larsen/Elizabeth Pomada Literary Agents, 1029 Jones St, San Francisco, CA 94109 *Tel:* 415-673-0939 *E-mail:* larsenpoma@aol.com *Web Site:* www.larsen-pomada.com, pg 639

Larson Publications, 4936 Rte 414, Burdett, NY 14818 *Tel:* 607-546-9342 *Toll Free Tel:* 800-828-2197 *Fax:* 607-546-9344 *E-mail:* larson@lightlink.com *Web Site:* www.larsonpublications.org, pg 149

The Maureen Lasher Agency/The LA Literary Agency, PO Box 46370, Los Angeles, CA 90046 *Tel:* 323-654-5288 *Fax:* 323-654-5388 *E-mail:* laliteraryag@aol. com, pg 639

Latin American Literary Review Press, 176 Penhurst Dr, Pittsburgh, PA 15235 *Tel:* 412-824-7903 *Fax:* 412-824-7909 *E-mail:* latin@angstrom.net *Web Site:* www. lalrp.org, pg 149

Laughing Elephant, 3645 Interlake Ave N, Seattle, WA 98103 *Tel:* 206-447-9229 *Toll Free Tel:* 800-354-0400 *Fax:* 206-447-9189 *E-mail:* mail@laughingelephant. com *Web Site:* www.laughingelephant.com, pg 149

James Laughlin Award, 588 Broadway, Suite 604, New York, NY 10012 *Tel:* 212-274-0343 *Fax:* 212-274-9427 *E-mail:* academy@poets.org *Web Site:* www. poets.org, pg 783

Laura Geringer Books, 1350 Avenue of Americas, 4th fl, New York, NY 10019 *Tel:* 212-261-6500 *Web Site:* www.harpercollins.com, pg 150

Laureate Press, PO Box 8125, Bangor, ME 04402-8125 *Toll Free Tel:* 800-946-2727 *Fax:* 207-884-8095, pg 150

LaurelTech Integrated Publishing Solutions, 1750 Elm St, Suite 201, Manchester, NH 03104 *Tel:* 603-606-5800 *Fax:* 603-606-5838 *E-mail:* sales@laureltech. com *Web Site:* www.laureltech.com, pg 604

Laurier Books Ltd, PO Box 2694, Sta D, Ottawa, ON K1P 5W6, Canada *Tel:* 613-738-2163 *Fax:* 613-247-0256 *E-mail:* educa@travel-net.com *Web Site:* www. travel-net.com/~educa/main.htm, pg 552

Law School Admission Council, 662 Penn St, Newtown, PA 18940 *Tel:* 215-968-1101 *Fax:* 215-968-1159 *E-mail:* wmargolis@lsac.org *Web Site:* www.lsac.org, pg 150

Law Tribune Books, 201 Ann St, 4th fl, Hartford, CT 06103 *Tel:* 860-527-7900 *Fax:* 860-527-7815 *E-mail:* lawtribune@amlaw.com *Web Site:* www.law. com/ct, pg 150

The Lawbook Exchange Ltd, 33 Terminal Ave, Clark, NJ 07066-1321 *Tel:* 732-382-1800 *Toll Free Tel:* 800-422-6686 *Fax:* 732-382-1887 *E-mail:* law@lawbookexchange.com *Web Site:* www. lawbookexchange.com, pg 150

Lawells Publishing, PO Box 1338, Royal Oak, MI 48068-1338 *Tel:* 248-543-5297 *Fax:* 248-543-5683 *Web Site:* www.lawells.net, pg 150

Lawrence Foundation Award, University of Nebraska, 201 Andrews Hall, Lincoln, NE 68588 *Tel:* 402-472-0911 *Web Site:* www.unl.edu/schooner/psmain.htm, pg 783

Frank Lawrence & Harriet Chappell Owsley Award, University of Georgia, Dept of History, Athens, GA 30602-1602 *Tel:* 706-542-8848 *Fax:* 706-542-2455 *Web Site:* www.uga.edu/~sha, pg 783

Merloyd Lawrence Inc, 102 Chestnut St, Boston, MA 02108 *Tel:* 617-523-5895 *Fax:* 617-252-5285, pg 150

Lawrenceville Press Inc, PO Box 704, Pennington, NJ 08534 *Tel:* 609-737-1148 *Fax:* 609-737-8564 *E-mail:* custserv@lvp.com *Web Site:* www.lvp.com, pg 150

Lawyers & Judges Publishing Co Inc, 917 N Swan Rd, Tucson, AZ 85711-1213 *Tel:* 520-323-1500 *Fax:* 520-323-0055 *E-mail:* sales@lawyersandjudges.com *Web Site:* www.lawyersandjudges.com, pg 150

The Lazear Agency Inc, 431 Second St, Suite 300, Hudson, WI 54016 *Tel:* 715-531-0012 *Fax:* 715-531-0016 *Web Site:* www.lazear.com, pg 639

Samuel Lazerow Fellowship for Research in Collections or Technical Services in Academic & Research Libraries, 50 E Huron St, Chicago, IL 60611 *Tel:* 312-280-2514 *Toll Free Tel:* 800-545-2433 (ext 2514) *Fax:* 312-280-2520 *Web Site:* www.ala.org/acrl, pg 783

Sarah Lazin Books, 126 Fifth Ave, Suite 300, New York, NY 10011 *Tel:* 212-989-5757 *Fax:* 212-989-1393, pg 640

LDA Award for Excellence, 42-46 209 St, Suite B-11, Bayside, NY 11361-2747 *Tel:* 718-224-9484 *Toll Free Tel:* 888-388-9887 *Fax:* 718-224-9487 *Web Site:* www. lilrc.org/~ncla1/awards.html, pg 783

LDA Publishers, 42-46 209 St, Bayside, NY 11361-2747 *Tel:* 718-224-9484 *Toll Free Tel:* 888-388-9887 *Fax:* 718-224-9487 *Web Site:* www.ldapublishers.com, pg 150

Anne Leach, 78240 Bonanza Dr, Palm Desert, CA 92211 *Tel:* 760-360-1432 *Fax:* 760-360-1432 *E-mail:* aleach@dc.rr.com, pg 604

Stephen Leacock Memorial Award for Humour, Box 854, Orillia, ON L3V 6K8, Canada *Tel:* 705-835-3218 *Fax:* 705-835-5171 *E-mail:* moonwood@simpatico.ca *Web Site:* www.leacock.ca/awards.html, pg 784

Leadership Directories Inc, 104 Fifth Ave, New York, NY 10011 *Tel:* 212-627-4140 *Fax:* 212-645-0931 *E-mail:* info@leadershipdirectories.com *Web Site:* www.leadershipdirectories.com, pg 150

Leadership Ministries Worldwide, 515 Airport Rd, Suite 111, Chattanooga, TN 37421 *Tel:* 423-855-2181 *Toll Free Tel:* 800-987-8790 *Fax:* 423-855-8616 *Toll Free Fax:* 800-987-8790 *E-mail:* info@outlinebible.org *Web Site:* www.outlinebible.org, pg 150

Leadership Publishers Inc, PO Box 8358, Des Moines, IA 50301-8358 *Tel:* 515-278-4765 *Toll Free Tel:* 800-814-3757 *Fax:* 515-270-8303, pg 150

Leading Edge Reports, 2171 Jericho Tpke, Suite 200, Commack, NY 11725 *Tel:* 631-462-5454 *Toll Free Tel:* 800-866-4648 *Fax:* 631-462-1842 *E-mail:* sales@ bta-ler.net *Web Site:* www.bta-ler.com, pg 151

League of Canadian Poets, 920 Yonge St, Suite 608, Toronto, ON M4W 3C7, Canada *Tel:* 416-504-1657 *Fax:* 416-504-0096 *E-mail:* info@poets.ca *Web Site:* www.poets.ca, pg 689

League of Vermont Writers, PO Box 172, Underhill Center, VT 05490 *Tel:* 802-253-9439 *Web Site:* www. leaguevtwriters.org, pg 689

League of Women Voters of the United States, 1730 "M" St NW, 10th fl, Washington, DC 20036 *Tel:* 202-429-1965 *Fax:* 202-429-0854; 202-429-4343 *E-mail:* lwv@ lwv.org *Web Site:* www.lwv.org, pg 690

Leap First Literary Agency, 1100 Melrose Ave, Elkins Park, PA 19027 *Tel:* 215-563-8050 *E-mail:* leapfirst@ aol.com, pg 640

Leapfrog Press, 95 Commercial St, Wellfleet, MA 02667-1495 *Tel:* 508-349-1925 *Fax:* 508-349-1180 *E-mail:* info@leapfrogpress.com *Web Site:* www. leapfrogpress.com, pg 151

Leaping Dog Press, PO Box 3316, San Jose, CA 95156-3316 *Toll Free Tel:* 877-570-6873 *Toll Free Fax:* 877-570-6873 *E-mail:* editor@leapingdogpress. com; sales@leapingdogpress.com *Web Site:* www. leapingdogpress.com, pg 151

The Learning Connection (TLC), 1901 Longleaf Blvd, Suite 300, Lake Wales, FL 33859 *Tel:* 863-676-4246 *Toll Free Tel:* 800-218-8489 *Fax:* 863-676-5216 *E-mail:* tlc@tlconnection.com *Web Site:* www. tlconnection.com, pg 151

Learning Links Inc, 2300 Marcus Ave, New Hyde Park, NY 11042 *Tel:* 516-437-9071 *Toll Free Tel:* 800-724-2616 *Fax:* 516-437-5392 *E-mail:* learning1x@aol.com *Web Site:* www.learninglinks.com, pg 151

Learning Resources Network (LERN), 208 S Main St, River Falls, WI 54022 *Tel:* 715-426-9777 *Toll Free Tel:* 800-678-5376 *Fax:* 715-426-5847 *Toll Free Fax:* 888-234-8633 *E-mail:* info@lern.org *Web Site:* www.lern.org, pg 151

The Learning Source Ltd, 644 Tenth St, Brooklyn, NY 11215 *Tel:* 718-768-0231 *Fax:* 718-369-3467 *E-mail:* info@learningsourceltd.com *Web Site:* www. learningsourceltd.com, pg 604

LearningExpress LLC, 55 Broadway, 8th fl, New York, NY 10006 *Tel:* 212-995-2566 *Toll Free Tel:* 800-295-9556 *Fax:* 212-995-5512 *E-mail:* customerservice@ learnatest.com (cust serv) *Web Site:* www.learnatest. com, pg 151

The Ned Leavitt Agency, 70 Wooster St, Suite 4-F, New York, NY 10012 *Tel:* 212-334-0999, pg 640

La Leche League International Inc, 1400 N Meacham Rd, Schaumburg, IL 60173 *Tel:* 847-519-7730 *Fax:* 847-519-0035 *E-mail:* llli@llli.org *Web Site:* www.lalecheleague.org, pg 151

Lectorum Publications Inc, 524 Broadway, New York, NY 10012 *Toll Free Tel:* 800-853-3291 (admin, mktg & sales); 800-345-5946 (orders) *Fax:* 212-727-3035 *Toll Free Fax:* 877-532-8676 *E-mail:* lectorum@ scholastic.com *Web Site:* www.lectorum.com, pg 151

Lederer Books, 6204 Park Heights Ave, Baltimore, MD 21215-3600 *Tel:* 410-358-6471 *Toll Free Tel:* 800-773-6574 *Fax:* 410-764-1376 *E-mail:* lederer@ messianicjewish.net; rightsandpermissions@ messianicjewidh.net (rights & perms) *Web Site:* messianicjewish.net, pg 151

Lee & Low Books Inc, 95 Madison Ave, New York, NY 10016 *Tel:* 212-779-4400 *Toll Free Tel:* 888-320-3190 ext 25 (orders only) *Fax:* 212-683-1894 (orders only); 212-532-6035 *E-mail:* info@leeandlow.com *Web Site:* www.leeandlow.com, pg 152

J & L Lee Co, Box 5575, Lincoln, NE 68505 *Tel:* 402-488-4416 *Toll Free Tel:* 888-665-0999 *Fax:* 402-489-2770 *E-mail:* info@leebooksellers.com *Web Site:* www.leebooksellers.com, pg 152

The Lee Shore Co Ltd, 7436 Washington Ave, Suite 100, Pittsburgh, PA 15218 *Tel:* 412-271-1100 *Toll Free Tel:* 800-898-7886 *Fax:* 412-271-1900 *E-mail:* info@ leeshoreagency.com *Web Site:* www.leeshoreagency. com, pg 640

Legal Education Publishing, 5302 Eastpark Blvd, Madison, WI 53718 *Toll Free Tel:* 800-957-4670 *Fax:* 608-257-5502 *E-mail:* service@wisbar.org *Web Site:* www.wisbar.org, pg 152

Legend Books, College Division, 69 Lansing St, Auburn, NY 13021 *Tel:* 315-258-8012, pg 152

Lehigh University Press, Linderman Library, 30 Library Dr, Bethlehem, PA 18015-3067 *Tel:* 610-758-3933 *Fax:* 610-758-6331 *E-mail:* inlup@lehigh.edu *Web Site:* fp1.cc.lehigh.edu/inlup, pg 152

Freda Leinwand, 463 West St, Studio 229G, New York, NY 10014 *Tel:* 212-691-0997, pg 604

Leisure Arts Inc, 5701 Ranch Dr, Little Rock, AR 72223 *Tel:* 501-868-8800 *Toll Free Tel:* 800-643-8030 *Fax:* 501-868-8937 *Web Site:* www.leisurearts.com, pg 152

James Leitch Gold Medal Award, 595 W Hartsdale Ave, White Plains, NY 10607 *Tel:* 914-761-1100 *Fax:* 914-761-3115 *E-mail:* smpte@smpte.org *Web Site:* www.smpte.org, pg 784

Lela Common Award for Canadian History, 320 S Shores Rd, Campbellford, ON K0L 1L0, Canada *Tel:* 705-653-0323 *Toll Free Tel:* 866-216-6222 *Fax:* 705-653-0593 *E-mail:* info@canauthors.org *Web Site:* www.canauthors.org, pg 784

Waldo G Leland Prize, 400 "A" St SE, Washington, DC 20003 *Tel:* 202-544-2422 *Fax:* 202-544-8307 *E-mail:* info@historians.org *Web Site:* www.historians.org, pg 784

Debra Lemonds, 468 E Providencia Ave, Suite A, Burbank, CA 91501-2475 *Tel:* 818-563-2928 *Fax:* 818-563-1680 *E-mail:* dlemonds@earthlink.net, pg 604

Leonardo Press, PO Box 1326, Camden, ME 04843-1326 *Tel:* 207-236-8649 *Fax:* 207-236-8649 *E-mail:* leonardo@spellingdoctor.com *Web Site:* www.spellingdoctor.com, pg 152

The Adele Leone Agency Inc, 26 Nantucket Place, Scarsdale, NY 10583 *Fax:* 212-866-0754, pg 640

Elizabeth J Leppman, 2466 Imperial Dr, St Cloud, MN 56301 *Tel:* 320-203-9894 *Fax:* 320-308-1660 *E-mail:* ejleppman@stcloudstate.edu, pg 604

Lerner Publications, 241 First Ave N, Minneapolis, MN 55401 *Tel:* 612-332-3344 *Toll Free Tel:* 800-328-4929 *Fax:* 612-332-7615 *Toll Free Fax:* 800-332-1132 *E-mail:* info@lernerbooks.com *Web Site:* www.lernerbooks.com, pg 152

Lerner Publishing Group, 241 First Ave N, Minneapolis, MN 55401 *Tel:* 612-332-3344 *Toll Free Tel:* 800-328-4929 *Fax:* 612-332-7615 *Toll Free Fax:* 800-332-1132 *E-mail:* info@lernerbooks.com *Web Site:* www.lernerbooks.com, pg 152

LernerClassroom, 241 First Ave N, Minneapolis, MN 55401 *Tel:* 612-332-3344 *Toll Free Tel:* 800-328-4929 *Fax:* 612-332-7615 *Toll Free Fax:* 800-332-1132 *E-mail:* info@lernerbooks.com *Web Site:* www.lernerbooks.com, pg 153

LernerSports, 241 First Ave N, Minneapolis, MN 55401 *Tel:* 612-332-3344 *Toll Free Tel:* 800-328-4929 *Fax:* 612-332-7615 *Toll Free Fax:* 800-332-1132 *E-mail:* info@lernerbooks.com *Web Site:* www.lernerbooks.com, pg 153

The Lescher Agency Inc, 47 E 19 St, New York, NY 10003 *Tel:* 212-529-1790 *Fax:* 212-529-2716, pg 640

Lescher & Lescher Ltd, 47 E 19 St, New York, NY 10003 *Tel:* 212-529-1790 *Fax:* 212-529-2716, pg 640

Lessiter Publications, PO Box 624, Brookfield, WI 53008-0624 *Tel:* 262-782-4480 *Fax:* 262-782-1252 *E-mail:* lessiter@lesspub.com *Web Site:* www.lesspub.com, pg 153

The Letter People®, 61 Mattatuck Heights Rd, Waterbury, CT 06705 *Tel:* 203-756-6562 *Toll Free Tel:* 800-227-9120; 800-874-0029 *Fax:* 203-756-2895 *Toll Free Fax:* 800-737-3322 *Web Site:* letterpeople.com, pg 153

LeveePressTwo, c/o Bolding, 330 Ft Pickens Rd, No 11A, Pensacola Beach, FL 32561 *Tel:* 850-934-1357 *Fax:* 850-932-1588 *E-mail:* HBOLD@worldnet.att.net *Web Site:* www.LeveeFiction.com, pg 572

Fenia & Yaakov Leviant Memorial Prize in Yiddish Culture, 26 Broadway, 3rd fl, New York, NY 10004-1789 *Tel:* 646-576-5141 *Fax:* 646-458-0030 *E-mail:* awards@mla.org *Web Site:* www.mla.org, pg 784

Harry Levin Prize, University of Texas, Program in Comparative Literature, One University Sta B5003, Austin, TX 78712-0196 *Tel:* 512-471-8020 *E-mail:* info@acla.org *Web Site:* www.acla.org, pg 784

Levine-Greenberg Literary Agency Inc, 307 Seventh Ave, Suite 1906, New York, NY 10001 *Tel:* 212-337-0934 *Fax:* 212-337-0948 *Web Site:* www.levinegreenberg.com, pg 640

Levinson Prize, 1030 N Clark St, Suite 420, Chicago, IL 60610 *Tel:* 312-787-7070 *Fax:* 312-787-6650 *E-mail:* poetry@poetrymagazine.org *Web Site:* www.poetrymagazine.org, pg 784

Lexington Books, 4501 Forbes Blvd, Lanham, MD 20706 *Tel:* 301-459-3366 *Fax:* 301-429-5748 *Web Site:* www.lexingtonbooks.com, pg 153

LexisNexis®, 701 E Water St, Charlottesville, VA 22902 *Tel:* 434-972-7600 *Toll Free Tel:* 800-446-3410; 800-828-8341 (orders) *E-mail:* customer.support@lexisnexis.com *Web Site:* www.lexisnexis.com, pg 153

LexisNexis Academic & Library Solutions, 7500 Old Georgetown Rd, Suite 1300, Bethesda, MD 20814-3389 *Tel:* 301-654-1550 *Toll Free Tel:* 800-638-8380 *Fax:* 301-654-4033; 301-657-3203 (sales) *E-mail:* academicinfo@lexisnexis.com *Web Site:* www.lexisnexis.com/academic, pg 153

LexisNexis Canada, 123 Commerce Valley Dr E, Suite 700, Markham, ON L3T 7W8, Canada *Tel:* 905-479-2665 *Toll Free Tel:* 800-668-6481 *Fax:* 905-479-2826 *Toll Free Fax:* 800-461-3275 *E-mail:* orders@lexisnexis.ca *Web Site:* www.lexisnexis.ca, pg 552

Leyerle Publications, 28 Stanley St, Mount Morris, NY 14510 *Tel:* 585-658-2193 *Fax:* 585-658-3298 *Web Site:* www.leyerlepublications.com, pg 153

Liberty Fund Inc, 8335 Allison Pointe Trail, Suite 300, Indianapolis, IN 46250-1684 *Tel:* 317-842-0880 *Toll Free Tel:* 800-955-8335 *Fax:* 317-579-6060 *E-mail:* books@libertyfund.org *Web Site:* www.libertyfund.org, pg 153

Libra Publishers Inc, 3089-C Clairemont Dr, PMB 383, San Diego, CA 92117 *Tel:* 858-571-1414 *Fax:* 858-571-1414, pg 154

Libraries Unlimited, 88 Post Rd W, Westport, CT 06881 *Toll Free Tel:* 800-225-5800 *Fax:* 203-222-1502; 603-431-2214 (orders) *E-mail:* lu-books@lu.com *Web Site:* www.lu.com, pg 154

Library & Archives Canada, 395 Wellington St, Ottawa, ON K1A 0N4, Canada *Tel:* 613-995-7969 (Publications); 613-996-5115 (General Inquiries); 613-992-6969 (TTY) *Toll Free Tel:* 866-578-7777 (Canada only); 866-299-1699 (Canada only) *Fax:* 613-991-9871 (Publications); 613-996-5115 (General Inquiries) *E-mail:* distribution@lac-bac.gc.ca; reference@lac-bac.gc.ca *Web Site:* www.collectionscanada.ca, pg 690

Library Association of Alberta, 80 Baker Crescent NW, Calgary, AB T2L 1R4, Canada *Tel:* 403-284-5818 *Toll Free Tel:* 877-522-5550 *Fax:* 403-282-6646 *Web Site:* www.laa.ab.ca, pg 690

Library Binding Institute, 70 E Lake, Suite 300, Chicago, IL 60601 *Tel:* 312-704-5020 *Fax:* 312-704-5025 *E-mail:* info@lbibinders.org *Web Site:* www.lbibinders.org, pg 690

The Library of America, 14 E 60 St, New York, NY 10022 *Tel:* 212-308-3360 *Fax:* 212-750-8352 *E-mail:* info@loa.org *Web Site:* www.loa.org; loaacademic.org, pg 154

Library of Virginia, 800 E Broad St, Richmond, VA 23219-8000 *Tel:* 804-692-3999 *Fax:* 804-692-3736 *Web Site:* www.lva.lib.va.us, pg 154

Lidec Inc, 4350 Ave de l'Hotel-de-Ville, Montreal, PQ H2W 2H5, Canada *Tel:* 514-843-5991 *Toll Free Tel:* 800-350-5991 (Canada Only) *Fax:* 514-843-5252 *E-mail:* lidec@lidec.qc.ca *Web Site:* www.lidec.qc.ca, pg 552

Robert Lieberman Agency, 400 Nelson Rd, Ithaca, NY 14850-9440 *Tel:* 607-273-8801 *Web Site:* www.people.cornell.edu/pages/RHL10/, pg 640

Mary Ann Liebert Inc, 2 Madison Ave, Larchmont, NY 10538 *Tel:* 914-834-3100 *Toll Free Tel:* 800-654-3237 *Fax:* 914-834-3771 *Web Site:* www.mliebert.com; liebertpub.com, pg 154

Life Cycle Books, LPO Box 1008, Niagara Falls, NY 14304-1008 *Tel:* 416-690-5860 *Toll Free Tel:* 800-214-5849 *Fax:* 416-690-8532 *E-mail:* orders@lifecyclebooks.com *Web Site:* www.lifecyclebooks.com, pg 154

Life Cycle Books Ltd, 421 Nugget Ave, Unit 8, Toronto, ON M1S 4L8, Canada *Tel:* 416-690-5860 *Toll Free Tel:* 866-880-5860 *Fax:* 416-690-8532 *Toll Free Fax:* 866-690-8532 *E-mail:* orders@lifecyclebooks.com *Web Site:* www.lifecyclebooks.com, pg 552

LifeQuest, 6404 S Calhoun St, Fort Wayne, IN 46807 *Toll Free Tel:* 800-774-3360 *E-mail:* dadoftia@aol.com, pg 154

Light-Beams Publishing, 10 Toon Lane, Lee, NH 03824 *Tel:* 603-659-1300 *Toll Free Tel:* 800-397-7641 *Fax:* 603-659-3399 *Web Site:* www.light-beams.com, pg 154

The Light Inc, 26 Worlds Fair Dr, Unit C, Somerset, NJ 08873 *Tel:* 732-868-0210 *Fax:* 732-868-0211 *E-mail:* info@thelightinc.com *Web Site:* www.thelightinc.com, pg 154

Light Technology Publishing, 4030 E Huntington Dr, Flagstaff, AZ 86004 *Tel:* 928-526-1345 *Toll Free Tel:* 800-450-0985 *Fax:* 928-714-1132 *E-mail:* publishing@lighttechnology.net, pg 154

LightSpeed Communications, 1240 Kroucher Dr, Bartonsville, PA 18321 *Tel:* 570-629-3495 *Fax:* 570-629-6252, pg 604

Ligonier Valley Writers Conference, PO Box B, Ligonier, PA 15658-1602 *Tel:* 724-537-3341 *Fax:* 724-537-0482 *E-mail:* sarshi@wpa.net, pg 744

Liguori Publications, One Liguori Dr, Liguori, MO 63057-9999 *Tel:* 636-464-2500 *Toll Free Tel:* 800-464-2555 *Fax:* 636-464-8449 *Web Site:* www.liguori.org, pg 154

The Ruth Lilly Poetry Prize, 1030 N Clark St, Suite 420, Chicago, IL 60610 *Tel:* 312-787-7070 *Fax:* 312-787-6650 *E-mail:* poetry@poetrymagazine.org *Web Site:* www.poetrymagazine.org, pg 784

Lilmur Publishing, 147 Brooke Ave, Toronto, ON M5M 2K3, Canada *Tel:* 416-486-0145 *Fax:* 416-486-5380, pg 552

Limelight Editions, 512 Newark Pompton Tpke, Pompton Plains, NJ 07444 *Tel:* 973-835-6375; 908-788-5753 (orders only) *Fax:* 973-835-6504; 908-237-2407 (orders only) *E-mail:* info@limelighteditions.com *Web Site:* www.limelighteditions.com, pg 155

Limulus Books Inc, 13742 Callington Dr, Wellington, FL 33414-8579 *Tel:* 561-793-3010 *Fax:* 561-793-0460, pg 155

Ray Lincoln Literary Agency, Elkins Park House, Suite 107-B, 7900 Old York Rd, Elkins Park, PA 19027 *Tel:* 215-635-0827 *Fax:* 215-782-8019, pg 640

Linden Publishing Company Inc, 2006 S Mary, Fresno, CA 93721 *Tel:* 559-233-6633 *Toll Free Tel:* 800-345-4447 (orders only) *Fax:* 559-233-6953 *Web Site:* lindenpub.com, pg 155

Lindisfarne Books, PO Box 58, Hudson, NY 12534 *Tel:* 413-528-8233 *Toll Free Tel:* 800-856-8664 (orders) *Fax:* 413-528-8826; 703-661-1501 (orders) *E-mail:* service@lindisfarne.com *Web Site:* www.lindisfarne.org, pg 155

Linguistic Society of America, 1325 18 St NW, Suite 211, Washington, DC 20036-6501 *Tel:* 202-835-1714 *Fax:* 202-835-1717 *E-mail:* lsa@lsadc.org *Web Site:* www.lsadc.org, pg 690

LinguiSystems Inc, 3100 Fourth Ave, East Moline, IL 61244 *Tel:* 309-755-2300 *Toll Free Tel:* 800-776-4332 *Fax:* 309-755-2377 *E-mail:* service@linguisystems.com *Web Site:* www.linguisystems.com, pg 155

Andrew S Linick PhD, The Copyologist®, Linick Bldg, 7 Putter Lane, Middle Island, NY 11953 *Tel:* 631-924-8555 *Fax:* 631-924-3890 *E-mail:* linickgrp@att.net *Web Site:* www.lgroup.addr.com, pg 604

The Linick Group Inc, Linick Bldg, 7 Putter Lane, Middle Island, NY 11953 *Tel:* 631-924-3888 *Fax:* 631-924-3890 *E-mail:* linickgrp@att.net *Web Site:* www.lgroup.addr.com, pg 155

Linns Stamp News-Ancillary Division, PO Box 29, Sidney, OH 45365-0029 Tel: 937-498-0801 (ext 197) Fax: 937-498-0807 Toll Free Fax: 800-488-5349 E-mail: cuserv@amospress.com Web Site: www. amosadvantage.com, pg 155

Linworth Publishing Inc, 480 E Wilson Bridge Rd, Suite L, Worthington, OH 43085-2372 Tel: 614-436-7107 Toll Free Tel: 800-786-5017 Fax: 614-436-9490 E-mail: linworth@linworthpublishing.com Web Site: www.linworth.com, pg 155

Elliot Linzer, 43-05 Crommelin St, Flushing, NY 11355 Tel: 718-353-1261 Fax: 208-279-5936 E-mail: elinzer@juno.com, pg 605

Lion Books Publisher, 210 Nelson Rd, Scarsdale, NY 10583 Tel: 914-725-2280 Fax: 914-725-3572, pg 155

LionHearted Publishing Inc, PO Box 618, Zephyr Cove, NV 89448-0618 Tel: 775-588-1388 Toll Free Tel: 888-546-6478 Toll Free Fax: 888-546-6478 E-mail: admin@lionhearted.com Web Site: www. lionhearted.com, pg 155

Wendy Lipkind Agency, 120 E 81 St, New York, NY 10028 Tel: 212-628-9653 Fax: 212-585-1306 E-mail: lipkindag@aol.com, pg 640

Joseph W Lippincott Award, 50 E Huron, Chicago, IL 60611 Tel: 312-280-3247 Toll Free Tel: 800-545-2433 (ext 3247) Fax: 312-944-3897 E-mail: awards@ala.org Web Site: www.ala.org, pg 784

Lippincott Williams & Wilkins, 530 Walnut St, 7th fl, Philadelphia, PA 19106 Tel: 215-521-8300 Toll Free Tel: 800-638-3030 (cust serv) Fax: 215-521-8902; 301-824-7390 (cust serv) E-mail: orders@lww.com Web Site: www.lww.com, pg 156

E Trina Lipton, 60 E Eighth St, No 15F, New York, NY 10003 Tel: 212-674-5558 (call first, messages); 212-674-3523 Fax: 212-674-3523 E-mail: trinalipton@ hotmail.com, pg 605

Eli & Gail Liss, 41 Viking Lane, Woodstock, NY 12498 Tel: 845-679-7173 E-mail: lissindex@aol.com, pg 605

Listen & Live Audio Inc, PO Box 817, Roseland, NJ 07068-0817 Tel: 973-781-1444 Toll Free Tel: 800-653-9400 Fax: 973-781-0333 Web Site: www.listenandlive. com, pg 156

LITA/Christian Larew Memorial Scholarship in Library & Information Technology, c/o American Library Association, 50 E Huron St, Chicago, IL 60611 Tel: 312-280-4269 Toll Free Tel: 800-545-2433 Fax: 312-280-3257 E-mail: lita@ala.org Web Site: www.lita.org, pg 784

LITA/LSSI Minority Scholarship in Library & Information Technology, c/o American Library Association, 50 E Huron St, Chicago, IL 60611-2795 Tel: 312-280-4269 Toll Free Tel: 800-545-2433 Fax: 312-280-3257 E-mail: lita@ala.org Web Site: www.lita.org, pg 784

LITA/OCLC Minority Scholarship in Library & Information Technology, c/o American Library Association, 50 E Huron St, Chicago, IL 60611-2795 Tel: 312-280-4269 Toll Free Tel: 800-545-2433 Fax: 312-280-3257 E-mail: lita@ala.org Web Site: www.lita.org, pg 785

LITA/SIRSI Scholarship in Library & Information Technology, c/o American Library Association, 50 E Huron St, Chicago, IL 60611 Tel: 312-280-4269 Toll Free Tel: 800-545-2433 Fax: 312-280-3257 E-mail: lita@ala.org Web Site: www.lita.org, pg 785

Literacy Institute for Education (LIFE) Inc, 84 Woodland Rd, Pleasantville, NY 10570 Tel: 914-741-1322 Fax: 914-741-1324 Web Site: bknelson.com, pg 156

The Literary Agency Ltd, 4942 Morrison Rd, Denver, CO 80219 Tel: 303-936-1978 Toll Free Tel: 800-261-1797 Fax: 303-936-1770 E-mail: peci4942@aol.com Web Site: www.peci.cc, pg 640

Literary & Creative Artists Inc, 3543 Albemarle St NW, Washington, DC 20008-4213 Tel: 202-362-4688 Fax: 202-362-8875 E-mail: query@lcadc.com (no attachments) Web Site: www.lcadc.com, pg 641

Literary Artists Representatives, 575 West End Ave, Suite GRC, New York, NY 10024-2711 Tel: 212-787-3808 Fax: 212-595-2098 E-mail: litartists@aol.com, pg 641

Literary Consultants LLC, 7542 Bear Canyon Rd NE, Albuquerque, NM 87109 Tel: 505-797-9397, pg 605

The Literary Group International, 270 Lafayette St, Suite 1505, New York, NY 10012 Tel: 212-274-1616 Fax: 212-274-9876 Web Site: www.theliterarygroup. com, pg 641

Literary Management Group Inc, 4238 Morriswood Dr, Nashville, TN 37204 Tel: 615-832-7231 Fax: 615-832-7231 Web Site: www.literarymanagementgroup.com; www.brucebarbour.com, pg 641

The Literary Press Group of Canada, 192 Spadina Ave, Suite 501, Toronto, ON M5T 2C2, Canada Tel: 416-483-1321 Fax: 416-483-2510 E-mail: info@lpg.ca Web Site: www.lpg.ca, pg 690

Literary Translation Projects, Nancy Hanks Ctr, 1100 Pennsylvania Ave NW, Rm 720, Washington, DC 20506-0001 Tel: 202-682-5428; 202-682-5034 (Literature Fellowships hotline) Web Site: www.arts. gov, pg 785

Literary Translators' Association of Canada, Concordia University, SB 335, 1455 De Maisonneuve West, Montreal, PQ H3G 1M8, Canada Tel: 514-848-8702 E-mail: info@attlc-ltac.org Web Site: www.attlc-ltac. org, pg 690

Little, Brown and Company Adult Trade Division, 1271 Avenue of the Americas, New York, NY 10020 Tel: 212-522-8700 Fax: 212-522-2067 Web Site: www. twbookmark.com, pg 156

Little, Brown and Company Books for Young Readers, 1271 Avenue of the Americas, New York, NY 10020 Tel: 212-522-8700 Toll Free Tel: 800-759-0190 Fax: 212-522-7997 Web Site: www.twbookmark.com, pg 156

Little Chicago Editorial Services, 154 Natural Tpke, Ripton, VT 05766 Tel: 802-388-9782 Fax: 802-388-6525, pg 605

Littleton-Griswold Prize in American Law & Society, 400 "A" St SE, Washington, DC 20003 Tel: 202-544-2422 Fax: 202-544-8307 E-mail: info@historians.org Web Site: www.historians.org, pg 785

Littleton-Griswold Research Grants, 400 "A" St SE, Washington, DC 20003 Tel: 202-544-2422 Fax: 202-544-8307 E-mail: info@historians.org Web Site: www. historians.org, pg 785

Barbara S Littlewood, 5109 Coney Weston Place, Madison, WI 53711 Tel: 608-273-1631 Fax: 608-273-9478 E-mail: barb_littlewood@compuserve.com, pg 605

Liturgical Press, St John's Abbey, Collegeville, MN 56321 Tel: 320-363-2213 Toll Free Tel: 800-858-5450 Fax: 320-363-3299 Toll Free Fax: 800-445-5899 E-mail: sales@litpress.org Web Site: www.litpress.org, pg 156

Liturgy Training Publications, 1800 N Hermitage Ave, Chicago, IL 60622-1101 Tel: 773-486-8970 Toll Free Tel: 800-933-1800 (US & Canada only) Fax: 773-486-7094 Toll Free Fax: 800-933-7094 (US & Canada only) E-mail: orders@ltp.org Web Site: www.ltp.org, pg 156

LitWest Group LLC, 379 Burning Tree Ct, Half Moon Bay, CA 94019 Web Site: www.litwest.com, pg 641

Livestock Publications Council, 910 Currie St, Fort Worth, TX 76107 Tel: 817-336-1130 Fax: 817-232-4820 Web Site: www.livestockpublications.com, pg 690

Living Language, 1745 Broadway, New York, NY 10019 Tel: 212-572-6148 Toll Free Tel: 800-726-0600 (orders) Fax: 212-940-7400 Toll Free Fax: 800-659-2436 E-mail: livinglanguage@randomhouse.com Web Site: www.livinglanguage.com, pg 157

Living Stream Ministry (LSM), 2431 W La Palima Ave, Anaheim, CA 92801 Tel: 714-991-4681 Fax: 714-991-4685 E-mail: books@lsm.org Web Site: www.lsm.org, pg 157

Livingston Press, University of West Alabama, Sta 22, Livingston, AL 35470 Tel: 205-652-3470 Fax: 205-652-3717 Web Site: www.livingstonpress.uwa.edu, pg 157

Llewellyn Publications, PO Box 64383, St Paul, MN 55164-0383 Tel: 651-291-1970 Toll Free Tel: 800-843-6666 Fax: 651-291-1908 E-mail: lwlpc@llewellyn. com Web Site: www.llewellyn.com, pg 157

The Local History Co, 112 N Woodland Rd, Pittsburgh, PA 15232 Tel: 412-362-2294 Toll Free Tel: 866-362-0789 Fax: 412-362-8192 E-mail: info@ thelocalhistorycompany.com Web Site: www. thelocalhistorycompany.com, pg 157

Local 7's Annual National Poetry Competition, PO Box 2409, Aptos, CA 95001 Tel: 831-784-4960 E-mail: bonnie.thomas@att.net Web Site: home. earthlinl.net/~nwu-local7/, pg 785

Locks Art Publications/Locks Gallery, 600 Washington Sq S, Philadelphia, PA 19106 Tel: 215-629-1000 Fax: 215-629-3868 E-mail: info@locksgallery.com Web Site: www.locksgallery.com, pg 157

Locus Awards, PO Box 13305, Oakland, CA 94661-0305 Tel: 510-339-9196 Fax: 510-339-8144 E-mail: locus@ locusmag.com Web Site: www.locusmag.com, pg 785

The Gerald Loeb Awards, Mullin Management Commons, Suite F-321B, 110 Westwood Plaza, Los Angeles, CA 90095-1481 Tel: 310-206-1877 Fax: 310-825-4479 E-mail: loeb@anderson.ucla.edu Web Site: www.loeb.anderson.ucla.edu, pg 785

Loft-Mentor Series in Poetry & Creative Prose, Open Book, Suite 200, 1011 Washington Ave S, Minneapolis, MN 55415 Tel: 612-215-2575 Fax: 612-215-2576 E-mail: loft@loft.org Web Site: www.loft. org, pg 785

Loft Press Inc, 181 Myra Lane, Fort Valley, VA 22652 Tel: 540-933-6210 Fax: 540-933-6523, pg 157

Auralie Phillips Logan, 42 Rocky Ridge, Cortlandt Manor, NY 10567-6530 Tel: 914-739-3469 Fax: 914-739-3469 E-mail: aplfgcnys@aol.com, pg 605

Wesley Logan Prize in African Diaspora History, 400 "A" St SE, Washington, DC 20003 Tel: 202-544-2422 Fax: 202-544-8307 E-mail: info@historians.org Web Site: www.historians.org, pg 785

Logos Bible Software, 1313 Commercial St, Bellingham, WA 98225-4372 Tel: 360-527-1700 Toll Free Tel: 800-875-6467 Fax: 360-527-1707 E-mail: info@logos.com Web Site: www.logos.com, pg 157

LokiWorks, 813-633 Bay St, Toronto, ON M5G 2G4, Canada Tel: 416-599-4303 Fax: 416-599-4308 E-mail: editor@lokiworks.com Web Site: www. lokiworks.com, pg 605

Lone Eagle Publishing, 1024 N Orange Dr, Los Angeles, CA 90038 Tel: 323-308-3411 Toll Free Tel: 800-815-0503 Fax: 323-468-7689 Web Site: www.hcdonline. com, pg 157

Lone Pine Publishing, 10145 81 Ave, Edmonton, AB T6E 1W9, Canada Tel: 780-433-9333 Toll Free Tel: 800-661-9017 Fax: 780-433-9646 Toll Free Fax: 800-424-7173 E-mail: info@lonepinepublishing. com Web Site: www.lonepinepublishing.com, pg 552

Lonely Planet Publications, 150 Linden St, Oakland, CA 94607 Tel: 510-893-8555 Toll Free Tel: 800-275-8555 (orders) Fax: 510-893-8972 E-mail: info@ lonelyplanet.com Web Site: www.lonelyplanet.com, pg 157

Longman Publishers, 1185 Avenue of the Americas, New York, NY 10036 Tel: 212-782-3300 Fax: 212-782-3311 Web Site: www.ablongman.com, pg 158

Longstreet Press, 325 N Milledge Ave, Athens, GA 30601 Tel: 706-543-5999 Fax: 706-543-5946 Web Site: www.longstreetpress.net, pg 158

Loompanics Unlimited, PO Box 1197, Port Townsend, WA 98368-0997 Tel: 360-385-5087 Toll Free Tel: 800-380-2230 (orders only) Fax: 360-385-7785 E-mail: editorial@loompanics.com; service@ loompanics.com Web Site: www.loompanics.com, pg 158

Looseleaf Law Publications Inc, 43-08 162 St, Flushing, NY 11358 *Tel:* 718-359-5559 *Toll Free Tel:* 800-647-5547 *Fax:* 718-539-0941 *E-mail:* llawpub@erols.com *Web Site:* www.LooseleafLaw.com, pg 158

Judy Lopez Memorial Award For Children's Literature, PO Box 7034, Beverly Hills, CA 90212-0034 *Tel:* 310-474-9917 *Fax:* 310-474-6436, pg 786

Lord John Press, 19073 Los Alimos St, Northridge, CA 91326 *Tel:* 818-363-6621 *Fax:* 818-366-6674 *Web Site:* lordjohnpress.com; lordjohnpress.net, pg 158

Lorenz Educational Publishers, PO Box 146340, Chicago, IL 60614-6340 *Tel:* 773-929-9847 *Fax:* 501-423-4158 *Web Site:* www.shkspr.com, pg 158

James Lorimer & Co Ltd, Publishers, 35 Britain St, 3rd fl, Toronto, ON M5A 1R7, Canada *Tel:* 416-362-4762 *Fax:* 416-362-3939 *E-mail:* info@lorimer.ca *Web Site:* www.lorimer.ca, pg 553

Los Angeles Literary Associates, 6324 Tahoe Dr, Los Angeles, CA 90068-1654 *Tel:* 323-464-6444 *Fax:* 323-464-6444, pg 641

Los Angeles Times Book Prizes, 202 W First St, 6th fl, Los Angeles, CA 90012 *Tel:* 213-237-5775 *Fax:* 213-346-3599 *Web Site:* www.latimes.com/bookprizes, pg 786

Lost Classics Book Co, PO Box 3429, Lake Wales, FL 33859-3429 *Tel:* 863-676-1920 *Toll Free Tel:* 800-283-3572 (wholesale orders); 888-211-2665 (educational) *Fax:* 863-676-1707 *E-mail:* mgeditor@lostclassicsbooks.com *Web Site:* www.lostclassicsbooks.com (retail site); www.lcbcbooks.com (wholesale site), pg 158

Lost Horse Press, 105 Lost Horse Lane, Sandpoint, ID 83864 *Tel:* 208-255-4410 *Fax:* 208-255-1560 *E-mail:* losthorsepress@mindspring.com *Web Site:* losthorsepress.org, pg 159

Lott Representatives, 11 E 47 St, 6th fl, New York, NY 10017 *Tel:* 212-755-5737, pg 666

Lotus Press, PO Box 325, Twin Lakes, WI 53181-0325 *Tel:* 262-889-8561 *Toll Free Tel:* 800-824-6396 (orders only) *Fax:* 262-889-8591 *E-mail:* lotuspress@lotuspress.com *Web Site:* www.lotuspress.com, pg 159

Louisiana Literature Poetry Prize, Southeastern Louisiana University, SLU Box 10792, Hammond, LA 70402 *Tel:* 985-549-5022 *E-mail:* lalit@selu.edu *Web Site:* www.louisianaliterature.org, pg 786

Louisiana State University Press, PO Box 25053, Baton Rouge, LA 70894-5053 *Tel:* 225-578-6294 *Toll Free Tel:* 800-861-3477 *Fax:* 225-578-6461 *Toll Free Fax:* 800-305-4416 *E-mail:* lsupress@lsu.edu *Web Site:* www.lsu.edu/guests/lsupress, pg 159

Louisiana State University, Writing Program, Dept of English, Baton Rouge, LA 70803 *Tel:* 225-578-3040 *Fax:* 225-578-4129 *Web Site:* www.lsu.edu, pg 752

Louisville Grawemeyer Award in Religion, 1044 Alta Vista Rd, Louisville, KY 40205-1798 *Tel:* 502-895-3411 *Toll Free Tel:* 800-264-1839 *Fax:* 502-894-2286 *E-mail:* grawemeyer@lpts.edu *Web Site:* www.grawemeyer.org, pg 786

Le Loup de Gouttiere Inc, 347 rue Sainte Paul, Quebec City, PQ G1K 3X1, Canada *Tel:* 418-694-2224 *Fax:* 418-694-2225 *E-mail:* loupgout@videotron.ca, pg 553

Love Creek Annual Short Play Festival, 2144 45 Ave, Long Island City, NY 11101 *Tel:* 212-714-9686 *E-mail:* creekread@aol.com, pg 786

Love Creek Mini Festivals, 2144 45 Ave, Long Island City, NY 11101 *Tel:* 212-714-9686 *E-mail:* creekread@aol.com, pg 786

Nancy Love Literary Agency, 250 E 65 St, Suite 4A, New York, NY 10021 *Tel:* 212-980-3499 *Fax:* 212-308-6405, pg 641

Love Publishing Co, 9101 E Kenyon Ave, Suite 2200, Denver, CO 80237 *Tel:* 303-221-7333 *Fax:* 303-221-7444 *E-mail:* lpc@lovepublishing.com *Web Site:* www.lovepublishing.com, pg 159

James Russell Lowell Prize, 26 Broadway, 3rd fl, New York, NY 10004-1789 *Tel:* 646-576-5141 *Fax:* 646-458-0030 *E-mail:* awards@mla.org *Web Site:* www.mla.org, pg 786

Lowenstein-Yost Associates Inc, 121 W 27 St, Suite 601, New York, NY 10001 *Tel:* 212-206-1630 *Fax:* 212-727-0280 *Web Site:* www.lowensteinyost.com, pg 641

Pat Lowther Memorial Award, 920 Yonge St, Suite 608, Toronto, ON M4W 3C7, Canada *Tel:* 416-504-1657 *Fax:* 416-504-0096 *E-mail:* info@poets.ca *Web Site:* www.poets.ca, pg 786

Loyola Press, 3441 N Ashland Ave, Chicago, IL 60657 *Tel:* 773-281-1818; 773-244-4429 *Toll Free Tel:* 800-621-1008 *Fax:* 773-281-0555; 773-281-0152 (trade) *E-mail:* editorial@loydapress.com *Web Site:* www.loyolapress.org, pg 159

LPD Press, 925 Salamanca NW, Albuquerque, NM 87107-5647 *Tel:* 505-344-9382 *Fax:* 505-345-5129 *E-mail:* info@nmsantos.com *Web Site:* www.nmsantos.com, pg 159

LRP Publications, 360 Hiatt Dr, Palm Beach Gardens, FL 33418 *Tel:* 215-784-0860 *Toll Free Tel:* 800-341-7874 *Fax:* 215-784-9639 *E-mail:* custserve@lrp.com *Web Site:* www.lrp.com, pg 159

LRS, 14214 S Figueroa St, Los Angeles, CA 90061-1034 *Tel:* 310-354-2610 *Toll Free Tel:* 800-255-5002 *Fax:* 310-354-2601 *E-mail:* lrsprint@aol.com *Web Site:* lrs-largeprint.com, pg 159

LTDBooks, 200 N Service Rd W, Unit 1, Suite 301, Oakville, ON L6M 2Y1, Canada *Tel:* 905-847-6060 *Fax:* 905-847-6060 *E-mail:* publisher@ltdbooks.com *Web Site:* www.ltdbooks.com, pg 553

Lucent Books Inc, 15822 Bernardo Center Dr, Suite C, San Diego, CA 92127 *Tel:* 858-485-7424 *Fax:* 858-485-9549 *E-mail:* info@gale.com *Web Site:* www.gale.com/lucent, pg 159

Lucky Press LLC, 126 S Maple St, Lancaster, OH 43130 *Tel:* 740-689-2950 (orders & editorial) *Fax:* 740-689-2951 (orders & editorial) *E-mail:* books@luckypress.com *Web Site:* www.luckypress.com, pg 160

Jeremiah Ludington Award, PO Box 1399, East Hampton, NY 11937-0709 *Tel:* 631-329-3315 *E-mail:* edupaperback@aol.com, pg 786

Ludwig von Mises Institute, 518 W Magnolia Ave, Auburn, AL 36832 *Tel:* 334-321-2100 *Fax:* 334-321-2119 *Web Site:* www.mises.org, pg 160

Lugus Publications, 48 Falcon St, Toronto, ON M4S 2P5, Canada *Tel:* 416-322-5113 *Fax:* 416-484-9512 *E-mail:* cymro43@hotmail.com, pg 553

Hugh J Luke Award, University of Nebraska, 201 Andrews Hall, Lincoln, NE 68588 *Tel:* 402-472-0911 *E-mail:* kgrey2@unl.edu *Web Site:* www.unl.edu/schooner/psmain.htm, pg 786

Lukeman Literary Management Ltd, 101 N Seventh St, Brooklyn, NY 11211 *Tel:* 718-599-8988 *Web Site:* www.lukeman.com, pg 641

Luna Bisonte Prods, 137 Leland Ave, Columbus, OH 43214 *Tel:* 614-846-4126, pg 160

Lyceum Books Inc, 5758 S Blackstone Ave, Chicago, IL 60637 *Tel:* 773-643-1902 *Fax:* 773-643-1903 *E-mail:* lyceum@lyceumbooks.com *Web Site:* www.lyceumbooks.com, pg 160

Lyndon B Johnson School of Public Affairs, University of Texas Austin, 2316 Red River St, Austin, TX 78705 *Tel:* 512-471-4218 *Fax:* 512-475-8867 *E-mail:* pubsinfo@uts.cc.utexas.edu *Web Site:* www.utexas.edu/lbj/pubs/, pg 160

Lynx House Press, 420 W 24 St, Spokane, WA 99203 *Tel:* 509-624-4894 *Fax:* 509-623-4238, pg 160

Western Literature Association: The Thomas J Lyon Book Award, 3200 Old Main Hill, College of Humanities, Arts & Social Sciences, Utah State University, Logan, UT 84322-0735 *Tel:* 435-797-3855 *Fax:* 435-797-4099 *Web Site:* www.usu.edu/westlit/tjlyonbookaward.html, pg 786

The Lyons Press, 246 Goose Lane, Guilford, CT 06437 *Tel:* 203-458-4500 *Toll Free Tel:* 800-243-0495 *Fax:* 203-458-4668 *Web Site:* www.lyonspress.com; www.globepequot.com, pg 160

Lyric Poetry Award, 15 Gramercy Park, New York, NY 10003 *Tel:* 212-254-9628 *Fax:* 212-673-2352 *Web Site:* www.poetrysociety.org, pg 786

Lyric Poetry Prizes, 65 Vermont, Rte 15, Jericho, VT 05465 *Tel:* 802-899-3993 *Fax:* 802-899-3993, pg 786

M R T S, PO Box 874402, Tempe, AZ 85287-4402 *Tel:* 480-727-6503 *Toll Free Tel:* 800-666-2211 *Fax:* 480-727-6505 *Toll Free Fax:* 800-688-2877 *E-mail:* mrts@asu.edu *Web Site:* www.asu.edu/clas/acmrs/mrts, pg 160

M S G-Haskell House Publishers Ltd, PO Box 190420, Brooklyn, NY 11219-0420 *Tel:* 718-435-7878 *Fax:* 718-633-7050, pg 160

Donald Maass Literary Agency, 160 W 95 St, Suite 1-B, New York, NY 10025 *Tel:* 212-866-8200 *Fax:* 212-866-8181 *E-mail:* dmla@mindspring.com, pg 641

MacAdam/Cage Publishing Inc, 155 Sansome St, Suite 550, San Francisco, CA 94104 *Tel:* 415-986-7502 *Toll Free Tel:* 866-986-7470 *Fax:* 415-986-7414 *E-mail:* info@macadamcage.com *Web Site:* www.macadamcage.com, pg 160

Macalester Park Publishing Co, 7317 Cahill Rd, Minneapolis, MN 55439-2067 *Tel:* 952-562-1234 *Toll Free Tel:* 800-407-9078 *Fax:* 952-941-3010 *E-mail:* publisher@mcchronicle.com *Web Site:* www.mcchronicle.com, pg 161

Gina Maccoby Literary Agency, PO Box 60, Chappaqua, NY 10514-0060 *Tel:* 914-238-5630 *Fax:* 914-238-5239, pg 642

Sir John A MacDonald Prize, 395 Wellington St, Ottawa, ON K1A 0N3, Canada *Tel:* 613-233-7885 *Fax:* 613-567-3110 *E-mail:* cha-shc@archives.ca *Web Site:* www.cha-shc.ca, pg 787

The MacDowell Colony, 100 High St, Peterborough, NH 03458 *Tel:* 603-924-3886 *Fax:* 603-924-9142 *E-mail:* info@macdowellcolony.org *Web Site:* www.macdowellcolony.org, pg 787

Donald MacLaren & Associates, 2021 46 St, Astoria, NY 11105 *Tel:* 718-932-7720 *Fax:* 718-932-7720, pg 605

Macmillan/McGraw-Hill, 2 Penn Plaza, New York, NY 10121 *Tel:* 212-904-2000, pg 161

Macmillan Reference USA™, 12 Lunar Dr, Woodbridge, CT 06525 *Tel:* 203-397-2600 *Toll Free Tel:* 800-444-0799 *Fax:* 203-392-3095 *Web Site:* www.gale.com, pg 161

Madison House Publishers, 4501 Forbes Blvd, Lanham, MD 20706 *Tel:* 301-459-3366 *Toll Free Tel:* 800-462-6420 *Fax:* 301-429-5748 *Web Site:* www.rowmanlittlefield.com, pg 161

Madison Press Books, 1000 Yonge St, Toronto, ON M4W 2K2, Canada *Tel:* 416-923-5027 *Fax:* 416-923-9708 *E-mail:* info@madisonpressbooks.com *Web Site:* www.madisonpressbooks.com, pg 553

Madison Square Press, 10 E 23 St, New York, NY 10010 *Tel:* 212-505-0950 *Fax:* 212-979-2207, pg 161

The Robert Madsen Literary Agency, 1331 E 34 St, Suite 1, Oakland, CA 94602 *Tel:* 510-223-2090, pg 642

Magazine Merit Awards, 8271 Beverly Blvd, Los Angeles, CA 90048 *Tel:* 323-782-1010 *Fax:* 323-782-1892 *E-mail:* membership@scbwi.org *Web Site:* www.scbwi.org, pg 787

The Magazine of the Year Award, The Lincoln Bldg, 60 E 42 St, Suite 721, New York, NY 10165 *Tel:* 212-983-8585 *Fax:* 212-983-2308 *E-mail:* mail@spd.org *Web Site:* www.spd.org, pg 787

Magazine Publishers of America, 810 Seventh Ave, New York, NY 10019 *Tel:* 212-872-3700 *Fax:* 212-888-4217 *E-mail:* infocenter@magazine.org *Web Site:* www.magazine.org, pg 690

Mage Publishers Inc, 1032 29 St NW, Washington, DC 20007 *Tel:* 202-342-1642 *Toll Free Tel:* 800-962-0922 *Fax:* 202-342-9269 *E-mail:* info@mage.com *Web Site:* www.mage.com, pg 161

Magick Mirror Communications, 511 Avenue of the Americas, PMB 173, New York, NY 10011-8436 *Tel:* 212-727-0002; 212-208-2951 (voice mail) *Toll Free Tel:* 800-356-6796 *Fax:* 212-208-2951 *E-mail:* MagickMirr@aol.com; Magickorders@aol. com *Web Site:* magickmirror.com, pg 572

The Magni Co, 7106 Wellington Point Rd, McKinney, TX 75070 *Tel:* 972-540-2050 *Fax:* 972-540-1057 *E-mail:* sales@magnico.com; info@magnico.com *Web Site:* www.magnico.com, pg 161

Maharishi University of Management Press, 1000 N Fourth St, Dept 1155, Fairfield, IA 52557-1155 *Tel:* 641-472-1101 *Toll Free Tel:* 800-831-6523 *Fax:* 641-472-1122 *E-mail:* mumpress@mum.edu *Web Site:* www.mumpress.com, pg 161

Maine Writers & Publishers Alliance, 1326 Washington St, Bath, ME 04530 *Tel:* 207-386-1400 *Fax:* 207-386-1401 *Web Site:* www.mainewriters.org, pg 690

Maisonneuve Press, PO Box 2980, Washington, DC 20013-2980 *Tel:* 301-277-7505 *Fax:* 301-277-2467 *Web Site:* www.maisonneuvepress.com, pg 161

J Russell Major Prize, 400 "A" St SE, Washington, DC 20003 *Tel:* 202-544-2422 *Fax:* 202-544-8307 *E-mail:* info@historians.org *Web Site:* www.historians. org, pg 787

Makeready Inc, 233 W 77 St, New York, NY 10024 *Tel:* 212-595-5083, pg 605

Management Advisory Services & Publications (MASP), PO Box 81151, Wellesley Hills, MA 02481-0001 *Tel:* 781-235-2895 *Fax:* 781-235-5446 *Web Site:* www. masp.com, pg 161

Management Concepts Inc, 8230 Leesburg Pike, Suite 800, Vienna, VA 22182 *Tel:* 703-790-9595 *Fax:* 703-790-1930 *E-mail:* publications@managementconcepts. com *Web Site:* www.managementconcepts.com, pg 161

Management Sciences for Health, 165 Allandale Rd, Boston, MA 02130-3400 *Tel:* 617-524-7799 *Fax:* 617-524-2825 *E-mail:* bookstore@msh.org *Web Site:* www. msh.org, pg 162

Manatee Publishing, 176 Fairview Ave, Cocoa, FL 32927 *Tel:* 321-632-2932 *Fax:* 321-632-2935 *E-mail:* fseasons@bellsouth.net, pg 162

Mandala Publishing, 17 Paul Dr, San Rafael, CA 94903 *Tel:* 415-883-4055 *Toll Free Tel:* 800-688-2218 (orders only) *Fax:* 415-884-0500 *E-mail:* mandala@mandala. org *Web Site:* www.mandala.org, pg 162

Manhattan Publishing Co, PO Box 850, Croton-on-Hudson, NY 10520-0850 *Tel:* 914-271-5194 *Toll Free Tel:* 888-686-7066 *Fax:* 914-271-5856 *Web Site:* www. manhattanpublishing.com, pg 162

Manic D Press, 250 Banks St, San Francisco, CA 94110 *Tel:* 415-648-8288 *Fax:* 415-648-8288 *E-mail:* info@ manicdpress.com *Web Site:* www.manicdpress.com, pg 162

Manitoba Arts Council, 525-93 Lombard Ave, Winnipeg, MB R3B 3B1, Canada *Tel:* 204-945-2237 *Toll Free Tel:* 866-994-2787 (in Manitoba) *Fax:* 204-945-5925 *E-mail:* info@artscouncil.mb.ca *Web Site:* www. artscouncil.mb.ca, pg 690

Manitoba Library Association, 600 100 Arthur St, Suite 416, Winnipeg, MB R3B 1H3, Canada *Tel:* 204-943-4567 *Fax:* 204-942-1555 *E-mail:* info@mla.mb.ca; mla@uwinnipeg.ca *Web Site:* www.mla.mb.ca, pg 690

The Manitoba Writers' Guild Inc, 206-100 Arthur St, Winnipeg, MB R3B 1H3, Canada *Tel:* 204-942-6134 *Toll Free Tel:* 888-637-5802 *Fax:* 204-942-5754 *E-mail:* info@mbwriter.mb.ca *Web Site:* www. mbwriter.mb.ca, pg 690

Carol Mann Agency, 55 Fifth Ave, New York, NY 10003 *Tel:* 212-206-5635 *Fax:* 212-675-4809, pg 642

Margaret Mann Citation, 50 E Huron St, Chicago, IL 60611 *Tel:* 312-280-5037 *Toll Free Tel:* 800-545-2433 *Fax:* 312-944-6131 *Web Site:* www.ala.org/alcts, pg 787

Phyllis Manner, 17 Springdale Rd, New Rochelle, NY 10804 *Tel:* 914-834-4707 *Fax:* 914-834-4707 *E-mail:* pmanner@aol.com, pg 605

Manning Publications Co, 209 Bruce Park Ave, Greenwich, CT 06830 *Tel:* 203-629-2211 *Fax:* 203-661-9018 *E-mail:* orders@manning.com *Web Site:* www.manning.com, pg 162

Freya Manston Associates Inc, 145 W 58 St, New York, NY 10019 *Tel:* 212-247-3075, pg 642

Manus & Associates Literary Agency Inc, 445 Park Ave, New York, NY 10022 *Tel:* 650-470-5151 (CA) *Fax:* 650-470-5159 (CA) *E-mail:* manuslit@manuslit. com *Web Site:* www.manuslit.com, pg 642

Many Voices Residencies, 2301 Franklin Ave E, Minneapolis, MN 55406 *Tel:* 612-332-7481 *Fax:* 612-332-6037 *E-mail:* info@pwcenter.org *Web Site:* www. pwcenter.org, pg 787

MapEasy Inc, PO Box 80, Wainscotte, NY 11975-0080 *Tel:* 631-537-6213 *Toll Free Tel:* 888-627-3279 *Fax:* 631-537-4541 *E-mail:* info@mapeasy.com *Web Site:* www.mapeasy.com, pg 162

Maple Tree Press Inc, 51 Front St E, Suite 200, Toronto, ON M5E 1B3, Canada *Tel:* 416-304-0702 *Fax:* 416-304-0525 *E-mail:* info@mapletreepress.com *Web Site:* www.mapletreepress.com, pg 553

Mapletree Publishing Co, 6233 Harvard Lane, Highlands Ranch, CO 80130-3773 *Tel:* 303-791-9024 *Toll Free Tel:* 800-537-0414 *Fax:* 303-791-9028 *E-mail:* mail@mapletreepublishing.com *Web Site:* www.mapletreepublishing.com, pg 163

MAR*CO Products Inc, 1443 Old York Rd, Warminster, PA 18974 *Tel:* 215-956-0313 *Toll Free Tel:* 800-448-2197 *Fax:* 215-956-9041 *E-mail:* marcoproducts@ comcast.net *Web Site:* www.marcoproducts.com; www. store.yahoo.com/marcoproducts, pg 163

Marathon Press, PO Box 407, Norfolk, NE 68702-0407 *Tel:* 402-371-5040 *Toll Free Tel:* 800-228-0629 *Fax:* 402-371-9382 *Web Site:* www.marathonpress. com, pg 163

MARC Publications, 800 W Chestnut Ave, Monrovia, CA 91016-3198 *Tel:* 626-303-8811 *Toll Free Tel:* 800-777-7752 (US only) *Fax:* 626-301-7786 *E-mail:* marcpubs@wvi.org *Web Site:* www. worldvisionresources.com, pg 163

March Street Press, 3413 Wilshire Dr, Greensboro, NC 27408 *Tel:* 336-282-9754 *Fax:* 336-282-9754 *Web Site:* www.marchstreetpress.com, pg 163

March Tenth Inc, 4 Myrtle St, Haworth, NJ 07641 *Tel:* 201-387-6551 *Fax:* 201-387-6552, pg 642

Denise Marcil Literary Agency Inc, 156 Fifth Ave, Suite 625, New York, NY 10010 *Tel:* 212-337-3402 *Fax:* 212-727-2688, pg 642

Danny Marcus Word Worker, 62 Washington St, Suite 2, Marblehead, MA 01945-3553 *Tel:* 781-631-3886 *Fax:* 781-631-3886 *E-mail:* danny@thecia.net, pg 605

Marian Library Medal, 300 College Park, Dayton, OH 45469-1390 *Tel:* 937-229-4214 *Fax:* 937-229-4258 *Web Site:* www.udayton.edu, pg 787

The Marilyn Hall Award, PO Box 39729, Los Angeles, CA 90039-0729, pg 787

Marine Education Textbooks Inc, 124 N Van Ave, Houma, LA 70363-5895 *Tel:* 985-879-3866 *Fax:* 985-879-3911 *E-mail:* namenet@triparish.net *Web Site:* www.marineeducationtextbooks.com, pg 163

Marine Techniques Publishing Inc, 126 Western Ave, Suite 266, Augusta, ME 04330-7252 *Tel:* 207-622-7984 *Fax:* 207-621-0821 *E-mail:* promariner@ midmaine.com; marinetechniques@midmaine. com *Web Site:* www.groups.yahoo.com/group/ marinetechniquespublishing, pg 163

Marion Street Press, 106 S Oak Park Ave, Oak Park, IL 60302 *Tel:* 708-445-8330 *Toll Free Tel:* 866-443-7987 *Fax:* 708-445-8648 *Web Site:* www.marionstreetpress. com, pg 163

Maritime Writers' Workshop, PO Box 4400, Fredericton, NB E3B 5A3, Canada *Tel:* 506-474-1144 *Fax:* 506-474-1144 (call first) *E-mail:* k4jc@unb.ca *Web Site:* www.unb.ca/extend/writers, pg 744

Mark Sonder Productions, 250 W 57 St, Suite 1830, New York, NY 10107 *Tel:* 212-262-4600 *Fax:* 212-246-0197 *E-mail:* msonder@marksondorproductions. com *Web Site:* www.marksonderproductions.com, pg 670

Market Data Retrieval, One Forest Pkwy, Shelton, CT 06484 *Tel:* 203-926-4800 *Toll Free Tel:* 800-333-8802 *Fax:* 203-926-0784 *E-mail:* mdrinfo@dnb.com *Web Site:* www.schooldata.com, pg 163

Marketscope Group Books LLC, PO Box 3118, Huntington Beach, CA 92605-3118 *Tel:* 714-375-9888 *Fax:* 714-375-9898, pg 163

Markowski International Publishers, One Oakglade Circle, Humelstown, PA 17036-9525 *Tel:* 717-566-0468 *Toll Free Tel:* 800-566-0534 (orders only) *Fax:* 717-566-6423 *E-mail:* possibilitypress@aol.com; posspress@aol.com, pg 164

Elaine Markson Literary Agency Inc, 44 Greenwich Ave, New York, NY 10011 *Tel:* 212-243-8480 *Fax:* 212-691-9014, pg 642

Marlor Press Inc, 4304 Brigadoon Dr, St Paul, MN 55126 *Tel:* 651-484-4600 *Toll Free Tel:* 800-669-4908 *Fax:* 651-490-1182 *E-mail:* marlor@minn.net, pg 164

Marlowe & Company, 245 W 17 St, 11th fl, New York, NY 10011-5300 *Tel:* 646-375-2570 *Fax:* 646-375-2571 *Web Site:* www.marlowepub.com, pg 164

Mildred Marmur Associates Ltd, 2005 Palmer Ave, PMB 127, Larchmont, NY 10538 *Tel:* 914-834-1170 *Fax:* 914-834-2840 *E-mail:* marmur@westnet.com, pg 642

Marquette University Press, Memorial Library, Rm 116, 1415 W Wisconsin Ave, Milwaukee, WI 53233 *Tel:* 414-288-1564 *Toll Free Tel:* 800-247-6553 *Fax:* 414-288-7813 *Web Site:* www.marquette.edu/ mupress/, pg 164

Marquis Who's Who, 562 Central Ave, New Providence, NJ 07974 *Tel:* 908-673-1001 *Toll Free Tel:* 800-473-7020 *Fax:* 908-673-1189 *Web Site:* www. marquiswhoswho.com, pg 164

Helen & Howard R Marraro Prize in Italian History, 400 "A" St SE, Washington, DC 20003 *Tel:* 202-544-2422 *Fax:* 202-544-8307 *E-mail:* info@historians.org *Web Site:* www.historians.org, pg 787

Howard R Marraro Prize, 26 Broadway, 3rd fl, New York, NY 10004-1789 *Tel:* 646-576-5141 *Fax:* 646-458-0030 *E-mail:* awards@mla.org *Web Site:* www. mla.org, pg 787

Marshall & Swift, 911 Wilshire Blvd, Suite 1800, Los Angeles, CA 90017 *Tel:* 213-683-9000 *Toll Free Tel:* 800-544-2678 *Fax:* 213-683-9043 (orders) *Web Site:* www.marshallswift.com, pg 164

Marshall Cavendish Corp, 99 White Plains Rd, Tarrytown, NY 10591-9001 *Tel:* 914-332-8888 *Fax:* 914-332-1888 *E-mail:* mcc@marshallcavendish. com *Web Site:* www.marshallcavendish.com, pg 164

The Evan Marshall Agency, 6 Tristam Place, Pine Brook, NJ 07058-9445 *Tel:* 973-882-1122 *Fax:* 973-882-3099 *Web Site:* www.thenovelist.com, pg 642

Lenore Marshall Poetry Prize, 588 Broadway, Suite 604, New York, NY 10012 *Tel:* 212-274-0343 *Fax:* 212-274-9427 *E-mail:* academy@poets.org *Web Site:* www. poets.org, pg 787

The Martell Agency, 545 Madison Ave, 7th fl, New York, NY 10022 *Tel:* 212-317-2672 *Fax:* 212-317-2676, pg 642

Frances Martin, 154 W 73 St, New York, NY 10023 *Tel:* 212-877-8160, pg 605

Martin Literary Management, 17328 Ventura Blvd, Suite 138, Encino, CA 91316 *Tel:* 818-595-1130 *Web Site:* www.martinliterarymanagement.com, pg 642

Martin-McLean Literary Associates, 1602 S Cerritos Dr, Suite D, Palm Springs, CA 92264 *Tel:* 760-320-4552 *Fax:* 760-323-8792 *E-mail:* martinmcleanlit@aol.com *Web Site:* www.martinmcleanlit.com; www.mcleanlit.com, pg 642

Martindale-Hubbell, 121 Chanlon Rd, New Providence, NJ 07974 *Tel:* 908-464-6800 *Toll Free Tel:* 800-526-4902 *Fax:* 908-464-3553 *E-mail:* info@martindale.com *Web Site:* www.martindale.com, pg 164

Martingale & Co, 20205 144 Ave NE, Woodinville, WA 98072 *Tel:* 425-483-3313 *Toll Free Tel:* 800-426-3126 *Fax:* 425-486-7596 *E-mail:* info@martingale-pub.com *Web Site:* www.martingale-pub.com, pg 164

Maryland Historical Society, 201 W Monument St, Baltimore, MD 21201 *Tel:* 410-685-3750 *Fax:* 410-385-2105 *Web Site:* www.mdhs.org, pg 164

Mason Crest Publishers, 370 Reed Rd, Suite 302, Broomall, PA 19008 *Tel:* 610-543-6200 *Toll Free Tel:* 866-MCP-BOOK (627-2665) *Fax:* 610-543-3878 *Web Site:* www.masoncrest.com, pg 165

Jack Mason Award, Baipa, PO Box E, Corte Madera, CA 94976 *Toll Free Tel:* 866-622-1325 *E-mail:* info@baipa.net *Web Site:* www.baipa.net, pg 788

Massachusetts Book Awards, Hampshire College MCB, 893 West St, Amherst, MA 01002 *Tel:* 413-559-5678 *Fax:* 413-559-5629 *E-mail:* massbook@hampshire.edu *Web Site:* www.massbook.org, pg 788

Massachusetts College of Art, Writing Children's Literature, 621 Huntington Ave, Boston, MA 02115 *Tel:* 617-879-7200 *Fax:* 617-879-7171 *E-mail:* continuing_education@massart.edu *Web Site:* www.massart.edu, pg 752

Massachusetts Historical Society, 1154 Boylston St, Boston, MA 02215 *Tel:* 617-536-1608 *Fax:* 617-859-0074 *E-mail:* publications@masshist.org *Web Site:* www.masshist.org, pg 165

Massachusetts Institute of Technology Libraries, 77 Mass Ave, Bldg 14, Rm 0551, Cambridge, MA 02139-4307 *Tel:* 617-253-7059 *Fax:* 617-253-1690 *E-mail:* docs@mit.edu *Web Site:* libraries.mit.edu/docs, pg 165

Master Books, PO Box 726, Green Forest, AR 72638-0726 *Tel:* 870-438-5288 *Fax:* 870-438-5120 *E-mail:* nlp@newleafpress.net *Web Site:* www.masterbooks.net, pg 165

Master Point Press, 331 Douglas Ave, Toronto, ON M5M 1H2, Canada *Tel:* 416-781-0351 *Fax:* 416-781-1831 *E-mail:* info@masterpointpress.com *Web Site:* www.masterpointpress.com, pg 553

Mastering Color for Print Production, 200 Deer Run Rd, Sewickley, PA 15143-2600 *Tel:* 412-741-6860 *Toll Free Tel:* 800-910-4283 *Fax:* 412-741-2311 *E-mail:* info@gain.net *Web Site:* www.gain.net, pg 744

Masters Literary Awards, PO Box 17897, Encino, CA 91416-7897 *Tel:* 818-377-4006 *E-mail:* titan.press@sbcglobal.net *Web Site:* www.titanpress.info, pg 788

Materials Research Society, 506 Keystone Dr, Warrendale, PA 15086 *Tel:* 724-779-3003 *Fax:* 724-779-8313 *E-mail:* info@mrs.org *Web Site:* www.mrs.org, pg 165

Math-Check, 3 Herbert St, Baldwin, NY 11510 *Tel:* 516-623-6898, pg 605

Math Teachers Press Inc, 4850 Park Glen Rd, Minneapolis, MN 55416 *Tel:* 952-545-6535 *Toll Free Tel:* 800-852-2435 *Fax:* 952-546-7502 *Web Site:* www.movingwithmath.com, pg 165

The Mathematical Association of America, 1529 18 St NW, Washington, DC 20036 *Tel:* 202-387-5200 *Toll Free Tel:* 800-331-1622 (orders) *Fax:* 202-265-2384 *E-mail:* ldouglas@pmds.com *Web Site:* www.maa.org, pg 165

Joy Matkowski, 773 Lee Lane, Enola, PA 17025 *Tel:* 717-732-8767 *E-mail:* jmatkowski1@comcast.net, pg 605

Harold Matson Co Inc, 276 Fifth Ave, New York, NY 10001 *Tel:* 212-679-4490 *Fax:* 212-545-1224 *E-mail:* hmatsco@aol.com, pg 643

Jed Mattes Inc, 2095 Broadway, Suite 302, New York, NY 10023-2895 *Tel:* 212-595-5228 *Fax:* 212-595-5232 *E-mail:* general@jedmattes.com, pg 643

Mature Women Scholarship Grant - Art/Letters/Music, c/o National Pen Women-Scholarship, Pen Arts Bldg, 1300 17 St NW, Washington, DC 20036-1973 *Tel:* 202-785-1997 *Web Site:* www.americanpenwomen.org, pg 788

Maupin House Publishing, 4445 SW 35 Terr, Suite 200, Gainesville, FL 32608 *Tel:* 352-373-5588 *Toll Free Tel:* 800-524-0634 (orders only) *Fax:* 352-373-5546 *E-mail:* sales@maupinhouse.com *Web Site:* www.maupinhouse.com, pg 165

Maval Publishing Inc, 567 Harrison St, Denver, CO 80206-4534 *Tel:* 303-338-8725 *Fax:* 303-745-6215 *E-mail:* maval@maval.com *Web Site:* www.maval.com, pg 165

Maverick Publications Inc, 63324 Nels Anderson Rd, Bend, OR 97701 *Tel:* 541-382-6978 *Fax:* 541-382-4831 *E-mail:* customerservice@maverickbooks.com *Web Site:* www.mavbooks.com, pg 165

Maximum Press, 605 Silverthorn Rd, Gulf Breeze, FL 32561 *Tel:* 850-934-0819 *Toll Free Tel:* 800-989-6733 *Fax:* 850-934-9981 *E-mail:* moreinfo@maxpress.com *Web Site:* www.maxpress.com, pg 166

Maxit Publishing Inc, PO Box 700, Lompoc, CA 93438-0700 *Tel:* 805-686-5100 *Toll Free Tel:* 866-686-5100 *Fax:* 805-686-5102 *Web Site:* www.maxitpublishing.com, pg 166

Peter Mayeux, RFD 1, Box 242 A3, Crete, NE 68333 *Tel:* 402-472-3046 *Fax:* 402-472-8403; 402-472-8597 *E-mail:* pmayeux1@unl.edu, pg 605

Mazda Publishers Inc, 2182 Dupont Dr, Suite 216, Irvine, CA 92612 *Tel:* 714-751-5252 *Fax:* 714-751-4805 *E-mail:* hello@mazdapub.com *Web Site:* www.mazdapub.com, pg 166

Maxim Mazumdar New Play Competition, One Curtain Up Alley, Buffalo, NY 14202-1911 *Tel:* 716-852-2600 *Fax:* 716-852-2266 *E-mail:* email@alleyway.com *Web Site:* alleyway.com, pg 788

MBA Publishing, 925 E St, Walla Walla, WA 99362 *Tel:* 509-529-0244 *Fax:* 509-529-8865 *E-mail:* mba@bmi.net *Web Site:* www.bmi.net/mba/, pg 572

MBH Book Services, 99 Willowbrook Blvd, Lewisburg, PA 17837 *Tel:* 570-523-8081, pg 605

McBooks Press Inc, 520 N Meadow St, Ithaca, NY 14850 *Tel:* 607-272-2114 *Toll Free Tel:* 888-266-5711 *Fax:* 607-273-6068 *E-mail:* mcbooks@mcbooks.com *Web Site:* www.mcbooks.com, pg 166

Margret McBride Literary Agency, 7744 Fay Ave, Suite 201, La Jolla, CA 92037 *Tel:* 858-454-1550 *Fax:* 858-454-2156 *E-mail:* staff@mcbridelit.com *Web Site:* www.mcbrideliterary.com, pg 643

Roger A McCaffrey Publishing, PO Box 1209, Ridgefield, CT 06877, pg 166

James H McCallum Jr, 29 Fletcher Rd, Monsey, NY 10952 *Tel:* 845-425-0882, pg 605

E J McCarthy Agency, 21 Columbus Ave, Suite 210, San Francisco, CA 94111 *Tel:* 415-296-7706 *Fax:* 415-296-7706 *E-mail:* ejmagency@mac.com, pg 643

Gerard McCauley Agency Inc, PO Box 844, Katonah, NY 10536-0844 *Tel:* 914-232-5700 *Fax:* 914-232-1506, pg 643

McClanahan Publishing House Inc, PO Box 100, Kuttawa, KY 42055-0100 *Tel:* 270-388-9388 *Toll Free Tel:* 800-544-6959 *Fax:* 270-388-6186 *E-mail:* books@kybooks.com *Web Site:* www.kybooks.com, pg 166

Anita D McClellan Associates, 50 Stearns St, Cambridge, MA 02138 *Tel:* 617-576-5960 *Fax:* 617-576-6950, pg 643

McClelland & Stewart Journey Prize, 90 Richmond St W, Suite 200, Toronto, ON M5C 1P1, Canada *Tel:* 416-504-8222 *Fax:* 416-504-9090 *E-mail:* info@writerstrust.com *Web Site:* www.writerstrust.com, pg 788

McClelland & Stewart Ltd, 481 University Ave, Suite 900, Toronto, ON M5G 2E9, Canada *Tel:* 416-598-1114 *Fax:* 416-598-7764 *E-mail:* mail@mcclelland.com *Web Site:* www.mcclelland.com, pg 553

McCormack's Guides Inc, 1734 Alhambra Ave, Martinez, CA 94553 *Tel:* 925-229-3581 *Toll Free Tel:* 800-222-3602 *Fax:* 925-228-7223 *E-mail:* bookinfo@mccormacks.com *Web Site:* www.mccormacks.com, pg 166

Kenya McCullum, 31 Wellington Ave, 2nd fl, Albany, NY 12203 *Tel:* 518-435-1307 *E-mail:* kmccullum@mindspring.com, pg 605

McCutchan Publishing Corp, 3220 Blume Dr, Suite 197, Richmond, CA 94806 *Tel:* 510-758-5510 *Toll Free Tel:* 800-227-1540 *Fax:* 510-758-6078 *E-mail:* mccutchanpublish@aol.com *Web Site:* www.mccutchanpublishing.com, pg 166

The McDonald & Woodward Publishing Co, 431-B E College St, Granville, OH 43023 *Tel:* 740-321-1140 *Toll Free Tel:* 800-233-8787 *Fax:* 740-321-1141 *E-mail:* mwpubco@mwpubco.com *Web Site:* www.mwpubco.com, pg 166

McDougal Littell, 909 Davis St, Evanston, IL 60201 *Tel:* 847-869-2300 *Toll Free Tel:* 800-462-6595 (orders) *Toll Free Fax:* 888-872-8380 *Web Site:* www.mcdougallittell.com, pg 166

McFarland & Co Inc Publishers, 960 Hwy 88 W, Jefferson, NC 28640 *Tel:* 336-246-4460 *Toll Free Tel:* 800-253-2187 (orders only) *Fax:* 336-246-5018; 336-246-4403 (orders) *E-mail:* info@mcfarlandpub.com *Web Site:* www.mcfarlandpub.com, pg 166

McGill-Queen's University Press, 3430 McTavish St, Montreal, PQ H3A 1X9, Canada *Tel:* 514-398-3750 *Fax:* 514-398-4333 *E-mail:* mqup@mqup.ca *Web Site:* www.mqup.mcgill.ca, pg 553

John H McGinnis Memorial Award, 307 Fondren Library W, 6404 Hilltop Lane, Dallas, TX 75275-0374 *Tel:* 214-768-1037 *Fax:* 214-768-1408 *E-mail:* swr@mail.smu.edu *Web Site:* www.southwestreview.org, pg 788

Helen McGrath & Associates, 1406 Idaho Ct, Concord, CA 94521 *Tel:* 925-672-6211 *Fax:* 925-672-6383 *E-mail:* hmcgrath_lit@yahoo.com, pg 643

Harold W McGraw Jr - Prize in Education, 1221 Avenue of the Americas, 47th fl, New York, NY 10020 *Tel:* 212-512-2435 *Fax:* 212-512-3611 *Web Site:* www.mcgraw-hill.com, pg 788

The McGraw-Hill Companies Inc, 1221 Avenue of the Americas, 50th fl, New York, NY 10020 *Tel:* 212-512-2000 *E-mail:* webmaster@mcgraw-hill.com *Web Site:* www.mcgraw-hill.com, pg 167

McGraw-Hill/Dushkin, 2460 Kerper Blvd, Dubuque, IA 52001 *Toll Free Tel:* 800-243-6532 *Web Site:* www.dushkin.com, pg 167

McGraw-Hill Education, 2 Penn Plaza, New York, NY 10121 *Tel:* 212-904-2000 *E-mail:* customer.service@mcgraw-hill.com *Web Site:* www.mheducation.com; www.mheducation.com/custserv.html, pg 167

McGraw-Hill Higher Education, 1333 Burr Ridge Pkwy, Burr Ridge, IL 60527 *Tel:* 630-789-4000 *Toll Free Tel:* 800-338-3987 (cust serv) *Fax:* 614-755-5645 (cust serv) *Web Site:* www.mhhe.com, pg 167

McGraw-Hill Humanities, Social Sciences, Languages, 2 Penn Plaza, 20th fl, New York, NY 10121 *Tel:* 212-904-2000 *Toll Free Tel:* 800-338-3987 (cust serv) *Fax:* 614-755-5645 (cust serv) *E-mail:* first name_last name@mcgraw-hill.com *Web Site:* www.mhhe.com, pg 168

McGraw-Hill International Publishing Group, 2 Penn Plaza, New York, NY 10121 *Tel:* 212-904-2000 *Web Site:* www.mcgrawhill.com, pg 168

McGraw-Hill/Irwin, 1333 Burr Ridge Pkwy, Burr Ridge, IL 60527 *Tel:* 630-789-4000 *Toll Free Tel:* 800-338-3987 (cust serv) *Fax:* 630-789-6942; 614-755-5645 (cust serv) *Web Site:* www.mhhe.com, pg 168

McGraw-Hill Learning Group, 8787 Orion Place, Columbus, OH 43240 *Tel:* 614-430-4000 *Fax:* 614-430-6621, pg 168

McGraw-Hill/Osborne, 2100 Powell St, 10th fl, Emeryville, CA 94608 *Tel:* 510-420-7700 *Toll Free Tel:* 800-227-0900 *Fax:* 510-420-7703 *Web Site:* shop.osborne.com/cgi-bin/osborne, pg 168

McGraw-Hill Primis Custom Publishing, 2460 Kerper Blvd, Dubuque, IA 52001 *Tel:* 563-588-1451 *Fax:* 563-589-4700 *E-mail:* first_last@mcgraw-hill.com *Web Site:* www.mhhe.com, pg 168

McGraw-Hill Professional, 2 Penn Plaza, New York, NY 10121 *Tel:* 212-904-2000 *Web Site:* www.books.mcgraw-hill.com, pg 168

McGraw-Hill Ryerson Ltd, 300 Water St, Whitby, ON L1N 9B6, Canada *Tel:* 905-430-5000 *Toll Free Tel:* 800-565-5758 (cust serv) *Fax:* 905-430-5020 *E-mail:* johnd@mcgrawhill.ca *Web Site:* www.mcgrawhill.ca, pg 554

McGraw-Hill Science, Engineering, Mathematics, 2460 Kerper Blvd, Dubuque, IA 52001 *Tel:* 563-588-1451 *Toll Free Tel:* 800-338-3987 (cust serv) *Fax:* 563-589-4700; 614-755-5645 (cust serv) *E-mail:* firstname_lastname@mcgraw-hill.com *Web Site:* www.mhhe.com, pg 169

McGraw-Hill Trade, 2 Penn Plaza, New York, NY 10121, pg 169

McHugh Literary Agency, 1033 Lyon Rd, Moscow, ID 83843-9167 *Tel:* 208-882-0107 *Fax:* 847-628-0146, pg 643

McHugh's Rights/Permissions Workshop™, PO Box 170665, Milwaukee, WI 53217-8056 *Tel:* 414-351-3056 *Fax:* 414-351-0666 *Web Site:* www.johnbmchugh.com, pg 744

McIntosh & Otis Inc, 353 Lexington Ave, Suite 1500, New York, NY 10016-0900 *Tel:* 212-687-7400 *Fax:* 212-687-6894 *E-mail:* info@mcintoshandotis.com, pg 643

Jenny McKean Moore Writer in Creative Writing, English Dept, The George Washington University, Washington, DC 20052 *Tel:* 202-994-6180 *Fax:* 202-994-7915 *Web Site:* www.gwu.edu/~english, pg 788

McKnight Advancement Grants, 2301 Franklin Ave E, Minneapolis, MN 55406 *Tel:* 612-332-7481 *Fax:* 612-332-6037 *E-mail:* info@pwcenter.org *Web Site:* www.pwcenter.org, pg 788

McKnight Artist Fellowship for Writers, Open Book, Suite 200, 1011 Washington Ave S, Minneapolis, MN 55415 *Tel:* 612-215-2575 *Fax:* 612-215-2576 *E-mail:* loft@loft.org *Web Site:* www.loft.org, pg 788

McKnight National Residency & Commission, 2301 Franklin Ave E, Minneapolis, MN 55406 *Tel:* 612-332-7481 *Fax:* 612-332-6037 *E-mail:* info@pwcenter.org *Web Site:* www.pwcenter.org, pg 788

Wil McKnight Associates Inc, 1801 W Hovey Ave, Suite A, Normal, IL 61761 *Tel:* 309-451-0000 *Fax:* 309-451-0000 *E-mail:* info@hardhatonline.com *Web Site:* www.hardhatonline.com, pg 169

Pamela Dittmer McKuen, 87 Tanglewood Dr, Glen Ellyn, IL 60137 *Tel:* 630-545-0867 *Fax:* 630-545-0868 *E-mail:* pmckuen@aol.com, pg 605

McLaren Memorial Comedy Playwriting Competition, 2000 W Wadley, Midland, TX 79705 *Tel:* 432-682-2544 *Fax:* 432-682-6136 *Web Site:* www.mctmidland.org, pg 789

Patricia A McLaughlin, 29331 Clear View Lane, Highland, CA 92346 *Tel:* 909-864-5491, pg 605

McLemore Prize, PO Box 571, Jackson, MS 39205-0571 *Tel:* 601-576-6850 *Fax:* 601-576-6975 *E-mail:* mhs@mdah.state.ms.us *Web Site:* www.mdah.state.ms.us, pg 789

Andrews McMeel Publishing, 4520 Main St, Suite 700, Kansas City, MO 64111-7701 *Tel:* 816-932-6700 *Toll Free Tel:* 800-851-8923 *Web Site:* www.universal.com/amp, pg 169

Sally Hill McMillan & Associates Inc, 429 E Kingston Ave, Charlotte, NC 28203 *Tel:* 704-334-0897 *Fax:* 704-334-1897 *E-mail:* mcmagency@aol.com, pg 643

Pat McNees, 10643 Weymouth St, Suite 204, Bethesda, MD 20814 *Tel:* 301-897-8557 *E-mail:* pmcnees@nasw.org *Web Site:* www.patmcnees.com, pg 605

McNeese State University, Writing Program, PO Box 92655, Lake Charles, LA 70609-0001 *Tel:* 337-475-5000; 337-475-5326 *Web Site:* www.mcneese.mfa.com, pg 753

McPherson & Co, 148 Smith Ave, Kingston, NY 12401 *Tel:* 845-331-5807 *Toll Free Tel:* 800-613-8219 *Fax:* 845-331-5807 *Toll Free Fax:* 800-613-8219 *Web Site:* www.mcphersonco.com, pg 169

McTavish & Nunn, 517 River Rd, Canmore, AB T1W 2E4, Canada *Tel:* 403-678-5859 *Fax:* 403-609-4072, pg 554

MDRT Center for Productivity, 325 W Touhy Ave, Park Ridge, IL 60068-4265 *Tel:* 847-692-6378 *Toll Free Tel:* 800-879-6378 *Fax:* 847-518-8921 *E-mail:* orders@mdrt.org *Web Site:* www.mdrt.org, pg 169

me+mi publishing inc, 128 S County Farm Rd, Wheaton, IL 60187 *Tel:* 630-752-9951 *Toll Free Tel:* 888-251-1444 *Fax:* 630-588-9804 *E-mail:* rw@rosawesley.com *Web Site:* www.memima.com, pg 169

Meadowbrook Press, 5451 Smetana Dr, Minnetonka, MN 55343 *Tel:* 952-930-1100 *Toll Free Tel:* 800-338-2232 *Fax:* 952-930-1940 *Web Site:* www.meadowbrookpress.com, pg 169

R S Means Co Inc, 63 Smiths Lane, Kingston, MA 02364-0800 *Tel:* 781-585-7880 *Toll Free Tel:* 800-448-8182 *Fax:* 781-585-8814 *Toll Free Fax:* 800-632-6732 *Web Site:* www.rsmeans.com, pg 169

P D Meany Publishers, 71 Fermanagh Ave, Toronto, ON M6R 1M1, Canada *Tel:* 416-516-2903 *Fax:* 416-516-7632 *E-mail:* info@pdmeany.com *Web Site:* www.pdmeany.com, pg 554

Medal of Honor for Literature, 15 Gramercy Park S, New York, NY 10003, pg 789

Medals of America Press, 114 Southchase Blvd, Fountain Inn, SC 29644 *Tel:* 864-862-6051 *Toll Free Tel:* 800-308-0849 *Fax:* 864-862-0256 *Toll Free Fax:* 800-407-8640 *E-mail:* press@usmedals.com *Web Site:* www.moapress.com, pg 170

MedBooks, 101 W Buckingham Rd, Richardson, TX 75081 *Tel:* 972-643-1802 *Toll Free Tel:* 800-443-7397 *Fax:* 972-994-0215 *E-mail:* medbooks@medbooks.com *Web Site:* www.medbooks.com, pg 170

Media Alliance, 942 Market St, Suite 503, San Francisco, CA 94102 *Tel:* 415-546-6334; 415-546-6491 *Fax:* 415-546-6218 *E-mail:* info@media-alliance.org *Web Site:* www.media-alliance.org, pg 691

Media & Methods, 1429 Walnut St, 10th fl, Philadelphia, PA 19102 *Tel:* 215-563-6005 *Toll Free Tel:* 800-555-5657 *Fax:* 215-587-9706 *Web Site:* www.media-methods.com, pg 170

Media Associates, PO Box 46, Wilton, CA 95693-0046 *Toll Free Tel:* 800-373-1897 (orders) *Fax:* 916-687-8711; 916-687-8711 *E-mail:* carlya777@hotmail.com *Web Site:* www.media-associates.co.nz, pg 170

Media Coalition Inc, 139 Fulton St, Suite 302, New York, NY 10038 *Tel:* 212-587-4025 *Fax:* 212-587-2436 *E-mail:* mediacoalition@mediacoalition.org *Web Site:* www.mediacoalition.org, pg 691

Media Credit Association (MCA), 84 Broad St, Milford, CT 06460 *Tel:* 203-876-2182 *Fax:* 203-876-5091 *Web Site:* www.mediacreditassociation.com, pg 691

Medical Group Management Association, 104 Inverness Terr E, Englewood, CO 80112 *Tel:* 303-799-1111 *Toll Free Tel:* 888-608-5601 *Fax:* 303-643-4439 *Web Site:* www.mgma.com, pg 170

Medical Physics Publishing Corp, 4513 Vernon Blvd, Madison, WI 53705-4964 *Tel:* 608-262-4021 *Toll Free Tel:* 800-442-5778 *Fax:* 608-265-2121 *E-mail:* mpp@medicalphysics.org *Web Site:* www.medicalphysics.org, pg 170

Medieval Institute Publications, 1903 W Michigan Ave, Kalamazoo, MI 49008-5432 *Tel:* 269-387-8755 (orders); 269-387-8754 *Fax:* 269-387-8750 *Web Site:* www.wmich.edu/medieval/mip, pg 170

MedMaster Inc, 3337 Hollywood Oaks Dr, Fort Lauderdale, FL 33312 *Tel:* 954-962-8414 *Toll Free Tel:* 800-335-3480 *Fax:* 954-962-4508 *E-mail:* mmbks@aol.com *Web Site:* www.medmaster.net, pg 170

Lucille Medwick Memorial Award, 15 Gramercy Park, New York, NY 10003 *Tel:* 212-254-9628 *Fax:* 212-673-2352 *Web Site:* www.poetrysociety.org, pg 789

MedWrite Associates, 31651 Auburn Dr, Beverly Hills, MI 48025 *Tel:* 248-646-2895 *Fax:* 248-647-7593, pg 605

The Russell Meerdink Co Ltd, 1555 S Park Ave, Neenah, WI 54956 *Tel:* 920-725-0955 *Toll Free Tel:* 800-635-6499 *Fax:* 920-725-0709 *Web Site:* www.horseinfo.com, pg 170

Mega Media Press, 1121 Hub Ct, El Cajon, CA 92020 *Tel:* 619-588-6846 *Toll Free Tel:* 800-803-9416 *Fax:* 619-588-6846 *Web Site:* www.imagetics.com, pg 170

Mehring Books Inc, PO Box 48377, Oak Park, MI 48237-5977 *Tel:* 248-967-2924 *Fax:* 248-967-3023 *E-mail:* inquiry@mehring.com; sales@mehring.com *Web Site:* www.mehring.com, pg 170

Mel Bay Publications Inc, 4 Industrial Dr, Pacific, MO 63069-0066 *Tel:* 636-257-3970 *Toll Free Tel:* 800-863-5229 *Fax:* 636-257-5062 *Toll Free Fax:* 800-660-9818 *E-mail:* email@melbay.com *Web Site:* www.melbay.com, pg 171

Melcher Book Award, 25 Beacon St, Boston, MA 02108-2800 *Tel:* 617-742-2100 (ext 303) *Fax:* 617-367-3237 *Web Site:* www.uua.org, pg 789

Frederic G Melcher Scholarship, 50 E Huron St, Chicago, IL 60611-2795 *Tel:* 312-280-2163 *Toll Free Tel:* 800-545-2433 *Fax:* 312-944-7671 *E-mail:* alsc@ala.org *Web Site:* www.ala.org/alsc/, pg 789

Barbara A Mele, 2525 Holland Ave, New York, NY 10467-8703 *Tel:* 718-654-8047 *Fax:* 718-654-8047 *E-mail:* bannmele@aol.com, pg 606

The Edwin Mellen Press, 415 Ridge St, Lewiston, NY 14092 *Tel:* 716-754-2266 (mgr acqs); 716-754-8566 (mktg); 716-754-2788 (order fulfillment) *Fax:* 716-754-4056; 716-754-1860 (order fulfillment) *E-mail:* mellen@wzrd.com; cs@wzrd.com (customer service, fulfillment) *Web Site:* www.mellenpress.com, pg 171

Tom Mellers Publishing Services (TMPS), 60 Second Ave, New York, NY 10003 *Tel:* 212-254-4958 *Fax:* 607-798-9988 *E-mail:* tmellers@clarityconnect.com, pg 606

The Melville Society, University of Minnesota, 140 Appleby Hall, Minneapolis, MN 55455 *Fax:* 612-625-0709, pg 691

Menasha Ridge Press Inc, 2204 First Ave S, Suite 102, Birmingham, AL 35233 *Tel:* 205-322-0439 *Fax:* 205-326-1012 *E-mail:* info@menasharidge.com *Web Site:* www.menasharidge.com, pg 171

MENC - The National Association for Music Education, 1806 Robert Fulton Dr, Reston, VA 20191 *Tel:* 703-860-4000 *Fax:* 703-860-9443 *E-mail:* franp@menc.org *Web Site:* www.menc.org, pg 171

Fred C Mench, Professor of Classics, 104 Iona Ave, Linwood, NJ 08221 *Tel:* 609-927-8430 *Fax:* 609-652-4550 *E-mail:* fmench@earthlink.net, pg 606

Claudia Menza Literary Agency, 1170 Broadway, Suite 807, New York, NY 10001 *Tel:* 212-889-6850 *E-mail:* menzacmla@aol.com, pg 643

MEP Publications, University of Minnesota, Physics Bldg, 116 Church St SE, Minneapolis, MN 55455-0112 *Tel:* 612-922-7993 *E-mail:* marqu002@tc.umn.edu *Web Site:* umn.edu/home/marqu002, pg 171

The Mercantile Library, 17 E 47 St, New York, NY 10017 *Tel:* 212-755-6710 *Fax:* 212-826-0831 *E-mail:* info@mercantilelibrary.org *Web Site:* www. mercantilelibrary.org, pg 691

Mercer University Press, 1400 Coleman Ave, Macon, GA 31207 *Tel:* 478-301-2880 *Toll Free Tel:* 800-637-2378 (ext 2880, outside GA); 800-342-0841 (ext 2880, GA) *Fax:* 478-301-2585 *E-mail:* mupressorders@ mercer.edu *Web Site:* www.mupress.org, pg 171

Scott Meredith Literary Agency LP, 200 W 57 St, Suite 904, New York, NY 10019 *Tel:* 646-274-1970 *Fax:* 212-977-5997 *Web Site:* www.writingtosell.com, pg 644

Merit Publishing International Inc, 5840 Corporate Way, Suite 200, West Palm Beach, FL 33407-2040 *Tel:* 561-637-1116 *Fax:* 561-477-4961 *E-mail:* meritpi@aol. com *Web Site:* www.meritpublishing.com, pg 171

Meriwether Publishing Ltd/Contemporary Drama Service, 885 Elkton Dr, Colorado Springs, CO 80907-3557 *Tel:* 719-594-4422 *Toll Free Tel:* 800-937-5297 *Fax:* 719-594-9916 *Toll Free Fax:* 888-594-4436 *E-mail:* merpcds@aol.com *Web Site:* www.meriwether. com, pg 171

Meisha Merlin Publishing Inc, 1702 Ronald Rd, Tucker, GA 30084 *Tel:* 770-414-4365 *Fax:* 770-414-4365 *E-mail:* email@meishamerlin.com; orders@ meishamerlin.com *Web Site:* www.meishamerlin.com, pg 172

Merriam Press, 218 Beech St, Bennington, VT 05201-2611 *Tel:* 802-447-0313 *Fax:* 802-217-1051 *Web Site:* www.merriam-press.com, pg 172

Merriam-Webster Inc, 47 Federal St, Springfield, MA 01102 *Tel:* 413-734-3134 *Toll Free Tel:* 800-828-1880 (orders & cust serv) *Fax:* 413-731-5979 *E-mail:* merriam_webster@merriam-webster.com *Web Site:* www.merriam-webster.com, pg 172

Merryant Publishers Inc, 7615 SW 257 St, Vashon, WA 98070 *Tel:* 206-463-3879 *Toll Free Tel:* 800-228-8958 *Fax:* 206-463-1604, pg 172

Barbara Mary Merson, 41 North St, Old Bridge, NJ 08857 *Tel:* 732-251-4604 *E-mail:* barbear28@aol.com, pg 606

Mesorah Publications Ltd, 4401 Second Ave, Brooklyn, NY 11232 *Tel:* 718-921-9000 *Toll Free Tel:* 800-637-6724 *Fax:* 718-680-1875 *E-mail:* artscroll@mesorah. com *Web Site:* www.artscroll.com; www.mesorah.com, pg 172

Messianic Jewish Publishers, 6204 Park Heights Ave, Baltimore, MD 21215-3600 *Tel:* 410-358-6471 *Toll Free Tel:* 800-773-6574 *Fax:* 410-764-1376 *E-mail:* lederer@messianicjewish.net; rightsandpermissions@messianicjewish.net (rights & perms) *Web Site:* messianicjewish.net, pg 172

META Publications Inc, PO Box 1910, Capitola, CA 95010-1910 *Tel:* 831-464-0254 *Fax:* 831-464-0517 *E-mail:* metapub@prodigy.net *Web Site:* www.meta-publications.com, pg 172

Metal Bulletin Inc, 1250 Broadway, 26th fl, New York, NY 10001 *Tel:* 212-213-6202 *Toll Free Tel:* 800-638-2525 *Fax:* 212-213-6273 *Web Site:* www.metbul.com, pg 172

Metal Powder Industries Federation, 105 College Rd E, Princeton, NJ 08540-6692 *Tel:* 609-452-7700 *Fax:* 609-987-8523 *E-mail:* info@mpif.org *Web Site:* www.mpif.org, pg 172

Metamorphous Press, 265 N Hancock St, Portland, OR 97227 *Tel:* 503-228-4972 *Toll Free Tel:* 800-937-7771 (orders only) *Fax:* 503-223-9117 *E-mail:* metabooks@ metamodels.com *Web Site:* www.metamodels.com, pg 172

Vicky Metcalf Award for Children's Literature, 90 Richmond St W, Suite 200, Toronto, ON M5C 1P1, Canada *Tel:* 416-504-8222 *Fax:* 416-504-9090 *E-mail:* info@writerstrust.com *Web Site:* www. writerstrust.com, pg 789

Metro Creative Graphics Inc, 519 Eighth Ave, New York, NY 10018 *Tel:* 212-947-5100 *Toll Free Tel:* 800-223-1600 *Web Site:* www. metrocreativegraphics.com, pg 173

Metropolitan Editorial & Writing Service, 4455 Douglas Ave, Riverdale, NY 10471 *Tel:* 718-549-5518, pg 606

Metropolitan Lithographers Association Inc, 950 Third Ave, 14th fl, New York, NY 10022 *Tel:* 212-644-1010 *Fax:* 212-644-1936, pg 691

The Metropolitan Museum of Art, 1000 Fifth Ave, New York, NY 10028 *Tel:* 212-879-5500; 212-535-7710 *Fax:* 212-396-5062 *E-mail:* info@metmuseum.org *Web Site:* www.metmuseum.org, pg 173

Mews Books Ltd, 20 Bluewater Hill, Westport, CT 06880 *Tel:* 203-227-1836 *Fax:* 203-227-1144 *E-mail:* mewsbooks@aol.com, pg 644

Helmut Meyer Literary Agency, 330 E 79 St, New York, NY 10021 *Tel:* 212-288-2421, pg 644

Jenny Meyer Literary Agency, 115 W 29 St, 10th fl, New York, NY 10001-5106 *Tel:* 212-564-9898 *Fax:* 212-564-6044 *E-mail:* jenny@meyerlit.com, pg 644

Meyerbooks Publisher, 235 W Main St, Glenwood, IL 60425 *Tel:* 708-757-4950, pg 173

MFA Publications, 465 Huntington Ave, Boston, MA 02115 *Tel:* 617-369-3438 *Fax:* 617-369-3459 *Web Site:* www.mfa-publications.org, pg 173

MGI Management Institute Inc, 701 Westchester Ave, Suite 308W, White Plains, NY 10604 *Tel:* 914-428-6500 *Toll Free Tel:* 800-932-0191 *Fax:* 914-428-0773 *E-mail:* mgiusa@aol.com *Web Site:* www.mgi.org, pg 173

Michael di Capua Books, 114 Fifth Ave, New York, NY 10011 *Tel:* 212-633-4400 *Fax:* 212-807-5880 *Web Site:* www.hyperionbooks.com, pg 173

Doris S Michaels Literary Agency Inc, 1841 Broadway, Suite 903, New York, NY 10023 *Tel:* 212-265-9474 *Fax:* 212-265-9480 *E-mail:* info@dsmagency.com *Web Site:* www.dsmagency.com, pg 644

Linda Michaels Ltd International Literary Agents, 344 Main St, Lakeville, CT 06039-0567 *Tel:* 860-435-1432 *Fax:* 860-435-1446 *E-mail:* lmlagency@aol.com, pg 644

Michelin Travel Publications, PO Box 19001, Greenville, SC 29602-9001 *Tel:* 864-458-5127 *Toll Free Tel:* 800-423-0485; 800-223-0987 *Fax:* 864-458-6674 *Toll Free Fax:* 866-297-0914 *E-mail:* michelin.travel-publications-us@us.michelin.com *Web Site:* www. viamichelin.com, pg 173

Michelin Travel Publications, 2540 Daniel Johnson, Suite 510, Laval, PQ H7T 2T9, Canada *Tel:* 450-978-4700 *Toll Free Tel:* 800-361-8236 (Canada) *Fax:* 450-978-1305 *Toll Free Fax:* 800-361-6937 (Canada) *E-mail:* michelin.travel-publications-canada@ca. michelin.com *Web Site:* www.michelin-travel.com, pg 554

Michigan Municipal League, 1675 Green Rd, Ann Arbor, MI 48105 *Tel:* 734-662-3246 *Toll Free Tel:* 800-653-2483 *Fax:* 734-663-4496 *Web Site:* www. mml.org, pg 173

Michigan State University Press (MSU Press), 1405 S Harrison Rd, Suite 25, East Lansing, MI 48823 *Tel:* 517-355-9543 *Fax:* 517-432-2611 *Toll Free Fax:* 800-678-2120 *E-mail:* msupress@msu.edu *Web Site:* www.msupress.msu.edu, pg 173

MicroMash, 6402 S Troy Circle, Englewood, CO 80111-6424 *Tel:* 303-799-0099 *Toll Free Tel:* 800-823-6039 *Fax:* 303-799-1425 *E-mail:* info@micromash.com *Web Site:* www.micromash.net, pg 173

Micromedia ProQuest, 20 Victoria St, Toronto, ON M5C 2N8, Canada *Tel:* 416-362-5211 *Toll Free Tel:* 800-387-2689 *Fax:* 416-362-6161 *E-mail:* info@ micromedia.ca *Web Site:* www.micromedia.ca, pg 554

Microsoft Press, One Microsoft Way, Redmond, WA 98052-6399 *Tel:* 425-882-8080 *Toll Free Tel:* 800-677-7377 *Fax:* 425-936-7329 *Web Site:* www.microsoft. com/presspass/exec/default.asp#qt, pg 173

Mid-List Press, 4324 12 Ave S, Minneapolis, MN 55407-3218 *Tel:* 612-822-3733 *Fax:* 612-823-8387 *E-mail:* guide@midlist.org *Web Site:* www.midlist.org, pg 174

Mid-List Press First Series Award for Creative Nonfiction, 4324 12 Ave S, Minneapolis, MN 55407-3218 *Tel:* 612-822-3733 *Fax:* 612-823-8387 *E-mail:* guide@midlist.org *Web Site:* www.midlist.org, pg 789

Mid-List Press First Series Award for Poetry, 4324 12 Ave S, Minneapolis, MN 55407-3218 *Tel:* 612-822-3733 *Fax:* 612-823-8387 *E-mail:* guide@midlist.org *Web Site:* www.midlist.org, pg 789

Mid-List Press First Series Award for Short Fiction, 4324 12 Ave S, Minneapolis, MN 55407-3218 *Tel:* 612-822-3733 *Fax:* 612-823-8387 *E-mail:* guide@ midlist.org *Web Site:* www.midlist.org, pg 789

Mid-List Press First Series Award for the Novel, 4324 12 Ave S, Minneapolis, MN 55407-3218 *Tel:* 612-822-3733 *Fax:* 612-823-8387 *E-mail:* guide@midlist.org *Web Site:* www.midlist.org, pg 789

Susan T Middleton, 366A Norton Hill Rd, Ashfield, MA 01330-9601 *Tel:* 413-628-4039 *E-mail:* smiddle@ crocker.com, pg 606

Midland Writers' Conference, 1710 W St Andrews, Midland, MI 48640 *Tel:* 989-837-3435 *Fax:* 989-837-3468, pg 744

Midmarch Arts Press, 300 Riverside Dr, New York, NY 10025-5239 *Tel:* 212-666-6990, pg 174

Midnight Marquee Press Inc, 9721 Britinay Lane, Baltimore, MD 21234 *Tel:* 410-665-1198 *Fax:* 410-665-9207 *E-mail:* mmarquee@aol.com *Web Site:* www.midmar.com, pg 174

MidWest Plan Service, 122 Davidson Hall, Iowa State University, Ames, IA 50011-3080 *Tel:* 515-294-4337 *Toll Free Tel:* 800-562-3618 *Fax:* 515-294-9589 *E-mail:* mwps@iastate.edu *Web Site:* www.mwpshq. org, pg 174

Midwest Traditions Inc, 3147 S Pennsylvania Ave, Milwaukee, WI 53207 *Tel:* 414-294-4319 *Toll Free Tel:* 800-736-9189 *Fax:* 414-962-3579, pg 174

Midwest Travel Writers Association, PO Box 83542, Lincoln, NE 68501-3542 *Tel:* 402-438-2253 *Fax:* 402-438-2253 *Web Site:* www.mtwa.org, pg 691

Mike Murach & Associates Inc, 3484 W Gettysburg Ave, Suite 101, Fresno, CA 93722-7801 *Tel:* 559-440-9071 *Toll Free Tel:* 800-221-5528 *Fax:* 559-440-0963 *E-mail:* murachbooks@murach.com *Web Site:* www. murach.com, pg 174

Mi'kmaq-Maliseet Institute, University of New Brunswick, PO Box 4400, Fredriction, NB E3B 6E3, Canada *Tel:* 506-453-4840 *Fax:* 506-453-4784 *E-mail:* micmac@unb.ca *Web Site:* www.unb.ca, pg 554

Milady Publishing, Executive Woods, 5 Maxwell Dr, Clifton Park, NY 12065-2919 *Tel:* 518-348-2300 (ext 2409) *Toll Free Tel:* 800-998-7498 *Fax:* 518-348-7000 *Web Site:* www.delmar.com; www.milady.com, pg 174

Robert J Milch, 9 Millbrook Dr, Stony Brook, NY 11790-2914 *Tel:* 631-689-8546 *Fax:* 631-689-8546 *E-mail:* milchedit@aol.com, pg 606

Kenneth W Mildenberger Prize, 26 Broadway, 3rd fl, New York, NY 10004-1789 *Tel:* 646-576-5141 *Fax:* 646-458-0030 *E-mail:* awards@mla.org *Web Site:* www.mla.org, pg 789

Military Info Publishing, PO Box 27640, Golden Valley, MN 55427 *Tel:* 763-533-8627 *Fax:* 763-533-8627 *E-mail:* publisher@military-info.com *Web Site:* www. military-info.com, pg 174

Military Living Publications, PO Box 2347, Falls Church, VA 22042-0347 *Tel:* 703-237-0203 *Fax:* 703-237-2233 *E-mail:* militaryliving@aol.com *Web Site:* www.militaryliving.com, pg 174

Milkweed Editions, 1011 Washington Ave S, Suite 300, Minneapolis, MN 55415 *Tel:* 612-332-3192 *Toll Free Tel:* 800-520-6455 *Fax:* 612-215-2550 *E-mail:* editor@milkweed.org *Web Site:* www. milkweed.org; www.worldashome.org, pg 174

Milkweed National Fiction Prize, 1011 Washington Ave S, Suite 300, Minneapolis, MN 55415 *Tel:* 612-332-3192 *Toll Free Tel:* 800-520-6455 *Fax:* 612-215-2550 *E-mail:* editor@milkweed.org *Web Site:* www.milkweed.org, pg 789

Mill Mountain Theatre, Center in the Square, 2nd fl, One Market Sq, Roanoke, VA 24011-1437 *Tel:* 540-342-5771 *Fax:* 540-342-5745 *E-mail:* outreach@millmountain.org *Web Site:* www.millmountain.org, pg 789

Martha Millard Literary Agency, 50 W 67 St, Suite 1-G, New York, NY 10023 *Tel:* 212-787-7769 *Fax:* 212-787-7867 *E-mail:* marmillink@aol.com, pg 644

The Millbrook Press Inc, 2 Old New Milford Rd, Brookfield, CT 06804 *Tel:* 203-740-2220 *Toll Free Tel:* 800-462-4703 *Fax:* 203-740-2526, pg 174

The Miller Agency Inc, One Sheridan Sq 7B, No 32, New York, NY 10014 *Tel:* 212-206-0913 *Fax:* 212-206-1473 *Web Site:* milleragency.net, pg 644

Richard K Miller Associates Inc, 4132 Atlanta Hwy, Suite 110-366, Loganville, GA 30052 *Tel:* 770-416-0006 *Fax:* 770-416-0052, pg 174

Robert Miller Gallery, 524 W 26 St, New York, NY 10001 *Tel:* 212-366-4774 *Fax:* 212-366-4454 *E-mail:* rmg@robertmillergallery.com *Web Site:* www.robertmillergallery.com, pg 175

Stephen M Miller, 15727 S Madison Dr, Olathe, KS 66062 *Tel:* 913-768-7997 *Fax:* 775-587-9195 *E-mail:* steve@miller-stephen.com *Web Site:* www.miller-stephen.com, pg 606

Milliken Publishing Co, 11643 Lilburn Park Dr, St Louis, MO 63146 *Tel:* 314-991-4220 *Toll Free Tel:* 800-325-4136 *Fax:* 314-991-4807 *Toll Free Fax:* 800-538-1319 *E-mail:* mpwebmaster@millikenpub.com *Web Site:* www.millikenpub.com, pg 175

Kathleen Mills Editorial & Production Services, PO Box 214, Chardon, OH 44024 *Tel:* 440-285-4347 *Fax:* 440-286-9213 *E-mail:* mills_edit@yahoo.com, pg 606

Milner Award, One Margaret Mitchell Sq NW, Atlanta, GA 30303 *Tel:* 404-730-1845 *Fax:* 404-730-1851, pg 790

Milton Dorfman Poetry Prize, 308 W Bloomfield St, Rome, NY 13440 *Tel:* 315-336-1040 *Fax:* 315-336-1090 *E-mail:* racc@borg.com, pg 790

The Minerals, Metals & Materials Society (TMS), 184 Thorn Hill Rd, Warrendale, PA 15086 *Tel:* 724-776-9000 *Toll Free Tel:* 800-759-4867 *Fax:* 724-776-3770 *E-mail:* publications@tms.org (orders) *Web Site:* www.tms.org (orders); www.tms.org/pubs/publications.html, pg 175

Miniature Book Society Inc, 402 York Ave, Delaware, OH 43015 *Web Site:* www.mbs.org, pg 691

Minnesota Historical Society Press, 345 Kellogg Blvd W, St Paul, MN 55102-1906 *Tel:* 651-296-2264 *Toll Free Tel:* 800-621-2736 *Fax:* 651-297-1345 *Toll Free Fax:* 800-621-8476 *Web Site:* www.mnhs.org/mhspress, pg 175

Mint Publishers Group, 62 June Rd, North Salem, NY 10560 *Tel:* 914-276-6576 *Fax:* 914-276-6579 *E-mail:* info@mintpub.com *Web Site:* www.mintpub.com, pg 175

Mississippi Review/University of Southern Mississippi, Center for Writers, Box 5144 USM, Hattiesburg, MS 39406 *Tel:* 601-266-5600 *Fax:* 601-266-5757 *E-mail:* rief@mississippireview.com *Web Site:* www.mississippireview.com; www.centerforwriters.com, pg 753

Mississippi River Writing Workshop, 720 Fourth Ave S, Riverview 101-D, St Cloud, MN 56301-4498 *Tel:* 320-308-3061; 320-308-4947 *Fax:* 320-308-5524, pg 744

Missouri Historical Society Press, PO Box 11940, St Louis, MO 63112-0040 *Tel:* 314-454-3150 *Fax:* 314-454-3162 *E-mail:* dtz@mohistory.org *Web Site:* www.mohistory.org, pg 175

MIT List Visual Arts Center, MIT E 15-109, 20 Ames St, Cambridge, MA 02139 *Tel:* 617-253-4680; 617-253-4400 (admission to exhibits) *Fax:* 617-258-7265 *E-mail:* hiroco@mit.edu *Web Site:* web.mit.edu/lvac, pg 175

The MIT Press, 5 Cambridge Ctr, Cambridge, MA 02142 *Tel:* 617-253-5646 *Toll Free Tel:* 800-405-1619 (orders only) *Fax:* 617-258-6779 *Web Site:* mitpress.mit.edu, pg 175

Mitchell Lane Publishers Inc, 1104 Kelly Dr, Newark, DE 19711 *Tel:* 302-234-9426 *Toll Free Tel:* 800-814-5484 *Fax:* 302-234-4742 *Toll Free Fax:* 866-834-4164 *E-mail:* mitchelllane@mitchelllane.com *Web Site:* www.mitchelllane.com, pg 176

W O Mitchell Literary Prize, 90 Richmond St W, Suite 200, Toronto, ON M5C 1P1, Canada *Tel:* 416-504-8222 *Fax:* 416-504-9090 *E-mail:* info@writerstrust.com *Web Site:* www.writerstrust.com, pg 790

MLA Prize for a Distinguished Bibliography, 26 Broadway, 3rd fl, New York, NY 10004-1789 *Tel:* 646-576-5141 *Fax:* 646-458-0030 *E-mail:* awards@mla.org *Web Site:* www.mla.org, pg 790

MLA Prize for Independent Scholars, 26 Broadway, 3rd fl, New York, NY 10004-1789 *Tel:* 646-576-5141 *Fax:* 646-458-0030 *E-mail:* awards@mla.org *Web Site:* www.mla.org, pg 790

MMB Music Inc, Contemporary Arts Bldg, 3526 Washington Ave, St Louis, MO 63103-1019 *Tel:* 314-531-9635 *Toll Free Tel:* 800-543-3771 *Fax:* 314-531-8384 *E-mail:* info@mmbmusic.com *Web Site:* www.mmbmusic.com, pg 176

Mobile Post Office Society, PO Box 427, Marstons Mills, MA 02648-0427 *Tel:* 508-428-9132 *Fax:* 508-428-2156 *E-mail:* dnc@math.uga.edu *Web Site:* www.eskimo.com/~rkunz/mposhome.html, pg 176

Mobility International USA, 45 W Broadway, Eugene, OR 97401 *Tel:* 541-343-1284 *Fax:* 541-343-6812 *E-mail:* info@miusa.org *Web Site:* www.miusa.org, pg 176

Sondra Mochson, 18 Overlook Dr, Port Washington, NY 11050 *Tel:* 516-883-0984, pg 606

Modern Curriculum Press, 299 Jefferson Rd, Parsippany, NJ 07054-0480 *Tel:* 973-739-8000 *Fax:* 973-739-8635 *Web Site:* www.pearsonlearning.com, pg 176

Modern Language Association of America (MLA), 26 Broadway, 3rd fl, New York, NY 10004-1789 *Tel:* 646-576-5000 *Fax:* 646-458-0030 *E-mail:* info@mla.org *Web Site:* www.mla.org, pg 176

Modern Language Association of America (MLA), 26 Broadway, 3rd fl, New York, NY 10004-1789 *Tel:* 646-576-5000 *Fax:* 646-458-0030 *E-mail:* convention@mla.org *Web Site:* www.mla.org, pg 691

Modern Language Association Prize for a Distinguished Scholarly Edition, 26 Broadway, 3rd fl, New York, NY 10004-1789 *Tel:* 646-576-5141 *Fax:* 646-458-0030 *E-mail:* awards@mla.org *Web Site:* www.mla.org, pg 790

Modern Language Association Prize for a First Book, 26 Broadway, 3rd fl, New York, NY 10004-1789 *Tel:* 646-576-5141 *Fax:* 646-458-0030 *E-mail:* awards@mla.org *Web Site:* www.mla.org, pg 790

Modern Language Association Prize in United States Latina & Latina & Latino & Chicana & Chicano Literary & Cultural Studies, 26 Broadway, 3rd fl, New York, NY 10004-1789 *Tel:* 646-576-5141 *Fax:* 646-458-0030 *E-mail:* awards@mla.org *Web Site:* www.mla.org, pg 790

Modern Publishing, 155 E 55 St, New York, NY 10022 *Tel:* 212-826-0850 *Fax:* 212-759-9069 *Web Site:* www.modernpublishing.com, pg 176

Modern Radio Laboratories, PO Box 14902, Minneapolis, MN 55414-0902 *Web Site:* www.modernradiolabs.com, pg 176

Modulo Editeur Inc, 233 Ave Dunbar, Rm 300, Mont Royal, PQ H3P 2H4, Canada *Tel:* 514-738-9818 *Toll Free Tel:* 888-738-9818 *Fax:* 514-738-5838 *Toll Free Fax:* 888-273-5247 *Web Site:* www.moduloediteur.com, pg 554

Modulo-Griffon Inc, 233 Dunbar Ave, Suite 300, Mont Royal, PQ H3P 2H4, Canada *Tel:* 514-738-9818 *Toll Free Tel:* 888-738-9818 *Fax:* 514-738-5838 *Toll Free Fax:* 888-273-5247 *Web Site:* www.moduloediteur.com, pg 554

Modus Vivendi Inc and Adventure Press, 5150 Saint Laurent, 2nd fl, Montreal, PQ H2T 1R8, Canada *Tel:* 514-272-0433 *Fax:* 514-272-7234 *E-mail:* enfo@modusadventure.com, pg 554

Moment Point Press Inc, 65 Rivard Rd, Needham, MA 02492 *Tel:* 781-449-9398 *Toll Free Tel:* 800-423-7087 (orders) *Fax:* 781-449-9397 *E-mail:* info@momentpoint.com *Web Site:* www.momentpoint.com, pg 176

MomsGuide.com Inc, 30 Doaks Lane, Marblehead, MA 01945 *Tel:* 781-639-7088 *Fax:* 781-639-7703 *E-mail:* mail@momsguide.com *Web Site:* www.momsguide.com; www.gametimeguides.com, pg 176

The Monacelli Press, 902 Broadway, 18th fl, New York, NY 10010 *Tel:* 212-777-0504 *Toll Free Tel:* 800-631-8571 (cust serv) *Fax:* 212-777-0514; 201-256-0000 (cust serv) *E-mail:* info@monacellipress.com; production@monacellipress.com; customerservice@penguinputnam.com *Web Site:* www.monacellipress.com, pg 177

Monday Morning Books Inc, PO Box 1134, Inverness, CA 94937-0034 *Tel:* 650-327-3374 *Toll Free Tel:* 800-255-6049 *Toll Free Fax:* 800-255-6048 *E-mail:* MMBooks@aol.com *Web Site:* www.mondaymorningbooks.com, pg 177

Mondia Editeurs Inc, 105 de Martigny Ouest, St-Jerome, PQ J7Y 2G2, Canada *Tel:* 450-438-8479 *Toll Free Tel:* 800-561-2371 (Canada) *Fax:* 450-432-3892 *E-mail:* info@mondiaduphare.net, pg 554

Mondo Publishing, 980 Avenue of the Americas, New York, NY 10018 *Tel:* 212-268-3560 *Toll Free Tel:* 800-242-3650 *Fax:* 212-268-3561 *E-mail:* mondopub@aol.com *Web Site:* www.mondopub.com, pg 177

Money Market Directories, 320 E Main St, Charlottesville, VA 22902 *Tel:* 434-977-1450 *Toll Free Tel:* 800-446-2810 *Fax:* 434-979-9962 *Web Site:* www.mmdwebaccess.com, pg 177

The Mongolia Society Inc, Indiana University, 322 Goodbody Hall, Bloomington, IN 47405-7005 *Tel:* 812-855-4078 *Fax:* 812-855-7500 *E-mail:* monsoc@indiana.edu *Web Site:* www.indiana.edu/~mongsoc, pg 177

Monogram Aviation Publications, PO Box 223, Sturbridge, MA 01566 *Tel:* 508-347-5574 *Fax:* 508-347-5772 *E-mail:* monogram@meganet.net *Web Site:* www.monogramaviation.com, pg 177

Montana Historical Society Press, 225 N Roberts St, Helena, MT 59620 *Tel:* 406-444-4741 (editorial); 406-444-2890 (ordering/marketing) *Toll Free Tel:* 800-243-9900 *Fax:* 406-444-2696 (ordering/marketing) *Web Site:* www.montanahistoricalsociety.org, pg 177

Lucy Maud Montgomery Literature for Children Prize, 115 Richmond St, Charlottetown, PE C1A 1H7, Canada *Tel:* 902-368-4410 *Fax:* 902-368-4418 *E-mail:* peiarts@peiartscouncil.com *Web Site:* www.peiartscouncil.com, pg 790

Monthly Review Press, 122 W 27 St, New York, NY 10001 *Tel:* 212-691-2555 *Toll Free Tel:* 800-670-9499 *Fax:* 212-727-3676 *E-mail:* mreview@igc.org *Web Site:* www.MonthlyReview.org, pg 177

Montreal-Contacts/The Rights Agency, PO Box 596-C, Montreal, PQ H2L 4K4, Canada *Tel:* 450-461-1575 *Fax:* 450-461-1505, pg 644

Moo Press Inc, PO Box 54, Warwick, NY 10990-0054 *Tel:* 845-987-7750 *Fax:* 845-987-7845 *E-mail:* info@moopress.com *Web Site:* www.moopress.com, pg 177

Moody Press, 820 N La Salle Blvd, Chicago, IL 60610 *Tel:* 312-329-2111 *Toll Free Tel:* 800-678-8812 *Fax:* 312-329-2019 *Web Site:* www.moodypress.org, pg 177

Moon Lady Press, PO Box 83, Marshfield Hills, MA 02051 *Tel:* 781-837-1618 *Toll Free Tel:* 800-840-0205 *Fax:* 781-837-7249 *Web Site:* www.donnagreen.com, pg 178

Moon Mountain Publishing, 80 Peachtree Rd, North Kingstown, RI 02852 *Tel:* 401-884-6703 *Toll Free Tel:* 800-353-5877 *Fax:* 401-884-7076 *E-mail:* hello@moonmountainpub.com *Web Site:* www.moonmountainpub.com, pg 178

Moonstone Press LLC, 7820 Oracle Place, Potomac, MD 20854 *Tel:* 301-765-1081 *Fax:* 301-765-0510 *E-mail:* mazeprod@erols.com *Web Site:* www.moonstonepress.net, pg 572

Moore Literary Agency, 10 State St, Suite 309, Newburyport, MA 01950 *Tel:* 978-465-9015 *Fax:* 978-465-8817, pg 644

Maureen Moran Agency, PO Box 20191, Park West Sta, New York, NY 10025-1518 *Tel:* 212-222-3838 *Fax:* 212-531-3464 *E-mail:* maureenm@erols.com, pg 644

Morehouse Publishing Co, PO Box 1321, Harrisburg, PA 17105-1321 *Tel:* 717-541-8130 *Toll Free Tel:* 800-877-0012 (orders only) *Fax:* 717-541-8136; 717-541-8128 (orders only) *E-mail:* morehouse@morehousegroup.com *Web Site:* www.morehousegroup.com, pg 178

Moreland Press Inc, 827 Christina Circle, Oldsmar, FL 34677 *Tel:* 813-891-0568 *Fax:* 813-891-0428 *E-mail:* morelandpress@aol.com *Web Site:* www.morelandpress.com, pg 178

Morgan Gaynin Inc, 194 Third Ave, New York, NY 10003 *Tel:* 212-475-0440 *Fax:* 212-353-8538 *E-mail:* info@morgangaynin.com *Web Site:* www.morgangaynin.com, pg 666

Morgan Kaufmann Publishers, 500 Sansome, Suite 400, San Francisco, CA 94111 *Tel:* 415-392-2665 *Fax:* 415-982-2665 *E-mail:* mkp@mkp.com *Web Site:* www.mkp.com, pg 178

Morgan Quinto Corp, PO Box 1656, Lawrence, KS 66044-8656 *Tel:* 785-841-3534 *Toll Free Tel:* 800-457-0742 *Fax:* 785-841-3568 *E-mail:* info@morganquinto.com *Web Site:* www.morganquinto.com, pg 178

Morgan Reynolds Publishing, 620 S Elm St, Suite 223, Greensboro, NC 27406 *Tel:* 336-275-1311 *Toll Free Tel:* 800-535-1504 *Fax:* 336-275-1152 *Toll Free Fax:* 800-535-5725 *E-mail:* editorial@morganreynolds.com *Web Site:* www.morganreynolds.com, pg 178

Howard Morhaim Literary Agency Inc, 11 John St, Suite 407, New York, NY 10038 *Tel:* 212-529-4433 *Fax:* 212-995-1112, pg 644

Morning Glory Press Inc, 6595 San Haroldo Way, Buena Park, CA 90620-3748 *Tel:* 714-828-1998 *Toll Free Tel:* 888-612-8254 *Fax:* 714-828-2049 *Toll Free Fax:* 888-327-4362 *E-mail:* info@morningglorypress.com *Web Site:* www.morningglorypress.com, pg 178

Morning Sun Books Inc, 9 Pheasant Lane, Scotch Plains, NJ 07076 *Tel:* 908-755-5454 *Fax:* 908-755-5455 *Web Site:* www.morningsunbooks.com, pg 178

Morningside Bookshop, 260 Oak St, Dayton, OH 45410 *Tel:* 937-461-6736 *Toll Free Tel:* 800-648-9710 *Fax:* 937-461-4260 *E-mail:* msbooks@erinet.com *Web Site:* www.morningsidebooks.com, pg 178

William Morris Agency, 1325 Avenue of the Americas, New York, NY 10019 *Tel:* 212-586-5100 *Fax:* 212-903-1418 *E-mail:* wma@interport.net *Web Site:* www.wma.com, pg 645

William Morris Society in the United States Fellowships, PO Box 53263, Washington, DC 20009 *Web Site:* www.morrissociety.org, pg 790

Henry Morrison Inc, PO Box 235, Bedford Hills, NY 10507-0235 *Tel:* 914-666-3500 *Fax:* 914-241-7846, pg 645

Samuel French Morse Poetry Prize, 406 Holmes, Boston, MA 02115 *Tel:* 617-373-4540 *Web Site:* www.casdn.neu.edu/~english, pg 790

Morton Publishing Co, 925 W Kenyon Ave, Unit 12, Englewood, CO 80110 *Tel:* 303-761-4805 *Fax:* 303-762-9923 *E-mail:* morton@morton-pub.com *Web Site:* www.morton-pub.com, pg 179

Mosaic Press, 358 Oliver Rd, Cincinnati, OH 45215 *Tel:* 513-761-5977 *Fax:* 513-761-5977 *Web Site:* www.mosaicpress.com, pg 179

Mosaic Press, DMB 145, 4500 Witmer Industrial Estates, Niagara Falls, NY 14305-1386 *Tel:* 905-825-2130 *Toll Free Tel:* 800-387-8992 *Fax:* 905-825-2130 *E-mail:* mosaicpress@on.aibn.com *Web Site:* www.mosaic-press.com, pg 179

Mosby Journal Division, 11830 Westline Industrial Dr, St Louis, MO 63146 *Tel:* 314-872-8370 *Toll Free Tel:* 800-325-4177 *Web Site:* www.elsevierhealth.com, pg 179

George L Mosse Prize, 400 "A" St SE, Washington, DC 20003 *Tel:* 202-544-2422 *Fax:* 202-544-8307 *E-mail:* info@historians.org *Web Site:* www.historians.org, pg 790

Motion Picture Association of America Inc (MPAA), 1600 "I" St NW, Washington, DC 20006 *Tel:* 202-293-1966 *Fax:* 202-293-7674 *Web Site:* www.mpaa.org, pg 691

Frank Luther Mott-Kappa Tau Alpha Research Award, University of Missouri, School of Journalism, Columbia, MO 65211-1200 *Tel:* 573-882-7685 *Fax:* 573-884-1720 *E-mail:* umcjourkta@missouri.edu, pg 791

Sheila Margaret Motton Prize, 16 Cornell St, Arlington, MA 02474 *Web Site:* www.nepoetryclub.org, pg 791

Mount Ida Press, 152 Washington Ave, Albany, NY 12210-2203 *Tel:* 518-426-5935 *Fax:* 518-426-4116 *E-mail:* info@mtidapress.com *Web Site:* www.mountidapress.com, pg 179

Mount Olive College Press, 634 Henderson St, Mount Olive, NC 28365 *Tel:* 919-658-2502 *Toll Free Tel:* 800-653-0854 *Fax:* 919-658-7180 *Web Site:* www.mountolivecollege.edu, pg 179

Mountain n' Air Books, 2947-A Honolulu Ave, La Crescenta, CA 91214 *Tel:* 818-248-9345 *Toll Free Tel:* 800-446-9696 *Fax:* 818-248-6516 *Toll Free Fax:* 800-303-5578 *Web Site:* www.mountain-n-air.com, pg 179

Mountain Press Publishing Co, 1301 S Third W, Missoula, MT 59801 *Tel:* 406-728-1900 *Toll Free Tel:* 800-234-5308 *Fax:* 406-728-1635 *E-mail:* info@mtnpress.com *Web Site:* www.mountain-press.com, pg 179

Mountain View Press, 19500 Skyline Blvd, La Honda, CA 94020 *Tel:* 650-747-0760 *Web Site:* www.theforthsource.com, pg 179

The Mountaineers Books, 1001 SW Klickitat Way, Suite 201, Seattle, WA 98134 *Tel:* 206-223-6303 *Toll Free Tel:* 800-553-4453 *Fax:* 206-223-6306 *Toll Free Fax:* 800-568-7604 *E-mail:* mbooks@mountaineers.org *Web Site:* www.mountaineersbooks.org, pg 179

Mouton de Gruyter, 500 Executive Blvd, Ossining, NY 10562 *Tel:* 914-762-5866 *Fax:* 914-762-0371 *E-mail:* info@degruyterny.com *Web Site:* www.degruyter.com, pg 179

Andrew Mowbray Inc Publishers, PO Box 460, Lincoln, RI 02865-0460 *Tel:* 401-726-8011 *Toll Free Tel:* 800-999-4697 *Fax:* 401-726-8061 *E-mail:* service@manatarmbooks.com *Web Site:* www.manatarmbooks.com, pg 180

Moyer Bell Ltd, 549 Old North Rd, Kingston, RI 02881 *Tel:* 401-783-5480 *Fax:* 401-284-0959 *E-mail:* acornalliance@yahoo.com *Web Site:* www.acornalliance.com, pg 180

Moznaim Publishing Corp, 4304 12 Ave, Brooklyn, NY 11219 *Tel:* 718-438-7680 *Toll Free Tel:* 800-364-5118 *Fax:* 718-438-1305, pg 180

MS Public Education Awards Program, 733 Third Ave, New York, NY 10017 *Tel:* 212-476-0436 *Fax:* 212-986-7981 *Web Site:* www.nationalmssociety.org, pg 791

M2 Pathways Inc, PO Box 733, Bozeman, MT 59771 *Tel:* 406-582-1009 *Fax:* 406-994-0496 *E-mail:* comments@m2pathways.com *Web Site:* www.m2pathways.com, pg 572

Mary Mueller, 516 Bartram Rd, Moorestown, NJ 08057 *Tel:* 856-778-4769 *E-mail:* mamam49@aol.com, pg 606

Multicultural Publications, 936 Slosson Ave, Akron, OH 44320 *Tel:* 330-865-9578 *Toll Free Tel:* 800-238-0297 *Fax:* 330-865-9578 *E-mail:* info@multiculturalpub.net *Web Site:* www.multiculturalpub.net, pg 180

Editions Multimondes, 930 rue Pouliot, Sainte-Foy, PQ G1V 3N9, Canada *Tel:* 418-651-3885 *Toll Free Tel:* 800-840-3029 *Fax:* 418-651-6822 *Toll Free Fax:* 888-303-5931 *E-mail:* multimondes@multim.com *Web Site:* www.multimondes.qc.ca, pg 555

Multnomah Publishers Inc, 204 W Adams Ave, Sisters, OR 97759 *Tel:* 541-549-1144 *Toll Free Tel:* 800-929-0910 *Fax:* 541-549-2044 (sales); 541-549-0432 (admin); 541-549-0260 (ed/prod); 541-549-8048 (mktg) *E-mail:* information@multnomahbooks.com *Web Site:* www.multnomahbooks.com, pg 180

Erika Mumford Prize, 16 Cornell St, Arlington, MA 02474 *Web Site:* www.nepoetryclub.org, pg 791

Munchweiler Press, 14217 Gale Dr, Victorville, CA 92394-7353 *Tel:* 760-245-9215 *Fax:* 760-245-9418 *E-mail:* publisher@munchweilerpress.com *Web Site:* www.munchweilerpress.com, pg 180

Mundania Press, 6470A Glenway Ave, Suite 109, Cincinnati, OH 45211-5222 *Tel:* 513-574-8902 *Fax:* 513-598-6800 *E-mail:* books@mundania.com *Web Site:* www.mundania.com, pg 180

Municipal Analysis Services Inc, PO Box 13453, Austin, TX 78711-3453 *Tel:* 512-327-3328 *Fax:* 413-740-1294 *E-mail:* munilysis@hotmail.com, pg 180

Muse Imagery LLC, 9811 W Charleston Blvd, Suite 2390, Las Vegas, NV 89117-7519 *Tel:* 702-233-5910 *Fax:* 702-233-1762 *E-mail:* publisher@museimagery.com *Web Site:* www.museimagery.com, pg 572

The Museum of Modern Art, 11 W 53 St, New York, NY 10019 *Tel:* 212-708-9443 *Fax:* 212-333-6575 *E-mail:* moma_publications@moma.org *Web Site:* www.moma.org, pg 180

Museum of New Mexico Press, 725 Camino Lejo, Santa Fe, NM 87501 *Tel:* 505-476-1158 *Toll Free Tel:* 800-249-7737 (orders) *Fax:* 505-476-1156 *Toll Free Fax:* 800-622-8667 (orders) *E-mail:* mnmpress@aol.com *Web Site:* www.mnmpress.org, pg 180

Music Publishers' Association of the United States, 2435 Fifth Ave, Suite 236, New York, NY 10016 *Tel:* 212-327-4044 *Fax:* 212-327-4044 *Web Site:* host.mpa.org; www.mpa.org, pg 691

Muska & Lipman Publishing, 25 Thomson Place, Boston, MA 02210 *Tel:* 617-757-7900 *Fax:* 513-924-9333 *Web Site:* www.muskalipman.com, pg 180

Mustang Publishing Co Inc, PO Box 770426, Memphis, TN 38177-0426 *Tel:* 901-684-1200 *Toll Free Tel:* 800-250-8713 *Fax:* 901-684-1256 *E-mail:* info@mustangpublishing.com *Web Site:* www.mustangpublishing.com, pg 181

My Chaotic Life™, 23062 La Cadena Dr, Laguna Hills, CA 92653 *Tel:* 949-380-7510 *Toll Free Tel:* 800-426-0099 *Fax:* 949-380-7575 *Web Site:* www.mychaoticlife.com, pg 181

Mysterious Content, 108 E 38 St, Suite 409, New York, NY 10016 *Tel:* 212-925-3721 *E-mail:* myscontent@aol.com, pg 645

Mystery Writers of America, 17 E 47 St, 6th fl, New York, NY 10017 *Tel:* 212-888-8171 *E-mail:* mwa@mysterywriters.org *Web Site:* www.mysterywriters.org, pg 691, 753

Mystic Ridge Books, PO Box 66930, Albuquerque, NM 87193 *Tel:* 505-899-2121 *E-mail:* publisher@mysticridgebooks.com *Web Site:* www.mysticridgebooks.com, pg 181

Mystic Seaport, PO Box 6000, Mystic, CT 06355-0990 *Tel:* 860-572-0711 *Fax:* 860-572-5321 *Web Site:* www.mysticseaport.org, pg 181

Mythopoeic Awards, PO Box 320486, San Francisco, CA 94132 *E-mail:* edith.crowe@sjsu.edu *Web Site:* www.mythsoc.org, pg 791

NACE International, 1440 S Creek Dr, Houston, TX 77084-4906 *Tel:* 281-228-6223 *Fax:* 281-228-6300 *E-mail:* pubs@mail.nace.org *Web Site:* www.nace.org, pg 181

NAFSA: Association of International Educators, 1307 New York Ave NW, 8th fl, Washington, DC 20005-4701 *Tel:* 202-737-3699 *Toll Free Tel:* 800-836-4994 (Book orders only) *Fax:* 202-737-3657 *E-mail:* inbox@nafsa.org *Web Site:* www.nafsa.org, pg 181

Jean V Naggar Literary Agency, 216 E 75 St, Suite 1-E, New York, NY 10021 *Tel:* 212-794-1082, pg 645

NAL, 375 Hudson St, New York, NY 10014 *Tel:* 212-366-2000 *E-mail:* online@penguinputnam.com *Web Site:* www.penguin.com, pg 181

Napa Valley Writers' Conference-Poetry & Fiction Sessions, Upper Valley Campus, 1088 College Ave, St Helena, CA 94574 *Tel:* 707-967-2900 (ext 1611) *Fax:* 707-967-2909 *E-mail:* writecon@napavalley.edu *Web Site:* www.napavalley.edu/writersconf, pg 745

Napa Writing Retreats, PO Box 3214, Napa, CA 94558 *Tel:* 707-252-1030 *Toll Free Tel:* 866-848-2961 *E-mail:* info@napawritingretreats.com *Web Site:* www.napawritingretreats.com, pg 745

NAPL, 75 W Century Rd, Paramus, NJ 07652 *Tel:* 201-634-9600 *Toll Free Tel:* 800-642-6275 *Fax:* 201-634-0324 *E-mail:* membership@napl.org; orders@napl.org *Web Site:* www.napl.org, pg 691

Napoleon Publishing/Rendezvous Press, 178 Willowdale Ave, Suite 201, Toronto, ON M2N 4Y8, Canada *Tel:* 416-730-9052 *Toll Free Tel:* 877-730-9052 *Fax:* 416-730-8096 *E-mail:* napoleonpublishing@transmedia95.com *Web Site:* www.transmedia95.com, pg 555

NAR Publications, State Rte 55, Barryville, NY 12719 *Tel:* 845-557-8713 *E-mail:* narpubs@aol.com, pg 181

Narada Press, 160 Columbia St W, Suite 147, Waterloo, ON N2L 3L3, Canada *Tel:* 519-886-1969, pg 555

The Narrative Press, 319 Salida Del Sol, Santa Barbara, CA 93109 *Tel:* 805-966-2186 *Fax:* 805-456-3915 *E-mail:* admin@narrativepress.com *Web Site:* www.narrativepress.com, pg 181

Nataraj Books, 7073 Brookfield Plaza, Springfield, VA 22150 *Tel:* 703-455-4996 *Fax:* 703-912-9052 *E-mail:* nataraj@erols.com *Web Site:* www.natarajbooks.com, pg 181

Nation Books, 245 W 17 St, 11th fl, New York, NY 10011-5300 *Tel:* 646-375-2570 *Fax:* 646-375-2571 *Web Site:* www.nationbooks.org, pg 182

National Academies Press, 500 Fifth St NW, Washington, DC 20001 *Tel:* 202-334-3313 *Toll Free Tel:* 800-624-6242 *Fax:* 202-334-2451 (orders) *Web Site:* www.nap.edu, pg 182

National Association of Black Journalists (NABJ), c/o University of Maryland, 8701 Adelphi Rd, Adelphi, MD 20783 *Tel:* 301-445-7100 *Fax:* 301-445-7101 *E-mail:* nabj@nabj.org *Web Site:* www.nabj.org, pg 692

National Association of Broadcasters (NAB), 1771 "N" St NW, Washington, DC 20036 *Tel:* 202-429-5300 *Toll Free Tel:* 800-368-5644 *Fax:* 202-775-3515 *Web Site:* www.nab.org, pg 182

National Association of Broadcasters (NAB), 1771 "N" St NW, Washington, DC 20036 *Tel:* 202-429-5300 *Toll Free Tel:* 800-368-5644 *Fax:* 202-429-3922 *E-mail:* nab@nab.org *Web Site:* www.nab.org, pg 692

National Association of College Stores (NACS), 500 E Lorain St, Oberlin, OH 44074 *Tel:* 440-775-7777 *Toll Free Tel:* 800-622-7498 *Fax:* 440-775-4769 *Web Site:* www.nacs.org, pg 692

National Association of Hispanic Publications Inc (NAHP), National Press Bldg, 529 14 St, Suite 1085, Washington, DC 20045 *Tel:* 202-662-7250 *Fax:* 202-662-7251, pg 692

National Association of Independent Publishers (NAIP), PO Box 430, Highland City, FL 33846-0430 *Tel:* 863-648-4420 *Fax:* 863-647-5951 *E-mail:* naip@aol.com *Web Site:* www.publishersreport.com, pg 692

National Association of Independent Publishers Representatives (NAIPR), Zeckendorf Towers, 111 E 14 St, PMB 157, New York, NY 10003 *Tel:* 207-832-7744 *Toll Free Tel:* 888-624-7779 *Fax:* 207-832-6073 *Toll Free Fax:* 800-416-2586 *E-mail:* naiprtwo@aol.com *Web Site:* www.naipr.org, pg 692

National Association of Insurance Commissioners, 2301 McGee, Suite 800, Kansas City, MO 64108 *Tel:* 816-842-3600; 816-783-8300 (Pubns) *Fax:* 816-471-7004 *Web Site:* www.naic.org, pg 182

National Association of Printing Ink Manufacturers (NAPIM), 581 Main St, Woodbridge, NJ 07095 *Tel:* 732-855-1525 *Fax:* 732-855-1838 *E-mail:* napim@napim.org *Web Site:* www.napim.org, pg 692

National Association of Real Estate Editors, 1003 NW Sixth Terr, Boca Raton, FL 33486-3455 *Tel:* 561-391-3599 *Fax:* 561-391-0099 *Web Site:* www.naree.org, pg 692

National Association of Science Writers (NASW), PO Box 890, Hedgesville, WV 25427 *Tel:* 304-754-5077 *Fax:* 304-754-5076 *Web Site:* www.nasw.org, pg 692

National Association of Secondary School Principals, 1904 Association Dr, Reston, VA 20191 *Tel:* 703-860-0200 *Toll Free Tel:* 800-253-7746 *Fax:* 703-476-5432 *Web Site:* www.principals.org, pg 182

National Association of Social Workers (NASW), 750 First St NE, Suite 700, Washington, DC 20002-4241 *Tel:* 301-317-8688 *Toll Free Tel:* 800-227-3590 *Fax:* 301-206-7989 *E-mail:* nasw@pmds.com *Web Site:* www.socialworkers.org, pg 182

National Awards for Education Reporting, 2122 "P" St NW, No 201, Washington, DC 20037 *Tel:* 202-452-9830 *Fax:* 202-452-9837 *E-mail:* ewa@ewa.org *Web Site:* www.ewa.org, pg 791

National Book Awards, 95 Madison Ave, Suite 709, New York, NY 10016 *Tel:* 212-685-0261 *Fax:* 212-213-6570 *E-mail:* nationalbook@national.org *Web Site:* www.nationalbook.org, pg 791

National Book Co, PO Box 8795, Portland, OR 97207-8795 *Tel:* 503-228-6345 *Fax:* 810-885-5811 *E-mail:* info@eralearning.com *Web Site:* www.eralearning.com, pg 182

National Braille Press, 88 Saint Stephen St, Boston, MA 02115 *Tel:* 617-266-6160 *Toll Free Tel:* 800-548-7323 (cust serv) *Fax:* 617-437-0456 *E-mail:* orders@nbp.org *Web Site:* www.nbp.org, pg 182

National Bureau of Economic Research Inc, 1050 Massachusetts Ave, Cambridge, MA 02138-5398 *Tel:* 617-868-3900 *Fax:* 617-868-2742 *E-mail:* op@nber.org *Web Site:* www.nber.org, pg 182

The National Business Book Award, Royal Trust Tower, TD Centre, Suite 3000, 77 King St W, Toronto, ON M5K 1G8, Canada *Tel:* 416-941-8383 *Fax:* 416-941-8345 *Web Site:* www.pwcglobal.com, pg 791

National Cable Telecommunications Association (NCTA), 1724 Massachusetts Ave NW, Washington, DC 20036 *Tel:* 202-775-3550 *Fax:* 202-775-3676 *Web Site:* www.ncta.com, pg 692

National Cartoonists Society (NCS), 1133 W Morse Blvd, Suite 201, Winter Park, FL 32789 *Tel:* 407-647-8839 *Fax:* 407-629-2502 *Web Site:* www.reuben.org, pg 692

National Catholic Educational Association, 1077 30 St NW, Suite 100, Washington, DC 20007-3852 *Tel:* 202-337-6232 *Fax:* 202-333-6706 *Web Site:* www.ncea.org, pg 182

National Center for Children in Poverty, 215 W 125 St, 3rd fl, New York, NY 10027 *Tel:* 646-284-9600 *Fax:* 646-284-9623 *E-mail:* nccp@columbia.edu *Web Site:* www.nccp.org, pg 183

National Center For Employee Ownership (NCEO), 1736 Franklin St, 8th fl, Oakland, CA 94612-3445 *Tel:* 510-208-1300 *Fax:* 510-272-9510 *E-mail:* nceo@nceo.org *Web Site:* www.nceo.org, pg 183

National Coalition Against Censorship (NCAC), 275 Seventh Ave, 9th fl, New York, NY 10001 *Tel:* 212-807-6222 *Fax:* 212-807-6245 *E-mail:* ncac@ncac.org *Web Site:* www.ncac.org, pg 692

National Coalition for Literacy, 50 E Huron St, Chicago, IL 60611 *Tel:* 312-280-3275 *Toll Free Tel:* 800-228-8813 *Fax:* 312-280-3256 *E-mail:* ncl@ala.org *Web Site:* www.ala.org, pg 693

National Communication Association, 1765 North St NW, Washington, DC 20036 *Tel:* 202-464-4622 *Fax:* 202-464-4600 *Web Site:* www.natcom.org, pg 693

The National Conference for Community & Justice, 475 Park Ave S, New York City, NY 10016 *Tel:* 212-545-1300 *Fax:* 212-545-8053 *Web Site:* www.nccj.org, pg 693

National Conference of Editorial Writers, 3899 N Front St, Harrisburg, PA 17110 *Tel:* 717-703-3015 *Fax:* 717-703-3014 *E-mail:* ncew@pa-news.org *Web Site:* www.ncew.org, pg 693

National Conference of State Legislatures, 7700 E First Place, Denver, CO 80230 *Tel:* 303-364-7700 *Fax:* 303-364-7812 *E-mail:* books@ncsl.org *Web Site:* www.ncsl.org, pg 183

National Council of Teachers of English (NCTE), 1111 W Kenyon Rd, Urbana, IL 61801-1096 *Tel:* 217-328-3870 *Toll Free Tel:* 800-369-6283; 877-369-6283 (cust serv) *Fax:* 217-328-0977 *E-mail:* orders@ncte.org *Web Site:* www.ncte.org, pg 183

National Council of Teachers of English (NCTE), 1111 W Kenyon Rd, Urbana, IL 61801-1096 *Tel:* 217-328-3870 *Toll Free Tel:* 877-369-6283; 877-369-6283 (cust serv) *Fax:* 217-328-0977 *E-mail:* public_info@ncte.org *Web Site:* www.ncte.org, pg 693

National Council of Teachers of Mathematics, 1906 Association Dr, Reston, VA 20191-1502 *Tel:* 703-620-9840 *Toll Free Tel:* 800-235-7566 *Fax:* 703-476-2970 *E-mail:* orders@nctm.org *Web Site:* www.nctm.org, pg 183

National Council on Radiation Protection & Measurements (NCRP), 7910 Woodmont Ave, Suite 400, Bethesda, MD 20814 *Tel:* 301-657-2652 *Toll Free Tel:* 800-229-2652 *Fax:* 301-907-8768 *E-mail:* ncrp@ncrp.com *Web Site:* www.ncrp.com, pg 183

National Crime Prevention Council, 1000 Connecticut Ave NW, 13th fl, Washington, DC 20036-5325 *Tel:* 202-466-6272 *Toll Free Tel:* 800-627-2911 (orders only) *Fax:* 202-296-1356 *Web Site:* www.ncpc.org, pg 183

National Education Association (NEA), 1201 16 St NW, Washington, DC 20036 *Tel:* 202-833-4000; 202-822-7207 (ed office) *Fax:* 202-822-7206 *Web Site:* www.nea.org, pg 183

National Education Association (NEA), 1201 16 St NW, Washington, DC 20036 *Tel:* 202-822-7200 *Fax:* 202-822-7206; 202-822-7292 *Web Site:* www.nea.org, pg 693

The National Endowment for the Arts, Nancy Hanks Ctr, 1100 Pennsylvania Ave NW, Room 720, Washington, DC 20506-0001 *Tel:* 202-682-5428 *Fax:* 202-682-5669 *Web Site:* www.arts.gov, pg 705

National Endowment for the Humanities Fellowships & Folger Longterm & Short-term Fellowships & Andrew W Mellon Foundations, c/o Fellowship Committee, 201 E Capitol St SE, Washington, DC 20003 *Tel:* 202-544-4600 (ext 348) *Fax:* 202-544-4623 *Web Site:* www.folger.edu, pg 791

National Federation of Abstracting & Information Services (NFAIS), 1518 Walnut St, Suite 1004, Philadelphia, PA 19102-3403 *Tel:* 215-893-1561 *Fax:* 215-893-1564 *E-mail:* nfais@nfais.org *Web Site:* www.nfais.org, pg 693

National Federation of Press Women Inc (NFPW), PO Box 5556, Arlington, VA 22205-0056 *Tel:* 703-534-2500 *Toll Free Tel:* 800-780-2715 *Fax:* 703-534-5751 *E-mail:* presswomen@aol.com *Web Site:* www.nfpw.org, pg 693

National Federation of State Poetry Societies Annual Poetry Contest, 13211 NW Holly Rd, Bremerton, WA 98312 *Web Site:* www.NFSPS.com, pg 791

National Gallery of Art, Fourth St & Constitution Ave, Landover, MD 20565 *Tel:* 202-842-6200 *Fax:* 202-408-8530 *Web Site:* www.nga.gov, pg 183

National Gallery of Canada, The Bookstore, 380 Sussex Dr, Ottawa, ON K1N 9N4, Canada *Tel:* 613-990-0962 (mail order sales) *Fax:* 613-990-1972 *E-mail:* ngcbook@gallery.ca *Web Site:* www.national.gallery.ca, pg 555

National Geographic Books, 1145 17 St NW, Washington, DC 20036 *Tel:* 202-857-7000 *Fax:* 202-857-7670 *Web Site:* www.nationalgeographics.com, pg 183

National Geographic Society, 1145 17 St NW, Washington, DC 20036 *Tel:* 202-857-7000 *Fax:* 202-429-5727 *Web Site:* www.nationalgeographic.com, pg 184

National Golf Foundation, 1150 S US Hwy One, Suite 401, Jupiter, FL 33477 *Tel:* 561-744-6006 *Toll Free Tel:* 800-733-6006 *Fax:* 561-744-6107 *E-mail:* ngf@ngf.org *Web Site:* www.ngf.org, pg 184

National Information Services Corp (NISC), Wyman Towers, 3100 Saint Paul St, Baltimore, MD 21218 *Tel:* 410-243-0797 *Fax:* 410-243-0982 *E-mail:* info@nisc.com; editor@nisc.com (comments); sales@nisc.com (sales); support@nisc.com (cust support) *Web Site:* www.nisc.com, pg 184

National Information Standards Organization, 4733 Bethesda Ave, Suite 300, Bethesda, MD 20814 *Tel:* 301-654-2512 *Fax:* 301-654-1721 *E-mail:* nisohq@niso.org *Web Site:* www.niso.org, pg 184, 693

National Institute for Trial Advocacy, University of Notre Dame, Notre Dame, IN 46556-6500 *Tel:* 574-271-8370 *Toll Free Tel:* 800-225-6482 *Fax:* 574-271-8375 *E-mail:* nita.1@nd.edu *Web Site:* www.nita.org, pg 184

National Jewish Book Award-Children's Literature, 15 E 26 St, 10th fl, New York, NY 10010-1579 *Tel:* 212-532-4949 (ext 297) *Fax:* 212-481-4174 *E-mail:* jbc@jewishbooks.org *Web Site:* www.jewishbookcouncil.org, pg 791

National Jewish Book Award-Children's Picture Book, 15 E 26 St, 10th fl, New York, NY 10010-1579 *Tel:* 212-532-4949 (ext 297) *Fax:* 212-481-4174 *E-mail:* jbc@jewishbooks.org *Web Site:* www.jewishbookcouncil.org, pg 791

National Jewish Book Award-Contemporary Jewish Life & Practices, 15 E 26 St, 10th fl, New York, NY 10010-1579 *Tel:* 212-532-4949 (ext 297) *Fax:* 212-481-4174 *E-mail:* jbc@jewishbooks.org *Web Site:* www.jewishbookcouncil.org, pg 792

National Jewish Book Award-Contemporary Jewish Thought & Experience, 15 E 26 St, 10th fl, New York, NY 10010-1579 *Tel:* 212-532-4949 (ext 297) *Fax:* 212-481-4174 *E-mail:* jbc@jewishbooks.org *Web Site:* www.jewishbookcouncil.org, pg 792

National Jewish Book Award-Jewish History, 15 E 26 St, 10th fl, New York, NY 10010-1579 *Tel:* 212-532-4949 (ext 297) *Fax:* 212-481-4174 *E-mail:* jbc@jewishbooks.org *Web Site:* www.jewishbookcouncil.org, pg 792

National Jewish Book Award-Scholarship, 15 E 26 St, 10th fl, New York, NY 10010-1579 *Tel:* 212-532-4949 (ext 297) *Fax:* 212-481-4174 *E-mail:* jbc@jewishbooks.org *Web Site:* www.jewishbookcouncil.org, pg 792

National Jewish Book Awards, 15 E 26 St, New York, NY 10010-1579 *Tel:* 212-532-4949 (ext 297) *Fax:* 212-481-4174 *E-mail:* jbc@jewishbooks.org *Web Site:* www.jewishbookcouncil.org, pg 792

National League of American Pen Women, c/o National Pen Women-Scholarship, Pen Arts Bldg, 1300 17 St NW, Washington, DC 20036-1973 *Web Site:* www.americanpenwomen.org, pg 693

National League of Cities, 1301 Pennsylvania Ave NW, Washington, DC 20004-1763 *Tel:* 202-626-3000 *Fax:* 202-626-3043 *Web Site:* www.nlc.org, pg 184

National Learning Corp, 212 Michael Dr, Syosset, NY 11791 *Tel:* 516-921-8888 *Toll Free Tel:* 800-645-6337 *Fax:* 516-921-8743 *Web Site:* www.passbooks.com, pg 184

National Mental Health Association, 2001 N Beauregard St, 12th fl, Alexandria, VA 22311 *Tel:* 703-684-7722 *Toll Free Tel:* 800-969-6642 *Fax:* 703-684-5968 *Web Site:* www.nmha.org, pg 694

The National Museum of Women in the Arts, 1250 New York Ave NW, Washington, DC 20005 *Tel:* 202-783-5000 *Toll Free Tel:* 800-222-7270 *Fax:* 202-393-3234 *Web Site:* www.nmwa.org, pg 184

National Music Publishers' Association (NMPA), 711 Third Ave, 8th fl, New York, NY 10017 *Tel:* 646-742-1651 *Fax:* 646-742-1779 *Web Site:* www.nmpa.org, pg 694

National Newspaper Association, University of Missouri, 127-129 Neff Annex, Columbia, MO 65211-1200 *Tel:* 573-882-5800 *Toll Free Tel:* 800-829-4662 *Fax:* 703-884-5490 *E-mail:* info@nna.org *Web Site:* www.nna.org, pg 694

National Newspaper Publishers Assn (NNPA), 3200 13 St NW, Washington, DC 20010 *Tel:* 202-588-8764 *Fax:* 202-588-8960 *E-mail:* info@blackpressusa.com *Web Site:* www.nnpa.org; www.blackpressusa.com, pg 694

National Notary Association, 9350 De Soto Ave, Chatsworth, CA 91311 *Tel:* 818-739-4000 *Toll Free Tel:* 800-876-6827 *Fax:* 818-700-0920 *E-mail:* nna@nationalnotary.org *Web Site:* www.nationalnotary.org, pg 184

National One-Act Playwriting Competition, 600 Wolfe St, Alexandria, VA 22314 *Tel:* 703-683-5778 *Fax:* 703-683-1378 *E-mail:* asklta@thelittletheatre.com *Web Site:* www.thelittletheatre.com, pg 792

National Outdoor Book Awards, 1065 S Eighth Ave, Pocatello, ID 83209 *Tel:* 208-236-3912 *Fax:* 208-236-4600 *Web Site:* www.isu.edu/outdoor/books/, pg 792

National Park Service Media Production, Harpers Ferry Ctr, Harpers Ferry, WV 25425 *Tel:* 304-535-6018 *Fax:* 304-535-6144 *Web Site:* www.nps.gov/hfc, pg 184

National Poetry Competition, PO Box 298, Thomaston, ME 04861 *Tel:* 207-354-0998 *E-mail:* cal@americanletters.org *Web Site:* www.americanletters.org, pg 792

National Poetry Series Open Competition, 57 Mountain Ave, Princeton, NJ 08540 *Tel:* 609-430-0999 *Fax:* 609-430-9933 *Web Site:* www.nationalpoetryseries.com, pg 792

National Press Club (NPC), 529 14 St NW, 13th fl, Washington, DC 20045 *Tel:* 202-662-7500 *Fax:* 202-662-7569 *E-mail:* infocenter@npcpress.org *Web Site:* www.press.org, pg 694

National Press Club of Canada, 150 Wellington St, 2nd fl, Ottawa, ON K1P 5A4, Canada *Tel:* 613-233-5641 *Fax:* 613-233-3511 *E-mail:* members@pressclub.on.ca *Web Site:* www.pressclub.on.ca, pg 694

The National Press Foundation, 1211 Connecticut Ave NW, Suite 310, Washington, DC 20036 *Tel:* 202-530-5355 *Fax:* 202-530-2855 *Web Site:* www.nationalpress.org, pg 694

National Press Photographers Association Inc (NPPA), 3200 Croasdaile Dr, Suite 306, Durham, NC 27705 *Tel:* 919-383-7246 *Fax:* 919-383-7261 *E-mail:* info@nppa.org *Web Site:* www.nppa.org, pg 694

National Publishing Co, 11311 Roosevelt Blvd, Philadelphia, PA 19154-2105 *Tel:* 215-676-1863 *Toll Free Tel:* 888-333-1863 *Fax:* 215-673-8069 *Web Site:* www.courier.com, pg 184

National Register Publishing, 562 Central Ave, New Providence, NJ 07974 *Tel:* 908-673-1001 *Toll Free Tel:* 800-473-7020 *Fax:* 909-673-1189 *Web Site:* www.nationalregisterpub.com, pg 185

National Resource Center for Youth Services (NRCYS), Schusterman Center, 4502 E 41 St, Bldg 4W, Tulsa, OK 74135-2512 *Tel:* 918-660-3700 *Toll Free Tel:* 800-274-2687 *Fax:* 918-660-3737 *Web Site:* www.nrcys.ou.edu, pg 185

National Science Teachers Association (NSTA), 1840 Wilson Blvd, Arlington, VA 22201-3000 *Tel:* 703-243-7100 *Toll Free Tel:* 800-722-NSTA (sales) *Fax:* 703-243-7177 *Web Site:* www.nsta.org, pg 185

The National Society of Newspaper Columnists (NSNC), Fillmore St, Suite 507, San Francisco, CA 94115 *Tel:* 415-541-5636 *Web Site:* www.columnists.com, pg 694

The National Society of Newspaper Columnists (NSNC), Courier-Journal Newspaper, 525 W Broadway, Louisville, KY 40201-7431 *Tel:* 502-582-4011 *Fax:* 502-582-4665 *Web Site:* www.courierjournal.com, pg 745

National State Publishing Association (NSPA), 207 Third Ave, Hattiesburg, MS 39401 *Tel:* 601-582-3330 *Fax:* 601-582-3354 *E-mail:* info@govpublishing.org *Web Site:* www.govpublishing.org, pg 694

National Ten-Minute Play Contest, 316 W Main St, Louisville, KY 40202-4218 *Tel:* 502-584-1265 *Web Site:* www.actorstheatre.org, pg 792

National Translation Award, Box 830688, Mail Sta JO51, Richardson, TX 75083-0688 *Tel:* 972-883-2093 *Fax:* 972-883-6303 *Web Site:* www.literarytranslators.org, pg 792

National Underwriter Co, 5081 Olympic Blvd, Erlanger, KY 41018 *Tel:* 859-692-2100 *Toll Free Tel:* 800-543-0874 *Fax:* 859-692-2289 *E-mail:* customerservice@nuco.com *Web Site:* www.nationalunderwriter.com, pg 185

National Writers Association, 3140 S Peoria, Suite 295, Aurora, CO 80014 *Tel:* 303-841-0246 *Fax:* 303-841-2607 *Web Site:* www.nationalwriters.com (magazine available on-line), pg 694

National Writers Association Novel Contest, 3140 S Peoria St, Suite 295, Aurora, CO 80014 *Tel:* 303-841-0246 *Fax:* 303-841-2607 *Web Site:* www.nationalwriters.com (magazine available on-line), pg 792

National Writers Union, 113 University Place, 6th fl, New York, NY 10003-4527 *Tel:* 212-254-0279 *Fax:* 212-254-0673 *E-mail:* nwu@nwu.org *Web Site:* www.nwu.org/, pg 694

The National Writer's Voice Project, 101 N Wacker Dr, Suite 1400, Chicago, IL 60606 *Tel:* 312-419-8658 *Toll Free Tel:* 800-USA-YMCA (800-872-9622) *Fax:* 312-977-4801 *Web Site:* www.ymca.net, pg 745

Native American Book Publishers, PO Box 510, Hamburg, MI 48139-0510 *Tel:* 810-231-3728 *Fax:* 810-231-3728, pg 185

Natural Heritage Books, PO Box 95, Sta O, Toronto, ON M4A 2M8, Canada *Tel:* 416-694-7907 *Toll Free Tel:* 800-725-9982 (orders only) *Fax:* 416-690-0819 *E-mail:* info@naturalheritagebooks.com *Web Site:* www.naturalheritagebooks.com, pg 555

Naturegraph Publishers Inc, 3543 Indian Creek Rd, Happy Camp, CA 96039 *Tel:* 530-493-5353 *Toll Free Tel:* 800-390-5353 *Fax:* 530-493-5240 *E-mail:* nature@sisqtel.net *Web Site:* www.naturegraph.com, pg 185

The Nautical & Aviation Publishing Co of America Inc, 2055 Middleburg Lane, Mount Pleasant, SC 29464 *Tel:* 843-856-0561 *Fax:* 843-856-3164 *E-mail:* nauticalaviationpublishing@att.net *Web Site:* www.nauticalaviation.com, pg 185

Nautilus Award, 109 N Beach Rd, Eastsound, WA 98245 *Tel:* 360-376-2702 *Toll Free Tel:* 800-367-1907 *Fax:* 360-376-2704 *E-mail:* napravision@napra.com *Web Site:* www.napra.com, pg 792

Naval Institute Press, 291 Wood Rd, Annapolis, MD 21402-5034 *Tel:* 410-268-6110 *Toll Free Tel:* 800-233-8764 *Fax:* 410-295-1084; 410-571-1703 (customer service) *E-mail:* webmaster@ navalinstitute.org; customer@navalinstitute.org (cust serv) *Web Site:* www.navalinstitute.org, pg 185

NavPress Publishing Group, 3820 N 30 St, Colorado Springs, CO 80904 *Tel:* 719-548-9222 *Toll Free Tel:* 800-366-7788 *Fax:* 719-260-7223 *Toll Free Fax:* 800-343-3902 *Web Site:* www.navpress.com, pg 185

NBM Publishing Inc, 555 Eighth Ave, Suite 1202, New York, NY 10018 *Tel:* 212-643-5407 *Toll Free Tel:* 800-886-1223 *Fax:* 212-643-1545 *E-mail:* admin@nbmpub.com *Web Site:* www.nbmpub. com, pg 185

NCCLS, 940 W Valley Rd, Suite 1400, Wayne, PA 19087-1898 *Tel:* 610-688-0100 *Fax:* 610-688-0700 *E-mail:* exoffice@nccls.org *Web Site:* www.nccls.org, pg 185

NDE Publishing, 15-30 Wertheim Ct, Richmond Hill, ON L4B 1B9, Canada *Tel:* 905-731-1288 *Toll Free Tel:* 800-675-1263 *Fax:* 905-731-5744 *E-mail:* info@ ndepublishing.com *Web Site:* www.ndepublishing.com, pg 555

Neal-Schuman Publishers Inc, 100 William St, Suite 2004, New York, NY 10038 *Tel:* 212-925-8650 *Toll Free Tel:* 866-672-6657 *Toll Free Fax:* 866-209-7932 *E-mail:* orders@neal-schuman.com *Web Site:* www. neal-schuman.com, pg 186

The Nebraska Review Awards, University of Nebraska-Omaha, WFAB 212, Omaha, NE 68182-0324 *Tel:* 402-554-3159 *Fax:* 402-614-2026 *Web Site:* www. zoopress.org/nebraskareview/, pg 793

E T Nedder Publishing, 9121 E Tanque Verde, Suite 105, PMB 299, Tucson, AZ 85749-8390 *Tel:* 520-760-2742 *Toll Free Tel:* 877-817-2742 *Fax:* 520-760-5883 *E-mail:* enedder@hotmail.com *Web Site:* nedderpublishing.com, pg 186

Neibauer Press, 20 Industrial Dr, Warminster, PA 18974 *Tel:* 215-322-6200 *Toll Free Tel:* 800-322-6203 *Fax:* 215-322-2495 *E-mail:* sales@neibauer.com *Web Site:* www.churchstewardship.com, pg 186

Nina Neimark Editorial Services, 543 Third St, Brooklyn, NY 11215 *Tel:* 718-499-6804 *E-mail:* pneimark@hotmail.com, pg 606

Nelson, 1120 Birchmount Rd, Scarborough, ON M1K 5G4, Canada *Tel:* 416-752-9448 *Toll Free Tel:* 800-268-2222 (cust serv); 800-430-4445 *Fax:* 416-752-8101 *E-mail:* inquire@nelson.com *Web Site:* www. nelson.com, pg 555

B K Nelson Inc Lecture Bureau, 84 Woodland Rd, Pleasantville, NY 10570 *Tel:* 914-741-1322; 212-889-0637 *Fax:* 914-741-1323 *E-mail:* bknelson4@cs.com *Web Site:* www.bknelson.com, pg 670

B K Nelson Inc Literary Agency, 1565 Paseo Vida, Palm Springs, CA 92264 *Tel:* 760-778-8800 *Fax:* 914-778-0034 *E-mail:* bknelson4@cs.com *Web Site:* www. bknelson.com, pg 645

Frank Nelson Doubleday Memorial Award, 2320 Capitol Ave, Cheyenne, WY 82002 *Tel:* 307-777-7742 *Fax:* 307-777-5499 *Web Site:* www.wyoarts.state.wy. us, pg 793

Nelson Information, 195 Broadway, 5th fl, New York, NY 10007 *Tel:* 646-822-2000 *Toll Free Tel:* 888-371-4575; 888-280-4864 (orders) *Fax:* 914-937-8590 *Web Site:* www.nelsoninformation.com, pg 186

Nelson Literary Agency LLC, 1020 15 St, Suite 26L, Denver, CO 80202 *Tel:* 303-463-5301 *Fax:* 720-384-0761 *E-mail:* query@nelsonagency.com *Web Site:* nelsonagency.com, pg 645

Nemmar Real Estate Training, 15 E Putnam Ave, Suite 151, Greenwich, CT 06830 *Fax:* 212-937-2122 *E-mail:* info@nemmar.com *Web Site:* www.nemmar. com, pg 186

Neo-Tech Publishing, PO Box 60906, Boulder City, NV 89006-0906 *Tel:* 702-293-5552 *Fax:* 702-293-4342 *Web Site:* www.neo-tech.com, pg 187

The Pablo Neruda Prize for Poetry, Nimrod Intl Journal, University of Tulsa, 600 S College, Tulsa, OK 74104 *Tel:* 918-631-3080 *Fax:* 918-631-3033 *E-mail:* nimrod@utulsa.edu *Web Site:* www.utulsa. edu/nimrod, pg 793

Nesbitt Graphics Inc, 555 Virginia Dr, Fort Washington, PA 19034 *Tel:* 215-591-9125 *Fax:* 215-591-9093 *Web Site:* www.Nesbittgraphics.com, pg 606

Neshui Publishing, 2838 Cherokee, St Louis, MO 63118 *Tel:* 314-772-3090 *E-mail:* neshui62@hotmail.com, pg 187

Networking Alternatives for Publishers, Retailers & Artists Inc (NAPRA), 109 North Beach Rd, Eastsound, WA 98245 *Tel:* 360-376-2702 *Toll Free Tel:* 800-367-1907 *Fax:* 360-376-2704 *E-mail:* napravision@napra.com *Web Site:* www.napra. com, pg 694

Neustadt International Prize for Literature, 630 Parrington Oval, Suite 110, Norman, OK 73019-4033 *Tel:* 405-325-4531 *Toll Free Tel:* 800-523-7363 *Fax:* 405-325-7495 *Web Site:* www.ou.edu/worldlit/, pg 793

Allan Nevins Prize, Columbia University, 603 Fayerweather Hall, MC 2538, New York, NY 10027, pg 793

Nevraumont Publishing Co, 71 Broadway, New York, NY 10006 *Tel:* 212-425-3270 *Fax:* 212-425-1818 *E-mail:* nevpub@cs.com, pg 187

New Age World Literary Services & Books, 6426 Valley View St, Space 49, Joshua Tree, CA 92252 *Tel:* 760-366-0117 *E-mail:* newagesphinx@yahoo.com *Web Site:* www.joshuatreevillage.com, pg 646

New Age World Publishing, 8345 NW 66 St, Suite 6344, Miami, FL 33166-2626 *Tel:* 305-735-8064 *Toll Free Fax:* 888-739-6129 *E-mail:* info@NAWPublishing.com *Web Site:* www.NAWPublishing.com, pg 187, 646

New Brand Agency Group, LLC, 3389 Sheridan St, Suite 317, Hollywood, FL 33021 *Tel:* 954-579-8900 *Fax:* 443-241-2568 *Web Site:* www.literaryagent.net, pg 646

New Brunswick Arts Board/Conseil des arts du NB, 634 Queen St, Suite 300, Fredericton, NB E3B 1C2, Canada *Tel:* 506-444-4444 *Fax:* 506-444-5543 *E-mail:* nbabcanb@artsnb.ca *Web Site:* www.artsnb.ca, pg 793

New Century Books, 213 Bay Club Dr, Santa Teresa, NM 88008 *Tel:* 505-589-1967 *Fax:* 505-589-1967 *E-mail:* newcentbks@elp.rr.com, pg 187

New City Press, 202 Cardinal Rd, Hyde Park, NY 12538 *Tel:* 845-229-0335 *Toll Free Tel:* 800-462-5980 (orders only) *Fax:* 845-229-0351 *E-mail:* info@newcitypress. com *Web Site:* www.newcitypress.com, pg 187

New Concepts Publishing, 5202 Humphreys Blvd, Lake Park, GA 31636 *Tel:* 229-257-0367 *Fax:* 229-219-1097 *E-mail:* newconcepts@newconceptspublishing. com *Web Site:* www.newconceptspublishing.com, pg 187

New Dimensions Publishing, 11248 N 11 St, Phoenix, AZ 85020 *Tel:* 602-861-2631 *Toll Free Tel:* 800-736-7367 *Fax:* 602-944-1235 *E-mail:* info@thedream.com *Web Site:* www.thedream.com, pg 187

New Directions Publishing Corp, 80 Eighth Ave, New York, NY 10011 *Tel:* 212-255-0230 *Toll Free Tel:* 800-233-4830 (PA) *Fax:* 212-255-0231 *E-mail:* newdirections@ndbooks.com *Web Site:* www. ndpublishing.com, pg 187

New England Book Awards, 1770 Massachusetts Ave, No 332, Cambridge, MA 02140 *Tel:* 617-576-3070 *Toll Free Tel:* 800-466-8711 *Fax:* 617-576-3091 *Web Site:* www.newenglandbooks.org, pg 793

New England Booksellers Association Inc (NEBA), 1770 Massachusetts Ave, No 332, Cambridge, MA 02140 *Tel:* 617-576-3070 *Toll Free Tel:* 800-466-8711 *Fax:* 617-576-3091 *Web Site:* www.newenglandbooks. org, pg 695

New England Poetry Club, 2 Farrar St, Cambridge, MA 02138 *Tel:* 781-643-0029, pg 695

The New England Press Inc, PO Box 575, Shelburne, VT 05482-0575 *Tel:* 802-863-2520 *Fax:* 802-863-1510 *E-mail:* nep@together.net *Web Site:* www.nepress.com, pg 188

New England Publishing Associates Inc, PO Box 5, Chester, CT 06412-0005 *Tel:* 860-345-READ (345-7323) *Fax:* 860-345-3660 *E-mail:* nepa@nepa.com *Web Site:* www.nepa.com, pg 646

New Falcon Publications/Falcon, 1739 E Broadway Rd, No 1-277, Tempe, AZ 85282 *Tel:* 602-708-1409 *Fax:* 602-708-1410 *E-mail:* info@newfalcon.com *Web Site:* www.newfalcon.com, pg 188

New Forums Press Inc, 1018 S Lewis St, Stillwater, OK 74074 *Tel:* 405-372-6158 *Toll Free Tel:* 800-606-3766 *Fax:* 405-377-2237 *E-mail:* info@newforums.com *Web Site:* www.newforums.com, pg 188

New Harbinger Publications Inc, 5674 Shattuck Ave, Oakland, CA 94609 *Tel:* 510-652-0215 *Toll Free Tel:* 800-748-6273 (orders only) *Fax:* 510-652-5472 *E-mail:* nhhelp@newharbinger.com *Web Site:* www. newharbinger.com, pg 188

New Horizon Press, PO Box 669, Far Hills, NJ 07931-0669 *Tel:* 908-604-6311 *Toll Free Tel:* 800-533-7978 (orders only) *Fax:* 908-604-6330 *E-mail:* nhp@ newhorizonpressbooks.com, pg 188

New Issues Poetry & Prose, Western Michigan University, Dept of English, 1903 W Michigan Ave, Kalamazoo, MI 49008-5331 *Tel:* 269-387-8185 *Fax:* 269-387-2562 *Web Site:* www.wmich. edu/newissues, pg 188

New Issues Poetry Prize, Western Michigan University, Dept of English, 1903 W Michigan Ave, Kalamazoo, MI 49008-5331 *Tel:* 269-387-8185 *Fax:* 269-387-2562 *Web Site:* www.wmich.edu/newissues, pg 793

New Jersey Council for the Humanities Book Award, 28 W State St, 6th fl, Trenton, NJ 08608 *Tel:* 609-695-4838 *Fax:* 609-695-4929 *E-mail:* njch@njch.org *Web Site:* www.njch.org, pg 793

New Jersey State Council on the Arts Fellowship Program (NJSCA), 225 W State St, 4th fl, Trenton, NJ 08608 *Tel:* 609-292-6130 *Fax:* 609-989-1440 *Web Site:* www.njartscouncil.org; www.midatlanticarts. org, pg 793

New Leaf Press Inc, PO Box 726, Green Forest, AR 72638-0726 *Tel:* 870-438-5288 *Toll Free Tel:* 800-643-9535 *Fax:* 870-438-5120 *E-mail:* nlp@newleafpress. net *Web Site:* www.newleafpress.net, pg 188

New Letters Literary Awards, 5101 Rockhill Rd, Kansas City, MO 64110-2499 *Tel:* 816-235-1168 *Fax:* 816-235-2611 *E-mail:* newletters@umkc.edu *Web Site:* www.newletters.org, pg 794

New Mexico Book Association (NMBA), 310 Read St, Santa Fe, NM 87504 *Tel:* 505-983-1412 *Fax:* 505-983-0899 *E-mail:* oceantree@earthlink.net *Web Site:* www. nmbook.org, pg 695

New Millennium Writings, PO Box 2463, Knoxville, TN 37901 *Tel:* 865-428-0389 *Fax:* 865-428-0389 *Web Site:* www.mach2.com, pg 794

New Orleans-Gulf South Booksellers Association, PO Box 750043, New Orleans, LA 70175-0043 *Tel:* 504-701-3417 *E-mail:* info@nogsba.com *Web Site:* www. nogsba.com, pg 695

New Past Press Inc, PO Box 558, Friendship, WI 53934-0558 *Tel:* 608-339-7191 *E-mail:* newpast@maqs.net *Web Site:* www.newpastpress.com, pg 188

New Play Development, 3828 Main St, Kansas City, MO 64111 *Tel:* 816-531-7529 ext 15 *Fax:* 816-531-0421 *Web Site:* www.unicorntheatre.org, pg 794

The New Press, 38 Greene St, 4th fl, New York, NY 10013 *Tel:* 212-629-8802 *Toll Free Tel:* 800-233-4830 (orders) *Fax:* 212-629-8617 *Toll Free Fax:* 800-458-6515 *E-mail:* newpress@thenewpress.com *Web Site:* www.thenewpress.com, pg 188

New Readers Press, 1320 Jamesville Ave, Syracuse, NY 13210 *Tel:* 315-422-9121 *Toll Free Tel:* 800-448-8878 *Fax:* 315-422-5561 *E-mail:* nrp@proliteracy.org *Web Site:* www.newreaderspress.com, pg 189

New Rivers Press, Minnesota State University Moorhead, 1104 Seventh Ave S, Moorhead, MN 56563 *Tel:* 218-477-5870 *Fax:* 218-477-2236 *E-mail:* nrp@mnstate.edu *Web Site:* www.newriverspress.com; www.mnstate.edu/newriverspress, pg 189

New Star Books Ltd, 107-3477 Commercial St, Vancouver, BC V5N 4E8, Canada *Tel:* 604-738-9429 *Fax:* 604-738-9332 *E-mail:* info@newstarbooks.com; orders@newstarbooks.com *Web Site:* www.newstarbooks.com, pg 555

New Strategist Publications Inc, 120 W State St, 4th fl, Ithaca, NY 14850 *Tel:* 607-273-0913 *Toll Free Tel:* 800-848-0842 *Fax:* 607-277-5009 *E-mail:* demographics@newstrategist.com *Web Site:* newstrategist.com, pg 189

New Victoria Publishers, 513 New Boston Rd, Norwich, VT 05055 *Tel:* 802-649-5297 *Toll Free Tel:* 800-326-5297 *Fax:* 802-649-5297 *Toll Free Fax:* 800-326-5297 *E-mail:* newvic@aol.com *Web Site:* www.newvictoria.com, pg 189

New Voices Publishing, 34 Salem St, Wilmington, MA 01887 *Tel:* 508-347-5669; 978-658-2131 *Fax:* 508-347-5669; 978-988-8833 *Web Site:* www.kidsterrain.com, pg 189

New Win Publishing Inc, 9682 Telstar Ave, Suite 110, El Monte, CA 91731 *Tel:* 626-448-4422 *Fax:* 626-602-3817 *Web Site:* www.newwinpublishing.com, pg 189

New World Library, 14 Pamaron Way, Novato, CA 94949 *Tel:* 415-884-2100 *Toll Free Tel:* 800-227-3900 (ext 52, retail orders) *Fax:* 415-884-2199 (ext 52, retail orders) *E-mail:* escort@newworldlibrary.com *Web Site:* www.newworldlibrary.com, pg 189

New World Publishing, PO Box 36075, Halifax, NS B3J 3S9, Canada *Toll Free Tel:* 877-211-3334 *Fax:* 902-576-2095 *E-mail:* nwp1@eastlink.ca *Web Site:* www.newworldpublishing.com, pg 555

New Writer Awards, 535 W William, Suite 301, Ann Arbor, MI 48103 *Tel:* 734-761-4833 *Fax:* 734-761-3939 *Web Site:* www.glca.org, pg 794

New York Academy of Sciences, 2 E 63 St, New York, NY 10021 *Tel:* 212-838-0230 *Toll Free Tel:* 800-843-6927 *Fax:* 212-888-2894 *E-mail:* publications@nyas.org *Web Site:* www.nyas.org, pg 189

The New York Botanical Garden Press, 200 St & Kazimiroff Blvd, Bronx, NY 10458-5126 *Tel:* 718-817-8721 *Fax:* 718-817-8842 *E-mail:* nybgpress@nybg.org *Web Site:* www.nybg.org, pg 189

New York City Book Awards, 53 E 79 St, New York, NY 10021 *Tel:* 212-288-6900 (ext 230) *Fax:* 212-988-4071 *E-mail:* events@nysoclib.org *Web Site:* www.nysoclib.org, pg 794

New York City College of Technology, 300 Jay St, Brooklyn, NY 11201 *Tel:* 718-260-5822; 718-260-5000 *Fax:* 718-260-5198 *E-mail:* connect@citytech.cuny.edu, pg 753

New York Public Library, Publications Office, Fifth Ave & 42 St, New York, NY 10018 *Tel:* 212-512-0202; 212-512-0201 *Fax:* 212-704-8620 *Web Site:* www.nypl.org, pg 190

The New York Public Library Helen Bernstein Book Award for Excellence in Journalism, Publications Office, Fifth Ave & 42 St, New York, NY 10018 *Tel:* 212-512-0202 *Fax:* 212-704-8620 *E-mail:* kvanwestering@nypl.org *Web Site:* www.nypl.org, pg 794

New York State Bar Association, One Elk St, Albany, NY 12207 *Tel:* 518-463-3200 *Toll Free Tel:* 800-582-2452 *Fax:* 518-463-8844 *Web Site:* www.nysba.org, pg 190

New York State Edith Wharton Citation of Merit for Fiction Writers, University at Albany, LE 320, Albany, NY 12222 *Tel:* 518-442-5620 *Fax:* 518-442-5621 *E-mail:* writers@uamail.albany.edu *Web Site:* www.albany.edu/writers-inst, pg 794

New York State Walt Whitman Citation of Merit for Poets, University at Albany, LE 320, Albany, NY 12222 *Tel:* 518-442-5620 *Fax:* 518-442-5621 *E-mail:* writers@uamail.albany.edu *Web Site:* www.albany.edu/writers-inst, pg 794

New York State Writers Institute, University at Albany, New Library 320, Albany, NY 12222 *Tel:* 518-442-5620 *Fax:* 518-442-5621 *E-mail:* writers@uamail.albany.edu *Web Site:* www.albany.edu/writers-inst/, pg 745

New York University, Center for Publishing, 11 W 42 St, Rm 400, New York, NY 10036 *Tel:* 212-992-3232 *Fax:* 212-992-3233 *E-mail:* pub.center@nyu.edu *Web Site:* www.scps.nyu.edu/publishing, pg 753

New York University Press, 838 Broadway, New York, NY 10003 *Tel:* 212-998-2575 (edit) *Toll Free Tel:* 800-996-6987 (orders) *Fax:* 212-995-3833 (orders) *E-mail:* feedback@nyupress.nyu.edu *Web Site:* www.nyupress.org, pg 190

John Newbery Medal, 50 E Huron St, Chicago, IL 60611-2795 *Tel:* 312-280-2163 *Toll Free Tel:* 800-545-2433 *Fax:* 312-944-7671 *E-mail:* alsc@ala.org *Web Site:* www.ala.org/alsc, pg 794

Newbridge Educational Publishing, One Beeman Rd, Northborough, MA 01532 *Tel:* 508-571-6500 *Toll Free Tel:* 800-867-0307 *Fax:* 508-571-6502 *Toll Free Fax:* 800-456-2419 *E-mail:* info@newbridgeonline.com *Web Site:* www.newbridgeonline.com; www.newbridgepub.com, pg 190

Newbury Street Press, 101 Newbury St, Boston, MA 02116 *Tel:* 617-536-5740 *Fax:* 617-536-7307 *Web Site:* www.newenglandancestors.org, pg 190

Newcomen-Harvard Book Award, c/o Business History Review, Harvard Business School, Soldiers Field Rd, Boston, MA 02163 *Tel:* 617-495-1003 *Fax:* 617-495-0594 *E-mail:* bhr@hbs.edu *Web Site:* www.newcomen.org, pg 794

NeWest Press, 8540 109 St, No 201, Edmonton, AB T6G 1E6, Canada *Tel:* 780-432-9427 *Toll Free Tel:* 866-796-5433 *Fax:* 780-433-3179 *E-mail:* info@newestpress.com *Web Site:* www.newestpress.com, pg 556

NewLife Publications, 375 Hwy 74 S, Peachtree City, GA 30269 *Tel:* 770-631-9940 *Toll Free Tel:* 800-235-7255 *Toll Free Fax:* 800-514-7072 *Web Site:* www.nlpdirect.com, pg 190

Newmarket Publishing & Communications, 18 E 48 St, New York, NY 10017 *Tel:* 212-832-3575 *Toll Free Tel:* 800-669-3903 *Fax:* 212-832-3629 *E-mail:* mailbox@newmarketpress.com *Web Site:* www.newmarketpress.com, pg 190

Newsletter & Electronic Publishers Association, 1501 Wilson Blvd, Suite 509, Arlington, VA 22209 *Tel:* 703-527-2333 *Toll Free Tel:* 800-356-9302 *Fax:* 703-841-0629 *Web Site:* www.newsletters.org, pg 695

NewSouth Books, 105 S Court St, Montgomery, AL 36104 *Tel:* 334-834-3556 *Fax:* 334-834-3557 *E-mail:* info@newsouthbooks.com *Web Site:* www.newsouthbooks.com, pg 190

NewSouth Inc, 105 S Court St, Montgomery, AL 36104 *Tel:* 334-834-3556 *Fax:* 334-834-3557 *E-mail:* info@newsouthbooks.com *Web Site:* www.newsouthbooks.com, pg 191

Newspaper Advertising Sales Association, 411 W Fifth St, Los Angeles, CA 90013, pg 695

Newspaper Association of America (NAA), 1921 Gallows Rd, Suite 600, Vienna, VA 22182 *Tel:* 703-902-1600 *Fax:* 703-917-0636 *Web Site:* www.naa.org, pg 695

The Newspaper Guild, 501 Third St NW, Washington, DC 20001-2760 *Tel:* 202-434-7173 *Fax:* 202-434-1472 *E-mail:* guild@swa-union.org *Web Site:* www.newsguild.org, pg 695

Next Decade Inc, 39 Old Farmstead Rd, Chester, NJ 07930 *Tel:* 908-879-6625 *Fax:* 908-879-2920 *E-mail:* info@nextdecade.com *Web Site:* www.nextdecade.com, pg 191

Nexus Press, 535 Means St, Atlanta, GA 30318 *Tel:* 404-577-3579 *Fax:* 404-577-5856 *E-mail:* nexusbooks@thecontemporary.org *Web Site:* www.thecontemporary.org, pg 191

Don & Gee Nicholl Fellowships in Screenwriting, 1313 N Vine St, Hollywood, CA 90028 *Tel:* 310-247-3059; 310-247-3010 *Fax:* 310-247-3794 *E-mail:* nicholl@oscars.org *Web Site:* www.oscars.org/nicholl, pg 794

Donald Nicholson-Smith, PO Box 272, Knickerbocker Sta, New York, NY 10002 *Tel:* 718-636-4732 *E-mail:* mnr.dns@verizon.net, pg 607

Nightengale Press, 1579 Nightengale Circle, Lindenhurst, IL 60046 *Tel:* 847-507-0274 *Fax:* 847-245-4167 *Web Site:* www.nightengalepress.com, pg 572

Nightingale-Conant, 6245 W Howard St, Niles, IL 60714 *Tel:* 847-647-0306; 847-647-0300 *Toll Free Tel:* 800-572-2770 *Fax:* 847-647-7145 *Web Site:* www.nightingale.com, pg 191

Coutts Nijhoff International West European Specialist Study Grant, 50 E Huron St, Chicago, IL 60611 *Tel:* 312-280-2514 *Toll Free Tel:* 800-545-2433 (ext 2514) *Fax:* 312-280-2520 *Web Site:* www.ala.org/acrl, pg 794

Nilgiri Press, 3600 Tomales Rd, Tomales, CA 94971 *Tel:* 707-878-2369 *Toll Free Tel:* 800-475-2369 *Fax:* 707-878-2375 *E-mail:* info@nilgiri.org *Web Site:* www.nilgiri.org, pg 191

Nimbus Publishing Ltd, 3731 Mackintosh St, Halifax, NS B3K 5A5, Canada *Tel:* 902-455-5304 *Toll Free Tel:* 800-646-2879 *Fax:* 902-455-5440 *E-mail:* customerservice@nimbus.ns.ca *Web Site:* www.nimbus.ns.ca, pg 556

John Frederick Nims Memorial Prize, 1030 N Clark St, Suite 420, Chicago, IL 60610 *Tel:* 312-787-7070 *Fax:* 312-787-6650 *E-mail:* poetry@poetrymagazine.org *Web Site:* www.poetrymagazine.org, pg 794

Nine Muses & Apollo Inc, 525 Broadway, Rm 201, New York, NY 10012 *Tel:* 212-431-2665, pg 647

Nixon Agency, 382 Audrey Dr, Suite 100, Loveland, CO 80537 *Tel:* 970-667-0920 *Fax:* 970-667-0920 *E-mail:* mcleanlit@aol.com *Web Site:* donnanixonagency.com, pg 647

NMMA Discover Boating Director's Award, 200 E Randolph Dr, Suite 5100, Chicago, IL 60601 *Tel:* 312-946-6200 *Fax:* 312-946-0388 *Web Site:* nmma.org, pg 795

No Starch Press Inc, 555 De Haro St, Suite 250, San Francisco, CA 94107-2192 *Tel:* 415-863-9900 *Toll Free Tel:* 800-420-7240 *Fax:* 415-863-9950 *E-mail:* info@nostarch.com *Web Site:* www.nostarch.com, pg 191

Noble Publishing Corp, 630 Pinnacle Ct, Norcross, GA 30071 *Tel:* 770-449-6774 *Fax:* 770-448-2839 *E-mail:* editor@noblepub.com; orders@noblepub.com *Web Site:* www.noblepub.com, pg 191

Regula Noetzli Literary Agent, 2344 County Rte 83, Pine Plains, NY 12567 *Tel:* 518-398-6260 *Fax:* 518-398-6258 *E-mail:* regula@taconic.net, pg 647

The Betsy Nolan Literary Agency, 224 W 29 St, 15th fl, New York, NY 10001 *Tel:* 212-967-8200 *Fax:* 212-967-7292, pg 647

Nolo, 950 Parker St, Berkeley, CA 94710 *Tel:* 510-549-1976 *Fax:* 510-548-5902 *E-mail:* info@nolo.com *Web Site:* www.nolo.com, pg 191

The Noontide Press, PO Box 2719, Newport Beach, CA 92659-1319 *Tel:* 949-631-1490 *Fax:* 949-631-0981 *E-mail:* orders@noontidepress.com *Web Site:* www.noontidepress.com, pg 191

Norman Publishing, 936-B Seventh St, PMB 238, Novato, CA 94945-3000 *Tel:* 415-892-3181 *Toll Free Tel:* 800-544-9359 *Fax:* 208-692-7446 *E-mail:* orders@jnorman.com *Web Site:* www.normanpublishing.com, pg 191

North American Agricultural Journalists, Texas A&M University, 201 Reed Macdonald, 2112 TAMU, College Station, TX 77843-2112 *Tel:* 979-845-2872 *Fax:* 979-845-2414 *E-mail:* ka-phillips@tamu.edu *Web Site:* naaj.tamu.edu, pg 695

North American Bookdealers Exchange, PO Box 606, Cottage Grove, OR 97424-0026 *Tel:* 541-942-7455 *Fax:* 561-258-2625 *E-mail:* nabe@bookmarketingprofits.com *Web Site:* bookmarketingprofits.com, pg 695

North American Graphic Arts Suppliers Association (NAGASA), 1604 New Hampshire Ave NW, Washington, DC 20009 *Tel:* 202-328-8441 *Fax:* 202-328-8513 *E-mail:* information@nagasa.org *Web Site:* www.nagasa.org, pg 695

North American Indian Prose Award, 233 N Eighth St, Lincoln, NE 68588-0255 *Tel:* 402-472-3581 *Fax:* 402-472-0308 *E-mail:* pressmail@unl.edu *Web Site:* www.nebraskapress.unl.edu, pg 795

North American Snowsports Journalists Association, 460 Sarsons Rd, Kelowna, BC V1W 1C2, Canada *Tel:* 250-764-2143 *Fax:* 250-764-2145 *E-mail:* nasja@shaw.ca *Web Site:* www.nasja.org, pg 695

North Atlantic Books, 1435 Fourth St, Berkeley, CA 94710 *Tel:* 510-559-8277 *Toll Free Tel:* 800-337-2665 (book orders only) *Fax:* 510-559-8279 *E-mail:* orders@northatlanticbooks.com *Web Site:* www.northatlanticbooks.com, pg 191

North Bay Books, 3110 Whitecliff Ct, Richmond, CA 94803 *Tel:* 510-758-4276 *Toll Free Tel:* 800-870-3194 *Fax:* 510-758-4659 *Web Site:* www.northbaybooks.com, pg 192

North Books, PO Box 1277, Wickford, RI 02852 *Tel:* 401-294-3682 *Fax:* 401-294-9491, pg 192

North Carolina Arts Council, Dept of Cultural Resources, Mail Service Ctr 4632, Raleigh, NC 27699-4632 *Tel:* 919-715-1519 *Fax:* 919-733-4834 *Web Site:* www.ncarts.org, pg 795

North Carolina Office of Archives & History, Historical Publ Sect, 4622 Mail Service Ctr, Raleigh, NC 27699-4622 *Tel:* 919-733-7442 *Fax:* 919-733-1439 *Web Site:* www.ncpublications.com, pg 192

North Carolina Writers' Network Annual Fall Conference, PO Box 954, Carrboro, NC 27510-0954 *Tel:* 919-967-9540 *Fax:* 919-929-0535 *E-mail:* mail@ncwriters.org *Web Site:* www.ncwriters.org, pg 745

North Country Books Inc, 311 Turner St, Utica, NY 13501-1729 *Tel:* 315-735-4877 *Fax:* 315-738-4342 *E-mail:* ncbooks@usadatanet.net *Web Site:* www.northcountrybooks.com, pg 192

North Country Press, RR1, Box 1395, Unity, ME 04988-1395 *Tel:* 207-948-2208 *Fax:* 207-948-9000 *E-mail:* info@ncpbooks.com *Web Site:* www.ncpbooks.com, pg 192

North Light Books, 4700 E Galbraith Rd, Cincinnati, OH 45236 *Tel:* 513-531-2690 *Toll Free Tel:* 800-666-0963 *Fax:* 513-891-7185 *Toll Free Fax:* 888-590-4082 *Web Site:* www.fwpublications.com, pg 192

North Point Press, 19 Union Sq W, New York, NY 10003 *Tel:* 212-741-6900 *Toll Free Tel:* 888-330-8477 *Fax:* 212-741-6973 *Web Site:* www.fsgbooks.com, pg 192

North River Press Publishing Corp, 321 Main St, Great Barrington, MA 01230 *Tel:* 413-528-0034 *Toll Free Tel:* 800-486-2665 *Fax:* 413-528-3163 *Toll Free Fax:* 800-BOOK-FAX (266-5329) *E-mail:* info@northriverpress.com *Web Site:* www.northriverpress.com, pg 192

North-South Center Press at the University of Miami, 1500 Monza Ave, Coral Gables, FL 33146 *Tel:* 305-284-6868 *Fax:* 305-284-6370 *Web Site:* www.miami.edu/nsc, pg 192

North-South Institute/Institut Nord-Sud, 55 Murray St, Suite 200, Ottawa, ON K1N 5M3, Canada *Tel:* 613-241-3535 *Fax:* 613-241-7435 *E-mail:* nsi@nsi-ins.ca *Web Site:* www.nsi-ins.ca, pg 556

North Star Press of Saint Cloud Inc, PO Box 451, St Cloud, MN 56302-0451 *Tel:* 320-558-9062 *Fax:* 320-558-9063 *E-mail:* nspress@cloudnet.com, pg 193

Northeast Midwest Institute, 218 "D" St SE, Washington, DC 20003 *Tel:* 202-544-5200 *Fax:* 202-544-0043 *Web Site:* www.nemw.org, pg 193

Northeast Texas Community College Annual Writers Conference, Continuing Education, PO Box 1307, Mount Pleasant, TX 75456-1307 *Tel:* 903-572-1911 *Fax:* 903-572-6712 *E-mail:* jbowers@ntcc.edu *Web Site:* www.ntcc.edu, pg 745

Northeastern Graphic Inc, 5 Emeline Dr, Hawthorne, NJ 07506 *Tel:* 973-221-0109 *Fax:* 973-221-0076 *Web Site:* www.northeasterngraphic.com, pg 607

Northern California Independent Booksellers Association (NCIBA), 37 Graham St, San Francisco, CA 94129 *Tel:* 415-561-7686 *Fax:* 415-561-7685 *E-mail:* office@nciba.com *Web Site:* www.nciba.com, pg 696

Northern California Translators Association, PO Box 14015, Berkeley, CA 94712-5015 *Tel:* 510-845-8712 *Fax:* 510-883-1355 *E-mail:* ncta@ncta.org *Web Site:* www.ncta.org, pg 696

Northern Canada Mission Distributors, PO Box 3030, Prince Albert, SK S6V 7V4, Canada *Tel:* 306-764-3388 *Fax:* 306-764-3390 *E-mail:* missiondist@ncem.ca *Web Site:* www.ncem.ca, pg 556

Northern Illinois University Press, 310 N Fifth St, De Kalb, IL 60115 *Tel:* 815-753-1826; 815-753-1075 *Fax:* 815-753-1845 *E-mail:* bberg@niu.edu *Web Site:* www.niu.edu/univ_press, pg 193

Northland Publishing Co, 2900 N Fort Valley Rd, Flagstaff, AZ 86001 *Tel:* 928-774-5251 *Toll Free Tel:* 800-346-3257 *Fax:* 928-774-0592 *E-mail:* info@northlandpub.com; design@northlandpub.com; editorial@northlandpub.com *Web Site:* www.northlandpub.com, pg 193

Northstone Publishing, 9025 Jim Bailey Rd, Kelowna, BC V4V 1R2, Canada *Tel:* 250-766-2778 *Toll Free Tel:* 800-299-2926 *Fax:* 250-766-2736 *Web Site:* www.joinhands.com, pg 556

Northwest Association of Book Publishers, PO Box 3786, Wilsonville, OR 97070-3786 *Tel:* 503-223-9055, pg 696

Northwest Territories Library Services, 75 Woodland Dr, Hay River, NT X0E 1G1, Canada *Tel:* 867-874-6531 *Toll Free Tel:* 866-297-0232 *Fax:* 867-874-3321 *Web Site:* www.nwtpls.gov.nt.ca, pg 696

Northwestern University Press, 625 Colfax St, Evanston, IL 60208 *Tel:* 847-491-2046 *Toll Free Tel:* 800-621-2736 (orders only) *Fax:* 847-491-8150 *E-mail:* nupress@northwestern.edu *Web Site:* www.nupress.northwestern.edu, pg 193

Northwoods Press, PO Box 298, Thomaston, ME 04861-0298 *Tel:* 207-354-0998 *E-mail:* cal@americanletters.org *Web Site:* www.americanletters.org, pg 193

Jeffrey Norton Publishers Inc, One Orchard Park Rd, Madison, CT 06443 *Tel:* 203-245-0195 *Toll Free Tel:* 800-243-1234 *Fax:* 203-245-0769 *Toll Free Fax:* 888-453-4329 *E-mail:* info@audioforum.com *Web Site:* www.audioforum.com, pg 193

W W Norton & Company Inc, 500 Fifth Ave, New York, NY 10110-0017 *Tel:* 212-354-5500 *Toll Free Tel:* 800-233-4830 (orders & cust serv) *Fax:* 212-869-0856 *Toll Free Fax:* 800-458-6515 *Web Site:* www.wwnorton.com, pg 193

Notable Wisconsin Authors, 5250 E Terrace Dr, Suite A-1, Madison, WI 53718-8345 *Tel:* 608-245-3640 *Fax:* 608-245-3646 *Web Site:* www.wla.lib.wi.us, pg 795

Nova Press, 11659 Mayfield Ave, Suite 1, Los Angeles, CA 90049 *Tel:* 310-207-4078 *Toll Free Tel:* 800-949-6175 *Fax:* 310-571-0908 *E-mail:* novapress@aol.com *Web Site:* www.novapress.net, pg 194

Nova Publishing Co, 1103 W College St, Carbondale, IL 62901 *Tel:* 618-457-3521 *Toll Free Tel:* 800-748-1175 *Fax:* 618-457-2541 *E-mail:* info@novapublishing.com *Web Site:* www.novapublishing.com, pg 194

Nova Science Publishers Inc, 400 Oset Ave, Suite 1600, Hauppauge, NY 11788 *Tel:* 631-231-7269 *Fax:* 631-231-8175 *E-mail:* novaeditorial@earthlink.net *Web Site:* www.novapublishers.com, pg 194

Novalis Publishing, 49 Front St E, 2nd fl, Toronto, ON M5E 1B3, Canada *Tel:* 416-363-3303 *Toll Free Tel:* 800-387-7164 *Fax:* 416-363-9409 *Toll Free Fax:* 800-204-4140 *E-mail:* novalis@interlog.com *Web Site:* www.novalis.ca, pg 556

NovelBooks Inc, PO Box 661, Douglas, MA 01516-0661 *Tel:* 508-476-1611 *Fax:* 508-476-3866 *E-mail:* publisher@novelbooksinc.com *Web Site:* www.novelbooksinc.com, pg 194

NPES The Association for Suppliers of Printing, Publishing & Converting Technologies, 1899 Preston White Dr, Reston, VA 20191-4367 *Tel:* 703-264-7200 *Fax:* 703-620-0994 *E-mail:* npes@npes.org *Web Site:* www.npes.org, pg 696

NPTA Alliance, 500 Bi-County Blvd, Suite 200E, Farmingdale, NY 11735 *Tel:* 631-777-2223 *Fax:* 631-777-2224 *Web Site:* www.gonpta.com, pg 696

nSight Inc, One Van de Graaff Dr, Suite 202, Burlington, MA 01803 *Tel:* 781-273-6300 *Fax:* 781-273-6301 *E-mail:* projects@nsightworks.com; consulting@nsightworks.com *Web Site:* www.nsightworks.com, pg 607

nursesbooks.org, The Publishing Program of ANA, 600 Maryland Ave SW, Suite 100-W, Washington, DC 20024-2571 *Tel:* 202-651-7000 *Toll Free Tel:* 800-637-0323 *Fax:* 202-651-7001 *E-mail:* anp@ana.org *Web Site:* www.nursesbooks.org, pg 194

NWAF Annual Conference, 3140 S Peoria St, PMB 295, Aurora, CO 80014 *Tel:* 303-841-0246 *Fax:* 303-841-2607 *Web Site:* www.nationalwriters.com, pg 745

Nystrom, 3333 Elston Ave, Chicago, IL 60618 *Tel:* 773-463-1144 *Toll Free Tel:* 800-621-8086 *Fax:* 773-463-0515 *E-mail:* info@nystromnet.com *Web Site:* www.nystromnet.com, pg 194

O Henry Award, 3700 Mockingbird Lane, Dallas, TX 75205 *Tel:* 512-245-2232 *Fax:* 512-745-7462 *Web Site:* www.stedwards.edu/newc/marks/til/awards_and_rules.htm, pg 795

OAG Worldwide, 3025 Highland Pkwy, Suite 200, Downers Grove, IL 60515 *Tel:* 630-515-5300 *Fax:* 630-515-5301 *Web Site:* www.oag.com, pg 194

Oak Knoll Press, 310 Delaware St, New Castle, DE 19720 *Tel:* 302-328-7232 *Toll Free Tel:* 800-996-2556 *Fax:* 302-328-7274 *E-mail:* oakknoll@oakknoll.com *Web Site:* www.oakknoll.com, pg 194

Oak Tree Publishing, 2743 S Veterans Pkwy, Suite 135, Springfield, IL 64704-6402 *Tel:* 217-879-2822 *Fax:* 217-879-2844 *E-mail:* oaktreepub@aol.com *Web Site:* www.oaktreebooks.com, pg 195

Oaklea Press, 6912 Three Chopt Rd, Suite B, Richmond, VA 23226 *Tel:* 804-281-5872 *Toll Free Tel:* 800-295-4066 *Fax:* 804-281-5686 *E-mail:* info@oakleapress.com *Web Site:* oakleapress.com, pg 195

Oakstone Medical Publishing, 6801 Cahaba Valley Rd, Birmingham, AL 35242 *Tel:* 205-991-5188 *Toll Free Tel:* 800-952-0690 *Fax:* 205-995-4656 *E-mail:* service@oakstonemedical.com *Web Site:* www.oakstonemedical.com, pg 195

Harold Ober Associates Inc, 425 Madison Ave, New York, NY 10017 *Tel:* 212-759-8600 *Fax:* 212-759-9428, pg 647

Oberlin College Press, 50 N Professor St, Oberlin, OH 44074-1095 *Tel:* 440-775-8408 *Fax:* 440-775-8124 *E-mail:* oc.press@oberlin.edu *Web Site:* www.oberlin.edu/ocpress, pg 556

Oberon Press, 350 Sparks St, Suite 400, Ottawa, ON K1R 7S8, Canada *Tel:* 613-238-3275 *Fax:* 613-238-3275 *E-mail:* oberon@sympatico.ca *Web Site:* www3.sympatico.ca/oberon, pg 556

Eli M Oboler Memorial Award, 50 E Huron St, Chicago, IL 60611 *Tel:* 312-280-4223; 312-280-4220 *Toll Free Tel:* 800-545-2433 *Fax:* 312-280-4227 *E-mail:* oif@ala.org *Web Site:* www.ala.org/ifrt, pg 795

Ocean Press, PO Box 1186, Old Chelsea Sta, New York, NY 10113-1186 *Tel:* 718-246-4160 *E-mail:* info@oceanbookscom.au *Web Site:* www.oceanbooks.com.au, pg 195

Ocean Publishing, PO Box 1080, Flagler Beach, FL 32136-1080 *Tel:* 386-517-1600 *Fax:* 386-517-2564 *E-mail:* publisher@cfl.rr.com *Web Site:* www.ocean-publishing.com, pg 195

Ocean Tree Books, 1325 Cerro Gordo Rd, Santa Fe, NM 87501 *Tel:* 505-983-1412 *Fax:* 505-983-0899 *E-mail:* oceantree@earthlink.net *Web Site:* www.oceantree.com, pg 195

Ocean View Books, PO Box 9249, Denver, CO 80209-0246 *Tel:* 303-756-5222 *Toll Free Tel:* 800-848-6222 (orders only) *Fax:* 303-756-3208 *E-mail:* ocean@probook.net *Web Site:* www.probook.net/ocean.html, pg 195

Oceana Publications Inc, 75 Main St, Dobbs Ferry, NY 10522-1601 *Tel:* 914-693-8100 *Toll Free Tel:* 800-831-0758 (orders only) *Fax:* 914-693-0402 *E-mail:* info@oceanalaw.com *Web Site:* www.oceanalaw.com, pg 195

The Flannery O'Connor Award for Short Fiction, 330 Research Dr, Athens, GA 30602-4901 *Tel:* 706-369-6130 (no phone queries accepted) *Fax:* 706-369-6131 *Web Site:* www.ugapress.org, pg 795

O'Connor Prize for Fiction (Descant Publication), TCU Box 297700, Fort Worth, TX 76129 *Tel:* 817-257-7240 / *Fax:* 817-257-7709 *E-mail:* descant@tcu.edu *Web Site:* www.eng.tcu.edu/journals/descant/index.html, pg 795

Octameron Associates, 1900 Mount Vernon Ave, Alexandria, VA 22301 *Tel:* 703-836-5480 *Fax:* 703-836-5650 *E-mail:* info@octameron.com *Web Site:* www.octameron.com, pg 196

Scott O'Dell Award for Historical Fiction, 1100 E 57 St, S-109, Chicago, IL 60637 *Tel:* 773-702-4085 *Fax:* 773-702-0775, pg 795

Odyssey: The Summer Fantasy Writing Workshop, 20 Levesque Lane, Mont Vernon, NH 03057 *Tel:* 603-673-6234 *Fax:* 603-673-6234 *Web Site:* www.sff.net/odyssey, pg 745

Of Dark & Stormy Nights, PO Box 6804, South Bend, IN 46660-6804 *Tel:* 212-888-8171 *Fax:* 212-888-8107 *Web Site:* www.mwamidwest.org, pg 745

Annual Off-Off-Broadway Original Short Play Festival, c/o Samuel Frenchz Inc, 45 W 25 St, New York, NY 10010 *Tel:* 212-206-8990 *Fax:* 212-206-1429 *E-mail:* samuelfrench@earthlink.net *Web Site:* www.samuelfrench.com, pg 795

Off the Page Press, PO Box 4880-J, Buena Vista, CO 81211 *Tel:* 719-395-9450 *Toll Free Tel:* 888-852-6402 *Fax:* 719-395-9453 *E-mail:* editor@yellowpagesage.com *Web Site:* www.yellowpagesage.com, pg 196

Howard O'Hagan Award for Short Fiction, 11759 Groat Rd, Edmonton, AB T5M 3K6, Canada *Tel:* 780-422-8174 *Toll Free Tel:* 800-665-5354 (Alberta only) *Fax:* 780-422-2663 *E-mail:* mail@writersguild.ab.ca *Web Site:* www.writersguild.ab.ca, pg 795

Ohio Genealogical Society, 713 S Main St, Mansfield, OH 44907-1644 *Tel:* 419-756-7294 *Fax:* 419-756-6861 *E-mail:* ogs@ogs.org *Web Site:* www.ogs.org, pg 196

Ohio State University Foreign Language Publications, 198 Hagerty Hall, 1775 College Rd, Columbus, OH 43210-1340 *Tel:* 614-292-3838 *Toll Free Tel:* 800-678-6999 *Fax:* 614-688-3355 *E-mail:* flpubs@osu.edu *Web Site:* nealrc.osu.edu/flpubs, pg 196

Ohio State University Press, 180 Pressey Hall, 1070 Carmack Rd, Columbus, OH 43210-1002 *Tel:* 614-292-6930 *Toll Free Tel:* 800-621-2736 *Fax:* 614-292-2065 *Toll Free Fax:* 800-621-8476 *E-mail:* ohiostatepress@osu.edu *Web Site:* ohiostatepress.org, pg 196

Ohio University, English Dept, Creative Writing Program, Ohio University, English Dept, Ellis Hall, Athens, OH 45701 *Tel:* 740-593-2838 *Fax:* 740-593-2818 *Web Site:* www.english.ohio.edu/index.html, pg 753

Ohio University Press, One Ohio University, Scott Quadrangle, Athens, OH 45701 *Tel:* 740-593-1155 *Toll Free Tel:* 800-621-2736 *Fax:* 740-593-4536 *Web Site:* www.ohio.edu/oupress/, pg 196

Ohioana Award for Children's Literature, 274 E First Ave, Suite 300, Columbus, OH 43201 *Tel:* 614-466-3831 *Fax:* 614-728-6974 *E-mail:* ohioana@sloma.state.oh.us *Web Site:* www.oplin.lib.us/ohioana, pg 795

Ohioana Book Awards, 274 E First Ave, Suite 300, Columbus, OH 43201 *Tel:* 614-466-3831 *Fax:* 614-728-6974 *E-mail:* ohioana@sloma.state.oh.us *Web Site:* www.oplin.lib.us/ohioana/, pg 795

Ohioana Career Award, 274 E First Ave, Suite 300, Columbus, OH 43201 *Tel:* 614-466-3831 *Fax:* 614-728-6974 *E-mail:* ohioana@sloma.state.oh.us *Web Site:* www.oplin.lib.us/ohioana, pg 796

Ohioana Citations, 274 E First Ave, Suite 300, Columbus, OH 43201 *Tel:* 614-466-3831 *Fax:* 614-728-6974 *E-mail:* ohioana@sloma.state.oh.us *Web Site:* www.oplin.lib.us/ohioana, pg 796

Ohioana Pegasus Award, 274 E First Ave, Suite 300, Columbus, OH 43201 *Tel:* 614-466-3831 *Fax:* 614-728-6974 *E-mail:* ohioana@sloma.state.oh.us *Web Site:* www.oplin.lib.us/ohioana, pg 796

Ohioana Poetry Award, 274 E First Ave, Suite 300, Columbus, OH 43201 *Tel:* 614-466-3831 *Fax:* 614-728-6974 *E-mail:* ohioana@sloma.state.oh.us *Web Site:* www.oplin.lib.us/ohioana, pg 796

Ohioana Walter Rumsey Marvin Grant, 274 E First Ave, Suite 300, Columbus, OH 43201 *Tel:* 614-466-3831 *Fax:* 614-728-6974 *E-mail:* ohioana@sloma.state.oh.us *Web Site:* www.oplin.lib.us/ohioana, pg 796

Old Barn Enterprises Inc, 600 Kelly Rd, Carthage, NC 28327 *Tel:* 910-947-2587 *Fax:* 910-947-5112, pg 196

Olde & Oppenheim Publishers, 3219 N Margate Place, Chandler, AZ 85224 *Tel:* 480-839-2280 *Fax:* 480-839-0241 *E-mail:* olde_oppenheim@hotmail.com, pg 196

Veronica Oliva, 26 Mizpah St, San Francisco, CA 94131 *Tel:* 415-469-0353 *Fax:* 415-469-0377 *E-mail:* olivasfca@aol.com, pg 607

The Oliver Press Inc, Charlotte Sq, 5707 W 36 St, Minneapolis, MN 55416-2510 *Tel:* 952-926-8981 *Fax:* 952-926-8965 *Web Site:* www.oliverpress.com, pg 196

Omni Publishers Inc, 29131 Bulverde Rd, San Antonio, TX 78260 *Tel:* 830-438-7110 *Fax:* 830-438-4645 *E-mail:* omnipub@gvtc.com *Web Site:* www.webbookstore.net, pg 196

Omnibus Press, 257 Park Ave S, 20th fl, New York, NY 10010 *Tel:* 212-254-2100 *Toll Free Tel:* 800-431-7187 *Fax:* 212-254-2013 *Toll Free Fax:* 800-345-6842 *E-mail:* info@musicsales.com *Web Site:* www.musicsales.com, pg 196

Omnidawn Publishing, 1632 Elm Ave, Richmond, CA 94805-1614 *Tel:* 510-237-5472 *Toll Free Tel:* 800-792-4957 *Fax:* 510-232-8525 *Web Site:* www.omnidawn.com, pg 196

Omnigraphics Inc, 615 Griswold St, Detroit, MI 48226 *Tel:* 313-961-1340 *Toll Free Tel:* 800-234-1340 (cust serv) *Fax:* 313-961-1383 *Toll Free Fax:* 800-875-1340 (cust serv) *E-mail:* info@omnigraphics.com *Web Site:* www.omnigraphics.com, pg 197

Omohundro Institute of Early American History & Culture, 109 Cary St, Williamsburg, VA 23185 *Tel:* 757-221-1114 *Fax:* 757-221-1047 *E-mail:* ieahc1@wm.edu *Web Site:* www.wm.edu/oieahc, pg 197

One Act Play Depot, 132 Memorial Dr, Spiritwood, SK S0J 2M0, Canada *E-mail:* plays@oneactplays.net; orders@oneactplays.net *Web Site:* oneactplays.net, pg 556

One Planet Publishing House, PO Box 19840, Seattle, WA 98109-1840 *Tel:* 206-282-9699 *Toll Free Tel:* 877-526-3814 (87-PLANET-14) *Fax:* 206-282-9699 *Toll Free Fax:* 877-526-3814 (87-PLANET-14) *E-mail:* info@oneplanetpublishinghouse.com *Web Site:* www.oneplanetpublishinghouse.com, pg 197

OneOnOne Computer Training, 2055 Army Trail Rd, Suite 100, Addison, IL 60101 *Tel:* 630-628-0500 *Toll Free Tel:* 800-424-8668 *E-mail:* oneonone@protrain.com *Web Site:* www.ooootraining.com, pg 197

OneSource, 300 Baker Ave, Concord, MA 01742 *Tel:* 978-318-4300 *Toll Free Tel:* 800-554-5501 (sales) *Fax:* 978-318-4690 *E-mail:* sales@onesource.com *Web Site:* www.onesource.com, pg 197

Online Training Solutions Inc, PO Box 2224, Redmond, WA 98073-2224 *Tel:* 425-885-1441 *Toll Free Tel:* 800-854-3344 *Fax:* 425-881-1642; 425-671-0640 *E-mail:* customerservice@otsi.com *Web Site:* www.otsi.com, pg 197

Ontario Library Association, 100 Lombard St, Suite 303, Toronto, ON M5C 1M3, Canada *Tel:* 416-363-3388 *Toll Free Tel:* 866-873-9867 *Fax:* 416-941-9581 *Toll Free Fax:* 800-387-1181 *Web Site:* www.accessola.com, pg 696

Oolichan Books, Box 10, Lantzville, BC V0R 2H0, Canada *Tel:* 250-390-4839 *Fax:* 250-390-4839 *E-mail:* oolichan@island.net *Web Site:* www.oolichan.com, pg 556

Open Court, SRA/McGraw-Hill, 332 S Michigan, Suite 1100, Chicago, IL 60604 *Tel:* 312-939-1500 *Toll Free Tel:* 800-815-2280 (orders only) *Fax:* 312-939-8150 *E-mail:* opencourt@caruspub.com *Web Site:* www.opencourtbooks.com, pg 197

Open Horizons Publishing Co, PO Box 205, Fairfield, IA 52556-0205 *Tel:* 641-472-6130 *Toll Free Tel:* 800-796-6130 *Fax:* 641-472-1560 *E-mail:* info@bookmarket.com *Web Site:* www.bookmarket.com, pg 197

Open Road Publishing, PO Box 284, Cold Spring Harbor, NY 11724-0284 *Tel:* 631-692-7172 *Fax:* 631-692-7193 *E-mail:* jopenroad@aol.com, pg 198

Opie Prize, Mershon Ctr, Ohio State University, 1501 Neil Ave, Columbus, OH 43201-2602 *Tel:* 614-292-3375 *Fax:* 614-292-2407, pg 796

OPIS/STALSBY Directories & Databases, Parkway 70 Plaza, 1255 Rt 70, Suite 32N, Lakewood, NJ 08701 *Tel:* 732-901-8800 *Toll Free Tel:* 800-275-0950 *Fax:* 732-901-9632 *Web Site:* www.opisnet.com, pg 198

Optical Society of America, 2010 Massachusetts Ave NW, Washington, DC 20036-1023 *Tel:* 202-223-8130 *Fax:* 202-223-1096 *E-mail:* custserv@osa.org *Web Site:* www.osa.org, pg 198

Optimization Software Inc, 10800 Savona Rd, Los Angeles, CA 90077 *Tel:* 310-472-2910 *Fax:* 310-472-2910 *E-mail:* aries@optipub.bizland.com *Web Site:* www.optipub.bizland, pg 198

Optometric Extension Program Foundation, 1921 E Carnegie Ave, Suite 3-L, Santa Ana, CA 92705-5510 *Tel:* 949-250-8070 *Fax:* 949-250-8157 *E-mail:* oep1@oep.org *Web Site:* www.oep.org, pg 198

Orange Frazer Press Inc, 37 1/2 W Main St, Wilmington, OH 45177 *Tel:* 937-382-3196 *Toll Free Tel:* 800-852-9332 *Fax:* 937-383-3159 *E-mail:* ofrazer@erinet.com *Web Site:* www.orangefrazer.com, pg 198

Orbis Books, Walsh Bldg, 75 Ryder Rd, Ossining, NY 10562 *Tel:* 914-941-7636 *Toll Free Tel:* 800-258-5838 (orders) *Fax:* 914-941-7005 (orders); 914-945-0670 (office) *E-mail:* orbisbooks@maryknoll.org *Web Site:* www.orbisbooks.com, pg 198

Orca Book Publishers, PO Box 468, Custer, WA 98240-0468 *Tel:* 250-380-1229 *Toll Free Tel:* 800-210-5277 *Fax:* 250-380-1892 *E-mail:* orca@orcabook.com *Web Site:* www.orcabook.com, pg 198

Orchises Press, PO Box 20602, Alexandria, VA 22320-1602 *Tel:* 703-683-1243 *Fax:* 703-993-1161 *Web Site:* mason.gmu.edu/~rlathbur/, pg 198

Order of the Cross, PO Box 2472, La Grange, IL 60525-8572 *Toll Free Tel:* 800-611-1361 *Toll Free Fax:* 800-611-1361 *E-mail:* meditate@interaccess.com, pg 198

Oregon Catholic Press, 5536 NE Hassalo, Portland, OR 97213 *Tel:* 503-281-1191 *Toll Free Tel:* 800-548-8749 *Fax:* 503-282-3486 *Toll Free Fax:* 800-843-8181 *E-mail:* liturgy@ocp.org *Web Site:* www.ocp.org, pg 198

Oregon Christian Writers, 1647 SW Pheasant Dr, Aloha, OR 97006 *Tel:* 503-642-9844 *Fax:* 503-848-3658 *E-mail:* miholer@viser.net *Web Site:* www.oregonchristianwriters.org, pg 696

Oregon Christian Writers Coaching Conference, 1647 SW Pheasant Dr, Aloha, OR 97006 *Tel:* 503-642-9844 *Fax:* 503-848-3658 *E-mail:* miholer@viser.net *Web Site:* www.oregonchristianwriters.org, pg 745

Oregon Christian Writers Seminar, 1647 SW Pheasant Dr, Aloha, OR 97006 *Tel:* 503-642-9844 *Fax:* 503-848-3658 *E-mail:* miholer@viser.net *Web Site:* www.oregonchristianwriters.org, pg 745

Oregon Historical Society Press, 1200 SW Park Ave, Portland, OR 97205-2483 *Tel:* 503-222-1741 *Fax:* 503-221-2035 *E-mail:* press@ohs.org *Web Site:* www.ohs.org, pg 199

Oregon State University Press, 102 Adams Hall, Corvallis, OR 97331 *Tel:* 541-737-3166 *Toll Free Tel:* 800-426-3797 (orders) *Fax:* 541-737-3170 *Toll Free Fax:* 800-426-3797 (orders) *E-mail:* osu.press@oregonstate.edu *Web Site:* oregonstate.edu/dept/press, pg 199

O'Reilly & Associates Inc, 1005 Gravenstein Hwy N, Sebastopol, CA 95472 *Tel:* 707-827-7000 *Toll Free Tel:* 800-998-9938 *Fax:* 707-829-0104 *E-mail:* info@oreilly.com *Web Site:* www.oreilly.com, pg 199

Organization for Economic Cooperation & Development, 2001 "L" St NW, Suite 650, Washington, DC 20036-4922 *Tel:* 202-785-6323 *Toll Free Tel:* 800-456-6323 *Fax:* 202-785-0350 *Web Site:* www.oecdwash.org; www.sourceoecd.org, pg 199

Organization of Book Publishers of Ontario, 720 Bathurst St, Suite 301, Toronto, ON M5S 2R4, Canada *Tel:* 416-536-7584 *Fax:* 416-536-7692 *E-mail:* obpo@interlog.com *Web Site:* www.ontariobooks.ca, pg 696

Oriental Institute Publications Sales, 1155 E 58 St, Chicago, IL 60637 *Tel:* 773-702-9514 *Fax:* 773-702-9853 *E-mail:* oi-publications@uchicago.edu; oi-museum@uchicago.edu; oi-administration@uchicago.edu *Web Site:* oi.uchicago.edu, pg 199

Orientation to the Graphic Arts, 200 Deer Run Rd, Sewickley, PA 15143-2600 *Tel:* 412-741-6860 *Toll Free Tel:* 800-910-4283 *Fax:* 412-741-2311 *E-mail:* info@gain.net *Web Site:* www.gain.net, pg 745

Original Publications, 22 E Mall, Plainview, NY 11803 *Tel:* 516-454-6809 *Fax:* 516-454-6829 *E-mail:* originalpub@aol.com, pg 199

Orion Book Services, 751 South St, West Brattleboro, VT 05301-4234 *Tel:* 802-254-2340 *Fax:* 802-254-2340 *E-mail:* gr8books@sover.net, pg 607

Naomi Ornest, 173 W 78 St, New York, NY 10024-6711 *Tel:* 212-873-9128, pg 607

Natalie Ornish Poetry Award, 3700 Mockingbird Lane, Dallas, TX 75205 *Tel:* 512-245-2232 *Fax:* 512-245-7462 *Web Site:* www.stedwards.edu/newc/marks/til/awards_and_rules.htm, pg 796

George Orwell Award, 1111 W Kenyon Rd, Urbana, IL 61801-1096 *Tel:* 217-328-3870 *Toll Free Tel:* 877-369-6283 *Fax:* 217-328-0977 *E-mail:* public_info@ncte.org *Web Site:* www.ncte.org, pg 796

Fifi Oscard Agency Inc, 110 W 40 St, New York, NY 10018 *Tel:* 212-764-1100 *Fax:* 212-840-5019 *E-mail:* agency@fifioscard.com *Web Site:* www.fifioscard.com, pg 647

Osprey Publishing Ltd, 443 Park Ave S, New York, NY 10016 *Tel:* 212-685-5560 *Fax:* 212-685-5836 *E-mail:* ospreyusa@aol.com *Web Site:* www.ospreypublishing.com, pg 199

Other Press LLC, 307 Seventh Ave, Suite 1807, New York, NY 10001 *Tel:* 212-414-0054 *Toll Free Tel:* 877-843-6843 *Fax:* 212-414-0939 *E-mail:* editor@otherpress.com; orders@otherpress.com *Web Site:* www.otherpress.com, pg 199

Other Press LLC, 307 Seventh Ave, Suite 1807, New York, NY 10001 *Tel:* 212-414-0054 *Toll Free Tel:* 877-THE-OTHER *Fax:* 212-414-0939 *E-mail:* orders@otherpress.com *Web Site:* www.otherpress.com, pg 573

Our Sunday Visitor Publishing, 200 Noll Plaza, Huntington, IN 46750 *Tel:* 800-348-2440 (orders) *Toll Free Tel:* 260-356-8400 *Toll Free Tel:* 260-356-8472 *Toll Free Fax:* 800-498-6709 *E-mail:* osvbooks@osv.com *Web Site:* www.osv.com, pg 199

Outcomes Unlimited Press Inc, 75 Cambridge Rd, Asheville, NC 28804 *Tel:* 828-712-1311 *Fax:* 828-258-1311 *Web Site:* www.drdossey.com, pg 200

Outdoor Empire Publishing Inc, 424 N 130 St, Seattle, WA 98133 *Tel:* 206-624-3845 *Toll Free Tel:* 800-645-5489 *Fax:* 206-695-8512 *E-mail:* hjudeh@outdoorempire.com *Web Site:* www.outdoorempire.com, pg 200

Outdoor Writers Association of America Conference, 158 Lower Georges Valley Rd, Spring Mills, PA 16875 *Tel:* 814-364-9557 *Fax:* 814-364-9558 *Web Site:* www.owaa.org, pg 745

The Overlook Press, 141 Wooster St, New York, NY 10012 *Tel:* 212-965-8400 *Fax:* 212-965-9834 *Web Site:* www.overlookny.com, pg 200

The Overmountain Press, PO Box 1261, Johnson City, TN 37605-1261 *Tel:* 423-926-2691 *Toll Free Tel:* 800-992-2691 *Fax:* 423-929-2464 *Web Site:* www.overmountainpress.com, pg 200

Overseas Press Club of America (OPC), 40 W 45 St, New York, NY 10036 *Tel:* 212-626-9220 *Fax:* 212-626-9210 *Web Site:* www.opcofamerica.org, pg 696

Richard C Owen Publishers Inc, PO Box 585, Katonah, NY 10536-0585 *Tel:* 914-232-3903 *Toll Free Tel:* 800-336-5588 *Fax:* 914-232-3977 *E-mail:* richardowen@rcowen.com *Web Site:* www.rcowen.com, pg 200

Oxbridge Communications Inc, 186 Fifth Ave, 6th fl, New York, NY 10010 *Tel:* 212-741-0231 *Toll Free Tel:* 800-955-0231 *Fax:* 212-633-2938 *E-mail:* info@oxbridge.com; custserv@oxbridge.com *Web Site:* www.mediafinder.com, pg 200

Oxford University Press Canada, 70 Wynford Dr, Don Mills, ON M3C 1J9, Canada *Tel:* 416-441-2941 *Toll Free Tel:* 800-387-8020 *Fax:* 416-444-0427 *Toll Free Fax:* 800-665-1771 *E-mail:* custserv@oupcan.com *Web Site:* www.oup.com/ca, pg 557

Oxford University Press, Inc, 198 Madison Ave, New York, NY 10016-4314 *Tel:* 212-726-6000 *Toll Free Tel:* 800-451-7556 (orders) *Web Site:* www.oup.com/us, pg 200

Oxmoor House Inc, 2100 Lakeshore Dr, Birmingham, AL 35209 *Tel:* 205-445-6000; 205-445-6560 *Toll Free Tel:* 800-366-4712 *Fax:* 205-445-6078 *Web Site:* www.oxmoorhouse.com, pg 201

Oyster River Press, 20 Riverview Rd, Durham, NH 03824-3313 *Tel:* 603-868-5006 *E-mail:* oysterriverpress@comcast.net *Web Site:* www.oysterriverpress.com, pg 201

Oyster River Press, 20 Riverview Rd, Durham, NH 03824-3313 *Tel:* 603-868-5006 *E-mail:* oysterriverpress@comcast.net *Web Site:* oysterriverpress.com, pg 607

Ozark Creative Writers Inc Annual Conference, 1818 N Taylor, Little Rock, AR 72207-4637 *E-mail:* carlj@mail.uca.edu; ozarkcreativewriters@earthlink.net *Web Site:* www.ozarkcreativewriters.org, pg 745

Ozark Mountain Publishing Inc, 276 Madison 2337, Huntsville, AR 72740 *Tel:* 479-738-2348 *Toll Free Tel:* 800-935-0045; 800-230-0312 *Fax:* 479-738-2348 *Toll Free Fax:* 800-935-0045; 800-230-0312 *Web Site:* www.ozarkmt.com, pg 201

Ozark Publishing Inc, PO Box 228, Prairie Grove, AR 72753-0228 *Tel:* 479-846-2793 *Toll Free Tel:* 800-321-5671 *Fax:* 479-846-2843 *E-mail:* msworkal@pgtc.net, pg 201

Jerome S Ozer Publisher Inc, 340 Tenafly Rd, Englewood, NJ 07631 *Tel:* 201-567-7040 *Fax:* 201-567-8134, pg 201

P & R Publishing Co, 1102 Marble Hill Rd, Phillipsburg, NJ 08865 *Tel:* 908-454-0505 *Toll Free Tel:* 800-631-0094 *Fax:* 908-859-2390 *E-mail:* per@prpbooks.com *Web Site:* prpbooks.com, pg 201

P R B Productions, 963 Peralta Ave, Albany, CA 94706-2144 *Tel:* 510-526-0722 *Fax:* 510-527-4763 *E-mail:* prbprdns@aol.com *Web Site:* www.prbmusic.com; www.prbpro.com, pg 201

P S M J Resources Inc, 10 Midland Ave, Newton, MA 02458 *Tel:* 617-965-0055 *Toll Free Tel:* 800-537-7765 *Fax:* 617-965-5152 *E-mail:* info@psmj.com *Web Site:* www.psmj.com, pg 201

Pace University, Master of Science in Publishing, Dept of Publishing, 551 Fifth Ave, Rm 805-E, New York, NY 10176 *Tel:* 212-346-1405 *Fax:* 212-661-8169 *Web Site:* www.pace.edu/dyson/mspub, pg 754

Pace University Press, 41 Park Row, Rm 1510, New York, NY 10038 *Tel:* 212-346-1405 *Fax:* 212-661-8169 *Web Site:* www.pace.edu/press, pg 201

Pacific Books, Publishers, 3427 Cork Oak Way, Palo Alto, CA 94303 *Tel:* 650-856-6400 *Fax:* 650-856-6400, pg 201

Pacific Educational Press, Faculty of Education, University of British Columbia, 6365 Biological Sciences Rd, Vancouver, BC V6T 1Z4, Canada *Tel:* 604-822-5385 *Fax:* 604-822-6603 *Web Site:* www.pep.educ.ubc.ca, pg 557

Pacific Literary Services, 1220 Club Ct, Richmond, CA 94803 *Tel:* 510-222-6555, pg 607

Pacific Northwest Book Awards, 317 W Broadway, Suite 214, Eugene, OR 97401-2890 *Tel:* 541-683-4363 *Fax:* 541-683-3910 *E-mail:* info@pnba.org *Web Site:* www.pnba.org/awards.htm, pg 796

Pacific Northwest Booksellers Association, 317 W Broadway, Suite 214, Eugene, OR 97401-2890 *Tel:* 541-683-4363 *Fax:* 541-683-3910 *E-mail:* info@pnba.org *Web Site:* www.pnba.org, pg 696

Pacific Northwest Children's Book Conference, 1633 SW Park Ave, Portland, OR 97207 *Tel:* 503-725-4186 *Toll Free Tel:* 800-547-8887 (ext 4186) *Fax:* 503-725-4840 *E-mail:* snydere@pdx.edu *Web Site:* www.haystack.pdx.edu/children, pg 745

Pacific Northwest Writers Conference, 23607 Hwy 99, Suite 2C, Edmonds, WA 98026 *Tel:* 425-673-2665 *E-mail:* staff@pnwa.org *Web Site:* www.pnwa.org, pg 746

Pacific Northwest Young Reader's Choice Award, Mary Gates Hall, Suite 370, Seattle, WA 98195-2840 *Tel:* 208-232-1263 (ext 28) *Fax:* 208-232-9266 *Web Site:* www.pnla.org, pg 796

Pacific Press Publishing Association, 1350 N Kings Rd, Nampa, ID 83687-3193 *Tel:* 208-465-2500 *Toll Free Tel:* 800-447-7377 *Fax:* 208-465-2531 *Web Site:* www.pacificpress.com, pg 201

Pacific Printing & Imaging Association, 1400 SW Fifth Ave, Suite 815, Portland, OR 97201 *Toll Free Tel:* 877-762-7742 *Toll Free Fax:* 800-824-1911 *E-mail:* info@pacprinting.org *Web Site:* www.pacprinting.org, pg 696

Pacific Publishing Services, PO Box 1150, Capitola, CA 95010-1150 *Tel:* 831-476-8284 *Fax:* 831-476-8294 *E-mail:* pacpub@attglobal.net, pg 607

Pacifica Military History, 1149 Grand Teton Dr, Pacifica, CA 94044 *Tel:* 650-355-6678 *Toll Free Tel:* 800-453-3152 (orders & inquiries) *E-mail:* mail@pacificamilitary.com *Web Site:* www.pacificamilitary.com, pg 202

Pact Publications, 1200 18 St NW, Suite 350, Washington, DC 20036 *Tel:* 202-466-5666 *Fax:* 202-466-5669 *E-mail:* books@pacthq.org *Web Site:* www.pactpublications.org, pg 202

Paladin Press, 7077 Winchester Circle, Boulder, CO 80301 *Tel:* 303-443-7250 *Toll Free Tel:* 800-392-2400 *Fax:* 303-442-8741 *E-mail:* service@paladin-press.com *Web Site:* www.paladin-press.com, pg 202

Palgrave Macmillan, 175 Fifth Ave, New York, NY 10010 *Tel:* 212-982-3900 *Fax:* 212-777-6359 *E-mail:* firstname.lastname@palgrave-usa.com *Web Site:* www.palgrave.com, pg 202

Palindrome Press, PO Box 65991, Washington, DC 20036-5991 *Tel:* 703-242-1734 *Fax:* 703-242-1734 *E-mail:* freedom@palindromepress.com *Web Site:* www.palindromepress.com, pg 202

Palladium Books Inc, 12455 Universal Dr, Taylor, MI 48180-4077 *Tel:* 734-946-2900 *Fax:* 734-946-1238 *Web Site:* www.palladiumbooks.com, pg 202

Palm Island Press, 411 Truman Ave, Key West, FL 33040 *Tel:* 305-294-7834 *Fax:* 305-296-3102 *E-mail:* pipress@earthlink.net *Web Site:* junekeith.com, pg 202

Palma Julia de Burgos, c/o Peter Bloch, 83 Park Terr W, Suite 6-A, New York, NY 10034 *Tel:* 212-942-2338 *Fax:* 718-367-0780 *Web Site:* www.buscapique.com, pg 796

Robert J Palmer, 209-14 Richland Ave, Oakland Gardens, NY 11364 *Tel:* 718-264-3021 *Fax:* 718-264-1824 *E-mail:* yanghao@okcom.net, pg 607

Pangaea Publications, 226 Wheeler St S, St Paul, MN 55105-1927 *Tel:* 651-690-3320 *Fax:* 651-690-3320 *E-mail:* info@pangaea.org *Web Site:* pangaea.org, pg 202

Karen L Pangallo, 27 Buffum St, Salem, MA 01970 *Tel:* 978-744-8796 *E-mail:* pangallo@noblenet.org, pg 607

Lucile Micheels Pannell Award for Excellence in Children's Bookselling, c/o Susannah Greenberg Public Relations, 2166 Broadway, Suite 9E, New York, NY 10024 *Tel:* 212-208-4629 *Fax:* 212-208-4629 *E-mail:* publicity@bookbuzz.com *Web Site:* www.wnba-books.org; www.wnba-books.org/awards, pg 796

Panoply Press Inc, PO Box 1885, Lake Oswego, OR 97035-0611 *Tel:* 503-697-7964 *Fax:* 503-636-5293 *E-mail:* panoplypress@aol.com, pg 202

Panoptic Enterprises, PO Box 11220, Burke, VA 22009-1220 *Tel:* 703-451-5953 *Toll Free Tel:* 800-594-4766 *Fax:* 703-451-5953 *Web Site:* www.fedgovcontracts.com, pg 202

Mildred & Albert Panowski Playwriting Award, Forest Roberts Theatre, Northern Michigan University, 1401 Presque Isle Ave, Marquette, MI 49855-5364 *Tel:* 906-227-2559 *Fax:* 906-227-2567 *Web Site:* www.nmu.edu/theatre, pg 797

Pantheon Books/Schocken Books, 1745 Broadway, New York, NY 10019 *Tel:* 212-751-2600 *Toll Free Tel:* 800-638-6460 *Fax:* 212-572-6030, pg 202

Panther Creek Press, 116 Tree Crest, Spring, TX 77393 *Tel:* 281-298-5772 *E-mail:* panthercreek3@hotmail.com *Web Site:* www.panthercreekpress.com, pg 203

Papyrus & Letterbox of London Publishers, 10501 Broom Hill Dr, Las Vegas, NV 89134-7339 *Tel:* 702-256-3838 *E-mail:* LB27383@earthlink.net *Web Site:* booksbyletterbox.com, pg 203

Para Publishing, PO Box 8206-R, Santa Barbara, CA 93118-8206 *Tel:* 805-968-7277 *Toll Free Tel:* 800-727-2782 *Fax:* 805-968-1379 *E-mail:* orders@parapublishing.com *Web Site:* www.parapublishing.com, pg 203

Parabola Books, 656 Broadway, Suite 615, New York, NY 10012 *Tel:* 212-505-6200 *Toll Free Tel:* 800-560-6984 *Fax:* 212-979-7325 *E-mail:* parabola@panix.com *Web Site:* www.parabola.org, pg 203

Parachute, 4060 Blvd St-Laurent, Bureau 501, Montreal, PQ H2W 1Y9, Canada *Tel:* 514-842-9805 *Fax:* 514-842-9319 *E-mail:* info@parachute.ca *Web Site:* www.parachute.ca, pg 557

Parachute Entertainment LLC, 156 Fifth Ave, Suite 302, New York, NY 10010 *Tel:* 212-691-1422 *Fax:* 212-645-8769 *Web Site:* www.parachutepublishing.com, pg 203

Parachute Publishing LLC, 156 Fifth Ave, Suite 302, New York, NY 10010 *Tel:* 212-691-1422 *Fax:* 212-645-8769 *Web Site:* www.parachutepublishing.com, pg 203

Paraclete Press, PO Box 1568, Orleans, MA 02653-1568 *Tel:* 508-255-4685 *Toll Free Tel:* 800-451-5006 *Fax:* 508-255-5705 *Web Site:* www.paracletepress.com, pg 203

Paradigm Publications, 202 Bendix Dr, Taos, NM 87571 *Tel:* 505-758-7758 *Toll Free Tel:* 800-873-3946 *Fax:* 505-758-7768 *Web Site:* www.paradigm-pubs.com; www.redwingbooks.com, pg 203

Paradise Cay Publications Inc, 550 S "G" St, No 12, Arcata, CA 95521 *Tel:* 707-822-9063 *Toll Free Tel:* 800-736-4509 *Fax:* 707-822-9163 *E-mail:* paracay@humboldt1.com *Web Site:* www.paracay.com, pg 203

Paragon House, 2285 University Ave W, Suite 200, St Paul, MN 55114-1635 *Tel:* 651-644-3087 *Toll Free Tel:* 800-447-3709 *Fax:* 651-644-0997 *Toll Free Fax:* 800-494-0997 *E-mail:* paragon@paragonhouse.com *Web Site:* www.paragonhouse.com, pg 204

Parallax Press, PO Box 7355, Berkeley, CA 94707-0355 *Tel:* 510-525-0101 *Fax:* 510-525-7129 *E-mail:* parallax@parallax.org *Web Site:* www.parallax.org, pg 204

Paraview Literary Agency, 40 Florence Circle, Bracey, VA 23919 *Tel:* 434-636-4138 *Fax:* 434-636-4138 *Web Site:* www.paraview.com, pg 647

Paraview Publishing, 191 Seventh Ave, Suite 2F, New York, NY 10011 *Tel:* 212-989-3616 *Fax:* 212-989-3662 *E-mail:* info@paraview.com; publisher@paraview.com *Web Site:* www.paraview.com, pg 204

Parenting Press Inc, 11065 Fifth Ave NE, Suite F, Seattle, WA 98125 *Tel:* 206-364-2900 *Toll Free Tel:* 800-99-BOOKS (992-6657) *Fax:* 206-364-0702 *E-mail:* office@parentingpress.com *Web Site:* www.parentingpress.com, pg 204

Paris-American Academy Writing Workshop, 277 Rue St Jacques, 75005 Paris, France *Tel:* 806-889-3533 *Fax:* 806-889-3533 *Web Site:* www.parisamericanacademy.edu; www.parisamericanacademy.fr, pg 746

Park Genealogical Books, PO Box 130968, Roseville, MN 55113-0968 *Tel:* 651-488-4416 *Fax:* 651-488-2653 *Web Site:* www.parkbooks.com, pg 204

Park Place Publications, 591 Lighthouse Ave, No 22, Pacific Grove, CA 93950 *Tel:* 831-649-6640 *Toll Free Tel:* 888-702-4500 *Fax:* 831-649-6649 *E-mail:* publisher@parkplace-publications.com; info@parkplace-publications.com *Web Site:* www.parkplace-publications.com, pg 204

Francis Parkman Prize, Columbia University, 603 Fayerweather Hall, MC 2538, New York, NY 10027, pg 797

The Richard Parks Agency, 138 E 16 St, Suite 5-B, New York, NY 10003 *Tel:* 212-254-9067 *Fax:* 212-228-1786 *E-mail:* rp@richardparksagency.com, pg 647

Parkway Publishers Inc, 421 Fairfield Lane, Blowing Rock, NC 28605 *Tel:* 828-265-3993 *Toll Free Tel:* 800-821-9155 *Fax:* 800-821-9155 *Toll Free Fax:* 800-821-9155 *E-mail:* parkwaypub@hotmail.com *Web Site:* www.parkwaypublishers.com, pg 204

Parlay International, 5835 Doyle St, Suite 111, Emeryville, CA 94608 *Tel:* 510-601-1000 *Toll Free Tel:* 800-457-2752 *Fax:* 510-601-1008 *E-mail:* info@parlay.com *Web Site:* www.parlay.com, pg 204

Parlay Press, PO Box 894, Superior, WI 54880 *Tel:* 218-834-2508 *E-mail:* mail@parlaypress.com *Web Site:* www.parlaypress.com, pg 204

Parsons School of Design, 66 Fifth Ave, New York, NY 10011 *Tel:* 212-229-8933 *Fax:* 212-229-5970 *Web Site:* www.parsons.edu/ce, pg 754

Passeggiata Press Inc, 420 W 14 St, Pueblo, CO 81003-2708 *Tel:* 719-544-1038 *Fax:* 719-544-7911 *E-mail:* passegpress@cs.com, pg 204

Passport Press Inc, PO Box 2543, Champlain, NY 12919-1346 *Tel:* 801-504-4385 *Fax:* 801-504-4385 *E-mail:* travelbook@yahoo.com, pg 204

Pastoral Press, 5536 NE Hassalo, Portland, OR 97213-3638 *Tel:* 503-281-1191 *Toll Free Tel:* 800-548-8749 *Fax:* 503-282-3486 *Toll Free Fax:* 800-462-7329 *E-mail:* liturgy@ocp.org *Web Site:* www.ocp.org, pg 205

Patchwork Press, PO Box 183, Bemidji, MN 56619-0183 *Tel:* 218-751-0759, pg 205

Path Press Inc, 1229 Emerson St, Evanston, IL 60201 *Tel:* 847-424-1620 *Fax:* 847-424-1623 *E-mail:* pathpressinc@aol.com, pg 205

Pathfinder Press, 4794 Clark Howell Hwy, College Park, GA 30349 *Tel:* 404-669-0600 (voice mail only) *Fax:* 707-667-1141 *E-mail:* pathfinder@pathfinderpress.com (edit); orders@pathfinderpress.com; permissions@pathfinderpress.com (permissions & copyright) *Web Site:* www.pathfinderpress.com, pg 205

Pathfinder Publishing Inc, 3600 Harbor Blvd, Suite 82, Oxnard, CA 93035 *Tel:* 800-977-2282 *Fax:* 805-985-3267 *Web Site:* www.pathfinderpublishing.com, pg 205

Pathways Publishing, 183 Guggins Lane, Boxborough, MA 01719 *Tel:* 978-264-4060 *Toll Free Tel:* 888-333-7284 *Fax:* 978-264-4069 *Web Site:* www.pathwayspub.com, pg 205

Patient-Centered Guides, 1005 Gravenstein Hwy N, Sebastopol, CA 95472 *Tel:* 707-829-0515 *Toll Free Tel:* 800-998-9938 *Fax:* 707-829-0104, pg 205

Kathi J Paton Literary Agency, 19 W 55 St, New York, NY 10019-4907 *Tel:* 212-265-6586; 908-647-2117 *E-mail:* kjplitbiz@optonline.net, pg 647

Diane Patrick, 140 Carver Loop, No 21A, Bronx, NY 10475-2954 *Tel:* 718-320-8251 *Fax:* 718-320-8251 *E-mail:* deepeedub@aol.com, pg 607

Patrick's Press, 2218 Wynnton Rd, Columbus, GA 31906 *Tel:* 706-322-1584 *Toll Free Tel:* 800-654-1052 *Fax:* 706-322-5806 *E-mail:* quizbowl@aol.com *Web Site:* www.patrickspress.com, pg 205

The Alicia Patterson Foundation Fellowship Program, 1730 Pennsylvania Ave, Suite 850, Washington, DC 20006 *Tel:* 202-393-5995 *Fax:* 301-951-8512 *E-mail:* info@aliciapatterson.org *Web Site:* www.aliciapatterson.org, pg 797

Sara Patton Book Production Services, 160 River Rd, Wailuku, HI 96793 *Tel:* 808-242-7838 *Toll Free Tel:* 800-433-4804 *Fax:* 808-242-6113, pg 607

Paul & Company, 140 Union St, Marshfield, MA 02050-6273 *Tel:* 781-834-9830 *Toll Free Tel:* 800-888-4741 (orders) *Fax:* 781-837-9996 *Web Site:* www.ipgbook.com, pg 205

Pauline Books & Media, 50 St Paul's Ave, Jamaica Plain, Boston, MA 02130 *Tel:* 617-522-8911 *Toll Free Tel:* 800-876-4463 (orders only) *Fax:* 617-541-9805 *E-mail:* businessoffice@pauline.org; orderentry@pauline.org *Web Site:* www.pauline.org, pg 205

Paulines, 5610 rue Beaubien est, Montreal, PQ H1T 1X5, Canada *Tel:* 514-253-5610 *Fax:* 514-253-1907 *E-mail:* paulines.editions@videotron.ca, pg 557

Paulist Press, 997 Macarthur Blvd, Mahwah, NJ 07430 *Tel:* 201-825-7300 *Toll Free Tel:* 800-218-1903 *Fax:* 201-825-8345 *Toll Free Fax:* 800-836-3161 (orders) *E-mail:* info@paulistpress.com *Web Site:* www.paulistpress.com, pg 206

Pavior Publishing, 2910 Camino Diablo, No 110, Walnut Creek, CA 94597 *Tel:* 925-295-0786 *Fax:* 925-935-7408 *E-mail:* editor@pavior.com *Web Site:* www.pavior.com, pg 573

Peabody Museum of Archaeology & Ethnology, Peabody Museum Press, 11 Divinity Ave, Cambridge, MA 02138 *Tel:* 617-495-3938 (Production); 617-496-9922 (Sales) *Fax:* 617-495-7535 *E-mail:* peapub@fas.harvard.edu *Web Site:* www.peabody.harvard.edu/publications, pg 206

Peace Hill Press, 18101 The Glebe Lane, Charles City, VA 23030 *Tel:* 804-829-5043 *Toll Free Tel:* 877-322-3445 (orders) *Fax:* 804-829-5704 *E-mail:* info@peacehillpress.net *Web Site:* www.peacehillpress.com, pg 206

Peachpit Press, 1249 Eighth St, Berkeley, CA 94710 *Tel:* 510-524-2178 *Fax:* 510-524-2221 *E-mail:* firstname.lastname@peachpit.com *Web Site:* www.peachpit.com, pg 206

Peachtree Publishers Ltd, 1700 Chattahoochee Ave, Atlanta, GA 30318 *Tel:* 404-876-8761 *Toll Free Tel:* 800-241-0113 *Fax:* 404-875-2578 *Toll Free Fax:* 800-875-8909 *E-mail:* hello@peachtree-online.com *Web Site:* www.peachtree-online.com, pg 206

Peanut Butter & Jelly Press LLC, PO Box 590239, Newton, MA 02459-0002 *Tel:* 617-630-0945 *Fax:* 617-630-0945 *E-mail:* info@pbjpress.com *Web Site:* www.publishinggame.com, pg 206

Pearson, 800 E 96 St, Indianapolis, IN 46240 *Tel:* 317-428-3000 *Toll Free Tel:* 800-545-5914 *Fax:* 317-581-4675 *Web Site:* www.macdigital.com, pg 206

Pearson Custom Publishing, 75 Arlington St, Suite 300, Boston, MA 02116 *Tel:* 617-848-6300 *Toll Free Tel:* 800-428-4466 (orders) *Fax:* 617-848-6358 *E-mail:* pcp@pearsoncustom.com *Web Site:* www.pearsoned.com, pg 206

Pearson Education, One Lake St, Upper Saddle River, NJ 07458 *Tel:* 201-236-7000 *Fax:* 201-236-3400 *E-mail:* firstname.lastname@pearsoned.com; communications@pearson.ed *Web Site:* www.pearsoned.com, pg 206

Pearson Education Canada Inc, 26 Prince Andrew Place, Don Mills, ON M3C 2T8, Canada *Tel:* 416-447-5101 *Toll Free Tel:* 800-567-3800; 800-387-8028 *Fax:* 416-443-0948 *Toll Free Fax:* 800-263-7733; 888-465-0536 *E-mail:* firstname.lastname@pearsoned.com *Web Site:* www.pearsoned.com, pg 557

Pearson Education - Elementary Group, 299 Jefferson Rd, Parsippany, NJ 07054-0480 *Tel:* 973-735-8000, pg 206

Pearson Education/ELT, 10 Bank St, 9th fl, White Plains, NY 10606 *Tel:* 914-993-5000 *Fax:* 914-993-8115 *E-mail:* firstname.lastname@pearsoned.com, pg 206

Pearson Education International Group, One Lake St, Upper Saddle River, NJ 07458 *Tel:* 201-236-7000, pg 206

Pearson Higher Education Division, One Lake St, Upper Saddle River, NJ 07458 *Tel:* 201-236-7000 *Fax:* 201-236-3381, pg 206

Pearson Professional Development, 1900 E Lake Ave, Glenview, IL 60025 *Tel:* 847-657-7450 *Toll Free Tel:* 800-348-4474 *Fax:* 847-486-3183 *E-mail:* info@pearsonpd.com *Web Site:* www.skylightedu.com; www.pearsonpd.com, pg 207

Pearson Technology Group (PTG), 201 W 103 St, Indianapolis, IN 46290 *Tel:* 317-581-3500 *Toll Free Tel:* 800-545-5914 *Fax:* 317-581-4675 *E-mail:* firstname.lastname@pearsoned.com *Web Site:* www.mcp.com, pg 207

Pearson Writers' Trust Non-Fiction Prize, 90 Richmond St W, Suite 200, Toronto, ON M5C 1P1, Canada *Tel:* 416-504-8222 *Fax:* 416-504-9090 *E-mail:* info@writerstrust.com *Web Site:* www.writerstrust.com, pg 797

William Peden Prize in Fiction, 1507 Hillcrest Hall, Columbia, MO 65211 *Tel:* 573-882-4474 *Toll Free Tel:* 800-949-2505 *Fax:* 573-884-4671 *E-mail:* tmr@moreview.com *Web Site:* www.missourireview.com, pg 797

T H Peek Publisher, PO Box 50123, Palo Alto, CA 94303-0123 *Tel:* 650-962-1010 *Toll Free Tel:* 800-962-9245 *Fax:* 650-962-1211 *E-mail:* thpeek@aol.com *Web Site:* www.thpeekpublisher.com, pg 207

Peel Productions Inc, PO Box 546, Columbus, NC 28722-0546 *Tel:* 828-859-3879 *Toll Free Tel:* 800-345-6665 *Fax:* 603-719-0067 *E-mail:* lmp@peelbooks.com *Web Site:* www.peelbooks.com, pg 207

Pelican Publishing Co Inc, 1000 Burmaster, Gretna, LA 70053 *Tel:* 504-368-1175 *Toll Free Tel:* 800-843-1724 *Fax:* 504-368-1195 *E-mail:* sales@pelicanpub.com (sales); office@pelicanpub.com (permission); promo@pelicanpub.com (publicity) *Web Site:* www.pelicanpub.com, pg 207

William Pell Agency, 22 Oak St, Southhampton, NY 11968 *Tel:* 631-204-0524 *Fax:* 631-287-4492 *E-mail:* wpellagency@hotmail.com, pg 647

Rodney Pelter, 129 E 61 St, New York, NY 10021 *Tel:* 212-838-3432, pg 647

Pema Browne Ltd, 11 Tena Place, Valley Cottage, NY 10989 *E-mail:* ppbltd@optonline.net *Web Site:* www.pemabrowneltd.com, pg 647

Pema Browne Ltd, 11 Tena Place, Valley Cottage, NY 10989 *E-mail:* info@pemabrowneltd.com *Web Site:* www.pemabrowneltd.com, pg 666

Pembroke Publishers Ltd, 538 Hood Rd, Markham, ON L3R 3K9, Canada *Tel:* 905-477-0650 *Fax:* 905-477-3691 *Web Site:* www.pembrokepublishers.com, pg 557

Pemmican Publications Inc, 150 Henry Ave, Winnipeg, MB R3B 0J7, Canada *Tel:* 204-589-6346 *Fax:* 204-589-2063 *E-mail:* pemmicanpublications@hotmail.com *Web Site:* www.pemmican.mb.ca, pg 557

Pen American Center, 588 Broadway, Suite 303, New York, NY 10012 *Tel:* 212-334-1660 *Fax:* 212-334-2181 *E-mail:* pen@pen.org *Web Site:* www.pen.org, pg 696

The PEN Award for Poetry in Translation, 588 Broadway, Suite 303, New York, NY 10012 *Tel:* 212-334-1660 *Fax:* 212-334-2181 *E-mail:* pen@pen.org *Web Site:* www.pen.org, pg 797

PEN Award for the Art of the Essay, 588 Broadway, Suite 303, New York, NY 10012 *Tel:* 212-334-1660 *Fax:* 212-334-2181 *E-mail:* pen@pen.org *Web Site:* www.pen.org, pg 797

PEN/Robert Bingham Fellowships for Writers, 588 Broadway, Suite 303, New York, NY 10012 *Tel:* 212-334-1660 *Fax:* 212-334-2181 *E-mail:* pen@pen.org *Web Site:* www.pen.org, pg 797

PEN Book-of-the-Month Translation Prize, 588 Broadway, Suite 303, New York, NY 10012 *Tel:* 212-334-1660 *Fax:* 212-334-2181 *E-mail:* pen@pen.org *Web Site:* www.pen.org, pg 797

PEN Canada, 24 Ryerson Ave, Suite 214, Toronto, ON M5T 2P3, Canada *Tel:* 416-703-8448 *Fax:* 416-703-3870 *E-mail:* pen@pencanada.ca *Web Site:* www.pencanada.ca, pg 696

PEN Center USA, 672 S Lafayette Park Place, Suite 42, Los Angeles, CA 90057 *Tel:* 213-365-8500 *Fax:* 213-365-9616 *E-mail:* pen@penusa.org *Web Site:* www.penusa.org, pg 697

PEN Center USA Literary Awards, 672 S Lafayette Park Place, Suite 42, Los Angeles, CA 90057 *Tel:* 213-365-8500 *Fax:* 213-365-9616 *E-mail:* awards@penusa.org *Web Site:* www.penusa.org, pg 797

PEN/Faulkner Award for Fiction, Folger Shakespeare Library, 201 E Capitol St SE, Washington, DC 20003 *Tel:* 202-675-0345 *Fax:* 202-608-1719 *Web Site:* www.penfaulkner.org, pg 797

PEN/Jerard Fund Award, 588 Broadway, Suite 303, New York, NY 10012 *Tel:* 212-334-1660 *Fax:* 212-334-2181 *E-mail:* pen@pen.org *Web Site:* www.pen.org, pg 797

PEN Martha Albrand Award for The Art of Memoir, 588 Broadway, Suite 303, New York, NY 10012 *Tel:* 212-334-1660 *Fax:* 212-334-2181 *E-mail:* pen@pen.org *Web Site:* www.pen.org, pg 798

PEN/Phyllis Naylor Working Writer Fellowship, 588 Broadway, Suite 303, New York, NY 10012 *Tel:* 212-334-1660 *Fax:* 212-334-2181 *E-mail:* pen@pen.org *Web Site:* www.pen.org, pg 798

The PEN/Ralph Manheim Medal for Translation, 588 Broadway, Suite 303, New York, NY 10012 *Tel:* 212-334-1660 *Fax:* 212-334-2181 *E-mail:* pen@pen.org *Web Site:* www.pen.org, pg 798

PEN Writers Fund, 588 Broadway, Suite 303, New York, NY 10012 *Tel:* 212-334-1660 *Fax:* 212-334-2181 *E-mail:* pen@pen.org *Web Site:* www.pen.org, pg 798

Pencil Point Press Inc, PO Box 634, New Hope, PA 18938 *Tel:* 215-862-8855 *Toll Free Tel:* 800-356-1299 *Fax:* 215-862-8857 *E-mail:* penpoint@ix.netcom.com *Web Site:* pencilpointpress.com, pg 207

Pendragon Press, 52 White Hill Lane, Hillsdale, NY 12529-5839 *Tel:* 518-325-6100 *Fax:* 518-325-6102 *E-mail:* penpress@taconic.net *Web Site:* www.pendragonpress.com, pg 207

Penfield Books, 215 Brown St, Iowa City, IA 52245 *Tel:* 319-337-9998 *Toll Free Tel:* 800-728-9998 *Fax:* 319-351-6846 *E-mail:* penfield@penfieldbooks.com *Web Site:* www.penfieldbooks.com, pg 207

Penguin Audiobooks, 375 Hudson St, New York, NY 10014 *Tel:* 212-366-2000 *E-mail:* online@penguin.com *Web Site:* www.penguin.com, pg 207

Penguin Books, 375 Hudson St, New York, NY 10014 *Tel:* 212-366-2000 *E-mail:* online@penguinputnam.com *Web Site:* www.penguin.com; www.penguinclassics.com, pg 207

Penguin Group (Canada), 10 Alcorn Ave, Suite 300, Toronto, ON M4V 3B2, Canada *Tel:* 416-925-2249 *Fax:* 416-925-0068 *Web Site:* www.penguin.ca, pg 557

Penguin Group (USA) Inc Sales, 375 Hudson St, New York, NY 10014 *Tel:* 212-366-2000 *E-mail:* online@penguinputnam.com *Web Site:* www.penguin.com, pg 207

Penguin Group (USA) Inc, 375 Hudson St, New York, NY 10014 *Tel:* 212-366-2000 *Fax:* 212-366-2666 *E-mail:* online@uspenguingroup.com *Web Site:* www.penguin.com, pg 208

Penguin Young Readers Group, 345 Hudson St, New York, NY 10014 *Tel:* 212-366-2000 *E-mail:* online@penguinputnam.com *Web Site:* www.penguin.com, pg 208

Penmarin Books Inc, 1044 Magnolia Way, Roseville, CA 95661 *Tel:* 916-771-5869 *Fax:* 916-771-5879 *E-mail:* penmarin@penmarin.com *Web Site:* www.penmarin.com, pg 208

Beth Penney Editorial Services, PO Box 604, Pacific Grove, CA 93950-0604 *Tel:* 831-372-7625, pg 607

Pennsylvania Council on the Arts Literature Program, 216 Finance Bldg, Harrisburg, PA 17120 *Tel:* 717-787-6883 *Fax:* 717-783-2538 *Web Site:* www.pacouncilonthearts.org, pg 798

Pennsylvania Historical & Museum Commission, Commonwealth Keystone Bldg, 400 North St, Harrisburg, PA 17120-0053 *Tel:* 717-783-2618 *Toll Free Tel:* 800-747-7790 *Fax:* 717-787-8312 *Web Site:* www.phmc.state.pa.us, pg 209

Pennsylvania State Data Center, Penn State Harrisburg, 777 W Harrisburg Pike, Middletown, PA 17057-4898 *Tel:* 717-948-6336 *Fax:* 717-948-6754 *E-mail:* pasdc@psu.edu *Web Site:* pasdc.hbg.psu.edu, pg 209

The Pennsylvania State University Press, 820 N University Dr, University Support Bldg 1, Suite C, University Park, PA 16802-1003 *Tel:* 814-865-1327 *Toll Free Tel:* 800-326-9180 *Fax:* 814-863-1408 *Toll Free Fax:* 877 7782665 *Web Site:* www.psupress.org, pg 209

PennWell Books & More, 1421 S Sheridan, Tulsa, OK 74112 *Tel:* 918-831-9421 *Toll Free Tel:* 800-752-9764 *Fax:* 918-832-9319 *E-mail:* sales@penwellbooks.com *Web Site:* www.penwellbooks.com, pg 209

PennWriters Conference, 5576 Edwards Rd, Murrysville, PA 15568 *Tel:* 724-327-2725 *Web Site:* www.pennwriters.org, pg 746

Penrose Press, 1333 Gough, Suite 8B, San Francisco, CA 94109 *Tel:* 415-567-4157 *Fax:* 415-567-4165 *E-mail:* info@penrose-press.com *Web Site:* www. penrose-press.com, pg 209

Pentecostal Publishing House, 8855 Dunn Rd, Hazelwood, MO 63042 *Tel:* 314-837-7300 *Fax:* 314-837-6574 *E-mail:* pphordersdept@upci.org (orders) *Web Site:* www.pentecostalpublishing.com, pg 209

Penton Overseas Inc, 2470 Impala Dr, Carlsbad, CA 92008-7226 *Tel:* 760-431-0060 *Toll Free Tel:* 800-748-5804 *Fax:* 760-431-8110 *E-mail:* info@ pentonoverseas.com *Web Site:* www.pentonoverseas. com, pg 209

PeopleSpeak, 25381G Alicia Pkwy, No 1, Laguna Hills, CA 92653 *Tel:* 949-581-6190 *Fax:* 949-581-4958 *E-mail:* pplspeak@norcov.com *Web Site:* www. detailsplease.com/peoplespeak, pg 607

Rebecca Pepper, 434 NE Floral Place, Portland, OR 97232 *Tel:* 503-236-5802 *E-mail:* rpepper@rpepper. net, pg 608

Per Annum Inc, 48 W 25 St, 10th fl, New York, NY 10010 *Tel:* 212-647-8700 *Toll Free Tel:* 800-548-1108 *Fax:* 212-647-8716 *E-mail:* info@perannum.com *Web Site:* www.perannum.com, pg 210

Peradam Press, PO Box 6, North San Juan, CA 95960-0006 *Tel:* 530-292-4266 *Toll Free Tel:* 800-241-8689 *Fax:* 530-292-4266 *Toll Free Fax:* 800-241-8689 *E-mail:* peradam@earthlink.net, pg 210

Dan Peragine Agency, 227 Beechwood Ave, Bogota, NJ 07603 *Tel:* 201-487-1296 *Fax:* 201-487-1433 *E-mail:* dpliterary@aol.com *Web Site:* www.writers. net, pg 648

Perfection Learning Corp, 10520 New York Ave, Des Moines, IA 50322 *Tel:* 515-278-0133 *Toll Free Tel:* 800-762-2999 *Fax:* 515-278-2980 *E-mail:* orders@perfectionlearning.com *Web Site:* perfectionlearning.com, pg 210

Perigee Books, 375 Hudson St, New York, NY 10014 *Tel:* 212-366-2000 *Fax:* 212-366-2365 *E-mail:* online@penguinputnam.com *Web Site:* www. penguin.com, pg 210

Periodical & Book Association of America Inc, 481 Eighth Ave, Suite 826, New York, NY 10001 *Tel:* 212-563-6502 *Fax:* 212-563-4098 *Web Site:* www. pbaa.net, pg 697

The Periodical Publications Assn Inc (PPA), PO Box 10669, Rockville, MD 20849-0669 *Tel:* 301-260-1646 *Fax:* 301-260-1647 *E-mail:* periodicalpubs@yahoo. com, pg 697

Periodical Writers' Association of Canada, 215 Spadina Ave, Suite 123, Toronto, ON M5T 2C7, Canada *Tel:* 416-504-1645 *Fax:* 416-913-2327 *E-mail:* pwac@ web.net; *Web Site:* www.pwac.ca; www. writers.ca, pg 697

The Permanent Press, 4170 Noyac Rd, Sag Harbor, NY 11963 *Tel:* 631-725-1101 *Fax:* 631-725-8215 *Web Site:* www.thepermanentpress.com, pg 210

The Permissions Group, 1247 Milwaukee Ave, Suite 303, Glenview, IL 60025 *Tel:* 847-635-6550 *Fax:* 847-635-6968 *E-mail:* info@permissionsgroup.com *Web Site:* www.permissionsgroup.com, pg 608

Philip A Perry, Freelance Editorial Services, 1311 Wesley Ave, Evanston, IL 60201-4117 *Tel:* 847-733-1270 *E-mail:* philaperry@aol.com, pg 608

Persea Books Inc, 853 Broadway, Suite 604, New York, NY 10003 *Tel:* 212-260-9256 *Fax:* 212-260-1902 *E-mail:* info@perseabooks.com *Web Site:* www. perseabooks.com, pg 210

The Perseus Books Group, 387 Park Ave S, 12th fl, New York, NY 10016 *Tel:* 212-340-8100 *Toll Free Tel:* 800-386-5656 (cust serv) *Fax:* 212-340-8115 *Web Site:* www.perseusbooksgroup.com, pg 210

Perspectives Press Inc: The Infertility & Adoption Publisher, PO Box 90318, Indianapolis, IN 46290-0318 *Tel:* 317-872-3055 *Web Site:* www. perspectivespress.com, pg 210

James Peter Associates Inc, PO Box 358, New Canaan, CT 06840 *Tel:* 203-972-1070 *Fax:* 203-972-1759, pg 648

Peter Pauper Press Inc, 202 Mamaroneck Ave, White Plains, NY 10601-5376 *Tel:* 914-681-0144 *Toll Free Tel:* 800-833-2311 *Fax:* 914-681-0389 *E-mail:* customerservice@peterpauper.com *Web Site:* www.peterpauper.com, pg 210

Gerald Peters Gallery, 1011 Paseo De Peralta, Santa Fe, NM 87501 *Tel:* 505-954-5700 *Fax:* 505-954-5754 *E-mail:* bookstore@gpgallery.com *Web Site:* www. gpgallery.com, pg 211

Elsa Peterson Ltd, 41 East Ave, Norwalk, CT 06851 *Tel:* 203-846-8331 *Fax:* 203-846-8049 *E-mail:* epltd@ earthlink.net, pg 608

Petroleum Extension Service (PETEX), University of Texas, One University Sta, R8100, Austin, TX 78712-1100 *Tel:* 512-471-5940 *Toll Free Tel:* 800-687-4132 *Fax:* 512-471-9410 *Toll Free Fax:* 800-687-7839 *E-mail:* rbpetex@mail.utexas.edu *Web Site:* www. utexas.edu/cee/petex, pg 211

Evelyn Walters Pettit, PO Box 3073, Winter Park, FL 32790-3073 *Tel:* 407-629-9289; 407-644-1711 *Fax:* 407-644-1099 *E-mail:* brandywine@ floridabooksellers.com, pg 608

Stephen Pevner Inc, 382 Lafayette St, Suite 8, New York, NY 10003 *Tel:* 212-674-8403 *Fax:* 212-529-3692, pg 648

Peytral Publications Inc, PO Box 1162, Minnetonka, MN 55345-0162 *Tel:* 952-949-8707 *Toll Free Tel:* 877-PEYTRAL (739-8725) *Fax:* 952-906-9777 *E-mail:* help@peytral.com *Web Site:* www.peytral.com, pg 211

Pfizer Award, University of Florida, 3310 Turlington Hall, Gainesville, FL 32611 *Tel:* 352-392-1677 *E-mail:* info@hssonline.org *Web Site:* www.hssonline. org, pg 798

Pflaum Publishing Group, 2621 Dryden Rd, Dayton, OH 45439 *Tel:* 937-293-1415 *Toll Free Tel:* 800-543-4383 *Fax:* 917-293-1310 *Toll Free Fax:* 800-370-4450 *Web Site:* www.pflaum.com, pg 211

Phaidon Press Inc, 180 Varick St, 14th fl, New York, NY 10014 *Tel:* 212-652-5400 *Toll Free Tel:* 800-759-0190 (cust serv) *Fax:* 212-652-5410 *Toll Free Fax:* 800-286-9471 (cust serv) *E-mail:* ussales@phaidon.com *Web Site:* www.phaidon.com, pg 211

James D Phelan Literary Award, 225 Bush St, Suite 500, San Francisco, CA 94104-4224 *Tel:* 415-733-8500 *Fax:* 415-477-2783 *Web Site:* www.sff.org, pg 798

Janice M Phelps, 126 S Maple St, Lancaster, OH 43130 *Tel:* 740-689-2950 *Fax:* 740-689-2951 *E-mail:* jmp@ janicephelps.com *Web Site:* www.janicephelps.com, pg 608

Phi Beta Kappa Award in Science, 1606 New Hampshire Ave NW, Washington, DC 20009 *Tel:* 202-265-3808 *Fax:* 202-986-1601 *Web Site:* www.pbk.org, pg 798

Phi Delta Kappa International, 408 N Union, Bloomington, IN 47401 *Tel:* 812-339-1156 *Toll Free Tel:* 800-766-1156 *Fax:* 812-339-0018 *E-mail:* information@pdkintl.org *Web Site:* www. pdkintl.org, pg 211

Philadelphia Museum of Art, 2525 Pennsylvania Ave, Philadelphia, PA 19130 *Tel:* 215-684-7250 *Fax:* 215-235-8715 *Web Site:* www.philamuseum.org, pg 211

Philadelphia Writers' Conference, PO Box 7171, Elkins Park, PA 19027-0171 *Tel:* 215-782-3288 *E-mail:* info@pwcwriters.org *Web Site:* pwcwriters. org, pg 746

Meredith Phillips, 4127 Old Adobe Rd, Palo Alto, CA 94306 *Tel:* 650-857-9555 *E-mail:* meredith.phillips@ gte.net, pg 608

Philosophy Documentation Center, PO Box 7147, Charlottesville, VA 22906-7147 *Toll Free Tel:* 800-444-2419 *E-mail:* order@pdcnet.org *Web Site:* www. pdcnet.org, pg 211

Phobos Books, 200 Park Ave S, Suite 1109, New York, NY 10003 *Tel:* 212-477-3225 *Fax:* 212-529-4223 *E-mail:* info@phobosweb.com *Web Site:* phobosweb. com, pg 211

Phoenix Learning Resources, 25 Third St, 2nd fl, Stamford, CT 06905 *Tel:* 203-353-1665 *Toll Free Tel:* 800-526-6581 *Fax:* 212-629-5648 *Web Site:* www. phoenixlr.com, pg 212

Phoenix Literary Agency, 216 S Yellowstone, Livingston, MT 59047 *Tel:* 902-232-2848; 520-404-4748 (cell), pg 648

Phoenix Society for Burn Survivors, 2153 Wealthy SE, Suite 215, E Grand Rapids, MI 49506 *Tel:* 616-458-2773 *Toll Free Tel:* 800-888-BURN (888-2876) *Fax:* 616-458-2831 *E-mail:* info@phoenix-society.org *Web Site:* www.phoenix-society.org, pg 212

PhotoEdit Inc, 235 E Broadway, Suite 1020, Long Beach, CA 90802 *Tel:* 562-435-2722 *Toll Free Tel:* 800-860-2098 *Fax:* 562-435-7161 *Toll Free Fax:* 800-804-3707 *E-mail:* sales@photoeditinc.com *Web Site:* www.photoeditinc.com, pg 608

Photographic Society of America Inc (PSA), 3000 United Founders Blvd, Suite 103, Oklahoma City, OK 73112-3940 *Tel:* 405-843-1437 *Fax:* 405-843-1438 *E-mail:* psahg@theshop.net; hq@psa-photo.org *Web Site:* www.psa-photo.org, pg 697

PIA/GATF (Graphic Arts Technical Foundation), 200 Deer Run Rd, Sewickley, PA 15143-2600 *Tel:* 412-741-6860 *Toll Free Tel:* 800-910-4283 *Fax:* 412-741-2311 *E-mail:* info@gain.net *Web Site:* www.gain.net, pg 212, 697

PIA/GATF (Graphic Arts Technical Foundation), 200 Deer Run Rd, Sewickley, PA 15143-2600 *Tel:* 412-741-6860 *Toll Free Tel:* 800-910-4283 *Fax:* 412-741-2311, pg 754

PIA/GATF/NAPL Sheetfed Executive of the Year, 200 Deer Run Rd, Sewickley, PA 15143-2600 *Tel:* 412-741-6860 *Toll Free Tel:* 800-910-4283 *Fax:* 412-741-2311 *E-mail:* info@gain.net *Web Site:* www.gain.net, pg 798

Piano Press, 1425 Ocean Ave, Suite 6, Del Mar, CA 92014 *Tel:* 619-884-1401 *Fax:* 858-459-3376 *E-mail:* pianopress@aol.com *Web Site:* www. pianopress.com, pg 212

Picador, 175 Fifth Ave, New York, NY 10010 *Tel:* 212-674-5151 *Fax:* 212-253-9627 *E-mail:* firstname. lastname@picadorusa.com *Web Site:* www.picadorusa. com, pg 212

Alison Picard Literary Agent, PO Box 2000, Cotuit, MA 02635 *Tel:* 508-477-7192 *Fax:* 508-477-7192 (call first) *E-mail:* ajpicard@aol.com, pg 648

Picasso Project, 1109 Geary Blvd, San Francisco, CA 94109 *Tel:* 415-292-6500 *Fax:* 415-292-6594 *E-mail:* editeur@earthlink.net *Web Site:* picasso@art-books.com (orders) *Web Site:* art-books.com, pg 212

Piccadilly Books Ltd, PO Box 25203, Colorado Springs, CO 80936-5203 *Tel:* 719-550-9887 *E-mail:* orders@ piccadillybooks.com *Web Site:* www.piccadillybooks. com, pg 212

Robert J Pickering Award for Playwriting Excellence, 89 Division, Coldwater, MI 49036 *Tel:* 517-279-7963, pg 798

Pickwick Publications, 215 Incline Way, San Jose, CA 95139-1526 *Tel:* 408-224-6777 *Fax:* 408-224-6686 *Web Site:* www.pickwickpublications.com, pg 212

Picton Press, PO Box 250, Rockport, ME 04856-0250 *Tel:* 207-236-6565 *Fax:* 207-236-6713 *E-mail:* sales@ pictonpress.com (orders) *Web Site:* www.pictonpress. com, pg 212

Pictorial Histories Publishing Co, 521 Bickford St, Missoula, MT 59801 *Tel:* 406-549-8488 *Toll Free Tel:* 888-763-8350 *Fax:* 406-728-9280 *E-mail:* phpc@montana.com *Web Site:* www. pictorialhistoriespublishing.com, pg 212

Pie in the Sky Publishing, 2511 S Dawson Way, Aurora, CO 80014 *Tel:* 303-751-2672 *Fax:* 303-751-2672 *E-mail:* pieintheskypublishing@msn.com *Web Site:* www.pieintheskypublishing.com, pg 212

Pieces of Learning, 1990 Market Rd, Marion, IL 62959-8976 Tel: 618-964-9426 Toll Free Tel: 800-729-5137 Toll Free Fax: 800-844-0455 E-mail: polmarion@midamer.net Web Site: www.piecesoflearning.com, pg 212

Lorne Pierce Medal, 283 Sparks St, Ottawa, ON K1R 7X9, Canada Tel: 613-991-6990 Fax: 613-991-6996 E-mail: adminrsc@rsc.ca Web Site: www.rsc.ca, pg 798

Pig Out Publications Inc, 207 E Gregory Blvd, Kansas City, MO 64114 Tel: 816-531-3119 Fax: 816-531-6113 Web Site: www.pigoutpublications.com, pg 213

Pilgrim Award & Pioneer Award, 6021 Grassmere, Corpus Christi, TX 78415 Tel: 530-752-1699 E-mail: sands@uwm.edu Web Site: www.sfra.org, pg 798

The Pilgrim Press/United Church Press, 700 Prospect Ave, Cleveland, OH 44115-1100 Tel: 216-736-3761 Toll Free Tel: 800-537-3394 (cust serv) Fax: 216-736-2207 E-mail: thepilgrimpress@thepilgrimpress.com Web Site: www.thepilgrimpress.com; www.theunitedchurchpress.com, pg 213

Pilgrim Publications, PO Box 66, Pasadena, TX 77501-0066 Tel: 713-477-4261; 713-477-2329 Fax: 713-477-7561 E-mail: pilgrimpub@aol.com Web Site: members.aol.com/pilgrimpub/; www.pilgrimpublications.com, pg 213

Pima Writers' Workshop, Pima College West Campus, 2202 W Anklam Rd, Tucson, AZ 85709-0170 Tel: 520-206-6084 Fax: 520-206-6020, pg 746

The Pimlico Agency Inc, PO Box 20447, Cherokee Sta, New York, NY 10021 Tel: 212-628-9729 Fax: 212-535-7861, pg 648

Caroline Pincus Book Midwife, 1237 Sixth Ave, San Francisco, CA 94122 Tel: 415-665-3200 Fax: 415-665-6502 E-mail: cpincus100@sbcglobal.net, pg 608

Marilyn Pincus Inc, 9645 E Holiday Way, Sun Lakes, AZ 85248 Tel: 408-883-1958 E-mail: MPscribe@aol.com, pg 608

Pinder Lane & Garon-Brooke Associates Ltd, 159 W 53 St, Suite 14-E, New York, NY 10019 Tel: 212-489-0880 Fax: 212-489-7104 E-mail: pinderl@interport.net, pg 648

Pine Barrens Press, 3959 Rte 563, Chatsworth, NJ 08019 Tel: 609-894-4415 Fax: 609-894-2350 E-mail: pbp@verizon.net, pg 213

Pine Forge Press, 2455 Teller Rd, Thousand Oaks, CA 91320 Tel: 805-499-4224 Fax: 805-499-0721 E-mail: info@sagepub.com Web Site: www.sagepub.com, pg 213

Pineapple Press Inc, PO Box 3889, Sarasota, FL 34230-3889 Tel: 941-359-0886 Toll Free Tel: 800-746-3275 (orders) Fax: 941-351-9988 E-mail: info@pineapplepress.com Web Site: www.pineapplepress.com, pg 213

Pioneer Publishing Co, Hwy 82 E, Carrolton, MS 38917 Tel: 662-237-6010 E-mail: pioneerse@tecinfo.com Web Site: www.pioneersoutheast.com, pg 213

Pippin Press, 229 E 85 St, New York, NY 10028 Tel: 212-288-4920 Fax: 908-237-2407, pg 213

Pippin Properties Inc, 155 E 38 St, Suite 2H, New York, NY 10016 Tel: 212-338-9310 Fax: 212-338-9579 E-mail: info@pippinproperties.com Web Site: www.pippinproperties.com, pg 648

Pippin Publishing Corp, 170 The Donway W, Toronto, ON M3C 2G3, Canada Tel: 416-510-2918 Toll Free Tel: 888-889-0001 Fax: 416-510-3359 Web Site: www.pippinpub.com, pg 557

Pir Publications Inc, 227 W Broadway, New York, NY 10013 Tel: 212-334-5212 Fax: 212-334-5214 E-mail: pirpress@ulster.net Web Site: www.sufibooks.com, pg 213

Pitspopany Press, 40 E 78 St, Suite 16-D, New York, NY 10021 Tel: 212-472-4959 Toll Free Tel: 800-232-2931 Fax: 212-472-6253 E-mail: pitspop@netvision.net.il; pitspopany@aol.com, pg 213

Pittenbruach Press, PO Box 553, Northampton, MA 01061-0553 Tel: 413-584-8547, pg 213

PJD Publications Ltd, PO Box 966, Westbury, NY 11590-0966 Tel: 516-626-0650 Fax: 516-626-5546 E-mail: pjdsankar@msn.com Web Site: www.pjdonline.com; www.pjdpublications.com, pg 214

Planners Press, 122 S Michigan Ave, Suite 1600, Chicago, IL 60603 Tel: 312-431-9100 Fax: 312-431-9985 Web Site: www.planning.org, pg 214

Planning/Communications, 7215 Oak Ave, River Forest, IL 60305-1935 Tel: 708-366-5200 Toll Free Tel: 888-366-5200 Fax: 708-366-5280 E-mail: info@planningcommunications.com Web Site: www.jobfindersonline.com, pg 214

Platinum One Publishing, 21W551 North Ave, Suite 132, Lombard, IL 60148 Tel: 630-935-7323 Fax: 203-651-1825 E-mail: customerservice@platinumonepublishing.com Web Site: www.platinumonepublishing.com, pg 573

Platinum Press Inc, 311 Crossways Park Dr, Woodbury, NY 11797 Tel: 516-364-1800 Fax: 516-364-1899, pg 214

Platypus Media LLC, 627 "A" St NE, Washington, DC 20002 Tel: 202-546-1674 Toll Free Tel: 877-872-8977 Fax: 202-546-2356 E-mail: info@platypusmedia.com Web Site: www.platypusmedia.com, pg 214

Playboy College Fiction Contest, 730 Fifth Ave, New York, NY 10019 Tel: 212-261-5000 Fax: 212-957-2900 Web Site: www.playboy.com, pg 799

Players Press Inc, PO Box 1132, Studio City, CA 91614-0132 Tel: 818-789-4980, pg 214

Playhouse on the Square, 51 S Cooper, Memphis, TN 38104 Tel: 901-725-0776 Fax: 901-272-7530, pg 799

Playhouse Publishing, 1566 Akron-Peninsula Rd, Akron, OH 44313 Tel: 330-926-1313 Toll Free Tel: 800-762-6775 Fax: 330-926-1315 E-mail: info@playhousepublishing.com Web Site: www.playhousepublishing.com, pg 214

PlayLabs, 2301 Franklin Ave E, Minneapolis, MN 55406 Tel: 612-332-7481 Fax: 612-332-6037 E-mail: info@pwcenter.org Web Site: www.pwcenter.org, pg 799

Playmore Inc, Publishers, 230 Fifth Ave, Suite 711, New York, NY 10001 Tel: 212-251-0600 Fax: 212-251-0966 Web Site: playmorebooks.com, pg 214

Playwright Discovery Award, 1300 Connecticut Ave NW, Suite 700, Washington, DC 20036 Tel: 202-628-2800 Toll Free Tel: 800-933-8721 Fax: 202-737-0725 Web Site: www.vsarts.org, pg 799

Playwrights Canada Press, 215 Spadina Ave, Sutie 230, Toronto, ON M5T 2C7, Canada Tel: 416-703-0013 Fax: 416-408-3402 E-mail: orders@playwrightscanada.com Web Site: www.playwrightscanada.com, pg 558

Playwrights Guild of Canada, 54 Wolseley St, 2nd fl, Toronto, ON M5T 1A5, Canada Tel: 416-703-0201 Fax: 416-703-0059 E-mail: info@playwrightsguild.ca Web Site: www.playwrightsguild.ca, pg 697

Playwrights Project, 450 "B" St, Suite 1020, San Diego, CA 92101-8093 Tel: 619-239-8222 Fax: 619-239-8225 E-mail: write@playwrightsproject.com Web Site: www.playwrightsproject.com, pg 799

Pleasant Company Publications, 8400 Fairway Place, Middleton, WI 53562 Tel: 608-836-4848 Fax: 608-257-3865 Web Site: www.americangirl.com, pg 214

Pleasure Boat Studio: A Literary Press, 201 W 89 St, Suite 6F, New York, NY 10024-1848 Tel: 212-362-8563 Toll Free Tel: 888-810-5308 Fax: 212-874-1158 Toll Free Fax: 800-810-5308 E-mail: pleasboat@nyc.rr.com Web Site: www.pbstudio.com, pg 214

Plexus Publishing Inc, 143 Old Marlton Pike, Medford, NJ 08055 Tel: 609-654-6500 Fax: 609-654-4309 E-mail: info@plexuspublishing.com Web Site: www.plexuspublishing.com, pg 214

Plimpton Prize, 541 E 72 St, New York, NY 10021 Tel: 212-861-0016 Fax: 212-861-4504 Web Site: www.theparisreview.org, pg 799

The Plough Publishing House, Spring Valley, Rte 381 N, Farmington, PA 15437 Tel: 724-329-1100 E-mail: contact@bruderhof.com Web Site: www.plough.com, pg 215

Ploughshares, Emerson College, 120 Boylston St, Boston, MA 02116 Tel: 617-824-8753 E-mail: pshares@emerson.edu Web Site: www.pshares.org, pg 215

Plume, 375 Hudson St, New York, NY 10014 Tel: 212-366-2000 Fax: 212-366-2666 E-mail: online@penguinputnam.com Web Site: www.penguin.com, pg 215

Plunkett Research Ltd, PO Drawer 541737, Houston, TX 77254-1737 Tel: 713-932-0000 Fax: 713-932-7080 E-mail: sales@plunkettresearch.com Web Site: www.plunkettresearch.com, pg 215

Plymouth Press/Plymouth Books, PO Box 2044, Miami Beach, FL 33140 Tel: 305-673-0771 Fax: 305-673-1014 (call first), pg 215

PMA Literary & Film Management Inc, PO Box 1817, Old Chelsea Sta, New York, NY 10011 Tel: 212-929-1222 Fax: 212-206-0238 E-mail: pmalitfilm@aol.com Web Site: www.pmalitfilm.com, pg 648

PMC Canadian Letters Award, 175 Bloor St E, South Tower, Suite 1007, Toronto, ON M4W 3R8, Canada Tel: 416-968-7218 Fax: 416-968-6182, pg 799

PNWA Literary Competition, 23607 Hwy 99, Suite 2C, Edmonds, WA 98026 Tel: 425-673-2665 E-mail: staff@pnwa.org Web Site: www.pnwa.org, pg 799

Joann "JP" Pochron, Writer for Hire, 830 Lake Orchid Circle, No 203, Vero Beach, FL 32962 Tel: 772-569-2967 E-mail: pageturn@bellsouth.net, pg 608

Pocket Books, 1230 Avenue of the Americas, New York, NY 10020 Toll Free Tel: 800-456-6798 Fax: 212-698-7284 E-mail: consumer.customerservice@simonandschuster.com Web Site: www.simonsays.com, pg 215

Pocket Press Inc, PO Box 25124, Portland, OR 97298 Toll Free Tel: 888-237-2110 Toll Free Fax: 877-643-3732 E-mail: sales@pocketpressinc.com Web Site: www.pocketpressinc.com, pg 215

Pocol Press, 6023 Pocol Dr, Clifton, VA 20124-1333 Tel: 703-830-5862 E-mail: chrisandtom@erols.com Web Site: www.pocolpress.com, pg 215

Poetry Center Book Award, 1600 Holloway Ave, San Francisco, CA 94132 Tel: 415-338-2227 Fax: 415-338-0966 E-mail: poetry@sfsu.edu Web Site: www.sfsu.edu/~poetry, pg 799

Poetry Flash at Cody's, 1450 Fourth St, Suite 4, Berkeley, CA 94710 Tel: 510-525-5476 Fax: 510-525-6752 E-mail: editor@poetryflash.org, pg 746

Poetry In Print, PO Box 30981, Albuquerque, NM 87190-0981 Tel: 505-888-3937 Fax: 505-888-3937 Web Site: www.poets.com/RobertEnglish.html, pg 799

Poetry Society of America (PSA), 15 Gramercy Park, New York, NY 10003 Tel: 212-254-9628 Toll Free Tel: 888-USA-POEM Fax: 212-673-2352 Web Site: www.poetrysociety.org, pg 697

Poets & Writers Inc, 72 Spring St, Suite 301, New York, NY 10012 Tel: 212-226-3586 Fax: 212-226-3963 Web Site: www.pw.org, pg 697

Pogo Press Inc, 4 Cardinal Lane, St Paul, MN 55127 Tel: 651-483-4692 Fax: 651-483-4692 E-mail: pogopres@minn.net Web Site: www.pogopress.com, pg 215

Poirot Literary Agency, 2685 Stephens Rd, Boulder, CO 80305 Tel: 303-494-0668 Fax: 303-494-9396 E-mail: poirotco@comcast.net, pg 648

Poisoned Pen Press Inc, 6962 E First Ave, Suite 103, Scottsdale, AZ 85251 Tel: 480-945-3375 ext 210 Fax: 480-949-1707 E-mail: info@poisonpenpress.com Web Site: www.poisonpenpress.com, pg 215

Polar Bear & Co, The Cascades, 8 Brook St, Solon, ME 04979 *Tel:* 207-643-2795 *E-mail:* polarbear@necsys. net *Web Site:* www.polarbearandco.com, pg 215

Polestar Book Publishers, 9050 Shaughnessy St, Vancouver, BC V6P 6E5, Canada *Tel:* 604-323-7100 *Toll Free Tel:* 800-663-5714 *Fax:* 604-323-2600 *Toll Free Fax:* 800-565-3770 *E-mail:* info@raincoast.com *Web Site:* www.raincoast.com, pg 558

Wendy Polhemus-Annibell, 4045 Bridge Lane, Cutchogue, NY 11935 *Tel:* 631-734-7239 *E-mail:* wannibel@suffolk.lib.ny.us, pg 608

Police Executive Research Forum, 1120 Connecticut Ave NW, Suite 930, Washington, DC 20036 *Tel:* 202-466-7820 *Toll Free Tel:* 888-202-4563 (cust serv) *Fax:* 202-466-7826 *E-mail:* perf@policeforum.org *Web Site:* www.policeforum.org, pg 216

The George Polk Awards, The Brooklyn Campus, University Plaza, Brooklyn, NY 11201 *Tel:* 718-488-1115 *Fax:* 718-246-6302, pg 799

Joan S Pollack, 890 West End Ave, Suite 14B, New York, NY 10025 *Tel:* 212-663-8143 *Fax:* 212-666-4219, pg 608

Polychrome Publishing Corp, 4509 N Francisco Ave, Chicago, IL 60625 *Tel:* 773-478-4455 *Fax:* 773-478-0786 *E-mail:* info@polychromebooks.com *Web Site:* www.polychromebooks.com, pg 216

Polyscience Publications Inc, PO Box 1606, Sta St-Martin, Laval, PQ H7V 3P8, Canada *Tel:* 450-688-8484 *Fax:* 450-688-1930 *E-mail:* info@polysciencepublications.com *Web Site:* www.polysciencepublications.com, pg 558

Pom Inc, 611 Broadway, No 907-B, New York, NY 10012 *Tel:* 212-673-3835 *Fax:* 212-673-4653 *E-mail:* pom-inc@att.net, pg 648

Pomegranate Communications, 775-A Southpoint Blvd, Petaluma, CA 94954-1495 *Tel:* 707-782-9000 *Toll Free Tel:* 800-227-1428 *Toll Free Fax:* 800-848-4376 *Web Site:* www.pomegranate.com, pg 216

Bella Pomer Agency Inc, 22 Shallmar Blvd, Penthouse 2, Toronto, ON M5N 2Z8, Canada *Tel:* 416-781-8597 *Fax:* 416-782-4196 *E-mail:* belpom@sympatico.ca, pg 649

Pontifical Institute of Mediaeval Studies, Dept of Publications, 59 Queens Park Crescent E, Toronto, ON M5S 2C4, Canada *Tel:* 416-926-7142 *Fax:* 416-926-7292 *E-mail:* pontifex@chass.utoronto.ca *Web Site:* www.pims.ca, pg 558

Poor Richards Award, 20 W 44 St, New York, NY 10036 *Tel:* 212-764-7021 *Fax:* 212-354-5365 *E-mail:* info@smallpress.org *Web Site:* www.smallpress.org, pg 799

Julie Popkin Literary Agency, 15340 Albright St, Suite 204, Pacific Palisades, CA 90272 *Tel:* 310-459-2834 *Fax:* 310-459-4128, pg 649

Popular Culture Inc, PO Box 110, Harbor Springs, MI 49740-0110 *Tel:* 231-439-9767 *Toll Free Tel:* 800-678-8828 *Fax:* 231-439-9767 *Toll Free Fax:* 800-678-8828, pg 216

Porcupine's Quill Inc, 68 Main St, Erin, ON N0B 1T0, Canada *Tel:* 519-833-9158 *Fax:* 519-833-9845 *E-mail:* pql@sentex.net *Web Site:* www.sentex.net/~pql, pg 558

Port Townsend Writers' Conference, PO Box 1158, Port Townsend, WA 98368-0958 *Tel:* 360-385-3102 *Toll Free Tel:* 800-733-3608 (ticket office) *Fax:* 360-385-2470 *E-mail:* centrum@centrum.org *Web Site:* www.centrum.org, pg 746

Portage & Main Press, 318 McDermot, Suite 100, Winnipeg, MB R3A 0A2, Canada *Tel:* 204-987-3500 *Toll Free Tel:* 800-667-9673 *Fax:* 204-947-0080 *Toll Free Fax:* 866-734-8477 *E-mail:* books@portageandmainpress.com *Web Site:* www.portageandmainpress.com, pg 558

Katherine Anne Porter Prize for Fiction, University of Tulsa, 600 S College, Tulsa, OK 74104 *Tel:* 918-631-3080 *Fax:* 918-631-3033 *E-mail:* nimrod@utulsa.edu *Web Site:* www.utulsa.edu/nimrod, pg 799

Porter Sargent Publishers Inc, 11 Beacon St, Suite 1400, Boston, MA 02108 *Tel:* 617-523-1670 *Toll Free Tel:* 800-342-7470 *Fax:* 617-523-1021 *E-mail:* info@portersargent.com *Web Site:* www.portersargent.com, pg 216

Portfolio Solutions, 2419 Rte 82, Suite 208, Billings, NY 12510-0074 *Tel:* 845-226-8401 *Fax:* 845-226-8937 *E-mail:* PSJDC@frontiernet.net, pg 666

PortSort.com, 490 Rockside Rd, Cleveland, OH 44131 *Tel:* 216-661-4222 *Toll Free Tel:* 800-486-1248 *Fax:* 216-661-2879 *E-mail:* woody@portsort.com *Web Site:* www.portsort.com, pg 666

Possibility Press, One Oakglade Circle, Hummelstown, PA 17036 *Tel:* 717-566-0468 *Toll Free Tel:* 800-566-0534 *Fax:* 717-566-6423 *E-mail:* posspress@aol.com, pg 216

Potlatch Publications Ltd, 30 Berry Hill, Waterdown, ON L0R 2H4, Canada *Tel:* 905-689-2104 *Fax:* 905-689-1632 *Web Site:* www.angelfire.com/on3/potlatch, pg 558

Pottersfield Press, 83 Leslie Rd, East Lawrencetown, NS B2Z 1P8, Canada *Toll Free Tel:* 800-NIMBUS9 (646-2879-orders only) *Toll Free Fax:* 888-253-3133 *Web Site:* www.pottersfieldpress.com, pg 558

powerHouse Books, 68 Charlton St, New York, NY 10014-4601 *Tel:* 212-604-9074 *Fax:* 212-366-5247 *E-mail:* info@powerhousebooks.com *Web Site:* www.powerhousebooks.com, pg 216

The Poynor Group, 444 E 82 St, Suite 28C, New York, NY 10028 *Tel:* 212-734-5909 *Fax:* 212-734-5909, pg 649

Practice Management Information Corp (PMIC), 4727 Wilshire Blvd, Suite 300, Los Angeles, CA 90010 *Tel:* 323-954-0224 *Fax:* 323-954-0253 *E-mail:* orders@medicalbookstore.com *Web Site:* www.pmiconline.com, pg 216

Practising Law Institute, 810 Seventh Ave, New York, NY 10019 *Tel:* 212-824-5700 *Toll Free Tel:* 800-260-4PLI (260-4754 customer service) *Fax:* 212-265-4742 *Toll Free Fax:* 800-321-0093 *E-mail:* info@pli.edu *Web Site:* www.pli.edu, pg 216

Prairie Schooner Readers' Choice Awards, University of Nebraska, 201 Andrews Hall, Lincoln, NE 68588 *Tel:* 402-472-0911 *E-mail:* kgrey2@unl.edu *Web Site:* www.unl.edu/schooner/psmain.htm, pg 800

Prairie Schooner Strousse Award, University of Nebraska, 201 Andrews Hall, Lincoln, NE 68588 *Tel:* 402-472-0911 *Fax:* 402-472-9771 *Web Site:* www.unl.edu/schooner/psmain.htm, pg 800

Prairie View Press, PR 205, Rosenort, MB R0G 1W0, Canada *Tel:* 204-746-2375 *Toll Free Tel:* 800-477-7377 *Fax:* 204-746-2667, pg 558

Prakken Publications Inc, 832 Phoenix Dr, Ann Arbor, MI 48108 *Tel:* 734-975-2800 *Toll Free Tel:* 800-530-9673 (orders only) *Fax:* 734-975-2787 *E-mail:* tdbooks@techdirections.com *Web Site:* www.techdirections.com; www.eddigest.com, pg 217

Helen F Pratt Inc Literary Agency, 1165 Fifth Ave, New York, NY 10029 *Tel:* 212-722-5081 *Fax:* 212-722-8569 *E-mail:* helenpratt@earthlink.net, pg 649

Prayer Book Press Inc, 1363 Fairfield Ave, Bridgeport, CT 06605 *Tel:* 203-384-2284 *Fax:* 203-579-9109, pg 217

Pre-Press Company Inc, 362 N Bedford St, East Bridgewater, MA 02333 *Tel:* 508-378-1100 (plant); 508-378-1101 (sales) *Fax:* 508-378-1105 *Web Site:* www.prepressco.com, pg 608

Precept Press, 1452 Second St, Santa Monica, CA 90401 *Tel:* 310-260-9400 *Fax:* 310-260-9494 *E-mail:* webmaster@bonusbooks.com *Web Site:* www.bonusbooks.com, pg 217

Prentice Hall Business Publishing, One Lake St, Upper Saddle River, NJ 07458 *Tel:* 201-236-7000, pg 217

Prentice Hall Career, Health, Education & Technology, One Lake St, Upper Saddle River, NJ 07458 *Tel:* 201-236-7000 *Fax:* 201-236-7755, pg 217

Prentice Hall Engineering/Science & Math, One Lake St, Upper Saddle River, NJ 07458 *Tel:* 201-236-7000, pg 217

Prentice Hall Humanities & Social Sciences, One Lake St, Upper Saddle River, NJ 07458 *Tel:* 201-236-7000, pg 217

Prentice Hall Press, 375 Hudson St, New York, NY 10014 *Tel:* 212-366-2000, pg 217

Prentice Hall School, One Lake St, Upper Saddle River, NJ 07458 *Tel:* 201-236-7000, pg 217

Linn Prentis, Literary Agent, 155 E 116 St, No 2F-2R, New York City, NY 10029 *Tel:* 212-876-8557 *Fax:* 212-876-5565 *E-mail:* linnprentis@earthlink.net, pg 649

PREP Publishing, 1110 1/2 Hay St, Fayetteville, NC 28305 *Tel:* 910-483-6611 *Toll Free Tel:* 800-533-2814 *Fax:* 910-483-2439 *E-mail:* preppub@aol.com *Web Site:* www.prep-pub.com, pg 217

Presbyterian Publishing Corp, 100 Witherspoon St, Louisville, KY 40202 *Tel:* 502-569-5052 *Toll Free Tel:* 800-227-2872 (US only) *Fax:* 502-569-8308 *Toll Free Fax:* 800-541-5113 (US only) *E-mail:* ppcmail@presbypub.com *Web Site:* www.ppcpub.com, pg 217

The Press at California State University, Fresno, 2380 E Keats, MB99, Fresno, CA 93740-8024 *Tel:* 559-278-3056 *Fax:* 559-278-6758 *E-mail:* press@csufresno.edu, pg 217, 573

Les Presses de l'Universite du Quebec, 2875 Boul Laurier, Bureau 450, Ste-Foy, PQ G1V 2M2, Canada *Tel:* 418-657-4399 *Fax:* 418-657-2096 *E-mail:* secretariat@puq.uquebec.ca; puq@puq.uquebec.ca *Web Site:* www.puq.ca, pg 558

Les Presses De L'Universite Laval, Maurice-Pollack House, Office 3103, University City, Sainte-Foy, PQ G1K 7P4, Canada *Tel:* 418-656-2803 *Fax:* 418-656-3305 *E-mail:* presses@pul.ulaval.ca *Web Site:* www.ulaval.ca/pul, pg 558

Prestel Publishing, 900 Broadway, Suite 603, New York, NY 10003 *Tel:* 212-995-2720 *Toll Free Tel:* 888-463-6110 (cust serv) *Fax:* 212-995-2733 *E-mail:* sales@prestel-usa.com *Web Site:* www.prestel.com, pg 217

Prestwick House Inc, PO Box 246, Cheswold, DE 19936-0246 *Tel:* 302-736-2665 *Fax:* 302-734-0549 *E-mail:* info@prestwickhouse.com *Web Site:* www.prestwickhouse.com, pg 218

Derek Price/Rod Webster Prize Award, University of Florida, 3310 Turlington Hall, Gainesville, FL 32611 *Tel:* 352-392-1677 *E-mail:* info@hssonline.org *Web Site:* www.hssonline.org, pg 800

Price Stern Sloan, 345 Hudson St, New York, NY 10014 *Tel:* 212-366-2000 *E-mail:* online@penguin.com *Web Site:* www.penguinputnam.com, pg 218

The Aaron M Priest Literary Agency Inc, 708 Third Ave, 23rd fl, New York, NY 10017 *Tel:* 212-818-0344 *Fax:* 212-573-9417, pg 649

Prima Games, 3000 Lava Ridge Ct, Roseville, CA 95661 *Tel:* 916-787-7000 *Toll Free Tel:* 800-632-8676 *Fax:* 916-787-7001 *Web Site:* www.primagames.com, pg 218

Primary Research Group, 224 W 30 St, Suite 802-1, New York, NY 10001 *Tel:* 212-736-2316 *Fax:* 212-412-9097 *E-mail:* primarydat@aol.com *Web Site:* www.primaryresearch.com, pg 218

PRIMEDIA Business Directories & Books, 9800 Metcalf Ave, Overland Park, KS 66212 *Tel:* 913-967-1719 *Toll Free Tel:* 800-453-9620; 800-262-1954 (cust serv) *Fax:* 913-967-1901 *Toll Free Fax:* 800-633-6219 *E-mail:* bookorders@primediabooks.com *Web Site:* www.primediabooks.com, pg 218

Primedia Business Magazine & Media, 9800 Metcalf Ave, Overland Park, KS 66212 *Tel:* 913-341-1300 *Toll Free Tel:* 800-262-1954 *Fax:* 913-967-1898 *Web Site:* www.primemediabusiness.com, pg 218

Primedia Consumer Magazine & Internet Group, 260 Madison Ave, New York, NY 10016 Tel: 212-726-4300 Toll Free Tel: 800-521-2885 Fax: 212-726-4310 E-mail: sgnews@primediasi.com Web Site: www.primediainc.com, pg 218

Princeton Architectural Press, 37 E Seventh St, New York, NY 10003 Tel: 212-995-9620 Toll Free Tel: 800-722-6657 (dist) Fax: 212-995-9454 E-mail: sales@papress.com Web Site: www.papress.com, pg 218

Princeton Book Co Publishers, PO Box 831, Hightstown, NJ 08520-0831 Tel: 609-426-0602 Toll Free Tel: 800-220-7149 Fax: 609-426-1344 E-mail: pbc@dancehorizons.com; elysian@aosi.com Web Site: www.dancehorizons.com, pg 218

The Princeton Review, 1745 Broadway, New York, NY 10019 Tel: 212-829-6928 Toll Free Tel: 800-733-3000 Fax: 212-940-7400 E-mail: princetonreview@randomhouse.com Web Site: www.princetonreview.com, pg 218

Princeton University Press, 41 William St, Princeton, NJ 08540 Tel: 609-258-4900 Toll Free Tel: 800-777-4726 Fax: 609-258-6305 Toll Free Fax: 800-999-1958 E-mail: orders@cpfsinc.com Web Site: www.pup.princeton.edu, pg 219

Print Buyers Association (Printing Industries of Northern Calif), 665 Third St, Suite 500, San Francisco, CA 94107 Tel: 415-495-8242 Fax: 415-543-7790 E-mail: info@pinc.org Web Site: www.pinc.org, pg 697

PrintImage International, 70 E Lake St, Suite 333, Chicago, IL 60601 Tel: 312-726-8015 Toll Free Tel: 800-234-0040 Fax: 312-726-8113 E-mail: info@printimage.org Web Site: www.printimage.org, pg 697

Printing Association of Florida Inc, 6275 Hazeltine National Dr, Orlando, FL 32822 Tel: 407-240-8009 Fax: 407-240-8333 Web Site: www.pafgraf.org, pg 697

Printing Brokerage/Buyers Association, PO Box 744, Palm Beach, FL 33480-0744 Tel: 561-586-9391 Toll Free Tel: 866-586-9391 Fax: 561-845-7130 E-mail: info@pbbai.net Web Site: www.pbbai.net, pg 697

Printing Industries of America Premier Print Award, 200 Deer Run Rd, Sewickley, PA 15143 Tel: 412-741-6860 Fax: 412-741-2311 Web Site: www.gain.net, pg 800

Printing Industries of Maryland, 2045 York Rd, 2nd fl, Timonium, MD 21093 Tel: 410-560-3300 Toll Free Tel: 800-560-3306 Fax: 410-560-3306 E-mail: pim@printmd.com Web Site: www.printmd.com, pg 698

Printing Industries of Wisconsin, 13005 W Bluemount Rd, Brooksfield, WI 53005 Tel: 262-785-7040 Fax: 262-785-7043 E-mail: info@piw.org Web Site: www.piw.org, pg 698

Printing Industry Association of the South, 305 Plus Park Blvd, Nashville, TN 37217 Tel: 615-366-1094 Toll Free Tel: 800-821-3138 Fax: 615-366-4192 E-mail: info@pias.org Web Site: www.pias.org, pg 698

Printlink Publishers Inc, 755 Main St, Monroe, CT 06468 Tel: 203-261-2977 Fax: 203-261-4331, pg 219

Michael L Printz Award, 50 E Huron St, Chicago, IL 60611 Tel: 312-280-4390 Toll Free Tel: 800-545-2433 (ext 4390) Fax: 312-664-7459 E-mail: yalsa@ala.org Web Site: www.ala.org/yalsa/printz, pg 800

Prise de Parole Inc, C P 550, Sudbury, ON P3E 4R2, Canada Tel: 705-675-6491 Fax: 705-673-1817 E-mail: prisedeparole@bellnet.ca, pg 558

Prism International Fiction Contest, University of British Columbia, Buch E462, 1866 Main Mall, Vancouver, BC V6T 1Z1, Canada Tel: 604-822-2514 Fax: 604-822-3616 E-mail: prism@interchange.ubc.ca Web Site: prism.arts.ubc.ca, pg 800

Prix Alvine-Belisle, 3414 Avenue Du Parc, Bureau 202, Montreal, PQ H2X 2H5, Canada Tel: 514-281-5012 Fax: 514-281-8219 E-mail: info@asted.org Web Site: www.asted.org, pg 800

Prix Champlain, Maison de la francophonie, 39, rue Dalhousie, Quebec, PQ G1K 8R8, Canada Tel: 418-646-9117 Fax: 418-644-7670 E-mail: cvfa@cvfa.ca Web Site: www.cvfa.ca, pg 800

Prize Stories: The O Henry Awards, Univ of Texas at Austin, One University Sta B 5000, Austin, TX 78712 Tel: 212-572-2016 Web Site: www.ohenryprizestories.com, pg 800

PRO-ED Inc, 8700 Shoal Creek Blvd, Austin, TX 78757-6897 Tel: 512-451-3246 Toll Free Tel: 800-897-3202 Fax: 512-451-8542 Toll Free Fax: 800-397-7633 E-mail: info@proedinc.com Web Site: www.proedinc.com, pg 219

Pro Lingua Associates Inc, 74 Cotton Mill Hill, Suite A-315, Brattleboro, VT 05301 Tel: 802-257-7779 Toll Free Tel: 800-366-4775 Fax: 802-257-5117 E-mail: orders@prolinguaassociates.com Web Site: www.prolinguaassociates.com, pg 219

Pro Quest Information & Learning, 300 N Zeeb Rd, Ann Arbor, MI 48106-1346 Tel: 734-761-4700 Toll Free Tel: 800-521-0600 Fax: 734-975-6486 Toll Free Fax: 800-864-0019 E-mail: info@il.proquest.com Web Site: www.il.proquest.com, pg 219

Procrustes/Sophia Editorial Services, 241 Bonita Los Trancos Woods, Portola Valley, CA 94028-8103 Tel: 650-851-1847 Fax: 650-210-9832, pg 608

Productive Publications, 1930 Younge St, 1210, Toronto, ON M4S 1G9, Canada Tel: 416-483-0634 Fax: 416-322-7434 Web Site: www.productivepublications.com, pg 559

Productivity Press, 444 Park Ave S, Suite 604, New York, NY 10016 Tel: 212-686-5900 Toll Free Tel: 888-319-5852 Fax: 212-686-5411 Toll Free Fax: 800-394-6286 E-mail: info@productivitypress.com Web Site: www.productivitypress.com, pg 219

Professional Communications Inc, 20968 State Rd 22, Caddo, OK 74729 Tel: 580-367-9838 Toll Free Tel: 800-337-9838 Fax: 580-367-9989 E-mail: info@pcibooks.com Web Site: www.pcibooks.com, pg 219

The Professional Education Group Inc, 12401 Minnetonka Blvd, Minnetonka, MN 55305-3994 Tel: 952-933-9990 Toll Free Tel: 800-229-2531 Fax: 952-933-7784 E-mail: orders@proedgroup.com Web Site: www.proedgroup.com, pg 219

Professional Publications, 1250 Fifth Ave, Belmont, CA 94002 Tel: 650-593-9119 Toll Free Tel: 800-426-1178 Fax: 650-592-4519 E-mail: info@passthatexam.com Web Site: www.passthatexam.com, pg 219

Professional Publishing, 1333 Burr Ridge Pkwy, Burr Ridge, IL 60527 Tel: 630-789-4000; 630-789-5500 Toll Free Tel: 800-2McGraw (262-4729) Fax: 630-789-6933 Web Site: www.books.mcgraw-hill.com, pg 220

Professional Resource Exchange Inc, 1891 Apex Rd, Sarasota, FL 34240 Tel: 941-343-9601 Toll Free Tel: 800-443-3364 Fax: 941-343-9201 Web Site: www.prpress.com, pg 220

The Professional Writer, PO Box 1631, Old Chelsea Sta, New York, NY 10113 Tel: 212-983-1951; 212-414-0188 E-mail: aprowrite@aol.com Web Site: www.theprofessionalwriter.com, pg 608

Progress in the Pressroom Seminar, PO Box 1086, White Stone, VA 22578-1086 Tel: 804-436-9922 Fax: 804-436-9511 E-mail: recouncil@rivnet.net Web Site: www.recouncil.org, pg 746

Prometheus Awards, 26 Partridge Hill, Honeye Falls, NY 14472 Tel: 585-582-1068 Web Site: www.lfs.org, pg 800

Prometheus Books, 59 John Glenn Dr, Amherst, NY 14228 Tel: 716-691-0133 Toll Free Tel: 800-421-0351 Fax: 716-691-0137 E-mail: marketing@prometheusbooks.com; editorial@prometheusbooks.com Web Site: www.Prometheusbooks.com, pg 220

Promissor Inc, 1007 Church St, Evanston, IL 60201 Tel: 847-866-2001 Toll Free Tel: 800-255-1312 Fax: 847-866-2002 E-mail: marketing@promissor.com Web Site: www.promissor.com, pg 220

Pronk&Associates Inc, 200 Yorkland Ave, Suite 500, Toronto, ON M2J 5C1, Canada Tel: 416-441-3760 Fax: 416-441-9991 E-mail: info@pronk.com Web Site: www.pronk.com, pg 608

Pro-Nouns Editorial Services Inc, 10835-62 Ave, Edmonton, AB T6H 1M9, Canada Tel: 780-436-0772 Fax: 780-438-7063 E-mail: info@pro-nouns.com Web Site: www.pro-nouns.com, pg 609

Proof Positive/Farrowlyne Associates Inc, 1620 Central St, Evanston, IL 60201 Tel: 847-866-9570 Fax: 847-866-9849, pg 609

ProStar Publications Inc, 3 Church Circle, Suite 109, Annapolis, MD 21401 Tel: 310-280-1010 Toll Free Tel: 800-481-6277 Fax: 310-280-1025 Toll Free Fax: 800-487-6277 E-mail: editor@prostarpublications.com Web Site: www.prostarpublications.com; www.nauticalbooks.com, pg 220

Protea Publishing, 5456 Peachtree Industrial Blvd, Suite 648, Atlanta, GA 30341 E-mail: southsky@earthlink.net Web Site: www.proteapublishing.com, pg 220

Protestant Church-Owned Publishers Association, 748 Crabthicket Lane, St Louis, MO 63131 Tel: 314-505-7237 Fax: 314-505-7760 E-mail: pcpa@pcpanews.org Web Site: www.pcpanews.org, pg 698

Susan Ann Protter Literary Agent, 110 W 40 St, Suite 1408, New York, NY 10018 Tel: 212-840-0480, pg 649

Providence Publishing Corp, 238 Seaboard Lane, Franklin, TN 37067 Tel: 615-771-2020 Toll Free Tel: 800-321-5692 Fax: 615-771-2002 E-mail: books@providencehouse.com Web Site: www.providencehouse.com, pg 220

Provincetown Arts Inc, 650 Commercial St, Provincetown, MA 02657 Tel: 508-487-3167 Web Site: www.provincetownarts.org, pg 220

The PRS Group Inc, 6320 Fly Rd, East Syracuse, NY 13057 Tel: 315-431-0511 Fax: 315-431-0200 E-mail: custserv@prsgroup.com Web Site: www.prsgroup.com, pg 220

Pruett Publishing Co, 7464 Arapahoe Rd, Unit A-9, Boulder, CO 80303 Tel: 303-449-4919 Toll Free Tel: 800-247-8224 Fax: 303-443-9019 Toll Free Fax: 800-527-9727 E-mail: pruettbks@aol.com Web Site: www.pruettpublishing.com, pg 220

PSD Associates, 7392 Palm Ave, Sebastopol, CA 95472-6705, pg 649

Psychological Assessment Resources Inc (PAR), 16204 N Florida Ave, Lutz, FL 33549 Tel: 813-968-3003 Toll Free Tel: 800-331-8378 Fax: 813-968-2598 Toll Free Fax: 800-727-9329 Web Site: www.parinc.com, pg 221

Psychology Press, 29 W 35 St, New York, NY 10001 Tel: 212-216-7800 Fax: 215-643-1430 Web Site: www.psypress.com, pg 221

The Psychology Society, 100 Beekman St, New York, NY 10038-1810 Tel: 212-285-1872 Fax: 212-285-1872, pg 221

PTG Software, 201 W 103 St, Indianapolis, IN 46920-1097 Tel: 317-581-3500; 317-581-3837 (tech support) Toll Free Tel: 800-858-7674 Fax: 317-581-3611 Web Site: www.macmillansoftware.com, pg 221

Public Citizen, 1600 20 St NW, Washington, DC 20009 Tel: 202-588-1000 Fax: 202-588-7798 E-mail: public_citizen@citizen.org Web Site: www.citizen.org, pg 221

Public Relations Society of America Inc, 33 Maiden Lane, 11th fl, New York, NY 10038-5150 Tel: 212-460-1400 Fax: 212-995-0757 E-mail: hq@prsa.org Web Site: www.prsa.org, pg 698

Public Utilities Reports Inc, 8229 Boone Blvd, Suite 400, Vienna, VA 22182 Tel: 703-847-7720 Toll Free Tel: 800-368-5001 Fax: 703-847-0683 E-mail: pur@pur.com Web Site: www.pur.com, pg 221

PublicAffairs, 250 W 57 St, Suite 1321, New York, NY 10107 Tel: 212-397-6666 Toll Free Tel: 800-242-7737 (orders) Fax: 212-397-4267 E-mail: publicaffairs@perseusbooks.com Web Site: www.publicaffairsbooks.com, pg 221

Quirk Books, 215 Church St, Philadelphia, PA 19106 *Tel:* 215-627-3581 *Fax:* 215-627-5220 *E-mail:* general@quirkbooks.com *Web Site:* www.quirkbooks.com, pg 224

Quite Specific Media Group Ltd, 7373 Pyramid Place, Hollywood, CA 90046 *Tel:* 323-851-5797 *Fax:* 323-851-5798 *E-mail:* info@quitespecificmedia.com *Web Site:* www.quitespecificmedia.com, pg 224

Quixote Press, 1854 345 Ave, Wever, IA 52658 *Tel:* 319-372-7480 *Toll Free Tel:* 800-571-BOOK *Fax:* 319-372-7485 *E-mail:* heartsntummies@hotmail.com, pg 224

QWF Prizes, 1200 Atwater Ave, Suite 3, Montreal, PQ H3Z 1X4, Canada *Tel:* 514-933-0878 *E-mail:* admin@qwf.org *Web Site:* www.qwf.org, pg 801

R D R Books, 2415 Woolsey St, Berkeley, CA 94705 *Tel:* 510-595-0595 *Fax:* 510-228-0300 *E-mail:* info@rdrbooks.com *Web Site:* www.rdrbooks.com, pg 224

R S V Products, PO Box 26, Hopkins, MN 55343-0026 *Tel:* 952-936-0400 *Fax:* 952-936-0400, pg 224

Susan Rabiner Literary Agent, 240 W 35 St, Suite 500, New York, NY 10001-2506 *Tel:* 212-279-0316 *Fax:* 212-279-0932 *E-mail:* susan@rabiner.net, pg 650

rada press inc, 715 Third Ave, Mendota Heights, MN 55118 *Tel:* 651-455-9695 *Fax:* 651-455-9675, pg 224

Thomas Head Raddall Atlantic Fiction Award, 1113 Marginal Rd, Halifax, NS B3H 4P7, Canada *Tel:* 902-423-8116 *Fax:* 902-422-0881 *E-mail:* talk@writers.ns.ca *Web Site:* www.writers.ns.ca, pg 801

Radix Press, 2314 Cheshire Lane, Houston, TX 77018-4023 *Tel:* 713-683-9076, pg 224

Jane Rafal Editing Associates, 325 Forest Ridge Dr, Scottsville, VA 24590 *Tel:* 434-286-6949 *Fax:* 434-286-6949 *E-mail:* janerafal@ntelos.net *Web Site:* www.cstone.net/~jrafaled/, pg 609

The Ragan Old North State Cup for Nonfiction, 4610 Mail Service Center, Raleigh, NC 27699-4610 *Tel:* 919-807-7290 *Fax:* 919-733-8807, pg 801

Ragged Bears, 413 Sixth Ave, Brooklyn, NY 11215-3310 *Tel:* 718-768-3696 *Fax:* 718-369-0844 *E-mail:* publisher@raggedbears.com *Web Site:* www.raggedbears.com, pg 224

Ragged Edge Press, 63 W Burd St, Shippensburg, PA 17257 *Tel:* 717-532-2237 *Toll Free Tel:* 888-948-6263 *Fax:* 717-532-6110 *E-mail:* marketing@whitemane.com, pg 224

Ragged Mountain Press, 485 Commercial St, Rockport, ME 04856 *Tel:* 207-236-4837 *Fax:* 207-236-6314 *Web Site:* www.raggedmountainpress.com, pg 225

Rainbow Books Inc, PO Box 430, Highland City, FL 33846-0430 *Tel:* 863-648-4420 *Toll Free Tel:* 800-431-1579 (orders only); 888-613-2665 *Fax:* 863-647-5951 *E-mail:* rbibooks@aol.com *Web Site:* www.rainbowbooksinc.com, pg 225

Rainbow Publishers, PO Box 261129, San Diego, CA 92196-1129 *Tel:* 858-668-3260 *Web Site:* www.rainbowpublishers.com, pg 225

Rainbow Studies International, 1950 S Shepard Ave, El Reno, OK 73036 *Tel:* 405-262-6826 *Toll Free Tel:* 800-242-5348 *Fax:* 405-262-7599 *E-mail:* rsimail@rainbowstudies.com *Web Site:* www.rainbowstudies.com, pg 225

Raincoast Publishing, 9050 Shaughnessy St, Vancouver, BC V6P 6E5, Canada *Tel:* 604-323-7100 *Toll Free Tel:* 800-663-5714 (Canada only) *Fax:* 604-323-2600 *Toll Free Tel:* 800-565-3700 *E-mail:* info@raincoast.com *Web Site:* www.raincoast.com, pg 559

Raines & Raines, 103 Kenyon Rd, Medusa, NY 12120 *Tel:* 518-239-8311 *Fax:* 518-239-6029, pg 650

Rainmaker Literary Agency, 25 NW 23 Place, Suite 6, PMB 460, Portland, OR 97210-5599 *Tel:* 503-222-2249 *E-mail:* info@rainmakerliterary.com *Web Site:* www.rainmakerliterary.com, pg 650

Diane Raintree, 360 W 21 St, New York, NY 10011 *Tel:* 212-242-2387, pg 650

Raiziss/de Palchi Fellowship, 588 Broadway, Suite 604, New York, NY 10012 *Tel:* 212-274-0343 *Fax:* 212-274-9427 *E-mail:* academy@poets.org *Web Site:* www.poets.org, pg 801

Raiziss/de Palchi Translation Award, 588 Broadway, Suite 604, New York, NY 10012 *Tel:* 212-274-0343 *Fax:* 212-274-9427 *E-mail:* academy@poets.org *Web Site:* www.poets.org, pg 801

Sir Walter Raleigh Award for Fiction, 4610 Mail Service Center, Raleigh, NC 27699-4610 *Tel:* 919-807-7290 *Fax:* 919-733-8807, pg 801

Jerry Ralya, 7909 Vermont Rte 14, Craftsbury Common, VT 05827 *Tel:* 802-586-2556 *Fax:* 802-586-2422 *E-mail:* ralya@earthlink.net, pg 610

Ram Publishing Co, 1881 W State St, Garland, TX 75042-6797 *Tel:* 972-494-6151 *Fax:* 972-494-1881 *Web Site:* www.garrett.com, pg 225

Ramsey & Ramsey, PO Box 1045, Fort Belvoir, VA 22060 *Tel:* 703-721-3630 *E-mail:* yellowspeak@yahoo.com, pg 670

RAND Corp, 1776 Main St, Santa Monica, CA 90407 *Tel:* 310-393-0411 *Fax:* 310-451-6996 *E-mail:* jane_ryan@rand.org *Web Site:* www.rand.org, pg 225

Rand McNally, 8255 Central Park Ave N, Skokie, IL 60076 *Tel:* 847-329-8100 *Toll Free Tel:* 800-333-0136 *Fax:* 847-673-0539 *Web Site:* www.randmcnally.com, pg 225

Random House Audio Publishing Group, 1745 Broadway, New York, NY 10019 *Tel:* 212-782-9720 *Fax:* 212-782-9600, pg 225

Random House Children's Books, 1745 Broadway, New York, NY 10019 *Tel:* 212-782-9000 *Toll Free Tel:* 800-200-3552 *Fax:* 212-782-9452 *Web Site:* www.randomhouse.com/kids, pg 225

Random House Direct Inc, 1745 Broadway, New York, NY 10019 *Tel:* 212-572-2604 *Fax:* 212-572-6018, pg 226

Random House Inc, 1745 Broadway, New York, NY 10019 *Tel:* 212-782-9000 *Toll Free Tel:* 800-726-0600 *Web Site:* www.randomhouse.com, pg 226

Random House International, 1745 Broadway, New York, NY 10019 *Tel:* 212-572-6106 *Fax:* 212-572-6045, pg 226

Random House Large Print, 1745 Broadway, New York, NY 10019 *Tel:* 212-782-9720 *Fax:* 212-782-9600, pg 227

Random House New Media Division, 1745 Broadway, New York, NY 10019 *Tel:* 212-782-9000, pg 227

Random House of Canada Ltd, One Toronto St, Unit 300, Toronto, ON M5C 2V6, Canada *Tel:* 416-364-4449 *Fax:* 416-364-6863 (edit & publicity); 416-364-6653 (subs rts) *Web Site:* www.randomhouse.ca, pg 559

Random House Publishing Group, 1745 Broadway, New York, NY 10019 *Toll Free Tel:* 800-200-3552 *Toll Free Fax:* 800-200-3552 *Web Site:* www.randomhouse.com, pg 227

Random House Reference, 1745 Broadway, New York, NY 10019 *Toll Free Tel:* 800-733-3000 *E-mail:* words@random.com; puzzles@random.com, pg 227

Random House Sales & Marketing, 1745 Broadway, New York, NY 10019 *Fax:* 212-782-9000, pg 227

Random House Value Publishing, 1745 Broadway, New York, NY 10019 *Tel:* 212-940-7422 *Fax:* 212-572-2114, pg 227

Rapids Christian Press Inc, 5777 Vista Dr, Ferndale, WA 98248 *Tel:* 360-384-1747 *Fax:* 360-384-1747, pg 227

Rational Island Publishers, 719 Second Ave N, Seattle, WA 98109 *Tel:* 206-284-0311 *Fax:* 206-284-8429 *E-mail:* ircc@rc.org *Web Site:* www.rc.org, pg 228

Rattapallax Press, 532 LaGuardia Place, Suite 353, New York, NY 10012 *Tel:* 212-560-7459 *Web Site:* www.rattapallax.com, pg 228

Raven Tree Press LLC, 200 S Washington St, Suite 306, Green Bay, WI 54301 *Tel:* 920-438-1605 *Toll Free Tel:* 877-256-0579 *Fax:* 920-438-1607 *E-mail:* raven@raventreepress.com *Web Site:* www.raventreepress.com, pg 228

Ravenhawk™ Books, 7739 E Broadway Blvd, No 95, Tucson, AZ 85710 *Tel:* 520-296-4491 *Fax:* 520-296-4491 *E-mail:* ravenhawk6dof@yahoo.com *Web Site:* ravenhawk.biz, pg 228

Charlotte Cecil Raymond, Literary Agent, 32 Bradlee Rd, Marblehead, MA 01945 *Tel:* 781-631-6722 *Fax:* 781-631-6722 *E-mail:* ccraymond@aol.com, pg 650

Rayve Productions Inc, PO Box 726, Windsor, CA 95492 *Tel:* 707-838-6200 *Toll Free Tel:* 800-852-4890 *Fax:* 707-838-2220 *E-mail:* rayvepro@aol.com *Web Site:* www.rayveproductions.com; www.foodandwinebooks.com, pg 228

RCL Resources for Christian Living, 200 E Bethany, Allen, TX 75002 *Tel:* 972-390-6300 *Toll Free Tel:* 800-527-5030 *Fax:* 972-390-6560 *Toll Free Fax:* 800-688-8356 *E-mail:* cservice@rcl-enterprises.com *Web Site:* www.rclweb.com, pg 228

The Rea Award for the Short Story, 53 W Church Hill Rd, Washington, CT 06794 *Web Site:* reaaward.org, pg 801

Read Only Productions, 399 Alameda de la Loma, Novato, CA 94947 *Tel:* 415-883-7583, pg 228

Reader's Digest Association (Canada) Ltd/Selection du Reader's Digest (Canada) Ltee, 1100 Rene Levesque Blvd W, Montreal, PQ H3B 5H5, Canada *Tel:* 514-940-0751 *Toll Free Tel:* 800-465-0780 *Fax:* 514-940-3637 (admin) *E-mail:* customer.service@readersdigest.ca *Web Site:* www.readersdigest.ca, pg 559

Reader's Digest Association Inc, Reader's Digest Rd, Pleasantville, NY 10570-7000 *Tel:* 914-238-1000 *Toll Free Tel:* 800-431-1726 *Fax:* 914-238-4559 *Web Site:* www.rd.com, pg 228

Reader's Digest Children's Books, Reader's Digest Rd, Pleasantville, NY 10570-7000 *Tel:* 914-244-4800 *Toll Free Tel:* 800-934-0977, pg 228

Reader's Digest General Books, Reader's Digest Rd, Pleasantville, NY 10570-7000 *Tel:* 914-238-1000 *Toll Free Tel:* 800-431-1726 *Fax:* 914-244-7436, pg 228

Reader's Digest Trade Books, Reader's Digest Rd, Pleasantville, NY 10570-7000 *Tel:* 914-244-7445 *Fax:* 914-244-7605, pg 229

Reader's Digest USA Select Editions, Reader's Digest Rd, Pleasantville, NY 10570-7000 *Tel:* 914-238-1000 *Toll Free Tel:* 800-310-6261 *Fax:* 914-238-4559, pg 229

The Reading Component, 1827 Ximeno Ave, PMB 195, Long Beach, CA 90815-5801 *Tel:* 310-521-6457 *Fax:* 562-597-0462, pg 610

Record Research Inc, PO Box 200, Menomonee Falls, WI 53052 *Tel:* 262-251-5408 *Toll Free Tel:* 800-827-9810 *Fax:* 262-251-9452 *E-mail:* books@recordresearch.com *Web Site:* www.recordresearch.com, pg 229

Recorded Books LLC, 270 Skipjack Rd, Prince Frederick, MD 20678 *Tel:* 410-535-5590 *Toll Free Tel:* 800-638-1304 *Fax:* 410-535-5499 *E-mail:* recordedbooks@recordedbooks.com *Web Site:* www.recordedbooks.com, pg 229

Red Crane Books Inc, PO Box 33950, Santa Fe, NM 87594-3950 *Tel:* 505-988-7070 *Fax:* 505-989-7476 *E-mail:* publish@redcrane.com *Web Site:* www.redcrane.com, pg 229

Red Dust Inc, Box 630, Gracie Sta, New York, NY 10028 *Tel:* 212-348-4388 *E-mail:* reddustjg@aol.com, pg 229

Red Hen Press, PO Box 3537, Granada Hills, CA 91394-0537 *Tel:* 818-831-0649 *Fax:* 818-831-6659 *E-mail:* editors@redhen.org *Web Site:* www.redhen.org, pg 229

Red Moon Press, PO Box 2461, Winchester, VA 22604-1661 *Tel:* 540-722-2156 *Fax:* 708-810-8992 *E-mail:* redmoon@shentel.net, pg 229

Red River Press, 3900 Roy Rd, Suite 37, Shreveport, LA 71107 *Tel:* 318-929-4196 *Fax:* 318-929-5125 *E-mail:* redriverpresskws@yahoo.com *Web Site:* www.achivalservices.com, pg 229

Red Rock Press, 459 Columbus Ave, Suite 114, New York, NY 10024 *Tel:* 212-362-6216 *Fax:* 212-362-6216 *E-mail:* info@redrockpress.com *Web Site:* www.redrockpress.com, pg 229

Red Sea Press Inc, 541 W Ingham Ave, Suite B, Trenton, NJ 08638 *Tel:* 609-695-3200 *Fax:* 609-695-6466 *E-mail:* awprsp@africanworld.com; awprsp@intac.com *Web Site:* www.africanworld.com, pg 230

Red Wheel/Weiser/Conari, 368 Congress St, 4th fl, Boston, MA 02210 *Tel:* 617-542-1324 *Toll Free Tel:* 800-423-7087 *Fax:* 617-482-9676 *Web Site:* www.redwheelweiser.com, pg 230

Redleaf Press, 10 Yorkton Ct, St Paul, MN 55117 *Tel:* 651-641-0305 *Toll Free Tel:* 800-423-8309 *Toll Free Fax:* 800-641-0115 *Web Site:* www.redleafpress.org, pg 230

Robert F Reed Technology Medal, 200 Deer Run Rd, Sewickley, PA 15143-2600 *Tel:* 412-741-6860 *Toll Free Tel:* 800-910-4283 *Fax:* 412-741-2311 *E-mail:* info@gain.net *Web Site:* www.gain.net, pg 801

Robert D Reed Publishers, PO Box 1992, Brandon, OR 97411-1192 *Tel:* 541-347-9882 *Fax:* 541-347-9883 *E-mail:* 4bobreed@msn.com *Web Site:* www.rdrpublishers.com, pg 230

Thomas Reed Publications Inc, 398 Columbus Ave, Box 302, Boston, MA 02116 *Tel:* 617-236-0465 *Toll Free Tel:* 800-995-4995 (customer service) *E-mail:* info@reedsalmanac.com; order@reedsalmanac.com *Web Site:* www.reedsalmanac.com, pg 230

Reedswain Inc, 562 Ridge Rd, Spring City, PA 19475 *Tel:* 610-469-6911 *Toll Free Tel:* 800-331-5191 *Fax:* 610-495-6632 *Web Site:* www.reedswain.com, pg 230

The Erin Reel Literary Agency (ERLA), 9006 Wilshire Blvd, Box 1, Beverly Hills, CA 90211 *Tel:* 818-706-3313 *Fax:* 818-706-3313 *E-mail:* erlaquery@sbcglobal.net *Web Site:* www.erinreel.com, pg 650

Helen Rees Literary Agency, 376 North St, Boston, MA 02113-2103 *Tel:* 617-227-9014 *Fax:* 617-227-8762, pg 650

Referee Books, 2017 Lathrop Ave, Racine, WI 53405 *Tel:* 262-632-8855 *Toll Free Tel:* 800-733-6100 *Fax:* 262-632-5460 *E-mail:* questions@referee.com *Web Site:* www.referee.com, pg 230

Reference & User Services Association, 50 E Huron St, Chicago, IL 60611 *Tel:* 312-944-6780 *Toll Free Tel:* 800-545-2433 *Fax:* 312-280-3224 *Web Site:* www.ala.org, pg 698

Reference Publications Inc, 218 Saint Clair River Dr, Algonac, MI 48001 *Tel:* 810-794-5722 *Fax:* 810-794-7463 *E-mail:* referencepub@sbcglobal.com, pg 230

Reference Service Press, 5000 Windplay Dr, Suite 4, El Dorado Hills, CA 95762-9600 *Tel:* 916-939-9620 *Fax:* 916-939-9626 *E-mail:* findaid@aol.com *Web Site:* www.rspfunding.com, pg 230

Reference Wordsmith, 29 Brooks Lane, Essex, CT 06426 *Tel:* 860-767-1551 *Fax:* 860-767-1288 *Web Site:* www.reference-wordsmith.com, pg 610

Reformation Heritage Books, 2919 Leonard St NE, Grand Rapids, MI 49525 *Tel:* 616-977-0599 *Fax:* 616-285-3246 *E-mail:* orders@heritagebooks.org *Web Site:* www.heritagebooks.org, pg 230

Regal Books, 1957 Eastman Ave, Ventura, CA 93003 *Tel:* 805-644-9721 *Toll Free Tel:* 800-446-7735 (orders) *Fax:* 805-644-9728 (editorial); 805-644-4729 (purchasing); 805-650-8713 (sales & corp serv); 805-658-3388 (orders) *Toll Free Fax:* 800-860-3109 (orders) *E-mail:* info@regalbooks.com *Web Site:* www.gospellight.com, pg 230

Regatta Press Ltd, 750 Cascadilla St, Ithaca, NY 14851 *Tel:* 607-277-2211 *Fax:* 607-277-6292 *Toll Free Fax:* 800-688-2877 *E-mail:* info@regattapress.com *Web Site:* www.regattapress.com, pg 230

Donna Regen, 401 Orchard Lane, Allen, TX 75002 *Tel:* 214-495-8007 *Fax:* 214-495-9229 *E-mail:* donna@dallasrelo.com, pg 610

Regina Medal Award, 100 North St, Suite 224, Pittsfield, MA 01201-5109 *Tel:* 413-443-2252 *Fax:* 413-442-2252 *E-mail:* cla@cathla.org *Web Site:* www.cathla.org, pg 801

Regnery Publishing Inc, One Massachusetts Ave, NW, Suite 600, Washington, DC 20001 *Tel:* 202-216-0600 *Toll Free Tel:* 888-219-4747 *Fax:* 202-216-0612 *E-mail:* editorial@regnery.com *Web Site:* www.regnery.com, pg 231

Regular Baptist Press, 1300 N Meacham Rd, Schaumburg, IL 60173-4806 *Tel:* 847-843-1600 *Toll Free Tel:* 800-727-4440 (orders only); 888-588-1600 *Fax:* 847-843-3757 *E-mail:* rbp@garbc.org *Web Site:* www.regularbaptistpress.org, pg 231

Rei America Inc, 10049 NW 89 Ave, No 13-14, Miami, FL 33178 *Tel:* 305-805-0771 *Toll Free Tel:* 800-726-5337 *Fax:* 305-887-4138 *Web Site:* www.reiamericainc.com, pg 231

The Naomi Reichstein Literary Agency, 5031 Foothills Rd, Rm G, Lake Oswego, OR 97034 *Tel:* 503-636-7575 *Fax:* 503-636-3957, pg 650

Kerry Reilly: Representatives, 1826 Asheville Place, Charlotte, NC 28203 *Tel:* 704-372-6007 *Fax:* 704-372-6007 *E-mail:* kerry@reillyreps.com *Web Site:* www.reillyreps.com, pg 667

Jody Rein Books Inc, 7741 S Ash Ct, Centennial, CO 80122 *Tel:* 303-694-4430 *Fax:* 303-694-0687 *Web Site:* www.jodyreinbooks.com, pg 650

Marian Reiner, 71 Disbrow Lane, New Rochelle, NY 10804 *Tel:* 914-235-7808 *Fax:* 914-576-1432 *E-mail:* mreinerlit@aol.com, pg 650

Reitt Editing Services, 591 Coles Meadow Rd, Northampton, MA 01060 *Tel:* 413-584-8779 *Fax:* 413-584-8779 *E-mail:* redits@comcast.net, pg 610

Remember the Magic Annual Summer Conference, PO Box 810, Gracie Sta, New York, NY 10028-0082 *Tel:* 212-737-7536 *Fax:* 212-737-9469 *E-mail:* iwwg@iwwg.org *Web Site:* www.iwwg.org, pg 746

Renaissance Alliance Publishing Inc, 8691 Ninth Ave, PMB 210, Port Arthur, TX 77642-8025 *Fax:* 409-727-4824 *E-mail:* regalcrest@gt.rr.com *Web Site:* www.rapbooks.biz; www.regalcrest.biz, pg 231

Renaissance House, 9400 Lloydcrest Dr, Beverly Hills, CA 90210 *Tel:* 310-860-9930 *Toll Free Tel:* 800-547-5113 *Fax:* 310-860-9902 *Web Site:* renaissancehouse.net, pg 231

Renaissance House, 9400 Lloydcrest Dr, Beverly Hills, CA 90210 *Tel:* 310-860-9930 *Toll Free Tel:* 800-547-5113 *Fax:* 310-860-9902 *E-mail:* laredo@renaissancehouse.net; info@renaissancehouse.net *Web Site:* renaissancehouse.net, pg 667

The Amy Rennert Agency Inc, 98 Main St, Suite 302, Tiburon, CA 94920 *Tel:* 415-789-8955 *Fax:* 415-789-8944 *E-mail:* arennert@pacbell.net, pg 651

Reporters Committee for Freedom of the Press, 1815 N Fort Myer Dr, Suite 900, Arlington, VA 22209-1817 *Tel:* 703-807-2100 *Toll Free Tel:* 800-336-4243 *Fax:* 703-807-2109 *E-mail:* rcfp@rcfp.org *Web Site:* www.rcfp.org, pg 698

Reprint Services Corp, PO Box 890820, Temecula, CA 92589-0820 *Toll Free Tel:* 800-273-6635 *Fax:* 909-767-0133, pg 231

Research & Education Association, 61 Ethel Rd W, Piscataway, NJ 08854 *Tel:* 732-819-8880 *Fax:* 732-819-8808 *E-mail:* info@rea.com *Web Site:* www.rea.com, pg 231

Research & Engineering Council of NAPL (National Association for Printing Leadership), PO Box 1086, White Stone, VA 22578-1086 *Tel:* 804-436-9922 *Fax:* 804-436-9511 *E-mail:* recouncil@rivnet.net *Web Site:* www.recouncil.org, pg 698

Research Press, 2612 N Mattis Ave, Champaign, IL 61822 *Tel:* 217-352-3273 *Toll Free Tel:* 800-519-2707 *Fax:* 217-352-1221 *E-mail:* rp@researchpress.com *Web Site:* www.researchpress.com, pg 231

Research Research, 240 E 27 St, Suite 20-K, New York, NY 10016 *Tel:* 212-779-9540, pg 610

Residency, 454 E Hill Rd, Austerlitz, NY 12017 *Tel:* 518-392-3103; 518-392-4144 *Fax:* 518-392-7664 *E-mail:* apply@millaycolony.org *Web Site:* www.millaycolony.org, pg 802

The Resource Centre, Box 190, Waterloo, ON N2J 3Z9, Canada *Tel:* 519-885-0826 *Toll Free Tel:* 800-923-0330 *Fax:* 519-747-5629 *E-mail:* resourcecentre@sympatico.ca *Web Site:* www.theresourcecentre.com, pg 559

Resource Publications Inc, 160 E Virginia St, Suite 290, San Jose, CA 95112-5876 *Tel:* 408-286-8505 *Fax:* 408-287-8748 *E-mail:* orders@rpinet.com *Web Site:* www.rpinet.com, pg 231

Resources for Rehabilitation, 22 Bonard Rd, Winchester, MA 01890 *Tel:* 781-368-9094 *Fax:* 781-368-9096 *E-mail:* info@rfr.org *Web Site:* www.frf.org, pg 231

Resources for the Future, 1616 "P" St NW, Washington, DC 20036-1400 *Tel:* 202-328-5086 *Fax:* 202-328-5137 *E-mail:* rffpress@rff.org *Web Site:* www.rffpress.org, pg 231

Paula Reuben, 291 W 22 St, Suite 103, San Pedro, CA 90731 *Tel:* 310-831-6057 *E-mail:* paulareuben@sbcglobal.net, pg 610

Fleming H Revell, PO Box 6287, Grand Rapids, MI 49516-6287 *Tel:* 616-676-9185 *Toll Free Tel:* 800-877-2665 *Fax:* 616-676-9573 *Web Site:* www.bakerbooks.com, pg 232

Review & Herald Publishing Association, 55 W Oak Ridge Dr, Hagerstown, MD 21740 *Tel:* 301-393-3000 *Toll Free Tel:* 800-234-7630 *Fax:* 301-393-4055 (periodicals); 301-393-3222 *E-mail:* editorial@rhpa.org *Web Site:* www.reviewandherald.org, pg 232

RGA Enterprises Inc, 135 Marrus Dr, Columbus, OH 43230 *Tel:* 614-471-6385 *E-mail:* rgaenterprises@msn.com, pg 610

The RGU Group, 560 W Southern Ave, Tempe, AZ 85282 *Tel:* 480-736-9862 *Toll Free Tel:* 800-266-5265 *Fax:* 480-736-9863 *Toll Free Fax:* 800-973-6694 *E-mail:* info@thergugroup.com *Web Site:* www.thergugroup.com, pg 232

Jodie Rhodes Literary Agency, 8840 Villa La Jolla Dr, Suite 315, La Jolla, CA 92037, pg 651

Rhodes Literary Agency, PO Box 89133, Honolulu, HI 96830-7133 *Tel:* 808-947-4689 (let phone ring at least six times; then leave message), pg 651

The Harold U Ribalow Prize, 50 W 58 St, New York, NY 10019 *Tel:* 212-451-6289 *Fax:* 212-451-6257 *E-mail:* imarks@hadassah.org *Web Site:* www.hadassah.org, pg 802

Evelyn Richardson Memorial Literary Trust Award, 1113 Marginal Rd, Halifax, NS B3H 4P7, Canada *Tel:* 902-423-8116 *Fax:* 902-422-0881 *E-mail:* talk@writers.ns.ca *Web Site:* www.writers.ns.ca, pg 802

Richland Agency, 2828 Donald Douglas Loop N, Santa Monica, CA 90405 *Tel:* 310-392-1195 *Fax:* 310-392-0395, pg 651

Lynne Rienner Publishers Inc, 1800 30 St, Suite 314, Boulder, CO 80301 *Tel:* 303-444-6684 *Fax:* 303-444-0824 *E-mail:* cservice@rienner.com *Web Site:* www.rienner.com, pg 232

Rigby, 10801 N MoPac Expressway, Austin, TX 78759 *Tel:* 512-343-8227 *Toll Free Tel:* 800-531-5015 *Toll Free Fax:* 800-699-9459 *E-mail:* ecare@harcourt.com *Web Site:* www.harcourtachieve.com, pg 232

Rights Unlimited Inc, 101 W 55 St, Suite 2D, New York, NY 10019 *Tel:* 212-246-0900 *Fax:* 212-246-2114 *E-mail:* faith@rightsunlimited.com *Web Site:* rightsunlimited.com, pg 651

John R Riina Literary Agency, 5905 Meadowood Rd, Baltimore, MD 21212 *Tel:* 410-433-2305 *E-mail:* jrriina@earthlink.net, pg 651

Linda L Rill Research, 21 Wingate St, Unit 404, Haverhill, MA 01832 *Tel:* 978-374-0931 *Fax:* 978-374-1008 *E-mail:* llrill@bellatlantic.net, pg 610

The Angela Rinaldi Literary Agency, PO Box 7877, Beverly Hills, CA 90212-7877 *Tel:* 310-842-7665 *Fax:* 310-837-8143, pg 651

Mary Roberts Rinehart Fund, George Mason Univ, English Dept, 4400 University Dr, Mail Stop Number 3E4, Fairfax, VA 22030-4444 *Tel:* 703-993-1185 *Web Site:* www.gmu.edu/depts/english, pg 802

Gwen Pharis Ringwood Award for Drama, 11759 Groat Rd, Edmonton, AB T5M 3K6, Canada *Tel:* 780-422-8174 *Toll Free Tel:* 800-665-5354 (Alberta only) *Fax:* 780-422-2663 *E-mail:* mail@writersguild.ab.ca *Web Site:* www.writersguild.ab.ca, pg 802

Rip Van Winkle Award, 252 Hudson Ave, Albany, NY 12210 *Tel:* 518-432-6952 (NY Libr Assn) *Web Site:* www.nyla.org, pg 802

Rising Sun Publishing, PO Box 70906, Marietta, GA 30007-0906 *Tel:* 770-518-0369 *Toll Free Tel:* 800-524-2813 *Fax:* 770-587-0862 *E-mail:* info@rspublishing.com *Web Site:* www.rspublishing.com, pg 232

Rising Tide Press, 526 E 16 St, Tucson, AZ 85701 *Toll Free Tel:* 800-311-3565, pg 232

Ann Rittenberg Literary Agency Inc, 1201 Broadway, Suite 708, New York, NY 10001 *Tel:* 212-684-6936 *Fax:* 212-684-6929 *Web Site:* www.rittlit.com, pg 651

Judith Riven Editorial Consultant, 250 W 16 St, Suite 4F, New York, NY 10011 *Tel:* 212-255-1009 *Fax:* 212-255-8547 *E-mail:* rivenlit@att.net, pg 610

Judith Riven Literary Agent/Editorial Consultant, 250 W 16 St, Suite 4F, New York, NY 10011 *Tel:* 212-255-1009 *Fax:* 212-255-8547 *E-mail:* rivenlit@att.net, pg 652

River City Publishing, LLC, 1719 Mulberry St, Montgomery, AL 36106 *Tel:* 334-265-6753 *Toll Free Tel:* 877-408-7078 *Fax:* 334-265-8880 *E-mail:* web@rivercitypublishing.com *Web Site:* www.rivercitypublishing.com, pg 232

River City Writing Awards, c/o University of Memphis, Dept English, Memphis, TN 38152 *Tel:* 901-678-4591 *Fax:* 901-678-2226 *E-mail:* rivercity@memphis.edu *Web Site:* www.people.memphis.edu/~rivercity/contests.html, pg 802

River City Writing Awards in Fiction, University of Memphis, Dept of English, Memphis, TN 38152 *Tel:* 901-678-4591 *Fax:* 901-678-2226 *E-mail:* rivercity@memphis.edu *Web Site:* www.people.memphis.edu/~rivercity/contests.html, pg 802

Riverhead Books (Hardcover), 375 Hudson St, New York, NY 10014 *Tel:* 212-366-2000 *E-mail:* online@penguinputnam.com *Web Site:* www.penguin.com, pg 232

Riverhead Books (Trade Paperback), 375 Hudson St, New York, NY 10014 *Tel:* 212-366-2000 *E-mail:* online@penguinputnam.com *Web Site:* www.penguin.com, pg 233

RiverOak Publishing, 4050 Lee Vance View, Colorado Springs, CO 80918 *Tel:* 719-536-0100 *Toll Free Tel:* 800-323-7543 *Web Site:* www.cookministries.com, pg 233

Riverside Book Co Inc, 150 W End Ave, No 11-H, New York, NY 10023 *Tel:* 212-595-0700 *Fax:* 212-559-0780 *Web Site:* www.riversidebook.com, pg 233

Riverside Literary Agency, 41 Simon Keets Rd, Leyden, MA 01337 *Tel:* 413-772-0067 *Fax:* 413-772-0969 *E-mail:* rivlit@sover.net, pg 652

The Riverside Publishing Co, 425 Spring Lake Dr, Itasca, IL 60143-2079 *Tel:* 630-467-7000 *Toll Free Tel:* 800-323-9540 *Fax:* 630-467-7192 (cust serv) *Web Site:* www.riverpub.com, pg 233

Rizzoli International Publications Inc, 300 Park Ave S, 3rd fl, New York, NY 10010-5399 *Tel:* 212-387-3400 *Toll Free Tel:* 800-522-6657 (orders only) *Fax:* 212-387-3535, pg 233

RLR Associates Ltd, 7 W 51 St, New York, NY 10019 *Tel:* 212-541-8641 *Fax:* 212-541-6052 *Web Site:* www.rlrassociates.net, pg 652

RMA, 612 Argyle Rd, Suite L5, Brooklyn, NY 11230 *Tel:* 718-434-1893 *Fax:* 718-434-2157 *E-mail:* ricia@ricia.com *Web Site:* www.ricia.com, pg 652

Roanoke-Chowan Award for Poetry, 4610 Mail Service Center, Raleigh, NC 27699-4610 *Tel:* 919-807-7290 *Fax:* 919-733-8807, pg 802

B J Robbins Literary Agency, 5130 Bellaire Ave, North Hollywood, CA 91607 *Tel:* 818-760-6602 *Fax:* 818-760-6616 *E-mail:* robbinsliterary@aol.com, pg 652

Robbins Office Inc, 405 Park Ave, 9th fl, New York, NY 10022 *Tel:* 212-223-0720 *Fax:* 212-223-2535, pg 652

The Roberts Group, 1530 Thomas Lake Pointe Rd, No 119, Eagan, MN 55122 *Tel:* 651-330-1457 *Fax:* 651-330-0892 *E-mail:* info@editorialservice.com *Web Site:* www.editorialservice.com, pg 610

Rochester Institute of Technology, School of Print Media, 69 Lomb Memorial Dr, Rochester, NY 14623-5603 *Tel:* 585-475-2727; 585-475-7223 *Fax:* 585-475-5336 *E-mail:* spmofc@rit.edu *Web Site:* www.rit.edu/~spms, pg 754

James A Rock & Co Publishers, 9710 Traville Gateway Dr, No 305, Rockville, MD 20850 *Toll Free Tel:* 800-411-2230 *Fax:* 301-294-1683 *E-mail:* jarock@sprintmail.com *Web Site:* rockpublishing.com, pg 233

Rockefeller University Press, 1114 First Ave, New York, NY 10021 *Tel:* 212-327-8572 *Fax:* 212-327-7944 *E-mail:* rupcd@rockefeller.edu *Web Site:* www.rupress.org, pg 233

Rockmill & Company, 647 Warren St, Brooklyn, NY 11217 *Tel:* 718-638-3990 *E-mail:* agentrockmill@yahoo.com, pg 652

Rockport Publishers, 33 Commercial St, Gloucester, MA 01930 *Tel:* 978-282-9590 *Fax:* 978-283-2742 *Web Site:* www.rockpub.com, pg 233

Rocky Mountain Book Award, PO Box 42, Lethbridge, AB T1J 3Y3, Canada *Tel:* 403-381-7164 *E-mail:* rockymountainbookaward@shaw.ca *Web Site:* www.lethsd.ab.ca/lvbookaward, pg 802

Rocky Mountain Books Ltd, 406-13 Ave NE, Calgary, AB T2E 1C2, Canada *Tel:* 403-249-9490 *Fax:* 403-249-2968 *Web Site:* www.rmbooks.com, pg 559

Rocky Mountain Mineral Law Foundation, 9191 Sheridan Blvd, Suite 203, Westminister, CO 80031 *Tel:* 303-321-8100 *Fax:* 303-321-7657 *E-mail:* info@rmmlf.org *Web Site:* www.rmmlf.org, pg 233

Rocky Mountain Publishing Professionals Guild (RMPPG), PO Box 17721, Boulder, CO 80308-7721 *Tel:* 303-447-0799 *Web Site:* RMPPG.org, pg 698

Rocky River Publishers LLC, PO Box 1679, Shepherdstown, WV 25443-1679 *Tel:* 304-876-2711 *Toll Free Tel:* 800-343-0686 *Fax:* 304-263-2949 *E-mail:* rockyriverpublishers@citlink.net *Web Site:* www.rockyriver.com, pg 233

Rod & Staff Publishers Inc, Hwy 172, Crockett, KY 41413-0003 *Tel:* 606-522-4348 *Toll Free Tel:* 800-643-1244 *Fax:* 606-522-4896 *Toll Free Fax:* 800-643-1244 (ordering in US) *Web Site:* www.anabaptistis.org, pg 233

Rodale Books, 400 S Tenth St, Emmaus, PA 18098-0099 *Tel:* 610-967-5171 *Fax:* 610-967-8961 *Web Site:* www.rodale.com, pg 233

Rodale Inc, 33 E Minor St, Emmaus, PA 18098-0099 *Tel:* 610-967-5171 *Fax:* 610-967-8962 *Web Site:* www.rodale.com, pg 234

Lillian R Rodberg & Associates, 1600 Lehigh Pkwy E, Rm 9F, Allentown, PA 18103-3035 *Tel:* 610-740-0662 *E-mail:* wpressinc@aol.com, pg 610

Rodnik Publishing Company, PO Box 46956, Seattle, WA 98146-0956 *Tel:* 206-937-5189 *Fax:* 206-937-3554 *E-mail:* rodnik2@comcast.net *Web Site:* www.rodnikpublishing.com, pg 573

Rodopi, One Rockefeller Plaza, Rm 1420, New York, NY 10020-2002 *Tel:* 212-265-6560 *Toll Free Tel:* 800-225-3998 (US only) *Fax:* 212-265-6402 *E-mail:* info@rodopi.nl *Web Site:* www.rodopi.nl, pg 234

The Roeher Institute, York University, Kinsmen Bldg, 4700 Keele St, North York, ON M3J 1P3, Canada *Tel:* 416-661-9611 *Fax:* 416-661-5701 *E-mail:* info@roeher.ca *Web Site:* www.roeher.ca, pg 560

Nicholas Roerich Poetry Prize, 2091 Suncrest Rd, Talent, OR 97540 *Tel:* 541-512-8792 *Fax:* 541-512-8793 *E-mail:* mail@storylinepress.com *Web Site:* www.storylinepress.com, pg 802

Rogers Writers' Trust Fiction Prize, 90 Richmond St W, Suite 200, Toronto, ON M5C 1P1, Canada *Tel:* 416-504-8222 *Fax:* 416-504-9090 *E-mail:* info@writerstrust.com *Web Site:* www.writerstrust.com, pg 802

Linda Roghaar Literary Agency Inc, 133 High Point Dr, Amherst, MA 01002 *Tel:* 413-256-1921 *Fax:* 413-256-2636 *E-mail:* contact@lindaroghaar.com *Web Site:* www.lindaroghaar.com, pg 652

The Roistacher Literary Agency, 545 W 111 St, New York, NY 10025 *Tel:* 212-222-1405, pg 652

Rolling Stone's Annual College Journalism Competition, 1290 Avenue of the Americas, 2nd fl, New York, NY 10104 *Tel:* 212-484-1616; 212-484-1636 *Fax:* 212-484-3434 *Web Site:* www.rollingstone.com, pg 802

Roman Catholic Books, PO Box 2286, Fort Collins, CO 80522-2286 *Tel:* 970-490-2735 *Fax:* 970-493-8781 *Web Site:* www.booksforcatholics.com, pg 234

Roman Studios, 814 Kaipii St, Kailua, HI 96734 *Tel:* 808-262-4708, pg 667

Romance Writers of America, 16000 Stuebner Airline, Suite 140, Spring, TX 77379 *Tel:* 832-717-5200 *Fax:* 832-717-5201 *E-mail:* info@rwanational.org *Web Site:* www.rwanational.org, pg 698

Romance Writers of America Awards, 16000 Stuebner Airline, Suite 140, Spring, TX 77379 *Tel:* 832-717-5200 *Fax:* 832-717-5201 *E-mail:* info@rwanational.org *Web Site:* www.rwanational.org, pg 803

Romance Writers of America National Conference, 16000 Stuebner Airline, Suite 140, Spring, TX 77379 *Tel:* 832-717-5200 *Fax:* 832-717-5201 *E-mail:* info@rwanational.org *Web Site:* www.rwanational.org, pg 746

Roncorp Inc, 732 Cascade Dr N, Mount Laurel, NJ 08054 *Tel:* 856-722-5993 *Fax:* 856-722-9252 *E-mail:* roncorp@comcast.net, pg 234

Ronin Publishing Inc, PO Box 22900, Oakland, CA 94609-5900 *Tel:* 510-420-3669 *Fax:* 510-420-3672 *E-mail:* askronin@roninpub.com *Web Site:* www.roninpub.com, pg 234

Ronsdale Press, 3350 W 21 Ave, Vancouver, BC V6S 1G7, Canada *Tel:* 604-738-4688 *Toll Free Tel:* 888-879-0919 *Fax:* 604-731-4548 *E-mail:* ronsdale@shaw.ca *Web Site:* ronsdalepress.com, pg 560

Peter Rooney, 332 Bleecker St, PMB X-6, New York, NY 10014-2980 *Tel:* 212-334-2042 *Fax:* 212-226-8047 *E-mail:* magnetix@ix.netcom.com *Web Site:* www.magneticreports.com, pg 610

Rosemont College, Dept of English, 1400 Montgomery Ave, Rosemont, PA 19010 *Tel:* 610-527-0200 (ext 2320) *Fax:* 610-526-2964 *Web Site:* www.rosemont.edu, pg 754

The Rosen Publishing Group Inc, 29 E 21 St, New York, NY 10010 *Tel:* 212-777-3017 *Toll Free Tel:* 800-237-9932 *Fax:* 212-777-0277 *E-mail:* info@rosenpublishing.com *Web Site:* www.rosenpublishing.com, pg 234

The Rosenberg Group, 23 Lincoln Ave, Marblehead, MA 01945 *Tel:* 781-990-1341 *Fax:* 781-990-1344 *Web Site:* www.rosenberggroup.com, pg 652

Rita Rosenkranz Literary Agency, 440 West End Ave, Suite 15D, New York, NY 10024-5358 *Tel:* 212-873-6333 *Fax:* 212-873-5225, pg 652

Rosenstone/Wender, 38 E 29 St, 10th fl, New York, NY 10016 *Tel:* 212-725-9445 *Fax:* 212-725-9447, pg 652

Rosenthal Represents, 3850 Eddingham Ave, Calabasas, CA 91302 *Tel:* 818-222-5445 *Fax:* 818-222-5650, pg 667

Ross Books, PO Box 4340, Berkeley, CA 94704-0340 *Tel:* 510-841-2474 *Toll Free Tel:* 800-367-0930 *Fax:* 510-841-2695 *E-mail:* staff@rossbooks.com *Web Site:* www.rossbooks.com, pg 234

Ross Publishing Inc, 330 W 58 St, Suite 306, New York, NY 10019-1827 *Tel:* 212-765-8200 *Fax:* 212-765-8296 *E-mail:* info@rosspub.com *Web Site:* www.rosspub.com, pg 234

The Roth Agency, 138 Bay State Rd, Rehoboth, MA 02769 *Tel:* 508-252-5818, pg 652

Carol Susan Roth Literary & Creative, PO Box 620337, Woodside, CA 94062 *Tel:* 650-323-3795 *E-mail:* carol@authorsbest.com, pg 652

Lois Roth Award for a Translation of a Literary Work, 26 Broadway, 3rd fl, New York, NY 10004-1789 *Tel:* 646-576-5141 *Fax:* 646-458-0030 *E-mail:* awards@mla.org *Web Site:* www.mla.org, pg 803

Rothstein Associates Inc, 4 Arapaho Rd, Brookfield, CT 06804-3104 *Tel:* 203-740-7444 *Toll Free Tel:* 888-768-4783 *Fax:* 203-740-7401 *E-mail:* info@rothstein.com *Web Site:* www.rothstein.com, pg 234

Jane Rotrosen Agency LLC, 318 E 51 St, New York, NY 10022 *Tel:* 212-593-4330 *Fax:* 212-935-6985, pg 653

Rough Guides, 345 Hudson St, New York, NY 10014 *Tel:* 212-414-3635 *Fax:* 212-414-3352 *E-mail:* mail@roughguides.com *Web Site:* www.roughguides.com, pg 234

The Rough Notes Co Inc, 11690 Technology Dr, Carmel, IN 46032-5600 *Tel:* 317-582-1600 *Toll Free Tel:* 800-428-4384 *Fax:* 317-816-1000 *Toll Free Fax:* 800-321-1909 *Web Site:* www.roughnotes.com, pg 235

Routledge, 29 W 35 St, New York, NY 10001-2299 *Tel:* 212-216-7800 *Fax:* 212-564-7854 (main) *E-mail:* info@taylorandfrancis.com *Web Site:* www.routledge-ny.com, pg 235

Damaris Rowland, 5 Peter Cooper Rd, No 13H, New York, NY 10010 *Tel:* 212-475-8942 *Fax:* 212-358-9411, pg 653

Rowman & Littlefield Publishers Inc, 4501 Forbes Blvd, Lanham, MD 20706 *Tel:* 301-459-3366 *Toll Free Tel:* 800-462-6420 *Fax:* 301-429-5748 *Web Site:* www.rowmanlittlefield.com, pg 235

Dick Rowson, 4701 Connecticut Ave NW, Suite 503, Washington, DC 20008 *Tel:* 202-244-8104 *Fax:* 202-244-8104 *E-mail:* rcrowson2@aol.com, pg 610

Roxbury Publishing Co, 2034 Cotner Ave, Los Angeles, CA 90025 *Tel:* 310-473-3312 *Fax:* 310-473-4490 *E-mail:* roxbury@roxbury.net *Web Site:* www.roxbury.net, pg 235

Royal Fireworks Press, First Ave, Unionville, NY 10988 *Tel:* 845-726-4444 *Fax:* 845-726-3824 *E-mail:* mail@rfwp.com *Web Site:* www.rfwp.com, pg 235

Royal Ontario Museum Publications, 100 Queen's Park, Toronto, ON M5S 2C6, Canada *Tel:* 416-586-5581 *Fax:* 416-586-5887 *E-mail:* info@rom.on.ca *Web Site:* www.rom.on.ca, pg 560

Royalton Press, 362 N Bedford St, East Bridgewater, MA 02333 *Tel:* 508-378-1110 *Fax:* 508-378-1105 *Web Site:* www.drummondpub.com, pg 235

Royalty Publishing Co, 1440 Church Camp Rd, Bedford, IN 47421 *Tel:* 812-278-8785 *Fax:* 812-278-8785 *E-mail:* neeto@admete.net *Web Site:* www.v-maximum-zone.com, pg 235

Royce Carlton Inc, 866 United Nations Plaza, Suite 587, New York, NY 10017-1880 *Tel:* 212-355-7700 *Toll Free Tel:* 800-LECTURE (532-8873) *Fax:* 212-888-8659 *E-mail:* info@roycecarlton.com *Web Site:* www.roycecarlton.com, pg 670

RSG Publishing, 217 County Hwy 1, Bainbridge, NY 13733-9307 *Tel:* 607-563-9000 *Fax:* 607-563-9000, pg 235

RT Edwards Inc, PO Box 27388, Philadelphia, PA 19118 *Tel:* 215-233-5046 *Fax:* 215-233-2421 *E-mail:* info@edwardspub.com *Web Site:* www.rtedwards.com, pg 236

RTP Publishing Group, PO Box 4501, Clifton Park, NY 12065 *Tel:* 518-383-6414 *Fax:* 518-383-6414 *E-mail:* rockytopbooks@aol.com *Web Site:* member.aol.com/rockytopbooks, pg 236

Peter Rubie Literary Agency, 240 W 35 St, Suite 500, New York, NY 10001 *Tel:* 212-279-1776 *Fax:* 212-279-0927 *E-mail:* pralit@aol.com *Web Site:* www.prlit.com, pg 653

William B Ruggles Journalism Scholarship, 5211 Port Royal Rd, Suite 510, Springfield, VA 22151 *Tel:* 703-321-9606 *Fax:* 703-321-7342 *E-mail:* research@nilrr.org *Web Site:* www.nilrr.org, pg 803

Runestone Press, 241 First Ave N, Minneapolis, MN 55401 *Tel:* 612-332-3344 *Toll Free Tel:* 800-328-4929; 800-332-1132 *Fax:* 612-332-7615 *E-mail:* info@lernerbooks.com *Web Site:* www.lernerbooks.com, pg 236

Running Press Book Publishers, 125 S 22 St, Philadelphia, PA 19103-4399 *Tel:* 215-567-5080 *Toll Free Tel:* 800-345-5359 (cust serv & orders) *Fax:* 215-568-2919 *Toll Free Fax:* 800-453-2884 *Web Site:* www.runningpress.com, pg 236

Russell & Volkening Inc, 50 W 29 St, Suite 7E, New York, NY 10001 *Tel:* 212-684-6050 *Fax:* 212-889-3026, pg 653

Russell Sage Foundation, 112 E 64 St, New York, NY 10021-7383 *Tel:* 212-750-6000 *Toll Free Tel:* 800-524-6401 *Fax:* 212-371-4761 *E-mail:* pubs@rsage.org *Web Site:* www.russellsage.org, pg 236

Russian Information Service Inc, PO Box 567, Montpelier, VT 05601 *Tel:* 802-223-4955 *Fax:* 802-223-6105 *Web Site:* www.rispubs.com, pg 236

Rutgers University Press, 100 Joyce Kilmer Ave, Piscataway, NJ 08854-8099 *Tel:* 732-445-7762 (edit); 732-445-7762 (ext 627, sales) *Toll Free Tel:* 800-446-9323 (orders only) *Fax:* 732-445-7039 (acqs, edit, mktg, perms, prodn); 732-445-1974 (fulfillment) *E-mail:* garyf@rci.rutgers.edu *Web Site:* rutgerspress.rutgers.edu, pg 236

Rutledge Hill Press, c/o Thomas Nelson Publishers, PO Box 141000, Nashville, TN 37214-1000 *Tel:* 615-902-2703 *Toll Free Tel:* 800-251-4000 (ext 2703) *Fax:* 615-902-2340 *Web Site:* www.rutledgehillpress.com, pg 236

The Cornelius Ryan Award, 40 W 45 St, New York, NY 10036 *Tel:* 212-626-9220 *Fax:* 212-626-9210 *Web Site:* www.opcofamerica.org, pg 803

Regina Ryan Publishing Enterprises Inc, 251 Central Park W, Suite 7D, New York, NY 10024 *Tel:* 212-787-5589 *E-mail:* queryreginaryanbooks@rcn.com, pg 653

Sable Publishing, 365 N Saturmino Dr, Suite 21, Palm Springs, CA 92262 *Tel:* 760-408-1881 *E-mail:* sablepublishing@aol.com *Web Site:* www.sablepublishing.com, pg 236

Sabre Foundation Inc, 872 Massachusetts Ave, Suite 2-1, Cambridge, MA 02139 *Tel:* 617-868-3510 *Fax:* 617-868-7916 *E-mail:* sabre@sabre.org *Web Site:* www.sabre.org, pg 705

Sachem Publishing Associates Inc, 271 Lake Ave, Greenwich, CT 06831 *Tel:* 203-661-3717 *Fax:* 203-661-0775 *E-mail:* sachempub@optonline.net, pg 610

William H Sadlier Inc, 9 Pine St, New York, NY 10005 *Tel:* 212-227-2120 *Toll Free Tel:* 800-221-5175 *Fax:* 212-312-6080 *Web Site:* www.sadlier.com; www.sadlier-oxford.com, pg 237

SAE (Society of Automotive Engineers International), 400 Commonwealth Dr, Warrendale, PA 15096-0001 *Tel:* 724-776-4841 *Toll Free Tel:* 877-606-7323 (cust serv) *Fax:* 724-776-0790 *E-mail:* publications@sae.org *Web Site:* www.sae.org, pg 237

Safari Press, 15621 Chemical Lane, Bldg B, Huntington Beach, CA 92649 *Tel:* 714-894-9080 *Toll Free Tel:* 800-451-4788 *Fax:* 714-894-4949 *E-mail:* info@safaripress.com *Web Site:* www.safaripress.com, pg 237

Safe Harbor Books, 504 Main St, New London, NH 03527 *Fax:* 603-526-3500 *E-mail:* safeharborbooks@aol.com, pg 573

Safer Society Foundation Inc, 8-10 Conant Sq, Brandon, VT 05733 *Tel:* 802-247-3132 *Fax:* 802-247-4233 *E-mail:* ssfi@sover.net *Web Site:* www.safersociety.org, pg 237

The Sagalyn Literary Agency, 7201 Wisconsin Ave, Suite 675, Bethesda, MD 20814 *Tel:* 301-718-6440 *Fax:* 301-718-6444 *E-mail:* agency@sagalyn.com *Web Site:* www.sagalyn.com, pg 653

Sagamore Publishing LLC, 804 N Neil St, Champaign, IL 61820 *Tel:* 217-359-5940 *Toll Free Tel:* 800-327-5557 (orders) *Fax:* 217-359-5975 *E-mail:* books@sagamorepub.com *Web Site:* www.sagamorepub.com, pg 237

Sage Publications, 2455 Teller Rd, Thousand Oaks, CA 91320 *Tel:* 805-499-0721 *Fax:* 805-499-0871 *E-mail:* info@sagepub.com *Web Site:* www.sagepub.com, pg 237

Saint Aedan's Press & Book Distributors Inc, PO Box 385, Hillsdale, NJ 07642-0385 *Tel:* 201-664-0127 *E-mail:* junius1920@yahoo.com *Web Site:* www.greatoldebooks.com; www.juniusbooks.com, pg 237

Saint Andrews College Press, 1700 Dogwood Mile, Laurinburg, NC 28352-5598 *Tel:* 910-277-5310 *Toll Free Tel:* 800-763-0198 *Fax:* 910-277-5020 *E-mail:* press@sapc.edu *Web Site:* www.sapc.edu, pg 237

St Anthony Messenger Press, 28 W Liberty St, Cincinnati, OH 45202 *Tel:* 513-241-5615 *Toll Free Tel:* 800-488-0488 *Fax:* 513-241-0399 *E-mail:* books@americancatholic.org *Web Site:* www.AmericanCatholic.org, pg 237

St Augustine's Press Inc, PO Box 2285, South Bend, IN 46680-2285 *Tel:* 773-702-7248 *Toll Free Tel:* 888-997-4994 *Fax:* 773-702-9756 *Web Site:* www.staugustine.net, pg 238

St Bede's Publications, 271 N Main St, Box 545, Petersham, MA 01366-0545 *Tel:* 978-724-3213 *Fax:* 978-724-3216, pg 238

St Herman Press, 10 Beegum Gorge Rd, Platina, CA 96076 *Tel:* 530-352-4430 *Fax:* 530-352-4432 *E-mail:* stherman@stherman.com *Web Site:* www.stherman.com, pg 238

St James Press, 27500 Drake Rd, Farmington Hills, MI 48331-3535 *Tel:* 248-699-4253 *Toll Free Tel:* 800-877-4253 *Fax:* 248-699-8061 *Toll Free Fax:* 800-414-5043 *Web Site:* www.gale.com, pg 238

Guy Saint-Jean editeur Inc, 3154 Blvd Industriel, Laval, PQ H7L 4P7, Canada *Tel:* 450-663-1777 *Fax:* 450-663-6666 *E-mail:* saint-jean.editeur@qc.aira.com *Web Site:* www.saint-jeanediteur.com, pg 560

St Johann Press, 315 Schraalenburgh Rd, Haworth, NJ 07641 *Tel:* 201-387-1529 *Fax:* 201-501-0698, pg 238

St Joseph's University Press, 5600 City Ave, Philadelphia, PA 19131 *Tel:* 610-660-3400 *Fax:* 610-660-3410 *E-mail:* sjupress@sju.edu *Web Site:* www.sju.edu, pg 238

St Jude's ImPress, 5537 Waterman Blvd, Suite 2W, St Louis, MO 63112 *Tel:* 314-454-0064 *E-mail:* stjudes1@mindspring.com, pg 238

Saint Louis Literary Award, 40 N Kingshighway Blvd, 10-J, St Louis, MO 63108 *Tel:* 314-361-1616 *Fax:* 314-361-0812, pg 803

St Martin's Press LLC, 175 Fifth Ave, New York, NY 10010 Tel: 212-674-5151 Fax: 212-420-9314 E-mail: firstname.lastname@stmartins.com Web Site: www.stmartins.com, pg 238

St Martin's Press Paperback and Reference Group, 175 Fifth Ave, New York, NY 10010 Fax: 212-995-2488 E-mail: firstname.lastname@stmartins.com, pg 239

St Martin's Press Trade Division, 175 Fifth Ave, New York, NY 10010 E-mail: firstname.lastname@stmartins.com Web Site: www.stmartins.com; www.minotaurbooks.com, pg 239

Saint Mary's Press, 702 Terrace Heights, Winona, MN 55987-1318 Tel: 507-457-7900 Toll Free Tel: 800-533-8095 Toll Free Fax: 800-344-9225 E-mail: smpress@smp.org Web Site: www.smp.org, pg 239

Saint Nectarios Press, 10300 Ashworth Ave N, Seattle, WA 98133-9410 Tel: 206-522-4471 Toll Free Tel: 800-643-4233 Fax: 206-523-0550 E-mail: orders@stnectariospress.com Web Site: www.stnectariospress.com, pg 239

Salem Press Inc, 2 University Plaza, Suite 121, Hackensack, NJ 07601 Tel: 201-968-9899 Toll Free Tel: 800-221-1592 Fax: 201-968-1411 E-mail: csr@salempress.com Web Site: www.salempress.com, pg 239

Barbara S Salz LLC Photo Research, 127 Prospect Place, South Orange, NJ 07079 Tel: 973-762-6486 Fax: 973-762-3089 E-mail: b.salz@verizon.net, pg 610

Salzman International, 824 Edwards St, Trinidad, CA 95570 Tel: 212-997-0115; 707-677-0241 Fax: 707-677-0242 Web Site: www.salzmaninternational.com, pg 667

Pat Samples, 7152 Unity Ave N, Brooklyn Center, MN 55429 Tel: 763-560-5199 Fax: 763-560-5298 E-mail: patsamples@patsamples.com Web Site: www.patsamples.com, pg 610

Paul Samuelson, 117 Oak Drive, San Rafael, CA 94901 Tel: 415-459-5352 Fax: 415-459-5352 E-mail: paul@storywrangler.com Web Site: www.storywrangler.com, pg 610

San Diego Christian Writers' Guild Conference, PO Box 270403, San Diego, CA 92198 Tel: 619-221-8183 Fax: 619-255-1131 E-mail: info@sandiegocwg.org Web Site: www.sandiegocwg.org, pg 746

San Diego State University Press, San Diego State University, 5500 Campanile Dr, San Diego, CA 92182-8141 Tel: 760-768-5536; 619-594-6220 (orders only) Fax: 760-768-5631 Web Site: www.rohan.sdsu.edu/dept/press/, pg 239

San Francisco Writers Conference 2005, 1029 Jones St, San Francisco, CA 94109 Tel: 415-673-0939 Toll Free Tel: 866-862-7392 Fax: 415-673-0367 E-mail: sfwriterscon@aol.com Web Site: www.sanfranciscowritersconference.com, pg 746

The Ernest Sandeen & Richard Sullivan Prizes in Fiction & Poetry, 356 O'Shaughnessy Hall, Notre Dame, IN 46556 Tel: 574-631-7526 E-mail: english.righter.1@nd.edu Web Site: www.nd.edu, pg 803

Victoria Sanders & Associates, 241 Avenue of the Americas, Suite 11H, New York, NY 10014 Tel: 212-633-8811 Fax: 212-633-0525 E-mail: queriesvsa@hotmail.com Web Site: www.victoriasanders.com, pg 653

Sandhills Writers' Conference, Languages, Literature & Communication, 2500 Walton Way, Augusta, GA 30904 Tel: 706-667-4437 Fax: 706-667-4770 Web Site: www.sandhills.aug.edu, pg 746

Sandlapper Publishing Inc, PO Drawer 730, Orangeburg, SC 29116-0730 Tel: 803-531-1658 Toll Free Tel: 800-849-7263 (orders only) Fax: 803-534-5223 Web Site: www.sandlapperpublishing.com, pg 239

Marie Sandoz Award, c/o Margaret Harding, PO Box 98, Crete, NE 68333-0098 Tel: 402-826-2636 Fax: 402-826-2636 E-mail: gh12521@alltel.net Web Site: www.nebraskalibraries.org, pg 803

Joanne Sandstrom, 1958 Manzanita Dr, Oakland, CA 94611 Tel: 510-643-6325; 510-339-1352 Fax: 510-643-7062 E-mail: joannes@socrates.berkeley.edu, pg 611

Sandum & Associates, 144 E 84 St, New York, NY 10028 Tel: 212-737-2011 Fax: 212-737-9296, pg 653

Santa Barbara Book Promotion Workshop, PO Box 8206-R, Santa Barbara, CA 93118-8206 Tel: 805-968-7277 Toll Free Tel: 800-727-2782 Fax: 805-968-1379 E-mail: orders@parapublishing.com Web Site: www.parapublishing.com, pg 746

Santa Monica Press LLC, 513 Wilshire Blvd, No 321, Santa Monica, CA 90401 Tel: 310-230-7759 Toll Free Tel: 800-784-9553 Fax: 310-230-7761 E-mail: books@santamonicapress.com Web Site: www.santamonicapress.com, pg 240

Santillana USA Publishing Co Inc, 2105 NW 86 Ave, Miami, FL 33122 Tel: 305-591-9522 Toll Free Tel: 800-245-8584 Fax: 305-591-9145 Toll Free Fax: 888-248-9518 E-mail: customerservice@santillanausa.com Web Site: www.santillanausa.com; www.alfaguara.net, pg 240

Sara Jordan Publishing, Sta "M", Box 160, Toronto, ON M6S 4T3, Canada Tel: 905-938-5050 Toll Free Tel: 800-567-7733 Fax: 905-938-9970 Toll Free Fax: 800-229-3855 Web Site: www.sara-jordan.com, pg 560

Sarabande Books Inc, 2234 Dundee Rd, Suite 200, Louisville, KY 40205 Tel: 502-458-4028 Fax: 502-458-4065 E-mail: info@sarabandebooks.org Web Site: www.sarabandebooks.org, pg 240

Karen E Sardinas-Wyssling, 6 Bradford Lane, Plainsboro, NJ 08536-2326 Tel: 609-275-9148 E-mail: starchild240@comcast.net, pg 611

May Sarton Award, 16 Cornell St, Arlington, MA 02474 Web Site: www.nepoetryclub.org, pg 803

SAS Publishing, SAS Campus Dr, Cary, NC 27513 Tel: 919-531-7447 Fax: 919-677-4444 E-mail: sasbbu@sas.com Web Site: www.sas.com, pg 240

Saskatchewan Arts Board, 2135 Broad St, Regina, SK S4P 3V7, Canada Tel: 306-787-4056 Toll Free Tel: 800-667-7526 (Saskatchewan only) Fax: 306-787-4199 E-mail: sab@artsboard.sk.ca Web Site: www.artsboard.sk.ca, pg 699

Sasquatch Books, 119 S Main, Suite 400, Seattle, WA 98104 Tel: 206-467-4300 Toll Free Tel: 800-775-0817 Fax: 206-467-4301 E-mail: books@sasquatchbooks.com Web Site: www.sasquatchbooks.com, pg 240

SATW Foundation Lowell Thomas Travel Journalism Competition, 1500 Sunday Dr, Suite 102, Raleigh, NC 27607 Tel: 919-861-5586; 713-532-6461 Fax: 919-787-4916 Web Site: www.satw.org, pg 803

Saunders College Publishing, The Public Ledger Bldg, 150 S Independence Mall W, Suite 1250, Philadelphia, PA 19106-3412 Tel: 215-238-5500 Fax: 215-238-5660 Web Site: www.hbcollege.com, pg 240

W B Saunders Ltd, 170 S Independence Mall W, Suite 300 E, Philadelphia, PA 19106-3399 Tel: 215-238-7800 Toll Free Tel: 800-545-2522 (cust serv) Fax: 215-238-7883 Web Site: www.elsevierhealth.com, pg 240

The Barbara Savage, 1001 SW Klickitat Way, Suite 201, Seattle, WA 98134 Tel: 206-223-6303 Fax: 206-223-6306 E-mail: mbooks@mountaineers.org Web Site: www.mountaineersbooks.org, pg 803

Savage Press, 1209 Lincoln St, Superior, WI 54880 Tel: 715-394-9513 Toll Free Tel: 800-732-3867 Fax: 715-394-9513 E-mail: mail@savpress.com Web Site: www.savpress.com, pg 240

Saxon, 10801 N MoPac Expressway, Austin, TX 78759 Tel: 512-343-8227 Toll Free Tel: 800-531-5015 Toll Free Fax: 800-699-9459 E-mail: ecare@harcourt.com Web Site: www.harcourtachieve.com, pg 240

Aldo & Jeanne Scaglione Prize for a Translation of a Literary Work, 26 Broadway, 3rd fl, New York, NY 10004-1789 Tel: 646-576-5141 Fax: 646-458-0030 E-mail: awards@mla.org Web Site: www.mla.org, pg 803

Aldo & Jeanne Scaglione Prize for a Translation of a Scholarly Study of Literature, 26 Broadway, 3rd fl, New York, NY 10004-1789 Tel: 646-576-5141 Fax: 646-458-0030 E-mail: awards@mla.org Web Site: www.mla.org, pg 803

Aldo & Jeanne Scaglione Prize for Comparative Literary Studies, 26 Broadway, 3rd fl, New York, NY 10004-1789 Tel: 646-576-5141 Fax: 646-458-0030 E-mail: awards@mla.org Web Site: www.mla.org, pg 804

Aldo & Jeanne Scaglione Prize for French & Francophone Studies, 26 Broadway, 3rd fl, New York, NY 10004-1789 Tel: 646-576-5141 Fax: 646-458-0030 E-mail: awards@mla.org Web Site: www.mla.org, pg 804

Aldo & Jeanne Scaglione Prize for Italian Studies, 26 Broadway, 3rd fl, New York, NY 10004-1789 Tel: 646-576-5141 Fax: 646-458-0030 E-mail: awards@mla.org Web Site: www.mla.org, pg 804

Aldo & Jeanne Scaglione Prize for Studies in Germanic Languages & Literature, 26 Broadway, 3rd fl, New York, NY 10004-1789 Tel: 646-576-5141 Fax: 646-458-0030 E-mail: awards@mla.org Web Site: www.mla.org, pg 804

Aldo & Jeanne Scaglione Prize for Studies in Slavic Languages & Literature, 26 Broadway, 3rd fl, New York, NY 10004-1789 Tel: 646-576-5141 Fax: 646-458-0030 E-mail: awards@mla.org Web Site: www.mla.org, pg 804

Aldo & Jeanne Scaglione Publication Award for a Manuscript in Italian Literary Studies, 26 Broadway, 3rd fl, New York, NY 10004-1789 Tel: 646-576-5141 Fax: 646-458-0030, pg 804

Jack Scagnetti Talent & Literary Agency, 5118 Vineland Ave, Suite 102, North Hollywood, CA 91601 Tel: 818-762-3871; 818-761-0580 Web Site: www.jackscagnetti.com, pg 653

William Sanders Scarborough Prize, 26 Broadway, 3rd fl, New York, NY 10004-1789 Tel: 646-576-5141 Fax: 646-458-0030 E-mail: awards@mla.org Web Site: www.mla.org, pg 804

Scarecrow Press/Government Institutes Div, 4501 Forbes Blvd, Suite 200, Lanham, MD 20706 Tel: 301-921-2304 Fax: 301-429-5747 Web Site: govinst.scarecrowpress.com, pg 240

Scarecrow Press Inc, 4501 Forbes Blvd, Suite 200, Lanham, MD 20706 Tel: 301-459-3366 Toll Free Tel: 800-462-6420 Fax: 301-429-5747 Toll Free Fax: 800-338-4550 Web Site: www.scarecrowpress.com, pg 240

SCBWI Work-In-Progress Grants, 8271 Beverly Blvd, Los Angeles, CA 90048 Tel: 323-782-1010 Fax: 323-782-1892 E-mail: membership@scbwi.org Web Site: www.scbwi.org, pg 804

Scepter Publishers, 8 W 38 St, New York, NY 10018 Tel: 212-354-0670 Toll Free Tel: 800-322-8773 Fax: 212-354-0736 Web Site: www.scepterpublishers.org, pg 241

William D Schaeffer Environmental Award, 200 Deer Run Rd, Sewickley, PA 15143-2600 Tel: 412-741-6860 Toll Free Tel: 800-910-4283 Fax: 412-741-2311 E-mail: info@gain.net Web Site: www.gain.net, pg 804

Robert Schalkenbach Foundation, 149 Madison Ave, Suite 601, New York, NY 10016-6713 Tel: 212-683-6424 Toll Free Tel: 800-269-9555 Fax: 212-683-6454 E-mail: staff@schalkenbach.org Web Site: www.schalkenbach.org, pg 241

C J Scheiner Books, 275 Linden Blvd, Suite B2, Brooklyn, NY 11226 Tel: 718-469-1089 Fax: 718-469-1089, pg 611

Schiavone Literary Agency Inc, 236 Trails End, West Palm Beach, FL 33413-2135 Tel: 561-966-9294 Fax: 561-966-9294 E-mail: profschia@aol.com Web Site: www.publishersmarketplace.com/members/profschia, pg 653

Schiffer Publishing Ltd, 4880 Lower Valley Rd, Atglen, PA 19310 *Tel:* 610-593-1777 *Fax:* 610-593-2002 *E-mail:* schifferbk@aol.com; schifferii@aol.com *Web Site:* schifferbooks.com, pg 241

Schirmer Trade Books, 25 Park Ave S, New York, NY 10010 *Tel:* 212-254-2100 *Toll Free Tel:* 800-431-7187 *Fax:* 212-254-2013 *Toll Free Fax:* 800-345-6842 *Web Site:* www.musicsales.com, pg 241

Wendy Schmalz Agency, PO Box 831, Hudson, NY 12534-0831 *Tel:* 518-672-7697 *Fax:* 518-672-7662 *E-mail:* wendy@schmalzagency.com, pg 654

Harold Schmidt Literary Agency, 415 W 23 St, Suite 6F, New York, NY 10011 *Tel:* 212-727-7473 *E-mail:* hslanyc@aol.com, pg 654

Bernadotte E Schmitt Grants, 400 "A" St SE, Washington, DC 20003 *Tel:* 202-544-2422 *Fax:* 202-544-8307 *E-mail:* info@historians.org *Web Site:* www.historians.org, pg 804

Scholars' Facsimiles & Reprints, PO Box 5934, Carefree, AZ 85377-5934 *Tel:* 480-575-9945 *Fax:* 480-575-9451 *E-mail:* maxinmin@umich.edu, pg 241

Scholastic Canada Ltd, 175 Hillmount Rd, Markham, ON L6C 1Z7, Canada *Tel:* 905-887-7323 *Toll Free Tel:* 800-268-3848 (Canada) *Fax:* 905-887-1131 *Toll Free Fax:* 800-387-4944; 866-346-1288 *Web Site:* www.scholastic.ca, pg 560

Scholastic Education, 524 Broadway, New York, NY 10012 *Tel:* 212-343-6100 *Fax:* 212-343-6189 *Web Site:* www.scholastic.com, pg 241

Scholastic Education Curriculum Publishing, 524 Broadway, New York, NY 10012 *Tel:* 212-343-6100 *Web Site:* www.scholastic.com, pg 241

Scholastic Entertainment Inc, 524 Broadway, New York, NY 10012 *Tel:* 212-343-7500 *Fax:* 212-965-7448, pg 241

Scholastic Inc, 557 Broadway, New York, NY 10012 *Tel:* 212-343-4469 *Toll Free Tel:* 800-scholastic *Fax:* 212-343-6930 *Web Site:* www.scholastic.com, pg 241

Scholastic International, 557 Broadway, New York, NY 10012 *Tel:* 212-343-6100 *Fax:* 212-343-4712, pg 242

Scholastic Library/Grolier National Library Week Grant, 50 E Huron St, Chicago, IL 60611 *Tel:* 312-280-4020 *Toll Free Tel:* 800-545-2433 (ext 4020) *Fax:* 312-944-8520 *E-mail:* pio@ala.org *Web Site:* www.ala.org, pg 804

Scholastic Library Publishing, 90 Old Sherman Tpke, Danbury, CT 06816 *Tel:* 203-797-3500 *Toll Free Tel:* 800-621-1115 *Fax:* 203-797-3657 *Web Site:* www.scholasticlibrary.com, pg 242

Scholastic Paperbacks, Teaching Resources & Reading Counts, 557 Broadway, New York, NY 10012-3999 *Tel:* 212-965-7241 *Fax:* 212-965-7487 *Web Site:* www.scholastic.com, pg 242

Scholastic Trade Division, 557 Broadway, New York, NY 10012 *Tel:* 212-343-6100; 212-343-4685 (export sales) *Fax:* 212-343-4714 (export sales) *Web Site:* www.scholastic.com, pg 242

Scholium International Inc, PO Box 1519, Port Washington, NY 11050-7519 *Tel:* 516-767-7171 *Fax:* 516-944-9824 *E-mail:* info@scholium.com; artcandido@cs.com *Web Site:* www.scholium.com, pg 242

Schonfeld & Associates Inc, 2830 Blackthorn Rd, Riverwood, IL 60015 *Tel:* 847-948-8080 *Toll Free Tel:* 800-205-0030 *Fax:* 847-948-8096 *E-mail:* saiinfo@saibooks.com *Web Site:* www.saibooks.com, pg 242

School of American Research Press, 660 Garcia St, Santa Fe, NM 87505 *Tel:* 505-954-7206 *Toll Free Tel:* 888-390-6070 *Fax:* 505-954-7241 *E-mail:* bkorders@sarsf.org *Web Site:* www.sarweb.org, pg 243

School of Government, University of North Carolina, CB 3330, Chapel Hill, NC 27599-3330 *Tel:* 919-966-4119 *Fax:* 919-962-2707 *E-mail:* khunt@iogmail.iog.unc.edu *Web Site:* www.sog.unc.edu, pg 243

School of Visual Arts, 209 E 23 St, New York, NY 10010 *Tel:* 212-592-2100 *Fax:* 212-592-2116 *Web Site:* www.schoolofvisualarts.edu, pg 754

School Zone Publishing Co, 1819 Industrial Dr, Grand Haven, MI 49417 *Tel:* 616-846-5030 *Toll Free Tel:* 800-253-0564 *Fax:* 616-846-6181 *Web Site:* www.schoolzone.com, pg 243

Schreiber Publishing Inc, 51 Monroe St, Suite 101, Rockville, MD 20850 *Tel:* 301-424-7737 *Toll Free Tel:* 800-822-3213 (sales) *Fax:* 301-424-2518 *E-mail:* books@schreibernet.com *Web Site:* schreiberpublishing.com, pg 243

Schroeder Indexing Services, 2606 Old Mill Lane, Suite 1, Rolling Meadows, IL 60008 *Tel:* 847-303-0989 *Fax:* 847-303-1559 *E-mail:* sanindex@schroederindexing.com *Web Site:* www.schroederindexing.com, pg 611

Franklin L Schulaner, PO Box 507, Kealakekua, HI 96750-0507 *Tel:* 808-322-3785 *E-mail:* tankay@hgea.org, pg 611

Susan Schulman, A Literary Agency, 454 W 44 St, New York, NY 10036 *Tel:* 212-713-1633 *Fax:* 212-581-8830 *E-mail:* schulman@aol.com *Web Site:* www.susanschulman.com, pg 654

Sherri Schultz Editorial Services, 1508 Tenth Ave E, Suite 302, Seattle, WA 98102 *Tel:* 206-325-3523 *E-mail:* sherrischultz@earthlink.net, pg 611

Henry & Ida Schuman Prize, University of Florida, 3310 Turlington Hall, Gainesville, FL 32611 *Tel:* 352-392-1677 *E-mail:* info@hssonline.org *Web Site:* www.hssonline.org, pg 804

The Schuna Group Inc, 1503 Briarknoll Dr, Arden Hills, MN 55112 *Tel:* 651-631-8480 *Fax:* 651-631-8458 *Web Site:* www.schunagroup.com, pg 667

A E Schwartz & Associates, PO Box 79228, Waverley, MA 02479-0228 *Tel:* 617-926-9111 *Fax:* 617-926-0660 *E-mail:* pgbs@aeschwartz.com *Web Site:* aeschwartz.com, pg 654

Laurens R Schwartz, Esquire, 5 E 22 St, Suite 15-D, New York, NY 10010-5325 *Tel:* 212-228-2614, pg 654

Ruth Schwartz Children's Book Award, c/o Ontario Arts Council Literature Office, 151 Bloor St W, 5th fl, Toronto, ON M5S 1T6, Canada *Tel:* 416-961-1660 (ext 7438) *Toll Free Tel:* 800-387-0058 (Canada) *Fax:* 416-961-7796 *E-mail:* info@arts.on.ca *Web Site:* www.arts.on.ca, pg 805

Science & Humanities Press, 1023 Stuyvesant Lane, Manchester, MO 63011-3601 *Tel:* 636-394-4950 *E-mail:* publisher@sciencehumanitiespress.com *Web Site:* sciencehumanitiespress.com; beachhousebooks.com; macroprintbooks.com; earlyeditionsbooks.com; heuristicsbooks.com, pg 243

Science Fiction & Fantasy Writers of America Inc, PO Box 877, Chestertown, MD 21620 *Toll Free Tel:* 888-322-7392 *E-mail:* execdir@sfwa.org *Web Site:* www.sfwa.org, pg 699

Science Fiction Research Association Inc, 6021 Grassmere, Corpus Christi, TX 78415 *Tel:* 512-855-9304, pg 699

Science in Society Journalism Awards, PO Box 890, Hedgesville, WV 25427 *Web Site:* www.nasw.org, pg 805

Science Publishers Inc, 234 May St, Enfield, NH 03748 *Tel:* 603-632-7377 *Fax:* 603-632-5611 *E-mail:* info@scipub.net *Web Site:* www.scipub.net, pg 243

Scientific Publishers Inc, 4460 SW 35 Terr, Suite 305, Gainesville, FL 32608 *Tel:* 352-373-5630 *Fax:* 352-373-3249 *E-mail:* scipub@aol.com *Web Site:* www.scipub.com, pg 243

SciTech Publishing, Inc, 7474 Creedmoor Rd, Raleigh, NC 27613 *Tel:* 919-866-1501 *Fax:* 919-844-5809 *E-mail:* info@scitechpub.com *Web Site:* www.scitechpub.com, pg 243

Scott Foresman, 1900 E Lake Ave, Glenview, IL 60025 *Tel:* 847-729-3000 *Toll Free Tel:* 800-535-4391 (Midwest) *Fax:* 847-729-8910 *E-mail:* firstname.lastname@scottforesman.com *Web Site:* www.scottforesman.com, pg 243

Freda Scott Inc, 383 Missouri St, San Francisco, CA 94107-2819 *Tel:* 415-398-9121 *Fax:* 415-550-9120 *E-mail:* info@fredascott.com, pg 667

Scott Jones Inc, PO Box 696, El Granada, CA 94018 *Tel:* 650-726-2436 *Fax:* 650-726-4693 *Web Site:* www.scottjonespub.com, pg 243

Scott Publications Inc, 801 W Norton, Suite 200, Muskegon, MI 49441 *Tel:* 231-733-9382 *Toll Free Tel:* 866-733-9382 *Fax:* 231-733-7635 *E-mail:* contactus@scottpublications.com *Web Site:* www.scottpublications.com, pg 243

Scott Publishing Co, 911 Vandemark Rd, Sidney, OH 45365 *Tel:* 937-498-0802 *Toll Free Tel:* 800-572-6885 *Fax:* 937-498-0807 *E-mail:* ssm@amospress.com *Web Site:* www.amosadvantage.com, pg 244

S©ott Treimel NY, 434 Lafayette St, New York, NY 10003-6943 *Tel:* 212-505-8353 *Fax:* 212-505-0664 *E-mail:* st.ny@verizon.net, pg 654

Scovil Chichak Galen Literary Agency Inc, 381 Park Ave S, Suite 1020, New York, NY 10016 *Tel:* 212-679-8686 *Fax:* 212-679-6710 *E-mail:* mailroom@scglit.com *Web Site:* www.scglit.com, pg 654

Screen Printing Technical Foundation, 10015 Main St, Fairfax, VA 22031-3489 *Tel:* 703-385-1335 *Fax:* 703-273-0456 *E-mail:* sgia@sgia.org *Web Site:* www.sgia.org, pg 699

Scribendi Inc, 153 Harvey St, Chatham, ON N7M 1M6, Canada *Fax:* 519-354-0192 *E-mail:* customerservice@scribendi.com *Web Site:* www.scribendi.com, pg 611

Scribner, 1230 Avenue of the Americas, New York, NY 10020, pg 244

Scripta Humanistica Publishing International, 1383 Kersey Lane, Potomac, MD 20854 *Tel:* 301-294-7949 *Fax:* 301-424-9584 *E-mail:* scripta@aol.com *Web Site:* www.scriptahumanistica.com, pg 244

Scriptural Research Center, PO Box 725, New Britain, CT 06050-0725 *Tel:* 203-272-1780 *Fax:* 203-272-2296 *E-mail:* scriptpublish@snet.net *Web Site:* www.scripturalresearch.com, pg 244

Scurlock Publishing Co Inc, 1293 Myrtle Springs Rd, Texarkana, TX 75503 *Tel:* 903-832-4726 *Toll Free Tel:* 800-228-6389 *Fax:* 903-831-3177 *E-mail:* scurlockpubl@txk.net *Web Site:* www.muzzmag.com; muzzleloadermag.com, pg 244

SDSU Writers' Conference, 5250 Campanile Dr, Rm 2503, San Diego, CA 92182-1920 *Tel:* 619-594-2517 *Fax:* 619-594-8566 *E-mail:* extended.std@sdsu.edu *Web Site:* www.ces.sdsu.edu, pg 747

Seal Books, One Toronto St, Suite 300, Toronto, ON M5C 2V6, Canada *Tel:* 416-364-4449 *Toll Free Tel:* 888-523-9292 (order desk) *Fax:* 416-957-1587 *Web Site:* www.randomhouse.ca, pg 560

Seal Press, 1400 65 St, Suite 250, Emeryville, CA 94608 *Tel:* 510-595-3664 *Fax:* 510-595-4228 *Web Site:* www.sealpress.com, pg 244

Hank Searls, 4435 Holly Lane NW, Gig Harbor, WA 98335 *Tel:* 253-851-9896 *Fax:* 253-851-9897 *E-mail:* hanksearls@harbornet.com *Web Site:* www.critiquemaster.com, pg 611

Hank Searls Authors Workshop, 4435 Holly Lane NW, Gig Harbor, WA 98335 *Tel:* 253-851-9897 *Fax:* 253-851-9897 *E-mail:* hanksearls@harbornet.com *Web Site:* critiquemaster.com, pg 747

Seascape Press Ltd, 1010 Roble Lane, Santa Barbara, CA 93103-2046 *Tel:* 805-965-4646 *Toll Free Tel:* 800-929-2906 *Fax:* 805-963-8188 *E-mail:* seapress@aol.com *Web Site:* www.seascapepress.com, pg 573

Sebastian Agency, 557 W Seventh St, Suite 2, St Paul, MN 55102 *Tel:* 651-224-6670 *Fax:* 651-224-6895 *Web Site:* www.sebastianagency.com, pg 654

Second Chance Press, 4170 Noyac Rd, Sag Harbor, NY 11963 *Tel:* 631-725-1101 *Fax:* 631-725-8215 *E-mail:* info@thepermanentpress.com *Web Site:* www.thepermanentpress.com, pg 244

Second Story Feminist Press, 720 Bathurst St, Suite 301, Toronto, ON M5S 2R4, Canada *Tel:* 416-537-7850 *Fax:* 416-537-0588 *E-mail:* info@secondstorypress.ca *Web Site:* www.secondstorypress.on.ca, pg 561

See Sharp Press, PO Box 1731, Tucson, AZ 85702-1731 *Tel:* 520-628-8720 *Fax:* 520-628-8720 *E-mail:* info@seesharppress.com *Web Site:* www.seesharppress.com, pg 244

Seedling Publications Inc, 520 E Bainbridge St, Elizabethtown, PA 17022 *Tel:* 614-267-7333 *Toll Free Tel:* 800-233-0759 *Fax:* 614-267-4205 *Toll Free Fax:* 888-834-1303 *E-mail:* sales@seedlingpub.com *Web Site:* www.seedlingpub.com, pg 244

The SeedSowers, PO Box 3317, Jacksonville, FL 32206-0317 *Tel:* 904-598-2345 *Toll Free Tel:* 800-228-2665 *Fax:* 904-598-3456 *E-mail:* books@seedsowers.com *Web Site:* seedsowers.com, pg 244

SelectiveHouse Publishers Inc, PO Box 10095, Gaithersburg, MD 20898 *Tel:* 301-990-2999 *Toll Free Tel:* 888-256-6399 (orders only) *Fax:* 301-990-2998 *E-mail:* sr@selectivehouse.com *Web Site:* www.selectivehouse.com, pg 244

Self-Counsel Press Inc, 1704 N State St, Bellingham, WA 98225 *Tel:* 360-676-4530 *Toll Free Tel:* 877-877-6490 *Fax:* 360-676-4549 *E-mail:* service@self-counsel.com *Web Site:* www.self-counsel.com, pg 245

Self-Counsel Press Inc, 1481 Charlotte Rd, North Vancouver, BC V7J 1H1, Canada *Tel:* 604-986-3366 *Toll Free Tel:* 800-663-3007 *Fax:* 604-986-3947 *E-mail:* service@self-counsel.com *Web Site:* www.self-counsel.com, pg 561

Lynn Seligman, 400 Highland Ave, Upper Montclair, NJ 07043 *Tel:* 973-783-3631 *E-mail:* seliglit@aol.com, pg 654

Selling to Hollywood, 269 S Beverly Dr, Suite 2600, Beverly Hills, CA 90212-3807 *Toll Free Tel:* 866-265-9091 *Toll Free Fax:* 866-265-9091 *E-mail:* asa@goasa.com *Web Site:* www.goasa.com, pg 747

Edythea Ginis Selman, Literary Agency Inc, 14 Washington Place, New York, NY 10003 *Tel:* 212-473-1874 *Fax:* 212-473-1875, pg 654

Richard Selman, 14 Washington Place, New York, NY 10003 *Tel:* 212-477-1874 *Fax:* 212-473-1875, pg 611

Alexa Selph, 4300 McClatchey Circle, Atlanta, GA 30342 *Tel:* 404-256-3717 *E-mail:* Lexal01@aol.com, pg 611

Sentient Publications LLC, 1113 Spruce St, Boulder, CO 80302 *Tel:* 303-443-2188 *Fax:* 303-381-2538 *E-mail:* contact@sentientpublications.com; salesmanager@sentientpublications.com *Web Site:* www.sentientpublications.com, pg 245

Sentner Memorial Short Story Award, 115 Richmond St, Charlottetown, PE C1A 1H7, Canada *Tel:* 902-368-4410 *Fax:* 902-368-4418 *E-mail:* peiarts@peiartscouncil.com *Web Site:* www.peiartscouncil.com, pg 805

Laurie S Senz, 2363 Deer Creek Trail, Deerfield Beach, FL 33442 *Tel:* 954-481-1930 *Fax:* 954-481-1939 *E-mail:* lsenz@aol.com, pg 611

Sepher-Hermon Press, 1153 45 St, Brooklyn, NY 11219 *Tel:* 718-972-9010 *Fax:* 718-972-6935, pg 245

Sequoyah Children's Book Award, 300 Hardy Dr, Edmond, OK 73013 *Tel:* 405-348-0506 *Fax:* 405-348-1629 *Web Site:* www.oklibs.org, pg 805

Sequoyah Young Adult Book Award, 300 Hardy Dr, Edmond, OK 73013 *Tel:* 405-348-0506 *Fax:* 405-348-1629 *Web Site:* www.oklibs.org, pg 805

Seraphine Publishing, 29 Queen St, Belleville, ON K8N 1T3, Canada *Tel:* 613-921-7636 *Fax:* 613-771-1737 *E-mail:* info@seraphinepublishing.com *Web Site:* www.seraphinepublishing.com, pg 611

Serindia Publications, PO Box 10335, Chicago, IL 60610-0335 *Tel:* 312-664-5531 *Fax:* 312-664-4389 *E-mail:* info@serindia.com *Web Site:* www.serindia.com, pg 245

Services Documentaires Multimedia Inc (SDM Inc), 5650 Rue D'Iberville, Bureau 620, Montreal, PQ H2G 2B3, Canada *Tel:* 514-382-0895 *Fax:* 514-384-9139 *E-mail:* info@sdm.qc.ca *Web Site:* www.sdm.qc.ca, pg 561

Seven Springs Press, 11150 Sanders Rd, Tensed, ID 83870 *Tel:* 208-274-2470 *E-mail:* sevenspringscc@aol.com, pg 574

Seven Stories Press, 140 Watts St, New York, NY 10013 *Tel:* 212-226-8760 *Toll Free Tel:* 800-283-3572 *Fax:* 212-226-1411 *E-mail:* info@sevenstories.com *Web Site:* www.sevenstories.com, pg 245

7 Ways to Make a Scene Sizzle, 708 Blossom Hill Rd, No 146, Los Gatos, CA 95032 *Tel:* 408-482-4678 *Fax:* 408-356-1798 *Web Site:* www.blockbusterplots.com, pg 747

Seventh Avenue Literary Agency, 1663 W Seventh Ave, Vancouver, BC V6J 1S4, Canada *Tel:* 604-734-3663 *Fax:* 604-734-8906 *Web Site:* www.seventhavenuelit.com, pg 655

Severn House Publishers Inc, 595 Madison Ave, 15th fl, New York, NY 10022 *Tel:* 212-888-4042 *Fax:* 212-759-5422 *E-mail:* editorial@severnhouse.com; sales@severnhouse.com *Web Site:* www.severnhouse.com, pg 245

Sewanee Writers' Conference, 310 St Lukes Hall, 735 University Ave, Sewanee, TN 37383-1000 *Tel:* 931-598-1141 *Web Site:* www.sewaneewriters.org, pg 747

Mary Sue Seymour, 475 Miner Street Rd, Canton, NY 13617 *Tel:* 315-386-1831 *Fax:* 315-386-1037 *E-mail:* marysue@slic.com *Web Site:* www.theseymouragency.com, pg 655

SF Canada, 10438 86 Ave, Edmonton, AB T6E 2M5, Canada *Tel:* 780-431-0562 *Web Site:* www.sfcanada.ca, pg 699

SFWA Nebula Awards, PO Box 877, Chestertown, MD 21620 *Toll Free Tel:* 888-322-7392 *E-mail:* execdir@sfwa.org *Web Site:* www.sfwa.org, pg 805

Doris P Shalley, 1093 General Sullivan Rd, Washington Crossing, PA 18977 *Tel:* 215-493-3521, pg 611

Shambhala Publications Inc, Horticultural Hall, 300 Massachusetts Ave, Boston, MA 02115 *Tel:* 617-424-0030 *Toll Free Tel:* 888-424-2329 (orders only) *Fax:* 617-236-1563; 303-665-5292 (orders only) *E-mail:* editors@shambhala.com *Web Site:* www.shambhala.com, pg 245

Shane-Armstrong Information Systems, 912 S Elmhurst Ave, Fayetteville, AR 72701 *Tel:* 479-521-8657 *Fax:* 479-521-8657, pg 611

M E Sharpe Inc, 80 Business Park Dr, Suite 202, Armonk, NY 10504 *Tel:* 914-273-1800 *Toll Free Tel:* 800-541-6563 *Fax:* 914-273-2106 *E-mail:* info@mesharpe.com *Web Site:* www.mesharpe.com, pg 246

Mina P Shaughnessy Prize, 26 Broadway, 3rd fl, New York, NY 10004-1789 *Tel:* 646-576-5141 *Fax:* 646-458-0030 *E-mail:* awards@mla.org *Web Site:* www.mla.org, pg 805

The Bernard Shaw Society, Box 1159, Madison Square Sta, New York, NY 10159-1159 *Tel:* 212-989-7833; 212-982-9885, pg 699

Charlotte Sheedy Literary Agency Inc, 65 Bleecker St, 12th fl, New York, NY 10012 *Tel:* 212-780-9800 *Fax:* 212-780-0308 *E-mail:* sheedy@sll.com, pg 655

The Sheep Meadow Press, PO Box 1345, Riverdale-on-Hudson, NY 10471 *Tel:* 718-548-5547 *Fax:* 718-884-0406 *E-mail:* poetry@sheepmeadowpress.com, pg 246

Sheetfed Offset Press Operating, 200 Deer Run Rd, Sewickley, PA 15143-2600 *Tel:* 412-741-6860 *Toll Free Tel:* 800-910-4283 *Fax:* 412-741-2311 *E-mail:* info@gain.net *Web Site:* www.gain.net, pg 747

Sheffield Publishing Co, 9009 Antioch Rd, Salem, WI 53168 *Tel:* 262-843-2281 *Fax:* 262-843-3683 *E-mail:* info@spcbooks.com *Web Site:* www.spcbooks.com, pg 246

Barry Sheinkopf, c/o The Writing Center, 601 Palisade Ave, Englewood Cliffs, NJ 07632 *Tel:* 201-567-4017 *Fax:* 201-567-7202 *E-mail:* 102100.1065@compuserve.com, pg 611

Shenandoah International Playwrights Retreat, 717 Quick's Mill Rd, Staunton, VA 24401 *Tel:* 540-248-4113 *Fax:* 540-248-4113 (call first) *E-mail:* sip@ntelos.net, pg 805

The Shepard Agency, 73 Kingswood Dr, Bethel, CT 06801 *Tel:* 203-790-4230; 203-790-1780 *Fax:* 203-798-2924 *E-mail:* shepardagcy@mindspring.com *Web Site:* home.mindspring.com/~shepardagcy, pg 655

The Robert E Shepard Agency, 1608 Dwight Way, Berkeley, CA 94703-1804 *Tel:* 510-849-3999 *E-mail:* query@shepardagency.com *Web Site:* www.shepardagency.com, pg 655

Sheridan House Inc, 145 Palisade St, Dobbs Ferry, NY 10522 *Tel:* 914-693-2410 *Fax:* 914-693-0776 *E-mail:* info@sheridanhouse.com *Web Site:* www.sheridanhouse.com, pg 246

Sherman Asher Publishing, PO Box 31725, Santa Fe, NM 87594-1725 *Tel:* 505-988-7214 *Fax:* 505-988-7214 *E-mail:* westernedge@santa-fe.net *Web Site:* www.shermanasher.com, pg 246

Ken Sherman & Associates, 9507 Santa Monica Blvd, Suite 211, Beverly Hills, CA 90210 *Tel:* 310-273-8840 *Fax:* 310-271-2875 *E-mail:* ksassociates@earthlink.net, pg 655

Wendy Sherman Associates Inc, 450 Seventh Ave, Suite 3004, New York, NY 10123 *Tel:* 212-279-9027 *Fax:* 212-279-8863, pg 655

Sheron Enterprises Inc, 1035 S Carley Ct, North Bellmore, NY 11710 *Tel:* 516-783-5885, pg 246

Shields Publications, PO Box 669, Eagle River, WI 54521-0669 *Tel:* 715-479-4810 *Fax:* 715-479-3905 *E-mail:* shields@nnex.net *Web Site:* www.wormbooks.com, pg 246

J Gordon Shillingford Publishing, RPO Corydon Ave, Winnipeg, MB R3M 3S3, Canada *Tel:* 204-779-6967 *Fax:* 204-779-6970 *Web Site:* www.jgshillingford.com, pg 561

ShipShape Publishing Inc, 12 Pine St, Chatham, NJ 07928 *Tel:* 973-635-3000 *Fax:* 973-635-4363 *E-mail:* ShipShapeBooks@aol.com *Web Site:* www.ShipShapePublishing.com, pg 574

Shirak, PO Box 414, Glendale, CA 91209-0414 *Tel:* 818-240-6540 *Fax:* 818-240-1295 *E-mail:* hratchh@yahoo.com, pg 246

The Shoe String Press Inc, 2 Linsley St, North Haven, CT 06473 *Tel:* 203-239-2702 *Fax:* 203-239-2568 *E-mail:* info@shoestringpress.com; books@shoestringpress.com *Web Site:* www.shoestringpress.com, pg 246

Shoemaker & Hoard, Publishers, 3704 Macomb St NW, Suite 4, Washington, DC 20016 *Tel:* 202-364-4464 *Fax:* 202-364-4484 *Web Site:* www.shoemakerhoard.com, pg 246

Monica Shoffman-Graves, 70 Transylvania Ave, Key Largo, FL 33037 *Tel:* 305-451-1462 *Fax:* 305-451-1462 *E-mail:* Keysmobill@earthlink.net, pg 611

Shoreline, 23 Sainte Anne, Ste Anne de Bellevue, PQ H9X 1L1, Canada *Tel:* 514-457-5733 *Fax:* 514-457-5733 *E-mail:* shoreline@sympatico.ca *Web Site:* www.shorelinepress.ca, pg 561

Short Mystery Fiction Society (SMFS), 1120 N 45 St, Waco, TX 76710 *Web Site:* groups.yahoo.com/group/shortmystery; www.shortmystery.net, pg 699

Short Story Award/Debut Author Award - The Blaggard Award, 101 W 23 St, Penthouse No 1, New York, NY 10011 *Tel:* 212-353-3495 *E-mail:* editorial@newmystery.tv *Web Site:* www.newmystery.tv, pg 805

Show What You Know® Publishing, 6344 Nicholas Dr, Columbus, OH 43234 *Tel:* 614-764-1211 *Toll Free Tel:* 877-PASSING (727-7464) *Fax:* 614-764-1311 *E-mail:* swyk@eapublishing.com *Web Site:* www.eapublishing.com, pg 246

SI International, 43 E 19 St, New York, NY 10003 *Tel:* 212-254-4996 *Fax:* 212-995-0911 *E-mail:* info@si-i.com *Web Site:* www.si-i.com, pg 667

Robert F Sibert Informational Book Award, 50 E Huron St, Chicago, IL 60611-2795 *Tel:* 312-280-2163 *Toll Free Tel:* 800-545-2433 *Fax:* 312-944-7671 *E-mail:* alsc@ala.org *Web Site:* www.ala.org/alsc, pg 805

Siddha Yoga Publications, 371 Brickman Rd, South Fallsburg, NY 12747 *Tel:* 845-434-2000 *Toll Free Tel:* 888-422-3334 (bookstore) *Fax:* 845-436-2131 *Toll Free Fax:* 888-422-3339 *E-mail:* info@siddhayoga.org; ebookstoreorders@syda.org *Web Site:* www.siddhayoga.org, pg 247

Bobbe Siegel Literary Agency, 41 W 83 St, New York, NY 10024 *Tel:* 212-877-4985 *Fax:* 212-877-4985 *E-mail:* bobbesiegelagency@yahoo.com, pg 655

Rosalie Siegel, International Literary Agent Inc, One Abey Dr, Pennington, NJ 08534 *Tel:* 609-737-1007 *Fax:* 609-737-3708 *E-mail:* rsiegel@ix.netcom.com, pg 655

Sierra Club Books, 85 Second St, 2nd fl, San Francisco, CA 94105 *Tel:* 415-977-5500 *Fax:* 415-977-5792 *E-mail:* books.publishing@sierraclub.org *Web Site:* www.sierraclub.org/books, pg 247

Sierra Club Books Adult Trade Division, 85 Second St, 2nd fl, San Francisco, CA 94105 *Tel:* 415-977-5500 *Fax:* 415-977-5792 *E-mail:* books.publishing@sierraclub.org *Web Site:* ww.sierraclub.org/books, pg 247

Sierra Press, 4988 Gold Leaf Dr, Mariposa, CA 95338 *Tel:* 209-966-5071 *Toll Free Tel:* 800-745-2631 *Fax:* 209-966-5073 *E-mail:* siepress@sti.net *Web Site:* www.nationalparksusa.com, pg 247

Signature Books Publishing LLC, 564 W 400 N, Salt Lake City, UT 84116-3411 *Tel:* 801-531-1483 *Toll Free Tel:* 800-356-5687 (orders) *Fax:* 801-531-1488 *E-mail:* people@signaturebooks.com *Web Site:* www.signaturebooks.com, pg 247

Signpost Books, 8912 192 St SW, Edmonds, WA 98026 *Tel:* 425-776-0370, pg 247

SIL International, 7500 W Camp Wisdom Rd, Dallas, TX 75236 *Tel:* 972-708-7404 *Fax:* 972-708-7363 *E-mail:* academic_books@sil.org *Web Site:* www.ethnologue.com, pg 247

Silicon Press, 25 Beverly Rd, Summit, NJ 07901 *Tel:* 908-273-8919 *Fax:* 908-273-6149 *E-mail:* info@silicon-press.com *Web Site:* www.silicon-press.com, pg 247

Silman-James Press, 3624 Shannon Rd, Los Angeles, CA 90027 *Tel:* 323-661-9922 *Toll Free Tel:* 877-SJP-BOOK (757-2665) *Fax:* 323-661-9933 *E-mail:* silmanjamespress@earthlink.net *Web Site:* www.silmanjamespress.com, pg 247

Dorothy Silver Playwriting Competition, 3505 Mayfield Rd, Cleveland Heights, OH 44118 *Tel:* 216-382-4000 (ext 215) *Fax:* 216-382-5401 *E-mail:* halletheatre@clevejcc.org *Web Site:* www.clevejcc.org, pg 805

Silver Lake Publishing, 11 S Mansfield Rd, Lansdowne, PA 19050 *Tel:* 610-626-8446 *E-mail:* publisher@silverlakepublishing.com *Web Site:* www.silverlakepublishing.com, pg 247

Silver Lake Publishing, 3501 W Sunset Blvd, Los Angeles, CA 90026 *Tel:* 323-663-3082 *Fax:* 323-663-3084 *E-mail:* theeditors@silverlakepub.com; results@silverlakepub.com *Web Site:* www.silverlakepub.com, pg 247

Silver Moon Press, 160 Fifth Ave, New York, NY 10010 *Tel:* 212-242-6499 *Toll Free Tel:* 800-874-3320 *Fax:* 212-242-6799 *E-mail:* mail@silvermoonpress.com *Web Site:* www.silvermoonpress.com, pg 247

Silver Pixel Press, 90 Oser Ave, Hauppauge, NY 11788 *Tel:* 631-645-2522 *Toll Free Tel:* 800-645-2522 *Fax:* 631-273-2557 *Web Site:* www.tiffen.com, pg 248

Silverback Books Inc, 55 New Montgomery St, Suite 503, San Francisco, CA 94105 *Tel:* 415-348-8595 *Toll Free Tel:* 866-348-8595 *Fax:* 415-348-8592 *E-mail:* info@silverbackbooks.com *Web Site:* www.silverbackbooks.com, pg 248

Esther T Silverman, 443 Vermont Place, Columbus, OH 43201 *Tel:* 614-299-1034 *Fax:* 614-299-1034 *E-mail:* esilver@columbus.rr.com, pg 611

Simba Information, 60 Long Ridge Rd, Suite 300, Stamford, CT 06902 *Tel:* 203-325-8193 *Fax:* 203-325-8915 *E-mail:* info@simbanet.com *Web Site:* www.simbanet.com, pg 248

Simcha Press, 3201 SW 15 St, Deerfield Beach, FL 33442-8190 *Tel:* 954-360-0909 ext 212 *Toll Free Tel:* 800-851-9100 ext 212 *Toll Free Fax:* 800-424-7652 *E-mail:* simchapress@hcibooks.com *Web Site:* www.simchapress.com, pg 248

Francis B Simkins Award, University of Georgia, Dept of History, Athens, GA 30602-1602 *Tel:* 706-542-8848 *Fax:* 706-542-2455 *Web Site:* www.uga.edu/~sha, pg 805

The John Simmons Short Fiction Award, Univ of Iowa, Writers Workshop, 102 Dey House, 507 N Clinton St, Iowa City, IA 52242 *Tel:* 319-335-0416 *Toll Free Tel:* 800-553-4692 (ext 0416) *Fax:* 319-335-0420, pg 806

Simon & Pierre Publishing Co Ltd, 8 Market St, 2nd fl, Toronto, ON M5E 1M6, Canada *Tel:* 416-214-5544 *Toll Free Tel:* 800-565-9523 (orders: Canada & US) *Fax:* 416-214-5556 *Toll Free Fax:* 800-221-9985 (orders) *E-mail:* info@dundurn.com *Web Site:* www.dundurn.com, pg 561

Simon & Schuster, 1230 Avenue of the Americas, New York, NY 10020 *Tel:* 212-698-7000 *Toll Free Tel:* 800-223-2348 (cust serv); 800-223-2336 (orders) *Toll Free Fax:* 800-943-9831 (orders) *Web Site:* www.simonsays.com, pg 248

Simon & Schuster Adult Publishing Group, 1230 Avenue of the Americas, New York, NY 10020 *Tel:* 212-698-7000 *Toll Free Tel:* 800-223-2336 (orders); 800-223-2348 (cust serv), pg 248

Simon & Schuster Audio, 1230 Avenue of the Americas, New York, NY 10020 *Tel:* 212-698-7664 *E-mail:* audiopub@simonandschuster.com *Web Site:* www.simonsaysaudio.com, pg 248

Simon & Schuster Children's Publishing, 1230 Avenue of the Americas, New York, NY 10020 *Tel:* 212-698-7000 *Web Site:* www.simonsayskids.com, pg 248

Simon & Schuster Inc, 1230 Avenue of the Americas, New York, NY 10020 *Tel:* 212-698-7000 *Fax:* 212-698-7007 *Web Site:* www.simonsays.com, pg 249

Simon & Schuster Online, 1230 Avenue of the Americas, New York, NY 10020 *Tel:* 212-698-7547 *Fax:* 212-632-8070 *E-mail:* ssonline@simonsays.com *Web Site:* www.simonsays.com; www.simonsayskids.com; www.simonsaysshop.com, pg 249

Simon & Schuster Sales & Distribution, 1230 Avenue of the Americas, New York, NY 10020 *Tel:* 212-698-7000, pg 249

Charlie May Simon Award, Arkansas Dept of Education, Rm 401-B, No 4 Capitol Mall, Little Rock, AR 72201 *Tel:* 501-682-4232 *Fax:* 501-682-4441 *Web Site:* arkedu.state.ar.us, pg 806

Sinauer Associates Inc, 23 Plumtree Rd, Sunderland, MA 01375-0407 *Tel:* 413-549-4300 *Fax:* 413-549-1118 *E-mail:* publish@sinauer.com *Web Site:* www.sinauer.com, pg 248

Evelyn Singer Agency Inc, PO Box 594, White Plains, NY 10602-0594 *Tel:* 914-949-1147 *Fax:* 914-948-5565, pg 655

Six Gallery Press, 4620 Los Feliz Blvd, Suite 1, Los Angeles, CA 90027 *E-mail:* sgpwc@yahoo.com *Web Site:* www.sixgallerypress.com, pg 249

Six Strings Music Publishing, PO Box 7718-151, Torrance, CA 90504-9118 *Toll Free Tel:* 800-784-0203 *Fax:* 310-362-8864 *Web Site:* www.sixstringsmusicpub.com, pg 249

SkillPath Publications, 6900 Squibb Rd, Mission, KS 66202 *Tel:* 913-362-3900 *Toll Free Tel:* 800-873-7545 *Fax:* 913-362-4264 *E-mail:* bookstore@skillpath.net *Web Site:* www.ourbookstore.com, pg 249

Skinner House Books, 25 Beacon St, Boston, MA 02108-2800 *Tel:* 617-742-2100 *Fax:* 617-742-7025 *E-mail:* skinner_house@uua.org *Web Site:* www.uua.org/skinner/index.html, pg 249

Skipping Stones Honor Awards, 1309 Lincoln St, Eugene, OR 97401 *Tel:* 541-342-4956 *E-mail:* info@skippingstones.org *Web Site:* www.skippingstones.org, pg 806

Irene Skolnick Literary Agency, 22 W 23 St, 5th fl, New York, NY 10010 *Tel:* 212-727-3648 *Fax:* 212-727-1024 *E-mail:* sirene35@aol.com, pg 656

Sky Oaks Productions Inc, 19544 Sky Oaks Way, Los Gatos, CA 95030 *Tel:* 408-395-7600 *Fax:* 408-395-8440 *E-mail:* tprworld@aol.com *Web Site:* www.tprworld.com, pg 250

Sky Publishing Corp, 49 Bay State Rd, Cambridge, MA 02138-1200 *Tel:* 617-864-7360 *Toll Free Tel:* 800-253-0245 *Fax:* 617-864-6117 *Web Site:* skyandtelescope.com, pg 250

SkyLight Paths Publishing, Sunset Farm Offices, Rte 4, Woodstock, VT 05091 *Tel:* 802-457-4000 *Toll Free Tel:* 800-962-4544 *Fax:* 802-457-4004 *E-mail:* editorial@skylightpaths.com *Web Site:* www.skylightpaths.com, pg 250

Skysong Press, 35 Peter St S, Orillia, ON L3V 5A8, Canada *E-mail:* skysong@bconnex.net *Web Site:* www.bconnex.net/~skysong/index.html, pg 561

SLA Annual Conference, 313 S Patrick St, Alexandria, VA 22314 *Tel:* 202-234-4700 *Fax:* 703-647-4901 *E-mail:* sla@sla.org *Web Site:* www.sla.org, pg 747

SLA Workshops, 313 S Patrick St, Alexandria, VA 22314 *Tel:* 703-647-4900 *Fax:* 703-647-4901 *E-mail:* sla@sla.org *Web Site:* www.sla.org, pg 747

Slack Incorporated, 6900 Grove Rd, Thorofare, NJ 08086-9447 *Tel:* 856-848-1000 *Toll Free Tel:* 800-257-8290 *Fax:* 856-853-5991 *Web Site:* www.slackbooks.com, pg 250

SLC Enterprises Inc, 6965 Oakbrook SE, Grand Rapids, MI 49546 *Tel:* 616-942-2665 (answering serv & voice mail) *Toll Free Tel:* 800-420-7222 *Toll Free Fax:* 800-420-7222 *E-mail:* candp5@comcast.net, pg 656

Sleeping Bear Press™, 310 N Main St, Suite 300, Chelsea, MI 48118 *Tel:* 734-475-4411 *Toll Free Tel:* 800-487-2323 *Fax:* 734-475-0787 *E-mail:* sleepingbear@thomson.com *Web Site:* www.sleepingbearpress.com, pg 250

Sligo Literary Agency LLC, 74-923 Hwy 111, Suite 173, Indian Wells, CA 92210 *Tel:* 760-340-6640 *Fax:* 760-340-4320 *E-mail:* ricsligo@aol.com, pg 656

Beverley Slopen Literary Agency, 131 Bloor St W, Suite 711, Toronto, ON M5S 1S3, Canada *Tel:* 416-964-9598 *Fax:* 416-921-7726 *E-mail:* beverley@slopenagency.ca *Web Site:* www.slopenagency.on.ca, pg 656

Bernice Slote Award, University of Nebraska, 201 Andrews Hall, Lincoln, NE 68588 *Tel:* 402-472-0911 *E-mail:* kgrey2@unl.edu *Web Site:* www.unl.edu/schooner/psmain.htm, pg 806

Small Press Center, 20 W 44 St, New York, NY 10036 *Tel:* 212-764-7021 *Fax:* 212-354-5365 *E-mail:* info@smallpress.org *Web Site:* www.smallpress.org, pg 699

Small Publishers, Artists & Writers Network (SPAWN), 323 E Matilija St, Suite 110, PMB 123, Ojai, CA 93023 *Tel:* 818-886-4281 *Fax:* 818-886-3320 *Web Site:* www.spawn.org, pg 699

Small Publishers Association of North America (SPAN), 425 Cedar St, Buena Vista, CO 81211 *Tel:* 719-395-4790 *Fax:* 719-395-8374 *E-mail:* span@spannet.org *Web Site:* www.spannet.org, pg 699, 747, 754

Smallwood Center for Newfoundland Studies, Memorial University of Newfoundland, St John's, NF A1C 5S7, Canada *Tel:* 709-737-7474 *Fax:* 709-737-7560 *E-mail:* iser@mun.ca *Web Site:* www.mun.ca/smallwood, pg 561

Smart Luck Publishers, PO Box 81770, Las Vegas, NV 89180-1770 *Tel:* 702-365-1818 *Toll Free Tel:* 800-945-4245 *Fax:* 850-937-6999 *Toll Free Fax:* 800-876-4245 *E-mail:* books@smartluck.com *Web Site:* www.smartluck.com, pg 574

Smith & Kraus Inc Publishers, 177 Lyme Rd, Hanover, NH 03755 *Tel:.*603-643-6431 (edit); 603-669-7032 (cust serv) *Toll Free Tel:* 800-288-2881 (orders only) *Fax:* 603-643-1831 *E-mail:* sandk@sover.net *Web Site:* www.smithkraus.com, pg 250

M Lee Smith Publishers LLC, 5201 Virginia Way, Brentwood, TN 37027 *Tel:* 615-373-7517 *Toll Free Tel:* 800-274-6774 *Fax:* 615-373-5183 *Web Site:* www.mleesmith.com, pg 250

Peter Smith Publisher Inc, 5 Lexington Ave, Magnolia, MA 01930 *Tel:* 978-525-3562 *Fax:* 978-525-3674, pg 250

The Smith Publishers, 69 Joralemon St, Brooklyn, NY 11201-4003 *Tel:* 718-834-1212 *Fax:* 718-834-1212 *E-mail:* thesmith1@aol.com; artsend@ma.ultranet.com *Web Site:* members.aol.com/thesmith1, pg 250

Roger W Smith, 59-67 58 Rd, Maspeth, NY 11378-3211 *Tel:* 718-416-1334 *E-mail:* roger.smith106@verizon.net, pg 611

Smith/Skolnik Literary Management, 963 Belvidere, Plainfield, NJ 07060 *Tel:* 908-822-1870 *Fax:* 908-822-1871, pg 656

Steve Smith Autosports, PO Box 11631, Santa Ana, CA 92711-1631 *Tel:* 714-639-7681 *Fax:* 714-639-9741 *E-mail:* sales@ssapubl.com *Web Site:* www.ssapubl.com, pg 250

Valerie Smith, Literary Agent, 1746 Rte 44-55, Modena, NY 12548 *Tel:* 845-883-5848, pg 656

Smithsonian Federal Series Section, 750 Ninth St NW, Suite 4300, Washington, DC 20560-0950 *Tel:* 202-275-2233 *Fax:* 202-275-2274, pg 251

Smithsonian Institution Press, 750 Ninth St NW, Suite 4300, Washington, DC 20560-0950 *Tel:* 202-275-2300 *Fax:* 202-275-2274 *E-mail:* inquiries@sipress.si.edu *Web Site:* www.sipress.si.edu, pg 251

Smokin' Donut Books, 381 Seaside Dr, Jamestown, RI 02835 *Tel:* 401-423-2400 *Toll Free Tel:* 877-474-8738 *Fax:* 401-423-2700 *E-mail:* info@smokindonut.com *Web Site:* www.smokindonut.com, pg 574

Smyth & Helwys Publishing Inc, 6316 Peake Rd, Macon, GA 31210 *Tel:* 478-757-1305 *Toll Free Tel:* 800-747-3016; 800-568-1248 *Fax:* 478-757-0564 *E-mail:* market@helwys.com *Web Site:* www.helwys.com, pg 251

Michael Snell Literary Agency, PO Box 1206, Truro, MA 02666-1206 *Tel:* 508-349-3718, pg 656

Kay Snow Literary Contest, 9045 SW Barbur Blvd, Suite 5-A, Portland, OR 97219 *Tel:* 503-452-1592 *Fax:* 503-452-0372 *E-mail:* wilwrite@willamettewriters.com *Web Site:* www.willamettewriters.com, pg 806

Snow Lion Publications Inc, 605 W State St, Ithaca, NY 14850 *Tel:* 607-273-8519 *Toll Free Tel:* 800-950-0313 *Fax:* 607-273-8508 *E-mail:* tibet@snowlionpub.com *Web Site:* www.snowlionpub.com, pg 251

Tom Snyder Productions, 80 Coolidge Hill Rd, Watertown, MA 02472-5003 *Tel:* 617-926-6000 *Toll Free Tel:* 800-342-0236 *Fax:* 617-926-6222 *E-mail:* ask@tomsnyder.com *Web Site:* www.tomsnyder.com, pg 251

Sobel Weber Associates Inc, 146 E 19 St, New York, NY 10003 *Tel:* 212-420-8585 *Fax:* 212-505-1017 *E-mail:* info@sobelweber.com *Web Site:* www.sobelweber.com, pg 656

Social Sciences & Humanities Research Council of Canada (SSHRC), 350 Albert St, Ottawa, ON K1P 6G4, Canada *Tel:* 613-992-0691 *Fax:* 613-992-1787 *E-mail:* z-info@sshrc.ca *Web Site:* www.sshrc.ca, pg 699

Society for Human Resource Management (SHRM), 1800 Duke St, Alexandria, VA 22314 *Tel:* 703-548-3440 *Toll Free Tel:* 800-444-5006 (orders) *Fax:* 703-836-0367; 770-442-9742 (orders) *E-mail:* shrm@shrm.org; shrmstore@shrm.org *Web Site:* www.shrm.org, pg 251

Society for Industrial & Applied Mathematics, 3600 University City Science Ctr, Philadelphia, PA 19104-2688 *Tel:* 215-382-9800 *Toll Free Tel:* 800-447-7426 *Fax:* 215-386-7999 *E-mail:* siam@siam.org *Web Site:* www.siam.org, pg 251

Society for Mining, Metallurgy & Exploration Inc, PO Box 277002, Littleton, CO 80127-7002 *Tel:* 303-973-9550 *Toll Free Tel:* 800-763-3132 *Fax:* 303-973-3845 *E-mail:* sme@smenet.org *Web Site:* www.smenet.org, pg 251

Society for Protective Coating, 40 24 St, 6th fl, Pittsburgh, PA 15222-4656 *Tel:* 412-281-2331 *Fax:* 412-281-9992 *E-mail:* books@sspc.org *Web Site:* www.sspc.org, pg 251

Society for Scholarly Publishing, 10200 W 44 Ave, Suite 304, Wheat Ridge, CO 80033-2840 *Tel:* 303-422-3914 *Fax:* 303-422-8894 *E-mail:* ssp@resourcecenter.com; info@sspnet.org *Web Site:* www.sspnet.org, pg 699

Society for Technical Communication, 901 N Stuart St, Suite 904, Arlington, VA 22203-1822 *Tel:* 703-522-4114 *Fax:* 703-522-2075 *E-mail:* stc@stc.org *Web Site:* www.stc.org, pg 699, 747

Society for the History of Authorship, Reading & Publishing Inc (SHARP), SHARP/University of South Carolina, PO Box 5816, Columbia, SC 29250 *Tel:* 803-777-5075 *Fax:* 803-782-0699 *E-mail:* membership@sharpweb.org *Web Site:* www.sharpweb.org, pg 700

Society of American Archivists, 527 S Wells St, 5th fl, Chicago, IL 60607 *Tel:* 312-922-0140 *Fax:* 312-347-1452 *E-mail:* info@archivists.org *Web Site:* www.archivists.org, pg 251

Society of American Business Editors & Writers Inc, Univ of Missouri, School of Journalism, 76 Gannett Hall, 134 Neff Annex, Columbia, MO 65211-1200 *Tel:* 573-882-7862 *Fax:* 573-884-1372 *E-mail:* sabew@missouri.edu *Web Site:* www.sabew.org, pg 700

Society of American Travel Writers Foundation, 1500 Sunday Dr, Suite 102, Raleigh, NC 27607 *Tel:* 919-861-5586 *Fax:* 919-787-4916 *E-mail:* satw@satw.org *Web Site:* www.satw.org, pg 700

Society of Biblical Literature, The Luce Ctr, Suite 350, 825 Houston Mill Rd, Atlanta, GA 30329 *Tel:* 404-727-2325 *Fax:* 802-864-7626 *E-mail:* sbl@sbl-site.org *Web Site:* www.sbl-site.org, pg 251

Society of Children's Book Writers & Illustrators (SCBWI), 8271 Beverly Blvd, Los Angeles, CA 90048 *Tel:* 323-782-1010 *Fax:* 323-782-1892 *E-mail:* membership@scbwi.org *Web Site:* www.scbwi.org, pg 700

Society of Environmental Toxicology & Chemistry, 1010 N 12 Ave, Pensacola, FL 32501-3370 *Tel:* 850-469-9777; 850-469-1500 *Fax:* 850-469-9778 *E-mail:* setac@setac.org *Web Site:* www.setac.org, pg 252

Society of Exploration Geophysicists, 8801 S Yale, Tulsa, OK 74137 *Tel:* 918-497-5500 *Fax:* 918-497-5557 *Web Site:* www.seg.org, pg 252

Society of Illustrators (SI), 128 E 63 St, New York, NY 10021-7303 *Tel:* 212-838-2560 *Fax:* 212-838-2561 *E-mail:* info@societyillustrators.org *Web Site:* www.societyillustrators.org, pg 700

Society of Manufacturing Engineers, One SME Dr, Dearborn, MI 48121 *Tel:* 313-271-1500 *Toll Free Tel:* 800-733-4763 (cust serv) *Fax:* 313-271-2861 *Web Site:* www.sme.org, pg 252

The Society of Midland Authors (SMA), PO Box 10419, Chicago, IL 60610-0419 *Tel:* 773-506-7578 *Fax:* 773-784-5900 *E-mail:* info@midlandauthors.com *Web Site:* www.midlandauthors.com, pg 700

The Society of Midland Authors Awards, PO Box 10419, Chicago, IL 60610-0419 *Tel:* 773-506-7578 *Fax:* 773-784-5900 *E-mail:* info@midlandauthors.com *Web Site:* www.midlandauthors.com, pg 806

Society of Motion Picture & Television Engineers (SMPTE), 595 W Hartsdale Ave, White Plains, NY 10607-1824 *Tel:* 914-761-1100 *Fax:* 914-761-3115 *E-mail:* smpte@smpte.org *Web Site:* www.smpte.org, pg 700

Society of National Association Publications (SNAP), 8405 Greensboro Dr, No 800, McLean, VA 22102 *Tel:* 703-506-3285 *Fax:* 703-506-3266 *E-mail:* snapinfo@snaponline.org *Web Site:* www.snaponline.org, pg 700

The Society of Naval Architects & Marine Engineers, 601 Pavonia Ave, Jersey City, NJ 07306-2907 *Tel:* 201-798-4800 *Toll Free Tel:* 800-798-2188 *Fax:* 201-798-4975 *Web Site:* www.sname.org, pg 252

The Society of Professional Journalists, Eugene S Pulliam National Journalism Ctr, 3909 N Meridian St, Indianapolis, IN 46208 *Tel:* 317-927-8000 *Fax:* 317-920-4789 *E-mail:* spj@spj.org *Web Site:* www.spj.org, pg 700

The Society of Southwestern Authors (SSA), PO Box 30355, Tucson, AZ 85751-0355 *Tel:* 520-546-9382 *Fax:* 520-296-0409 *E-mail:* wporter202@aol.com *Web Site:* www.azstarnet.com/nonprofit/ssa, pg 700

The Society of Southwestern Authors (SSA), PO Box 30355, Tucson, AZ 85751-0355 *Tel:* 520-546-9382 *Fax:* 520-296-0409 *Web Site:* www.azstarnet.com/nonprofit/ssa, pg 806

Society of Spanish & Spanish-American Studies, Univ Colorado, Society for Spanish & Spanish American Studies, Dept Spanish & Portuguese, Boulder, CO 80309-0278 *Tel:* 303-492-5900 *Fax:* 303-492-3699 *E-mail:* sssas@colorado.edu *Web Site:* www.colorado.edu/spanish/fpubs.html, pg 252

Socrates Media, 227 W Monroe St, Suite 500, Chicago, IL 60606 *Tel:* 312-762-5600 *Toll Free Tel:* 800-822-4566 *Web Site:* www.socrates.com, pg 252

Software & Information Industry Association (SIIA), 1090 Vermont Ave NW, 6th fl, Washington, DC 20005 *Tel:* 202-289-7442 *Fax:* 202-289-7097 *E-mail:* info@siia.net *Web Site:* www.siia.net, pg 700

Sogides Ltee, 955 rue Amherst, Montreal, PQ H2L 3K4, Canada *Tel:* 514-523-1182 *Toll Free Tel:* 800-361-4806 *Fax:* 514-597-0370 *Web Site:* www.sogides.com; www.edhomme.com, pg 561

Soho Press Inc, 853 Broadway, New York, NY 10003 *Tel:* 212-260-1900 *Fax:* 212-260-1902 *E-mail:* editor@sohopress.com *Web Site:* sohopress.com, pg 252

Soil Science Society of America, 677 S Segoe Rd, Madison, WI 53711-1086 *Tel:* 608-273-8095 *Fax:* 608-273-2021 *E-mail:* headquarters@soils.org *Web Site:* www.soils.org, pg 252

Solano Press Books, PO Box 773, Point Arena, CA 95468 *Tel:* 707-884-4508 *Toll Free Tel:* 800-931-9373 *Fax:* 707-884-4109 *E-mail:* spbooks@solano.com *Web Site:* www.solano.com, pg 252

Soli Deo Gloria Publications, 451 Millers Run Rd, Morgan, PA 15064 *Tel:* 412-221-1901 *Toll Free Tel:* 888-266-5734 *Fax:* 412-221-1902 *Web Site:* www.sdgbooks.com, pg 252

Solid Gold Marketing Design Workshops, PO Box 2373, La Mesa, CA 91943-2373 *Tel:* 858-569-6555 *Toll Free Tel:* 800-932-0973 *Fax:* 858-569-5924 *Web Site:* www.sparklepresentations.com, pg 747

Solucient, 10007 Church St, Suite 700, Evanston, IL 60201 *Tel:* 847-424-4400 *Toll Free Tel:* 800-366-7526 *Fax:* 847-332-1768 *E-mail:* pubs@solucient.com *Web Site:* www.solucient.com, pg 252

SOM Publishing, 163 Moon Valley Rd, Windyville, MO 65783 *Tel:* 417-345-8411 *Fax:* 417-345-6668 (call 417-345-8411 before faxing) *E-mail:* som@som.org *Web Site:* www.som.org, pg 252

Soncino Press, 123 Ditmas Ave, Brooklyn, NY 11218 *Tel:* 718-972-6200 *Toll Free Tel:* 800-972-6201 *Fax:* 718-972-6204 *E-mail:* info@soncino.com *Web Site:* www.soncino.com, pg 253

Mark Sonnenfeld, 45-08 Old Millstone Dr, East Windsor, NJ 08520 *Tel:* 609-443-0646 *Web Site:* experimentalpoet.com, pg 253

Sophia Institute Press, PO Box 5284, Manchester, NH 03108 *Tel:* 603-641-9344 *Toll Free Tel:* 800-888-9344 *Fax:* 603-641-8108 *Toll Free Fax:* 888-288-2259 *E-mail:* orders@sophiainstitute.com *Web Site:* www.sophiainstitute.com, pg 253

Sophie Kerr Prize, c/o College Relations Office, 300 Washington Ave, Chestertown, MD 21620 *Tel:* 410-778-2800 *Toll Free Tel:* 800-422-1782 *Fax:* 410-810-7150 *Web Site:* www.washcoll.edu, pg 806

Sopris West Educational Services, 4093 Specialty Place, Longmont, CO 80504 *Tel:* 303-651-2829 *Toll Free Tel:* 800-547-6747 *Fax:* 303-776-5934 *E-mail:* customerservice@sopriswest.com *Web Site:* www.sopriswest.com, pg 253

Sorin Books, 19113 Douglas Rd, Notre Dame, IN 46556 *Tel:* 574-287-2831 *Toll Free Tel:* 800-282-1865 *Fax:* 574-239-2904 *Toll Free Fax:* 800-282-5681 *E-mail:* sorinbk@nd.edu *Web Site:* www.sorinbooks.com, pg 253

SOS Publications, 43 De Normandie Ave, Fair Haven, NJ 07704-3303 *Tel:* 732-530-5896; 732-530-3199 *Fax:* 732-530-5896 *Web Site:* www.netlabs.net/hp/sosjs, pg 253

Gordon Soules Book Publishers Ltd, 1359 Ambleside Lane, West Vancouver, BC V7T 2Y9, Canada *Tel:* 604-922-6588; 604-688-5466 *Fax:* 604-688-5442 *E-mail:* books@gordonsoules.com *Web Site:* www.gordonsoules.com, pg 561

Sound & Vision, 359 Riverdale Ave, Toronto, ON M4J 1A4, Canada *Tel:* 416-465-2828 *Fax:* 416-465-0755 *Web Site:* www.soundandvision.com, pg 562

Soundprints, 353 Main Ave, Norwalk, CT 06851 *Tel:* 203-846-2274 *Toll Free Tel:* 800-228-7839; 800-577-2413, ext 118 (orders) *Fax:* 203-846-1776 *E-mail:* Soundprints@soundprints.com *Web Site:* www.soundprints.com, pg 253

Sourcebooks Inc, 1935 Brookdale Rd, Suite 139, Naperville, IL 60563 *Tel:* 630-961-3900 *Toll Free Tel:* 800-432-7444 *Fax:* 630-961-2168 *E-mail:* info@sourcebooks.com *Web Site:* www.sourcebooks.com, pg 253

South Carolina Bar, Continuing Legal Education Div, 950 Taylor St, Columbia, SC 29201 *Tel:* 803-771-0333 *Toll Free Tel:* 800-768-7787 *Fax:* 803-252-8427 *E-mail:* scbar-info@scbar.org *Web Site:* www.scbar.org, pg 254

South Carolina Dept of Archives & History, 8301 Parklane Rd, Columbia, SC 29223 *Tel:* 803-896-6100 *Fax:* 803-896-6198 *Web Site:* www.state.sc.us/scdah/, pg 254

South End Press, 7 Brookline St, No 1, Cambridge, MA 02139-4146 *Tel:* 617-547-4002 *Fax:* 617-547-1333 *E-mail:* southend@southendpress.org *Web Site:* www.southendpress.org, pg 254

South Platte Press, PO Box 163, David City, NE 68632-0163 *Tel:* 402-367-3554 *E-mail:* railroads@alltel.net *Web Site:* www.southplattepress.net, pg 254

South-Western, A Thomson Business, 5191 Natorp Blvd, Mason, OH 45040 *Tel:* 513-229-1000 *Toll Free Tel:* 800-543-0487 *Fax:* 513-229-1025 *Web Site:* www.thomson.com, pg 254

Southampton Writers' Conference, 239 Montauk Hwy, Southampton, NY 11968 *Tel:* 631-287-8175 *Fax:* 631-287-8253 *E-mail:* summer@southampton.liu.edu *Web Site:* www.southampton.liu.edu/summer, pg 747

Southeast Asia Publications, Northern Illinois University, Center for Southeast Asian Studies, Adams 412, DeKalb, IL 60115 *Tel:* 815-753-5790 *Fax:* 815-753-1776 *E-mail:* seap@niu.edu *Web Site:* www.niu.edu/cseas/seap, pg 254

Southeast Booksellers Association (SEBA), 2611 Forest Dr, Suite 124, Columbia, SC 29204 *Tel:* 803-779-0118 *Toll Free Tel:* 800-331-9617 *Fax:* 803-779-0113 *Web Site:* www.sebaweb.org; arts.sebaweb.org (authors round the south); tradeshow.sebaweb.org (virtual trade show), pg 700

Southeast Literary Agency, PO Box 910, Sharpes, FL 32959-0910 *Tel:* 321-632-5019, pg 656

Southeastern Theatre Conference New Play Project (SETC), 1114 Whitehall Rd, Murfreesboro, TN 37130 *Tel:* 336-272-3645 *Fax:* 336-272-8810 *E-mail:* setc@sectonline.com *Web Site:* www.setc.org, pg 806

Southern Books Competition, 1438 W Peachtree St NW, Suite 200, Atlanta, GA 30309-2955 *Tel:* 404-892-0943 *Fax:* 404-892-7879 *Web Site:* www.solinet.net, pg 806

Southern California Writers' Conference/Los Angeles/San Diego/Palm Springs, 1010 University Ave, Suite 54, San Diego, CA 92103 *Tel:* 619-233-4651 *Fax:* 253-390-8577 *E-mail:* wewrite@writersconference.com *Web Site:* www.writersconference.com, pg 747

Southern Historical Press Inc, 275 W Broad St, Greenville, SC 29601-2634 *Tel:* 864-233-2346 *Fax:* 864-233-2349, pg 254

Southern Illinois University Press, PO Box 3697, Carbondale, IL 62902-3697 *Tel:* 618-453-2281 *Toll Free Tel:* 800-346-2680 *Fax:* 618-453-1221 *Toll Free Fax:* 800-346-2681 *E-mail:* jstetter@siu.edu *Web Site:* www.siu.edu/~siupress, pg 254

Southern Methodist University Press, 314 Fondren Library W, 6404 Hill Top Lane, Dallas, TX 75275 *Tel:* 214-768-1430; 214-768-1432 *Fax:* 214-768-1428, pg 255

Southern Playwrights Competition, 700 Pelham Rd N, Jacksonville, AL 36265-1602 *Tel:* 256-782-5414 *Fax:* 256-782-5441 *Web Site:* www.jsu.edu/depart/english/southpla.htm, pg 806

The Southern Review/LSU Short Fiction Award, Louisiana State University, 43 Allen Hall, Baton Rouge, LA 70803-5005 *Tel:* 225-578-5108 *Fax:* 225-578-5098 *E-mail:* bmacon@lsu.edu *Web Site:* www.lsu.edu/thesouthernreview, pg 806

Southfarm Press, Publisher, PO Box 1296, Middletown, CT 06457-1296 *Tel:* 860-346-8798 *Fax:* 860-347-9931 *E-mail:* southfarm@ix.netcom.com *Web Site:* www.war-books.com; www.wandahaan.com, pg 255

SouthWest Writers Conference Series, 3721 Morris St NE, Suite A, Albuquerque, NM 87111-3611 *Tel:* 505-265-9485 *Fax:* 505-265-9483 *E-mail:* swriters@aol.com *Web Site:* www.southwestwriters.org, pg 747

Sovereign Award Outstanding Newspaper Story, Outstanding Feature Story, Woodbine Sales Pavilion, 555 Rexdale Blvd, Rexdale, ON M9W 5L2, Canada *Tel:* 416-675-7756 *Fax:* 416-675-6378 *E-mail:* jockeyclub@bellnet.ca *Web Site:* www.jockeyclubcanada.com, pg 806

The Sow's Ear Poetry Prize & The Sow's Ear Chapbook Prize, 355 Mount Lebanon Rd, Donalds, SC 29638-9115 *Tel:* 864-379-8061, pg 807

Soyfoods Center, PO Box 234, Lafayette, CA 94549-0234 *Tel:* 925-283-2991, pg 255

Spanish Evangelical Publishers Association (SEPA)/Asociacion de Editores Evangelicos Hispanos, 1370 NW 88 Ave, Miami, FL 33172 *Tel:* 305-592-6136 *Fax:* 786-331-7720 *E-mail:* sepa@bmsi.com *Web Site:* www.sepalit.org, pg 700

Speakers Guild, PO Box 1540, Sandwich, MA 02563-1540 *Tel:* 508-888-6702 *Fax:* 508-888-6771 *E-mail:* speakers@cape.com *Web Site:* www.speakersguild.com, pg 670

Special Libraries Association (SLA), 313 S Patrick St, Alexandria, VA 22314 *Tel:* 703-647-4900 *Fax:* 703-647-4901 *E-mail:* sla@sla.org *Web Site:* www.sla.org, pg 701

Specialized Systems Consultants Inc, PO Box 55549, Seattle, WA 98155-0549 *Tel:* 206-782-7733 *Fax:* 206-782-7191 *E-mail:* sales@ssc.com; info@ssc.com *Web Site:* www.ssc.com, pg 255

Speck Press, 1635 S Fairfax St, Denver, CO 80222 *Tel:* 303-777-0539 *Toll Free Tel:* 800-996-9783 *Fax:* 303-756-8011 *E-mail:* books@speckpress.com *Web Site:* www.speckpress.com, pg 255

Spectrum Literary Agency, 320 Central Park W, Suite 1-D, New York, NY 10025 *Tel:* 212-362-4323 *Fax:* 212-362-4562 *Web Site:* www.spectrumliteraryagency.com, pg 656

The Speech Bin Inc, 1965 25 Ave, Vero Beach, FL 32960 *Tel:* 772-770-0007 *Toll Free Tel:* 800-4-SPEECH (477-3324) *Fax:* 772-770-0006 *Toll Free Fax:* 888-FAX-2-BIN (329-2246) *E-mail:* info@speechbin.com *Web Site:* www.speechbin.com, pg 255

Robert Speller & Sons, Publishers Inc, Times Sq Sta, New York, NY 10108-0461 *Tel:* 212-473-0333, pg 255

Spence Publishing Co, 111 Cole St, Dallas, TX 75207 *Tel:* 214-939-1700 *Fax:* 214-939-1800 *Web Site:* www.spencepublishing.com, pg 255

Sphinx Publishing, 1935 Brookdale Rd, Suite 139, Naperville, IL 60563 *Tel:* 630-961-3900 *Toll Free Tel:* 800-43-bright *Fax:* 630-961-2168 *E-mail:* info@sourcebooks.com *Web Site:* www.sourcebooks.com, pg 255

SPIE, International Society for Optical Engineering, 1000 20 St, Bellingham, WA 98225 *Tel:* 360-676-3290 *Fax:* 360-647-1445 *E-mail:* spie@spie.org *Web Site:* www.spie.org, pg 255

The Spieler Agency, 154 W 57 St, 13th fl, Rm 135, New York, NY 10019 *Tel:* 212-757-4439 *Web Site:* spieleragency.com, pg 656

Spinsters Ink, 191 University Blvd, Suite 300, Denver, CO 80206 *Tel:* 303-761-5552 *Toll Free Tel:* 800-301-6860; 800-729-6423 (orders) *E-mail:* spinster@spinstersink.com *Web Site:* www.spinsters-ink.com, pg 255

SPIRAL Books, 70 Cider Mill Rd, Bedford, NH 03110-4200 *Tel:* 603-471-1917 *Fax:* 603-471-1977 *E-mail:* order@spiralbooks.com *Web Site:* www.spiralbooks.com, pg 255

Helen Spiroplaus, 4916 Amberton Dr, Powder Springs, GA 30127 *Tel:* 770-419-8308 *Fax:* 770-419-9836 *E-mail:* spiro@bellsouth.net, pg 611

Philip G Spitzer Literary Agency, 50 Talmage Farm Lane, East Hampton, NY 11937 *Tel:* 631-329-3650 *Fax:* 631-329-3651 *E-mail:* spitzer516@aol.com, pg 657

Spizzirri Press Inc, PO Box 9397, Rapid City, SD 57709-9397 *Tel:* 605-348-2749 *Toll Free Tel:* 800-325-9819 *Fax:* 605-348-6251 *Toll Free Fax:* 800-322-9819 *E-mail:* spizzpub@aol.com *Web Site:* www.spizzirri.com, pg 256

Split Rock Arts Program, 360 Coffey Hall, 1420 Eckles Ave, St Paul, MN 55108-6084 *Tel:* 612-625-8100 *Fax:* 612-624-6210 *E-mail:* srap@cce.umn.edu *Web Site:* www.cce.umn.edu/splitrockarts, pg 747

The Sporting News Publishing Co, A Vulcan Sports Media Company, 10176 Corporate Square Dr, Suite 200, St Louis, MO 63132 *Tel:* 314-997-7111 *Fax:* 314-993-7726 *Web Site:* www.sportingnews.com, pg 256

Sports Books Publisher Inc, 278 Robert St, Toronto, ON M5S 2K8, Canada *Tel:* 416-922-0860 *Fax:* 416-966-9022 *E-mail:* sbp@sportsbookpub.com *Web Site:* www.sportsbookspub.com, pg 562

Sports Publishing LLC, 804 N Neil St, Champaign, IL 61820 *Tel:* 217-363-2072 *Toll Free Tel:* 877-424-BOOK (424-2665) *Fax:* 217-363-2073 *E-mail:* marketing@sportspublishingllc.com *Web Site:* www.sportspublishingllc.com, pg 256

Spring Point Publishing Services, 4 The Ledges, Hallowell, ME 04347 *Tel:* 207-622-3973 *Fax:* 207-622-3973, pg 611

P Gregory Springer, 206 Wood St, Urbana, IL 61801 *Tel:* 217-239-4800 *Fax:* 775-459-4675 *Web Site:* 8am. com, pg 611

Springer Publishing Co Inc, 11 W 42 St, New York, NY 10036 *Tel:* 212-431-4370 *Toll Free Tel:* 877-687-7476 *Fax:* 212-941-7842 *E-mail:* springer@springerpub.com *Web Site:* www.springerpub.com, pg 256

Springer-Verlag New York Inc, 175 Fifth Ave, New York, NY 10010 *Tel:* 212-460-1500 *Toll Free Tel:* 800-777-4643 *Fax:* 212-473-6272 *Web Site:* www. springer-ny.com, pg 256

SPUR Awards, 1012 Fair St, Franklin, TN 37064 *Tel:* 615-791-1444 *Fax:* 615-791-1444 *Web Site:* www. westernwriters.org, pg 807

Square One Publishers, 115 Herricks Rd, Garden City Park, NY 11040 *Tel:* 516-535-2010 *Fax:* 516-535-2014 *E-mail:* sq1info@aol.com *Web Site:* squareonepublishers.com, pg 256

Squarebooks Inc, PO Box 6699, Santa Rosa, CA 95406 *Tel:* 707-545-1221 *Toll Free Tel:* 800-345-6699 *Fax:* 707-545-0909 *E-mail:* sales@fotobaron.com *Web Site:* fotobaron.com/squarebooks, pg 256

Squaw Valley Community of Writers Workshops, PO Box 1416, Nevada City, CA 95959 *Tel:* 530-470-8440 *E-mail:* brett@squawvalleywriters.org *Web Site:* www. squawvalleywriters.org, pg 748

SRA/McGraw-Hill, a Division of McGraw-Hill Learning Group, 8787 Orion Place, Columbus, OH 43240 *Tel:* 614-430-4000 *Fax:* 614-430-6621 *E-mail:* sra@ mcgraw-hill.com *Web Site:* www.sra-4kids.com, pg 256

SSR Inc, 116 Fourth St SE, Washington, DC 20003 *Tel:* 202-543-1800 *Fax:* 202-544-7432 *E-mail:* ssr@ ssrinc.com, pg 611

ST Publications Book Division, 407 Gilbert Ave, Cincinnati, OH 45202 *Tel:* 513-421-2050 *Toll Free Tel:* 800-925-1110 *Fax:* 513-421-5144 *E-mail:* books@stpubs.com *Web Site:* www.stpubs. com, pg 256

Stackler Editorial Agency, 555 Lincoln Ave, Alameda, CA 94501 *Tel:* 510-814-9694 *Fax:* 510-814-9694 *E-mail:* stackler@aol.com *Web Site:* www.fictioneditor. com, pg 612

Stackpole Books, 5067 Ritter Rd, Mechanicsburg, PA 17055 *Tel:* 717-796-0411 *Toll Free Tel:* 800-732-3669 *Fax:* 717-796-0412 *Web Site:* www.stackpolebooks. com, pg 257

The Edna Staebler Award for Creative Non-Fiction, 75 University Ave W, Waterloo, ON N2L 3C5, Canada *Tel:* 519-884-1970 (ext 3109) *Fax:* 519-884-8202, pg 807

Stairway Publications, PO Box 518, Huntington, NY 11743-0518 *Tel:* 631-423-4050 *Fax:* 631-351-2142 *E-mail:* publisher@stairwaypub.com *Web Site:* www. stairwaypub.com, pg 257

Stand! Publishing, 2744 Seneca St, No T-12, Wichita, KS 67207 *Tel:* 316-265-2880 *E-mail:* standbooks@ yahoo.com *Web Site:* www.standbooks.com, pg 257

Standard Educational Corp, 200 W Jackson, 7th fl, Chicago, IL 60606 *Tel:* 312-692-1000, pg 257

Standard Publications Inc, 903 Western Ave, Urbana, IL 61801 *Tel:* 217-898-7825 *E-mail:* spi@ standardpublications.com *Web Site:* www. standardpublications.com, pg 257

Standard Publishing Co, 8121 Hamilton Ave, Cincinnati, OH 45231 *Tel:* 513-931-4050 *Toll Free Tel:* 800-543-1301 *Fax:* 513-931-0950 *Toll Free Fax:* 877-867-5751 *E-mail:* customerservice@standardpub.com *Web Site:* www.standardpub.com, pg 257

Standard Publishing Corp, 155 Federal St, 13th fl, Boston, MA 02110 *Tel:* 617-457-0600 *Toll Free Tel:* 800-682-5759 *Fax:* 617-457-0608 *E-mail:* info@ spcpub.com *Web Site:* spcpub.com, pg 257

Stanford Creative Services, 7645 N Union Blvd, Suite 235, Colorado Springs, CO 80920 *Tel:* 719-599-7808 *Fax:* 719-590-7555 *Web Site:* www.stanfordcreative. com, pg 612

Stanford Publishing Courses at Stanford University, Green Library, Rm 245-B, 557 Escondidio Mall, Stanford, CA 94305-6004 *Tel:* 650-725-5311 *Fax:* 650-736-1904 *E-mail:* publishing.courses@ stanford.edu *Web Site:* publishingcourses.stanford.edu, pg 754

Stanford University Press, 1450 Page Mill Rd, Palo Alto, CA 94304-1124 *Tel:* 650-723-9434 *Fax:* 650-725-3457 *Web Site:* www.sup.org, pg 257

Stanley Drama Award, One Campus Rd, Staten Island, NY 10301 *Tel:* 718-390-3157 *Fax:* 718-390-3323, pg 807

Edward Stanley Award, University of Nebraska, 201 Andrews Hall, Lincoln, NE 68588 *Tel:* 402-472-0911 *Fax:* 402-472-9771 *E-mail:* kgrey2@unl.edu *Web Site:* www.unl.edu/schooner/psmain.htm, pg 807

Star Bright Books, The Star Bldg, Suite 2B, 42-26 28 St, Long Island City, NY 11101 *Tel:* 718-784-9112 *Toll Free Tel:* 800-788-4439 *Fax:* 718-784-9012 *E-mail:* info@starbrightbooks.com; orders@ starbrightbooks.com *Web Site:* www.starbrightbooks. com, pg 257

Star Publishing Co, 940 Emmett Ave, Belmont, CA 94002 *Tel:* 650-591-3505 *Fax:* 650-591-3898 *E-mail:* mail@starpublishing.com *Web Site:* www. starpublishing.com, pg 258

Starbooks Press, 1391 Blvd of the Arts, Sarasota, FL 34236-2904 *Tel:* 941-957-1281 *Fax:* 941-955-3829, pg 258

Starlite Inc, PO Box 20004, St Petersburg, FL 33742-0004 *Tel:* 727-392-2929 *Toll Free Tel:* 800-577-2929 *Fax:* 727-392-6161 *E-mail:* starlite@citebook.com *Web Site:* www.starlite-inc.com; www.citebook.com, pg 258

Agnes Lynch Starrett Poetry Prize, 3400 Forbes Ave, Pittsburgh, PA 15260 *Tel:* 412-383-2456 *Fax:* 412-383-2466 *Web Site:* www.pitt.edu/~press, pg 807

State Mutual Book & Periodical Service Ltd, PO Box 1199, Bridgehampton, NY 11932-1199 *Tel:* 631-537-1104 *Fax:* 631-537-0412, pg 258

State of Maine Writers' Conference, 16 Foley Ave, Saco, ME 04072 *Tel:* 207-284-4119 *Web Site:* www. suiteonedesign.com, pg 748

State University of New York Press, 90 State St, Suite 700, Albany, NY 12207-1707 *Tel:* 518-472-5000 *Toll Free Tel:* 800-666-2211 (orders) *Fax:* 518-472-5038 *Toll Free Fax:* 800-688-2877 (orders) *E-mail:* orderbook@cupserv.org; info@sunypress.edu *Web Site:* www.sunypress.edu, pg 258

Statistics Canada, R H Coats Bldg, Lobby, Holland Ave, Ottawa, ON K1A 0T6, Canada *Tel:* 613-951-8116 *Toll Free Tel:* 800-700-1033 (Canada & US); 800-267-6677 (orders) *Fax:* 613-951-1584 (local); 613-951-7277 (orders); 613-951-0581 (requests) *Toll Free Fax:* 800-889-9734; 877-287-4369 (orders) *E-mail:* order@statcan.ca; infostats@statcan.ca *Web Site:* www.statcan.ca, pg 562

Nancy Stauffer Associates, PO Box 1203, Darien, CT 06820 *Tel:* 203-655-3717 *Fax:* 203-655-3704 *E-mail:* nanstauf@optonline.net, pg 657

Steck-Vaughn, 10801 N MoPac Expressway, Austin, TX 78759 *Tel:* 512-343-8227 *Toll Free Tel:* 800-531-5015 *Toll Free Fax:* 800-699-9459 *E-mail:* ecare@harcourt. com *Web Site:* www.harcourtachieve.com, pg 258

Lyle Steele & Co Ltd Literary Agents, 511 E 73 St, Suite 6, New York, NY 10021 *Tel:* 212-288-2981, pg 657

Nancy Steele, 2210 Pine St, Philadelphia, PA 19103-6516 *Tel:* 215-732-5175 *E-mail:* NancyS1861@aol. com, pg 612

Steeple Hill Books, 233 Broadway, Suite 1001, New York, NY 10279 *Tel:* 212-553-4200 *Fax:* 212-227-8969 *E-mail:* customer_service@harlequin.ca *Web Site:* www.steeplehill.com, pg 258

Steerforth Press, 25 Lebanon St, Hanover, NH 03755 *Tel:* 603-643-4787 *Fax:* 603-643-4788 *E-mail:* info@ steerforth.com *Web Site:* www.steerforth.com, pg 258

Stegner Fellowship, Stanford Creative Writing Program, Mail Code 2087, Stanford, CA 94305-2087 *Tel:* 650-723-2637 *Fax:* 650-723-3679 *Web Site:* www.stanford. edu/dept/english/cw/fellowship.html, pg 807

Michael Steinberg Literary Agent, PO Box 274, Glencoe, IL 60022-0274 *Tel:* 847-835-4000 *Fax:* 847-835-8881 *E-mail:* michael14steinberg@comcast.net, pg 657

Steiner Books, PO Box 799, Great Barrington, MA 01230-0799 *Tel:* 413-528-8233 *Fax:* 413-528-8826 *E-mail:* service@anthropress.org *Web Site:* www. anthropress.org, pg 258

Stemmer House Publishers Inc, 4 White Brook Rd, Gilsum, NH 03448 *Tel:* 603-357-0236 *Toll Free Tel:* 800-345-6665 *Fax:* 603-357-2073 *E-mail:* pbs@ pathwaybook.com *Web Site:* www.stemmer.com, pg 259

Stenhouse Publishers, 477 Congress St, Suite 4B, Portland, ME 04101-3451 *Tel:* 207-253-1600 *Toll Free Tel:* 888-363-0566 *Fax:* 207-253-5121 *Toll Free Fax:* 800-833-9164 *E-mail:* info@stenhouse.com *Web Site:* www.stenhouse.com, pg 259

Stephan G Stephannson Award for Poetry, 11759 Groat Rd, Edmonton, AB T5M 3K6, Canada *Tel:* 780-422-8174 *Toll Free Tel:* 800-665-5354 (Alberta only) *Fax:* 780-422-2663 *E-mail:* mail@writersguild.ab.ca *Web Site:* www.writersguild.ab.ca, pg 807

Sterling Lord Literistic Inc, 65 Bleecker St, New York, NY 10012 *Tel:* 212-780-6050 *Fax:* 212-780-6095, pg 657

Sterling Publishing Co Inc, 387 Park Ave S, 5th fl, New York, NY 10016-8810 *Tel:* 212-532-7160 *Toll Free Tel:* 800-367-9692 *Fax:* 212-213-2495 *Web Site:* www. sterlingpub.com, pg 259

SterlingHouse Publisher Inc, 7436 Washington Ave, Suite 200, Pittsburgh, PA 15218 *Tel:* 412-271-8800 *Toll Free Tel:* 888-542-2665 *Fax:* 412-271-8600 *E-mail:* info@sterlinghousepublisher.com *Web Site:* www.sterlinghousepublisher.com, pg 259

Gloria Stern, 12535 Chandler Blvd, Suite 3, North Hollywood, CA 91607 *Tel:* 818-508-6296 *Fax:* 818-508-6296 *Web Site:* www.geocities.com/athens/1980/ writers.html, pg 657

Gloria Stern Agency, 2929 Buffalo Speedway, Suite 2111, Houston, TX 77098 *Tel:* 713-963-8360 *Fax:* 713-963-8460 *E-mail:* dstern1391@earthlink.net, pg 657

Miriam Stern, Attorney-at-Law/Literary Agent, 303 E 83 St, 20th fl, New York, NY 10028 *Tel:* 212-794-1289, pg 657

The Joan Stewart Agency, 800 Third Ave, 34th fl, New York, NY 10022 *Tel:* 212-418-7255 *Fax:* 212-486-6518, pg 657

Stewart, Tabori & Chang, 115 W 18 St, 5th fl, New York, NY 10011 *Tel:* 212-519-1200 *Fax:* 212-519-1210 *Web Site:* www.abramsbooks.com, pg 259

Jeff Stewart's Teaching Tools, PO Box 15308, Seattle, WA 98115 *Tel:* 425-486-4510 *Fax:* 425-486-4510, pg 260

H Stillman Publishers Inc, 21405 Woodchuck Lane, Boca Raton, FL 33428 *Tel:* 561-482-6343, pg 260

Stimola Literary Studio, 308 Chase Ct, Edgewater, NJ 07020 *Tel:* 201-945-9353 *Fax:* 201-945-9353 *E-mail:* LtryStudio@aol.com, pg 657

Stipes Publishing LLC, 204 W University, Champaign, IL 61820 *Tel:* 217-356-8391 *Fax:* 217-356-5753 *E-mail:* stipes@soltec.net *Web Site:* www.stipes.com, pg 260

Brooke C Stoddard, 101 N Columbus St, 4th fl, Alexandria, VA 22314 *Tel:* 703-838-1650 *Fax:* 703-836-3085 *E-mail:* brookecstoddard@cs.com, pg 612

Stoeger Publishing Co, 17603 Indian Head Hwy, Suite 200, Accokeek, MD 20607 *Tel:* 301-283-6300 *Fax:* 301-283-6986, pg 260

Jean Stoess, 500 Ryland St, Suite 150, Reno, NV 89502 *Tel:* 775-322-5326 *Fax:* 775-322-8271 *E-mail:* jstoess@aol.com, pg 612

Jeri L Stolk, 90 Bronson Terr, Springfield, MA 01108 *Tel:* 413-739-9585 *E-mail:* jeri.stolk@comcast.net, pg 612

Stone Bridge Press LLC, PO Box 8208, Berkeley, CA 94707-8208 *Tel:* 510-524-8732 *Toll Free Tel:* 800-947-7271 *Fax:* 510-524-8711 *E-mail:* sbp@stonebridge. com; sbpedit@stonebridge.com *Web Site:* www. stonebridge.com, pg 260

Stoneydale Press Publishing Co, 523 Main St, Stevensville, MT 59870 *Tel:* 406-777-2729 *Toll Free Tel:* 800-735-7006 *Fax:* 406-777-2521 *E-mail:* stoneydale@montana.com *Web Site:* www. stoneydale.com, pg 260

Storey Books, 210 Mass MoCA Way, North Adams, MA 01247 *Tel:* 413-346-2100 *Toll Free Tel:* 800-793-9396 *Fax:* 413-346-2253 *E-mail:* info@storey.com *Web Site:* www.storey.com, pg 260

Story Line Press, 2091 Suncrest Rd, Talent, OR 97540 *Tel:* 541-512-8792 *Fax:* 541-512-8793 *E-mail:* mail@ storylinepress.com *Web Site:* www.storylinepress.com, pg 260

Story Time Stories That Rhyme, PO Box 416, Denver, CO 80201-0416 *Tel:* 303-575-5676 *Fax:* 303-575-1187 *E-mail:* mail@storytimestoriesthatrhyme.org *Web Site:* www.storytimestoriesthatrhyme.org, pg 260

Elizabeth Matchett Stover Memorial Award, 307 Fondren Library W, 6404 Hilltop Lane, Dallas, TX 75275-0374 *Tel:* 214-768-1037 *Fax:* 214-768-1408 *E-mail:* swr@ mail.smu.edu *Web Site:* www.southwestreview.org, pg 807

Straight Line Editorial Development Inc, 3239 Sacramento St, San Francisco, CA 94115-2047 *Tel:* 415-864-2011 *Fax:* 415-864-2013 *E-mail:* sledinc@aol.com, pg 612

Strata Publishing Inc, PO Box 1303, State College, PA 16804 *Tel:* 814-234-8545; 814-234-2150 (sales) *Fax:* 814-238-7222 *E-mail:* editorial@stratapub.com *Web Site:* www.stratapub.com, pg 260

Stratford Publishing Services Inc, 70 Landmark Hill Dr, Brattleboro, VT 05301 *Tel:* 802-254-6073 *Toll Free Tel:* 800-451-4328 *Fax:* 802-254-5240 *Web Site:* www. stratfordpublishing.com, pg 612

Barbara Cohen Stratyner, 40 Lincoln Center Plaza, New York, NY 10023 *Tel:* 212-870-1830 *Fax:* 212-870-1870, pg 612

Robin Straus Agency Inc, 229 E 79 St, New York, NY 10021 *Tel:* 212-472-3282 *Fax:* 212-472-3833 *E-mail:* springbird@aol.com, pg 657

Marianne Strong Literary Agency, 65 E 96 St, New York, NY 10128 *Tel:* 212-249-1000 *Fax:* 212-831-3241 *E-mail:* stronglit@aol.com, pg 657

The Jesse Stuart Foundation, PO Box 669, Ashland, KY 41105-0669 *Tel:* 606-326-1667 *Fax:* 606-325-2519 *Web Site:* www.jsfbooks.com, pg 260

Barbara Ward Stuhlmann, Author's Representative, PO Box 276, Becket, MA 01223-0276 *Tel:* 413-623-5170, pg 658

Stylewriter Inc, 4395 N Windsor Dr, Provo, UT 84604-6301 *Tel:* 801-235-9462 *Toll Free Tel:* 866-997-9462 *E-mail:* customerservice@swinc.org; query@swinc.org *Web Site:* www.swinc.org; www.stylewriterinc.org, pg 260

Stylus Publishing LLC, 22883 Quicksilver Dr, Sterling, VA 20166-2012 *Tel:* 703-661-1504 (edit & sales) *Toll Free Tel:* 800-232-0223 *Fax:* 703-661-1547 *E-mail:* stylusmail@presswarehouse.com; stylusinfo@ styluspub.com *Web Site:* styluspub.com, pg 261

Success Advertising & Publishing, 3419 Dunham Rd, Warsaw, NY 14569 *Tel:* 585-786-5663, pg 261

The Sugarman Family Award for Jewish Children's Literature, 1529 16 St NW, Washington, DC 20036 *Tel:* 202-518-9400 *Fax:* 202-518-9420, pg 807

Joan G Sugarman Children's Book Award, 1851 Columbia Rd NW, No 205, Washington, DC 20009 *Tel:* 202-466-1344 *E-mail:* sugarman@lefund.org *Web Site:* www.washwriter.org, pg 807

Sherwood Sugden & Co, 315 Fifth St, Peru, IL 61354 *Tel:* 815-224-6651 *Fax:* 815-223-4486 *E-mail:* philomon1@netscape.net *Web Site:* monist. buffalo.edu, pg 261

Sumach Press, 1415 Bathurst St, Suite 302, Toronto, ON M5R 3H5, Canada *Tel:* 416-531-6250 *Fax:* 416-531-3892 *E-mail:* sumachpress@on.aibn.com *Web Site:* www.sumachpress.com, pg 562

Summa Publications, PO Box 660725, Birmingham, AL 35266-0725 *Tel:* 205-822-0463 *Fax:* 205-822-0463, pg 261

Summer Poetry in Idyllwild, 52500 Temecula Dr, Idyllwild, CA 92549 *Tel:* 909-659-2171 *Fax:* 909-659-4383 *Web Site:* www.idyllwildarts.org, pg 748

Summer Writers' Workshops, UCCE, 250 Hofstra University, Hempstead, NY 11549-2500 *Tel:* 516-463-7600 *Fax:* 516-463-4833 *E-mail:* uccelibarts@hofstra. edu *Web Site:* www.hofstra.edu/writers, pg 748

Summit Publications, PO Box 39128, Indianapolis, IN 46239 *Tel:* 317-862-3330 *Toll Free Tel:* 800-419-0200 *Fax:* 317-862-2599 *E-mail:* yogs@iquest.net *Web Site:* www.yogs.com, pg 261

Summit University Press, 558 Old Yellowstone Trail S, Corwin Springs, MT 59030-5000 *Tel:* 406-848-9295 *Toll Free Tel:* 800-245-5445 *Fax:* 406-848-9290 *E-mail:* info@summituniversitypress.com *Web Site:* www.hostmontana.com/supress; www. summituniversitypress.com, pg 261

Summy-Birchard Inc, 15800 NW 48 Ave, Miami, FL 33014 *Tel:* 305-620-1500 *Toll Free Tel:* 800-327-7643 *Fax:* 305-621-1094, pg 261

Sun & Moon Press, 6026 Wilshire Blvd, Suite 200A, Los Angeles, CA 90036 *Tel:* 323-857-1115 *Fax:* 323-857-0143 *E-mail:* sales@consortium.com *Web Site:* www.greeninteger.com, pg 261

Sun Books - Sun Publishing, PO Box 5588, Santa Fe, NM 87502-5588 *Tel:* 505-471-5177; 505-471-6151 *Fax:* 505-473-4458 *E-mail:* info@sunbooks.com *Web Site:* www.sunbooks.com, pg 261

Sunbelt Publications Inc, 1250 Fayette St, El Cajon, CA 92020-1511 *Tel:* 619-258-4911 *Toll Free Tel:* 800-626-6579 *Fax:* 619-258-4916 *E-mail:* mail@sunbeltpub. com *Web Site:* www.sunbeltbooks.com, pg 261

Sunburst Technology, 400 Columbus Ave, Suite 160E, Valhalla, NY 10595 *Tel:* 914-747-3310 *Toll Free Tel:* 800-338-3457 *Fax:* 914-747-4109 *Web Site:* www. sunburst.com, pg 262

Sundance Publishing, One Beeman Rd, Northborough, MA 01532 *Tel:* 508-571-6500 *Toll Free Tel:* 800-343-8204 *Fax:* 508-571-6510 *Toll Free Fax:* 800-456-2419 *E-mail:* info@sundancepub.com *Web Site:* www. sundancepub.com, pg 262

Sunset Books/Sunset Publishing Corp, 80 Willow Rd, Menlo Park, CA 94025-3691 *Tel:* 650-321-3600 *Toll Free Tel:* 800-227-7346; 800-321-0372 (California only) *Fax:* 650-324-1532 *Web Site:* sunset.com, pg 262

Sunstone Press, PO Box 2321, Santa Fe, NM 87504-2321 *Tel:* 505-988-4418 *Fax:* 505-988-1025 (orders only) *Web Site:* www.sunstonepress.com, pg 262

Surrey Books, 230 E Ohio St, Suite 120, Chicago, IL 60611 *Tel:* 312-751-7330 *Toll Free Tel:* 800-326-4430 *Fax:* 312-751-7334 *E-mail:* surreybk@aol.com *Web Site:* www.surreybooks.com, pg 262

Susquehanna University Press, Associated University Presses, 2010 Eastpark Blvd, Cranbury, NJ 08512 *Tel:* 609-655-4770 *Fax:* 609-655-8366 *E-mail:* aup440@aol.com, pg 262

Swagman Publishing Inc, PO Box 519, Castle Rock, CO 80104 *Tel:* 303-660-3307 *Toll Free Tel:* 800-660-5107 *Fax:* 303-688-4388 *E-mail:* mail@4wdbooks.com *Web Site:* www.4wdbooks.com, pg 262

Swallow Press, Scott Quadrangle, Athens, OH 45701 *Tel:* 740-593-1155 *Toll Free Tel:* 800-621-2736 (orders only) *Fax:* 740-593-4536 *Toll Free Fax:* 800-621-8476 (orders only) *Web Site:* www.ohiou.edu/oupress/, pg 262

Swan Isle Press, 11030 S Langley Ave, Chicago, IL 60628 *Tel:* 773-568-1550 *Toll Free Tel:* 800-621-2736 *Fax:* 773-660-2235 *Toll Free Fax:* 800-621-8476 *E-mail:* info@swanislepress.com *Web Site:* www. swanpress.com, pg 263

Carolyn Swayze Literary Agency Ltd, 15927 Pacific Place, White Rock, BC V4B 1S9, Canada *Tel:* 604-538-3478 *Fax:* 604-531-3022 *E-mail:* cswayze@direct. ca *Web Site:* www.swayzeagency.com, pg 658

Swedenborg Association, 278-A Meeting St, Charleston, SC 29401 *Tel:* 843-853-6211 *Fax:* 843-853-6226 *E-mail:* arcana@swedenborg.net; assn@swedenborg. net, pg 263

Swedenborg Foundation Publishers/Chrysalis Books, 320 N Church St, West Chester, PA 19380 *Tel:* 610-430-3222 *Toll Free Tel:* 800-355-3222 (cust serv) *Fax:* 610-430-7982 *E-mail:* info@swedenborg.com *Web Site:* www.swedenborg.com, pg 263

Sweetgrass Press LLC, PO Box 1862, Merrimack, NH 03054-1862 *Tel:* 603-883-7001 *Fax:* 603-883-7001 *Toll Free Fax:* 866-727-7757 *E-mail:* info@ sweetgrasspress.com *Web Site:* www.sweetgrasspress. com, pg 263

May Swenson Poetry Award, 7800 Old Main Hill, Logan, UT 84322-7800 *Tel:* 435-797-1362 *Fax:* 435-797-0313 *Web Site:* www.usu.edu/usupress, pg 807

SYBEX Inc, 1151 Marina Village Pkwy, Alameda, CA 94501 *Tel:* 510-523-8233 *Toll Free Tel:* 800-227-2346 *Fax:* 510-523-2373 *E-mail:* pressinfo@sybex.com *Web Site:* www.sybex.com, pg 263

Sydney Taylor Book Awards, 15 E 26 St, New York, NY 10010-1579 *Tel:* 212-725-5359 *Fax:* 212-481-4174 *E-mail:* ajl@jewishbooks.org *Web Site:* www. jewishlibraries.org, pg 807

Sydney Taylor Manuscript Award, 15 E 26 St, New York, NY 10010-1579 *Tel:* 212-725-5359 *Fax:* 212-678-9998 *E-mail:* ajl@jewishbooks.org *Web Site:* www.jewishlibraries.org, pg 808

Charles S Sydnor Award, University of Georgia, Dept of History, Athens, GA 30602-1602 *Tel:* 706-542-8848 *Fax:* 706-542-2455 *Web Site:* www.uga.edu/~sha, pg 808

Elvira C Sylve—Editorial & Secretarial Services, PO Box 870602, New Orleans, LA 70187 *Tel:* 504-244-8357 *Fax:* 504-244-8357 (call first) *E-mail:* elcsy58@ aol.com, pg 612

Synapse Information Resources Inc, 1247 Taft Ave, Endicott, NY 13760 *Tel:* 607-748-4145 *Toll Free Tel:* 888-SYN-CHEM *Fax:* 607-786-3966 *E-mail:* salesinfo@synapseinfo.com *Web Site:* www. synapseinfo.com, pg 263

Synaxis Press, 37323 Hawkins Pickle Rd, Dewdney, BC V0M 1H0, Canada *Tel:* 604-826-9336 *Fax:* 604-820-9758 *E-mail:* synaxis@new-ostrog.org *Web Site:* www. new-ostrog.org/synaxis, pg 562

SynergEbooks, 1235 Flat Shoals Rd, King, NC 27021 *Tel:* 336-994-2405 *Toll Free Tel:* 888-812-2533 *Fax:* 336-994-2405 *E-mail:* inquiries@synergebooks. com; synergebooks@aol.com *Web Site:* www. synergebooks.com, pg 263

Syracuse University Creative Writing Program, 401 Hall of Languages, Syracuse, NY 13244-1170 *Tel:* 315-443-2174 *Fax:* 315-443-3660 *Web Site:* www.syr.edu, pg 754

Syracuse University Press, 621 Skytop Rd, Syracuse, NY 13244-5290 *Tel:* 315-443-5534 *Toll Free Tel:* 800-365-8929 (orders only) *Fax:* 315-443-5545 *E-mail:* supress@syr.edu *Web Site:* syracuseuniversitypress.syr.edu, pg 263

Syracuse University, SI Newhouse School of Public Communications, 215 University Place, Syracuse, NY 13244-2100 *Tel:* 315-443-2301 *Fax:* 315-443-3946 *E-mail:* newhouse@syr.edu *Web Site:* www.newhouse. syr.edu, pg 754

The Systemsware Corp, 973 Russell Ave, Suite D, Gaithersburg, MD 20879 *Tel:* 301-948-4890 *Fax:* 301-926-4243 *Web Site:* www.systemswarecorp.com, pg 263

T & T Clark International, PO Box 1321, Harrisburg, PA 17105 *Tel:* 717-541-8130 *Toll Free Tel:* 800-877-0012 *Fax:* 717-541-8136 *Web Site:* www.tandtclarkinternational.com, pg 263

T J Publishers Inc, 817 Silver Spring Ave, Suite 206, Silver Spring, MD 20910-4617 *Tel:* 301-585-4440 *Toll Free Tel:* 800-999-1168 *Fax:* 301-585-5930 *E-mail:* TJPubinc@aol.com, pg 574

T S Eliot Prize for Poetry, 100 E Normal St, Kirksville, MO 63501-4221 *Tel:* 660-785-7336 *Toll Free Tel:* 800-916-6802 *Fax:* 660-785-4480 *E-mail:* tsup@truman.edu *Web Site:* tsup.truman.edu, pg 808

Robert E Tabian/Literary Agent, 31 E 32 St, Suite 300, New York, NY 10016 *Tel:* 212-481-8484 (ext 330) *Fax:* 212-481-9582 *E-mail:* retlit@mindspring.com, pg 658

Tafnews Press, 2570 El Camino Real, No 606, Mountain View, CA 94040 *Tel:* 650-948-8188 *Fax:* 650-948-9445 *E-mail:* biz@trackandfieldnews.com *Web Site:* www.trackandfieldnews.com, pg 264

Tag & Label Manufacturers Institute Inc, 40 Shuman Blvd, Suite 295, Naperville, IL 60563 *Tel:* 630-357-9222 *Fax:* 630-357-0192 *E-mail:* office@tlmi.com *Web Site:* www.tlmi.com, pg 701

Tahrike Tarsile Qur'an Inc, 80-08 51 Ave, Elmhurst, NY 11373 *Tel:* 718-446-6472 *Fax:* 718-446-4370 *E-mail:* orders@koranusa.org *Web Site:* www.koranusa.org, pg 264

Take the Panic Out of Plot, 708 Blossom Hill Rd, No 146, Los Gatos, CA 95032 *Tel:* 408-482-4678 *Fax:* 408-356-1798 *Web Site:* www.blockbusterplots.com, pg 748

Talisman House Publishers, PO Box 3157, Jersey City, NJ 07303-3157 *Tel:* 201-938-0698 *Fax:* 201-938-1693 *E-mail:* talismaned@aol.com *Web Site:* www.talismanpublishers.com, pg 264

Carol Talpers, 2738 Webster St, Berkeley, CA 94705 *Tel:* 510-549-9050, pg 612

Tamos Books Inc, 300 Wales Ave, Winnipeg, MB R2M 2S9, Canada *Tel:* 204-256-9204 *Fax:* 204-255-7845 *E-mail:* tamos@mts.net *Web Site:* www.escape.ca/~tamos, pg 562

TAN Books & Publishers Inc, 2020 Harrison Ave, Rockford, IL 61104 *Tel:* 815-226-7777 *Fax:* 815-226-7770 *E-mail:* tan@tanbooks.com; taneditor@tanbooks.com *Web Site:* www.tanbooks.com, pg 264

Tapestry Press Ltd, 19 Nashoba Rd, Littleton, MA 01460 *Tel:* 978-486-0200 *Toll Free Tel:* 800-535-2007 *Fax:* 978-486-0244 *E-mail:* publish@tapestrypress.com *Web Site:* www.tapestrypress.com, pg 264

Taplinger Publishing Co Inc, PO Box 175, Marlboro, NJ 07746-0175 *Tel:* 646-215-9003 *Fax:* 646-215-9560, pg 264

Tarascon Publishing, 1015 W Central Ave, Lompoc, CA 93436 *Tel:* 805-736-7000 *Toll Free Tel:* 800-929-9926 *Fax:* 805-736-6161 *Toll Free Fax:* 877-929-9926 *E-mail:* info@tarascon.com *Web Site:* www.tarascon.com, pg 264

Jeremy P Tarcher, 375 Hudson St, New York, NY 10014 *Tel:* 212-366-2000 *E-mail:* online@penguinputnam.com *Web Site:* www.penguin.com, pg 264

Roslyn Targ Literary Agency Inc, 105 W 13 St, Suite 15-E, New York, NY 10011 *Tel:* 212-206-9390 *Fax:* 212-989-6233 *E-mail:* roslyntarg@aol.com, pg 658

Taschen America, 6671 Sunset Blvd, Suite 1508, Los Angeles, CA 90028 *Tel:* 323-463-4441 *Toll Free Tel:* 888-TASCHEN (827-2436) *Fax:* 323-463-4442 *Web Site:* www.taschen.com, pg 264

The Taunton Press Inc, 63 S Main St, Newtown, CT 06470 *Tel:* 203-426-8171 *Toll Free Tel:* 800-283-7252; 800-888-8286 (orders) *Fax:* 203-426-3434 *Web Site:* www.taunton.com, pg 264

Taylor & Francis Editorial, Production & Manufacturing Division, 325 Chestnut St, Philadelphia, PA 19106 *Tel:* 215-625-8900 *Toll Free Tel:* 800-354-1420 *Fax:* 215-625-2940 *E-mail:* info@taylorandfrancis.com *Web Site:* www.taylorandfrancis.com, pg 264

Taylor & Francis Inc, 325 Chestnut St, Philadelphia, PA 19106 *Tel:* 215-625-8900 *Toll Free Tel:* 800-354-1420 *Fax:* 215-625-2940 *E-mail:* info@taylorandfrancis.com *Web Site:* www.taylorandfrancis.com, pg 264

Dawson Taylor Literary Agency, 4722 Holly Lake Dr, Lake Worth, FL 33463-5372 *Tel:* 561-965-4150 *Fax:* 561-641-9765 *E-mail:* dawsontaylo@aol.com, pg 658

Rennie Taylor-Alton Blakeslee Fellowships in Science Writing, PO Box 910, Hedgesville, WV 25427 *Tel:* 304-754-5077 *Fax:* 304-754-5076 *Web Site:* www.casw.org, pg 808

TCP Press, 9 Lobraico Lane, Whitchurch-Stouffville, ON L4A 7X5, Canada *Tel:* 905-640-8914 *Toll Free Tel:* 800-772-7765 *Fax:* 905-640-2922 *E-mail:* tcp@tcpnow.com *Web Site:* www.tcppress.com, pg 562

Teach Me Tapes Inc, 6016 Blue Circle Dr, Minnetonka, MN 55343 *Tel:* 952-933-8086 *Toll Free Tel:* 800-456-4656 *Fax:* 952-933-0512 *E-mail:* marie@teachmetapes.com *Web Site:* www.teachmetapes.com, pg 265

Teacher Created Materials Inc, 6421 Industry Way, Westminster, CA 92683 *Tel:* 714-891-7895 *Toll Free Tel:* 800-662-4321 *Fax:* 714-892-0283 *Toll Free Fax:* 800-525-1254 *E-mail:* tcminfo@teachercreated.com *Web Site:* www.teachercreated.com, pg 265

Teacher Ideas Press, 361 Hanover St, Portsmouth, NH 03801-3912 *Toll Free Tel:* 800-225-5800 *Fax:* 603-431-2214 *Toll Free Fax:* 800-934-2004 (perms & foreign rts) *E-mail:* custserv@teacherideaspress.com; permissions@teacherideaspress.com; foreignrights@teacherideaspress.com *Web Site:* www.teacherideaspress.com, pg 265

Teachers & Writers Collaborative, 5 Union Sq W, New York, NY 10003-3306 *Tel:* 212-691-6590 *Toll Free Tel:* 888-266-5789 *Fax:* 212-675-0171 *E-mail:* info@twc.org *Web Site:* www.twc.org, pg 265, 701

Teachers College Press, 1234 Amsterdam Ave, New York, NY 10027 *Tel:* 212-678-3929 *Fax:* 212-678-4149 *E-mail:* tcpress@tc.columbia.edu *Web Site:* www.teacherscollegepress.com, pg 265

Teacher's Discovery, 2741 Paldan Dr, Auburn Hills, MI 48326 *Tel:* 248-340-7220 ext 207 *Toll Free Tel:* 800-521-3897 *Fax:* 248-340-7212 *Toll Free Fax:* 888-987-2436 *Web Site:* www.teachersdiscovery.com, pg 265

Teachers of English to Speakers of Other Languages Inc (TESOL), 700 S Washington St, Suite 200, Alexandria, VA 22314-4287 *Tel:* 703-836-0774 *Fax:* 703-836-7864 *E-mail:* info@tesol.org *Web Site:* www.tesol.org, pg 265

Teaching & Learning Co, 1204 Buchanan St, Carthage, IL 62321-0010 *Tel:* 217-357-2591 *Fax:* 217-357-6789 *E-mail:* customerservice@teachinglearning.com *Web Site:* TeachingLearning.Com, pg 265

Teaching Strategies, PO Box 42243, Washington, DC 20015 *Tel:* 202-362-7543 *Toll Free Tel:* 800-637-3652 *Fax:* 202-364-7273 *E-mail:* info@teachingstrategies.com *Web Site:* www.teachingstrategies.com, pg 265

Patricia Teal Literary Agency, 2036 Vista del Rosa, Fullerton, CA 92831 *Tel:* 714-738-8333 *Fax:* 714-738-8333, pg 658

TechBooks Professional Publishing Group, 11150 Main St, Suite 402, Fairfax, VA 22030 *Tel:* 703-352-0001 *Fax:* 703-352-8862 *E-mail:* info@techbooks.com *Web Site:* www.techbooks.com, pg 612

Technical Association of the Graphic Arts (TAGA), 68 Lomb Memorial Dr, Rochester, NY 14623-5604 *Tel:* 585-475-7470 *Fax:* 585-475-2250 *E-mail:* tagaofc@aol.com *Web Site:* www.taga.org, pg 701

Technical Association of the Pulp & Paper Industry (TAPPI), 15 Technology Pkwy S, Norcross, GA 30092 *Tel:* 770-446-1400 *Toll Free Tel:* 800-332-8686 *Fax:* 770-446-6947 *E-mail:* webmaster@tappi.org *Web Site:* www.tappi.org, pg 266, 701

Technical Books for the Layperson Inc, PO Box 391, Lake Grove, NY 11755 *Tel:* 540-877-1477 *Fax:* 540-877-1477 *E-mail:* tbl_inc@yahoo.com *Web Site:* tblbooks.com, pg 266

Technology Training Systems Inc (TTS), 3131 S Vaughn Way, Suite 300, Aurora, CO 80014-3503 *Tel:* 303-368-0300 *Toll Free Tel:* 800-676-8871 *Fax:* 303-368-0312 *E-mail:* info@myplantstraining.com *Web Site:* www.myplantstraining.com, pg 266

Teddy Award for Children's Books, 1501 W Fifth St, Suite E-2, Austin, TX 78703 *Tel:* 512-499-8914 *Fax:* 512-499-0441 *E-mail:* wlt@writersleague.org *Web Site:* www.writersleague.org, pg 808

Temple University Press, 1601 N Broad St, 083-42, USB Room 306, Philadelphia, PA 19122-6099 *Tel:* 215-204-8787 *Toll Free Tel:* 800-447-1656 *Fax:* 215-204-4719 *E-mail:* tempress@temple.edu *Web Site:* www.temple.edu/tempress, pg 266

Templegate Publishers, 302 E Adams St, Springfield, IL 62701 *Tel:* 217-522-3353 (billing) *Toll Free Tel:* 800-367-4844 (orders only) *Fax:* 217-522-3362 *E-mail:* wisdom@templegate.com; orders@templegate.com (sales) *Web Site:* www.templegate.com, pg 266

Templeton Foundation Press, 5 Radnor Corporate Ctr, Suite 120, 100 Matsonford Rd, Radnor, PA 19087 *Tel:* 610-971-2670 *Toll Free Tel:* 800-561-3367 *Fax:* 610-971-2672 *E-mail:* tfp@templetonpress.org *Web Site:* www.templetonpress.org, pg 266

Temporal Mechanical Press, 6760 Hwy 7, Estes Park, CO 80517-6404 *Tel:* 970-586-4706 *E-mail:* enosmillscbn@earthlink.net *Web Site:* www.geocities.com/soho/nook/7587, pg 266

Ten Speed Press, PO Box 7123, Berkeley, CA 94707 *Tel:* 510-559-1600 *Toll Free Tel:* 800-841-Book *Fax:* 510-559-1629; 510-524-1052 (general) *E-mail:* order@tenspeed.com *Web Site:* www.tenspeed.com, pg 266

Tennessee Arts Commission Fellowships, 401 Charlotte Ave, Nashville, TN 37243-0780 *Tel:* 615-741-1701 (voice & TDD) *Fax:* 615-741-8559 *Web Site:* www.arts.state.tn.us, pg 808

Teora USA LLC, 2 Wisconsin Circle, Suite 870, Chevy Chase, MD 20815 *Tel:* 301-986-6990 *Toll Free Tel:* 800-358-3754 *Fax:* 301-986-6992 *Toll Free Fax:* 800-358-3754 *E-mail:* info@teora.com *Web Site:* www.teorausa.com, pg 266

Teton New Media, 4125 S Hwy 89, Suite 1, Jackson, WY 83001 *Tel:* 307-732-0028 *Toll Free Tel:* 877-306-9793 *Fax:* 307-734-0841, pg 267

Tetra Press, 3001 Commerce St, Blacksburg, VA 24060 *Tel:* 540-951-5400 *Toll Free Tel:* 800-526-0650 *Fax:* 540-951-5415 *E-mail:* consumer@tetra-fish.com *Web Site:* www.tetra-fish.com, pg 267

Texas A&M University Press, John H Lindsey Bldg, Lewis St, 4354 TAMU, College Station, TX 77843-4354 *Tel:* 979-845-1436 *Toll Free Tel:* 800-826-8911 (orders) *Fax:* 979-847-8752 *Toll Free Fax:* 888-617-2421 (orders) *E-mail:* fdl@tampress.tamu.edu *Web Site:* www.tamu.edu/upress/, pg 267

The Texas Bluebonnet Award, 3355 Bee Cave Rd, Suite 401, Austin, TX 78746 *Tel:* 512-328-1518 *Toll Free Tel:* 800-580-2852 *Fax:* 512-328-8852 *Web Site:* www.txla.org, pg 808

Texas Christian University Press, PO Box 298300, Fort Worth, TX 76129 *Tel:* 817-257-7822 *Toll Free Tel:* 800-826-8911 *Fax:* 817-257-5075 *Toll Free Fax:* 888-617-2421 *Web Site:* www.prs.tcu.edu/prs/, pg 267

Texas Institute of Letters, 3700 Mockingbird Lane, Dallas, TX 75205 *Tel:* 214-528-2655, pg 701

Texas Institute of Letters Awards, 3700 Mockingbird Lane, Dallas, TX 75205 *Tel:* 512-245-2232 *Fax:* 512-245-7462 *Web Site:* www.stedwards.edu/newc/marks/til/awards_and_rules.htm; www.english.swt.edu/css/til/rules.htm, pg 808

University of Texas Press, PO Box 7819, Austin, TX 78713-7819 *Tel:* 512-471-7233 *Fax:* 512-232-7178 *E-mail:* utpress@uts.cc.utexas.edu *Web Site:* www.utexas.edu/utpress, pg 267

Texas State Historical Association, University Sta, DO-901, Austin, TX 78712 *Tel:* 512-471-1525 *Fax:* 512-471-1551 *E-mail:* comments@tsha.utexas.edu *Web Site:* www.tsha.utexas.edu, pg 267

Texas Tech University Press, 2903 Fourth St, Lubbock, TX 79412 *Tel:* 806-742-2982 *Toll Free Tel:* 800-832-4042 *Fax:* 806-742-2979 *E-mail:* ttup@ttu.edu *Web Site:* www.ttup.ttu.edu, pg 267

Texas Western Press, c/o University of Texas at El Paso, 500 W University Ave, El Paso, TX 79968-0633 *Tel:* 915-747-5688 *Toll Free Tel:* 800-488-3789 *Fax:* 915-747-7515 *E-mail:* twpress@utep.edu *Web Site:* www.utep.edu/~twp, pg 267

Texere, 55 E 52 St, New York, NY 10055 *Tel:* 212-317-5511 *Fax:* 212-317-5178 *E-mail:* Firstname_Lastname@etexere.com *Web Site:* www.etexere.com; www.etexere.co.uk, pg 267

Text & Academic Authors Association Inc, PO Box 76477, St Petersburg, FL 33734-6477 *Tel:* 727-821-7277 *Fax:* 727-821-7271 *E-mail:* text@tampabay.rr.com *Web Site:* www.taaonline.net, pg 701

Textbook Writers Associates Inc, 12 Nathan Rd, Newton Centre, MA 02459 *Tel:* 617-630-8500 *Fax:* 617-630-8502 *E-mail:* info@textbookwriters.com *Web Site:* www.textbookwriters.com, pg 612

TFH Publications Inc, 61 Third Ave, Neptune City, NJ 07753 *Tel:* 732-988-8400 *Toll Free Tel:* 800-631-2188 *Fax:* 732-988-5466 *E-mail:* info@tfh.com *Web Site:* www.tfh.com, pg 268

Thames & Hudson, 500 Fifth Ave, New York, NY 10110 *Tel:* 212-354-3763 *Toll Free Tel:* 800-233-4830 *Fax:* 212-398-1252 *E-mail:* bookinfo@thames.wwnorton.com *Web Site:* www.thamesandhudsonusa.com, pg 268

Theatre Communications Group Inc, 520 Eighth Ave, New York, NY 10018 *Tel:* 212-609-5900 *Fax:* 212-609-5901 *E-mail:* tcg@tcg.org *Web Site:* www.tcg.org, pg 268

The Theatre Library Association Award, Queens College, CUNY, Flushing, NY 11367 *Tel:* 718-997-3762 *Fax:* 718-997-3753 *Web Site:* tla.library.unt.edu, pg 808

Theatre-Scriptworks, 216 Finance Bldg, Harrisburg, PA 17120 *Tel:* 717-787-6883 *Fax:* 717-783-2538 *Web Site:* www.pacouncilonthearts.org, pg 808

Theosophical Publishing House/Quest Books, 306 W Geneva Rd, Wheaton, IL 60187 *Tel:* 630-665-0130 *Toll Free Tel:* 800-669-9425 *Fax:* 630-665-8791 *E-mail:* questbooks@theosmail.net *Web Site:* www.questbooks.net, pg 268

Theosophical University Press, PO Box C, Pasadena, CA 91109-7107 *Tel:* 626-798-3378 *Fax:* 626-798-4749 *E-mail:* tupress@theosociety.org *Web Site:* www.theosociety.org, pg 268

Theta Reports, 1775 Broadway, Suite 511, New York, NY 10019 *Tel:* 212-262-8230 *Fax:* 212-262-8234 *Web Site:* www.thetareports.com, pg 268

Theytus Books Ltd, Lot 45, Green Mountain Rd, RR No 2, Site 50, Comp 8, Penticton, BC V2A 6J7, Canada *Tel:* 250-493-7181 *Fax:* 250-493-5302 *E-mail:* theytusbooks@vip.net *Web Site:* www.theytusbooks.ca, pg 563

Thieme New York, 333 Seventh Ave, 5th fl, New York, NY 10001 *Tel:* 212-760-0888 *Toll Free Tel:* 800-782-3488 *Fax:* 212-947-1112 *E-mail:* customerservice@thieme.com *Web Site:* www.thieme.com, pg 268

Thinkers' Press Inc, 1101 W Fourth St, Davenport, IA 52802 *Tel:* 563-323-7117 *Toll Free Tel:* 800-397-7117 *Fax:* 563-323-0511 *E-mail:* tpi@chessco.com *Web Site:* www.chessco.com, pg 268

Thinking Publications, 424 Galloway, Eau Claire, WI 54703 *Tel:* 715-832-2488 *Toll Free Tel:* 800-225-4769 *Fax:* 715-832-9082 *Toll Free Fax:* 800-828-8885 *E-mail:* custserv@thinkingpublications.com *Web Site:* www.thinkingpublications.com, pg 269

Third World Press, 7822 S Dobson Ave, Chicago, IL 60619 *Tel:* 773-651-0700 *Fax:* 773-651-7286 *E-mail:* twpress3@aol.com *Web Site:* www.thirdworldpressinc.com, pg 269

Thistledown Press Ltd, 633 Main St, Saskatoon, SK S7H 0J8, Canada *Tel:* 306-244-1722 *Fax:* 306-244-1762 *E-mail:* marketing@thistledown.sk.ca *Web Site:* www.thistledown.sk.ca, pg 563

Thomas Brothers Maps, 17731 Cowan, Irvine, CA 92614 *Tel:* 949-852-9189 *Fax:* 949-757-1564 *E-mail:* webmaster@thomas.com *Web Site:* www.randmcnally.com, pg 269

Charles C Thomas Publisher Ltd, 2600 S First St, Springfield, IL 62704 *Tel:* 217-789-8980 *Toll Free Tel:* 800-258-8980 *Fax:* 217-789-9130 *E-mail:* books@ccthomas.com *Web Site:* www.ccthomas.com, pg 269

Thomas Geale Publications Inc, PO Box 370540, Montara, CA 94037-0540 *Tel:* 650-728-5219 *Toll Free Tel:* 800-554-5457 *Fax:* 650-728-0918, pg 269

Thomas Nelson Inc, 501 Nelson Place, Nashville, TN 37214 *Tel:* 615-889-9000 *Toll Free Tel:* 800-251-4000 *Fax:* 615-902-1610 *E-mail:* publicity@thomasnelson.com *Web Site:* www.thomasnelson.com, pg 269

Thomas Publications, 3245 Fairfield Rd, Gettysburg, PA 17325 *Tel:* 717-642-6600 *Toll Free Tel:* 800-840-6782 *Fax:* 717-642-5555 *E-mail:* thomaspub@blazenet.net *Web Site:* www.thomaspublications.com, pg 269

William A Thomas Braille Bookstore, 3290 SE Slater St, Stuart, FL 34997 *Tel:* 772-286-8366 *Toll Free Tel:* 888-336-3142 *Fax:* 772-286-8909 *Web Site:* www.brailleintl.org, pg 269

Thompson Educational Publishing Inc, 6 Ripley Ave, Suite 200, Toronto, ON M6S 3N9, Canada *Tel:* 416-766-2763 (admin & orders) *Fax:* 416-766-0398 (admin & orders) *E-mail:* publisher@thompsonbooks.com *Web Site:* www.thompsonbooks.com, pg 563

Thomson Delmar Learning, 5 Maxwell Dr, Clifton Park, NY 12065-8007 *Tel:* 518-464-3500 *Toll Free Tel:* 800-347-7707 (cust serv); 800-998-7498 *Fax:* 518-464-0393 *Toll Free Fax:* 800-487-8488 (cust serv) *Web Site:* www.thomson.com; www.delmarlearning.com, pg 269

Thomson Financial Publishing, 4709 W Golf Rd, Suite 600, Skokie, IL 60076-1253 *Tel:* 847-676-9600; 847-677-8037 *Toll Free Tel:* 800-321-3373 *Fax:* 847-676-9616 *E-mail:* custservice@tfp.com *Web Site:* www.tfp.com; www.tgbr.com, pg 270

Thomson Gale, 27500 Drake Rd, Farmington Hills, MI 48331-3535 *Tel:* 248-699-4253 *Toll Free Tel:* 800-347-4253 *Fax:* 248-699-8070 *Toll Free Fax:* 800-414-5043 *E-mail:* galeord@gale.com *Web Site:* www.gale.com, pg 270

Thomson Learning Inc, 200 First Stamford Place, Suite 400, Stamford, CT 06902 *Tel:* 203-539-8000 *Fax:* 203-539-7581 *E-mail:* communications@thomsonlearning.com *Web Site:* www.thomson.com/learning, pg 270

Thomson Peterson's, 2000 Lenox Dr, Lawrenceville, NJ 08648 *Tel:* 609-896-1800 *Toll Free Tel:* 800-338-3282 *Toll Free Fax:* 800-772-2465 *E-mail:* sales@petersons.com *Web Site:* www.petersons.com, pg 270

Thorndike Press, 295 Kennedy Memorial Dr, Waterville, ME 04901-4517 *Tel:* 207-859-1026 *Toll Free Tel:* 800-233-1244 *Fax:* 207-859-1009 *Toll Free Fax:* 800-558-4676 (orders) *E-mail:* printorders@thomson.com; international@thomson.com (orders for customers outside US & CA) *Web Site:* www.gale.com/thorndike, pg 270

Susan Thornton, 5108 South St, Vermilion, OH 44089 *Tel:* 440-967-1757 *E-mail:* thornton@hbr.net, pg 612

ThorsonsElement US, 535 Albany St, 5th fl, Boston, MA 02118 *Tel:* 617-451-1533 *Fax:* 617-451-0971 *Web Site:* www.thorsons.com, pg 270

Three Day Novel Contest, 3495 Cambie St, Suite 364, Vancouver, BC V5Z 4R3, Canada *E-mail:* 3day@bluelakebooks.com *Web Site:* www.anvilpress.com, pg 808

The Three Oaks Prize in Fiction, 2091 Suncrest Rd, Talent, OR 97540 *Tel:* 541-512-8792 *Fax:* 541-512-8793 *E-mail:* mail@storylinepress.com *Web Site:* www.storylinepress.com, pg 808

3 Seas Literary Agency, PO Box 8571, Madison, WI 53708 *Tel:* 608-221-4306 *E-mail:* threeseaslit@aol.com *Web Site:* threeseaslit.com, pg 658

Through the Bible Publishers, 2643 Midpoint Dr, Fort Collins, CO 80524-3216 *Tel:* 970-484-8483 *Toll Free Tel:* 800-284-0158 *Fax:* 970-495-6700 *E-mail:* discipleland@throughthebible.com *Web Site:* www.throughthebible.com, pg 271

Thunder's Mouth Press, 245 W 17 St, 11th fl, New York, NY 10011-5300 *Tel:* 646-375-2570 *Fax:* 646-375-2571 *Web Site:* www.thundersmouth.com, pg 271

Thurber Prize for American Humor, 77 Jefferson Ave, Columbus, OH 43215 *Tel:* 614-464-1032 *Fax:* 614-280-3645 *E-mail:* thurberhouse@thurberhouse.org *Web Site:* www.thurberhouse.org, pg 808

Tia Chucha Press, 12737 Glen Oaks Blvd, Suite 22, Sylmar, CA 91342 *Tel:* 818-362-7060 *Fax:* 818-362-7102 *E-mail:* info@tiachucha.com *Web Site:* www.tiachucha.com, pg 271

Tiare Publications, PO Box 493, Lake Geneva, WI 53147-0493 *Tel:* 262-248-4845 *Toll Free Tel:* 800-420-0579 *Fax:* 262-249-0299 *E-mail:* info@tiare.com *Web Site:* www.tiare.com, pg 271

Tide-mark Press, 179 Broad St, Windsor, CT 06095 *Tel:* 860-683-4499 *Toll Free Tel:* 800-338-2508 *Fax:* 860-683-4055 *E-mail:* customerservice@tide-mark.com *Web Site:* www.tidemarkpress.com, pg 271

Tidewater Publishers, 101 Water Way, Centreville, MD 21617 *Tel:* 410-758-1075 *Toll Free Tel:* 800-638-7641 *Fax:* 410-758-6849 *E-mail:* editor@cornellmaritimepress.com *Web Site:* www.tidewaterpublishrs.com, pg 271

Tilbury House Publishers, 2 Mechanic St, No 3, Gardiner, ME 04345 *Tel:* 207-582-1899 *Toll Free Tel:* 800-582-1899 (orders) *Fax:* 207-582-8229 *E-mail:* tilbury@tilburyhouse.com *Web Site:* www.tilburyhouse.com, pg 271

Timber Press Inc, 133 SW Second Ave, Suite 450, Portland, OR 97204 *Tel:* 503-227-2878 *Toll Free Tel:* 800-327-5680 *Fax:* 503-227-3070 *E-mail:* mail@timberpress.com *Web Site:* www.timberpress.com, pg 271

Time Being Books, 10411 Clayton Rd, Suites 201-203, St Louis, MO 63131 *Tel:* 314-432-1771 *Toll Free Tel:* 866-840-4334 *Fax:* 314-432-7939 *Toll Free Fax:* 888-301-9121 *E-mail:* tbbooks@sbcglobal.net *Web Site:* www.timebeing.com, pg 271

Time Warner Audio Books, Sports Illustrated Bldg, 135 W 50 St, New York, NY 10020 *Tel:* 212-522-7334 *Fax:* 212-522-7994 *Web Site:* www.twbookmark.com/audiobooks, pg 271

Time Warner Book Group, 1271 Avenue of the Americas, New York, NY 10020 *Tel:* 212-522-7200 *Fax:* 212-522-7991 *Web Site:* www.twbookmark.com, pg 271

Times Change Press, 8453 Blackney Rd, Sebastopol, CA 95472 *Tel:* 707-824-9456, pg 272

Editions Pierre Tisseyre, 5757 Cypihot, St-Laurent, PQ H4S 1R3, Canada *Tel:* 514-334-2690 *Toll Free Tel:* 800-263-3678 *Fax:* 514-334-8395 *Toll Free Fax:* 800-643-4720 (Canada only) *E-mail:* ed.tisseyre@erpi.com, pg 563

TNG Canada/CWA, 7B-1050 Baxter Rd, Ottawa, ON K2C 3P1, Canada *Tel:* 613-820-9777 *Toll Free Tel:* 877-486-4292 *Fax:* 613-820-8188 *E-mail:* info@ tngcanada.org *Web Site:* www.tngcanada.org, pg 701

Toad Hall Inc, RR 2, Box 2090, Laceyville, PA 18623 *Tel:* 570-869-2942 *Fax:* 570-869-1031 *E-mail:* toadhallco@aol.com *Web Site:* www. laceyville.com/Toad-Hall, pg 272, 658

The Toby Press LLC, 2 Great Pasture Rd, Danbury, CT 06810 *Tel:* 203-830-8508 *Fax:* 203-830-8512 *E-mail:* toby@tobypress.com *Web Site:* www. tobypress.com, pg 272

Todd Publications, PO Box 635, Nyack, NY 10960-0635 *Tel:* 845-358-6213 *Fax:* 845-358-6213 *E-mail:* toddpub@aol.com *Web Site:* www. toddpublications.com, pg 272

Todd Publishing Inc, 1224 N Nokomis NE, Alexandria, MN 56308 *Tel:* 320-763-5190 *Fax:* 320-763-9290, pg 272

TODTRI Book Publishers, 4049 Broadway, Suite 153, New York, NY 10032 *Tel:* 212-695-6622 ext 10 *Toll Free Tel:* 800-696-7299 *Fax:* 212-695-6988 *Toll Free Fax:* 800-696-7482 *E-mail:* todtri@mindspring.com *Web Site:* TODTRI.com, pg 272

Mary F Tomaselli, 146-05 14 Ave, Whitestone, NY 11357 *Tel:* 718-767-3541 *E-mail:* indexer@aol.com *Web Site:* members.aol.com/indexer/indexer.htm, pg 612

The Tomasino Agency Inc, 70 Chestnut St, Dobbs Ferry, NY 10522 *Tel:* 914-674-9659 *Fax:* 914-693-0381 *E-mail:* BookNView@aol.com, pg 658

Tommy Nelson, PO Box 141000, Nashville, TN 37214-1000 *Tel:* 615-889-9000 *Toll Free Tel:* 800-251-4000 *Fax:* 615-902-3330 *Web Site:* www.tommynelson.com, pg 272

Jeanne Toomey Associates, 95 Belden St, Rte 126, Falls Village, CT 06031 *Tel:* 860-824-5469; 860-824-0831; 860-824-3020 *Fax:* 860-824-5460, pg 658

Top of the Mountain Publishing, PO Box 2244, Pinellas Park, FL 33780-2244 *Tel:* 727-391-3958 *Fax:* 727-391-4598 *E-mail:* tag@abcinfo.com *Web Site:* abcinfo. com; www.topofthemountain.com, pg 272

Torah Aura Productions, 4423 Fruitland Ave, Los Angeles, CA 90058 *Tel:* 323-585-7312 *Toll Free Tel:* 800-238-6724 *Fax:* 323-585-0327 *E-mail:* misrad@torahaura.com *Web Site:* www. torahaura.com, pg 272

Torah Umesorah Publications, 5723 18 Ave, Brooklyn, NY 11204 *Tel:* 718-259-1223 *Fax:* 718-259-1795 *E-mail:* mail@tupublications.com; publications@ tupublications.com, pg 272

Tormont/Brimar Publication Inc, 338 St Antoine E, 3rd fl, Montreal, PQ H2Y 1A3, Canada *Tel:* 514-954-1441 *Fax:* 514-954-1443 *E-mail:* info@tormont.ca, pg 563

Phyllis R Tornetta Literary Agency, 4 Kettle Lane, Mashpee, MA 02649 *Tel:* 508-539-8821 *E-mail:* phyl4@capecod.net, pg 658

Tortuga Press, 3919 Mayette Ave, Santa Rosa, CA 95405 *Tel:* 707-544-4720 *Fax:* 707-544-5609 *E-mail:* info@ tortugapress.com *Web Site:* www.tortugapress.com, pg 272

Total Power Publishing, 4274 Bay View Dr, Fernandina Beach, FL 32035 *Tel:* 904-321-1169 *Fax:* 904-321-2872 *E-mail:* stinger20007399@aol.com, pg 273

Totline Publications, 3195 Wilson Dr NW, Grand Rapids, MI 49544 *Toll Free Tel:* 800-417-3261 *Toll Free Fax:* 888-203-9361 *Web Site:* www.teacherspecialty. com, pg 273

Tower Publishing Co, 588 Saco Rd, Standish, ME 04084 *Tel:* 207-642-5400 *Toll Free Tel:* 800-969-8693 *Fax:* 207-642-5463 *E-mail:* info@towerpub.com *Web Site:* www.towerpub.com, pg 273

TowleHouse Publishing, 394 W Main St, Suite B-9, Hendersonville, TN 37075 *Tel:* 615-822-6405 *Fax:* 615-822-5535 *E-mail:* vermonte@aol.com *Web Site:* www.towlehouse.com, pg 273

Towngate Theatre Playwriting Contest, Stifel Fine Arts Ctr, 1330 National Rd, Wheeling, WV 26003 *Tel:* 304-242-7700 *Fax:* 304-242-7747, pg 808

Townson Publishing Co Ltd, PO Box 1404, Bentall Centre, Vancouver, BC V6C 2P7, Canada *Tel:* 604-263-0014 *Fax:* 604-263-0014 *E-mail:* info@townson. ca *Web Site:* www.townson.ca, pg 563

Towson University Prize for Literature, English Dept, 8000 York Rd, Towson, MD 21252 *Tel:* 410-704-2847 *Fax:* 410-704-6392 *Web Site:* www.towson.edu, pg 809

Traders Press Inc, 703 Laurens Rd, Greenville, SC 29607-1912 *Tel:* 864-298-0222 *Toll Free Tel:* 800-927-8222 *Fax:* 864-298-0221 *Web Site:* www.traderspress. com, pg 273

Tradewind Books, 1809 Maritime Mews, Vancouver, BC V6H 3W7, Canada *Tel:* 604-662-4405 *Fax:* 604-730-0154 *E-mail:* tradewindbooks@eudoramail.com *Web Site:* www.tradewindbooks.com, pg 563

Trafalgar Square, Howe Hill Rd, North Pomfret, VT 05053 *Tel:* 802-457-1911 *Toll Free Tel:* 800-423-4525 *Fax:* 802-457-1913 *E-mail:* tsquare@sover.net *Web Site:* www.trafalgarsquarebooks.com, pg 273

Trafton Publishing, 109 Barcliff Terr, Cary, NC 27511 *Tel:* 919-363-0999 *Web Site:* www.rogbates.com, pg 273

Trails Books, PO Box 317, Black Earth, WI 53515-0317 *Tel:* 608-767-8000 *Toll Free Tel:* 800-236-8088 *Fax:* 608-767-5444 *E-mail:* books@wistrails.com *Web Site:* www.trailsbooks.com, pg 273

Trails Illustrated, Division of National Geographic Maps, PO Box 4357, Evergreen, CO 80437-4357 *Tel:* 303-670-3457 *Toll Free Tel:* 800-962-1643 *Fax:* 303-670-3644 *Toll Free Fax:* 800-626-8676 *E-mail:* topomaps@aol.com *Web Site:* www. nationalgeographics.com, pg 273

Training Resource Network Inc (T R N), PO Box 439, St Augustine, FL 32085-0439 *Tel:* 904-823-9800 (cust serv); 904-824-7121 (edit off) *Toll Free Tel:* 800-280-7010 (orders) *Fax:* 904-823-3554 *E-mail:* customerservice@trninc.com *Web Site:* www. trninc.com, pg 273

Trakker Maps Inc, 8350 Parkline Blvd, Suite 360, Orlando, FL 32809 *Tel:* 407-447-6485 *Toll Free Tel:* 800-327-3108 *Fax:* 407-447-6488 *E-mail:* sales@ trakkermaps.com *Web Site:* www.trakkermaps.com, pg 273

Tralco Lingo Fun, 1030 Upper James St, Suite 101, Hamilton, ON L9C 6X6, Canada *Tel:* 905-575-5717 *Toll Free Tel:* 888-487-2526 *Fax:* 905-575-1783 *Toll Free Fax:* 866-487-2527 *E-mail:* sales@tralco.com *Web Site:* www.tralco.com, pg 563

Trans-Atlantic Publications Inc, 311 Bainbridge St, Philadelphia, PA 19147 *Tel:* 215-925-5083 *Fax:* 215-925-1912 *E-mail:* order@transatlanticpub. com *Web Site:* www.transatlanticpub.com; www. businesstitles.com, pg 274

Trans Tech Publications, c/o Enfield Distribution Co, 234 May St, Enfield, NH 03748 *Tel:* 603-632-7377 *Fax:* 603-632-5611 *E-mail:* usa-ttp@ttp.net; info@ enfiedbooks.com *Web Site:* www.ttp.net, pg 274

Transaction Publishers, Rutgers University, 35 Berrue Circle, Piscataway, NJ 08854 *Tel:* 732-445-2280 *Toll Free Tel:* 888-999-6778 *Fax:* 732-445-3138 *E-mail:* trans@transactionpub.com *Web Site:* www. transactionpub.com, pg 274

Transatlantic Arts Inc, PO Box 6086, Albuquerque, NM 87197-6086 *Tel:* 505-898-2289 *Fax:* 505-898-2289 *E-mail:* books@transatlantic.com *Web Site:* www. transatlantic.com/direct, pg 274

Transatlantic Literary Agency Inc, 72 Glengowan Rd, Toronto, ON M4N 1G4, Canada *Tel:* 416-488-9214 *Fax:* 416-488-4531 *E-mail:* info@tla1.com *Web Site:* www.tla1.com, pg 659

Transcontinental Music Publications, 633 Third Ave, New York, NY 10017 *Tel:* 212-650-4101 *Toll Free Tel:* 800-455-5223 *Fax:* 212-650-4109 *E-mail:* tmp@ uahc.org *Web Site:* www.transcontinentalmusic.com, pg 274

Translation Prize, 58 Park Ave, New York, NY 10016 *Tel:* 212-879-9779 *Fax:* 212-686-2115 *E-mail:* info@ amscan.org *Web Site:* www.amscan.org, pg 809

Transnational Publishers Inc, 410 Saw Mill River Rd, Suite 2045, Ardsley, NY 10502 *Tel:* 914-693-5100 *Toll Free Tel:* 800-914-8186 (orders only) *Fax:* 914-693-4430 *E-mail:* info@transnationalpubs.com *Web Site:* www.transnationalpubs.com, pg 274

Transportation Research Board, 500 Fifth St NW, Washington, DC 20001 *Tel:* 202-334-3213 *Fax:* 202-334-2519 *E-mail:* trbsales@nas.edu *Web Site:* trb.org, pg 274

Transportation Technical Service Inc, 500 Lafayette Blvd, Suite 230, Fredericksburg, VA 22401 *Tel:* 540-899-9872 *Toll Free Tel:* 888-ONLY-TTS (665-9887) *Fax:* 540-899-1948 *E-mail:* truckinfo@ttstrucks.com *Web Site:* www.ttstrucks.com, pg 274

Travel Keys, PO Box 160691, Sacramento, CA 95816-0691 *Tel:* 916-452-5200 *Fax:* 916-452-5200, pg 274

Travelers' Tales Inc, 330 Townsend St, Suite 208, San Francisco, CA 94107 *Tel:* 415-227-8600 *Fax:* 415-227-8605 *E-mail:* ttales@travelerstales.com *Web Site:* www.travelerstales.com, pg 275

Treasure Bay Inc, 17 Parkgrove Dr, South San Francisco, CA 94080 *Tel:* 650-589-7980 *Fax:* 650-589-7927 *E-mail:* webothread@comcast.net, pg 275

Treehaus Communications Inc, 906 W Loveland Ave, Loveland, OH 45140 *Tel:* 513-683-5716 *Toll Free Tel:* 800-638-4287 (orders) *Fax:* 513-683-2882 (orders) *E-mail:* treehaus@treehaus1.com *Web Site:* www.treehaus1.com, pg 275

Triad Publishing Co, PO Drawer 13355, Gainesville, FL 32604 *Tel:* 352-373-5800 *Fax:* 352-373-1488 *Toll Free Fax:* 800-854-4947 *Web Site:* www.triadpublishing. com, pg 275

Trident Inc, 885 Pierce Butler Rte, St Paul, MN 55104 *Tel:* 651-638-0077 *Fax:* 651-638-0084 *E-mail:* info@ atlas-games.com *Web Site:* www.atlas-games.com, pg 275

Trident Media Group LLC, 41 Madison Ave, 36th fl, New York, NY 10010 *Tel:* 212-262-4810 *Fax:* 212-725-4501 *Web Site:* www.tridentmediagroup.com, pg 659

Trident Media Inc, 801 N Pitt St, Suite 123, Alexandria, VA 22314 *Tel:* 703-684-6895 *Fax:* 703-684-0639 *E-mail:* info@samhost.net *Web Site:* www.edenplaza. com, pg 275

Trident Press International, 801 12 Ave S, Suite 400, Naples, FL 34102 *Tel:* 239-649-7077 *Toll Free Tel:* 800-593-3662 *Fax:* 239-649-5832 *Toll Free Fax:* 800-494-4226 *E-mail:* tridentpress@worldnet.att. net *Web Site:* www.trident-international.com, pg 275

Trillium Book Award/Prix Trillium, 175 Bloor St E, Suite 501, South Tower, Toronto, ON M4W 3R8, Canada *Tel:* 416-642-6698 *Fax:* 416-314-6876 *Web Site:* www.omdc.on.ca, pg 809

Trimarket Co, 2264 Bowdoin St, Palo Alto, CA 94306 *Tel:* 650-494-1406 *Fax:* 650-494-1413 *E-mail:* info@ trimarket.com *Web Site:* www.trimarket.com, pg 275

The Trinity Foundation, PO Box 68, Unicoi, TN 37692-0068 *Tel:* 423-743-0199 *Fax:* 423-743-2005 *Web Site:* www.trinityfoundation.org, pg 275

Trinity University Press, One Trinity Place, San Antonio, TX 78212-7200 *Tel:* 210-999-8884 *Fax:* 210-999-8838 *E-mail:* books@trinity.edu *Web Site:* www.trinity. edu/tupress, pg 275

TripBuilder Inc, 15 Oak St, Westport, CT 06880 *Tel:* 203-227-1255 *Toll Free Tel:* 800-525-9745 *Fax:* 203-227-1257 *E-mail:* info@tripbuilder.com *Web Site:* www.tripbuilder.com, pg 275

TriQuarterly Books, 2020 Ridge Ave, Evanston, IL 60208-4302 *Tel:* 847-491-3490 *Toll Free Tel:* 800-621-2736 (orders only) *Fax:* 847-467-2096 *E-mail:* nupress@northwestern.edu *Web Site:* www. nupress.northwestern.edu, pg 275

Tristan Publishing, 2300 Louisiana Ave, Suite B, Golden Valley, MN 55427 *Tel:* 763-545-1383 *Toll Free Tel:* 866-545-1383 *Fax:* 763-545-1387 *E-mail:* info@tristanpublishing.com *Web Site:* www.tristanpublishing.com, pg 276

Triumph Books, 601 S LaSalle St, Suite 500, Chicago, IL 60605 *Tel:* 312-939-3330 *Toll Free Tel:* 800-335-5323 *Fax:* 312-663-3557 *E-mail:* orders@triumphbooks.com *Web Site:* www.triumphbooks.com, pg 276

Triumph Learning, 333 E 38 St, 8th fl, New York, NY 10016 *Tel:* 212-652-0200 *Fax:* 212-652-0203 *Web Site:* www.triumphlearning.com, pg 276

Tropical Press Inc, PO Box 161174, Miami, FL 33116-1174 *Tel:* 305-971-1887 *Fax:* 305-378-1595 *E-mail:* tropicbook@aol.com *Web Site:* www.tropicalpress.com, pg 276

Troubleshooting Sheetfed Offset Press Problems, 200 Deer Run Rd, Sewickley, PA 15143-2600 *Tel:* 412-741-6860 *Toll Free Tel:* 800-910-4283 *Fax:* 412-741-2311 *E-mail:* info@gain.net *Web Site:* www.gain.net, pg 748

Harry S Truman Book Award, 500 W US Hwy 24, Independence, MO 64050-1798 *Tel:* 816-268-8248 *Fax:* 816-268-8295 *E-mail:* truman.library@nara.gov *Web Site:* www.trumanlibrary.org, pg 809

Truman State University Press, 100 E Normal St, Kirksville, MO 63501-4221 *Tel:* 660-785-7336 *Toll Free Tel:* 800-916-6802 *Fax:* 660-785-4480 *E-mail:* tsup@truman.edu *Web Site:* tsup.truman.edu, pg 276

Lynn Truppe, 15980 W Marietta Dr, New Berlin, WI 53151 *Tel:* 262-782-7482, pg 612

Trustus Playwrights' Festival, 520 Lady St, Columbia, SC 29201 *Tel:* 803-254-9732 *Fax:* 803-771-9153 *E-mail:* trustus@trustus.org *Web Site:* www.trustus.org, pg 809

TSAR Publications, PO Box 6996, Sta A, Toronto, ON M5W 1X7, Canada *Tel:* 416-483-7191 *Fax:* 416-486-0706 *E-mail:* treview@total.net *Web Site:* www.tsarbooks.com, pg 563

TSG Publishing Foundation Inc, 28641 N 63 Place, Cave Creek, AZ 85331 *Tel:* 480-502-1909 *Fax:* 480-502-0713 *E-mail:* info@tsgfoundation.org *Web Site:* www.tsgfoundation.org, pg 276

TSI Graphics, 1300 S Raney, Effingham, IL 62401 *Tel:* 217-347-7733 *Fax:* 217-342-9611 *Web Site:* www.tsigraphics.com, pg 612

Kate Tufts Discovery Award, 160 E Tenth St, Harper East B7, Claremont, CA 91711 *Tel:* 909-621-8974 *Web Site:* www.cgu.edu/tufts, pg 809

Kingsley Tufts Poetry Award, 160 E Tenth St, Harper E B7, Claremont, CA 91711-6165 *Tel:* 909-621-8974 *Web Site:* www.cgu.edu/tufts, pg 809

Tugeau 2 Inc, 2132-A Central SE, Suite 196, Albuquerque, NM 87106 *Tel:* 505-842-0922 *Web Site:* www.tugeau2.com, pg 667

Christina A Tugeau Artist Agent LLC, 3009 Margaret Jones Lane, Williamsburg, VA 23185 *Tel:* 757-221-0666 *E-mail:* chris@catugeau.com *Web Site:* www.CATugeau.com, pg 667

Tundra Books, 481 University Ave, Suite 900, Toronto, ON M5G 2E9, Canada *Tel:* 416-598-4786 *Fax:* 416-598-0247 *E-mail:* tundra@mcclelland.com *Web Site:* www.tundrabooks.com, pg 563

Tundra Books of Northern New York, PO Box 1030, Plattsburgh, NY 12901 *Tel:* 416-598-4786 *Fax:* 416-598-0247 *E-mail:* tundra@mcclelland.com *Web Site:* www.tundrabooks.com, pg 276

Melissa Turk & the Artist Network, 9 Babbling Brook Lane, Suffern, NY 10901 *Tel:* 845-368-8606 *Fax:* 845-368-8608 *E-mail:* melissa@melissaturk.com *Web Site:* www.melissaturk.com, pg 667

Nancy Byrd Turner Memorial, 100 N Berwick, Williamsburg, VA 23188 *Web Site:* www.poetrysocietyofvirginia.org, pg 809

Turnstone Press, 607-100 Arthur St, Winnipeg, MB R3B 1H3, Canada *Tel:* 204-947-1555 *Toll Free Tel:* 800-982-6472 *Fax:* 204-942-1555 *E-mail:* editor@turnstonepress.com; mktg@turnstonepress.com *Web Site:* www.turnstonepress.com, pg 564

Turtle Books Inc, 866 United Nations Plaza, Suite 525, New York, NY 10017 *Tel:* 212-644-2020 *Fax:* 212-223-4387 *E-mail:* turtlebook@aol.com *Web Site:* www.turtlebooks.com, pg 276

Turtle Point Press, 233 Broadway, Rm 946, New York, NY 10279 *Tel:* 212-285-1019 *Fax:* 212-285-1019 *E-mail:* countomega@aol.com *Web Site:* www.turtlepoint.com, pg 276

Tuttle Publishing, Airport Business Park, 364 Innovation Dr, North Clarendon, VT 05759-9436 *Tel:* 617-951-4080 (edit); 802-773-8930 *Toll Free Tel:* 800-526-2778 *Fax:* 617-951-4045 (edit); 802-773-6993 *Toll Free Fax:* 800-FAX-TUTL *E-mail:* info@tuttlepublishing.com *Web Site:* www.tuttlepublishing.com, pg 277

Twayne Publishers, 27500 Drake Rd, Famington Hills, MI 48331-3535 *Tel:* 248-699-4253 *Toll Free Tel:* 800-877-4253 *Web Site:* www.galegroup.com/twayne, pg 277

28th Appalachian Writers' Workshop, PO Box 844, Hindman, KY 41822-0844 *Tel:* 606-785-5475 *Fax:* 606-785-3499 *E-mail:* hss@tgtel.com *Web Site:* www.hindmansettlement.org, pg 748

Twenty-First Century King James Bible Publishers, 215 Main Ave, Gary, SD 57237 *Tel:* 605-272-5575 *Toll Free Tel:* 800-225-5521 *Fax:* 605-272-5306 *E-mail:* kj21@kj21.com *Web Site:* www.kj21.com, pg 277

The 25 Most "Censored" Stories of 2003, Sonoma State University, 1801 E Cotati Ave, Rohnert Park, CA 94928 *Tel:* 707-664-2500 *Fax:* 707-664-2108 *E-mail:* censored@sonoma.edu *Web Site:* www.projectcensored.org, pg 809

Twenty-Third Publications, 185 Willow St, Mystic, CT 06355 *Tel:* 860-536-2611 *Toll Free Tel:* 800-321-0411 (orders) *Fax:* 860-536-5674 (edit) *Toll Free Fax:* 800-572-0788, pg 277

Twilight Times Books, PO Box 3340, Kingsport, TN 37664-0340 *Tel:* 423-323-0183 *Fax:* 423-323-0183 *E-mail:* publisher@twilighttimes.com *Web Site:* www.twilighttimesbooks.com, pg 277

Twin Oaks Indexing, 138 Twin Oaks Rd, Louisa, VA 23093 *Tel:* 540-894-5126 *Fax:* 540-894-4112 *E-mail:* indexing@twinoaks.org, pg 612

Twin Peaks Press, PO Box 129, Vancouver, WA 98666-0129 *Tel:* 360-694-2462 *Fax:* 360-696-3210 *E-mail:* twinpeak@pacifier.com *Web Site:* www.pacifier.com/~twinpeak, pg 277

2M Communications Ltd, 121 W 27 St, Suite 601, New York, NY 10001 *Tel:* 212-741-1509 *Fax:* 212-691-4460 *Web Site:* www.2mcommunications.com, pg 659

Two Thousand Three Associates, 4180 Saxon Dr, New Smyrna Beach, FL 32169 *Tel:* 386-427-7876 *Fax:* 386-423-7523 *E-mail:* ttta@worldnet.att.net, pg 277

Tyndale House Publishers Inc, 351 Executive Dr, Carol Stream, IL 60188 *Tel:* 630-668-8303 *Toll Free Tel:* 800-323-9400 *Web Site:* www.tyndale.com, pg 277

Type & Archetype Press, PO Box 14285, Charleston, SC 29422-4285 *Tel:* 843-406-9113 *Toll Free Tel:* 800-447-8973 *Fax:* 843-406-9118 *E-mail:* info@typetemperament.com *Web Site:* www.typearchetype.com, pg 277

Tzipora Publications Inc, 175 E 96 St, Suite 10-O, New York, NY 10128 *Tel:* 212-427-5399 *Fax:* 413-638-9158 *E-mail:* tziporapub@msn.com *Web Site:* www.tziporapub.com, pg 277

UCI Extension Writers' Program, PO Box 6050, Irvine, CA 92616 *Tel:* 949-824-5990 *Fax:* 949-824-3651 *Web Site:* www.unex.uci.edu, pg 748

UCLA Fowler Museum of Cultural History, 1586 Fowler, Los Angeles, CA 90095-1549 *Tel:* 310-825-9672 *Fax:* 310-206-7007 *Web Site:* www.fmch.ucla.edu, pg 278

UCLA Latin American Center Publications, UCLA Latin American Ctr, 10343 Bunche Hall, Los Angeles, CA 90095 *Tel:* 310-825-6634 *Fax:* 310-206-6859 *E-mail:* lacpubs@international.ucla.edu *Web Site:* www.international.ucla.edu/lac, pg 278

Ucross Foundation Residency Program, 30 Big Red Lane, Clearmont, WY 82835 *Tel:* 307-737-2291 *Fax:* 307-737-2322 *E-mail:* info@ucross.org *Web Site:* www.ucrossfoundation.org, pg 809

Ugly Duckling Presse, 106 Ferris St, 2nd fl, Brooklyn, NY 11231 *Tel:* 718-852-5529 *E-mail:* udp_mailbox@yahoo.com *Web Site:* www.uglyducklingpresse.org, pg 278

UglyTown, 2148 1/2 W Sunset Blvd, Suite 204, Los Angeles, CA 90026-3148 *Tel:* 213-484-8334 *Fax:* 213-484-8333 *E-mail:* mayorsoffice@uglytown.com *Web Site:* www.uglytown.com, pg 278

ULI-The Urban Land Institute, 1025 Thomas Jefferson St NW, Suite 500 W, Washington, DC 20007-5201 *Tel:* 202-624-7000 *Toll Free Tel:* 800-321-5011 *Fax:* 202-624-7140; 410-626-7147 (orders only) *Toll Free Fax:* 800-248-4585 *E-mail:* bookstore@uli.org *Web Site:* www.uli.org, pg 278

Ultramarine Publishing Co Inc, 12 Washington Ave, Hastings-on-Hudson, NY 10706 *Tel:* 914-478-1339 *E-mail:* washbook@sprynet.com, pg 278

Ulysses Press, PO Box 3440, Berkeley, CA 94703-0440 *Tel:* 510-601-8301 *Toll Free Tel:* 800-377-2542 *Fax:* 510-601-8307 *E-mail:* ulysses@ulyssespress.com *Web Site:* www.ulyssespress.com, pg 278

Ulysses Travel Guides, 4176 Saint Denis, Montreal, PQ H2W 2M5, Canada *Tel:* 514-843-9447 *Fax:* 514-843-9448 *E-mail:* info@ulysses.ca *Web Site:* www.ulyssesguides.com, pg 564

Unarius Academy of Science Publications, 145 S Magnolia Ave, El Cajon, CA 92020-4522 *Tel:* 619-444-7062 *Toll Free Tel:* 800-475-7062 *Fax:* 619-447-9637 *E-mail:* uriel@unarius.org *Web Site:* www.unarius.org, pg 278

Undergraduate Paper Competition in Cryptology, Dept Math Sciences, US Military Academy, West Point, NY 10996 *Tel:* 845-938-3200 *Web Site:* www.dean.usma.edu/math/pubs/cryptologia, pg 809

Underwood Books Inc, PO Box 1609, Grass Valley, CA 95945-1609 *Fax:* 530-274-7179 *Web Site:* www.underwoodbooks.com, pg 278

Unicor Medical Inc, 4160 Carmichael Rd, Suite 101, Montgomery, AL 36106 *Tel:* 334-260-8150 *Toll Free Tel:* 800-825-7421 *Fax:* 334-272-1046 *Toll Free Fax:* 800-305-8030 *E-mail:* sales@unicormed.com *Web Site:* www.unicormed.com, pg 278

Union des Ecrivaines et Ecrivains Quebecois, 3492 avenue Laval, Montreal, PQ H2X 3C8, Canada *Tel:* 514-849-8540 *Toll Free Tel:* 888-849-8540 *Fax:* 514-271-6239 *E-mail:* ecrivez@uneq.qc.ca *Web Site:* www.uneq.qc.ca, pg 701

Union League Civic & Arts Foundation Poetry Prize, 1030 N Clark St, Suite 420, Chicago, IL 60610 *Tel:* 312-787-7070 *Fax:* 312-787-6650 *E-mail:* poetry@poetrymagazine.org *Web Site:* www.poetrymagazine.org, pg 809

Union Square Publishing, 857 Broadway, 3rd fl, New York, NY 10003 *Tel:* 212-255-6661 *Fax:* 212-255-6671 *E-mail:* cardozapub@aol.com *Web Site:* www.cardozapub.com, pg 278

Unique Publications Books & Videos, 4201 W Vanowen Place, Burbank, CA 91505 *Tel:* 818-845-2656 *Toll Free Tel:* 800-332-3330 *Fax:* 818-845-7761 *E-mail:* info@cfwenterprises.com *Web Site:* www.cfwenterprises.com, pg 279

The United Educators Inc, 900 N Shore Dr, Suite 140, Lake Bluff, IL 60044 *Tel:* 847-234-3700 *Fax:* 847-234-8705 *E-mail:* arslms@aol.com, pg 279

United Hospital Fund, 350 Fifth Ave, 23rd fl, New York, NY 10118-2399 *Tel:* 212-494-0700 *Fax:* 212-494-0800 *E-mail:* info@uhfnyc.org *Web Site:* www.uhfnyc.org, pg 279

United Nations Association of the United States of America Inc, 801 Second Ave, 2nd fl, New York, NY 10017 *Tel:* 212-907-1300 *Fax:* 212-682-9185 *E-mail:* unadc@unausa.org *Web Site:* www.unausa.org, pg 701

United Nations Publications, 2 United Nations Plaza, Rm DC2-0853, New York, NY 10017 *Tel:* 212-963-8302 *Toll Free Tel:* 800-253-9646 *Fax:* 212-963-3489 *E-mail:* publications@un.org *Web Site:* www.un.org/publications, pg 279

United States Holocaust Memorial Museum, 100 Raoul Wallenberg Place SW, Washington, DC 20024-2126 *Tel:* 202-488-6115; 202-488-6144 (orders) *Toll Free Tel:* 800-259-9998 (orders) *Fax:* 202-488-2684; 202-488-0438 (orders) *Web Site:* www.ushmm.org/, pg 279

United States Institute of Peace Press, 1200 17 St NW, Suite 200, Washington, DC 20036-3011 *Tel:* 202-457-1700 (edit); 703-661-1590 (cust serv) *Toll Free Tel:* 800-868-8064 (cust serv) *Fax:* 703-661-1501 (cust serv) *Web Site:* www.usip.org, pg 279

United States Pharmacopeia, 12601 Twinbrook Pkwy, Rockville, MD 20852 *Tel:* 301-881-0666 *Toll Free Tel:* 800-227-8772 *Fax:* 301-816-8148; 301-816-8236 (mktg) *E-mail:* marketing@usp.org *Web Site:* www.usp.org, pg 279

United States Tennis Association, 70 W Red Oak Lane, White Plains, NY 10604 *Tel:* 914-696-7000 *Fax:* 914-696-7027 *Web Site:* www.usta.com, pg 279

United Synagogue Book Service, 155 Fifth Ave, New York, NY 10010 *Tel:* 212-533-7800 (ext 2003) *Toll Free Tel:* 800-594-5617 (warehouse only) *Fax:* 212-253-5422 *E-mail:* booksvc@uscj.org *Web Site:* www.uscj.org/booksvc, pg 279

United Talent Agency, 9560 Wilshire Blvd, Suite 500, Beverly Hills, CA 90212 *Tel:* 310-273-6700 *Fax:* 310-247-1111, pg 659

United Tribes Media Inc, 240 W 35 St, Suite 500, New York, NY 10001 *Tel:* 212-244-4166; 212-534-7646 *E-mail:* janguerth@aol.com, pg 659

Unity House, 1901 NW Blue Pkwy, Unity Village, MO 64065-0001 *Tel:* 816-524-3550 (ext 3300); 816-251-3571 (sales) *Fax:* 816-251-3557 *E-mail:* unity@unityworldhq.org *Web Site:* www.unityonline.org, pg 280

Univelt Inc, PO Box 28130, San Diego, CA 92198-0130 *Tel:* 760-746-4005 *Fax:* 760-746-3139 *E-mail:* 76121.1532@compuserve.com *Web Site:* www.univelt.com, pg 280

Universe Publishing, 300 Park Ave S, 3rd fl, New York, NY 10010 *Tel:* 212-387-3400 *Fax:* 212-387-3535, pg 280

University College of Cape Breton Press Inc, 1250 Grand Lake Rd, Sydney, NS B1P 6L2, Canada *Tel:* 902-563-1604; 902-563-1421 *Fax:* 902-563-1177 *E-mail:* uucb_press@uccb.ca *Web Site:* www.uccbpress.ca, pg 564

University Council for Educational Administration, Univ of Missouri, 205 Hill Hall, Columbia, MO 65211-2185 *Tel:* 573-884-8300 *Fax:* 573-884-8302 *E-mail:* ucea@missouri.edu *Web Site:* www.ucea.org, pg 280

University Extension Press, 117 Science Place, Saskatoon, SK S7N 5C8, Canada *Tel:* 306-966-5558 *Fax:* 306-966-5567 *E-mail:* uep.books@usask.ca *Web Site:* www.uep.usask.ca, pg 564

The University of Akron Press, 374-B Bierce Library, Akron, OH 44325-1703 *Tel:* 330-972-5342 (ext 1703) *Toll Free Tel:* 877-827-7377 *Fax:* 330-972-8364 *E-mail:* uapress@uakron.edu *Web Site:* www.uakron.edu/uapress, pg 280

University of Alabama Press, Box 870380, Tuscaloosa, AL 35487-0380 *Tel:* 205-348-5180; 773-702-7000 (orders) *Fax:* 205-348-9201 *Web Site:* www.uapress.ua.edu, pg 280

University of Alabama Program in Creative Writing, PO Box 870244, Tuscaloosa, AL 35487-0244 *Tel:* 205-348-0766 *Fax:* 205-348-1388 *E-mail:* writeua@english.as.ua.edu *Web Site:* www.as.ua.edu/english, pg 755

University of Alaska Press, Eielson Bldg, Rm 104, Fairbanks, AK 99775-6240 *Tel:* 907-474-5831 *Toll Free Tel:* 888-252-6657 (US only) *Fax:* 907-474-5502 *E-mail:* fypress@uaf.edu *Web Site:* www.uaf.edu/uapress, pg 280

University of Alberta Press, Ring House 2, Edmonton, AB T6G 2E1, Canada *Tel:* 780-492-3662 *Fax:* 780-492-0719 *E-mail:* uap@ualberta.ca *Web Site:* www.uap.ualberta.ca, pg 564

The University of Arizona Press, 355 S Euclid Ave, Suite 103, Tucson, AZ 85719-6654 *Tel:* 520-621-1441 *Toll Free Tel:* 800-426-3797 (orders) *Fax:* 520-621-8899 *Toll Free Fax:* 800-426-3797 *E-mail:* uapress@uapress.arizona.edu *Web Site:* www.uapress.arizona.edu, pg 280

The University of Arkansas Press, McIlroy House, 201 Ozark Ave, Fayetteville, AR 72701 *Tel:* 479-575-3246 *Toll Free Tel:* 800-626-0090 *Fax:* 479-575-6044 *E-mail:* uapress@uark.edu *Web Site:* www.uapress.com, pg 280

University of Baltimore - Yale Gordon College of Liberal Arts, Ampersand Institute for Words & Images, 1420 N Charles St, Baltimore, MD 21201-5779 *Tel:* 410-837-6022 *Fax:* 410-837-6029 *Web Site:* raven.ubalt.edu, pg 755

University of British Columbia Press, 2029 West Mall, Vancouver, BC V6T 1Z2, Canada *Tel:* 604-822-5959 *Toll Free Tel:* 877-377-9378 *Fax:* 604-822-6083 *Toll Free Fax:* 800-668-0821 *E-mail:* info@ubcpress.ca *Web Site:* www.ubcpress.ca, pg 564

University of Calgary Press, 2500 University Dr NW, Calgary, AB T2N 1N4, Canada *Tel:* 403-220-7578 *Fax:* 403-282-0085 *E-mail:* whildebr@ucalgary.ca *Web Site:* www.uofcpress.com, pg 565

University of California Extension Professional Sequence in Copyediting & Courses in Publishing, 1995 University Ave, Suite 200, Berkeley, CA 94720-7002 *Tel:* 510-642-6362 *Fax:* 510-643-0599 *E-mail:* letters@unx.berkeley.edu *Web Site:* www.unex.berkeley.edu, pg 755

University of California Institute on Global Conflict & Cooperation, 9500 Gilman Dr, La Jolla, CA 92093-0518 *Tel:* 858-534-1979 *Fax:* 858-534-7655 *Web Site:* www-igcc.ucsd.edu, pg 280

University of California Press, 2120 Berkeley Way, Berkeley, CA 94720 *Tel:* 510-642-4247 *Toll Free Tel:* 800-777-4726 *Fax:* 510-643-7127 *Toll Free Fax:* 800-999-1958 *E-mail:* askucp@ucpress.edu *Web Site:* www.ucpress.edu, pg 281

University of Chicago, Graham School of General Studies, 1427 E 60 St, Chicago, IL 60637 *Tel:* 773-702-1682 *Fax:* 773-702-6814 *Web Site:* www.grahamschool.uchicago.edu, pg 755

The University of Connecticut, The Realities of Publishing, Dept of English, 337 Mansfield Rd, Rm 332, Storrs, CT 06269-1025 *Tel:* 860-486-2141 *Fax:* 203-486-1530 *E-mail:* halfyawk@aol.com (instructor) *Web Site:* www.uconn.edu (for university); www.sp.uconn.edu/~en291isi/wecometopublishing.html, pg 755

University of Delaware Press, Associated University Presses, 2010 Eastpark Blvd, Cranbury, NJ 08512 *Tel:* 609-655-4770 *Fax:* 609-655-8366 *E-mail:* aup440@aol.com, pg 281

University of Denver Center for Teaching International Relations Publications, University of Denver, CTIR/GSIS, 2201 S Gaylord St, Denver, CO 80208 *Tel:* 303-871-3106 *Toll Free Tel:* 800-967-2847 *Fax:* 303-871-2456 *Web Site:* www.du.edu/ctir, pg 281

University of Denver Publishing Institute, 2075 S University Blvd, D-114, Denver, CO 80210 *Tel:* 303-871-2570 *Fax:* 303-871-2501 *Web Site:* www.du.edu/pi, pg 755

University of Georgia Press, 330 Research Dr, Athens, GA 30602-4901 *Tel:* 706-369-6130 *Toll Free Tel:* 800-266-5842 (orders only) *Fax:* 706-369-6131 *E-mail:* books@ugapress.uga.edu *Web Site:* www.ugapress.org, pg 281

University of Hawaii, Bilger Hall, Rm 104, 2545 McCarthy Mall, Honolulu, HI 96822 *Tel:* 808-956-6660 *Fax:* 808-956-9170 *E-mail:* mwp@hawaii.edu *Web Site:* www.hawaii.edu/mwp, pg 755

University of Hawaii Press, 2840 Kolowalu St, Honolulu, HI 96822 *Tel:* 808-956-8255 *Toll Free Tel:* 888-847-7377 *Fax:* 808-988-6052 *Toll Free Fax:* 800-650-7811 *E-mail:* uhpbooks@hawaii.edu *Web Site:* www.uhpress.hawaii.edu, pg 281

University of Healing Press, 1101 Far Valley Rd, Campo, CA 91906-3213 *Tel:* 619-478-5111; 619-478-2506 *Toll Free Tel:* 888-463-8654 *Fax:* 619-478-5013 *E-mail:* unihealing@goduni.org *Web Site:* www.university-of-healing.edu, pg 281

University of Houston Creative Writing Program, 229 Roy Cullen Bldg, Houston, TX 77204-3015 *Tel:* 713-743-3015 *Fax:* 713-743-3697 *E-mail:* cwp@uh.edu *Web Site:* www.uh.edu/cwp, pg 755

University of Illinois at Chicago, Program for Writers, 601 S Morgan St, Chicago, IL 60607-7120 *Tel:* 312-413-2229; 312-413-2200 (English Dept) *Fax:* 312-413-1005, pg 755

University of Illinois, Dept of Journalism, Gregory Hall, Rm 120A, 810 S Wright St, Urbana, IL 61801 *Tel:* 217-333-0709 *Fax:* 217-333-7931 *E-mail:* journ@uiuc.edu *Web Site:* www.uiuc.edu/spike/index.pl, pg 755

University of Illinois Graduate School of Library & Information Science, 501 E Daniel St, Champaign, IL 61820-6211 *Tel:* 217-333-1359 *Fax:* 217-244-7329 *E-mail:* puboff@alexia.lis.uiuc.edu *Web Site:* www.lis.uiuc.edu/puboff/, pg 281

University of Illinois Press, 1325 S Oak, Champaign, IL 61820-6903 *Tel:* 217-333-0950; 212-577-5487 *Fax:* 217-244-8082; 410-516-6969 (orders) *E-mail:* uipress@uillinois.edu; journals@uillinois.edu *Web Site:* www.press.uillinois.edu, pg 281

University of Iowa Press, University of Iowa, 100 Kuhl House, Iowa City, IA 52242-1000 *Tel:* 319-335-2000 *Toll Free Tel:* 800-621-2736 (orders only) *Fax:* 319-335-2055 *Toll Free Fax:* 800-621-8476 (orders only) *E-mail:* uipress@uiowa.edu *Web Site:* www.uiowapress.org, pg 282

University of Iowa, Writer's Workshop, 102 Dey House, 507 N Clinton St, Iowa City, IA 52242 *Tel:* 319-335-0416 *Fax:* 319-335-0420, pg 809

University of Iowa, Writers' Workshop, Graduate Creative Writing Program, 102 Dey House, 507 N Clinton St, Iowa City, IA 52242-1000 *Tel:* 319-335-0416 *Toll Free Tel:* 800-553-4692 (ext 0416) *Fax:* 319-335-0420 *Web Site:* www.uiowa.edu/~iww/, pg 755

University of Louisiana at Lafayette, Center for Louisiana Studies, PO Box 40831, UL, Lafayette, LA 70504-0831 *Tel:* 337-482-6027 *Fax:* 337-482-6028 *E-mail:* ann@louisiana.edu *Web Site:* www.cls.louisiana.edu, pg 282

University of Manitoba Press, St Johns College, Winnipeg, MB R3T 2N2, Canada *Tel:* 204-474-9495 *Fax:* 204-474-7566 *Web Site:* www.umanitoba.ca/uofmpress, pg 565

University of Massachusetts Press, PO Box 429, Amherst, MA 01004-0429 *Tel:* 413-545-2217 *Toll Free Tel:* 800-537-5487 *Fax:* 413-545-1226; 410-516-6998 (fulfillment) *E-mail:* info@umpress.umass.edu; hfcustserv@mail.press.jhu.edu *Web Site:* www.umass.edu/umpress, pg 282

University of Michigan Center for Japanese Studies, 1085 Frieze Bldg, 1055 S State St, Ann Arbor, MI 48109-1285 *Tel:* 734-647-8885 *Fax:* 734-647-8886 *E-mail:* cjspubs@umich.edu *Web Site:* www.umich.edu/~iinet/cjs/, pg 282

University of Michigan Press, 839 Greene St, Ann Arbor, MI 48104-3209 *Tel:* 734-764-4388 *Fax:* 734-615-1540 *E-mail:* um.press@umich.edu *Web Site:* www.press.umich.edu, pg 282

University of Minnesota Press, 111 Third Ave S, Suite 290, Minneapolis, MN 55401-2520 *Tel:* 612-627-1970 *Fax:* 612-627-1980 *E-mail:* ump@tc.umn.edu *Web Site:* www.upress.umn.edu, pg 282

University of Missouri-Kansas City, New Letters Weekend Writers Conference, College of Arts & Sciences, Continuing Education Div, 5300 Rockhill Rd, Kansas City, MO 64110 *Tel:* 816-235-2736 *Fax:* 816-235-5279 *Web Site:* www.umkc.edu, pg 755

University of Missouri Press, 2910 Le Mone Blvd, Columbia, MO 65201 *Tel:* 573-882-7641 *Toll Free Tel:* 800-828-1894 (orders) *Fax:* 573-884-4498 *Web Site:* www.umsystem.edu/upress, pg 283

University of Montana, Environmental Writing Institute, Environmental Studies, University of Montana, Missoula, MT 59812 *Tel:* 406-243-2904 *Fax:* 406-243-6090 *E-mail:* evst@selway.umt.edu *Web Site:* www.umt.edu/ewi, pg 756

University of Nebraska at Omaha Center for Public Affairs Research, 6001 Dodge St, Omaha, NE 68182 *Tel:* 402-554-2134 *Fax:* 402-554-4946 *Web Site:* www.cpara.unomaha.edu/, pg 283

University of Nebraska Press, 233 N Eighth St, Lincoln, NE 68588-0255 *Tel:* 402-472-3581 *Toll Free Tel:* 800-755-1105 (orders) *Fax:* 402-472-0308 *Toll Free Fax:* 800-526-2617 *E-mail:* press@unl.edu *Web Site:* www.nebraskapress.unl.edu; www.bisonbooks.com, pg 283

University of Nevada Press, MS 166, Reno, NV 89557-0076 *Tel:* 775-784-6573 *Toll Free Tel:* 800-682-6657 *Fax:* 775-784-6200 *Toll Free Fax:* 877-682-6657 *Web Site:* www.nvbooks.nevada.edu, pg 283

University of New Mexico Press, 1720 Lomas Blvd NE, MSC01 1200, Albuquerque, NM 87131-0001 *Tel:* 505-277-2346; 505-277-4810 (order dept) *Toll Free Tel:* 800-249-7737 (orders only) *Fax:* 505-277-3350 *Toll Free Fax:* 800-622-8667 *E-mail:* unmpress@unm.edu; custserv@upress.unm.edu (order dept) *Web Site:* unmpress.com, pg 283

University of New Orleans Press, c/o UNO Foundation, 6601 Franklin Ave, New Orleans, LA 70122 *Tel:* 504-280-1375 *Fax:* 504-280-7339 *Web Site:* www.uno.edu, pg 283

The University of North Carolina Press, 116 S Boundary St, Chapel Hill, NC 27514-3808 *Tel:* 919-966-3561 *Toll Free Tel:* 800-848-6224 (orders only) *Fax:* 919-966-3829 *Toll Free Fax:* 800-272-6817 (orders) *E-mail:* uncpress@unc.edu *Web Site:* www.uncpress.unc.edu, pg 283

University of North Texas Press, 1820 Highland St, Bain Hall 101, Denton, TX 76201 *Tel:* 940-565-2142 *Fax:* 940-565-4590 *Web Site:* www.unt.edu/untpress, pg 284

University of Notre Dame Press, 310 Flanner Hall, Notre Dame, IN 46556 *Tel:* 574-631-6346 *Toll Free Tel:* 800-621-2736 (orders) *Fax:* 574-631-8148 *Toll Free Fax:* 800-621-8476 (orders) *E-mail:* nd.undpress.1@nd.edu *Web Site:* www.undpress.nd.edu, pg 284

University of Oklahoma Press, 4100 28 Ave NW, Norman, OK 73069-8218 *Tel:* 405-325-2000 *Toll Free Tel:* 800-627-7377 (orders) *Fax:* 405-364-5798 (orders) *Toll Free Fax:* 800-735-0476 (orders) *E-mail:* oupress@ou.edu *Web Site:* www.oupress.com, pg 284

University of Ottawa Press/Les Presses de l'Universite d'Ottawa, 542 King Edward Ave, Ottawa, ON K1N 6N5, Canada *Tel:* 613-562-5246 *Fax:* 613-562-5247 *E-mail:* press@uottawa.ca *Web Site:* www.uopress.uottawa.ca, pg 565

The University of Pennsylvania Museum of Archaeology & Anthropology, 3260 South St, Philadelphia, PA 19104-6324 *Tel:* 215-898-5723 *Fax:* 215-573-2497 *E-mail:* publications@museum.upenn.edu *Web Site:* www.museum.upenn.edu/publications, pg 284

University of Pennsylvania Press, 4200 Pine St, Philadelphia, PA 19104-4011 *Tel:* 215-898-6261 *Toll Free Tel:* 800-445-9880 (orders & cust serv only) *Fax:* 215-898-0404; 410-516-6998 (orders) *E-mail:* custserv@pobox.upenn.edu *Web Site:* www.upenn.edu/pennpress, pg 284

University of Pittsburgh Press, 3400 Forbes Ave, 5th fl, Pittsburgh, PA 15260 *Tel:* 412-383-2456 *Fax:* 412-383-2466 *E-mail:* press@pitt.edu *Web Site:* www.pitt.edu/~press, pg 284

University of Puerto Rico Press, Edificio EDUPR/Dialogo, Carr No 1, KM 12-0, Piso 2, Jardin Bota'nico Area Norte, San Juan, PR 00931 *Tel:* 787-758-6932; 787-758-8345 (sales); 787-250-0046; 787-250-0000 *Fax:* 787-753-9116; 787-751-8785 (sales dept), pg 284

University of Rochester Press, 668 Mt Hope Ave, Rochester, NY 14620 *Tel:* 585-275-0419 *Fax:* 585-271-8778 *E-mail:* boydell@boydellusa.net *Web Site:* boydellandbrewer.com, pg 285

University of Scranton Press, 445 Madison Ave, Scranton, PA 18510 *Tel:* 570-941-4228 *Toll Free Tel:* 800-941-3081 *Fax:* 570-941-6256 *Toll Free Fax:* 800-941-8804 *Web Site:* www.scrantonpress.com (Catalog), pg 285

University of South Carolina Press, 1600 Hampton St, 5th fl, Columbia, SC 29208 *Tel:* 803-777-5243 *Toll Free Tel:* 800-768-2500 (orders) *Fax:* 803-777-0160 *Toll Free Fax:* 800-868-0740 (orders) *Web Site:* www.sc.edu/uscpress/, pg 285

University of Southern California, Professional Writing Program, Waite Phillips Hall, Rm 404, Los Angeles, CA 90089-4034 *Tel:* 213-740-3252 *Fax:* 213-740-5775 *E-mail:* mpw@usc.edu *Web Site:* www.usc.edu/dept/LAS/mpw, pg 756

University of Tennessee Press, 110 Conference Center Bldg, Knoxville, TN 37996-4108 *Tel:* 865-974-3321 *Toll Free Tel:* 800-621-2736 (ordering) *Fax:* 865-974-3724 *E-mail:* custserv@utpress.org *Web Site:* www.utpress.org, pg 285

University of Texas at Arlington School of Urban & Public Affairs, University Hall, 5th fl, 601 S Naderman Dr, Arlington, TX 76010 *Tel:* 817-272-3071 *Fax:* 817-272-5008 *E-mail:* supapubs@uta.edu *Web Site:* www.uta.edu/supa, pg 285

University of Texas at Austin, Creative Writing Program, Dept of English, One University Sta, B5000, Austin, TX 78712-1164 *Tel:* 512-475-6356 *Fax:* 512-471-2898 *Web Site:* www.en.utexas.edu/grad/crwconc.html, pg 756

University of Texas at El Paso, Dept Creative Writing, MFA with Bilingual Option, 500 W University Ave, PMB 670, El Paso, TX 79968-9991 *Tel:* 915-747-5713 *Fax:* 915-747-5523 *E-mail:* mfadirector@utep.edu *Web Site:* www.utep.edu/cw, pg 756

University of Toronto Press Inc, 10 St Mary St, Suite 700, Toronto, ON M4Y 2W8, Canada *Tel:* 416-978-2239 (admin) *Fax:* 416-978-4738 (admin) *Web Site:* www.utpress.utoronto.ca, pg 565

The University of Utah Press, 1795 E South Campus Dr, Rm 101, Salt Lake City, UT 84112-9402 *Tel:* 801-581-6671 *Toll Free Tel:* 800-773-6672 *Fax:* 801-581-3365 *E-mail:* info@upress.utah.edu *Web Site:* www.uofupress.com, pg 285

The University of Virginia Press, PO Box 400318, Charlottesville, VA 22904-4318 *Tel:* 434-924-3468 (cust serv); 434-924-3469 (cust serv) *Toll Free Tel:* 800-831-3406 (cust serv) *Fax:* 434-982-2655 *Toll Free Fax:* 877-288-6400 *E-mail:* upressvirginia@virginia.edu *Web Site:* www.upressvirginia.edu, pg 285

University of Virginia Publishing & Communications Institute, 104 Midmont Lane, Charlottesville, VA 22904-4764 *Tel:* 434-982-5345 *Toll Free Tel:* 800-346-3882 *Fax:* 434-982-5239, pg 756

University of Washington Press, 1326 Fifth Ave, Suite 555, Seattle, WA 98101-2604 *Tel:* 206-543-4050; 206-543-8870 *Toll Free Tel:* 800-441-4115 (orders) *Fax:* 206-543-3932 *Toll Free Fax:* 800-669-7993 (orders) *E-mail:* uwpord@u.washington.edu *Web Site:* www.washington.edu/uwpress/, pg 286

University of Wisconsin Press, 1930 Monroe St, 3rd fl, Madison, WI 53711 *Tel:* 608-263-1110 *Toll Free Tel:* 800-621-2736 (Orders) *Fax:* 608-263-1120 *Toll Free Fax:* 800-621-8476 (Orders) *E-mail:* uwiscpress@uwpress.wisc.edu (Main Office) *Web Site:* www.wisc.edu/wisconsinpress/, pg 286

University of Wisconsin - Madison Liberal Studies & the Arts, 621 Lowell Hall, 610 Langdon St, Madison, WI 53703-1195 *Tel:* 608-262-3982 *Fax:* 608-265-2475 *Web Site:* www.dcs.wisc.edu/lsa, pg 756

University of Wisconsin-Milwaukee Center for Architecture & Urban Planning Research, PO Box 413, Milwaukee, WI 53201-0413 *Tel:* 414-229-2878 *Fax:* 414-229-6976 *E-mail:* caupr@uwm.edu *Web Site:* www.uwm.edu/SARUP, pg 286

University Press of America Inc, 4501 Forbes Blvd, Suite 200, Lanham, MD 20706 *Tel:* 301-459-3366 *Toll Free Tel:* 800-462-6420 *Fax:* 301-429-5748 *Toll Free Fax:* 800-338-4550 *Web Site:* www.univpress.com, pg 286

University Press of Colorado, 5589 Arapahoe Ave, Suite 206-C, Boulder, CO 80303 *Tel:* 720-406-8849 *Toll Free Tel:* 800-627-7377 *Fax:* 720-406-3443 *Web Site:* www.upcolorado.com, pg 286

University Press of Florida, 15 NW 15 St, Gainesville, FL 32611-2079 *Tel:* 352-392-1351 *Toll Free Tel:* 800-226-3822 (orders only) *Fax:* 352-392-7302 *Toll Free Fax:* 800-680-1955 (orders only) *E-mail:* info@upf.com *Web Site:* www.upf.com, pg 286

University Press of Kansas, 2501 W 15 St, Lawrence, KS 66049-3905 *Tel:* 785-864-4154; 785-864-4155 (orders) *Fax:* 785-864-4586 *E-mail:* upress@ku.edu *Web Site:* www.kansaspress.ku.edu, pg 287

The University Press of Kentucky, 663 S Limestone St, Lexington, KY 40508-4008 *Tel:* 859-257-8761; 859-257-8442 (mktg) *Toll Free Tel:* 800-839-6855 (orders) *Fax:* 859-323-1873 *Web Site:* www.kentuckypress.com, pg 287

University Press of Mississippi, 3825 Ridgewood Rd, Jackson, MS 39211-6492 *Tel:* 601-432-6205 *Toll Free Tel:* 800-737-7788 *Fax:* 601-432-6217 *E-mail:* press@ihl.state.ms.us *Web Site:* www.upress.state.ms.us, pg 287

University Press of New England, One Court St, Lebanon, NH 03766 *Tel:* 603-448-1533 *Toll Free Tel:* 800-421-1561 (orders only) *Fax:* 603-448-7006; 603-643-1540 *E-mail:* university.press@dartmouth.edu *Web Site:* www.upne.com, pg 287

University Publishing Co, 1134-A 28 St, Richmond, CA 94804 *E-mail:* unipub@earthlink.net, pg 287

University Publishing Group, 138 W Washington St, Suites 403-405, Hagerstown, MD 21740 *Tel:* 240-420-0036 *Toll Free Tel:* 800-654-8188 *Fax:* 240-420-0037 *E-mail:* editorial@upgbooks.com; orders@upgbooks.com *Web Site:* www.upgbooks.com, pg 287

University Publishing House, PO Box 1664, Mannford, OK 74044 *Tel:* 918-865-4726 *Fax:* 918-865-4726 *E-mail:* upub2@juno.com *Web Site:* www.universitypublishinghouse.com, pg 288

University Science Books, 55-D Gate Five Rd, Sausalito, CA 94965 *Tel:* 415-332-5390 *Fax:* 415-332-5393 *E-mail:* univscibks@igc.org *Web Site:* www.uscibooks.com, pg 288

UnKnownTruths.com Publishing Co, 8815 Conroy Windermere Rd, Suite 190, Orlando, FL 32835 *Tel:* 407-929-9207 *Fax:* 407-876-3933 *E-mail:* info@unknowntruths.com *Web Site:* unknowntruths.com, pg 288

Unlimited Publishing LLC, PO Box 3007, Bloomington, IN 47402 *Toll Free Tel:* 800-218-8877 *E-mail:* operations@unlimitedpublishing.com *Web Site:* www.unlimitedpublishing.com, pg 288

W E Upjohn Institute for Employment Research, 300 S Westnedge Ave, Kalamazoo, MI 49007-4686 *Tel:* 269-343-5541; 269-343-4330 (pubns) *Toll Free Tel:* 888-

227-8569 *Fax:* 269-343-7310 *E-mail:* publications@upjohninstitute.org *Web Site:* www.upjohninstitute.org, pg 288

Upper Midwest Booksellers Association (UMBA), 3407 W 44 St, Minneapolis, MN 55410 *Tel:* 612-926-5868 *Toll Free Tel:* 800-784-7522 *Fax:* 612-926-6657 *E-mail:* umbaoffice@aol.com *Web Site:* www.abookaday.com, pg 701

Upper Room Books, 1908 Grand Ave, Nashville, TN 37212 *Toll Free Tel:* 800-972-0433 *Fax:* 615-340-7266 *Web Site:* www.upperroom.org, pg 288

Upstart Books™, W5527 State Rd 106, Fort Atkinson, WI 53538-8428 *Tel:* 920-563-9571 *Toll Free Tel:* 800-448-4887 *Fax:* 920-563-7395 *Toll Free Fax:* 800-448-5828 *Web Site:* www.highsmith.com, pg 288

Upublish.com, 23331 Water Circle, Boca Raton, FL 33486-8540 *Tel:* 561-750-4344 *Toll Free Tel:* 800-636-8329 *Fax:* 561-750-6797 *E-mail:* info4@upublish.com *Web Site:* www.universal-publishers.com, pg 288

The Urban Institute Press, 2100 "M" St NW, Washington, DC 20037 *Tel:* 202-261-5687 *Toll Free Tel:* 877-UIPRESS (847-7377) *Fax:* 202-467-5775 *E-mail:* pubs@ui.urban.org *Web Site:* www.uipress.org, pg 288

Urban Land Institute, 1025 Thomas Jefferson St NW, Suite 500 W, Washington, DC 20007 *Tel:* 202-624-7000 *Toll Free Tel:* 800-321-5011 *Fax:* 410-626-7140 *E-mail:* Bookstore@uli.org *Web Site:* www.bookstore.uli.org, pg 288

Urim Publications, 3709 13 Ave, Brooklyn, NY 11218 *Tel:* 718-972-5449 *Fax:* 718-972-6307 *E-mail:* publisher@urimpublications.com *Web Site:* www.urimpublications.com, pg 288

URJ Press, 633 Third Ave, New York, NY 10017-6778 *Tel:* 212-650-4100 *Toll Free Tel:* 888-489-UAHC (489-8242) *Fax:* 212-650-4119 *E-mail:* press@urj.org *Web Site:* www.urjpress.com, pg 289

US Board on Books For Young People (USBBY), c/o IRA, 800 Barksdale Rd, Newark, DE 19714 *Tel:* 302-731-1600 (ext 297) *Fax:* 302-731-1057 *E-mail:* usbby@reading.org *Web Site:* www.usbby.org, pg 701

US Conference of Catholic Bishops, USCCB Publishing, 3211 Fourth St NE, Washington, DC 20017-1194 *Tel:* 202-541-3090 *Toll Free Tel:* 800-235-8722 (orders only) *Fax:* 202-541-3089 *Web Site:* www.usccb.org/publishing, pg 289

US Games Systems Inc, 179 Ludlow St, Stamford, CT 06902 *Tel:* 203-353-8400 *Toll Free Tel:* 800-544-2637 (800-54GAMES) *Fax:* 203-353-8431 *E-mail:* info@usgamesinc.com *Web Site:* www.usgamesinc.com, pg 289

US Government Printing Office, Superintendent of Documents, Washington, DC 20401 *Tel:* 202-512-1707 *Toll Free Tel:* 888-293-6498 (cust serv); 866-512-1800 (orders) *Fax:* 202-512-1655 (bibliographic info); 202-512-2250 (orders & pricing) *Toll Free Fax:* 866-512-1800 *E-mail:* orders@gpo.gov *Web Site:* bookstore.gpo.gov (sales); gpoaccess.gov, pg 289

U.S.A. Books Abroad Inc®, 46 Willow Dr, Briarcliff Manor, NY 10510 *Tel:* 914-762-2400 *Fax:* 914-762-2407 *E-mail:* booksabroad@optonline.net *Web Site:* www.usabooksabroad.com, pg 701

USBE: United States Book Exchange, 2969 W 25 St, Cleveland, OH 44113 *Tel:* 216-241-6960 *Fax:* 216-241-6966 *E-mail:* usbe@usbe.com *Web Site:* www.usbe.com, pg 701

Arlene S Uslander, 1920 Chestnut Ave, Apt 105, Glenview, IL 60025 *Tel:* 847-729-7757 *Fax:* 847-729-8677 *E-mail:* auslander@theramp.net *Web Site:* www.uslander.net, pg 612

Utah Geological Survey, 1594 W North Temple, Suite 3110, Salt Lake City, UT 84116 *Tel:* 801-537-3300 *Toll Free Tel:* 888-UTAH-MAP (882-4627 bookstore) *Fax:* 801-537-3400 *E-mail:* geostore@utah.gov *Web Site:* geology.utah.gov, pg 289

Utah Original Writers Competition, 617 E South Temple, Salt Lake City, UT 84102-1177 *Tel:* 801-236-7553 *Fax:* 801-236-7556 *Web Site:* www.arts.utah.gov, pg 810

Utah State University Press, 7800 Old Main Hill, Logan, UT 84322-7800 *Tel:* 435-797-1362 *Toll Free Tel:* 800-239-9974 *Fax:* 435-797-0313 *Web Site:* www.usu.edu/usupress, pg 289

VanDam Inc, 11 W 20 St, 4th fl, New York, NY 10011-3704 *Tel:* 212-929-0416 *Toll Free Tel:* 800-UNFOLDS (863-6537) *Fax:* 212-929-0426 *E-mail:* info@vandam.com *Web Site:* www.vandam.com, pg 289

Vandamere Press, 3580 Morris St N, Saint Petersburg, FL 33713 *Tel:* 727-556-0950 *Toll Free Tel:* 800-551-7776 *Fax:* 727-556-2560 *E-mail:* orders@vandamere.com *Web Site:* www.vandamere.com, pg 289

Vanderbilt University Press, 201 University Plaza Bldg, 112 21 Ave S, Nashville, TN 37203 *Tel:* 615-322-3585 *Toll Free Tel:* 800-627-7377 (orders only) *Fax:* 615-343-8823 *Toll Free Fax:* 800-735-0476 (orders only) *E-mail:* vupress@vanderbilt.edu *Web Site:* www.vanderbilt.edu/vupress, pg 289

Vanwell Publishing Ltd, One Northrup Cres, St Catharines, ON L2R 7S2, Canada *Tel:* 905-937-3100 *Toll Free Tel:* 800-661-6136 *Fax:* 905-937-1760 *E-mail:* sales@vanwell.com, pg 565

Daniel Varoujan Award, 16 Cornell St, Arlington, MA 02474 *Web Site:* www.nepoetryclub.org, pg 810

Samuel S Vaughan, 23 Inness Rd, Tenafly, NJ 07670 *Tel:* 201-568-9485 *Fax:* 201-568-7527 *E-mail:* samuelsvaughan@aol.com, pg 612

Vault.com Inc, 150 W 22 St, 5th fl, New York, NY 10011 *Tel:* 212-366-4212 ext 384 *Fax:* 212-366-6117 *E-mail:* feedback@staff.vault.com *Web Site:* www.vault.com, pg 289

Vedanta Press, 1946 Vedanta Place, Hollywood, CA 90068 *Tel:* 323-960-1727 *Fax:* 323-465-9568 *E-mail:* info@vedanta.org *Web Site:* www.vedanta.com, pg 290

Vehicule Press, 125 Place du Parc Sta, Montreal, PQ H2X 4A3, Canada *Tel:* 514-844-6073 *Fax:* 514-844-7543 *E-mail:* vp@vehiculepress.com *Web Site:* www.vehiculepress.com, pg 566

The Vendome Press, 1334 York Ave, 3rd fl, New York, NY 10021 *Tel:* 212-737-5297 *Fax:* 212-737-5340 *E-mail:* vendomepress@earthlink.net, pg 290

Venture Publishing Inc, 1999 Cato Ave, State College, PA 16801 *Tel:* 814-234-4561 *Fax:* 814-234-1651 *E-mail:* vpublish@venturepublish.com *Web Site:* www.venturepublish.com, pg 290

Verbatim Books, 4 Laurel Heights, Old Lyme, CT 06371 *Tel:* 860-434-2104 *Web Site:* www.verbatimbooks.com, pg 290

Vermont Arts Council Grants, 136 State St, Drawer 33, Montpelier, VT 05633-6001 *Tel:* 802-828-3291 *Fax:* 802-828-3363 *E-mail:* info@vermontartscouncil.org *Web Site:* www.vermontartscouncil.org, pg 810

Vermont College, MFA in Writing Program, 36 College St, Montpelier, VT 05602 *Tel:* 802-828-8840 *Fax:* 802-828-8649 *Web Site:* www.tui.edu/vermontcollege, pg 756

Vermont Studio Center, PO Box 613, Johnson, VT 05656 *Tel:* 802-635-2727 *Fax:* 802-635-2730 *E-mail:* info@vermontstudiocenter.org *Web Site:* www.vermontstudiocenter.org, pg 748

Vermont Studio Center Writer's Fellowships, PO Box 613, Johnson, VT 05656 *Tel:* 802-635-2727 *Fax:* 802-635-2730 *E-mail:* writing@vermontstudiocenter.org; info@vermontstudiocenter.org *Web Site:* www.vermontstudiocenter.org, pg 810

Verso, 180 Varick St, 10th fl, New York, NY 10014-4606 *Tel:* 212-807-9680 *Fax:* 212-807-9152 *E-mail:* versony@versobooks.com *Web Site:* www.versobooks.com, pg 290

Veterans of Foreign Wars of the US, 406 W 34 St, Kansas City, MO 64111 *Tel:* 816-756-3390 *Fax:* 816-968-1169 *E-mail:* info@vfw.org *Web Site:* www.vfw.org, pg 702

Ralph M Vicinanza Ltd, 303 W 18 St, New York, NY 10011 *Tel:* 212-924-7090 *Fax:* 212-691-9644 *E-mail:* ralphvic@aol.com, pg 659

Victoria School of Writing, 306-620 View St, Victoria, BC V8W 1J6, Canada *Tel:* 250-595-3000 *E-mail:* info@victoriaschoolofwriting.org *Web Site:* www.victoriaschoolofwriting.org, pg 748

Victory in Grace Printing, 60 Quentin Rd, Lake Zurich, IL 60047 *Tel:* 847-438-4494 *Toll Free Tel:* 800-784-7223 *Fax:* 847-438-4232 *Web Site:* www.victoryingrace.org, pg 290

Viking, 375 Hudson St, New York, NY 10014 *Tel:* 212-366-2000 *E-mail:* online@penguinputnam.com *Web Site:* www.penguin.com, pg 290

Viking Children's Books, 345 Hudson St, New York, NY 10014 *Tel:* 212-366-2000 *E-mail:* online@penguinputnam.com *Web Site:* www.penguin.com, pg 290

Viking Penguin, 375 Hudson St, New York, NY 10014 *Tel:* 212-366-2000 *E-mail:* online@penguinputnam.com *Web Site:* www.penguin.com, pg 290

Viking Studio, 375 Hudson St, New York, NY 10014 *Tel:* 212-366-2000 *E-mail:* online@penguinputnam.com *Web Site:* www.penguin.com, pg 290

The Vines Agency Inc, 648 Broadway, Suite 901, New York, NY 10012 *Tel:* 212-777-5522 *Fax:* 212-777-5978 *Web Site:* www.vinesagency.com, pg 659

Carl Vinson Institute of Government, University of Georgia, 201 N Milledge Ave, Athens, GA 30602 *Tel:* 706-542-2736 *Fax:* 706-542-6239 *Web Site:* www.cviog.uga.edu, pg 290

Vintage & Anchor Books, 1745 Broadway, New York, NY 10019 *Tel:* 212-751-2600 *Fax:* 212-572-6043, pg 291

Violet Crown Book Awards, 1501 W Fifth St, Suite E-2, Austin, TX 78703 *Tel:* 512-499-8914 *Fax:* 512-499-0441 *E-mail:* wlt@writersleague.org *Web Site:* www.writersleague.org, pg 810

Violet Prose Publications, PO Box 245, Victor, NY 14654 *Tel:* 585-924-3063 *Fax:* 585-924-4118 *E-mail:* VioletProsePubs@aol.com *Web Site:* www.VioletProsePubs.com, pg 574

Visible Ink Press, 43311 Joy Rd, Suite 414, Canton, MI 48187-2075 *Tel:* 734-667-3211 *Fax:* 734-667-4311 *E-mail:* inquiries@visibleink.com *Web Site:* www.visibleink.com, pg 291

Vision Books International, 775 E Blithedale Ave, No 342, Mill Valley, CA 94941 *Tel:* 415-383-0962 *Fax:* 415-383-4521 *E-mail:* publisher@vbipublishing.com *Web Site:* www.vbipublishing.com, pg 574

Vision Works Publishing, 47 Sheffield Rd, Suite A, Boxford, MA 01921 *Tel:* 978-887-3125 *Toll Free Tel:* 888-821-3135 *Fax:* 630-982-2134 *E-mail:* visionworksbooks@email.com, pg 291

Visions Communications, 200 E Tenth St, Suite 714, New York, NY 10003 *Tel:* 212-529-4029 *Fax:* 212-529-4029 *E-mail:* bayvisions@aol.com; info@visionsbooks.com, pg 291

Visiting Writers Series, English Dept, PO Box 755720, Fairbanks, AK 99775 *Tel:* 907-474-7193 *Fax:* 907-474-5247 *E-mail:* faengl@uaf.edu *Web Site:* www.uaf.edu/english/, pg 748

Vista Publishing Inc, 151 Delaware Ave, Oakhurst, NJ 07755 *E-mail:* info@vistapubl.com; sales@vistapubl.com *Web Site:* www.vistapubl.com, pg 291

Visual Artists & Galleries Association Inc (VAGA), 350 Fifth Ave, Suite 2820, New York City, NY 10118 *Tel:* 212-736-6666 *Fax:* 212-736-6767 *E-mail:* info@vagarights.com, pg 702

Visual Reference Publications Inc, 302 Fifth Ave, New York, NY 10001 *Tel:* 212-279-7000 *Toll Free Tel:* 800-251-4545 *Fax:* 212-279-7014 *Web Site:* www.visualrefernce.com, pg 291

Visuals Unlimited, 27 Meadow Dr, Hollis, NH 03049 *Tel:* 603-465-3340 *Fax:* 603-465-3360 *E-mail:* staff@ visualsunlimited.com *Web Site:* visualsunlimited.com, pg 612

Vital Health Publishing, 149 Old Branchville Rd, Ridgefield, CT 06877 *Tel:* 203-894-1882 *Toll Free Tel:* 877-848-2665 (orders) *Fax:* 203-894-1866 *E-mail:* info@vitalhealthbooks.com *Web Site:* www. vitalhealthbooks.com, pg 291

Viveca Smith Publishing, PMB 131, 3001 S Hardin Blvd, Suite 110, McKinney, TX 75070-9028 *Tel:* 214-793-0089 *Fax:* 972-562-7559 *E-mail:* vsmithpublishing@aol.com *Web Site:* www. vivecasmithpublishing.com, pg 574

VLB Editeur Inc, 955 Amherst St, Montreal, PQ H2L 3K4, Canada *Tel:* 514-523-1182 *Fax:* 514-282-7530 *E-mail:* vml@sogides.com *Web Site:* www.edvlb.com, pg 566

Vocabula Communications Co, 10 Grant Place, Lexington, MA 02420 *Tel:* 781-861-1515 *E-mail:* info@vocabula.com *Web Site:* www.vocabula. com, pg 613

Vocalis Ltd, 100 Avalon Circle, Waterbury, CT 06710 *Tel:* 203-753-5244 *Fax:* 203-574-5433 *E-mail:* vocalis@sbcglobal.net; info@vocalisesl.com *Web Site:* www.vocalisesl.com; www.vocalisfiction. com; www.vocalisltd.com, pg 291

Volcano Press Inc, 21496 National St, Volcano, CA 95689 *Tel:* 209-296-4991 *Toll Free Tel:* 800-879-9636 *Fax:* 209-296-4995 *E-mail:* sales@volcanopress.com *Web Site:* www.volcanopress.com, pg 291

Stephanie von Hirschberg Literary Agency LLC, 1290 Avenue of the Americas, 29th fl, New York, NY 10104 *Tel:* 212-660-3000, pg 659

Dina von Zweck, 80 Beekman St, No 6-K, New York, NY 10038 *Tel:* 212-732-1020, pg 613

Voyageur Press, 123 N Second St, Stillwater, MN 55082 *Tel:* 651-430-2210 *Toll Free Tel:* 800-888-9653 *Fax:* 651-430-2211 *E-mail:* books@voyageurpress.com *Web Site:* www.voyageurpress.com, pg 291

W Publishing Group, PO Box 141000, Nashville, TN 37214-1000 *Tel:* 615-889-9000 *Fax:* 615-902-2112 *Web Site:* www.wpublishinggroup.com, pg 292

Wadsworth Publishing, 10 Davis Dr, Belmont, CA 94002-3002 *Toll Free Tel:* 800-357-0092 *Fax:* 650-592-3342 *Toll Free Fax:* 800-522-4923 *Web Site:* www.wadsworth.com, pg 292

Wake Forest University Press, A5 Tribble Hall, Wake Forest University, Winston-Salem, NC 27109 *Tel:* 336-758-5448 *Fax:* 336-758-5636 *E-mail:* wfupress@wfu. edu *Web Site:* www.wfu.edu/wfupress, pg 292

J Weston Walch Publisher, 321 Valley St, Portland, ME 04104 *Tel:* 207-772-2846 *Toll Free Tel:* 800-341-6094 *Fax:* 207-772-3105 *Toll Free Fax:* 888-991-5755 *E-mail:* customerservice@mail.walch.com *Web Site:* www.walch.com, pg 292

Mary Jack Wald Associates Inc, 111 E 14 St, New York, NY 10003 *Tel:* 212-254-7842 *Fax:* 212-254-7842, pg 659

Wales Literary Agency Inc, PO Box 9428, Seattle, WA 98109-0428 *Tel:* 206-284-7114 *Fax:* 206-322-1033 *E-mail:* waleslit@waleslit.com *Web Site:* www. waleslit.com, pg 660

Walker & Co, 104 Fifth Ave, 7th fl, New York, NY 10011 *Tel:* 212-727-8300 *Toll Free Tel:* 800-289-2553 *Fax:* 212-727-0984 *Toll Free Fax:* 800-218-9367 *E-mail:* firstinitiallastname@walkerbooks.com *Web Site:* www.walkerbooks.com, pg 292

Jayne Walker Literary Services, 1406 Euclid Ave, Suite 1, Berkeley, CA 94708 *Tel:* 510-843-8265, pg 613

Stanley Walker Journalism Award, 3700 Mockingbird Lane, Dallas, TX 75205 *Tel:* 512-245-2232 *Fax:* 512-245-7462, pg 810

Wall & Emerson Inc, 6 O'Connor Dr, Toronto, ON M4K 2K1, Canada *Tel:* 416-467-8685 *Toll Free Tel:* 877-409-4601 *Fax:* 416-352-5368 *E-mail:* wall@ wallbooks.com *Web Site:* www.wallbooks.com, pg 566

Dorothy Wall, Writing Consultant, 3045 Telegraph Ave, Berkeley, CA 94705 *Tel:* 510-486-8008, pg 613

Bronwen Wallace Memorial Award, 90 Richmond St W, Suite 200, Toronto, ON M5C 1P1, Canada *Tel:* 416-504-8222 *Fax:* 416-504-9090 *E-mail:* info@ writerstrust.com *Web Site:* www.writerstrust.com, pg 810

Wallace Literary Agency Inc, 177 E 70 St, New York, NY 10021 *Tel:* 212-570-9090 *Fax:* 212-772-8979 *E-mail:* walliter@aol.com, pg 660

Edward Lewis Wallant Book Award, 3 Brighton Rd, West Hartford, CT 06117 *Tel:* 860-232-1421, pg 810

Russ Walter Publisher, 196 Tiffany Lane, Manchester, NH 03104-4782 *Tel:* 603-666-6644 *Fax:* 603-666-6644 *E-mail:* russ@secretfun.com *Web Site:* www.secretfun. com, pg 292

Wm K Walthers Inc, 5601 W Florist Ave, Milwaukee, WI 53218 *Tel:* 414-527-0770 *Toll Free Tel:* 800-877-7171 *Fax:* 414-527-4423 *E-mail:* comments@walthers. com *Web Site:* www.walthers.com, pg 292

Wambtac Communications, 17300 17 St, Suite J-276, Tustin, CA 92780 *Tel:* 714-954-0580 *Toll Free Tel:* 800-641-3936 *Fax:* 714-954-0793 *E-mail:* wambtac@wambtac.com *Web Site:* www. wambtac.com, pg 613

Wanderlust Publications, 2009 S Tenth St, McAllen, TX 78503-5405 *Tel:* 956-686-3601 *Fax:* 956-686-0732 *E-mail:* info@sanbornsinsurance.com *Web Site:* www. sanbornsinsurance.com, pg 292

WANT Publishing Co, 420 Lexington Ave, Suite 300, New York, NY 10170 *Tel:* 212-687-3774 *Fax:* 212-687-3779 *Web Site:* www.courts.com, pg 293

Theodore Ward Prize for Playwriting, Columbia College, Theater Dept, 72 E 11 St, Chicago, IL 60605 *Tel:* 312-344-6136 *Fax:* 312-344-8077, pg 810

John A Ware Literary Agency, 392 Central Park W, New York, NY 10025 *Tel:* 212-866-4733 *Fax:* 212-866-4734, pg 660

Frederick Warne, 345 Hudson St, New York, NY 10014 *Tel:* 212-366-2000 *E-mail:* online@penguinputnam. com *Web Site:* www.penguin.com, pg 293

Warner Books, 1271 Avenue of the Americas, New York, NY 10020 *Tel:* 212-522-7200 *Fax:* 212-522-7991 *Web Site:* www.twbookmark.com, pg 293

Warner Bros Publications Inc, 15800 NW 48 Ave, Miami, FL 33014 *Tel:* 305-620-1500 *Toll Free Tel:* 800-327-7643 *Fax:* 305-621-4869 *E-mail:* wbpsales@warnerchappell.com *Web Site:* www.warnerbrospublications.com, pg 293

Warner Bros Worldwide Publishing, 4000 Warner Blvd, Bldg 118, Burbank, CA 91522-1704 *Tel:* 818-954-5450 *Fax:* 818-954-5595 *Web Site:* www.warnerbros. com, pg 293

Warner Faith (Christian Book Division of Time Warner Book Group), 2 Creekside Crossing, 10 Cadillac Dr, Suite 220, Brentwood, TN 37027 *Tel:* 615-221-0996 *Fax:* 615-221-0962 *Web Site:* www.twbookmark.com, pg 293

Andrea Warren, 4908 W 71 St, Prairie Village, KS 66208 *Tel:* 913-722-2343 *Fax:* 913-722-4436 *E-mail:* awkansas@aol.com, pg 613

Warren Communications News, 2115 Ward Ct NW, Washington, DC 20037-1209 *Tel:* 202-872-9200 *Fax:* 202-293-3435 *E-mail:* info@warren-news.com *Web Site:* www.warren-news.com, pg 293

Warren, Gorham & Lamont, 395 Hudson St, New York, NY 10014 *Tel:* 212-367-6300 *Toll Free Tel:* 800-431-9025; 800-678-2185 (cust serv) *Fax:* 212-367-6305 *Web Site:* www.riahome.com, pg 293

Warren Wilson College, MFA Program for Writers, PO Box 9000, Asheville, NC 28815-9000 *Tel:* 828-771-3715 *Fax:* 828-771-7005 *E-mail:* mfa@warren-wilson. edu *Web Site:* www.warren-wilson.edu/~mfa, pg 756

Warwick Associates, 18340 Sonoma Hwy, Sonoma, CA 95476 *Tel:* 707-939-9212 *Fax:* 707-938-3515 *E-mail:* warwick@vom.com *Web Site:* www. warwickassociates.net, pg 660

Warwick Publishing Inc, 161 Frederick St, Toronto, ON M5A 4P3, Canada *Tel:* 416-596-1555 *Fax:* 416-596-1520 *Web Site:* www.warwickgp.com, pg 566

Washington Independent Writers (WIW), 733 15 St NW, Suite 220, Washington, DC 20005 *Tel:* 202-737-9500 *Fax:* 202-638-7800 *E-mail:* info@washwriter.org *Web Site:* www.washwriter.org, pg 702

Washington Researchers Ltd, 1655 N Fort Myer Dr, Suite 800, Arlington, VA 22209 *Tel:* 703-312-2863 *Fax:* 703-527-4586 *E-mail:* research@researchers.com *Web Site:* www.washingtonresearchers.com, pg 613

Washington State University Press, Cooper Publications Bldg, Grimes Way, Pullman, WA 99164-5910 *Tel:* 509-335-3518 *Toll Free Tel:* 800-354-7360 *Fax:* 509-335-8568 *E-mail:* wsupress@wsu.edu *Web Site:* wsupress.wsu.edu, pg 293

Harriet Wasserman Literary Agency Inc, 137 E 36 St, New York, NY 10016 *Tel:* 212-689-3257 *Fax:* 212-689-3257 *E-mail:* hawlainc@aol.com, pg 660

Water Environment Federation, 601 Wythe St, Alexandria, VA 22314-1994 *Tel:* 703-684-2400 *Toll Free Tel:* 800-666-0206 *Fax:* 703-684-2492 *E-mail:* csc@wef.org *Web Site:* www.wef.org, pg 294

Water Resources Publications LLC, PO Box 260026, Highlands Ranch, CO 80163-0026 *Tel:* 720-873-0171 *Fax:* 720-873-0173 *E-mail:* info@wrpllc.com *Web Site:* www.wrpllc.com, pg 294

Water Row Press, PO Box 438, Sudbury, MA 01776 *Tel:* 508-485-8515 *Fax:* 508-229-0885 *E-mail:* contact@waterrowbooks.com *Web Site:* www. waterrowbooks.com, pg 294

WaterBrook Press, 2375 Telstar Dr, Suite 160, Colorado Springs, CO 80920 *Tel:* 719-590-4999 *Toll Free Tel:* 800-603-7051 (orders) *Fax:* 719-590-8977 *Toll Free Fax:* 800-294-5686 (orders) *Web Site:* www. waterbrookpress.com, pg 294

Waterfront Books, 85 Crescent Rd, Burlington, VT 05401 *Tel:* 802-658-7477 *Toll Free Tel:* 800-639-6063 (orders) *Fax:* 802-860-1368 *E-mail:* helpkids@ waterfrontbooks.com *Web Site:* www.waterfrontbooks. com, pg 294

Waterloo Music Co Ltd, 3 Regina St N, Waterloo, ON N2J 4A5, Canada *Tel:* 519-886-4990 *Toll Free Tel:* 800-563-9683 (Canada & US) *Fax:* 519-886-4999 *E-mail:* info@waterloomusic.com *Web Site:* www. waterloomusic.com, pg 566

WaterPlow Press™, Amherst Office Park, 441 West Street, Suite G, Amherst, MA 01002 *Tel:* 413-253-1520 *Toll Free Tel:* 866-367-3300 (orders only) *Fax:* 413-253-1521 *E-mail:* sales@waterplowpress.com *Web Site:* www.waterplowpress.com, pg 294

Waterside Productions Inc, 2187 Newcastle Ave, Suite 204, Cardiff, CA 92007 *Tel:* 760-632-9190 *Fax:* 760-632-9295 *Web Site:* www.waterside.com, pg 660

Watkins Loomis Agency Inc, 133 E 35 St, Suite 1, New York, NY 10016 *Tel:* 212-532-0080 *Fax:* 212-889-0506, pg 660

Watson-Guptill Publications, 770 Broadway, New York, NY 10003 *Tel:* 646-654-5450 *Toll Free Tel:* 800-278-8477 (orders only) *Fax:* 646-654-5486; 646-654-5487 *E-mail:* info@watsonguptill.com *Web Site:* www. watsonguptill.com, pg 294

Watson Publishing International, PO Box 1240, Sagamore Beach, MA 02562-1240 *Tel:* 508-888-9113 *Fax:* 508-888-3733 *E-mail:* orders@watsonpublishing. com *Web Site:* www.watsonpublishing.com; www. shpusa.com, pg 294

Sandra Watt & Associates, 1750 N Sierra Bonita St, Los Angeles, CA 90046 *Tel:* 323-874-0791, pg 660

Waveland Press Inc, 4180 IL Rte 83, Suite 101, Long Grove, IL 60047-9580 *Tel:* 847-634-0081 *Fax:* 847-634-9501 *E-mail:* info@waveland.com *Web Site:* www.waveland.com, pg 294

Waxman Literary Agency, 80 Fifth Ave, Suite 1101, New York, NY 10011 *Tel:* 212-675-5556 *Fax:* 212-675-1381 *E-mail:* submit@waxmanagency.com *Web Site:* www.waxmanagency.com, pg 660

Wayne State University Press, Leonard N Simons Bldg, 4809 Woodward Ave, Detroit, MI 48201-1309 *Tel:* 313-577-4600 *Toll Free Tel:* 800-978-7323 *Fax:* 313-577-6131, pg 294

Wayside Publications, PO Box 318, Goreville, IL 62939 *Tel:* 618-995-1157 *Web Site:* www.waysidepublications.com, pg 295

Wayside Publishing, 11 Jan Sebastian Way, Suite 5, Sandwich, MA 02563 *Tel:* 508-833-5096 *Toll Free Tel:* 888-302-2519 *Fax:* 508-833-6284 *E-mail:* wayside@sprintmail.com *Web Site:* www.waysidepublishing.com, pg 295

Weatherhill Inc, 41 Monroe Tpke, Trumbull, CT 06611 *Tel:* 203-459-5090 *Toll Free Tel:* 800-437-7840 *Fax:* 203-459-5095 *Toll Free Fax:* 800-557-5601 *E-mail:* weatherhill@weatherhill.com *Web Site:* www.weatherhill.com, pg 295

Web Offset Association, 200 Deer Run Rd, Sewickley, PA 15143 *Tel:* 412-741-6860 *Toll Free Tel:* 800-910-4283 *Fax:* 412-741-2311 *Web Site:* www.gain.net, pg 702

Web Offset Press Operating, 200 Deer Run Rd, Sewickley, PA 15143-2600 *Tel:* 412-741-6860 *Toll Free Tel:* 800-910-4283 *Fax:* 412-741-2311 *E-mail:* info@gain.net *Web Site:* www.gain.net, pg 748

Web Printing Association, 100 Daingerfield Rd, Alexandria, VA 22314 *Tel:* 703-519-8100 *Toll Free Tel:* 800-742-2666 *Fax:* 703-519-7109 *Web Site:* www.gain.net, pg 702

Webb Research Group, Publishers, PO Box 314, Medford, OR 97501-0021 *Tel:* 541-664-5205 *Fax:* 541-664-9131 *E-mail:* pnwbooks@pnwbooks.com *Web Site:* www.pnorthwestbooks.com, pg 295

Wecksler-Incomco, 170 West End Ave, New York, NY 10023 *Tel:* 212-787-2239 *Fax:* 212-496-7035 *E-mail:* jacinny@aol.com, pg 660

Weidner & Sons Publishing, PO Box 2178 (Cinnaminson), Riverton, NJ 08077 *Tel:* 856-486-1755 *Fax:* 856-486-7583 *E-mail:* weidner@waterw.com *Web Site:* www.arlhs.com/weidnerpublishing, pg 295

Weigl Educational Publishers Ltd, 6325 Tenth St SE, Calgary, AB T2H 2Z9, Canada *Tel:* 403-233-7747 *Toll Free Tel:* 800-668-0766 *Fax:* 403-233-7769 *E-mail:* info@weigl.com *Web Site:* www.weigl.com, pg 566

Weil Publishing Co Inc, 150 Capitol St, Augusta, ME 04330 *Tel:* 207-621-0029 *Toll Free Tel:* 800-877-9345 *Fax:* 207-621-0069 *E-mail:* info@weilpublishing.com *Web Site:* www.weilpublishing.com, pg 295

The Wendy Weil Agency Inc, 232 Madison Ave, Suite 1300, New York, NY 10016 *Tel:* 212-685-0030 *Fax:* 212-685-0765, pg 660

Cherry Weiner Literary Agency, 28 Kipling Way, Manalapan, NJ 07726 *Tel:* 732-446-2096 *Fax:* 732-792-0506 *E-mail:* cherry8486@aol.com, pg 660

The Weingel-Fidel Agency, 310 E 46 St, Suite 21-E, New York, NY 10017 *Tel:* 212-599-2959 *Fax:* 212-286-1986 *E-mail:* wfagy@aol.com, pg 661

Ted Weinstein Literary Management, 35 Stillman St, Suite 203, San Francisco, CA 94107 *Web Site:* www.twliterary.com, pg 661

Weiss Ratings Inc, 15430 Endeavor Dr, Jupiter, FL 33478 *Tel:* 561-627-3300 *Toll Free Tel:* 800-289-9222 *Fax:* 561-625-6685 *E-mail:* wr@weissinc.com *Web Site:* www.weissratings.com, pg 295

Jesse A Weissman, 10 Shore Blvd, Suite 1-L, Brooklyn, NY 11235-4022 *Tel:* 718-646-2118 *Fax:* 718-646-0520 *E-mail:* jesseaw1@earthlink.net, pg 613

Anne Jones Weitzer, 60 Sutton Place S, Suite 9B South, New York, NY 10022-4168 *Tel:* 212-758-8149; 201-224-6931 *Fax:* 206-339-8149 *E-mail:* 47dehaven@msn.com; alas101@hotmail.com, pg 613

Welcome Books, 6 W 18 St, 3rd fl, New York, NY 10011 *Tel:* 212-989-3200 *Fax:* 212-989-3205 *E-mail:* info@welcomebooks.com *Web Site:* www.welcomebooks.com, pg 295

Welcome Rain Publishers LLC, 532 Laguardia Place, Suite 473, New York, NY 10012 *Tel:* 718-832-1607 *Fax:* 212-889-0869 *E-mail:* welcomrain@aol.com, pg 295

Rene Wellek Prize, University of Texas, Program in Comparative Literature, One University Sta B5003, Austin, TX 78712-0196 *Tel:* 512-471-8020 *E-mail:* info@acla.org *Web Site:* www.acla.org, pg 810

Wellington Press, 9601-30 Miccosukee Rd, Tallahassee, FL 32309 *Tel:* 850-878-6500 *E-mail:* booksuprint@aol.com; wellpress@aol.com *Web Site:* www.booksuprint.com, pg 295

Wellness Institute Inc, 1007 Whitney Ave, Gretna, LA 70056 *Tel:* 504-361-1845 *Fax:* 504-365-0114 *Web Site:* selfhelpbooks.com, pg 295

Wendy Lynn & Co, 504 Wilson Rd, Annapolis, MD 21401 *Tel:* 410-224-2729; 410-507-1059 *Fax:* 410-224-2183 *Web Site:* wendy-lynn.com, pg 667

Werbel Publishing Co Inc, 686 Deer Park Ave, Dix Hills, NY 11746-6219 *Tel:* 631-243-0032 *Toll Free Tel:* 800-293-7235 *Fax:* 631-243-0069 *E-mail:* info@werbel.com *Web Site:* www.werbel.com, pg 296

Eliot Werner Publications Inc, 31 Willow Lane, Clinton Corners, NY 12514 *Tel:* 845-266-4241 *Fax:* 845-266-3317 *E-mail:* ewerner@earthlink.net *Web Site:* www.eliotwerner.com, pg 296

Toby Wertheim, 240 E 76 St, New York, NY 10021 *Tel:* 212-472-8587 *E-mail:* feb298@aol.com, pg 613

Wescott Cove Publishing Co, PO Box 560989, Rockledge, FL 32956 *Tel:* 321-690-2224 *Fax:* 321-690-0853 *E-mail:* customerservice@wescottcovepublishing.com *Web Site:* www.wescottcovepublishing.com, pg 296

Wesleyan Publishing House, 13300 Olio Rd, Noblesville, IN 46060 *Tel:* 317-774-3853 *Toll Free Tel:* 800-493-7539 *Fax:* 317-774-3860 *Toll Free Fax:* 800-788-3535 *E-mail:* wph@wesleyan.org *Web Site:* www.wesleyan.org/wph, pg 296

Wesleyan University Press, 215 Long Lane, Middletown, CT 06459-0433 *Tel:* 860-685-7711 *Fax:* 860-685-7712 *Web Site:* www.wesleyan.edu/wespress, pg 296

Wesleyan Writers Conference, c/o Wesleyan University, 279 Court St, Middletown, CT 06459 *Tel:* 860-685-3604 *Fax:* 860-685-2441 *Web Site:* www.wesleyan.edu/writers, pg 748

West, A Thomson Business, 610 Opperman Dr, Eagan, MN 55123 *Tel:* 651-687-7000 *Toll Free Tel:* 800-328-9352 (sales); 800-328-4880 (cust serv) *Fax:* 651-687-7302 *Web Site:* www.west.com, pg 296

West Coast Book People Association, 27 McNear Dr, San Rafael, CA 94901-1545 *Tel:* 415-459-1227 *Fax:* 415-459-1227, pg 702

West Coast Ensemble Full Play Competition, PO Box 38728, Los Angeles, CA 90038 *Tel:* 323-876-9337 *Fax:* 323-876-8916, pg 810

West Coast Literary Associates, 951 Old County Rd, No 140, Belmont, CA 94002 *Tel:* 650-557-0438 *E-mail:* wstlit@aol.com, pg 661

The Westchester Literary Agency, 2533 Egret Lake Dr, West Palm Beach, FL 33413 *Tel:* 561-642-2908 *Fax:* 561-439-2228, pg 661

Westcliffe Publishers Inc, 2650 S Zuni St, Englewood, CO 80110-1145 *Tel:* 303-935-0900 *Toll Free Tel:* 800-523-3692 *Fax:* 303-935-0903 *E-mail:* sales@westcliffepublishers.com *Web Site:* www.westcliffepublishers.com, pg 296

Western Heritage Awards (Wrangler Award), 1700 NE 63 St, Oklahoma City, OK 73111 *Tel:* 405-478-2250 *Fax:* 405-478-4714 *Web Site:* www.nationalcowboymuseum.org, pg 810

Western Magazine Awards Foundation, Main PO Box 2131, Vancouver, BC V6B 3T8, Canada *Tel:* 604-669-3717 *Fax:* 604-204-9302 *E-mail:* wma@direct.ca *Web Site:* www.westernmagazineawards.com, pg 810

Western National Parks Association, 12880 N Vistoso Village Dr, Tucson, AZ 85737-8797 *Tel:* 520-622-1999 *Toll Free Tel:* 888-569-SPMA (orders only) *Fax:* 520-623-9519 *E-mail:* info@wnpa.org *Web Site:* www.wnpa.org, pg 296

Western New York Wares Inc, PO Box 733, Ellicott Sta, Buffalo, NY 14205 *Tel:* 716-832-6088 *E-mail:* buffalobooks@att.net *Web Site:* www.buffalobooks.com, pg 296

Western Pennsylvania Genealogical Society, 4400 Forbes Ave, Pittsburgh, PA 15213-4080 *Tel:* 412-687-6811 (answering machine) *E-mail:* info@wpgs.org *Web Site:* www.wpgs.org, pg 296

Western Reflections Publishing Co, 219 Main St, Montrose, CO 81401 *Tel:* 970-249-7180 *Toll Free Tel:* 800-993-4490 *Fax:* 970-249-7181 *E-mail:* westref@montrose.net *Web Site:* www.westernreflectionspub.com, pg 297

Western States Arts Federation, 1743 Wazee St, Suite 300, Denver, CO 80202 *Tel:* 303-629-1166 *Fax:* 303-629-9717 *E-mail:* staff@westaf.org *Web Site:* www.westaf.org, pg 705

Western US Book Design & Production Awards, 501 S Cherry St, Suite 320, Denver, CO 80246 *Tel:* 303-447-2320 *Fax:* 303-279-7111 *E-mail:* executivedirector@pubwest.org *Web Site:* www.pubwest.org, pg 811

Western Writers of America Inc, 1012 Fair St, Franklin, TN 37064 *Tel:* 615-791-1444 *Fax:* 615-791-1444 *Web Site:* www.westernwriters.org, pg 702

Westernlore Press, PO Box 35305, Tucson, AZ 85740-5305 *Tel:* 520-297-5491 *Fax:* 520-297-1722, pg 297

Westminster John Knox Press, 100 Witherspoon St, Louisville, KY 40202-1396 *Tel:* 502-569-5052 *Toll Free Tel:* 800-227-2872 (US only) *Fax:* 502-569-8308 *Toll Free Fax:* 800-541-5113 (US only) *E-mail:* wjk@wjkbooks.com *Web Site:* www.wjkbooks.com, pg 297

Westview Press, 5500 Central Ave, Boulder, CO 80301 *Tel:* 303-444-3541 *Toll Free Tel:* 800-386-5656 *Fax:* 720-406-7336 *E-mail:* westview.orders@perseusbooks.com *Web Site:* www.perseusbooksgroup.com; www.westviewpress.com, pg 297

Westwood Creative Artists Ltd, 94 Harbord St, Toronto, ON M5S 1G6, Canada *Tel:* 416-964-3302 *Fax:* 416-975-9209, pg 661

Rosemary Wetherold, 4507 Cliffstone Cove, Austin, TX 78735 *Tel:* 512-892-1606 *E-mail:* roses@ix.netcom.com, pg 613

WH&O International, 892 Worcester St, Suite 130, Wellesley, MA 02482 *Tel:* 781-239-0822 *Toll Free Tel:* 800-553-6678 *Fax:* 781-239-0822 *E-mail:* whobooks@hotmail.com *Web Site:* www.whobooks.com, pg 297

Wheatherstone Press, 10250 SW Greenburg Rd, No 125, Portland, OR 97223 *Tel:* 503-244-8929 *Toll Free Tel:* 800-980-0077 *Fax:* 503-244-9795 *E-mail:* relocntr@europa.com *Web Site:* www.wheatherstonepress.com, pg 297

Helen Rippier Wheeler, 1909 Cedar St, Suite 212, Berkeley, CA 94709-2037 *Tel:* 510-549-2970 *Fax:* 510-549-2970 *E-mail:* pen136@inreach.com, pg 613

Barbara Mlotek Whelehan, 7064 SE Cricket Ct, Stuart, FL 34997 *Tel:* 954-554-0765 (cell); 772-463-0818 (home) *E-mail:* barbarawhelehan@bellsouth.net, pg 613

Whereabouts Press, 1111 Eighth St, Suite D, Berkeley, CA 94710-1455 *Tel:* 510-527-8280 *Fax:* 510-527-8780 *E-mail:* mail@whereaboutspress.com *Web Site:* www.whereaboutspress.com, pg 297

Whitaker House, 30 Hunt Valley Circle, New Kensington, PA 15068 *Tel:* 724-334-7000 *Toll Free Tel:* 877-793-9800 *Fax:* 724-334-1200 *Toll Free Fax:* 800-765-1960 *E-mail:* sales@whitakerhouse.com, pg 297

Willow Creek Press, 9931 Hwy 70 W, Minocqua, WI 54548 Tel: 715-358-7010 Toll Free Tel: 800-850-9453 Fax: 715-358-2807 E-mail: info@willowcreekpress. com Web Site: www.willowcreekpress.com, pg 300

Wilshire Book Co, 12015 Sherman Rd, North Hollywood, CA 91605 Tel: 818-765-8579 Fax: 818-765-2922 Web Site: www.mpowers.com, pg 300

The Wilshire Literary Agency, 20 Barristers Walk, Dennis, MA 02638 Tel: 508-385-5200, pg 661

The Wilson Devereux Co, 5 Ledyard St, 2nd fl, Newport, RI 02840 Tel: 401-846-8081 E-mail: bdb4@wildev. com Web Site: www.wildev.com, pg 661

H W Wilson, 950 University Ave, Bronx, NY 10452-4224 Tel: 718-588-8400 Toll Free Tel: 800-367-6770 Fax: 718-590-1617 Toll Free Fax: 800-590-1617 E-mail: custserv@hwwilson.com Web Site: www. hwwilson.com, pg 300

H W Wilson Co Indexing Award, 10200 W 44 Ave, Suite 304, Wheat Ridge, CO 80033 Tel: 303-463-2887 Fax: 303-422-8894 E-mail: info@asindexing.org Web Site: www.asindexing.org, pg 811

H W Wilson Foundation, 950 University Ave, Bronx, NY 10452-4224 Tel: 718-588-8400 Toll Free Tel: 800-367-6770 Fax: 718-538-2716 Toll Free Fax: 800-367-6770 E-mail: custserv@hwwilson.com Web Site: www.hwwilson.com, pg 705

The H W Wilson Library Staff Development Grant, 50 E Huron St, Chicago, IL 60611 Tel: 312-280-3247 Toll Free Tel: 800-545-2433 (ext 3247) Fax: 312-944-3897 E-mail: awards@ala.org Web Site: www.ala.org, pg 812

Wimbledon Music Inc & Trigram Music Inc, 1801 Century Park E, Suite 2400, Los Angeles, CA 90067-2326 Tel: 310-556-9683 Fax: 310-277-1278 E-mail: webmaster@wimbtri.com Web Site: www. wimbtri.com, pg 300

Wimmer Cookbooks, 4650 Shelby Air Dr, Memphis, TN 38118 Tel: 901-362-8900 Toll Free Tel: 800-548-2537 Toll Free Fax: 800-794-9806 E-mail: wimmer@ wimmerco.com Web Site: www.wimmerco.com, pg 301

Wind Canyon Books Inc, PO Box 511, Brawley, CA 92227 Tel: 760-344-5545 Toll Free Tel: 800-952-7007 Fax: 760-344-8841 E-mail: books@windcanyon. com Web Site: www.windcanyon.com; www.aviation-heritage.com, pg 301

Windham Bay Press, PO Box 1198, Occidental, CA 95465 Tel: 707-823-7150 Fax: 707-823-7150, pg 301

Windhaven Press Editorial Services, 68 Hunting Rd, Auburn, NH 03032 Tel: 603-483-0929 Fax: 603-483-8022 E-mail: info@windhaven.com Web Site: www. windhaven.com, pg 613

Windsor Books, 141 John St, Babylon, NY 11702 Tel: 631-321-7830 Toll Free Tel: 800-321-5934 Fax: 631-321-1435 E-mail: windsor.books@att.net Web Site: www.windsorpublishing.com, pg 301

Windstorm Creative, PO Box 28, Port Orchard, WA 98366 Tel: 360-769-7174 E-mail: queries@ windstormcreative.com Web Site: www. windstormcreative.com, pg 301

Windswept House Publishers, 584 Sound Dr, Mount Desert, ME 04660 Tel: 207-244-5027 Fax: 207-244-3369 E-mail: windswt@acadia.net Web Site: www. booknotes.com/windswept/, pg 301

The Wine Appreciation Guild Ltd, 360 Swift Ave, Unit 30-40, South San Francisco, CA 94080 Tel: 650-866-3020 Toll Free Tel: 800-231-9463 Fax: 650-866-3513 E-mail: shannon@wineappreciation. com; info@wineappreciation.com Web Site: www. wineappreciation.com, pg 301

Wings Press, 627 E Guenther, San Antonio, TX 78210 Tel: 210-271-7805; 210-222-8449 Fax: 210-271-7805 Web Site: www.wingspress.com, pg 613

Audur H Winnan, 747 Tenth Ave, No 16-K, New York, NY 10019 Tel: 212-581-9766, pg 614

Winner Enterprises, 670 Nighthawk Circle, Winter Springs, FL 32708 Tel: 407-696-2103 Fax: 407-696-2103 Web Site: www.winnerenterprises.com, pg 301

Laurence L Winship Book Award, Emerson College, 120 Boylston St, Boston, MA 02116 Tel: 617-824-8820 E-mail: pen_ne@emerson.edu Web Site: www.pen-ne.org, pg 812

Justin Winsor Essay Prize, 50 E Huron St, Chicago, IL 60611 Tel: 312-280-4273 Toll Free Tel: 800-545-2433 (ext 4273) Fax: 312-280-4392 Web Site: www.ala.org, pg 812

Roberta H Winston, 15 Sabina Way, Belmont, MA 02478-2268 Tel: 617-489-4190, pg 614

Winter Springs Editorial Services, 2263 Turk Rd, Doylestown, PA 18901-2964 Tel: 215-340-9052 Fax: 215-340-9052, pg 614

Winters Publishing, 705 E Washington St, Greensburg, IN 47240 Tel: 812-663-4948 Toll Free Tel: 800-457-3230 Fax: 812-663-4948 Toll Free Fax: 800-457-3230, pg 301

Winterthur Museum, Garden & Library, Publications Division, Winterthur, DE 19735 Tel: 302-888-4613 Toll Free Tel: 800-448-3883 Fax: 302-888-4950 Web Site: www.winterthur.org, pg 301

Wisconsin Dept of Public Instruction, 125 S Webster St, Madison, WI 53702 Tel: 608-266-2188 Toll Free Tel: 800-243-8782 Fax: 608-267-9110 E-mail: pubsales@dpi.state.wi.us Web Site: www.dpi. state.wi.us, pg 301

Wisconsin Retreat, 15255 Turnberry Dr, Brookfield, WI 53005 Tel: 262-783-4890 Web Site: www.scbwi.org, pg 749

Wisdom Publications Inc, 199 Elm St, Somerville, MA 02144 Tel: 617-776-7416 Fax: 617-776-7841 E-mail: info@wisdompubs.org Web Site: www. wisdompubs.org, pg 301

Wish Publishing, PO Box 10337, Terre Haute, IN 47801-0337 Tel: 812-299-5700 Fax: 928-447-1836 Web Site: www.wishpublishing.com, pg 302

Wittenborn Art Books, 1109 Geary Blvd, San Francisco, CA 94109 Tel: 415-292-6500 Toll Free Tel: 800-660-6403 Fax: 415-292-6594 E-mail: wittenborn@art-books.com Web Site: art-books.com, pg 302

Paul A Witty Short Story Award, 800 Barksdale Rd, Newark, DE 19714 Tel: 302-731-1600 Fax: 302-731-1057 E-mail: pubinfo@reading.org Web Site: www. reading.org, pg 812

Wizards of the Coast Inc, PO Box 707, Renton, WA 98057-0707 Web Site: www.wizards.com/books, pg 302

WJ Fantasy Inc, 955 Connecticut Ave, Bridgeport, CT 06607 Tel: 203-333-5212 Toll Free Tel: 800-222-7529 (orders) Fax: 203-366-3826 Toll Free Fax: 800-200-3000 E-mail: wjfantasy.inc@snet.net Web Site: www. wjfantasy.com, pg 302

Alan Wofsy Fine Arts, 1109 Geary Blvd, San Francisco, CA 94109 Tel: 415-292-6500 Fax: 415-512-0130 (acctg); 415-292-6594 (off & cust serv) E-mail: beauxarts@earthlink.net (cust serv); editeur@ earthlink.net (edit); order@art-books.com (orders) Web Site: art-books.com, pg 302

Gary S Wohl Literary Agency, 400 Chambers St, Unit 28-H, New York, NY 10282-1019 Tel: 212-242-0125 E-mail: gwohl@earthlink.net, pg 661

Audrey R Wolf Literary Agency, 2510 Virginia Ave NW, Washington, DC 20037 Tel: 202-965-0405 Fax: 202-298-6966 E-mail: bigbad@earthlink.net, pg 661

Wolf Den Books, 5783 SW 40 St, Suite 221, Miami, FL 33155 Toll Free Tel: 877-667-9737 Fax: 305-667-7751 E-mail: info@wolfdenbooks.com Web Site: www. wolfdenbooks.com, pg 302

Deborah Wolfe Ltd, 731 N 24 St, Philadelphia, PA 19130 Tel: 215-232-6666 Fax: 215-232-6585 E-mail: info@illustrationonline.com Web Site: www. illustrationonline.com, pg 667

Thomas Wolfe Student Prize, 809 Gardner St, Raleigh, NC 27607 Tel: 919-834-6983 Fax: 919-515-7856 Web Site: www.thomaswolfe.org, pg 812

Nancy Wolff, 125 Gates Ave, No 14, Montclair, NJ 07042 Tel: 973-746-7415 E-mail: wolffindex@aol. com, pg 614

Wolters Kluwer US Corp, 2700 Lake Cook Rd, Riverwoods, IL 60015 Tel: 847-267-7000 Fax: 847-580-5192 Web Site: www.wolterskluwer.com, pg 302

Women In Production, 276 Bowery, New York, NY 10012 Tel: 212-334-2106 Fax: 212-431-5786 E-mail: office@wip.org Web Site: www.wip.org, pg 702

Women Who Write, PO Box 652, Madison, NJ 07940 Tel: 908-232-1640 Fax: 908-317-8105 E-mail: info@ womenwhowrite.org Web Site: www.womenwhowrite. org, pg 702

Women's Writing Conferences & Retreats, PO Box 810, Gracie Sta, New York, NY 10028-0082 Tel: 212-737-7536 Fax: 212-737-9469 E-mail: iwwg@iwwg.org Web Site: www.iwwg.org, pg 749

Women's National Book Association Award, c/o Susannah Greenberg Public Relations, 2166 Broadway, Suite 9-E, New York, NY 10024 Tel: 212-208-4629 Fax: 212-208-4629 E-mail: publicity@bookbuzz.com Web Site: www.wnba-books.org, pg 812

Women's National Book Association Inc, c/o Susannah Greenberg Public Relations, 2166 Broadway, Suite 9-E, New York, NY 10024 Tel: 212-208-4629 Fax: 212-208-4629 E-mail: publicity@bookbuzz.com Web Site: www.wnba-books.org, pg 702

Women's National Book Association/Los Angeles Chapter, PO Box 7034, Beverly Hills, CA 90212-0034 Tel: 310-474-9917 Fax: 310-474-6436, pg 749

Wood & Wood Book Services, 62 Great Ring Rd, Sandy Hook, CT 06482 Tel: 203-270-8206 Fax: 203-270-8362, pg 614

Wood Lake Books Inc, 9025 Jim Bailey Rd, Kelowna, BC V4V 1R2, Canada Tel: 250-766-2778 Toll Free Tel: 800-663-2775 (orders) Fax: 250-766-2736 Toll Free Fax: 888-841-9991 (orders) E-mail: info@ woodlake.com Web Site: www.woodlakebooks.com, pg 567

Woodbine House, 6510 Bells Mill Rd, Bethesda, MD 20817 Tel: 301-897-3570 Toll Free Tel: 800-843-7323 Fax: 301-897-5838 E-mail: info@woodbinehouse.com Web Site: www.woodbinehouse.com, pg 302

Woodland Publishing Inc, 448 E 800 N, Orem, UT 84097 Tel: 801-434-8113 Toll Free Tel: 800-777-2665 Fax: 801-334-1913 Web Site: www. woodlandpublishing.com, pg 302

Ralph Woodrow Evangelistic Association Inc, PO Box 21, Palm Springs, CA 92263-0021 Tel: 760-323-9882 Toll Free Tel: 877-664-1549 Fax: 760-323-3982 E-mail: ralphwoodrow@earthlink.net Web Site: www. ralphwoodrow.com, pg 302

The Woodrow Wilson Center Press, One Woodrow Wilson Plaza, 1300 Pennsylvania Ave NW, Washington, DC 20004-3027 Tel: 202-691-4000 Fax: 202-691-4001 E-mail: press@wwics.si.edu Web Site: wilsoncenter.org, pg 302

Carter G Woodson Book Awards, 8555 16 St, Suite 500, Silver Spring, MD 20910 Tel: 301-588-1800 Toll Free Tel: 800-296-7840 Fax: 301-588-2049 E-mail: excellence@ncss.org Web Site: www. socialstudies.org, pg 812

Word Works Washington Prize, 7129 Alger Rd, Falls Church, VA 22042 Fax: 703-527-9384 E-mail: editor@wordworksdc.com Web Site: www. wordworksdc.com, pg 812

Word Wrangler Publishing Inc, 332 Tobin Creek Rd, Livingston, MT 59047 Tel: 406-686-4230; 406-686-4417 Toll Free Tel: 866-896-2897 Fax: 406-686-4417 E-mail: wrdwranglr@aol.com Web Site: www. wordwrangler.com, pg 303

WordCo Indexing Services, 49 Church St, Norwich, CT 06360 Tel: 860-886-2532 Toll Free Tel: 877-967-3263 Fax: 860-886-1155 Web Site: www.wordco.com, pg 614

WordCrafters Editorial Services Inc, 22636 Glenn Dr, Suite 106, Sterling, VA 20164 *Tel:* 703-471-0160 *Fax:* 703-471-0693 *E-mail:* editors@ wordcrafterseditorial.com, pg 614

WordForce Communications, 206-264 Queen's Quay W, Toronto, ON M5J 1B5, Canada *Tel:* 416-970-6733 *Fax:* 416-260-2229 *E-mail:* info@wordforce.ca *Web Site:* www.wordforce.ca, pg 614

WordMaster & Associates LLC, 4317 W Farrand Rd, Clio, MI 48420 *Tel:* 810-686-2047 *Fax:* 810-564-9929 *E-mail:* wordmasterpub@comcast.net, pg 614

Words into Print, 200 W 86 St, Suite 14-1, New York, NY 10024 *Tel:* 212-877-3211 *Fax:* 212-873-3796 *E-mail:* sas22@ix.netcom.com *Web Site:* www. wordsintoprint.org, pg 614

Words That Work!, W7615 County Rd YY, Wautoma, WI 54982-8382 *Tel:* 920-787-2645 *Fax:* 920-787-2698, pg 614

Wordsworth Associates Editorial Services, 9 Tappan Rd, Wellesley, MA 02482 *Tel:* 781-237-4761 *Fax:* 781-237-4758, pg 614

Wordsworth Communication, PO Box 9781, Alexandria, VA 22304-0468 *Tel:* 703-642-8775 *Fax:* 703-642-8775, pg 614

Wordtree branching dictionary, 10876 Bradshaw W102, Overland Park, KS 66210-1148 *Tel:* 913-469-1010 *Web Site:* www.wordtree.com, pg 303

Wordware Publishing Inc, 2320 Los Rios Blvd, Suite 200, Plano, TX 75074 *Tel:* 972-423-0090 *Toll Free Tel:* 800-229-4949 *Fax:* 972-881-9147 *E-mail:* info@ wordware.com *Web Site:* www.wordware.com, pg 303

The Wordwatcher, 605-4854 Cote-des-Neiges, Montreal, PQ H3V 1G7, Canada *Tel:* 514-739-9274; 514-398-1511 *E-mail:* wordwatcher@vif.com *Web Site:* www. vif.com/users/wordwatcher/, pg 614

WordWitlox, 642 Chiron Crescent, Pickering, ON L1V 4T4, Canada *Tel:* 416-420-0669 *Web Site:* www. wordwitlox.com, pg 614

Workers Compensation Research Institute, 955 Massachusetts Ave, Cambridge, MA 02139 *Tel:* 617-661-9274 *Fax:* 617-661-9284 *E-mail:* wcri@wcinet. org *Web Site:* www.wcrinet.org, pg 303

Working With Words, 9720 SW Eagle Ct, Beaverton, OR 97008 *Tel:* 503-644-4317 *Fax:* 503-644-4317 *E-mail:* w3words@zzz.com, pg 614

Workman Publishing Co Inc, 708 Broadway, New York, NY 10003-9555 *Tel:* 212-254-5900 *Toll Free Tel:* 800-722-7202 *Fax:* 212-254-8098 *E-mail:* info@workman. com *Web Site:* www.workman.com, pg 303

World Almanac Books, 512 Seventh Ave, 22nd fl, New York, NY 10018 *Tel:* 646-312-6800 *Fax:* 646-312-6839 *E-mail:* info@wagroup.com *Web Site:* www. worldalmanac.com, pg 303

World Bank Publications, Office of the Publisher, 1818 "H" St NW, U-11-1104, Washington, DC 20433 *Tel:* 202-473-0393 (sales mgr) *Toll Free Tel:* 800-645-7247 (cust serv) *Fax:* 202-522-2631 *E-mail:* books@ worldbank.org; pubrights@worldbank.org (foreign rts) *Web Site:* www.worldbank.org/publications, pg 303

World Book Inc, 233 N Michigan, Suite 2000, Chicago, IL 60601 *Tel:* 312-729-5800 *Toll Free Tel:* 800-967-5325 (consumer sales, US); 800-463-8845 (consumer sales, Canada); 800-975-3250 (school & library sales, US); 800-837-5365 (school & library sales, Canada); 866-866-5200 (web sales) *Fax:* 312-729-5600; 312-729-5606 *Toll Free Fax:* 800-433-9330 (school & library sales, US); 888-690-4002 (school library sales, Canada) *Web Site:* www.worldbook.com, pg 303

World Book Inc Continuing Education Grant, 100 North St, Suite 224, Pittsfield, MA 01201-5109 *Tel:* 413-443-2252 *Fax:* 413-442-2252 *E-mail:* cla@cathla.org *Web Site:* www.cathla.org, pg 812

World Citizens, 96 La Verne Ave, Mill Valley, CA 94941 *Tel:* 415-380-8020 *Toll Free Tel:* 800-247-6553 (orders only) *Web Site:* soultosoulmedia.com; skateman.com, pg 303

World Class Speakers & Entertainers, 5200 Kanan Rd, Suite 210, Agoura Hills, CA 91301 *Tel:* 818-991-5400 *Fax:* 818-991-2226 *E-mail:* wcse@speak.com *Web Site:* www.speak.com, pg 670

World Eagle, 111 King St, Littleton, MA 01460-1527 *Tel:* 978-486-9180 *Toll Free Tel:* 800-854-8273 *Fax:* 978-486-9652 *E-mail:* iba@ibaradio.org *Web Site:* www.worldeagle.com; www.ibaradio.org, pg 304

World Leisure Corp, 177 Paris St, Boston, MA 02128 *Tel:* 617-569-1966 *Toll Free Tel:* 877-863-1966 *Web Site:* www.worldleisure.com, pg 304

World Publishing, 404 BNA Dr, Bldg 200, Suite 208, Nashville, TN 37217 *Tel:* 615-902-2395 *Toll Free Tel:* 800-363-0308 *Fax:* 615-902-2397 *Toll Free Fax:* 800-822-4271 (orders) *E-mail:* questions@ worldpublishing.com; orders@worldpublishing.com *Web Site:* www.worldpublishing.com, pg 304

World Resources Institute, 10 "G" St NE, Suite 800, Washington, DC 20002 *Tel:* 202-729-7600 *Toll Free Tel:* 800-822-0504 *Fax:* 202-729-7707 *E-mail:* publications@wri.org *Web Site:* www.wri. org/wri, pg 304

World Scientific Publishing Co Inc, 27 Warren St, Suite 401-402, Hackensack, NJ 07601 *Tel:* 201-487-9655 *Toll Free Tel:* 800-227-7562 *Fax:* 201-487-9656 *Toll Free Fax:* 888-977-2665 *E-mail:* wspc@wspc.com *Web Site:* www.wspc.com, pg 304

World Trade Press, 1450 Grant Ave, Suite 204, Novato, CA 94945 *Tel:* 415-898-1124 *Toll Free Tel:* 800-833-8586 *Fax:* 415-898-1080 *E-mail:* admin@ worldtradepress.com *Web Site:* www.worldtradepress. com, pg 304

World's Best Short-Short Story Contest, Dept of English, The Florida State University, Tallahassee, FL 32306-1036 *Tel:* 850-644-2773; 850-644-4230 *E-mail:* southeastreview@english.fsu.edu *Web Site:* www.english.fsu.edu/southeastreview/default. htm, pg 812

Worldwide Library, 225 Duncan Mill Rd, Don Mills, ON M3B 3K9, Canada *Tel:* 416-445-5860 *Fax:* 416-445-8655; 416-445-8736 *Web Site:* www.eharlequin.com, pg 567

Wrangling With Writing, PO Box 30355, Tucson, AZ 85751-0355 *Tel:* 520-575-9063 *Web Site:* www. azstarnet.com/nonprofit/ssa, pg 749

Ann Wright Representatives, 165 W 46 St, Suite 1105, New York, NY 10036-2501 *Tel:* 212-764-6770 *Fax:* 212-764-5125, pg 661

The Wright Group/McGraw-Hill, a Division of McGraw-Hill Learning Group, One Prudential Plaza, 130 E Randolph, 4th fl, Chicago, IL 60601 *Tel:* 312-233-6520 *Toll Free Tel:* 800-537-4740 *Fax:* 312-233-6605 *Web Site:* www.wrightgroup.com, pg 304

Write Stuff Enterprises Inc, 1001 S Andrew Ave, 2nd fl, Fort Lauderdale, FL 33316 *Tel:* 954-462-6657 *Toll Free Tel:* 800-900-2665 *Fax:* 954-463-2220 *E-mail:* legends@writestuffbooks.com *Web Site:* www. writestuffbooks.com, pg 304

The Write Watchman, 9151 Yellowwood Dr, Cincinnati, OH 45251-1948 *Tel:* 603-643-6416 *Toll Free Tel:* 800-768-0829 ext 6416 *Fax:* 603-643-6416 *E-mail:* lmk42@earthlink.net, pg 614

The Write Way, 2449 Goddard Rd, Toledo, OH 43606 *Tel:* 419-531-9203 *Fax:* 419-531-9203, pg 615

The Writer's Advocate/Literary Agenting & Editorial Services, 1675 Larimer St, Suite 410, Denver, CO 80202 *Tel:* 303-297-1233 *Fax:* 303-297-3997 *E-mail:* thewritersadvocate@thelightningfactory.com *Web Site:* www.thelightningfactory.com, pg 615, 661

Writers' Alliance of Newfoundland & Labrador, 155 Water St, Suite 102, St John's, NF A1C 6K1, Canada *Tel:* 709-739-5215 *Fax:* 709-739-5931 *E-mail:* wanl@ nfld.com *Web Site:* www.writersalliance.nf.ca, pg 702

Writers' Alliance of Newfoundland & Labrador, Box 2681, St Johns, NF A1C 6K1, Canada *Tel:* 709-739-5215 *Fax:* 709-739-5931 *E-mail:* wanl@nfld.com *Web Site:* www.writersalliance.nf.ca, pg 702

Writers Anonymous Inc, 1302 E Coronado Rd, Phoenix, AZ 85006 *Tel:* 602-256-2830 *Fax:* 602-256-2830 *Web Site:* writersanonymousinc.com, pg 615

Writer's AudioShop, 1316 Overland Stage Rd, Dripping Springs, TX 78620 *Tel:* 512-264-9210 *Toll Free Tel:* 800-88-WRITE (889-7483) *Fax:* 512-264-9210 *E-mail:* writersaudio@timberwdfinc.com; wrtaudshop@aol.com *Web Site:* www.writersaudio. com, pg 304

The Writers' Collective, 780 Reservoir Ave, Suite 243, Cranston, RI 02910 *Tel:* 401-537-9175 *E-mail:* info@ writerscollective.org *Web Site:* www.writerscollective. org, pg 305

The Writers Community, 101 N Wacker Dr, Chicago, IL 60606 *Toll Free Tel:* 800-USA-YMCA, Ext 6830 *Fax:* 312-977-1729 *E-mail:* jason.shinder@ymca.net *Web Site:* www.ymca.net, pg 812

Writer's Digest Books, 4700 E Galbraith Rd, Cincinnati, OH 45236 *Tel:* 513-531-2690 *Toll Free Tel:* 800-289-0963 *Fax:* 513-891-7185 *Web Site:* www.writersdigest. com, pg 305

Writer's Digest School, 4700 E Galbraith Rd, Cincinnati, OH 45236 *Tel:* 513-531-2690 *Toll Free Tel:* 800-759-0963 *Fax:* 513-531-0798 *E-mail:* wds@fwpubs.com *Web Site:* www.fwpubs.com, pg 756

Writer's Digest Writing Competition, 4700 E Galbraith Rd, Cincinnati, OH 45236 *Tel:* 513-531-2690 (ext 580) *Fax:* 513-531-0798 *E-mail:* writing-competition@fwpubs.com *Web Site:* www. writersdigest.com, pg 812

The Writer's Emergency Assistance Fund, 1501 Broadway, Suite 302, New York, NY 10036 *Tel:* 212-997-0947 *Fax:* 212-768-7414 *E-mail:* staff@asja.org *Web Site:* asja.org, pg 813

Writers Federation of Nova Scotia, 1113 Marginal Rd, Halifax, NS B3H 4P7, Canada *Tel:* 902-423-8116 *Fax:* 902-422-0881 *E-mail:* talk@writers.ns.ca *Web Site:* www.writers.ns.ca, pg 702

Writers' Fellowships, 417 W Roosevelt Ave, Phoenix, AZ 85003 *Tel:* 602-255-5882 *Fax:* 602-256-0282, pg 813

Writers: Free-Lance Inc, 167 Bluff Rd, Strasburg, VA 22657 *Tel:* 540-635-4617, pg 615

Writers Guild of Alberta Annual Awards Program, 11759 Groat Rd, Edmonton, AB T5M 3K6, Canada *Tel:* 780-422-8174 *Toll Free Tel:* 800-665-5354 (Alberta only) *Fax:* 780-422-2663 *E-mail:* mail@writersguild.ab.ca *Web Site:* www.writersguild.ab.ca, pg 813

Writers Guild of America Awards, 7000 W Third St, Los Angeles, CA 90048 *Tel:* 323-951-4000 *Fax:* 323-782-4802 *Web Site:* www.wga.org, pg 813

Writers Guild of America East Inc (WGAE), 555 W 57 St, New York, NY 10019 *Tel:* 212-767-7800 *Fax:* 212-582-1909 *E-mail:* info@wgaeast.org *Web Site:* www. wgaeast.org, pg 702

Writers Guild of America West Inc (WGAW), 7000 W Third St, Los Angeles, CA 90048 *Tel:* 323-951-4000 *Fax:* 323-782-4800 *Web Site:* www.wga.org, pg 703

Writers' Haven Writers (WHW), 2244 Fourth Ave, San Diego, CA 92101 *Tel:* 619-696-0569, pg 703

Writers House LLC, 21 W 26 St, New York, NY 10010 *Tel:* 212-685-2400 *Fax:* 212-685-1781, pg 662

Writers-In-Exile Center, American Branch, 42 Derby Ave, Orange, CT 06477 *Tel:* 203-397-1479 *Fax:* 203-785-4744; 203-397-5439, pg 703

Writers' Journal Annual Fiction Contest, PO Box 394, Perham, MN 56573 *Tel:* 218-346-7921 *Fax:* 218-346-7924 *E-mail:* writersjournal@lakesplus.com *Web Site:* www.writersjournal.com, pg 813

Writers' Journal Annual Horror/Ghost Contest, PO Box 394, Perham, MN 56573 *Tel:* 218-346-7921 *Fax:* 218-346-7924 *E-mail:* writersjournal@lakesplus.com *Web Site:* www.writersjournal.com, pg 813

Writers' Journal Annual Romance Contest, PO Box 394, Perham, MN 56573 *Tel:* 218-346-7921 *Fax:* 218-346-7924 *E-mail:* writersjournal@lakesplus.com *Web Site:* www.writersjournal.com, pg 813

Writers' Journal Annual Short Story Contest, PO Box 394, Perham, MN 56573 *Tel:* 218-346-7921 *Fax:* 218-346-7924 *E-mail:* writersjournal@lakesplus.com *Web Site:* www.writersjournal.com, pg 813

Writers' Journal Annual Travel Writing Contest, PO Box 394, Perham, MN 56573 *Tel:* 218-346-7921 *Fax:* 218-346-7924 *E-mail:* writersjournal@lakesplus.com *Web Site:* www.writersjournal.com, pg 813

Writers' Journal Annual Poetry Contest, PO Box 394, Perham, MN 56573 *Tel:* 218-346-7921 *Fax:* 218-346-7924 *E-mail:* writersjournal@lakesplus.com *Web Site:* www.writersjournal.com, pg 813

Writers' League of Texas, 1501 W Fifth St, Suite E-2, Austin, TX 78703 *Tel:* 512-499-8914 *Fax:* 512-499-0441 *E-mail:* wlt@writersleague.org *Web Site:* www.writersleague.org, pg 670, 703, 749

The Writer's Lifeline Inc, 518 S Fairfax Ave, Los Angeles, CA 90036 *Tel:* 323-932-0905 *Fax:* 323-932-0321 *E-mail:* questions@thewriterslifeline.com; comments@thewriterslifeline.com *Web Site:* www.thewriterslifeline.com, pg 615

Writers' Productions, PO Box 630, Westport, CT 06881-0630 *Tel:* 203-227-8199, pg 662

Writer's Relief, Inc, 245 Teaneck Rd, Ridgefield Park, NJ 07660 *Tel:* 201-641-3003 *Fax:* 201-641-1253 *Web Site:* www.wrelief.com, pg 615

Writers' Representatives LLC, 116 W 14 St, 11th fl, New York, NY 10011-7305 *Tel:* 212-620-9009 *Fax:* 212-620-0023 *E-mail:* transom@writersreps.com *Web Site:* www.writersreps.com, pg 662

Writers Retreat Workshop (WRW), 5721 Magazine St, Suite 161, New Orleans, LA 70115 *Toll Free Tel:* 800-642-2494 *E-mail:* wrw04@netscape.net *Web Site:* www.writersretreatworkshop.com, pg 749

Writers' Union of Canada, 90 Richmond St E, Suite 200, Toronto, ON M5C 1P1, Canada *Tel:* 416-703-8982 *Fax:* 416-504-9090 *E-mail:* info@writersunion.ca *Web Site:* www.writersunion.ca, pg 703

Writers Workshop in Children's Literature, 10305 SW 127 Ct, Miami, FL 33186 *Tel:* 305-382-2677, pg 749

Writers Workshop in Science Fiction, University of Kansas English Dept, 3114 Wescoe Hall, Lawrence, KS 66045-2350 *Tel:* 785-864-3380 *Fax:* 785-864-1159, pg 749

The Writing Center, 601 Palisade Ave, Englewood Cliffs, NJ 07632 *Tel:* 201-567-4017 *Fax:* 201-567-7202 *E-mail:* 102100.1065@compuserve.com, pg 749

The Writing for Children Founders Workshops, 814 Court St, Dept CF, Honesdale, PA 18431 *Tel:* 570-253-1192 *Fax:* 570-253-0179 *E-mail:* contact@highlightsfoundation.org *Web Site:* www.highlightsfoundation.org, pg 749

Writing Today, PO Box 549003, Birmingham, AL 35282-9765 *Tel:* 205-226-4921 *Toll Free Tel:* 800-523-5793 *Fax:* 205-226-4931 *E-mail:* dcwilson@bsc.edu *Web Site:* www.bsc.edu, pg 749

Writing Workshops, 1333 Research Park Dr, Davis, CA 95616 *Tel:* 530-754-5237 *Toll Free Tel:* 800-752-0881 *Fax:* 530-754-5105 *Web Site:* www.extension.ucdavis.edu, pg 749

The Writings of Mary Baker Eddy/Publisher, 175 Huntington Ave, Suite A-16-10, Boston, MA 02115 *Tel:* 617-450-3514; 617-450-2000 (Christian Science Church Boston) *Toll Free Tel:* 800-288-7090 *Fax:* 617-450-7334 *Web Site:* www.spirituality.com, pg 305

The Wylie Agency Inc, 250 W 57 St, Suite 2114, New York, NY 10107 *Tel:* 212-246-0069 *Fax:* 212-586-8953 *E-mail:* mail@wylieagency.com, pg 662

Wyndham Hall Press, 5050 Kerr Rd, Lima, OH 45806 *Tel:* 419-648-9124 *Toll Free Tel:* 866-895-0977 *Fax:* 419-648-9124; 413-208-2409 *E-mail:* whpbooks@wcoil.com *Web Site:* www.wyndhamhallpress.com, pg 305

Wyoming Arts Council Literature Fellowships, 2320 Capitol Ave, Cheyenne, WY 82002 *Tel:* 307-777-7742 *Fax:* 307-777-5499 *Web Site:* www.wyoarts.state.wy.us, pg 814

Wyrick & Co, 284-A Meeting St, Charleston, SC 29401 *Tel:* 843-722-0881 *Toll Free Tel:* 800-227-5898 *Fax:* 843-722-6771 *E-mail:* wyrickco@bellsouth.net, pg 305

XC Publishing, 931 E Avenida de las Flores, Thousand Oaks, CA 91360 *Tel:* 805-495-7768 *Fax:* 413-431-5515 *E-mail:* xuhl@xcpublishing.com *Web Site:* www.xcpublishing.com, pg 305

Xlibris Corp, 436 Walnut St, 11th fl, The Independence Bldg, Philadelphia, PA 19106 *Tel:* 215-923-4686 *Toll Free Tel:* 888-795-4274 *Fax:* 215-923-4685 *E-mail:* info@xlibris.com *Web Site:* www.xlibris.com, pg 305

XYZ Editeur, 1781 rue Saint-Hubert, Montreal, PQ H2L 3Z1, Canada *Tel:* 514-525-2170 *Fax:* 514-525-7537, pg 567

XYZ Publishing, 1781 Saint Hubert St, Montreal, PQ H2L 3Z1, Canada *Tel:* 514-252-2170 *Fax:* 514-525-7537 *E-mail:* info@xyzedit.qc.ca *Web Site:* www.xyzedit.qc.ca, pg 567

Yale Center for British Art, 1080 Chapel St, New Haven, CT 06520 *Tel:* 203-432-2800; 203-432-2850 *Fax:* 203-432-4530 *E-mail:* bacinfo@yale.edu *Web Site:* www.yale.edu/ycba, pg 305

Yale Series of Younger Poets, 302 Temple St, New Haven, CT 06511 *Tel:* 203-432-0900 *Fax:* 203-432-2394; 203-432-0948 *Web Site:* www.yale.edu/yup/, pg 814

Yale University Press, 302 Temple St, New Haven, CT 06511 *Tel:* 203-432-0960; 401-531-2800 (cust serv) *Toll Free Tel:* 800-405-1619 (cust serv) *Fax:* 203-432-0948; 401-531-2801 (cust serv) *Toll Free Fax:* 800-406-9145 (cust serv) *E-mail:* customer.care@trilateral.org (cust serv) *Web Site:* www.yale.edu/yup/, pg 305

Yard Dog Press, 710 W Redbud Lane, Alma, AR 72921-7247 *Tel:* 479-632-4693 *Fax:* 479-632-4693 *Web Site:* www.yarddogpress.com, pg 306

Yardbird Books, 601 Kennedy Rd, Airville, PA 17302 *Tel:* 717-927-6377 *Toll Free Tel:* 800-622-6044 (Sales) *Fax:* 717-927-6377 *E-mail:* info@yardbird.com *Web Site:* www.yardbird.com, pg 306

YBK Publishers Inc, 425 Broome St, New York, NY 10013 *Tel:* 212-219-0135 *Fax:* 212-219-0136 *E-mail:* info@ybkpublishers.com, pg 306

Ye Galleon Press, 107 E Main St, Fairfield, WA 99012 *Tel:* 509-283-2422 *Toll Free Tel:* 800-829-5586 (orders only) *Fax:* 509-283-2422, pg 306

Ye Olde Genealogie Shoppe, PO Box 39128, Indianapolis, IN 46239 *Tel:* 317-862-3330 *Toll Free Tel:* 800-419-0200 *Fax:* 317-862-2599 *E-mail:* yogs@iquest.net *Web Site:* www.yogs.com, pg 306

YES New Play Festival, 205 FA Theatre Dept, Nunn Dr, Highland Heights, KY 41099-1007 *Tel:* 859-572-6362 *Fax:* 859-572-6057, pg 814

Yeshiva University Press, 500 W 185 St, New York, NY 10033-3201 *Tel:* 212-960-5400 *Fax:* 212-960-0043 *E-mail:* yuadmit@yu.edu *Web Site:* www.yu.edu, pg 306

YMAA Publication Center, 4354 Washington St, Roslindale, MA 02131 *Tel:* 617-323-7215 *Toll Free Tel:* 800-669-8892 *Fax:* 617-323-7417 *E-mail:* ymaa@aol.com *Web Site:* www.ymaa.com, pg 306

York Press Inc, 9540 Deereco Rd, Timonium, MD 21093 *Tel:* 410-560-1557 *Toll Free Tel:* 800-962-2763 *Fax:* 410-560-6758 *E-mail:* york@abs.net *Web Site:* www.yorkpress.com, pg 306

York Press Ltd, 152 Boardwalk Dr, Toronto, ON M4L 3X4, Canada *Tel:* 416-690-3788 *Fax:* 416-690-3797 *E-mail:* yorkpress@sympatico.ca *Web Site:* www3.sympatico.ca/yorkpress, pg 567

Mary Yost Associates Inc, 59 E 54 St, Suite 73, New York, NY 10022 *Tel:* 212-980-4988 *Fax:* 212-935-3632 *E-mail:* yostbooks59@aol.com, pg 662

The Young Adult Canadian Book Award, 328 Frank St, Ottawa, ON K2P 0X8, Canada *Tel:* 613-232-9625 *Fax:* 613-563-9895 *Web Site:* www.cla.ca, pg 814

The Young Agency, 156 Fifth Ave, Suite 617, New York, NY 10010 *Tel:* 212-229-2612 *Fax:* 212-924-6609, pg 662

Donald Young, 166 E 61 St, Suite 3-C, New York, NY 10021 *Tel:* 212-593-0010 *E-mail:* numiscribe@aol.com, pg 615

Young Lions Fiction Award, Office of Development, Rm 73, Fifth Ave & 42 St, New York, NY 10018 *Tel:* 212-930-0887 *Fax:* 212-930-0983 *E-mail:* younglions@nypl.org *Web Site:* www2.nypl.org, pg 814

Young People's Press Inc (YPPI), 3033 Fifth Ave, Suite 200, San Diego, CA 92103 *Tel:* 619-688-9040 *Toll Free Tel:* 800-231-9774 *Fax:* 619-688-9044 *E-mail:* info@youngpeoplespress.com *Web Site:* www.youngpeoplespress.com, pg 306

Phyllis Smart Young Poetry Prize & Chris O'Malley Fiction Prize, University of Wisconsin - English Dept, 7193 HCW, 600 N Park St, Madison, WI 53706 *Tel:* 608-263-0566 *E-mail:* madreview@mail.studentorg.wisc.edu *Web Site:* mendota.english.wisc.edu/~MadRev/main.html, pg 814

Young Writer's Workshop, PO Box 408, Osterville, MA 02655 *Tel:* 508-375-0516 *E-mail:* ccw@capecod.net *Web Site:* www.capecodwriterscenter.com, pg 749

Yucca Tree Press, 270 Avenida de Mesilla, Las Cruces, NM 88005 *Tel:* 505-525-9707 *Toll Free Tel:* 888-817-1990 *Fax:* 505-525-9711 *E-mail:* thefolks@barbed-wire.net *Web Site:* www.barbed-wire.net, pg 306

YWAM Publishing, PO Box 55787, Seattle, WA 98155-0787 *Tel:* 425-771-1153 *Toll Free Tel:* 800-922-2143 *Fax:* 425-775-2383 *E-mail:* information@ywampublishing.com *Web Site:* www.ywampublishing.com, pg 306

Jane Shapiro Zacek, 104 Manning Blvd, Albany, NY 12203-1708 *Tel:* 518-489-7630; 518-388-6011 *Fax:* 518-388-6875 *E-mail:* zacekj@union.edu, pg 615

Zachary Shuster Harmsworth Agency, 1776 Broadway, New York, NY 10019 *Tel:* 212-765-6900 *Fax:* 212-765-6490 *Web Site:* www.zshliterary.com, pg 662

The Zack Company Inc, 243 W 70 St, Suite 8-D, New York, NY 10023-4366 *Tel:* 212-712-2400 *Fax:* 212-712-9110 *Web Site:* www.zackcompany.com, pg 662

Zagat Survey, 4 Columbus Circle, New York, NY 10019 *Tel:* 212-977-6000 *Toll Free Tel:* 800-333-3421 (gen inquiries); 888-371-5440 (orders); 800-540-9609 (corp sales) *Fax:* 212-977-9760; 802-864-9846 (order related) *E-mail:* corpsales@zagat.com; shop@zagat.com *Web Site:* www.zagat.com, pg 306

Zaner-Bloser Inc, 2200 W Fifth Ave, Columbus, OH 43215 *Tel:* 614-486-0221 *Toll Free Tel:* 800-421-3018 *Fax:* 614-487-2699 *Toll Free Fax:* 800-992-6087 *E-mail:* info@zaner-bloser.com *Web Site:* www.zaner-bloser.com, pg 306

Zebra Communications, 230 Deerchase Dr, Suite B, Woodstock, GA 30188 *Tel:* 770-924-0528 *Fax:* 770-592-7362 *Web Site:* www.zebraeditor.com, pg 615

Susan Zeckendorf Associates Inc, 171 W 57 St, Suite 11-B, New York, NY 10019 *Tel:* 212-245-2928, pg 663

Zeiders & Associates, PO Box 670, Lewisburg, PA 17837 *Tel:* 570-524-4315 *Fax:* 570-524-4315, pg 615

Zeig, Tucker & Theisen Inc, 3614 N 24 St, Phoenix, AZ 85016 *Tel:* 602-957-1270 *Toll Free Fax:* 800-688-2877 *E-mail:* zttorders@mindspring.com *Web Site:* www.zeigtucker.com, pg 307

Zephyr Press Catalog, 814 N Franklin St, Chicago, IL 60610 *Tel:* 312-337-5985 *Toll Free Tel:* 800-232-2187 *Fax:* 312-337-1651 *E-mail:* neways2learn@zephyrpress.com *Web Site:* www.zephyrpress.com, pg 307

George Ziegler, 40 E Norwich Ave, Columbus, OH 43201 *Tel:* 614-299-2845, pg 663

Barbara J Zitwer Agency, 525 West End Ave, Apt 11H, New York, NY 10024 *Tel:* 212-501-8423 *Fax:* 212-501-8462 *E-mail:* bjzitwerag@aol.com, pg 663

Robert Zolnerzak, 101 Clark St, Apt 20K, Brooklyn, NY 11201 *Tel:* 718-522-0591, pg 615

Zondervan, 5300 Patterson Ave SE, Grand Rapids, MI 49530 *Tel:* 616-698-6900 *Toll Free Tel:* 800-727-1309 (cust serv) *Fax:* 616-698-3439; 616-698-3255 (cust serv) *Web Site:* www.zondervan.com, pg 307

Zone Books, 1226 Prospect Ave, Brooklyn, NY 11218 *Tel:* 718-686-0048 *Toll Free Tel:* 800-405-1619 (orders & cust serv) *Fax:* 212-625-9772; 718-686-9045 *Toll Free Fax:* 800-406-9145 (orders) *E-mail:* urzone@zonebooks.org; mitpress-orders@mit.edu (orders), pg 307

Anna Zornio Memorial Children's Theatre Playwriting Award, Paul Creative Arts, 30 College Rd, D-22, Durham, NH 03824-3538 *Tel:* 603-862-3038 *Fax:* 603-862-0298, pg 814

Zumaya Publications, 403-366 Howard Ave, Burnaby, BC V5B 4Y2, Canada *Tel:* 604-299-8417 *E-mail:* editorial@zumayapublications.com *Web Site:* www.zumayapublications.com, pg 567

Industry Yellow Pages — Personnel Index

Included in this index are the personnel included in the entries in this volume of *LMP*, along with the page number(s) on which they appear. Not included in this index are those individuals associated with listings in the **Calendar of Book Trade & Promotional Events; Reference Books for the Trade** and **Magazines for the Trade** sections. Also, personnel associated with secondary addresses within listings (such as branch offices, sales offices, editorial offices, etc.) are not included.

Aaboe, Niels, M E Sharpe Inc, 80 Business Park Dr, Suite 202, Armonk, NY 10504 *Tel:* 914-273-1800 *Toll Free Tel:* 800-541-6563 *Fax:* 914-273-2106 *E-mail:* info@mesharpe.com *Web Site:* www.mesharpe.com, pg 246

Aanstad, Betty, Krause Publications, 700 E State St, Iola, WI 54990 *Tel:* 715-445-4612 ext 365 *Toll Free Tel:* 800-258-0929; 888-457-2873 *Fax:* 715-445-4087 *Web Site:* www.krause.com, pg 147

Abajian-Harvey, Ann Marie, Ashgate Publishing Co, 101 Cherry St, Suite 420, Burlington, VT 05401-4405 *Tel:* 802-865-7641 *Fax:* 802-865-7847 *E-mail:* info@ashgate.com *Web Site:* www.ashgate.com, pg 25

Abbate, Matthew, The MIT Press, 5 Cambridge Ctr, Cambridge, MA 02142 *Tel:* 617-253-5646 *Toll Free Tel:* 800-405-1619 (orders only) *Fax:* 617-258-6779 *Web Site:* mitpress.mit.edu, pg 175

Abbott, J L, Amber Quill Press LLC, PO Box 265, Indian Hills, CO 80454 *E-mail:* customer_service@amberquillpress.com *Web Site:* amberquill.com, pg 10

Abdo, Jim, Abdo Publishing, 4940 Viking Dr, Suite 622, Edina, MN 55435 *Tel:* 952-831-2120 (ext 223) *Toll Free Tel:* 800-800-1312 *Fax:* 952-831-1632 *E-mail:* info@abdopub.com *Web Site:* www.abdopub.com, pg 3

Abdo, Paul, Abdo Publishing, 4940 Viking Dr, Suite 622, Edina, MN 55435 *Tel:* 952-831-2120 (ext 223) *Toll Free Tel:* 800-800-1312 *Fax:* 952-831-1632 *E-mail:* info@abdopub.com *Web Site:* www.abdopub.com, pg 3

Abdulhamid, Abusolayman, The International Institute of Islamic Thought, 500 Grove St, Suite 200, Herndon, VA 20170 *Tel:* 703-471-1133 *Fax:* 703-471-3922 *E-mail:* iiit@iiit.org *Web Site:* www.iiit.org, pg 137

Abe, Carol, University of Hawaii Press, 2840 Kolowalu St, Honolulu, HI 96822 *Tel:* 808-956-8255 *Toll Free Tel:* 888-847-7377 *Fax:* 808-988-6052 *Toll Free Fax:* 800-650-7811 *E-mail:* uhpbooks@hawaii.edu *Web Site:* www.uhpress.hawaii.edu, pg 281

Abecassis, Andree, Ann Elmo Agency Inc, 60 E 42 St, New York, NY 10165 *Tel:* 212-661-2880; 212-661-2881 *Fax:* 212-661-2883, pg 629

Abeel, Tom, JIST Publishing Inc, 8902 Otis Ave, Indianapolis, IN 46216 *Tel:* 317-613-4200 *Toll Free Tel:* 800-648-5478 *Fax:* 317-613-4304 *Toll Free Fax:* 800-547-8329 *E-mail:* info@jist.com *Web Site:* www.jist.com, pg 141

Abel, Carole, Carole Abel Literary Agent, 160 W 87 St, New York, NY 10024 *Tel:* 212-724-1168 *Fax:* 212-724-1384 *E-mail:* caroleabel@aol.com, pg 617

Abel, Dominick, Dominick Abel Literary Agency Inc, 146 W 82 St, Suite 1-B, New York, NY 10024 *Tel:* 212-877-0710 *Fax:* 212-595-3133 *E-mail:* agency@dalainc.com, pg 617

Abel, Ken, ABELexpress, 601 Beechwood Ave, Carnegie, PA 15106 *Tel:* 412-279-0672 *Toll Free Tel:* 800-542-9001 *Fax:* 412-429-2911, pg 3

Abel, Marilyn J, Educational Paperback Association (EPA), PO Box 1399, East Hampton, NY 11937-0709 *Tel:* 631-329-3315 *E-mail:* edupaperback@aol.com *Web Site:* www.edupaperback.org, pg 686

Abel, Marilyn J, Jeremiah Ludington Award, PO Box 1399, East Hampton, NY 11937-0709 *Tel:* 631-329-3315 *E-mail:* edupaperback@aol.com, pg 786

Abel, Richard M, University Press of New England, One Court St, Lebanon, NH 03766 *Tel:* 603-448-1533 *Toll Free Tel:* 800-421-1561 (orders only) *Fax:* 603-448-7006; 603-643-1540 *E-mail:* university.press@dartmouth.edu *Web Site:* www.upne.com, pg 287

Aber, J Lawrence, National Center for Children in Poverty, 215 W 125 St, 3rd fl, New York, NY 10027 *Tel:* 646-284-9600 *Fax:* 646-284-9623 *E-mail:* nccp@columbia.edu *Web Site:* www.nccp.org, pg 183

Abisch, Roz, Boche Kaplan, 166 W Waukena Ave, Oceanside, NY 11572 *Tel:* 516-764-9828, pg 603

Abkemeier, Laurie, DeFiore & Co, Author Services, 72 Spring St, Suite 304, New York, NY 10012 *Tel:* 212-925-7744 *Fax:* 212-925-9803 *E-mail:* submissions@defioreandco.com *Web Site:* defioreandco.com, pg 627

Abou, Stephanie, The Joy Harris Literary Agency, 156 Fifth Ave, Suite 617, New York, NY 10010 *Tel:* 212-924-6269 *Fax:* 212-924-6609 *E-mail:* gen.office@jhlitagent.com, pg 634

Abraham, Jeff, Book Industry Standards & Communications, 19 W 21 St, Suite 905, New York, NY 10010 *Tel:* 646-336-7141 *Fax:* 646-336-6214 *E-mail:* info@bisg.org *Web Site:* www.bisg.org, pg 681

Abraham, Jeff, Book Industry Study Group Inc, 19 W 21 St, Suite 905, New York, NY 10010 *Tel:* 646-336-7141 *Fax:* 646-336-6214 *E-mail:* info@bisg.org *Web Site:* www.bisg.org, pg 681

Abrahams, Toni, Scholastic Library Publishing, 90 Old Sherman Tpke, Danbury, CT 06816 *Tel:* 203-797-3500 *Toll Free Tel:* 800-621-1115 *Fax:* 203-797-3657 *Web Site:* www.scholasticlibrary.com, pg 242

Abram, Stephen, Canadian Library Association (CLA), 328 Frank St, Ottawa, ON K2P 0X8, Canada *Tel:* 613-232-9625 *Fax:* 613-563-9895 *E-mail:* info@cla.ca *Web Site:* www.cla.ca/, pg 683

Abrams, Joanne, Square One Publishers, 115 Herricks Rd, Garden City Park, NY 11040 *Tel:* 516-535-2010 *Fax:* 516-535-2014 *E-mail:* sq1info@aol.com *Web Site:* squareonepublishers.com, pg 256

Abrams, Richard, URJ Press, 633 Third Ave, New York, NY 10017-6778 *Tel:* 212-650-4100 *Toll Free Tel:* 888-489-UAHC (489-8242) *Fax:* 212-650-4119 *E-mail:* press@urj.org *Web Site:* www.urjpress.com, pg 289

Abrams, Richard I, Abrams & Co Publishers Inc, 61 Mattatuck Heights Rd, Waterbury, CT 06705 *Tel:* 203-756-6562 *Toll Free Tel:* 800-227-9120 *Fax:* 203-756-2895 *Toll Free Fax:* 800-737-3322, pg 3

Abrams, Richard I, The Letter People®, 61 Mattatuck Heights Rd, Waterbury, CT 06705 *Tel:* 203-756-6562 *Toll Free Tel:* 800-227-9120; 800-874-0029 *Fax:* 203-756-2895 *Toll Free Fax:* 800-737-3322 *Web Site:* letterpeople.com, pg 153

Abrams, Rick, Tom Snyder Productions, 80 Coolidge Hill Rd, Watertown, MA 02472-5003 *Tel:* 617-926-6000 *Toll Free Tel:* 800-342-0236 *Fax:* 617-926-6222 *E-mail:* ask@tomsnyder.com *Web Site:* www.tomsnyder.com, pg 251

Abrams, Robert E, Abbeville Publishing Group, 116 W 23 St, Suite 500, New York, NY 10011 *Tel:* 646-375-2039 *Toll Free Tel:* 800-ART-BOOK (278-2665) *Fax:* 646-375-2040 *E-mail:* abbeville@abbeville.com *Web Site:* www.abbeville.com, pg 2

Abrams, Robert E, Artabras Inc, 116 W 23 St, Suite 500, New York, NY 10011 *Tel:* 646-375-2039 *Toll Free Tel:* 800-ART-BOOK *Fax:* 646-375-2040 *E-mail:* abbeville@abbeville.com *Web Site:* www.abbeville.com, pg 24

Abramson, Robert, United Synagogue Book Service, 155 Fifth Ave, New York, NY 10010 *Tel:* 212-533-7800 (ext 2003) *Toll Free Tel:* 800-594-5617 (warehouse only) *Fax:* 212-253-5422 *E-mail:* booksvc@uscj.org *Web Site:* www.uscj.org/booksvc, pg 279

Abrigana, Lani, Kamehameha Schools Press, 1887 Makuakane St, Honolulu, HI 96817-1887 *Tel:* 808-842-8719 *Fax:* 808-842-8895 *E-mail:* kspress@ksbe.edu *Web Site:* kspress.ksbe.edu, pg 144

Abrohms, Alison, Nesbitt Graphics Inc, 555 Virginia Dr, Fort Washington, PA 19034 *Tel:* 215-591-9125 *Fax:* 215-591-9093 *Web Site:* www.Nesbittgraphics.com, pg 606

Absolon, K B, Kabel Publishers, 11225 Huntover Dr, Rockville, MD 20852 *Tel:* 301-468-6463 *Toll Free Tel:* 800-543-3167 *Fax:* 301-468-6463 *E-mail:* kabelcomp@erols.com *Web Site:* www.erols.com/kabelcomp/index2.html, pg 143

Acacia, Rose, Writers House LLC, 21 W 26 St, New York, NY 10010 *Tel:* 212-685-2400 *Fax:* 212-685-1781, pg 662

Accordino, Michael, Simon & Schuster, 1230 Avenue of the Americas, New York, NY 10020 *Tel:* 212-698-7000 *Toll Free Tel:* 800-223-2348 (cust serv); 800-223-2336 (orders) *Toll Free Fax:* 800-943-9831 (orders) *Web Site:* www.simonsays.com, pg 248

Acheson, Alice B, Alice B Acheson's Workshops for Writers, Illustrators & Photographers, PO Box 735, Friday Harbor, WA 98250 *Tel:* 360-378-2815 *Fax:* 360-378-2841 *E-mail:* aliceba@aol.com, pg 741

Ackerman, Ellen, The Conference Board Inc, 845 Third Ave, New York, NY 10022 *Tel:* 212-759-0900 *Fax:* 212-980-7014 *E-mail:* info@conference-board.org *Web Site:* www.conference-board.org, pg 66

Ackerman, John G, Cornell University Press, 512 E State St, Ithaca, NY 14850 *Tel:* 607-277-2338 *Fax:* 607-277-2374 *E-mail:* cupressinfo@cornell.edu *Web Site:* www.cornellpress.cornell.edu, pg 68

Acton, Amy, Phoenix Society for Burn Survivors, 2153 Wealthy SE, Suite 215, E Grand Rapids, MI 49506 *Tel:* 616-458-2773 *Toll Free Tel:* 800-888-BURN (888-2876) *Fax:* 616-458-2831 *E-mail:* info@phoenix-society.org *Web Site:* www.phoenix-society.org, pg 212

Acuna, Melissa, South-Western, A Thomson Business, 5191 Natorp Blvd, Mason, OH 45040 *Tel:* 513-229-1000 *Toll Free Tel:* 800-543-0487 *Fax:* 513-229-1025 *Web Site:* www.thomson.com, pg 254

Adamo, John, Random House Children's Books, 1745 Broadway, New York, NY 10019 *Tel:* 212-782-9000 *Toll Free Tel:* 800-200-3552 *Fax:* 212-782-9452 *Web Site:* www.randomhouse.com/kids, pg 225

Adamonis, Richard, Penguin Group (USA) Inc Sales, 375 Hudson St, New York, NY 10014 *Tel:* 212-366-2000 *E-mail:* online@penguinputnam.com *Web Site:* www.penguin.com, pg 208

Adams, Barry, Temple University Press, 1601 N Broad St, 083-42, USB Room 306, Philadelphia, PA 19122-6099 *Tel:* 215-204-8787 *Toll Free Tel:* 800-447-1656 *Fax:* 215-204-4719 *E-mail:* tempress@temple.edu *Web Site:* www.temple.edu/tempress, pg 266

Adams, Bob, dbS Productions, University Sta, Charlottesville, VA 22903 *Tel:* 434-293-5502 *Toll Free Tel:* 800-745-1581 *Fax:* 434-293-5502 *E-mail:* info@dbs-sar.com *Web Site:* www.dbs-sar.com, pg 77

Adams, Brenda, University of Georgia Press, 330 Research Dr, Athens, GA 30602-4901 *Tel:* 706-369-6130 *Toll Free Tel:* 800-266-5842 (orders only) *Fax:* 706-369-6131 *E-mail:* books@ugapress.uga.edu *Web Site:* www.ugapress.org, pg 281

Adams, Cathy, Birkhauser Boston, 675 Massachusetts Ave, Cambridge, MA 02139 Tel: 617-876-2333 Toll Free Tel: 800-777-4643 (cust serv) Fax: 617-876-1272 E-mail: service@birkhauser.com Web Site: www. birkhauser.com, pg 39

Adams, Chuck, Algonquin Books of Chapel Hill, 127 Kingston Dr, Suite 105, Chapel Hill, NC 27514 Tel: 919-967-0108 Fax: 919-933-0272 E-mail: dialogue@algonquin.com Web Site: www. algonquin.com, pg 8

Adams, Garry, Ye Galleon Press, 107 E Main St, Fairfield, WA 99012 Tel: 509-283-2422 Toll Free Tel: 800-829-5586 (orders only) Fax: 509-283-2422, pg 306

Adams, Lisa, The Garamond Agency Inc, 12 Horton St, Newburyport, MA 01950 Tel: 978-462-5060 Fax: 978-462-6697 Web Site: www.garamondagency.com, pg 632

Adams, Michael, University of Texas at Austin, Creative Writing Program, Dept of English, One University Sta, B5000, Austin, TX 78712-1164 Tel: 512-475-6356 Fax: 512-471-2898 Web Site: www.en.utexas. edu/grad/crwconc.html, pg 756

Adams, Paul, Harvard University Press, 79 Garden St, Cambridge, MA 02138-1499 Tel: 617-495-2600; 401-531-2800 (international orders) Toll Free Tel: 800-405-1619 (orders) Fax: 617-495-5898 (general); 617-496-4677 (edit & rts); 401-531-2801 (international orders) Toll Free Fax: 800-406-9145 (orders) E-mail: firstname_lastname@harvard.edu Web Site: www.hup.harvard.edu, pg 117

Adams, Stephanie, Bonus Books Inc, 1452 Second St, Santa Monica, CA 90403 Tel: 310-260-9400 Toll Free Tel: 800-225-3775 E-mail: webmaster@bonusbooks. com Web Site: www.bonusbooks.com, pg 43

Adams, Terry, Little, Brown and Company Adult Trade Division, 1271 Avenue of the Americas, New York, NY 10020 Tel: 212-522-8700 Fax: 212-522-2067 Web Site: www.twbookmark.com, pg 156

Adams, William, University of South Carolina Press, 1600 Hampton St, 5th fl, Columbia, SC 29208 Tel: 803-777-5243 Toll Free Tel: 800-768-2500 (orders) Fax: 803-777-0160 Toll Free Fax: 800-868-0740 (orders) Web Site: www.sc.edu/uscpress/, pg 285

Adamson, Doug, American Bankers Association, 1120 Connecticut Ave NW, Washington, DC 20036 Tel: 202-663-5087 Toll Free Tel: 800-BANKERS (226-5377) Fax: 202-663-5087 (cust serv) Web Site: www.aba.com, pg 12

Addington, Nancy, Central Ohio Writers of Literature for Children, c/o St Joseph Montessori School, 933 Hamlet St, Columbus, OH 43201-3595 Tel: 614-291-8644 Fax: 614-291-7411 E-mail: cowriters@mail.com Web Site: www.sjms.net/conf, pg 742

Adel, Judith, J Adel Graphic Design, 586 Ramapo Rd, Teaneck, NJ 07666 Tel: 201-836-2606 E-mail: jadelnj@aol.com, pg 589

Adelman, Jennifer, ASM Press, 1752 "N" St NW, Washington, DC 20036-2904 Tel: 202-737-3600 Toll Free Tel: 800-546-2416 Fax: 202-942-9342 E-mail: books@asmusa.org Web Site: www.asmpress. org, pg 25

Adero, Malaika, Atria Books, 1230 Avenue of the Americas, New York, NY 10020 Tel: 212-698-7000 Fax: 212-698-7007 Web Site: www.simonsays.com, pg 27

Adkins, Lain, Association of American University Presses, 1427 E 60 St, Chicago, IL 60637 Tel: 773-702-7700; 773-702-7600 Toll Free Tel: 800-621-2736 (orders) Fax: 773-702-9756 (sales); 773-660-2235 (orders); 773-702-2708 E-mail: general@press. uchicago.edu Web Site: www.press.uchicago.edu, pg 26

Adlam, Laura, LTDBooks, 200 N Service Rd W, Unit 1, Suite 301, Oakville, ON L6M 2Y1, Canada Tel: 905-847-6060 Fax: 905-847-6060 E-mail: publisher@ ltdbooks.com Web Site: www.ltdbooks.com, pg 553

Adler, Allan R, Association of American Publishers (AAP), 71 Fifth Ave, 2nd fl, New York, NY 10003-3004 Tel: 212-255-0200 Fax: 212-255-7007 Web Site: www.publishers.org, pg 679

Adler, Karen, Pig Out Publications Inc, 207 E Gregory Blvd, Kansas City, MO 64114 Tel: 816-531-3119 Fax: 816-531-6113 Web Site: www.pigoutpublications. com, pg 213

Adlington, Scott, Dearborn Trade Publishing, 30 S Wacker Dr, Chicago, IL 60606-1719 Tel: 312-836-4400 Fax: 312-836-1021 E-mail: contactus@dearborn. com Web Site: www.dearborn.com, pg 78

Adzima, Katherine, Workman Publishing Co Inc, 708 Broadway, New York, NY 10003-9555 Tel: 212-254-5900 Toll Free Tel: 800-722-7202 Fax: 212-254-8098 E-mail: info@workman.com Web Site: www.workman. com, pg 303

Aghassi, Jeff, The Permanent Press, 4170 Noyac Rd, Sag Harbor, NY 11963 Tel: 631-725-1101 Fax: 631-725-8215 Web Site: www.thepermanentpress.com, pg 210

Aglialoro, Todd, Sophia Institute Press, PO Box 5284, Manchester, NH 03108 Tel: 603-641-9344 Toll Free Tel: 800-888-9344 Fax: 603-641-8108 Toll Free Fax: 888-288-2259 E-mail: orders@sophiainstitute. com Web Site: www.sophiainstitute.com, pg 253

Agnew, Tim, Concordia Publishing House, 3558 S Jefferson Ave, St Louis, MO 63118-3968 Tel: 314-268-1000 Toll Free Tel: 800-325-3040 Fax: 314-268-1329 Toll Free Fax: 800-490-9889 E-mail: cphorder@ cph.org Web Site: www.cph.org, pg 66

Agree, Peter A, University of Pennsylvania Press, 4200 Pine St, Philadelphia, PA 19104-4011 Tel: 215-898-6261 Toll Free Tel: 800-445-9880 (orders & cust serv only) Fax: 215-898-0404; 410-516-6998 (orders) E-mail: custserv@pobox.upenn.edu Web Site: www. upenn.edu/pennpress, pg 284

Aguilo, Maria Jesus, Berrett-Koehler Publishers Inc, 235 Montgomery St, Suite 650, San Francisco, CA 94104 Tel: 415-288-0260 Fax: 415-362-2512 E-mail: bkpub@bkpub.com Web Site: www. bkconnection.com, pg 37

Aguirre, Virginia, Transnational Publishers Inc, 410 Saw Mill River Rd, Suite 2045, Ardsley, NY 10502 Tel: 914-693-5100 Toll Free Tel: 800-914-8186 (orders only) Fax: 914-693-4430 E-mail: info@transnationalpubs.com Web Site: www. transnationalpubs.com, pg 274

Ahearn, Chris, ThorsonsElement US, 535 Albany St, 5th fl, Boston, MA 02118 Tel: 617-451-1533 Fax: 617-451-0971 Web Site: www.thorsons.com, pg 270

Ahearn, Pamela, Ahearn Agency Inc, 2021 Pine St, New Orleans, LA 70118 Tel: 504-861-8395 Fax: 504-866-6434, pg 618

Ahern, Rosemary, Other Press LLC, 307 Seventh Ave, Suite 1807, New York, NY 10001 Tel: 212-414-0054 Toll Free Tel: 877-THE-OTHER Fax: 212-414-0939 E-mail: orders@otherpress.com Web Site: www. otherpress.com, pg 573

Ahlrich, Loretta, The Century Foundation Press, 41 E 70 St, New York, NY 10021 Tel: 212-535-4441 Fax: 212-535-7534 E-mail: info@tcf.org Web Site: www.tcf.org, pg 58

Ahner, Betsy, American Society of Agronomy, 677 S Segoe Rd, Madison, WI 53711-1086 Tel: 608-273-8080 Fax: 608-273-2021 E-mail: headquarters@ agronomy.org Web Site: www.agronomy.org, pg 18

Ahner, Betsy, Soil Science Society of America, 677 S Segoe Rd, Madison, WI 53711-1086 Tel: 608-273-8095 Fax: 608-273-2021 E-mail: headquarters@soils. org Web Site: www.soils.org, pg 252

Ahrens, John, George T Bisel Co Inc, 710 S Washington Sq, Philadelphia, PA 19106 Tel: 215-922-5760 Toll Free Tel: 800-247-3526 Fax: 215-922-2235 E-mail: info@bisel.com Web Site: www.bisel.com, pg 39

Aiello, Gary, R R Bowker LLC, 630 Central Ave, New Providence, NJ 07974 Tel: 908-286-1090 Toll Free Tel: 888-269-5372; 888-269-5372 (cust serv - press 2 for returns) Fax: 908-219-0098 E-mail: orderinfo@ bowker.com Web Site: www.bowker.com, pg 44

Aiken, Paul, Authors Guild, 31 E 28 St, New York, NY 10016 Tel: 212-563-5904 Fax: 212-564-8363; 212-564-5363 E-mail: staff@authorsguild.org Web Site: www.authorsguild.org, pg 680

Aiken, Paul, The Authors League of America Inc, 31 E 28 St, New York, NY 10016 Tel: 212-564-8350 Fax: 212-564-8363 E-mail: staff@authorsguild.com Web Site: www.authorsguild.com, pg 681

Aiken, Paul, The Authors Registry Inc, 31 E 28 St, 10th fl, New York, NY 10016 Tel: 212-563-6920 Fax: 212-564-5363 E-mail: staff@authorsregistry.org Web Site: www.authorsregistry.org, pg 681

Aileen, Tami, Purple People Inc, PO Box 3194, Sedona, AZ 86340-3194 Tel: 928-204-6400 Toll Free Tel: 866-787-7535 Fax: 928-282-1662 E-mail: info@ purplepeople.com; sales@purplepeople.com (sales & orders); admin@purplepeople.com (billing) Web Site: www.purplepeople.com, pg 222

Ainsworth, Joanne S, Ainsworth Editorial Services, 43-01 12 St, Suite 339, Long Island City, NY 11101 Tel: 718-361-5254 Fax: 718-361-2837 E-mail: nycedit@aol.com, pg 589

Airoldi, Philip Jr, Puffin Books, 345 Hudson St, New York, NY 10014 Tel: 212-366-2000 E-mail: online@ penguinputnam.com Web Site: www.penguin.com, pg 222

Aitchison, Janet, Oxford University Press, Inc, 198 Madison Ave, New York, NY 10016-4314 Tel: 212-726-6000 Toll Free Tel: 800-451-7556 (orders) Web Site: www.oup.com/us, pg 200

Ajamian, Azad, Capital Books Inc, 22841 Quicksilver Dr, Sterling, VA 20166 Tel: 703-661-1571 Toll Free Tel: 800-758-3756 Fax: 703-661-1547 Web Site: www. capital-books.com, pg 52

Akeley, Jonathan, Cintas Fellowship Program, 809 United Nations Plaza, New York, NY 10017-3580 Tel: 212-984-5565 Fax: 212-984-5325 E-mail: cintas@iie.org Web Site: www.iie.org/cintas, pg 767

Akenson, Donald H, McGill-Queen's University Press, 3430 McTavish St, Montreal, PQ H3A 1X9, Canada Tel: 514-398-3750 Fax: 514-398-4333 E-mail: mqup@ mqup.ca Web Site: www.mqup.mcgill.ca, pg 553

Aker, J, Kabel Publishers, 11225 Huntover Dr, Rockville, MD 20852 Tel: 301-468-6463 Toll Free Tel: 800-543-3167 Fax: 301-468-6463 E-mail: kabelcomp@erols.com Web Site: www.erols. com/kabelcomp/index2.html, pg 143

Akers, Lane, Lawrence Erlbaum Associates Inc, 10 Industrial Ave, Mahwah, NJ 07430-2262 Tel: 201-236-2199 Toll Free Tel: 800-9-BOOKS-9 (926-6579) Fax: 201-760-3735 E-mail: orders@erlbaum.com Web Site: www.erlbaum.com, pg 91

Akin, Wanda M, Akin & Randolph Agency for Representation for Authors, Artists & Athletes (Literary Division), One Gateway Ctr, Suite 2600, Newark, NJ 07102 Tel: 973-623-6834 Toll Free Tel: 888-870-0765 Fax: 973-353-8417 Web Site: www. akinandrandolph.com, pg 618

Aks, Dan, Primedia Consumer Magazine & Internet Group, 260 Madison Ave, New York, NY 10016 Tel: 212-726-4300 Toll Free Tel: 800-521-2885 Fax: 212-726-4310 E-mail: sgnews@primediasi.com Web Site: www.primediainc.com, pg 218

Alain, Marc, Modus Vivendi Inc and Adventure Press, 5150 Saint Laurent, 2nd fl, Montreal, PQ H2T 1R8, Canada Tel: 514-272-0433 Fax: 514-272-7234 E-mail: enfo@modusadventure.com, pg 554

Alan, Dennis, CATALYST Creative Services, 619 Marion Plaza, Palo Alto, CA 94301-4251 Tel: 650-325-1500, pg 593

Alan, Ken, City & Regional Magazine Association, 4929 Wilshire Blvd, Suite 428, Los Angeles, CA 90010 Tel: 323-937-5514 Fax: 323-937-0959 Web Site: www. citymag.org, pg 685

Albee, Edward, William Flanagan Memorial Creative Persons Center, 14 Harrison St, New York, NY 10013 *Tel:* 212-226-2020 *E-mail:* info@albeefoundation.org *Web Site:* www.albeefoundation.org, pg 774

Albers, Donald J, The Mathematical Association of America, 1529 18 St NW, Washington, DC 20036 *Tel:* 202-387-5200 *Toll Free Tel:* 800-331-1622 (orders) *Fax:* 202-265-2384 *E-mail:* ldouglas@pmds.com *Web Site:* www.maa.org, pg 165

Albers, Wes, Southern California Writers' Conference/ Los Angeles/San Diego/Palm Springs, 1010 University Ave, Suite 54, San Diego, CA 92103 *Tel:* 619-233-4651 *Fax:* 253-390-8577 *E-mail:* wewrite@ writersconference.com *Web Site:* www.writersconference.com, pg 747

Albert, Janice, Albert Editorial Services, 565 Bellevue Ave, No 1704, Oakland, CA 94610 *Tel:* 510-839-1140, pg 589

Albert, Neale, Miniature Book Society Inc, 402 York Ave, Delaware, OH 43015 *Web Site:* www.mbs.org, pg 691

Albert, Ronald, Novalis Publishing, 49 Front St E, 2nd fl, Toronto, ON M5E 1B3, Canada *Tel:* 416-363-3303 *Toll Free Tel:* 800-387-7164 *Fax:* 416-363-9409 *Toll Free Fax:* 800-204-4140 *E-mail:* novalis@interlog.com *Web Site:* www.novalis.ca, pg 556

Alberti, Robert E, Impact Publishers Inc, PO Box 6016, Atascadero, CA 93423-6016 *Tel:* 805-466-5917 (opers & admin); 805-461-5911 (edit) *Toll Free Tel:* 800-246-7228 (orders) *Fax:* 805-466-5919 (opers & admin offices); 805-461-0554 (edit offices) *E-mail:* info@impactpublishers.com *Web Site:* www.impactpublishers.com; www.bibliotherapy.com, pg 131

Albi, Mary, The Continuum International Publishing Group, 15 E 26 St, Suite 1703, New York, NY 10010 *Tel:* 212-953-5858 *Toll Free Tel:* 800-561-7704 *Fax:* 212-953-5944 *E-mail:* info@continuum-books.com *Web Site:* www.continuumbooks.com, pg 67

Albrecht, Ms Geri, Heuer Publishing LLC, 211 First Ave SE, Cedar Rapids, IA 52401 *Tel:* 319-368-8008 *Toll Free Tel:* 800-950-7529 *Fax:* 319-364-1771 *E-mail:* editor@hitplays.com *Web Site:* www.hitplays.com, pg 122

Alcala, Rosa, University of Texas at El Paso, Dept Creative Writing, MFA with Bilingual Option, 500 W University Ave, PMB 670, El Paso, TX 79968-9991 *Tel:* 915-747-5713 *Fax:* 915-747-5523 *E-mail:* mfadirector@utep.edu *Web Site:* www.utep.edu/cw, pg 756

Alcosiba, Alissa, Kumu Kahua/UHM Theatre Dept Playwriting Contest, 46 Merchant St, Honolulu, HI 96813 *Tel:* 808-536-4222 *Fax:* 808-536-4226 *E-mail:* info@kumakahua.org *Web Site:* www.kumukahua.org, pg 783

Aldana, Patricia, Groundwood Books, 720 Bathurst St, Suite 500, Toronto, ON M5S 2R4, Canada *Tel:* 416-537-2501 *Fax:* 416-537-4647 *E-mail:* genmail@groundwood-dm.com *Web Site:* www.groundwoodbooks.com, pg 548

Aldana, Patsy, Douglas & McIntyre Publishing Group, 2323 Quebec St, Suite 201, Vancouver, BC V5T 4S7, Canada *Tel:* 604-254-7191 *Toll Free Tel:* 800-565-9523 (orders in Canada) *Fax:* 604-254-9099 *Toll Free Fax:* 800-221-9985 (orders in Canada) *E-mail:* dm@douglas-mcintyre.com *Web Site:* www.douglas-mcintyre.com, pg 542

Alden, Connie, Harcourt School Publishers, 6277 Sea Harbor Dr, Orlando, FL 32887 *Tel:* 407-345-2000 *Toll Free Tel:* 800-225-5425 (cust serv) *Fax:* 407-352-3445 *Toll Free Fax:* 800-874-6418 *E-mail:* hbspcs@hbschool.com *Web Site:* www.harcourtschool.com, pg 114

Alderson, Martha, 7 Ways to Make a Scene Sizzle, 708 Blossom Hill Rd, No 146, Los Gatos, CA 95032 *Tel:* 408-482-4678 *Fax:* 408-356-1798 *Web Site:* blockbusterplots.com, pg 747

Alderson, Martha, Take the Panic Out of Plot, 708 Blossom Hill Rd, No 146, Los Gatos, CA 95032 *Tel:* 408-482-4678 *Fax:* 408-356-1798 *Web Site:* blockbusterplots.com, pg 748

Aldinger, Joel, Hal Leonard Corp, 7777 W Bluemound Rd, Milwaukee, WI 53213 *Tel:* 414-774-3630 *Toll Free Tel:* 800-524-4425 *Fax:* 414-774-3259 *E-mail:* halinfo@halleonard.com *Web Site:* www.halleonard.com, pg 112

Aldrich, Peter C, National Bureau of Economic Research Inc, 1050 Massachusetts Ave, Cambridge, MA 02138-5398 *Tel:* 617-868-3900 *Fax:* 617-868-2742 *E-mail:* op@nber.org *Web Site:* www.nber.org, pg 182

Alenier, Karren L, Word Works Washington Prize, 7129 Alger Rd, Falls Church, VA 22042 *Fax:* 703-527-9384 *E-mail:* editor@wordworksdc.com *Web Site:* www.wordworksdc.com, pg 812

Alesse, Craig, Amherst Media Inc, 175 Rano St, Suite 200, Buffalo, NY 14207 *Tel:* 716-874-4450 *Fax:* 716-874-4508 *E-mail:* amherstmed@aol.com *Web Site:* www.amherstmedia.com, pg 19

Alewel, Rex, Marathon Press, PO Box 407, Norfolk, NE 68702-0407 *Tel:* 402-371-5040 *Toll Free Tel:* 800-228-0629 *Fax:* 402-371-9382 *Web Site:* www.marathonpress.com, pg 163

Alexander, Amy, Watson-Guptill Publications, 770 Broadway, New York, NY 10003 *Tel:* 646-654-5450 *Toll Free Tel:* 800-278-8477 (orders only) *Fax:* 646-654-5486; 646-654-5487 *E-mail:* info@watsonguptill.com *Web Site:* www.watsonguptill.com, pg 294

Alexander, Dr Florence, Ebon Research Systems Publishing LLC, 812 Sweetwater Club Blvd, Longwood, FL 32779 *Tel:* 407-786-9200 *Fax:* 407-682-2384 *E-mail:* ebonrs@prodigy.net *Web Site:* ebonresearchsystems.com, pg 86

Alexander, Francie, Scholastic Education, 524 Broadway, New York, NY 10012 *Tel:* 212-343-6100 *Fax:* 212-343-6189 *Web Site:* www.scholastic.com, pg 241

Alexander, Francie, Scholastic Education Curriculum Publishing, 524 Broadway, New York, NY 10012 *Tel:* 212-343-6100 *Web Site:* www.scholastic.com, pg 241

Alexander, Jill, Adams Media, An F+W Publications Co, 57 Littlefield St, 2nd fl, Avon, MA 02322 *Tel:* 508-427-7100 *Fax:* 508-427-6790 *Toll Free Fax:* 800-872-5628 *E-mail:* authors@adamsmedia.com; orders@adamsmedia.com *Web Site:* www.adamsmedia.com, pg 5

Alexander, Jo, Oregon State University Press, 102 Adams Hall, Corvallis, OR 97331 *Tel:* 541-737-3166 *Toll Free Tel:* 800-426-3797 (orders) *Fax:* 541-737-3170 *Toll Free Fax:* 800-426-3797 (orders) *E-mail:* osu.press@oregonstate.edu *Web Site:* oregonstate.edu/dept/press, pg 199

Alexander, Neil M, Abingdon Press, 201 Eighth Ave S, Nashville, TN 37203-3919 *Tel:* 615-749-6290 (publicist); 615-749-6000; 615-749-6451 (sales) *Toll Free Tel:* 800-251-3320 *Fax:* 615-749-6056 *Web Site:* www.abingdonpress.com, pg 3

Alexander, Pamela, The Field Poetry Prize, 50 N Professor St, Oberlin, OH 44074-1095 *Tel:* 440-775-8408 *Fax:* 440-775-8124 *E-mail:* oc.press@oberlin.edu *Web Site:* www.oberlin.edu/ocpress, pg 773

Alexander, Pamela, Oberlin College Press, 50 N Professor St, Oberlin, OH 44074-1095 *Tel:* 440-775-8408 *Fax:* 440-775-8124 *E-mail:* oc.press@oberlin.edu *Web Site:* www.oberlin.edu/ocpress, pg 195

Alexander, Susanne, Goose Lane Editions, 469 King St, Fredericton, NB E3B 1E5, Canada *Tel:* 506-450-4251 *Toll Free Tel:* 888-926-8377 *Fax:* 506-459-4991 *E-mail:* gooselane@gooselane.com *Web Site:* www.gooselane.com, pg 548

Alexander, Tracy, McLaren Memorial Comedy Playwriting Competition, 2000 W Wadley, Midland, TX 79705 *Tel:* 432-682-2544 *Fax:* 432-682-6136 *Web Site:* www.mctmidland.org, pg 789

Algar, Liza, Douglas & McIntyre Publishing Group, 2323 Quebec St, Suite 201, Vancouver, BC V5T 4S7, Canada *Tel:* 604-254-7191 *Toll Free Tel:* 800-565-9523 (orders in Canada) *Fax:* 604-254-9099 *Toll Free Fax:* 800-221-9985 (orders in Canada) *E-mail:* dm@douglas-mcintyre.com *Web Site:* www.douglas-mcintyre.com, pg 542

Alguire, Julie, Crabtree Publishing Co, 350 Fifth Ave, Suite 3308, PMB 16-A, New York, NY 10118 *Tel:* 212-496-5040 *Toll Free Tel:* 800-387-7650 *Toll Free Tel:* 800-355-7166 *E-mail:* letters@crabtreebooks.com *Web Site:* www.crabtreebooks.com, pg 71

Ali, Liaquat, Kazi Publications Inc, 3023 W Belmont Ave, Chicago, IL 60618 *Tel:* 773-267-7001 *Fax:* 773-267-7002 *E-mail:* info@kazi.org *Web Site:* www.kazi.org/, pg 144

Aljian, Nettie, Princeton Architectural Press, 37 E Seventh St, New York, NY 10003 *Tel:* 212-995-9620 *Toll Free Tel:* 800-722-6657 (dist) *Fax:* 212-995-9454 *E-mail:* sales@papress.com *Web Site:* www.papress.com, pg 218

Allan, Jessica G, Paul H Brookes Publishing Co, PO Box 10624, Baltimore, MD 21285-0624 *Tel:* 410-337-9580 *Toll Free Tel:* 800-638-3775 *Fax:* 410-337-8539 *E-mail:* custserv@brookespublishing.com *Web Site:* www.brookespublishing.com, pg 48

Allan, Richard, The Aaland Agency, PO Box 849, Inyokern, CA 93527-0849 *Tel:* 760-384-3910 *Fax:* 760-384-4435 *Web Site:* www.the-aaland-agency.com, pg 617

Allan, Robin, American Psychiatric Publishing Inc, 1000 Wilson Blvd, Suite 1825, Arlington, VA 22209 *Tel:* 703-907-7322 *Toll Free Tel:* 800-368-5777 *Fax:* 703-907-1091 *E-mail:* appi@psych.org *Web Site:* www.appi.org, pg 16

Allard, Jacques, Editions Hurtubise HMH Ltee, 1815 De Lorimier, Montreal, PQ H2K 3W6, Canada *Tel:* 514-523-1523 *Toll Free Tel:* 800-361-1664 (Canada only) *Fax:* 514-523-9969; 514-523-5955 (edit) *E-mail:* hurtubisehmh@hurtubisehmh.com *Web Site:* www.hurtubisehmh.com, pg 545

Allbritten, Drew, The Council for Exceptional Children, 1110 N Glebe Rd, Arlington, VA 22201-5704 *Tel:* 703-620-3660 *Toll Free Tel:* 800-224-6830 *Fax:* 703-264-9494 *E-mail:* service@cec.sped.org *Web Site:* www.cec.sped.org, pg 685

Allen, Andrew, W B Saunders Ltd, 170 S Independence Mall W, Suite 300 E, Philadelphia, PA 19106-3399 *Tel:* 215-238-7800 *Toll Free Tel:* 800-545-2522 (cust serv) *Fax:* 215-238-7883 *Web Site:* www.elsevierhealth.com, pg 240

Allen, Ann, Carl Vinson Institute of Government, University of Georgia, 201 N Milledge Ave, Athens, GA 30602 *Tel:* 706-542-2736 *Fax:* 706-542-6239 *Web Site:* www.cviog.uga.edu, pg 290

Allen, C Richard, The Sporting News Publishing Co, A Vulcan Sports Media Company, 10176 Corporate Square Dr, Suite 200, St Louis, MO 63132 *Tel:* 314-997-7111 *Fax:* 314-993-7726 *Web Site:* www.sportingnews.com, pg 256

Allen, Carin, Shambhala Publications Inc, Horticultural Hall, 300 Massachusetts Ave, Boston, MA 02115 *Tel:* 617-424-0030 *Toll Free Tel:* 888-424-2329 (orders only) *Fax:* 617-236-1563; 303-665-5292 (orders only) *E-mail:* editors@shambhala.com *Web Site:* www.shambhala.com, pg 245

Allen, David, The Millbrook Press Inc, 2 Old New Milford Rd, Brookfield, CT 06804 *Tel:* 203-740-2220 *Toll Free Tel:* 800-462-4703 *Fax:* 203-740-2526, pg 174

Allen, Deborah, Black Dome Press Corp, 1011 Rte 296, Hensonville, NY 12439 *Tel:* 518-734-6357 *Fax:* 518-734-5802 *E-mail:* blackdomep@aol.com *Web Site:* www.blackdomepress.com, pg 40

Allen, Ms Desmond Walls, Arkansas Research Inc, PO Box 303, Conway, AR 72033-0303 *Tel:* 501-470-1120 *Fax:* 501-470-1120 *Web Site:* www.arkansasresearch.com, pg 23

Allen, Frank, The Drummond Publishing Group, 362 N Bedford St, East Bridgewater, MA 02333 *Tel:* 508-378-1110 *Fax:* 508-378-1105 *Web Site:* www.drummondpub.com, pg 84

Allen, Frank, Royalton Press, 362 N Bedford St, East Bridgewater, MA 02333 *Tel:* 508-378-1110 *Fax:* 508-378-1105 *Web Site:* www.drummondpub.com, pg 235

Allen, George, Forward Movement Publications, 300 W Fourth St, Cincinnati, OH 45202 *Tel:* 513-721-6659 *Toll Free Tel:* 800-543-1813 *Fax:* 513-721-0729 *E-mail:* orders@forwarddaybyday.com *Web Site:* www.forwardmovement.org, pg 99

Allen, Inge, Crystal Publishers, 3460 Lost Hills Dr, Las Vegas, NV 89122 *Tel:* 702-434-3037 *Fax:* 702-434-3037 *Web Site:* www.crystalpub.com, pg 74

Allen, Jim, Canadian Publishers' Council (CPC), 250 Merton St, Suite 203, Toronto, ON M4S 1B1, Canada *Tel:* 416-322-7011 *Fax:* 416-322-6999 *E-mail:* pubadmin@pubcouncil.ca *Web Site:* www.pubcouncil.ca, pg 683

Allen, John, Blue Book Publications Inc, 8009 34 Ave S, Suite 175, Minneapolis, MN 55425 *Tel:* 952-854-5229 *Toll Free Tel:* 800-877-4867 *Fax:* 952-853-1486 *E-mail:* bluebook@bluebookinc.com *Web Site:* www.bluebookinc.com, pg 570

Allen, Lawrence, The Museum of Modern Art, 11 W 53 St, New York, NY 10019 *Tel:* 212-708-9443 *Fax:* 212-333-6575 *E-mail:* moma_publications@moma.org *Web Site:* www.moma.org, pg 180

Allen, Leonard, Palgrave Macmillan, 175 Fifth Ave, New York, NY 10010 *Tel:* 212-982-3900 *Fax:* 212-777-6359 *E-mail:* firstname.lastname@palgrave-usa.com *Web Site:* www.palgrave.com, pg 202

Allen, Linda, Abingdon Press, 201 Eighth Ave S, Nashville, TN 37203-3919 *Tel:* 615-749-6290 (publicist); 615-749-6000; 615-749-6451 (sales) *Toll Free Tel:* 800-251-3320 *Fax:* 615-749-6056 *Web Site:* www.abingdonpress.com, pg 3

Allen, Linda, Linda Allen Literary Agency, 1949 Green St, Suite 5, San Francisco, CA 94123 *Tel:* 415-921-6437 *Fax:* 415-921-3733, pg 618

Allen, Marc, New World Library, 14 Pamaron Way, Novato, CA 94949 *Tel:* 415-884-2100 *Toll Free Tel:* 800-227-3900 (ext 52, retail orders) *Fax:* 415-884-2199 (ext 52, retail orders) *E-mail:* escort@newworldlibrary.com *Web Site:* www.newworldlibrary.com, pg 189

Allen, Maria, Graphic Arts Association, 1100 Northbrook Dr, Suite 120, Trevose, PA 19053 *Tel:* 215-396-2300 *Fax:* 215-396-9890 *E-mail:* gaa@gaa1900.com *Web Site:* www.gaa1900.com, pg 752

Allen, Mavis, Harlequin Enterprises Ltd, 233 Broadway, Suite 1001, New York, NY 10279 *Tel:* 212-553-4200 *Fax:* 212-227-8969 *E-mail:* customer.ecare@harlequin.ca *Web Site:* www.eharlequin.com; www.luna-books.com; www.mirabooks.com; www.reddressink.com; www.steeplehill.com, pg 115

Allen, Mitch, AltaMira Press, 1630 N Main St, No 367, Walnut Creek, CA 94596 *Tel:* 925-938-7243 *Fax:* 925-933-9720 *E-mail:* explore@altamirapress.com *Web Site:* www.altamirapress.com, pg 9

Allen, Patrick, Hill Street Press LLC, 191 E Broad St, Suite 209, Athens, GA 30601-2848 *Tel:* 706-613-7200 *Fax:* 706-613-7204 *Web Site:* www.hillstreetpress.com, pg 122

Allen, Paula K, Warner Bros Worldwide Publishing, 4000 Warner Blvd, Bldg 118, Burbank, CA 91522-1704 *Tel:* 818-954-5450 *Fax:* 818-954-5595 *Web Site:* www.warnerbros.com, pg 293

Allen, Robert, Brands-to-Books Inc, 155 W 72 St, Suite 302, New York, NY 10023 *Tel:* 212-362-6957 *Fax:* 212-874-2892 *E-mail:* agents@brandstobooks.com *Web Site:* www.brandstobooks.com, pg 622

Allen, S, Starlite Inc, PO Box 20004, St Petersburg, FL 33742-0004 *Tel:* 727-392-2929 *Toll Free Tel:* 800-577-2929 *Fax:* 727-392-6161 *E-mail:* starlite@citebook.com *Web Site:* www.starlite-inc.com; www.citebook.com, pg 258

Allen, Scott, MacAdam/Cage Publishing Inc, 155 Sansome St, Suite 550, San Francisco, CA 94104 *Tel:* 415-986-7502 *Toll Free Tel:* 866-986-7470 *Fax:* 415-986-7414 *E-mail:* info@macadamcage.com *Web Site:* www.macadamcage.com, pg 160

Allen, Simon, McGraw-Hill International Publishing Group, 2 Penn Plaza, New York, NY 10121 *Tel:* 212-904-2000 *Web Site:* www.mcgrawhill.com, pg 168

Allen, Tina R, E-Digital Books LLC, 1155 S Havana St, Suite 11, PMB 364, Aurora, CO 80012 *Tel:* 303-745-4997 *Fax:* 303-745-4997 *E-mail:* edigital@edigitalbooks.com *Web Site:* www.edigitalbooks.com, pg 85

Allen, William L, National Geographic Society, 1145 17 St NW, Washington, DC 20036 *Tel:* 202-857-7000 *Fax:* 202-429-5727 *Web Site:* www.nationalgeographic.com, pg 184

Allen, Yvonne, Aristide D Caratzas, Publisher, PO Box 344-H, Scarsdale, NY 10583 *Tel:* 914-725-4847 *Toll Free Tel:* 800-204-2665 *Fax:* 914-725-4847 (call first) *E-mail:* info@caratzas.com *Web Site:* www.caratzas.com, pg 53

Allender, David, Workman Publishing Co Inc, 708 Broadway, New York, NY 10003-9555 *Tel:* 212-254-5900 *Toll Free Tel:* 800-722-7202 *Fax:* 212-254-8098 *E-mail:* info@workman.com *Web Site:* www.workman.com, pg 303

Alley, John, May Swenson Poetry Award, 7800 Old Main Hill, Logan, UT 84322-7800 *Tel:* 435-797-1362 *Fax:* 435-797-0313 *Web Site:* www.usu.edu/usupress, pg 807

Allinson, Richard, Criminal Justice Press, PO Box 249, Monsey, NY 10952-0249 *Tel:* 845-354-9139 *Toll Free Tel:* 800-914-3379 *Web Site:* www.criminaljusticepress.com, pg 72

Allison, Mark, Stackpole Books, 5067 Ritter Rd, Mechanicsburg, PA 17055 *Tel:* 717-796-0411 *Toll Free Tel:* 800-732-3669 *Fax:* 717-796-0412 *Web Site:* www.stackpolebooks.com, pg 257

Allison, Susan, Berkley Books, 375 Hudson St, New York, NY 10014 *Tel:* 212-366-2000 *Fax:* 212-366-2666 *E-mail:* online@penguinputnam.com *Web Site:* www.penguin.com, pg 36

Allison, Susan, Berkley Publishing Group, 375 Hudson St, New York, NY 10014 *Tel:* 212-366-2000 *E-mail:* online@penguinputnam.com *Web Site:* www.penguin.com, pg 37

Allman, Daniel J, New Directions Publishing Corp, 80 Eighth Ave, New York, NY 10011 *Tel:* 212-255-0230 *Toll Free Tel:* 800-233-4830 (PA) *Fax:* 212-255-0231 *E-mail:* newdirections@ndbooks.com *Web Site:* www.ndpublishing.com, pg 187

Allport, Susan, Cross Pond Editing Group, 333 Hook Rd, Katonah, NY 10536 *Tel:* 914-232-8687 *Fax:* 914-232-1258, pg 595

Allred, Kim, Allred & Allred Literary Agents, 7834 Alabama Ave, Canoga Park, CA 91304-4905 *Tel:* 818-346-4313 *Fax:* 818-346-4313, pg 618

Allred, Robert, Allred & Allred Literary Agents, 7834 Alabama Ave, Canoga Park, CA 91304-4905 *Tel:* 818-346-4313 *Fax:* 818-346-4313, pg 618

Allred, Robert, University Publishing Co, 1134-A 28 St, Richmond, CA 94804 *E-mail:* unipub@earthlink.net, pg 287

Allridge, Suzanne, Paul H Brookes Publishing Co, PO Box 10624, Baltimore, MD 21285-0624 *Tel:* 410-337-9580 *Toll Free Tel:* 800-638-3775 *Fax:* 410-337-8539 *E-mail:* custserv@brookespublishing.com *Web Site:* www.brookespublishing.com, pg 48

Allsup, Mike, Harcourt Inc, 6277 Sea Harbor Dr, Orlando, FL 32887 *Tel:* 407-345-2000 *Toll Free Tel:* 800-225-5425 (cust serv) *Fax:* 407-352-3445 (cust serv), pg 114

Alm, Michelle, Tyndale House Publishers Inc, 351 Executive Dr, Carol Stream, IL 60188 *Tel:* 630-668-8303 *Toll Free Tel:* 800-323-9400 *Web Site:* www.tyndale.com, pg 277

Almack, William, Christian Literature Crusade Inc, 701 Pennsylvania Ave, Fort Washington, PA 19034-8449 *Tel:* 215-542-1242 *Toll Free Tel:* 800-659-1240 (orders) *Fax:* 215-542-7580 *E-mail:* clcbooks@safeplace.net *Web Site:* www.clcpublications.com, pg 61

Almada, Jeanette, Almada & Associates, 627 W Roscoe, Unit 2-B, Chicago, IL 60657 *Tel:* 773-404-9350 *Fax:* 773-404-9278, pg 590

Almeida, Katherine, The MIT Press, 5 Cambridge Ctr, Cambridge, MA 02142 *Tel:* 617-253-5646 *Toll Free Tel:* 800-405-1619 (orders only) *Fax:* 617-258-6779 *Web Site:* mitpress.mit.edu, pg 175

Almquist, Curtis, Cowley Publications, 4 Brattle St, Cambridge, MA 02138 *Tel:* 617-441-0300 *Toll Free Tel:* 800-225-1534 *Fax:* 617-441-0120 *Toll Free Fax:* 877-225-6675 *E-mail:* cowley@cowley.org *Web Site:* www.cowley.org, pg 71

Alonzo, Anne-Marie, Editions Trois, 4882 Cherrier, Laval, PQ H7T 2Y9, Canada *Tel:* 450-978-5245 *Fax:* 450-978-0899 *E-mail:* ed3ama@videotron.ca, pg 546

Alperen, Jennifer, The Betsy Nolan Literary Agency, 224 W 29 St, 15th fl, New York, NY 10001 *Tel:* 212-967-8200 *Fax:* 212-967-7292, pg 647

Alsina, Marta Aponte, University of Puerto Rico Press, Edificio EDUPR/Dialogo, Carr No 1, KM 12-0, Piso 2, Jardin Bota'nico Area Norte, San Juan, PR 00931 *Tel:* 787-758-6932; 787-758-8345 (sales); 787-250-0046; 787-250-0000 *Fax:* 787-753-9116; 787-751-8785 (sales dept), pg 285

Alter, Judy, Texas Christian University Press, PO Box 298300, Fort Worth, TX 76129 *Tel:* 817-257-7822 *Toll Free Tel:* 800-826-8911 *Fax:* 817-257-5075 *Toll Free Fax:* 888-617-2421 *Web Site:* www.prs.tcu.edu/prs/, pg 267

Althouse, Janet, Possibility Press, One Oakglade Circle, Hummelstown, PA 17036 *Tel:* 717-566-0468 *Toll Free Tel:* 800-566-0534 *Fax:* 717-566-6423 *E-mail:* posspress@aol.com, pg 216

Altman, Rick, Pearson Education/ELT, 10 Bank St, 9th fl, White Plains, NY 10606 *Tel:* 914-993-5000 *Fax:* 914-993-8115 *E-mail:* firstname.lastname@pearsoned.com, pg 206

Alton, Tom, Alaska Native Language Center, PO Box 757680, Fairbanks, AK 99775-7680 *Tel:* 907-474-7874 *Fax:* 907-474-6586 *Web Site:* www.uaf.edu/anlc/, pg 7

Altreuter, Judith, Modern Language Association of America (MLA), 26 Broadway, 3rd fl, New York, NY 10004-1789 *Tel:* 646-576-5000 *Fax:* 646-458-0030 *E-mail:* info@mla.org *Web Site:* www.mla.org, pg 176

Altshuler, Miriam, Miriam Altshuler Literary Agency, 53 Old Post Rd N, Red Hook, NY 12571 *Tel:* 845-758-9408 *Fax:* 845-758-3118, pg 619

Altshuler, Miriam, Association of Authors' Representatives Inc (AAR), PO Box 237201, Ansonia Sta, New York, NY 10023 *E-mail:* aarinc@mindspring.com *Web Site:* www.aar-online.org, pg 679

Aluise, Victor, e-Scholastic, 568 Broadway, 9th fl, New York, NY 10012 *Tel:* 212-343-7100 *Fax:* 212-343-4949, pg 85

Aluri, Rao, Parkway Publishers Inc, 421 Fairfield Lane, Blowing Rock, NC 28605 *Tel:* 828-265-3993 *Toll Free Tel:* 800-821-9155 *Fax:* 828-265-3993 *Toll Free Fax:* 800-821-9155 *E-mail:* parkwaypub@hotmail.com *Web Site:* www.parkwaypublishers.com, pg 204

Alvare, Susan, Hartman Publishing Inc, 8529 Indian School Rd NE, Albuquerque, NM 87112 *Tel:* 505-291-1274 *Toll Free Tel:* 800-999-9534 *Fax:* 505-291-1284 *Toll Free Fax:* 800-474-6106 *E-mail:* orders@hartmanonline.com *Web Site:* www.hartmanonline.com, pg 116

Alvarez, Cindy, Simon & Schuster Children's Publishing, 1230 Avenue of the Americas, New York, NY 10020 *Tel:* 212-698-7000 *Web Site:* www.simonsayskids.com, pg 248

Alvarez, Lisa, Squaw Valley Community of Writers Workshops, PO Box 1416, Nevada City, CA 95959 *Tel:* 530-470-8440 *E-mail:* brett@squawvalleywriters.org *Web Site:* www.squawvalleywriters.org, pg 748

Amastae, Jon, Texas Western Press, c/o University of Texas at El Paso, 500 W University Ave, El Paso, TX 79968-0633 *Tel:* 915-747-5688 *Toll Free Tel:* 800-488-3789 *Fax:* 915-747-7515 *E-mail:* twpress@utep.edu *Web Site:* www.utep.edu/~twp, pg 267

Amato, Frank W, Frank Amato Publications Inc, PO Box 82112, Portland, OR 97282 *Tel:* 503-653-8108 *Toll Free Tel:* 800-541-9498 *Fax:* 503-653-2766 *Web Site:* www.amatobooks.com, pg 10

Amber, Arnold, TNG Canada/CWA, 7B-1050 Baxter Rd, Ottawa, ON K2C 3P1, Canada *Tel:* 613-820-9777 *Toll Free Tel:* 877-486-4292 *Fax:* 613-820-8188 *E-mail:* info@tngcanada.org *Web Site:* www.tngcanada.org, pg 701

Amen-ra, RaDine, Quantum Leap SLC Publications, 2740 Greenbriar Pkwy, Suite 201, Atlanta, GA 30308 *Toll Free Fax:* 877-571-9788 *E-mail:* distribution@blackamericanhandbook.com *Web Site:* www.blackamericanhandbook.com, pg 223

Ames, Michael, Vanderbilt University Press, 201 University Plaza Bldg, 112 21 Ave S, Nashville, TN 37203 *Tel:* 615-322-3585 *Toll Free Tel:* 800-627-7377 (orders only) *Fax:* 615-343-8823 *Toll Free Fax:* 800-735-0476 (orders only) *E-mail:* vupress@vanderbilt.edu *Web Site:* www.vanderbilt.edu/vupress, pg 289

Ames, Rosemarie, Passeggiata Press Inc, 420 W 14 St, Pueblo, CO 81003-2708 *Tel:* 719-544-1038 *Fax:* 719-544-7911 *E-mail:* passegpress@cs.com, pg 204

Ames, Steve, World Citizens, 96 La Verne Ave, Mill Valley, CA 94941 *Tel:* 415-380-8020 *Toll Free Tel:* 800-247-6553 (orders only) *Web Site:* soultosoulmedia.com; skateman.com, pg 304

Amitie, Julie, Simon & Schuster Children's Publishing, 1230 Avenue of the Americas, New York, NY 10020 *Tel:* 212-698-7000 *Web Site:* www.simonsayskids.com, pg 248

Ammer, Bonnie, Random House Inc, 1745 Broadway, New York, NY 10019 *Tel:* 212-782-9000 *Toll Free Tel:* 800-726-0600 *Web Site:* www.randomhouse.com, pg 226

Amorosino, Charles S Jr, Teachers of English to Speakers of Other Languages Inc (TESOL), 700 S Washington St, Suite 200, Alexandria, VA 22314-4287 *Tel:* 703-836-0774 *Fax:* 703-836-7864 *E-mail:* info@tesol.org *Web Site:* www.tesol.org, pg 265

Amoroso, Lisa, G P Putnam's Sons (Hardcover), 375 Hudson St, New York, NY 10014 *Tel:* 212-366-2000 *E-mail:* online@penguinputnam.com *Web Site:* www.penguin.com, pg 223

Amoroso, Nicole, Philadelphia Museum of Art, 2525 Pennsylvania Ave, Philadelphia, PA 19130 *Tel:* 215-684-7250 *Fax:* 215-235-8715 *Web Site:* www.philamuseum.org, pg 211

Amos, India, Seven Stories Press, 140 Watts St, New York, NY 10013 *Tel:* 212-226-8760 *Toll Free Tel:* 800-283-3572 *Fax:* 212-226-1411 *E-mail:* info@sevenstories.com *Web Site:* www.sevenstories.com, pg 245

Amos, Jennifer, National Golf Foundation, 1150 S US Hwy One, Suite 401, Jupiter, FL 33477 *Tel:* 561-744-6006 *Toll Free Tel:* 800-733-6006 *Fax:* 561-744-6107 *E-mail:* ngf@ngf.org *Web Site:* www.ngf.org, pg 184

Amparan-Close, Joann, Wecksler-Incomco, 170 West End Ave, New York, NY 10023 *Tel:* 212-787-2239 *Fax:* 212-496-7035 *E-mail:* jacinny@aol.com, pg 660

Amsel, Andrew, Hartmore House Inc, 304 E 49 St, New York, NY 10017 *Tel:* 203-384-2284; 212-319-6666 *Fax:* 203-579-9109, pg 116

Amsel, Andrew, Prayer Book Press Inc, 1363 Fairfield Ave, Bridgeport, CT 06605 *Tel:* 203-384-2284 *Fax:* 203-579-9109, pg 217

Amster, Betsy, Betsy Amster Literary Enterprises, PO Box 27788, Los Angeles, CA 90027-0788 *Tel:* 323-662-1987 *Fax:* 323-660-4015 *E-mail:* amsterlit@compuserve.com, pg 619

Andersen, Ashley, Soundprints, 353 Main Ave, Norwalk, CT 06851 *Tel:* 203-846-2274 *Toll Free Tel:* 800-228-7839; 800-577-2413, ext 118 (orders) *Fax:* 203-846-1776 *E-mail:* Soundprints@soundprints.com *Web Site:* www.soundprints.com, pg 253

Andersen, Mary, University of Washington Press, 1326 Fifth Ave, Suite 555, Seattle, WA 98101-2604 *Tel:* 206-543-4050; 206-543-8870 *Toll Free Tel:* 800-441-4115 (orders) *Fax:* 206-543-3932 *Toll Free Fax:* 800-669-7993 (orders) *E-mail:* uwpord@u.washington.edu *Web Site:* www.washington.edu/uwpress/, pg 286

Andersen, Peter, Alfred A Knopf, 1745 Broadway, New York, NY 10019 *Tel:* 212-751-2600 *Toll Free Tel:* 800-638-6460 *Fax:* 212-572-2593 *Web Site:* www.randomhouse.com/knopf, pg 146

Andersen, Polly, Meadowbrook Press, 5451 Smetana Dr, Minnetonka, MN 55343 *Tel:* 952-930-1100 *Toll Free Tel:* 800-338-2232 *Fax:* 952-930-1940 *Web Site:* www.meadowbrookpress.com, pg 169

Anderson, Alison, University of Pennsylvania Press, 4200 Pine St, Philadelphia, PA 19104-4011 *Tel:* 215-898-6261 *Toll Free Tel:* 800-445-9880 (orders & cust serv only) *Fax:* 215-898-0404; 410-516-6998 (orders) *E-mail:* custserv@pobox.upenn.edu *Web Site:* www.upenn.edu/pennpress, pg 284

Anderson, Ann-Marie, Temple University Press, 1601 N Broad St, 083-42, USB Room 306, Philadelphia, PA 19122-6099 *Tel:* 215-204-8787 *Toll Free Tel:* 800-447-1656 *Fax:* 215-204-4719 *E-mail:* tempress@temple.edu *Web Site:* www.temple.edu/tempress, pg 266

Anderson, Barbara, Lynx House Press, 420 W 24 St, Spokane, WA 99203 *Tel:* 509-624-4894 *Fax:* 509-623-4238, pg 160

Anderson, Barbara S, Barbara S Anderson, 706 W Davis, Ann Arbor, MI 48103-4855 *Tel:* 734-995-0125; 734-994-6182 *Fax:* 734-994-5207, pg 590

Anderson, Becky A, Gollehon Press Inc, 6157 28 St SE, Grand Rapids, MI 49546 *Tel:* 616-949-3515 *Fax:* 619-949-8674, pg 106

Anderson, Bill, Christian Booksellers Association (CBA), 9240 Explorer Dr, Colorado Springs, CO 80920 *Tel:* 719-265-9895 *Toll Free Tel:* 800-252-1950 *Fax:* 719-272-3510 *E-mail:* info@cbaonline.org *Web Site:* www.cbaonline.org, pg 685

Anderson, Bill, Crossway Books, 1300 Crescent St, Wheaton, IL 60187 *Tel:* 630-682-4300 *Fax:* 630-682-4785 *E-mail:* editorial@goodnews-crossway.org *Web Site:* www.crosswaybooks.org, pg 73

Anderson, Christiane, American Society of Plant Taxonomists, University of Michigan Herbarium, 3600 Varsity Dr, Ann Arbor, MI 48108-2287 *Tel:* 734-647-2812 *Fax:* 734-647-5719 *Web Site:* www.sysbot.org, pg 18

Anderson, Chuck, Rainbow Publishers, PO Box 261129, San Diego, CA 92196-1129 *Tel:* 858-668-3260 *Web Site:* www.rainbowpublishers.com, pg 225

Anderson, D Kamili, Howard University Press, 2225 Georgia Ave NW, Suite 718, Washington, DC 20059 *Tel:* 202-238-2570 *Fax:* 202-588-9849 *E-mail:* howardupress@howard.edu *Web Site:* www.hupress.howard.edu, pg 127

Anderson, David, Benoit & Associates, 279 S Schuyler Ave, Kankakee, IL 60901 *Tel:* 815-932-2582 *Fax:* 815-932-2594 *E-mail:* benoitart@aol.com, pg 665

Anderson, Deborah, Southeastern Theatre Conference New Play Project (SETC), 1114 Whitehall Rd, Murfreesboro, TN 37130 *Tel:* 336-272-3645 *Fax:* 336-272-8810 *E-mail:* setc@sectonline.com *Web Site:* www.setc.org, pg 806

Anderson, Denise, Scholastic Canada Ltd, 175 Hillmount Rd, Markham, ON L6C 1Z7, Canada *Tel:* 905-887-7323 *Toll Free Tel:* 800-268-3848 (Canada) *Fax:* 905-887-1131 *Toll Free Fax:* 800-387-4944; 866-346-1288 *Web Site:* www.scholastic.ca, pg 560

Anderson, Fran, G & S Editors, 410 Baylor, Austin, TX 78703-5312 *Tel:* 512-478-5341 *Fax:* 512-476-4756 *Web Site:* www.gstype.com, pg 599

Anderson, Frank J, Kitemaug Press, 229 Mohawk Dr, Spartanburg, SC 29301-2827 *Tel:* 864-576-3338 *E-mail:* kitemaugpresswhq@msn.com, pg 146

Anderson, Gordon L, Paragon House, 2285 University Ave W, Suite 200, St Paul, MN 55114-1635 *Tel:* 651-644-3087 *Toll Free Tel:* 800-447-3709 *Fax:* 651-644-0997 *Toll Free Fax:* 800-494-0997 *E-mail:* paragon@paragonhouse.com *Web Site:* www.paragonhouse.com, pg 204

Anderson, Kathleen, Anderson/Grinberg Literary Management Inc, 266 W 23 St, Suite 3, New York, NY 10011 *Tel:* 212-620-5883 *Fax:* 212-627-4725 *E-mail:* queries@andersongrinberg.com, pg 619

Anderson, Kathryn, Greenwich Publishing Group Inc, 929 Boston Post Rd, Suite 9, Old Saybrook, CT 06475 *Tel:* 860-388-9941 *E-mail:* info@greenwichpublishing.com *Web Site:* www.greenwichpublishing.com, pg 109

Anderson, Kelly, Gryphon House Inc, 10726 Tucker St, Beltsville, MD 20704 *Tel:* 301-595-9500 *Toll Free Tel:* 800-638-0928 *Fax:* 301-595-0051 *E-mail:* info@ghbooks.com *Web Site:* www.gryphonhouse.com, pg 110

Anderson, Leigh, Society of Biblical Literature, The Luce Ctr, Suite 350, 825 Houston Mill Rd, Atlanta, GA 30329 *Tel:* 404-727-2325 *Fax:* 802-864-7626 *E-mail:* sbl@sbl-site.org *Web Site:* www.sbl-site.org, pg 251

Anderson, Marc, Cambridge University Press, 40 W 20 St, New York, NY 10011-4211 *Tel:* 212-924-3900 *Toll Free Tel:* 800-899-5222 *Fax:* 212-691-3239 *Web Site:* www.cambridge.org, pg 52

Anderson, Megan, The Dawn Horse Press, 12040 N Seigler Rd, Middletown, CA 95461 *Tel:* 707-928-6590 *Toll Free Tel:* 877-770-0772 *Fax:* 707-928-5068 *E-mail:* dhp@adidam.org *Web Site:* www.dawnhorsepress.com, pg 77

Anderson, Norman, American Psychological Association, 750 First St NE, Washington, DC 20002-4242 *Tel:* 202-336-5500; 202-336-5540 *Toll Free Tel:* 800-374-2721 *Fax:* 202-336-5620 *E-mail:* order@apa.org *Web Site:* www.apa.org, pg 677

Anderson, Pat, Berrett-Koehler Publishers Inc, 235 Montgomery St, Suite 650, San Francisco, CA 94104 *Tel:* 415-288-0260 *Fax:* 415-362-2512 *E-mail:* bkpub@bkpub.com *Web Site:* www.bkconnection.com, pg 37

Anderson, Patricia PhD, Patricia Anderson, 1489 Marine Dr, Suite 515, West Vancouver, BC V7T 1B8, Canada *Tel:* 604-740-0805 *Fax:* 604-740-0805 *E-mail:* query@helpingyougetpublished.com *Web Site:* www.helpingyougetpublished.com, pg 590

Anderson, Peggy, Concordia Publishing House, 3558 S Jefferson Ave, St Louis, MO 63118-3968 *Tel:* 314-268-1000 *Toll Free Tel:* 800-325-3040 *Fax:* 314-268-1329 *Toll Free Fax:* 800-490-9889 *E-mail:* cphorder@cph.org *Web Site:* www.cph.org, pg 66

Anderson, Richard, Encyclopaedia Britannica Inc, 310 S Michigan Ave, Chicago, IL 60604 *Tel:* 312-347-7000 *Toll Free Tel:* 800-323-1229 *Fax:* 312-347-7399 *E-mail:* editor@eb.com *Web Site:* www.eb.com; www.britannica.com, pg 91

Anderson, Rick, Jerry B Jenkins Christian Writers Guild, PO Box 88196, Black Forest, CO 80908 *Toll Free Tel:* 866-495-5177 *Fax:* 719-495-5181 *E-mail:* contactus@christianwritersguild.com *Web Site:* www.christianwritersguild.com, pg 685

Anderson, Rob, Joan G Sugarman Children's Book Award, 1851 Columbia Rd NW, No 205, Washington, DC 20009 *Tel:* 202-466-1344 *E-mail:* sugarman@lefund.org *Web Site:* www.washwriter.org, pg 807

Anderson, Steve, Graphic Arts Center Publishing Co, 3019 NW Yeon Ave, Portland, OR 97210 *Tel:* 503-226-2402 *Toll Free Tel:* 800-452-3032 *Fax:* 503-223-1410 *Toll Free Fax:* 800-355-9685 *E-mail:* editorial@gacpc.com; sales@gacpc.com *Web Site:* www.gacpc.com, pg 107

Anderson, Sue, Altitude Publishing Canada Ltd, 1500 Railway Ave, Canmore, AB T1W 1P6, Canada *Tel:* 403-678-6888 *Toll Free Tel:* 800-957-6888 *Fax:* 403-678-6951 *Toll Free Fax:* 800-957-1477 *E-mail:* orderdesk@altitudepublishing.com; sales@ altitudepublishing.com (ordering) *Web Site:* www. altitudepublishing.com, pg 535

Anderson, Thomas, Dragon Moon Press, PO Box 64312, Calgary, AB T2K 6J7, Canada *Tel:* 403-277-2140 *Fax:* 403-277-3679 *E-mail:* publisher@ dragonmoonpress.com *Web Site:* www. dragonmoonpress.com, pg 543

Andes, Joyce, Simon & Schuster Inc, 1230 Avenue of the Americas, New York, NY 10020 *Tel:* 212-698-7000 *Fax:* 212-698-7007 *Web Site:* www.simonsays. com, pg 249

Andiman, Lori, Inkwell Management, 521 Fifth Ave, 26th fl, New York, NY 10175 *Tel:* 212-922-3500 *Fax:* 212-922-0535 *E-mail:* contact@ inkwellmanagement.com *Web Site:* www. inkwellmanagement.com, pg 635

Andonian, Mr Aramais, Blue Crane Books, PO Box 380291, Cambridge, MA 02238 *Tel:* 617-926-8989 *Fax:* 617-926-0982 *E-mail:* bluecrane@arrow1.com, pg 41

Andrashko, Faye, Illinois State Museum Society, 502 S Spring St, Springfield, IL 62706-5000 *Tel:* 217-782-7387 *Fax:* 217-782-1254 *E-mail:* editor@museum. state.il.us *Web Site:* www.museum.state.il.us, pg 131

Andreou, George, Alfred A Knopf, 1745 Broadway, New York, NY 10019 *Tel:* 212-751-2600 *Toll Free Tel:* 800-638-6460 *Fax:* 212-572-2593 *Web Site:* www. randomhouse.com/knopf, pg 146

Andreozzi, Lou, LexisNexis®, 701 E Water St, Charlottesville, VA 22902 *Tel:* 434-972-7600 *Toll Free Tel:* 800-446-3410; 800-828-8341 (orders) *E-mail:* customer.support@lexisnexis.com *Web Site:* www.lexisnexis.com, pg 153

Andres, Bill, OAG Worldwide, 3025 Highland Pkwy, Suite 200, Downers Grove, IL 60515 *Tel:* 630-515-5300 *Fax:* 630-515-5301 *Web Site:* www.oag.com, pg 194

Andrewes, Lancelot, Wittenborn Art Books, 1109 Geary Blvd, San Francisco, CA 94109 *Tel:* 415-292-6500 *Toll Free Tel:* 800-660-6403 *Fax:* 415-292-6594 *E-mail:* wittenborn@art-books.com *Web Site:* art-books.com, pg 302

Andrews, Bart, Bart Andrews & Associates Inc, 7510 Sunset Blvd, Suite 100, Los Angeles, CA 90046-3418 *Tel:* 310-271-9916, pg 619

Andrews, Gaylen, Copywriter's Council of America (CCA), CCA Bldg, 7 Putter Lane, Middle Island, NY 11953 *Tel:* 631-924-8555 *Fax:* 631-924-3890 *E-mail:* cca4dmcopy@att.net *Web Site:* www.lgroup. addr.com/CCA.htm, pg 685

Andrews, Hugh, Andrews McMeel Publishing, 4520 Main St, Suite 700, Kansas City, MO 64111-7701 *Tel:* 816-932-6700 *Toll Free Tel:* 800-851-8923 *Web Site:* www.universal.com/amp, pg 169

Andrews, Jean, Graphic Arts Center Publishing Co, 3019 NW Yeon Ave, Portland, OR 97210 *Tel:* 503-226-2402 *Toll Free Tel:* 800-452-3032 *Fax:* 503-223-1410 *Toll Free Fax:* 800-355-9685 *E-mail:* editorial@gacpc.com; sales@gacpc.com *Web Site:* www.gacpc.com, pg 107

Andrews, Karen, The Haworth Press Inc, 10 Alice St, Binghamton, NY 13904-1580 *Tel:* 607-722-5857 *Toll Free Tel:* 800-429-6784 *Fax:* 607-722-1424 *Toll Free Fax:* 800-895-0582 *E-mail:* getinfo@haworthpressinc. com *Web Site:* www.haworthpress.com, pg 118

Andrews, Kathleen W, Andrews McMeel Publishing, 4520 Main St, Suite 700, Kansas City, MO 64111-7701 *Tel:* 816-932-6700 *Toll Free Tel:* 800-851-8923 *Web Site:* www.universal.com/amp, pg 169

Andrews, Mary E, Ave Maria Press, 19113 Douglas Rd, Notre Dame, IN 46556 *Tel:* 574-287-2831 *Toll Free Tel:* 800-282-1865 *Fax:* 574-239-2904 *Toll Free Fax:* 800-282-5681 *E-mail:* avemariapress.1@nd.edu *Web Site:* www.avemariapress.com, pg 29

Andrews, Mary E, Sorin Books, 19113 Douglas Rd, Notre Dame, IN 46556 *Tel:* 574-287-2831 *Toll Free Tel:* 800-282-1865 *Fax:* 574-239-2904 *Toll Free Fax:* 800-282-5681 *E-mail:* sorinbk@nd.edu *Web Site:* www.sorinbooks.com, pg 253

Andrews, Meredith, National Book Awards, 95 Madison Ave, Suite 709, New York, NY 10016 *Tel:* 212-685-0261 *Fax:* 212-213-6570 *E-mail:* nationalbook@ national.org *Web Site:* www.nationalbook.org, pg 791

Andrews, Richard, Maharishi University of Management Press, 1000 N Fourth St, Dept 1155, Fairfield, IA 52557-1155 *Tel:* 641-472-1101 *Toll Free Tel:* 800-831-6523 *Fax:* 641-472-1122 *E-mail:* mumpress@mum. edu *Web Site:* www.mumpress.com, pg 161

Andrikanich, Chris, Gray & Company Publishers, 1588 E 40 St, Cleveland, OH 44103 *Tel:* 216-431-2665 *Toll Free Tel:* 800-915-3609 *E-mail:* info@grayco.com *Web Site:* www.grayco.com, pg 108

Andriulli, Tony, Bernstein & Andriulli Inc, 58 W 40 St, 6th fl, New York, NY 10018 *Tel:* 212-682-1490 *Fax:* 212-286-1890 *E-mail:* info@ba-reps.com *Web Site:* www.ba-reps.com, pg 665

Andrulevich, Bill, Fairchild Books, 7 W 34 St, New York, NY 10001 *Tel:* 212-630-3880 *Toll Free Tel:* 800-932-4724 *Fax:* 212-630-3868; 212-630-3898 *Web Site:* www.fairchildbooks.com, pg 94

Andrus, Dana, The MIT Press, 5 Cambridge Ctr, Cambridge, MA 02142 *Tel:* 617-253-5646 *Toll Free Tel:* 800-405-1619 (orders only) *Fax:* 617-258-6779 *Web Site:* mitpress.mit.edu, pg 175

Andujar, Julio I, Andujar Communication Technologies Inc, 7946 Ivanhoe Ave, Suite 314, La Jolla, CA 92037 *Tel:* 858-459-2673 *Fax:* 858-459-9768, pg 19

Anfuso, Dominick V, Free Press, 1230 Avenue of the Americas, New York, NY 10020 *Tel:* 212-698-7000 *Toll Free Tel:* 800-223-2345 (cust serv); 800-223-2336 (orders); 888-866-6631 (fulfillment), pg 100

Ang, Judith, Holiday House Inc, 425 Madison Ave, New York, NY 10017 *Tel:* 212-688-0085 *Fax:* 212-421-6134, pg 123

Angel, Ann, Wisconsin Retreat, 15255 Turnberry Dr, Brookfield, WI 53005 *Tel:* 262-783-4890 *Web Site:* www.scbwi.org, pg 749

Angelillo, Ed, Frog Ltd, 1435 Fourth St, Berkeley, CA 94710 *Tel:* 510-559-8277 *Toll Free Tel:* 800-337-2665 (book orders only) *Fax:* 510-559-8279 *E-mail:* orders@northatlanticbooks.com *Web Site:* www.northatlanticbooks.com, pg 101

Angelillo, Phillip A, Math-Check, 3 Herbert St, Baldwin, NY 11510 *Tel:* 516-623-6898, pg 605

Angelillo, Tom, Oxmoor House Inc, 2100 Lakeshore Dr, Birmingham, AL 35209 *Tel:* 205-445-6000; 205-445-6560 *Toll Free Tel:* 800-366-4712 *Fax:* 205-445-6078 *Web Site:* www.oxmoorhouse.com, pg 201

Angelini, Maria, Transnational Publishers Inc, 410 Saw Mill River Rd, Suite 2045, Ardsley, NY 10502 *Tel:* 914-693-5100 *Toll Free Tel:* 800-914-8186 (orders only) *Fax:* 914-693-4430 *E-mail:* info@transnationalpubs.com *Web Site:* www. transnationalpubs.com, pg 274

Angellili, Chris, Random House Children's Books, 1745 Broadway, New York, NY 10019 *Tel:* 212-782-9000 *Toll Free Tel:* 800-200-3552 *Fax:* 212-782-9452 *Web Site:* www.randomhouse.com/kids, pg 226

Angers, Shelly, Jewish Lights Publishing, Sunset Farm Offices, Rte 4, Woodstock, VT 05091 *Tel:* 802-457-4000 *Toll Free Tel:* 800-962-4544 *Fax:* 802-457-4004 *E-mail:* sales@jewishlights.com *Web Site:* www. jewishlights.com, pg 140

Angus, Julie, Hanser Gardner Publications, 6915 Valley Ave, Cincinnati, OH 45244-3029 *Tel:* 513-527-8977 *Toll Free Tel:* 800-950-8977 *Fax:* 513-527-8801 *Toll Free Fax:* 800-527-8801 *E-mail:* hgfeedback@ gardnerweb.com *Web Site:* www.hansergardner.com, pg 113

Anker, James D, Anker Publishing Co Inc, 176 Ballville Rd, Bolton, MA 01740-1255 *Tel:* 978-779-6190 *Fax:* 978-779-6366 *E-mail:* info@ankerpub.com *Web Site:* www.ankerpub.com, pg 20

Anker, Susan W, Anker Publishing Co Inc, 176 Ballville Rd, Bolton, MA 01740-1255 *Tel:* 978-779-6190 *Fax:* 978-779-6366 *E-mail:* info@ankerpub.com *Web Site:* www.ankerpub.com, pg 20

Anne, P, American Sciences Press Inc, 20 Cross Rd, Syracuse, NY 13224-2104, pg 17

Annear, Brent, Anson Jones MD Award, c/o Texas Medical Association, 401 W 15 St, Austin, TX 78701 *Tel:* 512-370-1300 *Fax:* 512-370-1629 *Web Site:* www. texmed.org, pg 781

Annechino, Christine, Peter Glenn Publications, 6040 NW 43 Terr, Boca Raton, FL 33496 *Tel:* 561-999-8930 *Toll Free Tel:* 888-332-6700 *Fax:* 561-999-8931 *E-mail:* lynn@pgdirect.com *Web Site:* www.pgdirect. com, pg 105

Ansell, Dorothy I, National Resource Center for Youth Services (NRCYS), Schusterman Center, 4502 E 41 St, Bldg 4W, Tulsa, OK 74135-2512 *Tel:* 918-660-3700 *Toll Free Tel:* 800-274-2687 *Fax:* 918-660-3737 *Web Site:* www.nrcys.ou.edu, pg 185

Anson-Turturro, Ginny, Penguin Young Readers Group, 345 Hudson St, New York, NY 10014 *Tel:* 212-366-2000 *E-mail:* online@penguinputnam.com *Web Site:* www.penguin.com, pg 208

Anthony, Alta H, The Johns Hopkins University Press, 2715 N Charles St, Baltimore, MD 21218-4363 *Tel:* 410-516-6900 *Toll Free Tel:* 800-537-5487 *Fax:* 410-516-6968 *Web Site:* www.press.jhu.edu, pg 141

Anthony, Mark, Huntington House Publishers, 104 Row 2, Suite A-1 & A-2, Lafayette, LA 70508 *Tel:* 337-237-7049; 337-749-4009 (sales); 337-237-3082 (opers) *Toll Free Tel:* 800-749-4009 (sales) *Fax:* 337-237-7060 *E-mail:* admin@alphapublishingonline.com; sales@alphapublishingonline.com *Web Site:* www. alphapublishingonline.com, pg 129

Antion, Thomas, Anchor Publishing, Virginia, PO Box 9558, Virginia Beach, VA 23450-9558 *Tel:* 757-431-1366 *Web Site:* www.antion.com, pg 19

Anton, Fred, Music Publishers' Association of the United States, 2435 Fifth Ave, Suite 236, New York, NY 10016 *Tel:* 212-327-4044 *Fax:* 212-327-4044 *Web Site:* host.mpa.org; www.mpa.org, pg 691

Anton, Fred S, Warner Bros Publications Inc, 15800 NW 48 Ave, Miami, FL 33014 *Tel:* 305-620-1500 *Toll Free Tel:* 800-327-7643 *Fax:* 305-621-4869 *E-mail:* wbpsales@warnerchappell.com *Web Site:* www.warnerbrospublications.com, pg 293

Antonetti, Martin, American Printing History Association, PO Box 4519, Grand Central Sta, New York, NY 10163-4519 *Tel:* 212-930-9220 *Fax:* 212-930-0079 *Web Site:* www.printinghistory.org, pg 677

Antonetti, Martin, American Printing History Association Award, PO Box 4519, Grand Central Sta, New York, NY 10163-4519 *Tel:* 212-930-9220 *Fax:* 212-930-0079 *Web Site:* www.printinghistory.org, pg 759

Antonsen, Lisa, Crabtree Publishing Co, 350 Fifth Ave, Suite 3308, PMB 16-A, New York, NY 10118 *Tel:* 212-496-5040 *Toll Free Tel:* 800-387-7650 *Toll Free Fax:* 800-355-7166 *E-mail:* letters@ crabtreebooks.com *Web Site:* www.crabtreebooks.com, pg 71

Antonsen, Lisa, Crabtree Publishing Co Ltd, 612 Welland Ave, St Catharines, ON L2M 5V6, Canada *Tel:* 905-682-5221 *Toll Free Tel:* 800-387-7650 *Fax:* 905-682-7166 *Toll Free Fax:* 800-355-7166 *E-mail:* custserv@crabtreebooks.com; sales@ crabtreebooks.com; orders@crabtreebooks.com *Web Site:* www.crabtreebooks.com, pg 541

Antony, Peter, The Metropolitan Museum of Art, 1000 Fifth Ave, New York, NY 10028 *Tel:* 212-879-5500; 212-535-7710 *Fax:* 212-396-5062 *E-mail:* info@ metmuseum.org *Web Site:* www.metmuseum.org, pg 173

Apatoff, Rob, Rand McNally, 8255 Central Park Ave N, Skokie, IL 60076 *Tel:* 847-329-8100 *Toll Free Tel:* 800-333-0136 *Fax:* 847-673-0539 *Web Site:* www. randmcnally.com, pg 225

Apeles, Christina L, PEN Center USA, 672 S Lafayette Park Place, Suite 42, Los Angeles, CA 90057 *Tel:* 213-365-8500 *Fax:* 213-365-9616 *E-mail:* pen@ penusa.org *Web Site:* www.penusa.org, pg 697

Apeles, Teena, PEN Center USA Literary Awards, 672 S Lafayette Park Place, Suite 42, Los Angeles, CA 90057 *Tel:* 213-365-8500 *Fax:* 213-365-9616 *E-mail:* awards@penusa.org *Web Site:* www.penusa. org, pg 797

Apelian, Bill, Bob Jones University Press, 1700 Wade Hampton Blvd, Greenville, SC 29614 *Tel:* 864-242-5100 *Toll Free Tel:* 800-845-5731 (orders only) *Fax:* 864-298-0268 *E-mail:* asmith@bju.edu *Web Site:* www.bjup.com, pg 142

Apilado, Myron, AIM Magazine Short Story Contest, PO Box 1174, Maywood, IL 60153-8174 *Tel:* 708-344-4414 *Fax:* 206-543-2746 (WA) *Web Site:* www. aimmagazine.org, pg 758

Apilado, Ruth, AIM Magazine Short Story Contest, PO Box 1174, Maywood, IL 60153-8174 *Tel:* 708-344-4414 *Fax:* 206-543-2746 (WA) *Web Site:* www. aimmagazine.org, pg 758

Aponte, Natalia, Tom Doherty Associates, LLC, 175 Fifth Ave, 14th fl, New York, NY 10010 *Tel:* 212-388-0100 *Toll Free Tel:* 800-455-0340 *Fax:* 212-388-0191 *E-mail:* firstname.lastname@tor.com *Web Site:* www. tor.com, pg 82

Applebaum, Irwyn, Bantam Dell Publishing Group, 1745 Broadway, New York, NY 10019 *Tel:* 212-782-9000 *Toll Free Tel:* 800-223-6834 *Fax:* 212-302-7985 *Web Site:* www.randomhouse.com/bantamdell, pg 31

Applebaum, Irwyn, Random House Inc, 1745 Broadway, New York, NY 10019 *Tel:* 212-782-9000 *Toll Free Tel:* 800-726-0600 *Web Site:* www.randomhouse.com, pg 226

Applebaum, Stuart, Random House Inc, 1745 Broadway, New York, NY 10019 *Tel:* 212-782-9000 *Toll Free Tel:* 800-726-0600 *Web Site:* www.randomhouse.com, pg 226

Aquilino, Joy, Watson-Guptill Publications, 770 Broadway, New York, NY 10003 *Tel:* 646-654-5450 *Toll Free Tel:* 800-278-8477 (orders only) *Fax:* 646-654-5486; 646-654-5487 *E-mail:* info@watsonguptill. com *Web Site:* www.watsonguptill.com, pg 294

Arab, Ranjit, University Press of Kansas, 2501 W 15 St, Lawrence, KS 66049-3905 *Tel:* 785-864-4154; 785-864-4155 (orders) *Fax:* 785-864-4586 *E-mail:* upress@ku.edu *Web Site:* www.kansaspress. ku.edu, pg 287

Arakawa, Yoichi, Six Strings Music Publishing, PO Box 7718-151, Torrance, CA 90504-9118 *Toll Free Tel:* 800-784-0203 *Fax:* 310-362-8864 *Web Site:* www. sixstringsmusicpub.com, pg 249

Arbogast, Ingrid, Amber Quill Press LLC, PO Box 265, Indian Hills, CO 80454 *E-mail:* customer_service@ amberquillpress.com *Web Site:* amberquill.com, pg 10

Archer, Ellen, Hyperion, 77 W 66 St, 11th fl, New York, NY 10023-6298 *Tel:* 212-456-0100 *Toll Free Tel:* 800-759-0190 (cust serv) *Fax:* 212-456-0157 *Web Site:* hyperionbooks.com, pg 129

Archer, Peter, Wizards of the Coast Inc, PO Box 707, Renton, WA 98057-0707 *Web Site:* www.wizards. com/books, pg 302

Areheart, Shaye, Crown Publishing Group, 1745 Broadway, New York, NY 10019 *Tel:* 212-782-9000 *Toll Free Tel:* 888-264-1745 *Fax:* 212-940-7408 *Web Site:* www.randomhouse.com/crown, pg 74

Arellano, Susan, Susan Rabiner Literary Agent, 240 W 35 St, Suite 500, New York, NY 10001-2506 *Tel:* 212-279-0316 *Fax:* 212-279-0932 *E-mail:* susan@rabiner. net, pg 650

Argiriou, Celia, Modern Curriculum Press, 299 Jefferson Rd, Parsippany, NJ 07054-0480 *Tel:* 973-739-8000 *Fax:* 973-739-8635 *Web Site:* www.pearsonlearning. com, pg 176

Argyle, Ray, PMC Canadian Letters Award, 175 Bloor St E, South Tower, Suite 1007, Toronto, ON M4W 3R8, Canada *Tel:* 416-968-7218 *Fax:* 416-968-6182, pg 799

Aridjis, Homero, Pen American Center, 588 Broadway, Suite 303, New York, NY 10012 *Tel:* 212-334-1660 *Fax:* 212-334-2181 *E-mail:* pen@pen.org *Web Site:* www.pen.org, pg 696

Aries, A B, Optimization Software Inc, 10800 Savona Rd, Los Angeles, CA 90077 *Tel:* 310-472-2910 *Fax:* 310-472-2910 *E-mail:* aries@optipub.bizland.com *Web Site:* www.optipub.bizland, pg 198

Aris, Anthony, Serindia Publications, PO Box 10335, Chicago, IL 60610-0335 *Tel:* 312-664-5531 *Fax:* 312-664-4389 *E-mail:* info@serindia.com *Web Site:* www. serindia.com, pg 245

Aristy, Jeffrey, Routledge, 29 W 35 St, New York, NY 10001-2299 *Tel:* 212-216-7800 *Fax:* 212-564-7854 (main) *E-mail:* info@taylorandfrancis.com *Web Site:* www.routledge-ny.com, pg 235

Ark, Daniel Vander, Christian Schools International, 3350 E Paris Ave SE, Grand Rapids, MI 49512-3054 *Tel:* 616-957-1070 *Toll Free Tel:* 800-635-8288 *Fax:* 616-957-5022 *E-mail:* info@csionline.org *Web Site:* www.csionline.org, pg 61

Arkin, Steve, Paulist Press, 997 Macarthur Blvd, Mahwah, NJ 07430 *Tel:* 201-825-7300 *Toll Free Tel:* 800-218-1903 *Fax:* 201-825-8345 *Toll Free Fax:* 800-836-3161 (orders) *E-mail:* info@paulistpress. com *Web Site:* www.paulistpress.com, pg 206

Arlinghaus, Sandra Lach, Institute of Mathematical Geography, 1964 Boulder Dr, Ann Arbor, MI 48104 *Tel:* 734-975-0246 *Web Site:* www. instituteofmathematicalgeography.org, pg 135

Arlington, William J, John Wiley & Sons Inc, 111 River St, Hoboken, NJ 07030 *Tel:* 201-748-6000 *Toll Free Tel:* 800-225-5945 (cust serv) *Fax:* 201-748-6088 *E-mail:* info@wiley.com *Web Site:* www.wiley.com, pg 299

Armato, Doug, University of Minnesota Press, 111 Third Ave S, Suite 290, Minneapolis, MN 55401-2520 *Tel:* 612-627-1970 *Fax:* 612-627-1980 *E-mail:* ump@ tc.umn.edu *Web Site:* www.upress.umn.edu, pg 282

Armbruster, Bruce, University Science Books, 55-D Gate Five Rd, Sausalito, CA 94965 *Tel:* 415-332-5390 *Fax:* 415-332-5393 *E-mail:* univscibks@igc.org *Web Site:* www.uscibooks.com, pg 288

Armbruster, Kathy, University Science Books, 55-D Gate Five Rd, Sausalito, CA 94965 *Tel:* 415-332-5390 *Fax:* 415-332-5393 *E-mail:* univscibks@igc.org *Web Site:* www.uscibooks.com, pg 288

Armengol, Norma C, Baptist Spanish Publishing House (d/b/a Casa Bautista de Publicaciones), 7000 Alabama St, El Paso, TX 79904 *Tel:* 915-566-9656 *Toll Free Tel:* 800-755-5958 (cust serv & orders); 800-985-9971 (Casa Bautista Miami) *Fax:* 915-562-6502; 915-565-9008 (orders) *E-mail:* cbpmail@casabautista.org *Web Site:* www.casabautista.org, pg 31

Arms, Gary, Dubuque Fine Arts Players, 1686 Lawndale St, Dubuque, IA 52001 *Tel:* 563-582-5502, pg 771

Armstead, Stacey L, The Johns Hopkins University Press, 2715 N Charles St, Baltimore, MD 21218-4363 *Tel:* 410-516-6900 *Toll Free Tel:* 800-537-5487 *Fax:* 410-516-6968 *Web Site:* www.press.jhu.edu, pg 141

Armstrong, Lynn, Shane-Armstrong Information Systems, 912 S Elmhurst Ave, Fayetteville, AR 72701 *Tel:* 479-521-8657 *Fax:* 479-521-8657, pg 611

Arnett, Mark, Krause Publications, 700 E State St, Iola, WI 54990 *Tel:* 715-445-4612 ext 365 *Toll Free Tel:* 800-258-0929; 888-457-2873 *Fax:* 715-445-4087 *Web Site:* www.krause.com, pg 147

Arnold, Beth, The Haworth Press Inc, 10 Alice St, Binghamton, NY 13904-1580 *Tel:* 607-722-5857 *Toll Free Tel:* 800-429-6784 *Fax:* 607-722-1424 *Toll Free Fax:* 800-895-0582 *E-mail:* getinfo@haworthpressinc. com *Web Site:* www.haworthpress.com, pg 118

Arnold, Clare, Edward Elgar Publishing Inc, 136 West St, Suite 202, Northampton, MA 01060 *Tel:* 413-584-5551 *Toll Free Tel:* 800-390-3149 (orders) *Fax:* 413-584-9933 *Web Site:* www.e-elgar.com, pg 89

Arnold, David, CarTech Inc, 39966 Grand Ave, North Branch, MN 55056 *Tel:* 651-277-1200 *Toll Free Tel:* 800-551-4754 *Fax:* 651-277-1203 *E-mail:* info@ cartechbooks.com *Web Site:* www.cartechbooks.com, pg 54

Arnold, John, M S G-Haskell House Publishers Ltd, PO Box 190420, Brooklyn, NY 11219-0420 *Tel:* 718-435-7878 *Fax:* 718-633-7050, pg 160

Arnovitz, Benton M, United States Holocaust Memorial Museum, 100 Raoul Wallenberg Place SW, Washington, DC 20024-2126 *Tel:* 202-488-6115; 202-488-6144 (orders) *Toll Free Tel:* 800-259-9998 (orders) *Fax:* 202-488-2684; 202-488-0438 (orders) *Web Site:* www.ushmm.org/, pg 279

Arnow, Ann, Bridge Publications Inc, 4751 Fountain Ave, Los Angeles, CA 90029 *Tel:* 323-953-3320 *Toll Free Tel:* 800-722-1733; 800-843-7389 (CA) *Fax:* 323-953-3328 *E-mail:* info@bridgepub.com *Web Site:* www.bridgepub.com, pg 47

Arnow, Don, Bridge Publications Inc, 4751 Fountain Ave, Los Angeles, CA 90029 *Tel:* 323-953-3320 *Toll Free Tel:* 800-722-1733; 800-843-7389 (CA) *Fax:* 323-953-3328 *E-mail:* info@bridgepub.com *Web Site:* www.bridgepub.com, pg 47

Aronoff, Phyllis, John Glassco Translation Prize, Concordia University, SB 335, 1455 De Maisonneuve West, Montreal, PQ H3G 1M8, Canada *Tel:* 514-848-8702 *E-mail:* info@attlc-ltac.org *Web Site:* www.attlc-ltac.org, pg 776

Aronoff, Phyllis, Literary Translators' Association of Canada, Concordia University, SB 335, 1455 De Maisonneuve West, Montreal, PQ H3G 1M8, Canada *Tel:* 514-848-8702 *E-mail:* info@attlc-ltac.org *Web Site:* www.attlc-ltac.org, pg 690

Aronson, Michael A, Harvard University Press, 79 Garden St, Cambridge, MA 02138-1499 *Tel:* 617-495-2600; 401-531-2800 (international orders) *Toll Free Tel:* 800-405-1619 (orders) *Fax:* 617-495-5898 (general); 617-496-4677 (edit & rts); 401-531-2801 (international orders) *Toll Free Fax:* 800-406-9145 (orders) *E-mail:* firstname_lastname@harvard.edu *Web Site:* www.hup.harvard.edu, pg 117

Aronstein, Mark, Association of School Business Officials International, 11401 North Shore Dr, Reston, VA 20190 *Tel:* 703-478-0405 *Fax:* 703-478-0205 *E-mail:* asboreq@asbointl.org *Web Site:* www.asbointl. org, pg 27

Arris, William Jr, Adams Media, An F+W Publications Co, 57 Littlefield St, 2nd fl, Avon, MA 02322 *Tel:* 508-427-7100 *Fax:* 508-427-6790 *Toll Free Fax:* 800-872-5628 *E-mail:* authors@adamsmedia. com; orders@adamsmedia.com *Web Site:* www. adamsmedia.com, pg 5

Arrow, Kevin P, Graphic World Publishing Services, 11687 Adie Rd, Maryland Heights, MO 63043 *Tel:* 314-567-9854 *Fax:* 314-567-0360, pg 600

Arroyo, Madeline, Stairway Publications, PO Box 518, Huntington, NY 11743-0518 *Tel:* 631-423-4050 *Fax:* 631-351-2142 *E-mail:* publisher@stairwaypub. com *Web Site:* www.stairwaypub.com, pg 257

Art, Pamela, Storey Books, 210 Mass MoCA Way, North Adams, MA 01247 *Tel:* 413-346-2100 *Toll Free Tel:* 800-793-9396 *Fax:* 413-346-2253 *E-mail:* info@ storey.com *Web Site:* www.storey.com, pg 260

Arthurs, Eugene, SPIE, International Society for Optical Engineering, 1000 20 St, Bellingham, WA 98225 *Tel:* 360-676-3290 *Fax:* 360-647-1445 *E-mail:* spie@ spie.org *Web Site:* www.spie.org, pg 255

Artigiani, Susan, Naval Institute Press, 291 Wood Rd, Annapolis, MD 21402-5034 *Tel:* 410-268-6110 *Toll Free Tel:* 800-233-8764 *Fax:* 410-295-1084; 410-

571-1703 (customer service) E-mail: webmaster@
navalinstitute.org; customer@navalinstitute.org (cust
serv) Web Site: www.navalinstitute.org, pg 185

Artis, Christopher, Bantam Dell Publishing Group,
1745 Broadway, New York, NY 10019 Tel: 212-782-
9000 Toll Free Tel: 800-223-6834 Fax: 212-302-7985
Web Site: www.randomhouse.com/bantamdell, pg 31

Asaro, Catherine, SFWA Nebula Awards, PO Box 877,
Chestertown, MD 21620 Toll Free Tel: 888-322-7392
E-mail: execdir@sfwa.org Web Site: www.sfwa.org,
pg 805

Asborno, Liz, Resource Publications Inc, 160 E Virginia
St, Suite 290, San Jose, CA 95112-5876 Tel: 408-286-
8505 Fax: 408-287-8748 E-mail: orders@rpinet.com
Web Site: www.rpinet.com, pg 231

Ascher, Allen, Pearson Education/ELT, 10 Bank St,
9th fl, White Plains, NY 10606 Tel: 914-993-5000
Fax: 914-993-8115 E-mail: firstname.lastname@
pearsoned.com, pg 206

Asciutto, Mary Anne, Asciutto Art Representatives Inc,
1712 E Butler Circle, Chandler, AZ 85225 Tel: 480-
899-0600 Fax: 480-899-3636 E-mail: aartreps@cox.
net, pg 665

Ash, Irene, Synapse Information Resources Inc, 1247
Taft Ave, Endicott, NY 13760 Tel: 607-748-4145
Toll Free Tel: 888-SYN-CHEM Fax: 607-786-3966
E-mail: salesinfo@synapseinfo.com Web Site: www.
synapseinfo.com, pg 263

Ash, Michael, Synapse Information Resources Inc, 1247
Taft Ave, Endicott, NY 13760 Tel: 607-748-4145
Toll Free Tel: 888-SYN-CHEM Fax: 607-786-3966
E-mail: salesinfo@synapseinfo.com Web Site: www.
synapseinfo.com, pg 263

Ashbach, Chip, B K Nelson Inc Lecture Bureau, 84
Woodland Rd, Pleasantville, NY 10570 Tel: 914-
741-1322; 212-889-0637 Fax: 914-741-1323
E-mail: bknelson4@cs.com Web Site: www.bknelson.
com, pg 670

Ashbach, Leonard, B K Nelson Inc Literary Agency,
1565 Paseo Vida, Palm Springs, CA 92264 Tel: 760-
778-8800 Fax: 914-778-0034 E-mail: bknelson4@cs.
com Web Site: www.bknelson.com, pg 645

Asher, Gary, Maverick Publications Inc, 63324 Nels
Anderson Rd, Bend, OR 97701 Tel: 541-382-6978
Fax: 541-382-4831 E-mail: customerservice@
maverickbooks.com Web Site: www.mavbooks.com,
pg 165

Asher, James, McClanahan Publishing House Inc, PO
Box 100, Kuttawa, KY 42055-0100 Tel: 270-388-
9388 Toll Free Tel: 800-544-6959 Fax: 270-388-6186
E-mail: books@kybooks.com Web Site: www.kybooks.
com, pg 166

Asher, Martin, Vintage & Anchor Books, 1745
Broadway, New York, NY 10019 Tel: 212-751-2600
Fax: 212-572-6043, pg 291

Asher, Virginia Lee, Sky Oaks Productions Inc, 19544
Sky Oaks Way, Los Gatos, CA 95030 Tel: 408-395-
7600 Fax: 408-395-8440 E-mail: tprworld@aol.com
Web Site: www.tpr-world.com, pg 250

Ashley, Susan, Gareth Stevens Inc, 330 W Olive St,
Suite 100, Milwaukee, WI 53212 Tel: 414-332-3520
Toll Free Tel: 800-542-2595 Fax: 414-332-3567
E-mail: info@gspub.com; info@worldalmaclibrary.
com Web Site: www.garethstevens.com; www.
worldalmanaclibrary.com, pg 102

Ashour, Savannah, Arcade Publishing Inc, 141 Fifth
Ave, New York, NY 10010 Tel: 212-475-2633
Fax: 212-353-8148 E-mail: arcadeinfo@arcadepub.
com Web Site: www.arcadepub.com, pg 22

Ashwell, Drew, College Press Publishing Co, 223
W Third St, Joplin, MO 64801 Tel: 417-623-6280
Toll Free Tel: 800-289-3300 Fax: 417-623-8250
E-mail: books@collegepress.com Web Site: www.
collegepress.com, pg 64

Asiaghi, Anthony, American Society of Mechanical
Engineers (ASME), 3 Park Ave, New York, NY 10016
Tel: 212-591-7000 Toll Free Tel: 800-843-2763 (cust

serv) Fax: 212-591-7674; 973-882-1717 (cust serv)
E-mail: infocentral@asme.org Web Site: www.asme.
org, pg 18

Asinugo, Samuel, Trident Media Inc, 801 N Pitt St,
Suite 123, Alexandria, VA 22314 Tel: 703-684-
6895 Fax: 703-684-0639 E-mail: info@samhost.net
Web Site: www.edenplaza.com, pg 275

Aspatore, Jonathan R, Aspatore Books, 264 Beacon
St, 2nd fl, Boston, MA 02116 Tel: 617-369-7017
Fax: 617-249-1970 E-mail: info@aspatore.com
Web Site: www.aspatore.com, pg 26

Aspinwall, Margaret, The Metropolitan Museum
of Art, 1000 Fifth Ave, New York, NY 10028
Tel: 212-879-5500; 212-535-7710 Fax: 212-396-
5062 E-mail: info@metmuseum.org Web Site: www.
metmuseum.org, pg 173

Assathiany, Pascal, Editions du Boreal Express, 4447 rue
St Denis, Montreal, PQ H2J 2L2, Canada Tel: 514-
287-7401 Fax: 514-287-7664 E-mail: boreal@
editionsboreal.qc.ca Web Site: www.editionsboreal.
qc.ca, pg 544

Asselin, David A, American Academy of Environmental
Engineers, 130 Holiday Ct, Suite 100, Annapolis,
MD 21401 Tel: 410-266-3311 Fax: 410-266-7653
E-mail: academy@aaee.net Web Site: www.aaee.net,
pg 11

Asselstine, Peter, Micromedia ProQuest, 20 Victoria
St, Toronto, ON M5C 2N8, Canada Tel: 416-362-
5211 Toll Free Tel: 800-387-2689 Fax: 416-362-
6161 E-mail: info@micromedia.ca Web Site: www.
micromedia.ca, pg 554

Aster, Howard, Mosaic Press, DMB 145, 4500 Witmer
Industrial Estates, Niagara Falls, NY 14305-1386
Tel: 905-825-2130 Toll Free Tel: 800-387-8992
Fax: 905-825-2130 E-mail: mosaicpress@on.aibn.com
Web Site: www.mosaic-press.com, pg 179

Aster, Steve, Primedia Consumer Magazine & Internet
Group, 260 Madison Ave, New York, NY 10016
Tel: 212-726-4300 Toll Free Tel: 800-521-2885
Fax: 212-726-4310 E-mail: sgnews@primediasi.com
Web Site: www.primediainc.com, pg 218

Astley, Roger, Cambridge University Press, 40 W 20
St, New York, NY 10011-4211 Tel: 212-924-3900
Toll Free Tel: 800-899-5222 Fax: 212-691-3239
Web Site: www.cambridge.org, pg 52

Astrupgaard, Lis, Bridge Publications Inc, 4751 Fountain
Ave, Los Angeles, CA 90029 Tel: 323-953-3320
Toll Free Tel: 800-722-1733; 800-843-7389 (CA)
Fax: 323-953-3328 E-mail: info@bridgepub.com
Web Site: www.bridgepub.com, pg 47

Atchity, Kenneth, AEI (Atchity Editorial/Entertainment
International Inc), 9601 Wilshire Blvd, No 1202,
Beverly Hills, CA 90210 Tel: 323-932-0407 Fax: 323-
932-0321 E-mail: submissions@aeionline.com
Web Site: www.aeionline.com, pg 618

Atchity, Kenneth, The Writer's Lifeline Inc, 518 S
Fairfax Ave, Los Angeles, CA 90036 Tel: 323-
932-0905 Fax: 323-932-0321 E-mail: questions@
thewriterslifeline.com; comments@thewriterslifeline.
com Web Site: www.thewriterslifeline.com, pg 615

Aten, Alison, Llewellyn Publications, PO Box 64383,
St Paul, MN 55164-0383 Tel: 651-291-1970 Toll Free
Tel: 800-843-6666 Fax: 651-291-1908 E-mail: lwlpc@
llewellyn.com Web Site: www.llewellyn.com, pg 157

Athearn, Lloyd, The American Alpine Club Press, 710
Tenth St, Suite 100, Golden, CO 80401 Tel: 303-
384-0110 Fax: 303-384-0111 E-mail: aacpress@
americanalpineclub.org Web Site: www.
americanalpineclub.org, pg 11

Atkin, Jennifer, Planning/Communications, 7215 Oak
Ave, River Forest, IL 60305-1935 Tel: 708-366-
5200 Toll Free Tel: 888-366-5200 Fax: 708-366-
5280 E-mail: info@planningcommunications.com
Web Site: www.jobfindersonline.com, pg 214

Atkins, Karen, The RGU Group, 560 W Southern
Ave, Tempe, AZ 85282 Tel: 480-736-9862 Toll Free
Tel: 800-266-5265 Fax: 480-736-9863 Toll Free
Fax: 800-973-6694 E-mail: info@thergugroup.com
Web Site: www.thergugroup.com, pg 232

Atkins, Todd, The RGU Group, 560 W Southern Ave,
Tempe, AZ 85282 Tel: 480-736-9862 Toll Free
Tel: 800-266-5265 Fax: 480-736-9863 Toll Free
Fax: 800-973-6694 E-mail: info@thergugroup.com
Web Site: www.thergugroup.com, pg 232

Atkinson, Sarah, Northern Illinois University Press, 310
N Fifth St, De Kalb, IL 60115 Tel: 815-753-1826;
815-753-1075 Fax: 815-753-1845 E-mail: bberg@niu.
edu Web Site: www.niu.edu/univ_press, pg 193

Atkocaitis, John, The Wright Group/McGraw-Hill,
a Division of McGraw-Hill Learning Group, One
Prudential Plaza, 130 E Randolph, 4th fl, Chicago, IL
60601 Tel: 312-233-6520 Toll Free Tel: 800-537-4740
Fax: 312-233-6605 Web Site: www.wrightgroup.com,
pg 304

Attenborough, Jon, Simon & Schuster Inc, 1230 Avenue
of the Americas, New York, NY 10020 Tel: 212-698-
7000 Fax: 212-698-7007 Web Site: www.simonsays.
com, pg 249

Attinello, Lauren, Jim Henson Publishing/Muppet Press,
117 E 69 St, New York, NY 10021 Tel: 212-794-
2400 Fax: 212-794-5157 Web Site: www.henson.com,
pg 141

Atwan, Helene, Beacon Press, 41 Mount Vernon St,
Boston, MA 02108 Tel: 617-742-2110 Toll Free
Tel: 800-225-3362 (orders only) Fax: 617-723-3097;
617-742-2290 Web Site: www.beacon.org, pg 34

Aubin, Patrick, National Gallery of Canada, The
Bookstore, 380 Sussex Dr, Ottawa, ON K1N
9N4, Canada Tel: 613-990-0962 (mail order sales)
Fax: 613-990-1972 E-mail: ngcbook@gallery.ca
Web Site: www.national.gallery.ca, pg 555

Aubrey, Quinn, Stand! Publishing, 2744 Seneca St,
No T-12, Wichita, KS 67207 Tel: 316-265-2880
E-mail: standbooks@yahoo.com Web Site: www.
standbooks.com, pg 257

Auclair, Kristen, The Graybill & English Literary
Agency LLC, 1875 Connecticut Ave, NW, Suite 712,
Washington, DC 20009 Tel: 202-588-9798 Fax: 202-
457-0662 Web Site: graybillandenglish.com, pg 633

Augenbraum, Harold, The Mercantile Library, 17 E
47 St, New York, NY 10017 Tel: 212-755-6710
Fax: 212-826-0831 E-mail: info@mercantilelibrary.org
Web Site: www.mercantilelibrary.org, pg 691

Auger, Lorraine, Guerin Editeur Ltee, 4501 rue Drolet,
Montreal, PQ H2T 2G2, Canada Tel: 514-842-3481
Toll Free Tel: 800-398-8337 Fax: 514-842-4923
Web Site: www.guerin-editeur.qc.ca, pg 549

Augerbraun, Harold, National Book Awards, 95 Madison
Ave, Suite 709, New York, NY 10016 Tel: 212-685-
0261 Fax: 212-213-6570 E-mail: nationalbook@
national.org Web Site: www.nationalbook.org, pg 791

Augustine, Peggy, Abingdon Press, 201 Eighth Ave
S, Nashville, TN 37203-3919 Tel: 615-749-6290
(publicist); 615-749-6000; 615-749-6451 (sales)
Toll Free Tel: 800-251-3320 Fax: 615-749-6056
Web Site: www.abingdonpress.com, pg 3

Auh, Jin, The Wylie Agency Inc, 250 W 57 St, Suite
2114, New York, NY 10107 Tel: 212-246-0069
Fax: 212-586-8953 E-mail: mail@wylieagency.com,
pg 662

Ault, Charles, Temple University Press, 1601 N Broad
St, 083-42, USB Room 306, Philadelphia, PA 19122-
6099 Tel: 215-204-8787 Toll Free Tel: 800-447-1656
Fax: 215-204-4719 E-mail: tempress@temple.edu
Web Site: www.temple.edu/tempress, pg 266

Ausenda, Marco, Rizzoli International Publications Inc,
300 Park Ave S, 3rd fl, New York, NY 10010-5399
Tel: 212-387-3400 Toll Free Tel: 800-522-6657 (orders
only) Fax: 212-387-3535, pg 233

Austin, Erik, Inter-University Consortium for Political
& Social Research, PO Box 1248, Ann Arbor, MI
48106-1248 Tel: 734-647-5000 Fax: 734-647-8200
E-mail: netmail@icpsr.umich.edu Web Site: www.
icpsr.umich.edu, pg 136

Austin, Kurt, National Council of Teachers of English
(NCTE), 1111 W Kenyon Rd, Urbana, IL 61801-
1096 Tel: 217-328-3870 Toll Free Tel: 800-369-

6283; 877-369-6283 (cust serv) *Fax:* 217-328-0977 *E-mail:* orders@ncte.org *Web Site:* www.ncte.org, pg 183

Austin, Nicole Diamond, The Creative Culture Inc, 72 Spring St, Suite 304, New York, NY 10012 *Tel:* 212-680-3510 *Fax:* 212-680-3509 *Web Site:* www.thecreativeculture.com, pg 626

Austin, Patricia, National Council of Teachers of English (NCTE), 1111 W Kenyon Rd, Urbana, IL 61801-1096 *Tel:* 217-328-3870 *Toll Free Tel:* 800-369-6283; 877-369-6283 (cust serv) *Fax:* 217-328-0977 *E-mail:* orders@ncte.org *Web Site:* www.ncte.org, pg 183

Avery, Laurie, Ohio State University Press, 180 Pressey Hall, 1070 Carmack Rd, Columbus, OH 43210-1002 *Tel:* 614-292-6930 *Toll Free Tel:* 800-621-2736 *Fax:* 614-292-2065 *Toll Free Fax:* 800-621-8476 *E-mail:* ohiostatepress@osu.edu *Web Site:* ohiostatepress.org, pg 196

Aviles, Marta Cecilia, United Nations Publications, 2 United Nations Plaza, Rm DC2-0853, New York, NY 10017 *Tel:* 212-963-8302 *Toll Free Tel:* 800-253-9646 *Fax:* 212-963-3489 *E-mail:* publications@un.org *Web Site:* www.un.org/publications, pg 279

Avis, Ed, Marion Street Press, 106 S Oak Park Ave, Oak Park, IL 60302 *Tel:* 708-445-8330 *Toll Free Tel:* 866-443-7987 *Fax:* 708-445-8648 *Web Site:* www.marionstreetpress.com, pg 163

Avrahami, Michal, Gefen Books, 600 Broadway, Lynbrook, NY 11563 *Tel:* 516-593-1234 *Toll Free Tel:* 800-477-5257 *Fax:* 516-295-2739 *E-mail:* gefenny@gefenpublishing.com *Web Site:* www.israelbooks.com, pg 103

Avramidis, Manny, American Management Association, 1601 Broadway, New York, NY 10019-7420 *Tel:* 212-586-8100.*Toll Free Tel:* 800-262-9699 *Fax:* 212-903-8168 *Web Site:* www.amanet.org, pg 677

Awalt, Barbe, LPD Press, 925 Salamanca NW, Albuquerque, NM 87107-5647 *Tel:* 505-344-9382 *Fax:* 505-345-5129 *E-mail:* info@nmsantos.com *Web Site:* www.nmsantos.com, pg 159

Axelrod, Glen, TFH Publications Inc, 61 Third Ave, Neptune City, NJ 07753 *Tel:* 732-988-8400 *Toll Free Tel:* 800-631-2188 *Fax:* 732-988-5466 *E-mail:* info@tfh.com *Web Site:* www.tfh.com, pg 268

Axelrod, Steven, The Axelrod Agency, 55 Main St, Chatham, NY 12037 *Tel:* 518-392-2100 *Fax:* 518-392-2944 *E-mail:* steve@axelrodagency.com, pg 620

Axford, Elizabeth C, Piano Press, 1425 Ocean Ave, Suite 6, Del Mar, CA 92014 *Tel:* 619-884-1401 *Fax:* 858-459-3376 *E-mail:* pianopress@aol.com *Web Site:* www.pianopress.com, pg 212

Axford, Liz, Piano Press, 1425 Ocean Ave, Suite 6, Del Mar, CA 92014 *Tel:* 619-884-1401 *Fax:* 858-459-3376 *E-mail:* pianopress@aol.com *Web Site:* www.pianopress.com, pg 212

Ayers, Sandra, Brandywine Press, 154 General Pulaski Walk, Naugatuck, CT 06770-2978 *Tel:* 203-729-7556 *Toll Free Tel:* 800-345-1776 *Fax:* 203-729-7567 *Web Site:* www.brandywinepress.com, pg 45

Aynesmith, Lawrence, White Cliffs Media Inc, PO Box 6083, Incline Village, NV 89450 *Tel:* 775-831-4899 *Toll Free Tel:* 800-345-6665 (orders only) *Fax:* 603-357-2073 *E-mail:* wcm@wcmedia.com *Web Site:* www.wcmedia.com, pg 298

Ayres, Ruth, Urban Land Institute, 1025 Thomas Jefferson St NW, Suite 500 W, Washington, DC 20007 *Tel:* 202-624-7000 *Toll Free Tel:* 800-321-5011 *Fax:* 410-626-7140 *E-mail:* Bookstore@uli.org *Web Site:* www.bookstore.uli.org, pg 288

Ayres, William, Harry Chapin Media Awards, 505 Eighth Ave, 21st fl, New York, NY 10018 *Tel:* 212-629-8850 *Toll Free Tel:* 800-5-HUNGRY (548-6479) *Fax:* 212-465-9274 *E-mail:* media@worldhungeryear.org *Web Site:* www.worldhungeryear.org, pg 766

Aytch, Cotrenia, APPA: The Association of Higher Education Facilities Officers, 1643 Prince St, Alexandria, VA 22314-2818 *Tel:* 703-684-1446 *Fax:* 703-549-2772 *Web Site:* www.appa.org, pg 21

Azar, Phyllis, Tom Doherty Associates, LLC, 175 Fifth Ave, 14th fl, New York, NY 10010 *Tel:* 212-388-0100 *Toll Free Tel:* 800-455-0340 *Fax:* 212-388-0191 *E-mail:* firstname.lastname@tor.com *Web Site:* www.tor.com, pg 81

Azevedo, Neil, The Nebraska Review Awards, University of Nebraska-Omaha, WFAB 212, Omaha, NE 68182-0324 *Tel:* 402-554-3159 *Fax:* 402-614-2026 *Web Site:* www.zoopress.org/nebraskareview/, pg 793

Aziz, Hanifa, Elsevier Science Inc, 360 Park Ave S, New York, NY 10010 *Tel:* 212-989-5800 *Fax:* 212-633-3965; 212-633-3990 *Web Site:* www.elsevier.com, pg 89

Aziz, Ms Nurjehan, TSAR Publications, PO Box 6996, Sta A, Toronto, ON M5W 1X7, Canada *Tel:* 416-483-7191 *Fax:* 416-486-0706 *E-mail:* treview@total.net *Web Site:* www.tsarbooks.com, pg 563

Baard, Paul P, Fordham University, Graduate School of Business Administration, Dept of Communications & Media Management, 113 W 60 St, New York, NY 10023 *Tel:* 212-636-6199 *Fax:* 212-765-5573, pg 752

Babbitt, Sherry, Philadelphia Museum of Art, 2525 Pennsylvania Ave, Philadelphia, PA 19130 *Tel:* 215-684-7250 *Fax:* 215-235-8715 *Web Site:* www.philamuseum.org, pg 211

Babler, Linda, Atwood Publishing, 2710 Atwood Ave, Madison, WI 53704 *Tel:* 608-242-7101 *Toll Free Tel:* 888-242-7101 *Fax:* 608-242-7102 *E-mail:* customerservice@atwoodpublishing.com *Web Site:* www.atwoodpublishing.com, pg 27

Bacak, Walter, American Translators Association (ATA), 225 Reinekers Lane, Suite 590, Alexandria, VA 22314 *Tel:* 703-683-6100 *Fax:* 703-683-6122 *E-mail:* ata@atanet.org *Web Site:* www.atanet.org, pg 678

Bacak, Walter, Lewis Galantiere Prize, 225 Reinekers Lane, Suite 590, Alexandria, VA 22314 *Tel:* 703-683-6100 *Fax:* 703-683-6122 *E-mail:* ata@atanet.org *Web Site:* www.atanet.org, pg 775

Bacak, Walter, Alexander Gode Medal, 225 Reinekers Lane, Suite 590, Alexandria, VA 22314 *Tel:* 703-683-6100 *Fax:* 703-683-6122 *E-mail:* ata@atanet.org *Web Site:* www.atanet.org, pg 776

Bacchi, Josephine A, John Wiley & Sons Inc, 111 River St, Hoboken, NJ 07030 *Tel:* 201-748-6000 *Toll Free Tel:* 800-225-5945 (cust serv) *Fax:* 201-748-6088 *E-mail:* info@wiley.com *Web Site:* www.wiley.com, pg 299

Bace, Marjan, Manning Publications Co, 209 Bruce Park Ave, Greenwich, CT 06830 *Tel:* 203-629-2211 *Fax:* 203-661-9018 *E-mail:* orders@manning.com *Web Site:* www.manning.com, pg 162

Bacher, Arlene, Rutgers University Press, 100 Joyce Kilmer Ave, Piscataway, NJ 08854-8099 *Tel:* 732-445-7762 (edit); 732-445-7762 (ext 627, sales) *Toll Free Tel:* 800-446-9323 (orders only) *Fax:* 732-445-7039 (acqs, edit, mktg, perms, prodn); 732-445-1974 (fulfillment) *E-mail:* garyf@rci.rutgers.edu *Web Site:* rutgerspress.rutgers.edu, pg 236

Bacher, Dana, Rodale Books, 400 S Tenth St, Emmaus, PA 18098-0099 *Tel:* 610-967-5171 *Fax:* 610-967-8961 *Web Site:* www.rodale.com, pg 233

Bacher, Thomas, Purdue University Press, S Campus Courts-E, 509 Harrison St, West Lafayette, IN 47907-2025 *Tel:* 765-494-2038 *Toll Free Tel:* 800-247-6553 (orders) *Fax:* 765-496-2442 *E-mail:* pupress@purdue.edu *Web Site:* www.thepress.purdue.edu, pg 222

Bachman, Margie K, University of Pittsburgh Press, 3400 Forbes Ave, 5th fl, Pittsburgh, PA 15260 *Tel:* 412-383-2456 *Fax:* 412-383-2466 *E-mail:* press@pitt.edu *Web Site:* www.pitt.edu/~press, pg 284

Backhus, Craig, American Society of Mechanical Engineers (ASME), 3 Park Ave, New York, NY 10016 *Tel:* 212-591-7000 *Toll Free Tel:* 800-843-2763 (cust serv) *Fax:* 212-591-7674; 973-882-1717 (cust serv) *E-mail:* infocentral@asme.org *Web Site:* www.asme.org, pg 18

Backing, Janis, Moody Press, 820 N La Salle Blvd, Chicago, IL 60610 *Tel:* 312-329-2111 *Toll Free Tel:* 800-678-8812 *Fax:* 312-329-2019 *Web Site:* www.moodypress.org, pg 177

Backman, Elizabeth H, Elizabeth H Backman, 86 Johnnycake Hollow Rd, Pine Plains, NY 12567 *Tel:* 518-398-9344 *Fax:* 518-398-6368 *E-mail:* bethcountry@taconic.net, pg 591

Backman, John, Backman Writing & Communications, 32 Hillview Ave, Rensselaer, NY 12144 *Tel:* 518-449-4985 *Fax:* 518-449-7273 *Web Site:* www.backwrite.com, pg 591

Backus, Charles, Texas A&M University Press, John H Lindsey Bldg, Lewis St, 4354 TAMU, College Station, TX 77843-4354 *Tel:* 979-845-1436 *Toll Free Tel:* 800-826-8911 (orders) *Fax:* 979-847-8752 *Toll Free Fax:* 888-617-2421 (orders) *E-mail:* fdl@tampress.tamu.edu *Web Site:* www.tamu.edu/upress/, pg 267

Bacon, Thorn, Bestseller Consultants, PO Box 922, Wilsonville, OR 97070 *Tel:* 503-694-5381 *Fax:* 503-694-5046, pg 591

Bacon, Ursula, Bestseller Consultants, PO Box 922, Wilsonville, OR 97070 *Tel:* 503-694-5381 *Fax:* 503-694-5046, pg 591

Badalian, Mrs Alvart, Blue Crane Books, PO Box 380291, Cambridge, MA 02238 *Tel:* 617-926-8989 *Fax:* 617-926-0982 *E-mail:* bluecrane@arrow1.com, pg 41

Bader, Bonnie, Grosset & Dunlap, 345 Hudson St, New York, NY 10014 *Tel:* 212-366-2000 *E-mail:* online@penguinputnam.com *Web Site:* www.penguin.com, pg 110

Badertscher, Nancy, The Association for Women In Communications, 780 Richie Hwy, Suite 28-S, Severna Park, MD 21146 *Tel:* 410-544-7442 *Fax:* 410-544-4640 *E-mail:* info@womcom.org *Web Site:* www.womcom.org, pg 741

Badger, Susan, Wadsworth Publishing, 10 Davis Dr, Belmont, CA 94002-3002 *Toll Free Tel:* 800-357-0092 *Fax:* 650-592-3342 *Toll Free Fax:* 800-522-4923 *Web Site:* www.wadsworth.com, pg 292

Baehrecke, Astrid, The MIT Press, 5 Cambridge Ctr, Cambridge, MA 02142 *Tel:* 617-253-5646 *Toll Free Tel:* 800-405-1619 (orders only) *Fax:* 617-258-6779 *Web Site:* mitpress.mit.edu, pg 175

Baen, James P, Baen Publishing Enterprises, PO Box 1403, Riverdale, NY 10471-0605 *Tel:* 919-570-1640 *Fax:* 919-570-1644 *Web Site:* baen.com, pg 30

Baensch, Robert, New York University, Center for Publishing, 11 W 42 St, Rm 400, New York, NY 10036 *Tel:* 212-992-3232 *Fax:* 212-992-3233 *E-mail:* pub.center@nyu.edu *Web Site:* www.scps.nyu.edu/publishing, pg 753

Baer, D Richard, Hollywood Film Archive, 8391 Beverly Blvd, PMB 321, Hollywood, CA 90048 *Tel:* 323-655-4968, pg 124

Baer, Marlene, Regal Books, 1957 Eastman Ave, Ventura, CA 93003 *Tel:* 805-644-9721 *Toll Free Tel:* 800-446-7735 (orders) *Fax:* 805-644-9728 (editorial); 805-644-4729 (purchasing); 805-650-8713 (sales & corp serv); 805-658-3388 (orders) *Toll Free Fax:* 800-860-3109 (orders) *E-mail:* info@regalbooks.com *Web Site:* www.gospellight.com, pg 230

Baffa, Grace, Mason Crest Publishers, 370 Reed Rd, Suite 302, Broomall, PA 19008 *Tel:* 610-543-6200 *Toll Free Tel:* 866-MCP-BOOK *Fax:* 610-543-3878 *Web Site:* www.masoncrest.com, pg 165

Bagnato, Judi Gowe, Summy-Birchard Inc, 15800 NW 48 Ave, Miami, FL 33014 *Tel:* 305-620-1500 *Toll Free Tel:* 800-327-7643 *Fax:* 305-621-1094, pg 261

Bagne, Mary, ABC-CLIO, 130 Cremona Dr, Santa Barbara, CA 93117 *Tel:* 805-968-1911 *Toll Free Tel:* 800-368-6868 *Fax:* 805-685-9685 *E-mail:* sales@abc-clio.com *Web Site:* www.abc-clio.com, pg 3

Bahamon, Claire, Management Sciences for Health, 165 Allandale Rd, Boston, MA 02130-3400 *Tel:* 617-524-7799 *Fax:* 617-524-2825 *E-mail:* bookstore@msh.org *Web Site:* www.msh.org, pg 162

Bahash, Robert J, The McGraw-Hill Companies Inc, 1221 Avenue of the Americas, 50th fl, New York, NY 10020 *Tel:* 212-512-2000 *E-mail:* webmaster@mcgraw-hill.com *Web Site:* www.mcgraw-hill.com, pg 167

Bahler, Shannon, Liberty Fund Inc, 8335 Allison Pointe Trail, Suite 300, Indianapolis, IN 46250-1684 *Tel:* 317-842-0880 *Toll Free Tel:* 800-955-8335 *Fax:* 317-579-6060 *E-mail:* books@libertyfund.org *Web Site:* www.libertyfund.org, pg 153

Bahr, Ed, Pacific Press Publishing Association, 1350 N Kings Rd, Nampa, ID 83687-3193 *Tel:* 208-465-2500 *Toll Free Tel:* 800-447-7377 *Fax:* 208-465-2531 *Web Site:* www.pacificpress.com, pg 202

Bahr, Robert, Factor Press, 5204 Dove Point Lane, Salisbury, MD 21801 *Tel:* 410-334-6111 *Toll Free Tel:* 888-334-6677 *Fax:* 410-334-6111 *E-mail:* factorpress@earthlink.net, pg 93

Baida, Mike, Micromedia ProQuest, 20 Victoria St, Toronto, ON M5C 2N8, Canada *Tel:* 416-362-5211 *Toll Free Tel:* 800-387-2689 *Fax:* 416-362-6161 *E-mail:* info@micromedia.ca *Web Site:* www.micromedia.ca, pg 554

Bailey, Anne G, Westernlore Press, PO Box 35305, Tucson, AZ 85740-5305 *Tel:* 520-297-5491 *Fax:* 520-297-1722, pg 297

Bailey, Brenda MLIS, Elvira C Sylve—Editorial & Secretarial Services, PO Box 870602, New Orleans, LA 70187 *Tel:* 504-244-8357 *Fax:* 504-244-8357 (call first) *E-mail:* elcsy58@aol.com, pg 612

Bailey, Bud, Easy Money Press, 5419 87 St, Lubbock, TX 79424 *Tel:* 806-543-5215 *E-mail:* easymoneypress@yahoo.com, pg 86

Bailey, Elizabeth E, National Bureau of Economic Research Inc, 1050 Massachusetts Ave, Cambridge, MA 02138-5398 *Tel:* 617-868-3900 *Fax:* 617-868-2742 *E-mail:* op@nber.org *Web Site:* www.nber.org, pg 182

Bailey, Laura, Mi'kmaq-Maliseet Institute, University of New Brunswick, PO Box 4400, Fredriction, NB E3B 6E3, Canada *Tel:* 506-453-4840 *Fax:* 506-453-4784 *E-mail:* micmac@unb.ca *Web Site:* www.unb.ca, pg 554

Bailey, Lynn R, Westernlore Press, PO Box 35305, Tucson, AZ 85740-5305 *Tel:* 520-297-5491 *Fax:* 520-297-1722, pg 297

Bailey, Michael, F A Davis Co, 1915 Arch St, Philadelphia, PA 19103 *Tel:* 215-568-2270 *Toll Free Tel:* 800-523-4049 *Fax:* 215-568-5065 *E-mail:* info@fadavis.com *Web Site:* www.fadavis.com, pg 76

Bailey, Michele, Vermont Arts Council Grants, 136 State St, Drawer 33, Montpelier, VT 05633-6001 *Tel:* 802-828-3291 *Fax:* 802-828-3363 *E-mail:* info@vermontartscouncil.org *Web Site:* www.vermontartscouncil.org, pg 810

Bailey, Rhonda, XYZ Publishing, 1781 Saint Hubert St, Montreal, PQ H2L 3Z1, Canada *Tel:* 514-252-2170 *Fax:* 514-525-7537 *E-mail:* info@xyzedit.qc.ca *Web Site:* www.xyzedit.qc.ca, pg 567

Bailey, Sarah, Susquehanna University Press, Associated University Presses, 2010 Eastpark Blvd, Cranbury, NJ 08512 *Tel:* 609-655-4770 *Fax:* 609-655-8366 *E-mail:* aup440@aol.com, pg 262

Bailey, Simon, Trident Press International, 801 12 Ave S, Suite 400, Naples, FL 34102 *Tel:* 239-649-7077 *Toll Free Tel:* 800-593-3662 *Fax:* 239-649-5832 *Toll Free Fax:* 800-494-4226 *E-mail:* tridentpress@worldnet.att. net *Web Site:* www.trident-international.com, pg 275

Baillie, Bernadette M, Advantage Publishers Group, 5880 Oberlin Dr, San Diego, CA 92121 *Tel:* 858-457-2500 *Toll Free Tel:* 800-284-3580 *Fax:* 858-812-6476 *Toll Free Fax:* 800-499-3822 *E-mail:* apgcuserv@advmkt.com *Web Site:* www.advantagebooksonline. com, pg 6

Bainbridge, Kelly, Providence Publishing Corp, 238 Seaboard Lane, Franklin, TN 37067 *Tel:* 615-771-2020 *Toll Free Tel:* 800-321-5692 *Fax:* 615-771-2002 *E-mail:* books@providencehouse.com *Web Site:* www.providencehouse.com, pg 220

Baird, Gail, Creative Bound International Inc, 151 Tansley Dr, Carp, ON K0A 1L0, Canada *Tel:* 613-831-3641 *Toll Free Tel:* 800-287-8610 (N America) *Fax:* 613-831-3643 *E-mail:* editor@creativebound.com *Web Site:* www.creativebound.com, pg 541

Bakamjian, Ted, Society of Exploration Geophysicists, 8801 S Yale, Tulsa, OK 74137 *Tel:* 918-497-5500 *Fax:* 918-497-5557 *Web Site:* www.seg.org, pg 252

Bakeman, Mary Hawker, Park Genealogical Books, PO Box 130968, Roseville, MN 55113-0968 *Tel:* 651-488-4416 *Fax:* 651-488-2653 *Web Site:* www.parkbooks. com, pg 204

Baker, Alice, St Martin's Press LLC, 175 Fifth Ave, New York, NY 10010 *Tel:* 212-674-5151 *Fax:* 212-420-9314 *E-mail:* firstname.lastname@stmartins *Web Site:* www.stmartins.com, pg 238

Baker, Bernadette, Beyond Words Publishing Inc, 20827 NW Cornell Rd, Suite 500, Hillsboro, OR 97124-9808 *Tel:* 503-531-8700 *Fax:* 503-531-8773 *Web Site:* www.beyondword.com, pg 38

Baker, Brian, W W Norton & Company Inc, 500 Fifth Ave, New York, NY 10110-0017 *Tel:* 212-354-5500 *Toll Free Tel:* 800-233-4830 (orders & cust serv) *Fax:* 212-869-0856 *Toll Free Fax:* 800-458-6515 *Web Site:* www.wwnorton.com, pg 193

Baker, Carolyn C, American Counseling Association, 5999 Stevenson Ave, Alexandria, VA 22304-3300 *Tel:* 703-823-9800 *Toll Free Tel:* 800-422-2648 (ext 222 - book orders only) *Fax:* 703-461-9260 *Toll Free Fax:* 800-473-2329 *Web Site:* www.counseling.org, pg 13

Baker, Charles, Arte Publico Press, University of Houston, 4800 Calhoun, Houston, TX 77204-2174 *Tel:* 713-743-2841 *Toll Free Tel:* 800-633-2783 *Fax:* 713-743-2847 *Web Site:* www.arte.uh.edu, pg 24

Baker, Daniel W, The Library of America, 14 E 60 St, New York, NY 10022 *Tel:* 212-308-3360 *Fax:* 212-750-8352 *E-mail:* info@loa.org *Web Site:* www.loa. org; www.loaacademic.org, pg 154

Baker, Doris, Filter Press LLC, PO Box 95, Palmer Lake, CO 80133 *Tel:* 719-481-2420 *Toll Free Tel:* 888-570-2663 *Fax:* 719-481-2420 *E-mail:* filter. press@prodigy.net *Web Site:* filterpressbooks.com, pg 96

Baker, Dwight, Baker Books, PO Box 6287, Grand Rapids, MI 49516-6287 *Tel:* 616-676-9185 *Toll Free Tel:* 800-877-2665; 800-679-1957 *Fax:* 616-676-9573 *Toll Free Fax:* 800-398-3110 *Web Site:* www.bakerpublishinggroup.com, pg 30

Baker, Dwight, Chosen Books, PO Box 6287, Grand Rapids, MI 49516-6287 *Tel:* 616-676-9185 *Toll Free Tel:* 800-877-2665 *Fax:* 616-676-2315 *Web Site:* www.bakerpublishinggroup.com, pg 61

Baker, Dwight, Fleming H Revell, PO Box 6287, Grand Rapids, MI 49516-6287 *Tel:* 616-676-9185 *Toll Free Tel:* 800-877-2665 *Fax:* 616-676-9573 *Web Site:* www.bakerbooks.com, pg 232

Baker, Greg, CTB/McGraw-Hill, 20 Ryan Ranch Rd, Monterey, CA 93940-5703 *Tel:* 831-393-0700 *Toll Free Tel:* 800-538-9547 *Fax:* 831-393-7825 *Web Site:* www.ctb.com, pg 74

Baker, Jason, Fine Communications, 322 Eighth Ave, 15th fl, New York, NY 10001 *Tel:* 212-595-3500 *Fax:* 212-595-3779, pg 96

Baker, John F, Barbara Braun Associates Inc, 104 Fifth Ave, 7th fl, New York, NY 10011 *Tel:* 212-604-9023 *Fax:* 212-604-9041 *E-mail:* bba230@earthlink.net *Web Site:* www.barbarabraunagency.com, pg 622

Baker, Karen, Temple University Press, 1601 N Broad St, 083-42, USB Room 306, Philadelphia, PA 19122-6099 *Tel:* 215-204-8787 *Toll Free Tel:* 800-447-1656 *Fax:* 215-204-4719 *E-mail:* tempress@temple.edu *Web Site:* www.temple.edu/tempress, pg 266

Baker, Lynn, Excelsior Cee Publishing, 1311 Cherry Stone, Norman, OK 73072 *Tel:* 405-329-3909 *Fax:* 405-329-6886 *E-mail:* ecp@oecadvantage.net *Web Site:* www.excelsiorcee.com, pg 93

Baker, Mary, Aerial Photography Services Inc, 2511 S Tryon St, Charlotte, NC 28203 *Tel:* 704-333-5143 *Fax:* 704-333-5148 *Toll Free Fax:* 800-204-4910 *E-mail:* aps@aps-1.com *Web Site:* www.aps-1.com, pg 6

Baker, Patricia, Hoover Institution Press, 424 Galvez Mall, Stanford, CA 94305-6010 *Tel:* 650-723-3373 *Toll Free Tel:* 800-935-2882 *Fax:* 650-723-8626 *E-mail:* digest@hoover.stanford.edu; hooverpress@hoover.stanford.edu *Web Site:* www.hoover.org, pg 125

Baker, Paula, Peachpit Press, 1249 Eighth St, Berkeley, CA 94710 *Tel:* 510-524-2178 *Fax:* 510-524-2221 *E-mail:* firstname.lastname@peachpit.com *Web Site:* www.peachpit.com, pg 206

Baker, Rhoda, National Resource Center for Youth Services (NRCYS), Schusterman Center, 4502 E 41 St, Bldg 4W, Tulsa, OK 74135-2512 *Tel:* 918-660-3700 *Toll Free Tel:* 800-274-2687 *Fax:* 918-660-3737 *Web Site:* www.nrcys.ou.edu, pg 185

Baker, Richard, Baker Books, PO Box 6287, Grand Rapids, MI 49516-6287 *Tel:* 616-676-9185 *Toll Free Tel:* 800-877-2665; 800-679-1957 *Fax:* 616-676-9573 *Toll Free Fax:* 800-398-3110 *Web Site:* www.bakerpublishinggroup.com, pg 30

Baker-Harris, Sharon, American Foundation for the Blind (AFB Press), 11 Penn Plaza, Suite 300, New York, NY 10001 *Tel:* 212-502-7600 *Toll Free Tel:* 800-232-3044 (orders) *Fax:* 212-502-7777 *E-mail:* afbinfo@afb.net *Web Site:* www.afb.org, pg 13

Bakhtiar, Mary, Kazi Publications Inc, 3023 W Belmont Ave, Chicago, IL 60618 *Tel:* 773-267-7001 *Fax:* 773-267-7002 *E-mail:* info@kazi.org *Web Site:* www.kazi. org/, pg 144

Bakke, Timothy O, Creative Homeowner, 24 Park Way, Upper Saddle River, NJ 07458-9960 *Tel:* 201-934-7100 *Toll Free Tel:* 800-631-7795 *Fax:* 201-934-8971 *E-mail:* info@creativehomeowner.com *Web Site:* www.creativehomeowner.com, pg 72

Baldacci, Matthew, St Martin's Press Trade Division, 175 Fifth Ave, New York, NY 10010 *E-mail:* firstname.lastname@stmartins.com *Web Site:* www.stmartins.com; www.minotaurbooks. com, pg 239

Baldi, Malaga, Malaga Baldi Literary Agency, 233 W 99, Suite 19C, New York, NY 10025 *Tel:* 212-222-3213 *E-mail:* mbaldi@nyc.rr.com, pg 620

Balding, David, Metamorphous Press, 265 N Hancock St, Portland, OR 97227 *Tel:* 503-228-4972 *Toll Free Tel:* 800-937-7771 (orders only) *Fax:* 503-223-9117 *E-mail:* metabooks@metamodels.com *Web Site:* www.metamodels.com, pg 172

Baldwin, Margo, Chelsea Green Publishing Co, PO Box 428, White River Junction, VT 05001-0428 *Tel:* 802-295-6300 *Toll Free Tel:* 800-639-4099 (cust serv & consumer orders); 800-807-6726 (trade & wholesale orders) *Fax:* 802-295-6444 *Web Site:* www.chelseagreen.com, pg 59

Baliszewsky, Robin, Prentice Hall Career, Health, Education & Technology, One Lake St, Upper Saddle River, NJ 07458 *Tel:* 201-236-7000 *Fax:* 201-236-7755, pg 217

Balkin, Richard A, The Balkin Agency Inc, PO Box 222, Amherst, MA 01004 *Tel:* 413-548-9835 *Fax:* 413-548-9836, pg 620

Ball, Andy, Alloy Entertainment, 151 W 26 St, 11th fl, New York, NY 10001 *Tel:* 212-244-4307, pg 9

Ball, John, DK Publishing Inc, 375 Hudson St, 2nd fl, New York, NY 10014-3672 *Tel:* 212-213-4800 *Toll Free Tel:* 877-342-5357 (cust serv) *Fax:* 212-213-5202 *Web Site:* www.dk.com, pg 81

Ball, Linda, Creative Publishing International Inc, 18705 Lake Dr E, Chanhassen, MN 55317 *Tel:* 952-936-4700 *Toll Free Tel:* 800-328-0590 (sales) *Fax:* 952-933-1456 *Web Site:* www.creativepub.com, pg 72

Ballantyne, Robert, Arsenal Pulp Press Book Publishers Ltd, 1014 Homer St, Suite 103, Vancouver, BC V6B 2W9, Canada *Tel:* 604-687-4233 *Toll Free Tel:* 888-600-PULP (600-7857) *Fax:* 604-687-4283 *E-mail:* contact@arsenalpulp.com *Web Site:* www. arsenalpulp.com, pg 536

Ballard, Amanda, Grace Associates, 945 Fourth Ave, Suite 200-A, Huntington, WV 25701 *Tel:* 304-697-3236 *Fax:* 304-697-3399 *E-mail:* publish@cloh.net *Web Site:* www.booksbygrace.com, pg 600

Ballard, John, World Citizens, 96 La Verne Ave, Mill Valley, CA 94941 *Tel:* 415-380-8020 *Toll Free Tel:* 800-247-6553 (orders only) *Web Site:* soultosoulmedia.com; skateman.com, pg 304

Ballard, Mike, Meadowbrook Press, 5451 Smetana Dr, Minnetonka, MN 55343 *Tel:* 952-930-1100 *Toll Free Tel:* 800-338-2232 *Fax:* 952-930-1940 *Web Site:* www. meadowbrookpress.com, pg 169

Ballast, Matthew, Bulfinch Press, 1271 Avenue of the Americas, New York, NY 10020 *Tel:* 212-522-8700 *Toll Free Tel:* 800-759-0190 *Fax:* 212-467-2886 *Web Site:* www.twbookmark.com, pg 50

Ballentine, Lee, Ocean View Books, PO Box 9249, Denver, CO 80209-0246 *Tel:* 303-756-5222 *Toll Free Tel:* 800-848-6222 (orders only) *Fax:* 303-756-3208 *E-mail:* ocean@probook.net *Web Site:* www.probook. net/ocean.html, pg 195

Balliett, Will, Avalon Publishing Group Inc, 1400 65 St, Suite 250, Emeryville, CA 94608 *Tel:* 510-595-3664 *Fax:* 510-535-4228 *Web Site:* www.avalonpub.com, pg 29

Balliett, Will, Carroll & Graf Publishers, 245 W 17 St, 11th fl, New York, NY 10011-5300 *Tel:* 646-375-2570 *Fax:* 646-375-2571 *Web Site:* www.carrollandgraf.com, pg 54

Ballinger, Malcolm, Ballinger Publishing, 41 N Jefferson St, Suite 300, Pensacola, FL 32501 *Tel:* 850-433-1166 *Fax:* 850-435-9174 *E-mail:* info@ballingerpublishing. com *Web Site:* www.ballingerpublishing.com, pg 31

Ballinger, Peter R, P R B Productions, 963 Peralta Ave, Albany, CA 94706-2144 *Tel:* 510-526-0722 *Fax:* 510-527-4763 *E-mail:* prbprdns@aol.com *Web Site:* www. prbmusic.com; www.prbpro.com, pg 201

Balmuth, Deborah, Storey Books, 210 Mass MoCA Way, North Adams, MA 01247 *Tel:* 413-346-2100 *Toll Free Tel:* 800-793-9396 *Fax:* 413-346-2253 *E-mail:* info@ storey.com *Web Site:* www.storey.com, pg 260

Balog, Dennis, Time Warner Book Group, 1271 Avenue of the Americas, New York, NY 10020 *Tel:* 212-522-7200 *Fax:* 212-522-7991 *Web Site:* www.twbookmark. com, pg 271

Balow, Dan, Tyndale House Publishers Inc, 351 Executive Dr, Carol Stream, IL 60188 *Tel:* 630-668-8303 *Toll Free Tel:* 800-323-9400 *Web Site:* www. tyndale.com, pg 277

Balsamo, Kathy, Pieces of Learning, 1990 Market Rd, Marion, IL 62959-8976 *Tel:* 618-964-9426 *Toll Free Tel:* 800-729-5137 *Toll Free Fax:* 800-844-0455 *E-mail:* polmarion@midamer.net *Web Site:* www. piecesoflearning.com, pg 212

Balsamo, Stan, Pieces of Learning, 1990 Market Rd, Marion, IL 62959-8976 *Tel:* 618-964-9426 *Toll Free Tel:* 800-729-5137 *Toll Free Fax:* 800-844-0455 *E-mail:* polmarion@midamer.net *Web Site:* www. piecesoflearning.com, pg 212

Balter, Katya, The Spieler Agency, 154 W 57 St, 13th fl, Rm 135, New York, NY 10019 *Tel:* 212-757-4439 *Web Site:* spieleragency.com, pg 656

Balvenie, K, One Act Play Depot, 132 Memorial Dr, Spiritwood, SK S0J 2M0, Canada *E-mail:* plays@ oneactplays.net; orders@oneactplays.net *Web Site:* oneactplays.net, pg 556

Balzer, Paula, Sarah Lazin Books, 126 Fifth Ave, Suite 300, New York, NY 10011 *Tel:* 212-989-5757 *Fax:* 212-989-1393, pg 640

Bamford, Chris, Lindisfarne Books, PO Box 58, Hudson, NY 12534 *Tel:* 413-528-8233 *Toll Free Tel:* 800-856-8664 (orders) *Fax:* 413-528-8826; 703-661-1501 (orders) *E-mail:* service@lindisfarne.org *Web Site:* www.lindisfarne.org, pg 155

Bamford, Christopher, Steiner Books, PO Box 799, Great Barrington, MA 01230-0799 *Tel:* 413-528-8233 *Fax:* 413-528-8826 *E-mail:* service@anthropress.org *Web Site:* www.anthropress.org, pg 258

Banchs, William H, Arts Recognition & Talent Search (ARTS), 444 Brickell Ave, Suite P14, Miami, FL 33131 *Tel:* 305-377-1140 *Toll Free Tel:* 800-970-2787 *Fax:* 305-377-1149 *E-mail:* nfaa@nfaa.org *Web Site:* www.artsawards.org, pg 760

Bancroft, Carol, Carol Bancroft & Friends, 121 Dodgingtown Rd, Bethel, CT 06801 *Tel:* 203-748-4823 *Toll Free Tel:* 800-720-7020 *Fax:* 203-748-4581 *E-mail:* artists@carolbancroft.com *Web Site:* www. carolbancroft.com, pg 665

Bandstra, Judy, Christian Schools International, 3350 E Paris Ave SE, Grand Rapids, MI 49512-3054 *Tel:* 616-957-1070 *Toll Free Tel:* 800-635-8288 *Fax:* 616-957-5022 *E-mail:* info@csionline.org *Web Site:* www. csionline.org, pg 61

Banis, Robert J, Science & Humanities Press, 1023 Stuyvesant Lane, Manchester, MO 63011-3601 *Tel:* 636-394-4950 *E-mail:* publisher@sciencehumanitiespress. com *Web Site:* sciencehumanitiespress.com; beachhousebooks.com; macroprintbooks.com; earlyeditionsbooks.com; heuristicsbooks.com, pg 243

Banker, Rhea, Pearson Education/ELT, 10 Bank St, 9th fl, White Plains, NY 10606 *Tel:* 914-993-5000 *Fax:* 914-993-8115 *E-mail:* firstname.lastname@ pearsoned.com, pg 206

Bankoff, Lisa, International Creative Management, 40 W 57 St, New York, NY 10019 *Tel:* 212-556-5600 *Fax:* 212-556-5665 *Web Site:* www.icmtalent.com, pg 635

Banks, Janet, JIST Publishing Inc, 8902 Otis Ave, Indianapolis, IN 46216 *Tel:* 317-613-4200 *Toll Free Tel:* 800-648-5478 *Fax:* 317-613-4304 *Toll Free Fax:* 800-547-8329 *E-mail:* info@jist.com *Web Site:* www.jist.com, pg 141

Banks, Leslie, Dearborn Trade Publishing, 30 S Wacker Dr, Chicago, IL 60606-1719 *Tel:* 312-836-4400 *Fax:* 312-836-1021 *E-mail:* contactus@dearborn.com *Web Site:* www.dearborn.com, pg 78

Banks, Toni, Lawrence Jordan Literary Agency, 345 W 121 St, New York, NY 10027 *Tel:* 212-662-7871 *Fax:* 212-662-8138 *E-mail:* ljlagency@aol.com, pg 636

Banner, Robert, CRC Publications, 2850 Kalamazoo Ave SE, Grand Rapids, MI 49560 *Tel:* 616-224-0819; 616-224-0728 *Toll Free Tel:* 800-333-8300 *Fax:* 616-224-0834 *E-mail:* sales@crcpublications.org *Web Site:* www.faithaliveresources.org, pg 72

Bannon, Joseph J Sr, Sagamore Publishing LLC, 804 N Neil St, Champaign, IL 61820 *Tel:* 217-359-5940 *Toll Free Tel:* 800-327-5557 (orders) *Fax:* 217-359-5975 *E-mail:* books@sagamorepub.com *Web Site:* www. sagamorepub.com, pg 237

Bannon, Joseph J Sr, Sports Publishing LLC, 804 N Neil St, Champaign, IL 61820 *Tel:* 217-363-2072 *Toll Free Tel:* 877-424-BOOK (424-2665) *Fax:* 217-363-2073 *E-mail:* marketing@sportspublishingllc.com *Web Site:* www.sportspublishingllc.com, pg 256

Bannon, Peter L, Sagamore Publishing LLC, 804 N Neil St, Champaign, IL 61820 *Tel:* 217-359-5940 *Toll Free Tel:* 800-327-5557 (orders) *Fax:* 217-359-5975 *E-mail:* books@sagamorepub.com *Web Site:* www. sagamorepub.com, pg 237

Bannon, Peter L, Sports Publishing LLC, 804 N Neil St, Champaign, IL 61820 *Tel:* 217-363-2072 *Toll Free Tel:* 877-424-BOOK (424-2665) *Fax:* 217-363-2073 *E-mail:* marketing@sportspublishingllc.com *Web Site:* www.sportspublishingllc.com, pg 256

Baraheni, Reza, PEN Canada, 24 Ryerson Ave, Suite 214, Toronto, ON M5T 2P3, Canada *Tel:* 416-703-8448 *Fax:* 416-703-3870 *E-mail:* pen@pencanada.ca *Web Site:* www.pencanada.ca, pg 696

Baran, Maya, Walker & Co, 104 Fifth Ave, 7th fl, New York, NY 10011 *Tel:* 212-727-8300 *Toll Free Tel:* 800-289-2553 *Fax:* 212-727-0984 *Toll Free Fax:* 800-218-9367 *E-mail:* firstinitiallastname@ walkerbooks.com *Web Site:* www.walkerbooks.com, pg 292

Baranofsky, Michael, Hendrickson Publishers Inc, PO Box 3473, Peabody, MA 01961-3473 *Tel:* 978-532-6546 *Toll Free Tel:* 800-358-3111 *Fax:* 978-531-8146 *E-mail:* orders@hendrickson.com *Web Site:* www. hendrickson.com, pg 121

Barba, Christine, Time Warner Book Group, 1271 Avenue of the Americas, New York, NY 10020 *Tel:* 212-522-7200 *Fax:* 212-522-7991 *Web Site:* www. twbookmark.com, pg 271

Barba, Greg, Harian Creative Books, 47 Hyde Blvd, Ballston Spa, NY 12020-1607 *Tel:* 518-885-6699; 518-885-7397, pg 115

Barba, Harry, Harian Creative Awards, 47 Hyde Blvd, Ballston Spa, NY 12020-1607 *Tel:* 518-885-6699; 518-885-7397, pg 777

Barba, Harry, Harian Creative Books, 47 Hyde Blvd, Ballston Spa, NY 12020-1607 *Tel:* 518-885-6699; 518-885-7397, pg 115

Barbee, Michael, Kalmbach Publishing Co, 21027 Crossroads Circle, Waukesha, WI 53187 *Tel:* 262-796-8776 *Toll Free Tel:* 800-533-6644 *Fax:* 262-796-1615 (sales & cust serv) *Web Site:* www.kalmbach.com, pg 143

Barber, A Richard, A Richard Barber & Associates, 554 E 82 St, New York, NY 10028 *Tel:* 212-737-7266 *Fax:* 212-879-0183 *E-mail:* barberrich@aol.com, pg 620

Barber, Edwin, W W Norton & Company Inc, 500 Fifth Ave, New York, NY 10110-0017 *Tel:* 212-354-5500 *Toll Free Tel:* 800-233-4830 (orders & cust serv) *Fax:* 212-869-0856 *Toll Free Fax:* 800-458-6515 *Web Site:* www.wwnorton.com, pg 193

Barber, Orion M, Orion Book Services, 751 South St, West Brattleboro, VT 05301-4234 *Tel:* 802-254-2340 *Fax:* 802-254-2340 *E-mail:* gr8books@sover.net, pg 607

Barber, Richard, Boydell & Brewer Inc, 668 Mount Hope Ave, University of Rochester, Rochester, NY 14620 *Tel:* 585-275-0419 *Fax:* 585-271-8778 *Web Site:* www.boydellandbrewer.co.uk, pg 45

Barber, Virginia, William Morris Agency, 1325 Avenue of the Americas, New York, NY 10019 *Tel:* 212-586-5100 *Fax:* 212-903-1418 *E-mail:* wma@interport.net *Web Site:* www.wma.com, pg 645

Barbor, Dave, Curtis Brown Ltd, 10 Astor Place, New York, NY 10003 *Tel:* 212-473-5400, pg 623

Barbour, Bruce R, Literary Management Group Inc, 4238 Morriswood Dr, Nashville, TN 37204 *Tel:* 615-832-7231 *Fax:* 615-832-7231 *Web Site:* www. literarymanagementgroup.com; www.brucebarbour. com, pg 641

Barbour, John, Playmore Inc, Publishers, 230 Fifth Ave, Suite 711, New York, NY 10001 *Tel:* 212-251-0600 *Fax:* 212-251-0966 *Web Site:* playmorebooks.com, pg 214

Barbour, Matthew, Omnigraphics Inc, 615 Griswold St, Detroit, MI 48226 *Tel:* 313-961-1340 *Toll Free Tel:* 800-234-1340 (cust serv) *Fax:* 313-961-1383 *Toll Free Fax:* 800-875-1340 (cust serv) *E-mail:* info@ omnigraphics.com *Web Site:* www.omnigraphics.com, pg 197

Barbour, Wanda, American Industrial Hygiene Association, 2700 Prosperity Ave, Suite 250, Fairfax, VA 22031-4319 *Tel:* 703-849-8888 *Fax:* 703-207-3561 *E-mail:* infonet@aiha.org *Web Site:* www.aiha.org, pg 14

Barcelona, James D, Pro Quest Information & Learning, 300 N Zeeb Rd, Ann Arbor, MI 48106-1346 Tel: 734-761-4700 Toll Free Tel: 800-521-0600 Fax: 734-975-6486 Toll Free Fax: 800-864-0019 E-mail: info@il.proquest.com Web Site: www.il.proquest.com, pg 219

Barchers, Suzanne, Teacher Ideas Press, 361 Hanover St, Portsmouth, NH 03801-3912 Toll Free Tel: 800-225-5800 Fax: 603-431-2214 Toll Free Fax: 800-354-2004 (perms & foreign rts) E-mail: custserv@teacherideaspress.com; permissions@teacherideaspress.com; foreignrights@teacherideaspress.com Web Site: www.teacherideaspress.com, pg 265

Barclay, Barbara, LexisNexis Academic & Library Solutions, 7500 Old Georgetown Rd, Suite 1300, Bethesda, MD 20814-3389 Tel: 301-654-1550 Toll Free Tel: 800-638-8380 Fax: 301-654-4033; 301-657-3203 (sales) E-mail: academicinfo@lexisnexis.com Web Site: www.lexisnexis.com/academic, pg 153

Barclay, Ellen, Fulbright Scholar Program, 3007 Tilden St NW, Suite 5-L, Washington, DC 20008-3009 Tel: 202-686-4000 Fax: 202-362-3442 E-mail: cieswebmaster@cies.iie.org Web Site: www.cies.org, pg 775

Bard, Scott, Longstreet Press, 325 N Milledge Ave, Athens, GA 30601 Tel: 706-543-5999 Fax: 706-543-5946 Web Site: www.longstreetpress.net, pg 158

Barden, Amy, Women's National Book Association Inc, c/o Susannah·Greenberg Public Relations, 2166 Broadway, Suite 9-E, New York, NY 10024 Tel: 212-208-4629 Fax: 212-208-4629 E-mail: publicity@bookbuzz.com Web Site: www.wnba-books.org, pg 702

Bareille, Marie, American Institute of Certified Public Accountants, Harborside Financial Ctr, 201 Plaza Three, Jersey City, NJ 07311-3881 Tel: 201-938-3000 Toll Free Tel: 888-777-7077 Fax: 201-938-3329 Web Site: www.aicpa.org, pg 15

Barendsma, Cecile, Janklow & Nesbit Associates, 445 Park Ave, New York, NY 10022 Tel: 212-421-1700 Fax: 212-980-3671 E-mail: postmaster@janklow.com, pg 636

Barer, Julie, Sanford J Greenburger Associates Inc, 55 Fifth Ave, 15th fl, New York, NY 10003 Tel: 212-206-5600 Fax: 212-463-8718 Web Site: www.greenburger.com, pg 633

Barer-Stein, Thelma PhD, Culture Concepts Books, 69 Ashmount Crescent, Toronto, ON M9R 1C9, Canada Tel: 416-245-8119 Fax: 416-245-3383 E-mail: cultureconcepts@sympatico.ca Web Site: www.cultureconcepts.ca, pg 595

Barger, Jack, Sophia Institute Press, PO Box 5284, Manchester, NH 03108 Tel: 603-641-9344 Toll Free Tel: 800-888-9344 Fax: 603-641-8108 Toll Free Fax: 888-288-2259 E-mail: orders@sophiainstitute.com Web Site: www.sophiainstitute.com, pg 253

Barger, John L, Sophia Institute Press, PO Box 5284, Manchester, NH 03108 Tel: 603-641-9344 Toll Free Tel: 800-888-9344 Fax: 603-641-8108 Toll Free Fax: 888-288-2259 E-mail: orders@sophiainstitute.com Web Site: www.sophiainstitute.com, pg 253

Barkan, Bebe, Cross-Cultural Communications, 239 Wynsum Ave, Merrick, NY 11566-4725 Tel: 516-868-5635 Fax: 516-379-1901 E-mail: cccpoetry@aol.com Web Site: www.cross-culturalcommunications.com, pg 73

Barkan, Stanley H, Cross-Cultural Communications, 239 Wynsum Ave, Merrick, NY 11566-4725 Tel: 516-868-5635 Fax: 516-379-1901 E-mail: cccpoetry@aol.com Web Site: www.cross-culturalcommunications.com, pg 73

Barke, William, Addison Wesley Higher Education Group, 75 Arlington St, Boston, MA 02116 Tel: 617-848-7500 Fax: 617-848-6016 E-mail: firstname.lastname@pearsoned.com Web Site: www.awl.com, pg 5

Barker, B D, The Wilson Devereux Co, 5 Ledyard St, 2nd fl, Newport, RI 02840 Tel: 401-846-8081 E-mail: bdb4@wildev.com Web Site: www.wildev.com, pg 661

Barker, David, The Continuum International Publishing Group, 15 E 26 St, Suite 1703, New York, NY 10010 Tel: 212-953-5858 Toll Free Tel: 800-561-7704 Fax: 212-953-5944 E-mail: info@continuum-books.com Web Site: www.continuumbooks.com, pg 67

Barker, Karen, IODE Book Award, 40 St Clair Ave E, Suite 205, Toronto, ON M4T 1M9, Canada Tel: 416-925-5078 Fax: 416-925-5127, pg 758

Barker, Laura J, WaterBrook Press, 2375 Telstar Dr, Suite 160, Colorado Springs, CO 80920 Tel: 719-590-4999 Toll Free Tel: 800-603-7051 (orders) Fax: 719-590-8977 Toll Free Fax: 800-294-5686 (orders) Web Site: www.waterbrookpress.com, pg 294

Barker, Rebeccah, Charisma House, 600 Rinehart Rd, Lake Mary, FL 32746 Tel: 407-333-0600 (all imprints) Toll Free Tel: 800-283-8494 (Charisma House, Siloam Press, Creation House Press); 800-665-1468 Fax: 407-333-7100 (all imprints) E-mail: webmaster@charismahouse.com; webmaster@creationhouse.com Web Site: www.charismamag.com; www.strang.com (all imprints), pg 58

Barker, Wayne G, Aegean Park Press, PO Box 2120, Walnut Creek, CA 94595 Tel: 925-947-2533 Toll Free Tel: 800-736-3587 (orders only) Fax: 925-947-2144 E-mail: books@aegeanparkpress.com Web Site: www.aegeanparkpress.com, pg 6

Barkman, Donna, Jane Addams Children's Book Award, 777 United Nations Plaza, New York, NY 10017 Tel: 212-682-8830 Fax: 212-682-8211 E-mail: japa@igc.org Web Site: www.janeaddamspeace.org, pg 757

Barksdale, Calvert, Arcade Publishing Inc, 141 Fifth Ave, New York, NY 10010 Tel: 212-475-2633 Fax: 212-353-8148 E-mail: arcadeinfo@arcadepub.com Web Site: www.arcadepub.com, pg 22

Barna, Matt, The Dawn Horse Press, 12040 N Seigler Rd, Middletown, CA 95461 Tel: 707-928-6590 Toll Free Tel: 877-770-0772 Fax: 707-928-5068 E-mail: dhp@adidam.org Web Site: www.dawnhorsepress.com, pg 77

Barnas, Ed, Cambridge University Press, 40 W 20 St, New York, NY 10011-4211 Tel: 212-924-3900 Toll Free Tel: 800-899-5222 Fax: 212-691-3239 Web Site: www.cambridge.org, pg 52

Barnes, Jacqueline, BuilderBooks.com, 1201 15 St NW, Washington, DC 20005-2800 Tel: 202-822-0200; 202-266-8200 Toll Free Tel: 800-223-2665 (orders); 800-368-5242 ext 8368 (editorial) Fax: 202-266-8096 (edit); 202-266-5889 (edit) Web Site: www.builderbooks.com, pg 49

Barnes, Janet, Bentley Publishers, 1734 Massachusetts Ave, Cambridge, MA 02138 Tel: 617-547-4170 Toll Free Tel: 800-423-4595 Fax: 617-876-9235 E-mail: sales@bentleypublishers.com Web Site: www.bentleypublishers.com, pg 36

Barnes, Jim, The Independent Publisher Book Awards, 400 W Front St, Suite 4-A, Traverse City, MI 49684 Tel: 231-933-0445 Toll Free Tel: 800-706-4636 Fax: 231-933-0448, pg 779

Barnes, Jim, Jenkins Group Inc, 400 W Front St, Suite 4-A, Traverse City, MI 49684 Tel: 231-933-0445 Toll Free Tel: 800-706-4636 Fax: 231-933-0448 E-mail: info@bookpublishing.com Web Site: www.bookpublishing.com, pg 602

Barnes, Juliet, Other Press LLC, 307 Seventh Ave, Suite 1807, New York, NY 10001 Tel: 212-414-0054 Toll Free Tel: 877-843-6843 Fax: 212-414-0939 E-mail: editor@otherpress.com; orders@otherpress.com Web Site: www.otherpress.com, pg 199

Barnes, Juliet, Other Press LLC, 307 Seventh Ave, Suite 1807, New York, NY 10001 Tel: 212-414-0054 Toll Free Tel: 877-THE-OTHER Fax: 212-414-0939 E-mail: orders@otherpress.com Web Site: www.otherpress.com, pg 573

Barnes, Mary M, Canyon Country Publications, PO Box 963, Moab, UT 84532-0963 Tel: 435-259-6700, pg 52

Barnett, John, The Shoe String Press Inc, 2 Linsley St, North Haven, CT 06473 Tel: 203-239-2702 Fax: 203-239-2568 E-mail: info@shoestringpress.com; books@shoestringpress.com Web Site: www.shoestringpress.com, pg 246

Barnett, Laura, Oakstone Medical Publishing, 6801 Cahaba Valley Rd, Birmingham, AL 35242 Tel: 205-991-5188 Toll Free Tel: 800-952-0690 Fax: 205-995-4656 E-mail: service@oakstonemedical.com Web Site: www.oakstonemedical.com, pg 195

Barnum, Prof Jill PhD, The Melville Society, University of Minnesota, 140 Appleby Hall, Minneapolis, MN 55455 Fax: 612-625-0709, pg 691

Barocci, Bob, Advertising Research Foundation, 641 Lexington Ave, New York, NY 10022 Tel: 212-751-5656 Fax: 212-319-5265 E-mail: info@thearf.org Web Site: www.thearf.org, pg 675

Baron, Carol, G P Putnam's Sons (Hardcover), 375 Hudson St, New York, NY 10014 Tel: 212-366-2000 E-mail: online@penguinputnam.com Web Site: www.penguin.com, pg 223

Baron, Carole, Dutton, 375 Hudson St, New York, NY 10014 Tel: 212-366-2000 Fax: 212-366-2262 E-mail: online@penguinputnam.com Web Site: www.penguin.com, pg 85

Baron, Carole, Penguin Group (USA) Inc, 375 Hudson St, New York, NY 10014 Tel: 212-366-2000 Fax: 212-366-2666 E-mail: online@uspenguingroup.com Web Site: www.penguin.com, pg 208

Baron, Ed, Sable Publishing, 365 N Saturmino Dr, Suite 21, Palm Springs, CA 92262 Tel: 760-408-1881 E-mail: sablepublishing@aol.com Web Site: www.sablepublishing.com, pg 236

Baron, Herman, DIANE Publishing Co, 330 Pusey Ave, Suite 3 rear, Collingdale, PA 19023 Tel: 610-461-6200 Toll Free Tel: 800-782-3833 Fax: 610-461-6130 E-mail: dianepub@comcast.net Web Site: www.dianepublishingcentral.com, pg 80

Baron, Robert C, Fulcrum Publishing Inc, 16100 Table Mountain Pkwy, Suite 300, Golden, CO 80403 Tel: 303-277-1623 Toll Free Tel: 800-992-2908 Fax: 303-279-7111 Toll Free Fax: 800-726-7112 E-mail: fulcrum@fulcrum-books.com Web Site: www.fulcrum-books.com, pg 101

Baror, Danny, Baror International Inc, 831 Mount Kisco Rd, Armonk, NY 10504 Tel: 914-273-9199 Fax: 914-273-5058 E-mail: barorint@aol.com, pg 620

Barr, Pamela, The Metropolitan Museum of Art, 1000 Fifth Ave, New York, NY 10028 Tel: 212-879-5500; 212-535-7710 Fax: 212-396-5062 E-mail: info@metmuseum.org Web Site: www.metmuseum.org, pg 173

Barr, Wayne, Barron's Educational Series Inc, 250 Wireless Blvd, Hauppauge, NY 11788 Tel: 631-434-3311 Toll Free Tel: 800-645-3476 Fax: 631-434-3723 E-mail: info@barronseduc.com Web Site: www.barronseduc.com (Books can be purchased online), pg 32

Barrable, Susan, Madison Press Books, 1000 Yonge St, Toronto, ON M4W 2K2, Canada Tel: 416-923-5027 Fax: 416-923-9708 E-mail: info@madisonpressbooks.com Web Site: www.madisonpressbooks.com, pg 553

Barras, Lise, Editions du renouveau Pedagogique Inc, 5757 rue Cypihot, St-Laurent, PQ H4S 1R3, Canada Tel: 514-334-2690 Toll Free Tel: 800-263-3678 Fax: 514-334-4720 Toll Free Fax: 800-643-4720 E-mail: erpidlm@erpi.com Web Site: www.erpi.com, pg 544

Barrett, Edward J, Chandler & Sharp Publishers Inc, 11 Commercial Blvd, Suite A, Novato, CA 94949 Tel: 415-883-2353 Fax: 415-440-5004 Web Site: www.chandlersharp.com, pg 58

Barrett, Laura G, Templeton Foundation Press, 5 Radnor Corporate Ctr, Suite 120, 100 Matsonford Rd, Radnor, PA 19087 Tel: 610-971-2670 Toll Free Tel: 800-561-3367 Fax: 610-971-2672 E-mail: tfp@templetonpress.org Web Site: www.templetonpress.org, pg 266

Barrett, Linda, The Fisherman Library, 1622 Beaver Dam Rd, Point Pleasant, NJ 08742 Tel: 732-295-8600 Fax: 732-295-4162, pg 97

Barrett, Loretta A, Loretta Barrett Books Inc, 101 Fifth Ave, New York, NY 10003 *Tel:* 212-242-3420 *Fax:* 212-807-9579, pg 620

Barrett, Mark, Blackwell Publishing Professional, 2121 State Ave, Ames, IA 50014 *Tel:* 515-292-0140 *Toll Free Tel:* 800-862-6657 (orders only) *Fax:* 515-292-3348 *Web Site:* www.blackwellprofessional.com, pg 40

Barrett, Paul, Socrates Media, 227 W Monroe St, Suite 500, Chicago, IL 60606 *Tel:* 312-762-5600 *Toll Free Tel:* 800-822-4566 *Web Site:* www.socrates.com, pg 252

Barrett, Pete, The Fisherman Library, 1622 Beaver Dam Rd, Point Pleasant, NJ 08742 *Tel:* 732-295-8600 *Fax:* 732-295-4162, pg 97

Barrett, Ruth Macauley, Templeton Foundation Press, 5 Radnor Corporate Ctr, Suite 120, 100 Matsonford Rd, Radnor, PA 19087 *Tel:* 610-971-2670 *Toll Free Tel:* 800-561-3367 *Fax:* 610-971-2672 *E-mail:* tfp@ templetonpress.org *Web Site:* www.templetonpress.org, pg 266

Barrett, Sheila, Harvard University Press, 79 Garden St, Cambridge, MA 02138-1499 *Tel:* 617-495-2600; 401-531-2800 (international orders) *Toll Free Tel:* 800-405-1619 (orders) *Fax:* 617-495-5898 (general); 617-496-4677 (edit & rts); 401-531-2801 (international orders) *Toll Free Fax:* 800-406-9145 (orders) *E-mail:* firstname_lastname@harvard.edu *Web Site:* www.hup.harvard.edu, pg 117

Barrick, Peter, BNI Publications Inc, 1612 S Clementine St, Anaheim, CA 92802 *Tel:* 714-517-0970 *Toll Free Tel:* 800-873-6397 *Fax:* 714-535-8078 *Web Site:* www.bnibooks.com, pg 42

Barriere, Marie-Clark, Editions de l'Hexagone, 1010, rue de la Gauchetiere Est, Montreal, PQ H2L 2N5, Canada *Tel:* 514-523-1182 *Fax:* 514-282-7530 *E-mail:* vml@sogides.com *Web Site:* www.edhexagone.com, pg 544

Barron, Don, Art Direction Book Co Inc, 456 Glenbrook Rd, Glenbrook, CT 06906 *Tel:* 203-353-1441 *Fax:* 203-353-1371, pg 24

Barron, Manuel H, Barron's Educational Series Inc, 250 Wireless Blvd, Hauppauge, NY 11788 *Tel:* 631-434-3311 *Toll Free Tel:* 800-645-3476 *Fax:* 631-434-3723 *E-mail:* info@barronseduc.com *Web Site:* www.barronseduc.com (Books can be purchased online), pg 32

Barrosse, Emily, McGraw-Hill Humanities, Social Sciences, Languages, 2 Penn Plaza, 20th fl, New York, NY 10121 *Tel:* 212-904-2000 *Toll Free Tel:* 800-338-3987 (cust serv) *Fax:* 614-755-5645 (cust serv) *E-mail:* first name_last name@mcgraw-hill.com *Web Site:* www.mhhe.com, pg 168

Barrosse, Emily, Saunders College Publishing, The Public Ledger Bldg, 150 S Independence Mall W, Suite 1250, Philadelphia, PA 19106-3412 *Tel:* 215-238-5500 *Fax:* 215-238-5660 *Web Site:* www.hbcollege.com, pg 240

Barry, Mindy, Paulist Press, 997 Macarthur Blvd, Mahwah, NJ 07430 *Tel:* 201-825-7300 *Toll Free Tel:* 800-218-1903 *Fax:* 201-825-8345 *Toll Free Fax:* 800-836-3161 (orders) *E-mail:* info@paulistpress.com *Web Site:* www.paulistpress.com, pg 206

Barry, Sheila, Kids Can Press Ltd, 29 Birch Ave, Toronto, ON M4V 1E2, Canada *Tel:* 416-925-5437 *Toll Free Tel:* 800-265-0884 *Fax:* 416-960-5437 *E-mail:* info@kidscan.com *Web Site:* kidscanpress.com, pg 552

Barry, Susan, The Barry-Swayne Literary Agency, 4 Manitou Rd, Garrison, NY 10524 *Tel:* 845-424-2448 *E-mail:* info@swayneagency.com *Web Site:* www.swayneagency.com, pg 620

Barry, William, DK Publishing Inc, 375 Hudson St, 2nd fl, New York, NY 10014-3672 *Tel:* 212-213-4800 *Toll Free Tel:* 877-342-5357 (cust serv) *Fax:* 212-213-5202 *Web Site:* www.dk.com, pg 81

Barslin, Janette, Socrates Media, 227 W Monroe St, Suite 500, Chicago, IL 60606 *Tel:* 312-762-5600 *Toll Free Tel:* 800-822-4566 *Web Site:* www.socrates.com, pg 252

Barsotti, Sylvia, e-Scholastic, 568 Broadway, 9th fl, New York, NY 10012 *Tel:* 212-343-7100 *Fax:* 212-343-4949, pg 85

Barstow, John, W W Norton & Company Inc, 500 Fifth Ave, New York, NY 10110-0017 *Tel:* 212-354-5500 *Toll Free Tel:* 800-233-4830 (orders & cust serv) *Fax:* 212-869-0856 *Toll Free Fax:* 800-458-6515 *Web Site:* www.wwnorton.com, pg 193

Bart, Istvan, Central European University Press, 400 W 59 St, New York, NY 10019 *Tel:* 212-547-6932 *Fax:* 646-557-2416 *Web Site:* www.ceupress.com, pg 57

Bartell, Dan, W W Norton & Company Inc, 500 Fifth Ave, New York, NY 10110-0017 *Tel:* 212-354-5500 *Toll Free Tel:* 800-233-4830 (orders & cust serv) *Fax:* 212-869-0856 *Toll Free Fax:* 800-458-6515 *Web Site:* www.wwnorton.com, pg 193

Barth, Ilene, Red Rock Press, 459 Columbus Ave, Suite 114, New York, NY 10024 *Tel:* 212-362-6216 *Fax:* 212-362-6216 *E-mail:* info@redrockpress.com *Web Site:* www.redrockpress.com, pg 229

Barth, Jennifer, Henry Holt and Company, LLC, 115 W 18 St, New York, NY 10011 *Tel:* 212-886-9200 *Toll Free Tel:* 888-330-8477 (orders) *Fax:* 212-633-0748 *E-mail:* publicity@hholt.com *Web Site:* www.henryholt.com, pg 124

Barthelme, Frederick, Mississippi Review/University of Southern Mississippi, Center for Writers, Box 5144 USM, Hattiesburg, MS 39406 *Tel:* 601-266-5600 *Fax:* 601-266-5757 *E-mail:* rief@mississippireview.com *Web Site:* www.mississippireview.com; www.centerforwriters.com, pg 753

Bartol, Nancy, Kalmbach Publishing Co, 21027 Crossroads Circle, Waukesha, WI 53187 *Tel:* 262-796-8776 *Toll Free Tel:* 800-533-6644 *Fax:* 262-796-1615 (sales & cust serv) *Web Site:* www.kalmbach.com, pg 143

Barton, Laurence, American College, 270 S Bryn Mawr Ave, Bryn Mawr, PA 19010 *Tel:* 610-526-1000 *Fax:* 610-526-1310 *Web Site:* www.amercoll.edu, pg 12

Barton, Linda, Black Rose Books Ltd, CP 1258 Succ Place de Parc, Montreal, PQ H2X 4A7, Canada *Tel:* 514-844-4076 *Toll Free Tel:* 800-565-9523 *Fax:* 514-849-4797 *Toll Free Fax:* 800-221-9985 *E-mail:* blackrose@web.net *Web Site:* www.web.net/blackrosebooks, pg 536

Barton, Rick, Leisure Arts Inc, 5701 Ranch Dr, Little Rock, AR 72223 *Tel:* 501-868-8800 *Toll Free Tel:* 800-643-8030 *Fax:* 501-868-8937 *Web Site:* www.leisurearts.com, pg 152

Barz, Otto, YBK Publishers Inc, 425 Broome St, New York, NY 10013 *Tel:* 212-219-0135 *Fax:* 212-219-0136 *E-mail:* info@ybkpublishers.com, pg 306

Barz, Otto H, Publishing Synthesis Ltd, 425 Broome St, New York, NY 10013 *Tel:* 212-219-0135 *Fax:* 212-219-0136 *E-mail:* info@pubsyn.com *Web Site:* www.pubsyn.com, pg 609

Barzinji, Dr Jaman, The International Institute of Islamic Thought, 500 Grove St, Suite 200, Herndon, VA 20170 *Tel:* 703-471-1133 *Fax:* 703-471-3922 *E-mail:* iiit@iiit.org *Web Site:* www.iiit.org, pg 137

Basart, Kate, Sasquatch Books, 119 S Main, Suite 400, Seattle, WA 98104 *Tel:* 206-467-4300 *Toll Free Tel:* 800-775-0817 *Fax:* 206-467-4301 *E-mail:* books@sasquatchbooks.com *Web Site:* www.sasquatchbooks.com, pg 240

Basch, Richard, Don Buchwald & Associates Inc, 6500 Wilshire Blvd, Suite 2200, Los Angeles, CA 90048 *Tel:* 323-655-7400 *Fax:* 323-655-7470 *Web Site:* www.donbuchwald.com, pg 623

Bash, Holly, Tom Doherty Associates, LLC, 175 Fifth Ave, 14th fl, New York, NY 10010 *Tel:* 212-388-0100 *Toll Free Tel:* 800-455-0340 *Fax:* 212-388-0191 *E-mail:* firstname.lastname@tor.com *Web Site:* www.tor.com, pg 82

Bash, Holly, St Martin's Press LLC, 175 Fifth Ave, New York, NY 10010 *Tel:* 212-674-5151 *Fax:* 212-420-9314 *E-mail:* firstname.lastname@stmartins.com *Web Site:* www.stmartins.com, pg 239

Baskin, John, Orange Frazer Press Inc, 37 1/2 W Main St, Wilmington, OH 45177 *Tel:* 937-382-3196 *Toll Free Tel:* 800-852-9332 *Fax:* 937-383-3159 *E-mail:* ofrazer@erinet.com *Web Site:* www.orangefrazer.com, pg 198

Basmajian, Nancy, Ohio University Press, One Ohio University, Scott Quadrangle, Athens, OH 45701 *Tel:* 740-593-1155 *Toll Free Tel:* 800-621-2736 *Fax:* 740-593-4536 *Web Site:* www.ohio.edu/oupress/, pg 196

Basmajian, Nancy, Swallow Press, Scott Quadrangle, Athens, OH 45701 *Tel:* 740-593-1155 *Toll Free Tel:* 800-621-2736 (orders only) *Fax:* 740-593-4536 *Toll Free Fax:* 800-621-8476 (orders only) *Web Site:* www.ohiou.edu/oupress/, pg 263

Bason, Robert, Capra Press, 155 Canon View Rd, Santa Barbara, CA 93108 *Tel:* 805-969-0203 *Fax:* 805-565-0724 *E-mail:* order@caprapress.com *Web Site:* www.caprapress.com, pg 52

Basore, Thomas, Web Offset Association, 200 Deer Run Rd, Sewickley, PA 15143 *Tel:* 412-741-6860 *Toll Free Tel:* 800-910-4283 *Fax:* 412-741-2311 *Web Site:* www.gain.net, pg 702

Basore, Thomas B, Web Printing Association, 100 Daingerfield Rd, Alexandria, VA 22314 *Tel:* 703-519-8100 *Toll Free Tel:* 800-742-2666 *Fax:* 703-519-7109 *Web Site:* www.gain.net, pg 702

Bass, Jeri, Antiquarian Booksellers Association of Canada (ABAC), 824 Fort St, Victoria, BC V8W 1H8, Canada *Tel:* 250-360-2929 *Fax:* 250-361-1812 *E-mail:* info@abac.org *Web Site:* www.abac.org, pg 678

Bass, Richard, The Alban Institute Inc, 2121 Cooperative Way, Suite 100, Herndon, VA 20171 *Tel:* 703-964-2700 *Toll Free Tel:* 800-486-1318 *Fax:* 703-964-0370 *E-mail:* webmaster@alban.org *Web Site:* www.alban.org, pg 7

Bassett, Marjory, Medal of Honor for Literature, 15 Gramercy Park S, New York, NY 10003, pg 789

Bast, Tom, Triumph Books, 601 S LaSalle St, Suite 500, Chicago, IL 60605 *Tel:* 312-939-3330 *Toll Free Tel:* 800-335-5323 *Fax:* 312-663-3557 *E-mail:* orders@triumphbooks.com *Web Site:* www.triumphbooks.com, pg 276

Batalion, Milton, Time Warner Book Group, 1271 Avenue of the Americas, New York, NY 10020 *Tel:* 212-522-7200 *Fax:* 212-522-7991 *Web Site:* www.twbookmark.com, pg 271

Batavick, Frank, Cambridge Educational, 2572 Brunswick Ave, Lawrenceville, NJ 08648-4128 *Toll Free Tel:* 800-468-4227 *Toll Free Fax:* 800-329-6687 *E-mail:* custserve@cambridgeeducational.com *Web Site:* www.cambridgeeducational.com, pg 51

Bateman, Lewis, Cambridge University Press, 40 W 20 St, New York, NY 10011-4211 *Tel:* 212-924-3900 *Toll Free Tel:* 800-899-5222 *Fax:* 212-691-3239 *Web Site:* www.cambridge.org, pg 52

Bateman, Roger, Trafton Publishing, 109 Barcliff Terr, Cary, NC 27511 *Tel:* 919-363-0999 *Web Site:* www.rogbates.com, pg 273

Bates, Greg, Common Courage Press, One Red Barn Rd, Monroe, ME 04951 *Tel:* 207-525-0900 *Toll Free Tel:* 800-497-3207 *Fax:* 207-525-3068 *E-mail:* orders-info@commoncouragepress.com *Web Site:* www.commoncouragepress.com, pg 65

Batitto, Lisa Ann, Harry Chapin Media Awards, 505 Eighth Ave, 21st fl, New York, NY 10018 *Tel:* 212-629-8850 *Toll Free Tel:* 800-5-HUNGRY (548-6479) *Fax:* 212-465-9274 *E-mail:* media@worldhungeryear.org *Web Site:* www.worldhungeryear.org, pg 766

Batmanglij, Mohammad, Mage Publishers Inc, 1032 29 St NW, Washington, DC 20007 *Tel:* 202-342-1642 *Toll Free Tel:* 800-962-0922 *Fax:* 202-342-9269 *E-mail:* info@mage.com *Web Site:* www.mage.com, pg 161

Batmanglij, Najmieh, Mage Publishers Inc, 1032 29 St NW, Washington, DC 20007 *Tel:* 202-342-1642 *Toll Free Tel:* 800-962-0922 *Fax:* 202-342-9269 *E-mail:* info@mage.com *Web Site:* www.mage.com, pg 161

Battaglia, Emi, Warner Books, 1271 Avenue of the Americas, New York, NY 10020 *Tel:* 212-522-7200 *Fax:* 212-522-7991 *Web Site:* www.twbookmark.com, pg 293

Battista, Garth, Breakaway Books, PO Box 24, Halcottsville, NY 12438-0024 *Tel:* 607-326-4805 *Toll Free:* 800-548-4348 (voicemail) *Fax:* 212-898-0408 *E-mail:* mail@breakawaybooks.com; orders@breakawaybooks.com; info@breakawaybooks.com *Web Site:* www.breakawaybooks.com, pg 46

Battle, Angela, Society of American Travel Writers Foundation, 1500 Sunday Dr, Suite 102, Raleigh, NC 27607 *Tel:* 919-861-5586 *Fax:* 919-787-4916 *E-mail:* satw@satw.org *Web Site:* www.satw.org, pg 700

Bauer, Judith A, Liguori Publications, One Liguori Dr, Liguori, MO 63057-9999 *Tel:* 636-464-2500 *Toll Free Tel:* 800-464-2555 *Fax:* 636-464-8449 *Web Site:* www.liguori.org, pg 155

Bauer, Libby, Bernan, 4611-F Assembly Dr, Lanham, MD 20706-4391 *Tel:* 301-459-2255; 301-459-7666 (cust serv) *Toll Free Tel:* 800-274-4447; 800-274-4888 (cust serv) *Fax:* 301-459-9235; 301-459-0056 (cust serv) *Toll Free Tel:* 800-865-3450 *E-mail:* info@bernan.com *Web Site:* www.bernan.com, pg 37

Bauer, Margaret, National Gallery of Art, Fourth St & Constitution Ave, Landover, MD 20565 *Tel:* 202-842-6200 *Fax:* 202-408-8530 *Web Site:* www.nga.gov, pg 183

Bauer, Susan Wise, Peace Hill Press, 18101 The Glebe Lane, Charles City, VA 23030 *Tel:* 804-829-5043 *Toll Free Tel:* 877-322-3445 (orders) *Fax:* 804-829-5704 *E-mail:* info@peacehillpress.net *Web Site:* www.peacehillpress.com, pg 206

Bauerle, Chris, Cumberland House Publishing Inc, 431 Harding Industrial Dr, Nashville, TN 37211 *Tel:* 615-832-1171 *Toll Free Tel:* 888-439-2665 *Fax:* 615-832-0633 *E-mail:* information@cumberlandhouse.com *Web Site:* www.cumberlandhouse.com, pg 74

Baugh, Kellye, Milner Award, One Margaret Mitchell Sq NW, Atlanta, GA 30303 *Tel:* 404-730-1845 *Fax:* 404-730-1851, pg 790

Baum, Beverly, University Press of America Inc, 4501 Forbes Blvd, Suite 200, Lanham, MD 20706 *Tel:* 301-459-3366 *Toll Free Tel:* 800-462-6420 *Fax:* 301-429-5748 *Toll Free Fax:* 800-338-4550 *Web Site:* www.univpress.com, pg 286

Baum, Michael, Guild Publishing, 931 E Main St, Madison, WI 53703-2955 *Tel:* 608-257-2590 *Toll Free Tel:* 800-930-1856 *Fax:* 608-257-2690 *E-mail:* artinfo@guild.com *Web Site:* www.guild.com, pg 111

Baumhauer, Marge, Graphic Arts Association, 1100 Northbrook Dr, Suite 120, Trevose, PA 19053 *Tel:* 215-396-2300 *Fax:* 215-396-9890 *E-mail:* gaa@gaa1900.com *Web Site:* www.gaa1900.com, pg 752

Baxter, Annabelle, Dupree, Miller & Associates Inc, 100 Highland Park Village, Suite 350, Dallas, TX 75205 *Tel:* 214-559-2665 *Fax:* 214-559-7243 *E-mail:* dmabook@aol.com, pg 628

Bay, Beth, Visions Communications, 200 E Tenth St, Suite 714, New York, NY 10003 *Tel:* 212-529-4029 *Fax:* 212-529-4029 *E-mail:* bayvisions@aol.com; info@visionsbooks.com, pg 291

Bay, William A, Mel Bay Publications Inc, 4 Industrial Dr, Pacific, MO 63069-0066 *Tel:* 636-257-3970 *Toll Free Tel:* 800-863-5229 *Fax:* 636-257-5062 *Toll Free Fax:* 800-660-9818 *E-mail:* email@melbay.com *Web Site:* www.melbay.com, pg 171

Bayer, Lisa, Redleaf Press, 10 Yorkton Ct, St Paul, MN 55117 *Tel:* 651-641-0305 *Toll Free Tel:* 800-423-8309 *Toll Free Fax:* 800-641-0115 *Web Site:* www.redleafpress.org, pg 230

Bayley, Pam, The Perseus Books Group, 387 Park Ave S, 12th fl, New York, NY 10016 *Tel:* 212-340-8100 *Toll Free Tel:* 800-386-5656 (cust serv) *Fax:* 212-340-8115 *Web Site:* www.perseusbooksgroup.com, pg 210

Bazzy, William M, Artech House Inc, 685 Canton St, Norwood, MA 02062 *Tel:* 781-769-9750 *Toll Free Tel:* 800-225-9977 *Fax:* 781-769-6334 *E-mail:* artech@artechhouse.com *Web Site:* www.artechhouse.com, pg 24

Beach, Kristen, Liberty Fund Inc, 8335 Allison Pointe Trail, Suite 300, Indianapolis, IN 46250-1684 *Tel:* 317-842-0880 *Toll Free Tel:* 800-955-8335 *Fax:* 317-579-6060 *E-mail:* books@libertyfund.org *Web Site:* www.libertyfund.org, pg 153

Beach, Sue, Tilbury House Publishers, 2 Mechanic St, No 3, Gardiner, ME 04345 *Tel:* 207-582-1899 *Toll Free Tel:* 800-582-1899 (orders) *Fax:* 207-582-8229 *E-mail:* tilbury@tilburyhouse.com *Web Site:* www.tilburyhouse.com, pg 271

Beacham, Deborah M, Beacham Publishing Corp, PO Box 1810, Nokomis, FL 34274-1810 *Tel:* 941-480-9644 *Toll Free Tel:* 800-466-9644 *Fax:* 941-480-9644 *E-mail:* beachampub@aol.com *Web Site:* www.beachampublishing.com, pg 34

Beacham, Walton, Beacham Publishing Corp, PO Box 1810, Nokomis, FL 34274-1810 *Tel:* 941-480-9644 *Toll Free Tel:* 800-466-9644 *Fax:* 941-480-9644 *E-mail:* beachampub@aol.com *Web Site:* www.beachampublishing.com, pg 34

Beacom, David, National Science Teachers Association (NSTA), 1840 Wilson Blvd, Arlington, VA 22201-3000 *Tel:* 703-243-7100 *Toll Free Tel:* 800-722-NSTA (sales) *Fax:* 703-243-7177 *Web Site:* www.nsta.org, pg 185

Beagell, Lori, The Haworth Press Inc, 10 Alice St, Binghamton, NY 13904-1580 *Tel:* 607-722-5857 *Toll Free Tel:* 800-429-6784 *Fax:* 607-722-1424 *Toll Free Fax:* 800-895-0582 *E-mail:* getinfo@haworthpressinc.com *Web Site:* www.haworthpress.com, pg 118

Beal, Aimee, Alice James Books, 238 Main St, Farmington, ME 04938 *Tel:* 207-778-7071 *Fax:* 207-778-7071 *E-mail:* ajb@umf.maine.edu *Web Site:* www.alicejamesbooks.org, pg 8

Beal, Ellen, Running Press Book Publishers, 125 S 22 St, Philadelphia, PA 19103-4399 *Tel:* 215-567-5080 *Toll Free Tel:* 800-345-5359 (cust serv & orders) *Fax:* 215-568-2919 *Toll Free Fax:* 800-453-2884 *Web Site:* www.runningpress.com, pg 236

Beal, Greg, Academy of Motion Picture Arts & Sciences (AMPAS), 1313 N Vine St, Hollywood, CA 90028 *Tel:* 310-247-3000 *Fax:* 310-859-9351 *E-mail:* ampas@oscars.org *Web Site:* www.oscars.org, pg 675

Beal, Greg, Don & Gee Nicholl Fellowships in Screenwriting, 1313 N Vine St, Hollywood, CA 90028 *Tel:* 310-247-3059; 310-247-3010 *Fax:* 310-247-3794 *E-mail:* nicholl@oscars.org *Web Site:* www.oscars.org/nicholl, pg 794

Beale, Steven, Davies Publishing Inc, 32 S Raymond Ave, Pasadena, CA 91105-1935 *Tel:* 626-792-3046 *Toll Free Tel:* 877-792-0005 *Fax:* 626-792-5308 *E-mail:* daviescorp@aol.com *Web Site:* www.daviespublishing.com, pg 76

Bean, Susan, Northern Illinois University Press, 310 N Fifth St, De Kalb, IL 60115 *Tel:* 815-753-1826; 815-753-1075 *Fax:* 815-753-1845 *E-mail:* bberg@niu.edu *Web Site:* www.niu.edu/univ_press, pg 193

Beard, Chris, Beard Books Inc, 306 N Market St, Frederick, MD 21701-5337 *Tel:* 240-629-3300 *Toll Free Tel:* 888-563-4573 (book orders) *Fax:* 240-629-3360 *E-mail:* info@beardbooks.com; order@beardbooks.com *Web Site:* www.beardbooks.com, pg 34

Beard, Michael, Macalester Park Publishing Co, 7317 Cahill Rd, Minneapolis, MN 55439-2067 *Tel:* 952-562-1234 *Toll Free Tel:* 800-407-9078 *Fax:* 952-941-3010 *E-mail:* publisher@mcchronicle.com *Web Site:* www.mcchronicle.com, pg 161

Bearnson, Lisa, Creating Keepsakes Books, 14901 S Heritagecrest Way, Bluffdale, UT 84065 *Tel:* 801-984-2070 *Toll Free Tel:* 800-815-3538 *Fax:* 801-984-2080 *Web Site:* www.creatingkeepsakes.com, pg 72

Bearse, Stacy V, Eclipse Press, 3101 Beaumont Centre Circle, Lexington, KY 40513 *Tel:* 859-278-2361 *Toll Free Tel:* 800-866-2361 *Fax:* 859-276-6868 *E-mail:* editorial@eclipsepress.com; marketing@eclipsepress.com *Web Site:* www.eclipsepress.com, pg 86

Beasley, Bruce, 49th Parallel Poetry Award, Mail Stop 9053, Western Washington University, Bellingham, WA 98225 *Tel:* 360-650-4863 *E-mail:* bhreview@cc.wwu.edu *Web Site:* www.wwu.edu/~bhreview, pg 774

Beasley, Malcolm, Professional Communications Inc, 20968 State Rd 22, Caddo, OK 74729 *Tel:* 580-367-9838 *Toll Free Tel:* 800-337-9838 *Fax:* 580-367-9989 *E-mail:* info@pcibooks.com *Web Site:* www.pcibooks.com, pg 219

Beasley, Sandra, Ralph Waldo Emerson Award, 1606 New Hampshire Ave NW, Washington, DC 20009 *Tel:* 202-265-3808 *Fax:* 202-986-1601 *Web Site:* www.pbk.org, pg 772

Beasley, Sandra, The Christian Gauss Award, 1606 New Hampshire Ave NW, Washington, DC 20009 *Tel:* 202-265-3808 *Fax:* 202-986-1601 *Web Site:* www.pbk.org, pg 775

Beasley, Sandra, Phi Beta Kappa Award in Science, 1606 New Hampshire Ave NW, Washington, DC 20009 *Tel:* 202-265-3808 *Fax:* 202-986-1601 *Web Site:* www.pbk.org, pg 798

Beaudoin, Andre, Les Editions Ganesha Inc, CP 484 Succursale Youville, Montreal, PQ H2P 2W1, Canada *Tel:* 450-641-2395 *Fax:* 450-641-2989 *E-mail:* courriel@editions-ganesha.qc.ca *Web Site:* editions-ganesha.qc.ca, pg 545

Beaufait, Fred W PhD, New York City College of Technology, 300 Jay St, Brooklyn, NY 11201 *Tel:* 718-260-5822; 718-260-5000 *Fax:* 718-260-5198 *E-mail:* connect@citytech.cuny.edu, pg 753

Beaulieu, Michelle, Georges Borchardt Inc, 136 E 57 St, New York, NY 10022 *Tel:* 212-753-5785 *Fax:* 212-838-6518 *E-mail:* georges@gbagency.com, pg 622

Beaumont, Nancy, Society of American Archivists, 527 S Wells St, 5th fl, Chicago, IL 60607 *Tel:* 312-922-0140 *Fax:* 312-347-1452 *E-mail:* info@archivists.org *Web Site:* www.archivists.org, pg 251

Beauregard, Alain, Corp professionnelle des traducteurs et interpretes agrees du quebec, 2021 Union Ave, Suite 1108, Montreal, PQ H3A 2S9, Canada *Tel:* 514-845-4411 *Fax:* 514-845-9903, pg 685

Beck, David, Kennedy Information, One Phoenix Mill Lane, 5th fl, Peterborough, NH 03458 *Tel:* 603-924-0900 *Toll Free Tel:* 800-531-0007 *Fax:* 603-924-4460 *E-mail:* office@kennedyinfo.com *Web Site:* www.kennedyinfo.com, pg 145

Beck, Robyn, Laureate Press, PO Box 8125, Bangor, ME 04402-8125 *Toll Free Tel:* 800-946-2727 *Fax:* 207-884-8095, pg 150

Becker, Adam, Association for the Export of Canadian Books, One Nicholas, Suite 504, Ottawa, ON K1N 7B7, Canada *Tel:* 613-562-2324 *Fax:* 613-562-2329 *E-mail:* aecb@aecb.org *Web Site:* www.aecb.org, pg 679

Becker, Cliff, Fellowships for Creative Writers, Nancy Hanks Ctr, 1100 Pennsylvania Ave NW, Rm 720, Washington, DC 20506-0001 *Tel:* 202-682-5428; 202-682-5034 (Literature Fellowships hotline) *Fax:* 202-682-5669 *Web Site:* www.arts.gov, pg 773

Becker, Cliff, Literary Translation Projects, Nancy Hanks Ctr, 1100 Pennsylvania Ave NW, Rm 720, Washington, DC 20506-0001 *Tel:* 202-682-5428; 202-682-5034 (Literature Fellowships hotline) *Web Site:* www.arts.gov, pg 785

Becker, Cliff, The National Endowment for the Arts, Nancy Hanks Ctr, 1100 Pennsylvania Ave NW, Room 720, Washington, DC 20506-0001 *Tel:* 202-682-5428 *Fax:* 202-682-5669 *Web Site:* www.arts.gov, pg 705

Becker, Steve, Bridge-Logos Publishers, 17310 NW 32 Ave, Newberry, FL 32669 *Tel:* 352-472-7900 *Toll Free Tel:* 800-631-5802 *Fax:* 352-472-7908 *Toll Free Fax:* 800-935-6467 *E-mail:* info@bridgelogos.com *Web Site:* www.bridgelogos.com, pg 47

Becker, Thomas M, Chautauqua Writers' Workshop, PO Box 28, Chautauqua, NY 14722-0408 *Tel:* 716-357-6200 *Toll Free Tel:* 800-836-ARTS (836-2787) *E-mail:* cpaul@chautauquava-inst.com *Web Site:* www.ciweb.org, pg 742

Becketti, Kevin, Backbeat Books, 600 Harrison St, San Francisco, CA 94107 *Tel:* 415-947-6615 *Toll Free Tel:* 866-222-5232 (orders only) *Fax:* 415-947-6015; 408-848-8294 (orders only) *E-mail:* books@musicplayer.com; books@cmp.com *Web Site:* www.backbeatbooks.com, pg 30

Beckingham, Dennis, Thomson Learning Inc, 200 First Stamford Place, Suite 400, Stamford, CT 06902 *Tel:* 203-539-8000 *Fax:* 203-539-7581 *E-mail:* communications@thomsonlearning.com *Web Site:* www.thomson.com/learning, pg 270

Beckley, Brent, William Andrew Publishing, 13 Eaton Ave, Norwich, NY 13815 *Tel:* 607-337-5000 *Toll Free Tel:* 800-932-7045 *Fax:* 607-337-5090 *E-mail:* publishing@williamandrew.com *Web Site:* www.williamandrew.com, pg 300

Beckner, Richard, Beacon Hill Press of Kansas City, PO Box 419527, Kansas City, MO 64141-6527 *Tel:* 816-931-1900 *Toll Free Tel:* 800-877-0700 (retail order) *Fax:* 816-753-4071 *Toll Free Fax:* 800-849-9827 (order) *Web Site:* www.beaconhillbooks.com, pg 34

Beckwith, Wes, Wordware Publishing Inc, 2320 Los Rios Blvd, Suite 200, Plano, TX 75074 *Tel:* 972-423-0090 *Toll Free Tel:* 800-229-4949 *Fax:* 972-881-9147 *E-mail:* info@wordware.com *Web Site:* www.wordware.com, pg 303

Bedell, Jack, Louisiana Literature Poetry Prize, Southeastern Louisiana University, SLU Box 10792, Hammond, LA 70402 *Tel:* 985-549-5022 *E-mail:* lalit@selu.edu *Web Site:* www.louisianaliterature.org, pg 786

Bednarik, Joseph, Copper Canyon Press, PO Box 271, Port Townsend, WA 98368 *Tel:* 360-385-4925 *Fax:* 360-385-4985 *E-mail:* poetry@coppercanyonpress.org *Web Site:* www.coppercanyonpress.org, pg 68

Bednarz, Kathryn, Astragal Press, PO Box 239, Mendham, NJ 07945-0239 *Tel:* 973-543-3045 *Fax:* 973-543-3044 *E-mail:* info@astragalpress.com *Web Site:* www.astragalpress.com, pg 27

Bedrick, Abigail, Enchanted Lion Books, 115 W 18 St, 6th fl, New York, NY 10011 *Tel:* 212-675-1959 *Fax:* 212-675-2142 *E-mail:* enchantedlionbooks@yahoo.com, pg 90

Bedrick, Claudia, Enchanted Lion Books, 115 W 18 St, 6th fl, New York, NY 10011 *Tel:* 212-675-1959 *Fax:* 212-675-2142 *E-mail:* enchantedlionbooks@yahoo.com, pg 90

Bedrick, Muriel, Enchanted Lion Books, 115 W 18 St, 6th fl, New York, NY 10011 *Tel:* 212-675-1959 *Fax:* 212-675-2142 *E-mail:* enchantedlionbooks@yahoo.com, pg 90

Bedrick, Peter, Enchanted Lion Books, 115 W 18 St, 6th fl, New York, NY 10011 *Tel:* 212-675-1959 *Fax:* 212-675-2142 *E-mail:* enchantedlionbooks@yahoo.com, pg 90

Beecher, Donald, Dovehouse Editions Inc, 1890 Fairmeadow Crescent, Ottawa, ON K1H 7B9, Canada *Tel:* 613-731-7601 *Fax:* 613-731-7601 *Web Site:* www.dovehouse.ca, pg 543

Beeke, Joel R, Reformation Heritage Books, 2919 Leonard St NE, Grand Rapids, MI 49525 *Tel:* 616-977-0599 *Fax:* 616-285-3246 *E-mail:* orders@heritagebooks.org *Web Site:* www.heritagebooks.org, pg 230

Beeler, Thomas T, Thomas T Beeler Publisher, 710 Main St, Suite 300, Rollinsford, NH 03869 *Tel:* 603-749-0392 *Toll Free Tel:* 800-818-7574 *Fax:* 603-749-0395 *Toll Free Fax:* 888-222-3396 *E-mail:* cservice@beelerpub.com *Web Site:* www.beelerpub.com, pg 35

Beer, Jeremy, ISI Books, PO Box 4431, 3901 Centerville Rd, Wilmington, DE 19807 *Tel:* 302-652-4600 *Toll Free Tel:* 800-526-7022 *Fax:* 302-652-1760 *E-mail:* bookstore@isi.org *Web Site:* www.isibooks.org, pg 139

Beer, Stephanie, Curtis Benjamin Award, 50 "F" St NW, Washington, DC 20001-1530 *Tel:* 202-347-3375 *Fax:* 202-347-3690 *Web Site:* www.publishers.org, pg 762

Beers, Ron, Tyndale House Publishers Inc, 351 Executive Dr, Carol Stream, IL 60188 *Tel:* 630-668-8303 *Toll Free Tel:* 800-323-9400 *Web Site:* www.tyndale.com, pg 277

Beetz, Kirk H, Beacham Publishing Corp, PO Box 1810, Nokomis, FL 34274-1810 *Tel:* 941-480-9644 *Toll Free Tel:* 800-466-9644 *Fax:* 941-480-9644 *E-mail:* beachampub@aol.com *Web Site:* www.beachampublishing.com, pg 34

Begell, William, Begell House Inc Publishers, 145 Madison Ave, Suite 601, New York, NY 10016 *Tel:* 212-725-1999 *Fax:* 212-213-8368 *E-mail:* orders@begellhouse.com *Web Site:* www.begellhouse.com, pg 35

Beggs, Pauline, First Folio Resource Group Inc, 10 King St E, Suite 801, Toronto, ON M5C 1C3, Canada *Tel:* 416-368-7668 *Fax:* 416-368-9363 *E-mail:* mail@firstfolio.com *Web Site:* www.firstfolio.com, pg 599

Begin, Nancy, Helen Exley Giftbooks, 185 Main St, Spencer, MA 01562 *Toll Free Tel:* 877-395-3942 *Toll Free Fax:* 800-807-7363 *E-mail:* helen.exleygiftbooks@verizon.net, pg 93

Begley, Charlotte, Clovernook Printing House for the Blind, 7000 Hamilton Ave, Cincinnati, OH 45231-5297 *Tel:* 513-522-3860 *Toll Free Tel:* 888-234-7156 *Fax:* 513-728-3946 (admin); 513-728-3950 (sales) *Web Site:* www.clovernook.org, pg 63

Behar, Tracy, Atria Books, 1230 Avenue of the Americas, New York, NY 10020 *Tel:* 212-698-7000 *Fax:* 212-698-7007 *Web Site:* www.simonsays.com, pg 27

Behm, Melissa A, Paul H Brookes Publishing Co, PO Box 10624, Baltimore, MD 21285-0624 *Tel:* 410-337-9580 *Toll Free Tel:* 800-638-3775 *Fax:* 410-337-8539 *E-mail:* custserv@brookespublishing.com *Web Site:* www.brookespublishing.com, pg 48

Behm, Melissa A, Health Professions Press, PO Box 10624, Baltimore, MD 21285-0624 *Tel:* 410-337-9585 *Toll Free Tel:* 888-337-8808 *Fax:* 410-337-8539 *E-mail:* custserv@healthpropress.com *Web Site:* www.healthpropress.com, pg 119

Behn, Robin, University of Alabama Program in Creative Writing, PO Box 870244, Tuscaloosa, AL 35487-0244 *Tel:* 205-348-0766 *Fax:* 205-348-1388 *E-mail:* writeua@english.as.ua.edu *Web Site:* www.as.ua.edu/english, pg 755

Behnke, Leonard, McGraw-Hill/Dushkin, 2460 Kerper Blvd, Dubuque, IA 52001 *Toll Free Tel:* 800-243-6532 *Web Site:* www.dushkin.com, pg 167

Behrman, David, Behrman House Inc, 11 Edison Place, Springfield, NJ 07081 *Tel:* 973-379-7200 *Fax:* 973-379-7280 *Web Site:* www.behrmanhouse.com, pg 35

Behrnd-Klodt, Menzi, Pleasant Company Publications, 8400 Fairway Place, Middleton, WI 53562 *Tel:* 608-836-4848 *Fax:* 608-257-3865 *Web Site:* www.americangirl.com, pg 214

Beier, Elizabeth, St Martin's Press Trade Division, 175 Fifth Ave, New York, NY 10010 *E-mail:* firstname.lastname@stmartins.com *Web Site:* www.stmartins.com; www.minotaurbooks.com, pg 239

Beil, Frederic C, Frederic C Beil Publisher Inc, 609 Whitaker St, Savannah, GA 31401 *Tel:* 912-233-2446 *Fax:* 912-233-6456 *E-mail:* beilbook@beil.com *Web Site:* www.beil.com, pg 35

Beilenson, Evelyn L, Peter Pauper Press Inc, 202 Mamaroneck Ave, White Plains, NY 10601-5376 *Tel:* 914-681-0144 *Toll Free Tel:* 800-833-2311

Fax: 914-681-0389 *E-mail:* customerservice@peterpauper.com *Web Site:* www.peterpauper.com, pg 210

Beilenson, Laurence, Peter Pauper Press Inc, 202 Mamaroneck Ave, White Plains, NY 10601-5376 *Tel:* 914-681-0144 *Toll Free Tel:* 800-833-2311 *Fax:* 914-681-0389 *E-mail:* customerservice@peterpauper.com *Web Site:* www.peterpauper.com, pg 210

Beilenson, Nick, Peter Pauper Press Inc, 202 Mamaroneck Ave, White Plains, NY 10601-5376 *Tel:* 914-681-0144 *Toll Free Tel:* 800-833-2311 *Fax:* 914-681-0389 *E-mail:* customerservice@peterpauper.com *Web Site:* www.peterpauper.com, pg 210

Beirl, Lynn, Writer's Digest School, 4700 E Galbraith Rd, Cincinnati, OH 45236 *Tel:* 513-531-2690 *Toll Free Tel:* 800-759-0963 *Fax:* 513-531-0798 *E-mail:* wds@fwpubs.com *Web Site:* www.fwpubs.com, pg 756

Beiser, Martin, Free Press, 1230 Avenue of the Americas, New York, NY 10020 *Tel:* 212-698-7000 *Toll Free Tel:* 800-223-2345 (cust serv); 800-223-2336 (orders); 888-866-6631 (fulfillment), pg 100

Beitzel, Tim, Kendall/Hunt Publishing Co, 4050 Westmark Dr, Dubuque, IA 52002 *Tel:* 563-589-1000 *Toll Free Tel:* 800-228-0810 (orders only) *Fax:* 563-589-1114 *Toll Free Fax:* 800-772-9165 *Web Site:* www.kendallhunt.com, pg 144

Belanger, Paul, Editions du Noroit Ltee, PO Box 156, Succersale de Lorimier, Montreal, PQ H2H 2N6, Canada *Tel:* 514-727-0005 *Fax:* 514-723-6660 *E-mail:* lenoroit@lenoroit.com *Web Site:* www.lenoroit.com, pg 544

Belasco, Leslie, ALI-ABA Committee on Continuing Professional Education, 4025 Chestnut St, Philadelphia, PA 19104 *Tel:* 215-243-1600 *Toll Free Tel:* 800-CLE-NEWS *Fax:* 215-243-1664; 215-243-1683 *Web Site:* www.ali-aba.org, pg 8

Belfiglio, Brian, Crown Publishing Group, 1745 Broadway, New York, NY 10019 *Tel:* 212-782-9000 *Toll Free Tel:* 888-264-1745 *Fax:* 212-940-7408 *Web Site:* www.randomhouse.com/crown, pg 74

Belfus, Linda, Elsevier, 11830 Westline Industrial Dr, St Louis, MO 63146 *Tel:* 314-872-8370 *Toll Free Tel:* 800-325-4177 *Fax:* 314-432-1380 *Web Site:* www.elsevier.com; www.elsevierhealth.com, pg 89

Belfus, Linda C, Hanley & Belfus, 170 S Independence Mall W, Suite 300 E, Philadelphia, PA 19106-3399 *Tel:* 215-238-7800 *Toll Free Tel:* 800-545-2522 (orders) *Fax:* 215-238-7883 *Web Site:* www.elsevierhealth.com, pg 113

Beliveau, Mathieu, Editions Sciences & Culture Inc, 5090 rue de Bellechasse, Montreal, PQ H1T 2A2, Canada *Tel:* 514-253-0403 *Fax:* 514-256-5078 *E-mail:* admin@sciences-culture.qc.ca *Web Site:* www.sciences-culture.qc.ca, pg 545

Bell, Britt, Moyer Bell Ltd, 549 Old North Rd, Kingston, RI 02881 *Tel:* 401-783-5480 *Fax:* 401-284-0959 *E-mail:* acornalliance@yahoo.com *Web Site:* www.acornalliance.com, pg 180

Bell, Cristine, Evan-Moor Educational Publishers, 18 Lower Ragsdale Dr, Monterey, CA 93940 *Tel:* 831-649-5901 *Toll Free Tel:* 800-777-4362 *Fax:* 831-649-6256 *E-mail:* customerservice@evan-moor.com *Web Site:* www.evan-moor.com, pg 92

Bell, John, Evan-Moor Educational Publishers, 18 Lower Ragsdale Dr, Monterey, CA 93940 *Tel:* 831-649-5901 *Toll Free Tel:* 800-777-4362 *Fax:* 831-649-6256 *E-mail:* customerservice@evan-moor.com *Web Site:* www.evan-moor.com, pg 92

Bell, Muriel, Stanford University Press, 1450 Page Mill Rd, Palo Alto, CA 94304-1124 *Tel:* 650-723-9434 *Fax:* 650-725-3457 *Web Site:* www.sup.org, pg 257

Bellamy, Linda, Home Planners LLC, 3275 W Ina Rd, Suite 220, Tucson, AZ 85741 *Tel:* 520-297-8200 *Toll Free Tel:* 800-322-6797 *Fax:* 520-297-6219 *Toll Free Fax:* 800-531-2555 *E-mail:* customerservice@eplans.com *Web Site:* www.eplans.com, pg 125

Bellanca, Dr Patricia, Harvard Summer Writing Program, 51 Brattle St, Dept S760, Cambridge, MA 02138-3722 *Tel:* 617-495-4024 *Fax:* 617-495-9176 *E-mail:* summer@hudce.harvard.edu *Web Site:* www.summer.harvard.edu, pg 743

Belleba, Ed, Microsoft Press, One Microsoft Way, Redmond, WA 98052-6399 *Tel:* 425-882-8080 *Toll Free Tel:* 800-677-7377 *Fax:* 425-936-7329 *Web Site:* www.microsoft.com/presspass/exec/default.asp#qt, pg 173

Bellemare, Gaston, Ecrits des Forges, 1497 La Violette, CP 335, Trois Rivieres, PQ G9A 1W5, Canada *Tel:* 819-379-9813 *Fax:* 819-376-0774 *E-mail:* ecrits.desforges@tr.cgocable.ca, pg 543

Beller, Laurence, Amsco School Publications Inc, 315 Hudson St, New York, NY 10013-1085 *Tel:* 212-886-6500; 212-886-6565 *Toll Free Tel:* 800-969-8398 *Fax:* 212-675-7010 *E-mail:* info@amscopub.com *Web Site:* www.amscopub.com, pg 19

Bellevue, James, Avid Reader Press, 6705 W Hwy 290, Suite 502-295, Austin, TX 78735 *Tel:* 512-288-5349 *Fax:* 512-288-0317 *E-mail:* info@avidreaderpress.com; orders@avidreaderpress.com *Web Site:* www.avidreaderpress.com, pg 29

Bellitto, Christopher, Paulist Press, 997 Macarthur Blvd, Mahwah, NJ 07430 *Tel:* 201-825-7300 *Toll Free Tel:* 800-218-1903 *Fax:* 201-825-8345 *Toll Free Fax:* 800-836-3161 (orders) *E-mail:* info@paulistpress.com *Web Site:* www.paulistpress.com, pg 206

Belyea, Jeff, State of Maine Writers' Conference, 16 Foley Ave, Saco, ME 04072 *Tel:* 207-284-4119 *Web Site:* www.suiteonedesign.com, pg 748

Bemis, Carol Stiles, W W Norton & Company Inc, 500 Fifth Ave, New York, NY 10110-0017 *Tel:* 212-354-5500 *Toll Free Tel:* 800-233-4830 (orders & cust serv) *Fax:* 212-869-0856 *Toll Free Fax:* 800-458-6515 *Web Site:* www.wwnorton.com, pg 193

Benard, Martine, La Courte Echelle, 5243 Saint Laurent Blvd, Montreal, PQ H2T 1S4, Canada *Tel:* 514-274-2004 *Toll Free Tel:* 800-387-6192 (orders only) *Fax:* 514-270-4160 *Toll Free Fax:* 800-450-0391 (orders only) *E-mail:* info@courteechelle.com, pg 541

Benatar, Raquel, Renaissance House, 9400 Lloydcrest Dr, Beverly Hills, CA 90210 *Tel:* 310-860-9930 *Toll Free Tel:* 800-547-5113 *Fax:* 310-860-9902 *Web Site:* renaissancehouse.net, pg 231

Benator, Gene A, Benator Publishing LLC, 1240 Johnson Ferry Place, Suite C-5, Marietta, GA 30068 *Tel:* 770-977-5750 *Fax:* 770-977-8464 *E-mail:* benpubl2@bellsouth.net *Web Site:* benatorpublishing.com, pg 35

Benbow, Ann E, American Geological Institute (AGI), 4220 King St, Alexandria, VA 22302-1507 *Tel:* 703-379-2480 *Fax:* 703-379-7563 *E-mail:* pubs@agiweb.org *Web Site:* www.agiweb.org, pg 14

Bender, Jody R, Glencoe/McGraw-Hill, 8787 Orion Place, Columbus, OH 43240 *Tel:* 614-430-4000 *Toll Free Tel:* 800-848-1567 *Web Site:* www.glencoe.com, pg 105

Bender, R J, R James Bender Publishing, PO Box 23456, San Jose, CA 95153-3456 *Tel:* 408-225-5777 *Fax:* 408-225-4739 *E-mail:* order@bender-publishing.com *Web Site:* www.bender-publishing.com, pg 36

Bender, Robert, Simon & Schuster, 1230 Avenue of the Americas, New York, NY 10020 *Tel:* 212-698-7000 *Toll Free Tel:* 800-223-2348 (cust serv); 800-223-2336 (orders) *Toll Free Fax:* 800-943-9831 (orders) *Web Site:* www.simonsays.com, pg 248

Bender, Roger, R James Bender Publishing, PO Box 23456, San Jose, CA 95153-3456 *Tel:* 408-225-5777 *Fax:* 408-225-4739 *E-mail:* order@bender-publishing.com *Web Site:* www.bender-publishing.com, pg 36

Benedetto, Alexander, Camex Books Inc, 535 Fifth Ave, New York, NY 10017 *Tel:* 212-682-8400 *Fax:* 212-808-4669, pg 52

Benedetto, Victor, Camex Books Inc, 535 Fifth Ave, New York, NY 10017 *Tel:* 212-682-8400 *Fax:* 212-808-4669, pg 52

Benedict, Holly, Quincannon Publishing Group, PO Box 8100, Glen Ridge, NJ 07028-8100 *Tel:* 973-669-8367 *E-mail:* editors@quincannongroup.com *Web Site:* www.quincannongroup.com, pg 224

Benedict, Julia, Helen F Pratt Inc Literary Agency, 1165 Fifth Ave, New York, NY 10029 *Tel:* 212-722-5081 *Fax:* 212-722-8569 *E-mail:* helenpratt@earthlink.net, pg 649

Benedict, Pinckney, Hollins University, Writing Program, English Dept, Roanoke, VA 24020 *Tel:* 540-362-6317 *Fax:* 540-362-6097 *E-mail:* creative.writing@hollins.edu *Web Site:* www.hollins.edu, pg 752

Benenson, Sharen, The Mercantile Library, 17 E 47 St, New York, NY 10017 *Tel:* 212-755-6710 *Fax:* 212-826-0831 *E-mail:* info@mercantilelibrary.org *Web Site:* www.mercantilelibrary.org, pg 691

Benevides, Beth A, The Catholic University of America Press, 240 Leahy Hall, 620 Michigan Ave NE, Washington, DC 20064 *Tel:* 202-319-5052 *Fax:* 202-319-4985 *E-mail:* cua-press@cua.edu *Web Site:* cuapress.cua.edu, pg 55

Benezra, Mark, Original Publications, 22 E Mall, Plainview, NY 11803 *Tel:* 516-454-6809 *Fax:* 516-454-6829 *E-mail:* originalpub@aol.com, pg 199

Bengal, Adam, KTAV Publishing House Inc, 930 Newark Ave, Jersey City, NJ 07306 *Tel:* 201-963-9524 *Fax:* 201-963-0102 *E-mail:* orders@ktav.com *Web Site:* www.ktav.com, pg 147

Benirschke, Ingrid, Cold Spring Harbor Laboratory Press, 500 Sunnyside Blvd, Woodbury, NY 11797-2924 *Tel:* 516-422-4100 *Toll Free Tel:* 800-843-4388 *Fax:* 516-422-4097 *E-mail:* cshpress@cshl.edu *Web Site:* www.cshlpress.com, pg 64

Benjamin, Dan, Do-It-Yourself Legal Publishers, 60 Park Place, Suite 1013, Newark, NJ 07102 *Tel:* 973-639-0400 *Fax:* 973-639-1801 *E-mail:* selfhelp1@yahoo.com, pg 81

Benjamin, Michelle, Polestar Book Publishers, 9050 Shaughnessy St, Vancouver, BC V6P 6E5, Canada *Tel:* 604-323-7100 *Toll Free Tel:* 800-663-5714 *Fax:* 604-323-2600 *Toll Free Fax:* 800-565-3770 *E-mail:* info@raincoast.com *Web Site:* www.raincoast.com, pg 558

Benjamin, Michelle, Raincoast Publishing, 9050 Shaughnessy St, Vancouver, BC V6P 6E5, Canada *Tel:* 604-323-7100 *Toll Free Tel:* 800-663-5714 (Canada only) *Fax:* 604-323-2600 *Toll Free Fax:* 800-565-3700 *E-mail:* info@raincoast.com *Web Site:* www.raincoast.com, pg 559

Benjamin, R Dyke, Bibliographical Society of America, PO Box 1537, Lenox Hill Sta, New York, NY 10021-0043 *Tel:* 212-452-2710 *Fax:* 212-452-2710 *E-mail:* bsa@bibsocamer.org *Web Site:* www.bibsocamer.org, pg 681

Benjamin, Vaughn P, Media Credit Association (MCA), 84 Broad St, Milford, CT 06460 *Tel:* 203-876-2182 *Fax:* 203-876-5091 *Web Site:* www.mediacreditassociation.com, pg 691

Benko, James S, ITA Institute, PO Box 281, Grand Blanc, MI 48439 *Tel:* 810-232-6482 *E-mail:* hq@itatkd.com *Web Site:* www.itatkd.com, pg 139

Bennaton, Gwendolyn K, Art from Latin America, Box 1948, Murray Hill Sta, New York, NY 10156-0612 *Tel:* 212-683-2136, pg 24

Bennett, Avie, McClelland & Stewart Ltd, 481 University Ave, Suite 900, Toronto, ON M5G 2E9, Canada *Tel:* 416-598-1114 *Fax:* 416-598-7764 *E-mail:* mail@mcclelland.com *Web Site:* mcclelland.com, pg 553

Bennett, Barbara, Kensington Publishing Corp, 850 Third Ave, New York, NY 10022 *Tel:* 212-407-1500 *Toll Free Tel:* 800-221-2647 *Fax:* 212-935-0699 *Web Site:* www.kensingtonbooks.com, pg 145

Bennett, David, Transatlantic Literary Agency Inc, 72 Glengowan Rd, Toronto, ON M4N 1G4, Canada *Tel:* 416-488-9214 *Fax:* 416-488-4531 *E-mail:* info@tla1.com *Web Site:* www.tla1.com, pg 659

Bennett, Douglas S, Pearson, 800 E 96 St, Indianapolis, IN 46240 *Tel:* 317-428-3000 *Toll Free Tel:* 800-545-5914 *Fax:* 317-581-4675 *Web Site:* www.macdigital.com, pg 206

Bennett, Gary, American Institute of Chemical Engineers (AICHE), 3 Park Ave, New York, NY 10016-5991 *Tel:* 212-591-7338 *Toll Free Tel:* 800-242-4363 *Fax:* 212-591-8888 *E-mail:* xpress@aiche.org *Web Site:* www.aiche.org, pg 15

Bennett, Henry, Kamehameha Schools Press, 1887 Makuakane St, Honolulu, HI 96817-1887 *Tel:* 808-842-8719 *Fax:* 808-842-8895 *E-mail:* kspress@ksbe.edu *Web Site:* kspress.ksbe.edu, pg 144

Bennett, John M, Luna Bisonte Prods, 137 Leland Ave, Columbus, OH 43214 *Tel:* 614-846-4126, pg 160

Bennett, Karen, Harcourt School Publishers, 6277 Sea Harbor Dr, Orlando, FL 32887 *Tel:* 407-345-2000 *Toll Free Tel:* 800-225-5425 (cust serv) *Fax:* 407-352-3445 *Toll Free Fax:* 800-874-6418 *E-mail:* hbspcs@hbschool.com *Web Site:* www.harcourtschool.com, pg 114

Bennett, Kathryn, University of Toronto Press Inc, 10 St Mary St, Suite 700, Toronto, ON M4Y 2W8, Canada *Tel:* 416-978-2239 (admin) *Fax:* 416-978-4738 (admin) *Web Site:* www.utpress.utoronto.ca, pg 565

Bennett, Lynn, Transatlantic Literary Agency Inc, 72 Glengowan Rd, Toronto, ON M4N 1G4, Canada *Tel:* 416-488-9214 *Fax:* 416-488-4531 *E-mail:* info@tla1.com *Web Site:* www.tla1.com, pg 659

Bennett, Michael, The Astronomical Society of the Pacific, 390 Ashton Ave, San Francisco, CA 94112 *Tel:* 415-337-1100 *Toll Free Tel:* 800-335-2624 (Cust Serv) *Fax:* 415-337-5205 *E-mail:* service@astrosociety.org *Web Site:* www.astrosociety.org, pg 27

Bennett, Nancy, NAR Publications, State Rte 55, Barryville, NY 12719 *Tel:* 845-557-8713 *E-mail:* narpubs@aol.com, pg 181

Bennett, Tim, Association for Computing Machinery, 1515 Broadway, New York, NY 10036 *Tel:* 212-869-7440 *Toll Free Tel:* 800-342-6626 *Fax:* 212-869-0481 *E-mail:* acmhelp@acm.org *Web Site:* www.acm.org, pg 26

Bennett, Tina, Janklow & Nesbit Associates, 445 Park Ave, New York, NY 10022 *Tel:* 212-421-1700 *Fax:* 212-980-3671 *E-mail:* postmaster@janklow.com, pg 636

Bennett, Tom, Michelin Travel Publications, 2540 Daniel Johnson, Suite 510, Laval, PQ H7T 2T9, Canada *Tel:* 450-978-4700 *Toll Free Tel:* 800-361-8236 (Canada) *Fax:* 450-978-1305 *Toll Free Fax:* 800-361-6937 (Canada) *E-mail:* michelin.travel-publications-canada@ca.michelin.com *Web Site:* www.michelin-travel.com, pg 554

Bennett, Twila, Fleming H Revell, PO Box 6287, Grand Rapids, MI 49516-6287 *Tel:* 616-676-9185 *Toll Free Tel:* 800-877-2665 *Fax:* 616-676-9573 *Web Site:* www.bakerbooks.com, pg 232

Bennie, Dale, University of Oklahoma Press, 4100 28 Ave NW, Norman, OK 73069-8218 *Tel:* 405-325-2000 *Toll Free Tel:* 800-627-7377 (orders) *Fax:* 405-364-5798 (orders) *Toll Free Fax:* 800-735-0476 (orders) *E-mail:* oupress@ou.edu *Web Site:* www.oupress.com, pg 284

Benoit, Michael J, Benoit & Associates, 279 S Schuyler Ave, Kankakee, IL 60901 *Tel:* 815-932-2582 *Fax:* 815-932-2594 *E-mail:* benoitart@aol.com, pg 665

Bensky, Dan, Eastland Press, 3257 16 Ave W, Suite 2, Seattle, WA 98119 *Tel:* 206-217-0204 *Toll Free Tel:* 800-453-3278 *Fax:* 206-217-0205 *Toll Free Fax:* 800-241-3329 (orders) *E-mail:* info@eastlandpress.com; orders@eastlandpress.com (orders-credit cards only) *Web Site:* www.eastlandpress.com, pg 86

Bensky, Lilian, Eastland Press, 3257 16 Ave W, Suite 2, Seattle, WA 98119 *Tel:* 206-217-0204 *Toll Free Tel:* 800-453-3278 (orders only) *Fax:* 206-217-0205 *Toll Free Fax:* 800-241-3329 (orders) *E-mail:* info@

eastlandpress.com; orders@eastlandpress.com (orders-credit cards only) *Web Site:* www.eastlandpress.com, pg 86

Benson, Frances, Cornell University Press, 512 E State St, Ithaca, NY 14850 *Tel:* 607-277-2338 *Fax:* 607-277-2374 *E-mail:* cupressinfo@cornell.edu *Web Site:* www.cornellpress.cornell.edu, pg 68

Benson, Jack, Water Environment Federation, 601 Wythe St, Alexandria, VA 22314-1994 *Tel:* 703-684-2400 *Toll Free Tel:* 800-666-0206 *Fax:* 703-684-2492 *E-mail:* csc@wef.org *Web Site:* www.wef.org, pg 294

Benson, John W, B K Nelson Inc Lecture Bureau, 84 Woodland Rd, Pleasantville, NY 10570 *Tel:* 914-741-1322; 212-889-0637 *Fax:* 914-741-1323 *E-mail:* bknelson4@cs.com *Web Site:* www.bknelson.com, pg 670

Benson, John W, B K Nelson Inc Literary Agency, 1565 Paseo Vida, Palm Springs, CA 92264 *Tel:* 760-778-8800 *Fax:* 914-778-0034 *E-mail:* bknelson4@cs.com *Web Site:* www.bknelson.com, pg 645

Benson, Vera, American Map Corp, 46-35 54 Rd, Maspeth, NY 11378 *Tel:* 718-784-0055 *Toll Free Tel:* 800-432-MAPS *Fax:* 718-784-0640 (admin); 718-784-1216 (sales & orders), pg 15

Benson, Vera, Hagstrom Map Co Inc, 46-35 54 Rd, Maspeth, NY 11378 *Tel:* 718-784-0055 *Toll Free Tel:* 800-432-MAPS (432-6277) *Fax:* 718-784-0640 (admin); 718-784-1216 (sales & orders) *Web Site:* www.americanmap.com, pg 111

Benson, Vera, Hammond World Atlas Corp, 95 Progress St, Union, NJ 07083 *Tel:* 908-206-1300 *Toll Free Tel:* 800-526-4953 *Fax:* 908-206-1104 *E-mail:* customerservice@hammondmap.com; feedback@hammondmap.com *Web Site:* www.hammondmap.com, pg 112

Benson-Armer, Richard, Thomson Learning Inc, 200 First Stamford Place, Suite 400, Stamford, CT 06902 *Tel:* 203-539-8000 *Fax:* 203-539-7581 *E-mail:* communications@thomsonlearning.com *Web Site:* www.thomson.com/learning, pg 270

Bent, Jenny, Trident Media Group LLC, 41 Madison Ave, 36th fl, New York, NY 10010 *Tel:* 212-262-4810 *Fax:* 212-725-4501 *Web Site:* www.tridentmediagroup.com, pg 659

Bentley, D M R, Canadian Poetry Press, Dept of English, University of Western Ontario, London, ON N6A 3K7, Canada *Tel:* 519-673-1164; 519-661-2111 (ext 85834) *Fax:* 519-661-3776 *Web Site:* www.canadianpoetry.ca, pg 539

Bentley, Michael, Bentley Publishers, 1734 Massachusetts Ave, Cambridge, MA 02138 *Tel:* 617-547-4170 *Toll Free Tel:* 800-423-4595 *Fax:* 617-876-9235 *E-mail:* sales@bentleypublishers.com *Web Site:* www.bentleypublishers.com, pg 36

Bentley, Peter, State Mutual Book & Periodical Service Ltd, PO Box 1199, Bridgehampton, NY 11932-1199 *Tel:* 631-537-1104 *Fax:* 631-537-0412, pg 258

Benton, Lori, Harcourt Trade Publishers, 525 "B" St, Suite 1900, San Diego, CA 92101 *Tel:* 619-231-6616 *Toll Free Tel:* 800-543-1918 (cust serv) *Toll Free Tel:* 800-235-0256 (cust serv) *Web Site:* www.harcourtbooks.com, pg 115

Benton, Margaret, Bantam Dell Publishing Group, 1745 Broadway, New York, NY 10019 *Tel:* 212-782-9000 *Toll Free Tel:* 800-223-6834 *Fax:* 212-302-7985 *Web Site:* www.randomhouse.com/bantamdell, pg 31

Ber-Donkor, Nina, Knopf Canada, One Toronto St, Suite 300, Toronto, ON M5C 2V6, Canada *Tel:* 416-364-4449 *Toll Free Tel:* 800-668-4247 (order desk) *Fax:* 416-364-0462 *Web Site:* www.randomhouse.ca, pg 552

Bera, Madeleine, Univelt Inc, PO Box 28130, San Diego, CA 92198-0130 *Tel:* 760-746-4005 *Fax:* 760-746-3139 *E-mail:* 76121.1532@compuserve.com *Web Site:* www.univelt.com, pg 280

Berberoglu, Hrayr, Food and Beverage Consultants, 39 Burnview Crescent, Toronto, ON M1H 1B4, Canada *Tel:* 416-431-2015 *Fax:* 416-431-2015 *E-mail:* h1rayr@netscape.com, pg 547

Bercholz, Hazel, Shambhala Publications Inc, Horticultural Hall, 300 Massachusetts Ave, Boston, MA 02115 *Tel:* 617-424-0030 *Toll Free Tel:* 888-424-2329 (orders only) *Fax:* 617-236-1563; 303-665-5292 (orders only) *E-mail:* editors@shambhala.com *Web Site:* www.shambhala.com, pg 245

Bercholz, Samuel, Shambhala Publications Inc, Horticultural Hall, 300 Massachusetts Ave, Boston, MA 02115 *Tel:* 617-424-0030 *Toll Free Tel:* 888-424-2329 (orders only) *Fax:* 617-236-1563; 303-665-5292 (orders only) *E-mail:* editors@shambhala.com *Web Site:* www.shambhala.com, pg 245

Berchowitz, Gillian, Ohio University Press, One Ohio University, Scott Quadrangle, Athens, OH 45701 *Tel:* 740-593-1155 *Toll Free Tel:* 800-621-2736 *Fax:* 740-593-4536 *Web Site:* www.ohio.edu/oupress/, pg 196

Berchowitz, Gillian, Swallow Press, Scott Quadrangle, Athens, OH 45701 *Tel:* 740-593-1155 *Toll Free Tel:* 800-621-2736 (orders only) *Fax:* 740-593-4536 *Toll Free Fax:* 800-621-8476 (orders only) *Web Site:* www.ohiou.edu/oupress/, pg 263

Beren, Peter, Mandala Publishing, 17 Paul Dr, San Rafael, CA 94903 *Tel:* 415-883-4055 *Toll Free Tel:* 800-688-2218 (orders only) *Fax:* 415-884-0500 *E-mail:* mandala@mandala.org *Web Site:* www.mandala.org, pg 162

Berendsen, Robert, Berendsen & Associates Inc, 2233 Kemper Lane, Cincinnati, OH 45206 *Tel:* 513-861-1400 *Fax:* 513-861-6420 *Web Site:* www.illustratorsrep.com; www.photographersrep.com; www.designersrep.com; www.stockartrep.com, pg 665

Bereny, Justin A, Business/Technology Books (B/T Books), PO Box 574, Orinda, CA 94563-0526 *Tel:* 925-299-1829 *Fax:* 925-299-0668 *E-mail:* btbooks@evinfo.com *Web Site:* www.evinfo.com, pg 50

Berg, Barbara, Northern Illinois University Press, 310 N Fifth St, De Kalb, IL 60115 *Tel:* 815-753-1826; 815-753-1075 *Fax:* 815-753-1845 *E-mail:* bberg@niu.edu *Web Site:* www.niu.edu/univ_press, pg 193

Berg, Ginny C, R J Berg/Destinations Press Ltd, 450 E 96 St, Suite 500, Indianapolis, IN 46290 *Toll Free Tel:* 800-638-3909 *Fax:* 317-251-5901 *E-mail:* r.j.berg@destinationspressltd.com *Web Site:* www.destinationspressltd.com, pg 36

Berg, Karen, Kabbalah Publishing, 155 E 48 St, New York, NY 10017 *Tel:* 212-644-0025 *Toll Free Tel:* 866-524-8723 *Fax:* 212-317-1264 *E-mail:* ny@kabbalah.com *Web Site:* www.kabbalah.com, pg 143

Berg, Michael, Kabbalah Publishing, 155 E 48 St, New York, NY 10017 *Tel:* 212-644-0025 *Toll Free Tel:* 866-524-8723 *Fax:* 212-317-1264 *E-mail:* ny@kabbalah.com *Web Site:* www.kabbalah.com, pg 143

Berg, Patty, Harcourt Trade Publishers, 525 "B" St, Suite 1900, San Diego, CA 92101 *Tel:* 619-231-6616 *Toll Free Tel:* 800-543-1918 (cust serv) *Toll Free Fax:* 800-235-0256 (cust serv) *Web Site:* www.harcourtbooks.com, pg 115

Berg, Rav S P, Kabbalah Publishing, 155 E 48 St, New York, NY 10017 *Tel:* 212-644-0025 *Toll Free Tel:* 866-524-8723 *Fax:* 212-317-1264 *E-mail:* ny@kabbalah.com *Web Site:* www.kabbalah.com, pg 143

Berg, Ray, R J Berg/Destinations Press Ltd, 450 E 96 St, Suite 500, Indianapolis, IN 46290 *Toll Free Tel:* 800-638-3909 *Fax:* 317-251-5901 *E-mail:* r.j.berg@destinationspressltd.com *Web Site:* www.destinationspressltd.com, pg 36

Bergan, Colleen, NCCLS, 940 W Valley Rd, Suite 1400, Wayne, PA 19087-1898 *Tel:* 610-688-0100 *Fax:* 610-688-0700 *E-mail:* exoffice@nccls.org *Web Site:* www.nccls.org, pg 185

Bergenfield, Merrill, St Martin's Press LLC, 175 Fifth Ave, New York, NY 10010 *Tel:* 212-674-5151 *Fax:* 212-420-9314 *E-mail:* firstname.lastname@stmartins.com *Web Site:* www.stmartins.com, pg 239

Berger, Douglas, The Direct Marketing Association Inc (The DMA), 1120 Avenue of the Americas, New York, NY 10036-6700 *Tel:* 212-768-7277

Fax: 212-768-4547 *E-mail:* dma@the-dma.org; customerservice@the-dma.org *Web Site:* www.the-dma.org, pg 80

Berger, Ellie, Scholastic Inc, 557 Broadway, New York, NY 10012 *Tel:* 212-343-4469 *Toll Free Tel:* 800-scholastic *Fax:* 212-343-6930 *Web Site:* www.scholastic.com, pg 242

Berger, Ellie, Scholastic Trade Division, 557 Broadway, New York, NY 10012 *Tel:* 212-343-6100; 212-343-4685 (export sales) *Fax:* 212-343-4714 (export sales) *Web Site:* www.scholastic.com, pg 242

Berger, Karen, Quality Medical Publishing Inc, 2248 Welsch Industrial Ct, St Louis, MO 63146-4222 *Tel:* 314-878-7808 *Toll Free Tel:* 800-423-6865 *Fax:* 314-878-9937 *E-mail:* qmp@qmp.com *Web Site:* www.qmp.com, pg 223

Berger, Marcella, Fireside & Touchstone, 1230 Avenue of the Americas, New York, NY 10020, pg 97

Berger, Marcella, Simon & Schuster, 1230 Avenue of the Americas, New York, NY 10020 *Tel:* 212-698-7000 *Toll Free Tel:* 800-223-2348 (cust serv); 800-223-2336 (orders) *Toll Free Fax:* 800-943-9831 (orders) *Web Site:* www.simonsays.com, pg 248

Berger, Mary, Penguin Group (USA) Inc Sales, 375 Hudson St, New York, NY 10014 *Tel:* 212-366-2000 *E-mail:* online@penguinputnam.com *Web Site:* www.penguin.com, pg 208

Berger, Mel, William Morris Agency, 1325 Avenue of the Americas, New York, NY 10019 *Tel:* 212-586-5100 *Fax:* 212-903-1418 *E-mail:* wma@interport.net *Web Site:* www.wma.com, pg 645

Berger, Pat, ABI Professional Publications, 3580 Morris St N, Saint Petersburg, FL 33713 *Tel:* 727-556-0950 *Toll Free Tel:* 800-551-7776 *Fax:* 727-556-2560 *E-mail:* abipropub@vandamere.com; orders@vandamere.com *Web Site:* www.abipropub.com, pg 3

Berger, Pat, Vandamere Press, 3580 Morris St N, Saint Petersburg, FL 33713 *Tel:* 727-556-0950 *Toll Free Tel:* 800-551-7776 *Fax:* 727-556-2560 *E-mail:* orders@vandamere.com *Web Site:* www.vandamere.com, pg 289

Bergfeld, Ellen, American Society of Agronomy, 677 S Segoe Rd, Madison, WI 53711-1086 *Tel:* 608-273-8080 *Fax:* 608-273-2021 *E-mail:* headquarters@agronomy.org *Web Site:* www.agronomy.org, pg 18

Berghahn, Marion, Berghahn Books, 150 Broadway, Suite 812, New York, NY 10038 *Tel:* 212-222-6502 *Fax:* 212-222-5209 *E-mail:* info@berghahnbooks.com *Web Site:* www.berghahnbooks.com, pg 36

Bergman, Marilyn, American Society of Composers, Authors & Publishers (ASCAP), One Lincoln Plaza, New York City, NY 10023 *Tel:* 212-621-6000 *Toll Free Tel:* 800-952-7227 *Fax:* 212-362-7328 *E-mail:* info@ascap.com *Web Site:* www.ascap.com, pg 677

Bergquist, George, Nelson, 1120 Birchmount Rd, Scarborough, ON M1K 5G4, Canada *Tel:* 416-752-9448 *Toll Free Tel:* 800-268-2222 (cust serv); 800-430-4445 *Fax:* 416-752-8101 *E-mail:* inquire@nelson.com *Web Site:* www.nelson.com, pg 555

Bergsten, C Fred, Institute for International Economics, 1750 Massachusetts Ave NW, Washington, DC 20036 *Tel:* 202-328-9000 *Toll Free Tel:* 800-522-9139 *Fax:* 202-328-5432 *E-mail:* orders@iie.com *Web Site:* www.iie.com, pg 134

Bergstrom, Barbara, Barbara Bergstrom, MA, 13 Stockton Way, Howell, NJ 07731 *Tel:* 732-363-8372, pg 591

Bergstrom, Betty, Promissor Inc, 1007 Church St, Evanston, IL 60201 *Tel:* 847-866-2000 *Toll Free Tel:* 800-255-1312 *Fax:* 847-866-2002 *E-mail:* marketing@promissor.com *Web Site:* www.promissor.com, pg 220

Bergstrom, Jen, Simon & Schuster Children's Publishing, 1230 Avenue of the Americas, New York, NY 10020 *Tel:* 212-698-7000 *Web Site:* www.simonsayskids.com, pg 248

Berke, Martin, Weatherhill Inc, 41 Monroe Tpke, Trumbull, CT 06611 *Tel:* 203-459-5090 *Toll Free Tel:* 800-437-7840 *Fax:* 203-459-5095 *Toll Free Fax:* 800-557-5601 *E-mail:* weatherhill@weatherhill. com *Web Site:* www.weatherhill.com, pg 295

Berke, Ruth, McGraw-Hill Higher Education, 1333 Burr Ridge Pkwy, Burr Ridge, IL 60527 *Tel:* 630-789-4000 *Toll Free Tel:* 800-338-3987 (cust serv) *Fax:* 614-755-5645 (cust serv) *Web Site:* www.mhhe.com, pg 167

Berkey, Jane Rotrosen, Jane Rotrosen Agency LLC, 318 E 51 St, New York, NY 10022 *Tel:* 212-593-4330 *Fax:* 212-935-6985, pg 653

Berki, Attila, Books for Everybody, 70 The Esplanade, Suite 210, Toronto, ON M5E 1R2, Canada *Tel:* 416-360-0044 *Fax:* 416-955-0794 *E-mail:* mail@booksforeverybody.com *Web Site:* www. booksforeverybody.com, pg 682

Berkower, Amy, Writers House LLC, 21 W 26 St, New York, NY 10010 *Tel:* 212-685-2400 *Fax:* 212-685-1781, pg 662

Berkowitz, Dana, Fairchild Books, 7 W 34 St, New York, NY 10001 *Tel:* 212-630-3880 *Toll Free Tel:* 800-932-4724 *Fax:* 212-630-3868; 212-630-3898 *Web Site:* www.fairchildbooks.com, pg 94

Berlin, Ann, John Wiley & Sons Inc Education Publishing Group, 111 River St, Hoboken, NJ 07030 *Tel:* 201-748-6000 *Fax:* 201-748-6088 *E-mail:* info@ wiley.com *Web Site:* www.wiley.com, pg 300

Berlin, Kenneth, Environmental Law Institute, 1616 "P" St NW, Suite 200, Washington, DC 20036 *Tel:* 202-939-3800 *Fax:* 202-939-3868 *E-mail:* law@eli.org *Web Site:* www.eli.org, pg 91

Berlin, Rachel, Facts on File Inc, 132 W 31 St, 17th fl, New York, NY 10001 *Tel:* 212-967-8800 *Toll Free Tel:* 800-322-8755 *Fax:* 212-967-9196 *Toll Free Fax:* 800-678-3633 *E-mail:* custserv@factsonfile.com *Web Site:* www.factsonfile.com, pg 94

Berliner, Don, Donald Keyhoe Journalism Award, PO Box 277, Mount Rainier, MD 20712 *Tel:* 703-684-6032 *Fax:* 703-684-6032 *Web Site:* www.fufor.com, pg 782

Berlow, Lawrence H, Berlow Technical Communications Inc, 9 Prairie Ave, Suffern, NY 10901 *Tel:* 845-357-8215 *E-mail:* bteccinc@yahoo.com, pg 591

Berlowitz, Leslie, American Academy of Arts & Sciences (AAAS), Norton's Woods, 136 Irving St, Cambridge, MA 02138-1996 *Tel:* 617-576-5000 *Fax:* 617-576-5050 *Web Site:* www.amacad.org, pg 675

Berman, Ed, Nelson, 1120 Birchmount Rd, Scarborough, ON M1K 5G4, Canada *Tel:* 416-752-9448 *Toll Free Tel:* 800-268-2222 (cust serv); 800-430-4445 *Fax:* 416-752-8101 *E-mail:* inquire@nelson.com *Web Site:* www.nelson.com, pg 555

Berman, Jan, Developmental Studies Center, 2000 Embarcadero, Suite 305, Oakland, CA 94606-5300 *Tel:* 510-533-0213 *Toll Free Tel:* 800-666-7270 *Fax:* 510-842-0348 *E-mail:* pubs@devstu.org *Web Site:* www.devstu.org, pg 79

Berman, Jeff, Warren Communications News, 2115 Ward Ct NW, Washington, DC 20037-1209 *Tel:* 202-872-9200 *Fax:* 202-293-3435 *E-mail:* info@warren-news. com *Web Site:* www.warren-news.com, pg 293

Berman, Sam, The Rough Notes Co Inc, 11690 Technology Dr, Carmel, IN 46032-5600 *Tel:* 317-582-1600 *Toll Free Tel:* 800-428-4384 *Fax:* 317-816-1000 *Toll Free Fax:* 800-321-1909 *Web Site:* www. roughnotes.com, pg 235

Bernabeo, Paul, Marshall Cavendish Corp, 99 White Plains Rd, Tarrytown, NY 10591-9001 *Tel:* 914-332-8888 *Fax:* 914-332-1888 *E-mail:* mcc@marshallcavendish.com *Web Site:* www. marshallcavendish.com, pg 164

Bernal, Peggy Park, Huntington Library Press, 1151 Oxford Rd, San Marino, CA 91108 *Tel:* 626-405-2138 *Fax:* 626-585-0794 *E-mail:* booksales@huntington.org *Web Site:* www.huntington.org/HLPress/HEHPubs. html, pg 129

Bernard, Alec, Puddingstone Literary, Authors' Agents, 11 Mabro Dr, Denville, NJ 07834-9607 *Tel:* 973-366-3622, pg 649

Bernard, Andre, Harcourt Inc, 6277 Sea Harbor Dr, Orlando, FL 32887 *Tel:* 407-345-2000 *Toll Free Tel:* 800-225-5425 (cust serv) *Fax:* 407-352-3445 (cust serv), pg 114

Bernard, Andre, Harcourt Trade Publishers, 525 "B" St, Suite 1900, San Diego, CA 92101 *Tel:* 619-231-6616 *Toll Free Tel:* 800-543-1918 (cust serv) *Toll Free Fax:* 800-235-0256 (cust serv) *Web Site:* www. harcourtbooks.com, pg 115

Bernfeld, Linda, Writers Workshop in Children's Literature, 10305 SW 127 Ct, Miami, FL 33186 *Tel:* 305-382-2677, pg 749

Berning, Shannon, Newmarket Publishing & Communications, 18 E 48 St, New York, NY 10017 *Tel:* 212-832-3575 *Toll Free Tel:* 800-669-3903 *Fax:* 212-832-3629 *E-mail:* mailbox@newmarketpress. com *Web Site:* www.newmarketpress.com, pg 190

Bernstein, Barbara, Hampton Press Inc, 23 Broadway, Cresskill, NJ 07626 *Tel:* 201-894-1686 *Toll Free Tel:* 800-894-8955 *Fax:* 201-894-8732 *E-mail:* hamptonpr1@aol.com *Web Site:* www. hamptonpress.com, pg 113

Bernstein, Jack, Interlingua Publishing, 423 S Pacific Coast Hwy, No 208, Redondo Beach, CA 90277 *Tel:* 310-792-3636 *Fax:* 509-479-8935 *E-mail:* interlingua@aol.com, pg 136

Bernstein, Jennifer C, The Metropolitan Museum of Art, 1000 Fifth Ave, New York, NY 10028 *Tel:* 212-879-5500; 212-535-7710 *Fax:* 212-396-5062 *E-mail:* info@metmuseum.org *Web Site:* www. metmuseum.org, pg 173

Bernstein, Meredith, Meredith G Bernstein, 2112 Broadway, Suite 503A, New York, NY 10023 *Tel:* 212-799-1007 *Fax:* 212-799-1145, pg 621

Bernstein, Rachel, Random House Publishing Group, 1745 Broadway, New York, NY 10019 *Toll Free Tel:* 800-200-3552 *Toll Free Fax:* 800-200-3552 *Web Site:* www.randomhouse.com, pg 227

Bernstein, Stacy, Federal Bar Association, 2215 "M" St NW, Washington, DC 20037 *Tel:* 202-785-1614 *Fax:* 202-785-1568 *E-mail:* fba@fedbar.org *Web Site:* www.fedbar.org, pg 95

Bernstein, Tracy, NAL, 375 Hudson St, New York, NY 10014 *Tel:* 212-366-2000 *E-mail:* online@ penguinputnam.com *Web Site:* www.penguin.com, pg 181

Berrent, Howard, Harcourt Interactive Technology, 99 Powerhouse Rd, Suite 106, Roslyn Heights, NY 11577 *Tel:* 516-625-6755 *Toll Free Tel:* 800-745-3276 *Fax:* 516-625-6789 *E-mail:* hit@harcourt.com *Web Site:* www.hit.iloli.com, pg 114

Berry, Gail, Open Horizons Publishing Co, PO Box 205, Fairfield, IA 52556-0205 *Tel:* 641-472-6130 *Toll Free Tel:* 800-796-6130 *Fax:* 641-472-1560 *E-mail:* info@ bookmarket.com *Web Site:* www.bookmarket.com, pg 197

Berry, Henry, Independent Publishing Agency, PO Box 176, Southport, CT 06890 *Tel:* 203-332-7629 *Fax:* 203-332-7629, pg 635

Berry, Joseph P, American Editing, 69 Lansing St, Auburn, NY 13021 *Tel:* 315-258-8012, pg 590

Berry, Joseph P, Legend Books, College Division, 69 Lansing St, Auburn, NY 13021 *Tel:* 315-258-8012, pg 152

Berry, Kathy, Global Travel Publishers Inc, 5353 N Federal Hwy, Suite 300, Fort Lauderdale, FL 33308 *Tel:* 954-491-8877 *Toll Free Tel:* 800-882-9453 *Fax:* 954-491-9060 *E-mail:* noltingaac@aol.com *Web Site:* www.africanadventure.com, pg 571

Berry, Leah M, Glory Bound Books, 6642 Marlette St, Suite 101, Marlette, MI 48453 *Tel:* 989-635-7520 *E-mail:* info@gloryboundenterprises.com *Web Site:* www.thegloryboundbookcompany.com, pg 106

Berry, R M, Fiction Collective Two Inc, Florida State University, FC2, Dept of English, Tallahassee, FL 32306-1580 *Tel:* 850-644-2260 *Fax:* 850-644-6808 *E-mail:* fc2@english.fsu.edu *Web Site:* fc2.org, pg 96

Berry, Tammy, University of Tennessee Press, 110 Conference Center Bldg, Knoxville, TN 37996-4108 *Tel:* 865-974-3321 *Toll Free Tel:* 800-621-2736 (ordering) *Fax:* 865-974-3724 *E-mail:* custserv@ utpress.org *Web Site:* www.utpress.org, pg 285

Berryhill, Dani, Oxmoor House Inc, 2100 Lakeshore Dr, Birmingham, AL 35209 *Tel:* 205-445-6000; 205-445-6560 *Toll Free Tel:* 800-366-4712 *Fax:* 205-445-6078 *Web Site:* www.oxmoorhouse.com, pg 201

Berset, David, Haights Cross Communications Inc, 10 New King St, White Plains, NY 10604 *Tel:* 914-289-9400 *Fax:* 914-289-9401 *E-mail:* info@haightscross. com *Web Site:* www.haightscross.com, pg 112

Berset, David, Recorded Books LLC, 270 Skipjack Rd, Prince Frederick, MD 20678 *Tel:* 410-535-5590 *Toll Free Tel:* 800-638-1304 *Fax:* 410-535-5499 *E-mail:* recordedbooks@recordedbooks.com *Web Site:* www.recordedbooks.com, pg 229

Bershtel, Sara, Henry Holt and Company, LLC, 115 W 18 St, New York, NY 10011 *Tel:* 212-886-9200 *Toll Free Tel:* 888-330-8477 (orders) *Fax:* 212-633-0748 *E-mail:* publicity@hholt.com *Web Site:* www. henryholt.com, pg 124

Berthold, Dennis, The Melville Society, University of Minnesota, 140 Appleby Hall, Minneapolis, MN 55455 *Fax:* 612-625-0709, pg 691

Bertin, Joan E, National Coalition Against Censorship (NCAC), 275 Seventh Ave, 9th fl, New York, NY 10001 *Tel:* 212-807-6222 *Fax:* 212-807-6245 *E-mail:* ncac@ncac.org *Web Site:* www.ncac.org, pg 692

Bertoli, Monique, Les Editions du Vermillon, 305 rue Saint-Patrick, Ottawa, ON K1N 5K4, Canada *Tel:* 613-241-4032 *Fax:* 613-241-3109 *E-mail:* leseditionsduvermillon@rogers.com *Web Site:* www.primatech.ca/vermillon/index.html; vermillon.info.ca, pg 545

Bertouille, Ariane, Prix Emile-Nelligan, 261 avenue Bloomfield, Outremont, PQ H2V 3R6, Canada *Tel:* 514-849-8540 *Fax:* 514-271-6239 *E-mail:* info@ fondation-nelligan.org *Web Site:* www.fondation-nelligan.org, pg 772

Bertouille, Ariane, Union des Ecrivaines et Ecrivains Quebecois, 3492 avenue Laval, Montreal, PQ H2X 3C8, Canada *Tel:* 514-849-8540 *Toll Free Tel:* 888-849-8540 *Fax:* 514-271-6239 *E-mail:* ecrivez@uneq. qc.ca *Web Site:* www.uneq.qc.ca, pg 701

Bertucci, Mary Lou, Swedenborg Foundation Publishers/ Chrysalis Books, 320 N Church St, West Chester, PA 19380 *Tel:* 610-430-3222 *Toll Free Tel:* 800-355-3222 (cust serv) *Fax:* 610-430-7982 *E-mail:* info@ swedenborg.com *Web Site:* www.swedenborg.com, pg 263

Berube, Margery, Houghton Mifflin Trade & Reference Division, 222 Berkeley St, Boston, MA 02116-3764 *Tel:* 617-351-5000 *Toll Free Tel:* 800-225-3362 *Web Site:* www.houghtonmifflinbooks.com, pg 126

Berzanskis, Andrew, The Flannery O'Connor Award for Short Fiction, 330 Research Dr, Athens, GA 30602-4901 *Tel:* 706-369-6130 (no phone queries accepted) *Fax:* 706-369-6131 *Web Site:* www.ugapress.org, pg 795

Besant, Todd, Turnstone Press, 607-100 Arthur St, Winnipeg, MB R3B 1H3, Canada *Tel:* 204-947-1555 *Toll Free Tel:* 800-982-6472 *Fax:* 204-942-1555 *E-mail:* editor@turnstonepress.com; mktg@ turnstonepress.com *Web Site:* www.turnstonepress.com, pg 564

Bimm, Bridget, Sovereign Award Outstanding Newspaper Story, Outstanding Feature Story, Woodbine Sales Pavilion, 555 Rexdale Blvd, Rexdale, ON M9W 5L2, Canada *Tel:* 416-675-7756 *Fax:* 416-675-6378 *E-mail:* jockeyclub@bellnet.ca *Web Site:* www.jockeyclubcanada.com, pg 807

Bingen, Lisa, Great Source Education Group, 181 Ballardvale St, Wilmington, MA 01887 *Tel:* 978-661-1300 *Toll Free Tel:* 800-289-4490 (orders), pg 108

Bingham, Joan, Grove/Atlantic Inc, 841 Broadway, 4th fl, New York, NY 10003-4793 *Tel:* 212-614-7850 *Toll Free Tel:* 800-521-0178 *Fax:* 212-614-7886 *Web Site:* www.groveatlantic.com, pg 110

Bingham, Ken, Rosemont College, Dept of English, 1400 Montgomery Ave, Rosemont, PA 19010 *Tel:* 610-527-0200 (ext 2320) *Fax:* 610-526-2964 *Web Site:* www.rosemont.edu, pg 754

Binney, Jan J, The Speech Bin Inc, 1965 25 Ave, Vero Beach, FL 32960 *Tel:* 772-770-0007 *Toll Free Tel:* 800-4-SPEECH (477-3324) *Fax:* 772-770-0006 *Toll Free Fax:* 888-FAX-2-BIN (329-2246) *E-mail:* speechbin@speechbin.com *Web Site:* www. speechbin.com, pg 255

Binyominson, Yerachmiel, Hachai Publications Inc, 156 Chester Ave, Brooklyn, NY 11218 *Tel:* 718-633-0100 *Toll Free Tel:* 800-50-HACHAI (504-2424) *Fax:* 718-633-0103 *E-mail:* info@hachai.com *Web Site:* www. hachai.com, pg 111

Biolchini, Bob, PennWell Books & More, 1421 S Sheridan, Tulsa, OK 74112 *Tel:* 918-831-9421 *Toll Free Tel:* 800-752-9764 *Fax:* 918-832-9319 *E-mail:* sales@penwellbooks.com *Web Site:* www. penwellbooks.com, pg 209

Birch, Susan, ASM Press, 1752 "N" St NW, Washington, DC 20036-2904 *Tel:* 202-737-3600 *Toll Free Tel:* 800-546-2416 *Fax:* 202-942-9342 *E-mail:* books@asmusa. org *Web Site:* www.asmpress.org, pg 25

Bird, Marcia, The Globe Pequot Press, 246 Goose Lane, Guilford, CT 06437 *Tel:* 203-458-4500 *Toll Free Tel:* 800-243-0495 (cust serv) *Fax:* 203-458-4601 *Toll Free Fax:* 800-820-2329 (orders & cust serv) *E-mail:* info@globepequot.com *Web Site:* www. globepequot.com, pg 106

Bird, Robin, Michelin Travel Publications, PO Box 19001, Greenville, SC 29602-9001 *Tel:* 864-458-5127 *Toll Free Tel:* 800-423-0485; 800-223-0987 *Fax:* 864-458-6674 *Toll Free Fax:* 866-297-0914 *E-mail:* michelin.travel-publications-us@us.michelin. com *Web Site:* www.viamichelin.com, pg 173

Birkholz, Linda, Peradam Press, PO Box 6, North San Juan, CA 95960-0006 *Tel:* 800-241-8689 *Fax:* 530-292-4266 *Toll Free Fax:* 800-241-8689 *E-mail:* peradam@earthlink.net, pg 210

Birks, Kristin, Freedom of Information Center, 133 Neff Annex, Columbia, MO 65211-0012 *Tel:* 573-882-4856 *Fax:* 573-884-6204 *E-mail:* foi@missouri.edu *Web Site:* foi.missouri.edu, pg 687

Birnbaum, Agnes, Bleecker Street Associates Inc, 532 LaGuardia Place, No 617, New York, NY 10012 *Tel:* 212-677-4492 *Fax:* 212-388-0001, pg 621

Birschel, Dee, International Foundation of Employee Benefit Plans, 18700 W Bluemound Rd, Brookfield, WI 53045 *Tel:* 262-786-6700 *Toll Free Tel:* 888-334-3327 *Fax:* 262-786-8780 *E-mail:* books@ifebp.org *Web Site:* www.ifebp.org, pg 137

Bisbee-Beek, Mary, University of Michigan Press, 839 Greene St, Ann Arbor, MI 48104-3209 *Tel:* 734-764-4388 *Fax:* 734-615-1540 *E-mail:* um.press@umich.edu *Web Site:* www.press.umich.edu, pg 282

Bischel, Dr Margaret, Apollo Managed Care Consultants, 860 Ladera Lane, Santa Barbara, CA 93108 *Tel:* 805-969-2606 *Fax:* 805-969-3749 *E-mail:* mail@apollomanagedcare.com *Web Site:* www.apollomanagedcare.com, pg 21

Bischoff, Karen, Harcourt Interactive Technology, 99 Powerhouse Rd, Suite 106, Roslyn Heights, NY 11577 *Tel:* 516-625-6755 *Toll Free Tel:* 800-745-3276 *Fax:* 516-625-6789 *E-mail:* hit@harcourt.com *Web Site:* www.hit.iloli.com, pg 114

Bishell, Bill, University of Texas Press, PO Box 7819, Austin, TX 78713-7819 *Tel:* 512-471-7233 *Fax:* 512-232-7178 *E-mail:* utpress@uts.cc.utexas.edu *Web Site:* www.utexas.edu/utpress, pg 267

Bishop, William F, The Johns Hopkins University Press, 2715 N Charles St, Baltimore, MD 21218-4363 *Tel:* 410-516-6900 *Toll Free Tel:* 800-537-5487 *Fax:* 410-516-6968 *Web Site:* www.press.jhu.edu, pg 141

Bissmeyer, Melynda, Levine-Greenberg Literary Agency Inc, 307 Seventh Ave, Suite 1906, New York, NY 10001 *Tel:* 212-337-0934 *Fax:* 212-337-0948 *Web Site:* www.levinegreenberg.com, pg 640

Bisso, Larry, Bookbuilders of Boston, 44 Highland Circle, Halifax, MA 02338 *Tel:* 781-293-8600 *Toll Free Tel:* 866-820-0469 *E-mail:* office@bbboston.org *Web Site:* www.bbboston.org, pg 682

Bisson, Michelle, Marshall Cavendish Corp, 99 White Plains Rd, Tarrytown, NY 10591-9001 *Tel:* 914-332-8888 *Fax:* 914-332-1888 *E-mail:* mcc@marshallcavendish.com *Web Site:* www. marshallcavendish.com, pg 164

Bix, Amy Sue, Edelstein Prize, Iowa State University, 603 Ross Hall, History Dept, Ames, IA 50011 *Tel:* 515-294-8469 *Fax:* 515-294-6390 *E-mail:* shot@ iastate.edu *Web Site:* www.shot.jhu.edu, pg 771

Bixby, Robert, March Street Press, 3413 Wilshire Dr, Greensboro, NC 27408 *Tel:* 336-282-9754 *Fax:* 336-282-9754 *Web Site:* www.marchstreetpress.com, pg 163

Bixler, Gina, University of Notre Dame Press, 310 Flanner Hall, Notre Dame, IN 46556 *Tel:* 574-631-6346 *Toll Free Tel:* 800-621-2736 (orders) *Fax:* 574-631-8148 *Toll Free Fax:* 800-621-8476 (orders) *E-mail:* nd.undpress.1@nd.edu *Web Site:* www. undpress.nd.edu, pg 284

Bizri, Jonmana, International Medical Publishing Inc, 1313 Dolly Madison Blvd, Suite 302, McLean, VA 22101 *Tel:* 703-356-2037 *Toll Free Tel:* 800-530-3142 *Fax:* 703-734-8987 *E-mail:* contact@ medicalpublishing.com *Web Site:* www. medicalpublishing.com, pg 137

Bjerke, John, Martingale & Co, 20205 144 Ave NE, Woodinville, WA 98072 *Tel:* 425-483-3313 *Toll Free Tel:* 800-426-3126 *Fax:* 425-486-7596 *E-mail:* info@ martingale-pub.com *Web Site:* www.martingale-pub. com, pg 164

Bjerke, Paisius, St Herman Press, 10 Beegum Gorge Rd, Platina, CA 96076 *Tel:* 530-352-4430 *Fax:* 530-352-4432 *E-mail:* stherman@stherman.com *Web Site:* www.stherman.com, pg 238

Bjorklund, Charles, Perigee Books, 375 Hudson St, New York, NY 10014 *Tel:* 212-366-2000 *Fax:* 212-366-2365 *E-mail:* online@penguinputnam.com *Web Site:* www.penguin.com, pg 210

Bjorklund, Charles, Riverhead Books (Trade Paperback), 375 Hudson St, New York, NY 10014 *Tel:* 212-366-2000 *E-mail:* online@penguinputnam.com *Web Site:* www.penguin.com, pg 233

Black, Cynthia, Beyond Words Publishing Inc, 20827 NW Cornell Rd, Suite 500, Hillsboro, OR 97124-9808 *Tel:* 503-531-8700 *Fax:* 503-531-8773 *Web Site:* www. beyondword.com, pg 38

Black, David, David Black Literary Agency, 156 Fifth Ave, Suite 608, New York, NY 10010 *Tel:* 212-242-5080 *Fax:* 212-924-6609, pg 621

Black, Debby, Dharma Publishing, 2910 San Pablo Ave, Berkeley, CA 94702 *Tel:* 510-548-5407 *Toll Free Tel:* 800-873-4276 *Fax:* 510-548-2230 *E-mail:* info@dharmapublishing.com *Web Site:* www. dharmapublishing.com, pg 79

Black, James, Emond Montgomery Publications Ltd, 60 Shaftesbury Ave, Toronto, ON M4T 1A3, Canada *Tel:* 416-975-3925 *Toll Free Tel:* 888-837-0815 *Fax:* 416-975-3924 *E-mail:* info@emp.ca; orders@ emp.ca *Web Site:* www.emp.ca, pg 546

Black, Jeff, Hollywood Creative Directory, 1024 N Orange Dr, Hollywood, CA 90038 *Tel:* 323-308-3490 *Toll Free Tel:* 800-815-0503 *Fax:* 323-308-3493 *Web Site:* www.hcdonline.com, pg 124

Black, Jeffrey, Lone Eagle Publishing, 1024 N Orange Dr, Los Angeles, CA 90038 *Tel:* 323-308-3411 *Toll Free Tel:* 800-815-0503 *Fax:* 323-468-7689 *Web Site:* www.hcdonline.com, pg 157

Black, Josephine L, Blue Dolphin Publishing Inc, 12428 Nevada City Hwy, Grass Valley, CA 95945 *Tel:* 530-265-6925 *Toll Free Tel:* 800-643-0765 *Fax:* 530-265-0787 *E-mail:* bdolphin@netshel.net *Web Site:* www. bluedolphinpublishing.com, pg 41

Black, Julie, Random House Sales & Marketing, 1745 Broadway, New York, NY 10019 *Fax:* 212-782-9000, pg 227

Black, Kathy, Vermont Studio Center, PO Box 613, Johnson, VT 05656 *Tel:* 802-635-2727 *Fax:* 802-635-2730 *E-mail:* info@vermontstudiocenter.org *Web Site:* www.vermontstudiocenter.org, pg 748

Black, Kim, National Council of Teachers of English (NCTE), 1111 W Kenyon Rd, Urbana, IL 61801-1096 *Tel:* 217-328-3870 *Toll Free Tel:* 800-369-6283; 877-369-6283 (cust serv) *Fax:* 217-328-0977 *E-mail:* orders@ncte.org *Web Site:* www.ncte.org, pg 183

Black, Peter, CCAB Inc, 90 Eglinton Ave E, Suite 980, Toronto, ON M4P 2Y3, Canada *Tel:* 416-487-2418 *Fax:* 416-487-6405 *E-mail:* info@bpai.com *Web Site:* www.bpai.com, pg 684

Blackhall, Gail, The Globe Pequot Press, 246 Goose Lane, Guilford, CT 06437 *Tel:* 203-458-4500 *Toll Free Tel:* 800-243-0495 (cust serv) *Fax:* 203-458-4601 *Toll Free Fax:* 800-820-2329 (orders & cust serv) *E-mail:* info@globepequot.com *Web Site:* www. globepequot.com, pg 106

Blackmer, Alice, Chelsea Green Publishing Co, PO Box 428, White River Junction, VT 05001-0428 *Tel:* 802-295-6300 *Toll Free Tel:* 800-639-4099 (cust serv & consumer orders); 800-807-6726 (trade & wholesale orders) *Fax:* 802-295-6444 *Web Site:* www. chelseagreen.com, pg 59

Blackstone, Anne, The Lazear Agency Inc, 431 Second St, Suite 300, Hudson, WI 54016 *Tel:* 715-531-0012 *Fax:* 715-531-0016 *Web Site:* www.lazear.com, pg 639

Blades, Joe, Broken Jaw Press Inc, 5-2004 York St, Fredericton, NB E3B 5A6, Canada *Tel:* 506-454-5127 *Fax:* 506-454-5127 *Web Site:* www.brokenjaw.com, pg 537

Blades, Joe, Random House Publishing Group, 1745 Broadway, New York, NY 10019 *Toll Free Tel:* 800-200-3552 *Toll Free Fax:* 800-200-3552 *Web Site:* www.randomhouse.com, pg 227

Blagden, Donna, Duke University Press, 905 W Main St, Suite 18-B, Durham, NC 27701 *Tel:* 919-687-3600 *Toll Free Tel:* 888-651-0122 (orders only) *Fax:* 919-688-4574 *Toll Free Fax:* 888-651-0124 *Web Site:* www.dukeupress.edu, pg 84

Blagowidow, George, Hippocrene Books Inc, 171 Madison Ave, New York, NY 10016 *Tel:* 212-685-4371 (edit); 718-454-2366 (sales & cust serv) *Fax:* 718-454-1391 (cust serv); 212-779-9338 (edit) *Toll Free Fax:* 800-809-3855 (sales) *E-mail:* orders@hippocrenebooks.com *Web Site:* www. hippocrenebooks.com, pg 123

Blagowidow, Ludmilla, Hippocrene Books Inc, 171 Madison Ave, New York, NY 10016 *Tel:* 212-685-4371 (edit); 718-454-2366 (sales & cust serv) *Fax:* 718-454-1391 (cust serv); 212-779-9338 (edit) *Toll Free Fax:* 800-809-3855 (sales) *E-mail:* orders@hippocrenebooks.com *Web Site:* www. hippocrenebooks.com, pg 123

Blagowidow, Nicholas, Hippocrene Books Inc, 171 Madison Ave, New York, NY 10016 *Tel:* 212-685-4371 (edit); 718-454-2366 (sales & cust serv) *Fax:* 718-454-1391 (cust serv); 212-779-9338 (edit) *Toll Free Fax:* 800-809-3855 (sales) *E-mail:* orders@hippocrenebooks.com *Web Site:* www. hippocrenebooks.com, pg 123

Blair, Alan, Abingdon Press, 201 Eighth Ave S, Nashville, TN 37203-3919 *Tel:* 615-749-6290 (publicist); 615-749-6000; 615-749-6451 (sales) *Toll Free Tel:* 800-251-3320 *Fax:* 615-749-6056 *Web Site:* www.abingdonpress.com, pg 3

Blair, Allan, Creative Homeowner, 24 Park Way, Upper Saddle River, NJ 07458-9960 *Tel:* 201-934-7100 *Toll Free Tel:* 800-631-7795 *Fax:* 201-934-8971 *E-mail:* info@creativehomeowner.com *Web Site:* www.creativehomeowner.com, pg 72

Blair, Susan, J Weston Walch Publisher, 321 Valley St, Portland, ME 04104 *Tel:* 207-772-2846 *Toll Free Tel:* 800-341-6094 *Fax:* 207-772-3105 *Toll Free Fax:* 888-991-5755 *E-mail:* customerservice@mail.walch.com *Web Site:* www.walch.com, pg 292

Blair, Susan A, Pathways Publishing, 183 Guggins Lane, Boxborough, MA 01719 *Tel:* 978-264-4060 *Toll Free Tel:* 888-333-7284 *Fax:* 978-264-4069 *Web Site:* www.pathwayspub.com, pg 205

Blake, Emerson, Milkweed Editions, 1011 Washington Ave S, Suite 300, Minneapolis, MN 55415 *Tel:* 612-332-3192 *Toll Free Tel:* 800-520-6455 *Fax:* 612-215-2550 *E-mail:* editor@milkweed.org *Web Site:* www.milkweed.org; www.worldashome.org, pg 174

Blake, Emerson, Milkweed National Fiction Prize, 1011 Washington Ave S, Suite 300, Minneapolis, MN 55415 *Tel:* 612-332-3192 *Toll Free Tel:* 800-520-6455 *Fax:* 612-215-2550 *E-mail:* editor@milkweed.org *Web Site:* www.milkweed.org, pg 789

Blake, Holly, Headlands Center for the Arts Residency for CA, NC, OH & NJ Writers, 944 Fort Barry, Sausalito, CA 94965 *Tel:* 415-331-2787 *Fax:* 415-331-3857 *Web Site:* www.headlands.org, pg 778

Blake, Robert, Fodor's Travel Publications, 1745 Broadway, New York, NY 10019 *Tel:* 212-572-8784 *Toll Free Tel:* 800-733-3000 *Fax:* 212-572-2248 *Web Site:* www.fodors.com, pg 98

Blake, Sylvia, Competency Press, PO Box 95, White Plains, NY 10605-0091 *Tel:* 914-948-6783 *Fax:* 914-761-7179 *E-mail:* studentcomp@aol.com, pg 66

Blake, Tammy, Clarkson Potter Publishers, 1745 Broadway, New York, NY 10019 *Tel:* 212-782-9000 *Toll Free Tel:* 888-264-1745 *Fax:* 212-572-6181 *Web Site:* www.clarksonpotter.com; www.randomhouse.com/crown/clarksonpotter, pg 63

Blakey, Sarabeth, Beyond Words Publishing Inc, 20827 NW Cornell Rd, Suite 500, Hillsboro, OR 97124-9808 *Tel:* 503-531-8700 *Fax:* 503-531-8773 *Web Site:* www.beyondword.com, pg 38

Blanchard, Andre, Les Editions Un Monde Different, 3925 Grande Allee, St-Hubert, PQ J4T 2V8, Canada *Tel:* 450-656-2660 *Fax:* 450-445-9098 *Web Site:* www.umd.ca, pg 546

Blanchard, James, Weil Publishing Co Inc, 150 Capitol St, Augusta, ME 04330 *Tel:* 207-621-0029 *Toll Free Tel:* 800-877-9345 *Fax:* 207-621-0069 *E-mail:* info@weilpublishing.com *Web Site:* www.weilpublishing.com, pg 295

Blanchard, Marshall, Hoover Institution Press, 424 Galvez Mall, Stanford, CA 94305-6010 *Tel:* 650-723-3373 *Toll Free Tel:* 800-935-2882 *Fax:* 650-723-8626 *E-mail:* digest@hoover.stanford.edu; hooverpress@hoover.stanford.edu *Web Site:* www.hoover.org, pg 125

Blanchard, Paula, Down East Books, PO Box 679, Camden, ME 04843 *Tel:* 207-594-9544 *Toll Free Tel:* 800-766-1670 (ME only) *Fax:* 207-594-7215 *Web Site:* www.downeastbooks.com, pg 83

Blanchette, Jean-Guy, Groupe Educalivres Inc, 955, rue Bergar, Laval, PQ H7L 4Z6, Canada *Tel:* 514-334-8466 *Toll Free Tel:* 800-567-3671 (Info Service) *Fax:* 514-334-8387 *E-mail:* commentaires@educalivres.com *Web Site:* www.educalivres.com, pg 548

Blanchette, Rick, Ball Publishing, 335 N River St, Batavia, IL 60510 *Tel:* 630-208-9080 *Fax:* 630-208-9350 *E-mail:* info@ballpublishing.com *Web Site:* www.ballpublishing.com, pg 30

Blanco, Alicia, Two Thousand Three Associates, 4180 Saxon Dr, New Smyrna Beach, FL 32169 *Tel:* 386-427-7876 *Fax:* 386-423-7523 *E-mail:* ttta@worldnet.att.net, pg 277

Bland, Jacqueline, Graphic Arts Marketing Information Service (GAMIS), 100 Daingerfield Rd, Alexandria, VA 22314 *Tel:* 703-519-8100; 703-519-8179 *Toll Free Tel:* 800-742-2666 *Fax:* 703-548-3227 *E-mail:* info@gamis.org *Web Site:* www.gamis.org, pg 687

Blankenship, Amy, The Direct Marketing Association Inc (The DMA), 1120 Avenue of the Americas, New York, NY 10036-6700 *Tel:* 212-768-7277 *Fax:* 212-768-4547 *E-mail:* dma@the-dma.org; customerservice@the-dma.org *Web Site:* www.the-dma.org, pg 80

Blanton, Sandra, Peter Lampack Agency Inc, 551 Fifth Ave, Suite 1613, New York, NY 10176 *Tel:* 212-687-9106 *Fax:* 212-687-9109 *E-mail:* lampackag@verizon.net (other correspondence), pg 639

Blasberg, Ann, Other Press LLC, 307 Seventh Ave, Suite 1807, New York, NY 10001 *Tel:* 212-414-0054 *Toll Free Tel:* 877-843-6843 *Fax:* 212-414-0939 *E-mail:* editor@otherpress.com; orders@otherpress.com *Web Site:* www.otherpress.com, pg 199

Blaschko, Tom, Idyll Arbor Inc, 25119 SE 262 St, Ravensdale, WA 98051 *Tel:* 425-432-3231 *Fax:* 425-432-3726 *E-mail:* sales@idyllarbor.com *Web Site:* www.idyllarbor.com, pg 130

Blasdell, Caitlin, Liza Dawson Associates, 240 W 35 St, Suite 500, New York, NY 10001 *Tel:* 212-465-9071, pg 626

Blate, Sam, Sam Blate Associates, LLC, 10331 Watkins Mill Dr, Montgomery Village, MD 20886-3950 *Tel:* 301-840-2248 *Fax:* 301-990-0707 *E-mail:* info@writephotopro.com *Web Site:* www.writephotopro.com, pg 592

Blauwkamp, Caroline H, Zondervan, 5300 Patterson Ave SE, Grand Rapids, MI 49530 *Tel:* 616-698-6900 *Toll Free Tel:* 800-727-1309 (cust serv) *Fax:* 616-698-3439; 616-698-3255 (cust serv) *Web Site:* www.zondervan.com, pg 307

Blazek, Diane, Ball Publishing, 335 N River St, Batavia, IL 60510 *Tel:* 630-208-9080 *Fax:* 630-208-9350 *E-mail:* info@ballpublishing.com *Web Site:* www.ballpublishing.com, pg 30

Bleecker, Isabelle, The Perseus Books Group, 387 Park Ave S, 12th fl, New York, NY 10016 *Tel:* 212-340-8100 *Toll Free Tel:* 800-386-5656 (cust serv) *Fax:* 212-340-8115 *Web Site:* www.perseusbooksgroup.com, pg 210

Blickers, Beth, Abrams Artists Agency, 275 Seventh Ave, 26th fl, New York, NY 10001 *Tel:* 646-486-4600 *Fax:* 646-486-2358, pg 617

Blie, Harrison, Dine College Press, Dine College, Tsaile, AZ 86556 *Tel:* 928-724-6635 *Fax:* 928-724-6637 *Web Site:* www.dinecollege.edu, pg 80

Bligh, Arthur, Humanics Publishing Group, 12 S Dixie Hwy, Suite 203, Lake Worth, FL 33460 *Tel:* 561-533-6231 *Toll Free Tel:* 800-874-8844 *Toll Free Fax:* 888-874-8844 *E-mail:* humanics@mindspring.com *Web Site:* humanicspub.com; humanicslearning.com; humanicsdealer.com, pg 128

Blischke, Alathea, McLaren Memorial Comedy Playwriting Competition, 2000 W Wadley, Midland, TX 79705 *Tel:* 432-682-2544 *Fax:* 432-682-6136 *Web Site:* www.mctmidland.org, pg 789

Bliss, Anthony A Jr, Aqua Quest Publications Inc, 18 Garvies Point Rd, Glen Cove, NY 11542 *Tel:* 516-759-0476 *Toll Free Tel:* 800-933-8989 *Fax:* 516-759-4519 *E-mail:* info@aquaquest.com *Web Site:* www.aquaquest.com, pg 22

Bliss, Corey, The Haworth Press Inc, 10 Alice St, Binghamton, NY 13904-1580 *Tel:* 607-722-5857 *Toll Free Tel:* 800-429-6784 *Fax:* 607-722-1424 *Toll Free Fax:* 800-895-0582 *E-mail:* getinfo@haworthpressinc.com *Web Site:* www.haworthpress.com, pg 118

Bliss, Josefina A, Aqua Quest Publications Inc, 18 Garvies Point Rd, Glen Cove, NY 11542 *Tel:* 516-759-0476 *Toll Free Tel:* 800-933-8989 *Fax:* 516-759-4519 *E-mail:* info@aquaquest.com *Web Site:* www.aquaquest.com, pg 22

Bloch, Charles, Bloch Publishing Co, 118 E 28 St, Suite 501-503, New York, NY 10016-8413 *Tel:* 212-532-3977 *Fax:* 212-779-9169 *E-mail:* blochpub@worldnet.att.net *Web Site:* www.blochpub.com, pg 41

Bloch, Peter, Palma Julia de Burgos, c/o Peter Bloch, 83 Park Terr W, Suite 6-A, New York, NY 10034 *Tel:* 212-942-2338 *Fax:* 718-367-0780 *Web Site:* www.buscapique.com, pg 796

Bloch, Sam, Herzl Press, 633 Third Ave, 21st fl, New York, NY 10017 *Tel:* 212-339-6020 *Fax:* 212-318-6176 *E-mail:* midstreamthf@aol.com *Web Site:* www.midstreamthf.com, pg 121

Block, A G, California Journal Press, 2101 "K" St, Sacramento, CA 95816-4920 *Tel:* 916-444-2840 *Fax:* 916-446-5369 *E-mail:* edit@statenet.com, pg 51

Block, Gwen M, Marine Education Textbooks Inc, 124 N Van Ave, Houma, LA 70363-5895 *Tel:* 985-879-3866 *Fax:* 985-879-3911 *E-mail:* namenet@triparish.net *Web Site:* www.marineeducationtextbooks.com, pg 163

Block, Richard A, Marine Education Textbooks Inc, 124 N Van Ave, Houma, LA 70363-5895 *Tel:* 985-879-3866 *Fax:* 985-879-3911 *E-mail:* namenet@triparish.net *Web Site:* www.marineeducationtextbooks.com, pg 163

Blom, Jeff, Blue Dove Press, 4204 Sorrento Valley Blvd, Suite K, San Diego, CA 92121 *Tel:* 858-623-3330 *Toll Free Tel:* 800-691-1008 (orders) *Fax:* 858-623-3325 *E-mail:* mail@bluedove.org *Web Site:* www.bluedove.org, pg 41

Blomberg, Keith, Human Kinetics Inc, PO Box 5076, Champaign, IL 61825-5076 *Tel:* 217-351-5076 *Toll Free Tel:* 800-747-4457 *Fax:* 217-351-1549 (orders/cust serv) *E-mail:* info@hkusa.com *Web Site:* www.humankinetics.com, pg 128

Blome, Scott, American Printing House for the Blind Inc, 1839 Frankfort Ave, Louisville, KY 40206 *Tel:* 502-895-2405 *Toll Free Tel:* 800-223-1839 (cust serv) *Fax:* 502-899-2274 *E-mail:* info@aph.org *Web Site:* www.aph.org, pg 16

Blood, Michael, Avisson Press Inc, 3007 Taliaferro Rd, Greensboro, NC 27408 *Tel:* 336-288-6989 *Fax:* 336-288-6989 *E-mail:* avisson4@aol.com, pg 29

Bloom, Brettne, Kneerim & Williams, c/o Fish & Richardson PC, 225 Franklin St, Boston, MA 02110 *Tel:* 617-542-5070 *Fax:* 617-542-8906 *Web Site:* www.fr.com, pg 638

Bloom, Carol, Bloom Ink Publishing Professionals, 122 S Ninth St, Lafayette, IN 47901-1652 *Tel:* 765-429-4888 *Fax:* 765-420-9597 *Web Site:* www.awbo.org/bloomink.htm, pg 592

Bloom, Floyd E, American Association for the Advancement of Science, 1200 New York Ave NW, Washington, DC 20005 *Tel:* 202-326-6400 *Fax:* 202-289-4021 *E-mail:* webmaster@aaas.org *Web Site:* www.aaas.org, pg 675

Bloom, Sue, Pact Publications, 1200 18 St NW, Suite 350, Washington, DC 20036 *Tel:* 202-466-5666 *Fax:* 202-466-5669 *E-mail:* books@pacthq.org *Web Site:* www.pactpublications.org, pg 202

Bloomer, Paul, Redleaf Press, 10 Yorkton Ct, St Paul, MN 55117 *Tel:* 651-641-0305 *Toll Free Tel:* 800-423-8309 *Toll Free Fax:* 800-641-0115 *Web Site:* www.redleafpress.org, pg 230

Bloomfield, Julia, Getty Publications, 1200 Getty Center Dr, Suite 500, Los Angeles, CA 90049-1682 *Tel:* 310-440-7365 *Fax:* 310-440-7758 *E-mail:* pubsinfo@getty.edu *Web Site:* www.getty.edu/bookstore, pg 104

Bloomquist, Max, Brilliance Audio, 1704 Eaton Dr, Grand Haven, MI 49417 *Tel:* 616-846-5256 *Toll Free Tel:* 800-648-2312 (orders only) *Fax:* 616-846-0630 *Web Site:* www.brillianceaudio.com, pg 48

Blosser, Dr Pam, SOM Publishing, 163 Moon Valley Rd, Windyville, MO 65783 *Tel:* 417-345-8411 *Fax:* 417-345-6668 (call 417-345-8411 before faxing) *E-mail:* som@som.org *Web Site:* www.som.org, pg 253

Blosser, Paul, SOM Publishing, 163 Moon Valley Rd, Windyville, MO 65783 *Tel:* 417-345-8411 *Fax:* 417-345-6668 (call 417-345-8411 before faxing) *E-mail:* som@som.org *Web Site:* www.som.org, pg 253

Blough, Heidi, Heidi Blough, Book Indexer, 502 Tanager Rd, St Augustine, FL 32086 *Tel:* 904-797-6572 *Fax:* 904-797-7617 *E-mail:* indexing@heidiblough. com *Web Site:* www.heidiblough.com, pg 592

Blough, Kathryn G, Association of American Publishers (AAP), 71 Fifth Ave, 2nd fl, New York, NY 10003-3004 *Tel:* 212-255-0200 *Fax:* 212-255-7007 *Web Site:* www.publishers.org, pg 679

Blount, Katie, McLemore Prize, PO Box 571, Jackson, MS 39205-0571 *Tel:* 601-576-6850 *Fax:* 601-576-6975 *E-mail:* mhs@mdah.state.ms.us *Web Site:* www.mdah. state.ms.us, pg 789

Bloxdorf, Kim, Record Research Inc, PO Box 200, Menomonee Falls, WI 53052 *Tel:* 262-251-5408 *Toll Free Tel:* 800-827-9810 *Fax:* 262-251-9452 *E-mail:* books@recordresearch.com *Web Site:* www. recordresearch.com, pg 229

Bludman, Helene, Jewish Publication Society, 2100 Arch St, 2nd fl, Philadelphia, PA 19103 *Tel:* 215-832-0600 *Toll Free Tel:* 800-234-3151 *Fax:* 215-568-2017 *E-mail:* jewishbook@jewishpub.org *Web Site:* www. jewishpub.org, pg 141

Blue, Anthony, Special Libraries Association (SLA), 313 S Patrick St, Alexandria, VA 22314 *Tel:* 703-647-4900 *Fax:* 703-647-4901 *E-mail:* sla@sla.org *Web Site:* www.sla.org, pg 701

Blue, Marian, Blue & Ude Writers' Services, PO Box 145, Clinton, WA 98236 *Tel:* 360-341-1630 *E-mail:* blueyude@whidbey.com *Web Site:* www. blueudewritersservices.com, pg 592

Blumenthal, Richard, Haights Cross Communications Inc, 10 New King St, White Plains, NY 10604 *Tel:* 914-289-9400 *Fax:* 914-289-9401 *E-mail:* info@ haightscross.com *Web Site:* www.haightscross.com, pg 112

Blundo, Joe, The National Society of Newspaper Columnists (NSNC), Fillmore St, Suite 507, San Francisco, CA 94115 *Tel:* 415-541-5636 *Web Site:* www.columnists.com, pg 694

Bluth, Winfried, Herald Press, 616 Walnut Ave, Scottdale, PA 15683-1999 *Tel:* 724-887-8500 *Toll Free Tel:* 800-245-7894 *Fax:* 724-887-3111 *E-mail:* hp@ mph.org *Web Site:* www.heraldpress.com, pg 121

Boadt, Lawrence, Paulist Press, 997 Macarthur Blvd, Mahwah, NJ 07430 *Tel:* 201-825-7300 *Toll Free Tel:* 800-218-1903 *Fax:* 201-825-8345 *Toll Free Fax:* 800-836-3161 (orders) *E-mail:* info@paulistpress. com *Web Site:* www.paulistpress.com, pg 206

Boals, Judy, Judy Boals Inc & Jim Flynn Agency, 208 W 30 St, Suite 401, New York, NY 10001 *Tel:* 212-868-1068; 212-868-0924 *Fax:* 212-868-1052, pg 621

Boates, Reid, Reid Boates Literary Agency, 69 Cooks Crossroad, Pittstown, NJ 08867-0328 *Tel:* 908-730-8523 *Fax:* 908-730-8931 *E-mail:* boatesliterary@att. net, pg 621

Boaz, David, Cato Institute, 1000 Massachusetts Ave NW, Washington, DC 20001-5403 *Tel:* 202-842-0200 *Toll Free Tel:* 800-767-1241 *Fax:* 202-842-3490 *E-mail:* books@cato.org *Web Site:* www.cato.org, pg 55

Boaz, John, Big Guy Books Inc, 7750 El Camino Real, Suite F, Carlsbad, CA 92009 *Tel:* 760-334-1222 *Toll Free Tel:* 866-210-5938 (Booksellers cust serv); 800-741-6493 (For parents, teachers, schools & libraries) *Fax:* 760-334-1225 *E-mail:* info@bigguybooks. com; orders@bigguybooks.com *Web Site:* www. bigguybooks.com, pg 38

Bobbitt, Michael D, Twilight Times Books, PO Box 3340, Kingsport, TN 37664-0340 *Tel:* 423-323-0183 *Fax:* 423-323-0183 *E-mail:* publisher@twilighttimes. com *Web Site:* www.twilighttimesbooks.com, pg 277

Bobco, Ann, Simon & Schuster Children's Publishing, 1230 Avenue of the Americas, New York, NY 10020 *Tel:* 212-698-7000 *Web Site:* www.simonsayskids.com, pg 248

Bobko, Jane, The Metropolitan Museum of Art, 1000 Fifth Ave, New York, NY 10028 *Tel:* 212-879-5500; 212-535-7710 *Fax:* 212-396-5062 *E-mail:* info@ metmuseum.org *Web Site:* www.metmuseum.org, pg 173

Bobley, Douglas, Bobley Harmann Corp, 311 Crossways Park Dr, Woodbury, NY 11797 *Tel:* 516-364-1800 *Fax:* 516-364-1899 *E-mail:* info@bobley.com *Web Site:* www.bobley.com, pg 43

Bobley, Mark, Bobley Harmann Corp, 311 Crossways Park Dr, Woodbury, NY 11797 *Tel:* 516-364-1800 *Fax:* 516-364-1899 *E-mail:* info@bobley.com *Web Site:* www.bobley.com, pg 42

Bobley, Peter M, Bobley Harmann Corp, 311 Crossways Park Dr, Woodbury, NY 11797 *Tel:* 516-364-1800 *Fax:* 516-364-1899 *E-mail:* info@bobley.com *Web Site:* www.bobley.com, pg 43

Bobley, Peter M, Platinum Press Inc, 311 Crossways Park Dr, Woodbury, NY 11797 *Tel:* 516-364-1800 *Fax:* 516-364-1899, pg 214

Bobrow, Deborah, Dorothy Silver Playwriting Competition, 3505 Mayfield Rd, Cleveland Heights, OH 44118 *Tel:* 216-382-4000 (ext 215) *Fax:* 216-382-5401 *E-mail:* halletheatre@clevejcc.org *Web Site:* www.clevejcc.org, pg 805

Bobst, Chuck, Pacific Press Publishing Association, 1350 N Kings Rd, Nampa, ID 83687-3193 *Tel:* 208-465-2500 *Toll Free Tel:* 800-447-7377 *Fax:* 208-465-2531 *Web Site:* www.pacificpress.com, pg 202

Boccuzzi, Ben, International Medical Publishing Inc, 1313 Dolly Madison Blvd, Suite 302, McLean, VA 22101 *Tel:* 703-356-2037 *Toll Free Tel:* 800-530-3142 *Fax:* 703-734-8987 *E-mail:* contact@ medicalpublishing.com *Web Site:* www. medicalpublishing.com, pg 137

Boczkowski, Tricia, Simon & Schuster Children's Publishing, 1230 Avenue of the Americas, New York, NY 10020 *Tel:* 212-698-7000 *Web Site:* www. simonsayskids.com, pg 248

Bodkin, Robin, Alan Wofsy Fine Arts, 1109 Geary Blvd, San Francisco, CA 94109 *Tel:* 415-292-6500 *Fax:* 415-512-0130 (acctg); 415-292-6594 (off & cust serv) *E-mail:* beauxarts@earthlink.net (cust serv); editeur@earthlink.net (edit); order@art-books.com (orders) *Web Site:* art-books.com, pg 302

Boedeker, Bill, Little, Brown and Company Books for Young Readers, 1271 Avenue of the Americas, New York, NY 10020 *Tel:* 212-522-8700 *Toll Free Tel:* 800-759-0190 *Fax:* 212-522-7997 *Web Site:* www. twbookmark.com, pg 156

Boehm, Ronald, ABC-CLIO, 130 Cremona Dr, Santa Barbara, CA 93117 *Tel:* 805-968-1911 *Toll Free Tel:* 800-368-6868 *Fax:* 805-685-9685 *E-mail:* sales@ abc-clio.com *Web Site:* www.abc-clio.com, pg 2

Boer, Faye, Folklore Publishing, 8025 102 St, Edmonton, AB T6E 4A2, Canada *Tel:* 780-910-6216 *Fax:* 780-433-9646 *Web Site:* www.folklorepublishing.com, pg 547

Boers, Jack, Baker Books, PO Box 6287, Grand Rapids, MI 49516-6287 *Tel:* 616-676-9185 *Toll Free Tel:* 800-877-2665; 800-679-1957 *Fax:* 616-676-9573 *Toll Free Fax:* 800-398-3110 *Web Site:* www. bakerpublishinggroup.com, pg 30

Boersma, Karen, Kids Can Press Ltd, 2250 Military Rd, Tonawanda, NY 14150 *Tel:* 416-925-5437 (Toronto, ON, Canada) *Toll Free Tel:* 800-265-0884; 866-481-5827 (orders) *Fax:* 416-960-5437 (Toronto, ON, Canada) *E-mail:* info@kidscan.com; lfyman@kidscan. com (orders) *Web Site:* www.kidscanpress.com, pg 145

Boersma, Karen, Kids Can Press Ltd, 29 Birch Ave, Toronto, ON M4V 1E2, Canada *Tel:* 416-925-5437 *Toll Free Tel:* 800-265-0884 *Fax:* 416-960-5437 *E-mail:* info@kidscan.com *Web Site:* kidscanpress. com, pg 552

Boes, Terri, Writer's Digest Writing Competition, 4700 E Galbraith Rd, Cincinnati, OH 45236 *Tel:* 513-531-2690 (ext 580) *Fax:* 513-531-0798 *E-mail:* writing-competition@fwpubs.com *Web Site:* www. writersdigest.com, pg 812

Boettcher, Gerald, Kalmbach Publishing Co, 21027 Crossroads Circle, Waukesha, WI 53187 *Tel:* 262-796-8776 *Toll Free Tel:* 800-533-6644 *Fax:* 262-796-1615 (sales & cust serv) *Web Site:* www.kalmbach.com, pg 143

Boga, Hiro, Oolichan Books, Box 10, Lantzville, BC V0R 2H0, Canada *Tel:* 250-390-4839 *Fax:* 250-390-4839 *E-mail:* oolichan@island.net *Web Site:* www. oolichan.com, pg 556

Bogaards, Paul, Alfred A Knopf, 1745 Broadway, New York, NY 10019 *Tel:* 212-751-2600 *Toll Free Tel:* 800-638-6460 *Fax:* 212-572-2593 *Web Site:* www. randomhouse.com/knopf, pg 146

Bogehold, Lindley, Black Dog & Leventhal Publishers Inc, 151 W 19 St, 12th fl, New York, NY 10011 *Tel:* 212-647-9336 *Fax:* 212-647-9332 *E-mail:* information@bdlev.com *Web Site:* www.bdlev. com, pg 39

Bogner, Hal, CyclopsMedia.com, 1076 Eagle Dr, Salinas, CA 93905 *Tel:* 831-776-9500 *Fax:* 831-422-5915 *E-mail:* custserv@cyclopsmedia.com *Web Site:* www. cyclopsmedia.com, pg 75

Bogstad, Janice, Pilgrim Award & Pioneer Award, 6021 Grassmere, Corpus Christi, TX 78415 *Tel:* 530-752-1699 *E-mail:* sands@uwm.edu *Web Site:* www.sfra. org, pg 799

Bogusky, Kathy, Fifth House Publishers, 1511 1800 Fourth St SW, Calgary, AB T2S 2S5, Canada *Tel:* 403-571-5230 *Toll Free Tel:* 800-387-9776 *Fax:* 403-571-5235 *Toll Free Fax:* 800-260-9777 *Web Site:* www.fitzhenry.ca/fifthhouse.htm, pg 546

Bohannon, Adam B, Fairchild Books, 7 W 34 St, New York, NY 10001 *Tel:* 212-630-3880 *Toll Free Tel:* 800-932-4724 *Fax:* 212-630-3868; 212-630-3898 *Web Site:* www.fairchildbooks.com, pg 94

Bohannon, Kendall, The Writer's Advocate/Literary Agenting & Editorial Services, 1675 Larimer St, Suite 410, Denver, CO 80202 *Tel:* 303-297-1233 *Fax:* 303-297-3997 *E-mail:* thewritersadvocate@ thelightningfactory.com *Web Site:* www. thelightningfactory.com, pg 661

Bohm, Fredric C, Michigan State University Press (MSU Press), 1405 S Harrison Rd, Suite 25, East Lansing, MI 48823 *Tel:* 517-355-9543 *Fax:* 517-432-2611 *Toll Free Fax:* 800-678-2120 *E-mail:* msupress@msu.edu *Web Site:* www.msupress.msu.edu, pg 173

Boies, Kay, Sequoyah Children's Book Award, 300 Hardy Dr, Edmond, OK 73013 *Tel:* 405-348-0506 *Fax:* 405-348-1629 *Web Site:* www.oklibs.org, pg 805

Boies, Kay, Sequoyah Young Adult Book Award, 300 Hardy Dr, Edmond, OK 73013 *Tel:* 405-348-0506 *Fax:* 405-348-1629 *Web Site:* www.oklibs.org, pg 805

Boilard, Amy, LaurelTech Integrated Publishing Solutions, 1750 Elm St, Suite 201, Manchester, NH 03104 *Tel:* 603-606-5800 *Fax:* 603-606-5838 *E-mail:* sales@laureltech.com *Web Site:* www. laureltech.com, pg 604

Boisseau, Michelle, BKMK Press of the University of Missouri-Kansas City, 5101 Rockhill Rd, Kansas City, MO 64110-2499 *Tel:* 816-235-2558 *Fax:* 816-235-2611 *E-mail:* bkmk@umkc.edu *Web Site:* www.umkc. edu/bkmk, pg 39

Boisseau, Michelle, G S Sharat Chandra Prize for Short Fiction, 5101 Rockhill Rd, Kansas City, MO 64110 *Tel:* 816-235-2558 *Fax:* 816-235-2611 *E-mail:* bkmk@ umkc.edu *Web Site:* www.umkc.edu/bkmk/, pg 766

Boisseau, Michelle, John Ciardi Prize for Poetry, 5101 Rockhill Rd, Kansas City, MO 64110 *Tel:* 816-235-2558 *Fax:* 816-235-2611 *E-mail:* bkmk@umkc.edu *Web Site:* www.umkc.edu/bkmk/, pg 767

Boitnott, Sally, Pelican Publishing Co Inc, 1000 Burmaster, Gretna, LA 70053 *Tel:* 504-368-1175 *Toll Free Tel:* 800-843-1724 *Fax:* 504-368-1195 *E-mail:* sales@pelicanpub.com (sales); office@ pelicanpub.com (permission); promo@pelicanpub.com (publicity) *Web Site:* www.pelicanpub.com, pg 207

Bol, Bob, Baker Books, PO Box 6287, Grand Rapids, MI 49516-6287 *Tel:* 616-676-9185 *Toll Free Tel:* 800-877-2665; 800-679-1957 *Fax:* 616-676-9573 *Toll Free Fax:* 800-398-3110 *Web Site:* www. bakerpublishinggroup.com, pg 30

Bol, Robert, Chosen Books, PO Box 6287, Grand Rapids, MI 49516-6287 *Tel:* 616-676-9185 *Toll Free Tel:* 800-877-2665 *Fax:* 616-676-2315 *Web Site:* www. bakerpublishinggroup.com, pg 61

Bol, Robert, Fleming H Revell, PO Box 6287, Grand Rapids, MI 49516-6287 *Tel:* 616-676-9185 *Toll Free Tel:* 800-877-2665 *Fax:* 616-676-9573 *Web Site:* www. bakerbooks.com, pg 232

Bolchazy, Ladislaus J, Bolchazy-Carducci Publishers Inc, 1000 Brown St, Unit 101, Wauconda, IL 60084 *Tel:* 847-526-4344 *Fax:* 847-526-2867 *Web Site:* www. bolchazy.com, pg 43

Bolchazy, Marie Carducci, Bolchazy-Carducci Publishers Inc, 1000 Brown St, Unit 101, Wauconda, IL 60084 *Tel:* 847-526-4344 *Fax:* 847-526-2867 *Web Site:* www. bolchazy.com, pg 43

Bolding, Sally, LeveePressTwo, c/o Bolding, 330 Ft Pickens Rd, No 11A, Pensacola Beach, FL 32561 *Tel:* 850-934-1357 *Fax:* 850-932-1588 *E-mail:* HBOLD@worldnet.att.net *Web Site:* www. LeveeFiction.com, pg 572

Boldrick, Nellie, Ignatius Press, 2515 McAllister St, San Francisco, CA 94118 *Tel:* 415-387-2324 *Toll Free Tel:* 877-320-9276 (book orders) *Fax:* 415-387-0896 *E-mail:* info@ignatius.com *Web Site:* www.ignatius. com, pg 131

Boldrick, Penelope, Ignatius Press, 2515 McAllister St, San Francisco, CA 94118 *Tel:* 415-387-2324 *Toll Free Tel:* 877-320-9276 (book orders) *Fax:* 415-387-0896 *E-mail:* info@ignatius.com *Web Site:* www.ignatius. com, pg 131

Bole, Bonnie, Princeton University Press, 41 William St, Princeton, NJ 08540 *Tel:* 609-258-4900 *Toll Free Tel:* 800-777-4726 *Fax:* 609-258-6305 *Toll Free Fax:* 800-999-1958 *E-mail:* orders@cpfsinc.com *Web Site:* www.pup.princeton.edu, pg 219

Bolger, Loretta, Quincannon Publishing Group, PO Box 8100, Glen Ridge, NJ 07028-8100 *Tel:* 973-669-8367 *E-mail:* editors@quincannongroup.com *Web Site:* www.quincannongroup.com, pg 224

Bolhuis, David, RAND Corp, 1776 Main St, Santa Monica, CA 90407 *Tel:* 310-393-0411 *Fax:* 310-451-6996 *E-mail:* jane_ryan@rand.org *Web Site:* www. rand.org, pg 225

Bolinao, Mela, HK Portfolio Inc, 10 E 29 St, 40G, New York, NY 10016 *Tel:* 212-689-7830 *Fax:* 212-689-7829 *Web Site:* www.hkportfolio.com, pg 666

Bolinder, Scott W, Zondervan, 5300 Patterson Ave SE, Grand Rapids, MI 49530 *Tel:* 616-698-6900 *Toll Free Tel:* 800-727-1309 (cust serv) *Fax:* 616-698-3439; 616-698-3255 (cust serv) *Web Site:* www.zondervan. com, pg 307

Boll, Dana, Emmis Books, 1700 Madison Rd, 2nd fl, Cincinnati, OH 45206 *Tel:* 513-861-4045 *Toll Free Tel:* 800-913-9563 *Fax:* 513-861-4430 *E-mail:* info@ emmis.com *Web Site:* www.emmisbooks.com, pg 90

Bollas, George, Cortina Learning International Inc, 7 Hollyhock Rd, Wilton, CT 06897-4414 *Tel:* 203-762-2510 *Toll Free Tel:* 800-245-2145 *Fax:* 203-762-2514 *E-mail:* info@cortina-languages.com; cortinainc@aol. com *Web Site:* www.cortina-languages.com (English language animation & sound); www.cursos-ingles-cortina.com (Spanish language animation & sound), pg 69

Bollas, George, Institute for Language Study, 7 Hollyhock Rd, Wilton, CT 06897 *Tel:* 203-762-2510 *Toll Free Tel:* 800-245-2145 *Fax:* 203-762-2514 *E-mail:* cortinainc@aol.com *Web Site:* www.cortina-languages.com; members.aol.com/cortinainc, pg 134

Bollinger, Eric, Sligo Literary Agency LLC, 74-923 Hwy 111, Suite 173, Indian Wells, CA 92210 *Tel:* 760-340-6640 *Fax:* 760-340-4320 *E-mail:* ricsligo@aol.com, pg 656

Bolm, Jennifer, Adventures Unlimited Press, One Adventure Place, Kempton, IL 60946 *Tel:* 815-253-6390 *Fax:* 815-253-6300 *E-mail:* auphq@frontiernet. net *Web Site:* www.adventuresunlimitedpress.com, pg 6

Bolotin, Susan, Workman Publishing Co Inc, 708 Broadway, New York, NY 10003-9555 *Tel:* 212-254-5900 *Toll Free Tel:* 800-722-7202 *Fax:* 212-254-8098 *E-mail:* info@workman.com *Web Site:* www.workman. com, pg 303

Bolson, Robert, Eclipse Press, 3101 Beaumont Centre Circle, Lexington, KY 40513 *Tel:* 859-278-2361 *Toll Free Tel:* 800-866-2361 *Fax:* 859-276-6868 *E-mail:* editorial@eclipsepress.com; marketing@ eclipsepress.com *Web Site:* www.eclipsepress.com, pg 86

Bolstad, Karen, Purich Publishing Ltd, PO Box 23032, Market Mall Postal Outlet, Saskatoon, SK S7J 5H3, Canada *Tel:* 306-373-5311 *Fax:* 306-373-5315 *E-mail:* purich@sasktel.net *Web Site:* www. purichpublishing.com, pg 559

Bolton, Catherine, Public Relations Society of America Inc, 33 Maiden Lane, 11th fl, New York, NY 10038-5150 *Tel:* 212-460-1400 *Fax:* 212-995-0757 *E-mail:* hq@prsa.org *Web Site:* www.prsa.org, pg 698

Bolton, Sharyn, Pacific Northwest Writers Conference, 23607 Hwy 99, Suite 2C, Edmonds, WA 98026 *Tel:* 425-673-2665 *E-mail:* staff@pnwa.org *Web Site:* www.pnwa.org, pg 746

Bolton, Sharyn, PNWA Literary Competition, 23607 Hwy 99, Suite 2C, Edmonds, WA 98026 *Tel:* 425-673-2665 *E-mail:* staff@pnwa.org *Web Site:* www.pnwa. org, pg 799

Bonacum, Leslie, CCH Inc, 2700 Lake Cook Rd, Riverwoods, IL 60015 *Tel:* 847-267-7000 *Toll Free Tel:* 888-224-7377 *Web Site:* www.cch.com, pg 56

Bond, Alison M, Alison M Bond Ltd, 155 W 72 St, Suite 302, New York, NY 10023 *Tel:* 212-874-2850 *Fax:* 212-874-2892 *E-mail:* mail@bondlit.com, pg 621

Bond, John H, Slack Incorporated, 6900 Grove Rd, Thorofare, NJ 08086-9447 *Tel:* 856-848-1000 *Toll Free Tel:* 800-257-8290 *Fax:* 856-853-5991 *Web Site:* www.slackbooks.com, pg 250

Bond, Sandra, Bond Literary Agency, 1430 E Bates Ave, Englewood, CO 80113 *Tel:* 303-781-9305 *Fax:* 303-783-9166, pg 621

Bonenberger, John, William H Sadlier Inc, 9 Pine St, New York, NY 10005 *Tel:* 212-227-2120 *Toll Free Tel:* 800-221-5175 *Fax:* 212-312-6080 *Web Site:* www. sadlier.com; www.sadlier-oxford.com, pg 237

Bonessi, Ed, Classroom Connect, 8000 Marina Blvd, Suite 400, Brisbane, CA 94005 *Tel:* 650-351-5100 *Toll Free Tel:* 800-638-1639 (cust support) *Fax:* 650-351-5300 *E-mail:* connect@classroom.com *Web Site:* www.classroom.com, pg 63

Bonk, Rich, Philadelphia Museum of Art, 2525 Pennsylvania Ave, Philadelphia, PA 19130 *Tel:* 215-684-7250 *Fax:* 215-235-8715 *Web Site:* www. philamuseum.org, pg 211

Bonoff, Steven, International Prepress Association, 7200 France Ave S, Suite 223, Edina, MN 55435 *Tel:* 952-896-1908 *Fax:* 952-896-0181 *E-mail:* info@ipa.org *Web Site:* www.ipa.org, pg 689

Bonomini, Michelle, South-Western, A Thomson Business, 5191 Natorp Blvd, Mason, OH 45040 *Tel:* 513-229-1000 *Toll Free Tel:* 800-543-0487 *Fax:* 513-229-1025 *Web Site:* www.thomson.com, pg 254

Bookman, Robert, Creative Artists Agency, 9830 Wilshire Blvd, Beverly Hills, CA 90212-1825 *Tel:* 310-288-4545 *Fax:* 310-288-4800 *Web Site:* www. caa.com, pg 626

Boone, Anne Q, Grafco Productions Inc, 291 Pat Mell Rd, Suite 101, Marietta, GA 30060 *Tel:* 770-436-1500 *Toll Free Tel:* 888-656-1500 *Fax:* 770-444-9357 *E-mail:* jabo@rightconnections.net *Web Site:* www. jackwboone.com, pg 107

Boone, Laurel, Goose Lane Editions, 469 King St, Fredericton, NB E3B 1E5, Canada *Tel:* 506-450-4251 *Toll Free Tel:* 888-926-8377 *Fax:* 506-459-4991 *E-mail:* gooselane@gooselane.com *Web Site:* www. gooselane.com, pg 548

Boorstein, Amy, Crown Publishing Group, 1745 Broadway, New York, NY 10019 *Tel:* 212-782-9000 *Toll Free Tel:* 888-264-1745 *Fax:* 212-940-7408 *Web Site:* www.randomhouse.com/crown, pg 74

Boos, Florence, William Morris Society in the United States Fellowships, PO Box 53263, Washington, DC 20009 *Web Site:* www.morrissociety.org, pg 790

Booth, Doris, Authorlink Press, 3720 Millswood Dr, Irving, TX 75062 *Tel:* 972-650-1986 *Fax:* 972-650-1622 *Web Site:* www.authorlink.com, pg 28

Booth, Linda, Herald Publishing House, 1001 W Walnut, Independence, MO 64051 *Tel:* 816-521-3015 *Toll Free Tel:* 800-767-8181 *Fax:* 816-521-3066 *E-mail:* marketing@heraldhouse.org *Web Site:* www. heraldhouse.org, pg 121

Booth, Tami, Rodale Books, 400 S Tenth St, Emmaus, PA 18098-0099 *Tel:* 610-967-5171 *Fax:* 610-967-8961 *Web Site:* www.rodale.com, pg 234

Booth, Tom, Oregon State University Press, 102 Adams Hall, Corvallis, OR 97331 *Tel:* 541-737-3166 *Toll Free Tel:* 800-426-3797 (orders) *Fax:* 541-737-3170 *Toll Free Fax:* 800-426-3797 (orders) *E-mail:* osu.press@ oregonstate.edu *Web Site:* oregonstate.edu/dept/press, pg 199

Borchardt, Anne, Georges Borchardt Inc, 136 E 57 St, New York, NY 10022 *Tel:* 212-753-5785 *Fax:* 212-838-6518 *E-mail:* georges@gbagency.com, pg 622

Borchardt, Georges, Georges Borchardt Inc, 136 E 57 St, New York, NY 10022 *Tel:* 212-753-5785 *Fax:* 212-838-6518 *E-mail:* georges@gbagency.com, pg 622

Borchardt, Valerie, Georges Borchardt Inc, 136 E 57 St, New York, NY 10022 *Tel:* 212-753-5785 *Fax:* 212-838-6518 *E-mail:* georges@gbagency.com, pg 622

Borden, Leslye, PhotoEdit Inc, 235 E Broadway, Suite 1020, Long Beach, CA 90802 *Tel:* 562-435-2722 *Toll Free Tel:* 800-860-2098 *Fax:* 562-435-7161 *Toll Free Fax:* 800-804-3707 *E-mail:* sales@photoeditinc.com *Web Site:* www.photoeditinc.com, pg 608

Bordewyk, Gordon, Christian Schools International, 3350 E Paris Ave SE, Grand Rapids, MI 49512-3054 *Tel:* 616-957-1070 *Toll Free Tel:* 800-635-8288 *Fax:* 616-957-5022 *E-mail:* info@csionline.org *Web Site:* www.csionline.org, pg 61

Borgenicht, David, Quirk Books, 215 Church St, Philadelphia, PA 19106 *Tel:* 215-627-3581 *Fax:* 215-627-5220 *E-mail:* general@quirkbooks.com *Web Site:* www.quirkbooks.com, pg 224

Borges, Michael, Empire State Award for Excellence in Literature for Young People, 252 Hudson Ave, Albany, NY 12210 *Tel:* 518-432-6952 *Fax:* 518-427-1697 *E-mail:* info@nyla.org *Web Site:* www.nyla.org, pg 772

Born, Bob, Pocket Press Inc, PO Box 25124, Portland, OR 97298 *Toll Free Tel:* 888-237-2110 *Toll Free Fax:* 877-643-3732 *E-mail:* sales@pocketpressinc.com *Web Site:* www.pocketpressinc.com, pg 215

Borneman, Adrian, American Film Institute (AFI), 2021 N Western Ave, Los Angeles, CA 90027 *Tel:* 323-856-7600 *Toll Free Tel:* 800-774-4234 (memberships) *Fax:* 323-467-4578 *E-mail:* info@afi. com *Web Site:* www.afi.com, pg 676

Borneman, Brooke, Dorchester Publishing Co Inc, 200 Madison Ave, Suite 2000, New York, NY 10016 *Tel:* 212-725-8811 *Toll Free Tel:* 800-481-9191 (order dept) *Fax:* 212-532-1054 *E-mail:* dorchedits@ dorchesterpub.com *Web Site:* www.dorchesterpub.com, pg 82

Borodyanskaya, Yulia, Newmarket Publishing & Communications, 18 E 48 St, New York, NY 10017 *Tel:* 212-832-3575 *Toll Free Tel:* 800-669-3903 *Fax:* 212-832-3629 *E-mail:* mailbox@newmarketpress. com *Web Site:* www.newmarketpress.com, pg 190

Borzumato, Theresa, Random House Children's Books, 1745 Broadway, New York, NY 10019 *Tel:* 212-782-9000 *Toll Free Tel:* 800-200-3552 *Fax:* 212-782-9452 *Web Site:* www.randomhouse.com/kids, pg 225

Bosio, Sue C, Carlsbad Publications, 3242 McKinley St, Carlsbad, CA 92008 *Tel:* 760-729-9543 *Fax:* 760-729-9543 *E-mail:* bunkobabe9@aol.com, pg 593

Boskey, Bennett C, American Law Institute, 4025 Chestnut St, Philadelphia, PA 19104-3099 *Tel:* 215-243-1600 *Toll Free Tel:* 800-253-6397 *Fax:* 215-243-1664; 215-243-1683 *Web Site:* www.ali.org, pg 15

Bosse, Suzanne, Association for the Export of Canadian Books, One Nicholas, Suite 504, Ottawa, ON K1N 7B7, Canada *Tel:* 613-562-2324 *Fax:* 613-562-2329 *E-mail:* aecb@aecb.org *Web Site:* www.aecb.org, pg 679

Bossert, Joan, Oxford University Press, Inc, 198 Madison Ave, New York, NY 10016-4314 *Tel:* 212-726-6000 *Toll Free Tel:* 800-451-7556 (orders) *Web Site:* www.oup.com/us, pg 200

Bossier, William, Louisiana State University Press, PO Box 25053, Baton Rouge, LA 70894-5053 *Tel:* 225-578-6294 *Toll Free Tel:* 800-861-3477 *Fax:* 225-578-6461 *Toll Free Fax:* 800-305-4416 *E-mail:* lsupress@ lsu.edu *Web Site:* www.lsu.edu/guests/lsupress, pg 159

Bost, Laura, University of Texas Press, PO Box 7819, Austin, TX 78713-7819 *Tel:* 512-471-7233 *Fax:* 512-232-7178 *E-mail:* utpress@uts.cc.utexas.edu *Web Site:* www.utexas.edu/utpress, pg 267

Bostley, SSJ, Jean R, Aggiornamento Award, 100 North St, Suite 224, Pittsfield, MA 01201-5109 *Tel:* 413-443-2252 *Fax:* 413-442-2252 *E-mail:* cla@cathla.org *Web Site:* www.cathla.org, pg 757

Bostley, SSJ, Jean R, Catholic Library Association, 100 North St, Suite 224, Pittsfield, MA 01201-5109 *Tel:* 413-443-2252 *Fax:* 413-442-2252 *E-mail:* cla@ cathla.org *Web Site:* www.cathla.org, pg 684

Bostley, SSJ, Jean R, Katharine Drexel Award, 100 North St, Suite 224, Pittsfield, MA 01201-5109 *Tel:* 413-443-2252 *Fax:* 413-442-2252 *E-mail:* cla@ cathla.org *Web Site:* www.cathla.org, pg 771

Bostley, SSJ, Jean R, Jerome Award, 100 North St, Suite 224, Pittsfield, MA 01201-5109 *Tel:* 413-443-2252 *Fax:* 413-442-2252 *E-mail:* cla@cathla.org *Web Site:* www.cathla.org, pg 781

Bostley, SSJ, Jean R, Regina Medal Award, 100 North St, Suite 224, Pittsfield, MA 01201-5109 *Tel:* 413-443-2252 *Fax:* 413-442-2252 *E-mail:* cla@cathla.org *Web Site:* www.cathla.org, pg 801

Bostley, SSJ, Jean R, World Book Inc Continuing Education Grant, 100 North St, Suite 224, Pittsfield, MA 01201-5109 *Tel:* 413-443-2252 *Fax:* 413-442-2252 *E-mail:* cla@cathla.org *Web Site:* www.cathla. org, pg 812

Boston, Ann, Hill Street Press LLC, 191 E Broad St, Suite 209, Athens, GA 30601-2848 *Tel:* 706-613-7200 *Fax:* 706-613-7204 *Web Site:* www.hillstreetpress.com, pg 122

Boston, Leslie Paul, The Boston Word Works, PO Box 56419, Sherman Oaks, CA 91413-1419 *Tel:* 818-904-9088 *Fax:* 818-787-1431, pg 592

Bosveld, Jennifer, Pudding House Poetry Chapbook Competition, 81 Shadymere Lane, Columbus, OH 43213 *Tel:* 614-986-1881 *E-mail:* info@puddinghouse. com *Web Site:* www.puddinghouse.com, pg 800

Bosveld, Jennifer, Pudding House Publications, 81 Shadymere Lane, Columbus, OH 43213 *Tel:* 614-986-1881 *E-mail:* info@puddinghouse.com *Web Site:* www.puddinghouse.com, pg 221

Boswell, Len, American Diabetes Association, 1701 N Beauregard St, Alexandria, VA 22311 *Tel:* 703-299-2046 *Toll Free Tel:* 800-232-6733 *Fax:* 908-806-2301 *Web Site:* www.diabetes.org, pg 13

Bothwell, Brenda, Goodheart-Willcox Publisher, 18604 W Creek Dr, Tinley Park, IL 60477-6243 *Tel:* 708-687-5000 *Toll Free Tel:* 800-323-0440 *Fax:* 708-687-0315 *Toll Free Fax:* 888-409-3900 *E-mail:* custserv@ g-w.com *Web Site:* www.g-w.com, pg 107

Botton, Maury, The New Press, 38 Greene St, 4th fl, New York, NY 10013 *Tel:* 212-629-8802 *Toll Free Tel:* 800-233-4830 (orders) *Fax:* 212-629-8617 *Toll Free Fax:* 800-458-6515 *E-mail:* newpress@ thenewpress.com *Web Site:* www.thenewpress.com, pg 188

Bottrell, Donna, The Wine Appreciation Guild Ltd, 360 Swift Ave, Unit 30-40, South San Francisco, CA 94080 *Tel:* 650-866-3020 *Toll Free Tel:* 800-231-9463 *Fax:* 650-866-3513 *E-mail:* shannon@ wineappreciation.com; info@wineappreciation.com *Web Site:* www.wineappreciation.com, pg 301

Bottum, Steven, Basic Books, 387 Park Ave S, 12th fl, New York, NY 10016-8810 *Tel:* 212-340-8100 *Toll Free Tel:* 800-242-7737 (orders) *Fax:* 212-340-8135 *E-mail:* basic.books@perseusbooks.com *Web Site:* www.basicbooks.com, pg 33

Botzman, Harvey, Cyclotour Guide Books, 160 Harvard St, Rochester, NY 14607 *Tel:* 585-244-6157 *Fax:* 585-244-6157 *E-mail:* cyclotour@cyclotour.com *Web Site:* www.cyclotour.com, pg 75

Bouchard, Jean, Cheneliere/McGraw-Hill, 7001 Saint Laurent Blvd, Montreal, PQ H2S 3E3, Canada *Tel:* 514-273-1066 *Fax:* 514-276-0324 *E-mail:* chene@dlcmcgrawhill.ca *Web Site:* www. dlcmcgrawhill.ca, pg 540

Bouchard, Robert, American Institute of Certified Public Accountants, Harborside Financial Ctr, 201 Plaza Three, Jersey City, NJ 07311-3881 *Tel:* 201-938-3000 *Toll Free Tel:* 888-777-7077 *Fax:* 201-938-3329 *Web Site:* www.aicpa.org, pg 15

Boucher, Pierre, Canadian Printing Industries Association, 75 Albert St, Suite 906, Ottawa, ON K1P 5E7, Canada *Tel:* 613-236-7208 *Fax:* 613-236-8169 *Web Site:* www.cpia-aci.ca, pg 683

Boudreau, Patricia, The Kane Press, 240 W 35 St, Suite 300, New York, NY 10001-2506 *Tel:* 212-268-1435 *Fax:* 212-268-2044 *Web Site:* www.kanepress.com, pg 144

Boudreaux, Lee, Random House Publishing Group, 1745 Broadway, New York, NY 10019 *Toll Free Tel:* 800-200-3552 *Toll Free Fax:* 800-200-3552 *Web Site:* www.randomhouse.com, pg 227

Boulder, Sharon, Top of the Mountain Publishing, PO Box 2244, Pinellas Park, FL 33780-2244 *Tel:* 727-391-3958 *Fax:* 727-391-4598 *E-mail:* tag@abcinfo. com *Web Site:* abcinfo.com; www.topofthemountain. com, pg 272

Boule, H James, Merryant Publishers Inc, 7615 SW 257 St, Vashon, WA 98070 *Tel:* 206-463-3879 *Toll Free Tel:* 800-228-8958 *Fax:* 206-463-1604, pg 172

Boule, Mary Null, Merryant Publishers Inc, 7615 SW 257 St, Vashon, WA 98070 *Tel:* 206-463-3879 *Toll Free Tel:* 800-228-8958 *Fax:* 206-463-1604, pg 172

Boulerice, Yvan, Art Image Publications, PO Box 160, Derby Line, VT 05830-0160 *Toll Free Tel:* 800-361-2598 *Toll Free Fax:* 800-559-2598 *E-mail:* info@ artimagepublications.com *Web Site:* www. artimagepublications.com, pg 24

Boulle, Philippe, White Wolf Publishing Inc, 1554 Litton Dr, Stone Mountain, GA 30083 *Tel:* 404-292-1819 *Toll Free Tel:* 800-454-9653 *Fax:* 678-382-3883 *Web Site:* www.white-wolf.com, pg 298

Bourassa-Chevrier, Madeleine, Institute of Psychological Research, Inc., 34 Fleury St W, Montreal, PQ H3L 1S9, Canada *Tel:* 514-382-3000 *Toll Free Tel:* 800-363-7800 *Fax:* 514-382-3007 *Toll Free Fax:* 888-382-3007 *E-mail:* info@i-p-r.ca *Web Site:* www.i-p-r.ca, pg 551

Bourdon, Pierre, Sogides Ltee, 955 rue Amherst, Montreal, PQ H2L 3K4, Canada *Tel:* 514-523-1182 *Toll Free Tel:* 800-361-4806 *Fax:* 514-597-0370 *Web Site:* www.sogides.com; www.edhomme.com, pg 561

Bouregy-Mickelsen, Ellen, Thomas Bouregy & Co Inc, 160 Madison Ave, New York, NY 10016 *Tel:* 212-598-0222 *Fax:* 212-979-1862 *E-mail:* customerservice@avalonbooks.com *Web Site:* avalonbooks.com, pg 44

Bourgue, Pauline, New Brunswick Arts Board/ Conseil des arts du NB, 634 Queen St, Suite 300, Fredericton, NB E3B 1C2, Canada *Tel:* 506-444-4444 *Fax:* 506-444-5543 *E-mail:* nbabcanb@artsnb.ca *Web Site:* www.artsnb.ca, pg 793

Bouris, Karen, Inner Ocean Publishing Inc, 1037 Makawao Ave, Makawao, Maui, HI 96768-1239 *Tel:* 808-573-8000 *Toll Free Tel:* 800-863-1449 *Fax:* 808-573-0700 *Toll Free Fax:* 800-755-4118 *E-mail:* info@innerocean.com *Web Site:* www. innerocean.com, pg 134

Bourne, Beebe, Music Publishers' Association of the United States, 2435 Fifth Ave, Suite 236, New York, NY 10016 *Tel:* 212-327-4044 *Fax:* 212-327-4044 *Web Site:* host.mpa.org; www.mpa.org, pg 691

Bourne, Nina, Alfred A Knopf, 1745 Broadway, New York, NY 10019 *Tel:* 212-751-2600 *Toll Free Tel:* 800-638-6460 *Fax:* 212-572-2593 *Web Site:* www. randomhouse.com/knopf, pg 146

Bourret, Michael, Dystel & Goderich Literary Management, One Union Sq W, Suite 904, New York, NY 10003 *Tel:* 212-627-9100 *Fax:* 212-627-9313 *Web Site:* www.dystel.com, pg 629

Bova, Barbara, The Barbara Bova Literary Agency, 3951 Gulfshore Blvd, Suite PH1-B, Naples, FL 34103 *Tel:* 239-649-7237 *Fax:* 239-649-7263 *E-mail:* bovab4@aol.com *Web Site:* barbarabovaliteraryagency.com, pg 622

Bovee, Renee, Artist Fellowships in Literature, 1380 Lawrence St, Suite 1200, Denver, CO 80204 *Tel:* 303-866-2723 *Fax:* 303-866-4266 *E-mail:* coloarts@state. co.us *Web Site:* www.coloarts.state.co.us, pg 760

Bovenschulte, Robert D, The American Chemical Society, 1155 16 St NW, Washington, DC 20036 *Tel:* 202-872-4600 *Toll Free Tel:* 800-227-5558 *Fax:* 202-872-6067 *Web Site:* www.acs.org; pubs.acs. org, pg 12

Bovis, Julia, Rough Guides, 345 Hudson St, New York, NY 10014 *Tel:* 212-414-3635 *Fax:* 212-414-3352 *E-mail:* mail@roughguides.com *Web Site:* www. roughguides.com, pg 235

Bowe, William J, Encyclopaedia Britannica Inc, 310 S Michigan Ave, Chicago, IL 60604 *Tel:* 312-347-7000 *Toll Free Tel:* 800-323-1229 *Fax:* 312-347-7399 *E-mail:* editor@eb.com *Web Site:* www.eb.com; www. britannica.com, pg 91

Bowen, Brenda, Hyperion Books for Children, 114 Fifth Ave, New York, NY 10011 *Tel:* 212-633-4400 *Toll Free Tel:* 800-807-5880 *Web Site:* www. hyperionbooksforchildren.com, pg 129

Bower, Alan, Pearson Technology Group (PTG), 201 W 103 St, Indianapolis, IN 46290 *Tel:* 317-581-3500 *Toll Free Tel:* 800-545-5914 *Fax:* 317-581-4675 *E-mail:* firstname.lastname@pearsoned.com *Web Site:* www.mcp.com, pg 207

Bower, Brenda, Disney Press, 114 Fifth Ave, New York, NY 10011 *Tel:* 212-633-4400 *Fax:* 212-807-5432 *Web Site:* www.disney.go.com, pg 81

Bower, Emily, Shambhala Publications Inc, Horticultural Hall, 300 Massachusetts Ave, Boston, MA 02115 *Tel:* 617-424-0030 *Toll Free Tel:* 888-424-2329 (orders only) *Fax:* 617-236-1563; 303-665-5292 (orders only) *E-mail:* editors@shambhala.com *Web Site:* www. shambhala.com, pg 245

Bowering, David, Jesperson Publishing, 100 Water St, 3rd fl, St John's, NF A1C 6E6, Canada *Tel:* 709-757-2216 *Fax:* 709-757-0708 *E-mail:* info@ jespersonpublishing.nf.net *Web Site:* www. jespersonpublishing.nf.net, pg 551

Bram, Larry, Teaching Strategies, PO Box 42243, Washington, DC 20015 *Tel:* 202-362-7543 *Toll Free Tel:* 800-637-3652 *Fax:* 202-364-7273 *E-mail:* info@teachingstrategies.com *Web Site:* www.teachingstrategies.com, pg 265

Bramson, Ann, Artisan, 708 Broadway, New York, NY 10003-9555 *Tel:* 212-254-5900 *Fax:* 212-254-8098 *E-mail:* artisaninfo@workman.com *Web Site:* www.artisanbooks.com, pg 25

Bramson, Scott B, Transaction Publishers, Rutgers University, 35 Berrue Circle, Piscataway, NJ 08854 *Tel:* 732-445-2280 *Toll Free Tel:* 888-999-6778 *Fax:* 732-445-3138 *E-mail:* trans@transactionpub.com *Web Site:* www.transactionpub.com, pg 274

Branagan, May, Authors Cooperative, 1700 Ben Franklin Dr, Suite 9E, Sarasota, FL 34236-2374 *Tel:* 941-388-5009 *E-mail:* authcoop@comcast.net *Web Site:* www.authorscooperative.com, pg 28

Brandel, Ms Dusty, American Auto Racing Writers & Broadcasters, 922 N Pass Ave, Burbank, CA 91505 *Tel:* 818-842-7005 *Fax:* 818-842-7020 *E-mail:* aarwba@compuserve.com *Web Site:* www.aarwba.org, pg 676

Brandenburgh, Greg, Element Books, 535 Albany St, 5th fl, Boston, MA 02118 *Tel:* 617-451-8984 *Web Site:* www.thorsons.com, pg 89

Brander, Jacob, Mesorah Publications Ltd, 4401 Second Ave, Brooklyn, NY 11232 *Tel:* 718-921-9000 *Toll Free Tel:* 800-637-6724 *Fax:* 718-680-1875 *E-mail:* artscroll@mesorah.com *Web Site:* www.artscroll.com; www.mesorah.com, pg 172

Brandl, Gary, New City Press, 202 Cardinal Rd, Hyde Park, NY 12538 *Tel:* 845-229-0335 *Toll Free Tel:* 800-462-5980 (orders only) *Fax:* 845-229-0351 *E-mail:* info@newcitypress.com *Web Site:* www.newcitypress.com, pg 187

Brandreth, Dale, Caissa Editions, PO Box 151, Yorklyn, DE 19736-0151 *Tel:* 302-239-4608, pg 51

Brandreth, Suzanne, The Cooke Agency Inc, 278 Bloor St E, Suite 305, Toronto, ON M4W 3M4, Canada *Tel:* 416-406-3390 *Fax:* 416-406-3389 *E-mail:* agents@cookeagency.ca, pg 625

Brandt, Carl, Brandt & Hochman Literary Agents Inc, 1501 Broadway, Suite 2310, New York, NY 10036 *Tel:* 212-840-5760 *Fax:* 212-840-5776, pg 622

Brandt, Joan, The Joan Brandt Agency, 788 Wesley Dr NW, Atlanta, GA 30305 *Tel:* 404-351-8877 *Fax:* 404-351-0068, pg 622

Brandt-Riske, Kris, American Federation of Astrologers Inc, 6535 S Rural Rd, Tempe, AZ 85283-3746 *Tel:* 480-838-1751 *Toll Free Tel:* 888-301-7630 *Fax:* 480-838-8293 *E-mail:* afa@msn.com *Web Site:* www.astrologers.com, pg 13

Branham, Sarah, Atria Books, 1230 Avenue of the Americas, New York, NY 10020 *Tel:* 212-698-7000 *Fax:* 212-698-7007 *Web Site:* www.simonsays.com, pg 27

Brann, Helen, The Helen Brann Agency Inc, 94 Curtis Rd, Bridgewater, CT 06752 *Tel:* 860-354-9580 *Fax:* 860-355-2572 *E-mail:* helenbrannagency@earthlink.net, pg 622

Brannigan, Jim, BBC Audiobooks America, One Lafayette Rd, Hampton, NH 03842 *Tel:* 603-926-8744 *Toll Free Tel:* 800-621-0182 *Fax:* 603-929-3890 *E-mail:* info@bbcaudiobooksamerica.com, pg 34

Brannon, Barbara A, Society for the History of Authorship, Reading & Publishing Inc (SHARP), SHARP/University of South Carolina, PO Box 5816, Columbia, SC 29250 *Tel:* 803-777-5075 *Fax:* 803-782-0699 *E-mail:* membership@sharpweb.org *Web Site:* www.sharpweb.org, pg 700

Brashear, Christina, Ellora's Cave Publishing Inc, 1337 Commerce Dr, Suite 13, Stow, OH 44224 *Tel:* 330-689-1118 *E-mail:* service@ellorascave.com *Web Site:* www.ellorascave.com, pg 89

Brasseaux, Dr Carl, University of Louisiana at Lafayette, Center for Louisiana Studies, PO Box 40831, UL, Lafayette, LA 70504-0831 *Tel:* 337-482-6027 *Fax:* 337-482-6028 *E-mail:* ann@louisiana.edu *Web Site:* www.cls.louisiana.edu, pg 282

Brastow, Scott, Chatsworth Press, 9135 Alabama Ave, Suite B, Chatsworth, CA 91311 *Tel:* 818-341-3156 *Toll Free Tel:* 800-262-7367 (US); 800-272-7367 (CA) *Fax:* 818-341-3562 *E-mail:* info@pac-media.com *Web Site:* pac-media.com, pg 59

Braswell, Calandra, World Scientific Publishing Co Inc, 27 Warren St, Suite 401-402, Hackensack, NJ 07601 *Tel:* 201-487-9655 *Toll Free Tel:* 800-227-7562 *Fax:* 201-487-9656 *Toll Free Fax:* 888-977-2665 *E-mail:* wspc@wspc.com *Web Site:* www.wspc.com, pg 304

Bratton, Chuck, EMC/Paradigm Publishing, 875 Montreal Way, St Paul, MN 55102 *Tel:* 651-290-2800 (corp) *Toll Free Tel:* 800-328-1452 *Fax:* 651-290-2899 *Toll Free Fax:* 800-328-4564 *E-mail:* educate@emcp.com *Web Site:* www.emcp.com, pg 90

Brault, Jean, Les Editions Brault et Bouthillier, 4823, rue Sherbrooke Ouest, bureau 275, Westmount, PQ H3Z 1G7, Canada *Tel:* 514-932-9466 *Toll Free Tel:* 800-668-1108 *Fax:* 514-932-5929 *E-mail:* editions@ebbp.ca, pg 543

Brault, Matt, Professional Publications Inc, 1250 Fifth Ave, Belmont, CA 94002 *Tel:* 650-593-9119 *Toll Free Tel:* 800-426-1178 *Fax:* 650-592-4519 *E-mail:* info@passthatexam.com *Web Site:* www.passthatexam.com, pg 220

Braun, Barbara, Barbara Braun Associates Inc, 104 Fifth Ave, 7th fl, New York, NY 10011 *Tel:* 212-604-9023 *Fax:* 212-604-9041 *E-mail:* bba230@earthlink.net *Web Site:* www.barbarabraunagency.com, pg 622

Braun, Mary Elizabeth, Oregon State University Press, 102 Adams Hall, Corvallis, OR 97331 *Tel:* 541-737-3166 *Toll Free Tel:* 800-426-3797 (orders) *Fax:* 541-737-3170 *Toll Free Fax:* 800-426-3797 (orders) *E-mail:* osu.press@oregonstate.edu *Web Site:* oregonstate.edu/dept/press, pg 199

Braunstein, Donna Lee, Donna Lee Braunstein Your Personal Researcher, 22848 Mesa Way, Lake Forest, CA 92630 *Tel:* 949-472-8538 *E-mail:* dlbraunstein@prodigy.net, pg 592

Bray, Melanie, Nova Publishing Co, 1103 W College St, Carbondale, IL 62901 *Tel:* 618-457-3521 *Toll Free Tel:* 800-748-1175 *Fax:* 618-457-2541 *E-mail:* info@novapublishing.com *Web Site:* www.novapublishing.com, pg 194

Braziller, George, George Braziller Inc, 171 Madison Ave, Suite 1105, New York, NY 10016 *Tel:* 212-889-0909 *Fax:* 212-689-5405 *E-mail:* georgebraziller@earthlink.net *Web Site:* www.georgebraziller.com, pg 46

Braziller, Karen, Persea Books Inc, 853 Broadway, Suite 604, New York, NY 10003 *Tel:* 212-260-9256 *Fax:* 212-260-1902 *E-mail:* info@perseabooks.com *Web Site:* www.perseabooks.com, pg 210

Braziller, Michael, Persea Books Inc, 853 Broadway, Suite 604, New York, NY 10003 *Tel:* 212-260-9256 *Fax:* 212-260-1902 *E-mail:* info@perseabooks.com *Web Site:* www.perseabooks.com, pg 210

Brchan, Cheryl, Colorado Geological Survey, 1313 Sherman St, Rm 715, Denver, CO 80203 *Tel:* 303-866-2611; 303-866-4762 (pubns) *Fax:* 303-866-2461 *E-mail:* cgspubs@state.co.us *Web Site:* www.geosurvey.state.co.us, pg 65

Brealey, Nicholas, Nicholas Brealey Publishing, 3704 Beard Ave N, Minneapolis, MN 55422 *Tel:* 763-208-3169 *Toll Free Tel:* 888-BREALEY (273-2539) *Fax:* 763-208-3170 *E-mail:* booksmatter@earthlink.net *Web Site:* www.nbrealey-books.com, pg 46

Brechner, Michael, Cypress House, 155 Cypress St, Fort Bragg, CA 95437 *Tel:* 707-964-9520 *Toll Free Tel:* 800-773-7782 *Fax:* 707-964-7531 *E-mail:* publishing@cypresshouse.com *Web Site:* www.cypresshouse.com, pg 596

Bree, Loris Theovin, Marlor Press Inc, 4304 Brigadoon Dr, St Paul, MN 55126 *Tel:* 651-484-4600 *Toll Free Tel:* 800-669-4908 *Fax:* 651-490-1182 *E-mail:* marlor@minn.net, pg 164

Bree, Marlin, Marlor Press Inc, 4304 Brigadoon Dr, St Paul, MN 55126 *Tel:* 651-484-4600 *Toll Free Tel:* 800-669-4908 *Fax:* 651-490-1182 *E-mail:* marlor@minn.net, pg 164

Breeskin, Andrea, Transportation Research Board, 500 Fifth St NW, Washington, DC 20001 *Tel:* 202-334-3213 *Fax:* 202-334-2519 *E-mail:* trbsales@nas.edu *Web Site:* trb.org, pg 274

Bregy, Terry, Down East Books, PO Box 679, Camden, ME 04843 *Tel:* 207-594-9544 *Toll Free Tel:* 800-766-1670 (ME only) *Fax:* 207-594-7215 *Web Site:* www.downeastbooks.com, pg 83

Breichner, William F, The Johns Hopkins University Press, 2715 N Charles St, Baltimore, MD 21218-4363 *Tel:* 410-516-6900 *Toll Free Tel:* 800-537-5487 *Fax:* 410-516-6968 *Web Site:* www.press.jhu.edu, pg 141

Breisach, Ernst, Cistercian Publications Inc, Editorial Office, WMU, 1903 W Michigan Ave, Kalamazoo, MI 49008 *Tel:* 269-387-8920 *Fax:* 269-387-8390 *E-mail:* cistpub@wmich.edu *Web Site:* www.spencerabbey.org/cistpub, pg 62

Breisacher, Ed, The Darwin Press Inc, 280 N Main St, Pennington, NJ 08534 *Tel:* 609-737-1349 *Fax:* 609-737-0929 *E-mail:* books@darwinpress.com *Web Site:* www.darwinpress.com, pg 76

Breitenbach, Laura A PhD, Harold W McGraw Jr - Prize in Education, 1221 Avenue of the Americas, 47th fl, New York, NY 10020 *Tel:* 212-512-2435 *Fax:* 212-512-3611 *Web Site:* www.mcgraw-hill.com, pg 788

Breiter, Marilyn, Indiana University Press, 601 N Morton St, Bloomington, IN 47404-3797 *Tel:* 812-855-8817 *Toll Free Tel:* 800-842-6796 (orders only) *Fax:* 812-855-7931 (orders only); 812-855-8507 *E-mail:* iupress@indiana.edu; iuorder@indiana.edu (orders) *Web Site:* www.iupress.indiana.edu, pg 132

Bremner, Joseph, Kennedy Information, One Phoenix Mill Lane, 5th fl, Peterborough, NH 03458 *Tel:* 603-924-0900 *Toll Free Tel:* 800-531-0007 *Fax:* 603-924-4460 *E-mail:* office@kennedyinfo.com *Web Site:* www.kennedyinfo.com, pg 145

Brennan, Maria, Foundation of American Women in Radio & Television, 8405 Greensboro Dr, Suite 800, McLean, VA 22102 *Tel:* 703-506-3290 *Fax:* 703-506-3266 *E-mail:* info@awrt.org *Web Site:* www.awrt.org, pg 687

Brennan, Maria E, Gracie Allen Awards®, 8405 Greensboro Dr, Suite 800, McLean, VA 22102 *Tel:* 703-506-3290 *Fax:* 703-506-3266 *E-mail:* info@awrt.org *Web Site:* www.awrt.org, pg 758

Brennan, Michael, Penguin Group (USA) Inc Sales, 375 Hudson St, New York, NY 10014 *Tel:* 212-366-2000 *E-mail:* online@penguinputnam.com *Web Site:* www.penguin.com, pg 208

Brennan, Norma, American Institute of Aeronautics & Astronautics, 1801 Alexander Bell Dr, Suite 500, Reston, VA 20191 *Tel:* 703-264-7500 *Toll Free Tel:* 800-639-2422 *Fax:* 703-264-7551 *E-mail:* custserv@aiaa.org *Web Site:* www.aiaa.org, pg 14

Brennan, Scott, American Translators Association (ATA), 225 Reinekers Lane, Suite 590, Alexandria, VA 22314 *Tel:* 703-683-6100 *Fax:* 703-683-6122 *E-mail:* ata@atanet.org *Web Site:* www.atanet.org, pg 678

Brennan, Scott, Lewis Galantiere Prize, 225 Reinekers Lane, Suite 590, Alexandria, VA 22314 *Tel:* 703-683-6100 *Fax:* 703-683-6122 *E-mail:* ata@atanet.org *Web Site:* www.atanet.org, pg 775

Brennan, Scott, Alexander Gode Medal, 225 Reinekers Lane, Suite 590, Alexandria, VA 22314 *Tel:* 703-683-6100 *Fax:* 703-683-6122 *E-mail:* ata@atanet.org *Web Site:* www.atanet.org, pg 776

Brennan, Susan, W H Freeman and Co, 41 Madison Ave, 37th fl, New York, NY 10010 *Tel:* 212-576-9400 *Fax:* 212-689-2383 *Web Site:* www.whfreeman.com, pg 100

Brenner, Carol, Brenner Information Group, 9282 Samantha Ct, San Diego, CA 92129 *Tel:* 858-538-0093 *Toll Free Tel:* 800-811-4337 *Fax:* 858-484-2599 *E-mail:* info@brennerbooks.com; sales@brennerbooks.com (ordering) *Web Site:* www.brennerbooks.com, pg 46

Brenner, Robert, Brenner Information Group, 9282 Samantha Ct, San Diego, CA 92129 *Tel:* 858-538-0093 *Toll Free Tel:* 800-811-4337 *Fax:* 858-484-2599 *E-mail:* info@brennerbooks.com; sales@brennerbooks.com (ordering) *Web Site:* www.brennerbooks.com, pg 46

Brent, Barbara, Two Thousand Three Associates, 4180 Saxon Dr, New Smyrna Beach, FL 32169 *Tel:* 386-427-7876 *Fax:* 386-423-7523 *E-mail:* ttta@worldnet.att.net, pg 277

Brent, Jonathan, Yale University Press, 302 Temple St, New Haven, CT 06511 *Tel:* 203-432-0960; 401-531-2800 (cust serv) *Toll Free Tel:* 800-405-1619 (cust serv) *Fax:* 203-432-0948; 401-531-2801 (cust serv) *Toll Free Fax:* 800-406-9145 (cust serv) *E-mail:* customer.care@trilateral.org (cust serv) *Web Site:* www.yale.edu/yup/, pg 305

Brent, T David, Association of American University Presses, 1427 E 60 St, Chicago, IL 60637 *Tel:* 773-702-7700; 773-702-7600 *Toll Free Tel:* 800-621-2736 (orders) *Fax:* 773-702-9756 (sales); 773-660-2235 (orders); 773-702-2708 *E-mail:* general@press.uchicago.edu *Web Site:* www.press.uchicago.edu, pg 26

Breschini, Gary PhD, Coyote Press, PO Box 3377, Salinas, CA 93912-3377 *Tel:* 831-422-4912 *Fax:* 831-422-4913 *E-mail:* coyote@coyotepress.com *Web Site:* www.coyotepress.com, pg 71

Breslof, Lisa, The John Burroughs List of Nature Books for Young Readers, 15 W 77 St, New York, NY 10024 *Tel:* 212-769-5169 *Fax:* 212-313-7182 *Web Site:* research.amnh.org/burroughs, pg 765

Breslof, Lisa, John Burroughs Medal, 15 W 77 St, New York, NY 10024 *Tel:* 212-769-5169 *Fax:* 212-313-7182 *Web Site:* research.amnh.org/burroughs, pg 765

Breslof, Lisa, John Burroughs Outstanding Published Nature Essay Award, 15 W 77 St, New York, NY 10024 *Tel:* 212-769-5169 *Fax:* 212-313-7182 *Web Site:* research.amnh.org/burroughs, pg 765

Bressler, Wendy, American Council on Education, One Dupont Circle NW, Washington, DC 20036 *Tel:* 202-939-9380; 202-939-9300 *Fax:* 202-939-9302 *Web Site:* www.acenet.edu, pg 13

Bressler, Wendy, American Council on Education, One Dupont Circle NW, Washington, DC 20036 *Tel:* 202-939-9300 *Fax:* 202-939-9302 *Web Site:* www.acenet.edu, pg 676

Brettrager, Cindy, Pearson Professional Development, 1900 E Lake Ave, Glenview, IL 60025 *Tel:* 847-657-7450 *Toll Free Tel:* 800-348-4474 *Fax:* 847-486-3183 *E-mail:* info@pearsonpd.com *Web Site:* www.skylightedu.com; www.pearsonpd.com, pg 207

Brettschneider, Cathie, The University of Virginia Press, PO Box 400318, Charlottesville, VA 22904-4318 *Tel:* 434-924-3468 (cust serv); 434-924-3469 (cust serv) *Toll Free Tel:* 800-831-3406 (cust serv) *Fax:* 434-982-2655 *Toll Free Fax:* 877-288-6400 *E-mail:* upressvirginia@virginia.edu *Web Site:* www.upressvirginia.edu, pg 285

Brewer, Andrew, University of California Press, 2120 Berkeley Way, Berkeley, CA 94720 *Tel:* 510-642-4247 *Toll Free Tel:* 800-777-4726 *Fax:* 510-643-7127 *Toll Free Fax:* 800-999-1958 *E-mail:* askucp@ucpress.edu *Web Site:* www.ucpress.edu, pg 281

Brey-Casiano, Carol, Margaret Mann Citation, 50 E Huron St, Chicago, IL 60611 *Tel:* 312-280-5037 *Toll Free Tel:* 800-545-2433 *Fax:* 312-944-6131 *Web Site:* www.ala.org/alcts, pg 787

Brey-Casiano, Carol, Reference & User Services Association, 50 E Huron St, Chicago, IL 60611 *Tel:* 312-944-6780 *Toll Free Tel:* 800-545-2433 *Fax:* 312-280-3224 *Web Site:* www.ala.org, pg 698

Bricker, Jim, Naval Institute Press, 291 Wood Rd, Annapolis, MD 21402-5034 *Tel:* 410-268-6110 *Toll Free Tel:* 800-233-8764 *Fax:* 410-295-1084; 410-571-1703 (customer service) *E-mail:* webmaster@navalinstitute.org; customer@navalinstitute.org (cust serv) *Web Site:* www.navalinstitute.org, pg 185

Brickhouse, Jamie, Basic Books, 387 Park Ave S, 12th fl, New York, NY 10016-8810 *Tel:* 212-340-8100 *Toll Free Tel:* 800-242-7737 (orders) *Fax:* 212-340-8135 *E-mail:* basic.books@perseusbooks.com *Web Site:* www.basicbooks.com, pg 33

Brickhouse, Jamie, Counterpoint Press, 387 Park Ave S, New York, NY 10016 *Tel:* 212-340-8100 *Fax:* 212-340-8135 (edit); 212-340-8115 *E-mail:* counterpointpress@perseusbooks.com *Web Site:* www.counterpointpress.com, pg 70

Briere, Guy, Tormont/Brimar Publication Inc, 338 St Antoine E, 3rd fl, Montreal, PQ H2Y 1A3, Canada *Tel:* 514-954-1441 *Fax:* 514-954-1443 *E-mail:* info@tormont.ca, pg 563

Briers, Jill, Scholastic Canada Ltd, 175 Hillmount Rd, Markham, ON L6C 1Z7, Canada *Tel:* 905-887-7323 *Toll Free Tel:* 800-268-3848 (Canada) *Fax:* 905-887-1131 *Toll Free Fax:* 800-387-4944; 866-346-1288 *Web Site:* www.scholastic.ca, pg 560

Brigg, Peter, Pilgrim Award & Pioneer Award, 6021 Grassmere, Corpus Christi, TX 78415 *Tel:* 530-752-1699 *E-mail:* sands@uwm.edu *Web Site:* www.sfra.org, pg 799

Brigg, Peter, Science Fiction Research Association Inc, 6021 Grassmere, Corpus Christi, TX 78415 *Tel:* 512-855-9304, pg 699

Briggs, Barbara L, University Press of New England, One Court St, Lebanon, NH 03766 *Tel:* 603-448-1533 *Toll Free Tel:* 800-421-1561 (orders only) *Fax:* 603-448-7006; 603-643-1540 *E-mail:* university.press@dartmouth.edu *Web Site:* www.upne.com, pg 287

Briggs, David, G P Putnam's Sons (Children's), 345 Hudson St, New York, NY 10014 *Tel:* 212-366-2000 *E-mail:* online@penguinputnam.com *Web Site:* www.penguin.com, pg 223

Briggs, Harry, M E Sharpe Inc, 80 Business Park Dr, Suite 202, Armonk, NY 10504 *Tel:* 914-273-1800 *Toll Free Tel:* 800-541-6563 *Fax:* 914-273-2106 *E-mail:* info@mesharpe.com *Web Site:* www.mesharpe.com, pg 246

Briggs, John H Jr, Holiday House Inc, 425 Madison Ave, New York, NY 10017 *Tel:* 212-688-0085 *Fax:* 212-421-6134, pg 123

Briggs, Kate H, Holiday House Inc, 425 Madison Ave, New York, NY 10017 *Tel:* 212-688-0085 *Fax:* 212-421-6134, pg 123

Briggs, Kim, Orbis Books, Walsh Bldg, 75 Ryder Rd, Ossining, NY 10562 *Tel:* 914-941-7636 *Toll Free Tel:* 800-258-5838 (orders) *Fax:* 914-941-7005 (orders); 914-945-0670 (office) *E-mail:* orbisbooks@maryknoll.org *Web Site:* www.orbisbooks.com, pg 198

Briggs, Laurie, Nolo, 950 Parker St, Berkeley, CA 94710 *Tel:* 510-549-1976 *Fax:* 510-548-5902 *E-mail:* info@nolo.com *Web Site:* www.nolo.com, pg 191

Briggs, M Courtney, M Courtney Briggs Esq, Authors Representative, 100 N Broadway Ave, 20th fl, Oklahoma City, OK 73102 *Tel:* 405-235-1900 *Fax:* 405-235-1995, pg 622

Briggs, Michael, University Press of Kansas, 2501 W 15 St, Lawrence, KS 66049-3905 *Tel:* 785-864-4154; 785-864-4155 (orders) *Fax:* 785-864-4586 *E-mail:* upress@ku.edu *Web Site:* www.kansaspress.ku.edu, pg 287

Bright, Cynthia F, Bright Mountain Books Inc, 206 Riva Ridge Dr, Fairview, NC 28730 *Tel:* 828-628-1768 *Toll Free Tel:* 800-437-3959 *Fax:* 828-628-1755 *E-mail:* booksbmb@charter.net, pg 47

Bright, Harry, Maharishi University of Management Press, 1000 N Fourth St, Dept 1155, Fairfield, IA 52557-1155 *Tel:* 641-472-1101 *Toll Free Tel:* 800-831-6523 *Fax:* 641-472-1122 *E-mail:* mumpress@mum.edu *Web Site:* www.mumpress.com, pg 161

Bright, Mary, Presbyterian Publishing Corp, 100 Witherspoon St, Louisville, KY 40202 *Tel:* 502-569-5052 *Toll Free Tel:* 800-227-2872 (US only) *Fax:* 502-569-8308 *Toll Free Fax:* 800-541-5113 (US only) *E-mail:* ppcmail@presbypub.com *Web Site:* www.ppcpub.com, pg 217

Bright, Mary, Westminster John Knox Press, 100 Witherspoon St, Louisville, KY 40202-1396 *Tel:* 502-569-5052 *Toll Free Tel:* 800-227-2872 (US only) *Fax:* 502-569-8308 *Toll Free Fax:* 800-541-5113 (US only) *E-mail:* wjk@wjkbooks.com *Web Site:* www.wjkbooks.com, pg 297

Brill, Chip, Barrytown/Station Hill Press, 120 Station Hill Rd, Barrytown, NY 12507 *Tel:* 845-758-5293 *E-mail:* publishers@stationhill.org *Web Site:* www.stationhill.org, pg 33

Brill, L Chip, Peter Glenn Publications, 6040 NW 43 Terr, Boca Raton, FL 33496 *Tel:* 561-999-8930 *Toll Free Tel:* 888-332-6700 *Fax:* 561-999-8931 *E-mail:* lynn@pgdirect.com *Web Site:* www.pgdirect.com, pg 105

Brill, Patricia, Harcourt School Publishers, 6277 Sea Harbor Dr, Orlando, FL 32887 *Tel:* 407-345-2000 *Toll Free Tel:* 800-225-5425 (cust serv) *Fax:* 407-352-3445 *Toll Free Fax:* 800-874-6418 *E-mail:* hbspcs@hbschool.com *Web Site:* www.harcourtschool.com, pg 114

Brill, Randi S, The Quarasan Group Inc, 405 W Superior St, Chicago, IL 60611 *Tel:* 312-981-2500 *Fax:* 312-981-2507 *E-mail:* info@quarasan.com *Web Site:* www.quarasan.com, pg 609

Brimmer, Andrew, National Bureau of Economic Research Inc, 1050 Massachusetts Ave, Cambridge, MA 02138-5398 *Tel:* 617-868-3900 *Fax:* 617-868-2742 *E-mail:* op@nber.org *Web Site:* www.nber.org, pg 182

Brinati, Teresa, Society of American Archivists, 527 S Wells St, 5th fl, Chicago, IL 60607 *Tel:* 312-922-0140 *Fax:* 312-347-1452 *E-mail:* info@archivists.org *Web Site:* www.archivists.org, pg 251

Brindisi, Marc, Sundance Publishing, One Beeman Rd, Northborough, MA 01532 *Tel:* 508-571-6500 *Toll Free Tel:* 800-343-8204 *Fax:* 508-571-6510 *Toll Free Fax:* 800-456-2419 *E-mail:* info@sundancepub.com *Web Site:* www.sundancepub.com, pg 262

Brink, Matthew H, Butte Publications Inc, PO Box 1328, Hillsboro, OR 97123-1328 *Tel:* 503-648-9791 *Toll Free Tel:* 866-312-8883 *Fax:* 503-693-9526 *E-mail:* service@buttepublications.com *Web Site:* www.buttepublications.com, pg 50

Brinker, Jane, International Broadcasting Services Ltd, 825 Cherry Lane, Penns Park, PA 18943 *Tel:* 215-598-3298 *Fax:* 215-598-3794 *E-mail:* hq@passband.com; mktg@passband.com *Web Site:* www.passband.com, pg 136

Brinkley, Alan, Columbia University Press, 61 W 62 St, New York, NY 10023 *Tel:* 212-459-0600 *Toll Free Tel:* 800-944-8648 *Fax:* 212-459-3678 *Web Site:* www.columbia.edu/cu/cup, pg 65

Brinley, Joseph F Jr, The Woodrow Wilson Center Press, One Woodrow Wilson Plaza, 1300 Pennsylvania Ave NW, Washington, DC 20004-3027 *Tel:* 202-691-4000 *Fax:* 202-691-4001 *E-mail:* press@wwics.si.edu *Web Site:* wilsoncenter.org, pg 302

Brintnall, Michael, American Political Science Association, 1527 New Hampshire Ave NW, Washington, DC 20036 *Tel:* 202-483-2512 *Fax:* 202-483-2657 *E-mail:* apsa@apsanet.org *Web Site:* www.apsanet.org, pg 677

Brissie, Gene, Ghosts & Collaborators International, PO Box 358, New Canaan, CT 06840 *Tel:* 203-972-1070 *Fax:* 203-972-1759, pg 632

Brissie, Gene, Kensington Publishing Corp, 850 Third Ave, New York, NY 10022 *Tel:* 212-407-1500 *Toll Free Tel:* 800-221-2647 *Fax:* 212-935-0699 *Web Site:* www.kensingtonbooks.com, pg 145

Brissie, Gene, James Peter Associates Inc, PO Box 358, New Canaan, CT 06840 *Tel:* 203-972-1070 *Fax:* 203-972-1759, pg 648

Bristol, Barbara K, Whiting Writers' Awards, 1133 Avenue of the Americas, 22nd fl, New York, NY 10036 Tel: 212-336-2138, pg 811

Bristol, James, Stratford Publishing Services Inc, 70 Landmark Hill Dr, Brattleboro, VT 05301 Tel: 802-254-6073 Toll Free Tel: 800-451-4328 Fax: 802-254-5240 Web Site: www.stratfordpublishing.com, pg 612

Britson, Lowell, Stanford University Press, 1450 Page Mill Rd, Palo Alto, CA 94304-1124 Tel: 650-723-9434 Fax: 650-725-3457 Web Site: www.sup.org, pg 257

Britt, Nadine, Penguin Young Readers Group, 345 Hudson St, New York, NY 10014 Tel: 212-366-2000 E-mail: online@penguinputnam.com Web Site: www.penguin.com, pg 208

Britton, Gregory M, Minnesota Historical Society Press, 345 Kellogg Blvd W, St Paul, MN 55102-1906 Tel: 651-296-2264 Toll Free Tel: 800-621-2736 Fax: 651-297-1345 Toll Free Fax: 800-621-8476 Web Site: www.mnhs.org/mhspress, pg 175

Brizel, Michael A, Reader's Digest Association Inc, Reader's Digest Rd, Pleasantville, NY 10570-7000 Tel: 914-238-1000 Toll Free Tel: 800-431-1726 Fax: 914-238-4559 Web Site: www.rd.com, pg 228

Brizel, Michael A, Reader's Digest Children's Books, Reader's Digest Rd, Pleasantville, NY 10570-7000 Tel: 914-244-4800 Toll Free Tel: 800-934-0977, pg 228

Brizel, Michael A, Reader's Digest General Books, Reader's Digest Rd, Pleasantville, NY 10570-7000 Tel: 914-238-1000 Toll Free Tel: 800-431-1726 Fax: 914-244-7436, pg 228

Brizel, Michael A, Reader's Digest Trade Books, Reader's Digest Rd, Pleasantville, NY 10570-7000 Tel: 914-244-7445 Fax: 914-244-7605, pg 229

Brizel, Michael A, Reader's Digest USA Select Editions, Reader's Digest Rd, Pleasantville, NY 10570-7000 Tel: 914-238-1000 Toll Free Tel: 800-310-6261 Fax: 914-238-4559, pg 229

Broadhurst, Jamie, Polestar Book Publishers, 9050 Shaughnessy St, Vancouver, BC V6P 6E5, Canada Tel: 604-323-7100 Toll Free Tel: 800-663-5714 Fax: 604-323-2600 Toll Free Fax: 800-565-3770 E-mail: info@raincoast.com Web Site: www.raincoast.com, pg 558

Broadhurst, Jamie, Raincoast Publishing, 9050 Shaughnessy St, Vancouver, BC V6P 6E5, Canada Tel: 604-323-7100 Toll Free Tel: 800-663-5714 (Canada only) Fax: 604-323-2600 Toll Free Fax: 800-565-3700 E-mail: info@raincoast.com Web Site: www.raincoast.com, pg 559

Brobeck, Carol, National Endowment for the Humanities Fellowships & Folger Longterm & Short-term Fellowships & Andrew W Mellon Foundations, c/o Fellowship Committee, 201 E Capitol St SE, Washington, DC 20003 Tel: 202-544-4600 (ext 348) Fax: 202-544-4623 Web Site: www.folger.edu, pg 791

Brockbank, Bray, Blackwell Publishing Professional, 2121 State Ave, Ames, IA 50014 Tel: 515-292-0140 Toll Free Tel: 800-862-6657 (orders only) Fax: 515-292-3348 Web Site: www.blackwellprofessional.com, pg 40

Brockett, Louise, W W Norton & Company Inc, 500 Fifth Ave, New York, NY 10110-0017 Tel: 212-354-5500 Toll Free Tel: 800-233-4830 (orders & cust serv) Fax: 212-869-0856 Toll Free Fax: 800-458-6515 Web Site: www.wwnorton.com, pg 193

Brockman, John, Brockman Inc, 5 E 59 St, New York, NY 10022 Tel: 212-935-8900 Fax: 212-935-5535 E-mail: rights@brockman.com, pg 623

Brodsky, Trilogy, Time Being Books, 10411 Clayton Rd, Suites 201-203, St Louis, MO 63131 Tel: 314-432-1771 Toll Free Tel: 866-840-4334 Fax: 314-432-7939 Toll Free Fax: 888-301-9121 E-mail: tbbooks@sbcglobal.net Web Site: www.timebeing.com, pg 271

Broesche, Jeffrey, Fine Communications, 322 Eighth Ave, 15th fl, New York, NY 10001 Tel: 212-595-3500 Fax: 212-595-3779, pg 96

Brogan, Frank, CMP Books, 600 Harrison St, San Francisco, CA 94107 Tel: 415-947-6615; 408-848-3854 (orders) Toll Free Tel: 800-500-6875 (orders) Fax: 415-947-6015; 408-848-5784 (orders) E-mail: books@cmp.com Web Site: www.cmpbooks.com, pg 63

Broida, Peter, Dewey Publications Inc, 2009 N 14 St, Suite 705, Arlington, VA 22201 Tel: 703-524-1355 Fax: 703-524-1463 E-mail: info@deweypub.com Web Site: www.deweypub.com, pg 79

Broido, Tom, Music Publishers' Association of the United States, 2435 Fifth Ave, Suite 236, New York, NY 10016 Tel: 212-327-4044 Fax: 212-327-4044 Web Site: host.mpa.org; www.mpa.org, pg 691

Brokering, Mark, O'Reilly & Associates Inc, 1005 Gravenstein Hwy N, Sebastopol, CA 95472 Tel: 707-827-7000 Toll Free Tel: 800-998-9938 Fax: 707-829-0104 E-mail: info@oreilly.com Web Site: www.oreilly.com, pg 199

Brommer, Richard C, Glencoe/McGraw-Hill, 8787 Orion Place, Columbus, OH 43240 Tel: 614-430-4000 Toll Free Tel: 800-848-1567 Web Site: www.glencoe.com, pg 105

Brondino, Jeanne, Hunter House Publishers, 1515 1/2 Park St, Alameda, CA 94501 Tel: 510-865-5282 Toll Free Tel: 800-266-5592 Fax: 510-865-4295 E-mail: acquisitions@hunterhouse.com Web Site: www.hunterhouse.com/, pg 129

Brondoli, Mike, Duke University Press, 905 W Main St, Suite 18-B, Durham, NC 27701 Tel: 919-687-3600 Toll Free Tel: 888-651-0122 (orders only) Fax: 919-688-4574 Toll Free Fax: 888-651-0124 Web Site: www.dukepress.edu, pg 84

Brontley, Jason, Counterpoint Press, 387 Park Ave S, New York, NY 10016 Tel: 212-340-8100 Fax: 212-340-8135 (edit); 212-340-8115 E-mail: counterpointpress@perseusbooks.com Web Site: www.counterpointpress.com, pg 70

Brook, Matt, Naval Institute Press, 291 Wood Rd, Annapolis, MD 21402-5034 Tel: 410-268-6110 Toll Free Tel: 800-233-8764 Fax: 410-295-1084; 410-571-1703 (customer service) E-mail: webmaster@navalinstitute.org; customer@navalinstitute.org (cust serv) Web Site: www.navalinstitute.org, pg 185

Brook, Susan T, Naval Institute Press, 291 Wood Rd, Annapolis, MD 21402-5034 Tel: 410-268-6110 Toll Free Tel: 800-233-8764 Fax: 410-295-1084; 410-571-1703 (customer service) E-mail: webmaster@navalinstitute.org; customer@navalinstitute.org (cust serv) Web Site: www.navalinstitute.org, pg 185

Brooke, Jerome, GoodSAMARitan Press, PO Box 803282, Santa Clarita, CA 91380 Tel: 661-799-0694, pg 107

Brookes, Jeff, Paul H Brookes Publishing Co, PO Box 10624, Baltimore, MD 21285-0624 Tel: 410-337-9580 Toll Free Tel: 800-638-3775 Fax: 410-337-8539 E-mail: custserv@brookespublishing.com Web Site: www.brookespublishing.com, pg 48

Brookes, Paul H, Paul H Brookes Publishing Co, PO Box 10624, Baltimore, MD 21285-0624 Tel: 410-337-9580 Toll Free Tel: 800-638-3775 Fax: 410-337-8539 E-mail: custserv@brookespublishing.com Web Site: www.brookespublishing.com, pg 48

Brooks, Anne, The Career Press Inc, 3 Tice Rd, Franklin Lakes, NJ 07417 Tel: 201-848-0310 Toll Free Tel: 800-CAREER-1 (227-3371) Fax: 201-848-1727 Web Site: www.careerpress.com, pg 53

Brooks, Catherine, The Pimlico Agency Inc, PO Box 20447, Cherokee Sta, New York, NY 10021 Tel: 212-628-9729 Fax: 212-535-7861, pg 648

Brooks, Eric, Penguin Group (USA) Inc, 375 Hudson St, New York, NY 10014 Tel: 212-366-2000 Fax: 212-366-2666 E-mail: online@uspenguingroup.com Web Site: www.penguin.com, pg 208

Brooks, Gabrielle T, Alfred A Knopf, 1745 Broadway, New York, NY 10019 Tel: 212-751-2600 Toll Free Tel: 800-638-6460 Fax: 212-572-2593 Web Site: www.randomhouse.com/knopf, pg 146

Brooks, Lane, Public Citizen, 1600 20 St NW, Washington, DC 20009 Tel: 202-588-1000 Fax: 202-588-7798 E-mail: public_citizen@citizen.org Web Site: www.citizen.org, pg 221

Brooks, Marshall, The Smith Publishers, 69 Joralemon St, Brooklyn, NY 11201-4003 Tel: 718-834-1212 Fax: 718-834-1212 E-mail: thesmith1@aol.com; artsend@ma.ultranet.com Web Site: members.aol.com/thesmith1, pg 250

Brooks, Michael, Northwestern University Press, 625 Colfax St, Evanston, IL 60208 Tel: 847-491-2046 Toll Free Tel: 800-621-2736 (orders only) Fax: 847-491-8150 E-mail: nupress@northwestern.edu Web Site: www.nupress.northwestern.edu, pg 193

Brooks, Phyllis, United Hospital Fund, 350 Fifth Ave, 23rd fl, New York, NY 10118-2399 Tel: 212-494-0700 Fax: 212-494-0800 E-mail: info@uhfnyc.org Web Site: www.uhfnyc.org, pg 279

Brooks, Randy, High/Coo Press, 3720 N Woodridge Dr, Decatur, IL 62526-1117 Tel: 217-877-2966 E-mail: brooksbooks@q-com.com Web Site: www.family-net.net/~brooksbooks, pg 122

Brooks, Regina, Writers Retreat Workshop (WRW), 5721 Magazine St, Suite 161, New Orleans, LA 70115 Toll Free Tel: 800-642-2494 E-mail: wrw04@netscape.net Web Site: www.writersretreatworkshop.com, pg 749

Brophy, Philippa, Sterling Lord Literistic Inc, 65 Bleecker St, New York, NY 10012 Tel: 212-780-6050 Fax: 212-780-6095, pg 657

Broquet, Antoine, Broquet Inc, 97B Montee des Bouleaux, St Constant, PQ J5A 1A9, Canada Tel: 450-638-3338 Fax: 450-638-4338 E-mail: info@broquet.qc.ca Web Site: www.broquet.qc.ca, pg 537

Broshack, Dorothy, Holiday House Inc, 425 Madison Ave, New York, NY 10017 Tel: 212-688-0085 Fax: 212-421-6134, pg 123

Brosius, Matthew E, Organization for Economic Cooperation & Development, 2001 "L" St NW, Suite 650, Washington, DC 20036-4922 Tel: 202-785-6323 Toll Free Tel: 800-456-6323 Fax: 202-785-0350 Web Site: www.oecdwash.org; www.sourceoecd.org, pg 199

Brothers, Connie, The Iowa Short Fiction Award, 102 Dey House, 507 N Clinton St, Iowa City, IA 52242 Tel: 319-335-0416 Fax: 319-335-0420, pg 780

Brothers, Ellen, Pleasant Company Publications, 8400 Fairway Place, Middleton, WI 53562 Tel: 608-836-4848 Fax: 608-257-3865 Web Site: www.americangirl.com, pg 214

Broude, Susan, Purple People Inc, PO Box 3194, Sedona, AZ 86340-3194 Tel: 928-204-6400 Toll Free Tel: 866-787-7535 Fax: 928-282-1662 E-mail: info@purplepeople.com; sales@purplepeople.com (sales & orders); admin@purplepeople.com (billing) Web Site: www.purplepeople.com, pg 222

Broughton, Paul, Life Cycle Books, LPO Box 1008, Niagara Falls, NY 14304-1008 Tel: 416-690-5860 Toll Free Tel: 800-214-5849 Fax: 416-690-8532 E-mail: orders@lifecyclebooks.com Web Site: www.lifecyclebooks.com, pg 154

Broughton, Paul, Life Cycle Books Ltd, 421 Nugget Ave, Unit 8, Toronto, ON M1S 4L8, Canada Tel: 416-690-5860 Toll Free Tel: 866-880-5860 Fax: 416-690-8532 Toll Free Fax: 866-690-8532 E-mail: orders@lifecyclebooks.com Web Site: www.lifecyclebooks.com, pg 552

Broussard, Michael, Dupree, Miller & Associates Inc, 100 Highland Park Village, Suite 350, Dallas, TX 75205 Tel: 214-559-2665 Fax: 214-559-7243 E-mail: dmabook@aol.com, pg 628

Brouwer, Joel, University of Alabama Program in Creative Writing, PO Box 870244, Tuscaloosa, AL 35487-0244 Tel: 205-348-0766 Fax: 205-348-1388 E-mail: writeua@english.as.ua.edu Web Site: www.as.ua.edu/english, pg 755

Brown, Terrence, Society of Illustrators (SI), 128 E 63 St, New York, NY 10021-7303 *Tel:* 212-838-2560 *Fax:* 212-838-2561 *E-mail:* info@societyillustrators. org *Web Site:* www.societyillustrators.org, pg 700

Brown, Therese, Catholic Book Publishers Association Inc, 8404 Jamesport Dr, Rockford, IL 61108 *Tel:* 815-332-3245 *Fax:* 815-332-3476 *E-mail:* cbpa3@aol.com *Web Site:* www.cbpa.org, pg 684

Brown, Tracy, Wendy Sherman Associates Inc, 450 Seventh Ave, Suite 3004, New York, NY 10123 *Tel:* 212-279-9027 *Fax:* 212-279-8863, pg 655

Brown, Tricia, Graphic Arts Center Publishing Co, 3019 NW Yeon Ave, Portland, OR 97210 *Tel:* 503-226-2402 *Toll Free Tel:* 800-452-3032 *Fax:* 503-223-1410 *Toll Free Fax:* 800-355-9685 *E-mail:* editorial@gacpc.com; sales@gacpc.com *Web Site:* www.gacpc.com, pg 107

Brown, Valerie, The Lyons Press, 246 Goose Lane, Guilford, CT 06437 *Tel:* 203-458-4500 *Toll Free Tel:* 800-243-0495 *Fax:* 203-458-4668 *Web Site:* www.lyonspress.com; www.globepequot.com, pg 160

Brown, Wendover, BrownTrout Publishers Inc, PO Box 280070, San Francisco, CA 94128-0070 *Tel:* 650-340-9800 *Toll Free Tel:* 800-777-7812 *Fax:* 310-316-1138 *E-mail:* sales@browntrout.com *Web Site:* www.browntrout.com, pg 49

Brown, William, Houghton Mifflin Co, 222 Berkeley St, Boston, MA 02116-3764 *Tel:* 617-351-5000 *Toll Free Tel:* 800-225-3362 (trade books); 800-733-2828 (text books); 800-225-1464 (college texts) *Fax:* 617-351-1125 *Web Site:* www.hmco.com, pg 126

Brown, William E, Waterside Productions Inc, 2187 Newcastle Ave, Suite 204, Cardiff, CA 92007 *Tel:* 760-632-9190 *Fax:* 760-632-9295 *Web Site:* www.waterside.com, pg 660

Browne, Chris, The Darwin Press Inc, 280 N Main St, Pennington, NJ 08534 *Tel:* 609-737-1349 *Fax:* 609-737-0929 *E-mail:* books@darwinpress.com *Web Site:* www.darwinpress.com, pg 76

Browne, Pema, Pema Browne Ltd, 11 Tena Place, Valley Cottage, NY 10989 *E-mail:* ppbltd@optonline.net *Web Site:* www.pemabrowneltd.com, pg 647

Browne, Pema, Pema Browne Ltd, 11 Tena Place, Valley Cottage, NY 10989 *E-mail:* info@pemabrowneltd.com *Web Site:* www.pemabrowneltd.com, pg 666

Browne, Perry J, Pema Browne Ltd, 11 Tena Place, Valley Cottage, NY 10989 *E-mail:* ppbltd@optonline. net *Web Site:* www.pemabrowneltd.com, pg 647

Browne, Perry J, Pema Browne Ltd, 11 Tena Place, Valley Cottage, NY 10989 *E-mail:* info@pemabrowneltd.com *Web Site:* www.pemabrowneltd.com, pg 666

Browne, Renni, The Editorial Department, LLC, 1710 S Olympic Club Dr, Tucson, AZ 85710 *Tel:* 520-546-9992 *Toll Free Tel:* 866-360-6996 *Fax:* 520-546-9993 *E-mail:* admin@editorialdepartment.net *Web Site:* www.editorialdepartment.net, pg 597

Browne, Ross, The Editorial Department, LLC, 1710 S Olympic Club Dr, Tucson, AZ 85710 *Tel:* 520-546-9992 *Toll Free Tel:* 866-360-6996 *Fax:* 520-546-9993 *E-mail:* admin@editorialdepartment.net *Web Site:* www.editorialdepartment.net, pg 597

Brownrigg, Deborah, Canadian Museum of Civilization, 100 Laurier St, Hull, PQ J8X 4H2, Canada *Tel:* 819-776-8387 *Toll Free Tel:* 800-555-5621 (North America only) *Fax:* 819-776-8300 *E-mail:* publications@civilization.ca (mail order) *Web Site:* www.civilization.ca, pg 539

Brownstein, Joanne, Association of Authors' Representatives Inc (AAR), PO Box 237201, Ansonia Sta, New York, NY 10023 *E-mail:* aarinc@mindspring.com *Web Site:* www.aar-online.org, pg 679

Brozak, Gary, Plume, 375 Hudson St, New York, NY 10014 *Tel:* 212-366-2000 *Fax:* 212-366-2666 *E-mail:* online@penguinputnam.com *Web Site:* www.penguin.com, pg 215

Bruccoli, Matthew J, Bruccoli Clark Layman Inc, 2006 Sumter St, Columbia, SC 29201 *Tel:* 803-771-4642 *Fax:* 803-799-6953, pg 49

Bruce, Sandra, Milady Publishing, Executive Woods, 5 Maxwell Dr, Clifton Park, NY 12065-2919 *Tel:* 518-348-2300 (ext 2409) *Toll Free Tel:* 800-998-7498 *Fax:* 518-348-7000 *Web Site:* www.delmar.com; www.milady.com, pg 174

Bruce, Thomas, Glencoe/McGraw-Hill, 8787 Orion Place, Columbus, OH 43240 *Tel:* 614-430-4000 *Toll Free Tel:* 800-848-1567 *Web Site:* www.glencoe.com, pg 105

Bruce, Thomas, St Anthony Messenger Press, 28 W Liberty St, Cincinnati, OH 45202 *Tel:* 513-241-5615 *Toll Free Tel:* 800-488-0488 *Fax:* 513-241-0399 *E-mail:* books@americancatholic.org *Web Site:* www.AmericanCatholic.org, pg 237

Bruckner, Al, Sage Publications, 2455 Teller Rd, Thousand Oaks, CA 91320 *Tel:* 805-499-0721 *Fax:* 805-499-0871 *E-mail:* info@sagepub.com *Web Site:* www.sagepub.com, pg 237

Bruckner, Carol, ICM Lecture Division, 40 W 57 St, New York, NY 10019 *Tel:* 212-556-5602 *Fax:* 212-556-6829 *Web Site:* www.icmtalent.com, pg 669

Brugger, Robert J, The Johns Hopkins University Press, 2715 N Charles St, Baltimore, MD 21218-4363 *Tel:* 410-516-6900 *Toll Free Tel:* 800-537-5487 *Fax:* 410-516-6968 *Web Site:* www.press.jhu.edu, pg 141

Brumley, Mark, Ignatius Press, 2515 McAllister St, San Francisco, CA 94118 *Tel:* 415-387-2324 *Toll Free Tel:* 877-320-9276 (book orders) *Fax:* 415-387-0896 *E-mail:* info@ignatius.com *Web Site:* www.ignatius.com, pg 131

Brummer, Andre, Ancestry Publishing, 360 W 4800 N, Provo, UT 84064 *Tel:* 801-705-7305 *Toll Free Tel:* 800-262-3787 *Fax:* 801-426-3501 *E-mail:* editor@ancestry.com; dealersales@ancestry-inc.com *Web Site:* www.ancestry.com, pg 19

Brun, Henry, Amsco School Publications Inc, 315 Hudson St, New York, NY 10013-1085 *Tel:* 212-886-6500; 212-886-6565 *Toll Free Tel:* 800-969-8398 *Fax:* 212-675-7010 *E-mail:* info@amscopub.com *Web Site:* www.amscopub.com, pg 19

Bruner, Kurt, Focus on the Family, 8605 Explorer Dr, Colorado Springs, CO 80920 *Tel:* 719-531-3400 *Fax:* 719-531-3484 *Web Site:* www.family.org, pg 97

Brunet, Denis, Services Documentaires Multimedia Inc (SDM Inc), 5650 Rue D'Iberville, Bureau 620, Montreal, PQ H2G 2B3, Canada *Tel:* 514-382-0895 *Fax:* 514-384-9139 *E-mail:* info@sdm.qc.ca *Web Site:* www.sdm.qc.ca, pg 561

Brunke, Pamela, Salem Press Inc, 2 University Plaza, Suite 121, Hackensack, NJ 07601 *Tel:* 201-968-9899 *Toll Free Tel:* 800-221-1592 *Fax:* 201-968-1411 *E-mail:* csr@salempress.com *Web Site:* www.salempress.com, pg 239

Bruscia, Kenneth E, Barcelona Publishers, Pathway Book Service, 4 White Brook Rd, Gilsum, NH 03448 *Tel:* 603-357-0236 *Toll Free Tel:* 800-345-6665 *Fax:* 603-357-2073 *E-mail:* pbs@pathwaybooks.com *Web Site:* barcelonapublishers.com, pg 32

Bryan, Deidre, University Press of Florida, 15 NW 15 St, Gainesville, FL 32611-2079 *Tel:* 352-392-1351 *Toll Free Tel:* 800-226-3822 (orders only) *Fax:* 352-392-7302 *Toll Free Fax:* 800-680-1955 (orders only) *E-mail:* info@upf.com *Web Site:* www.upf.com, pg 287

Bryan, Nancy, University of Texas Press, PO Box 7819, Austin, TX 78713-7819 *Tel:* 512-471-7233 *Fax:* 512-232-7178 *E-mail:* utpress@uts.cc.utexas.edu *Web Site:* www.utexas.edu/utpress, pg 267

Bryans, John, Information Today, Inc, 143 Old Marlton Pike, Medford, NJ 08055-8750 *Tel:* 609-654-6266 *Toll Free Tel:* 800-300-9868 (cust serv) *Fax:* 609-654-4309 *E-mail:* custserv@infotoday.com *Web Site:* www.infotoday.com, pg 133

Bryant, John, The Melville Society, University of Minnesota, 140 Appleby Hall, Minneapolis, MN 55455 *Fax:* 612-625-0709, pg 691

Bryant, Kay, Oxmoor House Inc, 2100 Lakeshore Dr, Birmingham, AL 35209 *Tel:* 205-445-6000; 205-445-6560 *Toll Free Tel:* 800-366-4712 *Fax:* 205-445-6078 *Web Site:* www.oxmoorhouse.com, pg 201

Bryant, Marcia, The Anisfield Wolf Book Award in Human Relations, 1422 Euclid Ave, Suite 1300, Cleveland, OH 44115-2001 *Tel:* 216-861-3810 *Fax:* 216-861-2229 *E-mail:* contactus@clevefdn.org, pg 759

Bryant, Peggy, Rainbow Books Inc, PO Box 430, Highland City, FL 33846-0430 *Tel:* 863-648-4420 *Toll Free Tel:* 800-431-1579 (orders only); 888-613-2665 *Fax:* 863-647-5951 *E-mail:* rbibooks@aol.com *Web Site:* www.rainbowbooksinc.com, pg 225

Bryant, Virginia V, The AEI Press, 1150 17 St NW, Washington, DC 20036 *Tel:* 202-862-5800 *Fax:* 202-862-7177 *Web Site:* www.aei.org, pg 6

Bryce, Mary, George Braziller Inc, 171 Madison Ave, Suite 1105, New York, NY 10016 *Tel:* 212-889-0909 *Fax:* 212-689-5405 *E-mail:* georgebraziller@earthlink.net *Web Site:* www.georgebraziller.com, pg 46

Bryfonski, Dedria, Thomson Gale, 27500 Drake Rd, Farmington Hills, MI 48331-3535 *Tel:* 248-699-4253 *Toll Free Tel:* 800-347-4253 *Fax:* 248-699-8070 *Toll Free Fax:* 800-414-5043 *E-mail:* galeord@gale.com *Web Site:* www.gale.com, pg 270

Buchanan, Mary (Ginger), Berkley Books, 375 Hudson St, New York, NY 10014 *Tel:* 212-366-2000 *Fax:* 212-366-2666 *E-mail:* online@penguinputnam.com *Web Site:* www.penguin.com, pg 36

Buchanan, Mary (Ginger), Berkley Publishing Group, 375 Hudson St, New York, NY 10014 *Tel:* 212-366-2000 *E-mail:* online@penguinputnam.com *Web Site:* www.penguin.com, pg 37

Buchholz, Theodore O, Saunders College Publishing, The Public Ledger Bldg, 150 S Independence Mall W, Suite 1250, Philadelphia, PA 19106-3412 *Tel:* 215-238-5500 *Fax:* 215-238-5660 *Web Site:* www.hbcollege.com, pg 240

Buchwald, Don, Don Buchwald & Associates Inc, 6500 Wilshire Blvd, Suite 2200, Los Angeles, CA 90048 *Tel:* 323-655-7400 *Fax:* 323-655-7470 *Web Site:* www.donbuchwald.com, pg 623

Buchwald, Shari, The Analytic Press, 101 West St, Hillsdale, NJ 07642 *Tel:* 201-358-9477; 201-236-9500 *Toll Free Tel:* 800-926-6579 (orders only); 800-627-0629 (journal orders) *Fax:* 201-358-4700 (edit); 201-760-3735 (orders only) *E-mail:* tap@analyticpress.com *Web Site:* www.analyticpress.com, pg 19

Buck, Bethany, Simon & Schuster Children's Publishing, 1230 Avenue of the Americas, New York, NY 10020 *Tel:* 212-698-7000 *Web Site:* www.simonsayskids.com, pg 248

Buck, Howard, Howard Buck Agency, 80 Eighth Ave, Suite 1107, New York, NY 10011 *Tel:* 212-924-9093, pg 623

Buckenstose, Tammy, Trails Illustrated, Division of National Geographic Maps, PO Box 4357, Evergreen, CO 80437-4357 *Tel:* 303-670-3457 *Toll Free Tel:* 800-962-1643 *Fax:* 303-670-3644 *Toll Free Fax:* 800-626-8676 *E-mail:* topomaps@aol.com *Web Site:* www.nationalgeographics.com, pg 273

Buckhalter, Edwin, Severn House Publishers Inc, 595 Madison Ave, 15th fl, New York, NY 10022 *Tel:* 212-888-4042 *Fax:* 212-759-5422 *E-mail:* editorial@severnhouse.com; sales@severnhouse.com *Web Site:* www.severnhouse.com, pg 245

Buckingham, Marcia, Denlinger's Publishers Ltd, PO Box 1030, Edgewater, FL 32132-1030 *Tel:* 386-424-1737 *Toll Free Tel:* 800-362-1810 *Fax:* 386-428-3534 *Toll Free Fax:* 800-589-1191 *E-mail:* editor@thebookden.com *Web Site:* www.thebookden.com, pg 79

Buckley, Carol, Piano Press, 1425 Ocean Ave, Suite 6, Del Mar, CA 92014 *Tel:* 619-884-1401 *Fax:* 858-459-3376 *E-mail:* pianopress@aol.com *Web Site:* www.pianopress.com, pg 212

Buckley, Cicely, Oyster River Press, 20 Riverview Rd, Durham, NH 03824-3313 *Tel:* 603-868-5006 *E-mail:* oysterriverpress@comcast.net *Web Site:* www.oysterriverpress.com, pg 201

Buckley, Cicely, Oyster River Press, 20 Riverview Rd, Durham, NH 03824-3313 *Tel:* 603-868-5006 *E-mail:* oysterriverpress@comcast.net *Web Site:* oysterriverpress.com, pg 607

Buckley, Jim, American Book Producers Association (ABPA), 160 Fifth Ave, Suite 622, New York, NY 10010 *Tel:* 212-645-2368 *Toll Free Tel:* 800-209-4575 *Fax:* 212-242-6499 *E-mail:* office@abpaonline.org *Web Site:* www.abpaonline.org, pg 676

Buckley, Jim, Book Producing: Making Books Happen, 160 Fifth Ave, New York, NY 10010-7003 *Tel:* 212-645-2368 *Toll Free Tel:* 800-209-4575 *Fax:* 212-242-6799 *E-mail:* office@abpaonline.org *Web Site:* www.abpaonline.org, pg 742

Buckley, Paul, Viking Penguin, 375 Hudson St, New York, NY 10014 *Tel:* 212-366-2000 *E-mail:* online@penguinputnam.com *Web Site:* www.penguin.com, pg 290

Buckner, Judith, Judith Buckner Literary Agency, 12721 Hart St, North Hollywood, CA 91605 *Tel:* 818-982-8202 *Fax:* 818-764-6844 *E-mail:* jbuckner@pacbell.net, pg 623

Budnick, Phil, Penguin Group (USA) Inc Sales, 375 Hudson St, New York, NY 10014 *Tel:* 212-366-2000 *E-mail:* online@penguinputnam.com *Web Site:* www.penguin.com, pg 208

Budoff, Milt, Brookline Books, PO Box 1209, Brookline, MA 02445 *Toll Free Tel:* 800-666-2665; 800-345-6665 (orders) *Fax:* 617-734-6772 *Web Site:* www.brooklinebooks.com, pg 49

Bufe, Charles, See Sharp Press, PO Box 1731, Tucson, AZ 85702-1731 *Tel:* 520-628-8720 *Fax:* 520-628-8720 *E-mail:* info@seesharppress.com *Web Site:* www.seesharppress.com, pg 244

Buffington, Peter, Peace Hill Press, 18101 The Glebe Lane, Charles City, VA 23030 *Tel:* 804-829-5043 *Toll Free Tel:* 877-322-3445 (orders) *Fax:* 804-829-5704 *E-mail:* info@peacehillpress.net *Web Site:* www.peacehillpress.com, pg 206

Buffington, Sara, Peace Hill Press, 18101 The Glebe Lane, Charles City, VA 23030 *Tel:* 804-829-5043 *Toll Free Tel:* 877-322-3445 (orders) *Fax:* 804-829-5704 *E-mail:* info@peacehillpress.net *Web Site:* www.peacehillpress.com, pg 206

Bui, Francoise, Random House Children's Books, 1745 Broadway, New York, NY 10019 *Tel:* 212-782-9000 *Toll Free Tel:* 800-200-3552 *Fax:* 212-782-9452 *Web Site:* www.randomhouse.com/kids, pg 226

Bukowski, Denise, The Bukowski Agency, 202-14 Prince Arthur Ave, Toronto, ON M5R 1A9, Canada *Tel:* 416-928-6728 *Fax:* 416-963-9978 *E-mail:* assistant@thebukowskiagency.com *Web Site:* www.thebukowskiagency.com, pg 623

Bull, James, Bull Publishing Co, PO Box 1377, Boulder, CO 80306-1377 *Tel:* 303-545-6350 *Toll Free Tel:* 800-676-2855 *Fax:* 303-545-6354 *E-mail:* bullpublishing@msn.com *Web Site:* www.bullpub.com, pg 50

Bull, Katie, Commonwealth Editions, 266 Cabot St, Beverly, MA 01915 *Tel:* 978-921-0747 *Fax:* 978-927-8195 *Web Site:* www.commonwealtheditions.com, pg 66

Bull, Webster, Commonwealth Editions, 266 Cabot St, Beverly, MA 01915 *Tel:* 978-921-0747 *Fax:* 978-927-8195 *Web Site:* www.commonwealtheditions.com, pg 66

Bullard, Anna, University of California Press, 2120 Berkeley Way, Berkeley, CA 94720 *Tel:* 510-642-4247 *Toll Free Tel:* 800-777-4726 *Fax:* 510-643-7127 *Toll Free Fax:* 800-999-1958 *E-mail:* askucp@ucpress.edu *Web Site:* www.ucpress.edu, pg 281

Bullas, Roz, Wilderness Press, 1200 Fifth St, Berkeley, CA 94710 *Tel:* 510-558-1666 *Toll Free Tel:* 800-443-7227 *Fax:* 510-558-1696 *E-mail:* info@wildernesspress.com *Web Site:* www.wildernesspress.com, pg 299

Bulzone, Marisa, Stewart, Tabori & Chang, 115 W 18 St, 5th fl, New York, NY 10011 *Tel:* 212-519-1200 *Fax:* 212-519-1210 *Web Site:* www.abramsbooks.com, pg 260

Bumps, Susan, North Atlantic Books, 1435 Fourth St, Berkeley, CA 94710 *Tel:* 510-559-8277 *Toll Free Tel:* 800-337-2665 (book orders only) *Fax:* 510-559-8279 *E-mail:* orders@northatlanticbooks.com *Web Site:* www.northatlanticbooks.com, pg 192

Bunce, Cindy, Cedar Fort Inc, 925 N Main St, Springville, UT 84663 *Tel:* 801-489-4084 *Toll Free Tel:* 800-759-2665 *Fax:* 801-489-1097 *E-mail:* skybook@cedarfort.com *Web Site:* www.cedarfort.com, pg 56

Bunch, Cindy, InterVarsity Press, 430 E Plaza Dr, Westmont, IL 60559-1234 *Tel:* 630-734-4000 *Toll Free Tel:* 800-843-7225 *Fax:* 630-734-4200 *E-mail:* mail@ivpress.com *Web Site:* www.ivpress.com, pg 138

Bundt, Dianne, Meriwether Publishing Ltd/Contemporary Drama Service, 885 Elkton Dr, Colorado Springs, CO 80907-3557 *Tel:* 719-594-4422 *Toll Free Tel:* 800-937-5297 *Fax:* 719-594-9916 *Toll Free Fax:* 888-594-4436 *E-mail:* merpcds@aol.com *Web Site:* www.meriwether.com, pg 171

Bunting, Jennifer, Tilbury House Publishers, 2 Mechanic St, No 3, Gardiner, ME 04345 *Tel:* 207-582-1899 *Toll Free Tel:* 800-582-1899 (orders) *Fax:* 207-582-8229 *E-mail:* tilbury@tilburyhouse.com *Web Site:* www.tilburyhouse.com, pg 271

Bunton, Jeannie, Corporation for Public Broadcasting (CPB), 401 Ninth St NW, Washington, DC 20004-2037 *Tel:* 202-879-9600 *Fax:* 202-879-9700 *E-mail:* info@cpb.org *Web Site:* www.cpb.org, pg 685

Bunzel, Mark, FineEdge.com, 14004 Biz Point Lane, Anacortes, WA 98221 *Tel:* 360-299-8500 *Fax:* 360-299-0535 *Web Site:* www.fineedge.com, pg 97

Burbank, Toni, Bantam Dell Publishing Group, 1745 Broadway, New York, NY 10019 *Tel:* 212-782-9000 *Toll Free Tel:* 800-223-6834 *Fax:* 212-302-7985 *Web Site:* www.randomhouse.com/bantamdell, pg 31

Burch, Marcia, Fireside & Touchstone, 1230 Avenue of the Americas, New York, NY 10020, pg 97

Burch, Martin, Ocean Tree Books, 1325 Cerro Gordo Rd, Santa Fe, NM 87501 *Tel:* 505-983-1412 *Fax:* 505-983-0899 *E-mail:* oceantree@earthlink.net *Web Site:* www.oceantree.com, pg 195

Burch, Michael E, Whitecap Books Ltd, 351 Lynn Ave, North Vancouver, BC V7J 2C4, Canada *Tel:* 604-980-9852 *Toll Free Tel:* 888-870-3442 ext 239 & 241 (cust serv) *Fax:* 604-980-8197 *Toll Free Fax:* 888-661-6630 (orders only) *E-mail:* whitecap@whitecap.ca *Web Site:* www.whitecap.ca, pg 567

Burchell, Robert, Center for Urban Policy Research, 33 Livingston Ave, Suite 400, New Brunswick, NJ 08901-1982 *Tel:* 732-932-3133 *Fax:* 732-932-2363 *Web Site:* www.policy.rutgers.edu/cupr, pg 57

Burford, Peter, Burford Books, 32 Morris Ave, Springfield, NJ 07081 *Tel:* 973-258-0960 *Fax:* 973-258-0113 *E-mail:* info@burfordbooks.com *Web Site:* www.burfordbooks.com, pg 50

Burg, Barb, Bantam Dell Publishing Group, 1745 Broadway, New York, NY 10019 *Tel:* 212-782-9000 *Toll Free Tel:* 800-223-6834 *Fax:* 212-302-7985 *Web Site:* www.randomhouse.com/bantamdell, pg 31

Burger, Dr Henry G, Wordtree branching dictionary, 10876 Bradshaw W102, Overland Park, KS 66210-1148 *Tel:* 913-469-1010 *Web Site:* www.wordtree.com, pg 303

Burger, Knox, Knox Burger Associates Ltd, 425 Madison Ave, New York, NY 10017 *Tel:* 212-759-8600 *Fax:* 212-759-9428, pg 623

Burger, Knox, Harold Ober Associates Inc, 425 Madison Ave, New York, NY 10017 *Tel:* 212-759-8600 *Fax:* 212-759-9428, pg 647

Burgess, Angela, IEEE Computer Society, 10662 Los Vaqueros Circle, Los Alamitos, CA 90720-1314 *Tel:* 714-821-8380 *Toll Free Tel:* 800-272-6657 *Fax:* 714-821-4010 *E-mail:* csbooks@computer.org *Web Site:* www.computer.org, pg 130

Burgess, Kathy, University Press of Mississippi, 3825 Ridgewood Rd, Jackson, MS 39211-6492 *Tel:* 601-432-6205 *Toll Free Tel:* 800-737-7788 *Fax:* 601-432-6217 *E-mail:* press@ihl.state.ms.us *Web Site:* www.upress.state.ms.us, pg 287

Burgess, Sue, SCBWI Work-In-Progress Grants, 8271 Beverly Blvd, Los Angeles, CA 90048 *Tel:* 323-782-1010 *Fax:* 323-782-1892 *E-mail:* membership@scbwi.org *Web Site:* www.scbwi.org, pg 804

Burgess, Susie, Chalice Press, 1221 Locust St, Suite 1200, St Louis, MO 63103 *Tel:* 314-231-8500 *Toll Free Tel:* 800-366-3383 *Fax:* 314-231-8524 *E-mail:* chalicepress@cbp21.com *Web Site:* www.cbp21.com; www.chalicepress.com, pg 58

Burgo, Kate, Adams Media, An F+W Publications Co, 57 Littlefield St, 2nd fl, Avon, MA 02322 *Tel:* 508-427-7100 *Fax:* 508-427-6790 *Toll Free Fax:* 800-872-5628 *E-mail:* authors@adamsmedia.com; orders@adamsmedia.com *Web Site:* www.adamsmedia.com, pg 5

Burgos, Jose A, University of Puerto Rico Press, Edificio EDUPR/Dialogo, Carr No 1, KM 12-0, Piso 2, Jardin Bota'nico Area Norte, San Juan, PR 00931 *Tel:* 787-758-6932; 787-758-8345 (sales); 787-250-0046; 787-250-0000 *Fax:* 787-753-9116; 787-751-8785 (sales dept), pg 285

Burk, Dale A, Stoneydale Press Publishing Co, 523 Main St, Stevensville, MT 59870 *Tel:* 406-777-2729 *Toll Free Tel:* 800-735-7006 *Fax:* 406-777-2521 *E-mail:* stoneydale@montana.com *Web Site:* www.stoneydale.com, pg 260

Burke, Alexander, Hofstra University, English Dept, 204 Calkins, Hempstead, NY 11549 *Tel:* 516-463-5454 *Fax:* 516-463-6395 *E-mail:* engpmu@hofstra.edu *Web Site:* www.hofstra.edu, pg 752

Burke, Alexander, Phoenix Learning Resources, 25 Third St, 2nd fl, Stamford, CT 06905 *Tel:* 203-353-1665 *Toll Free Tel:* 800-526-6581 *Fax:* 212-629-5648 *Web Site:* www.phoenixlr.com, pg 212

Burke, Barbara, Jonathan David Publishers Inc, 68-22 Eliot Ave, Middle Village, NY 11379 *Tel:* 718-456-8611 *Fax:* 718-894-2818 *E-mail:* info@jdbooks.com; jondavpub@aol.com *Web Site:* www.jdbooks.com, pg 142

Burke, Jennifer, Harmonie Park Press, 23630 Pinewood, Warren, MI 48091 *Tel:* 586-755-3080 *Toll Free Tel:* 800-886-3080 *Fax:* 586-755-4213 *E-mail:* info@harmonieparkpress.com *Web Site:* harmonieparkpress.com, pg 115

Burke, Katie, Pomegranate Communications, 775-A Southpoint Blvd, Petaluma, CA 94954-1495 *Tel:* 707-782-9000 *Toll Free Tel:* 800-227-1428 *Toll Free Fax:* 800-848-4376 *Web Site:* www.pomegranate.com, pg 216

Burke, Louise, Pocket Books, 1230 Avenue of the Americas, New York, NY 10020 *Toll Free Tel:* 800-456-6798 *Fax:* 212-698-7284 *E-mail:* consumer.customerservice@simonandschuster.com *Web Site:* www.simonsays.com, pg 215

Burke, Michael, Penguin Group (USA) Inc Sales, 375 Hudson St, New York, NY 10014 *Tel:* 212-366-2000 *E-mail:* online@penguinputnam.com *Web Site:* www.penguin.com, pg 208

Burke, Mindy, American Water Works Association, 6666 W Quincy Ave, Denver, CO 80235 *Tel:* 303-794-7711 *Toll Free Tel:* 800-926-7337 *Fax:* 303-347-0804 *Web Site:* www.awwa.org, pg 18

Burke, Sharon, Harvest House Publishers Inc, 990 Owen Loop N, Eugene, OR 97402 *Tel:* 541-343-0123 *Toll Free Tel:* 800-547-8979 *Fax:* 541-342-6410 *E-mail:* admin@harvesthousepublishers.com *Web Site:* www.harvesthousepublishers.com, pg 117

Burke, T Patrick, Calculator Training Center, 94 Buckingham Rd, New Milford, CT 06776 *Tel:* 860-355-8255 *E-mail:* c-t-c@att.net, pg 51

Burke, Terry, Health Communications Inc, 3201 SW 15 St, Deerfield Beach, FL 33442-8190 *Tel:* 954-360-0909 *Toll Free Tel:* 800-851-9100 (cust serv); 800-441-5569 (order entry) *Fax:* 954-360-0034 *Web Site:* www.hcibooks.com, pg 119

Burke, Therese, DK Publishing Inc, 375 Hudson St, 2nd fl, New York, NY 10014-3672 *Tel:* 212-213-4800 *Toll Free Tel:* 877-342-5357 (cust serv) *Fax:* 212-213-5202 *Web Site:* www.dk.com, pg 81

Burke, Thomas F, Pomegranate Communications, 775-A Southpoint Blvd, Petaluma, CA 94954-1495 *Tel:* 707-782-9000 *Toll Free Tel:* 800-227-1428 *Toll Free Fax:* 800-848-4376 *Web Site:* www.pomegranate.com, pg 216

Burke, William, Cummings & Hathaway Publishers, 395 Atlantic Ave, East Rockaway, NY 11518 *Tel:* 516-593-3607 *Fax:* 516-593-1401 *E-mail:* chpublish@aol.com, pg 74

Burkett, John W, Leadership Ministries Worldwide, 515 Airport Rd, Suite 111, Chattanooga, TN 37421 *Tel:* 423-855-2181 *Toll Free Tel:* 800-987-8790 *Fax:* 423-855-8616 *Toll Free Fax:* 800-987-8790 *E-mail:* info@outlinebible.org *Web Site:* www.outlinebible.org, pg 150

Burkin, Michael, Simon & Schuster Sales & Distribution, 1230 Avenue of the Americas, New York, NY 10020 *Tel:* 212-698-7000, pg 249

Burks, Patrick C, American Geological Institute (AGI), 4220 King St, Alexandria, VA 22302-1507 *Tel:* 703-379-2480 *Fax:* 703-379-7563 *E-mail:* pubs@agiweb.org *Web Site:* www.agiweb.org, pg 14

Burles, Kenneth T, Salem Press Inc, 2 University Plaza, Suite 121, Hackensack, NJ 07601 *Tel:* 201-968-9899 *Toll Free Tel:* 800-221-1592 *Fax:* 201-968-1411 *E-mail:* csr@salempress.com *Web Site:* www.salempress.com, pg 239

Burn, Geoffrey R H, Stanford University Press, 1450 Page Mill Rd, Palo Alto, CA 94304-1124 *Tel:* 650-723-9434 *Fax:* 650-725-3457 *Web Site:* www.sup.org, pg 257

Burnell, Greg, Thomson Delmar Learning, 5 Maxwell Dr, Clifton Park, NY 12065-8007 *Tel:* 518-464-3500 *Toll Free Tel:* 800-347-7707 (cust serv); 800-998-7498 *Fax:* 518-464-0393 *Toll Free Fax:* 800-487-8488 (cust serv) *Web Site:* www.thomson.com; www.delmarlearning.com, pg 269

Burner, David, Brandywine Press, 154 General Pulaski Walk, Naugatuck, CT 06770-2978 *Tel:* 203-729-7556 *Toll Free Tel:* 800-345-1776 *Fax:* 203-729-7567 *Web Site:* www.brandywinepress.com, pg 45

Burnett, Andrea, Chronicle Books LLC, 85 Second St, 6th fl, San Francisco, CA 94105 *Tel:* 415-537-4200 *Toll Free Tel:* 800-722-6657 (cust serv) *Fax:* 415-537-4460 *Toll Free Fax:* 800-858-7787 (orders) *E-mail:* frontdesk@chroniclebooks.com *Web Site:* www.chroniclebooks.com, pg 61

Burnett, Sheila, Barnes & Noble Books (Imports & Reprints), 4501 Forbes Blvd, Suite 200, Lanham, MD 20706 *Tel:* 301-459-3366 *Toll Free Tel:* 800-462-6420 (orders only) *Fax:* 301-429-5748 *Toll Free Fax:* 800-338-4550 (orders only) *Web Site:* www.rowmanlittlefield.com, pg 32

Burnett, Sheila, Rowman & Littlefield Publishers Inc, 4501 Forbes Blvd, Lanham, MD 20706 *Tel:* 301-459-3366 *Toll Free Tel:* 800-462-6420 *Fax:* 301-429-5748 *Web Site:* www.rowmanlittlefield.com, pg 235

Burnette, Terry, South Carolina Bar, Continuing Legal Education Div, 950 Taylor St, Columbia, SC 29201 *Tel:* 803-771-0333 *Toll Free Tel:* 800-768-7787 *Fax:* 803-252-8427 *E-mail:* scbar-info@scbar.org *Web Site:* www.scbar.org, pg 254

Burnham, Bill, Soundprints, 353 Main Ave, Norwalk, CT 06851 *Tel:* 203-846-2274 *Toll Free Tel:* 800-228-7839; 800-577-2413, ext 118 (orders) *Fax:* 203-846-1776 *E-mail:* Soundprints@soundprints.com *Web Site:* www.soundprints.com, pg 253

Burns, Carol Ann, Southern Illinois University Press, PO Box 3697, Carbondale, IL 62902-3697 *Tel:* 618-453-2281 *Toll Free Tel:* 800-346-2680 *Fax:* 618-453-1221 *Toll Free Fax:* 800-346-2681 *E-mail:* jstetter@siu.edu *Web Site:* www.siu.edu/~siupress, pg 254

Burns, Dayna K, Blackbirch Press®, 27500 Drake Rd, Farmington Hills, MI 48311-3535 *Toll Free Tel:* 800-877-4253 *Toll Free Fax:* 800-414-5043 (orders) *E-mail:* galeord@gale.com; customerservice@gale.com *Web Site:* www.gale.com, pg 40

Burns, Don, Faith Library Publications, 1025 W Kenosha St, Broken Arrow, OK 74012 *Tel:* 918-258-1588 (ext 2218) *Toll Free Tel:* 888-258-0999 (orders only) *Fax:* 918-251-8016 (orders) *Web Site:* www.rhema.org, pg 94

Burns, Heidi, Peter Lang Publishing Inc, 275 Seventh Ave, 28th fl, New York, NY 10001-6708 *Tel:* 212-647-7700 *Toll Free Tel:* 800-770-5264 (cust serv) *Fax:* 212-647-7707 *Web Site:* www.peterlangusa.com, pg 148

Burns, Scott, Oxford University Press, Inc, 198 Madison Ave, New York, NY 10016-4314 *Tel:* 212-726-6000 *Toll Free Tel:* 800-451-7556 (orders) *Web Site:* www.oup.com/us, pg 200

Burns, Vince, Greenwood Publishing Group Inc, 88 Post Rd W, Westport, CT 06880-4208 *Tel:* 203-226-3571 *Toll Free Tel:* 800-225-5800 *Fax:* 203-222-1502 *E-mail:* bookinfo@greenwood.com (general); firstintial&fulllastname@greenwood.com (individuals) *Web Site:* www.greenwood.com, pg 109

Burns, William, Resource Publications Inc, 160 E Virginia St, Suite 290, San Jose, CA 95112-5876 *Tel:* 408-286-8505 *Fax:* 408-287-8748 *E-mail:* orders@rpinet.com *Web Site:* www.rpinet.com, pg 231

Burnside, Yvonne, The Conference Board Inc, 845 Third Ave, New York, NY 10022 *Tel:* 212-759-0900 *Fax:* 212-980-7014 *E-mail:* info@conference-board.org *Web Site:* www.conference-board.org, pg 66

Burr, Andrea, Great Source Education Group, 181 Ballardvale St, Wilmington, MA 01887 *Tel:* 978-661-1300 *Toll Free Tel:* 800-289-4490 (orders), pg 108

Burr, Jim, University of Texas Press, PO Box 7819, Austin, TX 78713-7819 *Tel:* 512-471-7233 *Fax:* 512-232-7178 *E-mail:* utpress@uts.cc.utexas.edu *Web Site:* www.utexas.edu/utpress, pg 267

Burrell, Dean, Chronicle Books LLC, 85 Second St, 6th fl, San Francisco, CA 94105 *Tel:* 415-537-4200 *Toll Free Tel:* 800-722-6657 (cust serv) *Fax:* 415-537-4460 *Toll Free Fax:* 800-858-7787 (orders) *E-mail:* frontdesk@chroniclebooks.com *Web Site:* www.chroniclebooks.com, pg 61

Burri, Breht, Davies Publishing Inc, 32 S Raymond Ave, Pasadena, CA 91105-1935 *Tel:* 626-792-3046 *Toll Free Tel:* 877-792-0005 *Fax:* 626-792-5308 *E-mail:* daviescorp@aol.com *Web Site:* www.daviespublishing.com, pg 76

Burri, Peter, Industrial Press Inc, 200 Madison Ave, 21st fl, New York, NY 10016-4078 *Tel:* 212-889-6330 *Toll Free Tel:* 888-528-7852 *Fax:* 212-545-8327 *E-mail:* info@industrialpress.com *Web Site:* www.industrialpress.com, pg 132

Burrows, Arthur A, Pro Lingua Associates Inc, 74 Cotton Mill Hill, Suite A-315, Brattleboro, VT 05301 *Tel:* 802-257-7779 *Toll Free Tel:* 800-366-4775 *Fax:* 802-257-5117 *E-mail:* orders@prolinguaassociates.com *Web Site:* www.prolinguaassociates.com, pg 219

Burrows, Elise C, Pro Lingua Associates Inc, 74 Cotton Mill Hill, Suite A-315, Brattleboro, VT 05301 *Tel:* 802-257-7779 *Toll Free Tel:* 800-366-4775 *Fax:* 802-257-5117 *E-mail:* orders@prolinguaassociates.com *Web Site:* www.prolinguaassociates.com, pg 219

Burrows, Ralph, Doubleday Canada, One Toronto St, Suite 300, Toronto, ON M5C 2V6, Canada *Tel:* 416-364-4449 *Fax:* 416-957-1587 *Web Site:* www.randomhouse.ca, pg 542

Burrows, Ralph, Random House of Canada Ltd, One Toronto St, Unit 300, Toronto, ON M5C 2V6, Canada *Tel:* 416-364-4449 *Fax:* 416-364-6863 (edit & publicity); 416-364-6653 (subs rts) *Web Site:* www.randomhouse.ca, pg 559

Burrows, Ralph, Seal Books, One Toronto St, Suite 300, Toronto, ON M5C 2V6, Canada *Tel:* 416-364-4449 *Toll Free Tel:* 888-523-9292 (order desk) *Fax:* 416-957-1587 *Web Site:* www.randomhouse.ca, pg 560

Burrows, William R, Orbis Books, Walsh Bldg, 75 Ryder Rd, Ossining, NY 10562 *Tel:* 914-941-7636 *Toll Free Tel:* 800-258-5838 (orders) *Fax:* 914-941-7005 (orders); 914-945-0670 (office) *E-mail:* orbisbooks@maryknoll.org *Web Site:* www.orbisbooks.com, pg 198

Burton, Elizabeth K, Zumaya Publications, 403-366 Howard Ave, Burnaby, BC V5B 4Y2, Canada *Tel:* 604-299-8417 *E-mail:* editorial@zumayapublications.com *Web Site:* www.zumayapublications.com, pg 567

Burton, Harry, Newmarket Publishing & Communications, 18 E 48 St, New York, NY 10017 *Tel:* 212-832-3575 *Toll Free Tel:* 800-669-3903 *Fax:* 212-832-3629 *E-mail:* mailbox@newmarketpress.com *Web Site:* www.newmarketpress.com, pg 190

Burton, Julie, MacAdam/Cage Publishing Inc, 155 Sansome St, Suite 550, San Francisco, CA 94104 *Tel:* 415-986-7502 *Toll Free Tel:* 866-986-7470 *Fax:* 415-986-7414 *E-mail:* info@macadamcage.com *Web Site:* www.macadamcage.com, pg 161

Burton, Kermit, ALPHA Publications of America Inc, 4500 E Speedway Blvd, Suite 31, Tucson, AZ 85712-5325 *Tel:* 520-795-7100 *Toll Free Tel:* 800-528-3494 *Toll Free Fax:* 800-770-4329 *E-mail:* alphalegalkits@alphapublications.com *Web Site:* www.alphapublications.com, pg 9

Burton, Melissa, Princeton University Press, 41 William St, Princeton, NJ 08540 *Tel:* 609-258-4900 *Toll Free Tel:* 800-777-4726 *Fax:* 609-258-6305 *Toll Free Fax:* 800-999-1958 *E-mail:* orders@cpfsinc.com *Web Site:* www.pup.princeton.edu, pg 219

Burton, Michael, University Press of New England, One Court St, Lebanon, NH 03766 *Tel:* 603-448-1533 *Toll Free Tel:* 800-421-1561 (orders only) *Fax:* 603-448-7006; 603-643-1540 *E-mail:* university.press@dartmouth.edu *Web Site:* www.upne.com, pg 287

Burton, Nik, Coteau Books, 401-2206 Dewdney Ave, Regina, SK S4R 1H3, Canada *Tel:* 306-777-0170 *Toll Free Tel:* 800-440-4471 (Canada Only) *Fax:* 306-522-5152 *E-mail:* coteau@coteaubooks.com *Web Site:* www.coteaubooks.com, pg 541

Busa, Christopher, Provincetown Arts Inc, 650 Commercial St, Provincetown, MA 02657 *Tel:* 508-487-3167 *Web Site:* www.provincetownarts.org, pg 220

Busby, Mark, Brazo Bookstore (Houston Award), 3700 Mockingbird Lane, Dallas, TX 75205 *Tel:* 214-528-2655 *Web Site:* www.stedwards.edu/newc/marks/til/awards_and_rules.htm, pg 764

Busby, Mark, Carr P Collins Award, Center for the Study of the Southwest, Southwest Texas State University, San Marcos, TX 78666 *Tel:* 512-245-2232 *Fax:* 512-245-7462 *Web Site:* www.stedwards.edu/newc/marks/til/awards_and_rules.htm, pg 768

Busby, Mark, Soeurette Diehl Fraser Award, 3700 Mockingbird Lane, Dallas, TX 75205 *Tel:* 512-245-2232 *Fax:* 512-245-7462 *Web Site:* www.stedwards.edu/newc/marks/til/awards_and_rules.htm, pg 774

Busby, Mark, Friends of the Dallas Public Library Award, Center for the Study of the Southwest, Southwest Texas State University, San Marcos, TX 78666 *Tel:* 512-245-2232 *Fax:* 512-245-7462 *Web Site:* www.stedwards.edu/newc/marks/til/awards_and_rules.htm, pg 775

Busby, Mark, Jesse H Jones Award, 3700 Mockingbird Lane, Dallas, TX 75205 *Tel:* 214-528-2655 *Fax:* 512-245-7462 *Web Site:* www.stedwards.edu/newc/marks/til/awards_and_rules.htm, pg 781

Busby, Mark, O Henry Award, 3700 Mockingbird Lane, Dallas, TX 75205 *Tel:* 512-245-2232 *Fax:* 512-245-7462 *Web Site:* www.stedwards.edu/newc/marks/til/awards_and_rules.htm, pg 795

Byron, Arthur, Babbage Press, 8740 Penfield Ave, Northbridge, CA 91324-3224 *Tel:* 818-341-3161 *E-mail:* books@babbagepress.com *Web Site:* www. babbagepress.com, pg 30

Cabanis, Tracy, The Bookbinders' Guild of New York, Dunn & Co, 110 Grand Ave, Ridgefield Park, NJ 07660 *Tel:* 201-229-1888 *Fax:* 201-229-1755 *Web Site:* www.bookbindersguild.org, pg 682

Cabasin, Linda, Fodor's Travel Publications, 1745 Broadway, New York, NY 10019 *Tel:* 212-572-8784 *Toll Free Tel:* 800-733-3000 *Fax:* 212-572-2248 *Web Site:* www.fodors.com, pg 98

Cabaza, Becky, Crown Publishing Group, 1745 Broadway, New York, NY 10019 *Tel:* 212-782-9000 *Toll Free Tel:* 888-264-1745 *Fax:* 212-940-7408 *Web Site:* www.randomhouse.com/crown, pg 74

Cabezas, Sue, Applewood Books Inc, 128 The Great Rd, Bedford, MA 01730 *Tel:* 781-271-0055 *Fax:* 781-271-0056 *E-mail:* applewood@awb.com *Web Site:* www. awb.com, pg 22

Cabin, John, Vandamere Press, 3580 Morris St N, Saint Petersburg, FL 33713 *Tel:* 727-556-0950 *Toll Free Tel:* 800-551-7776 *Fax:* 727-556-2560 *E-mail:* orders@vandamere.com *Web Site:* www. vandamere.com, pg 289

Cabral, Louis, Association pour l'Avancement des Sciences et des Techniques de la Documentation, 3414 Avenue du Parc, Bureau 202, Montreal, PQ H2X 2H5, Canada *Tel:* 514-281-5012 *Fax:* 514-281-8219 *E-mail:* info@asted.org *Web Site:* www.asted.org, pg 536, 680

Cabral, Louis, Prix Alvine-Belisle, 3414 Avenue Du Parc, Bureau 202, Montreal, PQ H2X 2H5, Canada *Tel:* 514-281-5012 *Fax:* 514-281-8219 *E-mail:* info@ asted.org *Web Site:* www.asted.org, pg 800

Cacho, Kim, Doubleday Broadway Publishing Group, 1745 Broadway, New York, NY 10019 *Tel:* 212-782-9000 *Toll Free Tel:* 800-223-6834; 800-223-5780 (sales) *Fax:* 212-302-7985 (correspondence); 212-492-9862 (orders), pg 82

Caddigan, Nicole, Hamilton Books, 4501 Forbes Blvd, Suite 200, Lanham, MD 20706 *Tel:* 301-459-3366, pg 112

Cady, Beth, International Reading Association, 800 Barksdale Rd, Newark, DE 19714 *Tel:* 302-731-1600 *Fax:* 302-731-1057 *Web Site:* www.reading.org, pg 689

Cady, Beth, International Reading Association Children's Book Award, 800 Barksdale Rd, Newark, DE 19714 *Tel:* 302-731-1600 *Fax:* 302-731-1057 *Web Site:* www. reading.org, pg 780

Cady, Beth, International Reading Association Print Media Award, 800 Barksdale Rd, Newark, DE 19714 *Tel:* 302-731-1600 *Fax:* 302-731-1057 *E-mail:* pubinfo@reading.org *Web Site:* www.reading. org, pg 780

Cady, Donald, Wesleyan Publishing House, 13300 Olio Rd, Noblesville, IN 46060 *Tel:* 317-774-3853 *Toll Free Tel:* 800-493-7539 *Fax:* 317-774-3860 *Toll Free Fax:* 800-788-3535 *E-mail:* wph@wesleyan.org *Web Site:* www.wesleyan.org/wph, pg 296

Caeser, Dorothy, Hudson Park Press, Johnny Cake Hollow Rd, Pine Plains, NY 12567 *Tel:* 212-929-8898 *Fax:* 212-242-6137 *E-mail:* hudpark@aol.com *Web Site:* www.hudsonpark.com, pg 128

Caggiula, Sam, Running Press Book Publishers, 125 S 22 St, Philadelphia, PA 19103-4399 *Tel:* 215-567-5080 *Toll Free Tel:* 800-345-5359 (cust serv & orders) *Fax:* 215-568-2919 *Toll Free Fax:* 800-453-2884 *Web Site:* www.runningpress.com, pg 236

Caglioti, Carla, Southampton Writers' Conference, 239 Montauk Hwy, Southampton, NY 11968 *Tel:* 631-287-8175 *Fax:* 631-287-8253 *E-mail:* summer@ southampton.liu.edu *Web Site:* www.southampton.liu. edu/summer, pg 747

Cahill, Erin M, Paul H Brookes Publishing Co, PO Box 10624, Baltimore, MD 21285-0624 *Tel:* 410-337-9580 *Toll Free Tel:* 800-638-3775 *Fax:* 410-337-8539 *E-mail:* custserv@brookespublishing.com *Web Site:* www.brookespublishing.com, pg 48

Cahoon, Nancy Stauffer, Nancy Stauffer Associates, PO Box 1203, Darien, CT 06820 *Tel:* 203-655-3717 *Fax:* 203-655-3704 *E-mail:* nanstauf@optonline.net, pg 657

Cain, Diane, Penguin Young Readers Group, 345 Hudson St, New York, NY 10014 *Tel:* 212-366-2000 *E-mail:* online@penguinputnam.com *Web Site:* www. penguin.com, pg 208

Cain, Harlan, Read Only Productions, 399 Alameda de la Loma, Novato, CA 94947 *Tel:* 415-883-7583, pg 228

Cairns, Michael, R R Bowker LLC, 630 Central Ave, New Providence, NJ 07974 *Tel:* 908-286-1090 *Toll Free Tel:* 888-269-5372; 888-269-5372 (cust serv - press 2 for returns) *Fax:* 908-219-0098 *E-mail:* orderinfo@bowker.com *Web Site:* www. bowker.com, pg 44

Calamari, Liz, Farrar, Straus & Giroux, LLC, 19 Union Sq W, New York, NY 10003 *Tel:* 212-741-6900 *Fax:* 212-741-6973 *Web Site:* www.fsgbooks.com, pg 95

Calder, Moira, Pro-Nouns Editorial Services Inc, 10835-62 Ave, Edmonton, AB T6H 1M9, Canada *Tel:* 780-436-0772 *Fax:* 780-438-7063 *E-mail:* info@pro-nouns. com *Web Site:* www.pro-nouns.com, pg 609

Caldwell, Alexis, The Vines Agency Inc, 648 Broadway, Suite 901, New York, NY 10012 *Tel:* 212-777-5522 *Fax:* 212-777-5978 *Web Site:* www.vinesagency.com, pg 659

Caldwell, Lynn Borders, F A Davis Co, 1915 Arch St, Philadelphia, PA 19103 *Tel:* 215-568-2270 *Toll Free Tel:* 800-523-4049 *Fax:* 215-568-5065 *E-mail:* info@ fadavis.com *Web Site:* www.fadavis.com, pg 76

Caldwell, Vince, Society for Human Resource Management (SHRM), 1800 Duke St, Alexandria, VA 22314 *Tel:* 703-548-3440 *Toll Free Tel:* 800-444-5006 (orders) *Fax:* 703-836-0367; 770-442-9742 (orders) *E-mail:* shrm@shrm.org; shrmstore@shrm.org *Web Site:* www.shrm.org, pg 251

Calhoun, Arlene S, American Biographical Institute, 5126 Bur Oak Circle, Raleigh, NC 27612 *Tel:* 919-781-8710 *Fax:* 919-781-8712, pg 12

Calhoun, Chris, Sterling Lord Literistic Inc, 65 Bleecker St, New York, NY 10012 *Tel:* 212-780-6050 *Fax:* 212-780-6095, pg 657

Calhoun, Jack, South-Western, A Thomson Business, 5191 Natorp Blvd, Mason, OH 45040 *Tel:* 513-229-1000 *Toll Free Tel:* 800-543-0487 *Fax:* 513-229-1025 *Web Site:* www.thomson.com, pg 254

Calhoun, Milburn, Pelican Publishing Co Inc, 1000 Burmaster, Gretna, LA 70053 *Tel:* 504-368-1175 *Toll Free Tel:* 800-843-1724 *Fax:* 504-368-1195 *E-mail:* sales@pelicanpub.com (sales); office@ pelicanpub.com (permission); promo@pelicanpub.com (publicity) *Web Site:* www.pelicanpub.com, pg 207

Calicchio, Rosemary, William H Sadlier Inc, 9 Pine St, New York, NY 10005 *Tel:* 212-227-2120 *Toll Free Tel:* 800-221-5175 *Fax:* 212-312-6080 *Web Site:* www. sadlier.com; www.sadlier-oxford.com, pg 237

Call, Jerry, Time Being Books, 10411 Clayton Rd, Suites 201-203, St Louis, MO 63131 *Tel:* 314-432-1771 *Toll Free Tel:* 866-840-4334 *Fax:* 314-432-7939 *Toll Free Tel:* 888-301-9191 *E-mail:* tbbooks@ sbcglobal.net *Web Site:* www.timebeing.com, pg 271

Call, Pat, Wadsworth Publishing, 10 Davis Dr, Belmont, CA 94002-3002 *Toll Free Tel:* 800-357-0092 *Fax:* 650-592-3342 *Toll Free Fax:* 800-522-4923 *Web Site:* www.wadsworth.com, pg 292

Call, Susan, Jossey-Bass, 989 Market St, San Francisco, CA 94103-1741 *Tel:* 415-433-1740 *Toll Free Tel:* 800-956-7739 *Fax:* 415-433-0499 (edit/mktg) *Web Site:* www.josseybass.com; www.pfeiffer.com, pg 142

Callahan, Laurie, New Directions Publishing Corp, 80 Eighth Ave, New York, NY 10011 *Tel:* 212-255-0230 *Toll Free Tel:* 800-233-4830 (PA) *Fax:* 212-255-0231 *E-mail:* newdirections@ndbooks.com *Web Site:* www. ndpublishing.com, pg 187

Callahan, Mary Margaret, Penguin Group (USA) Inc Sales, 375 Hudson St, New York, NY 10014 *Tel:* 212-366-2000 *E-mail:* online@penguinputnam.com *Web Site:* www.penguin.com, pg 208

Callahan, Pat, University of South Carolina Press, 1600 Hampton St, 5th fl, Columbia, SC 29208 *Tel:* 803-777-5243 *Toll Free Tel:* 800-768-2500 (orders) *Fax:* 803-777-0160 *Toll Free Fax:* 800-868-0740 (orders) *Web Site:* www.sc.edu/uscpress/, pg 285

Callahan, Patrick, Getty Publications, 1200 Getty Center Dr, Suite 500, Los Angeles, CA 90049-1682 *Tel:* 310-440-7365 *Fax:* 310-440-7758 *E-mail:* pubsinfo@getty. edu *Web Site:* www.getty.edu/bookstore, pg 104

Callahan, Tirzah, Cardweb.com Inc, 10 N Jefferson St, Suite 301, Frederick, MD 21701 *Tel:* 301-631-9100 *Fax:* 301-631-9112 *E-mail:* cardservices@cardweb. com; cardstaff@cardweb.com *Web Site:* www.cardweb. com, pg 53

Callaway, Nicholas D, Callaway Editions Inc, 54 Seventh Ave S, New York, NY 10014 *Tel:* 212-929-5212 *Fax:* 212-929-8087 *Web Site:* www.callaway.com, pg 51

Callet, Bette, Lion Books Publisher, 210 Nelson Rd, Scarsdale, NY 10583 *Tel:* 914-725-2280 *Fax:* 914-725-3572, pg 155

Calligaro, Julie, Demery Publishing, 20600 Eureka, Suite 900, Taylor, MI 48180 *Tel:* 734-671-1275 *Fax:* 734-671-0107 *Web Site:* www.demerypub.com, pg 570

Calliotte, Catherine, Gryphon House Inc, 10726 Tucker St, Beltsville, MD 20704 *Tel:* 301-595-9500 *Toll Free Tel:* 800-638-0928 *Fax:* 301-595-0051 *E-mail:* info@ ghbooks.com *Web Site:* www.gryphonhouse.com, pg 110

Callipari, Linda, Chelsea House Publishers LLC, 2080 Cabot Blvd W, Suite 201, Langhorne, PA 19047-1813 *Tel:* 610-353-5166 *Toll Free Tel:* 800-848-BOOK (848-2665) *Fax:* 610-359-1439 *Toll Free Fax:* 877-780-7300 *E-mail:* sales@chelseahouse.com *Web Site:* www.chelseahouse.com, pg 59

Calloway, MaryKatherine, Louisiana State University Press, PO Box 25053, Baton Rouge, LA 70894-5053 *Tel:* 225-578-6294 *Toll Free Tel:* 800-861-3477 *Fax:* 225-578-6461 *Toll Free Fax:* 800-305-4416 *E-mail:* lsupress@lsu.edu *Web Site:* www.lsu. edu/guests/lsupress, pg 159

Calott, Reid, Educational Insights Inc, 18730 S Wilmington Ave, Suite 100, Rancho Dominguez, CA 90220 *Tel:* 310-884-2000 *Toll Free Tel:* 800-933-3277 *Fax:* 310-884-2015 *E-mail:* service@edin.com *Web Site:* www.educationalinsights.com, pg 88

Calvert, Stephen, AA's & PE's, 129 Third Ave, Benton, WI 53803-0072 *Tel:* 608-759-3303, pg 589

Calvo, Roque J, The Electrochemical Society Inc, 65 S Main St, Pennington, NJ 08534-2839 *Tel:* 609-737-1902 *Fax:* 609-737-2743 *E-mail:* ecs@electrochem.org *Web Site:* www.electrochem.org, pg 88

Camacho, Mia, Scholastic Trade Division, 557 Broadway, New York, NY 10012 *Tel:* 212-343-6100; 212-343-4685 (export sales) *Fax:* 212-343-4714 (export sales) *Web Site:* www.scholastic.com, pg 242

Camardi, Ben, Harold Matson Co Inc, 276 Fifth Ave, New York, NY 10001 *Tel:* 212-679-4490 *Fax:* 212-545-1224 *E-mail:* hmatsco@aol.com, pg 643

Cameron, Anthony, Cameron & Co, 680 Eighth St, Suite 205, San Francisco, CA 94103 *Tel:* 415-558-8455 *Toll Free Tel:* 800-779-5582 *Fax:* 415-558-8657 *Web Site:* www.abovebooks.com, pg 52

Cameron, Clifford, Signpost Books, 8912 192 St SW, Edmonds, WA 98026 *Tel:* 425-776-0370, pg 247

Cameron, Hamish, University of Toronto Press Inc, 10 St Mary St, Suite 700, Toronto, ON M4Y 2W8, Canada *Tel:* 416-978-2239 (admin) *Fax:* 416-978-4738 (admin) *Web Site:* www.utpress.utoronto.ca, pg 565

Cameron, John, Medical Physics Publishing Corp, 4513 Vernon Blvd, Madison, WI 53705-4964 *Tel:* 608-262-4021 *Toll Free Tel:* 800-442-5778 *Fax:* 608-265-2121 *E-mail:* mpp@medicalphysics.org *Web Site:* www.medicalphysics.org, pg 170

Cameron, Kimberley, Reece Halsey Agency/Reece Halsey North, 8733 Sunset Blvd, Suite 101, Los Angeles, CA 90069 *Tel:* 310-652-2409 *Fax:* 310-652-7595, pg 634

Cameron, Linda, University of Alberta Press, Ring House 2, Edmonton, AB T6G 2E1, Canada *Tel:* 780-492-3662 *Fax:* 780-492-0719 *E-mail:* uap@ualberta.ca *Web Site:* www.uap.ualberta.ca, pg 564

Cameron, Melissa, Fenn Publishing Co Ltd, 34 Nixon Rd, Bolton, ON L7E 1W2, Canada *Tel:* 905-951-6600 *Toll Free Tel:* 800-267-3366 (Canada only) *Fax:* 905-951-6601 *Toll Free Fax:* 800-465-3422 (Canada Only) *E-mail:* sales@hbfenn.com *Web Site:* www.hbfenn.com, pg 546

Cameron, Robert, Cameron & Co, 680 Eighth St, Suite 205, San Francisco, CA 94103 *Tel:* 415-558-8455 *Toll Free Tel:* 800-779-5582 *Fax:* 415-558-8657 *Web Site:* www.abovebooks.com, pg 52

Camhi, Elaine, American Institute of Aeronautics & Astronautics, 1801 Alexander Bell Dr, Suite 500, Reston, VA 20191 *Tel:* 703-264-7500 *Toll Free Tel:* 800-639-2422 *Fax:* 703-264-7551 *E-mail:* custserv@aiaa.org *Web Site:* www.aiaa.org, pg 14

Camp, Kristin, Steerforth Press, 25 Lebanon St, Hanover, NH 03755 *Tel:* 603-643-4787 *Fax:* 603-643-4788 *E-mail:* info@steerforth.com *Web Site:* www.steerforth.com, pg 258

Camp, Lisa, McFarland & Co Inc Publishers, 960 Hwy 88 W, Jefferson, NC 28640 *Tel:* 336-246-4460 *Toll Free Tel:* 800-253-2187 (orders only) *Fax:* 336-246-5018; 336-246-4403 (orders) *E-mail:* info@mcfarlandpub.com *Web Site:* www.mcfarlandpub.com, pg 166

Campanella, Joseph, Amsco School Publications Inc, 315 Hudson St, New York, NY 10013-1085 *Tel:* 212-886-6500; 212-886-6565 *Toll Free Tel:* 800-969-8398 *Fax:* 212-675-7010 *E-mail:* info@amscopub.com *Web Site:* www.amscopub.com, pg 19

Campanello, Kimberly, Black Warrior Review Literary Awards, University of Alabama, Tuscaloosa, AL 35486-0027 *Tel:* 205-348-4518 *E-mail:* bwr@ua.edu *Web Site:* www.webdelsol.com/bwr, pg 763

Campbell, Ann, Doubleday Broadway Publishing Group, 1745 Broadway, New York, NY 10019 *Tel:* 212-782-9000 *Toll Free Tel:* 800-223-6834; 800-223-5780 (sales) *Fax:* 212-302-7985 (correspondence); 212-492-9862 (orders), pg 83

Campbell, Barbara, Loyola Press, 3441 N Ashland Ave, Chicago, IL 60657 *Tel:* 773-281-1818; 773-244-4429 *Toll Free Tel:* 800-621-1008 *Fax:* 773-281-0555; 773-281-0152 (trade) *E-mail:* editorial@loydapress.com *Web Site:* www.loyolapress.org, pg 159

Campbell, Bruce, Capital Enquiry Inc, 1034 Emerald Bay Rd, No 435, South Lake Tahoe, CA 96150 *Tel:* 916-442-1434 *Fax:* 916-244-2704 *E-mail:* info@capenq.com *Web Site:* www.capenq.com, pg 52

Campbell, Colin, The Colonial Williamsburg Foundation, PO Box 1776, Williamsburg, VA 23187-1776 *Tel:* 757-229-1000 *Toll Free Tel:* 800-HISTORY *Fax:* 757-220-7325 *Web Site:* www.colonialwilliamsburg.org/publications, pg 65

Campbell, Jane, Chosen Books, PO Box 6287, Grand Rapids, MI 49516-6287 *Tel:* 616-676-9185 *Toll Free Tel:* 800-877-2665 *Fax:* 616-676-2315 *Web Site:* www.bakerpublishinggroup.com, pg 61

Campbell, Jennie, Water Resources Publications LLC, PO Box 260026, Highlands Ranch, CO 80163-0026 *Tel:* 720-873-0171 *Fax:* 720-873-0173 *E-mail:* info@wrpllc.com *Web Site:* www.wrpllc.com, pg 294

Campbell, Lakisha, BuilderBooks.com, 1201 15 St NW, Washington, DC 20005-2800 *Tel:* 202-822-0200; 202-266-8200 *Toll Free Tel:* 800-223-2665 (orders); 800-368-5242 ext 8368 (editorial) *Fax:* 202-266-8096 (edit); 202-266-5889 (edit) *Web Site:* www.builderbooks.com, pg 49

Campbell, Logan, Pearson Higher Education Division, One Lake St, Upper Saddle River, NJ 07458 *Tel:* 201-236-7000 *Fax:* 201-236-3381, pg 206

Campbell, Marie, Transatlantic Literary Agency Inc, 72 Glengowan Rd, Toronto, ON M4N 1G4, Canada *Tel:* 416-488-9214 *Fax:* 416-488-4531 *E-mail:* info@tla1.com *Web Site:* www.tla1.com, pg 659

Campbell, Marilyn A, Rutgers University Press, 100 Joyce Kilmer Ave, Piscataway, NJ 08854-8099 *Tel:* 732-445-7762 (edit); 732-445-7762 (ext 627, sales) *Toll Free Tel:* 800-446-9323 (orders only) *Fax:* 732-445-7039 (acqs, edit, mktg, perms, prodn); 732-445-1974 (fulfillment) *E-mail:* garyf@rci.rutgers.edu *Web Site:* rutgerspress.rutgers.edu, pg 236

Campbell, Rick, Anhinga Press, PO Box 10595, Tallahassee, FL 32302-2595 *Tel:* 850-442-1408 *Fax:* 850-442-6323 *E-mail:* info@anhinga.org *Web Site:* www.anhinga.org, pg 20

Campbell, Rick, Anhinga Prize for Poetry, PO Box 10595, Tallahassee, FL 32302-2595 *Tel:* 850-442-6323 *Fax:* 850-442-6323 *E-mail:* info@anhinga.org *Web Site:* www.anhinga.org, pg 759

Campos, Alexander, The Center for Book Arts, 28 W 27 St, 3rd fl, New York, NY 10001 *Tel:* 212-481-0295 *Fax:* 212-481-9853 (call before faxing) *E-mail:* info@centerforbookarts.org *Web Site:* www.centerforbookarts.org, pg 751

Campos, Mike, Read Only Productions, 399 Alameda de la Loma, Novato, CA 94947 *Tel:* 415-883-7583, pg 228

Canac-Marquis, Jean, Editions du Phare Inc, 105 rue de Martigny Ouest, St Jerome, PQ J7Y 2G2, Canada *Tel:* 450-438-8479 *Toll Free Tel:* 800-561-2371 (Canada) *Fax:* 450-432-3892 *E-mail:* info@mondiaduphare.net, pg 544

Canac-Marquis, Jean, Mondia Editeurs Inc, 105 de Martigny Ouest, St-Jerome, PQ J7Y 2G2, Canada *Tel:* 450-438-8479 *Toll Free Tel:* 800-561-2371 (Canada) *Fax:* 450-432-3892 *E-mail:* info@mondiaduphare.net, pg 554

Canada, Steve, Crop Circle Books Press, 1123 N Las Posas Ct, Ridgecrest, CA 93555 *Tel:* 760-446-1938 *E-mail:* cropcircles@webtv.net *Web Site:* www.cropcirclebooks.com, pg 72

Canavan, Susan, Houghton Mifflin Trade & Reference Division, 222 Berkeley St, Boston, MA 02116-3764 *Tel:* 617-351-5000 *Toll Free Tel:* 800-225-3362 *Web Site:* www.houghtonmifflinbooks.com, pg 126

Canavan, Susanne F, Christopher-Gordon Publishers Inc, 1502 Providence Hwy, Suite 12, Norwood, MA 02062 *Tel:* 781-762-5577 *Toll Free Tel:* 800-934-8322 *Fax:* 781-762-2110 *Web Site:* www.christopher-gordon.com, pg 61

Candage, Mellen, Howells House, PO Box 9546, Washington, DC 20016-9546 *Tel:* 202-333-2182 *Fax:* 202-333-2184 *E-mail:* hhi@ix.netcom.com, pg 127

Candido, Arthur A, Scholium International Inc, PO Box 1519, Port Washington, NY 11050-7519 *Tel:* 516-767-7171 *Fax:* 516-944-9824 *E-mail:* info@scholium.com; artcandido@cs.com *Web Site:* www.scholium.com, pg 242

Candido, Elena M, Scholium International Inc, PO Box 1519, Port Washington, NY 11050-7519 *Tel:* 516-767-7171 *Fax:* 516-944-9824 *E-mail:* info@scholium.com; artcandido@cs.com *Web Site:* www.scholium.com, pg 242

Canfield, Doug, The Mountaineers Books, 1001 SW Klickitat Way, Suite 201, Seattle, WA 98134 *Tel:* 206-223-6303 *Toll Free Tel:* 800-553-4453 *Fax:* 206-223-6306 *Toll Free Fax:* 800-568-7604 *E-mail:* mbooks@mountaineers.org *Web Site:* www.mountaineersbooks.org, pg 179

Canipos, Alexander, The Center for Book Arts, 28 W 27 St, 3rd fl, New York, NY 10001 *Tel:* 212-481-0295 *Fax:* 212-481-9853 (call before faxing) *E-mail:* info@centerforbookarts.org *Web Site:* www.centerforbookarts.org, pg 684

Cannizzo, Karen A, Pflaum Publishing Group, 2621 Dryden Rd, Dayton, OH 45439 *Tel:* 937-293-1415 *Toll Free Tel:* 800-543-4383 *Fax:* 917-293-1310 *Toll Free Fax:* 800-370-4450 *Web Site:* www.pflaum.com, pg 211

Cannon, Dolores, Ozark Mountain Publishing Inc, 276 Madison 2337, Huntsville, AR 72740 *Tel:* 479-738-2348 *Toll Free Tel:* 800-935-0045; 800-230-0312 *Fax:* 479-738-2348 *Toll Free Fax:* 800-935-0045; 800-230-0312 *Web Site:* www.ozarkmt.com, pg 201

Cannon, Linda, CTB/McGraw-Hill, 20 Ryan Ranch Rd, Monterey, CA 93940-5703 *Tel:* 831-393-0700 *Toll Free Tel:* 800-538-9547 *Fax:* 831-393-7825 *Web Site:* www.ctb.com, pg 74

Cannon, Pamela, Artisan, 708 Broadway, New York, NY 10003-9555 *Tel:* 212-254-5900 *Fax:* 212-254-8098 *E-mail:* artisaninfo@workman.com *Web Site:* www.artisanbooks.com, pg 25

Cannon, Preston, Warner Faith (Christian Book Division of Time Warner Book Group), 2 Creekside Crossing, 10 Cadillac Dr, Suite 220, Brentwood, TN 37027 *Tel:* 615-221-0996 *Fax:* 615-221-0962 *Web Site:* www.twbookmark.com, pg 293

Canton, Alan N, Adams-Blake Publishing, 8041 Sierra St, Suite 102, Fair Oaks, CA 95628 *Tel:* 916-962-9296 *E-mail:* info@adams-blake.com *Web Site:* www.adams-blake.com, pg 5

Cantor, Jacqueline, Bantam Dell Publishing Group, 1745 Broadway, New York, NY 10019 *Tel:* 212-782-9000 *Toll Free Tel:* 800-223-6834 *Fax:* 212-302-7985 *Web Site:* www.randomhouse.com/bantamdell, pg 31

Cantor-Adams, Deborah, The MIT Press, 5 Cambridge Ctr, Cambridge, MA 02142 *Tel:* 617-253-5646 *Toll Free Tel:* 800-405-1619 (orders only) *Fax:* 617-258-6779 *Web Site:* mitpress.mit.edu, pg 175

Caples, Debbi, Petroleum Extension Service (PETEX), University of Texas, One University Sta, R8100, Austin, TX 78712-1100 *Tel:* 512-471-5940 *Toll Free Tel:* 800-687-4132 *Fax:* 512-471-9410 *Toll Free Fax:* 800-687-7839 *E-mail:* rbpetex@mail.utexas.edu *Web Site:* www.utexas.edu/cee/petex, pg 211

Capozza, Shana, The Globe Pequot Press, 246 Goose Lane, Guilford, CT 06437 *Tel:* 203-458-4500 *Toll Free Tel:* 800-243-0495 (cust serv) *Fax:* 203-458-4601 *Toll Free Fax:* 800-820-2329 (orders & cust serv) *E-mail:* info@globepequot.com *Web Site:* www.globepequot.com, pg 105

Cappabianca, Rosemarie, McGraw-Hill Education, 2 Penn Plaza, New York, NY 10121 *Tel:* 212-904-2000 *E-mail:* customer.service@mcgraw-hill.com *Web Site:* www.mheducation.com; www.mheducation.com/custserv.html, pg 167

Capps, Karen, Concordia Publishing House, 3558 S Jefferson Ave, St Louis, MO 63118-3968 *Tel:* 314-268-1000 *Toll Free Tel:* 800-325-3040 *Fax:* 314-268-1329 *Toll Free Fax:* 800-490-9889 *E-mail:* cphorder@cph.org *Web Site:* www.cph.org, pg 66

Capron, Elise, Sandra Dijkstra Literary Agency, 1155 Camino del Mar, PMB 515, Del Mar, CA 92014-2605 *Tel:* 858-755-3115 *Fax:* 858-794-2822 *E-mail:* sdla@dijkstraagency.com, pg 627

Capshew, Jeff, St Martin's Press LLC, 175 Fifth Ave, New York, NY 10010 *Tel:* 212-674-5151 *Fax:* 212-420-9314 *E-mail:* firstname.lastname@stmartins.com *Web Site:* www.stmartins.com, pg 238

Caraballo, Mariann Donato, Penguin Group (USA) Inc Sales, 375 Hudson St, New York, NY 10014 *Tel:* 212-366-2000 *E-mail:* online@penguinputnam.com *Web Site:* www.penguin.com, pg 207

Carantza, Laura, Michigan State University Press (MSU Press), 1405 S Harrison Rd, Suite 25, East Lansing, MI 48823 *Tel:* 517-355-9543 *Fax:* 517-432-2611 *Toll Free Fax:* 800-678-2120 *E-mail:* msupress@msu.edu *Web Site:* www.msupress.msu.edu, pg 173

Caras, Kathryn, Indiana University Press, 601 N Morton St, Bloomington, IN 47404-3797 *Tel:* 812-855-8817 *Toll Free Tel:* 800-842-6796 (orders only) *Fax:* 812-855-7931 (orders only); 812-855-8507 *E-mail:* iupress@indiana.edu; iuorder@indiana.edu (orders) *Web Site:* www.iupress.indiana.edu, pg 132

Caratozzolo, Marie, Square One Publishers, 115 Herricks Rd, Garden City Park, NY 11040 *Tel:* 516-535-2010 *Fax:* 516-535-2014 *E-mail:* sq1info@aol.com *Web Site:* squareonepublishers.com, pg 256

Caratzas, Aristide D, Aristide D Caratzas, Publisher, PO Box 344-H, Scarsdale, NY 10583 *Tel:* 914-725-4847 *Toll Free Tel:* 800-204-2665 *Fax:* 914-725-4847 (call first) *E-mail:* info@caratzas.com *Web Site:* www.caratzas.com, pg 53

Carbone, Becky, Para Publishing, PO Box 8206-R, Santa Barbara, CA 93118-8206 *Tel:* 805-968-7277 *Toll Free Tel:* 800-727-2782 *Fax:* 805-968-1379 *E-mail:* orders@parapublishing.com *Web Site:* www.parapublishing.com, pg 203

Cardenas, Christi, The Lazear Agency Inc, 431 Second St, Suite 300, Hudson, WI 54016 *Tel:* 715-531-0012 *Fax:* 715-531-0016 *Web Site:* www.lazear.com, pg 639

Carder, Sarah, Jeremy P Tarcher, 375 Hudson St, New York, NY 10014 *Tel:* 212-366-2000 *E-mail:* online@penguinputnam.com *Web Site:* www.penguin.com, pg 264

Cardillo, Jessica, Time Warner Audio Books, Sports Illustrated Bldg, 135 W 50 St, New York, NY 10020 *Tel:* 212-522-7334 *Fax:* 212-522-7994 *Web Site:* www.twbookmark.com/audiobooks, pg 271

Cardoza, Avery, Cardoza Publishing, 857 Broadway, 3rd fl, New York, NY 10003 *Tel:* 212-255-6661 *Fax:* 212-255-6671 *E-mail:* cardozapub@aol.com *Web Site:* www.cardozapub.com, pg 53

Cardoza, Avery, Open Road Publishing, PO Box 284, Cold Spring Harbor, NY 11724-0284 *Tel:* 631-692-7172 *Fax:* 631-692-7193 *E-mail:* jopenroad@aol.com, pg 198

Cardoza, Avery, Union Square Publishing, 857 Broadway, 3rd fl, New York, NY 10003 *Tel:* 212-255-6661 *Fax:* 212-255-6671 *E-mail:* cardozapub@aol.com *Web Site:* www.cardozapub.com, pg 278

Carey, Andrea, Twenty-Third Publications, 185 Willow St, Mystic, CT 06355 *Tel:* 860-536-2611 *Toll Free Tel:* 800-321-0411 (orders) *Fax:* 860-536-5674 (edit) *Toll Free Fax:* 800-572-0788, pg 277

Carey, Christopher, McBooks Press Inc, 520 N Meadow St, Ithaca, NY 14850 *Tel:* 607-272-2114 *Toll Free Tel:* 888-266-5711 *Fax:* 607-273-6068 *E-mail:* mcbooks@mcbooks.com *Web Site:* www.mcbooks.com, pg 166

Carey, Jennifer, Mountain Press Publishing Co, 1301 S Third W, Missoula, MT 59801 *Tel:* 406-728-1900 *Toll Free Tel:* 800-234-5308 *Fax:* 406-728-1635 *E-mail:* info@mtnpress.com *Web Site:* www.mountain-press.com, pg 179

Cargill, Noreen, Bread Loaf Writers' Conference, Kirk Alumni Center, Middlebury, VT 05753 *Tel:* 802-443-5286 *Fax:* 802-443-2087 *E-mail:* blwc@middlebury.edu *Web Site:* www.middlebury.edu, pg 742

Cargill, Noreen, Bread Loaf Writers' Conference of Middlebury College, Middlebury College, Middlebury, VT 05753 *Tel:* 802-443-5286 *Fax:* 802-443-2087 *E-mail:* blwc@middlebury.edu *Web Site:* www.middlebury.edu/~blwc, pg 764

Cargill, Noreen, Fellowship & Scholarship Program for Writers, Middlebury College, Middlebury, VT 05753 *Tel:* 802-443-5286 *Fax:* 802-443-2087 *E-mail:* blwc@middlebury.edu *Web Site:* www.middlebury.edu/~blwc, pg 773

Carkhuff, R W, HRD Press, 22 Amherst Rd, Amherst, MA 01002 *Tel:* 413-253-3488 *Toll Free Tel:* 800-822-2801 *Fax:* 413-253-3490 *E-mail:* info@hrdpress.com; orders@hrdpress.com *Web Site:* www.hrdpress.com, pg 127

Carl, Polly K, McKnight National Residency & Commission, 2301 Franklin Ave E, Minneapolis, MN 55406 *Tel:* 612-332-7481 *Fax:* 612-332-6037 *E-mail:* info@pwcenter.org *Web Site:* www.pwcenter.org, pg 788

Carl-Hendrick, Judy, Intercultural Press Inc, PO Box 700, 374 US Rte One, Yarmouth, ME 04096 *Tel:* 207-846-5168 *Toll Free Tel:* 866-372-2665 *Fax:* 207-846-5181 *E-mail:* books@interculturalpress.com *Web Site:* www.interculturalpress.com, pg 136

Carleo, John F, Industrial Press Inc, 200 Madison Ave, 21st fl, New York, NY 10016-4078 *Tel:* 212-889-6330 *Toll Free Tel:* 888-528-7852 *Fax:* 212-545-8327 *E-mail:* info@industrialpress.com *Web Site:* www.industrialpress.com, pg 132

Carlevale, John M, Consortium Publishing, 640 Weaver Hill Rd, West Greenwich, RI 02817-2261 *Tel:* 401-397-9838 *Fax:* 401-392-1926, pg 67

Carley, Jennifer, The Drummond Publishing Group, 362 N Bedford St, East Bridgewater, MA 02333 *Tel:* 508-378-1110 *Fax:* 508-378-1105 *Web Site:* www.drummondpub.com, pg 84

Carley, Jennifer, Royalton Press, 362 N Bedford St, East Bridgewater, MA 02333 *Tel:* 508-378-1110 *Fax:* 508-378-1105 *Web Site:* www.drummondpub.com, pg 235

Carley, Michael, The University of Akron Press, 374-B Bierce Library, Akron, OH 44325-1703 *Tel:* 330-972-5342 (ext 1703) *Toll Free Tel:* 877-827-7377 *Fax:* 330-972-8364 *E-mail:* uapress@uakron.edu *Web Site:* www.uakron.edu/uapress, pg 280

Carlisle, John B, Carlisle Communications Ltd, 4242 Chavenelle Dr, Dubuque, IA 52002-2650 *Tel:* 563-557-1500 *Fax:* 563-557-1376 *E-mail:* carlisle@carcomm.com *Web Site:* www.carcomm.com, pg 593

Carlisle, Julie A, Carlisle Communications Ltd, 4242 Chavenelle Dr, Dubuque, IA 52002-2650 *Tel:* 563-557-1500 *Fax:* 563-557-1376 *E-mail:* carlisle@carcomm.com *Web Site:* www.carcomm.com, pg 593

Carlisle, Michael, Inkwell Management, 521 Fifth Ave, 26th fl, New York, NY 10175 *Tel:* 212-922-3500 *Fax:* 212-922-0535 *E-mail:* contact@inkwellmanagement.com *Web Site:* www.inkwellmanagement.com, pg 635

Carlisle, Tony, Carlisle Communications Ltd, 4242 Chavenelle Dr, Dubuque, IA 52002-2650 *Tel:* 563-557-1500 *Fax:* 563-557-1376 *E-mail:* carlisle@carcomm.com *Web Site:* www.carcomm.com, pg 593

Carlson, Anne, Scott O'Dell Award for Historical Fiction, 1100 E 57 St, S-109, Chicago, IL 60637 *Tel:* 773-702-4085 *Fax:* 773-702-0775, pg 795

Carlson, Bruce, Hearts & Tummies Cookbook Co, 1854 345 Ave, Wever, IA 52658 *Tel:* 319-372-7480 *Toll Free Tel:* 800-571-BOOK *Fax:* 319-372-7485 *E-mail:* heartsntummies@hotmail.com, pg 120

Carlson, Bruce, Quixote Press, 1854 345 Ave, Wever, IA 52658 *Tel:* 319-372-7480 *Toll Free Tel:* 800-571-BOOK *Fax:* 319-372-7485 *E-mail:* heartsntummies@hotmail.com, pg 224

Carlson, Carolyn, Viking, 375 Hudson St, New York, NY 10014 *Tel:* 212-366-2000 *E-mail:* online@penguinputnam.com *Web Site:* www.penguin.com, pg 290

Carlson, Constance, Hazelden Publishing & Educational Services, 15251 Pleasant Valley Rd, Center City, MN 55012-0176 *Tel:* 651-213-4470 *Toll Free Tel:* 800-328-9000 *Web Site:* www.hazelden.org, pg 118

Carlson, Dale, Bick Publishing House, 307 Neck Rd, Madison, CT 06443 *Tel:* 203-245-0073 *Fax:* 203-245-5990 *E-mail:* bickpubhse@aol.com *Web Site:* www.bickpubhouse.com, pg 38

Carlson, Dan, Bick Publishing House, 307 Neck Rd, Madison, CT 06443 *Tel:* 203-245-0073 *Fax:* 203-245-5990 *E-mail:* bickpubhse@aol.com *Web Site:* www.bickpubhouse.com, pg 38

Carlson, Erik, Association of American University Presses, 1427 E 60 St, Chicago, IL 60637 *Tel:* 773-702-7700; 773-702-7600 *Toll Free Tel:* 800-621-

2736 (orders) *Fax:* 773-702-9756 (sales); 773-660-2235 (orders); 773-702-2708 *E-mail:* general@press.uchicago.edu *Web Site:* www.press.uchicago.edu, pg 26

Carlson, Hannah, Bick Publishing House, 307 Neck Rd, Madison, CT 06443 *Tel:* 203-245-0073 *Fax:* 203-245-5990 *E-mail:* bickpubhse@aol.com *Web Site:* www.bickpubhouse.com, pg 38

Carlson, Jane, Southern Illinois University Press, PO Box 3697, Carbondale, IL 62902-3697 *Tel:* 618-453-2281 *Toll Free Tel:* 800-346-2680 *Fax:* 618-453-1221 *Toll Free Tel:* 800-346-2681 *E-mail:* jstetter@siu.edu *Web Site:* www.siu.edu/~siupress, pg 254

Carlson, Jennifer, Dunow & Carlson Literary Agency Inc, 27 W 20 St, Suite 1003, New York, NY 10011 *Tel:* 212-645-7606 *Fax:* 212-645-7614 *E-mail:* mail@dunowcarlson.com, pg 628

Carlson, Laura, Antioch Writers' Workshop, PO Box 494, Yellow Springs, OH 45387-0494 *Tel:* 937-475-7357; 937-767-2700 (Board of Trustees) *E-mail:* info@antiochwritersworkshop.com *Web Site:* www.antiochwritersworkshop.com, pg 741

Carlson, Linda, Parenting Press Inc, 11065 Fifth Ave NE, Suite F, Seattle, WA 98125 *Tel:* 206-364-2900 *Toll Free Tel:* 800-99-BOOKS (992-6657) *Fax:* 206-364-0702 *E-mail:* office@parentingpress.com *Web Site:* www.parentingpress.com, pg 204

Carlson, Lynn, Harper's Magazine Foundation, 666 Broadway, New York, NY 10012 *Tel:* 212-420-5720 *Fax:* 212-228-5889 *Web Site:* www.harpers.org, pg 116

Carlson, Tom, River City Writing Awards in Fiction, University of Memphis, Dept of English, Memphis, TN 38152 *Tel:* 901-678-4591 *Fax:* 901-678-2226 *E-mail:* rivercity@memphis.edu *Web Site:* www.people.memphis.edu/~rivercity/contests.html, pg 802

Carlton, Wendy, Riverhead Books (Hardcover), 375 Hudson St, New York, NY 10014 *Tel:* 212-366-2000 *E-mail:* online@penguinputnam.com *Web Site:* www.penguin.com, pg 233

Carman, Bill, IDRC Books/Les Editions du CRDI, PO Box 8500, Ottawa, ON K1G 3H9, Canada *Tel:* 613-236-6163 *Fax:* 613-563-2476 *E-mail:* pub@idrc.ca *Web Site:* www.idrc.ca, pg 550

Carman, Bill, International Development Research Centre, 250 Albert St, Ottawa, ON K1P 6M1, Canada *Tel:* 613-236-6163 *Fax:* 613-238-7230 *E-mail:* pub@idrc.ca *Web Site:* www.idrc.ca/booktique, pg 551

Carman, Peter, Paris-American Academy Writing Workshop, 277 Rue St Jacques, 75005 Paris, France *Tel:* 806-889-3533 *Fax:* 806-889-3533 *Web Site:* www.parisamericanacademy.edu; www.parisamericanacademy.fr, pg 746

Carmen, Pamela, Callawind Publications Inc, 3539 Saint Charles Blvd, Suite 179, Kirkland, PQ H9H 3C4, Canada *Tel:* 514-685-9109 *Fax:* 514-685-7952 *E-mail:* info@callawind.com *Web Site:* www.callawind.com, pg 538

Carnahan, Brian, Oxmoor House Inc, 2100 Lakeshore Dr, Birmingham, AL 35209 *Tel:* 205-445-6000; 205-445-6560 *Toll Free Tel:* 800-366-4712 *Fax:* 205-445-6078 *Web Site:* www.oxmoorhouse.com, pg 201

Carneal, Betty, The Writings of Mary Baker Eddy/Publisher, 175 Huntington Ave, Suite A-16-10, Boston, MA 02115 *Tel:* 617-450-3514; 617-450-2000 (Christian Science Church Boston) *Toll Free Tel:* 800-288-7090 *Fax:* 617-450-7334 *Web Site:* www.spirituality.com, pg 305

Carneal, Jeffrey J, Eagle Publishing Inc, One Massachusetts Ave NW, Washington, DC 20001 *Tel:* 202-216-0600 *Fax:* 202-216-0612 *Web Site:* www.regnery.com, pg 85

Carnes, Elizabeth, Half Halt Press Inc, 20042 Benevola Church Rd, Boonsboro, MD 21713 *Tel:* 301-733-7119 *Toll Free Tel:* 800-822-9635 (orders only) *Fax:* 301-733-7408 *E-mail:* gem@halfhaltpress.com *Web Site:* www.halfhaltpress.com, pg 112

Carnes, Mark, James Fenimore Cooper Prize, Columbia University, 603 Fayerweather Hall, MC 2538, New York, NY 10027, pg 768

Carnes, Mark, Allan Nevins Prize, Columbia University, 603 Fayerweather Hall, MC 2538, New York, NY 10027, pg 793

Carnes, Mark, Francis Parkman Prize, Columbia University, 603 Fayerweather Hall, MC 2538, New York, NY 10027, pg 797

Carney, Caroline Francis, Book Deals Inc, 244 Fifth Ave, Suite 2164, New York, NY 10001-7604 *Tel:* 212-252-2701 *Fax:* 212-591-6211 *E-mail:* bookdeals@aol.com *Web Site:* www.bookdealsinc.com, pg 621

Carney, Kevin, The Charles Bernheimer Prize, University of Texas, Program in Comparative Literature, One University Sta B5003, Austin, TX 78712-0196 *Tel:* 512-471-8020 *E-mail:* info@acla.org *Web Site:* www.acla.org, pg 766

Carney, Kevin, Harry Levin Prize, University of Texas, Program in Comparative Literature, One University Sta B5003, Austin, TX 78712-0196 *Tel:* 512-471-8020 *E-mail:* info@acla.org *Web Site:* www.acla.org, pg 784

Carney, Kevin, University of Texas at Austin, Creative Writing Program, Dept of English, One University Sta, B5000, Austin, TX 78712-1164 *Tel:* 512-475-6356 *Fax:* 512-471-2898 *Web Site:* www.en.utexas.edu/grad/crwconc.html, pg 756

Carney, Kevin, Rene Wellek Prize, University of Texas, Program in Comparative Literature, One University Sta B5003, Austin, TX 78712-0196 *Tel:* 512-471-8020 *E-mail:* info@acla.org *Web Site:* www.acla.org, pg 810

Carns, Tracy, The Overlook Press, 141 Wooster St, New York, NY 10012 *Tel:* 212-965-8400 *Fax:* 212-965-9834 *Web Site:* www.overlookny.com, pg 200

Carola, Leslie, Hugh Lauter Levin Associates Inc, 9 Burr Rd, Westport, CT 06880 *Tel:* 203-227-6422 *Fax:* 203-227-6717 *E-mail:* inquiries@hlla.com *Web Site:* www.hlla.com, pg 128

Caron, David, Houghton Mifflin Co, 222 Berkeley St, Boston, MA 02116-3764 *Tel:* 617-351-5000 *Toll Free Tel:* 800-225-3362 (trade books); 800-733-2828 (text books); 800-225-1464 (college texts) *Fax:* 617-351-1125 *Web Site:* www.hmco.com, pg 126

Caron, David, The Literary Press Group of Canada, 192 Spadina Ave, Suite 501, Toronto, ON M5T 2C2, Canada *Tel:* 416-483-1321 *Fax:* 416-483-2510 *E-mail:* info@lpg.ca *Web Site:* www.lpg.ca, pg 690

Carothers, Leslie, Environmental Law Institute, 1616 "P" St NW, Suite 200, Washington, DC 20036 *Tel:* 202-939-3800 *Fax:* 202-939-3868 *E-mail:* law@eli.org *Web Site:* www.eli.org, pg 91

Carpenter, Georgia, Cedar Fort Inc, 925 N Main St, Springville, UT 84663 *Tel:* 801-489-4084 *Toll Free Tel:* 800-759-2665 *Fax:* 801-489-1097 *E-mail:* skybook@cedarfort.com *Web Site:* www.cedarfort.com, pg 56

Carpenter, Ken, Houghton Mifflin Trade & Reference Division, 222 Berkeley St, Boston, MA 02116-3764 *Tel:* 617-351-5000 *Toll Free Tel:* 800-225-3362 *Web Site:* www.houghtonmifflinbooks.com, pg 126

Carpenter, Margot, Definition Press, 141 Greene St, New York, NY 10012 *Tel:* 212-777-4490 *Fax:* 212-777-4426 *E-mail:* mc@definitionpress.org *Web Site:* www.definitionpress.org, pg 570

Carpenter, Sarah, Dawbert Press Inc, PO Box 67, Duxbury, MA 02331 *Tel:* 781-934-7202 *Toll Free Tel:* 800-933-2923 *Fax:* 781-934-2945 *E-mail:* info@dawbert.com *Web Site:* www.dawbert.com; www.familiesonthego.com; www.petsonthego.com, pg 77

Carr, David, University of Manitoba Press, St Johns College, Winnipeg, MB R3T 2N2, Canada *Tel:* 204-474-9495 *Fax:* 204-474-7566 *Web Site:* www.umanitoba.ca/uofmpress, pg 565

Carr, Kelly, Standard Publishing Co, 8121 Hamilton Ave, Cincinnati, OH 45231 *Tel:* 513-931-4050 *Toll Free Tel:* 800-543-1301 *Fax:* 513-931-0950 *Toll Free Fax:* 877-867-5751 *E-mail:* customerservice@standardpub.com *Web Site:* www.standardpub.com, pg 257

Carr, Lloyd, New York City College of Technology, 300 Jay St, Brooklyn, NY 11201 *Tel:* 718-260-5822; 718-260-5000 *Fax:* 718-260-5198 *E-mail:* connect@citytech.cuny.edu, pg 753

Carr, Rosalyn, University of Hawaii Press, 2840 Kolowalu St, Honolulu, HI 96822 *Tel:* 808-956-8255 *Toll Free Tel:* 888-847-7377 *Fax:* 808-988-6052 *Toll Free Fax:* 800-650-7811 *E-mail:* uhpbooks@hawaii.edu *Web Site:* www.uhpress.hawaii.edu, pg 281

Carrerou, Maggie, Arts Recognition & Talent Search (ARTS), 444 Brickell Ave, Suite P14, Miami, FL 33131 *Tel:* 305-377-1140 *Toll Free Tel:* 800-970-2787 *Fax:* 305-377-1149 *E-mail:* nfaa@nfaa.org *Web Site:* www.artsawards.org, pg 760

Carrigan, Ellen, American Institute of Physics, 2 Huntington Quadrangle, Suite 1NO1, Melville, NY 11747-4502 *Tel:* 516-576-2477 *Fax:* 516-576-2474 *E-mail:* proceedings-mgr@aip.org *Web Site:* www.aip.org, pg 15

Carrigan, Henry, T & T Clark International, PO Box 1321, Harrisburg, PA 17105 *Tel:* 717-541-8130 *Toll Free Tel:* 800-877-0012 *Fax:* 717-541-8136 *Web Site:* www.tandtclarkinternational.com, pg 263

Carrion, Isabel, The French-American Foundation Translation Prize, 28 W 44 St, Suite 1420, New York, NY 10036 *Tel:* 212-829-8800 *Fax:* 212-829-8810 *E-mail:* info@frenchamerican.org *Web Site:* www.frenchamerican.org, pg 775

Carroll, Joe, Home Planners LLC, 3275 W Ina Rd, Suite 220, Tucson, AZ 85741 *Tel:* 520-297-8200 *Toll Free Tel:* 800-322-6797 *Fax:* 520-297-6219 *Toll Free Fax:* 800-531-2555 *E-mail:* customerservice@eplans.com *Web Site:* www.eplans.com, pg 125

Carroll, Mark T, ALI-ABA Committee on Continuing Professional Education, 4025 Chestnut St, Philadelphia, PA 19104 *Tel:* 215-243-1600 *Toll Free Tel:* 800-CLE-NEWS *Fax:* 215-243-1664; 215-243-1683 *Web Site:* www.ali-aba.org, pg 8

Carroll, Michael, Beach Holme Publishing, 409 Granville St, Suite 1010, Vancouver, BC V6C 1T2, Canada *Tel:* 604-733-4868 *Toll Free Tel:* 888-551-6655 (orders) *Fax:* 604-733-4860 *E-mail:* bhp@beachholme.bc.ca *Web Site:* www.beachholme.bc.ca, pg 536

Carroll, Patrick M, Princeton University Press, 41 William St, Princeton, NJ 08540 *Tel:* 609-258-4900 *Toll Free Tel:* 800-777-4726 *Fax:* 609-258-6305 *Toll Free Fax:* 800-999-1958 *E-mail:* orders@cpfsinc.com *Web Site:* www.pup.princeton.edu, pg 219

Carroll, William, Coda Publications, CR A-68, Bldg 92, Raton, NM 87740 *Tel:* 505-445-4455 *Fax:* 505-445-4455 *E-mail:* newmexicobooks@bacavalley.com; coda@bacavalley.com, pg 64

Carsch, R E, R E Carsch, MS-Consultant, 1453 Rhode Island St, San Francisco, CA 94107-3248 *Tel:* 415-641-1095 *Fax:* 415-641-1095 *E-mail:* recarsch@mzinfo.com, pg 593

Carson, Anne Conover, Anne Carson Associates, 3323 Nebraska Ave NW, Washington, DC 20016 *Tel:* 202-244-6679, pg 593

Carson, Carol, Alfred A Knopf, 1745 Broadway, New York, NY 10019 *Tel:* 212-751-2600 *Toll Free Tel:* 800-638-6460 *Fax:* 212-572-2593 *Web Site:* www.randomhouse.com/knopf, pg 146

Carson, Cheryl, University of Tennessee Press, 110 Conference Center Bldg, Knoxville, TN 37996-4108 *Tel:* 865-974-3321 *Toll Free Tel:* 800-621-2736 (ordering) *Fax:* 865-974-3724 *E-mail:* custserv@utpress.org *Web Site:* www.utpress.org, pg 285

Carson, Dina C, Iron Gate Publishing, PO Box 999, Niwot, CO 80544 *Tel:* 303-530-2551 *Fax:* 303-530-5273 *E-mail:* editor@irongate.com; booknews@reunionsolutions.com *Web Site:* www.irongate.com; www.reunionsolutions.com, pg 139

Carson, Ed, Pearson Education Canada Inc, 26 Prince Andrew Place, Don Mills, ON M3C 2T8, Canada *Tel:* 416-447-5101 *Toll Free Tel:* 800-567-3800; 800-387-8028 *Fax:* 416-443-0948 *Toll Free Fax:* 800-263-7733; 888-465-0536 *E-mail:* firstname.lastname@pearsoned.com *Web Site:* www.pearsoned.com, pg 557

Carson, Ed, Penguin Group (Canada), 10 Alcorn Ave, Suite 300, Toronto, ON M4V 3B2, Canada *Tel:* 416-925-2249 *Fax:* 416-925-0068 *Web Site:* www.penguin.ca, pg 557

Carson, H Glenn, Carson Enterprises Inc, PO Box 716, Dona Ana, NM 88032-0716 *Tel:* 505-541-1732, pg 54

Carstens, Harold H, Carstens Publications Inc, 108 Phil Hardin Rd, Newton, NJ 07860 *Tel:* 973-383-3355 *Fax:* 973-383-4064 *E-mail:* hal@carstens-publications.com *Web Site:* www.carstens-publications.com, pg 54

Carswell, Christine, Chronicle Books LLC, 85 Second St, 6th fl, San Francisco, CA 94105 *Tel:* 415-537-4200 *Toll Free Tel:* 800-722-6657 (cust serv) *Fax:* 415-537-4460 *Toll Free Fax:* 800-858-7787 (orders) *E-mail:* frontdesk@chroniclebooks.com *Web Site:* www.chroniclebooks.com, pg 61

Cartaino, Carol, White Oak Editions, 2000 Flat Run Rd, Seaman, OH 45679 *Tel:* 937-764-1303 *Fax:* 937-764-1303, pg 613

Carter, Brenda, Congressional Quarterly Press, 1255 22 St NW, Washington, DC 20037 *Tel:* 202-729-1800 *Toll Free Tel:* 866-427-7737 *Fax:* 202-729-1809 *Toll Free Fax:* 800-380-3810 *E-mail:* customerservice@cqpress.com *Web Site:* www.cq.com, pg 66

Carter, Cherie, UnKnownTruths.com Publishing Co, 8815 Conroy Windermere Rd, Suite 190, Orlando, FL 32835 *Tel:* 407-929-9207 *Fax:* 407-876-3933 *E-mail:* info@unknowntruths.com *Web Site:* unknowntruths.com, pg 288

Carter, Deborah, Louisiana State University Press, PO Box 25053, Baton Rouge, LA 70894-5053 *Tel:* 225-578-6294 *Toll Free Tel:* 800-861-3477 *Fax:* 225-578-6461 *Toll Free Fax:* 800-305-4416 *E-mail:* lsupress@lsu.edu *Web Site:* www.lsu.edu/guests/lsupress, pg 159

Carter, Deborah, Mysterious Content, 108 E 38 St, Suite 409, New York, NY 10016 *Tel:* 212-925-3721 *E-mail:* myscontent@aol.com, pg 645

Carter, Eric, Acrobat Books, PO Box 870, Venice, CA 90294-0870 *Tel:* 310-578-1055 *Fax:* 310-823-8447 *E-mail:* acrobooks@cs.com, pg 4

Carter, Jackie, Disney Publishing Worldwide, 500 S Buena Vista, Burbank, CA 91521 *Tel:* 212-633-4400 *Fax:* 212-633-4833 *Web Site:* www.disney.go.com/disneybooks, pg 81

Carter, Jackie, Jump at the Sun, 114 Fifth Ave, New York, NY 10011 *Tel:* 212-633-4400 *Fax:* 212-633-4809 *Web Site:* www.disney.com, pg 143

Carter, Jane, Harbor House, 111 Tenth St, Augusta, GA 30901 *Tel:* 706-738-0354 *Fax:* 706-738-0354 *E-mail:* harborbook@knology.net *Web Site:* harborhousebooks.com, pg 114

Carter, Jill, Crossway Books, 1300 Crescent St, Wheaton, IL 60187 *Tel:* 630-682-4300 *Fax:* 630-682-4785 *E-mail:* editorial@goodnews-crossway.org *Web Site:* www.crosswaybooks.org, pg 73

Carter, Leon, Productivity Press, 444 Park Ave S, Suite 604, New York, NY 10016 *Tel:* 212-686-5900 *Toll Free Tel:* 888-319-5852 *Fax:* 212-686-5411 *Toll Free Fax:* 800-394-6286 *E-mail:* info@productivitypress.com *Web Site:* www.productivitypress.com, pg 219

Carter, Richard E, ALI-ABA Committee on Continuing Professional Education, 4025 Chestnut St, Philadelphia, PA 19104 *Tel:* 215-243-1600 *Toll Free Tel:* 800-CLE-NEWS *Fax:* 215-243-1664; 215-243-1683 *Web Site:* www.ali-aba.org, pg 8

Carter, Virgil, American Society of Mechanical Engineers (ASME), 3 Park Ave, New York, NY 10016 *Tel:* 212-591-7000 *Toll Free Tel:* 800-843-2763 (cust serv) *Fax:* 212-591-7674; 973-882-1717 (cust serv) *E-mail:* infocentral@asme.org *Web Site:* www.asme.org, pg 18

Cartwright, Christopher, Wolters Kluwer US Corp, 2700 Lake Cook Rd, Riverwoods, IL 60015 *Tel:* 847-267-7000 *Fax:* 847-580-5192 *Web Site:* www.wolterskluwer.com, pg 302

Cartwright, Erin, Avalon Books, 160 Madison Ave, 5th fl, New York, NY 10016 *Tel:* 212-598-0222 *Fax:* 212-979-1862 *E-mail:* avalon@avalonbooks.com *Web Site:* www.avalonbooks.com, pg 28

Cartwright, Perry, Association of American University Presses, 1427 E 60 St, Chicago, IL 60637 *Tel:* 773-702-7700; 773-702-7600 *Toll Free Tel:* 800-621-2736 (orders) *Fax:* 773-702-9756 (sales); 773-660-2235 (orders); 773-702-2708 *E-mail:* general@press.uchicago.edu *Web Site:* www.press.uchicago.edu, pg 26

Cartwright-Niumata, Erin, Thomas Bouregy & Co Inc, 160 Madison Ave, New York, NY 10016 *Tel:* 212-598-0222 *Fax:* 212-979-1862 *E-mail:* customerservice@avalonbooks.com *Web Site:* avalonbooks.com, pg 44

Caruso, Wendy, New York Academy of Sciences, 2 E 63 St, New York, NY 10021 *Tel:* 212-838-0230 *Toll Free Tel:* 800-843-6927 *Fax:* 212-888-2894 *E-mail:* publications@nyas.org *Web Site:* www.nyas.org, pg 189

Caruthers, Gavin, Simon & Schuster Audio, 1230 Avenue of the Americas, New York, NY 10020 *Tel:* 212-698-7664 *E-mail:* audiopub@simonandschuster.com *Web Site:* www.simonsaysaudio.com, pg 248

Carvainis, Maria, Maria Carvainis Agency Inc, 1350 Avenue of the Americas, Suite 2905, New York, NY 10019 *Tel:* 212-245-6365 *Fax:* 212-245-7196 *E-mail:* mca@mariacarvainisagency.com, pg 624

Carver, Holly, University of Iowa Press, University of Iowa, 100 Kuhl House, Iowa City, IA 52242-1000 *Tel:* 319-335-2000 *Toll Free Tel:* 800-621-2736 (orders only) *Fax:* 319-335-2055 *Toll Free Fax:* 800-621-8476 (orders only) *E-mail:* uipress@uiowa.edu *Web Site:* www.uiowapress.org, pg 282

Cary, Andrew, The Haworth Press Inc, 10 Alice St, Binghamton, NY 13904-1580 *Tel:* 607-722-5857 *Toll Free Tel:* 800-429-6784 *Fax:* 607-722-1424 *Toll Free Fax:* 800-895-0582 *E-mail:* getinfo@haworthpressinc.com *Web Site:* www.haworthpress.com, pg 118

Casari, Stephen Cogil, SLC Enterprises Inc, 6965 Oakbrook SE, Grand Rapids, MI 49546 *Tel:* 616-942-2665 (answering serv & voice mail) *Toll Free Tel:* 800-420-7222 *Toll Free Fax:* 800-420-7222 *E-mail:* candp5@comcast.net, pg 656

Cascardi, Andrea, Transatlantic Literary Agency Inc, 72 Glengowan Rd, Toronto, ON M4N 1G4, Canada *Tel:* 416-488-9214 *Fax:* 416-488-4531 *E-mail:* info@tla1.com *Web Site:* www.tla1.com, pg 659

Case, Roger, Krause Publications, 700 E State St, Iola, WI 54990 *Tel:* 715-445-4612 ext 365 *Toll Free Tel:* 800-258-0929; 888-457-2873 *Fax:* 715-445-4087 *Web Site:* www.krause.com, pg 147

Caseburg, Sharon, Turnstone Press, 607-100 Arthur St, Winnipeg, MB R3B 1H3, Canada *Tel:* 204-947-1555 *Toll Free Tel:* 800-982-6472 *Fax:* 204-942-1555 *E-mail:* editor@turnstonepress.com; mktg@turnstonepress.com *Web Site:* www.turnstonepress.com, pg 564

Caseburg, Sharon, University of Manitoba Press, St Johns College, Winnipeg, MB R3T 2N2, Canada *Tel:* 204-474-9495 *Fax:* 204-474-7566 *Web Site:* www.umanitoba.ca/uofmpress, pg 565

Casella, Jean, The Feminist Press at The City University of New York, 365 Fifth Ave, Suite 5406, New York, NY 10016 *Tel:* 212-817-7926 *Fax:* 212-817-1593 *Web Site:* www.feministpress.org, pg 96

Casemore, Kristin, The Crossing Press, PO Box 7123, Berkeley, CA 94707 *Tel:* 510-559-1600 *Toll Free Tel:* 800-841-2665 (orders & cust serv) *Fax:* 510-524-1052 *E-mail:* publicity@tenspeed.com *Web Site:* tenspeed.com, pg 73

Casemore, Kristin, Ten Speed Press, PO Box 7123, Berkeley, CA 94707 *Tel:* 510-559-1600 *Toll Free Tel:* 800-841-Book *Fax:* 510-559-1629; 510-524-1052 (general) *E-mail:* order@tenspeed.com *Web Site:* www.tenspeed.com, pg 266

Casetti, Joanne, Running Press Book Publishers, 125 S 22 St, Philadelphia, PA 19103-4399 *Tel:* 215-567-5080 *Toll Free Tel:* 800-345-5359 (cust serv & orders) *Fax:* 215-568-2919 *Toll Free Fax:* 800-453-2884 *Web Site:* www.runningpress.com, pg 236

Casey, Maribeth, Algonquin Books of Chapel Hill, 127 Kingston Dr, Suite 105, Chapel Hill, NC 27514 *Tel:* 919-967-0108 *Fax:* 919-933-0272 *E-mail:* dialogue@algonquin.com *Web Site:* www.algonquin.com, pg 8

Casey, Maribeth, Artisan, 708 Broadway, New York, NY 10003-9555 *Tel:* 212-254-5900 *Fax:* 212-254-8098 *E-mail:* artisaninfo@workman.com *Web Site:* www.artisanbooks.com, pg 25

Casey, Maribeth, Storey Books, 210 Mass MoCA Way, North Adams, MA 01247 *Tel:* 413-346-2100 *Toll Free Tel:* 800-793-9396 *Fax:* 413-346-2253 *E-mail:* info@storey.com *Web Site:* www.storey.com, pg 260

Casey, Maribeth, Workman Publishing Co Inc, 708 Broadway, New York, NY 10003-9555 *Tel:* 212-254-5900 *Toll Free Tel:* 800-722-7202 *Fax:* 212-254-8098 *E-mail:* info@workman.com *Web Site:* www.workman.com, pg 303

Casey, Monica, CTB/McGraw-Hill, 20 Ryan Ranch Rd, Monterey, CA 93940-5703 *Tel:* 831-393-0700 *Toll Free Tel:* 800-538-9547 *Fax:* 831-393-7825 *Web Site:* www.ctb.com, pg 74

Cash, Amy Opperman, Larson Publications, 4936 Rte 414, Burdett, NY 14818 *Tel:* 607-546-9342 *Toll Free Tel:* 800-828-2197 *Fax:* 607-546-9344 *E-mail:* larson@lightlink.com *Web Site:* www.larsonpublications.org, pg 149

Cash, Ellen, W H Freeman and Co, 41 Madison Ave, 37th fl, New York, NY 10010 *Tel:* 212-576-9400 *Fax:* 212-689-2383 *Web Site:* www.whfreeman.com, pg 100

Cash, Mary, Holiday House Inc, 425 Madison Ave, New York, NY 10017 *Tel:* 212-688-0085 *Fax:* 212-421-6134, pg 123

Cash, Mary, International Reading Association Children's Book Award, 800 Barksdale Rd, Newark, DE 19714 *Tel:* 302-731-1600 *Fax:* 302-731-1057 *Web Site:* www.reading.org, pg 780

Cash, Mary, Paul A Witty Short Story Award, 800 Barksdale Rd, Newark, DE 19714 *Tel:* 302-731-1600 *Fax:* 302-731-1057 *E-mail:* pubinfo@reading.org *Web Site:* www.reading.org, pg 812

Cash, Paul, Larson Publications, 4936 Rte 414, Burdett, NY 14818 *Tel:* 607-546-9342 *Toll Free Tel:* 800-828-2197 *Fax:* 607-546-9344 *E-mail:* larson@lightlink.com *Web Site:* www.larsonpublications.org, pg 149

Cash, Susan L, Kent State University Press, PO Box 5190, Kent, OH 44242-0001 *Tel:* 330-672-7913; 330-672-8097 (sales office) *Toll Free Tel:* 800-247-6553 (orders) *Fax:* 330-672-3104 *Web Site:* www.kentstateuniversitypress.com, pg 145

Cashman, Ann, The Maureen Lasher Agency/The LA Literary Agency, PO Box 46370, Los Angeles, CA 90046 *Tel:* 323-654-5288 *Fax:* 323-654-5388 *E-mail:* laliteraryag@aol.com, pg 639

Caso, Adolph, Branden Publishing Co Inc, PO Box 812094, Wellesley, MA 02482-0013 *Tel:* 781-235-3634 *Fax:* 781-790-1056 *E-mail:* branden@branden.com *Web Site:* www.branden.com, pg 45

Caso, Adolph, Dante University of America Press Inc, PO Box 812158, Wellesley, MA 02482 *Tel:* 781-235-3634 *Fax:* 781-790-1056 *E-mail:* danteu@danteuniversity.org *Web Site:* www.danteuniversity.org, pg 76

Caso, Robert, Branden Publishing Co Inc, PO Box 812094, Wellesley, MA 02482-0013 *Tel:* 781-235-3634 *Fax:* 781-790-1056 *E-mail:* branden@branden.com *Web Site:* www.branden.com, pg 45

Casper, Rob, Council of Literary Magazines & Presses (CLMP), 154 Christopher St, Suite 3-C, New York, NY 10014-2839 *Tel:* 212-741-9110 *Fax:* 212-741-9112 *E-mail:* info@clmp.org *Web Site:* www.clmp.org, pg 686

Cassady, David, Smyth & Helwys Publishing Inc, 6316 Peake Rd, Macon, GA 31210 *Tel:* 478-757-1305 *Toll Free Tel:* 800-747-3016; 800-568-1248 *Fax:* 478-757-0564 *E-mail:* market@helwys.com *Web Site:* www.helwys.com, pg 251

Cassell, Dana, Florida State Writing Competition, Main St, North Stratford, NH 03590 *Tel:* 603-922-8338 *Fax:* 603-922-8339 *E-mail:* contest@writers-editors.com *Web Site:* www.writers-editors.com, pg 774

Cassell, Dana K, Florida Freelance Writers Association, Main St, North Stratford, NH 03590 *Tel:* 603-922-8338 *Fax:* 603-922-8339 *E-mail:* FFWA@writers-editors.com *Web Site:* www.writers-editors.com; www.ffwamembers.com, pg 687

Cassell, Jay, The Globe Pequot Press, 246 Goose Lane, Guilford, CT 06437 *Tel:* 203-458-4500 *Toll Free Tel:* 800-243-0495 (cust serv) *Fax:* 203-458-4601 *Toll Free Fax:* 800-820-2329 (orders & cust serv) *E-mail:* info@globepequot.com *Web Site:* www.globepequot.com, pg 105

Cassell, Jay, The Lyons Press, 246 Goose Lane, Guilford, CT 06437 *Tel:* 203-458-4500 *Toll Free Tel:* 800-243-0495 *Fax:* 203-458-4668 *Web Site:* www.lyonspress.com; www.globepequot.com, pg 160

Cassiday, Terry, Baha'i Publishing Trust, 415 Linden Ave, Wilmette, IL 60091 *Tel:* 847-425-7950 *Fax:* 847-425-7951 *E-mail:* bpt@usbnc.org, pg 30

Cassidy, Eileen D, Graphic Arts Education & Research Foundation (GAERF), 1899 Preston White Dr, Reston, VA 20191-4367 *Tel:* 703-264-7200 *Fax:* 703-620-3165 *E-mail:* gaerf@npes.org *Web Site:* www.npes.org, pg 705

Cassidy, John, Klutz, 455 Portage Ave, Palo Alto, CA 94306 *Tel:* 650-857-0888 *Fax:* 650-857-9110 *Web Site:* www.klutz.com, pg 146

Cassidy, Lynda, UnKnownTruths.com Publishing Co, 8815 Conroy Windermere Rd, Suite 190, Orlando, FL 32835 *Tel:* 407-929-9207 *Fax:* 407-876-3933 *E-mail:* info@unknowntruths.com *Web Site:* unknowntruths.com, pg 288

Cassin, Brian, Doubleday Canada, One Toronto St, Suite 300, Toronto, ON M5C 2V6, Canada *Tel:* 416-364-4449 *Fax:* 416-957-1587 *Web Site:* www.randomhouse.ca, pg 542

Cassin, Brian, Knopf Canada, One Toronto St, Suite 300, Toronto, ON M5C 2V6, Canada *Tel:* 416-364-4449 *Toll Free Tel:* 800-668-4247 (order desk) *Fax:* 416-364-0462 *Web Site:* www.randomhouse.ca, pg 552

Cassin, Brian, Random House of Canada Ltd, One Toronto St, Unit 300, Toronto, ON M5C 2V6, Canada *Tel:* 416-364-4449 *Fax:* 416-364-6863 (edit & publicity); 416-364-6653 (subs rts) *Web Site:* www.randomhouse.ca, pg 559

Cassin, Brian, Seal Books, One Toronto St, Suite 300, Toronto, ON M5C 2V6, Canada *Tel:* 416-364-4449 *Toll Free Tel:* 888-523-9292 (order desk) *Fax:* 416-957-1587 *Web Site:* www.randomhouse.ca, pg 560

Cassity, Brian, Bilingual Press/Editorial Bilingue, Hispanic Research Ctr, Arizona State Univ, Tempe, AZ 85287-2702 *Tel:* 480-965-3867 *Fax:* 480-965-8309 *E-mail:* brp@asu.edu *Web Site:* www.asu.edu/brp/brp, pg 38

Castiglia, Julie, Julie Castiglia Literary Agency, 1155 Camino Del Mar, Suite 510, Del Mar, CA 92014 *Tel:* 858-755-8761 *Fax:* 858-755-7063 *E-mail:* jaclagency@aol.com, pg 624

Castillo, J, American Research Press, PO Box 141, Rehoboth, NM 87322 *Web Site:* www.gallup.unm.edu/~smarandache, pg 17

Castillo, Tete, Wanderlust Publications, 2009 S Tenth St, McAllen, TX 78503-5405 *Tel:* 956-686-3601 *Fax:* 956-686-0732 *E-mail:* info@sanbornsinsurance.com *Web Site:* www.sanbornsinsurance.com, pg 292

Castonguay, Joan, American Management Association, 1601 Broadway, New York, NY 10019-7420 *Tel:* 212-586-8100 *Toll Free Tel:* 800-262-9699 *Fax:* 212-903-8168 *Web Site:* www.amanet.org, pg 677

Chan, Joanne, Heyday Books, 2054 University Ave, Berkeley, CA 94704 *Tel:* 510-549-3564 *Fax:* 510-549-1889 *E-mail:* heyday@heydaybooks.com *Web Site:* www.heydaybooks.com, pg 122

Chance, LaBron, Harcourt Inc, 6277 Sea Harbor Dr, Orlando, FL 32887 *Tel:* 407-345-2000 *Toll Free Tel:* 800-225-5425 (cust serv) *Fax:* 407-352-3445 (cust serv), pg 114

Chandler, Chad, Kendall/Hunt Publishing Co, 4050 Westmark Dr, Dubuque, IA 52002 *Tel:* 563-589-1000 *Toll Free Tel:* 800-228-0810 (orders only) *Fax:* 563-589-1114 *Toll Free Fax:* 800-772-9165 *Web Site:* www.kendallhunt.com, pg 144

Chaney, Margo, University of Illinois Press, 1325 S Oak, Champaign, IL 61820-6903 *Tel:* 217-333-0950; 212-577-5487 *Fax:* 217-244-8082; 410-516-6969 (orders) *E-mail:* uipress@uillinois.edu; journals@uillinois.edu *Web Site:* www.press.uillinois.edu, pg 282

Chang, Ginny, Shambhala Publications Inc, Horticultural Hall, 300 Massachusetts Ave, Boston, MA 02115 *Tel:* 617-424-0030 *Toll Free Tel:* 888-424-2329 (orders only) *Fax:* 617-236-1563; 303-665-5292 (orders only) *E-mail:* editors@shambhala.com *Web Site:* www.shambhala.com, pg 245

Chang, Melanie, Random House Children's Books, 1745 Broadway, New York, NY 10019 *Tel:* 212-782-9000 *Toll Free Tel:* 800-200-3552 *Fax:* 212-782-9452 *Web Site:* www.randomhouse.com/kids, pg 226

Chang, Susan, Tom Doherty Associates, LLC, 175 Fifth Ave, 14th fl, New York, NY 10010 *Tel:* 212-388-0100 *Toll Free Tel:* 800-455-0340 *Fax:* 212-388-0191 *E-mail:* firstname.lastname@tor.com *Web Site:* www.tor.com, pg 82

Changar, Amy, Bookbuilders West, PO Box 7046, San Francisco, CA 94120-9727 *Tel:* 415-273-5790 *Web Site:* www.bookbuilders.org, pg 682

Chao, David, Hamilton Books, 4501 Forbes Blvd, Suite 200, Lanham, MD 20706 *Tel:* 301-459-3366, pg 112

Chapell, Gary, Nightingale-Conant, 6245 W Howard St, Niles, IL 60714 *Tel:* 847-647-0306; 847-647-0300 *Toll Free Tel:* 800-572-2770 *Fax:* 847-647-7145 *Web Site:* www.nightingale.com, pg 191

Chapin, Amy, Avery Color Studios, 511 "D" Ave, Gwinn, MI 49841 *Tel:* 906-346-3908 *Toll Free Tel:* 800-722-9925 *Fax:* 906-346-3015 *E-mail:* avery@portup.com, pg 29

Chapin, Wells, Avery Color Studios, 511 "D" Ave, Gwinn, MI 49841 *Tel:* 906-346-3908 *Toll Free Tel:* 800-722-9925 *Fax:* 906-346-3015 *E-mail:* avery@portup.com, pg 29

Chaplin, Candice, Hyperion, 77 W 66 St, 11th fl, New York, NY 10023-6298 *Tel:* 212-456-0100 *Toll Free Tel:* 800-759-0190 (cust serv) *Fax:* 212-456-0157 *Web Site:* hyperionbooks.com, pg 129

Chapman, Ian, Simon & Schuster Inc, 1230 Avenue of the Americas, New York, NY 10020 *Tel:* 212-698-7000 *Fax:* 212-698-7007 *Web Site:* www.simonsays.com, pg 249

Chapman, James, Fugue State Press, PO Box 80, Cooper Sta, New York, NY 10276 *Tel:* 212-673-7922 *Fax:* 208-693-6152 *E-mail:* info@fuguestatepress.com *Web Site:* www.fuguestatepress.com, pg 101

Chapman, Woodrow, Hanser Gardner Publications, 6915 Valley Ave, Cincinnati, OH 45244-3029 *Tel:* 513-527-8977 *Toll Free Tel:* 800-950-8977 *Fax:* 513-527-8801 *Toll Free Tel:* 800-527-8801 *E-mail:* hgfeedback@gardnerweb.com *Web Site:* www.hansergardner.com, pg 113

Chappell, Chris, Stackpole Books, 5067 Ritter Rd, Mechanicsburg, PA 17055 *Tel:* 717-796-0411 *Toll Free Tel:* 800-732-3669 *Fax:* 717-796-0412 *Web Site:* www.stackpolebooks.com, pg 257

Chaput, Lucien, Les Editions du Ble, 340 Provencher Blvd, St Boniface, MB R2H 0G7, Canada *Tel:* 204-237-8200 *Fax:* 204-233-8182 *E-mail:* trigo@mb.sympatico.ca, pg 544

Chard, Lynn, Institute of Continuing Legal Education, 1020 Greene St, Ann Arbor, MI 48109-1444 *Tel:* 734-764-0533 *Toll Free Tel:* 877-229-4350 *Fax:* 734-763-2412 *Toll Free Fax:* 877-229-4351 *E-mail:* icle@umich.edu *Web Site:* www.icle.org/, pg 135

Charette, Francois, Association for the Export of Canadian Books, One Nicholas, Suite 504, Ottawa, ON K1N 7B7, Canada *Tel:* 613-562-2324 *Fax:* 613-562-2329 *E-mail:* aecb@aecb.org *Web Site:* www.aecb.org, pg 679

Charles, Kristi, National Resource Center for Youth Services (NRCYS), Schusterman Center, 4502 E 41 St, Bldg 4W, Tulsa, OK 74135-2512 *Tel:* 918-660-3700 *Toll Free Tel:* 800-274-2687 *Fax:* 918-660-3737 *Web Site:* www.nrcys.ou.edu, pg 185

Charles, William, A Abacus Group, PO Box 35, Ridgecrest, CA 93556 *Tel:* 760-375-5243 *Fax:* 760-375-1140 *E-mail:* gtd007@ridgenet.net *Web Site:* www.ridgenet.net/~gtd007, pg 617

Charlton, Robert, David R Godine Publisher Inc, 9 Hamilton Place, Boston, MA 02108 *Tel:* 617-451-9600 *Fax:* 617-350-0250 *E-mail:* info@godine.com *Web Site:* www.godine.com, pg 106

Charner, Kathleen, Gryphon House Inc, 10726 Tucker St, Beltsville, MD 20704 *Tel:* 301-595-9500 *Toll Free Tel:* 800-638-0928 *Fax:* 301-595-0051 *E-mail:* info@ghbooks.com *Web Site:* www.gryphonhouse.com, pg 110

Charnogursky, Michael, W W Norton & Company Inc, 500 Fifth Ave, New York, NY 10110-0017 *Tel:* 212-354-5500 *Toll Free Tel:* 800-233-4830 (orders & cust serv) *Fax:* 212-869-0856 *Toll Free Fax:* 800-458-6515 *Web Site:* www.wwnorton.com, pg 193

Charpentier, Julia, Twilight Times Books, PO Box 3340, Kingsport, TN 37664-0340 *Tel:* 423-323-0183 *Fax:* 423-323-0183 *E-mail:* publisher@twilighttimes.com *Web Site:* www.twilighttimesbooks.com, pg 277

Charters, Lisa, Doubleday Canada, One Toronto St, Suite 300, Toronto, ON M5C 2V6, Canada *Tel:* 416-364-4449 *Fax:* 416-957-1587 *Web Site:* www.randomhouse.ca, pg 542

Charters, Lisa, Knopf Canada, One Toronto St, Suite 300, Toronto, ON M5C 2V6, Canada *Tel:* 416-364-4449 *Toll Free Tel:* 800-668-4247 (order desk) *Fax:* 416-364-0462 *Web Site:* www.randomhouse.ca, pg 552

Charters, Lisa, Random House of Canada Ltd, One Toronto St, Unit 300, Toronto, ON M5C 2V6, Canada *Tel:* 416-364-4449 *Fax:* 416-364-6863 (edit & publicity); 416-364-6653 (subs rts) *Web Site:* www.randomhouse.ca, pg 559

Charters, Lisa, Seal Books, One Toronto St, Suite 300, Toronto, ON M5C 2V6, Canada *Tel:* 416-364-4449 *Toll Free Tel:* 888-523-9292 (order desk) *Fax:* 416-957-1587 *Web Site:* www.randomhouse.ca, pg 560

Chasan, Gail, Harlequin Enterprises Ltd, 233 Broadway, Suite 1001, New York, NY 10279 *Tel:* 212-553-4200 *Fax:* 212-227-8969 *E-mail:* customer.ecare@harlequin.ca *Web Site:* www.eharlequin.com; www.luna-books.com; www.mirabooks.com; www.reddressink.com; www.steeplehill.com, pg 115

Chase, Bob, Greenwood Publishing Group Inc, 88 Post Rd W, Westport, CT 06880-4208 *Tel:* 203-226-3571 *Toll Free Tel:* 800-225-5800 *Fax:* 203-222-1502 *E-mail:* bookinfo@greenwood.com (general); firstintial&fulllastname@greenwood.com (individuals) *Web Site:* www.greenwood.com, pg 109

Chasek, Ruth, Springer Publishing Co Inc, 11 W 42 St, New York, NY 10036 *Tel:* 212-431-4370 *Toll Free Tel:* 877-687-7476 *Fax:* 212-941-7842 *E-mail:* springer@springerpub.com *Web Site:* www.springerpub.com, pg 256

Chavan, Diane, Association of Graphic Communications, Graphic Arts Education Center, 330 Seventh Ave, 9th fl, New York, NY 10001-5010 *Tel:* 212-279-2100 *Fax:* 212-279-5381, pg 751

Chavers, Linda, The New Press, 38 Greene St, 4th fl, New York, NY 10013 *Tel:* 212-629-8802 *Toll Free Tel:* 800-233-4830 (orders) *Fax:* 212-629-8617

Toll Free Fax: 800-458-6515 *E-mail:* newpress@thenewpress.com *Web Site:* www.thenewpress.com, pg 188

Checkoway, Barbara, Boston University, 236 Bay State Rd, Boston, MA 02215 *Tel:* 617-353-2510 *Fax:* 617-353-3653 *Web Site:* www.bu.edu/writing/, pg 751

Cheers, Patricia, American College, 270 S Bryn Mawr Ave, Bryn Mawr, PA 19010 *Tel:* 610-526-1000 *Fax:* 610-526-1310 *Web Site:* www.amercoll.edu, pg 12

Chelius, Jane, Jane Chelius Literary Agency, Inc, 548 Second St, Brooklyn, NY 11215 *Tel:* 718-499-0236 *Fax:* 718-832-7335 *E-mail:* queries@janechelius.com *Web Site:* www.janechelius.com, pg 624

Chelius, Mark, Jane Chelius Literary Agency, Inc, 548 Second St, Brooklyn, NY 11215 *Tel:* 718-499-0236 *Fax:* 718-832-7335 *E-mail:* queries@janechelius.com *Web Site:* www.janechelius.com, pg 624

Chen, Catharine, Prism International Fiction Contest, University of British Columbia, Buch E462, 1866 Main Mall, Vancouver, BC V6T 1Z1, Canada *Tel:* 604-822-2514 *Fax:* 604-822-3616 *E-mail:* prism@interchange.ubc.ca *Web Site:* prism.arts.ubc.ca, pg 800

Chen, Cynthia, Pippin Publishing Corp, 170 The Donway W, Toronto, ON M3C 2G3, Canada *Tel:* 416-510-2918 *Toll Free Tel:* 888-889-0001 *Fax:* 416-510-3359 *Web Site:* www.pippinpub.com, pg 557

Cheney, Elyse, Sanford J Greenburger Associates Inc, 55 Fifth Ave, 15th fl, New York, NY 10003 *Tel:* 212-206-5600 *Fax:* 212-463-8718 *Web Site:* www.greenburger.com, pg 633

Cheney, Sally, Chelsea House Publishers LLC, 2080 Cabot Blvd W, Suite 201, Langhorne, PA 19047-1813 *Tel:* 610-353-5166 *Toll Free Tel:* 800-848-BOOK (848-2665) *Fax:* 610-359-1439 *Toll Free Fax:* 877-780-7300 *E-mail:* sales@chelseahouse.com *Web Site:* www.chelseahouse.com, pg 59

Cheney, Stephanie L, Intercultural Press Inc, PO Box 700, 374 US Rte One, Yarmouth, ME 04096 *Tel:* 207-846-5168 *Toll Free Tel:* 866-372-2665 *Fax:* 207-846-5181 *E-mail:* books@interculturalpress.com *Web Site:* www.interculturalpress.com, pg 136

Cheng, Jill, Cheng & Tsui Co Inc, 25 West St, 5th fl, Boston, MA 02111-1213 *Tel:* 617-988-2401 *Toll Free Tel:* 800-554-1963 *Fax:* 617-426-3669 *E-mail:* service@cheng-tsui.com *Web Site:* www.cheng-tsui.com, pg 59

Cheng, Kipp, American Association of Advertising Agencies (AAAA), 405 Lexington Ave, 18th fl, New York, NY 10174-1801 *Tel:* 212-682-2500 *Fax:* 212-682-8391 *Web Site:* www.aaaa.org, pg 676

Chernoff, Mitchell, Society for Industrial & Applied Mathematics, 3600 University City Science Ctr, Philadelphia, PA 19104-2688 *Tel:* 215-382-9800 *Toll Free Tel:* 800-447-7426 *Fax:* 215-386-7999 *E-mail:* siam@siam.org *Web Site:* www.siam.org, pg 251

Cherry, Amy, W W Norton & Company Inc, 500 Fifth Ave, New York, NY 10110-0017 *Tel:* 212-354-5500 *Toll Free Tel:* 800-233-4830 (orders & cust serv) *Fax:* 212-869-0856 *Toll Free Fax:* 800-458-6515 *Web Site:* www.wwnorton.com, pg 193

Cherry, Sheila, National Press Club (NPC), 529 14 St NW, 13th fl, Washington, DC 20045 *Tel:* 202-662-7500 *Fax:* 202-662-7569 *E-mail:* infocenter@npcpress.org *Web Site:* www.press.org, pg 694

Chesman, Andrea, Little Chicago Editorial Services, 154 Natural Tpke, Ripton, VT 05766 *Tel:* 802-388-9782 *Fax:* 802-388-6525, pg 605

Chester, Linda, Linda Chester & Associates, Rockefeller Ctr, 630 Fifth Ave, New York, NY 10111 *Tel:* 212-218-3350 *Fax:* 212-218-3343 *E-mail:* lcassoc@mindspring.com *Web Site:* www.lindachester.com, pg 624

Chetti, Carmen, M E Sharpe Inc, 80 Business Park Dr, Suite 202, Armonk, NY 10504 *Tel:* 914-273-1800 *Toll Free Tel:* 800-541-6563 *Fax:* 914-273-2106 *E-mail:* info@mesharpe.com *Web Site:* www.mesharpe.com, pg 246

Cheung, Anthony, Imprint Publications Inc, 230 E Ohio St, Suite 300, Chicago, IL 60611-3705 *Tel:* 312-337-9268 *Fax:* 312-337-9622 *E-mail:* imppub@aol.com, pg 132

Chevako, Anne W, Publishing Resources Inc, PO Box 41307, San Juan, PR 00940-1307 *Tel:* 787-727-1800 *Fax:* 787-727-1823 *E-mail:* pri@chevako.net, pg 609

Chevako, Ronald J, Publishing Resources Inc, PO Box 41307, San Juan, PR 00940-1307 *Tel:* 787-727-1800 *Fax:* 787-727-1823 *E-mail:* pri@chevako.net, pg 609

Chevrier, Robert, Institute of Psychological Research, Inc., 34 Fleury St W, Montreal, PQ H3L 1S9, Canada *Tel:* 514-382-3000 *Toll Free Tel:* 800-363-7800 *Fax:* 514-382-3007 *Toll Free Fax:* 888-382-3007 *E-mail:* info@i-p-r.ca *Web Site:* www.i-p-r.ca, pg 551

Chi, Y S, Random House Inc, 1745 Broadway, New York, NY 10019 *Tel:* 212-782-9000 *Toll Free Tel:* 800-726-0600 *Web Site:* www.randomhouse.com, pg 226

Chicorel, Marietta S, American Library Publishing Co, PO Box 4272, Sedona, AZ 86340-4272 *Tel:* 928-282-4922 *E-mail:* grace@sedonaarizona.com, pg 15

Childers, Kimberly B, Indiana University Press, 601 N Morton St, Bloomington, IN 47404-3797 *Tel:* 812-855-8817 *Toll Free Tel:* 800-842-6796 (orders only) *Fax:* 812-855-7931 (orders only); 812-855-8507 *E-mail:* iupress@indiana.edu; iuorder@indiana.edu (orders) *Web Site:* www.iupress.indiana.edu, pg 132

Childress, David H, Adventures Unlimited Press, One Adventure Place, Kempton, IL 60946 *Tel:* 815-253-6390 *Fax:* 815-253-6300 *E-mail:* auphq@frontiernet.net *Web Site:* www.adventuresunlimitedpress.com, pg 6

Childs, Faith Hampton, Faith Childs Literary Agency Inc, 915 Broadway, Suite 1009, New York, NY 10010 *Tel:* 212-995-9600 *Fax:* 212-995-9709 *E-mail:* faith@faithchildsliteraryagencyinc.com, pg 624

Childs, Jim, The Taunton Press Inc, 63 S Main St, Newtown, CT 06470 *Tel:* 203-426-8171 *Toll Free Tel:* 800-283-7252; 800-888-8286 (orders) *Fax:* 203-426-3434 *Web Site:* www.taunton.com, pg 264

Childs, John S, Optical Society of America, 2010 Massachusetts Ave NW, Washington, DC 20036-1023 *Tel:* 202-223-8130 *Fax:* 202-223-1096 *E-mail:* custserv@osa.org *Web Site:* www.osa.org, pg 198

Childs, Lucy, The Aaron M Priest Literary Agency Inc, 708 Third Ave, 23rd fl, New York, NY 10017 *Tel:* 212-818-0344 *Fax:* 212-573-9417, pg 649

Chilton, Lynne, Wood Lake Books Inc, 9025 Jim Bailey Rd, Kelowna, BC V4V 1R2, Canada *Tel:* 250-766-2778 *Toll Free Tel:* 800-663-2775 (orders) *Fax:* 250-766-2736 *Toll Free Fax:* 888-841-9991 (orders) *E-mail:* info@woodlake.com *Web Site:* www.woodlakebooks.com, pg 567

Chilton, Rob, National Publishing Co, 11311 Roosevelt Blvd, Philadelphia, PA 19154-2105 *Tel:* 215-676-1863 *Toll Free Tel:* 888-333-1863 *Fax:* 215-673-8069 *Web Site:* www.courier.com, pg 184

Chin, Kristina, American Institute of Chemical Engineers (AICHE), 3 Park Ave, New York, NY 10016-5991 *Tel:* 212-591-7338 *Toll Free Tel:* 800-242-4363 *Fax:* 212-591-8888 *E-mail:* xpress@aiche.org *Web Site:* www.aiche.org, pg 15

Chin, Sandra, W W Norton & Company Inc, 500 Fifth Ave, New York, NY 10110-0017 *Tel:* 212-354-5500 *Toll Free Tel:* 800-233-4830 (orders & cust serv) *Fax:* 212-869-0856 *Toll Free Fax:* 800-458-6515 *Web Site:* www.wwnorton.com, pg 193

China, Wanda C, University of Hawaii Press, 2840 Kolowalu St, Honolulu, HI 96822 *Tel:* 808-956-8255 *Toll Free Tel:* 888-847-7377 *Fax:* 808-988-6052 *Toll Free Fax:* 800-650-7811 *E-mail:* uhpbooks@hawaii.edu *Web Site:* www.uhpress.hawaii.edu, pg 281

Chiotti, Danielle, Adams Media, An F+W Publications Co, 57 Littlefield St, 2nd fl, Avon, MA 02322 *Tel:* 508-427-7100 *Fax:* 508-427-6790 *Toll Free*

Fax: 800-872-5628 *E-mail:* authors@adamsmedia.com; orders@adamsmedia.com *Web Site:* www.adamsmedia.com, pg 5

Chirico, Anthony, Alfred A Knopf, 1745 Broadway, New York, NY 10019 *Tel:* 212-751-2600 *Toll Free Tel:* 800-638-6460 *Fax:* 212-572-2593 *Web Site:* www.randomhouse.com/knopf, pg 146

Chittenden, Laurie, Dutton, 375 Hudson St, New York, NY 10014 *Tel:* 212-366-2000 *Fax:* 212-366-2262 *E-mail:* online@penguinputnam.com *Web Site:* www.penguin.com, pg 85

Chiu, Hungdah, East Asian Legal Studies Program, 500 W Baltimore St, Baltimore, MD 21201-1786 *Tel:* 410-706-3870 *Fax:* 410-706-1516 *E-mail:* eastasia@law.umaryland.edu, pg 85

Chmiel, Barbara R, The Blackburn Press, PO Box 287, Caldwell, NJ 07006-0287 *Tel:* 973-228-7077 *Fax:* 973-228-7276 *Web Site:* www.blackburnpress.com, pg 40

Cho, Moon, Phobos Books, 200 Park Ave S, Suite 1109, New York, NY 10003 *Tel:* 212-477-3225 *Fax:* 212-529-4223 *E-mail:* info@phobosweb.com *Web Site:* phobosweb.com, pg 211

Chodosh, Ellen, Oxford University Press, Inc, 198 Madison Ave, New York, NY 10016-4314 *Tel:* 212-726-6000 *Toll Free Tel:* 800-451-7556 (orders) *Web Site:* www.oup.com/us, pg 200

Cholak, Karin, Greenwood Publishing Group Inc, 88 Post Rd W, Westport, CT 06880-4208 *Tel:* 203-226-3571 *Toll Free Tel:* 800-225-5800 *Fax:* 203-222-1502 *E-mail:* bookinfo@greenwood.com (general); firstintial&fulllastname@greenwood.com (individuals) *Web Site:* www.greenwood.com, pg 109

Chon, Christopher, SelectiveHouse Publishers Inc, PO Box 10095, Gaithersburg, MD 20898 *Tel:* 301-990-2999 *Toll Free Tel:* 888-256-6399 (orders only) *Fax:* 301-990-2998 *E-mail:* sr@selectivehouse.com *Web Site:* www.selectivehouse.com, pg 244

Choquette, Claude, Montreal-Contacts/The Rights Agency, PO Box 596-C, Montreal, PQ H2L 4K4, Canada *Tel:* 450-461-1575 *Fax:* 450-461-1505, pg 644

Choron, Harry, March Tenth Inc, 4 Myrtle St, Haworth, NJ 07641 *Tel:* 201-387-6551 *Fax:* 201-387-6552, pg 642

Choron, Sandra, March Tenth Inc, 4 Myrtle St, Haworth, NJ 07641 *Tel:* 201-387-6551 *Fax:* 201-387-6552, pg 642

Chorpenning, Rev Joseph F, St Joseph's University Press, 5600 City Ave, Philadelphia, PA 19131 *Tel:* 610-660-3400 *Fax:* 610-660-3410 *E-mail:* sjupress@sju.edu *Web Site:* www.sju.edu, pg 238

Chou, Shelly, Agency Chicago, 28 E Jackson Blvd, 10th fl, Suite A-600, Chicago, IL 60604 *Tel:* 312-409-0205, pg 618

Chow, Fiona, Pippin Publishing Corp, 170 The Donway W, Toronto, ON M3C 2G3, Canada *Tel:* 416-510-2918 *Toll Free Tel:* 888-889-0001 *Fax:* 416-510-3359 *Web Site:* www.pippinpub.com, pg 557

Choyce, Lesley, Pottersfield Press, 83 Leslie Rd, East Lawrencetown, NS B2Z 1P8, Canada *Toll Free Tel:* 800-NIMBUS9 (646-2879-orders only) *Toll Free Fax:* 888-253-3133 *Web Site:* www.pottersfieldpress.com, pg 558

Choyke, Phyllis Ford, The Society of Midland Authors (SMA), PO Box 10419, Chicago, IL 60610-0419 *Tel:* 773-506-7578 *Fax:* 773-784-5900 *E-mail:* info@midlandauthors.com *Web Site:* www.midlandauthors.com, pg 700

Choyke, Phyllis Ford, The Society of Midland Authors Awards, PO Box 10419, Chicago, IL 60610-0419 *Tel:* 773-506-7578 *Fax:* 773-784-5900 *E-mail:* info@midlandauthors.com *Web Site:* www.midlandauthors.com, pg 806

Chrisman, Ronald, University of North Texas Press, 1820 Highland St, Bain Hall 101, Denton, TX 76201 *Tel:* 940-565-2142 *Fax:* 940-565-4590 *Web Site:* www.unt.edu/untpress, pg 284

Chrismer, Dianne, Fulcrum Publishing Inc, 16100 Table Mountain Pkwy, Suite 300, Golden, CO 80403 *Tel:* 303-277-1623 *Toll Free Tel:* 800-992-2908 *Fax:* 303-279-7111 *Toll Free Fax:* 800-726-7112 *E-mail:* fulcrum@fulcrum-books.com *Web Site:* www.fulcrum-books.com, pg 101

Christ, Carl F, National Bureau of Economic Research Inc, 1050 Massachusetts Ave, Cambridge, MA 02138-5398 *Tel:* 617-868-3900 *Fax:* 617-868-2742 *E-mail:* op@nber.org *Web Site:* www.nber.org, pg 182

Christel, Henry E, William H Sadlier Inc, 9 Pine St, New York, NY 10005 *Tel:* 212-227-2120 *Toll Free Tel:* 800-221-5175 *Fax:* 212-312-6080 *Web Site:* www.sadlier.com; www.sadlier-oxford.com, pg 237

Christensen, John, Our Sunday Visitor Publishing, 200 Noll Plaza, Huntington, IN 46750 *Tel:* 260-356-8400 *Toll Free Tel:* 800-348-2440 (orders) *Fax:* 260-356-8472 *Toll Free Fax:* 800-498-6709 *E-mail:* osvbooks@osv.com *Web Site:* www.osv.com, pg 200

Christian, Bryan, Free Press, 1230 Avenue of the Americas, New York, NY 10020 *Tel:* 212-698-7000 *Toll Free Tel:* 800-223-2345 (cust serv); 800-223-2336 (orders); 888-866-6631 (fulfillment), pg 100

Christian, Mark, Pentecostal Publishing House, 8855 Dunn Rd, Hazelwood, MO 63042 *Tel:* 314-837-7300 *Fax:* 314-837-6574 *E-mail:* pphordersdept@upci.org (orders) *Web Site:* www.pentecostalpublishing.com, pg 209

Christian, Rebecca, Perfection Learning Corp, 10520 New York Ave, Des Moines, IA 50322 *Tel:* 515-278-0133 *Toll Free Tel:* 800-762-2999 *Fax:* 515-278-2980 *E-mail:* orders@perfectionlearning.com *Web Site:* perfectionlearning.com, pg 210

Christiansen, Carol, Bantam Dell Publishing Group, 1745 Broadway, New York, NY 10019 *Tel:* 212-782-9000 *Toll Free Tel:* 800-223-6834 *Fax:* 212-302-7985 *Web Site:* www.randomhouse.com/bantamdell, pg 31

Christiansen, Carol, Doubleday Broadway Publishing Group, 1745 Broadway, New York, NY 10019 *Tel:* 212-782-9000 *Toll Free Tel:* 800-223-6834; 800-223-5780 (sales) *Fax:* 212-302-7985 (correspondence); 212-492-9862 (orders), pg 83

Christiansen, Gayla, Texas A&M University Press, John H Lindsey Bldg, Lewis St, 4354 TAMU, College Station, TX 77843-4354 *Tel:* 979-845-1436 *Toll Free Tel:* 800-826-8911 (orders) *Fax:* 979-847-8752 *Toll Free Fax:* 888-617-2421 (orders) *E-mail:* fdl@tampress.tamu.edu *Web Site:* www.tamu.edu/upress/, pg 267

Christianson, Dick, Kalmbach Publishing Co, 21027 Crossroads Circle, Waukesha, WI 53187 *Tel:* 262-796-8776 *Toll Free Tel:* 800-533-6644 *Fax:* 262-796-1615 (sales & cust serv) *Web Site:* www.kalmbach.com, pg 143

Christianson, Julie, University of California Press, 2120 Berkeley Way, Berkeley, CA 94720 *Tel:* 510-642-4247 *Toll Free Tel:* 800-777-4726 *Fax:* 510-643-7127 *Toll Free Fax:* 800-999-1958 *E-mail:* askucp@ucpress.edu *Web Site:* www.ucpress.edu, pg 281

Christianson, Kelli, Professional Publishing, 1333 Burr Ridge Pkwy, Burr Ridge, IL 60527 *Tel:* 630-789-4000; 630-789-5500 *Toll Free Tel:* 800-2McGraw (262-4729) *Fax:* 630-789-6933 *Web Site:* www.books.mcgraw-hill.com, pg 220

Christie, Peter, Benoit & Associates, 279 S Schuyler Ave, Kankakee, IL 60901 *Tel:* 815-932-2582 *Fax:* 815-932-2594 *E-mail:* benoitart@aol.com, pg 665

Christie, Susan, American Public Human Services Association, 810 First St NE, Suite 500, Washington, DC 20002 *Tel:* 202-682-0100 *Fax:* 202-289-6555 *E-mail:* pubs@aphsa.org *Web Site:* www.aphsa.org, pg 677

Christmas, Bobbie, Zebra Communications, 230 Deerchase Dr, Suite B, Woodstock, GA 30188 *Tel:* 770-924-0528 *Fax:* 770-592-7362 *Web Site:* www.zebraeditor.com, pg 615

Christoffersen, Hans, Liguori Publications, One Liguori Dr, Liguori, MO 63057-9999 *Tel:* 636-464-2500 *Toll Free Tel:* 800-464-2555 *Fax:* 636-464-8449 *Web Site:* www.liguori.org, pg 154

Christofferson, Andrea, University of Wisconsin Press, 1930 Monroe St, 3rd fl, Madison, WI 53711 *Tel:* 608-263-1110 *Toll Free Tel:* 800-621-2736 (Orders) *Fax:* 608-263-1120 *Toll Free Fax:* 800-621-8476 (Orders) *E-mail:* uwiscpress@uwpress.wisc.edu (Main Office) *Web Site:* www.wisc.edu/wisconsinpress/, pg 286

Christopher, Andre, The Annual Great American Tennis Writing Awards, 15 Elm Place, Rye, NY 10580 *Tel:* 914-967-4890 *Fax:* 914-967-8178 *E-mail:* tennisweek@tennisweek.com *Web Site:* www.tennisweek.com, pg 777

Christopher, Tom, Follett Higher Education Group, 1818 Swift Dr, Oak Grove, IL 60523 *Tel:* 630-279-2330 *Toll Free Tel:* 800-323-4506 *Fax:* 630-279-2569 *Web Site:* www.fheg.follett.com, pg 687

Christopher, William F (Bill), William F Christopher Publication Services, 410 Sutcliffe Place, Walnut Creek, CA 94598-3924 *Tel:* 925-943-5584 *Fax:* 925-943-5594 *E-mail:* billtmig@astound.net, pg 624

Christopherson, D Foy, Augsburg Fortress Publishers, Publishing House of the Evangelical Lutheran Church in America, 100 S Fifth St, Suite 700, Minneapolis, MN 55402 *Tel:* 612-330-3300 *Toll Free Tel:* 800-426-0115 (ext 639 subns); 800-328-4648 (orders); 800-421-0239 (perms) *Fax:* 612-330-3455 *Toll Free Fax:* 800-421-0239 (perms & copyrights) *E-mail:* customerservice@augsburgfortress.org; copyright@augsburgfortress.org (for reprint permission requests) *Web Site:* www.augsburgfortress.org, pg 28

Chromy, Adam, Artists & Artisans Inc, 45 W 21 St, 3rd fl, New York, NY 10010 *Tel:* 212-924-9619 *Fax:* 212-242-1114 *Web Site:* www.artistsandartisans.com, pg 619

Chu, Lily, Captus Press Inc, 1600 Steeles Ave W, Units 14-15, Concord, ON L4K 4M2, Canada *Tel:* 416-736-5537 *Fax:* 416-736-5793 *E-mail:* info@captus.com *Web Site:* www.captus.com, pg 539

Chu, Lynn, Writers' Representatives LLC, 116 W 14 St, 11th fl, New York, NY 10011-7305 *Tel:* 212-620-9009 *Fax:* 212-620-0023 *E-mail:* transom@writersreps.com *Web Site:* www.writersreps.com, pg 662

Chubet, Caroline T, Jones Hutton Literary Associates, 160 N Compo Rd, Westport, CT 06880 *Tel:* 203-226-2588 *Fax:* 509-356-5190 *Web Site:* www.marquiswhoswho.net/huttonandhutton, pg 636

Chudney, Steven, Marshall Cavendish Corp, 99 White Plains Rd, Tarrytown, NY 10591-9001 *Tel:* 914-332-8888 *Fax:* 914-332-1888 *E-mail:* mcc@marshallcavendish.com *Web Site:* www.marshallcavendish.com, pg 164

Chun, Fay Ann, Hawaii Award for Literature, 250 S Hotel St, 2nd fl, Honolulu, HI 96813 *Tel:* 808-586-0769 *Fax:* 808-586-0308 *E-mail:* sfca@sfca.state.hi.us *Web Site:* www.hawaii.gov/sfca, pg 778

Chun, Stephanie, University of Hawaii Press, 2840 Kolowalu St, Honolulu, HI 96822 *Tel:* 808-956-8255 *Toll Free Tel:* 888-847-7377 *Fax:* 808-988-6052 *Toll Free Fax:* 800-650-7811 *E-mail:* uhpbooks@hawaii.edu *Web Site:* www.uhpress.hawaii.edu, pg 281

Chun, Susan E, The Metropolitan Museum of Art, 1000 Fifth Ave, New York, NY 10028 *Tel:* 212-879-5500; 212-535-7710 *Fax:* 212-396-5062 *E-mail:* info@metmuseum.org *Web Site:* www.metmuseum.org, pg 173

Church, Barbara J, Ashgate Publishing Co, 101 Cherry St, Suite 420, Burlington, VT 05401-4405 *Tel:* 802-865-7641 *Fax:* 802-865-7847 *E-mail:* info@ashgate.com *Web Site:* www.ashgate.com, pg 25

Church, Dawson, Elite Books, 10 Hop Ranch Ct, Santa Rosa, CA 95407 *Tel:* 707-525-9292 *Fax:* 360-362-3634 *Web Site:* elitebooks.org, pg 89

Churko, Helen, Royce Carlton Inc, 866 United Nations Plaza, Suite 587, New York, NY 10017-1880 *Tel:* 212-355-7700 *Toll Free Tel:* 800-LECTURE (532-8873) *Fax:* 212-888-8659 *E-mail:* info@roycecarlton.com *Web Site:* www.roycecarlton.com, pg 670

Chutick, Mark, CCC Publications LLC, 9725 Lurline Ave, Chatsworth, CA 91311 *Tel:* 818-718-0507 *Toll Free Tel:* 800-248-LAFF (248-5233) *Fax:* 818-718-0655 *Web Site:* www.whyleavethehouse.com, pg 55

Ciccarelli, Louise A, NCCLS, 940 W Valley Rd, Suite 1400, Wayne, PA 19087-1898 *Tel:* 610-688-0100 *Fax:* 610-688-0700 *E-mail:* exoffice@nccls.org *Web Site:* www.nccls.org, pg 185

Cichy, Walt, Nystrom, 3333 Elston Ave, Chicago, IL 60618 *Tel:* 773-463-1144 *Toll Free Tel:* 800-621-8086 *Fax:* 773-463-0515 *E-mail:* info@nystromnet.com *Web Site:* www.nystromnet.com, pg 194

Ciecierski, Ande, Routledge, 29 W 35 St, New York, NY 10001-2299 *Tel:* 212-216-7800 *Fax:* 212-564-7854 (main) *E-mail:* info@taylorandfrancis.com *Web Site:* www.routledge-ny.com, pg 235

Ciecierski, Andrea, Brunner-Routledge, 270 Madison Ave, New York, NY 10016 *Tel:* 212-216-7800 *Toll Free Tel:* 800-634-7064 (orders); 800-797-3803 *Fax:* 212-643-1430, pg 49

Ciero, Louise, Oceana Publications Inc, 75 Main St, Dobbs Ferry, NY 10522-1601 *Tel:* 914-693-8100 *Toll Free Tel:* 800-831-0758 (orders only) *Fax:* 914-693-0402 *E-mail:* info@oceanalaw.com *Web Site:* www.oceanalaw.com, pg 195

Cifelli, Laura, NAL, 375 Hudson St, New York, NY 10014 *Tel:* 212-366-2000 *E-mail:* online@penguinputnam.com *Web Site:* www.penguin.com, pg 181

Cihlar, James, Redleaf Press, 10 Yorkton Ct, St Paul, MN 55117 *Tel:* 651-641-0305 *Toll Free Tel:* 800-423-8309 *Toll Free Fax:* 800-641-0115 *Web Site:* www.redleafpress.org, pg 230

Cilella, Salvatore G Jr, Indiana Historical Society Press, 450 W Ohio St, Indianapolis, IN 46202-3269 *Tel:* 317-233-9557 (sales); 317-234-2716 (editorial) *Toll Free Tel:* 800-447-1830 (orders only) *Fax:* 317-234-0562 (sales); 317-233-0857 (editorial) *E-mail:* ihspress@indianahistory.org; orders@indianahistory.org (orders) *Web Site:* www.indianahistory.org; shop.indianahistory.org (orders), pg 132

Cimino, Antoinette, Springer-Verlag New York Inc, 175 Fifth Ave, New York, NY 10010 *Tel:* 212-460-1500 *Toll Free Tel:* 800-777-4643 *Fax:* 212-473-6272 *Web Site:* www.springer-ny.com, pg 256

Cimino, Valerie, The Harvard Common Press, 535 Albany St, Boston, MA 02118 *Tel:* 617-423-5803 *Toll Free Tel:* 888-657-3755 *Fax:* 617-695-9794 *E-mail:* orders@harvardcommonpress.com *Web Site:* www.harvardcommonpress.com, pg 117

Cinque, Elaine, Princeton Book Co Publishers, PO Box 831, Hightstown, NJ 08520-0831 *Tel:* 609-426-0602 *Toll Free Tel:* 800-220-7149 *Fax:* 609-426-1344 *E-mail:* pbc@dancehorizons.com; elysian@aosi.com *Web Site:* www.dancehorizons.com, pg 218

Cioffe, Rosanne, Hospital & Healthcare Compensation Service, PO Box 376, Oakland, NJ 07436 *Tel:* 201-405-0075 *Fax:* 201-405-2110 *E-mail:* allinfo@hhcsinc.com *Web Site:* www.hhcsinc.com, pg 126

Ciommo, Dave, Educators Publishing Service Inc, 625 Mount Auburn St, Cambridge, MA 02139-9031 *Tel:* 617-547-6706 *Toll Free Tel:* 800-225-5750 *Fax:* 617-547-0412 *Toll Free Fax:* 888-440-2665 *E-mail:* epsbooks@epsbooks.com *Web Site:* www.epsbooks.com, pg 88

Ciotola, Andrew, Bucknell Seminar for Younger Poets, Bucknell University, Lewisburg, PA 17837 *Tel:* 570-577-1853 *Fax:* 570-577-3760 *E-mail:* stadlercenter@bucknell.edu *Web Site:* bucknell.edu/stadlercenter, pg 764

Cirillo, Andrea, Jane Rotrosen Agency LLC, 318 E 51 St, New York, NY 10022 *Tel:* 212-593-4330 *Fax:* 212-935-6985, pg 653

Cirkus, Jessika, The Sugarman Family Award for Jewish Children's Literature, 1529 16 St NW, Washington, DC 20036 *Tel:* 202-518-9400 *Fax:* 202-518-9420, pg 807

Cirone, Paul, The Aaron M Priest Literary Agency Inc, 708 Third Ave, 23rd fl, New York, NY 10017 *Tel:* 212-818-0344 *Fax:* 212-573-9417, pg 649

Citron, Christiane H, Colorado Book Awards, 2123 Downing St, Denver, CO 80205 *Tel:* 303-839-8320 *Fax:* 303-839-8319 *Web Site:* www.coloradobook.org, pg 768

Claassen, Dick, Awe-Struck E-Books Inc, 2458 Cherry St, Dubuque, IA 52001-5749 *E-mail:* editor@awe-struckebooks.net; tech@awestruckebooks.net *Web Site:* www.awe-struck.net (ordering), pg 30

Clague, Sue, Council for American Indian Education, 1240 Burlington Ave, Billings, MT 59102-4224 *Tel:* 406-248-3465 (PM); 406-652-7598 (AM) *Fax:* 406-248-1297 *E-mail:* cie@cie-mt.org *Web Site:* www.cie-mt.org, pg 70

Clapp, Sharon, John Deere Publishing, 5440 Corporate Park Dr, Davenport, IA 52807 *Toll Free Tel:* 800-522-7448 *Fax:* 563-355-3690 *E-mail:* johndeerepublishing@johndeere.com *Web Site:* www.deere.com, pg 141

Clapp, Steve, LifeQuest, 6404 S Calhoun St, Fort Wayne, IN 46807 *Toll Free Tel:* 800-774-3360 *E-mail:* dadoftia@aol.com, pg 154

Clark, Curtis L, University of South Carolina Press, 1600 Hampton St, 5th fl, Columbia, SC 29208 *Tel:* 803-777-5243 *Toll Free Tel:* 800-768-2500 (orders) *Fax:* 803-777-0160 *Toll Free Fax:* 800-868-0740 (orders) *Web Site:* www.sc.edu/uscpress/, pg 285

Clark, Denise, University of Washington Press, 1326 Fifth Ave, Suite 555, Seattle, WA 98101-2604 *Tel:* 206-543-4050; 206-543-8870 *Toll Free Tel:* 800-441-4115 (orders) *Fax:* 206-543-3932 *Toll Free Fax:* 800-669-7993 (orders) *E-mail:* uwpord@u.washington.edu *Web Site:* www.washington.edu/uwpress/, pg 286

Clark, Gary, Vermont Studio Center, PO Box 613, Johnson, VT 05656 *Tel:* 802-635-2727 *Fax:* 802-635-2730 *E-mail:* info@vermontstudiocenter.org *Web Site:* www.vermontstudiocenter.org, pg 748

Clark, Gary, Vermont Studio Center Writer's Fellowships, PO Box 613, Johnson, VT 05656 *Tel:* 802-635-2727 *Fax:* 802-635-2730 *E-mail:* writing@vermontstudiocenter.org; info@vermontstudiocenter.org *Web Site:* www.vermontstudiocenter.org, pg 810

Clark, Ginger, Writers House LLC, 21 W 26 St, New York, NY 10010 *Tel:* 212-685-2400 *Fax:* 212-685-1781, pg 662

Clark, I E, I E Clark Publications, PO Box 246, Schulenburg, TX 78956 *Tel:* 979-743-3232 *Fax:* 979-743-4765 *E-mail:* ieclark@cvtv.net *Web Site:* www.ieclark.com, pg 63

Clark, Ja'Lene, Wildcat Canyon Press, 2105 E 15 St, Suite B, Tulsa, OK 74104 *Toll Free Tel:* 800-247-8850 *E-mail:* order@counciloakbooks.com, pg 299

Clark, Ja-lene, Council Oak Books LLC, 2105 E 15 St, Suite B, Tulsa, OK 74104 *Tel:* 918-743-BOOK (743-2665) *Toll Free Tel:* 800-247-8850 *Fax:* 918-743-4288 *E-mail:* publicity@counciloakbooks.com; orders@counciloakbooks.com *Web Site:* www.counciloakbooks.com, pg 70

Clark, James, Thomas Wolfe Student Prize, 809 Gardner St, Raleigh, NC 27607 *Tel:* 919-834-6983 *Fax:* 919-515-7856 *Web Site:* www.thomaswolfe.org, pg 812

Clark, James C, Penguin Group (USA) Inc, 375 Hudson St, New York, NY 10014 *Tel:* 212-366-2000 *Fax:* 212-366-2666 *E-mail:* online@uspenguingroup.com *Web Site:* www.penguin.com, pg 208

Clark, Janice, American Mathematical Society, 201 Charles St, Providence, RI 02904-2294 *Tel:* 401-455-4000 *Toll Free Tel:* 800-321-4267 *Fax:* 401-331-3842; 401-455-4046 (cust serv) *E-mail:* ams@ams.org *Web Site:* www.ams.org, pg 16

Clark, Jim, The Greensboro Review Literary Award in Fiction & Poetry, University North Carolina at Greensboro, English Dept, McIver Bldg, Rm 134, Greensboro, NC 27402-6170 *Tel:* 336-334-5459 *Web Site:* www.uncg.edu/eng/mfa, pg 777

Clark, June, Peter Rubie Literary Agency, 240 W 35 St, Suite 500, New York, NY 10001 *Tel:* 212-279-1776 *Fax:* 212-279-0927 *E-mail:* pralit@aol.com *Web Site:* www.prlit.com, pg 653

Clark, Kate, Donald M Grant Publisher Inc, PO Box 187, Hampton Falls, NH 03844-0187 *Tel:* 603-778-7191 *Fax:* 603-778-7191 *E-mail:* grantbooks@aol.com *Web Site:* www.grantbooks.com, pg 107

Clark, Ken, One Planet Publishing House, PO Box 19840, Seattle, WA 98109-1840 *Tel:* 206-282-9699 *Toll Free Tel:* 877-526-3814 (87-PLANET-14) *Fax:* 206-282-9699 *Toll Free Fax:* 877-526-3814 (87-PLANET-14) *E-mail:* info@oneplanetpublishinghouse.com *Web Site:* www.oneplanetpublishinghouse.com, pg 197

Clark, Kevin, American Public Works Association, 2345 Grand Ave, Suite 500, Kansas City, MO 64108-2641 *Tel:* 816-472-6100 *Fax:* 816-472-1610 *E-mail:* apwa@apwa.net *Web Site:* www.apwa.net, pg 17

Clark, Larry, Comprehensive Health Education Foundation (CHEF), 22419 Pacific Hwy S, Seattle, WA 98198-5104 *Tel:* 206-824-2907 *Toll Free Tel:* 800-323-2433 *Fax:* 206-824-3072 *E-mail:* info@chef.org *Web Site:* www.chef.org, pg 66

Clark, Lila N, I E Clark Publications, PO Box 246, Schulenburg, TX 78956 *Tel:* 979-743-3232 *Fax:* 979-743-4765 *E-mail:* ieclark@cvtv.net *Web Site:* www.ieclark.com, pg 63

Clark, Margaret, Pocket Books, 1230 Avenue of the Americas, New York, NY 10020 *Toll Free Tel:* 800-456-6798 *Fax:* 212-698-7284 *E-mail:* consumer.customerservice@simonandschuster.com *Web Site:* www.simonsays.com, pg 215

Clark, Raymond C, Pro Lingua Associates Inc, 74 Cotton Mill Hill, Suite A-315, Brattleboro, VT 05301 *Tel:* 802-257-7779 *Toll Free Tel:* 800-366-4775 *Fax:* 802-257-5117 *E-mail:* orders@prolinguaassociates.com *Web Site:* www.prolinguaassociates.com, pg 219

Clark, Sandra, Kent State University Press, PO Box 5190, Kent, OH 44242-0001 *Tel:* 330-672-7913; 330-672-8097 (sales office) *Toll Free Tel:* 800-247-6553 (orders) *Fax:* 330-672-3104 *Web Site:* www.kentstateuniversitypress.com, pg 145

Clark, Sarah F, Yale University Press, 302 Temple St, New Haven, CT 06511 *Tel:* 203-432-0960; 401-531-2800 (cust serv) *Toll Free Tel:* 800-405-1619 (cust serv) *Fax:* 203-432-0948; 401-531-2801 (cust serv) *Toll Free Fax:* 800-406-9145 (cust serv) *E-mail:* customer.care@trilateral.org (cust serv) *Web Site:* www.yale.edu/yup/, pg 305

Clark, Stephen, Pathfinder Press, 4794 Clark Howell Hwy, College Park, GA 30349 *Tel:* 404-669-0600 (voice mail only) *Fax:* 707-667-1141 *E-mail:* pathfinder@pathfinderpress.com (edit); orders@pathfinderpress.com; permissions@pathfinderpress.com (permissions & copyright) *Web Site:* www.pathfinderpress.com, pg 205

Clark, William, Wm Clark Associates, 355 W 22 St, 4th fl, New York, NY 10011 *Tel:* 212-675-2784 *Toll Free Tel:* 866-828-4252 *E-mail:* query@wmclark.com *Web Site:* www.wmclark.com, pg 625

Clarke, Chandra, Scribendi Inc, 153 Harvey St, Chatham, ON N7M 1M6, Canada *Fax:* 519-354-0192 *E-mail:* customerservice@scribendi.com *Web Site:* www.scribendi.com, pg 611

Clarke, Harold, Reader's Digest Children's Books, Reader's Digest Rd, Pleasantville, NY 10570-7000 *Tel:* 914-244-4800 *Toll Free Tel:* 800-934-0977, pg 228

Clarke, Harold, Reader's Digest Trade Books, Reader's Digest Rd, Pleasantville, NY 10570-7000 *Tel:* 914-244-7445 *Fax:* 914-244-7605, pg 229

Clarke, Mia Barkan, Cross-Cultural Communications, 239 Wynsum Ave, Merrick, NY 11566-4725 *Tel:* 516-868-5635 *Fax:* 516-379-1901 *E-mail:* cccpoetry@aol.com *Web Site:* www.cross-culturalcommunications.com, pg 73

Clarry, Dale, Carswell, One Corporate Plaza, 2075 Kennedy Rd, Toronto, ON M1T 3V4, Canada *Tel:* 416-609-8000 *Toll Free Tel:* 800-387-5164 (Canada & US) *Fax:* 416-298-5094 (Toronto); 403-233-8159 (Calgary); 604-685-5343 (Vancouver); 514-985-6605 *Toll Free Fax:* 877-750-9041 *E-mail:* comments@carswell.com *Web Site:* www.carswell.com, pg 539

Classic, Lesley, Database Directories, 588 Dufferin Ave, London, ON N6B 2A4, Canada *Tel:* 519-433-1666 *Fax:* 519-430-1131 *E-mail:* info@databasedirectory.com; lclassic@databasedirectory.com *Web Site:* www.databasedirectory.com, pg 542

Clay, Michele, Barbour Publishing Inc, 1810 Barbour Dr, Uhrichsville, OH 44683 *Tel:* 740-922-6045 *Fax:* 740-922-5948 *E-mail:* info@barbourbooks.com *Web Site:* www.barbourbooks.com, pg 32

Clayton, Douglas, Harvard Education Publishing Group, 8 Story St, 1st fl, Cambridge, MA 02138 *Tel:* 617-495-3432 *Toll Free Tel:* 800-513-0763 *Fax:* 617-496-3584 *E-mail:* hepg@harvard.edu *Web Site:* gseweb.harvard.edu/hepg, pg 117

Cleary, David, Lone Pine Publishing, 10145 81 Ave, Edmonton, AB T6E 1W9, Canada *Tel:* 780-433-9333 *Toll Free Tel:* 800-661-9017 *Fax:* 780-433-9646 *Toll Free Fax:* 800-424-7173 *E-mail:* info@lonepinepublishing.com *Web Site:* www.lonepinepublishing.com, pg 553

Cleary, Donald, Jane Rotrosen Agency LLC, 318 E 51 St, New York, NY 10022 *Tel:* 212-593-4330 *Fax:* 212-935-6985, pg 653

Cleary, Patricia, Humana Press, 999 Riverview Dr, Suite 208, Totowa, NJ 07512 *Tel:* 973-256-1699 *Fax:* 973-256-8341 *E-mail:* humana@humanapr.com *Web Site:* humanapress.com, pg 128

Cleary, Patti, F A Davis Co, 1915 Arch St, Philadelphia, PA 19103 *Tel:* 215-568-2270 *Toll Free Tel:* 800-523-4049 *Fax:* 215-568-5065 *E-mail:* info@fadavis.com *Web Site:* www.fadavis.com, pg 76

Cleary, Rita, SPUR Awards, 1012 Fair St, Franklin, TN 37064 *Tel:* 615-791-1444 *Fax:* 615-791-1444 *Web Site:* www.westernwriters.org, pg 807

Cleary, Rita, Western Writers of America Inc, 1012 Fair St, Franklin, TN 37064 *Tel:* 615-791-1444 *Fax:* 615-791-1444 *Web Site:* www.westernwriters.org, pg 702

Clemens, Paul M, Blue Dolphin Publishing Inc, 12428 Nevada City Hwy, Grass Valley, CA 95945 *Tel:* 530-265-6925 *Toll Free Tel:* 800-643-0765 *Fax:* 530-265-0787 *E-mail:* bdolphin@netshel.net *Web Site:* www.bluedolphinpublishing.com, pg 41

Clement, Yolande, Centre Franco-Ontarien de Ressources en Alphabetisation, 432 Ave Westmount, Unit H, Sudbury, ON P3A 5Z8, Canada *Tel:* 705-524-3672 *Toll Free Tel:* 888-814-4422 (orders, Canada only) *Fax:* 705-524-8535 *E-mail:* info@centrefora.on.ca *Web Site:* www.centrefora.on.ca, pg 540

Clements, Pamela, Rutledge Hill Press, c/o Thomas Nelson Publishers, PO Box 141000, Nashville, TN 37214-1000 *Tel:* 615-902-2703 *Toll Free Tel:* 800-251-4000 (ext 2703) *Fax:* 615-902-2340 *Web Site:* www.rutledgehillpress.com, pg 236

Clements, Rob, Clements Publishing, 6021 Younge St, Suite 213, Toronto, ON M2M 3W2, Canada *Tel:* 416-558-9439 *Fax:* 416-352-5997 *E-mail:* info@clementspublishing.com *Web Site:* www.clementspublishing.com, pg 540

Clemmensen, Chris, Solucient, 10007 Church St, Suite 700, Evanston, IL 60201 *Tel:* 847-424-4400 *Toll Free Tel:* 800-366-7526 *Fax:* 847-332-1768 *E-mail:* pubs@solucient.com *Web Site:* www.solucient.com, pg 252

Clerkin, Kristine, Houghton Mifflin College Division, 222 Berkeley St, Boston, MA 02116-3764 *Tel:* 617-351-5000 *Toll Free Tel:* 800-225-1464 (orders) *Web Site:* www.college.hmco.com, pg 126

Clerkin, Tom, The MIT Press, 5 Cambridge Ctr, Cambridge, MA 02142 *Tel:* 617-253-5646 *Toll Free Tel:* 800-405-1619 (orders only) *Fax:* 617-258-6779 *Web Site:* mitpress.mit.edu, pg 175

Cleroux, Normand, Editions du renouveau Pedagogique Inc, 5757 rue Cypihot, St-Laurent, PQ H4S 1R3, Canada *Tel:* 514-334-2690 *Toll Free Tel:* 800-263-3678 *Fax:* 514-334-4720 *Toll Free Fax:* 800-643-4720 *E-mail:* erpidlm@erpi.com *Web Site:* www.erpi.com, pg 544

Clever, Glenn, Borealis Press Ltd, 110 Bloomingdale St, Ottawa, ON K2C 4A4, Canada *Tel:* 613-798-9299 *Fax:* 613-798-9747 *E-mail:* borealis@istar.ca *Web Site:* www.borealispress.com, pg 537

Cline, Susan, Nelson, 1120 Birchmount Rd, Scarborough, ON M1K 5G4, Canada *Tel:* 416-752-9448 *Toll Free Tel:* 800-268-2222 (cust serv); 800-430-4445 *Fax:* 416-752-8101 *E-mail:* inquire@nelson.com *Web Site:* www.nelson.com, pg 555

Clingham, Greg, Bucknell University Press, c/o Associated University Presses, 2010 Eastpark Blvd, Cranbury, NJ 08512 *Tel:* 609-655-4770 *Fax:* 609-655-8366 *E-mail:* aup440@aol.com, pg 49

Clockel, William, Educator's International Press, 18 Colleen Rd, Troy, NY 12180 *Tel:* 518-271-9886 *Fax:* 518-266-9422 *Web Site:* www.edint.com, pg 88

Cloquette, Claude, Health Communications Inc, 3201 SW 15 St, Deerfield Beach, FL 33442-8190 *Tel:* 954-360-0909 *Toll Free Tel:* 800-851-9100 (cust serv); 800-441-5569 (order entry) *Fax:* 954-360-0034 *Web Site:* www.hcibooks.com, pg 119

Close, Ann, Alfred A Knopf, 1745 Broadway, New York, NY 10019 *Tel:* 212-751-2600 *Toll Free Tel:* 800-638-6460 *Fax:* 212-572-2593 *Web Site:* www.randomhouse.com/knopf, pg 146

Closson, Marietta, Closson Press, 1935 Sampson Dr, Apollo, PA 15613-9208 *Tel:* 724-337-4482 *Fax:* 724-337-9484 *E-mail:* clossonpress@comcast.net *Web Site:* www.clossonpress.com, pg 63

Closson-Buck, Paula, Bucknell Seminar for Younger Poets, Bucknell University, Lewisburg, PA 17837 *Tel:* 570-577-1853 *Fax:* 570-577-3760 *E-mail:* stadlercenter@bucknell.edu *Web Site:* bucknell.edu/stadlercenter, pg 764

Cloud, Sanford Jr, The National Conference for Community & Justice, 475 Park Ave S, New York City, NY 10016 *Tel:* 212-545-1300 *Fax:* 212-545-8053 *Web Site:* www.nccj.org, pg 693

Clymer, Katie, Milkweed Editions, 1011 Washington Ave S, Suite 300, Minneapolis, MN 55415 *Tel:* 612-332-3192 *Toll Free Tel:* 800-520-6455 *Fax:* 612-215-2550 *E-mail:* editor@milkweed.org *Web Site:* www.milkweed.org; www.worldashome.org, pg 174

Cmich, Jennifer, Playhouse Publishing, 1566 Akron-Peninsula Rd, Akron, OH 44313 *Tel:* 330-926-1313 *Toll Free Tel:* 800-762-6775 *Fax:* 330-926-1315 *E-mail:* info@playhousepublishing.com *Web Site:* www.playhousepublishing.com, pg 214

Coady, Frances, Picador, 175 Fifth Ave, New York, NY 10010 *Tel:* 212-674-5151 *Fax:* 212-253-9627 *E-mail:* firstname.lastname@picadorusa.com *Web Site:* www.picadorusa.com, pg 212

Coakley, Dan, Abrams & Co Publishers Inc, 61 Mattatuck Heights Rd, Waterbury, CT 06705 *Tel:* 203-756-6562 *Toll Free Tel:* 800-227-9120 *Fax:* 203-756-2895 *Toll Free Fax:* 800-737-3322, pg 3

Coakley, Daniel, Graphic Learning, 61 Mattatuck Heights Rd, Waterbury, CT 06705 *Tel:* 203-756-6562 *Toll Free Tel:* 800-874-0029; 800-227-9120 *Fax:* 203-756-2895 *Toll Free Fax:* 800-737-3322, pg 108

Coakley, Daniel, The Letter People®, 61 Mattatuck Heights Rd, Waterbury, CT 06705 *Tel:* 203-756-6562 *Toll Free Tel:* 800-227-9120; 800-874-0029 *Fax:* 203-756-2895 *Toll Free Fax:* 800-737-3322 *Web Site:* letterpeople.com, pg 153

Coalson, Lance, Father & Son Publishing, 4909 N Monroe St, Tallahassee, FL 32303 *Tel:* 850-562-3927 *Toll Free Tel:* 800-741-2712 (orders only) *Fax:* 850-562-0916 *Web Site:* www.fatherson.com, pg 95

Coates, Dr Lawrence, Bowling Green State University, Creative Writing Program, 226 East Hall, Bowling Green, OH 43403 *Tel:* 419-372-8370 *Fax:* 419-372-6805 *E-mail:* mmcgowa@bgnet.bgsu.edu *Web Site:* www.bgsu.edu/departments/creative-writing, pg 751

Coates, W Paul, Black Classic Press, PO Box 13414, Baltimore, MD 21203 *Tel:* 410-358-0980 *Fax:* 410-358-0987 *E-mail:* bcp@charm.net *Web Site:* www.blackclassic.com, pg 39

Cobb, Jonathan, Island Press, 1718 Connecticut Ave NW, Suite 300, Washington, DC 20009 *Tel:* 202-232-7933 *Toll Free Tel:* 800-828-1302 *Fax:* 202-234-1328; 707-983-6414 (orders only) *E-mail:* info@islandpress.org *Web Site:* www.islandpress.org, pg 139

Cobb, Steve, WaterBrook Press, 2375 Telstar Dr, Suite 160, Colorado Springs, CO 80920 *Tel:* 719-590-4999 *Toll Free Tel:* 800-603-7051 (orders) *Fax:* 719-590-8977 *Toll Free Fax:* 800-294-5686 (orders) *Web Site:* www.waterbrookpress.com, pg 294

Coburn, Lora, Platinum One Publishing, 21W551 North Ave, Suite 132, Lombard, IL 60148 *Tel:* 630-935-7323 *Fax:* 203-651-1825 *E-mail:* customerservice@platinumonepublishing.com *Web Site:* www.platinumonepublishing.com, pg 573

Cochran, Wendy, Harcourt Canada Ltd, 55 Horner Ave, Toronto, ON M8Z 4X6, Canada *Tel:* 416-255-4491; 416-255-0177 (Voice Mail) *Toll Free Tel:* 800-387-7278 (North America); 800-387-7305 (North America) *Fax:* 416-255-6708 *Toll Free Fax:* 800-665-7307 (North America) *E-mail:* firstname_lastname@harcourt.com *Web Site:* www.harcourtcanada.com, pg 549

Cochran, Wendy, Harcourt School Publishers, 6277 Sea Harbor Dr, Orlando, FL 32887 *Tel:* 407-345-2000 *Toll Free Tel:* 800-225-5425 (cust serv) *Fax:* 407-352-3445 *Toll Free Fax:* 800-874-6418 *E-mail:* hbspcs@hbschool.com *Web Site:* www.harcourtschool.com, pg 114

Cochrane, Hank, Penguin Group (USA) Inc Sales, 375 Hudson St, New York, NY 10014 *Tel:* 212-366-2000 *E-mail:* online@penguinputnam.com *Web Site:* www.penguin.com, pg 208

Cochrane, Marnie, Da Capo Press Inc, 11 Cambridge Center, Cambridge, MA 02142 *Tel:* 617-252-5200 *Toll Free Tel:* 800-242-7737 (orders) *Fax:* 617-252-5285 *E-mail:* custserve@lrp.com *Web Site:* www.dacapopress.com, pg 75

Cochrane, Ruth B, SRA/McGraw-Hill, a Division of McGraw-Hill Learning Group, 8787 Orion Place, Columbus, OH 43240 *Tel:* 614-430-4000 *Fax:* 614-430-6621 *E-mail:* sra@mcgraw-hill.com *Web Site:* www.sra-4kids.com, pg 256

Cochrell, Christie, Stanford University Press, 1450 Page Mill Rd, Palo Alto, CA 94304-1124 *Tel:* 650-723-9434 *Fax:* 650-725-3457 *Web Site:* www.sup.org, pg 257

Coe, Karen, United States Holocaust Memorial Museum, 100 Raoul Wallenberg Place SW, Washington, DC 20024-2126 *Tel:* 202-488-6115; 202-488-6144 (orders) *Toll Free Tel:* 800-259-9998 (orders) *Fax:* 202-488-2684; 202-488-0438 (orders) *Web Site:* www.ushmm.org/, pg 279

Coe, Pennie, Oregon State University Press, 102 Adams Hall, Corvallis, OR 97331 *Tel:* 541-737-3166 *Toll Free Tel:* 800-426-3797 (orders) *Fax:* 541-737-3170 *Toll Free Fax:* 800-426-3797 (orders) *E-mail:* osu.press@oregonstate.edu *Web Site:* oregonstate.edu/dept/press, pg 199

Coe, Richard, Time Warner Book Group, 1271 Avenue of the Americas, New York, NY 10020 *Tel:* 212-522-7200 *Fax:* 212-522-7991 *Web Site:* www.twbookmark.com, pg 271

Coelho, Lu Ann, American Institute of Ultrasound in Medicine, 14750 Sweitzer Lane, Suite 100, Laurel, MD 20707-5906 *Tel:* 301-498-4100

Toll Free Tel: 800-638-5352 *Fax:* 301-498-4450 *E-mail:* publications@aium.org *Web Site:* www.aium.org, pg 15

Coffee, Margaret, Scholastic Trade Division, 557 Broadway, New York, NY 10012 *Tel:* 212-343-6100; 212-343-4685 (export sales) *Fax:* 212-343-4714 (export sales) *Web Site:* www.scholastic.com, pg 242

Coffey, Jessica, Oxford University Press Canada, 70 Wynford Dr, Don Mills, ON M3C 1J9, Canada *Tel:* 416-441-2941 *Toll Free Tel:* 800-387-8020 *Fax:* 416-444-0427 *Toll Free Fax:* 800-665-1771 *E-mail:* custserv@oupcan.com *Web Site:* www.oup.com/ca, pg 557

Coffey, Michele, Princeton Book Co Publishers, PO Box 831, Hightstown, NJ 08520-0831 *Tel:* 609-426-0602 *Toll Free Tel:* 800-220-7149 *Fax:* 609-426-1344 *E-mail:* pbc@dancehorizons.com; elysian@aosi.com *Web Site:* www.dancehorizons.com, pg 218

Coffey, Thomas P, Dimension Books Inc, PO Box 9, Starrucca, PA 18462 *Tel:* 570-727-2486 *Fax:* 570-727-2813, pg 80

Coffin, Andy, Waterloo Music Co Ltd, 3 Regina St N, Waterloo, ON N2J 4A5, Canada *Tel:* 519-886-4990 *Toll Free Tel:* 800-563-9683 (Canada & US) *Fax:* 519-886-4999 *E-mail:* info@waterloomusic.com *Web Site:* www.waterloomusic.com, pg 566

Coffin, Christina, Yale University Press, 302 Temple St, New Haven, CT 06511 *Tel:* 203-432-0960; 401-531-2800 (cust serv) *Toll Free Tel:* 800-405-1619 (cust serv) *Fax:* 203-432-0948; 401-531-2801 (cust serv) *Toll Free Fax:* 800-406-9145 (cust serv) *E-mail:* customer.care@trilateral.org (cust serv) *Web Site:* www.yale.edu/yup/, pg 305

Cogan Akmon, Nancy, Blushing Rose Publishing, 29 Katrina Rd, San Anselmo, CA 94960 *Tel:* 415-458-2090 *Toll Free Tel:* 800-898-2263 *Fax:* 415-458-2091 *E-mail:* info@blushingrose.com *Web Site:* www.blushingrose.com, pg 42

Coghlin, Marlene, Christian Booksellers Association of Canada, 155 Suffolk St W, Suite 15, Guelph, ON N1H 2J7, Canada *Tel:* 519-766-1683 *Fax:* 519-763-8184 *E-mail:* info@cbacanada.com *Web Site:* www.cbacanada.com, pg 685

Cohan, Maya, Acrobat Books, PO Box 870, Venice, CA 90294-0870 *Tel:* 310-578-1055 *Fax:* 310-823-8447 *E-mail:* acrobooks@cs.com, pg 4

Cohan, Tony, Acrobat Books, PO Box 870, Venice, CA 90294-0870 *Tel:* 310-578-1055 *Fax:* 310-823-8447 *E-mail:* acrobooks@cs.com, pg 4

Cohen, Bill, The Haworth Press Inc, 10 Alice St, Binghamton, NY 13904-1580 *Tel:* 607-722-5857 *Toll Free Tel:* 800-429-6784 *Fax:* 607-722-1424 *Toll Free Fax:* 800-895-0582 *E-mail:* getinfo@haworthpressinc.com *Web Site:* www.haworthpress.com, pg 118

Cohen, Brett, Quirk Books, 215 Church St, Philadelphia, PA 19106 *Tel:* 215-627-3581 *Fax:* 215-627-5220 *E-mail:* general@quirkbooks.com *Web Site:* www.quirkbooks.com, pg 224

Cohen, Christine, Virginia Kidd Agency Inc, 538 E Harford St, Milford, PA 18337 *Tel:* 570-296-6205 *Fax:* 570-296-7266 *Web Site:* vkagency.com, pg 637

Cohen, Cindy, Lonely Planet Publications, 150 Linden St, Oakland, CA 94607 *Tel:* 510-893-8555 *Toll Free Tel:* 800-275-8555 (orders) *Fax:* 510-893-8972 *E-mail:* info@lonelyplanet.com *Web Site:* www.lonelyplanet.com, pg 157

Cohen, Craig, powerHouse Books, 68 Charlton St, New York, NY 10014-4601 *Tel:* 212-604-9074 *Fax:* 212-366-5247 *E-mail:* info@powerhousebooks.com *Web Site:* www.powerhousebooks.com, pg 216

Cohen, David, Scholastic Trade Division, 557 Broadway, New York, NY 10012 *Tel:* 212-343-6100; 212-343-4685 (export sales) *Fax:* 212-343-4714 (export sales) *Web Site:* www.scholastic.com, pg 242

Cohen, David R, Oceana Publications Inc, 75 Main St, Dobbs Ferry, NY 10522-1601 *Tel:* 914-693-8100 *Toll Free Tel:* 800-831-0758 (orders only) *Fax:* 914-693-0402 *E-mail:* info@oceanalaw.com *Web Site:* www.oceanalaw.com, pg 195

Cohen, Eugenia, Puddingstone Literary, Authors' Agents, 11 Mabro Dr, Denville, NJ 07834-9607 *Tel:* 973-366-3622, pg 650

Cohen, Fran, First Folio Resource Group Inc, 10 King St E, Suite 801, Toronto, ON M5C 1C3, Canada *Tel:* 416-368-7668 *Fax:* 416-368-9363 *E-mail:* mail@firstfolio.com *Web Site:* www.firstfolio.com, pg 599

Cohen, Herbert J, Bobley Harmann Corp, 311 Crossways Park Dr, Woodbury, NY 11797 *Tel:* 516-364-1800 *Fax:* 516-364-1899 *E-mail:* info@bobley.com *Web Site:* www.bobley.com, pg 43

Cohen, Herbert J, Platinum Press Inc, 311 Crossways Park Dr, Woodbury, NY 11797 *Tel:* 516-364-1800 *Fax:* 516-364-1899, pg 214

Cohen, Howard, Emmis Books, 1700 Madison Rd, 2nd fl, Cincinnati, OH 45206 *Tel:* 513-861-4045 *Toll Free Tel:* 800-913-9563 *Fax:* 513-861-4430 *E-mail:* info@emmis.com *Web Site:* www.emmisbooks.com, pg 90

Cohen, Jeff, Silver Pixel Press, 90 Oser Ave, Hauppauge, NY 11788 *Tel:* 631-645-2522 *Toll Free Tel:* 800-645-2522 *Fax:* 631-273-2557 *Web Site:* www.tiffen.com, pg 248

Cohen, Jill, Bulfinch Press, 1271 Avenue of the Americas, New York, NY 10020 *Tel:* 212-522-8700 *Toll Free Tel:* 800-759-0190 *Fax:* 212-467-2886 *Web Site:* www.twbookmark.com, pg 50

Cohen, Jonathan, Kensington Publishing Corp, 850 Third Ave, New York, NY 10022 *Tel:* 212-407-1500 *Toll Free Tel:* 800-221-2647 *Fax:* 212-935-0699 *Web Site:* www.kensingtonbooks.com, pg 145

Cohen, Judith, Cascade Pass Inc, 4223 Glencoe Ave, Suite C-105, Marina Del Rey, CA 90292 *Tel:* 310-305-0210 *Toll Free Tel:* 888-837-0704 *Fax:* 310-305-7850 *Web Site:* www.cascadepass.com, pg 54

Cohen, Katia Segre, Geolytics Inc, PO Box 10, East Brunswick, NJ 08816 *Tel:* 732-651-2000 *Toll Free Tel:* 800-577-6717 *Fax:* 732-651-2721 *E-mail:* support@geolytics.com *Web Site:* www.geolytics.com, pg 104

Cohen, Kelly, Optical Society of America, 2010 Massachusetts Ave NW, Washington, DC 20036-1023 *Tel:* 202-223-8130 *Fax:* 202-223-1096 *E-mail:* custserv@osa.org *Web Site:* www.osa.org, pg 198

Cohen, Linda, R D R Books, 2415 Woolsey St, Berkeley, CA 94705 *Tel:* 510-595-0595 *Fax:* 510-228-0300 *E-mail:* info@rdrbooks.com *Web Site:* www.rdrbooks.com, pg 224

Cohen, Linda P, American Institute of Certified Public Accountants, Harborside Financial Ctr, 201 Plaza Three, Jersey City, NJ 07311-3881 *Tel:* 201-938-3000 *Toll Free Tel:* 888-777-7077 *Fax:* 201-938-3329 *Web Site:* www.aicpa.org, pg 15

Cohen, Lois, Oceana Publications Inc, 75 Main St, Dobbs Ferry, NY 10522-1601 *Tel:* 914-693-8100 *Toll Free Tel:* 800-831-0758 (orders only) *Fax:* 914-693-0402 *E-mail:* info@oceanalaw.com *Web Site:* www.oceanalaw.com, pg 195

Cohen, Lord, Alan Wofsy Fine Arts, 1109 Geary Blvd, San Francisco, CA 94109 *Tel:* 415-292-6500 *Fax:* 415-512-0130 (acctg); 415-292-6594 (off & cust serv) *E-mail:* beauxarts@earthlink.net (cust serv); editeur@earthlink.net (edit); order@art-books.com (orders) *Web Site:* art-books.com, pg 302

Cohen, M, Players Press Inc, PO Box 1132, Studio City, CA 91614-0132 *Tel:* 818-789-4980, pg 214

Cohen, Marcia, Bedford/St Martin's, 75 Arlington St, Boston, MA 02116 *Tel:* 617-399-4000 *Fax:* 617-426-8582 *Web Site:* www.bedfordstmartins.com, pg 35

Cohen, Mark E, CDL Press, PO Box 34454, Bethesda, MD 20854 *Tel:* 301-762-2066 *Fax:* 253-484-5542 *E-mail:* cdlpress@erols.com, pg 56

Cohen, Morton, Sunburst Technology, 400 Columbus Ave, Suite 160E, Valhalla, NY 10595 *Tel:* 914-747-3310 *Toll Free Tel:* 800-338-3457 *Fax:* 914-747-4109 *Web Site:* www.sunburst.com, pg 262

Cohen, Philip, Mason Crest Publishers, 370 Reed Rd, Suite 302, Broomall, PA 19008 *Tel:* 610-543-6200 *Toll Free Tel:* 866-MCP-BOOK (627-2665) *Fax:* 610-543-3878 *Web Site:* www.masoncrest.com, pg 165

Cohen, Stan, Pictorial Histories Publishing Co, 521 Bickford St, Missoula, MT 59801 *Tel:* 406-549-8488 *Toll Free Tel:* 888-763-8350 *Fax:* 406-728-9280 *E-mail:* phpc@montana.com *Web Site:* www.pictorialhistoriespublishing.com, pg 212

Cohen, Steve, St Martin's Press LLC, 175 Fifth Ave, New York, NY 10010 *Tel:* 212-674-5151 *Fax:* 212-420-9314 *E-mail:* firstname.lastname@stmartins.com *Web Site:* www.stmartins.com, pg 238

Cohen, Stuart, Baywood Publishing Co Inc, 26 Austin Ave, Amityville, NY 11701 *Tel:* 631-691-1270 *Toll Free Tel:* 800-638-7819 *Fax:* 631-691-1770 *E-mail:* baywood@baywood.com *Web Site:* www.baywood.com, pg 33

Cohen, Susan, Writers House LLC, 21 W 26 St, New York, NY 10010 *Tel:* 212-685-2400 *Fax:* 212-685-1781, pg 662

Cohen, Susan Lee, Riverside Literary Agency, 41 Simon Keets Rd, Leyden, MA 01337 *Tel:* 413-772-0067 *Fax:* 413-772-0969 *E-mail:* rivlit@sover.net, pg 652

Cohen, Susan Perlman, Rosenstone/Wender, 38 E 29 St, 10th fl, New York, NY 10016 *Tel:* 212-725-9445 *Fax:* 212-725-9447, pg 652

Cohen, Susie, BOA Editions Ltd, 260 East Ave, Rochester, NY 14604 *Tel:* 585-546-3410 *Fax:* 585-546-3913 *Web Site:* www.boaeditions.org, pg 42

Cohen, Warren, Modern Publishing, 155 E 55 St, New York, NY 10022 *Tel:* 212-826-0850 *Fax:* 212-759-9069 *Web Site:* www.modernpublishing.com, pg 176

Cohl, Claudia H, Scholastic Inc, 557 Broadway, New York, NY 10012 *Tel:* 212-343-4469 *Toll Free Tel:* 800-scholastic *Fax:* 212-343-6930 *Web Site:* www.scholastic.com, pg 242

Cohn, Richard E, Beyond Words Publishing Inc, 20827 NW Cornell Rd, Suite 500, Hillsboro, OR 97124-9808 *Tel:* 503-531-8700 *Fax:* 503-531-8773 *Web Site:* www.beyondword.com, pg 38

Cohn, Stephen, Duke University Press, 905 W Main St, Suite 18-B, Durham, NC 27701 *Tel:* 919-687-3600 *Toll Free Tel:* 888-651-0122 (orders only) *Fax:* 919-688-4574 *Toll Free Fax:* 888-651-0124 *Web Site:* www.dukepress.edu, pg 84

Cohn, Stuart G, Scott Foresman, 1900 E Lake Ave, Glenview, IL 60025 *Tel:* 847-729-3000 *Toll Free Tel:* 800-535-4391 (Midwest) *Fax:* 847-729-8910 *E-mail:* firstname.lastname@scottforesman.com *Web Site:* www.scottforesman.com, pg 243

Coker, Deborah, The Connor Literary Agency, 2911 W 71 St, Minneapolis, MN 55423 *Tel:* 612-866-1486 *Fax:* 612-866-1486 *E-mail:* coolmkc@aol.com, pg 625

Colbeck, J Richard, Robert J Pickering Award for Playwriting Excellence, 89 Division, Coldwater, MI 49036 *Tel:* 517-279-7963, pg 798

Colbert, Jaimee Wriston, Binghamton University Writing Program, c/o Dept of English, PO Box 6000, Binghamton, NY 13902-6000 *Tel:* 607-777-2168 *Fax:* 607-777-2408, pg 751

Colburn, Kerry, Chronicle Books LLC, 85 Second St, 6th fl, San Francisco, CA 94105 *Tel:* 415-537-4200 *Toll Free Tel:* 800-722-6657 (cust serv) *Fax:* 415-537-4460 *Toll Free Fax:* 800-858-7787 (orders) *E-mail:* frontdesk@chroniclebooks.com *Web Site:* www.chroniclebooks.com, pg 61

Colby, Gerard, National Writers Union, 113 University Place, 6th fl, New York, NY 10003-4527 *Tel:* 212-254-0279 *Fax:* 212-254-0673 *E-mail:* nwu@nwu.org *Web Site:* www.nwu.org/, pg 694

Colby, John T Jr, Brick Tower Press, 1230 Park Ave, New York, NY 10128 *Tel:* 212-427-7139 *Toll Free Tel:* 800-68-BRICK (682-7425) *Fax:* 212-860-8852 *E-mail:* bricktower@aol.com *Web Site:* www.bricktowerpress.com, pg 47

Cole, David, Empire Publishing Service, PO Box 1344, Studio City, CA 91614-0344 *Tel:* 818-784-8918, pg 90

Cole, John Y, The Center for the Book in the Library of Congress, The Library of Congress, 101 Independence Ave SE, Washington, DC 20540-4920 *Tel:* 202-707-5221 *Fax:* 202-707-0269 *E-mail:* cfbook@loc.gov *Web Site:* www.loc.gov/cfbook, pg 684

Cole, Marsha, The University of Akron Press, 374-B Bierce Library, Akron, OH 44325-1703 *Tel:* 330-972-5342 (ext 1703) *Toll Free Tel:* 877-827-7377 *Fax:* 330-972-8364 *E-mail:* uapress@uakron.edu *Web Site:* www.uakron.edu/uapress, pg 280

Cole, Richard L, University of Texas at Arlington School of Urban & Public Affairs, University Hall, 5th fl, 601 S Naderman Dr, Arlington, TX 76010 *Tel:* 817-272-3071 *Fax:* 817-272-5008 *E-mail:* supapubs@uta.edu *Web Site:* www.uta.edu/supa, pg 285

Cole, Steve, American Geophysical Union (AGU), 2000 Florida Ave NW, Washington, DC 20009 *Tel:* 202-462-6900 *Toll Free Tel:* 800-966-2481 (North America) *Fax:* 202-328-0566 *E-mail:* service@agu.org *Web Site:* www.agu.org, pg 14

Cole, Sue, Disney Press, 114 Fifth Ave, New York, NY 10011 *Tel:* 212-633-4400 *Fax:* 212-807-5432 *Web Site:* www.disney.go.com, pg 81

Cole, Sue, Disney Publishing Worldwide, 500 S Buena Vista, Burbank, CA 91521 *Tel:* 212-633-4400 *Fax:* 212-633-4833 *Web Site:* www.disney.go.com/disneybooks, pg 81

Coleburn, Carolyn, Viking, 375 Hudson St, New York, NY 10014 *Tel:* 212-366-2000 *E-mail:* online@penguinputnam.com *Web Site:* www.penguin.com, pg 290

Coleman, Beth, Law Tribune Books, 201 Ann St, 4th fl, Hartford, CT 06103 *Tel:* 860-527-7900 *Fax:* 860-527-7815 *E-mail:* lawtribune@amlaw.com *Web Site:* www.law.com/ct, pg 150

Coleman, DeVerne, Alomega Press, 4601 N Cleveland Ave, Kansas City, MO 64117 *Tel:* 816-454-0980 *Fax:* 816-454-0980, pg 9

Coleman, James E, National Association of Printing Ink Manufacturers (NAPIM), 581 Main St, Woodbridge, NJ 07095 *Tel:* 732-855-1525 *Fax:* 732-855-1838 *E-mail:* napim@napim.org *Web Site:* www.napim.org, pg 692

Coles, B, Renaissance Alliance Publishing Inc, 8691 Ninth Ave, PMB 210, Port Arthur, TX 77642-8025 *Fax:* 409-727-4824 *E-mail:* regalcrest@gt.rr.com *Web Site:* www.rapbooks.biz; www.regalcrest.biz, pg 231

Colgrass, Neal, Holloway House Publishing Co, 8060 Melrose Ave, Los Angeles, CA 90046-7082 *Tel:* 323-653-8060 *Fax:* 323-655-9452 *E-mail:* info@hollowayhousebooks.com *Web Site:* www.hollowayhousebooks.com, pg 124

Collette, Ann, Helen Rees Literary Agency, 376 North St, Boston, MA 02113-2103 *Tel:* 617-227-9014 *Fax:* 617-227-8762, pg 650

Collier, Diana G, Clarity Press Inc, 3277 Roswell Rd NE, Suite 469, Atlanta, GA 30305 *Toll Free Tel:* 800-729-6423 (orders); 877-613-1495 *Fax:* 404-231-3899 *Toll Free Fax:* 877-613-7868 *E-mail:* clarity@islandnet.com; claritypress@usa.net (editorial) *Web Site:* www.claritypress.com, pg 62

Collier, Dianna, Collier Associates, 37 Marina Gardens Dr, Palm Beach Gardens, FL 33410 *Tel:* 561-697-3541 *Fax:* 561-478-4316, pg 625

Collier, Harold, White Mane Kids, 63 W Burd St, Shippensburg, PA 17257 *Tel:* 717-532-2237 *Toll Free Tel:* 888-WHT-MANE (948-6263) *Fax:* 717-532-6110 *E-mail:* marketing@whitemane.com; editorial@whitemane.com, pg 298

Collier, Harold E, Ragged Edge Press, 63 W Burd St, Shippensburg, PA 17257 *Tel:* 717-532-2237 *Toll Free Tel:* 888-948-6263 *Fax:* 717-532-6110 *E-mail:* marketing@whitemane.com, pg 225

Collier, Harold E, White Mane Publishing Co Inc, 73 W Burd St, Shippensburg, PA 17257 *Tel:* 717-532-2237 *Toll Free Tel:* 888-948-6263 *Fax:* 717-532-6110 *E-mail:* marketing@whitemane.com; editorial@whitemane.com, pg 298

Collier, Jan, Jan Collier Represents Inc, PO Box 470818, Mill Valley, CA 94941 *Tel:* 415-383-9026 *Fax:* 415-383-9037 *E-mail:* jan@jan-collier-represents.com *Web Site:* www.jan-collier-represents.com, pg 665

Collier, Jennifer R, University of Alaska Press, Eielson Bldg, Rm 104, Fairbanks, AK 99775-6240 *Tel:* 907-474-5831 *Toll Free Tel:* 888-252-6657 (US only) *Fax:* 907-474-5502 *E-mail:* fypress@uaf.edu *Web Site:* www.uaf.edu/uapress, pg 280

Collier, Michael, Bread Loaf Writers' Conference, Kirk Alumni Center, Middlebury, VT 05753 *Tel:* 802-443-5286 *Fax:* 802-443-2087 *E-mail:* blwc@middlebury.edu *Web Site:* www.middlebury.edu, pg 742

Collier, Michael, Fellowship & Scholarship Program for Writers, Middlebury College, Middlebury, VT 05753 *Tel:* 802-443-5286 *Fax:* 802-443-2087 *E-mail:* blwc@middlebury.edu *Web Site:* www.middlebury.edu/~blwc, pg 773

Collier, Peter, Encounter Books, 665 Third St, Suite 330, San Francisco, CA 94107-1951 *Tel:* 415-538-1460 *Toll Free Tel:* 800-786-3839 *Fax:* 415-538-1461 *Toll Free Fax:* 877-811-1461 *E-mail:* read@encounterbooks.com *Web Site:* www.encounterbooks.com, pg 90

Collier, Sue, Mapletree Publishing Co, 6233 Harvard Lane, Highlands Ranch, CO 80130-3773 *Tel:* 303-791-9024 *Toll Free Tel:* 800-537-0414 *Fax:* 303-791-9028 *E-mail:* mail@mapletreepublishing.com *Web Site:* www.mapletreepublishing.com, pg 163

Colligan, Susan, National Bureau of Economic Research Inc, 1050 Massachusetts Ave, Cambridge, MA 02138-5398 *Tel:* 617-868-3900 *Fax:* 617-868-2742 *E-mail:* op@nber.org *Web Site:* www.nber.org, pg 182

Collin, Frances, Frances Collin Literary Agent, PO Box 33, Wayne, PA 19087-0033 *Tel:* 610-254-0555 *Fax:* 610-254-5029, pg 625

Collinge, Mike, Book & Periodical Council, 192 Spadina Ave, Suite 107, Toronto, ON M5T 2C2, Canada *Tel:* 416-975-9366 *Fax:* 416-975-1839 *E-mail:* bkper@interlog.com *Web Site:* www.freedomtoread.ca, pg 681

Collins, Debbie Justus, White Stone Books, 1501 S Florida Ave, Lakeland, FL 33803 *Toll Free Tel:* 866-253-8622 *Toll Free Fax:* 800-830-5688 *E-mail:* info@whitestonebooks.com *Web Site:* www.whitestonebooks.com, pg 574

Collins, Donald A, Association of American University Presses, 1427 E 60 St, Chicago, IL 60637 *Tel:* 773-702-7700; 773-702-7600 *Toll Free Tel:* 800-621-2736 (sales); 773-702-9756 (sales); 773-660-2235 (orders); 773-702-2708 *Fax:* general@press.uchicago.edu *Web Site:* www.press.uchicago.edu, pg 26

Collins, Gretchen, GSC Communications, 1761 S Columbia Ave, Tulsa, OK 74104-5820 *Tel:* 918-749-2360 *Fax:* 918-749-2360 *E-mail:* swwriter@juno.com, pg 601

Collins, Kim, Discovery House Publishers, 3000 Kraft SE, Grand Rapids, MI 49512 *Tel:* 616-942-9218; 616-974-2210 (cust serv) *Toll Free Tel:* 800-653-8333 *Fax:* 616-957-5741 *E-mail:* dhp@rbc.org *Web Site:* www.gospelcom.net/rbc/dhp/; www.rbc.net, pg 81

Collins, Martha, The Field Poetry Prize, 50 N Professor St, Oberlin, OH 44074-1095 *Tel:* 440-775-8408 *Fax:* 440-775-8124 *E-mail:* oc.press@oberlin.edu *Web Site:* www.oberlin.edu/ocpress, pg 773

Collins, Martha, Oberlin College Press, 50 N Professor St, Oberlin, OH 44074-1095 *Tel:* 440-775-8408 *Fax:* 440-775-8124 *E-mail:* oc.press@oberlin.edu *Web Site:* www.oberlin.edu/ocpress, pg 195

Collins Rosenberg, Barbara, The Rosenberg Group, 23 Lincoln Ave, Marblehead, MA 01945 *Tel:* 781-990-1341 *Fax:* 781-990-1344 *Web Site:* www.rosenberggroup.com, pg 652

Collins, Teresa, The University Press of Kentucky, 663 S Limestone St, Lexington, KY 40508-4008 *Tel:* 859-257-8761; 859-257-8442 (mktg) *Toll Free Tel:* 800-839-6855 (orders) *Fax:* 859-323-1873 *Web Site:* www.kentuckypress.com, pg 287

Colom, Nyani, Genesis Press Inc, PO Box 101, Columbus, MS 39703 *Tel:* 662-329-9927 *Toll Free Tel:* 888-463-4461 (orders only) *Fax:* 662-329-9399 *E-mail:* books@genesis-press.com *Web Site:* www.genesis-press.com, pg 104

Colon, Myrna Lee, University of Puerto Rico Press, Edificio EDUPR/Dialogo, Carr No 1, KM 12-0, Piso 2, Jardin Bota'nico Area Norte, San Juan, PR 00931 *Tel:* 787-758-6932; 787-758-8345 (sales); 787-250-0046; 787-250-0000 *Fax:* 787-753-9116; 787-751-8785 (sales dept), pg 285

Colona, Laura, The Direct Marketing Association Inc (The DMA), 1120 Avenue of the Americas, New York, NY 10036-6700 *Tel:* 212-768-7277 *Fax:* 212-768-4547 *E-mail:* dma@the-dma.org; customerservice@the-dma.org *Web Site:* www.the-dma.org, pg 80

Colonnese, Frank, Center for Thanatology Research & Education Inc, 391 Atlantic Ave, Brooklyn, NY 11217-1701 *Tel:* 718-858-3026 *Fax:* 718-852-1846 *Web Site:* www.thanatology.org, pg 57

Colquitt, Geoff, Rough Guides, 345 Hudson St, New York, NY 10014 *Tel:* 212-414-3635 *Fax:* 212-414-3352 *E-mail:* mail@roughguides.com *Web Site:* www.roughguides.com, pg 235

Colter, Amy L, International Universities Press Inc, 59 Boston Post Rd, Madison, CT 06443 *Tel:* 203-245-4000 *Toll Free Tel:* 800-835-3487 *Fax:* 203-245-0775 *E-mail:* orders@iup.com *Web Site:* www.iup.com, pg 138

Colton, Tim, Carolina Academic Press, 700 Kent St, Durham, NC 27701 *Tel:* 919-489-7486 *Toll Free Tel:* 800-489-7486 *Fax:* 919-493-5668 *E-mail:* cap@cap-press.com *Web Site:* www.cap-press.com; www.caplaw.com, pg 54

Columbus, Frank, Nova Science Publishers Inc, 400 Oset Ave, Suite 1600, Hauppauge, NY 11788 *Tel:* 631-231-7269 *Fax:* 631-231-8175 *E-mail:* novaeditorial@earthlink.net *Web Site:* www.novapublishers.com, pg 194

Columbus, Jay, Camex Books Inc, 535 Fifth Ave, New York, NY 10017 *Tel:* 212-682-8400 *Fax:* 212-808-4669, pg 52

Colvin, Rod, Addicus Books Inc, PO Box 45327, Omaha, NE 68145 *Tel:* 402-330-7493 *Toll Free Tel:* 800-352-2873 (orders) *Fax:* 402-330-1707 *E-mail:* info@addicusbooks.com; addicusbks@aol.com *Web Site:* www.addicusbooks.com, pg 5

Colvin, Theresa, Individual Artist Awards, 175 W Ostend St, Suite E, Baltimore, MD 21230 *Tel:* 410-767-6555 *Fax:* 410-333-1062 *Web Site:* www.msac.org, pg 779

Colzie, Dierdra, Teachers & Writers Collaborative, 5 Union Sq W, New York, NY 10003-3306 *Tel:* 212-691-6590 *Toll Free Tel:* 888-266-5789 *Fax:* 212-675-0171 *E-mail:* info@twc.org *Web Site:* www.twc.org, pg 265, 701

Combellick, Katherine A, Fordham University, Graduate School of Business Administration, Dept of Communications & Media Management, 113 W 60 St, New York, NY 10023 *Tel:* 212-636-6199 *Fax:* 212-765-5573, pg 752

Comins, Jane, Hyperion, 77 W 66 St, 11th fl, New York, NY 10023-6298 *Tel:* 212-456-0100 *Toll Free Tel:* 800-759-0190 (cust serv) *Fax:* 212-456-0157 *Web Site:* hyperionbooks.com, pg 129

Como, Maureen, Liturgy Training Publications, 1800 N Hermitage Ave, Chicago, IL 60622-1101 *Tel:* 773-486-8970 *Toll Free Tel:* 800-933-1800 (US & Canada only) *Fax:* 773-486-7094 *Toll Free Fax:* 800-933-7094 (US & Canada only) *E-mail:* orders@ltp.org *Web Site:* www.ltp.org, pg 156

Comparato, Frank E, Labyrinthos, 3064 Holline Ct, Lancaster, CA 93535-4910 *Tel:* 661-946-2726 *Fax:* 661-946-2726, pg 148

Compton, Denver, ABC-CLIO, 130 Cremona Dr, Santa Barbara, CA 93117 *Tel:* 805-968-1911 *Toll Free Tel:* 800-368-6868 *Fax:* 805-685-9685 *E-mail:* sales@abc-clio.com *Web Site:* www.abc-clio.com, pg 3

Compton, Ramona, Lee Jacobs Productions, PO Box 362, Pomeroy, OH 45769-0362 *Tel:* 740-992-5208 *Fax:* 740-992-0616 *E-mail:* ljacobs@frognet.net *Web Site:* www.leejacobsproductions.com, pg 140

Conant, Vic, Nightingale-Conant, 6245 W Howard St, Niles, IL 60714 *Tel:* 847-647-0306; 847-647-0300 *Toll Free Tel:* 800-572-2770 *Fax:* 847-647-7145 *Web Site:* www.nightingale.com, pg 191

Conary, Lori, Shubert Fendrich Memorial Playwriting Contest, PO Box 4267, Englewood, CO 80155-4267 *Tel:* 303-779-4035 *Toll Free Tel:* 800-333-7262 *Fax:* 303-779-4315 *E-mail:* playwrights@pioneerdrama.com *Web Site:* www.pioneerdrama.com, pg 773

Concepcion, Cristina, Don Congdon Associates Inc, 156 Fifth Ave, Suite 625, New York, NY 10010-7002 *Tel:* 212-645-1229 *Fax:* 212-727-2688 *E-mail:* dca@doncongdon.com, pg 625

Conde, Sidney, St Martin's Press LLC, 175 Fifth Ave, New York, NY 10010 *Tel:* 212-674-5151 *Fax:* 212-420-9314 *E-mail:* firstname.lastname@stmartins.com *Web Site:* www.stmartins.com, pg 238

Condello, Virginia, Rainbow Books Inc, PO Box 430, Highland City, FL 33846-0430 *Tel:* 863-648-4420 *Toll Free Tel:* 800-431-1579 (orders only); 888-613-2665 *Fax:* 863-647-5951 *E-mail:* rbibooks@aol.com *Web Site:* www.rainbowbooksinc.com, pg 225

Condon, Alicia, Dorchester Publishing Co Inc, 200 Madison Ave, Suite 2000, New York, NY 10016 *Tel:* 212-725-8811 *Toll Free Tel:* 800-481-9191 (order dept) *Fax:* 212-532-1054 *E-mail:* dorchedits@dorchesterpub.com *Web Site:* www.dorchesterpub.com, pg 82

Condon, Phil, University of Montana, Environmental Writing Institute, Environmental Studies, University of Montana, Missoula, MT 59812 *Tel:* 406-243-2904 *Fax:* 406-243-6090 *E-mail:* evst@selway.umt.edu *Web Site:* www.umt.edu/ewi, pg 756

Condron, Dr Barbara, SOM Publishing, 163 Moon Valley Rd, Windyville, MO 65783 *Tel:* 417-345-8411 *Fax:* 417-345-6668 (call 417-345-8411 before faxing) *E-mail:* som@som.org *Web Site:* www.som.org, pg 253

Conery, Leslie, International Society for Technology in Education, 480 Charnelton St, Eugene, OR 97401-2626 *Tel:* 541-302-3777 *Toll Free Tel:* 800-336-5191 (orders only) *Fax:* 541-302-3778 *E-mail:* iste@iste.org *Web Site:* www.iste.org, pg 138

Coney, Kristen, Ave Maria Press, 19113 Douglas Rd, Notre Dame, IN 46556 *Tel:* 574-287-2831 *Toll Free Tel:* 800-282-1865 *Fax:* 574-239-2904 *Toll Free Fax:* 800-282-5681 *E-mail:* avemariapress.1@nd.edu *Web Site:* www.avemariapress.com, pg 29

Confer, Nathan, J Weston Walch Publisher, 321 Valley St, Portland, ME 04104 *Tel:* 207-772-2846 *Toll Free Tel:* 800-341-6094 *Fax:* 207-772-3105 *Toll Free Fax:* 888-991-5755 *E-mail:* customerservice@mail.walch.com *Web Site:* www.walch.com, pg 292

Congdon, Don, Don Congdon Associates Inc, 156 Fifth Ave, Suite 625, New York, NY 10010-7002 *Tel:* 212-645-1229 *Fax:* 212-727-2688 *E-mail:* dca@doncongdon.com, pg 625

Congdon, Michael, Don Congdon Associates Inc, 156 Fifth Ave, Suite 625, New York, NY 10010-7002 *Tel:* 212-645-1229 *Fax:* 212-727-2688 *E-mail:* dca@doncongdon.com, pg 625

Conine, Nancy, Transaction Publishers, Rutgers University, 35 Berrue Circle, Piscataway, NJ 08854 *Tel:* 732-445-2280 *Toll Free Tel:* 888-999-6778 *Fax:* 732-445-3138 *E-mail:* trans@transactionpub.com *Web Site:* www.transactionpub.com, pg 274

Conklin, Elizabeth, The Taunton Press Inc, 63 S Main St, Newtown, CT 06470 *Tel:* 203-426-8171 *Toll Free Tel:* 800-283-7252; 800-888-8286 (orders) *Fax:* 203-426-3434 *Web Site:* www.taunton.com, pg 264

Conklin, Paul, Facts on File Inc, 132 W 31 St, 17th fl, New York, NY 10001 *Tel:* 212-967-8800 *Toll Free Tel:* 800-322-8755 *Fax:* 212-967-9196 *Toll Free Fax:* 800-678-3633 *E-mail:* custserv@factsonfile.com *Web Site:* www.factsonfile.com, pg 94

Conklin, Robert B, Timber Press Inc, 133 SW Second Ave, Suite 450, Portland, OR 97204 *Tel:* 503-227-2878 *Toll Free Tel:* 800-327-5680 *Fax:* 503-227-3070 *E-mail:* mail@timberpress.com *Web Site:* www.timberpress.com, pg 271

Conklin, Walter J, John Wiley & Sons Inc, 111 River St, Hoboken, NJ 07030 *Tel:* 201-748-6000 *Toll Free Tel:* 800-225-5945 (cust serv) *Fax:* 201-748-6088 *E-mail:* info@wiley.com *Web Site:* www.wiley.com, pg 299

Conlan, Don R, National Bureau of Economic Research Inc, 1050 Massachusetts Ave, Cambridge, MA 02138-5398 *Tel:* 617-868-3900 *Fax:* 617-868-2742 *E-mail:* op@nber.org *Web Site:* www.nber.org, pg 182

Conlan, Jennifer, Ambassador Books Inc, 91 Prescott St, Worcester, MA 01605 *Tel:* 508-756-2893 *Toll Free Tel:* 800-577-0909 *Fax:* 508-757-7055 *Web Site:* www.ambassadorbooks.com, pg 10

Conlan, Kate, Ambassador Books Inc, 91 Prescott St, Worcester, MA 01605 *Tel:* 508-756-2893 *Toll Free Tel:* 800-577-0909 *Fax:* 508-757-7055 *Web Site:* www.ambassadorbooks.com, pg 10

Conley, Cort, Idaho Fellowship, PO Box 83720, Boise, ID 83720-0008 *Tel:* 208-334-2119 *Toll Free Tel:* 800-ART-FUND (278-3863 within Idaho) *Fax:* 208-334-2488, pg 779

Conley, Cort, Idaho Writer in Residence, PO Box 83720, Boise, ID 83720-0008 *Tel:* 208-334-2119 *Toll Free Tel:* 800-ART-FUND (278-3863 within Idaho) *Fax:* 208-334-2488, pg 779

Conley, Susan, Arden Press Inc, PO Box 418, Denver, CO 80201-0418 *Tel:* 303-697-6766 *Fax:* 303-697-3443 *E-mail:* ardenpress@msn.com, pg 23

Conmy, Matt, Springer-Verlag New York Inc, 175 Fifth Ave, New York, NY 10010 *Tel:* 212-460-1500 *Toll Free Tel:* 800-777-4643 *Fax:* 212-473-6272 *Web Site:* www.springer-ny.com, pg 256

Connell, Leslie Anne, Oxford University Press Canada, 70 Wynford Dr, Don Mills, ON M3C 1J9, Canada *Tel:* 416-441-2941 *Toll Free Tel:* 800-387-8020 *Fax:* 416-444-0427 *Toll Free Fax:* 800-665-1771 *E-mail:* custserv@oupcan.com *Web Site:* www.oup.com/ca, pg 557

Connell, Steve, Alan Wofsy Fine Arts, 1109 Geary Blvd, San Francisco, CA 94109 *Tel:* 415-292-6500 *Fax:* 415-512-0130 (acctg); 415-292-6594 (off & cust serv) *E-mail:* beauxarts@earthlink.net (cust serv); editeur@earthlink.net (edit); order@art-books.com (orders) *Web Site:* art-books.com, pg 302

Connelly, Caroline, Blackwell Publishing Professional, 2121 State Ave, Ames, IA 50014 *Tel:* 515-292-0140 *Toll Free Tel:* 800-862-6657 (orders only) *Fax:* 515-292-3348 *Web Site:* www.blackwellprofessional.com, pg 40

Connelly, Claire, Connelly Editorial Services, 1630 Main St, Suite 41, Coventry, CT 06238 *Tel:* 860-742-5279 *Fax:* 860-742-5279 *E-mail:* angelsus@aol.com, pg 594

Connelly, Neil, McNeese State University, Writing Program, PO Box 92655, Lake Charles, LA 70609-0001 *Tel:* 337-475-5000; 337-475-5326 *Web Site:* www.mcneese.mfa.com, pg 753

Connelly, Valerie, Nightengale Press, 1579 Nightengale Circle, Lindenhurst, IL 60046 *Tel:* 847-507-0274 *Fax:* 847-245-4167 *Web Site:* www.nightengalepress.com, pg 572

Cook, Philip, B C Decker Inc, 20 Hughson St S, 10th fl, Hamilton, ON L8N 2A1, Canada *Tel:* 905-522-7017 *Toll Free Tel:* 800-568-7281 *Fax:* 905-522-7839 *E-mail:* info@bcdecker.com *Web Site:* www.bcdecker.com, pg 542

Cook, Tonya, Cornell University Press, 512 E State St, Ithaca, NY 14850 *Tel:* 607-277-2338 *Fax:* 607-277-2374 *E-mail:* cupressinfo@cornell.edu *Web Site:* www.cornellpress.cornell.edu, pg 68

Cook, W Richard, University of Alabama Press, Box 870380, Tuscaloosa, AL 35487-0380 *Tel:* 205-348-5180; 773-702-7000 (orders) *Fax:* 205-348-9201 *Web Site:* www.uapress.ua.edu, pg 280

Cook, William, The American Chemical Society, 1155 16 St NW, Washington, DC 20036 *Tel:* 202-872-4600 *Toll Free Tel:* 800-227-5558 *Fax:* 202-872-6067 *Web Site:* www.acs.org; pubs.acs.org, pg 12

Cooke, Dean, The Cooke Agency Inc, 278 Bloor St E, Suite 305, Toronto, ON M4W 3M4, Canada *Tel:* 416-406-3390 *Fax:* 416-406-3389 *E-mail:* agents@cookeagency.ca, pg 625

Cooke, Jacqueline, Prometheus Books, 59 John Glenn Dr, Amherst, NY 14228 *Tel:* 716-691-0133 *Toll Free Tel:* 800-421-0351 *Fax:* 716-691-0137 *E-mail:* marketing@prometheusbooks.com; editorial@prometheusbooks.com *Web Site:* www.Prometheusbooks.com, pg 220

Cookman, Whitney, Crown Publishing Group, 1745 Broadway, New York, NY 10019 *Tel:* 212-782-9000 *Toll Free Tel:* 888-264-1745 *Fax:* 212-940-7408 *Web Site:* www.randomhouse.com/crown, pg 74

Cool, Lisa Collier, American Society of Journalists & Authors (ASJA), 1501 Broadway, Suite 302, New York, NY 10036 *Tel:* 212-997-0947 *Fax:* 212-768-7414 *E-mail:* staff@asja.org *Web Site:* www.asja.org, pg 678

Cooley, Martha, Stanford University Press, 1450 Page Mill Rd, Palo Alto, CA 94304-1124 *Tel:* 650-723-9434 *Fax:* 650-725-3457 *Web Site:* www.sup.org, pg 257

Cooper, Ben, Franciscan Press, 1800 College Ave, Quincy, IL 62301-2699 *Tel:* 217-228-5670 *Fax:* 217-228-5672 *Web Site:* www.franciscanpress.com, pg 100

Cooper, Doris, Fireside & Touchstone, 1230 Avenue of the Americas, New York, NY 10020, pg 97

Cooper, Elizabeth, Milkweed Editions, 1011 Washington Ave S, Suite 300, Minneapolis, MN 55415 *Tel:* 612-332-3192 *Toll Free Tel:* 800-520-6455 *Fax:* 612-215-2550 *E-mail:* editor@milkweed.org *Web Site:* www.milkweed.org; www.worldashome.org, pg 174

Cooper, I L, Cooper Publishing Group, 2694 Garfield Rd N, No 26, Traverse City, MI 49686 *Tel:* 231-933-9958 *Fax:* 231-933-9964 *E-mail:* icooper100@aol.com, pg 68

Cooper, Jennifer, University of Louisiana at Lafayette, Center for Louisiana Studies, PO Box 40831, UL, Lafayette, LA 70504-0831 *Tel:* 337-482-6027 *Fax:* 337-482-6028 *E-mail:* ann@louisiana.edu *Web Site:* www.cls.louisiana.edu, pg 282

Cooper, Karen, Adams Media, An F+W Publications Co, 57 Littlefield St, 2nd fl, Avon, MA 02322 *Tel:* 508-427-7100 *Fax:* 508-427-6790 *Toll Free Tel:* 800-872-5628 *E-mail:* authors@adamsmedia.com; orders@adamsmedia.com *Web Site:* www.adamsmedia.com, pg 5

Cooper, Kathleen B, National Bureau of Economic Research Inc, 1050 Massachusetts Ave, Cambridge, MA 02138-5398 *Tel:* 617-868-3900 *Fax:* 617-868-2742 *E-mail:* op@nber.org *Web Site:* www.nber.org, pg 182

Cooper, Kathy, Hampton Roads Publishing Co Inc, 1125 Stoney Ridge Rd, Charlottesville, VA 22902 *Tel:* 434-296-2772 *Toll Free Tel:* 800-766-8009 (orders) *Fax:* 434-296-5096 *Toll Free Fax:* 800-766-9042 *E-mail:* hrpc@hrpub.com *Web Site:* www.hrpub.com, pg 113

Cooper, Marshall, Kennedy Information, One Phoenix Mill Lane, 5th fl, Peterborough, NH 03458 *Tel:* 603-924-0900 *Toll Free Tel:* 800-531-0007 *Fax:* 603-924-4460 *E-mail:* office@kennedyinfo.com *Web Site:* www.kennedyinfo.com, pg 145

Cooper, Petra, McGraw-Hill Ryerson Ltd, 300 Water St, Whitby, ON L1N 9B6, Canada *Tel:* 905-430-5000 *Toll Free Tel:* 800-565-5758 (cust serv) *Fax:* 905-430-5020 *E-mail:* johnd@mcgrawhill.ca *Web Site:* www.mcgrawhill.ca, pg 554

Cooper, Robin, Berkley Books, 375 Hudson St, New York, NY 10014 *Tel:* 212-366-2000 *Fax:* 212-366-2666 *E-mail:* online@penguinputnam.com *Web Site:* www.penguin.com, pg 36

Cooper, Robin, Berkley Publishing Group, 375 Hudson St, New York, NY 10014 *Tel:* 212-366-2000 *E-mail:* online@penguinputnam.com *Web Site:* www.penguin.com, pg 37

Cooper, Terry, Scholastic Paperbacks, Teaching Resources & Reading Counts, 557 Broadway, New York, NY 10012-3999 *Tel:* 212-965-7241 *Fax:* 212-965-7487 *Web Site:* www.scholastic.com, pg 242

Cooper, Tim, Harcourt Trade Publishers, 525 "B" St, Suite 1900, San Diego, CA 92101 *Tel:* 619-231-6616 *Toll Free Tel:* 800-543-1918 (cust serv) *Toll Free Fax:* 800-235-0256 (cust serv) *Web Site:* www.harcourtbooks.com, pg 115

Cooper, Vicki, Perfection Learning Corp, 10520 New York Ave, Des Moines, IA 50322 *Tel:* 515-278-0133 *Toll Free Tel:* 800-762-2999 *Fax:* 515-278-2980 *E-mail:* orders@perfectionlearning.com *Web Site:* perfectionlearning.com, pg 210

Coorpender, Bruce, Pocket Press Inc, PO Box 25124, Portland, OR 97298 *Toll Free Tel:* 888-237-2110 *Toll Free Fax:* 877-643-3732 *E-mail:* sales@pocketpressinc.com *Web Site:* www.pocketpressinc.com, pg 215

Coover, Doe, The Doe Coover Agency, PO Box 668, Winchester, MA 01890 *Tel:* 781-721-6000 *Fax:* 781-721-6727, pg 626

Cope, Eileen, Lowenstein-Yost Associates Inc, 121 W 27 St, Suite 601, New York, NY 10001 *Tel:* 212-206-1630 *Fax:* 212-727-0280 *Web Site:* www.lowensteinyost.com, pg 641

Copeland, Brenda, Atria Books, 1230 Avenue of the Americas, New York, NY 10020 *Tel:* 212-698-7000 *Fax:* 212-698-7007 *Web Site:* www.simonsays.com, pg 27

Copeland, Joelean, Eastern Washington University Press, Eastern Washington University, 705 W First Ave, Spokane, WA 99201 *Tel:* 509-623-4286 *Toll Free Tel:* 800-508-9095 *Fax:* 509-623-4283 *E-mail:* ewupress@ewu.edu *Web Site:* ewupress.ewu.edu, pg 86

Copella, Susan, Pennsylvania State Data Center, Penn State Harrisburg, 777 W Harrisburg Pike, Middletown, PA 17057-4898 *Tel:* 717-948-6336 *Fax:* 717-948-6754 *E-mail:* pasdc@psu.edu *Web Site:* pasdc.hbg.psu.edu, pg 209

Copp, Karen, University of Iowa Press, University of Iowa, 100 Kuhl House, Iowa City, IA 52242-1000 *Tel:* 319-335-2000 *Toll Free Tel:* 800-621-2736 (orders only) *Fax:* 319-335-2055 *Toll Free Fax:* 800-621-8476 (orders only) *E-mail:* uipress@uiowa.edu *Web Site:* www.uiowapress.org, pg 282

Coppenger, Loyd, Large Print, PO Box 5000, Yucaipa, CA 92399-1450 *Tel:* 909-795-8977 *Fax:* 909-795-8970 *E-mail:* lbw@lbwinc.org *Web Site:* www.lbwinc.org, pg 149

Coppola, Michelle, Dutton Children's Books, 345 Hudson St, New York, NY 10014 *Tel:* 212-366-2000 *E-mail:* online@penguinputnam.com *Web Site:* www.penguin.com, pg 85

Corbet, Kathleen A, The McGraw-Hill Companies Inc, 1221 Avenue of the Americas, 50th fl, New York, NY 10020 *Tel:* 212-512-2000 *E-mail:* webmaster@mcgraw-hill.com *Web Site:* www.mcgraw-hill.com, pg 167

Corcoran, Susan, Bantam Dell Publishing Group, 1745 Broadway, New York, NY 10019 *Tel:* 212-782-9000 *Toll Free Tel:* 800-223-6834 *Fax:* 212-302-7985 *Web Site:* www.randomhouse.com/bantamdell, pg 31

Corda, Jesse, VanDam Inc, 11 W 20 St, 4th fl, New York, NY 10011-3704 *Tel:* 212-929-0416 *Toll Free Tel:* 800-UNFOLDS (863-6537) *Fax:* 212-929-0426 *E-mail:* info@vandam.com *Web Site:* www.vandam.com, pg 289

Cordasco, Michael V, Saint Aedan's Press & Book Distributors Inc, PO Box 385, Hillsdale, NJ 07642-0385 *Tel:* 201-664-0127 *E-mail:* junius1920@yahoo.com *Web Site:* www.greatoldebooks.com; www.juniusbooks.com, pg 237

Cordero, Chris, Players Press Inc, PO Box 1132, Studio City, CA 91614-0132 *Tel:* 818-789-4980, pg 214

Corea, Fran, Penguin Group (USA) Inc Sales, 375 Hudson St, New York, NY 10014 *Tel:* 212-366-2000 *E-mail:* online@penguinputnam.com *Web Site:* www.penguin.com, pg 208

Corenswet, John, Paul Dry Books, 117 S 17 St, Suite 1102, Philadelphia, PA 19103 *Tel:* 215-231-9939 *Fax:* 215-231-9942 *E-mail:* editor@pauldrybooks.com *Web Site:* www.pauldrybooks.com, pg 84

Corey, Alla, Rowman & Littlefield Publishers Inc, 4501 Forbes Blvd, Lanham, MD 20706 *Tel:* 301-459-3366 *Toll Free Tel:* 800-462-6420 *Fax:* 301-429-5748 *Web Site:* www.rowmanlittlefield.com, pg 235

Corey, David, Berkshire House, 1206 Rte 12, Woodstock, VT 05091 *Tel:* 802-457-4826 *Toll Free Tel:* 800-245-4151 *Fax:* 802-457-1678 *Web Site:* www.countrymanpress.com, pg 37

Corey, David, The Countryman Press, 1206 Rte 12 N, Woodstock, VT 05091 *Tel:* 802-457-4826 *Toll Free Tel:* 800-245-4151 *Fax:* 802-457-1678 *E-mail:* countrymanpress@wwnorton.com *Web Site:* www.countrymanpress.com, pg 70

Corey, Paul, Prentice Hall Engineering/Science & Math, One Lake St, Upper Saddle River, NJ 07458 *Tel:* 201-236-7000, pg 217

Corey, Robin, Simon & Schuster Children's Publishing, 1230 Avenue of the Americas, New York, NY 10020 *Tel:* 212-698-7000 *Web Site:* www.simonsayskids.com, pg 248

Corless, Peter, Green Knight Publishing, 360 Chiquita Ave, No 4, Mountain View, CA 94041 *Tel:* 650-964-4276 *Fax:* 650-964-4276 *E-mail:* gawaine@greenknight.com *Web Site:* www.greenknight.com, pg 108

Corman, Judith A, Scholastic Inc, 557 Broadway, New York, NY 10012 *Tel:* 212-343-4469 *Toll Free Tel:* 800-scholastic *Fax:* 212-343-6930 *Web Site:* www.scholastic.com, pg 242

Cormier, Robin, EEI Communications, 66 Canal Center Plaza, Suite 200, Alexandria, VA 22314-5507 *Tel:* 703-683-0683 *Fax:* 703-683-4915 *E-mail:* info@eeicommunications.com *Web Site:* www.eeicommunications.com, pg 598

Cornacchia, Len, Routledge, 29 W 35 St, New York, NY 10001-2299 *Tel:* 212-216-7800 *Fax:* 212-564-7854 (main) *E-mail:* info@taylorandfrancis.com *Web Site:* www.routledge-ny.com, pg 235

Cornacchione, Enzo, Delano Greenidge Editions, 14 Mount Morris Park W, Suite 7, New York, NY 10027-6317 *Tel:* 917-492-8014 *Fax:* 917-492-0966 *E-mail:* dge@thing.net, pg 109

Cornelius, Casey, Morgan Reynolds Publishing, 620 S Elm St, Suite 223, Greensboro, NC 27406 *Tel:* 336-275-1311 *Toll Free Tel:* 800-535-1504 *Fax:* 336-275-1152 *Toll Free Fax:* 800-535-5725 *E-mail:* editorial@morganreynolds.com *Web Site:* www.morganreynolds.com, pg 178

Cornell, Chris, Down East Books, PO Box 679, Camden, ME 04843 *Tel:* 207-594-9544 *Toll Free Tel:* 800-766-1670 (ME only) *Fax:* 207-594-7215 *Web Site:* www.downeastbooks.com, pg 83

Cornell, Mary Beth, Technical Association of the Pulp & Paper Industry (TAPPI), 15 Technology Pkwy S, Norcross, GA 30092 *Tel:* 770-446-1400

Toll Free Tel: 800-332-8686 Fax: 770-446-6947 E-mail: webmaster@tappi.org Web Site: www.tappi. org, pg 266, 701

Cornell, Merial, Cornell & McCarthy LLC, 2-D Cross Hwy, Westport, CT 06880 Tel: 203-454-4210 Fax: 203-454-4258 Web Site: www. cornellandmccarthy.com, pg 665

Cornell, Vance, Polar Bear & Co, The Cascades, 8 Brook St, Solon, ME 04979 Tel: 207-643-2795 E-mail: polarbear@necsys.net Web Site: www. polarbearandco.com, pg 216

Cornell, Wayne, Caxton Press, 312 Main St, Caldwell, ID 83605-3299 Tel: 208-459-7421 Toll Free Tel: 800-657-6465 Fax: 208-459-7450 E-mail: publish@ caxtonpress.com Web Site: www.caxtonpress.com, pg 55

Cornett, Patricia L, MedWrite Associates, 31651 Auburn Dr, Beverly Hills, MI 48025 Tel: 248-646-2895 Fax: 248-647-7593, pg 606

Corngold, Sally Marshall, Optometric Extension Program Foundation, 1921 E Carnegie Ave, Suite 3-L, Santa Ana, CA 92705-5510 Tel: 949-250-8070 Fax: 949-250-8157 E-mail: oep1@oep.org Web Site: www.oep. org, pg 198

Coron, Dave, Saint Mary's Press, 702 Terrace Heights, Winona, MN 55987-1318 Tel: 507-457-7900 Toll Free Tel: 800-533-8095 Toll Free Fax: 800-344-9225 E-mail: smpress@smp.org Web Site: www.smp.org, pg 239

Correia, Peter R III, National Resource Center for Youth Services (NRCYS), Schusterman Center, 4502 E 41 St, Bldg 4W, Tulsa, OK 74135-2512 Tel: 918-660-3700 Toll Free Tel: 800-274-2687 Fax: 918-660-3737 Web Site: www.nrcys.ou.edu, pg 185

Corrigan, Anne Marie, University of Toronto Press Inc, 10 St Mary St, Suite 700, Toronto, ON M4Y 2W8, Canada Tel: 416-978-2239 (admin) Fax: 416-978-4738 (admin) Web Site: www.utpress.utoronto.ca, pg 565

Corrington, Paul, Corrington Indexing Services, 2638 E Kenwood, Mesa, AZ 85213 Tel: 480-827-8904 Fax: 480-827-1182, pg 595

Corsa, Bill, Osprey Publishing Ltd, 443 Park Ave S, New York, NY 10016 Tel: 212-685-5560 Fax: 212-685-5836 E-mail: ospreyusa@aol.com Web Site: www. ospreypublishing.com, pg 199

Corson, Maurice, National Jewish Book Awards, 15 E 26 St, New York, NY 10010-1579 Tel: 212-532-4949 (ext 297) Fax: 212-481-4174 E-mail: jbc@jewishbooks.org Web Site: www.jewishbookcouncil.org, pg 792

Cosay, Gary C, United Talent Agency, 9560 Wilshire Blvd, Suite 500, Beverly Hills, CA 90212 Tel: 310-273-6700 Fax: 310-247-1111, pg 659

Cosindas, Gia, Breakout Productions Inc, PO Box 1643, Port Townsend St, WA 98368-0129 Tel: 360-379-1965 Fax: 360-379-3794, pg 46

Cosindas, Gia, Loompanics Unlimited, PO Box 1197, Port Townsend, WA 98368-0997 Tel: 360-385-5087 Toll Free Tel: 800-380-2230 (orders only) Fax: 360-385-7785 E-mail: editorial@loompanics.com; service@loompanics.com Web Site: www.loompanics. com, pg 158

Costa, Cathy L, Paul H Brookes Publishing Co, PO Box 10624, Baltimore, MD 21285-0624 Tel: 410-337-9580 Toll Free Tel: 800-638-3775 Fax: 410-337-8539 E-mail: custserv@brookespublishing.com Web Site: www.brookespublishing.com, pg 48

Costantini, Lana, Straight Line Editorial Development Inc, 3239 Sacramento St, San Francisco, CA 94115-2047 Tel: 415-864-2011 Fax: 415-864-2013 E-mail: sledinc@aol.com, pg 612

Costanzo, Gerald, Carnegie Mellon University Press, 5032 Forbes Ave, Pittsburgh, PA 15289-1021 Tel: 412-268-2861 Fax: 412-268-8706 Web Site: www.cmu. edu/universitypress, pg 53

Costello, Gwen, Twenty-Third Publications, 185 Willow St, Mystic, CT 06355 Tel: 860-536-2611 Toll Free Tel: 800-321-0411 (orders) Fax: 860-536-5674 (edit) Toll Free Fax: 800-572-0788, pg 277

Costello, John, The MIT Press, 5 Cambridge Ctr, Cambridge, MA 02142 Tel: 617-253-5646 Toll Free Tel: 800-405-1619 (orders only) Fax: 617-258-6779 Web Site: mitpress.mit.edu, pg 175

Costello, Susan, Abbeville Publishing Group, 116 W 23 St, Suite 500, New York, NY 10011 Tel: 646-375-2039 Toll Free Tel: 800-ART-BOOK (278-2665) Fax: 646-375-2040 E-mail: abbeville@abbeville.com Web Site: www.abbeville.com, pg 2

Costello, Susan, Artabras Inc, 116 W 23 St, Suite 500, New York, NY 10011 Tel: 646-375-2039 Toll Free Tel: 800-ART-BOOK Fax: 646-375-2040 E-mail: abbeville@abbeville.com Web Site: www. abbeville.com, pg 24

Cote, Dan, nSight Inc, One Van de Graaff Dr, Suite 202, Burlington, MA 01803 Tel: 781-273-6300 Fax: 781-273-6301 E-mail: projects@nsightworks. com; consulting@nsightworks.com Web Site: www. nsightworks.com, pg 607

Cote, Marc, Cormorant Books Inc, 215 Spadina Ave, Studio 230, Toronto, ON M5T 2C7, Canada Tel: 416-929-4957 E-mail: cormorantbooksinc@bellnet.ca Web Site: www.cormorantbooks.com, pg 541

Cotter, Kelly, Standard Publishing Corp, 155 Federal St, 13th fl, Boston, MA 02110 Tel: 617-457-0600 Toll Free Tel: 800-682-5759 Fax: 617-457-0608 E-mail: info@spcpub.com Web Site: spcpub.com, pg 257

Cottle, Anna, Cine/Lit Representation, PO Box 802918, Santa Clarita, CA 91380-2918 Tel: 661-513-0268 Fax: 661-513-0951 E-mail: cinelit@msn.com, pg 625

Cottom, Robert, Maryland Historical Society, 201 W Monument St, Baltimore, MD 21201 Tel: 410-685-3750 Fax: 410-385-2105 Web Site: www.mdhs.org, pg 164

Cottrell, David, Metamorphous Press, 265 N Hancock St, Portland, OR 97227 Tel: 503-228-4972 Toll Free Tel: 800-937-7771 (orders only) Fax: 503-223-9117 E-mail: metabooks@metamodels.com Web Site: www. metamodels.com, pg 172

Cottrell, Sophie, Little, Brown and Company Adult Trade Division, 1271 Avenue of the Americas, New York, NY 10020 Tel: 212-522-8700 Fax: 212-522-2067 Web Site: www.twbookmark.com, pg 156

Cotts, Diane, University of Oklahoma Press, 4100 28 Ave NW, Norman, OK 73069-8218 Tel: 405-325-2000 Toll Free Tel: 800-627-7377 (orders) Fax: 405-364-5798 (orders) Toll Free Tel: 800-735-0476 (orders) E-mail: oupress@ou.edu Web Site: www.oupress.com, pg 284

Couch, Frank, World Publishing, 404 BNA Dr, Bldg 200, Suite 208, Nashville, TN 37217 Tel: 615-902-2395 Toll Free Tel: 800-363-0308 Fax: 615-902-2397 Toll Free Fax: 800-822-4271 (orders) E-mail: questions@worldpublishing.com; orders@ worldpublishing.com Web Site: www.worldpublishing. com, pg 304

Coughlan, Robert, Capstone Press, 151 Good Counsel Dr, Mankato, MN 56002 Toll Free Tel: 800-747-4992 Toll Free Fax: 888-262-0705 Web Site: www. capstonepress.com, pg 53

Coughlin, Michelle, Business Marketing Association, 400 N Michigan Ave, Suite 1510, Chicago, IL 60611 Tel: 312-822-0005 Toll Free Tel: 800-664-4262 Fax: 312-822-0054 E-mail: bma@marketing.org Web Site: www.marketing.org, pg 682

Coulas, Pam, Canadian Museum of Civilization, 100 Laurier St, Hull, PQ J8X 4H2, Canada Tel: 819-776-8387 Toll Free Tel: 800-555-5621 (North America only) Fax: 819-776-8300 E-mail: publications@ civilization.ca (mail order) Web Site: www.civilization. ca, pg 539

Coulson, Barbara, T H Peek Publisher, PO Box 50123, Palo Alto, CA 94303-0123 Tel: 650-962-1010 Toll Free Tel: 800-962-9245 Fax: 650-962-1211 E-mail: thpeek@aol.com Web Site: www. thpeekpublisher.com, pg 207

Coun, Rachel, Scholastic Trade Division, 557 Broadway, New York, NY 10012 Tel: 212-343-6100; 212-343-4685 (export sales) Fax: 212-343-4714 (export sales) Web Site: www.scholastic.com, pg 242

Counihan, Claire, Holiday House Inc, 425 Madison Ave, New York, NY 10017 Tel: 212-688-0085 Fax: 212-421-6134, pg 123

Cournoyer, Lucie, Les Editions Ganesha Inc, CP 484 Succursale Youville, Montreal, PQ H2P 2W1, Canada Tel: 450-641-2395 Fax: 450-641-2989 E-mail: courriel@editions-ganesha.qc.ca Web Site: editions-ganesha.qc.ca, pg 545

Courrier, Kathleen, The Urban Institute Press, 2100 "M" St NW, Washington, DC 20037 Tel: 202-261-5687 Toll Free Tel: 877-UIPRESS (847-7377) Fax: 202-467-5775 E-mail: pubs@ui.urban.org Web Site: www. uipress.org, pg 288

Court, Kathryn, Penguin Books, 375 Hudson St, New York, NY 10014 Tel: 212-366-2000 E-mail: online@ penguinputnam.com Web Site: www.penguin.com; www.penguinclassics.com, pg 207

Court, Kathryn, Penguin Group (USA) Inc, 375 Hudson St, New York, NY 10014 Tel: 212-366-2000 Fax: 212-366-2666 E-mail: online@uspenguingroup.com Web Site: www.penguin.com, pg 208

Court, Kathryn, Plume, 375 Hudson St, New York, NY 10014 Tel: 212-366-2000 Fax: 212-366-2666 E-mail: online@penguinputnam.com Web Site: www. penguin.com, pg 215

Court, Kathryn, Viking Penguin, 375 Hudson St, New York, NY 10014 Tel: 212-366-2000 E-mail: online@ penguinputnam.com Web Site: www.penguin.com, pg 290

Courtney, Barbara, Artist Trust Fellowship, 1835 12 Ave, Seattle, WA 98122 Tel: 206-467-8734 Fax: 206-467-9633 E-mail: info@artisttrust.org Web Site: www. artisttrust.org, pg 760

Courtney, Barbara, Grants for Artist Projects, 1835 12 Ave, Seattle, WA 98122 Tel: 206-467-8734 Fax: 206-467-9633 E-mail: info@artisttrust.org Web Site: www. artisttrust.org, pg 776

Cousens, Ellis, John Wiley & Sons Inc, 111 River St, Hoboken, NJ 07030 Tel: 201-748-6000 Toll Free Tel: 800-225-5945 (cust serv) Fax: 201-748-6088 E-mail: info@wiley.com Web Site: www.wiley.com, pg 299

Cousineau, Helene, Editions du renouveau Pedagogique Inc, 5757 rue Cypihot, St-Laurent, PQ H4S 1R3, Canada Tel: 514-334-2690 Toll Free Tel: 800-263-3678 Fax: 514-334-4720 Toll Free Fax: 800-643-4720 E-mail: erpidlm@erpi.com Web Site: www.erpi.com, pg 544

Covell, John, The MIT Press, 5 Cambridge Ctr, Cambridge, MA 02142 Tel: 617-253-5646 Toll Free Tel: 800-405-1619 (orders only) Fax: 617-258-6779 Web Site: mitpress.mit.edu, pg 175

Covelli-Hunt, Robyn, Sun Books - Sun Publishing, PO Box 5588, Santa Fe, NM 87502-5588 Tel: 505-471-5177; 505-471-6151 Fax: 505-473-4458 E-mail: info@sunbooks.com Web Site: www.sunbooks. com, pg 261

Covington, Heather, Disilgold Publishing Inc, 2739 Mickle Ave, Bronx, NY 10469 Tel: 917-757-1658 Fax: 718-547-0499 E-mail: disilgold@aol.com Web Site: www.disilgold.com, pg 571

Cowan, Linda, Harcourt Canada Ltd, 55 Horner Ave, Toronto, ON M8Z 4X6, Canada Tel: 416-255-4491; 416-255-0177 (Voice Mail) Toll Free Tel: 800-387-7278 (North America); 800-387-7305 (North America) Fax: 416-255-6708 Toll Free Fax: 800-665-7307 (North America) E-mail: firstname_lastname@ harcourt.com Web Site: www.harcourtcanada.com, pg 549

Cowden, Sue, McDougal Littell, 909 Davis St, Evanston, IL 60201 Tel: 847-869-2300 Toll Free Tel: 800-462-6595 (orders) Toll Free Fax: 888-872-8380 Web Site: www.mcdougallittell.com, pg 166

Cowles, Lauren, Cambridge University Press, 40 W 20 St, New York, NY 10011-4211 *Tel:* 212-924-3900 *Toll Free Tel:* 800-899-5222 *Fax:* 212-691-3239 *Web Site:* www.cambridge.org, pg 52

Cowles, William R, SkillPath Publications, 6900 Squibb Rd, Mission, KS 66202 *Tel:* 913-362-3900 *Toll Free Tel:* 800-873-7545 *Fax:* 913-362-4264 *E-mail:* bookstore@skillpath.net *Web Site:* www.ourbookstore.com, pg 249

Cox, Beth, McFarland & Co Inc Publishers, 960 Hwy 88 W, Jefferson, NC 28640 *Tel:* 336-246-4460 *Toll Free Tel:* 800-253-2187 (orders only) *Fax:* 336-246-5018; 336-246-4403 (orders) *E-mail:* info@mcfarlandpub.com *Web Site:* www.mcfarlandpub.com, pg 166

Cox, Erin, Scribner, 1230 Avenue of the Americas, New York, NY 10020, pg 244

Cox, Jeffrey, Snow Lion Publications Inc, 605 W State St, Ithaca, NY 14850 *Tel:* 607-273-8519 *Toll Free Tel:* 800-950-0313 *Fax:* 607-273-8508 *E-mail:* tibet@snowlionpub.com *Web Site:* www.snowlionpub.com, pg 251

Cox, Jennifer, Westminster John Knox Press, 100 Witherspoon St, Louisville, KY 40202-1396 *Tel:* 502-569-5052 *Toll Free Tel:* 800-227-2872 (US only) *Fax:* 502-569-8308 *Toll Free Fax:* 800-541-5113 (US only) *E-mail:* wjk@wjkbooks.com *Web Site:* www.wjkbooks.com, pg 297

Cox, Joyce, Online Training Solutions Inc, PO Box 2224, Redmond, WA 98073-2224 *Tel:* 425-885-1441 *Toll Free Tel:* 800-854-3344 *Fax:* 425-881-1642; 425-671-0640 *E-mail:* customerservice@otsi.com *Web Site:* www.otsi.com, pg 197

Cox, Kathleen, Corporation for Public Broadcasting (CPB), 401 Ninth St NW, Washington, DC 20004-2037 *Tel:* 202-879-9600 *Fax:* 202-879-9700 *E-mail:* info@cpb.org *Web Site:* www.cpb.org, pg 685

Cox, Michelle, Briefings Publishing Group, 1101 King St, Suite 110, Alexandria, VA 22314 *Tel:* 703-548-3800 *Toll Free Tel:* 800-888-2086 *Fax:* 703-684-2136 *E-mail:* customerservice@briefings.com *Web Site:* www.briefings.com, pg 47

Cox, Tom, Random House Children's Books, 1745 Broadway, New York, NY 10019 *Tel:* 212-782-9000 *Toll Free Tel:* 800-200-3552 *Fax:* 212-782-9452 *Web Site:* www.randomhouse.com/kids, pg 225

Cox, Tom, Random House Sales & Marketing, 1745 Broadway, New York, NY 10019 *Fax:* 212-782-9000, pg 227

Cozzaglio, Donna, I E Clark Publications, PO Box 246, Schulenburg, TX 78956 *Tel:* 979-743-3232 *Fax:* 979-743-4765 *E-mail:* ieclark@cvtv.net *Web Site:* www.ieclark.com, pg 63

Cozzi, Guy, Nemmar Real Estate Training, 15 E Putnam Ave, Suite 151, Greenwich, CT 06830 *Fax:* 212-937-2122 *E-mail:* info@nemmar.com *Web Site:* www.nemmar.com, pg 187

Crabtree, Andrea, Crabtree Publishing Co Ltd, 612 Welland Ave, St Catharines, ON L2M 5V6, Canada *Tel:* 905-682-5221 *Toll Free Tel:* 800-387-7650 *Fax:* 905-682-7166 *Toll Free Fax:* 800-355-7166 *E-mail:* custserv@crabtreebooks.com; sales@crabtreebooks.com; orders@crabtreebooks.com *Web Site:* www.crabtreebooks.com, pg 541

Crabtree, Peter A, Crabtree Publishing Co, 350 Fifth Ave, Suite 3308, PMB 16-A, New York, NY 10118 *Tel:* 212-496-5040 *Toll Free Tel:* 800-387-7650 *Toll Free Fax:* 800-355-7166 *E-mail:* letters@crabtreebooks.com *Web Site:* www.crabtreebooks.com, pg 71

Crabtree, Peter A, Crabtree Publishing Co Ltd, 612 Welland Ave, St Catharines, ON L2M 5V6, Canada *Tel:* 905-682-5221 *Toll Free Tel:* 800-387-7650 *Fax:* 905-682-7166 *Toll Free Fax:* 800-355-7166 *E-mail:* custserv@crabtreebooks.com; sales@crabtreebooks.com; orders@crabtreebooks.com *Web Site:* www.crabtreebooks.com, pg 541

Cracchiolo, Rachelle, Teacher Created Materials Inc, 6421 Industry Way, Westminster, CA 92683 *Tel:* 714-891-7895 *Toll Free Tel:* 800-662-4321 *Fax:* 714-892-0283 *Toll Free Fax:* 800-525-1254 *E-mail:* tcminfo@teachercreated.com *Web Site:* www.teachercreated.com, pg 265

Craft, Baird, Jones McClure Publishing Inc, 1113 Vine St, Suite 240, Houston, TX 77002 *Tel:* 713-223-2727 *Toll Free Tel:* 800-626-6667 *Fax:* 713-223-9393 *E-mail:* comments@jonesmcclure.com *Web Site:* www.jonesmcclure.com, pg 142

Craig, Bryce H, P & R Publishing Co, 1102 Marble Hill Rd, Phillipsburg, NJ 08865 *Tel:* 908-454-0505 *Toll Free Tel:* 800-631-0094 *Fax:* 908-859-2390 *E-mail:* per@prpbooks.com *Web Site:* prpbooks.com, pg 201

Craig, Carol L, Editing International LLC, 2123 Marlow Lane, Suite 21, Eugene, OR 97401-6431 *Tel:* 541-344-9118 *E-mail:* info@4-edit.com *Web Site:* www.4-edit.com, pg 597

Craig, Joanna, Kent State University Press, PO Box 5190, Kent, OH 44242-0001 *Tel:* 330-672-7913; 330-672-8097 (sales office) *Toll Free Tel:* 800-247-6553 (orders) *Fax:* 330-672-3104 *Web Site:* www.kentstateuniversitypress.com, pg 145

Craig, Joycelin, The Astronomical Society of the Pacific, 390 Ashton Ave, San Francisco, CA 94112 *Tel:* 415-337-1100 *Toll Free Tel:* 800-335-2624 (Cust Serv) *Fax:* 415-337-5205 *E-mail:* service@astrosociety.org *Web Site:* www.astrosociety.org, pg 27

Craig, Kathleen Rynne, AANS-American Association of Neurological Surgeons, 5550 Meadow Brook Dr, Rolling Meadows, IL 60008 *Tel:* 847-378-0500 *Fax:* 847-378-0600 *E-mail:* info@aans.org *Web Site:* www.neurosurgery.org, pg 2

Cramer, Cathy, Kalmbach Publishing Co, 21027 Crossroads Circle, Waukesha, WI 53187 *Tel:* 262-796-8776 *Toll Free Tel:* 800-533-6644 *Fax:* 262-796-1615 (sales & cust serv) *Web Site:* www.kalmbach.com, pg 143

Crandall, Mary Jo, Ave Maria Press, 19113 Douglas Rd, Notre Dame, IN 46556 *Tel:* 574-287-2831 *Toll Free Tel:* 800-282-1865 *Fax:* 574-239-2904 *Toll Free Fax:* 800-282-5681 *E-mail:* avemariapress.1@nd.edu *Web Site:* www.avemariapress.com, pg 29

Crandall, Mary Jo, Sorin Books, 19113 Douglas Rd, Notre Dame, IN 46556 *Tel:* 574-287-2831 *Toll Free Tel:* 800-282-1865 *Fax:* 574-239-2904 *Toll Free Fax:* 800-282-5681 *E-mail:* sorinbk@nd.edu *Web Site:* www.sorinbooks.com, pg 253

Crandall-Hollick, Martine L, World Eagle, 111 King St, Littleton, MA 01460-1527 *Tel:* 978-486-9180 *Toll Free Tel:* 800-854-8273 *Fax:* 978-486-9652 *E-mail:* iba@ibaradio.org *Web Site:* www.worldeagle.com; www.ibaradio.org, pg 304

Crandell, Leslie, O'Reilly & Associates Inc, 1005 Gravenstein Hwy N, Sebastopol, CA 95472 *Tel:* 707-827-7000 *Toll Free Tel:* 800-998-9938 *Fax:* 707-829-0104 *E-mail:* info@oreilly.com *Web Site:* www.oreilly.com, pg 199

Crane, Carla, Standard Publishing Co, 8121 Hamilton Ave, Cincinnati, OH 45231 *Tel:* 513-931-4050 *Toll Free Tel:* 800-543-1301 *Fax:* 513-931-0950 *Toll Free Fax:* 877-867-5751 *E-mail:* customerservice@standardpub.com *Web Site:* www.standardpub.com, pg 257

Crane, Edward H, Cato Institute, 1000 Massachusetts Ave NW, Washington, DC 20001-5403 *Tel:* 202-842-0200 *Toll Free Tel:* 800-767-1241 *Fax:* 202-842-3490 *E-mail:* books@cato.org *Web Site:* www.cato.org, pg 55

Crane, Edward M, Begell House Inc Publishers, 145 Madison Ave, Suite 601, New York, NY 10016 *Tel:* 212-725-1999 *Fax:* 212-213-8368 *E-mail:* orders@begellhouse.com *Web Site:* www.begellhouse.com, pg 35

Crane, Heidi T, Lawrenceville Press Inc, PO Box 704, Pennington, NJ 08534 *Tel:* 609-737-1148 *Fax:* 609-737-8564 *E-mail:* custserv@lvp.com *Web Site:* www.lvp.com, pg 150

Crane, Merissa, Loyola Press, 3441 N Ashland Ave, Chicago, IL 60657 *Tel:* 773-281-1818; 773-244-4429 *Toll Free Tel:* 800-621-1008 *Fax:* 773-281-0555; 773-281-0152 (trade) *E-mail:* editorial@loydapress.com *Web Site:* www.loyolapress.org, pg 159

Crary, Elizabeth, Parenting Press Inc, 11065 Fifth Ave NE, Suite F, Seattle, WA 98125 *Tel:* 206-364-2900 *Toll Free Tel:* 800-99-BOOKS (992-6657) *Fax:* 206-364-0702 *E-mail:* office@parentingpress.com *Web Site:* www.parentingpress.com, pg 204

Crary, Jonathan, Zone Books, 1226 Prospect Ave, Brooklyn, NY 11218 *Tel:* 718-686-0048 *Toll Free Tel:* 800-405-1619 (orders & cust serv) *Fax:* 212-625-9772; 718-686-9045 *Toll Free Fax:* 800-406-9145 (orders) *E-mail:* urzone@zonebooks.org; mitpressorders@mit.edu (orders), pg 307

Craven, Robert H Jr, F A Davis Co, 1915 Arch St, Philadelphia, PA 19103 *Tel:* 215-568-2270 *Toll Free Tel:* 800-523-4049 *Fax:* 215-568-5065 *E-mail:* info@fadavis.com *Web Site:* www.fadavis.com, pg 76

Craven, Robert H Sr, F A Davis Co, 1915 Arch St, Philadelphia, PA 19103 *Tel:* 215-568-2270 *Toll Free Tel:* 800-523-4049 *Fax:* 215-568-5065 *E-mail:* info@fadavis.com *Web Site:* www.fadavis.com, pg 76

Craven, Victoria, Watson-Guptill Publications, 770 Broadway, New York, NY 10003 *Tel:* 646-654-5450 *Toll Free Tel:* 800-278-8477 (orders only) *Fax:* 646-654-5486; 646-654-5487 *E-mail:* info@watsonguptill.com *Web Site:* www.watsonguptill.com, pg 294

Crawford, Ann, Geological Society of America (GSA), 3300 Penrose Place, Boulder, CO 80301 *Tel:* 303-447-2020 *Toll Free Tel:* 800-472-1988 *Fax:* 303-357-1070 *E-mail:* pubs@geosociety.org *Web Site:* www.geosociety.org, pg 104

Crawford, Betty-Anne, Rights Unlimited Inc, 101 W 55 St, Suite 2D, New York, NY 10019 *Tel:* 212-246-0900 *Fax:* 212-246-2114 *E-mail:* faith@rightsunlimited.com *Web Site:* rightsunlimited.com, pg 651

Crawford, Cam, The Roeher Institute, York University, Kinsmen Bldg, 4700 Keele St, North York, ON M3J 1P3, Canada *Tel:* 416-661-9611 *Fax:* 416-661-5701 *E-mail:* info@roeher.ca *Web Site:* www.roeher.ca, pg 560

Crawford, Christina, Seven Springs Press, 11150 Sanders Rd, Tensed, ID 83870 *Tel:* 208-274-2470 *E-mail:* sevenspringscc@aol.com, pg 574

Crawford, Hope, William Andrew Publishing, 13 Eaton Ave, Norwich, NY 13815 *Tel:* 607-337-5000 *Toll Free Tel:* 800-932-7045 *Fax:* 607-337-5090 *E-mail:* publishing@williamandrew.com *Web Site:* www.williamandrew.com, pg 300

Crawford, Ingrid, North American Bookdealers Exchange, PO Box 606, Cottage Grove, OR 97424-0026 *Tel:* 541-942-7455 *Fax:* 561-258-2625 *E-mail:* nabe@bookmarketingprofits.com *Web Site:* www.bookmarketingprofits.com, pg 695

Crawford, Lorne, Crawford Literary Agency, 94 Evans Rd, Barnstead, NH 03218 *Tel:* 603-269-5851 *Fax:* 603-269-2533 *E-mail:* crawfordlit@att.net, pg 626

Crawford, Maggie, Pocket Books, 1230 Avenue of the Americas, New York, NY 10020 *Toll Free Tel:* 800-456-6798 *Fax:* 212-698-7284 *E-mail:* consumer.customerservice@simonandschuster.com *Web Site:* www.simonsays.com, pg 215

Crawford, Susan, Crawford Literary Agency, 94 Evans Rd, Barnstead, NH 03218 *Tel:* 603-269-5851 *Fax:* 603-269-2533 *E-mail:* crawfordlit@att.net, pg 626

Crawford, Tad, Allworth Press, 10 E 23 St, Suite 510, New York, NY 10010 *Tel:* 212-777-8395 *Toll Free Tel:* 800-491-2808 *Fax:* 212-777-8261 *E-mail:* pub@allworth.com *Web Site:* www.allworth.com, pg 9

Crawford, Tom, Dover Publications Inc, 31 E Second St, Mineola, NY 11501 *Tel:* 516-294-7000 *Toll Free Tel:* 800-223-3130 (orders) *Fax:* 516-742-6953; 516-742-5049 (orders) *Web Site:* www.doverpublications.com; www.doverdirect.com, pg 83

Crouch, Orin, M Lee Smith Publishers LLC, 5201 Virginia Way, Brentwood, TN 37027 *Tel:* 615-373-7517 *Toll Free Tel:* 800-274-6774 *Fax:* 615-373-5183 *Web Site:* www.mleesmith.com, pg 250

Crouch, Tom, Los Angeles Times Book Prizes, 202 W First St, 6th fl, Los Angeles, CA 90012 *Tel:* 213-237-5775 *Fax:* 213-346-3599 *Web Site:* www.latimes.com/bookprizes, pg 786

Crow, Dennis, Maisonneuve Press, PO Box 2980, Washington, DC 20013-2980 *Tel:* 301-277-7505 *Fax:* 301-277-2467 *Web Site:* www.maisonneuvepress.com, pg 161

Crowe, Joey, Abingdon Press, 201 Eighth Ave S, Nashville, TN 37203-3919 *Tel:* 615-749-6290 (publicist); 615-749-6000; 615-749-6451 (sales) *Toll Free Tel:* 800-251-3320 *Fax:* 615-749-6056 *Web Site:* www.abingdonpress.com, pg 3

Crowe, Sara, Trident Media Group LLC, 41 Madison Ave, 36th fl, New York, NY 10010 *Tel:* 212-262-4810 *Fax:* 212-725-4501 *Web Site:* www.tridentmediagroup.com, pg 659

Crowe-Lile, Katie, Harcourt School Publishers, 6277 Sea Harbor Dr, Orlando, FL 32887 *Tel:* 407-345-2000 *Toll Free Tel:* 800-225-5425 (cust serv) *Fax:* 407-352-3445 *Toll Free Fax:* 800-874-6418 *E-mail:* hbspcs@hbschool.com *Web Site:* www.harcourtschool.com, pg 114

Crowell, Elizabeth, Rosalie Boyle/Norma Farber Award, 16 Cornell St, Arlington, MA 02474 *Web Site:* www.nepoetryclub.org, pg 764

Crowell, Elizabeth, Barbara Bradley Prize, 16 Cornell St, Arlington, MA 02474 *Web Site:* www.nepoetryclub.org, pg 764

Crowell, Elizabeth, Der-Hovanessian Translation Prize, 16 Cornell St, Arlington, MA 02474 *Web Site:* www.nepoetryclub.org, pg 769

Crowell, Elizabeth, Sheila Margaret Motton Prize, 16 Cornell St, Arlington, MA 02474 *Web Site:* www.nepoetryclub.org, pg 791

Crowell, Elizabeth, Erika Mumford Prize, 16 Cornell St, Arlington, MA 02474 *Web Site:* www.nepoetryclub.org, pg 791

Crowell, Elizabeth, May Sarton Award, 16 Cornell St, Arlington, MA 02474 *Web Site:* www.nepoetryclub.org, pg 803

Crowell, Elizabeth, Daniel Varoujan Award, 16 Cornell St, Arlington, MA 02474 *Web Site:* www.nepoetryclub.org, pg 810

Crowley, James M, Society for Industrial & Applied Mathematics, 3600 University City Science Ctr, Philadelphia, PA 19104-2688 *Tel:* 215-382-9800 *Toll Free Tel:* 800-447-7426 *Fax:* 215-386-7999 *E-mail:* siam@siam.org *Web Site:* www.siam.org, pg 251

Crowley, Louise, Vermont College, MFA in Writing Program, 36 College St, Montpelier, VT 05602 *Tel:* 802-828-8840 *Fax:* 802-828-8649 *Web Site:* www.tui.edu/vermontcollege, pg 756

Crowther, Duane S, Horizon Publishers & Distributors Inc, 50 S 500 W, Bountiful, UT 84010 *Tel:* 801-295-9451 *Toll Free Tel:* 800-759-2665 *Fax:* 801-489-1096 *E-mail:* horizonp@burgoyne.com *Web Site:* www.horizonpublishersbooks.com, pg 125

Crumley, Gene, Writing Workshops, 1333 Research Park Dr, Davis, CA 95616 *Tel:* 530-754-5237 *Toll Free Tel:* 800-752-0881 *Fax:* 530-754-5105 *Web Site:* www.extension.ucdavis.edu, pg 749

Crumly, Chuck, University of California Press, 2120 Berkeley Way, Berkeley, CA 94720 *Tel:* 510-642-4247 *Toll Free Tel:* 800-777-4726 *Fax:* 510-643-7127 *Toll Free Fax:* 800-999-1958 *E-mail:* askucp@ucpress.edu *Web Site:* www.ucpress.edu, pg 281

Crumrine, David, e-Scholastic, 568 Broadway, 9th fl, New York, NY 10012 *Tel:* 212-343-7100 *Fax:* 212-343-4949, pg 85

Crutcher, John, Bloomberg Press, PO Box 888, Princeton, NJ 08542-0888 *Tel:* 609-279-4600 *E-mail:* press@bloomberg.com *Web Site:* www.bloomberg.com/books, pg 41

Crutchfield, James A, SPUR Awards, 1012 Fair St, Franklin, TN 37064 *Tel:* 615-791-1444 *Fax:* 615-791-1444 *Web Site:* www.westernwriters.org, pg 807

Crutchfield, James A, Western Writers of America Inc, 1012 Fair St, Franklin, TN 37064 *Tel:* 615-791-1444 *Fax:* 615-791-1444 *Web Site:* www.westernwriters.org, pg 702

Cruz, Jason, Routledge, 29 W 35 St, New York, NY 10001-2299 *Tel:* 212-216-7800 *Fax:* 212-564-7854 (main) *E-mail:* info@taylorandfrancis.com *Web Site:* www.routledge-ny.com, pg 235

Cruz, John, American Bible Society, 1865 Broadway, New York, NY 10023-7505 *Tel:* 212-408-1200 *Toll Free Tel:* 800-322-4253 (orders only) *Fax:* 212-408-1259 *E-mail:* info@americanbible.org *Web Site:* www.americanbible.org, pg 12

Csontos, David, Frances Goldin Literary Agency, Inc, 57 E 11 St, Suite 5B, New York, NY 10003 *Tel:* 212-777-0047 *Fax:* 212-228-1660 *E-mail:* agency@goldinlit.com *Web Site:* www.goldinlit.com, pg 632

Cubberley, William, Practising Law Institute, 810 Seventh Ave, New York, NY 10019 *Tel:* 212-824-5700 *Toll Free Tel:* 800-260-4PLI (260-4754 customer service) *Fax:* 212-265-4742 *Toll Free Fax:* 800-321-0093 *E-mail:* info@pli.edu *Web Site:* www.pli.edu, pg 217

Cuccarese, Julia M, American Literary Press/Noble House, 8019 Belair Rd, Suite 10, Baltimore, MD 21236 *Tel:* 410-882-7700 *Fax:* 410-882-7703 *E-mail:* amerlit@americanliterarypress.com *Web Site:* www.americanliterarypress.com, pg 569

Cuevas, Jeannine, The Kiriyama Pacific Rim Book Prize, 650 Delancy St, Suite 101, San Francisco, CA 94107-2082 *Tel:* 415-777-1628 *Fax:* 415-777-1646 *Web Site:* www.kiriyamaprize.org, pg 782

Culhane, Sean M, Regatta Press Ltd, 750 Cascadilla St, Ithaca, NY 14851 *Tel:* 607-277-2211 *Fax:* 607-277-6292 *Toll Free Fax:* 800-688-2877 *E-mail:* info@regattapress.com *Web Site:* www.regattapress.com, pg 231

Cull, Mark E, Red Hen Press, PO Box 3537, Granada Hills, CA 91394-0537 *Tel:* 818-831-0649 *Fax:* 818-831-6659 *E-mail:* editors@redhen.org *Web Site:* www.redhen.org, pg 229

Cullers, Robert M, Writers: Free-Lance Inc, 167 Bluff Rd, Strasburg, VA 22657 *Tel:* 540-635-4617, pg 615

Cullerton, Jackie, Schreiber Publishing Inc, 51 Monroe St, Suite 101, Rockville, MD 20850 *Tel:* 301-424-7737 *Toll Free Tel:* 800-822-3213 (sales) *Fax:* 301-424-2518 *E-mail:* books@schreibernet.com *Web Site:* schreiberpublishing.com, pg 243

Culley, Joyce, University Press of America Inc, 4501 Forbes Blvd, Suite 200, Lanham, MD 20706 *Tel:* 301-459-3366 *Toll Free Tel:* 800-462-6420 *Fax:* 301-429-5748 *Toll Free Fax:* 800-338-4550 *Web Site:* www.univpress.com, pg 286

Culliford, Craig, Crabtree Publishing Co Ltd, 612 Welland Ave, St Catharines, ON L2M 5V6, Canada *Tel:* 905-682-5221 *Toll Free Tel:* 800-387-7650 *Fax:* 905-682-7166 *Toll Free Fax:* 800-355-7166 *E-mail:* custserv@crabtreebooks.com; sales@crabtreebooks.com; orders@crabtreebooks.com *Web Site:* www.crabtreebooks.com, pg 541

Culliton, Katie, LexisNexis Academic & Library Solutions, 7500 Old Georgetown Rd, Suite 1300, Bethesda, MD 20814-3389 *Tel:* 301-654-1550 *Toll Free Tel:* 800-638-8380 *Fax:* 301-654-4033; 301-657-3203 (sales) *E-mail:* academicinfo@lexisnexis.com *Web Site:* www.lexisnexis.com/academic, pg 153

Culp, Rick, Prentice Hall School, One Lake St, Upper Saddle River, NJ 07458 *Tel:* 201-236-7000, pg 217

Culpeper, Roy, North-South Institute/Institut Nord-Sud, 55 Murray St, Suite 200, Ottawa, ON K1N 5M3, Canada *Tel:* 613-241-3535 *Fax:* 613-241-7435 *E-mail:* nsi@nsi-ins.ca *Web Site:* www.nsi-ins.ca, pg 556

Culpepper, Steve, Garlinghouse Inc, 174 Oakwood Dr, Glastonbury, CT 06033 *Tel:* 860-659-5667 *Fax:* 860-659-5692 *E-mail:* info@garlinghouse.com *Web Site:* www.garlinghouse.com, pg 103

Culver, Julie, Lowenstein-Yost Associates Inc, 121 W 27 St, Suite 601, New York, NY 10001 *Tel:* 212-206-1630 *Fax:* 212-727-0280 *Web Site:* www.lowensteinyost.com, pg 641

Cummings, A E, Madison Press Books, 1000 Yonge St, Toronto, ON M4W 2K2, Canada *Tel:* 416-923-5027 *Fax:* 416-923-9708 *E-mail:* info@madisonpressbooks.com *Web Site:* www.madisonpressbooks.com, pg 553

Cummings, Gerry, Time Warner Book Group, 1271 Avenue of the Americas, New York, NY 10020 *Tel:* 212-522-7200 *Fax:* 212-522-7991 *Web Site:* www.twbookmark.com, pg 271

Cummings, Mark, Scholastic Library Publishing, 90 Old Sherman Tpke, Danbury, CT 06816 *Tel:* 203-797-3500 *Toll Free Tel:* 800-621-1115 *Fax:* 203-797-3657 *Web Site:* www.scholasticlibrary.com, pg 242

Cumpston, Copenhaver, University of Illinois Press, 1325 S Oak, Champaign, IL 61820-6903 *Tel:* 217-333-0950; 212-577-5487 *Fax:* 217-244-8082; 410-516-6969 (orders) *E-mail:* uipress@uillinois.edu; journals@uillinois.edu *Web Site:* www.press.uillinois.edu, pg 282

Cunningham, Frank J, Ave Maria Press, 19113 Douglas Rd, Notre Dame, IN 46556 *Tel:* 574-287-2831 *Toll Free Tel:* 800-282-1865 *Fax:* 574-239-2904 *Toll Free Fax:* 800-282-5681 *E-mail:* avemariapress.1@nd.edu *Web Site:* www.avemariapress.com, pg 29

Cunningham, Frank J, Sorin Books, 19113 Douglas Rd, Notre Dame, IN 46556 *Tel:* 574-287-2831 *Toll Free Tel:* 800-282-1865 *Fax:* 574-239-2904 *Toll Free Fax:* 800-282-5681 *E-mail:* sorinbk@nd.edu *Web Site:* www.sorinbooks.com, pg 253

Cunningham, Jennifer, University of Oklahoma Press, 4100 28 Ave NW, Norman, OK 73069-8218 *Tel:* 405-325-2000 *Toll Free Tel:* 800-627-7377 (orders) *Fax:* 405-364-5798 (orders) *Toll Free Fax:* 800-735-0476 (orders) *E-mail:* oupress@ou.edu *Web Site:* www.oupress.com, pg 284

Cunningham, John, St Martin's Press Trade Division, 175 Fifth Ave, New York, NY 10010 *E-mail:* firstname.lastname@stmartins.com *Web Site:* www.stmartins.com; www.minotaurbooks.com, pg 239

Cunningham, John D, Visuals Unlimited, 27 Meadow Dr, Hollis, NH 03049 *Tel:* 603-465-3340 *Fax:* 603-465-3360 *E-mail:* staff@visualsunlimited.com *Web Site:* visualsunlimited.com, pg 612

Cunningham, Judith, Oxford University Press, Inc, 198 Madison Ave, New York, NY 10016-4314 *Tel:* 212-726-6000 *Toll Free Tel:* 800-451-7556 (orders) *Web Site:* www.oup.com/us, pg 200

Cunningham, Paula, McClanahan Publishing House Inc, PO Box 100, Kuttawa, KY 42055-0100 *Tel:* 270-388-9388 *Toll Free Tel:* 800-544-6959 *Fax:* 270-388-6186 *E-mail:* books@kybooks.com *Web Site:* www.kybooks.com, pg 166

Cuprisin, Jim, The Academy of Producer Insurance Studies Inc, PO Box 27027, Austin, TX 78755-2027 *Tel:* 512-346-7050 *Toll Free Tel:* 800-526-2777 *Fax:* 512-343-2167 *E-mail:* alliance@scic.com *Web Site:* www.thenationalalliance.com, pg 4

Curchek, Sanatan, Aum Publications, 86-10 Parsons Blvd, Jamaica, NY 11432 *Tel:* 718-291-9757 *Fax:* 718-523-1423, pg 28

Curr, Judith, Atria Books, 1230 Avenue of the Americas, New York, NY 10020 *Tel:* 212-698-7000 *Fax:* 212-698-7007 *Web Site:* www.simonsays.com, pg 27

Curran, Geraldine, Marshall Cavendish Corp, 99 White Plains Rd, Tarrytown, NY 10591-9001 *Tel:* 914-332-8888 *Fax:* 914-332-1888 *E-mail:* mcc@marshallcavendish.com *Web Site:* www.marshallcavendish.com, pg 164

Daley, Gabriella, American Correctional Association, 4380 Forbes Blvd, Lanham, MD 20706-4322 *Tel:* 301-918-1800 *Toll Free Tel:* 800-222-5646 *Fax:* 301-918-1886 *Web Site:* www.aca.org, pg 13

Dalglish, Lucy, Reporters Committee for Freedom of the Press, 1815 N Fort Myer Dr, Suite 900, Arlington, VA 22209-1817 *Tel:* 703-807-2100 *Toll Free Tel:* 800-336-4243 *Fax:* 703-807-2109 *E-mail:* rcfp@rcfp.org *Web Site:* www.rcfp.org, pg 698

Dallek, Robert, James Fenimore Cooper Prize, Columbia University, 603 Fayerweather Hall, MC 2538, New York, NY 10027, pg 768

Dallek, Robert, Allan Nevins Prize, Columbia University, 603 Fayerweather Hall, MC 2538, New York, NY 10027, pg 793

Dallek, Robert, Francis Parkman Prize, Columbia University, 603 Fayerweather Hall, MC 2538, New York, NY 10027, pg 797

Dalton, Pat, Diamond Literary Agency Inc, 3063 S Kearney St, Denver, CO 80222 *Tel:* 303-753-6318 *E-mail:* diamondliteraryagency@yahoo.com, pg 627

Dalton, Sundar, Aum Publications, 86-10 Parsons Blvd, Jamaica, NY 11432 *Tel:* 718-291-9757 *Fax:* 718-523-1423, pg 28

Damen, Saskia, Michelin Travel Publications, PO Box 19001, Greenville, SC 29602-9001 *Tel:* 864-458-5127 *Toll Free Tel:* 800-423-0485; 800-223-0987 *Fax:* 864-458-6674 *Toll Free Fax:* 866-297-0914 *E-mail:* michelin.travel-publications-us@us.michelin.com *Web Site:* www.viamichelin.com, pg 173

Damiani, Bruno M, Scripta Humanistica Publishing International, 1383 Kersey Lane, Potomac, MD 20854 *Tel:* 301-294-7949 *Fax:* 301-424-9584 *E-mail:* scripta@aol.com *Web Site:* www.scriptahumanistica.com, pg 244

Damp, Dennis V, Bookhaven Press LLC, 249 Field Club Circle, McKees Rocks, PA 15136 *Tel:* 412-494-6926 *Toll Free Tel:* 800-782-7424 (orders only) *Fax:* 412-494-5749 *E-mail:* bookhaven@aol.com *Web Site:* members.aol.com/bookhaven, pg 44

Dams, Jeanne, Of Dark & Stormy Nights, PO Box 6804, South Bend, IN 46660-6804 *Tel:* 212-888-8171 *Fax:* 212-888-8107 *Web Site:* www.mwamidwest.org, pg 745

Dan, Barbara Griffin, Eden Publishing, PO Box 20176, Keizer, OR 97307-0176 *Tel:* 503-390-9013 *Fax:* 503-390-9013 *E-mail:* info@edenpublishing.com *Web Site:* www.edenpublishing.com, pg 87

Dana, Heather, Kluwer Academic Publishers, 101 Philip Dr, Assinippi Park, Norwell, MA 02061 *Tel:* 781-871-6600 *Fax:* 781-871-6528; 781-681-9045 (cust serv) *E-mail:* kluwer@wkap.com *Web Site:* www.wkap.nl, pg 146

Danato, Kris, Grade Finders Inc, 662 Exton Commons, Exton, PA 19341 *Tel:* 610-524-7070 *Fax:* 610-524-8912 *E-mail:* info@gradefinders.com *Web Site:* www.gradefinders.com, pg 107

Danbury, Richard S III, Dan River Press, PO Box 298, Thomaston, ME 04861 *Tel:* 207-354-0998 *E-mail:* cal@americanletter.org *Web Site:* www.americanletters.org, pg 75

Danbury, Richard S III, Northwoods Press, PO Box 298, Thomaston, ME 04861-0298 *Tel:* 207-354-0998 *E-mail:* cal@americanletters.org *Web Site:* www.americanletters.org, pg 193

Dane, M Stephen, Kluwer Academic Publishers, 101 Philip Dr, Assinippi Park, Norwell, MA 02061 *Tel:* 781-871-6600 *Fax:* 781-871-6528; 781-681-9045 (cust serv) *E-mail:* kluwer@wkap.com *Web Site:* www.wkap.nl, pg 146

Danforth, Scott, University of Tennessee Press, 110 Conference Center Bldg, Knoxville, TN 37996-4108 *Tel:* 865-974-3321 *Toll Free Tel:* 800-621-2736 (ordering) *Fax:* 865-974-3724 *E-mail:* custserv@utpress.org *Web Site:* www.utpress.org, pg 285

Daniel, John, John Daniel & Co, Publishers, PO Box 2790, McKinleyville, CA 95519 *Tel:* 707-839-3495 *Toll Free Tel:* 800-662-8351 *Fax:* 707-839-3242 *E-mail:* dandd@danielpublishing.com *Web Site:* www.danielpublishing.com, pg 75

Daniel, Nadia, College of General Studies Special Programs, University of Pennsylvania, 3440 Market St, Suite 100, Philadelphia, PA 19104-3335 *Tel:* 215-898-7326 *Fax:* 215-573-2053 *E-mail:* cgs@sas.upenn.edu *Web Site:* www.sas.upenn.edu/cgs, pg 751

Daniel, Susan, John Daniel & Co, Publishers, PO Box 2790, McKinleyville, CA 95519 *Tel:* 707-839-3495 *Toll Free Tel:* 800-662-8351 *Fax:* 707-839-3242 *E-mail:* dandd@danielpublishing.com *Web Site:* www.danielpublishing.com, pg 75

Daniels, Diana, Mason Crest Publishers, 370 Reed Rd, Suite 302, Broomall, PA 19008 *Tel:* 610-543-6200 *Toll Free Tel:* 866-MCP-BOOK (627-2665) *Fax:* 610-543-3878 *Web Site:* www.masoncrest.com, pg 165

Daniels, Leslie, The Joy Harris Literary Agency, 156 Fifth Ave, Suite 617, New York, NY 10010 *Tel:* 212-924-6269 *Fax:* 212-924-6609 *E-mail:* gen.office@jhlitagent.com, pg 634

Daniels, Ray, Brewers Publications, 736 Pearl St, Boulder, CO 80302 *Tel:* 303-447-0816 *Toll Free Tel:* 888-822-6273 (Canada & US) *Fax:* 303-447-2825 *Web Site:* www.beertown.org, pg 46

Dannenberg, Penelope, Artists' Fellowships, 155 Avenue of the Americas, 14th fl, New York, NY 10013-1507 *Tel:* 212-366-6900 *Fax:* 212-366-1778 *E-mail:* nyainfo@nyfa.org *Web Site:* www.nyfa.org, pg 760

Dannis, Joe, DawnSignPress, 6130 Nancy Ridge Dr, San Diego, CA 92121-3223 *Tel:* 858-625-0600 *Toll Free Tel:* 800-549-5350 *Fax:* 858-625-2336 *E-mail:* info@dawnsign.com *Web Site:* www.dawnsign.com, pg 77

Dano, Yvette, Penguin Group (USA) Inc, 375 Hudson St, New York, NY 10014 *Tel:* 212-366-2000 *Fax:* 212-366-2666 *E-mail:* online@uspenguingroup.com *Web Site:* www.penguin.com, pg 208

Danowski, Deb, Wm B Eerdmans Publishing Co, 255 Jefferson Ave SE, Grand Rapids, MI 49503 *Tel:* 616-459-4591 *Toll Free Tel:* 800-253-7521 *Fax:* 616-459-6540 *E-mail:* sales@eerdmans.com *Web Site:* www.eerdmans.com, pg 88

Darby, Timothy, BNA Books, 1231 25 St NW, Washington, DC 20037 *Tel:* 202-452-4343 *Toll Free Tel:* 800-960-1220 *Fax:* 202-452-4997 (editorial off); 732-346-1624 (cust serv) *E-mail:* books@bna.com *Web Site:* www.bnabooks.com, pg 42

Darden, Robert, Baylor University, Writing Program, One Baylor Place, Waco, TX 76798 *Tel:* 254-710-1768 *Fax:* 254-710-3894 *Web Site:* www.baylor.edu, pg 751

Dardick, Simon, Vehicule Press, 125 Place du Parc Sta, Montreal, PQ H2X 4A3, Canada *Tel:* 514-844-6073 *Fax:* 514-844-7543 *E-mail:* vp@vehiculepress.com *Web Site:* www.vehiculepress.com, pg 566

Darhansoff, Liz, Darhansoff, Verrill, Feldman Literary Agents, 236 W 26 St, Suite 802, New York, NY 10001-6736 *Tel:* 917-305-1300 *Fax:* 917-305-1400 *Web Site:* www.dvagency.com, pg 626

Darling, Daniel, Victory in Grace Printing, 60 Quentin Rd, Lake Zurich, IL 60047 *Tel:* 847-438-4494 *Toll Free Tel:* 800-784-7223 *Fax:* 847-438-4232 *Web Site:* www.victoryingrace.org, pg 290

Darling, Harold, Laughing Elephant, 3645 Interlake Ave N, Seattle, WA 98103 *Tel:* 206-447-9229 *Toll Free Tel:* 800-354-0400 *Fax:* 206-447-9189 *E-mail:* mail@laughingelephant.com *Web Site:* www.laughingelephant.com, pg 150

Darnton, Kate, PublicAffairs, 250 W 57 St, Suite 1321, New York, NY 10107 *Tel:* 212-397-6666 *Toll Free Tel:* 800-242-7737 (orders) *Fax:* 212-397-4267 *E-mail:* publicaffairs@perseusbooks.com *Web Site:* www.publicaffairsbooks.com, pg 221

Darrell, Eugene, The Mathematical Association of America, 1529 18 St NW, Washington, DC 20036 *Tel:* 202-387-5200 *Toll Free Tel:* 800-331-1622 (orders) *Fax:* 202-265-2384 *E-mail:* ldouglas@pmds.com *Web Site:* www.maa.org, pg 165

Darrell, Jose, Key Porter Books Ltd, 70 The Esplanade, 3rd fl, Toronto, ON M5E 1R2, Canada *Tel:* 416-862-7777 *Fax:* 416-862-2304 *E-mail:* info@keyporter.com *Web Site:* www.keyporter.com, pg 551

Darrock, Deb, Simon & Schuster, 1230 Avenue of the Americas, New York, NY 10020 *Tel:* 212-698-7000 *Toll Free Tel:* 800-223-2348 (cust serv); 800-223-2336 (orders) *Toll Free Fax:* 800-943-9831 (orders) *Web Site:* www.simonsays.com, pg 248

Dart, Tom, First Folio Resource Group Inc, 10 King St E, Suite 801, Toronto, ON M5C 1C3, Canada *Tel:* 416-368-7668 *Fax:* 416-368-9363 *E-mail:* mail@firstfolio.com *Web Site:* www.firstfolio.com, pg 599

Darwin, Tony, Starlite Inc, PO Box 20004, St Petersburg, FL 33742-0004 *Tel:* 727-392-2929 *Toll Free Tel:* 800-577-2929 *Fax:* 727-392-6161 *E-mail:* starlite@citebook.com *Web Site:* www.starlite-inc.com; www.citebook.com, pg 258

Dassopoulos, Catherine, Professional Publishing, 1333 Burr Ridge Pkwy, Burr Ridge, IL 60527 *Tel:* 630-789-4000; 630-789-5500 *Toll Free Tel:* 800-2McGraw (262-4729) *Fax:* 630-789-6933 *Web Site:* www.books.mcgraw-hill.com, pg 220

Dattila, Robert, Phoenix Literary Agency, 216 S Yellowstone, Livingston, MT 59047 *Tel:* 902-232-2848; 520-404-4748 (cell), pg 648

Daugherty, Chester, Concourse Press, PO Box 8265, Philadelphia, PA 19101-8265 *Tel:* 610-325-0313 *Fax:* 610-359-1953, pg 66

Daugherty, Shokoofeh, Concourse Press, PO Box 8265, Philadelphia, PA 19101-8265 *Tel:* 610-325-0313 *Fax:* 610-359-1953, pg 66

Davenport, Elaine, Writer's AudioShop, 1316 Overland Stage Rd, Dripping Springs, TX 78620 *Tel:* 512-264-9210 *Toll Free Tel:* 800-88-WRITE (889-7483) *Fax:* 512-264-9210 *E-mail:* writersaudio@timberwdfinc.com; wrtaudshop@aol.com *Web Site:* www.writersaudio.com, pg 304

Davenport, May, May Davenport Publishers, 26313 Purissima Rd, Los Altos Hills, CA 94022 *Tel:* 650-947-1275 *Fax:* 650-947-1373 *E-mail:* mdbooks@earthlink.net *Web Site:* www.maydavenportpublishers.com, pg 76

David, Jack, ECW Press, 2120 Queen St E, Suite 200, Toronto, ON M4E 1E2, Canada *Tel:* 416-694-3348 *Fax:* 416-698-9906 *E-mail:* info@ecwpress.com *Web Site:* www.ecwpress.com, pg 543

David, John, Oaklea Press, 6912 Three Chopt Rd, Suite B, Richmond, VA 23226 *Tel:* 804-281-5872 *Toll Free Tel:* 800-295-4066 *Fax:* 804-281-5686 *E-mail:* info@oakleapress.com *Web Site:* www.oakleapress.com, pg 195

David, Pierre, Editions du Phare Inc, 105 rue de Martigny Ouest, St Jerome, PQ J7Y 2G2, Canada *Tel:* 450-438-8479 *Toll Free Tel:* 800-561-2371 (Canada) *Fax:* 450-432-3892 *E-mail:* info@mondiaduphare.net, pg 544

David, Pierre, Mondia Editeurs Inc, 105 de Martigny Ouest, St-Jerome, PQ J7Y 2G2, Canada *Tel:* 450-438-8479 *Toll Free Tel:* 800-561-2371 (Canada) *Fax:* 450-432-3892 *E-mail:* info@mondiaduphare.net, pg 555

Davidar, David, Penguin Group (Canada), 10 Alcorn Ave, Suite 300, Toronto, ON M4V 3B2, Canada *Tel:* 416-925-2249 *Fax:* 416-925-0068 *Web Site:* www.penguin.ca, pg 557

Davidian, Marlena, Transaction Publishers, Rutgers University, 35 Berrue Circle, Piscataway, NJ 08854 *Tel:* 732-445-2280 *Toll Free Tel:* 888-999-6778 *Fax:* 732-445-3138 *E-mail:* trans@transactionpub.com *Web Site:* www.transactionpub.com, pg 274

Davidson, Andrew J, Harlan Davidson Inc/Forum Press Inc, 773 Glenn Ave, Wheeling, IL 60090-6000 *Tel:* 847-541-9720 *Fax:* 847-541-9830 *E-mail:* harlandavidson@harlandavidson.com *Web Site:* www.harlandavidson.com, pg 115

Davidson, Angela E, Harlan Davidson Inc/Forum Press Inc, 773 Glenn Ave, Wheeling, IL 60090-6000 *Tel:* 847-541-9720 *Fax:* 847-541-9830 *E-mail:* harlandavidson@harlandavidson.com *Web Site:* www.harlandavidson.com, pg 115

Davidson, Dayle, Group Publishing Inc, 1515 Cascade Ave, Loveland, CO 80538 *Tel:* 970-669-3836 *Toll Free Tel:* 800-447-1070 *Fax:* 970-678-4392 *E-mail:* innovatr@grouppublishing.com *Web Site:* www.grouppublishing.com, pg 110

Davidson, George, The Overlook Press, 141 Wooster St, New York, NY 10012 *Tel:* 212-965-8400 *Fax:* 212-965-9834 *Web Site:* www.overlookny.com, pg 200

Davidson, Leigh, Down There Press, 938 Howard St, Suite 101, San Francisco, CA 94103 *Tel:* 415-974-8985 *Fax:* 415-974-8989 *E-mail:* downtherepress@excite.com *Web Site:* www.goodvibes.com/dtp/dtp.html, pg 83

Davidson, Stuart, The Riverside Publishing Co, 425 Spring Lake Dr, Itasca, IL 60143-2079 *Tel:* 630-467-7000 *Toll Free Tel:* 800-323-9540 *Fax:* 630-467-7192 (cust serv) *Web Site:* www.riverpub.com, pg 233

Davie, Matt, Simon & Schuster Online, 1230 Avenue of the Americas, New York, NY 10020 *Tel:* 212-698-7547 *Fax:* 212-632-8070 *E-mail:* ssonline@simonsays.com *Web Site:* www.simonsays.com; www.simonsayskids.com; www.simonsaysshop.com, pg 249

Davies, A L, Davies Publishing Inc, 32 S Raymond Ave, Pasadena, CA 91105-1935 *Tel:* 626-792-3046 *Toll Free Tel:* 877-792-0005 *Fax:* 626-792-5308 *E-mail:* daviescorp@aol.com *Web Site:* www.daviespublishing.com, pg 76

Davies, Anne Lloyd, Simon & Schuster Inc, 1230 Avenue of the Americas, New York, NY 10020 *Tel:* 212-698-7000 *Fax:* 212-698-7007 *Web Site:* www.simonsays.com, pg 249

Davies, Elizabeth B, The Davies Group Publishers, PO Box 440140, Aurora, CO 80044-0140 *Tel:* 303-750-8374 *Fax:* 303-337-0952 *E-mail:* daviesgroup@msn.com, pg 76

Davies, Matt, Association of American Editorial Cartoonists, 1221 Stoneferry Lane, Raleigh, NC 27606 *Tel:* 919-859-5516 *Fax:* 919-859-3172, pg 679

Davies, Michael, Davies Publishing Inc, 32 S Raymond Ave, Pasadena, CA 91105-1935 *Tel:* 626-792-3046 *Toll Free Tel:* 877-792-0005 *Fax:* 626-792-5308 *E-mail:* daviescorp@aol.com *Web Site:* www.daviespublishing.com, pg 76

Davies, Vicki, University of Nevada Press, MS 166, Reno, NV 89557-0076 *Tel:* 775-784-6573 *Toll Free Tel:* 800-682-6657 *Fax:* 775-784-6200 *Toll Free Fax:* 877-682-6657 *Web Site:* www.nvbooks.nevada.edu, pg 283

Davis, Aida, American Institute of Aeronautics & Astronautics, 1801 Alexander Bell Dr, Suite 500, Reston, VA 20191 *Tel:* 703-264-7500 *Toll Free Tel:* 800-639-2422 *Fax:* 703-264-7551 *E-mail:* custserv@aiaa.org *Web Site:* www.aiaa.org, pg 14

Davis, Alan, New Rivers Press; Minnesota State University Moorhead, 1104 Seventh Ave S, Moorhead, MN 56563 *Tel:* 218-477-5870 *Fax:* 218-477-2236 *E-mail:* nrp@mnstate.edu *Web Site:* www.newriverspress.com; www.mnstate.edu/newriverspress, pg 189

Davis, Amanda, New York University Press, 838 Broadway, New York, NY 10003 *Tel:* 212-998-2575 (edit) *Toll Free Tel:* 800-996-6987 (orders) *Fax:* 212-995-3833 (orders) *E-mail:* feedback@nyupress.nyu.edu *Web Site:* www.nyupress.org, pg 190

Davis, Andrea, Warner Faith (Christian Book Division of Time Warner Book Group), 2 Creekside Crossing, 10 Cadillac Dr, Suite 220, Brentwood, TN 37027 *Tel:* 615-221-0996 *Fax:* 615-221-0962 *Web Site:* www.twbookmark.com, pg 293

Davis, Anne, The Pennsylvania State University Press, 820 N University Dr, University Support Bldg 1, Suite C, University Park, PA 16802-1003 *Tel:* 814-865-1327 *Toll Free Tel:* 800-326-9180 *Fax:* 814-863-1408 *Toll Free Fax:* 877 7782665 *Web Site:* www.psupress.org, pg 209

Davis, Bruce, Academy of Motion Picture Arts & Sciences (AMPAS), 1313 N Vine St, Hollywood, CA 90028 *Tel:* 310-247-3000 *Fax:* 310-859-9351 *E-mail:* ampas@oscars.org *Web Site:* www.oscars.org, pg 675

Davis, Candy, Editing International LLC, 2123 Marlow Lane, Suite 21, Eugene, OR 97401-6431 *Tel:* 541-344-9118 *E-mail:* info@4-edit.com *Web Site:* www.4-edit.com, pg 597

Davis, Carlos, McGraw-Hill International Publishing Group, 2 Penn Plaza, New York, NY 10121 *Tel:* 212-904-2000 *Web Site:* www.mcgrawhill.com, pg 168

Davis, Carlos A, Santillana USA Publishing Co Inc, 2105 NW 86 Ave, Miami, FL 33122 *Tel:* 305-591-9522 *Toll Free Tel:* 800-245-8584 *Fax:* 305-591-9145 *Toll Free Fax:* 888-248-9518 *E-mail:* customerservice@santillanausa.com *Web Site:* www.santillanausa.com; www.alfaguara.net, pg 240

Davis, Charles N, Freedom of Information Center, 133 Neff Annex, Columbia, MO 65211-0012 *Tel:* 573-882-4856 *Fax:* 573-884-6204 *E-mail:* foi@missouri.edu *Web Site:* foi.missouri.edu, pg 687

Davis, Christina, Teachers & Writers Collaborative, 5 Union Sq W, New York, NY 10003-3306 *Tel:* 212-691-6590 *Toll Free Tel:* 888-266-5789 *Fax:* 212-675-0171 *E-mail:* info@twc.org *Web Site:* www.twc.org, pg 265, 701

Davis, Coleen, Standard Publishing Co, 8121 Hamilton Ave, Cincinnati, OH 45231 *Tel:* 513-931-4050 *Toll Free Tel:* 800-543-1301 *Fax:* 513-931-0950 *Toll Free Fax:* 877-867-5751 *E-mail:* customerservice@standardpub.com *Web Site:* www.standardpub.com, pg 257

Davis, Debbie, Livingston Press, University of West Alabama, Sta 22, Livingston, AL 35470 *Tel:* 205-652-3470 *Fax:* 205-652-3717 *Web Site:* www.livingstonpress.uwa.edu, pg 157

Davis, Deena, Regal Books, 1957 Eastman Ave, Ventura, CA 93003 *Tel:* 805-644-9721 *Toll Free Tel:* 800-446-7735 (orders) *Fax:* 805-644-9728 (editorial); 805-644-4729 (purchasing); 805-650-8713 (sales & corp serv); 805-658-3388 (orders) *Toll Free Fax:* 800-860-3109 (orders) *E-mail:* info@regalbooks.com *Web Site:* www.gospellight.com, pg 230

Davis, Denise, Justin Winsor Essay Prize, 50 E Huron St, Chicago, IL 60611 *Tel:* 312-280-4273 *Toll Free Tel:* 800-545-2433 (ext 4273) *Fax:* 312-280-4392 *Web Site:* www.ala.org, pg 812

Davis, Gary, The Learning Source Ltd, 644 Tenth St, Brooklyn, NY 11215 *Tel:* 718-768-0231 *Fax:* 718-369-3467 *E-mail:* info@learningsourceltd.com *Web Site:* www.learningsourceltd.com, pg 604

Davis, George, ISA, 67 Alexander Dr, Research Triangle Park, NC 27709 *Tel:* 919-549-8411 *Fax:* 919-549-8288 *E-mail:* info@isa.org *Web Site:* www.isa.org, pg 139

Davis, Gloria, Frank Lawrence & Harriet Chappell Owsley Award, University of Georgia, Dept of History, Athens, GA 30602-1602 *Tel:* 706-542-8848 *Fax:* 706-542-2455 *Web Site:* www.uga.edu/~sha, pg 783

Davis, Gloria, Francis B Simkins Award, University of Georgia, Dept of History, Athens, GA 30602-1602 *Tel:* 706-542-8848 *Fax:* 706-542-2455 *Web Site:* www.uga.edu/~sha, pg 805

Davis, Gloria, Charles S Sydnor Award, University of Georgia, Dept of History, Athens, GA 30602-1602 *Tel:* 706-542-8848 *Fax:* 706-542-2455 *Web Site:* www.uga.edu/~sha, pg 808

Davis, J Madison, Gaylord College of Journalism & Mass Communication, Professional Writing Program, c/o University of Oklahoma, 860 Van Vleet Oval, Rm 101, Norman, OK 73019-0270 *Tel:* 405-325-2721 *Fax:* 405-325-7565, pg 752

Davis, James B, Practice Management Information Corp (PMIC), 4727 Wilshire Blvd, Suite 300, Los Angeles, CA 90010 *Tel:* 323-954-0224 *Fax:* 323-954-0253 *E-mail:* orders@medicalbookstore.com *Web Site:* www.pmiconline.com, pg 216

Davis, Jill, Viking Children's Books, 345 Hudson St, New York, NY 10014 *Tel:* 212-366-2000 *E-mail:* online@penguinputnam.com *Web Site:* www.penguin.com, pg 290

Davis, Joyce N, William Allen White Children's Book Awards, William Allen White Library, 1200 Commercial St, Emporia, KS 66801-5092 *Tel:* 620-341-5719 *Fax:* 620-341-6208 *Web Site:* waw.emporia.edu, pg 811

Davis, Kathryn, Ericson Books, 1614 Redbud St, Nacogdoches, TX 75965 *Tel:* 936-564-3625 *Fax:* 936-552-8999 *E-mail:* info@ericsonbooks.com *Web Site:* www.ericsonbooks.com, pg 91

Davis, Ken, Lone Pine Publishing, 10145 81 Ave, Edmonton, AB T6E 1W9, Canada *Tel:* 780-433-9333 *Toll Free Tel:* 800-661-9017 *Fax:* 780-433-9646 *Toll Free Fax:* 800-424-7173 *E-mail:* info@lonepinepublishing.com *Web Site:* www.lonepinepublishing.com, pg 552

Davis, Leigh, BradyGAMES Publishing, 800 E 96 St, 3rd fl, Indianapolis, IN 46240 *Tel:* 317-428-3000 *Toll Free Tel:* 800-545-5912; 800-571-5840 (cust serv) *E-mail:* bradyquestions@pearsoned.com *Web Site:* www.bradygames.com, pg 45

Davis, Linda Baron, Benjamin Cummings, 1301 Sansome St, San Francisco, CA 94111 *Tel:* 415-402-2500 *Fax:* 415-402-2591 *E-mail:* question@aw.com *Web Site:* www.aw-bc.com, pg 36

Davis, Mae, National League of Cities, 1301 Pennsylvania Ave NW, Washington, DC 20004-1763 *Tel:* 202-626-3000 *Fax:* 202-626-3043 *Web Site:* www.nlc.org, pg 184

Davis, Patti, The PRS Group Inc, 6320 Fly Rd, East Syracuse, NY 13057 *Tel:* 315-431-0511 *Fax:* 315-431-0200 *E-mail:* custserv@prsgroup.com *Web Site:* www.prsgroup.com, pg 220

Davis, Ruth, Standard Publishing Co, 8121 Hamilton Ave, Cincinnati, OH 45231 *Tel:* 513-931-4050 *Toll Free Tel:* 800-543-1301 *Fax:* 513-931-0950 *Toll Free Fax:* 877-867-5751 *E-mail:* customerservice@standardpub.com *Web Site:* www.standardpub.com, pg 257

Davis, Sam, American Management Association, 1601 Broadway, New York, NY 10019-7420 *Tel:* 212-586-8100 *Toll Free Tel:* 800-262-9699 *Fax:* 212-903-8168 *Web Site:* www.amanet.org, pg 677

Davis, Sheila, American Society of Electroneurodiagnostic Technologists Inc, 426 W 42 St, Kansas City, KS 64111 *Tel:* 816-931-1120 *Fax:* 816-931-1145 *E-mail:* info@aset.org *Web Site:* www.aset.org, pg 18

Davis, Wendy, The Learning Source Ltd, 644 Tenth St, Brooklyn, NY 11215 *Tel:* 718-768-0231 *Fax:* 718-369-3467 *E-mail:* info@learningsourceltd.com *Web Site:* www.learningsourceltd.com, pg 604

Davis-Undiano, Robert Con, Neustadt International Prize for Literature, 630 Parrington Oval, Suite 110, Norman, OK 73019-4033 *Tel:* 405-325-4531 *Toll Free Tel:* 800-523-7363 *Fax:* 405-325-7495 *Web Site:* www.ou.edu/worldlit/, pg 793

Davison, Russell, Society for Protective Coating, 40 24 St, 6th fl, Pittsburgh, PA 15222-4656 *Tel:* 412-281-2331 *Fax:* 412-281-9992 *E-mail:* books@sspc.org *Web Site:* www.sspc.org, pg 251

Davy, Diane, Key Porter Books Ltd, 70 The Esplanade, 3rd fl, Toronto, ON M5E 1R2, Canada *Tel:* 416-862-7777 *Fax:* 416-862-2304 *E-mail:* info@keyporter.com *Web Site:* www.keyporter.com, pg 551

Dawes, John, Piano Press, 1425 Ocean Ave, Suite 6, Del Mar, CA 92014 *Tel:* 619-884-1401 *Fax:* 858-459-3376 *E-mail:* pianopress@aol.com *Web Site:* www.pianopress.com, pg 212

Dawley, Harold, Wellness Institute Inc, 1007 Whitney Ave, Gretna, LA 70056 *Tel:* 504-361-1845 *Fax:* 504-365-0114 *Web Site:* selfhelpbooks.com, pg 295

Dawley, Nancy, FourWinds Press LLC, 4157 Crossgate Dr, Cincinnati, OH 47025 *Tel:* 513-891-0415 *Fax:* 513-891-1648 *Web Site:* www.fourwindspress. com, pg 571

Dawson, Dawn, Salem Press Inc, 2 University Plaza, Suite 121, Hackensack, NJ 07601 *Tel:* 201-968-9899 *Toll Free Tel:* 800-221-1592 *Fax:* 201-968-1411 *E-mail:* csr@salempress.com *Web Site:* www. salempress.com, pg 239

Dawson, G T, A Abacus Group, PO Box 35, Ridgecrest, CA 93556 *Tel:* 760-375-5243 *Fax:* 760-375-1140 *E-mail:* gtd007@ridgenet.net *Web Site:* www.ridgenet. net/~gtd007, pg 589, 617

Dawson, Hal, Ram Publishing Co, 1881 W State St, Garland, TX 75042-6797 *Tel:* 972-494-6151 *Fax:* 972-494-1881 *Web Site:* www.garrett.com, pg 225

Dawson, Kathryn, G P Putnam's Sons (Children's), 345 Hudson St, New York, NY 10014 *Tel:* 212-366-2000 *E-mail:* online@penguinputnam.com *Web Site:* www. penguin.com, pg 223

Dawson, Lee, Dark Horse Comics, 10956 SE Main St, Milwaukie, OR 97222 *Tel:* 503-652-8815 *Fax:* 503-654-9440 *E-mail:* dhcomics@darkhorsecomics.com *Web Site:* www.darkhorse.com, pg 76

Dawson, Liza, Liza Dawson Associates, 240 W 35 St, Suite 500, New York, NY 10001 *Tel:* 212-465-9071, pg 626

Day, Hope, Ageless Press, 3759 Collins St, Sarasota, FL 34232 *Tel:* 941-365-1367 *Fax:* 941-365-1367 *E-mail:* irishope@comcast.net *Web Site:* irisforrest. com, pg 6

Day, Jill, Teaching & Learning Co, 1204 Buchanan St, Carthage, IL 62321-0010 *Tel:* 217-357-2591 *Fax:* 217-357-6789 *E-mail:* customerservice@teachinglearning. com *Web Site:* TeachingLearning.Com, pg 265

Day, Karen, Oxford University Press, Inc, 198 Madison Ave, New York, NY 10016-4314 *Tel:* 212-726-6000 *Toll Free Tel:* 800-451-7556 (orders) *Web Site:* www. oup.com/us, pg 200

Day, Karen C, Charles Scribner's Sons, PO Box 9187, Farmington Hills, MI 48333-9187 *Toll Free Tel:* 800-877-4253 *Toll Free Fax:* 800-414-5043 *E-mail:* galeord@gale.com, pg 58

Day, Lawson, Amber Lotus, Strawberry Creek Design Ctr, 1250 Addison St, Studio 214, Berkeley, CA 94702 *Tel:* 510-225-0149 *Toll Free Tel:* 800-625-8378 (orders only) *Fax:* 510-665-6083 *E-mail:* info@ amberlotus.com *Web Site:* www.amberlotus.com, pg 10

Day, Richard, Self-Counsel Press Inc, 1704 N State St, Bellingham, WA 98225 *Tel:* 360-676-4530 *Toll Free Tel:* 877-877-6490 *Fax:* 360-676-4549 *E-mail:* service@self-counsel.com *Web Site:* www.self-counsel.com, pg 245

Day, Richard, Self-Counsel Press Inc, 1481 Charlotte Rd, North Vancouver, BC V7J 1H1, Canada *Tel:* 604-986-3366 *Toll Free Tel:* 800-663-3007 *Fax:* 604-986-3947 *E-mail:* service@self-counsel.com *Web Site:* www.self-counsel.com, pg 561

Day, Sharon, The University of Utah Press, 1795 E South Campus Dr, Rm 101, Salt Lake City, UT 84112-9402 *Tel:* 801-581-6671 *Toll Free Tel:* 800-773-6672 *Fax:* 801-581-3365 *E-mail:* info@upress.utah. edu *Web Site:* www.uofupress.com, pg 285

Dayus, Susan, Canadian Booksellers Association Author of the Year Award, 789 Don Mills Rd, Suite 700, Toronto, ON M3C 1T5, Canada *Tel:* 416-467-7883 *Fax:* 416-467-7886 *E-mail:* enquiries@cbabook.org *Web Site:* www.cbabook.org, pg 765

Dayus, Susan, Canadian Booksellers Association (CBA), 789 Don Mills Rd, Suite 700, Toronto, ON M3C 1T5, Canada *Tel:* 416-467-7883 *Toll Free Tel:* 866-788-0790 *Fax:* 416-467-7886 *E-mail:* enquiries@cbabook. org *Web Site:* www.cbabook.org, pg 683

Dayus, Susan, Canadian Booksellers Association Libris Awards, 789 Don Mills Rd, Suite 700, Toronto, ON M3C 1T5, Canada *Tel:* 416-467-7883 *Fax:* 416-467-7886 *E-mail:* enquiries@cbabook.org *Web Site:* www. cbabook.org, pg 765

De Angelis, Dr Catherine MD, American Medical Association, 515 N State St, Chicago, IL 60610 *Tel:* 312-464-5000 *Toll Free Tel:* 800-621-8335 *Fax:* 312-464-4184 *Web Site:* www.ama-assn.org, pg 677

De Boer, Rebecca, University of Notre Dame Press, 310 Flanner Hall, Notre Dame, IN 46556 *Tel:* 574-631-6346 *Toll Free Tel:* 800-621-2736 (orders) *Fax:* 574-631-8148 *Toll Free Fax:* 800-621-8476 (orders) *E-mail:* nd.undpress.1@nd.edu *Web Site:* www. undpress.nd.edu, pg 284

de Buerba, Jose, World Bank Publications, Office of the Publisher, 1818 "H" St NW, U-11-1104, Washington, DC 20433 *Tel:* 202-473-0393 (sales mgr) *Toll Free Tel:* 800-645-7247 (cust serv) *Fax:* 202-522-2631 *E-mail:* books@worldbank.org; pubrights@worldbank. org (foreign rts) *Web Site:* www.worldbank.org/ publications, pg 303

De Carlo, Janet, Portfolio Solutions, 2419 Rte 82, Suite 208, Billings, NY 12510-0074 *Tel:* 845-226-8401 *Fax:* 845-226-8937 *E-mail:* PSJDC@frontiernet.net, pg 666

De Courcey, Anne, Fulcrum Publishing Inc, 16100 Table Mountain Pkwy, Suite 300, Golden, CO 80403 *Tel:* 303-277-1623 *Toll Free Tel:* 800-992-2908 *Fax:* 303-279-7111 *Toll Free Fax:* 800-726-7112 *E-mail:* fulcrum@fulcrum-books.com *Web Site:* www. fulcrum-books.com, pg 101

De Echevarria, Ignacio, Fondo de Cultura Economica USA Inc, 2293 Verus St, San Diego, CA 92154 *Tel:* 619-429-0455 *Toll Free Tel:* 800-532-3872 *Fax:* 619-429-0827 *E-mail:* sales@fceusa.com *Web Site:* www.fceusa.com, pg 98

De Fabis, Sue, Five Star Publications Inc, 4696 W Tyson St, Dept LM, Chandler, AZ 85226 *Tel:* 480-940-8182 *Fax:* 480-940-8787 *E-mail:* info@fivestarpublications. com *Web Site:* www.fivestarpublications.com; www. authorsandexperts.com; www.youcanpublish.com; www.schoolbookings.com, pg 97

De Frank, Mike, Pennsylvania State Data Center, Penn State Harrisburg, 777 W Harrisburg Pike, Middletown, PA 17057-4898 *Tel:* 717-948-6336 *Fax:* 717-948-6754 *E-mail:* pasdc@psu.edu *Web Site:* pasdc.hbg.psu.edu, pg 209

de Gaspe Bonar, James, CCH Inc, 2700 Lake Cook Rd, Riverwoods, IL 60015 *Tel:* 847-267-7000 *Toll Free Tel:* 888-224-7377 *Web Site:* www.cch.com, pg 56

De George, Beverley J, Saint Mary's Press, 702 Terrace Heights, Winona, MN 55987-1318 *Tel:* 507-457-7900 *Toll Free Tel:* 800-533-8095 *Toll Free Fax:* 800-344-9225 *E-mail:* smpress@smp.org *Web Site:* www.smp. org, pg 239

De Giglio, Peter, Holtzbrinck Publishers, 175 Fifth Ave, New York, NY 10010 *Tel:* 212-674-5151 *Fax:* 212-420-9314 *E-mail:* firstname.lastname@hbpub.com *Web Site:* www.holtzbrinck.com, pg 125

De Gutis, Donna, Margret McBride Literary Agency, 7744 Fay Ave, Suite 201, La Jolla, CA 92037 *Tel:* 858-454-1550 *Fax:* 858-454-2156 *E-mail:* staff@ mcbridelit.com *Web Site:* www.mcbrideliterary.com, pg 643

de Guzman, Beth, Warner Books, 1271 Avenue of the Americas, New York, NY 10020 *Tel:* 212-522-7200 *Fax:* 212-522-7991 *Web Site:* www.twbookmark.com, pg 293

de Isasi, Cristina, Bilingual Press/Editorial Bilingue, Hispanic Research Ctr, Arizona State Univ, Tempe, AZ 85287-2702 *Tel:* 480-965-3867 *Fax:* 480-965-8309 *E-mail:* brp@asu.edu *Web Site:* www.asu.edu/brp/brp, pg 38

de Jonge, Christina, The Dawn Horse Press, 12040 N Seigler Rd, Middletown, CA 95461 *Tel:* 707-928-6590 *Toll Free Tel:* 877-770-0772 *Fax:* 707-928-5068 *E-mail:* dhp@adidam.org *Web Site:* www. dawnhorsepress.com, pg 77

de la Cheneliere, Michel, Cheneliere/McGraw-Hill, 7001 Saint Laurent Blvd, Montreal, PQ H2S 3E3, Canada *Tel:* 514-273-1066 *Fax:* 514-276-0324 *E-mail:* chene@dlcmcgrawhill.com *Web Site:* www. dlcmcgrawhill.ca, pg 540

de la Haba, Lois, The Lois de la Haba Agency Inc, 76-12 Grand Central Pkwy, Suite 4, New York, NY 11375 *Tel:* 718-544-2392 *Fax:* 718-544-2393 *E-mail:* habalit@aol.com, pg 627

De Lancy, Jennifer, David R Godine Publisher Inc, 9 Hamilton Place, Boston, MA 02108 *Tel:* 617-451-9600 *Fax:* 617-350-0250 *E-mail:* info@godine.com *Web Site:* www.godine.com, pg 106

De Maio, Frank, Newmarket Publishing & Communications, 18 E 48 St, New York, NY 10017 *Tel:* 212-832-3575 *Toll Free Tel:* 800-669-3903 *Fax:* 212-832-3629 *E-mail:* mailbox@newmarketpress. com *Web Site:* www.newmarketpress.com, pg 190

De Marco, Frank, Hampton Roads Publishing Co Inc, 1125 Stoney Ridge Rd, Charlottesville, VA 22902 *Tel:* 434-296-2772 *Toll Free Tel:* 800-766-8009 (orders) *Fax:* 434-296-5096 *Toll Free Fax:* 800-766-9042 *E-mail:* hrpc@hrpub.com *Web Site:* www.hrpub. com, pg 113

de Montebello, Philippe, The Metropolitan Museum of Art, 1000 Fifth Ave, New York, NY 10028 *Tel:* 212-879-5500; 212-535-7710 *Fax:* 212-396-5062 *E-mail:* info@metmuseum.org *Web Site:* www. metmuseum.org, pg 173

De Muth, Christopher C, The AEI Press, 1150 17 St NW, Washington, DC 20036 *Tel:* 202-862-5800 *Fax:* 202-862-7177 *Web Site:* www.aei.org, pg 6

De Pasquale, Georgette, Learning Links Inc, 2300 Marcus Ave, New Hyde Park, NY 11042 *Tel:* 516-437-9071 *Toll Free Tel:* 800-724-2616 *Fax:* 516-437-5392 *E-mail:* learning1x@aol.com *Web Site:* www. learninglinks.com, pg 151

De Pasture, Madris, New Concepts Publishing, 5202 Humphreys Blvd, Lake Park, GA 31636 *Tel:* 229-257-0367 *Fax:* 229-219-1097 *E-mail:* newconcepts@ newconceptspublishing.com *Web Site:* www. newconceptspublishing.com, pg 187

de Pree, Ariane, Stanford University Press, 1450 Page Mill Rd, Palo Alto, CA 94304-1124 *Tel:* 650-723-9434 *Fax:* 650-725-3457 *Web Site:* www.sup.org, pg 257

De Rosa, Maureen, American Academy of Pediatrics, 141 NW Point Blvd, Elk Grove Village, IL 60007-1098 *Tel:* 847-434-4000 *Toll Free Tel:* 888-227-1770 *Fax:* 847-228-1281 *E-mail:* pubs@aap.org *Web Site:* www.aap.org, pg 11

De Smet, Christine, University of Wisconsin - Madison Liberal Studies & the Arts, 621 Lowell Hall, 610 Langdon St, Madison, WI 53703-1195 *Tel:* 608-262-3982 *Fax:* 608-265-2475 *Web Site:* www.dcs.wisc. edu/lsa, pg 756

De Spelder, Lynne Ann, Pacific Publishing Services, PO Box 1150, Capitola, CA 95010-1150 *Tel:* 831-476-8284 *Fax:* 831-476-8294 *E-mail:* pacpub@attglobal. net, pg 607

de Spoelberch, Jacques, J de S Associates Inc, 9 Shagbark Rd, South Norwalk, CT 06854 *Tel:* 203-838-7571 *Fax:* 203-866-2713, pg 635

De Taeye, Inge, The Karpfinger Agency, 357 W 20 St, New York, NY 10011-3379 *Tel:* 212-691-2690 *Fax:* 212-691-7129, pg 637

de Tonnancour, Camille M, Current Clinical Strategies Publishing, 27071 Cabot Rd, Suite 126, Laguna Hills, CA 92653-7011 *Tel:* 949-348-8404 *Toll Free Tel:* 800-331-8227 *Fax:* 949-348-8404 *Toll Free Fax:* 800-965-9420 *E-mail:* info@ccpublishing.com *Web Site:* www. ccpublishing.com, pg 75

de Vinck, Jose M, Alleluia Press, 672 Franklin Tpke, Allendale, NJ 07401 *Tel:* 201-327-3513, pg 8

De Welt, Chris, College Press Publishing Co, 223 W Third St, Joplin, MO 64801 *Tel:* 417-623-6280 *Toll Free Tel:* 800-289-3300 *Fax:* 417-623-8250 *E-mail:* books@collegepress.com *Web Site:* www. collegepress.com, pg 64

De Young, Tim, Dorchester Publishing Co Inc, 200 Madison Ave, Suite 2000, New York, NY 10016 *Tel:* 212-725-8811 *Toll Free Tel:* 800-481-9191 (order dept) *Fax:* 212-532-1054 *E-mail:* dorchedits@ dorchesterpub.com *Web Site:* www.dorchesterpub.com, pg 82

Deal, Barbara, Copywriter's Council of America (CCA), CCA Bldg, 7 Putter Lane, Middle Island, NY 11953-0102 *Tel:* 631-924-8555 *Fax:* 631-924-3890 *E-mail:* cca4dmcopy@att.net *Web Site:* www.lgroup. addr.com/CCA.htm, pg 595

Deal, Barbara, Copywriter's Council of America (CCA), CCA Bldg, 7 Putter Lane, Middle Island, NY 11953 *Tel:* 631-924-8555 *Fax:* 631-924-3890 *E-mail:* cca4dmcopy@att.net *Web Site:* www.lgroup. addr.com/CCA.htm, pg 685

Dean, Barbara, Island Press, 1718 Connecticut Ave NW, Suite 300, Washington, DC 20009 *Tel:* 202-232-7933 *Toll Free Tel:* 800-828-1302 *Fax:* 202-234-1328; 707-983-6414 (orders only) *E-mail:* info@islandpress.org *Web Site:* www.islandpress.org, pg 139

Dean, Cathy, Author's Helper, 515 E Eighth St, Unit D, Davis, CA 95616 *Tel:* 530-759-2091 *E-mail:* info@ authorshelper.com *Web Site:* www.authorshelper.com, pg 591

Dean, John, Rizzoli International Publications Inc, 300 Park Ave S, 3rd fl, New York, NY 10010-5399 *Tel:* 212-387-3400 *Toll Free Tel:* 800-522-6657 (orders only) *Fax:* 212-387-3535, pg 233

Dean, Mary Catherine, Abingdon Press, 201 Eighth Ave S, Nashville, TN 37203-3919 *Tel:* 615-749-6290 (publicist); 615-749-6000; 615-749-6451 (sales) *Toll Free Tel:* 800-251-3320 *Fax:* 615-749-6056 *Web Site:* www.abingdonpress.com, pg 3

Dean, Otis, Blackwell Publishers, 350 Main St, Malden, MA 02148 *Tel:* 781-388-8200 *Fax:* 781-388-8210 *E-mail:* books@blackwellpublishing.com *Web Site:* www.blackwellpublishing.com, pg 40

Dearyan, Julie, Victory in Grace Printing, 60 Quentin Rd, Lake Zurich, IL 60047 *Tel:* 847-438-4494 *Toll Free Tel:* 800-784-7223 *Fax:* 847-438-4232 *Web Site:* www.victoryingrace.org, pg 290

Dearyan, Neal, Victory in Grace Printing, 60 Quentin Rd, Lake Zurich, IL 60047 *Tel:* 847-438-4494 *Toll Free Tel:* 800-784-7223 *Fax:* 847-438-4232 *Web Site:* www.victoryingrace.org, pg 290

DeBolt, Barbara Sue, Book World Inc/Blue Star Productions, 9666 E Riggs Rd, No 194, Sun Lakes, AZ 85248 *Tel:* 480-895-7995 *Fax:* 480-895-6991 *E-mail:* bsp@bluestarproductions.net *Web Site:* www.bluestarproductions.net, pg 44

Debow, Steve, McGraw-Hill Higher Education, 1333 Burr Ridge Pkwy, Burr Ridge, IL 60527 *Tel:* 630-789-4000 *Toll Free Tel:* 800-338-3987 (cust serv) *Fax:* 614-755-5645 (cust serv) *Web Site:* www.mhhe.com, pg 167

Debow, Steve, McGraw-Hill Humanities, Social Sciences, Languages, 2 Penn Plaza, 20th fl, New York, NY 10121 *Tel:* 212-904-2000 *Toll Free Tel:* 800-338-3987 (cust serv) *Fax:* 614-755-5645 (cust serv) *E-mail:* first name_last name@mcgraw-hill.com *Web Site:* www.mhhe.com, pg 168

Decalo, Sam, Florida Academic Press, PO Box 540, Gainesville, FL 32602-0540 *Tel:* 352-332-5104 *Fax:* 352-331-6003 *E-mail:* fapress@worldnet.att.net, pg 97

Decarie, Andre, Decarie, Editeur Inc, 233 Ave Dunbar, Ville Mont-Royal, PQ H3P 2H4, Canada *Tel:* 514-342-8500 *Fax:* 514-342-3982 *E-mail:* info@decarieediteur.com *Web Site:* www.decarieediteur.com, pg 542

Deck, Jo Ann, The Crossing Press, PO Box 7123, Berkeley, CA 94707 *Tel:* 510-559-1600 *Toll Free Tel:* 800-841-2665 (orders & cust serv) *Fax:* 510-524-1052 *E-mail:* publicity@tenspeed.com *Web Site:* www.tenspeed.com, pg 73

Deck, Joann, Ten Speed Press, PO Box 7123, Berkeley, CA 94707 *Tel:* 510-559-1600 *Toll Free Tel:* 800-841-Book *Fax:* 510-559-1629; 510-524-1052 (general) *E-mail:* order@tenspeed.com *Web Site:* www.tenspeed.com, pg 266

Deck, Jon, Fox Chapel Publishing Co Inc, 1970 Broad St, East Petersburg, PA 17520 *Tel:* 717-560-4703 *Toll Free Tel:* 800-457-9112 *Fax:* 717-560-4702 *E-mail:* custservice@foxchapelpublishing.com *Web Site:* www.foxchapelpublishing.com, pg 99

Decker, Brian C, B C Decker Inc, 20 Hughson St S, 10th fl, Hamilton, ON L8N 2A1, Canada *Tel:* 905-522-7017 *Toll Free Tel:* 800-568-7281 *Fax:* 905-522-7839 *E-mail:* info@bcdecker.com *Web Site:* www.bcdecker.com, pg 542

Decker-Lucke, Shirley, Hendrickson Publishers Inc, PO Box 3473, Peabody, MA 01961-3473 *Tel:* 978-532-6546 *Toll Free Tel:* 800-358-3111 *Fax:* 978-531-8146 *E-mail:* orders@hendrickson.com *Web Site:* www.hendrickson.com, pg 121

Deckter, Manny, Franklin Book Co Inc, 7804 Montgomery Ave, Elkins Park, PA 19027 *Tel:* 215-635-5252 *Fax:* 215-635-6155 *E-mail:* service@franklinbook.com *Web Site:* www.franklinbook.com, pg 100

DeCoff, Brandon, Ashgate Publishing Co, 101 Cherry St, Suite 420, Burlington, VT 05401-4405 *Tel:* 802-865-7641 *Fax:* 802-865-7847 *E-mail:* info@ashgate.com *Web Site:* www.ashgate.com, pg 25

DeCola, Angie, Morgan Reynolds Publishing, 620 S Elm St, Suite 223, Greensboro, NC 27406 *Tel:* 336-275-1311 *Toll Free Tel:* 800-535-1504 *Fax:* 336-275-1152 *Toll Free Fax:* 800-535-5725 *E-mail:* editorial@morganreynolds.com *Web Site:* www.morganreynolds.com, pg 178

Dee, Alexander, Ivan R Dee Publisher, 1332 N Halsted St, Chicago, IL 60622-2694 *Tel:* 312-787-6262 *Toll Free Tel:* 800-462-6420 (orders) *Fax:* 312-787-6269 *Toll Free Fax:* 800-338-4550 (orders) *E-mail:* elephant@ivanrdee.com *Web Site:* www.ivanrdee.com, pg 78

Dee, Ivan R, Ivan R Dee Publisher, 1332 N Halsted St, Chicago, IL 60622-2694 *Tel:* 312-787-6262 *Toll Free Tel:* 800-462-6420 (orders) *Fax:* 312-787-6269 *Toll Free Fax:* 800-338-4550 (orders) *E-mail:* elephant@ivanrdee.com *Web Site:* www.ivanrdee.com, pg 78

Deen, John, Universe Publishing, 300 Park Ave S, 3rd fl, New York, NY 10010 *Tel:* 212-387-3400 *Fax:* 212-387-3535, pg 280

Deer, Sherry Carr, Intercultural Development Research Association (IDRA), 5835 Callaghan Rd, Suite 350, San Antonio, TX 78228-1190 *Tel:* 210-444-1710 *Fax:* 210-444-1714 *E-mail:* contact@idra.org *Web Site:* www.idra.org, pg 136

Dees, Almena, Carolrhoda Books Inc, 241 First Ave N, Minneapolis, MN 55401 *Tel:* 612-332-3344 *Toll Free Tel:* 800-328-4929 *Fax:* 612-332-7615 *Toll Free Fax:* 800-332-1132 *E-mail:* info@lernerbooks.com *Web Site:* www.lernerbooks.com, pg 54

Dees, Almena, First Avenue Editions, 241 First Ave N, Minneapolis, MN 55401 *Tel:* 612-332-3344 *Toll Free Tel:* 800-328-4929 *Fax:* 612-332-7615 *Toll Free Fax:* 800-332-1132 *E-mail:* info@lernerbooks.com *Web Site:* www.lernerbooks.com, pg 97

Dees, Almena, Lerner Publishing Group, 241 First Ave N, Minneapolis, MN 55401 *Tel:* 612-332-3344 *Toll Free Tel:* 800-328-4929 *Fax:* 612-332-7615 *Toll Free Fax:* 800-332-1132 *E-mail:* info@lernerbooks.com *Web Site:* www.lernerbooks.com, pg 152

Dees, Almena, LernerSports, 241 First Ave N, Minneapolis, MN 55401 *Tel:* 612-332-3344 *Toll Free Tel:* 800-328-4929 *Fax:* 612-332-7615 *Toll Free Fax:* 800-332-1132 *E-mail:* info@lernerbooks.com *Web Site:* www.lernerbooks.com, pg 153

Dees, Almena, Runestone Press, 241 First Ave N, Minneapolis, MN 55401 *Tel:* 612-332-3344 *Toll Free Tel:* 800-328-4929; 800-332-1132 *Fax:* 612-332-7615 *E-mail:* info@lernerbooks.com *Web Site:* www.lernerbooks.com, pg 236

Deever, John, Resources for the Future, 1616 "P" St NW, Washington, DC 20036-1400 *Tel:* 202-328-5086 *Fax:* 202-328-5137 *E-mail:* rffpress@rff.org *Web Site:* www.rffpress.org, pg 231

DeFiore, Brian, DeFiore & Co, Author Services, 72 Spring St, Suite 304, New York, NY 10012 *Tel:* 212-925-7744 *Fax:* 212-925-9803 *E-mail:* submissions@defioreandco.com *Web Site:* defioreandco.com, pg 627

Degan, John, Periodical Writers' Association of Canada, 215 Spadina Ave, Suite 123, Toronto, ON M5T 2C7, Canada *Tel:* 416-504-1645 *Fax:* 416-913-2327 *E-mail:* pwac@web.net; info@pwac.ca *Web Site:* www.pwac.ca; www.writers.ca, pg 697

DeGennaro, Denise, Fodor's Travel Publications, 1745 Broadway, New York, NY 10019 *Tel:* 212-572-8784 *Toll Free Tel:* 800-733-3000 *Fax:* 212-572-2248 *Web Site:* www.fodors.com, pg 98

DeGennaro, Denise, The Princeton Review, 1745 Broadway, New York, NY 10019 *Tel:* 212-829-6928 *Toll Free Tel:* 800-733-3000 *Fax:* 212-940-7400 *E-mail:* princetonreview@randomhouse.com *Web Site:* www.princetonreview.com, pg 219

DeGennaro, Denise, Random House Reference, 1745 Broadway, New York, NY 10019 *Toll Free Tel:* 800-733-3000 *E-mail:* words@random.com; puzzles@random.com, pg 227

Deger, Steve, Fairview Press, 2450 Riverside Ave, Minneapolis, MN 55454 *Tel:* 612-672-4180 *Toll Free Tel:* 800-544-8207 *Fax:* 612-672-4980 *Web Site:* www.fairviewpress.org, pg 94

Dehmler, Mari Lynch, Fine Wordworking, PO Box 3041, Monterey, CA 93942-3041 *Tel:* 831-375-6278, pg 599

Deichert, Jerry, University of Nebraska at Omaha Center for Public Affairs Research, 6001 Dodge St, Omaha, NE 68182 *Tel:* 402-554-2134 *Fax:* 402-554-4946 *Web Site:* www.cpara.unomaha.edu/, pg 283

Deisinger, Robert D, American Technical Publishers Inc, 1155 W 175 St, Homewood, IL 60430-4600 *Tel:* 708-957-1100 *Toll Free Tel:* 800-323-3471 *Fax:* 708-957-1101 *E-mail:* service@americantech.net *Web Site:* www.go2atp.com, pg 18

Deitch, JoAnne W, Discovery Enterprises Ltd, 31 Laurelwood Dr, Carlisle, MA 01741 *Tel:* 978-287-5401 *Toll Free Tel:* 800-729-1720 *Fax:* 978-287-5402 *E-mail:* ushistorydocs@aol.com *Web Site:* www.ushistorydocs.com, pg 80

Deitch, Kenneth M, Discovery Enterprises Ltd, 31 Laurelwood Dr, Carlisle, MA 01741 *Tel:* 978-287-5401 *Toll Free Tel:* 800-729-1720 *Fax:* 978-287-5402 *E-mail:* ushistorydocs@aol.com *Web Site:* www.ushistorydocs.com, pg 80

Dejarlais, Natalie, Nolo, 950 Parker St, Berkeley, CA 94710 *Tel:* 510-549-1976 *Fax:* 510-548-5902 *E-mail:* info@nolo.com *Web Site:* www.nolo.com, pg 191

DeJesus, Dahlia, Begell House Inc Publishers, 145 Madison Ave, Suite 601, New York, NY 10016 *Tel:* 212-725-1999 *Fax:* 212-213-8368 *E-mail:* orders@begellhouse.com *Web Site:* www.begellhouse.com, pg 35

Dekker, David, Marcel Dekker Inc, 270 Madison Ave, New York, NY 10016 *Tel:* 212-696-9000 *Toll Free Tel:* 800-228-1160 (outside NY) *Fax:* 212-685-4540 *Web Site:* www.dekker.com, pg 78

Dekker, Marcel, Marcel Dekker Inc, 270 Madison Ave, New York, NY 10016 *Tel:* 212-696-9000 *Toll Free Tel:* 800-228-1160 (outside NY) *Fax:* 212-685-4540 *Web Site:* www.dekker.com, pg 78

Dekker, Russell, Marcel Dekker Inc, 270 Madison Ave, New York, NY 10016 *Tel:* 212-696-9000 *Toll Free Tel:* 800-228-1160 (outside NY) *Fax:* 212-685-4540 *Web Site:* www.dekker.com, pg 78

Deku, Prof Afrikadzata PhD, Continental Afrikan Publishers, 182 Stribling Circle, Spartanburg, SC 29301 *Tel:* 864-576-7992 *Fax:* 775-295-9699; 864-574-3399 *E-mail:* afrikalion@aol.com *Web Site:* www.bbean.com/afrika/index.html; www.bbean.com/afrika/books.html; www.writers.net/writers/22249; www.freeyellow.com/members3/mike//, pg 67

Del Busso, Antoine, Editions Fides, 165 rue Deslauriers, St-Laurent, PQ H4N 2S4, Canada *Tel:* 514-745-4290 *Toll Free Tel:* 800-363-1451 *Fax:* 514-745-4299 *E-mail:* editions@fides.qc.ca *Web Site:* www.editionsfides.com, pg 545

Del Villar, Brooke, Caribe Betania Editores, 501 Nelson Place, Nashville, TN 37214 *Tel:* 615-391-3937 *Toll Free Tel:* 800-322-7426 *Fax:* 615-883-9376 *E-mail:* caribe@editorecaribe.com *Web Site:* www.caribebetania.com, pg 53

Delacoste, Frederique, Cleis Press, PO Box 14684, San Francisco, CA 94114-0684 *Tel:* 415-575-4700 *Toll Free Tel:* 800-780-2279 (US) *Fax:* 415-575-4705 *E-mail:* cleis@cleispress.com *Web Site:* www.cleispress.com, pg 63

Delaine, John, University of Wisconsin Press, 1930 Monroe St, 3rd fl, Madison, WI 53711 *Tel:* 608-263-1110 *Toll Free Tel:* 800-621-2736 (Orders) *Fax:* 608-263-1120 *Toll Free Fax:* 800-621-8476 (Orders) *E-mail:* uwiscpress@uwpress.wisc.edu (Main Office) *Web Site:* www.wisc.edu/wisconsinpress/, pg 286

Delamar, Gloria, Philadelphia Writers' Conference, PO Box 7171, Elkins Park, PA 19027-0171 *Tel:* 215-782-3288 *E-mail:* info@pwcwriters.org *Web Site:* pwcwriters.org, pg 746

Delaney, Janice F, PEN/Faulkner Award for Fiction, Folger Shakespeare Library, 201 E Capitol St SE, Washington, DC 20003 *Tel:* 202-675-0345 *Fax:* 202-608-1719 *Web Site:* www.penfaulkner.org, pg 797

Delaney, Rachel, Northwestern University Press, 625 Colfax St, Evanston, IL 60208 *Tel:* 847-491-2046 *Toll Free Tel:* 800-621-2736 (orders only) *Fax:* 847-491-8150 *E-mail:* nupress@northwestern.edu *Web Site:* www.nupress.northwestern.edu, pg 193

Delanois, Angel, Editions Pierre Tisseyre, 5757 Cypihot, St-Laurent, PQ H4S 1R3, Canada *Tel:* 514-334-2690 *Toll Free Tel:* 800-263-3678 *Fax:* 514-334-8395 *Toll Free Fax:* 800-643-4720 (Canada only) *E-mail:* ed.tisseyre@erpi.com, pg 563

Delbourgo, Joelle, Joelle Delbourgo Associates, Inc Literary Management, 450 Seventh Ave, Suite 3004, New York, NY 10123 *Tel:* 212-279-9027 *Fax:* 212-279-8863 *E-mail:* info@delbourgo.com (queries) *Web Site:* www.delbourgo.com/about.htm, pg 627

Delea, Christine, Creative Writing Conference, Case Annex 467, 512 Lancaster Ave, Richmond, KY 40475-3102 *Tel:* 859-622-5861 *Fax:* 859-622-3156 *Web Site:* www.english.eku.edu, pg 743

Delffs, Dudley, WaterBrook Press, 2375 Telstar Dr, Suite 160, Colorado Springs, CO 80920 *Tel:* 719-590-4999 *Toll Free Tel:* 800-603-7051 (orders) *Fax:* 719-590-8977 *Toll Free Fax:* 800-294-5686 (orders) *Web Site:* www.waterbrookpress.com, pg 294

Delgadillo, Drustva, Washington Researchers Ltd, 1655 N Fort Myer Dr, Suite 800, Arlington, VA 22209 *Tel:* 703-312-2863 *Fax:* 703-527-4586 *E-mail:* research@researchers.com *Web Site:* www.washingtonresearchers.com, pg 613

Delk, Wade, Check Payment Systems Association, 2025 "M" St, Suite 800, Washington, DC 20036 *Tel:* 202-857-1144 *Fax:* 202-223-4579 *E-mail:* info@cpsa-checks.org *Web Site:* www.cpsa-checks.org, pg 684

Dellarocco, A, Brooklyn Writers Club, PO Box 184, Bath Beach Sta, Brooklyn, NY 11214-0184 *Tel:* 718-680-4084, pg 682, 742

Dellheim, Charles, Laura Gross Literary Agency Ltd, 75 Clinton Place, Newton Centre, MA 02459-1117 *Tel:* 617-964-2977 *Fax:* 617-964-3023 *E-mail:* lglitag@aol.com, pg 633

Dellon, Hope, St Martin's Press Trade Division, 175 Fifth Ave, New York, NY 10010 *E-mail:* firstname.lastname@stmartins.com *Web Site:* www.stmartins.com; www.minotaurbooks.com, pg 239

Delmontagne, Regis J, Graphic Arts Education & Research Foundation (GAERF), 1899 Preston White Dr, Reston, VA 20191-4367 *Tel:* 703-264-7200 *Fax:* 703-620-3165 *E-mail:* gaerf@npes.org *Web Site:* www.npes.org, pg 705

Delmontagne, Regis J, NPES The Association for Suppliers of Printing, Publishing & Converting Technologies, 1899 Preston White Dr, Reston, VA 20191-4367 *Tel:* 703-264-7200 *Fax:* 703-620-0994 *E-mail:* npes@npes.org *Web Site:* www.npes.org, pg 696

Delo, Paula, National Association of Social Workers (NASW), 750 First St NE, Suite 700, Washington, DC 20002-4241 *Tel:* 301-317-8688 *Toll Free Tel:* 800-227-3590 *Fax:* 301-206-7989 *E-mail:* nasw@pmds.com *Web Site:* www.socialworkers.org, pg 182

DeLong, Michaela, American Association of Cereal Chemists, 3340 Pilot Knob Rd, St Paul, MN 55121-2097 *Tel:* 651-454-7250 *Toll Free Tel:* 800-328-7560 *Fax:* 651-454-0766 *E-mail:* aacc@scisoc.org *Web Site:* www.aaccnet.org, pg 11

DeLong, Michaela, American Phytopathological Society, 3340 Pilot Knob Rd, St Paul, MN 55121-2097 *Tel:* 651-454-7250 *Toll Free Tel:* 800-328-7560 *Fax:* 651-454-0766 *E-mail:* aps@scisoc.org *Web Site:* www.apsnet.org, pg 16

DeMaio, M C Susan, Oceana Publications Inc, 75 Main St, Dobbs Ferry, NY 10522-1601 *Tel:* 914-693-8100 *Toll Free Tel:* 800-831-0758 (orders only) *Fax:* 914-693-0402 *E-mail:* info@oceanalaw.com *Web Site:* www.oceanalaw.com, pg 195

Demas, Jamie, Bedford/St Martin's, 75 Arlington St, Boston, MA 02116 *Tel:* 617-399-4000 *Fax:* 617-426-8582 *Web Site:* www.bedfordstmartins.com, pg 35

DeMayo, Joan, Random House Children's Books, 1745 Broadway, New York, NY 10019 *Tel:* 212-782-9000 *Toll Free Tel:* 800-200-3552 *Fax:* 212-782-9452 *Web Site:* www.randomhouse.com/kids, pg 225

DeMayo, Joan, Random House Sales & Marketing, 1745 Broadway, New York, NY 10019 *Fax:* 212-782-9000, pg 227

Demers, Elizabeth, North American Indian Prose Award, 233 N Eighth St, Lincoln, NE 68588-0255 *Tel:* 402-472-3581 *Fax:* 402-472-0308 *E-mail:* pressmail@unl.edu *Web Site:* www.nebraskapress.unl.edu, pg 795

DeMers, Martin, Algora Publishing, 222 Riverside Dr, Suite 16-D, New York, NY 10025-6809 *Tel:* 212-678-0232 *Toll Free Tel:* 888-405-0689 *Fax:* 212-666-3682 *E-mail:* editors@algora.com *Web Site:* www.algora.com, pg 8

Deming, Thomas, McDougal Littell, 909 Davis St, Evanston, IL 60201 *Tel:* 847-869-2300 *Toll Free Tel:* 800-462-6595 (orders) *Toll Free Fax:* 888-872-8380 *Web Site:* www.mcdougallittell.com, pg 166

Dempsey, PJ, M Evans & Co Inc, 216 E 49 St, New York, NY 10017 *Tel:* 212-688-2810 *Fax:* 212-486-4544 *E-mail:* editorial@mevans.com *Web Site:* www.mevans.com, pg 93

Denekamp, Hope, Kneerim & Williams, c/o Fish & Richardson PC, 225 Franklin St, Boston, MA 02110 *Tel:* 617-542-5070 *Fax:* 617-542-8906 *Web Site:* www.fr.com, pg 638

Denis, Everette E, Fordham University, Graduate School of Business Administration, 33 W 60 St, 4th fl, Off of Graduate Admissions, New York, NY 10023 *Tel:* 212-636-6200 *Fax:* 212-636-7076, pg 774

Denison, John, The Boston Mills Press, 132 Main St, Erin, ON N0B 1T0, Canada *Tel:* 519-833-2407 *Fax:* 519-833-2195 *E-mail:* books@bostonmillspress.com *Web Site:* www.bostonmillspress.com, pg 537

Denlinger Oehms, Diane, Denlinger's Publishers Ltd, PO Box 1030, Edgewater, FL 32132-1030 *Tel:* 386-424-1737 *Toll Free Tel:* 800-362-1810 *Fax:* 386-428-3534 *Toll Free Fax:* 800-589-1191 *E-mail:* editor@thebookden.com *Web Site:* www.thebookden.com, pg 79

Dennis, Deborah, Carol Guenzi Agents Inc, 865 Delaware, Denver, CO 80204 *Tel:* 303-820-2599 *Toll Free Tel:* 800-417-5120 *Fax:* 303-820-2598 *E-mail:* art@artagent.com *Web Site:* www.artagent.com, pg 666

Dennis, Everette P, Fordham University, Graduate School of Business Administration, Dept of Communications & Media Management, 113 W 60 St, New York, NY 10023 *Tel:* 212-636-6199 *Fax:* 212-765-5573, pg 752

Dennis, Franklin, Marion Boyars Publishers Inc, c/o The Feminist, 365 Fifth Ave, Suite 5406, New York, NY 10016 *Tel:* 212-697-9676 *Fax:* 212-808-0664 *Web Site:* www.marionboyars.co.uk, pg 45

Dennis, Lane T, Crossway Books, 1300 Crescent St, Wheaton, IL 60187 *Tel:* 630-682-4300 *Fax:* 630-682-4785 *E-mail:* editorial@goodnews-crossway.org *Web Site:* www.crosswaybooks.org, pg 73

Dennis, Neil, IEE, c/o Inspec, 379 Thornall St, Edison, NJ 08837-2225 *Tel:* 732-321-5575 *Fax:* 732-321-5702 *E-mail:* iee@inspecinc.com *Web Site:* www.iee.org/publishing, pg 130

Dennison, Eleanor, Norma Epstein Foundation, 15 King's College Circle, Toronto, ON M5S 3H7, Canada *Tel:* 416-978-8083 *Fax:* 416-971-2027 *Web Site:* www.utoronto.ca, pg 772

Dennison, Sally, Council Oak Books LLC, 2105 E 15 St, Suite B, Tulsa, OK 74104 *Tel:* 918-743-BOOK (743-2665) *Toll Free Tel:* 800-247-8850 *Fax:* 918-743-4288 *E-mail:* publicity@counciloakbooks.com; orders@counciloakbooks.com *Web Site:* www.counciloakbooks.com, pg 70

Dennys, Louise, Knopf Canada, One Toronto St, Suite 300, Toronto, ON M5C 2V6, Canada *Tel:* 416-364-4449 *Toll Free Tel:* 800-668-4247 (order desk) *Fax:* 416-364-0462 *Web Site:* www.randomhouse.ca, pg 552

Dent, Mary J, Resource Publications Inc, 160 E Virginia St, Suite 290, San Jose, CA 95112-5876 *Tel:* 408-286-8505 *Fax:* 408-287-8748 *E-mail:* orders@rpinet.com *Web Site:* www.rpinet.com, pg 231

Dente, Linda, Artist Fellowships, One Financial Plaza, 755 Main St, Hartford, CT 06103 *Tel:* 860-566-4770 *Fax:* 860-566-6462 *E-mail:* artsinfo@ctarts.org *Web Site:* www.ctarts.org, pg 760

Denton, Henry, Plymouth Press/Plymouth Books, PO Box 2044, Miami Beach, FL 33140 *Tel:* 305-673-0771 *Fax:* 305-673-1014 (call first), pg 215

Denton, James, University Press of Florida, 15 NW 15 St, Gainesville, FL 32611-2079 *Tel:* 352-392-1351 *Toll Free Tel:* 800-226-3822 (orders only) *Fax:* 352-392-7302 *Toll Free Fax:* 800-680-1955 (orders only) *E-mail:* info@upf.com *Web Site:* www.upf.com, pg 287

Deonarain, Renuka, The Brookings Institution Press, 1775 Massachusetts Ave NW, Washington, DC 20036-2188 *Tel:* 202-797-6000 *Toll Free Tel:* 800-275-1447 *Fax:* 202-797-6195 *E-mail:* bibooks@brook.edu *Web Site:* www.brookings.edu, pg 48

Der Hovanessian, Diana, Rosalie Boyle/Norma Farber Award, 16 Cornell St, Arlington, MA 02474 *Web Site:* www.nepoetryclub.org, pg 764

Der Hovanessian, Diana, Barbara Bradley Prize, 16 Cornell St, Arlington, MA 02474 *Web Site:* www.nepoetryclub.org, pg 764

Der Hovanessian, Diana, Der-Hovanessian Translation Prize, 16 Cornell St, Arlington, MA 02474 *Web Site:* www.nepoetryclub.org, pg 769

Der Hovanessian, Diana, Firman Houghton Prize, 16 Cornell St, Arlington, MA 02474 *Web Site:* www.nepoetryclub.org, pg 774

Der Hovanessian, Diana, Golden Rose Award, 16 Cornell St, Arlington, MA 02474 *Web Site:* www.nepoetryclub.org, pg 776

Der Hovanessian, Diana, Sheila Margaret Motton Prize, 16 Cornell St, Arlington, MA 02474 *Web Site:* www.nepoetryclub.org, pg 791

Der Hovanessian, Diana, Erika Mumford Prize, 16 Cornell St, Arlington, MA 02474 *Web Site:* www.nepoetryclub.org, pg 791

Der Hovanessian, Diana, New England Poetry Club, 2 Farrar St, Cambridge, MA 02138 *Tel:* 781-643-0029, pg 695

1009

di Capua, Michael, Michael di Capua Books, 114 Fifth Ave, New York, NY 10011 *Tel:* 212-633-4400 *Fax:* 212-807-5880 *Web Site:* www.hyperionbooks. com, pg 173

Di Chiera, Christina M, Fellowship Program, One Capital Hill, 3rd fl, Providence, RI 02908 *Tel:* 401-222-3880 *Fax:* 401-222-3018 *Web Site:* www.arts.ri. gov, pg 773

Di Marco, Cris, Windstorm Creative, PO Box 28, Port Orchard, WA 98366 *Tel:* 360-769-7174 *E-mail:* queries@windstormcreative.com *Web Site:* www.windstormcreative.com, pg 301

Diamond, Sam, Players Press Inc, PO Box 1132, Studio City, CA 91614-0132 *Tel:* 818-789-4980, pg 214

Diaz, Jorge E, Baptist Spanish Publishing House (d/b/a Casa Bautista de Publicaciones), 7000 Alabama St, El Paso, TX 79904 *Tel:* 915-566-9656 *Toll Free Tel:* 800-755-5958 (cust serv & orders); 800-985-9971 (Casa Bautista Miami) *Fax:* 915-562-6502; 915-565-9008 (orders) *E-mail:* cbpmail@casabautista.org *Web Site:* www.casabautista.org, pg 31

Diaz, Miryam, Baptist Spanish Publishing House (d/b/a Casa Bautista de Publicaciones), 7000 Alabama St, El Paso, TX 79904 *Tel:* 915-566-9656 *Toll Free Tel:* 800-755-5958 (cust serv & orders); 800-985-9971 (Casa Bautista Miami) *Fax:* 915-562-6502; 915-565-9008 (orders) *E-mail:* cbpmail@casabautista.org *Web Site:* www.casabautista.org, pg 31

Diaz, Nestor, Pureplay Press, 11353 Missouri Ave, Los Angeles, CA 90025 *Tel:* 310-479-8773 *Toll Free Tel:* 800-247-6553 (orders only) *Fax:* 310-473-9384 *E-mail:* info@cubanovel.com *Web Site:* www. pureplaypress.com, pg 222

DiBello, John, W W Norton & Company Inc, 500 Fifth Ave, New York, NY 10110-0017 *Tel:* 212-354-5500 *Toll Free Tel:* 800-233-4830 (orders & cust serv) *Fax:* 212-869-0856 *Toll Free Fax:* 800-458-6515 *Web Site:* www.wwnorton.com, pg 193

DiCicco, Mark, Tyndale House Publishers Inc, 351 Executive Dr, Carol Stream, IL 60188 *Tel:* 630-668-8303 *Toll Free Tel:* 800-323-9400 *Web Site:* www. tyndale.com, pg 277

Dickens, Allison, Random House Publishing Group, 1745 Broadway, New York, NY 10019 *Toll Free Tel:* 800-200-3552 *Toll Free Fax:* 800-200-3552 *Web Site:* www.randomhouse.com, pg 227

Dickensheid, Diane, Victoria Sanders & Associates, 241 Avenue of the Americas, Suite 11H, New York, NY 10014 *Tel:* 212-633-8811 *Fax:* 212-633-0525 *E-mail:* queriesvsa@hotmail.com *Web Site:* www. victoriasanders.com, pg 653

Dickerson, Donna, Peabody Museum of Archaeology & Ethnology, Peabody Museum Press, 11 Divinity Ave, Cambridge, MA 02138 *Tel:* 617-495-3938 (Production); 617-496-9922 (Sales) *Fax:* 617-495-7535 *E-mail:* peapub@fas.harvard.edu *Web Site:* www. peabody.harvard.edu/publications, pg 206

Dickerson, Terese, Oxford University Press, Inc, 198 Madison Ave, New York, NY 10016-4314 *Tel:* 212-726-6000 *Toll Free Tel:* 800-451-7556 (orders) *Web Site:* www.oup.com/us, pg 200

Dickinson, Christopher, Congressional Quarterly Press, 1255 22 St NW, Washington, DC 20037 *Tel:* 202-729-1800 *Toll Free Tel:* 866-427-7737 *Fax:* 202-729-1809 *Toll Free Fax:* 800-380-3810 *E-mail:* customerservice@cqpress.com *Web Site:* www.cq.com, pg 66

Dickinson, Greg, The Althouse Press, University of Western Ontario, 1137 Western Rd, London, ON N6G 1G7, Canada *Tel:* 519-661-2096 *Fax:* 519-661-3833 *E-mail:* press@uwo.ca *Web Site:* www.edu.uwo. ca/althousepress, pg 535

Dickinson, Jan, Wheatherstone Press, 10250 SW Greenburg Rd, No 125, Portland, OR 97223 *Tel:* 503-244-8929 *Toll Free Tel:* 800-980-0077 *Fax:* 503-244-9795 *E-mail:* relocntr@europa.com *Web Site:* www. wheatherstonepress.com, pg 297

Dickinson, Kathryn, White Bird Annual Playwriting Contest, 138 S Oxford St, Suite 3-A, Brooklyn, NY 11217 *Tel:* 718-398-3658 *Fax:* 718-398-3658 *E-mail:* info@whitebirdproductions.org *Web Site:* www.whitebirdproductions.org, pg 811

Dickson, Jan, Environmental Ethics Books, 1704 W Mulberry St, UNT, EESAT Bldg 370, Denton, TX 76201 *Tel:* 940-565-2727 *Toll Free Tel:* 800-264-9962 *Fax:* 940-565-4439 *Toll Free Fax:* 800-295-0536 *E-mail:* ee@unt.edu *Web Site:* www.cep.unt.edu, pg 91

Dickson, Jonathan Lovat, Pippin Publishing Corp, 170 The Donway W, Toronto, ON M3C 2G3, Canada *Tel:* 416-510-2918 *Toll Free Tel:* 888-889-0001 *Fax:* 416-510-3359 *Web Site:* www.pippinpub.com, pg 557

Dickstein, Alice, Brown Publishing Network Inc, 95 Sawyer Rd, Waltham, MA 02453 *Tel:* 781-237-7567 *Fax:* 781-237-8874 *Web Site:* www.brownpubnet.com, pg 593

Diedrick, Brice, JMW Group Inc, 5 W Cross St, Hawthorne, NY 10532 *Tel:* 914-769-6400 *Fax:* 914-769-0250, pg 141

Diehl, Dan, UnKnownTruths.com Publishing Co, 8815 Conroy Windermere Rd, Suite 190, Orlando, FL 32835 *Tel:* 407-929-9207 *Fax:* 407-876-3933 *E-mail:* info@unknowntruths.com *Web Site:* unknowntruths.com, pg 288

Diehl, Debra, University Press of Kansas, 2501 W 15 St, Lawrence, KS 66049-3905 *Tel:* 785-864-4154; 785-864-4155 (orders) *Fax:* 785-864-4586 *E-mail:* upress@ku.edu *Web Site:* www.kansaspress. ku.edu, pg 287

Diener, Matthew S, Loyola Press, 3441 N Ashland Ave, Chicago, IL 60657 *Tel:* 773-281-1818; 773-244-4429 *Toll Free Tel:* 800-621-1008 *Fax:* 773-281-0555; 773-281-0152 (trade) *E-mail:* editorial@loydapress.com *Web Site:* www.loyolapress.org, pg 159

Diep-Lang, JoAnn, Sasquatch Books, 119 S Main, Suite 400, Seattle, WA 98104 *Tel:* 206-467-4300 *Toll Free Tel:* 800-775-0817 *Fax:* 206-467-4301 *E-mail:* books@sasquatchbooks.com *Web Site:* www. sasquatchbooks.com, pg 240

Dietrich, Katherine, Clarkson Potter Publishers, 1745 Broadway, New York, NY 10019 *Tel:* 212-782-9000 *Toll Free Tel:* 888-264-1745 *Fax:* 212-572-6181 *Web Site:* www.clarksonpotter.com; www. randomhouse.com/crown/clarksonpotter, pg 63

Dietrich, Katherine, Crown Publishing Group, 1745 Broadway, New York, NY 10019 *Tel:* 212-782-9000 *Toll Free Tel:* 888-264-1745 *Fax:* 212-940-7408 *Web Site:* www.randomhouse.com/crown, pg 74

Diez, Barbara, Bloomberg Press, PO Box 888, Princeton, NJ 08542-0888 *Tel:* 609-279-4600 *E-mail:* press@ bloomberg.com *Web Site:* www.bloomberg.com/books, pg 41

Diez, Susan, Tropical Press Inc, PO Box 161174, Miami, FL 33116-1174 *Tel:* 305-971-1887 *Fax:* 305-378-1595 *E-mail:* tropicbook@aol.com *Web Site:* www. tropicalpress.com, pg 276

Diforio, Robert G, D4EO Literary Agency, 7 Indian Valley Rd, Weston, CT 06883 *Tel:* 203-544-7180; 203-545-7180 (cell phone) *Fax:* 203-544-7160 *E-mail:* d4eo@optionline.net *Web Site:* www. publishersmarketplace.com/members/d4eo, pg 627

Diggs, Anita, The Literary Group International, 270 Lafayette St, Suite 1505, New York, NY 10012 *Tel:* 212-274-1616 *Fax:* 212-274-9876 *Web Site:* www. theliterarygroup.com, pg 641

Dijkstra, Sandra, Sandra Dijkstra Literary Agency, 1155 Camino del Mar, PMB 515, Del Mar, CA 92014-2605 *Tel:* 858-755-3115 *Fax:* 858-794-2822 *E-mail:* sdla@ dijkstraagency.com, pg 627

DiLeo, Dale, Training Resource Network Inc (T R N), PO Box 439, St Augustine, FL 32085-0439 *Tel:* 904-823-9800 (cust serv); 904-824-7121 (edit off) *Toll Free Tel:* 800-280-7010 (orders) *Fax:* 904-823-3554 *E-mail:* customerservice@trninc.com *Web Site:* www. trninc.com, pg 273

Diley, Esther, Augsburg Fortress Publishers, Publishing House of the Evangelical Lutheran Church in America, 100 S Fifth St, Suite 700, Minneapolis, MN 55402 *Tel:* 612-330-3300 *Toll Free Tel:* 800-426-0115 (ext 639 subns); 800-328-4648 (orders); 800-421-0239 (perms) *Fax:* 612-330-3455 *Toll Free Fax:* 800-421-0239 (perms & copyrights) *E-mail:* customerservice@ augsburgfortress.org; copyright@augsburgfortress.org (for reprint permission requests) *Web Site:* www. augsburgfortress.org, pg 28

Dill, John, Canadian Publishers' Council (CPC), 250 Merton St, Suite 203, Toronto, ON M4S 1B1, Canada *Tel:* 416-322-7011 *Fax:* 416-322-6999 *E-mail:* pubadmin@pubcouncil.ca *Web Site:* www. pubcouncil.ca, pg 684

Dill, John, McGraw-Hill International Publishing Group, 2 Penn Plaza, New York, NY 10121 *Tel:* 212-904-2000 *Web Site:* www.mcgrawhill.com, pg 168

Dill, John, McGraw-Hill Ryerson Ltd, 300 Water St, Whitby, ON L1N 9B6, Canada *Tel:* 905-430-5000 *Toll Free Tel:* 800-565-5758 (cust serv) *Fax:* 905-430-5020 *E-mail:* johnd@mcgrawhill.ca *Web Site:* www. mcgrawhill.ca, pg 554

Dillahunt, Amy, Free Spirit Publishing Inc, 217 Fifth Ave N, Suite 200, Minneapolis, MN 55401-1299 *Tel:* 612-338-2068 *Toll Free Tel:* 800-735-7323 *Fax:* 612-337-5050 *E-mail:* help4kids@freespirit.com *Web Site:* www.freespirit.com, pg 100

Dillon, Sanyu, Random House Publishing Group, 1745 Broadway, New York, NY 10019 *Toll Free Tel:* 800-200-3552 *Toll Free Fax:* 800-200-3552 *Web Site:* www.randomhouse.com, pg 227

Dilworth, John R, Harcourt Assessment Inc, 19500 Bulverde Rd, San Antonio, TX 78259 *Tel:* 210-339-5000 *Toll Free Tel:* 800-211-8378 *Web Site:* www. harcourtassessment.com, pg 114

Dilworth, Mary E, ERIC Clearinghouse on Teaching & Teacher Education, 1307 New York Ave NW, Suite 300, Washington, DC 20005 *Tel:* 202-293-2450 *Toll Free Tel:* 800-799-3742 *Fax:* 202-457-8095 *Web Site:* www.ericsp.org, pg 686

DiMarco, Maureen, Houghton Mifflin Co, 222 Berkeley St, Boston, MA 02116-3764 *Tel:* 617-351-5000 *Toll Free Tel:* 800-225-3362 (trade books); 800-733-2828 (text books); 800-225-1464 (college texts) *Fax:* 617-351-1125 *Web Site:* www.hmco.com, pg 126

DiMartino, Christina, Christina DiMartino Literary Services, 59 W 119 St, Suite 2, New York City, NY 10026 *Tel:* 212-996-9086; 917-972-6012 *E-mail:* writealot@earthlink.net, pg 596

Dimnik, Michelle, Rocky Mountain Book Award, PO Box 42, Lethbridge, AB T1J 3Y3, Canada *Tel:* 403-381-7164 *E-mail:* rockymountainbookaward@shaw.ca *Web Site:* www.lethsd.ab.ca/lvbookaward, pg 802

Dimock, Peter, Columbia University Press, 61 W 62 St, New York, NY 10023 *Tel:* 212-459-0600 *Toll Free Tel:* 800-944-8648 *Fax:* 212-459-3678 *Web Site:* www. columbia.edu/cu/cup, pg 65

DiNardo, Doug, McGraw-Hill Science, Engineering, Mathematics, 2460 Kerper Blvd, Dubuque, IA 52001 *Tel:* 563-588-1451 *Toll Free Tel:* 800-338-3987 (cust serv) *Fax:* 563-589-4700; 614-755-5645 (cust serv) *E-mail:* firstname_lastname@mcgraw-hill.com *Web Site:* www.mhhe.com, pg 169

Ding, Kristine, University of Illinois Press, 1325 S Oak, Champaign, IL 61820-6903 *Tel:* 217-333-0950; 212-577-5487 *Fax:* 217-244-8082; 410-516-6969 (orders) *E-mail:* uipress@uillinois.edu; journals@uillinois.edu *Web Site:* www.press.uillinois.edu, pg 282

Dinger, Angela, William H Sadlier Inc, 9 Pine St, New York, NY 10005 *Tel:* 212-227-2120 *Toll Free Tel:* 800-221-5175 *Fax:* 212-312-6080 *Web Site:* www. sadlier.com; www.sadlier-oxford.com, pg 237

Dinger, Frank S, William H Sadlier Inc, 9 Pine St, New York, NY 10005 *Tel:* 212-227-2120 *Toll Free Tel:* 800-221-5175 *Fax:* 212-312-6080 *Web Site:* www. sadlier.com; www.sadlier-oxford.com, pg 237

Dinger, William S, William H Sadlier Inc, 9 Pine St, New York, NY 10005 *Tel:* 212-227-2120 *Toll Free Tel:* 800-221-5175 *Fax:* 212-312-6080 *Web Site:* www. sadlier.com; www.sadlier-oxford.com, pg 237

Dingledine, Kenneth, Samuel French Inc, 45 W 25 St, New York, NY 10010-2751 *Tel:* 212-206-8990 *Fax:* 212-206-1429 *E-mail:* samuelfrench@earthlink. net *Web Site:* www.samuelfrench.com, pg 101

Dingledine, Kenneth, Annual Off-Off-Broadway Original Short Play Festival, c/o Samuel Frenchz Inc, 45 W 25 St, New York, NY 10010 *Tel:* 212-206-8990 *Fax:* 212-206-1429 *E-mail:* samuelfrench@earthlink. net *Web Site:* www.samuelfrench.com, pg 795

Dingman, Beth, New Victoria Publishers, 513 New Boston Rd, Norwich, VT 05055 *Tel:* 802-649-5297 *Toll Free Tel:* 800-326-5297 *Fax:* 802-649-5297 *Toll Free Fax:* 800-326-5297 *E-mail:* newvic@aol.com *Web Site:* www.newvictoria.com, pg 189

Dingwall, Wendy, High Country Publishers Ltd, 197 New Market Center, No 135, Boone, NC 28607 *Tel:* 828-964-0590 *Fax:* 828-262-1973 *E-mail:* editor@highcountrypublishers.com *Web Site:* www.highcountrypublishers.com, pg 122

Dinstman, Lee, Agency For The Performing Arts Inc, 9200 Sunset Blvd, Suite 900, Los Angeles, CA 90069 *Tel:* 310-273-0744 *Fax:* 310-888-4242, pg 618

Dion, Denis, Les Presses De L'Universite Laval, Maurice-Pollack House, Office 3103, University City, Sainte-Foy, PQ G1K 7P4, Canada *Tel:* 418-656-2803 *Fax:* 418-656-3305 *E-mail:* presses@pul.ulaval.ca *Web Site:* www.ulaval.ca/pul, pg 558

Dion, Marc, Association pour l'Avancement des Sciences et des Techniques de la Documentation, 3414 Avenue du Parc, Bureau 202, Montreal, PQ H2X 2H5, Canada *Tel:* 514-281-5012 *Fax:* 514-281-8219 *E-mail:* info@ asted.org *Web Site:* www.asted.org, pg 680

Dion, Pierre, Reader's Digest Association (Canada) Ltd/Selection du Reader's Digest (Canada) Ltee, 1100 Rene Levesque Blvd W, Montreal, PQ H3B 5H5, Canada *Tel:* 514-940-0751 *Toll Free Tel:* 800-465-0780 *Fax:* 514-940-3637 (admin) *E-mail:* customer. service@readersdigest.ca *Web Site:* www.readersdigest. ca, pg 559

DiRusso, Gale, Chrysalis Publishing Group Inc, 34 Main St, Natick, MA 01760 *Tel:* 508-647-3730 *Toll Free Tel:* 877-922-1822 *Fax:* 508-653-3448 *E-mail:* info@chrysalispublishing.com *Web Site:* www. chrysalispublishing.com, pg 594

Diskant, George E, Diskant & Associates, 116 E De La Guerra St, Suite 9, Santa Barbara, CA 93101 *Tel:* 805-962-2961, pg 628

Dismuke, Charles, Oakstone Medical Publishing, 6801 Cahaba Valley Rd, Birmingham, AL 35242 *Tel:* 205-991-5188 *Toll Free Tel:* 800-952-0690 *Fax:* 205-995-4656 *E-mail:* service@oakstonemedical.com *Web Site:* www.oakstonemedical.com, pg 195

Disney, Connie, Signature Books Publishing LLC, 564 W 400 N, Salt Lake City, UT 84116-3411 *Tel:* 801-531-1483 *Toll Free Tel:* 800-356-5687 (orders) *Fax:* 801-531-1488 *E-mail:* people@signaturebooks. com *Web Site:* www.signaturebooks.com, pg 247

Dispirito, Mary Ann, League of Vermont Writers, PO Box 172, Underhill Center, VT 05490 *Tel:* 802-253-9439 *Web Site:* www.leaguevtwriters.org, pg 690

DiStefano, G, editions CERES Ltd/Le Moyen Francais, CP 1657 Succ B, 1250 University, Montreal, PQ H3B 3L3, Canada *Tel:* 514-937-7138 *Fax:* 514-937-9875 *Web Site:* www.editionsceres.ca, pg 543

Ditlefsen, Charles E, Cedco Publishing Co, 100 Pelican Way, San Rafael, CA 94901 *Tel:* 415-451-3000 *Toll Free Tel:* 800-227-6162 *Fax:* 415-457-4839 *E-mail:* sales@cedco.com *Web Site:* www.cedco.com, pg 56

Ditlow, Barbara, Writers Guild of America Awards, 7000 W Third St, Los Angeles, CA 90048 *Tel:* 323-951-4000 *Fax:* 323-782-4802 *Web Site:* www.wga.org, pg 813

Ditlow, Tim, Random House Audio Publishing Group, 1745 Broadway, New York, NY 10019 *Tel:* 212-782-9720 *Fax:* 212-782-9600, pg 225

Dittmer, Luther A, Institute of Mediaeval Music, PO Box 295, Henryville, PA 18332-0295 *Tel:* 570-629-1278 *Fax:* 613-225-9487 *Web Site:* members.rogers. com/mediaeval1, pg 135

Diver, Lucienne, Spectrum Literary Agency, 320 Central Park W, Suite 1-D, New York, NY 10025 *Tel:* 212-362-4323 *Fax:* 212-362-4562 *Web Site:* www. spectrumliteraryagency.com, pg 656

DiVietro, Philip, American Society of Mechanical Engineers (ASME), 3 Park Ave, New York, NY 10016 *Tel:* 212-591-7000 *Toll Free Tel:* 800-843-2763 (cust serv) *Fax:* 212-591-7674; 973-882-1717 (cust serv) *E-mail:* infocentral@asme.org *Web Site:* www.asme. org, pg 18

Dixon, Dan, University of California Press, 2120 Berkeley Way, Berkeley, CA 94720 *Tel:* 510-642-4247 *Toll Free Tel:* 800-777-4726 *Fax:* 510-643-7127 *Toll Free Fax:* 800-999-1958 *E-mail:* askucp@ucpress.edu *Web Site:* www.ucpress.edu, pg 281

Dixon, Lynn, Pacific Northwest Book Awards, 317 W Broadway, Suite 214, Eugene, OR 97401-2890 *Tel:* 541-683-4363 *Fax:* 541-683-3910 *E-mail:* info@ pnba.org *Web Site:* www.pnba.org/awards.htm, pg 796

Dixon, Mary, Portage & Main Press, 318 McDermot, Suite 100, Winnipeg, MB R3A 0A2, Canada *Tel:* 204-987-3500 *Toll Free Tel:* 800-667-9673 *Fax:* 204-947-0080 *Toll Free Fax:* 866-734-8477 *E-mail:* books@portageandmainpress.com *Web Site:* www.portageandmainpress.com, pg 558

Dixon, Shatera, University of Houston Creative Writing Program, 229 Roy Cullen Bldg, Houston, TX 77204-3015 *Tel:* 713-743-3015 *Fax:* 713-743-3697 *E-mail:* cwp@uh.edu *Web Site:* www.uh.edu/cwp, pg 755

Dixon, Susan, Antiquarian Booksellers' Association of America, 20 W 44 St, 4th fl, New York, NY 10036 *Tel:* 212-944-8291 *Fax:* 212-944-8293 *E-mail:* hq@ abaa.org *Web Site:* www.abaa.org, pg 678

Dlouhy, Caitlyn, Simon & Schuster Children's Publishing, 1230 Avenue of the Americas, New York, NY 10020 *Tel:* 212-698-7000 *Web Site:* www. simonsayskids.com, pg 248

Dobbin, Robert, Berkeley Hills Books, 1435 Fourth St, Berkeley, CA 94710 *Tel:* 510-559-8650 *Fax:* 510-559-8670 *Web Site:* www.berkeleyhills.com, pg 36

Doble, Elizabeth, John Wiley & Sons Inc Professional & Trade Group, 111 River St, Hoboken, NJ 07030 *Tel:* 201-748-6000 *Toll Free Tel:* 800-225-5945 (cust serv) *Fax:* 201-748-6088 *E-mail:* info@wiley.com *Web Site:* www.wiley.com, pg 300

Dobles, Gustavo, Aspen Publishers, A Wolters Kluwer Company, 1185 Avenue of the Americas, New York, NY 10036 *Tel:* 212-597-0200 *Toll Free Tel:* 800-234-1660 (cust serv); 800-447-1717 (orders); 800-950-5259 (legal educ); 800-LAW-PLGL (paralegal textbook); 800-317-3113 (bookstore sales); 800-364-2512 (Loislaw) *Web Site:* www.aspenpublishers.com, pg 26

Dobmeier, Charlene, Fifth House Publishers, 1511 1800 Fourth St SW, Calgary, AB T2S 2S5, Canada *Tel:* 403-571-5230 *Toll Free Tel:* 800-387-9776 *Fax:* 403-571-5235 *Toll Free Fax:* 800-260-9777 *Web Site:* www.fitzhenry.ca/fifthhouse.htm, pg 546

Dobrowolski, Thomas, Bantam Dell Publishing Group, 1745 Broadway, New York, NY 10019 *Tel:* 212-782-9000 *Toll Free Tel:* 800-223-6834 *Fax:* 212-302-7985 *Web Site:* www.randomhouse.com/bantamdell, pg 31

Dobson, Edward D, Traders Press Inc, 703 Laurens Rd, Greenville, SC 29607-1912 *Tel:* 864-298-0222 *Toll Free Tel:* 800-927-8222 *Fax:* 864-298-0221 *Web Site:* www.traderspress.com, pg 273

Dodd, Howell, Institute for Language Study, 7 Hollyhock Rd, Wilton, CT 06897 *Tel:* 203-762-2510 *Toll Free Tel:* 800-245-2145 *Fax:* 203-762-2514 *E-mail:* cortinainc@aol.com *Web Site:* www.cortina-languages.com; members.aol.com/cortinainc, pg 134

Doenges, Susann, Bureau of Economic Geology, University of Texas at Austin, 10100 Burnet Rd, Bldg 130, Austin, TX 78750 *Tel:* 512-471-7144 *Toll Free Tel:* 888-839-4365 *Fax:* 512-471-0140 *Toll Free Fax:* 888-839-6277 *E-mail:* pubsales@beg.utexas.edu *Web Site:* www.beg.utexas.edu, pg 50

Doering, Ron, Random House Publishing Group, 1745 Broadway, New York, NY 10019 *Toll Free Tel:* 800-200-3552 *Toll Free Fax:* 800-200-3552 *Web Site:* www.randomhouse.com, pg 227

Dohan, Blanche B, InfoServices International Inc, 313 Main St, Huntington, NY 11743 *Tel:* 631-549-0064 *Fax:* 631-549-6663 *E-mail:* typ@infoservices.com *Web Site:* www.infoservices.com, pg 133

Dohan, Michael R, InfoServices International Inc, 313 Main St, Huntington, NY 11743 *Tel:* 631-549-0064 *Fax:* 631-549-6663 *E-mail:* typ@infoservices.com *Web Site:* www.infoservices.com, pg 133

Doherty, Kathleen, Tom Doherty Associates, LLC, 175 Fifth Ave, 14th fl, New York, NY 10010 *Tel:* 212-388-0100 *Toll Free Tel:* 800-455-0340 *Fax:* 212-388-0191 *E-mail:* firstname.lastname@tor.com *Web Site:* www. tor.com, pg 81

Doherty, Tom, Tom Doherty Associates, LLC, 175 Fifth Ave, 14th fl, New York, NY 10010 *Tel:* 212-388-0100 *Toll Free Tel:* 800-455-0340 *Fax:* 212-388-0191 *E-mail:* firstname.lastname@tor.com *Web Site:* www. tor.com, pg 81

Doige, Lynda A, Mi'kmaq-Maliseet Institute, University of New Brunswick, PO Box 4400, Fredriction, NB E3B 6E3, Canada *Tel:* 506-453-4840 *Fax:* 506-453-4784 *E-mail:* micmac@unb.ca *Web Site:* www.unb.ca, pg 554

Dolan, Deirdre, The Countryman Press, 1206 Rte 12 N, Woodstock, VT 05091 *Tel:* 802-457-4826 *Toll Free Tel:* 800-245-4151 *Fax:* 802-457-1678 *E-mail:* countrymanpress@wwnorton.com *Web Site:* www.countrymanpress.com, pg 70

Dolan, Deirdre F, W W Norton & Company Inc, 500 Fifth Ave, New York, NY 10110-0017 *Tel:* 212-354-5500 *Toll Free Tel:* 800-233-4830 (orders & cust serv) *Fax:* 212-869-0856 *Toll Free Fax:* 800-458-6515 *Web Site:* www.wwnorton.com, pg 193

Dolger, Jonathan, The Jonathan Dolger Agency, 49 E 96 St, Suite 9-B, New York, NY 10128 *Tel:* 212-427-1853 *Fax:* 212-369-7118, pg 628

Dolgert, Paul, Humana Press, 999 Riverview Dr, Suite 208, Totowa, NJ 07512 *Tel:* 973-256-1699 *Fax:* 973-256-8341 *E-mail:* humana@humanapr.com *Web Site:* humanapress.com, pg 128

Dolgins, Stuart, American Map Corp, 46-35 54 Rd, Maspeth, NY 11378 *Tel:* 718-784-0055 *Toll Free Tel:* 800-432-MAPS *Fax:* 718-784-0640 (admin); 718-784-1216 (sales & orders), pg 15

Dolgins, Stuart, Hagstrom Map Co Inc, 46-35 54 Rd, Maspeth, NY 11378 *Tel:* 718-784-0055 *Toll Free Tel:* 800-432-MAPS (432-6277) *Fax:* 718-784-0640 (admin); 718-784-1216 (sales & orders) *Web Site:* www.americanmap.com, pg 111

Dolgins, Stuart, Hammond World Atlas Corp, 95 Progress St, Union, NJ 07083 *Tel:* 908-206-1300 *Toll Free Tel:* 800-526-4953 *Fax:* 908-206-1104 *E-mail:* customerservice@hammondmap.com; feedback@hammondmap.com *Web Site:* www. hammondmap.com, pg 112

Dolgins, Stuart, Langenscheidt Publishers Inc, 46-35 54 Rd, Maspeth, NY 11378 *Tel:* 718-784-0055 *Toll Free Tel:* 800-432-MAPS (732-6277) *Fax:* 718-784-0640 *Toll Free Fax:* 888-773-7979 *E-mail:* sales@ langenscheidt.com *Web Site:* www.langenscheidt.com, pg 149

Dolgins, Stuart, Trakker Maps Inc, 8350 Parkline Blvd, Suite 360, Orlando, FL 32809 *Tel:* 407-447-6485 *Toll Free Tel:* 800-327-3108 *Fax:* 407-447-6488 *E-mail:* sales@trakkermaps.com *Web Site:* www. trakkermaps.com, pg 273

Dolin, Lisa, Rodale Books, 400 S Tenth St, Emmaus, PA 18098-0099 *Tel:* 610-967-5171 *Fax:* 610-967-8961 *Web Site:* www.rodale.com, pg 233

Doling, Jennie, State University of New York Press, 90 State St, Suite 700, Albany, NY 12207-1707 *Tel:* 518-472-5000 *Toll Free Tel:* 800-666-2211 (orders) *Fax:* 518-472-5038 *Toll Free Fax:* 800-688-2877 (orders) *E-mail:* orderbook@cupserv.org; info@sunypress.edu *Web Site:* www.sunypress.edu, pg 258

Dollar, Douglas, New Forums Press Inc, 1018 S Lewis St, Stillwater, OK 74074 *Tel:* 405-372-6158 *Toll Free Tel:* 800-606-3766 *Fax:* 405-377-2237 *E-mail:* info@newforums.com *Web Site:* www.newforums.com, pg 188

Dollente, Sheila, San Diego State University Press, San Diego State University, 5500 Campanile Dr, San Diego, CA 92182-8141 *Tel:* 760-768-5536; 619-594-6220 (orders only) *Fax:* 760-768-5631 *Web Site:* www.rohan.sdsu.edu/dept/press/, pg 239

Dombos, Juliet, The Pilgrim Press/United Church Press, 700 Prospect Ave, Cleveland, OH 44115-1100 *Tel:* 216-736-3761 *Toll Free Tel:* 800-537-3394 (cust serv) *Fax:* 216-736-2207 *E-mail:* thepilgrimpress@thepilgrimpress.com *Web Site:* www.thepilgrimpress.com; www.theunitedchurchpress.com, pg 213

Dombrouski, Peter, Silverback Books Inc, 55 New Montgomery St, Suite 503, San Francisco, CA 94105 *Tel:* 415-348-8595 *Toll Free Tel:* 866-348-8595 *Fax:* 415-348-8592 *E-mail:* info@silverbackbooks.com *Web Site:* www.silverbackbooks.com, pg 248

Domenig, Kathleen, Strata Publishing Inc, PO Box 1303, State College, PA 16804 *Tel:* 814-234-8545; 814-234-2150 (sales) *Fax:* 814-238-7222 *E-mail:* editorial@stratapub.com *Web Site:* www.stratapub.com, pg 260

Domino, Kathleen, University of Alabama Press, Box 870380, Tuscaloosa, AL 35487-0380 *Tel:* 205-348-5180; 773-702-7000 (orders) *Fax:* 205-348-9201 *Web Site:* www.uapress.ua.edu, pg 280

Domnitz, Avin Mark, American Booksellers Association, 828 S Broadway, Tarrytown, NY 10591 *Tel:* 914-591-2665 *Toll Free Tel:* 800-637-0037 *Fax:* 914-591-2720 *E-mail:* editorial@booksense.com *Web Site:* www.booksense.com, pg 676

Domnitz, Avin Mark, Book Sense Book of the Year Award, 828 S Broadway, Tarrytown, NY 10591 *Tel:* 914-591-2665 *Toll Free Tel:* 800-637-0037 *Fax:* 914-591-2720 *Web Site:* www.bookweb.org, pg 763

Domras, Roger, American Psychiatric Publishing Inc, 1000 Wilson Blvd, Suite 1825, Arlington, VA 22209 *Tel:* 703-907-7322 *Toll Free Tel:* 800-368-5777 *Fax:* 703-907-1091 *E-mail:* appi@psych.org *Web Site:* www.appi.org, pg 16

Donaher, Edward, Alba House, 2187 Victory Blvd, Staten Island, NY 10314 *Tel:* 718-761-0047 (edit & prodn); 718-698-2759 (mktg & billing) *Toll Free Tel:* 800-343-2522 *Fax:* 718-761-0057 *E-mail:* albabooks@aol.com *Web Site:* www.albahouse.org, pg 7

Donahue, George, The Lyons Press, 246 Goose Lane, Guilford, CT 06437 *Tel:* 203-458-4500 *Toll Free Tel:* 800-243-0495 *Fax:* 203-458-4668 *Web Site:* www.lyonspress.com; www.globepequot.com, pg 160

Donahue, James, Augsburg Fortress Publishers, Publishing House of the Evangelical Lutheran Church in America, 100 S Fifth St, Suite 700, Minneapolis, MN 55402 *Tel:* 612-330-3300 *Toll Free Tel:* 800-426-0115 (ext 639 subns); 800-328-4648 (orders); 800-421-0239 (perms) *Fax:* 612-330-3455 *Toll Free Fax:* 800-421-0239 (perms & copyrights) *E-mail:* customerservice@augsburgfortress.org; copyright@augsburgfortress.org (for reprint permission requests) *Web Site:* www.augsburgfortress.org, pg 28

Donahue, Suzanne, Free Press, 1230 Avenue of the Americas, New York, NY 10020 *Tel:* 212-698-7000 *Toll Free Tel:* 800-223-2345 (cust serv); 800-223-2336 (orders); 888-866-6631 (fulfillment), pg 100

Donatich, John, Yale University Press, 302 Temple St, New Haven, CT 06511 *Tel:* 203-432-0960; 401-531-2800 (cust serv) *Toll Free Tel:* 800-405-1619 (cust serv) *Fax:* 203-432-0948; 401-531-2801 (cust serv) *Toll Free Fax:* 800-406-9145 (cust serv) *E-mail:* customer.care@trilateral.org (cust serv) *Web Site:* www.yale.edu/yup/, pg 305

Donato, Mariann, Penguin Young Readers Group, 345 Hudson St, New York, NY 10014 *Tel:* 212-366-2000 *E-mail:* online@penguinputnam.com *Web Site:* www.penguin.com, pg 208

Donegan, Fran, Creative Homeowner, 24 Park Way, Upper Saddle River, NJ 07458-9960 *Tel:* 201-934-7100 *Toll Free Tel:* 800-631-7795 *Fax:* 201-934-8971 *E-mail:* info@creativehomeowner.com *Web Site:* www.creativehomeowner.com, pg 72

Donelson, Andrew, Hickory Tales Publishing LLC, 841 Newberry St, Bowling Green, KY 42103 *Tel:* 270-791-3242, pg 571

Donica, Karen, Editorial Options Inc, 353 Lexington Ave, New York, NY 10016 *Tel:* 212-986-2888 *Fax:* 212-986-1194 *Web Site:* www.edop.com, pg 597

Donini, Graig, Sinauer Associates Inc, 23 Plumtree Rd, Sunderland, MA 01375-0407 *Tel:* 413-549-4300 *Fax:* 413-549-1118 *E-mail:* publish@sinauer.com *Web Site:* www.sinauer.com, pg 249

Donnaud, Janis A, Janis A Donnaud & Associates Inc, 525 Broadway, 2nd fl, New York, NY 10012 *Tel:* 212-431-2663 *Fax:* 212-431-2667 *E-mail:* JDonnaud@aol.com, pg 628

Donnelly, Katharine, Appalachian Mountain Club Books, 5 Joy St, Boston, MA 02108 *Tel:* 617-523-0655 *Fax:* 617-523-0722 *Web Site:* www.outdoors.org, pg 21

Donnelly, Margarita, Calyx Books, PO Box B, Corvallis, OR 97339-0539 *Tel:* 541-753-9384 *Fax:* 541-753-0515 *E-mail:* calyx@proaxis.com *Web Site:* www.proaxis.com/~calyx, pg 51

Donnelly, Maureen, Penguin Books, 375 Hudson St, New York, NY 10014 *Tel:* 212-366-2000 *E-mail:* online@penguinputnam.com *Web Site:* www.penguin.com; www.penguinclassics.com, pg 207

Donnelly, Maureen, Viking Studio, 375 Hudson St, New York, NY 10014 *Tel:* 212-366-2000 *E-mail:* online@penguinputnam.com *Web Site:* www.penguin.com, pg 290

Donnelly, Susan, Harvard University Press, 79 Garden St, Cambridge, MA 02138-1499 *Tel:* 617-495-2600; 401-531-2800 (international orders) *Toll Free Tel:* 800-405-1619 (orders) *Fax:* 617-495-5898 (general); 617-496-4677 (edit & rts); 401-531-2801 (international orders) *Toll Free Fax:* 800-406-9145 (orders) *E-mail:* firstname_lastname@harvard.edu *Web Site:* www.hup.harvard.edu, pg 117

Donner, Andrea, Willow Creek Press, 9931 Hwy 70 W, Minocqua, WI 54548 *Tel:* 715-358-7010 *Toll Free Tel:* 800-850-9453 *Fax:* 715-358-2807 *E-mail:* info@willowcreekpress.com *Web Site:* www.willowcreekpress.com, pg 300

Donovan, D, Celo Book Production Service, 160 Ohle Rd, Burnsville, NC 28714 *Tel:* 828-675-5918, pg 594

Donovan, Jim, Jim Donovan Literary, 4515 Prentice, Suite 109, Dallas, TX 75206 *Tel:* 214-696-9411 *Fax:* 214-696-9412, pg 628

Donovan, Lisa, Simon & Schuster Children's Publishing, 1230 Avenue of the Americas, New York, NY 10020 *Tel:* 212-698-7000 *Web Site:* www.simonsayskids.com, pg 248

Donovan, Robin, Berrett-Koehler Publishers Inc, 235 Montgomery St, Suite 650, San Francisco, CA 94104 *Tel:* 415-288-0260 *Fax:* 415-362-2512 *E-mail:* bkpub@bkpub.com *Web Site:* www.bkconnection.com, pg 37

Dooley, Virginia, Scholastic Paperbacks, Teaching Resources & Reading Counts, 557 Broadway, New York, NY 10012-3999 *Tel:* 212-965-7241 *Fax:* 212-965-7487 *Web Site:* www.scholastic.com, pg 242

Doolittle, Dara, Gerald Peters Gallery, 1011 Paseo De Peralta, Santa Fe, NM 87501 *Tel:* 505-954-5700 *Fax:* 505-954-5754 *E-mail:* bookstore@gpgallery.com *Web Site:* www.gpgallery.com, pg 211

Doornbos, Chris H, Zondervan, 5300 Patterson Ave SE, Grand Rapids, MI 49530 *Tel:* 616-698-6900 *Toll Free Tel:* 800-727-1309 (cust serv) *Fax:* 616-698-3439; 616-698-3255 (orders) *Web Site:* www.zondervan.com, pg 307

Dooven, K C Den, KC Publications Inc, PO Box 94558, Las Vegas, NV 89193-4558 *Tel:* 702-433-3415 *Toll Free Tel:* 800-626-9673 *Fax:* 702-433-3420 *E-mail:* kcp@kcpublications.com *Web Site:* www.kcpublications.com, pg 144

Dore, Faye, Epimetheus Books Inc, 2711 Centerville Rd, Suite 120-5336, Wilmington, DE 19808-1643 *Tel:* 646-345-2030 *E-mail:* epimetheus@att.net *Web Site:* www.epimetheusbooks.com, pg 91

Dorese, Alyss, The Dorese Agency Ltd, 37965 Palo Verde Dr, Cathedral City, CA 92234 *Tel:* 760-321-1115 *Fax:* 760-321-1049 *Web Site:* www.doreseagency.com, pg 628

Dorff, Patricia, Council on Foreign Relations Press, 58 E 68 St, New York, NY 10021 *Tel:* 212-434-9400 *Fax:* 212-434-9859 *E-mail:* publications@cfr.org; communications@cfr.org *Web Site:* www.cfr.org, pg 70

Dorfman, Debra, Grosset & Dunlap, 345 Hudson St, New York, NY 10014 *Tel:* 212-366-2000 *E-mail:* online@penguinputnam.com *Web Site:* www.penguin.com, pg 110

Dorfman, Debra, Price Stern Sloan, 345 Hudson St, New York, NY 10014 *Tel:* 212-366-2000 *E-mail:* online@penguin.com *Web Site:* www.penguinputnam.com, pg 218

Dorfman, Larry, The Globe Pequot Press, 246 Goose Lane, Guilford, CT 06437 *Tel:* 203-458-4500 *Toll Free Tel:* 800-243-0495 (cust serv) *Fax:* 203-458-4601 *Toll Free Fax:* 800-820-2329 (orders & cust serv) *E-mail:* info@globepequot.com *Web Site:* www.globepequot.com, pg 105

Dorfman, Peter, Wimbledon Music Inc & Trigram Music Inc, 1801 Century Park E, Suite 2400, Los Angeles, CA 90067-2326 *Tel:* 310-556-9683 *Fax:* 310-277-1278 *E-mail:* webmaster@wimbtri.com *Web Site:* www.wimbtri.com, pg 301

Dorio, Terrie, Judy Lopez Memorial Award For Children's Literature, PO Box 7034, Beverly Hills, CA 90212-0034 *Tel:* 310-474-9917 *Fax:* 310-474-6436, pg 786

Dorman, Jessica, The Historic New Orleans Collection, 533 Royal St, New Orleans, LA 70130 *Tel:* 504-523-4662 *Fax:* 504-598-7108 *E-mail:* hnocinfo@hnoc.org *Web Site:* www.hnoc.org, pg 123

Dorman, Pamela, Viking, 375 Hudson St, New York, NY 10014 *Tel:* 212-366-2000 *E-mail:* online@penguinputnam.com *Web Site:* www.penguin.com, pg 290

Dorr, Sharron, Theosophical Publishing House/Quest Books, 306 W Geneva Rd, Wheaton, IL 60187 *Tel:* 630-665-0130 *Toll Free Tel:* 800-669-9425 *Fax:* 630-665-8791 *E-mail:* questbooks@theosmail.net *Web Site:* www.questbooks.net, pg 268

Dorrance, Sam, Brassey's Inc, 22841 Quicksilver Dr, Dulles, VA 20166 *Tel:* 703-661-1548 *Toll Free Tel:* 800-775-2518 (orders only) *Fax:* 703-661-1547 *E-mail:* djacobs@booksintl.com *Web Site:* www.brasseysinc.com, pg 46

Dorsey, Candas Jane, Books Collective, 214-21 10405 Jasper Ave, Edmonton, AB T5J 3S2, Canada *Tel:* 780-448-0590 *Fax:* 780-448-0640 *E-mail:* river@bookscollective.com *Web Site:* www.bookscollective.com, pg 537

Dorsey, Candas Jane, SF Canada, 10438 86 Ave, Edmonton, AB T6E 2M5, Canada *Tel:* 780-431-0562 *Web Site:* www.sfcanada.ca, pg 699

Dosanjh, Achi, Springer-Verlag New York Inc, 175 Fifth Ave, New York, NY 10010 *Tel:* 212-460-1500 *Toll Free Tel:* 800-777-4643 *Fax:* 212-473-6272 *Web Site:* www.springer-ny.com, pg 256

Dossey, Dr Donald, Outcomes Unlimited Press Inc, 75 Cambridge Rd, Asheville, NC 28804 *Tel:* 828-712-1311 *Fax:* 828-258-1311 *Web Site:* www.drdossey.com, pg 200

Dotterer, Dick, Julie Harris Playwright Award Competition, PO Box 39729, Los Angeles, CA 90039-0729, pg 777

Doyle, Debbie Ann, J Russell Major Prize, 400 "A" St SE, Washington, DC 20003 *Tel:* 202-544-2422 *Fax:* 202-544-8307 *E-mail:* info@historians.org *Web Site:* www.historians.org, pg 787

Doyle, Debbie Ann, Helen & Howard R Marraro Prize in Italian History, 400 "A" St SE, Washington, DC 20003 *Tel:* 202-544-2422 *Fax:* 202-544-8307 *E-mail:* info@historians.org *Web Site:* www.historians. org, pg 787

Doyle, Debbie Ann, George L Mosse Prize, 400 "A" St SE, Washington, DC 20003 *Tel:* 202-544-2422 *Fax:* 202-544-8307 *E-mail:* info@historians.org *Web Site:* www.historians.org, pg 790

Doyle, Debbie Ann, Bernadotte E Schmitt Grants, 400 "A" St SE, Washington, DC 20003 *Tel:* 202-544-2422 *Fax:* 202-544-8307 *E-mail:* info@historians.org *Web Site:* www.historians.org, pg 804

Doyle, Judith, Curbstone Press, 321 Jackson St, Willimantic, CT 06226 *Tel:* 860-423-5110 *Fax:* 860-423-9242 *E-mail:* info@curbstone.org *Web Site:* www.curbstone.org, pg 74

Doyle, Kevin, C D Howe Institute, 125 Adelaide St E, Toronto, ON M5C 1L7, Canada *Tel:* 416-865-1904 *Fax:* 416-865-1866 *E-mail:* cdhowe@cdhowe.org *Web Site:* www.cdhowe.org, pg 550

Doyle, Linda J, Westcliffe Publishers Inc, 2650 S Zuni St, Englewood, CO 80110-1145 *Tel:* 303-935-0900 *Toll Free Tel:* 800-523-3692 *Fax:* 303-935-0903 *E-mail:* sales@westcliffepublishers.com *Web Site:* www.westcliffepublishers.com, pg 296

Doyle, Patricia, Barron's Educational Series Inc, 250 Wireless Blvd, Hauppauge, NY 11788 *Tel:* 631-434-3311 *Toll Free Tel:* 800-645-3476 *Fax:* 631-434-3723 *E-mail:* info@barronseduc.com *Web Site:* www.barronseduc.com (Books can be purchased online), pg 32

Doyle, Robert, Sunset Books/Sunset Publishing Corp, 80 Willow Rd, Menlo Park, CA 94025-3691 *Tel:* 650-321-3600 *Toll Free Tel:* 800-227-7346; 800-321-0372 (California only) *Fax:* 650-324-1532 *Web Site:* sunset.com, pg 262

Doyle-Kimball, Mary, National Association of Real Estate Editors, 1003 NW Sixth Terr, Boca Raton, FL 33486-3455 *Tel:* 561-391-3599 *Fax:* 561-391-0099 *Web Site:* www.naree.org, pg 692

Drake, David, Doubleday Broadway Publishing Group, 1745 Broadway, New York, NY 10019 *Tel:* 212-782-9000 *Toll Free Tel:* 800-223-6834; 800-223-5780 (sales) *Fax:* 212-302-7985 (correspondence); 212-492-9862 (orders), pg 82

Drake, Liz, Creativity Fellowship, Alden B Dow Creativity Center, 4000 Whiting Dr, Midland, MI 48640-2398 *Tel:* 989-837-4478 *Fax:* 989-837-4468 *E-mail:* creativity@northwood.edu *Web Site:* www.northwood.edu/abd, pg 769

Drake, O Burtch, American Association of Advertising Agencies (AAAA), 405 Lexington Ave, 18th fl, New York, NY 10174-1801 *Tel:* 212-682-2500 *Fax:* 212-682-8391 *Web Site:* www.aaaa.org, pg 676

Drake, Paul, Harbor Lights Press (HLP), PO Box 505, Gloucester City, NJ 08030-0505 *Tel:* 856-742-5810 *E-mail:* harborlightspress@yahoo.com *Web Site:* www.harborlightspress.com, pg 114

Drake-Johnson, Vanessa, W W Norton & Company Inc, 500 Fifth Ave, New York, NY 10110-0017 *Tel:* 212-354-5500 *Toll Free Tel:* 800-233-4830 (orders & cust serv) *Fax:* 212-869-0856 *Toll Free Fax:* 800-458-6515 *Web Site:* www.wwnorton.com, pg 193

Draughon, Terry, World Publishing, 404 BNA Dr, Bldg 200, Suite 208, Nashville, TN 37217 *Tel:* 615-902-2395 *Toll Free Tel:* 800-363-0308 *Fax:* 615-902-2397 *Toll Free Fax:* 800-822-4271 (orders) *E-mail:* questions@worldpublishing.com; orders@worldpublishing.com *Web Site:* www.worldpublishing.com, pg 304

Draves, William A, Learning Resources Network (LERN), 208 S Main St, River Falls, WI 54022 *Tel:* 715-426-9777 *Toll Free Tel:* 800-678-5376 *Fax:* 715-426-5847 *Toll Free Fax:* 888-234-8633 *E-mail:* info@lern.org *Web Site:* www.lern.org, pg 151

Drayton, John, University of Oklahoma Press, 4100 28 Ave NW, Norman, OK 73069-8218 *Tel:* 405-325-2000 *Toll Free Tel:* 800-627-7377 (orders) *Fax:* 405-364-5798 (orders) *Toll Free Fax:* 800-735-0476 (orders) *E-mail:* oupress@ou.edu *Web Site:* www.oupress.com, pg 284

Drayton, John N, The Angie Debo Prize, 1005 Asp Ave, Norman, OK 73019-6051 *Tel:* 405-325-2000 *Fax:* 405-325-4000 *Web Site:* www.oupress.com, pg 769

Draze, Dianne, Dandy Lion Publications, 3563 Sueldo, Suite L, San Luis Obispo, CA 93401 *Tel:* 805-543-3332 *Toll Free Tel:* 800-776-8032 *Fax:* 805-544-2823 *E-mail:* dandy@dandylionbooks.com *Web Site:* www.dandylionbooks.com, pg 75

Dregni, Michael, Voyageur Press, 123 N Second St, Stillwater, MN 55082 *Tel:* 651-430-2210 *Toll Free Tel:* 800-888-9653 *Fax:* 651-430-2211 *E-mail:* books@voyageurpress.com *Web Site:* www.voyageurpress.com, pg 291

Drennan, Christina L, Drennan Communications, 6 Robin Lane, East Kingston, NH 03827 *Tel:* 603-642-8002 *Fax:* 603-642-8002, pg 596

Drennan, Christina L, Drennan Literary Agency, 6 Robin Lane, East Kingston, NH 03827 *Tel:* 603-642-8002 *Fax:* 603-642-8002, pg 628

Drennan, William D, Drennan Communications, 6 Robin Lane, East Kingston, NH 03827 *Tel:* 603-642-8002 *Fax:* 603-642-8002, pg 596

Drennan, William D, Drennan Literary Agency, 6 Robin Lane, East Kingston, NH 03827 *Tel:* 603-642-8002 *Fax:* 603-642-8002, pg 628

Dresner, Joanne, Pearson Education/ELT, 10 Bank St, 9th fl, White Plains, NY 10606 *Tel:* 914-993-5000 *Fax:* 914-993-8115 *E-mail:* firstname.lastname@pearsoned.com, pg 206

Drew, Lisa, Scribner, 1230 Avenue of the Americas, New York, NY 10020, pg 244

Drew, Todd, American Civil Liberties Union, 125 Broad St, 18th fl, New York, NY 10004 *Tel:* 212-549-2500 *Toll Free Tel:* 800-775-ACLU (orders) *E-mail:* info@aclu.org *Web Site:* www.aclu.org, pg 676

Drexler, Patty, Psychological Assessment Resources Inc (PAR), 16204 N Florida Ave, Lutz, FL 33549 *Tel:* 813-968-3003 *Toll Free Tel:* 800-331-8378 *Fax:* 813-968-2598 *Toll Free Fax:* 800-727-9329 *Web Site:* www.parinc.com, pg 221

Drexler, Susan, Stackpole Books, 5067 Ritter Rd, Mechanicsburg, PA 17055 *Tel:* 717-796-0411 *Toll Free Tel:* 800-732-3669 *Fax:* 717-796-0412 *Web Site:* www.stackpolebooks.com, pg 257

Dreyer, Benjamin, Random House Publishing Group, 1745 Broadway, New York, NY 10019 *Toll Free Tel:* 800-200-3552 *Toll Free Fax:* 800-200-3552 *Web Site:* www.randomhouse.com, pg 227

Dreyfus, William Louis, Poetry Society of America (PSA), 15 Gramercy Park, New York, NY 10003 *Tel:* 212-254-9628 *Toll Free Tel:* 888-USA-POEM *Fax:* 212-673-2352 *Web Site:* www.poetrysociety.org, pg 697

Dreyfus, Brian, Paul Kohner Agency, 9300 Wilshire Blvd, Suite 555, Beverly Hills, CA 90212 *Tel:* 310-550-1060 *Fax:* 310-276-1083, pg 638

Dreyfuss, Robert, ASTM International, 100 Barr Harbor Dr, West Conshohocken, PA 19428 *Tel:* 610-832-9500 *Fax:* 610-832-9555 *E-mail:* service@astm.org *Web Site:* www.astm.org, pg 27

Driesler, Steve, Association of American Publishers (AAP), 71 Fifth Ave, 2nd fl, New York, NY 10003-3004 *Tel:* 212-255-0200 *Fax:* 212-255-7007 *Web Site:* www.publishers.org, pg 679

Driscoll, Denise, Lonely Planet Publications, 150 Linden St, Oakland, CA 94607 *Tel:* 510-893-8555 *Toll Free Tel:* 800-275-8555 (orders) *Fax:* 510-893-8972 *E-mail:* info@lonelyplanet.com *Web Site:* www.lonelyplanet.com, pg 157

Driscoll, Susan, iUniverse, 2021 Pine Lake Rd, Suite 100, Lincoln, NE 68512 *Tel:* 402-323-7800 *Toll Free Tel:* 877-288-4737 *Fax:* 402-323-7824 *E-mail:* firstname.lastname@iuniverse.com; general.inquiries@iuniverse.com *Web Site:* www.iuniverse.com, pg 140

Droege, Judith A, Paul H Brookes Publishing Co, PO Box 10624, Baltimore, MD 21285-0624 *Tel:* 410-337-9580 *Toll Free Tel:* 800-638-3775 *Fax:* 410-337-8539 *E-mail:* custserv@brookespublishing.com *Web Site:* www.brookespublishing.com, pg 48

Drost, Susie, The Mongolia Society Inc, Indiana University, 322 Goodbody Hall, Bloomington, IN 47405-7005 *Tel:* 812-855-4078 *Fax:* 812-855-7500 *E-mail:* monsoc@indiana.edu *Web Site:* www.indiana.edu/~mongsoc, pg 177

Druding, Harry F, Nesbitt Graphics Inc, 555 Virginia Dr, Fort Washington, PA 19034 *Tel:* 215-591-9125 *Fax:* 215-591-9093 *Web Site:* www.Nesbittgraphics.com, pg 606

Drugan, Wayne (Rusty), New England Book Awards, 1770 Massachusetts Ave, No 332, Cambridge, MA 02140 *Tel:* 617-576-3070 *Toll Free Tel:* 800-466-8711 *Fax:* 617-576-3091 *Web Site:* www.newenglandbooks.org, pg 793

Drugan, Wayne (Rusty), New England Booksellers Association Inc (NEBA), 1770 Massachusetts Ave, No 332, Cambridge, MA 02140 *Tel:* 617-576-3070 *Toll Free Tel:* 800-466-8711 *Fax:* 617-576-3091 *Web Site:* www.newenglandbooks.org, pg 695

Drummond, Siobhan, Drummond Books, 2111 Cleveland St, Evanston, IL 60202 *Tel:* 847-869-5305, pg 596

Drury, Patricia, Quincannon Publishing Group, PO Box 8100, Glen Ridge, NJ 07028-8100 *Tel:* 973-669-8367 *E-mail:* editors@quincannongroup.com *Web Site:* www.quincannongroup.com, pg 224

Dry, Paul, Paul Dry Books, 117 S 17 St, Suite 1102, Philadelphia, PA 19103 *Tel:* 215-231-9939 *Fax:* 215-231-9942 *E-mail:* editor@pauldrybooks.com *Web Site:* www.pauldrybooks.com, pg 84

Dryden, Emma, Simon & Schuster Children's Publishing, 1230 Avenue of the Americas, New York, NY 10020 *Tel:* 212-698-7000 *Web Site:* www.simonsayskids.com, pg 248

Du Bow, Wendy, The Writer's Advocate/Literary Agenting & Editorial Services, 1675 Larimer St, Suite 410, Denver, CO 80202 *Tel:* 303-297-1233 *Fax:* 303-297-3997 *E-mail:* thewritersadvocate@thelightningfactory.com *Web Site:* www.thelightningfactory.com, pg 661

Du Fresne, Albert H, Polyscience Publications Inc, PO Box 1606, Sta St-Martin, Laval, PQ H7V 3P8, Canada *Tel:* 450-688-8484 *Fax:* 450-688-1930 *E-mail:* info@polysciencepublications.com *Web Site:* www.polysciencepublications.com, pg 558

du Houx, Paul, Polar Bear & Co, The Cascades, 8 Brook St, Solon, ME 04979 *Tel:* 207-643-2795 *E-mail:* polarbear@necsys.net *Web Site:* www.polarbearandco.com, pg 215

du Houx, Ramona, Polar Bear & Co, The Cascades, 8 Brook St, Solon, ME 04979 *Tel:* 207-643-2795 *E-mail:* polarbear@necsys.net *Web Site:* www.polarbearandco.com, pg 215

Du Ross, Greg, North American Graphic Arts Suppliers Association (NAGASA), 1604 New Hampshire Ave NW, Washington, DC 20009 *Tel:* 202-328-8441 *Fax:* 202-328-8513 *E-mail:* information@nagasa.org *Web Site:* www.nagasa.org, pg 695

du Toit, Johan, Protea Publishing, 5456 Peachtree Industrial Blvd, Suite 648, Atlanta, GA 30341 *E-mail:* southsky@earthlink.net *Web Site:* www.proteapublishing.com, pg 220

Duane, Dick, Pinder Lane & Garon-Brooke Associates Ltd, 159 W 53 St, Suite 14-E, New York, NY 10019 *Tel:* 212-489-0880 *Fax:* 212-489-7104 *E-mail:* pinderl@interport.net, pg 648

Durakis, Tom, American Bible Society, 1865 Broadway, New York, NY 10023-7505 *Tel:* 212-408-1200 *Toll Free Tel:* 800-322-4253 (orders only) *Fax:* 212-408-1259 *E-mail:* info@americanbible.org *Web Site:* www.americanbible.org, pg 12

Durand, Amelia, Island Press, 1718 Connecticut Ave NW, Suite 300, Washington, DC 20009 *Tel:* 202-232-7933 *Toll Free Tel:* 800-828-1302 *Fax:* 202-234-1328; 707-983-6414 (orders only) *E-mail:* info@islandpress.org *Web Site:* www.islandpress.org, pg 139

Durante, Carolyn, Center for Migration Studies of New York Inc, 209 Flagg Place, Staten Island, NY 10304-1199 *Tel:* 718-351-8800 *Fax:* 718-667-4598 *E-mail:* cms@cmsny.org *Web Site:* www.cmsny.org, pg 57

Durbin, Jon, W W Norton & Company Inc, 500 Fifth Ave, New York, NY 10110-0017 *Tel:* 212-354-5500 *Toll Free Tel:* 800-233-4830 (orders & cust serv) *Fax:* 212-869-0856 *Toll Free Fax:* 800-458-6515 *Web Site:* www.wwnorton.com, pg 193

Durepos, Joseph, Loyola Press, 3441 N Ashland Ave, Chicago, IL 60657 *Tel:* 773-281-1818; 773-244-4429 *Toll Free Tel:* 800-621-1008 *Fax:* 773-281-0555; 773-281-0152 (trade) *E-mail:* editorial@loydapress.com *Web Site:* www.loyolapress.org, pg 159

Durie, Veronica, Zephyr Press Catalog, 814 N Franklin St, Chicago, IL 60610 *Tel:* 312-337-5985 *Toll Free Tel:* 800-232-2187 *Fax:* 312-337-1651 *E-mail:* neways2learn@zephyrpress.com *Web Site:* www.zephyrpress.com, pg 307

Durniak, Tony, Institute of Electrical & Electronics Engineers Inc, 445 Hoes Lane, Piscataway, NJ 08854 *Tel:* 732-981-0060 *Toll Free Tel:* 800-678-4333 *Fax:* 732-981-9334 *E-mail:* c.fadvska@ieee.org *Web Site:* www.ieee.org, pg 135

Durocher, Cort, American Institute of Aeronautics & Astronautics, 1801 Alexander Bell Dr, Suite 500, Reston, VA 20191 *Tel:* 703-264-7500 *Toll Free Tel:* 800-639-2422 *Fax:* 703-264-7551 *E-mail:* custserv@aiaa.org *Web Site:* www.aiaa.org, pg 14

Durr, Debbie, National Information Services Corp (NISC), Wyman Towers, 3100 Saint Paul St, Baltimore, MD 21218 *Tel:* 410-243-0797 *Fax:* 410-243-0982 *E-mail:* info@nisc.com; editor@nisc.com (comments); sales@nisc.com (sales); support@nisc.com (cust support) *Web Site:* www.nisc.com, pg 184

Dusek, Florence, Florida Academic Press, PO Box 540, Gainesville, FL 32602-0540 *Tel:* 352-332-5104 *Fax:* 352-331-6003 *E-mail:* fapress@worldnet.att.net, pg 97

Duster, Troy, American Sociological Association (ASA), 1307 New York Ave NW, Suite 700, Washington, DC 20005-4701 *Tel:* 202-383-9005 *Fax:* 202-638-0882 *E-mail:* executive.office@asanet.org *Web Site:* www.asanet.org, pg 678

Duverglas, Donna, Bantam Dell Publishing Group, 1745 Broadway, New York, NY 10019 *Tel:* 212-782-9000 *Toll Free Tel:* 800-223-6834 *Fax:* 212-302-7985 *Web Site:* www.randomhouse.com/bantamdell, pg 31

Dworkin, Sharon, Prayer Book Press Inc, 1363 Fairfield Ave, Bridgeport, CT 06605 *Tel:* 203-384-2284 *Fax:* 203-579-9109, pg 217

Dwyer, Caroline, University of Oklahoma Press, 4100 28 Ave NW, Norman, OK 73069-8218 *Tel:* 405-325-2000 *Toll Free Tel:* 800-627-7377 (orders) *Fax:* 405-364-5798 (orders) *Toll Free Fax:* 800-735-0476 (orders) *E-mail:* oupress@ou.edu *Web Site:* www.oupress.com, pg 284

Dwyer, Cecelia, North Star Press of Saint Cloud Inc, PO Box 451, St Cloud, MN 56302-0451 *Tel:* 320-558-9062 *Fax:* 320-558-9063 *E-mail:* nspress@cloudnet.com, pg 193

Dwyer, Corinne A, North Star Press of Saint Cloud Inc, PO Box 451, St Cloud, MN 56302-0451 *Tel:* 320-558-9062 *Fax:* 320-558-9063 *E-mail:* nspress@cloudnet.com, pg 193

Dwyer, Jeff, Dwyer & O'Grady Inc, 725 Third St, Cedar Key, FL 32625 *Tel:* 352-543-9307 *Fax:* 603-375-5373 *Web Site:* www.dwyerogrady.com, pg 628, 665

Dwyer, Joyce, Huntington House Publishers, 104 Row 2, Suite A-1 & A-2, Lafayette, LA 70508 *Tel:* 337-237-7049; 337-749-4009 (sales); 337-237-3082 (opers) *Toll Free Tel:* 800-749-4009 (sales) *Fax:* 337-237-7060 *E-mail:* admin@alphapublishingonline.com; sales@alphapublishingonline.com *Web Site:* www.alphapublishingonline.com, pg 129

Dwyer, Peter, Liturgical Press, St John's Abbey, Collegeville, MN 56321 *Tel:* 320-363-2213 *Toll Free Tel:* 800-858-5450 *Fax:* 320-363-3299 *Toll Free Fax:* 800-445-5899 *E-mail:* sales@litpress.org *Web Site:* www.litpress.org, pg 156

Dwyer, Susan, Thames & Hudson, 500 Fifth Ave, New York, NY 10110 *Tel:* 212-354-3763 *Toll Free Tel:* 800-233-4830 *Fax:* 212-398-1252 *E-mail:* bookinfo@thames.wwnorton.com *Web Site:* www.thamesandhudsonusa.com, pg 268

Dwyer, Susan T, Health Professions Press, PO Box 10624, Baltimore, MD 21285-0624 *Tel:* 410-337-9585 *Toll Free Tel:* 888-337-8808 *Fax:* 410-337-8539 *E-mail:* custserv@healthpropress.com *Web Site:* www.healthpropress.com, pg 119

Dyck, Bill, Northern Canada Mission Distributors, PO Box 3030, Prince Albert, SK S6V 7V4, Canada *Tel:* 306-764-3388 *Fax:* 306-764-3390 *E-mail:* missiondist@ncem.ca *Web Site:* www.ncem.ca, pg 556

Dye, Donna, McLemore Prize, PO Box 571, Jackson, MS 39205-0571 *Tel:* 601-576-6850 *Fax:* 601-576-6975 *E-mail:* mhs@mdah.state.ms.us *Web Site:* www.mdah.state.ms.us, pg 789

Dyer, Carolyn, Pro Quest Information & Learning, 300 N Zeeb Rd, Ann Arbor, MI 48106-1346 *Tel:* 734-761-4700 *Toll Free Tel:* 800-521-0600 *Fax:* 734-975-6486 *Toll Free Fax:* 800-864-0019 *E-mail:* info@il.proquest.com *Web Site:* www.il.proquest.com, pg 219

Dyer, Gord, McGraw-Hill Ryerson Ltd, 300 Water St, Whitby, ON L1N 9B6, Canada *Tel:* 905-430-5000 *Toll Free Tel:* 800-565-5758 (cust serv) *Fax:* 905-430-5020 *E-mail:* johnd@mcgrawhill.ca *Web Site:* www.mcgrawhill.ca, pg 554

Dyer, Gordon, McGraw-Hill International Publishing Group, 2 Penn Plaza, New York, NY 10121 *Tel:* 212-904-2000 *Web Site:* www.mcgrawhill.com, pg 168

Dyer, Jessica, Fulcrum Publishing Inc, 16100 Table Mountain Pkwy, Suite 300, Golden, CO 80403 *Tel:* 303-277-1623 *Toll Free Tel:* 800-992-2908 *Fax:* 303-279-7111 *Toll Free Fax:* 800-726-7112 *E-mail:* fulcrum@fulcrum-books.com *Web Site:* www.fulcrum-books.com, pg 101

Dyke, George, Earth Edit, PO Box 114, Maiden Rock, WI 54750 *Tel:* 715-448-3009, pg 596

Dykstra, LeeAnna, Broadview Press, 280 Perry St, Unit 5, Peterborough, ON K9J 2A8, Canada *Tel:* 705-743-8990 *Fax:* 705-743-8353 *E-mail:* customerservice@broadviewpress.com *Web Site:* www.broadviewpress.com, pg 537

Dykstra-Poel, Susan, University of Rochester Press, 668 Mt Hope Ave, Rochester, NY 14620 *Tel:* 585-275-0419 *Fax:* 585-271-8778 *E-mail:* boydell@boydellusa.net *Web Site:* boydellandbrewer.com, pg 285

Dynak, Sharon, Ucross Foundation Residency Program, 30 Big Red Lane, Clearmont, WY 82835 *Tel:* 307-737-2291 *Fax:* 307-737-2322 *E-mail:* info@ucross.org *Web Site:* www.ucrossfoundation.org, pg 809

Dyson, Cheryl, XC Publishing, 931 E Avenida de las Flores, Thousand Oaks, CA 91360 *Tel:* 805-495-7768 *Fax:* 413-431-5515 *E-mail:* xuhl@xcpublishing.com *Web Site:* www.xcpublishing.com, pg 305

Dyssegaard, Elisabeth, Random House Publishing Group, 1745 Broadway, New York, NY 10019 *Toll Free Tel:* 800-200-3552 *Toll Free Fax:* 800-200-3552 *Web Site:* www.randomhouse.com, pg 227

Dystel, Jane, Dystel & Goderich Literary Management, One Union Sq W, Suite 904, New York, NY 10003 *Tel:* 212-627-9100 *Fax:* 212-627-9313 *Web Site:* www.dystel.com, pg 629

Dzavik, Andrea, University Press of Florida, 15 NW 15 St, Gainesville, FL 32611-2079 *Tel:* 352-392-1351 *Toll Free Tel:* 800-226-3822 (orders only) *Fax:* 352-392-7302 *Toll Free Fax:* 800-680-1955 (orders only) *E-mail:* info@upf.com *Web Site:* www.upf.com, pg 287

Eadie, Wayne, Publishers Information Bureau (PIB), 810 Seventh Ave, 24th fl, New York, NY 10019 *Tel:* 212-872-3700 *Fax:* 212-888-4217 *E-mail:* pib@magazine.org *Web Site:* www.magazine.org, pg 698

Eads, George C, National Bureau of Economic Research Inc, 1050 Massachusetts Ave, Cambridge, MA 02138-5398 *Tel:* 617-868-3900 *Fax:* 617-868-2742 *E-mail:* op@nber.org *Web Site:* www.nber.org, pg 182

Eads, Valerie, Hungry Samurai, Grand Central Sta, PO Box 824, New York, NY 10163-0824 *Tel:* 212-865-7786 *Fax:* 212-865-7786 *E-mail:* mail@hungrysamurai.com *Web Site:* hungrysamurai.com, pg 601

Eagle, Theodora, John L Hochmann Books, 320 E 58 St, New York, NY 10022 *Tel:* 212-319-0505, pg 635

Eakin, Wendy, Dorset House Publishing Co Inc, 353 W 12 St, New York, NY 10014 *Tel:* 212-620-4053 *Toll Free Tel:* 800-DHBOOKS (342-6657 orders only) *Fax:* 212-727-1044 *E-mail:* info@dorsethouse.com; dhpubco@aol.com *Web Site:* www.dorsethouse.com, pg 82

Eanfar, Ferris, Maxit Publishing Inc, PO Box 700, Lompoc, CA 93438-0700 *Tel:* 805-686-5100 *Toll Free Tel:* 866-686-5100 *Fax:* 805-686-5102 *Web Site:* www.maxitpublishing.com, pg 166

Earl, Meryl, Kensington Publishing Corp, 850 Third Ave, New York, NY 10022 *Tel:* 212-407-1500 *Toll Free Tel:* 800-221-2647 *Fax:* 212-935-0699 *Web Site:* www.kensingtonbooks.com, pg 145

Earley, Joan, Carstens Publications Inc, 108 Phil Hardin Rd, Newton, NJ 07860 *Tel:* 973-383-3355 *Fax:* 973-383-4064 *E-mail:* hal@carstens-publications.com *Web Site:* www.carstens-publications.com, pg 54

Earnst, Collin, Houghton Mifflin Co, 222 Berkeley St, Boston, MA 02116-3764 *Tel:* 617-351-5000 *Toll Free Tel:* 800-225-3362 (trade books); 800-733-2828 (text books); 800-225-1464 (college texts) *Fax:* 617-351-1125 *Web Site:* www.hmco.com, pg 126

Easterly, John, The Southern Review/LSU Short Fiction Award, Louisiana State University, 43 Allen Hall, Baton Rouge, LA 70803-5005 *Tel:* 225-578-5108 *Fax:* 225-578-5098 *E-mail:* bmacon@lsu.edu *Web Site:* www.lsu.edu/thesouthernreview, pg 806

Eastmen, Shirley, Annual Cape Cod Writers' Conference, PO Box 408, Osterville, MA 02655 *Tel:* 508-420-0200 *E-mail:* ccwc@capecod.net *Web Site:* www.capecodwriterscenter.com, pg 742

Eastmen, Shirley, Young Writer's Workshop, PO Box 408, Osterville, MA 02655 *Tel:* 508-375-0516 *E-mail:* ccwc@capecod.net *Web Site:* www.capecodwriterscenter.com, pg 749

Easton, Emily, Walker & Co, 104 Fifth Ave, 7th fl, New York, NY 10011 *Tel:* 212-727-8300 *Toll Free Tel:* 800-289-2553 *Fax:* 212-727-0984 *Toll Free Fax:* 800-218-9367 *E-mail:* firstinitiallastname@walkerbooks.com *Web Site:* www.walkerbooks.com, pg 292

Eaton, Brenda, Interlink Publishing Group Inc, 46 Crosby St, Northampton, MA 01060 *Tel:* 413-582-7054 *Toll Free Tel:* 800-238-LINK (238-5465) *Fax:* 413-582-7057 *E-mail:* info@interlinkbooks.com *Web Site:* www.interlinkbooks.com, pg 136

Eaton, Jonathan, International Marine Publishing, 485 Commercial St, Rockport, ME 04856 *Tel:* 207-236-4837 *Fax:* 207-236-6314 *Web Site:* www.internationalmarine.com/im, pg 137

Eaton, Jonathan, Ragged Mountain Press, 485 Commercial St, Rockport, ME 04856 *Tel:* 207-236-4837 *Fax:* 207-236-6314 *Web Site:* www.raggedmountainpress.com, pg 225

Eerdmans, William B Jr, Wm B Eerdmans Publishing Co, 255 Jefferson Ave SE, Grand Rapids, MI 49503 *Tel:* 616-459-4591 *Toll Free Tel:* 800-253-7521 *Fax:* 616-459-6540 *E-mail:* sales@eerdmans.com *Web Site:* www.eerdmans.com, pg 88

Egan, Chris L, The University of North Carolina Press, 116 S Boundary St, Chapel Hill, NC 27514-3808 *Tel:* 919-966-3561 *Toll Free Tel:* 800-848-6224 (orders only) *Fax:* 919-966-3829 *Toll Free Fax:* 800-272-6817 (orders) *E-mail:* uncpress@unc.edu *Web Site:* www.uncpress.unc.edu, pg 283

Egan-Miller, Danielle, Browne & Miller Literary Associates, 410 S Michigan Ave, Suite 460, Chicago, IL 60605 *Tel:* 312-922-3063 *Fax:* 312-922-1905 *E-mail:* mail@browneandmiller.com *Web Site:* www.browneandmiller.com, pg 623

Egen, Maureen Mahon, Time Warner Book Group, 1271 Avenue of the Americas, New York, NY 10020 *Tel:* 212-522-7200 *Fax:* 212-522-7991 *Web Site:* www.twbookmark.com, pg 271

Eglash, Joel, Transcontinental Music Publications, 633 Third Ave, New York, NY 10017 *Tel:* 212-650-4101 *Toll Free Tel:* 800-455-5223 *Fax:* 212-650-4109 *E-mail:* tmp@uahc.org *Web Site:* www.transcontinentalmusic.com, pg 274

Egnotovich, Stephanie, Westminster John Knox Press, 100 Witherspoon St, Louisville, KY 40202-1396 *Tel:* 502-569-5052 *Toll Free Tel:* 800-227-2872 (US only) *Fax:* 502-569-8308 *Toll Free Fax:* 800-541-5113 (US only) *E-mail:* wjk@wjkbooks.com *Web Site:* www.wjkbooks.com, pg 297

Ehle, Robert, Stanford University Press, 1450 Page Mill Rd, Palo Alto, CA 94304-1124 *Tel:* 650-723-9434 *Fax:* 650-725-3457 *Web Site:* www.sup.org, pg 257

Ehman, Don, New Jersey State Council on the Arts Fellowship Program (NJSCA), 225 W State St, 4th fl, Trenton, NJ 08608 *Tel:* 609-292-6130 *Fax:* 609-989-1440 *Web Site:* www.njartscouncil.org; www.midatlanticarts.org, pg 793

Eichenberger, Jim, Standard Publishing Co, 8121 Hamilton Ave, Cincinnati, OH 45231 *Tel:* 513-931-4050 *Toll Free Tel:* 800-543-1301 *Fax:* 513-931-0950 *Toll Free Fax:* 877-867-5751 *E-mail:* customerservice@standardpub.com *Web Site:* www.standardpub.com, pg 257

Einerson, Alison, Gibbs Smith Publisher, 1877 E Gentile, Layton, UT 84040 *Tel:* 801-544-9800 *Toll Free Tel:* 800-748-5439 (orders only) *Fax:* 801-544-5582 *Toll Free Fax:* 800-213-3023 (orders only) *E-mail:* info@gibbs-smith.com *Web Site:* www.gibbs-smith.com, pg 104

Einhorn, Amy, Warner Books, 1271 Avenue of the Americas, New York, NY 10020 *Tel:* 212-522-7200 *Fax:* 212-522-7991 *Web Site:* www.twbookmark.com, pg 293

Eis, Arlene, Infosources Publishing, 140 Norma Rd, Teaneck, NJ 07666 *Tel:* 201-836-7072 *Web Site:* www.infosourcespub.com, pg 133

Eisenberg, Michael, Farrar, Straus & Giroux Books for Young Readers, 19 Union Sq W, New York, NY 10003 *Tel:* 212-741-6900 *Fax:* 212-633-2427 *E-mail:* childrens.marketing@fsgbooks.com; childrens.editorial@fsgbooks.com *Web Site:* www.fsgkids.com, pg 95

Eisenberg, Paul, Fodor's Travel Publications, 1745 Broadway, New York, NY 10019 *Tel:* 212-572-8784 *Toll Free Tel:* 800-733-3000 *Fax:* 212-572-2248 *Web Site:* www.fodors.com, pg 98

Eisenberg, Shauna, National Jewish Book Awards, 15 E 26 St, New York, NY 10010-1579 *Tel:* 212-532-4949 (ext 297) *Fax:* 212-481-4174 *E-mail:* jbc@jewishbooks.org *Web Site:* www.jewishbookcouncil.org, pg 792

Eisenbraun, James E, Eisenbrauns Inc, PO Box 275, Winona Lake, IN 46590-0275 *Tel:* 574-269-2011 *Fax:* 574-269-6788 *E-mail:* publisher@eisenbrauns.com *Web Site:* www.eisenbrauns.com/, pg 88

Eisinger, Eric, The Brookings Institution Press, 1775 Massachusetts Ave NW, Washington, DC 20036-2188 *Tel:* 202-797-6000 *Toll Free Tel:* 800-275-1447 *Fax:* 202-797-6195 *E-mail:* bibooks@brook.edu *Web Site:* www.brookings.edu, pg 48

El Mallakh, Dorothea H, International Research Center for Energy & Economic Development, 850 Willowbrook Rd, Boulder, CO 80302 *Tel:* 303-442-4014 *Fax:* 303-442-5042 *E-mail:* iceed@colorado.edu *Web Site:* www.iceed.org, pg 138

Elbe, Susan, John Wiley & Sons Inc Education Publishing Group, 111 River St, Hoboken, NJ 07030 *Tel:* 201-748-6000 *Fax:* 201-748-6088 *E-mail:* info@wiley.com *Web Site:* www.wiley.com, pg 300

Elchlepp, Ellen, Doubleday Broadway Publishing Group, 1745 Broadway, New York, NY 10019 *Tel:* 212-782-9000 *Toll Free Tel:* 800-223-6834; 800-223-5780 (sales) *Fax:* 212-302-7985 (correspondence); 212-492-9862 (orders), pg 82

Elder, E Rozanne, Cistercian Publications Inc, Editorial Office, WMU, 1903 W Michigan Ave, Kalamazoo, MI 49008 *Tel:* 269-387-8920 *Fax:* 269-387-8390 *E-mail:* cistpub@wmich.edu *Web Site:* www.spencerabbey.org/cistpub, pg 62

Elder, John B, Inner Ocean Publishing Inc, 1037 Makawao Ave, Makawao, Maui, HI 96768-1239 *Tel:* 808-573-8000 *Toll Free Tel:* 800-863-1449 *Fax:* 808-573-0700 *Toll Free Fax:* 800-755-4118 *E-mail:* info@innerocean.com *Web Site:* www.innerocean.com, pg 134

Eldridge, Betsy Palmer, Guild of Book Workers, 521 Fifth Ave, 17th fl, New York, NY 10175 *Tel:* 212-292-4444 *Web Site:* www.palimpsest.stanford.ed, pg 688

Eldridge, Jon, Aspen Publishers, A Wolters Kluwer Company, 1185 Avenue of the Americas, New York, NY 10036 *Tel:* 212-597-0200 *Toll Free Tel:* 800-234-1660 (cust serv); 800-447-1717 (orders); 800-950-5259 (legal educ); 800-LAW-PLGL (paralegal textbook); 800-317-3113 (bookstore sales); 800-364-2512 (Loislaw) *Web Site:* www.aspenpublishers.com, pg 26

Eldridge, Sherri, Harvest Hill Press, PO Box 55, Salisbury Cove, ME 04672 *Tel:* 207-288-8900 *Toll Free Tel:* 888-288-8900 *Fax:* 207-288-3611, pg 117

Eleftheriou, Michael, Creative Publishing International Inc, 18705 Lake Dr E, Chanhassen, MN 55317 *Tel:* 952-936-4700 *Toll Free Tel:* 800-328-0590 (sales) *Fax:* 952-933-1456 *Web Site:* www.creativepub.com, pg 72

Elfenbein, Reed, John Wiley & Sons Inc Scientific/Technical/Medical Publishing, 111 River St, Hoboken, NJ 07030 *Tel:* 201-748-6000 *Toll Free Tel:* 800-225-5945 (cust serv) *Fax:* 201-748-8728 *E-mail:* info@wiley.com *Web Site:* www.wiley.com, pg 300

Elfstrand, Rhonda, Moody Press, 820 N La Salle Blvd, Chicago, IL 60610 *Tel:* 312-329-2111 *Toll Free Tel:* 800-678-8812 *Fax:* 312-329-2019 *Web Site:* www.moodypress.org, pg 177

Eliel, Gerasim, St Herman Press, 10 Beegum Gorge Rd, Platina, CA 96076 *Tel:* 530-352-4430 *Fax:* 530-352-4432 *E-mail:* stherman@stherman.com *Web Site:* www.stherman.com, pg 238

Eliseo, Leigh Ann, David Black Literary Agency, 156 Fifth Ave, Suite 608, New York, NY 10010 *Tel:* 212-242-5080 *Fax:* 212-924-6609, pg 621

Elitzik, Paul, Lake View Press, Box 578279, Chicago, IL 60657-8279 *Tel:* 773-935-2694 *Web Site:* www.lakeviewpress.com, pg 148

Elkhadem, Dr S, York Press Ltd, 152 Boardwalk Dr, Toronto, ON M4L 3X4, Canada *Tel:* 416-690-3788 *Fax:* 416-690-3797 *E-mail:* yorkpress@sympatico.ca *Web Site:* www3.sympatico.ca/yorkpress, pg 567

Ellen, Joan, World Citizens, 96 La Verne Ave, Mill Valley, CA 94941 *Tel:* 415-380-8020 *Toll Free Tel:* 800-247-6553 (orders only) *Web Site:* soultosoulmedia.com; skateman.com, pg 304

Ellenberg, Ethan, Ethan Ellenberg Literary Agency, 548 Broadway, Suite 5-E, New York, NY 10012 *Tel:* 212-431-4554 *Fax:* 212-941-4652 *E-mail:* agent@ethanellenberg.com *Web Site:* www.ethanellenberg.com, pg 629

Ellenbogen, Ilene, W H Freeman and Co, 41 Madison Ave, 37th fl, New York, NY 10010 *Tel:* 212-576-9400 *Fax:* 212-689-2383 *Web Site:* www.whfreeman.com, pg 101

Eller, Beth, Walker & Co, 104 Fifth Ave, 7th fl, New York, NY 10011 *Tel:* 212-727-8300 *Toll Free Tel:* 800-289-2553 *Fax:* 212-727-0984 *Toll Free Fax:* 800-218-9367 *E-mail:* firstinitiallastname@walkerbooks.com *Web Site:* www.walkerbooks.com, pg 292

Ellerbeck, Brian, Teachers College Press, 1234 Amsterdam Ave, New York, NY 10027 *Tel:* 212-678-3929 *Fax:* 212-678-4149 *E-mail:* tcpress@tc.columbia.edu *Web Site:* www.teacherscollegepress.com, pg 265

Elling, Karla, Arizona State University, Creative Writing Program, Dept of English, Box 870302, Tempe, AZ 85287-0302 *Tel:* 480-965-7454; 480-965-3528 *Fax:* 480-965-3451 *Web Site:* www.asu.edu/clas/english/creativewriting, pg 751

Ellingham, Mark, Rough Guides, 345 Hudson St, New York, NY 10014 *Tel:* 212-414-3635 *Fax:* 212-414-3352 *E-mail:* mail@roughguides.com *Web Site:* www.roughguides.com, pg 235

Ellinson, Alexander Z, CIS Publishers & Distributors, 180 Park Ave S, Lakewood, NJ 08701 *Tel:* 732-905-3000 *Fax:* 732-367-6666, pg 62

Elliot, Allison, Dawbert Press Inc, PO Box 67, Duxbury, MA 02331 *Tel:* 781-934-7202 *Toll Free Tel:* 800-933-2923 *Fax:* 781-934-2945 *E-mail:* info@dawbert.com *Web Site:* www.dawbert.com; www.familiesonthego.com; www.petsonthego.com, pg 77

Elliott, Brad, Dufour Editions Inc, PO Box 7, Chester Springs, PA 19425-0007 *Tel:* 610-458-5005 *Toll Free Tel:* 800-869-5677 *Fax:* 610-458-7103 *E-mail:* info@dufoureditions.com *Web Site:* www.dufoureditions.com, pg 84

Elliott, Jennifer, International Linguistics Corp, 12220 Blue Ridge Blvd, Suite G, Grandview, MO 64030 *Tel:* 816-765-8855 *Toll Free Tel:* 800-237-1830 *Fax:* 816-765-2855 *E-mail:* info@learnables.com *Web Site:* www.learnables.com, pg 137

Elliott, Joe, Association for Supervision & Curriculum Development (ASCD), 1703 N Beauregaard St, Alexandria, VA 22311-1453 *Tel:* 703-578-9600 *Toll Free Tel:* 800-933-2723 *Fax:* 703-575-5400 *E-mail:* member@ascd.org *Web Site:* www.ascd.org, pg 26

Elliott, Paul, Wordsworth Communication, PO Box 9781, Alexandria, VA 22304-0468 *Tel:* 703-642-8775 *Fax:* 703-642-8775, pg 614

Elliott, Sarah, Bantam Dell Publishing Group, 1745 Broadway, New York, NY 10019 *Tel:* 212-782-9000 *Toll Free Tel:* 800-223-6834 *Fax:* 212-302-7985 *Web Site:* www.randomhouse.com/bantamdell, pg 31

Elliott, Shirley, Health Research, 62 Seventh St, Pomeroy, WA 99347 *Tel:* 509-843-2385 *Toll Free Tel:* 888-844-2386 *Fax:* 509-843-2387 *E-mail:* publish@pomeroy-wa.com *Web Site:* www.healthresearchbooks.com, pg 120

Elliott, Stephanie, Wesleyan University Press, 215 Long Lane, Middletown, CT 06459-0433 *Tel:* 860-685-7711 *Fax:* 860-685-7712 *Web Site:* www.wesleyan.edu/wespress, pg 296

Elliott, Stephen P, Sachem Publishing Associates Inc, 271 Lake Ave, Greenwich, CT 06831 *Tel:* 203-661-3717 *Fax:* 203-661-0775 *E-mail:* sachempub@optonline.net, pg 610

Ellis, Deb, Small Publishers Association of North America (SPAN), 425 Cedar St, Buena Vista, CO 81211 *Tel:* 719-395-4790 *Fax:* 719-395-8374 *E-mail:* span@spannet.org *Web Site:* www.spannet.org, pg 747

Ellis, Donald S, Creative Arts Book Co, 833 Bancroft Way, Berkeley, CA 94710 *Tel:* 510-848-4777 *Fax:* 510-848-4844 *E-mail:* staff@creativeartsbooks.com; capublisher@yahoo.com *Web Site:* www.creativeartsbooks.com, pg 72

Ellis, Drew, Neo-Tech Publishing, PO Box 60906, Boulder City, NV 89006-0906 *Tel:* 702-293-5552 *Fax:* 702-293-4342 *Web Site:* www.neo-tech.com, pg 187

Ellis, Elizabeth M, Creative Arts Book Co, 833 Bancroft Way, Berkeley, CA 94710 *Tel:* 510-848-4777 *Fax:* 510-848-4844 *E-mail:* staff@creativeartsbooks.com; capublisher@yahoo.com *Web Site:* www.creativeartsbooks.com, pg 72

Ellis, Glen, Royal Ontario Museum Publications, 100 Queen's Park, Toronto, ON M5S 2C6, Canada *Tel:* 416-586-5581 *Fax:* 416-586-5887 *E-mail:* info@rom.on.ca *Web Site:* www.rom.on.ca, pg 560

Ellis, Glenn, Random House Children's Books, 1745 Broadway, New York, NY 10019 *Tel:* 212-782-9000 *Toll Free Tel:* 800-200-3552 *Fax:* 212-782-9452 *Web Site:* www.randomhouse.com/kids, pg 225

Ellis, Glenn, Random House Sales & Marketing, 1745 Broadway, New York, NY 10019 *Fax:* 212-782-9000, pg 227

Ellis, Robert, Institute for Language Study, 7 Hollyhock Rd, Wilton, CT 06897 *Tel:* 203-762-2510 *Toll Free Tel:* 800-245-2145 *Fax:* 203-762-2514 *E-mail:* cortinainc@aol.com *Web Site:* www.cortina-languages.com; members.aol.com/cortinainc, pg 134

Ellison, Nicholas, Nicholas Ellison Inc, 55 Fifth Ave, New York, NY 10003 *Tel:* 212-206-6050 *Fax:* 212-463-8718 *Web Site:* www.greenburger.com, pg 629

Ellsberg, Robert, Orbis Books, Walsh Bldg, 75 Ryder Rd, Ossining, NY 10562 *Tel:* 914-941-7636 *Toll Free Tel:* 800-258-5838 (orders) *Fax:* 914-941-7005 (orders); 914-945-0670 (office) *E-mail:* orbisbooks@maryknoll.org *Web Site:* www.orbisbooks.com, pg 198

Ellsworth, Sara, The Narrative Press, 319 Salida Del Sol, Santa Barbara, CA 93109 *Tel:* 805-966-2186 *Fax:* 805-456-3915 *E-mail:* admin@narrativepress.com *Web Site:* www.narrativepress.com, pg 181

Elon, Lois, Outcomes Unlimited Press Inc, 75 Cambridge Rd, Asheville, NC 28804 *Tel:* 828-712-1311 *Fax:* 828-258-1311 *Web Site:* www.drdossey.com, pg 200

Elsworthy, Sam, Princeton University Press, 41 William St, Princeton, NJ 08540 *Tel:* 609-258-4900 *Toll Free Tel:* 800-777-4726 *Fax:* 609-258-6305 *Toll Free Fax:* 800-999-1958 *E-mail:* orders@cpfsinc.com *Web Site:* www.pup.princeton.edu, pg 219

Elwell, Jake, Wieser & Elwell Inc, 80 Fifth Ave, Suite 1101, New York, NY 10011 *Tel:* 212-260-0860 *Fax:* 212-675-1381 *E-mail:* jetwell8@earthlink.net, pg 661

Elwell, James, Tyndale House Publishers Inc, 351 Executive Dr, Carol Stream, IL 60188 *Tel:* 630-668-8303 *Toll Free Tel:* 800-323-9400 *Web Site:* www.tyndale.com, pg 277

Ely, Liz, PhotoEdit Inc, 235 E Broadway, Suite 1020, Long Beach, CA 90802 *Tel:* 562-435-2722 *Toll Free Tel:* 800-860-2098 *Fax:* 562-435-7161 *Toll Free Fax:* 800-804-3707 *E-mail:* sales@photoeditinc.com *Web Site:* www.photoeditinc.com, pg 608

Emerick, Ingrid, Seal Press, 1400 65 St, Suite 250, Emeryville, CA 94608 *Tel:* 510-595-3664 *Fax:* 510-595-4228 *Web Site:* www.sealpress.com, pg 244

Emerick, Ken, Aid to Individual Artists, 727 E Main St, Columbus, OH 43205-1796 *Tel:* 614-466-2613 *Fax:* 614-466-4494 *Web Site:* www.oac.state.oh.us, pg 758

Emerson, James C, The Emerson Co, 12342 Northup Way, Bellevue, WA 98005 *Tel:* 425-869-0655 *Fax:* 425-869-0746 *Web Site:* www.emersoncompany.com, pg 90

Emerson, Jessica, University of New Orleans Press, c/o UNO Foundation, 6601 Franklin Ave, New Orleans, LA 70122 *Tel:* 504-280-1375 *Fax:* 504-280-7339 *Web Site:* www.uno.edu, pg 283

Emery, Allan, Hendrickson Publishers Inc, PO Box 3473, Peabody, MA 01961-3473 *Tel:* 978-532-6546 *Toll Free Tel:* 800-358-3111 *Fax:* 978-531-8146 *E-mail:* orders@hendrickson.com *Web Site:* www.hendrickson.com, pg 121

Emery, Margaret, International Universities Press Inc, 59 Boston Post Rd, Madison, CT 06443 *Tel:* 203-245-4000 *Toll Free Tel:* 800-835-3487 *Fax:* 203-245-0775 *E-mail:* orders@iup.com *Web Site:* www.iup.com, pg 138

Emery, Nancy, Epimetheus Books Inc, 2711 Centerville Rd, Suite 120-5336, Wilmington, DE 19808-1643 *Tel:* 646-345-2030 *E-mail:* epimetheus@att.net *Web Site:* www.epimetheusbooks.com, pg 91

Emery, Sheila, Watson-Guptill Publications, 770 Broadway, New York, NY 10003 *Tel:* 646-654-5450 *Toll Free Tel:* 800-278-8477 (orders only) *Fax:* 646-654-5486; 646-654-5487 *E-mail:* info@watsonguptill.com *Web Site:* www.watsonguptill.com, pg 294

Emmerson, Richard K, John Nicholas Brown Prize, 104 Mount Auburn St, 5th fl, Cambridge, MA 02138 *Tel:* 617-491-1622 *Fax:* 617-492-3303 *E-mail:* speculum@medievalacademy.org *Web Site:* www.medievalacademy.org, pg 764

Emmerson, Richard K, Elliott Prize, 104 Mount Auburn St, 5th fl, Cambridge, MA 02138 *Tel:* 617-491-1622 *Fax:* 617-492-3303 *E-mail:* speculum@medievalacademy.org *Web Site:* www.medievalacademy.org, pg 772

Emmerson, Richard K, Haskins Medal Award, 104 Mount Auburn St, 5th fl, Cambridge, MA 02138 *Tel:* 617-491-1622 *Fax:* 617-492-3303 *E-mail:* speculum@medievalacademy.org *Web Site:* www.medievalacademy.org, pg 778

Emmrich, Terry, University of Wisconsin Press, 1930 Monroe St, 3rd fl, Madison, WI 53711 *Tel:* 608-263-1110 *Toll Free Tel:* 800-621-2736 (Orders) *Fax:* 608-263-1120 *Toll Free Fax:* 800-621-8476 (Orders) *E-mail:* uwiscpress@uwpress.wisc.edu (Main Office) *Web Site:* www.wisc.edu/wisconsinpress/, pg 286

Emond, D Paul, Emond Montgomery Publications Ltd, 60 Shaftesbury Ave, Toronto, ON M4T 1A3, Canada *Tel:* 416-975-3925 *Toll Free Tel:* 888-837-0815 *Fax:* 416-975-3924 *E-mail:* info@emp.ca; orders@emp.ca *Web Site:* www.emp.ca, pg 546

Enderlin, Jennifer, St Martin's Press Paperback and Reference Group, 175 Fifth Ave, New York, NY 10010 *Fax:* 212-995-2488 *E-mail:* firstname.lastname@stmartins.com, pg 239

Enderlin, Jennifer, St Martin's Press Trade Division, 175 Fifth Ave, New York, NY 10010 *E-mail:* firstname.lastname@stmartins.com *Web Site:* www.stmartins.com; www.minotaurbooks.com, pg 239

Endicott, Laura, University of Missouri Press, 2910 Le Mone Blvd, Columbia, MO 65201 *Tel:* 573-882-7641 *Toll Free Tel:* 800-828-1894 (orders) *Fax:* 573-884-4498 *Web Site:* www.umsystem.edu/upress, pg 283

Engel, Anne, Jean V Naggar Literary Agency, 216 E 75 St, Suite 1-E, New York, NY 10021 *Tel:* 212-794-1082, pg 645

Engel, Deborah, Houghton Mifflin Trade & Reference Division, 222 Berkeley St, Boston, MA 02116-3764 *Tel:* 617-351-5000 *Toll Free Tel:* 800-225-3362 *Web Site:* www.houghtonmifflinbooks.com, pg 126

Engel, Jacqueline, Penguin Group (USA) Inc Sales, 375 Hudson St, New York, NY 10014 *Tel:* 212-366-2000 *E-mail:* online@penguinputnam.com *Web Site:* www.penguin.com, pg 208

Engel, Margaret, The Alicia Patterson Foundation Fellowship Program, 1730 Pennsylvania Ave, Suite 850, Washington, DC 20006 *Tel:* 202-393-5995 *Fax:* 301-951-8512 *E-mail:* info@aliciapatterson.org *Web Site:* www.aliciapatterson.org, pg 797

Engelhardt, Sara L, The Foundation Center, 79 Fifth Ave, New York, NY 10003-3076 *Tel:* 212-807-3690 *Toll Free Tel:* 800-424-9836 *Fax:* 212-807-3691 *Web Site:* www.fdncenter.org, pg 99

Engineer, Dilshad, Oberon Press, 350 Sparks St, Suite 400, Ottawa, ON K1R 7S8, Canada *Tel:* 613-238-3275 *Fax:* 613-238-3275 *E-mail:* oberon@sympatico.ca *Web Site:* www3.sympatico.ca/oberon, pg 556

England, Claire, The Continuum International Publishing Group, 15 E 26 St, Suite 1703, New York, NY 10010 *Tel:* 212-953-5858 *Toll Free Tel:* 800-561-7704 *Fax:* 212-953-5944 *E-mail:* info@continuum-books.com *Web Site:* www.continuumbooks.com, pg 67

England, David, Simon & Schuster Inc, 1230 Avenue of the Americas, New York, NY 10020 *Tel:* 212-698-7000 *Fax:* 212-698-7007 *Web Site:* www.simonsays.com, pg 249

England, Karen, OPIS/STALSBY Directories & Databases, Parkway 70 Plaza, 1255 Rt 70, Suite 32N, Lakewood, NJ 08701 *Tel:* 732-901-8800 *Toll Free Tel:* 800-275-0950 *Fax:* 732-901-9632 *Web Site:* www.opisnet.com, pg 198

Englefield, Cynthia, Show What You Know® Publishing, 6344 Nicholas Dr, Columbus, OH 43234 *Tel:* 614-764-1211 *Toll Free Tel:* 877-PASSING (727-7464) *Fax:* 614-764-1311 *E-mail:* swyk@eapublishing.com *Web Site:* www.eapublishing.com, pg 246

English, Catherine, American Library Association (ALA), 50 E Huron St, Chicago, IL 60611 *Tel:* 312-944-6780 *Toll Free Tel:* 800-545-2433 *Fax:* 312-944-8741 *E-mail:* editionsmarketing@ala.org *Web Site:* www.ala.org, pg 15

English, Elaine, The Graybill & English Literary Agency LLC, 1875 Connecticut Ave, NW, Suite 712, Washington, DC 20009 *Tel:* 202-588-9798 *Fax:* 202-457-0662 *Web Site:* graybillandenglish.com, pg 633

English, Robert G, Poetry In Print, PO Box 30981, Albuquerque, NM 87190-0981 *Tel:* 505-888-3937 *Fax:* 505-888-3937 *Web Site:* www.poets.com/RobertEnglish.html, pg 799

Englund, Sheryl L, Cornell University Press, 512 E State St, Ithaca, NY 14850 *Tel:* 607-277-2338 *Fax:* 607-277-2374 *E-mail:* cupressinfo@cornell.edu *Web Site:* www.cornellpress.cornell.edu, pg 68

Enochs, Susan, The Monacelli Press, 902 Broadway, 18th fl, New York, NY 10010 *Tel:* 212-777-0504 *Toll Free Tel:* 800-631-8571 (cust serv) *Fax:* 212-777-0514; 201-256-0000 (cust serv) *E-mail:* info@monacellipress.com; production@monacellipress.com; customerservice@penguinputnam.com *Web Site:* www.monacellipress.com, pg 177

Enslow, Brian D, Enslow Publishers Inc, 40 Industrial Rd, Berkeley Heights, NJ 07922 *Tel:* 908-771-9400 *Toll Free Tel:* 800-398-2504 *Fax:* 908-771-0925 *Web Site:* www.myreportlinks.com; www.enslow.com, pg 91

Enslow, Mark, Enslow Publishers Inc, 40 Industrial Rd, Berkeley Heights, NJ 07922 *Tel:* 908-771-9400 *Toll Free Tel:* 800-398-2504 *Fax:* 908-771-0925 *Web Site:* www.myreportlinks.com; www.enslow.com, pg 91

Ensor, Kendra, Rand McNally, 8255 Central Park Ave N, Skokie, IL 60076 *Tel:* 847-329-8100 *Toll Free Tel:* 800-333-0136 *Fax:* 847-673-0539 *Web Site:* www.randmcnally.com, pg 225

Entrekin, Morgan, Grove/Atlantic Inc, 841 Broadway, 4th fl, New York, NY 10003-4793 *Tel:* 212-614-7850 *Toll Free Tel:* 800-521-0178 *Fax:* 212-614-7886 *Web Site:* www.groveatlantic.com, pg 110

Entricken, Kevin, Aspen Publishers, A Wolters Kluwer Company, 1185 Avenue of the Americas, New York, NY 10036 *Tel:* 212-597-0200 *Toll Free Tel:* 800-234-1660 (cust serv); 800-447-1717 (orders); 800-950-5259 (legal educ); 800-LAW-PLGL (paralegal textbook); 800-317-3113 (bookstore sales); 800-364-2512 (Loislaw) *Web Site:* www.aspenpublishers.com, pg 26

Ephraim, Elliot, Elliot's Books, PO Box 6, Northford, CT 06472-0006 *Tel:* 203-484-2184 *Fax:* 203-484-7644 *E-mail:* outofprintbooks@mindspring.com, pg 89

Epler, Barbara, New Directions Publishing Corp, 80 Eighth Ave, New York, NY 10011 *Tel:* 212-255-0230 *Toll Free Tel:* 800-233-4830 (PA) *Fax:* 212-255-0231 *E-mail:* newdirections@ndbooks.com *Web Site:* www. ndpublishing.com, pg 187

Epperson, Connie, Oakstone Medical Publishing, 6801 Cahaba Valley Rd, Birmingham, AL 35242 *Tel:* 205-991-5188 *Toll Free Tel:* 800-952-0690 *Fax:* 205-995-4656 *E-mail:* service@oakstonemedical.com *Web Site:* www.oakstonemedical.com, pg 195

Eppy, Pearl, Pearl Eppy, 201 E 79 St, New York, NY 10021 *Tel:* 212-737-0354, pg 598

Eprile, Paul, Between the Lines, 720 Bathurst St, No 404, Toronto, ON M5S 2R4, Canada *Tel:* 416-535-9914 *Toll Free Tel:* 800-718-7201 *Fax:* 416-535-1484 *E-mail:* btlbooks@web.ca *Web Site:* www.btlbooks. com, pg 536

Epstein, Don R, Greater Talent Network Inc, 437 Fifth Ave, New York, NY 10016 *Tel:* 212-645-4200 *Toll Free Tel:* 800-326-4211 *Fax:* 212-627-1471 *E-mail:* gtn@greatertalent.com *Web Site:* www. gtnspeakers.com, pg 669

Epstein, Kate, Adams Media, An F+W Publications Co, 57 Littlefield St, 2nd fl, Avon, MA 02322 *Tel:* 508-427-7100 *Fax:* 508-427-6790 *Toll Free Fax:* 800-872-5628 *E-mail:* authors@adamsmedia.com; orders@ adamsmedia.com *Web Site:* www.adamsmedia.com, pg 5

Epstein, Leslie, Boston University, 236 Bay State Rd, Boston, MA 02215 *Tel:* 617-353-2510 *Fax:* 617-353-3653 *Web Site:* www.bu.edu/writing/, pg 751

Epstein, Ron, Humana Press, 999 Riverview Dr, Suite 208, Totowa, NJ 07512 *Tel:* 973-256-1699 *Fax:* 973-256-8341 *E-mail:* humana@humanapr.com *Web Site:* humanapress.com, pg 128

Epstein, Theodore, Atlantic Law Book Co, 22 Grassmere Ave, West Hartford, CT 06110-1215 *Tel:* 860-231-9300 *Fax:* 860-231-9242 *E-mail:* atlanticlawbooks@ aol.com *Web Site:* www.atlntc.com, pg 27

Erdman, Margaret, Sleeping Bear Press™, 310 N Main St, Suite 300, Chelsea, MI 48118 *Tel:* 734-475-4411 *Toll Free Tel:* 800-487-2323 *Fax:* 734-475-0787 *E-mail:* sleepingbear@thomson.com *Web Site:* www. sleepingbearpress.com, pg 250

Erdmann, Bob, Columbine Communications & Publications Inc, 1293 Elizabeth Barcus Way, Fortuna, CA 95540 *Tel:* 707-726-9200 *Fax:* 707-726-9300 *E-mail:* cocompub@aol.com, pg 65

Erdner, Lisa, Advanced Sheetfed Press Operations, 200 Deer Run Rd, Sewickley, PA 15143-2600 *Tel:* 412-741-6860 *Toll Free Tel:* 800-910-4283 *Fax:* 412-741-2311 *E-mail:* info@gain.net *Web Site:* www.gain.net, pg 741

Erdner, Lisa, Naomi Berber Memorial Award, 200 Deer Run Rd, Sewickley, PA 15143-2600 *Tel:* 412-741-6860 *Toll Free Tel:* 800-910-4283 *Fax:* 412-741-2311 *E-mail:* info@gain.net *Web Site:* www.gain.net, pg 762

Erdner, Lisa, Color Management for the Pressroom, 200 Deer Run Rd, Sewickley, PA 15143-2600 *Tel:* 412-741-6860 *Toll Free Tel:* 800-910-4283 *Fax:* 412-741-2311 *E-mail:* info@gain.net *Web Site:* www.gain.net, pg 743

Erdner, Lisa, Education Awards of Excellence, 200 Deer Run Rd, Sewickley, PA 15143-2600 *Tel:* 412-741-6860 *Toll Free Tel:* 800-910-4283 *Fax:* 412-741-2311 *E-mail:* info@gain.net *Web Site:* www.gain.net, pg 771

Erdner, Lisa, Fine Tune Your CTP Installation, 200 Deer Run Rd, Sewickley, PA 15143-2600 *Tel:* 412-741-6860 *Toll Free Tel:* 800-910-4283 *Fax:* 412-741-2311 *E-mail:* info@gain.net *Web Site:* www.gain.net, pg 743

Erdner, Lisa, Graphic Arts Employers of America, 100 Daingerfield Rd, Alexandria, VA 22314 *Tel:* 703-519-8100; 703-519-8151 *Fax:* 703-548-3227 *Web Site:* www.gain.net, pg 687

Erdner, Lisa, Implementing Color Management, 200 Deer Run Rd, Sewickley, PA 15143-2600 *Tel:* 412-741-6860 *Toll Free Tel:* 800-910-4283 *Fax:* 412-741-2311 *E-mail:* info@gain.net *Web Site:* www.gain.net, pg 744

Erdner, Lisa, InterTech Technology Award, 200 Deer Run Rd, Sewickley, PA 15143-2600 *Tel:* 412-741-6860 *Toll Free Tel:* 800-910-4283 *Fax:* 412-741-2311 *E-mail:* info@gain.net *Web Site:* www.gain.net, pg 780

Erdner, Lisa, Frederick D Kagy Education Award of Excellence, 200 Deer Run Rd, Sewickley, PA 15143-2600 *Tel:* 412-741-6860 *Toll Free Tel:* 800-910-4283 *Fax:* 412-741-2311 *E-mail:* info@gain.net *Web Site:* www.gain.net, pg 782

Erdner, Lisa, Mastering Color for Print Production, 200 Deer Run Rd, Sewickley, PA 15143-2600 *Tel:* 412-741-6860 *Toll Free Tel:* 800-910-4283 *Fax:* 412-741-2311 *E-mail:* info@gain.net *Web Site:* www.gain.net, pg 744

Erdner, Lisa, Orientation to the Graphic Arts, 200 Deer Run Rd, Sewickley, PA 15143-2600 *Tel:* 412-741-6860 *Toll Free Tel:* 800-910-4283 *Fax:* 412-741-2311 *E-mail:* info@gain.net *Web Site:* www.gain.net, pg 745

Erdner, Lisa, PIA/GATF (Graphic Arts Technical Foundation), 200 Deer Run Rd, Sewickley, PA 15143-2600 *Tel:* 412-741-6860 *Toll Free Tel:* 800-910-4283 *Fax:* 412-741-2311 *E-mail:* info@gain.net *Web Site:* www.gain.net, pg 697

Erdner, Lisa, PIA/GATF (Graphic Arts Technical Foundation), 200 Deer Run Rd, Sewickley, PA 15143-2600 *Tel:* 412-741-6860 *Toll Free Tel:* 800-910-4283 *Fax:* 412-741-2311, pg 754

Erdner, Lisa, PIA/GATF/NAPL Sheetfed Executive of the Year, 200 Deer Run Rd, Sewickley, PA 15143-2600 *Tel:* 412-741-6860 *Toll Free Tel:* 800-910-4283 *Fax:* 412-741-2311 *E-mail:* info@gain.net *Web Site:* www.gain.net, pg 798

Erdner, Lisa, Robert F Reed Technology Medal, 200 Deer Run Rd, Sewickley, PA 15143-2600 *Tel:* 412-741-6860 *Toll Free Tel:* 800-910-4283 *Fax:* 412-741-2311 *E-mail:* info@gain.net *Web Site:* www.gain.net, pg 801

Erdner, Lisa, William D Schaeffer Environmental Award, 200 Deer Run Rd, Sewickley, PA 15143-2600 *Tel:* 412-741-6860 *Toll Free Tel:* 800-910-4283 *Fax:* 412-741-2311 *E-mail:* info@gain.net *Web Site:* www.gain.net, pg 804

Erdner, Lisa, Sheetfed Offset Press Operating, 200 Deer Run Rd, Sewickley, PA 15143-2600 *Tel:* 412-741-6860 *Toll Free Tel:* 800-910-4283 *Fax:* 412-741-2311 *E-mail:* info@gain.net *Web Site:* www.gain.net, pg 747

Erdner, Lisa, Troubleshooting Sheetfed Offset Press Problems, 200 Deer Run Rd, Sewickley, PA 15143-2600 *Tel:* 412-741-6860 *Toll Free Tel:* 800-910-4283 *Fax:* 412-741-2311 *E-mail:* info@gain.net *Web Site:* www.gain.net, pg 748

Erdner, Lisa, Web Offset Press Operating, 200 Deer Run Rd, Sewickley, PA 15143-2600 *Tel:* 412-741-6860 *Toll Free Tel:* 800-910-4283 *Fax:* 412-741-2311 *E-mail:* info@gain.net *Web Site:* www.gain.net, pg 748

Erickson, Kerry L, National Book Co, PO Box 8795, Portland, OR 97207-8795 *Tel:* 503-228-6345 *Fax:* 810-885-5811 *E-mail:* info@eralearning.com *Web Site:* www.eralearning.com, pg 182

Ericson, Carolyn, Ericson Books, 1614 Redbud St, Nacogdoches, TX 75965 *Tel:* 936-564-3625 *Fax:* 936-552-8999 *E-mail:* info@ericsonbooks.com *Web Site:* www.ericsonbooks.com, pg 91

Erinmore, Herbert, The Jonathan Dolger Agency, 49 E 96 St, Suite 9-B, New York, NY 10128 *Tel:* 212-427-1853 *Fax:* 212-369-7118, pg 628

Erlacher, Bill, Artists Associates, 4416 La Jolla Dr, Bradenton, FL 34210-3927 *Tel:* 941-756-8445 *Fax:* 941-727-8840, pg 665

Erlbaum, Lawrence, The Analytic Press, 101 West St, Hillsdale, NJ 07642 *Tel:* 201-358-9477; 201-236-9500 *Toll Free Tel:* 800-926-6579 (orders only); 800-627-0629 (journal orders) *Fax:* 201-358-4700 (edit); 201-760-3735 (orders only) *E-mail:* tap@analyticpress.com *Web Site:* www.analyticpress.com, pg 19

Erlbaum, Lawrence, Lawrence Erlbaum Associates Inc, 10 Industrial Ave, Mahwah, NJ 07430-2262 *Tel:* 201-236-2199 *Toll Free Tel:* 800-9-BOOKS-9 (926-6579) *Fax:* 201-760-3735 *E-mail:* orders@erlbaum.com *Web Site:* www.erlbaum.com, pg 91

Ermitage, Kathleen, Proof Positive/Farrowlyne Associates Inc, 1620 Central St, Evanston, IL 60201 *Tel:* 847-866-9570 *Fax:* 847-866-9849, pg 609

Ernsberger, George, Publishing Synthesis Ltd, 425 Broome St, New York, NY 10013 *Tel:* 212-219-0135 *Fax:* 212-219-0136 *E-mail:* info@pubsyn.com *Web Site:* www.pubsyn.com, pg 609

Ernst, Alex, Ernst Publishing Company LLC, 1937 Delaware Tpke, Clarksville, NY 12041 *Toll Free Tel:* 800-345-3822 *Toll Free Fax:* 800-252-0906 *Web Site:* www.ernst.cc, pg 92

Ernst, Christopher, Artech House Inc, 685 Canton St, Norwood, MA 02062 *Tel:* 781-769-9750 *Toll Free Tel:* 800-225-9977 *Fax:* 781-769-6334 *E-mail:* artech@artechhouse.com *Web Site:* www. artechhouse.com, pg 24

Ernzen, Brandy, CMP Books, 600 Harrison St, San Francisco, CA 94107 *Tel:* 415-947-6615; 408-848-3854 (orders) *Toll Free Tel:* 800-500-6875 (orders) *Fax:* 415-947-6015; 408-848-5784 (orders) *E-mail:* books@cmp.com *Web Site:* www.cmpbooks. com, pg 64

Errick, Steve, Foundation Press Inc, 395 Hudson St, New York, NY 10014 *Tel:* 212-367-6790 *Fax:* 212-367-6799 *Web Site:* www.foundation-press.com, pg 99

Erwin, Mary, University of Michigan Press, 839 Greene St, Ann Arbor, MI 48104-3209 *Tel:* 734-764-4388 *Fax:* 734-615-1540 *E-mail:* um.press@umich.edu *Web Site:* www.press.umich.edu, pg 282

Eshenour, Janet, BradyGAMES Publishing, 800 E 96 St, 3rd fl, Indianapolis, IN 46240 *Tel:* 317-428-3000 *Toll Free Tel:* 800-545-5912; 800-571-5840 (cust serv) *E-mail:* bradyquestions@pearsoned.com *Web Site:* www.bradygames.com, pg 45

Eskenazi, Brian, Riverside Book Co Inc, 150 W End Ave, No 11-H, New York, NY 10023 *Tel:* 212-595-0700 *Fax:* 212-559-0780 *Web Site:* www. riversidebook.com, pg 233

Eskenazi, Paul, Jim Henson Publishing/Muppet Press, 117 E 69 St, New York, NY 10021 *Tel:* 212-794-2400 *Fax:* 212-794-5157 *Web Site:* www.henson.com, pg 141

Eskenazi, Victor, Riverside Book Co Inc, 150 W End Ave, No 11-H, New York, NY 10023 *Tel:* 212-595-0700 *Fax:* 212-559-0780 *Web Site:* www. riversidebook.com, pg 233

Espelage, Arthur, Canon Law Society of America, 108 N Payne St, Suite C, Alexandria, VA 22314-2906 *Tel:* 703-739-2560 *Fax:* 703-739-2562 *E-mail:* coordinator@clsa.org *Web Site:* www.clsa.org, pg 52

Esposito, Michael, Marshall Cavendish Corp, 99 White Plains Rd, Tarrytown, NY 10591-9001 *Tel:* 914-332-8888 *Fax:* 914-332-1888 *E-mail:* mcc@marshallcavendish.com *Web Site:* www. marshallcavendish.com, pg 164

Essary, Loris, International Titles, 931 E 56 St, Austin, TX 78751-1724 *Tel:* 512-451-2221 *Fax:* 512-467-1330, pg 635

Essary, Loris, Quincannon Publishing Group, PO Box 8100, Glen Ridge, NJ 07028-8100 *Tel:* 973-669-8367 *E-mail:* editors@quincannongroup.com *Web Site:* www.quincannongroup.com, pg 224

Essex, Robert L, Review & Herald Publishing Association, 55 W Oak Ridge Dr, Hagerstown, MD 21740 *Tel:* 301-393-3000 *Toll Free Tel:* 800-234-7630 *Fax:* 301-393-4055 (periodicals); 301-393-3222 *E-mail:* editorial@rhpa.org *Web Site:* www. reviewandherald.com, pg 232

Estell, Ingrid, Mountain Press Publishing Co, 1301 S Third W, Missoula, MT 59801 *Tel:* 406-728-1900 *Toll Free Tel:* 800-234-5308 *Fax:* 406-728-1635 *E-mail:* info@mtnpress.com *Web Site:* www.mountain-press.com, pg 179

Estell, Twyla, Chitra Publications, 2 Public Ave, Montrose, PA 18801 *Tel:* 570-278-1984 *Toll Free Tel:* 800-628-8244 *Fax:* 570-278-2223 *E-mail:* chitra@epix.net *Web Site:* www.quilttownusa.com, pg 60

Estes, Jack, Pleasure Boat Studio: A Literary Press, 201 W 89 St, Suite 6F, New York, NY 10024-1848 *Tel:* 212-362-8563 *Toll Free Tel:* 888-810-5308 *Fax:* 212-874-1158 *Toll Free Fax:* 800-810-5308 *E-mail:* pleasboat@nyc.rr.com *Web Site:* www.pbstudio.com, pg 214

Estoppey, Carol, The Conference Board Inc, 845 Third Ave, New York, NY 10022 *Tel:* 212-759-0900 *Fax:* 212-980-7014 *E-mail:* info@conference-board.org *Web Site:* www.conference-board.org, pg 66

Estrin, Heidi, Sydney Taylor Book Awards, 15 E 26 St, New York, NY 10010-1579 *Tel:* 212-725-5359 *Fax:* 212-481-4174 *E-mail:* ajl@jewishbooks.org *Web Site:* www.jewishlibraries.org, pg 808

Etchemendy, Nancy, Horror Writers Association, PO Box 50577, Palo Alto, CA 94303 *E-mail:* hwa@horror.org *Web Site:* www.horror.org/, pg 688

Eth, Felicia, Felicia Eth Literary Representation, 555 Bryant St, Suite 350, Palo Alto, CA 94301 *Tel:* 650-401-8891; 650-375-1276 *Fax:* 650-401-8892 *E-mail:* feliciaeth@aol.com, pg 629

Etheridge, Shawn, PRIMEDIA Business Directories & Books, 9800 Metcalf Ave, Overland Park, KS 66212 *Tel:* 913-967-1719 *Toll Free Tel:* 800-453-9620; 800-262-1954 (cust serv) *Fax:* 913-967-1901 *Toll Free Fax:* 800-633-6219 *E-mail:* bookorders@primediabooks.com *Web Site:* www.primediabooks.com, pg 218

Ethridge, Will, Pearson Higher Education Division, One Lake St, Upper Saddle River, NJ 07458 *Tel:* 201-236-7000 *Fax:* 201-236-3381, pg 206

Etienne, Phil, Abbey Press, One Hill Dr, St Meinrad, IN 47577 *Tel:* 812-357-6611 *Toll Free Tel:* 800-962-4760 *Fax:* 812-357-8388 *E-mail:* dep@abbeypress.com *Web Site:* www.abbeypress.com, pg 2

Etra, Judith, Whittier Publications Inc, 64 Alabama Ave, Island Park, NY 11558 *Tel:* 516-432-8120 *Toll Free Tel:* 800-897-TEXT (897-8398) *Fax:* 516-889-0341 *E-mail:* info@whitbooks.com, pg 298

Ettinger, Andrew, Los Angeles Literary Associates, 6324 Tahoe Dr, Los Angeles, CA 90068-1654 *Tel:* 323-464-6444 *Fax:* 323-464-6444, pg 641

Eubanks, Georgann, Duke University Writers' Workshop, PO Box 90700, Durham, NC 27708-0700 *Tel:* 919-684-6259 *Fax:* 919-681-8235 *E-mail:* learnmore@duke.edu *Web Site:* www.learnmore.duke.edu, pg 743

Eulau, Dennis, Simon & Schuster Adult Publishing Group, 1230 Avenue of the Americas, New York, NY 10020 *Tel:* 212-698-7000 *Toll Free Tel:* 800-223-2336 (orders); 800-223-2348 (cust serv), pg 248

Evans, Anne, Napa Valley Writers' Conference-Poetry & Fiction Sessions, Upper Valley Campus, 1088 College Ave, St Helena, CA 94574 *Tel:* 707-967-2900 (ext 1611) *Fax:* 707-967-2909 *E-mail:* writecon@napavalley.edu *Web Site:* www.napavalley.edu/writersconf, pg 745

Evans, Chris, Stackpole Books, 5067 Ritter Rd, Mechanicsburg, PA 17055 *Tel:* 717-796-0411 *Toll Free Tel:* 800-732-3669 *Fax:* 717-796-0412 *Web Site:* www.stackpolebooks.com, pg 257

Evans, Elaine, Trident Press International, 801 12 Ave S, Suite 400, Naples, FL 34102 *Tel:* 239-649-7077 *Toll Free Tel:* 800-593-3662 *Fax:* 239-649-5832 *Toll Free Fax:* 800-494-4226 *E-mail:* tridentpress@worldnet.att.net *Web Site:* www.trident-international.com, pg 275

Evans, Gene, Merit Publishing International Inc, 5840 Corporate Way, Suite 200, West Palm Beach, FL 33407-2040 *Tel:* 561-637-1116 *Fax:* 561-477-4961 *E-mail:* meritpi@aol.com *Web Site:* www.meritpublishing.com, pg 171

Evans, Janet, A Abacus Group, PO Box 35, Ridgecrest, CA 93556 *Tel:* 760-375-5243 *Fax:* 760-375-1140 *E-mail:* gtd007@ridgenet.net *Web Site:* www.ridgenet.net/~gtd007, pg 617

Evans, Janet, Ivy House Publishing Group, 5122 Bur Oak Circle, Raleigh, NC 27612 *Tel:* 919-782-0281 *Toll Free Tel:* 800-948-2786 *Fax:* 919-781-9042 *E-mail:* thepublisher@ivyhousebooks.com *Web Site:* www.ivyhousebooks.com, pg 572

Evans, Janet M, American Biographical Institute, 5126 Bur Oak Circle, Raleigh, NC 27612 *Tel:* 919-781-8710 *Fax:* 919-781-8712, pg 12

Evans, Joni, William Morris Agency, 1325 Avenue of the Americas, New York, NY 10019 *Tel:* 212-586-5100 *Fax:* 212-903-1418 *E-mail:* wma@interport.net *Web Site:* www.wma.com, pg 645

Evans, Joy, Evan-Moor Educational Publishers, 18 Lower Ragsdale Dr, Monterey, CA 93940 *Tel:* 831-649-5901 *Toll Free Tel:* 800-777-4362 *Fax:* 831-649-6256 *E-mail:* customerservice@evan-moor.com *Web Site:* www.evan-moor.com, pg 92

Evans, Lamar F, National State Publishing Association (NSPA), 207 Third Ave, Hattiesburg, MS 39401 *Tel:* 601-582-3330 *Fax:* 601-582-3354 *E-mail:* info@govpublishing.org *Web Site:* www.govpublishing.org, pg 694

Evans, Lawrence, SFWA Nebula Awards, PO Box 877, Chestertown, MD 21620 *Toll Free Tel:* 888-322-7392 *E-mail:* execdir@sfwa.org *Web Site:* www.sfwa.org, pg 805

Evans, Mary, Mary Evans Inc, 242 E Fifth St, New York, NY 10003 *Tel:* 212-979-0880 *Fax:* 212-979-5344 *E-mail:* merrylit@aol.com, pg 629

Evans, Mary Selden, Syracuse University Press, 621 Skytop Rd, Syracuse, NY 13244-5290 *Tel:* 315-443-5534 *Toll Free Tel:* 800-365-8929 (orders only) *Fax:* 315-443-5545 *E-mail:* supress@syr.edu *Web Site:* www.syracuseuniversitypress.syr.edu, pg 263

Evans, Stephanie, Basic Health Publications Inc, 8200 Boulevard E, Suite 25-G, North Bergen, NJ 07047 *Tel:* 201-868-8336 *Toll Free Tel:* 800-575-8890 *Fax:* 201-868-8335, pg 33

Evans, Stephanie, Editions du Meridien, 1980 Sherbrooke Ouest, No 540, Montreal, PQ H3H 1E8, Canada *Tel:* 514-935-0464 *Fax:* 514-935-0458 *E-mail:* info@editionsdumeridien.com *Web Site:* www.editionsdumeridien.com, pg 544

Evans, Susan, The Society of Naval Architects & Marine Engineers, 601 Pavonia Ave, Jersey City, NJ 07306-2907 *Tel:* 201-798-4800 *Toll Free Tel:* 800-798-2188 *Fax:* 201-798-4975 *Web Site:* www.sname.org, pg 252

Evans, William, Evan-Moor Educational Publishers, 18 Lower Ragsdale Dr, Monterey, CA 93940 *Tel:* 831-649-5901 *Toll Free Tel:* 800-777-4362 *Fax:* 831-649-6256 *E-mail:* customerservice@evan-moor.com *Web Site:* www.evan-moor.com, pg 92

Everingham, Kate, Arcadia Publishing, 420 Wando Park Blvd, Mount Pleasant, SC 29464 *Tel:* 843-853-2070 *Toll Free Tel:* 888-313-2665 (orders only) *Fax:* 843-853-0044 *E-mail:* sales@arcadiapublishing.com *Web Site:* www.arcadiapublishing.com, pg 22

Everly-Warren, Jacqueline, Doubleday Broadway Publishing Group, 1745 Broadway, New York, NY 10019 *Tel:* 212-782-9000 *Toll Free Tel:* 800-223-6834; 800-223-5780 (sales) *Fax:* 212-302-7985 (correspondence); 212-492-9862 (orders), pg 82

Ewing, Jack, Jack Ewing Concepts & Copy, PO Box 571, Boise, ID 83701 *Tel:* 208-345-1782 *Fax:* 208-345-1782 (call first) *E-mail:* citzenew@aol.com, pg 598

Ewing, John H, American Mathematical Society, 201 Charles St, Providence, RI 02904-2294 *Tel:* 401-455-4000 *Toll Free Tel:* 800-321-4267 *Fax:* 401-331-3842; 401-455-4046 (cust serv) *E-mail:* ams@ams.org *Web Site:* www.ams.org, pg 16

Ewing, Peter, Standard Educational Corp, 200 W Jackson, 7th fl, Chicago, IL 60606 *Tel:* 312-692-1000, pg 257

Ewing, Peter, The United Educators Inc, 900 N Shore Dr, Suite 140, Lake Bluff, IL 60044 *Tel:* 847-234-3700 *Fax:* 847-234-8705 *E-mail:* arslms@aol.com, pg 279

Exley, Richard, Helen Exley Giftbooks, 185 Main St, Spencer, MA 01562 *Toll Free Tel:* 877-395-3942 *Toll Free Fax:* 800-807-7363 *E-mail:* helen.exleygiftbooks@verizon.net, pg 93

Eyler, Truman, Thomas Publications, 3245 Fairfield Rd, Gettysburg, PA 17325 *Tel:* 717-642-6600 *Toll Free Tel:* 800-840-6782 *Fax:* 717-642-5555 *E-mail:* thomaspub@blazenet.net *Web Site:* www.thomaspublications.com, pg 269

Ezzell, Emmy, Indiana University Press, 601 N Morton St, Bloomington, IN 47404-3797 *Tel:* 812-855-8817 *Toll Free Tel:* 800-842-6796 (orders only) *Fax:* 812-855-7931 (orders only); 812-855-8507 *E-mail:* iupress@indiana.edu; iuorder@indiana.edu (orders) *Web Site:* www.iupress.indiana.edu, pg 132

Fabrizi, Rich, Scott Foresman, 1900 E Lake Ave, Glenview, IL 60025 *Tel:* 847-729-3000 *Toll Free Tel:* 800-535-4391 (Midwest) *Fax:* 847-729-8910 *E-mail:* firstname.lastname@scottforesman.com *Web Site:* www.scottforesman.com, pg 243

Fackovec, William, Marian Library Medal, 300 College Park, Dayton, OH 45469-1390 *Tel:* 937-229-4214 *Fax:* 937-229-4258 *Web Site:* www.udayton.edu, pg 787

Factor, Sari, Macmillan/McGraw-Hill, 2 Penn Plaza, New York, NY 10121 *Tel:* 212-904-2000, pg 161

Fadlalla, Michelle, Simon & Schuster Children's Publishing, 1230 Avenue of the Americas, New York, NY 10020 *Tel:* 212-698-7000 *Web Site:* www.simonsayskids.com, pg 248

Faduska, Catherine, IEEE Press, 445 Hoes Lane, Piscataway, NJ 08854 *Tel:* 732-981-3418 *Fax:* 732-981-8062 *E-mail:* ieeepress@ieee.org *Web Site:* www.ieee.org/pubs/press/, pg 131

Faenza, Michael, National Mental Health Association, 2001 N Beauregard St, 12th fl, Alexandria, VA 22311 *Tel:* 703-684-7722 *Toll Free Tel:* 800-969-6642 *Fax:* 703-684-5968 *Web Site:* www.nmha.org, pg 694

Fagan, John, Penguin Books, 375 Hudson St, New York, NY 10014 *Tel:* 212-366-2000 *E-mail:* online@penguinputnam.com *Web Site:* www.penguin.com; www.penguinclassics.com, pg 207

Fagan, Ray, Harcourt Inc, 6277 Sea Harbor Dr, Orlando, FL 32887 *Tel:* 407-345-2000 *Toll Free Tel:* 800-225-5425 (cust serv) *Fax:* 407-352-3445 (cust serv), pg 114

Fagerness, Taryn, Sandra Dijkstra Literary Agency, 1155 Camino del Mar, PMB 515, Del Mar, CA 92014-2605 *Tel:* 858-755-3115 *Fax:* 858-794-2822 *E-mail:* sdla@dijkstraagency.com, pg 627

Faherty, Robert L, The Brookings Institution Press, 1775 Massachusetts Ave NW, Washington, DC 20036-2188 *Tel:* 202-797-6000 *Toll Free Tel:* 800-275-1447 *Fax:* 202-797-6195 *E-mail:* bibooks@brook.edu *Web Site:* www.brookings.edu, pg 48

Fahey, John, National Geographic Society, 1145 17 St NW, Washington, DC 20036 *Tel:* 202-857-7000 *Fax:* 202-429-5727 *Web Site:* www.nationalgeographic.com, pg 184

Fairweather, Gari, Editorial Options Inc, 353 Lexington Ave, New York, NY 10016 *Tel:* 212-986-2888 *Fax:* 212-986-1194 *Web Site:* www.edop.com, pg 597

Faiz, Mohamed, United Nations Publications, 2 United Nations Plaza, Rm DC2-0853, New York, NY 10017 *Tel:* 212-963-8302 *Toll Free Tel:* 800-253-9646 *Fax:* 212-963-3489 *E-mail:* publications@un.org *Web Site:* www.un.org/publications, pg 279

Falaster, Lisa, Southern Illinois University Press, PO Box 3697, Carbondale, IL 62902-3697 *Tel:* 618-453-2281 *Toll Free Tel:* 800-346-2680 *Fax:* 618-453-1221 *Toll Free Fax:* 800-346-2681 *E-mail:* jstetter@siu.edu *Web Site:* www.siu.edu/~siupress, pg 254

Falb, Mark C, Kendall/Hunt Publishing Co, 4050 Westmark Dr, Dubuque, IA 52002 *Tel:* 563-589-1000 *Toll Free Tel:* 800-228-0810 (orders only) *Fax:* 563-589-1114 *Toll Free Fax:* 800-772-9165 *Web Site:* www.kendallhunt.com, pg 144

Falk, Peter H, Falk Art Reference, 61 Beekman Place, Madison, CT 06443 *Tel:* 203-245-2246 *Web Site:* www.falkart.com, pg 94

Falkner, Jeannie, Nelson, 1120 Birchmount Rd, Scarborough, ON M1K 5G4, Canada *Tel:* 416-752-9448 *Toll Free Tel:* 800-268-2222 (cust serv); 800-430-4445 *Fax:* 416-752-8101 *E-mail:* inquire@nelson.com *Web Site:* www.nelson.com, pg 555

Falley, Don, Microsoft Press, One Microsoft Way, Redmond, WA 98052-6399 *Tel:* 425-882-8080 *Toll Free Tel:* 800-677-7377 *Fax:* 425-936-7329 *Web Site:* www.microsoft.com/presspass/exec/default.asp#qt, pg 173

Falvey, Bill, Westminster John Knox Press, 100 Witherspoon St, Louisville, KY 40202-1396 *Tel:* 502-569-5052 *Toll Free Tel:* 800-227-2872 (US only) *Fax:* 502-569-8308 *Toll Free Fax:* 800-541-5113 (US only) *E-mail:* wjk@wjkbooks.com *Web Site:* www.wjkbooks.com, pg 297

Famighetti, Robert, Gareth Stevens Inc, 330 W Olive St, Suite 100, Milwaukee, WI 53212 *Tel:* 414-332-3520 *Toll Free Tel:* 800-542-2595 *Fax:* 414-332-3567 *E-mail:* info@gspub.com; info@worldalmanaclibrary.com *Web Site:* www.garethstevens.com; www.worldalmanaclibrary.com, pg 102

Fang, Irving, rada press inc, 715 Third Ave, Mendota Heights, MN 55118 *Tel:* 651-455-9695 *Fax:* 651-455-9675, pg 224

Farace, Patrick, W H Freeman and Co, 41 Madison Ave, 37th fl, New York, NY 10010 *Tel:* 212-576-9400 *Fax:* 212-689-2383 *Web Site:* www.whfreeman.com, pg 100

Farah, Priscilla, The Metropolitan Museum of Art, 1000 Fifth Ave, New York, NY 10028 *Tel:* 212-879-5500; 212-535-7710 *Fax:* 212-396-5062 *E-mail:* info@metmuseum.org *Web Site:* www.metmuseum.org, pg 173

Faran, Ellen W, The MIT Press, 5 Cambridge Ctr, Cambridge, MA 02142 *Tel:* 617-253-5646 *Toll Free Tel:* 800-405-1619 (orders only) *Fax:* 617-258-6779 *Web Site:* mitpress.mit.edu, pg 175

Farber, Ann, Farber Literary Agency Inc, 14 E 75 St, New York, NY 10021 *Tel:* 212-861-7075 *Fax:* 212-861-7076 *E-mail:* farberlit@aol.com, pg 629

Farber, Donald C, Farber Literary Agency Inc, 14 E 75 St, New York, NY 10021 *Tel:* 212-861-7075 *Fax:* 212-861-7076 *E-mail:* farberlit@aol.com, pg 629

Farber, Gary, The Perseus Books Group, 387 Park Ave S, 12th fl, New York, NY 10016 *Tel:* 212-340-8100 *Toll Free Tel:* 800-386-5656 (cust serv) *Fax:* 212-340-8115 *Web Site:* www.perseusbooksgroup.com, pg 210

Farber, James P Jr, Half Halt Press Inc, 20042 Benevola Church Rd, Boonsboro, MD 21713 *Tel:* 301-733-7119 *Toll Free Tel:* 800-822-9635 (orders only) *Fax:* 301-733-7408 *E-mail:* gem@halfhaltpress.com *Web Site:* www.halfhaltpress.com, pg 112

Farber, Seth, Farber Literary Agency Inc, 14 E 75 St, New York, NY 10021 *Tel:* 212-861-7075 *Fax:* 212-861-7076 *E-mail:* farberlit@aol.com, pg 629

Farden, William J, Outdoor Empire Publishing Inc, 424 N 130 St, Seattle, WA 98133 *Tel:* 206-624-3845 *Toll Free Tel:* 800-645-5489 *Fax:* 206-695-8512 *E-mail:* hjudeh@outdoorempire.com *Web Site:* www.outdoorempire.com, pg 200

Fargnoli, A Nicholas, James Joyce Society, 26 Varick Ct, Rockville Centre, NY 11570 *Tel:* 516-764-3119 *Fax:* 516-255-9094 *E-mail:* info@joycesociety.org *Web Site:* www.joycesociety.org, pg 689

Farkas, Stacey, The Career Press Inc, 3 Tice Rd, Franklin Lakes, NJ 07417 *Tel:* 201-848-0310 *Toll Free Tel:* 800-CAREER-1 (227-3371) *Fax:* 201-848-1727 *Web Site:* www.careerpress.com, pg 53

Farley, Dan, Harcourt Trade Publishers, 525 "B" St, Suite 1900, San Diego, CA 92101 *Tel:* 619-231-6616 *Toll Free Tel:* 800-543-1918 (cust serv) *Toll Free Fax:* 800-235-0256 (cust serv) *Web Site:* www.harcourtbooks.com, pg 115

Farley, Richard, Marshall Cavendish Corp, 99 White Plains Rd, Tarrytown, NY 10591-9001 *Tel:* 914-332-8888 *Fax:* 914-332-1888 *E-mail:* mcc@marshallcavendish.com *Web Site:* www.marshallcavendish.com, pg 164

Farlow, Martha, The University of Virginia Press, PO Box 400318, Charlottesville, VA 22904-4318 *Tel:* 434-924-3468 (cust serv); 434-924-3469 (cust serv) *Toll Free Tel:* 800-831-3406 (cust serv) *Fax:* 434-982-2655 *Toll Free Fax:* 877-288-6400 *E-mail:* upressvirginia@virginia.edu *Web Site:* www.upressvirginia.edu, pg 285

Farmer, Annette C, W D Farmer Residence Designer Inc, 2007 Montreal Rd, Tucker, GA 30084 *Tel:* 770-934-7380 *Toll Free Tel:* 800-225-7526; 800-221-7526 (GA) *Fax:* 770-934-1700 *E-mail:* wdfarmer@wdfarmerplans.com *Web Site:* www.wdfarmerplans.com; www.homeplansbyfarmer.com, pg 95

Farmer, Brent, Charlesbridge Publishing Inc, 85 Main St, Watertown, MA 02472 *Tel:* 617-926-0329 *Toll Free Tel:* 800-225-3214 *Fax:* 617-926-5720 *E-mail:* books@charlesbridge.com *Web Site:* www.charlesbridge.com, pg 58

Farmer, W D, W D Farmer Residence Designer Inc, 2007 Montreal Rd, Tucker, GA 30084 *Tel:* 770-934-7380 *Toll Free Tel:* 800-225-7526; 800-221-7526 (GA) *Fax:* 770-934-1700 *E-mail:* wdfarmer@wdfarmerplans.com *Web Site:* www.wdfarmerplans.com; www.homeplansbyfarmer.com, pg 95

Farnam, William D, American Society of Civil Engineers (ASCE), 1801 Alexander Bell Dr, Reston, VA 20191-4400 *Tel:* 703-295-6200 *Toll Free Tel:* 800-548-2723 *Fax:* 703-295-6278 *E-mail:* marketing@asce.org *Web Site:* www.asce.org, pg 18

Farnol, Jane, Astor Indexers, PO Box 950, Kent, CT 06757 *Tel:* 860-927-3654 *Toll Free Tel:* 800-848-2328 *Fax:* 860-927-3654, pg 590

Farnsworth, David, Casemate Publishers, 2114 Darby Rd, Havertown, PA 19083 *Tel:* 610-853-9131 *Fax:* 610-853-9146 *E-mail:* casemate@casematepublishing.com *Web Site:* www.casematepublishing.com, pg 54

Farr, Jeff, Old Barn Enterprises Inc, 600 Kelly Rd, Carthage, NC 28327 *Tel:* 910-947-2587 *Fax:* 910-947-5112, pg 196

Farr, Michael, JIST Publishing Inc, 8902 Otis Ave, Indianapolis, IN 46216 *Tel:* 317-613-4200 *Toll Free Tel:* 800-648-5478 *Fax:* 317-613-4304 *Toll Free Fax:* 800-547-8329 *E-mail:* info@jist.com *Web Site:* www.jist.com, pg 141

Farrell, Dan, Antique Collectors Club Ltd, 116 Pleasant St, East Hampton, MA 01027 *Tel:* 413-529-0861 *Toll Free Tel:* 800-252-5231 *Fax:* 413-297-0862 *E-mail:* info@antiquecc.com *Web Site:* www.antiquecc.com, pg 20

Farrell, Eleanor M, Mythopoeic Awards, PO Box 320486, San Francisco, CA 94132 *E-mail:* edith.crowe@sjsu.edu *Web Site:* www.mythsoc.org, pg 791

Farrell, Tanya, Picador, 175 Fifth Ave, New York, NY 10010 *Tel:* 212-674-5151 *Fax:* 212-253-9627 *E-mail:* firstname.lastname@picadorusa.com *Web Site:* www.picadorusa.com, pg 212

Farrell, Tracy, Harlequin Enterprises Ltd, 233 Broadway, Suite 1001, New York, NY 10279 *Tel:* 212-553-4200 *Fax:* 212-227-8969 *E-mail:* customer.ecare@harlequin.ca *Web Site:* www.eharlequin.com; www.luna-books.com; www.mirabooks.com; www.reddressink.com; www.steeplehill.com, pg 115

Farricker, Bill, Tom Doherty Associates, LLC, 175 Fifth Ave, 14th fl, New York, NY 10010 *Tel:* 212-388-0100 *Toll Free Tel:* 800-455-0340 *Fax:* 212-388-0191 *E-mail:* firstname.lastname@tor.com *Web Site:* www.tor.com, pg 82

Farricker, Bill, St Martin's Press LLC, 175 Fifth Ave, New York, NY 10010 *Tel:* 212-674-5151 *Fax:* 212-420-9314 *E-mail:* firstname.lastname@stmartins.com *Web Site:* www.stmartins.com, pg 238

Farrington, Debra, Morehouse Publishing Co, PO Box 1321, Harrisburg, PA 17105-1321 *Tel:* 717-541-8130 *Toll Free Tel:* 800-877-0012 (orders only) *Fax:* 717-541-8136; 717-541-8128 (orders only) *E-mail:* morehouse@morehousegroup.com *Web Site:* www.morehousegroup.com, pg 178

Farris, Mike, Farris Literary Agency Inc, PO Box 570069, Dallas, TX 75357-0069 *Tel:* 972-203-8804 *E-mail:* farris1@airmail.net; agent@farrisliterary.com *Web Site:* www.farrisliterary.com, pg 630

Farris, Susan Morgan, Farris Literary Agency Inc, PO Box 570069, Dallas, TX 75357-0069 *Tel:* 972-203-8804 *E-mail:* farris1@airmail.net; agent@farrisliterary.com *Web Site:* www.farrisliterary.com, pg 630

Farstrup, Alan E, International Reading Association, 800 Barksdale Rd, Newark, DE 19714 *Tel:* 302-731-1600 *Fax:* 302-731-1057 *Web Site:* www.reading.org, pg 689

Farver, Jane, MIT List Visual Arts Center, MIT E 15-109, 20 Ames St, Cambridge, MA 02139 *Tel:* 617-253-4680; 617-253-4400 (admission to exhibits) *Fax:* 617-258-7265 *E-mail:* hiroco@mit.edu *Web Site:* web.mit.edu/lvac, pg 175

Fass, Carol, Fass Speakers Bureau, 26 W 17 St, Suite 802, New York, NY 10011 *Tel:* 212-691-9707 *Fax:* 212-691-5012 *E-mail:* fsb@fasspr.com *Web Site:* www.fasspr.com, pg 669

Fassbender, Tom, UglyTown, 2148 1/2 W Sunset Blvd, Suite 204, Los Angeles, CA 90026-3148 *Tel:* 213-484-8334 *Fax:* 213-484-8333 *E-mail:* mayorsoffice@uglytown.com *Web Site:* www.uglytown.com, pg 278

Fastiggi, Ray, Rockefeller University Press, 1114 First Ave, New York, NY 10021 *Tel:* 212-327-8572 *Fax:* 212-327-7944 *E-mail:* rupcd@rockefeller.edu *Web Site:* www.rupress.org, pg 233

Fattibene, James, BNA Books, 1231 25 St NW, Washington, DC 20037 *Tel:* 202-452-4343 *Toll Free Tel:* 800-960-1220 *Fax:* 202-452-4997 (editorial off); 732-346-1624 (cust serv) *E-mail:* books@bna.com *Web Site:* www.bnabooks.com, pg 42

Fauci, Julia, Northern Illinois University Press, 310 N Fifth St, De Kalb, IL 60115 *Tel:* 815-753-1826; 815-753-1075 *Fax:* 815-753-1845 *E-mail:* bberg@niu.edu *Web Site:* www.niu.edu/univ_press, pg 193

Fauley, Tim, Orange Frazer Press Inc, 37 1/2 W Main St, Wilmington, OH 45177 *Tel:* 937-382-3196 *Toll Free Tel:* 800-852-9332 *Fax:* 937-383-3159 *E-mail:* ofrazer@erinet.com *Web Site:* www.orangefrazer.com, pg 198

Faulhaber, Diana, American Dietetic Association, 120 S Riverside Plaza, Suite 2000, Chicago, IL 60606 *Tel:* 312-899-0040 *Fax:* 312-899-4757 *Web Site:* www.eatright.org, pg 13

Faulkner, Cassandra J, Blue Book Publications Inc, 8009 34 Ave S, Suite 175, Minneapolis, MN 55425 *Tel:* 952-854-5229 *Toll Free Tel:* 800-877-4867 *Fax:* 952-853-1486 *E-mail:* bluebook@bluebookinc.com *Web Site:* www.bluebookinc.com, pg 570

Faulkner, Donald, New York State Writers Institute, University at Albany, New Library 320, Albany, NY 12222 *Tel:* 518-442-5620 *Fax:* 518-442-5621 *E-mail:* writers@uamail.albany.edu *Web Site:* www.albany.edu/writers-inst/, pg 745

Faurot, Barbara, Whitecap Books Ltd, 351 Lynn Ave, North Vancouver, BC V7J 2C4, Canada *Tel:* 604-980-9852 *Toll Free Tel:* 888-870-3442 ext 239 & 241 (cust serv) *Fax:* 604-980-8197 *Toll Free Fax:* 888-661-6630 (orders only) *E-mail:* whitecap@whitecap.ca *Web Site:* www.whitecap.ca, pg 567

Fausset, Katherine, Watkins Loomis Agency Inc, 133 E 35 St, Suite 1, New York, NY 10016 *Tel:* 212-532-0080 *Fax:* 212-889-0506, pg 660

Faust, David, Standard Publishing Co, 8121 Hamilton Ave, Cincinnati, OH 45231 *Tel:* 513-931-4050 *Toll Free Tel:* 800-543-1301 *Fax:* 513-931-0950 *Toll Free Fax:* 877-867-5751 *E-mail:* customerservice@standardpub.com *Web Site:* www.standardpub.com, pg 257

Faust, Jessica, BookEnds LLC, 136 Long Hill Rd, Gillette, NJ 07933 *Tel:* 908-604-2652 *E-mail:* editor@ bookends-inc.com *Web Site:* www.bookends-inc.com, pg 622

Favreau, Marc, The New Press, 38 Greene St, 4th fl, New York, NY 10013 *Tel:* 212-629-8802 *Toll Free Tel:* 800-233-4830 (orders) *Fax:* 212-629-8617 *Toll Free Fax:* 800-458-6515 *E-mail:* newpress@ thenewpress.com *Web Site:* www.thenewpress.com, pg 188

Fay, Bill, Scott Publishing Co, 911 Vandemark Rd, Sidney, OH 45365 *Tel:* 937-498-0802 *Toll Free Tel:* 800-572-6885 *Fax:* 937-498-0807 *E-mail:* ssm@ amospress.com *Web Site:* www.amosadvantage.com, pg 244

Feal, Rosemary, Modern Language Association of America (MLA), 26 Broadway, 3rd fl, New York, NY 10004-1789 *Tel:* 646-576-5000 *Fax:* 646-458-0030 *E-mail:* info@mla.org *Web Site:* www.mla.org, pg 176

Feal, Rosemary, Modern Language Association of America (MLA), 26 Broadway, 3rd fl, New York, NY 10004-1789 *Tel:* 646-576-5000 *Fax:* 646-458-0030 *E-mail:* convention@mla.org *Web Site:* www.mla.org, pg 691

Fearon, Merrill, The Federation of British Columbia Writers, PO Box 3887, Sta Terminal, Vancouver, BC V6B 2Z3, Canada *Tel:* 604-683-2057 *Fax:* 604-608-5522 *E-mail:* fedoffice@bcwriters.com *Web Site:* www.bcwriters.com, pg 687

Feazel, R Michael, Warren Communications News, 2115 Ward Ct NW, Washington, DC 20037-1209 *Tel:* 202-872-9200 *Fax:* 202-293-3435 *E-mail:* info@warren-news.com *Web Site:* www.warren-news.com, pg 293

Fecych, Ruth, Simon & Schuster, 1230 Avenue of the Americas, New York, NY 10020 *Tel:* 212-698-7000 *Toll Free Tel:* 800-223-2348 (cust serv); 800-223-2336 (orders) *Toll Free Fax:* 800-943-9831 (orders) *Web Site:* www.simonsays.com, pg 248

Fedor, John, American Diabetes Association, 1701 N Beauregard St, Alexandria, VA 22311 *Tel:* 703-299-2046 *Toll Free Tel:* 800-232-6733 *Fax:* 908-806-2301 *Web Site:* www.diabetes.org, pg 13

Fedorko, Lauren, Book Builders LLC, 425 Madison Ave, 19th fl, New York, NY 10017 *Tel:* 212-371-1110 *Fax:* 212-893-8680 *E-mail:* mail@bookbuildersllc.com *Web Site:* www.bookbuildersllc.com, pg 592

Fedorko, Paul, Trident Media Group LLC, 41 Madison Ave, 36th fl, New York, NY 10010 *Tel:* 212-262-4810 *Fax:* 212-725-4501 *Web Site:* www.tridentmediagroup.com, pg 659

Feffer, Emily, Random House International, 1745 Broadway, New York, NY 10019 *Tel:* 212-572-6106 *Fax:* 212-572-6045, pg 227

Feher, Michel, Zone Books, 1226 Prospect Ave, Brooklyn, NY 11218 *Tel:* 718-686-0048 *Toll Free Tel:* 800-405-1619 (orders & cust serv) *Fax:* 212-625-9772; 718-686-9045 *Toll Free Fax:* 800-406-9145 (orders) *E-mail:* urzone@zonebooks.org; mitpress-orders@mit.edu (orders), pg 307

Feher-Gurewich, Judith, Other Press LLC, 307 Seventh Ave, Suite 1807, New York, NY 10001 *Tel:* 212-414-0054 *Toll Free Tel:* 877-843-6843 *Fax:* 212-414-0939 *E-mail:* editor@otherpress.com; orders@otherpress.com *Web Site:* www.otherpress.com, pg 199

Feher-Gurewich, Judith, Other Press LLC, 307 Seventh Ave, Suite 1807, New York, NY 10001 *Tel:* 212-414-0054 *Toll Free Tel:* 877-THE-OTHER *Fax:* 212-414-0939 *E-mail:* orders@otherpress.com *Web Site:* www.otherpress.com, pg 573

Fehl, Donna, Standard Publishing Co, 8121 Hamilton Ave, Cincinnati, OH 45231 *Tel:* 513-931-4050 *Toll Free Tel:* 800-543-1301 *Fax:* 513-931-0950 *Toll Free Fax:* 877-867-5751 *E-mail:* customerservice@ standardpub.com *Web Site:* www.standardpub.com, pg 257

Fehr, Don, Smithsonian Institution Press, 750 Ninth St NW, Suite 4300, Washington, DC 20560-0950 *Tel:* 202-275-2300 *Fax:* 202-275-2274 *E-mail:* inquiries@sipress.si.edu *Web Site:* www.sipress.si.edu, pg 251

Fehring, Julie G, Stairway Publications, PO Box 518, Huntington, NY 11743-0518 *Tel:* 631-423-4050 *Fax:* 631-351-2142 *E-mail:* publisher@stairwaypub.com *Web Site:* www.stairwaypub.com, pg 257

Feiden, Karyn, Karyn L Feiden Editorial Services, 392 Central Park W, Suite 10-P, New York, NY 10025 *Tel:* 212-663-4942, pg 599

Feider, Sarah, W W Norton & Company Inc, 500 Fifth Ave, New York, NY 10110-0017 *Tel:* 212-354-5500 *Toll Free Tel:* 800-233-4830 (orders & cust serv) *Fax:* 212-869-0856 *Toll Free Fax:* 800-458-6515 *Web Site:* www.wwnorton.com, pg 193

Feigen, Brenda, Feigen/Parrent Literary Management, 10158 Hollow Glen Circle, Bel Air, CA 90077 *Tel:* 310-271-4722 *Fax:* 310-274-0503 *E-mail:* feigenparrentlit@aol.com, pg 630

Feigenbaum, Laurie, Feigenbaum Publishing Consultants Inc, 61 Bounty Lane, Jericho, NY 11753 *Tel:* 516-647-8314 *Fax:* 516-681-9121 *E-mail:* readrover5@aol.com, pg 630

Feik, William R, Feik Indexers, 1623 Third Ave, Suite 29-K, New York, NY 10128-3638 *Tel:* 212-369-3480 *Fax:* 212-410-0927 *E-mail:* indexer@earthlink.net, pg 599

Feinberg, David E, EMC/Paradigm Publishing, 875 Montreal Way, St Paul, MN 55102 *Tel:* 651-290-2800 (corp) *Toll Free Tel:* 800-328-1452 *Fax:* 651-290-2899 *Toll Free Fax:* 800-328-4564 *E-mail:* educate@emcp.com *Web Site:* www.emcp.com, pg 90

Feinberg, Joan E, Bedford/St Martin's, 75 Arlington St, Boston, MA 02116 *Tel:* 617-399-4000 *Fax:* 617-426-8582 *Web Site:* www.bedfordstmartins.com, pg 35

Feist, Betsy, Betsy Feist Resources, 140 E 81 St, New York, NY 10028-1875 *Tel:* 212-861-2014 *Fax:* 212-861-8304 *E-mail:* bfresources@rcn.com, pg 599

Feiwel, Jean, Scholastic Inc, 557 Broadway, New York, NY 10012 *Tel:* 212-343-4469 *Toll Free Tel:* 800-scholastic *Fax:* 212-343-6930 *Web Site:* www.scholastic.com, pg 242

Feiwel, Jean, Scholastic Trade Division, 557 Broadway, New York, NY 10012 *Tel:* 212-343-6100; 212-343-4685 (export sales) *Fax:* 212-343-4714 (export sales) *Web Site:* www.scholastic.com, pg 242

Felber, John E, International Intertrade Index, 636 Buchanan St, Hillside, NJ 07205 *Tel:* 908-686-2382 *Fax:* 908-686-2382, pg 137

Feldcamp, John, Xlibris Corp, 436 Walnut St, 11th fl, The Independence Bldg, Philadelphia, PA 19106 *Tel:* 215-923-4686 *Toll Free Tel:* 888-795-4274 *Fax:* 215-923-4685 *E-mail:* info@xlibris.com *Web Site:* www.xlibris.com, pg 305

Felder, David, Wellington Press, 9601-30 Miccosukee Rd, Tallahassee, FL 32309 *Tel:* 850-878-6500 *E-mail:* booksuprint@aol.com; wellpress@aol.com *Web Site:* www.booksuprint.com, pg 295

Feldheim, Yitzchak, Philipp Feldheim Inc, 200 Airport Executive Park, Nanuet, NY 10954 *Tel:* 845-356-2282 *Toll Free Tel:* 800-237-7149 *Fax:* 845-425-1908 *E-mail:* sales@feldheim.com *Web Site:* www.feldheim.com, pg 95

Feldman, Gwen, Silman-James Press, 3624 Shannon Rd, Los Angeles, CA 90027 *Tel:* 323-661-9922 *Toll Free Tel:* 877-SJP-BOOK (757-2665) *Fax:* 323-661-9933 *E-mail:* silmanjamespress@earthlink.net *Web Site:* www.silmanjamespress.com, pg 247

Feldman, Jennifer, BBC Audiobooks America, One Lafayette Rd, Hampton, NH 03842 *Tel:* 603-926-8744 *Toll Free Tel:* 800-621-0182 *Fax:* 603-929-3890 *E-mail:* info@bbcaudiobooksamerica.com, pg 34

Feldman, Lawrence, Time Warner Book Group, 1271 Avenue of the Americas, New York, NY 10020 *Tel:* 212-522-7200 *Fax:* 212-522-7991 *Web Site:* www.twbookmark.com, pg 271

Feldman, Leigh, Darhansoff, Verrill, Feldman Literary Agents, 236 W 26 St, Suite 802, New York, NY 10001-6736 *Tel:* 917-305-1300 *Fax:* 917-305-1400 *Web Site:* www.dvagency.com, pg 626

Feldman, Nancy, Penguin Group (USA) Inc Sales, 375 Hudson St, New York, NY 10014 *Tel:* 212-366-2000 *E-mail:* online@penguinputnam.com *Web Site:* www.penguin.com, pg 208

Feldstein, Martin PhD, National Bureau of Economic Research Inc, 1050 Massachusetts Ave, Cambridge, MA 02138-5398 *Tel:* 617-868-3900 *Fax:* 617-868-2742 *E-mail:* op@nber.org *Web Site:* www.nber.org, pg 182

Feldstein, Paul, Trafalgar Square, Howe Hill Rd, North Pomfret, VT 05053 *Tel:* 802-457-1911 *Toll Free Tel:* 800-423-4525 *Fax:* 802-457-1913 *E-mail:* tsquare@sover.net *Web Site:* www.trafalgarsquarebooks.com, pg 273

Felhofer, Jim, DBI Books, 700 E State St, Iola, WI 54990-0001 *Tel:* 715-445-2214 *Toll Free Tel:* 888-457-2873 *Fax:* 715-445-4087 *Web Site:* www.krause.com, pg 77

Fellmeth, Michael, Dramatists Play Service Inc, 440 Park Ave S, New York, NY 10016 *Tel:* 212-683-8960 *Fax:* 212-213-1539 *E-mail:* postmaster@dramatists.com *Web Site:* www.dramatists.com, pg 84

Felt, Robert L, Paradigm Publications, 202 Bendix Dr, Taos, NM 87571 *Tel:* 505-758-7758 *Toll Free Tel:* 800-873-3946 *Fax:* 505-758-7768 *Web Site:* www.paradigm-pubs.com; www.redwingbooks.com, pg 203

Fendley, Christina, Beekman Publishers Inc, 2626 Rte 212, Woodstock, NY 12498 *Tel:* 845-679-2300 *Toll Free Tel:* 888-BEEKMAN (orders) *Fax:* 845-679-2301 *E-mail:* beekman@beekmanpublishers.com *Web Site:* www.beekmanpublishers.com, pg 35

Fendrich, Steven, Shubert Fendrich Memorial Playwriting Contest, PO Box 4267, Englewood, CO 80155-4267 *Tel:* 303-779-4035 *Toll Free Tel:* 800-333-7262 *Fax:* 303-779-4315 *E-mail:* playwrights@ pioneerdrama.com *Web Site:* www.pioneerdrama.com, pg 773

Fenn, Bradley, Fenn Publishing Co Ltd, 34 Nixon Rd, Bolton, ON L7E 1W2, Canada *Tel:* 905-951-6600 *Toll Free Tel:* 800-267-3366 (Canada only) *Fax:* 905-951-6601 *Toll Free Fax:* 800-465-3422 (Canada Only) *E-mail:* sales@hbfenn.com *Web Site:* www.hbfenn.com, pg 546

Fenn, Harold B, Fenn Publishing Co Ltd, 34 Nixon Rd, Bolton, ON L7E 1W2, Canada *Tel:* 905-951-6600 *Toll Free Tel:* 800-267-3366 (Canada only) *Fax:* 905-951-6601 *Toll Free Fax:* 800-465-3422 (Canada Only) *E-mail:* sales@hbfenn.com *Web Site:* www.hbfenn.com, pg 546

Fenn, Jordan, Fenn Publishing Co Ltd, 34 Nixon Rd, Bolton, ON L7E 1W2, Canada *Tel:* 905-951-6600 *Toll Free Tel:* 800-267-3366 (Canada only) *Fax:* 905-951-6601 *Toll Free Fax:* 800-465-3422 (Canada Only) *E-mail:* sales@hbfenn.com *Web Site:* www.hbfenn.com, pg 546

Fenn, Michael, Fenn Publishing Co Ltd, 34 Nixon Rd, Bolton, ON L7E 1W2, Canada *Tel:* 905-951-6600 *Toll Free Tel:* 800-267-3366 (Canada only) *Fax:* 905-951-6601 *Toll Free Fax:* 800-465-3422 (Canada Only) *E-mail:* sales@hbfenn.com *Web Site:* www.hbfenn.com, pg 546

Fensch, Thomas, New Century Books, 213 Bay Club Dr, Santa Teresa, NM 88008 *Tel:* 505-589-1967 *Fax:* 505-589-1967 *E-mail:* newcentbks@elp.rr.com, pg 187

Fenton, Heike, Transnational Publishers Inc, 410 Saw Mill River Rd, Suite 2045, Ardsley, NY 10502 *Tel:* 914-693-5100 *Toll Free Tel:* 800-914-8186 (orders only) *Fax:* 914-693-4430 *E-mail:* info@transnationalpubs.com *Web Site:* www.transnationalpubs.com, pg 274

Fenton, Jayne, Home Planners LLC, 3275 W Ina Rd, Suite 220, Tucson, AZ 85741 *Tel:* 520-297-8200 *Toll Free Tel:* 800-322-6797 *Fax:* 520-297-6219 *Toll Free Fax:* 800-531-2555 *E-mail:* customerservice@eplans.com *Web Site:* www.eplans.com, pg 125

Fenton, Matt, Springer Publishing Co Inc, 11 W 42 St, New York, NY 10036 *Tel:* 212-431-4370 *Toll Free Tel:* 877-687-7476 *Fax:* 212-941-7842 *E-mail:* springer@springerpub.com *Web Site:* www. springerpub.com, pg 256

Fenton, Robert L, Robert L Fenton PC; Entertainment Attorney & Literary Agent, 31800 Northwestern Hwy, Suite 204, Farmington Hills, MI 48334 *Tel:* 248-855-8780 *Fax:* 248-855-3302 *E-mail:* fenent@msn.com *Web Site:* www.robertlfenton.com, pg 630

Fenza, D W, Association of Writers & Writing Programs (AWP), George Mason University, MS-1E3, Fairfax, VA 22030-4444 *Tel:* 703-993-4301 *Fax:* 703-993-4302 *E-mail:* awp@awpwriter.org *Web Site:* www.awpwriter. org, pg 680

Fenza, D W, AWP Award Series, George Mason University, MS-1E3, Fairfax, VA 22030-4444 *Tel:* 703-993-4301 *Fax:* 703-993-4302 *E-mail:* awp@awpwriter. org *Web Site:* www.awpwriter.org, pg 760

Feresten, Nancy Laties, National Geographic Books, 1145 17 St NW, Washington, DC 20036 *Tel:* 202-857-7000 *Fax:* 202-857-7670 *Web Site:* www. nationalgeographics.com, pg 183

Ferguson, Archie, Pantheon Books/Schocken Books, 1745 Broadway, New York, NY 10019 *Tel:* 212-751-2600 *Toll Free Tel:* 800-638-6460 *Fax:* 212-572-6030, pg 202

Ferguson, Jill, American Academy of Pediatrics, 141 NW Point Blvd, Elk Grove Village, IL 60007-1098 *Tel:* 847-434-4000 *Toll Free Tel:* 888-227-1770 *Fax:* 847-228-1281 *E-mail:* pubs@aap.org *Web Site:* www.aap.org, pg 11

Ferguson, Margaret, Farrar, Straus & Giroux Books for Young Readers, 19 Union Sq W, New York, NY 10003 *Tel:* 212-741-6900 *Fax:* 212-633-2427 *E-mail:* childrens.marketing@fsgbooks.com; childrens. editorial@fsgbooks.com *Web Site:* www.fsgkidsbooks. com, pg 95

Ferguson, Marnie, Fenn Publishing Co Ltd, 34 Nixon Rd, Bolton, ON L7E 1W2, Canada *Tel:* 905-951-6600 *Toll Free Tel:* 800-267-3366 (Canada only) *Fax:* 905-951-6601 *Toll Free Fax:* 800-465-3422 (Canada Only) *E-mail:* sales@hbfenn.com *Web Site:* www.hbfenn. com, pg 546

Ferlinghetti, Lawrence, City Lights Books Inc, 261 Columbus Ave, San Francisco, CA 94133 *Tel:* 415-362-8193 *Fax:* 415-362-4921 *E-mail:* staff@citylights. com *Web Site:* www.citylights.com, pg 62

Ferm, Betty, PMA Literary & Film Management Inc, PO Box 1817, Old Chelsea Sta, New York, NY 10011 *Tel:* 212-929-1222 *Fax:* 212-206-0238 *E-mail:* pmalitfilm@aol.com *Web Site:* www. pmalitfilm.com, pg 648

Fernald, Tom, Chronicle Books LLC, 85 Second St, 6th fl, San Francisco, CA 94105 *Tel:* 415-537-4200 *Toll Free Tel:* 800-722-6657 (cust serv) *Fax:* 415-537-4460 *Toll Free Fax:* 800-858-7787 (orders) *E-mail:* frontdesk@chroniclebooks.com *Web Site:* www.chroniclebooks.com, pg 61

Fernandes, Leonard M, Printlink Publishers Inc, 755 Main St, Monroe, CT 06468 *Tel:* 203-261-2977 *Fax:* 203-261-4331, pg 219

Fernandez, Esteban, Spanish Evangelical Publishers Association (SEPA)/Asociacion de Editores Evangelicos Hispanos, 1370 NW 88 Ave, Miami, FL 33172 *Tel:* 305-592-6136 *Fax:* 786-331-7720 *E-mail:* sepa@bmsi.com *Web Site:* www.sepalit.org, pg 701

Ferrara, Mary Ann, Orbis Books, Walsh Bldg, 75 Ryder Rd, Ossining, NY 10562 *Tel:* 914-941-7636 *Toll Free Tel:* 800-258-5838 (orders) *Fax:* 914-941-7005 (orders); 914-945-0670 (office) *E-mail:* orbisbooks@ maryknoll.org *Web Site:* www.orbisbooks.com, pg 198

Ferrara, Virginia, Grove/Atlantic Inc, 841 Broadway, 4th fl, New York, NY 10003-4793 *Tel:* 212-614-7850 *Toll Free Tel:* 800-521-0178 *Fax:* 212-614-7886 *Web Site:* www.groveatlantic.com, pg 110

Ferrari-Adler, Jofie, Nation Books, 245 W 17 St, 11th fl, New York, NY 10011-5300 *Tel:* 646-375-2570 *Fax:* 646-375-2571 *Web Site:* www.nationbooks.org, pg 182

Ferrari-Adler, Jofie, Thunder's Mouth Press, 245 W 17 St, 11th fl, New York, NY 10011-5300 *Tel:* 646-375-2570 *Fax:* 646-375-2571 *Web Site:* www. thundersmouth.com, pg 271

Ferraro, Clare, Penguin Group (USA) Inc, 375 Hudson St, New York, NY 10014 *Tel:* 212-366-2000 *Fax:* 212-366-2666 *E-mail:* online@uspenguingroup.com *Web Site:* www.penguin.com, pg 208

Ferraro, Clare, Plume, 375 Hudson St, New York, NY 10014 *Tel:* 212-366-2000 *Fax:* 212-366-2666 *E-mail:* online@penguinputnam.com *Web Site:* www. penguin.com, pg 215

Ferraro, Clare, Viking, 375 Hudson St, New York, NY 10014 *Tel:* 212-366-2000 *E-mail:* online@ penguinputnam.com *Web Site:* www.penguin.com, pg 290

Ferraro, Clare, Viking Penguin, 375 Hudson St, New York, NY 10014 *Tel:* 212-366-2000 *E-mail:* online@ penguinputnam.com *Web Site:* www.penguin.com, pg 290

Ferrell, Mickee, Haynes Manuals Inc, 861 Lawrence Dr, Newbury Park, CA 91320 *Tel:* 805-498-6703 *Toll Free Tel:* 800-442-9637 *Fax:* 805-498-2867 *E-mail:* info@ haynes.com *Web Site:* www.haynes.com, pg 118

Ferreyra, Gonzalo, The Crossing Press, PO Box 7123, Berkeley, CA 94707 *Tel:* 510-559-1600 *Toll Free Tel:* 800-841-2665 (orders & cust serv) *Fax:* 510-524-1052 *E-mail:* publicity@tenspeed.com *Web Site:* www. tenspeed.com, pg 73

Ferrier, Ian, QWF Prizes, 1200 Atwater Ave, Suite 3, Montreal, PQ H3Z 1X4, Canada *Tel:* 514-933-0878 *E-mail:* admin@qwf.org *Web Site:* www.qwf.org, pg 801

Ferro, Bob, Watson-Guptill Publications, 770 Broadway, New York, NY 10003 *Tel:* 646-654-5450 *Toll Free Tel:* 800-278-8477 (orders only) *Fax:* 646-654-5486; 646-654-5487 *E-mail:* info@watsonguptill.com *Web Site:* www.watsonguptill.com, pg 294

Ferron, Michel, Les Editions Un Monde Different, 3925 Grande Allee, St-Hubert, PQ J4T 2V8, Canada *Tel:* 450-656-2660 *Fax:* 450-445-9098 *Web Site:* www. umd.ca, pg 546

Ferry, Prof David, Boston University, 236 Bay State Rd, Boston, MA 02215 *Tel:* 617-353-2510 *Fax:* 617-353-3653 *Web Site:* www.bu.edu/writing/, pg 751

Fertig, Howard, Howard Fertig Inc, Publisher, 80 E 11 St, New York, NY 10003 *Tel:* 212-982-7922 *Fax:* 212-982-1099, pg 96

Fessio, Joseph, Ignatius Press, 2515 McAllister St, San Francisco, CA 94118 *Tel:* 415-387-2324 *Toll Free Tel:* 877-320-9276 (book orders) *Fax:* 415-387-0896 *E-mail:* info@ignatius.com *Web Site:* www.ignatius. com, pg 131

Fetterman, Bonny V, Words into Print, 200 W 86 St, Suite 14-1, New York, NY 10024 *Tel:* 212-877-3211 *Fax:* 212-873-3796 *E-mail:* sas22@ix.netcom.com *Web Site:* www.wordsintoprint.org, pg 614

Fetty, Karen, Simon & Schuster Inc, 1230 Avenue of the Americas, New York, NY 10020 *Tel:* 212-698-7000 *Fax:* 212-698-7007 *Web Site:* www.simonsays.com, pg 249

Feuer, Lisa, Random House Publishing Group, 1745 Broadway, New York, NY 10019 *Toll Free Tel:* 800-200-3552 *Toll Free Fax:* 800-200-3552 *Web Site:* www.randomhouse.com, pg 227

Feulner, Edwin J Jr, The Heritage Foundation, 214 Massachusetts Ave NE, Washington, DC 20002-4999 *Tel:* 202-546-4400 *Fax:* 202-546-8328 *Web Site:* www. heritage.org, pg 705

Ficarra, Elise, Poetry Center Book Award, 1600 Holloway Ave, San Francisco, CA 94132 *Tel:* 415-338-2227 *Fax:* 415-338-0966 *E-mail:* poetry@sfsu.edu *Web Site:* www.sfsu.edu/~poetry, pg 799

Fickeisen, Cheryl, Chronicle Guidance Publications Inc, 66 Aurora St, Moravia, NY 13118 *Tel:* 315-497-0330 *Toll Free Tel:* 800-622-7284 *Fax:* 315-497-3359 *E-mail:* customerservice@chronicleguidance.com *Web Site:* www.chronicleguidance.com, pg 62

Fickeisen, Christopher D, Chronicle Guidance Publications Inc, 66 Aurora St, Moravia, NY 13118 *Tel:* 315-497-0330 *Toll Free Tel:* 800-622-7284 *Fax:* 315-497-3359 *E-mail:* customerservice@ chronicleguidance.com *Web Site:* www. chronicleguidance.com, pg 62

Fickeisen, Gary W, Chronicle Guidance Publications Inc, 66 Aurora St, Moravia, NY 13118 *Tel:* 315-497-0330 *Toll Free Tel:* 800-622-7284 *Fax:* 315-497-3359 *E-mail:* customerservice@chronicleguidance.com *Web Site:* www.chronicleguidance.com, pg 62

Fickling, David, Random House Children's Books, 1745 Broadway, New York, NY 10019 *Tel:* 212-782-9000 *Toll Free Tel:* 800-200-3552 *Fax:* 212-782-9452 *Web Site:* www.randomhouse.com/kids, pg 225

Fidler, Patricia, Yale University Press, 302 Temple St, New Haven, CT 06511 *Tel:* 203-432-0960; 401-531-2800 (cust serv) *Toll Free Tel:* 800-405-1619 (cust serv) *Fax:* 203-432-0948; 401-531-2801 (cust serv) *Toll Free Fax:* 800-406-9145 (cust serv) *E-mail:* customer.care@trilateral.org (cust serv) *Web Site:* www.yale.edu/yup/, pg 305

Field, Kim, Microsoft Press, One Microsoft Way, Redmond, WA 98052-6399 *Tel:* 425-882-8080 *Toll Free Tel:* 800-677-7377 *Fax:* 425-936-7329 *Web Site:* www.microsoft.com/presspass/exec/default. asp#qt, pg 173

Field, Nancy, Dog-Eared Publications, PO Box 620863, Middleton, WI 53562-0863 *Tel:* 608-831-1410 *Toll Free Tel:* 888-364-3277 *Fax:* 608-831-1410 *Toll Free Fax:* 888-364-3277 *Web Site:* www.dog-eared.com, pg 81

Field, Ty, Wadsworth Publishing, 10 Davis Dr, Belmont, CA 94002-3002 *Toll Free Tel:* 800-357-0092 *Fax:* 650-592-3342 *Toll Free Fax:* 800-522-4923 *Web Site:* www.wadsworth.com, pg 292

Fielder, John, Westcliffe Publishers Inc, 2650 S Zuni St, Englewood, CO 80110-1145 *Tel:* 303-935-0900 *Toll Free Tel:* 800-523-3692 *Fax:* 303-935-0903 *E-mail:* sales@westcliffepublishers.com *Web Site:* www.westcliffepublishers.com, pg 296

Fields, LeAnn, University of Michigan Press, 839 Greene St, Ann Arbor, MI 48104-3209 *Tel:* 734-764-4388 *Fax:* 734-615-1540 *E-mail:* um.press@umich.edu *Web Site:* www.press.umich.edu, pg 282

Fields, Michelle R, Harriet Wasserman Literary Agency Inc, 137 E 36 St, New York, NY 10016 *Tel:* 212-689-3257 *Fax:* 212-689-3257 *E-mail:* hawlainc@aol.com, pg 660

Fife, Bruce, Piccadilly Books Ltd, PO Box 25203, Colorado Springs, CO 80936-5203 *Tel:* 719-550-9887 *E-mail:* orders@piccadillybooks.com *Web Site:* www. piccadillybooks.com, pg 212

Figman, Elliot, Poets & Writers Inc, 72 Spring St, Suite 301, New York, NY 10012 *Tel:* 212-226-3586 *Fax:* 212-226-3963 *Web Site:* www.pw.org, pg 697

Figueroa, Miguel A, Neal-Schuman Publishers Inc, 100 William St, Suite 2004, New York, NY 10038 *Tel:* 212-925-8650 *Toll Free Tel:* 866-672-6657 *Toll Free Fax:* 866-209-7932 *E-mail:* orders@neal-schuman.com *Web Site:* www.neal-schuman.com, pg 186

Figurski, Daniel, Sunburst Technology, 400 Columbus Ave, Suite 160E, Valhalla, NY 10595 *Tel:* 914-747-3310 *Toll Free Tel:* 800-338-3457 *Fax:* 914-747-4109 *Web Site:* www.sunburst.com, pg 262

Files, Jeff, J Weston Walch Publisher, 321 Valley St, Portland, ME 04104 *Tel:* 207-772-2846 *Toll Free Tel:* 800-341-6094 *Fax:* 207-772-3105 *Toll Free Fax:* 888-991-5755 *E-mail:* customerservice@mail. walch.com *Web Site:* www.walch.com, pg 292

Files, Meg, Pima Writers' Workshop, Pima College West Campus, 2202 W Anklam Rd, Tucson, AZ 85709-0170 *Tel:* 520-206-6084 *Fax:* 520-206-6020, pg 746

Filippini, Michelle, University of Nevada Press, MS 166, Reno, NV 89557-0076 *Tel:* 775-784-6573 *Toll Free Tel:* 800-682-6657 *Fax:* 775-784-6200 *Toll Free Fax:* 877-682-6657 *Web Site:* www.nvbooks.nevada. edu, pg 283

Filling, Gregory, Pippin Press, 229 E 85 St, New York, NY 10028 *Tel:* 212-288-4920 *Fax:* 908-237-2407, pg 213

Fillingham, Ashley, Aspen Publishers, A Wolters Kluwer Company, 1185 Avenue of the Americas, New York, NY 10036 *Tel:* 212-597-0200 *Toll Free Tel:* 800-234-1660 (cust serv); 800-447-1717 (orders); 800-950-5259 (legal educ); 800-LAW-PLGL (paralegal textbook); 800-317-3113 (bookstore sales); 800-364-2512 (Loislaw) *Web Site:* www.aspenpublishers.com, pg 26

Fillion, Luke, Daisy Books, 991 King St W, Hamilton, ON L8S 4R5, Canada *Tel:* 905-526-0451 *Fax:* 905-526-0451 *E-mail:* admin@daisybooks.com *Web Site:* www.daisybooks.com, pg 542

Fillion, Sheilagh, Harcourt Canada Ltd, 55 Horner Ave, Toronto, ON M8Z 4X6, Canada *Tel:* 416-255-4491; 416-255-0177 (Voice Mail) *Toll Free Tel:* 800-387-7278 (North America); 800-387-7305 (North America) *Fax:* 416-255-6708 *Toll Free Fax:* 800-665-7307 (North America) *E-mail:* firstname_lastname@ harcourt.com *Web Site:* www.harcourtcanada.com, pg 549

Filucci, Sierra, University of California Press, 2120 Berkeley Way, Berkeley, CA 94720 *Tel:* 510-642-4247 *Toll Free Tel:* 800-777-4726 *Fax:* 510-643-7127 *Toll Free Fax:* 800-999-1958 *E-mail:* askucp@ucpress.edu *Web Site:* www.ucpress.edu, pg 281

Filyer, Lorraine, Ruth Schwartz Children's Book Award, c/o Ontario Arts Council Literature Office, 151 Bloor St W, 5th fl, Toronto, ON M5S 1T6, Canada *Tel:* 416-961-1660 (ext 7438) *Toll Free Tel:* 800-387-0058 (Canada) *Fax:* 416-961-7796 *E-mail:* info@arts.on.ca *Web Site:* www.arts.on.ca, pg 805

Finch, David, Rocky Mountain Books Ltd, 406-13 Ave NE, Calgary, AB T2E 1C2, Canada *Tel:* 403-249-9490 *Fax:* 403-249-2968 *Web Site:* www.rmbooks.com, pg 560

Fincher, Donna, AKTRIN Furniture Information Centre, 164 S Main St, Suite 307, High Point, NC 27260 *Tel:* 336-841-8535 *Fax:* 336-841-5435 *E-mail:* aktrin@aktrin.com (Canada); aktrinusa@ northstate.net (US) *Web Site:* www.aktrin.com, pg 7

Fine, Anton, Fine Communications, 322 Eighth Ave, 15th fl, New York, NY 10001 *Tel:* 212-595-3500 *Fax:* 212-595-3779, pg 96

Fine, Barry, Bridge Publications Inc, 4751 Fountain Ave, Los Angeles, CA 90029 *Tel:* 323-953-3320 *Toll Free Tel:* 800-722-1733; 800-843-7389 (CA) *Fax:* 323-953-3328 *E-mail:* info@bridgepub.com *Web Site:* www. bridgepub.com, pg 47

Fine, Cheryl, Management Concepts Inc, 8230 Leesburg Pike, Suite 800, Vienna, VA 22182 *Tel:* 703-790-9595 *Fax:* 703-790-1930 *E-mail:* publications@ managementconcepts.com *Web Site:* www. managementconcepts.com, pg 162

Fine, Debbie, Southeast Literary Agency, PO Box 910, Sharpes, FL 32959-0910 *Tel:* 321-632-5019, pg 656

Fine, Kaethe, Fine Communications, 322 Eighth Ave, 15th fl, New York, NY 10001 *Tel:* 212-595-3500 *Fax:* 212-595-3779, pg 96

Fine, Michael J, Fine Communications, 322 Eighth Ave, 15th fl, New York, NY 10001 *Tel:* 212-595-3500 *Fax:* 212-595-3779, pg 96

Finegan, Patrick G Jr, Palindrome Press, PO Box 65991, Washington, DC 20036-5991 *Tel:* 703-242-1734 *Fax:* 703-242-1734 *E-mail:* freedom@ palindromepress.com *Web Site:* www.palindromepress. com, pg 202

Fingerhut, Benjamin, St Augustine's Press Inc, PO Box 2285, South Bend, IN 46680-2285 *Tel:* 773-702-7248 *Toll Free Tel:* 888-997-4994 *Fax:* 773-702-9756 *Web Site:* www.staugustine.net, pg 238

Fingerhut, Bruce, St Augustine's Press Inc, PO Box 2285, South Bend, IN 46680-2285 *Tel:* 773-702-7248 *Toll Free Tel:* 888-997-4994 *Fax:* 773-702-9756 *Web Site:* www.staugustine.net, pg 238

Fink, Debra, Professional Resource Exchange Inc, 1891 Apex Rd, Sarasota, FL 34240 *Tel:* 941-343-9601 *Toll Free Tel:* 800-443-3364 *Fax:* 941-343-9201 *Web Site:* www.prpress.com, pg 220

Fink, Robin, Penguin Group (USA) Inc Sales, 375 Hudson St, New York, NY 10014 *Tel:* 212-366-2000 *E-mail:* online@penguinputnam.com *Web Site:* www. penguin.com, pg 208

Fink, Tom, IEEE Computer Society, 10662 Los Vaqueros Circle, Los Alamitos, CA 90720-1314 *Tel:* 714-821-8380 *Toll Free Tel:* 800-272-6657 *Fax:* 714-821-4010 *E-mail:* csbooks@computer.org *Web Site:* www. computer.org, pg 130

Finkelstein, Jesse, Polestar Book Publishers, 9050 Shaughnessy St, Vancouver, BC V6P 6E5, Canada *Tel:* 604-323-7100 *Toll Free Tel:* 800-663-5714 *Fax:* 604-323-2600 *Toll Free Fax:* 800-565-3770 *E-mail:* info@raincoast.com *Web Site:* www.raincoast. com, pg 558

Finkelstein, Jesse, Raincoast Publishing, 9050 Shaughnessy St, Vancouver, BC V6P 6E5, Canada *Tel:* 604-323-7100 *Toll Free Tel:* 800-663-5714 (Canada only) *Fax:* 604-323-2600 *Toll Free Fax:* 800-565-3700 *E-mail:* info@raincoast.com *Web Site:* www. raincoast.com, pg 559

Finley, Doug, CCH Canadian Limited, A Wolters Kluwer Company, 90 Sheppard Ave E, Suite 300, Toronto, ON M2N 6X1, Canada *Tel:* 416-224-2224 *Toll Free Tel:* 800-268-4522 (Canada & US cust serv) *Fax:* 416-224-2243 *Toll Free Fax:* 800-461-4131 *E-mail:* cservice@cch.ca (cust serv) *Web Site:* www. cch.ca, pg 539

Finman, Stephanie, The Martell Agency, 545 Madison Ave, 7th fl, New York, NY 10022 *Tel:* 212-317-2672 *Fax:* 212-317-2676, pg 642

Finn, James B, James B Finn Literary Agency Inc, PO Box 28227A, St Louis, MO 63132 *Tel:* 314-997-7133, pg 630

Finn, Magee, Random House Publishing Group, 1745 Broadway, New York, NY 10019 *Toll Free Tel:* 800-200-3552 *Toll Free Fax:* 800-200-3552 *Web Site:* www.randomhouse.com, pg 227

Firestein, Natalie, M Evans & Co Inc, 216 E 49 St, New York, NY 10017 *Tel:* 212-688-2810 *Fax:* 212-486-4544 *E-mail:* editorial@mevans.com *Web Site:* www. mevans.com, pg 93

Firing, Rob, HarperCollins Publishers Canada, 2 Bloor St E, 20th fl, Toronto, ON M4W 1A8, Canada *Tel:* 416-975-9334 *Fax:* 416-975-9884 (publishing); 416-975-5223 (sales) *E-mail:* hccanada@harpercollins. com *Web Site:* www.harpercanada.com, pg 549

Firstenberg, Jean Picker, American Film Institute (AFI), 2021 N Western Ave, Los Angeles, CA 90027 *Tel:* 323-856-7600 *Toll Free Tel:* 800-774-4234 (memberships) *Fax:* 323-467-4578 *E-mail:* info@afi. com *Web Site:* www.afi.com, pg 676

Fischbach, Christopher, Coffee House Press, 27 N Fourth St, Suite 400, Minneapolis, MN 55401 *Tel:* 612-338-0125 *Fax:* 612-338-4004 *Web Site:* www. coffeehousepress.org, pg 64

Fischer, Amy-Lynn, University of California Press, 2120 Berkeley Way, Berkeley, CA 94720 *Tel:* 510-642-4247 *Toll Free Tel:* 800-777-4726 *Fax:* 510-643-7127 *Toll Free Fax:* 800-999-1958 *E-mail:* askucp@ucpress.edu *Web Site:* www.ucpress.edu, pg 281

Fischer, Dena, The Amy Rennert Agency Inc, 98 Main St, Suite 302, Tiburon, CA 94920 *Tel:* 415-789-8955 *Fax:* 415-789-8944 *E-mail:* arennert@pacbell.net, pg 651

Fischer, Grada, The Fischer Ross Group Inc, 249 E 48 St, 15th fl, New York, NY 10017 *Tel:* 212-355-5777 *Fax:* 212-355-7820 *E-mail:* frgstaff@earthlink.net, pg 669

Fischer, Kathleen, Abrams & Co Publishers Inc, 61 Mattatuck Heights Rd, Waterbury, CT 06705 *Tel:* 203-756-6562 *Toll Free Tel:* 800-227-9120 *Fax:* 203-756-2895 *Toll Free Fax:* 800-737-3322, pg 3

Fischer, Kathleen, Graphic Learning, 61 Mattatuck Heights Rd, Waterbury, CT 06705 *Tel:* 203-756-6562 *Toll Free Tel:* 800-874-0029; 800-227-9120 *Fax:* 203-756-2895 *Toll Free Fax:* 800-737-3322, pg 108

Fischer, Kathleen, The Letter People®, 61 Mattatuck Heights Rd, Waterbury, CT 06705 *Tel:* 203-756-6562 *Toll Free Tel:* 800-227-9120; 800-874-0029 *Fax:* 203-756-2895 *Toll Free Fax:* 800-737-3322 *Web Site:* letterpeople.com, pg 153

Fischer, Lee, Golden West Publishers, 4113 N Longview, Phoenix, AZ 85014 *Tel:* 602-265-4392 *Toll Free Tel:* 800-658-5830 *Fax:* 602-279-6901 *Web Site:* www. goldenwestpublishers.com, pg 106

Fischer, Steve, ThorsonsElement US, 535 Albany St, 5th fl, Boston, MA 02118 *Tel:* 617-451-1533 *Fax:* 617-451-0971 *Web Site:* www.thorsons.com, pg 270

Fisher, Agnes, Simon & Schuster Inc, 1230 Avenue of the Americas, New York, NY 10020 *Tel:* 212-698-7000 *Fax:* 212-698-7007 *Web Site:* www.simonsays. com, pg 249

Fisher, Allan, P & R Publishing Co, 1102 Marble Hill Rd, Phillipsburg, NJ 08865 *Tel:* 908-454-0505 *Toll Free Tel:* 800-631-0094 *Fax:* 908-859-2390 *E-mail:* per@prpbooks.com *Web Site:* prpbooks.com, pg 201

Fisher, Anthony G, Brown Publishing Network Inc, 95 Sawyer Rd, Waltham, MA 02453 *Tel:* 781-237-7567 *Fax:* 781-237-8874 *Web Site:* www.brownpubnet.com, pg 593

Fisher, Brad, The Charles Press, Publishers, 117 S 17 St, Suite 310, Philadelphia, PA 19103 *Tel:* 215-496-9616; 215-496-9625 *Fax:* 215-496-9637 *E-mail:* mailbox@ charlespresspub.com *Web Site:* www.charlespresspub. com, pg 58

Fisher, George, Random House Sales & Marketing, 1745 Broadway, New York, NY 10019 *Fax:* 212-782-9000, pg 227

Fisher, John, Templegate Publishers, 302 E Adams St, Springfield, IL 62701 *Tel:* 217-522-3353 (edit & sales); 217-522-3354 (billing) *Toll Free Tel:* 800-367-4844 (orders only) *Fax:* 217-522-3362 *E-mail:* wisdom@templegate.com; orders@templegate. com (sales) *Web Site:* www.templegate.com, pg 266

Fisher, Maurice D, Gifted Education Press, 10201 Yuma Ct, Manassas, VA 20109 *Tel:* 703-369-5017 *Web Site:* www.giftededpress.com; www.giftedpress. com, pg 104

Fisher, Michael G, Harvard University Press, 79 Garden St, Cambridge, MA 02138-1499 *Tel:* 617-495-2600; 401-531-2800 (international orders) *Toll Free Tel:* 800-405-1619 (orders) *Fax:* 617-495-5898 (general); 617-496-4677 (edit & rts); 401-531-2801 (international orders) *Toll Free Fax:* 800-406-9145 (orders) *E-mail:* firstname_lastname@harvard.edu *Web Site:* www.hup.harvard.edu, pg 117

Fisher, Ryan, The Charles Bernheimer Prize, University of Texas, Program in Comparative Literature, One University Sta B5003, Austin, TX 78712-0196 *Tel:* 512-471-8020 *E-mail:* info@acla.org *Web Site:* www.acla.org, pg 766

Fisher, Tracy, William Morris Agency, 1325 Avenue of the Americas, New York, NY 10019 *Tel:* 212-586-5100 *Fax:* 212-903-1418 *E-mail:* wma@interport.net *Web Site:* www.wma.com, pg 645

Fishman, Aleisa, United States Holocaust Memorial Museum, 100 Raoul Wallenberg Place SW, Washington, DC 20024-2126 *Tel:* 202-488-6115; 202-488-6144 (orders) *Toll Free Tel:* 800-259-9998 (orders) *Fax:* 202-488-2684; 202-488-0438 (orders) *Web Site:* www.ushmm.org/, pg 279

Fisk, Raymond G, Down The Shore Publishing Corp, 638 Teal St, Cedar Run, NJ 08092 *Tel:* 609-978-1233 *Fax:* 609-597-0422 *E-mail:* shore@att.net *Web Site:* www.down-the-shore.com, pg 83

Fiske, Robert Hartwell, Vocabula Communications Co, 10 Grant Place, Lexington, MA 02420 Tel: 781-861-1515 E-mail: info@vocabula.com Web Site: www. vocabula.com, pg 613

Fisketjon, Gary, Alfred A Knopf, 1745 Broadway, New York, NY 10019 Tel: 212-751-2600 Toll Free Tel: 800-638-6460 Fax: 212-572-2593 Web Site: www. randomhouse.com/knopf, pg 146

Fitterling, Michael Alan, Lost Classics Book Co, PO Box 3429, Lake Wales, FL 33859-3429 Tel: 863-676-1920 Toll Free Tel: 800-283-3572 (wholesale orders); 888-211-2665 (educational) Fax: 863-676-1707 E-mail: mgeditor@lostclassicsbooks.com Web Site: www.lostclassicsbooks.com (retail site); www.lcbcbooks.com (wholesale site), pg 159

Fitzgerald, Brenda, The University of Virginia Press, PO Box 400318, Charlottesville, VA 22904-4318 Tel: 434-924-3468 (cust serv); 434-924-3469 (cust serv) Toll Free Tel: 800-831-3406 (cust serv) Fax: 434-982-2655 Toll Free Fax: 877-288-6400 E-mail: upressvirginia@virginia.edu Web Site: www.upressvirginia.edu, pg 285

Fitzgerald, Gary, Rutgers University Press, 100 Joyce Kilmer Ave, Piscataway, NJ 08854-8099 Tel: 732-445-7762 (edit); 732-445-7762 (ext 627, sales) Toll Free Tel: 800-446-9323 (orders only) Fax: 732-445-7039 (acqs, edit, mktg, perms, prodn); 732-445-1974 (fulfillment) E-mail: garyf@rci.rutgers.edu Web Site: rutgerspress.rutgers.edu, pg 236

Fitzgerald, Kevin, Rough Guides, 345 Hudson St, New York, NY 10014 Tel: 212-414-3635 Fax: 212-414-3352 E-mail: mail@roughguides.com Web Site: www. roughguides.com, pg 235

Fitzgerald, Susan Kelly, Kinship Books, 781 Rte 308, Rhinebeck, NY 12572 Tel: 845-876-4200 (orders); 845-876-4592 Toll Free Tel: 800-249-1109 (orders) E-mail: kinshipbooks@cs.com Web Site: www. kinshipny.com, pg 145

Fitzhenry, Sharon, Fitzhenry & Whiteside Limited, 195 Allstate Pkwy, Markham, ON L3R 4T8, Canada Tel: 905-477-9700 Toll Free Tel: 800-387-9776 Fax: 905-477-9179 Toll Free Tel: 800-260-9777 E-mail: godwit@fitzhenry.ca Web Site: www.fitzhenry. ca, pg 547

Fitzpatrick, Kathryn, Cold Spring Harbor Laboratory Press, 500 Sunnyside Blvd, Woodbury, NY 11797-2924 Tel: 516-422-4100 Toll Free Tel: 800-843-4388 Fax: 516-422-4097 E-mail: cshpress@cshl.edu Web Site: www.cshlpress.com, pg 64

Fitzpatrick, Lee, Manning Publications Co, 209 Bruce Park Ave, Greenwich, CT 06830 Tel: 203-629-2211 Fax: 203-661-9018 E-mail: orders@manning.com Web Site: www.manning.com, pg 162

Fitzpatrick, Lisa, Mandala Publishing, 17 Paul Dr, San Rafael, CA 94903 Tel: 415-883-4055 Toll Free Tel: 800-688-2218 (orders only) Fax: 415-884-0500 E-mail: mandala@mandala.org Web Site: www. mandala.org, pg 162

Fix, Jefferey J, Educational Communications Inc, 1701 Directors Blvd, Suite 920, Austin, TX 78744 Tel: 512-440-2705 Fax: 512-447-1687 Web Site: www. honoring.com, pg 87

Fjestad, S P, Blue Book Publications Inc, 8009 34 Ave S, Suite 175, Minneapolis, MN 55425 Tel: 952-854-5229 Toll Free Tel: 800-877-4867 Fax: 952-853-1486 E-mail: bluebook@bluebookinc.com Web Site: www. bluebookinc.com, pg 570

Flach, Andrew, Hatherleigh Press, 5-22 46 Ave, Suite 200, Long Island City, NY 11101 Tel: 718-786-5338 Toll Free Tel: 800-528-2550 Fax: 718-706-6087 E-mail: info@hatherleigh.com Web Site: www. getfitnow.com; www.hatherleighpress.com, pg 118

Flach, Frederic, Hatherleigh Press, 5-22 46 Ave, Suite 200, Long Island City, NY 11101 Tel: 718-786-5338 Toll Free Tel: 800-528-2550 Fax: 718-706-6087 E-mail: info@hatherleigh.com Web Site: www. getfitnow.com; www.hatherleighpress.com, pg 118

Flaherty, Nora, St Martin's Press LLC, 175 Fifth Ave, New York, NY 10010 Tel: 212-674-5151 Fax: 212-420-9314 E-mail: firstname.lastname@stmartins.com Web Site: www.stmartins.com, pg 238

Flaherty, Regis J, Emmaus Road Publishing Inc, 827 N Fourth St, Steubenville, OH 43952 Tel: 740-283-2484 Toll Free Tel: 800-398-5470 Fax: 740-283-4011 Web Site: www.emmausroad.org, pg 90

Flamand, Jacques, Les Editions du Vermillon, 305 rue Saint-Patrick, Ottawa, ON K1N 5K4, Canada Tel: 613-241-4032 Fax: 613-241-3109 E-mail: leseditionsduvermillon@rogers.com Web Site: www.primatech.ca/vermillon/index.html; vermillon.info.ca, pg 545

Flamini, Michael, St Martin's Press Trade Division, 175 Fifth Ave, New York, NY 10010 E-mail: firstname. lastname@stmartins.com Web Site: www.stmartins. com; www.minotaurbooks.com, pg 239

Flanagan, James B, HCPro, 200 Hoods Lane, Marblehead, MA 01945 Tel: 781-639-1872 Toll Free Tel: 800-650-6787 Fax: 781-639-2982 Toll Free Fax: 800-639-8511 E-mail: customer_service@hcpro. com Web Site: www.hcpro.com, pg 119

Flanagan, John F, Goodheart-Willcox Publisher, 18604 W Creek Dr, Tinley Park, IL 60477-6243 Tel: 708-687-5000 Toll Free Tel: 800-323-0440 Fax: 708-687-0315 Toll Free Fax: 888-409-3900 E-mail: custserv@ g-w.com Web Site: www.g-w.com, pg 107

Flanagan, Martin, Williamson Books, 535 Metroplex Dr, Suite 250, Nashville, TN 37211 Tel: 802-425-2713 (edit) Toll Free Tel: 800-586-2572 (sales & orders) Fax: 802-425-2714 (edit) Web Site: www. williamsonbooks.com, pg 300

Flanagan, Marty, Ideals Publications Inc, 535 Metroplex Dr, Suite 250, Nashville, TN 37211 Tel: 615-781-1427 Toll Free Tel: 800-558-4343 (customer service) Fax: 615-781-1447 Web Site: www.idealsbooks.com, pg 130

Flanders, Margaret, Judy Lopez Memorial Award For Children's Literature, PO Box 7034, Beverly Hills, CA 90212-0034 Tel: 310-474-9917 Fax: 310-474-6436, pg 786

Flanders, Margaret, Women's National Book Association/ Los Angeles Chapter, PO Box 7034, Beverly Hills, CA 90212-0034 Tel: 310-474-9917 Fax: 310-474-6436, pg 749

Flannery, Francis, Rights Unlimited Inc, 101 W 55 St, Suite 2D, New York, NY 10019 Tel: 212-246-0900 Fax: 212-246-2114 E-mail: faith@rightsunlimited.com Web Site: rightsunlimited.com, pg 651

Flannery, Jennifer, Flannery Literary, 1155 S Washington St, Suite 202, Naperville, IL 60540 Tel: 630-428-2682 Fax: 630-428-2683, pg 630

Flashman, Melissa, Trident Media Group LLC, 41 Madison Ave, 36th fl, New York, NY 10010 Tel: 212-262-4810 Fax: 212-725-4501 Web Site: www. tridentmediagroup.com, pg 659

Flaws, Robert, Blue Poppy Press, 5441 Western Ave, No 2, Boulder, CO 80301 Tel: 303-447-8372 Toll Free Tel: 800-487-9296 Fax: 303-245-8362 E-mail: info@ bluepoppy.com Web Site: www.bluepoppy.com, pg 42

Flax, Margery, Edgar Allan Poe Awards®, 17 E 47 St, 6th fl, New York, NY 10017 Tel: 212-888-8171 E-mail: mwa@mysterywriters.org Web Site: www. mysterywriters.org, pg 771

Flax, Margery, Robert L Fish Memorial Award, 17 E 47 St, 6th fl, New York, NY 10017 Tel: 212-888-8171 E-mail: mwa@mysterywriters.org Web Site: www. mysterywriters.org, pg 774

Flax, Margery, Mystery Writers of America, 17 E 47 St, 6th fl, New York, NY 10017 Tel: 212-888-8171 E-mail: mwa@mysterywriters.org Web Site: www. mysterywriters.org, pg 691, 753

Flaxman, Jill, Crown Publishing Group, 1745 Broadway, New York, NY 10019 Tel: 212-782-9000 Toll Free Tel: 888-264-1745 Fax: 212-940-7408 Web Site: www. randomhouse.com/crown, pg 74

Fleck, Robert D, Oak Knoll Press, 310 Delaware St, New Castle, DE 19720 Tel: 302-328-7232 Toll Free Tel: 800-996-2556 Fax: 302-328-7274 E-mail: oakknoll@oakknoll.com Web Site: www. oakknoll.com, pg 194

Fleenor, Harry M Jr, The Literary Agency Ltd, 4942 Morrison Rd, Denver, CO 80219 Tel: 303-936-1978 Toll Free Tel: 800-261-1797 Fax: 303-936-1770 E-mail: peci4942@aol.com Web Site: www.peci.cc, pg 640

Fleet, Jani, Signature Books Publishing LLC, 564 W 400 N, Salt Lake City, UT 84116-3411 Tel: 801-531-1483 Toll Free Tel: 800-356-5687 (orders) Fax: 801-531-1488 E-mail: people@signaturebooks.com Web Site: www.signaturebooks.com, pg 247

Fleet, Jennifer, BioTechniques Books, One Research Dr, Suite 400 A, Westborough, MA 01581 Tel: 508-614-1414 Fax: 508-616-2930 Web Site: www. biotechniques.com, pg 39

Fleischer, Chip, Steerforth Press, 25 Lebanon St, Hanover, NH 03755 Tel: 603-643-4787 Fax: 603-643-4788 E-mail: info@steerforth.com Web Site: www. steerforth.com, pg 258

Fleischner, Michael, Thomson Peterson's, 2000 Lenox Dr, Lawrenceville, NJ 08648 Tel: 609-896-1800 Toll Free Tel: 800-338-3282 Toll Free Fax: 800-772-2465 E-mail: sales@petersons.com Web Site: www. petersons.com, pg 270

Fleishman, Ernest B, Scholastic Inc, 557 Broadway, New York, NY 10012 Tel: 212-343-4469 Toll Free Tel: 800-scholastic Fax: 212-343-6930 Web Site: www.scholastic.com, pg 242

Fleishman, Samuel, Literary Artists Representatives, 575 West End Ave, Suite GRC, New York, NY 10024-2711 Tel: 212-787-3808 Fax: 212-595-2098 E-mail: litartists@aol.com, pg 641

Fleming, Adrian, Stackpole Books, 5067 Ritter Rd, Mechanicsburg, PA 17055 Tel: 717-796-0411 Toll Free Tel: 800-732-3669 Fax: 717-796-0412 Web Site: www. stackpolebooks.com, pg 257

Fleming, Antoinette, Mondo Publishing, 980 Avenue of the Americas, New York, NY 10018 Tel: 212-268-3560 Toll Free Tel: 800-242-3650 Fax: 212-268-3561 E-mail: mondopub@aol.com Web Site: www. mondopub.com, pg 177

Fleming, P, ICS Press, 3100 Harrison St, Oakland, CA 94611 Tel: 510-238-5010 Toll Free Tel: 800-326-0263 Fax: 510-238-8440 E-mail: mail@icspress.com Web Site: www.icspress.com, pg 130

Fleming, Peter, Peter Fleming Agency, PO Box 458, Pacific Palisades, CA 90272 Tel: 310-454-1373, pg 630

Fleming, Sue, Free Press, 1230 Avenue of the Americas, New York, NY 10020 Tel: 212-698-7000 Toll Free Tel: 800-223-2345 (cust serv); 800-223-2336 (orders); 888-866-6631 (fulfillment), pg 100

Fleming, Sue, Scribner, 1230 Avenue of the Americas, New York, NY 10020, pg 244

Fleming, Sue, Simon & Schuster Adult Publishing Group, 1230 Avenue of the Americas, New York, NY 10020 Tel: 212-698-7000 Toll Free Tel: 800-223-2336 (orders); 800-223-2348 (cust serv), pg 248

Fletcher, Jim, New Leaf Press Inc, PO Box 726, Green Forest, AR 72638-0726 Tel: 870-438-5288 Toll Free Tel: 800-643-9535 Fax: 870-438-5120 E-mail: nlp@ newleafpress.net Web Site: www.newleafpress.net, pg 188

Flicker, John, Bantam Dell Publishing Group, 1745 Broadway, New York, NY 10019 Tel: 212-782-9000 Toll Free Tel: 800-223-6834 Fax: 212-302-7985 Web Site: www.randomhouse.com/bantamdell, pg 31

Flint, John, Neo-Tech Publishing, PO Box 60906, Boulder City, NV 89006-0906 Tel: 702-293-5552 Fax: 702-293-4342 Web Site: www.neo-tech.com, pg 187

Flomenhaft, Marion, Summer Writers' Workshops, UCCE, 250 Hofstra University, Hempstead, NY 11549-2500 Tel: 516-463-7600 Fax: 516-463-4833 E-mail: uccelibarts@hofstra.edu Web Site: www. hofstra.edu/writers, pg 748

Flora, Debi, Small Publishers Association of North America (SPAN), 425 Cedar St, Buena Vista, CO 81211 Tel: 719-395-4790 Fax: 719-395-8374 E-mail: span@spannet.org Web Site: www.spannet.org, pg 699, 747, 754

Flora, Scott, About Books Inc, 425 Cedar St, Buena Vista, CO 81211-1500 Tel: 719-395-2459 Fax: 719-395-8374 E-mail: abi@about-books.com Web Site: www.about-books.com, pg 589

Flora, Scott, Small Publishers Association of North America (SPAN), 425 Cedar St, Buena Vista, CO 81211 Tel: 719-395-4790 Fax: 719-395-8374 E-mail: span@spannet.org Web Site: www.spannet.org, pg 699, 747, 754

Flores, Colleen M, Four Paws Press LLC, 2460 Garden Rd, Suite B, Monterey, CA 93940 Tel: 831-375-PAWS (375-7297) Fax: 831-649-8007 Web Site: www.fourpawspress.com, pg 99

Floridis, Tad, Grove/Atlantic Inc, 841 Broadway, 4th fl, New York, NY 10003-4793 Tel: 212-614-7850 Toll Free Tel: 800-521-0178 Fax: 212-614-7886 Web Site: www.groveatlantic.com, pg 110

Florio, Dr Charles, Northeast Texas Community College Annual Writers Conference, Continuing Education, PO Box 1307, Mount Pleasant, TX 75456-1307 Tel: 903-572-1911 Fax: 903-572-6712 E-mail: jbowers@ntcc.edu Web Site: www.ntcc.edu, pg 745

Florio, Marie, Fireside & Touchstone, 1230 Avenue of the Americas, New York, NY 10020, pg 97

Florio, Marie, Simon & Schuster, 1230 Avenue of the Americas, New York, NY 10020 Tel: 212-698-7000 Toll Free Tel: 800-223-2348 (cust serv); 800-223-2336 (orders) Toll Free Fax: 800-943-9831 (orders) Web Site: www.simonsays.com, pg 248

Florita, Kira, Country Music Foundation Press, 222 Fifth Ave S, Nashville, TN 37203 Tel: 615-416-2001 Fax: 615-255-2245 Web Site: www.countrymusichalloffame.com, pg 70

Flournoy, Heather, Vital Health Publishing, 149 Old Branchville Rd, Ridgefield, CT 06877 Tel: 203-894-1882 Toll Free Tel: 877-848-2665 (orders) Fax: 203-894-1866 E-mail: info@vitalhealthbooks.com Web Site: www.vitalhealthbooks.com, pg 291

Flower, Mary, Grove/Atlantic Inc, 841 Broadway, 4th fl, New York, NY 10003-4793 Tel: 212-614-7850 Toll Free Tel: 800-521-0178 Fax: 212-614-7886 Web Site: www.groveatlantic.com, pg 110

Flowers, Richard, C P A Book Publisher, 9205 SE Clackamas Rd, Clackamas, OR 97015 Tel: 503-668-4977 Fax: 503-668-8614 E-mail: cpabooks@hotmail.com, pg 51

Floyd, Cherrie, Stylewriter Inc, 4395 N Windsor Dr, Provo, UT 84604-6301 Tel: 801-235-9462 Toll Free Tel: 866-997-9462 E-mail: customerservice@swinc.org; query@swinc.org Web Site: www.swinc.org; www.stylewriterinc.org, pg 261

Floyd, Cindy Lee, Data Trace Publishing Co, 110 West Rd, Suite 227, Towson, MD 21204-2316 Tel: 410-494-4994 Toll Free Tel: 800-342-0454 (orders only) Fax: 410-494-0515 E-mail: info@datatrace.com Web Site: www.datatrace.com, pg 76

Floyd, Randall, Harbor House, 111 Tenth St, Augusta, GA 30901 Tel: 706-738-0354 Fax: 706-738-0354 E-mail: harborbook@knology.net Web Site: harborhousebooks.com, pg 114

Floyd, William, Stylewriter Inc, 4395 N Windsor Dr, Provo, UT 84604-6301 Tel: 801-235-9462 Toll Free Tel: 866-997-9462 E-mail: customerservice@swinc.org; query@swinc.org Web Site: www.swinc.org; www.stylewriterinc.org, pg 261

Fluck, Avery, The Bookbinders' Guild of New York, Dunn & Co, 110 Grand Ave, Ridgefield Park, NJ 07660 Tel: 201-229-1888 Fax: 201-229-1755 Web Site: www.bookbindersguild.org, pg 682

Flynn, Dan, State University of New York Press, 90 State St, Suite 700, Albany, NY 12207-1707 Tel: 518-472-5000 Toll Free Tel: 800-666-2211 (orders)

Fax: 518-472-5038 Toll Free Fax: 800-688-2877 (orders) E-mail: orderbook@cupserv.org; info@sunypress.edu Web Site: www.sunypress.edu, pg 258

Flynn, Jacquie, AMACOM Books, 1601 Broadway, New York, NY 10019-7406 Tel: 212-586-8100; 518-891-5510 (orders) Toll Free Tel: 800-262-9699 (cust serv) Fax: 212-903-8168; 518-891-2372 (orders) Web Site: www.amanet.org, pg 10

Flynn, Jim, Judy Boals Inc & Jim Flynn Agency, 208 W 30 St, Suite 401, New York, NY 10001 Tel: 212-868-1068; 212-868-0924 Fax: 212-868-1052, pg 621

Fochetta, Frank, Simon & Schuster Sales & Distribution, 1230 Avenue of the Americas, New York, NY 10020 Tel: 212-698-7000, pg 249

Fodor, Judith F, Passeggiata Press Inc, 420 W 14 St, Pueblo, CO 81003-2708 Tel: 719-544-1038 Fax: 719-544-7911 E-mail: passegpress@cs.com, pg 204

Fogarty, Kathleen, Tom Doherty Associates, LLC, 175 Fifth Ave, 14th fl, New York, NY 10010 Tel: 212-388-0100 Toll Free Tel: 800-455-0340 Fax: 212-388-0191 E-mail: firstname.lastname@tor.com Web Site: www.tor.com, pg 81

Fogelberg, Paul A, The Professional Education Group Inc, 12401 Minnetonka Blvd, Minnetonka, MN 55305-3994 Tel: 952-933-9990 Toll Free Tel: 800-229-2531 Fax: 952-933-7784 E-mail: orders@proedgroup.com Web Site: www.proedgroup.com, pg 219

Fogelman, Evan M, The Fogelman Literary Agency, 7515 Greenville Ave, Suite 712, Dallas, TX 75231 Tel: 214-361-9956 Fax: 214-361-9553 E-mail: info@fogelman.com Web Site: www.fogelman.com, pg 630

Fogelman, Sheldon, Sheldon Fogelman Agency Inc, 10 E 40 St, Suite 3800, New York, NY 10016 Tel: 212-532-7250 Fax: 212-685-8939 E-mail: fogelman@worldnet.att.net; agency@sheldonfogelmanagency.com, pg 630

Fogiel, Max, Research & Education Association, 61 Ethel Rd W, Piscataway, NJ 08854 Tel: 732-819-8880 Fax: 732-819-8808 E-mail: info@rea.com Web Site: www.rea.com, pg 231

Fogle, Linda, University of South Carolina Press, 1600 Hampton St, 5th fl, Columbia, SC 29208 Tel: 803-777-5243 Toll Free Tel: 800-768-2500 (orders) Fax: 803-777-0160 Toll Free Fax: 800-868-0740 (orders) Web Site: www.sc.edu/uscpress/, pg 285

Foley, Fiona, Elsevier, 11830 Westline Industrial Dr, St Louis, MO 63146 Tel: 314-872-8370 Toll Free Tel: 800-325-4177 Fax: 314-432-1380 Web Site: www.elsevier.com; www.elsevierhealth.com, pg 89

Foley, Fiona, W B Saunders Ltd, 170 S Independence Mall W, Suite 300 E, Philadelphia, PA 19106-3399 Tel: 215-238-7800 Toll Free Tel: 800-545-2522 (cust serv) Fax: 215-238-7883 Web Site: www.elsevierhealth.com, pg 240

Foley, Janet, Fodor's Travel Publications, 1745 Broadway, New York, NY 10019 Tel: 212-572-8784 Toll Free Tel: 800-733-3000 Fax: 212-572-2248 Web Site: www.fodors.com, pg 98

Foley, Joan, The Foley Agency, 34 E 38 St, New York, NY 10016 Tel: 212-686-6930, pg 630

Foley, Joseph, The Foley Agency, 34 E 38 St, New York, NY 10016 Tel: 212-686-6930, pg 630

Foley, Linda K, The Newspaper Guild, 501 Third St NW, Washington, DC 20001-2760 Tel: 202-434-7173 Fax: 202-434-1472 E-mail: guild@swa-union.org Web Site: www.newsguild.org, pg 695

Foley, Margaret, Royal Fireworks Press, First Ave, Unionville, NY 10988 Tel: 845-726-4444 Fax: 845-726-3824 E-mail: mail@rfwp.com Web Site: www.rfwp.com, pg 235

Foley, Rich, Thomson Gale, 27500 Drake Rd, Farmington Hills, MI 48331-3535 Tel: 248-699-4253 Toll Free Tel: 800-347-4253 Fax: 248-699-8070 Toll Free Fax: 800-414-5043 E-mail: galeord@gale.com Web Site: www.gale.com, pg 270

Foley, Sue, Illuminating Engineering Society of North America, 120 Wall St, 17th fl, New York, NY 10005-4001 Tel: 212-248-5000 Fax: 212-248-5017; 212-248-5018 Web Site: www.iesna.org, pg 131

Folgedalen, Gail, Gail's Guides, PO Box 70323, Bellevue, WA 98005 Tel: 425-917-0737 E-mail: guides@oz.net Web Site: www.gailsguides.com, pg 102

Folgedalen, Lee, Gail's Guides, PO Box 70323, Bellevue, WA 98005 Tel: 425-917-0737 E-mail: guides@oz.net Web Site: www.gailsguides.com, pg 102

Follmer, David C, Lyceum Books Inc, 5758 S Blackstone Ave, Chicago, IL 60637 Tel: 773-643-1902 Fax: 773-643-1903 E-mail: lyceum@lyceumbooks.com Web Site: www.lyceumbooks.com, pg 160

Follstad, Mark, National Association of Independent Publishers Representatives (NAIPR), Zeckendorf Towers, 111 E 14 St, PMB 157, New York, NY 10003 Tel: 207-832-7744 Toll Free Tel: 888-624-7779 Fax: 207-832-6073 Toll Free Fax: 800-416-2586 E-mail: naiprtwo@aol.com Web Site: www.naipr.org, pg 692

Foltz, Jill, Educator's Award, PO Box 1589, Austin, TX 78767-1589 Tel: 512-478-5748 Fax: 512-478-3961 E-mail: societyexec@deltakappagamma.org Web Site: www.deltakappagamma.org, pg 771

Folz, Robert, Visuals Unlimited, 27 Meadow Dr, Hollis, NH 03049 Tel: 603-465-3340 Fax: 603-465-3360 E-mail: staff@visualsunlimited.com Web Site: visualsunlimited.com, pg 613

Folz, Shelly, Visuals Unlimited, 27 Meadow Dr, Hollis, NH 03049 Tel: 603-465-3340 Fax: 603-465-3360 E-mail: staff@visualsunlimited.com Web Site: visualsunlimited.com, pg 613

Fonseca, Bryan, Basile Festival of Emerging American Theatre (FEAT), 749 N Park Ave, Indianapolis, IN 46202 Tel: 317-635-7529 Fax: 317-635-0010 E-mail: info@phoenixtheatre.org Web Site: www.phoenixtheatre.org, pg 761

Fontana, John, Doubleday Broadway Publishing Group, 1745 Broadway, New York, NY 10019 Tel: 212-782-9000 Toll Free Tel: 800-223-6834; 800-223-5780 (sales) Fax: 212-302-7985 (correspondence); 212-492-9862 (orders), pg 82

Fontana, Virginia, The University of Utah Press, 1795 E South Campus Dr, Rm 101, Salt Lake City, UT 84112-9402 Tel: 801-581-6671 Toll Free Tel: 800-773-6672 Fax: 801-581-3365 E-mail: info@upress.utah.edu Web Site: www.uofupress.com, pg 285

Foo, Bill, Other Press LLC, 307 Seventh Ave, Suite 1807, New York, NY 10001 Tel: 212-414-0054 Toll Free Tel: 877-THE-OTHER Fax: 212-414-0939 E-mail: orders@otherpress.com Web Site: www.otherpress.com, pg 573

Foot, Doug, Knopf Canada, One Toronto St, Suite 300, Toronto, ON M5C 2V6, Canada Tel: 416-364-4449 Toll Free Tel: 800-668-4247 (order desk) Fax: 416-364-0462 Web Site: www.randomhouse.ca, pg 552

Foot, Doug, Seal Books, One Toronto St, Suite 300, Toronto, ON M5C 2V6, Canada Tel: 416-364-4449 Toll Free Tel: 888-523-9292 (order desk) Fax: 416-957-1587 Web Site: www.randomhouse.ca, pg 560

Foot, Douglas, Doubleday Canada, One Toronto St, Suite 300, Toronto, ON M5C 2V6, Canada Tel: 416-364-4449 Fax: 416-957-1587 Web Site: www.randomhouse.ca, pg 542

Foot, Douglas, Random House of Canada Ltd, One Toronto St, Unit 300, Toronto, ON M5C 2V6, Canada Tel: 416-364-4449 Fax: 416-364-6863 (edit & publicity); 416-364-6653 (subs rts) Web Site: www.randomhouse.ca, pg 559

Foote, Wade, Breakwater Books Ltd, 100 Water St, St Johns, NF A1C 6E6, Canada Tel: 709-722-6680 Toll Free Tel: 800-563-3333 Fax: 709-753-0708 E-mail: info@breakwater.nf.net Web Site: www.breakwater.nf.net; www.breakwaterbooks.com, pg 537

Foraker, Chet, Sopris West Educational Services, 4093 Specialty Place, Longmont, CO 80504 Tel: 303-651-2829 Toll Free Tel: 800-547-6747 Fax: 303-776-5934 E-mail: customerservice@sopriswest.com Web Site: www.sopriswest.com, pg 253

Forbes, Arlene, Chatelaine Press, 6454 Honey Tree Ct, Burke, VA 22015 *Tel:* 703-569-2062 *Toll Free Tel:* 800-249-9527 *Fax:* 703-569-9610 *E-mail:* egmhelp@enterprise-government.com *Web Site:* www. chatpress.com; www.enterprise-government.com, pg 59

Ford, Adrianne, Unity House, 1901 NW Blue Pkwy, Unity Village, MO 64065-0001 *Tel:* 816-524-3550 (ext 3300); 816-251-3571 (sales) *Fax:* 816-251-3557 *E-mail:* unity@unityworldhq.org *Web Site:* www. unityonline.org, pg 280

Ford, Arden, McGill-Queen's University Press, 3430 McTavish St, Montreal, PQ H3A 1X9, Canada *Tel:* 514-398-3750 *Fax:* 514-398-4333 *E-mail:* mqup@ mqup.ca *Web Site:* www.mqup.mcgill.ca, pg 553

Ford, Beth, Scholastic Inc, 557 Broadway, New York, NY 10012 *Tel:* 212-343-4469 *Toll Free Tel:* 800-scholastic *Fax:* 212-343-6930 *Web Site:* www. scholastic.com, pg 242

Ford, Clifford, Clifford Ford Publications, 120 Walnut Ct, Unit 15, Ottawa, ON K1R 7W2, Canada *Tel:* 613-230-3666 *Fax:* 613-230-6725 *E-mail:* host@cliffordfordpublications.ca *Web Site:* cliffordfordpublications.ca, pg 687

Ford, David, Little, Brown and Company Books for Young Readers, 1271 Avenue of the Americas, New York, NY 10020 *Tel:* 212-522-8700 *Toll Free Tel:* 800-759-0190 *Fax:* 212-522-7997 *Web Site:* www. twbookmark.com, pg 156

Ford, Dennis, Noble Publishing Corp, 630 Pinnacle Ct, Norcross, GA 30071 *Tel:* 770-449-6774 *Fax:* 770-448-2839 *E-mail:* editor@noblepub.com; orders@noblepub. com *Web Site:* www.noblepub.com, pg 191

Ford, Elizabeth J, Kirchoff/Wohlberg Inc, 866 United Nations Plaza, Suite 525, New York, NY 10017 *Tel:* 212-644-2020 *Fax:* 212-223-4387 *E-mail:* kirchwohl@aol.com *Web Site:* www. kirchoffwohlberg.com, pg 603, 637, 666

Ford, Gregory L, Ugly Duckling Presse, 106 Ferris St, 2nd fl, Brooklyn, NY 11231 *Tel:* 718-852-5529 *E-mail:* udp_mailbox@yahoo.com *Web Site:* www. uglyducklingpresse.org, pg 278

Ford, Jon, Paladin Press, 7077 Winchester Circle, Boulder, CO 80301 *Tel:* 303-443-7250 *Toll Free Tel:* 800-392-2400 *Fax:* 303-442-8741 *E-mail:* service@paladin-press.com *Web Site:* www. paladin-press.com, pg 202

Ford, Julie, Organization of Book Publishers of Ontario, 720 Bathurst St, Suite 301, Toronto, ON M5S 2R4, Canada *Tel:* 416-536-7584 *Fax:* 416-536-7692 *E-mail:* obpo@interlog.com *Web Site:* www. ontariobooks.ca, pg 696

Ford, June, JFE Editorial Services, PO Box 122417, Fort Worth, TX 76121-2417 *Tel:* 817-560-7018 *E-mail:* jford@jfe-editorial.com, pg 602

Ford, Kenneth, AAAI Press, 445 Burgess Dr, Suite 100, Menlo Park, CA 94025-3496 *Tel:* 650-328-3123 *Fax:* 650-321-4457 *E-mail:* press@aaai.org *Web Site:* www.aaaipress.org, pg 2

Ford, Olivia, Frog Ltd, 1435 Fourth St, Berkeley, CA 94710 *Tel:* 510-559-8277 *Toll Free Tel:* 800-337-2665 (book orders only) *Fax:* 510-559-8279 *E-mail:* orders@northatlanticbooks.com *Web Site:* www.northatlanticbooks.com, pg 101

Ford, Olivia, North Atlantic Books, 1435 Fourth St, Berkeley, CA 94710 *Tel:* 510-559-8277 *Toll Free Tel:* 800-337-2665 (book orders only) *Fax:* 510-559-8279 *E-mail:* orders@northatlanticbooks.com *Web Site:* www.northatlanticbooks.com, pg 192

Forder, Reg, Caribbean Christian Writers Conference Cruise, PO Box 110390, Nashville, TN 37222 *Tel:* 615-834-0450 *Toll Free Tel:* 800-21-WRITE (219-7483) *Web Site:* www.acwriters.com, pg 742

Forder, Reg A, American Christian Writers, PO Box 110390, Nashville, TN 37222 *Tel:* 615-834-0450 *Toll Free Tel:* 800-21-WRITE (219-7483) *Fax:* 615-834-7736 *Web Site:* www.acwriters.com, pg 676

Forder, Reg A, Christian Writers' Conference, PO Box 110390, Nashville, TN 37222-0390 *Tel:* 615-834-0450 *Toll Free Tel:* 800-219-7483 *Fax:* 615-834-7736 *E-mail:* acwriters@aol.com *Web Site:* www.acwriters. com, pg 742

Forguson, Geoff, Oxford University Press Canada, 70 Wynford Dr, Don Mills, ON M3C 1J9, Canada *Tel:* 416-441-2941 *Toll Free Tel:* 800-387-8020 *Fax:* 416-444-0427 *Toll Free Fax:* 800-665-1771 *E-mail:* custserv@oupcan.com *Web Site:* www.oup. com/ca, pg 557

Forland, Emily, The Wendy Weil Agency Inc, 232 Madison Ave, Suite 1300, New York, NY 10016 *Tel:* 212-685-0030 *Fax:* 212-685-0765, pg 660

Forman, Deborah, Swedenborg Foundation Publishers/ Chrysalis Books, 320 N Church St, West Chester, PA 19380 *Tel:* 610-430-3222 *Toll Free Tel:* 800-355-3222 (cust serv) *Fax:* 610-430-7982 *E-mail:* info@ swedenborg.com *Web Site:* www.swedenborg.com, pg 263

Forman, Mark, Light-Beams Publishing, 10 Toon Lane, Lee, NH 03824 *Tel:* 603-659-1300 *Toll Free Tel:* 800-397-7641 *Fax:* 603-659-3399 *Web Site:* www.light-beams.com, pg 154

Forman, Sandra, YES New Play Festival, 205 FA Theatre Dept, Nunn Dr, Highland Heights, KY 41099-1007 *Tel:* 859-572-6362 *Fax:* 859-572-6057, pg 814

Forman, Stephen A, W W Norton & Company Inc, 500 Fifth Ave, New York, NY 10110-0017 *Tel:* 212-354-5500 *Toll Free Tel:* 800-233-4830 (orders & cust serv) *Fax:* 212-869-0856 *Toll Free Fax:* 800-458-6515 *Web Site:* www.wwnorton.com, pg 193

Formica, Ron, New England Publishing Associates Inc, PO Box 5, Chester, CT 06412-0005 *Tel:* 860-345-READ (345-7323) *Fax:* 860-345-3660 *E-mail:* nepa@ nepa.com *Web Site:* www.nepa.com, pg 646

Forpin, Jean-Louis, Association Nationale des Editeurs de Livres, 2514 boul Rosemont, Montreal, PQ H1Y 1K4, Canada *Tel:* 514-273-8130 *Fax:* 514-273-9657 *E-mail:* info@anel.org *Web Site:* www.anel.org, pg 679

Forrer, David, Inkwell Management, 521 Fifth Ave, 26th fl, New York, NY 10175 *Tel:* 212-922-3500 *Fax:* 212-922-0535 *E-mail:* contact@inkwellmanagement.com *Web Site:* www.inkwellmanagement.com, pg 635

Forrest, Iris, Ageless Press, 3759 Collins St, Sarasota, FL 34232 *Tel:* 941-365-1367 *Fax:* 941-365-1367 *E-mail:* irishope@comcast.net *Web Site:* irisforrest. com, pg 6

Forrey, Scott, The Urban Institute Press, 2100 "M" St NW, Washington, DC 20037 *Tel:* 202-261-5687 *Toll Free Tel:* 877-UIPRESS (847-7377) *Fax:* 202-467-5775 *E-mail:* pubs@ui.urban.org *Web Site:* www. uipress.org, pg 288

Forrie, Jackie, Thistledown Press Ltd, 633 Main St, Saskatoon, SK S7H 0J8, Canada *Tel:* 306-244-1722 *Fax:* 306-244-1762 *E-mail:* marketing@thistledown.sk. ca *Web Site:* www.thistledown.sk.ca, pg 563

Forristal, Patrick, The Dawn Horse Press, 12040 N Seigler Rd, Middletown, CA 95461 *Tel:* 707-928-6590 *Toll Free Tel:* 877-770-0772 *Fax:* 707-928-5068 *E-mail:* dhp@adidam.org *Web Site:* www. dawnhorsepress.com, pg 77

Forrister, Brad, M Lee Smith Publishers LLC, 5201 Virginia Way, Brentwood, TN 37027 *Tel:* 615-373-7517 *Toll Free Tel:* 800-274-6774 *Fax:* 615-373-5183 *Web Site:* www.mleesmith.com, pg 250

Forseth, Ron, Through the Bible Publishers, 2643 Midpoint Dr, Fort Collins, CO 80524-3216 *Tel:* 970-484-8483 *Toll Free Tel:* 800-284-0158 *Fax:* 970-495-6700 *E-mail:* discipleland@throughthebible.com *Web Site:* www.throughthebible.com, pg 271

Forte, Deborah, Scholastic Entertainment Inc, 524 Broadway, New York, NY 10012 *Tel:* 212-343-7500 *Fax:* 212-965-7448, pg 241

Forte, Deborah A, Scholastic Inc, 557 Broadway, New York, NY 10012 *Tel:* 212-343-4469 *Toll Free Tel:* 800-scholastic *Fax:* 212-343-6930 *Web Site:* www.scholastic.com, pg 242

Forte, Fran, The New Press, 38 Greene St, 4th fl, New York, NY 10013 *Tel:* 212-629-8802 *Toll Free Tel:* 800-233-4830 (orders) *Fax:* 212-629-8617 *Toll Free Fax:* 800-458-6515 *E-mail:* newpress@ thenewpress.com *Web Site:* www.thenewpress.com, pg 188

Forte, Henry S, Incentive Publications Inc, 3835 Cleghorn Ave, Nashville, TN 37215 *Tel:* 615-385-2934 *Toll Free Tel:* 800-421-2830 *Fax:* 615-385-2967 *E-mail:* comments@incentivepublications.com *Web Site:* www.incentivepublications.com, pg 132

Forte, Imogene, Incentive Publications Inc, 3835 Cleghorn Ave, Nashville, TN 37215 *Tel:* 615-385-2934 *Toll Free Tel:* 800-421-2830 *Fax:* 615-385-2967 *E-mail:* comments@incentivepublications.com *Web Site:* www.incentivepublications.com, pg 132

Fortenberry, Rie, Mississippi Review/University of Southern Mississippi, Center for Writers, Box 5144 USM, Hattiesburg, MS 39406 *Tel:* 601-266-5600 *Fax:* 601-266-5757 *E-mail:* rief@mississippireview. com *Web Site:* www.mississippireview.com; www. centerforwriters.com, pg 753

Fortgang, Adam, Princeton University Press, 41 William St, Princeton, NJ 08540 *Tel:* 609-258-4900 *Toll Free Tel:* 800-777-4726 *Fax:* 609-258-6305 *Toll Free Fax:* 800-999-1958 *E-mail:* orders@cpfsinc.com *Web Site:* www.pup.princeton.edu, pg 219

Fortin, Joe, Book Sales Inc, 114 Northfield Ave, Edison, NJ 08837 *Tel:* 732-225-0530 *Toll Free Tel:* 800-526-7257 *Fax:* 732-225-2257 *E-mail:* sales@ booksalesusa.com; customerservice@booksalesusa.com *Web Site:* www.booksalesusa.com, pg 43

Fortune, Gail, Berkley Books, 375 Hudson St, New York, NY 10014 *Tel:* 212-366-2000 *Fax:* 212-366-2666 *E-mail:* online@penguinputnam.com *Web Site:* www.penguin.com, pg 36

Fortune, Gail, Berkley Publishing Group, 375 Hudson St, New York, NY 10014 *Tel:* 212-366-2000 *E-mail:* online@penguinputnam.com *Web Site:* www. penguin.com, pg 37

Foster, Edward, Talisman House Publishers, PO Box 3157, Jersey City, NJ 07303-3157 *Tel:* 201-938-0698 *Fax:* 201-938-1693 *E-mail:* talismaned@aol.com *Web Site:* www.talismanpublishers.com, pg 264

Foster, Frances, Farrar, Straus & Giroux Books for Young Readers, 19 Union Sq W, New York, NY 10003 *Tel:* 212-741-6900 *Fax:* 212-633-2427 *E-mail:* childrens.marketing@fsgbooks.com; childrens. editorial@fsgbooks.com *Web Site:* www.fsgkidsbooks. com, pg 95

Foster, Frank, Medals of America Press, 114 Southchase Blvd, Fountain Inn, SC 29644 *Tel:* 864-862-6051 *Toll Free Tel:* 800-308-0849 *Fax:* 864-862-0256 *Toll Free Fax:* 800-407-8640 *E-mail:* press@usmedals.com *Web Site:* www.moapress.com, pg 170

Foster, Lee, Foster Travel Publishing, PO Box 5715, Berkeley, CA 94705-0715 *Tel:* 510-549-2202 *Fax:* 510-549-1131 *E-mail:* lee@fostertravel.com *Web Site:* www.fostertravel.com, pg 599

Foster, Pat, Pat Foster Artist Representative, 32 W 40 St, Suite 2 S, New York, NY 10018 *Tel:* 212-575-6887 *Fax:* 212-869-6871 *E-mail:* pfosterrep@aol.com *Web Site:* www.patfosterartrep.com, pg 666

Foster, Paul, Jossey-Bass, 989 Market St, San Francisco, CA 94103-1741 *Tel:* 415-433-1740 *Toll Free Tel:* 800-956-7739 *Fax:* 415-433-0499 (edit/mktg) *Web Site:* www.josseybass.com; www.pfeiffer.com, pg 142

Fotinos, Joel, G P Putnam's Sons (Hardcover), 375 Hudson St, New York, NY 10014 *Tel:* 212-366-2000 *E-mail:* online@penguinputnam.com *Web Site:* www. penguin.com, pg 223

Fotinos, Joel, Jeremy P Tarcher, 375 Hudson St, New York, NY 10014 *Tel:* 212-366-2000 *E-mail:* online@ penguinputnam.com *Web Site:* www.penguin.com, pg 264

Foulds, Nancy, Lone Pine Publishing, 10145 81 Ave, Edmonton, AB T6E 1W9, Canada *Tel:* 780-433-9333 *Toll Free Tel:* 800-661-9017

Fax: 780-433-9646 *Toll Free Fax:* 800-424-7173 *E-mail:* info@lonepinepublishing.com *Web Site:* www. lonepinepublishing.com, pg 553

Foulon, Herve, Editions Marcel Didier Inc, 1815 Ave de Lorimier, Montreal, PQ H2K 3W6, Canada *Tel:* 514-523-1523 *Toll Free Tel:* 800-361-1664 (Canada) *Fax:* 514-523-9969 *E-mail:* hurtubisehmh@ hurtubisehmh.com *Web Site:* www.hurtubisehmh.com, pg 544

Foulon, Herve, Editions Hurtubise HMH Ltee, 1815 De Lorimier, Montreal; PQ H2K 3W6, Canada *Tel:* 514-523-1523 *Toll Free Tel:* 800-361-1664 (Canada only) *Fax:* 514-523-9969; 514-523-5955 (edit) *E-mail:* hurtubisehmh@hurtubisehmh.com *Web Site:* www.hurtubisehmh.com, pg 545

Fountain, Katrina, Abingdon Press, 201 Eighth Ave S, Nashville, TN 37203-3919 *Tel:* 615-749-6290 (publicist); 615-749-6000; 615-749-6451 (sales) *Toll Free Tel:* 800-251-3320 *Fax:* 615-749-6056 *Web Site:* www.abingdonpress.com, pg 3

Fowler, Arnaud, Editions Hurtubise HMH Ltee, 1815 De Lorimier, Montreal, PQ H2K 3W6, Canada *Tel:* 514-523-1523 *Toll Free Tel:* 800-361-1664 (Canada only) *Fax:* 514-523-9969; 514-523-5955 (edit) *E-mail:* hurtubisehmh@hurtubisehmh.com *Web Site:* www.hurtubisehmh.com, pg 545

Fowler, Bill, Harrison House Publishers, 2448 E 81 St, Suite 4800, Tulsa, OK 74137-4256 *Tel:* 918-523-5700 *Toll Free Tel:* 800-888-4126 *Fax:* 918-494-5688 (sales) *Toll Free Fax:* 800-830-5688 *Web Site:* www. harrisonhouse.com, pg 116

Fowler, Judy, Holt, Rinehart and Winston, 10801 N MoPac Expy, Bldg 3, Austin, TX 78759 *Tel:* 512-721-7000 *Toll Free Tel:* 800-225-5425 (cust serv) *Fax:* 512-721-7833 (mktg); 512-721-7898 (edit) *Web Site:* www.hrw.com, pg 124

Fowler, Marjorie L, The University of North Carolina Press, 116 S Boundary St, Chapel Hill, NC 27514-3808 *Tel:* 919-966-3561 *Toll Free Tel:* 800-848-6224 (orders only) *Fax:* 919-966-3829 *Toll Free Fax:* 800-272-6817 (orders) *E-mail:* uncpress@unc.edu *Web Site:* www.uncpress.unc.edu, pg 283

Fowles, Cynthia, Bear & Co Inc, One Park St, Rochester, VT 05767 *Tel:* 802-767-3174 *Toll Free Tel:* 800-932-3277 *Fax:* 802-767-3726 *E-mail:* orders@InnerTraditions.com *Web Site:* InnerTraditions.com, pg 34

Fowles, Cynthia, Inner Traditions International Ltd, One Park St, Rochester, VT 05767 *Tel:* 802-767-3174 *Toll Free Tel:* 800-246-8648 *Fax:* 802-767-3726 *E-mail:* orders@InnerTraditions.com *Web Site:* www. InnerTraditions.com, pg 134

Fox, Anna, ChemTec Publishing, 38 Earswick Dr, Scarborough, ON M1E 1C6, Canada *Tel:* 416-265-2603 *Fax:* 416-265-1399 *E-mail:* info@chemtec.org; orderdesk@chemtec.org *Web Site:* www.chemtec.org, pg 540

Fox, Bob, Aid to Individual Artists, 727 E Main St, Columbus, OH 43205-1796 *Tel:* 614-466-2613 *Fax:* 614-466-4494 *Web Site:* www.oac.state.oh.us, pg 758

Fox, Buddy, Mark Sonder Productions, 250 W 57 St, Suite 1830, New York, NY 10107 *Tel:* 212-262-4600 *Fax:* 212-246-0197 *E-mail:* msonder@ marksonderproductions.com *Web Site:* www. marksonderproductions.com, pg 670

Fox, Carolyn, Aliform Publishing, 117 Warwick St SE, Minneapolis, MN 55414 *Tel:* 612-379-7639 *Fax:* 612-379-7639 *E-mail:* information@aliformgroup.com *Web Site:* www.aliformgroup.com, pg 569

Fox, Ed, Tafnews Press, 2570 El Camino Real, No 606, Mountain View, CA 94040 *Tel:* 650-948-8188 *Fax:* 650-948-9445 *E-mail:* biz@trackandfieldnews. com *Web Site:* www.trackandfieldnews.com, pg 264

Fox, Jim, HarperCollins Publishers, 10 E 53 St, New York, NY 10022 *Tel:* 212-207-7000 *Fax:* 212-207-7145 *Web Site:* www.harpercollins.com, pg 116

Fox, Jim, Silman-James Press, 3624 Shannon Rd, Los Angeles, CA 90027 *Tel:* 323-661-9922 *Toll Free Tel:* 877-SJP-BOOK (757-2665) *Fax:* 323-661-9933 *E-mail:* silmanjamespress@earthlink.net *Web Site:* www.silmanjamespress.com, pg 247

Fox, Joey, South End Press, 7 Brookline St, No 1, Cambridge, MA 02139-4146 *Tel:* 617-547-4002 *Fax:* 617-547-1333 *E-mail:* southend@southendpress. org *Web Site:* www.southendpress.org, pg 254

Fox, Kate Templeton, Ohioana Book Awards, 274 E First Ave, Suite 300, Columbus, OH 43201 *Tel:* 614-466-3831 *Fax:* 614-728-6974 *E-mail:* ohioana@ sloma.state.oh.us *Web Site:* www.oplin.lib.us/ohioana/, pg 796

Fox, Keith, McGraw-Hill Professional, 2 Penn Plaza, New York, NY 10121 *Tel:* 212-904-2000 *Web Site:* www.books.mcgraw-hill.com, pg 168

Fox, Larry, BuilderBooks.com, 1201 15 St NW, Washington, DC 20005-2800 *Tel:* 202-822-0200; 202-266-8200 *Toll Free Tel:* 800-223-2665 (orders); 800-368-5242 ext 8368 (editorial) *Fax:* 202-266-8096 (edit); 202-266-5889 (edit) *Web Site:* www. builderbooks.com, pg 49

Fox, Laurie, Linda Chester & Associates, Rockefeller Ctr, 630 Fifth Ave, New York, NY 10111 *Tel:* 212-218-3350 *Fax:* 212-218-3343 *E-mail:* lcassoc@ mindspring.com *Web Site:* www.lindachester.com, pg 624

Fox, Leonard, Swedenborg Association, 278-A Meeting St, Charleston, SC 29401 *Tel:* 843-853-6211 *Fax:* 843-853-6226 *E-mail:* arcana@swedenborg.net; assn@ swedenborg.net, pg 263

Fox, Lissa, Handprint Books Inc, 413 Sixth Ave, Brooklyn, NY 11215-3310 *Tel:* 718-768-3696 *Fax:* 718-369-0844 *E-mail:* publisher@ handprintbooks.com *Web Site:* www.handprintbooks. com, pg 113

Fox, Marilyn L, American Academy of Orthopaedic Surgeons, 6300 N River Rd, Rosemont, IL 60018-4262 *Tel:* 847-823-7186 *Toll Free Tel:* 800-346-2267 *Fax:* 847-823-8125 *Toll Free Fax:* 800-999-2939 *E-mail:* golembiewski@aaos.org *Web Site:* www.aaos. org, pg 11

Fox, Peggy L, New Directions Publishing Corp, 80 Eighth Ave, New York, NY 10011 *Tel:* 212-255-0230 *Toll Free Tel:* 800-233-4830 (PA) *Fax:* 212-255-0231 *E-mail:* newdirections@ndbooks.com *Web Site:* www. ndpublishing.com, pg 187

Fox, R K, American Press, 28 State St, Suite 1100, Boston, MA 02109 *Tel:* 617-247-0022 *Fax:* 617-247-0022 *E-mail:* ampress@flash.net *Web Site:* www. americanpressboston.com, pg 16

Fox, Robert, Human Kinetics Inc, PO Box 5076, Champaign, IL 61825-5076 *Tel:* 217-351-5076 *Toll Free Tel:* 800-747-4457 *Fax:* 217-351-1549 (orders/ cust serv) *E-mail:* info@hkusa.com *Web Site:* www. humankinetics.com, pg 128

Foxe, Jeanette, Scott Publications Inc, 801 W Norton, Suite 200, Muskegon, MI 49441 *Tel:* 231-733-9382 *Toll Free Tel:* 866-733-9382 *Fax:* 231-733-7635 *E-mail:* contactus@scottpublications.com *Web Site:* www.scottpublications.com, pg 244

Foy, Fritz, Holtzbrinck Publishers, 175 Fifth Ave, New York, NY 10010 *Tel:* 212-674-5151 *Fax:* 212-420-9314 *E-mail:* firstname.lastname@hbpub.com *Web Site:* www.holtzbrinck.com, pg 125

Foy, Fritz, St Martin's Press LLC, 175 Fifth Ave, New York, NY 10010 *Tel:* 212-674-5151 *Fax:* 212-420-9314 *E-mail:* firstname.lastname@stmartins.com *Web Site:* www.stmartins.com, pg 238

Foy, Pat, Health Forum Inc, One N Franklin St, 28th fl, Chicago, IL 60606 *Tel:* 312-893-6884 *Toll Free Tel:* 800-242-2626 *Fax:* 312-422-4600 *Web Site:* www. ahaonlinestore.com, pg 119

Fraire, Mark, Artist Fellowship Awards Program, 101 E Wilson St, 1st fl, Madison, WI 53702 *Tel:* 608-266-0190 *Fax:* 608-267-0380 *E-mail:* artsboard@arts.state. wi.us *Web Site:* www.arts.state.wi.us, pg 760

Frame, Randy, Judson Press, 588 N Gulph Rd, King of Prussia, PA 19406 *Tel:* 610-768-2118 *Toll Free Tel:* 800-458-3766 *Fax:* 610-768-2441 *Web Site:* www. judsonpress.com, pg 143

Franc, Mike, The Heritage Foundation, 214 Massachusetts Ave NE, Washington, DC 20002-4999 *Tel:* 202-546-4400 *Fax:* 202-546-8328 *Web Site:* www. heritage.org, pg 705

Francen, Merry, Printing Brokerage/Buyers Association, PO Box 744, Palm Beach, FL 33480-0744 *Tel:* 561-586-9391 *Toll Free Tel:* 866-586-9391 *Fax:* 561-845-7130 *E-mail:* info@pbbai.net *Web Site:* www.pbbai. net, pg 697

Francendese, Janet, Temple University Press, 1601 N Broad St, 083-42, USB Room 306, Philadelphia, PA 19122-6099 *Tel:* 215-204-8787 *Toll Free Tel:* 800-447-1656 *Fax:* 215-204-4719 *E-mail:* tempress@temple. edu *Web Site:* www.temple.edu/tempress, pg 266

Frances, Michael, Classic Books, PO Box 130, Murrieta, CA 92564-0130 *Toll Free Tel:* 888-265-3547 *Toll Free Fax:* 888-265-3550 *E-mail:* 4classic@gte.net, pg 63

Franceschelli, Christopher, Handprint Books Inc, 413 Sixth Ave, Brooklyn, NY 11215-3310 *Tel:* 718-768-3696 *Fax:* 718-369-0844 *E-mail:* publisher@ handprintbooks.com *Web Site:* www.handprintbooks. com, pg 113

Franceschelli, Christopher, Ragged Bears, 413 Sixth Ave, Brooklyn, NY 11215-3310 *Tel:* 718-768-3696 *Fax:* 718-369-0844 *E-mail:* publisher@raggedbears. com *Web Site:* www.raggedbears.com, pg 224

Francis, Barbara, Pippin Press, 229 E 85 St, New York, NY 10028 *Tel:* 212-288-4920 *Fax:* 908-237-2407, pg 213

Francis, Brad, Penguin Group (Canada), 10 Alcorn Ave, Suite 300, Toronto, ON M4V 3B2, Canada *Tel:* 416-925-2249 *Fax:* 416-925-0068 *Web Site:* www.penguin. ca, pg 557

Francis, Donna, Creative Book Publishing, 36 Austin St, St Johns, NF A1B 3T7, Canada *Tel:* 709-722-8500 *Toll Free Tel:* 877-722-1722 (Canada only) *Fax:* 709-579-7745 *E-mail:* nlbooks@transcontinental. ca *Web Site:* www.nfbooks.com, pg 541

Francis, Lowell, University of Notre Dame Press, 310 Flanner Hall, Notre Dame, IN 46556 *Tel:* 574-631-6346 *Toll Free Tel:* 800-621-2736 (orders) *Fax:* 574-631-8148 *Toll Free Fax:* 800-621-8476 (orders) *E-mail:* nd.undpress.1@nd.edu *Web Site:* www. undpress.nd.edu, pg 284

Francis, Mary, University of California Press, 2120 Berkeley Way, Berkeley, CA 94720 *Tel:* 510-642-4247 *Toll Free Tel:* 800-777-4726 *Fax:* 510-643-7127 *Toll Free Fax:* 800-999-1958 *E-mail:* askucp@ucpress.edu *Web Site:* www.ucpress.edu, pg 281

Francis, Ruth, New Mexico Book Association (NMBA), 310 Read St, Santa Fe, NM 87504 *Tel:* 505-983-1412 *Fax:* 505-983-0899 *E-mail:* oceantree@earthlink.net *Web Site:* www.nmbook.org, pg 695

Francis, Therese, Crossquarter Publishing Group, 1910 Sombra Ct, Santa Fe, NM 87505 *Tel:* 505-438-9846 *Fax:* 505-438-9846 *E-mail:* sales@crossquarter.com; info@crossquarter.com *Web Site:* www.crossquarter. com, pg 73

Francisco, Daisy, Springer-Verlag New York Inc, 175 Fifth Ave, New York, NY 10010 *Tel:* 212-460-1500 *Toll Free Tel:* 800-777-4643 *Fax:* 212-473-6272 *Web Site:* www.springer-ny.com, pg 256

Franco, Carol, Harvard Business School Press, 300 N Beacon St, Watertown, MA 02472 *Tel:* 617-783-7400 *Toll Free Tel:* 888-500-1016 *Fax:* 617-783-7664 *E-mail:* bookpublisher@mail1.hbsp.harvard.edu *Web Site:* www.hbsp.harvard.edu, pg 116

Frank, Ann W, Rainmaker Literary Agency, 25 NW 23 Place, Suite 6, PMB 460, Portland, OR 97210-5599 *Tel:* 503-222-2249 *E-mail:* info@rainmakerliterary.com *Web Site:* www.rainmakerliterary.com, pg 650

Frank, Charlotte, McGraw-Hill Education, 2 Penn Plaza, New York, NY 10121 *Tel:* 212-904-2000 *E-mail:* customer.service@mcgraw-hill.com *Web Site:* www.mheducation.com; www.mheducation. com/custserv.html, pg 167

Frank, Cynthia, Cypress House, 155 Cypress St, Fort Bragg, CA 95437 *Tel:* 707-964-9520 *Toll Free Tel:* 800-773-7782 *Fax:* 707-964-7531 *E-mail:* publishing@cypresshouse.com *Web Site:* www.cypresshouse.com, pg 596

Frank, Daniel, Pantheon Books/Schocken Books, 1745 Broadway, New York, NY 10019 *Tel:* 212-751-2600 *Toll Free Tel:* 800-638-6460 *Fax:* 212-572-6030, pg 202

Frank, Jerome, Branden Publishing Co Inc, PO Box 812094, Wellesley, MA 02482-0013 *Tel:* 781-235-3634 *Fax:* 781-790-1056 *E-mail:* branden@branden.com *Web Site:* www.branden.com, pg 45

Frank, Jerry, Vandamere Press, 3580 Morris St N, Saint Petersburg, FL 33713 *Tel:* 727-556-0950 *Toll Free Tel:* 800-551-7776 *Fax:* 727-556-2560 *E-mail:* orders@vandamere.com *Web Site:* www.vandamere.com, pg 289

Frank, Joanne, Delta Systems Co Inc, 1400 Miller Pkwy, McHenry, IL 60050-7030 *Tel:* 815-363-3582 *Toll Free Tel:* 800-323-8270 *Fax:* 815-363-2948 *Toll Free Fax:* 800-909-9901 *E-mail:* custsvc@delta-systems.com *Web Site:* www.delta-systems.com, pg 79

Frank, Rebecca, Massachusetts Book Awards, Hampshire College MCB, 893 West St, Amherst, MA 01002 *Tel:* 413-559-5678 *Fax:* 413-559-5629 *E-mail:* massbook@hampshire.edu *Web Site:* www.massbook.org, pg 788

Frank, Sandi, The New York Botanical Garden Press, 200 St & Kazimiroff Blvd, Bronx, NY 10458-5126 *Tel:* 718-817-8721 *Fax:* 718-817-8842 *E-mail:* nybgpress@nybg.org *Web Site:* www.nybg.org, pg 189

Frank-McNeil, Julia, American Psychological Association, 750 First St NE, Washington, DC 20002-4242 *Tel:* 202-336-5500 *Toll Free Tel:* 800-374-2721 *Fax:* 202-336-5620 *E-mail:* order@apa.org *Web Site:* www.apa.org/books, pg 17

Frankel, Bonnie, Frankel & Associates, 5120 Wright Terr, Skokie, IL 60077 *Tel:* 847-674-8417, pg 669

Frankel, David, The Museum of Modern Art, 11 W 53 St, New York, NY 10019 *Tel:* 212-708-9443 *Fax:* 212-333-6575 *E-mail:* moma_publications@moma.org *Web Site:* www.moma.org, pg 180

Frankel, Ellen, Jewish Publication Society, 2100 Arch St, 2nd fl, Philadelphia, PA 19103 *Tel:* 215-832-0600 *Toll Free Tel:* 800-234-3151 *Fax:* 215-568-2017 *E-mail:* jewishbook@jewishpub.org *Web Site:* www.jewishpub.org, pg 141

Frankel, Norman, Frankel & Associates, 5120 Wright Terr, Skokie, IL 60077 *Tel:* 847-674-8417, pg 669

Frankio, Philip, Speakers Guild, PO Box 1540, Sandwich, MA 02563-1540 *Tel:* 508-888-6702 *Fax:* 508-888-6771 *E-mail:* speakers@cape.com *Web Site:* www.speakersguild.com, pg 670

Frankl, Beth, Shambhala Publications Inc, Horticultural Hall, 300 Massachusetts Ave, Boston, MA 02115 *Tel:* 617-424-0030 *Toll Free Tel:* 888-424-2329 (orders only) *Fax:* 617-236-1563; 303-665-5292 (orders only) *E-mail:* editors@shambhala.com *Web Site:* www.shambhala.com, pg 245

Franklin, Lynn C, Lynn C Franklin Associates Ltd, 1350 Broadway, Suite 2015, New York, NY 10018 *Tel:* 212-868-6311 *Fax:* 212-868-6312 *E-mail:* agency@fsainc.com, pg 631

Franklin, Paul, Abingdon Press, 201 Eighth Ave S, Nashville, TN 37203-3919 *Tel:* 615-749-6290 (publicist); 615-749-6000; 615-749-6451 (sales) *Toll Free Tel:* 800-251-3320 *Fax:* 615-749-6056 *Web Site:* www.abingdonpress.com, pg 3

Franklin, Penelope, Words into Print, 200 W 86 St, Suite 14-1, New York, NY 10024 *Tel:* 212-877-3211 *Fax:* 212-873-3796 *E-mail:* sas22@ix.netcom.com *Web Site:* www.wordsintoprint.org, pg 614

Franklin, Robert, McFarland & Co Inc Publishers, 960 Hwy 88 W, Jefferson, NC 28640 *Tel:* 336-246-4460 *Toll Free Tel:* 800-253-2187 (orders only) *Fax:* 336-

246-5018; 336-246-4403 (orders) *E-mail:* info@mcfarlandpub.com *Web Site:* www.mcfarlandpub.com, pg 166

Frankos, Anthony J, American Medical Association, 515 N State St, Chicago, IL 60610 *Tel:* 312-464-5000 *Toll Free Tel:* 800-621-8335 (cust serv) *Fax:* 312-464-4184 *Web Site:* www.ama-assn.org, pg 16

Frantz, Kristen, Berrett-Koehler Publishers Inc, 235 Montgomery St, Suite 650, San Francisco, CA 94104 *Tel:* 415-288-0260 *Fax:* 415-362-2512 *E-mail:* bkpub@bkpub.com *Web Site:* www.bkconnection.com, pg 37

Franzak, George, University Press of America Inc, 4501 Forbes Blvd, Suite 200, Lanham, MD 20706 *Tel:* 301-459-3366 *Toll Free Tel:* 800-462-6420 *Fax:* 301-429-5748 *Toll Free Fax:* 800-338-4550 *Web Site:* www.univpress.com, pg 286

Fraser, Suzanne, Tamos Books Inc, 300 Wales Ave, Winnipeg, MB R2M 2S9, Canada *Tel:* 204-256-9204 *Fax:* 204-255-7845 *E-mail:* tamos@mts.net *Web Site:* www.escape.ca/~tamos, pg 562

Fraser, Warren, University of Alaska Press, Eielson Bldg, Rm 104, Fairbanks, AK 99775-6240 *Tel:* 907-474-5831 *Toll Free Tel:* 888-252-6657 (US only) *Fax:* 907-474-5502 *E-mail:* fypress@uaf.edu *Web Site:* www.uaf.edu/uapress, pg 280

Frautshi, Dylan, Iconografix Inc, 1830-A Hanley Rd, Hudson, WI 54016 *Tel:* 715-381-9755 *Toll Free Tel:* 800-289-3504 (orders only) *Fax:* 715-381-9756 *E-mail:* iconogfx@spacestar.net, pg 130

Frazier, Felicia, Random House Children's Books, 1745 Broadway, New York, NY 10019 *Tel:* 212-782-9000 *Toll Free Tel:* 800-200-3552 *Fax:* 212-782-9452 *Web Site:* www.randomhouse.com/kids, pg 225

Frazier, Felicia, Random House Sales & Marketing, 1745 Broadway, New York, NY 10019 *Fax:* 212-782-9000, pg 227

Frazier, J Warren, John Hawkins & Associates Inc, 71 W 23 St, Suite 1600, New York, NY 10010 *Tel:* 212-807-7040 *Fax:* 212-807-9555 *Web Site:* jhaliterary.com, pg 634

Frazier, Kathleen, Health Press NA Inc, 2920 Carlisle Blvd NE, Albuquerque, NM 87110 *Tel:* 505-888-1394 *Fax:* 505-888-1521 *E-mail:* goodbooks@healthpress.com *Web Site:* www.healthpress.com, pg 119

Frech, Linda H, University of Missouri Press, 2910 Le Mone Blvd, Columbia, MO 65201 *Tel:* 573-882-7641 *Toll Free Tel:* 800-828-1894 (orders) *Fax:* 573-884-4498 *Web Site:* www.umsystem.edu/upress, pg 283

Frechette, Jacques, Guy Saint-Jean editeur Inc, 3154 Blvd Industriel, Laval, PQ H7L 4P7, Canada *Tel:* 450-663-1777 *Fax:* 450-663-6666 *E-mail:* saint-jean.editeur@qc.aira.com *Web Site:* www.saint-jeanediteur.com, pg 560

Frederick, Dawn, Sebastian Agency, 557 W Seventh St, Suite 2, St Paul, MN 55102 *Tel:* 651-224-6670 *Fax:* 651-224-6895 *Web Site:* www.sebastianagency.com, pg 654

Frederick, Ruth, Standard Publishing Co, 8121 Hamilton Ave, Cincinnati, OH 45231 *Tel:* 513-931-4050 *Toll Free Tel:* 800-543-1301 *Fax:* 513-931-0950 *Toll Free Fax:* 877-867-5751 *E-mail:* customerservice@standardpub.com *Web Site:* www.standardpub.com, pg 257

Fredericks, Jeanne, Jeanne Fredericks Literary Agency Inc, 221 Benedict Hill Rd, New Canaan, CT 06840 *Tel:* 203-972-3011 *Fax:* 203-972-3011 *E-mail:* jfredrks@optonline.net (no unsol attachments), pg 631

Free, Liz, John Hawkins & Associates Inc, 71 W 23 St, Suite 1600, New York, NY 10010 *Tel:* 212-807-7040 *Fax:* 212-807-9555 *Web Site:* jhaliterary.com, pg 634

Freedman, Robert A, Robert A Freedman Dramatic Agency Inc, 1501 Broadway, Suite 2310, New York, NY 10036 *Tel:* 212-840-5760 *Fax:* 212-840-5776, pg 631

Freeman, Brad, Nexus Press, 535 Means St, Atlanta, GA 30318 *Tel:* 404-577-3579 *Fax:* 404-577-5856 *E-mail:* nexusbooks@thecontemporary.org *Web Site:* www.thecontemporary.org, pg 191

Freeman, Don, Hazelden Publishing & Educational Services, 15251 Pleasant Valley Rd, Center City, MN 55012-0176 *Tel:* 651-213-4470 *Toll Free Tel:* 800-328-9000 *Web Site:* www.hazelden.org, pg 118

Freeman, Julie, International Association of Business Communicators (IABC), One Hallidie Plaza, Suite 600, San Francisco, CA 94102 *Tel:* 415-544-4700 *Toll Free Tel:* 800-776-4222 *Fax:* 415-544-4747 *E-mail:* service_centre@iabc.com *Web Site:* www.iabc.com, pg 688

Freeman, Robert, Carswell, One Corporate Plaza, 2075 Kennedy Rd, Toronto, ON M1T 3V4, Canada *Tel:* 416-609-8000 *Toll Free Tel:* 800-387-5164 (Canada & US) *Fax:* 416-298-5094 (Toronto); 403-233-8159 (Calgary); 604-685-5343 (Vancouver); 514-985-6605 *Toll Free Fax:* 877-750-9041 *E-mail:* comments@carswell.com *Web Site:* www.carswell.com, pg 539

Freeny, Devon, Bonus Books Inc, 1452 Second St, Santa Monica, CA 90403 *Tel:* 310-260-9400 *Toll Free Tel:* 800-225-3775 *E-mail:* webmaster@bonusbooks.com *Web Site:* www.bonusbooks.com, pg 43

Freeny, Devon, Precept Press, 1452 Second St, Santa Monica, CA 90401 *Tel:* 310-260-9400 *Fax:* 310-260-9494 *E-mail:* webmaster@bonusbooks.com *Web Site:* www.bonusbooks.com, pg 217

Freeny, Phyllis Jones, Professional Communications Inc, 20968 State Rd 22, Caddo, OK 74729 *Tel:* 580-367-9838 *Toll Free Tel:* 800-337-9838 *Fax:* 580-367-9989 *E-mail:* info@pcibooks.com *Web Site:* www.pcibooks.com, pg 219

Freiert, Jeffrey, Plume, 375 Hudson St, New York, NY 10014 *Tel:* 212-366-2000 *Fax:* 212-366-2666 *E-mail:* online@penguinputnam.com *Web Site:* www.penguin.com, pg 215

Freilach, David, MIT List Visual Arts Center, MIT E 15-109, 20 Ames St, Cambridge, MA 02139 *Tel:* 617-253-4680; 617-253-4400 (admission to exhibits) *Fax:* 617-258-7265 *E-mail:* hiroco@mit.edu *Web Site:* web.mit.edu/lvac, pg 175

Frelick, Tim, Elm Street Publishing Services Inc, 828 N Elm St, Hinsdale, IL 60521 *Tel:* 630-789-2102 *Fax:* 630-789-2105 *E-mail:* esps@elmst.com *Web Site:* www.elmst.com, pg 598

Frelick, Tim, Saunders College Publishing, The Public Ledger Bldg, 150 S Independence Mall W, Suite 1250, Philadelphia, PA 19106-3412 *Tel:* 215-238-5500 *Fax:* 215-238-5660 *Web Site:* www.hbcollege.com, pg 240

Fremon, Celeste, PEN Center USA, 672 S Lafayette Park Place, Suite 42, Los Angeles, CA 90057 *Tel:* 213-365-8500 *Fax:* 213-365-9616 *E-mail:* pen@penusa.org *Web Site:* www.penusa.org, pg 697

French, Carolyn, Fifi Oscard Agency Inc, 110 W 40 St, New York, NY 10018 *Tel:* 212-764-1100 *Fax:* 212-840-5019 *E-mail:* agency@fifioscard.com *Web Site:* www.fifioscard.com, pg 647

Frenette, Guy, Groupe Beauchemin, Editeur Ltee, 3281 ave Jean Beraud, Laval, PQ H7T 2L2, Canada *Tel:* 514-334-5912 *Toll Free Tel:* 800-361-2598 (US & Canada); 800-361-4504 (Canada Only) *Fax:* 450-688-6269 *E-mail:* promotion@beauchemin.qc.ca *Web Site:* www.beauchemineediteur.com, pg 536

Frenkel, James, Tom Doherty Associates, LLC, 175 Fifth Ave, 14th fl, New York, NY 10010 *Tel:* 212-388-0100 *Toll Free Tel:* 800-455-0340 *Fax:* 212-388-0191 *E-mail:* firstname.lastname@tor.com *Web Site:* www.tor.com, pg 82

Frese, Alan, Pippin Press, 229 E 85 St, New York, NY 10028 *Tel:* 212-288-4920 *Fax:* 908-237-2407, pg 213

Frevert, Patricia, Skinner House Books, 25 Beacon St, Boston, MA 02108-2800 *Tel:* 617-742-2100 *Fax:* 617-742-7025 *E-mail:* skinner_house@uua.org *Web Site:* www.uua.org/skinner/index.html, pg 249

Fry, Ronald W, The Career Press Inc, 3 Tice Rd, Franklin Lakes, NJ 07417 *Tel:* 201-848-0310 *Toll Free Tel:* 800-CAREER-1 (227-3371) *Fax:* 201-848-1727 *Web Site:* www.careerpress.com, pg 53

Fry, Sonya, The Cornelius Ryan Award, 40 W 45 St, New York, NY 10036 *Tel:* 212-626-9220 *Fax:* 212-626-9210 *Web Site:* www.opcofamerica.org, pg 803

Fry, Sonya K, Overseas Press Club of America (OPC), 40 W 45 St, New York, NY 10036 *Tel:* 212-626-9220 *Fax:* 212-626-9210 *Web Site:* www.opcofamerica.org, pg 696

Fryling, Robert A, InterVarsity Press, 430 E Plaza Dr, Westmont, IL 60559-1234 *Tel:* 630-734-4000 *Toll Free Tel:* 800-843-7225 *Fax:* 630-734-4200 *E-mail:* mail@ivpress.com *Web Site:* www.ivpress.com, pg 138

Fryman, Alona, Bloomsbury Publishing, 175 Fifth Ave, Suite 300, New York, NY 10010 *Tel:* 212-674-5151 *Toll Free Tel:* 800-221-7945 *Fax:* 212-780-0115 *Web Site:* www.bloomsbury.com/usa, pg 41

Fuchs, Carl, Research & Education Association, 61 Ethel Rd W, Piscataway, NJ 08854 *Tel:* 732-819-8880 *Fax:* 732-819-8808 *E-mail:* info@rea.com *Web Site:* www.rea.com, pg 231

Fuchs, Penny Bender, American Association of Sunday & Feature Editors, College of Journalism, University of Maryland, Journalism Bldg, College Park, MD 20742-7111 *Tel:* 301-314-2631 *E-mail:* aasfe@jmail.umd.edu *Web Site:* www.aasfe.org, pg 676

Fuenfhausen, Christian, Milkweed Editions, 1011 Washington Ave S, Suite 300, Minneapolis, MN 55415 *Tel:* 612-332-3192 *Toll Free Tel:* 800-520-6455 *Fax:* 612-215-2550 *E-mail:* editor@milkweed.org *Web Site:* www.milkweed.org; www.worldashome.org, pg 174

Fuentecilla, Eric, Free Press, 1230 Avenue of the Americas, New York, NY 10020 *Tel:* 212-698-7000 *Toll Free Tel:* 800-223-2345 (cust serv); 800-223-2336 (orders); 888-866-6631 (fulfillment), pg 100

Fuentes, Vincent, M E Sharpe Inc, 80 Business Park Dr, Suite 202, Armonk, NY 10504 *Tel:* 914-273-1800 *Toll Free Tel:* 800-541-6563 *Fax:* 914-273-2106 *E-mail:* info@mesharpe.com *Web Site:* www.mesharpe.com, pg 246

Fuersich, Larry, Visual Reference Publications Inc, 302 Fifth Ave, New York, NY 10001 *Tel:* 212-279-7000 *Toll Free Tel:* 800-251-4545 *Fax:* 212-279-7014 *Web Site:* www.visualrefernce.com, pg 291

Fuerstein, Carol, The Metropolitan Museum of Art, 1000 Fifth Ave, New York, NY 10028 *Tel:* 212-879-5500; 212-535-7710 *Fax:* 212-396-5062 *E-mail:* info@metmuseum.org *Web Site:* www.metmuseum.org, pg 173

Fugate, David, Waterside Productions Inc, 2187 Newcastle Ave, Suite 204, Cardiff, CA 92007 *Tel:* 760-632-9190 *Fax:* 760-632-9295 *Web Site:* www.waterside.com, pg 660

Fugee, Thomas R, Transportation Technical Service Inc, 500 Lafayette Blvd, Suite 230, Fredericksburg, VA 22401 *Tel:* 540-899-9872 *Toll Free Tel:* 888-ONLY-TTS (665-9887) *Fax:* 540-899-1948 *E-mail:* truckinfo@ttstrucks.com *Web Site:* www.ttstrucks.com, pg 274

Fugere, Collette, Chelsea Green Publishing Co, PO Box 428, White River Junction, VT 05001-0428 *Tel:* 802-295-6300 *Toll Free Tel:* 800-639-4099 (cust serv & consumer orders); 800-807-6726 (trade & wholesale orders) *Fax:* 802-295-6444 *Web Site:* www.chelseagreen.com, pg 59

Fugolo, c s, Rev Joseph, Center for Migration Studies of New York Inc, 209 Flagg Place, Staten Island, NY 10304-1199 *Tel:* 718-351-8800 *Fax:* 718-667-4598 *E-mail:* cms@cmsny.org *Web Site:* www.cmsny.org, pg 56

Fuhrman, Candice, Candice Fuhrman Literary Agency, 60 Greenwood Way, Mill Valley, CA 94941 *Tel:* 415-383-6081 *Fax:* 415-384-0739 *E-mail:* candicef@pacbell.net, pg 632

Fukuda, Jeanine, The Wright Group/McGraw-Hill, a Division of McGraw-Hill Learning Group, One Prudential Plaza, 130 E Randolph, 4th fl, Chicago, IL 60601 *Tel:* 312-233-6520 *Toll Free Tel:* 800-537-4740 *Fax:* 312-233-6605 *Web Site:* www.wrightgroup.com, pg 304

Fulbrook, John, Scribner, 1230 Avenue of the Americas, New York, NY 10020, pg 244

Fuller, Barbara, editcetera, 2034 Blake St, Suite 5, Berkeley, CA 94704 *Tel:* 510-849-1110 *Fax:* 510-848-1448 *E-mail:* info@editcetera.com *Web Site:* www.editcetera.com, pg 597

Fuller, Diana, Squaw Valley Community of Writers Workshops, PO Box 1416, Nevada City, CA 95959 *Tel:* 530-470-8440 *E-mail:* brett@squawvalleywriters.org *Web Site:* www.squawvalleywriters.org, pg 748

Fuller, Karen, Gray & Company Publishers, 1588 E 40 St, Cleveland, OH 44103 *Tel:* 216-431-2665 *Toll Free Tel:* 800-915-3609 *E-mail:* info@grayco.com *Web Site:* www.grayco.com, pg 108

Fuller, Renee, Ball-Stick-Bird Publications Inc, PO Box 429, Williamstown, MA 01267-0429 *Tel:* 413-664-0002 *Fax:* 413-664-0002 *E-mail:* info@ballstickbird.com *Web Site:* www.ballstickbird.com, pg 31

Fuller, Susan, Backbeat Books, 600 Harrison St, San Francisco, CA 94107 *Tel:* 415-947-6615 *Toll Free Tel:* 866-222-5232 (orders only) *Fax:* 415-947-6015; 408-848-8294 (orders only) *E-mail:* books@musicplayer.com; books@cmp.com *Web Site:* www.backbeatbooks.com, pg 30

Fuller, Susan, CMP Books, 600 Harrison St, San Francisco, CA 94107 *Tel:* 415-947-6615; 408-848-3854 (orders) *Toll Free Tel:* 800-500-6875 (orders) *Fax:* 415-947-6015; 408-848-5784 (orders) *E-mail:* books@cmp.com *Web Site:* www.cmpbooks.com, pg 63

Fullman, Milton, SATW Foundation Lowell Thomas Travel Journalism Competition, 1500 Sunday Dr, Suite 102, Raleigh, NC 27607 *Tel:* 919-861-5586; 713-532-6461 *Fax:* 919-787-4916 *Web Site:* www.satw.org, pg 803

Fullman, Milton, Society of American Travel Writers Foundation, 1500 Sunday Dr, Suite 102, Raleigh, NC 27607 *Tel:* 919-861-5586 *Fax:* 919-787-4916 *E-mail:* satw@satw.org *Web Site:* www.satw.org, pg 700

Fulton, Len, Dustbooks, PO Box 100, Paradise, CA 95967-0222 *Tel:* 530-877-6110 *Toll Free Tel:* 800-477-6110 *Fax:* 530-877-0222 *E-mail:* publisher@dustbooks.com *Web Site:* www.dustbooks.com, pg 85

Fulton, Margaretta, Harvard University Press, 79 Garden St, Cambridge, MA 02138-1499 *Tel:* 617-495-2600; 401-531-2800 (international orders) *Toll Free Tel:* 800-405-1619 (orders) *Fax:* 617-495-5898 (general); 617-496-4677 (edit & rts); 401-531-2801 (international orders) *Toll Free Tel:* 800-406-9145 (orders) *E-mail:* firstname_lastname@harvard.edu *Web Site:* www.hup.harvard.edu, pg 117

Fulton, Richard, Richard Fulton Inc, 66 Richfield St, Plainview, NY 11803 *Tel:* 516-349-0407 *Fax:* 516-349-0407, pg 669

Fund, Ken, Rockport Publishers, 33 Commercial St, Gloucester, MA 01930 *Tel:* 978-282-9590 *Fax:* 978-283-2742 *Web Site:* www.rockpub.com, pg 233

Funk, Cameon, MAR*CO Products Inc, 1443 Old York Rd, Warminster, PA 18974 *Tel:* 215-956-0313 *Toll Free Tel:* 800-448-2197 *Fax:* 215-956-9041 *E-mail:* marcoproducts@comcast.net *Web Site:* www.marcoproducts.com; www.store.yahoo.com/marcoproducts, pg 163

Furbush, Helen, Harbor Island Books, 1214 W Boston Post Rd, No 245, Mamaroneck, NY 10543 *Tel:* 914-420-9782 *Fax:* 914-835-7897 *E-mail:* publisher@lyingawake.net *Web Site:* www.lyingawake.net, pg 571

Furl, Nate, Dalkey Archive Press, Illinois State University 8905, Normal, IL 61790-8905 *Tel:* 309-438-7555 *Fax:* 309-438-7422 *E-mail:* contact@dalkeyarchive.com *Web Site:* www.dalkeyarchive.com, pg 75

Furman, Laura, Prize Stories: The O Henry Awards, Univ of Texas at Austin, One University Sta B 5000, Austin, TX 78712 *Tel:* 212-572-2016 *Web Site:* www.ohenryprizestories.com, pg 800

Furman, Laura, University of Texas at Austin, Creative Writing Program, Dept of English, One University Sta, B5000, Austin, TX 78712-1164 *Tel:* 512-475-6356 *Fax:* 512-471-2898 *Web Site:* www.en.utexas.edu/grad/crwconc.html, pg 756

Furney, Laura, University Press of Colorado, 5589 Arapahoe Ave, Suite 206-C, Boulder, CO 80303 *Tel:* 720-406-8849 *Toll Free Tel:* 800-627-7377 *Fax:* 720-406-3443 *Web Site:* www.upcolorado.com, pg 286

Furnish, Ben, BKMK Press of the University of Missouri-Kansas City, 5101 Rockhill Rd, Kansas City, MO 64110-2499 *Tel:* 816-235-2558 *Fax:* 816-235-2611 *E-mail:* bkmk@umkc.edu *Web Site:* www.umkc.edu/bkmk, pg 39

Furnish, Ben, G S Sharat Chandra Prize for Short Fiction, 5101 Rockhill Rd, Kansas City, MO 64110 *Tel:* 816-235-2558 *Fax:* 816-235-2611 *E-mail:* bkmk@umkc.edu *Web Site:* www.umkc.edu/bkmk/, pg 766

Furnish, Ben, John Ciardi Prize for Poetry, 5101 Rockhill Rd, Kansas City, MO 64110 *Tel:* 816-235-2558 *Fax:* 816-235-2611 *E-mail:* bkmk@umkc.edu *Web Site:* www.umkc.edu/bkmk/, pg 767

Furse, Ray, Weatherhill Inc, 41 Monroe Tpke, Trumbull, CT 06611 *Tel:* 203-459-5090 *Toll Free Tel:* 800-437-7840 *Fax:* 203-459-5095 *Toll Free Fax:* 800-557-5601 *E-mail:* weatherhill@weatherhill.com *Web Site:* www.weatherhill.com, pg 295

Furst, Jerry, Liturgical Press, St John's Abbey, Collegeville, MN 56321 *Tel:* 320-363-2213 *Toll Free Tel:* 800-858-5450 *Fax:* 320-363-3299 *Toll Free Fax:* 800-445-5899 *E-mail:* sales@litpress.org *Web Site:* www.litpress.org, pg 156

Fusco, Antonia, Algonquin Books of Chapel Hill, 127 Kingston Dr, Suite 105, Chapel Hill, NC 27514 *Tel:* 919-967-0108 *Fax:* 919-933-0272 *E-mail:* dialogue@algonquin.com *Web Site:* www.algonquin.com, pg 8

Fusting, Donald W, Lanahan Publishers Inc, 324 Hawthorn Rd, Baltimore, MD 21210 *Tel:* 410-366-2434 *Toll Free Tel:* 866-354-1949 *Fax:* 410-366-8798 *Toll Free Fax:* 888-345-7257 *E-mail:* lanahan@aol.com *Web Site:* www.lanahanpublishers.com, pg 148

Futter, Deb, Doubleday Broadway Publishing Group, 1745 Broadway, New York, NY 10019 *Tel:* 212-782-9000 *Toll Free Tel:* 800-223-6834; 800-223-5780 (sales) *Fax:* 212-302-7985 (correspondence); 212-492-9862 (orders), pg 82

Fyerson, Dennis, Briefings Publishing Group, 1101 King St, Suite 110, Alexandria, VA 22314 *Tel:* 703-548-3800 *Toll Free Tel:* 800-888-2086 *Fax:* 703-684-2136 *E-mail:* customerservice@briefings.com *Web Site:* www.briefings.com, pg 47

Ga, Ellie, Ugly Duckling Presse, 106 Ferris St, 2nd fl, Brooklyn, NY 11231 *Tel:* 718-852-5529 *E-mail:* udp_mailbox@yahoo.com *Web Site:* www.uglyducklingpresse.org, pg 278

Gabbert, Doug, Multnomah Publishers Inc, 204 W Adams Ave, Sisters, OR 97759 *Tel:* 541-549-1144 *Toll Free Tel:* 800-929-0910 *Fax:* 541-549-2044 (sales); 541-549-0432 (admin); 541-549-0260 (ed/prod); 541-549-8048 (mktg) *E-mail:* information@multnomahbooks.com *Web Site:* www.multnomahbooks.com, pg 180

Gable, Dorothy, Medical Physics Publishing Corp, 4513 Vernon Blvd, Madison, WI 53705-4964 *Tel:* 608-262-4021 *Toll Free Tel:* 800-442-5778 *Fax:* 608-265-2121 *E-mail:* mpp@medicalphysics.org *Web Site:* www.medicalphysics.org, pg 170

Gabler, Betsy, Zephyr Press Catalog, 814 N Franklin St, Chicago, IL 60610 *Tel:* 312-337-5985 *Toll Free Tel:* 800-232-2187 *Fax:* 312-337-1651 *E-mail:* neways2learn@zephyrpress.com *Web Site:* www.zephyrpress.com, pg 307

Gabler, Edna, United States Tennis Association, 70 W Red Oak Lane, White Plains, NY 10604 *Tel:* 914-696-7000 *Fax:* 914-696-7027 *Web Site:* www.usta.com, pg 279

Gabriel, Ashala, Marlene Gabriel Agency, 333 W 56 St, Suite 8-A, 8th fl, New York, NY 10019 *Tel:* 212-397-8322 *E-mail:* mgalit@aol.com, pg 632

Gabriel, B J, Simon & Schuster Sales & Distribution, 1230 Avenue of the Americas, New York, NY 10020 *Tel:* 212-698-7000, pg 249

Gabriel, Tricia, Phaidon Press Inc, 180 Varick St, 14th fl, New York, NY 10014 *Tel:* 212-652-5400 *Toll Free Tel:* 800-759-0190 (cust serv) *Fax:* 212-652-5410 *Toll Free Fax:* 800-286-9471 (cust serv) *E-mail:* ussales@phaidon.com *Web Site:* www.phaidon.com, pg 211

Gabrielli, Edward, St Martin's Press Paperback and Reference Group, 175 Fifth Ave, New York, NY 10010 *Tel:* 212-995-2488 *E-mail:* firstname.lastname@stmartins.com, pg 239

Gadd, Laurence, North River Press Publishing Corp, 321 Main St, Great Barrington, MA 01230 *Tel:* 413-528-0034 *Toll Free Tel:* 800-486-2665 *Fax:* 413-528-3163 *Toll Free Fax:* 800-BOOK-FAX (266-5329) *E-mail:* info@northriverpress.com *Web Site:* www.northriverpress.com, pg 192

Gaden, Bill, Simon & Schuster Children's Publishing, 1230 Avenue of the Americas, New York, NY 10020 *Tel:* 212-698-7000 *Web Site:* www.simonsayskids.com, pg 248

Gades, Gwen, Dragon Moon Press, PO Box 64312, Calgary, AB T2K 6J7, Canada *Tel:* 403-277-2140 *Fax:* 403-277-3679 *E-mail:* publisher@dragonmoonpress.com *Web Site:* www.dragonmoonpress.com, pg 543

Gadja, Linda, Institute of Environmental Sciences and Technology - IEST, 5005 Newport Dr, Suite 506, Rolling Meadows, IL 60008 *Tel:* 847-255-1561 *Fax:* 847-255-1699 *E-mail:* publicationsales@iest.org *Web Site:* iest.org, pg 135

Gadler, Enrica, The Lyons Press, 246 Goose Lane, Guilford, CT 06437 *Tel:* 203-458-4500 *Toll Free Tel:* 800-243-0495 *Fax:* 203-458-4668 *Web Site:* www.lyonspress.com; www.globepequot.com, pg 160

Gadney, Alan, Film-Video Publications/Circus Source Publications, 7944 Capistrano Ave, West Hills, CA 91304 *Tel:* 818-340-0175 *Fax:* 818-340-6770 *E-mail:* circussource@aol.com, pg 96

Gadney, Mary M, Film-Video Publications/Circus Source Publications, 7944 Capistrano Ave, West Hills, CA 91304 *Tel:* 818-340-0175 *Fax:* 818-340-6770 *E-mail:* circussource@aol.com, pg 96

Gadsen, Cynthia, Abingdon Press, 201 Eighth Ave S, Nashville, TN 37203-3919 *Tel:* 615-749-6290 (publicist); 615-749-6000; 615-749-6451 (sales) *Toll Free Tel:* 800-251-3320 *Fax:* 615-749-6056 *Web Site:* www.abingdonpress.com, pg 3

Gaedhe, Nick, Educators Publishing Service Inc, 625 Mount Auburn St, Cambridge, MA 02139-9031 *Tel:* 617-547-6706 *Toll Free Tel:* 800-225-5750 *Fax:* 617-547-0412 *Toll Free Fax:* 888-440-2665 *E-mail:* epsbooks@epsbooks.com *Web Site:* www.epsbooks.com, pg 88

Gaeth, Lisa, W W Norton & Company Inc, 500 Fifth Ave, New York, NY 10110-0017 *Tel:* 212-354-5500 *Toll Free Tel:* 800-233-4830 (orders & cust serv) *Fax:* 212-869-0856 *Toll Free Fax:* 800-458-6515 *Web Site:* www.wwnorton.com, pg 193

Gaffin, Deborah, e-Scholastic, 568 Broadway, 9th fl, New York, NY 10012 *Tel:* 212-343-7100 *Fax:* 212-343-4949, pg 85

Gage, J Marshall, Kirkbride Bible Co Inc, 335 W Ninth St, Indianapolis, IN 46202 *Tel:* 317-633-1900 *Toll Free Tel:* 800-428-4385 *Fax:* 317-633-1444 *E-mail:* sales@kirkbride.com *Web Site:* www.kirkbride.com, pg 146

Gagel, Diane, Ohio Genealogical Society, 713 S Main St, Mansfield, OH 44907-1644 *Tel:* 419-756-7294 *Fax:* 419-756-6861 *E-mail:* ogs@ogs.org *Web Site:* www.ogs.org, pg 196

Gagne, Normand, Les Editions du Roseau, 6521 rue Louis-Hemon, Montreal, PQ H2G 2L1, Canada *Tel:* 514-725-7772 *Fax:* 514-725-5889 *E-mail:* editions@roseau.ca *Web Site:* www.roseau.ca, pg 544

Gagnon, Jean-Marc, Editions Multimondes, 930 rue Pouliot, Sainte-Foy, PQ G1V 3N9, Canada *Tel:* 418-651-3885 *Toll Free Tel:* 800-840-3029 *Fax:* 418-651-6822 *Toll Free Fax:* 888-303-5931 *E-mail:* multimondes@multim.com *Web Site:* www.multimondes.qc.ca, pg 555

Gagnon, Nicole, Warren, Gorham & Lamont, 395 Hudson St, New York, NY 10014 *Tel:* 212-367-6300 *Toll Free Tel:* 800-431-9025; 800-678-2185 (cust serv) *Fax:* 212-367-6305 *Web Site:* www.riahome.com, pg 293

Gaines, Karen, Productivity Press, 444 Park Ave S, Suite 604, New York, NY 10016 *Tel:* 212-686-5900 *Toll Free Tel:* 888-319-5852 *Fax:* 212-686-5411 *Toll Free Fax:* 800-394-6286 *E-mail:* info@productivitypress.com *Web Site:* www.productivitypress.com, pg 219

Gainsburg, Roy, St Martin's Press LLC, 175 Fifth Ave, New York, NY 10010 *Tel:* 212-674-5151 *Fax:* 212-420-9314 *E-mail:* firstname.lastname@stmartins.com *Web Site:* www.stmartins.com, pg 238

Galassi, Donna, Avalon Publishing Group Inc, 1400 65 St, Suite 250, Emeryville, CA 94608 *Tel:* 510-595-3664 *Fax:* 510-535-4228 *Web Site:* www.avalonpub.com, pg 29

Galassi, Donna, Avalon Travel Publishing, 1400 65 St, Suite 250, Emeryville, CA 94608 *Tel:* 510-595-3664 *Fax:* 510-535-4228 *E-mail:* info@travelmatters.com *Web Site:* www.travelmatters.com, pg 29

Galassi, Jonathan, Farrar, Straus & Giroux, LLC, 19 Union Sq W, New York, NY 10003 *Tel:* 212-741-6900 *Fax:* 212-741-6973 *Web Site:* www.fsgbooks.com, pg 95

Galasso, Al, North American Bookdealers Exchange, PO Box 606, Cottage Grove, OR 97424-0026 *Tel:* 541-942-7455 *Fax:* 561-258-2625 *E-mail:* nabe@bookmarketingprofits.com *Web Site:* www.bookmarketingprofits.com, pg 695

Galbraith, Judy, Free Spirit Publishing Inc, 217 Fifth Ave N, Suite 200, Minneapolis, MN 55401-1299 *Tel:* 612-338-2068 *Toll Free Tel:* 800-735-7323 *Fax:* 612-337-5050 *E-mail:* help4kids@freespirit.com *Web Site:* www.freespirit.com, pg 100

Gale, David, Simon & Schuster Children's Publishing, 1230 Avenue of the Americas, New York, NY 10020 *Tel:* 212-698-7000 *Web Site:* www.simonsayskids.com, pg 248

Gale, Kate, Red Hen Press, PO Box 3537, Granada Hills, CA 91394-0537 *Tel:* 818-831-0649 *Fax:* 818-831-6659 *E-mail:* editors@redhen.org *Web Site:* www.redhen.org, pg 229

Gale, Meighan, Zone Books, 1226 Prospect Ave, Brooklyn, NY 11218 *Tel:* 718-686-0048 *Toll Free Tel:* 800-405-1619 (orders & cust serv) *Fax:* 212-625-9772; 718-686-9045 *Toll Free Fax:* 800-406-9145 (orders) *E-mail:* urzone@zonebooks.org; mitpress-orders@mit.edu (orders), pg 307

Galen, Esther, Mehring Books Inc, PO Box 48377, Oak Park, MI 48237-5977 *Tel:* 248-967-2924 *Fax:* 248-967-3023 *E-mail:* inquiry@mehring.com; sales@mehring.com *Web Site:* www.mehring.com, pg 171

Galen, Russell, Scovil Chichak Galen Literary Agency Inc, 381 Park Ave S, Suite 1020, New York, NY 10016 *Tel:* 212-679-8686 *Fax:* 212-679-6710 *E-mail:* mailroom@scglit.com *Web Site:* www.scglit.com, pg 654

Gales, Tammie, Northland Publishing Co, 2900 N Fort Valley Rd, Flagstaff, AZ 86001 *Tel:* 928-774-5251 *Toll Free Tel:* 800-346-3257 *Fax:* 928-774-0592 *E-mail:* info@northlandpub.com; design@northlandpub.com; editorial@northlandpub.com *Web Site:* www.northlandpub.com, pg 193

Galian, Carl, Random House Publishing Group, 1745 Broadway, New York, NY 10019 *Toll Free Tel:* 800-200-3552 *Toll Free Fax:* 800-200-3552 *Web Site:* www.randomhouse.com, pg 227

Galimberti, Joseph, Institute of Public Administration of Canada, 1075 Bay St, Suite 401, Toronto, ON M5S 2B1, Canada *Tel:* 416-924-8787 *Fax:* 416-924-4992 *E-mail:* ntl@ipac.ca; ntl@iapc.ca *Web Site:* www.ipac.ca; www.iapc.ca, pg 551

Gall, John, Vintage & Anchor Books, 1745 Broadway, New York, NY 10019 *Tel:* 212-751-2600 *Fax:* 212-572-6043, pg 291

Gall, Robert, Blue Mountain Arts Inc, PO Box 4549, Boulder, CO 80306 *Tel:* 303-449-0536 *Toll Free Tel:* 800-473-2082 *Fax:* 303-417-6496 *Toll Free Fax:* 800-256-1213 *E-mail:* booksbma@mindspring.com; ordersbma@mindspring.com *Web Site:* www.sps.com, pg 41

Gallagher, Amy, North River Press Publishing Corp, 321 Main St, Great Barrington, MA 01230 *Tel:* 413-528-0034 *Toll Free Tel:* 800-486-2665 *Fax:* 413-528-3163 *Toll Free Fax:* 800-BOOK-FAX (266-5329) *E-mail:* info@northriverpress.com *Web Site:* www.northriverpress.com, pg 192

Gallagher, Derek, Western National Parks Association, 12880 N Vistoso Village Dr, Tucson, AZ 85737-8797 *Tel:* 520-622-1999 *Toll Free Tel:* 888-569-SPMA (orders only) *Fax:* 520-623-9519 *E-mail:* info@wnpa.org *Web Site:* www.wnpa.org, pg 296

Gallagher, Judith, Ligonier Valley Writers Conference, PO Box B, Ligonier, PA 15658-1602 *Tel:* 724-537-3341 *Fax:* 724-537-0482 *E-mail:* sarshi@wpa.net, pg 744

Gallagher, Kati, Upper Midwest Booksellers Association (UMBA), 3407 W 44 St, Minneapolis, MN 55410 *Tel:* 612-926-5868 *Toll Free Tel:* 800-784-7522 *Fax:* 612-926-6657 *E-mail:* umbaoffice@aol.com *Web Site:* www.abookaday.com, pg 701

Gallagher, Megan, Xlibris Corp, 436 Walnut St, 11th fl, The Independence Bldg, Philadelphia, PA 19106 *Tel:* 215-923-4686 *Toll Free Tel:* 888-795-4274 *Fax:* 215-923-4685 *E-mail:* info@xlibris.com *Web Site:* www.xlibris.com, pg 305

Gallagher, Pamela, Violet Downey Book Award, 40 Orchard View Blvd, Suite 254, Toronto, ON M4R 1B9, Canada *Tel:* 416-487-4416 *Fax:* 416-487-4417 *E-mail:* iode@bellnet.ca *Web Site:* www.iode.ca, pg 770

Gallagher, Patricia, Liberty Fund Inc, 8335 Allison Pointe Trail, Suite 300, Indianapolis, IN 46250-1684 *Tel:* 317-842-0880 *Toll Free Tel:* 800-955-8335 *Fax:* 317-579-6060 *E-mail:* books@libertyfund.org *Web Site:* www.libertyfund.org, pg 153

Gallagher, Patty, The Globe Pequot Press, 246 Goose Lane, Guilford, CT 06437 *Tel:* 203-458-4500 *Toll Free Tel:* 800-243-0495 (cust serv) *Fax:* 203-458-4601 *Toll Free Fax:* 800-820-2329 (orders & cust serv) *E-mail:* info@globepequot.com *Web Site:* www.globepequot.com, pg 106

Gallagher, Richard R, National Book Co, PO Box 8795, Portland, OR 97207-8795 *Tel:* 503-228-6345 *Fax:* 810-885-5811 *E-mail:* info@eralearning.com *Web Site:* www.eralearning.com, pg 182

Gallardo, Adriana, Chicano Latino Literary Contest, University of California, Dept Spanish & Portuguese, Irvine, CA 92697-5275 *Tel:* 949-824-5443 *Fax:* 949-824-2803 *E-mail:* cllp@uci.edu *Web Site:* www.humanities.uci.edu/spanishandportuguese/contest.html, pg 766

Gallegos, Anna, Museum of New Mexico Press, 725 Camino Lejo, Santa Fe, NM 87501 *Tel:* 505-476-1158 *Toll Free Tel:* 800-249-7737 (orders) *Fax:* 505-476-1156 *Toll Free Fax:* 800-622-8667 (orders) *E-mail:* mnmpress@aol.com *Web Site:* www.mnmpress.org, pg 180

Gallman, Amanda, Sandlapper Publishing Inc, PO Drawer 730, Orangeburg, SC 29116-0730 *Tel:* 803-531-1658 *Toll Free Tel:* 800-849-7263 (orders only) *Fax:* 803-534-5223 *Web Site:* www.sandlapperpublishing.com, pg 239

Gallo, Irene, Tom Doherty Associates, LLC, 175 Fifth Ave, 14th fl, New York, NY 10010 *Tel:* 212-388-0100 *Toll Free Tel:* 800-455-0340 *Fax:* 212-388-0191 *E-mail:* firstname.lastname@tor.com *Web Site:* www.tor.com, pg 81

Gallo, Vincent, William H Sadlier Inc, 9 Pine St, New York, NY 10005 *Tel:* 212-227-2120 *Toll Free Tel:* 800-221-5175 *Fax:* 212-312-6080 *Web Site:* www.sadlier.com; www.sadlier-oxford.com, pg 237

Gallotta, Trish, OPIS/STALSBY Directories & Databases, Parkway 70 Plaza, 1255 Rt 70, Suite 32N, Lakewood, NJ 08701 *Tel:* 732-901-8800 *Toll Free Tel:* 800-275-0950 *Fax:* 732-901-9632 *Web Site:* www.opisnet.com, pg 198

Galt, Jeffrey, Harcourt Assessment Inc, 19500 Bulverde Rd, San Antonio, TX 78259 *Tel:* 210-339-5000 *Toll Free Tel:* 800-211-8378 *Web Site:* www.harcourtassessment.com, pg 114

Galvin, Laura, Soundprints, 353 Main Ave, Norwalk, CT 06851 *Tel:* 203-846-2274 *Toll Free Tel:* 800-228-7839; 800-577-2413, ext 118 (orders) *Fax:* 203-846-1776 *E-mail:* Soundprints@soundprints.com *Web Site:* www.soundprints.com, pg 253

Galvin, Robert, EMC/Paradigm Publishing, 875 Montreal Way, St Paul, MN 55102 *Tel:* 651-290-2800 (corp) *Toll Free Tel:* 800-328-1452 *Fax:* 651-290-2899 *Toll Free Fax:* 800-328-4564 *E-mail:* educate@emcp.com *Web Site:* www.emcp.com, pg 90

Galvin, Tom, Health Communications Inc, 3201 SW 15 St, Deerfield Beach, FL 33442-8190 *Tel:* 954-360-0909 *Toll Free Tel:* 800-851-9100 (cust serv); 800-441-5569 (order entry) *Fax:* 954-360-0034 *Web Site:* www.hcibooks.com, pg 119

Gamarello, Paul, Workman Publishing Co Inc, 708 Broadway, New York, NY 10003-9555 *Tel:* 212-254-5900 *Toll Free Tel:* 800-722-7202 *Fax:* 212-254-8098 *E-mail:* info@workman.com *Web Site:* www.workman.com, pg 303

Gambardella, Lisa, Nelson Information, 195 Broadway, 5th fl, New York, NY 10007 *Tel:* 646-822-2000 *Toll Free Tel:* 888-371-4575; 888-280-4864 (orders) *Fax:* 914-937-8590 *Web Site:* www.nelsoninformation.com, pg 186

Gamboa, Sharon, Penguin Group (USA) Inc Sales, 375 Hudson St, New York, NY 10014 *Tel:* 212-366-2000 *E-mail:* online@penguinputnam.com *Web Site:* www.penguin.com, pg 208

Gambrel, Bryan, Indiana University Press, 601 N Morton St, Bloomington, IN 47404-3797 *Tel:* 812-855-8817 *Toll Free Tel:* 800-842-6796 (orders only) *Fax:* 812-855-7931 (orders only); 812-855-8507 *E-mail:* iupress@indiana.edu; iuorder@indiana.edu (orders) *Web Site:* www.iupress.indiana.edu, pg 132

Gammon, Kimberly, EDGE Science Fiction & Fantasy Publishing, PO Box 1714, Sta M, Calgary, AB T2P 2L7, Canada *Tel:* 403-254-0160 *Toll Free Tel:* 877-254-0115 *Fax:* 403-254-0456 *E-mail:* publisher@hadespublications.com *Web Site:* www.edgewebsite.com, pg 543

Gammons, Keith, Smyth & Helwys Publishing Inc, 6316 Peake Rd, Macon, GA 31210 *Tel:* 478-757-1305 *Toll Free Tel:* 800-747-3016; 800-568-1248 *Fax:* 478-757-0564 *E-mail:* market@helwys.com *Web Site:* www.helwys.com, pg 251

Gandiglio, Carla G, Hadronic Press Inc, 35246 US 19 N, No 215, Palm Harbor, FL 34684 *Tel:* 727-934-9593 *Fax:* 727-934-9275 *E-mail:* hadronic@tampabay.rr.com *Web Site:* www.hadronicpress.com, pg 111

Gandorf, James, The Mathematical Association of America, 1529 18 St NW, Washington, DC 20036 *Tel:* 202-387-5200 *Toll Free Tel:* 800-331-1622 (orders) *Fax:* 202-265-2384 *E-mail:* ldouglas@pmds.com *Web Site:* www.maa.org, pg 165

Gandrow, Kristen, Jerome Playwright-in-Residence Fellowship, 2301 Franklin Ave E, Minneapolis, MN 55406 *Tel:* 612-332-7481 *Fax:* 612-332-6037 *E-mail:* info@pwcenter.org *Web Site:* www.pwcenter.org, pg 781

Gandrow, Kristen, Many Voices Residencies, 2301 Franklin Ave E, Minneapolis, MN 55406 *Tel:* 612-332-7481 *Fax:* 612-332-6037 *E-mail:* info@pwcenter.org *Web Site:* www.pwcenter.org, pg 787

Gandrow, Kristen, McKnight Advancement Grants, 2301 Franklin Ave E, Minneapolis, MN 55406 *Tel:* 612-332-7481 *Fax:* 612-332-6037 *E-mail:* info@pwcenter.org *Web Site:* www.pwcenter.org, pg 788

Gandrow, Kristen, McKnight National Residency & Commission, 2301 Franklin Ave E, Minneapolis, MN 55406 *Tel:* 612-332-7481 *Fax:* 612-332-6037 *E-mail:* info@pwcenter.org *Web Site:* www.pwcenter.org, pg 788

Gandrow, Kristen, PlayLabs, 2301 Franklin Ave E, Minneapolis, MN 55406 *Tel:* 612-332-7481 *Fax:* 612-332-6037 *E-mail:* info@pwcenter.org *Web Site:* www.pwcenter.org, pg 799

Gann, Kirby, Sarabande Books Inc, 2234 Dundee Rd, Suite 200, Louisville, KY 40205 *Tel:* 502-458-4028 *Fax:* 502-458-4065 *E-mail:* info@sarabandebooks.org *Web Site:* www.sarabandebooks.org, pg 240

Gantz, Thomas W, Kendall/Hunt Publishing Co, 4050 Westmark Dr, Dubuque, IA 52002 *Tel:* 563-589-1000 *Toll Free Tel:* 800-228-0810 (orders only) *Fax:* 563-589-1114 *Toll Free Fax:* 800-772-9165 *Web Site:* www.kendallhunt.com, pg 144

Garabedian, Peter, Holtzbrinck Publishers, 175 Fifth Ave, New York, NY 10010 *Tel:* 212-674-5151 *Fax:* 212-420-9314 *E-mail:* firstname.lastname@hbpub.com *Web Site:* www.holtzbrinck.com, pg 124

Garano, Lorna, New Harbinger Publications Inc, 5674 Shattuck Ave, Oakland, CA 94609 *Tel:* 510-652-0215 *Toll Free Tel:* 800-748-6273 (orders only) *Fax:* 510-652-5472 *E-mail:* nhhelp@newharbinger.com *Web Site:* www.newharbinger.com, pg 188

Garcia, Carlos, American Institute of Ultrasound in Medicine, 14750 Sweitzer Lane, Suite 100, Laurel, MD 20707-5906 *Tel:* 301-498-4100 *Toll Free Tel:* 800-638-5352 *Fax:* 301-498-4450 *E-mail:* publications@aium.org *Web Site:* www.aium.org, pg 15

Garcia, Florencio Oscar, FOG Publications, 413 Pennsylvania NE, Albuquerque, NM 87108 *Tel:* 505-255-3096, pg 98

Garcia, Kathleen, Beta Computer Indexing, 61 S Kashong Dr, Geneva, NY 14456 *Tel:* 315-719-0486 *Fax:* 315-719-0487, pg 591

Garcia, Robert T, American Fantasy Press, 919 Tappan St, Woodstock, IL 60098 *Tel:* 815-338-5512 *Fax:* 815-338-5512 *E-mail:* garpubserv@aol.com *Web Site:* www.american-fantasy.com, pg 569

Gardenier, Polly, Binford & Mort Publishing Inc, 5245 NE Elam Young Pkwy, Suite C, Hillsboro, OR 97124 *Tel:* 503-844-4960 *Toll Free Tel:* 888-221-4514 *Fax:* 503-844-4959, pg 38

Gardiner, Eileen, Italica Press, 595 Main St, Suite 605, New York, NY 10044 *Tel:* 212-935-4230 *Fax:* 212-838-7812 *E-mail:* inquiries@italicapress.com *Web Site:* www.italicapress.com, pg 139

Gardner, Bensen, University of Wisconsin Press, 1930 Monroe St, 3rd fl, Madison, WI 53711 *Tel:* 608-263-1110 *Toll Free Tel:* 800-621-2736 (Orders) *Fax:* 608-263-1120 *Toll Free Fax:* 800-621-8476 (Orders) *E-mail:* uwiscpress@uwpress.wisc.edu (Main Office) *Web Site:* www.wisc.edu/wisconsinpress/, pg 286

Gardner, Joe, Child's Play, 67 Minot Ave, Auburn, ME 04210 *Toll Free Tel:* 800-472-0099; 800-639-6404 *Toll Free Fax:* 800-854-6989 *E-mail:* cplay@earthlink.net *Web Site:* www.childs-play.com, pg 60

Gardner, Richard S, Battery Press Inc, 1020 Fourth Ave S, Nashville, TN 37210 *Tel:* 615-298-1401 *Fax:* 615-298-1401 *E-mail:* batterybks@aol.com *Web Site:* www.batterypress.com, pg 33

Gardner, Thomas D, Reader's Digest General Books, Reader's Digest Rd, Pleasantville, NY 10570-7000 *Tel:* 914-238-1000 *Toll Free Tel:* 800-431-1726 *Fax:* 914-244-7436, pg 228

Gardner, Thomas D, Reader's Digest Trade Books, Reader's Digest Rd, Pleasantville, NY 10570-7000 *Tel:* 914-244-7445 *Fax:* 914-244-7605, pg 229

Gardner, Thomas D, Reader's Digest USA Select Editions, Reader's Digest Rd, Pleasantville, NY 10570-7000 *Tel:* 914-238-1000 *Toll Free Tel:* 800-310-6261 *Fax:* 914-238-4559, pg 229

Gardner, Tom, Reader's Digest Association Inc, Reader's Digest Rd, Pleasantville, NY 10570-7000 *Tel:* 914-238-1000 *Toll Free Tel:* 800-431-1726 *Fax:* 914-238-4559 *Web Site:* www.rd.com, pg 228

Gareffa, Peter, St James Press, 27500 Drake Rd, Farmington Hills, MI 48331-3535 *Tel:* 248-699-4253 *Toll Free Tel:* 800-877-4253 *Fax:* 248-699-8061 *Toll Free Fax:* 800-414-5043 *Web Site:* www.gale.com, pg 238

Garitone, Linda, Comprehensive Health Education Foundation (CHEF), 22419 Pacific Hwy S, Seattle, WA 98198-5104 *Tel:* 206-824-2907 *Toll Free Tel:* 800-323-2433 *Fax:* 206-824-3072 *E-mail:* info@chef.org *Web Site:* www.chef.org, pg 66

Garlick, Phil, OneSource, 300 Baker Ave, Concord, MA 01742 *Tel:* 978-318-4300 *Toll Free Tel:* 800-554-5501 (sales) *Fax:* 978-318-4690 *E-mail:* sales@onesource.com *Web Site:* www.onesource.com, pg 197

Garlock, Franklin L, Unarius Academy of Science Publications, 145 S Magnolia Ave, El Cajon, CA 92020-4522 *Tel:* 619-444-7062 *Toll Free Tel:* 800-475-7062 *Fax:* 619-447-9637 *E-mail:* uriel@unarius.org *Web Site:* www.unarius.org, pg 278

Garncarz, Barb, University of Wisconsin-Milwaukee Center for Architecture & Urban Planning Research, PO Box 413, Milwaukee, WI 53201-0413 *Tel:* 414-229-2878 *Fax:* 414-229-6976 *E-mail:* caupr@uwm.edu *Web Site:* www.uwm.edu/SARUP, pg 286

Garneau, Greg, National Press Photographers Association Inc (NPPA), 3200 Croasdaile Dr, Suite 306, Durham, NC 27705 *Tel:* 919-383-7246 *Fax:* 919-383-7261 *E-mail:* info@nppa.org *Web Site:* www.nppa.org, pg 694

Garneau, Luc, Editions du renouveau Pedagogique Inc, 5757 rue Cypihot, St-Laurent, PQ H4S 1R3, Canada *Tel:* 514-334-2690 *Toll Free Tel:* 800-263-3678 *Fax:* 514-334-4720 *Toll Free Fax:* 800-643-4720 *E-mail:* erpidlm@erpi.com *Web Site:* www.erpi.com, pg 544

Garner, Joan, Teacher Ideas Press, 361 Hanover St, Portsmouth, NH 03801-3912 *Toll Free Tel:* 800-225-5800 *Fax:* 603-431-2214 *Toll Free Fax:* 800-354-2004 (perms & foreign rts) *E-mail:* custserv@teacherideaspress.com; permissions@teacherideaspress.com; foreignrights@teacherideaspress.com *Web Site:* www.teacherideaspress.com, pg 265

Garner, Marion, Knopf Canada, One Toronto St, Suite 300, Toronto, ON M5C 2V6, Canada *Tel:* 416-364-4449 *Toll Free Tel:* 800-668-4247 (order desk) *Fax:* 416-364-0462 *Web Site:* www.randomhouse.ca, pg 552

Garneski, Sally, American College of Surgeons, 633 N Saint Clair St, Chicago, IL 60611-3211 *Tel:* 312-202-5000 *Toll Free Tel:* 800-621-4111 *Fax:* 312-202-5001 *E-mail:* postmaster@facs.org *Web Site:* www.facs.org, pg 13

Garone, Eugene A, Pencil Point Press Inc, PO Box 634, New Hope, PA 18938 *Tel:* 215-862-8855 *Toll Free Tel:* 800-356-1299 *Fax:* 215-862-8857 *E-mail:* penpoint@ix.netcom.com *Web Site:* pencilpointpress.com, pg 207

Garonzik, Joe, Genealogical Publishing Co Inc, 1001 N Calvert St, Baltimore, MD 21202 *Tel:* 410-837-8271 *Toll Free Tel:* 800-296-6687 *Fax:* 410-752-8492 *E-mail:* orders@genealogical.com *Web Site:* www.genealogical.com, pg 103

Garrard, Marcy, University of Washington Press, 1326 Fifth Ave, Suite 555, Seattle, WA 98101-2604 *Tel:* 206-543-4050; 206-543-8870 *Toll Free Tel:* 800-441-4115 (orders) *Fax:* 206-543-3932 *Toll Free Fax:* 800-669-7993 (orders) *E-mail:* uwpord@u.washington.edu *Web Site:* www.washington.edu/uwpress/, pg 286

Garretson, Robin, Success Advertising & Publishing, 3419 Dunham Rd, Warsaw, NY 14569 Tel: 585-786-5663, pg 261

Garrett, David, The University of Virginia Press, PO Box 400318, Charlottesville, VA 22904-4318 Tel: 434-924-3468 (cust serv); 434-924-3469 (cust serv) Toll Free Tel: 800-831-3406 (cust serv) Fax: 434-982-2655 Toll Free Fax: 877-288-6400 E-mail: upressvirginia@virginia.edu Web Site: www.upressvirginia.edu, pg 285

Garrett, Jane, Alfred A Knopf, 1745 Broadway, New York, NY 10019 Tel: 212-751-2600 Toll Free Tel: 800-638-6460 Fax: 212-572-2593 Web Site: www.randomhouse.com/knopf, pg 146

Garrett, Michael, How to be Published Workshops, PO Box 100031, Birmingham, AL 35210 Tel: 205-907-0140 Web Site: www.writing2sell.com, pg 744

Garrett, Paula, Pearson, 800 E 96 St, Indianapolis, IN 46240 Tel: 317-428-3000 Toll Free Tel: 800-545-5914 Fax: 317-581-4675 Web Site: www.macdigital.com, pg 206

Garrett, Paula, PTG Software, 201 W 103 St, Indianapolis, IN 46920-1097 Tel: 317-581-3500; 317-581-3837 (tech support) Toll Free Tel: 800-858-7674 Fax: 317-581-3611 Web Site: www.macmillansoftware.com, pg 221

Garrett, Shirley Stone, Harian Creative Books, 47 Hyde Blvd, Ballston Spa, NY 12020-1607 Tel: 518-885-6699; 518-885-7397, pg 115

Garrett, Susan R, Louisville Grawemeyer Award in Religion, 1044 Alta Vista Rd, Louisville, KY 40205-1798 Tel: 502-895-3411 Toll Free Tel: 800-264-1839 Fax: 502-894-2286 E-mail: grawemeyer@lpts.edu Web Site: www.grawemeyer.org, pg 786

Garrett, Suzanne, Andrews McMeel Publishing, 4520 Main St, Suite 700, Kansas City, MO 64111-7701 Tel: 816-932-6700 Toll Free Tel: 800-851-8923 Web Site: www.universal.com/amp, pg 169

Garrick, Kate, DeFiore & Co, Author Services, 72 Spring St, Suite 304, New York, NY 10012 Tel: 212-925-7744 Fax: 212-925-9803 E-mail: submissions@defioreandco.com Web Site: defioreandco.com, pg 627

Garrido, Marta, Merit Publishing International Inc, 5840 Corporate Way, Suite 200, West Palm Beach, FL 33407-2040 Tel: 561-637-1116 Fax: 561-477-4961 E-mail: meritpi@aol.com Web Site: www.meritpublishing.com, pg 171

Garrison, Deborah, Alfred A Knopf, 1745 Broadway, New York, NY 10019 Tel: 212-751-2600 Toll Free Tel: 800-638-6460 Fax: 212-572-2593 Web Site: www.randomhouse.com/knopf, pg 146

Garrison, Deborah, Pantheon Books/Schocken Books, 1745 Broadway, New York, NY 10019 Tel: 212-751-2600 Toll Free Tel: 800-638-6460 Fax: 212-572-6030, pg 203

Garrison, Karen, Primedia Business Magazine & Media, 9800 Metcalf Ave, Overland Park, KS 66212 Tel: 913-341-1300 Toll Free Tel: 800-262-1954 Fax: 913-967-1898 Web Site: www.primemediabusiness.com, pg 218

Garrison, Nancy, Ozark Mountain Publishing Inc, 276 Madison 2337, Huntsville, AR 72740 Tel: 479-738-2348 Toll Free Tel: 800-935-0045; 800-230-0312 Fax: 479-738-2348 Toll Free Fax: 800-935-0045; 800-230-0312 Web Site: www.ozarkmt.com, pg 201

Garrotto, Alfred J, Bridge Learning Systems Inc, 351 Los Altos, American Canyon, CA 94589 Tel: 925-228-3177 Toll Free Tel: 800-487-9868 Fax: 925-372-6099 E-mail: bridge@blsinc.com Web Site: www.blsinc.com, pg 47

Garry, Peggy, John Wiley & Sons Inc, 111 River St, Hoboken, NJ 07030 Tel: 201-748-6000 Toll Free Tel: 800-225-5945 (cust serv) Fax: 201-748-6088 E-mail: info@wiley.com Web Site: www.wiley.com, pg 299

Gartenberg, Max, Max Gartenberg Literary Agency, 12 Westminster Dr, Livingston, NJ 07039-1414 Tel: 973-994-4457 Fax: 973-994-4457 E-mail: gartenbook@att.net, pg 632

Garvey, Elaine, Templegate Publishers, 302 E Adams St, Springfield, IL 62701 Tel: 217-522-3353 (edit & sales); 217-522-3354 (billing) Toll Free Tel: 800-367-4844 (orders only) Fax: 217-522-3362 E-mail: wisdom@templegate.com; orders@templegate.com (sales) Web Site: www.templegate.com, pg 266

Garvey, Thomas M, Templegate Publishers, 302 E Adams St, Springfield, IL 62701 Tel: 217-522-3353 (edit & sales); 217-522-3354 (billing) Toll Free Tel: 800-367-4844 (orders only) Fax: 217-522-3362 E-mail: wisdom@templegate.com; orders@templegate.com (sales) Web Site: www.templegate.com, pg 266

Garych, Leslie, Scholastic Trade Division, 557 Broadway, New York, NY 10012 Tel: 212-343-6100; 212-343-4685 (export sales) Fax: 212-343-4714 (export sales) Web Site: www.scholastic.com, pg 242

Gasoi, Marta, University of California Press, 2120 Berkeley Way, Berkeley, CA 94720 Tel: 510-642-4247 Toll Free Tel: 800-777-4726 Fax: 510-643-7127 Toll Free Fax: 800-999-1958 E-mail: askucp@ucpress.edu Web Site: www.ucpress.edu, pg 281

Gaspard, Donald, Huntington House Publishers, 104 Row 2, Suite A-1 & A-2, Lafayette, LA 70508 Tel: 337-237-7049; 337-749-4009 (sales); 337-237-3082 (opers) Toll Free Tel: 800-749-4009 (sales) Fax: 337-237-7060 E-mail: admin@alphapublishingonline.com; sales@alphapublishingonline.com Web Site: www.alphapublishingonline.com, pg 129

Gaspers, Karen, Chicago Women in Publishing, PO Box 268107, Chicago, IL 60626 Tel: 312-641-6311 Fax: 312-645-1078 E-mail: mail@cwip.org Web Site: www.cwip.org, pg 684

Gates, Jennifer, Zachary Shuster Harmsworth Agency, 1776 Broadway, New York, NY 10019 Tel: 212-765-6900 Fax: 212-765-6490 Web Site: www.zshliterary.com, pg 662

Gates, Penny, Harian Creative Books, 47 Hyde Blvd, Ballston Spa, NY 12020-1607 Tel: 518-885-6699; 518-885-7397, pg 115

Gates, Rob, The Gaylactic Spectrum Awards, c/o Lambda Sci-Fi, PO Box 656, Washington, DC 20044 Tel: 202-483-6369 E-mail: info@spectrumawards.org Web Site: www.spectrumawards.org, pg 775

Gates, Tracy, Viking Children's Books, 345 Hudson St, New York, NY 10014 Tel: 212-366-2000 E-mail: online@penguinputnam.com Web Site: www.penguin.com, pg 290

Gatlin, Mark, Naval Institute Press, 291 Wood Rd, Annapolis, MD 21402-5034 Tel: 410-268-6110 Toll Free Tel: 800-233-8764 Fax: 410-295-1084; 410-571-1703 (customer service) E-mail: webmaster@navalinstitute.org; customer@navalinstitute.org (cust serv) Web Site: www.navalinstitute.org, pg 185

Gatt, Michelle, Slack Incorporated, 6900 Grove Rd, Thorofare, NJ 08086-9447 Tel: 856-848-1000 Toll Free Tel: 800-257-8290 Fax: 856-853-5991 Web Site: www.slackbooks.com, pg 250

Gatta, Gina, Damron Co, PO Box 422458, San Francisco, CA 94142-2458 Tel: 415-255-0404 Toll Free Tel: 800-462-6654 Fax: 415-703-9049 E-mail: editor@damron.com Web Site: www.damron.com, pg 75

Gaudioso, Gloria, William H Sadlier Inc, 9 Pine St, New York, NY 10005 Tel: 212-227-2120 Toll Free Tel: 800-221-5175 Fax: 212-312-6080 Web Site: www.sadlier.com; www.sadlier-oxford.com, pg 237

Gault, Erin, Maple Tree Press Inc, 51 Front St E, Suite 200, Toronto, ON M5E 1B3, Canada Tel: 416-304-0702 Fax: 416-304-0525 E-mail: info@mapletreepress.com Web Site: www.mapletreepress.com, pg 553

Gauntt, Ann, Ayer Company, Publishers Inc, One Lower Mill Rd, North Stratford, NH 03590 Tel: 603-669-7032 Fax: 603-669-7945 E-mail: ayerpub@yahoo.com Web Site: www.ayerpub.com, pg 30

Gauthier, David, Canadian Plains Research Center, University of Regina, Regina, SK S4S 0A2, Canada Tel: 306-585-4758; 306-585-4759 Fax: 306-585-4699 Web Site: www.cprc.uregina.ca, pg 539

Gautreaux, Gabrielle, University of New Orleans Press, c/o UNO Foundation, 6601 Franklin Ave, New Orleans, LA 70122 Tel: 504-280-1375 Fax: 504-280-7339 Web Site: www.uno.edu, pg 283

Gauvin, Rod, Pro Quest Information & Learning, 300 N Zeeb Rd, Ann Arbor, MI 48106-1346 Tel: 734-761-4700 Toll Free Tel: 800-521-0600 Fax: 734-975-6486 Toll Free Tel: 800-864-0019 E-mail: info@il.proquest.com Web Site: www.il.proquest.com, pg 219

Gavin, Tara, Harlequin Enterprises Ltd, 233 Broadway, Suite 1001, New York, NY 10279 Tel: 212-553-4200 Fax: 212-227-8969 E-mail: customer.ecare@harlequin.ca Web Site: www.eharlequin.com; www.luna-books.com; www.mirabooks.com; www.reddressink.com; www.steeplehill.com, pg 115

Gavin, Tara, Steeple Hill Books, 233 Broadway, Suite 1001, New York, NY 10279 Tel: 212-553-4200 Fax: 212-227-8969 E-mail: customer_service@harlequin.ca Web Site: www.steeplehill.com, pg 258

Gay, Pamela, Binghamton University Writing Program, c/o Dept of English, PO Box 6000, Binghamton, NY 13902-6000 Tel: 607-777-2168 Fax: 607-777-2408, pg 751

Gaynin, Gail, Morgan Gaynin Inc, 194 Third Ave, New York, NY 10003 Tel: 212-475-0440 Fax: 212-353-8538 E-mail: info@morgangaynin.com Web Site: www.morgangaynin.com, pg 666

Gaynor, Charlene F, The Association of Educational Publishers (AEP), 510 Heron Dr, Suite 309, Logan Township, NJ 08085 Tel: 856-241-7772 Fax: 856-241-0709 E-mail: mail@edpress.org Web Site: www.edpress.org, pg 680

Gayot, Alain, Gault Millau Inc/Gayot Publications, 4311 Wilshire Blvd, Suite 405, Los Angeles, CA 90010 Tel: 323-965-3529 Toll Free Tel: 800-LE BEST 1 Fax: 323-936-2883 E-mail: info@gayot.com Web Site: www.gayot.com, pg 103

Gayot, Andre, Gault Millau Inc/Gayot Publications, 4311 Wilshire Blvd, Suite 405, Los Angeles, CA 90010 Tel: 323-965-3529 Toll Free Tel: 800-LE BEST 1 Fax: 323-936-2883 E-mail: info@gayot.com Web Site: www.gayot.com, pg 103

Gazlay, Laura, The Library of America, 14 E 60 St, New York, NY 10022 Tel: 212-308-3360 Fax: 212-750-8352 E-mail: info@loa.org Web Site: www.loa.org; www.loaacademic.org, pg 154

Gazzolo, Paul, Martindale-Hubbell, 121 Chanlon Rd, New Providence, NJ 07974 Tel: 908-464-6800 Toll Free Tel: 800-526-4902 Fax: 908-464-3553 E-mail: info@martindale.com Web Site: www.martindale.com, pg 164

Geale, Nancy L, Thomas Geale Publications Inc, PO Box 370540, Montara, CA 94037-0540 Tel: 650-728-5219 Toll Free Tel: 800-554-5457 Fax: 650-728-0918, pg 269

Geary, Judith, High Country Publishers Ltd, 197 New Market Center, No 135, Boone, NC 28607 Tel: 828-964-0590 Fax: 828-262-1973 E-mail: editor@highcountrypublishers.com Web Site: www.highcountrypublishers.com, pg 122

Gebauer, Rudiger, Springer-Verlag New York Inc, 175 Fifth Ave, New York, NY 10010 Tel: 212-460-1500 Toll Free Tel: 800-777-4643 Fax: 212-473-6272 Web Site: www.springer-ny.com, pg 256

Gee, Connie, Be Puzzled, 2030 Harrison St, San Francisco, CA 94110 Tel: 415-503-1600 Toll Free Tel: 800-347-4818 Fax: 415-503-0085 E-mail: orders@areyougame.com Web Site: www.areyougame.com, pg 34

Gehani, Narain, Silicon Press, 25 Beverly Rd, Summit, NJ 07901 Tel: 908-273-8919 Fax: 908-273-6149 E-mail: info@silicon-press.com Web Site: www.silicon-press.com, pg 247

Geiger, Ellen, Curtis Brown Ltd, 10 Astor Place, New York, NY 10003 Tel: 212-473-5400, pg 623

Geiger, Lawrence, American Management Association, 1601 Broadway, New York, NY 10019-7420 *Tel:* 212-586-8100 *Toll Free Tel:* 800-262-9699 *Fax:* 212-903-8168 *Web Site:* www.amanet.org, pg 677

Geiogamah, Hanay, American Indian Studies Center Publications at UCLA, 3220 Campbell Hall, Los Angeles, CA 90095-1548 *Tel:* 310-825-7315; 310-206-7508 *Fax:* 310-206-7060 *E-mail:* aiscpubs@ucla.edu; aisc@ucla.edu *Web Site:* www.sscnet.ucla.edu, pg 14

Geiser, Elizabeth A, University of Denver Publishing Institute, 2075 S University Blvd, D-114, Denver, CO 80210 *Tel:* 303-871-2570 *Fax:* 303-871-2501 *Web Site:* www.du.edu/pi, pg 755

Geist, Ken, Scholastic Trade Division, 557 Broadway, New York, NY 10012 *Tel:* 212-343-6100; 212-343-4685 (export sales) *Fax:* 212-343-4714 (export sales) *Web Site:* www.scholastic.com, pg 242

Gelardi, Salvatore, Academic Press, 525 B St, Suite 1900, San Diego, CA 92101 *Tel:* 619-231-6616 *Toll Free Tel:* 800-321-5068 (cust serv) *Fax:* 619-699-6715 *E-mail:* firstinitiallastname@acad.com; firstinitial.lastname@elsevier.com *Web Site:* www.elsevier.com, pg 4

Gelber, Alexis, Overseas Press Club of America (OPC), 40 W 45 St, New York, NY 10036 *Tel:* 212-626-9220 *Fax:* 212-626-9210 *Web Site:* www.opcofamerica.org, pg 696

Gelbman, Leslie, Berkley Books, 375 Hudson St, New York, NY 10014 *Tel:* 212-366-2000 *Fax:* 212-366-2666 *E-mail:* online@penguinputnam.com *Web Site:* www.penguin.com, pg 36

Gelbman, Leslie, Berkley Publishing Group, 375 Hudson St, New York, NY 10014 *Tel:* 212-366-2000 *E-mail:* online@penguinputnam.com *Web Site:* www.penguin.com, pg 37

Gelbman, Leslie, Penguin Group (USA) Inc, 375 Hudson St, New York, NY 10014 *Tel:* 212-366-2000 *Fax:* 212-366-2666 *E-mail:* online@uspenguingroup.com *Web Site:* www.penguin.com, pg 208

Gelbman, Leslie, G P Putnam's Sons (Hardcover), 375 Hudson St, New York, NY 10014 *Tel:* 212-366-2000 *E-mail:* online@penguinputnam.com *Web Site:* www.penguin.com, pg 223

Gelfman, Jane, Gelfman Schneider Literary Agents Inc, 250 W 57 St, Suite 2515, New York, NY 10107 *Tel:* 212-245-1993 *Fax:* 212-245-8678 *E-mail:* mail@gelfmanschneider.com, pg 632

Gelinas, Robert E, ArcheBooks Publishing, 9101 W Sahara Ave, Suite 105-112, Las Vegas, NV 89117 *Tel:* 702-253-1338 *Toll Free Tel:* 800-358-8101 *Fax:* 561-868-2127 *E-mail:* publisher@archebooks.com *Web Site:* www.archebooks.com, pg 22

Geline, Deborah Weiss, Artisan, 708 Broadway, New York, NY 10003-9555 *Tel:* 212-254-5900 *Fax:* 212-254-8098 *E-mail:* artisaninfo@workman.com *Web Site:* www.artisanbooks.com, pg 25

Gelles, Heinz, Phoenix Learning Resources, 25 Third St, 2nd fl, Stamford, CT 06905 *Tel:* 203-353-1665 *Toll Free Tel:* 800-526-6581 *Fax:* 212-629-5648 *Web Site:* www.phoenixlr.com, pg 212

Gelles-Cole, Sandi, Gelles-Cole Literary Enterprises, PO Box 341, Woodstock, NY 12498-0341 *Tel:* 845-247-8111 *Web Site:* www.consulting-editors.com, pg 600

Geltzeiler, Michael S, Reader's Digest Association Inc, Reader's Digest Rd, Pleasantville, NY 10570-7000 *Tel:* 914-238-1000 *Toll Free Tel:* 800-431-1726 *Fax:* 914-238-4559 *Web Site:* www.rd.com, pg 228

Geltzeiler, Michael S, Reader's Digest Children's Books, Reader's Digest Rd, Pleasantville, NY 10570-7000 *Tel:* 914-244-4800 *Toll Free Tel:* 800-934-0977, pg 228

Geltzeiler, Michael S, Reader's Digest General Books, Reader's Digest Rd, Pleasantville, NY 10570-7000 *Tel:* 914-238-1000 *Toll Free Tel:* 800-431-1726 *Fax:* 914-244-7436, pg 228

Geltzeiler, Michael S, Reader's Digest Trade Books, Reader's Digest Rd, Pleasantville, NY 10570-7000 *Tel:* 914-244-7445 *Fax:* 914-244-7605, pg 229

Geltzeiler, Michael S, Reader's Digest USA Select Editions, Reader's Digest Rd, Pleasantville, NY 10570-7000 *Tel:* 914-238-1000 *Toll Free Tel:* 800-310-6261 *Fax:* 914-238-4559, pg 229

Gemignani, Nathan, Cornell University Press, 512 E State St, Ithaca, NY 14850 *Tel:* 607-277-2338 *Fax:* 607-277-2374 *E-mail:* cupressinfo@cornell.edu *Web Site:* www.cornellpress.cornell.edu, pg 68

Genao, Sobeira, Human Rights Watch, 350 Fifth Ave, 34th fl, New York, NY 10118 *Tel:* 212-290-4700 *Fax:* 212-736-1300 *E-mail:* hrwnyc@hrw.org *Web Site:* www.hrw.org, pg 128

Genna, Vicki, Hill & Wang, 19 Union Sq W, New York, NY 10003 *Tel:* 212-741-6900 *Fax:* 212-206-5340 *E-mail:* fsg.publicity@fsgbooks.com *Web Site:* www.fsgbooks.com, pg 122

Genna, Victoria, Farrar, Straus & Giroux, LLC, 19 Union Sq W, New York, NY 10003 *Tel:* 212-741-6900 *Fax:* 212-741-6973 *Web Site:* www.fsgbooks.com, pg 95

Gennaro, Denise, Living Language, 1745 Broadway, New York, NY 10019 *Tel:* 212-572-6148 *Toll Free Tel:* 800-726-0600 (orders) *Fax:* 212-940-7400 *Toll Free Fax:* 800-659-2436 *E-mail:* livinglanguage@randomhouse.com *Web Site:* www.livinglanguage.com, pg 157

Genner, Debra, The Denali Press, PO Box 021535, Juneau, AK 99802-1535 *Tel:* 907-586-6014 *Fax:* 907-463-6780 *E-mail:* denalipress@alaska.com *Web Site:* www.denalipress.com, pg 79

Genoways, Ted, Emily Clark Balch Prizes in Creative American Writing, One West Range, Charlottesville, VA 22903 *Tel:* 434-924-3124 *Fax:* 434-924-1397 *E-mail:* vqreview@virginia.edu *Web Site:* www.virginia.edu/vqr, pg 761

Gentel, Gary, Scholastic Trade Division, 557 Broadway, New York, NY 10012 *Tel:* 212-343-6100; 212-343-4685 (export sales) *Fax:* 212-343-4714 (export sales) *Web Site:* www.scholastic.com, pg 242

Gentillo, Eileen, Simon & Schuster Sales & Distribution, 1230 Avenue of the Americas, New York, NY 10020 *Tel:* 212-698-7000, pg 249

Georgakas, Dan, Ocean Press, PO Box 1186, Old Chelsea Sta, New York, NY 10113-1186 *Tel:* 718-246-4160 *E-mail:* info@oceanbookscom.au *Web Site:* www.oceanbooks.com.au, pg 195

George, Lee Anne, Association of Research Libraries, 21 Dupont Circle NW, Suite 800, Washington, DC 20036 *Tel:* 202-296-2296 *Fax:* 202-872-0884 *E-mail:* arlhq@arl.org *Web Site:* www.arl.org, pg 27

George, Lisa, Bantam Dell Publishing Group, 1745 Broadway, New York, NY 10019 *Tel:* 212-782-9000 *Toll Free Tel:* 800-223-6834 *Fax:* 212-302-7985 *Web Site:* www.randomhouse.com/bantamdell, pg 31

Gerardi, Jan, Random House Children's Books, 1745 Broadway, New York, NY 10019 *Tel:* 212-782-9000 *Toll Free Tel:* 800-200-3552 *Fax:* 212-782-9452 *Web Site:* www.randomhouse.com/kids, pg 226

Gerbasi, Catherine, Portage & Main Press, 318 McDermot, Suite 100, Winnipeg, MB R3A 0A2, Canada *Tel:* 204-987-3500 *Toll Free Tel:* 800-667-9673 *Fax:* 204-947-0080 *Toll Free Fax:* 866-734-8477 *E-mail:* books@portageandmainpress.com *Web Site:* www.portageandmainpress.com, pg 558

Gerbitz, Jacki, Legal Education Publishing, 5302 Eastpark Blvd, Madison, WI 53718 *Toll Free Tel:* 800-957-4670 *Fax:* 608-257-5502 *E-mail:* service@wisbar.org *Web Site:* www.wisbar.org, pg 152

Gerdeman, Martha, Vanderbilt University Press, 201 University Plaza Bldg, 112 21 Ave S, Nashville, TN 37203 *Tel:* 615-322-3585 *Toll Free Tel:* 800-627-7377 (orders only) *Fax:* 615-343-8823 *Toll Free Fax:* 800-735-0476 (orders only) *E-mail:* vupress@vanderbilt.edu *Web Site:* www.vanderbilt.edu/vupress, pg 289

Gerecke, Jeff, JCA Literary Agency Inc, 27 W 20 St, Suite 1103, New York, NY 10011 *Tel:* 212-807-0888 *Fax:* 212-807-0461 *Web Site:* www.jcalit.com, pg 636

Geringer, Laura, Laura Geringer Books, 1350 Avenue of Americas, 4th fl, New York, NY 10019 *Tel:* 212-261-6500 *Web Site:* www.harpercollins.com, pg 150

Gerken, Victoria, Alfred A Knopf, 1745 Broadway, New York, NY 10019 *Tel:* 212-751-2600 *Toll Free Tel:* 800-638-6460 *Fax:* 212-572-2593 *Web Site:* www.randomhouse.com/knopf, pg 146

Gerken, Victoria, Pantheon Books/Schocken Books, 1745 Broadway, New York, NY 10019 *Tel:* 212-751-2600 *Toll Free Tel:* 800-638-6460 *Fax:* 212-572-6030, pg 203

Germain, Sally, The Bureau For At-Risk Youth, 135 Dupont St, Plainview, NY 11803-0760 *Tel:* 516-349-5520 *Fax:* 516-349-5521 *E-mail:* info@at-risk.com *Web Site:* www.at-risk.com, pg 50

Germain, Sally, JayJo Books, 135 Dupont St, Plainview, NY 11803 *Tel:* 516-349-5520 *Fax:* 516-349-5521 *E-mail:* jayjobooks@guidancechannel.com *Web Site:* www.guidancechannel.com, pg 140

German, Andrew, Mystic Seaport, PO Box 6000, Mystic, CT 06355-0990 *Tel:* 860-572-0711 *Fax:* 860-572-5321 *Web Site:* www.mysticseaport.org, pg 181

Germano, William P, Routledge, 29 W 35 St, New York, NY 10001-2299 *Tel:* 212-216-7800 *Fax:* 212-564-7854 (main) *E-mail:* info@taylorandfrancis.com *Web Site:* www.routledge-ny.com, pg 235

Gerrain, Dawn, Milady Publishing, Executive Woods, 5 Maxwell Dr, Clifton Park, NY 12065-2919 *Tel:* 518-348-2300 (ext 2409) *Toll Free Tel:* 800-998-7498 *Fax:* 518-348-7000 *Web Site:* www.delmar.com; www.milady.com, pg 174

Gerrish, Nancy, McGraw-Hill Ryerson Ltd, 300 Water St, Whitby, ON L1N 9B6, Canada *Tel:* 905-430-5000 *Toll Free Tel:* 800-565-5758 (cust serv) *Fax:* 905-430-5020 *E-mail:* johnd@mcgrawhill.ca *Web Site:* www.mcgrawhill.ca, pg 554

Gerry, Cheryl, Down East Books, PO Box 679, Camden, ME 04843 *Tel:* 207-594-9544 *Toll Free Tel:* 800-766-1670 (ME only) *Fax:* 207-594-7215 *Web Site:* www.downeastbooks.com, pg 83

Gershel, Larry, A Richard Barber & Associates, 554 E 82 St, New York, NY 10028 *Tel:* 212-737-7266 *Fax:* 212-879-0183 *E-mail:* barberrich@aol.com, pg 620

Gershenowitz, Deborah, New York University Press, 838 Broadway, New York, NY 10003 *Tel:* 212-998-2575 (edit) *Toll Free Tel:* 800-996-6987 (orders) *Fax:* 212-995-3833 (orders) *E-mail:* feedback@nyupress.nyu.edu *Web Site:* www.nyupress.org, pg 190

Gerstl, Hugo N, Four Paws Press LLC, 2460 Garden Rd, Suite B, Monterey, CA 93940 *Tel:* 831-375-PAWS (375-7297) *Fax:* 831-649-8007 *Web Site:* www.fourpawspress.com, pg 99

Gerth, Anne, InterVarsity Press, 430 E Plaza Dr, Westmont, IL 60559-1234 *Tel:* 630-734-4000 *Toll Free Tel:* 800-843-7225 *Fax:* 630-734-4200 *E-mail:* mail@ivpress.com *Web Site:* www.ivpress.com, pg 138

Gertler, Joanna, Oxford University Press Canada, 70 Wynford Dr, Don Mills, ON M3C 1J9, Canada *Tel:* 416-441-2941 *Toll Free Tel:* 800-387-8020 *Fax:* 416-444-0427 *Toll Free Fax:* 800-665-1771 *E-mail:* custserv@oupcan.com *Web Site:* www.oup.com/ca, pg 557

Gervasio, Janet, HarperCollins Publishers, 10 E 53 St, New York, NY 10022 *Tel:* 212-207-7000 *Fax:* 212-207-7145 *Web Site:* www.harpercollins.com, pg 116

Gesin, Jay, Phaidon Press Inc, 180 Varick St, 14th fl, New York, NY 10014 *Tel:* 212-652-5400 *Toll Free Tel:* 800-759-0190 (cust serv) *Fax:* 212-652-5410 *Toll Free Fax:* 800-286-9471 (cust serv) *E-mail:* ussales@phaidon.com *Web Site:* www.phaidon.com, pg 211

Gesser, Kenneth, Transcontinental Music Publications, 633 Third Ave, New York, NY 10017 *Tel:* 212-650-4101 *Toll Free Tel:* 800-455-5223 *Fax:* 212-650-4109 *E-mail:* tmp@uahc.org *Web Site:* www.transcontinentalmusic.com, pg 274

Gesser, Kenneth, URJ Press, 633 Third Ave, New York, NY 10017-6778 *Tel:* 212-650-4100 *Toll Free Tel:* 888-489-UAHC (489-8242) *Fax:* 212-650-4119 *E-mail:* press@urj.org *Web Site:* www.urjpress.com, pg 289

Gesumaria, Samuel, Hampton-Brown Co Inc, 26385 Carmel Rancho Blvd, Carmel, CA 93923 *Tel:* 831-625-3666 *Toll Free Tel:* 800-933-3510 *Fax:* 831-625-8619 *E-mail:* customerservice@hampton-brown.com *Web Site:* www.hampton-brown.com, pg 113

Geyer, Raymond C, Golden West Books, 525 N Electric Ave, Alhambra, CA 91801 *Tel:* 626-458-8148 *Fax:* 626-458-8148, pg 106

Ghanoon-Parvar, M R, Concourse Press, PO Box 8265, Philadelphia, PA 19101-8265 *Tel:* 610-325-0313 *Fax:* 610-359-1953, pg 66

Ghavami, Parvaneh, ADASI Publishing Co, 6 Dover Point Rd, Suite B, Dover, NH 03820-4698 *Tel:* 727-488-7353 *E-mail:* info@adasi.com *Web Site:* www.adasi.com, pg 5

Ghazarian, Ms Salpi H, Blue Crane Books, PO Box 380291, Cambridge, MA 02238 *Tel:* 617-926-8989 *Fax:* 617-926-0982 *E-mail:* bluecrane@arrow1.com, pg 41

Ghazarian, Vivian, Artisan, 708 Broadway, New York, NY 10003-9555 *Tel:* 212-254-5900 *Fax:* 212-254-8098 *E-mail:* artisaninfo@workman.com *Web Site:* www.artisanbooks.com, pg 25

Ghose, Zulfikar, University of Texas at Austin, Creative Writing Program, Dept of English, One University Sta, B5000, Austin, TX 78712-1164 *Tel:* 512-475-6356 *Fax:* 512-471-2898 *Web Site:* www.en.utexas.edu/grad/crwconc.html, pg 756

Ghosh, Anna, Scovil Chichak Galen Literary Agency Inc, 381 Park Ave S, Suite 1020, New York, NY 10016 *Tel:* 212-679-8686 *Fax:* 212-679-6710 *E-mail:* mailroom@scglit.com *Web Site:* www.scglit.com, pg 654

Ghoura, Judy, Fitzhenry & Whiteside Limited, 195 Allstate Pkwy, Markham, ON L3R 4T8, Canada *Tel:* 905-477-9700 *Toll Free Tel:* 800-387-9776 *Fax:* 905-477-9179 *Toll Free Fax:* 800-260-9777 *E-mail:* godwit@fitzhenry.ca *Web Site:* www.fitzhenry.ca, pg 547

Ghublikian, Ann, Advantage Publishers Group, 5880 Oberlin Dr, San Diego, CA 92121 *Tel:* 858-457-2500 *Toll Free Tel:* 800-284-3580 *Fax:* 858-812-6476 *Toll Free Fax:* 800-499-3822 *E-mail:* apgcuserv@advmkt.com *Web Site:* www.advantagebooksonline.com, pg 6

Giagnocavo, Alan, Fox Chapel Publishing Co Inc, 1970 Broad St, East Petersburg, PA 17520 *Tel:* 717-560-4703 *Toll Free Tel:* 800-457-9112 *Fax:* 717-560-4702 *E-mail:* custservice@foxchapelpublishing.com *Web Site:* www.foxchapelpublishing.com, pg 99

Giamo, Sr Donna William, Pauline Books & Media, 50 St Paul's Ave, Jamaica Plain, Boston, MA 02130 *Tel:* 617-522-8911 *Toll Free Tel:* 800-876-4463 (orders only) *Fax:* 617-541-9805 *E-mail:* businessoffice@pauline.org; orderentry@pauline.org *Web Site:* www.pauline.org, pg 205

Giangrande, Greg, HarperCollins Publishers, 10 E 53 St, New York, NY 10022 *Tel:* 212-207-7000 *Fax:* 212-207-7145 *Web Site:* www.harpercollins.com, pg 116

Giarratano, Matt, Penguin Books, 375 Hudson St, New York, NY 10014 *Tel:* 212-366-2000 *E-mail:* online@penguinputnam.com *Web Site:* www.penguin.com; www.penguinclassics.com, pg 207

Gibaldi, Joseph, Modern Language Association of America (MLA), 26 Broadway, 3rd fl, New York, NY 10004-1789 *Tel:* 646-576-5000 *Fax:* 646-458-0030 *E-mail:* info@mla.org *Web Site:* www.mla.org, pg 176

Gibbs, Paul G, Teachers of English to Speakers of Other Languages Inc (TESOL), 700 S Washington St, Suite 200, Alexandria, VA 22314-4287 *Tel:* 703-836-0774 *Fax:* 703-836-7864 *E-mail:* info@tesol.org *Web Site:* www.tesol.org, pg 265

Gibeault, Francois, Editions Hurtubise HMH Ltee, 1815 De Lorimier, Montreal, PQ H2K 3W6, Canada *Tel:* 514-523-1523 *Toll Free Tel:* 800-361-1664

(Canada only) *Fax:* 514-523-9969; 514-523-5955 (edit) *E-mail:* hurtubisehmh@hurtubisehmh.com *Web Site:* www.hurtubisehmh.com, pg 545

Giblin, Brian, Soundprints, 353 Main Ave, Norwalk, CT 06851 *Tel:* 203-846-2274 *Toll Free Tel:* 800-228-7839; 800-577-2413, ext 118 (orders) *Fax:* 203-846-1776 *E-mail:* Soundprints@soundprints.com *Web Site:* www.soundprints.com, pg 253

Giblin, Jody, National Geographic Books, 1145 17 St NW, Washington, DC 20036 *Tel:* 202-857-7000 *Fax:* 202-857-7670 *Web Site:* www.nationalgeographics.com, pg 183

Gibson, Amy, The Graduate Group/Booksellers, 86 Norwood Rd, West Hartford, CT 06117-2236 *Tel:* 860-233-2330 *Toll Free Tel:* 800-484-7280 ext 3579 *Fax:* 860-233-2330 *E-mail:* graduategroup@hotmail.com *Web Site:* www.graduategroup.com, pg 107

Gibson, Chip, Random House Children's Books, 1745 Broadway, New York, NY 10019 *Tel:* 212-782-9000 *Toll Free Tel:* 800-200-3552 *Fax:* 212-782-9452 *Web Site:* www.randomhouse.com/kids, pg 225

Gibson, Chip, Random House Inc, 1745 Broadway, New York, NY 10019 *Tel:* 212-782-9000 *Toll Free Tel:* 800-726-0600 *Web Site:* www.randomhouse.com, pg 226

Gibson, George L, Walker & Co, 104 Fifth Ave, 7th fl, New York, NY 10011 *Tel:* 212-727-8300 *Toll Free Tel:* 800-289-2553 *Fax:* 212-727-0984 *Toll Free Fax:* 800-218-9367 *E-mail:* firstinitiallastname@walkerbooks.com *Web Site:* www.walkerbooks.com, pg 292

Gibson, Jane, Natural Heritage Books, PO Box 95, Sta O, Toronto, ON M4A 2M8, Canada *Tel:* 416-694-7907 *Toll Free Tel:* 800-725-9982 (orders only) *Fax:* 416-690-0819 *E-mail:* info@naturalheritagebooks.com *Web Site:* www.naturalheritagebooks.com, pg 555

Gibson, Karen, Blackwell Publishers, 350 Main St, Malden, MA 02148 *Tel:* 781-388-8200 *Fax:* 781-388-8210 *E-mail:* books@blackwellpublishing.com *Web Site:* www.blackwellpublishing.com, pg 40

Gibson, Leonora, Wesleyan University Press, 215 Long Lane, Middletown, CT 06459-0433 *Tel:* 860-685-7711 *Fax:* 860-685-7712 *Web Site:* www.wesleyan.edu/wespress, pg 296

Gibson, Paul, CCH Inc, 2700 Lake Cook Rd, Riverwoods, IL 60015 *Tel:* 847-267-7000 *Toll Free Tel:* 888-224-7377 *Web Site:* www.cch.com, pg 56

Gibson, Theresa, Manhattan Publishing Co, PO Box 850, Croton-on-Hudson, NY 10520-0850 *Tel:* 914-271-5194 *Toll Free Tel:* 888-686-7066 *Fax:* 914-271-5856 *Web Site:* www.manhattanpublishing.com, pg 162

Giddens, Mary, Steiner Books, PO Box 799, Great Barrington, MA 01230-0799 *Tel:* 413-528-8233 *Fax:* 413-528-8826 *E-mail:* service@anthropress.org *Web Site:* www.anthropress.org, pg 258

Gideonse, Ted, Ann Rittenberg Literary Agency Inc, 1201 Broadway, Suite 708, New York, NY 10001 *Tel:* 212-684-6936 *Fax:* 212-684-6929 *Web Site:* www.rittlit.com, pg 651

Gies, Janna O, Emily Clark Balch Prizes in Creative American Writing, One West Range, Charlottesville, VA 22903 *Tel:* 434-924-3124 *Fax:* 434-924-1397 *E-mail:* vqreview@virginia.edu *Web Site:* www.virginia.edu/vqr, pg 761

Gifford, James M, The Jesse Stuart Foundation, PO Box 669, Ashland, KY 41105-0669 *Tel:* 606-326-1667 *Fax:* 606-325-2519 *Web Site:* www.jsfbooks.com, pg 260

Giffuni, Cathe, Research Research, 240 E 27 St, Suite 20-K, New York, NY 10016 *Tel:* 212-779-9540, pg 610

Gift, Allison, A & B Publishers Group, 223 Duffield St, Brooklyn, NY 11201 *Tel:* 718-783-7808 *Fax:* 718-783-7267 *Web Site:* anbdonline.com, pg 1

Gift, Eric, A & B Publishers Group, 223 Duffield St, Brooklyn, NY 11201 *Tel:* 718-783-7808 *Fax:* 718-783-7267 *Web Site:* anbdonline.com, pg 1

Gift, Wendy, A & B Publishers Group, 223 Duffield St, Brooklyn, NY 11201 *Tel:* 718-783-7808 *Fax:* 718-783-7267 *Web Site:* anbdonline.com, pg 1

Gigante, Alex, Penguin Group (USA) Inc, 375 Hudson St, New York, NY 10014 *Tel:* 212-366-2000 *Fax:* 212-366-2666 *E-mail:* online@uspenguingroup.com *Web Site:* www.penguin.com, pg 208

Giggins, Isabelle, Warner Bros Worldwide Publishing, 4000 Warner Blvd, Bldg 118, Burbank, CA 91522-1704 *Tel:* 818-954-5450 *Fax:* 818-954-5595 *Web Site:* www.warnerbros.com, pg 293

Gilbert, Jon, Seven Stories Press, 140 Watts St, New York, NY 10013 *Tel:* 212-226-8760 *Toll Free Tel:* 800-283-3572 *Fax:* 212-226-1411 *E-mail:* info@sevenstories.com *Web Site:* www.sevenstories.com, pg 245

Gilbert, Larry A, Church Growth Institute, PO Box 7, Elkton, MD 21922-0007 *Tel:* 434-525-0022 *Toll Free Tel:* 800-553-4769 (orders only) *Fax:* 434-525-0608 *Toll Free Fax:* 800-644-4729 (orders only) *E-mail:* cgimail@churchgrowth.org *Web Site:* www.churchgrowth.org, pg 62

Gilbert, Nichole, Baker & Taylor Conference Grants, 50 E Huron St, Chicago, IL 60611 *Tel:* 312-280-4390 (ext 4391) *Toll Free Tel:* 800-545-2433 (ext 4390) *Fax:* 312-664-7459 *E-mail:* yalsa@ala.org *Web Site:* www.ala.org/yalsa/printz, pg 760

Gilbert, Nichole, Margaret A Edwards Award, 50 E Huron St, Chicago, IL 60611 *Tel:* 312-280-4390 *Toll Free Tel:* 800-545-2433 (ext 4390) *Fax:* 312-664-7459 *E-mail:* yalsa@ala.org *Web Site:* www.ala.org/yalsa/, pg 772

Gilbert, Nichole, Frances Henne YALSA/VOYA Research Grant, 50 E Huron St, Chicago, IL 60611 *Toll Free Tel:* 800-545-2433 (ext 4391) *Fax:* 312-664-7459 *E-mail:* yalsa@ala.org *Web Site:* www.ala.org/yalsa/printz, pg 778

Gilbert, Nichole, Michael L Printz Award, 50 E Huron St, Chicago, IL 60611 *Tel:* 312-280-4390 *Toll Free Tel:* 800-545-2433 (ext 4390) *Fax:* 312-664-7459 *E-mail:* yalsa@ala.org *Web Site:* www.ala.org/yalsa/printz, pg 800

Gilbert, Paul, Counterpoint Press, 387 Park Ave S, New York, NY 10016 *Tel:* 212-340-8100 *Fax:* 212-340-8135 (edit); 212-340-8115 *E-mail:* counterpointpress@perseusbooks.com *Web Site:* www.counterpointpress.com, pg 70

Gilbert, Richard, Ohio University Press, One Ohio University, Scott Quadrangle, Athens, OH 45701 *Tel:* 740-593-1155 *Toll Free Tel:* 800-621-2736 *Fax:* 740-593-4536 *Web Site:* www.ohio.edu/oupress/, pg 196

Gilbert, Richard, Swallow Press, Scott Quadrangle, Athens, OH 45701 *Tel:* 740-593-1155 *Toll Free Tel:* 800-621-2736 (orders only) *Fax:* 740-593-4536 *Toll Free Fax:* 800-621-8476 (orders only) *Web Site:* www.ohiou.edu/oupress/, pg 263

Gilbert, Sandra, Stewart, Tabori & Chang, 115 W 18 St, 5th fl, New York, NY 10011 *Tel:* 212-519-1200 *Fax:* 212-519-1210 *Web Site:* www.abramsbooks.com, pg 260

Gilbert, Sharon, Broadman & Holman Publishers, 127 Ninth Ave N, Nashville, TN 37234-0114 *Tel:* 615-251-2520 *Fax:* 615-251-5004 *Web Site:* www.broadmanholman.com, pg 48

Gilbert, Sheila E, DAW Books Inc, 375 Hudson St, 3rd fl, New York, NY 10014 *Tel:* 212-366-2096 *Fax:* 212-366-2090 *E-mail:* daw@us.penguingroup.com *Web Site:* www.dawbooks.com, pg 77

Gilbride, Tara, Crown Publishing Group, 1745 Broadway, New York, NY 10019 *Tel:* 212-782-9000 *Toll Free Tel:* 888-264-1745 *Fax:* 212-940-7408 *Web Site:* www.randomhouse.com/crown, pg 74

Gildea, Matthew, Adams Media, An F+W Publications Co, 57 Littlefield St, 2nd fl, Avon, MA 02322 *Tel:* 508-427-7100 *Fax:* 508-427-6790 *Toll Free*

Fax: 800-872-5628 E-mail: authors@adamsmedia. com; orders@adamsmedia.com Web Site: www. adamsmedia.com, pg 5

Gildenhuys, Faith, Editors' Association of Canada/ Association canadienne des reviseurs, 27 Carlton St, Suite 502, Toronto, ON M5B 1L2, Canada Tel: 416-975-1379 Toll Free Tel: 866-226-3348 Fax: 416-975-1637 E-mail: info@editors.ca Web Site: www.editors. ca; www.reviseurs.ca, pg 686

Giles, T E, Detselig Enterprises Ltd, 210, 1220 Kensington Rd NW, Calgary, AB T2N 3P5, Canada Tel: 403-283-0900 Fax: 403-283-6947 E-mail: temeron@telusplanet.net Web Site: www. temerondetselig.com, pg 542

Gill, Craig, University Press of Mississippi, 3825 Ridgewood Rd, Jackson, MS 39211-6492 Tel: 601-432-6205 Toll Free Tel: 800-737-7788 Fax: 601-432-6217 E-mail: press@ihl.state.ms.us Web Site: www. upress.state.ms.us, pg 287

Gill, Kay, Omnigraphics Inc, 615 Griswold St, Detroit, MI 48226 Tel: 313-961-1340 Toll Free Tel: 800-234-1340 (cust serv) Fax: 313-961-1383 Toll Free Fax: 800-875-1340 (cust serv) E-mail: info@ omnigraphics.com Web Site: www.omnigraphics.com, pg 197

Gill, Veronica, Blade Publishing, 4540 Kearny Villa Rd, Suite 103, San Diego, CA 92123 Tel: 619-440-2309 Fax: 619-334-7070 E-mail: bladeinternational@yahoo. com, pg 40

Gillan, Laura, Springer-Verlag New York Inc, 175 Fifth Ave, New York, NY 10010 Tel: 212-460-1500 Toll Free Tel: 800-777-4643 Fax: 212-473-6272 Web Site: www.springer-ny.com, pg 256

Gillan, Maria, Binghamton University Writing Program, c/o Dept of English, PO Box 6000, Binghamton, NY 13902-6000 Tel: 607-777-2168 Fax: 607-777-2408, pg 751

Gillerman, Gerald, Merloyd Lawrence Inc, 102 Chestnut St, Boston, MA 02108 Tel: 617-523-5895 Fax: 617-252-5285, pg 150

Gillespie, Christine, Fodor's Travel Publications, 1745 Broadway, New York, NY 10019 Tel: 212-572-8784 Toll Free Tel: 800-733-3000 Fax: 212-572-2248 Web Site: www.fodors.com, pg 98

Gillespie, Jennie, San Diego Christian Writers' Guild Conference, PO Box 270403, San Diego, CA 92198 Tel: 619-221-8183 Fax: 619-255-1131 E-mail: info@ sandiegocwg.org Web Site: www.sandiegocwg.org, pg 746

Gillespie, Robert, San Diego Christian Writers' Guild Conference, PO Box 270403, San Diego, CA 92198 Tel: 619-221-8183 Fax: 619-255-1131 E-mail: info@ sandiegocwg.org Web Site: www.sandiegocwg.org, pg 746

Gillette, Victoria, University of Texas at Arlington School of Urban & Public Affairs, University Hall, 5th fl, 601 S Naderman Dr, Arlington, TX 76010 Tel: 817-272-3071 Fax: 817-272-5008 E-mail: supapubs@uta. edu Web Site: www.uta.edu/supa, pg 285

Gillies, Paige, Publishers' Graphics Inc, 231 Judd Rd, Easton, CT 06612-1025 Tel: 203-445-1511 Fax: 203-445-1411 E-mail: sales@publishersgraphics.com Web Site: www.publishersgraphics.com, pg 666

Gilligan, ElizaBeth, SFWA Nebula Awards, PO Box 877, Chestertown, MD 21620 Toll Free Tel: 888-322-7392 E-mail: execdir@sfwa.org Web Site: www.sfwa.org, pg 805

Gilligan, Michael, American Catholic Press, 16565 S State St, South Holland, IL 60473 Tel: 708-331-5845 Fax: 708-331-5484 E-mail: acp@acpress.org Web Site: www.acpress.org, pg 12

Gilliland, Hap, Council for American Indian Education, 1240 Burlington Ave, Billings, MT 59102-4224 Tel: 406-248-3465 (PM); 406-652-7598 (AM) Fax: 406-248-1297 E-mail: cie@cie-mt.org Web Site: www.cie-mt.org, pg 69

Gillingham, Brian, Institute of Mediaeval Music, PO Box 295, Henryville, PA 18332-0295 Tel: 570-629-1278 Fax: 613-225-9487 Web Site: members.rogers. com/mediaeval1, pg 135

Gillis, Karen, St Martin's Press LLC, 175 Fifth Ave, New York, NY 10010 Tel: 212-674-5151 Fax: 212-420-9314 E-mail: firstname.lastname@stmartins.com Web Site: www.stmartins.com, pg 238

Gilliss, Sonya, Fitzhenry & Whiteside Limited, 195 Allstate Pkwy, Markham, ON L3R 4T8, Canada Tel: 905-477-9700 Toll Free Tel: 800-387-9776 Fax: 905-477-9179 Toll Free Fax: 800-260-9777 E-mail: godwit@fitzhenry.ca Web Site: www.fitzhenry. ca, pg 547

Gilly, Holly, Human Kinetics Inc, PO Box 5076, Champaign, IL 61825-5076 Tel: 217-351-5076 Toll Free Tel: 800-747-4457 Fax: 217-351-1549 (orders/ cust serv) E-mail: info@hkusa.com Web Site: www. humankinetics.com, pg 128

Gilman, Heather, Steeple Hill Books, 233 Broadway, Suite 1001, New York, NY 10279 Tel: 212-553-4200 Fax: 212-227-8969 E-mail: customer_service@ harlequin.ca Web Site: www.steeplehill.com, pg 258

Gilmartin, Ellen, New Voices Publishing, 34 Salem St, Wilmington, MA 01887 Tel: 508-347-5669; 978-658-2131 Fax: 508-347-5669; 978-988-8833 Web Site: www.kidsterrain.com, pg 189

Gilmer, E J, Amber Quill Press LLC, PO Box 265, Indian Hills, CO 80454 E-mail: customer_service@ amberquillpress.com Web Site: amberquill.com, pg 10

Gilmer, Linda, Oxmoor House Inc, 2100 Lakeshore Dr, Birmingham, AL 35209 Tel: 205-445-6000; 205-445-6560 Toll Free Tel: 800-366-4712 Fax: 205-445-6078 Web Site: www.oxmoorhouse.com, pg 201

Gilmore, Tom, St Martin's Press LLC, 175 Fifth Ave, New York, NY 10010 Tel: 212-674-5151 Fax: 212-420-9314 E-mail: firstname.lastname@stmartins.com Web Site: www.stmartins.com, pg 238

Gilpin, R Wayne, Future Horizons Inc, 721 W Abram St, Arlington, TX 76013 Tel: 817-277-0727 Toll Free Tel: 800-489-0727 Fax: 817-277-2270 E-mail: info@futurehorizons-autism.com Web Site: www.futurehorizons-autism.com, pg 102

Gilson, Kristin, Puffin Books, 345 Hudson St, New York, NY 10014 Tel: 212-366-2000 E-mail: online@ penguinputnam.com Web Site: www.penguin.com, pg 222

Gimbel, Despina P, New York University Press, 838 Broadway, New York, NY 10003 Tel: 212-998-2575 (edit) Toll Free Tel: 800-996-6987 (orders) Fax: 212-995-3833 (orders) E-mail: feedback@nyupress.nyu.edu Web Site: www.nyupress.org, pg 190

Ging, Mary, Elsevier, 11830 Westline Industrial Dr, St Louis, MO 63146 Tel: 314-872-8370 Toll Free Tel: 800-325-4177 Fax: 314-432-1380 Web Site: www. elsevier.com; www.elsevierhealth.com, pg 89

Ging, Mary, Mosby Journal Division, 11830 Westline Industrial Dr, St Louis, MO 63146 Tel: 314-872-8370 Toll Free Tel: 800-325-4177 Web Site: www. elsevierhealth.com, pg 179

Ging, Mary, W B Saunders Ltd, 170 S Independence Mall W, Suite 300 E, Philadelphia, PA 19106-3399 Tel: 215-238-7800 Toll Free Tel: 800-545-2522 (cust serv) Fax: 215-238-7883 Web Site: www. elsevierhealth.com, pg 240

Ginger, Helen, Teddy Award for Children's Books, 1501 W Fifth St, Suite E-2, Austin, TX 78703 Tel: 512-499-8914 Fax: 512-499-0441 E-mail: wlt@ writersleague.org Web Site: www.writersleague.org, pg 808

Ginger, Helen, Violet Crown Book Awards, 1501 W Fifth St, Suite E-2, Austin, TX 78703 Tel: 512-499-8914 Fax: 512-499-0441 E-mail: wlt@writersleague. org Web Site: www.writersleague.org, pg 810

Ginger, Helen, Writers' League of Texas, 1501 W Fifth St, Suite E-2, Austin, TX 78703 Tel: 512-499-8914 Fax: 512-499-0441 E-mail: wlt@writersleague.org Web Site: www.writersleague.org, pg 670, 703, 749

Gingold, Joel A, Key Curriculum Press, 1150 65 St, Emeryville, CA 94608 Tel: 510-595-7000 Toll Free Tel: 800-995-6284 Fax: 510-595-7040 Toll Free Fax: 800-541-2442 E-mail: customer.service@ keypress.com Web Site: www.keypress.com, pg 145

Ginnis, Patti, Encyclopaedia Britannica Inc, 310 S Michigan Ave, Chicago, IL 60604 Tel: 312-347-7000 Toll Free Tel: 800-323-1229 Fax: 312-347-7399 E-mail: editor@eb.com Web Site: www.eb.com; www. britannica.com, pg 91

Ginsberg, Peter L, Curtis Brown Ltd, 10 Astor Place, New York, NY 10003 Tel: 212-473-5400, pg 623

Ginsburg, Susan, Writers House LLC, 21 W 26 St, New York, NY 10010 Tel: 212-685-2400 Fax: 212-685-1781, pg 662

Giouvanos, Theophrastos, Hammond World Atlas Corp, 95 Progress St, Union, NJ 07083 Tel: 908-206-1300 Toll Free Tel: 800-526-4953 Fax: 908-206-1104 E-mail: customerservice@hammondmap. com; feedback@hammondmap.com Web Site: www. hammondmap.com, pg 112

Gipson, Scott, Caxton Press, 312 Main St, Caldwell, ID 83605-3299 Tel: 208-459-7421 Toll Free Tel: 800-657-6465 Fax: 208-459-7450 E-mail: publish@ caxtonpress.com Web Site: www.caxtonpress.com, pg 55

Giracca, Shaughna, Gracie Allen Awards®, 8405 Greensboro Dr, Suite 800, McLean, VA 22102 Tel: 703-506-3290 Fax: 703-506-3266 E-mail: info@ awrt.org Web Site: www.awrt.org, pg 759

Girard, Carole, Cheneliere/McGraw-Hill, 7001 Saint Laurent Blvd, Montreal, PQ H2S 3E3, Canada Tel: 514-273-1066 Fax: 514-276-0324 E-mail: chene@dlcmcgrawhill.ca Web Site: www. dlcmcgrawhill.ca, pg 540

Girod, Carlos V Jr, Society of Motion Picture & Television Engineers (SMPTE), 595 W Hartsdale Ave, White Plains, NY 10607-1824 Tel: 914-761-1100 Fax: 914-761-3115 E-mail: smpte@smpte.org Web Site: www.smpte.org, pg 700

Giron, Robert L, Gival Press LLC, PO Box 3812, Arlington, VA 22203 Tel: 703-351-0079 Fax: 703-351-0079 E-mail: givalpress@yahoo.com Web Site: www. givalpress.prodigybiz.com; www.givalpress.com, pg 105

Gisbert, Michele, Rutgers University Press, 100 Joyce Kilmer Ave, Piscataway, NJ 08854-8099 Tel: 732-445-7762 (edit); 732-445-7762 (ext 627, sales) Toll Free Tel: 800-446-9323 (orders only) Fax: 732-445-7039 (acqs, edit, mktg, perms, prodn); 732-445-1974 (fulfillment) E-mail: garyf@rci.rutgers.edu Web Site: rutgerspress.rutgers.edu, pg 236

Gislason, Barbara J, Blue Raven Press, 219 SE Main St, Suite 506, Minneapolis, MN 55414 Tel: 612-331-8039 Fax: 612-331-8115 Web Site: www.blueravenpress. com, pg 570

Gislason, Barbara J, The Gislason Agency, 219 SE Main St, Suite 506, Minneapolis, MN 55414 Tel: 612-331-8033 Fax: 612-331-8115 E-mail: gislasonbj@aol.com Web Site: www.TheGislasonAgency.com, pg 632

Gissinger, Beth, Adams Media, An F+W Publications Co, 57 Littlefield St, 2nd fl, Avon, MA 02322 Tel: 508-427-7100 Fax: 508-427-6790 Toll Free Fax: 800-872-5628 E-mail: authors@adamsmedia. com; orders@adamsmedia.com Web Site: www. adamsmedia.com, pg 5

Gissler, Sig, Pulitzer Prizes, 709 Journalism Bldg, New York, NY 10027 Tel: 212-854-3841 Fax: 212-854-3342 E-mail: pulitzer@pulitzer.org Web Site: www. pulitzer.org, pg 800

Giurglu, Mihaela, Fugue State Press, PO Box 80, Cooper Sta, New York, NY 10276 Tel: 212-673-7922 Fax: 208-693-6152 E-mail: info@fuguestatepress.com Web Site: www.fuguestatepress.com, pg 101

Givens, Bettye, Paris-American Academy Writing Workshop, 277 Rue St Jacques, 75005 Paris, France Tel: 806-889-3533 Fax: 806-889-3533 Web Site: www.parisamericanacademy.edu; www. parisamericanacademy.fr, pg 746

Givler, Peter J, AAUP Book, Jacket & Journal Design Show, 71 W 23 St, Suite 901, New York, NY 10010 *Tel:* 212-989-1010 *Fax:* 212-989-0275; 212-989-0176 *E-mail:* info@aaupnet.org *Web Site:* www.aaupnet.org, pg 757

Givler, Peter J, Association of American University Presses (AAUP), 71 W 23 St, Suite 901, New York City, NY 10010 *Tel:* 212-989-1010 *Fax:* 212-989-0275; 212-989-0176 *E-mail:* info@aaupnet.org *Web Site:* www.aaupnet.org, pg 679

Glad, Tom, National Press Club (NPC), 529 14 St NW, 13th fl, Washington, DC 20045 *Tel:* 202-662-7500 *Fax:* 202-662-7569 *E-mail:* infocenter@npcpress.org *Web Site:* www.press.org, pg 694

Gladden, Carolan, Gladden Unlimited, 3808 Georgia St, No 301, San Diego, CA 92103 *Tel:* 619-260-1544, pg 632

Gladstone, William, Waterside Productions Inc, 2187 Newcastle Ave, Suite 204, Cardiff, CA 92007 *Tel:* 760-632-9190 *Fax:* 760-632-9295 *Web Site:* www.waterside.com, pg 660

Glardon, Dave, The National Society of Newspaper Columnists (NSNC), Fillmore St, Suite 507, San Francisco, CA 94115 *Tel:* 415-541-5636 *Web Site:* www.columnists.com, pg 694

Glasner, Lynne, Associated Editors, 27 W 96 St, New York, NY 10025 *Tel:* 212-662-9703 *Fax:* 212-662-0549, pg 590

Glasoe, Maureen, Chicago Women in Publishing, PO Box 268107, Chicago, IL 60626 *Tel:* 312-641-6311 *Fax:* 312-645-1078 *E-mail:* mail@cwip.org *Web Site:* www.cwip.org, pg 684

Glass, Alan, Commonwealth Business Media, 400 Windsor Corporate Center, 50 Millstone Rd, Suite 200, East Windsor, NJ 08520-1415 *Tel:* 609-371-7700 *Toll Free Tel:* 800-221-5488; 888-215-6084 (orders) *Fax:* 609-371-7712 *Web Site:* www.cbizmedia.com, pg 65

Glass, Alex, Trident Media Group LLC, 41 Madison Ave, 36th fl, New York, NY 10010 *Tel:* 212-262-4810 *Fax:* 212-725-4501 *Web Site:* www.tridentmediagroup.com, pg 659

Glass, Kira, Harcourt Trade Publishers, 525 "B" St, Suite 1900, San Diego, CA 92101 *Tel:* 619-231-6616 *Toll Free Tel:* 800-543-1918 (cust serv) *Toll Free Fax:* 800-235-0256 (cust serv) *Web Site:* www.harcourtbooks.com, pg 115

Glass, Maureen, Health Administration Press, One N Franklin St, Suite 1700, Chicago, IL 60606-3491 *Tel:* 312-424-2800 *Fax:* 312-424-0014 *E-mail:* hap@ache.org *Web Site:* www.ache.org, pg 119

Glasser, Carla, The Betsy Nolan Literary Agency, 224 W 29 St, 15th fl, New York, NY 10001 *Tel:* 212-967-8200 *Fax:* 212-967-7292, pg 647

Glasser, Frederick, Barron's Educational Series Inc, 250 Wireless Blvd, Hauppauge, NY 11788 *Tel:* 631-434-3311 *Toll Free Tel:* 800-645-3476 *Fax:* 631-434-3723 *E-mail:* info@barronseduc.com *Web Site:* www.barronseduc.com (Books can be purchased online), pg 32

Glasser, Rachel K, Sydney Taylor Manuscript Award, 15 E 26 St, New York, NY 10010-1579 *Tel:* 212-725-5359 *Fax:* 212-678-8998 *E-mail:* ajl@jewishbooks.org *Web Site:* www.jewishlibraries.org, pg 808

Glassman, Bruce, Lucent Books Inc, 15822 Bernardo Center Dr, Suite C, San Diego, CA 92127 *Tel:* 858-485-7424 *Fax:* 858-485-9549 *E-mail:* info@gale.com *Web Site:* www.gale.com/lucent, pg 159

Glassman, Paul, Passport Press Inc, PO Box 2543, Champlain, NY 12919-1346 *Tel:* 801-504-4385 *Fax:* 801-504-4385 *E-mail:* travelbook@yahoo.com, pg 205

Glavash, Keith, Massachusetts Institute of Technology Libraries, 77 Mass Ave, Bldg 14, Rm 0551, Cambridge, MA 02139-4307 *Tel:* 617-253-7059 *Fax:* 617-253-1690 *E-mail:* docs@mit.edu *Web Site:* libraries.mit.edu/docs, pg 165

Glave, Thomas, Binghamton University Writing Program, c/o Dept of English, PO Box 6000, Binghamton, NY 13902-6000 *Tel:* 607-777-2168 *Fax:* 607-777-2408, pg 751

Glazer, Lori, Houghton Mifflin Trade & Reference Division, 222 Berkeley St, Boston, MA 02116-3764 *Tel:* 617-351-5000 *Toll Free Tel:* 800-225-3362 *Web Site:* www.houghtonmifflinbooks.com, pg 126

Glazner, Steve, APPA: The Association of Higher Education Facilities Officers, 1643 Prince St, Alexandria, VA 22314-2818 *Tel:* 703-684-1446 *Fax:* 703-549-2772 *Web Site:* www.appa.org, pg 21

Gleason, Carolyn, Smithsonian Institution Press, 750 Ninth St NW, Suite 4300, Washington, DC 20560-0950 *Tel:* 202-275-2300 *Fax:* 202-275-2274 *E-mail:* inquiries@sipress.si.edu *Web Site:* www.sipress.si.edu, pg 251

Gleason, Edward S, Forward Movement Publications, 300 W Fourth St, Cincinnati, OH 45202 *Tel:* 513-721-6659 *Toll Free Tel:* 800-543-1813 *Fax:* 513-721-0729 *E-mail:* orders@forwarddaybyday.com *Web Site:* www.forwardmovement.org, pg 99

Gleason, Laura, Louisiana State University Press, PO Box 25053, Baton Rouge, LA 70894-5053 *Tel:* 225-578-6294 *Toll Free Tel:* 800-861-3477 *Fax:* 225-578-6461 *Toll Free Fax:* 800-305-4416 *E-mail:* lsupress@lsu.edu *Web Site:* www.lsu.edu/guests/lsupress, pg 159

Gleason, Robert, Tom Doherty Associates, LLC, 175 Fifth Ave, 14th fl, New York, NY 10010 *Tel:* 212-388-0100 *Toll Free Tel:* 800-455-0340 *Fax:* 212-388-0191 *E-mail:* firstname.lastname@tor.com *Web Site:* www.tor.com, pg 82

Gleason, Ruth, American Society of Indexers Inc (ASI), 10200 W 44 Ave, Suite 304, Wheat Ridge, CO 80033 *Tel:* 303-463-2887 *Fax:* 303-422-8894 *E-mail:* info@asindexing.org *Web Site:* www.asindexing.org, pg 678

Gleichman, Jill, Paulist Press, 997 Macarthur Blvd, Mahwah, NJ 07430 *Tel:* 201-825-7300 *Toll Free Tel:* 800-218-1903 *Fax:* 201-825-8345 *Toll Free Fax:* 800-836-3161 (orders) *E-mail:* info@paulistpress.com *Web Site:* www.paulistpress.com, pg 206

Gleim, James, Krause Publications, 700 E State St, Iola, WI 54990 *Tel:* 715-445-4612 ext 365 *Toll Free Tel:* 800-258-0929; 888-457-2873 *Fax:* 715-445-4087 *Web Site:* www.krause.com, pg 147

Glenn, John, American Book Producers Association (ABPA), 160 Fifth Ave, Suite 622, New York, NY 10010 *Tel:* 212-645-2368 *Toll Free Tel:* 800-209-4575 *Fax:* 212-242-6499 *E-mail:* office@abpaonline.org *Web Site:* www.abpaonline.org, pg 676

Glenn, John, Book Producing: Making Books Happen, 160 Fifth Ave, New York, NY 10010-7003 *Tel:* 212-645-2368 *Toll Free Tel:* 800-209-4575 *Fax:* 212-242-6799 *E-mail:* office@abpaonline.org *Web Site:* www.abpaonline.org, pg 742

Glick, Mollie, Jean V Naggar Literary Agency, 216 E 75 St, Suite 1-E, New York, NY 10021 *Tel:* 212-794-1082, pg 645

Glick, Stacey, Dystel & Goderich Literary Management, One Union Sq W, Suite 904, New York, NY 10003 *Tel:* 212-627-9100 *Fax:* 212-627-9313 *Web Site:* www.dystel.com, pg 629

Glover, Angelika, Knopf Canada, One Toronto St, Suite 300, Toronto, ON M5C 2V6, Canada *Tel:* 416-364-4449 *Toll Free Tel:* 800-668-4247 (order desk) *Fax:* 416-364-0462 *Web Site:* www.randomhouse.ca, pg 552

Glover, Jay, CyclopsMedia.com, 1076 Eagle Dr, Salinas, CA 93905 *Tel:* 831-776-9500 *Fax:* 831-422-5915 *E-mail:* custserv@cyclopsmedia.com *Web Site:* www.cyclopsmedia.com, pg 75

Glover, Jennifer, John Milton Society for the Blind, 475 Riverside Dr, Rm 455, New York, NY 10027 *Tel:* 212-870-3335 *Fax:* 212-870-3229 *E-mail:* order@jmsblind.org *Web Site:* www.jmsblind.org, pg 141

Glover, Linda, W H Freeman and Co, 41 Madison Ave, 37th fl, New York, NY 10010 *Tel:* 212-576-9400 *Fax:* 212-689-2383 *Web Site:* www.whfreeman.com, pg 100

Glover, Rob, Standard Publishing Co, 8121 Hamilton Ave, Cincinnati, OH 45231 *Tel:* 513-931-4050 *Toll Free Tel:* 800-543-1301 *Fax:* 513-931-0950 *Toll Free Fax:* 877-867-5751 *E-mail:* customerservice@standardpub.com *Web Site:* www.standardpub.com, pg 257

Glover, Sally, Lynne Rienner Publishers Inc, 1800 30 St, Suite 314, Boulder, CO 80301 *Tel:* 303-444-6684 *Fax:* 303-444-0824 *E-mail:* cservice@rienner.com *Web Site:* www.rienner.com, pg 232

Gluck, Suzanne, William Morris Agency, 1325 Avenue of the Americas, New York, NY 10019 *Tel:* 212-586-5100 *Fax:* 212-903-1418 *E-mail:* wma@interport.net *Web Site:* www.wma.com, pg 645

Gluckman, Paul, Warren Communications News, 2115 Ward Ct NW, Washington, DC 20037-1209 *Tel:* 202-872-9200 *Fax:* 202-293-3435 *E-mail:* info@warren-news.com *Web Site:* www.warren-news.com, pg 293

Glueck, Michael Wells, EditAndPublishYourBook.com, PO Box 2965, Nantucket, MA 02584-2965 *E-mail:* michaeltheauthor@yahoo.com *Web Site:* www.editandpublishyourbook.com, pg 597

Glusman, John, Farrar, Straus & Giroux, LLC, 19 Union Sq W, New York, NY 10003 *Tel:* 212-741-6900 *Fax:* 212-741-6973 *Web Site:* www.fsgbooks.com, pg 95

Glynn, Diana, Basic Health Publications Inc, 8200 Boulevard E, Suite 25-G, North Bergen, NJ 07047 *Tel:* 201-868-8336 *Toll Free Tel:* 800-575-8890 *Fax:* 201-868-8335, pg 33

Goble, Sam, MicroMash, 6402 S Troy Circle, Englewood, CO 80111-6424 *Tel:* 303-799-0099 *Toll Free Tel:* 800-823-6039 *Fax:* 303-799-1425 *E-mail:* info@micromash.com *Web Site:* www.micromash.net, pg 173

Goc, Michael J, New Past Press Inc, PO Box 558, Friendship, WI 53934-0558 *Tel:* 608-339-7191 *E-mail:* newpast@maqs.net *Web Site:* newpastpress.com, pg 188

Goddy, David, Scholastic Education Curriculum Publishing, 524 Broadway, New York, NY 10012 *Tel:* 212-343-6100 *Web Site:* www.scholastic.com, pg 241

Godell, Trelawney N, Brown Publishing Network Inc, 95 Sawyer Rd, Waltham, MA 02453 *Tel:* 781-237-7567 *Fax:* 781-237-8874 *Web Site:* www.brownpubnet.com, pg 593

Goderich, Miriam, Dystel & Goderich Literary Management, One Union Sq W, Suite 904, New York, NY 10003 *Tel:* 212-627-9100 *Fax:* 212-627-9313 *Web Site:* www.dystel.com, pg 629

Godfrey, Bill, DC Comics, 1700 Broadway, New York, NY 10019 *Tel:* 212-636-5400 *Toll Free Tel:* 800-759-0190 (distribution) *Fax:* 212-636-5481 *Web Site:* dccomics.com; www.madmag.com, pg 77

Godfrey, Dave, Beach Holme Publishing, 409 Granville St, Suite 1010, Vancouver, BC V6C 1T2, Canada *Tel:* 604-733-4868 *Toll Free Tel:* 888-551-6655 (orders) *Fax:* 604-733-4860 *E-mail:* bhp@beachholme.bc.ca *Web Site:* www.beachholme.bc.ca, pg 536

Godfrey, Ellen, Beach Holme Publishing, 409 Granville St, Suite 1010, Vancouver, BC V6C 1T2, Canada *Tel:* 604-733-4868 *Toll Free Tel:* 888-551-6655 (orders) *Fax:* 604-733-4860 *E-mail:* bhp@beachholme.bc.ca *Web Site:* www.beachholme.bc.ca, pg 536

Godine, David R, David R Godine Publisher Inc, 9 Hamilton Place, Boston, MA 02108 *Tel:* 617-451-9600 *Fax:* 617-350-0250 *E-mail:* info@godine.com *Web Site:* www.godine.com, pg 106

Godlis, Eileen, Janklow & Nesbit Associates, 445 Park Ave, New York, NY 10022 *Tel:* 212-421-1700 *Fax:* 212-980-3671 *E-mail:* postmaster@janklow.com, pg 636

Godoff, Ann, Penguin Group (USA) Inc, 375 Hudson St, New York, NY 10014 *Tel:* 212-366-2000 *Fax:* 212-366-2666 *E-mail:* online@uspenguingroup.com *Web Site:* www.penguin.com, pg 208

Godwin, Laura, Henry Holt and Company, LLC, 115 W 18 St, New York, NY 10011 *Tel:* 212-886-9200 *Toll Free Tel:* 888-330-8477 (orders) *Fax:* 212-633-0748 *E-mail:* publicity@hholt.com *Web Site:* www.henryholt.com, pg 124

Godwin, Mary Jo, Scarecrow Press Inc, 4501 Forbes Blvd, Suite 200, Lanham, MD 20706 *Tel:* 301-459-3366 *Toll Free Tel:* 800-462-6420 *Fax:* 301-429-5747 *Toll Free Fax:* 800-338-4550 *Web Site:* www.scarecrowpress.com, pg 241

Goering, Karl, SAE (Society of Automotive Engineers International), 400 Commonwealth Dr, Warrendale, PA 15096-0001 *Tel:* 724-776-4841 *Toll Free Tel:* 877-606-7323 (cust serv) *Fax:* 724-776-0790 *E-mail:* publications@sae.org *Web Site:* www.sae.org, pg 237

Goering, Kevin, The Perseus Books Group, 387 Park Ave S, 12th fl, New York, NY 10016 *Tel:* 212-340-8100 *Toll Free Tel:* 800-386-5656 (cust serv) *Fax:* 212-340-8115 *Web Site:* www.perseusbooksgroup.com, pg 210

Goerlich, Shirley B, RSG Publishing, 217 County Hwy 1, Bainbridge, NY 13733-9307 *Tel:* 607-563-9000 *Fax:* 607-563-9000, pg 235

Goertz, Elena, American Society of Media Photographers (ASMP), 150 N Second St, Philadelphia, PA 19106 *Tel:* 215-451-2767 *Fax:* 215-451-0880 *E-mail:* info@asmp.org *Web Site:* www.asmp.org, pg 678

Goetsch, Lara, Cunningham Commission for Youth Theatre, 2135 N Kenmore, Chicago, IL 60614 *Tel:* 773-325-7938 *Fax:* 773-325-7920 *Web Site:* theatreschool.depaul.edu, pg 769

Goetz, Lisa, Bloomberg Press, PO Box 888, Princeton, NJ 08542-0888 *Tel:* 609-279-4600 *E-mail:* press@bloomberg.com *Web Site:* www.bloomberg.com/books, pg 41

Goff, Anthony, Time Warner Audio Books, Sports Illustrated Bldg, 135 W 50 St, New York, NY 10020 *Tel:* 212-522-7334 *Fax:* 212-522-7994 *Web Site:* www.twbookmark.com/audiobooks, pg 271

Goff, Raoul, Mandala Publishing, 17 Paul Dr, San Rafael, CA 94903 *Tel:* 415-883-4055 *Toll Free Tel:* 800-688-2218 (orders only) *Fax:* 415-884-0500 *E-mail:* mandala@mandala.org *Web Site:* www.mandala.org, pg 162

Goggins, Gerard E, Ambassador Books Inc, 91 Prescott St, Worcester, MA 01605 *Tel:* 508-756-2893 *Toll Free Tel:* 800-577-0909 *Fax:* 508-757-7055 *Web Site:* www.ambassadorbooks.com, pg 10

Gogo, Jeff, Crabtree Publishing Co, 350 Fifth Ave, Suite 3308, PMB 16-A, New York, NY 10118 *Tel:* 212-496-5040 *Toll Free Tel:* 800-387-7650 *Toll Free Fax:* 800-355-7166 *E-mail:* letters@crabtreebooks.com *Web Site:* www.crabtreebooks.com, pg 71

Golan, Joan Marlow, Harlequin Enterprises Ltd, 233 Broadway, Suite 1001, New York, NY 10279 *Tel:* 212-553-4200 *Fax:* 212-227-8969 *E-mail:* customer.ecare@harlequin.ca *Web Site:* www.eharlequin.com; www.luna-books.com; www.mirabooks.com; www.reddressink.com; www.steeplehill.com, pg 115

Golan, Joan Marlow, Steeple Hill Books, 233 Broadway, Suite 1001, New York, NY 10279 *Tel:* 212-553-4200 *Fax:* 212-227-8969 *E-mail:* customer_service@harlequin.ca *Web Site:* www.steeplehill.com, pg 258

Gold, Benjamin PhD, New Age World Publishing, 8345 NW 66 St, Suite 6344, Miami, FL 33166-2626 *Tel:* 305-735-8064 *Toll Free Fax:* 888-739-6129 *E-mail:* info@NAWPublishing.com *Web Site:* www.NAWPublishing.com, pg 187, 646

Gold, Edwin, University of Baltimore - Yale Gordon College of Liberal Arts, Ampersand Institute for Words & Images, 1420 N Charles St, Baltimore, MD 21201-5779 *Tel:* 410-837-6022 *Fax:* 410-837-6029 *Web Site:* raven.ubalt.edu, pg 755

Gold, Elizabeth, Guideposts Book & Inspirational Media Division, 16 E 34 St, New York, NY 10016 *Tel:* 212-251-8100 *Fax:* 212-684-0679 *Web Site:* www.guidepostsbooks.com, pg 111

Gold, Jennifer, Rough Guides, 345 Hudson St, New York, NY 10014 *Tel:* 212-414-3635 *Fax:* 212-414-3352 *E-mail:* mail@roughguides.com *Web Site:* www.roughguides.com, pg 235

Gold, Jerry, Black Heron Press, PO Box 95676, Seattle, WA 98145-2676 *Tel:* 206-363-5210 *Fax:* 206-363-5210 *Web Site:* www.blackheronpress.com, pg 40

Gold, Tanya, Oyster River Press, 20 Riverview Rd, Durham, NH 03824-3313 *Tel:* 603-868-5006 *E-mail:* oysterriverpress@comcast.net *Web Site:* www.oysterriverpress.com, pg 201

Gold, Tanya, Oyster River Press, 20 Riverview Rd, Durham, NH 03824-3313 *Tel:* 603-868-5006 *E-mail:* oysterriverpress@comcast.net *Web Site:* oysterriverpress.com, pg 607

Goldbaum, Milton J, Alan Wofsy Fine Arts, 1109 Geary Blvd, San Francisco, CA 94109 *Tel:* 415-292-6500 *Fax:* 415-512-0130 (acctg); 415-292-6594 (off & cust serv) *E-mail:* beauxarts@earthlink.net (cust serv); editeur@earthlink.net (edit); order@art-books.com (orders) *Web Site:* art-books.com, pg 302

Goldberg, Arthur, Abbeville Publishing Group, 116 W 23 St, Suite 500, New York, NY 10011 *Tel:* 646-375-2039 *Toll Free Tel:* 800-ART-BOOK (278-2665) *Fax:* 646-375-2040 *E-mail:* abbeville@abbeville.com *Web Site:* www.abbeville.com, pg 2

Goldberg, Arthur, Artabras Inc, 116 W 23 St, Suite 500, New York, NY 10011 *Tel:* 646-375-2039 *Toll Free Tel:* 800-ART-BOOK *Fax:* 646-375-2040 *E-mail:* abbeville@abbeville.com *Web Site:* www.abbeville.com, pg 24

Goldberg, Beverly, The Century Foundation Press, 41 E 70 St, New York, NY 10021 *Tel:* 212-535-4441 *Fax:* 212-535-7534 *E-mail:* info@tcf.org *Web Site:* www.tcf.org, pg 58

Goldberg, Beverly, The Century Foundation Press, 41 E 70 St, New York, NY 10021 *Tel:* 212-535-4441 *Fax:* 212-535-7534 *Web Site:* www.tcf.org, pg 705

Goldberg, Glenn S, The McGraw-Hill Companies Inc, 1221 Avenue of the Americas, 50th fl, New York, NY 10020 *Tel:* 212-512-2000 *E-mail:* webmaster@mcgraw-hill.com *Web Site:* www.mcgraw-hill.com, pg 167

Goldberg, Harriet, MedMaster Inc, 3337 Hollywood Oaks Dr, Fort Lauderdale, FL 33312 *Tel:* 954-962-8414 *Toll Free Tel:* 800-335-3480 *Fax:* 954-962-4508 *E-mail:* mmbks@aol.com *Web Site:* www.medmaster.net, pg 170

Goldberg, Marcia Lee, MMB Music Inc, Contemporary Arts Bldg, 3526 Washington Ave, St Louis, MO 63103-1019 *Tel:* 314-531-9635 *Toll Free Tel:* 800-543-3771 *Fax:* 314-531-8384 *E-mail:* info@mmbmusic.com *Web Site:* www.mmbmusic.com, pg 176

Goldberg, Matthew, Basic Books, 387 Park Ave S, 12th fl, New York, NY 10016-8810 *Tel:* 212-340-8100 *Toll Free Tel:* 800-242-7737 (orders) *Fax:* 212-340-8135 *E-mail:* basic.books@perseusbooks.com *Web Site:* www.basicbooks.com, pg 33

Goldberg, Matthew, Counterpoint Press, 387 Park Ave S, New York, NY 10016 *Tel:* 212-340-8100 *Fax:* 212-340-8135 (edit); 212-340-8115 *E-mail:* counterpointpress@perseusbooks.com *Web Site:* www.counterpointpress.com, pg 70

Goldberg, Matthew, Da Capo Press Inc, 11 Cambridge Center, Cambridge, MA 02142 *Tel:* 617-252-5200 *Toll Free Tel:* 800-242-7737 (orders) *Fax:* 617-252-5285 *E-mail:* custserve@lrp.com *Web Site:* www.dacapopress.com, pg 75

Goldberg, Matthew, The Perseus Books Group, 387 Park Ave S, 12th fl, New York, NY 10016 *Tel:* 212-340-8100 *Toll Free Tel:* 800-386-5656 (cust serv) *Fax:* 212-340-8115 *Web Site:* www.perseusbooksgroup.com, pg 210

Goldberg, Matthew, PublicAffairs, 250 W 57 St, Suite 1321, New York, NY 10107 *Tel:* 212-397-6666 *Toll Free Tel:* 800-242-7737 (orders) *Fax:* 212-397-4267 *E-mail:* publicaffairs@perseusbooks.com *Web Site:* www.publicaffairsbooks.com, pg 221

Goldberg, Matthew, Westview Press, 5500 Central Ave, Boulder, CO 80301 *Tel:* 303-444-3541 *Toll Free Tel:* 800-386-5656 *Fax:* 720-406-7336 *E-mail:* westview.orders@perseusbooks.com *Web Site:* www.perseusbooksgroup.com; www.westviewpress.com, pg 297

Goldberg, Matty, Running Press Book Publishers, 125 S 22 St, Philadelphia, PA 19103-4399 *Tel:* 215-567-5080 *Toll Free Tel:* 800-345-5359 (cust serv & orders) *Fax:* 215-568-2919 *Toll Free Fax:* 800-453-2884 *Web Site:* www.runningpress.com, pg 236

Goldberg, Michael, ASM Press, 1752 "N" St NW, Washington, DC 20036-2904 *Tel:* 202-737-3600 *Toll Free Tel:* 800-546-2416 *Fax:* 202-942-9342 *E-mail:* books@asmusa.org *Web Site:* www.asmpress.org, pg 25

Goldberg, Norman A, MMB Music Inc, Contemporary Arts Bldg, 3526 Washington Ave, St Louis, MO 63103-1019 *Tel:* 314-531-9635 *Toll Free Tel:* 800-543-3771 *Fax:* 314-531-8384 *E-mail:* info@mmbmusic.com *Web Site:* www.mmbmusic.com, pg 176

Goldberg, Randi, Globe Fearon, 299 Jefferson Rd, Parsippany, NJ 07054 *Tel:* 973-739-8000, pg 105

Goldberg, Stephen, MedMaster Inc, 3337 Hollywood Oaks Dr, Fort Lauderdale, FL 33312 *Tel:* 954-962-8414 *Toll Free Tel:* 800-335-3480 *Fax:* 954-962-4508 *E-mail:* mmbks@aol.com *Web Site:* www.medmaster.net, pg 170

Goldberger, Amy S, Publishing Services, 525 E 86 St, Suite 10-E, New York, NY 10028 *Tel:* 212-628-9127 *Fax:* 212-628-9128 *E-mail:* pubserv525@aol.com, pg 609, 649

Goldblatt, Deborah, Cambridge University Press, 40 W 20 St, New York, NY 10011-4211 *Tel:* 212-924-3900 *Toll Free Tel:* 800-899-5222 *Fax:* 212-691-3239 *Web Site:* www.cambridge.org, pg 52

Golden, James Jr, Mercer University Press, 1400 Coleman Ave, Macon, GA 31207 *Tel:* 478-301-2880 *Toll Free Tel:* 800-637-2378 (ext 2880, outside GA); 800-342-0841 (ext 2880, GA) *Fax:* 478-301-2585 *E-mail:* mupressorders@mercer.edu *Web Site:* www.mupress.org, pg 171

Golden, Lilly, The Lyons Press, 246 Goose Lane, Guilford, CT 06437 *Tel:* 203-458-4500 *Toll Free Tel:* 800-243-0495 *Fax:* 203-458-4668 *Web Site:* www.lyonspress.com; www.globepequot.com, pg 160

Golden, Lori, Health Communications Inc, 3201 SW 15 St, Deerfield Beach, FL 33442-8190 *Tel:* 954-360-0909 *Toll Free Tel:* 800-851-9100 (cust serv); 800-441-5569 (order entry) *Fax:* 954-360-0034 *Web Site:* www.hcibooks.com, pg 119

Golden, Marita, The Hurston/Wright Award for College Writers, 6525 Bellcrest Rd, Suite 531, Hyattsville, MD 20782 *Tel:* 301-683-2134 *Fax:* 301-277-1262 *E-mail:* info@hurston-wright.org *Web Site:* www.hurston-wright.org, pg 779

Golden, Marita, The Hurston/Wright Legacy Award, 6525 Bellcrest Rd, Suite 531, Hyattsville, MD 20782 *Tel:* 301-683-2134 *Fax:* 301-277-1262 *E-mail:* info@hurston-wright.org *Web Site:* www.hurston-wright.org, pg 779

Golden, Marita, The Hurston/Wright Writer's Week, 6525 Bellcrest Rd, Suite 531, Hyattsville, MD 20782 *Tel:* 301-683-2134 *Fax:* 301-277-1262 *E-mail:* info@hurston-wright.org *Web Site:* www.hurston-wright.org, pg 744

Golden, Winifred, Julie Castiglia Literary Agency, 1155 Camino Del Mar, Suite 510, Del Mar, CA 92014 *Tel:* 858-755-8761 *Fax:* 858-755-7063 *E-mail:* jaclagency@aol.com, pg 624

Goldfarb, Ronald L, Goldfarb & Associates, 721 Gibbon St, Alexandria, VA 22314 *Tel:* 202-466-3030 *Fax:* 703-836-5644 *E-mail:* rglawlit@aol.com, pg 632

Goodman, Gloria, Seal Books, One Toronto St, Suite 300, Toronto, ON M5C 2V6, Canada *Tel:* 416-364-4449 *Toll Free Tel:* 888-523-9292 (order desk) *Fax:* 416-957-1587 *Web Site:* www.randomhouse.ca, pg 560

Goodman, Dr Harold, Health Resources Press Inc, 8609 Second Ave, Suite 405B, Silver Spring, MD 20910 *Tel:* 301-565-2494 *Fax:* 301-565-2494 *Web Site:* www.healthresourcespress.com, pg 120

Goodman, Irene, Irene Goodman Literary Agency, 80 Fifth Ave, Suite 1101, New York, NY 10011 *Tel:* 212-604-0330 *Fax:* 212-675-1381 *E-mail:* igagency@aol.com, pg 633

Goodman, Peter, Stone Bridge Press LLC, PO Box 8208, Berkeley, CA 94707-8208 *Tel:* 510-524-8732 *Toll Free Tel:* 800-947-7271 *Fax:* 510-524-8711 *E-mail:* sbp@stonebridge.com; sbpedit@stonebridge.com *Web Site:* www.stonebridge.com, pg 260

Goodman, Sarah, Ralph M Vicinanza Ltd, 303 W 18 St, New York, NY 10011 *Tel:* 212-924-7090 *Fax:* 212-691-9644 *E-mail:* ralphvic@aol.com, pg 659

Goodman, Sasha, Goodman-Andrew Agency Inc, 6680 Colgate Ave, Los Angeles, CA 90048 *Tel:* 310-387-0242 *Fax:* 323-653-3457 *E-mail:* ukseg@aol.com, pg 633

Goodnough, Doris, Orbis Books, Walsh Bldg, 75 Ryder Rd, Ossining, NY 10562 *Tel:* 914-941-7636 *Toll Free Tel:* 800-258-5838 (orders) *Fax:* 914-941-7005 (orders); 914-945-0670 (office) *E-mail:* orbisbooks@maryknoll.org *Web Site:* www.orbisbooks.com, pg 198

Goodrow, Tina, Rutledge Hill Press, c/o Thomas Nelson Publishers, PO Box 141000, Nashville, TN 37214-1000 *Tel:* 615-902-2703 *Toll Free Tel:* 800-251-4000 (ext 2703) *Fax:* 615-902-2340 *Web Site:* www.rutledgehillpress.com, pg 236

Goodson, Connie, Concordia Publishing House, 3558 S Jefferson Ave, St Louis, MO 63118-3968 *Tel:* 314-268-1000 *Toll Free Tel:* 800-325-3040 *Fax:* 314-268-1329 *Toll Free Fax:* 800-490-9889 *E-mail:* cphorder@cph.org *Web Site:* www.cph.org, pg 66

Goodwin, Daniel H, Dixon Ryan Fox Manuscript Prize, Lake Rd, Cooperstown, NY 13326 *Tel:* 607-547-1491 *Fax:* 607-547-1405 *E-mail:* hennessy10@hotmail.com, pg 770

Goodwin, Elinor, Storey Books, 210 Mass MoCA Way, North Adams, MA 01247 *Tel:* 413-346-2100 *Toll Free Tel:* 800-793-9396 *Fax:* 413-346-2253 *E-mail:* info@storey.com *Web Site:* www.storey.com, pg 260

Goodwin, George Ann, Southern Methodist University Press, 314 Fondren Library W, 6404 Hill Top Lane, Dallas, TX 75275 *Tel:* 214-768-1430; 214-768-1432 *Fax:* 214-768-1428, pg 255

Goody, Margo, Audio Renaissance, 175 Fifth Ave, New York, NY 10010 *Tel:* 212-674-5151 *Toll Free Tel:* 888-330-8477 (cust serv) *Fax:* 917-534-0980 *E-mail:* firstname.lastname@hbpub.com *Web Site:* www.audiorenaissance.com, pg 27

Gooldy, Patricia, Summit Publications, PO Box 39128, Indianapolis, IN 46239 *Tel:* 317-862-3330 *Toll Free Tel:* 800-419-0200 *Fax:* 317-862-2599 *E-mail:* yogs@iquest.net *Web Site:* www.yogs.com, pg 261

Gooldy, Patricia, Ye Olde Genealogie Shoppe, PO Box 39128, Indianapolis, IN 46239 *Tel:* 317-862-3330 *Toll Free Tel:* 800-419-0200 *Fax:* 317-862-2599 *E-mail:* yogs@iquest.net *Web Site:* www.yogs.com, pg 306

Goossen, Chester, Prairie View Press, PR 205, Rosenort, MB R0G 1W0, Canada *Tel:* 204-746-2375 *Toll Free Tel:* 800-477-7377 *Fax:* 204-746-2667, pg 558

Goossen, Dalen, Prairie View Press, PR 205, Rosenort, MB R0G 1W0, Canada *Tel:* 204-746-2375 *Toll Free Tel:* 800-477-7377 *Fax:* 204-746-2667, pg 558

Gordijn, Peggy, Jane Rotrosen Agency LLC, 318 E 51 St, New York, NY 10022 *Tel:* 212-593-4330 *Fax:* 212-935-6985, pg 653

Gordon, Annette, Clarity Press Inc, 3277 Roswell Rd NE, Suite 469, Atlanta, GA 30305 *Toll Free Tel:* 800-729-6423 (orders); 877-613-1495 *Fax:* 404-231-

3899 *Toll Free Fax:* 877-613-7868 *E-mail:* clarity@islandnet.com; claritypress@usa.net (editorial) *Web Site:* www.claritypress.com, pg 62

Gordon, Ashley, River City Publishing, LLC, 1719 Mulberry St, Montgomery, AL 36106 *Tel:* 334-265-6753 *Toll Free Tel:* 877-408-7078 *Fax:* 334-265-8880 *E-mail:* web@rivercitypublishing.com *Web Site:* www.rivercitypublishing.com, pg 232

Gordon, Douglas C, P M Gordon Associates Inc, 2115 Wallace St, Philadelphia, PA 19130 *Tel:* 215-769-2525 *Fax:* 215-769-5354 *E-mail:* pmga@pond.com, pg 600

Gordon, Kathryn B, Simon & Schuster Online, 1230 Avenue of the Americas, New York, NY 10020 *Tel:* 212-698-7547 *Fax:* 212-632-8070 *E-mail:* ssonline@simonsays.com *Web Site:* www.simonsays.com; www.simonsayskids.com; www.simonsaysshop.com, pg 249

Gordon, Marilyn, Baker Books, PO Box 6287, Grand Rapids, MI 49516-6287 *Tel:* 616-676-9185 *Toll Free Tel:* 800-877-2665; 800-679-1957 *Fax:* 616-676-9573 *Toll Free Fax:* 800-398-3110 *Web Site:* www.bakerpublishinggroup.com, pg 30

Gordon, Marilyn, Chosen Books, PO Box 6287, Grand Rapids, MI 49516-6287 *Tel:* 616-676-9185 *Toll Free Tel:* 800-877-2665 *Fax:* 616-676-2315 *Web Site:* www.bakerpublishinggroup.com, pg 61

Gordon, Marilyn, Fleming H Revell, PO Box 6287, Grand Rapids, MI 49516-6287 *Tel:* 616-676-9185 *Toll Free Tel:* 800-877-2665 *Fax:* 616-676-9573 *Web Site:* www.bakerbooks.com, pg 232

Gordon, Peggy M, P M Gordon Associates Inc, 2115 Wallace St, Philadelphia, PA 19130 *Tel:* 215-769-2525 *Fax:* 215-769-5354 *E-mail:* pmga@pond.com, pg 600

Gordon, Peter, Cambridge University Press, 40 W 20 St, New York, NY 10011-4211 *Tel:* 212-924-3900 *Toll Free Tel:* 800-899-5222 *Fax:* 212-691-3239 *Web Site:* www.cambridge.org, pg 52

Gordon, Robert, Players Press Inc, PO Box 1132, Studio City, CA 91614-0132 *Tel:* 818-789-4980, pg 214

Gordon, Rose Corbett, Corbett Gordon Co, 6 Fort Rachel Place, Mystic, CT 06355 *Tel:* 860-536-4108 *Fax:* 860-536-3732, pg 595

Gordon, Russell, Simon & Schuster Children's Publishing, 1230 Avenue of the Americas, New York, NY 10020 *Tel:* 212-698-7000 *Web Site:* www.simonsayskids.com, pg 248

Gordon, Tim, General Store Publishing House, 499 O'Brien Rd, Renfrew, ON K7V 4A6, Canada *Tel:* 613-432-7697 *Toll Free Tel:* 800-465-6072 *Fax:* 613-432-7184 *Web Site:* www.gsph.com, pg 548

Gore, Dorothy, Christian Booksellers Association (CBA), 9240 Explorer Dr, Colorado Springs, CO 80920 *Tel:* 719-265-9895 *Toll Free Tel:* 800-252-1950 *Fax:* 719-272-3510 *E-mail:* info@cbaonline.org *Web Site:* www.cbaonline.org, pg 685

Gorelick, Richard, Graphic Arts Sales Foundation (GASF), 113 E Evans St, West Chester, PA 19380 *Tel:* 610-431-9780 *Fax:* 610-436-5238 *E-mail:* info@gasf.org *Web Site:* www.gasf.org, pg 688

Gorham, Sarah, Sarabande Books Inc, 2234 Dundee Rd, Suite 200, Louisville, KY 40205 *Tel:* 502-458-4028 *Fax:* 502-458-4065 *E-mail:* info@sarabandebooks.org *Web Site:* www.sarabandebooks.org, pg 240

Gorlinsky, Raelene, Ellora's Cave Publishing Inc, 1337 Commerce Dr, Suite 13, Stow, OH 44224 *Tel:* 330-689-1118 *E-mail:* service@ellorascave.com *Web Site:* www.ellorascave.com, pg 89

Gorman, Maire, Houghton Mifflin Trade & Reference Division, 222 Berkeley St, Boston, MA 02116-3764 *Tel:* 617-351-5000 *Toll Free Tel:* 800-225-3362 *Web Site:* www.houghtonmifflinbooks.com, pg 126

Gormley, Jim, National Academies Press, 500 Fifth St NW, Washington, DC 20001 *Tel:* 202-334-3313 *Toll Free Tel:* 800-624-6242 *Fax:* 202-334-2451 (orders) *Web Site:* www.nap.edu, pg 182

Gormley, Patricia, e-Scholastic, 568 Broadway, 9th fl, New York, NY 10012 *Tel:* 212-343-7100 *Fax:* 212-343-4949, pg 85

Gorzelski, Elaine, Harmonie Park Press, 23630 Pinewood, Warren, MI 48091 *Tel:* 586-755-3080 *Toll Free Tel:* 800-886-3080 *Fax:* 586-755-4213 *E-mail:* info@harmonieparkpress.com *Web Site:* harmonieparkpress.com, pg 115

Gosnell, Lynn, Trinity University Press, One Trinity Place, San Antonio, TX 78212-7200 *Tel:* 210-999-8884 *Fax:* 210-999-8838 *E-mail:* books@trinity.edu *Web Site:* www.trinity.edu/tupress, pg 275

Goss, Linda, RTP Publishing Group, PO Box 4501, Clifton Park, NY 12065 *Tel:* 518-383-6414 *Fax:* 518-383-6414 *E-mail:* rockytopbooks@aol.com *Web Site:* member.aol.com/rockytopbooks, pg 236

Gosse, Jonathan F, American Technical Publishers Inc, 1155 W 175 St, Homewood, IL 60430-4600 *Tel:* 708-957-1100 *Toll Free Tel:* 800-323-3471 *Fax:* 708-957-1101 *E-mail:* service@americantech.net *Web Site:* www.go2atp.com, pg 18

Gosse, Liz, Fulcrum Publishing Inc, 16100 Table Mountain Pkwy, Suite 300, Golden, CO 80403 *Tel:* 303-277-1623 *Toll Free Tel:* 800-992-2908 *Fax:* 303-279-7111 *Toll Free Fax:* 800-726-7112 *E-mail:* fulcrum@fulcrum-books.com *Web Site:* www.fulcrum-books.com, pg 101

Gossett, Bruce, American Society of Civil Engineers (ASCE), 1801 Alexander Bell Dr, Reston, VA 20191-4400 *Tel:* 703-295-6200 *Toll Free Tel:* 800-548-2723 *Fax:* 703-295-6278 *E-mail:* marketing@asce.org *Web Site:* www.asce.org, pg 18

Gott, Jeff, Thomas Nelson Inc, 501 Nelson Place, Nashville, TN 37214 *Tel:* 615-889-9000 *Toll Free Tel:* 800-251-4000 *Fax:* 615-902-1610 *E-mail:* publicity@thomasnelson.com *Web Site:* www.thomasnelson.com, pg 269

Gotta, Iazamir, Trident Media Group LLC, 41 Madison Ave, 36th fl, New York, NY 10010 *Tel:* 212-262-4810 *Fax:* 212-725-4501 *Web Site:* www.tridentmediagroup.com, pg 659

Gottfried, Chet, C+S Gottfried, 619 Cricklewood Dr, State College, PA 16803 *Tel:* 631-563-2841 *E-mail:* cs@lookoutnow.com *Web Site:* www.lookoutnow.com/dtp, pg 600

Gottfried, Glenn, Thomson Financial Publishing, 4709 W Golf Rd, Suite 600, Skokie, IL 60076-1253 *Tel:* 847-676-9600; 847-677-8037 *Toll Free Tel:* 800-321-3373 *Fax:* 847-676-9616 *E-mail:* custservice@tfp.com *Web Site:* www.tfp.com; www.tgbr.com, pg 270

Gottfried, Susan, C+S Gottfried, 619 Cricklewood Dr, State College, PA 16803 *Tel:* 631-563-2841 *E-mail:* cs@lookoutnow.com *Web Site:* www.lookoutnow.com/dtp, pg 600

Gotthelf, Cheryl, Scholastic Entertainment Inc, 524 Broadway, New York, NY 10012 *Tel:* 212-343-7500 *Fax:* 212-965-7448, pg 241

Gottlieb, Richard, Grey House Publishing Inc, 185 Millerton Rd, Millerton, NY 12546 *Tel:* 518-789-8700 *Toll Free Tel:* 800-562-2139 *Fax:* 518-789-0556 *E-mail:* books@greyhouse.com *Web Site:* www.greyhouse.com, pg 109

Gottlieb, Robert, Trident Media Group LLC, 41 Madison Ave, 36th fl, New York, NY 10010 *Tel:* 212-262-4810 *Fax:* 212-725-4501 *Web Site:* www.tridentmediagroup.com, pg 659

Gottlieb, Sherry, Sherry Gottlieb, 4900 Dunes St, Oxnard, CA 93035 *Tel:* 805-382-3425 *Fax:* 805-658-8601 *E-mail:* writer@wordservices.com *Web Site:* www.wordservices.com, pg 600

Gottstein, Adam, Volcano Press Inc, 21496 National St, Volcano, CA 95689 *Tel:* 209-296-4991 *Toll Free Tel:* 800-879-9636 *Fax:* 209-296-4995 *E-mail:* sales@volcanopress.com *Web Site:* www.volcanopress.com, pg 291

Granger, Elizabeth, Midwest Travel Writers Association, PO Box 83542, Lincoln, NE 68501-3542 *Tel:* 402-438-2253 *Fax:* 402-438-2253 *Web Site:* www.mtwa.org, pg 691

Graninger, Matt, Marketscope Group Books LLC, PO Box 3118, Huntington Beach, CA 92605-3118 *Tel:* 714-375-9888 *Fax:* 714-375-9898, pg 163

Grann, Phyllis, Doubleday Broadway Publishing Group, 1745 Broadway, New York, NY 10019 *Tel:* 212-782-9000 *Toll Free Tel:* 800-223-6834; 800-223-5780 (sales) *Fax:* 212-302-7985 (correspondence); 212-492-9862 (orders), pg 83

Grant, Cherise, Fireside & Touchstone, 1230 Avenue of the Americas, New York, NY 10020, pg 97

Grant, Donald M, Donald M Grant Publisher Inc, PO Box 187, Hampton Falls, NH 03844-0187 *Tel:* 603-778-7191 *Fax:* 603-778-7191 *E-mail:* grantbooks@aol.com *Web Site:* www.grantbooks.com, pg 107

Grant, Janet Kobobel, Books & Such, 4788 Carissa Ave, Santa Rosa, CA 95405 *Tel:* 707-538-4184 *Fax:* 707-538-3937 *E-mail:* janet@janetgrant.com *Web Site:* janetgrant.com, pg 622

Grant, Jerome, Prentice Hall Business Publishing, One Lake St, Upper Saddle River, NJ 07458 *Tel:* 201-236-7000, pg 217

Grant, Kathy, Health Communications Inc, 3201 SW 15 St, Deerfield Beach, FL 33442-8190 *Tel:* 954-360-0909 *Toll Free Tel:* 800-851-9100 (cust serv); 800-441-5569 (order entry) *Fax:* 954-360-0034 *Web Site:* www.hcibooks.com, pg 119

Grant, Lisa, The Writers' Collective, 780 Reservoir Ave, Suite 243, Cranston, RI 02910 *Tel:* 401-537-9175 *E-mail:* info@writerscollective.org *Web Site:* www.writerscollective.org, pg 305

Grant, Nancy, Houghton Mifflin Trade & Reference Division, 222 Berkeley St, Boston, MA 02116-3764 *Tel:* 617-351-5000 *Toll Free Tel:* 800-225-3362 *Web Site:* www.houghtonmifflinbooks.com, pg 126

Grant, Penny, Sinauer Associates Inc, 23 Plumtree Rd, Sunderland, MA 01375-0407 *Tel:* 413-549-4300 *Fax:* 413-549-1118 *E-mail:* publish@sinauer.com *Web Site:* www.sinauer.com, pg 249

Grantham, Charles E, Contemporary Publishing Co of Raleigh Inc, 6001-101 Chapel Hill Rd, Raleigh, NC 27607 *Tel:* 919-851-8221 *Fax:* 919-851-6666 *E-mail:* questions@contemporarypublishing.com *Web Site:* www.contemporarypublishing.com, pg 67

Grantham, Dean, Graphic World Publishing Services, 11687 Adie Rd, Maryland Heights, MO 63043 *Tel:* 314-567-9854 *Fax:* 314-567-0360, pg 600

Granville-Callahan, Cynthia, Love Creek Annual Short Play Festival, 2144 45 Ave, Long Island City, NY 11101 *Tel:* 212-714-9686 *E-mail:* creekread@aol.com, pg 786

Granville-Callahan, Cynthia, Love Creek Mini Festivals, 2144 45 Ave, Long Island City, NY 11101 *Tel:* 212-714-9686 *E-mail:* creekread@aol.com, pg 786

Grassie, Jill, Creative Bound International Inc, 151 Tansley Dr, Carp, ON K0A 1L0, Canada *Tel:* 613-831-3641 *Toll Free Tel:* 800-287-8610 (N America) *Fax:* 613-831-3643 *E-mail:* editor@creativebound.com *Web Site:* www.creativebound.com, pg 541

Grathwohl, Jeff, The University of Utah Press, 1795 E South Campus Dr, Rm 101, Salt Lake City, UT 84112-9402 *Tel:* 801-581-6671 *Toll Free Tel:* 800-773-6672 *Fax:* 801-581-3365 *E-mail:* info@upress.utah.edu *Web Site:* www.uofupress.com, pg 285

Gratz, Mike, Olde & Oppenheim Publishers, 3219 N Margate Place, Chandler, AZ 85224 *Tel:* 480-839-2280 *Fax:* 480-839-0241 *E-mail:* olde_oppenheim@hotmail.com, pg 196

Grau, Julie, Riverhead Books (Hardcover), 375 Hudson St, New York, NY 10014 *Tel:* 212-366-2000 *E-mail:* online@penguinputnam.com *Web Site:* www.penguin.com, pg 233

Graul, Donald O Jr, Washington Independent Writers (WIW), 733 15 St NW, Suite 220, Washington, DC 20005 *Tel:* 202-737-9500 *Fax:* 202-638-7800 *E-mail:* info@washwriter.org *Web Site:* www.washwriter.org, pg 702

Grauman, Judith, The Guilford Press, 72 Spring St, New York, NY 10012 *Tel:* 212-431-9800 *Toll Free Tel:* 800-365-7006 (orders) *Fax:* 212-966-6708 *E-mail:* orders@guilford.com *Web Site:* www.guilford.com, pg 111

Gravel, Sophie, Les Publications du Quebec, 1500 rue Jean-Talon Nord, 1 etage, Ste Foy, PQ G1N 2E5, Canada *Tel:* 418-644-1342 *Toll Free Tel:* 800-463-2100 (Quebec province only) *Fax:* 418-644-7813 *E-mail:* service.clientele@mrci.gouv.qc.ca *Web Site:* www.publicationsduquebec.gouv.qc.ca, pg 559

Graveline, Pierre, Editions de l'Hexagone, 1010, rue de la Gauchetiere Est, Montreal, PQ H2L 2N5, Canada *Tel:* 514-523-1182 *Fax:* 514-282-7530 *E-mail:* vml@sogides.com *Web Site:* www.edhexagone.com, pg 544

Graveline, Pierre, VLB Editeur Inc, 955 Amherst St, Montreal, PQ H2L 3K4, Canada *Tel:* 514-523-1182 *Fax:* 514-282-7530 *E-mail:* vml@sogides.com *Web Site:* www.edvlb.com, pg 566

Graves, Michael, Sage Publications, 2455 Teller Rd, Thousand Oaks, CA 91320 *Tel:* 805-499-0721 *Fax:* 805-499-0871 *E-mail:* info@sagepub.com *Web Site:* www.sagepub.com, pg 237

Gravesande, Doreen, International Standard Book Numbering (ISBN) US Agency, A Cambridge Information Group Co, 630 Central Ave, New Providence, NJ 07974 *Toll Free Tel:* 877-310-7333 *Fax:* 908-219-0188 *E-mail:* ISBN-SAN@bowker.com *Web Site:* www.isbn.org, pg 689

Gray, Beverley, LokiWorks, 813-633 Bay St, Toronto, ON M5G 2G4, Canada *Tel:* 416-599-4303 *Fax:* 416-599-4308 *E-mail:* editor@lokiworks.com *Web Site:* www.lokiworks.com, pg 605

Gray, Brian, National Catholic Educational Association, 1077 30 St NW, Suite 100, Washington, DC 20007-3852 *Tel:* 202-337-6232 *Fax:* 202-333-6706 *Web Site:* www.ncea.org, pg 182

Gray, Corey, Taylor & Francis Editorial, Production & Manufacturing Division, 325 Chestnut St, Philadelphia, PA 19106 *Tel:* 215-625-8900 *Toll Free Tel:* 800-354-1420 *Fax:* 215-625-2940 *E-mail:* info@taylorandfrancis.com *Web Site:* www.taylorandfrancis.com, pg 264

Gray, Corey, Taylor & Francis Inc, 325 Chestnut St, Philadelphia, PA 19106 *Tel:* 215-625-8900 *Toll Free Tel:* 800-354-1420 *Fax:* 215-625-2940 *E-mail:* info@taylorandfrancis.com *Web Site:* www.taylorandfrancis.com, pg 265

Gray, David, Gray & Company Publishers, 1588 E 40 St, Cleveland, OH 44103 *Tel:* 216-431-2665 *Toll Free Tel:* 800-915-3609 *E-mail:* info@grayco.com *Web Site:* www.grayco.com, pg 108

Gray, Lisa, Broadview Press, 280 Perry St, Unit 5, Peterborough, ON K9J 2A8, Canada *Tel:* 705-743-8990 *Fax:* 705-743-8353 *E-mail:* customerservice@broadviewpress.com *Web Site:* www.broadviewpress.com, pg 537

Gray, Tracy, Paul H Brookes Publishing Co, PO Box 10624, Baltimore, MD 21285-0624 *Tel:* 410-337-9580 *Toll Free Tel:* 800-638-3775 *Fax:* 410-337-8539 *E-mail:* custserv@brookespublishing.com *Web Site:* www.brookespublishing.com, pg 48

Graybill, Nina, The Graybill & English Literary Agency LLC, 1875 Connecticut Ave, NW, Suite 712, Washington, DC 20009 *Tel:* 202-588-9798 *Fax:* 202-457-0662 *Web Site:* graybillandenglish.com, pg 633

Grayson, Ashley, Ashley Grayson Literary Agency, 1342 18 St, San Pedro, CA 90732 *Tel:* 310-548-4672 *Fax:* 310-514-1148 *E-mail:* graysonagent@earthlink.net, pg 633

Grayson, Carolyn, Ashley Grayson Literary Agency, 1342 18 St, San Pedro, CA 90732 *Tel:* 310-548-4672 *Fax:* 310-514-1148 *E-mail:* graysonagent@earthlink.net, pg 633

Grayson, Nancy, The Flannery O'Connor Award for Short Fiction, 330 Research Dr, Athens, GA 30602-4901 *Tel:* 706-369-6130 (no phone queries accepted) *Fax:* 706-369-6131 *Web Site:* www.ugapress.org, pg 795

Grayson, Nancy, University of Georgia Press, 330 Research Dr, Athens, GA 30602-4901 *Tel:* 706-369-6130 *Toll Free Tel:* 800-266-5842 (orders only) *Fax:* 706-369-6131 *E-mail:* books@ugapress.uga.edu *Web Site:* www.ugapress.org, pg 281

Grebenar, Sandy, Harcourt Trade Publishers, 525 "B" St, Suite 1900, San Diego, CA 92101 *Tel:* 619-231-6616 *Toll Free Tel:* 800-543-1918 (cust serv) *Toll Free Fax:* 800-235-0256 (cust serv) *Web Site:* www.harcourtbooks.com, pg 115

Greco, Al, Random House Children's Books, 1745 Broadway, New York, NY 10019 *Tel:* 212-782-9000 *Toll Free Tel:* 800-726-0600 *Fax:* 212-782-9452 *Web Site:* www.randomhouse.com/kids, pg 225

Greco, Al, Random House Sales & Marketing, 1745 Broadway, New York, NY 10019 *Tel:* 212-782-9000, pg 227

Greco, Albert N, Fordham University, Graduate School of Business Administration, Dept of Communications & Media Management, 113 W 60 St, New York, NY 10023 *Tel:* 212-636-6199 *Fax:* 212-765-5573, pg 752

Greco, John Jr, The Direct Marketing Association Inc (The DMA), 1120 Avenue of the Americas, New York, NY 10036-6700 *Tel:* 212-768-7277 *Fax:* 212-768-4547 *E-mail:* dma@the-dma.org; customerservice@the-dma.org *Web Site:* www.the-dma.org, pg 80

Greco, John Jr, The Direct Marketing Association Inc (The DMA), 1120 Avenue of the Americas, New York, NY 10036-6700 *Tel:* 212-768-7277 *Fax:* 212-768-4547 *E-mail:* dma@the-dma.org *Web Site:* www.the-dma.org, pg 686

Greco, Joseph, The Lois de la Haba Agency Inc, 76-12 Grand Central Pkwy, Suite 4, New York, NY 11375 *Tel:* 718-544-2392 *Fax:* 718-544-2393 *E-mail:* habalit@aol.com, pg 627

Green, Annie, Hackney Literary Awards, Birmingham-Southern College, Box 549003, Birmingham, AL 35254 *Tel:* 205-226-4921 *Toll Free Tel:* 800-523-5793 *Fax:* 205-226-3072 *E-mail:* dcwilson@bsc.edu *Web Site:* www.bsc.edu, pg 777

Green, Annie, Writing Today, PO Box 549003, Birmingham, AL 35282-9765 *Tel:* 205-226-4921 *Toll Free Tel:* 800-523-5793 *Fax:* 205-226-4931 *E-mail:* dcwilson@bsc.edu *Web Site:* www.bsc.edu, pg 749

Green, Ashbel, Alfred A Knopf, 1745 Broadway, New York, NY 10019 *Tel:* 212-751-2600 *Toll Free Tel:* 800-638-6460 *Fax:* 212-572-2593 *Web Site:* www.randomhouse.com/knopf, pg 146

Green, Caroline, Phaidon Press Inc, 180 Varick St, 14th fl, New York, NY 10014 *Tel:* 212-652-5400 *Toll Free Tel:* 800-759-0190 (cust serv) *Fax:* 212-652-5410 *Toll Free Fax:* 800-286-9471 (cust serv) *E-mail:* ussales@phaidon.com *Web Site:* www.phaidon.com, pg 211

Green, Dan, NMMA Discover Boating Director's Award, 200 E Randolph Dr, Suite 5100, Chicago, IL 60601 *Tel:* 312-946-6200 *Fax:* 312-946-0388 *Web Site:* nmma.org, pg 795

Green, Dan, Pom Inc, 611 Broadway, No 907-B, New York, NY 10012 *Tel:* 212-673-3835 *Fax:* 212-673-4653 *E-mail:* pom-inc@att.net, pg 648

Green, Donna, Moon Lady Press, PO Box 83, Marshfield Hills, MA 02051 *Tel:* 781-837-1618 *Toll Free Tel:* 800-840-0205 *Fax:* 781-837-7249 *Web Site:* www.donnagreen.com, pg 178

Green, Elizabeth, Tarascon Publishing, 1015 W Central Ave, Lompoc, CA 93436 *Tel:* 805-736-7000 *Toll Free Tel:* 800-929-9926 *Fax:* 805-736-6161 *Toll Free Fax:* 877-929-9926 *E-mail:* info@tarascon.com *Web Site:* www.tarascon.com, pg 264

Green, Frank, Bard Society, 1358 Tiber Ave, Jacksonville, FL 32207 *Tel:* 904-398-5352, pg 742

Green, George, America West Publishers, PO Box 2208, Carson City, NV 89702-2208 *Tel:* 775-885-0700 *Toll Free Tel:* 800-729-4131 *Toll Free Fax:* 877-726-2632, pg 10

Green, James A, Greenwood Research Books & Software, PO Box 12102, Wichita, KS 67277-2102 *Tel:* 316-214-5103 *E-mail:* grnwdrsch@hotmail.com *Web Site:* grnwd.tripod.com, pg 109

Green, Jonathan, Shambhala Publications Inc, Horticultural Hall, 300 Massachusetts Ave, Boston, MA 02115 *Tel:* 617-424-0030 *Toll Free Tel:* 888-424-2329 (orders only) *Fax:* 617-236-1563; 303-665-5292 (orders only) *E-mail:* editors@shambhala.com *Web Site:* www.shambhala.com, pg 245

Green, Joyce R, Warren H Green Inc, 8356 Olive Blvd, St Louis, MO 63132 *Tel:* 314-991-1335 *Toll Free Tel:* 800-537-0655 *Fax:* 314-997-1788 *E-mail:* whgreen@inlink.com *Web Site:* www. whgreen.com, pg 108

Green, Mary, Martingale & Co, 20205 144 Ave NE, Woodinville, WA 98072 *Tel:* 425-483-3313 *Toll Free Tel:* 800-426-3126 *Fax:* 425-486-7596 *E-mail:* info@ martingale-pub.com *Web Site:* www.martingale-pub. com, pg 164

Green, Nancy N, W W Norton & Company Inc, 500 Fifth Ave, New York, NY 10110-0017 *Tel:* 212-354-5500 *Toll Free Tel:* 800-233-4830 (orders & cust serv) *Fax:* 212-869-0856 *Toll Free Fax:* 800-458-6515 *Web Site:* www.wwnorton.com, pg 193

Green, Nat, Phaidon Press Inc, 180 Varick St, 14th fl, New York, NY 10014 *Tel:* 212-652-5400 *Toll Free Tel:* 800-759-0190 (cust serv) *Fax:* 212-652-5410 *Toll Free Fax:* 800-286-9471 (cust serv) *E-mail:* ussales@ phaidon.com *Web Site:* www.phaidon.com, pg 211

Green, Richard, Creative Artists Agency, 9830 Wilshire Blvd, Beverly Hills, CA 90212-1825 *Tel:* 310-288-4545 *Fax:* 310-288-4800 *Web Site:* www.caa.com, pg 626

Green, Sally, Brooding Heron Press, 101 Bookmonger Rd, Waldron Island, WA 98297 *Tel:* 360-202-6621, pg 48

Green, Sam, Brooding Heron Press, 101 Bookmonger Rd, Waldron Island, WA 98297 *Tel:* 360-202-6621, pg 48

Green, Simon, Pom Inc, 611 Broadway, No 907-B, New York, NY 10012 *Tel:* 212-673-3835 *Fax:* 212-673-4653 *E-mail:* pom-inc@att.net, pg 648

Green, Susan E, Huntington Library Press, 1151 Oxford Rd, San Marino, CA 91108 *Tel:* 626-405-2138 *Fax:* 626-585-0794 *E-mail:* booksales@huntington.org *Web Site:* www.huntington.org/HLPress/HEHPubs. html, pg 129

Greenbaum, Arlynn, Authors Unlimited Inc, 31 E 32 St, Suite 300, New York, NY 10016 *Tel:* 212-481-8484 (ext 336) *Fax:* 212-481-9582 *Web Site:* www. authorsunlimited.com, pg 669

Greenberg, Daniel, Levine-Greenberg Literary Agency Inc, 307 Seventh Ave, Suite 1906, New York, NY 10001 *Tel:* 212-337-0934 *Fax:* 212-337-0948 *Web Site:* www.levinegreenberg.com, pg 640

Greenberg, Ellen, Random House Children's Books, 1745 Broadway, New York, NY 10019 *Tel:* 212-782-9000 *Toll Free Tel:* 800-200-3552 *Fax:* 212-782-9452 *Web Site:* www.randomhouse.com/kids, pg 226

Greenberg, Jeff, AAA Photos, 401 Ocean Dr, Miami Beach, FL 33139 *Tel:* 305-534-0804 *Web Site:* www. PhotosPhotos.net, pg 589

Greenberg, Mark, Getty Publications, 1200 Getty Center Dr, Suite 500, Los Angeles, CA 90049-1682 *Tel:* 310-440-7365 *Fax:* 310-440-7758 *E-mail:* pubsinfo@getty. edu *Web Site:* www.getty.edu/bookstore, pg 104

Greenberg, Zeke, Alan Wofsy Fine Arts, 1109 Geary Blvd, San Francisco, CA 94109 *Tel:* 415-292-6500 *Fax:* 415-512-0130 (acctg); 415-292-6594 (off & cust serv) *E-mail:* beauxarts@earthlink.net (cust serv); editeur@earthlink.net (edit); order@art-books.com (orders) *Web Site:* art-books.com, pg 302

Greenblatt, Susan L, Resources for Rehabilitation, 22 Bonard Rd, Winchester, MA 01890 *Tel:* 781-368-9094 *Fax:* 781-368-9096 *E-mail:* info@rfr.org *Web Site:* www.rfr.org, pg 231

Greene, Anne, Wesleyan Writers Conference, c/o Wesleyan University, 279 Court St, Middletown, CT 06459 *Tel:* 860-685-3604 *Fax:* 860-685-2441 *Web Site:* www.wesleyan.edu/writers, pg 748

Greene, Cheryll Y, Cheryll Y Greene Editorial Services, 158-18 Riverside Dr W, Suite 6E, New York, NY 10032 *Tel:* 212-740-6003 *Fax:* 212-740-6003 *E-mail:* editorseye@mindspring.com, pg 600

Greene, Grace Worcester, Dorothy Canfield Fisher Children's Book Award, 109 State St, Montpelier, VT 05609-0601 *Tel:* 802-828-6954 *Fax:* 802-828-2199 *E-mail:* cbec@dol.state.vt.us *Web Site:* www.dcfaward. org; dol.state.vt.us, pg 774

Greene, Kristin, St Martin's Press LLC, 175 Fifth Ave, New York, NY 10010 *Tel:* 212-674-5151 *Fax:* 212-420-9314 *E-mail:* firstname.lastname@stmartins.com *Web Site:* www.stmartins.com, pg 238

Greene, Mary, R S Means Co Inc, 63 Smiths Lane, Kingston, MA 02364-0800 *Tel:* 781-585-7880 *Toll Free Tel:* 800-448-8182 *Fax:* 781-585-8814 *Toll Free Fax:* 800-632-6732 *Web Site:* www.rsmeans.com, pg 170

Greene, Thomas J, Greene Bark Press Inc, PO Box 1108, Bridgeport, CT 06601-1108 *Tel:* 203-372-4861 *Fax:* 203-371-5856 *E-mail:* greenebark@aol.com *Web Site:* www.greenebarkpress.com, pg 108

Greenfeld, Beth, Makeready Inc, 233 W 77 St, New York, NY 10024 *Tel:* 212-595-5083, pg 605

Greenfield, George M, CreativeWell Inc, PO Box 3130, Memorial Sta, Upper Montclair, NJ 07043 *Tel:* 973-783-7575 *Fax:* 973-783-7530 *E-mail:* info@ creativewell.com *Web Site:* www.creativewell.com, pg 626, 669

Greenfield, Ilan, Gefen Books, 600 Broadway, Lynbrook, NY 11563 *Tel:* 516-593-1234 *Toll Free Tel:* 800-477-5257 *Fax:* 516-295-2739 *E-mail:* gefenny@ gefenpublishing.com *Web Site:* www.israelbooks.com, pg 103

Greenfield, Steven, The Century Foundation Press, 41 E 70 St, New York, NY 10021 *Tel:* 212-535-4441 *Fax:* 212-535-7534 *E-mail:* info@tcf.org *Web Site:* www.tcf.org, pg 58

Greengrass, Linda, Irma S & James H Black Award, 610 W 112 St, New York, NY 10025 *Tel:* 212-875-4400 *Fax:* 212-875-4558 *Web Site:* streetcat.bankstreet. edu/html/isb.html, pg 762

Greenhut, Carol, Schonfeld & Associates Inc, 2830 Blackthorn Rd, Riverwood, IL 60015 *Tel:* 847-948-8080 *Toll Free Tel:* 800-205-0030 *Fax:* 847-948-8096 *E-mail:* saiinfo@saibooks.com *Web Site:* www. saibooks.com, pg 242

Greenidge, Delano, Delano Greenidge Editions, 14 Mount Morris Park W, Suite 7, New York, NY 10027-6317 *Tel:* 917-492-8014 *Fax:* 917-492-0966 *E-mail:* dge@thing.net, pg 109

Greenland, Paul R, Paul Greenland Editorial Services, 608 Dawson Ave, Rockford, IL 61107 *Tel:* 815-519-2588 *E-mail:* paul@paulgreenland.com, pg 601

Greenleaf, Clinton T III, Greenleaf Book Group LLC, Longhorn Bldg, Suite 600, 3rd fl, 4425 Mopac S, Austin, TX 78735 *Tel:* 512-891-6100 *Toll Free Tel:* 800-932-5420 *Fax:* 512-891-6150 *E-mail:* email@greenleafbookgroup.com *Web Site:* www.greenleafbookgroup.com, pg 109

Greeno, Gayle, Persea Books Inc, 853 Broadway, Suite 604, New York, NY 10003 *Tel:* 212-260-9256 *Fax:* 212-260-1902 *E-mail:* info@perseabooks.com *Web Site:* www.perseabooks.com, pg 210

Greenspan, Elizabeth, Society for Industrial & Applied Mathematics, 3600 University City Science Ctr, Philadelphia, PA 19104-2688 *Tel:* 215-382-9800 *Toll Free Tel:* 800-447-7426 *Fax:* 215-386-7999 *E-mail:* siam@siam.org *Web Site:* www.siam.org, pg 251

Greenspan Regan, Linda, Prometheus Books, 59 John Glenn Dr, Amherst, NY 14228 *Tel:* 716-691-0133 *Toll Free Tel:* 800-421-0351 *Fax:* 716-691-0137 *E-mail:* marketing@prometheusbooks.com; editorial@prometheusbooks.com *Web Site:* www. Prometheusbooks.com, pg 220

Greenspan, Shari Dash, Urim Publications, 3709 13 Ave, Brooklyn, NY 11218 *Tel:* 718-972-5449 *Fax:* 718-972-6307 *E-mail:* publisher@urimpublications.com *Web Site:* www.urimpublications.com, pg 288

Greenstein, Ruth, Words into Print, 200 W 86 St, Suite 14-1, New York, NY 10024 *Tel:* 212-877-3211 *Fax:* 212-873-3796 *E-mail:* sas22@ix.netcom.com *Web Site:* www.wordsintoprint.org, pg 614

Greenwald, Martin, Central European University Press, 400 W 59 St, New York, NY 10019 *Tel:* 212-547-6932 *Fax:* 646-557-2416 *Web Site:* www.ceupress. com, pg 57

Greenwood, Daphne, ASM Press, 1752 "N" St NW, Washington, DC 20036-2904 *Tel:* 202-737-3600 *Toll Free Tel:* 800-546-2416 *Fax:* 202-942-9342 *E-mail:* books@asmusa.org *Web Site:* www.asmpress. org, pg 25

Greenwood, Loren, Wizards of the Coast Inc, PO Box 707, Renton, WA 98057-0707 *Web Site:* www.wizards. com/books, pg 302

Greenwood, Susan G, Association of Graphic Communications, 330 Seventh Ave, 9th fl, New York, NY 10001-5010 *Tel:* 212-279-2100 *Fax:* 212-279-5381 *Web Site:* www.agcomm.org, pg 680

Greevy, Doug, American Institute of Aeronautics & Astronautics, 1801 Alexander Bell Dr, Suite 500, Reston, VA 20191 *Tel:* 703-264-7500 *Toll Free Tel:* 800-639-2422 *Fax:* 703-264-7551 *E-mail:* custserv@aiaa.org *Web Site:* www.aiaa.org, pg 14

Grefe, Richard, American Institute of Graphic Arts (AIGA), 164 Fifth Ave, New York, NY 10010 *Tel:* 212-807-1990 *Toll Free Tel:* 800-548-1634 *Fax:* 212-807-1799 *E-mail:* aiga@aiga.org *Web Site:* www.aiga.org, pg 676

Greg, Laura, Seascape Press Ltd, 1010 Roble Lane, Santa Barbara, CA 93103-2046 *Tel:* 805-965-4646 *Toll Free Tel:* 800-929-2906 *Fax:* 805-963-8188 *E-mail:* seapress@aol.com *Web Site:* www. seascapepress.com, pg 573

Gregg, Jon, Vermont Studio Center, PO Box 613, Johnson, VT 05656 *Tel:* 802-635-2727 *Fax:* 802-635-2730 *E-mail:* info@vermontstudiocenter.org *Web Site:* www.vermontstudiocenter.org, pg 748

Gregory, Alexis, The Vendome Press, 1334 York Ave, 3rd fl, New York, NY 10021 *Tel:* 212-737-5297 *Fax:* 212-737-5340 *E-mail:* vendomepress@earthlink. net, pg 290

Gregory, Kathy, Sierra Press, 4988 Gold Leaf Dr, Mariposa, CA 95338 *Tel:* 209-966-5071 *Toll Free Tel:* 800-745-2631 *Fax:* 209-966-5073 *E-mail:* siepress@sti.net *Web Site:* www. nationalparksusa.com, pg 247

Gregory, Keith, Southern Methodist University Press, 314 Fondren Library W, 6404 Hill Top Lane, Dallas, TX 75275 *Tel:* 214-768-1430; 214-768-1432 *Fax:* 214-768-1428, pg 255

Gregory, Lynda C, Blanche C Gregory Inc, 2 Tudor City Place, New York, NY 10017 *Tel:* 212-697-0828 *Fax:* 212-697-0828 *E-mail:* bcgliteraryagent@aol.com *Web Site:* www.bcgliteraryagency.com, pg 633

Gregory, Maia, Maia Gregory Associates, 311 E 72 St, New York, NY 10021 *Tel:* 212-288-0310, pg 633

Gregory, Michael, Southern California Writers' Conference/Los Angeles/San Diego/Palm Springs, 1010 University Ave, Suite 54, San Diego, CA 92103 *Tel:* 619-233-4651 *Fax:* 253-390-8577 *E-mail:* wewrite@writersconference.com *Web Site:* www.writersconference.com, pg 747

Gregory, Michael Steven, Writers' Haven Writers (WHW), 2244 Fourth Ave, San Diego, CA 92101 *Tel:* 619-696-0569, pg 703

Gregory, Thomas West, Concourse Press, PO Box 8265, Philadelphia, PA 19101-8265 *Tel:* 610-325-0313 *Fax:* 610-359-1953, pg 66

Gregson, Sheryl, Richard Ivey School of Business, University of Western Ontario, London, ON N6A 3K7, Canada *Tel:* 519-661-3208 *Toll Free Tel:* 800-649-6355 *Fax:* 519-661-3882 *E-mail:* cases@ivey.uwo. ca *Web Site:* www.ivey.uwo.ca/cases, pg 551

Greig, Bill T III, Regal Books, 1957 Eastman Ave, Ventura, CA 93003 *Tel:* 805-644-9721 *Toll Free Tel:* 800-446-7735 (orders) *Fax:* 805-644-9728 (editorial); 805-644-4729 (purchasing); 805-650-8713 (sales & corp serv); 805-658-3388 (orders) *Toll Free Fax:* 800-860-3109 (orders) *E-mail:* info@regalbooks. com *Web Site:* www.gospellight.com, pg 230

Greig, William T Jr, Regal Books, 1957 Eastman Ave, Ventura, CA 93003 *Tel:* 805-644-9721 *Toll Free Tel:* 800-446-7735 (orders) *Fax:* 805-644-9728 (editorial); 805-644-4729 (purchasing); 805-650-8713 (sales & corp serv); 805-658-3388 (orders) *Toll Free Fax:* 800-860-3109 (orders) *E-mail:* info@regalbooks. com *Web Site:* www.gospellight.com, pg 230

Greipo, Jennifer, Joelle Delbourgo Associates, Inc Literary Management, 450 Seventh Ave, Suite 3004, New York, NY 10123 *Tel:* 212-279-9027 *Fax:* 212-279-8863 *E-mail:* info@delbourgo.com (queries) *Web Site:* www.delbourgo.com/about.htm, pg 627

Grenawalt, Christa, Phaidon Press Inc, 180 Varick St, 14th fl, New York, NY 10014 *Tel:* 212-652-5400 *Toll Free Tel:* 800-759-0190 (cust serv) *Fax:* 212-652-5410 *Toll Free Fax:* 800-286-9471 (cust serv) *E-mail:* ussales@phaidon.com *Web Site:* www. phaidon.com, pg 211

Grench, Charles, The University of North Carolina Press, 116 S Boundary St, Chapel Hill, NC 27514-3808 *Tel:* 919-966-3561 *Toll Free Tel:* 800-848-6224 (orders only) *Fax:* 919-966-3829 *Toll Free Fax:* 800-272-6817 (orders) *E-mail:* uncpress@unc.edu *Web Site:* www. uncpress.unc.edu, pg 283

Gretchen, Mary, Vocalis Ltd, 100 Avalon Circle, Waterbury, CT 06710 *Tel:* 203-753-5244 *Fax:* 203-574-5433 *E-mail:* vocalis@sbcglobal.net; info@ vocalisesl.com *Web Site:* www.vocalisesl.com; www. vocalisfiction.com; www.vocalisltd.com, pg 291

Greuel, David, Wayside Publishing, 11 Jan Sebastian Way, Suite 5, Sandwich, MA 02563 *Tel:* 508-833-5096 *Toll Free Tel:* 888-302-2519 *Fax:* 508-833-6284 *E-mail:* wayside@sprintmail.com *Web Site:* www. waysidepublishing.com, pg 295

Gridgeman, Neal, The Resource Centre, Box 190, Waterloo, ON N2J 3Z9, Canada *Tel:* 519-885-0826 *Toll Free Tel:* 800-923-0330 *Fax:* 519-747-5629 *E-mail:* resourcecentre@sympatico.ca *Web Site:* www. theresourcecentre.com, pg 559

Grieman, Pamela, American Indian Studies Center Publications at UCLA, 3220 Campbell Hall, Los Angeles, CA 90095-1548 *Tel:* 310-825-7315; 310-206-7508 *Fax:* 310-206-7060 *E-mail:* aiscpubs@ucla.edu; aisc@ucla.edu *Web Site:* www.sscnet.ucla.edu, pg 14

Griffes, Peter L, ProStar Publications Inc, 3 Church Circle, Suite 109, Annapolis, MD 21401 *Tel:* 310-280-1010 *Toll Free Tel:* 800-481-6277 *Fax:* 310-280-1025 *Toll Free Fax:* 800-487-6277 *E-mail:* editor@prostarpublications.com *Web Site:* www.prostarpublications.com; www. nauticalbooks.com, pg 220

Griffin, Jean, Bulfinch Press, 1271 Avenue of the Americas, New York, NY 10020 *Tel:* 212-522-8700 *Toll Free Tel:* 800-759-0190 *Fax:* 212-467-2886 *Web Site:* www.twbookmark.com, pg 50

Griffin, Jean, Little, Brown and Company Adult Trade Division, 1271 Avenue of the Americas, New York, NY 10020 *Tel:* 212-522-8700 *Fax:* 212-522-2067 *Web Site:* www.twbookmark.com, pg 156

Griffin, Jean, Time Warner Book Group, 1271 Avenue of the Americas, New York, NY 10020 *Tel:* 212-522-7200 *Fax:* 212-522-7991 *Web Site:* www.twbookmark. com, pg 271

Griffin, Jean, Warner Books, 1271 Avenue of the Americas, New York, NY 10020 *Tel:* 212-522-7200 *Fax:* 212-522-7991 *Web Site:* www.twbookmark.com, pg 293

Griffin, Jennifer, Workman Publishing Co Inc, 708 Broadway, New York, NY 10003-9555 *Tel:* 212-254-5900 *Toll Free Tel:* 800-722-7202 *Fax:* 212-254-8098 *E-mail:* info@workman.com *Web Site:* www.workman. com, pg 303

Griffin, Louise, Liturgy Training Publications, 1800 N Hermitage Ave, Chicago, IL 60622-1101 *Tel:* 773-486-8970 *Toll Free Tel:* 800-933-1800 (US & Canada only) *Fax:* 773-486-7094 *Toll Free Fax:* 800-933-7094 (US & Canada only) *E-mail:* orders@ltp.org *Web Site:* www.ltp.org, pg 156

Griffin, Regina, Holiday House Inc, 425 Madison Ave, New York, NY 10017 *Tel:* 212-688-0085 *Fax:* 212-421-6134, pg 123

Griffin, Susan, Carter G Woodson Book Awards, 8555 16 St, Suite 500, Silver Spring, MD 20910 *Tel:* 301-588-1800 *Toll Free Tel:* 800-296-7840 *Fax:* 301-588-2049 *E-mail:* excellence@ncss.org *Web Site:* www. socialstudies.org, pg 812

Griffis, Steve, Texas A&M University Press, John H Lindsey Bldg, Lewis St, 4354 TAMU, College Station, TX 77843-4354 *Tel:* 979-845-1436 *Toll Free Tel:* 800-826-8911 (orders) *Fax:* 979-847-8752 *Toll Free Fax:* 888-617-2421 (orders) *E-mail:* fdl@tampress. tamu.edu *Web Site:* www.tamu.edu/upress/, pg 267

Griffith, Cathy, Standard Publishing Co, 8121 Hamilton Ave, Cincinnati, OH 45231 *Tel:* 513-931-4050 *Toll Free Tel:* 800-543-1301 *Fax:* 513-931-0950 *Toll Free Fax:* 877-867-5751 *E-mail:* customerservice@ standardpub.com *Web Site:* www.standardpub.com, pg 257

Griffith, Suzette, University of Alabama Press, Box 870380, Tuscaloosa, AL 35487-0380 *Tel:* 205-348-5180; 773-702-7000 (orders) *Fax:* 205-348-9201 *Web Site:* www.uapress.ua.edu, pg 280

Grile, Harry, Liguori Publications, One Liguori Dr, Liguori, MO 63057-9999 *Tel:* 636-464-2500 *Toll Free Tel:* 800-464-2555 *Fax:* 636-464-8449 *Web Site:* www. liguori.org, pg 154

Grilliot, Bob, JIST Publishing Inc, 8902 Otis Ave, Indianapolis, IN 46216 *Tel:* 317-613-4200 *Toll Free Tel:* 800-648-5478 *Fax:* 317-613-4304 *Toll Free Fax:* 800-547-8329 *E-mail:* info@jist.com *Web Site:* www.jist.com, pg 141

Grima, Tony, National Braille Press, 88 Saint Stephen St, Boston, MA 02115 *Tel:* 617-266-6160 *Toll Free Tel:* 800-548-7323 (cust serv) *Fax:* 617-437-0456 *E-mail:* orders@nbp.org *Web Site:* www.nbp.org, pg 182

Grimaldi, Jennifer, The Century Foundation Press, 41 E 70 St, New York, NY 10021 *Tel:* 212-535-4441 *Fax:* 212-535-7534 *E-mail:* info@tcf.org *Web Site:* www.tcf.org, pg 58

Grimes, Johanna, The University of North Carolina Press, 116 S Boundary St, Chapel Hill, NC 27514-3808 *Tel:* 919-966-3561 *Toll Free Tel:* 800-848-6224 (orders only) *Fax:* 919-966-3829 *Toll Free Fax:* 800-272-6817 (orders) *E-mail:* uncpress@unc.edu *Web Site:* www.uncpress.unc.edu, pg 283

Grimes, Julie, The Society of Professional Journalists, Eugene S Pulliam National Journalism Ctr, 3909 N Meridian St, Indianapolis, IN 46208 *Tel:* 317-927-8000 *Fax:* 317-920-4789 *E-mail:* spj@spj.org *Web Site:* www.spj.org, pg 700

Grimes, Mark, American Academy of Pediatrics, 141 NW Point Blvd, Elk Grove Village, IL 60007-1098 *Tel:* 847-434-4000 *Toll Free Tel:* 888-227-1770 *Fax:* 847-228-1281 *E-mail:* pubs@aap.org *Web Site:* www.aap.org, pg 11

Grimes, Mary, Cardoza Publishing, 857 Broadway, 3rd fl, New York, NY 10003 *Tel:* 212-255-6661 *Fax:* 212-255-6671 *E-mail:* cardozapub@aol.com *Web Site:* www.cardozapub.com, pg 53

Grimes, Mary, Union Square Publishing, 857 Broadway, 3rd fl, New York, NY 10003 *Tel:* 212-255-6661 *Fax:* 212-255-6671 *E-mail:* cardozapub@aol.com *Web Site:* www.cardozapub.com, pg 278

Grimm, Amy, Warren Wilson College, MFA Program for Writers, PO Box 9000, Asheville, NC 28815-9000 *Tel:* 828-771-3715 *Fax:* 828-771-7005 *E-mail:* mfa@ warren-wilson.edu *Web Site:* www.warren-wilson. edu/~mfa, pg 756

Grimshaw, Shaun, Red River Press, 3900 Roy Rd, Suite 37, Shreveport, LA 71107 *Tel:* 318-929-4196 *Fax:* 318-929-5125 *E-mail:* redriverpresskws@yahoo. com *Web Site:* www.achivalservices.com, pg 229

Grinberg, Jill, Anderson/Grinberg Literary Management Inc, 266 W 23 St, Suite 3, New York, NY 10011 *Tel:* 212-620-5883 *Fax:* 212-627-4725 *E-mail:* queries@andersongrinberg.com, pg 619

Grisanti, Alfred C, Kendall/Hunt Publishing Co, 4050 Westmark Dr, Dubuque, IA 52002 *Tel:* 563-589-1000 *Toll Free Tel:* 800-228-0810 (orders only) *Fax:* 563-589-1114 *Toll Free Fax:* 800-772-9165 *Web Site:* www.kendallhunt.com, pg 144

Groell, Anne, Bantam Dell Publishing Group, 1745 Broadway, New York, NY 10019 *Tel:* 212-782-9000 *Toll Free Tel:* 800-223-6834 *Fax:* 212-302-7985 *Web Site:* www.randomhouse.com/bantamdell, pg 31

Groffsky, Maxine, Maxine Groffsky Literary Agency, 853 Broadway, Suite 708, New York, NY 10003 *Tel:* 212-979-1500 *Fax:* 212-979-1405, pg 633

Groleau, Micheline, Decarie, Editeur Inc, 233 Ave Dunbar, Ville Mont-Royal, PQ H3P 2H4, Canada *Tel:* 514-342-8500 *Fax:* 514-342-3982 *E-mail:* info@ decarieediteur.com *Web Site:* www.decarieediteur.com, pg 542

Gromling, Frank, Ocean Publishing, PO Box 1080, Flagler Beach, FL 32136-1080 *Tel:* 386-517-1600 *Fax:* 386-517-2564 *E-mail:* publisher@cfl.rr.com *Web Site:* www.ocean-publishing.com, pg 195

Groner, Judyth, Kar-Ben Publishing, 1251 Washington Ave N, Minneapolis, MN 55401 *Tel:* 612-332-3344 *Toll Free Tel:* 800-4-KARBEN (452-7236) *Toll Free Fax:* 800-332-1132 *E-mail:* kar-ben@lernerbooks.com *Web Site:* www.karben.com, pg 144

Groner, Shneur, Mesorah Publications Ltd, 4401 Second Ave, Brooklyn, NY 11232 *Tel:* 718-921-9000 *Toll Free Tel:* 800-637-6724 *Fax:* 718-680-1875 *E-mail:* artscroll@mesorah.com *Web Site:* www. artscroll.com; www.mesorah.com, pg 172

Gronholm, Diane, Panoply Press Inc, PO Box 1885, Lake Oswego, OR 97035-0611 *Tel:* 503-697-7964 *Fax:* 503-636-5293 *E-mail:* panoplypress@aol.com, pg 202

Grooms, Nadia, Writers House LLC, 21 W 26 St, New York, NY 10010 *Tel:* 212-685-2400 *Fax:* 212-685-1781, pg 662

Groppi, June, Association of American University Presses, 1427 E 60 St, Chicago, IL 60637 *Tel:* 773-702-7700; 773-702-7600 *Toll Free Tel:* 800-621-2736 (orders) *Fax:* 773-702-9756 (sales); 773-660-2235 (orders); 773-702-2708 *E-mail:* general@press. uchicago.edu *Web Site:* www.press.uchicago.edu, pg 26

Groseth, Michael, Oxford University Press, Inc, 198 Madison Ave, New York, NY 10016-4314 *Tel:* 212-726-6000 *Toll Free Tel:* 800-451-7556 (orders) *Web Site:* www.oup.com/us, pg 200

Grosjean, Jill, Jill Grosjean Literary Agency, 1390 Millstone Rd, Sag Harbor, NY 11963 *Tel:* 631-725-7419 *Fax:* 631-725-8632 *E-mail:* jill6981@aol.com, pg 633

Groskreutz, Candace, Underwood Books Inc, PO Box 1609, Grass Valley, CA 95945-1609 *Fax:* 530-274-7179 *Web Site:* www.underwoodbooks.com, pg 278

Gross, Arlene C, Gerald Gross Associates LLC, 63 Grand St, Croton-on-Hudson, NY 10520-2518 *Tel:* 914-271-8705 *Fax:* 914-271-1239 *E-mail:* grosassoc@aol.com *Web Site:* www.bookdocs. com/jgross.html, pg 601

Gross, Jacob, Sepher-Hermon Press, 1153 45 St, Brooklyn, NY 11219 *Tel:* 718-972-9010 *Fax:* 718-972-6935, pg 245

Gross, Jerry, Gerald Gross Associates LLC, 63 Grand St, Croton-on-Hudson, NY 10520-2518 *Tel:* 914-271-8705 *Fax:* 914-271-1239 *E-mail:* grosassoc@aol.com *Web Site:* www.bookdocs.com/jgross.html, pg 601

Gross, Laura, Laura Gross Literary Agency Ltd, 75 Clinton Place, Newton Centre, MA 02459-1117 *Tel:* 617-964-2977 *Fax:* 617-964-3023 *E-mail:* lglitag@aol.com, pg 633

Gross, Margaret, Sepher-Hermon Press, 1153 45 St, Brooklyn, NY 11219 *Tel:* 718-972-9010 *Fax:* 718-972-6935, pg 245

Gross, Samuel, Sepher-Hermon Press, 1153 45 St, Brooklyn, NY 11219 *Tel:* 718-972-9010 *Fax:* 718-972-6935, pg 245

Gross, Susan, Red River Press, 3900 Roy Rd, Suite 37, Shreveport, LA 71107 *Tel:* 318-929-4196 *Fax:* 318-929-5125 *E-mail:* redriverpresskws@yahoo.com *Web Site:* www.achivalservices.com, pg 229

Grossgart, Chris, International Association of Business Communicators (IABC), One Hallidie Plaza, Suite 600, San Francisco, CA 94102 *Tel:* 415-544-4700 *Toll Free Tel:* 800-776-4222 *Fax:* 415-544-4747 *E-mail:* service_centre@iabc.com *Web Site:* www.iabc.com, pg 688

Grossinger, Richard, Frog Ltd, 1435 Fourth St, Berkeley, CA 94710 *Tel:* 510-559-8277 *Toll Free Tel:* 800-337-2665 (book orders only) *Fax:* 510-559-8279 *E-mail:* orders@northatlanticbooks.com *Web Site:* www.northatlanticbooks.com, pg 101

Grossinger, Richard, North Atlantic Books, 1435 Fourth St, Berkeley, CA 94710 *Tel:* 510-559-8277 *Toll Free Tel:* 800-337-2665 (book orders only) *Fax:* 510-559-8279 *E-mail:* orders@northatlanticbooks.com *Web Site:* www.northatlanticbooks.com, pg 192

Grosskopf, Bill M, G & S Editors, 410 Baylor, Austin, TX 78703-5312 *Tel:* 512-478-5341 *Fax:* 512-476-4756 *Web Site:* www.gstype.com, pg 599

Grossman, Dina, Tzipora Publications Inc, 175 E 96 St, Suite 10-O, New York, NY 10128 *Tel:* 212-427-5399 *Fax:* 413-638-9158 *E-mail:* tziporapub@msn.com *Web Site:* www.tziporapub.com, pg 277

Grossman, Lawrence, American Jewish Committee, 165 E 56 St, New York, NY 10022 *Tel:* 212-751-4000 *Fax:* 212-891-1492 *Web Site:* www.ajc.org, pg 676

Grosz-Ngate, Maria, Indiana University African Studies Program, Indiana University, 221 Woodburn Hall, Bloomington, IN 47405 *Tel:* 812-855-8254 *Fax:* 812-855-6734 *E-mail:* afrist@indiana.edu *Web Site:* www.indiana.edu/~afrist, pg 132

Grote, Bill, Craftsman Book Co, 6058 Corte Del Cedro, Carlsbad, CA 92009 *Tel:* 760-438-7828 *Toll Free Tel:* 800-829-8123 *Fax:* 760-438-0398 *Web Site:* www.craftsman-book.com, pg 71

Groth, Gary, Fantagraphics Books, 7563 Lake City Way NE, Seattle, WA 98115 *Tel:* 206-524-1967 *Toll Free Tel:* 800-657-1100 *Fax:* 206-524-2104 *E-mail:* ffbicomix@fantagraphics.com *Web Site:* www.fantagraphics.com, pg 95

Groth, Rick, Krause Publications, 700 E State St, Iola, WI 54990 *Tel:* 715-445-4612 ext 365 *Toll Free Tel:* 800-258-0929; 888-457-2873 *Fax:* 715-445-4087 *Web Site:* www.krause.com, pg 147

Groton, John, Random House Inc, 1745 Broadway, New York, NY 10019 *Tel:* 212-782-9000 *Toll Free Tel:* 800-726-0600 *Web Site:* www.randomhouse.com, pg 226

Groton, John, Random House Sales & Marketing, 1745 Broadway, New York, NY 10019 *Fax:* 212-782-9000, pg 227

Grove, Clarica, Specialized Systems Consultants Inc, PO Box 55549, Seattle, WA 98155-0549 *Tel:* 206-782-7733 *Fax:* 206-782-7191 *E-mail:* sales@ssc.com; info@ssc.com *Web Site:* www.ssc.com, pg 255

Groves, Jenny, Gryphon House Inc, 10726 Tucker St, Beltsville, MD 20704 *Tel:* 301-595-9500 *Toll Free Tel:* 800-638-0928 *Fax:* 301-595-0051 *E-mail:* info@ghbooks.com *Web Site:* www.gryphonhouse.com, pg 110

Grows, Penelope, Wilfrid Laurier University Press, 75 University Ave W, Waterloo, ON N2L 3C5, Canada *Tel:* 519-884-0710 (ext 6124) *Fax:* 519-725-1399 *E-mail:* press@wlu.ca *Web Site:* www.press.wlu.ca, pg 567

Grubbauer, Melinda, De Vorss & Co, 553 Constitution Ave, Camarillo, CA 93012-8510 *Tel:* 805-322-9010 *Toll Free Tel:* 800-843-5743 *Fax:* 805-322-9011 *E-mail:* service@devorss.com *Web Site:* www.devorss.com, pg 78

Gruber, Sharon, University of New Orleans Press, c/o UNO Foundation, 6601 Franklin Ave, New Orleans, LA 70122 *Tel:* 504-280-1375 *Fax:* 504-280-7339 *Web Site:* www.uno.edu, pg 283

Grubin, Eve, George Bogin Memorial Award, 15 Gramercy Park, New York, NY 10003 *Tel:* 212-254-9628 *Fax:* 212-673-2352 *Web Site:* www.poetrysociety.org, pg 763

Grucelski, John, University of Michigan Press, 839 Greene St, Ann Arbor, MI 48104-3209 *Tel:* 734-764-4388 *Fax:* 734-615-1540 *E-mail:* um.press@umich.edu *Web Site:* www.press.umich.edu, pg 282

Gruenberg, Leif, Omnigraphics Inc, 615 Griswold St, Detroit, MI 48226 *Tel:* 313-961-1340 *Toll Free Tel:* 800-234-1340 (cust serv) *Fax:* 313-961-1383 *Toll Free Fax:* 800-875-1340 (cust serv) *E-mail:* info@omnigraphics.com *Web Site:* www.omnigraphics.com, pg 197

Gruhn, Cathy Lee, Rodale Books, 400 S Tenth St, Emmaus, PA 18098-0099 *Tel:* 610-967-5171 *Fax:* 610-967-8961 *Web Site:* www.rodale.com, pg 233

Grunden, Nola, Regal Books, 1957 Eastman Ave, Ventura, CA 93003 *Tel:* 805-644-9721 *Toll Free Tel:* 800-446-7735 (orders) *Fax:* 805-644-9728 (editorial); 805-644-4729 (purchasing); 805-650-8713 (sales & corp serv); 805-658-3388 (sales) *Toll Free Fax:* 800-860-3109 (orders) *E-mail:* info@regalbooks.com *Web Site:* www.gospellight.com, pg 230

Grunewald, Nancy, Washington State University Press, Cooper Publications Bldg, Grimes Way, Pullman, WA 99164-5910 *Tel:* 509-335-3518 *Toll Free Tel:* 800-354-7360 *Fax:* 509-335-8568 *E-mail:* wsupress@wsu.edu *Web Site:* wsupress.wsu.edu, pg 293

Grupper, Beth, Kaplan Publishing, 1230 Avenue of the Americas, New York, NY 10020 *Tel:* 212-632-4973 *Web Site:* www.simonsays.com, pg 144

Guadango, Joe, Sterling Publishing Co Inc, 387 Park Ave S, 5th fl, New York, NY 10016-8810 *Tel:* 212-532-7160 *Toll Free Tel:* 800-367-9692 *Fax:* 212-213-2495 *Web Site:* www.sterlingpub.com, pg 259

Guaracao, Hernan, National Association of Hispanic Publications Inc (NAHP), National Press Bldg, 529 14 St, Suite 1085, Washington, DC 20045 *Tel:* 202-662-7250 *Fax:* 202-662-7251, pg 692

Guararra, Rosanne, Grosset & Dunlap, 345 Hudson St, New York, NY 10014 *Tel:* 212-366-2000 *E-mail:* online@penguinputnam.com *Web Site:* www.penguin.com, pg 110

Guarnaschelli, Maria, W W Norton & Company Inc, 500 Fifth Ave, New York, NY 10110-0017 *Tel:* 212-354-5500 *Toll Free Tel:* 800-233-4830 (orders & cust serv) *Fax:* 212-869-0856 *Toll Free Fax:* 800-458-6515 *Web Site:* www.wwnorton.com, pg 193

Gubins, Samuel, Annual Reviews, 4139 El Camino Way, Palo Alto, CA 94306 *Tel:* 650-493-4400 *Toll Free Tel:* 800-523-8635 *Fax:* 650-855-9815 *E-mail:* service@annualreviews.org *Web Site:* www.annualreviews.org, pg 20

Gudmundson, Wayne, New Rivers Press, Minnesota State University Moorhead, 1104 Seventh Ave S, Moorhead, MN 56563 *Tel:* 218-477-5870 *Fax:* 218-477-2236 *E-mail:* nrp@mnstate.edu *Web Site:* www.newriverspress.com; www.mnstate.edu/newriverspress, pg 189

Guenzi, Carol, Carol Guenzi Agents Inc, 865 Delaware, Denver, CO 80204 *Tel:* 303-820-2599 *Toll Free Tel:* 800-417-5120 *Fax:* 303-820-2598 *E-mail:* art@artagent.com *Web Site:* www.artagent.com, pg 666

Guerin, Marc-Aime, Guerin Editeur Ltee, 4501 rue Drolet, Montreal, PQ H2T 2G2, Canada *Tel:* 514-842-3481 *Toll Free Tel:* 800-398-8337 *Fax:* 514-842-4923 *Web Site:* www.guerin-editeur.qc.ca, pg 549

Guerin, Reine Bertrand, Services Documentaires Multimedia Inc (SDM Inc), 5650 Rue D'Iberville, Bureau 620, Montreal, PQ H2G 2B3, Canada *Tel:* 514-382-0895 *Fax:* 514-384-9139 *E-mail:* info@sdm.qc.ca *Web Site:* www.sdm.qc.ca, pg 561

Guerra, Michael, National Catholic Educational Association, 1077 30 St NW, Suite 100, Washington, DC 20007-3852 *Tel:* 202-337-6232 *Fax:* 202-333-6706 *Web Site:* www.ncea.org, pg 182

Guerrero, Laura, Feral House, PO Box 39910, Los Angeles, CA 90039 *Tel:* 323-666-3311 *Fax:* 323-666-3330 *E-mail:* info@feralhouse.com *Web Site:* www.feralhouse.com, pg 96

Guerth, Jan-Erik, United Tribes Media Inc, 240 W 35 St, Suite 500, New York, NY 10001 *Tel:* 212-244-4166; 212-534-7646 *E-mail:* janguerth@aol.com, pg 659

Guevara, Linda, All About Kids Publishing, 117 Bernal Rd, No 70, PMB 405, San Jose, CA 95119 *Tel:* 408-846-1833 *Fax:* 408-846-1835 (ordering) *Web Site:* www.aakp.com, pg 8

Guevin, John R, Biographical Publishing Co, 35 Clark Hill Rd, Prospect, CT 06712-1011 *Tel:* 203-758-3661 *Fax:* 253-793-2618 *E-mail:* biopub@aol.com *Web Site:* members.aol.com/biopub, pg 39

Guidera, Rachel, Verso, 180 Varick St, 10th fl, New York, NY 10014-4606 *Tel:* 212-807-9680 *Fax:* 212-807-9152 *E-mail:* versony@versobooks.com *Web Site:* www.versobooks.com, pg 290

Guido, Umberto III, Peter Glenn Publications, 6040 NW 43 Terr, Boca Raton, FL 33496 *Tel:* 561-999-8930 *Toll Free Tel:* 888-332-6700 *Fax:* 561-999-8931 *E-mail:* lynn@pgdirect.com *Web Site:* www.pgdirect.com, pg 105

Guild, Ed, NAR Publications, State Rte 55, Barryville, NY 12719 *Tel:* 845-557-8713 *E-mail:* narpubs@aol.com, pg 181

Guimdom, Bernard, Editions Vents d'Ouest, 185 rue Eddy, Hull, PQ J8X 2X2, Canada *Tel:* 819-770-6377 *Fax:* 819-770-0559 *E-mail:* info@ventsdouest.ca, pg 546

Gulan, Mike, Champion Press Ltd, 4308 Blueberry Rd, Fredonia, WI 53021 *Tel:* 262-692-3897 *Toll Free Tel:* 877-250-3354 *Fax:* 262-692-3342 *E-mail:* info@championpress.com *Web Site:* www.championpress.com, pg 58

Gulierrez, Victoria, Bridge Publications Inc, 4751 Fountain Ave, Los Angeles, CA 90029 *Tel:* 323-953-3320 *Toll Free Tel:* 800-722-1733; 800-843-7389 (CA) *Fax:* 323-953-3328 *E-mail:* info@bridgepub.com *Web Site:* www.bridgepub.com, pg 47

Guma, Matthew, Inkwell Management, 521 Fifth Ave, 26th fl, New York, NY 10175 *Tel:* 212-922-3500 *Fax:* 212-922-0535 *E-mail:* contact@inkwellmanagement.com *Web Site:* www.inkwellmanagement.com, pg 635

Gunderson, Joanna, Red Dust Inc, Box 630, Gracie Sta, New York, NY 10028 *Tel:* 212-348-4388 *E-mail:* reddustjg@aol.com, pg 229

Gunderson, Wilfred E, Rapids Christian Press Inc, 5777 Vista Dr, Ferndale, WA 98248 *Tel:* 360-384-1747 *Fax:* 360-384-1747, pg 227

Gunn, James, Writers Workshop in Science Fiction, University of Kansas English Dept, 3114 Wescoe Hall, Lawrence, KS 66045-2350 *Tel:* 785-864-3380 *Fax:* 785-864-1159, pg 749

Gunnison, John P, Adventure House, 914 Laredo Rd, Silver Spring, MD 20901 *Tel:* 301-754-1589 *Fax:* 978-215-7412 *Web Site:* www.adventurehouse.com, pg 6

Gunsser, Margo, The Kane Press, 240 W 35 St, Suite 300, New York, NY 10001-2506 *Tel:* 212-268-1435 *Fax:* 212-268-2044 *Web Site:* www.kanepress.com, pg 144

Gupta, Anita, TechBooks Professional Publishing Group, 11150 Main St, Suite 402, Fairfax, VA 22030 *Tel:* 703-352-0001 *Fax:* 703-352-8862 *E-mail:* info@techbooks.com *Web Site:* www.techbooks.com, pg 612

Gurewitz, Brian, Books on Tape®, Customer Service, 400 Hahn Rd, Westminster, MD 21157 *Toll Free Tel:* 800-733-3000 *Toll Free Fax:* 800-659-2436 *E-mail:* botlib@booksontape.com *Web Site:* library.booksontape.com, pg 44

Gurock, Jeffrey, Yeshiva University Press, 500 W 185 St, New York, NY 10033-3201 *Tel:* 212-960-5400 *Fax:* 212-960-0043 *E-mail:* yuadmit@yu.edu *Web Site:* www.yu.edu, pg 306

Gusay, Charlotte, The Charlotte Gusay Literary Agency, 10532 Blythe Ave, Los Angeles, CA 90064 *Tel:* 310-559-0831 *Fax:* 310-559-2639 *E-mail:* gusay1@aol.com (for queries only) *Web Site:* www.mediastudio.com/gusay, pg 666

Gustafson, Katie, Impressions Book & Journal Services Inc, 2016 Winnebago St, Madison, WI 53704 *Tel:* 608-244-6218 *Fax:* 608-244-7050 *E-mail:* info@impressions.com *Web Site:* www.impressions.com, pg 602

Gustafson, Susan, Whole Person Associates Inc, 210 W Michigan St, Duluth, MN 55802-1908 *Tel:* 218-727-0500 *Toll Free Tel:* 800-247-6789 *Fax:* 218-727-0505 *E-mail:* books@wholeperson.com *Web Site:* www.wholeperson.com, pg 298

Guthrie, Ulrike, The Pilgrim Press/United Church Press, 700 Prospect Ave, Cleveland, OH 44115-1100 *Tel:* 216-736-3761 *Toll Free Tel:* 800-537-3394 (cust serv) *Fax:* 216-736-2207 *E-mail:* thepilgrimpress@thepilgrimpress.com *Web Site:* www.thepilgrimpress.com; www.theunitedchurchpress.com, pg 213

Gutmann, Myron, Inter-University Consortium for Political & Social Research, PO Box 1248, Ann Arbor, MI 48106-1248 *Tel:* 734-647-5000 *Fax:* 734-647-8200 *E-mail:* netmail@icpsr.umich.edu *Web Site:* www.icpsr.umich.edu, pg 136

Gutrich, Richard, Albert Whitman & Co, 6340 Oakton St, Morton Grove, IL 60053-2723 *Tel:* 847-581-0033 *Toll Free Tel:* 800-255-7675 *Fax:* 847-581-0039 *E-mail:* mail@awhitmanco.com *Web Site:* www.albertwhitman.com, pg 298

Gutting, Mary, Cottonwood Press Inc, 109-B Cameron Dr, Fort Collins, CO 80525 *Tel:* 970-204-0715 *Toll Free Tel:* 800-864-4297 *Fax:* 970-204-0761 *E-mail:* cottonwood@cottonwoodpress.com *Web Site:* www.cottonwoodpress.com, pg 69

Guttman, Naomi, Hamilton College, English/Creative Writing, Dept of English, 198 College Hill Rd, Clinton, NY 13323 *Tel:* 315-859-4370 *Fax:* 315-859-4390 *Web Site:* www.hamilton.edu, pg 752

Guy, Melody, Random House Publishing Group, 1745 Broadway, New York, NY 10019 *Toll Free Tel:* 800-200-3552 *Toll Free Fax:* 800-200-3552 *Web Site:* www.randomhouse.com, pg 227

Guzman, Vivianna, American Management Association, 1601 Broadway, New York, NY 10019-7420 *Tel:* 212-586-8100 *Toll Free Tel:* 800-262-9699 *Fax:* 212-903-8168 *Web Site:* www.amanet.org, pg 677

Guzowski, Bruce, HCPro, 200 Hoods Lane, Marblehead, MA 01945 *Tel:* 781-639-1872 *Toll Free Tel:* 800-650-6787 *Fax:* 781-639-2982 *Toll Free Fax:* 800-639-8511 *E-mail:* customer_service@hcpro.com *Web Site:* www.hcpro.com, pg 119

Gyorgyey, Clara, Writers-In-Exile Center, American Branch, 42 Derby Ave, Orange, CT 06477 *Tel:* 203-397-1479 *Fax:* 203-785-4744; 203-397-5439, pg 703

Gyorkos, Monica, Parachute, 4060 Blvd St-Laurent, Bureau 501, Montreal, PQ H2W 1Y9, Canada *Tel:* 514-842-9805 *Fax:* 514-842-9319 *E-mail:* info@parachute.ca *Web Site:* www.parachute.ca, pg 557

Gyurke, Jim, Psychological Assessment Resources Inc (PAR), 16204 N Florida Ave, Lutz, FL 33549 *Tel:* 813-968-3003 *Toll Free Tel:* 800-331-8378 *Fax:* 813-968-2598 *Toll Free Fax:* 800-727-9329 *Web Site:* www.parinc.com, pg 221

Haan, Walter J, Southfarm Press, Publisher, PO Box 1296, Middletown, CT 06457-1296 *Tel:* 860-346-8798 *Fax:* 860-347-9931 *E-mail:* southfarm@ix.netcom.com *Web Site:* www.war-books.com; www.wandahaan.com, pg 255

Haas, Kevin, Creative Publishing International Inc, 18705 Lake Dr E, Chanhassen, MN 55317 *Tel:* 952-936-4700 *Toll Free Tel:* 800-328-0590 (sales) *Fax:* 952-933-1456 *Web Site:* www.creativepub.com, pg 72

Haas, Margaret, University of Michigan Press, 839 Greene St, Ann Arbor, MI 48104-3209 *Tel:* 734-764-4388 *Fax:* 734-615-1540 *E-mail:* um.press@umich.edu *Web Site:* www.press.umich.edu, pg 282

Haas, Mary Beth, Indiana University Press, 601 N Morton St, Bloomington, IN 47404-3797 *Tel:* 812-855-8817 *Toll Free Tel:* 800-842-6796 (orders only) *Fax:* 812-855-7931 (orders only); 812-855-8507 *E-mail:* iupress@indiana.edu; iuorder@indiana.edu (orders) *Web Site:* www.iupress.indiana.edu, pg 132

Haase, H W, Quintessence Publishing Co Inc, 551 Kimberly Dr, Carol Stream, IL 60188 *Tel:* 630-682-3223 *Toll Free Tel:* 800-621-0387 *Fax:* 630-682-3288 *E-mail:* contact@quintbook.com *Web Site:* www.quintpub.com, pg 224

Haavik, Amy, American Association of Collegiate Registrars & Admissions Officers, One Dupont Circle NW, Suite 520, Washington, DC 20036-1135 *Tel:* 202-293-9161 *Toll Free Tel:* 877-338-3733 *Fax:* 202-872-8857 *E-mail:* info@aacrao.org *Web Site:* www.aacrao.org, pg 11

Habecker, Eugene B, American Bible Society, 1865 Broadway, New York, NY 10023-7505 *Tel:* 212-408-1200 *Toll Free Tel:* 800-322-4253 (orders only) *Fax:* 212-408-1259 *E-mail:* info@americanbible.org *Web Site:* www.americanbible.org, pg 12

Habegger, Larry, Travelers' Tales Inc, 330 Townsend St, Suite 208, San Francisco, CA 94107 *Tel:* 415-227-8600 *Fax:* 415-227-8605 *E-mail:* ttales@travelerstales.com *Web Site:* www.travelerstales.com, pg 275

Haber, Pierre C, The Psychology Society, 100 Beekman St, New York, NY 10038-1810 *Tel:* 212-285-1872 *Fax:* 212-285-1872, pg 221

Habgood, Robert P, Dawbert Press Inc, PO Box 67, Duxbury, MA 02331 *Tel:* 781-934-7202 *Toll Free Tel:* 800-933-2923 *Fax:* 781-934-2945 *E-mail:* info@dawbert.com *Web Site:* www.dawbert.com; www.familiesonthego.com; www.petsonthego.com, pg 77

Hackett, Emily, Internet Alliance (IA), 1111 19 St NW, Suite 1180, Washington, DC 20036 *Tel:* 202-955-8091; 202-861-2476 *Fax:* 202-955-8081 *E-mail:* ia@internetalliance.org *Web Site:* www.internetalliance.org, pg 689

Hackinson, Frank, FJH Music Co Inc, 2525 Davie Rd, Suite 360, Fort Lauderdale, FL 33317 *Tel:* 954-382-6061 *Toll Free Tel:* 800-262-8744 *Fax:* 954-382-3073 *E-mail:* custserv@fjhmusic.com *Web Site:* www.fjhmusic.com, pg 97

Hackinson, Kyle, FJH Music Co Inc, 2525 Davie Rd, Suite 360, Fort Lauderdale, FL 33317 *Tel:* 954-382-6061 *Toll Free Tel:* 800-262-8744 *Fax:* 954-382-3073 *E-mail:* custserv@fjhmusic.com *Web Site:* www.fjhmusic.com, pg 97

Hades, Brian, EDGE Science Fiction & Fantasy Publishing, PO Box 1714, Sta M, Calgary, AB T2P 2L7, Canada *Tel:* 403-254-0160 *Toll Free Tel:* 877-254-0115 *Fax:* 403-254-0456 *E-mail:* publisher@hadespublications.com *Web Site:* www.edgewebsite.com, pg 543

Hadidian, Dikran Y, Pickwick Publications, 215 Incline Way, San Jose, CA 95139-1526 *Tel:* 408-224-6777 *Fax:* 408-224-6686 *Web Site:* www.pickwickpublications.com, pg 212

Hadidian, Jean W, Pickwick Publications, 215 Incline Way, San Jose, CA 95139-1526 *Tel:* 408-224-6777 *Fax:* 408-224-6686 *Web Site:* www.pickwickpublications.com, pg 212

Hadley, Bridget, Holt, Rinehart and Winston, 10801 N MoPac Expy, Bldg 3, Austin, TX 78759 *Tel:* 512-721-7000 *Toll Free Tel:* 800-225-5425 (cust serv) *Fax:* 512-721-7833 (mktg); 512-721-7898 (edit) *Web Site:* www.hrw.com, pg 124

Haessner, Elaine C, Aztex Corp, PO Box 50046, Tucson, AZ 85703-1046 *Tel:* 520-882-4656 *Fax:* 520-792-8501 *Web Site:* www.aztexcorp.com, pg 30

Haessner, Walter R, Aztex Corp, PO Box 50046, Tucson, AZ 85703-1046 *Tel:* 520-882-4656 *Fax:* 520-792-8501 *Web Site:* www.aztexcorp.com, pg 30

Hagadorn, Barbara, Markus Wiener Publishers Inc, 231 Nassau St, Princeton, NJ 08542 *Tel:* 609-921-1141; 609-921-7686 (orders) *Fax:* 609-921-1140; 609-279-0657 (orders) *E-mail:* publisher@markuswiener.com; orders@markuswiener.com *Web Site:* www.markuswiener.com, pg 299

Hagan, Lisa, Paraview Literary Agency, 40 Florence Circle, Bracey, VA 23919 *Tel:* 434-636-4138 *Fax:* 434-636-4138 *Web Site:* www.paraview.com, pg 647

Hagelin, Rebecca, The Heritage Foundation, 214 Massachusetts Ave NE, Washington, DC 20002-4999 *Tel:* 202-546-4400 *Fax:* 202-546-8328 *Web Site:* www.heritage.org, pg 705

Hagen, Donald H, Bernan, 4611-F Assembly Dr, Lanham, MD 20706-4391 *Tel:* 301-459-2255; 301-459-7666 (cust serv) *Toll Free Tel:* 800-274-4447; 800-274-4888 (cust serv) *Fax:* 301-459-9235; 301-459-0056 (cust serv) *Toll Free Fax:* 800-865-3450 *E-mail:* info@bernan.com *Web Site:* www.bernan.com, pg 37

Hagen, James, InterVarsity Press, 430 E Plaza Dr, Westmont, IL 60559-1234 *Tel:* 630-734-4000 *Toll Free Tel:* 800-843-7225 *Fax:* 630-734-4200 *E-mail:* mail@ivpress.com *Web Site:* www.ivpress.com, pg 138

Hager, David L, American Health Publishing Co, Texas Star Pkwy, Suite 120, Euless, TX 76040 *Tel:* 817-545-4500 *Toll Free Tel:* 800-LEARN41 *Fax:* 817-545-2211 *E-mail:* contact@thelifestylecompany.com *Web Site:* www.thelifestylecompany.com, pg 14

Hager, Hal, Hal Hager & Associates, 15 N Richards Ave, Somerville, NJ 08876-2717 *Tel:* 908-231-9407 *Fax:* 908-725-0979 *E-mail:* halhager@verizon.net, pg 601

Haggerty, Kathy, Reader's Digest USA Select Editions, Reader's Digest Rd, Pleasantville, NY 10570-7000 *Tel:* 914-238-1000 *Toll Free Tel:* 800-310-6261 *Fax:* 914-238-4559, pg 229

Hagood, Louis, Oxbridge Communications Inc, 186 Fifth Ave, 6th fl, New York, NY 10010 *Tel:* 212-741-0231 *Toll Free Tel:* 800-955-0231 *Fax:* 212-633-2938 *E-mail:* info@oxbridge.com; custserv@oxbridge.com *Web Site:* www.mediafinder.com, pg 200

Hagood, Patricia, Oxbridge Communications Inc, 186 Fifth Ave, 6th fl, New York, NY 10010 *Tel:* 212-741-0231 *Toll Free Tel:* 800-955-0231 *Fax:* 212-633-2938 *E-mail:* info@oxbridge.com; custserv@oxbridge.com *Web Site:* www.mediafinder.com, pg 200

Hagopian, Lori, Hal Leonard Corp, 7777 W Bluemound Rd, Milwaukee, WI 53213 *Tel:* 414-774-3630 *Toll Free Tel:* 800-524-4425 *Fax:* 414-774-3259 *E-mail:* halinfo@halleonard.com *Web Site:* www.halleonard.com, pg 112

Hague, Stacy, Other Press LLC, 307 Seventh Ave, Suite 1807, New York, NY 10001 *Tel:* 212-414-0054 *Toll Free Tel:* 877-843-6843 *Fax:* 212-414-0939 *E-mail:* editor@otherpress.com; orders@otherpress.com *Web Site:* www.otherpress.com, pg 199

Hahn, Hannelore, The International Women's Writing Guild (IWWG), PO Box 810, Gracie Sta, New York, NY 10028-0082 *Tel:* 212-737-7536 *Fax:* 212-737-9469 *E-mail:* iwwg@iwwg.org *Web Site:* www.iwwg.org, pg 689

Hamill, Sam, Copper Canyon Press, PO Box 271, Port Townsend, WA 98368 *Tel:* 360-385-4925 *Fax:* 360-385-4985 *E-mail:* poetry@coppercanyonpress.org *Web Site:* www.coppercanyonpress.org, pg 68

Hamill, Sam, Port Townsend Writers' Conference, PO Box 1158, Port Townsend, WA 98368-0958 *Tel:* 360-385-3102 *Toll Free Tel:* 800-733-3608 (ticket office) *Fax:* 360-385-2470 *E-mail:* centrum@centrum.org *Web Site:* www.centrum.org, pg 746

Hamilton, Andrew, Andrew Hamilton Literary Agency, PO Box 604118, Cleveland, OH 44104-0118 *Tel:* 216-299-8809 *Fax:* 760-875-7292 *E-mail:* bkagent22@yahoo.com *Web Site:* www.andrewhamiltonliterary.com, pg 634

Hamilton, Carol, AAAI Press, 445 Burgess Dr, Suite 100, Menlo Park, CA 94025-3496 *Tel:* 650-328-3123 *Fax:* 650-321-4457 *E-mail:* press@aaai.org *Web Site:* www.aaaipress.org, pg 2

Hamilton, Carol, American Association of Colleges for Teacher Education (AACTE), 1307 New York Ave NW, Suite 300, Washington, DC 20005-4701 *Tel:* 202-293-2450 *Fax:* 202-457-8095 *E-mail:* aacte@aacte.org *Web Site:* www.aacte.org, pg 11

Hamilton, David, AAAI Press, 445 Burgess Dr, Suite 100, Menlo Park, CA 94025-3496 *Tel:* 650-328-3123 *Fax:* 650-321-4457 *E-mail:* press@aaai.org *Web Site:* www.aaaipress.org, pg 2

Hamilton, David, First Folio Resource Group Inc, 10 King St E, Suite 801, Toronto, ON M5C 1C3, Canada *Tel:* 416-368-7668 *Fax:* 416-368-9363 *E-mail:* mail@firstfolio.com *Web Site:* www.firstfolio.com, pg 599

Hamilton, Dennis, WH&O International, 892 Worcester St, Suite 130, Wellesley, MA 02482 *Tel:* 781-239-0822 *Toll Free Tel:* 800-553-6678 *Fax:* 781-239-0822 *E-mail:* whobooks@hotmail.com *Web Site:* www.whobooks.com, pg 297

Hamilton, Jen, Beach Holme Publishing, 409 Granville St, Suite 1010, Vancouver, BC V6C 1T2, Canada *Tel:* 604-733-4868 *Toll Free Tel:* 888-551-6655 (orders) *Fax:* 604-733-4860 *E-mail:* bhp@beachholme.bc.ca *Web Site:* www.beachholme.bc.ca, pg 536

Hamilton, Marilyn, Bunting Fellowship, 34 Concord Ave, Cambridge, MA 02138 *Tel:* 617-495-8212; 617-495-8237 (personnel contact) *Fax:* 617-495-8136 *Web Site:* www.radcliffe.edu, pg 764

Hamilton, Mark, Neo-Tech Publishing, PO Box 60906, Boulder City, NV 89006-0906 *Tel:* 702-293-5552 *Fax:* 702-293-4342 *Web Site:* www.neo-tech.com, pg 187

Hamilton, Michaela, Kensington Publishing Corp, 850 Third Ave, New York, NY 10022 *Tel:* 212-407-1500 *Toll Free Tel:* 800-221-2647 *Fax:* 212-935-0699 *Web Site:* www.kensingtonbooks.com, pg 145

Hamilton, Patricia, Park Place Publications, 591 Lighthouse Ave, No 22, Pacific Grove, CA 93950 *Tel:* 831-649-6640 *Toll Free Tel:* 888-702-4500 *Fax:* 831-649-6649 *E-mail:* publisher@parkplace-publications.com; info@parkplace-publications.com *Web Site:* www.parkplace-publications.com, pg 204

Hamilton, William, University of Hawaii Press, 2840 Kolowalu St, Honolulu, HI 96822 *Tel:* 808-956-8255 *Toll Free Tel:* 888-847-7377 *Fax:* 808-988-6052 *Toll Free Fax:* 800-650-7811 *E-mail:* uhpbooks@hawaii.edu *Web Site:* www.uhpress.hawaii.edu, pg 281

Hamlin, Faith, Sanford J Greenburger Associates Inc, 55 Fifth Ave, 15th fl, New York, NY 10003 *Tel:* 212-206-5600 *Fax:* 212-463-8718 *Web Site:* www.greenburger.com, pg 633

Hamlin, Rick, Guideposts Young Writers Contest, 16 E 34 St, New York, NY 10016 *Tel:* 212-251-8100 *Toll Free Tel:* 800-932-2145 *Fax:* 212-684-0679 *Web Site:* www.guidepostsbooks.com, pg 777

Hamm, Wanda K, Unicor Medical Inc, 4160 Carmichael Rd, Suite 101, Montgomery, AL 36106 *Tel:* 334-260-8150 *Toll Free Tel:* 800-825-7421 *Fax:* 334-272-1046 *Toll Free Fax:* 800-305-8030 *E-mail:* sales@unicormed.com *Web Site:* www.unicormed.com, pg 278

Hamma, Robert, Ave Maria Press, 19113 Douglas Rd, Notre Dame, IN 46556 *Tel:* 574-287-2831 *Toll Free Tel:* 800-282-1865 *Fax:* 574-239-2904 *Toll Free Fax:* 800-282-5681 *E-mail:* avemariapress.1@nd.edu *Web Site:* www.avemariapress.com, pg 29

Hamma, Robert, Sorin Books, 19113 Douglas Rd, Notre Dame, IN 46556 *Tel:* 574-287-2831 *Toll Free Tel:* 800-282-1865 *Fax:* 574-239-2904 *Toll Free Fax:* 800-282-5681 *E-mail:* sorinbk@nd.edu *Web Site:* www.sorinbooks.com, pg 253

Hamman, Kathleen, North-South Center Press at the University of Miami, 1500 Monza Ave, Coral Gables, FL 33146 *Tel:* 305-284-6868 *Fax:* 305-284-6370 *Web Site:* www.miami.edu/nsc, pg 192

Hammeken, Peggy A, Peytral Publications Inc, PO Box 1162, Minnetonka, MN 55345-0162 *Tel:* 952-949-8707 *Toll Free Tel:* 877-PEYTRAL (739-8725) *Fax:* 952-906-9777 *E-mail:* help@peytral.com *Web Site:* www.peytral.com, pg 211

Hammeken, Roberto, Peytral Publications Inc, PO Box 1162, Minnetonka, MN 55345-0162 *Tel:* 952-949-8707 *Toll Free Tel:* 877-PEYTRAL (739-8725) *Fax:* 952-906-9777 *E-mail:* help@peytral.com *Web Site:* www.peytral.com, pg 211

Hammel, Eric, Pacifica Military History, 1149 Grand Teton Dr, Pacifica, CA 94044 *Tel:* 650-355-6678 *Toll Free Tel:* 800-453-3152 (orders & inquiries) *E-mail:* mail@pacificamilitary.com *Web Site:* www.pacificamilitary.com, pg 202

Hammell, William M, Temple University Press, 1601 N Broad St, 083-42, USB Room 306, Philadelphia, PA 19122-6099 *Tel:* 215-204-8787 *Toll Free Tel:* 800-447-1656 *Fax:* 215-204-4719 *E-mail:* tempress@temple.edu *Web Site:* www.temple.edu/tempress, pg 266

Hammer, Alex, HSC Publications, 360-A W Merrick Rd, Suite 40, Valley Stream, NY 11580 *Tel:* 516-256-0223 *E-mail:* hscpub@aol.com *Web Site:* www.hscpub.com, pg 128

Hammer, Jennifer, New York University Press, 838 Broadway, New York, NY 10003 *Tel:* 212-998-2575 (edit) *Toll Free Tel:* 800-996-6987 (orders) *Fax:* 212-995-3833 (orders) *E-mail:* feedback@nyupress.nyu.edu *Web Site:* www.nyupress.org, pg 190

Hammerslough, Nancy, Brown Barn Books, 119 Kettle Creek Rd, Weston, CT 06883 *Tel:* 203-227-3387 *Toll Free Tel:* 888-227-3308 *Fax:* 203-222-9673 *E-mail:* editorial@brownbarnbooks.com *Web Site:* www.brownbarnbooks.com, pg 49

Hammond, Dosier D, The Countryman Press, 1206 Rte 12 N, Woodstock, VT 05091 *Tel:* 802-457-4826 *Toll Free Tel:* 800-245-4151 *Fax:* 802-457-1678 *E-mail:* countrymanpress@wwnorton.com *Web Site:* www.countrymanpress.com, pg 70

Hammond, Dosier D, W W Norton & Company Inc, 500 Fifth Ave, New York, NY 10110-0017 *Tel:* 212-354-5500 *Toll Free Tel:* 800-233-4830 (orders & cust serv) *Fax:* 212-869-0856 *Toll Free Fax:* 800-458-6515 *Web Site:* www.wwnorton.com, pg 193

Hammond, Robert, Marianne Strong Literary Agency, 65 E 96 St, New York, NY 10128 *Tel:* 212-249-1000 *Fax:* 212-831-3241 *E-mail:* stronglit@aol.com, pg 657

Hammond, Sharon, American Industrial Hygiene Association, 2700 Prosperity Ave, Suite 250, Fairfax, VA 22031-4319 *Tel:* 703-849-8888 *Fax:* 703-207-3561 *E-mail:* infonet@aiha.org *Web Site:* www.aiha.org, pg 14

Hamon, Donna L, Triad Publishing Co, PO Drawer 13355, Gainesville, FL 32604 *Tel:* 352-373-5800 *Fax:* 352-373-1488 *Toll Free Fax:* 800-854-4947 *Web Site:* www.triadpublishing.com, pg 275

Hamparian, Anahid, Marshall Cavendish Corp, 99 White Plains Rd, Tarrytown, NY 10591-9001 *Tel:* 914-332-8888 *Fax:* 914-332-1888 *E-mail:* mcc@marshallcavendish.com *Web Site:* www.marshallcavendish.com, pg 164

Hampel, Matt, Bancroft Prizes, 517 Butler Library, 535 W 114 St, New York, NY 10027 *Tel:* 212-854-4746 *Fax:* 212-854-9099 *Web Site:* www.columbia.edu/cu/lweb/eguides/amerihist/bancroft.html, pg 761

Hampton, Debra, John F Blair Publisher, 1406 Plaza Dr, Winston-Salem, NC 27103 *Tel:* 336-768-1374 *Toll Free Tel:* 800-222-9796 *Fax:* 336-768-9194 *E-mail:* blairpub@blairpub.com *Web Site:* www.blairpub.com, pg 41

Hamrick, Dave, University of Texas Press, PO Box 7819, Austin, TX 78713-7819 *Tel:* 512-471-7233 *Fax:* 512-232-7178 *E-mail:* utpress@uts.cc.utexas.edu *Web Site:* www.utexas.edu/utpress, pg 267

Hamza, Dr M H, ACTA Press/IASTED, 4500 16 Ave NW, No 80, Calgary, AB T3B 0M6, Canada *Tel:* 403-288-1195 *Fax:* 403-247-6851 *E-mail:* comments@actapress.com *Web Site:* www.actapress.com, pg 535

Hanby-Robie, Sharon, BigScore Productions, PO Box 4575, Lancaster, PA 17604 *Tel:* 717-293-0247 *Fax:* 717-293-1945 *E-mail:* bigscore@bigscoreproductions.com *Web Site:* www.bigscoreproductions.com, pg 621

Hancock, David, Hancock House Publishers, 1431 Harrison Ave, Blaine, WA 98230-5005 *Tel:* 604-538-1114 *Toll Free Tel:* 800-938-1114 *Fax:* 604-538-2262 *Toll Free Fax:* 800-983-2262 *E-mail:* sales@hancockhouse.com *Web Site:* www.hancockhouse.com, pg 113

Hancock, David, Hancock House Publishers Ltd, 19313 Zero Ave, Surrey, BC V3S 9R9, Canada *Tel:* 604-538-1114 *Toll Free Tel:* 800-938-1114 *Fax:* 604-538-2262 *Toll Free Fax:* 800-983-2262 *E-mail:* promo@hancockwildlife.org; sales@hancockhouse.com *Web Site:* www.hancockhouse.com, pg 549

Hancock, Nancy, Fireside & Touchstone, 1230 Avenue of the Americas, New York, NY 10020, pg 97

Handberg, Ryan, The Learning Connection (TLC), 1901 Longleaf Blvd, Suite 300, Lake Wales, FL 33859 *Tel:* 863-676-4246 *Toll Free Tel:* 800-218-8489 *Fax:* 863-676-5216 *E-mail:* tlc@tlconnection.com *Web Site:* www.tlconnection.com, pg 151

Handberg Sasman, Irene, The Learning Connection (TLC), 1901 Longleaf Blvd, Suite 300, Lake Wales, FL 33859 *Tel:* 863-676-4246 *Toll Free Tel:* 800-218-8489 *Fax:* 863-676-5216 *E-mail:* tlc@tlconnection.com *Web Site:* www.tlconnection.com, pg 151

Hane, Ron, CEF Press, PO Box 348, Warrenton, MO 63383-0348 *Tel:* 636-456-4380 *Toll Free Tel:* 800-748-7710 *Fax:* 636-456-4321 *Web Site:* www.cefonline.com, pg 56

Hanesalo, Bruce A, Military Info Publishing, PO Box 27640, Golden Valley, MN 55427 *Tel:* 763-533-8627 *Fax:* 763-533-8627 *E-mail:* publisher@military-info.com *Web Site:* www.military-info.com, pg 174

Hanfling, Renita, AMACOM Books, 1601 Broadway, New York, NY 10019-7406 *Tel:* 212-586-8100; 518-891-5510 (orders) *Toll Free Tel:* 800-262-9699 (cust serv) *Fax:* 212-903-8168; 518-891-2372 (orders) *Web Site:* www.amanet.org, pg 10

Hanger, Linda, Nolo, 950 Parker St, Berkeley, CA 94710 *Tel:* 510-549-1976 *Fax:* 510-548-5902 *E-mail:* info@nolo.com *Web Site:* www.nolo.com, pg 191

Hanger, Nancy C, Windhaven Press Editorial Services, 68 Hunting Rd, Auburn, NH 03032 *Tel:* 603-483-0929 *Fax:* 603-483-8022 *E-mail:* info@windhaven.com *Web Site:* www.windhaven.com, pg 613

Hankshaw, Hank, Two Thousand Three Associates, 4180 Saxon Dr, New Smyrna Beach, FL 32169 *Tel:* 386-427-7876 *Fax:* 386-423-7523 *E-mail:* ttta@worldnet.att.net, pg 277

Hanlon, Debbie, Jesperson Publishing, 100 Water St, 3rd fl, St John's, NF A1C 6E6, Canada *Tel:* 709-757-2216 *Fax:* 709-757-0708 *E-mail:* info@jespersonpublishing.nf.net *Web Site:* www.jespersonpublishing.nf.net, pg 551

Hanna, Bill, Acacia House Publishing Services Ltd, 51 Acacia Rd, Toronto, ON M4S 2K6, Canada *Tel:* 416-484-8356; 416-484-1430 *Fax:* 416-484-8356, pg 617

Hantz, Sara, Web Offset Press Operating, 200 Deer Run Rd, Sewickley, PA 15143-2600 *Tel:* 412-741-6860 *Toll Free Tel:* 800-910-4283 *Fax:* 412-741-2311 *E-mail:* info@gain.net *Web Site:* www.gain.net, pg 748

Hanus, Ed, Productivity Press, 444 Park Ave S, Suite 604, New York, NY 10016 *Tel:* 212-686-5900 *Toll Free Tel:* 888-319-5852 *Fax:* 212-686-5411 *Toll Free Fax:* 800-394-6286 *E-mail:* info@productivitypress. com *Web Site:* www.productivitypress.com, pg 219

Haproff, David, Russell Sage Foundation, 112 E 64 St, New York, NY 10021-7383 *Tel:* 212-750-6000 *Toll Free Tel:* 800-524-6401 *Fax:* 212-371-4761 *E-mail:* pubs@rsage.org *Web Site:* www.russellsage. org, pg 236

Harbeck, Thomas, Rodale Inc, 33 E Minor St, Emmaus, PA 18098-0099 *Tel:* 610-967-5171 *Fax:* 610-967-8962 *Web Site:* www.rodale.com, pg 234

Harcar, Christina, Tom Doherty Associates, LLC, 175 Fifth Ave, 14th fl, New York, NY 10010 *Tel:* 212-388-0100 *Toll Free Tel:* 800-455-0340 *Fax:* 212-388-0191 *E-mail:* firstname.lastname@tor.com *Web Site:* www. tor.com, pg 82

Harcar, Christina, St Martin's Press LLC, 175 Fifth Ave, New York, NY 10010 *Tel:* 212-674-5151 *Fax:* 212-420-9314 *E-mail:* firstname.lastname@stmartins.com *Web Site:* www.stmartins.com, pg 239

Harcar, Christina, St Martin's Press Trade Division, 175 Fifth Ave, New York, NY 10010 *E-mail:* firstname. lastname@stmartins.com *Web Site:* www.stmartins. com; www.minotaurbooks.com, pg 239

Hardin, James, Camden House, 668 Mount Hope Ave, Rochester, NY 14620 *Tel:* 585-273-5709; 585-275-0419 *Fax:* 585-271-8778 *E-mail:* boydell@boydellusa. net *Web Site:* www.boydell.co.uk/camdenfr.htm; www. camden-house.com, pg 593

Hardin, Judy, Encounter Books, 665 Third St, Suite 330, San Francisco, CA 94107-1951 *Tel:* 415-538-1460 *Toll Free Tel:* 800-786-3839 *Fax:* 415-538-1461 *Toll Free Fax:* 877-811-1461 *E-mail:* read@encounterbooks.com *Web Site:* www.encounterbooks.com, pg 90

Harding, Elizabeth, Curtis Brown Ltd, 10 Astor Place, New York, NY 10003 *Tel:* 212-473-5400, pg 623

Harding, Margaret, Marie Sandoz Award, c/o Margaret Harding, PO Box 98, Crete, NE 68333-0098 *Tel:* 402-826-2636 *Fax:* 402-826-2636 *E-mail:* gh12521@alltel. net *Web Site:* www.nebraskalibraries.org, pg 803

Harding, Sally, Seventh Avenue Literary Agency, 1663 W Seventh Ave, Vancouver, BC V6J 1S4, Canada *Tel:* 604-734-3663 *Fax:* 604-734-8906 *Web Site:* www. seventhavenuelit.com, pg 655

Harding, Sandy, Coronet Books & Publications, PO Box 957, Eagle Point, OR 97524 *Tel:* 541-858-5585 *Fax:* 541-858-5595 *E-mail:* lionspaw@country.net, pg 69

Hardjowirogo, Jono, Association for Computing Machinery, 1515 Broadway, New York, NY 10036 *Tel:* 212-869-7440 *Toll Free Tel:* 800-342-6626 *Fax:* 212-869-0481 *E-mail:* acmhelp@acm.org *Web Site:* www.acm.org, pg 26

Hardwick, Marjorie, The MIT Press, 5 Cambridge Ctr, Cambridge, MA 02142 *Tel:* 617-253-5646 *Toll Free Tel:* 800-405-1619 (orders only) *Fax:* 617-258-6779 *Web Site:* mitpress.mit.edu, pg 175

Hardy, Gordon, Houghton Mifflin Trade & Reference Division, 222 Berkeley St, Boston, MA 02116-3764 *Tel:* 617-351-5000 *Toll Free Tel:* 800-225-3362 *Web Site:* www.houghtonmifflinbooks.com, pg 126

Hare, Robbie Anna, Goldfarb & Associates, 721 Gibbon St, Alexandria, VA 22314 *Tel:* 202-466-3030 *Fax:* 703-836-5644 *E-mail:* rglawlit@aol.com, pg 632

Hargrove, Eugene C, Environmental Ethics Books, 1704 W Mulberry St, UNT, EESAT Bldg 370, Denton, TX 76201 *Tel:* 940-565-2727 *Toll Free Tel:* 800-264-9962 *Fax:* 940-565-4439 *Toll Free Fax:* 800-295-0536 *E-mail:* ee@unt.edu *Web Site:* www.cep.unt.edu, pg 91

Haringa, Steven T, Arrow Map Inc, 58 Norfolk Ave, Unit 4, South Easton, MA 02375 *Tel:* 508-230-2112 *Toll Free Tel:* 800-343-7500 *Fax:* 508-230-8186 *E-mail:* amisales@arrowmap.com *Web Site:* www. arrowmap.com, pg 24

Harkness, Holly, Pathfinder Press, 4794 Clark Howell Hwy, College Park, GA 30349 *Tel:* 404-669-0600 (voice mail only) *Fax:* 707-667-1141 *E-mail:* pathfinder@pathfinderpress.com (edit); orders@pathfinderpress.com; permissions@ pathfinderpress.com (permissions & copyright) *Web Site:* www.pathfinderpress.com, pg 205

Harland, Cisco, Water Row Press, PO Box 438, Sudbury, MA 01776 *Tel:* 508-485-8515 *Fax:* 508-229-0885 *E-mail:* contact@waterrowbooks.com *Web Site:* www. waterrowbooks.com, pg 294

Harley, Glory, Sable Publishing, 365 N Saturnino Dr, Suite 21, Palm Springs, CA 92262 *Tel:* 760-408-1881 *E-mail:* sablepublishing@aol.com *Web Site:* www. sablepublishing.com, pg 236

Harling, Prof Philip, British Council Prize in the Humanities, University of Kentucky, History Dept, Lexington, KY 40506-0027 *Tel:* 859-257-1246 *Fax:* 859-323-3885 *Web Site:* www.nacbs.org, pg 764

Harlow, Victoria, New England Publishing Associates Inc, PO Box 5, Chester, CT 06412-0005 *Tel:* 860-345-READ (345-7323) *Fax:* 860-345-3660 *E-mail:* nepa@ nepa.com *Web Site:* www.nepa.com, pg 646

Harman, Vincent, Bobley Harmann Corp, 311 Crossways Park Dr, Woodbury, NY 11797 *Tel:* 516-364-1800 *Fax:* 516-364-1899 *E-mail:* info@bobley.com *Web Site:* www.bobley.com, pg 43

Harmon, Charles T, Neal-Schuman Publishers Inc, 100 William St, Suite 2004, New York, NY 10038 *Tel:* 212-925-8650 *Toll Free Tel:* 866-672-6657 *Toll Free Fax:* 866-209-7932 *E-mail:* orders@neal-schuman.com *Web Site:* www.neal-schuman.com, pg 186

Harmsworth, Esmond, Zachary Shuster Harmsworth Agency, 1776 Broadway, New York, NY 10019 *Tel:* 212-765-6900 *Fax:* 212-765-6490 *Web Site:* www. zshliterary.com, pg 662

Harnish, Tom, Naval Institute Press, 291 Wood Rd, Annapolis, MD 21402-5034 *Tel:* 410-268-6110 *Toll Free Tel:* 800-233-8764 *Fax:* 410-295-1084; 410-571-1703 (customer service) *E-mail:* webmaster@ navalinstitute.org; customer@navalinstitute.org (cust serv) *Web Site:* www.navalinstitute.org, pg 185

Harnum, Bill, University of Toronto Press Inc, 10 St Mary St, Suite 700, Toronto, ON M4Y 2W8, Canada *Tel:* 416-978-2239 (admin) *Fax:* 416-978-4738 (admin) *Web Site:* www.utpress.utoronto.ca, pg 565

Harper, Calvin W, Woodland Publishing Inc, 448 E 800 N, Orem, UT 84097 *Tel:* 801-434-8113 *Toll Free Tel:* 800-777-2665 *Fax:* 801-334-1913 *Web Site:* www. woodlandpublishing.com, pg 302

Harper, Dennis, KC Publications Inc, PO Box 94558, Las Vegas, NV 89193-4558 *Tel:* 702-433-3415 *Toll Free Tel:* 800-626-9673 *Fax:* 702-433-3420 *E-mail:* kcp@kcpublications.com *Web Site:* www. kcpublications.com, pg 144

Harper, Gil, Penguin Group (USA) Inc, 375 Hudson St, New York, NY 10014 *Tel:* 212-366-2000 *Fax:* 212-366-2666 *E-mail:* online@uspenguingroup.com *Web Site:* www.penguin.com, pg 208

Harper, Jacquelin, Scholastic Trade Division, 557 Broadway, New York, NY 10012 *Tel:* 212-343-6100; 212-343-4685 (export sales) *Fax:* 212-343-4714 (export sales) *Web Site:* www.scholastic.com, pg 242

Harper, Laurie, Sebastian Agency, 557 W Seventh St, Suite 2, St Paul, MN 55102 *Tel:* 651-224-6670 *Fax:* 651-224-6895 *Web Site:* www.sebastianagency. com, pg 654

Harper, Matthew, M Evans & Co Inc, 216 E 49 St, New York, NY 10017 *Tel:* 212-688-2810 *Fax:* 212-486-4544 *E-mail:* editorial@mevans.com *Web Site:* www. mevans.com, pg 93

Harper, Suzanne, Simon & Schuster Children's Publishing, 1230 Avenue of the Americas, New York, NY 10020 *Tel:* 212-698-7000 *Web Site:* www. simonsayskids.com, pg 248

Harper, Terrance G, The Society of Professional Journalists, Eugene S Pulliam National Journalism Ctr, 3909 N Meridian St, Indianapolis, IN 46208 *Tel:* 317-927-8000 *Fax:* 317-920-4789 *E-mail:* spj@spj.org *Web Site:* www.spj.org, pg 700

Harper, Wendy, Central Ohio Writers of Literature for Children, c/o St Joseph Montessori School, 933 Hamlet St, Columbus, OH 43201-3595 *Tel:* 614-291-8644 *Fax:* 614-291-7411 *E-mail:* cowriters@mail.com *Web Site:* www.sjms.net/conf, pg 742

Harrell, Dawn, Hendrickson Publishers Inc, PO Box 3473, Peabody, MA 01961-3473 *Tel:* 978-532-6546 *Toll Free Tel:* 800-358-3111 *Fax:* 978-531-8146 *E-mail:* orders@hendrickson.com *Web Site:* www. hendrickson.com, pg 121

Harriet, Sydney H, Agents Inc for Medical & Mental Health Professionals, PO Box 4956, Fresno, CA 93744-4956 *Tel:* 559-438-1883 *Fax:* 559-438-1883, pg 618

Harrigan, Pat, Classroom Connect, 8000 Marina Blvd, Suite 400, Brisbane, CA 94005 *Tel:* 650-351-5100 *Toll Free Tel:* 800-638-1639 (cust support) *Fax:* 650-351-5300 *E-mail:* connect@classroom.com *Web Site:* www.classroom.com, pg 63

Harrington, Denis J, Denis J Harrington Publishers, 6207 Fushsimi Ct, Burke, VA 22015-3451 *Tel:* 703-440-8920 *Fax:* 703-440-8929, pg 116

Harrington, Rev Jeremy OFM, St Anthony Messenger Press, 28 W Liberty St, Cincinnati, OH 45202 *Tel:* 513-241-5615 *Toll Free Tel:* 800-488-0488 *Fax:* 513-241-0399 *E-mail:* books@americancatholic. org *Web Site:* www.AmericanCatholic.org, pg 237

Harrington, John P, Denis J Harrington Publishers, 6207 Fushsimi Ct, Burke, VA 22015-3451 *Tel:* 703-440-8920 *Fax:* 703-440-8929, pg 116

Harrington, Joyce, Adams & Ambrose Publishing, PO Box 259684, Madison, WI 53725-9684 *Tel:* 608-257-5700 *Fax:* 608-257-5719 *E-mail:* info@adamsambrose. com, pg 5

Harrington, Karen, Friends of American Writers Award, 680 N Lake Shore Dr, Suite L208, Chicago, IL 60611 *Tel:* 312-664-5628, pg 775

Harrington, Karen, Juvenile Literary Awards/Young People's Literature Awards, 680 N Lake Shore Dr-L208, Chicago, IL 60611 *Tel:* 312-664-5628, pg 782

Harrington, Mary A, Denis J Harrington Publishers, 6207 Fushsimi Ct, Burke, VA 22015-3451 *Tel:* 703-440-8920 *Fax:* 703-440-8929, pg 116

Harrington, Roby, W W Norton & Company Inc, 500 Fifth Ave, New York, NY 10110-0017 *Tel:* 212-354-5500 *Toll Free Tel:* 800-233-4830 (orders & cust serv) *Fax:* 212-869-0856 *Toll Free Fax:* 800-458-6515 *Web Site:* www.wwnorton.com, pg 193

Harrington, Sean P, Denis J Harrington Publishers, 6207 Fushsimi Ct, Burke, VA 22015-3451 *Tel:* 703-440-8920 *Fax:* 703-440-8929, pg 116

Harrington, Walt, University of Illinois, Dept of Journalism, Gregory Hall, Rm 120A, 810 S Wright St, Urbana, IL 61801 *Tel:* 217-333-0709 *Fax:* 217-333-7931 *E-mail:* journ@uiuc.edu *Web Site:* www. uiuc.edu/spike/index.pl, pg 755

Harris, Alec, GIA Publications, Inc, 7404 S Mason Ave, Chicago, IL 60638 *Tel:* 708-496-3800 *Toll Free Tel:* 800-442-1358 *Fax:* 708-496-3828 *E-mail:* custserv@giamusic.com *Web Site:* www. giamusic.com, pg 104

Harris, Alyza, Peanut Butter & Jelly Press LLC, PO Box 590239, Newton, MA 02459-0002 *Tel:* 617-630-0945 *Fax:* 617-630-0945 *E-mail:* info@pbjpress.com *Web Site:* www.publishinggame.com, pg 206

Harris, Alyza, The Publishing Game, PO Box 590239, Newton, MA 02459-0002 *Tel:* 617-630-0945 *E-mail:* info@publishinggame.com *Web Site:* www. publishinggame.com, pg 746

Harris, Ann, Bantam Dell Publishing Group, 1745 Broadway, New York, NY 10019 *Tel:* 212-782-9000 *Toll Free Tel:* 800-223-6834 *Fax:* 212-302-7985 *Web Site:* www.randomhouse.com/bantamdell, pg 31

Harris, Barbara, Harris Literary Agency, PO Box 6023, San Diego, CA 92166 *Tel:* 619-697-0600 *Fax:* 619-697-0610 *E-mail:* hlit@adnc.com *Web Site:* harrisliterary.com, pg 634

Harris, Barbara J, Harris Literary Agency, PO Box 6023, San Diego, CA 92166 *Tel:* 619-697-0600 *Fax:* 619-697-0610 *E-mail:* hlit@adnc.com *Web Site:* harrisliterary.com, pg 634

Harris, Carl, Kluwer Academic Publishers, 101 Philip Dr, Assinippi Park, Norwell, MA 02061 *Tel:* 781-871-6600 *Fax:* 781-871-6528; 781-681-9045 (cust serv) *E-mail:* kluwer@wkap.com *Web Site:* www.wkap.nl, pg 146

Harris, Chris, MapEasy Inc, PO Box 80, Wainscotte, NY 11975-0080 *Tel:* 631-537-6213 *Toll Free Tel:* 888-627-3279 *Fax:* 631-537-4541 *E-mail:* info@mapeasy.com *Web Site:* www.mapeasy.com, pg 162

Harris, David, American Jewish Committee, 165 E 56 St, New York, NY 10022 *Tel:* 212-751-4000 *Fax:* 212-891-1492 *Web Site:* www.ajc.org, pg 676

Harris, David, Bob Jones University Press, 1700 Wade Hampton Blvd, Greenville, SC 29614 *Tel:* 864-242-5100 *Toll Free Tel:* 800-845-5731 (orders only) *Fax:* 864-298-0268 *E-mail:* asmith@bju.edu *Web Site:* www.bjup.com, pg 142

Harris, Dorothy, House of Collectibles, 1745 Broadway, New York, NY 10019 *Tel:* 212-782-9000 *Fax:* 212-572-4997 *E-mail:* houseofcollectibles@randomhouse.com *Web Site:* www.houseofcollectibles.com; www.randomhouse.com, pg 126

Harris, Dorothy, Random House Reference, 1745 Broadway, New York, NY 10019 *Toll Free Tel:* 800-733-3000 *E-mail:* words@random.com; puzzles@random.com, pg 227

Harris, Elizabeth, Peanut Butter & Jelly Press LLC, PO Box 590239, Newton, MA 02459-0002 *Tel:* 617-630-0945 *Fax:* 617-630-0945 *E-mail:* info@pbjpress.com *Web Site:* www.publishinggame.com, pg 206

Harris, Elizabeth, University of Texas at Austin, Creative Writing Program, Dept of English, One University Sta, B5000, Austin, TX 78712-1164 *Tel:* 512-475-6356 *Fax:* 512-471-2898 *Web Site:* www.en.utexas.edu/grad/crwconc.html, pg 756

Harris, Ellen, Aperture Books, 20 E 23 St, New York, NY 10010 *Tel:* 212-505-5555 *Toll Free Tel:* 800-929-2323 *Fax:* 212-598-4015 *E-mail:* info@aperture.org *Web Site:* www.aperture.org, pg 21

Harris, Janet, Storey Books, 210 Mass MoCA Way, North Adams, MA 01247 *Tel:* 413-346-2100 *Toll Free Tel:* 800-793-9396 *Fax:* 413-346-2253 *E-mail:* info@storey.com *Web Site:* www.storey.com, pg 260

Harris, Joy, The Joy Harris Literary Agency, 156 Fifth Ave, Suite 617, New York, NY 10010 *Tel:* 212-924-6269 *Fax:* 212-924-6609 *E-mail:* gen.office@jhlitagent.com, pg 634

Harris, Leo J, Pogo Press Inc, 4 Cardinal Lane, St Paul, MN 55127 *Tel:* 651-483-4692 *Fax:* 651-483-4692 *E-mail:* pogopres@minn.net *Web Site:* www.pogopress.com, pg 215

Harris, Marilyn, Houghton Mifflin Trade & Reference Division, 222 Berkeley St, Boston, MA 02116-3764 *Tel:* 617-351-5000 *Toll Free Tel:* 800-225-3362 *Web Site:* www.houghtonmifflinbooks.com, pg 126

Harris, Melissa, Aperture Books, 20 E 23 St, New York, NY 10010 *Tel:* 212-505-5555 *Toll Free Tel:* 800-929-2323 *Fax:* 212-598-4015 *E-mail:* info@aperture.org *Web Site:* www.aperture.org, pg 21

Harris, Moira F, Pogo Press Inc, 4 Cardinal Lane, St Paul, MN 55127 *Tel:* 651-483-4692 *Fax:* 651-483-4692 *E-mail:* pogopres@minn.net *Web Site:* www.pogopress.com, pg 215

Harris, Patricia, National Information Standards Organization, 4733 Bethesda Ave, Suite 300, Bethesda, MD 20814 *Tel:* 301-654-2512 *Fax:* 301-654-1721 *E-mail:* nisohq@niso.org *Web Site:* www.niso.org, pg 184

Harris, Patricia R, National Information Standards Organization, 4733 Bethesda Ave, Suite 300, Bethesda, MD 20814 *Tel:* 301-654-2512 *Fax:* 301-654-1721 *E-mail:* nisohq@niso.org *Web Site:* www.niso.org, pg 693

Harris, Richard K, New Mexico Book Association (NMBA), 310 Read St, Santa Fe, NM 87504 *Tel:* 505-983-1412 *Fax:* 505-983-0899 *E-mail:* oceantree@earthlink.net *Web Site:* www.nmbook.org, pg 695

Harris, Samantha, American Book Publishing, 325 E 2400 S, Salt Lake City, UT 84115 *Tel:* 801-486-8639 *E-mail:* info@american-book.com *Web Site:* www.american-book.com, pg 12

Harris, Sloan, International Creative Management, 40 W 57 St, New York, NY 10019 *Tel:* 212-556-5600 *Fax:* 212-556-5665 *Web Site:* www.icmtalent.com, pg 635

Harris, Virginia S, The Writings of Mary Baker Eddy/Publisher, 175 Huntington Ave, Suite A-16-10, Boston, MA 02115 *Tel:* 617-450-3514; 617-450-2000 (Christian Science Church Boston) *Toll Free Tel:* 800-288-7090 *Fax:* 617-450-7334 *Web Site:* www.spirituality.com, pg 305

Harris, Wendy A, The Johns Hopkins University Press, 2715 N Charles St, Baltimore, MD 21218-4363 *Tel:* 410-516-6900 *Toll Free Tel:* 800-537-5487 *Fax:* 410-516-6968 *Web Site:* www.press.jhu.edu, pg 141

Harrison, Colin, Scribner, 1230 Avenue of the Americas, New York, NY 10020, pg 244

Harrison, G H, Media Associates, PO Box 46, Wilton, CA 95693-0046 *Toll Free Tel:* 800-373-1897 (orders) *Fax:* 916-687-8711; 916-687-8711 *E-mail:* carlya777@hotmail.com *Web Site:* www.media-associates.co.nz, pg 170

Harrison, Heather, Lonely Planet Publications, 150 Linden St, Oakland, CA 94607 *Tel:* 510-893-8555 *Toll Free Tel:* 800-275-8555 (orders) *Fax:* 510-893-8972 *E-mail:* info@lonelyplanet.com *Web Site:* www.lonelyplanet.com, pg 157

Harrison, Jack, University of Massachusetts Press, PO Box 429, Amherst, MA 01004-0429 *Tel:* 413-545-2217 *Toll Free Tel:* 800-537-5487 *Fax:* 413-545-1226; 410-516-6998 (fulfillment) *E-mail:* info@umpress.umass.edu; hfcustserv@mail.press.jhu.edu *Web Site:* www.umass.edu/umpress, pg 282

Harrison, Joyce, The University Press of Kentucky, 663 S Limestone St, Lexington, KY 40508-4008 *Tel:* 859-257-8761; 859-257-8442 (mktg) *Toll Free Tel:* 800-839-6855 (orders) *Fax:* 859-323-1873 *Web Site:* www.kentuckypress.com, pg 287

Harrison, Kate, E T Nedder Publishing, 9121 E Tanque Verde, Suite 105, PMB 299, Tucson, AZ 85749-8390 *Tel:* 520-760-2742 *Toll Free Tel:* 877-817-2742 *Fax:* 520-760-5883 *E-mail:* enedder@hotmail.com *Web Site:* nedderpublishing.com, pg 186

Harrison, Michael, Broadview Press, 280 Perry St, Unit 5, Peterborough, ON K9J 2A8, Canada *Tel:* 705-743-8990 *Fax:* 705-743-8353 *E-mail:* customerservice@broadviewpress.com *Web Site:* www.broadviewpress.com, pg 537

Harriss, Clarinda, BrickHouse Books Inc, 306 Suffolk Rd, Baltimore, MD 21218 *Tel:* 410-704-2869; 410-235-7690 *Fax:* 410-704-3999; 410-235-7690 *Web Site:* www.towson.edu; www.brickhousebooks.edu, pg 47

Harry, Isobel, PEN Canada, 24 Ryerson Ave, Suite 214, Toronto, ON M5T 2P3, Canada *Tel:* 416-703-8448 *Fax:* 416-703-3870 *E-mail:* pen@pencanada.ca *Web Site:* www.pencanada.ca, pg 696

Hart, A L, The Fox Chase Agency Inc, 701 Lee Rd, Suite 102, Chesterbrook, PA 19087 *Tel:* 610-640-7560 *Fax:* 610-640-7562, pg 631

Hart, Alexander, ALI-ABA Committee on Continuing Professional Education, 4025 Chestnut St, Philadelphia, PA 19104 *Tel:* 215-243-1600 *Toll Free Tel:* 800-CLE-NEWS *Fax:* 215-243-1664; 215-243-1683 *Web Site:* www.ali-aba.org, pg 8

Hart, Jo C, The Fox Chase Agency Inc, 701 Lee Rd, Suite 102, Chesterbrook, PA 19087 *Tel:* 610-640-7560 *Fax:* 610-640-7562, pg 631

Hart, Margaret, Louisiana State University Press, PO Box 25053, Baton Rouge, LA 70894-5053 *Tel:* 225-578-6294 *Toll Free Tel:* 800-861-3477 *Fax:* 225-578-6461 *Toll Free Fax:* 800-305-4416 *E-mail:* lsupress@lsu.edu *Web Site:* www.lsu.edu/guests/lsupress, pg 159

Hart, Margaret, Transatlantic Literary Agency Inc, 72 Glengowan Rd, Toronto, ON M4N 1G4, Canada *Tel:* 416-488-9214 *Fax:* 416-488-4531 *E-mail:* info@tla1.com *Web Site:* www.tla1.com, pg 659

Harte, Lawrence, Althos Publishing, 106 W Vance St, Fuquay-Varina, NC 27526 *Tel:* 919-557-2260 *Toll Free Tel:* 800-227-9681 *Fax:* 919-557-2261 *E-mail:* info@althos.com *Web Site:* www.althosbooks.com; www.telecomdefinitions.com, pg 10

Hartjens, Elisabeth M, Imagefinders Inc, 6101 Utah Ave NW, Washington, DC 20015 *Tel:* 202-244-4456 *Fax:* 202-244-3237, pg 602

Hartley, Glen, Writers' Representatives LLC, 116 W 14 St, 11th fl, New York, NY 10011-7305 *Tel:* 212-620-9009 *Fax:* 212-620-0023 *E-mail:* transom@writersreps.com *Web Site:* www.writersreps.com, pg 662

Hartley, John, Peter Pauper Press Inc, 202 Mamaroneck Ave, White Plains, NY 10601-5376 *Tel:* 914-681-0144 *Toll Free Tel:* 800-833-2311 *Fax:* 914-681-0389 *E-mail:* customerservice@peterpauper.com *Web Site:* www.peterpauper.com, pg 210

Hartman, Christopher, Newbury Street Press, 101 Newbury St, Boston, MA 02116 *Tel:* 617-536-5740 *Fax:* 617-536-7307 *Web Site:* www.newenglandancestors.org, pg 190

Hartman, Doug, CTB/McGraw-Hill, 20 Ryan Ranch Rd, Monterey, CA 93940-5703 *Tel:* 831-393-0700 *Toll Free Tel:* 800-538-9547 *Fax:* 831-393-7825 *Web Site:* www.ctb.com, pg 74

Hartman, Ken, CharismaLife Publishers, 600 Rinehart Rd, Lake Mary, FL 32746 *Tel:* 407-333-0600 *Toll Free Tel:* 800-451-4598 *Fax:* 407-333-7100 *E-mail:* charismalife@strang.com *Web Site:* www.charismamag.com, pg 58

Hartman, Mark, Hartman Publishing Inc, 8529 Indian School Rd NE, Albuquerque, NM 87112 *Tel:* 505-291-1274 *Toll Free Tel:* 800-999-9534 *Fax:* 505-291-1284 *Toll Free Fax:* 800-474-6106 *E-mail:* orders@hartmanonline.com *Web Site:* www.hartmanonline.com, pg 116

Hartman, William, Quintessence Publishing Co Inc, 551 Kimberly Dr, Carol Stream, IL 60188 *Tel:* 630-682-3223 *Toll Free Tel:* 800-621-0387 *Fax:* 630-682-3288 *E-mail:* contact@quintbook.com *Web Site:* www.quintpub.com, pg 224

Hartman-Seeskin, Sara, Free Spirit Publishing Inc, 217 Fifth Ave N, Suite 200, Minneapolis, MN 55401-1299 *Tel:* 612-338-2068 *Toll Free Tel:* 800-735-7323 *Fax:* 612-337-5050 *E-mail:* help4kids@freespirit.com *Web Site:* www.freespirit.com, pg 100

Hartmann, Patti, The University of Arizona Press, 355 S Euclid Ave, Suite 103, Tucson, AZ 85719-6654 *Tel:* 520-621-1441 *Toll Free Tel:* 800-426-3797 (orders) *Fax:* 520-621-8899 *Toll Free Fax:* 800-426-3797 *E-mail:* uapress@uapress.arizona.edu *Web Site:* www.uapress.arizona.edu, pg 280

Hartnett, Teresa, Hartnett Publishing Agency, 4301 S 36 St, Arlington, VA 22206 *Tel:* 703-998-0412 *Fax:* 801-730-2939 *E-mail:* hartnettinc@mindspring.com, pg 634

Hartshorn, Ted S, Martingale & Co, 20205 144 Ave NE, Woodinville, WA 98072 *Tel:* 425-483-3313 *Toll Free Tel:* 800-426-3126 *Fax:* 425-486-7596 *E-mail:* info@martingale-pub.com *Web Site:* www.martingale-pub.com, pg 164

Hartsock, Marcia, Association of Medical Illustrators (AMI), 6660 Delmonico Dr, Suite D-107, Colorado Springs, CO 80919 *Tel:* 719-598-8622 *E-mail:* hq@ami.org *Web Site:* www.ami.org, pg 680

Hartstein, Sam, Yeshiva University Press, 500 W 185 St, New York, NY 10033-3201 *Tel:* 212-960-5400 *Fax:* 212-960-0043 *E-mail:* yuadmit@yu.edu *Web Site:* www.yu.edu, pg 306

Hartwell, David, Tom Doherty Associates, LLC, 175 Fifth Ave, 14th fl, New York, NY 10010 *Tel:* 212-388-0100 *Toll Free Tel:* 800-455-0340 *Fax:* 212-388-0191 *E-mail:* firstname.lastname@tor.com *Web Site:* www.tor.com, pg 82

Hartwig, Elinor L, York Press Inc, 9540 Deereco Rd, Timonium, MD 21093 *Tel:* 410-560-1557 *Toll Free Tel:* 800-962-2763 *Fax:* 410-560-6758 *E-mail:* york@abs.net *Web Site:* www.yorkpress.com, pg 306

Harty, Pamela, The Knight Agency Inc, 577 S Main St, Madison, GA 30650 *Tel:* 706-752-0096 *E-mail:* knightagency@msn.com; knightagent@aol.com (queries) *Web Site:* www.knightagency.net, pg 638

Hartzler, John, Christian Light Publications Inc, 1066 Chicago Ave, Harrisonburg, VA 22802 *Tel:* 540-434-0768, pg 61

Harvey, Alan, Stanford University Press, 1450 Page Mill Rd, Palo Alto, CA 94304-1124 *Tel:* 650-723-9434 *Fax:* 650-725-3457 *Web Site:* www.sup.org, pg 257

Harvey, Ms Brett, American Society of Journalists & Authors (ASJA), 1501 Broadway, Suite 302, New York, NY 10036 *Tel:* 212-997-0947 *Fax:* 212-768-7414 *E-mail:* staff@asja.org *Web Site:* www.asja.org, pg 678

Harvey, Ms Brett, American Society of Journalists & Authors Writers Conference, 1501 Broadway, Suite 302, New York, NY 10036 *Tel:* 212-997-0947 *Fax:* 212-768-7414 *E-mail:* staff@asja.org *Web Site:* www.asja.org, pg 741

Harvey, Ms Brett, The Writer's Emergency Assistance Fund, 1501 Broadway, Suite 302, New York, NY 10036 *Tel:* 212-997-0947 *Fax:* 212-768-7414 *E-mail:* staff@asja.org *Web Site:* asja.org, pg 813

Harvey, Charmian, Editions Yvon Blais, 137 John, CP 180, Cowansville, PQ J2K 1W9, Canada *Tel:* 450-266-1086 *Fax:* 450-263-9256 *E-mail:* commandes@editionsyvonblais.qc.ca *Web Site:* www.editionsyvonblais.qc.ca, pg 546

Harvey, Daniel, G P Putnam's Sons (Hardcover), 375 Hudson St, New York, NY 10014 *Tel:* 212-366-2000 *E-mail:* online@penguinputnam.com *Web Site:* www.penguin.com, pg 223

Harvey, David, Maria Carvainis Agency Inc, 1350 Avenue of the Americas, Suite 2905, New York, NY 10019 *Tel:* 212-245-6365 *Fax:* 212-245-7196 *E-mail:* mca@mariacarvainisagency.com, pg 624

Harvey, Glen F, The American Ceramic Society, 735 Ceramic Place, Westerville, OH 43081-8720 *Tel:* 614-794-5890 *Fax:* 614-794-5892 *E-mail:* info@ceramics.org *Web Site:* www.ceramics.org, pg 12

Harvey, Pat, Bear & Co Inc, One Park St, Rochester, VT 05767 *Tel:* 802-767-3174 *Toll Free Tel:* 800-932-3277 *Fax:* 802-767-3726 *E-mail:* orders@InnerTraditions.com *Web Site:* InnerTraditions.com, pg 34

Harvey, Pat, Inner Traditions International Ltd, One Park St, Rochester, VT 05767 *Tel:* 802-767-3174 *Toll Free Tel:* 800-246-8648 *Fax:* 802-767-3726 *E-mail:* orders@InnerTraditions.com *Web Site:* www.InnerTraditions.com, pg 134

Harvey, Rhea, Pacific Press Publishing Association, 1350 N Kings Rd, Nampa, ID 83687-3193 *Tel:* 208-465-2500 *Toll Free Tel:* 800-447-7377 *Fax:* 208-465-2531 *Web Site:* www.pacificpress.com, pg 202

Harvey, Susan, Pacific Press Publishing Association, 1350 N Kings Rd, Nampa, ID 83687-3193 *Tel:* 208-465-2500 *Toll Free Tel:* 800-447-7377 *Fax:* 208-465-2531 *Web Site:* www.pacificpress.com, pg 202

Harwood, Diane Trout, Photographic Society of America Inc (PSA), 3000 United Founders Blvd, Suite 103, Oklahoma City, OK 73112-3940 *Tel:* 405-843-1437 *Fax:* 405-843-1438 *E-mail:* psahg@theshop.net; hq@psa-photo.org *Web Site:* www.psa-photo.org, pg 697

Hasenmueller, Joe, Graphic World Publishing Services, 11687 Adie Rd, Maryland Heights, MO 63043 *Tel:* 314-567-9854 *Fax:* 314-567-0360, pg 600

Hass, Robert, Squaw Valley Community of Writers Workshops, PO Box 1416, Nevada City, CA 95959 *Tel:* 530-470-8440 *E-mail:* brett@squawvalleywriters.org *Web Site:* www.squawvalleywriters.org, pg 748

Hassan, Alyssa, South End Press, 7 Brookline St, No 1, Cambridge, MA 02139-4146 *Tel:* 617-547-4002 *Fax:* 617-547-1333 *E-mail:* southend@southendpress.org *Web Site:* www.southendpress.org, pg 254

Hassan, Yuksel, Scholastic Canada Ltd, 175 Hillmount Rd, Markham, ON L6C 1Z7, Canada *Tel:* 905-887-7323 *Toll Free Tel:* 800-268-3848 (Canada) *Fax:* 905-887-1131 *Toll Free Fax:* 800-387-4944; 866-346-1288 *Web Site:* www.scholastic.ca, pg 560

Hassel, Robert, Harcourt School Publishers, 6277 Sea Harbor Dr, Orlando, FL 32887 *Tel:* 407-345-2000 *Toll Free Tel:* 800-225-5425 (cust serv) *Fax:* 407-352-3445 *Toll Free Fax:* 800-874-6418 *E-mail:* hbspcs@hbschool.com *Web Site:* www.harcourtschool.com, pg 114

Hasselberger, Rich, Berkley Books, 375 Hudson St, New York, NY 10014 *Tel:* 212-366-2000 *Fax:* 212-366-2666 *E-mail:* online@penguinputnam.com *Web Site:* www.penguin.com, pg 36

Hasselberger, Rich, Berkley Publishing Group, 375 Hudson St, New York, NY 10014 *Tel:* 212-366-2000 *E-mail:* online@penguinputnam.com *Web Site:* www.penguin.com, pg 37

Hasselberger, Rich, Dutton, 375 Hudson St, New York, NY 10014 *Tel:* 212-366-2000 *Fax:* 212-366-2262 *E-mail:* online@penguinputnam.com *Web Site:* www.penguin.com, pg 85

Hasselberger, Rich, NAL, 375 Hudson St, New York, NY 10014 *Tel:* 212-366-2000 *E-mail:* online@penguinputnam.com *Web Site:* www.penguin.com, pg 181

Hassinger, Mary, Instructional Fair Group, 3195 Wilson Dr NW, Grand Rapids, MI 49544 *Tel:* 616-802-3000 *Toll Free Tel:* 800-417-3261 *Fax:* 616-802-3007 *Toll Free Fax:* 888-203-9361 *Web Site:* elementary-educators.teacherspecialty.com/Instructional_Fair/, pg 135

Hastings, Deborah, Federal Street Press, 2513 Old Kings Hwy N, Darien, CT 06820 *Tel:* 203-852-1280 *Fax:* 203-852-1389, pg 95

Hastings, Lyn Barris, Random House Direct Inc, 1745 Broadway, New York, NY 10019 *Tel:* 212-572-2604 *Fax:* 212-572-6018, pg 226

Hasychak, Sue, Agnes Lynch Starrett Poetry Prize, 3400 Forbes Ave, Pittsburgh, PA 15260 *Tel:* 412-383-2456 *Fax:* 412-383-2466 *Web Site:* www.pitt.edu/~press, pg 807

Hatch, Jerry, HPBooks, 375 Hudson St, New York, NY 10014 *Tel:* 212-366-2000 *E-mail:* online@penguinputnam.com *Web Site:* www.penguin.com, pg 127

Hatch, Ronald, Ronsdale Press, 3350 W 21 Ave, Vancouver, BC V6S 1G7, Canada *Tel:* 604-738-4688 *Toll Free Tel:* 888-879-0919 *Fax:* 604-731-4548 *E-mail:* ronsdale@shaw.ca *Web Site:* ronsdalepress.com, pg 560

Hatch, Veronica, Ronsdale Press, 3350 W 21 Ave, Vancouver, BC V6S 1G7, Canada *Tel:* 604-738-4688 *Toll Free Tel:* 888-879-0919 *Fax:* 604-731-4548 *E-mail:* ronsdale@shaw.ca *Web Site:* ronsdalepress.com, pg 560

Hatcher, Lori, Urban Land Institute, 1025 Thomas Jefferson St NW, Suite 500 W, Washington, DC 20007 *Tel:* 202-624-7000 *Toll Free Tel:* 800-321-5011 *Fax:* 410-626-7140 *E-mail:* Bookstore@uli.org *Web Site:* www.bookstore.uli.org, pg 288

Hathaway, Bill, Record Research Inc, PO Box 200, Menomonee Falls, WI 53052 *Tel:* 262-251-5408 *Toll Free Tel:* 800-827-9810 *Fax:* 262-251-9452 *E-mail:* books@recordresearch.com *Web Site:* www.recordresearch.com, pg 229

Hathaway, Connie, Penmarin Books Inc, 1044 Magnolia Way, Roseville, CA 95661 *Tel:* 916-771-5869 *Fax:* 916-771-5879 *E-mail:* penmarin@penmarin.com *Web Site:* www.penmarin.com, pg 208

Hathaway, Michael, Farrar, Straus & Giroux, LLC, 19 Union Sq W, New York, NY 10003 *Tel:* 212-741-6900 *Fax:* 212-741-6973 *Web Site:* www.fsgbooks.com, pg 95

Hatsopoulos, George, National Bureau of Economic Research Inc, 1050 Massachusetts Ave, Cambridge, MA 02138-5398 *Tel:* 617-868-3900 *Fax:* 617-868-2742 *E-mail:* op@nber.org *Web Site:* www.nber.org, pg 182

Hatter, Richard W, John Simon Guggenheim Memorial Foundation, 90 Park Ave, New York, NY 10016 *Tel:* 212-687-4470 *Fax:* 212-697-3248 *E-mail:* fellowships@gf.org *Web Site:* www.gf.org, pg 705

Hatton, Valerie, Firefly Books Ltd, 66 Leek Crescent, Richmond Hill, ON L4B 1H1, Canada *Tel:* 416-499-8412 *Toll Free Tel:* 800-387-5085 *Fax:* 416-499-1142 *Toll Free Fax:* 800-565-6034 *E-mail:* service@fireflybooks.com *Web Site:* www.fireflybooks.com, pg 547

Hattori, April L, McGraw-Hill Education, 2 Penn Plaza, New York, NY 10121 *Tel:* 212-904-2000 *E-mail:* customer.service@mcgraw-hill.com *Web Site:* www.mheducation.com; www.mheducation.com/custserv.html, pg 167

Hauck, Robert, American Political Science Association, 1527 New Hampshire Ave NW, Washington, DC 20036 *Tel:* 202-483-2512 *Fax:* 202-483-2657 *E-mail:* apsa@apsanet.org *Web Site:* www.apsanet.org, pg 677

Haught, Robert, The National Society of Newspaper Columnists (NSNC), Fillmore St, Suite 507, San Francisco, CA 94115 *Tel:* 415-541-5636 *Web Site:* www.columnists.com, pg 694

Hauser, Barb, Barb Hauser Another Girl Rep, PO Box 421443, San Francisco, CA 94142-1443 *Tel:* 415-647-5660 *Fax:* 415-546-4180 *E-mail:* barb@girlrep.com *Web Site:* www.girlrep.com, pg 666

Haut, Judith, Random House Children's Books, 1745 Broadway, New York, NY 10019 *Tel:* 212-782-9000 *Toll Free Tel:* 800-200-3552 *Fax:* 212-782-9452 *Web Site:* www.randomhouse.com/kids, pg 225

Haveman, Gerda, Zumaya Publications, 403-366 Howard Ave, Burnaby, BC V5B 4Y2, Canada *Tel:* 604-299-8417 *E-mail:* editorial@zumayapublications.com *Web Site:* www.zumayapublications.com, pg 567

Haven, Dr Steve, Ashland Poetry Press, Ashland University, 401 College Ave, Ashland, OH 44805 *Tel:* 419-289-5110 *Fax:* 419-289-5638 *Web Site:* www.ashland.edu/aupoetry, pg 25

Haver, Thomas M, William K Bradford Publishing Co Inc, 35 Forest Ridge Rd, Concord, MA 01742 *Tel:* 978-402-5300 *Toll Free Tel:* 800-421-2009 *Fax:* 978-318-9500 *E-mail:* wkb@wkbradford.com *Web Site:* www.wkbradford.com, pg 300

Haverkamp, Jim, National Press Photographers Association Inc (NPPA), 3200 Croasdaile Dr, Suite 306, Durham, NC 27705 *Tel:* 919-383-7246 *Fax:* 919-383-7261 *E-mail:* info@nppa.org *Web Site:* www.nppa.org, pg 694

Hawes, Peter, Greenwich Publishing Group Inc, 929 Boston Post Rd, Suite 9, Old Saybrook, CT 06475 *Tel:* 860-388-9941 *E-mail:* info@greenwichpublishing.com *Web Site:* www.greenwichpublishing.com, pg 109

Hawke, Anthony, Hounslow Press, 8 Market St, 2nd fl, Toronto, ON M5E 1M6, Canada *Tel:* 416-214-5544 *Fax:* 416-214-5556 *E-mail:* info@dundurn.com *Web Site:* www.dundurn.com, pg 550

Hecker, Helen, Twin Peaks Press, PO Box 129, Vancouver, WA 98666-0129 *Tel:* 360-694-2462 *Fax:* 360-696-3210 *E-mail:* twinpeak@pacifier.com *Web Site:* www.pacifier.com/~twinpeak, pg 277

Hecker, John, Stipes Publishing LLC, 204 W University, Champaign, IL 61820 *Tel:* 217-356-8391 *Fax:* 217-356-5753 *E-mail:* stipes@soltec.net *Web Site:* www.stipes.com, pg 260

Hecker, Mel, United States Holocaust Memorial Museum, 100 Raoul Wallenberg Place SW, Washington, DC 20024-2126 *Tel:* 202-488-6115; 202-488-6144 (orders) *Toll Free Tel:* 800-259-9998 (orders) *Fax:* 202-488-2684; 202-488-0438 (orders) *Web Site:* www.ushmm.org/, pg 279

Hector, Alfonso, US Games Systems Inc, 179 Ludlow St, Stamford, CT 06902 *Tel:* 203-353-8400 *Toll Free Tel:* 800-544-2637 (800-54GAMES) *Fax:* 203-353-8431 *E-mail:* info@usgamesinc.com *Web Site:* www.usgamesinc.com, pg 289

Heddle, Jennifer, Pocket Books, 1230 Avenue of the Americas, New York, NY 10020 *Toll Free Tel:* 800-456-6798 *Fax:* 212-698-7284 *E-mail:* consumer.customerservice@simonandschuster.com *Web Site:* www.simonsays.com, pg 215

Hedman, Judith, Augsburg Fortress Publishers, Publishing House of the Evangelical Lutheran Church in America, 100 S Fifth St, Suite 700, Minneapolis, MN 55402 *Tel:* 612-330-3300 *Toll Free Tel:* 800-426-0115 (ext 639 subns); 800-328-4648 (orders); 800-421-0239 (perms) *Fax:* 612-330-3455 *Toll Free Fax:* 800-421-0239 (perms & copyrights) *E-mail:* customerservice@augsburgfortress.org; copyright@augsburgfortress.org (for reprint permission requests) *Web Site:* www.augsburgfortress.org, pg 28

Hedman, Kevin, The Gislason Agency, 219 SE Main St, Suite 506, Minneapolis, MN 55414 *Tel:* 612-331-8033 *Fax:* 612-331-8115 *E-mail:* gislasonbj@aol.com *Web Site:* www.TheGislasonAgency.com, pg 632

Heer, Brian, McGraw-Hill Education, 2 Penn Plaza, New York, NY 10121 *Tel:* 212-904-2000 *E-mail:* customer.service@mcgraw-hill.com *Web Site:* www.mheducation.com; www.mheducation.com/custserv.html, pg 167

Heer, Brian, McGraw-Hill International Publishing Group, 2 Penn Plaza, New York, NY 10121 *Tel:* 212-904-2000 *Web Site:* www.mcgrawhill.com, pg 168

Heffernan, Dick, Penguin Group (USA) Inc Sales, 375 Hudson St, New York, NY 10014 *Tel:* 212-366-2000 *E-mail:* online@penguinputnam.com *Web Site:* www.penguin.com, pg 207

Heffernan, Dick, Penguin Group (USA) Inc, 375 Hudson St, New York, NY 10014 *Tel:* 212-366-2000 *Fax:* 212-366-2666 *E-mail:* online@uspenguingroup.com *Web Site:* www.penguin.com, pg 208

Heffron, Jack, Emmis Books, 1700 Madison Rd, 2nd fl, Cincinnati, OH 45206 *Tel:* 513-861-4045 *Toll Free Tel:* 800-913-9563 *Fax:* 513-861-4430 *E-mail:* info@emmis.com *Web Site:* www.emmisbooks.com, pg 90

Heflin, Mark, American Illustration/American Photography, 126 Fifth Ave, Suite 14B, New York, NY 10011 *Tel:* 212-243-5262 *Fax:* 212-243-5201 *E-mail:* aiap@skyweb.net *Web Site:* www.ai-ap.com, pg 759

Hegeman, Ann, Rutgers University Press, 100 Joyce Kilmer Ave, Piscataway, NJ 08854-8099 *Tel:* 732-445-7762 (edit); 732-445-7762 (ext 627, sales) *Toll Free Tel:* 800-446-9323 (orders only) *Fax:* 732-445-7039 (acqs, edit, mktg, perms, prodn); 732-445-1974 (fulfillment) *E-mail:* garyf@rci.rutgers.edu *Web Site:* rutgerspress.rutgers.edu, pg 236

Hegg, Chris, Goodheart-Willcox Publisher, 18604 W Creek Dr, Tinley Park, IL 60477-6243 *Tel:* 708-687-5000 *Toll Free Tel:* 800-323-0440 *Fax:* 708-687-0315 *Toll Free Fax:* 888-409-3900 *E-mail:* custserv@g-w.com *Web Site:* www.g-w.com, pg 107

Heider, Joe, John Wiley & Sons Inc Education Publishing Group, 111 River St, Hoboken, NJ 07030 *Tel:* 201-748-6000 *Fax:* 201-748-6088 *E-mail:* info@wiley.com *Web Site:* www.wiley.com, pg 300

Heifetz, Merrilee, Writers House LLC, 21 W 26 St, New York, NY 10010 *Tel:* 212-685-2400 *Fax:* 212-685-1781, pg 662

Heimbouch, Hollis, Harvard Business School Press, 300 N Beacon St, Watertown, MA 02472 *Tel:* 617-783-7400 *Toll Free Tel:* 888-500-1016 *Fax:* 617-783-7664 *E-mail:* bookpublisher@mail1.hbsp.harvard.edu *Web Site:* www.hbsp.harvard.edu, pg 116

Heimburger, Donald J, Heimburger House Publishing Co, 7236 W Madison St, Forest Park, IL 60130 *Tel:* 708-366-1973 *Fax:* 708-366-1973 *Web Site:* www.heimburgerhouse.com, pg 120

Heimert, Laura, Yale University Press, 302 Temple St, New Haven, CT 06511 *Tel:* 203-432-0960; 401-531-2800 (cust serv) *Toll Free Tel:* 800-405-1619 (cust serv) *Fax:* 203-432-0948; 401-531-2801 (cust serv) *Toll Free Fax:* 800-406-9145 (cust serv) *E-mail:* customer.care@trilateral.org (cust serv) *Web Site:* www.yale.edu/yup/, pg 305

Hein, William S Jr, William S Hein & Co Inc, 1285 Main St, Buffalo, NY 14209-1987 *Tel:* 716-882-2600 *Toll Free Tel:* 800-828-7571 *Fax:* 716-883-8100 *E-mail:* mail@wshein.com *Web Site:* www.wshein.com, pg 120

Heindel, DeAnna, Georges Borchardt Inc, 136 E 57 St, New York, NY 10022 *Tel:* 212-753-5785 *Fax:* 212-838-6518 *E-mail:* georges@gbagency.com, pg 622

Heinle, Charles, Educators Publishing Service Inc, 625 Mount Auburn St, Cambridge, MA 02139-9031 *Tel:* 617-547-6706 *Toll Free Tel:* 800-225-5750 *Fax:* 617-547-0412 *Toll Free Fax:* 888-440-2665 *E-mail:* epsbooks@epsbooks.com *Web Site:* www.epsbooks.com, pg 88

Heiser, Chris, Association of American University Presses, 1427 E 60 St, Chicago, IL 60637 *Tel:* 773-702-7700; 773-702-7600 *Toll Free Tel:* 800-621-2736 (orders) *Fax:* 773-702-9756 (sales); 773-660-2235 (orders); 773-702-2708 *E-mail:* general@press.uchicago.edu *Web Site:* www.press.uchicago.edu, pg 26

Heiserman, Alice, American Correctional Association, 4380 Forbes Blvd, Lanham, MD 20706-4322 *Tel:* 301-918-1800 *Toll Free Tel:* 800-222-5646 *Fax:* 301-918-1886 *Web Site:* www.aca.org, pg 13

Heiss, Beth, Carolrhoda Books Inc, 241 First Ave N, Minneapolis, MN 55401 *Tel:* 612-332-3344 *Toll Free Tel:* 800-328-4929 *Fax:* 612-332-7615 *Toll Free Fax:* 800-332-1132 *E-mail:* info@lernerbooks.com *Web Site:* www.lernerbooks.com, pg 54

Heiss, Beth, First Avenue Editions, 241 First Ave N, Minneapolis, MN 55401 *Tel:* 612-332-3344 *Toll Free Tel:* 800-328-4929 *Fax:* 612-332-7615 *Toll Free Fax:* 800-332-1132 *E-mail:* info@lernerbooks.com *Web Site:* www.lernerbooks.com, pg 97

Heiss, Beth, Lerner Publications, 241 First Ave N, Minneapolis, MN 55401 *Tel:* 612-332-3344 *Toll Free Tel:* 800-328-4929 *Fax:* 612-332-7615 *Toll Free Fax:* 800-332-1132 *E-mail:* info@lernerbooks.com *Web Site:* www.lernerbooks.com, pg 152

Heiss, Beth, Lerner Publishing Group, 241 First Ave N, Minneapolis, MN 55401 *Tel:* 612-332-3344 *Toll Free Tel:* 800-328-4929 *Fax:* 612-332-7615 *Toll Free Fax:* 800-332-1132 *E-mail:* info@lernerbooks.com *Web Site:* www.lernerbooks.com, pg 152

Heiss, Beth, LernerSports, 241 First Ave N, Minneapolis, MN 55401 *Tel:* 612-332-3344 *Toll Free Tel:* 800-328-4929 *Fax:* 612-332-7615 *Toll Free Fax:* 800-332-1132 *E-mail:* info@lernerbooks.com *Web Site:* www.lernerbooks.com, pg 153

Heiss, Beth, Runestone Press, 241 First Ave N, Minneapolis, MN 55401 *Tel:* 612-332-3344 *Toll Free Tel:* 800-328-4929; 800-332-1132 *Fax:* 612-332-7615 *E-mail:* info@lernerbooks.com *Web Site:* www.lernerbooks.com, pg 236

Heisz, Janet, Westcliffe Publishers Inc, 2650 S Zuni St, Englewood, CO 80110-1145 *Tel:* 303-935-0900 *Toll Free Tel:* 800-523-3692 *Fax:* 303-935-0903 *E-mail:* sales@westcliffepublishers.com *Web Site:* www.westcliffepublishers.com, pg 296

Heitowit, Henry, Inter-University Consortium for Political & Social Research, PO Box 1248, Ann Arbor, MI 48106-1248 *Tel:* 734-647-5000 *Fax:* 734-647-8200 *E-mail:* netmail@icpsr.umich.edu *Web Site:* www.icpsr.umich.edu, pg 136

Helbert, Kristen Leverton, LifeQuest, 6404 S Calhoun St, Fort Wayne, IN 46807 *Toll Free Tel:* 800-774-3360 *E-mail:* dadoftia@aol.com, pg 154

Held, Ivan, Warner Books, 1271 Avenue of the Americas, New York, NY 10020 *Tel:* 212-522-7200 *Fax:* 212-522-7991 *Web Site:* www.twbookmark.com, pg 293

Held, Michael J, Rockefeller University Press, 1114 First Ave, New York, NY 10021 *Tel:* 212-327-8572 *Fax:* 212-327-7944 *E-mail:* rupcd@rockefeller.edu *Web Site:* www.rupress.org, pg 233

Helfand, Debra, Farrar, Straus & Giroux, LLC, 19 Union Sq W, New York, NY 10003 *Tel:* 212-741-6900 *Fax:* 212-741-6973 *Web Site:* www.fsgbooks.com, pg 95

Helferty, Molly, Groundwood Books, 720 Bathurst St, Suite 500, Toronto, ON M5S 2R4, Canada *Tel:* 416-537-2501 *Fax:* 416-537-4647 *E-mail:* genmail@groundwood-dm.com *Web Site:* www.groundwoodbooks.com, pg 548

Helgesen, Charles, The Oliver Press Inc, Charlotte Sq, 5707 W 36 St, Minneapolis, MN 55416-2510 *Tel:* 952-926-8981 *Fax:* 952-926-8965 *Web Site:* www.oliverpress.com, pg 196

Helgesen, Jeff, Research Press, 2612 N Mattis Ave, Champaign, IL 61822 *Tel:* 217-352-3273 *Toll Free Tel:* 800-519-2707 *Fax:* 217-352-1221 *E-mail:* rp@researchpress.com *Web Site:* www.researchpress.com, pg 231

Hellegers, Louisa, Cambridge University Press, 40 W 20 St, New York, NY 10011-4211 *Tel:* 212-924-3900 *Toll Free Tel:* 800-899-5222 *Fax:* 212-691-3239 *Web Site:* www.cambridge.org, pg 52

Heller, Brian, Tom Doherty Associates, LLC, 175 Fifth Ave, 14th fl, New York, NY 10010 *Tel:* 212-388-0100 *Toll Free Tel:* 800-455-0340 *Fax:* 212-388-0191 *E-mail:* firstname.lastname@tor.com *Web Site:* www.tor.com, pg 81

Heller, Brian, St Martin's Press LLC, 175 Fifth Ave, New York, NY 10010 *Tel:* 212-674-5151 *Fax:* 212-420-9314 *E-mail:* firstname.lastname@stmartins.com *Web Site:* www.stmartins.com, pg 238

Heller, Sarah, The Authors League Fund, 31 E 28 St, New York, NY 10016 *Tel:* 212-268-1208 *Fax:* 212-564-5363 *E-mail:* authlgfund@aol.com *Web Site:* www.authorsleaguefund.org, pg 681

Helm, James, Helm Editorial Services, 707 SW Eighth Way, Fort Lauderdale, FL 33315 *Tel:* 954-525-5626 *Fax:* 954-525-5626 (call first) *E-mail:* helmls@aol.com, pg 601

Helm, Lynne, Helm Editorial Services, 707 SW Eighth Way, Fort Lauderdale, FL 33315 *Tel:* 954-525-5626 *Fax:* 954-525-5626 (call first) *E-mail:* helmls@aol.com, pg 601

Helms, Russell, Menasha Ridge Press Inc, 2204 First Ave S, Suite 102, Birmingham, AL 35233 *Tel:* 205-322-0439 *Fax:* 205-326-1012 *E-mail:* info@menasharidge.com *Web Site:* www.menasharidge.com, pg 171

Hemley, Robin, 49th Parallel Poetry Award, Mail Stop 9053, Western Washington University, Bellingham, WA 98225 *Tel:* 360-650-4863 *E-mail:* bhreview@cc.wwu.edu *Web Site:* www.wwu.edu/~bhreview, pg 774

Hemmerly, Sylvia, The Florida Publishers Association Inc, PO Box 430, Highland City, FL 33846-0430 *Tel:* 863-647-5951 *Fax:* 863-647-5951 *E-mail:* fpabooks@aol.com *Web Site:* www.flbookpub.org, pg 687

Hemperly, Becky S, Candlewick Press, 2067 Massachusetts Ave, Cambridge, MA 02140 *Tel:* 617-661-3330 *Fax:* 617-661-0565 *E-mail:* bigbear@candlewick.com *Web Site:* www.candlewick.com, pg 52

Hempseed, Sonja, Harmonie Park Press, 23630 Pinewood, Warren, MI 48091 *Tel:* 586-755-3080 *Toll Free Tel:* 800-886-3080 *Fax:* 586-755-4213 *E-mail:* info@harmonieparkpress.com *Web Site:* harmonieparkpress.com, pg 115

Hench, John B, American Antiquarian Society, 185 Salisbury St, Worcester, MA 01609-1634 *Tel:* 508-755-5221 *Fax:* 508-754-9069 *Web Site:* www.americanantiquarian.org, pg 675

Henche, Rosa, University of Puerto Rico Press, Edificio EDUPR/Dialogo, Carr No 1, KM 12-0, Piso 2, Jardin Bota'nico Area Norte, San Juan, PR 00931 *Tel:* 787-758-6932; 787-758-8345 (sales); 787-250-0046; 787-250-0000 *Fax:* 787-753-9116; 787-751-8785 (sales dept), pg 285

Hendee, Bill, South-Western, A Thomson Business, 5191 Natorp Blvd, Mason, OH 45040 *Tel:* 513-229-1000 *Toll Free Tel:* 800-543-0487 *Fax:* 513-229-1025 *Web Site:* www.thomson.com, pg 254

Hendel, Richard, The University of North Carolina Press, 116 S Boundary St, Chapel Hill, NC 27514-3808 *Tel:* 919-966-3561 *Toll Free Tel:* 800-848-6224 (orders only) *Fax:* 919-966-3829 *Toll Free Fax:* 800-272-6817 (orders) *E-mail:* uncpress@unc.edu *Web Site:* www.uncpress.unc.edu, pg 283

Henderson, Albert, Chess Combination Inc, PO Box 2423, Noble Sta, Bridgeport, CT 06608-0423 *Tel:* 203-301-0791 *Toll Free Tel:* 800-354-4083 *Fax:* 203-301-0792 *Web Site:* chessNIC.com, pg 60

Henderson, Allison, Scholastic Library Publishing, 90 Old Sherman Tpke, Danbury, CT 06816 *Tel:* 203-797-3500 *Toll Free Tel:* 800-621-1115 *Fax:* 203-797-3657 *Web Site:* www.scholasticlibrary.com, pg 242

Henderson, Bill, Pushcart Press, PO Box 380, Wainscott, NY 11975-0380 *Tel:* 631-324-9300, pg 222

Henderson, Bill, Pushcart Prize: Best of the Small Presses, PO Box 380, Wainscott, NY 11975-0380 *Tel:* 631-324-9300, pg 801

Henderson, Brian, Wilfrid Laurier University Press, 75 University Ave W, Waterloo, ON N2L 3C5, Canada *Tel:* 519-884-0710 (ext 6124) *Fax:* 519-725-1399 *E-mail:* press@wlu.ca *Web Site:* www.press.wlu.ca, pg 567

Henderson, Carol, North Carolina Writers' Network Annual Fall Conference, PO Box 954, Carrboro, NC 27510-0954 *Tel:* 919-967-9540 *Fax:* 919-929-0535 *E-mail:* mail@ncwriters.org *Web Site:* www.ncwriters.org, pg 745

Henderson, Charlotte, A K Peters Ltd, 888 Worcester St, Suite 230, Wellesley, MA 02482 *Tel:* 781-416-2888 *Fax:* 781-416-2889 *E-mail:* service@akpeters.com *Web Site:* www.akpeters.com, pg 1

Henderson, Diane, Homestead Publishing, PO Box 193, Moose, WY 83012-0193 *Tel:* 307-733-6248 *Fax:* 307-733-6248 *Web Site:* www.homesteadpublishing.net, pg 125

Henderson, Doug, Scholastic Trade Division, 557 Broadway, New York, NY 10012 *Tel:* 212-343-6100; 212-343-4685 (export sales) *Fax:* 212-343-4714 (export sales) *Web Site:* www.scholastic.com, pg 242

Henderson, Homer, Parenting Press Inc, 11065 Fifth Ave NE, Suite F, Seattle, WA 98125 *Tel:* 206-364-2900 *Toll Free Tel:* 800-99-BOOKS (992-6657) *Fax:* 206-364-0702 *E-mail:* office@parentingpress.com *Web Site:* www.parentingpress.com, pg 204

Henderson, Jesse, New York University Press, 838 Broadway, New York, NY 10003 *Tel:* 212-998-2575 (edit) *Toll Free Tel:* 800-996-6987 (orders) *Fax:* 212-995-3833 (orders) *E-mail:* feedback@nyupress.nyu.edu *Web Site:* www.nyupress.org, pg 190

Henderson, John, H & M Productions II Inc, 226-06 56 Ave, Bayside, NY 11361 *Tel:* 718-357-6707 *Fax:* 718-357-8920 *E-mail:* handm@mft.com, pg 111

Henderson, Paul, US Conference of Catholic Bishops, USCCB Publishing, 3211 Fourth St NE, Washington, DC 20017-1194 *Tel:* 202-541-3090 *Toll Free Tel:* 800-235-8722 (orders only) *Fax:* 202-541-3089 *Web Site:* www.usccb.org/publishing, pg 289

Henderson, Robyn, The Pilgrim Press/United Church Press, 700 Prospect Ave, Cleveland, OH 44115-1100 *Tel:* 216-736-3761 *Toll Free Tel:* 800-537-3394 (cust serv) *Fax:* 216-736-2207 *E-mail:* thepilgrimpress@thepilgrimpress.com *Web Site:* www.thepilgrimpress.com; www.theunitedchurchpress.com, pg 213

Hendin, David, DH Literary Inc, PO Box 990, Nyack, NY 10960 *Tel:* 212-753-7942 *E-mail:* dhendin@aol.com, pg 627

Hendrex, Jerry, ANR Publications University of California, 6701 San Pablo Ave, 2nd fl, Oakland, CA 94608-1239 *Tel:* 510-642-2431 *Toll Free Tel:* 800-994-8849 *Fax:* 510-643-5470 *E-mail:* danrcs@ucdavis.edu *Web Site:* anrcatalog.ucdavis.edu, pg 20

Hendricks, Kathy, Impressions Book & Journal Services Inc, 2016 Winnebago St, Madison, WI 53704 *Tel:* 608-244-6218 *Fax:* 608-244-7050 *E-mail:* info@impressions.com *Web Site:* www.impressions.com, pg 602

Hendrickson, Stephen J, Hendrickson Publishers Inc, PO Box 3473, Peabody, MA 01961-3473 *Tel:* 978-532-6546 *Toll Free Tel:* 800-358-3111 *Fax:* 978-531-8146 *E-mail:* orders@hendrickson.com *Web Site:* www.hendrickson.com, pg 121

Hendrickson, V Leslie, Columbia Publishing Course at Columbia University, 2950 Broadway, MC 3801, New York, NY 10027 *Tel:* 212-854-1898 *Fax:* 212-854-7618 *E-mail:* publishing@jrn.columbia.edu *Web Site:* www.jrn.columbia.edu/publishing, pg 752

Hendriks, Peter, Kluwer Academic Publishers, 101 Philip Dr, Assinippi Park, Norwell, MA 02061 *Tel:* 781-871-6600 *Fax:* 781-871-6528; 781-681-9045 (cust serv) *E-mail:* kluwer@wkap.com *Web Site:* www.wkap.nl, pg 146

Hendrix, Laura, Black Warrior Review Literary Awards, University of Alabama, Tuscaloosa, AL 35486-0027 *Tel:* 205-348-4518 *E-mail:* bwr@ua.edu *Web Site:* www.webdelsol.com/bwr, pg 763

Henkin, Andrey, Translation Prize, 58 Park Ave, New York, NY 10016 *Tel:* 212-879-9779 *Fax:* 212-686-2115 *E-mail:* info@amscan.org *Web Site:* www.amscan.org, pg 809

Henkin, Carole, Blackwell Publishing/Futura, 3 W Main St, Elmsford, NY 10523 *Tel:* 914-593-0731 *Toll Free Tel:* 800-759-6102 *Fax:* 914-593-0732 *E-mail:* jbellhouse@ny.blackwellpublishing.com *Web Site:* www.blackwellpublishing.com/futura; www.blackwellfutura.com, pg 40

Henning, Rick, Edward Elgar Publishing Inc, 136 West St, Suite 202, Northampton, MA 01060 *Tel:* 413-584-5551 *Toll Free Tel:* 800-390-3149 (orders) *Fax:* 413-584-9933 *Web Site:* www.e-elgar.com, pg 89

Henningsen, Pamela, Binford & Mort Publishing Inc, 5245 NE Elam Young Pkwy, Suite C, Hillsboro, OR 97124 *Tel:* 503-844-4960 *Toll Free Tel:* 888-221-4514 *Fax:* 503-844-4959, pg 38

Henoch, Larissa, Health Communications Inc, 3201 SW 15 St, Deerfield Beach, FL 33442-8190 *Tel:* 954-360-0909 *Toll Free Tel:* 800-851-9100 (cust serv); 800-441-5569 (order entry) *Fax:* 954-360-0034 *Web Site:* www.hcibooks.com, pg 119

Henriquez, Ana, Phaidon Press Inc, 180 Varick St, 14th fl, New York, NY 10014 *Tel:* 212-652-5400 *Toll Free Tel:* 800-759-0190 (cust serv) *Fax:* 212-652-5410 *Toll Free Fax:* 800-286-9471 (cust serv) *E-mail:* ussales@phaidon.com *Web Site:* www.phaidon.com, pg 211

Henry, Christie, Association of American University Presses, 1427 E 60 St, Chicago, IL 60637 *Tel:* 773-702-7700; 773-702-7600 *Toll Free Tel:* 800-621-2736 (orders) *Fax:* 773-702-9756 (sales); 773-660-2235 (orders); 773-702-2708 *E-mail:* general@press.uchicago.edu *Web Site:* www.press.uchicago.edu, pg 26

Henry, Gray, Fons Vitae, 49 Mockingbird Valley Dr, Louisville, KY 40207-1366 *Tel:* 502-897-3641 *Fax:* 502-893-7373 *E-mail:* fonsvitaeky@aol.com *Web Site:* www.fonsvitae.com, pg 98

Henry, Jack, World Citizens, 96 La Verne Ave, Mill Valley, CA 94941 *Tel:* 415-380-8020 *Toll Free Tel:* 800-247-6553 (orders only) *Web Site:* soultosoulmedia.com; skateman.com, pg 304

Henry, Karen, Bedford/St Martin's, 75 Arlington St, Boston, MA 02116 *Tel:* 617-399-4000 *Fax:* 617-426-8582 *Web Site:* www.bedfordstmartins.com, pg 35

Henry, Linda, Cameron & Co, 680 Eighth St, Suite 205, San Francisco, CA 94103 *Tel:* 415-558-8455 *Toll Free Tel:* 800-779-5582 *Fax:* 415-558-8657 *Web Site:* www.abovebooks.com, pg 52

Henry, Lynn, Polestar Book Publishers, 9050 Shaughnessy St, Vancouver, BC V6P 6E5, Canada *Tel:* 604-323-7100 *Toll Free Tel:* 800-663-5714 *Fax:* 604-323-2600 *Toll Free Fax:* 800-565-3770 *E-mail:* info@raincoast.com *Web Site:* www.raincoast.com, pg 558

Hensley, Todd, C & T Publishing Inc, 1651 Challenge Dr, Concord, CA 94520 *Tel:* 925-677-0377 *Toll Free Tel:* 800-284-1114 *Fax:* 925-677-0373 *E-mail:* ctinfo@ctpub.com *Web Site:* www.ctpub.com, pg 51

Hensley, Tony, C & T Publishing Inc, 1651 Challenge Dr, Concord, CA 94520 *Tel:* 925-677-0377 *Toll Free Tel:* 800-284-1114 *Fax:* 925-677-0373 *E-mail:* ctinfo@ctpub.com *Web Site:* www.ctpub.com, pg 51

Henze, Jason, SterlingHouse Publisher Inc, 7436 Washington Ave, Suite 200, Pittsburgh, PA 15218 *Tel:* 412-271-8800 *Toll Free Tel:* 888-542-2665 *Fax:* 412-271-8600 *E-mail:* info@sterlinghousepublisher.com *Web Site:* www.sterlinghousepublisher.com, pg 259

Heppner, John B, Scientific Publishers Inc, 4460 SW 35 Terr, Suite 305, Gainesville, FL 32608 *Tel:* 352-373-5630 *Fax:* 352-373-3249 *E-mail:* scipub@aol.com *Web Site:* www.scipub.com, pg 243

Herbeck, Jaime, Disney Publishing Worldwide, 500 S Buena Vista, Burbank, CA 91521 *Tel:* 212-633-4400 *Fax:* 212-633-4833 *Web Site:* www.disney.go.com/disneybooks, pg 81

Herbig, Alice, University of Washington Press, 1326 Fifth Ave, Suite 555, Seattle, WA 98101-2604 *Tel:* 206-543-4050; 206-543-8870 *Toll Free Tel:* 800-441-4115 (orders) *Fax:* 206-543-3932 *Toll Free Fax:* 800-669-7993 (orders) *E-mail:* uwpord@u.washington.edu *Web Site:* www.washington.edu/uwpress/, pg 286

Herbst, Peggy Smith, Harcourt School Publishers, 6277 Sea Harbor Dr, Orlando, FL 32887 *Tel:* 407-345-2000 *Toll Free Tel:* 800-225-5425 (cust serv) *Fax:* 407-352-3445 *Toll Free Fax:* 800-874-6418 *E-mail:* hbspcs@hbschool.com *Web Site:* www.harcourtschool.com, pg 114

Herbst, Peter, Society for Technical Communication, 901 N Stuart St, Suite 904, Arlington, VA 22203-1822 *Tel:* 703-522-4114 *Fax:* 703-522-2075 *E-mail:* stc@stc.org *Web Site:* www.stc.org, pg 699, 747

Herdeck, Donald E, Passeggiata Press Inc, 420 W 14 St, Pueblo, CO 81003-2708 *Tel:* 719-544-1038 *Fax:* 719-544-7911 *E-mail:* passegpress@cs.com, pg 204

Herdeck, Margaret, Passeggiata Press Inc, 420 W 14 St, Pueblo, CO 81003-2708 *Tel:* 719-544-1038 *Fax:* 719-544-7911 *E-mail:* passegpress@cs.com, pg 204

Herder, Gwendolin, The Crossroad Publishing Company, 16 Penn Plaza, Suite 1550, New York, NY 10001 *Tel:* 212-868-1801 *Toll Free Tel:* 800-395-0690 (orders) *Fax:* 212-868-2171 *Toll Free Fax:* 800-462-6420 (orders) *E-mail:* ask@crossroadpublishing.com *Web Site:* www.crossroadpublishing.com, pg 73

Herendeen, Kevin, Harris InfoSource, 2057 E Aurora Rd, Twinsburg, OH 44087 *Tel:* 330-425-9000 *Toll Free Tel:* 800-888-5900 *Fax:* 330-425-7150 *Toll Free Fax:* 800-643-5997 *Web Site:* www.harrisinfo.com, pg 116

Herling, Lisa, HarperCollins Publishers, 10 E 53 St, New York, NY 10022 *Tel:* 212-207-7000 *Fax:* 212-207-7145 *Web Site:* www.harpercollins.com, pg 116

Hermalyn, Dr Gary, The Bronx County Historical Society, 3309 Bainbridge Ave, Bronx, NY 10467 *Tel:* 718-881-8900 *Fax:* 718-881-4827 *Web Site:* www. bronxhistoricalsociety.org, pg 48

Herman, Cheryl, Books on Tape®, Customer Service, 400 Hahn Rd, Westminster, MD 21157 *Toll Free Tel:* 800-733-3000 *Toll Free Fax:* 800-659-2436 *E-mail:* botlib@booksontape.com *Web Site:* library. booksontape.com, pg 44

Herman, Craig, Atria Books, 1230 Avenue of the Americas, New York, NY 10020 *Tel:* 212-698-7000 *Fax:* 212-698-7007 *Web Site:* www.simonsays.com, pg 27

Herman, Craig, Pocket Books, 1230 Avenue of the Americas, New York, NY 10020 *Toll Free Tel:* 800-456-6798 *Fax:* 212-698-7284 *E-mail:* consumer.customerservice@simonandschuster. com *Web Site:* www.simonsays.com, pg 215

Herman, Craig, Simon & Schuster, 1230 Avenue of the Americas, New York, NY 10020 *Tel:* 212-698-7000 *Toll Free Tel:* 800-223-2348 (cust serv); 800-223-2336 (orders) *Toll Free Fax:* 800-943-9831 (orders) *Web Site:* www.simonsays.com, pg 248

Herman, Craig, Simon & Schuster Adult Publishing Group, 1230 Avenue of the Americas, New York, NY 10020 *Tel:* 212-698-7000 *Toll Free Tel:* 800-223-2336 (orders); 800-223-2348 (cust serv), pg 248

Herman, Edith, Warren Communications News, 2115 Ward Ct NW, Washington, DC 20037-1209 *Tel:* 202-872-9200 *Fax:* 202-293-3435 *E-mail:* info@warren-news.com *Web Site:* www.warren-news.com, pg 293

Herman, Jeffrey H, The Jeff Herman Agency LLC, 9 South St, Stockbridge, MA 01262 *Tel:* 413-298-0077 *Fax:* 413-298-8188 *Web Site:* www.jeffherman.com, pg 634

Herman, Rhonda, McFarland & Co Inc Publishers, 960 Hwy 88 W, Jefferson, NC 28640 *Tel:* 336-246-4460 *Toll Free Tel:* 800-253-2187 (orders only) *Fax:* 336-246-5018; 336-246-4403 (orders) *E-mail:* info@ mcfarlandpub.com *Web Site:* www.mcfarlandpub.com, pg 166

Herman, Ronnie Ann, Herman Agency, 350 Central Park W, New York, NY 10025 *Tel:* 212-749-4907 *Fax:* 212-662-5151 *E-mail:* hermanagen@aol.com *Web Site:* www.hermanagencyinc.com, pg 666

Hermance, David, Columbine Communications & Publications Inc, 1293 Elizabeth Barcus Way, Fortuna, CA 95540 *Tel:* 707-726-9200 *Fax:* 707-726-9300 *E-mail:* cocompub@aol.com, pg 65

Hernandez, Prospero, Smithsonian Institution Press, 750 Ninth St NW, Suite 4300, Washington, DC 20560-0950 *Tel:* 202-275-2300 *Fax:* 202-275-2274 *E-mail:* inquiries@sipress.si.edu *Web Site:* www. sipress.si.edu, pg 251

Hernandez, Robert, National Geographic Society, 1145 17 St NW, Washington, DC 20036 *Tel:* 202-857-7000 *Fax:* 202-429-5727 *Web Site:* www.nationalgeographic. com, pg 184

Herner, Susan, Susan Herner Rights Agency Inc, PO Box 57, Pound Ridge, NY 10576 *Tel:* 914-234-2864 *Fax:* 914-234-2866 *E-mail:* sherneragency@optonline. net, pg 634

Herrera, Margot, Workman Publishing Co Inc, 708 Broadway, New York, NY 10003-9555 *Tel:* 212-254-5900 *Toll Free Tel:* 800-722-7202 *Fax:* 212-254-8098 *E-mail:* info@workman.com *Web Site:* www.workman. com, pg 303

Herrin, Deborah, Optical Society of America, 2010 Massachusetts Ave NW, Washington, DC 20036-1023 *Tel:* 202-223-8130 *Fax:* 202-223-1096 *E-mail:* custserv@osa.org *Web Site:* www.osa.org, pg 198

Herrmann, F S, Concourse Press, PO Box 8265, Philadelphia, PA 19101-8265 *Tel:* 610-325-0313 *Fax:* 610-359-1953, pg 66

Hersch, Vallerie, TFH Publications Inc, 61 Third Ave, Neptune City, NJ 07753 *Tel:* 732-988-8400 *Toll Free Tel:* 800-631-2188 *Fax:* 732-988-5466 *E-mail:* info@ tfh.com *Web Site:* www.tfh.com, pg 268

Herscher, Charlotte, Random House Publishing Group, 1745 Broadway, New York, NY 10019 *Toll Free Tel:* 800-200-3552 *Toll Free Fax:* 800-200-3552 *Web Site:* www.randomhouse.com, pg 227

Hersh, Mary Claire, The Society of Midland Authors (SMA), PO Box 10419, Chicago, IL 60610-0419 *Tel:* 773-506-7578 *Fax:* 773-784-5900 *E-mail:* info@ midlandauthors.com *Web Site:* www.midlandauthors. com, pg 700

Hersh, Mary Claire, The Society of Midland Authors Awards, PO Box 10419, Chicago, IL 60610-0419 *Tel:* 773-506-7578 *Fax:* 773-784-5900 *E-mail:* info@ midlandauthors.com *Web Site:* www.midlandauthors. com, pg 806

Hershey, Jennifer, G P Putnam's Sons (Hardcover), 375 Hudson St, New York, NY 10014 *Tel:* 212-366-2000 *E-mail:* online@penguinputnam.com *Web Site:* www. penguin.com, pg 223

Hershon, Robert, Hanging Loose Press, 231 Wyckoff St, Brooklyn, NY 11217 *Tel:* 212-206-8465 *Fax:* 212-243-7499 *E-mail:* print225@aol.com *Web Site:* www. hangingloosepress.com, pg 113

Hertz, Amy, Doubleday Broadway Publishing Group, 1745 Broadway, New York, NY 10019 *Tel:* 212-782-9000 *Toll Free Tel:* 800-223-6834; 800-223-5780 (sales) *Fax:* 212-302-7985 (correspondence); 212-492-9862 (orders), pg 82

Herz, Lucy A, Harlan Davidson Inc/Forum Press Inc, 773 Glenn Ave, Wheeling, IL 60090-6000 *Tel:* 847-541-9720 *Fax:* 847-541-9830 *E-mail:* harlandavidson@harlandavidson.com *Web Site:* www.harlandavidson.com, pg 115

Herz, Suzanne, Doubleday Broadway Publishing Group, 1745 Broadway, New York, NY 10019 *Tel:* 212-782-9000 *Toll Free Tel:* 800-223-6834; 800-223-5780 (sales) *Fax:* 212-302-7985 (correspondence); 212-492-9862 (orders), pg 82

Hess, Barbara, ShipShape Publishing Inc, 12 Pine St, Chatham, NJ 07928 *Tel:* 973-635-3000 *Fax:* 973-635-4363 *E-mail:* ShipShapeBooks@aol.com *Web Site:* www.ShipShapePublishing.com, pg 574

Hess, Charles, South-Western, A Thomson Business, 5191 Natorp Blvd, Mason, OH 45040 *Tel:* 513-229-1000 *Toll Free Tel:* 800-543-0487 *Fax:* 513-229-1025 *Web Site:* www.thomson.com, pg 254

Hess, Diane, Scholastic Trade Division, 557 Broadway, New York, NY 10012 *Tel:* 212-343-6100; 212-343-4685 (export sales) *Fax:* 212-343-4714 (export sales) *Web Site:* www.scholastic.com, pg 242

Hess, Errol, The Sow's Ear Poetry Prize & The Sow's Ear Chapbook Prize, 355 Mount Lebanon Rd, Donalds, SC 29638-9115 *Tel:* 864-379-8061, pg 807

Hess, Lindy, Columbia Publishing Course at Columbia University, 2950 Broadway, MC 3801, New York, NY 10027 *Tel:* 212-854-1898 *Fax:* 212-854-7618 *E-mail:* publishing@jrn.columbia.edu *Web Site:* www. jrn.columbia.edu/publishing, pg 752

Hess, Virginia, Stegner Fellowship, Stanford Creative Writing Program, Mail Code 2087, Stanford, CA 94305-2087 *Tel:* 650-723-2637 *Fax:* 650-723-3679 *Web Site:* www.stanford.edu/dept/english/cw/ fellowship.html, pg 807

Hessel, Carolyn Starman, National Jewish Book Award-Children's Literature, 15 E 26 St, 10th fl, New York, NY 10010-1579 *Tel:* 212-532-4949 (ext 297) *Fax:* 212-481-4174 *E-mail:* jbc@jewishbooks.org *Web Site:* www.jewishbookcouncil.org, pg 791

Hessel, Carolyn Starman, National Jewish Book Award-Children's Picture Book, 15 E 26 St, 10th fl, New York, NY 10010-1579 *Tel:* 212-532-4949 (ext 297) *Fax:* 212-481-4174 *E-mail:* jbc@jewishbooks.org *Web Site:* www.jewishbookcouncil.org, pg 791

Hessel, Carolyn Starman, National Jewish Book Award-Contemporary Jewish Life & Practices, 15 E 26 St, 10th fl, New York, NY 10010-1579 *Tel:* 212-532-4949 (ext 297) *Fax:* 212-481-4174 *E-mail:* jbc@ jewishbooks.org *Web Site:* www.jewishbookcouncil. org, pg 792

Hessel, Carolyn Starman, National Jewish Book Award-Contemporary Jewish Thought & Experience, 15 E 26 St, 10th fl, New York, NY 10010-1579 *Tel:* 212-532-4949 (ext 297) *Fax:* 212-481-4174 *E-mail:* jbc@ jewishbooks.org *Web Site:* www.jewishbookcouncil. org, pg 792

Hessel, Carolyn Starman, National Jewish Book Award-Jewish History, 15 E 26 St, 10th fl, New York, NY 10010-1579 *Tel:* 212-532-4949 (ext 297) *Fax:* 212-481-4174 *E-mail:* jbc@jewishbooks.org *Web Site:* www.jewishbookcouncil.org, pg 792

Hessel, Carolyn Starman, National Jewish Book Award-Scholarship, 15 E 26 St, 10th fl, New York, NY 10010-1579 *Tel:* 212-532-4949 (ext 297) *Fax:* 212-481-4174 *E-mail:* jbc@jewishbooks.org *Web Site:* www.jewishbookcouncil.org, pg 792

Hessel, Carolyn Starman, National Jewish Book Awards, 15 E 26 St, New York, NY 10010-1579 *Tel:* 212-532-4949 (ext 297) *Fax:* 212-481-4174 *E-mail:* jbc@ jewishbooks.org *Web Site:* www.jewishbookcouncil. org, pg 792

Hester, M L, Avisson Press Inc, 3007 Taliaferro Rd, Greensboro, NC 27408 *Tel:* 336-288-6989 *Fax:* 336-288-6989 *E-mail:* avisson4@aol.com, pg 29

Hetrick, J Thomas, Pocol Press, 6023 Pocol Dr, Clifton, VA 20124-1333 *Tel:* 703-830-5862 *E-mail:* chrisandtom@erols.com *Web Site:* www. pocolpress.com, pg 215

Hettler, Kurt, Oxford University Press, Inc, 198 Madison Ave, New York, NY 10016-4314 *Tel:* 212-726-6000 *Toll Free Tel:* 800-451-7556 (orders) *Web Site:* www. oup.com/us, pg 200

Hewett, Miles M, Empire Press Media/Avant-Guide, 444 Madison Ave, 35th fl, New York, NY 10122 *Tel:* 212-563-1003 *Fax:* 212-536-2419 *E-mail:* info@avantguide.com; editor@avantguide.com *Web Site:* www.avantguide.com, pg 90

Hewitt, Heather, Los Angeles Literary Associates, 6324 Tahoe Dr, Los Angeles, CA 90068-1654 *Tel:* 323-464-6444 *Fax:* 323-464-6444, pg 641

Heyden, Eric, Thomas Nelson Inc, 501 Nelson Place, Nashville, TN 37214 *Tel:* 615-889-9000 *Toll Free Tel:* 800-251-4000 *Fax:* 615-902-1610 *E-mail:* publicity@thomasnelson.com *Web Site:* www. thomasnelson.com, pg 269

Heywood, Leslie, Binghamton University Writing Program, c/o Dept of English, PO Box 6000, Binghamton, NY 13902-6000 *Tel:* 607-777-2168 *Fax:* 607-777-2408, pg 751

Hibbert, Edward, Donadio & Olson Inc Literary Representatives, 121 W 27 St, Suite 704, New York, NY 10001 *Tel:* 212-691-8077 *Fax:* 212-633-2837 *E-mail:* mail@donadio.com, pg 628

Hickey, Adrienne, AMACOM Books, 1601 Broadway, New York, NY 10019-7406 *Tel:* 212-586-8100; 518-891-5510 (orders) *Toll Free Tel:* 800-262-9699 (cust serv) *Fax:* 212-903-8168; 518-891-2372 (orders) *Web Site:* www.amanet.org, pg 10

Hicks, Joe, Smart Luck Publishers, PO Box 81770, Las Vegas, NV 89180-1770 *Tel:* 702-365-1818 *Toll Free Tel:* 800-945-4245 *Fax:* 850-937-6999 *Toll Free Fax:* 800-876-4245 *E-mail:* books@smartluck.com *Web Site:* www.smartluck.com, pg 574

Hicks, Kim, Workman Publishing Co Inc, 708 Broadway, New York, NY 10003-9555 *Tel:* 212-254-5900 *Toll Free Tel:* 800-722-7202 *Fax:* 212-254-8098 *E-mail:* info@workman.com *Web Site:* www.workman. com, pg 303

Hicks, Patricia, Peradam Press, PO Box 6, North San Juan, CA 95960-0006 *Tel:* 530-292-4266 *Toll Free Tel:* 800-241-8689 *Fax:* 530-292-4266 *Toll Free Fax:* 800-241-8689 *E-mail:* peradam@earthlink.net, pg 210

Hicks, Tyler G, International Wealth Success Inc, PO Box 186, Merrick, NY 11566-0186 *Tel:* 516-766-5850 *Toll Free Tel:* 800-323-0548 *Fax:* 516-766-5919 *E-mail:* admin@iwsmoney.com *Web Site:* www. iwsmoney.com, pg 138

Hicks, William, River City Publishing, LLC, 1719 Mulberry St, Montgomery, AL 36106 *Tel:* 334-265-6753 *Toll Free Tel:* 877-408-7078 *Fax:* 334-265-8880 *E-mail:* web@rivercitypublishing.com *Web Site:* www.rivercitypublishing.com, pg 232

Hietala, Johnna, Jody Rein Books Inc, 7741 S Ash Ct, Centennial, CO 80122 *Tel:* 303-694-4430 *Fax:* 303-694-0687 *Web Site:* www.jodyreinbooks.com, pg 650

Higgins, Diane, St Martin's Press Trade Division, 175 Fifth Ave, New York, NY 10010 *E-mail:* firstname.lastname@stmartins.com *Web Site:* www.stmartins.com; www.minotaurbooks.com, pg 239

Higgins-Jacob, Coleen, John Simon Guggenheim Memorial Foundation, 90 Park Ave, New York, NY 10016 *Tel:* 212-687-4470 *Fax:* 212-697-3248 *E-mail:* fellowships@gf.org *Web Site:* www.gf.org, pg 705

Higgs, Lisa, The Gislason Agency, 219 SE Main St, Suite 506, Minneapolis, MN 55414 *Tel:* 612-331-8033 *Fax:* 612-331-8115 *E-mail:* gislasonbj@aol.com *Web Site:* www.TheGislasonAgency.com, pg 632

Higgs, Stephanie, Random House Publishing Group, 1745 Broadway, New York, NY 10019 *Toll Free Tel:* 800-200-3552 *Toll Free Fax:* 800-200-3552 *Web Site:* www.randomhouse.com, pg 227

Highfill, David, G P Putnam's Sons (Hardcover), 375 Hudson St, New York, NY 10014 *Tel:* 212-366-2000 *E-mail:* online@penguinputnam.com *Web Site:* www.penguin.com, pg 223

Highsmith, Bonnie, Waveland Press Inc, 4180 IL Rte 83, Suite 101, Long Grove, IL 60047-9580 *Tel:* 847-634-0081 *Fax:* 847-634-9501 *E-mail:* info@waveland.com *Web Site:* www.waveland.com, pg 294

Hilario, Kim, Faber & Faber Inc, 19 Union Sq W, New York, NY 10003 *Tel:* 212-741-6900 *Toll Free Tel:* 888-330-8477 *Fax:* 212-633-9385 *Web Site:* www.fsgbooks.com/faberandfaber.htm, pg 93

Hildebrandt, Walter, University of Calgary Press, 2500 University Dr NW, Calgary, AB T2N 1N4, Canada *Tel:* 403-220-7578 *Fax:* 403-282-0085 *E-mail:* whildebr@ucalgary.ca *Web Site:* www.uofcpress.com, pg 565

Hildreth, Mary Anne, Tower Publishing Co, 588 Saco Rd, Standish, ME 04084 *Tel:* 207-642-5400 *Toll Free Tel:* 800-969-8693 *Fax:* 207-642-5463 *E-mail:* info@towerpub.com *Web Site:* www.towerpub.com, pg 273

Hildreth, Shirley, Muse Imagery LLC, 9811 W Charleston Blvd, Suite 2390, Las Vegas, NV 89117-7519 *Tel:* 702-233-5910 *Fax:* 702-233-1762 *E-mail:* publisher@museimagery.com *Web Site:* www.museimagery.com, pg 572

Hiles, Wendy, IEE, c/o Inspec, 379 Thornall St, Edison, NJ 08837-2225 *Tel:* 732-321-5575 *Fax:* 732-321-5702 *E-mail:* iee@inspecinc.com *Web Site:* www.iee.org/publishing, pg 130

Hilferty, Daniel, Mason Crest Publishers, 370 Reed Rd, Suite 302, Broomall, PA 19008 *Tel:* 610-543-6200 *Toll Free Tel:* 866-MCP-BOOK (627-2665) *Fax:* 610-543-3878 *Web Site:* www.masoncrest.com, pg 165

Hilgers, Thomas, University of Hawaii, Bilger Hall, Rm 104, 2545 McCarthy Mall, Honolulu, HI 96822 *Tel:* 808-956-6660 *Fax:* 808-956-9170 *E-mail:* mwp@hawaii.edu *Web Site:* www.hawaii.edu/mwp, pg 755

Hill, Bob, The National Society of Newspaper Columnists (NSNC), Courier-Journal Newspaper, 525 W Broadway, Louisville, KY 40201-7431 *Tel:* 502-582-4011 *Fax:* 502-582-4665 *Web Site:* www.courierjournal.com, pg 745

Hill, Chip, Total Power Publishing, 4274 Bay View Dr, Fernandina Beach, FL 32035 *Tel:* 904-321-1169 *Fax:* 904-321-2872 *E-mail:* stinger20007399@aol.com, pg 273

Hill, David, Kregel Publications, 733 Wealthy St SE, Grand Rapids, MI 49503-5553 *Tel:* 616-451-4775 *Toll Free Tel:* 800-733-2607 *Fax:* 616-451-9330 *E-mail:* kregelbooks@kregel.com *Web Site:* www.kregelpublications.com, pg 147

Hill, Frances, Emerging Playwright Award, 17 E 47 St, New York, NY 10017 *Tel:* 212-421-1380 *Fax:* 212-421-1387 *E-mail:* urbanstage@aol.com *Web Site:* www.urbanstages.org, pg 772

Hill, Frederick, Frederick Hill Bonnie Nadell Literary Agency, 1842 Union St, San Francisco, CA 94123 *Tel:* 415-921-2910 *Fax:* 415-921-2802, pg 634

Hill, Janet, Doubleday Broadway Publishing Group, 1745 Broadway, New York, NY 10019 *Tel:* 212-782-9000 *Toll Free Tel:* 800-223-6834; 800-223-5780 (sales) *Tel:* 212-302-7985 (correspondence); 212-492-9862 (orders), pg 82

Hill, Joann, Clarion Books, 215 Park Ave S, New York, NY 10003 *Tel:* 212-420-5800 *Toll Free Tel:* 800-225-3362 (orders) *Fax:* 212-420-5855 *Web Site:* www.clarion.com, pg 62

Hill, Joanna V, Templeton Foundation Press, 5 Radnor Corporate Ctr, Suite 120, 100 Matsonford Rd, Radnor, PA 19087 *Tel:* 610-971-2670 *Toll Free Tel:* 800-561-3367 *Fax:* 610-971-2672 *E-mail:* tfp@templetonpress.org *Web Site:* www.templetonpress.org, pg 266

Hill, Joe, Total Power Publishing, 4274 Bay View Dr, Fernandina Beach, FL 32035 *Tel:* 904-321-1169 *Fax:* 904-321-2872 *E-mail:* stinger20007399@aol.com, pg 273

Hill, Karen, Elm Street Publishing Services Inc, 828 N Elm St, Hinsdale, IL 60521 *Tel:* 630-789-2102 *Fax:* 630-789-2105 *E-mail:* esps@elmst.com *Web Site:* www.elmst.com, pg 598

Hill, Michael, American Association of University Women Award for Juvenile Literature, 4610 Mail Service Center, Raleigh, NC 27699-4610 *Tel:* 919-807-7290 *Fax:* 919-733-8807, pg 759

Hill, Michael, The Ragan Old North State Cup for Nonfiction, 4610 Mail Service Center, Raleigh, NC 27699-4610 *Tel:* 919-807-7290 *Fax:* 919-733-8807, pg 801

Hill, Michael, Sir Walter Raleigh Award for Fiction, 4610 Mail Service Center, Raleigh, NC 27699-4610 *Tel:* 919-807-7290 *Fax:* 919-733-8807, pg 801

Hill, Michael, Roanoke-Chowan Award for Poetry, 4610 Mail Service Center, Raleigh, NC 27699-4610 *Tel:* 919-807-7290 *Fax:* 919-733-8807, pg 802

Hill, Pam, Carson-Dellosa Publishing Co Inc, PO Box 35665, Greensboro, NC 27425-5665 *Tel:* 336-632-0084 *Fax:* 336-632-0087 *Web Site:* www.carsondellosa.com, pg 54

Hill, Richard, AHA Press, One N Franklin, Suite 2800, Chicago, IL 60606 *Tel:* 312-893-6800 *Fax:* 312-422-4500 *Web Site:* www.hospitalconnect.com; www.ahaonlinestore.com (orders), pg 7

Hill, Richard, American Society for Information Science & Technology (ASIS), 1320 Fenwick Lane, Suite 510, Silver Spring, MD 20910 *Tel:* 301-495-0900 *Fax:* 301-495-0810 *E-mail:* asis@asis.org *Web Site:* www.asis.org, pg 677

Hill, Rick, Health Forum Inc, One N Franklin St, 28th fl, Chicago, IL 60606 *Tel:* 312-893-6884 *Toll Free Tel:* 800-242-2626 *Fax:* 312-422-4600 *Web Site:* www.ahaonlinestore.com, pg 119

Hill, Stephen W, Kiva Publishing Inc, 21731 E Buckskin Dr, Walnut, CA 91789 *Tel:* 909-595-6833 *Toll Free Tel:* 800-634-5482 *Fax:* 909-860-5424 *E-mail:* kivapub@aol.com *Web Site:* www.kivapub.com, pg 146

Hill, Van, Celebrity Press, 1501 County Hospital Rd, Nashville, TN 37218 *Tel:* 615-254-2450 *Toll Free Tel:* 800-327-5113 *Fax:* 615-254-2408, pg 56

Hillebrand, Eileen, Scholastic Paperbacks, Teaching Resources & Reading Counts, 557 Broadway, New York, NY 10012-3999 *Tel:* 212-965-7241 *Fax:* 212-965-7487 *Web Site:* www.scholastic.com, pg 242

Hilliard, Elbert, McLemore Prize, PO Box 571, Jackson, MS 39205-0571 *Tel:* 601-576-6850 *Fax:* 601-576-6975 *E-mail:* mhs@mdah.state.ms.us *Web Site:* www.mdah.state.ms.us, pg 789

Hillman, Dennis, Kregel Publications, 733 Wealthy St SE, Grand Rapids, MI 49503-5553 *Tel:* 616-451-4775 *Toll Free Tel:* 800-733-2607 *Fax:* 616-451-9330 *E-mail:* kregelbooks@kregel.com *Web Site:* www.kregelpublications.com, pg 147

Hillman, Jesse, P & R Publishing Co, 1102 Marble Hill Rd, Phillipsburg, NJ 08865 *Tel:* 908-454-0505 *Toll Free Tel:* 800-631-0094 *Fax:* 908-859-2390 *E-mail:* per@prpbooks.com *Web Site:* prpbooks.com, pg 201

Hills, Fred W, Free Press, 1230 Avenue of the Americas, New York, NY 10020 *Tel:* 212-698-7000 *Toll Free Tel:* 800-223-2345 (cust serv); 800-223-2336 (orders); 888-866-6631 (fulfillment), pg 100

Hillsman, Sally T, American Sociological Association (ASA), 1307 New York Ave NW, Suite 700, Washington, DC 20005-4701 *Tel:* 202-383-9005 *Fax:* 202-638-0882 *E-mail:* executive.office@asanet.org *Web Site:* www.asanet.org, pg 678

Hilzen, Natalie, American Foundation for the Blind (AFB Press), 11 Penn Plaza, Suite 300, New York, NY 10001 *Tel:* 212-502-7600 *Toll Free Tel:* 800-232-3044 (orders) *Fax:* 212-502-7777 *E-mail:* afbinfo@afb.net *Web Site:* www.afb.org, pg 13

Himmel, Eric, Harry N Abrams Inc, 100 Fifth Ave, New York, NY 10011 *Tel:* 212-206-7715 *Toll Free Tel:* 800-345-1359 *Fax:* 212-645-8437 *E-mail:* webmaster@abramsbooks.com *Web Site:* www.abramsbooks.com, pg 3

Himmler, Robert C, Custom Editorial Productions Inc (CEP), 546 W Liberty St, Cincinnati, OH 45214 *Tel:* 513-723-1100 *Fax:* 513-723-1103 *E-mail:* cep@customeditorial.com *Web Site:* www.customeditorial.com, pg 596

Hinckley, Joseph A, Brown Publishing Network Inc, 95 Sawyer Rd, Waltham, MA 02453 *Tel:* 781-237-7567 *Fax:* 781-237-8874 *Web Site:* www.brownpubnet.com, pg 593

Hindmar, James, American Film Institute (AFI), 2021 N Western Ave, Los Angeles, CA 90027 *Tel:* 323-856-7600 *Toll Free Tel:* 800-774-4234 (memberships) *Fax:* 323-467-4578 *E-mail:* info@afi.com *Web Site:* www.afi.com, pg 676

Hines, Thomas M, Summa Publications, PO Box 660725, Birmingham, AL 35266-0725 *Tel:* 205-822-0463 *Fax:* 205-822-0463, pg 261

Hiney, Harlan, Golden West Books, 525 N Electric Ave, Alhambra, CA 91801 *Tel:* 626-458-8148 *Fax:* 626-458-8148, pg 106

Hiniker, Mary, Institute of Continuing Legal Education, 1020 Greene St, Ann Arbor, MI 48109-1444 *Tel:* 734-764-0533 *Toll Free Tel:* 877-229-4350 *Fax:* 734-763-2412 *Toll Free Fax:* 877-229-4351 *E-mail:* icle@umich.edu *Web Site:* www.icle.org/, pg 135

Hinkel, Nancy, Random House Children's Books, 1745 Broadway, New York, NY 10019 *Tel:* 212-782-9000 *Toll Free Tel:* 800-200-3552 *Fax:* 212-782-9452 *Web Site:* www.randomhouse.com/kids, pg 226

Hinkelman, Edward G, World Trade Press, 1450 Grant Ave, Suite 204, Novato, CA 94945 *Tel:* 415-898-1124 *Toll Free Tel:* 800-833-8586 *Fax:* 415-898-1080 *E-mail:* admin@worldtradepress.com *Web Site:* www.worldtradepress.com, pg 304

Hinkley, John, Moody Press, 820 N La Salle Blvd, Chicago, IL 60610 *Tel:* 312-329-2111 *Toll Free Tel:* 800-678-8812 *Fax:* 312-329-2019 *Web Site:* www.moodypress.org, pg 177

Hinojosa-Smith, Rolando, University of Texas at Austin, Creative Writing Program, Dept of English, One University Sta, B5000, Austin, TX 78712-1164 *Tel:* 512-475-6356 *Fax:* 512-471-2898 *Web Site:* www.en.utexas.edu/grad/crwconc.html, pg 756

Hintz, Roxanne, Samuel French Inc, 45 W 25 St, New York, NY 10010-2751 *Tel:* 212-206-8990 *Fax:* 212-206-1429 *E-mail:* samuelfrench@earthlink.net *Web Site:* www.samuelfrench.com, pg 101

Hipkins, Jason, Cardweb.com Inc, 10 N Jefferson St, Suite 301, Frederick, MD 21701 *Tel:* 301-631-9100 *Fax:* 301-631-9112 *E-mail:* cardservices@cardweb. com; cardstaff@cardweb.com *Web Site:* www.cardweb. com, pg 53

Hirashima, Steve, University of Hawaii Press, 2840 Kolowalu St, Honolulu, HI 96822 *Tel:* 808-956-8255 *Toll Free Tel:* 888-847-7377 *Fax:* 808-988-6052 *Toll Free Fax:* 800-650-7811 *E-mail:* uhpbooks@hawaii. edu *Web Site:* www.uhpress.hawaii.edu, pg 281

Hirsch, Cheryl, Basic Health Publications Inc, 8200 Boulevard E, Suite 25-G, North Bergen, NJ 07047 *Tel:* 201-868-8336 *Toll Free Tel:* 800-575-8890 *Fax:* 201-868-8335, pg 33

Hirsch, Ed, Frankel & Associates, 5120 Wright Terr, Skokie, IL 60077 *Tel:* 847-674-8417, pg 669

Hirsch, Edward, John Simon Guggenheim Memorial Foundation, 90 Park Ave, New York, NY 10016 *Tel:* 212-687-4470 *Fax:* 212-697-3248 *E-mail:* fellowships@gf.org *Web Site:* www.gf.org, pg 705

Hirsch, Robert F, Avalon Books, 160 Madison Ave, 5th fl, New York, NY 10016 *Tel:* 212-598-0222 *Fax:* 212-979-1862 *E-mail:* avalon@avalonbooks.com *Web Site:* www.avalonbooks.com, pg 28

Hirsch, Robert F, Thomas Bouregy & Co Inc, 160 Madison Ave, New York, NY 10016 *Tel:* 212-598-0222 *Fax:* 212-979-1862 *E-mail:* customerservice@ avalonbooks.com *Web Site:* avalonbooks.com, pg 44

Hirsch, Tom, Basic Health Publications Inc, 8200 Boulevard E, Suite 25-G, North Bergen, NJ 07047 *Tel:* 201-868-8336 *Toll Free Tel:* 800-575-8890 *Fax:* 201-868-8335, pg 33

Hirschberg, Henry, The McGraw-Hill Companies Inc, 1221 Avenue of the Americas, 50th fl, New York, NY 10020 *Tel:* 212-512-2000 *E-mail:* webmaster@ mcgraw-hill.com *Web Site:* www.mcgraw-hill.com, pg 167

Hirschberg, Henry, McGraw-Hill Education, 2 Penn Plaza, New York, NY 10121 *Tel:* 212-904-2000 *E-mail:* customer.service@mcgraw-hill.com *Web Site:* www.mheducation.com; www.mheducation. com/custserv.html, pg 167

Hirschfeld, Amy, Brill Academic Publishers Inc, 112 Water St, Suite 601, Boston, MA 02109 *Tel:* 617-263-2323 *Toll Free Tel:* 800-962-4406 *Fax:* 617-263-2324 *E-mail:* cs@brillusa.com *Web Site:* www.brill.nl, pg 47

Hirst, John, B C Decker Inc, 20 Hughson St S, 10th fl, Hamilton, ON L8N 2A1, Canada *Tel:* 905-522-7017 *Toll Free Tel:* 800-568-7281 *Fax:* 905-522-7839 *E-mail:* info@bcdecker.com *Web Site:* www.bcdecker. com, pg 542

Hisbrook, David, Xlibris Corp, 436 Walnut St, 11th fl, The Independence Bldg, Philadelphia, PA 19106 *Tel:* 215-923-4686 *Toll Free Tel:* 888-795-4274 *Fax:* 215-923-4685 *E-mail:* info@xlibris.com *Web Site:* www.xlibris.com, pg 305

Hitchcock, Barbara W, Monogram Aviation Publications, PO Box 223, Sturbridge, MA 01566 *Tel:* 508-347-5574 *Fax:* 508-347-5772 *E-mail:* monogram@ meganet.net *Web Site:* www.monogramaviation.com, pg 177

Hitchcock, Joanna, University of Texas Press, PO Box 7819, Austin, TX 78713-7819 *Tel:* 512-471-7233 *Fax:* 512-232-7178 *E-mail:* utpress@uts.cc.utexas.edu *Web Site:* www.utexas.edu/utpress, pg 267

Hitchcock, Thomas H, Monogram Aviation Publications, PO Box 223, Sturbridge, MA 01566 *Tel:* 508-347-5574 *Fax:* 508-347-5772 *E-mail:* monogram@ meganet.net *Web Site:* www.monogramaviation.com, pg 177

Hivnor, Margaret, Association of American University Presses, 1427 E 60 St, Chicago, IL 60637 *Tel:* 773-702-7700; 773-702-7600 *Toll Free Tel:* 800-621-2736 (orders) *Fax:* 773-702-9756 (sales); 773-660-2235 (orders); 773-702-2708 *E-mail:* general@press. uchicago.edu *Web Site:* www.press.uchicago.edu, pg 26

Hjelmgaard, Kim, Justin, Charles & Co, Publishers, 20 Park Plaza, Suite 909, Boston, MA 02116 *Tel:* 617-426-4406 *Fax:* 617-426-4408 *E-mail:* info@ justincharlesbooks.com *Web Site:* www. justincharlesbooks.com, pg 143

Hoagland, Michael, American Forest & Paper Association, 1111 19 St NW, Suite 800, Washington, DC 20036 *Tel:* 202-463-2700 *Toll Free Tel:* 800-878-8878 *Fax:* 202-463-4703 *E-mail:* info@afandpa.org *Web Site:* www.afandpa.org, pg 676

Hoard, Trish, Shoemaker & Hoard, Publishers, 3704 Macomb St NW, Suite 4, Washington, DC 20016 *Tel:* 202-364-4464 *Fax:* 202-364-4484 *Web Site:* www. shoemakerhoard.com, pg 246

Hobbs, Neda, C A P Publishing & Literary Co LLC, 17471 Jefferson Davis Hwy, Dumfries, VA 22026 *Tel:* 703-441-3500 *Fax:* 301-499-8844, pg 50

Hoce, Larry, McDougal Littell, 909 Davis St, Evanston, IL 60201 *Tel:* 847-869-2300 *Toll Free Tel:* 800-462-6595 (orders) *Toll Free Fax:* 888-872-8380 *Web Site:* www.mcdougallittell.com, pg 166

Hocherman, Riva, Henry Holt and Company, LLC, 115 W 18 St, New York, NY 10011 *Tel:* 212-886-9200 *Toll Free Tel:* 888-330-8477 (orders) *Fax:* 212-633-0748 *E-mail:* publicity@hholt.com *Web Site:* www. henryholt.com, pg 124

Hochman, Gail, Association of Authors' Representatives Inc (AAR), PO Box 237201, Ansonia Sta, New York, NY 10023 *E-mail:* aarinc@mindspring.com *Web Site:* www.aar-online.org, pg 679

Hochman, Gail, Brandt & Hochman Literary Agents Inc, 1501 Broadway, Suite 2310, New York, NY 10036 *Tel:* 212-840-5760 *Fax:* 212-840-5776, pg 622

Hochmann, John L, John L Hochmann Books, 320 E 58 St, New York, NY 10022 *Tel:* 212-319-0505, pg 635

Hock, Zarina M, National Council of Teachers of English (NCTE), 1111 W Kenyon Rd, Urbana, IL 61801-1096 *Tel:* 217-328-3870 *Toll Free Tel:* 800-369-6283; 877-369-6283 (cust serv) *Fax:* 217-328-0977 *E-mail:* orders@ncte.org *Web Site:* www.ncte.org, pg 183

Hodapp, Angie, Nelson Literary Agency LLC, 1020 15 St, Suite 26L, Denver, CO 80202 *Tel:* 303-463-5301 *Fax:* 720-384-0761 *E-mail:* query@nelsonagency.com *Web Site:* nelsonagency.com, pg 645

Hodge, Richard C, Institute of Police Technology & Management, University Ctr, 12000 Alumni Dr, Jacksonville, FL 32224-2678 *Tel:* 904-620-4786 *Fax:* 904-620-2453, pg 135

Hodges, Michael, LaurelTech Integrated Publishing Solutions, 1750 Elm St, Suite 201, Manchester, NH 03104 *Tel:* 603-606-5800 *Fax:* 603-606-5838 *E-mail:* sales@laureltech.com *Web Site:* www. laureltech.com, pg 604

Hodgin, Jere Lee, Mill Mountain Theatre, Center in the Square, 2nd fl, One Market Sq, Roanoke, VA 24011-1437 *Tel:* 540-342-5771 *Fax:* 540-342-5745 *E-mail:* outreach@millmountain.org *Web Site:* www. millmountain.org, pg 789

Hodgkins, Priscilla, Bennington Writing Seminars, One College Dr, Bennington, VT 05201 *Tel:* 802-440-4452 *Fax:* 802-440-4453 *E-mail:* writing@bennington.edu *Web Site:* www.bennington.edu/graduateprogram, pg 742

Hodgman, George, Henry Holt and Company, LLC, 115 W 18 St, New York, NY 10011 *Tel:* 212-886-9200 *Toll Free Tel:* 888-330-8477 (orders) *Fax:* 212-633-0748 *E-mail:* publicity@hholt.com *Web Site:* www. henryholt.com, pg 124

Hodgman, Sandy, Robbins Office Inc, 405 Park Ave, 9th fl, New York, NY 10022 *Tel:* 212-223-0720 *Fax:* 212-223-2535, pg 652

Hoefling, Pat, University of Illinois Press, 1325 S Oak, Champaign, IL 61820-6903 *Tel:* 217-333-0950; 212-577-5487 *Fax:* 217-244-8082; 410-516-6969 (orders) *E-mail:* uipress@uillinois.edu; journals@uillinois.edu *Web Site:* www.press.uillinois.edu, pg 282

Hoehner, Jane, Wayne State University Press, Leonard N Simons Bldg, 4809 Woodward Ave, Detroit, MI 48201-1309 *Tel:* 313-577-4600 *Toll Free Tel:* 800-978-7323 *Fax:* 313-577-6131, pg 294

Hoerenz, Tina, The New York Public Library Helen Bernstein Book Award for Excellence in Journalism, Publications Office, Fifth Ave & 42 St, New York, NY 10018 *Tel:* 212-512-0202 *Fax:* 212-704-8620 *E-mail:* kvanwestering@nypl.org *Web Site:* www.nypl. org, pg 794

Hofeldt, Sara E, Tapestry Press Ltd, 19 Nashoba Rd, Littleton, MA 01460 *Tel:* 978-486-0200 *Toll Free Tel:* 800-535-2007 *Fax:* 978-486-0244 *E-mail:* publish@tapestrypress.com *Web Site:* www. tapestrypress.com, pg 264

Hoff, Jean, Pontifical Institute of Mediaeval Studies, Dept of Publications, 59 Queens Park Crescent E, Toronto, ON M5S 2C4, Canada *Tel:* 416-926-7142 *Fax:* 416-926-7292 *E-mail:* pontifex@chass.utoronto. ca *Web Site:* www.pims.ca, pg 558

Hoffbuhr, Jack W, American Water Works Association, 6666 W Quincy Ave, Denver, CO 80235 *Tel:* 303-794-7711 *Toll Free Tel:* 800-926-7337 *Fax:* 303-347-0804 *Web Site:* www.awwa.org, pg 18

Hoffman, Antonia, Authors Marketing Services Ltd, 2336 Bloor St W, Box 84668, Toronto, ON M6S 4Z7, Canada *Tel:* 416-763-8797 *Fax:* 416-763-1504, pg 620

Hoffman, Barry, Gauntlet Press, 5307 Arroyo St, Colorado Springs, CO 80922 *Tel:* 719-591-5566 *Fax:* 719-591-6676 *E-mail:* info@gauntletpress.com *Web Site:* www.gauntletpress.com, pg 103

Hoffman, Beth, The Foundation for Economic Education Inc, 30 S Broadway, Irvington-on-Hudson, NY 10533 *Tel:* 914-591-7230 *Toll Free Tel:* 800-960-4FEE (960-4333) *Fax:* 914-591-8910 *E-mail:* fee@fee.org *Web Site:* www.fee.org, pg 99

Hoffman, Carrie, Mississippi Review/University of Southern Mississippi, Center for Writers, Box 5144 USM, Hattiesburg, MS 39406 *Tel:* 601-266-5600 *Fax:* 601-266-5757 *E-mail:* rief@mississippireview. com *Web Site:* www.mississippireview.com; www. centerforwriters.com, pg 753

Hoffman, Hillary, Merriam-Webster Inc, 47 Federal St, Springfield, MA 01102 *Tel:* 413-734-3134 *Toll Free Tel:* 800-828-1880 (orders & cust serv) *Fax:* 413-731-5979 *E-mail:* merriam_webster@merriam-webster.com *Web Site:* www.merriam-webster.com, pg 172

Hoffman, Joan, School Zone Publishing Co, 1819 Industrial Dr, Grand Haven, MI 49417 *Tel:* 616-846-5030 *Toll Free Tel:* 800-253-0564 *Fax:* 616-846-6181 *Web Site:* www.schoolzone.com, pg 243

Hoffman, Larry, Authors Marketing Services Ltd, 2336 Bloor St W, Box 84668, Toronto, ON M6S 4Z7, Canada *Tel:* 416-763-8797 *Fax:* 416-763-1504, pg 620

Hoffman, Mary, Oakstone Medical Publishing, 6801 Cahaba Valley Rd, Birmingham, AL 35242 *Tel:* 205-991-5188 *Toll Free Tel:* 800-952-0690 *Fax:* 205-995-4656 *E-mail:* service@oakstonemedical.com *Web Site:* www.oakstonemedical.com, pg 195

Hoffman, Mitch, Dutton, 375 Hudson St, New York, NY 10014 *Tel:* 212-366-2000 *Fax:* 212-366-2262 *E-mail:* online@penguinputnam.com *Web Site:* www. penguin.com, pg 85

Hoffman, Nina, National Geographic Books, 1145 17 St NW, Washington, DC 20036 *Tel:* 202-857-7000 *Fax:* 202-857-7670 *Web Site:* www. nationalgeographics.com, pg 183

Hoffman, Nina, National Geographic Society, 1145 17 St NW, Washington, DC 20036 *Tel:* 202-857-7000 *Fax:* 202-429-5727 *Web Site:* www.nationalgeographic. com, pg 184

Hoffman, Peter, RAND Corp, 1776 Main St, Santa Monica, CA 90407 *Tel:* 310-393-0411 *Fax:* 310-451-6996 *E-mail:* jane_ryan@rand.org *Web Site:* www. rand.org, pg 225

Hoffman, Randy, Captus Press Inc, 1600 Steeles Ave W, Units 14-15, Concord, ON L4K 4M2, Canada *Tel:* 416-736-5537 *Fax:* 416-736-5793 *E-mail:* info@ captus.com *Web Site:* www.captus.com, pg 539

Hoffman, Ronald, Jamestown Prize, 109 Cary St, Williamsburg, VA 23185 *Tel:* 757-221-1114 *Fax:* 757-221-1047 *E-mail:* ieahc1@wm.edu *Web Site:* www. wm.edu/oieahc, pg 781

Hoffman, Ronald, Omohundro Institute of Early American History & Culture, 109 Cary St, Williamsburg, VA 23185 *Tel:* 757-221-1114 *Fax:* 757-221-1047 *E-mail:* ieahc1@wm.edu *Web Site:* www. wm.edu/oieahc, pg 197

Hoffman, Scott, PMA Literary & Film Management Inc, PO Box 1817, Old Chelsea Sta, New York, NY 10011 *Tel:* 212-929-1222 *Fax:* 212-206-0238 *E-mail:* pmalitfilm@aol.com *Web Site:* www. pmalitfilm.com, pg 648

Hoffman, Stuart A, Star Publishing Co, 940 Emmett Ave, Belmont, CA 94002 *Tel:* 650-591-3505 *Fax:* 650-591-3898 *E-mail:* mail@starpublishing.com *Web Site:* www.starpublishing.com, pg 258

Hoffnagle, Jerry, Rizzoli International Publications Inc, 300 Park Ave S, 3rd fl, New York, NY 10010-5399 *Tel:* 212-387-3400 *Toll Free Tel:* 800-522-6657 (orders only) *Fax:* 212-387-3535, pg 233

Hogan, Erin, Association of American University Presses, 1427 E 60 St, Chicago, IL 60637 *Tel:* 773-702-7700; 773-702-7600 *Toll Free Tel:* 800-621-2736 (orders) *Fax:* 773-702-9756 (sales); 773-660-2235 (orders); 773-702-2708 *E-mail:* general@press. uchicago.edu *Web Site:* www.press.uchicago.edu, pg 26

Hogan, Florence, United States Pharmacopeia, 12601 Twinbrook Pkwy, Rockville, MD 20852 *Tel:* 301-881-0666 *Toll Free Tel:* 800-227-8772 *Fax:* 301-816-8148; 301-816-8236 (mktg) *E-mail:* marketing@usp.org *Web Site:* www.usp.org, pg 279

Hogan, Mary S, Plexus Publishing Inc, 143 Old Marlton Pike, Medford, NJ 08055 *Tel:* 609-654-6500 *Fax:* 609-654-4309 *E-mail:* info@plexuspublishing.com *Web Site:* www.plexuspublishing.com, pg 214

Hogan, Thomas Jr, Information Today, Inc, 143 Old Marlton Pike, Medford, NJ 08055-8750 *Tel:* 609-654-6266 *Toll Free Tel:* 800-300-9868 (cust serv) *Fax:* 609-654-4309 *E-mail:* custserv@infotoday.com *Web Site:* www.infotoday.com, pg 133

Hogan, Thomas Jr, Plexus Publishing Inc, 143 Old Marlton Pike, Medford, NJ 08055 *Tel:* 609-654-6500 *Fax:* 609-654-4309 *E-mail:* info@plexuspublishing. com *Web Site:* www.plexuspublishing.com, pg 214

Hogan, Thomas, Plexus Publishing Inc, 143 Old Marlton Pike, Medford, NJ 08055 *Tel:* 609-654-6500 *Fax:* 609-654-4309 *E-mail:* info@plexuspublishing.com *Web Site:* www.plexuspublishing.com, pg 214

Hogan, Thomas H, Information Today, Inc, 143 Old Marlton Pike, Medford, NJ 08055-8750 *Tel:* 609-654-6266 *Toll Free Tel:* 800-300-9868 (cust serv) *Fax:* 609-654-4309 *E-mail:* custserv@infotoday.com *Web Site:* www.infotoday.com, pg 133

Hoge, Steve, W W Norton & Company Inc, 500 Fifth Ave, New York, NY 10110-0017 *Tel:* 212-354-5500 *Toll Free Tel:* 800-233-4830 (orders & cust serv) *Fax:* 212-869-0856 *Toll Free Fax:* 800-458-6515 *Web Site:* www.wwnorton.com, pg 194

Hogenson, Barbara, The Barbara Hogenson Agency Inc, 165 West End Ave, Suite 19-C, New York, NY 10023 *Tel:* 212-874-8084 *Fax:* 212-362-3011 *E-mail:* bhogenson@aol.com, pg 635

Hoggan, Kathy D, K H Marketing Communications, 16205 NE Sixth St, Bellevue, WA 98008 *Tel:* 425-562-0417 *Fax:* 425-746-4406, pg 602

Hoggard, Jim, Brazo Bookstore (Houston Award), 3700 Mockingbird Lane, Dallas, TX 75205 *Tel:* 214-528-2655 *Fax:* 512-245-7462 *Web Site:* www.stedwards.edu/newc/marks/til/awards_and_rules.htm, pg 764

Hoggard, Jim, Carr P Collins Award, Center for the Study of the Southwest, Southwest Texas State University, San Marcos, TX 78666 *Tel:* 512-245-2232 *Fax:* 512-245-7462 *Web Site:* www.stedwards.edu/newc/marks/til/awards_and_rules.htm, pg 768

Hoggard, Jim, Soeurette Diehl Fraser Award, 3700 Mockingbird Lane, Dallas, TX 75205 *Tel:* 512-245-2232 *Fax:* 512-245-7462 *Web Site:* www.stedwards.edu/newc/marks/til/awards_and_rules.htm, pg 774

Hoggard, Jim, Friends of the Dallas Public Library Award, Center for the Study of the Southwest, Southwest Texas State University, San Marcos, TX 78666 *Tel:* 512-245-2232 *Fax:* 512-245-7462 *Web Site:* www.stedwards.edu/newc/marks/til/awards_and_rules.htm, pg 775

Hoggard, Jim, Jesse H Jones Award, 3700 Mockingbird Lane, Dallas, TX 75205 *Tel:* 214-528-2655 *Fax:* 512-245-7462 *Web Site:* www.stedwards.edu/newc/marks/til/awards_and_rules.htm, pg 781

Hoggard, Jim, O Henry Award, 3700 Mockingbird Lane, Dallas, TX 75205 *Tel:* 512-245-2232 *Fax:* 512-245-7462 *Web Site:* www.stedwards.edu/newc/marks/til/awards_and_rules.htm, pg 795

Hoggard, Jim, Natalie Ornish Poetry Award, 3700 Mockingbird Lane, Dallas, TX 75205 *Tel:* 512-245-2232 *Fax:* 512-245-7462 *Web Site:* www.stedwards.edu/newc/marks/til/awards_and_rules.htm, pg 796

Hoggard, Jim, Texas Institute of Letters, 3700 Mockingbird Lane, Dallas, TX 75205 *Tel:* 214-528-2655, pg 701

Hoggard, Jim, Texas Institute of Letters Awards, 3700 Mockingbird Lane, Dallas, TX 75205 *Tel:* 512-245-2232 *Fax:* 512-245-7462 *Web Site:* www.stedwards.edu/newc/marks/til/awards_and_rules.htm; www. english.swt.edu/css/til/rules.htm, pg 808

Hoggard, Jim, Stanley Walker Journalism Award, 3700 Mockingbird Lane, Dallas, TX 75205 *Tel:* 512-245-2232 *Fax:* 512-245-7462, pg 810

Hogrefe, Christine, Hogrefe & Huber Publishers, 875 Massachusetts Ave, 7th fl, Cambridge, MA 02139 *Toll Free Tel:* 800-228-3749; 866-823-4726 *Fax:* 617-354-6875 *E-mail:* hh@hhpub.com *Web Site:* www.hhpub. com, pg 123

Hohle, Carol, The Writings of Mary Baker Eddy/ Publisher, 175 Huntington Ave, Suite A-16-10, Boston, MA 02115 *Tel:* 617-450-3514; 617-450-2000 (Christian Science Church Boston) *Toll Free Tel:* 800-288-7090 *Fax:* 617-450-7334 *Web Site:* www. spirituality.com, pg 305

Hohman, Dave, Voyageur Press, 123 N Second St, Stillwater, MN 55082 *Tel:* 651-430-2210 *Toll Free Tel:* 800-888-9653 *Fax:* 651-430-2211 *E-mail:* books@voyageurpress.com *Web Site:* www. voyageurpress.com, pg 291

Hoiberg, Dale, Encyclopaedia Britannica Inc, 310 S Michigan Ave, Chicago, IL 60604 *Tel:* 312-347-7000 *Toll Free Tel:* 800-323-1229 *Fax:* 312-347-7399 *E-mail:* editor@eb.com *Web Site:* www.eb.com; www. britannica.com, pg 91

Holava, Carol, Syracuse University Press, 621 Skytop Rd, Syracuse, NY 13244-5290 *Tel:* 315-443-5534 *Toll Free Tel:* 800-365-8929 (orders only) *Fax:* 315-443-5545 *E-mail:* supress@syr.edu *Web Site:* syracuseuniversitypress.syr.edu, pg 263

Holcomb, Abbie, Avalon Books, 160 Madison Ave, 5th fl, New York, NY 10016 *Tel:* 212-598-0222 *Fax:* 212-979-1862 *E-mail:* avalon@avalonbooks.com *Web Site:* www.avalonbooks.com, pg 28

Holden, John, American Business Media, 675 Third Ave, Suite 415, New York, NY 10017 *Tel:* 212-661-6360 *Fax:* 212-370-0736 *E-mail:* info@abmmail.com *Web Site:* www.americanbusinessmedia.com, pg 676

Holder, Greg, Standard Publishing Co, 8121 Hamilton Ave, Cincinnati, OH 45231 *Tel:* 513-931-4050 *Toll Free Tel:* 800-543-1301 *Fax:* 513-931-0950 *Toll Free Fax:* 877-867-5751 *E-mail:* customerservice@ standardpub.com *Web Site:* www.standardpub.com, pg 257

Holder, Jakob, William Flanagan Memorial Creative Persons Center, 14 Harrison St, New York, NY 10013 *Tel:* 212-226-2020 *E-mail:* info@albeefoundation.org *Web Site:* www.albeefoundation.org, pg 774

Holder, Jennifer, Standard Publishing Co, 8121 Hamilton Ave, Cincinnati, OH 45231 *Tel:* 513-931-4050 *Toll Free Tel:* 800-543-1301 *Fax:* 513-931-0950 *Toll Free Fax:* 877-867-5751 *E-mail:* customerservice@ standardpub.com *Web Site:* www.standardpub.com, pg 257

Holding, Brian, Human Kinetics Inc, PO Box 5076, Champaign, IL 61825-5076 *Tel:* 217-351-5076 *Toll Free Tel:* 800-747-4457 *Fax:* 217-351-1549 (orders/ cust serv) *E-mail:* info@hkusa.com *Web Site:* www. humankinetics.com, pg 128

Holdridge, Jefferson, Wake Forest University Press, A5 Tribble Hall, Wake Forest University, Winston-Salem, NC 27109 *Tel:* 336-758-5448 *Fax:* 336-758-5636 *E-mail:* wfupress@wfu.edu *Web Site:* www.wfu. edu/wfupress, pg 292

Holey, Steve, Bethany House Publishers/Baker Bookhouse, PO Box 6287, Grand Rapids, MI 49516-6287 *Tel:* 616-676-9185 *Toll Free Tel:* 800-877-2665 *Web Site:* www.bethanyhouse.com; www. bakerpublishinggroup.com, pg 37

Hollahan, Patricia, Medieval Institute Publications, 1903 W Michigan Ave, Kalamazoo, MI 49008-5432 *Tel:* 269-387-8755 (orders); 269-387-8754 *Fax:* 269-387-8750 *Web Site:* www.wmich.edu/medieval/mip, pg 170

Hollaman, Keith, Newmarket Publishing & Communications, 18 E 48 St, New York, NY 10017 *Tel:* 212-832-3575 *Toll Free Tel:* 800-669-3903 *Fax:* 212-832-3629 *E-mail:* mailbox@newmarketpress. com *Web Site:* www.newmarketpress.com, pg 190

Holland, Cherene, The Pennsylvania State University Press, 820 N University Dr, University Support Bldg 1, Suite C, University Park, PA 16802-1003 *Tel:* 814-865-1327 *Toll Free Tel:* 800-326-9180 *Fax:* 814-863-1408 *Toll Free Fax:* 877 7782665 *Web Site:* www. psupress.org, pg 209

Holland, David, Harlequin Enterprises Ltd, 225 Duncan Mill Rd, Don Mills, ON M3B 3K9, Canada *Tel:* 416-445-5860 *Fax:* 416-445-8655 *Web Site:* www. eharlequin.com; www.luna-books.com; www. mirabooks.com; www.reddressink.com; www. steeplehill.com, pg 549

Holland, Edward, Cinco Puntos Press, 701 Texas Ave, El Paso, TX 79901 *Tel:* 915-838-1625 *Toll Free Tel:* 800-566-9072 *Fax:* 915-838-1635 *E-mail:* info@ cincopuntos.com *Web Site:* www.cincopuntos.com, pg 62

Holland, Jessica, William K Bradford Publishing Co Inc, 35 Forest Ridge Rd, Concord, MA 01742 *Tel:* 978-402-5300 *Toll Free Tel:* 800-421-2009 *Fax:* 978-318-9500 *E-mail:* wkb@wkbradford.com *Web Site:* www. wkbradford.com, pg 300

Holland, Ken, Tom Doherty Associates, LLC, 175 Fifth Ave, 14th fl, New York, NY 10010 *Tel:* 212-388-0100 *Toll Free Tel:* 800-455-0340 *Fax:* 212-388-0191 *E-mail:* firstname.lastname@tor.com *Web Site:* www. tor.com, pg 82

Holland, Ken, St Martin's Press LLC, 175 Fifth Ave, New York, NY 10010 *Tel:* 212-674-5151 *Fax:* 212-420-9314 *E-mail:* firstname.lastname@stmartins.com *Web Site:* www.stmartins.com, pg 238

Holland, Larry V, Scholastic Inc, 557 Broadway, New York, NY 10012 *Tel:* 212-343-4469 *Toll Free Tel:* 800-scholastic *Fax:* 212-343-6930 *Web Site:* www.scholastic.com, pg 242

Holland, Lori, Current Medicine, 400 Market St, Suite 700, Philadelphia, PA 19106 *Tel:* 215-574-2266 *Toll Free Tel:* 800-427-1796 *Fax:* 215-574-2270 *E-mail:* info@phl.cursci.com, pg 75

Holland, Mark, Rocky Mountain Mineral Law Foundation, 9191 Sheridan Blvd, Suite 203, Westminister, CO 80031 *Tel:* 303-321-8100 *Fax:* 303-321-7657 *E-mail:* info@rmmlf.org *Web Site:* www. rmmlf.org, pg 233

Holland, Rebecca, Doubleday Broadway Publishing Group, 1745 Broadway, New York, NY 10019 *Tel:* 212-782-9000 *Toll Free Tel:* 800-223-6834; 800-223-5780 (sales) *Fax:* 212-302-7985 (correspondence); 212-492-9862 (orders), pg 83

Holland, Tom, Oriental Institute Publications Sales, 1155 E 58 St, Chicago, IL 60637 *Tel:* 773-702-9514 *Fax:* 773-702-9853 *E-mail:* oi-publications@uchicago.edu; oi-museum@uchicago.edu; oi-administration@uchicago.edu *Web Site:* oi.uchicago.edu, pg 199

Hollander, Eli, Philipp Feldheim Inc, 200 Airport Executive Park, Nanuet, NY 10954 *Tel:* 845-356-2282 *Toll Free Tel:* 800-237-7149 *Fax:* 845-425-1908 *E-mail:* sales@feldheim.com *Web Site:* www.feldheim.com, pg 95

Hollander, Joe, Scholastic Library Publishing, 90 Old Sherman Tpke, Danbury, CT 06816 *Tel:* 203-797-3500 *Toll Free Tel:* 800-621-1115 *Fax:* 203-797-3657 *Web Site:* www.scholasticlibrary.com, pg 242

Hollander, Lisa, Workman Publishing Co Inc, 708 Broadway, New York, NY 10003-9555 *Tel:* 212-254-5900 *Toll Free Tel:* 800-722-7202 *Fax:* 212-254-8098 *E-mail:* info@workman.com *Web Site:* www.workman.com, pg 303

Holley, Joe, Brazo Bookstore (Houston Award), 3700 Mockingbird Lane, Dallas, TX 75205 *Tel:* 214-528-2655 *Web Site:* www.stedwards.edu/newc/marks/til/awards_and_rules.htm, pg 764

Holley, Joe, Carr P Collins Award, Center for the Study of the Southwest, Southwest Texas State University, San Marcos, TX 78666 *Tel:* 512-245-2232 *Fax:* 512-245-7462 *Web Site:* www.stedwards.edu/newc/marks/til/awards_and_rules.htm, pg 768

Holley, Joe, Soeurette Diehl Fraser Award, 3700 Mockingbird Lane, Dallas, TX 75205 *Tel:* 512-245-2232 *Fax:* 512-245-7462 *Web Site:* www.stedwards.edu/newc/marks/til/awards_and_rules.htm, pg 774

Holley, Joe, Friends of the Dallas Public Library Award, Center for the Study of the Southwest, Southwest Texas State University, San Marcos, TX 78666 *Tel:* 512-245-2232 *Fax:* 512-245-7462 *Web Site:* www.stedwards.edu/newc/marks/til/awards_and_rules.htm, pg 775

Holley, Joe, Jesse H Jones Award, 3700 Mockingbird Lane, Dallas, TX 75205 *Tel:* 214-528-2655 *Fax:* 512-245-7462 *Web Site:* www.stedwards.edu/newc/marks/til/awards_and_rules.htm, pg 781

Holley, Joe, O Henry Award, 3700 Mockingbird Lane, Dallas, TX 75205 *Tel:* 512-245-2232 *Fax:* 512-245-7462 *Web Site:* www.stedwards.edu/newc/marks/til/awards_and_rules.htm, pg 795

Holley, Joe, Natalie Ornish Poetry Award, 3700 Mockingbird Lane, Dallas, TX 75205 *Tel:* 512-245-2232 *Fax:* 512-245-7462 *Web Site:* www.stedwards.edu/newc/marks/til/awards_and_rules.htm, pg 796

Holley, Joe, Texas Institute of Letters, 3700 Mockingbird Lane, Dallas, TX 75205 *Tel:* 214-528-2655, pg 701

Holley, Joe, Texas Institute of Letters Awards, 3700 Mockingbird Lane, Dallas, TX 75205 *Tel:* 512-245-2232 *Fax:* 512-245-7462 *Web Site:* www.stedwards.edu/newc/marks/til/awards_and_rules.htm; www.english.swt.edu/css/til/rules.htm, pg 808

Holley, Joe, Stanley Walker Journalism Award, 3700 Mockingbird Lane, Dallas, TX 75205 *Tel:* 512-245-2232 *Fax:* 512-245-7462, pg 810

Hollick, Linda, Routledge, 29 W 35 St, New York, NY 10001-2299 *Tel:* 212-216-7800 *Fax:* 212-564-7854 (main) *E-mail:* info@taylorandfrancis.com *Web Site:* www.routledge-ny.com, pg 235

Holliday, Monica, Association of American University Presses, 1427 E 60 St, Chicago, IL 60637 *Tel:* 773-702-7700; 773-702-7600 *Toll Free Tel:* 800-621-2736 (orders) *Fax:* 773-702-9756 (sales); 773-660-2235 (orders); 773-702-2708 *E-mail:* general@press.uchicago.edu *Web Site:* www.press.uchicago.edu, pg 26

Holliday, Sara, New York City Book Awards, 53 E 79 St, New York, NY 10021 *Tel:* 212-288-6900 (ext 230) *Fax:* 212-988-4071 *E-mail:* events@nysoclib.org *Web Site:* www.nysoclib.org, pg 794

Hollister, Dean, Martindale-Hubbell, 121 Chanlon Rd, New Providence, NJ 07974 *Tel:* 908-464-6800 *Toll Free Tel:* 800-526-4902 *Fax:* 908-464-3553 *E-mail:* info@martindale.com *Web Site:* www.martindale.com, pg 164

Holloway, J David, American Technical Publishers Inc, 1155 W 175 St, Homewood, IL 60430-4600 *Tel:* 708-957-1100 *Toll Free Tel:* 800-323-3471 *Fax:* 708-957-1101 *E-mail:* service@americantech.net *Web Site:* www.go2atp.com, pg 18

Hollowell, Jennifer, JMH Creative Solutions, PO Box 2443, Lewiston, ME 04241-2443 *Tel:* 207-784-9138 *E-mail:* poemwriter@midmaine.com; poemwriter1@yahoo.com *Web Site:* www.jmhcreativesolutions.com, pg 602

Hollway, Johanna, University Press of New England, One Court St, Lebanon, NH 03766 *Tel:* 603-448-1533 *Toll Free Tel:* 800-421-1561 (orders only) *Fax:* 603-448-7006; 603-643-1540 *E-mail:* university.press@dartmouth.edu *Web Site:* www.upne.com, pg 287

Holmes, Henry, Henry Holmes Literary Agent/Book Publicist, PO Box 433, Swansea, MA 02777 *Tel:* 508-672-2258, pg 601, 635

Holmes, J D, Holmes Publishing Group, PO Box 623, Edmonds, WA 98020-0623 *Tel:* 425-771-2701 *Fax:* 425-771-5651, pg 124

Holmes, Janet, Ahsahta Press, Boise State University, Dept of English, Boise, ID 83725 *Tel:* 208-426-2195 *Fax:* 208-426-4373, pg 7

Holmes, Jean Elizabeth, National League of American Pen Women, c/o National Pen Women-Scholarship, Pen Arts Bldg, 1300 17 St NW, Washington, DC 20036-1973 *Web Site:* www.americanpenwomen.org, pg 693

Holmes, Lori A, SRA/McGraw-Hill, a Division of McGraw-Hill Learning Group, 8787 Orion Place, Columbus, OH 43240 *Tel:* 614-430-4000 *Fax:* 614-430-6621 *E-mail:* sra@mcgraw-hill.com *Web Site:* www.sra-4kids.com, pg 256

Holmes, Miriam H, Holmes & Meier Publishers Inc, 160 Broadway, East Bldg, New York, NY 10038 *Tel:* 212-374-0100 *Fax:* 212-374-1313 *E-mail:* info@holmesandmeier.com *Web Site:* www.holmesandmeier.com, pg 124

Holmgren, Karin, Little, Brown and Company Books for Young Readers, 1271 Avenue of the Americas, New York, NY 10020 *Tel:* 212-522-8700 *Toll Free Tel:* 800-759-0190 *Fax:* 212-522-7997 *Web Site:* www.twbookmark.com, pg 156

Holmstrom, Krista, Travelers' Tales Inc, 330 Townsend St, Suite 208, San Francisco, CA 94107 *Tel:* 415-227-8600 *Fax:* 415-227-8605 *E-mail:* ttales@travelerstales.com *Web Site:* www.travelerstales.com, pg 275

Holquist, Carol, Discovery House Publishers, 3000 Kraft SE, Grand Rapids, MI 49512 *Tel:* 616-942-9218; 616-974-2210 (cust serv) *Toll Free Tel:* 800-653-8333 *Fax:* 616-957-5741 *E-mail:* dhp@rbc.org *Web Site:* www.gospelcom.net/rbc/dhp/; www.rbc.net, pg 80

Holston, Kim R, American Institute for CPCU & Insurance Institute of America, 720 Providence Rd, Malvern, PA 19355-0716 *Tel:* 610-644-2100 *Toll Free Tel:* 800-644-2101 *Fax:* 610-640-9576; 610-644-7629 *E-mail:* cserv@cpcuiia.org *Web Site:* www.aicpcu.org, pg 14

Holt, Joan K, The Metropolitan Museum of Art, 1000 Fifth Ave, New York, NY 10028 *Tel:* 212-879-5500; 212-535-7710 *Fax:* 212-396-5062 *E-mail:* info@metmuseum.org *Web Site:* www.metmuseum.org, pg 173

Holt, Russell, Pacific Press Publishing Association, 1350 N Kings Rd, Nampa, ID 83687-3193 *Tel:* 208-465-2500 *Toll Free Tel:* 800-447-7377 *Fax:* 208-465-2531 *Web Site:* www.pacificpress.com, pg 202

Holtby, David V, University of New Mexico Press, 1720 Lomas Blvd NE, MSC01 1200, Albuquerque, NM 87131-0001 *Tel:* 505-277-2346; 505-277-4810 (order dept) *Toll Free Tel:* 800-249-7737 (orders only) *Fax:* 505-277-3350 *Toll Free Fax:* 800-622-8667 *E-mail:* unmpress@unm.edu; custserv@upress.unm.edu (order dept) *Web Site:* unmpress.com, pg 283

Holtmeier, Jeffrey, ASM Press, 1752 "N" St NW, Washington, DC 20036-2904 *Tel:* 202-737-3600 *Toll Free Tel:* 800-546-2416 *Fax:* 202-942-9342 *E-mail:* books@asmusa.org *Web Site:* www.asmpress.org, pg 25

Holton, Lisa, Disney Press, 114 Fifth Ave, New York, NY 10011 *Tel:* 212-633-4400 *Fax:* 212-807-5432 *Web Site:* www.disney.go.com, pg 81

Holton, Lisa, Disney Publishing Worldwide, 500 S Buena Vista, Burbank, CA 91521 *Tel:* 212-633-4400 *Fax:* 212-633-4833 *Web Site:* www.disney.go.com/disneybooks, pg 81

Holton, Lisa, Hyperion Books for Children, 114 Fifth Ave, New York, NY 10011 *Tel:* 212-633-4400 *Fax:* 212-807-5880 *Web Site:* www.hyperionbooksforchildren.com, pg 129

Holton, Loralee, Order of the Cross, PO Box 2472, La Grange, IL 60525-8572 *Toll Free Tel:* 800-611-1361 *Toll Free Fax:* 800-611-1361 *E-mail:* meditate@interaccess.com, pg 198

Holtzman, Bob, Moon Mountain Publishing, 80 Peachtree Rd, North Kingstown, RI 02852 *Tel:* 401-884-6703 *Toll Free Tel:* 800-353-5877 *Fax:* 401-884-7076 *E-mail:* hello@moonmountainpub.com *Web Site:* www.moonmountainpub.com, pg 178

Holub, Dennis, Artist Grants, 800 Governors Dr, Pierre, SD 57501-2294 *Tel:* 605-773-3131 *Fax:* 605-773-6962 *E-mail:* sdac@state.sd.us *Web Site:* www.sdarts.org, pg 760

Holway, Richard, The University of Virginia Press, PO Box 400318, Charlottesville, VA 22904-4318 *Tel:* 434-924-3468 (cust serv); 434-924-3469 (cust serv) *Toll Free Tel:* 800-831-3406 (cust serv) *Fax:* 434-982-2655 *Toll Free Fax:* 877-288-6400 *E-mail:* upressvirginia@virginia.edu *Web Site:* www.upressvirginia.edu, pg 285

Holwitz, Stanley, University of California Press, 2120 Berkeley Way, Berkeley, CA 94720 *Tel:* 510-642-4247 *Toll Free Tel:* 800-777-4726 *Fax:* 510-643-7127 *Toll Free Fax:* 800-999-1958 *E-mail:* askucp@ucpress.edu *Web Site:* www.ucpress.edu, pg 281

Holzapfel, Cynthia, Book Publishing Co, 415 Farm Rd, Summertown, TN 38483 *Tel:* 931-964-3571 *Toll Free Tel:* 888-260-8458 *Fax:* 931-964-3518 *E-mail:* info@bookpubco.com *Web Site:* www.bookpubco.com, pg 43

Holzapfel, Robert, Book Publishing Co, 415 Farm Rd, Summertown, TN 38483 *Tel:* 931-964-3571 *Toll Free Tel:* 888-260-8458 *Fax:* 931-964-3518 *E-mail:* info@bookpubco.com *Web Site:* www.bookpubco.com, pg 43

Holzer, Harold, The Metropolitan Museum of Art, 1000 Fifth Ave, New York, NY 10028 *Tel:* 212-879-5500; 212-535-7710 *Fax:* 212-396-5062 *E-mail:* info@metmuseum.org *Web Site:* www.metmuseum.org, pg 173

Holzman, Alex, Temple University Press, 1601 N Broad St, 083-42, USB Room 306, Philadelphia, PA 19122-6099 *Tel:* 215-204-8787 *Toll Free Tel:* 800-447-1656 *Fax:* 215-204-4719 *E-mail:* tempress@temple.edu *Web Site:* www.temple.edu/tempress, pg 266

Homer, Sandra, The Boston Mills Press, 132 Main St, Erin, ON N0B 1T0, Canada *Tel:* 519-833-2407 *Fax:* 519-833-2195 *E-mail:* books@bostonmillspress.com *Web Site:* www.bostonmillspress.com, pg 537

Homoleski, Brian, SIL International, 7500 W Camp Wisdom Rd, Dallas, TX 75236 *Tel:* 972-708-7404 *Fax:* 972-708-7363 *E-mail:* academic_books@sil.org *Web Site:* www.ethnologue.com, pg 247

Homsher, Deborah, Cornell University Southeast Asia Program Publications, 640 Stewart Ave, Ithaca, NY 14850 *Tel:* 607-255-8038 *Fax:* 607-277-1904; 607-255-7534 *E-mail:* seap-pubs@cornell.edu *Web Site:* www.einaudi.cornell.edu/southeastasia.publications/SEAP, pg 69

Honeycutt, Banks, Oxford University Press, Inc, 198 Madison Ave, New York, NY 10016-4314 *Tel:* 212-726-6000 *Toll Free Tel:* 800-451-7556 (orders) *Web Site:* www.oup.com/us, pg 200

Hong, Bob, Rapids Christian Press Inc, 5777 Vista Dr, Ferndale, WA 98248 *Tel:* 360-384-1747 *Fax:* 360-384-1747, pg 227

Hong, Jae S, Cambridge University Press, 40 W 20 St, New York, NY 10011-4211 *Tel:* 212-924-3900 *Toll Free Tel:* 800-899-5222 *Fax:* 212-691-3239 *Web Site:* www.cambridge.org, pg 52

Hook, Diana H, Norman Publishing, 936-B Seventh St, PMB 238, Novato, CA 94945-3000 *Tel:* 415-892-3181 *Toll Free Tel:* 800-544-9359 *Fax:* 208-692-7446 *E-mail:* orders@jnorman.com *Web Site:* www.normanpublishing.com, pg 191

Hooker, Dan, Ashley Grayson Literary Agency, 1342 18 St, San Pedro, CA 90732 *Tel:* 310-548-4672 *Fax:* 310-514-1148 *E-mail:* graysonagent@earthlink.net, pg 633

Hoole, Brunson, Algonquin Books of Chapel Hill, 127 Kingston Dr, Suite 105, Chapel Hill, NC 27514 *Tel:* 919-967-0108 *Fax:* 919-933-0272 *E-mail:* dialogue@algonquin.com *Web Site:* www.algonquin.com, pg 8

Hoolihan, Katie, University of Minnesota Press, 111 Third Ave S, Suite 290, Minneapolis, MN 55401-2520 *Tel:* 612-627-1970 *Fax:* 612-627-1980 *E-mail:* ump@tc.umn.edu *Web Site:* www.upress.umn.edu, pg 282

Hooper, Kevin, Humanics Publishing Group, 12 S Dixie Hwy, Suite 203, Lake Worth, FL 33460 *Tel:* 561-533-6231 *Toll Free Tel:* 800-874-8844 *Toll Free Fax:* 888-874-8844 *E-mail:* humanics@mindspring.com *Web Site:* humanicspub.com; humanicslearning.com; humanicsdealer.com, pg 128

Hooper, Niels, Verso, 180 Varick St, 10th fl, New York, NY 10014-4606 *Tel:* 212-807-9680 *Fax:* 212-807-9152 *E-mail:* versony@versobooks.com *Web Site:* versobooks.com, pg 290

Hoover, James, InterVarsity Press, 430 E Plaza Dr, Westmont, IL 60559-1234 *Tel:* 630-734-4000 *Toll Free Tel:* 800-843-7225 *Fax:* 630-734-4200 *E-mail:* mail@ivpress.com *Web Site:* www.ivpress.com, pg 138

Hoover, Peggy, MBH Book Services, 99 Willowbrook Blvd, Lewisburg, PA 17837 *Tel:* 570-523-8081, pg 605

Hopcroft, Jennifer, Cowley Publications, 4 Brattle St, Cambridge, MA 02138 *Tel:* 617-441-0300 *Toll Free Tel:* 800-225-1534 *Fax:* 617-441-0120 *Toll Free Fax:* 877-225-6675 *E-mail:* cowley@cowley.org *Web Site:* www.cowley.org, pg 71

Hopen, Bob, Martindale-Hubbell, 121 Chanlon Rd, New Providence, NJ 07974 *Tel:* 908-464-6800 *Toll Free Tel:* 800-526-4902 *Fax:* 908-464-3553 *E-mail:* info@martindale.com *Web Site:* www.martindale.com, pg 164

Hopkin, James, Jossey-Bass, 989 Market St, San Francisco, CA 94103-1741 *Tel:* 415-433-1740 *Toll Free Tel:* 800-956-7739 *Fax:* 415-433-0499 (edit/mktg) *Web Site:* www.josseybass.com; www.pfeiffer.com, pg 142

Hopkins, Michael, Glencoe/McGraw-Hill, 8787 Orion Place, Columbus, OH 43240 *Tel:* 614-430-4000 *Toll Free Tel:* 800-848-1567 *Web Site:* www.glencoe.com, pg 105

Hopkins, Mike, Graphic Arts Center Publishing Co, 3019 NW Yeon Ave, Portland, OR 97210 *Tel:* 503-226-2402 *Toll Free Tel:* 800-452-3032 *Fax:* 503-223-1410 *Toll Free Fax:* 800-355-9685 *E-mail:* editorial@gacpc.com; sales@gacpc.com *Web Site:* www.gacpc.com, pg 107

Hoppe, Joy, AGS Publishing, 4201 Woodland Rd, Circle Pines, MN 55014-1716 *Tel:* 651-287-7220 *Toll Free Tel:* 800-328-2560 *Toll Free Fax:* 800-471-8457 *E-mail:* agsmail@agsnet.com *Web Site:* www.agsnet.com, pg 7

Horak, Kelly, National Bureau of Economic Research Inc, 1050 Massachusetts Ave, Cambridge, MA 02138-5398 *Tel:* 617-868-3900 *Fax:* 617-868-2742 *E-mail:* op@nber.org *Web Site:* www.nber.org, pg 182

Horbaczewski, Henry, Harcourt Inc, 6277 Sea Harbor Dr, Orlando, FL 32887 *Tel:* 407-345-2000 *Toll Free Tel:* 800-225-5425 (cust serv) *Fax:* 407-352-3445 (cust serv), pg 114

Horch, Cheryl, Chicago Book Clinic, 5443 N Broadway, Suite 101, Chicago, IL 60640 *Tel:* 773-561-4150 *Fax:* 773-561-1343 *Web Site:* www.chicagobookclinic.org, pg 684

Horch, Cheryl, Chicago Book Clinic Annual Book Show Awards, 5443 N Broadway, Suite 101, Chicago, IL 60640 *Tel:* 773-561-4150 *Fax:* 773-561-1343 *Web Site:* www.chicagobookclinic.org, pg 766

Horch, Cheryl, Chicago Book Clinic Distinguished Service Award, 5443 N Broadway, Suite 101, Chicago, IL 60640 *Tel:* 773-561-4150 *Fax:* 773-561-1343 *Web Site:* www.chicagobookclinic.org, pg 766

Horch, Cheryl, Chicago Book Clinic Seminars, 5443 N Broadway, Suite 101, Chicago, IL 60640 *Tel:* 773-561-4150 *Fax:* 773-561-1343 *Web Site:* www.chicagobookclinic.org, pg 751

Horhota, Wendy, Vanwell Publishing Ltd, One Northrup Cres, St Catharines, ON L2R 7S2, Canada *Tel:* 905-937-3100 *Toll Free Tel:* 800-661-6136 *Fax:* 905-937-1760 *E-mail:* sales@vanwell.com, pg 565

Horinstein, Regine, Corporation of Professional Librarians of Quebec, 353, rue Sainte Niclas, Suite 103, Montreal, PQ H2Y 2P1, Canada *Tel:* 514-845-3327 *Fax:* 514-845-1618 *E-mail:* info@cbpq.qc.ca *Web Site:* www.cbpq.qc.ca, pg 685

Horler, Fred, Kids Can Press Ltd, 2250 Military Rd, Tonawanda, NY 14150 *Tel:* 416-925-5437 (Toronto, ON, Canada) *Toll Free Tel:* 800-265-0884; 866-481-5827 (orders) *Fax:* 416-960-5437 (Toronto, ON, Canada) *E-mail:* info@kidscan.com; lfyman@kidscan.com (orders) *Web Site:* www.kidscanpress.com, pg 145

Horler, Fred, Kids Can Press Ltd, 29 Birch Ave, Toronto, ON M4V 1E2, Canada *Tel:* 416-925-5437 *Toll Free Tel:* 800-265-0884 *Fax:* 416-960-5437 *E-mail:* info@kidscan.com *Web Site:* kidscanpress.com, pg 552

Horn, Karen N, National Bureau of Economic Research Inc, 1050 Massachusetts Ave, Cambridge, MA 02138-5398 *Tel:* 617-868-3900 *Fax:* 617-868-2742 *E-mail:* op@nber.org *Web Site:* www.nber.org, pg 182

Horn, Sharon, IEE, c/o Inspec, 379 Thornall St, Edison, NJ 08837-2225 *Tel:* 732-321-5575 *Fax:* 732-321-5702 *E-mail:* iee@inspecinc.com *Web Site:* www.iee.org/publishing, pg 130

Hornburg, Michael, Grove/Atlantic Inc, 841 Broadway, 4th fl, New York, NY 10003-4793 *Tel:* 212-614-7850 *Toll Free Tel:* 800-521-0178 *Fax:* 212-614-7886 *Web Site:* www.groveatlantic.com, pg 110

Horne, Barbara, University of Illinois Press, 1325 S Oak, Champaign, IL 61820-6903 *Tel:* 217-333-0950; 212-577-5487 *Fax:* 217-244-8082; 410-516-6969 (orders) *E-mail:* uipress@uillinois.edu; journals@uillinois.edu *Web Site:* www.press.uillinois.edu, pg 282

Horne, Beverly, Writers' League of Texas, 1501 W Fifth St, Suite E-2, Austin, TX 78703 *Tel:* 512-499-8914 *Fax:* 512-499-0441 *E-mail:* wlt@writersleague.org *Web Site:* www.writersleague.org, pg 670

Hornfischer, Jim, Hornfischer Literary Management Inc, PO Box 50544, Austin, TX 78763 *Tel:* 512-472-0011 *Fax:* 512-472-0077 *E-mail:* queries@hornfischerlit.com *Web Site:* www.hornfischerlit.com, pg 635

Hornik, Laura, Dial Books for Young Readers, 345 Hudson St, New York, NY 10014 *Tel:* 212-366-2000 *Fax:* 212-414-3396 *E-mail:* online@penguinputnam.com *Web Site:* www.penguinusa.com, pg 80

Horning, Joel, Multnomah Publishers Inc, 204 W Adams Ave, Sisters, OR 97759 *Tel:* 541-549-1144 *Toll Free Tel:* 800-929-0910 *Fax:* 541-549-2044 (sales); 541-549-0432 (admin); 541-549-0260 (ed/prod); 541-549-8048 (mktg) *E-mail:* information@multnomahbooks.com *Web Site:* www.multnomahbooks.com, pg 180

Hornstein, Gabriel, AMS Press Inc, Brooklyn Navy Yard, Bldg 292, Suite 417, 63 Flushing Ave, New York, NY 11205 *Tel:* 212-777-4700; 718-875-8100 *Fax:* 212-995-5413 *E-mail:* amserve@earthlink.net, pg 19

Hornyak, Kim, Jenkins Group Inc, 400 W Front St, Suite 4-A, Traverse City, MI 49684 *Tel:* 231-933-0445 *Toll Free Tel:* 800-706-4636 *Fax:* 231-933-0448 *E-mail:* info@bookpublishing.com *Web Site:* www.bookpublishing.com, pg 602

Horowitz, Beverly, Random House Children's Books, 1745 Broadway, New York, NY 10019 *Tel:* 212-782-9000 *Toll Free Tel:* 800-200-3552 *Fax:* 212-782-9452 *Web Site:* www.randomhouse.com/kids, pg 225

Horowitz, David, Media Coalition Inc, 139 Fulton St, Suite 302, New York, NY 10038 *Tel:* 212-587-4025 *Fax:* 212-587-2436 *E-mail:* mediacoalition@mediacoalition.org *Web Site:* www.mediacoalition.org, pg 691

Horowitz, Irving Louis, Transaction Publishers, Rutgers University, 35 Berrue Circle, Piscataway, NJ 08854 *Tel:* 732-445-2280 *Toll Free Tel:* 888-999-6778 *Fax:* 732-445-3138 *E-mail:* trans@transactionpub.com *Web Site:* www.transactionpub.com, pg 274

Horowitz, Mitchell, Jeremy P Tarcher, 375 Hudson St, New York, NY 10014 *Tel:* 212-366-2000 *E-mail:* online@penguinputnam.com *Web Site:* www.penguin.com, pg 264

Horowitz, Shel, Accurate Writing & More, PO Box 1164, Northampton, MA 01061-1164 *Tel:* 413-586-2388 *Toll Free Tel:* 800-683-9673 *Fax:* 617-249-0153 *Web Site:* www.accuratewriting.com, pg 589

Horowitz, Valerie, The Lawbook Exchange Ltd, 33 Terminal Ave, Clark, NJ 07066-1321 *Tel:* 732-382-1800 *Toll Free Tel:* 800-422-6686 *Fax:* 732-382-1887 *E-mail:* law@lawbookexchange.com *Web Site:* www.lawbookexchange.com, pg 150

Horsfall, Stuart, Sopris West Educational Services, 4093 Specialty Place, Longmont, CO 80504 *Tel:* 303-651-2829 *Toll Free Tel:* 800-547-6747 *Fax:* 303-776-5934 *E-mail:* customerservice@sopriswest.com *Web Site:* www.sopriswest.com, pg 253

Horwich, Jon, Playmore Inc, Publishers, 230 Fifth Ave, Suite 711, New York, NY 10001 *Tel:* 212-251-0600 *Fax:* 212-251-0966 *Web Site:* playmorebooks.com, pg 214

Hoskins, Jim, Maximum Press, 605 Silverthorn Rd, Gulf Breeze, FL 32561 *Tel:* 850-934-0819 *Toll Free Tel:* 800-989-6733 *Fax:* 850-934-9981 *E-mail:* moreinfo@maxpress.com *Web Site:* www.maxpress.com, pg 166

Hossain, Mossadaq, Amirah Publishing, IBTS, 22-55 31 St, Long Island City, NY 11105 *Tel:* 718-721-4246 (IBTS) *Toll Free Tel:* 800-337-4287 (IBTS) *Fax:* 718-721-6108 (IBTS) *E-mail:* amirahpbco@aol.com; information@ibtsonline.com, pg 19

Hostetter, Christina, National Press Club (NPC), 529 14 St NW, 13th fl, Washington, DC 20045 *Tel:* 202-662-7500 *Fax:* 202-662-7569 *E-mail:* infocenter@npcpress.org *Web Site:* www.press.org, pg 694

Hostnik, W John Jr, Greenwich Publishing Group Inc, 929 Boston Post Rd, Suite 9, Old Saybrook, CT 06475 *Tel:* 860-388-9941 *E-mail:* info@greenwichpublishing.com *Web Site:* www.greenwichpublishing.com, pg 109

Hostrop, Leeona, ETC Publications, 700 E Vereda del Sur, Palm Springs, CA 92262 *Tel:* 760-325-5332 *Toll Free Tel:* 800-382-7869 *Fax:* 760-325-8841 *E-mail:* etcbooks@earthlink.net, pg 92

Hostrop, Richard W, ETC Publications, 700 E Vereda del Sur, Palm Springs, CA 92262 *Tel:* 760-325-5332 *Toll Free Tel:* 800-382-7869 *Fax:* 760-325-8841 *E-mail:* etcbooks@earthlink.net, pg 92

Hottensen, Judy, Grove/Atlantic Inc, 841 Broadway, 4th fl, New York, NY 10003-4793 *Tel:* 212-614-7850 *Toll Free Tel:* 800-521-0178 *Fax:* 212-614-7886 *Web Site:* www.groveatlantic.com, pg 110

Houdek, Diane, St Anthony Messenger Press, 28 W Liberty St, Cincinnati, OH 45202 *Tel:* 513-241-5615 *Toll Free Tel:* 800-488-0488 *Fax:* 513-241-0399 *E-mail:* books@americancatholic.org *Web Site:* www.AmericanCatholic.org, pg 237

Hough, Lindy, Frog Ltd, 1435 Fourth St, Berkeley, CA 94710 *Tel:* 510-559-8277 *Toll Free Tel:* 800-337-2665 (book orders only) *Fax:* 510-559-8279 *E-mail:* orders@northatlanticbooks.com *Web Site:* www.northatlanticbooks.com, pg 101

Hough, Lindy, North Atlantic Books, 1435 Fourth St, Berkeley, CA 94710 *Tel:* 510-559-8277 *Toll Free Tel:* 800-337-2665 (book orders only) *Fax:* 510-559-8279 *E-mail:* orders@northatlanticbooks.com *Web Site:* www.northatlanticbooks.com, pg 192

Houghton, B, Passport Press Inc, PO Box 2543, Champlain, NY 12919-1346 *Tel:* 801-504-4385 *Fax:* 801-504-4385 *E-mail:* travelbook@yahoo.com, pg 205

Houghton, Harmon, Clear Light Publishers, 823 Don Diego, Santa Fe, NM 87505 *Tel:* 505-989-9590 *Toll Free Tel:* 888-253-2747 (orders) *Fax:* 505-989-9519 *E-mail:* market@clearlightbooks.com *Web Site:* www.clearlightbooks.com, pg 63

Houk, Randy, The Benefactory, PO Box 128, Cohasset, MA 02025 *Tel:* 781-383-8027 *Toll Free Tel:* 800-729-7251 *Fax:* 781-383-8026 *E-mail:* thebenefactory@aol.com *Web Site:* www.readplay.com, pg 36

Houle, Phyllis, League of Vermont Writers, PO Box 172, Underhill Center, VT 05490 *Tel:* 802-253-9439 *Web Site:* www.leaguevtwriters.org, pg 690

Houlihan, Molly, Random House Publishing Group, 1745 Broadway, New York, NY 10019 *Toll Free Tel:* 800-200-3552 *Toll Free Fax:* 800-200-3552 *Web Site:* www.randomhouse.com, pg 227

Hoult, Peter J, Canadian Institute of Chartered Accountants, 277 Wellington St W, Toronto, ON M5V 3H2, Canada *Tel:* 416-977-3222 *Toll Free Tel:* 800-268-3793 (Canadian orders) *Fax:* 416-977-8585 *E-mail:* orders@cica.ca *Web Site:* www.cica.ca, pg 538

Hourigan, Katherine, Alfred A Knopf, 1745 Broadway, New York, NY 10019 *Tel:* 212-751-2600 *Toll Free Tel:* 800-638-6460 *Fax:* 212-572-2593 *Web Site:* www.randomhouse.com/knopf, pg 146

House, Carrie Nelson, University of Nevada Press, MS 166, Reno, NV 89557-0076 *Tel:* 775-784-6573 *Toll Free Tel:* 800-682-6657 *Fax:* 775-784-6200 *Toll Free Fax:* 877-682-6657 *Web Site:* www.nvbooks.nevada.edu, pg 283

House, Jackson, Townson Publishing Co Ltd, PO Box 1404, Bentall Centre, Vancouver, BC V6C 2P7, Canada *Tel:* 604-263-0014 *Fax:* 604-263-0014 *E-mail:* info@townson.ca *Web Site:* www.townson.ca, pg 563

House, Jenny, Classroom Connect, 8000 Marina Blvd, Suite 400, Brisbane, CA 94005 *Tel:* 650-351-5100 *Toll Free Tel:* 800-638-1639 (cust support) *Fax:* 650-351-5300 *E-mail:* connect@classroom.com *Web Site:* www.classroom.com, pg 63

Houseman, Donna, Linns Stamp News-Ancillary Division, PO Box 29, Sidney, OH 45365-0029 *Tel:* 937-498-0801 (ext 197) *Fax:* 937-498-0807 *Toll Free Fax:* 800-488-5349 *E-mail:* cuserv@amospress.com *Web Site:* www.amosadvantage.com, pg 155

Housley, Jim, Facts on File Inc, 132 W 31 St, 17th fl, New York, NY 10001 *Tel:* 212-967-8800 *Toll Free Tel:* 800-322-8755 *Fax:* 212-967-9196 *Toll Free Fax:* 800-678-3633 *E-mail:* custserv@factsonfile.com *Web Site:* www.factsonfile.com, pg 93

Houston, Brant, Investigative Reporters & Editors, 138 Neff Annex, UMC School of Journalism, Columbia, MO 65211 *Tel:* 573-882-2042 *Fax:* 573-882-5431 *E-mail:* info@ire.org *Web Site:* www.ire.org, pg 689

Houtz, Julie, Association for Supervision & Curriculum Development (ASCD), 1703 N Beauregard St, Alexandria, VA 22311-1453 *Tel:* 703-578-9600 *Toll Free Tel:* 800-933-2723 *Fax:* 703-575-5400 *E-mail:* member@ascd.org *Web Site:* www.ascd.org, pg 26

Hovemann, Glenn, Dawn Publications Inc, 12402 Bitney Springs Rd, Nevada City, CA 95959 *Tel:* 530-274-7775 *Toll Free Tel:* 800-545-7475 *Fax:* 530-274-7778 *E-mail:* nature@dawnpub.com *Web Site:* www.dawnpub.com, pg 77

Hovey, Kimberly, Random House Publishing Group, 1745 Broadway, New York, NY 10019 *Toll Free Tel:* 800-200-3552 *Toll Free Fax:* 800-200-3552 *Web Site:* www.randomhouse.com, pg 227

Howard, Chandra, Lucent Books Inc, 15822 Bernardo Center Dr, Suite C, San Diego, CA 92127 *Tel:* 858-485-7424 *Fax:* 858-485-9549 *E-mail:* info@gale.com *Web Site:* www.gale.com/lucent, pg 159

Howard, Eric, Northland Publishing Co, 2900 N Fort Valley Rd, Flagstaff, AZ 86001 *Tel:* 928-774-5251 *Toll Free Tel:* 800-346-3257 *Fax:* 928-774-0592 *E-mail:* info@northlandpub.com; design@northlandpub.com; editorial@northlandpub.com *Web Site:* www.northlandpub.com, pg 193

Howard, Gail, Smart Luck Publishers, PO Box 81770, Las Vegas, NV 89180-1770 *Tel:* 702-365-1818 *Toll Free Tel:* 800-945-4245 *Fax:* 850-937-6999 *Toll Free Fax:* 800-876-4245 *E-mail:* books@smartluck.com *Web Site:* www.smartluck.com, pg 574

Howard, Gerald, Doubleday Broadway Publishing Group, 1745 Broadway, New York, NY 10019 *Tel:* 212-782-9000 *Toll Free Tel:* 800-223-6834; 800-223-5780 (sales) *Fax:* 212-302-7985 (correspondence); 212-492-9862 (orders), pg 82

Howard, Hiram G, Christopher-Gordon Publishers Inc, 1502 Providence Hwy, Suite 12, Norwood, MA 02062 *Tel:* 781-762-5577 *Toll Free Tel:* 800-934-8322 *Fax:* 781-762-2110 *Web Site:* www.christopher-gordon.com, pg 61

Howard, J Kirk, Simon & Pierre Publishing Co Ltd, 8 Market St, 2nd fl, Toronto, ON M5E 1M6, Canada *Tel:* 416-214-5544 *Toll Free Tel:* 800-565-9523 (orders: Canada & US) *Fax:* 416-214-5556 *Toll Free Fax:* 800-221-9985 (orders) *E-mail:* info@dundurn.com *Web Site:* www.dundurn.com, pg 561

Howard, John, Howard Publishing, 3117 N Seventh St, West Monroe, LA 71291 *Tel:* 318-396-3122 *Toll Free Tel:* 800-858-4109 *Fax:* 318-397-1882 *E-mail:* info@howardpublishing.com *Web Site:* howardpublishing.com, pg 127

Howard, Jon, Editorial Services Group Inc, 2990 Heidelberg Dr, Boulder, CO 80305 *Tel:* 303-494-4197 *E-mail:* editor@boulder.net *Web Site:* www.emsotw.com, pg 598

Howard, Kathleen, The Metropolitan Museum of Art, 1000 Fifth Ave, New York, NY 10028 *Tel:* 212-879-5500; 212-535-7710 *Fax:* 212-396-5062 *E-mail:* info@metmuseum.org *Web Site:* www.metmuseum.org, pg 173

Howard, Kirk, Dundurn Press Ltd, 8 Market St, 2nd fl, Toronto, ON M5E 1M6, Canada *Tel:* 416-214-5544 *Fax:* 416-214-5556 *E-mail:* info@dundurn.com *Web Site:* www.dundurn.com, pg 543

Howard, Marilyn, Creative Freelancers Inc, 99 Park Ave, No 210-A, New York, NY 10016 *Tel:* 203-532-2924 *Toll Free Tel:* 800-398-9544; 888-398-9500 *Fax:* 203-532-2927 *E-mail:* cfonline@freelancers.com *Web Site:* www.freelancers.com, pg 595

Howard, Mary, MicroMash, 6402 S Troy Circle, Englewood, CO 80111-6424 *Tel:* 303-799-0099 *Toll Free Tel:* 800-823-6039 *Fax:* 303-799-1425 *E-mail:* info@micromash.com *Web Site:* www.micromash.net, pg 173

Howard, Meredith, Columbia University Press, 61 W 62 St, New York, NY 10023 *Tel:* 212-459-0600 *Toll Free Tel:* 800-944-8648 *Fax:* 212-459-3678 *Web Site:* www.columbia.edu/cu/cup, pg 65

Howard, Mike, Rainbow Studies International, 1950 S Shepard Ave, El Reno, OK 73036 *Tel:* 405-262-6826 *Toll Free Tel:* 800-242-5348 *Fax:* 405-262-7599 *E-mail:* rsimail@rainbowstudies.com *Web Site:* www.rainbowstudies.com, pg 225

Howard, Richard, Bernard F Conners Prize for Poetry, 541 E 72 St, New York, NY 10021 *Tel:* 212-861-0016 *Fax:* 212-861-4504 *Web Site:* www.theparisreview.org, pg 768

Howard, Roberta, Center for Strategic & International Studies, 1800 "K" St NW, Washington, DC 20006 *Tel:* 202-775-3119 *Fax:* 202-775-3199 *E-mail:* books@csis.org *Web Site:* www.csis.org, pg 57

Howe, Mark, Thomson Delmar Learning, 5 Maxwell Dr, Clifton Park, NY 12065-8007 *Tel:* 518-464-3500 *Toll Free Tel:* 800-347-7707 (cust serv); 800-998-7498 *Fax:* 518-464-0393 *Toll Free Fax:* 800-487-8488 (cust serv) *Web Site:* www.thomson.com; www.delmarlearning.com, pg 269

Howell, Christopher, Lynx House Press, 420 W 24 St, Spokane, WA 99203 *Tel:* 509-624-4894 *Fax:* 509-623-4238, pg 160

Howell, Chuck, Broadcast Pioneers Library of American Broadcasting, Hornbake Library, University of Maryland, College Park, MD 20742 *Tel:* 301-405-9160 *Fax:* 301-314-2634 *E-mail:* bp50@umail.umd.edu *Web Site:* www.lib.umd.edu/LAB, pg 682

Howell, Elinor, Howell Press Inc, 1713-2D Allied Lane, Charlottesville, VA 22903 *Tel:* 434-977-4006 *Toll Free Tel:* 800-868-4512 *Fax:* 434-971-7204 *Toll Free Fax:* 888-971-7204 *E-mail:* custserv@howellpress.com *Web Site:* www.howellpress.com, pg 127

Howell, Rebecca, Kentucky Women Writers Conference, University of Kentucky, 113 Bowman Hall, Lexington, KY 40506-0059 *Tel:* 859-257-8734; 859-257-6420; 859-257-8451 *Fax:* 859-257-8737 *E-mail:* kywwc@hotmail.com *Web Site:* www.uky.edu/conferences/kywwc, pg 744

Howell, Ross A Jr, Howell Press Inc, 1713-2D Allied Lane, Charlottesville, VA 22903 *Tel:* 434-977-4006 *Toll Free Tel:* 800-868-4512 *Fax:* 434-971-7204 *Toll Free Fax:* 888-971-7204 *E-mail:* custserv@howellpress.com *Web Site:* www.howellpress.com, pg 127

Howell, Theresa, Northland Publishing Co, 2900 N Fort Valley Rd, Flagstaff, AZ 86001 *Tel:* 928-774-5251 *Toll Free Tel:* 800-346-3257 *Fax:* 928-774-0592 *E-mail:* info@northlandpub.com; design@northlandpub.com; editorial@northlandpub.com *Web Site:* www.northlandpub.com, pg 193

Howells, W D, Howells House, PO Box 9546, Washington, DC 20016-9546 *Tel:* 202-333-2182 *Fax:* 202-333-2184 *E-mail:* hhi@ix.netcom.com, pg 127

Howes, Chuck, The Writings of Mary Baker Eddy/Publisher, 175 Huntington Ave, Suite A-16-10, Boston, MA 02115 *Tel:* 617-450-3514; 617-450-2000 (Christian Science Church Boston) *Toll Free Tel:* 800-288-7090 *Fax:* 617-450-7334 *Web Site:* www.spirituality.com, pg 305

Howes, Victor, New England Poetry Club, 2 Farrar St, Cambridge, MA 02138 *Tel:* 781-643-0029, pg 695

Howey, Linda, National Geographic Books, 1145 17 St NW, Washington, DC 20036 *Tel:* 202-857-7000 *Fax:* 202-857-7670 *Web Site:* www.nationalgeographics.com, pg 183

Howie, Dianne, Fulcrum Publishing Inc, 16100 Table Mountain Pkwy, Suite 300, Golden, CO 80403 *Tel:* 303-277-1623 *Toll Free Tel:* 800-992-2908 *Fax:* 303-279-7111 *Toll Free Fax:* 800-726-7112 *E-mail:* fulcrum@fulcrum-books.com *Web Site:* www.fulcrum-books.com, pg 101

Howitt, Jeff, American Society of Mechanical Engineers (ASME), 3 Park Ave, New York, NY 10016 *Tel:* 212-591-7000 *Toll Free Tel:* 800-843-2763 (cust serv) *Fax:* 212-591-7674; 973-882-1717 (cust serv) *E-mail:* infocentral@asme.org *Web Site:* www.asme.org, pg 18

Howland, Anna, Ivy House Publishing Group, 5122 Bur Oak Circle, Raleigh, NC 27612 *Tel:* 919-782-0281 *Toll Free Tel:* 800-948-2786 *Fax:* 919-781-9042 *E-mail:* thepublisher@ivyhousebooks.com *Web Site:* www.ivyhousebooks.com, pg 572

Howland, Barry, DawnSignPress, 6130 Nancy Ridge Dr, San Diego, CA 92121-3223 *Tel:* 858-625-0600 *Toll Free Tel:* 800-549-5350 *Fax:* 858-625-2336 *E-mail:* info@dawnsign.com *Web Site:* www.dawnsign.com, pg 77

Howson, Barbara, Kids Can Press Ltd, 2250 Military Rd, Tonawanda, NY 14150 *Tel:* 416-925-5437 (Toronto, ON, Canada) *Toll Free Tel:* 800-265-0884; 866-481-5827 (orders) *Fax:* 416-960-5437 (Toronto, ON, Canada) *E-mail:* info@kidscan.com; lfyman@kidscan.com (orders) *Web Site:* www.kidscanpress.com, pg 145

Howson, Barbara, Kids Can Press Ltd, 29 Birch Ave, Toronto, ON M4V 1E2, Canada *Tel:* 416-925-5437 *Toll Free Tel:* 800-265-0884 *Fax:* 416-960-5437 *E-mail:* info@kidscan.com *Web Site:* kidscanpress.com, pg 552

Hoy, Michael, Loompanics Unlimited, PO Box 1197, Port Townsend, WA 98368-0997 *Tel:* 360-385-5087 *Toll Free Tel:* 800-380-2230 (orders only) *Fax:* 360-385-7785 *E-mail:* editorial@loompanics.com; service@loompanics.com *Web Site:* www.loompanics.com, pg 158

Hoy, Mike, Breakout Productions Inc, PO Box 1643, Port Townsend St, WA 98368-0129 *Tel:* 360-379-1965 *Fax:* 360-379-3794, pg 46

Hoyem, Andrew, The Arion Press, The Presidio, 1802 Hays St, San Francisco, CA 94129 *Tel:* 415-561-2542 *Fax:* 415-561-2545 *E-mail:* arionpress@arionpress.com *Web Site:* www.arionpress.com, pg 23

Hoyle, Karen, Ezra Jack Keats Memorial Fellowship, University of Minnesota, 113 Andersen Library, 222 21 Ave S, Minneapolis, MN 55455 *Tel:* 612-624-4576 *Fax:* 612-625-5525 *E-mail:* clrc@tc.umn.edu *Web Site:* www.ezra-jack-keats.org; special.lib.umn.edu/clrc/, pg 782

Hoyt, Alex, Regnery Publishing Inc, One Massachusetts Ave, NW, Suite 600, Washington, DC 20001 *Tel:* 202-216-0600 *Toll Free Tel:* 888-219-4747 *Fax:* 202-216-0612 *E-mail:* editorial@regnery.com *Web Site:* www.regnery.com, pg 231

Hoyt, Debra Morton, W W Norton & Company Inc, 500 Fifth Ave, New York, NY 10110-0017 *Tel:* 212-354-5500 *Toll Free Tel:* 800-233-4830 (orders & cust serv) *Fax:* 212-869-0856 *Toll Free Fax:* 800-458-6515 *Web Site:* www.wwnorton.com, pg 193

Hrabluik, Allison, Writers' Union of Canada, 90 Richmond St E, Suite 200, Toronto, ON M5C 1P1, Canada *Tel:* 416-703-8982 *Fax:* 416-504-9090 *E-mail:* info@writersunion.ca *Web Site:* www.writersunion.ca, pg 703

Hronek, Janet, Blackwell Publishing Professional, 2121 State Ave, Ames, IA 50014 *Tel:* 515-292-0140 *Toll Free Tel:* 800-862-6657 (orders only) *Fax:* 515-292-3348 *Web Site:* www.blackwellprofessional.com, pg 40

Hruska, Laura M C, Soho Press Inc, 853 Broadway, New York, NY 10003 *Tel:* 212-260-1900 *Fax:* 212-260-1902 *E-mail:* editor@sohopress.com *Web Site:* sohopress.com, pg 252

Hruska, Richard, Humana Press, 999 Riverview Dr, Suite 208, Totowa, NJ 07512 *Tel:* 973-256-1699 *Fax:* 973-256-8341 *E-mail:* humana@humanapr.com *Web Site:* humanapress.com, pg 128

Hsiao, Andy, The New Press, 38 Greene St, 4th fl, New York, NY 10013 *Tel:* 212-629-8802 *Toll Free Tel:* 800-233-4830 (orders) *Fax:* 212-629-8617 *Toll Free Fax:* 800-458-6515 *E-mail:* newpress@thenewpress.com *Web Site:* www.thenewpress.com, pg 188

Hsu, Ellen, InterVarsity Press, 430 E Plaza Dr, Westmont, IL 60559-1234 *Tel:* 630-734-4000 *Toll Free Tel:* 800-843-7225 *Fax:* 630-734-4200 *E-mail:* mail@ivpress.com *Web Site:* www.ivpress.com, pg 138

Hu, Elizabeth, University of British Columbia Press, 2029 West Mall, Vancouver, BC V6T 1Z2, Canada *Tel:* 604-822-5959 *Toll Free Tel:* 877-377-9378 *Fax:* 604-822-6083 *Toll Free Fax:* 800-668-0821 *E-mail:* info@ubcpress.ca *Web Site:* www.ubcpress.ca, pg 564

Hubbard, Loretta W, Crystal Productions, 1812 Johns Dr, Glenview, IL 60025 *Tel:* 847-657-8144 *Toll Free Tel:* 800-255-8629 *Fax:* 847-657-8149 *Toll Free Fax:* 800-657-8149 *E-mail:* custserv@crystalproductions.com *Web Site:* www.crystalproductions.com, pg 74

Hubbard, Thomas N, Crystal Productions, 1812 Johns Dr, Glenview, IL 60025 *Tel:* 847-657-8144 *Toll Free Tel:* 800-255-8629 *Fax:* 847-657-8149 *Toll Free Fax:* 800-657-8149 *E-mail:* custserv@crystalproductions.com *Web Site:* www.crystalproductions.com, pg 74

Hubbs, Roger A, Cornell University Press, 512 E State St, Ithaca, NY 14850 *Tel:* 607-277-2338 *Fax:* 607-277-2374 *E-mail:* cupressinfo@cornell.edu *Web Site:* www.cornellpress.cornell.edu, pg 68

Huber, Fred, Penguin Group (USA) Inc Sales, 375 Hudson St, New York, NY 10014 *Tel:* 212-366-2000 *E-mail:* online@penguinputnam.com *Web Site:* www.penguin.com, pg 208

Huberman, Jack, The Continuing Legal Education Society of British Columbia, 845 Cambie, Suite 300, Vancouver, BC V6B 5T2, Canada *Tel:* 604-669-3544 *Toll Free Tel:* 800-663-0437 *Fax:* 604-669-9260 *Web Site:* www.cle.bc.ca, pg 541

Hudak, Frank, Manatee Publishing, 176 Fairview Ave, Cocoa, FL 32927 *Tel:* 321-632-2932 *Fax:* 321-632-2935 *E-mail:* fseasons@bellsouth.net, pg 162

Hudson, Christopher, Getty Publications, 1200 Getty Center Dr, Suite 500, Los Angeles, CA 90049-1682 *Tel:* 310-440-7365 *Fax:* 310-440-7758 *E-mail:* pubsinfo@getty.edu *Web Site:* www.getty.edu/bookstore, pg 104

Hudson, Jeanne-Marie, Audio Renaissance, 175 Fifth Ave, New York, NY 10010 *Tel:* 212-674-5151 *Toll Free Tel:* 800-330-8477 (cust serv) *Fax:* 917-534-0980 *E-mail:* firstname.lastname@hbpub.com *Web Site:* www.audiorenaissance.com, pg 27

Hudson, Marilyn E, Kindred Productions, 4-169 Riverton Ave, Winnipeg, MB R2L 2E5, Canada *Tel:* 204-669-6575 *Toll Free Tel:* 800-545-7322 *Fax:* 204-654-1865 *E-mail:* kindred@mbconf.ca *Web Site:* www.kindredproductions.com, pg 552

Hudson, Patrick, Tormont/Brimar Publication Inc, 338 St Antoine E, 3rd fl, Montreal, PQ H2Y 1A3, Canada *Tel:* 514-954-1441 *Fax:* 514-954-1443 *E-mail:* info@tormont.ca, pg 563

Hudson, Sandra, University of Georgia Press, 330 Research Dr, Athens, GA 30602-4901 *Tel:* 706-369-6130 *Toll Free Tel:* 800-266-5842 (orders only) *Fax:* 706-369-6131 *E-mail:* books@ugapress.uga.edu *Web Site:* www.ugapress.org, pg 281

Hudson, Travis L, American Geological Institute (AGI), 4220 King St, Alexandria, VA 22302-1507 *Tel:* 703-379-2480 *Fax:* 703-379-7563 *E-mail:* pubs@agiweb.org *Web Site:* www.agiweb.org, pg 14

Hudson-Miller, Joan, LRS, 14214 S Figueroa St, Los Angeles, CA 90061-1034 *Tel:* 310-354-2610 *Toll Free Tel:* 800-255-5002 *Fax:* 310-354-2601 *E-mail:* lrsprint@aol.com *Web Site:* lrs-largeprint.com, pg 159

Huelsing, Kristi, Coaches Choice, 4 Justin Ct, Monterey, CA 93940 *Toll Free Tel:* 888-229-5745 *Fax:* 831-372-6075 *E-mail:* info@coacheschoice.com *Web Site:* www.coacheschoice.com, pg 64

Huey-Heck, Lois, Wood Lake Books Inc, 9025 Jim Bailey Rd, Kelowna, BC V4V 1R2, Canada *Tel:* 250-766-2778 *Toll Free Tel:* 800-663-2775 (orders) *Fax:* 250-766-2736 *Toll Free Fax:* 888-841-9991 (orders) *E-mail:* info@woodlake.com *Web Site:* www.woodlakebooks.com, pg 567

Huff, Bill, Augsburg Fortress Publishers, Publishing House of the Evangelical Lutheran Church in America, 100 S Fifth St, Suite 700, Minneapolis, MN 55402 *Tel:* 612-330-3300 *Toll Free Tel:* 800-426-0115 (ext 639 subns); 800-328-4648 (orders); 800-421-0239 (perms) *Fax:* 612-330-3455 *Toll Free Fax:* 800-421-0239 (perms & copyrights) *E-mail:* customerservice@augsburgfortress.org; copyright@augsburgfortress.org (for reprint permission requests) *Web Site:* www.augsburgfortress.org, pg 28

Huffer, Donna, National Park Service Media Production, Harpers Ferry Ctr, Harpers Ferry, WV 25425 *Tel:* 304-535-6018 *Fax:* 304-535-6144 *Web Site:* www.nps.gov/hfc, pg 184

Hughes, Andrew, Alfred A Knopf, 1745 Broadway, New York, NY 10019 *Tel:* 212-751-2600 *Toll Free Tel:* 800-638-6460 *Fax:* 212-572-2593 *Web Site:* www.randomhouse.com/knopf, pg 146

Hughes, Brigid, Aga Khan Prize for Fiction, 541 E 72 St, New York, NY 10021 *Tel:* 212-861-0016 *Fax:* 212-861-4504 *Web Site:* www.theparisreview.org, pg 782

Hughes, Eileen, The Brookings Institution Press, 1775 Massachusetts Ave NW, Washington, DC 20036-2188 *Tel:* 202-797-6000 *Toll Free Tel:* 800-275-1447 *Fax:* 202-797-6195 *E-mail:* bibooks@brook.edu *Web Site:* www.brookings.edu, pg 48

Hughes, Georgia, New World Library, 14 Pamaron Way, Novato, CA 94949 *Tel:* 415-884-2100 *Toll Free Tel:* 800-227-3900 (ext 52, retail orders) *Fax:* 415-884-2199 (ext 52, retail orders) *E-mail:* escort@newworldlibrary.com *Web Site:* www.newworldlibrary.com, pg 189

Hughes, Gerald T Jr, Houghton Mifflin Co, 222 Berkeley St, Boston, MA 02116-3764 *Tel:* 617-351-5000 *Toll Free Tel:* 800-225-3362 (trade books); 800-733-2828 (text books); 800-225-1464 (college texts) *Fax:* 617-351-1125 *Web Site:* www.hmco.com, pg 126

Hughes, Gordon T II, American Business Media, 675 Third Ave, Suite 415, New York, NY 10017 *Tel:* 212-661-6360 *Fax:* 212-370-0736 *E-mail:* info@abmmail.com *Web Site:* www.americanbusinessmedia.com, pg 676

Hughes, Heather, Sleeping Bear Press™, 310 N Main St, Suite 300, Chelsea, MI 48118 *Tel:* 734-475-4411 *Toll Free Tel:* 800-487-2323 *Fax:* 734-475-0787 *E-mail:* sleepingbear@thomson.com *Web Site:* www.sleepingbearpress.com, pg 250

Hughes, Jennifer, Capital Books Inc, 22841 Quicksilver Dr, Sterling, VA 20166 *Tel:* 703-661-1571 *Toll Free Tel:* 800-758-3756 *Fax:* 703-661-1547 *Web Site:* www.capital-books.com, pg 52

Hughes, John, Basic Books, 387 Park Ave S, 12th fl, New York, NY 10016-8810 *Tel:* 212-340-8100 *Toll Free Tel:* 800-242-7737 (orders) *Fax:* 212-340-8135 *E-mail:* basic.books@perseusbooks.com *Web Site:* www.basicbooks.com, pg 33

Hughes, Kathleen, Capital Books Inc, 22841 Quicksilver Dr, Sterling, VA 20166 *Tel:* 703-661-1571 *Toll Free Tel:* 800-758-3756 *Fax:* 703-661-1547 *Web Site:* www.capital-books.com, pg 52

Hughes, Patricia, St Martin's Press LLC, 175 Fifth Ave, New York, NY 10010 *Tel:* 212-674-5151 *Fax:* 212-420-9314 *E-mail:* firstname.lastname@stmartins.com *Web Site:* www.stmartins.com, pg 238

Hughes, Phil, Specialized Systems Consultants Inc, PO Box 55549, Seattle, WA 98155-0549 *Tel:* 206-782-7733 *Fax:* 206-782-7191 *E-mail:* sales@ssc.com; info@ssc.com *Web Site:* www.ssc.com, pg 255

Huisingh, Rosemary, LinguiSystems Inc, 3100 Fourth Ave, East Moline, IL 61244 *Tel:* 309-755-2300 *Toll Free Tel:* 800-776-4332 *Fax:* 309-755-2377 *E-mail:* service@linguisystems.com *Web Site:* www.linguisystems.com, pg 155

Huisman, Violaine, Seven Stories Press, 140 Watts St, New York, NY 10013 *Tel:* 212-226-8760 *Toll Free Tel:* 800-283-3572 *Fax:* 212-226-1411 *E-mail:* info@sevenstories.com *Web Site:* www.sevenstories.com, pg 245

Hulbert, Jonathan, Wadsworth Publishing, 10 Davis Dr, Belmont, CA 94002-3002 *Toll Free Tel:* 800-357-0092 *Fax:* 650-592-3342 *Toll Free Fax:* 800-522-4923 *Web Site:* www.wadsworth.com, pg 292

Hulburt, Stephen, Prestel Publishing, 900 Broadway, Suite 603, New York, NY 10003 *Tel:* 212-995-2720 *Toll Free Tel:* 888-463-6110 (cust serv) *Fax:* 212-995-2733 *E-mail:* sales@prestel-usa.com *Web Site:* www.prestel.com, pg 218

Hulkower, Lynda, Midmarch Arts Press, 300 Riverside Dr, New York, NY 10025-5239 *Tel:* 212-666-6990, pg 174

Hull, Darrell, E & J Proofreading, 162 W Washington St, Hagerstown, MD 21740 *Tel:* 240-313-9250 *Fax:* 240-313-9250 *E-mail:* ejproofreading@yahoo. com, pg 596

Hull, Stephen P, Justin, Charles & Co, Publishers, 20 Park Plaza, Suite 909, Boston, MA 02116 *Tel:* 617-426-4406 *Fax:* 617-426-4408 *E-mail:* info@ justincharlesbooks.com *Web Site:* www. justincharlesbooks.com, pg 143

Hull-Du Pont, Lonnie, Fleming H Revell, PO Box 6287, Grand Rapids, MI 49516-6287 *Tel:* 616-676-9185 *Toll Free Tel:* 800-877-2665 *Fax:* 616-676-9573 *Web Site:* www.bakerbooks.com, pg 232

Hullett, James, Hackett Publishing Co Inc, PO Box 44937, Indianapolis, IN 46244-0937 *Tel:* 317-635-9250; 617-497-6306 *Fax:* 317-635-9292 *Toll Free Fax:* 800-783-9213 *E-mail:* customer@ hackettpublishing.com *Web Site:* www. hackettpublishing.com, pg 111

Hullinger, Margret S, BNA Books, 1231 25 St NW, Washington, DC 20037 *Tel:* 202-452-4343 *Toll Free Tel:* 800-960-1220 *Fax:* 202-452-4997 (editorial off); 732-346-1624 (cust serv) *E-mail:* books@bna.com *Web Site:* www.bnabooks.com, pg 42

Hulse, Heather, Broadman & Holman Publishers, 127 Ninth Ave N, Nashville, TN 37234-0114 *Tel:* 615-251-2520 *Fax:* 615-251-5004 *Web Site:* www. broadmanholman.com, pg 48

Hulsebosch, Betsy, Bantam Dell Publishing Group, 1745 Broadway, New York, NY 10019 *Tel:* 212-782-9000 *Toll Free Tel:* 800-223-6834 *Fax:* 212-302-7985 *Web Site:* www.randomhouse.com/bantamdell, pg 31

Hultenschmidt, Leah, Dorchester Publishing Co Inc, 200 Madison Ave, Suite 2000, New York, NY 10016 *Tel:* 212-725-8811 *Toll Free Tel:* 800-481-9191 (order dept) *Fax:* 212-532-1054 *E-mail:* dorchedits@ dorchesterpub.com *Web Site:* www.dorchesterpub.com, pg 82

Hultgren, Kellie, The Gislason Agency, 219 SE Main St, Suite 506, Minneapolis, MN 55414 *Tel:* 612-331-8033 *Fax:* 612-331-8115 *E-mail:* gislasonbj@aol.com *Web Site:* www.TheGislasonAgency.com, pg 632

Hultz, Alex, Barron's Educational Series Inc, 250 Wireless Blvd, Hauppauge, NY 11788 *Tel:* 631-434-3311 *Toll Free Tel:* 800-645-3476 *Fax:* 631-434-3723 *E-mail:* info@barronseduc.com *Web Site:* www. barronseduc.com (Books can be purchased online), pg 32

Humbert, Kaye, Health Administration Press, One N Franklin St, Suite 1700, Chicago, IL 60606-3491 *Tel:* 312-424-2800 *Fax:* 312-424-0014 *E-mail:* hap@ ache.org *Web Site:* www.ache.org, pg 119

Humes, Suzanne, Nautilus Award, 109 N Beach Rd, Eastsound, WA 98245 *Tel:* 360-376-2702 *Toll Free Tel:* 800-367-1907 *Fax:* 360-376-2704 *E-mail:* napravision@napra.com *Web Site:* www.napra. com, pg 793

Humes, Suzanne, Networking Alternatives for Publishers, Retailers & Artists Inc (NAPRA), 109 North Beach Rd, Eastsound, WA 98245 *Tel:* 360-376-2702 *Toll Free Tel:* 800-367-1907 *Fax:* 360-376-2704 *E-mail:* napravision@napra.com *Web Site:* www.napra. com, pg 695

Hummel, Kermit, Berkshire House, 1206 Rte 12, Woodstock, VT 05091 *Tel:* 802-457-4826 *Toll Free Tel:* 800-245-4151 *Fax:* 802-457-1678 *Web Site:* www. countrymanpress.com, pg 37

Hummel, Kermit, The Countryman Press, 1206 Rte 12 N, Woodstock, VT 05091 *Tel:* 802-457-4826 *Toll Free Tel:* 800-245-4151 *Fax:* 802-457-1678 *E-mail:* countrymanpress@wwnorton.com *Web Site:* www.countrymanpress.com, pg 70

Hummel, Sr Roberta, Pauline Books & Media, 50 St Paul's Ave, Jamaica Plain, Boston, MA 02130 *Tel:* 617-522-8911 *Toll Free Tel:* 800-876-4463 (orders only) *Fax:* 617-541-9805 *E-mail:* businessoffice@ pauline.org; orderentry@pauline.org *Web Site:* www. pauline.org, pg 205

Hummelsheim, Pam, Liguori Publications, One Liguori Dr, Liguori, MO 63057-9999 *Tel:* 636-464-2500 *Toll Free Tel:* 800-464-2555 *Fax:* 636-464-8449 *Web Site:* www.liguori.org, pg 155

Humphrey, Bob, Leisure Arts Inc, 5701 Ranch Dr, Little Rock, AR 72223 *Tel:* 501-868-8800 *Toll Free Tel:* 800-643-8030 *Fax:* 501-868-8937 *Web Site:* www. leisurearts.com, pg 152

Humphrey, Doug, Cambridge Educational, 2572 Brunswick Ave, Lawrenceville, NJ 08648-4128 *Toll Free Tel:* 800-468-4227 *Toll Free Fax:* 800-329-6687 *E-mail:* custserve@cambridgeeducational.com *Web Site:* www.cambridgeeducational.com, pg 51

Humphrey, John H, Journal of Roman Archaeology LLC, 95 Peleg Rd, Portsmouth, RI 02871 *Tel:* 401-683-1955 *Fax:* 401-683-1975 *E-mail:* jra@journalofromanarch. com *Web Site:* www.journalofromanarch.com, pg 142

Humphrey, Megan, Scholastic Library/Grolier National Library Week Grant, 50 E Huron St, Chicago, IL 60611 *Tel:* 312-280-4020 *Toll Free Tel:* 800-545-2433 (ext 4020) *Fax:* 312-944-8520 *E-mail:* pio@ala.org *Web Site:* www.ala.org, pg 804

Humphrey, Shonna, Maine Writers & Publishers Alliance, 1326 Washington St, Bath, ME 04530 *Tel:* 207-386-1400 *Fax:* 207-386-1401 *Web Site:* www. mainewriters.org, pg 690

Hundley, Amy, Grove/Atlantic Inc, 841 Broadway, 4th fl, New York, NY 10003-4793 *Tel:* 212-614-7850 *Toll Free Tel:* 800-521-0178 *Fax:* 212-614-7886 *Web Site:* www.groveatlantic.com, pg 110

Hung, David, Rapids Christian Press Inc, 5777 Vista Dr, Ferndale, WA 98248 *Tel:* 360-384-1747 *Fax:* 360-384-1747, pg 227

Hung, Helena, Penguin Group (Canada), 10 Alcorn Ave, Suite 300, Toronto, ON M4V 3B2, Canada *Tel:* 416-925-2249 *Fax:* 416-925-0068 *Web Site:* www.penguin. ca, pg 557

Hunnicutt, Jessie, G & S Editors, 410 Baylor, Austin, TX 78703-5312 *Tel:* 512-478-5341 *Fax:* 512-476-4756 *Web Site:* www.gstype.com, pg 599

Hunt, Katrina W, School of Government, University of North Carolina, CB 3330, Chapel Hill, NC 27599-3330 *Tel:* 919-966-4119 *Fax:* 919-962-2707 *E-mail:* khunt@iogmail.iog.unc.edu *Web Site:* www. sog.unc.edu, pg 243

Hunt, Kevin, Klutz, 455 Portage Ave, Palo Alto, CA 94306 *Tel:* 650-857-0888 *Fax:* 650-857-9110 *Web Site:* www.klutz.com, pg 146

Hunt, Margaret, Purdue University Press, S Campus Courts-E, 509 Harrison St, West Lafayette, IN 47907-2025 *Tel:* 765-494-2038 *Toll Free Tel:* 800-247-6553 (orders) *Fax:* 765-496-2442 *E-mail:* pupress@purdue. edu *Web Site:* www.thepress.purdue.edu, pg 222

Hunt, Maurice, Baylor University, Writing Program, One Baylor Place, Waco, TX 76798 *Tel:* 254-710-1768 *Fax:* 254-710-3894 *Web Site:* www.baylor.edu, pg 751

Hunt, Paula, Evan-Moor Educational Publishers, 18 Lower Ragsdale Dr, Monterey, CA 93940 *Tel:* 831-649-5901 *Toll Free Tel:* 800-777-4362 *Fax:* 831-649-6256 *E-mail:* customerservice@evan-moor.com *Web Site:* www.evan-moor.com, pg 92

Hunt, Richard, Emmis Books, 1700 Madison Rd, 2nd fl, Cincinnati, OH 45206 *Tel:* 513-861-4045 *Toll Free Tel:* 800-913-9563 *Fax:* 513-861-4430 *E-mail:* info@ emmis.com *Web Site:* www.emmisbooks.com, pg 90

Hunter, Ann, AAH Graphics Inc, 187 Myra Lane, Fort Valley, VA 22652 *Tel:* 540-933-6210 *Fax:* 540-933-6523 *Web Site:* www.aahgraphics.com, pg 589

Hunter, Ann A, Loft Press Inc, 181 Myra Lane, Fort Valley, VA 22652 *Tel:* 540-933-6210 *Fax:* 540-933-6523, pg 157

Hunter, Debra S, Jossey-Bass, 989 Market St, San Francisco, CA 94103-1741 *Tel:* 415-433-1740 *Toll Free Tel:* 800-956-7739 *Fax:* 415-433-0499 (edit/ mktg) *Web Site:* www.josseybass.com; www.pfeiffer. com, pg 142

Hunter, Diana, Consumer Press, 13326 SW 28 St, Suite 102, Fort Lauderdale, FL 33330-1102 *Tel:* 954-370-9153 *Fax:* 954-472-1008 *E-mail:* bookguest@aol.com *Web Site:* consumerpress.com, pg 67

Hunter, Diana, ProStar Publications Inc, 3 Church Circle, Suite 109, Annapolis, MD 21401 *Tel:* 310-280-1010 *Toll Free Tel:* 800-481-6277 *Fax:* 310-280-1025 *Toll Free Fax:* 800-487-6277 *E-mail:* editor@ prostarpublications.com *Web Site:* www. prostarpublications.com; www.nauticalbooks.com, pg 220

Hunter, Michael, Hunter Publishing Inc, 130 Campus Dr, Edison, NJ 08818 *Tel:* 732-225-1900 (orders) *Toll Free Tel:* 800-255-0343 *Fax:* 732-417-1744 *E-mail:* comments@hunterpublishing.com *Web Site:* www.hunterpublishing.com, pg 129

Hunter, Mike R, University College of Cape Breton Press Inc, 1250 Grand Lake Rd, Sydney, NS B1P 6L2, Canada *Tel:* 902-563-1604; 902-563-1421 *Fax:* 902-563-1177 *E-mail:* uucb_press@uccb.ca *Web Site:* www.uccbpress.ca, pg 564

Hunter, Stephen R, Loft Press Inc, 181 Myra Lane, Fort Valley, VA 22652 *Tel:* 540-933-6210 *Fax:* 540-933-6523, pg 157

Hunting, Constance, Puckerbrush Press, 76 Main St, Orono, ME 04473 *Tel:* 207-866-4868; 207-581-3832, pg 221

Huntting, Nancy, Definition Press, 141 Greene St, New York, NY 10012 *Tel:* 212-777-4490 *Fax:* 212-777-4426 *E-mail:* mc@definitionpress.org *Web Site:* www. definitionpress.org, pg 570

Hupping, Carol, Jewish Publication Society, 2100 Arch St, 2nd fl, Philadelphia, PA 19103 *Tel:* 215-832-0600 *Toll Free Tel:* 800-234-3151 *Fax:* 215-568-2017 *E-mail:* jewishbook@jewishpub.org *Web Site:* www. jewishpub.org, pg 141

Hurdle, Priscilla, Cornell University Press, 512 E State St, Ithaca, NY 14850 *Tel:* 607-277-2338 *Fax:* 607-277-2374 *E-mail:* cupressinfo@cornell.edu *Web Site:* www.cornellpress.cornell.edu, pg 68

Hurlburt, Carol, Graphic Communications Council, 1899 Preston White Dr, Reston, VA 20191-4367 *Tel:* 703-648-1768 *Fax:* 703-620-0994 *E-mail:* edcouncil@npes. org *Web Site:* www.npes.org/edcouncil, pg 688

Hurlburt, Carol J, NPES The Association for Suppliers of Printing, Publishing & Converting Technologies, 1899 Preston White Dr, Reston, VA 20191-4367 *Tel:* 703-264-7200 *Fax:* 703-620-0994 *E-mail:* npes@ npes.org *Web Site:* www.npes.org, pg 696

Hurley, Cheryl, The Library of America, 14 E 60 St, New York, NY 10022 *Tel:* 212-308-3360 *Fax:* 212-750-8352 *E-mail:* info@loa.org *Web Site:* www.loa. org; www.loaacademic.org, pg 154

Hurley, Elsa, Candice Fuhrman Literary Agency, 60 Greenwood Way, Mill Valley, CA 94941 *Tel:* 415-383-6081 *Fax:* 415-384-0739 *E-mail:* candicef@pacbell. net, pg 632

Hurley, Kevin, Elsevier, 11830 Westline Industrial Dr, St Louis, MO 63146 *Tel:* 314-872-8370 *Toll Free Tel:* 800-325-4177 *Fax:* 314-432-1380 *Web Site:* www. elsevier.com; www.elsevierhealth.com, pg 89

Hurley, Kevin, Mosby Journal Division, 11830 Westline Industrial Dr, St Louis, MO 63146 *Tel:* 314-872-8370 *Toll Free Tel:* 800-325-4177 *Web Site:* www. elsevierhealth.com, pg 179

Hurley, Kevin, W B Saunders Ltd, 170 S Independence Mall W, Suite 300 E, Philadelphia, PA 19106-3399 *Tel:* 215-238-7800 *Toll Free Tel:* 800-545-2522 (cust serv) *Fax:* 215-238-7883 *Web Site:* www. elsevierhealth.com, pg 240

Hurston, Vernita, The Guilford Press, 72 Spring St, New York, NY 10012 *Tel:* 212-431-9800 *Toll Free Tel:* 800-365-7006 (orders) *Fax:* 212-966-6708 *E-mail:* orders@guilford.com *Web Site:* www.guilford. com, pg 111

Hurvitz, David J, Leadership Directories Inc, 104 Fifth Ave, New York, NY 10011 *Tel:* 212-627-4140 *Fax:* 212-645-0931 *E-mail:* info@ leadershipdirectories.com *Web Site:* www. leadershipdirectories.com, pg 150

Huseman, Beth, Stewart, Tabori & Chang, 115 W 18 St, 5th fl, New York, NY 10011 *Tel:* 212-519-1200 *Fax:* 212-519-1210 *Web Site:* www.abramsbooks.com, pg 260

Hushion, Jacqueline, Canadian Publishers' Council (CPC), 250 Merton St, Suite 203, Toronto, ON M4S 1B1, Canada *Tel:* 416-322-7011 *Fax:* 416-322-6999 *E-mail:* pubadmin@pubcouncil.ca *Web Site:* www. pubcouncil.ca, pg 683

Huss, Sandy, University of Alabama Program in Creative Writing, PO Box 870244, Tuscaloosa, AL 35487-0244 *Tel:* 205-348-0766 *Fax:* 205-348-1388 *E-mail:* writeua@english.as.ua.edu *Web Site:* www.as. ua.edu/english, pg 755

Hussey, Mark, Pace University Press, 41 Park Row, Rm 1510, New York, NY 10038 *Tel:* 212-346-1405 *Fax:* 212-661-8169 *Web Site:* www.pace.edu/press, pg 201

Hussey, Mary Theresa, Harlequin Enterprises Ltd, 233 Broadway, Suite 1001, New York, NY 10279 *Tel:* 212-553-4200 *Fax:* 212-227-8969 *E-mail:* customer. ecare@harlequin.ca *Web Site:* www.eharlequin.com; www.luna-books.com; www.mirabooks.com; www. reddressink.com; www.steeplehill.com, pg 115

Hussey, Penny, NovelBooks Inc, PO Box 661, Douglas, MA 01516-0661 *Tel:* 508-476-1611 *Fax:* 508-476-3866 *E-mail:* publisher@novelbooksinc.com *Web Site:* www.novelbooksinc.com, pg 194

Hussey, Valerie, Kids Can Press Ltd, 2250 Military Rd, Tonawanda, NY 14150 *Tel:* 416-925-5437 (Toronto, ON, Canada) *Toll Free Tel:* 800-265-0884; 866-481-5827 (orders) *Fax:* 416-960-5437 (Toronto, ON, Canada) *E-mail:* info@kidscan.com; lfyman@kidscan. com (orders) *Web Site:* www.kidscanpress.com, pg 145

Hussey, Valerie, Kids Can Press Ltd, 29 Birch Ave, Toronto, ON M4V 1E2, Canada *Tel:* 416-925-5437 *Toll Free Tel:* 800-265-0884 *Fax:* 416-960-5437 *E-mail:* info@kidscan.com *Web Site:* kidscanpress. com, pg 552

Hustad, Megan, Counterpoint Press, 387 Park Ave S, New York, NY 10016 *Tel:* 212-340-8100 *Fax:* 212-340-8135 (edit); 212-340-8115 *E-mail:* counterpointpress@perseusbooks.com *Web Site:* www.counterpointpress.com, pg 70

Hutchings, Linda, The Fairmont Press Inc, 700 Indian Trail, Lilburn, GA 30047 *Tel:* 770-925-9388 *Fax:* 770-381-9865 *Web Site:* www.fairmontpress.com, pg 94

Hutchings, Stephen, Altitude Publishing Canada Ltd, 1500 Railway Ave, Canmore, AB T1W 1P6, Canada *Tel:* 403-678-6888 *Toll Free Tel:* 800-957-6888 *Fax:* 403-678-6951 *Toll Free Fax:* 800-957-1477 *E-mail:* orderdesk@altitudepublishing.com; sales@ altitudepublishing.com (ordering) *Web Site:* www. altitudepublishing.com, pg 535

Hutchinson, Charles, Geoscience Press Inc, PO Box 42948, Tuscon, AZ 85733-2948 *Tel:* 520-529-1567 *Fax:* 520-529-1567 *E-mail:* geobook@ix.netcom.com, pg 104

Hutchinson, Robert, BrownTrout Publishers Inc, PO Box 280070, San Francisco, CA 94128-0070 *Tel:* 650-340-9800 *Toll Free Tel:* 800-777-7812 *Fax:* 310-316-1138 *E-mail:* sales@browntrout.com *Web Site:* www. browntrout.com, pg 49

Hutchinson-Cleaves, Geoffrey, Papyrus & Letterbox of London Publishers, 10501 Broom Hill Dr, Las Vegas, NV 89134-7339 *Tel:* 702-256-3838 *E-mail:* LB27383@earthlink.net *Web Site:* booksbyletterbox.com, pg 203

Hutchison, Garrison Flint, G F Hutchison Press, 319 S Block Ave, Suite 17, Fayetteville, AR 72701 *Tel:* 479-587-1726 *E-mail:* drwriterguy@netscape.net *Web Site:* www.familypress.com, pg 129

Hutchison, Margot, Waterside Productions Inc, 2187 Newcastle Ave, Suite 204, Cardiff, CA 92007 *Tel:* 760-632-9190 *Fax:* 760-632-9295 *Web Site:* www. waterside.com, pg 660

Hutto, Alicia, South Carolina Bar, Continuing Legal Education Div, 950 Taylor St, Columbia, SC 29201 *Tel:* 803-771-0333 *Toll Free Tel:* 800-768-7787 *Fax:* 803-252-8427 *E-mail:* scbar-info@scbar.org *Web Site:* www.scbar.org, pg 253

Hutton, Caroline Du Bois, Jones Hutton Literary Associates, 160 N Compo Rd, Westport, CT 06880 *Tel:* 203-226-2588 *Fax:* 509-356-5190 *Web Site:* www. marquiswhoswho.net/huttonandhutton, pg 636

Hutton, Eileen, Brilliance Audio, 1704 Eaton Dr, Grand Haven, MI 49417 *Tel:* 616-846-5256 *Toll Free Tel:* 800-648-2312 (orders only) *Fax:* 616-846-0630 *Web Site:* www.brillianceaudio.com, pg 48

Hutton, Paul Andrew, SPUR Awards, 1012 Fair St, Franklin, TN 37064 *Tel:* 615-791-1444 *Fax:* 615-791-1444 *Web Site:* www.westernwriters.org, pg 807

Hutton, Virginia DuBois, Jones Hutton Literary Associates, 160 N Compo Rd, Westport, CT 06880 *Tel:* 203-226-2588 *Fax:* 509-356-5190 *Web Site:* www. marquiswhoswho.net/huttonandhutton, pg 636

Huxley, Michael, Starbooks Press, 1391 Blvd of the Arts, Sarasota, FL 34236-2904 *Tel:* 941-957-1281 *Fax:* 941-955-3829, pg 258

Huyghe, Patrick, Paraview Publishing, 191 Seventh Ave, Suite 2F, New York, NY 10011 *Tel:* 212-989-3616 *Fax:* 212-989-3662 *E-mail:* info@paraview.com; publisher@paraview.com *Web Site:* www.paraview. com, pg 204

Hwang, Cindy, Berkley Books, 375 Hudson St, New York, NY 10014 *Tel:* 212-366-2000 *Fax:* 212-366-2666 *E-mail:* online@penguinputnam.com *Web Site:* www.penguin.com, pg 36

Hwang, Cindy, Berkley Publishing Group, 375 Hudson St, New York, NY 10014 *Tel:* 212-366-2000 *E-mail:* online@penguinputnam.com *Web Site:* www. penguin.com, pg 37

Hwang, Phoebe, Seven Stories Press, 140 Watts St, New York, NY 10013 *Tel:* 212-226-8760 *Toll Free Tel:* 800-283-3572 *Fax:* 212-226-1411 *E-mail:* info@ sevenstories.com *Web Site:* www.sevenstories.com, pg 245

Hyatt, Carrie, Practice Management Information Corp (PMIC), 4727 Wilshire Blvd, Suite 300, Los Angeles, CA 90010 *Tel:* 323-954-0224 *Fax:* 323-954-0253 *E-mail:* orders@medicalbookstore.com *Web Site:* www.pmiconline.com, pg 216

Hyatt, Michael, Thomas Nelson Inc, 501 Nelson Place, Nashville, TN 37214 *Tel:* 615-889-9000 *Toll Free Tel:* 800-251-4000 *Fax:* 615-902-1610 *E-mail:* publicity@thomasnelson.com *Web Site:* www. thomasnelson.com, pg 269

Hyde, Dara, Grove/Atlantic Inc, 841 Broadway, 4th fl, New York, NY 10003-4793 *Tel:* 212-614-7850 *Toll Free Tel:* 800-521-0178 *Fax:* 212-614-7886 *Web Site:* www.groveatlantic.com, pg 110

Hyman, Alan, Picasso Project, 1109 Geary Blvd, San Francisco, CA 94109 *Tel:* 415-292-6500 *Fax:* 415-292-6594 *E-mail:* editeur@earthlink.net (editorial); picasso@art-books.com (orders) *Web Site:* art-books. com, pg 212

Hyman, Alan, Wittenborn Art Books, 1109 Geary Blvd, San Francisco, CA 94109 *Tel:* 415-292-6500 *Toll Free Tel:* 800-660-6403 *Fax:* 415-292-6594 *E-mail:* wittenborn@art-books.com *Web Site:* art-books.com, pg 302

Hyman, Lisa, IMG Literary, 825 Seventh Ave, 9th fl, New York, NY 10019 *Tel:* 212-774-6900 *Fax:* 212-246-1118 *Web Site:* www.imgworld.com, pg 635

Hyman, Mark, Wittenborn Art Books, 1109 Geary Blvd, San Francisco, CA 94109 *Tel:* 415-292-6500 *Toll Free Tel:* 800-660-6403 *Fax:* 415-292-6594 *E-mail:* wittenborn@art-books.com *Web Site:* art-books.com, pg 302

Iacofano, Judy, Teacher's Discovery, 2741 Paldan Dr, Auburn Hills, MI 48326 *Tel:* 248-340-7220 ext 207 *Toll Free Tel:* 800-521-3897 *Fax:* 248-340-7212 *Toll Free Fax:* 888-987-2436 *Web Site:* www. teachersdiscovery.com, pg 265

Iadanza, Patricia, The Haworth Press Inc, 10 Alice St, Binghamton, NY 13904-1580 *Tel:* 607-722-5857 *Toll Free Tel:* 800-429-6784 *Fax:* 607-722-1424 *Toll Free Fax:* 800-895-0582 *E-mail:* getinfo@haworthpressinc. com *Web Site:* www.haworthpress.com, pg 118

Ianello, George, Cambridge University Press, 40 W 20 St, New York, NY 10011-4211 *Tel:* 212-924-3900 *Toll Free Tel:* 800-899-5222 *Fax:* 212-691-3239 *Web Site:* www.cambridge.org, pg 52

Ibarra, Allan, Key Porter Books Ltd, 70 The Esplanade, 3rd fl, Toronto, ON M5E 1R2, Canada *Tel:* 416-862-7777 *Fax:* 416-862-2304 *E-mail:* info@keyporter.com *Web Site:* www.keyporter.com, pg 551

Ibeiss, Dennis, Garland Science Publishing, 270 Madison Ave, New York, NY 10016 *Tel:* 212-216-7800 *Fax:* 212-947-3027 *E-mail:* info@garland.com *Web Site:* www.garlandscience.com, pg 102

Igoe, Robert B Jr, North Country Books Inc, 311 Turner St, Utica, NY 13501-1729 *Tel:* 315-735-4877 *Fax:* 315-738-4342 *E-mail:* ncbooks@usadatanet.net *Web Site:* www.northcountrybooks.com, pg 192

Iguchi, Yasuyo, The MIT Press, 5 Cambridge Ctr, Cambridge, MA 02142 *Tel:* 617-253-5646 *Toll Free Tel:* 800-405-1619 (orders only) *Fax:* 617-258-6779 *Web Site:* mitpress.mit.edu, pg 175

Ihrig, Chris, All Wild-Up Productions, 303 Fourth Ave SE, Puyallup, WA 98372 *Tel:* 206-457-1949 *Fax:* 206-457-1949 *E-mail:* mail@allwildup.com *Web Site:* www.allwildup.com, pg 8

Ikeda, Masako, University of Hawaii Press, 2840 Kolowalu St, Honolulu, HI 96822 *Tel:* 808-956-8255 *Toll Free Tel:* 888-847-7377 *Fax:* 808-988-6052 *Toll Free Fax:* 800-650-7811 *E-mail:* uhpbooks@hawaii. edu *Web Site:* www.uhpress.hawaii.edu, pg 281

Ikler, Jeffrey, Prentice Hall School, One Lake St, Upper Saddle River, NJ 07458 *Tel:* 201-236-7000, pg 217

Illig, Linda, ASM Press, 1752 "N" St NW, Washington, DC 20036-2904 *Tel:* 202-737-3600 *Toll Free Tel:* 800-546-2416 *Fax:* 202-942-9342 *E-mail:* books@asmusa. org *Web Site:* www.asmpress.org, pg 25

Illingworth, John, Scholastic Trade Division, 557 Broadway, New York, NY 10012 *Tel:* 212-343-6100; 212-343-4685 (export sales) *Fax:* 212-343-4714 (export sales) *Web Site:* www.scholastic.com, pg 242

Imber-Black, Evan, Family Process Institute Inc, c/o Eldredge, Fox & Porretti, 180 Canal View Blvd, Suite 100, Rochester, NY 14623 *Tel:* 716-879-4900 (ext 153) *Fax:* 212-744-0206 *E-mail:* info@familyprocess. org *Web Site:* www.familyprocess.org, pg 95

Imelli, Bryan, The Wine Appreciation Guild Ltd, 360 Swift Ave, Unit 30-40, South San Francisco, CA 94080 *Tel:* 650-866-3020 *Toll Free Tel:* 800-231-9463 *Fax:* 650-866-3513 *E-mail:* shannon@ wineappreciation.com; info@wineappreciation.com *Web Site:* www.wineappreciation.com, pg 301

Imig, David G, American Association of Colleges for Teacher Education (AACTE), 1307 New York Ave NW, Suite 300, Washington, DC 20005-4701 *Tel:* 202-293-2450 *Fax:* 202-457-8095 *E-mail:* aacte@aacte.org *Web Site:* www.aacte.org, pg 11

Imperati, Annette, Springer Publishing Co Inc, 11 W 42 St, New York, NY 10036 *Tel:* 212-431-4370 *Toll Free Tel:* 877-687-7476 *Fax:* 212-941-7842 *E-mail:* springer@springerpub.com *Web Site:* www. springerpub.com, pg 256

Ina, Beth, University of Nebraska Press, 233 N Eighth St, Lincoln, NE 68588-0255 *Tel:* 402-472-3581 *Toll Free Tel:* 800-755-1105 (orders) *Fax:* 402-472-0308 *Toll Free Fax:* 800-526-2617 *E-mail:* press@unl. edu *Web Site:* www.nebraskapress.unl.edu; www. bisonbooks.com, pg 283

Ingalls, Barbara, High Country Publishers Ltd, 197 New Market Center, No 135, Boone, NC 28607 *Tel:* 828-964-0590 *Fax:* 828-262-1973 *E-mail:* editor@ highcountrypublishers.com *Web Site:* www. highcountrypublishers.com, pg 122

Ingalls, Johanna, Akashic Books, PO Box 1456, New York, NY 10009 *Tel:* 212-433-1875 *Fax:* 212-414-3199 *E-mail:* akashic7@aol.com *Web Site:* www. akashicbooks.com, pg 7

Ingalls, Robert, High Country Publishers Ltd, 197 New Market Center, No 135, Boone, NC 28607 *Tel:* 828-964-0590 *Fax:* 828-262-1973 *E-mail:* editor@ highcountrypublishers.com *Web Site:* www. highcountrypublishers.com, pg 122

Ingle, Stephen, WordCo Indexing Services, 49 Church St, Norwich, CT 06360 *Tel:* 860-886-2532 *Toll Free Tel:* 877-967-3263 *Fax:* 860-886-1155 *Web Site:* www. wordco.com, pg 614

Inglis, John, Cold Spring Harbor Laboratory Press, 500 Sunnyside Blvd, Woodbury, NY 11797-2924 *Tel:* 516-422-4100 *Toll Free Tel:* 800-843-4388 *Fax:* 516-422-4097 *E-mail:* cshpress@cshl.edu *Web Site:* www. cshlpress.com, pg 64

Ingram, Sheila, Chosen Books, PO Box 6287, Grand Rapids, MI 49516-6287 *Tel:* 616-676-9185 *Toll Free Tel:* 800-877-2665 *Fax:* 616-676-2315 *Web Site:* www. bakerpublishinggroup.com, pg 61

Ingram, Sheila, Fleming H Revell, PO Box 6287, Grand Rapids, MI 49516-6287 *Tel:* 616-676-9185 *Toll Free Tel:* 800-877-2665 *Fax:* 616-676-9573 *Web Site:* www. bakerbooks.com, pg 232

Inkei, Peter, Central European University Press, 400 W 59 St, New York, NY 10019 *Tel:* 212-547-6932 *Fax:* 646-557-2416 *Web Site:* www.ceupress.com, pg 57

Inkster, Tim, Porcupine's Quill Inc, 68 Main St, Erin, ON N0B 1T0, Canada *Tel:* 519-833-9158 *Fax:* 519-833-9845 *E-mail:* pql@sentex.net *Web Site:* www. sentex.net/~pql, pg 558

Innes, Christine, Doubleday Canada, One Toronto St, Suite 300, Toronto, ON M5C 2V6, Canada *Tel:* 416-364-4449 *Fax:* 416-957-1587 *Web Site:* www. randomhouse.ca, pg 542

Innes, Christine, Seal Books, One Toronto St, Suite 300, Toronto, ON M5C 2V6, Canada *Tel:* 416-364-4449 *Toll Free Tel:* 888-523-9292 (order desk) *Fax:* 416-957-1587 *Web Site:* www.randomhouse.ca, pg 560

Inskeep, Evelyn, Money Market Directories, 320 E Main St, Charlottesville, VA 22902 *Tel:* 434-977-1450 *Toll Free Tel:* 800-446-2810 *Fax:* 434-979-9962 *Web Site:* www.mmdwebaccess.com, pg 177

Ippolito, Andrew V, LDA Award for Excellence, 42-46 209 St, Suite B-11, Bayside, NY 11361-2747 *Tel:* 718-224-9484 *Toll Free Tel:* 888-388-9887 *Fax:* 718-224-9487 *Web Site:* www.lilrc.org/~ncla1/awards.html, pg 784

Ippolito, Andrew V, LDA Publishers, 42-46 209 St, Bayside, NY 11361-2747 *Tel:* 718-224-9484 *Toll Free Tel:* 888-388-9887 *Fax:* 718-224-9487 *Web Site:* www. ldapublishers.com, pg 150

Ippolito, Chris, W W Norton & Company Inc, 500 Fifth Ave, New York, NY 10110-0017 *Tel:* 212-354-5500 *Toll Free Tel:* 800-233-4830 (orders & cust serv) *Fax:* 212-869-0856 *Toll Free Fax:* 800-458-6515 *Web Site:* www.wwnorton.com, pg 193

Ireland, Pauline, Cambridge University Press, 40 W 20 St, New York, NY 10011-4211 *Tel:* 212-924-3900 *Toll Free Tel:* 800-899-5222 *Fax:* 212-691-3239 *Web Site:* www.cambridge.org, pg 52

Irons, David, Holt, Rinehart and Winston, 10801 N MoPac Expy, Bldg 3, Austin, TX 78759 *Tel:* 512-721-7000 *Toll Free Tel:* 800-225-5425 (cust serv) *Fax:* 512-721-7833 (mktg); 512-721-7898 (edit) *Web Site:* www.hrw.com, pg 124

Irvine, Dominique, Reference Publications Inc, 218 Saint Clair River Dr, Algonac, MI 48001 *Tel:* 810-794-5722 *Fax:* 810-794-7463 *E-mail:* referencepub@sbcglobal. com, pg 230

Irvine, Marie Aline, Reference Publications Inc, 218 Saint Clair River Dr, Algonac, MI 48001 *Tel:* 810-794-5722 *Fax:* 810-794-7463 *E-mail:* referencepub@ sbcglobal.com, pg 230

Irwin, Elizabeth, Trident Media Inc, 801 N Pitt St, Suite 123, Alexandria, VA 22314 *Tel:* 703-684-6895 *Fax:* 703-684-0639 *E-mail:* info@samhost.net *Web Site:* www.edenplaza.com, pg 275

Irwin, Miriam, Mosaic Press, 358 Oliver Rd, Cincinnati, OH 45215 *Tel:* 513-761-5977 *Fax:* 513-761-5977 *Web Site:* www.mosaicpress.com, pg 179

Isaacs, Stephen, Professional Publishing, 1333 Burr Ridge Pkwy, Burr Ridge, IL 60527 *Tel:* 630-789-4000; 630-789-5500 *Toll Free Tel:* 800-2McGraw (262-4729) *Fax:* 630-789-6933 *Web Site:* www.books.mcgraw-hill.com, pg 220

Isaacson, Dana, Random House Publishing Group, 1745 Broadway, New York, NY 10019 *Tel:* 800-200-3552 *Toll Free Fax:* 800-200-3552 *Web Site:* www.randomhouse.com, pg 227

Isenberg, Joy, Farrar, Straus & Giroux, LLC, 19 Union Sq W, New York, NY 10003 *Tel:* 212-741-6900 *Fax:* 212-741-6973 *Web Site:* www.fsgbooks.com, pg 95

Isherwood, Judith, Shoreline, 23 Sainte Anne, Ste Anne de Bellevue, PQ H9X 1L1, Canada *Tel:* 514-457-5733 *Fax:* 514-457-5733 *E-mail:* shoreline@sympatico.ca *Web Site:* www.shorelinepress.ca, pg 561

Ishii, Larry, Jossey-Bass, 989 Market St, San Francisco, CA 94103-1741 *Tel:* 415-433-1740 *Toll Free Tel:* 800-956-7739 *Fax:* 415-433-0499 (edit/mktg) *Web Site:* www.josseybass.com; www.pfeiffer.com, pg 142

Island, David J, Oregon Catholic Press, 5536 NE Hassalo, Portland, OR 97213 *Tel:* 503-281-1191 *Toll Free Tel:* 800-548-8749 *Fax:* 503-282-3486 *Toll Free Fax:* 800-843-8181 *E-mail:* liturgy@ocp.org *Web Site:* www.ocp.org, pg 198

Island MBA, David, Pastoral Press, 5536 NE Hassalo, Portland, OR 97213-3638 *Tel:* 503-281-1191 *Toll Free Tel:* 800-548-8749 *Fax:* 503-282-3486 *Toll Free Fax:* 800-462-7329 *E-mail:* liturgy@ocp.org *Web Site:* www.ocp.org, pg 205

Israel, Claire, Simon & Schuster Online, 1230 Avenue of the Americas, New York, NY 10020 *Tel:* 212-698-7547 *Fax:* 212-632-8070 *E-mail:* ssonline@ simonsays.com *Web Site:* www.simonsays.com; www. simonsayskids.com; www.simonsaysshop.com, pg 249

Issac, Joanne, American Numismatic Society, 26 Fulton St, New York, NY 10038 *Tel:* 212-571-4470 *Fax:* 212-571-4479 *E-mail:* info@amnumsoc.org; info@ numismatics.org *Web Site:* www.amnumsoc.org; www. numismatics.org, pg 16

Isselhardt, Tordis Ilg, Images from the Past Inc, 155 W Main St, Bennington, VT 05201-2105 *Tel:* 802-442-3204 *Toll Free Tel:* 888-442-3204 *Fax:* 802-442-3204 *E-mail:* info@imagesfromthepast.com; sales@imagesfromthepast.com *Web Site:* www. imagesfromthepast.com, pg 131

Itskevich, Jennifer, Barricade Books Inc, 185 Bridge Plaza N, Suite 308A, Fort Lee, NJ 07024 *Tel:* 201-944-7600 *Fax:* 201-944-6363 *E-mail:* customerservice@barricadebooks.com *Web Site:* www.barricadebooks.com, pg 32

Iucolano, Donna, e-Scholastic, 568 Broadway, 9th fl, New York, NY 10012 *Tel:* 212-343-7100 *Fax:* 212-343-4949, pg 85

Iucolano, Donna, Scholastic Inc, 557 Broadway, New York, NY 10012 *Tel:* 212-343-4469 *Toll Free Tel:* 800-scholastic *Fax:* 212-343-6930 *Web Site:* www.scholastic.com, pg 242

Ivers, Mitchell, Pocket Books, 1230 Avenue of the Americas, New York, NY 10020 *Toll Free Tel:* 800-456-6798 *Fax:* 212-698-7284 *E-mail:* consumer.customerservice@simonandschuster. com *Web Site:* www.simonsays.com, pg 215

Ivester, Stan, University of Tennessee Press, 110 Conference Center Bldg, Knoxville, TN 37996-4108 *Tel:* 865-974-3321 *Toll Free Tel:* 800-621-2736 (ordering) *Fax:* 865-974-3724 *E-mail:* custserv@ utpress.org *Web Site:* www.utpress.org, pg 285

Jabbari, Ahmad, Mazda Publishers Inc, 2182 Dupont Dr, Suite 216, Irvine, CA 92612 *Tel:* 714-751-5252 *Fax:* 714-751-4805 *E-mail:* hello@mazdapub.com *Web Site:* www.mazdapub.com, pg 166

Jablonowski, Cindy, Metal Powder Industries Federation, 105 College Rd E, Princeton, NJ 08540-6692 *Tel:* 609-452-7700 *Fax:* 609-987-8523 *E-mail:* info@ mpif.org *Web Site:* www.mpif.org, pg 172

Jablonski, Brian, William S Hein & Co Inc, 1285 Main St, Buffalo, NY 14209-1987 *Tel:* 716-882-2600 *Toll Free Tel:* 800-828-7571 *Fax:* 716-883-8100 *E-mail:* mail@wshein.com *Web Site:* www.wshein. com, pg 120

Jablonski, Sr Patricia Edward, Pauline Books & Media, 50 St Paul's Ave, Jamaica Plain, Boston, MA 02130 *Tel:* 617-522-8911 *Toll Free Tel:* 800-876-4463 (orders only) *Fax:* 617-541-9805 *E-mail:* businessoffice@ pauline.org; orderentry@pauline.org *Web Site:* www. pauline.org, pg 205

Jackson, Bobby L, Multicultural Publications, 936 Slosson Ave, Akron, OH 44320 *Tel:* 330-865-9578 *Toll Free Tel:* 800-238-0297 *Fax:* 330-865-9578 *E-mail:* info@multiculturalpub.net *Web Site:* www. multiculturalpub.net, pg 180

Jackson, D'Ann, Krause Publications, 700 E State St, Iola, WI 54990 *Tel:* 715-445-4612 ext 365 *Toll Free Tel:* 800-258-0929; 888-457-2873 *Fax:* 715-445-4087 *Web Site:* www.krause.com, pg 147

Jackson, David B, Stanford University Press, 1450 Page Mill Rd, Palo Alto, CA 94304-1124 *Tel:* 650-723-9434 *Fax:* 650-725-3457 *Web Site:* www.sup.org, pg 257

Jackson, Ernestine, Central Ohio Writers of Literature for Children, c/o St Joseph Montessori School, 933 Hamlet St, Columbus, OH 43201-3595 *Tel:* 614-291-8644 *Fax:* 614-291-7411 *E-mail:* cowriters@mail.com *Web Site:* www.sjms.net/conf, pg 742

Jackson, Guida M, Panther Creek Press, 116 Tree Crest, Spring, TX 77393 *Tel:* 281-298-5772 *E-mail:* panthercreek3@hotmail.com *Web Site:* www. panthercreekpress.com, pg 203

Jackson, Heather, St Martin's Press Paperback and Reference Group, 175 Fifth Ave, New York, NY 10010 *Fax:* 212-995-2488 *E-mail:* firstname. lastname@stmartins.com, pg 239

Jackson, Jennifer, Donald Maass Literary Agency, 160 W 95 St, Suite 1-B, New York, NY 10025 *Tel:* 212-866-8200 *Fax:* 212-866-8181 *E-mail:* dmla@ mindspring.com, pg 641

Jackson, Kate, HarperCollins Children's Books Group, 1350 Sixth Ave, New York, NY 10019 *Tel:* 212-261-6500 *Web Site:* www.harperchildrens.com, pg 115

Jackson, Michael, University of Nevada Press, MS 166, Reno, NV 89557-0076 *Tel:* 775-784-6573 *Toll Free Tel:* 800-682-6657 *Fax:* 775-784-6200 *Toll Free Fax:* 877-682-6657 *Web Site:* www.nvbooks.nevada. edu, pg 283

Jackson, Nancy, ShipShape Publishing Inc, 12 Pine St, Chatham, NJ 07928 *Tel:* 973-635-3000 *Fax:* 973-635-4363 *E-mail:* ShipShapeBooks@aol.com *Web Site:* www.ShipShapePublishing.com, pg 574

Jackson, Onshelle, Association of American University Presses, 1427 E 60 St, Chicago, IL 60637 *Tel:* 773-702-7700; 773-702-7600 *Toll Free Tel:* 800-621-2736 (orders) *Fax:* 773-702-9756 (sales); 773-660-2235 (orders); 773-702-2708 *E-mail:* general@press. uchicago.edu *Web Site:* www.press.uchicago.edu, pg 26

Jackson, Rem, Classroom Connect, 8000 Marina Blvd, Suite 400, Brisbane, CA 94005 *Tel:* 650-351-5100 *Toll Free Tel:* 800-638-1639 (cust support) *Fax:* 650-351-5300 *E-mail:* connect@classroom.com *Web Site:* www.classroom.com, pg 63

Jackson, Richard, Simon & Schuster Children's Publishing, 1230 Avenue of the Americas, New York, NY 10020 *Tel:* 212-698-7000 *Web Site:* www. simonsayskids.com, pg 248

Jackson, Sherri, Seraphine Publishing, 29 Queen St, Belleville, ON K8N 1T3, Canada *Tel:* 613-921-7636 *Fax:* 613-771-1737 *E-mail:* info@seraphinepublishing. com *Web Site:* www.seraphinepublishing.com, pg 611

Jacob, Mary Ann, Texas A&M University Press, John H Lindsey Bldg, Lewis St, 4354 TAMU, College Station, TX 77843-4354 *Tel:* 979-845-1436 *Toll Free Tel:* 800-826-8911 (orders) *Fax:* 979-847-8752 *Toll Free Fax:* 888-617-2421 (orders) *E-mail:* fdl@ tampress.tamu.edu *Web Site:* www.tamu.edu/upress/, pg 267

Jacob, Maryann, National Book Awards, 95 Madison Ave, Suite 709, New York, NY 10016 *Tel:* 212-685-0261 *Fax:* 212-213-6570 *E-mail:* nationalbook@ national.org *Web Site:* www.nationalbook.org, pg 791

Jacobs, Andrea, The Globe Pequot Press, 246 Goose Lane, Guilford, CT 06437 *Tel:* 203-458-4500 *Toll Free Tel:* 800-243-0495 (cust serv) *Fax:* 203-458-4601 *Toll Free Fax:* 800-820-2329 (orders & cust serv) *E-mail:* info@globepequot.com *Web Site:* www. globepequot.com, pg 106

Jacobs, Dale W, World Book Inc, 233 N Michigan, Suite 2000, Chicago, IL 60601 *Tel:* 312-729-5800 *Toll Free Tel:* 800-967-5325 (consumer sales, US); 800-463-8845 (consumer sales, Canada); 800-975-3250 (school & library sales, US); 800-837-5365 (school & library sales, Canada); 866-866-5200 (web sales) *Fax:* 312-729-5600; 312-729-5606 *Toll Free Fax:* 800-433-9330 (school & library sales, US); 888-690-4002 (school library sales, Canada) *Web Site:* www.worldbook.com, pg 303

Jacobs, Dr Dorri, Dorri Jacobs/Consulting & Editorial Services, 784 Columbus Ave, Suite 1C, New York, NY 10025 *Tel:* 212-222-4606 *E-mail:* dorrija@aol. com *Web Site:* members.aol.com/dorrija/yourwriter. htm; members.aol.com/domediate; endespair.com, pg 602

Jacobs, Elaine, The Westchester Literary Agency, 2533 Egret Lake Dr, West Palm Beach, FL 33413 *Tel:* 561-642-2908 *Fax:* 561-439-2228, pg 661

Jacobs, Jeff, Michelin Travel Publications, PO Box 19001, Greenville, SC 29602-9001 *Tel:* 864-458-5127 *Toll Free Tel:* 800-423-0485; 800-223-0987 *Fax:* 864-458-6674 *Toll Free Fax:* 866-297-0914 *E-mail:* michelin.travel-publications-us@us.michelin. com *Web Site:* www.viamichelin.com, pg 173

Jacobs, Kathy, Crossway Books, 1300 Crescent St, Wheaton, IL 60187 *Tel:* 630-682-4300 *Fax:* 630-682-4785 *E-mail:* editorial@goodnews-crossway.org *Web Site:* www.crosswaybooks.org, pg 73

Jacobs, Laurence, Craftsman Book Co, 6058 Corte Del Cedro, Carlsbad, CA 92009 *Tel:* 760-438-7828 *Toll Free Tel:* 800-829-8123 *Fax:* 760-438-0398 *Web Site:* www.craftsman-book.com, pg 71

Jacobs, Madeline, The American Chemical Society, 1155 16 St NW, Washington, DC 20036 *Tel:* 202-872-4600 *Toll Free Tel:* 800-227-5558 *Fax:* 202-872-6067 *Web Site:* www.acs.org; pubs.acs.org, pg 12

Jacobs, Mark, Providence Publishing Corp, 238 Seaboard Lane, Franklin, TN 37067 *Tel:* 615-771-2020 *Toll Free Tel:* 800-321-5692 *Fax:* 615-771-2002 *E-mail:* books@providencehouse.com *Web Site:* www. providencehouse.com, pg 220

Jacobs, Michael, Harry N Abrams Inc, 100 Fifth Ave, New York, NY 10011 *Tel:* 212-206-7715 *Toll Free Tel:* 800-345-1359 *Fax:* 212-645-8437 *E-mail:* webmaster@abramsbooks.com *Web Site:* www.abramsbooks.com, pg 3

Jacobs, Robert H, Univelt Inc, PO Box 28130, San Diego, CA 92198-0130 *Tel:* 760-746-4005 *Fax:* 760-746-3139 *E-mail:* 76121.1532@compuserve.com *Web Site:* www.univelt.com, pg 280

Jacobs, Robert Lee, Lee Jacobs Productions, PO Box 362, Pomeroy, OH 45769-0362 *Tel:* 740-992-5208 *Fax:* 740-992-0616 *E-mail:* ljacobs@frognet.net *Web Site:* www.leejacobsproductions.com, pg 140

Jacobsen, Jodi R, Sheffield Publishing Co, 9009 Antioch St, Salem, WI 53168 *Tel:* 262-843-2281 *Fax:* 262-843-3683 *E-mail:* info@spcbooks.com *Web Site:* www.spcbooks.com, pg 246

Jacobson, Clare, Princeton Architectural Press, 37 E Seventh St, New York, NY 10003 *Tel:* 212-995-9620 *Toll Free Tel:* 800-722-6657 (dist) *Fax:* 212-995-9454 *E-mail:* sales@papress.com *Web Site:* www.papress. com, pg 218

Jacobson, Donald C, Multnomah Publishers Inc, 204 W Adams Ave, Sisters, OR 97759 *Tel:* 541-549-1144 *Toll Free Tel:* 800-929-0910 *Fax:* 541-549-2044 (sales); 541-549-0432 (admin); 541-549-0260 (ed/prod); 541-549-8048 (mktg) *E-mail:* information@multnomahbooks.com *Web Site:* www.multnomahbooks.com, pg 180

Jacobson, Emilie, Curtis Brown Ltd, 10 Astor Place, New York, NY 10003 *Tel:* 212-473-5400, pg 623

Jacobson, Kathryn, Landauer Books, 12251 Maffitt Rd, Cumming, IA 50061 *Tel:* 515-287-2144 *Toll Free Tel:* 800-557-2144 *Fax:* 515-287-1530 *E-mail:* landaucor@aol.com, pg 148

Jacobson, Tanjam, The Brookings Institution Press, 1775 Massachusetts Ave NW, Washington, DC 20036-2188 *Tel:* 202-797-6000 *Toll Free Tel:* 800-275-1447 *Fax:* 202-797-6195 *E-mail:* bibooks@brook.edu *Web Site:* www.brookings.edu, pg 48

Jacoby, Judy, Doubleday Broadway Publishing Group, 1745 Broadway, New York, NY 10019 *Tel:* 212-782-9000 *Toll Free Tel:* 800-223-6834; 800-223-5780 (sales) *Fax:* 212-302-7985 (correspondence); 212-492-9862 (orders), pg 82

Jacoby, Melissa, Plume, 375 Hudson St, New York, NY 10014 *Tel:* 212-366-2000 *Fax:* 212-366-2666 *E-mail:* online@penguinputnam.com *Web Site:* www. penguin.com, pg 215

Jacques, Leo, Les Presses De L'Universite Laval, Maurice-Pollack House, Office 3103, University City, Sainte-Foy, PQ G1K 7P4, Canada *Tel:* 418-656-2803 *Fax:* 418-656-3305 *E-mail:* presses@pul.ulaval.ca *Web Site:* www.ulaval.ca/pul, pg 558

Jaeger, Ana, American Mathematical Society, 201 Charles St, Providence, RI 02904-2294 *Tel:* 401-455-4000 *Toll Free Tel:* 800-321-4267 *Fax:* 401-331-3842; 401-455-4046 (cust serv) *E-mail:* ams@ams.org *Web Site:* www.ams.org, pg 16

Jaeggi, Chris, Pearson Professional Development, 1900 E Lake Ave, Glenview, IL 60025 *Tel:* 847-657-7450 *Toll Free Tel:* 800-348-4474 *Fax:* 847-486-3183 *E-mail:* info@pearsonpd.com *Web Site:* www. skylightedu.com; www.pearsonpd.com, pg 207

Jaffe, Gary, Linda Chester & Associates, Rockefeller Ctr, 630 Fifth Ave, New York, NY 10111 *Tel:* 212-218-3350 *Fax:* 212-218-3343 *E-mail:* lcassoc@mindspring. com *Web Site:* www.lindachester.com, pg 624

Jaffe, Susanne, Thurber Prize for American Humor, 77 Jefferson Ave, Columbus, OH 43215 *Tel:* 614-464-1032 *Fax:* 614-280-3645 *E-mail:* thurberhouse@ thurberhouse.org *Web Site:* www.thurberhouse.org, pg 808

Jahns, Randy, Crossway Books, 1300 Crescent St, Wheaton, IL 60187 *Tel:* 630-682-4300 *Fax:* 630-682-4785 *E-mail:* editorial@goodnews-crossway.org *Web Site:* www.crosswaybooks.org, pg 73

Jain, Mukesh, Jain Publishing Co, PO Box 3523, Fremont, CA 94539 *Tel:* 510-659-8272 *Fax:* 510-659-0501 *E-mail:* mail@jainpub.com *Web Site:* www. jainpub.com, pg 140

James, Art, Ide House Inc, c/o Publishers Associates, PO Box 408, Radcliffe, IA 50230-0408 *Tel:* 515-899-2300 *Fax:* 515-899-2315 *E-mail:* orders@publishers-associates.com *Web Site:* www.publishers-associates. com, pg 130

James, Elisabeth, Sandra Dijkstra Literary Agency, 1155 Camino del Mar, PMB 515, Del Mar, CA 92014-2605 *Tel:* 858-755-3115 *Fax:* 858-794-2822 *E-mail:* sdla@ dijkstraagency.com, pg 627

James, Everett, Institute of Police Technology & Management, University Ctr, 12000 Alumni Dr, Jacksonville, FL 32224-2678 *Tel:* 904-620-4786 *Fax:* 904-620-2453, pg 135

James, Gethin, Lugus Publications, 48 Falcon St, Toronto, ON M4S 2P5, Canada *Tel:* 416-322-5113 *Fax:* 416-484-9512 *E-mail:* cymro43@hotmail.com, pg 553

James, Gregory, Peter Glenn Publications, 6040 NW 43 Terr, Boca Raton, FL 33496 *Tel:* 561-999-8930 *Toll Free Tel:* 888-332-6700 *Fax:* 561-999-8931 *E-mail:* lynn@pgdirect.com *Web Site:* www.pgdirect. com, pg 105

James, Jacqueline, Lugus Publications, 48 Falcon St, Toronto, ON M4S 2P5, Canada *Tel:* 416-322-5113 *Fax:* 416-484-9512 *E-mail:* cymro43@hotmail.com, pg 553

James, Marsha, Perfection Learning Corp, 10520 New York Ave, Des Moines, IA 50322 *Tel:* 515-278-0133 *Toll Free Tel:* 800-762-2999 *Fax:* 515-278-2980 *E-mail:* orders@perfectionlearning.com *Web Site:* perfectionlearning.com, pg 210

James, Michael, Unique Publications Books & Videos, 4201 W Vanowen Place, Burbank, CA 91505 *Tel:* 818-845-2656 *Toll Free Tel:* 800-332-3330 *Fax:* 818-845-7761 *E-mail:* info@cfwenterprises.com *Web Site:* www.cfwenterprises.com, pg 279

James, Selena, Pocket Books, 1230 Avenue of the Americas, New York, NY 10020 *Toll Free Tel:* 800-456-6798 *Fax:* 212-698-7284 *E-mail:* consumer. customerservice@simonandschuster.com *Web Site:* www.simonsays.com, pg 215

James, Wendy, Stratford Publishing Services Inc, 70 Landmark Hill Dr, Brattleboro, VT 05301 *Tel:* 802-254-6073 *Toll Free Tel:* 800-451-4328 *Fax:* 802-254-5240 *Web Site:* www.stratfordpublishing.com, pg 612

Jameson, Amy, Janklow & Nesbit Associates, 445 Park Ave, New York, NY 10022 *Tel:* 212-421-1700 *Fax:* 212-980-3671 *E-mail:* postmaster@janklow.com, pg 636

Jameson, W C, Ozark Creative Writers Inc Annual Conference, 1818 N Taylor, Little Rock, AR 72207-4637 *E-mail:* carlj@mail.uca.edu; ozarkcreativewriters@earthlink.net *Web Site:* www. ozarkcreativewriters.org, pg 745

Jamison, Mark, Canadian Magazine Publishers Association, 425 Adelaide St W, Suite 700, Toronto, ON M5V 3C1, Canada *Tel:* 416-504-0274 *Fax:* 416-504-0437 *E-mail:* cmpainfo@cmpa.ca *Web Site:* www. cmpa.ca/; www.magomania.com, pg 683

Janecke, Roger, Visible Ink Press, 43311 Joy Rd, Suite 414, Canton, MI 48187-2075 *Tel:* 734-667-3211 *Fax:* 734-667-4311 *E-mail:* inquiries@visibleink.com *Web Site:* www.visibleink.com, pg 291

Janeway, Brant, Plume, 375 Hudson St, New York, NY 10014 *Tel:* 212-366-2000 *Fax:* 212-366-2666 *E-mail:* online@penguinputnam.com *Web Site:* www. penguin.com, pg 215

Janeway, Carol B, Alfred A Knopf, 1745 Broadway, New York, NY 10019 *Tel:* 212-751-2600 *Toll Free Tel:* 800-638-6460 *Fax:* 212-572-2593 *Web Site:* www. randomhouse.com/knopf, pg 146

Janis, Larry, OneOnOne Computer Training, 2055 Army Trail Rd, Suite 100, Addison, IL 60101 *Tel:* 630-628-0500 *Toll Free Tel:* 800-424-8668 *E-mail:* oneonone@ protrain.com *Web Site:* www.oootraining.com, pg 197

Janke, Rolf, Sage Publications, 2455 Teller Rd, Thousand Oaks, CA 91320 *Tel:* 805-499-0721 *Fax:* 805-499-0871 *E-mail:* info@sagepub.com *Web Site:* www.sagepub.com, pg 237

Janklow, Lucas W, Janklow & Nesbit Associates, 445 Park Ave, New York, NY 10022 *Tel:* 212-421-1700 *Fax:* 212-980-3671 *E-mail:* postmaster@janklow.com, pg 636

Janklow, Morton L, Janklow & Nesbit Associates, 445 Park Ave, New York, NY 10022 *Tel:* 212-421-1700 *Fax:* 212-980-3671 *E-mail:* postmaster@janklow.com, pg 636

Janney-Pace, Priscilla, Antioch Writers' Workshop, PO Box 494, Yellow Springs, OH 45387-0494 *Tel:* 937-475-7357; 937-767-2700 (Board of Trustees) *E-mail:* info@antiochwritersworkshop.com *Web Site:* www.antiochwritersworkshop.com, pg 741

Jannsohn, Aimee, The Pilgrim Press/United Church Press, 700 Prospect Ave, Cleveland, OH 44115-1100 *Tel:* 216-736-3761 *Toll Free Tel:* 800-537-3394 (cust serv) *Fax:* 216-736-2207 *E-mail:* thepilgrimpress@ thepilgrimpress.com *Web Site:* www.thepilgrimpress. com; www.theunitedchurchpress.com, pg 213

Janos, Susan, Harrison House Publishers, 2448 E 81 St, Suite 4800, Tulsa, OK 74137-4256 *Tel:* 918-523-5700 *Toll Free Tel:* 800-888-4126 *Fax:* 918-494-5688 (sales) *Toll Free Fax:* 800-830-5688 *Web Site:* www. harrisonhouse.com, pg 116

Janson, Karen, Barefoot Books, 2067 Massachusetts Ave, 5th fl, Cambridge, MA 02140 *Tel:* 617-576-0660 *Fax:* 617-576-0049 *E-mail:* ussales@barefootbooks. com; help@barefootbooks.com *Web Site:* www. barefootbooks.com, pg 32

Janssen, Karl, University Press of Kansas, 2501 W 15 St, Lawrence, KS 66049-3905 *Tel:* 785-864-4154; 785-864-4155 (orders) *Fax:* 785-864-4586 *E-mail:* upress@ku.edu *Web Site:* www.kansaspress. ku.edu, pg 287

Januska, Michael, Tundra Books of Northern New York, PO Box 1030, Plattsburgh, NY 12901 *Tel:* 416-598-4786 *Fax:* 416-598-0247 *E-mail:* tundra@mcclelland. com *Web Site:* www.tundrabooks.com, pg 276

Jao, Jonathan, Random House Publishing Group, 1745 Broadway, New York, NY 10019 *Toll Free Tel:* 800-200-3552 *Toll Free Fax:* 800-200-3552 *Web Site:* www.randomhouse.com, pg 227

Japikse, Carl, Ariel Press, 90 Steve Tate Hwy, Suite 201, Marble Hill, GA 30148 *Tel:* 770-894-4226 *Fax:* 706-579-1865 (orders), pg 23

Jaquith, George, Wind Canyon Books Inc, PO Box 511, Brawley, CA 92227 *Tel:* 760-344-5545 *Toll Free Tel:* 800-952-7007 *Fax:* 760-344-8841 *E-mail:* books@windcanyon.com *Web Site:* www. windcanyon.com; www.aviation-heritage.com, pg 301

Jaramillo, Raquel, Henry Holt and Company, LLC, 115 W 18 St, New York, NY 10011 *Tel:* 212-886-9200 *Toll Free Tel:* 888-330-8477 (orders) *Fax:* 212-633-0748 *E-mail:* publicity@hholt.com *Web Site:* www. henryholt.com, pg 124

Jarashow, Amy, Random House Children's Books, 1745 Broadway, New York, NY 10019 *Tel:* 212-782-9000 *Toll Free Tel:* 800-200-3552 *Fax:* 212-782-9452 *Web Site:* www.randomhouse.com/kids, pg 226

Jarrell, Timothy, Fodor's Travel Publications, 1745 Broadway, New York, NY 10019 *Tel:* 212-572-8784 *Toll Free Tel:* 800-733-3000 *Fax:* 212-572-2248 *Web Site:* www.fodors.com, pg 98

Jarrett, Beverly, University of Missouri Press, 2910 Le Mone Blvd, Columbia, MO 65201 *Tel:* 573-882-7641 *Toll Free Tel:* 800-828-1894 (orders) *Fax:* 573-884-4498 *Web Site:* www.umsystem.edu/upress, pg 283

Jarvis, Ann, Midland Writers' Conference, 1710 W St Andrews, Midland, MI 48640 *Tel:* 989-837-3435 *Fax:* 989-837-3468, pg 744

Jarvis, Michael, Chain Store Guide, 3922 Coconut Palm Dr, Tampa, FL 33619 *Tel:* 813-627-6800 *Toll Free Tel:* 800-927-9292 *Fax:* 813-627-6882 *E-mail:* info@ csgis.com *Web Site:* www.csgis.com, pg 58

Jarvis, Sharon, Toad Hall Inc, RR 2, Box 2090, Laceyville, PA 18623 *Tel:* 570-869-2942 *Fax:* 570-869-1031 *E-mail:* toadhallco@aol.com *Web Site:* www.laceyville.com/Toad-Hall, pg 272, 658

Jasmine, Katherine, Newbridge Educational Publishing, One Beeman Rd, Northborough, MA 01532 *Tel:* 508-571-6500 *Toll Free Tel:* 800-867-0307 *Fax:* 508-571-6502 *Toll Free Fax:* 800-456-2419 *E-mail:* info@ newbridgeonline.com *Web Site:* www.newbridgeonline. com; www.newbridgepub.com, pg 190

Jasmine, Katherine, Sundance Publishing, One Beeman Rd, Northborough, MA 01532 *Tel:* 508-571-6500 *Toll Free Tel:* 800-343-8204 *Fax:* 508-571-6510 *Toll Free Fax:* 800-456-2419 *E-mail:* info@sundancepub.com *Web Site:* www.sundancepub.com, pg 262

Jauk, Liesl, Western Magazine Awards Foundation, Main PO Box 2131, Vancouver, BC V6B 3T8, Canada *Tel:* 604-669-3717 *Fax:* 604-204-9302 *E-mail:* wma@ direct.ca *Web Site:* www.westernmagazineawards.com, pg 810

Jayne, Julie, Cumberland House Publishing Inc, 431 Harding Industrial Dr, Nashville, TN 37211 *Tel:* 615-832-1171 *Toll Free Tel:* 888-439-2665 *Fax:* 615-832-0633 *E-mail:* information@cumberlandhouse.com *Web Site:* www.cumberlandhouse.com, pg 74

Jayo, James, Arcade Publishing Inc, 141 Fifth Ave, New York, NY 10010 *Tel:* 212-475-2633 *Fax:* 212-353-8148 *E-mail:* arcadeinfo@arcadepub.com *Web Site:* www.arcadepub.com, pg 22

Jeffers, Dawn, Raven Tree Press LLC, 200 S Washington St, Suite 306, Green Bay, WI 54301 *Tel:* 920-438-1605 *Toll Free Tel:* 877-256-0579 *Fax:* 920-438-1607 *E-mail:* raven@raventreepress.com *Web Site:* www. raventreepress.com, pg 228

Jeffrey, Douglas A, Hillsdale College Press, 33 E College St, Hillsdale, MI 49242 *Tel:* 517-437-7341 *Toll Free Tel:* 800-437-2268 *Fax:* 517-437-3923 *E-mail:* news@hillsdale.edu *Web Site:* www.hillsdale. edu, pg 123

Jeglinski, Melissa, Harlequin Enterprises Ltd, 233 Broadway, Suite 1001, New York, NY 10279 *Tel:* 212-553-4200 *Fax:* 212-227-8969 *E-mail:* customer. ecare@harlequin.ca *Web Site:* www.eharlequin.com; www.luna-books.com; www.mirabooks.com; www. reddressink.com; www.steeplehill.com, pg 115

Jellinek, Roger, Jellinek & Murray Literary Agency, 2024 Mauna Place, Honolulu, HI 96822 *Tel:* 808-521-4057 *Fax:* 808-521-4058 *E-mail:* jellinek@lava.net, pg 636

Jenkins, Jan, Indiana University Press, 601 N Morton St, Bloomington, IN 47404-3797 *Tel:* 812-855-8817 *Toll Free Tel:* 800-842-6796 (orders only) *Fax:* 812-855-7931 (orders only); 812-855-8507 *E-mail:* iupress@indiana.edu; iuorder@indiana.edu (orders) *Web Site:* www.iupress.indiana.edu, pg 132

Jenkins, Jean, Writers' Haven Writers (WHW), 2244 Fourth Ave, San Diego, CA 92101 *Tel:* 619-696-0569, pg 703

Jenkins, Jerrold R, The Independent Publisher Book Awards, 400 W Front St, Suite 4-A, Traverse City, MI 49684 *Tel:* 231-933-0445 *Toll Free Tel:* 800-706-4636 *Fax:* 231-933-0448, pg 779

Jenkins, Jerrold R, Jenkins Group Inc, 400 W Front St, Suite 4-A, Traverse City, MI 49684 *Tel:* 231-933-0445 *Toll Free Tel:* 800-706-4636 *Fax:* 231-933-0448 *E-mail:* info@bookpublishing.com *Web Site:* www. bookpublishing.com, pg 602

Jenkins, Jerry B, Jerry B Jenkins Christian Writers Guild, PO Box 88196, Black Forest, CO 80908 *Toll Free Tel:* 866-495-5177 *Fax:* 719-495-5181 *E-mail:* contactus@christianwritersguild.com *Web Site:* www.christianwritersguild.com, pg 685

Jenkins, John, Congressional Quarterly Press, 1255 22 St NW, Washington, DC 20037 *Tel:* 202-729-1800 *Toll Free Tel:* 866-427-7737 *Fax:* 202-729-1809 *Toll Free Fax:* 800-380-3810 *E-mail:* customerservice@cqpress. com *Web Site:* www.cq.com, pg 66

Jenkins, John, CQ Press, 1255 22 St NW, Suite 400, Washington, DC 20037 *Tel:* 202-729-1800 *Toll Free Tel:* 866-427-7737 *Fax:* 202-729-1923 *Toll Free Fax:* 800-380-3810 *E-mail:* customerservice@cqpress. com *Web Site:* www.cqpress.com, pg 71

Jenkins, John, The MIT Press, 5 Cambridge Ctr, Cambridge, MA 02142 *Tel:* 617-253-5646 *Toll Free Tel:* 800-405-1619 (orders only) *Fax:* 617-258-6779 *Web Site:* mitpress.mit.edu, pg 175

Jenkins, Joyce, Bay Area Book Reviewers Association Book Awards, c/o Poetry Flash, 1450 Fourth St, Suite 4, Berkeley, CA 94710 *Tel:* 510-525-5476 *Fax:* 510-525-6752 *E-mail:* babra@poetryflash.org; editor@ poetryflash.org *Web Site:* www.poetryflash.org, pg 761

Jenkins, Joyce, Fred Cody Award, c/o Poetry Flash, 1450 Fourth St, Suite 4, Berkeley, CA 94710 *Tel:* 510-525-5476 *Fax:* 510-525-6752 *E-mail:* babra@poetryflash. org; editor@poetryflash.org *Web Site:* www. poetryflash.org, pg 768

Jenkins, Joyce, Poetry Flash at Cody's, 1450 Fourth St, Suite 4, Berkeley, CA 94710 *Tel:* 510-525-5476 *Fax:* 510-525-6752 *E-mail:* editor@poetryflash.org, pg 746

Jenkins, Linda, Primedia Consumer Magazine & Internet Group, 260 Madison Ave, New York, NY 10016 *Tel:* 212-726-4300 *Toll Free Tel:* 800-521-2885 *Fax:* 212-726-4310 *E-mail:* sgnews@primediasi.com *Web Site:* www.primediainc.com, pg 218

Jenness, Morgan, Abrams Artists Agency, 275 Seventh Ave, 26th fl, New York, NY 10001 *Tel:* 646-486-4600 *Fax:* 646-486-2358, pg 617

Jenney, David, Northland Publishing Co, 2900 N Fort Valley Rd, Flagstaff, AZ 86001 *Tel:* 928-774-5251 *Toll Free Tel:* 800-346-3257 *Fax:* 928-774-0592 *E-mail:* info@northlandpub.com; design@ northlandpub.com; editorial@northlandpub.com *Web Site:* www.northlandpub.com, pg 193

Jennings, Marc, Aspen Publishers, A Wolters Kluwer Company, 1185 Avenue of the Americas, New York, NY 10036 *Tel:* 212-597-0200 *Toll Free Tel:* 800-234-1660 (cust serv); 800-447-1717 (orders); 800-950-5259 (legal educ); 800-LAW-PLGL (paralegal textbook); 800-317-3113 (bookstore sales); 800-364-2512 (Loislaw) *Web Site:* www.aspenpublishers.com, pg 26

Jennings, Vicki, The MIT Press, 5 Cambridge Ctr, Cambridge, MA 02142 *Tel:* 617-253-5646 *Toll Free Tel:* 800-405-1619 (orders only) *Fax:* 617-258-6779 *Web Site:* mitpress.mit.edu, pg 175

Jensen, Allan, Executive Excellence Publishing, 1366 E 1120 S, Provo, UT 84606 *Tel:* 801-375-4060 *Toll Free Tel:* 800-304-9782 *Fax:* 801-377-5960 *Web Site:* www. eep.com, pg 629

Jensen, Bobby John, Ide House Inc, c/o Publishers Associates, PO Box 408, Radcliffe, IA 50230-0408 *Tel:* 515-899-2300 *Fax:* 515-899-2315 *E-mail:* orders@publishers-associates.com *Web Site:* www.publishers-associates.com, pg 130

Jensen, Connie, Saint Mary's Press, 702 Terrace Heights, Winona, MN 55987-1318 *Tel:* 507-457-7900 *Toll Free Tel:* 800-533-8095 *Toll Free Fax:* 800-344-9225 *E-mail:* smpress@smp.org *Web Site:* www.smp.org, pg 239

Jensen, Jack, Chronicle Books LLC, 85 Second St, 6th fl, San Francisco, CA 94105 *Tel:* 415-537-4200 *Toll Free Tel:* 800-722-6657 (cust serv) *Fax:* 415-537-4460 *Toll Free Fax:* 800-858-7787 (orders) *E-mail:* frontdesk@chroniclebooks.com *Web Site:* www.chroniclebooks.com, pg 61

Jensen, Kirk, Cambridge University Press, 40 W 20 St, New York, NY 10011-4211 *Tel:* 212-924-3900 *Toll Free Tel:* 800-899-5222 *Fax:* 212-691-3239 *Web Site:* www.cambridge.org, pg 52

Jensen, Sandy, Paul H Brookes Publishing Co, PO Box 10624, Baltimore, MD 21285-0624 *Tel:* 410-337-9580 *Toll Free Tel:* 800-638-3775 *Fax:* 410-337-8539 *E-mail:* custserv@brookespublishing.com *Web Site:* www.brookespublishing.com, pg 48

Jenson, Jen, Chelsea House Publishers LLC, 2080 Cabot Blvd W, Suite 201, Langhorne, PA 19047-1813 *Tel:* 610-353-5166 *Toll Free Tel:* 800-848-BOOK (848-2665) *Fax:* 610-359-1439 *Toll Free Fax:* 877-780-7300 *E-mail:* sales@chelseahouse.com *Web Site:* www.chelseahouse.com, pg 59

Jermini, Dr Ellen, University of Healing Press, 1101 Far Valley Rd, Campo, CA 91906-3213 *Tel:* 619-478-5111; 619-478-2506 *Toll Free Tel:* 888-463-8654 *Fax:* 619-478-5013 *E-mail:* unihealing@goduni.org *Web Site:* www.university-of-healing.edu, pg 281

Jersild, Devon, Bread Loaf Writers' Conference, Kirk Alumni Center, Middlebury, VT 05753 *Tel:* 802-443-5286 *Fax:* 802-443-2087 *E-mail:* blwc@middlebury. edu *Web Site:* www.middlebury.edu, pg 742

Jersild, Devon, Fellowship & Scholarship Program for Writers, Middlebury College, Middlebury, VT 05753 *Tel:* 802-443-5286 *Fax:* 802-443-2087 *E-mail:* blwc@ middlebury.edu *Web Site:* www.middlebury.edu/~blwc, pg 773

Jessen, Joanne, American Speech-Language-Hearing Association (ASHA), 10801 Rockville Pike, Rockville, MD 20852 *Tel:* 301-897-5700 *Toll Free Tel:* 800-638-8255 *Fax:* 301-571-0457 *Web Site:* www.asha.org, pg 678

Jewell, Cathy, Etruscan Press, PO Box 9685, Silver Spring, MD 20916-9685 *Tel:* 301-946-6228 *Fax:* 301-946-5838 *E-mail:* info@etruscanpress.org *Web Site:* www.etruscanpress.com, pg 92

Jewell, Jane, Science Fiction & Fantasy Writers of America Inc, PO Box 877, Chestertown, MD 21620 *Toll Free Tel:* 888-322-7392 *E-mail:* execdir@sfwa.org *Web Site:* www.sfwa.org, pg 699

Jewell, Jane, SFWA Nebula Awards, PO Box 877, Chestertown, MD 21620 *Toll Free Tel:* 888-322-7392 *E-mail:* execdir@sfwa.org *Web Site:* www.sfwa.org, pg 805

Jewell, Lee, Panoply Press Inc, PO Box 1885, Lake Oswego, OR 97035-0611 *Tel:* 503-697-7964 *Fax:* 503-636-5293 *E-mail:* panoplypress@aol.com, pg 202

Jewell, Wanda, Southeast Booksellers Association (SEBA), 2611 Forest Dr, Suite 124, Columbia, SC 29204 *Tel:* 803-779-0118 *Toll Free Tel:* 800-331-9617 *Fax:* 803-779-0113 *Web Site:* www.sebaweb.org; arts.sebaweb.org (authors round the south); tradeshow.sebaweb.org (virtual trade show), pg 700

Joas, Pat, Canadian Booksellers Association Author of the Year Award, 789 Don Mills Rd, Suite 700, Toronto, ON M3C 1T5, Canada *Tel:* 416-467-7883 *Fax:* 416-467-7886 *E-mail:* enquiries@cbabook.org *Web Site:* www.cbabook.org, pg 765

Joas, Pat, Canadian Booksellers Association (CBA), 789 Don Mills Rd, Suite 700, Toronto, ON M3C 1T5, Canada *Tel:* 416-467-7883 *Toll Free Tel:* 866-788-0790 *Fax:* 416-467-7886 *E-mail:* enquiries@cbabook.org *Web Site:* www.cbabook.org, pg 683

Joas, Pat, Canadian Booksellers Association Libris Awards, 789 Don Mills Rd, Suite 700, Toronto, ON M3C 1T5, Canada *Tel:* 416-467-7883 *Fax:* 416-467-7886 *E-mail:* enquiries@cbabook.org *Web Site:* www.cbabook.org, pg 765

Joel, Richard, Yeshiva University Press, 500 W 185 St, New York, NY 10033-3201 *Tel:* 212-960-5400 *Fax:* 212-960-0043 *E-mail:* yuadmit@yu.edu *Web Site:* www.yu.edu, pg 306

Johannson, Catharine, Hybrid Publishing Co-op Ltd, 860 Mountain Ave, Winnipeg, MB R2X 1C3, Canada *Tel:* 204-589-4257 *Fax:* 204-589-4257 *E-mail:* mail@hybrid-publishing.ca *Web Site:* www.hybrid-publishing.ca, pg 550

Johns, Jorun, Ariadne Press, 270 Goins Ct, Riverside, CA 92507 *Tel:* 951-684-9202 *Fax:* 951-779-0449 *E-mail:* ariadnepress@aol.com *Web Site:* ariadnepress.com, pg 23

Johns, Joseph, Cornell Maritime Press Inc, PO Box 456, Centreville, MD 21617 *Tel:* 410-758-1075 *Toll Free Tel:* 800-638-7641 *Fax:* 410-758-6849 *E-mail:* editor@cornellmaritimepress.com *Web Site:* www.cornellmaritimepress.com, pg 68

Johns, Joseph, Tidewater Publishers, 101 Water Way, Centreville, MD 21617 *Tel:* 410-758-1075 *Toll Free Tel:* 800-638-7641 *Fax:* 410-758-6849 *E-mail:* editor@cornellmaritimepress.com *Web Site:* www.tidewaterpublishrs.com, pg 271

Johnson, Amanda, Palgrave Macmillan, 175 Fifth Ave, New York, NY 10010 *Tel:* 212-982-3900 *Fax:* 212-777-6359 *E-mail:* firstname.lastname@palgrave-usa.com *Web Site:* www.palgrave.com, pg 202

Johnson, Amy Crane, Raven Tree Press LLC, 200 S Washington St, Suite 306, Green Bay, WI 54301 *Tel:* 920-438-1605 *Toll Free Tel:* 877-256-0579 *Fax:* 920-438-1607 *E-mail:* raven@raventreepress.com *Web Site:* www.raventreepress.com, pg 228

Johnson, Andre, Empire Press Media/Avant-Guide, 444 Madison Ave, 35th fl, New York, NY 10122 *Tel:* 212-563-1003 *Fax:* 212-536-2419 *E-mail:* info@avantguide.com; editor@avantguide.com *Web Site:* www.avantguide.com, pg 90

Johnson, Annette R, AllWrite Advertising & Publishing, PO Box 2363, Atlanta, GA 30301 *Tel:* 404-723-8872 *Fax:* 404-420-2604 *E-mail:* editor@e-allwrite.com *Web Site:* www.e-allwrite.com, pg 590

Johnson, Bennett J, Path Press Inc, 1229 Emerson St, Evanston, IL 60201 *Tel:* 847-424-1620 *Fax:* 847-424-1623 *E-mail:* pathpressinc@aol.com, pg 205

Johnson, Beryl-Ann, Tilbury House Publishers, 2 Mechanic St, No 3, Gardiner, ME 04345 *Tel:* 207-582-1899 *Toll Free Tel:* 800-582-1899 (orders) *Fax:* 207-582-8229 *E-mail:* tilbury@tilburyhouse.com *Web Site:* www.tilburyhouse.com, pg 271

Johnson, Bill, Kay Snow Literary Contest, 9045 SW Barbur Blvd, Suite 5-A, Portland, OR 97219 *Tel:* 503-452-1592 *Fax:* 503-452-0372 *E-mail:* wilwrite@willamettewriters.com *Web Site:* www.willamettewriters.com, pg 806

Johnson, Bill, Willamette Writers, 9045 SW Barbur Blvd, Suite 5-A, Portland, OR 97219 *Tel:* 503-452-1592 *Fax:* 503-452-0372 *E-mail:* wilwrite@willamettewriters.com *Web Site:* www.willamettewriters.com, pg 702

Johnson, Bill, Willamette Writers' Conference, 9045 SW Barbur Blvd, Suite 5-A, Portland, OR 97219 *Tel:* 503-452-1592 *Fax:* 503-452-1592 *E-mail:* wilwrite@willamettewriters.com *Web Site:* www.willamettewriters.com, pg 749

Johnson, Billie, Oak Tree Publishing, 2743 S Veterans Pkwy, Suite 135, Springfield, IL 64704-6402 *Tel:* 217-879-2822 *Fax:* 217-879-2844 *E-mail:* oaktreepub@aol.com *Web Site:* www.oaktreebooks.com, pg 195

Johnson, Blanche, Wilderness Adventures Press Inc, 45 Buckskin Rd, Belgrade, MT 59714 *Tel:* 406-388-0112 *Toll Free Tel:* 800-925-3339 *Fax:* 406-388-0120 *Toll Free Fax:* 800-390-7558 *E-mail:* books@wildadv.com *Web Site:* www.wildadv.com, pg 299

Johnson, Carol, Bethany House Publishers/Baker Bookhouse, PO Box 6287, Grand Rapids, MI 49516-6287 *Tel:* 616-676-9185 *Toll Free Tel:* 800-877-2665 *Web Site:* www.bethanyhouse.com; www.bakerpublishinggroup.com, pg 37

Johnson, Chuck, Wilderness Adventures Press Inc, 45 Buckskin Rd, Belgrade, MT 59714 *Tel:* 406-388-0112 *Toll Free Tel:* 800-925-3339 *Fax:* 406-388-0120 *Toll Free Fax:* 800-390-7558 *E-mail:* books@wildadv.com *Web Site:* www.wildadv.com, pg 299

Johnson, Cliff, Cliff Johnson & Associates, 10867 Fruitland Dr, Studio City, CA 91604 *Tel:* 818-761-5665 *Fax:* 818-761-9501 *E-mail:* quest@pacificnet.net, pg 602

Johnson, Cliff, Tyndale House Publishers Inc, 351 Executive Dr, Carol Stream, IL 60188 *Tel:* 630-668-8303 *Toll Free Tel:* 800-323-9400 *Web Site:* www.tyndale.com, pg 277

Johnson, Connie, Double Play, PO Box 22481, Kansas City, MO 64113 *Tel:* 816-651-7118 *Fax:* 816-822-2521, pg 596

Johnson, Dale E, Timber Press Inc, 133 SW Second Ave, Suite 450, Portland, OR 97204 *Tel:* 503-227-2878 *Toll Free Tel:* 800-327-5680 *Fax:* 503-227-3070 *E-mail:* mail@timberpress.com *Web Site:* www.timberpress.com, pg 271

Johnson, Dan, Thomas Nelson Inc, 501 Nelson Place, Nashville, TN 37214 *Tel:* 615-889-9000 *Toll Free Tel:* 800-251-4000 *Fax:* 615-902-1610 *E-mail:* publicity@thomasnelson.com *Web Site:* www.thomasnelson.com, pg 269

Johnson, David, Concordia Publishing House, 3558 S Jefferson Ave, St Louis, MO 63118-3968 *Tel:* 314-268-1000 *Toll Free Tel:* 800-325-3040 *Fax:* 314-268-1329 *Toll Free Fax:* 800-490-9889 *E-mail:* cphorder@cph.org *Web Site:* www.cph.org, pg 66

Johnson, Diane, Livestock Publications Council, 910 Currie St, Fort Worth, TX 76107 *Tel:* 817-336-1130 *Fax:* 817-232-4820 *Web Site:* www.livestockpublications.com, pg 690

Johnson, Elaine, Graphic Arts Show Company, 1899 Preston White Dr, Reston, VA 20191 *Tel:* 703-264-7200 *Fax:* 703-620-9187 *E-mail:* info@gasc.org *Web Site:* www.gasc.org, pg 688

Johnson, Ellen, American Atheist Press, PO Box 5733, Parsippany, NJ 07054-6733 *Tel:* 908-276-7300 *Fax:* 908-276-7402 *E-mail:* info@atheists.org *Web Site:* www.atheists.org, pg 12

Johnson, Gary L, Bethany House Publishers/Baker Bookhouse, PO Box 6287, Grand Rapids, MI 49516-6287 *Tel:* 616-676-9185 *Toll Free Tel:* 800-877-2665 *Web Site:* www.bethanyhouse.com; www.bakerpublishinggroup.com, pg 37

Johnson, George F, Information Age Publishing Inc, 80 Mason St, Greenwich, CT 06830 *Tel:* 203-661-7602 *Fax:* 203-661-7952 *E-mail:* infoage@infoagepub.com *Web Site:* www.infoagepub.com, pg 133

Johnson, Gerardine, National Bureau of Economic Research Inc, 1050 Massachusetts Ave, Cambridge, MA 02138-5398 *Tel:* 617-868-3900 *Fax:* 617-868-2742 *E-mail:* op@nber.org *Web Site:* www.nber.org, pg 182

Johnson, Heidi, Center for Publishing Fellowships, 11 W 42 St, Rm 400, New York, NY 10036 *Tel:* 212-992-3232 *Fax:* 212-992-3233 *E-mail:* pub.center@nyu.edu *Web Site:* www.scps.nyu.edu/publishing, pg 766

Johnson, Heidi, New York University, Center for Publishing, 11 W 42 St, Rm 400, New York, NY 10036 *Tel:* 212-992-3232 *Fax:* 212-992-3233 *E-mail:* pub.center@nyu.edu *Web Site:* www.scps.nyu.edu/publishing, pg 753

Johnson, Jacqueline, Walker & Co, 104 Fifth Ave, 7th fl, New York, NY 10011 *Tel:* 212-727-8300 *Toll Free Tel:* 800-289-2553 *Fax:* 212-727-0984 *Toll Free Fax:* 800-218-9367 *E-mail:* firstinitiallastname@walkerbooks.com *Web Site:* www.walkerbooks.com, pg 292

Johnson, Jan, Red Wheel/Weiser/Conari, 368 Congress St, 4th fl, Boston, MA 02210 *Tel:* 617-542-1324 *Toll Free Tel:* 800-423-7087 *Fax:* 617-482-9676 *Web Site:* www.redwheelweiser.com, pg 230

Johnson, Jeanette, Review & Herald Publishing Association, 55 W Oak Ridge Dr, Hagerstown, MD 21740 *Tel:* 301-393-3000 *Toll Free Tel:* 800-234-7630 *Fax:* 301-393-4055 (periodicals); 301-393-3222 *E-mail:* editorial@rhpa.org *Web Site:* www.reviewandherald.com, pg 232

Johnson, Jeff, Tyndale House Publishers Inc, 351 Executive Dr, Carol Stream, IL 60188 *Tel:* 630-668-8303 *Toll Free Tel:* 800-323-9400 *Web Site:* www.tyndale.com, pg 277

Johnson, Jennifer, Craftsman Book Co, 6058 Corte Del Cedro, Carlsbad, CA 92009 *Tel:* 760-438-7828 *Toll Free Tel:* 800-829-8123 *Fax:* 760-438-0398 *Web Site:* www.craftsman-book.com, pg 71

Johnson, John, Selling to Hollywood, 269 S Beverly Dr, Suite 2600, Beverly Hills, CA 90212-3807 *Toll Free Tel:* 866-265-9091 *Toll Free Fax:* 866-265-9091 *E-mail:* asa@goasa.com *Web Site:* www.goasa.com, pg 747

Johnson, Joy, Centering Corp, 7230 Maple St, Omaha, NE 68134 *Tel:* 402-553-1200 *Fax:* 402-553-0507 *E-mail:* j1200@aol.com *Web Site:* www.centering.org, pg 57

Johnson, June, Medical Physics Publishing Corp, 4513 Vernon Blvd, Madison, WI 53705-4964 *Tel:* 608-262-4021 *Toll Free Tel:* 800-442-5778 *Fax:* 608-265-2121 *E-mail:* mpp@medicalphysics.org *Web Site:* www.medicalphysics.org, pg 170

Johnson, Kurt, J & S Publishing Co Inc, 1300 Bishop Lane, Alexandria, VA 22302 *Tel:* 703-823-9833 *Fax:* 703-823-9834 *E-mail:* jandspub@hotmail.com *Web Site:* www.jandspub.com, pg 140

Johnson, Leonidas, Crystal Fountain Publications, 500-A N Golden Springs Dr, Diamond Bar, CA 91765 *Tel:* 909-396-1201 *Fax:* 909-860-7803 *Web Site:* www.crystalfountain.org, pg 74

Johnson, Lisa, Dutton, 375 Hudson St, New York, NY 10014 *Tel:* 212-366-2000 *Fax:* 212-366-2262 *E-mail:* online@penguinputnam.com *Web Site:* www. penguin.com, pg 85

Johnson, Lise, South-Western, A Thomson Business, 5191 Natorp Blvd, Mason, OH 45040 *Tel:* 513-229-1000 *Toll Free Tel:* 800-543-0487 *Fax:* 513-229-1025 *Web Site:* www.thomson.com, pg 254

Johnson, Lloyd, Double Play, PO Box 22481, Kansas City, MO 64113 *Tel:* 816-651-7118 *Fax:* 816-822-2521, pg 596

Johnson, Lynette, Augsburg Fortress Publishers, Publishing House of the Evangelical Lutheran Church in America, 100 S Fifth St, Suite 700, Minneapolis, MN 55402 *Tel:* 612-330-3300 *Toll Free Tel:* 800-426-0115 (ext 639 subns); 800-328-4648 (orders); 800-421-0239 (perms) *Fax:* 612-330-3455 *Toll Free Fax:* 800-421-0239 (perms & copyrights) *E-mail:* customerservice@augsburgfortress.org; copyright@augsburgfortress.org (for reprint permission requests) *Web Site:* www.augsburgfortress.org, pg 28

Johnson, Margaret, Pact Publications, 1200 18 St NW, Suite 350, Washington, DC 20036 *Tel:* 202-466-5666 *Fax:* 202-466-5669 *E-mail:* books@pacthq.org *Web Site:* www.pactpublications.org, pg 202

Johnson, Mark, R S V Products, PO Box 26, Hopkins, MN 55343-0026 *Tel:* 952-936-0400 *Fax:* 952-936-0400, pg 224

Johnson, Dr Marv, Centering Corp, 7230 Maple St, Omaha, NE 68134 *Tel:* 402-553-1200 *Fax:* 402-553-0507 *E-mail:* j1200@aol.com *Web Site:* www. centering.org, pg 57

Johnson, Michael, Wadsworth Publishing, 10 Davis Dr, Belmont, CA 94002-3002 *Toll Free Tel:* 800-357-0092 *Fax:* 650-592-3342 *Toll Free Fax:* 800-522-4923 *Web Site:* www.wadsworth.com, pg 292

Johnson, Navorn, Hyperion, 77 W 66 St, 11th fl, New York, NY 10023-6298 *Tel:* 212-456-0100 *Toll Free Tel:* 800-759-0190 (cust serv) *Fax:* 212-456-0157 *Web Site:* hyperionbooks.com, pg 129

Johnson, Pamela J, The Pilgrim Press/United Church Press, 700 Prospect Ave, Cleveland, OH 44115-1100 *Tel:* 216-736-3761 *Toll Free Tel:* 800-537-3394 (cust serv) *Fax:* 216-736-2207 *E-mail:* thepilgrimpress@ thepilgrimpress.com *Web Site:* www.thepilgrimpress. com; www.theunitedchurchpress.com, pg 213

Johnson, Patricia, Alfred A Knopf, 1745 Broadway, New York, NY 10019 *Tel:* 212-751-2600 *Toll Free Tel:* 800-638-6460 *Fax:* 212-572-2593 *Web Site:* www. randomhouse.com/knopf, pg 146

Johnson, Phil, North American Snowsports Journalists Association, 460 Sarsons Rd, Kelowna, BC V1W 1C2, Canada *Tel:* 250-764-2143 *Fax:* 250-764-2145 *E-mail:* nasja@shaw.ca *Web Site:* www.nasja.org, pg 695

Johnson, Rich, DC Comics, 1700 Broadway, New York, NY 10019 *Tel:* 212-636-5400 *Toll Free Tel:* 800-759-0190 (distribution) *Fax:* 212-636-5481 *Web Site:* www. dccomics.com; www.madmag.com, pg 77

Johnson, Richard, Concordia Publishing House, 3558 S Jefferson Ave, St Louis, MO 63118-3968 *Tel:* 314-268-1000 *Toll Free Tel:* 800-325-3040 *Fax:* 314-268-1329 *Toll Free Fax:* 800-490-9889 *E-mail:* cphorder@ cph.org *Web Site:* www.cph.org, pg 66

Johnson, Robert G, Todd Publishing Inc, 1224 N Nokomis NE, Alexandria, MN 56308 *Tel:* 320-763-5190 *Fax:* 320-763-9290, pg 272

Johnson, Sandra, University of Nebraska Press, 233 N Eighth St, Lincoln, NE 68588-0255 *Tel:* 402-472-3581 *Toll Free Tel:* 800-755-1105 (orders) *Fax:* 402-472-0308 *Toll Free Fax:* 800-526-2617 *E-mail:* press@ unl.edu *Web Site:* www.nebraskapress.unl.edu; www. bisonbooks.com, pg 283

Johnson, Steven D, PrintImage International, 70 E Lake St, Suite 333, Chicago, IL 60601 *Tel:* 312-726-8015 *Toll Free Tel:* 800-234-0040 *Fax:* 312-726-8113 *E-mail:* info@printimage.org *Web Site:* www. printimage.org, pg 697

Johnson, Terence, Scribendi Inc, 153 Harvey St, Chatham, ON N7M 1M6, Canada *Fax:* 519-354-0192 *E-mail:* customerservice@scribendi.com *Web Site:* www.scribendi.com, pg 611

Johnson, Thomas, University Press of New England, One Court St, Lebanon, NH 03766 *Tel:* 603-448-1533 *Toll Free Tel:* 800-421-1561 (orders only) *Fax:* 603-448-7006; 603-643-1540 *E-mail:* university.press@ dartmouth.edu *Web Site:* www.upne.com, pg 287

Johnson, Thomas A, Manhattan Publishing Co, PO Box 850, Croton-on-Hudson, NY 10520-0850 *Tel:* 914-271-5194 *Toll Free Tel:* 888-686-7066 *Fax:* 914-271-5856 *Web Site:* www.manhattanpublishing.com, pg 162

Johnson, Thomas D, Business Research Services Inc, 4701 Sangamore Rd, Suite S155, Bethesda, MD 20816 *Tel:* 301-229-5561 *Toll Free Tel:* 800-845-8420 *Fax:* 301-229-6133 *E-mail:* brspubs@sba8a.com *Web Site:* www.sba8a.com; wwww.setasidealert.com, pg 50

Johnson, Tonya, Oregon Christian Writers, 1647 SW Pheasant Dr, Aloha, OR 97006 *Tel:* 503-642-9844 *Fax:* 503-848-3658 *E-mail:* miholer@viser.net *Web Site:* www.oregonchristianwriters.org, pg 696

Johnson-Schwartz, Kathryn, Playwrights Project, 450 "B" St, Suite 1020, San Diego, CA 92101-8093 *Tel:* 619-239-8222 *Fax:* 619-239-8225 *E-mail:* write@ playwrightsproject.com *Web Site:* www. playwrightsproject.com, pg 799

Johnston, Allyn, Harcourt Trade Publishers, 525 "B" St, Suite 1900, San Diego, CA 92101 *Tel:* 619-231-6616 *Toll Free Tel:* 800-543-1918 (cust serv) *Toll Free Fax:* 800-235-0256 (cust serv) *Web Site:* www. harcourtbooks.com, pg 115

Johnston, Becky, Landauer Books, 12251 Maffitt Rd, Cumming, IA 50061 *Tel:* 515-287-2144 *Toll Free Tel:* 800-557-2144 *Fax:* 515-287-1530 *E-mail:* landaucor@aol.com, pg 148

Johnston, Camille, Rodale Inc, 33 E Minor St, Emmaus, PA 18098-0099 *Tel:* 610-967-5171 *Fax:* 610-967-8962 *Web Site:* www.rodale.com, pg 234

Johnston, Cheryl, Morehouse Publishing Co, PO Box 1321, Harrisburg, PA 17105-1321 *Tel:* 717-541-8130 *Toll Free Tel:* 800-877-0012 (orders only) *Fax:* 717-541-8136; 717-541-8128 (orders only) *E-mail:* morehouse@morehousegroup.com *Web Site:* www.morehousegroup.com, pg 178

Johnston, Dillon, Wake Forest University Press, A5 Tribble Hall, Wake Forest University, Winston-Salem, NC 27109 *Tel:* 336-758-5448 *Fax:* 336-758-5636 *E-mail:* wfupress@wfu.edu *Web Site:* www.wfu. edu/wfupress, pg 292

Johnston, Mada, Abingdon Press, 201 Eighth Ave S, Nashville, TN 37203-3919 *Tel:* 615-749-6290 (publicist); 615-749-6000; 615-749-6451 (sales) *Toll Free Tel:* 800-251-3320 *Fax:* 615-749-6056 *Web Site:* www.abingdonpress.com, pg 3

Johnston, Patricia Irwin, Perspectives Press Inc: The Infertility & Adoption Publisher, PO Box 90318, Indianapolis, IN 46290-0318 *Tel:* 317-872-3055 *Web Site:* www.perspectivespress.com, pg 210

Johnston, Dr Richard, Stephen Leacock Memorial Award for Humour, Box 854, Orillia, ON L3V 6K8, Canada *Tel:* 705-835-3218 *Fax:* 705-835-5171 *E-mail:* moonwood@simpatico.ca *Web Site:* www. leacock.ca/awards.html, pg 784

Johnston, Tim, Emond Montgomery Publications Ltd, 60 Shaftesbury Ave, Toronto, ON M4T 1A3, Canada *Tel:* 416-975-3925 *Toll Free Tel:* 888-837-0815 *Fax:* 416-975-3924 *E-mail:* info@emp.ca; orders@ emp.ca *Web Site:* www.emp.ca, pg 546

Johnstone, Vicki, Harbour Publishing Co Ltd, 4437 Rondeview Rd, Madeira Park, BC V0N 2H0, Canada *Tel:* 604-883-2730 *Toll Free Tel:* 800-667-2988; 800-667-2988 *Fax:* 604-883-9451 *Toll Free Fax:* 877-604-9449 *E-mail:* info@harbourpublishing.com *Web Site:* www.harbourpublishing.com, pg 549

Joiner, Jackie, The Bukowski Agency, 202-14 Prince Arthur Ave, Toronto, ON M5R 1A9, Canada *Tel:* 416-928-6728 *Fax:* 416-963-9978 *E-mail:* assistant@thebukowskiagency.com *Web Site:* www.thebukowskiagency.com, pg 623

Joiner, Susan, Best Publishing Co, PO Box 30100, Flagstaff, AZ 86003-0100 *Tel:* 928-527-1055 *Toll Free Tel:* 800-468-1055 *Fax:* 928-526-0370 *E-mail:* divebooks@bestpub.com *Web Site:* www. bestpub.com, pg 37

Jolley, Carl, Penguin Group (USA) Inc, 375 Hudson St, New York, NY 10014 *Tel:* 212-366-2000 *Fax:* 212-366-2666 *E-mail:* online@uspenguingroup.com *Web Site:* www.penguin.com, pg 208

Jolley, Marc Jr, Mercer University Press, 1400 Coleman Ave, Macon, GA 31207 *Tel:* 478-301-2880 *Toll Free Tel:* 800-637-2378 (ext 2880, outside GA); 800-342-0841 (ext 2880, GA) *Fax:* 478-301-2585 *E-mail:* mupressorders@mercer.edu *Web Site:* www. mupress.org, pg 171

Jonas, Darrell, PublicAffairs, 250 W 57 St, Suite 1321, New York, NY 10107 *Tel:* 212-397-6666 *Toll Free Tel:* 800-242-7737 (orders) *Fax:* 212-397-4267 *E-mail:* publicaffairs@perseusbooks.com *Web Site:* www.publicaffairsbooks.com, pg 221

Jonas, Patrick, Aio Publishing Co LLC, PO Box 30788, Charleston, SC 29417 *Tel:* 843-225-3698 *Toll Free Tel:* 888-287-9888 *Web Site:* www.aiopublishing.com, pg 7

Jonas, Tiffany, Aio Publishing Co LLC, PO Box 30788, Charleston, SC 29417 *Tel:* 843-225-3698 *Toll Free Tel:* 888-287-9888 *Web Site:* www.aiopublishing.com, pg 7

Jones, Alan H, Caddo Gap Press, 3145 Geary Blvd, PMB 275, San Francisco, CA 94118 *Tel:* 415-666-3012 *Fax:* 415-666-3552 *E-mail:* caddogap@aol.com *Web Site:* www.caddogap.com, pg 51

Jones, Alice, Apogee Press, 2308 Sixth St, Berkeley, CA 94710 *E-mail:* editors@agopeepress.com *Web Site:* www.agopeepress.com, pg 21

Jones, Arnita, American Historical Association, 400 "A" St SE, Washington, DC 20003 *Tel:* 202-544-2422 *Fax:* 202-544-8307 *E-mail:* aha@historians.org *Web Site:* www.historians.org, pg 14

Jones, Bill, The American Ceramic Society, 735 Ceramic Place, Westerville, OH 43081-8720 *Tel:* 614-794-5890 *Fax:* 614-794-5892 *E-mail:* info@ceramics.org *Web Site:* www.ceramics.org, pg 12

Jones, Bill, Running Press Book Publishers, 125 S 22 St, Philadelphia, PA 19103-4399 *Tel:* 215-567-5080 *Toll Free Tel:* 800-345-5359 (cust serv & orders) *Fax:* 215-568-2919 *Toll Free Fax:* 800-453-2884 *Web Site:* www.runningpress.com, pg 236

Jones, Ms Brett Hall, Squaw Valley Community of Writers Workshops, PO Box 1416, Nevada City, CA 95959 *Tel:* 530-470-8440 *E-mail:* brett@ squawvalleywriters.org *Web Site:* www. squawvalleywriters.org, pg 748

Jones, Candide, Wake Forest University Press, A5 Tribble Hall, Wake Forest University, Winston-Salem, NC 27109 *Tel:* 336-758-5448 *Fax:* 336-758-5636 *E-mail:* wfupress@wfu.edu *Web Site:* www.wfu. edu/wfupress, pg 292

Jones, Cathy, William B Ruggles Journalism Scholarship, 5211 Port Royal Rd, Suite 510, Springfield, VA 22151 *Tel:* 703-321-9606 *Fax:* 703-321-7342 *E-mail:* research@nilrr.org *Web Site:* www. nilrr.org, pg 803

Jones, Christian, Davies Publishing Inc, 32 S Raymond Ave, Pasadena, CA 91105-1935 *Tel:* 626-792-3046 *Toll Free Tel:* 877-792-0005 *Fax:* 626-792-5308 *E-mail:* daviescorp@aol.com *Web Site:* www. daviespublishing.com, pg 76

Jones, Clayton E, Jones & Bartlett Publishers Inc, 40 Tall Pine Dr, Sudbury, MA 01776 *Tel:* 978-443-5000 *Toll Free Tel:* 800-832-0034 *Fax:* 978-443-8000 *E-mail:* info@jbpub.com *Web Site:* www.jbpub.com, pg 142

Jones, Deborah, William H Sadlier Inc, 9 Pine St, New York, NY 10005 *Tel:* 212-227-2120 *Toll Free Tel:* 800-221-5175 *Fax:* 212-312-6080 *Web Site:* www. sadlier.com; www.sadlier-oxford.com, pg 237

Jones, Diane W, The United Educators Inc, 900 N Shore Dr, Suite 140, Lake Bluff, IL 60044 *Tel:* 847-234-3700 *Fax:* 847-234-8705 *E-mail:* arslms@aol.com, pg 279

Jones, Donald W Jr, Jones & Bartlett Publishers Inc, 40 Tall Pine Dr, Sudbury, MA 01776 *Tel:* 978-443-5000 *Toll Free Tel:* 800-832-0034 *Fax:* 978-443-8000 *E-mail:* info@jbpub.com *Web Site:* www.jbpub.com, pg 142

Jones, Donna, Oxford University Press, Inc, 198 Madison Ave, New York, NY 10016-4314 *Tel:* 212-726-6000 *Toll Free Tel:* 800-451-7556 (orders) *Web Site:* www.oup.com/us, pg 200

Jones, Doug, Crown Publishing Group, 1745 Broadway, New York, NY 10019 *Tel:* 212-782-9000 *Toll Free Tel:* 888-264-1745 *Fax:* 212-940-7408 *Web Site:* www. randomhouse.com/crown, pg 74

Jones, Enid Ford, Jones Hutton Literary Associates, 160 N Compo Rd, Westport, CT 06880 *Tel:* 203-226-2588 *Fax:* 509-356-5190 *Web Site:* www.marquiswhoswho. net/huttonandhutton, pg 636

Jones, Frankie, Random House Publishing Group, 1745 Broadway, New York, NY 10019 *Toll Free Tel:* 800-200-3552 *Toll Free Fax:* 800-200-3552 *Web Site:* www.randomhouse.com, pg 227

Jones, Georgia, LadybugPress, 16964 Columbia River Dr, Sonora, CA 95370 *Tel:* 209-694-8340 *Toll Free Tel:* 888-892-5000 *Fax:* 209-694-8916 *E-mail:* ladybugpress@ladybugbooks.com *Web Site:* www.ladybugbooks.com, pg 148

Jones, Greg, China Books & Periodicals Inc, 2929 24 St, San Francisco, CA 94110-4126 *Tel:* 415-282-2994 *Toll Free Tel:* 800-818-2017 *Fax:* 415-282-0994 *E-mail:* info@chinabooks.com *Web Site:* www. chinabooks.com, pg 60

Jones, Greg, Signature Books Publishing LLC, 564 W 400 N, Salt Lake City, UT 84116-3411 *Tel:* 801-531-1483 *Toll Free Tel:* 800-356-5687 (orders) *Fax:* 801-531-1488 *E-mail:* people@signaturebooks.com *Web Site:* www.signaturebooks.com, pg 247

Jones, Hawk, KotaPress, PO Box 514, Vashon Island, WA 98070-0514 *Tel:* 206-251-6706 *E-mail:* editor@ kotapress.com *Web Site:* www.kotapress.com, pg 147

Jones, Holly, Providence Publishing Corp, 238 Seaboard Lane, Franklin, TN 37067 *Tel:* 615-771-2020 *Toll Free Tel:* 800-321-5692 *Fax:* 615-771-2002 *E-mail:* books@providencehouse.com *Web Site:* www. providencehouse.com, pg 220

Jones, Jennifer, Nilgiri Press, 3600 Tomales Rd, Tomales, CA 94971 *Tel:* 707-878-2369 *Toll Free Tel:* 800-475-2369 *Fax:* 707-878-2375 *E-mail:* info@ nilgiri.org *Web Site:* www.nilgiri.org, pg 191

Jones, Jennifer J, American Occupational Therapy Association Inc, 4720 Montgomery Lane, Bethesda, MD 20824 *Tel:* 301-652-2682 *Fax:* 301-652-7711 *Web Site:* www.aota.org, pg 16

Jones, John, The Crossroad Publishing Company, 16 Penn Plaza, Suite 1550, New York, NY 10001 *Tel:* 212-868-1801 *Toll Free Tel:* 800-395-0690 (orders) *Fax:* 212-868-2171 *Toll Free Fax:* 800-462-6420 (orders) *E-mail:* ask@crossroadpublishing.com *Web Site:* www.crossroadpublishing.com, pg 73

Jones, Jordan, Leaping Dog Press, PO Box 3316, San Jose, CA 95156-3316 *Toll Free Tel:* 877-570-6873 *Toll Free Fax:* 877-570-6873 *E-mail:* editor@ leapingdogpress.com; sales@leapingdogpress.com *Web Site:* www.leapingdogpress.com, pg 151

Jones, Judith, Alfred A Knopf, 1745 Broadway, New York, NY 10019 *Tel:* 212-751-2600 *Toll Free Tel:* 800-638-6460 *Fax:* 212-572-2593 *Web Site:* www. randomhouse.com/knopf, pg 146

Jones, Kara L C, KotaPress, PO Box 514, Vashon Island, WA 98070-0514 *Tel:* 206-251-6706 *E-mail:* editor@ kotapress.com *Web Site:* www.kotapress.com, pg 147

Jones, Keasley, Peachpit Press, 1249 Eighth St, Berkeley, CA 94710 *Tel:* 510-524-2178 *Fax:* 510-524-2221 *E-mail:* firstname.lastname@peachpit.com *Web Site:* www.peachpit.com, pg 206

Jones, Keiko, Signature Books Publishing LLC, 564 W 400 N, Salt Lake City, UT 84116-3411 *Tel:* 801-531-1483 *Toll Free Tel:* 800-356-5687 (orders) *Fax:* 801-531-1488 *E-mail:* people@signaturebooks.com *Web Site:* www.signaturebooks.com, pg 247

Jones, Lee, Houghton Mifflin Co, 222 Berkeley St, Boston, MA 02116-3764 *Tel:* 617-351-5000 *Toll Free Tel:* 800-225-3362 (trade books); 800-733-2828 (text books); 800-225-1464 (college texts) *Fax:* 617-351-1125 *Web Site:* www.hmco.com, pg 126

Jones, Lee, The Riverside Publishing Co, 425 Spring Lake Dr, Itasca, IL 60143-2079 *Tel:* 630-467-7000 *Toll Free Tel:* 800-323-9540 *Fax:* 630-467-7192 (cust serv) *Web Site:* www.riverpub.com, pg 233

Jones, Les, Standard Publishing Co, 8121 Hamilton Ave, Cincinnati, OH 45231 *Tel:* 513-931-4050 *Toll Free Tel:* 800-543-1301 *Fax:* 513-931-0950 *Toll Free Fax:* 877-867-5751 *E-mail:* customerservice@ standardpub.com *Web Site:* www.standardpub.com, pg 257

Jones, Linda, Enfield Publishing & Distribution Co, 234 May St, Enfield, NH 03748 *Tel:* 603-632-7377 *Fax:* 603-632-5611 *E-mail:* info@enfieldbooks.com *Web Site:* www.enfielddistribution.com, pg 91

Jones, Linda, Science Publishers Inc, 234 May St, Enfield, NH 03748 *Tel:* 603-632-7377 *Fax:* 603-632-5611 *E-mail:* info@scipub.net *Web Site:* www.scipub. net, pg 243

Jones, Linda, Trans Tech Publications, c/o Enfield Distribution Co, 234 May St, Enfield, NH 03748 *Tel:* 603-632-7377 *Fax:* 603-632-5611 *E-mail:* usa-ttp@ttp.net; info@enfiedbooks.com *Web Site:* www. ttp.net, pg 274

Jones, Lindsay, Knopf Canada, One Toronto St, Suite 300, Toronto, ON M5C 2V6, Canada *Tel:* 416-364-4449 *Toll Free Tel:* 800-668-4247 (order desk) *Fax:* 416-364-0462 *Web Site:* www.randomhouse.ca, pg 552

Jones, Lorena, Ten Speed Press, PO Box 7123, Berkeley, CA 94707 *Tel:* 510-559-1600 *Toll Free Tel:* 800-841-Book *Fax:* 510-559-1629; 510-524-1052 (general) *E-mail:* order@tenspeed.com *Web Site:* www.tenspeed. com, pg 266

Jones, Louis B, Squaw Valley Community of Writers Workshops, PO Box 1416, Nevada City, CA 95959 *Tel:* 530-470-8440 *E-mail:* brett@squawvalleywriters. org *Web Site:* www.squawvalleywriters.org, pg 748

Jones, Marcia, Betterway Books, 4700 E Galbraith Rd, Cincinnati, OH 45236 *Tel:* 513-531-2690 *Toll Free Tel:* 800-666-0963 *Fax:* 513-891-7185 *Toll Free Fax:* 888-590-4082 *Web Site:* www.fwpublications. com, pg 38

Jones, Marcia, North Light Books, 4700 E Galbraith Rd, Cincinnati, OH 45236 *Tel:* 513-531-2690 *Toll Free Tel:* 800-666-0963 *Fax:* 513-891-7185 *Toll Free Fax:* 888-590-4082 *Web Site:* www.fwpublications. com, pg 192

Jones, Marjorie Gillette, Baldwin Literary Services, 935 Hayes St, Baldwin, NY 11510-4834 *Tel:* 516-546-8338 *Fax:* 516-867-6850, pg 591

Jones, Marsha E, DAW Books Inc, 375 Hudson St, 3rd fl, New York, NY 10014 *Tel:* 212-366-2096 *Fax:* 212-366-2090 *E-mail:* daw@us.penguingroup. com *Web Site:* www.dawbooks.com, pg 77

Jones, Michael P, Crumb Elbow Publishing, PO Box 294, Rhododendron, OR 97049-0294 *Tel:* 503-622-4798, pg 74

Jones, Mike, Graphic Arts Center Publishing Co, 3019 NW Yeon Ave, Portland, OR 97210 *Tel:* 503-226-2402 *Toll Free Tel:* 800-452-3032 *Fax:* 503-223-1410 *Toll Free Fax:* 800-355-9685 *E-mail:* editorial@gacpc.com; sales@gacpc.com *Web Site:* www.gacpc.com, pg 107

Jones, Peder, Straight Line Editorial Development Inc, 3239 Sacramento St, San Francisco, CA 94115-2047 *Tel:* 415-864-2011 *Fax:* 415-864-2013 *E-mail:* sledinc@aol.com, pg 612

Jones, Peter, LRS, 14214 S Figueroa St, Los Angeles, CA 90061-1034 *Tel:* 310-354-2610 *Toll Free Tel:* 800-255-5002 *Fax:* 310-354-2601 *E-mail:* lrsprint@aol. com *Web Site:* lrs-largeprint.com, pg 159

Jones, Richard, Scott Jones Inc, PO Box 696, El Granada, CA 94018 *Tel:* 650-726-2436 *Fax:* 650-726-4693 *Web Site:* www.scottjonespub.com, pg 243

Jones, Sharon, Vision Books International, 775 E Blithedale Ave, No 342, Mill Valley, CA 94941 *Tel:* 415-383-0962 *Fax:* 415-383-4521 *E-mail:* publisher@vbipublishing.com *Web Site:* www. vbipublishing.com, pg 574

Jones, Sheila, Discipleship Publications International (DPI), 2 Sterling Rd, Billerica, MA 01862-2595 *Tel:* 978-670-8840 *Toll Free Tel:* 888-DPI-Book *Fax:* 978-670-8485 *E-mail:* dpibooks@icoc.org *Web Site:* www.dpibooks.org, pg 80

Jones, Tina, Livingston Press, University of West Alabama, Sta 22, Livingston, AL 35470 *Tel:* 205-652-3470 *Fax:* 205-652-3717 *Web Site:* www. livingstonpress.uwa.edu, pg 157

Jones, Tommie L, One Planet Publishing House, PO Box 19840, Seattle, WA 98109-1840 *Tel:* 206-282-9699 *Toll Free Tel:* 877-526-3814 (87-PLANET-14) *Fax:* 206-282-9699 *Toll Free Fax:* 877-526-3814 (87-PLANET-14) *E-mail:* info@oneplanetpublishinghouse. com *Web Site:* www.oneplanetpublishinghouse.com, pg 197

Jones, Tony, International Broadcasting Services Ltd, 825 Cherry Lane, Penns Park, PA 18943 *Tel:* 215-598-3298 *Fax:* 215-598-3794 *E-mail:* hq@passband.com; mktg@passband.com *Web Site:* www.passband.com, pg 136

Jones, Warren W, Solano Press Books, PO Box 773, Point Arena, CA 95468 *Tel:* 707-884-4508 *Toll Free Tel:* 800-931-9373 *Fax:* 707-884-4109 *E-mail:* spbooks@solano.com *Web Site:* www.solano. com, pg 252

Jordan, Dina, M Evans & Co Inc, 216 E 49 St, New York, NY 10017 *Tel:* 212-688-2810 *Fax:* 212-486-4544 *E-mail:* editorial@mevans.com *Web Site:* www. mevans.com, pg 93

Jordan, Elaine, Aztex Corp, PO Box 50046, Tucson, AZ 85703-1046 *Tel:* 520-882-4656 *Fax:* 520-792-8501 *Web Site:* www.aztexcorp.com, pg 30

Jordan, Jim, Columbia University Press, 61 W 62 St, New York, NY 10023 *Tel:* 212-459-0600 *Toll Free Tel:* 800-944-8648 *Fax:* 212-459-3678 *Web Site:* www. columbia.edu/cu/cup, pg 65

Jordan, Lawrence, Lawrence Jordan Literary Agency, 345 W 121 St, New York, NY 10027 *Tel:* 212-662-7871 *Fax:* 212-662-8138 *E-mail:* ljlagency@aol.com, pg 636

Jordan, Mark, Fine Communications, 322 Eighth Ave, 15th fl, New York, NY 10001 *Tel:* 212-595-3500 *Fax:* 212-595-3779, pg 96

Jordan, Sam, The Rosen Publishing Group Inc, 29 E 21 St, New York, NY 10010 *Tel:* 212-777-3017 *Toll Free Tel:* 800-237-9932 *Fax:* 212-777-0277 *E-mail:* info@ rosenpub.com *Web Site:* www.rosenpublishing.com, pg 234

Jorgensen, Muriel, Grove/Atlantic Inc, 841 Broadway, 4th fl, New York, NY 10003-4793 *Tel:* 212-614-7850 *Toll Free Tel:* 800-521-0178 *Fax:* 212-614-7886 *Web Site:* www.groveatlantic.com, pg 110

Joseph, Brian, Linguistic Society of America, 1325 18 St NW, Suite 211, Washington, DC 20036-6501 *Tel:* 202-835-1714 *Fax:* 202-835-1717 *E-mail:* lsa@lsadc.org *Web Site:* www.lsadc.org, pg 690

Joseph, Heather, Society for Scholarly Publishing, 10200 W 44 Ave, Suite 304, Wheat Ridge, CO 80033-2840 *Tel:* 303-422-3914 *Fax:* 303-422-8894 *E-mail:* ssp@ resourcecenter.com; info@sspnet.org *Web Site:* www. sspnet.org, pg 699

Joseph, Jennifer, Manic D Press, 250 Banks St, San Francisco, CA 94110 *Tel:* 415-648-8288 *Fax:* 415-648-8288 *E-mail:* info@manicdpress.com *Web Site:* www.manicdpress.com, pg 162

Joseph, Rolande, Warner Books, 1271 Avenue of the Americas, New York, NY 10020 *Tel:* 212-522-7200 *Fax:* 212-522-7991 *Web Site:* www.twbookmark.com, pg 293

Josephy, Jennifer, Doubleday Broadway Publishing Group, 1745 Broadway, New York, NY 10019 *Tel:* 212-782-9000 *Toll Free Tel:* 800-223-6834; 800-223-5780 (sales) *Fax:* 212-302-7985 (correspondence); 212-492-9862 (orders), pg 82

Joslyn, Jo, University of Pennsylvania Press, 4200 Pine St, Philadelphia, PA 19104-4011 *Tel:* 215-898-6261 *Toll Free Tel:* 800-445-9880 (orders & cust serv only) *Fax:* 215-898-0404; 410-516-6998 (orders) *E-mail:* custserv@pobox.upenn.edu *Web Site:* www.upenn.edu/pennpress, pg 284

Jovanovich, Peter, Pearson Education, One Lake St, Upper Saddle River, NJ 07458 *Tel:* 201-236-7000 *Fax:* 201-236-3400 *E-mail:* firstname.lastname@pearsoned.com; communications@pearson.ed *Web Site:* www.pearsoned.com, pg 206

Joyce, John, Joyce Media Inc, 2654 Diamond St, Rosamond, CA 93560 *Tel:* 661-269-1169 *Fax:* 661-269-2139 *E-mail:* joycemed@pacbell.net *Web Site:* www.joycemediainc.com, pg 142

Joyce, Rick, Running Press Book Publishers, 125 S 22 St, Philadelphia, PA 19103-4399 *Tel:* 215-567-5080 *Toll Free Tel:* 800-345-5359 (cust serv & orders) *Fax:* 215-568-2919 *Toll Free Fax:* 800-453-2884 *Web Site:* www.runningpress.com, pg 236

Ju, Ms Gloria, Alexander Hamilton Institute, 70 Hilltop Rd, Ramsey, NJ 07446-1119 *Tel:* 201-825-3377 *Toll Free Tel:* 800-879-2441 *Fax:* 201-825-8696 *E-mail:* editorial@ahipubs.com *Web Site:* www.ahipubs.com, pg 112

Juarez, Benny, Ross Books, PO Box 4340, Berkeley, CA 94704-0340 *Tel:* 510-841-2474 *Toll Free Tel:* 800-367-0930 *Fax:* 510-841-2695 *E-mail:* staff@rossbooks.com *Web Site:* www.rossbooks.com, pg 234

Jud, Brian, Book Marketing Works LLC, 50 Lovely St, Avon, CT 06001 *Tel:* 860-675-1344 *Toll Free Tel:* 800-562-4357 *Fax:* 203-729-5335 *Web Site:* www.bookmarketingworks.com, pg 43

Jud, Brian, Connecticut Authors & Publishers Association (CAPA), PO Box 715, Avon, CT 06001-0715 *Tel:* 203-729-5335 *Fax:* 203-729-5335 *E-mail:* labriol200@aol.com *Web Site:* www.aboutcapa.com, pg 685

Judd, Darrell, Artech House Inc, 685 Canton St, Norwood, MA 02062 *Tel:* 781-769-9750 *Toll Free Tel:* 800-225-9977 *Fax:* 781-769-6334 *E-mail:* artech@artechhouse.com *Web Site:* www.artechhouse.com, pg 24

Judson, Nancy, TripBuilder Inc, 15 Oak St, Westport, CT 06880 *Tel:* 203-227-1255 *Toll Free Tel:* 800-525-9745 *Fax:* 203-227-1257 *E-mail:* info@tripbuilder.com *Web Site:* www.tripbuilder.com, pg 275

Juhren, David, Society of Motion Picture & Television Engineers (SMPTE), 595 W Hartsdale Ave, White Plains, NY 10607-1824 *Tel:* 914-761-1100 *Fax:* 914-761-3115 *E-mail:* smpte@smpte.org *Web Site:* www.smpte.org, pg 700

Julien, Ria, Seven Stories Press, 140 Watts St, New York, NY 10013 *Tel:* 212-226-8760 *Toll Free Tel:* 800-283-3572 *Fax:* 212-226-1411 *E-mail:* info@sevenstories.com *Web Site:* www.sevenstories.com, pg 245

Juliot, Brent, Faith & Fellowship Press, 1020 Alcott Ave W, Fergus Falls, MN 56537 *Tel:* 218-736-7357 *Toll Free Tel:* 800-332-9232 *Fax:* 218-736-2200 *E-mail:* ffpress@clba.org *Web Site:* www.faithandfellowship.org, pg 94

June, Gary, Pearson Technology Group (PTG), 201 W 103 St, Indianapolis, IN 46290 *Tel:* 317-581-3500 *Toll Free Tel:* 800-545-5914 *Fax:* 317-581-4675 *E-mail:* firstname.lastname@pearsoned.com *Web Site:* www.mcp.com, pg 207

Junior, Michael, McGraw-Hill Higher Education, 1333 Burr Ridge Pkwy, Burr Ridge, IL 60527 *Tel:* 630-789-4000 *Toll Free Tel:* 800-338-3987 (cust serv) *Fax:* 614-755-5645 (cust serv) *Web Site:* www.mhhe.com, pg 167

Jurjevics, Juris, Soho Press Inc, 853 Broadway, New York, NY 10003 *Tel:* 212-260-1900 *Fax:* 212-260-1902 *E-mail:* editor@sohopress.com *Web Site:* sohopress.com, pg 252

Jutkowitz, Edward, Camino Books Inc, PO Box 59026, Philadelphia, PA 19102-9026 *Tel:* 215-413-1917 *Fax:* 215-413-3255 *E-mail:* camino@caminobooks.com *Web Site:* www.caminobooks.com, pg 52

Jutras, Luc, Health Communications Inc, 3201 SW 15 St, Deerfield Beach, FL 33442-8190 *Tel:* 954-360-0909 *Toll Free Tel:* 800-851-9100 (cust serv); 800-441-5569 (order entry) *Fax:* 954-360-0034 *Web Site:* www.hcibooks.com, pg 119

Jutras, Luc, Montreal-Contacts/The Rights Agency, PO Box 596-C, Montreal, PQ H2L 4K4, Canada *Tel:* 450-461-1575 *Fax:* 450-461-1505, pg 644

Kacian, Jim, Red Moon Press, PO Box 2461, Winchester, VA 22604-1661 *Tel:* 540-722-2156 *Fax:* 708-810-8992 *E-mail:* redmoon@shentel.net, pg 229

Kadetz, Stuart, Bhaktivedanta Book Publishing Inc, 9701 Vencie Blvd, Unit 3, Los Angeles, CA 90034 *Tel:* 310-559-4455 *Toll Free Tel:* 800-927-4152 *Fax:* 310-837-1056 *E-mail:* bbt2@webcom.com *Web Site:* www.krishna.com, pg 38

Kadin, Ellen, AMACOM Books, 1601 Broadway, New York, NY 10019-7406 *Tel:* 212-586-8100; 518-891-5510 (orders) *Toll Free Tel:* 800-262-9699 (cust serv) *Fax:* 212-903-8168; 518-891-2372 (orders) *Web Site:* www.amanet.org, pg 10

Kadushin, Raphael, University of Wisconsin Press, 1930 Monroe St, 3rd fl, Madison, WI 53711 *Tel:* 608-263-1110 *Toll Free Tel:* 800-621-2736 (Orders) *Fax:* 608-263-1120 *Toll Free Fax:* 800-621-8476 (Orders) *E-mail:* uwiscpress@uwpress.wisc.edu (Main Office) *Web Site:* www.wisc.edu/wisconsinpress/, pg 286

Kaemmer, Beverly, University of Minnesota Press, 111 Third Ave S, Suite 290, Minneapolis, MN 55401-2520 *Tel:* 612-627-1970 *Fax:* 612-627-1980 *E-mail:* ump@tc.umn.edu *Web Site:* www.upress.umn.edu, pg 282

Kaemmerling, Teressa, National Resource Center for Youth Services (NRCYS), Schusterman Center, 4502 E 41 St, Bldg 4W, Tulsa, OK 74135-2512 *Tel:* 918-660-3700 *Toll Free Tel:* 800-274-2687 *Fax:* 918-660-3737 *Web Site:* www.nrcys.ou.edu, pg 185

Kaeser, Scott, Tide-mark Press, 179 Broad St, Windsor, CT 06095 *Tel:* 860-683-4499 *Toll Free Tel:* 800-338-2508 *Fax:* 860-683-4055 *E-mail:* customerservice@tide-mark.com *Web Site:* www.tidemarkpress.com, pg 271

Kafka, Vincent, Effective Learning Systems, 805 Ocean Ave, Point Richmond, CA 94801-3735 *Tel:* 510-232-8218 *Fax:* 510-965-0134, pg 88

Kagan, Abby, Farrar, Straus & Giroux, LLC, 19 Union Sq W, New York, NY 10003 *Tel:* 212-741-6900 *Fax:* 212-741-6973 *Web Site:* www.fsgbooks.com, pg 95

Kagan, Heidi, Penguin Group (USA) Inc, 375 Hudson St, New York, NY 10014 *Tel:* 212-366-2000 *Fax:* 212-366-2666 *E-mail:* online@uspenguingroup.com *Web Site:* www.penguin.com, pg 208

Kagan, Ute Wartenberg, American Numismatic Society, 26 Fulton St, New York, NY 10038 *Tel:* 212-571-4470 *Fax:* 212-571-4479 *E-mail:* info@amnumsoc.org; info@numismatics.org *Web Site:* www.amnumsoc.org; www.numismatics.org, pg 16

Kageff, Karl, Southern Illinois University Press, PO Box 3697, Carbondale, IL 62902-3697 *Tel:* 618-453-2281 *Toll Free Tel:* 800-346-2680 *Fax:* 618-453-1221 *Toll Free Fax:* 800-346-2681 *E-mail:* jstetter@siu.edu *Web Site:* www.siu.edu/~siupress, pg 254

Kahan, Alan, Entomological Society of America, 9301 Annapolis Rd, Lanham, MD 20706-3115 *Tel:* 301-731-4535 *Fax:* 301-731-4538 *E-mail:* pubs@entsoc.org *Web Site:* www.entsoc.org, pg 91

Kahan, Marlene, American Society of Magazine Editors, 810 Seventh Ave, 24th fl, New York, NY 10019 *Tel:* 212-872-3700 *Fax:* 212-906-0128 *E-mail:* asme@magazine.org *Web Site:* www.asme.magazine.org, pg 678

Kahaunaele, Maile, Marketscope Group Books LLC, PO Box 3118, Huntington Beach, CA 92605-3118 *Tel:* 714-375-9888 *Fax:* 714-375-9898, pg 163

Kahla, Keith, St Martin's Press Trade Division, 175 Fifth Ave, New York, NY 10010 *E-mail:* firstname.lastname@stmartins.com *Web Site:* www.stmartins.com; www.minotaurbooks.com, pg 239

Kahn, Alan, Barnes & Noble Books (Imports & Reprints), 4501 Forbes Blvd, Suite 200, Lanham, MD 20706 *Tel:* 301-459-3366 *Toll Free Tel:* 800-462-6420 (orders only) *Fax:* 301-429-5748 *Toll Free Fax:* 800-338-4550 (orders only) *Web Site:* www.rowmanlittlefield.com, pg 32

Kahn, Kenneth F, The Dartnell Corp, 360 Hiatt Dr, Palm Beach Gardens, FL 33418 *Tel:* 561-622-6520 *Toll Free Tel:* 800-621-5463 *Fax:* 561-622-2423 *Web Site:* www.dartnellcorp.com, pg 76

Kahn, Kenneth F, LRP Publications, 360 Hiatt Dr, Palm Beach Gardens, FL 33418 *Tel:* 215-784-0860 *Toll Free Tel:* 800-341-7874 *Fax:* 215-784-9639 *E-mail:* custserve@lrp.com *Web Site:* www.lrp.com, pg 159

Kahn, Linda, Scholastic Entertainment Inc, 524 Broadway, New York, NY 10012 *Tel:* 212-343-7500 *Fax:* 212-965-7448, pg 241

Kahn, Yamile, The Woodrow Wilson Center Press, One Woodrow Wilson Plaza, 1300 Pennsylvania Ave NW, Washington, DC 20004-3027 *Tel:* 202-691-4000 *Fax:* 202-691-4001 *E-mail:* press@wwics.si.edu *Web Site:* wilsoncenter.org, pg 302

Kaibni, Kate, Vault.com Inc, 150 W 22 St, 5th fl, New York, NY 10011 *Tel:* 212-366-4212 ext 384 *Fax:* 212-366-6117 *E-mail:* feedback@staff.vault.com *Web Site:* www.vault.com, pg 289

Kaiman, Ken, Square One Publishers, 115 Herricks Rd, Garden City Park, NY 11040 *Tel:* 516-535-2010 *Fax:* 516-535-2014 *E-mail:* sq1info@aol.com *Web Site:* squareonepublishers.com, pg 256

Kaiman, Kenneth, Basic Health Publications Inc, 8200 Boulevard E, Suite 25-G, North Bergen, NJ 07047 *Tel:* 201-868-8336 *Toll Free Tel:* 800-575-8890 *Fax:* 201-868-8335, pg 33

Kaiser, Drake H M, Swedenborg Association, 278-A Meeting St, Charleston, SC 29401 *Tel:* 843-853-6211 *Fax:* 843-853-6226 *E-mail:* arcana@swedenborg.net; assn@swedenborg.net, pg 263

Kaiser, Jackie, Westwood Creative Artists Ltd, 94 Harbord St, Toronto, ON M5S 1G6, Canada *Tel:* 416-964-3302 *Fax:* 416-975-9209, pg 661

Kaiser, Julene, Twenty-First Century King James Bible Publishers, 215 Main Ave, Gary, SD 57237 *Tel:* 605-272-5575 *Toll Free Tel:* 800-225-5521 *Fax:* 605-272-5306 *E-mail:* kj21@kj21.com *Web Site:* www.kj21.com, pg 277

Kaiser, Laura, Commonwealth Business Media, 400 Windsor Corporate Center, 50 Millstone Rd, Suite 200, East Windsor, NJ 08520-1415 *Tel:* 609-371-7700 *Toll Free Tel:* 800-221-5488; 888-215-6084 (orders) *Fax:* 609-371-7712 *Web Site:* www.cbizmedia.com, pg 65

Kaiserlian, Penelope J, The University of Virginia Press, PO Box 400318, Charlottesville, VA 22904-4318 *Tel:* 434-924-3468 (cust serv); 434-924-3469 (cust serv) *Toll Free Tel:* 800-831-3406 (cust serv) *Fax:* 434-982-2655 *Toll Free Fax:* 877-288-6400 *E-mail:* upressvirginia@virginia.edu *Web Site:* www.upressvirginia.edu, pg 285

Karns, Judith, WordMaster & Associates LLC, 4317 W Farrand Rd, Clio, MI 48420 *Tel:* 810-686-2047 *Fax:* 810-564-9929 *E-mail:* wordmasterpub@comcast. net, pg 614

Karp, Jonathan, Random House Publishing Group, 1745 Broadway, New York, NY 10019 *Toll Free Tel:* 800-200-3552 *Toll Free Fax:* 800-200-3552 *Web Site:* www.randomhouse.com, pg 227

Karper, Altie, Pantheon Books/Schocken Books, 1745 Broadway, New York, NY 10019 *Tel:* 212-751-2600 *Toll Free Tel:* 800-638-6460 *Fax:* 212-572-6030, pg 203

Karpfinger, Barney M, The Karpfinger Agency, 357 W 20 St, New York, NY 10011-3379 *Tel:* 212-691-2690 *Fax:* 212-691-7129, pg 637

Karrel, Dean, John Wiley & Sons Inc Professional & Trade Group, 111 River St, Hoboken, NJ 07030 *Tel:* 201-748-6000 *Toll Free Tel:* 800-225-5945 (cust serv) *Fax:* 201-748-6088 *E-mail:* info@wiley.com *Web Site:* www.wiley.com, pg 300

Karshner, Roger, Dramaline® Publications, 36-851 Palm View Rd, Rancho Mirage, CA 92270-2417 *Tel:* 760-770-6076 *Fax:* 760-770-4507 *E-mail:* drama.line@ verizon.net *Web Site:* dramaline.com, pg 83

Karst, Gerry D, Review & Herald Publishing Association, 55 W Oak Ridge Dr, Hagerstown, MD 21740 *Tel:* 301-393-3000 *Toll Free Tel:* 800-234-7630 *Fax:* 301-393-4055 (periodicals); 301-393-3222 *E-mail:* editorial@rhpa.org *Web Site:* www. reviewandherald.com, pg 232

Kartofels, Stephanie, BAR/BRI Group, 111 W Jackson Blvd, Chicago, IL 60604 *Tel:* 312-894-1688 *Toll Free Tel:* 800-328-9352 *Fax:* 312-360-1842 *Toll Free Fax:* 800-430-9378 (orders) *Web Site:* www.gilbertlaw. com, pg 32

Karton, Carol K, Proof Positive/Farrowlyne Associates Inc, 1620 Central St, Evanston, IL 60201 *Tel:* 847-866-9570 *Fax:* 847-866-9849, pg 609

Kartsaklis, Lee, Simon & Schuster Inc, 1230 Avenue of the Americas, New York, NY 10020 *Tel:* 212-698-7000 *Fax:* 212-698-7007 *Web Site:* www.simonsays. com, pg 249

Kartsev, Vladimir, Fort Ross Inc, 26 Arthur Place, Yonkers, NY 10701 *Tel:* 914-375-6448 *Fax:* 914-375-6439 *E-mail:* fort.ross@verizon.net *Web Site:* www. fortross.net, pg 99

Kartsev, Dr Vladimir P, Fort Ross Inc - International Rights, 26 Arthur Place, Yonkers, NY 10701 *Tel:* 914-375-6448 *Fax:* 914-375-6439 *E-mail:* fort.ross@ verizon.net *Web Site:* www.fortross.net, pg 631, 665

Kasabian, Robert J, International Newspaper Financial Executives, 21525 Ridgetop Circle, Suite 200, Sterling, VA 20166 *Tel:* 703-421-4060 *Web Site:* www. infe.org, pg 688

Kasal, Marilyn H, The Sporting News Publishing Co, A Vulcan Sports Media Company, 10176 Corporate Square Dr, Suite 200, St Louis, MO 63132 *Tel:* 314-997-7111 *Fax:* 314-993-7726 *Web Site:* www. sportingnews.com, pg 256

Kasdin, Steven, Harcourt Trade Publishers, 525 "B" St, Suite 1900, San Diego, CA 92101 *Tel:* 619-231-6616 *Toll Free Tel:* 800-543-1918 (cust serv) *Toll Free Fax:* 800-235-0256 (cust serv) *Web Site:* www. harcourtbooks.com, pg 115

Kasdorf, William E, Impressions Book & Journal Services Inc, 2016 Winnebago St, Madison, WI 53704 *Tel:* 608-244-6218 *Fax:* 608-244-7050 *E-mail:* info@ impressions.com *Web Site:* www.impressions.com, pg 602

Kase, Josef, Papyrus & Letterbox of London Publishers, 10501 Broom Hill Dr, Las Vegas, NV 89134-7339 *Tel:* 702-256-3838 *E-mail:* LB27383@earthlink.net *Web Site:* booksbyletterbox.com, pg 203

Kasel, David, Sports Publishing LLC, 804 N Neil St, Champaign, IL 61820 *Tel:* 217-363-2072 *Toll Free Tel:* 877-424-BOOK (424-2665) *Fax:* 217-363-2073 *E-mail:* marketing@sportspublishingllc.com *Web Site:* www.sportspublishingllc.com, pg 256

Kaser, Richard T, Information Today, Inc, 143 Old Marlton Pike, Medford, NJ 08055-8750 *Tel:* 609-654-6266 *Toll Free Tel:* 800-300-9868 (cust serv) *Fax:* 609-654-4309 *E-mail:* custserv@infotoday.com *Web Site:* www.infotoday.com, pg 133

Kasha, Vivan, QPB/New Visions Award, Time & Life Bldg, 1271 Avenue of the Americas, New York, NY 10020 *Tel:* 212-522-4200 *Fax:* 212-467-0239 *E-mail:* pr@bookspan.com *Web Site:* www.bookspan. com, pg 801

Kasha, Vivan, QPB/New Voices Award, Time & Life Bldg, 1271 Avenue of the Americas, New York, NY 10020 *Tel:* 212-522-4200 *Fax:* 212-467-0239 *E-mail:* pr@bookspan.com *Web Site:* www.bookspan. com, pg 801

Kasher, Robert, Database Directories, 588 Dufferin Ave, London, ON N6B 2A4, Canada *Tel:* 519-433-1666 *Fax:* 519-430-1131 *E-mail:* info@databasedirectory. com; lclassic@databasedirectory.com *Web Site:* www. databasedirectory.com, pg 542

Kasper, Carol, Association of American University Presses, 1427 E 60 St, Chicago, IL 60637 *Tel:* 773-702-7700; 773-702-7600 *Toll Free Tel:* 800-621-2736 (orders) *Fax:* 773-702-9756 (sales); 773-660-2235 (orders); 773-702-2708 *E-mail:* general@press. uchicago.edu *Web Site:* www.press.uchicago.edu, pg 26

Kass, Francine, Simon & Schuster Children's Publishing, 1230 Avenue of the Americas, New York, NY 10020 *Tel:* 212-698-7000 *Web Site:* www.simonsayskids.com, pg 248

Kassahun, Checole, Africa World Press Inc, 541 W Ingham Ave, Suite B, Trenton, NJ 08638 *Tel:* 609-695-3200 *Fax:* 609-695-6466 *E-mail:* awprsp@africanworld.com; awprsp@intar.com *Web Site:* africanworld.com, pg 6

Kassahun, Checole, Red Sea Press Inc, 541 W Ingham Ave, Suite B, Trenton, NJ 08638 *Tel:* 609-695-3200 *Fax:* 609-695-6466 *E-mail:* awprsp@africanworld. com; awprsp@intac.com *Web Site:* www.africanworld. com, pg 230

Kassahun, Senait, Red Sea Press Inc, 541 W Ingham Ave, Suite B, Trenton, NJ 08638 *Tel:* 609-695-3200 *Fax:* 609-695-6466 *E-mail:* awprsp@africanworld. com; awprsp@intac.com *Web Site:* www.africanworld. com, pg 230

Kastely, Jay, University of Houston Creative Writing Program, 229 Roy Cullen Bldg, Houston, TX 77204-3015 *Tel:* 713-743-3015 *Fax:* 713-743-3697 *E-mail:* cwp@uh.edu *Web Site:* www.uh.edu/cwp, pg 755

Kastenmeier, Edward, Vintage & Anchor Books, 1745 Broadway, New York, NY 10019 *Tel:* 212-751-2600 *Fax:* 212-572-6043, pg 291

Katula, Ken, Gareth Stevens Inc, 330 W Olive St, Suite 100, Milwaukee, WI 53212 *Tel:* 414-332-3520 *Toll Free Tel:* 800-542-2595 *Fax:* 414-332-3567 *E-mail:* info@gspub.com; info@worldalmaclibrary. com *Web Site:* www.garethstevens.com; www. worldalmaclibrary.com, pg 102

Katz, Colleen, American Institute of Certified Public Accountants, Harborside Financial Ctr, 201 Plaza Three, Jersey City, NJ 07311-3881 *Tel:* 201-938-3000 *Toll Free Tel:* 888-777-7077 *Fax:* 201-938-3329 *Web Site:* www.aicpa.org, pg 15

Katz, David, American Book Producers Association (ABPA), 160 Fifth Ave, Suite 622, New York, NY 10010 *Tel:* 212-645-2368 *Toll Free Tel:* 800-209-4575 *Fax:* 212-242-6499 *E-mail:* office@abpaonline.org *Web Site:* www.abpaonline.org, pg 676

Katz, David, Book Producing: Making Books Happen, 160 Fifth Ave, New York, NY 10010-7003 *Tel:* 212-645-2368 *Toll Free Tel:* 800-209-4575 *Fax:* 212-242-6799 *E-mail:* office@abpaonline.org *Web Site:* www. abpaonline.org, pg 742

Katz, David, Cascade Pass Inc, 4223 Glencoe Ave, Suite C-105, Marina Del Rey, CA 90292 *Tel:* 310-305-0210 *Toll Free Tel:* 888-837-0704 *Fax:* 310-305-7850 *Web Site:* www.cascadepass.com, pg 54

Katz, David, Silver Moon Press, 160 Fifth Ave, New York, NY 10010 *Tel:* 212-242-6499 *Toll Free Tel:* 800-874-3320 *Fax:* 212-242-6799 *E-mail:* mail@ silvermoonpress.com *Web Site:* www.silvermoonpress. com, pg 247

Katz, Herbert M, Herbert M Katz Inc, 151 E 83 St, New York, NY 10028 *Tel:* 212-861-5460, pg 637

Katz, Jeremy, Rodale Books, 400 S Tenth St, Emmaus, PA 18098-0099 *Tel:* 610-967-5171 *Fax:* 610-967-8961 *Web Site:* www.rodale.com, pg 234

Katz, Joseph M, Limulus Books Inc, 13742 Callington Dr, Wellington, FL 33414-8579 *Tel:* 561-793-3010 *Fax:* 561-793-0460, pg 155

Katz, Laurie, Facts on File Inc, 132 W 31 St, 17th fl, New York, NY 10001 *Tel:* 212-967-8800 *Toll Free Tel:* 800-322-8755 *Fax:* 212-967-9196 *Toll Free Fax:* 800-678-3633 *E-mail:* custserv@factsonfile.com *Web Site:* www.factsonfile.com, pg 93

Katz, Michael, Tradewind Books, 1809 Maritime Mews, Vancouver, BC V6H 3W7, Canada *Tel:* 604-662-4405 *Fax:* 604-730-0154 *E-mail:* tradewindbooks@ eudoramail.com *Web Site:* www.tradewindbooks.com, pg 563

Katz, Nancy B, Herbert M Katz Inc, 151 E 83 St, New York, NY 10028 *Tel:* 212-861-5460, pg 637

Katz, Peter, Elsevier Engineering Information Inc (Ei), One Castle Point Terr, Hoboken, NJ 07030 *Tel:* 201-356-6800 *Toll Free Tel:* 800-221-1044 *Fax:* 201-356-6801 *Web Site:* www.ei.org, pg 89

Katz, Stephanie, Alfred A Knopf, 1745 Broadway, New York, NY 10019 *Tel:* 212-751-2600 *Toll Free Tel:* 800-638-6460 *Fax:* 212-572-2593 *Web Site:* www. randomhouse.com/knopf, pg 146

Katz, Stephanie, Pantheon Books/Schocken Books, 1745 Broadway, New York, NY 10019 *Tel:* 212-751-2600 *Toll Free Tel:* 800-638-6460 *Fax:* 212-572-6030, pg 203

Katz, Stewart, Carswell, One Corporate Plaza, 2075 Kennedy Rd, Toronto, ON M1T 3V4, Canada *Tel:* 416-609-8000 *Toll Free Tel:* 800-387-5164 (Canada & US) *Fax:* 416-298-5094 (Toronto); 403-233-8159 (Calgary); 604-685-5343 (Vancouver); 514-985-6605 *Toll Free Fax:* 877-750-9041 *E-mail:* comments@carswell.com *Web Site:* www. carswell.com, pg 539

Katz, Susan, HarperCollins Children's Books Group, 1350 Sixth Ave, New York, NY 10019 *Tel:* 212-261-6500 *Web Site:* www.harperchildrens.com, pg 115

Katzenberger, Elaine, City Lights Books Inc, 261 Columbus Ave, San Francisco, CA 94133 *Tel:* 415-362-8193 *Fax:* 415-362-4921 *E-mail:* staff@citylights. com *Web Site:* www.citylights.com, pg 62

Kau, Elvira, W D Hoard & Sons Co, 28 W Milwaukee Ave, Fort Atkinson, WI 53538-0801 *Tel:* 920-563-5551 *Fax:* 920-563-7298 *E-mail:* hoards@hoards.com *Web Site:* www.hoards.com, pg 123

Kauff, Amanda, Alfred A Knopf, 1745 Broadway, New York, NY 10019 *Tel:* 212-751-2600 *Toll Free Tel:* 800-638-6460 *Fax:* 212-572-2593 *Web Site:* www. randomhouse.com/knopf, pg 146

Kaufman, Brian, Anvilpress Inc, PO Box 3008, Vancouver, BC V6B 3X5, Canada *Tel:* 604-876-8710 *Toll Free Tel:* 800-565-9523 (ordering) *Fax:* 604-879-2667 *E-mail:* info@anvilpress.com *Web Site:* www. anvilpress.com, pg 535

Kaufman, Debra, Duke University Press, 905 W Main St, Suite 18-B, Durham, NC 27701 *Tel:* 919-687-3600 *Toll Free Tel:* 888-651-0122 (orders only) *Fax:* 919-688-4574 *Toll Free Fax:* 888-651-0124 *Web Site:* www.dukeupress.edu, pg 84

Kaufman, Jason, Doubleday Broadway Publishing Group, 1745 Broadway, New York, NY 10019 *Tel:* 212-782-9000 *Toll Free Tel:* 800-223-6834; 800-223-5780 (sales) *Fax:* 212-302-7985 (correspondence); 212-492-9862 (orders), pg 83

Keene, Mary B, Glenbridge Publishing Ltd, 19923 E Long Ave, Centennial, CO 80016-1969 Tel: 720-870-8381 Toll Free Tel: 800-986-4135 (orders) Fax: 720-870-5598 E-mail: glenbr@eazy.net Web Site: www.glenbridgepublishing.com, pg 105

Keenley, James R, World Almanac Books, 512 Seventh Ave, 22nd fl, New York, NY 10018 Tel: 646-312-6800 Fax: 646-312-6839 E-mail: info@waegroup.com Web Site: www.worldalmanac.com, pg 303

Keeslar, Christopher, Dorchester Publishing Co Inc, 200 Madison Ave, Suite 2000, New York, NY 10016 Tel: 212-725-8811 Toll Free Tel: 800-481-9191 (order dept) Fax: 212-532-1054 E-mail: dorchedits@dorchesterpub.com Web Site: www.dorchesterpub.com, pg 82

Keesler, Darin, Picador, 175 Fifth Ave, New York, NY 10010 Tel: 212-674-5151 Fax: 212-253-9627 E-mail: firstname.lastname@picadorusa.com Web Site: www.picadorusa.com, pg 212

Keessen, Robert, Scott Publications Inc, 801 W Norton, Suite 200, Muskegon, MI 49441 Tel: 231-733-9382 Toll Free Tel: 866-733-9382 Fax: 231-733-7635 E-mail: contactus@scottpublications.com Web Site: www.scottpublications.com, pg 244

Kefauver, Will, e-Scholastic, 568 Broadway, 9th fl, New York, NY 10012 Tel: 212-343-7100 Fax: 212-343-4949, pg 85

Kehoe, Michael, University of Michigan Press, 839 Greene St, Ann Arbor, MI 48104-3209 Tel: 734-764-4388 Fax: 734-615-1540 E-mail: um.press@umich.edu Web Site: www.press.umich.edu, pg 282

Kehrer, Daniel, BizBest Media Corp, 860 Via de la Paz, Suite D-4, Pacific Palisades, CA 90272 Tel: 310-230-6868 Toll Free Tel: 800-873-5205; 877-424-9237 Fax: 310-454-6130 E-mail: info@bizbest.com Web Site: www.bizbest.com, pg 39

Keim, Betty, Keim Publishing, 301 E 61 St, New York, NY 10021 Tel: 212-753-4404, pg 603

Keim, Lisa, Atria Books, 1230 Avenue of the Americas, New York, NY 10020 Tel: 212-698-7000 Fax: 212-698-7007 Web Site: www.simonsays.com, pg 27

Keim, Lisa, Pocket Books, 1230 Avenue of the Americas, New York, NY 10020 Toll Free Tel: 800-456-6798 Fax: 212-698-7284 E-mail: consumer.customerservice@simonandschuster.com Web Site: www.simonsays.com, pg 215

Kelada, Sami, Aquila Communications Inc, 2642 Diab St, St Laurent, PQ H4S 1E8, Canada Tel: 514-338-1065 Toll Free Tel: 800-667-7071 Fax: 514-338-1948 Toll Free Fax: 866-338-1948 E-mail: aquila@aquilacommunications.com Web Site: www.aquilacommunications.com, pg 536

Kelaher, Christopher, The Brookings Institution Press, 1775 Massachusetts Ave NW, Washington, DC 20036-2188 Tel: 202-797-6000 Toll Free Tel: 800-275-1447 Fax: 202-797-6195 E-mail: bibooks@brook.edu Web Site: www.brookings.edu, pg 48

Keller, Bob, Harcourt School Publishers, 6277 Sea Harbor Dr, Orlando, FL 32887 Tel: 407-345-2000 Toll Free Tel: 800-225-5425 (cust serv) Fax: 407-352-3445 Toll Free Fax: 800-874-6418 E-mail: hbspcs@hbschool.com Web Site: www.harcourtschool.com, pg 114

Keller, Debbie, Upper Room Books, 1908 Grand Ave, Nashville, TN 37212 Toll Free Tel: 800-972-0433 Fax: 615-340-7266 Web Site: www.upperroom.org, pg 288

Keller, Donald D, World Book Inc, 233 N Michigan, Suite 2000, Chicago, IL 60601 Tel: 312-729-5800 Toll Free Tel: 800-967-5325 (consumer sales, US); 800-463-8845 (consumer sales, Canada); 800-975-3250 (school & library sales, US); 800-837-5365 (school & library sales, Canada); 866-866-5200 (web sales) Fax: 312-729-5600; 312-729-5606 Toll Free Fax: 800-433-9330 (school & library sales, US); 888-690-4002 (school library sales, Canada) Web Site: www.worldbook.com, pg 303

Keller, Gary D, Bilingual Press/Editorial Bilingue, Hispanic Research Ctr, Arizona State Univ, Tempe, AZ 85287-2702 Tel: 480-965-3867 Fax: 480-965-8309 E-mail: brp@asu.edu Web Site: www.asu.edu/brp/brp, pg 38

Keller, Jack, Presbyterian Publishing Corp, 100 Witherspoon St, Louisville, KY 40202 Tel: 502-569-5052 Toll Free Tel: 800-227-2872 (US only) Fax: 502-569-8308 Toll Free Fax: 800-541-5113 (US only) E-mail: ppcmail@presbypub.com Web Site: www.ppcpub.com, pg 217

Keller, Dr Jack A Jr, Westminster John Knox Press, 100 Witherspoon St, Louisville, KY 40202-1396 Tel: 502-569-5052 Toll Free Tel: 800-227-2872 (US only) Fax: 502-569-8308 Toll Free Fax: 800-541-5113 (US only) E-mail: wjk@wjkbooks.com Web Site: www.wjkbooks.com, pg 297

Keller, James J, J J Keller & Associates, Inc, 3003 W Breezewood Lane, Neenah, WI 54957 Tel: 920-722-2848 Toll Free Tel: 800-327-6868 Toll Free Fax: 800-727-7516 E-mail: sales@jjkeller.com Web Site: www.jjkeller.com/jjk, pg 144

Keller, Meg, Resources for the Future, 1616 "P" St NW, Washington, DC 20036-1400 Tel: 202-328-5086 Fax: 202-328-5137 E-mail: rffpress@rff.org Web Site: www.rffpress.org, pg 231

Keller, Robert L, J J Keller & Associates, Inc, 3003 W Breezewood Lane, Neenah, WI 54957 Tel: 920-722-2848 Toll Free Tel: 800-327-6868 Toll Free Fax: 800-727-7516 E-mail: sales@jjkeller.com Web Site: www.jjkeller.com/jjk, pg 144

Keller, Wendy L, Forthwrite Literary Agency & Speakers Bureau, 23852 W Pacific Coast Hwy, Suite 701, Malibu, CA 90265 Tel: 310-394-9840 Toll Free Tel: 866-62WRITE (629-7483) Fax: 310-394-9857 E-mail: agent@kellermedia.com Web Site: www.KellerMedia.com, pg 631

Kelley, Allison, Romance Writers of America, 16000 Stuebner Airline, Suite 140, Spring, TX 77379 Tel: 832-717-5200 Fax: 832-717-5201 E-mail: info@rwanational.org Web Site: www.rwanational.org, pg 699

Kelley, Allison, Romance Writers of America Awards, 16000 Stuebner Airline, Suite 140, Spring, TX 77379 Tel: 832-717-5200 Fax: 832-717-5201 E-mail: info@rwanational.org Web Site: www.rwanational.org, pg 803

Kelley, Allison, Romance Writers of America National Conference, 16000 Stuebner Airline, Suite 140, Spring, TX 77379 Tel: 832-717-5200 Fax: 832-717-5201 E-mail: info@rwanational.org Web Site: www.rwanational.org, pg 746

Kelley, Cheryl, Wil McKnight Associates Inc, 1801 W Hovey Ave, Suite A, Normal, IL 61761 Tel: 309-451-0000 Fax: 309-451-0000 E-mail: info@hardhatonline.com Web Site: www.hardhatonline.com, pg 169

Kelley, Courtenay, Metamorphous Press, 265 N Hancock St, Portland, OR 97227 Tel: 503-228-4972 Toll Free Tel: 800-937-7771 (orders only) Fax: 503-223-9117 E-mail: metabooks@metamodels.com Web Site: www.metamodels.com, pg 172

Kelley, Marguerite, Pavior Publishing, 2910 Camino Diablo, No 110, Walnut Creek, CA 94597 Tel: 925-295-0786 Fax: 925-935-7408 E-mail: editor@pavior.com Web Site: www.pavior.com, pg 573

Kelley, Michael G, Neal-Schuman Publishers Inc, 100 William St, Suite 2004, New York, NY 10038 Tel: 212-925-8650 Fax: 866-672-6657 Toll Free Fax: 866-209-7932 E-mail: orders@neal-schuman.com Web Site: www.neal-schuman.com, pg 186

Kelley, Nancy, Northwest Association of Book Publishers, PO Box 3786, Wilsonville, OR 97070-3786 Tel: 503-223-9055, pg 696

Kelley, Pam, University of Hawaii Press, 2840 Kolowalu St, Honolulu, HI 96822 Tel: 808-956-8255 Toll Free Tel: 888-847-7377 Fax: 808-988-6052 Toll Free Fax: 800-650-7811 E-mail: uhpbooks@hawaii.edu Web Site: www.uhpress.hawaii.edu, pg 281

Kelley, Rich, New York Academy of Sciences, 2 E 63 St, New York, NY 10021 Tel: 212-838-0230 Toll Free Tel: 800-843-6927 Fax: 212-888-2894 E-mail: publications@nyas.org Web Site: www.nyas.org, pg 189

Kelley, Vera, Twayne Publishers, 27500 Drake Rd, Famington Hills, MI 48331-3535 Tel: 248-699-4253 Toll Free Tel: 800-877-4253 Web Site: www.galegroup.com/twayne, pg 277

Kellman, Tony, Sandhills Writers' Conference, Languages, Literature & Communication, 2500 Walton Way, Augusta, GA 30904 Tel: 706-667-4437 Fax: 706-667-4770 Web Site: www.sandhills.aug.edu, pg 746

Kellock, Alan C, The Kellock Co, 18811 Cypress Bend Ct, Boca Raton, FL 33498 Tel: 561-558-8603 E-mail: kellock@aol.com, pg 637

Kellock, Loren, The Kellock Co, 18811 Cypress Bend Ct, Boca Raton, FL 33498 Tel: 561-558-8603 E-mail: kellock@aol.com, pg 637

Kellogg, David, Council on Foreign Relations Press, 58 E 68 St, New York, NY 10021 Tel: 212-434-9400 Fax: 212-434-9859 E-mail: publications@cfr.org; communications@cfr.org Web Site: www.cfr.org, pg 70

Kelly, Barbara, PJD Publications Ltd, PO Box 966, Westbury, NY 11590-0966 Tel: 516-626-0650 Fax: 516-626-5546 E-mail: pjdsankar@msn.com Web Site: www.pjdonline.com; www.pjdpublications.com, pg 214

Kelly, Bill, St Martin's Press LLC, 175 Fifth Ave, New York, NY 10010 Tel: 212-674-5151 Fax: 212-420-9314 E-mail: firstname.lastname@stmartins.com Web Site: www.stmartins.com, pg 238

Kelly, Donna E, North Carolina Office of Archives & History, Historical Publ Sect, 4622 Mail Service Ctr, Raleigh, NC 27699-4622 Tel: 919-733-7442 Fax: 919-733-1439 Web Site: www.ncpublications.com, pg 192

Kelly, Gilbert B, Omohundro Institute of Early American History & Culture, 109 Cary St, Williamsburg, VA 23185 Tel: 757-221-1114 Fax: 757-221-1047 E-mail: ieahc1@wm.edu Web Site: www.wm.edu/oieahc, pg 197

Kelly, Janet, Columbia University Press, 61 W 62 St, New York, NY 10023 Tel: 212-459-0600 Toll Free Tel: 800-944-8648 Fax: 212-459-3678 Web Site: www.columbia.edu/cu/cup, pg 65

Kelly, Jim, McGraw-Hill Higher Education, 1333 Burr Ridge Pkwy, Burr Ridge, IL 60527 Tel: 630-789-4000 Toll Free Tel: 800-338-3987 (cust serv) Fax: 614-755-5645 (cust serv) Web Site: www.mhhe.com, pg 167

Kelly, Judith, Ivan R Dee Publisher, 1332 N Halsted St, Chicago, IL 60622-2694 Tel: 312-787-6262 Toll Free Tel: 800-462-6420 (orders) Fax: 312-787-6269 Toll Free Fax: 800-338-4550 (orders) E-mail: elephant@ivanrdee.com Web Site: www.ivanrdee.com, pg 78

Kelly, Kathryn, ARE Press, 215 67 St, Virginia Beach, VA 23451 Tel: 757-428-3588 Toll Free Tel: 800-333-4499 Fax: 757-491-0689 E-mail: are@edgarcayce.org Web Site: www.edgarcayce.org, pg 23

Kelly, Laura, Reader's Digest USA Select Editions, Reader's Digest Rd, Pleasantville, NY 10570-7000 Tel: 914-238-1000 Toll Free Tel: 800-310-6261 Fax: 914-238-4559, pg 229

Kelly, Melinda, University of Pennsylvania Press, 4200 Pine St, Philadelphia, PA 19104-4011 Tel: 215-898-6261 Toll Free Tel: 800-445-9880 (orders & cust serv only) Fax: 215-898-0404; 410-516-6998 (orders) E-mail: custserv@pobox.upenn.edu Web Site: www.upenn.edu/pennpress, pg 284

Kelly, Michael, Adams Media, An F+W Publications Co, 57 Littlefield St, 2nd fl, Avon, MA 02322 Tel: 508-427-7100 Fax: 508-427-6790 Toll Free Fax: 800-872-5628 E-mail: authors@adamsmedia.com; orders@adamsmedia.com Web Site: www.adamsmedia.com, pg 5

Kelly, Mike, Reprint Services Corp, PO Box 890820, Temecula, CA 92589-0820 Toll Free Tel: 800-273-6635 Fax: 909-767-0133, pg 231

Kelly, Neil K, F A Davis Co, 1915 Arch St, Philadelphia, PA 19103 *Tel:* 215-568-2270 *Toll Free Tel:* 800-523-4049 *Fax:* 215-568-5065 *E-mail:* info@ fadavis.com *Web Site:* www.fadavis.com, pg 76

Kelly, Robert, Goodheart-Willcox Publisher, 18604 W Creek Dr, Tinley Park, IL 60477-6243 *Tel:* 708-687-5000 *Toll Free Tel:* 800-323-0440 *Fax:* 708-687-0315 *Toll Free Fax:* 888-409-3900 *E-mail:* custserv@g-w. com *Web Site:* www.g-w.com, pg 107

Kelly, Susana, Sorin Books, 19113 Douglas Rd, Notre Dame, IN 46556 *Tel:* 574-287-2831 *Toll Free Tel:* 800-282-1865 *Fax:* 574-239-2904 *Toll Free Fax:* 800-282-5681 *E-mail:* sorinbk@nd.edu *Web Site:* www.sorinbooks.com, pg 253

Kelly, Susana J, Ave Maria Press, 19113 Douglas Rd, Notre Dame, IN 46556 *Tel:* 574-287-2831 *Toll Free Tel:* 800-282-1865 *Fax:* 574-239-2904 *Toll Free Fax:* 800-282-5681 *E-mail:* avemariapress.1@nd.edu *Web Site:* www.avemariapress.com, pg 29

Kelly, Theresa, Houghton Mifflin Co, 222 Berkeley St, Boston, MA 02116-3764 *Tel:* 617-351-5000 *Toll Free Tel:* 800-225-3362 (trade books); 800-733-2828 (text books); 800-225-1464 (college texts) *Fax:* 617-351-1125 *Web Site:* www.hmco.com, pg 126

Kelly, Theresa, Houghton Mifflin Trade & Reference Division, 222 Berkeley St, Boston, MA 02116-3764 *Tel:* 617-351-5000 *Toll Free Tel:* 800-225-3362 *Web Site:* www.houghtonmifflinbooks.com, pg 126

Kelly, Timothy T, National Geographic Society, 1145 17 St NW, Washington, DC 20036 *Tel:* 202-857-7000 *Fax:* 202-429-5727 *Web Site:* www.nationalgeographic. com, pg 184

Kelly, Virginia A, Dorland Healthcare Information, 1500 Walnut St, Suite 1000, Philadelphia, PA 19102 *Tel:* 215-875-1212 *Toll Free Tel:* 800-784-2332 *Fax:* 215-735-3966 *E-mail:* info@dorlandhealth.com *Web Site:* www.dorlandhealth.com, pg 82

Kelsey, Matthew, Backbeat Books, 600 Harrison St, San Francisco, CA 94107 *Tel:* 415-947-6615 *Toll Free Tel:* 866-222-5232 (orders only) *Fax:* 415-947-6015; 408-848-8294 (orders only) *E-mail:* books@ musicplayer.com; books@cmp.com *Web Site:* www. backbeatbooks.com, pg 30

Kelsey, Matthew, CMP Books, 600 Harrison St, San Francisco, CA 94107 *Tel:* 415-947-6615; 408-848-3854 (orders) *Toll Free Tel:* 800-500-6875 (orders) *Fax:* 415-947-6015; 408-848-5784 (orders) *E-mail:* books@cmp.com *Web Site:* www.cmpbooks. com, pg 63

Kelty, John, Copywriter's Council of America (CCA), CCA Bldg, 7 Putter Lane, Middle Island, NY 11953-0102 *Tel:* 631-924-3888 *Fax:* 631-924-3890 *E-mail:* cca4dmcopy@att.net *Web Site:* www.lgroup. addr.com/CCA.htm, pg 68

Kemmerer, Janette, The Haworth Press Inc, 10 Alice St, Binghamton, NY 13904-1580 *Tel:* 607-722-5857 *Toll Free Tel:* 800-429-6784 *Fax:* 607-722-1424 *Toll Free Fax:* 800-895-0582 *E-mail:* getinfo@haworthpressinc. com *Web Site:* www.haworthpress.com, pg 118

Kemnitz, T M, Royal Fireworks Press, First Ave, Unionville, NY 10988 *Tel:* 845-726-4444 *Fax:* 845-726-3824 *E-mail:* mail@rfwp.com *Web Site:* www. rfwp.com, pg 235

Kemp-Jones, Diana, Zumaya Publications, 403-366 Howard Ave, Burnaby, BC V5B 4Y2, Canada *Tel:* 604-299-8417 *E-mail:* editorial@ zumayapublications.com *Web Site:* www. zumayapublications.com, pg 567

Kemper, Jacob, Howell Press Inc, 1713-2D Allied Lane, Charlottesville, VA 22903 *Tel:* 434-977-4006 *Toll Free Tel:* 800-868-4512 *Fax:* 434-971-7204 *Toll Free Fax:* 888-971-7204 *E-mail:* custserv@howellpress.com *Web Site:* www.howellpress.com, pg 127

Kemper, Jennifer, American Marketing Association, 311 S Wacker Dr, Suite 5800, Chicago, IL 60606-2266 *Tel:* 312-542-9000 *Toll Free Tel:* 800-262-1150 *Fax:* 312-542-9001 *E-mail:* info@ama.org *Web Site:* www.marketingpower.com, pg 15, 677

Kempker, Debra, Prima Games, 3000 Lava Ridge Ct, Roseville, CA 95661 *Tel:* 916-787-7000 *Toll Free Tel:* 800-632-8676 *Fax:* 916-787-7001 *Web Site:* www. primagames.com, pg 218

Kendell, Joshua, Picador, 175 Fifth Ave, New York, NY 10010 *Tel:* 212-674-5151 *Fax:* 212-253-9627 *E-mail:* firstname.lastname@picadorusa.com *Web Site:* www.picadorusa.com, pg 212

Kendler, Bernhard, Cornell University Press, 512 E State St, Ithaca, NY 14850 *Tel:* 607-277-2338 *Fax:* 607-277-2374 *E-mail:* cupressinfo@cornell.edu *Web Site:* www.cornellpress.cornell.edu, pg 68

Kendrick, Michele, AAPG (American Association of Petroleum Geologists), 1444 S Boulder Ave, Tulsa, OK 74119 *Tel:* 918-584-2555 *Toll Free Tel:* 800-364-AAPG (364-2274) *Fax:* 918-560-2632 *Toll Free Fax:* 800-898-2274 *E-mail:* bookstore@aapg.org *Web Site:* www.aapg.org, pg 2

Kendzia, Mary Carol, Twenty-Third Publications, 185 Willow St, Mystic, CT 06355 *Tel:* 860-536-2611 *Toll Free Tel:* 800-321-0411 (orders) *Fax:* 860-536-5674 (edit) *Toll Free Fax:* 800-572-0788, pg 277

Kenelly, John, The Mathematical Association of America, 1529 18 St NW, Washington, DC 20036 *Tel:* 202-387-5200 *Toll Free Tel:* 800-331-1622 (orders) *Fax:* 202-265-2384 *E-mail:* ldouglas@pmds. com *Web Site:* www.maa.org, pg 165

Kenneally, Christopher, Beyond the Book, 222 Rosewood Dr, Danvers, MA 01923 *Toll Free Tel:* 800-928-3887 (ext 2420) *Fax:* 978-750-4250 *E-mail:* beyondthebook@copyright.com *Web Site:* www.copyright.com, pg 742

Kennedy, Christopher, Syracuse University Creative Writing Program, 401 Hall of Languages, Syracuse, NY 13244-1170 *Tel:* 315-443-2174 *Fax:* 315-443-3660 *Web Site:* www.syr.edu, pg 754

Kennedy, Daniel W, Whitehorse Press, 107 E Conway Rd, Center Conway, NH 03813 *Tel:* 603-356-6556 *Toll Free Tel:* 800-531-1133 *Fax:* 603-356-6590 *E-mail:* customerservice@whitehorsepress.com *Web Site:* www.whitehorsepress.com, pg 298

Kennedy, Elaine, Square One Publishers, 115 Herricks Rd, Garden City Park, NY 11040 *Tel:* 516-535-2010 *Fax:* 516-535-2014 *E-mail:* sq1info@aol.com *Web Site:* squareonepublishers.com, pg 256

Kennedy, George, Prakken Publications Inc, 832 Phoenix Dr, Ann Arbor, MI 48108 *Tel:* 734-975-2800 *Toll Free Tel:* 800-530-9673 (orders only) *Fax:* 734-975-2787 *E-mail:* tdbooks@techdirections.com *Web Site:* www. techdirections.com; www.eddigest.com, pg 217

Kennedy, Geraldine, PEN Center USA, 672 S Lafayette Park Place, Suite 42, Los Angeles, CA 90057 *Tel:* 213-365-8500 *Fax:* 213-365-9616 *E-mail:* pen@ penusa.org *Web Site:* www.penusa.org, pg 697

Kennedy, Grant, Lone Pine Publishing, 10145 81 Ave, Edmonton, AB T6E 1W9, Canada *Tel:* 780-433-9333 *Toll Free Tel:* 800-661-9017 *Fax:* 780-433-9646 *Toll Free Fax:* 800-424-7173 *E-mail:* info@lonepinepublishing.com *Web Site:* www. lonepinepublishing.com, pg 552

Kennedy, Hank, American Management Association, 1601 Broadway, New York, NY 10019-7420 *Tel:* 212-586-8100 *Toll Free Tel:* 800-262-9699 *Fax:* 212-903-8168 *Web Site:* www.amanet.org, pg 677

Kennedy, Harold V, AMACOM Books, 1601 Broadway, New York, NY 10019-7406 *Tel:* 212-586-8100; 518-891-5510 (orders) *Toll Free Tel:* 800-262-9699 (cust serv) *Fax:* 212-903-8168; 518-891-2372 (orders) *Web Site:* www.amanet.org, pg 10

Kennedy, Jewell, Harcourt Canada Ltd, 55 Horner Ave, Toronto, ON M8Z 4X6, Canada *Tel:* 416-255-4491; 416-255-0177 (Voice Mail) *Toll Free Tel:* 800-387-7278 (North America); 800-387-7305 (North America) *Fax:* 416-255-6708 *Toll Free Fax:* 800-665-7307 (North America) *E-mail:* firstname_lastname@ harcourt.com *Web Site:* www.harcourtcanada.com, pg 549

Kennedy, Judith M, Whitehorse Press, 107 E Conway Rd, Center Conway, NH 03813 *Tel:* 603-356-6556 *Toll Free Tel:* 800-531-1133 *Fax:* 603-356-6590 *E-mail:* customerservice@whitehorsepress.com *Web Site:* www.whitehorsepress.com, pg 298

Kennedy, Linda, The Globe Pequot Press, 246 Goose Lane, Guilford, CT 06437 *Tel:* 203-458-4500 *Toll Free Tel:* 800-243-0495 (cust serv) *Fax:* 203-458-4601 *Toll Free Tel:* 800-820-2329 (orders & cust serv) *E-mail:* info@globepequot.com *Web Site:* www. globepequot.com, pg 105

Kennedy, Mary, Institute of Intergovernmental Relations, Queen's University, Rm 301, Policy Studies Bldg, Kingston, ON K7L 3N6, Canada *Tel:* 613-533-2080 *Fax:* 613-533-6868 *E-mail:* iigr@iigr.ca *Web Site:* www.iigr.ca, pg 551

Kennedy, Mary Anne, Houghton Mifflin School Division, 222 Berkeley St, Boston, MA 02116-3764, pg 126

Kennedy, Megan, Rough Guides, 345 Hudson St, New York, NY 10014 *Tel:* 212-414-3635 *Fax:* 212-414-3352 *E-mail:* mail@roughguides.com *Web Site:* www. roughguides.com, pg 235

Kennedy, Shane, Lone Pine Publishing, 10145 81 Ave, Edmonton, AB T6E 1W9, Canada *Tel:* 780-433-9333 *Toll Free Tel:* 800-661-9017 *Fax:* 780-433-9646 *Toll Free Fax:* 800-424-7173 *E-mail:* info@lonepinepublishing.com *Web Site:* www. lonepinepublishing.com, pg 553

Kennedy, Susan Petersen, Penguin Group (USA) Inc, 375 Hudson St, New York, NY 10014 *Tel:* 212-366-2000 *Fax:* 212-366-2666 *E-mail:* online@ uspenguingroup.com *Web Site:* www.penguin.com, pg 208

Kennedy, Susan Petersen, Riverhead Books (Hardcover), 375 Hudson St, New York, NY 10014 *Tel:* 212-366-2000 *E-mail:* online@penguinputnam.com *Web Site:* www.penguin.com, pg 233

Kennedy, Terry, The Greensboro Review Literary Award in Fiction & Poetry, University North Carolina at Greensboro, English Dept, McIver Bldg, Rm 134, Greensboro, NC 27402-6170 *Tel:* 336-334-5459 *Web Site:* www.uncg.edu/eng/mfa, pg 777

Kennedy, William, New York State Edith Wharton Citation of Merit for Fiction Writers, University at Albany, LE 320, Albany, NY 12222 *Tel:* 518-442-5620 *Fax:* 518-442-5621 *E-mail:* writers@uamail. albany.edu *Web Site:* www.albany.edu/writers-inst, pg 794

Kennedy, William, New York State Walt Whitman Citation of Merit for Poets, University at Albany, LE 320, Albany, NY 12222 *Tel:* 518-442-5620 *Fax:* 518-442-5621 *E-mail:* writers@uamail.albany.edu *Web Site:* www.albany.edu/writers-inst, pg 794

Kennedy, William, New York State Writers Institute, University at Albany, New Library 320, Albany, NY 12222 *Tel:* 518-442-5620 *Fax:* 518-442-5621 *E-mail:* writers@uamail.albany.edu *Web Site:* www. albany.edu/writers-inst/, pg 745

Kenney, Mary, North Country Press, RR1, Box 1395, Unity, ME 04988-1395 *Tel:* 207-948-2208 *Fax:* 207-948-9000 *E-mail:* info@ncpbooks.com *Web Site:* www.ncpbooks.com, pg 192

Kent, Amy, Wm B Eerdmans Publishing Co, 255 Jefferson Ave SE, Grand Rapids, MI 49503 *Tel:* 616-459-4591 *Toll Free Tel:* 800-253-7521 *Fax:* 616-459-6540 *E-mail:* sales@eerdmans.com *Web Site:* www. eerdmans.com, pg 88

Kent, David, HarperCollins Publishers Canada, 2 Bloor St E, 20th fl, Toronto, ON M4W 1A8, Canada *Tel:* 416-975-9334 *Fax:* 416-975-9884 (publishing); 416-975-5223 (sales) *E-mail:* hccanada@harpercollins. com *Web Site:* www.harpercanada.com, pg 549

Kent, Norma, American Association of Community Colleges (AACC), One Dupont Circle NW, Suite 410, Washington, DC 20036 *Tel:* 202-728-0200; 301-490-8116 (orders) *Toll Free Tel:* 800-250-6557 *Fax:* 202-223-9390 (edit); 301-604-0158 (orders) *E-mail:* aaccpub@pmds.com (orders) *Web Site:* www. aacc.nche.edu, pg 11

Kent, Stephen J, Writer's Digest Books, 4700 E Galbraith Rd, Cincinnati, OH 45236 *Tel:* 513-531-2690 *Toll Free Tel:* 800-289-0963 *Fax:* 513-891-7185 *Web Site:* www.writersdigest.com, pg 305

Kentwell, Richard, Reedswain Inc, 562 Ridge Rd, Spring City, PA 19475 *Tel:* 610-469-6911 *Toll Free Tel:* 800-331-5191 *Fax:* 610-495-6632 *Web Site:* www.reedswain.com, pg 230

Kenyon, Lucy, Scribner, 1230 Avenue of the Americas, New York, NY 10020, pg 244

Kephart, Sheri, Easy Money Press, 5419 87 St, Lubbock, TX 79424 *Tel:* 806-543-5215 *E-mail:* easymoneypress@yahoo.com, pg 86

Kepler, Tasha, MacAdam/Cage Publishing Inc, 155 Sansome St, Suite 550, San Francisco, CA 94104 *Tel:* 415-986-7502 *Toll Free Tel:* 866-986-7470 *Fax:* 415-986-7414 *E-mail:* info@macadamcage.com *Web Site:* www.macadamcage.com, pg 161

Kerber, Michael, Red Wheel/Weiser/Conari, 368 Congress St, 4th fl, Boston, MA 02210 *Tel:* 617-542-1324 *Toll Free Tel:* 800-423-7087 *Fax:* 617-482-9676 *Web Site:* www.redwheelweiser.com, pg 230

Keresty, Laura, Wilderness Press, 1200 Fifth St, Berkeley, CA 94710 *Tel:* 510-558-1666 *Toll Free Tel:* 800-443-7227 *Fax:* 510-558-1696 *E-mail:* info@wildernesspress.com *Web Site:* www.wildernesspress.com, pg 299

Kerfoot, Karen, The Continuing Legal Education Society of British Columbia, 845 Cambie, Suite 300, Vancouver, BC V6B 5T2, Canada *Tel:* 604-669-3544 *Toll Free Tel:* 800-663-0437 *Fax:* 604-669-9260 *Web Site:* www.cle.bc.ca, pg 541

Kerkstra, Allen R, Zondervan, 5300 Patterson Ave SE, Grand Rapids, MI 49530 *Tel:* 616-698-6900 *Toll Free Tel:* 800-727-1309 (cust serv) *Fax:* 616-698-3439; 616-698-3255 (cust serv) *Web Site:* www.zondervan.com, pg 307

Kerkstra, Elizabeth, US Games Systems Inc, 179 Ludlow St, Stamford, CT 06902 *Tel:* 203-353-8400 *Toll Free Tel:* 800-544-2637 (800-54GAMES) *Fax:* 203-353-8431 *E-mail:* info@usgamesinc.com *Web Site:* www.usgamesinc.com, pg 289

Kern, Natasha, Natasha Kern Literary Agency Inc, PO Box 2908, Portland, OR 97208-2908 *Tel:* 503-297-6190 *Fax:* 503-297-8241 *E-mail:* natasha@natashakern.com *Web Site:* www.natashakern.com, pg 637

Kerner, Diane, Scholastic Canada Ltd, 175 Hillmount Rd, Markham, ON L6C 1Z7, Canada *Tel:* 905-887-7323 *Toll Free Tel:* 800-268-3848 (Canada) *Fax:* 905-887-1131 *Toll Free Tel:* 800-387-4944; 866-346-1288 *Web Site:* www.scholastic.ca, pg 560

Keros, Leslie, Association of American University Presses, 1427 E 60 St, Chicago, IL 60637 *Tel:* 773-702-7700; 773-702-7600 *Toll Free Tel:* 800-621-2736 (orders) *Fax:* 773-702-9756 (sales); 773-660-2235 (orders); 773-702-2708 *E-mail:* general@press.uchicago.edu *Web Site:* www.press.uchicago.edu, pg 26

Kerr, Elisabeth, W W Norton & Company Inc, 500 Fifth Ave, New York, NY 10110-0017 *Tel:* 212-354-5500 *Toll Free Tel:* 800-233-4830 (orders & cust serv) *Fax:* 212-869-0856 *Toll Free Fax:* 800-458-6515 *Web Site:* www.wwnorton.com, pg 193

Kerr, Lorraine, Baylor University Press, Baylor University, Waco, TX 76798-7363 *Tel:* 254-710-3164 *Toll Free Tel:* 800-710-3217 *Fax:* 254-710-3440 *Web Site:* www.baylorpress.com, pg 33

Kerr, Mark, Inner Ocean Publishing Inc, 1037 Makawao Ave, Makawao, Maui, HI 96768-1239 *Tel:* 808-573-8000 *Toll Free Tel:* 800-863-1449 *Fax:* 808-573-0700 *Toll Free Fax:* 800-755-4118 *E-mail:* info@innerocean.com *Web Site:* www.innerocean.com, pg 134

Kesh, Tom, ATL Press Inc, PO Box 4563 "T" Sta, Shrewsbury, MA 01545-7563 *Tel:* 508-898-2290 *Fax:* 508-898-2063 *E-mail:* atlpress@compuserve.com *Web Site:* www.atlpress.com, pg 27

Keshavarz, Talieh, ATL Press Inc, PO Box 4563 "T" Sta, Shrewsbury, MA 01545-7563 *Tel:* 508-898-2290 *Fax:* 508-898-2063 *E-mail:* atlpress@compuserve.com *Web Site:* www.atlpress.com, pg 27

Kessel-Hendricks, Greer, Atria Books, 1230 Avenue of the Americas, New York, NY 10020 *Tel:* 212-698-7000 *Fax:* 212-698-7007 *Web Site:* www.simonsays.com, pg 27

Kessinger, Roger A, Kessinger Publishing Co, PO Box 4587, Whitefish, MT 59937 *E-mail:* message@kessinger.net *Web Site:* www.kessinger.net, pg 145

Kessler, Ellen Terry, Kessler Communications, 280 W 86 St, New York, NY 10024 *Tel:* 212-724-8610 *E-mail:* lmp@etk.mailshell.com *Web Site:* www.kesslercommunications.com, pg 603

Kessler, Erika, Contemporary Publishing Co of Raleigh Inc, 6001-101 Chapel Hill Rd, Raleigh, NC 27607 *Tel:* 919-851-8221 *Fax:* 919-851-6666 *E-mail:* questions@contemporarypublishing.com *Web Site:* www.contemporarypublishing.com, pg 67

Kessler, John, Association of American University Presses, 1427 E 60 St, Chicago, IL 60637 *Tel:* 773-702-7700; 773-702-7600 *Toll Free Tel:* 800-621-2736 (orders) *Fax:* 773-702-9756 (sales); 773-660-2235 (orders); 773-702-2708 *E-mail:* general@press.uchicago.edu *Web Site:* www.press.uchicago.edu, pg 26

Kessler, Joseph I, World Class Speakers & Entertainers, 5200 Kanan Rd, Suite 210, Agoura Hills, CA 91301 *Tel:* 818-991-5400 *Fax:* 818-991-2226 *E-mail:* wcse@speak.com *Web Site:* www.speak.com, pg 670

Kessler, Rikki, Learning Links Inc, 2300 Marcus Ave, New Hyde Park, NY 11042 *Tel:* 516-437-9071 *Toll Free Tel:* 800-724-2616 *Fax:* 516-437-5392 *E-mail:* learning1x@aol.com *Web Site:* www.learninglinks.com, pg 151

Kessler, Robert J, Pendragon Press, 52 White Hill Lane, Hillsdale, NY 12529-5839 *Tel:* 518-325-6100 *Fax:* 518-325-6102 *E-mail:* penpress@taconic.net *Web Site:* www.pendragonpress.com, pg 207

Kessler, Sabine, American Institute of Physics, 2 Huntington Quadrangle, Suite 1NO1, Melville, NY 11747-4502 *Tel:* 516-576-2477 *Fax:* 516-576-2474 *E-mail:* proceedings-mgr@aip.org *Web Site:* www.aip.org, pg 15

Kestenbaum, Erika, Fodor's Travel Publications, 1745 Broadway, New York, NY 10019 *Tel:* 212-572-8784 *Toll Free Tel:* 800-733-3000 *Fax:* 212-572-2248 *Web Site:* www.fodors.com, pg 98

Ketay, Joyce, The Joyce Ketay Agency, 630 Ninth Ave, Suite 706, New York, NY 10036 *Tel:* 212-354-6825 *Fax:* 212-354-6732, pg 637

Ketterman, Kathleen, The University of North Carolina Press, 116 S Boundary St, Chapel Hill, NC 27514-3808 *Tel:* 919-966-3561 *Toll Free Tel:* 800-848-6224 (orders only) *Fax:* 919-966-3829 *Toll Free Fax:* 800-272-6817 (orders) *E-mail:* uncpress@unc.edu *Web Site:* www.uncpress.unc.edu, pg 283

Kettlewell, John, Adirondack Mountain Club, 814 Goggins Rd, Lake George, NY 12845-4117 *Tel:* 518-668-4447 *Toll Free Tel:* 800-395-8080 *Fax:* 518-668-3746 *E-mail:* adkinfo@adk.org *Web Site:* www.adk.org, pg 5

Kettyls, Roger, Self-Counsel Press Inc, 1704 N State St, Bellingham, WA 98225 *Tel:* 360-676-4530 *Toll Free Tel:* 877-877-6490 *Fax:* 360-676-4549 *E-mail:* service@self-counsel.com *Web Site:* www.self-counsel.com, pg 245

Kettyls, Roger, Self-Counsel Press Inc, 1481 Charlotte Rd, North Vancouver, BC V7J 1H1, Canada *Tel:* 604-986-3366 *Toll Free Tel:* 800-663-3007 *Fax:* 604-986-3947 *E-mail:* service@self-counsel.com *Web Site:* www.self-counsel.com, pg 561

Ketz, Louise B, Louise B Ketz Agency, 1485 First Ave, Suite 4-B, New York, NY 10021 *Tel:* 212-535-9259 *Fax:* 212-249-3103 *E-mail:* ketzagency@aol.com, pg 637

Keyes, Guy, Cold Spring Harbor Laboratory Press, 500 Sunnyside Blvd, Woodbury, NY 11797-2924 *Tel:* 516-422-4100 *Toll Free Tel:* 800-843-4388 *Fax:* 516-422-4097 *E-mail:* cshpress@cshl.edu *Web Site:* www.cshlpress.com, pg 64

Keyishian, Harry, Fairleigh Dickinson University Press, c/o Associated University Presses, 2010 Eastpark Blvd, Cranbury, NJ 08512 *Tel:* 609-655-4770 *Fax:* 609-655-8366 *E-mail:* aup440@aol.com, pg 94

Keyl, Anne, The University of Arizona Press, 355 S Euclid Ave, Suite 103, Tucson, AZ 85719-6654 *Tel:* 520-621-1441 *Toll Free Tel:* 800-426-3797 (orders) *Fax:* 520-621-8899 *Toll Free Fax:* 800-426-3797 *E-mail:* uapress@uapress.arizona.edu *Web Site:* www.uapress.arizona.edu, pg 280

Khalfan, Aunali M, Tahrike Tarsile Qur'an Inc, 80-08 51 Ave, Elmhurst, NY 11373 *Tel:* 718-446-6472 *Fax:* 718-446-4370 *E-mail:* orders@koranusa.org *Web Site:* www.koranusa.org, pg 264

Khan, Olive, HarperCollins Publishers Canada, 2 Bloor St E, 20th fl, Toronto, ON M4W 1A8, Canada *Tel:* 416-975-9334 *Fax:* 416-975-9884 (publishing); 416-975-5223 (sales) *E-mail:* hccanada@harpercollins.com *Web Site:* www.harpercanada.com, pg 549

Khan, Saeed, E-Z Publications, 1932 Ambassador Dr, Windsor, ON N9C 3R5, Canada *Tel:* 519-250-5138; 519-972-3962 *Fax:* 519-972-5256; 519-250-6588 *E-mail:* ezpublications@hotmail.com *Web Site:* www.ezpublications.com, pg 543

Kheradi, Cyrus, Simon & Schuster Sales & Distribution, 1230 Avenue of the Americas, New York, NY 10020 *Tel:* 212-698-7000, pg 249

Kheradi, Irene, Simon & Schuster, 1230 Avenue of the Americas, New York, NY 10020 *Tel:* 212-698-7000 *Toll Free Tel:* 800-223-2348 (cust serv); 800-223-2336 (orders) *Toll Free Fax:* 800-943-9831 (orders) *Web Site:* www.simonsays.com, pg 248

Kheradi, Irene, Simon & Schuster Adult Publishing Group, 1230 Avenue of the Americas, New York, NY 10020 *Tel:* 212-698-7000 *Toll Free Tel:* 800-223-2336 (orders); 800-223-2348 (cust serv), pg 248

Kianerney, AnnaMarie, American Society for Photogrammetry & Remote Sensing, 5410 Grosvenor Lane, Suite 210, Bethesda, MD 20814-2160 *Tel:* 301-493-0290 *Fax:* 301-493-0208 *E-mail:* asprs@asprs.org *Web Site:* www.asprs.org, pg 17

Kibbey, H, Panoply Press Inc, PO Box 1885, Lake Oswego, OR 97035-0611 *Tel:* 503-697-7964 *Fax:* 503-636-5293 *E-mail:* panoplypress@aol.com, pg 202

Kichline, Linda, ImaJinn Books, PO Box 545, Canon City, CO 81215 *Tel:* 719-275-0060 *Toll Free Tel:* 877-625-3592 *Fax:* 719-276-0741 *E-mail:* orders@imajinnbooks.com *Web Site:* www.imajinnbooks.com, pg 131

Kidder, Laura, Fodor's Travel Publications, 1745 Broadway, New York, NY 10019 *Tel:* 212-572-8784 *Toll Free Tel:* 800-733-3000 *Fax:* 212-572-2248 *Web Site:* www.fodors.com, pg 98

Kielhorn, Margot, Michigan State University Press (MSU Press), 1405 S Harrison Rd, Suite 25, East Lansing, MI 48823 *Tel:* 517-355-9543 *Fax:* 517-432-2611 *Toll Free Fax:* 800-678-2120 *E-mail:* msupress@msu.edu *Web Site:* www.msupress.msu.edu, pg 173

Kieling, Jared, Bloomberg Press, PO Box 888, Princeton, NJ 08542-0888 *Tel:* 609-279-4600 *E-mail:* press@bloomberg.com *Web Site:* www.bloomberg.com/books, pg 41

Kiely, Garrett, Palgrave Macmillan, 175 Fifth Ave, New York, NY 10010 *Tel:* 212-982-3900 *Fax:* 212-777-6359 *E-mail:* firstname.lastname@palgrave-usa.com *Web Site:* www.palgrave.com, pg 202

Kier, Mary Alice, Cine/Lit Representation, PO Box 802918, Santa Clarita, CA 91380-2918 *Tel:* 661-513-0268 *Fax:* 661-513-0951 *E-mail:* cinelit@msn.com, pg 625

Kiessling, Kathy, Children's Literature Association Book Award, PO Box 138, Battle Creek, MI 49016-0138 *Tel:* 269-965-8180 *Fax:* 269-965-3568 *Web Site:* www.childlitassn.org, pg 766

Kingsland, Phyllis, Association of American University Presses, 1427 E 60 St, Chicago, IL 60637 Tel: 773-702-7700; 773-702-7600 Toll Free Tel: 800-621-2736 (orders) Fax: 773-702-9756 (sales); 773-660-2235 (orders); 773-702-2708 E-mail: general@press.uchicago.edu Web Site: www.press.uchicago.edu, pg 26

Kinney, Erika Q, Paul H Brookes Publishing Co, PO Box 10624, Baltimore, MD 21285-0624 Tel: 410-337-9580 Toll Free Tel: 800-638-3775 Fax: 410-337-8539 E-mail: custserv@brookespublishing.com Web Site: www.brookespublishing.com, pg 48

Kinney, Noreen, International Cook Book & Culinary Arts Awards, 7500 Sunshine Skyway Lane, Unit T8, St Petersburg, FL 33711 Tel: 727-347-2437 E-mail: cordondor@aol.com Web Site: www.cordondorcuisine.com; www.goldribboncookery.com, pg 780

Kintigh, Cynthia, ANR Publications University of California, 6701 San Pablo Ave, 2nd fl, Oakland, CA 94608-1239 Tel: 510-642-2431 Toll Free Tel: 800-994-8849 Fax: 510-643-5470 E-mail: danrcs@ucdavis.edu Web Site: anrcatalog.ucdavis.edu, pg 20

Kintz, Bruce, Concordia Publishing House, 3558 S Jefferson Ave, St Louis, MO 63118-3968 Tel: 314-268-1000 Toll Free Tel: 800-325-3040 Fax: 314-268-1329 Toll Free Fax: 800-490-9889 E-mail: cphorder@cph.org Web Site: www.cph.org, pg 66

Kinzer, Mitchell, Warner Books, 1271 Avenue of the Americas, New York, NY 10020 Tel: 212-522-7200 Fax: 212-522-7991 Web Site: www.twbookmark.com, pg 293

Kipfer, Barbara Ann, Reference Wordsmith, 29 Brooks Lane, Essex, CT 06426 Tel: 860-767-1551 Fax: 860-767-1288 Web Site: www.reference-wordsmith.com, pg 610

Kipfer, Marci, Central Ohio Writers of Literature for Children, c/o St Joseph Montessori School, 933 Hamlet St, Columbus, OH 43201-3595 Tel: 614-291-8644 Fax: 614-291-7411 E-mail: cowriters@mail.com Web Site: www.sjms.net/conf, pg 742

Kiple, Cindy, InterVarsity Press, 430 E Plaza Dr, Westmont, IL 60559-1234 Tel: 630-734-4000 Toll Free Tel: 800-843-7225 Fax: 630-734-4200 E-mail: mail@ivpress.com Web Site: www.ivpress.com, pg 138

Kippur, Stephen A, John Wiley & Sons Inc, 111 River St, Hoboken, NJ 07030 Tel: 201-748-6000 Toll Free Tel: 800-225-5945 (cust serv) Fax: 201-748-6088 E-mail: info@wiley.com Web Site: www.wiley.com, pg 299

Kippur, Stephen A, John Wiley & Sons Inc Professional & Trade Group, 111 River St, Hoboken, NJ 07030 Tel: 201-748-6000 Toll Free Tel: 800-225-5945 (cust serv) Fax: 201-748-6088 E-mail: info@wiley.com Web Site: www.wiley.com, pg 300

Kirby, Judy, National Crime Prevention Council, 1000 Connecticut Ave NW, 13th fl, Washington, DC 20036-5325 Tel: 202-466-6272 Toll Free Tel: 800-627-2911 (orders only) Fax: 202-296-1356 Web Site: www.ncpc.org, pg 183

Kirchner, Harry, Groundwood Books, 720 Bathurst St, Suite 500, Toronto, ON M5S 2R4, Canada Tel: 416-537-2501 Fax: 416-537-4647 E-mail: genmail@groundwood-dm.com Web Site: www.groundwoodbooks.com, pg 548

Kirchoff, Mary, Wizards of the Coast Inc, PO Box 707, Renton, WA 98057-0707 Web Site: www.wizards.com/books, pg 302

Kirchoff, Morris A, Kirchoff/Wohlberg Inc, 866 United Nations Plaza, Suite 525, New York, NY 10017 Tel: 212-644-2020 Fax: 212-223-4387 E-mail: kirchwohl@aol.com Web Site: www.kirchoffwohlberg.com, pg 603, 637, 666

Kirchoff, Morris A, Turtle Books Inc, 866 United Nations Plaza, Suite 525, New York, NY 10017 Tel: 212-644-2020 Fax: 212-223-4387 E-mail: turtlebook@aol.com Web Site: www.turtlebooks.com, pg 276

Kirk, Kara, Getty Publications, 1200 Getty Center Dr, Suite 500, Los Angeles, CA 90049-1682 Tel: 310-440-7365 Fax: 310-440-7758 E-mail: pubsinfo@getty.edu Web Site: www.getty.edu/bookstore, pg 104

Kirk, Lindsay, The Magni Co, 7106 Wellington Point Rd, McKinney, TX 75070 Tel: 972-540-2050 Fax: 972-540-1057 E-mail: sales@magnico.com; info@magnico.com Web Site: www.magnico.com, pg 161

Kirk, Liza, River City Writing Awards in Fiction, University of Memphis, Dept of English, Memphis, TN 38152 Tel: 901-678-4591 Fax: 901-678-2226 E-mail: rivercity@memphis.edu Web Site: www.people.memphis.edu/~rivercity/contests.html, pg 802

Kirklin, Dan, Liberty Fund Inc, 8335 Allison Pointe Trail, Suite 300, Indianapolis, IN 46250-1684 Tel: 317-842-0880 Toll Free Tel: 800-955-8335 Fax: 317-579-6060 E-mail: books@libertyfund.org Web Site: www.libertyfund.org, pg 153

Kirkpatrick, Douglas J, Heldref Publications, 1319 18 St NW, Washington, DC 20036 Tel: 202-296-6267 Toll Free Tel: 800-365-9753 Fax: 202-293-6130 E-mail: subscribe@heldref.org Web Site: www.heldref.org, pg 705

Kirn, Wayne, Workman Publishing Co Inc, 708 Broadway, New York, NY 10003-9555 Tel: 212-254-5900 Toll Free Tel: 800-722-7202 Fax: 212-254-8098 E-mail: info@workman.com Web Site: www.workman.com, pg 303

Kirschbaum, Betsy, Water Row Press, PO Box 438, Sudbury, MA 01776 Tel: 508-485-8515 Fax: 508-229-0885 E-mail: contact@waterrowbooks.com Web Site: www.waterrowbooks.com, pg 294

Kirshbaum, Laurence J, Time Warner Book Group, 1271 Avenue of the Americas, New York, NY 10020 Tel: 212-522-7200 Fax: 212-522-7991 Web Site: www.twbookmark.com, pg 271

Kirshman, Deborah, University of California Press, 2120 Berkeley Way, Berkeley, CA 94720 Tel: 510-642-4247 Toll Free Tel: 800-777-4726 Fax: 510-643-7127 Toll Free Fax: 800-999-1958 E-mail: askucp@ucpress.edu Web Site: www.ucpress.edu, pg 281

Kirshner, Bob, American Forest & Paper Association, 1111 19 St NW, Suite 800, Washington, DC 20036 Tel: 202-463-2700 Toll Free Tel: 800-878-8878 Fax: 202-463-4703 E-mail: info@afandpa.org Web Site: www.afandpa.org, pg 676

Kirshner, Sandi, Allyn & Bacon, 75 Arlington St, Suite 300, Boston, MA 02116 Tel: 617-848-6000 Fax: 617-848-6016 E-mail: AandBpub@aol.com Web Site: www.ablongman.com, pg 9

Kisch, Nora, University Press of America Inc, 4501 Forbes Blvd, Suite 200, Lanham, MD 20706 Tel: 301-459-3366 Toll Free Tel: 800-462-6420 Fax: 301-429-5748 Toll Free Fax: 800-338-4550 Web Site: www.univpress.com, pg 286

Kiser, Kristin, Crown Publishing Group, 1745 Broadway, New York, NY 10019 Tel: 212-782-9000 Toll Free Tel: 888-264-1745 Fax: 212-940-7408 Web Site: www.randomhouse.com/crown, pg 74

Kisilinsky, Stuart, Association of American University Presses, 1427 E 60 St, Chicago, IL 60637 Tel: 773-702-7700; 773-702-7600 Toll Free Tel: 800-621-2736 (orders) Fax: 773-702-9756 (sales); 773-660-2235 (orders); 773-702-2708 E-mail: general@press.uchicago.edu Web Site: www.press.uchicago.edu, pg 26

Kisly, Lorraine, Parabola Books, 656 Broadway, Suite 615, New York, NY 10012 Tel: 212-505-6200 Toll Free Tel: 800-560-6984 Fax: 212-979-7325 E-mail: parabola@panix.com Web Site: www.parabola.org, pg 203

Kissling, Mark, ST Publications Book Division, 407 Gilbert Ave, Cincinnati, OH 45202 Tel: 513-421-2050 Toll Free Tel: 800-925-1110 Fax: 513-421-5144 E-mail: books@stpubs.com Web Site: www.stpubs.com, pg 257

Kistler, Don, Soli Deo Gloria Publications, 451 Millers Run Rd, Morgan, PA 15064 Tel: 412-221-1901 Toll Free Tel: 888-266-5734 Fax: 412-221-1902 Web Site: www.sdgbooks.com, pg 252

Kistler, Vivian, Columba Publishing Co Inc, 2003 W Market St, Akron, OH 44313 Tel: 330-836-2619 Toll Free Tel: 800-999-7491 Fax: 330-836-9659 Web Site: www.columbapublishing.com, pg 65

Kitter, Sharon, Hyperion, 77 W 66 St, 11th fl, New York, NY 10023-6298 Tel: 212-456-0100 Toll Free Tel: 800-759-0190 (cust serv) Fax: 212-456-0157 Web Site: hyperionbooks.com, pg 129

Kittle, Barbara, Prentice Hall Humanities & Social Sciences, One Lake St, Upper Saddle River, NJ 07458 Tel: 201-236-7000, pg 217

Kittrell, Kaye, BizBest Media Corp, 860 Via de la Paz, Suite D-4, Pacific Palisades, CA 90272 Tel: 310-230-6868 Toll Free Tel: 800-873-5205; 877-424-9237 Fax: 310-454-6130 E-mail: info@bizbest.com Web Site: www.bizbest.com, pg 39

Kjoller, Maria L, Farrar, Straus & Giroux Books for Young Readers, 19 Union Sq W, New York, NY 10003 Tel: 212-741-6900 Fax: 212-633-2427 E-mail: childrens.marketing@fsgbooks.com; childrens.editorial@fsgbooks.com Web Site: www.fsgkidsbooks.com, pg 95

Klappert, Helene, Oxford University Press, Inc, 198 Madison Ave, New York, NY 10016-4314 Tel: 212-726-6000 Toll Free Tel: 800-451-7556 (orders) Web Site: www.oup.com/us, pg 200

Klausner, Ron, Copley Publishing Group, 138 Great Rd, Acton, MA 01720 Tel: 978-263-9090 Toll Free Tel: 800-562-2147 Fax: 978-263-9190 E-mail: publish@copleycustom.com; textbook@copleypublishing.com Web Site: www.copleycustom.com; www.copleypublishing.com; www.copleyeditions.com, pg 68

Klausner, Ron, Pro Quest Information & Learning, 300 N Zeeb Rd, Ann Arbor, MI 48106-1346 Tel: 734-761-4700 Toll Free Tel: 800-521-0600 Fax: 734-975-6486 Toll Free Fax: 800-864-0019 E-mail: info@il.proquest.com Web Site: www.il.proquest.com, pg 219

Klaviter, Helen, Frederick Bock Prize, 1030 N Clark St, Suite 420, Chicago, IL 60610 Tel: 312-787-7070 Fax: 312-787-6650 E-mail: poetry@poetrymagazine.org Web Site: www.poetrymagazine.org, pg 763

Klaviter, Helen, Bess Hokin Prize, 1030 N Clark St, Suite 420, Chicago, IL 60610 Tel: 312-787-7070 Fax: 312-787-6650 E-mail: poetry@poetrymagazine.org Web Site: www.poetrymagazine.org, pg 778

Klaviter, Helen, The J Howard & Barbara M J Wood Prize, 1030 N Clark St, Suite 420, Chicago, IL 60610 Tel: 312-787-7070 Fax: 312-787-6650 E-mail: poetry@poetrymagazine.org Web Site: www.poetrymagazine.org, pg 779

Klaviter, Helen, Levinson Prize, 1030 N Clark St, Suite 420, Chicago, IL 60610 Tel: 312-787-7070 Fax: 312-787-6650 E-mail: poetry@poetrymagazine.org Web Site: www.poetrymagazine.org, pg 784

Klaviter, Helen, The Ruth Lilly Poetry Prize, 1030 N Clark St, Suite 420, Chicago, IL 60610 Tel: 312-787-7070 Fax: 312-787-6650 E-mail: poetry@poetrymagazine.org Web Site: www.poetrymagazine.org, pg 784

Klaviter, Helen, John Frederick Nims Memorial Prize, 1030 N Clark St, Suite 420, Chicago, IL 60610 Tel: 312-787-7070 Fax: 312-787-6650 E-mail: poetry@poetrymagazine.org Web Site: www.poetrymagazine.org, pg 794

Klaviter, Helen, Union League Civic & Arts Foundation Poetry Prize, 1030 N Clark St, Suite 420, Chicago, IL 60610 Tel: 312-787-7070 Fax: 312-787-6650 E-mail: poetry@poetrymagazine.org Web Site: www.poetrymagazine.org, pg 809

Klavora, Peter, Sports Books Publisher Inc, 278 Robert St, Toronto, ON M5S 2K8, Canada Tel: 416-922-0860 Fax: 416-966-9022 E-mail: sbp@sportsbookpub.com Web Site: www.sportsbookspub.com, pg 562

Klavora, Tania, Sports Books Publisher Inc, 278 Robert St, Toronto, ON M5S 2K8, Canada *Tel:* 416-922-0860 *Fax:* 416-966-9022 *E-mail:* sbp@sportsbookpub.com *Web Site:* www.sportsbookspub.com, pg 562

Klebanoff, Arthur M, Scott Meredith Literary Agency LP, 200 W 57 St, Suite 904, New York, NY 10019 *Tel:* 646-274-1970 *Fax:* 212-977-5997 *Web Site:* www.writingtosell.com, pg 644

Klein, Barry, Todd Publications, PO Box 635, Nyack, NY 10960-0635 *Tel:* 845-358-6213 *Fax:* 845-358-6213 *E-mail:* toddpub@aol.com *Web Site:* www.toddpublications.com, pg 272

Klein, Bernard, B Klein Publications, 6037 W Atlantic Ave, Delray Beach, FL 33482 *Tel:* 561-496-3316 *Fax:* 561-496-5546, pg 146

Klein, Chris, Saunders College Publishing, The Public Ledger Bldg, 150 S Independence Mall W, Suite 1250, Philadelphia, PA 19106-3412 *Tel:* 215-238-5500 *Fax:* 215-238-5660 *Web Site:* www.hbcollege.com, pg 240

Klein, Cynthia, Seascape Press Ltd, 1010 Roble Lane, Santa Maria, CA 93103-2046 *Tel:* 805-965-4646 *Toll Free Tel:* 800-929-2906 *Fax:* 805-963-8188 *E-mail:* seapress@aol.com *Web Site:* www.seascapepress.com, pg 573

Klein, Kathie, Society of Biblical Literature, The Luce Ctr, Suite 350, 825 Houston Mill Rd, Atlanta, GA 30329 *Tel:* 404-727-2325 *Fax:* 802-864-7626 *E-mail:* sbl@sbl-site.org *Web Site:* www.sbl-site.org, pg 251

Klein, Lara, International Creative Management, 40 W 57 St, New York, NY 10019 *Tel:* 212-556-5600 *Fax:* 212-556-5665 *Web Site:* www.icmtalent.com, pg 635

Klein, Sharon, Knopf Canada, One Toronto St, Suite 300, Toronto, ON M5C 2V6, Canada *Tel:* 416-364-4449 *Toll Free Tel:* 800-668-4247 (order desk) *Fax:* 416-364-0462 *Web Site:* www.randomhouse.ca, pg 552

Kleinberg, Naomi, Random House Children's Books, 1745 Broadway, New York, NY 10019 *Tel:* 212-782-9000 *Toll Free Tel:* 800-200-3552 *Fax:* 212-782-9452 *Web Site:* www.randomhouse.com/kids, pg 226

Kleiner, Karen, Clear Concepts, 1329 Federal Ave, Suite 6, Los Angeles, CA 90025 *Tel:* 310-473-5453, pg 594

Kleinert, Ian, The Literary Group International, 270 Lafayette St, Suite 1505, New York, NY 10012 *Tel:* 212-274-1616 *Fax:* 212-274-9876 *Web Site:* www.theliterarygroup.com, pg 641

Kleinman, Jeffrey, The Graybill & English Literary Agency LLC, 1875 Connecticut Ave, NW, Suite 712, Washington, DC 20009 *Tel:* 202-588-9798 *Fax:* 202-457-0662 *Web Site:* graybillandenglish.com, pg 633

Kleinschmidt, L, The Write Watchman, 9151 Yellowwood Dr, Cincinnati, OH 45251-1948 *Tel:* 603-643-6416 *Toll Free Tel:* 800-768-0829 ext 6416 *Fax:* 603-643-6416 *E-mail:* lmk42@earthlink.net, pg 614

Kleit, Micah, Temple University Press, 1601 N Broad St, 083-42, USB Room 306, Philadelphia, PA 19122-6099 *Tel:* 215-204-8787 *Toll Free Tel:* 800-447-1656 *Fax:* 215-204-4719 *E-mail:* tempress@temple.edu *Web Site:* www.temple.edu/tempress, pg 266

Klemens, Mark, Boydell & Brewer Inc, 668 Mount Hope Ave, University of Rochester, Rochester, NY 14620 *Tel:* 585-275-0419 *Fax:* 585-271-8778 *Web Site:* www.boydellandbrewer.co.uk, pg 45

Kliment, Edward, Pulitzer Prizes, 709 Journalism Bldg, New York, NY 10027 *Tel:* 212-854-3841 *Fax:* 212-854-3342 *E-mail:* pulitzer@pulitzer.org *Web Site:* www.pulitzer.org, pg 800

Klimo, Kate, Random House Children's Books, 1745 Broadway, New York, NY 10019 *Tel:* 212-782-9000 *Toll Free Tel:* 800-200-3552 *Fax:* 212-782-9452 *Web Site:* www.randomhouse.com/kids, pg 225

Klimt, Bill, Klimt Represents, 15 W 72 St, Suite 7-U, New York, NY 10023 *Tel:* 212-799-2231 *Fax:* 212-799-2362 *E-mail:* klimt@nyc.rr.com *Web Site:* klimtreps.com, pg 666

Klimt, Maurine, Klimt Represents, 15 W 72 St, Suite 7-U, New York, NY 10023 *Tel:* 212-799-2231 *Fax:* 212-799-2362 *E-mail:* klimt@nyc.rr.com *Web Site:* klimtreps.com, pg 666

Kline, Amy, Teachers College Press, 1234 Amsterdam Ave, New York, NY 10027 *Tel:* 212-678-3929 *Fax:* 212-678-4149 *E-mail:* tcpress@tc.columbia.edu *Web Site:* www.teacherscollegepress.com, pg 265

Kline, Daisy, Random House Children's Books, 1745 Broadway, New York, NY 10019 *Tel:* 212-782-9000 *Toll Free Tel:* 800-200-3552 *Fax:* 212-782-9452 *Web Site:* www.randomhouse.com/kids, pg 225

Kline, Jean, Heldref Publications, 1319 18 St NW, Washington, DC 20036 *Tel:* 202-296-6267 *Toll Free Tel:* 800-365-9753 *Fax:* 202-293-6130 *E-mail:* subscribe@heldref.org *Web Site:* www.heldref.org, pg 705

Klinger, Harvey, Harvey Klinger Inc, 301 W 53 St, New York, NY 10019 *Tel:* 212-581-7068 *Fax:* 212-315-3823 *E-mail:* queries@harveyklinger.com, pg 637

Kliot, Jules, Lacis Publications, 3163 Adeline St, Berkeley, CA 94703 *Tel:* 510-843-7178 *Fax:* 510-843-5018 *E-mail:* staff@lacis.com *Web Site:* www.lacis.com, pg 148

Klockner, Karen, Transatlantic Literary Agency Inc, 72 Glengowan Rd, Toronto, ON M4N 1G4, Canada *Tel:* 416-488-9214 *Fax:* 416-488-4531 *E-mail:* info@tla1.com *Web Site:* www.tla1.com, pg 659

Kloetzel, James E, Scott Publishing Co, 911 Vandemark Rd, Sidney, OH 45365 *Tel:* 937-498-0802 *Toll Free Tel:* 800-572-6885 *Fax:* 937-498-0807 *E-mail:* ssm@amospress.com *Web Site:* www.amosadvantage.com, pg 244

Klopfenstein, Gloria, Global Training Center Inc, 7801 N Dixie Dr, Dayton, OH 45414-2779 *Tel:* 937-454-5044 *Toll Free Tel:* 800-860-5030 *Fax:* 937-454-5099 *E-mail:* xportnow@aol.com *Web Site:* www.globaltrainingcenter.com, pg 105

Klose, Tory, Viking, 375 Hudson St, New York, NY 10014 *Tel:* 212-366-2000 *E-mail:* online@penguinputnam.com *Web Site:* www.penguin.com, pg 290

Kloske, Geoff, Simon & Schuster, 1230 Avenue of the Americas, New York, NY 10020 *Tel:* 212-698-7000 *Toll Free Tel:* 800-223-2348 (cust serv); 800-223-2336 (orders) *Toll Free Fax:* 800-943-9831 (orders) *Web Site:* www.simonsays.com, pg 248

Klug, Scott, Trails Books, PO Box 317, Black Earth, WI 53515-0317 *Tel:* 608-767-8000 *Toll Free Tel:* 800-236-8088 *Fax:* 608-767-5444 *E-mail:* books@wistrails.com *Web Site:* www.trailsbooks.com, pg 273

Knapp, James, Creative Homeowner, 24 Park Way, Upper Saddle River, NJ 07458-9960 *Tel:* 201-934-7100 *Toll Free Tel:* 800-631-7795 *Fax:* 201-934-8971 *E-mail:* info@creativehomeowner.com *Web Site:* www.creativehomeowner.com, pg 72

Knapp, Lucy, Warren H Green Inc, 8356 Olive Blvd, St Louis, MO 63132 *Tel:* 314-991-1335 *Toll Free Tel:* 800-537-0655 *Fax:* 314-997-1788 *E-mail:* whgreen@inlink.com *Web Site:* www.whgreen.com, pg 108

Knapp, Renee, Canadian Scholars' Press Inc, 180 Bloor St W, Suite 801, Toronto, ON M5S 2V6, Canada *Tel:* 416-929-2774 *Fax:* 416-929-1926 *E-mail:* info@cspi.org *Web Site:* www.cspi.org; www.womenspress.ca, pg 539

Knappman, Edward W, New England Publishing Associates Inc, PO Box 5, Chester, CT 06412-0005 *Tel:* 860-345-READ (345-7323) *Fax:* 860-345-3660 *E-mail:* nepa@nepa.com *Web Site:* www.nepa.com, pg 646

Knaupp, Andrew, Stylewriter Inc, 4395 N Windsor Dr, Provo, UT 84604-6301 *Tel:* 801-235-9462 *Toll Free Tel:* 866-997-9462 *E-mail:* customerservice@swinc.org; query@swinc.org *Web Site:* www.swinc.org; www.stylewriterinc.org, pg 261

Knecht, Mary Jane, Copper Canyon Press, PO Box 271, Port Townsend, WA 98368 *Tel:* 360-385-4925 *Fax:* 360-385-4985 *E-mail:* poetry@coppercanyonpress.org *Web Site:* www.coppercanyonpress.org, pg 68

Kneerim, Jill, Kneerim & Williams, c/o Fish & Richardson PC, 225 Franklin St, Boston, MA 02110 *Tel:* 617-542-5070 *Fax:* 617-542-8906 *Web Site:* www.fr.com, pg 638

Knezek, Don, International Society for Technology in Education, 480 Charnelton St, Eugene, OR 97401-2626 *Tel:* 541-302-3777 *Toll Free Tel:* 800-336-5191 (orders only) *Fax:* 541-302-3778 *E-mail:* iste@iste.org *Web Site:* www.iste.org, pg 138

Knickerbocker, Alzada, Northern California Independent Booksellers Association (NCIBA), 37 Graham St, San Francisco, CA 94129 *Tel:* 415-561-7686 *Fax:* 415-561-7685 *E-mail:* office@nciba.com *Web Site:* www.nciba.com, pg 696

Knickerbocker, Andrea, Lee Allan Agency, 7464 N 107 St, Milwaukee, WI 53224-3706 *Tel:* 414-357-7708, pg 618

Knight, Cindy, Abingdon Press, 201 Eighth Ave S, Nashville, TN 37203-3919 *Tel:* 615-749-6290 (publicist); 615-749-6000; 615-749-6451 (sales) *Toll Free Tel:* 800-251-3320 *Fax:* 615-749-6056 *Web Site:* www.abingdonpress.com, pg 3

Knight, Deidre, The Knight Agency Inc, 577 S Main St, Madison, GA 30650 *Tel:* 706-752-0096 *E-mail:* knightagency@msn.com; knightagent@aol.com (queries) *Web Site:* www.knightagency.net, pg 638

Knight, Denise, Eagle's View Publishing, 168W 12 St, Ogden, UT 84404 *Tel:* 801-393-4555; 801-745-0905 (edit) *Toll Free Tel:* 800-547-3364 (orders over $100) *Fax:* 801-745-0903 *E-mail:* eglcrafts@aol.com *Web Site:* eaglefeathertradingpost.com, pg 85

Knight, Judson, The Knight Agency Inc, 577 S Main St, Madison, GA 30650 *Tel:* 706-752-0096 *E-mail:* knightagency@msn.com; knightagent@aol.com (queries) *Web Site:* www.knightagency.net, pg 638

Knill, Ellen, Bellerophon Books, PO Box 21307, Santa Barbara, CA 93121-1307 *Tel:* 805-965-7034 *Toll Free Tel:* 800-253-9943 *Fax:* 805-965-8286 *E-mail:* sales@bellerophonbooks.com *Web Site:* www.bellerophonbooks.com, pg 35

Knitzer, Jane, National Center for Children in Poverty, 215 W 125 St, 3rd fl, New York, NY 10027 *Tel:* 646-284-9600 *Fax:* 646-284-9623 *E-mail:* nccp@columbia.edu *Web Site:* www.nccp.org, pg 183

Knobloch, Jamie, Thorndike Press, 295 Kennedy Memorial Dr, Waterville, ME 04901-4517 *Tel:* 207-859-1026 *Toll Free Tel:* 800-233-1244 *Fax:* 207-859-1009 *Toll Free Fax:* 800-558-4676 (orders) *E-mail:* printorders@thomson.com; international@thomson.com (orders for customers outside US & CA) *Web Site:* www.gale.com/thorndike, pg 270

Knoche, Grace F, Theosophical University Press, PO Box C, Pasadena, CA 91109-7107 *Tel:* 626-798-3378 *Fax:* 626-798-4749 *E-mail:* tupress@theosociety.org *Web Site:* www.theosociety.org, pg 268

Knoll, Elizabeth, Harvard University Press, 79 Garden St, Cambridge, MA 02138-1499 *Tel:* 617-495-2600; 401-531-2800 (international orders) *Toll Free Tel:* 800-405-1619 (orders) *Fax:* 617-495-5898 (general); 617-496-4677 (edit & rts); 401-531-2801 (international orders) *Toll Free Fax:* 800-406-9145 (orders) *E-mail:* firstname_lastname@harvard.edu *Web Site:* www.hup.harvard.edu, pg 117

Knope, Matthew, Prakken Publications Inc, 832 Phoenix Dr, Ann Arbor, MI 48108 *Tel:* 734-975-2800 *Toll Free Tel:* 800-530-9673 (orders only) *Fax:* 734-975-2787 *E-mail:* tdbooks@techdirections.com *Web Site:* www.techdirections.com; www.eddigest.com, pg 217

Knopf, Jerald D, Thomas Reed Publications Inc, 398 Columbus Ave, Box 302, Boston, MA 02116 *Tel:* 617-236-0465 *Toll Free Tel:* 800-995-4995 (customer

service) *E-mail:* info@reedsalmanac.com; order@
reedsalmanac.com *Web Site:* www.reedsalmanac.com,
pg 230

Knopf, Susan, American Book Producers Association
(ABPA), 160 Fifth Ave, Suite 622, New York, NY
10010 *Tel:* 212-645-2368 *Toll Free Tel:* 800-209-4575
Fax: 212-242-6499 *E-mail:* office@abpaonline.org
Web Site: www.abpaonline.org, pg 676

Knopf, Susan, Book Producing: Making Books Happen,
160 Fifth Ave, New York, NY 10010-7003 *Tel:* 212-
645-2368 *Toll Free Tel:* 800-209-4575 *Fax:* 212-242-
6799 *E-mail:* office@abpaonline.org *Web Site:* www.
abpaonline.org, pg 742

Knopf, Susan, Parachute Publishing LLC, 156 Fifth
Ave, Suite 302, New York, NY 10010 *Tel:* 212-
691-1422 *Fax:* 212-645-8769 *Web Site:* www.
parachutepublishing.com, pg 203

Knopp, Bryon, R D R Books, 2415 Woolsey St,
Berkeley, CA 94705 *Tel:* 510-595-0595 *Fax:* 510-228-
0300 *E-mail:* info@rdrbooks.com *Web Site:* www.
rdrbooks.com, pg 224

Knott, Ronald, Andrews University Press, Andrews
University Press, 213 Information Services Bldg,
Berrien Springs, MI 49104-1700 *Tel:* 269-471-6915
Toll Free Tel: 800-467-6369 (Visa & MC orders only)
Fax: 269-471-6224 *E-mail:* aupress@andrews.edu
Web Site: www.andrewsuniversitypress.com; www.
ancrews.edu/universitypress, pg 19

Knowles, Jack W, Management Concepts Inc, 8230
Leesburg Pike, Suite 800, Vienna, VA 22182 *Tel:* 703-
790-9595 *Fax:* 703-790-1930 *E-mail:* publications@
managementconcepts.com *Web Site:* www.
managementconcepts.com, pg 162

Knowlton, Cindy, Glory Bound Books, 6642 Marlette
St, Suite 101, Marlette, MI 48453 *Tel:* 989-635-
7520 *E-mail:* info@gloryboundenterprises.com
Web Site: www.thegloryboundbookcompany.com,
pg 106

Knowlton, Ginger, Curtis Brown Ltd, 10 Astor Place,
New York, NY 10003 *Tel:* 212-473-5400, pg 623

Knowlton, Kristy, Bandido Books, 9806 Heaton Ct,
Orlando, FL 32817 *Tel:* 407-657-9707 *Toll Free
Tel:* 877-814-6824 (pin 1174) *Fax:* 407-677-9796
E-mail: publish@bandidobooks.com *Web Site:* www.
bandidobooks.com, pg 31

Knowlton, Perry H, Curtis Brown Ltd, 10 Astor Place,
New York, NY 10003 *Tel:* 212-473-5400, pg 623

Knowlton, Timothy F, Curtis Brown Ltd, 10 Astor Place,
New York, NY 10003 *Tel:* 212-473-5400, pg 623

Knox, Douglas, Tyndale House Publishers Inc, 351
Executive Dr, Carol Stream, IL 60188 *Tel:* 630-668-
8303 *Toll Free Tel:* 800-323-9400 *Web Site:* www.
tyndale.com, pg 277

Knox, Robert, Concordia Publishing House, 3558 S
Jefferson Ave, St Louis, MO 63118-3968 *Tel:* 314-
268-1000 *Toll Free Tel:* 800-325-3040 *Fax:* 314-268-
1329 *Toll Free Fax:* 800-490-9889 *E-mail:* cphorder@
cph.org *Web Site:* www.cph.org, pg 66

Knutson, Rod, University of Wisconsin Press, 1930
Monroe St, 3rd fl, Madison, WI 53711 *Tel:* 608-263-
1110 *Toll Free Tel:* 800-621-2736 (Orders) *Fax:* 608-
263-1120 *Toll Free Fax:* 800-621-8476 (Orders)
E-mail: uwiscpress@uwpress.wisc.edu (Main Office)
Web Site: www.wisc.edu/wisconsinpress/, pg 286

Kobasa, Paul, World Book Inc, 233 N Michigan, Suite
2000, Chicago, IL 60601 *Tel:* 312-729-5800 *Toll Free
Tel:* 800-967-5325 (consumer sales, US); 800-463-
8845 (consumer sales, Canada); 800-975-3250 (school
& library sales, US); 800-837-5365 (school & library
sales, Canada); 866-866-5200 (web sales) *Fax:* 312-
729-5600; 312-729-5606 *Toll Free Fax:* 800-433-9330
(school & library sales, US); 888-690-4002 (school
library sales, Canada) *Web Site:* www.worldbook.com,
pg 303

Kobres, Jane, University of Georgia Press, 330
Research Dr, Athens, GA 30602-4901 *Tel:* 706-
369-6130 *Toll Free Tel:* 800-266-5842 (orders only)
Fax: 706-369-6131 *E-mail:* books@ugapress.uga.edu
Web Site: www.ugapress.org, pg 281

Kobrin, Eleanor Starke, The Analytic Press, 101 West St,
Hillsdale, NJ 07642 *Tel:* 201-358-9477; 201-236-9500
Toll Free Tel: 800-926-6579 (orders only); 800-627-
0629 (journal orders) *Fax:* 201-358-4700 (edit); 201-
760-3735 (orders only) *E-mail:* tap@analyticpress.com
Web Site: www.analyticpress.com, pg 19

Koch, Charles, Hammond World Atlas Corp, 95
Progress St, Union, NJ 07083 *Tel:* 908-206-1300
Toll Free Tel: 800-526-4953 *Fax:* 908-206-1104
E-mail: customerservice@hammondmap.com;
feedback@hammondmap.com *Web Site:* www.
hammondmap.com, pg 112

Koch, Laura, Penguin Group (USA) Inc Sales, 375
Hudson St, New York, NY 10014 *Tel:* 212-366-2000
E-mail: online@penguinputnam.com *Web Site:* www.
penguin.com, pg 208

Koch, Pat, McGraw-Hill Primis Custom Publishing, 2460
Kerper Blvd, Dubuque, IA 52001 *Tel:* 563-588-1451
Fax: 563-589-4700 *E-mail:* first_last@mcgraw-hill.
com *Web Site:* www.mhhe.com, pg 168

Koch, W John, Books by W John Koch Publishing,
11666-72 Ave, Edmonton, AB T6G 0C1,
Canada *Tel:* 780-436-0581 *Fax:* 780-430-1672
E-mail: wjohnkoch@wjkochpublishing.com
Web Site: www.wjkochpublishing.com, pg 570

Kochan, Susan, G P Putnam's Sons (Children's), 345
Hudson St, New York, NY 10014 *Tel:* 212-366-2000
E-mail: online@penguinputnam.com *Web Site:* www.
penguin.com, pg 223

Koecher, Molly, CarTech Inc, 39966 Grand Ave, North
Branch, MN 55056 *Tel:* 651-277-1200 *Toll Free
Tel:* 800-551-4754 *Fax:* 651-277-1203 *E-mail:* info@
cartechbooks.com *Web Site:* www.cartechbooks.com,
pg 54

Koehler, H Dirk, World Bank Publications, Office of the
Publisher, 1818 "H" St NW, U-11-1104, Washington,
DC 20433 *Tel:* 202-473-0393 (sales mgr) *Toll Free
Tel:* 800-645-7247 (cust serv) *Fax:* 202-522-2631
E-mail: books@worldbank.org; pubrights@worldbank.
org (foreign rts) *Web Site:* www.worldbank.org/
publications, pg 303

Koelsch, Han S, Springer-Verlag New York Inc, 175
Fifth Ave, New York, NY 10010 *Tel:* 212-460-1500
Toll Free Tel: 800-777-4643 *Fax:* 212-473-6272
Web Site: www.springer-ny.com, pg 256

Koenig, Hardy, Southeastern Theatre Conference
New Play Project (SETC), 1114 Whitehall Rd,
Murfreesboro, TN 37130 *Tel:* 336-272-3645
Fax: 336-272-8810 *E-mail:* setc@sectonline.com
Web Site: www.setc.org, pg 806

Koffler, Lionel, Firefly Books Ltd, 66 Leek Crescent,
Richmond Hill, ON L4B 1H1, Canada *Tel:* 416-499-
8412 *Toll Free Tel:* 800-387-5085 *Fax:* 416-499-
1142 *Toll Free Fax:* 800-565-6034 *E-mail:* service@
fireflybooks.com *Web Site:* www.fireflybooks.com,
pg 546

Kohler, Frank, Academy of Television Arts & Sciences
(ATAS), 5220 Lankershim Blvd, North Hollywood,
CA 91601-3109 *Tel:* 818-754-2800 *Fax:* 818-761-2827
Web Site: www.emmys.tv, pg 675

Kohler, Ina, Quite Specific Media Group Ltd, 7373
Pyramid Place, Hollywood, CA 90046 *Tel:* 323-
851-5797 *Fax:* 323-851-5798 *E-mail:* info@
quitespecificmedia.com *Web Site:* www.
quitespecificmedia.com, pg 224

Kohn, Paul, Pearson Education/ELT, 10 Bank St, 9th fl,
White Plains, NY 10606 *Tel:* 914-993-5000 *Fax:* 914-
993-8115 *E-mail:* firstname.lastname@pearsoned.com,
pg 206

Koize, John, St Anthony Messenger Press, 28 W
Liberty St, Cincinnati, OH 45202 *Tel:* 513-241-5615
Toll Free Tel: 800-488-0488 *Fax:* 513-241-0399
E-mail: books@americancatholic.org *Web Site:* www.
AmericanCatholic.org, pg 237

Kok, John H, Dordt College Press, 498 Fourth Ave
NE, Sioux Center, IA 51250 *Tel:* 712-722-6420
Fax: 712-722-1185 *E-mail:* dordtpress@dordt.edu
Web Site: www.dordt.edu/dordt_press, pg 82

Kolatch, Alfred J, Jonathan David Publishers Inc, 68-22
Eliot Ave, Middle Village, NY 11379 *Tel:* 718-456-
8611 *Fax:* 718-894-2818 *E-mail:* info@jdbooks.com;
jondavpub@aol.com *Web Site:* www.jdbooks.com,
pg 142

Kolatch, David, Jonathan David Publishers Inc, 68-22
Eliot Ave, Middle Village, NY 11379 *Tel:* 718-456-
8611 *Fax:* 718-894-2818 *E-mail:* info@jdbooks.com;
jondavpub@aol.com *Web Site:* www.jdbooks.com,
pg 142

Kolatch, Thelma R, Jonathan David Publishers Inc, 68-
22 Eliot Ave, Middle Village, NY 11379 *Tel:* 718-456-
8611 *Fax:* 718-894-2818 *E-mail:* info@jdbooks.com;
jondavpub@aol.com *Web Site:* www.jdbooks.com,
pg 142

Kolb, Patricia A, M E Sharpe Inc, 80 Business Park
Dr, Suite 202, Armonk, NY 10504 *Tel:* 914-273-
1800 *Toll Free Tel:* 800-541-6563 *Fax:* 914-273-
2106 *E-mail:* info@mesharpe.com *Web Site:* www.
mesharpe.com, pg 246

Kolby, Jeff, Nova Press, 11659 Mayfield Ave, Suite
1, Los Angeles, CA 90049 *Tel:* 310-207-4078
Toll Free Tel: 800-949-6175 *Fax:* 310-571-0908
E-mail: novapress@aol.com *Web Site:* www.novapress.
net, pg 194

Kollar, Holly, University of British Columbia Press,
2029 West Mall, Vancouver, BC V6T 1Z2, Canada
Tel: 604-822-5959 *Toll Free Tel:* 877-377-9378
Fax: 604-822-6083 *Toll Free Fax:* 800-668-0821
E-mail: info@ubcpress.ca *Web Site:* www.ubcpress.ca,
pg 564

Kolota, Michelle, Key Curriculum Press, 1150 65
St, Emeryville, CA 94608 *Tel:* 510-595-7000 *Toll
Free Tel:* 800-995-6284 *Fax:* 510-595-7040 *Toll
Free Fax:* 800-541-2442 *E-mail:* customer.service@
keypress.com *Web Site:* www.keypress.com, pg 145

Koltes, Joanne, Dimension Creative, 1500 McAndrews
Rd W, Suite 217, Burnsville, MN 55337 *Tel:* 952-
201-3981 *Fax:* 952-892-1722 *Web Site:* www.
dimensioncreative.com, pg 665

Komorowski, Diane, Heritage House Publishing Co Ltd,
17665 66 "A" Ave, No 108, Surrey, BC V3S 2A7,
Canada *Tel:* 604-574-7067 *Toll Free Tel:* 800-665-
3302 *Fax:* 604-574-9942 *Toll Free Fax:* 800-566-
3336 *E-mail:* publisher@heritagehouse.ca; editorial@
heritagehouse.ca; distribution@heritagehouse.ca
Web Site: www.heritagehouse.ca, pg 550

Kondras, Holly, Wish Publishing, PO Box 10337, Terre
Haute, IN 47801-0337 *Tel:* 812-299-5700 *Fax:* 928-
447-1836 *Web Site:* www.wishpublishing.com, pg 302

Kondrick, Maureen, Marquette University Press,
Memorial Library, Rm 116, 1415 W Wisconsin Ave,
Milwaukee, WI 53233 *Tel:* 414-288-1564 *Toll Free
Tel:* 800-247-6553 *Fax:* 414-288-7813 *Web Site:* www.
marquette.edu/mupress/, pg 164

Konecky, Sean, William S Konecky Associates Inc, 72
Ayers Pt Rd, Old Saybrook, CT 06475 *Tel:* 860-388-
0878 *Fax:* 860-388-0273, pg 147

Kong, Molly, Disney Press, 114 Fifth Ave, New York,
NY 10011 *Tel:* 212-633-4400 *Fax:* 212-807-5432
Web Site: www.disney.go.com, pg 81

Konner, Linda, Linda Konner Literary Agency, 10 W 15
St, Suite 1918, New York, NY 10011 *Tel:* 212-691-
3419 *Fax:* 212-691-0935, pg 638

Kontzias, Olga T, Fairchild Books, 7 W 34 St, New
York, NY 10001 *Tel:* 212-630-3880 *Toll Free
Tel:* 800-932-4724 *Fax:* 212-630-3868; 212-630-3898
Web Site: www.fairchildbooks.com, pg 94

Koohi-Kamali, Farideh, Palgrave Macmillan, 175
Fifth Ave, New York, NY 10010 *Tel:* 212-982-3900
Fax: 212-777-6359 *E-mail:* firstname.lastname@
palgrave-usa.com *Web Site:* www.palgrave.com,
pg 202

Kooij, Nina, Pelican Publishing Co Inc, 1000 Burmaster,
Gretna, LA 70053 *Tel:* 504-368-1175 *Toll Free
Tel:* 800-843-1724 *Fax:* 504-368-1195 *E-mail:* sales@

pelicanpub.com (sales); office@pelicanpub.com (permission); promo@pelicanpub.com (publicity) *Web Site:* www.pelicanpub.com, pg 207

Koons, Abigail, Nicholas Ellison Inc, 55 Fifth Ave, New York, NY 10003 *Tel:* 212-206-6050 *Fax:* 212-463-8718 *Web Site:* www.greenburger.com, pg 629

Koontz, Wanda, University Publishing Group, 138 W Washington St, Suites 403-405, Hagerstown, MD 21740 *Tel:* 240-420-0036 *Toll Free Tel:* 800-654-8188 *Fax:* 240-420-0037 *E-mail:* editorial@upgbooks.com; orders@upgbooks.com *Web Site:* www.upgbooks.com, pg 287

Koop, Alison, The Mountaineers Books, 1001 SW Klickitat Way, Suite 201, Seattle, WA 98134 *Tel:* 206-223-6303 *Toll Free Tel:* 800-553-4453 *Fax:* 206-223-6306 *Toll Free Fax:* 800-568-7604 *E-mail:* mbooks@mountaineers.org *Web Site:* www.mountaineersbooks.org, pg 179

Koos, Jeff, Rainbow Studies International, 1950 S Shepard Ave, El Reno, OK 73036 *Tel:* 405-262-6826 *Toll Free Tel:* 800-242-5348 *Fax:* 405-262-7599 *E-mail:* rsimail@rainbowstudies.com *Web Site:* www.rainbowstudies.com, pg 225

Kooter, Ben, Vanwell Publishing Ltd, One Northrup Cres, St Catharines, ON L2R 7S2, Canada *Tel:* 905-937-3100 *Toll Free Tel:* 800-661-6136 *Fax:* 905-937-1760 *E-mail:* sales@vanwell.com, pg 565

Kooter, Diane, Vanwell Publishing Ltd, One Northrup Cres, St Catharines, ON L2R 7S2, Canada *Tel:* 905-937-3100 *Toll Free Tel:* 800-661-6136 *Fax:* 905-937-1760 *E-mail:* sales@vanwell.com, pg 565

Kooter, Simon, Vanwell Publishing Ltd, One Northrup Cres, St Catharines, ON L2R 7S2, Canada *Tel:* 905-937-3100 *Toll Free Tel:* 800-661-6136 *Fax:* 905-937-1760 *E-mail:* sales@vanwell.com, pg 565

Kopernick, James, International Plate Printers', Die Stampers' & Engravers' Union of North America, 3957 Smoke Rd, Doylestown, PA 18901 *Tel:* 215-340-2843, pg 689

Kopf, Dorothy, Harlan Davidson Inc/Forum Press Inc, 773 Glenn Ave, Wheeling, IL 60090-6000 *Tel:* 847-541-9720 *Fax:* 847-541-9830 *E-mail:* harlandavidson@harlandavidson.com *Web Site:* www.harlandavidson.com, pg 115

Koplow, Michael, Association of American University Presses, 1427 E 60 St, Chicago, IL 60637 *Tel:* 773-702-7700; 773-702-7600 *Toll Free Tel:* 800-621-2736 (orders) *Fax:* 773-702-9756 (sales); 773-660-2235 (orders); 773-702-2708 *E-mail:* general@press.uchicago.edu *Web Site:* www.press.uchicago.edu, pg 26

Kopp, Linda, Simba Information, 60 Long Ridge Rd, Suite 300, Stamford, CT 06902 *Tel:* 203-325-8193 *Fax:* 203-325-8915 *E-mail:* info@simbanet.com *Web Site:* www.simbanet.com, pg 248

Kopp, Nancy, Christopher Publishing House, 24 Rockland St, Hanover, MA 02339 *Tel:* 781-826-7474; 781-826-5494 *Fax:* 781-826-5556 *E-mail:* cph@atigroupinc.com, pg 61

Koppel, Holly L, ASM Press, 1752 "N" St NW, Washington, DC 20036-2904 *Tel:* 202-737-3600 *Toll Free Tel:* 800-546-2416 *Fax:* 202-942-9342 *E-mail:* books@asmusa.org *Web Site:* www.asmpress.org, pg 25

Koppelman, Dorothy, Definition Press, 141 Greene St, New York, NY 10012 *Tel:* 212-777-4490 *Fax:* 212-777-4426 *E-mail:* mc@definitionpress.org *Web Site:* www.definitionpress.org, pg 570

Korda, Michael V, Simon & Schuster, 1230 Avenue of the Americas, New York, NY 10020 *Tel:* 212-698-7000 *Toll Free Tel:* 800-223-2348 (cust serv); 800-223-2336 (orders) *Toll Free Fax:* 800-943-9831 (orders) *Web Site:* www.simonsays.com, pg 248

Korman, Keith, Raines & Raines, 103 Kenyon Rd, Medusa, NY 12120 *Tel:* 518-239-8311 *Fax:* 518-239-6029, pg 650

Korn, Steven E, Blackwell Publishing/Futura, 3 W Main St, Elmsford, NY 10523 *Tel:* 914-593-0731 *Toll Free Tel:* 800-759-6102 *Fax:* 914-593-0732

E-mail: jbellhouse@ny.blackwellpublishing.com *Web Site:* www.blackwellpublishing.com/futura; www.blackwellfutura.com, pg 40

Kornblum, Allan, Coffee House Press, 27 N Fourth St, Suite 400, Minneapolis, MN 55401 *Tel:* 612-338-0125 *Fax:* 612-338-4004 *Web Site:* www.coffeehousepress.org, pg 64

Korper, Phyllis, Peter Lang Publishing Inc, 275 Seventh Ave, 28th fl, New York, NY 10001-6708 *Tel:* 212-647-7700 *Toll Free Tel:* 800-770-5264 (cust serv) *Fax:* 212-647-7707 *Web Site:* www.peterlangusa.com, pg 148

Kortekamp, Jeanne A, St Anthony Messenger Press, 28 W Liberty St, Cincinnati, OH 45202 *Tel:* 513-241-5615 *Toll Free Tel:* 800-488-0488 *Fax:* 513-241-0399 *E-mail:* books@americancatholic.org *Web Site:* www.AmericanCatholic.org, pg 237

Korytowski, Jack, Smithsonian Federal Series Section, 750 Ninth St NW, Suite 4300, Washington, DC 20560-0950 *Tel:* 202-275-2233 *Fax:* 202-275-2274, pg 251

Kosharek, Daniel, Museum of New Mexico Press, 725 Camino Lejo, Santa Fe, NM 87501 *Tel:* 505-476-1158 *Toll Free Tel:* 800-249-7737 (orders) *Fax:* 505-476-1156 *Toll Free Fax:* 800-622-8667 (orders) *E-mail:* mnmpress@aol.com *Web Site:* www.mnmpress.org, pg 180

Koster, Elaine, Elaine Koster Literary Agency LLC, 55 Central Park West, Suite 6, New York, NY 10023 *Tel:* 212-362-9488 *Fax:* 212-712-0164 *E-mail:* elainekost@aol.com, pg 639

Kostman, Lynne, UCLA Fowler Museum of Cultural History, 1586 Fowler, Los Angeles, CA 90095-1549 *Tel:* 310-825-9672 *Fax:* 310-206-7007 *Web Site:* www.fmch.ucla.edu, pg 278

Kostovski, Aleksandra, Nelson Algren Awards, Tribune Tower, LL2, 435 N Michigan Ave, Chicago, IL 60611 *Fax:* 312-222-5816 *Web Site:* www.chicagotribune.com, pg 758

Kosturko, Robert, Beacon Press, 41 Mount Vernon St, Boston, MA 02108 *Tel:* 617-742-2110 *Toll Free Tel:* 800-225-3362 (orders only) *Fax:* 617-723-3097; 617-742-2290 *Web Site:* www.beacon.org, pg 34

Kot, Rick, Viking, 375 Hudson St, New York, NY 10014 *Tel:* 212-366-2000 *E-mail:* online@penguinputnam.com *Web Site:* www.penguin.com, pg 290

Kothawala, Anne, Canadian Newspaper Association, 890 Yonge St, Suite 200, Toronto, ON M4W 3P4, Canada *Tel:* 416-923-3567 *Fax:* 416-923-7206 *Web Site:* www.cna-acj.ca, pg 683

Kothe, Barbara, Hanser Gardner Publications, 6915 Valley Ave, Cincinnati, OH 45244-3029 *Tel:* 513-527-8977 *Toll Free Tel:* 800-950-8977 *Fax:* 513-527-8801 *Toll Free Fax:* 800-527-8801 *E-mail:* hgfeedback@gardnerweb.com *Web Site:* www.hansergardner.com, pg 113

Kouner, Bruce, The AEI Press, 1150 17 St NW, Washington, DC 20036 *Tel:* 202-862-5800 *Fax:* 202-862-7177 *Web Site:* www.aei.org, pg 6

Kourmadas, Jim, McGraw-Hill/Irwin, 1333 Burr Ridge Pkwy, Burr Ridge, IL 60527 *Tel:* 630-789-4000 *Toll Free Tel:* 800-338-3987 (cust serv) *Fax:* 630-789-6942; 614-755-5645 (cust serv) *Web Site:* www.mhhe.com, pg 168

Kouts, Barbara S, Barbara S Kouts Literary Agency LLC, PO Box 560, Bellport, NY 11713 *Tel:* 631-286-1278 *Fax:* 631-286-1538 *E-mail:* bkouts@aol.com, pg 639

Kouwenberg, Dorothy, Springer Publishing Co Inc, 11 W 42 St, New York, NY 10036 *Tel:* 212-431-4370 *Toll Free Tel:* 877-687-7476 *Fax:* 212-941-7842 *E-mail:* springer@springerpub.com *Web Site:* www.springerpub.com, pg 256

Kowal, Harvey-Jane, Time Warner Book Group, 1271 Avenue of the Americas, New York, NY 10020 *Tel:* 212-522-7200 *Fax:* 212-522-7991 *Web Site:* www.twbookmark.com, pg 271

Kowalski, Edward, Abingdon Press, 201 Eighth Ave S, Nashville, TN 37203-3919 *Tel:* 615-749-6290 (publicist); 615-749-6000; 615-749-6451 (sales) *Toll Free Tel:* 800-251-3320 *Fax:* 615-749-6056 *Web Site:* www.abingdonpress.com, pg 3

Kowit, Mary, Blue Dove Press, 4204 Sorrento Valley Blvd, Suite K, San Diego, CA 92121 *Tel:* 858-623-3330 *Toll Free Tel:* 800-691-1008 (orders) *Fax:* 858-623-3325 *E-mail:* mail@bluedove.org *Web Site:* www.bluedove.org, pg 41

Koyanis, Melinda, Harvard University Press, 79 Garden St, Cambridge, MA 02138-1499 *Tel:* 617-495-2600; 401-531-2800 (international orders) *Toll Free Tel:* 800-405-1619 (orders) *Fax:* 617-495-5898 (general); 617-496-4677 (edit & rts); 401-531-2801 (international orders) *Toll Free Fax:* 800-406-9145 (orders) *E-mail:* firstname_lastname@harvard.edu *Web Site:* www.hup.harvard.edu, pg 117

Kozlova, Sonya, Emerging Playwright Award, 17 E 47 St, New York, NY 10017 *Tel:* 212-421-1380 *Fax:* 212-421-1387 *E-mail:* urbanstage@aol.com *Web Site:* www.urbanstages.org, pg 772

Kozlowski, Paul, Random House Sales & Marketing, 1745 Broadway, New York, NY 10019 *Fax:* 212-782-9000, pg 227

Kozodoy, Ruth, The Metropolitan Museum of Art, 1000 Fifth Ave, New York, NY 10028 *Tel:* 212-879-5500; 212-535-7710 *Fax:* 212-396-5062 *E-mail:* info@metmuseum.org *Web Site:* www.metmuseum.org, pg 173

Kraas, Ashley, Kraas Literary Agency, 13514 Winter Creek Ct, Houston, TX 77077 *Tel:* 281-870-9770 *Fax:* 281-870-9770 *Web Site:* www.kraasliterarygency.com, pg 639

Kraas, Irene, Kraas Literary Agency, 13514 Winter Creek Ct, Houston, TX 77077 *Tel:* 281-870-9770 *Fax:* 281-870-9770 *Web Site:* www.kraasliterarygency.com, pg 639

Kracht, Peter, Greenwood Publishing Group Inc, 88 Post Rd W, Westport, CT 06880-4208 *Tel:* 203-226-3571 *Toll Free Tel:* 800-225-5800 *Fax:* 203-222-1502 *E-mail:* bookinfo@greenwood.com (general); firstintial&fulllastname@greenwood.com (individuals) *Web Site:* www.greenwood.com, pg 109

Kraft, Eric, Kraft & Kraft, 100 Fourth Ave S, Suite 201, St Petersburg, FL 33701 *Tel:* 727-821-1627 *Web Site:* www.erickraft.com/kraftkraft, pg 604

Kraft, Madeline, Kraft & Kraft, 100 Fourth Ave S, Suite 201, St Petersburg, FL 33701 *Tel:* 727-821-1627 *Web Site:* www.erickraft.com/kraftkraft, pg 604

Kraft, Wolfgang, EMC/Paradigm Publishing, 875 Montreal Way, St Paul, MN 55102 *Tel:* 651-290-2800 (corp) *Toll Free Tel:* 800-328-1452 *Fax:* 651-290-2899 *Toll Free Fax:* 800-328-4564 *E-mail:* educate@emcp.com *Web Site:* www.emcp.com, pg 90

Kral, David M, Soil Science Society of America, 677 S Segoe Rd, Madison, WI 53711-1086 *Tel:* 608-273-8095 *Fax:* 608-273-2021 *E-mail:* headquarters@soils.org *Web Site:* www.soils.org, pg 252

Kramer, Gary, Temple University Press, 1601 N Broad St, 083-42, USB Room 306, Philadelphia, PA 19122-6099 *Tel:* 215-204-8787 *Toll Free Tel:* 800-447-1656 *Fax:* 215-204-4719 *E-mail:* tempress@temple.edu *Web Site:* www.temple.edu/tempress, pg 266

Kramer, H J, H J Kramer Inc, PO Box 1082, Tiburon, CA 94920-7002 *Tel:* 415-435-5367 *Fax:* 415-435-5364 *E-mail:* hjkramer@jps.net *Web Site:* www.newworldlibrary.com, pg 147

Kramer, Jill, Hay House Inc, 2776 Loker Ave W, Carlsbad, CA 92008 *Tel:* 760-431-7695 *Toll Free Tel:* 800-650-5115; 800-654-5126 (orders) *Fax:* 760-431-6948 *E-mail:* info@hayhouse.com *Web Site:* www.hayhouse.com, pg 118

Kramer, Jill, University of Alabama Press, Box 870380, Tuscaloosa, AL 35487-0380 *Tel:* 205-348-5180; 773-702-7000 (orders) *Fax:* 205-348-9201 *Web Site:* www.uapress.ua.edu, pg 280

Kramer, Linda, H J Kramer Inc, PO Box 1082, Tiburon, CA 94920-7002 *Tel:* 415-435-5367 *Fax:* 415-435-5364 *E-mail:* hjkramer@jps.net *Web Site:* www.newworldlibrary.com, pg 147

Kramer, Sarah, IEE, c/o Inspec, 379 Thornall St, Edison, NJ 08837-2225 *Tel:* 732-321-5575 *Fax:* 732-321-5702 *E-mail:* iee@inspecinc.com *Web Site:* www.iee.org/publishing, pg 130

Kramer, Sidney B, Mews Books Ltd, 20 Bluewater Hill, Westport, CT 06880 *Tel:* 203-227-1836 *Fax:* 203-227-1144 *E-mail:* mewsbooks@aol.com, pg 644

Kramer, Sydelle, Frances Goldin Literary Agency, Inc, 57 E 11 St, Suite 5B, New York, NY 10003 *Tel:* 212-777-0047 *Fax:* 212-228-1660 *E-mail:* agency@goldinlit.com *Web Site:* www.goldinlit.com, pg 632

Krames, Jeffrey, Professional Publishing, 1333 Burr Ridge Pkwy, Burr Ridge, IL 60527 *Tel:* 630-789-4000; 630-789-5500 *Toll Free Tel:* 800-2McGraw (262-4729) *Fax:* 630-789-6933 *Web Site:* www.books.mcgraw-hill.com, pg 220

Kranabetter, Karen, Wood Lake Books Inc, 9025 Jim Bailey Rd, Kelowna, BC V4V 1R2, Canada *Tel:* 250-766-2778 *Toll Free Tel:* 800-663-2775 (orders) *Fax:* 250-766-2736 *Toll Free Fax:* 888-841-9991 (orders) *E-mail:* info@woodlake.com *Web Site:* www.woodlakebooks.com, pg 567

Krannich, Ronald, Impact Publications, 9104 Manassas Dr, Suite N, Manassas Park, VA 20111-5211 *Tel:* 703-361-7300 *Fax:* 703-335-9486 *E-mail:* info@impactpublications.com *Web Site:* www.impactpublications.com; www.ishoparoundtheworld.com, pg 131

Krattenmaker, Kathleen, Philadelphia Museum of Art, 2525 Pennsylvania Ave, Philadelphia, PA 19130 *Tel:* 215-684-7250 *Fax:* 215-235-8715 *Web Site:* www.philamuseum.org, pg 211

Kraus, Donald, Oxford University Press, Inc, 198 Madison Ave, New York, NY 10016-4314 *Tel:* 212-726-6000 *Toll Free Tel:* 800-451-7556 (orders) *Web Site:* www.oup.com/us, pg 200

Kraus, Maribeth T, Modern Language Association of America (MLA), 26 Broadway, 3rd fl, New York, NY 10004-1789 *Tel:* 646-576-5000 *Fax:* 646-458-0030 *E-mail:* info@mla.org *Web Site:* www.mla.org, pg 176

Kraus, Maribeth T, Modern Language Association of America (MLA), 26 Broadway, 3rd fl, New York, NY 10004-1789 *Tel:* 646-576-5000 *Fax:* 646-458-0030 *E-mail:* convention@mla.org *Web Site:* www.mla.org, pg 691

Kraus, Marisa Smith, Smith & Kraus Inc Publishers, 177 Lyme Rd, Hanover, NH 03755 *Tel:* 603-643-6431 (edit); 603-669-7032 (cust serv) *Toll Free Tel:* 800-288-2881 (orders only) *Fax:* 603-643-1831 *E-mail:* sandk@sover.net *Web Site:* www.smithkraus.com, pg 250

Krause, Bill, Antique Trader Books, c/o Krause Publications, 700 E State St, Iola, WI 54990-0001 *Tel:* 715-445-2214 *Toll Free Tel:* 888-457-2873 *Fax:* 715-445-4087 *Web Site:* www.krause.com, pg 20

Krause, Bill, DBI Books, 700 E State St, Iola, WI 54990-0001 *Tel:* 715-445-2214 *Toll Free Tel:* 888-457-2873 *Fax:* 715-445-4087 *Web Site:* www.krause.com, pg 77

Krause, Bill, Krause Publications, 700 E State St, Iola, WI 54990 *Tel:* 715-445-4612 ext 365 *Toll Free Tel:* 800-258-0929; 888-457-2873 *Fax:* 715-445-4087 *Web Site:* www.krause.com, pg 147

Krause, Bruce, Homestore Plans & Publications, 213 E Fourth St, Suite 400, St Paul, MN 55101 *Tel:* 651-602-5000 *Toll Free Tel:* 888-626-2026 *Fax:* 651-602-5001 *Web Site:* homeplans.com, pg 125

Krause, Chester L, Krause Publications, 700 E State St, Iola, WI 54990 *Tel:* 715-445-4612 ext 365 *Toll Free Tel:* 800-258-0929; 888-457-2873 *Fax:* 715-445-4087 *Web Site:* www.krause.com, pg 147

Krause, Helgard K, Rockport Publishers, 33 Commercial St, Gloucester, MA 01930 *Tel:* 978-282-9590 *Fax:* 978-283-2742 *Web Site:* www.rockpub.com, pg 233

Krause, Mike, Bollix Books, 1609 W Callender Ave, Peoria, IL 61606 *Tel:* 309-453-4903 *Fax:* 309-676-6558 *E-mail:* editor@bollixbooks.com *Web Site:* www.bollixbooks.com, pg 43

Krause, Staley, Bollix Books, 1609 W Callender Ave, Peoria, IL 61606 *Tel:* 309-453-4903 *Fax:* 309-676-6558 *E-mail:* editor@bollixbooks.com *Web Site:* www.bollixbooks.com, pg 43

Krauss, Pamela, Clarkson Potter Publishers, 1745 Broadway, New York, NY 10019 *Tel:* 212-782-9000 *Toll Free Tel:* 888-264-1745 *Fax:* 212-572-6181 *Web Site:* www.clarksonpotter.com; www.randomhouse.com/crown/clarksonpotter, pg 63

Krausz, Keira, Reader's Digest General Books, Reader's Digest Rd, Pleasantville, NY 10570-7000 *Tel:* 914-238-1000 *Toll Free Tel:* 800-431-1726 *Fax:* 914-244-7436, pg 228

Kraut, Diane, DK Research Inc, 14 Mohegan Lane, Commack, NY 11725 *Tel:* 631-543-5537 *Fax:* 631-543-5549, pg 596

Kravitz, James, American Showcase Inc, 915 Broadway, New York, NY 10010 *Tel:* 212-673-6600 *Toll Free Tel:* 800-894-7469 *Fax:* 212-673-9795 *E-mail:* info@amshow.com *Web Site:* www.amshow.com, pg 17

Kravitz, Richard H, Aspen Publishers, A Wolters Kluwer Company, 1185 Avenue of the Americas, New York, NY 10036 *Tel:* 212-597-0200 *Toll Free Tel:* 800-234-1660 (cust serv); 800-447-1717 (orders); 800-950-5259 (legal educ); 800-LAW-PLGL (paralegal textbook); 800-317-3113 (bookstore sales); 800-364-2512 (Loislaw) *Web Site:* www.aspenpublishers.com, pg 26

Krayson, Allan E, Bancroft-Sage Publishing, 3943 Meadowbrook Rd, Minneapolis, MN 55426 *Tel:* 952-938-9330 *Toll Free Tel:* 800-846-7027 *Fax:* 952-938-7353 *E-mail:* feedback@finney-hobar.com *Web Site:* www.finney-hobar.com, pg 31

Krebs, Gary M, Adams Media, An F+W Publications Co, 57 Littlefield St, 2nd fl, Avon, MA 02322 *Tel:* 508-427-7100 *Fax:* 508-427-6790 *Toll Free Fax:* 800-872-5628 *E-mail:* authors@adamsmedia.com; orders@adamsmedia.com *Web Site:* www.adamsmedia.com, pg 5

Kregel, James R, Editorial Portavoz, 733 Wealthy St SE, Grand Rapids, MI 49503-5553 *Tel:* 616-451-4775 *Toll Free Tel:* 800-733-2607 *Fax:* 616-451-9330 *E-mail:* portavoz@portavoz.com *Web Site:* www.kregel.com; www.portavoz.com, pg 87

Kregel, James R, Kregel Publications, 733 Wealthy St SE, Grand Rapids, MI 49503-5553 *Tel:* 616-451-4775 *Toll Free Tel:* 800-733-2607 *Fax:* 616-451-9330 *E-mail:* kregelbooks@kregel.com *Web Site:* www.kregelpublications.com, pg 147

Kregel, Jerold W, Kregel Publications, 733 Wealthy St SE, Grand Rapids, MI 49503-5553 *Tel:* 616-451-4775 *Toll Free Tel:* 800-733-2607 *Fax:* 616-451-9330 *E-mail:* kregelbooks@kregel.com *Web Site:* www.kregelpublications.com, pg 147

Kreit, Eileen, Puffin Books, 345 Hudson St, New York, NY 10014 *Tel:* 212-366-2000 *E-mail:* online@penguinputnam.com *Web Site:* www.penguin.com, pg 222

Krell, Henry, Springer-Verlag New York Inc, 175 Fifth Ave, New York, NY 10010 *Tel:* 212-460-1500 *Toll Free Tel:* 800-777-4643 *Fax:* 212-473-6272 *Web Site:* www.springer-ny.com, pg 256

Kremer, John, Open Horizons Publishing Co, PO Box 205, Fairfield, IA 52556-0205 *Tel:* 641-472-6130 *Toll Free Tel:* 800-796-6130 *Fax:* 641-472-1560 *E-mail:* info@bookmarket.com *Web Site:* www.bookmarket.com, pg 197

Krempa, Julie, Baywood Publishing Co Inc, 26 Austin Ave, Amityville, NY 11701 *Tel:* 631-691-1270 *Toll Free Tel:* 800-638-7819 *Fax:* 631-691-1770 *E-mail:* baywood@baywood.com *Web Site:* www.baywood.com, pg 33

Kress, Rick, William Carey Library, PO Box 40129, Pasadena, CA 91114-7129 *Tel:* 626-798-0819 *Toll Free Tel:* 866-732-6657 *E-mail:* publishing@wclbooks.com *Web Site:* www.wclbooks.com, pg 53

Kress, Steven, The Pennsylvania State University Press, 820 N University Dr, University Support Bldg 1, Suite C, University Park, PA 16802-1003 *Tel:* 814-865-1327 *Toll Free Tel:* 800-326-9180 *Fax:* 814-863-1408 *Toll Free Fax:* 877 7782665 *Web Site:* www.psupress.org, pg 209

Kretschmer, Doris, University of California Press, 2120 Berkeley Way, Berkeley, CA 94720 *Tel:* 510-642-4247 *Toll Free Tel:* 800-777-4726 *Fax:* 510-643-7127 *Toll Free Fax:* 800-999-1958 *E-mail:* askucp@ucpress.edu *Web Site:* www.ucpress.edu, pg 281

Kretzer, Marilyn, Sterling Publishing Co Inc, 387 Park Ave S, 5th fl, New York, NY 10016-8810 *Tel:* 212-532-7160 *Toll Free Tel:* 800-367-9692 *Fax:* 212-213-2495 *Web Site:* www.sterlingpub.com, pg 259

Kretzschmer, Karla, Thomson Gale, 27500 Drake Rd, Farmington Hills, MI 48331-3535 *Tel:* 248-699-4253 *Toll Free Tel:* 800-347-4253 *Fax:* 248-699-8070 *Toll Free Fax:* 800-414-5043 *E-mail:* galeord@gale.com *Web Site:* www.gale.com, pg 270

Krieger, Abe, Current Medicine, 400 Market St, Suite 700, Philadelphia, PA 19106 *Tel:* 215-574-2266 *Toll Free Tel:* 800-427-1796 *Fax:* 215-574-2270 *E-mail:* info@phl.cursci.com, pg 75

Krieger, Donald E, Krieger Publishing Co, PO Box 9542, Melbourne, FL 32902-9542 *Tel:* 321-724-9542 *Toll Free Tel:* 800-724-0025 *Fax:* 321-951-3671 *E-mail:* info@krieger-publishing.com *Web Site:* www.krieger-publishing.com, pg 147

Krieger, Ellen, Simon & Schuster Children's Publishing, 1230 Avenue of the Americas, New York, NY 10020 *Tel:* 212-698-7000 *Web Site:* www.simonsayskids.com, pg 248

Krieger, Maxine D, Krieger Publishing Co, PO Box 9542, Melbourne, FL 32902-9542 *Tel:* 321-724-9542 *Toll Free Tel:* 800-724-0025 *Fax:* 321-951-3671 *E-mail:* info@krieger-publishing.com *Web Site:* www.krieger-publishing.com, pg 147

Krieger, Robert E, Krieger Publishing Co, PO Box 9542, Melbourne, FL 32902-9542 *Tel:* 321-724-9542 *Toll Free Tel:* 800-724-0025 *Fax:* 321-951-3671 *E-mail:* info@krieger-publishing.com *Web Site:* www.krieger-publishing.com, pg 147

Krier, Nicole, Theosophical Publishing House/Quest Books, 306 W Geneva Rd, Wheaton, IL 60187 *Tel:* 630-665-0130 *Toll Free Tel:* 800-669-9425 *Fax:* 630-665-8791 *E-mail:* questbooks@theosmail.net *Web Site:* www.questbooks.com, pg 268

Krijgsman, Alexandra, Random House Publishing Group, 1745 Broadway, New York, NY 10019 *Toll Free Tel:* 800-200-3552 *Toll Free Fax:* 800-200-3552 *Web Site:* www.randomhouse.com, pg 227

Krinsky, Santosh, Lotus Press, PO Box 325, Twin Lakes, WI 53181-0325 *Tel:* 262-889-8561 *Toll Free Tel:* 800-824-6396 (orders only) *Fax:* 262-889-8591 *E-mail:* lotuspress@lotuspress.com *Web Site:* www.lotuspress.com, pg 159

Krische, Hildegard, The Wilshire Literary Agency, 20 Barristers Walk, Dennis, MA 02638 *Tel:* 508-385-5200, pg 661

Krishock, David, Scholastic Inc, 557 Broadway, New York, NY 10012 *Tel:* 212-343-4469 *Toll Free Tel:* 800-scholastic *Fax:* 212-343-6930 *Web Site:* www.scholastic.com, pg 242

Krisko, Marla, Scholastic Canada Ltd, 175 Hillmount Rd, Markham, ON L6C 1Z7, Canada *Tel:* 905-887-7323 *Toll Free Tel:* 800-268-3848 (Canada) *Fax:* 905-887-1131 *Toll Free Fax:* 800-387-4944; 866-346-1288 *Web Site:* www.scholastic.ca, pg 560

Kritzer, Eddie, EKP Productions Inc, 8484 Wilshire Blvd, Suite 205, Beverly Hills, CA 90211 *Tel:* 323-655-5696 *Fax:* 323-655-5173 *E-mail:* producedby@aol.com *Web Site:* eddiekritzer.com, pg 669

Kroffe, Kerry, Association of American University Presses, 1427 E 60 St, Chicago, IL 60637 *Tel:* 773-702-7700; 773-702-7600 *Toll Free Tel:* 800-621-2736 (orders) *Fax:* 773-702-9756 (sales); 773-660-2235 (orders); 773-702-2708 *E-mail:* general@press.uchicago.edu *Web Site:* www.press.uchicago.edu, pg 26

Kroll, Edite, Edite Kroll Literary Agency Inc, 12 Grayhurst Park, Portland, ME 04102 *Tel:* 207-773-4922 *Fax:* 207-773-3936, pg 639

Kroll, Jonathan, Libra Publishers Inc, 3089-C Clairemont Dr, PMB 383, San Diego, CA 92117 *Tel:* 858-571-1414 *Fax:* 858-571-1414, pg 154

Kroll, Judith, University of Texas at Austin, Creative Writing Program, Dept of English, One University Sta, B5000, Austin, TX 78712-1164 *Tel:* 512-475-6356 *Fax:* 512-471-2898 *Web Site:* www.en.utexas.edu/grad/crwconc.html, pg 756

Kroll, William, Libra Publishers Inc, 3089-C Clairemont Dr, PMB 383, San Diego, CA 92117 *Tel:* 858-571-1414 *Fax:* 858-571-1414, pg 154

Kromback, Serena Leigh, Lexington Books, 4501 Forbes Blvd, Lanham, MD 20706 *Tel:* 301-459-3366 *Fax:* 301-429-5748 *Web Site:* www.lexingtonbooks.com, pg 153

Kronzek, Lynn C, Lynn C Kronzek & Richard A Flom, 145 S Glenoaks Blvd, Suite 240, Burbank, CA 91502 *Tel:* 818-843-2625 *E-mail:* lckronzek@earthlink.net, pg 604

Kroupa, Melanie, Farrar, Straus & Giroux Books for Young Readers, 19 Union Sq W, New York, NY 10003 *Tel:* 212-741-6900 *Fax:* 212-633-2427 *E-mail:* childrens.marketing@fsgbooks.com; childrens.editorial@fsgbooks.com *Web Site:* www.fsgkidsbooks.com, pg 95

Krueger, Jo Ann, The Aaland Agency, PO Box 849, Inyokern, CA 93527-0849 *Tel:* 760-384-3910 *Fax:* 760-384-4435 *Web Site:* www.the-aaland-agency.com, pg 617

Kruger, Leanne Flett, Theytus Books Ltd, Lot 45, Green Mountain Rd, RR No 2, Site 50, Comp 8, Penticton, BC V2A 6J7, Canada *Tel:* 250-493-7181 *Fax:* 250-493-5302 *E-mail:* theytusbooks@vip.net *Web Site:* www.theytusbooks.ca, pg 563

Kruger, Linda M, The Fogelman Literary Agency, 7515 Greenville Ave, Suite 712, Dallas, TX 75231 *Tel:* 214-361-9956 *Fax:* 214-361-9553 *E-mail:* info@fogelman.com *Web Site:* www.fogelman.com, pg 630

Krule, Lawrence, Jewish Book Council, 15 E 26 St, 10th fl, New York, NY 10010-1579 *Tel:* 212-532-4949 (ext 297) *Fax:* 212-481-4174 *E-mail:* jbc@jewishbooks.org *Web Site:* www.jewishbookcouncil.org, pg 689

Krumpfer, Jorie, W W Norton & Company Inc, 500 Fifth Ave, New York, NY 10110-0017 *Tel:* 212-354-5500 *Toll Free Tel:* 800-233-4830 (orders & cust serv) *Fax:* 212-869-0856 *Toll Free Fax:* 800-458-6515 *Web Site:* www.wwnorton.com, pg 194

Krup, Agnes, The Karpfinger Agency, 357 W 20 St, New York, NY 10011-3379 *Tel:* 212-691-2690 *Fax:* 212-691-7129, pg 637

Krupp, Michael R, Acropolis Books Inc, 8601 Dunwoody Place, Suite 303, Atlanta, GA 30350 *Tel:* 770-643-1118 *Toll Free Tel:* 800-773-9923 *Fax:* 770-643-1170 *E-mail:* acropolisbooks@mindspring.com *Web Site:* www.acropolisbooks.com, pg 569

Krusi, Beth, Appalachian Mountain Club Books, 5 Joy St, Boston, MA 02108 *Tel:* 617-523-0655 *Fax:* 617-523-0722 *Web Site:* www.outdoors.org, pg 21

Kruszynski, Rob, Raven Tree Press LLC, 200 S Washington St, Suite 306, Green Bay, WI 54301 *Tel:* 920-438-1605 *Toll Free Tel:* 877-256-0579 *Fax:* 920-438-1607 *E-mail:* raven@raventreepress.com *Web Site:* www.raventreepress.com, pg 228

Krysan, Alan, Anacus Press, 3943 Meadowbrook Rd, Minneapolis, MN 55426-4505 *Tel:* 952-938-9330 *Toll Free Tel:* 800-846-7027 *Fax:* 952-938-7353 *E-mail:* feedback@finney-hobar.com *Web Site:* www.anacus.com, pg 19

Kubik, John Milan, Foto Expression International (Toronto), 27 Saint Clair Ave E, Suite 1268, Toronto, ON M4T 2P4, Canada *Tel:* 705-745-5770 *Fax:* 705-745-9459 *E-mail:* operations@fotopressnews.org *Web Site:* www.fotopressnews.org, pg 666

Kucharczyk, Emily, Blackbirch Press®, 27500 Drake Rd, Farmington Hills, MI 48311-3535 *Toll Free Tel:* 800-877-4253 *Toll Free Fax:* 800-414-5043 (orders) *E-mail:* galeord@gale.com; customerservice@gale.com *Web Site:* www.gale.com, pg 40

Kuciak, Michael, AEI (Atchity Editorial/Entertainment International Inc), 9601 Wilshire Blvd, No 1202, Beverly Hills, CA 90210 *Tel:* 323-932-0407 *Fax:* 323-932-0321 *E-mail:* submissions@aeionline.com *Web Site:* www.aeionline.com, pg 618

Kuehl, Kathy, The Guilford Press, 72 Spring St, New York, NY 10012 *Tel:* 212-431-9800 *Toll Free Tel:* 800-365-7006 (orders) *Fax:* 212-966-6708 *E-mail:* orders@guilford.com *Web Site:* www.guilford.com, pg 111

Kuhne, Dave, Betsy Colquitt Award for Poetry, TCU Box 297700, Fort Worth, TX 76129 *Tel:* 817-257-7240 *Fax:* 817-257-7709 *E-mail:* descant@tcu.edu *Web Site:* www.eng.tcu.edu/journals/descant/index.html, pg 768

Kuhne, Dave, O'Connor Prize for Fiction (Descant Publication), TCU Box 297700, Fort Worth, TX 76129 *Tel:* 817-257-7240 *Fax:* 817-257-7709 *E-mail:* descant@tcu.edu *Web Site:* www.eng.tcu.edu/journals/descant/index.html, pg 795

Kuka, Ronald, Phyllis Smart Young Poetry Prize & Chris O'Malley Fiction Prize, University of Wisconsin - English Dept, 7193 HCW, 600 N Park St, Madison, WI 53706 *Tel:* 608-263-0566 *E-mail:* madreview@mail.studentorg.wisc.edu *Web Site:* mendota.english.wisc.edu/~MadRev/main.html, pg 814

Kukkonen, Susie, Inscape Publishing, 6465 Wayzata Blvd, Suite 800, St Louis Park, MN 55426 *Tel:* 763-765-2222 *Fax:* 763-765-2277 *Web Site:* www.inscapepublishing.com, pg 134

Kulibert, Brenda, Explorers Guide Publishing, 4843 Apperson Dr, Rhinelander, WI 54501 *Tel:* 715-362-6029 *Toll Free Tel:* 800-487-6029 *E-mail:* comment@explorers-guide.com *Web Site:* www.explorers-guide.com, pg 93

Kulibert, Gary, Explorers Guide Publishing, 4843 Apperson Dr, Rhinelander, WI 54501 *Tel:* 715-362-6029 *Toll Free Tel:* 800-487-6029 *E-mail:* comment@explorers-guide.com *Web Site:* www.explorers-guide.com, pg 93

Kulick, John, Eckankar, PO Box 27300, Minneapolis, MN 55427 *Tel:* 952-380-2200 *Toll Free Tel:* 866-485-5556 (CN orders); 888-408-0301 (US orders) *Fax:* 952-380-2395 *Toll Free Fax:* 866-485-6665 (CN orders) *E-mail:* eckbooks@eckankar.org *Web Site:* www.eckankar.org, pg 86

Kulin, Joseph, Parabola Books, 656 Broadway, Suite 615, New York, NY 10012 *Tel:* 212-505-6200 *Toll Free Tel:* 800-560-6984 *Fax:* 212-979-7325 *E-mail:* parabola@panix.com *Web Site:* www.parabola.org, pg 203

Kulka, John, Yale Series of Younger Poets, 302 Temple St, New Haven, CT 06511 *Tel:* 203-432-0900 *Fax:* 203-432-2394; 203-432-0948 *Web Site:* www.yale.edu/yup/, pg 814

Kulka, John, Yale University Press, 302 Temple St, New Haven, CT 06511 *Tel:* 203-432-0960; 401-531-2800 (cust serv) *Toll Free Tel:* 800-405-1619 (cust serv) *Fax:* 203-432-0948; 401-531-2801 (cust serv) *Toll Free Fax:* 800-406-9145 (cust serv) *E-mail:* customer.care@trilateral.org (cust serv) *Web Site:* www.yale.edu/yup/, pg 305

Kull, Irene Imperio, Temple University Press, 1601 N Broad St, 083-42, USB Room 306, Philadelphia, PA 19122-6099 *Tel:* 215-204-8787 *Toll Free Tel:* 800-447-1656 *Fax:* 215-204-4719 *E-mail:* tempress@temple.edu *Web Site:* www.temple.edu/tempress, pg 266

Kull, Matthew, Temple University Press, 1601 N Broad St, 083-42, USB Room 306, Philadelphia, PA 19122-6099 *Tel:* 215-204-8787 *Toll Free Tel:* 800-447-1656 *Fax:* 215-204-4719 *E-mail:* tempress@temple.edu *Web Site:* www.temple.edu/tempress, pg 266

Kundert, Beth, McGraw-Hill/Dushkin, 2460 Kerper Blvd, Dubuque, IA 52001 *Toll Free Tel:* 800-243-6532 *Web Site:* www.dushkin.com, pg 167

Kundert, Beth, McGraw-Hill Primis Custom Publishing, 2460 Kerper Blvd, Dubuque, IA 52001 *Tel:* 563-588-1451 *Fax:* 563-589-4700 *E-mail:* first_last@mcgraw-hill.com *Web Site:* www.mhhe.com, pg 168

Kunjufu, Jawanza, African American Images, 1909 W 95 St, Chicago, IL 60643 *Tel:* 773-445-0322 *Toll Free Tel:* 800-552-1991 *Fax:* 773-445-9844 *E-mail:* customer@africanamericanimages.com *Web Site:* africanamericanimages.com, pg 6

Kunstling, Frances W, North Carolina Office of Archives & History, Historical Publ Sect, 4622 Mail Service Ctr, Raleigh, NC 27699-4622 *Tel:* 919-733-7442 *Fax:* 919-733-1439 *Web Site:* www.ncpublications.com, pg 192

Kuny, Greg, American Psychiatric Publishing Inc, 1000 Wilson Blvd, Suite 1825, Arlington, VA 22209 *Tel:* 703-907-7322 *Toll Free Tel:* 800-368-5777 *Fax:* 703-907-1091 *E-mail:* appi@psych.org *Web Site:* www.appi.org, pg 16

Kuong, Jay, Management Advisory Services & Publications (MASP), PO Box 81151, Wellesley Hills, MA 02481-0001 *Tel:* 781-235-2895 *Fax:* 781-235-5446 *Web Site:* www.masp.com, pg 161

Kuong, Richard, Management Advisory Services & Publications (MASP), PO Box 81151, Wellesley Hills, MA 02481-0001 *Tel:* 781-235-2895 *Fax:* 781-235-5446 *Web Site:* www.masp.com, pg 161

Kupetz, Marilyn, Teachers of English to Speakers of Other Languages Inc (TESOL), 700 S Washington St, Suite 200, Alexandria, VA 22314-4287 *Tel:* 703-836-0774 *Fax:* 703-836-7864 *E-mail:* info@tesol.org *Web Site:* www.tesol.org, pg 265

Kurdi, Paula, International Standard Book Numbering (ISBN) US Agency, A Cambridge Information Group Co, 630 Central Ave, New Providence, NJ 07974 *Toll Free Tel:* 877-310-7333 *Fax:* 908-219-0188 *E-mail:* ISBN-SAN@bowker.com *Web Site:* www.isbn.org, pg 689

Kurdyla, Edward, Scarecrow Press/Government Institutes Div, 4501 Forbes Blvd, Suite 200, Lanham, MD 20706 *Tel:* 301-921-2300 *Fax:* 301-429-5747 *Web Site:* govinst.scarecrowpress.com, pg 240

Kurdyla, Edward, Scarecrow Press Inc, 4501 Forbes Blvd, Suite 200, Lanham, MD 20706 *Tel:* 301-459-3366 *Toll Free Tel:* 800-462-6420 *Fax:* 301-429-5747 *Toll Free Fax:* 800-338-4550 *Web Site:* www.scarecrowpress.com, pg 241

Kurian, George, International Encyclopedia Society, PO Box 519, Baldwin Place, NY 10505-0519 *Tel:* 914-962-3287 *Fax:* 914-962-3287 *Web Site:* encyclopediasociety.com, pg 688

Kurian, George, George Kurian Reference Books, PO Box 519, Baldwin Place, NY 10505-0519 *Tel:* 914-962-3287 *Fax:* 914-962-3287 *Web Site:* www.encyclopediasociety.com, pg 148

Kuris, Gary, Greenwood Publishing Group Inc, 88 Post Rd W, Westport, CT 06880-4208 *Tel:* 203-226-3571 *Toll Free Tel:* 800-225-5800 *Fax:* 203-222-1502 *E-mail:* bookinfo@greenwood.com (general); firstintial&fulllastname@greenwood.com (individuals) *Web Site:* www.greenwood.com, pg 109

Kurklis, Jackie, The Fairmont Press Inc, 700 Indian Trail, Lilburn, GA 30047 *Tel:* 770-925-9388 *Fax:* 770-381-9865 *Web Site:* www.fairmontpress.com, pg 94

Kurman, Raymond, JB Communications Inc, 101 W 55 St, Suite 2-D, New York, NY 10019 *Tel:* 212-246-0900 *Fax:* 212-246-2114, pg 140

Kurman, Raymond, Rights Unlimited Inc, 101 W 55 St, Suite 2D, New York, NY 10019 *Tel:* 212-246-0900 *Fax:* 212-246-2114 *E-mail:* faith@rightsunlimited.com *Web Site:* rightsunlimited.com, pg 651

Kurmey, Bev, City of Toronto Book Award, Protocol Office, 100 Queen St W, 10th fl, West Tower, Toronto, ON M5H 2N2, Canada *Tel:* 416-392-8191 *Fax:* 416-392-1247, pg 767

Kurst, Charlotte A, Cornell Maritime Press Inc, PO Box 456, Centreville, MD 21617 *Tel:* 410-758-1075 *Toll Free Tel:* 800-638-7641 *Fax:* 410-758-6849 *E-mail:* editor@cornellmaritimepress.com *Web Site:* www.cornellmaritimepress.com, pg 68

Kurst, Charlotte A, Tidewater Publishers, 101 Water Way, Centreville, MD 21617 *Tel:* 410-758-1075 *Toll Free Tel:* 800-638-7641 *Fax:* 410-758-6849 *E-mail:* editor@cornellmaritimepress.com *Web Site:* www.tidewaterpublishrs.com, pg 271

Kurtz, Gretchen, Prometheus Books, 59 John Glenn Dr, Amherst, NY 14228 *Tel:* 716-691-0133 *Toll Free Tel:* 800-421-0351 *Fax:* 716-691-0137 *E-mail:* marketing@prometheusbooks.com; editorial@prometheusbooks.com *Web Site:* www.Prometheusbooks.com, pg 220

Kurtz, Jill M, Our Sunday Visitor Publishing, 200 Noll Plaza, Huntington, IN 46750 *Tel:* 260-356-8400 *Toll Free Tel:* 800-348-2440 (orders) *Fax:* 260-356-8472 *Toll Free Fax:* 800-498-6709 *E-mail:* osvbooks@osv.com *Web Site:* www.osv.com, pg 200

Kurtz, Jonathan, Prometheus Books, 59 John Glenn Dr, Amherst, NY 14228 *Tel:* 716-691-0133 *Toll Free Tel:* 800-421-0351 *Fax:* 716-691-0137 *E-mail:* marketing@prometheusbooks.com; editorial@prometheusbooks.com *Web Site:* www.Prometheusbooks.com, pg 220

Kurtz, Louise, Artabras Inc, 116 W 23 St, Suite 500, New York, NY 10011 *Tel:* 646-375-2039 *Toll Free Tel:* 800-ART-BOOK *Fax:* 646-375-2040 *E-mail:* abbeville@abbeville.com *Web Site:* www.abbeville.com, pg 24

Kurtz, Paul, Prometheus Books, 59 John Glenn Dr, Amherst, NY 14228 *Tel:* 716-691-0133 *Toll Free Tel:* 800-421-0351 *Fax:* 716-691-0137 *E-mail:* marketing@prometheusbooks.com; editorial@prometheusbooks.com *Web Site:* www.Prometheusbooks.com, pg 220

Kury, Gloria, The Pennsylvania State University Press, 820 N University Dr, University Support Bldg 1, Suite C, University Park, PA 16802-1003 *Tel:* 814-865-1327 *Toll Free Tel:* 800-326-9180 *Fax:* 814-863-1408 *Toll Free Fax:* 877 7782665 *Web Site:* www.psupress.org, pg 209

Kurz, Norman, Lowenstein-Yost Associates Inc, 121 W 27 St, Suite 601, New York, NY 10001 *Tel:* 212-206-1630 *Fax:* 212-727-0280 *Web Site:* www.lowensteinyost.com, pg 641

Kuyper, Mark, Evangelical Christian Publishers Association, 4816 S Ash Ave, Suite 101, Tempe, AZ 85282-7735 *Tel:* 480-966-3998 *Fax:* 480-966-1944 *E-mail:* info@ecpa.org *Web Site:* www.ecpa.org, pg 686

Kuyper, Mark, General Trade Publishing & Retailing, 4816 S Ash Ave, Suite 101, Tempe, AZ 85282-7735 *Tel:* 480-966-3998 *Fax:* 480-966-1944 *Web Site:* www.ecpa.org, pg 743

Kuyper, Mark, Gold Medallion Book Awards, 4816 S Ash Ave, Suite 101, Tempe, AZ 85282-7735 *Tel:* 480-966-3998 *Fax:* 480-966-1944 *Web Site:* www.ecpa.org, pg 776

Kuyper, Mark, Introducing ECPA Publishing University, 4816 S Ash Ave, Suite 101, Tempe, AZ 85282-7735 *Tel:* 480-966-3998 *Fax:* 480-966-1944 *Web Site:* www.ecpa.org, pg 744

Kwan, Andrea, University of British Columbia Press, 2029 West Mall, Vancouver, BC V6T 1Z2, Canada *Tel:* 604-822-5959 *Toll Free Tel:* 877-377-9378 *Fax:* 604-822-6083 *Toll Free Fax:* 800-668-0821 *E-mail:* info@ubcpress.ca *Web Site:* www.ubcpress.ca, pg 564

Kwan, Lai, Cheng & Tsui Co Inc, 25 West St, 5th fl, Boston, MA 02111-1213 *Tel:* 617-988-2401 *Toll Free Tel:* 800-554-1963 *Fax:* 617-426-3669 *E-mail:* service@cheng-tsui.com *Web Site:* www.cheng-tsui.com, pg 59

Kwoleck, Katherine, In Audio, PO Box 3168, Falls Church, VA 22043 *Tel:* 540-722-2535 *Toll Free Tel:* 800-643-0295 *Fax:* 540-722-0903 *E-mail:* commuterslib@worldnet.att.net *Web Site:* inaudio.biz, pg 132

Kye, Maura, Denise Marcil Literary Agency Inc, 156 Fifth Ave, Suite 625, New York, NY 10010 *Tel:* 212-337-3402 *Fax:* 212-727-2688, pg 642

Kyllo, Blaine, Arsenal Pulp Press Book Publishers Ltd, 1014 Homer St, Suite 103, Vancouver, BC V6B 2W9, Canada *Tel:* 604-687-4233 *Toll Free Tel:* 888-600-PULP (600-7857) *Fax:* 604-687-4283 *E-mail:* contact@arsenalpulp.com *Web Site:* www.arsenalpulp.com, pg 536

Kyriakodis, Harry, ALI-ABA Committee on Continuing Professional Education, 4025 Chestnut St, Philadelphia, PA 19104 *Tel:* 215-243-1600 *Toll Free Tel:* 800-CLE-NEWS *Fax:* 215-243-1664; 215-243-1683 *Web Site:* www.ali-aba.org, pg 8

Kyriakodis, Harry, American Law Institute, 4025 Chestnut St, Philadelphia, PA 19104-3099 *Tel:* 215-243-1600 *Toll Free Tel:* 800-253-6397 *Fax:* 215-243-1664; 215-243-1683 *Web Site:* www.ali.org, pg 15

Kyte, Robert, Pacific Press Publishing Association, 1350 N Kings Rd, Nampa, ID 83687-3193 *Tel:* 208-465-2500 *Toll Free Tel:* 800-447-7377 *Fax:* 208-465-2531 *Web Site:* www.pacificpress.com, pg 202

L'Abbe, Pierre, P D Meany Publishers, 71 Fermanagh Ave, Toronto, ON M6R 1M1, Canada *Tel:* 416-516-2903 *Fax:* 416-516-7632 *E-mail:* info@pdmeany.com *Web Site:* www.pdmeany.com, pg 554

L'Engle, Madeleine, The Authors League Fund, 31 E 28 St, New York, NY 10016 *Tel:* 212-268-1208 *Fax:* 212-564-5363 *E-mail:* authlgfund@aol.com *Web Site:* www.authorsleaguefund.org, pg 681

L'Heureux, Christine, Chouette Publishing, 4710 St Ambroise, Bureau 225, Montreal, PQ H4C 2C7, Canada *Tel:* 514-925-3325 *Toll Free Tel:* 877-926-3325 *Fax:* 514-925-3323 *E-mail:* info@editions-chouette.com *Web Site:* www.chouettepublishing.com, pg 540

La Borde, Meg, Greenleaf Book Group LLC, Longhorn Bldg, Suite 600, 3rd fl, 4425 Mopac S, Austin, TX 78735 *Tel:* 512-891-6100 *Toll Free Tel:* 800-932-5420 *Fax:* 512-891-6150 *E-mail:* email@greenleafbookgroup.com *Web Site:* www.greenleafbookgroup.com, pg 109

La Brie, Sandra, Kane/Miller Book Publishers, PO Box 8515, La Jolla, CA 92038-8515 *Tel:* 858-456-0540 *Toll Free Tel:* 800-968-1930 *Fax:* 858-456-9641 *E-mail:* info@kanemiller.com *Web Site:* www.kanemiller.com, pg 144

La Gasse, Robert, Garden Writers Association of America, 10210 Leatherleaf Ct, Manassas, VA 20111 *Tel:* 703-257-1032 *Fax:* 703-257-0213 *E-mail:* info@gwaa.org *Web Site:* www.gwaa.org, pg 687

La Liberte, Robert, Editions de l'Hexagone, 1010, rue de la Gauchetiere Est, Montreal, PQ H2L 2N5, Canada *Tel:* 514-523-1182 *Fax:* 514-282-7530 *E-mail:* vml@sogides.com *Web Site:* www.edhexagone.com, pg 544

La Mattina, Elaine, White Pine Press, PO Box 236, Buffalo, NY 14201-0236 *Tel:* 716-627-4665 *Fax:* 716-627-4665 *E-mail:* wpine@whitepine.org *Web Site:* www.whitepine.org, pg 298

La Montagne, Lisa, BoardSource, 1828 "L" St NW, Suite 900, Washington, DC 20036-5104 *Tel:* 202-452-6262 *Toll Free Tel:* 800-883-6262 *Fax:* 202-452-6299 *E-mail:* mail@boardsource.org *Web Site:* www.boardsource.org, pg 42

La Rosa, Suzanne, NewSouth Books, 105 S Court St, Montgomery, AL 36104 *Tel:* 334-834-3556 *Fax:* 334-834-3557 *E-mail:* info@newsouthbooks.com *Web Site:* www.newsouthbooks.com, pg 190

La Salle, Peter, University of Texas at Austin, Creative Writing Program, Dept of English, One University Sta, B5000, Austin, TX 78712-1164 *Tel:* 512-475-6356 *Fax:* 512-471-2898 *Web Site:* www.en.utexas.edu/grad/crwconc.html, pg 756

La Via, Carmen, Fifi Oscard Agency Inc, 110 W 40 St, New York, NY 10018 *Tel:* 212-764-1100 *Fax:* 212-840-5019 *E-mail:* agency@fifioscard.com *Web Site:* www.fifioscard.com, pg 647

Labbe, Eric, Les Publications du Quebec, 1500 rue Jean-Talon Nord, 1 etage, Ste Foy, PQ G1N 2E5, Canada *Tel:* 418-644-1342 *Toll Free Tel:* 800-463-2100 (Quebec province only) *Fax:* 418-644-7813 *E-mail:* service.clientele@mrci.gouv.qc.ca *Web Site:* www.publicationsduquebec.gouv.qc.ca, pg 559

Labbe, Stephan, Editions du Trecarre, 7 chemin Bates, Outremont, PQ H2V 4V7, Canada *Tel:* 514-270-6860 *Fax:* 514-276-2533 *E-mail:* edition@trecarre.com *Web Site:* www.total-publishing.com, pg 545

Labbe, Stephane, Editions Total Publishing, 7 Bates Rd, Outremont, PQ H2V 4A7, Canada *Tel:* 514-276-2520 *Fax:* 514-276-2533 *Web Site:* www.total-publishing.com, pg 545

Laberge, Marc, Editions du Trecarre, 7 chemin Bates, Outremont, PQ H2V 4V7, Canada *Tel:* 514-270-6860 *Fax:* 514-276-2533 *E-mail:* edition@trecarre.com *Web Site:* www.total-publishing.com, pg 545

Labrie, Roger, Simon & Schuster, 1230 Avenue of the Americas, New York, NY 10020 *Tel:* 212-698-7000 *Toll Free Tel:* 800-223-2348 (cust serv); 800-223-2336 (orders) *Toll Free Fax:* 800-943-9831 (orders) *Web Site:* www.simonsays.com, pg 248

Lachance, Yvon, Association des Libraires du Quebec, 1001, de Maisonneuve Est, Bureau 580, Montreal, PQ H2L 4P9, Canada *Tel:* 514-526-3349 *Fax:* 514-526-3340 *E-mail:* info@alq.qc.ca *Web Site:* www.alq.qc.ca, pg 679

Lachapelle, Jean, Editions Marie-France, 9900 avenue des Laurentides, Montreal-Nord, PQ H1H 4V1, Canada *Tel:* 514-329-3700 *Toll Free Tel:* 800-563-6644 *Fax:* 514-329-0630 *E-mail:* editions@marie-france.qc.ca *Web Site:* www.marie-france.qc.ca, pg 545

Lachina, Jeffrey A, Lachina Publishing Services Inc, 3793 S Green Rd, Beachwood, OH 44122 *Tel:* 216-292-7959 *Fax:* 216-292-3639 *Web Site:* www.lachina.com, pg 604

Lacombe, Joanne, Editions Marie-France, 9900 avenue des Laurentides, Montreal-Nord, PQ H1H 4V1, Canada *Tel:* 514-329-3700 *Toll Free Tel:* 800-563-6644 *Fax:* 514-329-0630 *E-mail:* editions@marie-france.qc.ca *Web Site:* www.marie-france.qc.ca, pg 545

Lacy, Andy, Quality Education Data, Inc, 1625 Broadway, Suite 250, Denver, CO 80202 *Tel:* 303-209-9400 *Toll Free Tel:* 800-525-5811 *Fax:* 303-209-9444 *E-mail:* info@qeddata.com *Web Site:* www.qeddata.com, pg 223

Lacy, Linda M, Carolina Academic Press, 700 Kent St, Durham, NC 27701 *Tel:* 919-489-7486 *Toll Free Tel:* 800-489-7486 *Fax:* 919-493-5668 *E-mail:* cap@cap-press.com *Web Site:* www.cap-press.com; www.caplaw.com, pg 54

Laddin, Michael O, Whitston Publishing Co Inc, 1717 Central Ave, Suite 201, Albany, NY 12205 *Tel:* 518-452-1900 *Toll Free Tel:* 877-571-1900 *Fax:* 518-452-1777 *E-mail:* whitston@capital.net *Web Site:* www.whitston.com, pg 298

LaFitte, Dwayne, Creative Book Publishing, 36 Austin St, St Johns, NF A1B 3T7, Canada *Tel:* 709-722-8500 *Toll Free Tel:* 877-722-1722 (Canada only) *Fax:* 709-579-7745 *E-mail:* nlbooks@transcontinental.ca *Web Site:* www.nfbooks.com, pg 541

Lafontaine, Monique, Centre Franco-Ontarien de Ressources en Alphabetisation, 432 Ave Westmount, Unit H, Sudbury, ON P3A 5Z8, Canada *Tel:* 705-524-3672 *Toll Free Tel:* 888-814-4422 (orders, Canada only) *Fax:* 705-524-8535 *E-mail:* info@centrefora.on.ca *Web Site:* www.centrefora.on.ca, pg 540

Lagos, N, Management Advisory Services & Publications (MASP), PO Box 81151, Wellesley Hills, MA 02481-0001 *Tel:* 781-235-2895 *Fax:* 781-235-5446 *Web Site:* www.masp.com, pg 161

Lance, Suzanne, New York State Writers Institute, University at Albany, New Library 320, Albany, NY 12222 *Tel:* 518-442-5620 *Fax:* 518-442-5621 *E-mail:* writers@uamail.albany.edu *Web Site:* www.albany.edu/writers-inst/, pg 745

Land, Dudley, McGraw-Hill Primis Custom Publishing, 2460 Kerper Blvd, Dubuque, IA 52001 *Tel:* 563-588-1451 *Fax:* 563-589-4700 *E-mail:* first_last@mcgraw-hill.com *Web Site:* www.mhhe.com, pg 168

Land, Robert D, Land on Demand, 20 Long Crescent Dr, Bristol, VA 24201 *Tel:* 276-642-1007; 423-366-0513 *Fax:* 760-437-4511 *E-mail:* landondemand@cs.com, pg 604

Landau, David, Pureplay Press, 11353 Missouri Ave, Los Angeles, CA 90025 *Tel:* 310-479-8773 *Toll Free Tel:* 800-247-6553 (orders only) *Fax:* 310-473-9384 *E-mail:* info@cubanovel.com *Web Site:* www.pureplaypress.com, pg 222

Landauer, Jeramy, Landauer Books, 12251 Maffitt Rd, Cumming, IA 50061 *Tel:* 515-287-2144 *Toll Free Tel:* 800-557-2144 *Fax:* 515-287-1530 *E-mail:* landaucor@aol.com, pg 148

Lande, Debra, Chronicle Books LLC, 85 Second St, 6th fl, San Francisco, CA 94105 *Tel:* 415-537-4200 *Toll Free Tel:* 800-722-6657 (cust serv) *Fax:* 415-537-4460 *Toll Free Fax:* 800-858-7787 (orders) *E-mail:* frontdesk@chroniclebooks.com *Web Site:* www.chroniclebooks.com, pg 61

Landes, Ronald, Landes Bioscience, 810 S Church St, Georgetown, TX 78626 *Tel:* 512-863-7762 *Toll Free Tel:* 800-736-9948 *Fax:* 512-863-0081 *Web Site:* www.landesbioscience.com, pg 148

Landesman, Cliff, W W Norton & Company Inc, 500 Fifth Ave, New York, NY 10110-0017 *Tel:* 212-354-5500 *Toll Free Tel:* 800-233-4830 (orders & cust serv) *Fax:* 212-869-0856 *Toll Free Fax:* 800-458-6515 *Web Site:* www.wwnorton.com, pg 193

Landoe, Gene, CCH Inc, 2700 Lake Cook Rd, Riverwoods, IL 60015 *Tel:* 847-267-7000 *Toll Free Tel:* 888-224-7377 *Web Site:* www.cch.com, pg 55

Landon, Hut, Northern California Independent Booksellers Association (NCIBA), 37 Graham St, San Francisco, CA 94129 *Tel:* 415-561-7686 *Fax:* 415-561-7685 *E-mail:* office@nciba.com *Web Site:* www.nciba.com, pg 696

Landow, Kalen, Publishers Association of the West, PO Box 18157, Denver, CO 80218 *Tel:* 303-447-2320 *Fax:* 303-279-7111 *E-mail:* executivedirector@pubwest.org *Web Site:* www.pubwest.org, pg 698

Landow, Kalen, Western US Book Design & Production Awards, 501 S Cherry St, Suite 320, Denver, CO 80246 *Tel:* 303-447-2320 *Fax:* 303-279-7111 *E-mail:* executivedirector@pubwest.org *Web Site:* www.pubwest.org, pg 811

Landrigan, John, University Press of New England, One Court St, Lebanon, NH 03766 *Tel:* 603-448-1533 *Toll Free Tel:* 800-421-1561 (orders only) *Fax:* 603-448-7006; 603-643-1540 *E-mail:* university.press@dartmouth.edu *Web Site:* www.upne.com, pg 287

Landrum, Sherrye, American Diabetes Association, 1701 N Beauregard St, Alexandria, VA 22311 *Tel:* 703-299-2046 *Toll Free Tel:* 800-232-6733 *Fax:* 908-806-2301 *Web Site:* www.diabetes.org, pg 13

Landskroener, Marcia, Sophie Kerr Prize, c/o College Relations Office, 300 Washington Ave, Chestertown, MD 21620 *Tel:* 410-778-2800 *Toll Free Tel:* 800-422-1782 *Fax:* 410-810-7150 *Web Site:* www.washcoll.edu, pg 806

Lane, Barbara, California Book Awards, 595 Market St, San Francisco, CA 94105 *Tel:* 415-597-6700 *Fax:* 415-597-6729 *E-mail:* bookawards@commonwealthclub.org *Web Site:* www.commonwealthclub.org/bookawards, pg 765

Lane, Edmund C, Alba House, 2187 Victory Blvd, Staten Island, NY 10314 *Tel:* 718-761-0047 (edit & prodn); 718-698-2759 (mktg & billing) *Toll Free Tel:* 800-343-2522 *Fax:* 718-761-0057 *E-mail:* albabooks@aol.com *Web Site:* www.albahouse.org, pg 7

Lane, George A, Loyola Press, 3441 N Ashland Ave, Chicago, IL 60657 *Tel:* 773-281-1818; 773-244-4429 *Toll Free Tel:* 800-621-1008 *Fax:* 773-281-0555; 773-281-0152 (trade) *E-mail:* editorial@loydapress.com *Web Site:* www.loyolapress.org, pg 159

Lane, Mary Ann, Harvard University Press, 79 Garden St, Cambridge, MA 02138-1499 *Tel:* 617-495-2600; 401-531-2800 (international orders) *Toll Free Tel:* 800-405-1619 (orders) *Fax:* 617-495-5898 (general); 617-496-4677 (edit & rts); 401-531-2801 (international orders) *Toll Free Fax:* 800-406-9145 (orders) *E-mail:* firstname_lastname@harvard.edu *Web Site:* www.hup.harvard.edu, pg 117

Lang, George, University of Pennsylvania Press, 4200 Pine St, Philadelphia, PA 19104-4011 *Tel:* 215-898-6261 *Toll Free Tel:* 800-445-9880 (orders & cust serv only) *Fax:* 215-898-0404; 410-516-6998 (orders) *E-mail:* custserv@pobox.upenn.edu *Web Site:* www.upenn.edu/pennpress, pg 284

Lang, Kathryn, Southern Methodist University Press, 314 Fondren Library W, 6404 Hill Top Lane, Dallas, TX 75275 *Tel:* 214-768-1430; 214-768-1432 *Fax:* 214-768-1428, pg 255

Lang, Kristin, Darhansoff, Verrill, Feldman Literary Agents, 236 W 26 St, Suite 802, New York, NY 10001-6736 *Tel:* 917-305-1300 *Fax:* 917-305-1400 *Web Site:* www.dvagency.com, pg 626

Langdon, Chic, Langdon Enterprises, 16902 N Hardesty, Colbert, WA 99005 *Tel:* 509-238-4745 *Fax:* 509-238-1181, pg 149

Langdon, Robert P, Children's Book Press, 2211 Mission St, San Francisco, CA 94110 *Tel:* 415-821-3080 *Fax:* 415-821-3081 *E-mail:* info@childrensbookpress.org *Web Site:* www.cbookpress.org, pg 60

Lange, April, W W Norton & Company Inc, 500 Fifth Ave, New York, NY 10110-0017 *Tel:* 212-354-5500 *Toll Free Tel:* 800-233-4830 (orders & cust serv) *Fax:* 212-869-0856 *Toll Free Fax:* 800-458-6515 *Web Site:* www.wwnorton.com, pg 193

Lange, Heide, Sanford J Greenburger Associates Inc, 55 Fifth Ave, 15th fl, New York, NY 10003 *Tel:* 212-206-5600 *Fax:* 212-463-8718 *Web Site:* www.greenburger.com, pg 633

Lange, Michael, McGraw-Hill Science, Engineering, Mathematics, 2460 Kerper Blvd, Dubuque, IA 52001 *Tel:* 563-588-1451 *Toll Free Tel:* 800-338-3987 (cust serv) *Fax:* 563-589-4700; 614-755-5645 (cust serv) *E-mail:* firstname_lastname@mcgraw-hill.com *Web Site:* www.mhhe.com, pg 169

Langeland, Dierdre, Marshall Cavendish Corp, 99 White Plains Rd, Tarrytown, NY 10591-9001 *Tel:* 914-332-8888 *Fax:* 914-332-1888 *E-mail:* mcc@marshallcavendish.com *Web Site:* www.marshallcavendish.com, pg 164

Langenfeld, Joseph, In Audio, PO Box 3168, Falls Church, VA 22043 *Tel:* 540-722-2535 *Toll Free Tel:* 800-643-0295 *Fax:* 540-722-0903 *E-mail:* commuterslib@worldnet.att.net *Web Site:* inaudio.biz, pg 132

Langenscheidt, Andreas, American Map Corp, 46-35 54 Rd, Maspeth, NY 11378 *Tel:* 718-784-0055 *Toll Free Tel:* 800-432-MAPS *Fax:* 718-784-0640 (admin); 718-784-1216 (sales & orders), pg 15

Langenscheidt, Andreas, Hagstrom Map Co Inc, 46-35 54 Rd, Maspeth, NY 11378 *Tel:* 718-784-0055 *Toll Free Tel:* 800-432-MAPS (432-6277) *Fax:* 718-784-0640 (admin); 718-784-1216 (sales & orders) *Web Site:* www.americanmap.com, pg 111

Langenscheidt, Andreas, Langenscheidt Publishers Inc, 46-35 54 Rd, Maspeth, NY 11378 *Tel:* 718-784-0055 *Toll Free Tel:* 800-432-MAPS (732-6277) *Fax:* 718-784-0640 *Toll Free Fax:* 888-773-7979 *E-mail:* sales@langenscheidt.com *Web Site:* www.langenscheidt.com, pg 149

Langenscheidt, Andreas, Trakker Maps Inc, 8350 Parkline Blvd, Suite 360, Orlando, FL 32809 *Tel:* 407-447-6485 *Toll Free Tel:* 800-327-3108 *Fax:* 407-447-6488 *E-mail:* sales@trakkermaps.com *Web Site:* www.trakkermaps.com, pg 273

Langenscheidt, Karl, Trakker Maps Inc, 8350 Parkline Blvd, Suite 360, Orlando, FL 32809 *Tel:* 407-447-6485 *Toll Free Tel:* 800-327-3108 *Fax:* 407-447-6488 *E-mail:* sales@trakkermaps.com *Web Site:* www.trakkermaps.com, pg 273

Langer, Dr Steven, Abbott, Langer & Associates, 548 First St, Crete, IL 60417 *Tel:* 708-672-4200 *Fax:* 708-672-4674 *E-mail:* sales@abbott-langer.com *Web Site:* www.abbott-langer.com, pg 2

Langford, Jeff, International Publishing Management Association (IPMA), 1205 W College St, Liberty, MO 64068-3733 *Tel:* 816-781-1111 *Fax:* 816-781-2790 *E-mail:* ipmainfo@ipma.org *Web Site:* www.ipma.org, pg 689

Langhammer Law, Lee, Davies-Black Publishing, 3803 E Bayshore Rd, Palo Alto, CA 94303 *Tel:* 650-969-8901 *Toll Free Tel:* 800-624-1765 *Fax:* 650-623-9271 *Web Site:* www.daviesblack.com, pg 76

Langille, Donald, Palm Island Press, 411 Truman Ave, Key West, FL 33040 *Tel:* 305-294-7834 *Fax:* 305-296-3102 *E-mail:* pipress@earthlink.net *Web Site:* junekeith.com, pg 202

Langlois, Joanne, Andrew Mowbray Inc Publishers, PO Box 460, Lincoln, RI 02865-0460 *Tel:* 401-726-8011 *Toll Free Tel:* 800-999-4697 *Fax:* 401-726-8061 *E-mail:* service@manatarmbooks.com *Web Site:* www.manatarmbooks.com, pg 180

Langman, Joe, Schiffer Publishing Ltd, 4880 Lower Valley Rd, Atglen, PA 19310 *Tel:* 610-593-1777 *Fax:* 610-593-2002 *E-mail:* schifferbk@aol.com; schifferii@aol.com *Web Site:* schifferbooks.com, pg 241

Langstaff, Margaret, Literary Management Group Inc, 4238 Morriswood Dr, Nashville, TN 37204 *Tel:* 615-832-7231 *Fax:* 615-832-7231 *Web Site:* www.literarymanagementgroup.com; www.brucebarbour.com, pg 641

Langston, Jay, Stoeger Publishing Co, 17603 Indian Head Hwy, Suite 200, Accokeek, MD 20607 *Tel:* 301-283-6300 *Fax:* 301-283-6986, pg 260

Langston, John, University Press of Mississippi, 3825 Ridgewood Rd, Jackson, MS 39211-6492 *Tel:* 601-432-6205 *Toll Free Tel:* 800-737-7788 *Fax:* 601-432-6217 *E-mail:* press@ihl.state.ms.us *Web Site:* www.upress.state.ms.us, pg 287

Langton, Dawn, Training Resource Network Inc (T R N), PO Box 439, St Augustine, FL 32085-0439 *Tel:* 904-823-9800 (cust serv); 904-824-7121 (edit off) *Toll Free Tel:* 800-280-7010 (orders) *Fax:* 904-823-3554 *E-mail:* customerservice@trninc.com *Web Site:* www.trninc.com, pg 273

Lanigan, Julia, Humana Press, 999 Riverview Dr, Suite 208, Totowa, NJ 07512 *Tel:* 973-256-1699 *Fax:* 973-256-8341 *E-mail:* humana@humanapr.com *Web Site:* humanapress.com, pg 128

Lanigan, Thomas Sr, Humana Press, 999 Riverview Dr, Suite 208, Totowa, NJ 07512 *Tel:* 973-256-1699 *Fax:* 973-256-8341 *E-mail:* humana@humanapr.com *Web Site:* humanapress.com, pg 128

Lanigan, Thomas B Jr, Humana Press, 999 Riverview Dr, Suite 208, Totowa, NJ 07512 *Tel:* 973-256-1699 *Fax:* 973-256-8341 *E-mail:* humana@humanapr.com *Web Site:* humanapress.com, pg 128

Lankiewicz, Don, Holt, Rinehart and Winston, 10801 N MoPac Expy, Bldg 3, Austin, TX 78759 *Tel:* 512-721-7000 *Toll Free Tel:* 800-225-5425 (cust serv) *Fax:* 512-721-7833 (mktg); 512-721-7898 (edit) *Web Site:* www.hrw.com, pg 124

Lanoue, Marie Claude, Les Publications du Quebec, 1500 rue Jean-Talon Nord, 1 etage, Ste Foy, PQ G1N 2E5, Canada *Tel:* 418-644-1342 *Toll Free Tel:* 800-463-2100 (Quebec province only) *Fax:* 418-644-7813 *E-mail:* service.clientele@mrci.gouv.qc.ca *Web Site:* www.publicationsduquebec.gouv.qc.ca, pg 559

Lauer, Brett, Poetry Society of America (PSA), 15 Gramercy Park, New York, NY 10003 *Tel:* 212-254-9628 *Toll Free Tel:* 888-USA-POEM *Fax:* 212-673-2352 *Web Site:* www.poetrysociety.org, pg 697

Lauffer, Andy, Theosophical Publishing House/Quest Books, 306 W Geneva Rd, Wheaton, IL 60187 *Tel:* 630-665-0130 *Toll Free Tel:* 800-669-9425 *Fax:* 630-665-8791 *E-mail:* questbooks@theosmail.net *Web Site:* www.questbooks.net, pg 268

Laughlin, Matthew R, The Crossroad Publishing Company, 16 Penn Plaza, Suite 1550, New York, NY 10001 *Tel:* 212-868-1801 *Toll Free Tel:* 800-395-0690 (orders) *Fax:* 212-868-2171 *Toll Free Fax:* 800-462-6420 (orders) *E-mail:* ask@crossroadpublishing.com *Web Site:* www.crossroadpublishing.com, pg 73

Laughlin, Philip G, Cambridge University Press, 40 W 20 St, New York, NY 10011-4211 *Tel:* 212-924-3900 *Toll Free Tel:* 800-899-5222 *Fax:* 212-691-3239 *Web Site:* www.cambridge.org, pg 52

Laughman, Robert, Jane's Information Group, 110 N Royal St, Suite 200, Alexandria, VA 22314-1651 *Tel:* 703-683-3700 *Toll Free Tel:* 800-824-0768 (sales) *Fax:* 703-836-0297 *Toll Free Fax:* 800-836-0297 *E-mail:* info.us@janes.com *Web Site:* www.janes.com, pg 140

Laur, Mary, Association of American University Presses, 1427 E 60 St, Chicago, IL 60637 *Tel:* 773-702-7700; 773-702-7600 *Toll Free Tel:* 800-621-2736 (orders) *Fax:* 773-702-9756 (sales); 773-660-2235 (orders); 773-702-2708 *E-mail:* general@press.uchicago.edu *Web Site:* www.press.uchicago.edu, pg 26

Laurent, Huguette, Sogides Ltee, 955 rue Amherst, Montreal, PQ H2L 3K4, Canada *Tel:* 514-523-1182 *Toll Free Tel:* 800-361-4806 *Fax:* 514-597-0370 *Web Site:* www.sogides.com; www.edhomme.com, pg 561

Laurenzo, Diane, American Management Association, 1601 Broadway, New York, NY 10019-7420 *Tel:* 212-586-8100 *Toll Free Tel:* 800-262-9699 *Fax:* 212-903-8168 *Web Site:* www.amanet.org, pg 677

Laurie, Douglas, The Bernard Shaw Society, Box 1159, Madison Square Sta, New York, NY 10159-1159 *Tel:* 212-989-7833; 212-982-9885, pg 699

Laurino, Anthony J, Penguin Group (USA) Inc, 375 Hudson St, New York, NY 10014 *Tel:* 212-366-2000 *Fax:* 212-366-2666 *E-mail:* online@uspenguingroup.com *Web Site:* www.penguin.com, pg 208

Laurita, Raymond, Leonardo Press, PO Box 1326, Camden, ME 04843-1326 *Tel:* 207-236-8649 *Fax:* 207-236-8649 *E-mail:* leonardo@spellingdoctor.com *Web Site:* www.spellingdoctor.com, pg 152

Lauterbach, Nancy, Five Star Speakers & Trainers LLC, 8685 W 96 St, Overland Park, KS 66212 *Tel:* 913-648-6480 *Fax:* 913-648-6484 *E-mail:* fivestar@fivestarspeakers.com *Web Site:* www.fivestarspeakers.com, pg 669

Lauterbach, William, Five Star Speakers & Trainers LLC, 8685 W 96 St, Overland Park, KS 66212 *Tel:* 913-648-6480 *Fax:* 913-648-6484 *E-mail:* fivestar@fivestarspeakers.com *Web Site:* www.fivestarspeakers.com, pg 669

Lauziere, Marcel, The Canadian Council on Social Development, 309 Cooper St, 5th fl, Ottawa, ON K2P 0G5, Canada *Tel:* 613-236-8977 *Fax:* 613-236-2750 *E-mail:* council@ccsd.ca *Web Site:* www.ccsd.ca, pg 538

Lauzzana, Raymond, Penrose Press, 1333 Gough, Suite 8B, San Francisco, CA 94109 *Tel:* 415-567-4157 *Fax:* 415-567-4165 *E-mail:* info@penrose-press.com *Web Site:* www.penrose-press.com, pg 209

LaVacca, John, Pearson Education International Group, One Lake St, Upper Saddle River, NJ 07458 *Tel:* 201-236-7000, pg 206

Lavender, John, CRC Press LLC, 2000 NW Corporate Blvd, Boca Raton, FL 33431 *Tel:* 561-994-0555 *Toll Free Tel:* 800-272-7737 *Fax:* 561-997-7249 (edit); 561-998-8491 (mfg); 561-361-6057 (acctg); 561-994-0313 *Toll Free Fax:* 800-643-9428 (sales); 800-374-3401 (orders) *E-mail:* orders@crcpress.com *Web Site:* www.crcpress.com, pg 71

Laventhall, Don, Harold Ober Associates Inc, 425 Madison Ave, New York, NY 10017 *Tel:* 212-759-8600 *Fax:* 212-759-9428, pg 647

Lavery, Michael J, Audit Bureau of Circulations (ABC), 900 N Meacham Rd, Schaumburg, IL 60173-4968 *Tel:* 847-605-0909 *Fax:* 847-605-0483 *Web Site:* www.accessabc.com, pg 680

Lavoie, Thomas, The University of Arkansas Press, McIlroy House, 201 Ozark Ave, Fayetteville, AR 72701 *Tel:* 479-575-3246 *Toll Free Tel:* 800-626-0090 *Fax:* 479-575-6044 *E-mail:* uapress@uark.edu *Web Site:* www.uapress.com, pg 280

LaVorne, Roberta L, Paulist Press, 997 Macarthur Blvd, Mahwah, NJ 07430 *Tel:* 201-825-7300 *Toll Free Tel:* 800-218-1903 *Fax:* 201-825-8345 *Toll Free Fax:* 800-836-3161 (orders) *E-mail:* info@paulistpress.com *Web Site:* www.paulistpress.com, pg 206

Law, Elizabeth, Simon & Schuster Children's Publishing, 1230 Avenue of the Americas, New York, NY 10020 *Tel:* 212-698-7000 *Web Site:* www.simonsayskids.com, pg 248

Law, Elizabeth, Frederick Warne, 345 Hudson St, New York, NY 10014 *Tel:* 212-366-2000 *E-mail:* online@penguinputnam.com *Web Site:* www.penguin.com, pg 293

Law, Gordon, The Drummond Publishing Group, 362 N Bedford St, East Bridgewater, MA 02333 *Tel:* 508-378-1110 *Fax:* 508-378-1105 *Web Site:* www.drummondpub.com, pg 84

Law, Gordon, Royalton Press, 362 N Bedford St, East Bridgewater, MA 02333 *Tel:* 508-378-1110 *Fax:* 508-378-1105 *Web Site:* www.drummondpub.com, pg 235

Lawler, J George, The Continuum International Publishing Group, 15 E 26 St, Suite 1703, New York, NY 10010 *Tel:* 212-953-5858 *Toll Free Tel:* 800-561-7704 *Fax:* 212-953-5944 *E-mail:* info@continuumbooks.com *Web Site:* www.continuumbooks.com, pg 67

Lawler, John A IV, Martindale-Hubbell, 121 Chanlon Rd, New Providence, NJ 07974 *Tel:* 908-464-6800 *Toll Free Tel:* 800-526-4902 *Fax:* 908-464-3553 *E-mail:* info@martindale.com *Web Site:* www.martindale.com, pg 164

Lawner, Kathleen, ALI-ABA Committee on Continuing Professional Education, 4025 Chestnut St, Philadelphia, PA 19104 *Tel:* 215-243-1600 *Toll Free Tel:* 800-CLE-NEWS *Fax:* 215-243-1664; 215-243-1683 *Web Site:* www.ali-aba.org, pg 8

Lawner, Kathleen H, American Law Institute, 4025 Chestnut St, Philadelphia, PA 19104-3099 *Tel:* 215-243-1600 *Toll Free Tel:* 800-253-6397 *Fax:* 215-243-1664; 215-243-1683 *Web Site:* www.ali.org, pg 15

Lawrence, Derek, Speck Press, 1635 S Fairfax St, Denver, CO 80222 *Tel:* 303-777-0539 *Toll Free Tel:* 800-996-9783 *Fax:* 303-756-8011 *E-mail:* books@speckpress.com *Web Site:* www.speckpress.com, pg 255

Lawrence, Eileen, Alexander Street Press LLC, 3212 Duke St, Alexandria, VA 22314 *Tel:* 703-212-8520 *Toll Free Tel:* 800-889-5937 *Fax:* 240-465-0561 *E-mail:* sales@alexanderstreet.com *Web Site:* www.alexanderstreet.com, pg 8

Lawrence, Karen, Technical Association of the Graphic Arts (TAGA), 68 Lomb Memorial Dr, Rochester, NY 14623-5604 *Tel:* 585-475-7470 *Fax:* 585-475-2250 *E-mail:* tagaofc@aol.com *Web Site:* www.taga.org, pg 701

Lawrence, Kristin Harpster, Wayne State University Press, Leonard N Simons Bldg, 4809 Woodward Ave, Detroit, MI 48201-1309 *Tel:* 313-577-4600 *Toll Free Tel:* 800-978-7323 *Fax:* 313-577-6131, pg 294

Lawrence, Merloyd Ludington, Merloyd Lawrence Inc, 102 Chestnut St, Boston, MA 02108 *Tel:* 617-523-5895 *Fax:* 617-252-5285, pg 150

Lawrence, Michael E, The Pilgrim Press/United Church Press, 700 Prospect Ave, Cleveland, OH 44115-1100 *Tel:* 216-736-3761 *Toll Free Tel:* 800-537-3394 (cust serv) *Fax:* 216-736-2207 *E-mail:* thepilgrimpress@thepilgrimpress.com *Web Site:* www.thepilgrimpress.com; www.theunitedchurchpress.com, pg 213

Lawrence, Nancy, Melcher Book Award, 25 Beacon St, Boston, MA 02108-2800 *Tel:* 617-742-2100 (ext 303) *Fax:* 617-367-3237 *Web Site:* www.uua.org, pg 789

Lawrence, Pat, Six Gallery Press, 4620 Los Feliz Blvd, Suite 1, Los Angeles, CA 90027 *E-mail:* sgpwc@yahoo.com *Web Site:* www.sixgallerypress.com, pg 249

Lawrence, Priscilla, The Historic New Orleans Collection, 533 Royal St, New Orleans, LA 70130 *Tel:* 504-523-4662 *Fax:* 504-598-7108 *E-mail:* hnocinfo@hnoc.org *Web Site:* www.hnoc.org, pg 123

Lawrence, Richard, Eaton Literary Associates Literary Awards, PO Box 49795, Sarasota, FL 34230-6795 *Tel:* 941-366-6589 *Fax:* 941-365-4679 *E-mail:* eatonlit@aol.com *Web Site:* www.eatonliterary.com, pg 771

Lawrence, Starling R, W W Norton & Company Inc, 500 Fifth Ave, New York, NY 10110-0017 *Tel:* 212-354-5500 *Toll Free Tel:* 800-233-4830 (orders & cust serv) *Fax:* 212-869-0856 *Toll Free Fax:* 800-458-6515 *Web Site:* www.wwnorton.com, pg 193

Lawrence, Virginia, Small Publishers, Artists & Writers Network (SPAWN), 323 E Matilija St, Suite 110, PMB 123, Ojai, CA 93023 *Tel:* 818-886-4281 *Fax:* 818-886-3320 *Web Site:* www.spawn.org, pg 699

Lawry, Pat, Alexander Street Press LLC, 3212 Duke St, Alexandria, VA 22314 *Tel:* 703-212-8520 *Toll Free Tel:* 800-889-5937 *Fax:* 240-465-0561 *E-mail:* sales@alexanderstreet.com *Web Site:* www.alexanderstreet.com, pg 8

Lawson, Pamela, Harlequin Enterprises Ltd, 233 Broadway, Suite 1001, New York, NY 10279 *Tel:* 212-553-4200 *Fax:* 212-227-8969 *E-mail:* customer.ecare@harlequin.ca *Web Site:* www.eharlequin.com; www.luna-books.com; www.mirabooks.com; www.reddressink.com; www.steeplehill.com, pg 115

Lawson, Steven, Regal Books, 1957 Eastman Ave, Ventura, CA 93003 *Tel:* 805-644-9721 *Toll Free Tel:* 800-446-7735 (orders) *Fax:* 805-644-9728 (editorial); 805-644-4729 (purchasing); 805-650-8713 (sales & corp serv); 805-658-3388 (orders) *Toll Free Fax:* 800-860-3109 (orders) *E-mail:* info@regalbooks.com *Web Site:* www.gospellight.com, pg 230

Lawson, Vance, Thomas Nelson Inc, 501 Nelson Place, Nashville, TN 37214 *Tel:* 615-889-9000 *Toll Free Tel:* 800-251-4000 *Fax:* 615-902-1610 *E-mail:* publicity@thomasnelson.com *Web Site:* www.thomasnelson.com, pg 269

Lawson, Wayne P, Aid to Individual Artists, 727 E Main St, Columbus, OH 43205-1796 *Tel:* 614-466-2613 *Fax:* 614-466-4494 *Web Site:* www.oac.state.oh.us, pg 758

Lawton, Caryn, Washington State University Press, Cooper Publications Bldg, Grimes Way, Pullman, WA 99164-5910 *Tel:* 509-335-3518 *Toll Free Tel:* 800-354-7360 *Fax:* 509-335-8568 *E-mail:* wsupress@wsu.edu *Web Site:* wsupress.wsu.edu, pg 293

Lawton, John, Penguin Group (USA) Inc Sales, 375 Hudson St, New York, NY 10014 *Tel:* 212-366-2000 *E-mail:* online@penguinputnam.com *Web Site:* www.penguin.com, pg 208

Layfield, Benny, University Press of Florida, 15 NW 15 St, Gainesville, FL 32611-2079 *Tel:* 352-392-1351 *Toll Free Tel:* 800-226-3822 (orders only) *Fax:* 352-392-7302 *Toll Free Fax:* 800-680-1955 (orders only) *E-mail:* info@upf.com *Web Site:* www.upf.com, pg 287

Layman, Richard, Bruccoli Clark Layman Inc, 2006 Sumter St, Columbia, SC 29201 *Tel:* 803-771-4642 *Fax:* 803-799-6953, pg 49

Lazar, Harvey, Institute of Intergovernmental Relations, Queen's University, Rm 301, Policy Studies Bldg, Kingston, ON K7L 3N6, Canada *Tel:* 613-533-2080 *Fax:* 613-533-6868 *E-mail:* iigr@iigr.ca *Web Site:* www.iigr.ca, pg 551

387-8028 *Fax:* 416-443-0948 *Toll Free Fax:* 800-263-7733; 888-465-0536 *E-mail:* firstname.lastname@pearsoned.com *Web Site:* www.pearsoned.com, pg 557

Lee, Don, Ploughshares, Emerson College, 120 Boylston St, Boston, MA 02116 *Tel:* 617-824-8753 *E-mail:* pshares@emerson.edu *Web Site:* www.pshares.org, pg 215

Lee, Fred, Berkshire House, 1206 Rte 12, Woodstock, VT 05091 *Tel:* 802-457-4826 *Toll Free Tel:* 800-245-4151 *Fax:* 802-457-1678 *Web Site:* www.countrymanpress.com, pg 37

Lee, Fred, The Countryman Press, 1206 Rte 12 N, Woodstock, VT 05091 *Tel:* 802-457-4826 *Toll Free Tel:* 800-245-4151 *Fax:* 802-457-1678 *E-mail:* countrymanpress@wwnorton.com *Web Site:* www.countrymanpress.com, pg 70

Lee, Gail, Writers Guild of America East Inc (WGAE), 555 W 57 St, New York, NY 10019 *Tel:* 212-767-7800 *Fax:* 212-582-1909 *E-mail:* info@wgaeast.org *Web Site:* www.wgaeast.org, pg 703

Lee, Gary, MMB Music Inc, Contemporary Arts Bldg, 3526 Washington Ave, St Louis, MO 63103-1019 *Tel:* 314-531-9635 *Toll Free Tel:* 800-543-3771 *Fax:* 314-531-8384 *E-mail:* info@mmbmusic.com *Web Site:* www.mmbmusic.com, pg 176

Lee, James W, Texas Christian University Press, PO Box 298300, Fort Worth, TX 76129 *Tel:* 817-257-7822 *Toll Free Tel:* 800-826-8911 *Fax:* 817-257-5075 *Toll Free Fax:* 888-617-2421 *Web Site:* www.prs.tcu.edu/prs/, pg 267

Lee, Jovita Ador, GoodSAMARitan Press, PO Box 803282, Santa Clarita, CA 91380 *Tel:* 661-799-0694, pg 107

Lee, Ken, Michael Wiese Productions, 11288 Ventura Blvd, Suite 621, Studio City, CA 91604 *Tel:* 818-379-8799 *Toll Free Tel:* 800-379-8808 *Fax:* 818-986-3408 *Web Site:* www.mwp.com, pg 299

Lee, Lettie, Ann Elmo Agency Inc, 60 E 42 St, New York, NY 10165 *Tel:* 212-661-2880; 212-661-2881 *Fax:* 212-661-2883, pg 629

Lee, Linda, Law School Admission Council, 662 Penn St, Newtown, PA 18940 *Tel:* 215-968-1101 *Fax:* 215-968-1159 *E-mail:* wmargolis@lsac.org *Web Site:* www.lsac.org, pg 150

Lee, Nancy, Walter Foster Publishing Inc, 23062 La Cadena Dr, Laguna Hills, CA 92653 *Tel:* 949-380-7510 *Toll Free Tel:* 800-426-0099 *Fax:* 949-380-7575 *Web Site:* www.walterfoster.com, pg 99

Lee, Nancy, My Chaotic Life™, 23062 La Cadena Dr, Laguna Hills, CA 92653 *Tel:* 949-380-7510 *Toll Free Tel:* 800-426-0099 *Fax:* 949-380-7575 *Web Site:* www.mychaoticlife.com, pg 181

Lee, Philip, Lee & Low Books Inc, 95 Madison Ave, New York, NY 10016 *Tel:* 212-779-4400 *Toll Free Tel:* 888-320-3190 ext 25 (orders only) *Fax:* 212-683-1894 (orders only); 212-532-6035 *E-mail:* info@leeandlow.com *Web Site:* www.leeandlow.com, pg 152

Lee, Ray, Master Point Press, 331 Douglas Ave, Toronto, ON M5M 1H2, Canada *Tel:* 416-781-0351 *Fax:* 416-781-1831 *E-mail:* info@masterpointpress.com *Web Site:* www.masterpointpress.com, pg 553

Lee, Ron, WaterBrook Press, 2375 Telstar Dr, Suite 160, Colorado Springs, CO 80920 *Tel:* 719-590-4999 *Toll Free Tel:* 800-603-7051 (orders) *Fax:* 719-590-8977 *Toll Free Fax:* 800-294-5686 (orders) *Web Site:* www.waterbrookpress.com, pg 294

Lee, Sandra, Abingdon Press, 201 Eighth Ave S, Nashville, TN 37203-3919 *Tel:* 615-749-6290 (publicist); 615-749-6000; 615-749-6451 (sales) *Toll Free Tel:* 800-251-3320 *Fax:* 615-749-6056 *Web Site:* www.abingdonpress.com, pg 3

Lee, Simone, Fifth House Publishers, 1511 1800 Fourth St SW, Calgary, AB T2S 2S5, Canada *Tel:* 403-571-5230 *Toll Free Tel:* 800-387-9776 *Fax:* 403-571-5235 *Toll Free Fax:* 800-260-9777 *Web Site:* www.fitzhenry.ca/fifthhouse.htm, pg 546

Lee, Spencer, Farrar, Straus & Giroux, LLC, 19 Union Sq W, New York, NY 10003 *Tel:* 212-741-6900 *Fax:* 212-741-6973 *Web Site:* www.fsgbooks.com, pg 95

Lee, Stephanie, Manus & Associates Literary Agency Inc, 445 Park Ave, New York, NY 10022 *Tel:* 650-470-5151 (CA) *Fax:* 650-470-5159 (CA) *E-mail:* manuslit@manuslit.com *Web Site:* www.manuslit.com, pg 642

Leech, Lynn, The James Boatwright III Prize for Poetry, Washington & Lee University, Mattingly House, 2 Lee Ave, Lexington, VA 24450-0303 *Tel:* 540-458-8765 *Fax:* 540-458-8461 *Web Site:* www.shenandoah.wlu.edu, pg 763

Leech, Lynn, The Thomas H Carter Award For The Essay, Washington & Lee University, Mattingly House, 2 Lee Ave, Lexington, VA 24450-0303 *Tel:* 540-458-8765 *Fax:* 540-458-8461 *Web Site:* www.shenandoah.wlu.edu, pg 766

Leech, Lynn, The Goodheart Prize For Fiction, Washington & Lee University, Mattingly House, 2 Lee Ave, Lexington, VA 24450-0303 *Tel:* 540-458-8765 *Fax:* 540-458-8461 *Web Site:* www.shenandoah.wlu.edu, pg 776

Leers, Peter, Hastings House/Daytrips Publishers, 2601 Wells Ave, Suite 161, Fern Park, FL 32730 *Tel:* 407-339-3600 *Toll Free Tel:* 800-206-7822 *Fax:* 407-339-5900 *E-mail:* hastings_daytrips@earthlink.net *Web Site:* www.hastingshousebooks.com; www.daytripsbooks.com, pg 117

Lefebure, Guy, Prix Champlain, Maison de la francophonie, 39, rue Dalhousie, Quebec, PQ G1K 8R8, Canada *Tel:* 418-646-9117 *Fax:* 418-644-7670 *E-mail:* cvfa@cvfa.ca *Web Site:* www.cvfa.ca, pg 800

Lefort, Dominique, Modulo Editeur Inc, 233 Ave Dunbar, Rm 300, Mont Royal, PQ H3P 2H4, Canada *Tel:* 514-738-9818 *Toll Free Tel:* 888-738-9818 *Fax:* 514-738-5838 *Toll Free Fax:* 888-273-5247 *Web Site:* www.moduloediteur.com, pg 554

Lefort, Dominique, Modulo-Griffon Inc, 233 Dunbar Ave, Suite 300, Mont Royal, PQ H3P 2H4, Canada *Tel:* 514-738-9818 *Toll Free Tel:* 888-738-9818 *Fax:* 514-738-5838 *Toll Free Fax:* 888-273-5247 *Web Site:* www.moduloediteur.com, pg 554

Legaspi, Joseph O, Pulitzer Prizes, 709 Journalism Bldg, New York, NY 10027 *Tel:* 212-854-3841 *Fax:* 212-854-3342 *E-mail:* pulitzer@pulitzer.org *Web Site:* www.pulitzer.org, pg 800

Legault, Claude, Lidec Inc, 4350 Ave de l'Hotel-de-Ville, Montreal, PQ H2W 2H5, Canada *Tel:* 514-843-5991 *Toll Free Tel:* 800-350-5991 (Canada Only) *Fax:* 514-843-5252 *E-mail:* lidec@lidec.qc.ca *Web Site:* www.lidec.qc.ca, pg 552

Legget, Jenny, Banff Centre National Arts Award, 107 Tunnel Mountain Dr, Banff, AB T1L 1H5, Canada *Tel:* 403-762-6154 *Toll Free Tel:* 800-413-8368 *Fax:* 403-762-6158 *E-mail:* communications@banffcentre.ca *Web Site:* www.banffcentre.ca, pg 761

Leggett, John, Napa Valley Writers' Conference-Poetry & Fiction Sessions, Upper Valley Campus, 1088 College Ave, St Helena, CA 94574 *Tel:* 707-967-2900 (ext 1611) *Fax:* 707-967-2909 *E-mail:* writecon@napavalley.edu *Web Site:* www.napavalley.edu/writersconf, pg 745

Lehman, Susannah, Optical Society of America, 2010 Massachusetts Ave NW, Washington, DC 20036-1023 *Tel:* 202-223-8130 *Fax:* 202-223-1096 *E-mail:* custserv@osa.org *Web Site:* www.osa.org, pg 198

Lehmann, Stephanie, Elaine Koster Literary Agency LLC, 55 Central Park West, Suite 6, New York, NY 10023 *Tel:* 212-362-9488 *Fax:* 212-712-0164 *E-mail:* elainekost@aol.com, pg 639

Lehnhoff, Lisa, Heart Math, 14700 W Park Ave, Boulder Creek, CA 95006 *Tel:* 831-338-2161 *Toll Free Tel:* 800-450-9111 *Fax:* 831-338-9861 *Web Site:* www.heartmath.com, pg 120

Lehr, Donald, The Betsy Nolan Literary Agency, 224 W 29 St, 15th fl, New York, NY 10001 *Tel:* 212-967-8200 *Fax:* 212-967-7292, pg 647

Leichum, Laura, Northwestern University Press, 625 Colfax St, Evanston, IL 60208 *Tel:* 847-491-2046 *Toll Free Tel:* 800-621-2736 (orders only) *Fax:* 847-491-8150 *E-mail:* nupress@northwestern.edu *Web Site:* www.nupress.northwestern.edu, pg 193

Leider, Anna, Octameron Associates, 1900 Mount Vernon Ave, Alexandria, VA 22301 *Tel:* 703-836-5480 *Fax:* 703-836-5650 *E-mail:* info@octameron.com *Web Site:* www.octameron.com, pg 196

Leifso, Brenda, Prism International Fiction Contest, University of British Columbia, Buch E462, 1866 Main Mall, Vancouver, BC V6T 1Z1, Canada *Tel:* 604-822-2514 *Fax:* 604-822-3616 *E-mail:* prism@interchange.ubc.ca *Web Site:* prism.arts.ubc.ca, pg 800

Leight, Warren, Writers Guild of America East Inc (WGAE), 555 W 57 St, New York, NY 10019 *Tel:* 212-767-7800 *Fax:* 212-582-1909 *E-mail:* info@wgaeast.org *Web Site:* www.wgaeast.org, pg 703

Leinheiser, Francine, Simon & Schuster Inc, 1230 Avenue of the Americas, New York, NY 10020 *Tel:* 212-698-7000 *Fax:* 212-698-7007 *Web Site:* www.simonsays.com, pg 249

Leiper, Esther M, Writers' Journal Poetry Contest, PO Box 394, Perham, MN 56573 *Tel:* 218-346-7921 *Fax:* 218-346-7924 *E-mail:* writersjournal@lakesplus.com *Web Site:* www.writersjournal.com, pg 813

Leipold, Denise, Society of Manufacturing Engineers, One SME Dr, Dearborn, MI 48121 *Tel:* 313-271-1500 *Toll Free Tel:* 800-733-4763 (cust serv) *Fax:* 313-271-2861 *Web Site:* www.sme.org, pg 252

Leisy, James F Jr, Franklin, Beedle & Associates Inc, 8536 SW St Helens Dr, Suite D, Wilsonville, OR 97070 *Tel:* 503-682-7668 *Toll Free Tel:* 800-322-2665 *Fax:* 503-682-7638 *Web Site:* www.fbeedle.com, pg 100

Lelchuk, Alan, Steerforth Press, 25 Lebanon St, Hanover, NH 03755 *Tel:* 603-643-4787 *Fax:* 603-643-4788 *E-mail:* info@steerforth.com *Web Site:* www.steerforth.com, pg 258

Leman, Jim, Independent Writers of Chicago (IWOC), 5465 Grand Ave, Suite 100, PMB 119, Gurnee, IL 60031 *Tel:* 847-855-6670 *Fax:* 847-855-4502 *E-mail:* info@iwoc.org *Web Site:* www.iwoc.org, pg 688

Lemberg Rothenberg, Natalie, The Insiders System for Writers, 1223 Wilshire Blvd, No 336, Santa Monica, CA 90403 *Tel:* 310-899-9775 *Toll Free Tel:* 800-397-2615 *Fax:* 310-899-9775 *E-mail:* insiderssystem@msn.com *Web Site:* www.insiderssystem.com, pg 635

Lemenager, Brian, Adventures Unlimited Press, One Adventure Place, Kempton, IL 60946 *Tel:* 815-253-6390 *Fax:* 815-253-6300 *E-mail:* auphq@frontiernet.net *Web Site:* www.adventuresunlimitedpress.com, pg 6

Lemmert, Brenda, Teacher's Discovery, 2741 Paldan Dr, Auburn Hills, MI 48326 *Tel:* 248-340-7220 ext 207 *Toll Free Tel:* 800-521-3897 *Fax:* 248-340-7212 *Toll Free Fax:* 888-987-2436 *Web Site:* www.teachersdiscovery.com, pg 265

Lemmons, Thom, ACU Press, 1648 Campus Ct, Abilene, TX 79601 *Tel:* 325-674-2720 *Toll Free Tel:* 800-444-4228 *Fax:* 325-674-6471 *E-mail:* acupress@acu.edu *Web Site:* www.acu.edu/acupress, pg 5

Lemon, Carolyn, Ignatius Press, 2515 McAllister St, San Francisco, CA 94118 *Tel:* 415-387-2324 *Toll Free Tel:* 877-320-9276 (book orders) *Fax:* 415-387-0896 *E-mail:* info@ignatius.com *Web Site:* www.ignatius.com, pg 131

Lengyel, Heather, The Johns Hopkins University Press, 2715 N Charles St, Baltimore, MD 21218-4363 *Tel:* 410-516-6900 *Toll Free Tel:* 800-537-5487 *Fax:* 410-516-6968 *Web Site:* www.press.jhu.edu, pg 141

Lenhardt, Alfonso, National Crime Prevention Council, 1000 Connecticut Ave NW, 13th fl, Washington, DC 20036-5325 *Tel:* 202-466-6272 *Toll Free Tel:* 800-627-2911 (orders only) *Fax:* 202-296-1356 *Web Site:* www.ncpc.org, pg 183

LeValley, Jim, Microsoft Press, One Microsoft Way, Redmond, WA 98052-6399 *Tel:* 425-882-8080 *Toll Free Tel:* 800-677-7377 *Fax:* 425-936-7329 *Web Site:* www.microsoft.com/presspass/exec/default. asp#qt, pg 173

Leventhal, J P, Black Dog & Leventhal Publishers Inc, 151 W 19 St, 12th fl, New York, NY 10011 *Tel:* 212-647-9336 *Fax:* 212-647-9332 *E-mail:* information@ bdlev.com *Web Site:* www.bdlev.com, pg 39

Lever, Donna, Martingale & Co, 20205 144 Ave NE, Woodinville, WA 98072 *Tel:* 425-483-3313 *Toll Free Tel:* 800-426-3126 *Fax:* 425-486-7596 *E-mail:* info@ martingale-pub.com *Web Site:* www.martingale-pub. com, pg 164

Leverence, John, Academy of Television Arts & Sciences (ATAS), 5220 Lankershim Blvd, North Hollywood, CA 91601-3109 *Tel:* 818-754-2800 *Fax:* 818-761-2827 *Web Site:* www.emmys.tv, pg 675

Levering, Marcy, Standard Publishing Co, 8121 Hamilton Ave, Cincinnati, OH 45231 *Tel:* 513-931-4050 *Toll Free Tel:* 800-543-1301 *Fax:* 513-931-0950 *Toll Free Fax:* 877-867-5751 *E-mail:* customerservice@standardpub.com *Web Site:* www.standardpub.com, pg 257

Leverton, Yossi, Hachai Publications Inc, 156 Chester Ave, Brooklyn, NY 11218 *Tel:* 718-633-0100 *Toll Free Tel:* 800-50-HACHAI (504-2424) *Fax:* 718-633-0103 *E-mail:* info@hachai.com *Web Site:* www.hachai. com, pg 111

Levesque, Gaetan, XYZ Editeur, 1781 rue Saint-Hubert, Montreal, PQ H2L 3Z1, Canada *Tel:* 514-525-2170 *Fax:* 514-525-7537, pg 567

Levesque, Gaetan, XYZ Publishing, 1781 Saint Hubert St, Montreal, PQ H2L 3Z1, Canada *Tel:* 514-252-2170 *Fax:* 514-525-7537 *E-mail:* info@xyzedit.qc.ca *Web Site:* www.xyzedit.qc.ca, pg 567

Levin, Clarice, ibooks Inc, 24 W 25 St, 11th fl, New York, NY 10010 *Tel:* 212-645-9870 *Fax:* 212-645-9874 *Web Site:* www.bpvp.com; www.ibooks.net, pg 130

Levin, Hugh, Hugh Lauter Levin Associates Inc, 9 Burr Rd, Westport, CT 06880 *Tel:* 203-227-6422 *Fax:* 203-227-6717 *E-mail:* inquiries@hlla.com *Web Site:* www. hlla.com, pg 128

Levin, Janet Z, C & T Publishing Inc, 1651 Challenge Dr, Concord, CA 94520 *Tel:* 925-677-0377 *Toll Free Tel:* 800-284-1114 *Fax:* 925-677-0373 *E-mail:* ctinfo@ctpub.com *Web Site:* www.ctpub.com, pg 51

Levin, Martha K, Free Press, 1230 Avenue of the Americas, New York, NY 10020 *Tel:* 212-698-7000 *Toll Free Tel:* 800-223-2345 (cust serv); 800-223-2336 (orders); 888-866-6631 (fulfillment), pg 100

Levin, Neal, Bobley Harmann Corp, 311 Crossways Park Dr, Woodbury, NY 11797 *Tel:* 516-364-1800 *Fax:* 516-364-1899 *E-mail:* info@bobley.com *Web Site:* www.bobley.com, pg 42

Levine, Alice, Rocky Mountain Publishing Professionals Guild (RMPPG), PO Box 17721, Boulder, CO 80308-7721 *Tel:* 303-447-0799 *Web Site:* RMPPG.org, pg 698

Levine, Arthur A, Scholastic Trade Division, 557 Broadway, New York, NY 10012 *Tel:* 212-343-6100; 212-343-4685 (export sales) *Fax:* 212-343-4714 (export sales) *Web Site:* www.scholastic.com, pg 242

Levine, Barbara, Aslan Publishing, 2490 Black Rock Tpke, Fairfield, CT 06432 *Tel:* 203-372-0300 *Toll Free Tel:* 800-786-5427 *Fax:* 203-374-4766 *E-mail:* info@ aslanpublishing.com *Web Site:* www.aslanpublishing. com, pg 25

Levine, Daniel, Empire Press Media/Avant-Guide, 444 Madison Ave, 35th fl, New York, NY 10122 *Tel:* 212-563-1003 *Fax:* 212-536-2419 *E-mail:* info@avantguide.com; editor@avantguide.com *Web Site:* www.avantguide.com, pg 90

Levine, Deborah, The Jeff Herman Agency LLC, 9 South St, Stockbridge, MA 01262 *Tel:* 413-298-0077 *Fax:* 413-298-8188 *Web Site:* www.jeffherman.com, pg 634

Levine, Ellen, Trident Media Group LLC, 41 Madison Ave, 36th fl, New York, NY 10010 *Tel:* 212-262-4810 *Fax:* 212-725-4501 *Web Site:* www.tridentmediagroup. com, pg 659

Levine, Harold, Aslan Publishing, 2490 Black Rock Tpke, Fairfield, CT 06432 *Tel:* 203-372-0300 *Toll Free Tel:* 800-786-5427 *Fax:* 203-374-4766 *E-mail:* info@ aslanpublishing.com *Web Site:* www.aslanpublishing. com, pg 25

Levine, James, Levine-Greenberg Literary Agency Inc, 307 Seventh Ave, Suite 1906, New York, NY 10001 *Tel:* 212-337-0934 *Fax:* 212-337-0948 *Web Site:* www. levinegreenberg.com, pg 640

Levine, Jonathan D, Hartmore House Inc, 304 E 49 St, New York, NY 10017 *Tel:* 203-384-2284; 212-319-6666 *Fax:* 203-579-9109, pg 116

Levine, Jonathan D, Prayer Book Press Inc, 1363 Fairfield Ave, Bridgeport, CT 06605 *Tel:* 203-384-2284 *Fax:* 203-579-9109, pg 217

Levine, Michael, Westwood Creative Artists Ltd, 94 Harbord St, Toronto, ON M5S 1G6, Canada *Tel:* 416-964-3302 *Fax:* 416-975-9209, pg 661

Levine, Sheila, University of California Press, 2120 Berkeley Way, Berkeley, CA 94720 *Tel:* 510-642-4247 *Toll Free Tel:* 800-777-4726 *Fax:* 510-643-7127 *Toll Free Fax:* 800-999-1958 *E-mail:* askucp@ucpress.edu *Web Site:* www.ucpress.edu, pg 281

Levins, Michael, innovative Kids™, 18 Ann St, Norwalk, CT 06854 *Tel:* 203-838-6400 *Fax:* 203-855-5582 *E-mail:* info@innovativekids.com *Web Site:* www. innovativekids.com, pg 134

Levinson, Diane, Cleis Press, PO Box 14684, San Francisco, CA 94114-0684 *Tel:* 415-575-4700 *Toll Free Tel:* 800-780-2279 (US) *Fax:* 415-575-4705 *E-mail:* cleis@cleispress.com *Web Site:* www. cleispress.com, pg 63

Levinson, Sara, Rodale Inc, 33 E Minor St, Emmaus, PA 18098-0099 *Tel:* 610-967-5171 *Fax:* 610-967-8962 *Web Site:* www.rodale.com, pg 234

Levitan, Jeanie, Bear & Co Inc, One Park St, Rochester, VT 05767 *Tel:* 802-767-3174 *Toll Free Tel:* 800-932-3277 *Fax:* 802-767-3726 *E-mail:* orders@ InnerTraditions.com *Web Site:* InnerTraditions.com, pg 34

Levitan, Jeanie, Inner Traditions International Ltd, One Park St, Rochester, VT 05767 *Tel:* 802-767-3174 *Toll Free Tel:* 800-246-8648 *Fax:* 802-767-3726 *E-mail:* orders@InnerTraditions.com *Web Site:* www. InnerTraditions.com, pg 134

Levitt, Rachelle, ULI-The Urban Land Institute, 1025 Thomas Jefferson St NW, Suite 500 W, Washington, DC 20007-5201 *Tel:* 202-624-7000 *Toll Free Tel:* 800-321-5011 *Fax:* 202-624-7140; 410-626-7147 (orders only) *Toll Free Fax:* 800-248-4585 *E-mail:* bookstore@uli.org *Web Site:* www.uli.org, pg 278

Levitt, Rachelle, Urban Land Institute, 1025 Thomas Jefferson St NW, Suite 500 W, Washington, DC 20007 *Tel:* 202-624-7000 *Toll Free Tel:* 800-321-5011 *Fax:* 410-626-7140 *E-mail:* Bookstore@uli.org *Web Site:* www.bookstore.uli.org, pg 288

Levitt, Rich, Teacher Created Materials Inc, 6421 Industry Way, Westminster, CA 92683 *Tel:* 714-891-7895 *Toll Free Tel:* 800-662-4321 *Fax:* 714-892-0283 *Toll Free Fax:* 800-525-1254 *E-mail:* tcminfo@ teachercreated.com *Web Site:* www.teachercreated.com, pg 265

Levitz, Paul, DC Comics, 1700 Broadway, New York, NY 10019 *Tel:* 212-636-5400 *Toll Free Tel:* 800-759-0190 (distribution) *Fax:* 212-636-5481 *Web Site:* www. dccomics.com; www.madmag.com, pg 77

Levy, Arthur, American Management Association, 1601 Broadway, New York, NY 10019-7420 *Tel:* 212-586-8100 *Toll Free Tel:* 800-262-9699 *Fax:* 212-903-8168 *Web Site:* www.amanet.org, pg 677

Levy, Diana, IEE, c/o Inspec, 379 Thornall St, Edison, NJ 08837-2225 *Tel:* 732-321-5575 *Fax:* 732-321-5702 *E-mail:* iee@inspecinc.com *Web Site:* www.iee. org/publishing, pg 130

Levy, Ed, Girl Scouts of the USA, 420 Fifth Ave, New York, NY 10018-2798 *Tel:* 212-852-8000 *Toll Free Tel:* 800-478-7248 *Fax:* 212-852-6511 *Web Site:* www. girlscouts.org, pg 105

Lew, Roberta, Heinemann, 361 Hanover St, Portsmouth, NH 03801-3912 *Tel:* 603-431-7894 *Toll Free Tel:* 800-225-5800 *Fax:* 603-431-4971; 603-431-7840 *E-mail:* info@heinemann.com *Web Site:* www. heinemann.com, pg 120

Lewandoski, Joyce, University of Texas Press, PO Box 7819, Austin, TX 78713-7819 *Tel:* 512-471-7233 *Fax:* 512-232-7178 *E-mail:* utpress@uts.cc.utexas.edu *Web Site:* www.utexas.edu/utpress, pg 267

Lewent, Judy C, National Bureau of Economic Research Inc, 1050 Massachusetts Ave, Cambridge, MA 02138-5398 *Tel:* 617-868-3900 *Fax:* 617-868-2742 *E-mail:* op@nber.org *Web Site:* www.nber.org, pg 182

Lewis, Amanda, The Doe Coover Agency, PO Box 668, Winchester, MA 01890 *Tel:* 781-721-6000 *Fax:* 781-721-6727, pg 626

Lewis, Beth A, Augsburg Fortress Publishers, Publishing House of the Evangelical Lutheran Church in America, 100 S Fifth St, Suite 700, Minneapolis, MN 55402 *Tel:* 612-330-3300 *Toll Free Tel:* 800-426-0115 (ext 639 subns); 800-328-4648 (orders); 800-421-0239 (perms) *Fax:* 612-330-3455 *Toll Free Fax:* 800-421-0239 (perms & copyrights) *E-mail:* customerservice@ augsburgfortress.org; copyright@augsburgfortress.org (for reprint permission requests) *Web Site:* www. augsburgfortress.org, pg 28

Lewis, Darrell, Standard Publishing Co, 8121 Hamilton Ave, Cincinnati, OH 45231 *Tel:* 513-931-4050 *Toll Free Tel:* 800-543-1301 *Fax:* 513-931-0950 *Toll Free Fax:* 877-867-5751 *E-mail:* customerservice@ standardpub.com *Web Site:* www.standardpub.com, pg 257

Lewis, Dave, Baker Books, PO Box 6287, Grand Rapids, MI 49516-6287 *Tel:* 616-676-9185 *Toll Free Tel:* 800-877-2665; 800-679-1957 *Fax:* 616-676-9573 *Toll Free Fax:* 800-398-3110 *Web Site:* www. bakerpublishinggroup.com, pg 30

Lewis, Dave, Bethany House Publishers/Baker Bookhouse, PO Box 6287, Grand Rapids, MI 49516-6287 *Tel:* 616-676-9185 *Toll Free Tel:* 800-877-2665 *Web Site:* www.bethanyhouse.com; www. bakerpublishinggroup.com, pg 37

Lewis, David, Betterway Books, 4700 E Galbraith Rd, Cincinnati, OH 45236 *Tel:* 513-531-2690 *Toll Free Tel:* 800-666-0963 *Fax:* 513-891-7185 *Toll Free Fax:* 888-590-4082 *Web Site:* www.fwpublications. com, pg 38

Lewis, David, North Light Books, 4700 E Galbraith Rd, Cincinnati, OH 45236 *Tel:* 513-531-2690 *Toll Free Tel:* 800-666-0963 *Fax:* 513-891-7185 *Toll Free Fax:* 888-590-4082 *Web Site:* www.fwpublications. com, pg 192

Lewis, David, Writer's Digest Books, 4700 E Galbraith Rd, Cincinnati, OH 45236 *Tel:* 513-531-2690 *Toll Free Tel:* 800-289-0963 *Fax:* 513-891-7185 *Web Site:* www. writersdigest.com, pg 305

Lewis, Dorothy, National Academies Press, 500 Fifth St NW, Washington, DC 20001 *Tel:* 202-334-3313 *Toll Free Tel:* 800-624-6242 *Fax:* 202-334-2451 (orders) *Web Site:* www.nap.edu, pg 182

Lewis, J Brinley, Eagle Publishing Inc, One Massachusetts Ave NW, Washington, DC 20001 *Tel:* 202-216-0600 *Fax:* 202-216-0612 *Web Site:* www. regnery.com, pg 85

Lewis, Josee, VLB Editeur Inc, 955 Amherst St, Montreal, PQ H2L 3K4, Canada *Tel:* 514-523-1182 *Fax:* 514-282-7530 *E-mail:* vml@sogides.com *Web Site:* www.edvlb.com, pg 566

Lewis, Josipp, Editions de l'Hexagone, 1010, rue de la Gauchetiere Est, Montreal, PQ H2L 2N5, Canada *Tel:* 514-523-1182 *Fax:* 514-282-7530 *E-mail:* vml@ sogides.com *Web Site:* www.edhexagone.com, pg 544

Lewis, Kevin, Simon & Schuster Children's Publishing, 1230 Avenue of the Americas, New York, NY 10020 *Tel:* 212-698-7000 *Web Site:* www.simonsayskids.com, pg 248

Lewis, Kristen, Association for Information & Image Management International, 1100 Wayne Ave, Suite 1100, Silver Spring, MD 20910 *Tel:* 301-587-8202 *Toll Free Tel:* 800-477-2446 *Fax:* 240-494-2661 *E-mail:* aiim@aiim.org *Web Site:* www.aiim.org, pg 679

Lewis, Lydia, AMACOM Books, 1601 Broadway, New York, NY 10019-7406 *Tel:* 212-586-8100; 518-891-5510 (orders) *Toll Free Tel:* 800-262-9699 (cust serv) *Fax:* 212-903-8168; 518-891-2372 (orders) *Web Site:* www.amanet.org, pg 10

Lewis, Marc, Westminster John Knox Press, 100 Witherspoon St, Louisville, KY 40202-1396 *Tel:* 502-569-5052 *Toll Free Tel:* 800-227-2872 (US only) *Fax:* 502-569-8308 *Toll Free Fax:* 800-541-5113 (US only) *E-mail:* wjk@wjkbooks.com *Web Site:* www.wjkbooks.com, pg 297

Lewis, Mary, Technical Books for the Layperson Inc, PO Box 391, Lake Grove, NY 11755 *Tel:* 540-877-1477 *Fax:* 540-877-1477 *E-mail:* tbl_inc@yahoo.com *Web Site:* tblbooks.com, pg 266

Lewis, Michael, The Career Press Inc, 3 Tice Rd, Franklin Lakes, NJ 07417 *Tel:* 201-848-0310 *Toll Free Tel:* 800-CAREER-1 (227-3371) *Fax:* 201-848-1727 *Web Site:* www.careerpress.com, pg 53

Lewis, Rick, CCH Canadian Limited, A Wolters Kluwer Company, 90 Sheppard Ave E, Suite 300, Toronto, ON M2N 6X1, Canada *Tel:* 416-224-2224 *Toll Free Tel:* 800-268-4522 (Canada & US cust serv) *Fax:* 416-224-2243 *Toll Free Fax:* 800-461-4131 *E-mail:* cservice@cch.ca (cust serv) *Web Site:* www.cch.ca, pg 539

Lewis, Roslyn, Abingdon Press, 201 Eighth Ave S, Nashville, TN 37203-3919 *Tel:* 615-749-6290 (publicist); 615-749-6000; 615-749-6451 (sales) *Toll Free Tel:* 800-251-3320 *Fax:* 615-749-6056 *Web Site:* www.abingdonpress.com, pg 3

Lewis, S, Starlite Inc, PO Box 20004, St Petersburg, FL 33742-0004 *Tel:* 727-392-2929 *Toll Free Tel:* 800-577-2929 *Fax:* 727-392-6161 *E-mail:* starlite@citebook.com *Web Site:* www.starlite-inc.com; www.citebook.com, pg 258

Lewis, Sherry, The Overmountain Press, PO Box 1261, Johnson City, TN 37605-1261 *Tel:* 423-926-2691 *Toll Free Tel:* 800-992-2691 *Fax:* 423-929-2464 *Web Site:* www.overmountainpress.com, pg 200

Lewis, Stacey, City Lights Books Inc, 261 Columbus Ave, San Francisco, CA 94133 *Tel:* 415-362-8193 *Fax:* 415-362-4921 *E-mail:* staff@citylights.com *Web Site:* www.citylights.com, pg 62

Lewis, Sue, Jossey-Bass, 989 Market St, San Francisco, CA 94103-1741 *Tel:* 415-433-1740 *Toll Free Tel:* 800-956-7739 *Fax:* 415-433-0499 (orders) *Web Site:* www.josseybass.com; www.pfeiffer.com, pg 142

Lewis, Susan, Empire Press Media/Avant-Guide, 444 Madison Ave, 35th fl, New York, NY 10122 *Tel:* 212-563-1003 *Fax:* 212-536-2419 *E-mail:* info@avantguide.com; editor@avantguide.com *Web Site:* www.avantguide.com, pg 90

Lewis, Sylvia, Planners Press, 122 S Michigan Ave, Suite 1600, Chicago, IL 60603 *Tel:* 312-431-9100 *Fax:* 312-431-9985 *Web Site:* www.planning.org, pg 214

Lewy, Michelle, Scholastic Trade Division, 557 Broadway, New York, NY 10012 *Tel:* 212-343-6100; 212-343-4685 (export sales) *Fax:* 212-343-4714 (export sales) *Web Site:* www.scholastic.com, pg 242

Leyerle, William D, Leyerle Publications, 28 Stanley St, Mount Morris, NY 14510 *Tel:* 585-658-2193 *Fax:* 585-658-3298 *Web Site:* www.leyerlepublications.com, pg 153

Leyland, Winston, Gay Sunshine Press/Leyland Publications, PO Box 410690, San Francisco, CA 94141 *Tel:* 415-626-1935 *Fax:* 415-626-1802 *Web Site:* www.gaysunshine.com, pg 103

Li, Cherylynne, Fireside & Touchstone, 1230 Avenue of the Americas, New York, NY 10020, pg 97

Li, Yufan, East Asian Legal Studies Program, 500 W Baltimore St, Baltimore, MD 21201-1786 *Tel:* 410-706-3870 *Fax:* 410-706-1516 *E-mail:* eastasia@law.umaryland.edu, pg 85

Liang, Maureen, Outdoor Empire Publishing Inc, 424 N 130 St, Seattle, WA 98133 *Tel:* 206-624-3845 *Toll Free Tel:* 800-645-5489 *Fax:* 206-695-8512 *E-mail:* hjudeh@outdoorempire.com *Web Site:* www.outdoorempire.com, pg 200

Liberati, Jeannie, Hay House Inc, 2776 Loker Ave W, Carlsbad, CA 92008 *Tel:* 760-431-7695 *Toll Free Tel:* 800-650-5115; 800-654-5126 (orders) *Fax:* 760-431-6948 *E-mail:* info@hayhouse.com *Web Site:* www.hayhouse.com, pg 118

Liberator, Jennifer, Marlene Gabriel Agency, 333 W 56 St, Suite 8-A, 8th fl, New York, NY 10019 *Tel:* 212-397-8322 *E-mail:* mgalit@aol.com, pg 632

Liberatore, Arlette, Society for Industrial & Applied Mathematics, 3600 University City Science Ctr, Philadelphia, PA 19104-2688 *Tel:* 215-382-9800 *Toll Free Tel:* 800-447-7426 *Fax:* 215-386-7999 *E-mail:* siam@siam.org *Web Site:* www.siam.org, pg 251

Lidofsky, Norman, Penguin Group (USA) Inc Sales, 375 Hudson St, New York, NY 10014 *Tel:* 212-366-2000 *E-mail:* online@penguinputnam.com *Web Site:* www.penguin.com, pg 207

Lidofsky, Norman, Penguin Group (USA) Inc, 375 Hudson St, New York, NY 10014 *Tel:* 212-366-2000 *Fax:* 212-366-2666 *E-mail:* online@uspenguingroup.com *Web Site:* www.penguin.com, pg 208

Lidstone, Rob, The Literary Press Group of Canada, 192 Spadina Ave, Suite 501, Toronto, ON M5T 2C2, Canada *Tel:* 416-483-1321 *Fax:* 416-483-2510 *E-mail:* info@lpg.ca *Web Site:* www.lpg.ca, pg 690

Lieber, Dave, The National Society of Newspaper Columnists (NSNC), Fillmore St, Suite 507, San Francisco, CA 94115 *Tel:* 415-541-5636 *Web Site:* www.columnists.com, pg 694

Lieberman, Bonnie, John Wiley & Sons Inc, 111 River St, Hoboken, NJ 07030 *Tel:* 201-748-6000 *Toll Free Tel:* 800-225-5945 (cust serv) *Fax:* 201-748-6088 *E-mail:* info@wiley.com *Web Site:* www.wiley.com, pg 299

Lieberman, Bonnie, John Wiley & Sons Inc Education Publishing Group, 111 River St, Hoboken, NJ 07030 *Tel:* 201-748-6000 *Fax:* 201-748-6088 *E-mail:* info@wiley.com *Web Site:* www.wiley.com, pg 300

Lieberman, Robert, Robert Lieberman Agency, 400 Nelson Rd, Ithaca, NY 14850-9440 *Tel:* 607-273-8801 *Web Site:* www.people.cornell.edu/pages/RHL10/, pg 640

Liebman, Lance, American Law Institute, 4025 Chestnut St, Philadelphia, PA 19104-3099 *Tel:* 215-243-1600 *Toll Free Tel:* 800-253-6397 *Fax:* 215-243-1664; 215-243-1683 *Web Site:* www.ali.org, pg 15

Liebmann, Nicholas, St Herman Press, 10 Beegum Gorge Rd, Platina, CA 96076 *Tel:* 530-352-4430 *Fax:* 530-352-4432 *E-mail:* stherman@stherman.com *Web Site:* www.stherman.com, pg 238

Liebmann, Ruth, Random House Inc, 1745 Broadway, New York, NY 10019 *Tel:* 212-782-9000 *Toll Free Tel:* 800-726-0600 *Web Site:* www.randomhouse.com, pg 226

Liedloff, Kristen, Penguin Group (USA) Inc Sales, 375 Hudson St, New York, NY 10014 *Tel:* 212-366-2000 *E-mail:* online@penguinputnam.com *Web Site:* www.penguin.com, pg 208

Liese, Donna, Rutgers University Press, 100 Joyce Kilmer Ave, Piscataway, NJ 08854-8099 *Tel:* 732-445-7762 (edit); 732-445-7762 (ext 627, sales) *Toll Free Tel:* 800-446-9323 (orders only) *Fax:* 732-445-7039 (acqs, edit, mktg, perms, prodn); 732-445-1974 (fulfillment) *E-mail:* garyf@rci.rutgers.edu *Web Site:* rutgerspress.rutgers.edu, pg 236

Liffring-Zug Bourret, Joan, Penfield Books, 215 Brown St, Iowa City, IA 52245 *Tel:* 319-337-9998 *Toll Free Tel:* 800-728-9998 *Fax:* 319-351-6846 *E-mail:* penfield@penfieldbooks.com *Web Site:* www.penfieldbooks.com, pg 207

Lightstone, Libbie, Annick Press Ltd, 15 Patricia Ave, Toronto, ON M2M 1H9, Canada *Tel:* 416-221-4802 *Fax:* 416-221-8400 *E-mail:* annick@annickpress.com *Web Site:* www.annickpress.com, pg 535

Ligon, Linda, Interweave Press, 201 E Fourth St, Loveland, CO 80537 *Tel:* 970-669-7672 *Toll Free Tel:* 800-272-2193 *Fax:* 970-667-8317 *E-mail:* customerservice@interweave.com *Web Site:* www.interweave.com, pg 138

Ligrano, Ron, ProStar Publications Inc, 3 Church Circle, Suite 109, Annapolis, MD 21401 *Tel:* 310-280-1010 *Toll Free Tel:* 800-481-6277 *Fax:* 310-280-1025 *Toll Free Fax:* 800-487-6277 *E-mail:* editor@prostarpublications.com *Web Site:* www.prostarpublications.com; www.nauticalbooks.com, pg 220

Liguori, Nancy, The Analytic Press, 101 West St, Hillsdale, NJ 07642 *Tel:* 201-358-9477; 201-236-9500 *Toll Free Tel:* 800-926-6579 (orders only); 800-627-0629 (journal orders) *Fax:* 201-358-4700 (edit); 201-760-3735 (orders only) *E-mail:* tap@analyticpress.com *Web Site:* www.analyticpress.com, pg 19

Likoff, Laurie, Facts on File Inc, 132 W 31 St, 17th fl, New York, NY 10001 *Tel:* 212-967-8800 *Toll Free Tel:* 800-322-8755 *Fax:* 212-967-9196 *Toll Free Fax:* 800-678-3633 *E-mail:* custserv@factsonfile.com *Web Site:* www.factsonfile.com, pg 94

Lillebo, Karin, Silver Moon Press, 160 Fifth Ave, New York, NY 10010 *Tel:* 212-242-6499 *Toll Free Tel:* 800-874-3320 *Fax:* 212-242-6799 *E-mail:* mail@silvermoonpress.com *Web Site:* www.silvermoonpress.com, pg 247

Limb, John, Pastoral Press, 5536 NE Hassalo, Portland, OR 97213-3638 *Tel:* 503-281-1191 *Toll Free Tel:* 800-548-8749 *Fax:* 503-282-3486 *Toll Free Fax:* 800-462-7329 *E-mail:* liturgy@ocp.org *Web Site:* www.ocp.org, pg 205

Lin, Tracy, China Books & Periodicals Inc, 2929 24 St, San Francisco, CA 94110-4126 *Tel:* 415-282-2994 *Toll Free Tel:* 800-818-2017 *Fax:* 415-282-0994 *E-mail:* info@chinabooks.com *Web Site:* www.chinabooks.com, pg 60

Lincoln, Jerome A, Ray Lincoln Literary Agency, Elkins Park House, Suite 107-B, 7900 Old York Rd, Elkins Park, PA 19027 *Tel:* 215-635-0827 *Fax:* 215-782-8019, pg 640

Lincoln, Mary L, Northern Illinois University Press, 310 N Fifth St, De Kalb, IL 60115 *Tel:* 815-753-1826; 815-753-1075 *Fax:* 815-753-1845 *E-mail:* bberg@niu.edu *Web Site:* www.niu.edu/univ_press, pg 193

Lincoln, Mrs Ray, Ray Lincoln Literary Agency, Elkins Park House, Suite 107-B, 7900 Old York Rd, Elkins Park, PA 19027 *Tel:* 215-635-0827 *Fax:* 215-782-8019, pg 640

Lindeburg, Michael, Professional Publications Inc, 1250 Fifth Ave, Belmont, CA 94002 *Tel:* 650-593-9119 *Toll Free Tel:* 800-426-1178 *Fax:* 650-592-4519 *E-mail:* info@passthatexam.com *Web Site:* www.passthatexam.com, pg 220

Lindeman, Glen, Washington State University Press, Cooper Publications Bldg, Grimes Way, Pullman, WA 99164-5910 *Tel:* 509-335-3518 *Toll Free Tel:* 800-354-7360 *Fax:* 509-335-8568 *E-mail:* wsupress@wsu.edu *Web Site:* wsupress.wsu.edu, pg 293

Lindeman, Susan, Pennsylvania Historical & Museum Commission, Commonwealth Keystone Bldg, 400 North St, Harrisburg, PA 17120-0053 *Tel:* 717-783-2618 *Toll Free Tel:* 800-747-7790 *Fax:* 717-787-8312 *Web Site:* www.phmc.state.pa.us, pg 209

Lindemann, Ina, Springer-Verlag New York Inc, 175 Fifth Ave, New York, NY 10010 *Tel:* 212-460-1500 *Toll Free Tel:* 800-777-4643 *Fax:* 212-473-6272 *Web Site:* www.springer-ny.com, pg 256

Linder, Bertram, Educational Design Services Inc, 7238 Treviso Lane, Boynton Beach, FL 33437-7338 *Tel:* 561-739-9402, pg 629

Linder, Bertram L, Educational Design Services Inc, 7238 Treviso Lane, Boynton Beach, FL 33437-7338 *Tel:* 561-739-9402, pg 629

Linder, Gretchen, Association of American University Presses, 1427 E 60 St, Chicago, IL 60637 *Tel:* 773-702-7700; 773-702-7600 *Toll Free Tel:* 800-621-2736 (orders) *Fax:* 773-702-9756 (sales); 773-660-2235 (orders); 773-702-2708 *E-mail:* general@press.uchicago.edu *Web Site:* www.press.uchicago.edu, pg 26

Lindley, David, Harcourt Achieve, 10801 N MoPac Expressway, Austin, TX 78759 *Tel:* 512-343-8227 *Toll Free Tel:* 800-531-5015 *Toll Free Fax:* 800-699-9459 *E-mail:* ecare@harcourt.com *Web Site:* www.harcourtachieve.com, pg 114

Lindley, David, Rigby, 10801 N MoPac Expressway, Austin, TX 78759 *Tel:* 512-343-8227 *Toll Free Tel:* 800-531-5015 *Toll Free Fax:* 800-699-9459 *E-mail:* ecare@harcourt.com *Web Site:* www.harcourtachieve.com, pg 232

Lindley, David, Steck-Vaughn, 10801 N MoPac Expressway, Austin, TX 78759 *Tel:* 512-343-8227 *Toll Free Tel:* 800-531-5015 *Toll Free Fax:* 800-699-9459 *E-mail:* ecare@harcourt.com *Web Site:* www.harcourtachieve.com, pg 258

Lindquist, Laura, University of Pennsylvania Press, 4200 Pine St, Philadelphia, PA 19104-4011 *Tel:* 215-898-6261 *Toll Free Tel:* 800-445-9880 (orders & cust serv only) *Fax:* 215-898-0404; 410-516-6998 (orders) *E-mail:* custserv@pobox.upenn.edu *Web Site:* www.upenn.edu/pennpress, pg 284

Lindsay, Diana, Sunbelt Publications Inc, 1250 Fayette St, El Cajon, CA 92020-1511 *Tel:* 619-258-4911 *Toll Free Tel:* 800-626-6579 *Fax:* 619-258-4916 *E-mail:* mail@sunbeltpub.com *Web Site:* www.sunbeltbooks.com, pg 262

Lindsay, Jeanne, Morning Glory Press Inc, 6595 San Haroldo Way, Buena Park, CA 90620-3748 *Tel:* 714-828-1998 *Toll Free Tel:* 888-612-8254 *Fax:* 714-828-2049 *Toll Free Fax:* 888-327-4362 *E-mail:* info@morninggloorypress.com *Web Site:* www.morninggloorypress.com, pg 178

Lindsay, Lowell, Sunbelt Publications Inc, 1250 Fayette St, El Cajon, CA 92020-1511 *Tel:* 619-258-4911 *Toll Free Tel:* 800-626-6579 *Fax:* 619-258-4916 *E-mail:* mail@sunbeltpub.com *Web Site:* www.sunbeltbooks.com, pg 262

Lindsay, William A, Harvard University Press, 79 Garden St, Cambridge, MA 02138-1499 *Tel:* 617-495-2600; 401-531-2800 (international orders) *Toll Free Tel:* 800-405-1619 (orders); 617-495-5898 (general); 617-496-4677 (edit & rts); 401-531-2801 (international orders) *Toll Free Fax:* 800-406-9145 (orders) *E-mail:* firstname_lastname@harvard.edu *Web Site:* www.hup.harvard.edu, pg 117

Lindsey, Christine, Acropolis Books Inc, 8601 Dunwoody Place, Suite 303, Atlanta, GA 30350 *Tel:* 770-643-1118 *Toll Free Tel:* 800-773-9923 *Fax:* 770-643-1170 *E-mail:* acropolisbooks@mindspring.com *Web Site:* www.acropolisbooks.com, pg 569

Lindsey, Kathryn, Jim Donovan Literary, 4515 Prentice, Suite 109, Dallas, TX 75206 *Tel:* 214-696-9411 *Fax:* 214-696-9412, pg 628

Lindstrom, Ann, Proof Positive/Farrowlyne Associates Inc, 1620 Central St, Evanston, IL 60201 *Tel:* 847-866-9570 *Fax:* 847-866-9849, pg 609

Linebaugh, Andy, National Education Association (NEA), 1201 16 St NW, Washington, DC 20036 *Tel:* 202-822-7200 *Fax:* 202-822-7206; 202-822-7292 *Web Site:* www.nea.org, pg 693

Linebaugh, Nina, Teacher's Discovery, 2741 Paldan Dr, Auburn Hills, MI 48326 *Tel:* 248-340-7220 ext 207 *Toll Free Tel:* 800-521-3897 *Fax:* 248-340-7212 *Toll Free Fax:* 888-987-2436 *Web Site:* www.teachersdiscovery.com, pg 265

Lineman, Stacy, Mason Crest Publishers, 370 Reed Rd, Suite 302, Broomall, PA 19008 *Tel:* 610-543-6200 *Toll Free Tel:* 866-MCP-BOOK (627-2665) *Fax:* 610-543-3878 *Web Site:* www.masoncrest.com, pg 165

Linick, Andrew S PhD, Copywriter's Council of America (CCA), CCA Bldg, 7 Putter Lane, Middle Island, NY 11953-0102 *Tel:* 631-924-3888 *Fax:* 631-924-3890 *E-mail:* cca4dmcopy@att.net *Web Site:* www.lgroup.addr.com/CCA.htm, pg 68

Linick, Andrew S PhD, Copywriter's Council of America (CCA), CCA Bldg, 7 Putter Lane, Middle Island, NY 11953-0102 *Tel:* 631-924-8555 *Fax:* 631-924-3890 *E-mail:* cca4dmcopy@att.net *Web Site:* www.lgroup.addr.com/CCA.htm, pg 595

Linick, Andrew S PhD, Copywriter's Council of America (CCA), CCA Bldg, 7 Putter Lane, Middle Island, NY 11953 *Tel:* 631-924-8555 *Fax:* 631-924-3890 *E-mail:* cca4dmcopy@att.net *Web Site:* www.lgroup.addr.com/CCA.htm, pg 685

Linick, Andrew S PhD, Andrew S Linick PhD, The Copyologist®, Linick Bldg, 7 Putter Lane, Middle Island, NY 11953 *Tel:* 631-924-8555 *Fax:* 631-924-3890 *E-mail:* linickgrp@att.net *Web Site:* www.lgroup.addr.com, pg 604

Link, Rev Fred OFM, St Anthony Messenger Press, 28 W Liberty St, Cincinnati, OH 45202 *Tel:* 513-241-5615 *Toll Free Tel:* 800-488-0488 *Fax:* 513-241-0399 *E-mail:* books@americancatholic.org *Web Site:* www.AmericanCatholic.org, pg 237

Link, Nina B, Magazine Publishers of America, 810 Seventh Ave, New York, NY 10019 *Tel:* 212-872-3700 *Fax:* 212-888-4217 *E-mail:* infocenter@magazine.org *Web Site:* www.magazine.org, pg 690

Linka, Ruth, NeWest Press, 8540 109 St, No 201, Edmonton, AB T6G 1E6, Canada *Tel:* 780-432-9427 *Toll Free Tel:* 866-796-5433 *Fax:* 780-433-3179 *E-mail:* info@newestpress.com *Web Site:* www.newestpress.com, pg 556

Linstedt, Toni, Elsevier, 11830 Westline Industrial Dr, St Louis, MO 63146 *Tel:* 314-872-8370 *Toll Free Tel:* 800-325-4177 *Fax:* 314-432-1380 *Web Site:* www.elsevier.com; www.elsevierhealth.com, pg 89

Linstedt, Toni, W B Saunders Ltd, 170 S Independence Mall W, Suite 300 E, Philadelphia, PA 19106-3399 *Tel:* 215-238-7800 *Toll Free Tel:* 800-545-2522 (cust serv) *Fax:* 215-238-7883 *Web Site:* www.elsevierhealth.com, pg 240

Linton, Anita, Corwin Press, 2455 Teller Rd, Thousand Oaks, CA 91320 *Tel:* 805-499-9734 *Fax:* 805-499-5323 *Toll Free Fax:* 800-417-2466 *E-mail:* info@corwinpress.com *Web Site:* www.corwinpress.com, pg 69

Lintott, Judi, Michigan Municipal League, 1675 Green Rd, Ann Arbor, MI 48105 *Tel:* 734-662-3246 *Toll Free Tel:* 800-653-2483 *Fax:* 734-663-4496 *Web Site:* www.mml.org, pg 173

Linz, Werner Mark, The Continuum International Publishing Group, 15 E 26 St, Suite 1703, New York, NY 10010 *Tel:* 212-953-5858 *Toll Free Tel:* 800-561-7704 *Fax:* 212-953-5944 *E-mail:* info@continuumbooks.com *Web Site:* www.continuumbooks.com, pg 67

Linzy, Jan, Camino E E & Book Co, c/o Jan Linzy, PO Box 6400, Incline Village, NV 89450 *Tel:* 530-546-7053 *Fax:* 530-546-7053 *E-mail:* info@camino-books.com *Web Site:* www.camino-books.com, pg 52

Lionetti, Kim, BookEnds LLC, 136 Long Hill Rd, Gillette, NJ 07933 *Tel:* 908-604-2652 *E-mail:* editor@bookends-inc.com *Web Site:* www.bookends-inc.com, pg 622

Lipkin, Randie, Fugue State Press, PO Box 80, Cooper Sta, New York, NY 10276 *Tel:* 212-673-7922 *Fax:* 208-693-6152 *E-mail:* info@fuguestatepress.com *Web Site:* www.fuguestatepress.com, pg 101

Lipkind, Wendy, Wendy Lipkind Agency, 120 E 81 St, New York, NY 10028 *Tel:* 212-628-9653 *Fax:* 212-585-1306 *E-mail:* lipkindag@aol.com, pg 640

Lipkowski, Elena, Avid Reader Press, 6705 W Hwy 290, Suite 502-295, Austin, TX 78735 *Tel:* 512-288-5349 *Fax:* 512-288-0317 *E-mail:* info@avidreaderpress.com; orders@avidreaderpress.com *Web Site:* www.avidreaderpress.com, pg 29

Lipner, Roy, Dearborn Trade Publishing, 30 S Wacker Dr, Chicago, IL 60606-1719 *Tel:* 312-836-4400 *Fax:* 312-836-1021 *E-mail:* contactus@dearborn.com *Web Site:* www.dearborn.com, pg 78

Lippel, Rosalind, Scribner, 1230 Avenue of the Americas, New York, NY 10020, pg 244

Lippert, Kevin C, Princeton Architectural Press, 37 E Seventh St, New York, NY 10003 *Tel:* 212-995-9620 *Toll Free Tel:* 800-722-6657 (dist) *Fax:* 212-995-9454 *E-mail:* sales@papress.com *Web Site:* www.papress.com, pg 218

Lippincott, John, Council for Advancement & Support of Education (CASE), 1307 New York Ave NW, Suite 1000, Washington, DC 20005 *Tel:* 202-328-5900 *Fax:* 202-387-4973 *E-mail:* info@case.org *Web Site:* www.case.org, pg 685

Lippincott, Kim, Graphic Arts Employers of America, 100 Daingerfield Rd, Alexandria, VA 22314 *Tel:* 703-519-8100; 703-519-8151 *Fax:* 703-548-3227 *Web Site:* www.gain.net, pg 687

Lippincott, Walter, Princeton University Press, 41 William St, Princeton, NJ 08540 *Tel:* 609-258-4900 *Toll Free Tel:* 800-777-4726 *Fax:* 609-258-6305 *Toll Free Fax:* 800-999-1958 *E-mail:* orders@cpfsinc.com *Web Site:* www.pup.princeton.edu, pg 219

Lippman, Barry, LearningExpress LLC, 55 Broadway, 8th fl, New York, NY 10006 *Tel:* 212-995-2566 *Toll Free Tel:* 800-295-9556 *Fax:* 212-995-5512 *E-mail:* customerservice@learnatest.com (cust serv) *Web Site:* www.learnatest.com, pg 151

Lippman, David, Publishers Resource Group, 307 Camp Craft Rd, Austin, TX 78746 *Tel:* 512-328-7007 *Fax:* 512-328-9480 *E-mail:* info@prgaustin.com *Web Site:* www.prgaustin.com, pg 609

Lipschultz, Dale, National Coalition for Literacy, 50 E Huron St, Chicago, IL 60611 *Tel:* 312-280-3275 *Toll Free Tel:* 800-228-8813 *Fax:* 312-280-3256 *E-mail:* ncl@ala.org *Web Site:* www.ala.org, pg 693

Lipscombe, Trevor C, The Johns Hopkins University Press, 2715 N Charles St, Baltimore, MD 21218-4363 *Tel:* 410-516-6900 *Toll Free Tel:* 800-537-5487 *Fax:* 410-516-6968 *Web Site:* www.press.jhu.edu, pg 141

Lipsitz, Howard, Educational Technology Publications, 700 Palisade Ave, Englewood Cliffs, NJ 07632-0564 *Tel:* 201-871-4007 *Toll Free Tel:* 800-952-2665 *Fax:* 201-871-4009 *E-mail:* edtecpubs@aol.com *Web Site:* www.bookstoread.com/etp, pg 88

Lipsitz, Lawrence, Educational Technology Publications, 700 Palisade Ave, Englewood Cliffs, NJ 07632-0564 *Tel:* 201-871-4007 *Toll Free Tel:* 800-952-2665 *Fax:* 201-871-4009 *E-mail:* edtecpubs@aol.com *Web Site:* www.bookstoread.com/etp, pg 88

Lipskar, Simon, Writers House LLC, 21 W 26 St, New York, NY 10010 *Tel:* 212-685-2400 *Fax:* 212-685-1781, pg 662

Lipsky, John, National Bureau of Economic Research Inc, 1050 Massachusetts Ave, Cambridge, MA 02138-5398 *Tel:* 617-868-3900 *Fax:* 617-868-2742 *E-mail:* op@nber.org *Web Site:* www.nber.org, pg 182

Lipson, Kim, The Bureau For At-Risk Youth, 135 Dupont St, Plainview, NY 11803-0760 *Tel:* 516-349-5520 *Fax:* 516-349-5521 *E-mail:* info@at-risk.com *Web Site:* www.at-risk.com, pg 50

Lipton, Frances, Humana Press, 999 Riverview Dr, Suite 208, Totowa, NJ 07512 *Tel:* 973-256-1699 *Fax:* 973-256-8341 *E-mail:* humana@humanapr.com *Web Site:* humanapress.com, pg 128

Lipton, Irene, Provincetown Arts Inc, 650 Commercial St, Provincetown, MA 02657 *Tel:* 508-487-3167 *Web Site:* www.provincetownarts.org, pg 220

Lish, Theo E, Munchweiler Press, 14217 Gale Dr, Victorville, CA 92394-7353 *Tel:* 760-245-9215 *Fax:* 760-245-9418 *E-mail:* publisher@munchweilerpress.com *Web Site:* www.munchweilerpress.com, pg 180

Lisman, Sharon, Scholastic Entertainment Inc, 524 Broadway, New York, NY 10012 *Tel:* 212-343-7500 *Fax:* 212-965-7448, pg 241

Liss, Bob, Berrett-Koehler Publishers Inc, 235 Montgomery St, Suite 650, San Francisco, CA 94104 *Tel:* 415-288-0260 *Fax:* 415-362-2512 *E-mail:* bkpub@bkpub.com *Web Site:* www.bkconnection.com, pg 37

Liss, Eli, Eli & Gail Liss, 41 Viking Lane, Woodstock, NY 12498 *Tel:* 845-679-7173 *E-mail:* lissindex@aol.com, pg 605

Liss, Gail, Eli & Gail Liss, 41 Viking Lane, Woodstock, NY 12498 *Tel:* 845-679-7173 *E-mail:* lissindex@aol.com, pg 605

Liss, Laurie, Sterling Lord Literistic Inc, 65 Bleecker St, New York, NY 10012 *Tel:* 212-780-6050 *Fax:* 212-780-6095, pg 657

Listokin, David, Center for Urban Policy Research, 33 Livingston Ave, Suite 400, New Brunswick, NJ 08901-1982 *Tel:* 732-932-3133 *Fax:* 732-932-2363 *Web Site:* www.policy.rutgers.edu/cupr, pg 57

Lit, Susan B, Sky Publishing Corp, 49 Bay State Rd, Cambridge, MA 02138-1200 *Tel:* 617-864-7360 *Toll Free Tel:* 800-253-0245 *Fax:* 617-864-6117 *Web Site:* skyandtelescope.com, pg 250

Litchfield, Malcolm, Ohio State University Press, 180 Pressey Hall, 1070 Carmack Rd, Columbus, OH 43210-1002 *Tel:* 614-292-6930 *Toll Free Tel:* 800-621-2736 *Fax:* 614-292-2065 *Toll Free Fax:* 800-621-8476 *E-mail:* ohiostatepress@osu.edu *Web Site:* ohiostatepress.org, pg 196

Littell, Amelie, St Martin's Press Trade Division, 175 Fifth Ave, New York, NY 10010 *E-mail:* firstname.lastname@stmartins.com *Web Site:* www.stmartins.com; www.minotaurbooks.com, pg 239

Little, Celine, Georges Borchardt Inc, 136 E 57 St, New York, NY 10022 *Tel:* 212-753-5785 *Fax:* 212-838-6518 *E-mail:* georges@gbagency.com, pg 622

Little, Joseph, American Literacy Council, 148 W 117 St, New York, NY 10026 *Tel:* 212-663-4200 *Toll Free Tel:* 800-781-9985 *E-mail:* fyi@americanliteracy.com *Web Site:* www.americanliteracy.com, pg 677

Little, Josie, Braille Co Inc, 65-B Town Hall Sq, Falmouth, MA 02540-2754 *Tel:* 508-540-0800 *Fax:* 508-548-6116 *E-mail:* braillinc@capecod.net *Web Site:* home.capecod.net/~braillinc, pg 45

Littlefield, Barb, Thorndike Press, 295 Kennedy Memorial Dr, Waterville, ME 04901-4517 *Tel:* 207-859-1026 *Toll Free Tel:* 800-233-1244 *Fax:* 207-859-1009 *Toll Free Fax:* 800-558-4676 (orders) *E-mail:* printorders@thomson.com; international@thomson.com (orders for customers outside US & CA) *Web Site:* www.gale.com/thorndike, pg 270

Littlehale, David, McGraw-Hill/Irwin, 1333 Burr Ridge Pkwy, Burr Ridge, IL 60527 *Tel:* 630-789-4000 *Toll Free Tel:* 800-338-3987 (cust serv) *Fax:* 630-789-6942; 614-755-5645 (cust serv) *Web Site:* www.mhhe.com, pg 168

Littlehales, Alexandra, Moonstone Press LLC, 7820 Oracle Place, Potomac, MD 20854 *Tel:* 301-765-1081 *Fax:* 301-765-0510 *E-mail:* mazeprod@erols.com *Web Site:* www.moonstonepress.net, pg 572

Littleton, Jeff, NACE International, 1440 S Creek Dr, Houston, TX 77084-4906 *Tel:* 281-228-6223 *Fax:* 281-228-6300 *E-mail:* pubs@mail.nace.org *Web Site:* www.nace.org, pg 181

Litts, Matt, Smithsonian Institution Press, 750 Ninth St NW, Suite 4300, Washington, DC 20560-0950 *Tel:* 202-275-2300 *Fax:* 202-275-2274 *E-mail:* inquiries@sipress.si.edu *Web Site:* www.sipress.si.edu, pg 251

Litwack, Lisa, Pocket Books, 1230 Avenue of the Americas, New York, NY 10020 *Toll Free Tel:* 800-456-6798 *Fax:* 212-698-7284 *E-mail:* consumer.customerservice@simonandschuster.com *Web Site:* www.simonsays.com, pg 215

Litwack, Sherry, Sundance Publishing, One Beeman Rd, Northborough, MA 01532 *Tel:* 508-571-6500 *Toll Free Tel:* 800-343-8204 *Fax:* 508-571-6510 *Toll Free Fax:* 800-456-2419 *E-mail:* info@sundancepub.com *Web Site:* www.sundancepub.com, pg 262

Litz, Theresa A, Syracuse University Press, 621 Skytop Rd, Syracuse, NY 13244-5290 *Tel:* 315-443-5534 *Toll Free Tel:* 800-365-8929 (orders only) *Fax:* 315-443-5545 *E-mail:* supress@syr.edu *Web Site:* syracuseuniversitypress.syr.edu, pg 263

Litzky, Paula, Harbor Press Inc, 5713 Wollochet Dr NW, PO Box 1656, Gig Harbor, WA 98335 *Tel:* 253-851-5190 *Fax:* 253-851-5191 *E-mail:* info@harborpress.com *Web Site:* harborpress.com, pg 114

Liu, Stephanie N L, Golden Meteorite Press, PO Box 1223 Main Post Office, Edmonton, AB T5J 2M4, Canada *Tel:* 780-378-0063, pg 548

Lively, John, The Taunton Press Inc, 63 S Main St, Newtown, CT 06470 *Tel:* 203-426-8171 *Toll Free Tel:* 800-283-7252; 800-888-8286 (orders) *Fax:* 203-426-3434 *Web Site:* www.taunton.com, pg 264

Livesey, Magdalen B, Cortina Learning International Inc, 7 Hollyhock Rd, Wilton, CT 06897-4414 *Tel:* 203-762-2510 *Toll Free Tel:* 800-245-2145 *Fax:* 203-762-2514 *E-mail:* info@cortina-languages.com; cortinainc@aol.com *Web Site:* www.cortina-languages.com (English language animation & sound); www.cursos-ingles-cortina.com (Spanish language animation & sound), pg 69

Livesey, Magdalen B, Institute for Language Study, 7 Hollyhock Rd, Wilton, CT 06897 *Tel:* 203-762-2510 *Toll Free Tel:* 800-245-2145 *Fax:* 203-762-2514 *E-mail:* cortinainc@aol.com *Web Site:* www.cortina-languages.com; members.aol.com/cortinainc, pg 134

Livesey, Robert E, Cortina Learning International Inc, 7 Hollyhock Rd, Wilton, CT 06897-4414 *Tel:* 203-762-2510 *Toll Free Tel:* 800-245-2145 *Fax:* 203-762-2514 *E-mail:* info@cortina-languages.com; cortinainc@aol.com *Web Site:* www.cortina-languages.com (English language animation & sound); www.cursos-ingles-cortina.com (Spanish language animation & sound), pg 69

Livesey, Robert E, Institute for Language Study, 7 Hollyhock Rd, Wilton, CT 06897 *Tel:* 203-762-2510 *Toll Free Tel:* 800-245-2145 *Fax:* 203-762-2514 *E-mail:* cortinainc@aol.com *Web Site:* www.cortina-languages.com; members.aol.com/cortinainc, pg 134

Livesey, Sharon, Fordham University, Graduate School of Business Administration, Dept of Communications & Media Management, 113 W 60 St, New York, NY 10023 *Tel:* 212-636-6199 *Fax:* 212-765-5573, pg 752

Livingston, Jeffrey B, McGraw-Hill Learning Group, 8787 Orion Place, Columbus, OH 43240 *Tel:* 614-430-4000 *Fax:* 614-430-6621, pg 168

Lizza, Arthur M Jr, Lawrence Erlbaum Associates Inc, 10 Industrial Ave, Mahwah, NJ 07430-2262 *Tel:* 201-236-2199 *Toll Free Tel:* 800-9-BOOKS-9 (926-6579) *Fax:* 201-760-3735 *E-mail:* orders@erlbaum.com *Web Site:* www.erlbaum.com, pg 91

Lizzi, Marian, Perigee Books, 375 Hudson St, New York, NY 10014 *Tel:* 212-366-2000 *Fax:* 212-366-2365 *E-mail:* online@penguinputnam.com *Web Site:* www.penguin.com, pg 210

Lloreda, Christine, Fireside & Touchstone, 1230 Avenue of the Americas, New York, NY 10020, pg 97

Lloyd, Dennis, University of Pittsburgh Press, 3400 Forbes Ave, 5th fl, Pittsburgh, PA 15260 *Tel:* 412-383-2456 *Fax:* 412-383-2466 *E-mail:* press@pitt.edu *Web Site:* www.pitt.edu/~press, pg 284

Lloyd, Leigh, Simon & Schuster, 1230 Avenue of the Americas, New York, NY 10020 *Tel:* 212-698-7000 *Toll Free Tel:* 800-223-2348 (cust serv); 800-223-2336 (orders) *Toll Free Fax:* 800-943-9831 (orders) *Web Site:* www.simonsays.com, pg 248

Lloyd, Timothy, Opie Prize, Mershon Ctr, Ohio State University, 1501 Neil Ave, Columbus, OH 43201-2602 *Tel:* 614-292-3375 *Fax:* 614-292-2407, pg 796

Loberg, Kristin, Silver Lake Publishing, 3501 W Sunset Blvd, Los Angeles, CA 90026 *Tel:* 323-663-3082 *Fax:* 323-663-3084 *E-mail:* theeditors@silverlakepub.com; results@silverlakepub.com *Web Site:* www.silverlakepub.com, pg 247

Lobl, Howard P, Paul H Brookes Publishing Co, PO Box 10624, Baltimore, MD 21285-0624 *Tel:* 410-337-9580 *Toll Free Tel:* 800-638-3775 *Fax:* 410-337-8539 *E-mail:* custserv@brookespublishing.com *Web Site:* www.brookespublishing.com, pg 48

Lobo, Lance C, Laureate Press, PO Box 8125, Bangor, ME 04402-8125 *Toll Free Tel:* 800-946-2727 *Fax:* 207-884-8095, pg 150

Loch, Katherine, McGraw-Hill/Osborne, 2100 Powell St, 10th fl, Emeryville, CA 94608 *Tel:* 510-420-7700 *Toll Free Tel:* 800-227-0900 *Fax:* 510-420-7703 *Web Site:* shop.osborne.com/cgi-bin/osborne, pg 168

Lochner, Wendy, Columbia University Press, 61 W 62 St, New York, NY 10023 *Tel:* 212-459-0600 *Toll Free Tel:* 800-944-8648 *Fax:* 212-459-3678 *Web Site:* www.columbia.edu/cu/cup, pg 65

Locke, Terry, Loyola Press, 3441 N Ashland Ave, Chicago, IL 60657 *Tel:* 773-281-1818; 773-244-4429 *Toll Free Tel:* 800-621-1008 *Fax:* 773-281-0555; 773-281-0152 (trade) *E-mail:* editorial@loydapress.com *Web Site:* www.loyolapress.org, pg 159

Lockhart, Robert, University of Pennsylvania Press, 4200 Pine St, Philadelphia, PA 19104-4011 *Tel:* 215-898-6261 *Toll Free Tel:* 800-445-9880 (orders & cust serv only) *Fax:* 215-898-0404; 410-516-6998 (orders) *E-mail:* custserv@pobox.upenn.edu *Web Site:* www.upenn.edu/pennpress, pg 284

Locklin, Amy, Indiana University Writers' Conference, Indiana University, Dept of English, 464 Ballantine Hall, Bloomington, IN 47405 *Tel:* 812-855-1877 *Fax:* 812-855-9535 *E-mail:* writecon@indiana.edu *Web Site:* www.indiana.edu/~writecon/, pg 744

Lockridge, Jack D, Federal Bar Association, 2215 "M" St NW, Washington, DC 20037 *Tel:* 202-785-1614 *Fax:* 202-785-1568 *E-mail:* fba@fedbar.org *Web Site:* www.fedbar.org, pg 95

Locks, Sueyun, Locks Art Publications/Locks Gallery, 600 Washington Sq S, Philadelphia, PA 19106 *Tel:* 215-629-1000 *Fax:* 215-629-3868 *E-mail:* info@locksgallery.com *Web Site:* www.locksgallery.com, pg 157

Lockwood, Hal, Penmarin Books Inc, 1044 Magnolia Way, Roseville, CA 95661 *Tel:* 916-771-5869 *Fax:* 916-771-5879 *E-mail:* penmarin@penmarin.com *Web Site:* www.penmarin.com, pg 208

Lockwood, Nancy, Harcourt School Publishers, 6277 Sea Harbor Dr, Orlando, FL 32887 *Tel:* 407-345-2000 *Toll Free Tel:* 800-225-5425 (cust serv) *Fax:* 407-352-3445 *Toll Free Fax:* 800-874-6418 *E-mail:* hbspcs@hbschool.com *Web Site:* www.harcourtschool.com, pg 114

Loeber, Justin, Atria Books, 1230 Avenue of the Americas, New York, NY 10020 *Tel:* 212-698-7000 *Fax:* 212-698-7007 *Web Site:* www.simonsays.com, pg 27

Loehnen, Ben, Random House Publishing Group, 1745 Broadway, New York, NY 10019 *Toll Free Tel:* 800-200-3552 *Toll Free Fax:* 800-200-3552 *Web Site:* www.randomhouse.com, pg 227

Loehr, Julie L, Michigan State University Press (MSU Press), 1405 S Harrison Rd, Suite 25, East Lansing, MI 48823 *Tel:* 517-355-9543 *Fax:* 517-432-2611 *Toll Free Fax:* 800-678-2120 *E-mail:* msupress@msu.edu *Web Site:* www.msupress.msu.edu, pg 173

Loehr, Mallory, Random House Children's Books, 1745 Broadway, New York, NY 10019 *Tel:* 212-782-9000 *Toll Free Tel:* 800-200-3552 *Fax:* 212-782-9452 *Web Site:* www.randomhouse.com/kids, pg 225

Loeppke, Larry, McGraw-Hill/Dushkin, 2460 Kerper Blvd, Dubuque, IA 52001 *Toll Free Tel:* 800-243-6532 *Web Site:* www.dushkin.com, pg 167

Loeppke, Larry, McGraw-Hill Primis Custom Publishing, 2460 Kerper Blvd, Dubuque, IA 52001 *Tel:* 563-588-1451 *Fax:* 563-589-4700 *E-mail:* first_last@mcgraw-hill.com *Web Site:* www.mhhe.com, pg 168

Loertscher, David V, Hi Willow Research & Publishing, 312 S 1000 East, Salt Lake City, UT 84102 *Toll Free Tel:* 800-873-3043 *Fax:* 936-271-4560 *E-mail:* sales@lmcsource.com *Web Site:* www.lmcsource.com, pg 122

Loewen, Darleen, Prairie View Press, PR 205, Rosenort, MB R0G 1W0, Canada *Tel:* 204-746-2375 *Toll Free Tel:* 800-477-7377 *Fax:* 204-746-2667, pg 558

Loewenthal, Linda, David Black Literary Agency, 156 Fifth Ave, Suite 608, New York, NY 10010 *Tel:* 212-242-5080 *Fax:* 212-924-6609, pg 621

Lofquist, Jen, Stylus Publishing LLC, 22883 Quicksilver Dr, Sterling, VA 20166-2012 *Tel:* 703-661-1504 (edit & sales) *Toll Free Tel:* 800-232-0223 *Fax:* 703-661-1547 *E-mail:* stylusmail@presswarehouse.com; stylusinfo@styluspub.com *Web Site:* styluspub.com, pg 261

Logan, Drew, FourWinds Press LLC, 4157 Crossgate Dr, Cincinnati, OH 47025 *Tel:* 513-891-0415 *Fax:* 513-891-1648 *Web Site:* www.fourwindspress.com, pg 571

Loggia, Wendy, Random House Children's Books, 1745 Broadway, New York, NY 10019 *Tel:* 212-782-9000 *Toll Free Tel:* 800-200-3552 *Fax:* 212-782-9452 *Web Site:* www.randomhouse.com/kids, pg 226

Loggins, Bob, Abingdon Press, 201 Eighth Ave S, Nashville, TN 37203-3919 *Tel:* 615-749-6290 (publicist); 615-749-6000; 615-749-6451 (sales) *Toll Free Tel:* 800-251-3320 *Fax:* 615-749-6056 *Web Site:* www.abingdonpress.com, pg 3

Logiudice, Carolyn, LinguiSystems Inc, 3100 Fourth Ave, East Moline, IL 61244 *Tel:* 309-755-2300 *Toll Free Tel:* 800-776-4332 *Fax:* 309-755-2377 *E-mail:* service@linguisystems.com *Web Site:* www.linguisystems.com, pg 155

Loiselle, Louise, Flammarion Quebec, 375 Ave Laurier ouest, Montreal, PQ H2V 2K3, Canada *Tel:* 514-277-8807 *Fax:* 514-278-2085 *E-mail:* info@flammarion.qc.ca *Web Site:* www.flammarion.qc.ca, pg 547

Lomas, Theresa, Manitoba Library Association, 600 100 Arthur St, Suite 416, Winnipeg, MB R3B 1H3, Canada *Tel:* 204-943-4567 *Fax:* 204-942-1555 *E-mail:* info@mla.mb.ca; mla@uwinnipeg.ca *Web Site:* www.mla.mb.ca, pg 690

Lombardi, Janet, Girl Scouts of the USA, 420 Fifth Ave, New York, NY 10018-2798 *Tel:* 212-852-8000 *Toll Free Tel:* 800-478-7248 *Fax:* 212-852-6511 *Web Site:* www.girlscouts.org, pg 105

Lombardi, Terri, Hyperion, 77 W 66 St, 11th fl, New York, NY 10023-6298 *Tel:* 212-456-0100 *Toll Free Tel:* 800-759-0190 (cust serv) *Fax:* 212-456-0157 *Web Site:* hyperionbooks.com, pg 129

Lombardino, Kelly, Center for Creative Leadership, One Leadership Place, Greensboro, NC 27438-6300 *Tel:* 336-288-7210 *Fax:* 336-288-3999 *Web Site:* www.ccl.org/publications, pg 56

Lomke, Evander, The Continuum International Publishing Group, 15 E 26 St, Suite 1703, New York, NY 10010 *Tel:* 212-953-5858 *Toll Free Tel:* 800-561-7704 *Fax:* 212-953-5944 *E-mail:* info@continuumbooks.com *Web Site:* www.continuumbooks.com, pg 67

London, Dr Herb, Hudson Institute, 1015 18 St NW, Suite 300, Washington, DC 20036 *Tel:* 202-223-7770 *Fax:* 202-223-8537 *E-mail:* info@hudson.org *Web Site:* www.hudson.org, pg 128

London, Robin, The Joy Harris Literary Agency, 156 Fifth Ave, Suite 617, New York, NY 10010 *Tel:* 212-924-6269 *Fax:* 212-924-6609 *E-mail:* gen.office@jhlitagent.com, pg 634

Loney, Brian, Canada Law Book Inc, 240 Edward St, Aurora, ON L4G 3S9, Canada *Tel:* 905-841-6472 *Toll Free Tel:* 800-263-2037 *Fax:* 905-841-5085 *Web Site:* www.canadalawbook.ca, pg 538

Loney, Glenn, Norma Epstein Foundation, 15 King's College Circle, Toronto, ON M5S 3H7, Canada *Tel:* 416-978-8083 *Fax:* 416-971-2027 *Web Site:* www.utoronto.ca, pg 772

Long, Bob, Thinkers' Press Inc, 1101 W Fourth St, Davenport, IA 52802 *Tel:* 563-323-7117 *Toll Free Tel:* 800-397-7117 *Fax:* 563-323-0511 *E-mail:* tpi@chessco.com *Web Site:* www.chessco.com, pg 269

Long, Donna, HRD Press, 22 Amherst Rd, Amherst, MA 01002 *Tel:* 413-253-3488 *Toll Free Tel:* 800-822-2801 *Fax:* 413-253-3490 *E-mail:* info@hrdpress.com; orders@hrdpress.com *Web Site:* www.hrdpress.com, pg 127

Long, Erin, Florida Individual Artist Fellowships, 1001 DeSoto Park Dr, Tallahassee, FL 32301 *Tel:* 850-245-6470 *Fax:* 850-245-6492 *Web Site:* www.florida-arts.org, pg 774

Long, Greg, Holt, Rinehart and Winston, 10801 N MoPac Expy, Bldg 3, Austin, TX 78759 *Tel:* 512-721-7000 *Toll Free Tel:* 800-225-5425 (cust serv) *Fax:* 512-721-7833 (mktg); 512-721-7898 (edit) *Web Site:* www.hrw.com, pg 124

Long, Jennifer, NAL, 375 Hudson St, New York, NY 10014 *Tel:* 212-366-2000 *E-mail:* online@penguinputnam.com *Web Site:* www.penguin.com, pg 181

Long, Judy, Hill Street Press LLC, 191 E Broad St, Suite 209, Athens, GA 30601-2848 *Tel:* 706-613-7200 *Fax:* 706-613-7204 *Web Site:* www.hillstreetpress.com, pg 122

Long, Kathleen E, Business & Legal Reports Inc, 141 Mill Rock Rd, Old Saybrook, CT 06475-6001 *Tel:* 860-510-0100 *Toll Free Tel:* 800-727-5257 *Fax:* 860-510-7223 *E-mail:* blrblr@aol.com *Web Site:* www.blr.com, pg 50

Long, Michael, Hendrick-Long Publishing Co, 10635 Tower Oaks, Suite D, Houston, TX 77070 *Tel:* 832-912-READ (912-7323) *Fax:* 832-912-7353 *E-mail:* hendrick-long@worldnet.att.net *Web Site:* www.hendricklongpublishing.com, pg 121

Long, Sherry, Hampton-Brown Co Inc, 26385 Carmel Rancho Blvd, Carmel, CA 93923 *Tel:* 831-625-3666 *Toll Free Tel:* 800-933-3510 *Fax:* 831-625-8619 *E-mail:* customerservice@hampton-brown.com *Web Site:* www.hampton-brown.com, pg 113

Long, Travis, Association of College & University Printers, Penn State University, 101 Business Services Bldg, University Park, PA 16802 *Tel:* 814-865-7544 *Fax:* 814-863-6376, pg 680

Long, Vilma, Hendrick-Long Publishing Co, 10635 Tower Oaks, Suite D, Houston, TX 77070 *Tel:* 832-912-READ (912-7323) *Fax:* 832-912-7353 *E-mail:* hendrick-long@worldnet.att.net *Web Site:* www.hendricklongpublishing.com, pg 121

Longe, Ron, Routledge, 29 W 35 St, New York, NY 10001-2299 *Tel:* 212-216-7800 *Fax:* 212-564-7854 (main) *E-mail:* info@taylorandfrancis.com *Web Site:* www.routledge-ny.com, pg 235

Longo, Edward, Recorded Books LLC, 270 Skipjack Rd, Prince Frederick, MD 20678 *Tel:* 410-535-5590 *Toll Free Tel:* 800-638-1304 *Fax:* 410-535-5499 *E-mail:* recordedbooks@recordedbooks.com *Web Site:* www.recordedbooks.com, pg 229

Longo, Rick, School of Visual Arts, 209 E 23 St, New York, NY 10010 *Tel:* 212-592-2100 *Fax:* 212-592-2116 *Web Site:* www.schoolofvisualarts.edu, pg 754

Longworth, Jay, Clovernook Printing House for the Blind, 7000 Hamilton Ave, Cincinnati, OH 45231-5297 *Tel:* 513-522-3860 *Toll Free Tel:* 888-234-7156 *Fax:* 513-728-3946 (admin); 513-728-3950 (sales) *Web Site:* www.clovernook.org, pg 63

Lonnborg, Barbara, Boys Town Press, 14100 Crawford St, Boys Town, NE 68010 *Tel:* 402-498-1320 *Toll Free Tel:* 800-282-6657 *Fax:* 402-498-1310 *E-mail:* btpress@boystown.org *Web Site:* www.boystownpress.org, pg 45

Loo, Beverly Jane, University of Virginia Publishing & Communications Institute, 104 Midmont Lane, Charlottesville, VA 22904-4764 *Tel:* 434-982-5345 *Toll Free Tel:* 800-346-3882 *Fax:* 434-982-5239, pg 756

Loo, Patricia, M E Sharpe Inc, 80 Business Park Dr, Suite 202, Armonk, NY 10504 *Tel:* 914-273-1800 *Toll Free Tel:* 800-541-6563 *Fax:* 914-273-2106 *E-mail:* info@mesharpe.com *Web Site:* www.mesharpe.com, pg 246

Loomis, Bob, Random House Publishing Group, 1745 Broadway, New York, NY 10019 *Toll Free Tel:* 800-200-3552 *Toll Free Fax:* 800-200-3552 *Web Site:* www.randomhouse.com, pg 227

Loomis, Gloria, Watkins Loomis Agency Inc, 133 E 35 St, Suite 1, New York, NY 10016 *Tel:* 212-532-0080 *Fax:* 212-889-0506, pg 660

Loomis, Michael J, Graphic World Publishing Services, 11687 Adie Rd, Maryland Heights, MO 63043 *Tel:* 314-567-9854 *Fax:* 314-567-0360, pg 600

Looney, Dennis, Springer-Verlag New York Inc, 175 Fifth Ave, New York, NY 10010 *Tel:* 212-460-1500 *Toll Free Tel:* 800-777-4643 *Fax:* 212-473-6272 *Web Site:* www.springer-ny.com, pg 256

Lopez, Diana, University of Southern California, Professional Writing Program, Waite Phillips Hall, Rm 404, Los Angeles, CA 90089-4034 *Tel:* 213-740-3252 *Fax:* 213-740-5775 *E-mail:* mpw@usc.edu *Web Site:* www.usc.edu/dept/LAS/mpw, pg 756

Lopez-Franco, Edna, Morgan Kaufmann Publishers, 500 Sansome, Suite 400, San Francisco, CA 94111 *Tel:* 415-392-2665 *Fax:* 415-982-2665 *E-mail:* mkp@mkp.com *Web Site:* www.mkp.com, pg 178

Lopotukhin, Maina, Newmarket Publishing & Communications, 18 E 48 St, New York, NY 10017 *Tel:* 212-832-3575 *Toll Free Tel:* 800-669-3903 *Fax:* 212-832-3629 *E-mail:* mailbox@newmarketpress.com *Web Site:* www.newmarketpress.com, pg 190

Lorand, Susan, Markus Wiener Publishers Inc, 231 Nassau St, Princeton, NJ 08542 *Tel:* 609-921-1141; 609-921-7686 (orders) *Fax:* 609-921-1140; 609-279-0657 (orders) *E-mail:* publisher@markuswiener.com; orders@markuswiener.com *Web Site:* www.markuswiener.com, pg 299

Lord, Melissa, Bantam Dell Publishing Group, 1745 Broadway, New York, NY 10019 *Tel:* 212-782-9000 *Toll Free Tel:* 800-223-6834 *Fax:* 212-302-7985 *Web Site:* www.randomhouse.com/bantamdell, pg 31

Lord, Sara, Landes Bioscience, 810 S Church St, Georgetown, TX 78626 *Tel:* 512-863-7762 *Toll Free Tel:* 800-736-9948 *Fax:* 512-863-0081 *Web Site:* www.landesbioscience.com, pg 148

Lord, Sterling, Sterling Lord Literistic Inc, 65 Bleecker St, New York, NY 10012 *Tel:* 212-780-6050 *Fax:* 212-780-6095, pg 657

Lore, Matthew, Marlowe & Company, 245 W 17 St, 11th fl, New York, NY 10011-5300 *Tel:* 646-375-2570 *Fax:* 646-375-2571 *Web Site:* www.marlowepub.com, pg 164

Loren, Allan, Dun & Bradstreet, 103 JFK Pkwy, Short Hills, NJ 07078 *Tel:* 973-921-5500 *Toll Free Tel:* 800-526-0651 *E-mail:* custserv@dnb.com *Web Site:* www.dnb.com, pg 84

Loren, Cary, Book Beat Ltd, 26010 Greenfield, Oak Park, MI 48237 *Tel:* 248-968-1190 *Fax:* 248-968-3102 *E-mail:* bookbeat@aol.com *Web Site:* www.thebookbeat.com, pg 43

Lorenz, Laura, Management Sciences for Health, 165 Allandale Rd, Boston, MA 02130-3400 *Tel:* 617-524-7799 *Fax:* 617-524-2825 *E-mail:* bookstore@msh.org *Web Site:* www.msh.org, pg 162

Lorenz, Tom, Cottonwood Press, University of Kansas, Kansas Union, Rm 400, 1301 Jayhawk Blvd, Lawrence, KS 66045 *Tel:* 785-864-3777, pg 69

Lorimer, James, James Lorimer & Co Ltd, Publishers, 35 Britain St, 3rd fl, Toronto, ON M5A 1R7, Canada *Tel:* 416-362-4762 *Fax:* 416-362-3939 *E-mail:* info@lorimer.ca *Web Site:* www.lorimer.ca, pg 553

Lorimer, Rowland, Canadian Centre for Studies in Publishing, Simon Fraser University at Harbour Centre, 515 W Hastings St, Vancouver, BC V6B 5K3, Canada *Tel:* 604-291-5242 *Fax:* 604-291-5239 *E-mail:* ccsp-info@sfu.ca *Web Site:* www.harbour.sfu.ca/ccsp/, pg 683

Loring, Jacqueline, Young Writer's Workshop, PO Box 408, Osterville, MA 02655 *Tel:* 508-375-0516 *E-mail:* ccwc@capecod.net *Web Site:* www.capecodwriterscenter.com, pg 749

Loring, Jacqueline M, Annual Cape Cod Writers' Conference, PO Box 408, Osterville, MA 02655 *Tel:* 508-420-0200 *E-mail:* ccwc@capecod.net *Web Site:* www.capecodwriterscenter.com, pg 742

Lorraine, Walter, Houghton Mifflin Trade & Reference Division, 222 Berkeley St, Boston, MA 02116-3764 *Tel:* 617-351-5000 *Toll Free Tel:* 800-225-3362 *Web Site:* www.houghtonmifflinbooks.com, pg 126

Lorusso, Mike, National Publishing Co, 11311 Roosevelt Blvd, Philadelphia, PA 19154-2105 *Tel:* 215-676-1863 *Toll Free Tel:* 888-333-1863 *Fax:* 215-673-8069 *Web Site:* www.courier.com, pg 184

Lotman, Lynda, A+ English/ManuscriptEditing.com, 1830 Guinevere St, Arlington, TX 76014-2521 *Tel:* 817-467-7127 *E-mail:* editor@manuscriptediting.com *Web Site:* www.manuscriptediting.com; www.englishedit.com; www.queryletters.com; www.scifieditor.com; www.writingnetwork.com; www.book-editing.com; www.dissertationadvisors.com; www.thesisproofreader.com; www.statisticstutors.com; www.apawriting.com, pg 589

Lott, Ileo, MDRT Center for Productivity, 325 W Touhy Ave, Park Ridge, IL 60068-4265 *Tel:* 847-692-6378 *Toll Free Tel:* 800-879-6378 *Fax:* 847-518-8921 *E-mail:* orders@mdrt.org *Web Site:* www.mdrt.org, pg 169

Lott, Peter, Lott Representatives, 11 E 47 St, 6th fl, New York, NY 10017 *Tel:* 212-755-5737, pg 666

Lotts, Christopher, Ralph M Vicinanza Ltd, 303 W 18 St, New York, NY 10011 *Tel:* 212-924-7090 *Fax:* 212-691-9644 *E-mail:* ralphvic@aol.com, pg 659

Lotz, Amy B, Foundation of American Women in Radio & Television, 8405 Greensboro Dr, Suite 800, McLean, VA 22102 *Tel:* 703-506-3290 *Fax:* 703-506-3266 *E-mail:* info@awrt.org *Web Site:* www.awrt.org, pg 687

Lotz, Karen, Candlewick Press, 2067 Massachusetts Ave, Cambridge, MA 02140 *Tel:* 617-661-3330 *Fax:* 617-661-0565 *E-mail:* bigbear@candlewick.com *Web Site:* www.candlewick.com, pg 52

Loughlin, Tom, American Society of Mechanical Engineers (ASME), 3 Park Ave, New York, NY 10016 *Tel:* 212-591-7000 *Toll Free Tel:* 800-843-2763 (cust serv) *Fax:* 212-591-7674; 973-882-1717 (cust serv) *E-mail:* infocentral@asme.org *Web Site:* www.asme.org, pg 18

Loughrey, Mary, Looseleaf Law Publications Inc, 43-08 162 St, Flushing, NY 11358 *Tel:* 718-359-5559 *Toll Free Tel:* 800-647-5547 *Fax:* 718-539-0941 *E-mail:* llawpub@erols.com *Web Site:* www.LooseleafLaw.com, pg 158

Loughrey, Michael L, Looseleaf Law Publications Inc, 43-08 162 St, Flushing, NY 11358 *Tel:* 718-359-5559 *Toll Free Tel:* 800-647-5547 *Fax:* 718-539-0941 *E-mail:* llawpub@erols.com *Web Site:* www.LooseleafLaw.com, pg 158

Louie, Yook, Bantam Dell Publishing Group, 1745 Broadway, New York, NY 10019 *Tel:* 212-782-9000 *Toll Free Tel:* 800-223-6834 *Fax:* 212-302-7985 *Web Site:* www.randomhouse.com/bantamdell, pg 31

Lourie, Dick, Hanging Loose Press, 231 Wyckoff St, Brooklyn, NY 11217 *Tel:* 212-206-8465 *Fax:* 212-243-7499 *E-mail:* print225@aol.com *Web Site:* www.hangingloosepress.com, pg 113

Lourie, Iven, Gateways Books & Tapes, PO Box 370, Nevada City, CA 95959 *Tel:* 530-477-8101 *Toll Free Tel:* 800-869-0658 *Fax:* 530-272-0184 *E-mail:* info@gatewaysbooksandtapes.com *Web Site:* www.gatewaysbooksandtapes.com; www.retrosf.com, pg 103

Love, Karen, Lyndon B Johnson School of Public Affairs, University of Texas Austin, 2316 Red River St, Austin, TX 78705 *Tel:* 512-471-4218 *Fax:* 512-475-8867 *E-mail:* pubsinfo@uts.cc.utexas.edu *Web Site:* www.utexas.edu/lbj/pubs/, pg 160

Love, Nancy, Nancy Love Literary Agency, 250 E 65 St, Suite 4A, New York, NY 10021 *Tel:* 212-980-3499 *Fax:* 212-308-6405, pg 641

Love, Phyllis, F A Davis Co, 1915 Arch St, Philadelphia, PA 19103 *Tel:* 215-568-2270 *Toll Free Tel:* 800-523-4049 *Fax:* 215-568-5065 *E-mail:* info@fadavis.com *Web Site:* www.fadavis.com, pg 76

Love, Robert, Square One Publishers, 115 Herricks Rd, Garden City Park, NY 11040 *Tel:* 516-535-2010 *Fax:* 516-535-2014 *E-mail:* sq1info@aol.com *Web Site:* squareonepublishers.com, pg 256

Love, Stanley F, Love Publishing Co, 9101 E Kenyon Ave, Suite 2200, Denver, CO 80237 *Tel:* 303-221-7333 *Fax:* 303-221-7444 *E-mail:* lpc@lovepublishing.com *Web Site:* www.lovepublishing.com, pg 159

Lovell, Deborah, Taylor & Francis Editorial, Production & Manufacturing Division, 325 Chestnut St, Philadelphia, PA 19106 *Tel:* 215-625-8900 *Toll Free Tel:* 800-354-1420 *Fax:* 215-625-2940 *E-mail:* info@taylorandfrancis.com *Web Site:* www.taylorandfrancis.com, pg 264

Lovell, Deborah, Taylor & Francis Inc, 325 Chestnut St, Philadelphia, PA 19106 *Tel:* 215-625-8900 *Toll Free Tel:* 800-354-1420 *Fax:* 215-625-2940 *E-mail:* info@taylorandfrancis.com *Web Site:* www.taylorandfrancis.com, pg 265

Lovett, Steve, American Forest & Paper Association, 1111 19 St NW, Suite 800, Washington, DC 20036 *Tel:* 202-463-2700 *Toll Free Tel:* 800-878-8878 *Fax:* 202-463-4703 *E-mail:* info@afandpa.org *Web Site:* www.afandpa.org, pg 676

Lovig, Gail, Company's Coming Publishing Ltd, 2311 96 St, Edmonton, AB T6N 1G3, Canada *Tel:* 780-450-6223 *Toll Free Tel:* 800-875-7108 (US & Canada) *Fax:* 780-450-1857 *E-mail:* info@companyscoming.com *Web Site:* www.companyscoming.com, pg 541

Lovig, Grant, Company's Coming Publishing Ltd, 2311 96 St, Edmonton, AB T6N 1G3, Canada *Tel:* 780-450-6223 *Toll Free Tel:* 800-875-7108 (US & Canada) *Fax:* 780-450-1857 *E-mail:* info@companyscoming.com *Web Site:* www.companyscoming.com, pg 541

Lovisi, Gary, Gryphon Books, PO Box 209, Brooklyn, NY 11228 *Web Site:* www.gryphonbooks.com, pg 110

Low, Craig, Lee & Low Books Inc, 95 Madison Ave, New York, NY 10016 *Tel:* 212-779-4400 *Toll Free Tel:* 888-320-3190 ext 25 (orders only) *Fax:* 212-683-1894 (orders only); 212-532-6035 *E-mail:* info@leeandlow.com *Web Site:* www.leeandlow.com, pg 152

Low, Jason, Lee & Low Books Inc, 95 Madison Ave, New York, NY 10016 *Tel:* 212-779-4400 *Toll Free Tel:* 888-320-3190 ext 25 (orders only) *Fax:* 212-683-1894 (orders only); 212-532-6035 *E-mail:* info@leeandlow.com *Web Site:* www.leeandlow.com, pg 152

Lowder, James, Green Knight Publishing, 360 Chiquita Ave, No 4, Mountain View, CA 94041 *Tel:* 650-964-4276 *Fax:* 650-964-4276 *E-mail:* gawaine@greenknight.com *Web Site:* www.greenknight.com, pg 108

Lowe, Herb, National Association of Black Journalists (NABJ), c/o University of Maryland, 8701 Adelphi Rd, Adelphi, MD 20783 *Tel:* 301-445-7100 *Fax:* 301-445-7101 *E-mail:* nabj@nabj.org *Web Site:* www.nabj.org, pg 692

Lowe, Mary Ann, The Gerald Loeb Awards, Mullin Management Commons, Suite F-321B, 110 Westwood Plaza, Los Angeles, CA 90095-1481 *Tel:* 310-206-1877 *Fax:* 310-825-4479 *E-mail:* loeb@anderson.ucla.edu *Web Site:* www.loeb.anderson.ucla.edu, pg 785

Lowe, Monitta, The Pilgrim Press/United Church Press, 700 Prospect Ave, Cleveland, OH 44115-1100 *Tel:* 216-736-3761 *Toll Free Tel:* 800-537-3394 (cust serv) *Fax:* 216-736-2207 *E-mail:* thepilgrimpress@thepilgrimpress.com *Web Site:* www.thepilgrimpress.com; www.theunitedchurchpress.com, pg 213

Lowe, Rod, Children's Book Press, 2211 Mission St, San Francisco, CA 94110 *Tel:* 415-821-3080 *Fax:* 415-821-3081 *E-mail:* info@childrensbookpress.org *Web Site:* www.cbookpress.org, pg 60

Lowenstein, Barbara, Lowenstein-Yost Associates Inc, 121 W 27 St, Suite 601, New York, NY 10001 *Tel:* 212-206-1630 *Fax:* 212-727-0280 *Web Site:* www.lowensteinyost.com, pg 641

Lowenstein, Carole, Random House Publishing Group, 1745 Broadway, New York, NY 10019 *Toll Free Tel:* 800-200-3552 *Toll Free Fax:* 800-200-3552 *Web Site:* www.randomhouse.com, pg 227

Lowinger, Kathy, Tundra Books, 481 University Ave, Suite 900, Toronto, ON M5G 2E9, Canada *Tel:* 416-598-4786 *Fax:* 416-598-0247 *E-mail:* tundra@mcclelland.com *Web Site:* www.tundrabooks.com, pg 564

Lowman, Alfred, Authors & Artists Group Inc, 41 E 11 St, 11th fl, New York, NY 10003 *Tel:* 212-944-9898 *Fax:* 212-944-6484, pg 620

Lownds, Steven D, Trails Illustrated, Division of National Geographic Maps, PO Box 4357, Evergreen, CO 80437-4357 *Tel:* 303-670-3457 *Toll Free Tel:* 800-962-1643 *Fax:* 303-670-3644 *Toll Free Fax:* 800-626-8676 *E-mail:* topomaps@aol.com *Web Site:* www.nationalgeographics.com, pg 273

Lowry, Ann, University of Illinois Press, 1325 S Oak, Champaign, IL 61820-6903 *Tel:* 217-333-0950; 212-577-5487 *Fax:* 217-244-8082; 410-516-6969 (orders) *E-mail:* uipress@uillinois.edu; journals@uillinois.edu *Web Site:* www.press.uillinois.edu, pg 282

Lozier, Richard, University of Massachusetts Press, PO Box 429, Amherst, MA 01004-0429 *Tel:* 413-545-2217 *Toll Free Tel:* 800-537-5487 *Fax:* 413-545-1226; 410-516-6998 (fulfillment) *E-mail:* info@umpress.umass.edu; hfcustserv@mail.press.jhu.edu *Web Site:* www.umass.edu/umpress, pg 282

Lucas, Amy, New Letters Literary Awards, 5101 Rockhill Rd, Kansas City, MO 64110-2499 *Tel:* 816-235-1168 *Fax:* 816-235-2611 *E-mail:* newletters@umkc.edu *Web Site:* www.newletters.org, pg 794

Lucas, George, Inkwell Management, 521 Fifth Ave, 26th fl, New York, NY 10175 *Tel:* 212-922-3500 *Fax:* 212-922-0535 *E-mail:* contact@inkwellmanagement.com *Web Site:* www.inkwellmanagement.com, pg 635

Lucas, Joan, Harcourt School Publishers, 6277 Sea Harbor Dr, Orlando, FL 32887 *Tel:* 407-345-2000 *Toll Free Tel:* 800-225-5425 (cust serv) *Fax:* 407-352-3445 *Toll Free Fax:* 800-874-6418 *E-mail:* hbspcs@hbschool.com *Web Site:* www.harcourtschool.com, pg 114

Lucas, LaBruce M S, Southern Historical Press Inc, 275 W Broad St, Greenville, SC 29601-2634 *Tel:* 864-233-2346 *Fax:* 864-233-2349, pg 254

Lucas, Ling, Nine Muses & Apollo Inc, 525 Broadway, Rm 201, New York, NY 10012 *Tel:* 212-431-2665, pg 647

Lucas, Sandy, Presbyterian Publishing Corp, 100 Witherspoon St, Louisville, KY 40202 *Tel:* 502-569-5052 *Toll Free Tel:* 800-227-2872 (US only) *Fax:* 502-569-8308 *Toll Free Fax:* 800-541-5113 (US only) *E-mail:* ppcmail@presbypub.com *Web Site:* www.ppcpub.com, pg 217

Lucchese, Iole, Scholastic Canada Ltd, 175 Hillmount Rd, Markham, ON L6C 1Z7, Canada *Tel:* 905-887-7323 *Toll Free Tel:* 800-268-3848 (Canada) *Fax:* 905-887-1131 *Toll Free Fax:* 800-387-4944; 866-346-1288 *Web Site:* www.scholastic.ca, pg 560

Luce, Diana, The Creative Crayon Award, 13500 SW Pacific Hwy, Suite 129, Tigard, OR 97223 *Tel:* 503-670-1153 *Fax:* 503-213-5889 *Web Site:* www.thisnewworld.com, pg 769

Luce, Keisha, Festival of Poetry, Ridge Rd, Franconia, NH 03580 *Tel:* 603-823-5510 *E-mail:* rfrost@nci.net *Web Site:* www.frostplace.org, pg 743

Lucero, Jay, Scholastic Paperbacks, Teaching Resources & Reading Counts, 557 Broadway, New York, NY 10012-3999 *Tel:* 212-965-7241 *Fax:* 212-965-7487 *Web Site:* www.scholastic.com, pg 242

Lucero, Br Robert A OFM, St Anthony Messenger Press, 28 W Liberty St, Cincinnati, OH 45202 *Tel:* 513-241-5615 *Toll Free Tel:* 800-488-0488 *Fax:* 513-241-0399 *E-mail:* books@americancatholic. org *Web Site:* www.AmericanCatholic.org, pg 237

Luchars, Alex, Industrial Press Inc, 200 Madison Ave, 21st fl, New York, NY 10016-4078 *Tel:* 212-889-6330 *Toll Free Tel:* 888-528-7852 *Fax:* 212-545-8327 *E-mail:* info@industrialpress.com *Web Site:* www. industrialpress.com, pg 132

Luchetti, Lynn, Oxford University Press, Inc, 198 Madison Ave, New York, NY 10016-4314 *Tel:* 212-726-6000 *Toll Free Tel:* 800-451-7556 (orders) *Web Site:* www.oup.com/us, pg 200

Luciano, Jeannie, W W Norton & Company Inc, 500 Fifth Ave, New York, NY 10110-0017 *Tel:* 212-354-5500 *Toll Free Tel:* 800-233-4830 (orders & cust serv) *Fax:* 212-869-0856 *Toll Free Fax:* 800-458-6515 *Web Site:* www.wwnorton.com, pg 193

Lucido, Chet, Scott Foresman, 1900 E Lake Ave, Glenview, IL 60025 *Tel:* 847-729-3000 *Toll Free Tel:* 800-535-4391 (Midwest) *Fax:* 847-729-8910 *E-mail:* firstname.lastname@scottforesman.com *Web Site:* www.scottforesman.com, pg 243

Lucio, Paul, ATL Press Inc, PO Box 4563 "T" Sta, Shrewsbury, MA 01545-7563 *Tel:* 508-898-2290 *Fax:* 508-898-2063 *E-mail:* atlpress@compuserve.com *Web Site:* www.atlpress.com, pg 27

Lucke, Ann, Getty Publications, 1200 Getty Center Dr, Suite 500, Los Angeles, CA 90049-1682 *Tel:* 310-440-7365 *Fax:* 310-440-7758 *E-mail:* pubsinfo@getty.edu *Web Site:* www.getty.edu/bookstore, pg 104

Lucke, Ann, The Metropolitan Museum of Art, 1000 Fifth Ave, New York, NY 10028 *Tel:* 212-879-5500; 212-535-7710 *Fax:* 212-396-5062 *E-mail:* info@ metmuseum.org *Web Site:* www.metmuseum.org, pg 173

Luckert, David, Lynx House Press, 420 W 24 St, Spokane, WA 99203 *Tel:* 509-624-4894 *Fax:* 509-623-4238, pg 160

Lucki, Donna, Houghton Mifflin School Division, 222 Berkeley St, Boston, MA 02116-3764, pg 126

Ludden, Debbie, Thorndike Press, 295 Kennedy Memorial Dr, Waterville, ME 04901-4517 *Tel:* 207-859-1026 *Toll Free Tel:* 800-233-1244 *Fax:* 207-859-1009 *Toll Free Fax:* 800-558-4676 (orders) *E-mail:* printorders@thomson.com; international@ thomson.com (orders for customers outside US & CA) *Web Site:* www.gale.com/thorndike, pg 270

Ludwig, Jenny, American Eagle Publications Inc, 35610 Highway, Show Low, AZ 85901 *Tel:* 623-556-2925 *Toll Free Tel:* 866-764-2925 *Fax:* 623-556-2926 *E-mail:* custservice@ameaglepubs.com *Web Site:* www.ameaglepubs.com, pg 13

Ludwig, Mark A, American Eagle Publications Inc, 35610 Highway, Show Low, AZ 85901 *Tel:* 623-556-2925 *Toll Free Tel:* 866-764-2925 *Fax:* 623-556-2926 *E-mail:* custservice@ameaglepubs.com *Web Site:* www.ameaglepubs.com, pg 13

Luers, William H, United Nations Association of the United States of America Inc, 801 Second Ave, 2nd fl, New York, NY 10017 *Tel:* 212-907-1300 *Fax:* 212-682-9185 *E-mail:* unadc@unausa.org *Web Site:* www. unausa.org, pg 701

Lufers, Ingrid, Hancock House Publishers Ltd, 19313 Zero Ave, Surrey, BC V3S 9R9, Canada *Tel:* 604-538-1114 *Toll Free Tel:* 800-938-1114 *Fax:* 604-538-2262 *Toll Free Fax:* 800-983-2262 *E-mail:* promo@ hancockwildlife.org; sales@hancockhouse.com *Web Site:* www.hancockhouse.com, pg 549

Luger, Diane, Warner Books, 1271 Avenue of the Americas, New York, NY 10020 *Tel:* 212-522-7200 *Fax:* 212-522-7991 *Web Site:* www.twbookmark.com, pg 293

Lui, Brenna, AEI (Atchity Editorial/Entertainment International Inc), 9601 Wilshire Blvd, No 1202, Beverly Hills, CA 90210 *Tel:* 323-932-0407 *Fax:* 323-932-0321 *E-mail:* submissions@aeionline.com *Web Site:* www.aeionline.com, pg 618

Luke, Gary, Sasquatch Books, 119 S Main, Suite 400, Seattle, WA 98104 *Tel:* 206-467-4300 *Toll Free Tel:* 800-775-0817 *Fax:* 206-467-4301 *E-mail:* books@sasquatchbooks.com *Web Site:* www. sasquatchbooks.com, pg 240

Lukeman, Noah T, Lukeman Literary Management Ltd, 101 N Seventh St, Brooklyn, NY 11211 *Tel:* 718-599-8988 *Web Site:* www.lukeman.com, pg 641

Lull, Edward, J Franklin Dew Award, 100 N Berwick, Williamsburg, VA 23188 *Tel:* 757-258-5582 *Web Site:* www.poetrysocietyofvirginia.org, pg 769

Lum, Roxanne, Ignatius Press, 2515 McAllister St, San Francisco, CA 94118 *Tel:* 415-387-2324 *Toll Free Tel:* 877-320-9276 (book orders) *Fax:* 415-387-0896 *E-mail:* info@ignatius.com *Web Site:* www.ignatius. com, pg 131

Lumpee, Cynthia, Psychological Assessment Resources Inc (PAR), 16204 N Florida Ave, Lutz, FL 33549 *Tel:* 813-968-3003 *Toll Free Tel:* 800-331-8378 *Fax:* 813-968-2598 *Toll Free Tel:* 800-727-9329 *Web Site:* www.parinc.com, pg 221

Lumpkin, Ross, Thieme New York, 333 Seventh Ave, 5th fl, New York, NY 10001 *Tel:* 212-760-0888 *Toll Free Tel:* 800-782-3488 *Fax:* 212-947-1112 *E-mail:* customerservice@thieme.com *Web Site:* www. thieme.com, pg 268

Luna, Sr Carlos Gonzalez, University of Puerto Rico Press, Edificio EDUPR/Dialogo, Carr No 1, KM 12-0, Piso 2, Jardin Bota'nico Area Norte, San Juan, PR 00931 *Tel:* 787-758-6932; 787-758-8345 (sales); 787-250-0046; 787-250-0000 *Fax:* 787-753-9116; 787-751-8785 (sales dept), pg 284

Luna, Ramon, Texas Tech University Press, 2903 Fourth St, Lubbock, TX 79412 *Tel:* 806-742-2982 *Toll Free Tel:* 800-832-4042 *Fax:* 806-742-2979 *E-mail:* ttup@ ttu.edu *Web Site:* www.ttup.ttu.edu, pg 267

Lund, Peder C, Paladin Press, 7077 Winchester Circle, Boulder, CO 80301 *Tel:* 303-443-7250 *Toll Free Tel:* 800-392-2400 *Fax:* 303-442-8741 *E-mail:* service@paladin-press.com *Web Site:* www. paladin-press.com, pg 202

Lundahl, Jennifer, Sleeping Bear Press™, 310 N Main St, Suite 300, Chelsea, MI 48118 *Tel:* 734-475-4411 *Toll Free Tel:* 800-487-2323 *Fax:* 734-475-0787 *E-mail:* sleepingbear@thomson.com *Web Site:* www. sleepingbearpress.com, pg 250

Lundell, Michael, Indiana University Press, 601 N Morton St, Bloomington, IN 47404-3797 *Tel:* 812-855-8817 *Toll Free Tel:* 800-842-6796 (orders only) *Fax:* 812-855-7931 (orders only); 812-855-8507 *E-mail:* iupress@indiana.edu; iuorder@indiana.edu (orders) *Web Site:* www.iupress.indiana.edu, pg 132

Lundy, Daniel, Penguin Group (USA) Inc Sales, 375 Hudson St, New York, NY 10014 *Tel:* 212-366-2000 *E-mail:* online@penguinputnam.com *Web Site:* www. penguin.com, pg 208

Lupo, Thomas, Money Market Directories, 320 E Main St, Charlottesville, VA 22902 *Tel:* 434-977-1450 *Toll Free Tel:* 800-446-2810 *Fax:* 434-979-9962 *Web Site:* www.mmdwebaccess.com, pg 177

Lupoff, Ken, Berrett-Koehler Publishers Inc, 235 Montgomery St, Suite 650, San Francisco, CA 94104 *Tel:* 415-288-0260 *Fax:* 415-362-2512 *E-mail:* bkpub@bkpub.com *Web Site:* www. bkconnection.com, pg 37

Luppert, Sandi, Writer's Digest Writing Competition, 4700 E Galbraith Rd, Cincinnati, OH 45236 *Tel:* 513-531-2690 (ext 580) *Fax:* 513-531-0798 *E-mail:* writing-competition@fwpubs.com *Web Site:* www.writersdigest.com, pg 812

Luquire, Jerry, Brentwood Christian Press, 4000 Beallwood Ave, Columbus, GA 31904 *Tel:* 706-576-5787 *Toll Free Tel:* 800-334-8861 *E-mail:* brentwood@aol.com *Web Site:* www. brentwoodbooks.com, pg 46

Lurie, Stephanie, Dutton Children's Books, 345 Hudson St, New York, NY 10014 *Tel:* 212-366-2000 *E-mail:* online@penguinputnam.com *Web Site:* www. penguin.com, pg 85

Lurie, Susan, Parachute Publishing LLC, 156 Fifth Ave, Suite 302, New York, NY 10010 *Tel:* 212-691-1422 *Fax:* 212-645-8769 *Web Site:* www. parachutepublishing.com, pg 203

Luski, Michael, University of Alberta Press, Ring House 2, Edmonton, AB T6G 2E1, Canada *Tel:* 780-492-3662 *Fax:* 780-492-0719 *E-mail:* uap@ualberta.ca *Web Site:* www.uap.ualberta.ca, pg 564

Lutfy, Michael, HPBooks, 375 Hudson St, New York, NY 10014 *Tel:* 212-366-2000 *E-mail:* online@ penguinputnam.com *Web Site:* www.penguin.com, pg 127

Luther, John, Harian Creative Books, 47 Hyde Blvd, Ballston Spa, NY 12020-1607 *Tel:* 518-885-6699; 518-885-7397, pg 115

Luttinger, Selma, Robert A Freedman Dramatic Agency Inc, 1501 Broadway, Suite 2310, New York, NY 10036 *Tel:* 212-840-5760 *Fax:* 212-840-5776, pg 631

Lybolt, Peter, Toad Hall Inc, RR 2, Box 2090, Laceyville, PA 18623 *Tel:* 570-869-2942 *Fax:* 570-869-1031 *E-mail:* toadhallco@aol.com *Web Site:* www.laceyville.com/Toad-Hall, pg 658

Lydon, Tom, OneOnOne Computer Training, 2055 Army Trail Rd, Suite 100, Addison, IL 60101 *Tel:* 630-628-0500 *Toll Free Tel:* 800-424-8668 *E-mail:* oneonone@ protrain.com *Web Site:* www.ooootraining.com, pg 197

Lyle, Jane, Indiana University Press, 601 N Morton St, Bloomington, IN 47404-3797 *Tel:* 812-855-8817 *Toll Free Tel:* 800-842-6796 (orders only) *Fax:* 812-855-7931 (orders only); 812-855-8507 *E-mail:* iupress@indiana.edu; iuorder@indiana.edu (orders) *Web Site:* www.iupress.indiana.edu, pg 132

Lyman, Frank, John Wiley & Sons Inc Education Publishing Group, 111 River St, Hoboken, NJ 07030 *Tel:* 201-748-6000 *Fax:* 201-748-6088 *E-mail:* info@ wiley.com *Web Site:* www.wiley.com, pg 300

Lyman, Liz, Mapletree Publishing Co, 6233 Harvard Lane, Highlands Ranch, CO 80130-3773 *Tel:* 303-791-9024 *Toll Free Tel:* 800-537-0414 *Fax:* 303-791-9028 *E-mail:* mail@mapletreepublishing.com *Web Site:* www.mapletreepublishing.com, pg 163

Lynch, Catharine, G P Putnam's Sons (Hardcover), 375 Hudson St, New York, NY 10014 *Tel:* 212-366-2000 *E-mail:* online@penguinputnam.com *Web Site:* www. penguin.com, pg 223

Lynch, Chris, Simon & Schuster Audio, 1230 Avenue of the Americas, New York, NY 10020 *Tel:* 212-698-7664 *E-mail:* audiopub@simonandschuster.com *Web Site:* www.simonsaysaudio.com, pg 248

Lynch, Chris, Simon & Schuster Inc, 1230 Avenue of the Americas, New York, NY 10020 *Tel:* 212-698-7000 *Fax:* 212-698-7007 *Web Site:* www.simonsays.com, pg 249

Lynch, Claire, Facts on File Inc, 132 W 31 St, 17th fl, New York, NY 10001 *Tel:* 212-967-8800 *Toll Free Tel:* 800-322-8755 *Fax:* 212-967-9196 *Toll Free Fax:* 800-678-3633 *E-mail:* custserv@factsonfile.com *Web Site:* www.factsonfile.com, pg 94

Lynch, Dan, Tommy Nelson, PO Box 141000, Nashville, TN 37214-1000 *Tel:* 615-889-9000 *Toll Free Tel:* 800-251-4000 *Fax:* 615-902-3330 *Web Site:* www. tommynelson.com, pg 272

Lynch, Kevin, The Globe Pequot Press, 246 Goose Lane, Guilford, CT 06437 *Tel:* 203-458-4500 *Toll Free Tel:* 800-243-0495 (cust serv) *Fax:* 203-458-4601 *Toll Free Fax:* 800-820-2329 (orders & cust serv) *E-mail:* info@globepequot.com *Web Site:* www. globepequot.com, pg 106

Mackenzie, Leslie, Grey House Publishing Inc, 185 Millerton Rd, Millerton, NY 12546 *Tel:* 518-789-8700 *Toll Free Tel:* 800-562-2139 *Fax:* 518-789-0556 *E-mail:* books@greyhouse.com *Web Site:* www.greyhouse.com, pg 109

Macker, John, Gerald Peters Gallery, 1011 Paseo De Peralta, Santa Fe, NM 87501 *Tel:* 505-954-5700 *Fax:* 505-954-5754 *E-mail:* bookstore@gpgallery.com *Web Site:* www.gpgallery.com, pg 211

Mackey, Elliott, The Wine Appreciation Guild Ltd, 360 Swift Ave, Unit 30-40, South San Francisco, CA 94080 *Tel:* 650-866-3020 *Toll Free Tel:* 800-231-9463 *Fax:* 650-866-3513 *E-mail:* shannon@wineappreciation.com; info@wineappreciation.com *Web Site:* www.wineappreciation.com, pg 301

Macklem, Michael, Oberon Press, 350 Sparks St, Suite 400, Ottawa, ON K1R 7S8, Canada *Tel:* 613-238-3275 *Fax:* 613-238-3275 *E-mail:* oberon@sympatico.ca *Web Site:* www3.sympatico.ca/oberon, pg 556

Macklem, Nicholas, Oberon Press, 350 Sparks St, Suite 400, Ottawa, ON K1R 7S8, Canada *Tel:* 613-238-3275 *Fax:* 613-238-3275 *E-mail:* oberon@sympatico.ca *Web Site:* www3.sympatico.ca/oberon, pg 556

Mackross, Valerie, Amsco School Publications Inc, 315 Hudson St, New York, NY 10013-1085 *Tel:* 212-886-6500; 212-886-6565 *Toll Free Tel:* 800-969-8398 *Fax:* 212-675-7010 *E-mail:* info@amscopub.com *Web Site:* www.amscopub.com, pg 19

Mackwood, Robert, Seventh Avenue Literary Agency, 1663 W Seventh Ave, Vancouver, BC V6J 1S4, Canada *Tel:* 604-734-3663 *Fax:* 604-734-8906 *Web Site:* www.seventhavenuelit.com, pg 655

MacLachlan, Jim, LokiWorks, 813-633 Bay St, Toronto, ON M5G 2G4, Canada *Tel:* 416-599-4303 *Fax:* 416-599-4308 *E-mail:* editor@lokiworks.com *Web Site:* www.lokiworks.com, pg 605

MacLaren, Donald, Donald MacLaren & Associates, 2021 46 St, Astoria, NY 11105 *Tel:* 718-932-7720 *Fax:* 718-932-7720, pg 605

MacLaren, Donald S, BooksCraft Inc, 4909 Eastbourne Dr, Indianapolis, IN 46226 *Tel:* 317-542-8327 *Fax:* 317-591-9809 *E-mail:* bookscraft@comcast.net *Web Site:* www.bookscraft.com, pg 592

Maclean, Alison, Centennial College Press, c/o Centennial College, PO Box 631, Sta A, Scarborough, ON M1K 5E9, Canada *Tel:* 416-289-5000 (ext 8606) *Fax:* 416-289-5106 *E-mail:* ccpress@centennialcollege.ca *Web Site:* www.centennialcollege.ca, pg 540

MacLean, Brian, Novalis Publishing, 49 Front St E, 2nd fl, Toronto, ON M5E 1B3, Canada *Tel:* 416-363-3303 *Toll Free Tel:* 800-387-7164 *Fax:* 416-363-9409 *Toll Free Fax:* 800-204-4140 *E-mail:* novalis@interlog.com *Web Site:* www.novalis.ca, pg 556

MacLean, Tammy, IBFD Publications USA Inc (International Bureau of Fiscal Documentation), PO Box 805, Valatie, NY 12184 *Tel:* 518-758-2245 *Fax:* 518-784-2963 *E-mail:* info@ibfd.org *Web Site:* www.ibfd.org, pg 130

MacLellan, Lila, Western Magazine Awards Foundation, Main PO Box 2131, Vancouver, BC V6B 3T8, Canada *Tel:* 604-669-3717 *Fax:* 604-204-9302 *E-mail:* wma@direct.ca *Web Site:* www.westernmagazineawards.com, pg 810

Maclennan, Robert, The Anglican Book Centre, 80 Hayden St, Toronto, ON M4Y 3G2, Canada *Tel:* 416-924-1332 *Toll Free Tel:* 800-268-1168 (Canada only) *Fax:* 416-924-2760 *E-mail:* abc@nationalanglican.com *Web Site:* www.anglicanbookcentre.com, pg 535

MacMillan, Colleen, Annick Press Ltd, 15 Patricia Ave, Toronto, ON M2M 1H9, Canada *Tel:* 416-221-4802 *Fax:* 416-221-8400 *E-mail:* annick@annickpress.com *Web Site:* www.annickpress.com, pg 535

MacNeil, Mary, The University of Virginia Press, PO Box 400318, Charlottesville, VA 22904-4318 *Tel:* 434-924-3468 (cust serv); 434-924-3469 (cust serv) *Toll Free Tel:* 800-831-3406 (cust serv) *Fax:* 434-982-2655 *Toll Free Fax:* 877-288-6400 *E-mail:* upressvirginia@virginia.edu *Web Site:* www.upressvirginia.edu, pg 285

Macomber, Jennifer, American Psychological Association, 750 First St NE, Washington, DC 20002-4242 *Tel:* 202-336-5500 *Toll Free Tel:* 800-374-2721 *Fax:* 202-336-5620 *E-mail:* order@apa.org *Web Site:* www.apa.org/books, pg 17

Macrae, John, Henry Holt and Company, LLC, 115 W 18 St, New York, NY 10011 *Tel:* 212-886-9200 *Toll Free Tel:* 888-330-8477 (orders) *Fax:* 212-633-0748 *E-mail:* publicity@hholt.com *Web Site:* www.henryholt.com, pg 124

Macredie, Leslie, Wilfrid Laurier University Press, 75 University Ave W, Waterloo, ON N2L 3C5, Canada *Tel:* 519-884-0710 (ext 6124) *Fax:* 519-725-1399 *E-mail:* press@wlu.ca *Web Site:* www.press.wlu.ca, pg 567

Macy, Tom, Bedford/St Martin's, 75 Arlington St, Boston, MA 02116 *Tel:* 617-399-4000 *Fax:* 617-426-8582 *Web Site:* www.bedfordstmartins.com, pg 35

Madan, Neeti, Sterling Lord Literistic Inc, 65 Bleecker St, New York, NY 10012 *Tel:* 212-780-6050 *Fax:* 212-780-6095, pg 657

Madden, Glenda, University of New Mexico Press, 1720 Lomas Blvd NE, MSC01 1200, Albuquerque, NM 87131-0001 *Tel:* 505-277-2346; 505-277-4810 (order dept) *Toll Free Tel:* 800-249-7737 (orders only) *Fax:* 505-277-3350 *Toll Free Fax:* 800-622-8667 *E-mail:* unmpress@unm.edu; custserv@upress.unm.edu (order dept) *Web Site:* unmpress.com, pg 283

Maddison, George, University of British Columbia Press, 2029 West Mall, Vancouver, BC V6T 1Z2, Canada *Tel:* 604-822-5959 *Toll Free Tel:* 877-377-9378 *Fax:* 604-822-6083 *Toll Free Fax:* 800-668-0821 *E-mail:* info@ubcpress.ca *Web Site:* www.ubcpress.ca, pg 564

Maddox, Christine, The Fairmont Press Inc, 700 Indian Trail, Lilburn, GA 30047 *Tel:* 770-925-9388 *Fax:* 770-381-9865 *Web Site:* www.fairmontpress.com, pg 94

Madhubuti, Haki R, Third World Press, 7822 S Dobson Ave, Chicago, IL 60619 *Tel:* 773-651-0700 *Fax:* 773-651-7286 *E-mail:* twpress3@aol.com *Web Site:* www.thirdworldpressinc.com, pg 269

Madia, Nancy Green, Coffee House Press, 27 N Fourth St, Suite 400, Minneapolis, MN 55401 *Tel:* 612-338-0125 *Fax:* 612-338-4004 *Web Site:* www.coffeehousepress.org, pg 64

Madigan, Margaret, Makeready Inc, 233 W 77 St, New York, NY 10024 *Tel:* 212-595-5083, pg 605

Madigan, Timothy, University of Rochester Press, 668 Mt Hope Ave, Rochester, NY 14620 *Tel:* 585-275-0419 *Fax:* 585-271-8778 *E-mail:* boydell@boydellusa.net *Web Site:* boydellandbrewer.com, pg 285

Madison, Gabriele, Harcourt Achieve, 10801 N MoPac Expressway, Austin, TX 78759 *Tel:* 512-343-8227 *Toll Free Tel:* 800-531-5015 *Toll Free Fax:* 800-699-9459 *E-mail:* ecare@harcourt.com *Web Site:* www.harcourtachieve.com, pg 114

Madison, Gabriele, Steck-Vaughn, 10801 N MoPac Expressway, Austin, TX 78759 *Tel:* 512-343-8227 *Toll Free Tel:* 800-531-5015 *Toll Free Fax:* 800-699-9459 *E-mail:* ecare@harcourt.com *Web Site:* www.harcourtachieve.com, pg 258

Madison, Gabrielle, Rigby, 10801 N MoPac Expressway, Austin, TX 78759 *Tel:* 512-343-8227 *Toll Free Tel:* 800-531-5015 *Toll Free Fax:* 800-699-9459 *E-mail:* ecare@harcourt.com *Web Site:* www.harcourtachieve.com, pg 232

Madole, Michael, Allworth Press, 10 E 23 St, Suite 510, New York, NY 10010 *Tel:* 212-777-8395 *Toll Free Tel:* 800-491-2808 *Fax:* 212-777-8261 *E-mail:* pub@allworth.com *Web Site:* www.allworth.com, pg 9

Madsen, Liz, The Robert Madsen Literary Agency, 1331 E 34 St, Suite 1, Oakland, CA 94602 *Tel:* 510-223-2090, pg 642

Madson, Patricia, Penguin Group (USA) Inc Sales, 375 Hudson St, New York, NY 10014 *Tel:* 212-366-2000 *E-mail:* online@penguinputnam.com *Web Site:* www.penguin.com, pg 208

Maegraith, Michael, The Museum of Modern Art, 11 W 53 St, New York, NY 10019 *Tel:* 212-708-9443 *Fax:* 212-333-6575 *E-mail:* moma_publications@moma.org *Web Site:* www.moma.org, pg 180

Maerker, Jenevieve, Hackett Publishing Co Inc, PO Box 44937, Indianapolis, IN 46244-0937 *Tel:* 317-635-9250; 617-497-6306 *Fax:* 317-635-9292 *Toll Free Fax:* 800-783-9213 *E-mail:* customer@hackettpublishing.com *Web Site:* www.hackettpublishing.com, pg 111

Mafchir, James, New Mexico Book Association (NMBA), 310 Read St, Santa Fe, NM 87504 *Tel:* 505-983-1412 *Fax:* 505-983-0899 *E-mail:* oceantree@earthlink.net *Web Site:* www.nmbook.com, pg 695

Mafchir, James, Sherman Asher Publishing, PO Box 31725, Santa Fe, NM 87594-1725 *Tel:* 505-988-7214 *Fax:* 505-988-7214 *E-mail:* westernedge@santa-fe.net *Web Site:* www.shermanasher.com, pg 246

Magee, Connie, Impact Publishers Inc, PO Box 6016, Atascadero, CA 93423-6016 *Tel:* 805-466-5917 (opers & admin); 805-461-5911 (edit) *Toll Free Tel:* 800-246-7228 (orders) *Fax:* 805-466-5919 (opers & admin offices); 805-461-0554 (edit offices) *E-mail:* info@impactpublishers.com *Web Site:* www.impactpublishers.com; www.bibliotherapy.com, pg 131

Magill, James L, Salem Press Inc, 2 University Plaza, Suite 121, Hackensack, NJ 07601 *Tel:* 201-968-9899 *Toll Free Tel:* 800-221-1592 *Fax:* 201-968-1411 *E-mail:* csr@salempress.com *Web Site:* www.salempress.com, pg 239

Magill, William H, Reader's Digest Association Inc, Reader's Digest Rd, Pleasantville, NY 10570-7000 *Tel:* 914-238-1000 *Toll Free Tel:* 800-431-1726 *Fax:* 914-238-4559 *Web Site:* www.rd.com, pg 228

Magill, William H, Reader's Digest Children's Books, Reader's Digest Rd, Pleasantville, NY 10570-7000 *Tel:* 914-244-4800 *Toll Free Tel:* 800-934-0977, pg 228

Magill, William H, Reader's Digest General Books, Reader's Digest Rd, Pleasantville, NY 10570-7000 *Tel:* 914-238-1000 *Toll Free Tel:* 800-431-1726 *Fax:* 914-244-7436, pg 228

Magill, William H, Reader's Digest Trade Books, Reader's Digest Rd, Pleasantville, NY 10570-7000 *Tel:* 914-244-7445 *Fax:* 914-244-7605, pg 229

Magill, William H, Reader's Digest USA Select Editions, Reader's Digest Rd, Pleasantville, NY 10570-7000 *Tel:* 914-238-1000 *Toll Free Tel:* 800-310-6261 *Fax:* 914-238-4559, pg 229

Magne, Lawrence, International Broadcasting Services Ltd, 825 Cherry Lane, Penns Park, PA 18943 *Tel:* 215-598-3298 *Fax:* 215-598-3794 *E-mail:* hq@passband.com; mktg@passband.com *Web Site:* www.passband.com, pg 136

Magnon, Debbie, EDC Publishing, 10302 E 55 Place, Tulsa, OK 74146-6515 *Tel:* 918-622-4522 *Toll Free Tel:* 800-475-4522 *Fax:* 918-665-7919 *Toll Free Fax:* 800-747-4509 *E-mail:* edc@edcpub.com *Web Site:* www.edcpub.com, pg 86

Magnus, Mary H, Health Professions Press, PO Box 10624, Baltimore, MD 21285-0624 *Tel:* 410-337-9585 *Toll Free Tel:* 888-337-8808 *Fax:* 410-337-8539 *E-mail:* custserv@healthpropress.com *Web Site:* www.healthpropress.com, pg 119

Magnuson, James, University of Texas at Austin, Creative Writing Program, Dept of English, One University Sta, B5000, Austin, TX 78712-1164 *Tel:* 512-475-6356 *Fax:* 512-471-2898 *Web Site:* www.en.utexas.edu/grad/crwconc.html, pg 756

Magnuson, Steve, Sterling Publishing Co Inc, 387 Park Ave S, 5th fl, New York, NY 10016-8810 *Tel:* 212-532-7160 *Toll Free Tel:* 800-367-9692 *Fax:* 212-213-2495 *Web Site:* www.sterlingpub.com, pg 259

Magowan, Mark, The Vendome Press, 1334 York Ave, 3rd fl, New York, NY 10021 *Tel:* 212-737-5297 *Fax:* 212-737-5340 *E-mail:* vendomepress@earthlink.net, pg 290

Malden, Cheryl, The H W Wilson Library Staff Development Grant, 50 E Huron St, Chicago, IL 60611 *Tel:* 312-280-3247 *Toll Free Tel:* 800-545-2433 (ext 3247) *Fax:* 312-944-3897 *E-mail:* awards@ala.org *Web Site:* www.ala.org, pg 812

Malden, Cheryl M, Joseph W Lippincott Award, 50 E Huron, Chicago, IL 60611 *Tel:* 312-280-3247 *Toll Free Tel:* 800-545-2433 (ext 3247) *Fax:* 312-944-3897 *E-mail:* awards@ala.org *Web Site:* www.ala.org, pg 784

Maldonado, Alice, Juniper Prize for Poetry, Juniper Prize, University of Massachusetts Press, Amherst, MA 01003 *Tel:* 413-545-2217 *Fax:* 413-545-1226 *E-mail:* info@umpress.umass.edu *Web Site:* www.umass.edu/umpress, pg 782

Maleri, Jayna, Writers House LLC, 21 W 26 St, New York, NY 10010 *Tel:* 212-685-2400 *Fax:* 212-685-1781, pg 662

Malinowski, Edward A, U.S.A. Books Abroad Inc®, 46 Willow Dr, Briarcliff Manor, NY 10510 *Tel:* 914-762-2400 *Fax:* 914-762-2407 *E-mail:* booksabroad@optonline.net *Web Site:* www.usabooksabroad.com, pg 701

Malk, Steven, Writers House LLC, 21 W 26 St, New York, NY 10010 *Tel:* 212-685-2400 *Fax:* 212-685-1781, pg 662

Malkawi, Sathi, The International Institute of Islamic Thought, 500 Grove St, Suite 200, Herndon, VA 20170 *Tel:* 703-471-1133 *Fax:* 703-471-3922 *E-mail:* iiit@iiit.org *Web Site:* www.iiit.org, pg 137

Mallardi, Vincent, Printing Brokerage/Buyers Association, PO Box 744, Palm Beach, FL 33480-0744 *Tel:* 561-586-9391 *Toll Free Tel:* 866-586-9391 *Fax:* 561-845-7130 *E-mail:* info@pbbai.net *Web Site:* www.pbbai.net, pg 697

Mallea, Sara Velez, University of Nevada Press, MS 166, Reno, NV 89557-0076 *Tel:* 775-784-6573 *Toll Free Tel:* 800-682-6657 *Fax:* 775-784-6200 *Toll Free Fax:* 877-682-6657 *Web Site:* www.nvbooks.nevada.edu, pg 283

Malley, Lawrence, The University of Arkansas Press, McIlroy House, 201 Ozark Ave, Fayetteville, AR 72701 *Tel:* 479-575-3246 *Toll Free Tel:* 800-626-0090 *Fax:* 479-575-6044 *E-mail:* uapress@uark.edu *Web Site:* www.uapress.com, pg 280

Mallin, Michelle, The Perseus Books Group, 387 Park Ave S, 12th fl, New York, NY 10016 *Tel:* 212-340-8100 *Toll Free Tel:* 800-386-5656 (cust serv) *Fax:* 212-340-8115 *Web Site:* www.perseusbooksgroup.com, pg 210

Mallin, Michelle, Westview Press, 5500 Central Ave, Boulder, CO 80301 *Tel:* 303-444-3541 *Toll Free Tel:* 800-386-5656 *Fax:* 720-406-7336 *E-mail:* westview.orders@perseusbooks.com *Web Site:* www.perseusbooksgroup.com; www.westviewpress.com, pg 297

Malmud, Deborah A, W W Norton & Company Inc, 500 Fifth Ave, New York, NY 10110-0017 *Tel:* 212-354-5500 *Toll Free Tel:* 800-233-4830 (orders & cust serv) *Fax:* 212-869-0856 *Toll Free Fax:* 800-458-6515 *Web Site:* www.wwnorton.com, pg 193

Maloch, David, Arkansas State University Printing Program, PO Box 1930, Dept of Journalism & Printing, State University, AR 72467-1930 *Tel:* 870-972-2072 *Fax:* 870-910-8001 *Web Site:* www.astate.edu, pg 751
*

Malone, Robert J, Watson Davis & Helen Miles Davis Prize, University of Florida, 3310 Turlington Hall, Gainesville, FL 32611 *Tel:* 352-392-1677 *E-mail:* info@hssonline.org *Web Site:* www.hssonline.org, pg 769

Malone, Robert J, Pfizer Award, University of Florida, 3310 Turlington Hall, Gainesville, FL 32611 *Tel:* 352-392-1677 *E-mail:* info@hssonline.org *Web Site:* www.hssonline.org, pg 798

Malone, Robert J, Derek Price/Rod Webster Prize Award, University of Florida, 3310 Turlington Hall, Gainesville, FL 32611 *Tel:* 352-392-1677 *E-mail:* info@hssonline.org *Web Site:* www.hssonline.org, pg 800

Malone, Robert J, Henry & Ida Schuman Prize, University of Florida, 3310 Turlington Hall, Gainesville, FL 32611 *Tel:* 352-392-1677 *E-mail:* info@hssonline.org *Web Site:* www.hssonline.org, pg 805

Maloney, Dennis, White Pine Press, PO Box 236, Buffalo, NY 14201-0236 *Tel:* 716-627-4665 *Fax:* 716-627-4665 *E-mail:* wpine@whitepine.org *Web Site:* www.whitepine.org, pg 298

Maloney, Elaine, Canadian Circumpolar Institute (CCI) Press, University of Alberta, Campus Tower, Suite 308, 8625 112 St, Edmonton, AB T6H 0H1, Canada *Tel:* 780-492-4512 *Fax:* 780-492-1153 *E-mail:* ccinst@gpu.srv.ualberta.ca *Web Site:* www.ualberta.ca/~ccinst/, pg 538

Maloney, J, Southern Playwrights Competition, 700 Pelham Rd N, Jacksonville, AL 36265-1602 *Tel:* 256-782-5414 *Fax:* 256-782-5441 *Web Site:* www.jsu.edu/depart/english/southpla.htm, pg 806

Maloney, Karen A, Scholastic Inc, 557 Broadway, New York, NY 10012 *Tel:* 212-343-4469 *Toll Free Tel:* 800-scholastic *Fax:* 212-343-6930 *Web Site:* www.scholastic.com, pg 242

Malovany, Marti, Harry N Abrams Inc, 100 Fifth Ave, New York, NY 10011 *Tel:* 212-206-7715 *Toll Free Tel:* 800-345-1359 *Fax:* 212-645-8437 *E-mail:* webmaster@abramsbooks.com *Web Site:* www.abramsbooks.com, pg 3

Malpas, Pamela, Knox Burger Associates Ltd, 425 Madison Ave, New York, NY 10017 *Tel:* 212-759-8600 *Fax:* 212-759-9428, pg 623

Malpas, Pamela, Harold Ober Associates Inc, 425 Madison Ave, New York, NY 10017 *Tel:* 212-759-8600 *Fax:* 212-759-9428, pg 647

Maluccio, Paul, Blue Note Publications, 400 W Cocoa Beach Causeway, Suite 3, Cocoa Beach, FL 32931 *Tel:* 321-799-2583 *Toll Free Tel:* 800-624-0401 *Fax:* 321-799-1942 *E-mail:* order@bluenotebooks.com *Web Site:* www.bluenotebooks.com, pg 41

Malyil, Stacy, The Feminist Press at The City University of New York, 365 Fifth Ave, Suite 5406, New York, NY 10016 *Tel:* 212-817-7926 *Fax:* 212-817-1593 *Web Site:* www.feministpress.org, pg 96

Malzberg, Barry, Scott Meredith Literary Agency LP, 200 W 57 St, Suite 904, New York, NY 10019 *Tel:* 646-274-1970 *Fax:* 212-977-5997 *Web Site:* www.writingtosell.com, pg 644

Manaktala, Gita, The MIT Press, 5 Cambridge Ctr, Cambridge, MA 02142 *Tel:* 617-253-5646 *Toll Free Tel:* 800-405-1619 (orders only) *Fax:* 617-258-6779 *Web Site:* mitpress.mit.edu, pg 175

Manassah, Edward E, The National Society of Newspaper Columnists (NSNC), Courier-Journal Newspaper, 525 W Broadway, Louisville, KY 40201-7431 *Tel:* 502-582-4011 *Fax:* 502-582-4665 *Web Site:* www.courierjournal.com, pg 745

Manasse, Henri R Jr, American Society of Health-System Pharmacists, 7272 Wisconsin Ave, Bethesda, MD 20814 *Tel:* 301-657-3000 *Toll Free Tel:* 866-279-0681 (orders) *Fax:* 301-664-8867 *E-mail:* info@ashp.org *Web Site:* www.ashp.org, pg 18

Mancini, Gerard, Puffin Books, 345 Hudson St, New York, NY 10014 *Tel:* 212-366-2000 *E-mail:* online@penguinputnam.com *Web Site:* www.penguin.com, pg 222

Mancini, Gerard, Viking Children's Books, 345 Hudson St, New York, NY 10014 *Tel:* 212-366-2000 *E-mail:* online@penguinputnam.com *Web Site:* www.penguin.com, pg 290

Mancini, Rebecca J, Clarion Books, 215 Park Ave S, New York, NY 10003 *Tel:* 212-420-5800 *Toll Free Tel:* 800-225-3362 (orders) *Fax:* 212-420-5855 *Web Site:* www.clarion.com, pg 62

Mancuso, Leslie, JHPIEGO, 1615 Thames St, Suite 200, Baltimore, MD 21231-3492 *Tel:* 410-537-1825 *Fax:* 410-537-1474 *E-mail:* info@jhpiego.net; orders@jhpiego.net *Web Site:* www.jhpiego.org, pg 141

Mancuso, Robert, Basic Books, 387 Park Ave S, 12th fl, New York, NY 10016-8810 *Tel:* 212-340-8100 *Toll Free Tel:* 800-242-7737 (orders) *Fax:* 212-340-8135 *E-mail:* basic.books@perseusbooks.com *Web Site:* www.basicbooks.com, pg 33

Mancuso, Robert, Westview Press, 5500 Central Ave, Boulder, CO 80301 *Tel:* 303-444-3541 *Toll Free Tel:* 800-386-5656 *Fax:* 720-406-7336 *E-mail:* westview.orders@perseusbooks.com *Web Site:* www.perseusbooksgroup.com; www.westviewpress.com, pg 297

Mandel, Daniel, Sanford J Greenburger Associates Inc, 55 Fifth Ave, 15th fl, New York, NY 10003 *Tel:* 212-206-5600 *Fax:* 212-463-8718 *Web Site:* www.greenburger.com, pg 633

Mandel, Jay, William Morris Agency, 1325 Avenue of the Americas, New York, NY 10019 *Tel:* 212-586-5100 *Fax:* 212-903-1418 *E-mail:* wma@interport.net *Web Site:* www.wma.com, pg 645

Mandel, Jenny, Workman Publishing Co Inc, 708 Broadway, New York, NY 10003-9555 *Tel:* 212-254-5900 *Toll Free Tel:* 800-722-7202 *Fax:* 212-254-8098 *E-mail:* info@workman.com *Web Site:* www.workman.com, pg 303

Mandel, Phyllis, Random House Inc, 1745 Broadway, New York, NY 10019 *Tel:* 212-782-9000 *Toll Free Tel:* 800-726-0600 *Web Site:* www.randomhouse.com, pg 226

Mandel, Robert, University of Wisconsin Press, 1930 Monroe St, 3rd fl, Madison, WI 53711 *Tel:* 608-263-1110 *Toll Free Tel:* 800-621-2736 (Orders) *Fax:* 608-263-1120 *Toll Free Fax:* 800-621-8476 (Orders) *E-mail:* uwiscpress@uwpress.wisc.edu (Main Office) *Web Site:* www.wisc.edu/wisconsinpress/, pg 286

Mandelbaum, Mark, Association for Computing Machinery, 1515 Broadway, New York, NY 10036 *Tel:* 212-869-7440 *Toll Free Tel:* 800-342-6626 *Fax:* 212-869-0481 *E-mail:* acmhelp@acm.org *Web Site:* www.acm.org, pg 26

Mandeville, Craig, Simon & Schuster Adult Publishing Group, 1230 Avenue of the Americas, New York, NY 10020 *Tel:* 212-698-7000 *Toll Free Tel:* 800-223-2336 (orders); 800-223-2348 (cust serv), pg 248

Maner, Ron, The University of North Carolina Press, 116 S Boundary St, Chapel Hill, NC 27514-3808 *Tel:* 919-966-3561 *Toll Free Tel:* 800-848-6224 (orders only) *Fax:* 919-966-3829 *Toll Free Fax:* 800-272-6817 (orders) *E-mail:* uncpress@unc.edu *Web Site:* www.uncpress.unc.edu, pg 283

Mangan, Joe, Counterpoint Press, 387 Park Ave S, New York, NY 10016 *Tel:* 212-340-8100 *Fax:* 212-340-8135 (edit); 212-340-8115 *E-mail:* counterpointpress@perseusbooks.com *Web Site:* www.counterpointpress.com, pg 70

Mangan, Joe, Da Capo Press Inc, 11 Cambridge Center, Cambridge, MA 02142 *Tel:* 617-252-5200 *Toll Free Tel:* 800-242-7737 (orders) *Fax:* 617-252-5285 *E-mail:* custserve@lrp.com *Web Site:* www.dacapopress.com, pg 75

Mangan, Mona, Writers Guild of America East Inc (WGAE), 555 W 57 St, New York, NY 10019 *Tel:* 212-767-7800 *Fax:* 212-582-1909 *E-mail:* info@wgaeast.org *Web Site:* www.wgaeast.org, pg 703

Mangar, Joseph, The Perseus Books Group, 387 Park Ave S, 12th fl, New York, NY 10016 *Tel:* 212-340-8100 *Toll Free Tel:* 800-386-5656 (cust serv) *Fax:* 212-340-8115 *Web Site:* www.perseusbooksgroup.com, pg 210

Mangin, Daniel, Compass American Guides, 1745 Broadway, New York, NY 10019, pg 66

Mangouni, Norman, Caravan Books, PO Box 5934, Carefree, AZ 85377-5934 *Tel:* 480-575-9945 *Fax:* 480-575-9451 *E-mail:* maxinmin@umich.edu, pg 53

Marinacci, Barbara, The Bookmill, 22000 Mt Eden Rd, Saratoga, CA 95070-9729 *Tel:* 408-867-9450 *Fax:* 408-867-9450 *E-mail:* bookmill@ix.netcom.com *Web Site:* www.marinacci.com/Bookmill, pg 592

Marinacci, Rudy, The Bookmill, 22000 Mt Eden Rd, Saratoga, CA 95070-9729 *Tel:* 408-867-9450 *Fax:* 408-867-9450 *E-mail:* bookmill@ix.netcom.com *Web Site:* www.marinacci.com/Bookmill, pg 592

Marinaccio, Fran M, Woodbine House, 6510 Bells Mill Rd, Bethesda, MD 20817 *Tel:* 301-897-3570 *Toll Free Tel:* 800-843-7323 *Fax:* 301-897-5838 *E-mail:* info@ woodbinehouse.com *Web Site:* www.woodbinehouse. com, pg 302

Marinelli, Alyssa D, American Mathematical Society, 201 Charles St, Providence, RI 02904-2294 *Tel:* 401-455-4000 *Toll Free Tel:* 800-321-4267 *Fax:* 401-331-3842; 401-455-4046 (cust serv) *E-mail:* ams@ams.org *Web Site:* www.ams.org, pg 16

Marinelli, Janet, Brooklyn Botanic Garden, 1000 Washington Ave, Brooklyn, NY 11225-1099 *Tel:* 718-623-7200 *Toll Free Tel:* 800-367-9692 (orders) *Fax:* 718-622-7839 *Toll Free Fax:* 800-542-7567 (orders) *E-mail:* publications@bbg.org *Web Site:* www.bbg.org, pg 49

Mark, Tara, RLR Associates Ltd, 7 W 51 St, New York, NY 10019 *Tel:* 212-541-8641 *Fax:* 212-541-6052 *Web Site:* www.rlrassociates.net, pg 652

Markevich, Fenton, CRC Press LLC, 2000 NW Corporate Blvd, Boca Raton, FL 33431 *Tel:* 561-994-0555 *Toll Free Tel:* 800-272-7737 *Fax:* 561-997-7249 (edit); 561-998-8491 (mfg); 561-361-6057 (acctg); 561-994-0313 *Toll Free Fax:* 800-643-9428 (sales); 800-374-3401 (orders) *E-mail:* orders@crcpress.com *Web Site:* www.crcpress.com, pg 71

Markevich, Fenton, Garland Science Publishing, 270 Madison Ave, New York, NY 10016 *Tel:* 212-216-7800 *Fax:* 212-947-3027 *E-mail:* info@garland.com *Web Site:* www.garlandscience.com, pg 102

Markevich, Fenton, Routledge, 29 W 35 St, New York, NY 10001-2299 *Tel:* 212-216-7800 *Fax:* 212-564-7854 (main) *E-mail:* info@taylorandfrancis.com *Web Site:* www.routledge-ny.com, pg 235

Markham, Ann, Communication Creativity, 209 Church St, Buena Vista, CO 81211 *Tel:* 719-395-8659 *Toll Free Tel:* 800-331-8355 *Fax:* 719-633-1526 *Web Site:* www.communicationcreativity.com, pg 66

Markham, Judy, Discovery House Publishers, 3000 Kraft SE, Grand Rapids, MI 49512 *Tel:* 616-942-9218; 616-974-2210 (cust serv) *Toll Free Tel:* 800-653-8333 *Fax:* 616-957-5741 *E-mail:* dhp@rbc.org *Web Site:* www.gospelcom.net/rbc/dhp/; www.rbc.net, pg 81

Markland, Marcia, St Martin's Press Trade Division, 175 Fifth Ave, New York, NY 10010 *E-mail:* firstname. lastname@stmartins.com *Web Site:* www.stmartins. com; www.minotaurbooks.com, pg 239

Markman, Ahuta, Aum Publications, 86-10 Parsons Blvd, Jamaica, NY 11432 *Tel:* 718-291-9757 *Fax:* 718-523-1423, pg 28

Markman, Ericka, National Geographic Books, 1145 17 St NW, Washington, DC 20036 *Tel:* 202-857-7000 *Fax:* 202-857-7670 *Web Site:* www. nationalgeographics.com, pg 183

Markovac, Jasna, Academic Press, 525 B St, Suite 1900, San Diego, CA 92101 *Tel:* 619-231-6616 *Toll Free Tel:* 800-321-5068 (cust serv) *Fax:* 619-699-6715 *E-mail:* firstinitiallastname@acad.com; firstinitial. lastname@elsevier.com *Web Site:* www.elsevier.com, pg 4

Markowski, Marjorie L, Possibility Press, One Oakglade Circle, Hummelstown, PA 17036 *Tel:* 717-566-0468 *Toll Free Tel:* 800-566-0534 *Fax:* 717-566-6423 *E-mail:* posspress@aol.com, pg 216

Markowski, Michael A, Possibility Press, One Oakglade Circle, Hummelstown, PA 17036 *Tel:* 717-566-0468 *Toll Free Tel:* 800-566-0534 *Fax:* 717-566-6423 *E-mail:* posspress@aol.com, pg 216

Marks, Fred, Marquis Who's Who, 562 Central Ave, New Providence, NJ 07974 *Tel:* 908-673-1001 *Toll Free Tel:* 800-473-7020 *Fax:* 908-673-1189 *Web Site:* www.marquiswhoswho.com, pg 164

Marks, Fred, National Register Publishing, 562 Central Ave, New Providence, NJ 07974 *Tel:* 908-673-1001 *Toll Free Tel:* 800-473-7020 *Fax:* 909-673-1189 *Web Site:* www.nationalregisterpub.com, pg 185

Marks, Jim, Lambda Literary Awards (Lammys), 1217 11 St NW, Washington, DC 20001 *Tel:* 202-682-0952 *Fax:* 202-682-0955 *E-mail:* lbreditor@lambdalit.org *Web Site:* www.lambdalit.org, pg 783

Marks, Kevin, Multnomah Publishers Inc, 204 W Adams Ave, Sisters, OR 97759 *Tel:* 541-549-1144 *Toll Free Tel:* 800-929-0910 *Fax:* 541-549-2044 (sales); 541-549-0432 (admin); 541-549-0260 (ed/prod); 541-549-8048 (mktg) *E-mail:* information@multnomahbooks. com *Web Site:* www.multnomahbooks.com, pg 180

Marks, Linda, The National Museum of Women in the Arts, 1250 New York Ave NW, Washington, DC 20005 *Tel:* 202-783-5000 *Toll Free Tel:* 800-222-7270 *Fax:* 202-393-3234 *Web Site:* www.nmwa.org, pg 184

Marks, Patty, Ellora's Cave Publishing Inc, 1337 Commerce Dr, Suite 13, Stow, OH 44224 *Tel:* 330-689-1118 *E-mail:* service@ellorascave.com *Web Site:* www.ellorascave.com, pg 89

Marks, Vic, Hartley & Marks Publishers Ltd, 3661 W Broadway, Vancouver, BC V6R 2B8, Canada *Tel:* 604-739-1771 *Toll Free Tel:* 800-277-5887 *Fax:* 604-738-1913 *Toll Free Fax:* 800-707-5887 *E-mail:* pbdesk@ hartleyandmarks.com *Web Site:* www.hartleyandmarks. com, pg 549

Markson, Elaine, Elaine Markson Literary Agency Inc, 44 Greenwich Ave, New York, NY 10011 *Tel:* 212-243-8480 *Fax:* 212-691-9014, pg 642

Markus, Julia, Hofstra University, English Dept, 204 Calkins, Hempstead, NY 11549 *Tel:* 516-463-5454 *Fax:* 516-463-6395 *E-mail:* engpmu@hofstra.edu *Web Site:* www.hofstra.edu, pg 752

Marler, Don C, Dogwood Press, HC 53 Box 345, Hemphill, TX 75948-0345 *Tel:* 409-579-2184 *Fax:* 409-579-2184 *Web Site:* dogwoodpress.myriad. net/, pg 81

Marmion, Bridget, Houghton Mifflin Trade & Reference Division, 222 Berkeley St, Boston, MA 02116-3764 *Tel:* 617-351-5000 *Toll Free Tel:* 800-225-3362 *Web Site:* www.houghtonmifflinbooks.com, pg 126

Marmion, Kevin M, William S Hein & Co Inc, 1285 Main St, Buffalo, NY 14209-1987 *Tel:* 716-882-2600 *Toll Free Tel:* 800-828-7571 *Fax:* 716-883-8100 *E-mail:* mail@wshein.com *Web Site:* www.wshein. com, pg 120

Marmur, Mildred, Mildred Marmur Associates Ltd, 2005 Palmer Ave, PMB 127, Larchmont, NY 10538 *Tel:* 914-834-1170 *Fax:* 914-834-2840 *E-mail:* marmur@westnet.com, pg 642

Marquez, Manny, Davies Publishing Inc, 32 S Raymond Ave, Pasadena, CA 91105-1935 *Tel:* 626-792-3046 *Toll Free Tel:* 877-792-0005 *Fax:* 626-792-5308 *E-mail:* daviescorp@aol.com *Web Site:* www. daviespublishing.com, pg 76

Marquis, Paul, Starbooks Press, 1391 Blvd of the Arts, Sarasota, FL 34236-2904 *Tel:* 941-957-1281 *Fax:* 941-955-3829, pg 258

Marquit, Doris G, MEP Publications, University of Minnesota, Physics Bldg, 116 Church St SE, Minneapolis, MN 55455-0112 *Tel:* 612-922-7993 *E-mail:* marqu002@tc.umn.edu *Web Site:* umn. edu/home/marqu002, pg 171

Marquit, Erwin, MEP Publications, University of Minnesota, Physics Bldg, 116 Church St SE, Minneapolis, MN 55455-0112 *Tel:* 612-922-7993 *E-mail:* marqu002@tc.umn.edu *Web Site:* umn. edu/home/marqu002, pg 171

Marr, Marie, United States Institute of Peace Press, 1200 17 St NW, Suite 200, Washington, DC 20036-3011 *Tel:* 202-457-1700 (edit); 703-661-1590 (cust serv) *Toll Free Tel:* 800-868-8064 (cust serv) *Fax:* 703-661-1501 (cust serv) *Web Site:* www.usip.org, pg 279

Marrelli, Nancy, Vehicule Press, 125 Place du Parc Sta, Montreal, PQ H2X 4A3, Canada *Tel:* 514-844-6073 *Fax:* 514-844-7543 *E-mail:* vp@vehiculepress.com *Web Site:* www.vehiculepress.com, pg 566

Marrow, Linda, Random House Publishing Group, 1745 Broadway, New York, NY 10019 *Toll Free Tel:* 800-200-3552 *Toll Free Fax:* 800-200-3552 *Web Site:* www.randomhouse.com, pg 227

Mars, Laura, Grey House Publishing Inc, 185 Millerton Rd, Millerton, NY 12546 *Tel:* 518-789-8700 *Toll Free Tel:* 800-562-2139 *Fax:* 518-789-0556 *E-mail:* books@greyhouse.com *Web Site:* www. greyhouse.com, pg 109

Marsello, Greg, Learning Resources Network (LERN), 208 S Main St, River Falls, WI 54022 *Tel:* 715-426-9777 *Toll Free Tel:* 800-678-5376 *Fax:* 715-426-5847 *Toll Free Fax:* 888-234-8633 *E-mail:* info@lern.org *Web Site:* www.lern.org, pg 151

Marsh, Carole, Gallopade International Inc, 665 Hwy 74 S, Suite 600, Peachtree City, GA 30269 *Tel:* 770-631-4222 *Toll Free Tel:* 800-536-2GET (536-2438) *Fax:* 770-631-4810 *Toll Free Fax:* 800-871-2979 *E-mail:* info@gallopade.com *Web Site:* www. gallopade.com, pg 102

Marsh, Courtney, Dramaline® Publications, 36-851 Palm View Rd, Rancho Mirage, CA 92270-2417 *Tel:* 760-770-6076 *Fax:* 760-770-4507 *E-mail:* drama.line@ verizon.net *Web Site:* dramaline.com, pg 83

Marsh, Michael, Gallopade International Inc, 665 Hwy 74 S, Suite 600, Peachtree City, GA 30269 *Tel:* 770-631-4222 *Toll Free Tel:* 800-536-2GET (536-2438) *Fax:* 770-631-4810 *Toll Free Fax:* 800-871-2979 *E-mail:* info@gallopade.com *Web Site:* www. gallopade.com, pg 102

Marshall, Evan, The Evan Marshall Agency, 6 Tristam Place, Pine Brook, NJ 07058-9445 *Tel:* 973-882-1122 *Fax:* 973-882-3099 *Web Site:* www.thenovelist.com, pg 642

Marshall, J C, Excelsior Cee Publishing, 1311 Cherry Stone, Norman, OK 73072 *Tel:* 405-329-3909 *Fax:* 405-329-6886 *E-mail:* ecp@oecadvantage.net *Web Site:* www.excelsiorcee.com, pg 93

Marshall, Julie, Home Planners LLC, 3275 W Ina Rd, Suite 220, Tucson, AZ 85741 *Tel:* 520-297-8200 *Toll Free Tel:* 800-322-6797 *Fax:* 520-297-6219 *Toll Free Fax:* 800-531-2555 *E-mail:* customerservice@eplans. com *Web Site:* www.eplans.com, pg 125

Marshall, Len, HarperCollins General Books Group, 10 E 53 St, New York, NY 10022 *Tel:* 212-207-7000 *Fax:* 212-207-7633, pg 115

Marshall, Lisa, NavPress Publishing Group, 3820 N 30 St, Colorado Springs, CO 80904 *Tel:* 719-548-9222 *Toll Free Tel:* 800-366-7788 *Fax:* 719-260-7223 *Toll Free Fax:* 800-343-3902 *Web Site:* www.navpress.com, pg 185

Marshall, Mary, Greenwood Publishing Group Inc, 88 Post Rd W, Westport, CT 06880-4208 *Tel:* 203-226-3571 *Toll Free Tel:* 800-225-5800 *Fax:* 203-222-1502 *E-mail:* bookinfo@greenwood.com (general); firstintial&fulllastname@greenwood.com (individuals) *Web Site:* www.greenwood.com, pg 109

Marshall, Mary Lou, Krause Publications, 700 E State St, Iola, WI 54990 *Tel:* 715-445-4612 ext 365 *Toll Free Tel:* 800-258-0929; 888-457-2873 *Fax:* 715-445-4087 *Web Site:* www.krause.com, pg 147

Marson, Amy, C & T Publishing Inc, 1651 Challenge Dr, Concord, CA 94520 *Tel:* 925-677-0377 *Toll Free Tel:* 800-284-1114 *Fax:* 925-677-0373 *E-mail:* ctinfo@ctpub.com *Web Site:* www.ctpub.com, pg 51

Martell, Alice Fried, The Martell Agency, 545 Madison Ave, 7th fl, New York, NY 10022 *Tel:* 212-317-2672 *Fax:* 212-317-2676, pg 642

Martens, Julie S, Human Kinetics Inc, PO Box 5076, Champaign, IL 61825-5076 *Tel:* 217-351-5076 *Toll Free Tel:* 800-747-4457 *Fax:* 217-351-1549 (orders/ cust serv) *E-mail:* info@hkusa.com *Web Site:* www. humankinetics.com, pg 128

Martens, Pat, Boys Town Press, 14100 Crawford St, Boys Town, NE 68010 *Tel:* 402-498-1320 *Toll Free Tel:* 800-282-6657 *Fax:* 402-498-1310 *E-mail:* btpress@boystown.org *Web Site:* www.boystownpress.org, pg 45

Martens, Rainer, Human Kinetics Inc, PO Box 5076, Champaign, IL 61825-5076 *Tel:* 217-351-5076 *Toll Free Tel:* 800-747-4457 *Fax:* 217-351-1549 (orders/cust serv) *E-mail:* info@hkusa.com *Web Site:* www.humankinetics.com, pg 128

Martenz, Arden, MAR*CO Products Inc, 1443 Old York Rd, Warminster, PA 18974 *Tel:* 215-956-0313 *Toll Free Tel:* 800-448-2197 *Fax:* 215-956-9041 *E-mail:* marcoproducts@comcast.net *Web Site:* www.marcoproducts.com; www.store.yahoo.com/marcoproducts, pg 163

Marthaler, Beth, Blue Book Publications Inc, 8009 34 Ave S, Suite 175, Minneapolis, MN 55425 *Tel:* 952-854-5229 *Toll Free Tel:* 800-877-4867 *Fax:* 952-853-1486 *E-mail:* bluebook@bluebookinc.com *Web Site:* www.bluebookinc.com, pg 570

Marthe, L, Laurier Books Ltd, PO Box 2694, Sta D, Ottawa, ON K1P 5W6, Canada *Tel:* 613-738-2163 *Fax:* 613-247-0256 *E-mail:* educa@travel-net.com *Web Site:* www.travel-net.com/~educa/main.htm, pg 552

Martin, Andrea, Reader's Digest Association (Canada) Ltd/Selection du Reader's Digest (Canada) Ltee, 1100 Rene Levesque Blvd W, Montreal, PQ H3B 5H5, Canada *Tel:* 514-940-0751 *Toll Free Tel:* 800-465-0780 *Fax:* 514-940-3637 (admin) *E-mail:* customer.service@readersdigest.ca *Web Site:* www.readersdigest.ca, pg 559

Martin, Andrew, Sterling Publishing Co Inc, 387 Park Ave S, 5th fl, New York, NY 10016-8810 *Tel:* 212-532-7160 *Toll Free Tel:* 800-367-9692 *Fax:* 212-213-2495 *Web Site:* www.sterlingpub.com, pg 259

Martin, Barbara, Southern Illinois University Press, PO Box 3697, Carbondale, IL 62902-3697 *Tel:* 618-453-2281 *Toll Free Tel:* 800-346-2680 *Fax:* 618-453-1221 *Toll Free Fax:* 800-346-2681 *E-mail:* jstetter@siu.edu *Web Site:* www.siu.edu/~siupress, pg 254

Martin, Betty Woo, DiscoverGuides, 631 N Stephanie St, No 138, Henderson, NV 89014 *Tel:* 702-407-8777 *Fax:* 209-532-2699 *E-mail:* discoverguides@earthlink.net, pg 80

Martin, Bill, Agent Research & Evaluation Inc, 25 Barrow St, New York, NY 10014 *Tel:* 212-924-9942 *Fax:* 212-924-1864 *E-mail:* info@agentresearch.com *Web Site:* www.agentresearch.biz, pg 618

Martin, Brad, Doubleday Canada, One Toronto St, Suite 300, Toronto, ON M5C 2V6, Canada *Tel:* 416-364-4449 *Fax:* 416-957-1587 *Web Site:* www.randomhouse.ca, pg 542

Martin, Brad, Knopf Canada, One Toronto St, Suite 300, Toronto, ON M5C 2V6, Canada *Tel:* 416-364-4449 *Toll Free Tel:* 800-668-4247 (order desk) *Fax:* 416-364-0462 *Web Site:* www.randomhouse.ca, pg 552

Martin, Brad, Random House of Canada Ltd, One Toronto St, Unit 300, Toronto, ON M5C 2V6, Canada *Tel:* 416-364-4449 *Fax:* 416-364-6863 (edit & publicity); 416-364-6653 (subs rts) *Web Site:* www.randomhouse.ca, pg 559

Martin, Brad, Seal Books, One Toronto St, Suite 300, Toronto, ON M5C 2V6, Canada *Tel:* 416-364-4449 *Toll Free Tel:* 888-523-9292 (order desk) *Fax:* 416-957-1587 *Web Site:* www.randomhouse.ca, pg 560

Martin, Candice, Metamorphous Press, 265 N Hancock St, Portland, OR 97227 *Tel:* 503-228-4972 *Toll Free Tel:* 800-937-7771 (orders only) *Fax:* 503-223-9117 *E-mail:* metabooks@metamodels.com *Web Site:* www.metamodels.com, pg 172

Martin, Carolyn, American Historical Press, 10755 Sherman Way, Suite 2, Sun Valley, CA 91352 *Tel:* 818-503-0133 *Toll Free Tel:* 800-550-5750 *Fax:* 818-503-9081 *E-mail:* ahp@amhistpress.com *Web Site:* www.amhistpress.com, pg 14

Martin, Charles, The Arion Press, The Presidio, 1802 Hays St, San Francisco, CA 94129 *Tel:* 415-561-2542 *Fax:* 415-561-2545 *E-mail:* arionpress@arionpress.com *Web Site:* www.arionpress.com, pg 23

Martin, Colleen, The Writers' Collective, 780 Reservoir Ave, Suite 243, Cranston, RI 02910 *Tel:* 401-537-9175 *E-mail:* info@writerscollective.org *Web Site:* www.writerscollective.org, pg 305

Martin, Daniel B, Inter-American Development Bank, 1300 New York Ave NW, Washington, DC 20577 *Tel:* 202-623-1000 *Fax:* 202-623-3096 *E-mail:* idb-books@iadb.org; idbcc@iadb.org *Web Site:* www.iadb.org/pub, pg 135

Martin, Deborah, Magazine Publishers of America, 810 Seventh Ave, New York, NY 10019 *Tel:* 212-872-3700 *Fax:* 212-888-4217 *E-mail:* infocenter@magazine.org *Web Site:* www.magazine.org, pg 690

Martin, Denise Taylor, Dawson Taylor Literary Agency, 4722 Holly Lake Dr, Lake Worth, FL 33463-5372 *Tel:* 561-965-4150 *Fax:* 561-641-9765 *E-mail:* dawsontaylo@aol.com, pg 658

Martin, Denny, Piano Press, 1425 Ocean Ave, Suite 6, Del Mar, CA 92014 *Tel:* 619-884-1401 *Fax:* 858-459-3376 *E-mail:* pianopress@aol.com *Web Site:* www.pianopress.com, pg 212

Martin, Diane, Knopf Canada, One Toronto St, Suite 300, Toronto, ON M5C 2V6, Canada *Tel:* 416-364-4449 *Toll Free Tel:* 800-668-4247 (order desk) *Fax:* 416-364-0462 *Web Site:* www.randomhouse.ca, pg 552

Martin, Don W, DiscoverGuides, 631 N Stephanie St, No 138, Henderson, NV 89014 *Tel:* 702-407-8777 *Fax:* 209-532-2699 *E-mail:* discoverguides@earthlink.net, pg 80

Martin, Elizabeth, Sumach Press, 1415 Bathurst St, Suite 302, Toronto, ON M5R 3H5, Canada *Tel:* 416-531-6250 *Fax:* 416-531-3892 *E-mail:* sumachpress@on.aibn.com *Web Site:* www.sumachpress.com, pg 562

Martin, Forrest, Excelsior Cee Publishing, 1311 Cherry Stone, Norman, OK 73072 *Tel:* 405-329-3909 *Fax:* 405-329-6886 *E-mail:* ecp@oecadvantage.net *Web Site:* www.excelsiorcee.com, pg 93

Martin, Francois, Editions du Meridien, 1980 Sherbrooke Ouest, No 540, Montreal, PQ H3H 1E8, Canada *Tel:* 514-935-0464 *Fax:* 514-935-0458 *E-mail:* info@editionsdumeridien.com *Web Site:* www.editionsdumeridien.com, pg 544

Martin, George T, American Bankers Association, 1120 Connecticut Ave NW, Washington, DC 20036 *Tel:* 202-663-5087 *Toll Free Tel:* 800-BANKERS (226-5377) *Fax:* 202-663-5087 (cust serv) *Web Site:* www.aba.com, pg 12

Martin, Jehu, Money Market Directories, 320 E Main St, Charlottesville, VA 22902 *Tel:* 434-977-1450 *Toll Free Tel:* 800-446-2810 *Fax:* 434-979-9962 *Web Site:* www.mmdwebaccess.com, pg 177

Martin, John, Capstone Press, 151 Good Counsel Dr, Mankato, MN 56002 *Toll Free Tel:* 800-747-4992 *Toll Free Fax:* 888-262-0705 *Web Site:* www.capstonepress.com, pg 53

Martin, Lesley, Aperture Books, 20 E 23 St, New York, NY 10010 *Tel:* 212-505-5555 *Toll Free Tel:* 800-929-2323 *Fax:* 212-598-4015 *E-mail:* info@aperture.org *Web Site:* www.aperture.org, pg 21

Martin, Linda, Oolichan Books, Box 10, Lantzville, BC V0R 2H0, Canada *Tel:* 250-390-4839 *Fax:* 250-390-4839 *E-mail:* oolichan@island.net *Web Site:* www.oolichan.com, pg 556

Martin, Lisa Ann, Martin-McLean Literary Associates, 1602 S Cerritos Dr, Suite D, Palm Springs, CA 92264 *Tel:* 760-320-4552 *Fax:* 760-323-8792 *E-mail:* martinmcleanlit@aol.com *Web Site:* www.martinmcleanlit.com; www.mcleanlit.com, pg 642

Martin, Louis, Groupe Educalivres Inc, 955, rue Bergar, Laval, PQ H7L 4Z6, Canada *Tel:* 514-334-8466 *Toll Free Tel:* 800-567-3671 (Info Service) *Fax:* 514-334-8387 *E-mail:* commentaires@educalivres.com *Web Site:* www.educalivres.com, pg 548

Martin, Mary Jane, Kirchoff/Wohlberg Inc, 866 United Nations Plaza, Suite 525, New York, NY 10017 *Tel:* 212-644-2020 *Fax:* 212-223-4387 *E-mail:* kirchwohl@aol.com *Web Site:* www.kirchoffwohlberg.com, pg 603

Martin, Matthew, Bantam Dell Publishing Group, 1745 Broadway, New York, NY 10019 *Tel:* 212-782-9000 *Toll Free Tel:* 800-223-6834 *Fax:* 212-302-7985 *Web Site:* www.randomhouse.com/bantamdell, pg 31

Martin, Maurice, Society for Technical Communication, 901 N Stuart St, Suite 904, Arlington, VA 22203-1822 *Tel:* 703-522-4114 *Fax:* 703-522-2075 *E-mail:* stc@stc.org *Web Site:* www.stc.org, pg 699, 747

Martin, Michele, Carroll & Graf Publishers, 245 W 17 St, 11th fl, New York, NY 10011-5300 *Tel:* 646-375-2570 *Fax:* 646-375-2571 *Web Site:* www.carrollandgraf.com, pg 54

Martin, Michele, Marlowe & Company, 245 W 17 St, 11th fl, New York, NY 10011-5300 *Tel:* 646-375-2570 *Fax:* 646-375-2571 *Web Site:* www.marlowepub.com, pg 164

Martin, Michele, Nation Books, 245 W 17 St, 11th fl, New York, NY 10011-5300 *Tel:* 646-375-2570 *Fax:* 646-375-2571 *Web Site:* www.nationbooks.org, pg 182

Martin, Michele, Thunder's Mouth Press, 245 W 17 St, 11th fl, New York, NY 10011-5300 *Tel:* 646-375-2570 *Fax:* 646-375-2571 *Web Site:* www.thundersmouth.com, pg 271

Martin, Michelle, Avalon Publishing Group Inc, 1400 65 St, Suite 250, Emeryville, CA 94608 *Tel:* 510-595-3664 *Fax:* 510-535-4228 *Web Site:* www.avalonpub.com, pg 28

Martin, Philip, Midwest Traditions Inc, 3147 S Pennsylvania Ave, Milwaukee, WI 53207 *Tel:* 414-294-4319 *Toll Free Tel:* 800-736-9189 *Fax:* 414-962-3579, pg 174

Martin, S H, Oaklea Press, 6912 Three Chopt Rd, Suite B, Richmond, VA 23226 *Tel:* 804-281-5872 *Toll Free Tel:* 800-295-4066 *Fax:* 804-281-5686 *E-mail:* info@oakleapress.com *Web Site:* oakleapress.com, pg 195

Martin, Shari, Focus on the Family, 8605 Explorer Dr, Colorado Springs, CO 80920 *Tel:* 719-531-3400 *Fax:* 719-531-3484 *Web Site:* www.family.org, pg 97

Martin, Shari, University of British Columbia Press, 2029 West Mall, Vancouver, BC V6T 1Z2, Canada *Tel:* 604-822-5959 *Toll Free Tel:* 877-377-9378 *Fax:* 604-822-6083 *Toll Free Fax:* 800-668-0821 *E-mail:* info@ubcpress.ca *Web Site:* www.ubcpress.ca, pg 564

Martin, Sharlene, Martin Literary Management, 17328 Ventura Blvd, Suite 138, Encino, CA 91316 *Tel:* 818-595-1130 *Web Site:* www.martinliterarymanagement.com, pg 642

Martin, Sue, South-Western, A Thomson Business, 5191 Natorp Blvd, Mason, OH 45040 *Tel:* 513-229-1000 *Toll Free Tel:* 800-543-0487 *Fax:* 513-229-1025 *Web Site:* www.thomson.com, pg 254

Martin, Wayne, Tetra Press, 3001 Commerce St, Blacksburg, VA 24060 *Tel:* 540-951-5408 *Toll Free Tel:* 800-526-0650 *Fax:* 540-951-5415 *E-mail:* consumer@tetra-fish.com *Web Site:* www.tetra-fish.com, pg 267

Martin-Quittman, Beth, CreativeWell Inc, PO Box 3130, Memorial Sta, Upper Montclair, NJ 07043 *Tel:* 973-783-7575 *Fax:* 973-783-7530 *E-mail:* info@creativewell.com *Web Site:* www.creativewell.com, pg 626

Martinelli, Theresa, Wayne State University Press, Leonard N Simons Bldg, 4809 Woodward Ave, Detroit, MI 48201-1309 *Tel:* 313-577-4600 *Toll Free Tel:* 800-978-7323 *Fax:* 313-577-6131, pg 294

Martinez, Acacia, JIST Publishing Inc, 8902 Otis Ave, Indianapolis, IN 46216 *Tel:* 317-613-4200 *Toll Free Tel:* 800-648-5478 *Fax:* 317-613-4304 *Toll Free Fax:* 800-547-8329 *E-mail:* info@jist.com *Web Site:* www.jist.com, pg 141

Martinez, Elizabeth, Council for Exceptional Children, 1110 N Glebe Rd, Suite 300, Arlington, VA 22201 *Tel:* 703-620-3660 *Toll Free Tel:* 888-232-7733 (cust serv) *Fax:* 703-264-9494 *E-mail:* service@cec.sped.org *Web Site:* www.cec.sped.org, pg 70

Martinez, Evelyn, Vocalis Ltd, 100 Avalon Circle, Waterbury, CT 06710 *Tel:* 203-753-5244 *Fax:* 203-574-5433 *E-mail:* vocalis@sbcglobal.net; info@vocalisesl.com *Web Site:* www.vocalisesl.com; www.vocalisfiction.com; www.vocalisltd.com, pg 291

Martinez, Richard, Building News, 502 Maple Ave W, Vienna, VA 22180 *Tel:* 703-319-0498 *Toll Free Tel:* 888-264-2665 *Fax:* 703-319-9158 *E-mail:* sales@bnibooks.com *Web Site:* www.bnibooks.com, pg 49

Martinez, William H, Writers' Haven Writers (WHW), 2244 Fourth Ave, San Diego, CA 92101 *Tel:* 619-696-0569, pg 703

Martini, John, Association of Medical Illustrators (AMI), 6660 Delmonico Dr, Suite D-107, Colorado Springs, CO 80919 *Tel:* 719-598-8622 *E-mail:* hq@ami.org *Web Site:* www.ami.org, pg 680

Martino, Alfred, Listen & Live Audio Inc, PO Box 817, Roseland, NJ 07068-0817 *Tel:* 973-781-1444 *Toll Free Tel:* 800-653-9400 *Fax:* 973-781-0333 *Web Site:* www.listenandlive.com, pg 156

Martino, Vincent, Warner Bros Publications Inc, 15800 NW 48 Ave, Miami, FL 33014 *Tel:* 305-620-1500 *Toll Free Tel:* 800-327-7643 *Fax:* 305-621-4869 *E-mail:* wbpsales@warnerchappell.com *Web Site:* www.warnerbrospublications.com, pg 293

Martins, Tim H, Barbour Publishing Inc, 1810 Barbour Dr, Uhrichsville, OH 44683 *Tel:* 740-922-6045 *Fax:* 740-922-5948 *E-mail:* info@barbourbooks.com *Web Site:* www.barbourbooks.com, pg 32

Martone, Michael, University of Alabama Program in Creative Writing, PO Box 870244, Tuscaloosa, AL 35487-0244 *Tel:* 205-348-0766 *Fax:* 205-348-1388 *E-mail:* writeua@english.as.ua.edu *Web Site:* www.as.ua.edu/english, pg 755

Maruhn, Elaine, University of Nebraska Press, 233 N Eighth St, Lincoln, NE 68588-0255 *Tel:* 402-472-3581 *Toll Free Tel:* 800-755-1105 (orders) *Fax:* 402-472-0308 *Toll Free Fax:* 800-526-2617 *E-mail:* press@unl.edu *Web Site:* www.nebraskapress.unl.edu; www.bisonbooks.com, pg 283

Marvin, Sally, Random House Publishing Group, 1745 Broadway, New York, NY 10019 *Toll Free Tel:* 800-200-3552 *Toll Free Fax:* 800-200-3552 *Web Site:* www.randomhouse.com, pg 227

Marwell, Josh, HarperCollins Publishers, 10 E 53 St, New York, NY 10022 *Tel:* 212-207-7000 *Fax:* 212-207-7145 *Web Site:* www.harpercollins.com, pg 116

Marwell, Josh, HarperCollins Publishers Sales, 10 E 53 St, New York, NY 10022 *Fax:* 212-207-7826 *Web Site:* www.harpercollins.com, pg 116

Marx, Tracy, Bantam Dell Publishing Group, 1745 Broadway, New York, NY 10019 *Tel:* 212-782-9000 *Toll Free Tel:* 800-223-6834 *Fax:* 212-302-7985 *Web Site:* www.randomhouse.com/bantamdell, pg 31

Marzano, Vincent M, Scholastic Inc, 557 Broadway, New York, NY 10012 *Tel:* 212-343-6100 *Toll Free Tel:* 800-scholastic *Fax:* 212-343-6930 *Web Site:* www.scholastic.com, pg 242

Marzilli, Gina, Adams Media, An F+W Publications Co, 57 Littlefield St, 2nd fl, Avon, MA 02322 *Tel:* 508-427-7100 *Fax:* 508-427-6790 *Toll Free Fax:* 800-872-5628 *E-mail:* authors@adamsmedia.com; orders@adamsmedia.com *Web Site:* www.adamsmedia.com, pg 5

Masch, Travis, Parallax Press, PO Box 7355, Berkeley, CA 94707-0355 *Tel:* 510-525-0101 *Fax:* 510-525-7129 *E-mail:* parallax@parallax.org *Web Site:* www.parallax.org, pg 204

Mason, Alane, W W Norton & Company Inc, 500 Fifth Ave, New York, NY 10110-0017 *Tel:* 212-354-5500 *Toll Free Tel:* 800-233-4830 (orders & cust serv) *Fax:* 212-869-0856 *Toll Free Fax:* 800-458-6515 *Web Site:* www.wwnorton.com, pg 193

Mason, Cindy, Canadian Circumpolar Institute (CCI) Press, University of Alberta, Campus Tower, Suite 308, 8625 112 St, Edmonton, AB T6H 0H1, Canada *Tel:* 780-492-4512 *Fax:* 780-492-1153 *E-mail:* ccinst@gpu.srv.ualberta.ca *Web Site:* www.ualberta.ca/~ccinst/, pg 538

Mason, James, The Aaland Agency, PO Box 849, Inyokern, CA 93527-0849 *Tel:* 760-384-3910 *Fax:* 760-384-4435 *Web Site:* www.the-aaland-agency.com, pg 617

Mason, John, Scholastic Trade Division, 557 Broadway, New York, NY 10012 *Tel:* 212-343-6100; 212-343-4685 (export sales) *Fax:* 212-343-4714 (export sales) *Web Site:* www.scholastic.com, pg 242

Mason, Sally D, Jamestown Prize, 109 Cary St, Williamsburg, VA 23185 *Tel:* 757-221-1114 *Fax:* 757-221-1047 *E-mail:* ieahc1@wm.edu *Web Site:* www.wm.edu/oieahc, pg 781

Mason, Thomas A, Indiana Historical Society Press, 450 W Ohio St, Indianapolis, IN 46202-3269 *Tel:* 317-233-9557 (sales); 317-234-2716 (editorial) *Toll Free Tel:* 800-447-1830 (orders only) *Fax:* 317-234-0562 (sales); 317-233-0857 (editorial) *E-mail:* ihspress@indianahistory.org; orders@indianahistory.org (orders) *Web Site:* www.indianahistory.org; shop.indianahistory.org (orders), pg 132

Masquida, Stephane, Sogides Ltee, 955 rue Amherst, Montreal, PQ H2L 3K4, Canada *Tel:* 514-523-1182 *Toll Free Tel:* 800-361-4806 *Fax:* 514-597-0370 *Web Site:* www.sogides.com; www.edhomme.com, pg 561

Masse, Michel, CCH Canadian Limited, A Wolters Kluwer Company, 90 Sheppard Ave E, Suite 300, Toronto, ON M2N 6X1, Canada *Tel:* 416-224-2224 *Toll Free Tel:* 800-268-4522 (Canada & US cust serv) *Fax:* 416-224-2243 *Toll Free Fax:* 800-461-4131 *E-mail:* cservice@cch.ca (cust serv) *Web Site:* www.cch.ca, pg 539

Massey, Bill, Bantam Dell Publishing Group, 1745 Broadway, New York, NY 10019 *Tel:* 212-782-9000 *Toll Free Tel:* 800-223-6834 *Fax:* 212-302-7985 *Web Site:* www.randomhouse.com/bantamdell, pg 31

Massey, Lynne, Editors' Association of Canada/Association canadienne des reviseurs, 27 Carlton St, Suite 502, Toronto, ON M5B 1L2, Canada *Tel:* 416-975-1379 *Toll Free Tel:* 866-226-3348 *Fax:* 416-975-1637 *E-mail:* info@editors.ca *Web Site:* www.editors.ca; www.reviseurs.ca, pg 686

Massey-Garrison, Nicholas, Doubleday Canada, One Toronto St, Suite 300, Toronto, ON M5C 2V6, Canada *Tel:* 416-364-4449 *Fax:* 416-957-1587 *Web Site:* www.randomhouse.ca, pg 542

Massie, Maria, Inkwell Management, 521 Fifth Ave, 26th fl, New York, NY 10175 *Tel:* 212-922-3500 *Fax:* 212-922-0535 *E-mail:* contact@inkwellmanagement.com *Web Site:* www.inkwellmanagement.com, pg 635

Massiscotte, Celine, Sogides Ltee, 955 rue Amherst, Montreal, PQ H2L 3K4, Canada *Tel:* 514-523-1182 *Toll Free Tel:* 800-361-4806 *Fax:* 514-597-0370 *Web Site:* www.sogides.com; www.edhomme.com, pg 561

Mastarovitz, Mandy, Nexus Press, 535 Means St, Atlanta, GA 30318 *Tel:* 404-577-3579 *Fax:* 404-577-5856 *E-mail:* nexuspress@thecontemporary.org *Web Site:* www.thecontemporary.org, pg 191

Masterson, Amanda, Bureau of Economic Geology, University of Texas at Austin, 10100 Burnet Rd, Bldg 130, Austin, TX 78750 *Tel:* 512-471-7144 *Toll Free Tel:* 888-839-4365 *Fax:* 512-471-0140 *Toll Free Fax:* 888-839-6277 *E-mail:* pubsales@beg.utexas.edu *Web Site:* www.beg.utexas.edu, pg 50

Masterson, Pete, Jack Mason Award, Baipa, PO Box E, Corte Madera, CA 94976 *Toll Free Tel:* 866-622-1325 *E-mail:* info@baipa.net *Web Site:* www.baipa.net, pg 788

Masterson, Dr Thomas, International Medical Publishing Inc, 1313 Dolly Madison Blvd, Suite 302, McLean, VA 22101 *Tel:* 703-356-2037 *Toll Free Tel:* 800-530-3142 *Fax:* 703-734-8987 *E-mail:* contact@medicalpublishing.com *Web Site:* www.medicalpublishing.com, pg 137

Mastria, Louis, The Direct Marketing Association Inc (The DMA), 1120 Avenue of the Americas, New York, NY 10036-6700 *Tel:* 212-768-7277 *Fax:* 212-768-4547 *E-mail:* dma@the-dma.org; customerservice@the-dma.org *Web Site:* www.the-dma.org, pg 80

Mastrocola, Phaedra, Square One Publishers, 115 Herricks Rd, Garden City Park, NY 11040 *Tel:* 516-535-2010 *Fax:* 516-535-2014 *E-mail:* sq1info@aol.com *Web Site:* squareonepublishers.com, pg 256

Mastropieri, Allison G, Jonathan David Publishers Inc, 68-22 Eliot Ave, Middle Village, NY 11379 *Tel:* 718-456-8611 *Fax:* 718-894-2818 *E-mail:* info@jdbooks.com; jondavpub@aol.com *Web Site:* www.jdbooks.com, pg 142

Masullo, Jim, Greenwood Publishing Group Inc, 88 Post Rd W, Westport, CT 06880-4208 *Tel:* 203-226-3571 *Toll Free Tel:* 800-225-5800 *Fax:* 203-222-1502 *E-mail:* bookinfo@greenwood.com (general); firstintial&fulllastname@greenwood.com (individuals) *Web Site:* www.greenwood.com, pg 109

Matcha, Anita, Trails Books, PO Box 317, Black Earth, WI 53515-0317 *Tel:* 608-767-8000 *Toll Free Tel:* 800-236-8088 *Fax:* 608-767-5444 *E-mail:* books@wistrails.com *Web Site:* www.trailsbooks.com, pg 273

Matheson, Ed, Colophon Group, 1306 Rousseau Cres, Greely, ON K4P 1B3, Canada *Tel:* 613-821-0066 *Fax:* 613-821-9987 *E-mail:* colophongroup@rogers.com, pg 594

Mathews, Janet, Moreland Press Inc, 827 Christina Circle, Oldsmar, FL 34677 *Tel:* 813-891-0568 *Fax:* 813-891-0428 *E-mail:* morelandpress@aol.com *Web Site:* www.morelandpress.com, pg 178

Mathews, Steven C, PRO-ED Inc, 8700 Shoal Creek Blvd, Austin, TX 78757-6897 *Tel:* 512-451-3246 *Toll Free Tel:* 800-897-3202 *Fax:* 512-451-8542 *Toll Free Fax:* 800-397-7633 *E-mail:* info@proedinc.com *Web Site:* www.proedinc.com, pg 219

Mathis, Michael, Epimetheus Books Inc, 2711 Centerville Rd, Suite 120-5336, Wilmington, DE 19808-1643 *Tel:* 646-345-2030 *E-mail:* epimetheus@att.net *Web Site:* www.epimetheusbooks.com, pg 91

Matlins, Stuart M, Association of Jewish Book Publishers, c/o Jewish Lights Publishing Sunset Farm Offices, PO Box 237, Woodstock, VT 05091 *Tel:* 802-457-4000 *Fax:* 802-457-4004 *Web Site:* www.jewishlights.com, pg 680

Matlins, Stuart M, GemStone Press, Sunset Farm Offices, Rte 4, Woodstock, VT 05091 *Tel:* 802-457-4000 *Toll Free Tel:* 800-962-4544 *Fax:* 802-457-4004 *E-mail:* sales@gemstonepress.com *Web Site:* www.gemstonepress.com, pg 103

Matlins, Stuart M, Jewish Lights Publishing, Sunset Farm Offices, Rte 4, Woodstock, VT 05091 *Tel:* 802-457-4000 *Toll Free Tel:* 800-962-4544 *Fax:* 802-457-4004 *E-mail:* sales@jewishlights.com *Web Site:* www.jewishlights.com, pg 140

Matlins, Stuart M, SkyLight Paths Publishing, Sunset Farm Offices, Rte 4, Woodstock, VT 05091 *Tel:* 802-457-4000 *Toll Free Tel:* 800-962-4544 *Fax:* 802-457-4004 *E-mail:* editorial@skylightpaths.com *Web Site:* www.skylightpaths.com, pg 250

Matloff, Robert, The Guilford Press, 72 Spring St, New York, NY 10012 *Tel:* 212-431-9800 *Toll Free Tel:* 800-365-7006 (orders) *Fax:* 212-966-6708 *E-mail:* orders@guilford.com *Web Site:* www.guilford.com, pg 111

Matson, Jonathan, Harold Matson Co Inc, 276 Fifth Ave, New York, NY 10001 *Tel:* 212-679-4490 *Fax:* 212-545-1224 *E-mail:* hmatsco@aol.com, pg 643

Matson, Katinka, Brockman Inc, 5 E 59 St, New York, NY 10022 *Tel:* 212-935-8900 *Fax:* 212-935-5535 *E-mail:* rights@brockman.com, pg 623

Matson, Peter, Sterling Lord Literistic Inc, 65 Bleecker St, New York, NY 10012 *Tel:* 212-780-6050 *Fax:* 212-780-6095, pg 657

Mattachione, Faye, The National Business Book Award, Royal Trust Tower, TD Centre, Suite 3000, 77 King St W, Toronto, ON M5K 1G8, Canada *Tel:* 416-941-8383 *Fax:* 416-941-8345 *Web Site:* www.pwcglobal.com, pg 791

Mattawa, Khaled, University of Texas at Austin, Creative Writing Program, Dept of English, One University Sta, B5000, Austin, TX 78712-1164 *Tel:* 512-475-6356 *Fax:* 512-471-2898 *Web Site:* www.en.utexas.edu/grad/crwconc.html, pg 756

Matteo, Steve, Barron's Educational Series Inc, 250 Wireless Blvd, Hauppauge, NY 11788 *Tel:* 631-434-3311 *Toll Free Tel:* 800-645-3476 *Fax:* 631-434-3723 *E-mail:* info@barronseduc.com *Web Site:* www.barronseduc.com (Books can be purchased online), pg 32

Matthews, Linda H, Chicago Review Press, 814 N Franklin St, Chicago, IL 60610 *Tel:* 312-337-0747 *Toll Free Tel:* 800-888-4741 *Fax:* 312-337-5110 *E-mail:* editorial@ipgbook.com, pg 60

Matthews, Rex, Society of Biblical Literature, The Luce Ctr, Suite 350, 825 Houston Mill Rd, Atlanta, GA 30329 *Tel:* 404-727-2325 *Fax:* 802-864-7626 *E-mail:* sbl@sbl-site.org *Web Site:* www.sbl-site.org, pg 251

Matthews, Scott, Books on Tape®, Customer Service, 400 Hahn Rd, Westminster, MD 21157 *Toll Free Tel:* 800-733-3000 *Toll Free Fax:* 800-659-2436 *E-mail:* botlib@booksontape.com *Web Site:* library.booksontape.com, pg 44

Matthews, Scott, Random House Audio Publishing Group, 1745 Broadway, New York, NY 10019 *Tel:* 212-782-9720 *Fax:* 212-782-9600, pg 225

Matthews, Scott, Random House Large Print, 1745 Broadway, New York, NY 10019 *Tel:* 212-782-9720 *Fax:* 212-782-9600, pg 227

Matthias, Lee A, Lee Allan Agency, 7464 N 107 St, Milwaukee, WI 53224-3706 *Tel:* 414-357-7708, pg 618

Mattil, Debby, Teacher Ideas Press, 361 Hanover St, Portsmouth, NH 03801-3912 *Toll Free Tel:* 800-225-5800 *Fax:* 603-431-2214 *Toll Free Fax:* 800-354-2004 (perms & foreign rts) *E-mail:* custserv@teacherideaspress.com; permissions@teacherideaspress.com; foreignrights@teacherideaspress.com *Web Site:* www.teacherideaspress.com, pg 265

Mattura, Cat, McGraw-Hill Primis Custom Publishing, 2460 Kerper Blvd, Dubuque, IA 52001 *Tel:* 563-588-1451 *Fax:* 563-589-4700 *E-mail:* first_last@mcgraw-hill.com *Web Site:* www.mhhe.com, pg 168

Matut, Silvia, Santillana USA Publishing Co Inc, 2105 NW 86 Ave, Miami, FL 33122 *Tel:* 305-591-9522 *Toll Free Tel:* 800-245-8584 *Fax:* 305-591-9145 *Toll Free Fax:* 888-248-9518 *E-mail:* customerservice@santillanausa.com *Web Site:* www.santillanausa.com; www.alfaguara.net, pg 240

Matyi, Rita, Congressional Quarterly Press, 1255 22 St NW, Washington, DC 20037 *Tel:* 202-729-1800 *Toll Free Tel:* 866-427-7737 *Fax:* 202-729-1809 *Toll Free Fax:* 800-380-3810 *E-mail:* customerservice@cqpress.com *Web Site:* www.cq.com, pg 66

Matysko, Harriet I, Mary Ann Liebert Inc, 2 Madison Ave, Larchmont, NY 10538 *Tel:* 914-834-3100 *Toll Free Tel:* 800-654-3237 *Fax:* 914-834-3771 *Web Site:* www.mliebert.com; www.liebertpub.com, pg 154

Mauceri, Peter, Time Warner Book Group, 1271 Avenue of the Americas, New York, NY 10020 *Tel:* 212-522-7200 *Fax:* 212-522-7991 *Web Site:* www.twbookmark.com, pg 271

Mauer, Tzvi, Urim Publications, 3709 13 Ave, Brooklyn, NY 11218 *Tel:* 718-972-5449 *Fax:* 718-972-6307 *E-mail:* publisher@urimpublications.com *Web Site:* www.urimpublications.com, pg 288

Maule, Brewster, Educators Publishing Service Inc, 625 Mount Auburn St, Cambridge, MA 02139-9031 *Tel:* 617-547-6706 *Toll Free Tel:* 800-225-5750 *Fax:* 617-547-0412 *Toll Free Fax:* 888-440-2665 *E-mail:* epsbooks@epsbooks.com *Web Site:* www.epsbooks.com, pg 88

Maurer, Ann, Bick Publishing House, 307 Neck Rd, Madison, CT 06443 *Tel:* 203-245-0073 *Fax:* 203-245-5990 *E-mail:* bickpubhse@aol.com *Web Site:* www.bickpubhouse.com, pg 38

Maurer, Ann, Writers House LLC, 21 W 26 St, New York, NY 10010 *Tel:* 212-685-2400 *Fax:* 212-685-1781, pg 662

Maurer, Rolf, New Star Books Ltd, 107-3477 Commercial St, Vancouver, BC V5N 4E8, Canada *Tel:* 604-738-9429 *Fax:* 604-738-9332 *E-mail:* info@newstarbooks.com; orders@newstarbooks.com *Web Site:* www.newstarbooks.com, pg 555

Mausser, Therese, AMACOM Books, 1601 Broadway, New York, NY 10019-7406 *Tel:* 212-586-8100; 518-891-5510 (orders) *Toll Free Tel:* 800-262-9699 (cust serv) *Fax:* 212-903-8168; 518-891-2372 (orders) *Web Site:* www.amanet.org, pg 10

Mautner, Stephen, National Academies Press, 500 Fifth St NW, Washington, DC 20001 *Tel:* 202-334-3313 *Toll Free Tel:* 800-624-6242 *Fax:* 202-334-2451 (orders) *Web Site:* www.nap.edu, pg 182

Maves, Dr Michael, American Medical Association, 515 N State St, Chicago, IL 60610 *Tel:* 312-464-5000 *Toll Free Tel:* 800-621-8335 *Fax:* 312-464-4184 *Web Site:* www.ama-assn.org, pg 677

Mavjee, Maya, Doubleday Canada, One Toronto St, Suite 300, Toronto, ON M5C 2V6, Canada *Tel:* 416-364-4449 *Fax:* 416-957-1587 *Web Site:* www.randomhouse.ca, pg 542

Mavjee, Maya, Seal Books, One Toronto St, Suite 300, Toronto, ON M5C 2V6, Canada *Tel:* 416-364-4449 *Toll Free Tel:* 888-523-9292 (order desk) *Fax:* 416-957-1587 *Web Site:* www.randomhouse.ca, pg 560

Maxwell, Linda, Blue Dolphin Publishing Inc, 12428 Nevada City Hwy, Grass Valley, CA 95945 *Tel:* 530-265-6925 *Toll Free Tel:* 800-643-0765 *Fax:* 530-265-0787 *E-mail:* bdolphin@netshel.net *Web Site:* www.bluedolphinpublishing.com, pg 41

Maxwell, Nancy, Ariel Press, 90 Steve Tate Hwy, Suite 201, Marble Hill, GA 30148 *Tel:* 770-894-4226 *Fax:* 706-579-1865 (orders), pg 23

May, Christopher, Dufour Editions Inc, PO Box 7, Chester Springs, PA 19425-0007 *Tel:* 610-458-5005 *Toll Free Tel:* 800-869-5677 *Fax:* 610-458-7103 *E-mail:* info@dufoureditions.com *Web Site:* www.dufoureditions.com, pg 84

May, Linda, Greenwood Publishing Group Inc, 88 Post Rd W, Westport, CT 06880-4208 *Tel:* 203-226-3571 *Toll Free Tel:* 800-225-5800 *Fax:* 203-222-1502 *E-mail:* bookinfo@greenwood.com (general); firstintial&fulllastname@greenwood.com (individuals) *Web Site:* www.greenwood.com, pg 109

May, Louise, Lee & Low Books Inc, 95 Madison Ave, New York, NY 10016 *Tel:* 212-779-4400 *Toll Free Tel:* 888-320-3190 ext 25 (orders only) *Fax:* 212-683-1894 (orders only); 212-532-6035 *E-mail:* info@leeandlow.com *Web Site:* www.leeandlow.com, pg 152

May, Maura, Productivity Press, 444 Park Ave S, Suite 604, New York, NY 10016 *Tel:* 212-686-5900 *Toll Free Tel:* 888-319-5852 *Fax:* 212-686-5411 *Toll Free Fax:* 800-394-6286 *E-mail:* info@productivitypress.com *Web Site:* www.productivitypress.com, pg 219

May, Theresa, University of Texas Press, PO Box 7819, Austin, TX 78713-7819 *Tel:* 512-471-7233 *Fax:* 512-232-7178 *E-mail:* utpress@uts.cc.utexas.edu *Web Site:* www.utexas.edu/utpress, pg 267

Maya, Judith, Abrams & Co Publishers Inc, 61 Mattatuck Heights Rd, Waterbury, CT 06705 *Tel:* 203-756-6562 *Toll Free Tel:* 800-227-9120 *Fax:* 203-756-2895 *Toll Free Fax:* 800-737-3322, pg 3

Maya, Judith, Graphic Learning, 61 Mattatuck Heights Rd, Waterbury, CT 06705 *Tel:* 800-874-0029; 800-227-9120 *Fax:* 203-756-2895 *Toll Free Fax:* 800-737-3322, pg 108

Maya, Judith, The Letter People®, 61 Mattatuck Heights Rd, Waterbury, CT 06705 *Tel:* 203-756-6562 *Toll Free Tel:* 800-227-9120; 800-874-0029 *Fax:* 203-756-2895 *Toll Free Fax:* 800-737-3322 *Web Site:* letterpeople.com, pg 153

Mayberry, Debra, Columbia Books Inc, 1825 Connecticut Ave NW, Suite 625, Washington, DC 20009 *Tel:* 202-464-1662 *Toll Free Tel:* 888-265-0600 (cust serv) *Fax:* 202-464-1775; 240-646-7020 (cust serv) *E-mail:* info@columbiabooks.com *Web Site:* www.columbiabooks.com, pg 65

Maybury, Margaret, Greenwood Publishing Group Inc, 88 Post Rd W, Westport, CT 06880-4208 *Tel:* 203-226-3571 *Toll Free Tel:* 800-225-5800 *Fax:* 203-222-1502 *E-mail:* bookinfo@greenwood.com (general); firstintial&fulllastname@greenwood.com (individuals) *Web Site:* www.greenwood.com, pg 109

Mayer, Andy, Everyday Wisdom Press, 11010 Northup Way, Bellevue, WA 98004 *Tel:* 425-822-1950; 425-827-7120 *Toll Free Tel:* 866-319-5900 *Fax:* 425-828-9659 *E-mail:* everydaywisdom@everydaywisdom.net *Web Site:* everydaywisdom.net, pg 93

Mayer, Barbara, Cross Pond Editing Group, 333 Hook Rd, Katonah, NY 10536 *Tel:* 914-232-8687 *Fax:* 914-232-1258, pg 595

Mayer, Daniel, Vanderbilt University Press, 201 University Plaza Bldg, 112 21 Ave S, Nashville, TN 37203 *Tel:* 615-322-3585 *Toll Free Tel:* 800-627-7377 (orders only) *Fax:* 615-343-8823 *Toll Free Fax:* 800-735-0476 (orders only) *E-mail:* vupress@vanderbilt.edu *Web Site:* www.vanderbilt.edu/vupress, pg 289

Mayer, Karen, Penguin Group (USA) Inc, 375 Hudson St, New York, NY 10014 *Tel:* 212-366-2000 *Fax:* 212-366-2666 *E-mail:* online@uspenguingroup.com *Web Site:* www.penguin.com, pg 208

Mayer, Kristy, Carol Mann Agency, 55 Fifth Ave, New York, NY 10003 *Tel:* 212-206-5635 *Fax:* 212-675-4809, pg 642

Mayer, Loomis, Fordham University Press, 2546 Belmont Ave, Bronx, NY 10458-5172 *Tel:* 718-817-4780 *Toll Free Tel:* 800-247-6553 (orders) *Fax:* 718-817-4785 *Web Site:* www.fordhampress.com, pg 98

Mayer, Margery, Scholastic Education, 524 Broadway, New York, NY 10012 *Tel:* 212-343-6100 *Fax:* 212-343-6189 *Web Site:* www.scholastic.com, pg 241

Mayer, Margery, Scholastic Education Curriculum Publishing, 524 Broadway, New York, NY 10012 *Tel:* 212-343-6100 *Web Site:* www.scholastic.com, pg 241

Mayer, Margery, Scholastic Inc, 557 Broadway, New York, NY 10012 *Tel:* 212-343-4469 *Toll Free Tel:* 800-scholastic; 212-343-6930 *Web Site:* www.scholastic.com, pg 242

Mayer, Peter, The Overlook Press, 141 Wooster St, New York, NY 10012 *Tel:* 212-965-8400 *Fax:* 212-965-9834 *Web Site:* www.overlookny.com, pg 200

Mayer, Sandor, National Book Co, PO Box 8795, Portland, OR 97207-8795 *Tel:* 503-228-6345 *Fax:* 810-885-5811 *E-mail:* info@eralearning.com *Web Site:* www.eralearning.com, pg 182

Mayerski, Alfred, Gem Guides Book Co, 315 Cloverleaf Dr, Suite F, Baldwin Park, CA 91706 *Tel:* 626-855-1611 *Fax:* 626-855-1610 *E-mail:* gembooks@aol.com, pg 103

Mayerski, Kathy, Gem Guides Book Co, 315 Cloverleaf Dr, Suite F, Baldwin Park, CA 91706 *Tel:* 626-855-1611 *Fax:* 626-855-1610 *E-mail:* gembooks@aol.com, pg 103

Mayhew, Alice E, Simon & Schuster, 1230 Avenue of the Americas, New York, NY 10020 *Tel:* 212-698-7000 *Fax:* 800-223-2348 (cust serv); 800-223-2336 (orders) *Toll Free Fax:* 800-943-9831 (orders) *Web Site:* www.simonsays.com, pg 248

Maynard, Audrey, Tilbury House Publishers, 2 Mechanic St, No 3, Gardiner, ME 04345 *Tel:* 207-582-1899 *Toll Free Tel:* 800-582-1899 (orders) *Fax:* 207-582-8229 *E-mail:* tilbury@tilburyhouse.com *Web Site:* www.tilburyhouse.com, pg 271

Maynard, Garret C, The Gary-Paul Agency, 1549 Main St, Stratford, CT 00615 *Tel:* 203-375-2636 *Fax:* 203-375-2636 *Web Site:* www.thegarypaulagency.com, pg 600

Maynard, Jane, Quicksilver Productions, PO Box 340, Ashland, OR 97520-0012 *Tel:* 541-482-5343 *Fax:* 541-482-0960 *E-mail:* celestialcalendars@e-mail.com *Web Site:* www.quicksilverproductions.com, pg 224

Maynard, Jim, Quicksilver Productions, PO Box 340, Ashland, OR 97520-0012 *Tel:* 541-482-5343 *Fax:* 541-482-0960 *E-mail:* celestialcalendars@e-mail.com *Web Site:* www.quicksilverproductions.com, pg 224

Mayo, Jon, Miniature Book Society Inc, 402 York Ave, Delaware, OH 43015 *Web Site:* www.mbs.org, pg 691

Mayo, Julie, The Lazear Agency Inc, 431 Second St, Suite 300, Hudson, WI 54016 *Tel:* 715-531-0012 *Fax:* 715-531-0016 *Web Site:* www.lazear.com, pg 639

Mayotte, Alain, Prise de Parole Inc, C P 550, Sudbury, ON P3E 4R2, Canada *Tel:* 705-675-6491 *Fax:* 705-673-1817 *E-mail:* prisedeparole@bellnet.ca, pg 558

Mays, Barbara, Friends United Press, 101 Quaker Hill Dr, Richmond, IN 47374 *Tel:* 765-962-7573 *Toll Free Tel:* 800-537-8839 *Fax:* 765-966-1293 *E-mail:* friendspress@fum.org *Web Site:* www.fum.org, pg 101

Mays, Stedman, Clausen Mays & Tahan Literary Agency LLC, PO Box 1015, Cooper Sta, New York, NY 10276-1015 *Tel:* 212-714-8181 *Fax:* 212-714-8282 *E-mail:* cmtassist@aol.com, pg 625

Mays, Wendy, Wendy Lynn & Co, 504 Wilson Rd, Annapolis, MD 21401 *Tel:* 410-224-2729; 410-507-1059 *Fax:* 410-224-2183 *Web Site:* wendy-lynn.com, pg 667

Maze, Stephanie, Moonstone Press LLC, 7820 Oracle Place, Potomac, MD 20854 *Tel:* 301-765-1081 *Fax:* 301-765-0510 *E-mail:* mazeprod@erols.com *Web Site:* www.moonstonepress.net, pg 572

Mazia, Judith, Alan Wofsy Fine Arts, 1109 Geary Blvd, San Francisco, CA 94109 *Tel:* 415-292-6500 *Fax:* 415-512-0130 (acctg); 415-292-6594 (off & cust serv) *E-mail:* beauxarts@earthlink.net (cust serv); editeur@earthlink.net (edit); order@art-books.com (orders) *Web Site:* art-books.com, pg 302

Mazour, Elena, NDE Publishing, 15-30 Wertheim Ct, Richmond Hill, ON L4B 1B9, Canada *Tel:* 905-731-1288 *Toll Free Tel:* 800-675-1263 *Fax:* 905-731-5744 *E-mail:* info@ndepublishing.com *Web Site:* www.ndepublishing.com, pg 555

Mazza, Merrily, McGraw-Hill/Irwin, 1333 Burr Ridge Pkwy, Burr Ridge, IL 60527 *Tel:* 630-789-4000 *Toll Free Tel:* 800-338-3987 (cust serv) *Fax:* 630-789-6942; 614-755-5645 (cust serv) *Web Site:* www.mhhe.com, pg 168

Mazzilli-Blount, Tricia, Peter Glenn Publications, 6040 NW 43 Terr, Boca Raton, FL 33496 *Tel:* 561-999-8930 *Toll Free Tel:* 888-332-6700 *Fax:* 561-999-8931 *E-mail:* lynn@pgdirect.com *Web Site:* www.pgdirect.com, pg 105

McAbee, Gail, NovelBooks Inc, PO Box 661, Douglas, MA 01516-0661 *Tel:* 508-476-1611 *Fax:* 508-476-3866 *E-mail:* publisher@novelbooksinc.com *Web Site:* www.novelbooksinc.com, pg 194

McAdam, Susanne, McGill-Queen's University Press, 3430 McTavish St, Montreal, PQ H3A 1X9, Canada *Tel:* 514-398-3750 *Fax:* 514-398-4333 *E-mail:* mqup@mqup.ca *Web Site:* www.mqup.mcgill.ca, pg 553

McAdoo, Lynne, Andrews McMeel Publishing, 4520 Main St, Suite 700, Kansas City, MO 64111-7701 *Tel:* 816-932-6700 *Toll Free Tel:* 800-851-8923 *Web Site:* www.universal.com/amp, pg 169

McAliley, Kevin, Haights Cross Communications Inc, 10 New King St, White Plains, NY 10604 *Tel:* 914-289-9400 *Fax:* 914-289-9401 *E-mail:* info@haightscross.com *Web Site:* www.haightscross.com, pg 112

McAliley, Kevin, Triumph Learning, 333 E 38 St, 8th fl, New York, NY 10016 *Tel:* 212-652-0200 *Fax:* 212-652-0203 *Web Site:* www.triumphlearning.com, pg 276

McAllister, David, Boson Books, 3905 Meadow Field Lane, Raleigh, NC 27606 *Tel:* 919-233-8164 *Fax:* 919-233-8578 *E-mail:* boson@bosonbooks.com *Web Site:* www.bosonbooks.com, pg 44

McAllister, David, C & M Online Media Inc, 3905 Meadow Field Lane, Raleigh, NC 27606 *Tel:* 919-233-8164 *Fax:* 919-233-8578 *E-mail:* cm@cmonline.com *Web Site:* www.cmonline.com, pg 51

McAllister, Nancy, Boson Books, 3905 Meadow Field Lane, Raleigh, NC 27606 *Tel:* 919-233-8164 *Fax:* 919-233-8578 *E-mail:* boson@bosonbooks.com *Web Site:* www.bosonbooks.com, pg 44

McAllister, Nancy, C & M Online Media Inc, 3905 Meadow Field Lane, Raleigh, NC 27606 *Tel:* 919-233-8164 *Fax:* 919-233-8578 *E-mail:* cm@cmonline.com *Web Site:* www.cmonline.com, pg 51

McAloon, Hugh, Krause Publications, 700 E State St, Iola, WI 54990 *Tel:* 715-445-4612 ext 365 *Toll Free Tel:* 800-258-0929; 888-457-2873 *Fax:* 715-445-4087 *Web Site:* www.krause.com, pg 147

McAndless, Janet, Association of Medical Illustrators (AMI), 6660 Delmonico Dr, Suite D-107, Colorado Springs, CO 80919 *Tel:* 719-598-8622 *E-mail:* hq@ami.org *Web Site:* www.ami.org, pg 680

McAweeney, Terry, MFA Publications, 465 Huntington Ave, Boston, MA 02115 *Tel:* 617-369-3438 *Fax:* 617-369-3459 *Web Site:* www.mfa-publications.org, pg 173

McBride, Jason, Coach House Books, 401 Huron St, Rear, Toronto, ON M5S 2G5, Canada *Tel:* 416-979-2217 *Toll Free Tel:* 800-367-6360 *Fax:* 416-977-1158 *E-mail:* mail@chbooks.com *Web Site:* www.chbooks.com, pg 540

McBride, Kate, Adams Media, An F+W Publications Co, 57 Littlefield St, 2nd fl, Avon, MA 02322 *Tel:* 508-427-7100 *Fax:* 508-427-6790 *Toll Free Tel:* 800-872-5628 *E-mail:* authors@adamsmedia.com; orders@adamsmedia.com *Web Site:* www.adamsmedia.com, pg 5

McBride, Margret, Margret McBride Literary Agency, 7744 Fay Ave, Suite 201, La Jolla, CA 92037 *Tel:* 858-454-1550 *Fax:* 858-454-2156 *E-mail:* staff@mcbridelit.com *Web Site:* www.mcbrideliterary.com, pg 643

McCabe, Allison, Berkley Books, 375 Hudson St, New York, NY 10014 *Tel:* 212-366-2000 *Fax:* 212-366-2666 *E-mail:* online@penguinputnam.com *Web Site:* www.penguin.com, pg 36

McCabe, Allison, Berkley Publishing Group, 375 Hudson St, New York, NY 10014 *Tel:* 212-366-2000 *E-mail:* online@penguinputnam.com *Web Site:* www.penguin.com, pg 37

McCabe, Don, AVKO Dyslexia & Spelling Research Foundation Inc, 3084 W Willard Rd, Clio, MI 48420 *Tel:* 810-686-9283 *Toll Free Tel:* 866-285-6612 *Fax:* 810-686-1101 *E-mail:* avkoemail@aol.com *Web Site:* www.avko.org, pg 29

McCabe, Michael, IEE, c/o Inspec, 379 Thornall St, Edison, NJ 08837-2225 *Tel:* 732-321-5575 *Fax:* 732-321-5702 *E-mail:* iee@inspecinc.com *Web Site:* www.iee.org/publishing, pg 130

McCaffrey, Philip, W H Freeman and Co, 41 Madison Ave, 37th fl, New York, NY 10010 *Tel:* 212-576-9400 *Fax:* 212-689-2383 *Web Site:* www.whfreeman.com, pg 100

McCaffrey, Roger, Roman Catholic Books, PO Box 2286, Fort Collins, CO 80522-2286 *Tel:* 970-490-2735 *Fax:* 970-493-8781 *Web Site:* www.booksforcatholics.com, pg 234

McCaffrey, Roger A, Roger A McCaffrey Publishing, PO Box 1209, Ridgefield, CT 06877, pg 166

McCahon, Kristin, The Fraser Institute, 1770 Burrard St, 4th fl, Vancouver, BC V6J 3G7, Canada *Tel:* 604-688-0221 *Toll Free Tel:* 800-665-3558 *Fax:* 604-688-8539 *E-mail:* sales@fraserinstitute.ca *Web Site:* www.fraserinstitute.ca, pg 547

McCain, Paul T, Concordia Publishing House, 3558 S Jefferson Ave, St Louis, MO 63118-3968 *Tel:* 314-268-1000 *Toll Free Tel:* 800-325-3040 *Fax:* 314-268-1329 *Toll Free Fax:* 800-490-9889 *E-mail:* cphorder@cph.org *Web Site:* www.cph.org, pg 66

McCall, Linda, AAUP Book, Jacket & Journal Design Show, 71 W 23 St, Suite 901, New York, NY 10010 *Tel:* 212-989-1010 *Fax:* 212-989-0275; 212-989-0176 *E-mail:* info@aaupnet.org *Web Site:* www.aaupnet.org, pg 757

McCall, Linda, Association of American University Presses (AAUP), 71 W 23 St, Suite 901, New York City, NY 10010 *Tel:* 212-989-1010 *Fax:* 212-989-0275; 212-989-0176 *E-mail:* info@aaupnet.org *Web Site:* www.aaupnet.org, pg 679

McCall, Timothy, Penguin Group (USA) Inc Sales, 375 Hudson St, New York, NY 10014 *Tel:* 212-366-2000 *E-mail:* online@penguinputnam.com *Web Site:* www.penguin.com, pg 208

McCandless, Sarah, Dark Horse Comics, 10956 SE Main St, Milwaukie, OR 97222 *Tel:* 503-652-8815 *Fax:* 503-654-9440 *E-mail:* dhcomics@darkhorsecomics.com *Web Site:* www.darkhorse.com, pg 76

McCann, Anna, Dimension Books Inc, PO Box 9, Starrucca, PA 18462 *Tel:* 570-727-2486 *Fax:* 570-727-2813, pg 80

McCann, Christopher, Angelus Press, 2915 Forest Ave, Kansas City, MO 64109 *Tel:* 816-753-3150 *Toll Free Tel:* 800-966-7337 *Fax:* 816-753-3557 *Toll Free Fax:* 888-855-9022 *E-mail:* info@angeluspress.org *Web Site:* www.angeluspress.org, pg 20

McCann, Moira, Running Press Book Publishers, 125 S 22 St, Philadelphia, PA 19103-4399 *Tel:* 215-567-5080 *Toll Free Tel:* 800-345-5359 (cust serv & orders) *Fax:* 215-568-2919 *Toll Free Fax:* 800-453-2884 *Web Site:* www.runningpress.com, pg 236

McCann, Nancy, Autumn Authors' Affair, 1507 Burnham Ave, Calumet City, IL 60409 *Tel:* 708-862-9797 *E-mail:* exchbook@aol.com *Web Site:* www.rendezvousreviews.com, pg 741

McCann, Sharon, Nicholas Roerich Poetry Prize, 2091 Suncrest Rd, Talent, OR 97540 *Tel:* 541-512-8792 *Fax:* 541-512-8793 *E-mail:* mail@storylinepress.com *Web Site:* www.storylinepress.com, pg 802

McCann, Sharon, Story Line Press, 2091 Suncrest Rd, Talent, OR 97540 *Tel:* 541-512-8792 *Fax:* 541-512-8793 *E-mail:* mail@storylinepress.com *Web Site:* www.storylinepress.com, pg 260

McCann, Sharon, The Three Oaks Prize in Fiction, 2091 Suncrest Rd, Talent, OR 97540 *Tel:* 541-512-8792 *Fax:* 541-512-8793 *E-mail:* mail@storylinepress.com *Web Site:* www.storylinepress.com, pg 808

McCardell, Michelle, Upstart Books™, W5527 State Rd 106, Fort Atkinson, WI 53538-8428 *Tel:* 920-563-9571 *Toll Free Tel:* 800-448-4887 *Fax:* 920-563-7395 *Toll Free Fax:* 800-448-5828 *Web Site:* www.highsmith.com, pg 288

McCarter, Robert, Jodie Rhodes Literary Agency, 8840 Villa La Jolla Dr, Suite 315, La Jolla, CA 92037, pg 651

McCarthy, Ari, Skinner House Books, 25 Beacon St, Boston, MA 02108-2800 *Tel:* 617-742-2100 *Fax:* 617-742-7025 *E-mail:* skinner_house@uua.org *Web Site:* www.uua.org/skinner/index.html, pg 249

McCarthy, Brian, The Library of America, 14 E 60 St, New York, NY 10022 *Tel:* 212-308-3360 *Fax:* 212-750-8352 *E-mail:* info@loa.org *Web Site:* www.loa.org; www.loaacademic.org, pg 154

McCarthy, Charles, Yardbird Books, 601 Kennedy Rd, Airville, PA 17302 *Tel:* 717-927-6377 *Toll Free:* 800-622-6044 (Sales) *Fax:* 717-927-6377 *E-mail:* info@yardbird.com *Web Site:* www.yardbird.com, pg 306

McCarthy, Dan, Primedia Consumer Magazine & Internet Group, 260 Madison Ave, New York, NY 10016 *Tel:* 212-726-4300 *Toll Free Tel:* 800-521-2885 *Fax:* 212-726-4310 *E-mail:* sgnews@primediasi.com *Web Site:* www.primediainc.com, pg 218

McCarthy, E J, E J McCarthy Agency, 21 Columbus Ave, Suite 210, San Francisco, CA 94111 *Tel:* 415-296-7706 *Fax:* 415-296-7706 *E-mail:* ejmagency@mac.com, pg 643

McCarthy, Jim, Dystel & Goderich Literary Management, One Union Sq W, Suite 904, New York, NY 10003 *Tel:* 212-627-9100 *Fax:* 212-627-9313 *Web Site:* www.dystel.com, pg 629

McCarthy, Pat, Cornell & McCarthy LLC, 2-D Cross Hwy, Westport, CT 06880 *Tel:* 203-454-4210 *Fax:* 203-454-4258 *Web Site:* www.cornellandmccarthy.com, pg 665

McCarthy, Peter, Penguin Group (USA) Inc, 375 Hudson St, New York, NY 10014 *Tel:* 212-366-2000 *Fax:* 212-366-2666 *E-mail:* online@uspenguingroup.com *Web Site:* www.penguin.com, pg 208

McCarthy, Thomas, Marshall Cavendish Corp, 99 White Plains Rd, Tarrytown, NY 10591-9001 *Tel:* 914-332-8888 *Fax:* 914-332-1888 *E-mail:* mcc@marshallcavendish.com *Web Site:* www.marshallcavendish.com, pg 164

McCarthy, Tom, The Globe Pequot Press, 246 Goose Lane, Guilford, CT 06437 *Tel:* 203-458-4500 *Toll Free Tel:* 800-243-0495 (cust serv) *Fax:* 203-458-4601 *Toll Free Fax:* 800-820-2329 (orders & cust serv) *E-mail:* info@globepequot.com *Web Site:* www.globepequot.com, pg 105

McCarthy, Tom, The Lyons Press, 246 Goose Lane, Guilford, CT 06437 *Tel:* 203-458-4500 *Toll Free Tel:* 800-243-0495 *Fax:* 203-458-4668 *Web Site:* www.lyonspress.com; www.globepequot.com, pg 160

McCartin Associates, Sally Ann, Soho Press Inc, 853 Broadway, New York, NY 10003 *Tel:* 212-260-1900 *Fax:* 212-260-1902 *E-mail:* editor@sohopress.com *Web Site:* sohopress.com, pg 252

McCarty, Darlene, Charles C Thomas Publisher Ltd, 2600 S First St, Springfield, IL 62704 *Tel:* 217-789-8980 *Toll Free Tel:* 800-258-8980 *Fax:* 217-789-9130 *E-mail:* books@ccthomas.com *Web Site:* www.ccthomas.com, pg 269

McCauley, Gerard, Gerard McCauley Agency Inc, PO Box 844, Katonah, NY 10536-0844 *Tel:* 914-232-5700 *Fax:* 914-232-1506, pg 643

McCauley, Kay, The Pimlico Agency Inc, PO Box 20447, Cherokee Sta, New York, NY 10021 *Tel:* 212-628-9729 *Fax:* 212-535-7861, pg 648

McCauley, Kirby, The Pimlico Agency Inc, PO Box 20447, Cherokee Sta, New York, NY 10021 *Tel:* 212-628-9729 *Fax:* 212-535-7861, pg 648

McClane, Joseph, US Government Printing Office, Superintendent of Documents, Washington, DC 20401 *Tel:* 202-512-1707 *Toll Free Tel:* 888-293-6498 (cust serv); 866-512-1800 (orders) *Fax:* 202-512-1655 (bibliographic info); 202-512-2250 (orders & pricing) *Toll Free Fax:* 866-512-1800 *E-mail:* orders@gpo.gov *Web Site:* bookstore.gpo.gov (sales); gpoaccess.gov, pg 289

McCleary, Carol, The Wilshire Literary Agency, 20 Barristers Walk, Dennis, MA 02638 *Tel:* 508-385-5200, pg 661

McClellan, Anita, Anita D McClellan Associates, 50 Stearns St, Cambridge, MA 02138 *Tel:* 617-576-5960 *Fax:* 617-576-6950, pg 643

McClellan, Dennis, DC Press, 2445 River Tree, Sanford, FL 32771 *Tel:* 407-688-1156 *Toll Free Tel:* 866-602-1476 *Fax:* 407-688-1135 *E-mail:* info@focusonethics.com *Web Site:* www.focusonethics.com, pg 77

McClelland, Anne, Canadian Copyright Institute, 192 Spadina Ave, Suite 107, Toronto, ON M5T 2C2, Canada *Tel:* 416-975-1756 *Fax:* 416-975-1839 *E-mail:* bkper@interlog.com, pg 683

McClenand, Ann, Book & Periodical Council, 192 Spadina Ave, Suite 107, Toronto, ON M5T 2C2, Canada *Tel:* 416-975-9366 *Fax:* 416-975-1839 *E-mail:* bkper@interlog.com *Web Site:* www.freedomtoread.ca, pg 681

McClendon, Carole, Waterside Productions Inc, 2187 Newcastle Ave, Suite 204, Cardiff, CA 92007 *Tel:* 760-632-9190 *Fax:* 760-632-9295 *Web Site:* www.waterside.com, pg 660

McClintock, David, Dorset House Publishing Co Inc, 353 W 12 St, New York, NY 10014 *Tel:* 212-620-4053 *Toll Free Tel:* 800-DHBOOKS (342-6657 orders only) *Fax:* 212-727-1044 *E-mail:* info@dorsethouse.com; dhpubco@aol.com *Web Site:* www.dorsethouse.com, pg 82

McClinton, Susan, William S Hein & Co Inc, 1285 Main St, Buffalo, NY 14209-1987 *Tel:* 716-882-2600 *Toll Free Tel:* 800-828-7571 *Fax:* 716-883-8100 *E-mail:* mail@wshein.com *Web Site:* www.wshein.com, pg 120

McCloskey, Nanci, Virginia Kidd Agency Inc, 538 E Harford St, Milford, PA 18337 *Tel:* 570-296-6205 *Fax:* 570-296-7266 *Web Site:* vkagency.com, pg 637

McCloskey, Sue, Marlowe & Company, 245 W 17 St, 11th fl, New York, NY 10011-5300 *Tel:* 646-375-2570 *Fax:* 646-375-2571 *Web Site:* www.marlowepub.com, pg 164

McCluney, Richard, The Colonial Williamsburg Foundation, PO Box 1776, Williamsburg, VA 23187-1776 *Tel:* 757-229-1000 *Toll Free Tel:* 800-HISTORY *Fax:* 757-220-7325 *Web Site:* www.colonialwilliamsburg.org/publications, pg 65

McClung, Steven E, Glencoe/McGraw-Hill, 8787 Orion Place, Columbus, OH 43240 *Tel:* 614-430-4000 *Toll Free Tel:* 800-848-1567 *Web Site:* www.glencoe.com, pg 105

McClure, Cameron, Donald Maass Literary Agency, 160 W 95 St, Suite 1-B, New York, NY 10025 *Tel:* 212-866-8200 *Fax:* 212-866-8181 *E-mail:* dmla@mindspring.com, pg 641

McClure, Roger E, Cave Books, 277 Clamer Rd, Trenton, NJ 08628 *Tel:* 609-490-6359 (ed); 937-233-3561 (publr); 937-233-3561 (edit) *Web Site:* www.cavebooks.com, pg 55

McCluskey, Dr Neil G, The Westchester Literary Agency, 2533 Egret Lake Dr, West Palm Beach, FL 33413 *Tel:* 561-642-2908 *Fax:* 561-439-2228, pg 661

McConnell, David, Hillsdale Educational Publishers Inc, 39 North St, Hillsdale, MI 49242 *Tel:* 517-437-3179 *Fax:* 517-437-0531 *E-mail:* davestory@aol.com *Web Site:* hillsdalepublishers.com; michbooks.com, pg 123

McConnell, Gerald, Madison Square Press, 10 E 23 St, New York, NY 10010 *Tel:* 212-505-0950 *Fax:* 212-979-2207, pg 161

McConnell, Susan, Nolo, 950 Parker St, Berkeley, CA 94710 *Tel:* 510-549-1976 *Fax:* 510-548-5902 *E-mail:* info@nolo.com *Web Site:* www.nolo.com, pg 191

McConnell, Sylvia, Napoleon Publishing/Rendezvous Press, 178 Willowdale Ave, Suite 201, Toronto, ON M2N 4Y8, Canada *Tel:* 416-730-9052 *Toll Free Tel:* 877-730-9052 *Fax:* 416-730-8096 *E-mail:* napoleonpublishing@transmedia95.com *Web Site:* www.transmedia95.com, pg 555

McConville, Sarah, Harvard Business School Press, 300 N Beacon St, Watertown, MA 02472 *Tel:* 617-783-7400 *Toll Free Tel:* 888-500-1016 *Fax:* 617-783-7664 *E-mail:* bookpublisher@mail1.hbsp.harvard.edu *Web Site:* www.hbsp.harvard.edu, pg 116

McCormack, Don, McCormack's Guides Inc, 1734 Alhambra Ave, Martinez, CA 94553 *Tel:* 925-229-3581 *Toll Free Tel:* 800-222-3602 *Fax:* 925-228-7223 *E-mail:* bookinfo@mccormacks.com *Web Site:* www.mccormacks.com, pg 166

McCormick, Diane, Shambhala Publications Inc, Horticultural Hall, 300 Massachusetts Ave, Boston, MA 02115 *Tel:* 617-424-0030 *Toll Free Tel:* 888-424-2329 (orders only) *Fax:* 617-236-1563; 303-665-5292 (orders only) *E-mail:* editors@shambhala.com *Web Site:* www.shambhala.com, pg 245

McCoy, Anne, Columbia University Press, 61 W 62 St, New York, NY 10023 *Tel:* 212-459-0600 *Toll Free Tel:* 800-944-8648 *Fax:* 212-459-3678 *Web Site:* www.columbia.edu/cu/cup, pg 65

McCoy, Beverly, Eisenbrauns Inc, PO Box 275, Winona Lake, IN 46590-0275 *Tel:* 574-269-2011 *Fax:* 574-269-6788 *E-mail:* publisher@eisenbrauns.com *Web Site:* www.eisenbrauns.com/, pg 88

McCrae, Fiona, Graywolf Press, 2402 University Ave, Suite 203, St Paul, MN 55114 *Tel:* 651-641-0077 *Fax:* 651-641-0036 *E-mail:* wolves@graywolfpress.org *Web Site:* www.graywolfpress.org, pg 108

McCrary, J, The Perseus Books Group, 387 Park Ave S, 12th fl, New York, NY 10016 *Tel:* 212-340-8100 *Toll Free Tel:* 800-386-5656 (cust serv) *Fax:* 212-340-8115 *Web Site:* www.perseusbooksgroup.com, pg 210

McCraw, Thomas K, Newcomen-Harvard Book Award, c/o Business History Review, Harvard Business School, Soldiers Field Rd, Boston, MA 02163 *Tel:* 617-495-1003 *Fax:* 617-495-0594 *E-mail:* bhr@hbs.edu *Web Site:* www.newcomen.org, pg 794

McCready, Carolyn, Harvest House Publishers Inc, 990 Owen Loop N, Eugene, OR 97402 *Tel:* 541-343-0123 *Toll Free Tel:* 800-547-8979 *Fax:* 541-342-6410 *E-mail:* admin@harvesthousepublishers.com *Web Site:* www.harvesthousepublishers.com, pg 117

McCreight, Tim, American Institute of Chemical Engineers (AICHE), 3 Park Ave, New York, NY 10016-5991 *Tel:* 212-591-7338 *Toll Free Tel:* 800-242-4363 *Fax:* 212-591-8888 *E-mail:* xpress@aiche.org *Web Site:* www.aiche.org, pg 15

McCrosson, Steven, Herald Publishing House, 1001 W Walnut, Independence, MO 64051 *Tel:* 816-521-3015 *Toll Free Tel:* 800-767-8181 *Fax:* 816-521-3066 *E-mail:* marketing@heraldhouse.org *Web Site:* www.heraldhouse.org, pg 121

McCuen, Marnie, GEM Publications, 411 Mallalieu Dr, Hudson, WI 54016 *Tel:* 715-386-7113 *Toll Free Tel:* 800-290-6128 *Fax:* 715-386-7113 *E-mail:* gem@spacestar.net *Web Site:* www.spacestar.com/users/gem, pg 103

McCullough, Carrie, Harbor House, 111 Tenth St, Augusta, GA 30901 *Tel:* 706-738-0354 *Fax:* 706-738-0354 *E-mail:* harborbook@knology.net *Web Site:* harborhousebooks.com, pg 114

McCullough, Colin, Sabre Foundation Inc, 872 Massachusetts Ave, Suite 2-1, Cambridge, MA 02139 *Tel:* 617-868-3510 *Fax:* 617-868-7916 *E-mail:* sabre@sabre.org *Web Site:* www.sabre.org, pg 705

McCullough, Harry, M Evans & Co Inc, 216 E 49 St, New York, NY 10017 *Tel:* 212-688-2810 *Fax:* 212-486-4544 *E-mail:* editorial@mevans.com *Web Site:* www.mevans.com, pg 93

McCullough, Jay, The Lyons Press, 246 Goose Lane, Guilford, CT 06437 *Tel:* 203-458-4500 *Toll Free Tel:* 800-243-0495 *Fax:* 203-458-4668 *Web Site:* www.lyonspress.com; www.globepequot.com, pg 160

McCullough, Mark S, Wyndham Hall Press, 5050 Kerr Rd, Lima, OH 45806 *Tel:* 419-648-9124 *Toll Free Tel:* 866-895-0977 *Fax:* 419-648-9124; 413-208-2409 *E-mail:* whpbooks@wcoil.com *Web Site:* www.wyndhamhallpress.com, pg 305

McCullough, Michael, Duke University Press, 905 W Main St, Suite 18-B, Durham, NC 27701 *Tel:* 919-687-3600 *Toll Free Tel:* 888-651-0122 (orders only) *Fax:* 919-688-4574 *Toll Free Fax:* 888-651-0124 *Web Site:* www.dukepress.edu, pg 84

McCullough, Robert, Whitecap Books Ltd, 351 Lynn Ave, North Vancouver, BC V7J 2C4, Canada *Tel:* 604-980-9852 *Toll Free Tel:* 888-870-3442 ext 239 & 241 (cust serv) *Fax:* 604-980-8197 *Toll Free Fax:* 888-661-6630 (orders only) *E-mail:* whitecap@whitecap.ca *Web Site:* www.whitecap.ca, pg 567

McCune, Sara Miller, Sage Publications, 2455 Teller Rd, Thousand Oaks, CA 91320 *Tel:* 805-499-0721 *Fax:* 805-499-0871 *E-mail:* info@sagepub.com *Web Site:* www.sagepub.com, pg 237

McCurdy, Laura, Second Story Feminist Press, 720 Bathurst St, Suite 301, Toronto, ON M5S 2R4, Canada *Tel:* 416-537-7850 *Fax:* 416-537-0588 *E-mail:* info@secondstorypress.ca *Web Site:* www.secondstorypress.on.ca, pg 561

McCurdy, Wendy, Bantam Dell Publishing Group, 1745 Broadway, New York, NY 10019 *Tel:* 212-782-9000 *Toll Free Tel:* 800-223-6834 *Fax:* 212-302-7985 *Web Site:* www.randomhouse.com/bantamdell, pg 31

McCusker, Paul, Focus on the Family, 8605 Explorer Dr, Colorado Springs, CO 80920 *Tel:* 719-531-3400 *Fax:* 719-531-3484 *Web Site:* www.family.org, pg 97

McCutcheon, Clark, Jodie Rhodes Literary Agency, 8840 Villa La Jolla Dr, Suite 315, La Jolla, CA 92037, pg 651

McDaniel, Earl, BajonHouse Publishing, 609 Broad Ave, Belle Vernon, PA 15012 *Tel:* 724-929-5997 *Fax:* 724-929-5997, pg 30

McDaniel, Ron, EDC Publishing, 10302 E 55 Place, Tulsa, OK 74146-6515 *Tel:* 918-622-4522 *Toll Free Tel:* 800-475-4522 *Fax:* 918-665-7919 *Toll Free Fax:* 800-747-4509 *E-mail:* edc@edcpub.com *Web Site:* www.edcpub.com, pg 86

McDermott, Diana, M E Sharpe Inc, 80 Business Park Dr, Suite 202, Armonk, NY 10504 *Tel:* 914-273-1800 *Toll Free Tel:* 800-541-6563 *Fax:* 914-273-2106 *E-mail:* info@mesharpe.com *Web Site:* www.mesharpe.com, pg 246

McDermott, Jeanne T, Farrar, Straus & Giroux Books for Young Readers, 19 Union Sq W, New York, NY 10003 *Tel:* 212-741-6900 *Fax:* 212-633-2427 *E-mail:* childrens.marketing@fsgbooks.com; childrens.editorial@fsgbooks.com *Web Site:* www.fsgkidsbooks.com, pg 95

McDermott, Kathleen, Harvard University Press, 79 Garden St, Cambridge, MA 02138-1499 *Tel:* 617-495-2600; 401-531-2800 (international orders) *Toll Free Tel:* 800-405-1619 (orders) *Fax:* 617-495-5898 (general); 617-496-4677 (edit & rts); 401-531-2801 (international orders) *Toll Free Fax:* 800-406-9145 (orders) *E-mail:* firstname_lastname@harvard.edu *Web Site:* www.hup.harvard.edu, pg 117

McDiarmid, Mark, Penguin Group (USA) Inc Sales, 375 Hudson St, New York, NY 10014 *Tel:* 212-366-2000 *E-mail:* online@penguinputnam.com *Web Site:* www.penguin.com, pg 208

McDonald, Erroll, Pantheon Books/Schocken Books, 1745 Broadway, New York, NY 10019 *Tel:* 212-751-2600 *Toll Free Tel:* 800-638-6460 *Fax:* 212-572-6030, pg 202

McDonald, Jarom, Bartleby Press, 11141 Georgia Ave, Suite A-3, Silver Spring, MD 20902 *Tel:* 301-949-2443 *Fax:* 301-949-2205 *E-mail:* inquiries@bartlebythepublisher.com *Web Site:* www.bartlebythepublisher.com, pg 33

McDonald, Jennie, Developmental Studies Center, 2000 Embarcadero, Suite 305, Oakland, CA 94606-5300 *Tel:* 510-533-0213 *Toll Free Tel:* 800-666-7270 *Fax:* 510-842-0348 *E-mail:* pubs@devstu.org *Web Site:* www.devstu.org, pg 79

McDonald, Jerry N, The McDonald & Woodward Publishing Co, 431-B E College St, Granville, OH 43023 *Tel:* 740-321-1140 *Toll Free Tel:* 800-233-8787 *Fax:* 740-321-1141 *E-mail:* mwpubco@mwpubco.com *Web Site:* www.mwpubco.com, pg 166

McDonald, Jill, Blackwell Publishing Professional, 2121 State Ave, Ames, IA 50014 *Tel:* 515-292-0140 *Toll Free Tel:* 800-862-6657 (orders only) *Fax:* 515-292-3348 *Web Site:* www.blackwellprofessional.com, pg 40

McDonald, Mary, American Philosophical Society, 104 S Fifth St, Philadelphia, PA 19106 *Tel:* 215-440-3425 *Fax:* 215-440-3450 *Web Site:* www.amphilsoc.org, pg 16

McDonald, Sean, Riverhead Books (Hardcover), 375 Hudson St, New York, NY 10014 *Tel:* 212-366-2000 *E-mail:* online@penguinputnam.com *Web Site:* www.penguin.com, pg 233

McDonnell, Mark, Facts on File Inc, 132 W 31 St, 17th fl, New York, NY 10001 *Tel:* 212-967-8800 *Toll Free Tel:* 800-322-8755 *Fax:* 212-967-9196 *Toll Free Fax:* 800-678-3633 *E-mail:* custserv@factsonfile.com *Web Site:* www.factsonfile.com, pg 93

McDonough, Liz, University of California Extension Professional Sequence in Copyediting & Courses in Publishing, 1995 University Ave, Suite 200, Berkeley, CA 94720-7002 *Tel:* 510-642-6362 *Fax:* 510-643-0599 *E-mail:* letters@unx.berkeley.edu *Web Site:* www.unex.berkeley.edu, pg 755

McDougal, Harriet, Tom Doherty Associates, LLC, 175 Fifth Ave, 14th fl, New York, NY 10010 *Tel:* 212-388-0100 *Toll Free Tel:* 800-455-0340 *Fax:* 212-388-0191 *E-mail:* firstname.lastname@tor.com *Web Site:* www.tor.com, pg 82

McDougal, Nick, Bear & Co Inc, One Park St, Rochester, VT 05767 *Tel:* 802-767-3174 *Toll Free Tel:* 800-932-3277 *Fax:* 802-767-3726 *E-mail:* orders@InnerTraditions.com *Web Site:* InnerTraditions.com, pg 34

McDougal, Nick, Inner Traditions International Ltd, One Park St, Rochester, VT 05767 *Tel:* 802-767-3174 *Toll Free Tel:* 800-246-8648 *Fax:* 802-767-3726 *E-mail:* orders@InnerTraditions.com *Web Site:* InnerTraditions.com, pg 134

McDougall, Karen Sue, Cistercian Publications Inc, Editorial Office, WMU, 1903 W Michigan Ave, Kalamazoo, MI 49008 *Tel:* 269-387-8920 *Fax:* 269-387-8390 *E-mail:* cistpub@wmich.edu *Web Site:* www.spencerabbey.org/cistpub, pg 62

McDowell, Ella, Carter G Woodson Book Awards, 8555 16 St, Suite 500, Silver Spring, MD 20910 *Tel:* 301-588-1800 *Toll Free Tel:* 800-296-7840 *Fax:* 301-588-2049 *E-mail:* excellence@ncss.org *Web Site:* www.socialstudies.org, pg 812

McDowell, Paul, Carswell, One Corporate Plaza, 2075 Kennedy Rd, Toronto, ON M1T 3V4, Canada *Tel:* 416-609-8000 *Toll Free Tel:* 800-387-5164 (Canada & US) *Fax:* 416-298-5094 (Toronto); 403-233-8159 (Calgary); 604-685-5343 (Vancouver); 514-985-6605 *Toll Free Fax:* 877-750-9041 *E-mail:* comments@carswell.com *Web Site:* www.carswell.com, pg 539

McDowell, Robert, Nicholas Roerich Poetry Prize, 2091 Suncrest Rd, Talent, OR 97540 *Tel:* 541-512-8792 *Fax:* 541-512-8793 *E-mail:* mail@storylinepress.com *Web Site:* www.storylinepress.com, pg 802

McDowell, Robert, Story Line Press, 2091 Suncrest Rd, Talent, OR 97540 *Tel:* 541-512-8792 *Fax:* 541-512-8793 *E-mail:* mail@storylinepress.com *Web Site:* www.storylinepress.com, pg 260

McDowell, Robert, The Three Oaks Prize in Fiction, 2091 Suncrest Rd, Talent, OR 97540 *Tel:* 541-512-8792 *Fax:* 541-512-8793 *E-mail:* mail@storylinepress.com *Web Site:* www.storylinepress.com, pg 808

McDuffie, John, American Psychiatric Publishing Inc, 1000 Wilson Blvd, Suite 1825, Arlington, VA 22209 *Tel:* 703-907-7322 *Toll Free Tel:* 800-368-5777 *Fax:* 703-907-1091 *E-mail:* appi@psych.org *Web Site:* www.appi.org, pg 16

McEachern, Alec, Canadian Authors Association Awards for Poetry & Drama, 320 S Shores Rd, Campbellford, ON K0L 1L0, Canada *Tel:* 866-216-6222 *Fax:* 705-653-0593 *E-mail:* info@canauthors.org *Web Site:* www.canauthors.org, pg 765

McEachern, Alec, Canadian Authors Association (CAA), 320 S Shores Rd, Campbellford, ON K0L 1L0, Canada *Tel:* 705-653-0323 *Toll Free Tel:* 866-216-6222 *Fax:* 705-653-0593 *E-mail:* info@canauthors.org *Web Site:* www.CanAuthors.org, pg 683

McElvene, Clyde, The Hurston/Wright Award for College Writers, 6525 Bellcrest Rd, Suite 531, Hyattsville, MD 20782 *Tel:* 301-683-2134 *Fax:* 301-277-1262 *E-mail:* info@hurston-wright.org *Web Site:* www.hurston-wright.org, pg 779

McElvene, Clyde, The Hurston/Wright Legacy Award, 6525 Bellcrest Rd, Suite 531, Hyattsville, MD 20782 *Tel:* 301-683-2134 *Fax:* 301-277-1262 *E-mail:* info@hurston-wright.org *Web Site:* www.hurston-wright.org, pg 779

McElvene, Clyde, The Hurston/Wright Writer's Week, 6525 Bellcrest Rd, Suite 531, Hyattsville, MD 20782 *Tel:* 301-683-2134 *Fax:* 301-277-1262 *E-mail:* info@hurston-wright.org *Web Site:* www.hurston-wright.org, pg 744

McEvoy, Nion, Chronicle Books LLC, 85 Second St, 6th fl, San Francisco, CA 94105 *Tel:* 415-537-4200 *Toll Free Tel:* 800-722-6657 (cust serv) *Fax:* 415-537-4460 *Toll Free Fax:* 800-858-7787 (orders) *E-mail:* frontdesk@chroniclebooks.com *Web Site:* www.chroniclebooks.com, pg 61

McEvoy, Tim, Wordware Publishing Inc, 2320 Los Rios Blvd, Suite 200, Plano, TX 75074 *Tel:* 972-423-0090 *Toll Free Tel:* 800-229-4949 *Fax:* 972-881-9147 *E-mail:* info@wordware.com *Web Site:* www.wordware.com, pg 303

McEvoy, William, The Guilford Press, 72 Spring St, New York, NY 10012 *Tel:* 212-431-9800 *Toll Free Tel:* 800-365-7006 (orders) *Fax:* 212-966-6708 *E-mail:* orders@guilford.com *Web Site:* www.guilford.com, pg 111

McEwen, Laura, Reader's Digest Association Inc, Reader's Digest Rd, Pleasantville, NY 10570-7000 *Tel:* 914-238-1000 *Toll Free Tel:* 800-431-1726 *Fax:* 914-238-4559 *Web Site:* www.rd.com, pg 228

McEwen, Laura, Reader's Digest Children's Books, Reader's Digest Rd, Pleasantville, NY 10570-7000 *Tel:* 914-244-4800 *Toll Free Tel:* 800-934-0977, pg 228

McEwen, Laura, Reader's Digest Trade Books, Reader's Digest Rd, Pleasantville, NY 10570-7000 *Tel:* 914-244-7445 *Fax:* 914-244-7605, pg 229

McEwen, Laura, Reader's Digest USA Select Editions, Reader's Digest Rd, Pleasantville, NY 10570-7000 *Tel:* 914-238-1000 *Toll Free Tel:* 800-310-6261 *Fax:* 914-238-4559, pg 229

McEwen, Tim, Haights Cross Communications Inc, 10 New King St, White Plains, NY 10604 *Tel:* 914-289-9400 *Fax:* 914-289-9401 *E-mail:* info@haightscross.com *Web Site:* www.haightscross.com, pg 111

McEwen, Tim, Harcourt Achieve, 10801 N MoPac Expressway, Austin, TX 78759 *Tel:* 512-343-8227 *Toll Free Tel:* 800-531-5015 *Toll Free Fax:* 800-699-9459 *E-mail:* ecare@harcourt.com *Web Site:* www.harcourtachieve.com, pg 114

McEwen, Tim, Rigby, 10801 N MoPac Expressway, Austin, TX 78759 *Tel:* 512-343-8227 *Toll Free Tel:* 800-531-5015 *Toll Free Fax:* 800-699-9459 *E-mail:* ecare@harcourt.com *Web Site:* www.harcourtachieve.com, pg 232

McEwen, Tim, Steck-Vaughn, 10801 N MoPac Expressway, Austin, TX 78759 *Tel:* 512-343-8227 *Toll Free Tel:* 800-531-5015 *Toll Free Fax:* 800-699-9459 *E-mail:* ecare@harcourt.com *Web Site:* www.harcourtachieve.com, pg 258

McFadden, Lee, OneOnOne Computer Training, 2055 Army Trail Rd, Suite 100, Addison, IL 60101 *Tel:* 630-628-0500 *Toll Free Tel:* 800-424-8668 *E-mail:* oneonone@protrain.com *Web Site:* www.oootraining.com, pg 197

McFadden, Patricia, University of Minnesota Press, 111 Third Ave S, Suite 290, Minneapolis, MN 55401-2520 *Tel:* 612-627-1970 *Fax:* 612-627-1980 *E-mail:* ump@tc.umn.edu *Web Site:* www.upress.umn.edu, pg 282

McFadden, Virginia, FaithWalk Publishing, 333 Jackson St, Grand Haven, MI 49417 *Tel:* 616-846-9360 *Toll Free Tel:* 800-335-7177 *Fax:* 616-846-0072 *E-mail:* customerservice@faithwalkpub.com *Web Site:* www.faithwalkpub.com, pg 94

McFadden, Wendy, Brethren Press, 1451 Dundee Ave, Elgin, IL 60120-1694 *Tel:* 847-742-5100 *Toll Free Tel:* 800-323-8039 *Fax:* 847-742-1407 *Web Site:* www. brethrenpress.com, pg 46

McFall, Paul, Scott Foresman, 1900 E Lake Ave, Glenview, IL 60025 *Tel:* 847-729-3000 *Toll Free Tel:* 800-535-4391 (Midwest) *Fax:* 847-729-8910 *E-mail:* firstname.lastname@scottforesman.com *Web Site:* www.scottforesman.com, pg 243

McFarland, Beverly, Calyx Books, PO Box B, Corvallis, OR 97339-0539 *Tel:* 541-753-9384 *Fax:* 541-753-0515 *E-mail:* calyx@proaxis.com *Web Site:* www.proaxis.com/~calyx, pg 51

McFarland, Fred W, W W Norton & Company Inc, 500 Fifth Ave, New York, NY 10110-0017 *Tel:* 212-354-5500 *Toll Free Tel:* 800-233-4830 (orders & cust serv) *Fax:* 212-869-0856 *Toll Free Fax:* 800-458-6515 *Web Site:* www.wwnorton.com, pg 193

McFeely, W Drake, The Countryman Press, 1206 Rte 12 N, Woodstock, VT 05091 *Tel:* 802-457-4826 *Toll Free Tel:* 800-245-4151 *Fax:* 802-457-1678 *E-mail:* countrymanpress@wwnorton.com *Web Site:* www.countrymanpress.com, pg 70

McFeely, W Drake, W W Norton & Company Inc, 500 Fifth Ave, New York, NY 10110-0017 *Tel:* 212-354-5500 *Toll Free Tel:* 800-233-4830 (orders & cust serv) *Fax:* 212-869-0856 *Toll Free Fax:* 800-458-6515 *Web Site:* www.wwnorton.com, pg 193

McGandy, Michael, W W Norton & Company Inc, 500 Fifth Ave, New York, NY 10110-0017 *Tel:* 212-354-5500 *Toll Free Tel:* 800-233-4830 (orders & cust serv) *Fax:* 212-869-0856 *Toll Free Fax:* 800-458-6515 *Web Site:* www.wwnorton.com, pg 193

McGanghey, Sarah, MFA Publications, 465 Huntington Ave, Boston, MA 02115 *Tel:* 617-369-3438 *Fax:* 617-369-3459 *Web Site:* www.mfa-publications.org, pg 173

McGarry, Steve, National Cartoonists Society (NCS), 1133 W Morse Blvd, Suite 201, Winter Park, FL 32789 *Tel:* 407-647-8839 *Fax:* 407-629-2502 *Web Site:* www.reuben.org, pg 692

McGaughey, Eileen, Author Author Literary Agency Ltd, Lougheed Mall RPO, 9855 Austin Ave, No 236, Burnaby, BC V3J 7W2, Canada *Tel:* 604-415-0056 *Web Site:* www.authorauthorliteraryagency.com, pg 619

McGeary, Jennifer, NCCLS, 940 W Valley Rd, Suite 1400, Wayne, PA 19087-1898 *Tel:* 610-688-0100 *Fax:* 610-688-0700 *E-mail:* exoffice@nccls.org *Web Site:* www.nccls.org, pg 185

McGee, Don, Running Press Book Publishers, 125 S 22 St, Philadelphia, PA 19103-4399 *Tel:* 215-567-5080 *Toll Free Tel:* 800-345-5359 (cust serv & orders) *Fax:* 215-568-2919 *Toll Free Fax:* 800-453-2884 *Web Site:* www.runningpress.com, pg 236

McGee, Linda, Mason Crest Publishers, 370 Reed Rd, Suite 302, Broomall, PA 19008 *Tel:* 610-543-6200 *Toll Free Tel:* 866-MCP-BOOK (627-2665) *Fax:* 610-543-3878 *Web Site:* www.masoncrest.com, pg 165

McGee, Mary, PennWell Books & More, 1421 S Sheridan, Tulsa, OK 74112 *Tel:* 918-831-9421 *Toll Free Tel:* 800-752-9764 *Fax:* 918-832-9319 *E-mail:* sales@penwellbooks.com *Web Site:* www.penwellbooks.com, pg 209

McGee, Sheila, Abingdon Press, 201 Eighth Ave S, Nashville, TN 37203-3919 *Tel:* 615-749-6290 (publicist); 615-749-6000; 615-749-6451 (sales) *Toll Free Tel:* 800-251-3320 *Fax:* 615-749-6056 *Web Site:* www.abingdonpress.com, pg 3

McGeveran, William, World Almanac Books, 512 Seventh Ave, 22nd fl, New York, NY 10018 *Tel:* 646-312-6800 *Fax:* 646-312-6839 *E-mail:* info@waegroup.com *Web Site:* www.worldalmanac.com, pg 303

McGhee, Holly M, Pippin Properties Inc, 155 E 38 St, Suite 2H, New York, NY 10016 *Tel:* 212-338-9310 *Fax:* 212-338-9579 *E-mail:* info@pippinproperties.com *Web Site:* www.pippinproperties.com, pg 648

McGill, Deborah, North Carolina Arts Council, Dept of Cultural Resources, Mail Service Ctr 4632, Raleigh, NC 27699-4632 *Tel:* 919-715-1519 *Fax:* 919-733-4834 *Web Site:* www.ncarts.org, pg 795

McGinley, Brian, WaterBrook Press, 2375 Telstar Dr, Suite 160, Colorado Springs, CO 80920 *Tel:* 719-590-4999 *Toll Free Tel:* 800-603-7051 (orders) *Fax:* 719-590-8977 *Toll Free Fax:* 800-294-5686 (orders) *Web Site:* www.waterbrookpress.com, pg 294

McGinley, Jean, Disney Press, 114 Fifth Ave, New York, NY 10011 *Tel:* 212-633-4400 *Fax:* 212-807-5432 *Web Site:* www.disney.go.com, pg 81

McGinley, Jean, Disney Publishing Worldwide, 500 S Buena Vista, Burbank, CA 91521 *Tel:* 212-633-4400 *Fax:* 212-633-4833 *Web Site:* www.disney.go.com/disneybooks, pg 81

McGinnis, Mimi, F A Davis Co, 1915 Arch St, Philadelphia, PA 19103 *Tel:* 215-568-2270 *Toll Free Tel:* 800-523-4049 *Fax:* 215-568-5065 *E-mail:* info@fadavis.com *Web Site:* www.fadavis.com, pg 76

McGonagle, David J, The Catholic University of America Press, 240 Leahy Hall, 620 Michigan Ave NE, Washington, DC 20064 *Tel:* 202-319-5052 *Fax:* 202-319-4985 *E-mail:* cua-press@cua.edu *Web Site:* cuapress.cua.edu, pg 55

McGovern, Donna, Allen D Bragdon Publishers Inc, 252 Great Western Rd, South Yarmouth, MA 02664-2210 *Tel:* 508-398-4440 *Toll Free Tel:* 877-8-SMARTS (876-2787) *Fax:* 508-760-2397 *E-mail:* admin@brainwaves.com *Web Site:* www.brainwaves.com, pg 9

McGovern, Gene, Marquis Who's Who, 562 Central Ave, New Providence, NJ 07974 *Tel:* 908-673-1001 *Toll Free Tel:* 800-473-7020 *Fax:* 908-673-1189 *Web Site:* www.marquiswhoswho.com, pg 164

McGovern, Gene, National Register Publishing, 562 Central Ave, New Providence, NJ 07974 *Tel:* 908-673-1001 *Toll Free Tel:* 800-473-7020 *Fax:* 909-673-1189 *Web Site:* www.nationalregisterpub.com, pg 185

McGovern, Owen P, Catholic Book Awards, 3555 Veterans Memorial Hwy, Unit "O", Ronkonkoma, NY 11779 *Tel:* 631-471-4730 *Fax:* 631-471-4804 *E-mail:* cathjourn@aol.com *Web Site:* www.catholicpress.org, pg 766

McGovern, Owen P, Catholic Press Association of the US & Canada, 3555 Veterans Memorial Hwy, Unit O, Ronkonkoma, NY 11779 *Tel:* 631-471-4730 *Fax:* 631-471-4804 *E-mail:* cathjourn@aol.com *Web Site:* www.catholicpress.org, pg 684

McGovern, Owen P, Catholic Press Association of the US & Canada Journalism Awards, 3555 Veterans Memorial Hwy, Unit "O", Ronkonkoma, NY 11779 *Tel:* 631-471-4730 *Fax:* 631-471-4804 *E-mail:* cathjourn@aol.com *Web Site:* www.catholicpress.org, pg 766

McGowan, Mary, Bowling Green State University, Creative Writing Program, 226 East Hall, Bowling Green, OH 43403 *Tel:* 419-372-8370 *Fax:* 419-372-6805 *E-mail:* mmcgowa@bgnet.bgsu.edu *Web Site:* www.bgsu.edu/departments/creative-writing, pg 751

McGowan, Matt, Frances Goldin Literary Agency, Inc, 57 E 11 St, Suite 5B, New York, NY 10003 *Tel:* 212-777-0047 *Fax:* 212-228-1660 *E-mail:* agency@goldinlit.com *Web Site:* www.goldinlit.com, pg 632

McGrath, Beverly, The Foundation Center, 79 Fifth Ave, New York, NY 10003-3076 *Tel:* 212-807-3690 *Toll Free Tel:* 800-424-9836 *Fax:* 212-807-3691 *Web Site:* www.fdncenter.org, pg 99

McGrath, Helen, Helen McGrath & Associates, 1406 Idaho Ct, Concord, CA 94521 *Tel:* 925-672-6211 *Fax:* 925-672-6383 *E-mail:* hmcgrath_lit@yahoo.com, pg 643

McGrath, John H, WJ Fantasy Inc, 955 Connecticut Ave, Bridgeport, CT 06607 *Tel:* 203-333-5212 *Toll Free Tel:* 800-222-7529 (orders) *Fax:* 203-366-3826 *Toll Free Fax:* 800-200-3000 *E-mail:* wjfantasy.inc@snet.net *Web Site:* www.wjfantasy.com, pg 302

McGrath, Kat, Empire State Award for Excellence in Literature for Young People, 252 Hudson Ave, Albany, NY 12210 *Tel:* 518-432-6952 *Fax:* 518-427-1697 *E-mail:* info@nyla.org *Web Site:* www.nyla.org, pg 772

McGrath, Marty, Random House Sales & Marketing, 1745 Broadway, New York, NY 10019 *Fax:* 212-782-9000, pg 227

McGrath, Nancy C, The Shoe String Press Inc, 2 Linsley St, North Haven, CT 06473 *Tel:* 203-239-2702 *Fax:* 203-239-2568 *E-mail:* info@shoestringpress.com; books@shoestringpress.com *Web Site:* www.shoestringpress.com, pg 246

McGrath, Sarah, Scribner, 1230 Avenue of the Americas, New York, NY 10020, pg 244

McGraw, Brian, Prentice Hall Engineering/Science & Math, One Lake St, Upper Saddle River, NJ 07458 *Tel:* 201-236-7000, pg 217

McGraw, Harold W (Terry) III, The McGraw-Hill Companies Inc, 1221 Avenue of the Americas, 50th fl, New York, NY 10020 *Tel:* 212-512-2000 *E-mail:* webmaster@mcgraw-hill.com *Web Site:* www.mcgraw-hill.com, pg 167

McGraw, Kathy, The SeedSowers, PO Box 3317, Jacksonville, FL 32206-0317 *Tel:* 904-598-2345 *Toll Free Tel:* 800-228-2665 *Fax:* 904-598-3456 *E-mail:* books@seedsowers.com *Web Site:* seedsowers.com, pg 244

McGray, JoAnne, American Research Press, PO Box 141, Rehoboth, NM 87322 *Web Site:* www.gallup.unm.edu/~smarandache, pg 17

McGuigan, Peter, Sanford J Greenburger Associates Inc, 55 Fifth Ave, 15th fl, New York, NY 10003 *Tel:* 212-206-5600 *Fax:* 212-463-8718 *Web Site:* www.greenburger.com, pg 633

McGuire, Beverly, Coastside Editorial, 1111 Date St, Montara, CA 94037 *Tel:* 650-728-0902 *Fax:* 650-728-0905, pg 594

McGuire, Ginger, Scholastic Entertainment Inc, 524 Broadway, New York, NY 10012 *Tel:* 212-343-7500 *Fax:* 212-965-7448, pg 241

McGuire, Dr Jerry, Deep South Writers Festival, University of Louisiana at Lafayette, 104 University Circle, Lafayette, LA 70504 *Tel:* 337-482-5478 (Direct), pg 769

McGuire, Jim, Center for Migration Studies of New York Inc, 209 Flagg Place, Staten Island, NY 10304-1199 *Tel:* 718-351-8800 *Fax:* 718-667-4598 *E-mail:* cms@cmsny.org *Web Site:* www.cmsny.org, pg 57

McGuire, Libby, Random House Publishing Group, 1745 Broadway, New York, NY 10019 *Toll Free Tel:* 800-200-3552 *Toll Free Fax:* 800-200-3552 *Web Site:* www.randomhouse.com, pg 227

McGuire, Liz, Counterpoint Press, 387 Park Ave S, New York, NY 10016 *Tel:* 212-340-8100 *Fax:* 212-340-8135 (edit); 212-340-8115 *E-mail:* counterpointpress@perseusbooks.com *Web Site:* www.counterpointpress.com, pg 70

McGuire, Marilyn, Nautilus Award, 109 N Beach Rd, Eastsound, WA 98245 *Tel:* 360-376-2702 *Toll Free Tel:* 800-367-1907 *Fax:* 360-376-2704 *E-mail:* napravision@napra.com *Web Site:* www.napra.com, pg 793

McGuire, Marilyn, Networking Alternatives for Publishers, Retailers & Artists Inc (NAPRA), 109 North Beach Rd, Eastsound, WA 98245 *Tel:* 360-376-2702 *Toll Free Tel:* 800-367-1907 *Fax:* 360-376-2704 *E-mail:* napravision@napra.com *Web Site:* www.napra.com, pg 695

McGurgan, Diane, The Victor Cohn Prize for Excellence in Medical Science Reporting, PO Box 910, Hedgesville, WV 25427 *Tel:* 304-754-5077 *Fax:* 304-754-5076 *Web Site:* www.casw.org, pg 768

McGurgan, Diane, National Association of Science Writers (NASW), PO Box 890, Hedgesville, WV 25427 *Tel:* 304-754-5077 *Fax:* 304-754-5076 *Web Site:* www.nasw.org, pg 692

McGurgan, Diane, Science in Society Journalism Awards, PO Box 890, Hedgesville, WV 25427 *Web Site:* www.nasw.org, pg 805

McHale, Joe, Harcourt Achieve, 10801 N MoPac Expressway, Austin, TX 78759 *Tel:* 512-343-8227 *Toll Free Tel:* 800-531-5015 *Toll Free Fax:* 800-699-9459 *E-mail:* ecare@harcourt.com *Web Site:* www.harcourtachieve.com, pg 114

McHale, Joe, Rigby, 10801 N MoPac Expressway, Austin, TX 78759 *Tel:* 512-343-8227 *Toll Free Tel:* 800-531-5015 *Toll Free Fax:* 800-699-9459 *E-mail:* ecare@harcourt.com *Web Site:* www.harcourtachieve.com, pg 232

McHale, Joe, Steck-Vaughn, 10801 N MoPac Expressway, Austin, TX 78759 *Tel:* 512-343-8227 *Toll Free Tel:* 800-531-5015 *Toll Free Fax:* 800-699-9459 *E-mail:* ecare@harcourt.com *Web Site:* www.harcourtachieve.com, pg 258

McHale, John P, SRA/McGraw-Hill, a Division of McGraw-Hill Learning Group, 8787 Orion Place, Columbus, OH 43240 *Tel:* 614-430-4000 *Fax:* 614-430-6621 *E-mail:* sra@mcgraw-hill.com *Web Site:* www.sra-4kids.com, pg 256

McHugh, Elisabet, McHugh Literary Agency, 1033 Lyon Rd, Moscow, ID 83843-9167 *Tel:* 208-882-0107 *Fax:* 847-628-0146, pg 643

McHugh, John B, McHugh's Rights/Permissions Workshop™, PO Box 170665, Milwaukee, WI 53217-8056 *Tel:* 414-351-3056 *Fax:* 414-351-0666 *Web Site:* www.johnbmchugh.com, pg 744

McHugh, Michael J, Christian Liberty Press, 502 W Euclid Ave, Arlington Heights, IL 60004 *Tel:* 847-259-4444 *Fax:* 847-259-2941 *Web Site:* www.christianlibertypress.com, pg 61

McInerney, Seana, Kneerim & Williams, c/o Fish & Richardson PC, 225 Franklin St, Boston, MA 02110 *Tel:* 617-542-5070 *Fax:* 617-542-8906 *Web Site:* www.fr.com, pg 638

McIntire, Paul, American Society for Nondestructive Testing, 1711 Arlingate Lane, Columbus, OH 43228-0518 *Tel:* 614-274-6003 *Toll Free Tel:* 800-222-2768 *Fax:* 614-274-6899 *E-mail:* webmaster@asnt.org *Web Site:* www.asnt.org, pg 17

McIntosh, Madeline, Random House Inc, 1745 Broadway, New York, NY 10019 *Tel:* 212-782-9000 *Toll Free Tel:* 800-726-0600 *Web Site:* www.randomhouse.com, pg 226

McIntosh, Madeline, Random House Sales & Marketing, 1745 Broadway, New York, NY 10019 *Fax:* 212-782-9000, pg 227

McIntosh, Susan, Douglas & McIntyre Publishing Group, 2323 Quebec St, Suite 201, Vancouver, BC V5T 4S7, Canada *Tel:* 604-254-7191 *Toll Free Tel:* 800-565-9523 (orders in Canada) *Fax:* 604-254-9099 *Toll Free Fax:* 800-221-9985 (orders in Canada) *E-mail:* dm@douglas-mcintyre.com *Web Site:* www.douglas-mcintyre.com, pg 542

McIntosh, Susan, Greystone Books, 2323 Quebec St, Suite 201, Vancouver, BC V5T 4S7, Canada *Tel:* 604-254-7191 *Toll Free Tel:* 800-667-6902 *Fax:* 604-254-9099, pg 548

McIntosh, Susan, Groundwood Books, 720 Bathurst St, Suite 500, Toronto, ON M5S 2R4, Canada *Tel:* 416-537-2501 *Fax:* 416-537-4647 *E-mail:* genmail@groundwood-dm.com *Web Site:* www.groundwoodbooks.com, pg 548

McIntyre, Devin, Mary Evans Inc, 242 E Fifth St, New York, NY 10003 *Tel:* 212-979-0880 *Fax:* 212-979-5344 *E-mail:* merrylit@aol.com, pg 629

McIntyre, Gerry, Canadian Publishers' Council (CPC), 250 Merton St, Suite 203, Toronto, ON M4S 1B1, Canada *Tel:* 416-322-7011 *Fax:* 416-322-6999 *E-mail:* pubadmin@pubcouncil.ca *Web Site:* www.pubcouncil.ca, pg 684

McIntyre, Ione, Patchwork Press, PO Box 183, Bemidji, MN 56619-0183 *Tel:* 218-751-0759, pg 205

McIntyre, Sandra, Nimbus Publishing Ltd, 3731 Mackintosh St, Halifax, NS B3K 5A5, Canada *Tel:* 902-455-5304 *Toll Free Tel:* 800-646-2879 *Fax:* 902-455-5440 *E-mail:* customerservice@nimbus.ns.ca *Web Site:* www.nimbus.ns.ca, pg 556

McIntyre, Scott, Douglas & McIntyre Publishing Group, 2323 Quebec St, Suite 201, Vancouver, BC V5T 4S7, Canada *Tel:* 604-254-7191 *Toll Free Tel:* 800-565-9523 (orders in Canada) *Fax:* 604-254-9099 *Toll Free Fax:* 800-221-9985 (orders in Canada) *E-mail:* dm@douglas-mcintyre.com *Web Site:* www.douglas-mcintyre.com, pg 542

McIntyre, William S, International Risk Management Institute Inc, 12222 Merit Dr, Suite 1450, Dallas, TX 75251-2276 *Tel:* 972-960-7693 *Toll Free Tel:* 800-827-4242 *Fax:* 972-371-5120 *E-mail:* info@irmi.com *Web Site:* www.irmi.com, pg 138

McKay, Diane, Corp professionnelle des traducteurs et interpretes agrees du quebec, 2021 Union Ave, Suite 1108, Montreal, PQ H3A 2S9, Canada *Tel:* 514-845-4411 *Fax:* 514-845-9903, pg 685

McKay, Matt, New Harbinger Publications Inc, 5674 Shattuck Ave, Oakland, CA 94609 *Tel:* 510-652-0215 *Toll Free Tel:* 800-748-6273 (orders only) *Fax:* 510-652-5472 *E-mail:* nhhelp@newharbinger.com *Web Site:* www.newharbinger.com, pg 188

McKay, Tammy, Orange Frazer Press Inc, 37 1/2 W Main St, Wilmington, OH 45177 *Tel:* 937-382-3196 *Toll Free Tel:* 800-852-9332 *Fax:* 937-383-3159 *E-mail:* ofrazer@erinet.com *Web Site:* www.orangefrazer.com, pg 198

McKee, Barney, Quail Ridge Press, 101 Brooks Dr, Brandon, MS 39042 *Tel:* 601-825-2063 *Toll Free Tel:* 800-343-1583 *Fax:* 601-825-3091 *E-mail:* info@quailridge.com *Web Site:* quailridge.com, pg 223

McKee, Gwen, Quail Ridge Press, 101 Brooks Dr, Brandon, MS 39042 *Tel:* 601-825-2063 *Toll Free Tel:* 800-343-1583 *Fax:* 601-825-3091 *E-mail:* info@quailridge.com *Web Site:* quailridge.com, pg 223

McKee, James L, J & L Lee Co, Box 5575, Lincoln, NE 68505 *Tel:* 402-488-4416 *Toll Free Tel:* 888-665-0999 *Fax:* 402-489-2770 *E-mail:* info@leebooksellers.com *Web Site:* www.leebooksellers.com, pg 152

McKeever, Daniel P, Porter Sargent Publishers Inc, 11 Beacon St, Suite 1400, Boston, MA 02108 *Tel:* 617-523-1670 *Toll Free Tel:* 800-342-7470 *Fax:* 617-523-1021 *E-mail:* info@portersargent.com *Web Site:* portersargent.com, pg 216

McKenna, Debbie, Moore Literary Agency, 10 State St, Suite 309, Newburyport, MA 01950 *Tel:* 978-465-9015 *Fax:* 978-465-8817, pg 644

McKenna, Gwen, Mountain Press Publishing Co, 1301 S Third W, Missoula, MT 59801 *Tel:* 406-728-1900 *Toll Free Tel:* 800-234-5308 *Fax:* 406-728-1635 *E-mail:* info@mtnpress.com *Web Site:* www.mountain-press.com, pg 179

McKenna, Kate, Associated Press Broadcasters, 1825 "K" St NW, Suite 800, Washington, DC 20006 *Tel:* 202-736-1100 *Fax:* 202-736-1199 *Web Site:* www.ap.org, pg 679

McKenna, Lauren, Pocket Books, 1230 Avenue of the Americas, New York, NY 10020 *Toll Free Tel:* 800-456-6798 *Fax:* 212-698-7284 *E-mail:* consumer.customerservice@simonandschuster.com *Web Site:* www.simonsays.com, pg 215

McKenzie, Phyllis Corbett, Capital Speakers Inc, 2200 Wilson Blvd, Suite 850, Arlington, VA 22201 *Tel:* 703-894-0604 *Toll Free Tel:* 800-799-2629 *Fax:* 703-894-0605 *E-mail:* ideas@capitalspeakers.com *Web Site:* www.capitalspeakers.com, pg 669

McKeon, Clare, Key Porter Books Ltd, 70 The Esplanade, 3rd fl, Toronto, ON M5E 1R2, Canada *Tel:* 416-862-7777 *Fax:* 416-862-2304 *E-mail:* info@keyporter.com *Web Site:* www.keyporter.com, pg 551

McKeon, Don, Brassey's Inc, 22841 Quicksilver Dr, Dulles, VA 20166 *Tel:* 703-661-1548 *Toll Free Tel:* 800-775-2518 (orders only) *Fax:* 703-661-1547 *E-mail:* djacobs@booksintl.com *Web Site:* www.brasseysinc.com, pg 46

McKeon, Hilary, Looseleaf Law Publications Inc, 43-08 162 St, Flushing, NY 11358 *Tel:* 718-359-5559 *Toll Free Tel:* 800-647-5547 *Fax:* 718-539-0941 *E-mail:* llawpub@erols.com *Web Site:* www.LooseleafLaw.com, pg 158

McKeown, Andrea, The Writer's Lifeline Inc, 518 S Fairfax Ave, Los Angeles, CA 90036 *Tel:* 323-932-0905 *Fax:* 323-932-0321 *E-mail:* questions@thewriterslifeline.com; comments@thewriterslifeline.com *Web Site:* www.thewriterslifeline.com, pg 615

McKeown, Jack, Basic Books, 387 Park Ave S, 12th fl, New York, NY 10016-8810 *Tel:* 212-340-8100 *Toll Free Tel:* 800-242-7737 (orders) *Fax:* 212-340-8135 *E-mail:* basic.books@perseusbooks.com *Web Site:* www.basicbooks.com, pg 33

McKeown, Jack, Westview Press, 5500 Central Ave, Boulder, CO 80301 *Tel:* 303-444-3541 *Toll Free Tel:* 800-386-5656 *Fax:* 720-406-7336 *E-mail:* westview.orders@perseusbooks.com *Web Site:* www.perseusbooksgroup.com; www.westviewpress.com, pg 297

McKey, Ellen, Translation Prize, 58 Park Ave, New York, NY 10016 *Tel:* 212-879-9779 *Fax:* 212-686-2115 *E-mail:* info@amscan.org *Web Site:* www.amscan.org, pg 809

McKiernan, Tricia, Graphic Artists Guild Inc, 90 John St, Rm 403, New York, NY 10038 *Tel:* 212-791-3400 *Fax:* 212-791-0333 *E-mail:* execdir@gag.org *Web Site:* www.gag.org, pg 687

McKinley, Catherine, Publishing Certificate Program at City College, Division of Humanities NAC 5225, City College of New York, New York, NY 10031 *Tel:* 212-650-7925 *Fax:* 212-650-7912 *E-mail:* ccnypub@aol.com *Web Site:* www.ccny.cuny.edu/publishing_certificate/index.html, pg 754

McKinley, Nancy, Thinking Publications, 424 Galloway, Eau Claire, WI 54703 *Tel:* 715-832-2488 *Toll Free Tel:* 800-225-4769 *Fax:* 715-832-9082 *Toll Free Fax:* 800-828-8885 *E-mail:* custserv@thinkingpublications.com *Web Site:* www.thinkingpublications.com, pg 269

McKinley, Robert B, Cardweb.com Inc, 10 N Jefferson St, Suite 301, Frederick, MD 21701 *Tel:* 301-631-9100 *Fax:* 301-631-9112 *E-mail:* cardservices@cardweb.com; cardstaff@cardweb.com *Web Site:* www.cardweb.com, pg 53

McKinney, Anne, PREP Publishing, 1110 1/2 Hay St, Fayetteville, NC 28305 *Tel:* 910-483-6611 *Toll Free Tel:* 800-533-2814 *Fax:* 910-483-2439 *E-mail:* preppub@aol.com *Web Site:* www.prep-pub.com, pg 217

McKinney, Betty, Alpine Publications Inc, PO Box 7027, Loveland, CO 80537-0027 *Tel:* 970-667-2017 *Toll Free Tel:* 800-777-7257 (orders only) *Fax:* 970-667-9157 *E-mail:* alpinecsr@aol.com *Web Site:* www.alpinepub.com, pg 9

McKinney, David, The Metropolitan Museum of Art, 1000 Fifth Ave, New York, NY 10028 *Tel:* 212-879-5500; 212-535-7710 *Fax:* 212-396-5062 *E-mail:* info@metmuseum.org *Web Site:* www.metmuseum.org, pg 173

McKinnon, Tanya, Mary Evans Inc, 242 E Fifth St, New York, NY 10003 *Tel:* 212-979-0880 *Fax:* 212-979-5344 *E-mail:* merrylit@aol.com, pg 629

McKinstry, Robert, ABI Professional Publications, 3580 Morris St N, Saint Petersburg, FL 33713 *Tel:* 727-556-0950 *Toll Free Tel:* 800-551-7776 *Fax:* 727-556-2560 *E-mail:* abipropub@vandamere.com; orders@vandamere.com *Web Site:* www.abipropub.com, pg 3

McKnight, Linda, Westwood Creative Artists Ltd, 94 Harbord St, Toronto, ON M5S 1G6, Canada *Tel:* 416-964-3302 *Fax:* 416-975-9209, pg 661

McKnight, Wil, Wil McKnight Associates Inc, 1801 W Hovey Ave, Suite A, Normal, IL 61761 *Tel:* 309-451-0000 *Fax:* 309-451-0000 *E-mail:* info@hardhatonline.com *Web Site:* www.hardhatonline.com, pg 169

McRee, Judith, Aspen Publishers, A Wolters Kluwer Company, 1185 Avenue of the Americas, New York, NY 10036 *Tel:* 212-597-0200 *Toll Free Tel:* 800-234-1660 (cust serv); 800-447-1717 (orders); 800-950-5259 (legal educ); 800-LAW-PLGL (paralegal textbook); 800-317-3113 (bookstore sales); 800-364-2512 (Loislaw) *Web Site:* www.aspenpublishers.com, pg 26

McShane, Amy, Slack Incorporated, 6900 Grove Rd, Thorofare, NJ 08086-9447 *Tel:* 856-848-1000 *Toll Free Tel:* 800-257-8290 *Fax:* 856-853-5991 *Web Site:* www.slackbooks.com, pg 250

McShane, Kevin D, Fifi Oscard Agency Inc, 110 W 40 St, New York, NY 10018 *Tel:* 212-764-1100 *Fax:* 212-840-5019 *E-mail:* agency@fifioscard.com *Web Site:* www.fifioscard.com, pg 647

McSheffrey, Ken, Statistics Canada, R H Coats Bldg, Lobby, Holland Ave, Ottawa, ON K1A 0T6, Canada *Tel:* 613-951-8116 *Toll Free Tel:* 800-700-1033 (Canada & US); 800-267-6677 (orders) *Fax:* 613-951-1584 (local); 613-951-7277 (orders); 613-951-0581 (requests) *Toll Free Fax:* 800-889-9734; 877-287-4369 (orders) *E-mail:* order@statcan.ca; infostats@statcan.ca *Web Site:* www.statcan.ca, pg 562

McSweeney, Joyelle, University of Alabama Program in Creative Writing, PO Box 870244, Tuscaloosa, AL 35487-0244 *Tel:* 205-348-0766 *Fax:* 205-348-1388 *E-mail:* writeua@english.as.ua.edu *Web Site:* www.as.ua.edu/english, pg 755

McTavish, Carol, McTavish & Nunn, 517 River Rd, Canmore, AB T1W 2E4, Canada *Tel:* 403-678-5859 *Fax:* 403-609-4072, pg 554

McVay, Barry, Panoptic Enterprises, PO Box 11220, Burke, VA 22009-1220 *Tel:* 703-451-5953 *Toll Free Tel:* 800-594-4766 *Fax:* 703-451-5953 *Web Site:* www.fedgovcontracts.com, pg 202

McVay, Vivina H, Panoptic Enterprises, PO Box 11220, Burke, VA 22009-1220 *Tel:* 703-451-5953 *Toll Free Tel:* 800-594-4766 *Fax:* 703-451-5953 *Web Site:* www.fedgovcontracts.com, pg 202

McWilliams, Sandy, Harbor Press Inc, 5713 Wollochet Dr NW, PO Box 1656, Gig Harbor, WA 98335 *Tel:* 253-851-5190 *Fax:* 253-851-5191 *E-mail:* info@harborpress.com *Web Site:* harborpress.com, pg 114

Meacham, Beth, Tom Doherty Associates, LLC, 175 Fifth Ave, 14th fl, New York, NY 10010 *Tel:* 212-388-0100 *Toll Free Tel:* 800-455-0340 *Fax:* 212-388-0191 *E-mail:* firstname.lastname@tor.com *Web Site:* www.tor.com, pg 82

Mead, Linda, LitWest Group LLC, 379 Burning Tree Ct, Half Moon Bay, CA 94019 *Web Site:* www.litwest.com, pg 641

Meade, Fionn, Artist Trust Fellowship, 1835 12 Ave, Seattle, WA 98122 *Tel:* 206-467-8734 *Fax:* 206-467-9633 *E-mail:* info@artisttrust.org *Web Site:* www.artisttrust.org, pg 760

Meade, Fionn, Grants for Artist Projects, 1835 12 Ave, Seattle, WA 98122 *Tel:* 206-467-8734 *Fax:* 206-467-9633 *E-mail:* info@artisttrust.org *Web Site:* www.artisttrust.org, pg 776

Meader, James, Picador, 175 Fifth Ave, New York, NY 10010 *Tel:* 212-674-5151 *Fax:* 212-253-9627 *E-mail:* firstname.lastname@picadorusa.com *Web Site:* www.picadorusa.com, pg 212

Meadors, Alyce, Abingdon Press, 201 Eighth Ave S, Nashville, TN 37203-3919 *Tel:* 615-749-6290 (publicist); 615-749-6000; 615-749-6451 (sales) *Toll Free Tel:* 800-251-3320 *Fax:* 615-749-6056 *Web Site:* www.abingdonpress.com, pg 3

Meadows, Rob, Bear & Co Inc, One Park St, Rochester, VT 05767 *Tel:* 802-767-3174 *Toll Free Tel:* 800-932-3277 *Fax:* 802-767-3726 *E-mail:* orders@InnerTraditions.com *Web Site:* InnerTraditions.com, pg 34

Meadows, Rob, Inner Traditions International Ltd, One Park St, Rochester, VT 05767 *Tel:* 802-767-3174 *Toll Free Tel:* 800-246-8648 *Fax:* 802-767-3726 *E-mail:* orders@InnerTraditions.com *Web Site:* www.InnerTraditions.com, pg 134

Meals, Joyce C, America's Health Insurance Plans (AHIP), South Bldg, 601 Pennsylvania Ave NW, Suite 500, Washington, DC 20004 *Tel:* 202-778-3200 *Fax:* 202-861-6354 *Web Site:* www.insuranceeducation.org, pg 18

Meaney, Carol, Dover Publications Inc, 31 E Second St, Mineola, NY 11501 *Tel:* 516-294-7000 *Toll Free Tel:* 800-223-3130 (orders) *Fax:* 516-742-6953; 516-742-5049 (orders) *Web Site:* www.doverpublications.com; www.doverdirect.com, pg 83

Mecadon, Patricia, University of Scranton Press, 445 Madison Ave, Scranton, PA 18510 *Tel:* 570-941-4228 *Toll Free Tel:* 800-941-3081 *Fax:* 570-941-6256 *Toll Free Fax:* 800-941-8804 *Web Site:* www.scrantonpress.com (Catalog), pg 285

Mecartea, Shauna, Cotsen Institute of Archaeology at UCLA, PO Box 951510, Los Angeles, CA 90095-1510 *Tel:* 310-825-7411 *Fax:* 310-206-4723 *E-mail:* ioapubs@ucla.edu *Web Site:* www.sscnet.ucla.edu/ioa, pg 69

Mecklenborg, Mark, The American Ceramic Society, 735 Ceramic Place, Westerville, OH 43081-8720 *Tel:* 614-794-5890 *Fax:* 614-794-5892 *E-mail:* info@ceramics.org *Web Site:* www.ceramics.org, pg 12

Medalla, Leandro, Cortina Learning International Inc, 7 Hollyhock Rd, Wilton, CT 06897-4414 *Tel:* 203-762-2510 *Toll Free Tel:* 800-245-2145 *Fax:* 203-762-2514 *E-mail:* info@cortina-languages.com; cortinainc@aol.com *Web Site:* www.cortina-languages.com (English language animation & sound); www.cursos-ingles-cortina.com (Spanish language animation & sound), pg 69

Medeot, William, Orbis Books, Walsh Bldg, 75 Ryder Rd, Ossining, NY 10562 *Tel:* 914-941-7636 *Toll Free Tel:* 800-258-5838 (orders) *Fax:* 914-941-7005 (orders); 914-945-0670 (office) *E-mail:* orbisbooks@maryknoll.org *Web Site:* www.orbisbooks.com, pg 198

Medill, Dawn, Standard Publishing Co, 8121 Hamilton Ave, Cincinnati, OH 45231 *Tel:* 513-931-4050 *Toll Free Tel:* 800-543-1301 *Fax:* 513-931-0950 *Toll Free Fax:* 877-867-5751 *E-mail:* customerservice@standardpub.com *Web Site:* www.standardpub.com, pg 257

Medina, Kate, Random House Publishing Group, 1745 Broadway, New York, NY 10019 *Toll Free Tel:* 800-200-3552 *Toll Free Fax:* 800-200-3552 *Web Site:* www.randomhouse.com, pg 227

Medlock, Stephanie, University of Chicago, Graham School of General Studies, 1427 E 60 St, Chicago, IL 60637 *Tel:* 773-702-1682 *Fax:* 773-702-6814 *Web Site:* www.grahamschool.uchicago.edu, pg 755

Mednick, Robert, National Bureau of Economic Research Inc, 1050 Massachusetts Ave, Cambridge, MA 02138-5398 *Tel:* 617-868-3900 *Fax:* 617-868-2742 *E-mail:* op@nber.org *Web Site:* www.nber.org, pg 182

Medved, Patricia, Doubleday Broadway Publishing Group, 1745 Broadway, New York, NY 10019 *Tel:* 212-782-9000 *Toll Free Tel:* 800-223-6834; 800-223-5780 (sales) *Fax:* 212-302-7985 (correspondence); 212-492-9862 (orders), pg 83

Meehan, Larry, ALI-ABA Committee on Continuing Professional Education, 4025 Chestnut St, Philadelphia, PA 19104 *Tel:* 215-243-1600 *Toll Free Tel:* 800-CLE-NEWS 1x•s: 215-243-1664; 215-243-1683 *Web Site:* www.ali-aba.org, pg 8

Meehan, Patrick, Houghton Mifflin Co, 222 Berkeley St, Boston, MA 02116-3764 *Tel:* 617-351-5000 *Toll Free Tel:* 800-225-3362 (trade books); 800-733-2828 (text books); 800-225-1464 (college texts) *Fax:* 617-351-1125 *Web Site:* www.hmco.com, pg 126

Meerdink, Jan, The Russell Meerdink Co Ltd, 1555 S Park Ave, Neenah, WI 54956 *Tel:* 920-725-0955 *Toll Free Tel:* 800-635-6499 *Fax:* 920-725-0709 *Web Site:* www.horseinfo.com, pg 170

Meese, Al, Modern Curriculum Press, 299 Jefferson Rd, Parsippany, NJ 07054-0480 *Tel:* 973-739-8000 *Fax:* 973-739-8635 *Web Site:* www.pearsonlearning.com, pg 176

Megargee, Moira, Interlink Publishing Group Inc, 46 Crosby St, Northampton, MA 01060 *Tel:* 413-582-7054 *Toll Free Tel:* 800-238-LINK (238-5465) *Fax:* 413-582-7057 *E-mail:* info@interlinkbooks.com *Web Site:* www.interlinkbooks.com, pg 136

Meglin, Pat, Baldwin Literary Services, 935 Hayes St, Baldwin, NY 11510-4834 *Tel:* 516-546-8338 *Fax:* 516-867-6850, pg 591

Mehrabani, Mostafa, The McGraw-Hill Companies Inc, 1221 Avenue of the Americas, 50th fl, New York, NY 10020 *Tel:* 212-512-2000 *E-mail:* webmaster@mcgraw-hill.com *Web Site:* www.mcgraw-hill.com, pg 167

Mehta, Sonny, Alfred A Knopf, 1745 Broadway, New York, NY 10019 *Tel:* 212-751-2600 *Toll Free Tel:* 800-638-6460 *Fax:* 212-572-2593 *Web Site:* www.randomhouse.com/knopf, pg 146

Mehta, Sonny, Random House Inc, 1745 Broadway, New York, NY 10019 *Tel:* 212-782-9000 *Toll Free Tel:* 800-726-0600 *Web Site:* www.randomhouse.com, pg 226

Meier, Manuela, Cobblestone Publishing Co, 30 Grove St, Suite C, Peterborough, NH 03458 *Tel:* 603-924-7209 *Toll Free Tel:* 800-821-0115 *Fax:* 603-924-7380 *E-mail:* custsvc@cobblestone.mv.com *Web Site:* www.cobblestonepub.com, pg 64

Meinholz, Matt, American Society for Quality, 600 N Plankinton Ave, Milwaukee, WI 53203 *Tel:* 414-272-8575 *Toll Free Tel:* 800-248-1946 *Fax:* 414-272-1734 *E-mail:* cs@asq.org *Web Site:* www.asq.org, pg 17

Meisel, Susan Lee, Educational Media Co/TMA, 18740 Paseo Nuevo Dr, Tarzana, CA 91356 *Tel:* 818-708-0962 *Fax:* 818-345-2980 *Web Site:* educationalmediacompany.com, pg 598

Meissner, Bill, Mississippi River Writing Workshop, 720 Fourth Ave S, Riverview 101-D, St Cloud, MN 56301-4498 *Tel:* 320-308-3061; 320-308-4947 *Fax:* 320-308-5524, pg 744

Meisterich, Catherine, Leadership Directories Inc, 104 Fifth Ave, New York, NY 10011 *Tel:* 212-627-4140 *Fax:* 212-645-0931 *E-mail:* info@leadershipdirectories.com *Web Site:* www.leadershipdirectories.com, pg 150

Mejia, Bess, Prentice Hall Humanities & Social Sciences, One Lake St, Upper Saddle River, NJ 07458 *Tel:* 201-236-7000, pg 217

Meland, Sheba, Maple Tree Press Inc, 51 Front St E, Suite 200, Toronto, ON M5E 1B3, Canada *Tel:* 416-304-0702 *Fax:* 416-304-0525 *E-mail:* info@mapletreepress.com *Web Site:* www.mapletreepress.com, pg 553

Melando, Ed, John Wiley & Sons Inc, 111 River St, Hoboken, NJ 07030 *Tel:* 201-748-6000 *Toll Free Tel:* 800-225-5945 (cust serv) *Fax:* 201-748-6088 *E-mail:* info@wiley.com *Web Site:* www.wiley.com, pg 299

Melaragno, Renzo, Brandywine Press, 154 General Pulaski Walk, Naugatuck, CT 06770-2978 *Tel:* 203-729-7556 *Toll Free Tel:* 800-345-1776 *Fax:* 203-729-7567 *Web Site:* www.brandywinepress.com, pg 45

Mell, Donald, University of Delaware Press, Associated University Presses, 2010 Eastpark Blvd, Cranbury, NJ 08512 *Tel:* 609-655-4770 *Fax:* 609-655-8366 *E-mail:* aup440@aol.com, pg 281

Mello, Felice, The Countryman Press, 1206 Rte 12 N, Woodstock, VT 05091 *Tel:* 802-457-4826 *Toll Free Tel:* 800-245-4151 *Fax:* 802-457-1678 *E-mail:* countrymanpress@wwnorton.com *Web Site:* www.countrymanpress.com, pg 70

Mello, Felice, W W Norton & Company Inc, 500 Fifth Ave, New York, NY 10110-0017 *Tel:* 212-354-5500 *Toll Free Tel:* 800-233-4830 (orders & cust serv) *Fax:* 212-869-0856 *Toll Free Fax:* 800-458-6515 *Web Site:* www.wwnorton.com, pg 193

Mello, Kerriebeth, Fine Communications, 322 Eighth Ave, 15th fl, New York, NY 10001 *Tel:* 212-595-3500 *Fax:* 212-595-3779, pg 96

Metz, Isabel, University Press of Mississippi, 3825 Ridgewood Rd, Jackson, MS 39211-6492 *Tel:* 601-432-6205 *Toll Free Tel:* 800-737-7788 *Fax:* 601-432-6217 *E-mail:* press@ihl.state.ms.us *Web Site:* www. upress.state.ms.us, pg 287

Metz, Mary, The Mountaineers Books, 1001 SW Klickitat Way, Suite 201, Seattle, WA 98134 *Tel:* 206-223-6303 *Toll Free Tel:* 800-553-4453 *Fax:* 206-223-6306 *Toll Free Fax:* 800-568-7604 *E-mail:* mbooks@ mountaineers.org *Web Site:* www.mountaineersbooks. org, pg 179

Metz, Mary, The Barbara Savage, 1001 SW Klickitat Way, Suite 201, Seattle, WA 98134 *Tel:* 206-223-6303 *Fax:* 206-223-6306 *E-mail:* mbooks@mountaineers.org *Web Site:* www.mountaineersbooks.org, pg 803

Metzgar, Allen, Factor Press, 5204 Dove Point Lane, Salisbury, MD 21801 *Tel:* 410-334-6111 *Toll Free Tel:* 888-334-6677 *Fax:* 410-334-6111 *E-mail:* factorpress@earthlink.net, pg 93

Metzger, Michael, Northern California Translators Association, PO Box 14015, Berkeley, CA 94712-5015 *Tel:* 510-845-8712 *Fax:* 510-883-1355 *E-mail:* ncta@ncta.org *Web Site:* www.ncta.org, pg 696

Metzger, Philip A, Lehigh University Press, Linderman Library, 30 Library Dr, Bethlehem, PA 18015-3067 *Tel:* 610-758-3933 *Fax:* 610-758-6331 *E-mail:* inlup@ lehigh.edu *Web Site:* fp1.cc.lehigh.edu/inlup, pg 152

Metzger, Ted, PRIMEDIA Business Directories & Books, 9800 Metcalf Ave, Overland Park, KS 66212 *Tel:* 913-967-1719 *Toll Free Tel:* 800-453-9620; 800-262-1954 (cust serv) *Fax:* 913-967-1901 *Toll Free Fax:* 800-633-6219 *E-mail:* bookorders@ primediabooks.com *Web Site:* www.primediabooks. com, pg 218

Metzler, Michael, Action Publishing LLC, PO Box 391, Glendale, CA 91209 *Tel:* 323-478-1667 *Toll Free Tel:* 800-705-7482 *Fax:* 323-478-1767 *E-mail:* info@ actionpublishing.com *Web Site:* www.actionpublishing. com, pg 5

Meunier, Christiane, Chitra Publications, 2 Public Ave, Montrose, PA 18801 *Tel:* 570-278-1984 *Toll Free Tel:* 800-628-8244 *Fax:* 570-278-2223 *E-mail:* chitra@ epix.net *Web Site:* www.quilttownusa.com, pg 60

Meyer, Alan, Protestant Church-Owned Publishers Association, 748 Crabthicket Lane, St Louis, MO 63131 *Tel:* 314-505-7237 *Fax:* 314-505-7760 *E-mail:* pcpa@pcpanews.org *Web Site:* www. pcpanews.org, pg 698

Meyer, Audrey, University of Washington Press, 1326 Fifth Ave, Suite 555, Seattle, WA 98101-2604 *Tel:* 206-543-4050; 206-543-8870 *Toll Free Tel:* 800-441-4115 (orders) *Fax:* 206-543-3932 *Toll Free Fax:* 800-669-7993 (orders) *E-mail:* uwpord@u. washington.edu *Web Site:* www.washington.edu/ uwpress/, pg 286

Meyer, Brian, Western New York Wares Inc, PO Box 733, Ellicott Sta, Buffalo, NY 14205 *Tel:* 716-832-6088 *E-mail:* buffalobooks@att.net *Web Site:* www. buffalobooks.com, pg 296

Meyer, Christina, Penguin Group (USA) Inc Sales, 375 Hudson St, New York, NY 10014 *Tel:* 212-366-2000 *E-mail:* online@penguinputnam.com *Web Site:* www. penguin.com, pg 208

Meyer, David, Meyerbooks Publisher, 235 W Main St, Glenwood, IL 60425 *Tel:* 708-757-4950, pg 173

Meyer, Don, The Dorese Agency Ltd, 37965 Palo Verde Dr, Cathedral City, CA 92234 *Tel:* 760-321-1115 *Fax:* 760-321-1049 *Web Site:* www.doreseagency.com, pg 628

Meyer, Helmut, Helmut Meyer Literary Agency, 330 E 79 St, New York, NY 10021 *Tel:* 212-288-2421, pg 644

Meyer, Hilary, Ivan R Dee Publisher, 1332 N Halsted St, Chicago, IL 60622-2694 *Tel:* 312-787-6262 *Toll Free Tel:* 800-462-6420 (orders) *Fax:* 312-787-6269 *Toll Free Fax:* 800-338-4550 (orders) *E-mail:* elephant@ ivanrdee.com *Web Site:* www.ivanrdee.com, pg 78

Meyer, Jenny, Smithsonian Institution Press, 750 Ninth St NW, Suite 4300, Washington, DC 20560-0950 *Tel:* 202-275-2300 *Fax:* 202-275-2274 *E-mail:* inquiries@sipress.si.edu *Web Site:* www. sipress.si.edu, pg 251

Meyer, Joel, Fairview Press, 2450 Riverside Ave, Minneapolis, MN 55454 *Tel:* 612-672-4180 *Toll Free Tel:* 800-544-8207 *Fax:* 612-672-4980 *Web Site:* www. fairviewpress.org, pg 94

Meyer, Kathleen, Duquesne University Press, 600 Forbes Ave, Pittsburgh, PA 15282 *Tel:* 412-396-6610 *Toll Free Tel:* 800-666-2211 *Fax:* 412-396-5984 *Web Site:* www.dupress.duq.edu, pg 84

Meyer, Michael A, Hebrew Union College Press, 3101 Clifton Ave, Cincinnati, OH 45220 *Tel:* 513-221-1875 *Fax:* 513-221-0321 *E-mail:* hucpress@huc.edu *Web Site:* www.huc.edu, pg 120

Meyer, Peter, Pen American Center, 588 Broadway, Suite 303, New York, NY 10012 *Tel:* 212-334-1660 *Fax:* 212-334-2181 *E-mail:* pen@pen.org *Web Site:* www.pen.org, pg 696

Meyer, Peter, The PEN Award for Poetry in Translation, 588 Broadway, Suite 303, New York, NY 10012 *Tel:* 212-334-1660 *Fax:* 212-334-2181 *E-mail:* pen@ pen.org *Web Site:* www.pen.org, pg 797

Meyer, Peter, PEN Award for the Art of the Essay, 588 Broadway, Suite 303, New York, NY 10012 *Tel:* 212-334-1660 *Fax:* 212-334-2181 *E-mail:* pen@pen.org *Web Site:* www.pen.org, pg 797

Meyer, Peter, PEN/Robert Bingham Fellowships for Writers, 588 Broadway, Suite 303, New York, NY 10012 *Tel:* 212-334-1660 *Fax:* 212-334-2181 *E-mail:* pen@pen.org *Web Site:* www.pen.org, pg 797

Meyer, Peter, PEN Book-of-the-Month Translation Prize, 588 Broadway, Suite 303, New York, NY 10012 *Tel:* 212-334-1660 *Fax:* 212-334-2181 *E-mail:* pen@ pen.org *Web Site:* www.pen.org, pg 797

Meyer, Peter, PEN/Jerard Fund Award, 588 Broadway, Suite 303, New York, NY 10012 *Tel:* 212-334-1660 *Fax:* 212-334-2181 *E-mail:* pen@pen.org *Web Site:* www.pen.org, pg 797

Meyer, Peter, PEN Martha Albrand Award for The Art of Memoir, 588 Broadway, Suite 303, New York, NY 10012 *Tel:* 212-334-1660 *Fax:* 212-334-2181 *E-mail:* pen@pen.org *Web Site:* www.pen.org, pg 798

Meyer, Peter, PEN/Phyllis Naylor Working Writer Fellowship, 588 Broadway, Suite 303, New York, NY 10012 *Tel:* 212-334-1660 *Fax:* 212-334-2181 *E-mail:* pen@pen.org *Web Site:* www.pen.org, pg 798

Meyer, Peter, The PEN/Ralph Manheim Medal for Translation, 588 Broadway, Suite 303, New York, NY 10012 *Tel:* 212-334-1660 *Fax:* 212-334-2181 *E-mail:* pen@pen.org *Web Site:* www.pen.org, pg 798

Meyer, Victoria, Simon & Schuster, 1230 Avenue of the Americas, New York, NY 10020 *Tel:* 212-698-7000 *Toll Free Tel:* 800-223-2348 (cust serv); 800-223-2336 (orders) *Toll Free Fax:* 800-943-9831 (orders) *Web Site:* www.simonsays.com, pg 248

Meyer-Spacks, Patricia, American Academy of Arts & Sciences (AAAS), Norton's Woods, 136 Irving St, Cambridge, MA 02138-1996 *Tel:* 617-576-5000 *Fax:* 617-576-5050 *Web Site:* www.amacad.org, pg 675

Meyers, Annette, International Association of Crime Writers Inc, North American Branch, PO Box 8674, New York, NY 10116-8674 *Tel:* 212-243-8966 *Fax:* 815-361-1477, pg 688

Meyers, Bob, The National Press Foundation, 1211 Connecticut Ave NW, Suite 310, Washington, DC 20036 *Tel:* 202-530-5355 *Fax:* 202-530-2855 *Web Site:* www.nationalpress.org, pg 694

Meyers, Elaina, Standard Publishing Co, 8121 Hamilton Ave, Cincinnati, OH 45231 *Tel:* 513-931-4050 *Toll Free Tel:* 800-543-1301 *Fax:* 513-931-0950 *Toll Free Fax:* 877-867-5751 *E-mail:* customerservice@ standardpub.com *Web Site:* www.standardpub.com, pg 257

Meyers, Erik, Environmental Law Institute, 1616 "P" St NW, Suite 200, Washington, DC 20036 *Tel:* 202-939-3800 *Fax:* 202-939-3868 *E-mail:* law@eli.org *Web Site:* www.eli.org, pg 91

Meyers, Janet, The Wright Group/McGraw-Hill, a Division of McGraw-Hill Learning Group, One Prudential Plaza, 130 E Randolph, 4th fl, Chicago, IL 60601 *Tel:* 312-233-6520 *Toll Free Tel:* 800-537-4740 *Fax:* 312-233-6605 *Web Site:* www.wrightgroup.com, pg 304

Meyers, Tona Pierce, New World Library, 14 Pamaron Way, Novato, CA 94949 *Tel:* 415-884-2100 *Toll Free Tel:* 800-227-3900 (ext 52, retail orders) *Fax:* 415-884-2199 (ext 52, retail orders) *E-mail:* escort@ newworldlibrary.com *Web Site:* www.newworldlibrary. com, pg 189

Miao, Lillian, Paraclete Press, PO Box 1568, Orleans, MA 02653-1568 *Tel:* 508-255-4685 *Toll Free Tel:* 800-451-5006 *Fax:* 508-255-5705 *Web Site:* www. paracletepress.com, pg 203

Miawer, Boris, Basic Health Publications Inc, 8200 Boulevard E, Suite 25-G, North Bergen, NJ 07047 *Tel:* 201-868-8336 *Toll Free Tel:* 800-575-8890 *Fax:* 201-868-8335, pg 33

Micallef, Joseph, McGraw-Hill Education, 2 Penn Plaza, New York, NY 10121 *Tel:* 212-904-2000 *E-mail:* customer.service@mcgraw-hill.com *Web Site:* www.mheducation.com; www.mheducation. com/custserv.html, pg 167

Miccolis, Dominic J, World Book Inc, 233 N Michigan, Suite 2000, Chicago, IL 60601 *Tel:* 312-729-5800 *Toll Free Tel:* 800-967-5325 (consumer sales, US); 800-463-8845 (consumer sales, Canada); 800-975-3250 (school & library sales, US); 800-837-5365 (school & library sales, Canada); 866-866-5200 (web sales) *Fax:* 312-729-5600; 312-729-5606 *Toll Free Fax:* 800-433-9330 (school & library sales, US); 888-690-4002 (school library sales, Canada) *Web Site:* www. worldbook.com, pg 303

Michaels, Bernice, Leonardo Press, PO Box 1326, Camden, ME 04843-1326 *Tel:* 207-236-8649 *Fax:* 207-236-8649 *E-mail:* leonardo@spellingdoctor. com *Web Site:* www.spellingdoctor.com, pg 152

Michaels, Doris S, Doris S Michaels Literary Agency Inc, 1841 Broadway, Suite 903, New York, NY 10023 *Tel:* 212-265-9474 *Fax:* 212-265-9480 *E-mail:* info@ dsmagency.com *Web Site:* www.dsmagency.com, pg 644

Michaels, Kenneth J, McGraw-Hill Education, 2 Penn Plaza, New York, NY 10121 *Tel:* 212-904-2000 *E-mail:* customer.service@mcgraw-hill.com *Web Site:* www.mheducation.com; www.mheducation. com/custserv.html, pg 167

Michaels, Linda, Linda Michaels Ltd International Literary Agents, 344 Main St, Lakeville, CT 06039-0567 *Tel:* 860-435-1432 *Fax:* 860-435-1446 *E-mail:* lmlagency@aol.com, pg 644

Michaels, Melisa, Embiid Publishing, 600 Fouts St, Upham, ND 58789 *E-mail:* info@embiid.net; us@ embiid.net; submissions@embiid.net *Web Site:* www. embiid.net, pg 89

Michaels, Richard, Bluewood Books, 38 South "B" St, Suite 202, San Mateo, CA 94401 *Tel:* 650-548-0754 *Fax:* 650-548-0654 *E-mail:* bluewoodb@aol.com, pg 42

Michaels, Richard, Embiid Publishing, 600 Fouts St, Upham, ND 58789 *E-mail:* info@embiid.net; us@ embiid.net; submissions@embiid.net *Web Site:* www. embiid.net, pg 89

Michaelson, Paul, EMC/Paradigm Publishing, 875 Montreal Way, St Paul, MN 55102 *Tel:* 651-290-2800 (corp) *Toll Free Tel:* 800-328-1452 *Fax:* 651-290-2899 *Toll Free Fax:* 800-328-4564 *E-mail:* educate@emcp. com *Web Site:* www.emcp.com, pg 90

Michalicek, Steven S, Heuer Publishing LLC, 211 First Ave SE, Cedar Rapids, IA 52401 *Tel:* 319-368-8008 *Toll Free Tel:* 800-950-7529 *Fax:* 319-364-1771 *E-mail:* editor@hitplays.com *Web Site:* www.hitplays. com, pg 122

E-mail: info@gspub.com; info@worldalmanaclibrary. com *Web Site:* www.garethstevens.com; www. worldalmanaclibrary.com, pg 102

Miller, David, HCPro, 200 Hoods Lane, Marblehead, MA 01945 *Tel:* 781-639-1872 *Toll Free Tel:* 800-650-6787 *Fax:* 781-639-2982 *Toll Free Fax:* 800-639-8511 *E-mail:* customer_service@hcpro.com *Web Site:* www. hcpro.com, pg 119

Miller, Erin, RAND Corp, 1776 Main St, Santa Monica, CA 90407 *Tel:* 310-393-0411 *Fax:* 310-451-6996 *E-mail:* jane_ryan@rand.org *Web Site:* www.rand.org, pg 225

Miller, Fredericka, The Artists Agency, 1180 S Beverly Dr, Suite 400, Los Angeles, CA 90035 *Tel:* 310-277-7779 *Fax:* 310-785-9338, pg 619

Miller, Heather, Ohio State University Press, 180 Pressey Hall, 1070 Carmack Rd, Columbus, OH 43210-1002 *Tel:* 614-292-6930 *Toll Free Tel:* 800-621-2736 *Fax:* 614-292-2065 *Toll Free Fax:* 800-621-8476 *E-mail:* ohiostatepress@osu.edu *Web Site:* ohiostatepress.org, pg 196

Miller, Irene, The Edwin Mellen Press, 415 Ridge St, Lewiston, NY 14092 *Tel:* 716-754-2266 (mgr acqs); 716-754-8566 (mktg); 716-754-2788 (order fulfillment) *Fax:* 716-754-4056; 716-754-1860 (order fulfillment) *E-mail:* mellen@wzrd.com; cs@wzrd. com (customer service, fulfillment) *Web Site:* www. mellenpress.com, pg 171

Miller, James, American Academy of Arts & Sciences (AAAS), Norton's Woods, 136 Irving St, Cambridge, MA 02138-1996 *Tel:* 617-576-5000 *Fax:* 617-576-5050 *Web Site:* www.amacad.org, pg 675

Miller, Jan, Dupree, Miller & Associates Inc, 100 Highland Park Village, Suite 350, Dallas, TX 75205 *Tel:* 214-559-2665 *Fax:* 214-559-7243 *E-mail:* dmabook@aol.com, pg 628

Miller, Janice, Management Sciences for Health, 165 Allandale Rd, Boston, MA 02130-3400 *Tel:* 617-524-7799 *Fax:* 617-524-2825 *E-mail:* bookstore@msh.org *Web Site:* www.msh.org, pg 162

Miller, Jeffrey, Cadmus Editions, PO Box 126, Belvedere-Tiburon, CA 94920-0126 *Tel:* 707-762-0510 *Web Site:* www.cadmus-editions.com, pg 51

Miller, Jeffrey, Irwin Law Inc, 347 Bay St, Suite 501, Toronto, ON M5H 2R7, Canada *Tel:* 416-862-7690 *Toll Free Tel:* 888-314-9014 *Fax:* 416-862-9236 *Web Site:* www.irwinlaw.com, pg 551

Miller, Jo Ann, Basic Books, 387 Park Ave S, 12th fl, New York, NY 10016-8810 *Tel:* 212-340-8100 *Toll Free Tel:* 800-242-7737 (orders) *Fax:* 212-340-8135 *E-mail:* basic.books@perseusbooks.com *Web Site:* www.basicbooks.com, pg 33

Miller, JoAnn E, Upper Room Books, 1908 Grand Ave, Nashville, TN 37212 *Toll Free Tel:* 800-972-0433 *Fax:* 615-340-7266 *Web Site:* www.upperroom.org, pg 288

Miller, John, The Taunton Press Inc, 63 S Main St, Newtown, CT 06470 *Tel:* 203-426-8171 *Toll Free Tel:* 800-283-7252; 800-888-8286 (orders) *Fax:* 203-426-3434 *Web Site:* www.taunton.com, pg 264

Miller, Jordan, Academy Chicago Publishers, 363 W Erie St, Chicago, IL 60610 *Tel:* 312-751-7300 *Toll Free Tel:* 800-248-7323 *Fax:* 312-751-7306 *E-mail:* info@academychicago.com *Web Site:* www. academychicago.com, pg 4

Miller, Lee, The Globe Pequot Press, 246 Goose Lane, Guilford, CT 06437 *Tel:* 203-458-4500 *Toll Free Tel:* 800-243-0495 (cust serv) *Fax:* 203-458-4601 *Toll Free Fax:* 800-820-2329 (orders & cust serv) *E-mail:* info@globepequot.com *Web Site:* www. globepequot.com, pg 106

Miller, Leslie, Seal Press, 1400 65 St, Suite 250, Emeryville, CA 94608 *Tel:* 510-595-3664 *Fax:* 510-595-4228 *Web Site:* www.sealpress.com, pg 244

Miller, Levi, Herald Press, 616 Walnut Ave, Scottdale, PA 15683-1999 *Tel:* 724-887-8500 *Toll Free Tel:* 800-245-7894 *Fax:* 724-887-3111 *E-mail:* hp@mph.org *Web Site:* www.heraldpress.com, pg 121

Miller, Levi, Herald Press, 490 Dutton Dr, Unit C-8, Waterloo, ON N2L 6H7, Canada *Tel:* 519-747-5722 *Toll Free Tel:* 800-245-7894 (Canada & US) *Fax:* 519-747-5721 *E-mail:* hp@mph.org *Web Site:* www. heraldpress.com, pg 550

Miller, Marilee, Anchorage Press Plays Inc, PO Box 2901, Louisville, KY 40201-2901 *Tel:* 502-583-2288 *E-mail:* applays@bellsouth.net *Web Site:* applays.com, pg 19

Miller, Matthew, The Toby Press LLC, 2 Great Pasture Rd, Danbury, CT 06810 *Tel:* 203-830-8508 *Fax:* 203-830-8512 *E-mail:* toby@tobypress.com *Web Site:* www.tobypress.com, pg 272

Miller, Nancy, Random House Publishing Group, 1745 Broadway, New York, NY 10019 *Toll Free Tel:* 800-200-3552 *Toll Free Fax:* 800-200-3552 *Web Site:* www.randomhouse.com, pg 227

Miller, Peter, PMA Literary & Film Management Inc, PO Box 1817, Old Chelsea Sta, New York, NY 10011 *Tel:* 212-929-1222 *Fax:* 212-206-0238 *E-mail:* pmalitfilm@aol.com *Web Site:* www. pmalitfilm.com, pg 648

Miller, Richard K, Richard K Miller Associates Inc, 4132 Atlanta Hwy, Suite 110-366, Loganville, GA 30052 *Tel:* 770-416-0006 *Fax:* 770-416-0052, pg 174

Miller, Robert, Central Ohio Writers of Literature for Children, c/o St Joseph Montessori School, 933 Hamlet St, Columbus, OH 43201-3595 *Tel:* 614-291-8644 *Fax:* 614-291-7411 *E-mail:* cowriters@mail.com *Web Site:* www.sjms.net/conf, pg 742

Miller, Robert, Hyperion, 77 W 66 St, 11th fl, New York, NY 10023-6298 *Tel:* 212-456-0100 *Toll Free Tel:* 800-759-0190 (cust serv) *Fax:* 212-456-0157 *Web Site:* hyperionbooks.com, pg 208

Miller, Scott, Trident Media Group LLC, 41 Madison Ave, 36th fl, New York, NY 10010 *Tel:* 212-262-4810 *Fax:* 212-725-4501 *Web Site:* www.tridentmediagroup. com, pg 659

Miller, Shawn, Artists' Fellowships, 155 Avenue of the Americas, 14th fl, New York, NY 10013-1507 *Tel:* 212-366-6900 *Fax:* 212-366-1778 *E-mail:* nyainfo@nyfa.org *Web Site:* www.nyfa.org, pg 760

Miller, Stuart, Federal Buyers Guide Inc, 718-B State St, Santa Barbara, CA 93101 *Tel:* 805-963-7470 *Fax:* 805-963-7478 *Web Site:* www.gov-world.com, pg 95

Miller, Sylvia, Routledge, 29 W 35 St, New York, NY 10001-2299 *Tel:* 212-216-7800 *Fax:* 212-564-7854 (main) *E-mail:* info@taylorandfrancis.com *Web Site:* www.routledge-ny.com, pg 235

Miller, Tim, Six Gallery Press, 4620 Los Feliz Blvd, Suite 1, Los Angeles, CA 90027 *E-mail:* sgpwc@ yahoo.com *Web Site:* www.sixgallerypress.com, pg 249

Miller, Tina, Great Source Education Group, 181 Ballardvale St, Wilmington, MA 01887 *Tel:* 978-661-1300 *Toll Free Tel:* 800-289-4490 (orders), pg 108

Miller, William, Mary Roberts Rinehart Fund, George Mason Univ, English Dept, 4400 University Dr, Mail Stop Number 3E4, Fairfax, VA 22030-4444 *Tel:* 703-993-1185 *Web Site:* www.gmu.edu/depts/english, pg 802

Miller, Yvette E, Latin American Literary Review Press, 176 Penhurst Dr, Pittsburgh, PA 15235 *Tel:* 412-824-7903 *Fax:* 412-824-7909 *E-mail:* latin@angstrom.net *Web Site:* www.lalrp.org, pg 149

Miller-Baum, Rebecca, The Haworth Press Inc, 10 Alice St, Binghamton, NY 13904-1580 *Tel:* 607-722-5857 *Toll Free Tel:* 800-429-6784 *Fax:* 607-722-1424 *Toll Free Fax:* 800-895-0582 *E-mail:* getinfo@ haworthpressinc.com *Web Site:* www.haworthpress. com, pg 118

Millholland, Valerie, Duke University Press, 905 W Main St, Suite 18-B, Durham, NC 27701 *Tel:* 919-687-3600 *Toll Free Tel:* 888-651-0122 (orders only) *Fax:* 919-688-4574 *Toll Free Fax:* 888-651-0124 *Web Site:* www.dukeupress.edu, pg 84

Millichap, Paulette, Council Oak Books LLC, 2105 E 15 St, Suite B, Tulsa, OK 74104 *Tel:* 918-743-BOOK (743-2665) *Toll Free Tel:* 800-247-8850 *Fax:* 918-743-4288 *E-mail:* publicity@counciloakbooks.com; orders@counciloakbooks.com *Web Site:* www. counciloakbooks.com, pg 70

Milligan, Bryce, Wings Press, 627 E Guenther, San Antonio, TX 78210 *Tel:* 210-271-7805; 210-222-8449 *Fax:* 210-271-7805 *Web Site:* www.wingspress.com, pg 613

Milliken, Jean Mellichamp, Lyric Poetry Prizes, 65 Vermont, Rte 15, Jericho, VT 05465 *Tel:* 802-899-3993 *Fax:* 802-899-3993, pg 786

Milliken, Linda H, Edupress Inc, 208 Avenida Fabricante, Suite 200, San Clemente, CA 92672-7538 *Tel:* 949-366-9499 *Toll Free Tel:* 800-835-7978 *Fax:* 949-366-9441 *E-mail:* info@edupressinc.com *Web Site:* www.edupressinc.com, pg 88

Milling, Marcus, American Geological Institute (AGI), 4220 King St, Alexandria, VA 22302-1507 *Tel:* 703-379-2480 *Fax:* 703-379-7563 *E-mail:* pubs@agiweb. org *Web Site:* www.agiweb.org, pg 14

Millington, Jennifer A, Milton Dorfman Poetry Prize, 308 W Bloomfield St, Rome, NY 13440 *Tel:* 315-336-1040 *Fax:* 315-336-1090 *E-mail:* racc@borg.com, pg 790

Millman, Michael, Penguin Books, 375 Hudson St, New York, NY 10014 *Tel:* 212-366-2000 *E-mail:* online@ penguinputnam.com *Web Site:* www.penguin.com; www.penguinclassics.com, pg 207

Millman, Norman N, Summit University Press, 558 Old Yellowstone Trail S, Corwin Springs, MT 59030-5000 *Tel:* 406-848-9295 *Toll Free Tel:* 800-245-5445 *Fax:* 406-848-9290 *E-mail:* info@ summituniversitypress.com *Web Site:* www. hostmontana.com/supress; www.summitunuversitypress. com, pg 261

Milloy, Marilyn, National Education Association (NEA), 1201 16 St NW, Washington, DC 20036 *Tel:* 202-833-4000; 202-822-7207 (ed office) *Fax:* 202-822-7206 *Web Site:* www.nea.org, pg 183

Mills, Brenda, Fiction Collective Two Inc, Florida State University, FC2, Dept of English, Tallahassee, FL 32306-1580 *Tel:* 850-644-2260 *Fax:* 850-644-6808 *E-mail:* fc2@english.fsu.edu *Web Site:* fc2.org, pg 96

Mills, Douglas, Pearson, 800 E 96 St, Indianapolis, IN 46240 *Tel:* 317-428-3000 *Toll Free Tel:* 800-545-5914 *Fax:* 317-581-4675 *Web Site:* www.macdigital.com, pg 206

Mills, Elizabeth, John H McGinnis Memorial Award, 307 Fondren Library W, 6404 Hilltop Lane, Dallas, TX 75275-0374 *Tel:* 214-768-1037 *Fax:* 214-768-1408 *E-mail:* swr@mail.smu.edu *Web Site:* www. southwestreview.org, pg 788

Mills, Elizabeth, Elizabeth Matchett Stover Memorial Award, 307 Fondren Library W, 6404 Hilltop Lane, Dallas, TX 75275-0374 *Tel:* 214-768-1037 *Fax:* 214-768-1408 *E-mail:* swr@mail.smu.edu *Web Site:* www. southwestreview.org, pg 807

Mills, Elizabeth, Temporal Mechanical Press, 6760 Hwy 7, Estes Park, CO 80517-6404 *Tel:* 970-586-4706 *E-mail:* enosmillscbn@earthlink.net *Web Site:* www. geocities.com/soho/nook/7587, pg 266

Mills, Eryn, Temporal Mechanical Press, 6760 Hwy 7, Estes Park, CO 80517-6404 *Tel:* 970-586-4706 *E-mail:* enosmillscbn@earthlink.net *Web Site:* www. geocities.com/soho/nook/7587, pg 266

Mills, Kathleen, Kathleen Mills Editorial & Production Services, PO Box 214, Chardon, OH 44024 *Tel:* 440-285-4347 *Fax:* 440-286-9213 *E-mail:* mills_edit@ yahoo.com, pg 606

Mills, Nancy J, The University of Virginia Press, PO Box 400318, Charlottesville, VA 22904-4318 *Tel:* 434-924-3468 (cust serv); 434-924-3469 (cust serv) *Toll Free Tel:* 800-831-3406 (cust serv) *Fax:* 434-982-2655 *Toll Free Fax:* 877-288-6400 *E-mail:* upressvirginia@ virginia.edu *Web Site:* www.upressvirginia.edu, pg 285

Mills, Nancy L, Pie in the Sky Publishing, 2511 S Dawson Way, Aurora, CO 80014 *Tel:* 303-751-2672 *Fax:* 303-751-2672 *E-mail:* pieintheskypublishing@ msn.com *Web Site:* www.pieintheskypublishing.com, pg 212

Mills, Sharon, Texas A&M University Press, John H Lindsey Bldg, Lewis St, 4354 TAMU, College Station, TX 77843-4354 *Tel:* 979-845-1436 *Toll Free Tel:* 800-826-8911 (orders) *Fax:* 979-847-8752 *Toll Free Fax:* 888-617-2421 (orders) *E-mail:* fdl@tampress. tamu.edu *Web Site:* www.tamu.edu/upress/, pg 267

Milne, Teddy, Pittenbruach Press, PO Box 553, Northampton, MA 01061-0553 *Tel:* 413-584-8547, pg 214

Milner, Fran, Paladin Press, 7077 Winchester Circle, Boulder, CO 80301 *Tel:* 303-443-7250 *Toll Free Tel:* 800-392-2400 *Fax:* 303-442-8741 *E-mail:* service@paladin-press.com *Web Site:* www. paladin-press.com, pg 202

Milroy, Peter, University of British Columbia Press, 2029 West Mall, Vancouver, BC V6T 1Z2, Canada *Tel:* 604-822-5959 *Toll Free Tel:* 877-377-9378 *Fax:* 604-822-6083 *Toll Free Fax:* 800-668-0821 *E-mail:* info@ubcpress.ca *Web Site:* www.ubcpress.ca, pg 564

Milstein, Richard, Cambridge University Press, 40 W 20 St, New York, NY 10011-4211 *Tel:* 212-924-3900 *Toll Free Tel:* 800-899-5222 *Fax:* 212-691-3239 *Web Site:* www.cambridge.org, pg 52

Milton, Christina, University of Michigan Press, 839 Greene St, Ann Arbor, MI 48104-3209 *Tel:* 734-764-4388 *Fax:* 734-615-1540 *E-mail:* um.press@umich.edu *Web Site:* www.press.umich.edu, pg 282

Milton, Penny, Canadian Education Association/ Association canadienne d'education, 317 Adelaide St W, Suite 300, Toronto, ON M5V 1P9, Canada *Tel:* 416-591-6300 *Fax:* 416-591-5345 *E-mail:* info@ cea.ace.ca *Web Site:* www.cea-ace.ca, pg 538, 683

Minch, Mary, Art Institute of Chicago, 111 S Michigan Ave, Chicago, IL 60603-6110 *Tel:* 312-443-3600; 312-443-3540 (pubns) 312-443-3533 (sales & orders) *Fax:* 312-443-0849; 312-443-1334 (pubns) *E-mail:* webmaster@artic.edu *Web Site:* www.artic. edu, pg 24

Mindlin, Ivy, The Ivy League of Artists Inc, 10 E 39 St, 7th fl, New York, NY 10016 *Tel:* 212-545-7766 *Fax:* 212-545-9437 *E-mail:* ilartists@aol.com, pg 666

Mineault, Joanne, Albert B Corey Prize, 395 Wellington St, Ottawa, ON K1A 0N3, Canada *Tel:* 613-233-7885 *Fax:* 613-567-3110 *E-mail:* cha-shc@archives.ca *Web Site:* www.theaha.org/prizes, pg 768

Mineault, Joanne, Francois-Xavier Garneau Medal, 395 Wellington St, Ottawa, ON K1A 0N3, Canada *Tel:* 613-233-7885 *Fax:* 613-567-3110 *E-mail:* cha-shc@archives.ca *Web Site:* www.cha-shc.ca, pg 775

Mineault, Joanne, Sir John A MacDonald Prize, 395 Wellington St, Ottawa, ON K1A 0N3, Canada *Tel:* 613-233-7885 *Fax:* 613-567-3110 *E-mail:* cha-shc@archives.ca *Web Site:* www.cha-shc.ca, pg 787

Miner, Sydny, Simon & Schuster, 1230 Avenue of the Americas, New York, NY 10020 *Tel:* 212-698-7000 *Toll Free Tel:* 800-223-2348 (cust serv); 800-223-2336 (orders) *Toll Free Fax:* 800-943-9831 (orders) *Web Site:* www.simonsays.com, pg 248

Minkkinen, Sandra, The MIT Press, 5 Cambridge Ctr, Cambridge, MA 02142 *Tel:* 617-253-5646 *Toll Free Tel:* 800-405-1619 (orders only) *Fax:* 617-258-6779 *Web Site:* mitpress.mit.edu, pg 175

Minnerly, Lee, Baha'i Publishing Trust, 415 Linden Ave, Wilmette, IL 60091 *Tel:* 847-425-7950 *Fax:* 847-425-7951 *E-mail:* bpt@usbnc.org, pg 30

Minor, David, Federal Buyers Guide Inc, 718-B State St, Santa Barbara, CA 93101 *Tel:* 805-963-7470 *Fax:* 805-963-7478 *Web Site:* www.gov-world.com, pg 95

Mint, Morton, Mint Publishers Group, 62 June Rd, North Salem, NY 10560 *Tel:* 914-276-6576 *Fax:* 914-276-6579 *E-mail:* info@mintpub.com *Web Site:* www. mintpub.com, pg 175

Mintz, Carol, Newspaper Advertising Sales Association, 411 W Fifth St, Los Angeles, CA 90013, pg 695

Mintz, Jack, C D Howe Institute, 125 Adelaide St E, Toronto, ON M5C 1L7, Canada *Tel:* 416-865-1904 *Fax:* 416-865-1866 *E-mail:* cdhowe@cdhowe.org *Web Site:* www.cdhowe.org, pg 550

Mintz, Laurence, Transaction Publishers, Rutgers University, 35 Berrue Circle, Piscataway, NJ 08854 *Tel:* 732-445-2280 *Toll Free Tel:* 888-999-6778 *Fax:* 732-445-3138 *E-mail:* trans@transactionpub.com *Web Site:* www.transactionpub.com, pg 274

Minz, James, Tom Doherty Associates, LLC, 175 Fifth Ave, 14th fl, New York, NY 10010 *Tel:* 212-388-0100 *Toll Free Tel:* 800-455-0340 *Fax:* 212-388-0191 *E-mail:* firstname.lastname@tor.com *Web Site:* www. tor.com, pg 82

Miracle, Tracy, Cooper Square Press, 5360 Manhattan Circle, Suite 101, Boulder, CO 80303 *Tel:* 303-543-7835 *Fax:* 303-543-0043 *E-mail:* tradeeditorial@ rowman.com *Web Site:* www.coopersquarepress.com, pg 68

Miranda, Bob, Cognizant Communication Corp, 3 Hartsdale Rd, Elmsford, NY 10523-3701 *Tel:* 914-592-7720 *Fax:* 914-592-8981 *E-mail:* cogcomm@aol. com *Web Site:* www.cognizantcommunication.com, pg 64

Mirensky, Gabriela, AIGA 50 Books/50 Covers, 164 Fifth Ave, New York, NY 10010 *Tel:* 212-807-1990 *Toll Free Tel:* 800-548-1634 *Fax:* 212-807-1799 *E-mail:* competitions@aiga.org *Web Site:* www.aiga. org, pg 758

Mirkin, Cheryl, Markus Wiener Publishers Inc, 231 Nassau St, Princeton, NJ 08542 *Tel:* 609-921-1141; 609-921-7686 (orders) *Fax:* 609-921-1140; 609-279-0657 (orders) *E-mail:* publisher@markuswiener. com; orders@markuswiener.com *Web Site:* www. markuswiener.com, pg 299

Misher, Randi, Chelsea House Publishers LLC, 2080 Cabot Blvd W, Suite 201, Langhorne, PA 19047-1813 *Tel:* 610-353-5166 *Toll Free Tel:* 800-848-BOOK (848-2665) *Fax:* 610-359-1439 *Toll Free Fax:* 877-780-7300 *E-mail:* sales@chelseahouse.com *Web Site:* www.chelseahouse.com, pg 59

Miskin, Lucy, Copley Publishing Group, 138 Great Rd, Acton, MA 01720 *Tel:* 978-263-9090 *Toll Free Tel:* 800-562-2147 *Fax:* 978-263-9190 *E-mail:* publish@copleycustom.com; textbook@ copleypublishing.com *Web Site:* www.copleycustom. com; www.copleypublishing.com; www.copleyeditions. com, pg 68

Miskin, Michael J, Tapestry Press Ltd, 19 Nashoba Rd, Littleton, MA 01460 *Tel:* 978-486-0200 *Toll Free Tel:* 800-535-2007 *Fax:* 978-486-0244 *E-mail:* publish@tapestrypress.com *Web Site:* www. tapestrypress.com, pg 264

Miskowiec, Jay, Aliform Publishing, 117 Warwick St SE, Minneapolis, MN 55414 *Tel:* 612-379-7639 *Fax:* 612-379-7639 *E-mail:* information@ aliformgroup.com *Web Site:* www.aliformgroup.com, pg 569

Mitchell, Barbara J, Mitchell Lane Publishers Inc, 1104 Kelly Dr, Newark, DE 19711 *Tel:* 302-234-9426 *Toll Free Tel:* 800-814-5484 *Fax:* 302-234-4742 *Toll Free Fax:* 866-834-4164 *E-mail:* mitchelllane@mitchelllane. com *Web Site:* www.mitchelllane.com, pg 176

Mitchell, Betsy, Random House Publishing Group, 1745 Broadway, New York, NY 10019 *Toll Free Tel:* 800-200-3552 *Toll Free Fax:* 800-200-3552 *Web Site:* www.randomhouse.com, pg 227

Mitchell, Brian, Tommy Nelson, PO Box 141000, Nashville, TN 37214-1000 *Tel:* 615-889-9000 *Toll Free Tel:* 800-251-4000 *Fax:* 615-902-3330 *Web Site:* www.tommynelson.com, pg 272

Mitchell, Carine, Cambridge University Press, 40 W 20 St, New York, NY 10011-4211 *Tel:* 212-924-3900 *Toll Free Tel:* 800-899-5222 *Fax:* 212-691-3239 *Web Site:* www.cambridge.org, pg 52

Mitchell, Carmen, Justin, Charles & Co, Publishers, 20 Park Plaza, Suite 909, Boston, MA 02116 *Tel:* 617-426-4406 *Fax:* 617-426-4408 *E-mail:* info@ justincharlesbooks.com *Web Site:* www. justincharlesbooks.com, pg 143

Mitchell, Catherine, Tundra Books, 481 University Ave, Suite 900, Toronto, ON M5G 2E9, Canada *Tel:* 416-598-4786 *Fax:* 416-598-0247 *E-mail:* tundra@ mcclelland.com *Web Site:* www.tundrabooks.com, pg 564

Mitchell, Catherine, Tundra Books of Northern New York, PO Box 1030, Plattsburgh, NY 12901 *Tel:* 416-598-4786 *Fax:* 416-598-0247 *E-mail:* tundra@ mcclelland.com *Web Site:* www.tundrabooks.com, pg 276

Mitchell, Cynthia, Hampton Roads Publishing Co Inc, 1125 Stoney Ridge Rd, Charlottesville, VA 22902 *Tel:* 434-296-2772 *Toll Free Tel:* 800-766-8009 (orders) *Fax:* 434-296-5096 *Toll Free Fax:* 800-766-9042 *E-mail:* hrpc@hrpub.com *Web Site:* www.hrpub. com, pg 113

Mitchell, David, The Guilford Press, 72 Spring St, New York, NY 10012 *Tel:* 212-431-9800 *Toll Free Tel:* 800-365-7006 (orders) *Fax:* 212-966-6708 *E-mail:* orders@guilford.com *Web Site:* www.guilford. com, pg 111

Mitchell, Douglas C, Association of American University Presses, 1427 E 60 St, Chicago, IL 60637 *Tel:* 773-702-7700; 773-702-7600 *Toll Free Tel:* 800-621-2736 (orders) *Fax:* 773-702-9756 (sales); 773-660-2235 (orders); 773-702-2708 *E-mail:* general@press. uchicago.edu *Web Site:* www.press.uchicago.edu, pg 26

Mitchell, Elizabeth, Del Rey Books, 1745 Broadway, New York, NY 10019 *E-mail:* delrey@randomhouse. com *Web Site:* www.randomhouse.com, pg 78

Mitchell, Francis, New World Publishing, PO Box 36075, Halifax, NS B3J 3S9, Canada *Toll Free Tel:* 877-211-3334 *Fax:* 902-576-2095 *E-mail:* nwp1@ eastlink.ca *Web Site:* www.newworldpublishing.com, pg 556

Mitchell, Gwendolyn, Third World Press, 7822 S Dobson Ave, Chicago, IL 60619 *Tel:* 773-651-0700 *Fax:* 773-651-7286 *E-mail:* twpress3@aol.com *Web Site:* www. thirdworldpressinc.com, pg 269

Mitchell, Hal, Golden West Publishers, 4113 N Longview, Phoenix, AZ 85014 *Tel:* 602-265-4392 *Toll Free Tel:* 800-658-5830 *Fax:* 602-279-6901 *Web Site:* www.goldenwestpublishers.com, pg 106

Mitchell, Hellan, Michelin Travel Publications, PO Box 19001, Greenville, SC 29602-9001 *Tel:* 864-458-5127 *Toll Free Tel:* 800-423-0485; 800-223-0987 *Fax:* 864-458-6674 *Toll Free Fax:* 866-297-0914 *E-mail:* michelin.travel-publications-us@us.michelin. com *Web Site:* www.viamichelin.com, pg 173

Mitchell, Jack, The Drummond Publishing Group, 362 N Bedford St, East Bridgewater, MA 02333 *Tel:* 508-378-1110 *Fax:* 508-378-1105 *Web Site:* www. drummondpub.com, pg 84

Mitchell, Jack, Pre-Press Company Inc, 362 N Bedford St, East Bridgewater, MA 02333 *Tel:* 508-378-1100 (plant); 508-378-1101 (sales) *Fax:* 508-378-1105 *Web Site:* www.prepressco.com, pg 608

Mitchell, Jack, Royalton Press, 362 N Bedford St, East Bridgewater, MA 02333 *Tel:* 508-378-1110 *Fax:* 508-378-1105 *Web Site:* www.drummondpub.com, pg 235

Mitchell, Jason, Quirk Books, 215 Church St, Philadelphia, PA 19106 *Tel:* 215-627-3581 *Fax:* 215-627-5220 *E-mail:* general@quirkbooks.com *Web Site:* www.quirkbooks.com, pg 224

Mitchell, JoAnn, Oceana Publications Inc, 75 Main St, Dobbs Ferry, NY 10522-1601 *Tel:* 914-693-8100 *Toll Free Tel:* 800-831-0758 (orders only) *Fax:* 914-693-0402 *E-mail:* info@oceanalaw.com *Web Site:* www. oceanalaw.com, pg 195

Mitchell, Karen, A & B Publishers Group, 223 Duffield St, Brooklyn, NY 11201 *Tel:* 718-783-7808 *Fax:* 718-783-7267 *Web Site:* anbdonline.com, pg 1

Mitchell, Mary, Scholastic Education, 524 Broadway, New York, NY 10012 *Tel:* 212-343-6100 *Fax:* 212-343-6189 *Web Site:* www.scholastic.com, pg 241

Mitchell, Melanie, MacAdam/Cage Publishing Inc, 155 Sansome St, Suite 550, San Francisco, CA 94104 *Tel:* 415-986-7502 *Toll Free Tel:* 866-986-7470 *Fax:* 415-986-7414 *E-mail:* info@macadamcage.com *Web Site:* www.macadamcage.com, pg 161

Mitchell, Michaelyn, American Federation of Arts, 41 E 65 St, New York, NY 10021 *Tel:* 212-988-7700 *Toll Free Tel:* 800-232-0270 *Fax:* 212-861-2487 *E-mail:* publicat@afaweb.org *Web Site:* www.afaweb.org, pg 13

Mitchell, Mike, Thomas Nelson Inc, 501 Nelson Place, Nashville, TN 37214 *Tel:* 615-889-9000 *Toll Free Tel:* 800-251-4000 *Fax:* 615-902-1610 *E-mail:* publicity@thomasnelson.com *Web Site:* www.thomasnelson.com, pg 269

Mitchell, Nicole, University of Georgia Press, 330 Research Dr, Athens, GA 30602-4901 *Tel:* 706-369-6130 *Toll Free Tel:* 800-266-5842 (orders only) *Fax:* 706-369-6131 *E-mail:* books@ugapress.uga.edu *Web Site:* www.ugapress.org, pg 281

Mitchell, Patricia, The Pennsylvania State University Press, 820 N University Dr, University Support Bldg 1, Suite C, University Park, PA 16802-1003 *Tel:* 814-865-1327 *Toll Free Tel:* 800-326-9180 *Fax:* 814-863-1408 *Toll Free Fax:* 877 7782665 *Web Site:* www.psupress.org, pg 209

Mitchell, Robert P, Mitchell Lane Publishers Inc, 1104 Kelly Dr, Newark, DE 19711 *Tel:* 302-234-9426 *Toll Free Tel:* 800-814-5484 *Fax:* 302-234-4742 *Toll Free Fax:* 866-834-4164 *E-mail:* mitchelllane@mitchelllane.com *Web Site:* www.mitchelllane.com, pg 176

Mitchell, Rosemary, Standard Publishing Co, 8121 Hamilton Ave, Cincinnati, OH 45231 *Tel:* 513-931-4050 *Toll Free Tel:* 800-543-1301 *Fax:* 513-931-0950 *Toll Free Fax:* 877-867-5751 *E-mail:* customerservice@standardpub.com *Web Site:* www.standardpub.com, pg 257

Mitchell, Steve, Sopris West Educational Services, 4093 Specialty Place, Longmont, CO 80504 *Tel:* 303-651-2829 *Toll Free Tel:* 800-547-6747 *Fax:* 303-776-5934 *E-mail:* customerservice@sopriswest.com *Web Site:* www.sopriswest.com, pg 253

Mitchell, Steven L, Prometheus Books, 59 John Glenn Dr, Amherst, NY 14228 *Tel:* 716-691-0133 *Toll Free Tel:* 800-421-0351 *Fax:* 716-691-0137 *E-mail:* marketing@prometheusbooks.com; editorial@prometheusbooks.com *Web Site:* www.Prometheusbooks.com, pg 220

Mitchell, Susan, Farrar, Straus & Giroux, LLC, 19 Union Sq W, New York, NY 10003 *Tel:* 212-741-6900 *Fax:* 212-741-6973 *Web Site:* www.fsgbooks.com, pg 95

Mitchem, Gary, McFarland & Co Inc Publishers, 960 Hwy 88 W, Jefferson, NC 28640 *Tel:* 336-246-4460 *Toll Free Tel:* 800-253-2187 (orders only) *Fax:* 336-246-5018; 336-246-4403 (orders) *E-mail:* info@mcfarlandpub.com *Web Site:* www.mcfarlandpub.com, pg 166

Mitchner, Leslie, Rutgers University Press, 100 Joyce Kilmer Ave, Piscataway, NJ 08854-8099 *Tel:* 732-445-7762 (edit); 732-445-7762 (ext 627, sales) *Toll Free Tel:* 800-446-9323 (orders only) *Fax:* 732-445-7039 (acqs, edit, mktg, perms, prodn); 732-445-1974 (fulfillment) *E-mail:* garyf@rci.rutgers.edu *Web Site:* rutgerspress.rutgers.edu, pg 236

Mitoulis, Caliann, Media & Methods, 1429 Walnut St, 10th fl, Philadelphia, PA 19102 *Tel:* 215-563-6005 *Toll Free Tel:* 800-555-5657 *Fax:* 215-587-9706 *Web Site:* www.media-methods.com, pg 170

Mlawer, Teresa, Lectorum Publications Inc, 524 Broadway, New York, NY 10012 *Toll Free Tel:* 800-853-3291 (admin, mktg & sales); 800-345-5946 (orders) *Fax:* 212-727-3035 *Toll Free Fax:* 877-532-8676 *E-mail:* lectorum@scholastic.com *Web Site:* www.lectorum.com, pg 151

Mlazgar, Brian, Canadian Plains Research Center, University of Regina, Regina, SK S4S 0A2, Canada *Tel:* 306-585-4758; 306-585-4759 *Fax:* 306-585-4699 *Web Site:* www.cprc.uregina.ca, pg 539

Mobley, Lee, Ohio State University Press, 180 Pressey Hall, 1070 Carmack Rd, Columbus, OH 43210-1002 *Tel:* 614-292-6930 *Toll Free Tel:* 614-292-2065 *Toll Free Fax:* 800-621-8476 *E-mail:* ohiostatepress@osu.edu *Web Site:* ohiostatepress.org, pg 196

Moburg, Janelle, Doubleday Broadway Publishing Group, 1745 Broadway, New York, NY 10019 *Tel:* 212-782-9000 *Toll Free Tel:* 800-223-6834; 800-223-5780 (sales) *Fax:* 212-302-7985 (correspondence); 212-492-9862 (orders), pg 82

Modrak, Nancy, Association for Supervision & Curriculum Development (ASCD), 1703 N Beaureguard St, Alexandria, VA 22311-1453 *Tel:* 703-578-9600 *Toll Free Tel:* 800-933-2723 *Fax:* 703-575-5400 *E-mail:* member@ascd.org *Web Site:* www.ascd.org, pg 26

Moen, Jeff, University of Minnesota Press, 111 Third Ave S, Suite 290, Minneapolis, MN 55401-2520 *Tel:* 612-627-1970 *Fax:* 612-627-1980 *E-mail:* ump@tc.umn.edu *Web Site:* www.upress.umn.edu, pg 282

Moffat, Virginia, McGraw-Hill Higher Education, 1333 Burr Ridge Pkwy, Burr Ridge, IL 60527 *Tel:* 630-789-4000 *Toll Free Tel:* 800-338-3987 (cust serv) *Fax:* 614-755-5645 (cust serv) *Web Site:* www.mhhe.com, pg 167

Moffat, Virginia, McGraw-Hill Primis Custom Publishing, 2460 Kerper Blvd, Dubuque, IA 52001 *Tel:* 563-588-1451 *Fax:* 563-589-4700 *E-mail:* first_last@mcgraw-hill.com *Web Site:* www.mhhe.com, pg 168

Moggy, Dianne, Worldwide Library, 225 Duncan Mill Rd, Don Mills, ON M3B 3K9, Canada *Tel:* 416-445-5860 *Fax:* 416-445-8655; 416-445-8736 *Web Site:* www.eharlequin.com, pg 567

Moghari, Francesca, National Academies Press, 500 Fifth St NW, Washington, DC 20001 *Tel:* 202-334-3313 *Toll Free Tel:* 800-624-6242 *Fax:* 202-334-2451 (orders) *Web Site:* www.nap.edu, pg 182

Mohammed, Feroze, Gold Eagle, 225 Duncan Mill Rd, Don Mills, ON M3B 3K9, Canada *Tel:* 416-445-5860 *Fax:* 416-445-8655; 416-445-8736, pg 548

Mohammed, Feroze, Worldwide Library, 225 Duncan Mill Rd, Don Mills, ON M3B 3K9, Canada *Tel:* 416-445-5860 *Fax:* 416-445-8655; 416-445-8736 *Web Site:* www.eharlequin.com, pg 567

Mohan, Ann L, WordCrafters Editorial Services Inc, 22636 Glenn Dr, Suite 106, Sterling, VA 20164 *Tel:* 703-471-0160 *Fax:* 703-471-0693 *E-mail:* editors@wordcrafterseditorial.com, pg 614

Mohr, Dana, Manitoba Arts Council, 525-93 Lombard Ave, Winnipeg, MB R3B 3B1, Canada *Tel:* 204-945-2237 *Toll Free Tel:* 866-994-2787 (in Manitoba) *Fax:* 204-945-5925 *E-mail:* info@artscouncil.mb.ca *Web Site:* www.artscouncil.mb.ca, pg 690

Mohyde, Colleen, The Doe Coover Agency, PO Box 668, Winchester, MA 01890 *Tel:* 781-721-6000 *Fax:* 781-721-6727, pg 626

Mokotoff, Gary, Avotaynu Inc, 155 N Washington Ave, Bergenfield, NJ 07621 *Tel:* 201-387-7200 *Toll Free Tel:* 800-286-8296 *Fax:* 201-387-2855 *E-mail:* info@avotaynu.com *Web Site:* www.avotaynu.com, pg 29

Moldow, Susan, Scribner, 1230 Avenue of the Americas, New York, NY 10020, pg 244

Mole, Alan, American Literacy Council, 148 W 117 St, New York, NY 10026 *Tel:* 212-663-4200 *Toll Free Tel:* 800-781-9985 *E-mail:* fyi@americanliteracy.com *Web Site:* www.americanliteracy.com, pg 677

Molendyk, Sophia, Hospital & Healthcare Compensation Service, PO Box 376, Oakland, NJ 07436 *Tel:* 201-405-0075 *Fax:* 201-405-2110 *E-mail:* allinfo@hhcsinc.com *Web Site:* www.hhcsinc.com, pg 126

Molho, Deborah, French & European Publications Inc, Rockefeller Center Promenade, 610 Fifth Ave, New York, NY 10020-2497 *Tel:* 212-581-8810 *Fax:* 212-265-1094 *E-mail:* livresny@aol.com *Web Site:* www.frencheuropean.com, pg 101

Molho, Emanuel, French & European Publications Inc, Rockefeller Center Promenade, 610 Fifth Ave, New York, NY 10020-2497 *Tel:* 212-581-8810 *Fax:* 212-265-1094 *E-mail:* livresny@aol.com *Web Site:* www.frencheuropean.com, pg 101

Molina, Deirdre, Knopf Canada, One Toronto St, Suite 300, Toronto, ON M5C 2V6, Canada *Tel:* 416-364-4449 *Toll Free Tel:* 800-668-4247 (order desk) *Fax:* 416-364-0462 *Web Site:* www.randomhouse.ca, pg 552

Molinaro, J A, Canadian Speakers & Writers' Service Ltd, 44 Douglas Crescent, Toronto, ON M4W 2E7, Canada *Tel:* 416-921-4443 *Fax:* 416-922-9691 *E-mail:* pmmj@idirect.com, pg 624

Molinaro, Matie, Canadian Speakers & Writers' Service Ltd, 44 Douglas Crescent, Toronto, ON M4W 2E7, Canada *Tel:* 416-921-4443 *Fax:* 416-922-9691 *E-mail:* pmmj@idirect.com, pg 624

Molinaro, Paul, Canadian Speakers & Writers' Service Ltd, 44 Douglas Crescent, Toronto, ON M4W 2E7, Canada *Tel:* 416-921-4443 *Fax:* 416-922-9691 *E-mail:* pmmj@idirect.com, pg 624

Moll, Kay, Standard Publishing Co, 8121 Hamilton Ave, Cincinnati, OH 45231 *Tel:* 513-931-4050 *Toll Free Tel:* 800-543-1301 *Fax:* 513-931-0950 *Toll Free Fax:* 877-867-5751 *E-mail:* customerservice@standardpub.com *Web Site:* www.standardpub.com, pg 257

Moller, Marilyn, W W Norton & Company Inc, 500 Fifth Ave, New York, NY 10110-0017 *Tel:* 212-354-5500 *Toll Free Tel:* 800-233-4830 (orders & cust serv) *Fax:* 212-869-0856 *Toll Free Fax:* 800-458-6515 *Web Site:* www.wwnorton.com, pg 193

Molstad, Dorothy, Voyageur Press, 123 N Second St, Stillwater, MN 55082 *Tel:* 651-430-2210 *Toll Free Tel:* 800-888-9653 *Fax:* 651-430-2211 *E-mail:* books@voyageurpress.com *Web Site:* www.voyageurpress.com, pg 292

Molter, Gene, Adams Media, An F+W Publications Co, 57 Littlefield St, 2nd fl, Avon, MA 02322 *Tel:* 508-427-7100 *Fax:* 508-427-6790 *Toll Free Tel:* 800-872-5628 *E-mail:* authors@adamsmedia.com; orders@adamsmedia.com *Web Site:* www.adamsmedia.com, pg 5

Monacelli, Gianfranco, The Monacelli Press, 902 Broadway, 18th fl, New York, NY 10010 *Tel:* 212-777-0504 *Toll Free Tel:* 800-631-8571 (cust serv) *Fax:* 212-777-0514; 201-256-0000 (cust serv) *E-mail:* info@monacellipress.com; production@monacellipress.com; customerservice@penguinputnam.com *Web Site:* www.monacellipress.com, pg 177

Monaco, Lauren, Random House Sales & Marketing, 1745 Broadway, New York, NY 10019 *Fax:* 212-782-9000, pg 227

Monaco, Richard, The Adele Leone Agency Inc, 26 Nantucket Place, Scarsdale, NY 10583 *Fax:* 212-866-0754, pg 640

Monaghan, Katherine, Picador, 175 Fifth Ave, New York, NY 10010 *Tel:* 212-674-5151 *Fax:* 212-253-9627 *E-mail:* firstname.lastname@picadorusa.com *Web Site:* www.picadorusa.com, pg 212

Monaghan, Kelly, The Intrepid Traveler, 371 Walden Green Rd, Branford, CT 06405 *Tel:* 203-488-5341 *Fax:* 203-488-7677 *E-mail:* info@intrepidtraveler.com *Web Site:* www.intrepidtraveler.com, pg 139

Monagle, Ed, Scholastic Trade Division, 557 Broadway, New York, NY 10012 *Tel:* 212-343-6100; 212-343-4685 (export sales) *Fax:* 212-343-4714 (export sales) *Web Site:* www.scholastic.com, pg 242

Monahan, Patrick, CCAB Inc, 90 Eglinton Ave E, Suite 980, Toronto, ON M4P 2Y3, Canada *Tel:* 416-487-2418 *Fax:* 416-487-6405 *E-mail:* info@bpai.com *Web Site:* www.bpai.com, pg 684

Moore, Sam, Thomas Nelson Inc, 501 Nelson Place, Nashville, TN 37214 *Tel:* 615-889-9000 *Toll Free Tel:* 800-251-4000 *Fax:* 615-902-1610 *E-mail:* publicity@thomasnelson.com *Web Site:* www.thomasnelson.com, pg 269

Moore, Sam, Tommy Nelson, PO Box 141000, Nashville, TN 37214-1000 *Tel:* 615-889-9000 *Toll Free Tel:* 800-251-4000 *Fax:* 615-902-3330 *Web Site:* www.tommynelson.com, pg 272

Moore, Sandy, Simon & Schuster Audio, 1230 Avenue of the Americas, New York, NY 10020 *Tel:* 212-698-7664 *E-mail:* audiopub@simonandschuster.com *Web Site:* www.simonsaysaudio.com, pg 248

Moore, Stephen, Paul Kohner Agency, 9300 Wilshire Blvd, Suite 555, Beverly Hills, CA 90212 *Tel:* 310-550-1060 *Fax:* 310-276-1083, pg 638

Moore, Sylvia, Midmarch Arts Press, 300 Riverside Dr, New York, NY 10025-5239 *Tel:* 212-666-6990, pg 174

Moore, Thomas M, Milliken Publishing Co, 11643 Lilburn Park Dr, St Louis, MO 63146 *Tel:* 314-991-4220 *Toll Free Tel:* 800-325-4136 *Fax:* 314-991-4807 *Toll Free Fax:* 800-538-1319 *E-mail:* mpwebmaster@millikenpub.com *Web Site:* www.millikenpub.com, pg 175

Moore, Tim, Financial Times/Prentice Hall, One Lake St, Upper Saddle River, NJ 07458 *Tel:* 201-236-7000 *Toll Free Tel:* 800-922-0579 (orders) *Web Site:* www.phptr.com, pg 96

Moore, W Henson, American Forest & Paper Association, 1111 19 St NW, Suite 800, Washington, DC 20036 *Tel:* 202-463-2700 *Toll Free Tel:* 800-878-8878 *Fax:* 202-463-4703 *E-mail:* info@afandpa.org *Web Site:* www.afandpa.org, pg 676

Moorehead, Harold, Stanford University Press, 1450 Page Mill Rd, Palo Alto, CA 94304-1124 *Tel:* 650-723-9434 *Fax:* 650-725-3457 *Web Site:* www.sup.org, pg 257

Moorhouse, Jennifer, Association of American University Presses, 1427 E 60 St, Chicago, IL 60637 *Tel:* 773-702-7700; 773-702-7600 *Toll Free Tel:* 800-621-2736 (orders) *Fax:* 773-702-9756 (sales); 773-660-2235 (orders); 773-702-2708 *E-mail:* general@press.uchicago.edu *Web Site:* www.press.uchicago.edu, pg 26

Mooser, Steve, The Don Freeman Memorial Grant-In-Aid, 8271 Beverly Blvd, Los Angeles, CA 90048 *Tel:* 323-782-1010 *Fax:* 323-782-1892 *E-mail:* membership@scbwi.org *Web Site:* www.scbwi.org, pg 775

Mooser, Steve, Golden Kite Awards, 8271 Beverly Blvd, Los Angeles, CA 90048 *Tel:* 323-782-1010 *Fax:* 323-782-1892 *E-mail:* scbwi@scbwi.org *Web Site:* www.scbwi.org, pg 776

Mooser, Steve, Magazine Merit Awards, 8271 Beverly Blvd, Los Angeles, CA 90048 *Tel:* 323-782-1010 *Fax:* 323-782-1892 *E-mail:* membership@scbwi.org *Web Site:* www.scbwi.org, pg 787

Mooser, Steve, SCBWI Work-In-Progress Grants, 8271 Beverly Blvd, Los Angeles, CA 90048 *Tel:* 323-782-1010 *Fax:* 323-782-1892 *E-mail:* membership@scbwi.org *Web Site:* www.scbwi.org, pg 804

Mooser, Steve, Society of Children's Book Writers & Illustrators (SCBWI), 8271 Beverly Blvd, Los Angeles, CA 90048 *Tel:* 323-782-1010 *Fax:* 323-782-1892 *E-mail:* membership@scbwi.org *Web Site:* www.scbwi.org, pg 700

Mopsik, Eugene, American Society of Media Photographers (ASMP), 150 N Second St, Philadelphia, PA 19106 *Tel:* 215-451-2767 *Fax:* 215-451-0880 *E-mail:* info@asmp.org *Web Site:* www.asmp.org, pg 678

Morales, Lisa, Holiday House Inc, 425 Madison Ave, New York, NY 10017 *Tel:* 212-688-0085 *Fax:* 212-421-6134, pg 123

Morales, Rocio, Wanderlust Publications, 2009 S Tenth St, McAllen, TX 78503-5405 *Tel:* 956-686-3601 *Fax:* 956-686-0732 *E-mail:* info@sanbornsinsurance.com *Web Site:* www.sanbornsinsurance.com, pg 292

Moran, Amanda, Stanford University Press, 1450 Page Mill Rd, Palo Alto, CA 94304-1124 *Tel:* 650-723-9434 *Fax:* 650-725-3457 *Web Site:* www.sup.org, pg 257

Moran, Kevin, The Continuum International Publishing Group, 15 E 26 St, Suite 1703, New York, NY 10010 *Tel:* 212-953-5858 *Toll Free Tel:* 800-561-7704 *Fax:* 212-953-5944 *E-mail:* info@continuum-books.com *Web Site:* www.continuumbooks.com, pg 67

Moran, Kevin J, Hatherleigh Press, 5-22 46 Ave, Suite 200, Long Island City, NY 11101 *Tel:* 718-786-5338 *Toll Free Tel:* 800-528-2550 *Fax:* 718-706-6087 *E-mail:* info@hatherleigh.com *Web Site:* www.getfitnow.com; www.hatherleighpress.com, pg 118

Moran, Kris, Scholastic Trade Division, 557 Broadway, New York, NY 10012 *Tel:* 212-343-6100; 212-343-4685 (export sales) *Fax:* 212-343-4714 (export sales) *Web Site:* www.scholastic.com, pg 242

Moran, Martha, Hudson Park Press, Johnny Cake Hollow Rd, Pine Plains, NY 12567 *Tel:* 212-929-8898 *Fax:* 212-242-6137 *E-mail:* hudpark@aol.com *Web Site:* www.hudsonpark.com, pg 128

Moran, Maureen, Maureen Moran Agency, PO Box 20191, Park West Sta, New York, NY 10025-1518 *Tel:* 212-222-3838 *Fax:* 212-531-3464 *E-mail:* maureenm@erols.com, pg 644

Moran, Pat, Stackpole Books, 5067 Ritter Rd, Mechanicsburg, PA 17055 *Tel:* 717-796-0411 *Toll Free Tel:* 800-732-3669 *Fax:* 717-796-0412 *Web Site:* www.stackpolebooks.com, pg 257

Moran, Patrick R, Pro Lingua Associates Inc, 74 Cotton Mill Hill, Suite A-315, Brattleboro, VT 05301 *Tel:* 802-257-7779 *Toll Free Tel:* 800-366-4775 *Fax:* 802-257-5117 *E-mail:* orders@prolinguaassociates.com *Web Site:* www.prolinguaassociates.com, pg 219

Morehouse, Jim, Paradise Cay Publications Inc, 550 S "G" St, No 12, Arcata, CA 95521 *Tel:* 707-822-9063 *Toll Free Tel:* 800-736-4509 *Fax:* 707-822-9163 *E-mail:* paracay@humboldt1.com *Web Site:* www.paracay.com, pg 203

Morehouse, Matt, Paradise Cay Publications Inc, 550 S "G" St, No 12, Arcata, CA 95521 *Tel:* 707-822-9063 *Toll Free Tel:* 800-736-4509 *Fax:* 707-822-9163 *E-mail:* paracay@humboldt1.com *Web Site:* www.paracay.com, pg 203

Morehouse, Ward, The Apex Press, 777 United Nations Plaza, Suite 3-C, New York, NY 10017 *Tel:* 914-271-6500 *Toll Free Tel:* 800-316-2739 *Fax:* 914-271-6500 *Toll Free Tel:* 800-316-2739 *E-mail:* cipany@igc.org *Web Site:* www.cipa-apex.org, pg 21

Morel, Madeleine, 2M Communications Ltd, 121 W 27 St, Suite 601, New York, NY 10001 *Tel:* 212-741-1509 *Fax:* 212-691-4460 *Web Site:* www.2mcommunications.com, pg 659

Moreno, Fred, New York Academy of Sciences, 2 E 63 St, New York, NY 10021 *Tel:* 212-838-0230 *Toll Free Tel:* 800-843-6927 *Fax:* 212-888-2894 *E-mail:* publications@nyas.org *Web Site:* www.nyas.org, pg 189

Morgan, Alison, Tundra Books, 481 University Ave, Suite 900, Toronto, ON M5G 2E9, Canada *Tel:* 416-598-4786 *Fax:* 416-598-0247 *E-mail:* tundra@mcclelland.com *Web Site:* www.tundrabooks.com, pg 564

Morgan, Alison, Tundra Books of Northern New York, PO Box 1030, Plattsburgh, NY 12901 *Tel:* 416-598-4786 *Fax:* 416-598-0247 *E-mail:* tundra@mcclelland.com *Web Site:* www.tundrabooks.com, pg 276

Morgan, Carol, Harry N Abrams Inc, 100 Fifth Ave, New York, NY 10011 *Tel:* 212-206-7715 *Toll Free Tel:* 800-345-1359 *Fax:* 212-645-8437 *E-mail:* webmaster@abramsbooks.com *Web Site:* www.abramsbooks.com, pg 3

Morgan, Jeremy, Saskatchewan Arts Board, 2135 Broad St, Regina, SK S4P 3V7, Canada *Tel:* 306-787-4056 *Toll Free Tel:* 800-667-7526 (Saskatchewan only) *Fax:* 306-787-4199 *E-mail:* sab@artsboard.sk.ca *Web Site:* www.artsboard.sk.ca, pg 699

Morgan, Jill, Purple House Press, 8138 US Hwy 62 E, Cynthiana, KY 41031 *Tel:* 859-235-9970 *Fax:* 859-235-9970 *E-mail:* phpress@earthlink.net *Web Site:* www.purplehousepress.com, pg 222

Morgan, Kathleen, Morgan Quinto Corp, PO Box 1656, Lawrence, KS 66044-8656 *Tel:* 785-841-3534 *Toll Free Tel:* 800-457-0742 *Fax:* 785-841-3568 *E-mail:* info@morganquinto.com *Web Site:* www.morganquinto.com, pg 178

Morgan, Lael, Epicenter Press Inc, PO Box 82368, Kenmore, WA 98028 *Tel:* 425-485-6822 *Fax:* 425-481-8253 *E-mail:* info@epicenterpress.com *Web Site:* www.epicenterpress.com, pg 91

Morgan, Marisa, Arts Recognition & Talent Search (ARTS), 444 Brickell Ave, Suite P14, Miami, FL 33131 *Tel:* 305-377-1140 *Toll Free Tel:* 800-970-2787 *Fax:* 305-377-1149 *E-mail:* nfaa@nfaa.org *Web Site:* www.artsawards.org, pg 760

Morgan, Melissa, Elm Street Publishing Services Inc, 828 N Elm St, Hinsdale, IL 60521 *Tel:* 630-789-2102 *Fax:* 630-789-2105 *E-mail:* esps@elmst.com *Web Site:* www.elmst.com, pg 598

Morgan, Scott E, Morgan Quinto Corp, PO Box 1656, Lawrence, KS 66044-8656 *Tel:* 785-841-3534 *Toll Free Tel:* 800-457-0742 *Fax:* 785-841-3568 *E-mail:* info@morganquinto.com *Web Site:* www.morganquinto.com, pg 178

Morgan, Vicki, Morgan Gaynin Inc, 194 Third Ave, New York, NY 10003 *Tel:* 212-475-0440 *Fax:* 212-353-8538 *E-mail:* info@morgangaynin.com *Web Site:* www.morgangaynin.com, pg 666

Morgenstein, Leslie, Alloy Entertainment, 151 W 26 St, 11th fl, New York, NY 10001 *Tel:* 212-244-4307, pg 9

Morgenthaler, Lynelle, Harcourt Achieve, 10801 N MoPac Expressway, Austin, TX 78759 *Tel:* 512-343-8227 *Toll Free Tel:* 800-531-5015 *Toll Free Fax:* 800-699-9459 *E-mail:* ecare@harcourt.com *Web Site:* www.harcourtachieve.com, pg 114

Morgenthaler, Lynelle, Rigby, 10801 N MoPac Expressway, Austin, TX 78759 *Tel:* 512-343-8227 *Toll Free Tel:* 800-531-5015 *Toll Free Fax:* 800-699-9459 *E-mail:* ecare@harcourt.com *Web Site:* www.harcourtachieve.com, pg 232

Morgenthaler, Lynelle, Steck-Vaughn, 10801 N MoPac Expressway, Austin, TX 78759 *Tel:* 512-343-8227 *Toll Free Tel:* 800-531-5015 *Toll Free Fax:* 800-699-9459 *E-mail:* ecare@harcourt.com *Web Site:* www.harcourtachieve.com, pg 258

Morhaim, Howard, Howard Morhaim Literary Agency Inc, 11 John St, Suite 407, New York, NY 10038 *Tel:* 212-529-4433 *Fax:* 212-995-1112, pg 644

Moriarty, J P, MacAdam/Cage Publishing Inc, 155 Sansome St, Suite 550, San Francisco, CA 94104 *Tel:* 415-986-7502 *Toll Free Tel:* 866-986-7470 *Fax:* 415-986-7414 *E-mail:* info@macadamcage.com *Web Site:* www.macadamcage.com, pg 161

Morin, Petra, Penguin Group (Canada), 10 Alcorn Ave, Suite 300, Toronto, ON M4V 3B2, Canada *Tel:* 416-925-2249 *Fax:* 416-925-0068 *Web Site:* www.penguin.ca, pg 557

Morin-Spatz, Patrice, MedBooks, 101 W Buckingham Rd, Richardson, TX 75081 *Tel:* 972-643-1802 *Toll Free Tel:* 800-443-7397 *Fax:* 972-994-0215 *E-mail:* medbooks@medbooks.com *Web Site:* www.medbooks.com, pg 170

Morin-Spatz, Trish, MedBooks, 101 W Buckingham Rd, Richardson, TX 75081 *Tel:* 972-643-1802 *Toll Free Tel:* 800-443-7397 *Fax:* 972-994-0215 *E-mail:* medbooks@medbooks.com *Web Site:* www.medbooks.com, pg 170

Morneau, Claude, Ulysses Travel Guides, 4176 Saint Denis, Montreal, PQ H2W 2M5, Canada *Tel:* 514-843-9447 *Fax:* 514-843-9448 *E-mail:* info@ulysses.ca *Web Site:* www.ulyssesguides.com, pg 564

Morreale, Sherry, National Communication Association, 1765 North St NW, Washington, DC 20036 *Tel:* 202-464-4622 *Fax:* 202-464-4600 *Web Site:* www.natcom. org, pg 693

Morrell, Guy J, Bridge-Logos Publishers, 17310 NW 32 Ave, Newberry, FL 32669 *Tel:* 352-472-7900 *Toll Free Tel:* 800-631-5802 *Fax:* 352-472-7908 *Toll Free Fax:* 800-935-6467 *E-mail:* info@bridgelogos.com *Web Site:* www.bridgelogos.com, pg 47

Morris, Aaron, Self-Counsel Press Inc, 1704 N State St, Bellingham, WA 98225 *Tel:* 360-676-4530 *Toll Free Tel:* 877-877-6490 *Fax:* 360-676-4549 *E-mail:* service@self-counsel.com *Web Site:* www.self-counsel.com, pg 245

Morris, Carrington, Parabola Books, 656 Broadway, Suite 615, New York, NY 10012 *Tel:* 212-505-6200 *Toll Free Tel:* 800-560-6984 *Fax:* 212-979-7325 *E-mail:* parabola@panix.com *Web Site:* www.parabola. org, pg 203

Morris, David, Guideposts Book & Inspirational Media Division, 16 E 34 St, New York, NY 10016 *Tel:* 212-251-8100 *Fax:* 212-684-0679 *Web Site:* www. guidepostsbooks.com, pg 111

Morris, Fred, Jed Mattes Inc, 2095 Broadway, Suite 302, New York, NY 10023-2895 *Tel:* 212-595-5228 *Fax:* 212-595-5232 *E-mail:* general@jedmattes.com, pg 643

Morris, Gary, David Black Literary Agency, 156 Fifth Ave, Suite 608, New York, NY 10010 *Tel:* 212-242-5080 *Fax:* 212-924-6609, pg 621

Morris, Jean S, Western Pennsylvania Genealogical Society, 4400 Forbes Ave, Pittsburgh, PA 15213-4080 *Tel:* 412-687-6811 (answering machine) *E-mail:* info@ wpgs.org *Web Site:* www.wpgs.org, pg 296

Morris, Jessica, Gareth Stevens Inc, 330 W Olive St, Suite 100, Milwaukee, WI 53212 *Tel:* 414-332-3520 *Toll Free Tel:* 800-542-2595 *Fax:* 414-332-3567 *E-mail:* info@gspub.com; info@worldalmaniclibrary. com *Web Site:* www.garethstevens.com; www. worldalmaniclibrary.com, pg 102

Morris, Joyce Caughman, Caughman Associates, 1094 New DeHaven St, Suite 100, West Conshohocken, PA 19428-2713 *Tel:* 610-558-3734 *Toll Free Tel:* 877-BUY BOOK *Fax:* 610-558-5001; 610-941-9999, pg 570

Morris, Lisa, Association for Information & Image Management International, 1100 Wayne Ave, Suite 1100, Silver Spring, MD 20910 *Tel:* 301-587-8202 *Toll Free Tel:* 800-477-2446 *Fax:* 240-494-2661 *E-mail:* aiim@aiim.org *Web Site:* www.aiim.org, pg 679

Morris, Mary, Kluwer Academic Publishers, 101 Philip Dr, Assinippi Park, Norwell, MA 02061 *Tel:* 781-871-6600 *Fax:* 781-871-6528; 781-681-9045 (cust serv) *E-mail:* kluwer@wkap.com *Web Site:* www.wkap.nl, pg 146

Morris, Michael, Cornell University Press, 512 E State St, Ithaca, NY 14850 *Tel:* 607-277-2338 *Fax:* 607-277-2374 *E-mail:* cupressinfo@cornell.edu *Web Site:* www.cornellpress.cornell.edu, pg 68

Morris, Paul, Writers' Fellowships, 417 W Roosevelt Ave, Phoenix, AZ 85003 *Tel:* 602-255-5882 *Fax:* 602-256-0282, pg 813

Morris, Raymond A, SAE (Society of Automotive Engineers International), 400 Commonwealth Dr, Warrendale, PA 15096-0001 *Tel:* 724-776-4841 *Toll Free Tel:* 877-606-7323 (cust serv) *Fax:* 724-776-0790 *E-mail:* publications@sae.org *Web Site:* www.sae.org, pg 237

Morris, Richard, Janklow & Nesbit Associates, 445 Park Ave, New York, NY 10022 *Tel:* 212-421-1700 *Fax:* 212-980-3671 *E-mail:* postmaster@janklow.com, pg 636

Morris, Rita, National Conference of State Legislatures, 7700 E First Place, Denver, CO 80230 *Tel:* 303-364-7700 *Fax:* 303-364-7812 *E-mail:* books@ncsl.org *Web Site:* www.ncsl.org, pg 183

Morris-Babb, Meredith, University Press of Florida, 15 NW 15 St, Gainesville, FL 32611-2079 *Tel:* 352-392-1351 *Toll Free Tel:* 800-226-3822 (orders only) *Fax:* 352-392-7302 *Toll Free Fax:* 800-680-1955 (orders only) *E-mail:* info@upf.com *Web Site:* www. upf.com, pg 287

Morrison, Henry, Henry Morrison Inc, PO Box 235, Bedford Hills, NY 10507-0235 *Tel:* 914-666-3500 *Fax:* 914-241-7846, pg 645

Morrison, Michael, HarperCollins General Books Group, 10 E 53 St, New York, NY 10022 *Tel:* 212-207-7000 *Fax:* 212-207-7633, pg 115

Morrison, Paula, Frog Ltd, 1435 Fourth St, Berkeley, CA 94710 *Tel:* 510-559-8277 *Toll Free Tel:* 800-337-2665 (book orders only) *Fax:* 510-559-8279 *E-mail:* orders@northatlanticbooks.com *Web Site:* www.northatlanticbooks.com, pg 101

Morrison, Paula, North Atlantic Books, 1435 Fourth St, Berkeley, CA 94710 *Tel:* 510-559-8277 *Toll Free Tel:* 800-337-2665 (book orders only) *Fax:* 510-559-8279 *E-mail:* orders@northatlanticbooks.com *Web Site:* www.northatlanticbooks.com, pg 192

Morrison, Richard, University of Minnesota Press, 111 Third Ave S, Suite 290, Minneapolis, MN 55401-2520 *Tel:* 612-627-1970 *Fax:* 612-627-1980 *E-mail:* ump@ tc.umn.edu *Web Site:* www.upress.umn.edu, pg 282

Morrison, Rusty, Omnidawn Publishing, 1632 Elm Ave, Richmond, CA 94805-1614 *Tel:* 510-237-5472 *Toll Free Tel:* 800-792-4957 *Fax:* 510-232-8525 *Web Site:* www.omnidawn.com, pg 196

Morrison, Steve, Penguin Books, 375 Hudson St, New York, NY 10014 *Tel:* 212-366-2000 *E-mail:* online@ penguinputnam.com *Web Site:* www.penguin.com; www.penguinclassics.com, pg 207

Morriss, Bentley, Holloway House Publishing Co, 8060 Melrose Ave, Los Angeles, CA 90046-7082 *Tel:* 323-653-8060 *Fax:* 323-655-9452 *E-mail:* info@ hollowayhousebooks.com *Web Site:* www. hollowayhousebooks.com, pg 124

Morriss, Ian, TriQuarterly Books, 2020 Ridge Ave, Evanston, IL 60208-4302 *Tel:* 847-491-3490 *Toll Free Tel:* 800-621-2736 (orders only) *Fax:* 847-467-2096 *E-mail:* nupress@northwestern.edu *Web Site:* www. nupress.northwestern.edu, pg 275

Morrissey, Jake, Riverhead Books (Hardcover), 375 Hudson St, New York, NY 10014 *Tel:* 212-366-2000 *E-mail:* online@penguinputnam.com *Web Site:* www. penguin.com, pg 233

Morrissey, Kevin, Minnesota Historical Society Press, 345 Kellogg Blvd W, St Paul, MN 55102-1906 *Tel:* 651-296-2264 *Toll Free Tel:* 800-621-2736 *Fax:* 651-297-1345 *Toll Free Fax:* 800-621-8476 *Web Site:* www.mnhs.org/mhspress, pg 175

Morrissey, Steve, e-Scholastic, 568 Broadway, 9th fl, New York, NY 10012 *Tel:* 212-343-7100 *Fax:* 212-343-4949, pg 85

Morrow, Mark, American Society for Training & Development (ASTD), 1640 King St, Alexandria, VA 22313-2043 *Tel:* 703-683-8100 *Toll Free Tel:* 800-628-2783 *Fax:* 703-683-1523 *E-mail:* publications@astd. org *Web Site:* www.astd.org, pg 17

Morrow, Robert, eSchool News, 7920 Norfolk Ave, Suite 900, Bethesda, MD 20814 *Tel:* 301-913-0115 *Toll Free Tel:* 800-394-0115 *Fax:* 301-913-0119 *Web Site:* www. eschoolnews.com, pg 92

Morse, John M, Merriam-Webster Inc, 47 Federal St, Springfield, MA 01102 *Tel:* 413-734-3134 *Toll Free Tel:* 800-828-1880 (orders & cust serv) *Fax:* 413-731-5979 *E-mail:* merriam_webster@merriam-webster.com *Web Site:* www.merriam-webster.com, pg 172

Morse, Scott, FedEx Trade Networks, 220 Montgomery St, Suite 448, San Francisco, CA 94104-3410 *Tel:* 415-391-7501 *Toll Free Tel:* 800-556-9334 *Fax:* 415-391-7537 (Fax/Modem) *E-mail:* info@ worldtariff.com *Web Site:* www.worldtariff.com, pg 95

Mortensen, Dee, Indiana University Press, 601 N Morton St, Bloomington, IN 47404-3797 *Tel:* 812-855-8817 *Toll Free Tel:* 800-842-6796 (orders only)

Fax: 812-855-7931 (orders only); 812-855-8507 *E-mail:* iupress@indiana.edu; iuorder@indiana.edu (orders) *Web Site:* www.iupress.indiana.edu, pg 132

Mortensen, Vivien, Friends of American Writers Award, 680 N Lake Shore Dr, Suite L208, Chicago, IL 60611 *Tel:* 312-664-5628, pg 775

Mortensen, Vivien, Juvenile Literary Awards/Young People's Literature Awards, 680 N Lake Shore Dr-L208, Chicago, IL 60611 *Tel:* 312-664-5628, pg 782

Morteo, Renata, United Nations Publications, 2 United Nations Plaza, Rm DC2-0853, New York, NY 10017 *Tel:* 212-963-8302 *Toll Free Tel:* 800-253-9646 *Fax:* 212-963-3489 *E-mail:* publications@un.org *Web Site:* www.un.org/publications, pg 279

Mortimer, Lyle, Cedar Fort Inc, 925 N Main St, Springville, UT 84663 *Tel:* 801-489-4084 *Toll Free Tel:* 800-759-2665 *Fax:* 801-489-1097 *E-mail:* skybook@cedarfort.com *Web Site:* www. cedarfort.com, pg 56

Morton, Bonnie L, William S Hein & Co Inc, 1285 Main St, Buffalo, NY 14209-1987 *Tel:* 716-882-2600 *Toll Free Tel:* 800-828-7571 *Fax:* 716-883-8100 *E-mail:* mail@wshein.com *Web Site:* www.wshein. com, pg 120

Morton, David, Rizzoli International Publications Inc, 300 Park Ave S, 3rd fl, New York, NY 10010-5399 *Tel:* 212-387-3400 *Toll Free Tel:* 800-522-6657 (orders only) *Fax:* 212-387-3535, pg 233

Morton, Doug, Morton Publishing Co, 925 W Kenyon Ave, Unit 12, Englewood, CO 80110 *Tel:* 303-761-4805 *Fax:* 303-762-9923 *E-mail:* morton@morton-pub.com *Web Site:* www.morton-pub.com, pg 179

Mosa, Kaila, Altitude Publishing Canada Ltd, 1500 Railway Ave, Canmore, AB T1W 1P6, Canada *Tel:* 403-678-6888 *Toll Free Tel:* 800-957-6888 *Fax:* 403-678-6951 *Toll Free Fax:* 800-957-1477 *E-mail:* orderdesk@altitudepublishing.com; sales@ altitudepublishing.com (ordering) *Web Site:* www. altitudepublishing.com, pg 535

Mosbrook, Bill, Pathfinder Publishing Inc, 3600 Harbor Blvd, Suite 82, Oxnard, CA 93035 *Tel:* 805-984-7756 *Toll Free Tel:* 800-977-2282 *Fax:* 805-985-3267 *Web Site:* www.pathfinderpublishing.com, pg 205

Mosbrook, Evelyn, Pathfinder Publishing Inc, 3600 Harbor Blvd, Suite 82, Oxnard, CA 93035 *Tel:* 805-984-7756 *Toll Free Tel:* 800-977-2282 *Fax:* 805-985-3267 *Web Site:* www.pathfinderpublishing.com, pg 205

Mosbrucker, Sharon, Sundance Publishing, One Beeman Rd, Northborough, MA 01532 *Tel:* 508-571-6500 *Toll Free Tel:* 800-343-8204 *Fax:* 508-571-6510 *Toll Free Fax:* 800-456-2419 *E-mail:* info@sundancepub.com *Web Site:* www.sundancepub.com, pg 262

Moschovakis, Anna, Ugly Duckling Presse, 106 Ferris St, 2nd fl, Brooklyn, NY 11231 *Tel:* 718-852-5529 *E-mail:* udp_mailbox@yahoo.com *Web Site:* www. uglyducklingpresse.org, pg 278

Moscowitz, Faye, Jenny McKean Moore Writer in Creative Writing, English Dept, The George Washington University, Washington, DC 20052 *Tel:* 202-994-6180 *Fax:* 202-994-7915 *Web Site:* www. gwu.edu/~english, pg 788

Moselle, Gary, Craftsman Book Co, 6058 Corte Del Cedro, Carlsbad, CA 92009 *Tel:* 760-438-7828 *Toll Free Tel:* 800-829-8123 *Fax:* 760-438-0398 *Web Site:* www.craftsman-book.com, pg 71

Moselle, Trudy, Craftsman Book Co, 6058 Corte Del Cedro, Carlsbad, CA 92009 *Tel:* 760-438-7828 *Toll Free Tel:* 800-829-8123 *Fax:* 760-438-0398 *Web Site:* www.craftsman-book.com, pg 71

Moser, Nellie M, Abingdon Press, 201 Eighth Ave S, Nashville, TN 37203-3919 *Tel:* 615-749-6290 (publicist); 615-749-6000; 615-749-6451 (sales) *Toll Free Tel:* 800-251-3320 *Fax:* 615-749-6056 *Web Site:* www.abingdonpress.com, pg 3

Moser, Philip, Biblo & Tannen Booksellers & Publishers Inc, PO Box 302, Cheshire, CT 06410-0302 *Tel:* 203-250-1647 *Toll Free Tel:* 800-272-8778 *Fax:* 203-250-1647 *Toll Free Fax:* 800-272-8778 *E-mail:* biblo. moser@snet.net, pg 38

Moses, Daniel, Sierra Club Books Adult Trade Division, 85 Second St, 2nd fl, San Francisco, CA 94105 *Tel:* 415-977-5500 *Fax:* 415-977-5792 *E-mail:* books. publishing@sierraclub.org *Web Site:* ww.sierraclub. org/books, pg 247

Moses, Danny, Sierra Club Books, 85 Second St, 2nd fl, San Francisco, CA 94105 *Tel:* 415-977-5500 *Fax:* 415-977-5792 *E-mail:* books.publishing@ sierraclub.org *Web Site:* www.sierraclub.org/books, pg 247

Moses, James, Primary Research Group, 224 W 30 St, Suite 802-1, New York, NY 10001 *Tel:* 212-736-2316 *Fax:* 212-412-9097 *E-mail:* primarydat@aol.com *Web Site:* www.primaryresearch.com, pg 218

Moses, Laura, Wyrick & Co, 284-A Meeting St, Charleston, SC 29401 *Tel:* 843-722-0881 *Toll Free Tel:* 800-227-5898 *Fax:* 843-722-6771 *E-mail:* wyrickco@bellsouth.net, pg 305

Moskow, Michael H, National Bureau of Economic Research Inc, 1050 Massachusetts Ave, Cambridge, MA 02138-5398 *Tel:* 617-868-3900 *Fax:* 617-868-2742 *E-mail:* op@nber.org *Web Site:* www.nber.org, pg 182

Mosley, Christine, Penguin Group (USA) Inc Sales, 375 Hudson St, New York, NY 10014 *Tel:* 212-366-2000 *E-mail:* online@penguinputnam.com *Web Site:* www. penguin.com, pg 208

Moss, Jeremy, McGraw-Hill International Publishing Group, 2 Penn Plaza, New York, NY 10121 *Tel:* 212-904-2000 *Web Site:* www.mcgrawhill.com, pg 168

Moss, Melanie, Cornell University Southeast Asia Program Publications, 640 Stewart Ave, Ithaca, NY 14850 *Tel:* 607-255-8038 *Fax:* 607-277-1904; 607-255-7534 *E-mail:* seap-pubs@cornell.edu *Web Site:* www.einaudi.cornell.edu/southeastasia. publications/SEAP, pg 69

Moss, Paul, Upstart Books™, W5527 State Rd 106, Fort Atkinson, WI 53538-8428 *Tel:* 920-563-9571 *Toll Free Tel:* 800-448-4887 *Fax:* 920-563-7395 *Toll Free Fax:* 800-448-5828 *Web Site:* www.highsmith.com, pg 288

Moss, Sherry, Gallopade International Inc, 665 Hwy 74 S, Suite 600, Peachtree City, GA 30269 *Tel:* 770-631-4222 *Toll Free Tel:* 800-536-2GET (536-2438) *Fax:* 770-631-4810 *Toll Free Fax:* 800-871-2979 *E-mail:* info@gallopade.com *Web Site:* www. gallopade.com, pg 102

Moss, Stanley, The Sheep Meadow Press, PO Box 1345, Riverdale-on-Hudson, NY 10471 *Tel:* 718-548-5547 *Fax:* 718-884-0406 *E-mail:* poetry@ sheepmeadowpress.com, pg 246

Mossey, Jeanne, Swagman Publishing Inc, PO Box 519, Castle Rock, CO 80104 *Tel:* 303-660-3307 *Toll Free Tel:* 800-660-5107 *Fax:* 303-688-4388 *E-mail:* mail@ 4wdbooks.com *Web Site:* www.4wdbooks.com, pg 262

Mossey, Peter, Swagman Publishing Inc, PO Box 519, Castle Rock, CO 80104 *Tel:* 303-660-3307 *Toll Free Tel:* 800-660-5107 *Fax:* 303-688-4388 *E-mail:* mail@ 4wdbooks.com *Web Site:* www.4wdbooks.com, pg 262

Mossinger, Paul, The Invisible College Press LLC, 3703 Del Mar Dr, Woodbridge, VA 22193-0209 *Tel:* 703-590-4005 *E-mail:* sales@invispress.com *Web Site:* www.invispress.com, pg 139

Mosure, Jeanne, Disney Publishing Worldwide, 500 S Buena Vista, Burbank, CA 91521 *Tel:* 212-633-4400 *Fax:* 212-633-4833 *Web Site:* www.disney.go. com/disneybooks, pg 81

Motherwell, Elizabeth, University of Alabama Press, Box 870380, Tuscaloosa, AL 35487-0380 *Tel:* 205-348-5180; 773-702-7000 (orders) *Fax:* 205-348-9201 *Web Site:* www.uapress.ua.edu, pg 280

Motika, Stephen, PEN Writers Fund, 588 Broadway, Suite 303, New York, NY 10012 *Tel:* 212-334-1660 *Fax:* 212-334-2181 *E-mail:* pen@pen.org *Web Site:* www.pen.org, pg 798

Motl, Mary Lou, Custom Editorial Productions Inc (CEP), 546 W Liberty St, Cincinnati, OH 45214 *Tel:* 513-723-1100 *Fax:* 513-723-1103 *E-mail:* cep@ customeditorial.com *Web Site:* www.customeditorial. com, pg 596

Motts, Frederick C, James Leitch Gold Medal Award, 595 W Hartsdale Ave, White Plains, NY 10607 *Tel:* 914-761-1100 *Fax:* 914-761-3115 *E-mail:* smpte@smpte.org *Web Site:* www.smpte.org, pg 784

Motts, Frederick C, Society of Motion Picture & Television Engineers (SMPTE), 595 W Hartsdale Ave, White Plains, NY 10607-1824 *Tel:* 914-761-1100 *Fax:* 914-761-3115 *E-mail:* smpte@smpte.org *Web Site:* www.smpte.org, pg 700

Motu, Nick, Hazelden Publishing & Educational Services, 15251 Pleasant Valley Rd, Center City, MN 55012-0176 *Tel:* 651-213-4470 *Toll Free Tel:* 800-328-9000 *Web Site:* www.hazelden.org, pg 118

Mougrabi, Said, The Pilgrim Press/United Church Press, 700 Prospect Ave, Cleveland, OH 44115-1100 *Tel:* 216-736-3761 *Toll Free Tel:* 800-537-3394 (cust serv) *Fax:* 216-736-2207 *E-mail:* thepilgrimpress@ thepilgrimpress.com *Web Site:* www.thepilgrimpress. com; www.theunitedchurchpress.com, pg 213

Moulter, Larry, Helen Rees Literary Agency, 376 North St, Boston, MA 02113-2103 *Tel:* 617-227-9014 *Fax:* 617-227-8762, pg 650

Moulton, Anita, Milkweed Editions, 1011 Washington Ave S, Suite 300, Minneapolis, MN 55415 *Tel:* 612-332-3192 *Toll Free Tel:* 800-520-6455 *Fax:* 612-215-2550 *E-mail:* editor@milkweed.org *Web Site:* www. milkweed.org; www.worldashome.org, pg 174

Moulton, Tyler, Covenant Communications Inc, 920 E State Rd, Suite F, American Fork, UT 84003-0416 *Tel:* 801-756-9966 *Toll Free Tel:* 800-662-9545 *Fax:* 801-756-1049 *E-mail:* sales@covenant-lds.com *Web Site:* www.covenant-lds.com, pg 71

Mount, Ingrid, Elm Street Publishing Services Inc, 828 N Elm St, Hinsdale, IL 60521 *Tel:* 630-789-2102 *Fax:* 630-789-2105 *E-mail:* esps@elmst.com *Web Site:* www.elmst.com, pg 598

Mousa, Ed, Wadsworth Publishing, 10 Davis Dr, Belmont, CA 94002-3002 *Toll Free Tel:* 800-357-0092 *Fax:* 650-592-3342 *Toll Free Fax:* 800-522-4923 *Web Site:* www.wadsworth.com, pg 292

Moushabeck, Michel, Interlink Publishing Group Inc, 46 Crosby St, Northampton, MA 01060 *Tel:* 413-582-7054 *Toll Free Tel:* 800-238-LINK (238-5465) *Fax:* 413-582-7057 *E-mail:* info@interlinkbooks.com *Web Site:* www.interlinkbooks.com, pg 136

Mowbray, Stuart, Andrew Mowbray Inc Publishers, PO Box 460, Lincoln, RI 02865-0460 *Tel:* 401-726-8011 *Toll Free Tel:* 800-999-4697 *Fax:* 401-726-8061 *E-mail:* service@manatarmbooks.com *Web Site:* www. manatarmbooks.com, pg 180

Mower, Steve, Thomson Learning Inc, 200 First Stamford Place, Suite 400, Stamford, CT 06902 *Tel:* 203-539-8000 *Fax:* 203-539-7581 *E-mail:* communications@thomsonlearning.com *Web Site:* www.thomson.com/learning, pg 270

Moyle, Joann, Mint Publishers Group, 62 June Rd, North Salem, NY 10560 *Tel:* 914-276-6576 *Fax:* 914-276-6579 *E-mail:* info@mintpub.com *Web Site:* www. mintpub.com, pg 175

Mroczkowski, Manfred, Hay House Inc, 2776 Loker Ave W, Carlsbad, CA 92008 *Tel:* 760-431-7695 *Toll Free Tel:* 800-650-5115; 800-654-5126 (orders) *Fax:* 760-431-6948 *E-mail:* info@hayhouse.com *Web Site:* www.hayhouse.com, pg 118

Mroczkowski, Manfred, InterLicense Ltd, 110 Country Club Dr, Suite A, Mill Valley, CA 94941 *Tel:* 415-381-9780 *Fax:* 415-381-6485 *E-mail:* ilicense@aol. com, pg 635

Muccie, Mary, Society for Industrial & Applied Mathematics, 3600 University City Science Ctr, Philadelphia, PA 19104-2688 *Tel:* 215-382-9800 *Toll Free Tel:* 800-447-7426 *Fax:* 215-386-7999 *E-mail:* siam@siam.org *Web Site:* www.siam.org, pg 251

Muckley, Paul K, Barbour Publishing Inc, 1810 Barbour Dr, Uhrichsville, OH 44683 *Tel:* 740-922-6045 *Fax:* 740-922-5948 *E-mail:* info@barbourbooks.com *Web Site:* www.barbourbooks.com, pg 32

Mudd, Gary, American Printing House for the Blind Inc, 1839 Frankfort Ave, Louisville, KY 40206 *Tel:* 502-895-2405 *Toll Free Tel:* 800-223-1839 (cust serv) *Fax:* 502-899-2274 *E-mail:* info@aph.org *Web Site:* www.aph.org, pg 16

Mudditt, Alison, Sage Publications, 2455 Teller Rd, Thousand Oaks, CA 91320 *Tel:* 805-499-0721 *Fax:* 805-499-0871 *E-mail:* info@sagepub.com *Web Site:* www.sagepub.com, pg 237

Mueller, Marjorie, Oxford University Press, Inc, 198 Madison Ave, New York, NY 10016-4314 *Tel:* 212-726-6000 *Toll Free Tel:* 800-451-7556 (orders) *Web Site:* www.oup.com/us, pg 200

Mugmon, Karyn, Art Direction Book Co Inc, 456 Glenbrook Rd, Glenbrook, CT 06906 *Tel:* 203-353-1441 *Fax:* 203-353-1371, pg 24

Muhlenkamp, Monique, H J Kramer Inc, PO Box 1082, Tiburon, CA 94920-7002 *Tel:* 415-435-5367 *Fax:* 415-435-5364 *E-mail:* hjkramer@jps.net *Web Site:* www. newworldlibrary.com, pg 147

Mukalla, Claudette, International Book Centre Inc, 2391 Auburn Rd, Shelby Township, MI 48317 *Tel:* 248-879-8436; 586-254-7230 *Fax:* 586-254-7230; 248-879-8436 *E-mail:* ibc@ibcbooks.com *Web Site:* www. ibcbooks.com, pg 136

Mulder, David, American Products Publishing Co, 10950 SW Fifth St, Suite 155, Beaverton, OR 97005-4782 *Tel:* 503-672-7502 *Toll Free Tel:* 800-668-8181 *Fax:* 503-672-7104 *E-mail:* info@american-products. com *Web Site:* www.american-products.com, pg 16

Mulder, Gary, CRC Publications, 2850 Kalamazoo Ave SE, Grand Rapids, MI 49560 *Tel:* 616-224-0819; 616-224-0728 *Toll Free Tel:* 800-333-8300 *Fax:* 616-224-0834 *E-mail:* sales@crcpublications.org *Web Site:* www.faithaliveresources.org, pg 72

Mulder, Matt, Upstart Books™, W5527 State Rd 106, Fort Atkinson, WI 53538-8428 *Tel:* 920-563-9571 *Toll Free Tel:* 800-448-4887 *Fax:* 920-563-7395 *Toll Free Fax:* 800-448-5828 *Web Site:* www.highsmith.com, pg 288

Mulert, Carl, The Joyce Ketay Agency, 630 Ninth Ave, Suite 706, New York, NY 10036 *Tel:* 212-354-6825 *Fax:* 212-354-6732, pg 637

Mulhern, Molly, Ragged Mountain Press, 485 Commercial St, Rockport, ME 04856 *Tel:* 207-236-4837 *Fax:* 207-236-6314 *Web Site:* www. raggedmountainpress.com, pg 225

Mull, Steve, The Donning Co/Publishers, 184 Business Park Dr, Suite 206, Virginia Beach, VA 23462 *Tel:* 757-497-1789; 660-376-3543 (Missouri office) *Toll Free Tel:* 800-296-8572 *Fax:* 757-497-2542 *Web Site:* www.donning.com, pg 82

Mullane, Deirdre, The Spieler Agency, 154 W 57 St, 13th fl, Rm 135, New York, NY 10019 *Tel:* 212-757-4439 *Web Site:* spieleragency.com, pg 656

Mullane, Margaret, Lawrence Erlbaum Associates Inc, 10 Industrial Ave, Mahwah, NJ 07430-2262 *Tel:* 201-236-2199 *Toll Free Tel:* 800-9-BOOKS-9 (926-6579) *Fax:* 201-760-3735 *E-mail:* orders@erlbaum.com *Web Site:* www.erlbaum.com, pg 91

Mullauer, Marion, The American Chemical Society, 1155 16 St NW, Washington, DC 20036 *Tel:* 202-872-4600 *Toll Free Tel:* 800-227-5558 *Fax:* 202-872-6067 *Web Site:* www.acs.org; pubs.acs.org, pg 12

Mullen, Carrie, University of Minnesota Press, 111 Third Ave S, Suite 290, Minneapolis, MN 55401-2520 *Tel:* 612-627-1970 *Fax:* 612-627-1980 *E-mail:* ump@ tc.umn.edu *Web Site:* www.upress.umn.edu, pg 282

Mullen, Teresa, Association of American University Presses, 1427 E 60 St, Chicago, IL 60637 *Tel:* 773-702-7700; 773-702-7600 *Toll Free Tel:* 800-621-2736 (orders) *Fax:* 773-702-9756 (sales); 773-660-2235 (orders); 773-702-2708 *E-mail:* general@press. uchicago.edu *Web Site:* www.press.uchicago.edu, pg 26

Mullendore, Nick, Loretta Barrett Books Inc, 101 Fifth Ave, New York, NY 10003 *Tel:* 212-242-3420 *Fax:* 212-807-9579, pg 620

Muller, Pete, Crown Publishing Group, 1745 Broadway, New York, NY 10019 *Tel:* 212-782-9000 *Toll Free Tel:* 888-264-1745 *Fax:* 212-940-7408 *Web Site:* www.randomhouse.com/crown, pg 73

Muller, Peter, Random House Reference, 1745 Broadway, New York, NY 10019 *Toll Free Tel:* 800-733-3000 *E-mail:* words@random.com; puzzles@random.com, pg 227

Mulligan, Julia, Marcel Dekker Inc, 270 Madison Ave, New York, NY 10016 *Tel:* 212-696-9000 *Toll Free Tel:* 800-228-1160 (outside NY) *Fax:* 212-685-4540 *Web Site:* www.dekker.com, pg 78

Mullins, Mike, 28th Appalachian Writers' Workshop, PO Box 844, Hindman, KY 41822-0844 *Tel:* 606-785-5475 *Fax:* 606-785-3499 *E-mail:* hss@tgtel.com *Web Site:* www.hindmansettlement.org, pg 748

Mullins, Sherry, Briefings Publishing Group, 1101 King St, Suite 110, Alexandria, VA 22314 *Tel:* 703-548-3800 *Toll Free Tel:* 800-888-2086 *Fax:* 703-684-2136 *E-mail:* customerservice@briefings.com *Web Site:* www.briefings.com, pg 47

Mullins-Mitchell, Kimberly, MFA Publications, 465 Huntington Ave, Boston, MA 02115 *Tel:* 617-369-3438 *Fax:* 617-369-3459 *Web Site:* www.mfa-publications.org, pg 173

Mulrane, Patricia, Peter Lang Publishing Inc, 275 Seventh Ave, 28th fl, New York, NY 10001-6708 *Tel:* 212-647-7700 *Toll Free Tel:* 800-770-5264 (cust serv) *Fax:* 212-647-7707 *Web Site:* www.peterlangusa.com, pg 148

Mulroy, Kevin, National Geographic Books, 1145 17 St NW, Washington, DC 20036 *Tel:* 202-857-7000 *Fax:* 202-857-7670 *Web Site:* www.nationalgeographics.com, pg 183

Mulroy, Kevin, National Geographic Society, 1145 17 St NW, Washington, DC 20036 *Tel:* 202-857-7000 *Fax:* 202-429-5727 *Web Site:* www.nationalgeographic.com, pg 184

Mummery, Alexandra, Hunter House Publishers, 1515 1/2 Park St, Alameda, CA 94501 *Tel:* 510-865-5282 *Toll Free Tel:* 800-266-5592 *Fax:* 510-865-4295 *E-mail:* acquisitions@hunterhouse.com *Web Site:* www.hunterhouse.com/, pg 129

Munari, Donna, American Medical Writers Association, 40 W Gude Dr, Suite 101, Rockville, MD 20850-1192 *Tel:* 301-294-5303 *Fax:* 301-294-9006 *E-mail:* info@amwa.org *Web Site:* www.amwa.org, pg 677

Muncy, Michell, Spence Publishing Co, 111 Cole St, Dallas, TX 75207 *Tel:* 214-939-1700 *Fax:* 214-939-1800 *Web Site:* www.spencepublishing.com, pg 255

Mundy, Linus, Abbey Press, One Hill Dr, St Meinrad, IN 47577 *Tel:* 812-357-6611 *Toll Free Tel:* 800-962-4760 *Fax:* 812-357-8388 *E-mail:* dep@abbeypress.com *Web Site:* www.abbeypress.com, pg 2

Munier, Paula V, Adams Media, An F+W Publications Co, 57 Littlefield St, 2nd fl, Avon, MA 02322 *Tel:* 508-427-7100 *Fax:* 508-427-6790 *Toll Free Fax:* 800-872-5628 *E-mail:* authors@adamsmedia.com; orders@adamsmedia.com *Web Site:* www.adamsmedia.com, pg 5

Munk, Laurel, American Association of Blood Banks, 8101 Glenbrook Rd, Bethesda, MD 20814-2749 *Tel:* 301-907-6977 *Toll Free Tel:* 866-222-2498 (sales) *Fax:* 301-907-6895 *E-mail:* aabb@aabb.org; sales@aabb.org (ordering) *Web Site:* www.aabb.org, pg 11

Munoz, Julio E, Inter American Press Association (IAPA), 1801 SW Third Ave, Miami, FL 33129 *Tel:* 305-634-2465 *Fax:* 305-635-2272 *E-mail:* info@sipiapa.org *Web Site:* www.sipiapa.org, pg 688

Munro, Susan, The Continuing Legal Education Society of British Columbia, 845 Cambie, Suite 300, Vancouver, BC V6B 5T2, Canada *Tel:* 604-669-3544 *Toll Free Tel:* 800-663-0437 *Fax:* 604-669-9260 *Web Site:* www.cle.bc.ca, pg 541

Munson, Carol H, Winter Springs Editorial Services, 2263 Turk Rd, Doylestown, PA 18901-2964 *Tel:* 215-340-9052 *Fax:* 215-340-9052, pg 614

Munson, Lowell, Winter Springs Editorial Services, 2263 Turk Rd, Doylestown, PA 18901-2964 *Tel:* 215-340-9052 *Fax:* 215-340-9052, pg 614

Munson, Richard, Northeast Midwest Institute, 218 "D" St SE, Washington, DC 20003 *Tel:* 202-544-5200 *Fax:* 202-544-0043 *Web Site:* www.nemw.org, pg 193

Murach, Georgia, Mike Murach & Associates Inc, 3484 W Gettysburg Ave, Suite 101, Fresno, CA 93722-7801 *Tel:* 559-440-9071 *Toll Free Tel:* 800-221-5528 *Fax:* 559-440-0963 *E-mail:* murachbooks@murach.com *Web Site:* www.murach.com, pg 174

Muranaka, Royden, University of Hawaii Press, 2840 Kolowalu St, Honolulu, HI 96822 *Tel:* 808-956-8255 *Toll Free Tel:* 888-847-7377 *Fax:* 808-988-6052 *Toll Free Fax:* 800-650-7811 *E-mail:* uhpbooks@hawaii.edu *Web Site:* www.uhpress.hawaii.edu, pg 281

Murcray, Colin, American Water Works Association, 6666 W Quincy Ave, Denver, CO 80235 *Tel:* 303-794-7711 *Toll Free Tel:* 800-926-7337 *Fax:* 303-347-0804 *Web Site:* www.awwa.org, pg 18

Murgolo, Karen, Bulfinch Press, 1271 Avenue of the Americas, New York, NY 10020 *Tel:* 212-522-8700 *Toll Free Tel:* 800-759-0190 *Fax:* 212-467-2886 *Web Site:* www.twbookmark.com, pg 50

Murphy, Barbara, The MIT Press, 5 Cambridge Ctr, Cambridge, MA 02142 *Tel:* 617-253-5646 *Toll Free Tel:* 800-405-1619 (orders only) *Fax:* 617-258-6779 *Web Site:* mitpress.mit.edu, pg 175

Murphy, Chris, Scholastic Trade Division, 557 Broadway, New York, NY 10012 *Tel:* 212-343-6100; 212-343-4685 (export sales) *Fax:* 212-343-4714 (export sales) *Web Site:* www.scholastic.com, pg 242

Murphy, Christopher, NAFSA: Association of International Educators, 1307 New York Ave NW, 8th fl, Washington, DC 20005-4701 *Tel:* 202-737-3699 *Toll Free Tel:* 800-836-4994 (Book orders only) *Fax:* 202-737-3657 *E-mail:* inbox@nafsa.org *Web Site:* www.nafsa.org, pg 181

Murphy, David L, The McGraw-Hill Companies Inc, 1221 Avenue of the Americas, 50th fl, New York, NY 10020 *Tel:* 212-512-2000 *E-mail:* webmaster@mcgraw-hill.com *Web Site:* www.mcgraw-hill.com, pg 167

Murphy, Edward P, National Music Publishers' Association (NMPA), 711 Third Ave, 8th fl, New York, NY 10017 *Tel:* 646-742-1651 *Fax:* 646-742-1779 *Web Site:* www.nmpa.org, pg 694

Murphy, Jerald A, T J Publishers Inc, 817 Silver Spring Ave, Suite 206, Silver Spring, MD 20910-4617 *Tel:* 301-585-4440 *Toll Free Tel:* 800-999-1168 *Fax:* 301-585-5930 *E-mail:* TJPubinc@aol.com, pg 574

Murphy, John, St Martin's Press Paperback and Reference Group, 175 Fifth Ave, New York, NY 10010 *Fax:* 212-995-2488 *E-mail:* firstname.lastname@stmartins.com, pg 239

Murphy, John, St Martin's Press Trade Division, 175 Fifth Ave, New York, NY 10010 *E-mail:* firstname.lastname@stmartins.com *Web Site:* www.stmartins.com; www.minotaurbooks.com, pg 239

Murphy, Kevin, Meisha Merlin Publishing Inc, 1702 Ronald Rd, Tucker, GA 30084 *Tel:* 770-414-4365 *Fax:* 770-414-4365 *E-mail:* email@meishamerlin.com; orders@meishamerlin.com *Web Site:* www.meishamerlin.com, pg 172

Murphy, Liza, Cambridge University Press, 40 W 20 St, New York, NY 10011-4211 *Tel:* 212-924-3900 *Toll Free Tel:* 800-899-5222 *Fax:* 212-691-3239 *Web Site:* www.cambridge.org, pg 52

Murphy, Lora, The Center for Learning, 24600 Detroit Rd, Suite 201, Westlake, OH 44145 *Tel:* 440-250-9341 *Fax:* 440-250-9715 *Web Site:* www.centerforlearning.org, pg 56

Murphy, Marilyn, Interweave Press, 201 E Fourth St, Loveland, CO 80537 *Tel:* 970-669-7672 *Toll Free Tel:* 800-272-2193 *Fax:* 970-667-8317 *E-mail:* customerservice@interweave.com *Web Site:* www.interweave.com, pg 138

Murphy, Megan, Canadian Energy Research Institute, 3512 33 St NW, Suite 150, Calgary, AB T2L 2A6, Canada *Tel:* 403-282-1231 *Fax:* 403-284-4181 *E-mail:* ceri@ceri.ca *Web Site:* www.ceri.ca, pg 538

Murphy, Michael, Jessie Bernard Award, 1307 New York Ave NW, Suite 700, Washington, DC 20005 *Tel:* 202-383-9005 *Fax:* 202-638-0882 *E-mail:* governance@asanet.org *Web Site:* www.asanet.org, pg 762

Murphy, Michael, Betterway Books, 4700 E Galbraith Rd, Cincinnati, OH 45236 *Tel:* 513-531-2690 *Toll Free Tel:* 800-666-0963 *Fax:* 513-891-7185 *Toll Free Fax:* 888-590-4082 *Web Site:* www.fwpublications.com, pg 38

Murphy, Michael, Distinguished Scholarly Publication Award, 1307 New York Ave NW, Suite 700, Washington, DC 20005 *Tel:* 202-383-9005 *Fax:* 202-638-0882 *E-mail:* governance@asanet.org *Web Site:* www.asanet.org, pg 770

Murphy, Michael, Krause Publications, 700 E State St, Iola, WI 54990 *Tel:* 715-445-4612 ext 365 *Toll Free Tel:* 800-258-0929; 888-457-2873 *Fax:* 715-445-4087 *Web Site:* www.krause.com, pg 147

Murphy, Michael, North Light Books, 4700 E Galbraith Rd, Cincinnati, OH 45236 *Tel:* 513-531-2690 *Toll Free Tel:* 800-666-0963 *Fax:* 513-891-7185 *Toll Free Fax:* 888-590-4082 *Web Site:* www.fwpublications.com, pg 192

Murphy, Michael, Writer's Digest Books, 4700 E Galbraith Rd, Cincinnati, OH 45236 *Tel:* 513-531-2690 *Toll Free Tel:* 800-289-0963 *Fax:* 513-891-7185 *Web Site:* www.writersdigest.com, pg 305

Murphy, Richard, CCAB Inc, 90 Eglinton Ave E, Suite 980, Toronto, ON M4P 2Y3, Canada *Tel:* 416-487-2418 *Fax:* 416-487-6405 *E-mail:* info@bpai.com *Web Site:* www.bpai.com, pg 684

Murphy, Ryan, Academy of American Poets Fellowship, 588 Broadway, Suite 604, New York, NY 10012 *Tel:* 212-274-0343 *Fax:* 212-274-9427 *E-mail:* academy@poets.org *Web Site:* www.poets.org, pg 757

Murphy, Ryan, The Academy of American Poets Inc, 588 Broadway, Suite 604, New York, NY 10012 *Tel:* 212-274-0343 *Fax:* 212-274-9427 *E-mail:* academy@poets.org *Web Site:* www.poets.org, pg 675

Murphy, Ryan, Harold Morton Landon Translation Award, 588 Broadway, Suite 604, New York, NY 10012 *Tel:* 212-274-0343 *Fax:* 212-274-9427 *E-mail:* academy@poets.org *Web Site:* www.poets.org, pg 783

Murphy, Ryan, James Laughlin Award, 588 Broadway, Suite 604, New York, NY 10012 *Tel:* 212-274-0343 *Fax:* 212-274-9427 *E-mail:* academy@poets.org *Web Site:* www.poets.org, pg 783

Murphy, Ryan, Lenore Marshall Poetry Prize, 588 Broadway, Suite 604, New York, NY 10012 *Tel:* 212-274-0343 *Fax:* 212-274-9427 *E-mail:* academy@poets.org *Web Site:* www.poets.org, pg 787

Murphy, Ryan, Raiziss/de Palchi Fellowship, 588 Broadway, Suite 604, New York, NY 10012 *Tel:* 212-274-0343 *Fax:* 212-274-9427 *E-mail:* academy@poets.org *Web Site:* www.poets.org, pg 801

Murphy, Ryan, Raiziss/de Palchi Translation Award, 588 Broadway, Suite 604, New York, NY 10012 *Tel:* 212-274-0343 *Fax:* 212-274-9427 *E-mail:* academy@poets.org *Web Site:* www.poets.org, pg 801

Murphy, Ryan, Walt Whitman Award, 588 Broadway, Suite 604, New York, NY 10012 *Tel:* 212-274-0343 *Fax:* 212-274-9427 *E-mail:* academy@poets.org *Web Site:* www.poets.org, pg 811

Murphy, Steven, Rodale Inc, 33 E Minor St, Emmaus, PA 18098-0099 *Tel:* 610-967-5171 *Fax:* 610-967-8962 *Web Site:* www.rodale.com, pg 234

Murphy, Steven Pleshette, Rodale Books, 400 S Tenth St, Emmaus, PA 18098-0099 *Tel:* 610-967-5171 *Fax:* 610-967-8961 *Web Site:* www.rodale.com, pg 233

Murphy, Suzanne, Simon & Schuster Children's Publishing, 1230 Avenue of the Americas, New York, NY 10020 *Tel:* 212-698-7000 *Web Site:* www. simonsayskids.com, pg 248

Murphy, Trace, Doubleday Broadway Publishing Group, 1745 Broadway, New York, NY 10019 *Tel:* 212-782-9000 *Toll Free Tel:* 800-223-6834; 800-223-5780 (sales) *Fax:* 212-302-7985 (correspondence); 212-492-9862 (orders), pg 82

Murphy, Will, Random House Publishing Group, 1745 Broadway, New York, NY 10019 *Toll Free Tel:* 800-200-3552 *Toll Free Fax:* 800-200-3552 *Web Site:* www.randomhouse.com, pg 227

Murray, Amanda, Simon & Schuster, 1230 Avenue of the Americas, New York, NY 10020 *Tel:* 212-698-7000 *Toll Free Tel:* 800-223-2348 (cust serv); 800-223-2336 (orders) *Toll Free Fax:* 800-943-9831 (orders) *Web Site:* www.simonsays.com, pg 248

Murray, Barb, University of Calgary Press, 2500 University Dr NW, Calgary, AB T2N 1N4, Canada *Tel:* 403-220-7578 *Fax:* 403-282-0085 *E-mail:* whildebr@ucalgary.ca *Web Site:* www. uofcpress.com, pg 565

Murray, Brian, HarperCollins Publishers, 10 E 53 St, New York, NY 10022 *Tel:* 212-207-7000 *Fax:* 212-207-7145 *Web Site:* www.harpercollins.com, pg 116

Murray, David, Piano Press, 1425 Ocean Ave, Suite 6, Del Mar, CA 92014 *Tel:* 619-884-1401 *Fax:* 858-459-3376 *E-mail:* pianopress@aol.com *Web Site:* www. pianopress.com, pg 212

Murray, Eden-Lee, Jellinek & Murray Literary Agency, 2024 Mauna Place, Honolulu, HI 96822 *Tel:* 808-521-4057 *Fax:* 808-521-4058 *E-mail:* jellinek@lava.net, pg 636

Murray, Mary, McGraw-Hill Professional, 2 Penn Plaza, New York, NY 10121 *Tel:* 212-904-2000 *Web Site:* www.books.mcgraw-hill.com, pg 168

Murray, Mary K, Pro Quest Information & Learning, 300 N Zeeb Rd, Ann Arbor, MI 48106-1346 *Tel:* 734-761-4700 *Toll Free Tel:* 800-521-0600 *Fax:* 734-975-6486 *Toll Free Fax:* 800-864-0019 *E-mail:* info@il. proquest.com *Web Site:* www.il.proquest.com, pg 219

Murray, Pat, Park Place Publications, 591 Lighthouse Ave, No 22, Pacific Grove, CA 93950 *Tel:* 831-649-6640 *Toll Free Tel:* 888-702-4500 *Fax:* 831-649-6649 *E-mail:* publisher@parkplace-publications.com; info@ parkplace-publications.com *Web Site:* www.parkplace-publications.com, pg 204

Murray, William D G, Type & Archetype Press, PO Box 14285, Charleston, SC 29422-4285 *Tel:* 843-406-9113 *Toll Free Tel:* 800-447-8973 *Fax:* 843-406-9118 *E-mail:* info@typetemperament.com *Web Site:* www. typearchetype.com, pg 277

Murry, Elizabeth, The MIT Press, 5 Cambridge Ctr, Cambridge, MA 02142 *Tel:* 617-253-5646 *Toll Free Tel:* 800-405-1619 (orders only) *Fax:* 617-258-6779 *Web Site:* mitpress.mit.edu, pg 175

Muschett, James, Hugh Lauter Levin Associates Inc, 9 Burr Rd, Westport, CT 06880 *Tel:* 203-227-6422 *Fax:* 203-227-6717 *E-mail:* inquiries@hlla.com *Web Site:* www.hlla.com, pg 128

Muse, Jane, Houghton Mifflin College Division, 222 Berkeley St, Boston, MA 02116-3764 *Tel:* 617-351-5000 *Toll Free Tel:* 800-225-1464 (orders) *Web Site:* www.college.hmco.com, pg 126

Musgari, Sally, Milton Dorfman Poetry Prize, 308 W Bloomfield St, Rome, NY 13440 *Tel:* 315-336-1040 *Fax:* 315-336-1090 *E-mail:* racc@borg.com, pg 790

Musto, Ronald G, Italica Press, 595 Main St, Suite 605, New York, NY 10044 *Tel:* 212-935-4230 *Fax:* 212-838-7812 *E-mail:* inquiries@italicapress.com *Web Site:* www.italicapress.com, pg 139

Musty, Sherrill N, Waterfront Books, 85 Crescent Rd, Burlington, VT 05401 *Tel:* 802-658-7477 *Toll Free Tel:* 800-639-6063 (orders) *Fax:* 802-860-1368 *E-mail:* helpkids@waterfrontbooks.com *Web Site:* www.waterfrontbooks.com, pg 294

Mutean, Eva, Ignatius Press, 2515 McAllister St, San Francisco, CA 94118 *Tel:* 415-387-2324 *Toll Free Tel:* 877-320-9276 (book orders) *Fax:* 415-387-0896 *E-mail:* info@ignatius.com *Web Site:* www.ignatius. com, pg 131

Muzinic, Jason, American Dietetic Association, 120 S Riverside Plaza, Suite 2000, Chicago, IL 60606 *Tel:* 312-899-0040 *Fax:* 312-899-4757 *Web Site:* www. eatright.org, pg 13

Muzzarelli, Linda, Consumer Press, 13326 SW 28 St, Suite 102, Fort Lauderdale, FL 33330-1102 *Tel:* 954-370-9153 *Fax:* 954-472-1008 *E-mail:* bookguest@aol. com *Web Site:* consumerpress.com, pg 67

Mydlowski, Gene, Random House Publishing Group, 1745 Broadway, New York, NY 10019 *Toll Free Tel:* 800-200-3552 *Toll Free Fax:* 800-200-3552 *Web Site:* www.randomhouse.com, pg 227

Myers, Christopher S, Peter Lang Publishing Inc, 275 Seventh Ave, 28th fl, New York, NY 10001-6708 *Tel:* 212-647-7700 *Toll Free Tel:* 800-770-5264 (cust serv) *Fax:* 212-647-7707 *Web Site:* www.peterlangusa. com, pg 148

Myers, Garry, Classroom Publishers Association (CPA), c/o Highlights for Children, 1800 Watermark Dr, Columbus, OH 43216 *Tel:* 614-487-2601 *Fax:* 614-324-7946, pg 685

Myers, Gary, Howard Publishing, 3117 N Seventh St, West Monroe, LA 71291 *Tel:* 318-396-3122 *Toll Free Tel:* 800-858-4109 *Fax:* 318-397-1882 *E-mail:* info@ howardpublishing.com *Web Site:* howardpublishing. com, pg 127

Myers, Heather, Scholastic Inc, 557 Broadway, New York, NY 10012 *Tel:* 212-343-4469 *Toll Free Tel:* 800-scholastic *Fax:* 212-343-6930 *Web Site:* www.scholastic.com, pg 242

Myers, Irv, University Press of America Inc, 4501 Forbes Blvd, Suite 200, Lanham, MD 20706 *Tel:* 301-459-3366 *Toll Free Tel:* 800-462-6420 *Fax:* 301-429-5748 *Toll Free Fax:* 800-338-4550 *Web Site:* www. univpress.com, pg 286

Myers, Janice, Wm B Eerdmans Publishing Co, 255 Jefferson Ave SE, Grand Rapids, MI 49503 *Tel:* 616-459-4591 *Toll Free Tel:* 800-253-7521 *Fax:* 616-459-6540 *E-mail:* sales@eerdmans.com *Web Site:* www. eerdmans.com, pg 88

Myers, Jim, American Industrial Hygiene Association, 2700 Prosperity Ave, Suite 250, Fairfax, VA 22031-4319 *Tel:* 703-849-8888 *Fax:* 703-207-3561 *E-mail:* infonet@aiha.org *Web Site:* www.aiha.org, pg 14

Myers, Katharine, Princeton Architectural Press, 37 E Seventh St, New York, NY 10003 *Tel:* 212-995-9620 *Toll Free Tel:* 800-722-6657 (dist) *Fax:* 212-995-9454 *E-mail:* sales@papress.com *Web Site:* www.papress. com, pg 218

Myers, Kathy, American Institute for CPCU & Insurance Institute of America, 720 Providence Rd, Malvern, PA 19355-0716 *Tel:* 610-644-2100 *Toll Free Tel:* 800-644-2101 *Fax:* 610-640-9576; 610-644-7629 *E-mail:* cserv@cpcuiia.org *Web Site:* www.aicpcu.org, pg 14

Myers, Kelly, Sligo Literary Agency LLC, 74-923 Hwy 111, Suite 173, Indian Wells, CA 92210 *Tel:* 760-340-6640 *Fax:* 760-340-4320 *E-mail:* ricsligo@aol.com, pg 656

Myers, Nancy, Discovery Enterprises Ltd, 31 Laurelwood Dr, Carlisle, MA 01741 *Tel:* 978-287-5401 *Toll Free Tel:* 800-729-1720 *Fax:* 978-287-5402 *E-mail:* ushistorydocs@aol.com *Web Site:* www. ushistorydocs.com, pg 80

Myers, Patricia, Stanford University Press, 1450 Page Mill Rd, Palo Alto, CA 94304-1124 *Tel:* 650-723-9434 *Fax:* 650-725-3457 *Web Site:* www.sup.org, pg 257

Myles, Tom, Standard Educational Corp, 200 W Jackson, 7th fl, Chicago, IL 60606 *Tel:* 312-692-1000, pg 257

Myrick, Susan, Copley Publishing Group, 138 Great Rd, Acton, MA 01720 *Tel:* 978-263-9090 *Toll Free Tel:* 800-562-2147 *Fax:* 978-263-9190 *E-mail:* publish@copleycustom.com; textbook@ copleypublishing.com *Web Site:* www.copleycustom. com; www.copleypublishing.com; www.copleyeditions. com, pg 68

Nachbaur, Frederic, Routledge, 29 W 35 St, New York, NY 10001-2299 *Tel:* 212-216-7800 *Fax:* 212-564-7854 (main) *E-mail:* info@taylorandfrancis.com *Web Site:* www.routledge-ny.com, pg 235

Nachbaur, Fredric, New York University Press, 838 Broadway, New York, NY 10003 *Tel:* 212-998-2575 (edit) *Toll Free Tel:* 800-996-6987 (orders) *Fax:* 212-995-3833 (orders) *E-mail:* feedback@nyupress.nyu.edu *Web Site:* www.nyupress.org, pg 190

Naddaff, Ramona, Zone Books, 1226 Prospect Ave, Brooklyn, NY 11218 *Tel:* 718-686-0048 *Toll Free Tel:* 800-405-1619 (orders & cust serv) *Fax:* 212-625-9772; 718-686-9045 *Toll Free Fax:* 800-406-9145 (orders) *E-mail:* urzone@zonebooks.org; mitpress-orders@mit.edu (orders), pg 307

Nadeau, Pierre, Edimag, CP 325, Succ Rosemont, Montreal, PQ H1X 3B8, Canada *Tel:* 514-522-2244 *Fax:* 514-522-6301 *Web Site:* www.edimag.com, pg 543

Nadell, Bonnie, Frederick Hill Bonnie Nadell Literary Agency, 1842 Union St, San Francisco, CA 94123 *Tel:* 415-921-2910 *Fax:* 415-921-2802, pg 634

Naffin, Michelle, Altitude Publishing Canada Ltd, 1500 Railway Ave, Canmore, AB T1W 1P6, Canada *Tel:* 403-678-6888 *Toll Free Tel:* 800-957-6888 *Fax:* 403-678-6951 *Toll Free Fax:* 800-957-1477 *E-mail:* orderdesk@altitudepublishing.com; sales@ altitudepublishing.com (ordering) *Web Site:* www. altitudepublishing.com, pg 535

Naggar, David, Fodor's Travel Publications, 1745 Broadway, New York, NY 10019 *Tel:* 212-572-8784 *Toll Free Tel:* 800-733-3000 *Fax:* 212-572-2248 *Web Site:* www.fodors.com, pg 98

Naggar, David, Living Language, 1745 Broadway, New York, NY 10019 *Tel:* 212-572-6148 *Toll Free Tel:* 800-726-0600 (orders) *Fax:* 212-940-7400 *Toll Free Fax:* 800-659-2436 *E-mail:* livinglanguage@ randomhouse.com *Web Site:* www.livinglanguage.com, pg 157

Naggar, David, The Princeton Review, 1745 Broadway, New York, NY 10019 *Tel;* 212-829-6928 *Toll Free Tel:* 800-733-3000 *Fax:* 212-940-7400 *E-mail:* princetonreview@randomhouse.com *Web Site:* www.princetonreview.com, pg 218

Naggar, David, Random House Audio Publishing Group, 1745 Broadway, New York, NY 10019 *Tel:* 212-782-9720 *Fax:* 212-782-9600, pg 225

Naggar, David, Random House Inc, 1745 Broadway, New York, NY 10019 *Tel:* 212-782-9000 *Toll Free Tel:* 800-726-0600 *Web Site:* www.randomhouse.com, pg 226

Naggar, David, Random House Large Print, 1745 Broadway, New York, NY 10019 *Tel:* 212-782-9720 *Fax:* 212-782-9600, pg 227

Naggar, David, Random House Reference, 1745 Broadway, New York, NY 10019 *Toll Free Tel:* 800-733-3000 *E-mail:* words@random.com; puzzles@ random.com, pg 227

Naggar, David, Random House Value Publishing, 1745 Broadway, New York, NY 10019 *Tel:* 212-940-7422 *Fax:* 212-572-2114, pg 227

Naggar, Jean, Jean V Naggar Literary Agency, 216 E 75 St, Suite 1-E, New York, NY 10021 *Tel:* 212-794-1082, pg 645

Nagy, Maureen, The Overlook Press, 141 Wooster St, New York, NY 10012 *Tel:* 212-965-8400 *Fax:* 212-965-9834 *Web Site:* www.overlookny.com, pg 200

Naiburg, Irving B Jr, Ardent Media Inc, 522 E 82 St, Suite 1, New York, NY 10028 *Tel:* 212-861-1501 *Fax:* 212-861-0998 *E-mail:* ivyboxer@aol.com, pg 23

Nail, Dawson B, Warren Communications News, 2115 Ward Ct NW, Washington, DC 20037-1209 *Tel:* 202-872-9200 *Fax:* 202-293-3435 *E-mail:* info@warren-news.com *Web Site:* www.warren-news.com, pg 293

Nairin, Brian, Elsevier, 11830 Westline Industrial Dr, St Louis, MO 63146 *Tel:* 314-872-8370 *Toll Free Tel:* 800-325-4177 *Fax:* 314-432-1380 *Web Site:* www.elsevier.com; www.elsevierhealth.com, pg 89

Nairin, Brian, Mosby Journal Division, 11830 Westline Industrial Dr, St Louis, MO 63146 *Tel:* 314-872-8370 *Toll Free Tel:* 800-325-4177 *Web Site:* www.elsevierhealth.com, pg 179

Nairin, Brian, W B Saunders Ltd, 170 S Independence Mall W, Suite 300 E, Philadelphia, PA 19106-3399 *Tel:* 215-238-7800 *Toll Free Tel:* 800-545-2522 (cust serv) *Fax:* 215-238-7883 *Web Site:* www.elsevierhealth.com, pg 240

Nanavati, Madhu, Lilmur Publishing, 147 Brooke Ave, Toronto, ON M5M 2K3, Canada *Tel:* 416-486-0145 *Fax:* 416-486-5380, pg 552

Nance, Brett, The Jesse Stuart Foundation, PO Box 669, Ashland, KY 41105-0669 *Tel:* 606-326-1667 *Fax:* 606-325-2519 *Web Site:* www.jsfbooks.com, pg 260

Nantier, Terry, NBM Publishing Inc, 555 Eighth Ave, Suite 1202, New York, NY 10018 *Tel:* 212-643-5407 *Toll Free Tel:* 800-886-1223 *Fax:* 212-643-1545 *E-mail:* admin@nbmpub.com *Web Site:* www.nbmpub.com, pg 185

Naoum, Nadine, Groupe Beauchemin, Editeur Ltee, 3281 ave Jean Beraud, Laval, PQ H7T 2L2, Canada *Tel:* 514-334-5912 *Toll Free Tel:* 800-361-2598 (US & Canada); 800-361-4504 (Canada Only) *Fax:* 450-688-6269 *E-mail:* promotion@beauchemin.qc.ca *Web Site:* www.beaucheminediteur.com, pg 536

Naples, Mary Ann, The Creative Culture Inc, 72 Spring St, Suite 304, New York, NY 10012 *Tel:* 212-680-3510 *Fax:* 212-680-3509 *Web Site:* www.thecreativeculture.com, pg 626

Napoli, Philip, Fordham University, Graduate School of Business Administration, Dept of Communications & Media Management, 113 W 60 St, New York, NY 10023 *Tel:* 212-636-6199 *Fax:* 212-765-5573, pg 752

Napoli, Tony, Bluewood Books, 38 South "B" St, Suite 202, San Mateo, CA 94401 *Tel:* 650-548-0754 *Fax:* 650-548-0654 *E-mail:* bluewoodb@aol.com, pg 42

Nardone, Gay, Anna Zornio Memorial Children's Theatre Playwriting Award, Paul Creative Arts, 30 College Rd, D-22, Durham, NH 03824-3538 *Tel:* 603-862-3038 *Fax:* 603-862-0298, pg 814

Naselli, Mara, Association of American University Presses, 1427 E 60 St, Chicago, IL 60637 *Tel:* 773-702-7700; 773-702-7600 *Toll Free Tel:* 800-621-2736 (orders) *Fax:* 773-702-9756 (sales); 773-660-2235 (orders); 773-702-2708 *E-mail:* general@press.uchicago.edu *Web Site:* www.press.uchicago.edu, pg 26

Nash, Dave, C & T Publishing Inc, 1651 Challenge Dr, Concord, CA 94520 *Tel:* 925-677-0377 *Toll Free Tel:* 800-284-1114 *Fax:* 925-677-0373 *E-mail:* ctinfo@ctpub.com *Web Site:* www.ctpub.com, pg 51

Nash, Leanne, Christian History Project, 10333 178 St, Edmonton, AB T5N 2H7, Canada *Tel:* 780-443-4775 *Toll Free Tel:* 800-853-5402 *Fax:* 780-454-9298 *E-mail:* orders@christianhistoryproject.com *Web Site:* www.christianhistoryproject.com, pg 540

Nason, Beverly, Bawn Publishers Inc, 8877 Meadowview Dr, West Chester, OH 45069-3545 *Tel:* 513-759-6288 *Fax:* 513-759-6299 *E-mail:* bawn@one.net *Web Site:* www.bawnagency.com, pg 620

Nason, Willie, Bawn Publishers Inc, 8877 Meadowview Dr, West Chester, OH 45069-3545 *Tel:* 513-759-6288 *Fax:* 513-759-6299 *E-mail:* bawn@one.net *Web Site:* www.bawnagency.com, pg 620

Nassis, Christopher, Diverse Talent Group, 1875 Century Park E, Suite 2250, Los Angeles, CA 90067 *Tel:* 310-201-6565 *Fax:* 310-201-6572, pg 628

Nassise, Joseph, Horror Writers Association, PO Box 50577, Palo Alto, CA 94303 *E-mail:* hwa@horror.org *Web Site:* www.horror.org/, pg 688

Nathan, Jan, Benjamin Franklin Book Awards, 627 Aviation Way, Manhattan Beach, CA 90266 *Tel:* 310-372-2732 *Fax:* 310-374-3342 *E-mail:* info@pma-online.org *Web Site:* www.pma-online.org, pg 762

Nathan, Jan, Publishers Marketing Association (PMA), 627 Aviation Way, Manhattan Beach, CA 90266 *Tel:* 310-372-2732 *Fax:* 310-374-3342 *E-mail:* info@pma-online.org *Web Site:* www.pma-online.org, pg 698

Nathan, Rhoda, The Bernard Shaw Society, Box 1159, Madison Square Sta, New York, NY 10159-1159 *Tel:* 212-989-7833; 212-982-9885, pg 699

Nathan, Terry, Publishers Marketing Association (PMA), 627 Aviation Way, Manhattan Beach, CA 90266 *Tel:* 310-372-2732 *Fax:* 310-374-3342 *E-mail:* info@pma-online.org *Web Site:* www.pma-online.org, pg 698

Nathanson, Paul Alan, The Wordwatcher, 605-4854 Cote-des-Neiges, Montreal, PQ H3V 1G7, Canada *Tel:* 514-739-9274; 514-398-1511 *E-mail:* wordwatcher@vif.com *Web Site:* www.vif.com/users/wordwatcher/, pg 614

Nauf, Pat, Teacher's Discovery, 2741 Paldan Dr, Auburn Hills, MI 48326 *Tel:* 248-340-7220 ext 207 *Toll Free Tel:* 800-521-3897 *Fax:* 248-340-7212 *Toll Free Fax:* 888-987-2436 *Web Site:* www.teachersdiscovery.com, pg 265

Naughton, Diane, HarperCollins Children's Books Group, 1350 Sixth Ave, New York, NY 10019 *Tel:* 212-261-6500 *Web Site:* www.harperchildrens.com, pg 115

Naughton, Marjorie, Clarion Books, 215 Park Ave S, New York, NY 10003 *Tel:* 212-420-5800 *Toll Free Tel:* 800-225-3362 (orders) *Fax:* 212-420-5855 *Web Site:* www.clarion.com, pg 62

Nault, Jennifer, Banff Centre Press, 107 Tunnel Mountain Dr, Box 1020, Banff, AB T1L 1H5, Canada *Tel:* 403-762-7532 *Fax:* 403-762-6699 *E-mail:* press@banffcentre.ca *Web Site:* www.banffcentre.ca/press, pg 536

Nava, Lucille, Chrysalis Publishing Group Inc, 34 Main St, Natick, MA 01760 *Tel:* 508-647-3730 *Toll Free Tel:* 877-922-1822 *Fax:* 508-653-3448 *E-mail:* info@chrysalispublishing.com *Web Site:* www.chrysalispublishing.com, pg 594

Nave, Lisa, Douglas & McIntyre Publishing Group, 2323 Quebec St, Suite 201, Vancouver, BC V5T 4S7, Canada *Tel:* 604-254-7191 *Toll Free Tel:* 800-565-9523 (orders in Canada) *Fax:* 604-254-9099 *Toll Free Fax:* 800-221-9985 (orders in Canada) *E-mail:* dm@douglas-mcintyre.com *Web Site:* www.douglas-mcintyre.com, pg 542

Navera, Dorothy, Chelsea House Publishers LLC, 2080 Cabot Blvd W, Suite 201, Langhorne, PA 19047-1813 *Tel:* 610-353-5166 *Toll Free Tel:* 800-848-BOOK (848-2665) *Fax:* 610-359-1439 *Toll Free Fax:* 877-780-7300 *E-mail:* sales@chelseahouse.com *Web Site:* www.chelseahouse.com, pg 59

Navratil, Chris, Chronicle Books LLC, 85 Second St, 6th fl, San Francisco, CA 94105 *Tel:* 415-537-4200 *Toll Free Tel:* 800-722-6657 (cust serv) *Fax:* 415-537-4460 *Toll Free Fax:* 800-858-7787 (orders) *E-mail:* frontdesk@chroniclebooks.com *Web Site:* www.chroniclebooks.com, pg 61

Nawrocki, Sarah, Trinity University Press, One Trinity Place, San Antonio, TX 78212-7200 *Tel:* 210-999-8884 *Fax:* 210-999-8838 *E-mail:* books@trinity.edu *Web Site:* www.trinity.edu/tupress, pg 275

Nayer, Rick, Berkley Books, 375 Hudson St, New York, NY 10014 *Tel:* 212-366-2000 *Fax:* 212-366-2666 *E-mail:* online@penguinputnam.com *Web Site:* www.penguin.com, pg 36

Nayer, Rick, Berkley Publishing Group, 375 Hudson St, New York, NY 10014 *Tel:* 212-366-2000 *E-mail:* online@penguinputnam.com *Web Site:* www.penguin.com, pg 37

Nayer, Rick, NAL, 375 Hudson St, New York, NY 10014 *Tel:* 212-366-2000 *E-mail:* online@penguinputnam.com *Web Site:* www.penguin.com, pg 181

Naziruddin, Ali M, American Trust Publications, 745 McClintock Dr, Suite 114, Burr Ridge, IL 60527 *Tel:* 630-789-9191 *Toll Free Tel:* 888-319-5858 *Fax:* 630-789-9455 *Web Site:* www.nait.net, pg 18

Nead, Mary Ann, RCL Resources for Christian Living, 200 E Bethany, Allen, TX 75002 *Tel:* 972-390-6300 *Toll Free Tel:* 800-527-5030 *Fax:* 972-390-6560 *Toll Free Fax:* 800-688-8356 *E-mail:* cservice@rcl-enterprises.com *Web Site:* www.rclweb.com, pg 228

Neaderland, Louise, International Society of Copier Artists Ltd (ISCA), 759 President St, Suite 2H, Brooklyn, NY 11215 *Tel:* 718-638-3264 *E-mail:* isca4art2b@aol.com, pg 689

Neal, John Vincent, Neal-Schuman Publishers Inc, 100 William St, Suite 2004, New York, NY 10038 *Tel:* 212-925-8650 *Toll Free Tel:* 866-672-6657 *Toll Free Fax:* 866-209-7932 *E-mail:* orders@neal-schuman.com *Web Site:* www.neal-schuman.com, pg 186

Neal, June, Harcourt Inc, 6277 Sea Harbor Dr, Orlando, FL 32887 *Tel:* 407-345-2000 *Toll Free Tel:* 800-225-5425 (cust serv) *Fax:* 407-352-3445 (cust serv), pg 114

Neal, Mitchell, Holloway House Publishing Co, 8060 Melrose Ave, Los Angeles, CA 90046-7082 *Tel:* 323-653-8060 *Fax:* 323-655-9452 *E-mail:* info@hollowayhousebooks.com *Web Site:* www.hollowayhousebooks.com, pg 124

Neal, Rae, Multicultural Publications, 936 Slosson Ave, Akron, OH 44320 *Tel:* 330-865-9578 *Toll Free Tel:* 800-238-0297 *Fax:* 330-865-9578 *E-mail:* info@multiculturalpub.net *Web Site:* www.multiculturalpub.net, pg 180

Neale, John, Doubleday Canada, One Toronto St, Suite 300, Toronto, ON M5C 2V6, Canada *Tel:* 416-364-4449 *Fax:* 416-957-1587 *Web Site:* www.randomhouse.ca, pg 542

Neale, John, Knopf Canada, One Toronto St, Suite 300, Toronto, ON M5C 2V6, Canada *Tel:* 416-364-4449 *Toll Free Tel:* 800-668-4247 (order desk) *Fax:* 416-364-0462 *Web Site:* www.randomhouse.ca, pg 552

Neale, John, Random House of Canada Ltd, One Toronto St, Unit 300, Toronto, ON M5C 2V6, Canada *Tel:* 416-364-4449 *Fax:* 416-364-6863 (edit & publicity); 416-364-6653 (subs rts) *Web Site:* www.randomhouse.ca, pg 559

Neale, John, Seal Books, One Toronto St, Suite 300, Toronto, ON M5C 2V6, Canada *Tel:* 416-364-4449 *Toll Free Tel:* 888-523-9292 (order desk) *Fax:* 416-957-1587 *Web Site:* www.randomhouse.ca, pg 560

Nealeigh, Robert, Warner Faith (Christian Book Division of Time Warner Book Group), 2 Creekside Crossing, 10 Cadillac Dr, Suite 220, Brentwood, TN 37027 *Tel:* 615-221-0996 *Fax:* 615-221-0962 *Web Site:* www.twbookmark.com, pg 293

Necarsulmer, Edward IV, McIntosh & Otis Inc, 353 Lexington Ave, Suite 1500, New York, NY 10016-0900 *Tel:* 212-687-7400 *Fax:* 212-687-6894 *E-mail:* info@mcintoshandotis.com, pg 643

Necker, Rachel, Stylus Publishing LLC, 22883 Quicksilver Dr, Sterling, VA 20166-2012 *Tel:* 703-661-1504 (edit & sales) *Toll Free Tel:* 800-232-0223 *Fax:* 703-661-1547 *E-mail:* stylusmail@presswarehouse.com; stylusinfo@styluspub.com *Web Site:* styluspub.com, pg 261

Nedder, Ernie, E T Nedder Publishing, 9121 E Tanque Verde, Suite 105, PMB 299, Tucson, AZ 85749-8390 *Tel:* 520-760-2742 *Toll Free Tel:* 877-817-2742 *Fax:* 520-760-5883 *E-mail:* enedder@hotmail.com *Web Site:* nedderpublishing.com, pg 186

Nedder, Kathy, E T Nedder Publishing, 9121 E Tanque Verde, Suite 105, PMB 299, Tucson, AZ 85749-8390 *Tel:* 520-760-2742 *Toll Free Tel:* 877-817-2742 *Fax:* 520-760-5883 *E-mail:* enedder@hotmail.com *Web Site:* nedderpublishing.com, pg 186

Nedelcu, Maria, Teora USA LLC, 2 Wisconsin Circle, Suite 870, Chevy Chase, MD 20815 *Tel:* 301-986-6990 *Toll Free Tel:* 800-358-3754 *Fax:* 301-986-6992 *Toll Free Fax:* 800-358-3754 *E-mail:* info@teora.com *Web Site:* www.teorausa.com, pg 266

Nederveld, Faith, CRC Publications, 2850 Kalamazoo Ave SE, Grand Rapids, MI 49560 *Tel:* 616-224-0819; 616-224-0728 *Toll Free Tel:* 800-333-8300 *Fax:* 616-224-0834 *E-mail:* sales@crcpublications.org *Web Site:* www.faithaliveresources.org, pg 72

Nee, John, DC Comics, 1700 Broadway, New York, NY 10019 *Tel:* 212-636-5400 *Toll Free Tel:* 800-759-0190 (distribution) *Fax:* 212-636-5481 *Web Site:* www.dccomics.com; www.madmag.com, pg 77

Needham, Beryl, Random House Sales & Marketing, 1745 Broadway, New York, NY 10019 *Fax:* 212-782-9000, pg 227

Needham, Susan, The Catholic University of America Press, 240 Leahy Hall, 620 Michigan Ave NE, Washington, DC 20064 *Tel:* 202-319-5052 *Fax:* 202-319-4985 *E-mail:* cua-press@cua.edu *Web Site:* cuapress.cua.edu, pg 55

Neel, Thomas Stephen, Ohio Genealogical Society, 713 S Main St, Mansfield, OH 44907-1644 *Tel:* 419-756-7294 *Fax:* 419-756-6861 *E-mail:* ogs@ogs.org *Web Site:* www.ogs.org, pg 196

Neely, Judith Illov, F A Davis Co, 1915 Arch St, Philadelphia, PA 19103 *Tel:* 215-568-2270 *Toll Free Tel:* 800-523-4049 *Fax:* 215-568-5065 *E-mail:* info@fadavis.com *Web Site:* www.fadavis.com, pg 76

Neesemann, Cynthia, CS International Literary Agency, 43 W 39 St, New York, NY 10018 *Tel:* 212-921-1610 *E-mail:* csliterary@verizon.net, pg 595

Negri, Alexandre, Black Rose Books Ltd, CP 1258 Succ Place de Parc, Montreal, PQ H2X 4A7, Canada *Tel:* 514-844-4076 *Toll Free Tel:* 800-565-9523 *Fax:* 514-849-4797 *Toll Free Fax:* 800-221-9985 *E-mail:* blackrose@web.net *Web Site:* www.web.net/blackrosebooks, pg 536

Negri, Paul, Dover Publications Inc, 31 E Second St, Mineola, NY 11501 *Tel:* 516-294-7000 *Toll Free Tel:* 800-223-3130 (orders) *Fax:* 516-742-6953; 516-742-5049 (orders) *Web Site:* www.doverpublications.com; www.doverdirect.com, pg 83

Nehmer, Kathy, Educators Progress Service Inc, 214 Center St, Randolph, WI 53956 *Tel:* 920-326-3126 *Toll Free Tel:* 888-951-4469 *Fax:* 920-326-3127 *E-mail:* epsinc@centurytel.net, pg 88

Neibauer, Nathan, Neibauer Press, 20 Industrial Dr, Warminster, PA 18974 *Tel:* 215-322-6200 *Toll Free Tel:* 800-322-6203 *Fax:* 215-322-2495 *E-mail:* sales@neibauer.com *Web Site:* www.churchstewardship.com, pg 186

Neimark, Nina, Nina Neimark Editorial Services, 543 Third St, Brooklyn, NY 11215 *Tel:* 718-499-6804 *E-mail:* pneimark@hotmail.com, pg 606

Neimark-Hussain, Tanya, Pearson, 800 E 96 St, Indianapolis, IN 46240 *Tel:* 317-428-3000 *Toll Free Tel:* 800-545-5914 *Fax:* 317-581-4675 *Web Site:* www.macdigital.com, pg 206

Neister, Scott, Crawford Literary Agency, 94 Evans Rd, Barnstead, NH 03218 *Tel:* 603-269-5851 *Fax:* 603-269-2533 *E-mail:* crawfordlit@att.net, pg 626

Nellis, Muriel G, Literary & Creative Artists Inc, 3543 Albemarle St NW, Washington, DC 20008-4213 *Tel:* 202-362-4688 *Fax:* 202-362-8875 *E-mail:* query@lcadc.com (no attachments) *Web Site:* www.lcadc.com, pg 641

Nelson, Andrea, Warner Bros Publications Inc, 15800 NW 48 Ave, Miami, FL 33014 *Tel:* 305-620-1500 *Toll Free Tel:* 800-327-7643 *Fax:* 305-621-4869 *E-mail:* wbpsales@warnerchappell.com *Web Site:* www.warnerbrospublications.com, pg 293

Nelson, Bonita K, Literacy Institute for Education (LIFE) Inc, 84 Woodland Rd, Pleasantville, NY 10570 *Tel:* 914-741-1322 *Fax:* 914-741-1324 *Web Site:* bknelson.com, pg 156

Nelson, Bonita K, B K Nelson Inc Lecture Bureau, 84 Woodland Rd, Pleasantville, NY 10570 *Tel:* 914-741-1322; 212-889-0637 *Fax:* 914-741-1323 *E-mail:* bknelson4@cs.com *Web Site:* www.bknelson.com, pg 670

Nelson, Bonita K, B K Nelson Inc Literary Agency, 1565 Paseo Vida, Palm Springs, CA 92264 *Tel:* 760-778-8800 *Fax:* 914-778-0034 *E-mail:* bknelson4@cs.com *Web Site:* www.bknelson.com, pg 645

Nelson, Dan, Print Buyers Association (Printing Industries of Northern Calif), 665 Third St, Suite 500, San Francisco, CA 94107 *Tel:* 415-495-8242 *Fax:* 415-543-7790 *E-mail:* info@pinc.org *Web Site:* www.pinc.org, pg 697

Nelson, David, Impressions Book & Journal Services Inc, 2016 Winnebago St, Madison, WI 53704 *Tel:* 608-244-6218 *Fax:* 608-244-7050 *E-mail:* info@impressions.com *Web Site:* www.impressions.com, pg 602

Nelson, Eileen M, Redleaf Press, 10 Yorkton Ct, St Paul, MN 55117 *Tel:* 651-641-0305 *Toll Free Tel:* 800-423-8309 *Toll Free Fax:* 800-641-0115 *Web Site:* www.redleafpress.org, pg 230

Nelson, Jandy, Manus & Associates Literary Agency Inc, 445 Park Ave, New York, NY 10022 *Tel:* 650-470-5151 (CA) *Fax:* 650-470-5159 (CA) *E-mail:* manuslit@manuslit.com *Web Site:* www.manuslit.com, pg 642

Nelson, Jeffrey O, ISI Books, PO Box 4431, 3901 Centerville Rd, Wilmington, DE 19807 *Tel:* 302-652-4600 *Toll Free Tel:* 800-526-7022 *Fax:* 302-652-1760 *E-mail:* bookstore@isi.org *Web Site:* www.isibooks.org, pg 139

Nelson, Jennifer W, B K Nelson Inc Lecture Bureau, 84 Woodland Rd, Pleasantville, NY 10570 *Tel:* 914-741-1322; 212-889-0637 *Fax:* 914-741-1323 *E-mail:* bknelson4@cs.com *Web Site:* www.bknelson.com, pg 670

Nelson, Karen, Sterling Publishing Co Inc, 387 Park Ave S, 5th fl, New York, NY 10016-8810 *Tel:* 212-532-7160 *Toll Free Tel:* 800-367-9692 *Fax:* 212-213-2495 *Web Site:* www.sterlingpub.com, pg 259

Nelson, Kristin, Nelson Literary Agency LLC, 1020 15 St, Suite 26L, Denver, CO 80202 *Tel:* 303-463-5301 *Fax:* 720-384-0761 *E-mail:* query@nelsonagency.com *Web Site:* nelsonagency.com, pg 645

Nelson, Patricia, Kneerim & Williams, c/o Fish & Richardson PC, 225 Franklin St, Boston, MA 02110 *Tel:* 617-542-5070 *Fax:* 617-542-8906 *Web Site:* www.fr.com, pg 638

Nelson, Paul L, Modern Radio Laboratories, PO Box 14902, Minneapolis, MN 55414-0902 *Web Site:* www.modernradiolabs.com, pg 176

Nelson, Stephen R, Sheffield Publishing Co, 9009 Antioch Rd, Salem, WI 53168 *Tel:* 262-843-2281 *Fax:* 262-843-3683 *E-mail:* info@spcbooks.com *Web Site:* www.spcbooks.com, pg 246

Nelson, Steve, APS Press, 3340 Pilot Knob Rd, St Paul, MN 55121-2097 *Tel:* 651-454-7250 *Toll Free Tel:* 800-328-7560 *Fax:* 651-454-0766 *E-mail:* aps@scisoc.org *Web Site:* www.shopapspress.org, pg 22

Nelson, Steve, Eagan Press, 3340 Pilot Knob Rd, St Paul, MN 55121-2097 *Tel:* 651-454-7250 *Toll Free Tel:* 800-328-7560 *Fax:* 651-454-0766 *E-mail:* aacc@scisoc.org *Web Site:* www.aaccnet.org, pg 85

Nelson, Steven, American Phytopathological Society, 3340 Pilot Knob Rd, St Paul, MN 55121-2097 *Tel:* 651-454-7250 *Toll Free Tel:* 800-328-7560 *Fax:* 651-454-0766 *E-mail:* aps@scisoc.org *Web Site:* www.apsnet.org, pg 16

Nelson, Steven C, American Association of Cereal Chemists, 3340 Pilot Knob Rd, St Paul, MN 55121-2097 *Tel:* 651-454-7250 *Toll Free Tel:* 800-328-7560 *Fax:* 651-454-0766 *E-mail:* aacc@scisoc.org *Web Site:* www.aaccnet.org, pg 11

Nelson, Zachary, Heyday Books, 2054 University Ave, Berkeley, CA 94704 *Tel:* 510-549-3564 *Fax:* 510-549-1889 *E-mail:* heyday@heydaybooks.com *Web Site:* www.heydaybooks.com, pg 122

Nemeth, Terence, Theatre Communications Group Inc, 520 Eighth Ave, New York, NY 10018 *Tel:* 212-609-5900 *Fax:* 212-609-5901 *E-mail:* tcg@tcg.org *Web Site:* www.tcg.org, pg 268

Nephew, John, Trident Inc, 885 Pierce Butler Rte, St Paul, MN 55104 *Tel:* 651-638-0077 *Fax:* 651-638-0084 *E-mail:* info@atlas-games.com *Web Site:* www.atlas-games.com, pg 275

Nero, Laura, The RGU Group, 560 W Southern Ave, Tempe, AZ 85282 *Tel:* 480-736-9862 *Toll Free Tel:* 800-266-5265 *Fax:* 480-736-9863 *Toll Free Fax:* 800-973-6694 *E-mail:* info@thergugroup.com *Web Site:* www.thergugroup.com, pg 232

Nesbit, Glenda, David W & Beatrice C Evans Biography & Handcart Awards, 0735 Old Main Hill, Logan, UT 84322-0735 *Tel:* 435-797-3630 *Fax:* 435-797-3899 *E-mail:* mwc@cc.usu.edu *Web Site:* www.usu.edu/mountainwest, pg 772

Nesbit, Lynn, Janklow & Nesbit Associates, 445 Park Ave, New York, NY 10022 *Tel:* 212-421-1700 *Fax:* 212-980-3671 *E-mail:* postmaster@janklow.com, pg 636

Nesbitt, Bruce, Nesbitt Graphics Inc, 555 Virginia Dr, Fort Washington, PA 19034 *Tel:* 215-591-9125 *Fax:* 215-591-9093 *Web Site:* www.Nesbittgraphics.com, pg 606

Nesbitt, Harry J III, Nesbitt Graphics Inc, 555 Virginia Dr, Fort Washington, PA 19034 *Tel:* 215-591-9125 *Fax:* 215-591-9093 *Web Site:* www.Nesbittgraphics.com, pg 606

Neshui, Mr, Neshui Publishing, 2838 Cherokee, St Louis, MO 63118 *Tel:* 314-772-3090 *E-mail:* neshui62@hotmail.com, pg 187

Nessen, Cortney, Gibbs Smith Publisher, 1877 E Gentile, Layton, UT 84040 *Tel:* 801-544-9800 *Toll Free Tel:* 800-748-5439 (orders only) *Fax:* 801-544-5582 *Toll Free Fax:* 800-213-3023 (orders only) *E-mail:* info@gibbs-smith.com *Web Site:* www.gibbs-smith.com, pg 104

Nettles, Olin, American Psychological Association, 750 First St NE, Washington, DC 20002-4242 *Tel:* 202-336-5500 *Toll Free Tel:* 800-374-2721 *Fax:* 202-336-5620 *E-mail:* order@apa.org *Web Site:* www.apa.org/books, pg 17

Nettleton, Kathleen Calhoun, Pelican Publishing Co Inc, 1000 Burmaster, Gretna, LA 70053 *Tel:* 504-368-1175 *Toll Free Tel:* 800-843-1724 *Fax:* 504-368-1195 *E-mail:* sales@pelicanpub.com (sales); office@pelicanpub.com (permission); promo@pelicanpub.com (publicity) *Web Site:* www.pelicanpub.com, pg 207

Neubauer, Mrs H, Papyrus & Letterbox of London Publishers, 10501 Broom Hill Dr, Las Vegas, NV 89134-7339 *Tel:* 702-256-3838 *E-mail:* LB27383@earthlink.net *Web Site:* booksbyletterbox.com, pg 203

Neuburger, Rebecca, Police Executive Research Forum, 1120 Connecticut Ave NW, Suite 930, Washington, DC 20036 *Tel:* 202-466-7820 *Toll Free Tel:* 888-202-4563 (cust serv) *Fax:* 202-466-7826 *E-mail:* perf@policeforum.org *Web Site:* www.policeforum.org, pg 216

Neufeld, J, Safari Press, 15621 Chemical Lane, Bldg B, Huntington Beach, CA 92649 *Tel:* 714-894-9080 *Toll Free Tel:* 800-451-4788 *Fax:* 714-894-4949 *E-mail:* info@safaripress.com *Web Site:* www.safaripress.com, pg 237

Neumann, Rachel, Parallax Press, PO Box 7355, Berkeley, CA 94707-0355 *Tel:* 510-525-0101 *Fax:* 510-525-7129 *E-mail:* parallax@parallax.org *Web Site:* www.parallax.org, pg 204

Neville, Joanna, Maupin House Publishing, 4445 SW 35 Terr, Suite 200, Gainesville, FL 32608 *Tel:* 352-373-5588 *Toll Free Tel:* 800-524-0634 (orders only) *Fax:* 352-373-5546 *E-mail:* sales@maupinhouse.com *Web Site:* www.maupinhouse.com, pg 165

Nevins, Alan, The Firm, 9465 Wilshire Blvd, Beverly Hills, CA 90212 *Tel:* 310-860-8000 *Fax:* 310-860-8132, pg 630

Nevins, Linda M, Christopher-Gordon Publishers Inc, 1502 Providence Hwy, Suite 12, Norwood, MA 02062 *Tel:* 781-762-5577 *Toll Free Tel:* 800-934-8322 *Fax:* 781-762-2110 *Web Site:* www.christopher-gordon.com, pg 61

Nevo, Susan, Learning Links Inc, 2300 Marcus Ave, New Hyde Park, NY 11042 *Tel:* 516-437-9071 *Toll Free Tel:* 800-724-2616 *Fax:* 516-437-5392 *E-mail:* learning1x@aol.com *Web Site:* www.learninglinks.com, pg 151

Nevraumont, Peter N, Nevraumont Publishing Co, 71 Broadway, New York, NY 10006 *Tel:* 212-425-3270 *Fax:* 212-425-1818 *E-mail:* nevpub@cs.com, pg 187

New, Carol, Cambridge University Press, 40 W 20 St, New York, NY 10011-4211 *Tel:* 212-924-3900 *Toll Free Tel:* 800-899-5222 *Fax:* 212-691-3239 *Web Site:* www.cambridge.org, pg 52

Newberg, Esther, International Creative Management, 40 W 57 St, New York, NY 10019 *Tel:* 212-556-5600 *Fax:* 212-556-5665 *Web Site:* www.icmtalent.com, pg 635

Newborn, Barry, JIST Publishing Inc, 8902 Otis Ave, Indianapolis, IN 46216 *Tel:* 317-613-4200 *Toll Free Tel:* 800-648-5478 *Fax:* 317-613-4304 *Toll Free Fax:* 800-547-8329 *E-mail:* info@jist.com *Web Site:* www.jist.com, pg 141

Newborn, Sasha Briar, Bandanna Books, 1212 Punta Gorda St, Suite 13, Santa Barbara, CA 93103 *Tel:* 805-899-2145 *Fax:* 805-899-2145 *E-mail:* bandanna@cox.net *Web Site:* www.beachcollege.net/bookstore, pg 31

Newborn, Tangie, National Association of Black Journalists (NABJ), c/o University of Maryland, 8701 Adelphi Rd, Adelphi, MD 20783 *Tel:* 301-445-7100 *Fax:* 301-445-7101 *E-mail:* nabj@nabj.org *Web Site:* www.nabj.org, pg 692

Newcomb, Trish, The McDonald & Woodward Publishing Co, 431-B E College St, Granville, OH 43023 *Tel:* 740-321-1140 *Toll Free Tel:* 800-233-8787 *Fax:* 740-321-1141 *E-mail:* mwpubco@mwpubco.com *Web Site:* www.mwpubco.com, pg 166

Newell, Patricia, North Country Press, RR1, Box 1395, Unity, ME 04988-1395 *Tel:* 207-948-2208 *Fax:* 207-948-9000 *E-mail:* info@ncpbooks.com *Web Site:* www.ncpbooks.com, pg 192

Newlin, Bill, Avalon Publishing Group Inc, 1400 65 St, Suite 250, Emeryville, CA 94608 *Tel:* 510-595-3664 *Fax:* 510-535-4228 *Web Site:* www.avalonpub.com, pg 29

Newlin, Bill, Avalon Travel Publishing, 1400 65 St, Suite 250, Emeryville, CA 94608 *Tel:* 510-595-3664 *Fax:* 510-535-4228 *E-mail:* info@travelmatters.com *Web Site:* www.travelmatters.com, pg 29

Newman, Dr Al, River City Publishing, LLC, 1719 Mulberry St, Montgomery, AL 36106 *Tel:* 334-265-6753 *Toll Free Tel:* 877-408-7078 *Fax:* 334-265-8880 *E-mail:* web@rivercitypublishing.com *Web Site:* www.rivercitypublishing.com, pg 232

Newman, Barbara, Frederick Fell Publishers Inc, 2131 Hollywood Blvd, Suite 305, Hollywood, FL 33020 *Tel:* 954-925-5242 *Toll Free Tel:* 800-771-FELL (771-3355) *Fax:* 954-925-5244 *E-mail:* info@fellpub.com *Web Site:* www.fellpub.com, pg 100

Newman, Carey C, Baylor University Press, Baylor University, Waco, TX 76798-7363 *Tel:* 254-710-3164 *Toll Free Tel:* 800-710-3217 *Fax:* 254-710-3440 *Web Site:* www.baylorpress.com, pg 33

Newman, Carolyn, River City Publishing, LLC, 1719 Mulberry St, Montgomery, AL 36106 *Tel:* 334-265-6753 *Toll Free Tel:* 877-408-7078 *Fax:* 334-265-8880 *E-mail:* web@rivercitypublishing.com *Web Site:* www.rivercitypublishing.com, pg 232

Newman, Felice, Cleis Press, PO Box 14684, San Francisco, CA 94114-0684 *Tel:* 415-575-4700 *Toll Free Tel:* 800-780-2279 (US) *Fax:* 415-575-4705 *E-mail:* cleis@cleispress.com *Web Site:* www.cleispress.com, pg 63

Newman, James F, Oceana Publications Inc, 75 Main St, Dobbs Ferry, NY 10522-1601 *Tel:* 914-693-8100 *Toll Free Tel:* 800-831-0758 (orders only) *Fax:* 914-693-0402 *E-mail:* info@oceanalaw.com *Web Site:* www.oceanalaw.com, pg 195

Newman, Judith, Scholastic Trade Division, 557 Broadway, New York, NY 10012 *Tel:* 212-343-6100; 212-343-4685 (export sales) *Fax:* 212-343-4714 (export sales) *Web Site:* www.scholastic.com, pg 242

Newman, Judy, Scholastic Inc, 557 Broadway, New York, NY 10012 *Tel:* 212-343-6100 *Toll Free Tel:* 800-scholastic *Fax:* 212-343-6930 *Web Site:* www.scholastic.com, pg 242

Newman, Leslie, ST Publications Book Division, 407 Gilbert Ave, Cincinnati, OH 45202 *Tel:* 513-421-2050 *Toll Free Tel:* 800-925-1110 *Fax:* 513-421-5144 *E-mail:* books@stpubs.com *Web Site:* www.stpubs.com, pg 257

Newman, Megan, Avery, 375 Hudson St, New York, NY 10014 *Tel:* 212-366-2000 *Fax:* 212-366-2643 *E-mail:* online@penguinputnam.com *Web Site:* www.penguinputnam.com, pg 29

Newman, Megan, Viking Studio, 375 Hudson St, New York, NY 10014 *Tel:* 212-366-2000 *E-mail:* online@penguinputnam.com *Web Site:* www.penguin.com, pg 290

Newsom, Lori Michele, International Monetary Fund (IMF), 700 19 St NW, Suite 12-607, Washington, DC 20431 *Tel:* 202-623-7430 *Fax:* 202-623-7201 *E-mail:* publications@imf.org *Web Site:* www.imf.org, pg 137

Newton, Greg, Metal Bulletin Inc, 1250 Broadway, 26th fl, New York, NY 10001 *Tel:* 212-213-6202 *Toll Free Tel:* 800-638-2525 *Fax:* 212-213-6273 *Web Site:* www.metbul.com, pg 172

Newton, Marit, Emerald Books, PO Box 635, Lynnwood, WA 98046 *Tel:* 425-771-1153 *Toll Free Tel:* 800-922-2143 *Fax:* 425-775-2383 *E-mail:* emeraldbooks@seanet.com *Web Site:* www.ywampublishing.com, pg 90

Neylon, Sheila, Educators Publishing Service Inc, 625 Mount Auburn St, Cambridge, MA 02139-9031 *Tel:* 617-547-6706 *Toll Free Tel:* 800-225-5750 *Fax:* 617-547-0412 *Toll Free Fax:* 888-440-2665 *E-mail:* epsbooks@epsbooks.com *Web Site:* www.epsbooks.com, pg 88

Nguyen, Diep, Narada Press, 160 Columbia St W, Suite 147, Waterloo, ON N2L 3L3, Canada *Tel:* 519-886-1969, pg 555

Nguyen, Tuan, Encounter Books, 665 Third St, Suite 330, San Francisco, CA 94107-1951 *Tel:* 415-538-1460 *Toll Free Tel:* 800-786-3839 *Fax:* 415-538-1461 *Toll Free Fax:* 877-811-1461 *E-mail:* read@encounterbooks.com *Web Site:* www.encounterbooks.com, pg 90

Niambi, Kateria, e-Scholastic, 568 Broadway, 9th fl, New York, NY 10012 *Tel:* 212-343-7100 *Fax:* 212-343-4949, pg 85

Nicholaou, Mary, Eros Books, 463 Barlow Ave, Staten Island, NY 10308 *Tel:* 718-317-7484 *Web Site:* www.geocities.com/marynicholaou/classic_blue.html, pg 92

Nicholas, Jeff, Sierra Press, 4988 Gold Leaf Dr, Mariposa, CA 95338 *Tel:* 209-966-5071 *Toll Free Tel:* 800-745-2631 *Fax:* 209-966-5073 *E-mail:* siepress@sti.net *Web Site:* www.nationalparksusa.com, pg 247

Nicholls, David, Modern Language Association of America (MLA), 26 Broadway, 3rd fl, New York, NY 10004-1789 *Tel:* 646-576-5000 *Fax:* 646-458-0030 *E-mail:* info@mla.org *Web Site:* www.mla.org, pg 176

Nicholls, David, Modern Language Association of America (MLA), 26 Broadway, 3rd fl, New York, NY 10004-1789 *Tel:* 646-576-5000 *Fax:* 646-458-0030 *E-mail:* convention@mla.org *Web Site:* www.mla.org, pg 691

Nicholls, David G, Committee On Scholarly Editions, c/o Modern Language Association of America, 26 Broadway, 3rd fl, New York, NY 10004-1789 *Tel:* 646-576-5040 *Fax:* 646-458-0030 *Web Site:* www.mla.org, pg 685

Nichols, Bruce, Free Press, 1230 Avenue of the Americas, New York, NY 10020 *Tel:* 212-698-7000 *Toll Free Tel:* 800-223-2345 (cust serv); 800-223-2336 (orders); 888-866-6631 (fulfillment), pg 100

Nichols, George Q, National Publishing Co, 11311 Roosevelt Blvd, Philadelphia, PA 19154-2105 *Tel:* 215-676-1863 *Toll Free Tel:* 888-333-1863 *Fax:* 215-673-8069 *Web Site:* www.courier.com, pg 184

Nichols, Jackie, Playhouse on the Square, 51 S Cooper, Memphis, TN 38104 *Tel:* 901-725-0776 *Fax:* 901-272-7530, pg 799

Nichols, Joel J, Texas Tech University Press, 2903 Fourth St, Lubbock, TX 79412 *Tel:* 806-742-2982 *Toll Free Tel:* 800-832-4042 *Fax:* 806-742-2979 *E-mail:* ttup@ttu.edu *Web Site:* www.ttup.ttu.edu, pg 267

Nichols, Robby, Covenant Communications Inc, 920 E State Rd, Suite F, American Fork, UT 84003-0416 *Tel:* 801-756-9966 *Toll Free Tel:* 800-662-9545 *Fax:* 801-756-1049 *E-mail:* sales@covenant-lds.com *Web Site:* www.covenant-lds.com, pg 71

Nichols, Sally, University of Massachusetts Press, PO Box 429, Amherst, MA 01004-0429 *Tel:* 413-545-2217 *Toll Free Tel:* 800-537-5487 *Fax:* 413-545-1226; 410-516-6998 (fulfillment) *E-mail:* info@umpress.umass.edu; hfcustserv@mail.press.jhu.edu *Web Site:* www.umass.edu/umpress, pg 282

Nichols, Su-Lin, Newspaper Association of America (NAA), 1921 Gallows Rd, Suite 600, Vienna, VA 22182 *Tel:* 703-902-1600 *Fax:* 703-917-0636 *Web Site:* www.naa.org, pg 695

Nichols, Suzanne, Russell Sage Foundation, 112 E 64 St, New York, NY 10021-7383 *Tel:* 212-750-6000 *Toll Free Tel:* 800-524-6401 *Fax:* 212-371-4761 *E-mail:* pubs@rsage.org *Web Site:* www.russellsage.org, pg 236

Nicholson, George, Sterling Lord Literistic Inc, 65 Bleecker St, New York, NY 10012 *Tel:* 212-780-6050 *Fax:* 212-780-6095, pg 657

Nicholson, James G, The Riverside Publishing Co, 425 Spring Lake Dr, Itasca, IL 60143-2079 *Tel:* 630-467-7000 *Toll Free Tel:* 800-323-9540 *Fax:* 630-467-7192 (cust serv) *Web Site:* www.riverpub.com, pg 233

Nicholson, Wanda R, Association of American Editorial Cartoonists, 1221 Stoneferry Lane, Raleigh, NC 27606 *Tel:* 919-859-5516 *Fax:* 919-859-3172, pg 679

Nickelson, Ron, Standard Publishing Co, 8121 Hamilton Ave, Cincinnati, OH 45231 *Tel:* 513-931-4050 *Toll Free Tel:* 800-543-1301 *Fax:* 513-931-0950 *Toll Free Fax:* 877-867-5751 *E-mail:* customerservice@standardpub.com *Web Site:* www.standardpub.com, pg 257

Nickerson, Agnes Wong, Duke University Press, 905 W Main St, Suite 18-B, Durham, NC 27701 *Tel:* 919-687-3600 *Toll Free Tel:* 888-651-0122 (orders only) *Fax:* 919-688-4574 *Toll Free Fax:* 888-651-0124 *Web Site:* www.dukeupress.edu, pg 84

Nickless, Tracy, The Center for Exhibition Industry Research, 2301 S Lakeshore Dr, Suite E-1002, Chicago, IL 60616 *Tel:* 312-808-2347 *Fax:* 312-949-3472 *E-mail:* mceir@mpea.com *Web Site:* www.ceir.org, pg 684

Nickson, Richard, The Bernard Shaw Society, Box 1159, Madison Square Sta, New York, NY 10159-1159 *Tel:* 212-989-7833; 212-982-9885, pg 699

Nicotra, Maria, Gingerbread House, 602 Montauk Hwy, Westhampton Beach, NY 11978-1806 *Tel:* 631-288-5119 *Fax:* 631-288-5179 *E-mail:* ghbooks@optonline.net *Web Site:* gingerbreadbooks.com, pg 105

Nidy, Ellen, Universe Publishing, 300 Park Ave S, 3rd fl, New York, NY 10010 *Tel:* 212-387-3400 *Fax:* 212-387-3535, pg 280

Niefeld, Elaine M, Paul H Brookes Publishing Co, PO Box 10624, Baltimore, MD 21285-0624 *Tel:* 410-337-9580 *Toll Free Tel:* 800-638-3775 *Fax:* 410-337-8539 *E-mail:* custserv@brookespublishing.com *Web Site:* www.brookespublishing.com, pg 48

Niegowski, Bob, Free Press, 1230 Avenue of the Americas, New York, NY 10020 *Tel:* 212-698-7000 *Toll Free Tel:* 800-223-2345 (cust serv); 800-223-2336 (orders); 888-866-6631 (fulfillment), pg 100

Niegowski, Bob, Scribner, 1230 Avenue of the Americas, New York, NY 10020, pg 244

Nielsen, Robert F, Potlatch Publications Ltd, 30 Berry Hill, Waterdown, ON L0R 2H4, Canada *Tel:* 905-689-2104 *Fax:* 905-689-1632 *Web Site:* www.angelfire.com/on3/potlatch, pg 558

Nieman, Jim, Standard Publishing Co, 8121 Hamilton Ave, Cincinnati, OH 45231 *Tel:* 513-931-4050 *Toll Free Tel:* 800-543-1301 *Fax:* 513-931-0950 *Toll Free Fax:* 877-867-5751 *E-mail:* customerservice@standardpub.com *Web Site:* www.standardpub.com, pg 257

Niemirow, Herb, Springer-Verlag New York Inc, 175 Fifth Ave, New York, NY 10010 *Tel:* 212-460-1500 *Toll Free Tel:* 800-777-4643 *Fax:* 212-473-6272 *Web Site:* www.springer-ny.com, pg 256

Nikolic, Maja, Bridge Works Publishing, PO Box 1798, Bridgehampton, NY 11932-1798 *Tel:* 631-537-3418 *Fax:* 631-537-5092 *E-mail:* bap@hamptons.com, pg 47

Nikolic, Maja, Writers House LLC, 21 W 26 St, New York, NY 10010 *Tel:* 212-685-2400 *Fax:* 212-685-1781, pg 662

Niles, Jenifer L, Charles River Media, 10 Downer Ave, Hingham, MA 02043 *Tel:* 781-740-0400 (edit offices) *Toll Free Tel:* 800-382-8505 (orders) *Fax:* 781-740-8816; 703-996-1010 (orders) *E-mail:* info@charlesriver.com *Web Site:* www.charlesriver.com, pg 58

Nirkind, Bob, Watson-Guptill Publications, 770 Broadway, New York, NY 10003 *Tel:* 646-654-5450 *Toll Free Tel:* 800-278-8477 (orders only) *Fax:* 646-654-5486; 646-654-5487 *E-mail:* info@watsonguptill.com *Web Site:* www.watsonguptill.com, pg 294

Nisbet, Lynette, Prometheus Books, 59 John Glenn Dr, Amherst, NY 14228 *Tel:* 716-691-0133 *Toll Free Tel:* 800-421-0351 *Fax:* 716-691-0137 *E-mail:* marketing@prometheusbooks.com; editorial@prometheusbooks.com *Web Site:* www.Prometheusbooks.com, pg 220

Nitsche, David, TSI Graphics, 1300 S Raney, Effingham, IL 62401 *Tel:* 217-347-7733 *Fax:* 217-342-9611 *Web Site:* www.tsigraphics.com, pg 612

Nix, Jennifer, Chelsea Green Publishing Co, PO Box 428, White River Junction, VT 05001-0428 *Tel:* 802-295-6300 *Toll Free Tel:* 800-639-4099 (cust serv & consumer orders); 800-807-6726 (trade & wholesale orders) *Fax:* 802-295-6444 *Web Site:* chelseagreen.com, pg 59

Nixon, Donna McLean, Nixon Agency, 382 Audrey Dr, Suite 100, Loveland, CO 80537 *Tel:* 970-667-0920 *Fax:* 970-667-0920 *E-mail:* mcleanlit@aol.com *Web Site:* donnanixonagency.com, pg 647

Nobisso, Josephine, Gingerbread House, 602 Montauk Hwy, Westhampton Beach, NY 11978-1806 *Tel:* 631-288-5119 *Fax:* 631-288-5179 *E-mail:* ghbooks@optonline.net *Web Site:* gingerbreadbooks.com, pg 105

Noble, Bettie, Copley Publishing Group, 138 Great Rd, Acton, MA 01720 *Tel:* 978-263-9090 *Toll Free Tel:* 800-562-2147 *Fax:* 978-263-9190 *E-mail:* publish@copleycustom.com; textbook@copleypublishing.com *Web Site:* www.copleycustom.com; www.copleypublishing.com; www.copleyeditions.com, pg 68

Noble, Karen, Running Press Book Publishers, 125 S 22 St, Philadelphia, PA 19103-4399 *Tel:* 215-567-5080 *Toll Free Tel:* 800-345-5359 (cust serv & orders) *Fax:* 215-568-2919 *Toll Free Fax:* 800-453-2884 *Web Site:* www.runningpress.com, pg 236

Noble, Kathleen, FourWinds Press LLC, 4157 Crossgate Dr, Cincinnati, OH 47025 *Tel:* 513-891-0415 *Fax:* 513-891-1648 *Web Site:* www.fourwindspress.com, pg 571

Noel, Brook, Champion Press Ltd, 4308 Blueberry Rd, Fredonia, WI 53021 *Tel:* 262-692-3897 *Toll Free Tel:* 877-250-3354 *Fax:* 262-692-3342 *E-mail:* info@championpress.com *Web Site:* www.championpress.com, pg 58

Noel, Jesse, Money Market Directories, 320 E Main St, Charlottesville, VA 22902 *Tel:* 434-977-1450 *Toll Free Tel:* 800-446-2810 *Fax:* 434-979-9962 *Web Site:* www.mmdwebaccess.com, pg 177

Nolan, Betsy, The Betsy Nolan Literary Agency, 224 W 29 St, 15th fl, New York, NY 10001 *Tel:* 212-967-8200 *Fax:* 212-967-7292, pg 647

Nolan, Courtney, Adams Media, An F+W Publications Co, 57 Littlefield St, 2nd fl, Avon, MA 02322 *Tel:* 508-427-7100 *Fax:* 508-427-6790 *Toll Free Fax:* 800-872-5628 *E-mail:* authors@adamsmedia.com; orders@adamsmedia.com *Web Site:* www.adamsmedia.com, pg 5

Nolan, Pat, Penguin Group (USA) Inc Sales, 375 Hudson St, New York, NY 10014 *Tel:* 212-366-2000 *E-mail:* online@penguinputnam.com *Web Site:* www.penguin.com, pg 208

Nolan, Robert, Chalice Press, 1221 Locust St, Suite 1200, St Louis, MO 63103 *Tel:* 314-231-8500 *Toll Free Tel:* 800-366-3383 *Fax:* 314-231-8524 *E-mail:* chalicepress@cbp21.com *Web Site:* www.cbp21.com; www.chalicepress.com, pg 58

Nolden, Jacqueline A, ASTM International, 100 Barr Harbor Dr, West Conshohocken, PA 19428 *Tel:* 610-832-9500 *Fax:* 610-832-9555 *E-mail:* service@astm.org *Web Site:* www.astm.org, pg 27

Nolin, Leslie, Fairwinds Press, 200 Isleview Place, Lions Bay, BC V0N 2E0, Canada *Tel:* 604-913-0649 *Fax:* 604-913-0648 *E-mail:* info@izzoconsultants.com *Web Site:* www.izzoconsultants.com, pg 546

Nolting, Mark, Global Travel Publishers Inc, 5353 N Federal Hwy, Suite 300, Fort Lauderdale, FL 33308 *Tel:* 954-491-8877 *Toll Free Tel:* 800-882-9453 *Fax:* 954-491-9060 *E-mail:* noltingaac@aol.com *Web Site:* www.africanadventure.com, pg 571

Noon, Scott, Classroom Connect, 8000 Marina Blvd, Suite 400, Brisbane, CA 94005 *Tel:* 650-351-5100 *Toll Free Tel:* 800-638-1639 (cust support) *Fax:* 650-351-5300 *E-mail:* connect@classroom.com *Web Site:* www.classroom.com, pg 63

Noonan, Margaret, Fordham University Press, 2546 Belmont Ave, Bronx, NY 10458-5172 *Tel:* 718-817-4780 *Toll Free Tel:* 800-247-6553 (orders) *Fax:* 718-817-4785 *Web Site:* www.fordhampress.com, pg 98

Noone, Michele, Marshall Cavendish Corp, 99 White Plains Rd, Tarrytown, NY 10591-9001 *Tel:* 914-332-8888 *Fax:* 914-332-1888 *E-mail:* mcc@marshallcavendish.com *Web Site:* www.marshallcavendish.com, pg 164

Nora, Marianne, Mid-List Press, 4324 12 Ave S, Minneapolis, MN 55407-3218 *Tel:* 612-822-3733 *Fax:* 612-823-8387 *E-mail:* guide@midlist.org *Web Site:* www.midlist.org, pg 174

Nora, Marianne, Mid-List Press First Series Award for Creative Nonfiction, 4324 12 Ave S, Minneapolis, MN 55407-3218 *Tel:* 612-822-3733 *Fax:* 612-823-8387 *E-mail:* guide@midlist.org *Web Site:* www.midlist.org, pg 789

Nora, Marianne, Mid-List Press First Series Award for Poetry, 4324 12 Ave S, Minneapolis, MN 55407-3218 *Tel:* 612-822-3733 *Fax:* 612-823-8387 *E-mail:* guide@midlist.org *Web Site:* www.midlist.org, pg 789

Nora, Marianne, Mid-List Press First Series Award for Short Fiction, 4324 12 Ave S, Minneapolis, MN 55407-3218 *Tel:* 612-822-3733 *Fax:* 612-823-8387 *E-mail:* guide@midlist.org *Web Site:* www.midlist.org, pg 789

Nora, Marianne, Mid-List Press First Series Award for the Novel, 4324 12 Ave S, Minneapolis, MN 55407-3218 *Tel:* 612-822-3733 *Fax:* 612-823-8387 *E-mail:* guide@midlist.org *Web Site:* www.midlist.org, pg 789

Nordstedt, Jeff J, Barricade Books Inc, 185 Bridge Plaza N, Suite 308A, Fort Lee, NJ 07024 *Tel:* 201-944-7600 *Fax:* 201-944-6363 *E-mail:* customerservice@barricadebooks.com *Web Site:* www.barricadebooks.com, pg 32

Norell, Randy, American Historical Association, 400 "A" St SE, Washington, DC 20003 *Tel:* 202-544-2422 *Fax:* 202-544-8307 *E-mail:* aha@historians.org *Web Site:* www.historians.org, pg 14

Nori, Don Jr, Destiny Image, 167 Walnut Bottom Rd, Shippensburg, PA 17257-0310 *Tel:* 717-532-3040 *Toll Free Tel:* 800-722-6774 (orders only) *Fax:* 717-532-9291 *E-mail:* gates@destinyimage.com *Web Site:* www.destinyimage.com, pg 79

Nori, Don Sr, Destiny Image, 167 Walnut Bottom Rd, Shippensburg, PA 17257-0310 *Tel:* 717-532-3040 *Toll Free Tel:* 800-722-6774 (orders only) *Fax:* 717-532-9291 *E-mail:* gates@destinyimage.com *Web Site:* www.destinyimage.com, pg 79

Noriega, Jennifer, International Council for Adult Education, UQAM Faculty of Education, PO Box 8888, Downtown Branch, Montreal, PQ H3C 3P8, Canada *Tel:* 514-987-0029 *Fax:* 514-987-6753 *E-mail:* icae@er.uqam.ca *Web Site:* www.icae.org.uy, pg 688

Norman, Jeremy, Norman Publishing, 936-B Seventh St, PMB 238, Novato, CA 94945-3000 *Tel:* 415-892-3181 *Toll Free Tel:* 800-544-9359 *Fax:* 208-692-7446 *E-mail:* orders@jnorman.com *Web Site:* www.normanpublishing.com, pg 191

Norman, Robin, Jewish Publication Society, 2100 Arch St, 2nd fl, Philadelphia, PA 19103 *Tel:* 215-832-0600 *Toll Free Tel:* 800-234-3151 *Fax:* 215-568-2017 *E-mail:* jewishbook@jewishpub.org *Web Site:* www.jewishpub.org, pg 141

Norris, Mary, The Globe Pequot Press, 246 Goose Lane, Guilford, CT 06437 *Tel:* 203-458-4500 *Toll Free Tel:* 800-243-0495 (cust serv) *Fax:* 203-458-4601 *Toll Free Fax:* 800-820-2329 (orders & cust serv) *E-mail:* info@globepequot.com *Web Site:* www.globepequot.com, pg 105

Northrop, Jeffrey, Heinemann, 361 Hanover St, Portsmouth, NH 03801-3912 *Tel:* 603-431-7894 *Toll Free Tel:* 800-225-5800 *Fax:* 603-431-4971; 603-431-7840 *E-mail:* info@heinemann.com *Web Site:* www.heinemann.com, pg 120

Northup, Richard, Zaner-Bloser Inc, 2200 W Fifth Ave, Columbus, OH 43215 *Tel:* 614-486-0221 *Toll Free Tel:* 800-421-3018 *Fax:* 614-487-2699 *Toll Free Fax:* 800-992-6087 *E-mail:* info@zaner-bloser.com *Web Site:* www.zaner-bloser.com, pg 307

Norton, Jeffrey, Jeffrey Norton Publishers Inc, One Orchard Park Rd, Madison, CT 06443 *Tel:* 203-245-0195 *Toll Free Tel:* 800-243-1234 *Fax:* 203-245-0769 *Toll Free Fax:* 888-453-4329 *E-mail:* info@audioforum.com *Web Site:* www.audioforum.com, pg 193

Norton, Jennifer, The Pennsylvania State University Press, 820 N University Dr, University Support Bldg 1, Suite C, University Park, PA 16802-1003 *Tel:* 814-865-1327 *Toll Free Tel:* 800-326-9180 *Fax:* 814-863-1408 *Toll Free Fax:* 877 7782665 *Web Site:* www.psupress.org, pg 209

Norton, Lawrence, Simon & Schuster Inc, 1230 Avenue of the Americas, New York, NY 10020 *Tel:* 212-698-7000 *Fax:* 212-698-7007 *Web Site:* www.simonsays.com, pg 249

O'Connor, Patricia, Eastland Press, 3257 16 Ave W, Suite 2, Seattle, WA 98119 *Tel:* 206-217-0204 *Toll Free Tel:* 800-453-3278 (orders only) *Fax:* 206-217-0205 *Toll Free Fax:* 800-241-3329 (orders) *E-mail:* info@eastlandpress.com; orders@eastlandpress.com (orders-credit cards only) *Web Site:* www.eastlandpress.com, pg 86

O'Connor, Patricia, Harmonie Park Press, 23630 Pinewood, Warren, MI 48091 *Tel:* 586-755-3080 *Toll Free Tel:* 800-886-3080 *Fax:* 586-755-4213 *E-mail:* info@harmonieparkpress.com *Web Site:* harmonieparkpress.com, pg 115

O'Connor, Siobhan, Writers' Union of Canada, 90 Richmond St E, Suite 200, Toronto, ON M5C 1P1, Canada *Tel:* 416-703-8982 *Fax:* 416-504-9090 *E-mail:* info@writersunion.ca *Web Site:* www.writersunion.ca, pg 703

O'Day, Brian, PrintImage International, 70 E Lake St, Suite 333, Chicago, IL 60601 *Tel:* 312-726-8015 *Toll Free Tel:* 800-234-0040 *Fax:* 312-726-8113 *E-mail:* info@printimage.org *Web Site:* www.printimage.org, pg 697

O'Day, Tom, Agatha Awards, PO Box 31137, Bethesda, MD 20824-1137 *Tel:* 703-751-4444 *Web Site:* www.malicedomestic.org, pg 757

O'Donnell, Joan, Harvard University Press, 79 Garden St, Cambridge, MA 02138-1499 *Tel:* 617-495-2600; 401-531-2800 (international orders) *Toll Free Tel:* 800-405-1619 (orders) *Fax:* 617-495-5898 (general); 617-496-4677 (edit & rts); 401-531-2801 (international orders) *Toll Free Fax:* 800-406-9145 (orders) *E-mail:* firstname_lastname@harvard.edu *Web Site:* www.hup.harvard.edu, pg 117

O'Donnell, Kevin, William H Sadlier Inc, 9 Pine St, New York, NY 10005 *Tel:* 212-227-2120 *Toll Free Tel:* 800-221-5175 *Fax:* 212-312-6080 *Web Site:* www.sadlier.com; www.sadlier-oxford.com, pg 237

O'Donnell, Patrick, Goose Lane Editions, 469 King St, Fredericton, NB E3B 1E5, Canada *Tel:* 506-450-4251 *Toll Free Tel:* 888-926-8377 *Fax:* 506-459-4991 *E-mail:* gooselane@gooselane.com *Web Site:* www.gooselane.com, pg 548

O'Donohue, Jennifer, Penguin Group (USA) Inc Sales, 375 Hudson St, New York, NY 10014 *Tel:* 212-366-2000 *E-mail:* online@penguinputnam.com *Web Site:* www.penguin.com, pg 208

O'Grady, Elizabeth, Dwyer & O'Grady Inc, 725 Third St, Cedar Key, FL 32625 *Tel:* 352-543-9307 *Fax:* 603-375-5373 *Web Site:* www.dwyerogrady.com, pg 628, 665

O'Grady, Tom, The Thomas Grady Agency, 209 Bassett St, Petaluma, CA 94952-2668 *Tel:* 707-765-6229 *Fax:* 707-765-6810 *Web Site:* www.tgrady.com, pg 633

O'Halloran, Mark, Walter Foster Publishing Inc, 23062 La Cadena Dr, Laguna Hills, CA 92653 *Tel:* 949-380-7510 *Toll Free Tel:* 800-426-0099 *Fax:* 949-380-7575 *Web Site:* www.walterfoster.com, pg 99

O'Halloran, Mark, My Chaotic Life™, 23062 La Cadena Dr, Laguna Hills, CA 92653 *Tel:* 949-380-7510 *Toll Free Tel:* 800-426-0099 *Fax:* 949-380-7575 *Web Site:* www.mychaoticlife.com, pg 181

O'Halloran, Paul, Free Press, 1230 Avenue of the Americas, New York, NY 10020 *Tel:* 212-698-7000 *Toll Free Tel:* 800-223-2345 (cust serv); 800-223-2336 (orders); 888-866-6631 (fulfillment), pg 100

O'Halloran, Paul, Scribner, 1230 Avenue of the Americas, New York, NY 10020, pg 244

O'Hanian, Hunter, Fine Arts Work Center in Provincetown, 24 Pearl St, Provincetown, MA 02657 *Tel:* 508-487-9960 *Fax:* 508-487-8873 *E-mail:* general@fawc.org *Web Site:* www.fawc.org, pg 774

O'Hara, Lisa, Wilkinson Studios Inc, 901 W Jackson Blvd, Suite 201, Chicago, IL 60607 *Tel:* 312-226-0007 *Fax:* 312-226-0404 *Web Site:* www.wilkinsonstudios.com, pg 667

O'Hara, Lynne, Chelsea Green Publishing Co, PO Box 428, White River Junction, VT 05001-0428 *Tel:* 802-295-6300 *Toll Free Tel:* 800-639-4099 (cust serv & consumer orders); 800-807-6726 (trade & wholesale orders) *Fax:* 802-295-6444 *Web Site:* www.chelseagreen.com, pg 59

O'Hare, Joanne, University of Nevada Press, MS 166, Reno, NV 89557-0076 *Tel:* 775-784-6573 *Toll Free Tel:* 800-682-6657 *Fax:* 775-784-6200 *Toll Free Fax:* 877-682-6657 *Web Site:* www.nvbooks.nevada.edu, pg 283

O'Hare, Patricia A, Intercultural Press Inc, PO Box 700, 374 US Rte One, Yarmouth, ME 04096 *Tel:* 207-846-5168 *Toll Free Tel:* 866-372-2665 *Fax:* 207-846-5181 *E-mail:* books@interculturalpress.com *Web Site:* www.interculturalpress.com, pg 136

O'Hearn, Steve, Pearson Education Canada Inc, 26 Prince Andrew Place, Don Mills, ON M3C 2T8, Canada *Tel:* 416-447-5101 *Toll Free Tel:* 800-567-3800; 800-387-8028 *Fax:* 416-443-0948 *Toll Free Fax:* 800-263-7733; 888-465-0536 *E-mail:* firstname.lastname@pearsoned.com *Web Site:* www.pearsoned.com, pg 557

O'Hehir, Kathy, Modern Publishing, 155 E 55 St, New York, NY 10022 *Tel:* 212-826-0850 *Fax:* 212-759-9069 *Web Site:* www.modernpublishing.com, pg 176

O'Keefe, Martin, Institute of Jesuit Sources, 3601 Lindell Blvd, St Louis, MO 63108 *Tel:* 314-977-7257 *Fax:* 314-977-7263 *E-mail:* ijs@slu.edu *Web Site:* www.jesuitsources.com, pg 135

O'Leary, M J, John Wiley & Sons Inc Education Publishing Group, 111 River St, Hoboken, NJ 07030 *Tel:* 201-748-6000 *Fax:* 201-748-6088 *E-mail:* info@wiley.com *Web Site:* www.wiley.com, pg 300

O'Mahony, Kieran, EduCare Press, PO Box 17222, Seattle, WA 98127 *Tel:* 206-782-4797 *Fax:* 206-782-4802 *E-mail:* educarepress@hotmail.com *Web Site:* www.educarepress.com, pg 87

O'Mahony, Timothy K, EduCare Press, PO Box 17222, Seattle, WA 98127 *Tel:* 206-782-4797 *Fax:* 206-782-4802 *E-mail:* educarepress@hotmail.com *Web Site:* www.educarepress.com, pg 87

O'Malley, Brendan, Palgrave Macmillan, 175 Fifth Ave, New York, NY 10010 *Tel:* 212-982-3900 *Fax:* 212-777-6359 *E-mail:* firstname.lastname@palgrave-usa.com *Web Site:* www.palgrave.com, pg 202

O'Malley, Ed, Yale University Press, 302 Temple St, New Haven, CT 06511 *Tel:* 203-432-0960; 401-531-2800 (cust serv) *Toll Free Tel:* 800-405-1619 (cust serv) *Fax:* 203-432-0948; 401-531-2801 (cust serv) *Toll Free Fax:* 800-406-9145 (cust serv) *E-mail:* customer.care@trilateral.org (cust serv) *Web Site:* www.yale.edu/yup/, pg 305

O'Malley, Peg, Morgan Kaufmann Publishers, 500 Sansome, Suite 400, San Francisco, CA 94111 *Tel:* 415-392-2665 *Fax:* 415-982-2665 *E-mail:* mkp@mkp.com *Web Site:* www.mkp.com, pg 178

O'Moore-Klopf, Katharine, KOK Edit, 15 Hare Lane, East Setauket, NY 11733-3606 *Tel:* 631-474-1170 *Fax:* 631-474-9849 *E-mail:* editor@kokedit.com *Web Site:* www.kokedit.com, pg 604

O'Neal, David, Shambhala Publications Inc, Horticultural Hall, 300 Massachusetts Ave, Boston, MA 02115 *Tel:* 617-424-0030 *Toll Free Tel:* 888-424-2329 (orders only) *Fax:* 617-236-1563; 303-665-5292 (orders only) *E-mail:* editors@shambhala.com *Web Site:* www.shambhala.com, pg 245

O'Neal, Eilis, The Pablo Neruda Prize for Poetry, Nimrod Intl Journal, University of Tulsa, 600 S College, Tulsa, OK 74104 *Tel:* 918-631-3080 *Fax:* 918-631-3033 *E-mail:* nimrod@utulsa.edu *Web Site:* www.utulsa.edu/nimrod, pg 793

O'Neal, Eilis, Katherine Anne Porter Prize for Fiction, University of Tulsa, 600 S College, Tulsa, OK 74104 *Tel:* 918-631-3080 *Fax:* 918-631-3033 *E-mail:* nimrod@utulsa.edu *Web Site:* www.utulsa.edu/nimrod, pg 799

O'Neal, Maureen, Random House Publishing Group, 1745 Broadway, New York, NY 10019 *Toll Free Tel:* 800-200-3552 *Toll Free Fax:* 800-200-3552 *Web Site:* www.randomhouse.com, pg 227

O'Neall-Smith, Brenda, Blackwell Publishing Professional, 2121 State Ave, Ames, IA 50014 *Tel:* 515-292-0140 *Toll Free Tel:* 800-862-6657 (orders only) *Fax:* 515-292-3348 *Web Site:* www.blackwellprofessional.com, pg 40

O'Neil, John J, Food & Nutrition Press Inc (FNP), 6527 Main St, Trumbull, CT 06611 *Tel:* 203-261-8587 *Fax:* 203-261-9724 *E-mail:* foodpress@worldnet.att.net *Web Site:* www.foodscipress.com, pg 98

O'Neil, Lillian M, Food & Nutrition Press Inc (FNP), 6527 Main St, Trumbull, CT 06611 *Tel:* 203-261-8587 *Fax:* 203-261-9724 *E-mail:* foodpress@worldnet.att.net *Web Site:* www.foodscipress.com, pg 98

O'Neil, Tim, Society for Mining, Metallurgy & Exploration Inc, PO Box 277002, Littleton, CO 80127-7002 *Tel:* 303-973-9550 *Toll Free Tel:* 800-763-3132 *Fax:* 303-973-3845 *E-mail:* sme@smenet.org *Web Site:* www.smenet.org, pg 251

O'Neill, Albertha, Barricade Books Inc, 185 Bridge Plaza N, Suite 308A, Fort Lee, NJ 07024 *Tel:* 201-944-7600 *Fax:* 201-944-6363 *E-mail:* customerservice@barricadebooks.com *Web Site:* www.barricadebooks.com, pg 32

O'Neill, Colleen, Canadian Publishers' Council (CPC), 250 Merton St, Suite 203, Toronto, ON M4S 1B1, Canada *Tel:* 416-322-7011 *Fax:* 416-322-6999 *E-mail:* pubadmin@pubcouncil.ca *Web Site:* www.pubcouncil.ca, pg 684

O'Neill, Donna, Pocket Books, 1230 Avenue of the Americas, New York, NY 10020 *Toll Free Tel:* 800-456-6798 *Fax:* 212-698-7284 *E-mail:* consumer.customerservice@simonandschuster.com *Web Site:* www.simonsays.com, pg 215

O'Neill, George D Jr, Lost Classics Book Co, PO Box 3429, Lake Wales, FL 33859-3429 *Tel:* 863-676-1920 *Toll Free Tel:* 800-283-3572 (wholesale orders); 888-211-2665 (educational) *Fax:* 863-676-1707 *E-mail:* mgeditor@lostclassicsbooks.com *Web Site:* www.lostclassicsbooks.com (retail site); www.lcbcbooks.com (wholesale site), pg 159

O'Neill, Jill, Miles Conrad Memorial Lecture, 1518 Walnut St, Suite 1004, Philadelphia, PA 19102-3403 *Tel:* 215-893-1561 *Fax:* 215-893-1564 *E-mail:* nfais@nfais.org *Web Site:* www.nfais.org, pg 768

O'Neill, Jill, National Federation of Abstracting & Information Services (NFAIS), 1518 Walnut St, Suite 1004, Philadelphia, PA 19102-3403 *Tel:* 215-893-1561 *Fax:* 215-893-1564 *E-mail:* nfais@nfais.org *Web Site:* www.nfais.org, pg 693

O'Neill, John, Hamilton College, English/Creative Writing, Dept of English, 198 College Hill Rd, Clinton, NY 13323 *Tel:* 315-859-4370 *Fax:* 315-859-4390 *Web Site:* www.hamilton.edu, pg 752

O'Neill, John P, The Metropolitan Museum of Art, 1000 Fifth Ave, New York, NY 10028 *Tel:* 212-879-5500; 212-535-7710 *Fax:* 212-396-5062 *E-mail:* info@metmuseum.org *Web Site:* www.metmuseum.org, pg 173

O'Neill, Mark, Canadian Museum of Civilization, 100 Laurier St, Hull, PQ J8X 4H2, Canada *Tel:* 819-776-8387 *Toll Free Tel:* 800-555-5621 (North America only) *Fax:* 819-776-8300 *E-mail:* publications@civilization.ca (mail order) *Web Site:* www.civilization.ca, pg 538

O'Neill, Mary Ellen, Hyperion, 77 W 66 St, 11th fl, New York, NY 10023-6298 *Tel:* 212-456-0100 *Toll Free Tel:* 800-759-0190 (cust serv) *Fax:* 212-456-0157 *Web Site:* hyperionbooks.com, pg 129

O'Neill, Quinn, Vintage & Anchor Books, 1745 Broadway, New York, NY 10019 *Tel:* 212-751-2600 *Fax:* 212-572-6043, pg 291

O'Neill, Robert J Jr, International City/County Management Association, 777 N Capitol St NE, Suite 500, Washington, DC 20002 *Tel:* 202-289-4262 *Fax:* 202-962-3500 *E-mail:* pubs@icma.org *Web Site:* icma.org, pg 137

O'Neill, Suzanne, Atria Books, 1230 Avenue of the Americas, New York, NY 10020 *Tel:* 212-698-7000 *Fax:* 212-698-7007 *Web Site:* www.simonsays.com, pg 27

O'Reilly, James, Travelers' Tales Inc, 330 Townsend St, Suite 208, San Francisco, CA 94107 *Tel:* 415-227-8600 *Fax:* 415-227-8605 *E-mail:* ttales@travelerstales. com *Web Site:* www.travelerstales.com, pg 275

O'Reilly, Tim, O'Reilly & Associates Inc, 1005 Gravenstein Hwy N, Sebastopol, CA 95472 *Tel:* 707-827-7000 *Toll Free Tel:* 800-998-9938 *Fax:* 707-829-0104 *E-mail:* info@oreilly.com *Web Site:* www.oreilly. com, pg 199

O'Rourke, Kevin, Phaidon Press Inc, 180 Varick St, 14th fl, New York, NY 10014 *Tel:* 212-652-5400 *Toll Free Tel:* 800-759-0190 (cust serv) *Fax:* 212-652-5410 *Toll Free Fax:* 800-286-9471 (cust serv) *E-mail:* ussales@ phaidon.com *Web Site:* www.phaidon.com, pg 211

O'Rourke, Patrick, Thistledown Press Ltd, 633 Main St, Saskatoon, SK S7H 0J8, Canada *Tel:* 306-244-1722 *Fax:* 306-244-1762 *E-mail:* marketing@thistledown.sk. ca *Web Site:* www.thistledown.sk.ca, pg 563

O'Rourke, T Patrick, T J Publishers Inc, 817 Silver Spring Ave, Suite 206, Silver Spring, MD 20910-4617 *Tel:* 301-585-4440 *Toll Free Tel:* 800-999-1168 *Fax:* 301-585-5930 *E-mail:* TJPubinc@aol.com, pg 574

O'Rourke, William, The Ernest Sandeen & Richard Sullivan Prizes in Fiction & Poetry, 356 O'Shaughnessy Hall, Notre Dame, IN 46556 *Tel:* 574-631-7526 *E-mail:* english.righter.1@nd.edu *Web Site:* www.nd.edu, pg 803

O'Shaughnessy, Marianne, Red Crane Books Inc, PO Box 33950, Santa Fe, NM 87594-3950 *Tel:* 505-988-7070 *Fax:* 505-989-7476 *E-mail:* publish@redcrane. com *Web Site:* www.redcrane.com, pg 229

O'Shaughnessy, Michael, Red Crane Books Inc, PO Box 33950, Santa Fe, NM 87594-3950 *Tel:* 505-988-7070 *Fax:* 505-989-7476 *E-mail:* publish@redcrane.com *Web Site:* www.redcrane.com, pg 229

O'Shea, Barbara, Penguin Group (USA) Inc Sales, 375 Hudson St, New York, NY 10014 *Tel:* 212-366-2000 *E-mail:* online@penguinputnam.com *Web Site:* www. penguin.com, pg 207

O'Sullivan, Denise, Harlequin Enterprises Ltd, 233 Broadway, Suite 1001, New York, NY 10279 *Tel:* 212-553-4200 *Fax:* 212-227-8969 *E-mail:* customer. ecare@harlequin.ca *Web Site:* www.eharlequin.com; www.luna-books.com; www.mirabooks.com; www. reddressink.com; www.steeplehill.com, pg 115

O'Toole, Christian, Phobos Books, 200 Park Ave S, Suite 1109, New York, NY 10003 *Tel:* 212-477-3225 *Fax:* 212-529-4223 *E-mail:* info@phobosweb.com *Web Site:* phobosweb.com, pg 211

Oakes, John, Avalon Publishing Group Inc, 1400 65 St, Suite 250, Emeryville, CA 94608 *Tel:* 510-595-3664 *Fax:* 510-535-4228 *Web Site:* www.avalonpub.com, pg 29

Oakes, John, Four Walls Eight Windows, 245 W 17 St, 11th fl, New York, NY 10011 *Tel:* 646-375-2570 *Fax:* 646-375-2571 *Web Site:* www.4w8w.com, pg 99

Oakes, John, Nation Books, 245 W 17 St, 11th fl, New York, NY 10011-5300 *Tel:* 646-375-2570 *Fax:* 646-375-2571 *Web Site:* www.nationbooks.org, pg 182

Oakes, John, Thunder's Mouth Press, 245 W 17 St, 11th fl, New York, NY 10011-5300 *Tel:* 646-375-2570 *Fax:* 646-375-2571 *Web Site:* www.thundersmouth. com, pg 271

Oakes, Roger B, Adams & Ambrose Publishing, PO Box 259684, Madison, WI 53725-9684 *Tel:* 608-257-5700 *Fax:* 608-257-5719 *E-mail:* info@adamsambrose.com, pg 5

Oakes, Sheila Curry, St Martin's Press Trade Division, 175 Fifth Ave, New York, NY 10010 *E-mail:* firstname.lastname@stmartins.com *Web Site:* www.stmartins.com; www.minotaurbooks. com, pg 239

Oakley, Eric, Haynes Manuals Inc, 861 Lawrence Dr, Newbury Park, CA 91320 *Tel:* 805-498-6703 *Toll Free Tel:* 800-442-9637 *Fax:* 805-498-2867 *E-mail:* info@ haynes.com *Web Site:* www.haynes.com, pg 118

Oare, Gail A, Materials Research Society, 506 Keystone Dr, Warrendale, PA 15086 *Tel:* 724-779-3003 *Fax:* 724-779-8313 *E-mail:* info@mrs.org *Web Site:* www.mrs.org, pg 165

Oates, Gabriela, Menasha Ridge Press Inc, 2204 First Ave S, Suite 102, Birmingham, AL 35233 *Tel:* 205-322-0439 *Fax:* 205-326-1012 *E-mail:* info@ menasharidge.com *Web Site:* www.menasharidge.com, pg 171

Ober, Stuart A, Beekman Publishers Inc, 2626 Rte 212, Woodstock, NY 12498 *Tel:* 845-679-2300 *Toll Free Tel:* 888-BEEKMAN (orders) *Fax:* 845-679-2301 *E-mail:* beekman@beekmanpublishers.com *Web Site:* www.beekmanpublishers.com, pg 35

Oberoi, Angel, Gossamer Books LLC, 2112 Gossamer Ave, Redwood Shores, CA 94065 *Tel:* 650-257-4058 *Fax:* 650-257-4058 *E-mail:* info@gossamerbooks.com *Web Site:* www.gossamerbooks.com, pg 107

Oberweger, Lorin, Writers Retreat Workshop (WRW), 5721 Magazine St, Suite 161, New Orleans, LA 70115 *Toll Free Tel:* 800-642-2494 *E-mail:* wrw04@netscape. net *Web Site:* www.writersretreatworkshop.com, pg 749

Oblack, Linda, Indiana University Press, 601 N Morton St, Bloomington, IN 47404-3797 *Tel:* 812-855-8817 *Toll Free Tel:* 800-842-6796 (orders only) *Fax:* 812-855-7931 (orders only); 812-855-8507 *E-mail:* iupress@indiana.edu; iuorder@indiana.edu (orders) *Web Site:* www.iupress.indiana.edu, pg 132

Ochs, John P, The American Chemical Society, 1155 16 St NW, Washington, DC 20036 *Tel:* 202-872-4600 *Toll Free Tel:* 800-227-5558 *Fax:* 202-872-6067 *Web Site:* www.acs.org; pubs.acs.org, pg 12

OConnor, William, IEEE Press, 445 Hoes Lane, Piscataway, NJ 08854 *Tel:* 732-981-3418 *Fax:* 732-981-8062 *E-mail:* ieeepress@ieee.org *Web Site:* www. ieee.org/pubs/press/, pg 131

Odland, Julie, American Academy of Political & Social Science, 3814 Walnut St, Philadelphia, PA 19104 *Tel:* 215-746-6500 *Fax:* 215-898-1202 *Web Site:* www. aapss.org, pg 675

Oey, Eric, Tuttle Publishing, Airport Business Park, 364 Innovation Dr, North Clarendon, VT 05759-9436 *Tel:* 617-951-4080 (edit); 802-773-8930 *Toll Free Tel:* 800-526-2778 *Fax:* 617-951-4045 (edit); 802-773-6993 *Toll Free Fax:* 800-FAX-TUTL *E-mail:* info@ tuttlepublishing.com *Web Site:* www.tuttlepublishing. com, pg 277

Offit, Sidney, The Authors League Fund, 31 E 28 St, New York, NY 10016 *Tel:* 212-268-1208 *Fax:* 212-564-5363 *E-mail:* authlgfund@aol.com *Web Site:* www.authorsleaguefund.org, pg 681

Offit, Sidney, The George Polk Awards, The Brooklyn Campus, University Plaza, Brooklyn, NY 11201 *Tel:* 718-488-1115 *Fax:* 718-246-6302, pg 799

Ogilvie, Donald G, American Bankers Association, 1120 Connecticut Ave NW, Washington, DC 20036 *Tel:* 202-663-5087 *Toll Free Tel:* 800-BANKERS (226-5377) *Fax:* 202-663-5087 (cust serv) *Web Site:* www.aba.com, pg 12

Ogilvie, Michelle M, American Mathematical Society, 201 Charles St, Providence, RI 02904-2294 *Tel:* 401-455-4000 *Toll Free Tel:* 800-321-4267 *Fax:* 401-331-3842; 401-455-4046 (cust serv) *E-mail:* ams@ams.org *Web Site:* www.ams.org, pg 16

Ognibene, Peter E, Breakthrough Publications Inc, 326 Main St, Emmaus, PA 18049 *Tel:* 610-965-3200 *Toll Free Tel:* 800-824-5000 *Fax:* 610-965-5836 *Web Site:* www.booksonhorses.com, pg 46

Ogren, Rhonda, Llewellyn Publications, PO Box 64383, St Paul, MN 55164-0383 *Tel:* 651-291-1970 *Toll Free Tel:* 800-843-6666 *Fax:* 651-291-1908 *E-mail:* lwlpc@ llewellyn.com *Web Site:* www.llewellyn.com, pg 157

Ogroske, John, Writers' Journal Annual Fiction Contest, PO Box 394, Perham, MN 56573 *Tel:* 218-346-7921 *Fax:* 218-346-7924 *E-mail:* writersjournal@lakesplus. com *Web Site:* www.writersjournal.com, pg 813

Ogroske, John, Writers' Journal Annual Horror/Ghost Contest, PO Box 394, Perham, MN 56573 *Tel:* 218-346-7921 *Fax:* 218-346-7924 *E-mail:* writersjournal@ lakesplus.com *Web Site:* www.writersjournal.com, pg 813

Ogroske, John, Writers' Journal Annual Romance Contest, PO Box 394, Perham, MN 56573 *Tel:* 218-346-7921 *Fax:* 218-346-7924 *E-mail:* writersjournal@ lakesplus.com *Web Site:* www.writersjournal.com, pg 813

Ogroske, John, Writers' Journal Annual Short Story Contest, PO Box 394, Perham, MN 56573 *Tel:* 218-346-7921 *Fax:* 218-346-7924 *E-mail:* writersjournal@ lakesplus.com *Web Site:* www.writersjournal.com, pg 813

Ogroske, John, Writers' Journal Poetry Contest, PO Box 394, Perham, MN 56573 *Tel:* 218-346-7921 *Fax:* 218-346-7924 *E-mail:* writersjournal@lakesplus.com *Web Site:* www.writersjournal.com, pg 813

Ogroske, Leon, Writers' Journal Annual Fiction Contest, PO Box 394, Perham, MN 56573 *Tel:* 218-346-7921 *Fax:* 218-346-7924 *E-mail:* writersjournal@lakesplus. com *Web Site:* www.writersjournal.com, pg 813

Ogroske, Leon, Writers' Journal Annual Horror/Ghost Contest, PO Box 394, Perham, MN 56573 *Tel:* 218-346-7921 *Fax:* 218-346-7924 *E-mail:* writersjournal@ lakesplus.com *Web Site:* www.writersjournal.com, pg 813

Ogroske, Leon, Writers' Journal Annual Romance Contest, PO Box 394, Perham, MN 56573 *Tel:* 218-346-7921 *Fax:* 218-346-7924 *E-mail:* writersjournal@ lakesplus.com *Web Site:* www.writersjournal.com, pg 813

Ogroske, Leon, Writers' Journal Annual Short Story Contest, PO Box 394, Perham, MN 56573 *Tel:* 218-346-7921 *Fax:* 218-346-7924 *E-mail:* writersjournal@ lakesplus.com *Web Site:* www.writersjournal.com, pg 813

Ogroske, Leon, Writers' Journal Annual Travel Writing Contest, PO Box 394, Perham, MN 56573 *Tel:* 218-346-7921 *Fax:* 218-346-7924 *E-mail:* writersjournal@ lakesplus.com *Web Site:* www.writersjournal.com, pg 813

Ogroske, Leon, Writers' Journal Poetry Contest, PO Box 394, Perham, MN 56573 *Tel:* 218-346-7921 *Fax:* 218-346-7924 *E-mail:* writersjournal@lakesplus.com *Web Site:* www.writersjournal.com, pg 813

Ohl, Helaine, St Martin's Press LLC, 175 Fifth Ave, New York, NY 10010 *Tel:* 212-674-5151 *Fax:* 212-420-9314 *E-mail:* firstname.lastname@stmartins.com *Web Site:* www.stmartins.com, pg 238

Oja, Vivien, Split Rock Arts Program, 360 Coffey Hall, 1420 Eckles Ave, St Paul, MN 55108-6084 *Tel:* 612-625-8100 *Fax:* 612-624-6210 *E-mail:* srap@cce.umn. edu *Web Site:* www.cce.umn.edu/splitrockarts, pg 748

Okadigwe, Melanie, Lawrence Jordan Literary Agency, 345 W 121 St, New York, NY 10027 *Tel:* 212-662-7871 *Fax:* 212-662-8138 *E-mail:* ljlagency@aol.com, pg 636

Okun, Andy, Cherry Lane Music Co, 6 E 32 St, 11th fl, New York, NY 10016 *Tel:* 212-561-3000 *Fax:* 212-679-8157 *E-mail:* publishing@cherrylane.com *Web Site:* www.cherrylane.com, pg 60

Olbrych, John S, Cobblestone Publishing Co, 30 Grove St, Suite C, Peterborough, NH 03458 *Tel:* 603-924-7209 *Toll Free Tel:* 800-821-0115 *Fax:* 603-924-7380 *E-mail:* custsvc@cobblestone.mv.com *Web Site:* www. cobblestonepub.com, pg 64

Oldenbrook, Christine, National Underwriter Co, 5081 Olympic Blvd, Erlanger, KY 41018 *Tel:* 859-692-2100 *Toll Free Tel:* 800-543-0874 *Fax:* 859-692-2289 *E-mail:* customerservice@nuco.com *Web Site:* www. nationalunderwriter.com, pg 185

Oldfield, James Jr, Abacus, 5130 Patterson SE, Grand Rapids, MI 49512 *Tel:* 616-698-0330 *Toll Free Tel:* 800-451-4319 *Fax:* 616-698-0325 *E-mail:* info@abacuspub.com *Web Site:* www.abacuspub.com, pg 2

Oldsey, William, Pearson Education International Group, One Lake St, Upper Saddle River, NJ 07458 *Tel:* 201-236-7000, pg 206

Oldsey, William F, McGraw-Hill Education, 2 Penn Plaza, New York, NY 10121 *Tel:* 212-904-2000 *E-mail:* customer.service@mcgraw-hill.com *Web Site:* www.mheducation.com; www.mheducation.com/custserv.html, pg 167

Olexa, Keith, Phobos Books, 200 Park Ave S, Suite 1109, New York, NY 10003 *Tel:* 212-477-3225 *Fax:* 212-529-4223 *E-mail:* info@phobosweb.com *Web Site:* phobosweb.com, pg 211

Olinger, Chauncey G Jr, Metropolitan Editorial & Writing Service, 4455 Douglas Ave, Riverdale, NY 10471 *Tel:* 718-549-5518, pg 606

Oliveira, Mariha, Florida Funding Publications Inc, PO Box 561565, Miami, FL 33256 *Tel:* 305-251-2203 *Fax:* 305-251-2773 *E-mail:* info@floridafunding.com *Web Site:* www.floridafunding.com, pg 97

Oliver, Deborah, Ragged Mountain Press, 485 Commercial St, Rockport, ME 04856 *Tel:* 207-236-4837 *Fax:* 207-236-6314 *Web Site:* www.raggedmountainpress.com, pg 225

Oliver, Lin, The Don Freeman Memorial Grant-In-Aid, 8271 Beverly Blvd, Los Angeles, CA 90048 *Tel:* 323-782-1010 *Fax:* 323-782-1892 *E-mail:* membership@scbwi.org *Web Site:* www.scbwi.org, pg 775

Oliver, Lin, SCBWI Work-In-Progress Grants, 8271 Beverly Blvd, Los Angeles, CA 90048 *Tel:* 323-782-1010 *Fax:* 323-782-1892 *E-mail:* membership@scbwi.org *Web Site:* www.scbwi.org, pg 804

Oliver, Lin, Society of Children's Book Writers & Illustrators (SCBWI), 8271 Beverly Blvd, Los Angeles, CA 90048 *Tel:* 323-782-1010 *Fax:* 323-782-1892 *E-mail:* membership@scbwi.org *Web Site:* www.scbwi.org, pg 700

Olivieri, John, Abbeville Publishing Group, 116 W 23 St, Suite 500, New York, NY 10011 *Tel:* 646-375-2039 *Toll Free Tel:* 800-ART-BOOK (278-2665) *Fax:* 646-375-2040 *E-mail:* abbeville@abbeville.com *Web Site:* www.abbeville.com, pg 2

Olivieri, John, Artabras Inc, 116 W 23 St, Suite 500, New York, NY 10011 *Tel:* 646-375-2039 *Toll Free Tel:* 800-ART-BOOK *Fax:* 646-375-2040 *E-mail:* abbeville@abbeville.com *Web Site:* www.abbeville.com, pg 24

Olmsted, Elaine B, National Poetry Competition, PO Box 298, Thomaston, ME 04861 *Tel:* 207-354-0998 *E-mail:* cal@americanletters.org *Web Site:* www.americanletters.org, pg 792

Olmsted, Robert W, Dan River Press, PO Box 298, Thomaston, ME 04861 *Tel:* 207-354-0998 *E-mail:* cal@americanletter.org *Web Site:* www.americanletters.org, pg 75

Olmsted, Robert W, National Poetry Competition, PO Box 298, Thomaston, ME 04861 *Tel:* 207-354-0998 *E-mail:* cal@americanletters.org *Web Site:* www.americanletters.org, pg 792

Olmsted, Robert W, Northwoods Press, PO Box 298, Thomaston, ME 04861-0298 *Tel:* 207-354-0998 *E-mail:* cal@americanletters.org *Web Site:* www.americanletters.org, pg 193

Olsen, David, Summy-Birchard Inc, 15800 NW 48 Ave, Miami, FL 33014 *Tel:* 305-620-1500 *Toll Free Tel:* 800-327-7643 *Fax:* 305-621-1094, pg 261

Olsen, David, Warner Bros Publications Inc, 15800 NW 48 Ave, Miami, FL 33014 *Tel:* 305-620-1500 *Toll Free Tel:* 800-327-7643 *Fax:* 305-621-4869 *E-mail:* wbpsales@warnerchappell.com *Web Site:* www.warnerbrospublications.com, pg 293

Olsen, Jon, Geological Society of America (GSA), 3300 Penrose Place, Boulder, CO 80301 *Tel:* 303-447-2020 *Toll Free Tel:* 800-472-1988 *Fax:* 303-357-1070 *E-mail:* pubs@geosociety.org *Web Site:* www.geosociety.org, pg 104

Olsen, Kevin, W W Norton & Company Inc, 500 Fifth Ave, New York, NY 10110-0017 *Tel:* 212-354-5500 *Toll Free Tel:* 800-233-4830 (orders & cust serv) *Fax:* 212-869-0856 *Toll Free Fax:* 800-458-6515 *Web Site:* www.wwnorton.com, pg 193

Olsen, Lance, Fiction Collective Two Inc, Florida State University, FC2, Dept of English, Tallahassee, FL 32306-1580 *Tel:* 850-644-2260 *Fax:* 850-644-6808 *E-mail:* fc2@english.fsu.edu *Web Site:* fc2.org, pg 96

Olsen, Larry, John Wiley & Sons Inc Professional & Trade Group, 111 River St, Hoboken, NJ 07030 *Tel:* 201-748-6000 *Toll Free Tel:* 800-225-5945 (cust serv) *Fax:* 201-748-6088 *E-mail:* info@wiley.com *Web Site:* www.wiley.com, pg 300

Olsen, Leona, National State Publishing Association (NSPA), 207 Third Ave, Hattiesburg, MS 39401 *Tel:* 601-582-3330 *Fax:* 601-582-3354 *E-mail:* info@govpublishing.org *Web Site:* www.govpublishing.org, pg 694

Olsen, Richard, Harry N Abrams Inc, 100 Fifth Ave, New York, NY 10011 *Tel:* 212-206-7715 *Toll Free Tel:* 800-345-1359 *Fax:* 212-645-8437 *E-mail:* webmaster@abramsbooks.com *Web Site:* www.abramsbooks.com, pg 3

Olshan, Rickie, Don Buchwald & Associates Inc, 6500 Wilshire Blvd, Suite 2200, Los Angeles, CA 90048 *Tel:* 323-655-7400 *Fax:* 323-655-7470 *Web Site:* www.donbuchwald.com, pg 623

Olson, Allison, The Career Press Inc, 3 Tice Rd, Franklin Lakes, NJ 07417 *Tel:* 201-848-0310 *Toll Free Tel:* 800-CAREER-1 (227-3371) *Fax:* 201-848-1727 *Web Site:* www.careerpress.com, pg 53

Olson, Carol, Domhan Books, 9511 Shore Rd, Suite 514, Brooklyn, NY 11209 *Tel:* 718-680-4362 *Toll Free Fax:* 888-823-4770 *E-mail:* domhan@att.net *Web Site:* www.domhanbooks.com, pg 82

Olson, Harriett Jane, Abingdon Press, 201 Eighth Ave S, Nashville, TN 37203-3919 *Tel:* 615-749-6290 (publicist); 615-749-6000; 615-749-6451 (sales) *Toll Free Tel:* 800-251-3320 *Fax:* 615-749-6056 *Web Site:* www.abingdonpress.com, pg 3

Olson, Kay, Capstone Press, 151 Good Counsel Dr, Mankato, MN 56002 *Toll Free Tel:* 800-747-4992 *Toll Free Fax:* 888-262-0705 *Web Site:* www.capstonepress.com, pg 53

Olson, Kris, The Gislason Agency, 219 SE Main St, Suite 506, Minneapolis, MN 55414 *Tel:* 612-331-8033 *Fax:* 612-331-8115 *E-mail:* gislasonbj@aol.com *Web Site:* www.TheGislasonAgency.com, pg 632

Olson, Neil, Donadio & Olson Inc Literary Representatives, 121 W 27 St, Suite 704, New York, NY 10001 *Tel:* 212-691-8077 *Fax:* 212-633-2837 *E-mail:* mail@donadio.com, pg 628

Olson, Norman A, Regular Baptist Press, 1300 N Meacham Rd, Schaumburg, IL 60173-4806 *Tel:* 847-843-1600 *Toll Free Tel:* 800-727-4440 (orders only); 888-588-1600 *Fax:* 847-843-3757 *E-mail:* rbp@garbc.org *Web Site:* www.regularbaptistpress.org, pg 231

Olson, Peter, Random House Inc, 1745 Broadway, New York, NY 10019 *Tel:* 212-782-9000 *Toll Free Tel:* 800-726-0600 *Web Site:* www.randomhouse.com, pg 226

Olson, Sarah, Academy Chicago Publishers, 363 W Erie St, Chicago, IL 60610 *Tel:* 312-751-7300 *Toll Free Tel:* 800-248-7323 *Fax:* 312-751-7306 *E-mail:* info@academychicago.com *Web Site:* www.academychicago.com, pg 4

Olver, Julie, Vincent Astor Memorial Leadership Essay Contest, 291 Wood Rd, Annapolis, MD 21402-5034 *Tel:* 410-268-6110 *Toll Free Tel:* 800-233-8764 *Fax:* 410-295-1049 *E-mail:* articlesubmission@navalinstitute.org *Web Site:* www.navalinstitute.org, pg 760

Olver, Julie, Arleigh Burke Essay Contest, 291 Wood Rd, Annapolis, MD 21402-5034 *Tel:* 410-268-6110 *Toll Free Tel:* 800-233-8764 *Fax:* 410-295-1049 *E-mail:* essays@navalinstitute.org *Web Site:* www.navalinstitute.org, pg 764

Onken, Janice, Wendy Lynn & Co, 504 Wilson Rd, Annapolis, MD 21401 *Tel:* 410-224-2729; 410-507-1059 *Fax:* 410-224-2183 *Web Site:* wendy-lynn.com, pg 667

Ooka, Diane, Heian International Inc, 20655 S Western Ave, Suite 105, Torrance, CA 90501 *Tel:* 310-328-7200 *Fax:* 310-328-7676 *E-mail:* heianemail@earthlink.net *Web Site:* heian.com, pg 120

Oosterholt-Arnill, H, Carswell, One Corporate Plaza, 2075 Kennedy Rd, Toronto, ON M1T 3V4, Canada *Tel:* 416-609-8000 *Toll Free Tel:* 800-387-5164 (Canada & US) *Fax:* 416-298-5094 (Toronto); 403-233-8159 (Calgary); 604-685-5343 (Vancouver); 514-985-6605 *Toll Free Fax:* 877-750-9041 *E-mail:* comments@carswell.com *Web Site:* www.carswell.com, pg 539

Oppedisano, Robert, Fordham University Press, 2546 Belmont Ave, Bronx, NY 10458-5172 *Tel:* 718-817-4780 *Toll Free Tel:* 800-247-6553 (orders) *Fax:* 718-817-4785 *Web Site:* www.fordhampress.com, pg 98

Oppel, Frank, Book Sales Inc, 114 Northfield Ave, Edison, NJ 08837 *Tel:* 732-225-0530 *Toll Free Tel:* 800-526-7257 *Fax:* 732-225-2257 *E-mail:* sales@booksalesusa.com; customerservice@booksalesusa.com *Web Site:* www.booksalesusa.com, pg 43

Oppenheim, Steve, G P Putnam's Sons (Hardcover), 375 Hudson St, New York, NY 10014 *Tel:* 212-366-2000 *E-mail:* online@penguinputnam.com *Web Site:* www.penguin.com, pg 223

Oppenheimer, Henry, MGI Management Institute Inc, 701 Westchester Ave, Suite 308W, White Plains, NY 10604 *Tel:* 914-428-6500 *Toll Free Tel:* 800-932-0191 *Fax:* 914-428-0773 *E-mail:* mgiusa@aol.com *Web Site:* www.mgi.org, pg 173

Orange, Satia, Coretta Scott King Awards, ALA Office for Literacy & Outreach Services, 50 E Huron St, Chicago, IL 60611 *Tel:* 312-280-4295; 312-280-4294 *Fax:* 312-280-3256 *E-mail:* olos@ala.org *Web Site:* www.ala.org/olos, pg 782

Oranski, Michele M, The Catholic Health Association of the United States, 4455 Woodson Rd, St Louis, MO 63134-3797 *Tel:* 314-427-2500 *Fax:* 314-253-3540 *Web Site:* www.chausa.org, pg 55

Orchard, Karen, Oregon State University Press, 102 Adams Hall, Corvallis, OR 97331 *Tel:* 541-737-3166 *Toll Free Tel:* 800-426-3797 (orders) *Fax:* 541-737-3170 *Toll Free Fax:* 800-426-3797 (orders) *E-mail:* osu.press@oregonstate.edu *Web Site:* oregonstate.edu/dept/press, pg 199

Ordaz, Jason S, School of American Research Press, 660 Garcia St, Santa Fe, NM 87505 *Tel:* 505-954-7206 *Toll Free Tel:* 888-390-6070 *Fax:* 505-954-7241 *E-mail:* bkorders@sarsf.org *Web Site:* www.sarweb.org, pg 243

Oresick, Peter, PIA/GATF (Graphic Arts Technical Foundation), 200 Deer Run Rd, Sewickley, PA 15143-2600 *Tel:* 412-741-6860 *Toll Free Tel:* 800-910-4283 *Fax:* 412-741-2311 *E-mail:* info@gain.net *Web Site:* www.gain.net, pg 697

Oresick, Peter M, PIA/GATF (Graphic Arts Technical Foundation), 200 Deer Run Rd, Sewickley, PA 15143-2600 *Tel:* 412-741-6860 *Toll Free Tel:* 800-910-4283 *Fax:* 412-741-2311 *E-mail:* info@gain.net *Web Site:* www.gain.net, pg 212

Orfanos, Minnie, Friends of American Writers Award, 680 N Lake Shore Dr, Suite L208, Chicago, IL 60611 *Tel:* 312-664-5628, pg 775

Orfanos, Minnie, Juvenile Literary Awards/Young People's Literature Awards, 680 N Lake Shore Dr-L208, Chicago, IL 60611 *Tel:* 312-664-5628, pg 782

Orff, Joy, Speakers Guild, PO Box 1540, Sandwich, MA 02563-1540 *Tel:* 508-888-6702 *Fax:* 508-888-6771 *E-mail:* speakers@cape.com *Web Site:* www.speakersguild.com, pg 670

Orjala, Todd, University of Minnesota Press, 111 Third Ave S, Suite 290, Minneapolis, MN 55401-2520 *Tel:* 612-627-1970 *Fax:* 612-627-1980 *E-mail:* ump@tc.umn.edu *Web Site:* www.upress.umn.edu, pg 282

Orlando, Andrew, Penguin Group (USA) Inc, 375 Hudson St, New York, NY 10014 *Tel:* 212-366-2000 *Fax:* 212-366-2666 *E-mail:* online@uspenguingroup.com *Web Site:* www.penguin.com, pg 208

Orlin, Sheila, North Country Books Inc, 311 Turner St, Utica, NY 13501-1729 *Tel:* 315-735-4877 *Fax:* 315-738-4342 *E-mail:* ncbooks@usadatanet.net *Web Site:* www.northcountrybooks.com, pg 192

Orloff, Erica, The Poynor Group, 444 E 82 St, Suite 28C, New York, NY 10028 *Tel:* 212-734-5909 *Fax:* 212-734-5909, pg 649

Orlowski, Eugenia, Blue Dove Press, 4204 Sorrento Valley Blvd, Suite K, San Diego, CA 92121 *Tel:* 858-623-3330 *Toll Free Tel:* 800-691-1008 (orders) *Fax:* 858-623-3325 *E-mail:* mail@bluedove.org *Web Site:* www.bluedove.org, pg 41

Orner, Lita, Scarecrow Press Inc, 4501 Forbes Blvd, Suite 200, Lanham, MD 20706 *Tel:* 301-459-3366 *Toll Free Tel:* 800-462-6420 *Fax:* 301-429-5747 *Fax:* 800-338-4550 *Web Site:* www.scarecrowpress.com, pg 241

Ornstein, Karen B, Transaction Publishers, Rutgers University, 35 Berrue Circle, Piscataway, NJ 08854 *Tel:* 732-445-2280 *Toll Free Tel:* 888-999-6778 *Fax:* 732-445-3138 *E-mail:* trans@transactionpub.com *Web Site:* www.transactionpub.com, pg 274

Orozco, Kristian, Aperture Books, 20 E 23 St, New York, NY 10010 *Tel:* 212-505-5555 *Toll Free Tel:* 800-929-2323 *Fax:* 212-598-4015 *E-mail:* info@aperture.org *Web Site:* www.aperture.org, pg 21

Orphee, Matanya, Editions Orphee Inc, 1240 Clubview Blvd N, Columbus, OH 43235 *Tel:* 614-846-9517 *Fax:* 614-846-9794 *Web Site:* www.orphee.com, pg 87

Orr, Allan, CCH Canadian Limited, A Wolters Kluwer Company, 90 Sheppard Ave E, Suite 300, Toronto, ON M2N 6X1, Canada *Tel:* 416-224-2224 *Toll Free Tel:* 800-268-4522 (Canada & US cust serv) *Fax:* 416-224-2243 *Toll Free Fax:* 800-461-4131 *E-mail:* cservice@cch.ca (cust serv) *Web Site:* www.cch.ca, pg 539

Orr, John, Lynx House Press, 420 W 24 St, Spokane, WA 99203 *Tel:* 509-624-4894 *Fax:* 509-623-4238, pg 160

Orr, Katherine, Harlequin Enterprises Ltd, 225 Duncan Mill Rd, Don Mills, ON M3B 3K9, Canada *Tel:* 416-445-5860 *Fax:* 416-445-8655 *Web Site:* www.eharlequin.com; www.luna-books.com; www.mirabooks.com; www.reddressink.com; www.steeplehill.com, pg 549

Orrmont, Arthur, Literary Consultants LLC, 7542 Bear Canyon Rd NE, Albuquerque, NM 87109 *Tel:* 505-797-9397, pg 605

Orso, Allen, Advantage Publishers Group, 5880 Oberlin Dr, San Diego, CA 92121 *Tel:* 858-457-2500 *Toll Free Tel:* 800-284-3580 *Fax:* 858-812-6476 *Toll Free Fax:* 800-499-3822 *E-mail:* apgcuserv@avdmkt.com *Web Site:* www.advantagebooksonline.com, pg 6

Ortner, Renee, OPIS/STALSBY Directories & Databases, Parkway 70 Plaza, 1255 Rt 70, Suite 32N, Lakewood, NJ 08701 *Tel:* 732-901-8800 *Toll Free Tel:* 800-275-0950 *Fax:* 732-901-9632 *Web Site:* www.opisnet.com, pg 198

Osborn, Carolyn, Stanley Walker Journalism Award, 3700 Mockingbird Lane, Dallas, TX 75205 *Tel:* 512-245-2232 *Fax:* 512-245-7462, pg 810

Osborn, Jenelle, ABC-CLIO, 130 Cremona Dr, Santa Barbara, CA 93117 *Tel:* 805-968-1911 *Toll Free Tel:* 800-368-6868 *Fax:* 805-685-9685 *E-mail:* sales@abc-clio.com *Web Site:* www.abc-clio.com, pg 3

Oscard, Fifi, Fifi Oscard Agency Inc, 110 W 40 St, New York, NY 10018 *Tel:* 212-764-1100 *Fax:* 212-840-5019 *E-mail:* agency@fifioscard.com *Web Site:* www.fifioscard.com, pg 647

Oshinsky, Carole, National Center for Children in Poverty, 215 W 125 St, 3rd fl, New York, NY 10027 *Tel:* 646-284-9600 *Fax:* 646-284-9623 *E-mail:* nccp@columbia.edu *Web Site:* www.nccp.org, pg 183

Osier, Jill, Vermont Studio Center Writer's Fellowships, PO Box 613, Johnson, VT 05656 *Tel:* 802-635-2727 *Fax:* 802-635-2730 *E-mail:* writing@vermontstudiocenter.org; info@vermontstudiocenter.org *Web Site:* www.vermontstudiocenter.org, pg 810

Osing, Gordon, River City Writing Awards in Fiction, University of Memphis, Dept of English, Memphis, TN 38152 *Tel:* 901-678-4591 *Fax:* 901-678-2226 *E-mail:* rivercity@memphis.edu *Web Site:* www.people.memphis.edu/~rivercity/contests.html, pg 802

Osmun, Marion, Oxford University Press, Inc, 198 Madison Ave, New York, NY 10016-4314 *Tel:* 212-726-6000 *Toll Free Tel:* 800-451-7556 (orders) *Web Site:* www.oup.com/us, pg 200

Osnos, Peter, PublicAffairs, 250 W 57 St, Suite 1321, New York, NY 10107 *Tel:* 212-397-6666 *Toll Free Tel:* 800-242-7737 (orders) *Fax:* 212-397-4267 *E-mail:* publicaffairs@perseusbooks.com *Web Site:* www.publicaffairsbooks.com, pg 221

Ossmann, April, Alice James Books, 238 Main St, Farmington, ME 04938 *Tel:* 207-778-7071 *Fax:* 207-778-7071 *E-mail:* ajb@umf.maine.edu *Web Site:* www.alicejamesbooks.org, pg 8

Osteguy McIntyre, Suzanne, The Institute for Research on Public Policy, 1470 Peel, Suite 200, Montreal, PQ H3A 1T1, Canada *Tel:* 514-985-2461 *Fax:* 514-985-2559 *E-mail:* irpp@irpp.org *Web Site:* www.irpp.org, pg 551

Osterhoudt, Elmer G, Modern Radio Laboratories, PO Box 14902, Minneapolis, MN 55414-0902 *Web Site:* www.modernradiolabs.com, pg 176

Ostow, Micol, Grosset & Dunlap, 345 Hudson St, New York, NY 10014 *Tel:* 212-366-2000 *E-mail:* online@penguinputnam.com *Web Site:* www.penguin.com, pg 110

Ostroff, Bill, Rodale Inc, 33 E Minor St, Emmaus, PA 18098-0099 *Tel:* 610-967-5171 *Fax:* 610-967-8962 *Web Site:* www.rodale.com, pg 234

Osuszek, Alex, Harlequin Enterprises Ltd, 225 Duncan Mill Rd, Don Mills, ON M3B 3K9, Canada *Tel:* 416-445-5860 *Fax:* 416-445-8655 *Web Site:* www.eharlequin.com; www.luna-books.com; www.mirabooks.com; www.reddressink.com; www.steeplehill.com, pg 549

Oswald, Dan, M Lee Smith Publishers LLC, 5201 Virginia Way, Brentwood, TN 37027 *Tel:* 615-373-7517 *Toll Free Tel:* 800-274-6774 *Fax:* 615-373-5183 *Web Site:* www.mleesmith.com, pg 250

Oswald, Denise, Faber & Faber Inc, 19 Union Sq W, New York, NY 10003 *Tel:* 212-741-6900 *Toll Free Tel:* 888-330-8477 *Fax:* 212-633-9385 *Web Site:* www.fsgbooks.com/faberandfaber.htm, pg 93

Oswald, Rudolph A, National Bureau of Economic Research Inc, 1050 Massachusetts Ave, Cambridge, MA 02138-5398 *Tel:* 617-868-3900 *Fax:* 617-868-2742 *E-mail:* op@nber.org *Web Site:* www.nber.org, pg 182

Otis, Martha, Bulfinch Press, 1271 Avenue of the Americas, New York, NY 10020 *Tel:* 212-522-8700 *Toll Free Tel:* 800-759-0190 *Fax:* 212-467-2886 *Web Site:* www.twbookmark.com, pg 50

Otis, Martha, Little, Brown and Company Adult Trade Division, 1271 Avenue of the Americas, New York, NY 10020 *Tel:* 212-522-8700 *Fax:* 212-522-2067 *Web Site:* www.twbookmark.com, pg 156

Otis, Martha, Time Warner Book Group, 1271 Avenue of the Americas, New York, NY 10020 *Tel:* 212-522-7200 *Fax:* 212-522-7991 *Web Site:* www.twbookmark.com, pg 271

Otis, Randy, Impressions Book & Journal Services Inc, 2016 Winnebago St, Madison, WI 53704 *Tel:* 608-244-6218 *Fax:* 608-244-7050 *E-mail:* info@impressions.com *Web Site:* www.impressions.com, pg 602

Ottaviano, Christy, Henry Holt and Company, LLC, 115 W 18 St, New York, NY 10011 *Tel:* 212-886-9200 *Toll Free Tel:* 888-330-8477 (orders) *Fax:* 212-633-0748 *E-mail:* publicity@hholt.com *Web Site:* www.henryholt.com, pg 124

Otto, Laura, Indiana University Writers' Conference, Indiana University, Dept of English, 464 Ballantine Hall, Bloomington, IN 47405 *Tel:* 812-855-1877 *Fax:* 812-855-9535 *E-mail:* writecon@indiana.edu *Web Site:* www.indiana.edu/~writecon/, pg 744

Otto, Patrick, Howell Press Inc, 1713-2D Allied Lane, Charlottesville, VA 22903 *Tel:* 434-977-4006 *Toll Free Tel:* 800-868-4512 *Fax:* 434-971-7204 *Toll Free Fax:* 888-971-7204 *E-mail:* custserv@howellpress.com *Web Site:* www.howellpress.com, pg 127

Otzenberger, Stephen, College & University Professional Association for Human Resources, Tyson Place, 2607 Kingston Pike, Suite 250, Knoxville, TN 37919 *Tel:* 865-637-7673 *Fax:* 865-637-7674 *E-mail:* communications@cupahr.org *Web Site:* www.cupahr.org, pg 64

Ouimet, Mark, Frog Ltd, 1435 Fourth St, Berkeley, CA 94710 *Tel:* 510-559-8277 *Toll Free Tel:* 800-337-2665 (book orders only) *Fax:* 510-559-8279 *E-mail:* orders@northatlanticbooks.com *Web Site:* www.northatlanticbooks.com, pg 101

Ouimet, Mark, North Atlantic Books, 1435 Fourth St, Berkeley, CA 94710 *Tel:* 510-559-8277 *Toll Free Tel:* 800-337-2665 (book orders only) *Fax:* 510-559-8279 *E-mail:* orders@northatlanticbooks.com *Web Site:* www.northatlanticbooks.com, pg 192

Outhwaite, Tony, JCA Literary Agency Inc, 27 W 20 St, Suite 1103, New York, NY 10011 *Tel:* 212-807-0888 *Fax:* 212-807-0461 *Web Site:* www.jcalit.com, pg 636

Outland, Barbara, Louisiana State University Press, PO Box 25053, Baton Rouge, LA 70894-5053 *Tel:* 225-578-6294 *Toll Free Tel:* 800-861-3477 *Fax:* 225-578-6461 *Toll Free Fax:* 800-305-4416 *E-mail:* lsupress@lsu.edu *Web Site:* www.lsu.edu/guests/lsupress, pg 159

Ovedovitz, Nancy, Yale University Press, 302 Temple St, New Haven, CT 06511 *Tel:* 203-432-0960; 401-531-2800 (cust serv) *Toll Free Tel:* 800-405-1619 (cust serv) *Fax:* 203-432-0948; 401-531-2801 (cust serv) *Toll Free Fax:* 800-406-9145 (cust serv) *E-mail:* customer.care@trilateral.org (cust serv) *Web Site:* www.yale.edu/yup/, pg 305

Oveis, Frank, The Continuum International Publishing Group, 15 E 26 St, Suite 1703, New York, NY 10010 *Tel:* 212-953-5858 *Toll Free Tel:* 800-561-7704 *Fax:* 212-953-5944 *E-mail:* info@continuum-books.com *Web Site:* www.continuumbooks.com, pg 67

Overton, Kay L, Wyrick & Co, 284-A Meeting St, Charleston, SC 29401 *Tel:* 843-722-0881 *Toll Free Tel:* 800-227-5898 *Fax:* 843-722-6771 *E-mail:* wyrickco@bellsouth.net, pg 305

Owen, Audrey, Audrey Owen, 494 Eaglecrest Dr, Gibsons, BC V0N 1V8, Canada *E-mail:* editor@writershelper.com *Web Site:* www.writershelper.com, pg 590

Owen, Charlyce Jones, Prentice Hall Humanities & Social Sciences, One Lake St, Upper Saddle River, NJ 07458 *Tel:* 201-236-7000, pg 217

Owen, Richard C, Richard C Owen Publishers Inc, PO Box 585, Katonah, NY 10536-0585 *Tel:* 914-232-3903 *Toll Free Tel:* 800-336-5588 *Fax:* 914-232-3977 *E-mail:* richardowen@rcowen.com *Web Site:* www.rcowen.com, pg 200

Owens, Betsy, Rand McNally, 8255 Central Park Ave N, Skokie, IL 60076 *Tel:* 847-329-8100 *Toll Free Tel:* 800-333-0136 *Fax:* 847-673-0539 *Web Site:* www.randmcnally.com, pg 225

Owens, Crystal C, The American Chemical Society, 1155 16 St NW, Washington, DC 20036 *Tel:* 202-872-4600 *Toll Free Tel:* 800-227-5558 *Fax:* 202-872-6067 *Web Site:* www.acs.org; pubs.acs.org, pg 12

Owsiany, Dick, Graphic Arts Center Publishing Co, 3019 NW Yeon Ave, Portland, OR 97210 *Tel:* 503-226-2402 *Toll Free Tel:* 800-452-3032 *Fax:* 503-223-1410 *Toll Free Fax:* 800-355-9685 *E-mail:* editorial@gacpc.com; sales@gacpc.com *Web Site:* www.gacpc.com, pg 107

Oyama, Susan, Running Press Book Publishers, 125 S 22 St, Philadelphia, PA 19103-4399 *Tel:* 215-567-5080 *Toll Free Tel:* 800-345-5359 (cust serv & orders) *Fax:* 215-568-2919 *Toll Free Fax:* 800-453-2884 *Web Site:* www.runningpress.com, pg 236

Ozer, Harriet, Jerome S Ozer Publisher Inc, 340 Tenafly Rd, Englewood, NJ 07631 *Tel:* 201-567-7040 *Fax:* 201-567-8134, pg 201

Ozer, Jerome S, Jerome S Ozer Publisher Inc, 340 Tenafly Rd, Englewood, NJ 07631 *Tel:* 201-567-7040 *Fax:* 201-567-8134, pg 201

Pabley, Sonia, Rosenstone/Wender, 38 E 29 St, 10th fl, New York, NY 10016 *Tel:* 212-725-9445 *Fax:* 212-725-9447, pg 652

Pace, John, ASTM International, 100 Barr Harbor Dr, West Conshohocken, PA 19428 *Tel:* 610-832-9500 *Fax:* 610-832-9555 *E-mail:* service@astm.org *Web Site:* www.astm.org, pg 27

Pace, Kaye, John Wiley & Sons Inc Education Publishing Group, 111 River St, Hoboken, NJ 07030 *Tel:* 201-748-6000 *Fax:* 201-748-6088 *E-mail:* info@wiley.com *Web Site:* www.wiley.com, pg 300

Pacheco-Anderson, Joanie, Chronicle Books LLC, 85 Second St, 6th fl, San Francisco, CA 94105 *Tel:* 415-537-4200 *Toll Free Tel:* 800-722-6657 (cust serv) *Fax:* 415-537-4460 *Toll Free Fax:* 800-858-7787 (orders) *E-mail:* frontdesk@chroniclebooks.com *Web Site:* www.chroniclebooks.com, pg 61

Packard, Amy, Encounter Books, 665 Third St, Suite 330, San Francisco, CA 94107-1951 *Tel:* 415-538-1460 *Toll Free Tel:* 800-786-3839 *Fax:* 415-538-1461 *Toll Free Fax:* 877-811-1461 *E-mail:* read@encounterbooks.com *Web Site:* www.encounterbooks.com, pg 90

Padberg, John W, Institute of Jesuit Sources, 3601 Lindell Blvd, St Louis, MO 63108 *Tel:* 314-977-7257 *Fax:* 314-977-7263 *E-mail:* ijs@slu.edu *Web Site:* www.jesuitsources.com, pg 135

Paddio, Martin, Monthly Review Press, 122 W 27 St, New York, NY 10001 *Tel:* 212-691-2555 *Toll Free Tel:* 800-670-9499 *Fax:* 212-727-3676 *E-mail:* mreview@igc.org *Web Site:* www.MonthlyReview.org, pg 177

Paden, Carrie M, Society of American Business Editors & Writers Inc, Univ of Missouri, School of Journalism, 76 Gannett Hall, 134 Neff Annex, Columbia, MO 65211-1200 *Tel:* 573-882-7862 *Fax:* 573-884-1372 *E-mail:* sabew@missouri.edu *Web Site:* www.sabew.org, pg 700

Padgett, JoAnn, Advantage Publishers Group, 5880 Oberlin Dr, San Diego, CA 92121 *Tel:* 858-457-2500 *Toll Free Tel:* 800-284-3580 *Fax:* 858-812-6476 *Toll Free Fax:* 800-499-3822 *E-mail:* apgcuserv@advmkt.com *Web Site:* www.advantagebooksonline.com, pg 6

Padgett, Marvin, Crossway Books, 1300 Crescent St, Wheaton, IL 60187 *Tel:* 630-682-4300 *Fax:* 630-682-4785 *E-mail:* editorial@goodnews-crossway.org *Web Site:* www.crosswaybooks.org, pg 73

Padilla, Jessica, Creative Arts Book Co, 833 Bancroft Way, Berkeley, CA 94710 *Tel:* 510-848-4777 *Fax:* 510-848-4844 *E-mail:* staff@creativeartsbooks.com; capublisher@yahoo.com *Web Site:* www.creativeartsbooks.com, pg 72

Padley, Kristi, Four Paws Press LLC, 2460 Garden Rd, Suite B, Monterey, CA 93940 *Tel:* 831-375-PAWS (375-7297) *Fax:* 831-649-8007 *Web Site:* www.fourpawspress.com, pg 99

Padua, N J, Blacksmith Corp, PO Box 280, North Hampton, OH 45349-0280 *Tel:* 937-969-8389 *Toll Free Tel:* 800-531-2665 *Fax:* 937-969-8399 *E-mail:* sales@blacksmithcorp.com *Web Site:* www.blacksmithcorp.com, pg 40

Pagan, Eilenn, Walker & Co, 104 Fifth Ave, 7th fl, New York, NY 10011 *Tel:* 212-727-8300 *Toll Free Tel:* 800-289-2553 *Fax:* 212-727-0984 *Toll Free Fax:* 800-218-9367 *E-mail:* firstinitiallastname@walkerbooks.com *Web Site:* www.walkerbooks.com, pg 292

Pagan, Zena, Advertising Research Foundation, 641 Lexington Ave, New York, NY 10022 *Tel:* 212-751-5656 *Fax:* 212-319-5265 *E-mail:* info@thearf.org *Web Site:* www.thearf.org, pg 675

Page, Edita, Gerald Lampert Memorial Award, 920 Yonge St, Suite 608, Toronto, ON M4W 3C7, Canada *Tel:* 416-504-1657 *Fax:* 416-504-0096 *E-mail:* info@poets.ca *Web Site:* www.poets.ca, pg 783

Page, Edita, League of Canadian Poets, 920 Yonge St, Suite 608, Toronto, ON M4W 3C7, Canada *Tel:* 416-504-1657 *Fax:* 416-504-0096 *E-mail:* info@poets.ca *Web Site:* www.poets.ca, pg 689

Page, Edita, Pat Lowther Memorial Award, 920 Yonge St, Suite 608, Toronto, ON M4W 3C7, Canada *Tel:* 416-504-1657 *Fax:* 416-504-0096 *E-mail:* info@poets.ca *Web Site:* www.poets.ca, pg 786

Page, Linda, Healthy Healing Publications, PO Box 436, Carmel Valley, CA 93924 *Tel:* 831-659-8324 *Fax:* 831-659-4044 *E-mail:* customerservice@healthyhealing.com *Web Site:* www.healthyhealing.com, pg 120

Page, Robert, Zaner-Bloser Inc, 2200 W Fifth Ave, Columbus, OH 43215 *Tel:* 614-486-0221 *Toll Free Tel:* 800-421-3018 *Fax:* 614-487-2699 *Toll Free Fax:* 800-992-6087 *E-mail:* info@zaner-bloser.com *Web Site:* www.zaner-bloser.com, pg 307

Pagel, Stephen, Meisha Merlin Publishing Inc, 1702 Ronald Rd, Tucker, GA 30084 *Tel:* 770-414-4365 *Fax:* 770-414-4365 *E-mail:* email@meishamerlin.com; orders@meishamerlin.com *Web Site:* www.meishamerlin.com, pg 172

Pagonzzi, Michelle, The RGU Group, 560 W Southern Ave, Tempe, AZ 85282 *Tel:* 480-736-9862 *Toll Free Tel:* 800-266-5265 *Fax:* 480-736-9863 *Toll Free Fax:* 800-973-6694 *E-mail:* info@thergugroup.com *Web Site:* www.thergugroup.com, pg 232

Painchaud, Kathy, Thistledown Press Ltd, 633 Main St, Saskatoon, SK S7H 0J8, Canada *Tel:* 306-244-1722 *Fax:* 306-244-1762 *E-mail:* marketing@thistledown.sk.ca *Web Site:* www.thistledown.sk.ca, pg 563

Palassis, Neketas S, Saint Nectarios Press, 10300 Ashworth Ave N, Seattle, WA 98133-9410 *Tel:* 206-522-4471 *Toll Free Tel:* 800-643-4233 *Fax:* 206-523-0550 *E-mail:* orders@stnectariospress.com *Web Site:* www.stnectariospress.com, pg 239

Palatka, Andy, Business Forms Management Association (BFMA), 319 SW Washington St, Suite 710, Portland, OR 97204 *Tel:* 503-227-3393 *Fax:* 503-274-7667 *E-mail:* bfma@bfma.org *Web Site:* www.bfma.org, pg 682

Palatucci, Pat, Plexus Publishing Inc, 143 Old Marlton Pike, Medford, NJ 08055 *Tel:* 609-654-6500 *Fax:* 609-654-4309 *E-mail:* info@plexuspublishing.com *Web Site:* www.plexuspublishing.com, pg 214

Palgon, Michael, Doubleday Broadway Publishing Group, 1745 Broadway, New York, NY 10019 *Tel:* 212-782-9000 *Toll Free Tel:* 800-223-6834; 800-223-5780 (sales) *Fax:* 212-302-7985 (correspondence); 212-492-9862 (orders), pg 82

Palladino, Linda, Random House Children's Books, 1745 Broadway, New York, NY 10019 *Tel:* 212-782-9000 *Toll Free Tel:* 800-200-3552 *Fax:* 212-782-9452 *Web Site:* www.randomhouse.com/kids, pg 226

Pallai, David F, Charles River Media, 10 Downer Ave, Hingham, MA 02043 *Tel:* 781-740-0400 (edit offices) *Toll Free Tel:* 800-382-8505 (orders) *Fax:* 781-740-8816; 703-996-1010 (orders) *E-mail:* info@charlesriver.com *Web Site:* www.charlesriver.com, pg 58

Palmer, William, The Haworth Press Inc, 10 Alice St, Binghamton, NY 13904-1580 *Tel:* 607-722-5857 *Toll Free Tel:* 800-429-6784 *Fax:* 607-722-1424 *Toll Free Fax:* 800-895-0582 *E-mail:* getinfo@haworthpressinc.com *Web Site:* www.haworthpress.com, pg 118

Palmieri, Marco, Pocket Books, 1230 Avenue of the Americas, New York, NY 10020 *Toll Free Tel:* 800-456-6798 *Fax:* 212-698-7284 *E-mail:* consumer.customerservice@simonandschuster.com *Web Site:* www.simonsays.com, pg 215

Palmore, Dennis O, New Directions Publishing Corp, 80 Eighth Ave, New York, NY 10011 *Tel:* 212-255-0230 *Toll Free Tel:* 800-233-4830 (PA) *Fax:* 212-255-0231 *E-mail:* newdirections@ndbooks.com *Web Site:* www.ndpublishing.com, pg 187

Palmquist, Nancy K, W W Norton & Company Inc, 500 Fifth Ave, New York, NY 10110-0017 *Tel:* 212-354-5500 *Toll Free Tel:* 800-233-4830 (orders & cust serv) *Fax:* 212-869-0856 *Toll Free Fax:* 800-458-6515 *Web Site:* www.wwnorton.com, pg 193

Palumbo, Maryann, Mint Publishers Group, 62 June Rd, North Salem, NY 10560 *Tel:* 914-276-6576 *Fax:* 914-276-6579 *E-mail:* info@mintpub.com *Web Site:* www.mintpub.com, pg 175

Pampel, Birte, Allworth Press, 10 E 23 St, Suite 510, New York, NY 10010 *Tel:* 212-777-8395 *Toll Free Tel:* 800-491-2808 *Fax:* 212-777-8261 *E-mail:* pub@allworth.com *Web Site:* www.allworth.com, pg 9

Panec, Don, Treasure Bay Inc, 17 Parkgrove Dr, South San Francisco, CA 94080 *Tel:* 650-589-7980 *Fax:* 650-589-7927 *E-mail:* webothread@comcast.net, pg 275

Panico, Neil, The Dawn Horse Press, 12040 N Seigler Rd, Middletown, CA 95461 *Tel:* 707-928-6590 *Toll Free Tel:* 877-770-0772 *Fax:* 707-928-5068 *E-mail:* dhp@adidam.org *Web Site:* www.dawnhorsepress.com, pg 77

Pankoff, Jay, Technology Training Systems Inc (TTS), 3131 S Vaughn Way, Suite 300, Aurora, CO 80014-3503 *Tel:* 303-368-0300 *Toll Free Tel:* 800-676-8871 *Fax:* 303-368-0312 *E-mail:* info@myplantstraining.com *Web Site:* www.myplantstraining.com, pg 266

Pannell, James, Brook Street Press LLC, 200 Plantation Chase, Saint Simons Island, GA 31522 *Tel:* 912-638-0264 *Fax:* 912-638-0265 *E-mail:* info@brookstreetpress.com *Web Site:* www.brookstreetpress.com, pg 48

Pantano, Merry K (Gregory), Blanche C Gregory Inc, 2 Tudor City Place, New York, NY 10017 *Tel:* 212-697-0828 *Fax:* 212-697-0828 *E-mail:* bcgliteraryagent@aol.com *Web Site:* www.bcgliteraryagency.com, pg 633

Pantazopoulos, Theresa, Simon & Schuster Audio, 1230 Avenue of the Americas, New York, NY 10020 *Tel:* 212-698-7664 *E-mail:* audiopub@simonandschuster.com *Web Site:* www.simonsaysaudio.com, pg 248

Panzer, Robert, Visual Artists & Galleries Association Inc (VAGA), 350 Fifth Ave, Suite 2820, New York City, NY 10118 *Tel:* 212-736-6666 *Fax:* 212-736-6767 *E-mail:* info@vagarights.com, pg 702

Paola, Suzanne, 49th Parallel Poetry Award, Mail Stop 9053, Western Washington University, Bellingham, WA 98225 *Tel:* 360-650-4863 *E-mail:* bhreview@cc.wwu.edu *Web Site:* www.wwu.edu/~bhreview, pg 774

Paonessa, Bruce, Time Warner Book Group, 1271 Avenue of the Americas, New York, NY 10020 *Tel:* 212-522-7200 *Fax:* 212-522-7991 *Web Site:* www.twbookmark.com, pg 272

Pape, Don, WaterBrook Press, 2375 Telstar Dr, Suite 160, Colorado Springs, CO 80920 *Tel:* 719-590-4999 *Toll Free Tel:* 800-603-7051 (orders) *Fax:* 719-590-8977 *Toll Free Fax:* 800-294-5686 (orders) *Web Site:* www.waterbrookpress.com, pg 294

Papin, Jessica, Dystel & Goderich Literary Management, One Union Sq W, Suite 904, New York, NY 10003 *Tel:* 212-627-9100 *Fax:* 212-627-9313 *Web Site:* www.dystel.com, pg 629

Pappas, Evangeline A, ASIS International, 1625 Prince St, Alexandria, VA 22314 *Tel:* 703-518-1475 *Fax:* 703-518-1517, pg 25

Pappas, Joseph J, Consumer Press, 13326 SW 28 St, Suite 102, Fort Lauderdale, FL 33330-1102 *Tel:* 954-370-9153 *Fax:* 954-472-1008 *E-mail:* bookguest@aol.com *Web Site:* consumerpress.com, pg 67

Pappenheimer, Andrea, HarperCollins Publishers Sales, 10 E 53 St, New York, NY 10022 *Fax:* 212-207-7826 *Web Site:* www.harpercollins.com, pg 116

Paquin, Pierre-Marie, Editions Hurtubise HMH Ltee, 1815 De Lorimier, Montreal, PQ H2K 3W6, Canada *Tel:* 514-523-1523 *Toll Free Tel:* 800-361-1664 (Canada only) *Fax:* 514-523-9969; 514-523-5955 (edit) *E-mail:* hurtubisehmh@hurtubisehmh.com *Web Site:* www.hurtubisehmh.com, pg 545

Paradis, Lucille, Paulines, 5610 rue Beaubien est, Montreal, PQ H1T 1X5, Canada *Tel:* 514-253-5610 *Fax:* 514-253-1907 *E-mail:* paulines.editions@videotron.ca, pg 557

Paradis, Michelle, Modulo Editeur Inc, 233 Ave Dunbar, Rm 300, Mont Royal, PQ H3P 2H4, Canada *Tel:* 514-738-9818 *Toll Free Tel:* 888-738-9818 *Fax:* 514-738-5838 *Toll Free Fax:* 888-273-5247 *Web Site:* www.moduloediteur.com, pg 554

Paradis, Michelle, Modulo-Griffon Inc, 233 Dunbar Ave, Suite 300, Mont Royal, PQ H3P 2H4, Canada *Tel:* 514-738-9818 *Toll Free Tel:* 888-738-9818 *Fax:* 514-738-5838 *Toll Free Fax:* 888-273-5247 *Web Site:* www.moduloediteur.com, pg 554

Paradise, Connie, American Industrial Hygiene Association, 2700 Prosperity Ave, Suite 250, Fairfax, VA 22031-4319 *Tel:* 703-849-8888 *Fax:* 703-207-3561 *E-mail:* infonet@aiha.org *Web Site:* www.aiha.org, pg 14

Paraskevopoulos, D Jane, Forward Movement Publications, 300 W Fourth St, Cincinnati, OH 45202 *Tel:* 513-721-6659 *Toll Free Tel:* 800-543-1813 *Fax:* 513-721-0729 *E-mail:* orders@forwarddaybyday.com *Web Site:* www.forwardmovement.org, pg 99

Pardue, Whitney, Printing Industry Association of the South, 305 Plus Park Blvd, Nashville, TN 37217 *Tel:* 615-366-1094 *Toll Free Tel:* 800-821-3138 *Fax:* 615-366-4192 *E-mail:* info@pias.org *Web Site:* www.pias.org, pg 698

Pare, Cathy, Holt, Rinehart and Winston, 10801 N MoPac Expy, Bldg 3, Austin, TX 78759 *Tel:* 512-721-7000 *Toll Free Tel:* 800-225-5425 (cust serv) *Fax:* 512-721-7833 (mktg); 512-721-7898 (edit) *Web Site:* www.hrw.com, pg 124

Pare, Robert, Cheneliere/McGraw-Hill, 7001 Saint Laurent Blvd, Montreal, PQ H2S 3E3, Canada *Tel:* 514-273-1066 *Fax:* 514-276-0324 *E-mail:* chene@dlcmcgrawhill.ca *Web Site:* www.dlcmcgrawhill.ca, pg 540

Parent, Marie-Helene, Prix Alvine-Belisle, 3414 Avenue Du Parc, Bureau 202, Montreal, PQ H2X 2H5, Canada *Tel:* 514-281-5012 *Fax:* 514-281-8219 *E-mail:* info@asted.org *Web Site:* www.asted.org, pg 800

Parets, Meredith, ALSC BWI/Summer Reading Program Grant, 50 E Huron St, Chicago, IL 60611-2795 *Tel:* 312-280-2163 *Toll Free Tel:* 800-545-2433 *Fax:* 312-944-7671 *E-mail:* alsc@ala.org *Web Site:* www.ala.org/alsc, pg 759

Parfitt, Gerilyn, Eclipse Press, 3101 Beaumont Centre Circle, Lexington, KY 40513 *Tel:* 859-278-2361 *Toll Free Tel:* 800-866-2361 *Fax:* 859-276-6868 *E-mail:* editorial@eclipsepress.com; marketing@eclipsepress.com *Web Site:* www.eclipsepress.com, pg 86

Parfrey, Adam, Feral House, PO Box 39910, Los Angeles, CA 90039 *Tel:* 323-666-3311 *Fax:* 323-666-3330 *E-mail:* info@feralhouse.com *Web Site:* www.feralhouse.com, pg 96

Parisi, Rose, Illinois Arts Council Artists Fellowships, James R Thompson Ctr, 100 W Randolph, Suite 10-500, Chicago, IL 60601 *Tel:* 312-814-6750 *Toll Free Tel:* 800-237-6994 (IL only) *Fax:* 312-814-1471 *E-mail:* info@arts.state.il.us *Web Site:* www.state.il.us/agency/iac, pg 779

Park, Charlie, Peace Hill Press, 18101 The Glebe Lane, Charles City, VA 23030 *Tel:* 804-829-5043 *Toll Free Tel:* 877-322-3445 (orders) *Fax:* 804-829-5704 *E-mail:* info@peacehillpress.net *Web Site:* www.peacehillpress.com, pg 206

Park, Drew, Christian Publications Inc, 3825 Hartzdale Dr, Camp Hill, PA 17011 *Tel:* 717-761-7044 *Toll Free Tel:* 800-233-4443 (orders) *Fax:* 717-761-7273 *E-mail:* editorial@christianpublications.com *Web Site:* www.christianpublications.com, pg 61

Park, Gilman, Hudson Park Press, Johnny Cake Hollow Rd, Pine Plains, NY 12567 *Tel:* 212-929-8898 *Fax:* 212-242-6137 *E-mail:* hudpark@aol.com *Web Site:* www.hudsonpark.com, pg 128

Park, Jerry, Thomas Nelson Inc, 501 Nelson Place, Nashville, TN 37214 *Tel:* 615-889-9000 *Toll Free Tel:* 800-251-4000 *Fax:* 615-902-1610 *E-mail:* publicity@thomasnelson.com *Web Site:* www.thomasnelson.com, pg 269

Park, Kenneth, World Almanac Books, 512 Seventh Ave, 22nd fl, New York, NY 10018 *Tel:* 646-312-6800 *Fax:* 646-312-6839 *E-mail:* info@waegroup.com *Web Site:* www.worldalmanac.com, pg 303

Park, Lynn, Creative Arts Book Co, 833 Bancroft Way, Berkeley, CA 94710 *Tel:* 510-848-4777 *Fax:* 510-848-4844 *E-mail:* staff@creativeartsbooks.com; capublisher@yahoo.com *Web Site:* www.creativeartsbooks.com, pg 72

Park, Theresa, Sanford J Greenburger Associates Inc, 55 Fifth Ave, 15th fl, New York, NY 10003 *Tel:* 212-206-5600 *Fax:* 212-463-8718 *Web Site:* www.greenburger.com, pg 633

Parker, Blake, Incentive Publications Inc, 3835 Cleghorn Ave, Nashville, TN 37215 *Tel:* 615-385-2934 *Toll Free Tel:* 800-421-2830 *Fax:* 615-385-2967 *E-mail:* comments@incentivepublications.com *Web Site:* www.incentivepublications.com, pg 132

Parker, Brian, Scott Foresman, 1900 E Lake Ave, Glenview, IL 60025 *Tel:* 847-729-3000 *Toll Free Tel:* 800-535-4391 (Midwest) *Fax:* 847-729-8910 *E-mail:* firstname.lastname@scottforesman.com *Web Site:* www.scottforesman.com, pg 243

Parker, Dara P, Howell Press Inc, 1713-2D Allied Lane, Charlottesville, VA 22903 *Tel:* 434-977-4006 *Toll Free Tel:* 800-868-4512 *Fax:* 434-971-7204 *Toll Free Fax:* 888-971-7204 *E-mail:* custserv@howellpress.com *Web Site:* www.howellpress.com, pg 127

Parker, Harvey, A D D Warehouse, 300 NW 70 Ave, Suite 102, Plantation, FL 33317 *Tel:* 954-792-8100 *Toll Free Tel:* 800-233-9273 *Fax:* 954-792-8545 *E-mail:* websales@addwarehouse.com *Web Site:* www.addwarehouse.com, pg 1

Parker, Jim, Do It Now Foundation, 2750 S Hardy Dr, Suite 2, Tempe, AZ 85282 *Tel:* 480-736-0599 *Fax:* 480-736-0771 *E-mail:* doitnow@quest.net *Web Site:* www.doitnow.org, pg 81

Parker, Joyce, H D I Publishers, 2424 Elmen St, Houston, TX 77019-6710 *Tel:* 713-526-6900 *Toll Free Tel:* 800-321-7037 *Fax:* 713-526-7787 *Web Site:* www.hdipub.com, pg 111

Parker, Katie, Emmis Books, 1700 Madison Rd, 2nd fl, Cincinnati, OH 45206 *Tel:* 513-861-4045 *Toll Free Tel:* 800-913-9563 *Fax:* 513-861-4430 *E-mail:* info@emmis.com *Web Site:* www.emmisbooks.com, pg 90

Parker, Peyton, Parlay Press, PO Box 894, Superior, WI 54880 *Tel:* 218-834-2508 *E-mail:* mail@parlaypress.com *Web Site:* www.parlaypress.com, pg 204

Parker, Sonya, Greenhaven Press®, 15822 Bernardo Center Dr, Suite C, San Diego, CA 92127 *Tel:* 858-485-7424 *Toll Free Tel:* 800-877-4253 (cust serv & orders) *Fax:* 858-485-9549; 248-699-8051 (cust serv) *Toll Free Fax:* 800-414-5043 (orders only) *E-mail:* customerservice@gale.com; galeord@gale.com (orders) *Web Site:* www.gale.com/greenhaven, pg 109

Parker, Sonya, Lucent Books Inc, 15822 Bernardo Center Dr, Suite C, San Diego, CA 92127 *Tel:* 858-485-7424 *Fax:* 858-485-9549 *E-mail:* info@gale.com *Web Site:* www.gale.com/lucent, pg 159

Parker, William, Liguori Publications, One Liguori Dr, Liguori, MO 63057-9999 *Tel:* 636-464-2500 *Toll Free Tel:* 800-464-2555 *Fax:* 636-464-8449 *Web Site:* www.liguori.org, pg 154

Parkerson, Ami, New World Library, 14 Pamaron Way, Novato, CA 94949 *Tel:* 415-884-2100 *Toll Free Tel:* 800-227-3900 (ext 52, retail orders) *Fax:* 415-884-2199 (ext 52, retail orders) *E-mail:* escort@newworldlibrary.com *Web Site:* www.newworldlibrary.com, pg 189

Parkhurst, Liz Smith, August House Publishers Inc, 201 E Markham, Little Rock, AR 72201 *Tel:* 501-372-5450 *Toll Free Tel:* 800-284-8784 *Fax:* 501-372-5579 *Toll Free Fax:* 800-284-8784 (orders) *E-mail:* ahinfo@augusthouse.com *Web Site:* www.augusthouse.com, pg 28

Parkhurst, Ted, August House Publishers Inc, 201 E Markham, Little Rock, AR 72201 *Tel:* 501-372-5450 *Toll Free Tel:* 800-284-8784 *Fax:* 501-372-5579 *Toll Free Fax:* 800-284-8784 (orders) *E-mail:* ahinfo@augusthouse.com *Web Site:* www.augusthouse.com, pg 28

Parkin, Laurie, Kensington Publishing Corp, 850 Third Ave, New York, NY 10022 *Tel:* 212-407-1500 *Toll Free Tel:* 800-221-2647 *Fax:* 212-935-0699 *Web Site:* www.kensingtonbooks.com, pg 145

Parkinson, A O, Research Press, 2612 N Mattis Ave, Champaign, IL 61822 *Tel:* 217-352-3273 *Toll Free Tel:* 800-519-2707 *Fax:* 217-352-1221 *E-mail:* rp@researchpress.com *Web Site:* www.researchpress.com, pg 231

Parks, Richard, The Richard Parks Agency, 138 E 16 St, Suite 5-B, New York, NY 10003 *Tel:* 212-254-9067 *Fax:* 212-228-1786 *E-mail:* rp@richardparksagency.com, pg 647

Parks, Tricia, Menasha Ridge Press Inc, 2204 First Ave S, Suite 102, Birmingham, AL 35233 *Tel:* 205-322-0439 *Fax:* 205-326-1012 *E-mail:* info@menasharidge.com *Web Site:* www.menasharidge.com, pg 171

Parks, Walter, UnKnownTruths.com Publishing Co, 8815 Conroy Windermere Rd, Suite 190, Orlando, FL 32835 *Tel:* 407-929-9207 *Fax:* 407-876-3933 *E-mail:* info@unknowntruths.com *Web Site:* unknowntruths.com, pg 288

Parmiter, Tara, Seven Stories Press, 140 Watts St, New York, NY 10013 *Tel:* 212-226-8760 *Toll Free Tel:* 800-283-3572 *Fax:* 212-226-1411 *E-mail:* info@sevenstories.com *Web Site:* www.sevenstories.com, pg 245

Parnell, Byron, Kane/Miller Book Publishers, PO Box 8515, La Jolla, CA 92038-8515 *Tel:* 858-456-0540 *Toll Free Tel:* 800-968-1930 *Fax:* 858-456-9641 *E-mail:* info@kanemiller.com *Web Site:* www.kanemiller.com, pg 144

Parr, Steve, Stewart, Tabori & Chang, 115 W 18 St, 5th fl, New York, NY 10011 *Tel:* 212-519-1200 *Fax:* 212-519-1210 *Web Site:* www.abramsbooks.com, pg 259

Parrent, Joanne, Feigen/Parrent Literary Management, 10158 Hollow Glen Circle, Bel Air, CA 90077 *Tel:* 310-271-4722 *Fax:* 310-274-0503 *E-mail:* feigenparrentlit@aol.com, pg 630

Parrinello, Anna, Maria Carvainis Agency Inc, 1350 Avenue of the Americas, Suite 2905, New York, NY 10019 *Tel:* 212-245-6365 *Fax:* 212-245-7196 *E-mail:* mca@mariacarvainisagency.com, pg 624

Parris, Scott, Cambridge University Press, 40 W 20 St, New York, NY 10011-4211 *Tel:* 212-924-3900 *Toll Free Tel:* 800-899-5222 *Fax:* 212-691-3239 *Web Site:* www.cambridge.org, pg 52

Parrish, Rodney, Society of Environmental Toxicology & Chemistry, 1010 N 12 Ave, Pensacola, FL 32501-3370 *Tel:* 850-469-9777; 850-469-1500 *Fax:* 850-469-9778 *E-mail:* setac@setac.org *Web Site:* www.setac.org, pg 252

Parry, Joseph, Hamilton Books, 4501 Forbes Blvd, Suite 200, Lanham, MD 20706 *Tel:* 301-459-3366, pg 112

Parry, Robert T, National Bureau of Economic Research Inc, 1050 Massachusetts Ave, Cambridge, MA 02138-5398 *Tel:* 617-868-3900 *Fax:* 617-868-2742 *E-mail:* op@nber.org *Web Site:* www.nber.org, pg 182

Parsons, Edward, Cambridge University Press, 40 W 20 St, New York, NY 10011-4211 *Tel:* 212-924-3900 *Toll Free Tel:* 800-899-5222 *Fax:* 212-691-3239 *Web Site:* www.cambridge.org, pg 52

Parsons, Noel, Texas Tech University Press, 2903 Fourth St, Lubbock, TX 79412 *Tel:* 806-742-2982 *Toll Free Tel:* 800-832-4042 *Fax:* 806-742-2979 *E-mail:* ttup@ttu.edu *Web Site:* www.ttup.ttu.edu, pg 267

Parsons, Sue, Canadian Institute of Resources Law, University of Calgary, Murray Fraser Hall, Rm 3330, 2500 University Dr NW, Calgary, AB T2N 1N4, Canada *Tel:* 403-220-3200 *Fax:* 403-282-6182 *E-mail:* cirl@ucalgary.ca *Web Site:* www.cirl.ca, pg 538

Partland, J P, Editorial Freelancers Association (EFA), 71 W 23 St, New York, NY 10010 *Tel:* 212-929-5400 *Fax:* 212-929-5439 *E-mail:* info@the-efa.org *Web Site:* www.the-efa.org, pg 686

Parupia, Iqbal, International Association of Business Communicators (IABC), One Hallidie Plaza, Suite 600, San Francisco, CA 94102 *Tel:* 415-544-4700 *Toll Free Tel:* 800-776-4222 *Fax:* 415-544-4747 *E-mail:* service_centre@iabc.com *Web Site:* www.iabc.com, pg 688

Pasanen, Jane S, The Chelsea Forum Inc, 377 Rector Place, No 12-I, New York, NY 10280 *Tel:* 212-945-3100 *Fax:* 212-945-3101 *Web Site:* www.chelseaforum.com, pg 669

Pasanen, Jennifer, Scholastic Trade Division, 557 Broadway, New York, NY 10012 *Tel:* 212-343-6100; 212-343-4685 (export sales) *Fax:* 212-343-4714 (export sales) *Web Site:* www.scholastic.com, pg 242

Pascal, Naomi B, University of Washington Press, 1326 Fifth Ave, Suite 555, Seattle, WA 98101-2604 *Tel:* 206-543-4050; 206-543-8870 *Toll Free Tel:* 800-441-4115 (orders) *Fax:* 206-543-3932 *Toll Free Fax:* 800-669-7993 (orders) *E-mail:* uwpord@u.washington.edu *Web Site:* www.washington.edu/uwpress/, pg 286

Paschal, Allen W, Thomson Gale, 27500 Drake Rd, Farmington Hills, MI 48331-3535 *Tel:* 248-699-4253 *Toll Free Tel:* 800-347-4253 *Fax:* 248-699-8070 *Toll Free Fax:* 800-414-5043 *E-mail:* galeord@gale.com *Web Site:* www.gale.com, pg 270

Pascocello, Rick, Berkley Books, 375 Hudson St, New York, NY 10014 *Tel:* 212-366-2000 *Fax:* 212-366-2666 *E-mail:* online@penguinputnam.com *Web Site:* www.penguin.com, pg 36

Pascocello, Rick, Berkley Publishing Group, 375 Hudson St, New York, NY 10014 *Tel:* 212-366-2000 *E-mail:* online@penguinputnam.com *Web Site:* www.penguin.com, pg 37

Pascocello, Rick, NAL, 375 Hudson St, New York, NY 10014 *Tel:* 212-366-2000 *E-mail:* online@penguinputnam.com *Web Site:* www.penguin.com, pg 181

Pascoe, Jim, UglyTown, 2148 1/2 W Sunset Blvd, Suite 204, Los Angeles, CA 90026-3148 *Tel:* 213-484-8334 *Fax:* 213-484-8333 *E-mail:* mayorsoffice@uglytown.com *Web Site:* www.uglytown.com, pg 278

Pashman, Arlene, Center for Urban Policy Research, 33 Livingston Ave, Suite 400, New Brunswick, NJ 08901-1982 *Tel:* 732-932-3133 *Fax:* 732-932-2363 *Web Site:* www.policy.rutgers.edu/cupr, pg 57

Passaro, Lanny, E B P Latin America Group Inc, 175 E Delaware Place, Suite 8806, Chicago, IL 60611 *Tel:* 312-397-9590 *Fax:* 312-397-9593 *Web Site:* www.barsa.com, pg 85

Paster, Gail Kern, National Endowment for the Humanities Fellowships & Folger Longterm & Short-term Fellowships & Andrew W Mellon Foundations, c/o Fellowship Committee, 201 E Capitol St SE, Washington, DC 20003 *Tel:* 202-544-4600 (ext 348) *Fax:* 202-544-4623 *Web Site:* www.folger.edu, pg 791

Pastore, Susan, Kluwer Academic Publishers, 101 Philip Dr, Assinippi Park, Norwell, MA 02061 *Tel:* 781-871-6600 *Fax:* 781-871-6528; 781-681-9045 (cust serv) *E-mail:* kluwer@wkap.com *Web Site:* www.wkap.nl, pg 146

Pastorius, Edward W, Thomson Gale, 27500 Drake Rd, Farmington Hills, MI 48331-3535 *Tel:* 248-699-4253 *Toll Free Tel:* 800-347-4253 *Fax:* 248-699-8070 *Toll Free Fax:* 800-414-5043 *E-mail:* galeord@gale.com *Web Site:* www.gale.com, pg 270

Patchin, Richard R, Delta Systems Co Inc, 1400 Miller Pkwy, McHenry, IL 60050-7030 *Tel:* 815-363-3582 *Toll Free Tel:* 800-323-8270 *Fax:* 815-363-2948 *Toll Free Fax:* 800-909-9901 *E-mail:* custsvc@delta-systems.com *Web Site:* www.delta-systems.com, pg 79

Patenaude, Mike, Incentive Publications Inc, 3835 Cleghorn Ave, Nashville, TN 37215 *Tel:* 615-385-2934 *Toll Free Tel:* 800-421-2830 *Fax:* 615-385-2967 *E-mail:* comments@incentivepublications.com *Web Site:* www.incentivepublications.com, pg 132

Paton, Kathi J, Kathi J Paton Literary Agency, 19 W 55 St, New York, NY 10019-4907 *Tel:* 212-265-6586; 908-647-2117 *E-mail:* kjplitbiz@optonline.net, pg 647

Paton, Ken, Christian Publications Inc, 3825 Hartzdale Dr, Camp Hill, PA 17011 *Tel:* 717-761-7044 *Toll Free Tel:* 800-233-4443 *Fax:* 717-761-7273 *E-mail:* editorial@christianpublications.com *Web Site:* www.christianpublications.com, pg 61

Patota, Anne, The Guilford Press, 72 Spring St, New York, NY 10012 *Tel:* 212-431-9800 *Toll Free Tel:* 800-365-7006 (orders) *Fax:* 212-966-6708 *E-mail:* orders@guilford.com *Web Site:* www.guilford.com, pg 111

Patrick, Amy, Sleeping Bear Press™, 310 N Main St, Suite 300, Chelsea, MI 48118 *Tel:* 734-475-4411 *Toll Free Tel:* 800-487-2323 *Fax:* 734-475-0787 *E-mail:* sleepingbear@thomson.com *Web Site:* www.sleepingbearpress.com, pg 250

Patrick, Jean, Diamond Literary Agency Inc, 3063 S Kearney St, Denver, CO 80222 *Tel:* 303-753-6318 *E-mail:* diamondliteraryagency@yahoo.com, pg 627

Patrick, Philip, Crown Publishing Group, 1745 Broadway, New York, NY 10019 *Tel:* 212-782-9000 *Toll Free Tel:* 888-264-1745 *Fax:* 212-940-7408 *Web Site:* www.randomhouse.com/crown, pg 74

Patrusky, Ben, Rennie Taylor-Alton Blakeslee Fellowships in Science Writing, PO Box 910, Hedgesville, WV 25427 *Tel:* 304-754-5077 *Fax:* 304-754-5076 *Web Site:* www.casw.org, pg 808

Patten, Amanda, Fireside & Touchstone, 1230 Avenue of the Americas, New York, NY 10020, pg 97

Patten, Drake, Residency, 454 E Hill Rd, Austerlitz, NY 12017 *Tel:* 518-392-3103; 518-392-4144 *Fax:* 518-392-7664 *E-mail:* apply@millaycolony.org *Web Site:* www.millaycolony.org, pg 802

Patterson, Elaine, Arcadia Enterprises Inc, PO Box 206, Fruitland, MD 21826 *Tel:* 410-742-2682 *Toll Free Tel:* 877-742-2682 *Fax:* 410-742-2708 *Web Site:* www.buyarcadiabooks.com, pg 22

Patterson, Emma, The Wendy Weil Agency Inc, 232 Madison Ave, Suite 1300, New York, NY 10016 *Tel:* 212-685-0030 *Fax:* 212-685-0765, pg 660

Patterson, Kathleen, Optometric Extension Program Foundation, 1921 E Carnegie Ave, Suite 3-L, Santa Ana, CA 92705-5510 *Tel:* 949-250-8070 *Fax:* 949-250-8157 *E-mail:* oep1@oep.org *Web Site:* www.oep.org, pg 198

Patterson, Monique, St Martin's Press Paperback and Reference Group, 175 Fifth Ave, New York, NY 10010 *Fax:* 212-995-2488 *E-mail:* firstname.lastname@stmartins.com, pg 239

Patterson, P J, Chalice Press, 1221 Locust St, Suite 1200, St Louis, MO 63103 *Tel:* 314-231-8500 *Toll Free Tel:* 800-366-3383 *Fax:* 314-231-8524 *E-mail:* chalicepress@cbp21.com *Web Site:* www.cbp21.com; www.chalicepress.com, pg 58

Patterson, Sandra, American Psychiatric Publishing Inc, 1000 Wilson Blvd, Suite 1825, Arlington, VA 22209 *Tel:* 703-907-7322 *Toll Free Tel:* 800-368-5777 *Fax:* 703-907-1091 *E-mail:* appi@psych.org *Web Site:* www.appi.org, pg 16

Patterson, Tracy, Stackpole Books, 5067 Ritter Rd, Mechanicsburg, PA 17055 *Tel:* 717-796-0411 *Toll Free Tel:* 800-732-3669 *Fax:* 717-796-0412 *Web Site:* www.stackpolebooks.com, pg 257

Patton, Sara, Sara Patton Book Production Services, 160 River Rd, Wailuku, HI 96793 *Tel:* 808-242-7838 *Toll Free Tel:* 800-433-4804 *Fax:* 808-242-6113, pg 607

Pattow, Sara, Champion Press Ltd, 4308 Blueberry Rd, Fredonia, WI 53021 *Tel:* 262-692-3897 *Toll Free Tel:* 877-250-3354 *Fax:* 262-692-3342 *E-mail:* info@championpress.com *Web Site:* www.championpress.com, pg 58

Pattrick, Roy, Self-Counsel Press Inc, 1704 N State St, Bellingham, WA 98225 *Tel:* 360-676-4530 *Toll Free Tel:* 877-877-6490 *Fax:* 360-676-4549 *E-mail:* service@self-counsel.com *Web Site:* www.self-counsel.com, pg 245

Paul, Alexia, The Joy Harris Literary Agency, 156 Fifth Ave, Suite 617, New York, NY 10010 *Tel:* 212-924-6269 *Fax:* 212-924-6609 *E-mail:* gen.office@jhlitagent.com, pg 634

Paul, Beverly, Beautiful America Publishing Co, 2600 Progress Way, Woodburn, OR 97071 *Tel:* 503-982-4616 *Toll Free Tel:* 800-874-1233 *Fax:* 503-982-2825 *E-mail:* bapco@beautifulamericapub.com *Web Site:* www.beautifulamericapub.com, pg 34

Paul, Nancy Gray, Woodbine House, 6510 Bells Mill Rd, Bethesda, MD 20817 *Tel:* 301-897-3570 *Toll Free Tel:* 800-843-7323 *Fax:* 301-897-5838 *E-mail:* info@woodbinehouse.com *Web Site:* www.woodbinehouse.com, pg 302

Paulicelli, Rosemarie, M Evans & Co Inc, 216 E 49 St, New York, NY 10017 *Tel:* 212-688-2810 *Fax:* 212-486-4544 *E-mail:* editorial@mevans.com *Web Site:* www.mevans.com, pg 93

Paull, Richard Cary, Green Nature Books, 5290 SE 11 Dr, Bushnell, FL 33585 *Tel:* 352-793-5496 *E-mail:* info@greennaturebooks.com *Web Site:* www.greennaturebooks.com, pg 108

Paull, Shawnde, Patient-Centered Guides, 1005 Gravenstein Hwy N, Sebastopol, CA 95472 *Tel:* 707-829-0515 *Toll Free Tel:* 800-998-9938 *Fax:* 707-829-0104, pg 205

Paulsell, Mary, Jackie White Memorial National Children's Playwriting Contest, 309 Parkade Blvd, Columbia, MO 65202 *Tel:* 573-874-5628 *Web Site:* cec.missouri.org, pg 811

Paulsen, Nancy, Dial Books for Young Readers, 345 Hudson St, New York, NY 10014 *Tel:* 212-366-2000 *Fax:* 212-414-3396 *E-mail:* online@penguinputnam.com *Web Site:* www.penguinusa.com, pg 80

Paulsen, Nancy, G P Putnam's Sons (Children's), 345 Hudson St, New York, NY 10014 *Tel:* 212-366-2000 *E-mail:* online@penguinputnam.com *Web Site:* www.penguin.com, pg 223

Paulson, Jamis, The Manitoba Writers' Guild Inc, 206-100 Arthur St, Winnipeg, MB R3B 1H3, Canada *Tel:* 204-942-6134 *Toll Free Tel:* 888-637-5802 *Fax:* 204-942-5754 *E-mail:* info@mbwriter.mb.ca *Web Site:* www.mbwriter.mb.ca, pg 691

Pavilionis, Peter, United States Institute of Peace Press, 1200 17 St NW, Suite 200, Washington, DC 20036-3011 *Tel:* 202-457-1700 (edit); 703-661-1590 (cust serv) *Toll Free Tel:* 800-868-8064 (cust serv) *Fax:* 703-661-1501 (cust serv) *Web Site:* www.usip.org, pg 279

Pavlin, Jordan, Alfred A Knopf, 1745 Broadway, New York, NY 10019 *Tel:* 212-751-2600 *Toll Free Tel:* 800-638-6460 *Fax:* 212-572-2593 *Web Site:* www.randomhouse.com/knopf, pg 74

Pawlak, Mark, Hanging Loose Press, 231 Wyckoff St, Brooklyn, NY 11217 *Tel:* 212-206-8465 *Fax:* 212-243-7499 *E-mail:* print225@aol.com *Web Site:* www.hangingloosepress.com, pg 113

Pember, Arlyn, Gospel Publishing House, 1445 Boonville Ave, Springfield, MO 65802-1894 *Tel:* 417-831-8000 *Toll Free Tel:* 800-641-4310 *Fax:* 417-863-1874; 417-862-7566 *Web Site:* www.gospelpublishing. com, pg 107

Pempel, T J, Institute of East Asian Studies, University of California, IEAS Publications, 2223 Fulton St, Berkeley, CA 94720-2318 *Tel:* 510-643-6325 *Fax:* 510-643-7062 *E-mail:* easia@uclink.berkeley.edu *Web Site:* ieas.berkeley.edu/publications, pg 135

Pena, Carmen, Arte Publico Press, University of Houston, 4800 Calhoun, Houston, TX 77204-2174 *Tel:* 713-743-2841 *Toll Free Tel:* 800-633-2783 *Fax:* 713-743-2847 *Web Site:* www.arte.uh.edu, pg 24

Pencarski, Lydia, Canadian Publishers' Council (CPC), 250 Merton St, Suite 203, Toronto, ON M4S 1B1, Canada *Tel:* 416-322-7011 *Fax:* 416-322-6999 *E-mail:* pubadmin@pubcouncil.ca *Web Site:* www. pubcouncil.ca, pg 684

Pence, Russell E, Research Press, 2612 N Mattis Ave, Champaign, IL 61822 *Tel:* 217-352-3273 *Toll Free Tel:* 800-519-2707 *Fax:* 217-352-1221 *E-mail:* rp@ researchpress.com *Web Site:* www.researchpress.com, pg 231

Pendergrass, Renee, Monthly Review Press, 122 W 27 St, New York, NY 10001 *Tel:* 212-691-2555 *Toll Free Tel:* 800-670-9499 *Fax:* 212-727-3676 *E-mail:* mreview@igc.org *Web Site:* www. MonthlyReview.org, pg 177

Penhale, Barry L, Natural Heritage Books, PO Box 95, Sta O, Toronto, ON M4A 2M8, Canada *Tel:* 416-694-7907 *Toll Free Tel:* 800-725-9982 (orders only) *Fax:* 416-690-0819 *E-mail:* info@ naturalheritagebooks.com *Web Site:* www. naturalheritagebooks.com, pg 555

Penn, Suzanna, Girl Scouts of the USA, 420 Fifth Ave, New York, NY 10018-2798 *Tel:* 212-852-8000 *Toll Free Tel:* 800-478-7248 *Fax:* 212-852-6511 *Web Site:* www.girlscouts.org, pg 105

Pennell, Linda, Judith Riven Literary Agent/Editorial Consultant, 250 W 16 St, Suite 4F, New York, NY 10011 *Tel:* 212-255-1009 *Fax:* 212-255-8547 *E-mail:* rivenlit@att.net, pg 652

Penney, Beth, Beth Penney Editorial Services, PO Box 604, Pacific Grove, CA 93950-0604 *Tel:* 831-372-7625, pg 607

Penrose, Denise, Penrose Press, 1333 Gough, Suite 8B, San Francisco, CA 94109 *Tel:* 415-567-4157 *Fax:* 415-567-4165 *E-mail:* info@penrose-press.com *Web Site:* www.penrose-press.com, pg 209

Penton, Hugh V Jr, Penton Overseas Inc, 2470 Impala Dr, Carlsbad, CA 92008-7226 *Tel:* 760-431-0060 *Toll Free Tel:* 800-748-5804 *Fax:* 760-431-8110 *E-mail:* info@pentonoverseas.com *Web Site:* www. pentonoverseas.com, pg 209

Penton, Hugh V Sr, Penton Overseas Inc, 2470 Impala Dr, Carlsbad, CA 92008-7226 *Tel:* 760-431-0060 *Toll Free Tel:* 800-748-5804 *Fax:* 760-431-8110 *E-mail:* info@pentonoverseas.com *Web Site:* www. pentonoverseas.com, pg 209

Pepe, Christine, G P Putnam's Sons (Hardcover), 375 Hudson St, New York, NY 10014 *Tel:* 212-366-2000 *E-mail:* online@penguinputnam.com *Web Site:* www. penguin.com, pg 223

Pepe, Paolo, Atria Books, 1230 Avenue of the Americas, New York, NY 10020 *Tel:* 212-698-7000 *Fax:* 212-698-7007 *Web Site:* www.simonsays.com, pg 27

Pepe, Paolo, Pocket Books, 1230 Avenue of the Americas, New York, NY 10020 *Toll Free Tel:* 800-456-6798 *Fax:* 212-698-7284 *E-mail:* consumer. customerservice@simonandschuster.com *Web Site:* www.simonsays.com, pg 215

Pepper, Douglas, McClelland & Stewart Ltd, 481 University Ave, Suite 900, Toronto, ON M5G 2E9, Canada *Tel:* 416-598-1114 *Fax:* 416-598-7764 *E-mail:* mail@mcclelland.com *Web Site:* www. mcclelland.com, pg 553

Pepper, Eric, SPIE, International Society for Optical Engineering, 1000 20 St, Bellingham, WA 98225 *Tel:* 360-676-3290 *Fax:* 360-647-1445 *E-mail:* spie@ spie.org *Web Site:* www.spie.org, pg 255

Peragine, Dan, Dan Peragine Agency, 227 Beechwood Ave, Bogota, NJ 07603 *Tel:* 201-487-1296 *Fax:* 201-487-1433 *E-mail:* dpliterary@aol.com *Web Site:* www. writers.net, pg 648

Peragine, Karen A, Dan Peragine Agency, 227 Beechwood Ave, Bogota, NJ 07603 *Tel:* 201-487-1296 *Fax:* 201-487-1433 *E-mail:* dpliterary@aol.com *Web Site:* www.writers.net, pg 648

Peranteau, Paul, John Benjamins Publishing Co, 821 Bethlehem Pike, Erdenheim, PA 19038 *Tel:* 215-836-1200 *Toll Free Tel:* 800-562-5666 *Fax:* 215-836-1204 *E-mail:* service@benjamins.com *Web Site:* www. benjamins.com, pg 36

Perdue, Amy, HTC One-Act Playwriting Competition, PO Box 27032, Richmond, VA 23273-7032 *Tel:* 804-501-5138 *Fax:* 804-501-5284, pg 779

Pereyra-Suarez, Hector, Book Developers Inc, 930 Forest Ave, Palo Alto, CA 94301 *Tel:* 650-322-4595; 650-322-4379 *Fax:* 650-322-4379 *E-mail:* customerservice@bookdevelopers.com *Web Site:* www.bookdevelopers.com, pg 592

Perez, Amy, University of Texas at El Paso, Dept Creative Writing, MFA with Bilingual Option, 500 W University Ave, PMB 670, El Paso, TX 79968-9991 *Tel:* 915-747-5713 *Fax:* 915-747-5523 *E-mail:* mfadirector@utep.edu *Web Site:* www.utep. edu/cw, pg 756

Perez, Danielle, Bantam Dell Publishing Group, 1745 Broadway, New York, NY 10019 *Tel:* 212-782-9000 *Toll Free Tel:* 800-223-6834 *Fax:* 212-302-7985 *Web Site:* www.randomhouse.com/bantamdell, pg 31

Perez, Margie, The Amy Rennert Agency Inc, 98 Main St, Suite 302, Tiburon, CA 94920 *Tel:* 415-789-8955 *Fax:* 415-789-8944 *E-mail:* arennert@pacbell.net, pg 651

Perez, Milena, Rough Guides, 345 Hudson St, New York, NY 10014 *Tel:* 212-414-3635 *Fax:* 212-414-3352 *E-mail:* mail@roughguides.com *Web Site:* www. roughguides.com, pg 235

Perez, Minh L, American Research Press, PO Box 141, Rehoboth, NM 87322 *Web Site:* www.gallup.unm. edu/~smarandache, pg 17

Perez, Nanette, John Phillip Immroth Memorial Award for Intellectual Freedom, 50 E Huron St, Chicago, IL 60611 *Tel:* 312-280-4223; 312-280-4220 *Toll Free Tel:* 800-545-2433 *Fax:* 312-280-4227 *E-mail:* oif@ ala.org *Web Site:* www.ala.org/ifrt, pg 779

Perez, Nanette, Eli M Oboler Memorial Award, 50 E Huron St, Chicago, IL 60611 *Tel:* 312-280-4223; 312-280-4220 *Toll Free Tel:* 800-545-2433 *Fax:* 312-280-4227 *E-mail:* oif@ala.org *Web Site:* www.ala.org/ifrt, pg 795

Perkins, David M, Georgetown University Press, 3240 Prospect St NW, Washington, DC 20007 *Tel:* 202-687-6251 (acq); 202-687-5889 (busn); 202-687-5641 (mktg); 410-516-6956 (orders) *Toll Free Tel:* 800-537-5487 *Fax:* 202-687-6340 (edit); 410-516-6998 (orders) *E-mail:* gupress@georgetown.edu *Web Site:* www. press.georgetown.edu, pg 104

Perkins, Davis, Presbyterian Publishing Corp, 100 Witherspoon St, Louisville, KY 40202 *Tel:* 502-569-5052 *Toll Free Tel:* 800-227-2872 (US only) *Fax:* 502-569-8308 *Toll Free Fax:* 800-541-5113 (US only) *E-mail:* ppcmail@presbypub.com *Web Site:* www. ppcpub.com, pg 217

Perkins, Davis, Westminster John Knox Press, 100 Witherspoon St, Louisville, KY 40202-1396 *Tel:* 502-569-5052 *Toll Free Tel:* 800-227-2872 (US only) *Fax:* 502-569-8308 *Toll Free Fax:* 800-541-5113 (US only) *E-mail:* wjk@wjkbooks.com *Web Site:* www. wjkbooks.com, pg 297

Perkins, Dorothy, DIANE Publishing Co, 330 Pusey Ave, Suite 3 rear, Collingdale, PA 19023 *Tel:* 610-461-6200 *Toll Free Tel:* 800-782-3833 *Fax:* 610-461-6130 *E-mail:* dianepub@comcast.net *Web Site:* www. dianepublishingcentral.com, pg 80

Perkins, Gareth K, Berkeley Slavic Specialties, PO Box 3034, Oakland, CA 94609-0034 *Tel:* 510-653-8048 *Fax:* 510-653-6313 *E-mail:* 71034.456@compuserve. com *Web Site:* www.berkslav.com, pg 36

Perkins, Jane, Elm Street Publishing Services Inc, 828 N Elm St, Hinsdale, IL 60521 *Tel:* 630-789-2102 *Fax:* 630-789-2105 *E-mail:* esps@elmst.com *Web Site:* www.elmst.com, pg 598

Perkins, Nancy, The Canadian Council on Social Development, 309 Cooper St, 5th fl, Ottawa, ON K2P 0G5, Canada *Tel:* 613-236-8977 *Fax:* 613-236-2750 *E-mail:* council@ccsd.ca *Web Site:* www.ccsd.ca, pg 538

Perkins, Pat A, Paul H Brookes Publishing Co, PO Box 10624, Baltimore, MD 21285-0624 *Tel:* 410-337-9580 *Toll Free Tel:* 800-638-3775 *Fax:* 410-337-8539 *E-mail:* custserv@brookespublishing.com *Web Site:* www.brookespublishing.com, pg 48

Perkins, Randall, Hudson Hills Press LLC, 74-2 Union St, Manchester, VT 05254 *Tel:* 802-362-6450 *Fax:* 802-362-6459 *E-mail:* artbooks@hudsonhills.com *Web Site:* www.hudsonhills.com, pg 128

Perl, Liz, Berkley Books, 375 Hudson St, New York, NY 10014 *Tel:* 212-366-2000 *Fax:* 212-366-2666 *E-mail:* online@penguinputnam.com *Web Site:* www. penguin.com, pg 36

Perl, Liz, Berkley Publishing Group, 375 Hudson St, New York, NY 10014 *Tel:* 212-366-2000 *E-mail:* online@penguinputnam.com *Web Site:* www. penguin.com, pg 37

Perl, Liz, NAL, 375 Hudson St, New York, NY 10014 *Tel:* 212-366-2000 *E-mail:* online@penguinputnam. com *Web Site:* www.penguin.com, pg 181

Perl, Liz, Penguin Group (USA) Inc, 375 Hudson St, New York, NY 10014 *Tel:* 212-366-2000 *Fax:* 212-366-2666 *E-mail:* online@uspenguingroup.com *Web Site:* www.penguin.com, pg 208

Perlman, Jim, Holy Cow! Press, Mount Royal Sta, Duluth, MN 55803 *Tel:* 218-724-1653 *Fax:* 218-724-1653 *E-mail:* holycow@cpinternet.com *Web Site:* www.holycowpress.org, pg 125

Perlman, Nancy, Penguin Group (USA) Inc, 375 Hudson St, New York, NY 10014 *Tel:* 212-366-2000 *Fax:* 212-366-2666 *E-mail:* online@uspenguingroup.com *Web Site:* www.penguin.com, pg 208

Perlowitz, Efraim, Mesorah Publications Ltd, 4401 Second Ave, Brooklyn, NY 11232 *Tel:* 718-921-9000 *Toll Free Tel:* 800-637-6724 *Fax:* 718-680-1875 *E-mail:* artscroll@mesorah.com *Web Site:* www. artscroll.com; www.mesorah.com, pg 172

Perlstein, Jeffrey, Media Alliance, 942 Market St, Suite 503, San Francisco, CA 94102 *Tel:* 415-546-6334; 415-546-6491 *Fax:* 415-546-6218 *E-mail:* info@ media-alliance.org *Web Site:* www.media-alliance.org, pg 691

Perlstein, Jill, Book Sense Book of the Year Award, 828 S Broadway, Tarrytown, NY 10591 *Tel:* 914-591-2665 *Toll Free Tel:* 800-637-0037 *Fax:* 914-591-2720 *Web Site:* www.bookweb.org, pg 763

Permingeat, Max, Editions de Mortagne, BP 116, Boucherville, PQ J4B 5E6, Canada *Tel:* 450-641-2387 *Fax:* 450-655-6092 *E-mail:* edm@editionsdemortagne. qc.ca, pg 544

Perney, Suzanne, HCPro, 200 Hoods Lane, Marblehead, MA 01945 *Tel:* 781-639-1872 *Toll Free Tel:* 800-650-6787 *Fax:* 781-639-2982 *Toll Free Fax:* 800-639-8511 *E-mail:* customer_service@hcpro.com *Web Site:* www. hcpro.com, pg 119

Perreault, Russell, Vintage & Anchor Books, 1745 Broadway, New York, NY 10019 *Tel:* 212-751-2600 *Fax:* 212-572-6043, pg 291

Perrini, Ann J, Nevraumont Publishing Co, 71 Broadway, New York, NY 10006 *Tel:* 212-425-3270 *Fax:* 212-425-1818 *E-mail:* nevpub@cs.com, pg 187

Perrizo, Mira, Johnson Books, 1880 S 57 Ct, Boulder, CO 80301 *Tel:* 303-443-9766 *Toll Free Tel:* 800-258-5830 *Fax:* 303-998-7594 *E-mail:* books@ jpcolorado.com *Web Site:* www.jpcolorado.com; www.johnsonbooks.com, pg 141

Perron, Manon, Editions du Septentrion, 1300 ave Maguire, Sillery, PQ G1T 1Z3, Canada *Tel:* 418-688-3556 *Fax:* 418-527-4978 *E-mail:* sept@septentrion.qc.ca *Web Site:* www.septentrion.qc.ca, pg 544

Perron, Michel C, Groupe Beauchemin, Editeur Ltee, 3281 ave Jean Beraud, Laval, PQ H7T 2L2, Canada *Tel:* 514-334-5912 *Toll Free Tel:* 800-361-2598 (US & Canada); 800-361-4504 (Canada Only) *Fax:* 450-688-6269 *E-mail:* promotion@beauchemin.qc.ca *Web Site:* www.beaucheminediteur.com, pg 536

Perrone, Madeline, Literary Artists Representatives, 575 West End Ave, Suite GRC, New York, NY 10024-2711 *Tel:* 212-787-3808 *Fax:* 212-595-2098 *E-mail:* litartists@aol.com, pg 641

Perry, Ava, Circlet Press Inc, 1770 Massachusetts Ave, Suite 278, Cambridge, MA 02140 *Tel:* 617-864-0492 *Toll Free Tel:* 800-729-6423 (orders) *Fax:* 617-864-0663 *E-mail:* info@circlet.com *Web Site:* www.circlet.com, pg 62

Perry, Bonnie, Beacon Hill Press of Kansas City, PO Box 419527, Kansas City, MO 64141-6527 *Tel:* 816-931-1900 *Toll Free Tel:* 800-877-0700 (retail order) *Fax:* 816-753-4071 *Toll Free Fax:* 800-849-9827 (order) *Web Site:* www.beaconhillbooks.com, pg 34

Perry, Cheryl, Northstone Publishing, 9025 Jim Bailey Rd, Kelowna, BC V4V 1R2, Canada *Tel:* 250-766-2778 *Toll Free Tel:* 800-299-2926 *Fax:* 250-766-2736 *Web Site:* www.joinhands.com, pg 556

Perry, David, The University of North Carolina Press, 116 S Boundary St, Chapel Hill, NC 27514-3808 *Tel:* 919-966-3561 *Toll Free Tel:* 800-848-6224 (orders only) *Fax:* 919-966-3829 *Toll Free Fax:* 800-272-6817 (orders) *E-mail:* uncpress@unc.edu *Web Site:* www.uncpress.unc.edu, pg 283

Perry, Janelle, The Overlook Press, 141 Wooster St, New York, NY 10012 *Tel:* 212-965-8400 *Fax:* 212-965-9834 *Web Site:* www.overlookny.com, pg 200

Perry, Lisa, Collectors Press Inc, 15655 SW 74 Ave, Suite 200, Tigard, OR 97224 *Tel:* 503-684-3030 *Toll Free Tel:* 800-423-1848 *Fax:* 503-684-3777 *Web Site:* www.collectorspress.com, pg 64

Perry, Michael, Library Association of Alberta, 80 Baker Crescent NW, Calgary, AB T2L 1R4, Canada *Tel:* 403-284-5818 *Toll Free Tel:* 877-522-5550 *Fax:* 403-282-6646 *Web Site:* www.laa.ab.ca, pg 690

Perry, Michael C, Encore Performance Publishing, 2181 W California Ave, Suite 250, Salt Lake City, UT 84104 *Tel:* 801-485-5012 *Fax:* 801-485-4365 *E-mail:* encoreplay@aol.com *Web Site:* www.encoreplay.com, pg 90

Perry, Nancy, Bedford/St Martin's, 75 Arlington St, Boston, MA 02116 *Tel:* 617-399-4000 *Fax:* 617-426-8582 *Web Site:* www.bedfordstmartins.com, pg 35

Perry, Philip A, Philip A Perry, Freelance Editorial Services, 1311 Wesley Ave, Evanston, IL 60201-4117 *Tel:* 847-733-1270 *E-mail:* philaperry@aol.com, pg 608

Perry, Richard, Collectors Press Inc, 15655 SW 74 Ave, Suite 200, Tigard, OR 97224 *Tel:* 503-684-3030 *Toll Free Tel:* 800-423-1848 *Fax:* 503-684-3777 *Web Site:* www.collectorspress.com, pg 64

Perry, Ronald, Sheron Enterprises Inc, 1035 S Carley Ct, North Bellmore, NY 11710 *Tel:* 516-783-5885, pg 246

Perry, Sharon, Hanley-Wood LLC, 426 S Westgate St, Addison, IL 60101 *Tel:* 630-543-0870 *Toll Free Tel:* 800-837-0870 *Fax:* 630-543-3112 *Web Site:* www.hanleywood.com, pg 113

Perry, Sheila M, Sophia Institute Press, PO Box 5284, Manchester, NH 03108 *Tel:* 603-641-9344 *Toll Free Tel:* 800-888-9344 *Fax:* 603-641-8108 *Toll Free Fax:* 888-288-2259 *E-mail:* orders@sophiainstitute.com *Web Site:* www.sophiainstitute.com, pg 253

Perry, Sheryl, Sheron Enterprises Inc, 1035 S Carley Ct, North Bellmore, NY 11710 *Tel:* 516-783-5885, pg 246

Perry, Thomas, Random House Publishing Group, 1745 Broadway, New York, NY 10019 *Tel:* 800-200-3552 *Toll Free Fax:* 800-200-3552 *Web Site:* www.randomhouse.com, pg 227

Pershing, John, Hackett Publishing Co Inc, PO Box 44937, Indianapolis, IN 46244-0937 *Tel:* 317-635-9250; 617-497-6306 *Fax:* 317-635-9292 *Toll Free Fax:* 800-783-9213 *E-mail:* customer@ hackettpublishing.com *Web Site:* www.hackettpublishing.com, pg 111

Person, Hara, URJ Press, 633 Third Ave, New York, NY 10017-6778 *Tel:* 212-650-4100 *Toll Free Tel:* 888-489-UAHC (489-8242) *Fax:* 212-650-4119 *E-mail:* press@urj.org *Web Site:* www.urjpress.com, pg 289

Pervin, David, Palgrave Macmillan, 175 Fifth Ave, New York, NY 10010 *Tel:* 212-982-3900 *Fax:* 212-777-6359 *E-mail:* firstname.lastname@palgrave-usa.com *Web Site:* www.palgrave.com, pg 202

Pesce, William J, John Wiley & Sons Inc, 111 River St, Hoboken, NJ 07030 *Tel:* 201-748-6000 *Toll Free Tel:* 800-225-5945 (cust serv) *Fax:* 201-748-6088 *E-mail:* info@wiley.com *Web Site:* www.wiley.com, pg 299

Peskin, Joy, Viking Children's Books, 345 Hudson St, New York, NY 10014 *Tel:* 212-366-2000 *E-mail:* online@penguinputnam.com *Web Site:* www.penguin.com, pg 290

Pester, John, Living Stream Ministry (LSM), 2431 W La Palima Ave, Anaheim, CA 92801 *Tel:* 714-991-4681 *Fax:* 714-991-4685 *E-mail:* books@lsm.org *Web Site:* www.lsm.org, pg 157

Peter, Ernest, Barcelona Publishers, Pathway Book Service, 4 White Brook Rd, Gilsum, NH 03448 *Tel:* 603-357-0236 *Toll Free Tel:* 800-345-6665 *Fax:* 603-357-2073 *E-mail:* pbs@pathwaybooks.com *Web Site:* www.barcelonapublishers.com, pg 32

Peter, Ernest, Stemmer House Publishers Inc, 4 White Brook Rd, Gilsum, NH 03448 *Tel:* 603-357-0236 *Toll Free Tel:* 800-345-6665 *Fax:* 603-357-2073 *E-mail:* pbs@pathwaybook.com *Web Site:* www.stemmer.com, pg 259

Peterfreund, Michael, Oceana Publications Inc, 75 Main St, Dobbs Ferry, NY 10522-1601 *Tel:* 914-693-8100 *Toll Free Tel:* 800-831-0758 (orders only) *Fax:* 914-693-0402 *E-mail:* info@oceanalaw.com *Web Site:* www.oceanalaw.com, pg 195

Peters, Alice, A K Peters Ltd, 888 Worcester St, Suite 230, Wellesley, MA 02482 *Tel:* 781-416-2888 *Fax:* 781-416-2889 *E-mail:* service@akpeters.com *Web Site:* www.akpeters.com, pg 1

Peters, Barbara, Poisoned Pen Press Inc, 6962 E First Ave, Suite 103, Scottsdale, AZ 85251 *Tel:* 480-945-3375 ext 210 *Fax:* 480-949-1707 *E-mail:* info@poisonpenpress.com *Web Site:* www.poisonpenpress.com, pg 215

Peters, Cheri, Sewanee Writers' Conference, 310 St Lukes Hall, 735 University Ave, Sewanee, TN 37383-1000 *Tel:* 931-598-1141 *Web Site:* www.sewaneewriters.org, pg 747

Peters, Dave, Bridge Publications Inc, 4751 Fountain Ave, Los Angeles, CA 90029 *Tel:* 323-953-3320 *Toll Free Tel:* 800-722-1733; 800-843-7389 (CA) *Fax:* 323-953-3328 *E-mail:* info@bridgepub.com *Web Site:* www.bridgepub.com, pg 47

Peters, Gerald P, Gerald Peters Gallery, 1011 Paseo De Peralta, Santa Fe, NM 87501 *Tel:* 505-954-5700 *Fax:* 505-954-5754 *E-mail:* bookstore@gpgallery.com *Web Site:* www.gpgallery.com, pg 211

Peters, Jamie, Rainbow Books Inc, PO Box 430, Highland City, FL 33846-0430 *Tel:* 863-648-4420 *Toll Free Tel:* 800-431-1579 (orders only); 888-613-2665 *Fax:* 863-647-5951 *E-mail:* rbibooks@aol.com *Web Site:* www.rainbowbooksinc.com, pg 225

Peters, Klaus, A K Peters Ltd, 888 Worcester St, Suite 230, Wellesley, MA 02482 *Tel:* 781-416-2888 *Fax:* 781-416-2889 *E-mail:* service@akpeters.com *Web Site:* www.akpeters.com, pg 1

Peters, Michelle, Association of Manitoba Book Publishers, 100 Arthur St, Suite 404, Winnipeg, MB R3B 1H3, Canada *Tel:* 204-947-3335 *Fax:* 204-956-4689 *E-mail:* assocpub@mb.sympatico.ca *Web Site:* www.bookpublishers.mb.ca, pg 680

Peters, Nancy J, City Lights Books Inc, 261 Columbus Ave, San Francisco, CA 94133 *Tel:* 415-362-8193 *Fax:* 415-362-4921 *E-mail:* staff@citylights.com *Web Site:* www.citylights.com, pg 62

Peters, Sally, The Bernard Shaw Society, Box 1159, Madison Square Sta, New York, NY 10159-1159 *Tel:* 212-989-7833; 212-982-9885, pg 699

Peters, Dr Steven, Wichita State University Playwriting Contest, 1845 Fairmount St, Wichita, KS 67260-0153 *Tel:* 316-978-3368 *Fax:* 316-978-3202 *Web Site:* www.wichita.edu, pg 811

Peterseil, Yaacov, Pitspopany Press, 40 E 78 St, Suite 16-D, New York, NY 10021 *Tel:* 212-472-4959 *Toll Free Tel:* 800-232-2931 *Fax:* 212-472-6253 *E-mail:* pitspop@netvision.net.il; pitspopany@aol.com, pg 213

Petersen, Joan, Springer-Verlag New York Inc, 175 Fifth Ave, New York, NY 10010 *Tel:* 212-460-1500 *Toll Free Tel:* 800-777-4643 *Fax:* 212-473-6272 *Web Site:* www.springer-ny.com, pg 256

Petersen, Karen, Paladin Press, 7077 Winchester Circle, Boulder, CO 80301 *Tel:* 303-443-7250 *Toll Free Tel:* 800-392-2400 *Fax:* 303-442-8741 *E-mail:* service@paladin-press.com *Web Site:* www.paladin-press.com, pg 202

Petersen Kennedy, Susan J, Viking Penguin, 375 Hudson St, New York, NY 10014 *Tel:* 212-366-2000 *E-mail:* online@penguinputnam.com *Web Site:* www.penguin.com, pg 290

Petersen, Sheryl, Don Buchwald & Associates Inc, 6500 Wilshire Blvd, Suite 2200, Los Angeles, CA 90048 *Tel:* 323-655-7400 *Fax:* 323-655-7470 *Web Site:* www.donbuchwald.com, pg 623

Petersen, Shirley, Editorial Options Inc, 353 Lexington Ave, New York, NY 10016 *Tel:* 212-986-2888 *Fax:* 212-986-1194 *Web Site:* www.edop.com, pg 597

Peterson, Anna, Columbia University School of the Arts, Writing Division, 415 Dodge Hall, School of the Arts, Columbia University, 2960 Broadway, New York, NY 10027 *Tel:* 212-854-4391 *Fax:* 212-854-7704 *E-mail:* writing@columbia.edu *Web Site:* www.columbia.edu/cu/arts/writing, pg 752

Peterson, Arthur O, Abrams & Co Publishers Inc, 61 Mattatuck Heights Rd, Waterbury, CT 06705 *Tel:* 203-756-6562 *Toll Free Tel:* 800-227-9120 *Fax:* 203-756-2895 *Toll Free Fax:* 800-737-3322, pg 3

Peterson, Arthur O, Graphic Learning, 61 Mattatuck Heights Rd, Waterbury, CT 06705 *Tel:* 203-756-6562 *Toll Free Tel:* 800-874-0029; 800-227-9120 *Fax:* 203-756-2895 *Toll Free Fax:* 800-737-3322, pg 108

Peterson, Arthur O, The Letter People®, 61 Mattatuck Heights Rd, Waterbury, CT 06705 *Tel:* 203-756-6562 *Toll Free Tel:* 800-227-9120; 800-874-0029 *Fax:* 203-756-2895 *Toll Free Fax:* 800-737-3322 *Web Site:* letterpeople.com, pg 153

Peterson, Carol, Penguin Group (USA) Inc, 375 Hudson St, New York, NY 10014 *Tel:* 212-366-2000 *Fax:* 212-366-2666 *E-mail:* online@uspenguingroup.com *Web Site:* www.penguin.com, pg 208

Peterson, James, Coaches Choice, 4 Justin Ct, Monterey, CA 93940 *Toll Free Tel:* 888-229-5745 *Fax:* 831-372-6075 *E-mail:* info@coacheschoice.com *Web Site:* www.coacheschoice.com, pg 64

Peterson, Janet T, World Book Inc, 233 N Michigan, Suite 2000, Chicago, IL 60601 *Tel:* 312-729-5800 *Toll Free Tel:* 800-967-5325 (consumer sales, US); 800-463-8845 (consumer sales, Canada); 800-975-3250 (school & library sales, US); 800-837-5365 (school & library sales, Canada); 866-866-5200 (web sales) *Fax:* 312-729-5600; 312-729-5606 *Toll Free Fax:* 800-

433-9330 (school & library sales, US); 888-690-4002 (school library sales, Canada) *Web Site:* www.worldbook.com, pg 303

Peterson, Jeff, Foil Stamping & Embossing Association, 2150 SW Westport Dr, Suite 101, Topeka, KS 66614 *Tel:* 785-271-5816 *Fax:* 785-271-6404 *Web Site:* www.fsea.com, pg 687

Peterson, Jim, Recorded Books LLC, 270 Skipjack Rd, Prince Frederick, MD 20678 *Tel:* 410-535-5590 *Toll Free Tel:* 800-638-1304 *Fax:* 410-535-5499 *E-mail:* recordedbooks@recordedbooks.com *Web Site:* www.recordedbooks.com, pg 229

Peterson, Laura Blake, Curtis Brown Ltd, 10 Astor Place, New York, NY 10003 *Tel:* 212-473-5400, pg 623

Peterson, Lenny, Hazelden Publishing & Educational Services, 15251 Pleasant Valley Rd, Center City, MN 55012-0176 *Tel:* 651-213-4470 *Toll Free Tel:* 800-328-9000 *Web Site:* www.hazelden.org, pg 118

Peterson, Leslie, Warner Faith (Christian Book Division of Time Warner Book Group), 2 Creekside Crossing, 10 Cadillac Dr, Suite 220, Brentwood, TN 37027 *Tel:* 615-221-0996 *Fax:* 615-221-0962 *Web Site:* www.twbookmark.com, pg 293

Peterson, Marcia, Simon & Schuster Adult Publishing Group, 1230 Avenue of the Americas, New York, NY 10020 *Tel:* 212-698-7000 *Toll Free Tel:* 800-223-2336 (orders); 800-223-2348 (cust serv), pg 248

Peterson, Marilee, Editorial & Graphics Awards Competition-EXCEL Awards, 8405 Greensboro Dr, No 800, McLean, VA 22102 *Tel:* 703-506-3285 *Fax:* 703-506-3266 *E-mail:* info@snaponline.org *Web Site:* www.snaponline.org, pg 771

Peterson, Marilee, Society of National Association Publications (SNAP), 8405 Greensboro Dr, No 800, McLean, VA 22102 *Tel:* 703-506-3285 *Fax:* 703-506-3266 *E-mail:* snapinfo@snaponline.org *Web Site:* www.snaponline.org, pg 700

Peterson, Mike, The Child's World Inc, PO Box 326, Chanhassen, MN 55317-0326 *Tel:* 952-906-3939 *Toll Free Tel:* 800-599-READ (599-7323) *Fax:* 952-906-3940 *E-mail:* info@childsworld.com *Web Site:* www.childsworld.com, pg 60

Peterson, Patti McGill, Fulbright Scholar Program, 3007 Tilden St NW, Suite 5-L, Washington, DC 20008-3009 *Tel:* 202-686-4000 *Fax:* 202-362-3442 *E-mail:* cieswebmaster@cies.iie.org *Web Site:* www.cies.org, pg 775

Peterson, Peter G, National Bureau of Economic Research Inc, 1050 Massachusetts Ave, Cambridge, MA 02138-5398 *Tel:* 617-868-3900 *Fax:* 617-868-2742 *E-mail:* op@nber.org *Web Site:* www.nber.org, pg 182

Peterson, Stacy, National Notary Association, 9350 De Soto Ave, Chatsworth, CA 91311 *Tel:* 818-739-4000 *Toll Free Tel:* 800-876-6827 *Fax:* 818-700-0920 *E-mail:* nna@nationalnotary.org *Web Site:* www.nationalnotary.org, pg 184

Peterson, Susan, Coaches Choice, 4 Justin Ct, Monterey, CA 93940 *Toll Free Tel:* 888-229-5745 *Fax:* 831-372-6075 *E-mail:* info@coacheschoice.com *Web Site:* www.coacheschoice.com, pg 64

Peterson, Tom, The Creative Co, 123 S Broad St, Mankato, MN 56001 *Tel:* 507-388-6273 *Toll Free Tel:* 800-445-6209 *Fax:* 507-388-2746 *E-mail:* creativeco@aol.com, pg 72

Petilos, Randolph, Association of American University Presses, 1427 E 60 St, Chicago, IL 60637 *Tel:* 773-702-7700; 773-702-7600 *Toll Free Tel:* 800-621-2736 (orders) *Fax:* 773-702-9756 (sales); 773-660-2235 (orders); 773-702-2708 *E-mail:* general@press.uchicago.edu *Web Site:* www.press.uchicago.edu, pg 26

Petitt, Tracey, Rizzoli International Publications Inc, 300 Park Ave S, 3rd fl, New York, NY 10010-5399 *Tel:* 212-387-3400 *Toll Free Tel:* 800-522-6657 (orders only) *Fax:* 212-387-3535, pg 233

Petranker, Jack, Dharma Publishing, 2910 San Pablo Ave, Berkeley, CA 94702 *Tel:* 510-548-5407 *Toll Free Tel:* 800-873-4276 *Fax:* 510-548-2230 *E-mail:* info@dharmapublishing.com *Web Site:* www.dharmapublishing.com, pg 79

Petre, Kelly, Discipleship Publications International (DPI), 2 Sterling Rd, Billerica, MA 01862-2595 *Tel:* 978-670-8840 *Toll Free Tel:* 888-DPI-Book *Fax:* 978-670-8485 *E-mail:* dpibooks@icoc.org *Web Site:* www.dpibooks.org, pg 80

Petrie, Jeremy, Willow Creek Press, 9931 Hwy 70 W, Minocqua, WI 54548 *Tel:* 715-358-7010 *Toll Free Tel:* 800-850-9453 *Fax:* 715-358-2807 *E-mail:* info@willowcreekpress.com *Web Site:* www.willowcreekpress.com, pg 300

Petrie, Tom, Willow Creek Press, 9931 Hwy 70 W, Minocqua, WI 54548 *Tel:* 715-358-7010 *Toll Free Tel:* 800-850-9453 *Fax:* 715-358-2807 *E-mail:* info@willowcreekpress.com *Web Site:* www.willowcreekpress.com, pg 300

Petrillo, Al, Wrangling With Writing, PO Box 30355, Tucson, AZ 85751-0355 *Tel:* 520-575-9063 *Web Site:* www.azstarnet.com/nonprofit/ssa, pg 749

Petrillo, Alan M, Excalibur Publications, PO Box 89667, Tucson, AZ 85752-9667 *Tel:* 520-575-9057 *Fax:* 520-575-9068 *E-mail:* excalibureditor@earthlink.net, pg 93

Petrillo, Ernest, Penguin Group (USA) Inc Sales, 375 Hudson St, New York, NY 10014 *Tel:* 212-366-2000 *E-mail:* online@penguinputnam.com *Web Site:* www.penguin.com, pg 208

Petrillo, Luis, Lectorum Publications Inc, 524 Broadway, New York, NY 10012 *Toll Free Tel:* 800-853-3291 (admin, mktg & sales); 800-345-5946 (orders) *Fax:* 212-727-3035 *Toll Free Fax:* 877-532-8676 *E-mail:* lectorum@scholastic.com *Web Site:* www.lectorum.com, pg 151

Petrowski, Joseph, Lawrence Erlbaum Associates Inc, 10 Industrial Ave, Mahwah, NJ 07430-2262 *Tel:* 201-236-2199 *Toll Free Tel:* 800-9-BOOKS-9 (926-6579) *Fax:* 201-760-3735 *E-mail:* orders@erlbaum.com *Web Site:* www.erlbaum.com, pg 91

Petry, Richard, Workman Publishing Co Inc, 708 Broadway, New York, NY 10003-9555 *Tel:* 212-254-5900 *Toll Free Tel:* 800-722-7202 *Fax:* 212-254-8098 *E-mail:* info@workman.com *Web Site:* www.workman.com, pg 303

Pettey, Susan, Texas A&M University Press, John H Lindsey Bldg, Lewis St, 4354 TAMU, College Station, TX 77843-4354 *Tel:* 979-845-1436 *Toll Free Tel:* 800-826-8911 (orders) *Fax:* 979-847-8752 *Toll Free Fax:* 888-617-2421 (orders) *E-mail:* fdl@tampress.tamu.edu *Web Site:* www.tamu.edu/upress/, pg 267

Pettinato, Bernice, Beehive Production Services, 3 Fairview St, East Stroudsburg, PA 18301-2501 *Tel:* 570-421-3076 *Fax:* 570-421-3076 *E-mail:* beehive@ptd.net, pg 591

Petty, Jill, South End Press, 7 Brookline St, No 1, Cambridge, MA 02139-4146 *Tel:* 617-547-4002 *Fax:* 617-547-1333 *E-mail:* southend@southendpress.org *Web Site:* www.southendpress.org, pg 254

Pevner, Stephen, Stephen Pevner Inc, 382 Lafayette St, Suite 8, New York, NY 10003 *Tel:* 212-674-8403 *Fax:* 212-529-3692, pg 648

Pevsher, Stella, The Society of Midland Authors (SMA), PO Box 10419, Chicago, IL 60610-0419 *Tel:* 773-506-7578 *Fax:* 773-784-5900 *E-mail:* info@midlandauthors.com *Web Site:* www.midlandauthors.com, pg 700

Pevsher, Stella, The Society of Midland Authors Awards, PO Box 10419, Chicago, IL 60610-0419 *Tel:* 773-506-7578 *Fax:* 773-784-5900 *E-mail:* info@midlandauthors.com *Web Site:* www.midlandauthors.com, pg 806

Peyton, Mary, Harian Creative Awards, 47 Hyde Blvd, Ballston Spa, NY 12020-1607 *Tel:* 518-885-6699; 518-885-7397, pg 777

Peyton, Mary, Harian Creative Books, 47 Hyde Blvd, Ballston Spa, NY 12020-1607 *Tel:* 518-885-6699; 518-885-7397, pg 115

Pfaff, Kasey, PublicAffairs, 250 W 57 St, Suite 1321, New York, NY 10107 *Tel:* 212-397-6666 *Toll Free Tel:* 800-242-7737 (orders) *Fax:* 212-397-4267 *E-mail:* publicaffairs@perseusbooks.com *Web Site:* www.publicaffairsbooks.com, pg 221

Pfeiffer, Alice Randel, Syracuse University Press, 621 Skytop Rd, Syracuse, NY 13244-5290 *Tel:* 315-443-5534 *Toll Free Tel:* 800-365-8929 (orders only) *Fax:* 315-443-5545 *E-mail:* supress@syr.edu *Web Site:* syracuseuniversitypress.syr.edu, pg 263

Pfeiffer, Douglas A, Graphic Arts Center Publishing Co, 3019 NW Yeon Ave, Portland, OR 97210 *Tel:* 503-226-2402 *Toll Free Tel:* 800-452-3032 *Fax:* 503-223-1410 *Toll Free Fax:* 800-355-9685 *E-mail:* editorial@gacpc.com; sales@gacpc.com *Web Site:* www.gacpc.com, pg 107

Pfenning, Sharon, Academic Printing & Publishing, 9-3151 Lakeshore Rd, Suite 403, Kelowna, BC V1W 3S9, Canada *Tel:* 250-764-6427 *Fax:* 250-464-6428 *E-mail:* app@silk.net *Web Site:* www.academicprintingandpublishing.com, pg 535

Pflum, Patricia A, Young People's Press Inc (YPPI), 3033 Fifth Ave, Suite 200, San Diego, CA 92103 *Tel:* 619-688-9040 *Toll Free Tel:* 800-231-9774 *Fax:* 619-688-9044 *E-mail:* info@youngpeoplespress.com *Web Site:* www.youngpeoplespress.com, pg 306

Pfund, Niko, Oxford University Press, Inc, 198 Madison Ave, New York, NY 10016-4314 *Tel:* 212-726-6000 *Toll Free Tel:* 800-451-7556 (orders) *Web Site:* www.oup.com/us, pg 200

Phelps, Betsey, Medical Physics Publishing Corp, 4513 Vernon Blvd, Madison, WI 53705-4964 *Tel:* 608-262-4021 *Toll Free Tel:* 800-442-5778 *Fax:* 608-265-2121 *E-mail:* mpp@medicalphysics.org *Web Site:* www.medicalphysics.org, pg 170

Phelps, Janice, Lucky Press LLC, 126 S Maple St, Lancaster, OH 43130 *Tel:* 740-689-2950 (orders & editorial) *Fax:* 740-689-2951 (orders & editorial) *E-mail:* books@luckypress.com *Web Site:* www.luckypress.com, pg 160

Phelps, Joan E, Lucky Press LLC, 126 S Maple St, Lancaster, OH 43130 *Tel:* 740-689-2950 (orders & editorial) *Fax:* 740-689-2951 (orders & editorial) *E-mail:* books@luckypress.com *Web Site:* www.luckypress.com, pg 160

Phelps, Max, The Globe Pequot Press, 246 Goose Lane, Guilford, CT 06437 *Tel:* 203-458-4500 *Toll Free Tel:* 800-243-0495 (cust serv) *Fax:* 203-458-4601 *Toll Free Fax:* 800-820-2329 (orders & cust serv) *E-mail:* info@globepequot.com *Web Site:* www.globepequot.com, pg 106

Philips, Ian, Damron Co, PO Box 422458, San Francisco, CA 94142-2458 *Tel:* 415-255-0404 *Toll Free Tel:* 800-462-6654 *Fax:* 415-703-9049 *E-mail:* editor@damron.com *Web Site:* www.damron.com, pg 75

Phillips, Adrienne, Knopf Canada, One Toronto St, Suite 300, Toronto, ON M5C 2V6, Canada *Tel:* 416-364-4449 *Toll Free Tel:* 800-668-4247 (order desk) *Fax:* 416-364-0462 *Web Site:* www.randomhouse.ca, pg 552

Phillips, Andrew, John Wiley & Sons Inc Scientific/Technical/Medical Publishing, 111 River St, Hoboken, NJ 07030 *Tel:* 201-748-6000 *Toll Free Tel:* 800-225-5945 (cust serv) *Fax:* 201-748-8728 *E-mail:* info@wiley.com *Web Site:* www.wiley.com, pg 300

Phillips, Andrew V, Windhaven Press Editorial Services, 68 Hunting Rd, Auburn, NH 03032 *Tel:* 603-483-0929 *Fax:* 603-483-8022 *E-mail:* info@windhaven.com *Web Site:* www.windhaven.com, pg 613

Phillips, Barbara, Bridge Works Publishing, PO Box 1798, Bridgehampton, NY 11932-1798 *Tel:* 631-537-3418 *Fax:* 631-537-5092 *E-mail:* bap@hamptons.com, pg 47

Phillips, Betsy, Vanderbilt University Press, 201 University Plaza Bldg, 112 21 Ave S, Nashville, TN 37203 *Tel:* 615-322-3585 *Toll Free Tel:* 800-627-7377 (orders only) *Fax:* 615-343-8823 *Toll Free Fax:* 800-735-0476 (orders only) *E-mail:* vupress@vanderbilt.edu *Web Site:* www.vanderbilt.edu/vupress, pg 289

Phillips, Betsy, Jackie White Memorial National Children's Playwriting Contest, 309 Parkade Blvd, Columbia, MO 65202 *Tel:* 573-874-5628 *Web Site:* cec.missouri.org, pg 811

Phillips, David P, Rocky Mountain Mineral Law Foundation, 9191 Sheridan Blvd, Suite 203, Westminister, CO 80031 *Tel:* 303-321-8100 *Fax:* 303-321-7657 *E-mail:* info@rmmlf.org *Web Site:* www.rmmlf.org, pg 233

Phillips, James, The Crossroad Publishing Company, 16 Penn Plaza, Suite 1550, New York, NY 10001 *Tel:* 212-868-1801 *Toll Free Tel:* 800-395-0690 (orders) *Fax:* 212-868-2171 *Toll Free Fax:* 800-462-6420 (orders) *E-mail:* ask@crossroadpublishing.com *Web Site:* www.crossroadpublishing.com, pg 73

Phillips, Kathleen, North American Agricultural Journalists, Texas A&M University, 201 Reed Macdonald, 2112 TAMU, College Station, TX 77843-2112 *Tel:* 979-845-2872 *Fax:* 979-845-2414 *E-mail:* ka-phillips@tamu.edu *Web Site:* naaj.tamu.edu, pg 695

Phillips, Linda, American Psychiatric Publishing Inc, 1000 Wilson Blvd, Suite 1825, Arlington, VA 22209 *Tel:* 703-907-7322 *Toll Free Tel:* 800-368-5777 *Fax:* 703-907-1091 *E-mail:* appi@psych.org *Web Site:* www.appi.org, pg 16

Phillips, Lisa Faith, Random House Direct Inc, 1745 Broadway, New York, NY 10019 *Tel:* 212-572-2604 *Fax:* 212-572-6018, pg 226

Phillips, Dr Patricia A, Carl Hertzog Book Design Award, University of Texas at El Paso, University Library, El Paso, TX 79968-0582 *Tel:* 915-747-5683 *Fax:* 915-747-5345 *E-mail:* llimas@libr.utep.edu *Web Site:* libraryweb.utep.edu, pg 778

Phillips, Peter, The 25 Most "Censored" Stories of 2003, Sonoma State University, 1801 E Cotati Ave, Rohnert Park, CA 94928 *Tel:* 707-664-2500 *Fax:* 707-664-2108 *E-mail:* censored@sonoma.edu *Web Site:* www.projectcensored.org, pg 809

Phillips, Ted, United States Holocaust Memorial Museum, 100 Raoul Wallenberg Place SW, Washington, DC 20024-2126 *Tel:* 202-488-6115; 202-488-6144 (orders) *Toll Free Tel:* 800-259-9998 (orders) *Fax:* 202-488-2684; 202-488-0438 (orders) *Web Site:* www.ushmm.org/, pg 279

Phillips, Warren, Bridge Works Publishing, PO Box 1798, Bridgehampton, NY 11932-1798 *Tel:* 631-537-3418 *Fax:* 631-537-5092 *E-mail:* bap@hamptons.com, pg 47

Philpotts, Jacqueline, Fordham University Press, 2546 Belmont Ave, Bronx, NY 10458-5172 *Tel:* 718-817-4780 *Toll Free Tel:* 800-247-6553 (orders) *Fax:* 718-817-4785 *Web Site:* www.fordhampress.com, pg 98

Phipps, Jennie L, ASJA Writer Referral Service, 1501 Broadway, Suite 302, New York, NY 10036 *Tel:* 212-398-1934 *Fax:* 212-768-7414 *E-mail:* writers@asja.org *Web Site:* www.asja.org, pg 590

Phua, K K, World Scientific Publishing Co Inc, 27 Warren St, Suite 401-402, Hackensack, NJ 07601 *Tel:* 201-487-9655 *Toll Free Tel:* 800-227-7562 *Fax:* 201-487-9656 *Toll Free Fax:* 888-977-2665 *E-mail:* wspc@wspc.com *Web Site:* www.wspc.com, pg 304

Piazzi, Remo D, The United Educators Inc, 900 N Shore Dr, Suite 140, Lake Bluff, IL 60044 *Tel:* 847-234-3700 *Fax:* 847-234-8705 *E-mail:* arslms@aol.com, pg 279

Pichel, John, Hampton-Brown Co Inc, 26385 Carmel Rancho Blvd, Carmel, CA 93923 *Tel:* 831-625-3666 *Toll Free Tel:* 800-933-3510 *Fax:* 831-625-8619 *E-mail:* customerservice@hampton-brown.com *Web Site:* www.hampton-brown.com, pg 113

Pickett, Patty, Thomson Financial Publishing, 4709 W Golf Rd, Suite 600, Skokie, IL 60076-1253 *Tel:* 847-676-9600; 847-677-8037 *Toll Free Tel:* 800-321-3373 *Fax:* 847-676-9616 *E-mail:* custservice@tfp.com *Web Site:* www.tfp.com; www.tgbr.com, pg 270

Pieklo, Dave, McDougal Littell, 909 Davis St, Evanston, IL 60201 *Tel:* 847-869-2300 *Toll Free Tel:* 800-462-6595 (orders) *Toll Free Fax:* 888-872-8380 *Web Site:* www.mcdougallittell.com, pg 166

Piemme, Jennifer, The Lee Shore Co Ltd, 7436 Washington Ave, Suite 100, Pittsburgh, PA 15218 *Tel:* 412-271-1100 *Toll Free Tel:* 800-898-7886 *Fax:* 412-271-1900 *E-mail:* info@leeshoreagency.com *Web Site:* www.leeshoreagency.com, pg 640

Pierce, Carol, National Federation of Press Women Inc (NFPW), PO Box 5556, Arlington, VA 22205-0056 *Tel:* 703-534-2500 *Toll Free Tel:* 800-780-2715 *Fax:* 703-534-5751 *E-mail:* presswomen@aol.com *Web Site:* www.nfpw.org, pg 693

Pierce, Gregory, ACTA Publications, 4848 N Clark St, Chicago, IL 60640-4711 *Tel:* 773-271-1030 *Toll Free Tel:* 800-397-2282 *Fax:* 773-271-7399 *Toll Free Fax:* 800-397-0079 *E-mail:* actapublications@aol.com *Web Site:* www.actapublications.com, pg 4

Pierpont, Amy, Pocket Books, 1230 Avenue of the Americas, New York, NY 10020 *Toll Free Tel:* 800-456-6798 *Fax:* 212-698-7284 *E-mail:* consumer.customerservice@simonandschuster.com *Web Site:* www.simonsays.com, pg 215

Pierre-Pierre, Valerie, Canadian Education Association/Association canadienne d'éducation, 317 Adelaide St W, Suite 300, Toronto, ON M5V 1P9, Canada *Tel:* 416-591-6300 *Fax:* 416-591-5345 *E-mail:* info@cea.ace.ca *Web Site:* www.cea-ace.ca, pg 538, 683

Piersanti, Steven, Berrett-Koehler Publishers Inc, 235 Montgomery St, Suite 650, San Francisco, CA 94104 *Tel:* 415-288-0260 *Fax:* 415-362-2512 *E-mail:* bkpub@bkpub.com *Web Site:* www.bkconnection.com, pg 37

Pierson, Caryl K, Math Teachers Press Inc, 4850 Park Glen Rd, Minneapolis, MN 55416 *Tel:* 952-545-6535 *Toll Free Tel:* 800-852-2435 *Fax:* 952-546-7502 *Web Site:* www.movingwithmath.com, pg 165

Pierson, Frank, Academy of Motion Picture Arts & Sciences (AMPAS), 1313 N Vine St, Hollywood, CA 90028 *Tel:* 310-247-3000 *Fax:* 310-859-9351 *E-mail:* ampas@oscars.org *Web Site:* www.oscars.org, pg 675

Pierson, Jean Marie, G P Putnam's Sons (Hardcover), 375 Hudson St, New York, NY 10014 *Tel:* 212-366-2000 *E-mail:* online@penguinputnam.com *Web Site:* www.penguin.com, pg 223

Pierson, Jennifer, Rizzoli International Publications Inc, 300 Park Ave S, 3rd fl, New York, NY 10010-5399 *Tel:* 212-387-3400 *Toll Free Tel:* 800-522-6657 (orders only) *Fax:* 212-387-3535, pg 233

Pietsch, Michael, Little, Brown and Company Adult Trade Division, 1271 Avenue of the Americas, New York, NY 10020 *Tel:* 212-522-8700 *Fax:* 212-522-2067 *Web Site:* www.twbookmark.com, pg 156

Piguet, Patrice, United Nations Publications, 2 United Nations Plaza, Rm DC2-0853, New York, NY 10017 *Tel:* 212-963-8302 *Toll Free Tel:* 800-253-9646 *Fax:* 212-963-3489 *E-mail:* publications@un.org *Web Site:* www.un.org/publications, pg 279

Pigza, Jessica M, University of Pennsylvania Press, 4200 Pine St, Philadelphia, PA 19104-4011 *Tel:* 215-898-6261 *Toll Free Tel:* 800-445-9880 (orders & cust serv only) *Fax:* 215-898-0404; 410-516-6998 (orders) *E-mail:* custserv@pobox.upenn.edu *Web Site:* www.upenn.edu/pennpress, pg 284

Pike, Bryan, The BC Book Prizes, 207 W Hastings St, Suite 902, Vancouver, BC V6B 1H7, Canada *Tel:* 604-687-2405 *Fax:* 604-669-3701 *E-mail:* info@bcbookprizes.ca *Web Site:* www.bcbookprizes.ca, pg 761

Pike, Bryan, Western Magazine Awards Foundation, Main PO Box 2131, Vancouver, BC V6B 3T8, Canada *Tel:* 604-669-3717 *Fax:* 604-204-9302 *E-mail:* wma@direct.ca *Web Site:* www.westernmagazineawards.com, pg 810

Pike, Lindsay, Creative Bound International Inc, 151 Tansley Dr, Carp, ON K0A 1L0, Canada *Tel:* 613-831-3641 *Toll Free Tel:* 800-287-8610 (N America) *Fax:* 613-831-3643 *E-mail:* editor@creativebound.com *Web Site:* www.creativebound.com, pg 541

Pike, Lois, Sumach Press, 1415 Bathurst St, Suite 302, Toronto, ON M5R 3H5, Canada *Tel:* 416-531-6250 *Fax:* 416-531-3892 *E-mail:* sumachpress@on.aibn.com *Web Site:* www.sumachpress.com, pg 562

Pilcher, John, C & T Publishing Inc, 1651 Challenge Dr, Concord, CA 94520 *Tel:* 925-677-0377 *Toll Free Tel:* 800-284-1114 *Fax:* 925-677-0373 *E-mail:* ctinfo@ctpub.com *Web Site:* www.ctpub.com, pg 51

Pilon, Greg, Nelson, 1120 Birchmount Rd, Scarborough, ON M1K 5G4, Canada *Tel:* 416-752-9448 *Toll Free Tel:* 800-268-2222 (cust serv); 800-430-4445 *Fax:* 416-752-8101 *E-mail:* inquire@nelson.com *Web Site:* www.nelson.com, pg 555

Pilson, Barry, American Geophysical Union (AGU), 2000 Florida Ave NW, Washington, DC 20009 *Tel:* 202-462-6900 *Toll Free Tel:* 800-966-2481 (North America) *Fax:* 202-328-0566 *E-mail:* service@agu.org *Web Site:* www.agu.org, pg 14

Pimentel, Alejandro, CRC Publications, 2850 Kalamazoo Ave SE, Grand Rapids, MI 49560 *Tel:* 616-224-0819; 616-224-0728 *Toll Free Tel:* 800-333-8300 *Fax:* 616-224-0834 *E-mail:* sales@crcpublications.org *Web Site:* www.faithaliveresources.org, pg 72

Pincich, Theresa, Liturgy Training Publications, 1800 N Hermitage Ave, Chicago, IL 60622-1101 *Tel:* 773-486-8970 *Toll Free Tel:* 800-933-1800 (US & Canada only) *Fax:* 773-486-7094 *Toll Free Fax:* 800-933-7094 (US & Canada only) *E-mail:* orders@ltp.org *Web Site:* www.ltp.org, pg 156

Pincus, Caroline, Caroline Pincus Book Midwife, 1237 Sixth Ave, San Francisco, CA 94122 *Tel:* 415-665-3200 *Fax:* 415-665-6502 *E-mail:* cpincus100@sbcglobal.net, pg 608

Pincus, Marilyn, Marilyn Pincus Inc, 9645 E Holiday Way, Sun Lakes, AZ 85248 *Tel:* 408-883-1958 *E-mail:* MPscribe@aol.com, pg 608

Pine, Barbra, MIT List Visual Arts Center, MIT E 15-109, 20 Ames St, Cambridge, MA 02139 *Tel:* 617-253-4680; 617-253-4400 (admission to exhibits) *Fax:* 617-258-7265 *E-mail:* hiroco@mit.edu *Web Site:* web.mit.edu/lvac, pg 175

Pine, Ralph, Quite Specific Media Group Ltd, 7373 Pyramid Place, Hollywood, CA 90046 *Tel:* 323-851-5797 *Fax:* 323-851-5798 *E-mail:* info@quitespecificmedia.com *Web Site:* www.quitespecificmedia.com, pg 224

Pine, Richard S, Inkwell Management, 521 Fifth Ave, 26th fl, New York, NY 10175 *Tel:* 212-922-3500 *Fax:* 212-922-0535 *E-mail:* contact@inkwellmanagement.com *Web Site:* www.inkwellmanagement.com, pg 635

Pines, Sue, JIST Publishing Inc, 8902 Otis Ave, Indianapolis, IN 46216 *Tel:* 317-613-4200 *Toll Free Tel:* 800-648-5478 *Fax:* 317-613-4304 *Toll Free Fax:* 800-547-8329 *E-mail:* info@jist.com *Web Site:* www.jist.com, pg 141

Pingry, Pat, Williamson Books, 535 Metroplex Dr, Suite 250, Nashville, TN 37211 *Tel:* 802-425-2713 (edit) *Toll Free Tel:* 800-586-2572 (sales & orders) *Fax:* 802-425-2714 (edit) *Web Site:* www.williamsonbooks.com, pg 300

Pingry, Patricia, Ideals Publications Inc, 535 Metroplex Dr, Suite 250, Nashville, TN 37211 *Tel:* 615-781-1427 *Toll Free Tel:* 800-558-4343 (customer service) *Fax:* 615-781-1447 *Web Site:* www.idealsbooks.com, pg 130

Pinkerton, Allen, Canadian Magazine Publishers Association, 425 Adelaide St W, Suite 700, Toronto, ON M5V 3C1, Canada *Tel:* 416-504-0274 *Fax:* 416-504-0437 *E-mail:* cmpainfo@cmpa.ca *Web Site:* www.cmpa.ca/; www.magomania.com, pg 683

Pinkerton, Jennifer, The University of Arizona Press, 355 S Euclid Ave, Suite 103, Tucson, AZ 85719-6654 *Tel:* 520-621-1441 *Toll Free Tel:* 800-426-3797 (orders) *Fax:* 520-621-8899 *Toll Free Fax:* 800-426-3797 *E-mail:* uapress@uapress.arizona.edu *Web Site:* www.uapress.arizona.edu, pg 280

Pinkerton, Joan, Phoenix Learning Resources, 25 Third St, 2nd fl, Stamford, CT 06905 *Tel:* 203-353-1665 *Toll Free Tel:* 800-526-6581 *Fax:* 212-629-5648 *Web Site:* www.phoenixlr.com, pg 212

Pinkney, Andrea, Houghton Mifflin Trade & Reference Division, 222 Berkeley St, Boston, MA 02116-3764 *Tel:* 617-351-5000 *Toll Free Fax:* 800-225-3362 *Web Site:* www.houghtonmifflinbooks.com, pg 126

Pinkus, Linda, ShipShape Publishing Inc, 12 Pine St, Chatham, NJ 07928 *Tel:* 973-635-3000 *Fax:* 973-635-4363 *E-mail:* ShipShapeBooks@aol.com *Web Site:* www.ShipShapePublishing.com, pg 574

Pinkus, Samuel L, McIntosh & Otis Inc, 353 Lexington Ave, Suite 1500, New York, NY 10016-0900 *Tel:* 212-687-7400 *Fax:* 212-687-6894 *E-mail:* info@mcintoshandotis.com, pg 643

Pinsky, Prof Robert, Boston University, 236 Bay State Rd, Boston, MA 02215 *Tel:* 617-353-2510 *Fax:* 617-353-3653 *Web Site:* www.bu.edu/writing/, pg 751

Pinzow, Anne P, Toad Hall Inc, RR 2, Box 2090, Laceyville, PA 18623 *Tel:* 570-869-2942 *Fax:* 570-869-1031 *E-mail:* toadhallco@aol.com *Web Site:* www.laceyville.com/Toad-Hall, pg 272, 658

Piraneo, Josephine, Amber Quill Press LLC, PO Box 265, Indian Hills, CO 80454 *E-mail:* customer_service@amberquillpress.com *Web Site:* amberquill.com, pg 10

Pirooz, Patti, Penguin Audiobooks, 375 Hudson St, New York, NY 10014 *Tel:* 212-366-2000 *E-mail:* online@penguin.com *Web Site:* www.penguin.com, pg 207

Pirooz, Patti, Putnam Berkley Audio, 375 Hudson St, New York, NY 10014 *Tel:* 212-366-2000 *Fax:* 212-366-2666 *E-mail:* online@penguinputnam.com *Web Site:* www.penguin.com, pg 222

Pistner, Patricia, Miniature Book Society Inc, 402 York Ave, Delaware, OH 43015 *Web Site:* www.mbs.org, pg 691

Pitcher, Angela, Creative Book Publishing, 36 Austin St, St Johns, NF A1B 3T7, Canada *Tel:* 709-722-8500 *Toll Free Tel:* 877-722-1722 (Canada only) *Fax:* 709-579-7745 *E-mail:* nlbooks@transcontinental.ca *Web Site:* www.nfbooks.com, pg 541

Pitkin, Ronald E, Cumberland House Publishing Inc, 431 Harding Industrial Dr, Nashville, TN 37211 *Tel:* 615-832-1171 *Toll Free Tel:* 888-439-2665 *Fax:* 615-832-0633 *E-mail:* information@cumberlandhouse.com *Web Site:* www.cumberlandhouse.com, pg 74

Pitt, Nick, Warwick Publishing Inc, 161 Frederick St, Toronto, ON M5A 4P3, Canada *Tel:* 416-596-1555 *Fax:* 416-596-1520 *Web Site:* www.warwickgp.com, pg 566

Pitts, John, Doubleday Broadway Publishing Group, 1745 Broadway, New York, NY 10019 *Tel:* 212-782-9000 *Toll Free Tel:* 800-223-6834; 800-223-5780 (sales) *Fax:* 212-302-7985 (correspondence); 212-492-9862 (orders), pg 82

Pizzo, Marilyn, Poisoned Pen Press Inc, 6962 E First Ave, Suite 103, Scottsdale, AZ 85251 *Tel:* 480-945-3375 ext 210 *Fax:* 480-949-1707 *E-mail:* info@poisonpenpress.com *Web Site:* www.poisonpenpress.com, pg 215

Plantier, Paula, EditAmerica, 115 Jacobs Creek Rd, Ewing, NJ 08628 *Tel:* 609-882-5852 *Fax:* 609-882-5851 *E-mail:* editamerica@usa.com *Web Site:* www.editamerica.com, pg 597

Plass, Cheryl, Liguori Publications, One Liguori Dr, Liguori, MO 63057-9999 *Tel:* 636-464-2500 *Toll Free Tel:* 800-464-2555 *Fax:* 636-464-8449 *Web Site:* www.liguori.org, pg 155

Plastine, James, The Darwin Press Inc, 280 N Main St, Pennington, NJ 08534 *Tel:* 609-737-1349 *Fax:* 609-737-0929 *E-mail:* books@darwinpress.com *Web Site:* www.darwinpress.com, pg 76

Platt, Judith, Curtis Benjamin Award, 50 "F" St NW, Washington, DC 20001-1530 *Tel:* 202-347-3375 *Fax:* 202-347-3690 *Web Site:* www.publishers.org, pg 762

Platt, Julie M, SAS Publishing, SAS Campus Dr, Cary, NC 27513 *Tel:* 919-531-7447 *Fax:* 919-677-4444 *E-mail:* sasbbu@sas.com *Web Site:* www.sas.com, pg 240

Playter, Wayne, HarperCollins Publishers Canada, 2 Bloor St E, 20th fl, Toronto, ON M4W 1A8, Canada *Tel:* 416-975-9334 *Fax:* 416-975-9884 (publishing); 416-975-5223 (sales) *E-mail:* hccanada@harpercollins.com *Web Site:* www.harpercanada.com, pg 549

Pleasanton, Kristin, Delaware Division of the Arts Individual Artist Fellowships, 820 N French St, Wilmington, DE 19801 *Tel:* 302-577-8278 *Fax:* 302-577-6561 *Web Site:* www.artsdel.org, pg 769

Plog, Helen, St Martin's Press LLC, 175 Fifth Ave, New York, NY 10010 *Tel:* 212-674-5151 *Fax:* 212-420-9314 *E-mail:* firstname.lastname@stmartins.com *Web Site:* www.stmartins.com, pg 239

Plotkin, Martha, Police Executive Research Forum, 1120 Connecticut Ave NW, Suite 930, Washington, DC 20036 *Tel:* 202-466-7820 *Toll Free Tel:* 888-202-4563 (cust serv) *Fax:* 202-466-7826 *E-mail:* perf@policeforum.org *Web Site:* www.policeforum.org, pg 216

Plotnick, Stanley, Phobos Books, 200 Park Ave S, Suite 1109, New York, NY 10003 *Tel:* 212-477-3225 *Fax:* 212-529-4223 *E-mail:* info@phobosweb.com *Web Site:* phobosweb.com, pg 211

Plotnick, Stanley D, University Press of America Inc, 4501 Forbes Blvd, Suite 200, Lanham, MD 20706 *Tel:* 301-459-3366 *Toll Free Tel:* 800-462-6420 *Fax:* 301-429-5748 *Toll Free Fax:* 800-338-4550 *Web Site:* www.univpress.com, pg 286

Plumeri, James, Bantam Dell Publishing Group, 1745 Broadway, New York, NY 10019 *Tel:* 212-782-9000 *Toll Free Tel:* 800-223-6834 *Fax:* 212-302-7985 *Web Site:* www.randomhouse.com/bantamdell, pg 31

Plummer, Judy L, CQ Press, 1255 22 St NW, Suite 400, Washington, DC 20037 *Tel:* 202-729-1800 *Toll Free Tel:* 866-427-7737 *Fax:* 202-729-1923 *Toll Free Fax:* 800-380-3810 *E-mail:* customerservice@cqpress.com *Web Site:* www.cqpress.com, pg 71

Plunkett, Jack W, Plunkett Research Ltd, PO Drawer 541737, Houston, TX 77254-1737 *Tel:* 713-932-0000 *Fax:* 713-932-7080 *E-mail:* sales@plunkettresearch.com *Web Site:* www.plunkettresearch.com, pg 215

Poblocka, Joanna, League of Canadian Poets, 920 Yonge St, Suite 608, Toronto, ON M4W 3C7, Canada *Tel:* 416-504-1657 *Fax:* 416-504-0096 *E-mail:* info@poets.ca *Web Site:* www.poets.ca, pg 689

Pochoda, Phil M, University of Michigan Press, 839 Greene St, Ann Arbor, MI 48104-3209 *Tel:* 734-764-4388 *Fax:* 734-615-1540 *E-mail:* um.press@umich.edu *Web Site:* www.press.umich.edu, pg 282

Pochron, Joann "JP", Joann "JP" Pochron, Writer for Hire, 830 Lake Orchid Circle, No 203, Vero Beach, FL 32962 *Tel:* 772-569-2967 *E-mail:* pageturn@bellsouth.net, pg 608

Pockell, Les, Warner Books, 1271 Avenue of the Americas, New York, NY 10020 *Tel:* 212-522-7200 *Fax:* 212-522-7991 *Web Site:* www.twbookmark.com, pg 293

Podoll, Carol Ann, New Past Press Inc, PO Box 558, Friendship, WI 53934-0558 *Tel:* 608-339-7191 *E-mail:* newpast@maqs.net *Web Site:* www.newpastpress.com, pg 188

Poehlman, George, Augsburg Fortress Publishers, Publishing House of the Evangelical Lutheran Church in America, 100 S Fifth St, Suite 700, Minneapolis, MN 55402 *Tel:* 612-330-3300 *Toll Free Tel:* 800-426-0115 (ext 639 subns); 800-328-4648 (orders); 800-421-0239 (perms) *Fax:* 612-330-3455 *Toll Free Fax:* 800-421-0239 (perms & copyrights) *E-mail:* customerservice@augsburgfortress.org; copyright@augsburgfortress.org (for reprint permission requests) *Web Site:* www.augsburgfortress.org, pg 28

Poggie Chin, Lynn, Springer Publishing Co Inc, 11 W 42 St, New York, NY 10036 *Tel:* 212-431-4370 *Toll Free Tel:* 877-687-7476 *Fax:* 212-941-7842 *E-mail:* springer@springerpub.com *Web Site:* www.springerpub.com, pg 256

Pohja, Sue, Langenscheidt Publishers Inc, 46-35 54 Rd, Maspeth, NY 11378 *Tel:* 718-784-0055 *Toll Free Tel:* 800-432-MAPS (732-6277) *Fax:* 718-784-0640 *Toll Free Fax:* 888-773-7979 *E-mail:* sales@langenscheidt.com *Web Site:* www.langenscheidt.com, pg 149

Pohlen, Jerome, Zephyr Press Catalog, 814 N Franklin St, Chicago, IL 60610 *Tel:* 312-337-5985 *Toll Free Tel:* 800-232-2187 *Fax:* 312-337-1651 *E-mail:* neways2learn@zephyrpress.com *Web Site:* www.zephyrpress.com, pg 307

Poindexter, David, MacAdam/Cage Publishing Inc, 155 Sansome St, Suite 550, San Francisco, CA 94104 *Tel:* 415-986-7502 *Toll Free Tel:* 866-986-7470 *Fax:* 415-986-7414 *E-mail:* info@macadamcage.com *Web Site:* www.macadamcage.com, pg 160

Poirier, Pierre, Institute of Psychological Research, Inc., 34 Fleury St W, Montreal, PQ H3L 1S9, Canada *Tel:* 514-382-3000 *Toll Free Tel:* 800-363-7800 *Fax:* 514-382-3007 *Toll Free Fax:* 888-382-3007 *E-mail:* info@i-p-r.ca *Web Site:* www.i-p-r.ca, pg 551

Poirot, Henry M, Poirot Literary Agency, 2685 Stephens Rd, Boulder, CO 80305 *Tel:* 303-494-0668 *Fax:* 303-494-9396 *E-mail:* poirotco@comcast.net, pg 648

Poitras, Danielle, Les Publications Graficor 1989 Inc, 7001 boul Saint-Laurent, Montreal, PQ H2S 3E3, Canada *Tel:* 514-273-1066 *Toll Free Tel:* 800-565-5531 *Fax:* 514-276-0324 *Toll Free Fax:* 800-814-0324 *E-mail:* graficor@gmorin.qc.ca *Web Site:* www.graficor.qc.ca, pg 559

Polansky, Debra, Reader's Digest Children's Books, Reader's Digest Rd, Pleasantville, NY 10570-7000 *Tel:* 914-244-4800 *Toll Free Tel:* 800-934-0977, pg 228

Polese, Richard, New Mexico Book Association (NMBA), 310 Read St, Santa Fe, NM 87504 *Tel:* 505-983-1412 *Fax:* 505-983-0899 *E-mail:* oceantree@earthlink.net *Web Site:* www.nmbook.org, pg 695

Polese, Richard, Ocean Tree Books, 1325 Cerro Gordo Rd, Santa Fe, NM 87501 *Tel:* 505-983-1412 *Fax:* 505-983-0899 *E-mail:* oceantree@earthlink.net *Web Site:* www.oceantree.com, pg 195

Polishuk, Paul, Information Gatekeepers Inc, 320 Washington St, Suite 302, Boston, MA 02135 *Tel:* 617-782-5033 *Toll Free Tel:* 800-323-1088 *Fax:* 617-782-5735 *E-mail:* info@igigroup.com *Web Site:* www.igigroup.com, pg 133

Polizzotti, Mark, MFA Publications, 465 Huntington Ave, Boston, MA 02115 *Tel:* 617-369-3438 *Fax:* 617-369-3459 *Web Site:* www.mfa-publications.org, pg 173

Polkinhorn, Harry, San Diego State University Press, San Diego State University, 5500 Campanile Dr, San Diego, CA 92182-8141 *Tel:* 760-768-5536; 619-594-6220 (orders only) *Fax:* 760-768-5631 *Web Site:* www.rohan.sdsu.edu/dept/press/, pg 239

Pollak, Fran, Mews Books Ltd, 20 Bluewater Hill, Westport, CT 06880 *Tel:* 203-227-1836 *Fax:* 203-227-1144 *E-mail:* mewsbooks@aol.com, pg 644

Pollak, Marty, Astragal Press, PO Box 239, Mendham, NJ 07945-0239 *Tel:* 973-543-3045 *Fax:* 973-543-3044 *E-mail:* info@astragalpress.com *Web Site:* www.astragalpress.com, pg 27

Pollard, Dr Douglas, Highway Book Shop, RR 1, Cobalt, ON P0J 1C0, Canada *Tel:* 705-679-8375 *Fax:* 705-679-8511 *E-mail:* bookshop@nt.net *Web Site:* www.abebooks.com/home/highwaybooks, pg 550

Polley, Kathi, Bush Artist Fellows Program, 332 Minnesota St, E-900, St Paul, MN 55101 *Tel:* 651-227-5222 *Toll Free Tel:* 800-605-7315 *Fax:* 651-297-6485 *Web Site:* www.bushfoundation.org, pg 765

Pollock, Catherine, Doubleday Broadway Publishing Group, 1745 Broadway, New York, NY 10019 *Tel:* 212-782-9000 *Toll Free Tel:* 800-223-6834; 800-223-5780 (sales) *Fax:* 212-302-7985 (correspondence); 212-492-9862 (orders), pg 82

Pollock, William, No Starch Press Inc, 555 De Haro St, Suite 250, San Francisco, CA 94107-2192 *Tel:* 415-863-9900 *Toll Free Tel:* 800-420-7240 *Fax:* 415-863-9950 *E-mail:* info@nostarch.com *Web Site:* www.nostarch.com, pg 191

Pomada, Elizabeth, Michael Larsen/Elizabeth Pomada Literary Agents, 1029 Jones St, San Francisco, CA 94109 *Tel:* 415-673-0939 *E-mail:* larsenpoma@aol.com *Web Site:* www.larsen-pomada.com, pg 639

Pomada, Elizabeth, San Francisco Writers Conference 2005, 1029 Jones St, San Francisco, CA 94109 *Tel:* 415-673-0939 *Toll Free Tel:* 866-862-7392 *Fax:* 415-673-0367 *E-mail:* sfwriterscon@aol.com *Web Site:* www.sanfranciscowritersconference.com, pg 746

Pomer, Bella, Bella Pomer Agency Inc, 22 Shallmar Blvd, Penthouse 2, Toronto, ON M5N 2Z8, Canada *Tel:* 416-781-8597 *Fax:* 416-782-4196 *E-mail:* belpom@sympatico.ca, pg 649

Pomes, Anthony, Square One Publishers, 115 Herricks Rd, Garden City Park, NY 11040 *Tel:* 516-535-2010 *Fax:* 516-535-2014 *E-mail:* sq1info@aol.com *Web Site:* squareonepublishers.com, pg 256

Ponleithner, Henry, Pacific Books, Publishers, 3427 Cork Oak Way, Palo Alto, CA 94303 *Tel:* 650-856-6400 *Fax:* 650-856-6400, pg 201

Pontbriand, Chantal, Parachute, 4060 Blvd St-Laurent, Bureau 501, Montreal, PQ H2W 1Y9, Canada *Tel:* 514-842-9805 *Fax:* 514-842-9319 *E-mail:* info@parachute.ca *Web Site:* www.parachute.ca, pg 557

Poole, Don, J Weston Walch Publisher, 321 Valley St, Portland, ME 04104 *Tel:* 207-772-2846 *Toll Free Tel:* 800-341-6094 *Fax:* 207-772-3105 *Toll Free Fax:* 888-991-5755 *E-mail:* customerservice@mail.walch.com *Web Site:* www.walch.com, pg 292

Poorman, Michael, Association of College & University Printers, Penn State University, 101 Business Services Bldg, University Park, PA 16802 *Tel:* 814-865-7544 *Fax:* 814-863-6376, pg 680

Pop, Sorina, M E Sharpe Inc, 80 Business Park Dr, Suite 202, Armonk, NY 10504 *Tel:* 914-273-1800 *Toll Free Tel:* 800-541-6563 *Fax:* 914-273-2106 *E-mail:* info@mesharpe.com *Web Site:* www.mesharpe.com, pg 246

Pope, Anna, Book Publishing Co, 415 Farm Rd, Summertown, TN 38483 *Tel:* 931-964-3571 *Toll Free Tel:* 888-260-8458 *Fax:* 931-964-3518 *E-mail:* info@bookpubco.com *Web Site:* www.bookpubco.com, pg 43

Pope, Barbara Kline, National Academies Press, 500 Fifth St NW, Washington, DC 20001 *Tel:* 202-334-3313 *Toll Free Tel:* 800-624-6242 *Fax:* 202-334-2451 (orders) *Web Site:* www.nap.edu, pg 182

Pope, Jennifer, AEI (Atchity Editorial/Entertainment International Inc), 9601 Wilshire Blvd, No 1202, Beverly Hills, CA 90210 *Tel:* 323-932-0407 *Fax:* 323-932-0321 *E-mail:* submissions@aeionline.com *Web Site:* www.aeionline.com, pg 618

Pope, Norris, Stanford University Press, 1450 Page Mill Rd, Palo Alto, CA 94304-1124 *Tel:* 650-723-9434 *Fax:* 650-725-3457 *Web Site:* www.sup.org, pg 257

Popelars, Craig, Algonquin Books of Chapel Hill, 127 Kingston Dr, Suite 105, Chapel Hill, NC 27514 *Tel:* 919-967-0108 *Fax:* 919-933-0272 *E-mail:* dialogue@algonquin.com *Web Site:* www.algonquin.com, pg 8

Popkin, Julie, Julie Popkin Literary Agency, 15340 Albright St, Suite 204, Pacific Palisades, CA 90272 *Tel:* 310-459-2834 *Fax:* 310-459-4128, pg 649

Poploff, Michelle, Random House Children's Books, 1745 Broadway, New York, NY 10019 *Tel:* 212-782-9000 *Toll Free Tel:* 800-200-3552 *Fax:* 212-782-9452 *Web Site:* www.randomhouse.com/kids, pg 225

Popson, Glenn, The Urban Institute Press, 2100 "M" St NW, Washington, DC 20037 *Tel:* 202-261-5687 *Toll Free Tel:* 877-UIPRESS (847-7377) *Fax:* 202-467-5775 *E-mail:* pubs@ui.urban.org *Web Site:* www.uipress.org, pg 288

Poris, Betsy, Scholastic Trade Division, 557 Broadway, New York, NY 10012 *Tel:* 212-343-6100; 212-343-4685 (export sales) *Fax:* 212-343-4714 (export sales) *Web Site:* www.scholastic.com, pg 242

Porter, Anna, Key Porter Books Ltd, 70 The Esplanade, 3rd fl, Toronto, ON M5E 1R2, Canada *Tel:* 416-862-7777 *Fax:* 416-862-2304 *E-mail:* info@keyporter.com *Web Site:* www.keyporter.com, pg 551

Porter, Barry, Pocket Books, 1230 Avenue of the Americas, New York, NY 10020 *Toll Free Tel:* 800-456-6798 *Fax:* 212-698-7284 *E-mail:* consumer.customerservice@simonandschuster.com *Web Site:* www.simonsays.com, pg 215

Porter, Carolyn, Film-Video Publications/Circus Source Publications, 7944 Capistrano Ave, West Hills, CA 91304 *Tel:* 818-340-0175 *Fax:* 818-340-6770 *E-mail:* circussource@aol.com, pg 96

Porter, Karen, Summer Poetry in Idyllwild, 52500 Temecula Dr, Idyllwild, CA 92549 *Tel:* 909-659-2171 *Fax:* 909-659-4383 *Web Site:* www.idyllwildarts.org, pg 748

Porter, Penny, The Society of Southwestern Authors (SSA), PO Box 30355, Tucson, AZ 85751-0355 *Tel:* 520-546-9382 *Fax:* 520-296-0409 *Web Site:* www.azstarnet.com/nonprofit/ssa, pg 806

Porter, Robert, Allworth Press, 10 E 23 St, Suite 510, New York, NY 10010 *Tel:* 212-777-8395 *Toll Free Tel:* 800-491-2808 *Fax:* 212-777-8261 *E-mail:* pub@allworth.com *Web Site:* www.allworth.com, pg 9

Porter, Susanna, Random House Publishing Group, 1745 Broadway, New York, NY 10019 *Toll Free Tel:* 800-200-3552 *Toll Free Fax:* 800-200-3552 *Web Site:* www.randomhouse.com, pg 227

Portman, Janet, Nolo, 950 Parker St, Berkeley, CA 94710 *Tel:* 510-549-1976 *Fax:* 510-548-5902 *E-mail:* info@nolo.com *Web Site:* www.nolo.com, pg 191

Portnoy, Lynn, Diamond Publishers, 29260 Franklin Rd, Southfield, MI 48034 *Tel:* 248-353-2900 *Toll Free Tel:* 888-386-9688 *Fax:* 248-357-0102 *E-mail:* info@goinglikelynn.com *Web Site:* www.goinglikelynn.com, pg 571

Posner, Dena, Peanut Butter & Jelly Press LLC, PO Box 590239, Newton, MA 02459-0002 *Tel:* 617-630-0945 *Fax:* 617-630-0945 *E-mail:* info@pbjpress.com *Web Site:* www.publishinggame.com, pg 206

Posner-Sanchez, Andrea, Random House Children's Books, 1745 Broadway, New York, NY 10019 *Tel:* 212-782-9000 *Toll Free Tel:* 800-200-3552 *Fax:* 212-782-9452 *Web Site:* www.randomhouse.com/kids, pg 226

Post, Ana, Carter G Woodson Book Awards, 8555 16 St, Suite 500, Silver Spring, MD 20910 *Tel:* 301-588-1800 *Toll Free Tel:* 800-296-7840 *Fax:* 301-588-2049 *E-mail:* excellence@ncss.org *Web Site:* www.socialstudies.org, pg 812

Post, Chad, Dalkey Archive Press, Illinois State University 8905, Normal, IL 61790-8905 *Tel:* 309-438-7555 *Fax:* 309-438-7422 *E-mail:* contact@dalkeyarchive.com *Web Site:* www.dalkeyarchive.com, pg 75

Post, Thomas J, Mobile Post Office Society, PO Box 427, Marstons Mills, MA 02648-0427 *Tel:* 508-428-9132 *Fax:* 508-428-2156 *E-mail:* dnc@math.uga.edu *Web Site:* www.eskimo.com/~rkunz/mposhome.html, pg 176

Post, Tom, University of Tennessee Press, 110 Conference Center Bldg, Knoxville, TN 37996-4108 *Tel:* 865-974-3321 *Toll Free Tel:* 800-621-2736 (ordering) *Fax:* 865-974-3724 *E-mail:* custserv@utpress.org *Web Site:* www.utpress.org, pg 285

Poster, Kendra, Farrar, Straus & Giroux, LLC, 19 Union Sq W, New York, NY 10003 *Tel:* 212-741-6900 *Fax:* 212-741-6973 *Web Site:* www.fsgbooks.com, pg 95

Posternak, Jeffrey, The Wylie Agency Inc, 250 W 57 St, Suite 2114, New York, NY 10107 *Tel:* 212-246-0069 *Fax:* 212-586-8953 *E-mail:* mail@wylieagency.com, pg 662

Postreich, Gustav, Denlinger's Publishers Ltd, PO Box 1030, Edgewater, FL 32132-1030 *Tel:* 386-424-1737 *Toll Free Tel:* 800-362-1810 *Fax:* 386-428-3534 *Toll Free Fax:* 800-589-1191 *E-mail:* editor@thebookden.com *Web Site:* www.thebookden.com, pg 79

Potia, Zeenat, Harvard Business School Press, 300 N Beacon St, Watertown, MA 02472 *Tel:* 617-783-7400 *Toll Free Tel:* 888-500-1016 *Fax:* 617-783-7664 *E-mail:* bookpublisher@mail1.hbsp.harvard.edu *Web Site:* www.hbsp.harvard.edu, pg 116

Pott, Jon, Wm B Eerdmans Publishing Co, 255 Jefferson Ave SE, Grand Rapids, MI 49503 *Tel:* 616-459-4591 *Toll Free Tel:* 800-253-7521 *Fax:* 616-459-6540 *E-mail:* sales@eerdmans.com *Web Site:* www.eerdmans.com, pg 88

Pottebaum, Gerard A, Treehaus Communications Inc, 906 W Loveland Ave, Loveland, OH 45140 *Tel:* 513-683-5716 *Toll Free Tel:* 800-638-4287 (orders) *Fax:* 513-683-2882 (orders) *E-mail:* treehaus@treehaus1.com *Web Site:* www.treehaus1.com, pg 275

Potter, Al, Smallwood Center for Newfoundland Studies, Memorial University of Newfoundland, St John's, NF A1C 5S7, Canada *Tel:* 709-737-7474 *Fax:* 709-737-7560 *E-mail:* iser@mun.ca *Web Site:* www.mun.ca/smallwood, pg 561

Potter, Beverly, Ronin Publishing Inc, PO Box 22900, Oakland, CA 94609-5900 *Tel:* 510-420-3669 *Fax:* 510-420-3672 *E-mail:* askronin@roninpub.com *Web Site:* www.roninpub.com, pg 234

Potter, Donn King, Elizabeth H Backman, 86 Johnnycake Hollow Rd, Pine Plains, NY 12567 *Tel:* 518-398-9344 *Fax:* 518-398-6368 *E-mail:* bethcountry@taconic.net, pg 620

Potter, James E, Bridge Learning Systems Inc, 351 Los Altos, American Canyon, CA 94589 *Tel:* 925-228-3177 *Toll Free Tel:* 800-487-9868 *Fax:* 925-372-6099 *E-mail:* bridge@blsinc.com *Web Site:* www.blsinc.com, pg 47

Potter, Nicole, Allworth Press, 10 E 23 St, Suite 510, New York, NY 10010 *Tel:* 212-777-8395 *Toll Free Tel:* 800-491-2808 *Fax:* 212-777-8261 *E-mail:* pub@allworth.com *Web Site:* www.allworth.com, pg 9

Potter, Peter, The Pennsylvania State University Press, 820 N University Dr, University Support Bldg 1, Suite C, University Park, PA 16802-1003 *Tel:* 814-865-1327 *Toll Free Tel:* 800-326-9180 *Fax:* 814-863-1408 *Toll Free Fax:* 877 7782665 *Web Site:* www.psupress.org, pg 209

Potter, Ray, Princeton University Press, 41 William St, Princeton, NJ 08540 *Tel:* 609-258-4900 *Toll Free Tel:* 800-777-4726 *Fax:* 609-258-6305 *Toll Free Fax:* 800-999-1958 *E-mail:* orders@cpfsinc.com *Web Site:* www.pup.princeton.edu, pg 219

Potter, Sue, The Metropolitan Museum of Art, 1000 Fifth Ave, New York, NY 10028 *Tel:* 212-879-5500; 212-535-7710 *Fax:* 212-396-5062 *E-mail:* info@metmuseum.org *Web Site:* www.metmuseum.org, pg 173

Pottle, Peggy, Pacific Press Publishing Association, 1350 N Kings Rd, Nampa, ID 83687-3193 *Tel:* 208-465-2500 *Toll Free Tel:* 800-447-7377 *Fax:* 208-465-2531 *Web Site:* www.pacificpress.com, pg 202

Potts, Patricia, BuilderBooks.com, 1201 15 St NW, Washington, DC 20005-2800 *Tel:* 202-822-0200; 202-266-8200 *Toll Free Tel:* 800-223-2665 (orders); 800-368-5242 ext 8368 (editorial) *Fax:* 202-266-8096 (edit); 202-266-5889 (edit) *Web Site:* www.builderbooks.com, pg 49

Poulin, Joseph, Scriptural Research Center, PO Box 725, New Britain, CT 06050-0725 *Tel:* 203-272-1780 *Fax:* 203-272-2296 *E-mail:* scriptpublish@snet.net *Web Site:* www.scripturalresearch.com, pg 244

Poulson, Kevin, Sierra Press, 4988 Gold Leaf Dr, Mariposa, CA 95338 *Tel:* 209-966-5071 *Toll Free Tel:* 800-745-2631 *Fax:* 209-966-5073 *E-mail:* siepress@sti.net *Web Site:* www.nationalparksusa.com, pg 247

Pound, William, National Conference of State Legislatures, 7700 E First Place, Denver, CO 80230 *Tel:* 303-364-7700 *Fax:* 303-364-7812 *E-mail:* books@ncsl.org *Web Site:* www.ncsl.org, pg 183

Poupard, Dennis, Thomson Gale, 27500 Drake Rd, Farmington Hills, MI 48331-3535 *Tel:* 248-699-4253 *Toll Free Tel:* 800-347-4253 *Fax:* 248-699-8070 *Toll Free Fax:* 800-414-5043 *E-mail:* galeord@gale.com *Web Site:* www.gale.com, pg 270

Powall, Dominic, The Firm, 9465 Wilshire Blvd, Beverly Hills, CA 90212 *Tel:* 310-860-8000 *Fax:* 310-860-8132, pg 630

Powell, Craig, American Society for Quality, 600 N Plankinton Ave, Milwaukee, WI 53203 *Tel:* 414-272-8575 *Toll Free Tel:* 800-248-1946 *Fax:* 414-272-1734 *E-mail:* cs@asq.org *Web Site:* www.asq.org, pg 17

Powell, Judith, Top of the Mountain Publishing, PO Box 2244, Pinellas Park, FL 33780-2244 *Tel:* 727-391-3958 *Fax:* 727-391-4598 *E-mail:* tag@abcinfo.com *Web Site:* abcinfo.com; www.topofthemountain.com, pg 272

Powell, Judy, University of Calgary Press, 2500 University Dr NW, Calgary, AB T2N 1N4, Canada *Tel:* 403-220-7578 *Fax:* 403-282-0085 *E-mail:* whildebr@ucalgary.ca *Web Site:* www.uofcpress.com, pg 565

Powell, Rebecca, Globe Fearon, 299 Jefferson Rd, Parsippany, NJ 07054 *Tel:* 973-739-8000, pg 105

Powell, Sherri, Contemporary Publishing Co of Raleigh Inc, 6001-101 Chapel Hill Rd, Raleigh, NC 27607 *Tel:* 919-851-8221 *Fax:* 919-851-6666 *E-mail:* questions@contemporarypublishing.com *Web Site:* www.contemporarypublishing.com, pg 67

Powell, Tag, Top of the Mountain Publishing, PO Box 2244, Pinellas Park, FL 33780-2244 *Tel:* 727-391-3958 *Fax:* 727-391-4598 *E-mail:* tag@abcinfo.com *Web Site:* abcinfo.com; www.topofthemountain.com, pg 272

Power, Christine Taylor, Dawson Taylor Literary Agency, 4722 Holly Lake Dr, Lake Worth, FL 33463-5372 *Tel:* 561-965-4150 *Fax:* 561-641-9765 *E-mail:* dawsontaylo@aol.com, pg 658

Power, Daniel, powerHouse Books, 68 Charlton St, New York, NY 10014-4601 *Tel:* 212-604-9074 *Fax:* 212-366-5247 *E-mail:* info@powerhousebooks.com *Web Site:* www.powerhousebooks.com, pg 216

Power, Niall, Printing Industries of Wisconsin, 13005 W Bluemount Rd, Brooksfield, WI 53005 *Tel:* 262-785-7040 *Fax:* 262-785-7043 *E-mail:* info@piw.org *Web Site:* www.piw.org, pg 698

Powers, Amy, Boydell & Brewer Inc, 668 Mount Hope Ave, University of Rochester, Rochester, NY 14620 *Tel:* 585-275-0419 *Fax:* 585-271-8778 *Web Site:* www.boydellandbrewer.co.uk, pg 45

Powers, Bob, Rodnik Publishing Company, PO Box 46956, Seattle, WA 98146-0956 *Tel:* 206-937-5189 *Fax:* 206-937-3554 *E-mail:* rodnik2@comcast.net *Web Site:* www.rodnikpublishing.com, pg 573

Powers, Joe, Thomas Nelson Inc, 501 Nelson Place, Nashville, TN 37214 *Tel:* 615-889-9000 *Toll Free Tel:* 800-251-4000 *Fax:* 615-902-1610 *E-mail:* publicity@thomasnelson.com *Web Site:* www.thomasnelson.com, pg 269

Powers, John G, Scepter Publishers, 8 W 38 St, New York, NY 10018 *Tel:* 212-354-0670 *Toll Free Tel:* 800-322-8773 *Fax:* 212-354-0736 *Web Site:* scepterpublishers.org, pg 241

Powers, Melvin, Wilshire Book Co, 12015 Sherman Rd, North Hollywood, CA 91605 *Tel:* 818-765-8579 *Fax:* 818-765-2922 *Web Site:* www.mpowers.com, pg 300

Powers, Thomas, Steerforth Press, 25 Lebanon St, Hanover, NH 03755 *Tel:* 603-643-4787 *Fax:* 603-643-4788 *E-mail:* info@steerforth.com *Web Site:* www.steerforth.com, pg 258

Powers, Will, Minnesota Historical Society Press, 345 Kellogg Blvd W, St Paul, MN 55102-1906 *Tel:* 651-296-2264 *Toll Free Tel:* 800-621-2736 *Fax:* 651-297-1345 *Toll Free Fax:* 800-621-8476 *Web Site:* www.mnhs.org/mhspress, pg 175

Poynor, Jay, The Poynor Group, 444 E 82 St, Suite 28C, New York, NY 10028 *Tel:* 212-734-5909 *Fax:* 212-734-5909, pg 649

Poynter, Dan, Para Publishing, PO Box 8206-R, Santa Barbara, CA 93118-8206 *Tel:* 805-968-7277 *Toll Free Tel:* 800-727-2782 *Fax:* 805-968-1379 *E-mail:* orders@parapublishing.com *Web Site:* www.parapublishing.com, pg 203

Poynter, Dan, Santa Barbara Book Promotion Workshop, PO Box 8206-R, Santa Barbara, CA 93118-8206 *Tel:* 805-968-7277 *Toll Free Tel:* 800-727-2782 *Fax:* 805-968-1379 *E-mail:* orders@parapublishing.com *Web Site:* www.parapublishing.com, pg 747

Prabaharan, S R, World Book Inc, 233 N Michigan, Suite 2000, Chicago, IL 60601 *Tel:* 312-729-5800 *Toll Free Tel:* 800-967-5325 (consumer sales, US); 800-463-8845 (consumer sales, Canada); 800-975-3250 (school & library sales, US); 800-837-5365 (school & library sales, Canada); 866-866-5200 (web sales) *Fax:* 312-729-5600; 312-729-5606 *Toll Free Fax:* 800-433-9330 (school & library sales, US); 888-690-4002 (school library sales, Canada) *Web Site:* www.worldbook.com, pg 303

Pracht, Diane, The United Educators Inc, 900 N Shore Dr, Suite 140, Lake Bluff, IL 60044 *Tel:* 847-234-3700 *Fax:* 847-234-8705 *E-mail:* arslms@aol.com, pg 279

Praeger, Marta, Robert A Freedman Dramatic Agency Inc, 1501 Broadway, Suite 2310, New York, NY 10036 *Tel:* 212-840-5760 *Fax:* 212-840-5776, pg 631

Pranger, Linda, Aio Publishing Co LLC, PO Box 30788, Charleston, SC 29417 *Tel:* 843-225-3698 *Toll Free Tel:* 888-287-9888 *Web Site:* www.aiopublishing.com, pg 7

Prasad, Sheo, Augsburg Fortress Publishers, Publishing House of the Evangelical Lutheran Church in America, 100 S Fifth St, Suite 700, Minneapolis, MN 55402 *Tel:* 612-330-3300 *Toll Free Tel:* 800-426-0115 (ext 639 subns); 800-328-4648 (orders); 800-421-0239 (perms) *Fax:* 612-330-3455 *Toll Free Fax:* 800-421-0239 (perms & copyrights) *E-mail:* customerservice@augsburgfortress.org; copyright@augsburgfortress.org (for reprint permission requests) *Web Site:* www.augsburgfortress.org, pg 28

Prast, John, MDRT Center for Productivity, 325 W Touhy Ave, Park Ridge, IL 60068-4265 *Tel:* 847-692-6378 *Toll Free Tel:* 800-879-6378 *Fax:* 847-518-8921 *E-mail:* orders@mdrt.org *Web Site:* www.mdrt.org, pg 169

Prather, Linda, Hyperion, 77 W 66 St, 11th fl, New York, NY 10023-6298 *Tel:* 212-456-0100 *Toll Free Tel:* 800-759-0190 (cust serv) *Fax:* 212-456-0157 *Web Site:* hyperionbooks.com, pg 129

Prather, Miranda N, PublishAmerica, PO Box 151, Frederick, MD 21705-0151 *Tel:* 240-529-1031 *Fax:* 301-631-9073 *E-mail:* writers@publishamerica.com *Web Site:* www.publishamerica.com, pg 221

Pratt, Charles, George Bennett Fellowship, 20 Main St, Exeter, NH 03833-2460 *Tel:* 603-772-4311 *Web Site:* www.exeter.edu, pg 762

Pratt, Darrin, University Press of Colorado, 5589 Arapahoe Ave, Suite 206-C, Boulder, CO 80303 *Tel:* 720-406-8849 *Toll Free Tel:* 800-627-7377 *Fax:* 720-406-3443 *Web Site:* www.upcolorado.com, pg 286

Pratt, Helen F, Helen F Pratt Inc Literary Agency, 1165 Fifth Ave, New York, NY 10029 *Tel:* 212-722-5081 *Fax:* 212-722-8569 *E-mail:* helenpratt@earthlink.net, pg 649

Pratt, Linda, Sheldon Fogelman Agency Inc, 10 E 40 St, Suite 3800, New York, NY 10016 *Tel:* 212-532-7250 *Fax:* 212-685-8939 *E-mail:* fogelman@worldnet.att.net; agency@sheldonfogelmanagency.com, pg 630

Pratt, Stan, Boyds Mills Press, 815 Church St, Honesdale, PA 18431 *Tel:* 570-253-1164 *Toll Free Tel:* 877-512-8366 *Fax:* 570-253-0179 *Web Site:* www.boydsmillspress.com, pg 45

Prbylowski, Doug, Comex Systems Inc, 5 Cold Hill Rd, Suite 24, Mendham, NJ 07945 *Tel:* 973-543-2862 *Toll Free Tel:* 800-543-6959 *Fax:* 973-543-9644 *Web Site:* www.comexsystems.com, pg 65

Preiss, Byron, ibooks Inc, 24 W 25 St, 11th fl, New York, NY 10010 *Tel:* 212-645-9870 *Fax:* 212-645-9874 *Web Site:* www.bpvp.com; www.ibooks.net, pg 130

Prentiss, Winnie, Rockport Publishers, 33 Commercial St, Gloucester, MA 01930 *Tel:* 978-282-9590 *Fax:* 978-283-2742 *Web Site:* www.rockpub.com, pg 233

Preppernau, Joan, Online Training Solutions Inc, PO Box 2224, Redmond, WA 98073-2224 *Tel:* 425-885-1441 *Toll Free Tel:* 800-854-3344 *Fax:* 425-881-1642; 425-671-0640 *E-mail:* customerservice@otsi.com *Web Site:* www.otsi.com, pg 197

Prescott, Peter S, The Authors League Fund, 31 E 28 St, New York, NY 10016 *Tel:* 212-268-1208 *Fax:* 212-564-5363 *E-mail:* authlgfund@aol.com *Web Site:* www.authorsleaguefund.org, pg 668

Preskill, Robert, LitWest Group LLC, 379 Burning Tree Ct, Half Moon Bay, CA 94019 *Web Site:* www.litwest.com, pg 641

Presley, Bruce W, Lawrenceville Press Inc, PO Box 704, Pennington, NJ 08534 *Tel:* 609-737-1148 *Fax:* 609-737-8564 *E-mail:* custserv@lvp.com *Web Site:* www.lvp.com, pg 150

Press, David, Gareth Stevens Inc, 330 W Olive St, Suite 100, Milwaukee, WI 53212 *Tel:* 414-332-3520 *Toll Free Tel:* 800-542-2595 *Fax:* 414-332-3567 *E-mail:* info@gspub.com; info@worldalmanaclibrary.com *Web Site:* www.garethstevens.com; www.worldalmanaclibrary.com, pg 102

Prestigiacomo, Dana, Thomson Learning Inc, 200 First Stamford Place, Suite 400, Stamford, CT 06902 *Tel:* 203-539-8000 *Fax:* 203-539-7581 *E-mail:* communications@thomsonlearning.com *Web Site:* www.thomson.com/learning, pg 270

Preston, Frances, BMI, 320 W 57 St, New York, NY 10019 *Tel:* 212-586-2000 *Fax:* 212-246-2163 *Web Site:* www.bmi.com, pg 681

Preston, Marcia, ByLine Magazine & Press, PO Box 5240, Edmond, OK 73083-5240 *Tel:* 405-348-5591 *Web Site:* www.bylinemag.com, pg 765

Preston, Mark, United States Tennis Association, 70 W Red Oak Lane, White Plains, NY 10604 *Tel:* 914-696-7000 *Fax:* 914-696-7027 *Web Site:* www.usta.com, pg 279

Pretty, M, Golden Meteorite Press, PO Box 1223 Main Post Office, Edmonton, AB T5J 2M4, Canada *Tel:* 780-378-0063, pg 548

Price, Bernadette, Orbis Books, Walsh Bldg, 75 Ryder Rd, Ossining, NY 10562 *Tel:* 914-941-7636 *Toll Free Tel:* 800-258-5838 (orders) *Fax:* 914-941-7005 (orders); 914-945-0670 (office) *E-mail:* orbisbooks@maryknoll.org *Web Site:* www.orbisbooks.com, pg 198

Price, Bruce, Marathon Press, PO Box 407, Norfolk, NE 68702-0407 *Tel:* 402-371-5040 *Toll Free Tel:* 800-228-0629 *Fax:* 402-371-9382 *Web Site:* www.marathonpress.com, pg 163

Price, Eric, Grove/Atlantic Inc, 841 Broadway, 4th fl, New York, NY 10003-4793 *Tel:* 212-614-7850 *Toll Free Tel:* 800-521-0178 *Fax:* 212-614-7886 *Web Site:* www.groveatlantic.com, pg 110

Price, Fiona, Verso, 180 Varick St, 10th fl, New York, NY 10014-4606 *Tel:* 212-807-9680 *Fax:* 212-807-9152 *E-mail:* versony@versobooks.com *Web Site:* www.versobooks.com, pg 290

Puppo, Andrea, International Development Research Centre, 250 Albert St, Ottawa, ON K1P 6M1, Canada *Tel:* 613-236-6163 *Fax:* 613-238-7230 *E-mail:* pub@idrc.ca *Web Site:* www.idrc.ca/booktique, pg 551

Purich, Donald, Purich Publishing Ltd, PO Box 23032, Market Mall Postal Outlet, Saskatoon, SK S7J 5H3, Canada *Tel:* 306-373-5311 *Fax:* 306-373-5315 *E-mail:* purich@sasktel.net *Web Site:* www.purichpublishing.com, pg 559

Purr, Diane, Jonathan David Publishers Inc, 68-22 Eliot Ave, Middle Village, NY 11379 *Tel:* 718-456-8611 *Fax:* 718-894-2818 *E-mail:* info@jdbooks.com; jondavpub@aol.com *Web Site:* www.jdbooks.com, pg 142

Pursell, Robert, American Psychiatric Publishing Inc, 1000 Wilson Blvd, Suite 1825, Arlington, VA 22209 *Tel:* 703-907-7322 *Toll Free Tel:* 800-368-5777 *Fax:* 703-907-1091 *E-mail:* appi@psych.org *Web Site:* www.appi.org, pg 16

Purtell, April, Hewitt Homeschooling Resources, 2103 "B" St, Washougal, WA 98671 *Tel:* 360-835-8708 *Toll Free Tel:* 800-348-1750 *Fax:* 360-835-8697 *E-mail:* info@hewitthomeschooling.com *Web Site:* hewitthomeschooling.com, pg 122

Putzi, Sibylla M, World Trade Press, 1450 Grant Ave, Suite 204, Novato, CA 94945 *Tel:* 415-898-1124 *Toll Free Tel:* 800-833-8586 *Fax:* 415-898-1080 *E-mail:* admin@worldtradepress.com *Web Site:* www.worldtradepress.com, pg 304

Puzzo, Audrey, DK Publishing Inc, 375 Hudson St, 2nd fl, New York, NY 10014-3672 *Tel:* 212-213-4800 *Toll Free Tel:* 877-342-5357 (cust serv) *Fax:* 212-213-5202 *Web Site:* www.dk.com, pg 81

Pyles, Cindy, International Publishing Management Association (IPMA), 1205 W College St, Liberty, MO 64068-3733 *Tel:* 816-781-1111 *Fax:* 816-781-2790 *E-mail:* ipmainfo@ipma.org *Web Site:* www.ipma.org, pg 689

Pynn, Ronald E, Text & Academic Authors Association Inc, PO Box 76477, St Petersburg, FL 33734-6477 *Tel:* 727-821-7277 *Fax:* 727-821-7271 *E-mail:* text@tampabay.rr.com *Web Site:* www.taaonline.net, pg 701

Qualben, Lois, LangMarc Publishing, PO Box 90488, Austin, TX 78709-0488 *Tel:* 512-394-0989 *Toll Free Tel:* 800-864-1648 *Fax:* 512-394-0829 *E-mail:* langmarc@booksails.com *Web Site:* www.langmarc.com; www.booksails.com, pg 149

Qualben, Michael, LangMarc Publishing, PO Box 90488, Austin, TX 78709-0488 *Tel:* 512-394-0989 *Toll Free Tel:* 800-864-1648 *Fax:* 512-394-0829 *E-mail:* langmarc@booksails.com *Web Site:* www.langmarc.com; www.booksails.com, pg 149

Quam, Kathryn, MicroMash, 6402 S Troy Circle, Englewood, CO 80111-6424 *Tel:* 303-799-0099 *Toll Free Tel:* 800-823-6039 *Fax:* 303-799-1425 *E-mail:* info@micromash.com *Web Site:* www.micromash.net, pg 173

Quanbeck, Barbara, Word Wrangler Publishing Inc, 332 Tobin Creek Rd, Livingston, MT 59047 *Tel:* 406-686-4230; 406-686-4417 *Toll Free Tel:* 866-896-2897 *Fax:* 406-686-4417 *E-mail:* wrdwranglr@aol.com *Web Site:* www.wordwrangler.com, pg 303

Quandt, Peter, Haights Cross Communications Inc, 10 New King St, White Plains, NY 10604 *Tel:* 914-289-9400 *Fax:* 914-289-9401 *E-mail:* info@haightscross.com *Web Site:* www.haightscross.com, pg 111

Quasha, George, Barrytown/Station Hill Press, 120 Station Hill Rd, Barrytown, NY 12507 *Tel:* 845-758-5293 *E-mail:* publishers@stationhill.org *Web Site:* www.stationhill.org, pg 33

Queen, Lisa, IMG Literary, 825 Seventh Ave, 9th fl, New York, NY 10019 *Tel:* 212-774-6900 *Fax:* 212-246-1118 *Web Site:* www.imgworld.com, pg 635

Quick, Angie, Quick Publishing, 1610 Long Leaf Circle, St Louis, MO 63146 *Tel:* 314-432-3435 *Toll Free Tel:* 888-782-5474 *Fax:* 314-993-4485 *E-mail:* quickpublishing@sbcglobal.net *Web Site:* www.quickpublishing.com, pg 223

Quigley, Christine, Georgetown University Press, 3240 Prospect St NW, Washington, DC 20007 *Tel:* 202-687-6251 (acq); 202-687-5889 (busn); 202-687-5641 (mktg); 410-516-6956 (orders) *Toll Free Tel:* 800-537-5487 *Fax:* 202-687-6340 (edit); 410-516-6998 (orders) *E-mail:* gupress@georgetown.edu *Web Site:* www.press.georgetown.edu, pg 104

Quigley, Darcy, John Milton Society for the Blind, 475 Riverside Dr, Rm 455, New York, NY 10027 *Tel:* 212-870-3335 *Fax:* 212-870-3229 *E-mail:* order@jmsblind.org *Web Site:* www.jmsblind.org, pg 141

Quigley, Hannelore, American Fisheries Society, 5410 Grosvenor Lane, Suite 110, Bethesda, MD 20814-2199 *Tel:* 301-897-8616 *Fax:* 301-897-8096 *E-mail:* main@fisheries.org *Web Site:* www.fisheries.org, pg 13

Quigley, Kenneth, The Continuum International Publishing Group, 15 E 26 St, Suite 1703, New York, NY 10010 *Tel:* 212-953-5858 *Toll Free Tel:* 800-561-7704 *Fax:* 212-953-5944 *E-mail:* info@continuumbooks.com *Web Site:* www.continuumbooks.com, pg 67

Quigley, Kenneth, Morehouse Publishing Co, PO Box 1321, Harrisburg, PA 17105-1321 *Tel:* 717-541-8130 *Toll Free Tel:* 800-877-0012 (orders only) *Fax:* 717-541-8136; 717-541-8128 (orders only) *E-mail:* morehouse@morehousegroup.com *Web Site:* www.morehousegroup.com, pg 178

Quillen, Lida E, Twilight Times Books, PO Box 3340, Kingsport, TN 37664-0340 *Tel:* 423-323-0183 *Fax:* 423-323-0183 *E-mail:* publisher@twilighttimes.com *Web Site:* www.twilighttimesbooks.com, pg 277

Quincannon, Alan, Quincannon Publishing Group, PO Box 8100, Glen Ridge, NJ 07028-8100 *Tel:* 973-669-8367 *E-mail:* editors@quincannongroup.com *Web Site:* www.quincannongroup.com, pg 224

Quinlin, Margaret M, Peachtree Publishers Ltd, 1700 Chattahoochee Ave, Atlanta, GA 30318 *Tel:* 404-876-8761 *Toll Free Tel:* 800-241-0113 *Fax:* 404-875-2578 *Toll Free Fax:* 800-875-8909 *E-mail:* hello@peachtree-online.com *Web Site:* www.peachtree-online.com, pg 206

Quinn, Alice, Louise Louis & Emily F Bourne Student Poetry Award, 15 Gramercy Park, New York, NY 10003 *Tel:* 212-254-9628 *Fax:* 212-673-2352 *Web Site:* www.poetrysociety.org, pg 763

Quinn, Alice, Alice Fay Di Castagnola Award, 15 Gramercy Park, New York, NY 10003 *Tel:* 212-254-9628 *Fax:* 212-673-2352 *Web Site:* www.poetrysociety.org, pg 770

Quinn, Alice, Emily Dickinson Award, 15 Gramercy Park, New York, NY 10003 *Tel:* 212-254-9628 *Fax:* 212-673-2352 *Web Site:* www.poetrysociety.org, pg 772

Quinn, Alice, Norma Farber First Book Award, 15 Gramercy Park, New York, NY 10003 *Tel:* 212-254-9628 *Fax:* 212-673-2352 *Web Site:* www.poetrysociety.org, pg 773

Quinn, Alice, Cecil Hemley Memorial Award, 15 Gramercy Park, New York, NY 10003 *Tel:* 212-254-9628 *Fax:* 212-673-2352 *Web Site:* www.poetrysociety.org, pg 778

Quinn, Alice, Lyric Poetry Award, 15 Gramercy Park, New York, NY 10003 *Tel:* 212-254-9628 *Fax:* 212-673-2352 *Web Site:* www.poetrysociety.org, pg 786

Quinn, Alice, Lucille Medwick Memorial Award, 15 Gramercy Park, New York, NY 10003 *Tel:* 212-254-9628 *Fax:* 212-673-2352 *Web Site:* www.poetrysociety.org, pg 789

Quinn, Alice, Poetry Society of America (PSA), 15 Gramercy Park, New York, NY 10003 *Tel:* 212-254-9628 *Toll Free Tel:* 888-USA-POEM *Fax:* 212-673-2352 *Web Site:* www.poetrysociety.org, pg 697

Quinn, Alice, William Carlos Williams Award, 15 Gramercy Park, New York, NY 10003 *Tel:* 212-254-9628 *Fax:* 212-673-2352 *Web Site:* www.poetrysociety.org, pg 811

Quinn, Ann, Annick Press Ltd, 15 Patricia Ave, Toronto, ON M2M 1H9, Canada *Tel:* 416-221-4802 *Fax:* 416-221-8400 *E-mail:* annick@annickpress.com *Web Site:* www.annickpress.com, pg 535

Quinn, Ann, Firefly Books Ltd, 66 Leek Crescent, Richmond Hill, ON L4B 1H1, Canada *Tel:* 416-499-8412 *Toll Free Tel:* 800-387-5085 *Fax:* 416-499-1142 *Toll Free Tel:* 800-565-6034 *E-mail:* service@fireflybooks.com *Web Site:* www.fireflybooks.com, pg 547

Quinn, Kristy, A Abacus Group, PO Box 35, Ridgecrest, CA 93556 *Tel:* 760-375-5243 *Fax:* 760-375-1140 *E-mail:* gtd007@ridgenet.net *Web Site:* www.ridgenet.net/~gtd007, pg 617

Quinn, Laura, Little, Brown and Company Adult Trade Division, 1271 Avenue of the Americas, New York, NY 10020 *Tel:* 212-522-8700 *Fax:* 212-522-2067 *Web Site:* www.twbookmark.com, pg 156

Quinn, Lori, Warner Faith (Christian Book Division of Time Warner Book Group), 2 Creekside Crossing, 10 Cadillac Dr, Suite 220, Brentwood, TN 37027 *Tel:* 615-221-0996 *Fax:* 615-221-0962 *Web Site:* www.twbookmark.com, pg 293

Quinn, Martin, St Martin's Press LLC, 175 Fifth Ave, New York, NY 10010 *Tel:* 212-674-5151 *Fax:* 212-420-9314 *E-mail:* firstname.lastname@stmartins.com *Web Site:* www.stmartins.com, pg 238

Quinn, Marysarah, Clarkson Potter Publishers, 1745 Broadway, New York, NY 10019 *Tel:* 212-782-9000 *Toll Free Tel:* 888-264-1745 *Fax:* 212-572-6181 *Web Site:* www.clarksonpotter.com; www.randomhouse.com/crown/clarksonpotter, pg 63

Quinn, Michelle, Herald Press, 616 Walnut Ave, Scottdale, PA 15683-1999 *Tel:* 724-887-8500 *Toll Free Tel:* 800-245-7894 *Fax:* 724-887-3111 *E-mail:* hp@mph.org *Web Site:* www.heraldpress.com, pg 121

Quinn, Sarah, Groundwood Books, 720 Bathurst St, Suite 500, Toronto, ON M5S 2R4, Canada *Tel:* 416-537-2501 *Fax:* 416-537-4647 *E-mail:* genmail@groundwood-dm.com *Web Site:* www.groundwoodbooks.com, pg 548

Quinn, Steve, Adams Media, An F+W Publications Co, 57 Littlefield St, 2nd fl, Avon, MA 02322 *Tel:* 508-427-7100 *Fax:* 508-427-6790 *Toll Free Tel:* 800-872-5628 *E-mail:* authors@adamsmedia.com; orders@adamsmedia.com *Web Site:* www.adamsmedia.com, pg 5

Quinn, Susan, Sasquatch Books, 119 S Main, Suite 400, Seattle, WA 98104 *Tel:* 206-467-4300 *Toll Free Tel:* 800-775-0817 *Fax:* 206-467-4301 *E-mail:* books@sasquatchbooks.com *Web Site:* www.sasquatchbooks.com, pg 240

Quinn, Timothy, Liturgy Training Publications, 1800 N Hermitage Ave, Chicago, IL 60622-1101 *Tel:* 773-486-8970 *Toll Free Tel:* 800-933-1800 (US & Canada only) *Fax:* 773-486-7094 *Toll Free Fax:* 800-933-7094 (US & Canada only) *E-mail:* orders@ltp.org *Web Site:* www.ltp.org, pg 156

Quint, Paula, The Children's Book Council (CBC), 12 W 37 St, 2nd fl, New York, NY 10118-7480 *Tel:* 212-966-1990 *Toll Free Tel:* 800-999-2160 (orders only) *Fax:* 212-966-2073 *Toll Free Fax:* 888-807-9355 (orders only) *E-mail:* info@cbcbooks.org *Web Site:* www.cbcbooks.org, pg 684

Quintin, Michel, Editions Michel Quintin, PO Box 340, Waterloo, PQ J0E 2N0, Canada *Tel:* 450-539-3774 *Fax:* 450-539-4905 *E-mail:* info@michelquintin.ca, pg 559

Quinton, Linda, Tom Doherty Associates, LLC, 175 Fifth Ave, 14th fl, New York, NY 10010 *Tel:* 212-388-0100 *Toll Free Tel:* 800-455-0340 *Fax:* 212-388-0191 *E-mail:* firstname.lastname@tor.com *Web Site:* www.tor.com, pg 81

Quirk, Anne, Boston Globe-Horn Book Award, 56 Roland St, Suite 200, Boston, MA 02129 *Tel:* 617-628-0225 *Toll Free Tel:* 800-325-1170 *Fax:* 617-628-0882 *E-mail:* info@hbook.com *Web Site:* www.hbook.com, pg 763

Raines, Theron, Raines & Raines, 103 Kenyon Rd, Medusa, NY 12120 *Tel:* 518-239-8311 *Fax:* 518-239-6029, pg 650

Rainey, Alison A, G & S Editors, 410 Baylor, Austin, TX 78703-5312 *Tel:* 512-478-5341 *Fax:* 512-476-4756 *Web Site:* www.gstype.com, pg 599

Raisch, Charles A III, Short Story Award/Debut Author Award - The Blaggard Award, 101 W 23 St, Penthouse No 1, New York, NY 10011 *Tel:* 212-353-3495 *E-mail:* editorial@newmystery.tv *Web Site:* www.newmystery.tv, pg 805

Raitcheva, Raya, Prestel Publishing, 900 Broadway, Suite 603, New York, NY 10003 *Tel:* 212-995-2720 *Toll Free Tel:* 888-463-6110 (cust serv) *Fax:* 212-995-2733 *E-mail:* sales@prestel-usa.com *Web Site:* www.prestel.com, pg 218

Ramage, Ken, DBI Books, 700 E State St, Iola, WI 54990-0001 *Tel:* 715-445-2214 *Toll Free Tel:* 888-457-2873 *Fax:* 715-445-4087 *Web Site:* www.krause.com, pg 77

Ramaker, Wayne, Homestore Plans & Publications, 213 E Fourth St, Suite 400, St Paul, MN 55101 *Tel:* 651-602-5000 *Toll Free Tel:* 888-626-2026 *Fax:* 651-602-5001 *Web Site:* homeplans.com, pg 125

Ramer, Susan, Don Congdon Associates Inc, 156 Fifth Ave, Suite 625, New York, NY 10010-7002 *Tel:* 212-645-1229 *Fax:* 212-727-2688 *E-mail:* dca@doncongdon.com, pg 625

Ramey, Ardella R, Hellgate Press, 1375 Upper River Rd, Gold Hill, OR 97525 *Tel:* 541-855-5566 *Toll Free Tel:* 800-795-4059 *Fax:* 541-855-1360 *E-mail:* info@psi-research.com *Web Site:* www.psi-research.com, pg 121

Ramey, Emmett, Hellgate Press, 1375 Upper River Rd, Gold Hill, OR 97525 *Tel:* 541-855-5566 *Toll Free Tel:* 800-795-4059 *Fax:* 541-855-1360 *E-mail:* info@psi-research.com *Web Site:* www.psi-research.com, pg 121

Ramey, Missy, Fulcrum Publishing Inc, 16100 Table Mountain Pkwy, Suite 300, Golden, CO 80403 *Tel:* 303-277-1623 *Toll Free Tel:* 800-992-2908 *Fax:* 303-279-7111 *Toll Free Fax:* 800-726-7112 *E-mail:* fulcrum@fulcrum-books.com *Web Site:* www.fulcrum-books.com, pg 101

Ramirez, Virginia B, Food & Nutrition Press Inc (FNP), 6527 Main St, Trumbull, CT 06611 *Tel:* 203-261-8587 *Fax:* 203-261-9724 *E-mail:* foodpress@worldnet.att.net *Web Site:* www.foodscipress.com, pg 98

Ramos, Jose, Kirchoff/Wohlberg Inc, 866 United Nations Plaza, Suite 525, New York, NY 10017 *Tel:* 212-644-2020 *Fax:* 212-223-4387 *E-mail:* kirchwohl@aol.com *Web Site:* www.kirchoffwohlberg.com, pg 603

Ramos, Luis Arturo, University of Texas at El Paso, Dept Creative Writing, MFA with Bilingual Option, 500 W University Ave, PMB 670, El Paso, TX 79968-9991 *Tel:* 915-747-5713 *Fax:* 915-747-5523 *E-mail:* mfadirector@utep.edu *Web Site:* www.utep.edu/cw, pg 756

Ramsey, Diane, Pemmican Publications Inc, 150 Henry Ave, Winnipeg, MB R3B 0J7, Canada *Tel:* 204-589-6346 *Fax:* 204-589-2063 *E-mail:* pemmicanpublications@hotmail.com *Web Site:* www.pemmican.mb.ca, pg 557

Ramsey, Donna E, Ramsey & Ramsey, PO Box 1045, Fort Belvoir, VA 22060 *Tel:* 703-721-3630 *E-mail:* yellowspeak@yahoo.com, pg 670

Rana, Kiran S, Hunter House Publishers, 1515 1/2 Park St, Alameda, CA 94501 *Tel:* 510-865-5282 *Toll Free Tel:* 800-266-5592 *Fax:* 510-865-4295 *E-mail:* acquisitions@hunterhouse.com *Web Site:* www.hunterhouse.com/, pg 129

Rand, Bonnie, Ohio University Press, One Ohio University, Scott Quadrangle, Athens, OH 45701 *Tel:* 740-593-1155 *Toll Free Tel:* 800-621-2736 *Fax:* 740-593-4536 *Web Site:* www.ohio.edu/oupress/, pg 196

Rand, Bonnie, Swallow Press, Scott Quadrangle, Athens, OH 45701 *Tel:* 740-593-1155 *Toll Free Tel:* 800-621-2736 (orders only) *Fax:* 740-593-4536 *Toll Free Fax:* 800-621-8476 (orders only) *Web Site:* www.ohiou.edu/oupress/, pg 263

Randall, Michele E, Bibliographical Society of America, PO Box 1537, Lenox Hill Sta, New York, NY 10021-0043 *Tel:* 212-452-2710 *Fax:* 212-452-2710 *E-mail:* bsa@bibsocamer.org *Web Site:* www.bibsocamer.org, pg 681

Randall, Veronica, Ten Speed Press, PO Box 7123, Berkeley, CA 94707 *Tel:* 510-559-1600 *Toll Free Tel:* 800-841-Book *Fax:* 510-559-1629; 510-524-1052 (general) *E-mail:* order@tenspeed.com *Web Site:* www.tenspeed.com, pg 266

Randolph, Micaelia, Classroom Connect, 8000 Marina Blvd, Suite 400, Brisbane, CA 94005 *Tel:* 650-351-5100 *Toll Free Tel:* 800-638-1639 (cust support) *Fax:* 650-351-5300 *E-mail:* connect@classroom.com *Web Site:* www.classroom.com, pg 63

Randolph, Susan, Winterthur Museum, Garden & Library, Publications Division, Winterthur, DE 19735 *Tel:* 302-888-4613 *Toll Free Tel:* 800-448-3883 *Fax:* 302-888-4950 *Web Site:* www.winterthur.org, pg 301

Raney, Candace, Watson-Guptill Publications, 770 Broadway, New York, NY 10003 *Tel:* 646-654-5450 *Toll Free Tel:* 800-278-8477 (orders only) *Fax:* 646-654-5486; 646-654-5487 *E-mail:* info@watsonguptill.com *Web Site:* www.watsonguptill.com, pg 294

Rankin, Charles, The Angie Debo Prize, 1005 Asp Ave, Norman, OK 73019-6051 *Tel:* 405-325-2000 *Fax:* 405-325-4000 *Web Site:* www.oupress.com, pg 769

Rankin, Charles, University of Oklahoma Press, 4100 28 Ave NW, Norman, OK 73069-8218 *Tel:* 405-325-2000 *Toll Free Tel:* 800-627-7377 (orders) *Fax:* 405-364-5798 (orders) *Toll Free Tel:* 800-735-0476 (orders) *E-mail:* oupress@ou.edu *Web Site:* www.oupress.com, pg 284

Rankin, Jim, Dry Bones Press Inc, PO Box 597, Roseville, CA 95678 *Tel:* 916-435-8355 *Fax:* 916-435-8355 *E-mail:* drybones@drybones.com *Web Site:* www.drybones.com, pg 84

Rankin, Marcia, Florida Writers Association Conference, 10615 Limewood Dr, Jacksonville, FL 32257 *Tel:* 904-343-4188 *Toll Free Fax:* 800-536-5919 *Web Site:* www.floridawriters.net, pg 743

Rao, Rakhi, Ten Speed Press, PO Box 7123, Berkeley, CA 94707 *Tel:* 510-559-1600 *Toll Free Tel:* 800-841-Book *Fax:* 510-559-1629; 510-524-1052 (general) *E-mail:* order@tenspeed.com *Web Site:* www.tenspeed.com, pg 266

Rapisarda, Lisa, Health Professions Press, PO Box 10624, Baltimore, MD 21285-0624 *Tel:* 410-337-9585 *Toll Free Tel:* 888-337-8808 *Fax:* 410-337-8539 *E-mail:* custserv@healthpropress.com *Web Site:* www.healthpropress.com, pg 119

Rapisarda, Lisa P, Paul H Brookes Publishing Co, PO Box 10624, Baltimore, MD 21285-0624 *Tel:* 410-337-9580 *Toll Free Tel:* 800-638-3775 *Fax:* 410-337-8539 *E-mail:* custserv@brookespublishing.com *Web Site:* www.brookespublishing.com, pg 48

Rapkin, Michelle, Doubleday Broadway Publishing Group, 1745 Broadway, New York, NY 10019 *Tel:* 212-782-9000 *Toll Free Tel:* 800-223-6834; 800-223-5780 (sales) *Fax:* 212-302-7985 (correspondence); 212-492-9862 (orders), pg 82

Rapoport, Roger, R D R Books, 2415 Woolsey St, Berkeley, CA 94705 *Tel:* 510-595-0595 *Fax:* 510-228-0300 *E-mail:* info@rdrbooks.com *Web Site:* www.rdrbooks.com, pg 224

Rapp, Alan, Chronicle Books LLC, 85 Second St, 6th fl, San Francisco, CA 94105 *Tel:* 415-537-4200 *Toll Free Tel:* 800-722-6657 (cust serv) *Fax:* 415-537-4460 *Toll Free Fax:* 800-858-7787 (orders) *E-mail:* frontdesk@chroniclebooks.com *Web Site:* www.chroniclebooks.com, pg 61

Rapp, Gerald, Gerald & Cullen Rapp Inc, 420 Lexington Ave, Suite 3100, New York, NY 10170 *Tel:* 212-889-3337 *Fax:* 212-889-3341 *E-mail:* gerald@rappart.com *Web Site:* www.rappart.com, pg 666

Rapson, Judith, Stephen Leacock Memorial Award for Humour, Box 854, Orillia, ON L3V 6K8, Canada *Tel:* 705-835-3218 *Fax:* 705-835-5171 *E-mail:* moonwood@simpatico.ca *Web Site:* www.leacock.ca/awards.html, pg 784

Ras, Barbara, Trinity University Press, One Trinity Place, San Antonio, TX 78212-7200 *Tel:* 210-999-8884 *Fax:* 210-999-8838 *E-mail:* books@trinity.edu *Web Site:* www.trinity.edu/tupress, pg 275

Rashbaum, Beth, Bantam Dell Publishing Group, 1745 Broadway, New York, NY 10019 *Tel:* 212-782-9000 *Toll Free Tel:* 800-223-6834 *Fax:* 212-302-7985 *Web Site:* www.randomhouse.com/bantamdell, pg 31

Raskin, Sherman, Pace University, Master of Science in Publishing, Dept of Publishing, 551 Fifth Ave, Rm 805-E, New York, NY 10176 *Tel:* 212-346-1405 *Fax:* 212-661-8169 *Web Site:* www.pace.edu/dyson/mspub, pg 754

Raskin, Sherman, Pace University Press, 41 Park Row, Rm 1510, New York, NY 10038 *Tel:* 212-346-1405 *Fax:* 212-661-8169 *Web Site:* www.pace.edu/press, pg 201

Rasmussen, Steve, Key Curriculum Press, 1150 65 St, Emeryville, CA 94608 *Tel:* 510-595-7000 *Toll Free Tel:* 800-995-6284 *Fax:* 510-595-7040 *Toll Free Fax:* 800-541-2442 *E-mail:* customer.service@keypress.com *Web Site:* www.keypress.com, pg 145

Ratcliff, Robert, Abingdon Press, 201 Eighth Ave S, Nashville, TN 37203-3919 *Tel:* 615-749-6290 (publicist); 615-749-6000; 615-749-6451 (sales) *Toll Free Tel:* 800-251-3320 *Fax:* 615-749-6056 *Web Site:* www.abingdonpress.com, pg 3

Ratliff, Sr Madonna, Pauline Books & Media, 50 St Paul's Ave, Jamaica Plain, Boston, MA 02130 *Tel:* 617-522-8911 *Toll Free Tel:* 800-876-4463 (orders only) *Fax:* 617-541-9805 *E-mail:* businessoffice@pauline.org; orderentry@pauline.org *Web Site:* www.pauline.org, pg 205

Ratner, Elaine, Developmental Studies Center, 2000 Embarcadero, Suite 305, Oakland, CA 94606-5300 *Tel:* 510-533-0213 *Toll Free Tel:* 800-666-7270 *Fax:* 510-842-0348 *E-mail:* pubs@devstu.org *Web Site:* www.devstu.org, pg 79

Ratzlaff, Cindy, Rodale Books, 400 S Tenth St, Emmaus, PA 18098-0099 *Tel:* 610-967-5171 *Fax:* 610-967-8961 *Web Site:* www.rodale.com, pg 233

Ratzlaff, Marilyn, Rainbow Books Inc, PO Box 430, Highland City, FL 33846-0430 *Tel:* 863-648-4420 *Toll Free Tel:* 800-431-1579 (orders only); 888-613-2665 *Fax:* 863-647-5951 *E-mail:* rbibooks@aol.com *Web Site:* www.rainbowbooksinc.com, pg 225

Rau, Adam, Michael di Capua Books, 114 Fifth Ave, New York, NY 10011 *Tel:* 212-633-4400 *Fax:* 212-807-5880 *Web Site:* www.hyperionbooks.com, pg 173

Rauch, Brandon, The Greensboro Review Literary Award in Fiction & Poetry, University North Carolina at Greensboro, English Dept, McIver Bldg, Rm 134, Greensboro, NC 27402-6170 *Tel:* 336-334-5459 *Web Site:* www.uncg.edu/eng/mfa, pg 777

Rausch, Brenda, Hazelden Publishing & Educational Services, 15251 Pleasant Valley Rd, Center City, MN 55012-0176 *Tel:* 651-213-4470 *Toll Free Tel:* 800-328-9000 *Web Site:* www.hazelden.org, pg 118

Ravenscroft, Anthony, Crossquarter Publishing Group, 1910 Sombra Ct, Santa Fe, NM 87505 *Tel:* 505-438-9846 *Fax:* 505-438-9846 *E-mail:* sales@crossquarter.com; info@crossquarter.com *Web Site:* www.crossquarter.com, pg 73

Ravielli, Joanne, Home Planners LLC, 3275 W Ina Rd, Suite 220, Tucson, AZ 85741 *Tel:* 520-297-8200 *Toll Free Tel:* 800-322-6797 *Fax:* 520-297-6219 *Toll Free Fax:* 800-531-2555 *E-mail:* customerservice@eplans.com *Web Site:* www.eplans.com, pg 125

Rawle, Molly, Gestalt Journal Press, PO Box 278, Gouldsboro, ME 04607-0278 *Tel:* 845-691-7192 *Fax:* 775-254-1855 *E-mail:* tgjournal@gestalt.org *Web Site:* www.gestalt.org, pg 104

Rawlings, Wendy, University of Alabama Program in Creative Writing, PO Box 870244, Tuscaloosa, AL 35487-0244 *Tel:* 205-348-0766 *Fax:* 205-348-1388 *E-mail:* writeua@english.as.ua.edu *Web Site:* www.as. ua.edu/english, pg 755

Ray, Adrian, Excelsior Cee Publishing, 1311 Cherry Stone, Norman, OK 73072 *Tel:* 405-329-3909 *Fax:* 405-329-6886 *E-mail:* ecp@oecadvantage.net *Web Site:* www.excelsiorcee.com, pg 93

Ray, Anna, FPMI Solutions Inc, 4901 University Sq, Suite 3, Huntsville, AL 35816 *Tel:* 256-539-1850 *Fax:* 256-539-0911 *E-mail:* books@fpmi.com *Web Site:* www.fpmisolutions.com, pg 100

Ray, Barbara F, Rayve Productions Inc, PO Box 726, Windsor, CA 95492 *Tel:* 707-838-6200 *Toll Free:* 800-852-4890 *Fax:* 707-838-2220 *E-mail:* rayvepro@aol.com *Web Site:* www. rayveproductions.com; www.foodandwinebooks.com, pg 228

Ray, Bill, Technical Association of the Graphic Arts (TAGA), 68 Lomb Memorial Dr, Rochester, NY 14623-5604 *Tel:* 585-475-7470 *Fax:* 585-475-2250 *E-mail:* tagaofc@aol.com *Web Site:* www.taga.org, pg 701

Ray, Jo Anne, Canadian Centre for Studies in Publishing, Simon Fraser University at Harbour Centre, 515 W Hastings St, Vancouver, BC V6B 5K3, Canada *Tel:* 604-291-5242 *Fax:* 604-291-5239 *E-mail:* ccsp-info@sfu.ca *Web Site:* www.harbour.sfu. ca/ccsp/, pg 683

Ray, Laura, PortSort.com, 490 Rockside Rd, Cleveland, OH 44131 *Tel:* 216-661-4222 *Toll Free Tel:* 800-486-1248 *Fax:* 216-661-2879 *E-mail:* woody@portsort.com *Web Site:* www.portsort.com, pg 666

Ray, Norm, Rayve Productions Inc, PO Box 726, Windsor, CA 95492 *Tel:* 707-838-6200 *Toll Free Tel:* 800-852-4890 *Fax:* 707-838-2220 *E-mail:* rayvepro@aol.com *Web Site:* www. rayveproductions.com; www.foodandwinebooks.com, pg 228

Ray, Randy, Moment Point Press Inc, 65 Rivard Rd, Needham, MA 02492 *Tel:* 781-449-9398 *Toll Free Tel:* 800-423-7087 (orders) *Fax:* 781-449-9397 *E-mail:* info@momentpoint.com *Web Site:* www. momentpoint.com, pg 176

Ray, Susan, Moment Point Press Inc, 65 Rivard Rd, Needham, MA 02492 *Tel:* 781-449-9398 *Toll Free Tel:* 800-423-7087 (orders) *Fax:* 781-449-9397 *E-mail:* info@momentpoint.com *Web Site:* www. momentpoint.com, pg 176

Ray, Susannah, Paul H Brookes Publishing Co, PO Box 10624, Baltimore, MD 21285-0624 *Tel:* 410-337-9580 *Toll Free Tel:* 800-638-3775 *Fax:* 410-337-8539 *E-mail:* custserv@brookespublishing.com *Web Site:* www.brookespublishing.com, pg 48

Ray, Susannah, Health Professions Press, PO Box 10624, Baltimore, MD 21285-0624 *Tel:* 410-337-9585 *Toll Free Tel:* 888-337-8808 *Fax:* 410-337-8539 *E-mail:* custserv@healthpropress.com *Web Site:* www. healthpropress.com, pg 119

Ray, Terresa, Quail Ridge Press, 101 Brooks Dr, Brandon, MS 39042 *Tel:* 601-825-2063 *Toll Free Tel:* 800-343-1583 *Fax:* 601-825-3091 *E-mail:* info@ quailridge.com *Web Site:* quailridge.com, pg 223

Rayburn, Ann, Word Works Washington Prize, 7129 Alger Rd, Falls Church, VA 22042 *Fax:* 703-527-9384 *E-mail:* editor@wordworksdc.com *Web Site:* www. wordworksdc.com, pg 812

Raymond, Carl, DK Publishing Inc, 375 Hudson St, 2nd fl, New York, NY 10014-3672 *Tel:* 212-213-4800 *Toll Free Tel:* 877-342-5357 (cust serv) *Fax:* 212-213-5202 *Web Site:* www.dk.com, pg 81

Raymond, Katie, Fulcrum Publishing Inc, 16100 Table Mountain Pkwy, Suite 300, Golden, CO 80403 *Tel:* 303-277-1623 *Toll Free Tel:* 800-992-2908 *Fax:* 303-279-7111 *Toll Free Fax:* 800-726-7112 *E-mail:* fulcrum@fulcrum-books.com *Web Site:* www. fulcrum-books.com, pg 101

Raymond, Mary, Penguin Group (USA) Inc Sales, 375 Hudson St, New York, NY 10014 *Tel:* 212-366-2000 *E-mail:* online@penguinputnam.com *Web Site:* www. penguin.com, pg 208

Raz, Hilda, Virginia Faulkner Award for Excellence in Writing, University of Nebraska, 201 Andrews Hall, Lincoln, NE 68588 *Tel:* 402-472-0911 *E-mail:* kgrey2@unl.edu *Web Site:* www.unl.edu/ schooner/psmain.htm, pg 773

Raz, Hilda, Lawrence Foundation Award, University of Nebraska, 201 Andrews Hall, Lincoln, NE 68588 *Tel:* 402-472-0911 *Web Site:* www.unl.edu/schooner/ psmain.htm, pg 783

Raz, Hilda, Hugh J Luke Award, University of Nebraska, 201 Andrews Hall, Lincoln, NE 68588 *Tel:* 402-472-0911 *E-mail:* kgrey2@unl.edu *Web Site:* www.unl. edu/schooner/psmain.htm, pg 786

Raz, Hilda, Prairie Schooner Readers' Choice Awards, University of Nebraska, 201 Andrews Hall, Lincoln, NE 68588 *Tel:* 402-472-0911 *E-mail:* kgrey2@unl.edu *Web Site:* www.unl.edu/schooner/psmain.htm, pg 800

Raz, Hilda, Prairie Schooner Strousse Award, University of Nebraska, 201 Andrews Hall, Lincoln, NE 68588 *Tel:* 402-472-0911 *Fax:* 402-472-9771 *Web Site:* www. unl.edu/schooner/psmain.htm, pg 800

Raz, Hilda, Bernice Slote Award, University of Nebraska, 201 Andrews Hall, Lincoln, NE 68588 *Tel:* 402-472-0911 *E-mail:* kgrey2@unl.edu *Web Site:* www.unl.edu/schooner/psmain.htm, pg 806

Raz, Hilda, Edward Stanley Award, University of Nebraska, 201 Andrews Hall, Lincoln, NE 68588 *Tel:* 402-472-0911 *Fax:* 402-472-9771 *E-mail:* kgrey2@unl.edu *Web Site:* www.unl.edu/ schooner/psmain.htm, pg 807

Rea, Elizabeth R, The Rea Award for the Short Story, 53 W Church Hill Rd, Washington, CT 06794 *Web Site:* reaaward.org, pg 801

Reagan, Clare, Technical Association of the Pulp & Paper Industry (TAPPI), 15 Technology Pkwy S, Norcross, GA 30092 *Tel:* 770-446-1400 *Toll Free Tel:* 800-332-8686 *Fax:* 770-446-6947 *E-mail:* webmaster@tappi.org *Web Site:* www.tappi. org, pg 701

Reamer, Jodi, Writers House LLC, 21 W 26 St, New York, NY 10010 *Tel:* 212-685-2400 *Fax:* 212-685-1781, pg 662

Rebeck, Victoria, Abingdon Press, 201 Eighth Ave S, Nashville, TN 37203-3919 *Tel:* 615-749-6290 (publicist); 615-749-6000; 615-749-6451 (sales) *Toll Free Tel:* 800-251-3320 *Fax:* 615-749-6056 *Web Site:* www.abingdonpress.com, pg 3

Rebeiro, Angela, Playwrights Canada Press, 215 Spadina Ave, Sutie 230, Toronto, ON M5T 2C7, Canada *Tel:* 416-703-0013 *Fax:* 416-408-3402 *E-mail:* orders@playwrightscanada.com *Web Site:* www.playwrightscanada.com, pg 558

Reckert, Nicholas, Cambridge University Press, 40 W 20 St, New York, NY 10011-4211 *Tel:* 212-924-3900 *Toll Free Tel:* 800-899-5222 *Fax:* 212-691-3239 *Web Site:* www.cambridge.org, pg 52

Rector, Liam, Bennington Writing Seminars, One College Dr, Bennington, VT 05201 *Tel:* 802-440-4452 *Fax:* 802-440-4453 *E-mail:* writing@bennington.edu *Web Site:* www.bennington.edu/graduateprogram, pg 742

Reddig, Jill, Abingdon Press, 201 Eighth Ave S, Nashville, TN 37203-3919 *Tel:* 615-749-6290 (publicist); 615-749-6000; 615-749-6451 (sales) *Toll Free Tel:* 800-251-3320 *Fax:* 615-749-6056 *Web Site:* www.abingdonpress.com, pg 3

Redding, Cassandra, Northstone Publishing, 9025 Jim Bailey Rd, Kelowna, BC V4V 1R2, Canada *Tel:* 250-766-2778 *Toll Free Tel:* 800-299-2926 *Fax:* 250-766-2736 *Web Site:* www.joinhands.com, pg 556

Redding, Cassandra, Wood Lake Books Inc, 9025 Jim Bailey Rd, Kelowna, BC V4V 1R2, Canada *Tel:* 250-766-2778 *Toll Free Tel:* 800-663-2775 (orders)

Fax: 250-766-2736 *Toll Free Fax:* 888-841-9991 (orders) *E-mail:* info@woodlake.com *Web Site:* www. woodlakebooks.com, pg 567

Redditt, Jamie, William A Thomas Braille Bookstore, 3290 SE Slater St, Stuart, FL 34997 *Tel:* 772-286-8366 *Toll Free Tel:* 888-336-3142 *Fax:* 772-286-8909 *Web Site:* www.brailleintl.org, pg 269

Redfern, Stan, American Showcase Inc, 915 Broadway, New York, NY 10010 *Tel:* 212-673-6600 *Toll Free Tel:* 800-894-7469 *Fax:* 212-673-9795 *E-mail:* info@ amshow.com *Web Site:* www.amshow.com, pg 17

Redfern, Stanley, Harry N Abrams Inc, 100 Fifth Ave, New York, NY 10011 *Tel:* 212-206-7715 *Toll Free Tel:* 800-345-1359 *Fax:* 212-645-8437 *E-mail:* webmaster@abramsbooks.com *Web Site:* www.abramsbooks.com, pg 3

Redfield, Amy, Aio Publishing Co LLC, PO Box 30788, Charleston, SC 29417 *Tel:* 843-225-3698 *Toll Free Tel:* 888-287-9888 *Web Site:* www.aiopublishing.com, pg 7

Redford, Margie, Standard Publishing Co, 8121 Hamilton Ave, Cincinnati, OH 45231 *Tel:* 513-931-4050 *Toll Free Tel:* 800-543-1301 *Fax:* 513-931-0950 *Toll Free Fax:* 877-867-5751 *E-mail:* customerservice@standardpub.com *Web Site:* www.standardpub.com, pg 257

Rediger, Nancy, T S Eliot Prize for Poetry, 100 E Normal St, Kirksville, MO 63501-4221 *Tel:* 660-785-7336 *Toll Free Tel:* 800-916-6802 *Fax:* 660-785-4480 *E-mail:* tsup@truman.edu *Web Site:* tsup.truman.edu, pg 808

Rediger, Nancy, Truman State University Press, 100 E Normal St, Kirksville, MO 63501-4221 *Tel:* 660-785-7336 *Toll Free Tel:* 800-916-6802 *Fax:* 660-785-4480 *E-mail:* tsup@truman.edu *Web Site:* tsup.truman.edu, pg 276

Redkin, Andy, Alan Wofsy Fine Arts, 1109 Geary Blvd, San Francisco, CA 94109 *Tel:* 415-292-6500 *Fax:* 415-512-0130 (acctg); 415-292-6594 (off & cust serv) *E-mail:* beauxarts@earthlink.net (cust serv); editeur@earthlink.net (edit); order@art-books.com (orders) *Web Site:* art-books.com, pg 302

Redpath, Don, Penguin Group (USA) Inc Sales, 375 Hudson St, New York, NY 10014 *Tel:* 212-366-2000 *E-mail:* online@penguinputnam.com *Web Site:* www. penguin.com, pg 208

Reece, Jo Ann, University of Oklahoma Press, 4100 28 Ave NW, Norman, OK 73069-8218 *Tel:* 405-325-2000 *Toll Free Tel:* 800-627-7377 (orders) *Fax:* 405-364-5798 (orders) *Toll Free Fax:* 800-735-0476 (orders) *E-mail:* oupress@ou.edu *Web Site:* www.oupress.com, pg 284

Reed, Adrienne, Wales Literary Agency Inc, PO Box 9428, Seattle, WA 98109-0428 *Tel:* 206-284-7114 *Fax:* 206-322-1033 *E-mail:* waleslit@waleslit.com *Web Site:* www.waleslit.com, pg 660

Reed, Amber, Abbeville Publishing Group, 116 W 23 St, Suite 500, New York, NY 10011 *Tel:* 646-375-2039 *Toll Free Tel:* 800-ART-BOOK (278-2665) *Fax:* 646-375-2040 *E-mail:* abbeville@abbeville.com *Web Site:* www.abbeville.com, pg 2

Reed, Amber, Artabras Inc, 116 W 23 St, Suite 500, New York, NY 10011 *Tel:* 646-375-2039 *Toll Free Tel:* 800-ART-BOOK *Fax:* 646-375-2040 *E-mail:* abbeville@abbeville.com *Web Site:* www. abbeville.com, pg 24

Reed, Corp, B K Nelson Inc Lecture Bureau, 84 Woodland Rd, Pleasantville, NY 10570 *Tel:* 914-741-1322; 212-889-0637 *Fax:* 914-741-1323 *E-mail:* bknelson4@cs.com *Web Site:* www.bknelson. com, pg 670

Reed, Corp, B K Nelson Inc Literary Agency, 1565 Paseo Vida, Palm Springs, CA 92264 *Tel:* 760-778-8800 *Fax:* 914-778-0034 *E-mail:* bknelson4@cs.com *Web Site:* www.bknelson.com, pg 645

Reed, Diane B, Pennsylvania Historical & Museum Commission, Commonwealth Keystone Bldg, 400 North St, Harrisburg, PA 17120-0053 *Tel:* 717-783-2618 *Toll Free Tel:* 800-747-7790 *Fax:* 717-787-8312 *Web Site:* www.phmc.state.pa.us, pg 209

Reed, Frances, The Blackburn Press, PO Box 287, Caldwell, NJ 07006-0287 *Tel:* 973-228-7077 *Fax:* 973-228-7276 *Web Site:* www.blackburnpress. com, pg 40

Reed, Marc, Lee Allan Agency, 7464 N 107 St, Milwaukee, WI 53224-3706 *Tel:* 414-357-7708, pg 618

Reed, Rachel, The Alexander Graham Bell Association for the Deaf & Hard of Hearing, 3417 Volta Place NW, Washington, DC 20007-2778 *Tel:* 202-337-5220 *Fax:* 202-337-8314 *Web Site:* www.agbell.org, pg 8

Reed, Robert, Concourse Press, PO Box 8265, Philadelphia, PA 19101-8265 *Tel:* 610-325-0313 *Fax:* 610-359-1953, pg 66

Reed, Robert D, Robert D Reed Publishers, PO Box 1992, Brandon, OR 97411-1192 *Tel:* 541-347-9882 *Fax:* 541-347-9883 *E-mail:* 4bobreed@msn.com *Web Site:* www.rdrpublishers.com, pg 230

Reed, Ron, Nelson, 1120 Birchmount Rd, Scarborough, ON M1K 5G4, Canada *Tel:* 416-752-9448 *Toll Free Tel:* 800-268-2222 (cust serv); 800-430-4445 *Fax:* 416-752-8101 *E-mail:* inquire@nelson.com *Web Site:* www.nelson.com, pg 555

Reed, Ron, Publishers Resource Group, 307 Camp Craft Rd, Austin, TX 78746 *Tel:* 512-328-7007 *Fax:* 512-328-9480 *E-mail:* info@prgaustin.com *Web Site:* www.prgaustin.com, pg 609

Reed, Sally G, Friends of Libraries USA, 1420 Walnut St, Suite 450, Philadelphia, PA 19102-4017 *Tel:* 215-790-1674 *Toll Free Tel:* 800-936-5872 *Fax:* 215-545-3821 *E-mail:* folusa@folusa.org *Web Site:* www. folusa.org, pg 687

Reed-Morrisson, Laura, The Pennsylvania State University Press, 820 N University Dr, University Support Bldg 1, Suite C, University Park, PA 16802-1003 *Tel:* 814-865-1327 *Toll Free Tel:* 800-326-9180 *Fax:* 814-863-1408 *Toll Free Fax:* 877 7782665 *Web Site:* www.psupress.org, pg 209

Reeder-Kearns, Martha Joh, M2 Pathways Inc, PO Box 733, Bozeman, MT 59771 *Tel:* 406-582-1009 *Fax:* 406-994-0496 *E-mail:* comments@m2pathways. com *Web Site:* www.m2pathways.com, pg 572

Reehl, Jean, Rising Tide Press, 526 E 16 St, Tucson, AZ 85701 *Toll Free Tel:* 800-311-3565, pg 232

Reel, Erin, The Erin Reel Literary Agency (ERLA), 9006 Wilshire Blvd, Box 1, Beverly Hills, CA 90211 *Tel:* 818-706-3313 *Fax:* 818-706-3313 *E-mail:* erlaquery@sbcglobal.net *Web Site:* www. erinreel.com, pg 650

Reel, Fletcher, The Erin Reel Literary Agency (ERLA), 9006 Wilshire Blvd, Box 1, Beverly Hills, CA 90211 *Tel:* 818-706-3313 *Fax:* 818-706-3313 *E-mail:* erlaquery@sbcglobal.net *Web Site:* www. erinreel.com, pg 650

Rees, Helen, Helen Rees Literary Agency, 376 North St, Boston, MA 02113-2103 *Tel:* 617-227-9014 *Fax:* 617-227-8762, pg 650

Rees, Lorin, Helen Rees Literary Agency, 376 North St, Boston, MA 02113-2103 *Tel:* 617-227-9014 *Fax:* 617-227-8762, pg 650

Reese, Alan C, American Literary Press/Noble House, 8019 Belair Rd, Suite 10, Baltimore, MD 21236 *Tel:* 410-882-7700 *Fax:* 410-882-7703 *E-mail:* amerlit@americanliterarypress.com *Web Site:* www.americanliterarypress.com, pg 569

Reese, Bob, A R O Publishing Co, 398 S 1100 W, Provo, UT 84601 *Tel:* 801-377-8218 *Fax:* 801-818-0616 *E-mail:* aro@yahoo.com *Web Site:* www. aropublishing.com, pg 2

Reeves, Christian, Editions Marcel Didier Inc, 1815 Ave de Lorimier, Montreal, PQ H2K 3W6, Canada *Tel:* 514-523-1523 *Toll Free Tel:* 800-361-1664 (Canada) *Fax:* 514-523-9969 *E-mail:* hurtubisehmh@ hurtubisehmh.com *Web Site:* www.hurtubisehmh.com, pg 544

Reeves, Christian, Editions Hurtubise HMH Ltee, 1815 De Lorimier, Montreal, PQ H2K 3W6, Canada *Tel:* 514-523-1523 *Toll Free Tel:* 800-361-1664

(Canada only) *Fax:* 514-523-9969; 514-523-5955 (edit) *E-mail:* hurtubisehmh@hurtubisehmh.com *Web Site:* www.hurtubisehmh.com, pg 545

Reeves, F Dale, Standard Publishing Co, 8121 Hamilton Ave, Cincinnati, OH 45231 *Tel:* 513-931-4050 *Toll Free Tel:* 800-543-1301 *Fax:* 513-931-0950 *Toll Free Fax:* 877-867-5751 *E-mail:* customerservice@ standardpub.com *Web Site:* www.standardpub.com, pg 257

Reeves, Hilary, Milkweed Editions, 1011 Washington Ave S, Suite 300, Minneapolis, MN 55415 *Tel:* 612-332-3192 *Toll Free Tel:* 800-520-6455 *Fax:* 612-215-2550 *E-mail:* editor@milkweed.org *Web Site:* www. milkweed.org; www.worldashome.org, pg 174

Reeves, Hillary, Milkweed National Fiction Prize, 1011 Washington Ave S, Suite 300, Minneapolis, MN 55415 *Tel:* 612-332-3192 *Toll Free Tel:* 800-520-6455 *Fax:* 612-215-2550 *E-mail:* editor@milkweed.org *Web Site:* www.milkweed.org, pg 789

Reeves, Howard, Harry N Abrams Inc, 100 Fifth Ave, New York, NY 10011 *Tel:* 212-206-7715 *Toll Free Tel:* 800-345-1359 *Fax:* 212-645-8437 *E-mail:* webmaster@abramsbooks.com *Web Site:* www.abramsbooks.com, pg 3

Regan, Ann, Minnesota Historical Society Press, 345 Kellogg Blvd W, St Paul, MN 55102-1906 *Tel:* 651-296-2264 *Toll Free Tel:* 800-621-2736 *Fax:* 651-297-1345 *Toll Free Fax:* 800-621-8476 *Web Site:* www. mnhs.org/mhspress, pg 175

Regan, Clare, Technical Association of the Pulp & Paper Industry (TAPPI), 15 Technology Pkwy S, Norcross, GA 30092 *Tel:* 770-446-1400 *Toll Free Tel:* 800-332-8686 *Fax:* 770-446-6947 *E-mail:* webmaster@tappi. org *Web Site:* www.tappi.org, pg 266

Regan, Harold, H W Wilson, 950 University Ave, Bronx, NY 10452-4224 *Tel:* 718-588-8400 *Toll Free Tel:* 800-367-6770 *Fax:* 718-590-1617 *Toll Free Fax:* 800-590-1617 *E-mail:* custserv@hwwilson.com *Web Site:* www.hwwilson.com, pg 300

Regan, Monica, High Tide Press, 3650 W 183 St, Homewood, IL 60430 *Tel:* 708-206-2054 *Fax:* 708-206-2044 *Web Site:* www.hightidepress.com, pg 122

Regan, Tracy, Association for Supervision & Curriculum Development (ASCD), 1703 N Beaureguard St, Alexandria, VA 22311-1453 *Tel:* 703-578-9600 *Toll Free Tel:* 800-933-2723 *Fax:* 703-575-5400 *E-mail:* member@ascd.org *Web Site:* www.ascd.org, pg 26

Regas, Angela, Printing Association of Florida Inc, 6275 Hazeltine National Dr, Orlando, FL 32822 *Tel:* 407-240-8009 *Fax:* 407-240-8333 *Web Site:* www.pafgraf. org, pg 697

Reggio, Chris, Reader's Digest Trade Books, Reader's Digest Rd, Pleasantville, NY 10570-7000 *Tel:* 914-244-7445 *Fax:* 914-244-7605, pg 229

Regier, Willis G, University of Illinois Press, 1325 S Oak, Champaign, IL 61820-6903 *Tel:* 217-333-0950; 212-577-5487 *Fax:* 217-244-8082; 410-516-6969 (orders) *E-mail:* uipress@uillinois.edu; journals@ uillinois.edu *Web Site:* www.press.uillinois.edu, pg 282

Rehl, Beatrice, Cambridge University Press, 40 W 20 St, New York, NY 10011-4211 *Tel:* 212-924-3900 *Toll Free Tel:* 800-899-5222 *Fax:* 212-691-3239 *Web Site:* www.cambridge.org, pg 52

Rehm, Jerry, United States Holocaust Memorial Museum, 100 Raoul Wallenberg Place SW, Washington, DC 20024-2126 *Tel:* 202-488-6115; 202-488-6144 (orders) *Toll Free Tel:* 800-259-9998 (orders) *Fax:* 202-488-2684; 202-488-0438 (orders) *Web Site:* www.ushmm.org/, pg 279

Rehou, Maja, WordForce Communications, 206-264 Queen's Quay W, Toronto, ON M5J 1B5, Canada *Tel:* 416-970-6733 *Fax:* 416-260-2229 *E-mail:* info@ wordforce.ca *Web Site:* www.wordforce.ca, pg 614

Reich, Susan, Avalon Publishing Group Inc, 1400 65 St, Suite 250, Emeryville, CA 94608 *Tel:* 510-595-3664 *Fax:* 510-535-4228 *Web Site:* www.avalonpub.com, pg 28

Reicherter, Derek, Chelsea House Publishers LLC, 2080 Cabot Blvd W, Suite 201, Langhorne, PA 19047-1813 *Tel:* 610-353-5166 *Toll Free Tel:* 800-848-BOOK (848-2665) *Fax:* 610-359-1439 *Toll Free Fax:* 877-780-7300 *E-mail:* sales@chelseahouse.com *Web Site:* www.chelseahouse.com, pg 59

Reichlin, Jennifer, University of Georgia Press, 330 Research Dr, Athens, GA 30602-4901 *Tel:* 706-369-6130 *Toll Free Tel:* 800-266-5842 (orders only) *Fax:* 706-369-6131 *E-mail:* books@ugapress.uga.edu *Web Site:* www.ugapress.org, pg 281

Reichstein, Naomi, The Naomi Reichstein Literary Agency, 5031 Foothills Rd, Rm G, Lake Oswego, OR 97034 *Tel:* 503-636-7575 *Fax:* 503-636-3957, pg 650

Reid, Daniel, InterVarsity Press, 430 E Plaza Dr, Westmont, IL 60559-1234 *Tel:* 630-734-4000 *Toll Free Tel:* 800-843-7225 *Fax:* 630-734-4200 *E-mail:* mail@ ivpress.com *Web Site:* www.ivpress.com, pg 138

Reidhead, Julia, W W Norton & Company Inc, 500 Fifth Ave, New York, NY 10110-0017 *Tel:* 212-354-5500 *Toll Free Tel:* 800-233-4830 (orders & cust serv) *Fax:* 212-869-0856 *Toll Free Fax:* 800-458-6515 *Web Site:* www.wwnorton.com, pg 193

Reidy, Carolyn K, Simon & Schuster Adult Publishing Group, 1230 Avenue of the Americas, New York, NY 10020 *Tel:* 212-698-7000 *Toll Free Tel:* 800-223-2336 (orders); 800-223-2348 (cust serv), pg 248

Reidy, Carolyn K, Simon & Schuster Inc, 1230 Avenue of the Americas, New York, NY 10020 *Tel:* 212-698-7000 *Fax:* 212-698-7007 *Web Site:* www.simonsays. com, pg 249

Reighard, Jessica, Paul H Brookes Publishing Co, PO Box 10624, Baltimore, MD 21285-0624 *Tel:* 410-337-9580 *Toll Free Tel:* 800-638-3775 *Fax:* 410-337-8539 *E-mail:* custserv@brookespublishing.com *Web Site:* www.brookespublishing.com, pg 48

Reilly, Edward T, American Management Association, 1601 Broadway, New York, NY 10019-7420 *Tel:* 212-586-8100 *Toll Free Tel:* 800-262-9699 *Fax:* 212-903-8168 *Web Site:* www.amanet.org, pg 677

Reilly, Jack, Pearson Higher Education Division, One Lake St, Upper Saddle River, NJ 07458 *Tel:* 201-236-7000 *Fax:* 201-236-3381, pg 206

Reilly, Jonathan, Rutgers University Press, 100 Joyce Kilmer Ave, Piscataway, NJ 08854-8099 *Tel:* 732-445-7762 (edit); 732-445-7762 (ext 627, sales) *Toll Free Tel:* 800-446-9323 (orders only) *Fax:* 732-445-7039 (acqs, edit, mktg, perms, prodn); 732-445-1974 (fulfillment) *E-mail:* garyf@rci.rutgers.edu *Web Site:* rutgerspress.rutgers.edu, pg 236

Reilly, Julie, Standard Publishing Corp, 155 Federal St, 13th fl, Boston, MA 02110 *Tel:* 617-457-0600 *Toll Free Tel:* 800-682-5759 *Fax:* 617-457-0608 *E-mail:* info@spcpub.com *Web Site:* spcpub.com, pg 257

Reilly, T L, Emerging Playwright Award, 17 E 47 St, New York, NY 10017 *Tel:* 212-421-1380 *Fax:* 212-421-1387 *E-mail:* urbanstage@aol.com *Web Site:* www.urbanstages.org, pg 772

Reimer, John, IEEE Computer Society, 10662 Los Vaqueros Circle, Los Alamitos, CA 90720-1314 *Tel:* 714-821-8380 *Toll Free Tel:* 800-272-6657 *Fax:* 714-821-4010 *E-mail:* csbooks@computer.org *Web Site:* www.computer.org, pg 130

Rein, Jody, Jody Rein Books Inc, 7741 S Ash Ct, Centennial, CO 80122 *Tel:* 303-694-4430 *Fax:* 303-694-0687 *Web Site:* www.jodyreinbooks.com, pg 650

Reina, Randall, McGraw-Hill Learning Group, 8787 Orion Place, Columbus, OH 43240 *Tel:* 614-430-4000 *Fax:* 614-430-6621, pg 168

Reinertsen, Claire, W W Norton & Company Inc, 500 Fifth Ave, New York, NY 10110-0017 *Tel:* 212-354-5500 *Toll Free Tel:* 800-233-4830 (orders & cust serv) *Fax:* 212-869-0856 *Toll Free Fax:* 800-458-6515 *Web Site:* www.wwnorton.com, pg 193

Rex, Claudia, Association of American University Presses, 1427 E 60 St, Chicago, IL 60637 *Tel:* 773-702-7700; 773-702-7600 *Toll Free Tel:* 800-621-2736 (orders) *Fax:* 773-702-9756 (sales); 773-660-2235 (orders); 773-702-2708 *E-mail:* general@press.uchicago.edu *Web Site:* www.press.uchicago.edu, pg 26

Reyes, Christina, The National Conference for Community & Justice, 475 Park Ave S, New York City, NY 10016 *Tel:* 212-545-1300 *Fax:* 212-545-8053 *Web Site:* www.nccj.org, pg 693

Reynolds, Allan, Pearson Education Canada Inc, 26 Prince Andrew Place, Don Mills, ON M3C 2T8, Canada *Tel:* 416-447-5101 *Toll Free Tel:* 800-567-3800; 800-387-8028 *Fax:* 416-443-0948 *Toll Free Fax:* 800-263-7733; 888-465-0536 *E-mail:* firstname.lastname@pearsoned.com *Web Site:* www.pearsoned.com, pg 557

Reynolds, Carolyn, The Texas Bluebonnet Award, 3355 Bee Cave Rd, Suite 401, Austin, TX 78746 *Tel:* 512-328-1518 *Toll Free Tel:* 800-580-2852 *Fax:* 512-328-8852 *Web Site:* www.txla.org, pg 808

Reynolds, Dan, Storey Books, 210 Mass MoCA Way, North Adams, MA 01247 *Tel:* 413-346-2100 *Toll Free Tel:* 800-793-9396 *Fax:* 413-346-2253 *E-mail:* info@storey.com *Web Site:* www.storey.com, pg 260

Reynolds, Darlene, The Magni Co, 7106 Wellington Point Rd, McKinney, TX 75070 *Tel:* 972-540-2050 *Fax:* 972-540-1057 *E-mail:* sales@magnico.com; info@magnico.com *Web Site:* www.magnico.com, pg 161

Reynolds, Eric, Fantagraphics Books, 7563 Lake City Way NE, Seattle, WA 98115 *Tel:* 206-524-1967 *Toll Free Tel:* 800-657-1100 *Fax:* 206-524-2104 *E-mail:* ffbicomix@fantagraphics.com *Web Site:* www.fantagraphics.com, pg 95

Reynolds, Evan B, The Magni Co, 7106 Wellington Point Rd, McKinney, TX 75070 *Tel:* 972-540-2050 *Fax:* 972-540-1057 *E-mail:* sales@magnico.com; info@magnico.com *Web Site:* www.magnico.com, pg 161

Reynolds, Jean E, The Millbrook Press Inc, 2 Old New Milford Rd, Brookfield, CT 06804 *Tel:* 203-740-2220 *Toll Free Tel:* 800-462-4703 *Fax:* 203-740-2526, pg 174

Reynolds, Jill, The Linick Group Inc, Linick Bldg, 7 Putter Lane, Middle Island, NY 11953 *Tel:* 631-924-3888 *Fax:* 631-924-3890 *E-mail:* linickgrp@att.net *Web Site:* www.lgroup.addr.com, pg 155

Reynolds, Judy, Evergreen Pacific Publishing Ltd, 18002 15 Ave NE, Suite B, Shoreline, WA 98155-3838 *Tel:* 206-368-8157 *Fax:* 206-368-7968 *Web Site:* www.evergreenpacific.com, pg 93

Reynolds, Larry, Evergreen Pacific Publishing Ltd, 18002 15 Ave NE, Suite B, Shoreline, WA 98155-3838 *Tel:* 206-368-8157 *Fax:* 206-368-7968 *Web Site:* www.evergreenpacific.com, pg 93

Reynolds, Margaret, Association of Book Publishers of British Columbia, 100 W Pender, Suite 107, Vancouver, BC V6B 1R8, Canada *Tel:* 604-684-0228 *Fax:* 604-684-5788 *E-mail:* admin@books.bc.ca *Web Site:* www.books.bc.ca, pg 679

Reynolds, Margaret W, Linguistic Society of America, 1325 18 St NW, Suite 211, Washington, DC 20036-6501 *Tel:* 202-835-1714 *Fax:* 202-835-1717 *E-mail:* lsa@lsadc.org *Web Site:* www.lsadc.org, pg 690

Reynolds, Patrick, Louisiana State University Press, PO Box 25053, Baton Rouge, LA 70894-5053 *Tel:* 225-578-6294 *Toll Free Tel:* 800-861-3477 *Fax:* 225-578-6461 *Toll Free Fax:* 800-305-4416 *E-mail:* lsupress@lsu.edu *Web Site:* www.lsu.edu/guests/lsupress, pg 159

Reynolds, Phillip, The Invisible College Press LLC, 3703 Del Mar Dr, Woodbridge, VA 22193-0209 *Tel:* 703-590-4005 *E-mail:* sales@invispress.com *Web Site:* www.invispress.com, pg 139

Reynolds, Sara, Dutton Children's Books, 345 Hudson St, New York, NY 10014 *Tel:* 212-366-2000 *E-mail:* online@penguinputnam.com *Web Site:* www.penguin.com, pg 85

Rhetts, Paul, LPD Press, 925 Salamanca NW, Albuquerque, NM 87107-5647 *Tel:* 505-344-9382 *Fax:* 505-345-5129 *E-mail:* info@nmsantos.com *Web Site:* www.nmsantos.com, pg 159

Rhie, Gene S, Hollym International Corp, 18 Donald Place, Elizabeth, NJ 07208 *Tel:* 908-353-1655 *Fax:* 908-353-0255 *E-mail:* hollym2@optonline.net *Web Site:* www.hollym.com, pg 124

Rhind, Ian, CCH Canadian Limited, A Wolters Kluwer Company, 90 Sheppard Ave E, Suite 300, Toronto, ON M2N 6X1, Canada *Tel:* 416-224-2224 *Toll Free Tel:* 800-268-4522 (Canada & US cust serv) *Fax:* 416-224-2243 *Toll Free Fax:* 800-461-4131 *E-mail:* cservice@cch.ca (cust serv) *Web Site:* www.cch.ca, pg 539

Rhind-Tutt, Stephen, Alexander Street Press LLC, 3212 Duke St, Alexandria, VA 22314 *Tel:* 703-212-8520 *Toll Free Tel:* 800-889-5937 *Fax:* 240-465-0561 *E-mail:* sales@alexanderstreet.com *Web Site:* www.alexanderstreet.com, pg 8

Rhoden, Cheryl, Writers Guild of America Awards, 7000 W Third St, Los Angeles, CA 90048 *Tel:* 323-951-4000 *Fax:* 323-782-4802 *Web Site:* www.wga.org, pg 813

Rhoden, Cheryl, Writers Guild of America West Inc (WGAW), 7000 W Third St, Los Angeles, CA 90048 *Tel:* 323-951-4000 *Fax:* 323-782-4800 *Web Site:* www.wga.org, pg 703

Rhodes, Amy, Rodale Books, 400 S Tenth St, Emmaus, PA 18098-0099 *Tel:* 610-967-5171 *Fax:* 610-967-8961 *Web Site:* www.rodale.com, pg 233

Rhodes, David R, Pyncheon House, 6 University Dr, Suite 105, Amherst, MA 01002, pg 223

Rhodes, Frank, American Philosophical Society, 104 S Fifth St, Philadelphia, PA 19106 *Tel:* 215-440-3425 *Fax:* 215-440-3450 *Web Site:* www.amphilsoc.org, pg 16

Rhodes, Jodie, Jodie Rhodes Literary Agency, 8840 Villa La Jolla Dr, Suite 315, La Jolla, CA 92037, pg 651

Rhone, Mitzi, The Aaland Agency, PO Box 849, Inyokern, CA 93527-0849 *Tel:* 760-384-3910 *Fax:* 760-384-4435 *Web Site:* www.the-aaland-agency.com, pg 617

Ribble, Anne, Bibliographical Society of the University of Virginia, c/o Alderman Library, University of Virginia, McCormick Rd, Charlottesville, VA 22904 *Tel:* 434-924-7013 *Fax:* 434-924-1431 *E-mail:* bibsoc@virginia.edu *Web Site:* etext.lib.virginia.edu/bsuva/, pg 681

Ribesky, Mary, University of Washington Press, 1326 Fifth Ave, Suite 555, Seattle, WA 98101-2604 *Tel:* 206-543-4050; 206-543-8870 *Toll Free Tel:* 800-441-4115 (orders) *Fax:* 206-543-3932 *Toll Free Fax:* 800-669-7993 (orders) *E-mail:* uwpord@u.washington.edu *Web Site:* www.washington.edu/uwpress/, pg 286

Ricciardi, George, F A Davis Co, 1915 Arch St, Philadelphia, PA 19103 *Tel:* 215-568-2270 *Toll Free Tel:* 800-523-4049 *Fax:* 215-568-5065 *E-mail:* info@fadavis.com *Web Site:* www.fadavis.com, pg 76

Ricciato, Daniel, The New Press, 38 Greene St, 4th fl, New York, NY 10013 *Tel:* 212-629-8802 *Toll Free Tel:* 800-233-4830 (orders) *Fax:* 212-629-8617 *Toll Free Fax:* 800-458-6515 *E-mail:* newpress@thenewpress.com *Web Site:* www.thenewpress.com, pg 188

Rice, Catherine, Association of American University Presses, 1427 E 60 St, Chicago, IL 60637 *Tel:* 773-702-7700; 773-702-7600 *Toll Free Tel:* 800-621-2736 (orders) *Fax:* 773-702-9756 (sales); 773-660-2235 (orders); 773-702-2708 *E-mail:* general@press.uchicago.edu *Web Site:* www.press.uchicago.edu, pg 26

Rice, Patty, Andrews McMeel Publishing, 4520 Main St, Suite 700, Kansas City, MO 64111-7701 *Tel:* 816-932-6700 *Toll Free Tel:* 800-851-8923 *Web Site:* www.universal.com/amp, pg 169

Rice, Valentia, Penguin Group (USA) Inc Sales, 375 Hudson St, New York, NY 10014 *Tel:* 212-366-2000 *E-mail:* online@penguinputnam.com *Web Site:* www.penguin.com, pg 208

Rich, Alison, Doubleday Broadway Publishing Group, 1745 Broadway, New York, NY 10019 *Tel:* 212-782-9000 *Toll Free Tel:* 800-223-6834; 800-223-5780 (sales) *Fax:* 212-302-7985 (correspondence); 212-492-9862 (orders), pg 82

Rich, Dan, NavPress Publishing Group, 3820 N 30 St, Colorado Springs, CO 80904 *Tel:* 719-548-9222 *Toll Free Tel:* 800-366-7788 *Fax:* 719-260-7223 *Toll Free Fax:* 800-343-3902 *Web Site:* www.navpress.com, pg 185

Rich, Daniel, Book Sales Inc, 114 Northfield Ave, Edison, NJ 08837 *Tel:* 732-225-0530 *Toll Free Tel:* 800-526-7257 *Fax:* 732-225-2257 *E-mail:* sales@booksalesusa.com; customerservice@booksalesusa.com *Web Site:* www.booksalesusa.com, pg 43

Rich, Marvin, National Coalition Against Censorship (NCAC), 275 Seventh Ave, 9th fl, New York, NY 10001 *Tel:* 212-807-6222 *Fax:* 212-807-6245 *E-mail:* ncac@ncac.org *Web Site:* www.ncac.org, pg 692

Richard, Barbara, Vintage & Anchor Books, 1745 Broadway, New York, NY 10019 *Tel:* 212-751-2600 *Fax:* 212-572-6043, pg 291

Richard, David, Vital Health Publishing, 149 Old Branchville Rd, Ridgefield, CT 06877 *Tel:* 203-894-1882 *Toll Free Tel:* 877-848-2665 (orders) *Fax:* 203-894-1866 *E-mail:* info@vitalhealthbooks.com *Web Site:* www.vitalhealthbooks.com, pg 291

Richards, John, Perfection Learning Corp, 10520 New York Ave, Des Moines, IA 50322 *Tel:* 515-278-0133 *Toll Free Tel:* 800-762-2999 *Fax:* 515-278-2980 *E-mail:* orders@perfectionlearning.com *Web Site:* perfectionlearning.com, pg 210

Richards, Kent H, Society of Biblical Literature, The Luce Ctr, Suite 350, 825 Houston Mill Rd, Atlanta, GA 30329 *Tel:* 404-727-2325 *Fax:* 802-864-7626 *E-mail:* sbl@sbl-site.org *Web Site:* www.sbl-site.org, pg 251

Richards, Maggie, Henry Holt and Company, LLC, 115 W 18 St, New York, NY 10011 *Tel:* 212-886-9200 *Toll Free Tel:* 888-330-8477 (orders) *Fax:* 212-633-0748 *E-mail:* publicity@hholt.com *Web Site:* www.henryholt.com, pg 124

Richards, Robert, William H Sadlier Inc, 9 Pine St, New York, NY 10005 *Tel:* 212-227-2120 *Toll Free Tel:* 800-221-5175 *Fax:* 212-312-6080 *Web Site:* www.sadlier.com; www.sadlier-oxford.com, pg 237

Richards, Steve, Houghton Mifflin Co, 222 Berkeley St, Boston, MA 02116-3764 *Tel:* 617-351-5000 *Toll Free Tel:* 800-225-3362 (trade books); 800-733-2828 (text books); 800-225-1464 (college texts) *Fax:* 617-351-1125 *Web Site:* www.hmco.com, pg 126

Richardson, Anita, Morgan Reynolds Publishing, 620 S Elm St, Suite 223, Greensboro, NC 27406 *Tel:* 336-275-1311 *Toll Free Tel:* 800-535-1504 *Fax:* 336-275-1152 *Toll Free Fax:* 800-535-5725 *E-mail:* editorial@morganreynolds.com *Web Site:* www.morganreynolds.com, pg 178

Richardson, Anne, Yale University Press, 302 Temple St, New Haven, CT 06511 *Tel:* 203-432-0960; 401-531-2800 (cust serv) *Toll Free Tel:* 800-405-1619 (cust serv) *Fax:* 203-432-0948; 401-531-2801 (cust serv) *Toll Free Fax:* 800-406-9145 (cust serv) *E-mail:* customer.care@trilateral.org (cust serv) *Web Site:* www.yale.edu/yup/, pg 305

Richardson, Beth, Upper Room Books, 1908 Grand Ave, Nashville, TN 37212 *Toll Free Tel:* 800-972-0433 *Fax:* 615-340-7266 *Web Site:* www.upperroom.org, pg 288

Richardson, Carol, Broadview Press, 280 Perry St, Unit 5, Peterborough, ON K9J 2A8, Canada *Tel:* 705-743-8990 *Fax:* 705-743-8353 *E-mail:* customerservice@broadviewpress.com *Web Site:* www.broadviewpress.com, pg 537

Richardson, Faith, Fox Song Books, 2315 Glendale Blvd, Unit B, Los Angeles, CA 90039 *Toll Free Tel:* 888-369-2769 *Toll Free Fax:* 888-309-5063 *E-mail:* fox@foxsongbooks.com *Web Site:* foxsongbooks.com, pg 100

Richardson, Heather, The Overmountain Press, PO Box 1261, Johnson City, TN 37605-1261 *Tel:* 423-926-2691 *Toll Free Tel:* 800-992-2691 *Fax:* 423-929-2464 *Web Site:* www.overmountainpress.com, pg 200

Richardson, Herbert, The Edwin Mellen Press, 415 Ridge St, Lewiston, NY 14092 *Tel:* 716-754-2266 (mgr acqs); 716-754-8566 (mktg); 716-754-2788 (order fulfillment) *Fax:* 716-754-4056; 716-754-1860 (order fulfillment) *E-mail:* mellen@wzrd.com; cs@wzrd.com (customer service, fulfillment) *Web Site:* www.mellenpress.com, pg 171

Richardson, Julia, Simon & Schuster Children's Publishing, 1230 Avenue of the Americas, New York, NY 10020 *Tel:* 212-698-7000 *Web Site:* www.simonsayskids.com, pg 248

Richardson, Michael, Dark Horse Comics, 10956 SE Main St, Milwaukie, OR 97222 *Tel:* 503-652-8815 *Fax:* 503-654-9440 *E-mail:* dhcomics@darkhorsecomics.com *Web Site:* www.darkhorse.com, pg 76

Richardson, Norma, J Franklin Dew Award, 100 N Berwick, Williamsburg, VA 23188 *Tel:* 757-258-5582 *Web Site:* www.poetrysocietyofvirginia.org, pg 769

Richardson, Norma, Handy Andy Prize, 100 N Berwick, Williamsburg, VA 23188 *Web Site:* www.poetrysocietyofvirginia.org, pg 777

Richardson, Norma, Brodie Herndon Memorial, 100 N Berwick, Williamsburg, VA 23188 *Tel:* 757-258-5582 *Web Site:* www.poetrysocietyofvirginia.org, pg 778

Richardson, Norma, Nancy Byrd Turner Memorial, 100 N Berwick, Williamsburg, VA 23188 *Web Site:* www.poetrysocietyofvirginia.org, pg 809

Richardson, Paul E, Russian Information Service Inc, PO Box 567, Montpelier, VT 05601 *Tel:* 802-223-4955 *Fax:* 802-223-6105 *Web Site:* www.rispubs.com, pg 236

Richardson, Robyn, Benator Publishing LLC, 1240 Johnson Ferry Place, Suite C-5, Marietta, GA 30068 *Tel:* 770-977-5750 *Fax:* 770-977-8464 *E-mail:* benpubl2@bellsouth.net *Web Site:* benatorpublishing.com, pg 35

Richardson, Sally, St Martin's Press LLC, 175 Fifth Ave, New York, NY 10010 *Tel:* 212-674-5151 *Fax:* 212-420-9314 *E-mail:* firstname.lastname@stmartins.com *Web Site:* www.stmartins.com, pg 238

Richardson, Sally, St Martin's Press Paperback and Reference Group, 175 Fifth Ave, New York, NY 10010 *Fax:* 212-995-2488 *E-mail:* firstname.lastname@stmartins.com, pg 239

Richardson, Sally, St Martin's Press Trade Division, 175 Fifth Ave, New York, NY 10010 *E-mail:* firstname.lastname@stmartins.com *Web Site:* www.stmartins.com; www.minotaurbooks.com, pg 239

Richardson, Scott, Knopf Canada, One Toronto St, Suite 300, Toronto, ON M5C 2V6, Canada *Tel:* 416-364-4449 *Toll Free Tel:* 800-668-4247 (order desk) *Fax:* 416-364-0462 *Web Site:* www.randomhouse.ca, pg 552

Richardson, Vincent, Fox Song Books, 2315 Glendale Blvd, Unit B, Los Angeles, CA 90039 *Toll Free Tel:* 888-369-2769 *Toll Free Fax:* 888-309-5063 *E-mail:* fox@foxsongbooks.com *Web Site:* foxsongbooks.com, pg 100

Richason, Brad, Lerner Publishing Group, 241 First Ave N, Minneapolis, MN 55401 *Tel:* 612-332-3344 *Toll Free Tel:* 800-328-4929 *Fax:* 612-332-7615 *Toll Free Fax:* 800-332-1132 *E-mail:* info@lernerbooks.com *Web Site:* www.lernerbooks.com, pg 152

Richert, David, American Judicature Society, 2700 University Ave, Des Moines, IA 50311 *Tel:* 515-271-2281 *Fax:* 515-279-3090 *Web Site:* www.ajs.org, pg 15

Richland, Daniel, Richland Agency, 2828 Donald Douglas Loop N, Santa Monica, CA 90405 *Tel:* 310-392-1195 *Fax:* 310-392-0395, pg 651

Richman, Jordan, Writers Anonymous Inc, 1302 E Coronado Rd, Phoenix, AZ 85006 *Tel:* 602-256-2830 *Fax:* 602-256-2830 *Web Site:* writersanonymousinc.com, pg 615

Richman, Vita, Writers Anonymous Inc, 1302 E Coronado Rd, Phoenix, AZ 85006 *Tel:* 602-256-2830 *Fax:* 602-256-2830 *Web Site:* writersanonymousinc.com, pg 615

Richmond-Garza, Elizabeth, The Charles Bernheimer Prize, University of Texas, Program in Comparative Literature, One University Sta B5003, Austin, TX 78712-0196 *Tel:* 512-471-8020 *E-mail:* info@acla.org *Web Site:* www.acla.org, pg 766

Richmond-Garza, Elizabeth, Harry Levin Prize, University of Texas, Program in Comparative Literature, One University Sta B5003, Austin, TX 78712-0196 *Tel:* 512-471-8020 *E-mail:* info@acla.org *Web Site:* www.acla.org, pg 784

Richmond-Garza, Elizabeth, Rene Wellek Prize, University of Texas, Program in Comparative Literature, One University Sta B5003, Austin, TX 78712-0196 *Tel:* 512-471-8020 *E-mail:* info@acla.org *Web Site:* www.acla.org, pg 810

Richter, Bill, Nolo, 950 Parker St, Berkeley, CA 94710 *Tel:* 510-549-1976 *Fax:* 510-548-5902 *E-mail:* info@nolo.com *Web Site:* www.nolo.com, pg 191

Richter, Rich, Simon & Schuster Children's Publishing, 1230 Avenue of the Americas, New York, NY 10020 *Tel:* 212-698-7000 *Web Site:* www.simonsayskids.com, pg 248

Richter, Rick, Simon & Schuster Inc, 1230 Avenue of the Americas, New York, NY 10020 *Tel:* 212-698-7000 *Fax:* 212-698-7007 *Web Site:* www.simonsays.com, pg 249

Rickard, Joan, Author Author Literary Agency Ltd, Lougheed Mall RPO, 9855 Austin Ave, No 236, Burnaby, BC V3J 7W2, Canada *Tel:* 604-415-0056 *Web Site:* www.authorauthorliteraryagency.com, pg 619

Ricke, Margaret, Harcourt Interactive Technology, 99 Powerhouse Rd, Suite 106, Roslyn Heights, NY 11577 *Tel:* 516-625-6755 *Toll Free Tel:* 800-745-3276 *Fax:* 516-625-6789 *E-mail:* hit@harcourt.com *Web Site:* www.hit.iloli.com, pg 114

Rickman, Rebecca, Kneerim & Williams, c/o Fish & Richardson PC, 225 Franklin St, Boston, MA 02110 *Tel:* 617-542-5070 *Fax:* 617-542-8906 *Web Site:* www.fr.com, pg 638

Riconda, Margaret, LDA Publishers, 42-46 209 St, Bayside, NY 11361-2747 *Tel:* 718-224-9484 *Toll Free Tel:* 888-388-9887 *Fax:* 718-224-9487 *Web Site:* www.ldapublishers.com, pg 150

Ridder, Myles, Catholic News Publishing Co Inc, 210 North Ave, New Rochelle, NY 10801 *Tel:* 914-632-7771 *Toll Free Tel:* 800-433-7771 *Fax:* 914-632-3412 *Web Site:* www.graduateguide.com, pg 55

Riddle, Karen, University of South Carolina Press, 1600 Hampton St, 5th fl, Columbia, SC 29208 *Tel:* 803-777-5243 *Toll Free Tel:* 800-768-2500 (orders) *Fax:* 803-777-0160 *Toll Free Fax:* 800-868-0740 (orders) *Web Site:* www.sc.edu/uscpress/, pg 285

Ridker, Norman, BowTie Press, 3 Burroughs, Irvine, CA 92618 *Tel:* 949-855-8822 *Toll Free Tel:* 800-426-2516 *Fax:* 949-458-3856 *Web Site:* www.bowtiepress.com, pg 45

Rieck, Donald, Penguin Group (USA) Inc Sales, 375 Hudson St, New York, NY 10014 *Tel:* 212-366-2000 *E-mail:* online@penguinputnam.com *Web Site:* www.penguin.com, pg 208

Riegel, Joan, The Analytic Press, 101 West St, Hillsdale, NJ 07642 *Tel:* 201-358-9477; 201-236-9500 *Toll Free Tel:* 800-926-6579 (orders only); 800-627-0629 (journal orders) *Fax:* 201-358-4700 (edit); 201-760-3735 (orders only) *E-mail:* tap@analyticpress.com *Web Site:* www.analyticpress.com, pg 19

Riegert, Ray, Ulysses Press, PO Box 3440, Berkeley, CA 94703-0440 *Tel:* 510-601-8301 *Toll Free Tel:* 800-377-2542 *Fax:* 510-601-8307 *E-mail:* ulysses@ulyssespress.com *Web Site:* www.ulyssespress.com, pg 278

Rienner, Lynne, Lynne Rienner Publishers Inc, 1800 30 St, Suite 314, Boulder, CO 80301 *Tel:* 303-444-6684 *Fax:* 303-444-0824 *E-mail:* cservice@rienner.com *Web Site:* www.rienner.com, pg 232

Riensche, Rachel, Augsburg Fortress Publishers, Publishing House of the Evangelical Lutheran Church in America, 100 S Fifth St, Suite 700, Minneapolis, MN 55402 *Tel:* 612-330-3300 *Toll Free Tel:* 800-426-0115 (ext 639 subns); 800-328-4648 (orders); 800-421-0239 (perms) *Fax:* 612-330-3455 *Toll Free Fax:* 800-421-0239 (perms & copyrights) *E-mail:* customerservice@augsburgfortress.org; copyright@augsburgfortress.org (for reprint permission requests) *Web Site:* www.augsburgfortress.org, pg 28

Rieth, Kerry, Cebulash Associates, 10245 E Via Linda Ave, Suite 221, Scottsdale, AZ 85258 *Tel:* 480-451-8400 *Fax:* 480-451-0848 *E-mail:* cebulash@att.net, pg 594

Rife, Douglas M, Corwin Press, 2455 Teller Rd, Thousand Oaks, CA 91320 *Tel:* 805-499-9734 *Fax:* 805-499-5323 *Toll Free Fax:* 800-417-2466 *E-mail:* info@corwinpress.com *Web Site:* www.corwinpress.com, pg 69

Rifenberick, Adam, Sleeping Bear Press™, 310 N Main St, Suite 300, Chelsea, MI 48118 *Tel:* 734-475-4411 *Toll Free Tel:* 800-487-2323 *Fax:* 734-475-0787 *E-mail:* sleepingbear@thomson.com *Web Site:* www.sleepingbearpress.com, pg 250

Rifkin, Josh, Pomegranate Communications, 775-A Southpoint Blvd, Petaluma, CA 94954-1495 *Tel:* 707-782-9000 *Toll Free Tel:* 800-227-1428 *Toll Free Fax:* 800-848-4376 *Web Site:* www.pomegranate.com, pg 216

Rigas, Maia, Association of American University Presses, 1427 E 60 St, Chicago, IL 60637 *Tel:* 773-702-7700; 773-702-7600 *Toll Free Tel:* 800-621-2736 (orders) *Fax:* 773-702-9756 (sales); 773-660-2235 (orders); 773-702-2708 *E-mail:* general@press.uchicago.edu *Web Site:* www.press.uchicago.edu, pg 26

Rigg, Michael, Paladin Press, 7077 Winchester Circle, Boulder, CO 80301 *Tel:* 303-443-7250 *Toll Free Tel:* 800-392-2400 *Fax:* 303-442-8741 *E-mail:* service@paladin-press.com *Web Site:* www.paladin-press.com, pg 202

Riggle, Lynn, Tropical Press Inc, PO Box 161174, Miami, FL 33116-1174 *Tel:* 305-971-1887 *Fax:* 305-378-1595 *E-mail:* tropicbook@aol.com *Web Site:* www.tropicalpress.com, pg 276

Riggs, Rollin A, Mustang Publishing Co Inc, PO Box 770426, Memphis, TN 38177-0426 *Tel:* 901-684-1200 *Toll Free Tel:* 800-250-8713 *Fax:* 901-684-1256 *E-mail:* info@mustangpublishing.com *Web Site:* www.mustangpublishing.com, pg 181

Rihel, Bethany Coffey, Huntington Press Publishing, 3687 S Procyon Ave, Las Vegas, NV 89103 *Tel:* 702-252-0655 *Toll Free Tel:* 800-244-2224 *Fax:* 702-252-0675 *E-mail:* books@huntingtonpress.com *Web Site:* www.huntingtonpress.com, pg 129

Riker, Edie, East End Publishing Services Inc, 916 Sound Shore Rd, Riverhead, NY 11901 *Tel:* 631-722-3921 *Fax:* 631-722-3921, pg 597

Rikhoff, James C, The Amwell Press, Ridge Plaza, 2004 Rte 31 & Cregar Rd, Clinton, NJ 08809 *Tel:* 908-638-9033 *Fax:* 908-638-4728, pg 19

Riley, Elizabeth, W W Norton & Company Inc, 500 Fifth Ave, New York, NY 10110-0017 *Tel:* 212-354-5500 *Toll Free Tel:* 800-233-4830 (orders & cust serv) *Fax:* 212-869-0856 *Toll Free Fax:* 800-458-6515 *Web Site:* www.wwnorton.com, pg 193

Riley, Erika, Warner Books, 1271 Avenue of the Americas, New York, NY 10020 *Tel:* 212-522-7200 *Fax:* 212-522-7991 *Web Site:* www.twbookmark.com, pg 293

Riley, Jocelyn, Her Own Words, PO Box 5264, Madison, WI 53705-0264 *Tel:* 608-271-7083 *Fax:* 608-271-0209 *E-mail:* herownword@aol.com *Web Site:* www.herownwords.com, pg 121

Riley, Joe, Liturgical Press, St John's Abbey, Collegeville, MN 56321 *Tel:* 320-363-2213 *Toll Free Tel:* 800-858-5450 *Fax:* 320-363-3299 *Toll Free Fax:* 800-445-5899 *E-mail:* sales@litpress.org *Web Site:* www.litpress.org, pg 156

Riley, John, Morgan Reynolds Publishing, 620 S Elm St, Suite 223, Greensboro, NC 27406 *Tel:* 336-275-1311 *Toll Free Tel:* 800-535-1504 *Fax:* 336-275-1152 *Toll Free Fax:* 800-535-5725 *E-mail:* editorial@morganreynolds.com *Web Site:* www.morganreynolds.com, pg 178

Rimel, John, Mountain Press Publishing Co, 1301 S Third W, Missoula, MT 59801 *Tel:* 406-728-1900 *Toll Free Tel:* 800-234-5308 *Fax:* 406-728-1635 *E-mail:* info@mtnpress.com *Web Site:* www.mountain-press.com, pg 179

Rinaldi, Angela, The Angela Rinaldi Literary Agency, PO Box 7877, Beverly Hills, CA 90212-7877 *Tel:* 310-842-7665 *Fax:* 310-837-8143, pg 651

Rinck, Gary, John Wiley & Sons Inc, 111 River St, Hoboken, NJ 07030 *Tel:* 201-748-6000 *Toll Free Tel:* 800-225-5945 (cust serv) *Fax:* 201-748-6088 *E-mail:* info@wiley.com *Web Site:* www.wiley.com, pg 299

Rinehart, Rick, Cooper Square Press, 5360 Manhattan Circle, Suite 101, Boulder, CO 80303 *Tel:* 303-543-7835 *Fax:* 303-543-0043 *E-mail:* tradeeditorial@rowman.com *Web Site:* www.coopersquarepress.com, pg 68

Rinehart, Rick, Publishers Association of the West, PO Box 18157, Denver, CO 80218 *Tel:* 303-447-2320 *Fax:* 303-279-7111 *E-mail:* executivedirector@pubwest.org *Web Site:* www.pubwest.org, pg 698

Rinehart, Rick, Western US Book Design & Production Awards, 501 S Cherry St, Suite 320, Denver, CO 80246 *Tel:* 303-447-2320 *Fax:* 303-279-7111 *E-mail:* executivedirector@pubwest.org *Web Site:* www.pubwest.org, pg 811

Ringel, Jonathan, ICC Publishing Inc, 156 Fifth Ave, Suite 417, New York, NY 10010 *Tel:* 212-206-1150 *Fax:* 212-633-6025 *E-mail:* info@iccpub.net *Web Site:* www.iccbooksusa.com, pg 130

Ringer, Nancy, Basic Health Publications Inc, 8200 Boulevard E, Suite 25-G, North Bergen, NJ 07047 *Tel:* 201-868-8336 *Toll Free Tel:* 800-575-8890 *Fax:* 201-868-8335, pg 33

Ringer, Paul, Simba Information, 60 Long Ridge Rd, Suite 300, Stamford, CT 06902 *Tel:* 203-325-8193 *Fax:* 203-325-8915 *E-mail:* info@simbanet.com *Web Site:* www.simbanet.com, pg 248

Ringold, Francine PhD, The Pablo Neruda Prize for Poetry, Nimrod Intl Journal, University of Tulsa, 600 S College, Tulsa, OK 74104 *Tel:* 918-631-3080 *Fax:* 918-631-3033 *E-mail:* nimrod@utulsa.edu *Web Site:* www.utulsa.edu/nimrod, pg 793

Ringold, Francine PhD, Katherine Anne Porter Prize for Fiction, University of Tulsa, 600 S College, Tulsa, OK 74104 *Tel:* 918-631-3080 *Fax:* 918-631-3033 *E-mail:* nimrod@utulsa.edu *Web Site:* www.utulsa.edu/nimrod, pg 799

Rinker, Lowell, Cistercian Publications Inc, Editorial Office, WMU, 1903 W Michigan Ave, Kalamazoo, MI 49008 *Tel:* 269-387-8920 *Fax:* 269-387-8390 *E-mail:* cistpub@wmich.edu *Web Site:* www.spencerabbey.org/cistpub, pg 62

Ripianzi, David, YMAA Publication Center, 4354 Washington St, Roslindale, MA 02131 *Tel:* 617-323-7215 *Toll Free Tel:* 800-669-8892 *Fax:* 617-323-7417 *E-mail:* ymaa@aol.com *Web Site:* www.ymaa.com, pg 306

Rippeteau, Erika Kuebler, University of Nebraska Press, 233 N Eighth St, Lincoln, NE 68588-0255 *Tel:* 402-472-3581 *Toll Free Tel:* 800-755-1105 (orders)

Fax: 402-472-0308 *Toll Free Fax:* 800-526-2617 *E-mail:* press@un1.edu *Web Site:* www.nebraskapress.unl.edu; www.bisonbooks.com, pg 283

Rippin, Allyn, Thames & Hudson, 500 Fifth Ave, New York, NY 10110 *Tel:* 212-354-3763 *Toll Free Tel:* 800-233-4830 *Fax:* 212-398-1252 *E-mail:* bookinfo@thames.wwnorton.com *Web Site:* www.thamesandhudsonusa.com, pg 268

Rippon, Laurie, HarperCollins General Books Group, 10 E 53 St, New York, NY 10022 *Tel:* 212-207-7000 *Fax:* 212-207-7633, pg 115

Ritchie, Adele, Canadian Newspaper Association, 890 Yonge St, Suite 200, Toronto, ON M4W 3P4, Canada *Tel:* 416-923-3567 *Fax:* 416-923-7206 *Web Site:* www.cna-acj.ca, pg 683

Ritchie, Charles, Leading Edge Reports, 2171 Jericho Tpke, Suite 200, Commack, NY 11725 *Tel:* 631-462-5454 *Toll Free Tel:* 800-866-4648 *Fax:* 631-462-1842 *E-mail:* sales@bta-ler.net *Web Site:* www.bta-ler.com, pg 151

Ritchie, Marcelyn, The University of Utah Press, 1795 E South Campus Dr, Rm 101, Salt Lake City, UT 84112-9402 *Tel:* 801-581-6671 *Toll Free Tel:* 800-773-6672 *Fax:* 801-581-3365 *E-mail:* info@upress.utah.edu *Web Site:* www.uofupress.com, pg 285

Ritt, Judith W, Professional Resource Exchange Inc, 1891 Apex Rd, Sarasota, FL 34240 *Tel:* 941-343-9601 *Toll Free Tel:* 800-443-3364 *Fax:* 941-343-9201 *Web Site:* www.prpress.com, pg 220

Ritt, Lawrence G, Professional Resource Exchange Inc, 1891 Apex Rd, Sarasota, FL 34240 *Tel:* 941-343-9601 *Toll Free Tel:* 800-443-3364 *Fax:* 941-343-9201 *Web Site:* www.prpress.com, pg 220

Rittenberg, Ann, Association of Authors' Representatives Inc (AAR), PO Box 237201, Ansonia Sta, New York, NY 10023 *E-mail:* aarinc@mindspring.com *Web Site:* www.aar-online.org, pg 679

Rittenberg, Ann, Ann Rittenberg Literary Agency Inc, 1201 Broadway, Suite 708, New York, NY 10001 *Tel:* 212-684-6936 *Fax:* 212-684-6929 *Web Site:* www.rittlit.com, pg 651

Ritter, David, Stackpole Books, 5067 Ritter Rd, Mechanicsburg, PA 17055 *Tel:* 717-796-0411 *Toll Free Tel:* 800-732-3669 *Fax:* 717-796-0412 *Web Site:* www.stackpolebooks.com, pg 257

Ritter, Richard G, Gryphon Editions, 515 Madison Ave, Suite 3200, New York, NY 10022 *Tel:* 212-750-1048 *Toll Free Tel:* 800-633-8911 *Fax:* 212-644-6828 *E-mail:* gryphonnyc@aol.com *Web Site:* www.gryphoneditions.com, pg 110

Rivellese, Richard L, W W Norton & Company Inc, 500 Fifth Ave, New York, NY 10110-0017 *Tel:* 212-354-5500 *Toll Free Tel:* 800-233-4830 (orders & cust serv) *Fax:* 212-869-0856 *Toll Free Fax:* 800-458-6515 *Web Site:* www.wwnorton.com, pg 193

Rivelli, Cynthia, Allworth Press, 10 E 23 St, Suite 510, New York, NY 10010 *Tel:* 212-777-8395 *Toll Free Tel:* 800-491-2808 *Fax:* 212-777-8261 *E-mail:* pub@allworth.com *Web Site:* www.allworth.com, pg 9

Riven, Judith, Judith Riven Editorial Consultant, 250 W 16 St, Suite 4F, New York, NY 10011 *Tel:* 212-255-1009 *Fax:* 212-255-8547 *E-mail:* rivenlit@att.net, pg 610

Riven, Judith, Judith Riven Literary Agent/Editorial Consultant, 250 W 16 St, Suite 4F, New York, NY 10011 *Tel:* 212-255-1009 *Fax:* 212-255-8547 *E-mail:* rivenlit@att.net, pg 652

Rivera, Carmen, Lectorum Publications Inc, 524 Broadway, New York, NY 10012 *Toll Free Tel:* 800-853-3291 (admin, mktg & sales); 800-345-5946 (orders) *Fax:* 212-727-3035 *Toll Free Fax:* 877-532-8676 *E-mail:* lectorum@scholastic.com *Web Site:* www.lectorum.com, pg 151

Rivera Rodriguez, Michelle, Neal-Schuman Publishers Inc, 100 William St, Suite 2004, New York, NY 10038 *Tel:* 212-925-8650 *Fax:* 866-672-6657

Toll Free Fax: 866-209-7932 *E-mail:* orders@neal-schuman.com *Web Site:* www.neal-schuman.com, pg 186

Rivers, Alison, ABC-CLIO, 130 Cremona Dr, Santa Barbara, CA 93117 *Tel:* 805-968-1911 *Toll Free Tel:* 800-368-6868 *Fax:* 805-685-9685 *E-mail:* sales@abc-clio.com *Web Site:* www.abc-clio.com, pg 3

Rivkin, Charles, Jim Henson Publishing/Muppet Press, 117 E 69 St, New York, NY 10021 *Tel:* 212-794-2400 *Fax:* 212-794-5157 *Web Site:* www.henson.com, pg 141

Rivlin, Elisa, Simon & Schuster Inc, 1230 Avenue of the Americas, New York, NY 10020 *Tel:* 212-698-7000 *Fax:* 212-698-7007 *Web Site:* www.simonsays.com, pg 249

Rizzi, Judi, The Apex Press, 777 United Nations Plaza, Suite 3-C, New York, NY 10017 *Tel:* 914-271-6500 *Toll Free Tel:* 800-316-2739 *Fax:* 914-271-6500 *Toll Free Fax:* 800-316-2739 *E-mail:* cipany@igc.org *Web Site:* www.cipa-apex.org, pg 21

Rizzo, Heather, Little, Brown and Company Adult Trade Division, 1271 Avenue of the Americas, New York, NY 10020 *Tel:* 212-522-8700 *Fax:* 212-522-2067 *Web Site:* www.twbookmark.com, pg 156

Rizzo, Joel, Writers' Haven Writers (WHW), 2244 Fourth Ave, San Diego, CA 92101 *Tel:* 619-696-0569, pg 703

Rizzo, Kate, Robbins Office Inc, 405 Park Ave, 9th fl, New York, NY 10022 *Tel:* 212-223-0720 *Fax:* 212-223-2535, pg 652

Roach, Brian, Brunner-Routledge, 270 Madison Ave, New York, NY 10016 *Tel:* 212-216-7800 *Toll Free Tel:* 800-634-7064 (orders); 800-797-3803 *Fax:* 212-643-1430, pg 49

Robbins, B J, B J Robbins Literary Agency, 5130 Bellaire Ave, North Hollywood, CA 91607 *Tel:* 818-760-6602 *Fax:* 818-760-6616 *E-mail:* robbinsliterary@aol.com, pg 652

Robbins, Betsy, International Creative Management, 40 W 57 St, New York, NY 10019 *Tel:* 212-556-5600 *Fax:* 212-556-5665 *Web Site:* www.icmtalent.com, pg 635

Robbins, Caroline, Trafalgar Square, Howe Hill Rd, North Pomfret, VT 05053 *Tel:* 802-457-1911 *Toll Free Tel:* 800-423-4525 *Fax:* 802-457-1913 *E-mail:* tsquare@sover.net *Web Site:* www.trafalgarsquarebooks.com, pg 273

Robbins, Christopher, Gibbs Smith Publisher, 1877 E Gentile, Layton, UT 84040 *Tel:* 801-544-9800 *Toll Free Tel:* 800-748-5439 (orders only) *Fax:* 801-544-5582 *Toll Free Fax:* 800-213-3023 (orders only) *E-mail:* info@gibbs-smith.com *Web Site:* www.gibbs-smith.com, pg 104

Robbins, Dr John, The Trinity Foundation, PO Box 68, Unicoi, TN 37692-0068 *Tel:* 423-743-0199 *Fax:* 423-743-2005 *Web Site:* www.trinityfoundation.org, pg 275

Robbins, Kathy P, Robbins Office Inc, 405 Park Ave, 9th fl, New York, NY 10022 *Tel:* 212-223-0720 *Fax:* 212-223-2535, pg 652

Robelet, Michelle, Scott Jones Inc, PO Box 696, El Granada, CA 94018 *Tel:* 650-726-2436 *Fax:* 650-726-4693 *Web Site:* www.scottjonespub.com, pg 243

Roberson, Nancy K, Thomson Delmar Learning, 5 Maxwell Dr, Clifton Park, NY 12065-8007 *Tel:* 518-464-3500 *Toll Free Tel:* 800-347-7707 (cust serv); 800-998-7498 *Fax:* 518-464-0393 *Toll Free Fax:* 800-487-8488 (cust serv) *Web Site:* www.thomson.com; www.delmarlearning.com, pg 269

Roberts, Claire, Doubleday Broadway Publishing Group, 1745 Broadway, New York, NY 10019 *Tel:* 212-782-9000 *Toll Free Tel:* 800-223-6834; 800-223-5780 (sales) *Fax:* 212-302-7985 (correspondence); 212-492-9862 (orders), pg 82

Roberts, Gebrina, Allworth Press, 10 E 23 St, Suite 510, New York, NY 10010 *Tel:* 212-777-8395 *Toll Free Tel:* 800-491-2808 *Fax:* 212-777-8261 *E-mail:* pub@allworth.com *Web Site:* www.allworth.com, pg 9

Roberts, Jane F, Literary & Creative Artists Inc, 3543 Albemarle St NW, Washington, DC 20008-4213 *Tel:* 202-362-4688 *Fax:* 202-362-8875 *E-mail:* query@lcadc.com (no attachments) *Web Site:* www.lcadc.com, pg 641

Roberts, Nancy, Prentice Hall Humanities & Social Sciences, One Lake St, Upper Saddle River, NJ 07458 *Tel:* 201-236-7000, pg 217

Roberts, Nicole, Piano Press, 1425 Ocean Ave, Suite 6, Del Mar, CA 92014 *Tel:* 619-884-1401 *Fax:* 858-459-3376 *E-mail:* pianopress@aol.com *Web Site:* www.pianopress.com, pg 212

Roberts, Ray, Viking, 375 Hudson St, New York, NY 10014 *Tel:* 212-366-2000 *E-mail:* online@penguinputnam.com *Web Site:* www.penguin.com, pg 290

Roberts, Sherry, The Roberts Group, 1530 Thomas Lake Pointe Rd, No 119, Eagan, MN 55122 *Tel:* 651-330-1457 *Fax:* 651-330-0892 *E-mail:* info@editorialservice.com *Web Site:* www.editorialservice.com, pg 610

Roberts, Tony, The Roberts Group, 1530 Thomas Lake Pointe Rd, No 119, Eagan, MN 55122 *Tel:* 651-330-1457 *Fax:* 651-330-0892 *E-mail:* info@editorialservice.com *Web Site:* www.editorialservice.com, pg 610

Roberts, Tony, University of Oklahoma Press, 4100 28 Ave NW, Norman, OK 73069-8218 *Tel:* 405-325-2000 *Toll Free Tel:* 800-627-7377 (orders) *Fax:* 405-364-5798 (orders) *Toll Free Fax:* 800-735-0476 (orders) *E-mail:* oupress@ou.edu *Web Site:* www.oupress.com, pg 284

Robertson, Bruce, University Publishing House, PO Box 1664, Mannford, OK 74044 *Tel:* 918-865-4726 *Fax:* 918-865-4726 *E-mail:* upub2@juno.com *Web Site:* www.universitypublishinghouse.com, pg 288

Robertson, Michael, Digital Printing & Imaging Association, 10015 Main St, Fairfax, VA 22031-3489 *Tel:* 703-385-1339 *Toll Free Tel:* 888-385-3588 *Fax:* 703-273-0456 *E-mail:* dpi@dpia.org *Web Site:* www.dpia.org, pg 686

Robertson, Mike, Screen Printing Technical Foundation, 10015 Main St, Fairfax, VA 22031-3489 *Tel:* 703-385-1335 *Fax:* 703-273-0456 *E-mail:* sgia@sgia.org *Web Site:* www.sgia.org, pg 699

Robertson, Tom, Basile Festival of Emerging American Theatre (FEAT), 749 N Park Ave, Indianapolis, IN 46202 *Tel:* 317-635-7529 *Fax:* 317-635-0010 *E-mail:* info@phoenixtheatre.org *Web Site:* www.phoenixtheatre.org, pg 761

Robey, Annelise, Jane Rotrosen Agency LLC, 318 E 51 St, New York, NY 10022 *Tel:* 212-593-4330 *Fax:* 212-935-6985, pg 653

Robie, David A, BigScore Productions, PO Box 4575, Lancaster, PA 17604 *Tel:* 717-293-0247 *Fax:* 717-293-1945 *E-mail:* bigscore@bigscoreproductions.com *Web Site:* www.bigscoreproductions.com, pg 621

Robillard, Scott, Legal Education Publishing, 5302 Eastpark Blvd, Madison, WI 53718 *Toll Free Tel:* 800-957-4670 *Fax:* 608-257-5502 *E-mail:* service@wisbar.org *Web Site:* www.wisbar.org, pg 152

Robinson, Carol M, Unarius Academy of Science Publications, 145 S Magnolia Ave, El Cajon, CA 92020-4522 *Tel:* 619-444-7062 *Toll Free Tel:* 800-475-7062 *Fax:* 619-447-9637 *E-mail:* uriel@unarius.org *Web Site:* www.unarius.org, pg 278

Robinson, Colin, The New Press, 38 Greene St, 4th fl, New York, NY 10013 *Tel:* 212-629-8802 *Toll Free Tel:* 800-233-4830 (orders) *Tel:* 212-629-8617 *Toll Free Fax:* 800-458-6515 *E-mail:* newpress@thenewpress.com *Web Site:* www.thenewpress.com, pg 188

Robinson, Esther, Tom Doherty Associates, LLC, 175 Fifth Ave, 14th fl, New York, NY 10010 *Tel:* 212-388-0100 *Toll Free Tel:* 800-455-0340 *Fax:* 212-388-0191 *E-mail:* firstname.lastname@tor.com *Web Site:* www.tor.com, pg 82

Robinson, Esther, St Martin's Press LLC, 175 Fifth Ave, New York, NY 10010 *Tel:* 212-674-5151 *Fax:* 212-420-9314 *E-mail:* firstname.lastname@stmartins.com *Web Site:* www.stmartins.com, pg 239

Robinson, Jim, Harlequin Enterprises Ltd, 225 Duncan Mill Rd, Don Mills, ON M3B 3K9, Canada *Tel:* 416-445-5860 *Fax:* 416-445-8655 *Web Site:* www.eharlequin.com; www.luna-books.com; www.mirabooks.com; www.reddressink.com; www.steeplehill.com, pg 549

Robinson, Joe, EEI Communications, 66 Canal Center Plaza, Suite 200, Alexandria, VA 22314-5507 *Tel:* 703-683-7453 *Fax:* 703-683-7310 *E-mail:* train@eeicom.com *Web Site:* www.eeicommunications.com, pg 752

Robinson, Julie, Teacher's Discovery, 2741 Paldan Dr, Auburn Hills, MI 48326 *Tel:* 248-340-7220 ext 207 *Toll Free Tel:* 800-521-3897 *Fax:* 248-340-7212 *Toll Free Fax:* 888-987-2436 *Web Site:* www.teachersdiscovery.com, pg 265

Robinson, Kim, Oxford University Press, Inc, 198 Madison Ave, New York, NY 10016-4314 *Tel:* 212-726-6000 *Toll Free Tel:* 800-451-7556 (orders) *Web Site:* www.oup.com/us, pg 200

Robinson, Marian, The Guilford Press, 72 Spring St, New York, NY 10012 *Tel:* 212-431-9800 *Toll Free Tel:* 800-365-7006 (orders) *Fax:* 212-966-6708 *E-mail:* orders@guilford.com *Web Site:* www.guilford.com, pg 111

Robinson, Marileta, Highlights for Children Fiction Contest, 803 Church St, Honesdale, PA 18431 *Tel:* 570-253-1080 *Fax:* 570-251-7847 *E-mail:* eds@highlights-corp.com *Web Site:* www.highlights.com, pg 778

Robinson, Matt, League of Canadian Poets, 920 Yonge St, Suite 608, Toronto, ON M4W 3C7, Canada *Tel:* 416-504-1657 *Fax:* 416-504-0096 *E-mail:* info@poets.ca *Web Site:* www.poets.ca, pg 689

Robinson, Richard, Scholastic Inc, 557 Broadway, New York, NY 10012 *Tel:* 212-343-4469 *Toll Free Tel:* 800-scholastic *Fax:* 212-343-6930 *Web Site:* www.scholastic.com, pg 241

Robinson, Rose, University of California Press, 2120 Berkeley Way, Berkeley, CA 94720 *Tel:* 510-642-4247 *Toll Free Tel:* 800-777-4726 *Fax:* 510-643-7127 *Toll Free Fax:* 800-999-1958 *E-mail:* askucp@ucpress.edu *Web Site:* www.ucpress.edu, pg 281

Robitaille, Diane, New England Poetry Club, 2 Farrar St, Cambridge, MA 02138 *Tel:* 781-643-0029, pg 695

Robitz, Kathie, Creative Homeowner, 24 Park Way, Upper Saddle River, NJ 07458-9960 *Tel:* 201-934-7100 *Toll Free Tel:* 800-631-7795 *Fax:* 201-934-8971 *E-mail:* info@creativehomeowner.com *Web Site:* www.creativehomeowner.com, pg 72

Robson, Brian, Canadian Publishers' Council (CPC), 250 Merton St, Suite 203, Toronto, ON M4S 1B1, Canada *Tel:* 416-322-7011 *Fax:* 416-322-6999 *E-mail:* pubadmin@pubcouncil.ca *Web Site:* www.pubcouncil.ca, pg 684

Roche, Mary Beth, Audio Renaissance, 175 Fifth Ave, New York, NY 10010 *Tel:* 212-674-5151 *Toll Free Tel:* 888-330-8477 (cust serv) *Fax:* 917-534-0980 *E-mail:* firstname.lastname@hbpub.com *Web Site:* www.audiorenaissance.com, pg 27

Roche, Michael, South-Western, A Thomson Business, 5191 Natorp Blvd, Mason, OH 45040 *Tel:* 513-229-1000 *Toll Free Tel:* 800-543-0487 *Fax:* 513-229-1025 *Web Site:* www.thomson.com, pg 254

Roche, Tom, The Bookbinders' Guild of New York, Dunn & Co, 110 Grand Ave, Ridgefield Park, NJ 07660 *Tel:* 201-229-1888 *Fax:* 201-229-1755 *Web Site:* www.bookbindersguild.org, pg 682

Rochman, Hazel, Scott O'Dell Award for Historical Fiction, 1100 E 57 St, S-109, Chicago, IL 60637 *Tel:* 773-702-4085 *Fax:* 773-702-0775, pg 795

Rochon, Diane, Association pour l'Avancement des Sciences et des Techniques de la Documentation, 3414 Avenue du Parc, Bureau 202, Montreal, PQ

H2X 2H5, Canada *Tel:* 514-281-5012 *Fax:* 514-281-8219 *E-mail:* info@asted.org *Web Site:* www.asted.org, pg 680

Rochon, Peter, Library & Archives Canada, 395 Wellington St, Ottawa, ON K1A 0N4, Canada *Tel:* 613-995-7969 (Publications); 613-996-5115 (General Inquiries); 613-992-6969 (TTY) *Toll Free Tel:* 866-578-7777 (Canada only); 866-299-1699 (Canada only) *Fax:* 613-991-9871 (Publications); 613-996-5115 (General Inquiries) *E-mail:* distribution@lac-bac.gc.ca; reference@lac-bac.gc.ca *Web Site:* www.collectionscanada.ca, pg 690

Rock, Ed, Newbridge Educational Publishing, One Beeman Rd, Northborough, MA 01532 *Tel:* 508-571-6500 *Toll Free Tel:* 800-867-0307 *Fax:* 508-571-6502 *Toll Free Fax:* 800-456-2419 *E-mail:* info@newbridgeonline.com *Web Site:* www.newbridgeonline.com; www.newbridgepub.com, pg 190

Rock, Edward A, Sundance Publishing, One Beeman Rd, Northborough, MA 01532 *Tel:* 508-571-6500 *Toll Free Tel:* 800-343-8204 *Fax:* 508-571-6510 *Toll Free Fax:* 800-456-2419 *E-mail:* info@sundancepub.com *Web Site:* www.sundancepub.com, pg 262

Rock, Joanne, Binding Industries Association (BIA), 100 Daingerfield Rd, Alexandria, VA 22314 *Tel:* 703-519-8137 *Fax:* 703-548-3227 *E-mail:* bparrott@printing.org *Web Site:* www.gain.net, pg 681

Rock, Joanne, Library Binding Institute, 70 E Lake, Suite 300, Chicago, IL 60601 *Tel:* 312-704-5020 *Fax:* 312-704-5025 *E-mail:* info@lbibinders.org *Web Site:* www.lbibinders.org, pg 690

Rock, Maya, Writers House LLC, 21 W 26 St, New York, NY 10010 *Tel:* 212-685-2400 *Fax:* 212-685-1781, pg 662

Rock, Victoria, Chronicle Books LLC, 85 Second St, 6th fl, San Francisco, CA 94105 *Tel:* 415-537-4200 *Toll Free Tel:* 800-722-6657 (cust serv) *Fax:* 415-537-4460 *Toll Free Fax:* 800-858-7787 (orders) *E-mail:* frontdesk@chroniclebooks.com *Web Site:* www.chroniclebooks.com, pg 61

Rockefeller, Kirwan PhD, UCI Extension Writers' Program, PO Box 6050, Irvine, CA 92616 *Tel:* 949-824-5990 *Fax:* 949-824-3651 *Web Site:* www.unex.uci.edu, pg 748

Rockmill, Jayne, Rockmill & Company, 647 Warren St, Brooklyn, NY 11217 *Tel:* 718-638-3990 *E-mail:* agentrockmill@yahoo.com, pg 652

Rockwell, Llewellyn H Jr, Ludwig von Mises Institute, 518 W Magnolia Ave, Auburn, AL 36832 *Tel:* 334-321-2100 *Fax:* 334-321-2119 *Web Site:* www.mises.org, pg 160

Rodale, Ardath, Rodale Inc, 33 E Minor St, Emmaus, PA 18098-0099 *Tel:* 610-967-5171 *Fax:* 610-967-8962 *Web Site:* www.rodale.com, pg 234

Rodale, Maria, Rodale Inc, 33 E Minor St, Emmaus, PA 18098-0099 *Tel:* 610-967-5171 *Fax:* 610-967-8962 *Web Site:* www.rodale.com, pg 234

Rodberg, Lillian R, Lillian R Rodberg & Associates, 1600 Lehigh Pkwy E, Rm 9F, Allentown, PA 18103-3035 *Tel:* 610-740-0662 *E-mail:* wpressinc@aol.com, pg 610

Roddy, Carol, James P Barry Ohioana Award for Editorial Excellence, 274 E First Ave, Suite 300, Columbus, OH 43201 *Tel:* 614-466-3831 *Fax:* 614-728-6974 *E-mail:* ohioana@sloma.state.oh.us *Web Site:* www.oplin.lib.oh.us/ohioana, pg 761

Roddy, Carol, Ohioana Award for Children's Literature, 274 E First Ave, Suite 300, Columbus, OH 43201 *Tel:* 614-466-3831 *Fax:* 614-728-6974 *E-mail:* ohioana@sloma.state.oh.us *Web Site:* www.oplin.lib.oh.us/ohioana, pg 795

Roddy, Carol, Ohioana Book Awards, 274 E First Ave, Suite 300, Columbus, OH 43201 *Tel:* 614-466-3831 *Fax:* 614-728-6974 *E-mail:* ohioana@sloma.state.oh.us *Web Site:* www.oplin.lib.us/ohioana/, pg 795

Roddy, Carol, Ohioana Career Award, 274 E First Ave, Suite 300, Columbus, OH 43201 *Tel:* 614-466-3831 *Fax:* 614-728-6974 *E-mail:* ohioana@sloma.state.oh.us *Web Site:* www.oplin.lib.oh.us/ohioana, pg 796

Roddy, Carol, Ohioana Citations, 274 E First Ave, Suite 300, Columbus, OH 43201 *Tel:* 614-466-3831 *Fax:* 614-728-6974 *E-mail:* ohioana@sloma.state.oh.us *Web Site:* www.oplin.lib.oh.us/ohioana, pg 796

Roddy, Carol, Ohioana Pegasus Award, 274 E First Ave, Suite 300, Columbus, OH 43201 *Tel:* 614-466-3831 *Fax:* 614-728-6974 *E-mail:* ohioana@sloma.state.oh.us *Web Site:* www.oplin.lib.oh.us/ohioana, pg 796

Roddy, Carol, Ohioana Poetry Award, 274 E First Ave, Suite 300, Columbus, OH 43201 *Tel:* 614-466-3831 *Fax:* 614-728-6974 *E-mail:* ohioana@sloma.state.oh.us *Web Site:* www.oplin.lib.oh.us/ohioana, pg 796

Roddy, Carol, Ohioana Walter Rumsey Marvin Grant, 274 E First Ave, Suite 300, Columbus, OH 43201 *Tel:* 614-466-3831 *Fax:* 614-728-6974 *E-mail:* ohioana@sloma.state.oh.us *Web Site:* www.oplin.lib.oh.us/ohioana, pg 796

Rodenberger, Jean, Lippincott Williams & Wilkins, 530 Walnut St, 7th fl, Philadelphia, PA 19106 *Tel:* 215-521-8300 *Toll Free Tel:* 800-638-3030 (cust serv) *Fax:* 215-521-8902; 301-824-7390 (cust serv) *E-mail:* orders@lww.com *Web Site:* www.lww.com, pg 156

Rodergen, Jeffrey L, Write Stuff Enterprises Inc, 1001 S Andrew Ave, 2nd fl, Fort Lauderdale, FL 33316 *Tel:* 954-462-6657 *Toll Free Tel:* 800-900-2665 *Fax:* 954-463-2220 *E-mail:* legends@writestuffbooks.com *Web Site:* www.writestuffbooks.com, pg 304

Rodger, Ellen, Crabtree Publishing Co, 350 Fifth Ave, Suite 3308, PMB 16-A, New York, NY 10118 *Tel:* 212-496-5040 *Toll Free Tel:* 800-387-7650 *Toll Free Fax:* 800-355-7166 *E-mail:* letters@crabtreebooks.com *Web Site:* www.crabtreebooks.com, pg 71

Rodgers, Mary, First Avenue Editions, 241 First Ave N, Minneapolis, MN 55401 *Tel:* 612-332-3344 *Toll Free Tel:* 800-328-4929 *Fax:* 612-332-7615 *Toll Free Fax:* 800-332-1132 *E-mail:* info@lernerbooks.com *Web Site:* www.lernerbooks.com, pg 97

Rodgers, Mary, Lerner Publications, 241 First Ave N, Minneapolis, MN 55401 *Tel:* 612-332-3344 *Toll Free Tel:* 800-328-4929 *Fax:* 612-332-7615 *Toll Free Fax:* 800-332-1132 *E-mail:* info@lernerbooks.com *Web Site:* www.lernerbooks.com, pg 152

Rodgers, Mary, Lerner Publishing Group, 241 First Ave N, Minneapolis, MN 55401 *Tel:* 612-332-3344 *Toll Free Tel:* 800-328-4929 *Fax:* 612-332-7615 *Toll Free Fax:* 800-332-1132 *E-mail:* info@lernerbooks.com *Web Site:* www.lernerbooks.com, pg 152

Rodgers, Mary, LernerClassroom, 241 First Ave N, Minneapolis, MN 55401 *Tel:* 612-332-3344 *Toll Free Tel:* 800-328-4929 *Fax:* 612-332-7615 *Toll Free Fax:* 800-332-1132 *E-mail:* info@lernerbooks.com *Web Site:* www.lernerbooks.com, pg 153

Rodgers, Mary, LernerSports, 241 First Ave N, Minneapolis, MN 55401 *Tel:* 612-332-3344 *Toll Free Tel:* 800-328-4929 *Fax:* 612-332-7615 *Toll Free Fax:* 800-332-1132 *E-mail:* info@lernerbooks.com *Web Site:* www.lernerbooks.com, pg 153

Rodgers, Mary, Runestone Press, 241 First Ave N, Minneapolis, MN 55401 *Tel:* 612-332-3344 *Toll Free Tel:* 800-328-4929; 800-332-1132 *Fax:* 612-332-7615 *E-mail:* info@lernerbooks.com *Web Site:* www.lernerbooks.com, pg 236

Rodgers, Mary M, Carolrhoda Books Inc, 241 First Ave N, Minneapolis, MN 55401 *Tel:* 612-332-3344 *Toll Free Tel:* 800-328-4929 *Fax:* 612-332-7615 *Toll Free Fax:* 800-332-1132 *E-mail:* info@lernerbooks.com *Web Site:* www.lernerbooks.com, pg 54

Rodgers, Ruth, Golden West Books, 525 N Electric Ave, Alhambra, CA 91801 *Tel:* 626-458-8148 *Fax:* 626-458-8148, pg 106

Rodgers, Sherry, Dynamic Graphics Training, 6000 N Forest Park Dr, Peoria, IL 61614-3556 *Tel:* 309-687-0141 *Fax:* 309-688-8515 *Web Site:* www.dgusa.com, pg 752

Rodin, Clifford, American Society of Civil Engineers (ASCE), 1801 Alexander Bell Dr, Reston, VA 20191-4400 *Tel:* 703-295-6200 *Toll Free Tel:* 800-548-2723 *Fax:* 703-295-6278 *E-mail:* marketing@asce.org *Web Site:* www.asce.org, pg 18

Rodriguez, Adam, Harcourt Interactive Technology, 99 Powerhouse Rd, Suite 106, Roslyn Heights, NY 11577 *Tel:* 516-625-6755 *Toll Free Tel:* 800-745-3276 *Fax:* 516-625-6789 *E-mail:* hit@harcourt.com *Web Site:* www.hit.iloli.com, pg 114

Rodriguiz, Luis, Tia Chucha Press, 12737 Glen Oaks Blvd, Suite 22, Sylmar, CA 91342 *Tel:* 818-362-7060 *Fax:* 818-362-7102 *E-mail:* info@tiachucha.com *Web Site:* www.tiachucha.com, pg 271

Roe, Rosanne, nursesbooks.org, The Publishing Program of ANA, 600 Maryland Ave SW, Suite 100-W, Washington, DC 20024-2571 *Tel:* 202-651-7000 *Toll Free Tel:* 800-637-0323 *Fax:* 202-651-7001 *E-mail:* anp@ana.org *Web Site:* www.nursesbooks.org, pg 194

Roebling, Karl, Dynapress, PO Box 150217, Altamonte Springs, FL 32715-0217 *Tel:* 407-331-5550 *Fax:* 407-331-5550 (call first) *E-mail:* itsdifferent@dynapress.com *Web Site:* www.dynapress.com, pg 571

Roerig-Blong, Janice, McGraw-Hill Science, Engineering, Mathematics, 2460 Kerper Blvd, Dubuque, IA 52001 *Tel:* 563-588-1451 *Toll Free Tel:* 800-338-3987 (cust serv) *Fax:* 563-589-4700; 614-755-5645 (cust serv) *E-mail:* firstname_lastname@mcgraw-hill.com *Web Site:* www.mhhe.com, pg 169

Roets, Lois, Leadership Publishers Inc, PO Box 8358, Des Moines, IA 50301-8358 *Tel:* 515-278-4765 *Toll Free Tel:* 800-814-3757 *Fax:* 515-270-8303, pg 151

Rogalski, Michael, Quirk Books, 215 Church St, Philadelphia, PA 19106 *Tel:* 215-627-3581 *Fax:* 215-627-5220 *E-mail:* general@quirkbooks.com *Web Site:* www.quirkbooks.com, pg 224

Rogatz, Mitch, Triumph Books, 601 S LaSalle St, Suite 500, Chicago, IL 60605 *Tel:* 312-939-3330 *Toll Free Tel:* 800-335-5323 *Fax:* 312-663-3557 *E-mail:* orders@triumphbooks.com *Web Site:* www.triumphbooks.com, pg 276

Rogers, Chris, Oxford University Press, Inc, 198 Madison Ave, New York, NY 10016-4314 *Tel:* 212-726-6000 *Toll Free Tel:* 800-451-7556 (orders) *Web Site:* www.oup.com/us, pg 200

Rogers, Cindy-Joy, National Newspaper Association, University of Missouri, 127-129 Neff Annex, Columbia, MO 65211-1200 *Tel:* 573-882-5800 *Toll Free Tel:* 800-829-4662 *Fax:* 703-884-5490 *E-mail:* info@nna.org *Web Site:* www.nna.org, pg 694

Rogers, Elaine, Kneerim & Williams, c/o Fish & Richardson PC, 225 Franklin St, Boston, MA 02110 *Tel:* 617-542-5070 *Fax:* 617-542-8906 *Web Site:* www.fr.com, pg 638

Rogers, Elizabeth-Anne, Denlinger's Publishers Ltd, PO Box 1030, Edgewater, FL 32132-1030 *Tel:* 386-424-1737 *Toll Free Tel:* 800-362-1810 *Fax:* 386-428-3534 *Toll Free Fax:* 800-589-1191 *E-mail:* editor@thebookden.com *Web Site:* www.thebookden.com, pg 79

Rogers, Janet, Begell House Inc Publishers, 145 Madison Ave, Suite 601, New York, NY 10016 *Tel:* 212-725-1999 *Fax:* 212-213-8368 *E-mail:* orders@begellhouse.com *Web Site:* www.begellhouse.com, pg 35

Rogers, John, Basic Books, 387 Park Ave S, 12th fl, New York, NY 10016-8810 *Tel:* 212-340-8100 *Toll Free Tel:* 800-242-7737 (orders) *Fax:* 212-340-8135 *E-mail:* basic.books@perseusbooks.com *Web Site:* www.basicbooks.com, pg 33

Rogers, Kelly, Barnes & Noble Books (Imports & Reprints), 4501 Forbes Blvd, Suite 200, Lanham, MD 20706 *Tel:* 301-459-3366 *Toll Free Tel:* 800-462-6420 (orders only) *Fax:* 301-429-5748 *Toll Free Fax:* 800-338-4550 (orders only) *Web Site:* www.rowmanlittlefield.com, pg 32

Rogers, Kelly, Rowman & Littlefield Publishers Inc, 4501 Forbes Blvd, Lanham, MD 20706 *Tel:* 301-459-3366 *Toll Free Tel:* 800-462-6420 *Fax:* 301-429-5748 *Web Site:* www.rowmanlittlefield.com, pg 235

Rogers, Kelly, Scarecrow Press Inc, 4501 Forbes Blvd, Suite 200, Lanham, MD 20706 *Tel:* 301-459-3366 *Toll Free Tel:* 800-462-6420 (orders only) *Fax:* 301-429-5747 *Toll Free Fax:* 800-338-4550 *Web Site:* www.scarecrowpress.com, pg 241

Rogers, Kelly L, University Press of America Inc, 4501 Forbes Blvd, Suite 200, Lanham, MD 20706 *Tel:* 301-459-3366 *Toll Free Tel:* 800-462-6420 *Fax:* 301-429-5748 *Toll Free Fax:* 800-338-4550 *Web Site:* www.univpress.com, pg 286

Rogers, Marcia, Prometheus Books, 59 John Glenn Dr, Amherst, NY 14228 *Tel:* 716-691-0133 *Toll Free Tel:* 800-421-0351 *Fax:* 716-691-0137 *E-mail:* marketing@prometheusbooks.com; editorial@prometheusbooks.com *Web Site:* www.Prometheusbooks.com, pg 220

Rogers, Marian Hartman, Bibliogenesis, 152 Coddington Rd, Ithaca, NY 14850 *Tel:* 607-277-9660 *Fax:* 607-277-6661, pg 592

Rogers, Savannah, FC&A Publishing, 103 Clover Green, Peachtree City, GA 30269 *Tel:* 770-487-6307 *Toll Free Tel:* 800-537-1275 *Fax:* 770-631-4357 *E-mail:* customer_service@fca.com *Web Site:* www.fca.com, pg 95

Rogers, Scott, McGraw-Hill/Osborne, 2100 Powell St, 10th fl, Emeryville, CA 94608 *Tel:* 510-420-7700 *Toll Free Tel:* 800-227-0900 *Fax:* 510-420-7703 *Web Site:* shop.osborne.com/cgi-bin/osborne, pg 168

Rogge, Robie, The Metropolitan Museum of Art, 1000 Fifth Ave, New York, NY 10028 *Tel:* 212-879-5500; 212-535-7710 *Fax:* 212-396-5062 *E-mail:* info@metmuseum.org *Web Site:* www.metmuseum.org, pg 173

Roghaar, Linda L, Linda Roghaar Literary Agency Inc, 133 High Point Dr, Amherst, MA 01002 *Tel:* 413-256-1921 *Fax:* 413-256-2636 *E-mail:* contact@lindaroghaar.com *Web Site:* www.lindaroghaar.com, pg 652

Roginsky, Gwen, The Metropolitan Museum of Art, 1000 Fifth Ave, New York, NY 10028 *Tel:* 212-879-5500; 212-535-7710 *Fax:* 212-396-5062 *E-mail:* info@metmuseum.org *Web Site:* www.metmuseum.org, pg 173

Rohd, Brian, Data Trace Publishing Co, 110 West Rd, Suite 227, Towson, MD 21204-2316 *Tel:* 410-494-4994 *Toll Free Tel:* 800-342-0454 (orders only) *Fax:* 410-494-0515 *E-mail:* info@datatrace.com *Web Site:* www.datatrace.com, pg 76

Rohmann, Eric, Princeton University Press, 41 William St, Princeton, NJ 08540 *Tel:* 609-258-4900 *Toll Free Tel:* 800-777-4726 *Fax:* 609-258-6305 *Toll Free Fax:* 800-999-1958 *E-mail:* orders@cpfsinc.com *Web Site:* www.pup.princeton.edu, pg 219

Rohmer, Harriet, Children's Book Press, 2211 Mission St, San Francisco, CA 94110 *Tel:* 415-821-3080 *Fax:* 415-821-3081 *E-mail:* info@childrensbookpress.org *Web Site:* www.cbookpress.org, pg 60

Rohrig, Mike, St Martin's Press LLC, 175 Fifth Ave, New York, NY 10010 *Tel:* 212-674-5151 *Fax:* 212-420-9314 *E-mail:* firstname.lastname@stmartins.com *Web Site:* www.stmartins.com, pg 238

Roider, David, Oceana Publications Inc, 75 Main St, Dobbs Ferry, NY 10522-1601 *Tel:* 914-693-8100 *Toll Free Tel:* 800-831-0758 (orders only) *Fax:* 914-693-0402 *E-mail:* info@oceanalaw.com *Web Site:* www.oceanalaw.com, pg 195

Roistacher, Robert E, The Roistacher Literary Agency, 545 W 111 St, New York, NY 10025 *Tel:* 212-222-1405, pg 652

Rojas, M, Scientific Publishers Inc, 4460 SW 35 Terr, Suite 305, Gainesville, FL 32608 *Tel:* 352-373-5630 *Fax:* 352-373-3249 *E-mail:* scipub@aol.com *Web Site:* www.scipub.com, pg 243

Roland, Leonard, Dover Publications Inc, 31 E Second St, Mineola, NY 11501 *Tel:* 516-294-7000 *Toll Free Tel:* 800-223-3130 (orders) *Fax:* 516-742-6953; 516-742-5049 (orders) *Web Site:* www.doverpublications.com; www.doverdirect.com, pg 83

Rosenberg, Linda, Farrar, Straus & Giroux, LLC, 19 Union Sq W, New York, NY 10003 *Tel:* 212-741-6900 *Fax:* 212-741-6973 *Web Site:* www.fsgbooks.com, pg 95

Rosenberg, Liz, Binghamton University Writing Program, c/o Dept of English, PO Box 6000, Binghamton, NY 13902-6000 *Tel:* 607-777-2168 *Fax:* 607-777-2408, pg 751

Rosenberg, Shirley Sirota, SSR Inc, 116 Fourth St SE, Washington, DC 20003 *Tel:* 202-543-1800 *Fax:* 202-544-7432 *E-mail:* ssr@ssrinc.com, pg 611

Rosenblat, Arney, MS Public Education Awards Program, 733 Third Ave, New York, NY 10017 *Tel:* 212-476-0436 *Fax:* 212-986-7981 *Web Site:* www.nationalmssociety.org, pg 791

Rosenfeld, Dina, Hachai Publications Inc, 156 Chester Ave, Brooklyn, NY 11218 *Tel:* 718-633-0100 *Toll Free Tel:* 800-50-HACHAI (504-2424) *Fax:* 718-633-0103 *E-mail:* info@hachai.com *Web Site:* www.hachai.com, pg 111

Rosenfeld, Ellen, B K Nelson Inc Literary Agency, 1565 Paseo Vida, Palm Springs, CA 92264 *Tel:* 760-778-8800 *Fax:* 914-778-0034 *E-mail:* bknelson4@cs.com *Web Site:* www.bknelson.com, pg 645

Rosenfeld, Erv, Literacy Institute for Education (LIFE) Inc, 84 Woodland Rd, Pleasantville, NY 10570 *Tel:* 914-741-1322 *Fax:* 914-741-1324 *Web Site:* bknelson.com, pg 156

Rosenfeld, Erwin, B K Nelson Inc Literary Agency, 1565 Paseo Vida, Palm Springs, CA 92264 *Tel:* 760-778-8800 *Fax:* 914-778-0034 *E-mail:* bknelson4@cs.com *Web Site:* www.bknelson.com, pg 645

Rosenfeld, Nancy, AAA Books Unlimited, 88 Greenbrier E Dr, Deerfield, IL 60015 *Tel:* 847-945-0315 *Fax:* 847-444-1220 *Web Site:* www.aaabooksunlimited.com, pg 617

Rosenfeld, Theodore, Walker & Co, 104 Fifth Ave, 7th fl, New York, NY 10011 *Tel:* 212-727-8300 *Toll Free Tel:* 800-289-2553 *Fax:* 212-727-0984 *Toll Free Fax:* 800-218-9367 *E-mail:* firstinitiallastname@walkerbooks.com *Web Site:* www.walkerbooks.com, pg 292

Rosenfeld, Theodore D, Taplinger Publishing Co Inc, PO Box 175, Marlboro, NJ 07746-0175 *Tel:* 646-215-9003 *Fax:* 646-215-9560, pg 264

Rosenheim, Kellye, Whiting Writers' Awards, 1133 Avenue of the Americas, 22nd fl, New York, NY 10036 *Tel:* 212-336-2138, pg 811

Rosenkranz, Rita, Rita Rosenkranz Literary Agency, 440 West End Ave, Suite 15D, New York, NY 10024-5358 *Tel:* 212-873-6333 *Fax:* 212-873-5225, pg 652

Rosenstein, Natalee, Berkley Books, 375 Hudson St, New York, NY 10014 *Tel:* 212-366-2000 *Fax:* 212-366-2666 *E-mail:* online@penguinputnam.com *Web Site:* www.penguin.com, pg 36

Rosenstein, Natalee, Berkley Publishing Group, 375 Hudson St, New York, NY 10014 *Tel:* 212-366-2000 *E-mail:* online@penguinputnam.com *Web Site:* www.penguin.com, pg 37

Rosenstiel, Leonie, Literary Consultants LLC, 7542 Bear Canyon Rd NE, Albuquerque, NM 87109 *Tel:* 505-797-9397, pg 605

Rosenthal, David, Simon & Schuster, 1230 Avenue of the Americas, New York, NY 10020 *Tel:* 212-698-7000 *Toll Free Tel:* 800-223-2348 (cust serv); 800-223-2336 (orders) *Toll Free Fax:* 800-943-9831 (orders) *Web Site:* www.simonsays.com, pg 248

Rosenthal, Elise, Rosenthal Represents, 3850 Eddingham Ave, Calabasas, CA 91302 *Tel:* 818-222-5445 *Fax:* 818-222-5650, pg 667

Rosenthal, Tom, Morgan Kaufmann Publishers, 500 Sansome, Suite 400, San Francisco, CA 94111 *Tel:* 415-392-2665 *Fax:* 415-982-2665 *E-mail:* mkp@mkp.com *Web Site:* www.mkp.com, pg 178

Rosenwald, Robert, Poisoned Pen Press Inc, 6962 E First Ave, Suite 103, Scottsdale, AZ 85251 *Tel:* 480-945-3375 ext 210 *Fax:* 480-949-1707 *E-mail:* info@poisonpenpress.com *Web Site:* www.poisonpenpress.com, pg 215

Rosenwasser, Rena, Kelsey Street Press, 50 Northgate, Berkeley, CA 94708 *Tel:* 510-845-2260 *Fax:* 510-548-9185 *E-mail:* info@kelseyst.com *Web Site:* www.kelseyst.com, pg 144

Rosett, Richard N, National Bureau of Economic Research Inc, 1050 Massachusetts Ave, Cambridge, MA 02138-5398 *Tel:* 617-868-3900 *Fax:* 617-868-2742 *E-mail:* op@nber.org *Web Site:* www.nber.org, pg 182

Rosetti, Chip, Basic Books, 387 Park Ave S, 12th fl, New York, NY 10016-8810 *Tel:* 212-340-8100 *Toll Free Tel:* 800-242-7737 (orders) *Fax:* 212-340-8135 *E-mail:* basic.books@perseusbooks.com *Web Site:* www.basicbooks.com, pg 33

Rosinger, Joyce M, RGA Enterprises Inc, 135 Marrus Dr, Columbus, OH 43230 *Tel:* 614-471-6385 *E-mail:* rgaenterprises@msn.com, pg 610

Rosko, Kathryn, Princeton University Press, 41 William St, Princeton, NJ 08540 *Tel:* 609-258-4900 *Toll Free Tel:* 800-777-4726 *Fax:* 609-258-6305 *Toll Free Fax:* 800-999-1958 *E-mail:* orders@cpfsinc.com *Web Site:* www.pup.princeton.edu, pg 219

Ross, Andy M, LexisNexis Academic & Library Solutions, 7500 Old Georgetown Rd, Suite 1300, Bethesda, MD 20814-3389 *Tel:* 301-654-1550 *Toll Free Tel:* 800-638-8380 *Fax:* 301-654-4033; 301-657-3203 (sales) *E-mail:* academicinfo@lexisnexis.com *Web Site:* www.lexisnexis.com/academic, pg 153

Ross, Bob, Pilgrim Publications, PO Box 66, Pasadena, TX 77501-0066 *Tel:* 713-477-4261; 713-477-2329 *Fax:* 713-477-7561 *E-mail:* pilgrimpub@aol.com *Web Site:* members.aol.com/pilgrimpub/; www.pilgrimpublications.com, pg 213

Ross, Carol Fein, Time Warner Book Group, 1271 Avenue of the Americas, New York, NY 10020 *Tel:* 212-522-7200 *Fax:* 212-522-7991 *Web Site:* www.twbookmark.com, pg 271

Ross, Daniel, University of Alabama Press, Box 870380, Tuscaloosa, AL 35487-0380 *Tel:* 205-348-5180; 773-702-7000 (orders) *Fax:* 205-348-9201 *Web Site:* uapress.ua.edu, pg 280

Ross, Franz, Ross Books, PO Box 4340, Berkeley, CA 94704-0340 *Tel:* 510-841-2474 *Toll Free Tel:* 800-367-0930 *Fax:* 510-841-2695 *E-mail:* staff@rossbooks.com *Web Site:* www.rossbooks.com, pg 234

Ross, Harriet, Lion Books Publisher, 210 Nelson Rd, Scarsdale, NY 10583 *Tel:* 914-725-2280 *Fax:* 914-725-3572, pg 155

Ross, Krystyna, McClelland & Stewart Ltd, 481 University Ave, Suite 900, Toronto, ON M5G 2E9, Canada *Tel:* 416-598-1114 *Fax:* 416-598-7764 *E-mail:* mail@mcclelland.com *Web Site:* www.mcclelland.com, pg 553

Ross, Laura, Black Dog & Leventhal Publishers Inc, 151 W 19 St, 12th fl, New York, NY 10011 *Tel:* 212-647-9336 *Fax:* 212-647-9332 *E-mail:* information@bdlev.com *Web Site:* www.bdlev.com, pg 39

Ross, Linda, Time Warner Audio Books, Sports Illustrated Bldg, 135 W 50 St, New York, NY 10020 *Tel:* 212-522-7334 *Fax:* 212-522-7994 *Web Site:* www.twbookmark.com/audiobooks, pg 271

Ross, Lisa M, The Spieler Agency, 154 W 57 St, 13th fl, Rm 135, New York, NY 10019 *Tel:* 212-757-4439 *Web Site:* spieleragency.com, pg 656

Ross, Lois, North-South Institute/Institut Nord-Sud, 55 Murray St, Suite 200, Ottawa, ON K1N 5M3, Canada *Tel:* 613-241-3535 *Fax:* 613-241-7435 *E-mail:* nsi@nsi-ins.ca *Web Site:* www.nsi-ins.ca, pg 556

Ross, Marilyn, Communication Creativity, 209 Church St, Buena Vista, CO 81211 *Tel:* 719-395-8659 *Toll Free Tel:* 800-331-8355 *Fax:* 719-633-1526 *Web Site:* www.communicationcreativity.com, pg 66

Ross, Marji, Regnery Publishing Inc, One Massachusetts Ave, NW, Suite 600, Washington, DC 20001 *Tel:* 202-216-0600 *Toll Free Tel:* 888-219-4747 *Fax:* 202-216-0612 *E-mail:* editorial@regnery.com *Web Site:* www.regnery.com, pg 231

Ross, Marjory, Eagle Publishing Inc, One Massachusetts Ave NW, Washington, DC 20001 *Tel:* 202-216-0600 *Fax:* 202-216-0612 *Web Site:* www.regnery.com, pg 85

Ross, Michael, Encyclopaedia Britannica Inc, 310 S Michigan Ave, Chicago, IL 60604 *Tel:* 312-347-7000 *Toll Free Tel:* 800-323-1229 *Fax:* 312-347-7399 *E-mail:* editor@eb.com *Web Site:* www.eb.com; www.britannica.com, pg 91

Ross, Michael, St Martin's Press LLC, 175 Fifth Ave, New York, NY 10010 *Tel:* 212-674-5151 *Fax:* 212-420-9314 *E-mail:* firstname.lastname@stmartins.com *Web Site:* www.stmartins.com, pg 238

Ross, Mimi, Henry Holt and Company, LLC, 115 W 18 St, New York, NY 10011 *Tel:* 212-886-9200 *Toll Free Tel:* 888-330-8477 (orders) *Fax:* 212-633-0748 *E-mail:* publicity@hholt.com *Web Site:* www.henryholt.com, pg 124

Ross, Mona, Southern Illinois University Press, PO Box 3697, Carbondale, IL 62902-3697 *Tel:* 618-453-2281 *Toll Free Tel:* 800-346-2680 *Fax:* 618-453-1221 *Toll Free Fax:* 800-346-2681 *E-mail:* jstetter@siu.edu *Web Site:* www.siu.edu/~siupress, pg 254

Ross, Nancy, Lion Books Publisher, 210 Nelson Rd, Scarsdale, NY 10583 *Tel:* 914-725-2280 *Fax:* 914-725-3572, pg 155

Ross, Norman A, Ross Publishing Inc, 330 W 58 St, Suite 306, New York, NY 10019-1827 *Tel:* 212-765-8200 *Fax:* 212-765-8296 *E-mail:* info@rosspub.com *Web Site:* www.rosspub.com, pg 234

Ross, Patrick, Warren Communications News, 2115 Ward Ct NW, Washington, DC 20037-1209 *Tel:* 202-872-9200 *Fax:* 202-293-3435 *E-mail:* info@warren-news.com *Web Site:* www.warren-news.com, pg 293

Ross, Priscilla, State University of New York Press, 90 State St, Suite 700, Albany, NY 12207-1707 *Tel:* 518-472-5000 *Toll Free Tel:* 800-666-2211 (orders) *Fax:* 518-472-5038 *Toll Free Fax:* 800-688-2877 (orders) *E-mail:* orderbook@cupserv.org; info@sunypress.edu *Web Site:* www.sunypress.edu, pg 258

Ross, Rachel, Art Image Publications, PO Box 160, Derby Line, VT 05830-0160 *Toll Free Tel:* 800-361-2598 *Toll Free Fax:* 800-559-2598 *E-mail:* info@artimagepublications.com *Web Site:* www.artimagepublications.com, pg 24

Ross, Sayre, Lion Books Publisher, 210 Nelson Rd, Scarsdale, NY 10583 *Tel:* 914-725-2280 *Fax:* 914-725-3572, pg 155

Ross, Steve, Crown Publishing Group, 1745 Broadway, New York, NY 10019 *Tel:* 212-782-9000 *Toll Free Tel:* 888-264-1745 *Fax:* 212-940-7408 *Web Site:* www.randomhouse.com/crown, pg 74

Ross, Terrence, The Aaland Agency, PO Box 849, Inyokern, CA 93527-0849 *Tel:* 760-384-3910 *Fax:* 760-384-4435 *Web Site:* www.the-aaland-agency.com, pg 617

Rossbach, Catherine, Sage Publications, 2455 Teller Rd, Thousand Oaks, CA 91320 *Tel:* 805-499-0721 *Fax:* 805-499-0871 *E-mail:* info@sagepub.com *Web Site:* www.sagepub.com, pg 237

Rossen, Susan F, Art Institute of Chicago, 111 S Michigan Ave, Chicago, IL 60603-6110 *Tel:* 312-443-3600; 312-443-3540 (pubns); 312-443-3533 (sales & orders) *Fax:* 312-443-0849; 312-443-1334 (pubns) *E-mail:* webmaster@artic.edu *Web Site:* www.artic.edu, pg 24

Rossi, Dominick F Jr, Reader's Digest General Books, Reader's Digest Rd, Pleasantville, NY 10570-7000 *Tel:* 914-238-1000 *Toll Free Tel:* 800-431-1726 *Fax:* 914-244-7436, pg 228

Rossi, Janice, Kensington Publishing Corp, 850 Third Ave, New York, NY 10022 *Tel:* 212-407-1500 *Toll Free Tel:* 800-221-2647 *Fax:* 212-935-0699 *Web Site:* www.kensingtonbooks.com, pg 145

Rossman, Jessica, Book Industry Standards & Communications, 19 W 21 St, Suite 905, New York, NY 10010 *Tel:* 646-336-7141 *Fax:* 646-336-6214 *E-mail:* info@bisg.org *Web Site:* www.bisg.org, pg 681

Rosso, Don, Waveland Press Inc, 4180 IL Rte 83, Suite 101, Long Grove, IL 60047-9580 *Tel:* 847-634-0081 *Fax:* 847-634-9501 *E-mail:* info@waveland.com *Web Site:* www.waveland.com, pg 294

Rostan, Stephanie, Levine-Greenberg Literary Agency Inc, 307 Seventh Ave, Suite 1906, New York, NY 10001 *Tel:* 212-337-0934 *Fax:* 212-337-0948 *Web Site:* www.levinegreenberg.com, pg 640

Rotella, Guy, Samuel French Morse Poetry Prize, 406 Holmes, Boston, MA 02115 *Tel:* 617-373-4540 *Web Site:* www.casdn.neu.edu/~english, pg 790

Roter, Benjamin, Rodale Inc, 33 E Minor St, Emmaus, PA 18098-0099 *Tel:* 610-967-5171 *Fax:* 610-967-8962 *Web Site:* www.rodale.com, pg 234

Roth, Karen, Standard Publishing Co, 8121 Hamilton Ave, Cincinnati, OH 45231 *Tel:* 513-931-4050 *Toll Free Tel:* 800-543-1301 *Fax:* 513-931-0950 *Toll Free Fax:* 877-867-5751 *E-mail:* customerservice@standardpub.com *Web Site:* www.standardpub.com, pg 257

Roth, Pamela, SPIRAL Books, 70 Cider Mill Rd, Bedford, NH 03110-4200 *Tel:* 603-471-1917 *Fax:* 603-471-1977 *E-mail:* order@spiralbooks.com *Web Site:* www.spiralbooks.com, pg 255

Roth, Shelley, The Roth Agency, 138 Bay State Rd, Rehoboth, MA 02769 *Tel:* 508-252-5818, pg 652

Rothberg, Adam, Simon & Schuster Inc, 1230 Avenue of the Americas, New York, NY 10020 *Tel:* 212-698-7000 *Fax:* 212-698-7007 *Web Site:* www.simonsays.com, pg 249

Rothenberg, David, Nolo, 950 Parker St, Berkeley, CA 94710 *Tel:* 510-549-1976 *Fax:* 510-548-5902 *E-mail:* info@nolo.com *Web Site:* www.nolo.com, pg 191

Rothenberg, Jill, Westview Press, 5500 Central Ave, Boulder, CO 80301 *Tel:* 303-444-3541 *Toll Free Tel:* 800-386-5656 *Fax:* 720-406-7336 *E-mail:* westview.orders@perseusbooks.com *Web Site:* www.perseusbooksgroup.com; www.westviewpress.com, pg 297

Rothermich, John A, Phoenix Learning Resources, 25 Third St, 2nd fl, Stamford, CT 06905 *Tel:* 203-353-1665 *Toll Free Tel:* 800-526-6581 *Fax:* 212-629-5648 *Web Site:* www.phoenixlr.com, pg 212

Rothfarb, Michele, The Bookbinders' Guild of New York, Dunn & Co, 110 Grand Ave, Ridgefield Park, NJ 07660 *Tel:* 201-229-1888 *Fax:* 201-229-1755 *Web Site:* www.bookbindersguild.org, pg 682

Rothman, Cynthia, Kirchoff/Wohlberg Inc, 866 United Nations Plaza, Suite 525, New York, NY 10017 *Tel:* 212-644-2020 *Fax:* 212-223-4387 *E-mail:* kirchwohl@aol.com *Web Site:* www.kirchoffwohlberg.com, pg 603

Rothman, Judith, Hamilton Books, 4501 Forbes Blvd, Suite 200, Lanham, MD 20706 *Tel:* 301-459-3366, pg 112

Rothman, Judith, Lexington Books, 4501 Forbes Blvd, Lanham, MD 20706 *Tel:* 301-459-3366 *Fax:* 301-429-5748 *Web Site:* www.lexingtonbooks.com, pg 153

Rothman, Judith L, University Press of America Inc, 4501 Forbes Blvd, Suite 200, Lanham, MD 20706 *Tel:* 301-459-3366 *Toll Free Tel:* 800-462-6420 *Fax:* 301-429-5748 *Toll Free Fax:* 800-338-4550 *Web Site:* www.univpress.com, pg 286

Rothstein, Audrey, American Occupational Therapy Association Inc, 4720 Montgomery Lane, Bethesda, MD 20824 *Tel:* 301-652-2682 *Fax:* 301-652-7711 *Web Site:* www.aota.org, pg 16

Rothstein, Philip Jan, Rothstein Associates Inc, 4 Arapaho Rd, Brookfield, CT 06804-3104 *Tel:* 203-740-7444 *Toll Free Tel:* 888-768-4783 *Fax:* 203-740-7401 *E-mail:* info@rothstein.com *Web Site:* www.rothstein.com, pg 234

Rotondo, Andrea, Schirmer Trade Books, 25 Park Ave S, New York, NY 10010 *Tel:* 212-254-2100 *Toll Free Tel:* 800-431-7187 *Fax:* 212-254-2013 *Toll Free Fax:* 800-345-6842 *Web Site:* www.musicsales.com, pg 241

Rounds, John, St Martin's Press Paperback and Reference Group, 175 Fifth Ave, New York, NY 10010 *Fax:* 212-995-2488 *E-mail:* firstname.lastname@stmartins.com, pg 239

Rountree, Joseph N, The Colonial Williamsburg Foundation, PO Box 1776, Williamsburg, VA 23187-1776 *Tel:* 757-229-1000 *Toll Free Tel:* 800-HISTORY *Fax:* 757-220-7325 *Web Site:* www.colonialwilliamsburg.org/publications, pg 65

Roush, Sheryl, Solid Gold Marketing Design Workshops, PO Box 2373, La Mesa, CA 91943-2373 *Tel:* 858-569-6555 *Toll Free Tel:* 800-932-0973 *Fax:* 858-569-5924 *Web Site:* www.sparklepresentations.com, pg 747

Rousseau, S J, Richard W, University of Scranton Press, 445 Madison Ave, Scranton, PA 18510 *Tel:* 570-941-4228 *Toll Free Tel:* 800-941-3081 *Fax:* 570-941-6256 *Toll Free Fax:* 800-941-8804 *Web Site:* www.scrantonpress.com (Catalog), pg 285

Routledge, Brent, Micromedia ProQuest, 20 Victoria St, Toronto, ON M5C 2N8, Canada *Tel:* 416-362-5211 *Toll Free Tel:* 800-387-2689 *Fax:* 416-362-6161 *E-mail:* info@micromedia.ca *Web Site:* www.micromedia.ca, pg 554

Routy, Gilda, Editions Fides, 165 rue Deslauriers, St-Laurent, PQ H4N 2S4, Canada *Tel:* 514-745-4290 *Toll Free Tel:* 800-363-1451 *Fax:* 514-745-4299 *E-mail:* editions@fides.qc.ca *Web Site:* www.editionsfides.com, pg 545

Roux, Jacques, Black Rose Books Ltd, CP 1258 Succ Place de Parc, Montreal, PQ H2X 4A7, Canada *Tel:* 514-844-4076 *Toll Free Tel:* 800-565-9523 *Fax:* 514-849-4797 *Toll Free Fax:* 800-221-9985 *E-mail:* blackrose@web.net *Web Site:* www.web.net/blackrosebooks, pg 536

Rovins, Michael, McGraw-Hill Professional, 2 Penn Plaza, New York, NY 10121 *Tel:* 212-904-2000 *Web Site:* www.books.mcgraw-hill.com, pg 168

Rowan, Scott, Triumph Books, 601 S LaSalle St, Suite 500, Chicago, IL 60605 *Tel:* 312-939-3330 *Toll Free Tel:* 800-335-5323 *Fax:* 312-663-3557 *E-mail:* orders@triumphbooks.com *Web Site:* www.triumphbooks.com, pg 276

Rowe, Alan, Torah Aura Productions, 4423 Fruitland Ave, Los Angeles, CA 90058 *Tel:* 323-585-7312 *Toll Free Tel:* 800-238-6724 *Fax:* 323-585-0327 *E-mail:* misrad@torahaura.com *Web Site:* www.torahaura.com, pg 272

Rowe, Carol, Waveland Press Inc, 4180 IL Rte 83, Suite 101, Long Grove, IL 60047-9580 *Tel:* 847-634-0081 *Fax:* 847-634-9501 *E-mail:* info@waveland.com *Web Site:* www.waveland.com, pg 294

Rowe, Lisa, Greenwood Publishing Group Inc, 88 Post Rd W, Westport, CT 06880-4208 *Tel:* 203-226-3571 *Toll Free Tel:* 800-225-5800 *Fax:* 203-222-1502 *E-mail:* bookinfo@greenwood.com (general); firstintial&fulllastname@greenwood.com (individuals) *Web Site:* www.greenwood.com, pg 109

Rowe, Martin, Lantern Books, One Union Square W, Suite 201, New York, NY 10003 *Tel:* 212-414-2275 *Toll Free Tel:* 800-856-8664 *Fax:* 212-414-2412 *E-mail:* editorial@lanternbooks.com *Web Site:* www.lanternbooks.com, pg 149

Rowe, Neil, Waveland Press Inc, 4180 IL Rte 83, Suite 101, Long Grove, IL 60047-9580 *Tel:* 847-634-0081 *Fax:* 847-634-9501 *E-mail:* info@waveland.com *Web Site:* www.waveland.com, pg 294

Rowe, Peter, The National Society of Newspaper Columnists (NSNC), Fillmore St, Suite 507, San Francisco, CA 94115 *Tel:* 415-541-5636 *Web Site:* www.columnists.com, pg 694

Rowell, Edmon L Jr, Mercer University Press, 1400 Coleman Ave, Macon, GA 31207 *Tel:* 478-301-2880 *Toll Free Tel:* 800-637-2378 (ext 2880, outside GA);

800-342-0841 (ext 2880, GA) *Fax:* 478-301-2585 *E-mail:* mupressorders@mercer.edu *Web Site:* www.mupress.org, pg 171

Rowland, Melissa, Levine-Greenberg Literary Agency Inc, 307 Seventh Ave, Suite 1906, New York, NY 10001 *Tel:* 212-337-0934 *Fax:* 212-337-0948 *Web Site:* www.levinegreenberg.com, pg 640

Rowles, Mary, Chicago Review Press, 814 N Franklin St, Chicago, IL 60610 *Tel:* 312-337-0747 *Toll Free Tel:* 800-888-4741 *Fax:* 312-337-5110 *E-mail:* editorial@ipgbook.com, pg 60

Roxanis, Dean, Hamilton Books, 4501 Forbes Blvd, Suite 200, Lanham, MD 20706 *Tel:* 301-459-3366, pg 112

Roxanis, Dean, Lexington Books, 4501 Forbes Blvd, Lanham, MD 20706 *Tel:* 301-459-3366 *Fax:* 301-429-5748 *Web Site:* www.lexingtonbooks.com, pg 153

Roxburgh, Stephen, Front Street Inc, 862 Haywood Rd, Asheville, NC 28806 *Tel:* 828-254-8300 *Fax:* 828-221-2112 *E-mail:* contactus@frontstreetbooks.com *Web Site:* www.frontstreetbooks.com, pg 101

Roy, Bruno, Union des Ecrivaines et Ecrivains Quebecois, 3492 avenue Laval, Montreal, PQ H2X 3C8, Canada *Tel:* 514-849-8540 *Toll Free Tel:* 888-849-8540 *Fax:* 514-271-6239 *E-mail:* ecrivez@uneq.qc.ca *Web Site:* www.uneq.qc.ca, pg 701

Roy, Denise, Simon & Schuster, 1230 Avenue of the Americas, New York, NY 10020 *Tel:* 212-698-7000 *Toll Free Tel:* 800-223-2348 (cust serv); 800-223-2336 (orders) *Toll Free Fax:* 800-943-9831 (orders) *Web Site:* www.simonsays.com, pg 248

Royster, Paul, University of Nebraska Press, 233 N Eighth St, Lincoln, NE 68588-0255 *Tel:* 402-472-3581 *Toll Free Tel:* 800-755-1105 (orders) *Fax:* 402-472-0308 *Toll Free Fax:* 800-526-2617 *E-mail:* press@unl.edu *Web Site:* www.nebraskapress.unl.edu; www.bisonbooks.com, pg 283

Rozier, Adriane, Scholastic Paperbacks, Teaching Resources & Reading Counts, 557 Broadway, New York, NY 10012-3999 *Tel:* 212-965-7241 *Fax:* 212-965-7487 *Web Site:* www.scholastic.com, pg 242

Rubenstein, Sally, Minnesota Historical Society Press, 345 Kellogg Blvd W, St Paul, MN 55102-1906 *Tel:* 651-296-2264 *Toll Free Tel:* 800-621-2736 *Fax:* 651-297-1345 *Toll Free Fax:* 800-621-8476 *Web Site:* www.mnhs.org/mhspress, pg 175

Rubert, Cathy, Traders Press Inc, 703 Laurens Rd, Greenville, SC 29607-1912 *Tel:* 864-298-0222 *Toll Free Tel:* 800-927-8222 *Fax:* 864-298-0221 *Web Site:* www.traderspress.com, pg 273

Rubie, Peter, Peter Rubie Literary Agency, 240 W 35 St, Suite 500, New York, NY 10001 *Tel:* 212-279-1776 *Fax:* 212-279-0927 *E-mail:* pralit@aol.com *Web Site:* www.prlit.com, pg 653

Rubiera, Saundra, Writers Workshop in Children's Literature, 10305 SW 127 Ct, Miami, FL 33186 *Tel:* 305-382-2677, pg 749

Rubillo, Jim, National Council of Teachers of Mathematics, 1906 Association Dr, Reston, VA 20191-1502 *Tel:* 703-620-9840 *Toll Free Tel:* 800-235-7566 *Fax:* 703-476-2970 *E-mail:* orders@nctm.org *Web Site:* www.nctm.org, pg 183

Rubin, Barry, Jewish New Testament Publications Inc, PO Box 615, Clarksville, MD 21029 *Tel:* 410-764-6144 *Fax:* 410-764-1376 *E-mail:* jntp@messianicjewish.net; rightsandpermissions@messianicjewish.net (rights & perms) *Web Site:* www.messianicjewish.net/jntp, pg 140

Rubin, Barry, Lederer Books, 6204 Park Heights Ave, Baltimore, MD 21215-3600 *Tel:* 410-358-6471 *Toll Free Tel:* 800-773-6574 *Fax:* 410-764-1376 *E-mail:* lederer@messianicjewish.net; rightsandpermissions@messianicjewidh.net (rights & perms) *Web Site:* messianicjewish.net, pg 151

Rubin, Barry, Messianic Jewish Publishers, 6204 Park Heights Ave, Baltimore, MD 21215-3600 *Tel:* 410-358-6471 *Toll Free Tel:* 800-773-6574 *Fax:* 410-

764-1376 *E-mail:* lederer@messianicjewish.net; rightsandpermissions@messianicjewish.net (rights & perms) *Web Site:* messianicjewish.net, pg 172

Rubin, Cheryl, DC Comics, 1700 Broadway, New York, NY 10019 *Tel:* 212-636-5400 *Toll Free Tel:* 800-759-0190 (distribution) *Fax:* 212-636-5481 *Web Site:* www.dccomics.com; www.madmag.com, pg 77

Rubin, David M, Syracuse University, SI Newhouse School of Public Communications, 215 University Place, Syracuse, NY 13244-2100 *Tel:* 315-443-2301 *Fax:* 315-443-3946 *E-mail:* newhouse@syr.edu *Web Site:* www.newhouse.syr.edu, pg 754

Rubin, Donald S, The McGraw-Hill Companies Inc, 1221 Avenue of the Americas, 50th fl, New York, NY 10020 *Tel:* 212-512-2000 *E-mail:* webmaster@mcgraw-hill.com *Web Site:* www.mcgraw-hill.com, pg 167

Rubin, Ellen, Rip Van Winkle Award, 252 Hudson Ave, Albany, NY 12210 *Tel:* 518-432-6952 (NY Libr Assn) *Web Site:* www.nyla.org, pg 802

Rubin, Hanna, Peter Rubie Literary Agency, 240 W 35 St, Suite 500, New York, NY 10001 *Tel:* 212-279-1776 *Fax:* 212-279-0927 *E-mail:* pralit@aol.com *Web Site:* www.prlit.com, pg 653

Rubin, Irene, Amsco School Publications Inc, 315 Hudson St, New York, NY 10013-1085 *Tel:* 212-886-6500; 212-886-6565 *Toll Free Tel:* 800-969-8398 *Fax:* 212-675-7010 *E-mail:* info@amscopub.com *Web Site:* www.amscopub.com, pg 19

Rubin, Lorna, Triad Publishing Co, PO Drawer 13355, Gainesville, FL 32604 *Tel:* 352-373-5800 *Fax:* 352-373-1488 *Toll Free Fax:* 800-854-4947 *Web Site:* www.triadpublishing.com, pg 275

Rubin, Melvin L, Triad Publishing Co, PO Drawer 13355, Gainesville, FL 32604 *Tel:* 352-373-5800 *Fax:* 352-373-1488 *Toll Free Fax:* 800-854-4947 *Web Site:* www.triadpublishing.com, pg 275

Rubin, Michelle, Writers House LLC, 21 W 26 St, New York, NY 10010 *Tel:* 212-685-2400 *Fax:* 212-685-1781, pg 662

Rubin, Reka, Quirk Books, 215 Church St, Philadelphia, PA 19106 *Tel:* 215-627-3581 *Fax:* 215-627-5220 *E-mail:* general@quirkbooks.com *Web Site:* www.quirkbooks.com, pg 224

Rubin, Stan Sanvel, The Brockport Writers' Forum, 350 New Campus Dr, Brockport, NY 14420-2968 *Tel:* 585-395-5713 *Fax:* 585-395-2391 *Web Site:* www.acs.brockport.edu/~wforum/Main.html, pg 742

Rubin, Stephen, Doubleday Broadway Publishing Group, 1745 Broadway, New York, NY 10019 *Tel:* 212-782-9000 *Toll Free Tel:* 800-223-6834; 800-223-5780 (sales) *Fax:* 212-302-7985 (correspondence); 212-492-9862 (orders), pg 82

Rubin, Stephen, Random House Inc, 1745 Broadway, New York, NY 10019 *Tel:* 212-782-9000 *Toll Free Tel:* 800-726-0600 *Web Site:* www.randomhouse.com, pg 226

Rubino, Holly, The Lyons Press, 246 Goose Lane, Guilford, CT 06437 *Tel:* 203-458-4500 *Toll Free Tel:* 800-243-0495 *Fax:* 203-458-4668 *Web Site:* www.lyonspress.com; www.globepequot.com, pg 160

Rubino, Dr Joseph, Vision Works Publishing, 47 Sheffield Rd, Suite A, Boxford, MA 01921 *Tel:* 978-887-3125 *Toll Free Tel:* 888-821-3135 *Fax:* 630-982-2134 *E-mail:* visionworksbooks@email.com, pg 291

Rubino, Victor J, Practising Law Institute, 810 Seventh Ave, New York, NY 10019 *Tel:* 212-824-5700 *Toll Free Tel:* 800-260-4PLI (260-4754 customer service) *Fax:* 212-265-4742 *Toll Free Fax:* 800-321-0093 *E-mail:* info@pli.edu *Web Site:* www.pli.edu, pg 217

Ruby, Brenda A, Woodbine House, 6510 Bells Mill Rd, Bethesda, MD 20817 *Tel:* 301-897-3570 *Toll Free Tel:* 800-843-7323 *Fax:* 301-897-5838 *E-mail:* info@woodbinehouse.com *Web Site:* www.woodbinehouse.com, pg 302

Rucci, Marysue, Simon & Schuster, 1230 Avenue of the Americas, New York, NY 10020 *Tel:* 212-698-7000 *Toll Free Tel:* 800-223-2348 (cust serv); 800-223-2336 (orders) *Toll Free Fax:* 800-943-9831 (orders) *Web Site:* www.simonsays.com, pg 248

Rucci, Shawn, Prometheus Books, 59 John Glenn Dr, Amherst, NY 14228 *Tel:* 716-691-0133 *Toll Free Tel:* 800-421-0351 *Fax:* 716-691-0137 *E-mail:* marketing@prometheusbooks.com; editorial@prometheusbooks.com *Web Site:* www.Prometheusbooks.com, pg 220

Rudansky, Jill, American Medical Publishers Association, 14 Fort Hill Rd, Huntington, NY 11743 *Tel:* 631-423-0075 *Fax:* 631-423-0075 *E-mail:* info@ampaonline.org *Web Site:* www.ampaonline.org, pg 677

Rudd, Alexandra, Random House Publishing Group, 1745 Broadway, New York, NY 10019 *Tel:* 800-200-3552 *Toll Free Fax:* 800-200-3552 *Web Site:* www.randomhouse.com, pg 227

Ruddell, Gary, Hobby House Press Inc, One Corporate Dr, Grantsville, MD 21536 *Tel:* 301-895-3792 *Toll Free Tel:* 800-554-1447 *Fax:* 301-895-5029 *E-mail:* email@hobbyhouse.com *Web Site:* www.hobbyhouse.com, pg 123

Rudenberg, Norman, Harris Literary Agency, PO Box 6023, San Diego, CA 92166 *Tel:* 619-697-0600 *Fax:* 619-697-0610 *E-mail:* hlit@adnc.com *Web Site:* harrisliterary.com, pg 634

Ruder, Zvi, Kluwer Academic Publishers, 101 Philip Dr, Assinippi Park, Norwell, MA 02061 *Tel:* 781-871-6600 *Fax:* 781-871-6528; 781-681-9045 (cust serv) *E-mail:* kluwer@wkap.com *Web Site:* www.wkap.nl, pg 146

Rudes, Jerome, Fifi Oscard Agency Inc, 110 W 40 St, New York, NY 10018 *Tel:* 212-764-1100 *Fax:* 212-840-5019 *E-mail:* agency@fifioscard.com *Web Site:* www.fifioscard.com, pg 647

Rudin, Alexa, Zagat Survey, 4 Columbus Circle, New York, NY 10019 *Tel:* 212-977-6000 *Toll Free Tel:* 800-333-3421 (gen inquiries); 888-371-5440 (orders); 800-540-9609 (corp sales) *Fax:* 212-977-9760; 802-864-9846 (order related) *E-mail:* corpsales@zagat.com; shop@zagat.com *Web Site:* www.zagat.com, pg 306

Rudin, Max, The Library of America, 14 E 60 St, New York, NY 10022 *Tel:* 212-308-3360 *Fax:* 212-750-8352 *E-mail:* info@loa.org *Web Site:* www.loa.org; www.loaacademic.org, pg 154

Rudman, Frances, National Learning Corp, 212 Michael Dr, Syosset, NY 11791 *Tel:* 516-921-8888 *Toll Free Tel:* 800-645-6337 *Fax:* 516-921-8743 *Web Site:* www.passbooks.com, pg 184

Rudman, Michael P, National Learning Corp, 212 Michael Dr, Syosset, NY 11791 *Tel:* 516-921-8888 *Toll Free Tel:* 800-645-6337 *Fax:* 516-921-8743 *Web Site:* www.passbooks.com, pg 184

Rudolph, Heather, Information Today, Inc, 143 Old Marlton Pike, Medford, NJ 08055-8750 *Tel:* 609-654-6266 *Toll Free Tel:* 800-300-9868 (cust serv) *Fax:* 609-654-4309 *E-mail:* custserv@infotoday.com *Web Site:* www.infotoday.com, pg 133

Rudolph, John, G P Putnam's Sons (Children's), 345 Hudson St, New York, NY 10014 *Tel:* 212-366-2000 *E-mail:* online@penguinputnam.com *Web Site:* www.penguin.com, pg 223

Rue, Robin, Writers House LLC, 21 W 26 St, New York, NY 10010 *Tel:* 212-685-2400 *Fax:* 212-685-1781, pg 662

Ruebelman, Martha, EDCO Publishing Inc, 2648 Lapeer Rd, Auburn Hills, MI 48326 *Tel:* 248-475-4678 *Toll Free Tel:* 888-510-3326 *Fax:* 248-475-9122 *E-mail:* info@edcopublishing.com *Web Site:* www.edcopublishing.com, pg 87

Ruenzel, Nancy, Peachpit Press, 1249 Eighth St, Berkeley, CA 94710 *Tel:* 510-524-2178 *Fax:* 510-524-2221 *E-mail:* firstname.lastname@peachpit.com *Web Site:* www.peachpit.com, pg 206

Ruetschlin, David, Phi Delta Kappa International, 408 N Union, Bloomington, IN 47401 *Tel:* 812-339-1156 *Toll Free Tel:* 800-766-1156 *Fax:* 812-339-0018 *E-mail:* information@pdkintl.org *Web Site:* www.pdkintl.org, pg 211

Ruff, Felicia J, Stanley Drama Award, One Campus Rd, Staten Island, NY 10301 *Tel:* 718-390-3157 *Fax:* 718-390-3323, pg 807

Ruffenach, Pascal, Twenty-Third Publications, 185 Willow St, Mystic, CT 06355 *Tel:* 860-536-2611 *Toll Free Tel:* 800-321-0411 (orders) *Fax:* 860-536-5674 (edit) *Toll Free Fax:* 800-572-0788, pg 277

Ruffner, Frederick G, Omnigraphics Inc, 615 Griswold St, Detroit, MI 48226 *Tel:* 313-961-1340 *Toll Free Tel:* 800-234-1340 (cust serv) *Fax:* 313-961-1383 *Toll Free Fax:* 800-875-1340 (cust serv) *E-mail:* info@omnigraphics.com *Web Site:* www.omnigraphics.com, pg 197

Ruffner, Peter E, Omnigraphics Inc, 615 Griswold St, Detroit, MI 48226 *Tel:* 313-961-1340 *Toll Free Tel:* 800-234-1340 (cust serv) *Fax:* 313-961-1383 *Toll Free Fax:* 800-875-1340 (cust serv) *E-mail:* info@omnigraphics.com *Web Site:* www.omnigraphics.com, pg 197

Ruggere, Christine A, Bibliographical Society of America, PO Box 1537, Lenox Hill Sta, New York, NY 10021-0043 *Tel:* 212-452-2710 *Fax:* 212-452-2710 *E-mail:* bsa@bibsocamer.org *Web Site:* www.bibsocamer.org, pg 681

Ruggiero, Greg, Seven Stories Press, 140 Watts St, New York, NY 10013 *Tel:* 212-226-8760 *Toll Free Tel:* 800-283-3572 *Fax:* 212-226-1411 *E-mail:* info@sevenstories.com *Web Site:* www.sevenstories.com, pg 245

Ruggiero, Vincenzo, Penguin Group (USA) Inc, 375 Hudson St, New York, NY 10014 *Tel:* 212-366-2000 *Fax:* 212-366-2666 *E-mail:* online@uspenguingroup.com *Web Site:* www.penguin.com, pg 208

Rugland, Trudy, Theosophical University Press, PO Box C, Pasadena, CA 91109-7107 *Tel:* 626-798-3378 *Fax:* 626-798-4749 *E-mail:* tupress@theosociety.org *Web Site:* www.theosociety.org, pg 268

Ruiz, Hari, Central Ohio Writers of Literature for Children, c/o St Joseph Montessori School, 933 Hamlet St, Columbus, OH 43201-3595 *Tel:* 614-291-8644 *Fax:* 614-291-7411 *E-mail:* cowriters@mail.com *Web Site:* www.sjms.net/conf, pg 742

Ruiz, Karen, House to House Publications, 1924 W Main St, Ephrata, PA 17522 *Tel:* 717-738-3751 *Toll Free Tel:* 800-848-5892 *Fax:* 717-738-0656 *E-mail:* H2HP@dcfi.org *Web Site:* www.dcfi.org, pg 127

Rukkila, Roy, M R T S, PO Box 874402, Tempe, AZ 85287-4402 *Tel:* 480-727-6503 *Toll Free Tel:* 800-666-2211 *Fax:* 480-727-6505 *Toll Free Fax:* 800-688-2877 *E-mail:* mrts@asu.edu *Web Site:* www.asu.edu/clas/acmrs/mrts, pg 160

Rule, Scott, The Donning Co/Publishers, 184 Business Park Dr, Suite 206, Virginia Beach, VA 23462 *Tel:* 757-497-1789; 660-376-3543 (Missouri office) *Toll Free Tel:* 800-296-8572 *Fax:* 757-497-2542 *Web Site:* www.donning.com, pg 82

Ruley, Margaret, Jane Rotrosen Agency LLC, 318 E 51 St, New York, NY 10022 *Tel:* 212-593-4330 *Fax:* 212-935-6985, pg 653

Rulon-Miller, Rob, Antiquarian Booksellers' Association of America, 20 W 44 St, 4th fl, New York, NY 10036 *Tel:* 212-944-8291 *Fax:* 212-944-8293 *E-mail:* hq@abaa.org *Web Site:* www.abaa.org, pg 678

Rumble, Brant, Scribner, 1230 Avenue of the Americas, New York, NY 10020, pg 244

Rundall, Nick, Whitecap Books Ltd, 351 Lynn Ave, North Vancouver, BC V7J 2C4, Canada *Tel:* 604-980-9852 *Toll Free Tel:* 800-870-3442 ext 239 & 241 (cust serv) *Fax:* 604-980-8197 *Toll Free Fax:* 888-661-6630 (orders only) *E-mail:* whitecap@whitecap.ca *Web Site:* www.whitecap.ca, pg 567

Runde, Rich, Carlisle Communications Ltd, 4242 Chavenelle Dr, Dubuque, IA 52002-2650 *Tel:* 563-557-1500 *Fax:* 563-557-1376 *E-mail:* carlisle@ carcomm.com *Web Site:* www.carcomm.com, pg 593

Runge, Gailen, C & T Publishing Inc, 1651 Challenge Dr, Concord, CA 94520 *Tel:* 925-677-0377 *Toll Free Tel:* 800-284-1114 *Fax:* 925-677-0373 *E-mail:* ctinfo@ctpub.com *Web Site:* www.ctpub.com, pg 51

Runyon, Nancy, McCutchan Publishing Corp, 3220 Blume Dr, Suite 197, Richmond, CA 94806 *Tel:* 510-758-5510 *Toll Free Tel:* 800-227-1540 *Fax:* 510-758-6078 *E-mail:* mccutchanpublish@aol.com *Web Site:* www.mccutchanpublishing.com, pg 166

Rupnow, John, The Edwin Mellen Press, 415 Ridge St, Lewiston, NY 14092 *Tel:* 716-754-2266 (mgr acqs); 716-754-8566 (mktg); 716-754-2788 (order fulfillment) *Fax:* 716-754-4056; 716-754-1860 (order fulfillment) *E-mail:* mellen@wzrd.com; cs@wzrd. com (customer service, fulfillment) *Web Site:* www. mellenpress.com, pg 171

Rupp-Rivers, Sharon, Westview Press, 5500 Central Ave, Boulder, CO 80301 *Tel:* 303-444-3541 *Toll Free Tel:* 800-386-5656 *Fax:* 720-406-7336 *E-mail:* westview.orders@perseusbooks.com *Web Site:* www.perseusbooksgroup.com; www. westviewpress.com, pg 297

Ruppel, Philip, McGraw-Hill Professional, 2 Penn Plaza, New York, NY 10121 *Tel:* 212-904-2000 *Web Site:* www.books.mcgraw-hill.com, pg 168

Ruppel, Philip, McGraw-Hill Trade, 2 Penn Plaza, New York, NY 10121, pg 169

Rusch, Robert D, Cadence Jazz Books, Cadence Bldg, Redwood, NY 13679 *Tel:* 315-287-2852 *Fax:* 315-287-2860 *E-mail:* cjb@cadencebuilding. com; cadence@cadencebuilding.com *Web Site:* www. cadencebuilding.com, pg 51

Rusch, Tom, Silman-James Press, 3624 Shannon Rd, Los Angeles, CA 90027 *Tel:* 323-661-9922 *Toll Free Tel:* 877-SJP-BOOK (757-2665) *Fax:* 323-661-9933 *E-mail:* silmanjamespress@earthlink.net *Web Site:* www.silmanjamespress.com, pg 247

Rush, Deborah, Coteau Books, 401-2206 Dewdney Ave, Regina, SK S4R 1H3, Canada *Tel:* 306-777-0170 *Toll Free Tel:* 800-440-4471 (Canada Only) *Fax:* 306-522-5152 *E-mail:* coteau@coteaubooks.com *Web Site:* www.coteaubooks.com, pg 541

Rush, Deborah, Indiana University Press, 601 N Morton St, Bloomington, IN 47404-3797 *Tel:* 812-855-8817 *Toll Free Tel:* 800-842-6796 (orders only) *Fax:* 812-855-7931 (orders only); 812-855-8507 *E-mail:* iupress@indiana.edu; iuorder@indiana.edu (orders) *Web Site:* www.iupress.indiana.edu, pg 132

Rushdie, Salman, Pen American Center, 588 Broadway, Suite 303, New York, NY 10012 *Tel:* 212-334-1660 *Fax:* 212-334-2181 *E-mail:* pen@pen.org *Web Site:* www.pen.org, pg 696

Rusin, William F, W W Norton & Company Inc, 500 Fifth Ave, New York, NY 10110-0017 *Tel:* 212-354-5500 *Toll Free Tel:* 800-233-4830 (orders & cust serv) *Fax:* 212-869-0856 *Toll Free Fax:* 800-458-6515 *Web Site:* www.wwnorton.com, pg 193

Russ, Steve, Medals of America Press, 114 Southchase Blvd, Fountain Inn, SC 29644 *Tel:* 864-862-6051 *Toll Free Tel:* 800-308-0849 *Fax:* 864-862-0256 *Toll Free Fax:* 800-407-8640 *E-mail:* press@usmedals.com *Web Site:* www.moapress.com, pg 170

Russell, Barry, Beacon Hill Press of Kansas City, PO Box 419527, Kansas City, MO 64141-6527 *Tel:* 816-931-1900 *Toll Free Tel:* 800-877-0700 (retail order) *Fax:* 816-753-4071 *Toll Free Fax:* 800-849-9827 (order) *Web Site:* www.beaconhillbooks.com, pg 34

Russell, Cheryl, New Strategist Publications Inc, 120 W State St, 4th fl, Ithaca, NY 14850 *Tel:* 607-273-0913 *Toll Free Tel:* 800-848-0842 *Fax:* 607-277-5009 *E-mail:* demographics@newstrategist.com *Web Site:* newstrategist.com, pg 189

Russell, Cindy, Mint Publishers Group, 62 June Rd, North Salem, NY 10560 *Tel:* 914-276-6576 *Fax:* 914-276-6579 *E-mail:* info@mintpub.com *Web Site:* www. mintpub.com, pg 175

Russell, Evie, Kentucky Women Writers Conference, University of Kentucky, 113 Bowman Hall, Lexington, KY 40506-0059 *Tel:* 859-257-8734; 859-257-6420; 859-257-8451 *Fax:* 859-257-8737 *E-mail:* kywwc@ hotmail.com *Web Site:* www.uky.edu/conferences/ kywwc, pg 744

Russell, James, Amy Writing Awards, PO Box 16091, Lansing, MI 48901-6091 *Tel:* 517-323-6233 *Fax:* 517-321-2572 *E-mail:* amyfoundtn@aol.com *Web Site:* www.amyfound.org, pg 759

Russell, Kenn, Henry Holt and Company, LLC, 115 W 18 St, New York, NY 10011 *Tel:* 212-886-9200 *Toll Free Tel:* 888-330-8477 (orders) *Fax:* 212-633-0748 *E-mail:* publicity@hholt.com *Web Site:* www. henryholt.com, pg 124

Russell, Marianne, Marcel Dekker Inc, 270 Madison Ave, New York, NY 10016 *Tel:* 212-696-9000 *Toll Free Tel:* 800-228-1160 (outside NY) *Fax:* 212-685-4540 *Web Site:* www.dekker.com, pg 78

Russell, Susan, A Abacus Group, PO Box 35, Ridgecrest, CA 93556 *Tel:* 760-375-5243 *Fax:* 760-375-1140 *E-mail:* gtd007@ridgenet.net *Web Site:* www.ridgenet.net/~gtd007, pg 617

Russell, Susan, Southeast Asia Publications, Northern Illinois University, Center for Southeast Asian Studies, Adams 412, DeKalb, IL 60115 *Tel:* 815-753-5790 *Fax:* 815-753-1776 *E-mail:* seap@niu.edu *Web Site:* www.niu.edu/cseas/seap, pg 254

Russell, Tom, Living Language, 1745 Broadway, New York, NY 10019 *Tel:* 212-572-6148 *Toll Free Tel:* 800-726-0600 (orders) *Fax:* 212-940-7400 *Toll Free Fax:* 800-659-2436 *E-mail:* livinglanguage@ randomhouse.com *Web Site:* www.livinglanguage.com, pg 157

Russell, Tom, The Princeton Review, 1745 Broadway, New York, NY 10019 *Tel:* 212-829-6928 *Toll Free Tel:* 800-733-3000 *Fax:* 212-940-7400 *E-mail:* princetonreview@randomhouse.com *Web Site:* www.princetonreview.com, pg 218

Russo, Kat, American Society for Training & Development (ASTD), 1640 King St, Alexandria, VA 22313-2043 *Tel:* 703-683-8100 *Toll Free Tel:* 800-628-2783 *Fax:* 703-683-1523 *E-mail:* publications@astd. org *Web Site:* www.astd.org, pg 17

Russo, Sarah, Other Press LLC, 307 Seventh Ave, Suite 1807, New York, NY 10001 *Tel:* 212-414-0054 *Toll Free Tel:* 877-THE-OTHER *Fax:* 212-414-0939 *E-mail:* orders@otherpress.com *Web Site:* www. otherpress.com, pg 573

Russo, Seth, Scholastic International, 557 Broadway, New York, NY 10012 *Tel:* 212-343-6100 *Fax:* 212-343-4712, pg 242

Rustad, Sharon, DBI Books, 700 E State St, Iola, WI 54990-0001 *Tel:* 715-445-2214 *Toll Free Tel:* 888-457-2873 *Fax:* 715-445-4087 *Web Site:* www.krause.com, pg 77

Rutberg, Steve, Lawrence Erlbaum Associates Inc, 10 Industrial Ave, Mahwah, NJ 07430-2262 *Tel:* 201-236-2199 *Toll Free Tel:* 800-9-BOOKS-9 (926-6579) *Fax:* 201-760-3735 *E-mail:* orders@erlbaum.com *Web Site:* www.erlbaum.com, pg 92

Ruth, Gary, American Bible Society, 1865 Broadway, New York, NY 10023-7505 *Tel:* 212-408-1200 *Toll Free Tel:* 800-322-4253 (orders only) *Fax:* 212-408-1259 *E-mail:* info@americanbible.org *Web Site:* www. americanbible.org, pg 12

Rutherford, Laura, Allyn & Bacon, 75 Arlington St, Suite 300, Boston, MA 02116 *Tel:* 617-848-6000 *Fax:* 617-848-6016 *E-mail:* AandBpub@aol.com *Web Site:* www.ablongman.com, pg 9

Rutkoff, Jane Brailove, New Jersey Council for the Humanities Book Award, 28 W State St, 6th fl, Trenton, NJ 08608 *Tel:* 609-695-4838 *Fax:* 609-695-4929 *E-mail:* njch@njch.org *Web Site:* www.njch.org, pg 793

Rutkowski, Larry, AGS Publishing, 4201 Woodland Rd, Circle Pines, MN 55014-1716 *Tel:* 651-287-7220 *Toll Free Tel:* 800-328-2560 *Toll Free Fax:* 800-471-8457 *E-mail:* agsmail@agsnet.com *Web Site:* www.agsnet. com, pg 7

Rutland, Amanda, Amon Carter Museum, 3501 Camp Bowie Blvd, Fort Worth, TX 76107-2631 *Tel:* 817-738-1933 (ext 625) *Toll Free Tel:* 800-573-1933 *Fax:* 817-336-1123 *Web Site:* www.cartermuseum.org, pg 54

Rutledge, Hugh, International Press of Boston Inc, PO Box 43502, Somerville, MA 02143 *Tel:* 617-623-3016 *Fax:* 617-623-3101 *E-mail:* orders@intlpress.com; journals@intlpress.com *Web Site:* www.intlpress.com, pg 137

Rutledge, Linda, Agatha Awards, PO Box 31137, Bethesda, MD 20824-1137 *Tel:* 703-751-4444 *Web Site:* www.malicedomestic.org, pg 757

Rutledge, Melanuie, Canada Council for the Arts, 350 Albert St, Ottawa, ON K1P 5V8, Canada *Tel:* 613-566-4414 *Toll Free Tel:* 800-263-5588 (Canada only) *Fax:* 613-566-4410 *Web Site:* www.canadacouncil.ca, pg 682

Rutledge, Pat, Pacific Northwest Booksellers Association, 317 W Broadway, Suite 214, Eugene, OR 97401-2890 *Tel:* 541-683-4363 *Fax:* 541-683-3910 *E-mail:* info@ pnba.org *Web Site:* www.pnba.org, pg 696

Rutman, Jim, Sterling Lord Literistic Inc, 65 Bleecker St, New York, NY 10012 *Tel:* 212-780-6050 *Fax:* 212-780-6095, pg 657

Rutsky, Alan, Rizzoli International Publications Inc, 300 Park Ave S, 3rd fl, New York, NY 10010-5399 *Tel:* 212-387-3400 *Toll Free Tel:* 800-522-6657 (orders only) *Fax:* 212-387-3535, pg 233

Rutter, Meredith, Publicom Inc, 60 Aberdeen Ave, Cambridge, MA 02138 *Tel:* 617-714-0300 *Fax:* 617-714-0268 *E-mail:* info@publicom1.com *Web Site:* www.publicom1.com, pg 609

Rutter, Sandy, American Society of Agricultural Engineers, 2950 Niles Rd, St Joseph, MI 49085-9659 *Tel:* 269-429-0300 *Fax:* 269-429-3852 *E-mail:* hq@ asae.org *Web Site:* www.asae.org, pg 18

Rutz, Kathryn, The Haworth Press Inc, 10 Alice St, Binghamton, NY 13904-1580 *Tel:* 607-722-5857 *Toll Free Tel:* 800-429-6784 *Fax:* 607-722-1424 *Toll Free Fax:* 800-895-0582 *E-mail:* getinfo@haworthpressinc. com *Web Site:* www.haworthpress.com, pg 118

Ruwe, Stephen, Literary & Creative Artists Inc, 3543 Albemarle St NW, Washington, DC 20008-4213 *Tel:* 202-362-4688 *Fax:* 202-362-8875 *E-mail:* query@ lcadc.com (no attachments) *Web Site:* www.lcadc.com, pg 641

Rux, Sandra, Connecticut Academy of Arts & Sciences, PO Box 208211, New Haven, CT 06520-8211 *Tel:* 203-432-3113 *Fax:* 203-432-5712 *E-mail:* caas@ yale.edu *Web Site:* www.yale.edu/caas, pg 67

Ryan, Anthony J, Ignatius Press, 2515 McAllister St, San Francisco, CA 94118 *Tel:* 415-387-2324 *Toll Free Tel:* 877-320-9276 (book orders) *Fax:* 415-387-0896 *E-mail:* info@ignatius.com *Web Site:* www.ignatius. com, pg 131

Ryan, Barbara, Editorial Options Inc, 353 Lexington Ave, New York, NY 10016 *Tel:* 212-986-2888 *Fax:* 212-986-1194 *Web Site:* www.edop.com, pg 597

Ryan, Becky, SDSU Writers' Conference, 5250 Campanile Dr, Rm 2503, San Diego, CA 92182-1920 *Tel:* 619-594-2517 *Fax:* 619-594-8566 *E-mail:* extended.std@sdsu.edu *Web Site:* www.ces. sdsu.edu, pg 747

Ryan, Edward, Cambridge University Press, 40 W 20 St, New York, NY 10011-4211 *Tel:* 212-924-3900 *Toll Free Tel:* 800-899-5222 *Fax:* 212-691-3239 *Web Site:* www.cambridge.org, pg 52

Ryan, Elaine M, American Public Human Services Association, 810 First St NE, Suite 500, Washington, DC 20002 *Tel:* 202-682-0100 *Fax:* 202-289-6555 *E-mail:* pubs@aphsa.org *Web Site:* www.aphsa.org, pg 677

Ryan, George, PIA/GATF (Graphic Arts Technical Foundation), 200 Deer Run Rd, Sewickley, PA 15143-2600 *Tel:* 412-741-6860 *Toll Free Tel:* 800-910-4283 *Fax:* 412-741-2311 *E-mail:* info@gain.net *Web Site:* www.gain.net, pg 697

Ryan, Jane, RAND Corp, 1776 Main St, Santa Monica, CA 90407 *Tel:* 310-393-0411 *Fax:* 310-451-6996 *E-mail:* jane_ryan@rand.org *Web Site:* www.rand.org, pg 225

Ryan, John, National Learning Corp, 212 Michael Dr, Syosset, NY 11791 *Tel:* 516-921-8888 *Toll Free Tel:* 800-645-6337 *Fax:* 516-921-8743 *Web Site:* www.passbooks.com, pg 184

Ryan, Karen, American Society of Civil Engineers (ASCE), 1801 Alexander Bell Dr, Reston, VA 20191-4400 *Tel:* 703-295-6200 *Toll Free Tel:* 800-548-2723 *Fax:* 703-295-6278 *E-mail:* marketing@asce.org *Web Site:* www.asce.org, pg 18

Ryan, Mark D, New Brand Agency Group, LLC, 3389 Sheridan St, Suite 317, Hollywood, FL 33021 *Tel:* 954-579-8900 *Fax:* 443-241-2568 *Web Site:* www.literaryagent.net, pg 646

Ryan, Maureen, Ivan R Dee Publisher, 1332 N Halsted St, Chicago, IL 60622-2694 *Tel:* 312-787-6262 *Toll Free Tel:* 800-462-6420 (orders) *Fax:* 312-787-6269 *Toll Free Fax:* 800-338-4550 (orders) *E-mail:* elephant@ivanrdee.com *Web Site:* www.ivanrdee.com, pg 78

Ryan, Regina Sara, Hohm Press, PO Box 2501, Prescott, AZ 86302 *Tel:* 928-778-9189 *Toll Free Tel:* 800-381-2700 *Fax:* 928-717-1779 *E-mail:* hppublisher@cableone.net *Web Site:* www.hohmpress.com, pg 123

Ryan, Sean, Sky Publishing Corp, 49 Bay State Rd, Cambridge, MA 02138-1200 *Tel:* 617-864-7360 *Toll Free Tel:* 800-253-0245 *Fax:* 617-864-6117 *Web Site:* skyandtelescope.com, pg 250

Ryba, Richard, The Candace Lake Agency, 9200 Sunset Blvd, Suite 820, Los Angeles, CA 90069 *Tel:* 310-247-2115 *Fax:* 310-247-2116 *E-mail:* clagency@bwkliterary.com, pg 624

Ryder, Thomas, Reader's Digest Association Inc, Reader's Digest Rd, Pleasantville, NY 10570-7000 *Tel:* 914-238-1000 *Toll Free Tel:* 800-431-1726 *Fax:* 914-238-4559 *Web Site:* www.rd.com, pg 228

Ryder, Thomas O, Reader's Digest Children's Books, Reader's Digest Rd, Pleasantville, NY 10570-7000 *Tel:* 914-244-4800 *Toll Free Tel:* 800-934-0977, pg 228

Ryder, Thomas O, Reader's Digest General Books, Reader's Digest Rd, Pleasantville, NY 10570-7000 *Tel:* 914-238-1000 *Toll Free Tel:* 800-431-1726 *Fax:* 914-244-7436, pg 228

Ryder, Thomas O, Reader's Digest Trade Books, Reader's Digest Rd, Pleasantville, NY 10570-7000 *Tel:* 914-244-7445 *Fax:* 914-244-7605, pg 229

Ryder, Thomas O, Reader's Digest USA Select Editions, Reader's Digest Rd, Pleasantville, NY 10570-7000 *Tel:* 914-238-1000 *Toll Free Tel:* 800-310-6261 *Fax:* 914-238-4559, pg 229

Ryskamp, Bruce E, Zondervan, 5300 Patterson Ave SE, Grand Rapids, MI 49530 *Tel:* 616-698-6900 *Toll Free Tel:* 800-727-1309 (cust serv) *Fax:* 616-698-3439; 616-698-3255 (cust serv) *Web Site:* www.zondervan.com, pg 307

Rzasa, Cate, Elm Street Publishing Services Inc, 828 N Elm St, Hinsdale, IL 60521 *Tel:* 630-789-2102 *Fax:* 630-789-2105 *E-mail:* esps@elmst.com *Web Site:* www.elmst.com, pg 598

Sabene, Mauricio, Scholastic International, 557 Broadway, New York, NY 10012 *Tel:* 212-343-6100 *Fax:* 212-343-4712, pg 242

Sabia, Mary Ann, Charlesbridge Publishing Inc, 85 Main St, Watertown, MA 02472 *Tel:* 617-926-0329 *Toll Free Tel:* 800-225-3214 *Fax:* 617-926-5720 *E-mail:* books@charlesbridge.com *Web Site:* www.charlesbridge.com, pg 58

Sabiston, Pat, Publishers Association of the South (PAS), 4412 Fletcher St, Panama City, FL 32405-1017 *Tel:* 850-914-0766 *Fax:* 850-769-4348 *E-mail:* executive@pubsouth.org *Web Site:* www.pubsouth.org, pg 698

Sablone, Frank, Tag & Label Manufacturers Institute Inc, 40 Shuman Blvd, Suite 295, Naperville, IL 60563 *Tel:* 630-357-9222 *Fax:* 630-357-0192 *E-mail:* office@tlmi.com *Web Site:* www.tlmi.com, pg 701

Sach, Jacky, BookEnds LLC, 136 Long Hill Rd, Gillette, NJ 07933 *Tel:* 908-604-2652 *E-mail:* editor@bookends-inc.com *Web Site:* www.bookends-inc.com, pg 622

Sachdev, Rachana, Susquehanna University Press, Associated University Presses, 2010 Eastpark Blvd, Cranbury, NJ 08512 *Tel:* 609-655-4770 *Fax:* 609-655-8366 *E-mail:* aup440@aol.com, pg 262

Sachner, Heidi, Newmarket Publishing & Communications, 18 E 48 St, New York, NY 10017 *Tel:* 212-832-3575 *Toll Free Tel:* 800-669-3903 *Fax:* 212-832-3629 *E-mail:* mailbox@newmarketpress.com *Web Site:* www.newmarketpress.com, pg 190

Sachner, Mark, Gareth Stevens Inc, 330 W Olive St, Suite 100, Milwaukee, WI 53212 *Tel:* 414-332-3520 *Toll Free Tel:* 800-542-2595 *Fax:* 414-332-3567 *E-mail:* info@gspub.com; info@worldalmanaclibrary.com *Web Site:* www.garethstevens.com; www.worldalmanaclibrary.com, pg 102

Sachs, Robert, National Cable Telecommunications Association (NCTA), 1724 Massachusetts Ave NW, Washington, DC 20036 *Tel:* 202-775-3550 *Fax:* 202-775-3676 *Web Site:* www.ncta.com, pg 692

Sacilotto, Loriana, Harlequin Enterprises Ltd, 225 Duncan Mill Rd, Don Mills, ON M3B 3K9, Canada *Tel:* 416-445-5860 *Fax:* 416-445-8655 *Web Site:* www.eharlequin.com; www.luna-books.com; www.mirabooks.com; www.reddressink.com; www.steeplehill.com, pg 549

Sacilotto, Loriana, Worldwide Library, 225 Duncan Mill Rd, Don Mills, ON M3B 3K9, Canada *Tel:* 416-445-5860 *Fax:* 416-445-8655; 416-445-8736 *Web Site:* www.eharlequin.com, pg 567

Sacks, Marvin, Epimetheus Books Inc, 2711 Centerville Rd, Suite 120-5336, Wilmington, DE 19808-1643 *Tel:* 646-345-2030 *E-mail:* epimetheus@att.net *Web Site:* www.epimetheusbooks.com, pg 91

Sacramento, Anthony R, The United Educators Inc, 900 N Shore Dr, Suite 140, Lake Bluff, IL 60044 *Tel:* 847-234-3700 *Fax:* 847-234-8705 *E-mail:* arslms@aol.com, pg 279

Sader, Pam, Scholastic Library Publishing, 90 Old Sherman Tpke, Danbury, CT 06816 *Tel:* 203-797-3500 *Toll Free Tel:* 800-621-1115 *Fax:* 203-797-3657 *Web Site:* www.scholasticlibrary.com, pg 242

Sadler, Dutch, PRIMEDIA Business Directories & Books, 9800 Metcalf Ave, Overland Park, KS 66212 *Tel:* 913-967-1719 *Toll Free Tel:* 800-453-9620; 800-262-1954 (cust serv) *Fax:* 913-967-1901 *Toll Free Fax:* 800-633-6219 *E-mail:* bookorders@primediabooks.com *Web Site:* www.primediabooks.com, pg 218

Sadler, Kim Martin, The Pilgrim Press/United Church Press, 700 Prospect Ave, Cleveland, OH 44115-1100 *Tel:* 216-736-3761 *Toll Free Tel:* 800-537-3394 (cust serv) *Fax:* 216-736-2207 *E-mail:* thepilgrimpress@thepilgrimpress.com *Web Site:* www.thepilgrimpress.com; www.theunitedchurchpress.com, pg 213

Sadowski, Frank, Alba House, 2187 Victory Blvd, Staten Island, NY 10314 *Tel:* 718-761-0047 (edit & prodn); 718-698-2759 (mktg & billing) *Toll Free Tel:* 800-343-2522 *Fax:* 718-761-0057 *E-mail:* albabooks@aol.com *Web Site:* www.albahouse.org, pg 7

Sadowski, Michael, Harvard Education Publishing Group, 8 Story St, 1st fl, Cambridge, MA 02138 *Tel:* 617-495-3432 *Toll Free Tel:* 800-513-0763 *Fax:* 617-496-3584 *E-mail:* hepg@harvard.edu *Web Site:* gseweb.harvard.edu/hepg, pg 117

Saenz, Benjamin, University of Texas at El Paso, Dept Creative Writing, MFA with Bilingual Option, 500 W University Ave, PMB 670, El Paso, TX 79968-9991 *Tel:* 915-747-5713 *Fax:* 915-747-5523 *E-mail:* mfadirector@utep.edu *Web Site:* www.utep.edu/cw, pg 756

Saffel, Steve, Del Rey Books, 1745 Broadway, New York, NY 10019 *E-mail:* delrey@randomhouse.com *Web Site:* www.randomhouse.com, pg 78

Saffel, Steve, Random House Publishing Group, 1745 Broadway, New York, NY 10019 *Toll Free Tel:* 800-200-3552 *Toll Free Fax:* 800-200-3552 *Web Site:* www.randomhouse.com, pg 227

Sagalyn, Raphael, The Sagalyn Literary Agency, 7201 Wisconsin Ave, Suite 675, Bethesda, MD 20814 *Tel:* 301-718-6440 *Fax:* 301-718-6444 *E-mail:* agency@sagalyn.com *Web Site:* www.sagalyn.com, pg 653

Sagstetter, Karen, National Gallery of Art, Fourth St & Constitution Ave, Landover, MD 20565 *Tel:* 202-842-6200 *Fax:* 202-408-8530 *Web Site:* www.nga.gov, pg 183

Sahatdjian, David, Girl Scouts of the USA, 420 Fifth Ave, New York, NY 10018-2798 *Tel:* 212-852-8000 *Toll Free Tel:* 800-478-7248 *Fax:* 212-852-6511 *Web Site:* www.girlscouts.org, pg 105

Saielli, Robert J, Young People's Press Inc (YPPI), 3033 Fifth Ave, Suite 200, San Diego, CA 92103 *Tel:* 619-688-9040 *Toll Free Tel:* 800-231-9774 *Fax:* 619-688-9044 *E-mail:* info@youngpeoplespress.com *Web Site:* www.youngpeoplespress.com, pg 306

Saikia-Wilson, Rebecca, Houghton Mifflin Trade & Reference Division, 222 Berkeley St, Boston, MA 02116-3764 *Tel:* 617-351-5000 *Toll Free Tel:* 800-225-3362 *Web Site:* www.houghtonmifflinbooks.com, pg 126

Saint-Jean, Guy, Guy Saint-Jean editeur Inc, 3154 Blvd Industriel, Laval, PQ H7L 4P7, Canada *Tel:* 450-663-1777 *Fax:* 450-663-6666 *E-mail:* saint-jean.editeur@qc.aira.com *Web Site:* www.saint-jeanediteur.com, pg 560

Saint-Jean, Marie-Claire, Guy Saint-Jean editeur Inc, 3154 Blvd Industriel, Laval, PQ H7L 4P7, Canada *Tel:* 450-663-1777 *Fax:* 450-663-6666 *E-mail:* saint-jean.editeur@qc.aira.com *Web Site:* www.saint-jeanediteur.com, pg 560

Saint-Jean, Nicole, Guy Saint-Jean editeur Inc, 3154 Blvd Industriel, Laval, PQ H7L 4P7, Canada *Tel:* 450-663-1777 *Fax:* 450-663-6666 *E-mail:* saint-jean.editeur@qc.aira.com *Web Site:* www.saint-jeanediteur.com, pg 560

Sakamoto, Tim, IN-D Press, PO Box 642556, Los Angeles, CA 90064 *Tel:* 310-445-9326 *Fax:* 310-694-0222 *E-mail:* info@in-d.com *Web Site:* www.in-d.com, pg 132

Sakoian, Carol, Scholastic International, 557 Broadway, New York, NY 10012 *Tel:* 212-343-6100 *Fax:* 212-343-4712, pg 242

Sakowski, Carolyn, John F Blair Publisher, 1406 Plaza Dr, Winston-Salem, NC 27103 *Tel:* 336-768-1374 *Toll Free Tel:* 800-222-9796 *Fax:* 336-768-9194 *E-mail:* blairpub@blairpub.com *Web Site:* www.blairpub.com, pg 41

Saladino, Linda, The Conference Board Inc, 845 Third Ave, New York, NY 10022 *Tel:* 212-759-0900 *Fax:* 212-980-7014 *E-mail:* info@conference-board.org *Web Site:* www.conference-board.org, pg 66

Salamie, David E, InfoWorks Development Group, 2801 Cook Creek Dr, Ann Arbor, MI 48103-8962 *Tel:* 734-327-9669 *Fax:* 734-327-9686, pg 602

Salem, Deborah, Humane Society Press, 2100 L St NW, Washington, DC 20037 *Tel:* 202-452-1100 *Fax:* 301-258-3082 *Web Site:* www.hsus.org, pg 572

Salem, Lynn, Seedling Publications Inc, 520 E Bainbridge St, Elizabethtown, PA 17022 *Tel:* 614-267-7333 *Toll Free Tel:* 800-233-0759 *Fax:* 614-267-4205 *Toll Free Fax:* 888-834-1303 *E-mail:* sales@seedlingpub.com *Web Site:* www.seedlingpub.com, pg 244

Salemson, Steve, University of Wisconsin Press, 1930 Monroe St, 3rd fl, Madison, WI 53711 Tel: 608-263-1110 Toll Free Tel: 800-621-2736 (Orders) Fax: 608-263-1120 Toll Free Fax: 800-621-8476 (Orders) E-mail: uwiscpress@uwpress.wisc.edu (Main Office) Web Site: www.wisc.edu/wisconsinpress/, pg 286

Salender, Bruce, Jeffrey Norton Publishers Inc, One Orchard Park Rd, Madison, CT 06443 Tel: 203-245-0195 Toll Free Tel: 800-243-1234 Fax: 203-245-0769 Toll Free Fax: 888-453-4329 E-mail: info@audioforum.com Web Site: www.audioforum.com, pg 193

Saletan, Rebecca, Harcourt Trade Publishers, 525 "B" St, Suite 1900, San Diego, CA 92101 Tel: 619-231-6616 Toll Free Tel: 800-543-1918 (cust serv) Toll Free Fax: 800-235-0256 (cust serv) Web Site: www.harcourtbooks.com, pg 115

Saliba, Brian, Union Square Publishing, 857 Broadway, 3rd fl, New York, NY 10003 Tel: 212-255-6661 Fax: 212-255-6671 E-mail: cardozapub@aol.com Web Site: www.cardozapub.com, pg 278

Salisbury, Leila, The University Press of Kentucky, 663 S Limestone St, Lexington, KY 40508-4008 Tel: 859-257-8761; 859-257-8442 (mktg) Toll Free Tel: 800-839-6855 (orders) Fax: 859-323-1873 Web Site: www.kentuckypress.com, pg 287

Salitros, Linda, Texas A&M University Press, John H Lindsey Bldg, Lewis St, 4354 TAMU, College Station, TX 77843-4354 Tel: 979-845-1436 Toll Free Tel: 800-826-8911 (orders) Fax: 979-847-8752 Toll Free Fax: 888-617-2421 (orders) E-mail: fdl@tampress.tamu.edu Web Site: www.tamu.edu/upress/, pg 267

Salkanskas, Jill, McGraw-Hill/Osborne, 2100 Powell St, 10th fl, Emeryville, CA 94608 Tel: 510-420-7700 Toll Free Tel: 800-227-0900 Fax: 510-420-7703 Web Site: shop.osborne.com/cgi-bin/osborne, pg 168

Saller, Carol, Association of American University Presses, 1427 E 60 St, Chicago, IL 60637 Tel: 773-702-7700; 773-702-7600 Toll Free Tel: 800-621-2736 (orders) Fax: 773-702-9756 (sales); 773-660-2235 (orders); 773-702-2708 E-mail: general@press.uchicago.edu Web Site: www.press.uchicago.edu, pg 26

Salo, Gay, Piano Press, 1425 Ocean Ave, Suite 6, Del Mar, CA 92014 Tel: 619-884-1401 Fax: 858-459-3376 E-mail: pianopress@aol.com Web Site: www.pianopress.com, pg 212

Salser, Carl W, National Book Co, PO Box 8795, Portland, OR 97207-8795 Tel: 503-228-6345 Fax: 810-885-5811 E-mail: info@eralearning.com Web Site: www.eralearning.com, pg 182

Salser, Mark R, National Book Co, PO Box 8795, Portland, OR 97207-8795 Tel: 503-228-6345 Fax: 810-885-5811 E-mail: info@eralearning.com Web Site: www.eralearning.com, pg 182

Salt, Gary, The University of Arizona Press, 355 S Euclid Ave, Suite 103, Tucson, AZ 85719-6654 Tel: 520-621-1441 Toll Free Tel: 800-426-3797 (orders) Fax: 520-621-8899 Toll Free Fax: 800-426-3797 E-mail: uapress@uapress.arizona.edu Web Site: www.uapress.arizona.edu, pg 280

Salter, Janet, Julie Harris Playwright Award Competition, PO Box 39729, Los Angeles, CA 90039-0729, pg 777

Salter, Janet, The Marilyn Hall Award, PO Box 39729, Los Angeles, CA 90039-0729, pg 787

Saltman, Julie, Plume, 375 Hudson St, New York, NY 10014 Tel: 212-366-2000 Fax: 212-366-2666 E-mail: online@penguinputnam.com Web Site: www.penguin.com, pg 215

Saltz, Carole, Teachers College Press, 1234 Amsterdam Ave, New York, NY 10027 Tel: 212-678-3929 Fax: 212-678-4149 E-mail: tcpress@tc.columbia.edu Web Site: www.teacherscollegepress.com, pg 265

Salvador, Vanda, Paulines, 5610 rue Beaubien est, Montreal, PQ H1T 1X5, Canada Tel: 514-253-5610 Fax: 514-253-1907 E-mail: paulines.editions@videotron.ca, pg 557

Salvaille, Janick, Guerin Editeur Ltee, 4501 rue Drolet, Montreal, PQ H2T 2G2, Canada Tel: 514-842-3481 Toll Free Tel: 800-398-8337 Fax: 514-842-4923 Web Site: www.guerin-editeur.qc.ca, pg 549

Salvat-Golik, Marta, Ediciones Universal, 3090 SW Eighth St, Miami, FL 33135 Tel: 305-642-3355 Fax: 305-642-7978 E-mail: ediciones@ediciones.com Web Site: www.ediciones.com, pg 87

Salvatorelli, Tom, M E Sharpe Inc, 80 Business Park Dr, Suite 202, Armonk, NY 10504 Tel: 914-273-1800 Toll Free Tel: 800-541-6563 Fax: 914-273-2106 E-mail: info@mesharpe.com Web Site: www.mesharpe.com, pg 246

Salyards, Gail, Research Press, 2612 N Mattis Ave, Champaign, IL 61822 Tel: 217-352-3273 Toll Free Tel: 800-519-2707 Fax: 217-352-1221 E-mail: rp@researchpress.com Web Site: www.researchpress.com, pg 231

Salzer, Deborah, Playwrights Project, 450 "B" St, Suite 1020, San Diego, CA 92101-8093 Tel: 619-239-8222 Fax: 619-239-8225 E-mail: write@playwrightsproject.com Web Site: www.playwrightsproject.com, pg 799

Salzfass, Art, Book Marketing Works LLC, 50 Lovely St, Avon, CT 06001 Tel: 860-675-1344 Toll Free Tel: 800-562-4357 Fax: 203-729-5335 Web Site: www.bookmarketingworks.com, pg 43

Salzman, Richard, Salzman International, 824 Edwards St, Trinidad, CA 95570 Tel: 212-997-0115; 707-677-0241 Fax: 707-677-0242 Web Site: www.salzmaninternational.com, pg 667

Salzmann, Marianne, Brunswick Publishing Corp, 1386 Lawrenceville Plank Rd, Lawrenceville, VA 23868 Tel: 434-848-3865 Fax: 434-848-0607 E-mail: brunswickbooks@earthlink.net Web Site: www.brunswickbooks.com, pg 49

Salzmann, Oliver, Madison Press Books, 1000 Yonge St, Toronto, ON M4W 2K2, Canada Tel: 416-923-5027 Fax: 416-923-9708 E-mail: info@madisonpressbooks.com Web Site: www.madisonpressbooks.com, pg 553

Samen, Anita, Association of American University Presses, 1427 E 60 St, Chicago, IL 60637 Tel: 773-702-7700; 773-702-7600 Toll Free Tel: 800-621-2736 (orders) Fax: 773-702-9756 (sales); 773-660-2235 (orders); 773-702-2708 E-mail: general@press.uchicago.edu Web Site: www.press.uchicago.edu, pg 26

Samios, Craig, W B Saunders Ltd, 170 S Independence Mall W, Suite 300 E, Philadelphia, PA 19106-3399 Tel: 215-238-7800 Toll Free Tel: 800-545-2522 (cust serv) Fax: 215-238-7883 Web Site: www.elsevierhealth.com, pg 240

Samms, Robert L, Rapids Christian Press Inc, 5777 Vista Dr, Ferndale, WA 98248 Tel: 360-384-1747 Fax: 360-384-1747, pg 227

Samper, Marjorie, Lectorum Publications Inc, 524 Broadway, New York, NY 10012 Toll Free Tel: 800-853-3291 (admin, mktg & sales); 800-345-5946 (orders) Fax: 212-727-3035 Toll Free Fax: 877-532-8676 E-mail: lectorum@scholastic.com Web Site: www.lectorum.com, pg 151

Sample, Stephen, National Press Photographers Association Inc (NPPA), 3200 Croasdaile Dr, Suite 306, Durham, NC 27705 Tel: 919-383-7246 Fax: 919-383-7261 E-mail: info@nppa.org Web Site: www.nppa.org, pg 694

Samsa, George, Creative Arts Book Co, 833 Bancroft Way, Berkeley, CA 94710 Tel: 510-848-4777 Fax: 510-848-4844 E-mail: staff@creativeartsbooks.com; capublisher@yahoo.com Web Site: www.creativeartsbooks.com, pg 72

Samuels, Linda, Headlands Center for the Arts Residency for CA, NC, OH & NJ Writers, 944 Fort Barry, Sausalito, CA 94965 Tel: 415-331-2787 Fax: 415-331-3857 Web Site: www.headlands.org, pg 778

Samuelson, Bruce, Bernan, 4611-F Assembly Dr, Lanham, MD 20706-4391 Tel: 301-459-2255; 301-459-7666 (cust serv) Toll Free Tel: 800-274-4447;

800-274-4888 (cust serv) Fax: 301-459-9235; 301-459-0056 (cust serv) Toll Free Fax: 800-865-3450 E-mail: info@bernan.com Web Site: www.bernan.com, pg 37

Samuelson, Paul, Creative Arts Book Co, 833 Bancroft Way, Berkeley, CA 94710 Tel: 510-848-4777 Fax: 510-848-4844 E-mail: staff@creativeartsbooks.com; capublisher@yahoo.com Web Site: www.creativeartsbooks.com, pg 72

Sanchez, Julia, Cotsen Institute of Archaeology at UCLA, PO Box 951510, Los Angeles, CA 90095-1510 Tel: 310-825-7411 Fax: 310-206-4723 E-mail: ioapubs@ucla.edu Web Site: www.sscnet.ucla.edu/ioa, pg 69

Sand, Michael, Bulfinch Press, 1271 Avenue of the Americas, New York, NY 10020 Tel: 212-522-8700 Toll Free Tel: 800-759-0190 Fax: 212-467-2886 Web Site: www.twbookmark.com, pg 50

Sand, Thomas, Health Communications Inc, 3201 SW 15 St, Deerfield Beach, FL 33442-8190 Tel: 954-360-0909 Toll Free Tel: 800-851-9100 (cust serv); 800-441-5569 (order entry) Fax: 954-360-0034 Web Site: www.hcibooks.com, pg 119

Sandberg, Kirsten, Harvard Business School Press, 300 N Beacon St, Watertown, MA 02472 Tel: 617-783-7400 Toll Free Tel: 888-500-1016 Fax: 617-783-7664 E-mail: bookpublisher@mail1.hbsp.harvard.edu Web Site: www.hbsp.harvard.edu, pg 116

Sande, Avril, MacAdam/Cage Publishing Inc, 155 Sansome St, Suite 550, San Francisco, CA 94104 Tel: 415-986-7502 Toll Free Tel: 866-986-7470 Fax: 415-986-7414 E-mail: info@macadamcage.com Web Site: www.macadamcage.com, pg 161

Sanders, Bob, Mundania Press, 6470A Glenway Ave, Suite 109, Cincinnati, OH 45211-5222 Tel: 513-574-8902 Fax: 513-598-6800 E-mail: books@mundania.com Web Site: www.mundania.com, pg 180

Sanders, David, Ohio University Press, One Ohio University, Scott Quadrangle, Athens, OH 45701 Tel: 740-593-1155 Toll Free Tel: 800-621-2736 Fax: 740-593-4536 Web Site: www.ohio.edu/oupress/, pg 196

Sanders, David, Swallow Press, Scott Quadrangle, Athens, OH 45701 Tel: 740-593-1155 Toll Free Tel: 800-621-2736 (orders only) Fax: 740-593-4536 Toll Free Fax: 800-621-8476 (orders only) Web Site: www.ohiou.edu/oupress/, pg 263

Sanders, Doug, Sagamore Publishing LLC, 804 N Neil St, Champaign, IL 61820 Tel: 217-359-5940 Toll Free Tel: 800-327-5557 (orders) Fax: 217-359-5975 E-mail: books@sagamorepub.com Web Site: www.sagamorepub.com, pg 237

Sanders, Janna, Purple Pomegranate Productions, 84 Page St, San Francisco, CA 94102-5914 Tel: 415-864-2600 Fax: 415-864-3995 E-mail: info@jewsforjesus.org Web Site: www.jewsforjesus.org, pg 222

Sanders, Keith, Frank Luther Mott-Kappa Tau Alpha Research Award, University of Missouri, School of Journalism, Columbia, MO 65211-1200 Tel: 573-882-7685 Fax: 573-884-1720 E-mail: umcjourkta@missouri.edu, pg 791

Sanders, Pat, University of Manitoba Press, St Johns College, Winnipeg, MB R3T 2N2, Canada Tel: 204-474-9495 Fax: 204-474-7566 Web Site: www.umanitoba.ca/uofmpress, pg 565

Sanders, Ray, Purple House Press, 8138 US Hwy 62 E, Cynthiana, KY 41031 Tel: 859-235-9970 Fax: 859-235-9970 E-mail: phpress@earthlink.net Web Site: www.purplehousepress.com, pg 222

Sanders, Rob, Douglas & McIntyre Publishing Group, 2323 Quebec St, Suite 201, Vancouver, BC V5T 4S7, Canada Tel: 604-254-7191 Toll Free Tel: 800-565-9523 (orders in Canada) Fax: 604-254-9099 Toll Free Fax: 800-221-9985 (orders in Canada) E-mail: dm@douglas-mcintyre.com Web Site: www.douglas-mcintyre.com, pg 542

Sanders, Rob, Greystone Books, 2323 Quebec St, Suite 201, Vancouver, BC V5T 4S7, Canada Tel: 604-254-7191 Toll Free Tel: 800-667-6902 Fax: 604-254-9099, pg 548

Sanders, Susan, LexisNexis Canada, 123 Commerce Valley Dr E, Suite 700, Markham, ON L3T 7W8, Canada *Tel:* 905-479-2665 *Toll Free Tel:* 800-668-6481 *Fax:* 905-479-2826 *Toll Free Fax:* 800-461-3275 *E-mail:* orders@lexisnexis.ca *Web Site:* www.lexisnexis.ca, pg 552

Sanders, Victoria, Victoria Sanders & Associates, 241 Avenue of the Americas, Suite 11H, New York, NY 10014 *Tel:* 212-633-8811 *Fax:* 212-633-0525 *E-mail:* queriesvsa@hotmail.com *Web Site:* www.victoriasanders.com, pg 653

Sanderson, Camilla, Penguin Young Readers Group, 345 Hudson St, New York, NY 10014 *Tel:* 212-366-2000 *E-mail:* online@penguinputnam.com *Web Site:* www.penguin.com, pg 208

Sandifer, Glen, Red River Press, 3900 Roy Rd, Suite 37, Shreveport, LA 71107 *Tel:* 318-929-4196 *Fax:* 318-929-5125 *E-mail:* redriverpresskws@yahoo.com *Web Site:* www.achivalservices.com, pg 229

Sandifer, Kevin, Red River Press, 3900 Roy Rd, Suite 37, Shreveport, LA 71107 *Tel:* 318-929-4196 *Fax:* 318-929-5125 *E-mail:* redriverpresskws@yahoo.com *Web Site:* www.achivalservices.com, pg 229

Sandler, Joseph B, United Synagogue Book Service, 155 Fifth Ave, New York, NY 10010 *Tel:* 212-533-7800 (ext 2003) *Toll Free Tel:* 800-594-5617 (warehouse only) *Fax:* 212-253-5422 *E-mail:* booksvc@uscj.org *Web Site:* www.uscj.org/booksvc, pg 279

Sandler, Stanley, American Institute of Chemical Engineers (AICHE), 3 Park Ave, New York, NY 10016-5991 *Tel:* 212-591-7338 *Toll Free Tel:* 800-242-4363 *Fax:* 212-591-8888 *E-mail:* xpress@aiche.org *Web Site:* www.aiche.org, pg 15

Sandoval, Manuel G, University of Puerto Rico Press, Edificio EDUPR/Dialogo, Carr No 1, KM 12-0, Piso 2, Jardin Bota'nico Area Norte, San Juan, PR 00931 *Tel:* 787-758-6932; 787-758-8345 (sales); 787-250-0046; 787-250-0000 *Fax:* 787-753-9116; 787-751-8785 (sales dept), pg 284

Sands, Katharine, Sarah Jane Freymann Literary Agency, 59 W 71 St, Suite 9B, New York, NY 10023 *Tel:* 212-362-9277 *Fax:* 212-501-8240 *E-mail:* sjfs@aol.com, pg 631

Sandstrom, Joanne, Institute of East Asian Studies, University of California, IEAS Publications, 2223 Fulton St, Berkeley, CA 94720-2318 *Tel:* 510-643-6325 *Fax:* 510-643-7062 *E-mail:* easia@uclink.berkeley.edu *Web Site:* ieas.berkeley.edu/publications, pg 135

Sandum, Howard E, Sandum & Associates, 144 E 84 St, New York, NY 10028 *Tel:* 212-737-2011 *Fax:* 212-737-9296, pg 653

Sanek, Larry, Quality Education Data, Inc, 1625 Broadway, Suite 250, Denver, CO 80202 *Tel:* 303-209-9400 *Toll Free Tel:* 800-525-5811 *Fax:* 303-209-9444 *E-mail:* info@qeddata.com *Web Site:* www.qeddata.com, pg 223

Sanfilippo, Tony, The Pennsylvania State University Press, 820 N University Dr, University Support Bldg 1, Suite C, University Park, PA 16802-1003 *Tel:* 814-865-1327 *Toll Free Tel:* 800-326-9180 *Fax:* 814-863-1408 *Toll Free Fax:* 877 7782665 *Web Site:* www.psupress.org, pg 209

Sanford, David, Bantam Dell Publishing Group, 1745 Broadway, New York, NY 10019 *Tel:* 212-782-9000 *Toll Free Tel:* 800-223-6834 *Fax:* 212-302-7985 *Web Site:* www.randomhouse.com/bantamdell, pg 31

Sanford, Linda, Newbridge Educational Publishing, One Beeman Rd, Northborough, MA 01532 *Tel:* 508-571-6500 *Toll Free Tel:* 800-867-0307 *Fax:* 508-571-6502 *Toll Free Fax:* 800-456-2419 *E-mail:* info@newbridgeonline.com *Web Site:* www.newbridgeonline.com; www.newbridgepub.com, pg 190

Sanford, Sharon, Market Data Retrieval, One Forest Pkwy, Shelton, CT 06484 *Tel:* 203-926-4800 *Toll Free Tel:* 800-333-8802 *Fax:* 203-926-0784 *E-mail:* mdrinfo@dnb.com *Web Site:* www.schooldata.com, pg 163

Sangar, Puja, Stanford University Press, 1450 Page Mill Rd, Palo Alto, CA 94304-1124 *Tel:* 650-723-9434 *Fax:* 650-725-3457 *Web Site:* www.sup.org, pg 257

Sankar, Siva, PJD Publications Ltd, PO Box 966, Westbury, NY 11590-0966 *Tel:* 516-626-0650 *Fax:* 516-626-5546 *E-mail:* pjdsankar@msn.com *Web Site:* www.pjdonline.com; www.pjdpublications.com, pg 214

Sanmartin, Cristina, The MIT Press, 5 Cambridge Ctr, Cambridge, MA 02142 *Tel:* 617-253-5646 *Toll Free Tel:* 800-405-1619 (orders only) *Fax:* 617-258-6779 *Web Site:* mitpress.mit.edu, pg 175

Sanner, Cynthia, e-Scholastic, 568 Broadway, 9th fl, New York, NY 10012 *Tel:* 212-343-7100 *Fax:* 212-343-4949, pg 85

Sanny, Bob, Open Horizons Publishing Co, PO Box 205, Fairfield, IA 52556-0205 *Tel:* 641-472-6130 *Toll Free Tel:* 800-796-6130 *Fax:* 641-472-1560 *E-mail:* info@bookmarket.com *Web Site:* www.bookmarket.com, pg 197

Sansevere, John, Rights Unlimited Inc, 101 W 55 St, Suite 2D, New York, NY 10019 *Tel:* 212-246-0900 *Fax:* 212-246-2114 *E-mail:* faith@rightsunlimited.com *Web Site:* rightsunlimited.com, pg 651

Sansone, Jill, Hyperion, 77 W 66 St, 11th fl, New York, NY 10023-6298 *Tel:* 212-456-0100 *Toll Free Tel:* 800-759-0190 (cust serv) *Fax:* 212-456-0157 *Web Site:* hyperionbooks.com, pg 129

Santa, Shelley, Martingale & Co, 20205 144 Ave NE, Woodinville, WA 98072 *Tel:* 425-483-3313 *Toll Free Tel:* 800-426-3126 *Fax:* 425-486-7596 *E-mail:* info@martingale-pub.com *Web Site:* www.martingale-pub.com, pg 164

Santa, Rev Thomas, E T Nedder Publishing, 9121 E Tanque Verde, Suite 105, PMB 299, Tucson, AZ 85749-8390 *Tel:* 520-760-2742 *Toll Free Tel:* 877-817-2742 *Fax:* 520-760-5883 *E-mail:* enedder@hotmail.com *Web Site:* nedderpublishing.com, pg 186

Santarossa, Lauretta, Novalis Publishing, 49 Front St E, 2nd fl, Toronto, ON M5E 1B3, Canada *Tel:* 416-363-3303 *Toll Free Tel:* 800-387-7164 *Fax:* 416-363-9409 *Toll Free Fax:* 800-204-4140 *E-mail:* novalis@interlog.com *Web Site:* www.novalis.ca, pg 556

Santee, Mark, LearningExpress LLC, 55 Broadway, 8th fl, New York, NY 10006 *Tel:* 212-995-2566 *Toll Free Tel:* 800-295-9556 *Fax:* 212-995-5512 *E-mail:* customerservice@learnatest.com (cust serv) *Web Site:* www.learnatest.com, pg 151

Santek, Jerod, Loft-Mentor Series in Poetry & Creative Prose, Open Book, Suite 200, 1011 Washington Ave S, Minneapolis, MN 55415 *Tel:* 612-215-2575 *Fax:* 612-215-2576 *E-mail:* loft@loft.org *Web Site:* www.loft.org, pg 785

Santek, Jerod, McKnight Artist Fellowship for Writers, Open Book, Suite 200, 1011 Washington Ave S, Minneapolis, MN 55415 *Tel:* 612-215-2575 *Fax:* 612-215-2576 *E-mail:* loft@loft.org *Web Site:* www.loft.org, pg 788

Santi, Pat, Dog Writers' Association of America Inc (DWAA), 173 Union Rd, Coatesville, PA 19320 *Tel:* 610-384-2436 *Fax:* 610-384-2471 *E-mail:* dwaa@dwaa.org *Web Site:* www.dwaa.org, pg 686

Santi, Pat, Dog Writers' Association of America Inc (DWAA) Annual Awards, 173 Union Rd, Coatesville, PA 19320 *Tel:* 610-384-2436 *Fax:* 610-384-2471 *E-mail:* dwaa@dwaa.org; rhydowen@aol.com *Web Site:* www.dwaa.org, pg 770

Santiago, Ariel Selwyn, Vocalis Ltd, 100 Avalon Circle, Waterbury, CT 06710 *Tel:* 203-753-5244 *Fax:* 203-574-5433 *E-mail:* vocalis@sbcglobal.net; info@vocalisesl.com *Web Site:* www.vocalisesl.com; www.vocalisltd.com; www.vocalisfiction.com, pg 291

Santini, Robert, Prentice Hall Humanities & Social Sciences, One Lake St, Upper Saddle River, NJ 07458 *Tel:* 201-236-7000, pg 217

Santos-Gainer, Nancy, Fulbright Scholar Program, 3007 Tilden St NW, Suite 5-L, Washington, DC 20008-3009 *Tel:* 202-686-4000 *Fax:* 202-362-3442 *E-mail:* cieswebmaster@cies.iie.org *Web Site:* www.cies.org, pg 775

Santucci, Ernest, Agency Chicago, 28 E Jackson Blvd, 10th fl, Suite A-600, Chicago, IL 60604 *Tel:* 312-409-0205, pg 618

Sapir, Marc, The Museum of Modern Art, 11 W 53 St, New York, NY 10019 *Tel:* 212-708-9443 *Fax:* 212-333-6575 *E-mail:* moma_publications@moma.org *Web Site:* www.moma.org, pg 180

Sarada, Uma, Writers Guild of America East Inc (WGAE), 555 W 57 St, New York, NY 10019 *Tel:* 212-767-7800 *Fax:* 212-582-1909 *E-mail:* info@wgaeast.org *Web Site:* www.wgaeast.org, pg 703

Sarantos, DeLacy, Theosophical Publishing House/Quest Books, 306 W Geneva Rd, Wheaton, IL 60187 *Tel:* 630-665-0130 *Toll Free Tel:* 800-669-9425 *Fax:* 630-665-8791 *E-mail:* questbooks@theosmail.net *Web Site:* www.questbooks.net, pg 268

Saravese, Carolyn, Westview Press, 5500 Central Ave, Boulder, CO 80301 *Tel:* 303-444-3541 *Toll Free Tel:* 800-386-5656 *Fax:* 720-406-7336 *E-mail:* westview.orders@perseusbooks.com *Web Site:* www.perseusbooksgroup.com; www.westviewpress.com, pg 297

Saraydarian, Gita, TSG Publishing Foundation Inc, 28641 N 63 Place, Cave Creek, AZ 85331 *Tel:* 480-502-1909 *Fax:* 480-502-0713 *E-mail:* info@tsgfoundation.org *Web Site:* www.tsgfoundation.org, pg 276

Sargent, Brad, Inner Traditions International Ltd, One Park St, Rochester, VT 05767 *Tel:* 802-767-3174 *Toll Free Tel:* 800-246-8648 *Fax:* 802-767-3726 *E-mail:* orders@InnerTraditions.com *Web Site:* www.InnerTraditions.com, pg 134

Sargent, Brandi, Bear & Co Inc, One Park St, Rochester, VT 05767 *Tel:* 802-767-3174 *Toll Free Tel:* 800-932-3277 *Fax:* 802-767-3726 *E-mail:* orders@InnerTraditions.com *Web Site:* InnerTraditions.com, pg 34

Sargent, Dai, Ozark Publishing Inc, PO Box 228, Prairie Grove, AR 72753-0228 *Tel:* 479-846-2793 *Toll Free Tel:* 800-321-5671 *Fax:* 479-846-2843 *E-mail:* msworkal@pgtc.net, pg 201

Sargent, Dave, Ozark Publishing Inc, PO Box 228, Prairie Grove, AR 72753-0228 *Tel:* 479-846-2793 *Toll Free Tel:* 800-321-5671 *Fax:* 479-846-2843 *E-mail:* msworkal@pgtc.net, pg 201

Sargent, Herb, Writers Guild of America East Inc (WGAE), 555 W 57 St, New York, NY 10019 *Tel:* 212-767-7800 *Fax:* 212-582-1909 *E-mail:* info@wgaeast.org *Web Site:* www.wgaeast.org, pg 703

Sargent, John, Holtzbrinck Publishers, 175 Fifth Ave, New York, NY 10010 *Tel:* 212-674-5151 *Fax:* 212-420-9314 *E-mail:* firstname.lastname@hbpub.com *Web Site:* www.holtzbrinck.com, pg 124

Sargent, John, St Martin's Press LLC, 175 Fifth Ave, New York, NY 10010 *Tel:* 212-674-5151 *Fax:* 212-420-9314 *E-mail:* firstname.lastname@stmartins.com *Web Site:* www.stmartins.com, pg 238

Sargent, Michael, Tuttle Publishing, Airport Business Park, 364 Innovation Dr, North Clarendon, VT 05759-9436 *Tel:* 617-951-4080 (edit); 802-773-8930 *Toll Free Tel:* 800-526-2778 *Fax:* 617-951-4045 (edit); 802-773-6993 *Toll Free Fax:* 800-FAX-TUTL *E-mail:* info@tuttlepublishing.com *Web Site:* www.tuttlepublishing.com, pg 277

Sari, Paula, Wadsworth Publishing, 10 Davis Dr, Belmont, CA 94002-3002 *Tel:* 800-357-0092 *Fax:* 650-592-3342 *Toll Free Fax:* 800-522-4923 *Web Site:* www.wadsworth.com, pg 292

Sarma, Mukti H, Adenine Press Inc, 2066 Central Ave, Schenectady, NY 12304 *Tel:* 518-456-0784 *Fax:* 518-452-4955 *E-mail:* info@adeninepress.com *Web Site:* www.adeninepress.com, pg 5

Sarma, R H, Adenine Press Inc, 2066 Central Ave, Schenectady, NY 12304 *Tel:* 518-456-0784 *Fax:* 518-452-4955 *E-mail:* info@adeninepress.com *Web Site:* www.adeninepress.com, pg 5

Sarnoff, Richard, Random House Inc, 1745 Broadway, New York, NY 10019 *Tel:* 212-782-9000 *Toll Free Tel:* 800-726-0600 *Web Site:* www.randomhouse.com, pg 226

Sarracino, Ross, Walter Foster Publishing Inc, 23062 La Cadena Dr, Laguna Hills, CA 92653 *Tel:* 949-380-7510 *Toll Free Tel:* 800-426-0099 *Fax:* 949-380-7575 *Web Site:* www.walterfoster.com, pg 99

Sarracino, Ross, My Chaotic Life™, 23062 La Cadena Dr, Laguna Hills, CA 92653 *Tel:* 949-380-7510 *Toll Free Tel:* 800-426-0099 *Fax:* 949-380-7575 *Web Site:* www.mychaoticlife.com, pg 181

Sarrazin, Wendy, Tormont/Brimar Publication Inc, 338 St Antoine E, 3rd fl, Montreal, PQ H2Y 1A3, Canada *Tel:* 514-954-1441 *Fax:* 514-954-1443 *E-mail:* info@tormont.ca, pg 563

Sarris, Shirley, Salem Press Inc, 2 University Plaza, Suite 121, Hackensack, NJ 07601 *Tel:* 201-968-9899 *Toll Free Tel:* 800-221-1592 *Fax:* 201-968-1411 *E-mail:* csr@salempress.com *Web Site:* www.salempress.com, pg 239

Sarvetnick, Lois, Women Who Write, PO Box 652, Madison, NJ 07940 *Tel:* 908-232-1640 *Fax:* 908-317-8105 *E-mail:* info@womenwhowrite.org *Web Site:* www.womenwhowrite.org, pg 702

Saslow, Carl, Great Source Education Group, 181 Ballardvale St, Wilmington, MA 01887 *Tel:* 978-661-1300 *Toll Free Tel:* 800-289-4490 (orders), pg 108

Sassaman, Marcus, Pacific Printing & Imaging Association, 1400 SW Fifth Ave, Suite 815, Portland, OR 97201 *Toll Free Tel:* 877-762-7742 *Toll Free Fax:* 800-824-1911 *E-mail:* info@pacprinting.org *Web Site:* www.pacprinting.org, pg 696

Sather, Jan, Pine Forge Press, 2455 Teller Rd, Thousand Oaks, CA 91320 *Tel:* 805-499-4224 *Fax:* 805-499-0721 *E-mail:* info@sagepub.com *Web Site:* www.sagepub.com, pg 213

Satoh, Margaret, Society of Manufacturing Engineers, One SME Dr, Dearborn, MI 48121 *Tel:* 313-271-1500 *Toll Free Tel:* 800-733-4763 (cust serv) *Fax:* 313-271-2861 *Web Site:* www.sme.org, pg 252

Saunders, Margaret, The Drummond Publishing Group, 362 N Bedford St, East Bridgewater, MA 02333 *Tel:* 508-378-1110 *Fax:* 508-378-1105 *Web Site:* www.drummondpub.com, pg 84

Saunders, Margaret, Pre-Press Company Inc, 362 N Bedford St, East Bridgewater, MA 02333 *Tel:* 508-378-1100 (plant); 508-378-1101 (sales) *Fax:* 508-378-1105 *Web Site:* www.prepressco.com, pg 608

Saunders, Mark, The University of Virginia Press, PO Box 400318, Charlottesville, VA 22904-4318 *Tel:* 434-924-3468 (cust serv); 434-924-3469 (cust serv) *Toll Free Tel:* 800-831-3406 (cust serv) *Fax:* 434-982-2655 *Toll Free Fax:* 877-288-6400 *E-mail:* upressvirginia@virginia.edu *Web Site:* www.upressvirginia.edu, pg 285

Saunders, Neil, Publicom Inc, 60 Aberdeen Ave, Cambridge, MA 02138 *Tel:* 617-714-0300 *Fax:* 617-714-0268 *E-mail:* info@publicom1.com *Web Site:* www.publicom1.com, pg 609

Saunders, Peter, Garamond Press Ltd, 63 Mahogany Ct, Aurora, ON L4G 6M8, Canada *Tel:* 905-841-1460 *Toll Free Tel:* 800-898-9535 *Fax:* 905-841-3031 *E-mail:* garamond@web.ca *Web Site:* www.garamond.ca, pg 547

Saunders, Susan, Makeready Inc, 233 W 77 St, New York, NY 10024 *Tel:* 212-595-5083, pg 605

Saurer, Simon, Editions de l'Hexagone, 1010, rue de la Gauchetiere Est, Montreal, PQ H2L 2N5, Canada *Tel:* 514-523-1182 *Fax:* 514-282-7530 *E-mail:* vml@sogides.com *Web Site:* www.edhexagone.com, pg 544

Sautter, R Craig, The Society of Midland Authors (SMA), PO Box 10419, Chicago, IL 60610-0419 *Tel:* 773-506-7578 *Fax:* 773-784-5900 *E-mail:* info@midlandauthors.com *Web Site:* www.midlandauthors.com, pg 700

Sautter, R Craig, The Society of Midland Authors Awards, PO Box 10419, Chicago, IL 60610-0419 *Tel:* 773-506-7578 *Fax:* 773-784-5900 *E-mail:* info@midlandauthors.com *Web Site:* www.midlandauthors.com, pg 806

Savage, Eric, Neo-Tech Publishing, PO Box 60906, Boulder City, NV 89006-0906 *Tel:* 702-293-5552 *Fax:* 702-293-4342 *Web Site:* www.neo-tech.com, pg 187

Savage, Geoffrey, Sound & Vision, 359 Riverdale Ave, Toronto, ON M4J 1A4, Canada *Tel:* 416-465-2828 *Fax:* 416-465-0755 *Web Site:* www.soundandvision.com, pg 562

Savage, Jack, Whitehorse Press, 107 E Conway Rd, Center Conway, NH 03813 *Tel:* 603-356-6556 *Toll Free Tel:* 800-531-1133 *Fax:* 603-356-6590 *E-mail:* customerservice@whitehorsepress.com *Web Site:* www.whitehorsepress.com, pg 298

Savage, Michael P, Savage Press, 1209 Lincoln St, Superior, WI 54880 *Tel:* 715-394-9513 *Toll Free Tel:* 800-732-3867 *Fax:* 715-394-9513 *E-mail:* mail@savpress.com *Web Site:* www.savpress.com, pg 240

Savage, Roth, BizBest Media Corp, 860 Via de la Paz, Suite D-4, Pacific Palisades, CA 90272 *Tel:* 310-230-6868 *Toll Free Tel:* 800-873-5205; 877-424-9237 *Fax:* 310-454-6130 *E-mail:* info@bizbest.com *Web Site:* www.bizbest.com, pg 39

Savarese, Carolyn, Basic Books, 387 Park Ave S, 12th fl, New York, NY 10016-8810 *Tel:* 212-340-8100 *Toll Free Tel:* 800-242-7737 (orders) *Fax:* 212-340-8135 *E-mail:* basic.books@perseusbooks.com *Web Site:* www.basicbooks.com, pg 33

Savarese, Carolyn, Counterpoint Press, 387 Park Ave S, New York, NY 10016 *Tel:* 212-340-8100 *Fax:* 212-340-8135 (edit); 212-340-8115 *E-mail:* counterpointpress@perseusbooks.com *Web Site:* www.counterpointpress.com, pg 70

Savarese, Carolyn, Da Capo Press Inc, 11 Cambridge Center, Cambridge, MA 02142 *Tel:* 617-252-5200 *Toll Free Tel:* 800-242-7737 (orders) *Fax:* 617-252-5285 *E-mail:* custserve@lrp.com *Web Site:* www.dacapopress.com, pg 75

Savarese, Carolyn, Merloyd Lawrence Inc, 102 Chestnut St, Boston, MA 02108 *Tel:* 617-523-5895 *Fax:* 617-252-5285, pg 150

Savarese, Carolyn, The Perseus Books Group, 387 Park Ave S, 12th fl, New York, NY 10016 *Tel:* 212-340-8100 *Toll Free Tel:* 800-386-5656 (cust serv) *Fax:* 212-340-8115 *Web Site:* www.perseusbooksgroup.com, pg 210

Savarese, Carolyn, PublicAffairs, 250 W 57 St, Suite 1321, New York, NY 10107 *Tel:* 212-397-6666 *Toll Free Tel:* 800-242-7737 (orders) *Fax:* 212-397-4267 *E-mail:* publicaffairs@perseusbooks.com *Web Site:* www.publicaffairsbooks.com, pg 221

Savitt, Charles C, Island Press, 1718 Connecticut Ave NW, Suite 300, Washington, DC 20009 *Tel:* 202-232-7933 *Toll Free Tel:* 800-828-1302 *Fax:* 202-234-1328; 707-983-6414 (orders only) *E-mail:* info@islandpress.org *Web Site:* www.islandpress.org, pg 139

Savoy, Michelle Bisson, Bookbuilders West, PO Box 7046, San Francisco, CA 94120-9727 *Tel:* 415-273-5790 *Web Site:* www.bookbuilders.org, pg 682

Sawlor, Rhona, Maritime Writers' Workshop, PO Box 4400, Fredericton, NB E3B 5A3, Canada *Tel:* 506-474-1144 *Fax:* 506-474-1144 (call first) *E-mail:* k4jc@unb.ca *Web Site:* www.unb.ca/extend/writers, pg 744

Sawyer, Eleanor, CHA (Canadian Healthcare Association) Press, 17 York St, Suite 100, Ottawa, ON K1N 9J6, Canada *Tel:* 613-241-8005 (ext 264) *Fax:* 613-241-5055 *E-mail:* chapress@cha.ca *Web Site:* www.cha.ca, pg 540

Sawyer, John, Polestar Book Publishers, 9050 Shaughnessy St, Vancouver, BC V6P 6E5, Canada *Tel:* 604-323-7100 *Toll Free Tel:* 800-663-5714 *Fax:* 604-323-2600 *Toll Free Fax:* 800-565-3770 *E-mail:* info@raincoast.com *Web Site:* www.raincoast.com, pg 558

Sawyer, Kathy, Friends United Press, 101 Quaker Hill Dr, Richmond, IN 47374 *Tel:* 765-962-7573 *Toll Free Tel:* 800-537-8839 *Fax:* 765-966-1293 *E-mail:* friendspress@fum.org *Web Site:* www.fum.org, pg 101

Sawyer, Peter, Fifi Oscard Agency Inc, 110 W 40 St, New York, NY 10018 *Tel:* 212-764-1100 *Fax:* 212-840-5019 *E-mail:* agency@fifioscard.com *Web Site:* www.fifioscard.com, pg 647

Sayeski, Peter F, McGraw-Hill Learning Group, 8787 Orion Place, Columbus, OH 43240 *Tel:* 614-430-4000 *Fax:* 614-430-6621, pg 168

Sayle, Kim, Time Warner Audio Books, Sports Illustrated Bldg, 135 W 50 St, New York, NY 10020 *Tel:* 212-522-7334 *Fax:* 212-522-7994 *Web Site:* www.twbookmark.com/audiobooks, pg 271

Sayles, Patricia, Arte Publico Press, University of Houston, 4800 Calhoun, Houston, TX 77204-2174 *Tel:* 713-743-2841 *Toll Free Tel:* 800-633-2783 *Fax:* 713-743-2847 *Web Site:* www.arte.uh.edu, pg 24

Saylor, David, Scholastic Trade Division, 557 Broadway, New York, NY 10012 *Tel:* 212-343-6100; 212-343-4685 (export sales) *Fax:* 212-343-4714 (export sales) *Web Site:* www.scholastic.com, pg 242

Saylor, Janice, American Institute of Aeronautics & Astronautics, 1801 Alexander Bell Dr, Suite 500, Reston, VA 20191 *Tel:* 703-264-7500 *Toll Free Tel:* 800-639-2422 *Fax:* 703-264-7551 *E-mail:* custserv@aiaa.org *Web Site:* www.aiaa.org, pg 14

Sayre, C B, Hudson Park Press, Johnny Cake Hollow Rd, Pine Plains, NY 12567 *Tel:* 212-929-8898 *Fax:* 212-242-6137 *E-mail:* hudpark@aol.com *Web Site:* www.hudsonpark.com, pg 128

Sayre, Dan, Island Press, 1718 Connecticut Ave NW, Suite 300, Washington, DC 20009 *Tel:* 202-232-7933 *Toll Free Tel:* 800-828-1302 *Fax:* 202-234-1328; 707-983-6414 (orders only) *E-mail:* info@islandpress.org *Web Site:* www.islandpress.org, pg 139

Scagnetti, Jack, Jack Scagnetti Talent & Literary Agency, 5118 Vineland Ave, Suite 102, North Hollywood, CA 91601 *Tel:* 818-762-3871; 818-761-0580 *Web Site:* www.jackscagnetti.com, pg 653

Scanlan, Brian, Thieme New York, 333 Seventh Ave, 5th fl, New York, NY 10001 *Tel:* 212-760-0888 *Toll Free Tel:* 800-782-3488 *Fax:* 212-947-1112 *E-mail:* customerservice@thieme.com *Web Site:* www.thieme.com, pg 268

Scanlan, Mary E, The American Chemical Society, 1155 16 St NW, Washington, DC 20036 *Tel:* 202-872-4600 *Toll Free Tel:* 800-227-5558 *Fax:* 202-872-6067 *Web Site:* www.acs.org; pubs.acs.org, pg 12

Scanlon, Joanne, Insurance Institute of America Inc, 720 Providence Rd, Malvern, PA 19355 *Tel:* 610-644-2100 *Toll Free Tel:* 800-644-2101 *Fax:* 610-640-9576 *E-mail:* cserv@cpcuiia.org *Web Site:* www.aicpcu.org, pg 135

Scanlon, Matt, Association of Writers & Writing Programs (AWP), George Mason University, MS-1E3, Fairfax, VA 22030-4444 *Tel:* 703-993-4301 *Fax:* 703-993-4302 *E-mail:* awp@awpwriter.org *Web Site:* www.awpwriter.org, pg 680

Scanlon, Sally, The Intrepid Traveler, 371 Walden Green Rd, Branford, CT 06405 *Tel:* 203-488-5341 *Fax:* 203-488-7677 *E-mail:* info@intrepidtraveler.com *Web Site:* www.intrepidtraveler.com, pg 139

Scannell, Christy, Rainbow Publishers, PO Box 261129, San Diego, CA 92196-1129 *Tel:* 858-668-3260 *Web Site:* www.rainbowpublishers.com, pg 225

Scarbrough, Carl W, David R Godine Publisher Inc, 9 Hamilton Place, Boston, MA 02108 *Tel:* 617-451-9600 *Fax:* 617-350-0250 *E-mail:* info@godine.com *Web Site:* www.godine.com, pg 106

Scarlott, Melisa, Louisville Grawemeyer Award in Religion, 1044 Alta Vista Rd, Louisville, KY 40205-1798 *Tel:* 502-895-3411 *Toll Free Tel:* 800-264-1839 *Fax:* 502-894-2286 *E-mail:* grawemeyer@lpts.edu *Web Site:* www.grawemeyer.org, pg 786

Scarpulla, Zina, Facts on File Inc, 132 W 31 St, 17th fl, New York, NY 10001 *Tel:* 212-967-8800 *Toll Free Tel:* 800-322-8755 *Fax:* 212-967-9196 *Toll Free Fax:* 800-678-3633 *E-mail:* custserv@factsonfile.com *Web Site:* www.factsonfile.com, pg 94

Scartz, Sara, Teton New Media, 4125 S Hwy 89, Suite 1, Jackson, WY 83001 *Tel:* 307-732-0028 *Toll Free Tel:* 877-306-9793 *Fax:* 307-734-0841, pg 267

Scavotto, Marie, Sinauer Associates Inc, 23 Plumtree Rd, Sunderland, MA 01375-0407 *Tel:* 413-549-4300 *Fax:* 413-549-1118 *E-mail:* publish@sinauer.com *Web Site:* www.sinauer.com, pg 249

Schacterle, Lisa, Theta Reports, 1775 Broadway, Suite 511, New York, NY 10019 *Tel:* 212-262-8230 *Fax:* 212-262-8234 *Web Site:* www.thetareports.com, pg 268

Schader, Karen, Childswork/Childsplay LLC, 135 Dupont St, Plainview, NY 11803 *Tel:* 516-349-5520 *Toll Free Tel:* 800-962-1141 (cust serv) *Fax:* 516-349-5521 *Toll Free Fax:* 800-262-1886 (orders) *E-mail:* info@childswork.com *Web Site:* www.childswork.com, pg 60

Schaefer, Jay, Chronicle Books LLC, 85 Second St, 6th fl, San Francisco, CA 94105 *Tel:* 415-537-4200 *Toll Free Tel:* 800-722-6657 (cust serv) *Fax:* 415-537-4460 *Toll Free Fax:* 800-858-7787 (orders) *E-mail:* frontdesk@chroniclebooks.com *Web Site:* www.chroniclebooks.com, pg 61

Schaefer, Jill, Guild Publishing, 931 E Main St, Madison, WI 53703-2955 *Tel:* 608-257-2590 *Toll Free Tel:* 800-930-1856 *Fax:* 608-257-2690 *E-mail:* artinfo@guild.com *Web Site:* www.guild.com, pg 111

Schaefer, Leslye, Scholastic Entertainment Inc, 524 Broadway, New York, NY 10012 *Tel:* 212-343-7500 *Fax:* 212-965-7448, pg 241

Schaefer, Rita H, Houghton Mifflin Co, 222 Berkeley St, Boston, MA 02116-3764·*Tel:* 617-351-5000 *Toll Free Tel:* 800-225-3362 (trade books); 800-733-2828 (text books); 800-225-1464 (college texts) *Fax:* 617-351-1125 *Web Site:* www.hmco.com, pg 126

Schaefer, Rita H, McDougal Littell, 909 Davis St, Evanston, IL 60201 *Tel:* 847-869-2300 *Toll Free Tel:* 800-462-6595 (orders) *Toll Free Fax:* 888-872-8380 *Web Site:* www.mcdougallittell.com, pg 166

Schaeffer, Dave, Simon & Schuster Inc, 1230 Avenue of the Americas, New York, NY 10020 *Tel:* 212-698-7000 *Fax:* 212-698-7007 *Web Site:* www.simonsays.com, pg 249

Schafer, Ben, Da Capo Press Inc, 11 Cambridge Center, Cambridge, MA 02142 *Tel:* 617-252-5200 *Toll Free Tel:* 800-242-7737 (orders) *Fax:* 617-252-5285 *E-mail:* custserve@lrp.com *Web Site:* www.dacapopress.com, pg 75

Schaffer, Rose, The Center for Learning, 24600 Detroit Rd, Suite 201, Westlake, OH 44145 *Tel:* 440-250-9341 *Fax:* 440-250-9715 *Web Site:* www.centerforlearning.org, pg 56

Schaffner, Melanie, The Johns Hopkins University Press, 2715 N Charles St, Baltimore, MD 21218-4363 *Tel:* 410-516-6900 *Toll Free Tel:* 800-537-5487 *Fax:* 410-516-6968 *Web Site:* www.press.jhu.edu, pg 141

Schaffrath, Susan D, McDougal Littell, 909 Davis St, Evanston, IL 60201 *Tel:* 847-869-2300 *Toll Free Tel:* 800-462-6595 (orders) *Toll Free Fax:* 888-872-8380 *Web Site:* www.mcdougallittell.com, pg 166

Schaller, Doug, Locks Art Publications/Locks Gallery, 600 Washington Sq S, Philadelphia, PA 19106 *Tel:* 215-629-1000 *Fax:* 215-629-3868 *E-mail:* info@locksgallery.com *Web Site:* www.locksgallery.com, pg 157

Schaller-Linn, Sarah, Upper Room Books, 1908 Grand Ave, Nashville, TN 37212 *Toll Free Tel:* 800-972-0433 *Fax:* 615-340-7266 *Web Site:* www.upperroom.org, pg 288

Schamus, Martin, Sterling Publishing Co Inc, 387 Park Ave S, 5th fl, New York, NY 10016-8810 *Tel:* 212-532-7160 *Toll Free Tel:* 800-367-9692 *Fax:* 212-213-2495 *Web Site:* www.sterlingpub.com, pg 259

Schanck, D, Garland Science Publishing, 270 Madison Ave, New York, NY 10016 *Tel:* 212-216-7800 *Fax:* 212-947-3027 *E-mail:* info@garland.com *Web Site:* www.garlandscience.com, pg 102

Schapera, Vivien, FourWinds Press LLC, 4157 Crossgate Dr, Cincinnati, OH 47025 *Tel:* 513-891-0415 *Fax:* 513-891-1648 *Web Site:* www.fourwindspress.com, pg 571

Scharfstein, Bernard, KTAV Publishing House Inc, 930 Newark Ave, Jersey City, NJ 07306 *Tel:* 201-963-9524 *Fax:* 201-963-0102 *E-mail:* orders@ktav.com *Web Site:* www.ktav.com, pg 147

Scharfstein, Sol, KTAV Publishing House Inc, 930 Newark Ave, Jersey City, NJ 07306 *Tel:* 201-963-9524 *Fax:* 201-963-0102 *E-mail:* orders@ktav.com *Web Site:* www.ktav.com, pg 147

Scharlatt, Elisabeth, Algonquin Books of Chapel Hill, 127 Kingston Dr, Suite 105, Chapel Hill, NC 27514 *Tel:* 919-967-0108 *Fax:* 919-933-0272 *E-mail:* dialogue@algonquin.com *Web Site:* www.algonquin.com, pg 8

Schaub, Patricia, University of Texas at Austin, Creative Writing Program, Dept of English, One University Sta, B5000, Austin, TX 78712-1164 *Tel:* 512-475-6356 *Fax:* 512-471-2898 *Web Site:* www.en.utexas.edu/grad/crwconc.html, pg 756

Schaub, Thom, Phyllis Smart Young Poetry Prize & Chris O'Malley Fiction Prize, University of Wisconsin - English Dept, 7193 HCW, 600 N Park St, Madison, WI 53706 *Tel:* 608-263-0566 *E-mail:* madreview@mail.studentorg.wisc.edu *Web Site:* mendota.english.wisc.edu/~MadRev/main.html, pg 814

Schauer, David A, National Council on Radiation Protection & Measurements (NCRP), 7910 Woodmont Ave, Suite 400, Bethesda, MD 20814 *Tel:* 301-657-2652 *Toll Free Tel:* 800-229-2652 *Fax:* 301-907-8768 *E-mail:* ncrp@ncrp.com *Web Site:* www.ncrp.com, pg 183

Schaut, Diane, University of Notre Dame Press, 310 Flanner Hall, Notre Dame, IN 46556 *Tel:* 574-631-6346 *Toll Free Tel:* 800-621-2736 (orders) *Fax:* 574-631-8148 *Toll Free Fax:* 800-621-8476 (orders) *E-mail:* nd.undpress.1@nd.edu *Web Site:* www.undpress.nd.edu, pg 284

Schecter, Deborah, Scholastic Paperbacks, Teaching Resources & Reading Counts, 557 Broadway, New York, NY 10012-3999 *Tel:* 212-965-7241 *Fax:* 212-965-7487 *Web Site:* www.scholastic.com, pg 242

Scheel, Joanne, TNG Canada/CWA, 7B-1050 Baxter Rd, Ottawa, ON K2C 3P1, Canada *Tel:* 613-820-9777 *Toll Free Tel:* 877-486-4292 *Fax:* 613-820-8188 *E-mail:* info@tngcanada.org *Web Site:* www.tngcanada.org, pg 701

Scheffers, Todd, Goodheart-Willcox Publisher, 18604 W Creek Dr, Tinley Park, IL 60477-6243 *Tel:* 708-687-5000 *Toll Free Tel:* 800-323-0440 *Fax:* 708-687-0315 *Toll Free Fax:* 888-409-3900 *E-mail:* custserv@g-w.com *Web Site:* www.g-w.com, pg 107

Scheffler, Eckart A, Walter de Gruyter, Inc, 500 Executive Blvd, Ossining, NY 10562 *Tel:* 914-762-5866 *Fax:* 914-762-0371 *E-mail:* info@degruyterny.com *Web Site:* www.degruyter.com, pg 78

Scheffler, Eckart A, Mouton de Gruyter, 500 Executive Blvd, Ossining, NY 10562 *Tel:* 914-762-5866 *Fax:* 914-762-0371 *E-mail:* info@degruyterny.com *Web Site:* www.degruyter.com, pg 179

Scheibe, Amy, Free Press, 1230 Avenue of the Americas, New York, NY 10020 *Tel:* 212-698-7000 *Toll Free Tel:* 800-223-2345 (cust serv); 800-223-2336 (orders); 888-866-6631 (fulfillment), pg 100

Scheiner, C J, C J Scheiner Books, 275 Linden Blvd, Suite B2, Brooklyn, NY 11226 *Tel:* 718-469-1089 *Fax:* 718-469-1089, pg 611

Schell, Rick Lain, M Evans & Co Inc, 216 E 49 St, New York, NY 10017 *Tel:* 212-688-2810 *Fax:* 212-486-4544 *E-mail:* editorial@mevans.com *Web Site:* www.mevans.com, pg 93

Schellenberg, Michael, Knopf Canada, One Toronto St, Suite 300, Toronto, ON M5C 2V6, Canada *Tel:* 416-364-4449 *Toll Free Tel:* 800-668-4247 (order desk) *Fax:* 416-364-0462 *Web Site:* www.randomhouse.ca, pg 552

Schelling, Christopher, Ralph M Vicinanza Ltd, 303 W 18 St, New York, NY 10011 *Tel:* 212-924-7090 *Fax:* 212-691-9644 *E-mail:* ralphvic@aol.com, pg 659

Schellinger, Paul, Impressions Book & Journal Services Inc, 2016 Winnebago St, Madison, WI 53704 *Tel:* 608-244-6218 *Fax:* 608-244-7050 *E-mail:* info@impressions.com *Web Site:* www.impressions.com, pg 602

Schenck, Robert B, F A Davis Co, 1915 Arch St, Philadelphia, PA 19103 *Tel:* 215-568-2270 *Toll Free Tel:* 800-523-4049 *Fax:* 215-568-5065 *E-mail:* info@fadavis.com *Web Site:* www.fadavis.com, pg 76

Scherman, Nosson, Mesorah Publications Ltd, 4401 Second Ave, Brooklyn, NY 11232 *Tel:* 718-921-9000 *Toll Free Tel:* 800-637-6724 *Fax:* 718-680-1875 *E-mail:* artscroll@mesorah.com *Web Site:* www.artscroll.com; www.mesorah.com, pg 172

Schiano, Rita, New Voices Publishing, 34 Salem St, Wilmington, MA 01887 *Tel:* 508-347-5669; 978-658-2131 *Fax:* 508-347-5669; 978-988-8833 *Web Site:* www.kidsterrain.com, pg 189

Schiavenato, Martin, Bandido Books, 9806 Heaton Ct, Orlando, FL 32817 *Tel:* 407-657-9707 *Toll Free Tel:* 877-814-6824 (pin 1174) *Fax:* 407-677-9796 *E-mail:* publish@bandidobooks.com *Web Site:* www.bandidobooks.com, pg 31

Schiavi, Kristine, New England Publishing Associates Inc, PO Box 5, Chester, CT 06412-0005 *Tel:* 860-345-READ (345-7323) *Fax:* 860-345-3660 *E-mail:* nepa@nepa.com *Web Site:* www.nepa.com, pg 646

Schiavone, James, Schiavone Literary Agency Inc, 236 Trails End, West Palm Beach, FL 33413-2135 *Tel:* 561-966-9294 *Fax:* 561-966-9294 *E-mail:* profschia@aol.com *Web Site:* www.publishersmarketplace.com/members/profschia, pg 653

Schiebel, Elaine, Stewart, Tabori & Chang, 115 W 18 St, 5th fl, New York, NY 10011 *Tel:* 212-519-1200 *Fax:* 212-519-1210 *Web Site:* www.abramsbooks.com, pg 260

Schiff, Robbin, Random House Publishing Group, 1745 Broadway, New York, NY 10019 *Toll Free Tel:* 800-200-3552 *Toll Free Fax:* 800-200-3552 *Web Site:* www.randomhouse.com, pg 227

Schiff-Estess, Patricia, The Writer's Emergency Assistance Fund, 1501 Broadway, Suite 302, New York, NY 10036 *Tel:* 212-997-0947 *Fax:* 212-768-7414 *E-mail:* staff@asja.org *Web Site:* asja.org, pg 813

Schiffer, Nancy, Schiffer Publishing Ltd, 4880 Lower Valley Rd, Atglen, PA 19310 *Tel:* 610-593-1777 *Fax:* 610-593-2002 *E-mail:* schifferbk@aol.com; schifferii@aol.com *Web Site:* schifferbooks.com, pg 241

Schiffer, Peter, Schiffer Publishing Ltd, 4880 Lower Valley Rd, Atglen, PA 19310 *Tel:* 610-593-1777 *Fax:* 610-593-2002 *E-mail:* schifferbk@aol.com; schifferii@aol.com *Web Site:* schifferbooks.com, pg 241

Schiffrin, Andre, The New Press, 38 Greene St, 4th fl, New York, NY 10013 *Tel:* 212-629-8802 *Toll Free Tel:* 800-233-4830 (orders) *Fax:* 212-629-8617 *Toll Free Fax:* 800-458-6515 *E-mail:* newpress@thenewpress.com *Web Site:* www.thenewpress.com, pg 188

Schilhab, Ashley, Wimmer Cookbooks, 4650 Shelby Air Dr, Memphis, TN 38118 *Tel:* 901-362-8900 *Toll Free Tel:* 800-548-2537 *Toll Free Fax:* 800-794-9806 *E-mail:* wimmer@wimmerco.com *Web Site:* www.wimmerco.com, pg 301

Schiller, Alexandra, Galt Press, 1725 Clearwater-Largo Rd S, Clearwater, FL 33756 *Tel:* 727-581-8685 *Fax:* 727-585-8423 *E-mail:* galt@warda.net *Web Site:* www.warda.net/GaltPress.html; www.galtpress.com, pg 102

Schiller, Howard, Hollywood Film Archive, 8391 Beverly Blvd, PMB 321, Hollywood, CA 90048 *Tel:* 323-655-4968, pg 124

Schillig, Chris, Andrews McMeel Publishing, 4520 Main St, Suite 700, Kansas City, MO 64111-7701 *Tel:* 816-932-6700 *Toll Free Tel:* 800-851-8923 *Web Site:* www.universal.com/amp, pg 169

Schilling, Derick, The Library of America, 14 E 60 St, New York, NY 10022 *Tel:* 212-308-3360 *Fax:* 212-750-8352 *E-mail:* info@loa.org *Web Site:* www.loa.org; www.loaacademic.org, pg 154

Schilling, Julie, University of Pennsylvania Press, 4200 Pine St, Philadelphia, PA 19104-4011 *Tel:* 215-898-6261 *Toll Free Tel:* 800-445-9880 (orders & cust serv only) *Fax:* 215-898-0404; 410-516-6998 (orders) *E-mail:* custserv@pobox.upenn.edu *Web Site:* www.upenn.edu/pennpress, pg 284

Schilling, Linda, Great Source Education Group, 181 Ballardvale St, Wilmington, MA 01887 *Tel:* 978-661-1300 *Toll Free Tel:* 800-289-4490 (orders), pg 108

Schindel, Michael C, SAE (Society of Automotive Engineers International), 400 Commonwealth Dr, Warrendale, PA 15096-0001 *Tel:* 724-776-4841 *Toll Free Tel:* 877-606-7323 (cust serv) *Fax:* 724-776-0790 *E-mail:* publications@sae.org *Web Site:* www.sae.org, pg 237

Schipp, Carol, Abbey Press, One Hill Dr, St Meinrad, IN 47577 *Tel:* 812-357-6611 *Toll Free Tel:* 800-962-4760 *Fax:* 812-357-8388 *E-mail:* dep@abbeypress.com *Web Site:* www.abbeypress.com, pg 2

Schir, Sabine, Editions de l'Hexagone, 1010, rue de la Gauchetiere Est, Montreal, PQ H2L 2N5, Canada *Tel:* 514-523-1182 *Fax:* 514-282-7530 *E-mail:* vml@sogides.com *Web Site:* www.edhexagone.com, pg 544

Schlachter, Gail, Reference Service Press, 5000 Windplay Dr, Suite 4, El Dorado Hills, CA 95762-9600 *Tel:* 916-939-9620 *Fax:* 916-939-9626 *E-mail:* findaid@aol.com *Web Site:* www.rspfunding.com, pg 230

Schlageter, Mark, Warren, Gorham & Lamont, 395 Hudson St, New York, NY 10014 *Tel:* 212-367-6300 *Toll Free Tel:* 800-431-9025; 800-678-2185 (cust serv) *Fax:* 212-367-6305 *Web Site:* www.riahome.com, pg 293

Schlau, W Hank, EdiType, 84 Ashley Ave, Charleston, SC 29401 *Tel:* 843-853-2214 *Fax:* 843-853-2214, pg 598

Schlenski, Ted, The Heritage Foundation, 214 Massachusetts Ave NE, Washington, DC 20002-4999 *Tel:* 202-546-4400 *Fax:* 202-546-8328 *Web Site:* www.heritage.org, pg 705

Schlesinger, Edward, Pocket Books, 1230 Avenue of the Americas, New York, NY 10020 *Toll Free Tel:* 800-456-6798 *Fax:* 212-698-7284 *E-mail:* consumer.customerservice@simonandschuster.com *Web Site:* www.simonsays.com, pg 215

Schlesinger, Jim, Orbis Books, Walsh Bldg, 75 Ryder Rd, Ossining, NY 10562 *Tel:* 914-941-7636 *Toll Free Tel:* 800-258-5838 (orders) *Fax:* 914-941-7005 (orders); 914-945-0670 (office) *E-mail:* orbisbooks@maryknoll.org *Web Site:* www.orbisbooks.com, pg 198

Schlesinger, Keith, Soil Science Society of America, 677 S Segoe Rd, Madison, WI 53711-1086 *Tel:* 608-273-8095 *Fax:* 608-273-2021 *E-mail:* headquarters@soils.org *Web Site:* www.soils.org, pg 252

Schlesinger, Laurie, Jewish Publication Society, 2100 Arch St, 2nd fl, Philadelphia, PA 19103 *Tel:* 215-832-0600 *Toll Free Tel:* 800-234-3151 *Fax:* 215-568-2017 *E-mail:* jewishbook@jewishpub.org *Web Site:* www.jewishpub.org, pg 141

Schlessiger, Charles, Brandt & Hochman Literary Agents Inc, 1501 Broadway, Suite 2310, New York, NY 10036 *Tel:* 212-840-5760 *Fax:* 212-840-5776, pg 622

Schline, John, Penguin Group (USA) Inc, 375 Hudson St, New York, NY 10014 *Tel:* 212-366-2000 *Fax:* 212-366-2666 *E-mail:* online@uspenguingroup.com *Web Site:* www.penguin.com, pg 208

Schlosser, Bonnie, Northstone Publishing, 9025 Jim Bailey Rd, Kelowna, BC V4V 1R2, Canada *Tel:* 250-766-2778 *Toll Free Tel:* 800-299-2926 *Fax:* 250-766-2736 *Web Site:* www.joinhands.com, pg 556

Schlosser, Bonnie, Wood Lake Books Inc, 9025 Jim Bailey Rd, Kelowna, BC V4V 1R2, Canada *Tel:* 250-766-2778 *Toll Free Tel:* 800-663-2775 (orders) *Fax:* 250-766-2736 *Toll Free Fax:* 888-841-9991 (orders) *E-mail:* info@woodlake.com *Web Site:* www.woodlakebooks.com, pg 567

Schlosser, Ronald H, Thomson Learning Inc, 200 First Stamford Place, Suite 400, Stamford, CT 06902 *Tel:* 203-539-8000 *Fax:* 203-539-7581 *E-mail:* communications@thomsonlearning.com *Web Site:* www.thomson.com/learning, pg 270

Schluep, Chris, Del Rey Books, 1745 Broadway, New York, NY 10019 *E-mail:* delrey@randomhouse.com *Web Site:* www.randomhouse.com, pg 78

Schluep, Christopher, Random House Publishing Group, 1745 Broadway, New York, NY 10019 *Toll Free Tel:* 800-200-3552 *Toll Free Fax:* 800-200-3552 *Web Site:* www.randomhouse.com, pg 227

Schmalz, Wendy, Wendy Schmalz Agency, PO Box 831, Hudson, NY 12534-0831 *Tel:* 518-672-7697 *Fax:* 518-672-7662 *E-mail:* wendy@schmalzagency.com, pg 654

Schmenger, Jackie, The Association of Educational Publishers (AEP), 510 Heron Dr, Suite 309, Logan Township, NJ 08085 *Tel:* 856-241-7772 *Fax:* 856-241-0709 *E-mail:* mail@edpress.org *Web Site:* www.edpress.org, pg 680

Schmidgal, Erik, Baker Books, PO Box 6287, Grand Rapids, MI 49516-6287 *Tel:* 616-676-9185 *Toll Free Tel:* 800-877-2665; 800-679-1957 *Fax:* 616-676-9573 *Toll Free Fax:* 800-398-3110 *Web Site:* www.bakerpublishinggroup.com, pg 30

Schmidt, Alfred, Windsor Books, 141 John St, Babylon, NY 11702 *Tel:* 631-321-7830 *Toll Free Tel:* 800-321-5934 *Fax:* 631-321-1435 *E-mail:* windsor.books@att.net *Web Site:* www.windsorpublishing.com, pg 301

Schmidt, Clint, Blue Book Publications Inc, 8009 34 Ave S, Suite 175, Minneapolis, MN 55425 *Tel:* 952-854-5229 *Toll Free Tel:* 800-877-4867 *Fax:* 952-853-1486 *E-mail:* bluebook@bluebookinc.com *Web Site:* www.bluebookinc.com, pg 570

Schmidt, Harold D, Harold Schmidt Literary Agency, 415 W 23 St, Suite 6F, New York, NY 10011 *Tel:* 212-727-7473 *E-mail:* hslanyc@aol.com, pg 654

Schmidt, Helga, Steerforth Press, 25 Lebanon St, Hanover, NH 03755 *Tel:* 603-643-4787 *Fax:* 603-643-4788 *E-mail:* info@steerforth.com *Web Site:* www.steerforth.com, pg 258

Schmidt, Holly, Fair Winds Press, 33 Commercial St, Gloucester, MA 01930 *Tel:* 978-282-9590 *Fax:* 978-283-2742 *Web Site:* www.rockpub.com; www.fairwindspress.com, pg 94

Schmidt, Jeff, Windsor Books, 141 John St, Babylon, NY 11702 *Tel:* 631-321-7830 *Toll Free Tel:* 800-321-5934 *Fax:* 631-321-1435 *E-mail:* windsor.books@att.net *Web Site:* www.windsorpublishing.com, pg 301

Schmidt, Jim, Recorded Books LLC, 270 Skipjack Rd, Prince Frederick, MD 20678 *Tel:* 410-535-5590 *Toll Free Tel:* 800-638-1304 *Fax:* 410-535-5499 *E-mail:* recordedbooks@recordedbooks.com *Web Site:* www.recordedbooks.com, pg 229

Schmidt, Karen, Getty Publications, 1200 Getty Center Dr, Suite 500, Los Angeles, CA 90049-1682 *Tel:* 310-440-7365 *Fax:* 310-440-7758 *E-mail:* pubsinfo@getty.edu *Web Site:* www.getty.edu/bookstore, pg 104

Schmidt, Linda, Fodor's Travel Publications, 1745 Broadway, New York, NY 10019 *Tel:* 212-572-8784 *Toll Free Tel:* 800-733-3000 *Fax:* 212-572-2248 *Web Site:* www.fodors.com, pg 98

Schmidt, R Marilyn, Pine Barrens Press, 3959 Rte 563, Chatsworth, NJ 08019 *Tel:* 609-894-4415 *Fax:* 609-894-2350 *E-mail:* pbp@verizon.net, pg 213

Schmitz, Barbara, Writer's Digest Books, 4700 E Galbraith Rd, Cincinnati, OH 45236 *Tel:* 513-531-2690 *Toll Free Tel:* 800-289-0963 *Fax:* 513-891-7185 *Web Site:* www.writersdigest.com, pg 305

Schmitz, Elisabeth, Grove/Atlantic Inc, 841 Broadway, 4th fl, New York, NY 10003-4793 *Tel:* 212-614-7850 *Toll Free Tel:* 800-521-0178 *Fax:* 212-614-7886 *Web Site:* www.groveatlantic.com, pg 110

Schnee, Stuart, The Toby Press LLC, 2 Great Pasture Rd, Danbury, CT 06810 *Tel:* 203-830-8508 *Fax:* 203-830-8512 *E-mail:* toby@tobypress.com *Web Site:* www.tobypress.com, pg 272

Schneider, Amy J, Words That Work!, W7615 County Rd YY, Wautoma, WI 54982-8382 *Tel:* 920-787-2645 *Fax:* 920-787-2698, pg 614

Schneider, Carol, Random House Publishing Group, 1745 Broadway, New York, NY 10019 *Toll Free Tel:* 800-200-3552 *Toll Free Fax:* 800-200-3552 *Web Site:* www.randomhouse.com, pg 227

Schneider, Deborah, Gelfman Schneider Literary Agents Inc, 250 W 57 St, Suite 2515, New York, NY 10107 *Tel:* 212-245-1993 *Fax:* 212-245-8678 *E-mail:* mail@gelfmanschneider.com, pg 632

Schneider, Dr Diana M, Demos Medical Publishing LLC, 386 Park Ave S, Suite 201, New York, NY 10016 *Tel:* 212-683-0072 *Toll Free Tel:* 800-532-8663 *Fax:* 212-683-0118 *E-mail:* info@demospub.com *Web Site:* www.demosmedpub.com, pg 79

Schneider, Don, Review & Herald Publishing Association, 55 W Oak Ridge Dr, Hagerstown, MD 21740 *Tel:* 301-393-3000 *Toll Free Tel:* 800-234-7630 *Fax:* 301-393-4055 (periodicals); 301-393-3222 *E-mail:* editorial@rhpa.org *Web Site:* www.reviewandherald.com, pg 232

Schneider, Douglas, ISI Books, PO Box 4431, 3901 Centerville Rd, Wilmington, DE 19807 *Tel:* 302-652-4600 *Toll Free Tel:* 800-526-7022 *Fax:* 302-652-1760 *E-mail:* bookstore@isi.org *Web Site:* www.isibooks.org, pg 139

Schneider, Leslie, Rodale Books, 400 S Tenth St, Emmaus, PA 18098-0099 *Tel:* 610-967-5171 *Fax:* 610-967-8961 *Web Site:* www.rodale.com, pg 233

Schneider, Naomi, University of California Press, 2120 Berkeley Way, Berkeley, CA 94720 *Tel:* 510-642-4247 *Toll Free Tel:* 800-777-4726 *Fax:* 510-643-7127 *Toll Free Fax:* 800-999-1958 *E-mail:* askucp@ucpress.edu *Web Site:* www.ucpress.edu, pg 281

Schnell, Judith, Stackpole Books, 5067 Ritter Rd, Mechanicsburg, PA 17055 *Tel:* 717-796-0411 *Toll Free Tel:* 800-732-3669 *Fax:* 717-796-0412 *Web Site:* www.stackpolebooks.com, pg 257

Schnell, Ulla, The Continuum International Publishing Group, 15 E 26 St, Suite 1703, New York, NY 10010 *Tel:* 212-953-5858 *Toll Free Tel:* 800-561-7704 *Fax:* 212-953-5944 *E-mail:* info@continuum-books.com *Web Site:* www.continuumbooks.com, pg 67

Schnier, Maaret, Action Publishing LLC, PO Box 391, Glendale, CA 91209 *Tel:* 323-478-1667 *Toll Free Tel:* 800-705-7482 *Fax:* 323-478-1767 *E-mail:* info@actionpublishing.com *Web Site:* www.actionpublishing.com, pg 5

Schnittman, Evan, Oxford University Press, Inc, 198 Madison Ave, New York, NY 10016-4314 *Tel:* 212-726-6000 *Toll Free Tel:* 800-451-7556 (orders) *Web Site:* www.oup.com/us, pg 200

Schober, Sara, Random House Audio Publishing Group, 1745 Broadway, New York, NY 10019 *Tel:* 212-782-9720 *Fax:* 212-782-9600, pg 225

Schoen, Conny, Book Sales Inc, 114 Northfield Ave, Edison, NJ 08837 *Tel:* 732-225-0530 *Toll Free Tel:* 800-526-7257 *Fax:* 732-225-2257 *E-mail:* sales@booksalesusa.com; customerservice@booksalesusa.com *Web Site:* www.booksalesusa.com, pg 43

Schoenberg, Corrie, The Overlook Press, 141 Wooster St, New York, NY 10012 *Tel:* 212-965-8400 *Fax:* 212-965-9834 *Web Site:* www.overlookny.com, pg 200

Schoener, Debbie, Saint Mary's Press, 702 Terrace Heights, Winona, MN 55987-1318 *Tel:* 507-457-7900 *Toll Free Tel:* 800-533-8095 *Toll Free Fax:* 800-344-9225 *E-mail:* smpress@smp.org *Web Site:* www.smp.org, pg 239

Schoening, Eric E, Our Sunday Visitor Publishing, 200 Noll Plaza, Huntington, IN 46750 *Tel:* 260-356-8400 *Toll Free Tel:* 800-348-2440 (orders) *Fax:* 260-356-8472 *Toll Free Fax:* 800-498-6709 *E-mail:* osvbooks@osv.com *Web Site:* www.osv.com, pg 200

Schofield, Deniece, Mapletree Publishing Co, 6233 Harvard Lane, Highlands Ranch, CO 80130-3773 *Tel:* 303-791-9024 *Toll Free Tel:* 800-537-0414 *Fax:* 303-791-9028 *E-mail:* mail@mapletreepublishing.com *Web Site:* www.mapletreepublishing.com, pg 163

Schofield, William, Paul Dry Books, 117 S 17 St, Suite 1102, Philadelphia, PA 19103 *Tel:* 215-231-9939 *Fax:* 215-231-9942 *E-mail:* editor@pauldrybooks.com *Web Site:* www.pauldrybooks.com, pg 84

Scholder, Amy, Verso, 180 Varick St, 10th fl, New York, NY 10014-4606 *Tel:* 212-807-9680 *Fax:* 212-807-9152 *E-mail:* versony@versobooks.com *Web Site:* www.versobooks.com, pg 290

Scholl, Roger, Doubleday Broadway Publishing Group, 1745 Broadway, New York, New York, NY 10019 *Tel:* 212-782-9000 *Toll Free Tel:* 800-223-6834; 800-223-5780 (sales) *Fax:* 212-302-7985 (correspondence); 212-492-9862 (orders), pg 82

Scholl, Steven, White Cloud Press, PO Box 3400, Ashland, OR 97520 *Tel:* 541-488-6415 *Toll Free Tel:* 800-380-8286 *Fax:* 541-482-7708 *Web Site:* www.whitecloudpress.com, pg 298

Scholz, Alba M, Continuing Education Press, 1633 SW Park, Portland, OR 97201 *Tel:* 503-725-4891 *Toll Free Tel:* 866-647-7377 *Fax:* 503-725-4840 *E-mail:* press@pdx.edu *Web Site:* www.cep.pdx.edu, pg 67

Schorr, Alan Edward, The Denali Press, PO Box 021535, Juneau, AK 99802-1535 *Tel:* 907-586-6014 *Fax:* 907-463-6780 *E-mail:* denalipress@alaska.com *Web Site:* www.denalipress.com, pg 79

Schott, Abby, Allen A Knoll Publishers, 200 W Victoria St, 2nd fl, Suite A, Santa Barbara, CA 93101-3627 *Tel:* 805-564-3377 *Toll Free Tel:* 800-777-7623 *Fax:* 805-966-6657 *E-mail:* bookinfo@knollpublishers.com *Web Site:* www.knollpublishers.com, pg 146

Schott, Susan, University Press of Kansas, 2501 W 15 St, Lawrence, KS 66049-3905 *Tel:* 785-864-4154; 785-864-4155 (orders) *Fax:* 785-864-4586 *E-mail:* upress@ku.edu *Web Site:* www.kansaspress.ku.edu, pg 287

Schotter, Prof Richard, Boston University, 236 Bay State Rd, Boston, MA 02215 *Tel:* 617-353-2510 *Fax:* 617-353-3653 *Web Site:* www.bu.edu/writing/, pg 751

Schram, Christopher, Arts Recognition & Talent Search (ARTS), 444 Brickell Ave, Suite P14, Miami, FL 33131 *Tel:* 305-377-1140 *Toll Free Tel:* 800-970-2787 *Fax:* 305-377-1149 *E-mail:* nfaa@nfaa.org *Web Site:* www.artsawards.org, pg 760

Schrank, Ben, Alloy Entertainment, 151 W 26 St, 11th fl, New York, NY 10001 *Tel:* 212-244-4307, pg 9

Schrefer, John, Elsevier, 11830 Westline Industrial Dr, St Louis, MO 63146 *Tel:* 314-872-8370 *Toll Free Tel:* 800-325-4177 *Fax:* 314-432-1380 *Web Site:* www.elsevier.com; www.elsevierhealth.com, pg 89

Schrefer, John, W B Saunders Ltd, 170 S Independence Mall W, Suite 300 E, Philadelphia, PA 19106-3399 *Tel:* 215-238-7800 *Toll Free Tel:* 800-545-2522 (cust serv) *Fax:* 215-238-7883 *Web Site:* www.elsevierhealth.com, pg 89

Schrefer, Sally, Elsevier, 11830 Westline Industrial Dr, St Louis, MO 63146 *Tel:* 314-872-8370 *Toll Free Tel:* 800-325-4177 *Fax:* 314-432-1380 *Web Site:* www.elsevier.com; www.elsevierhealth.com, pg 89

Schrefer, Sally, W B Saunders Ltd, 170 S Independence Mall W, Suite 300 E, Philadelphia, PA 19106-3399 *Tel:* 215-238-7800 *Toll Free Tel:* 800-545-2522 (cust serv) *Fax:* 215-238-7883 *Web Site:* www.elsevierhealth.com, pg 240

Schreiber, James G, Zondervan, 5300 Patterson Ave SE, Grand Rapids, MI 49530 *Tel:* 616-698-6900 *Toll Free Tel:* 800-727-1309 (cust serv) *Fax:* 616-698-3439; 616-698-3255 (cust serv) *Web Site:* www.zondervan.com, pg 307

Schreiber, Linda, Thinking Publications, 424 Galloway, Eau Claire, WI 54703 *Tel:* 715-832-2488 *Toll Free Tel:* 800-225-4769 *Fax:* 715-832-9082 *Toll Free Fax:* 800-828-8885 *E-mail:* custserv@thinkingpublications.com *Web Site:* www.thinkingpublications.com, pg 269

Schreiber, Mordecai, Schreiber Publishing Inc, 51 Monroe St, Suite 101, Rockville, MD 20850 *Tel:* 301-424-7737 *Toll Free Tel:* 800-822-3213 (sales) *Fax:* 301-424-2518 *E-mail:* books@schreibernet.com *Web Site:* schreiberpublishing.com, pg 243

Schreiber, Ron, Hanging Loose Press, 231 Wyckoff St, Brooklyn, NY 11217 *Tel:* 212-206-8465 *Fax:* 212-243-7499 *E-mail:* print225@aol.com *Web Site:* www.hangingloosepress.com, pg 113

Schreier, Carl, Homestead Publishing, PO Box 193, Moose, WY 83012-0193 *Tel:* 307-733-6248 *Fax:* 307-733-6248 *Web Site:* www.homesteadpublishing.net, pg 125

Schreier, Daniela E, One Planet Publishing House, PO Box 19840, Seattle, WA 98109-1840 *Tel:* 206-282-9699 *Toll Free Tel:* 877-526-3814 (87-PLANET-14) *Fax:* 206-282-9699 *Toll Free Fax:* 877-526-3814 (87-PLANET-14) *E-mail:* info@oneplanetpublishinghouse.com *Web Site:* www.oneplanetpublishinghouse.com, pg 197

Schreiner, Tim, The Taunton Press Inc, 63 S Main St, Newtown, CT 06470 *Tel:* 203-426-8171 *Toll Free Tel:* 800-283-7252; 800-888-8286 (orders) *Fax:* 203-426-3434 *Web Site:* www.taunton.com, pg 264

Schrier, Eric, Reader's Digest General Books, Reader's Digest Rd, Pleasantville, NY 10570-7000 *Tel:* 914-238-1000 *Toll Free Tel:* 800-431-1726 *Fax:* 914-244-7436, pg 228

Schrier, Jack, The Copy Shoppe, PO Box 304, Mendham, NJ 07945 *Tel:* 973-543-2679 *Fax:* 973-543-9090 *E-mail:* catalogistics@juno.com, pg 595

Schroder, Heather, International Creative Management, 40 W 57 St, New York, NY 10019 *Tel:* 212-556-5600 *Fax:* 212-556-5665 *Web Site:* www.icmtalent.com, pg 635

Schroeder, Meredith, American Quilter's Society, 5801 Kentucky Dam Rd, Paducah, KY 42002 *Tel:* 270-898-7903 *Toll Free Tel:* 800-626-5420 (orders) *Fax:* 270-898-8890 *E-mail:* info@aqsquilt.com *Web Site:* www.aqsquilt.com, pg 17

Schroeder, Patricia S, Association of American Publishers (AAP), 71 Fifth Ave, 2nd fl, New York, NY 10003-3004 *Tel:* 212-255-0200 *Fax:* 212-255-7007 *Web Site:* www.publishers.org, pg 679

Schroeder, Sandi, Schroeder Indexing Services, 2606 Old Mill Lane, Suite 1, Rolling Meadows, IL 60008 *Tel:* 847-303-0989 *Fax:* 847-303-1559 *E-mail:* sanindex@schroederindexing.com *Web Site:* www.schroederindexing.com, pg 611

Schroeter, Alice, University of Washington Press, 1326 Fifth Ave, Suite 555, Seattle, WA 98101-2604 *Tel:* 206-543-4050; 206-543-8870 *Toll Free Tel:* 800-441-4115 (orders) *Fax:* 206-543-3932 *Toll Free Fax:* 800-669-7993 (orders) *E-mail:* uwpord@u.washington.edu *Web Site:* www.washington.edu/uwpress/, pg 286

Schrott, Cathy, Professional Publications Inc, 1250 Fifth Ave, Belmont, CA 94002 *Tel:* 650-593-9119 *Toll Free Tel:* 800-426-1178 *Fax:* 650-592-4519 *E-mail:* info@passthatexam.com *Web Site:* www.passthatexam.com, pg 220

Schube, Peter Esq, Jim Henson Publishing/Muppet Press, 117 E 69 St, New York, NY 10021 *Tel:* 212-794-2400 *Fax:* 212-794-5157 *Web Site:* www.henson.com, pg 141

Schubert, Lawrence, Alba House, 2187 Victory Blvd, Staten Island, NY 10314 *Tel:* 718-761-0047 (edit & prodn); 718-698-2759 (mktg & billing) *Toll Free Tel:* 800-343-2522 *Fax:* 718-761-0057 *E-mail:* albabooks@aol.com *Web Site:* www.albahouse.org, pg 7

Schubert, Lori, Quebec Writers' Federation, 1200 Atwater Ave, Suite 3, Montreal, PQ H3Z 1X4, Canada *Tel:* 514-933-0878 *E-mail:* admin@qwf.org *Web Site:* www.qwf.org, pg 698

Schubert, Lori, QWF Prizes, 1200 Atwater Ave, Suite 3, Montreal, PQ H3Z 1X4, Canada *Tel:* 514-933-0878 *E-mail:* admin@qwf.org *Web Site:* www.qwf.org, pg 801

Schueneman, Martha, Editorial Freelancers Association (EFA), 71 W 23 St, New York, NY 10010 *Tel:* 212-929-5400 *Fax:* 212-929-5439 *E-mail:* info@the-efa.org *Web Site:* www.the-efa.org, pg 686

Schuessler, Heidi, Sasquatch Books, 119 S Main, Suite 400, Seattle, WA 98104 *Tel:* 206-467-4300 *Toll Free Tel:* 800-775-0817 *Fax:* 206-467-4301 *E-mail:* books@sasquatchbooks.com *Web Site:* www.sasquatchbooks.com, pg 240

Schuetz, Richard, University of New Mexico Press, 1720 Lomas Blvd NE, MSC01 1200, Albuquerque, NM 87131-0001 *Tel:* 505-277-2346; 505-277-4810 (order dept) *Toll Free Tel:* 800-249-7737 (orders only) *Fax:* 505-277-3350 *Toll Free Fax:* 800-622-8667 *E-mail:* unmpress@unm.edu; custserv@upress.unm.edu (order dept) *Web Site:* unmpress.com, pg 283

Schulberg, Sandra, Phobos Books, 200 Park Ave S, Suite 1109, New York, NY 10003 *Tel:* 212-477-3225 *Fax:* 212-529-4223 *E-mail:* info@phobosweb.com *Web Site:* phobosweb.com, pg 211

Schulhafer, Joan, Kensington Publishing Corp, 850 Third Ave, New York, NY 10022 *Tel:* 212-407-1500 *Toll Free Tel:* 800-221-2647 *Fax:* 212-935-0699 *Web Site:* www.kensingtonbooks.com, pg 145

Schulman, Janet, Random House Children's Books, 1745 Broadway, New York, NY 10019 *Tel:* 212-782-9000 *Toll Free Tel:* 800-200-3552 *Fax:* 212-782-9452 *Web Site:* www.randomhouse.com/kids, pg 226

Schulman, Marla, Schreiber Publishing Inc, 51 Monroe St, Suite 101, Rockville, MD 20850 *Tel:* 301-424-7737 *Toll Free Tel:* 800-822-3213 (sales) *Fax:* 301-424-2518 *E-mail:* books@schreibernet.com *Web Site:* schreiberpublishing.com, pg 243

Schulman, Susan, Susan Schulman, A Literary Agency, 454 W 44 St, New York, NY 10036 *Tel:* 212-713-1633 *Fax:* 212-581-8830 *E-mail:* schulman@aol.com *Web Site:* www.susanschulman.com, pg 654

Schulte, Rainer, American Literary Translators Association (ALTA), PO Box 830688, Mail Sta MC 35, Richardson, TX 75083-0688 *Tel:* 972-883-2093 *Fax:* 972-883-6303 *Web Site:* www.literarytranslators.org, pg 677

Schulte, Rainer PhD, National Translation Award, Box 830688, Mail Sta JO51, Richardson, TX 75083-0688 *Tel:* 972-883-2093 *Fax:* 972-883-6303 *Web Site:* www.literarytranslators.org, pg 792

Schultheiss, Tom, Popular Culture Inc, PO Box 110, Harbor Springs, MI 49740-0110 *Tel:* 231-439-9767 *Toll Free Tel:* 800-678-8828 *Fax:* 231-439-9767 *Toll Free Fax:* 800-678-8828, pg 216

Schultz, Bill, Regal Books, 1957 Eastman Ave, Ventura, CA 93003 *Tel:* 805-644-9721 *Toll Free Tel:* 800-446-7735 (orders) *Fax:* 805-644-9728 (editorial); 805-644-4729 (purchasing); 805-650-8713 (sales & corp serv); 805-658-3388 (orders) *Toll Free Fax:* 800-860-3109 (orders) *E-mail:* info@regalbooks.com *Web Site:* www.gospellight.com, pg 230

Schultz, Coreena, Facts on File Inc, 132 W 31 St, 17th fl, New York, NY 10001 *Tel:* 212-967-8800 *Toll Free Tel:* 800-322-8755 *Fax:* 212-967-9196 *Toll Free Fax:* 800-678-3633 *E-mail:* custserv@factsonfile.com *Web Site:* www.factsonfile.com, pg 94

Schultz, Hugh, Abingdon Press, 201 Eighth Ave S, Nashville, TN 37203-3919 *Tel:* 615-749-6290 (publicist); 615-749-6000; 615-749-6451 (sales) *Toll Free Tel:* 800-251-3320 *Fax:* 615-749-6056 *Web Site:* www.abingdonpress.com, pg 3

Schultz, Jonathan, Concordia Publishing House, 3558 S Jefferson Ave, St Louis, MO 63118-3968 *Tel:* 314-268-1000 *Toll Free Tel:* 800-325-3040 *Fax:* 314-268-1329 *Toll Free Fax:* 800-490-9889 *E-mail:* cphorder@cph.org *Web Site:* www.cph.org, pg 66

Schultz, Patricia, The Edwin Mellen Press, 415 Ridge St, Lewiston, NY 14092 *Tel:* 716-754-2266 (mgr acqs); 716-754-8566 (mktg); 716-754-2788 (order fulfillment) *Fax:* 716-754-4056; 716-754-1860 (order fulfillment) *E-mail:* mellen@wzrd.com; cs@wzrd. com (customer service, fulfillment) *Web Site:* www. mellenpress.com, pg 171

Schultz, Thom, Group Publishing Inc, 1515 Cascade Ave, Loveland, CO 80538 *Tel:* 970-669-3836 *Toll Free Tel:* 800-447-1070 *Fax:* 970-678-4392 *E-mail:* innovatr@grouppublishing.com *Web Site:* www.grouppublishing.com, pg 110

Schultze, Michael, H W Wilson, 950 University Ave, Bronx, NY 10452-4224 *Tel:* 718-588-8400 *Toll Free Tel:* 800-367-6770 *Fax:* 718-590-1617 *Toll Free Fax:* 800-590-1617 *E-mail:* custserv@hwwilson.com *Web Site:* www.hwwilson.com, pg 300

Schulz, Sue, Houghton Mifflin School Division, 222 Berkeley St, Boston, MA 02116-3764, pg 126

Schumacher, George, Penguin Young Readers Group, 345 Hudson St, New York, NY 10014 *Tel:* 212-366-2000 *E-mail:* online@penguinputnam.com *Web Site:* www.penguin.com, pg 208

Schuman, Patricia Glass, Neal-Schuman Publishers Inc, 100 William St, Suite 2004, New York, NY 10038 *Tel:* 212-925-8650 *Toll Free Tel:* 866-672-6657 *Toll Free Fax:* 866-209-7932 *E-mail:* orders@neal-schuman.com *Web Site:* www.neal-schuman.com, pg 186

Schuna, JoAnne, The Schuna Group Inc, 1503 Briarknoll Dr, Arden Hills, MN 55112 *Tel:* 651-631-8480 *Fax:* 651-631-8458 *Web Site:* www.schunagroup.com, pg 667

Schuneman, Robert, ECS Publishing, 138 Ipswich St, Boston, MA 02215 *Tel:* 617-236-1935 *Toll Free Tel:* 800-777-1919 *Fax:* 617-236-0261 *E-mail:* office@ecspub.com *Web Site:* www.ecspub.com, pg 86

Schupf, Hillary, Pocket Books, 1230 Avenue of the Americas, New York, NY 10020 *Toll Free Tel:* 800-456-6798 *Fax:* 212-698-7284 *E-mail:* consumer.customerservice@simonandschuster. com *Web Site:* www.simonsays.com, pg 215

Schupf, Margot, Rodale Books, 400 S Tenth St, Emmaus, PA 18098-0099 *Tel:* 610-967-5171 *Fax:* 610-967-8961 *Web Site:* www.rodale.com, pg 234

Schustack, Marjorie, John Wiley & Sons Inc Professional & Trade Group, 111 River St, Hoboken, NJ 07030 *Tel:* 201-748-6000 *Toll Free Tel:* 800-225-5945 (cust serv) *Fax:* 201-748-6088 *E-mail:* info@wiley.com *Web Site:* www.wiley.com, pg 300

Schuster, Maria, Yucca Tree Press, 270 Avenida de Mesilla, Las Cruces, NM 88005 *Tel:* 505-525-9707 *Toll Free Tel:* 888-817-1990 *Fax:* 505-525-9711 *E-mail:* thefolks@barbed-wire.net *Web Site:* www. barbed-wire.net, pg 306

Schwab, Christine, Association of American University Presses, 1427 E 60 St, Chicago, IL 60637 *Tel:* 773-702-7700; 773-702-7600 *Toll Free Tel:* 800-621-2736 (orders) 773-702-9756 (sales); 773-660-2235 (orders); 773-702-2708 *E-mail:* general@press. uchicago.edu *Web Site:* www.press.uchicago.edu, pg 26

Schwabinger, Jennifer, Penguin Group (USA) Inc Sales, 375 Hudson St, New York, NY 10014 *Tel:* 212-366-2000 *E-mail:* online@penguinputnam.com *Web Site:* www.penguin.com, pg 208

Schwalbe, Russell, Impressions Book & Journal Services Inc, 2016 Winnebago St, Madison, WI 53704 *Tel:* 608-244-6218 *Fax:* 608-244-7050 *E-mail:* info@impressions.com *Web Site:* www.impressions.com, pg 602

Schwalbe, Will, Hyperion, 77 W 66 St, 11th fl, New York, NY 10023-6298 *Tel:* 212-456-0100 *Toll Free Tel:* 800-759-0190 (cust serv) *Fax:* 212-456-0157 *Web Site:* hyperionbooks.com, pg 129

Schwartz, Alex, Association of American University Presses, 1427 E 60 St, Chicago, IL 60637 *Tel:* 773-702-7700; 773-702-7600 *Toll Free Tel:* 800-621-2736 (orders) *Fax:* 773-702-9756 (sales); 773-660-2235 (orders); 773-702-2708 *E-mail:* general@press. uchicago.edu *Web Site:* www.press.uchicago.edu, pg 26

Schwartz, Andres, Editorial Portavoz, 733 Wealthy St SE, Grand Rapids, MI 49503-5553 *Tel:* 616-451-4775 *Toll Free Tel:* 800-733-2607 *Fax:* 616-451-9330 *E-mail:* portavoz@portavoz.com *Web Site:* www. kregel.com; www.portavoz.com, pg 87

Schwartz, Andrew E, A E Schwartz & Associates, PO Box 79228, Waverley, MA 02479-0228 *Tel:* 617-926-9111 *Fax:* 617-926-0660 *E-mail:* pgbs@aeschwartz. com *Web Site:* aeschwartz.com, pg 654

Schwartz, Anne, Simon & Schuster Children's Publishing, 1230 Avenue of the Americas, New York, NY 10020 *Tel:* 212-698-7000 *Web Site:* www. simonsayskids.com, pg 248

Schwartz, Eric, The Bookbinders' Guild of New York, Dunn & Co, 110 Grand Ave, Ridgefield Park, NJ 07660 *Tel:* 201-229-1888 *Fax:* 201-229-1755 *Web Site:* www.bookbindersguild.org, pg 682

Schwartz, Harold L, MEP Publications, University of Minnesota, Physics Bldg, 116 Church St SE, Minneapolis, MN 55455-0112 *Tel:* 612-922-7993 *E-mail:* marqu002@tc.umn.edu *Web Site:* umn. edu/home/marqu002, pg 171

Schwartz, Marilyn, University of California Press, 2120 Berkeley Way, Berkeley, CA 94720 *Tel:* 510-642-4247 *Toll Free Tel:* 800-777-4726 *Fax:* 510-643-7127 *Toll Free Fax:* 800-999-1958 *E-mail:* askucp@ucpress.edu *Web Site:* www.ucpress.edu, pg 281

Schwartz, Philip, St Martin's Press LLC, 175 Fifth Ave, New York, NY 10010 *Tel:* 212-674-5151 *Fax:* 212-420-9314 *E-mail:* firstname.lastname@stmartins.com *Web Site:* www.stmartins.com, pg 238

Schwartz, Rick, HarperCollins Publishers, 10 E 53 St, New York, NY 10022 *Tel:* 212-207-7000 *Fax:* 212-207-7145 *Web Site:* www.harpercollins.com, pg 116

Schwartz, Steven, Witter Bynner Foundation for Poetry, PO Box 10169, Santa Fe, NM 87504 *Tel:* 505-988-3251 *Fax:* 505-986-8222 *E-mail:* bynnerfoundation@aol.com *Web Site:* www.bynnerfoundation.org, pg 765

Schwartz, Steven, Sarah Jane Freymann Literary Agency, 59 W 71 St, Suite 9B, New York, NY 10023 *Tel:* 212-362-9277 *Fax:* 212-501-8240 *E-mail:* sjfs@aol.com, pg 631

Schwartz, Susan, Dutton, 375 Hudson St, New York, NY 10014 *Tel:* 212-366-2000 *Fax:* 212-366-2262 *E-mail:* online@penguinputnam.com *Web Site:* www. penguin.com, pg 85

Schwartz, Susan A, Words into Print, 200 W 86 St, Suite 14-1, New York, NY 10024 *Tel:* 212-877-3211 *Fax:* 212-873-3796 *E-mail:* sas22@ix.netcom.com *Web Site:* www.wordsintoprint.org, pg 614

Schwartz, Susan H, Surrey Books, 230 E Ohio St, Suite 120, Chicago, IL 60611 *Tel:* 312-751-7330 *Toll Free Tel:* 800-326-4430 *Fax:* 312-751-7334 *E-mail:* surreybk@aol.com *Web Site:* www. surreybooks.com, pg 262

Schwartzentruber, Mike, Northstone Publishing, 9025 Jim Bailey Rd, Kelowna, BC V4V 1R2, Canada *Tel:* 250-766-2778 *Toll Free Tel:* 800-299-2926 *Fax:* 250-766-2736 *Web Site:* www.joinhands.com, pg 556

Schwartzentruber, Mike, Wood Lake Books Inc, 9025 Jim Bailey Rd, Kelowna, BC V4V 1R2, Canada *Tel:* 250-766-2778 *Toll Free Tel:* 800-663-2775 (orders) *Fax:* 250-766-2736 *Toll Free Fax:* 888-841-9991 (orders) *E-mail:* info@woodlake.com *Web Site:* www.woodlakebooks.com, pg 567

Schwarz, Evelya Lee, Prestel Publishing, 900 Broadway, Suite 603, New York, NY 10003 *Tel:* 212-995-2720 *Toll Free Tel:* 888-463-6110 (cust serv) *Fax:* 212-995-2733 *E-mail:* sales@prestel-usa.com *Web Site:* www. prestel.com, pg 218

Schwarz, Helena, Columbia University Press, 61 W 62 St, New York, NY 10023 *Tel:* 212-459-0600 *Toll Free Tel:* 800-944-8648 *Fax:* 212-459-3678 *Web Site:* www. columbia.edu/cu/cup, pg 65

Schwarz, Tim, Carolrhoda Books Inc, 241 First Ave N, Minneapolis, MN 55401 *Tel:* 612-332-3344 *Toll Free Tel:* 800-328-4929 *Fax:* 612-332-7615 *Toll Free Fax:* 800-332-1132 *E-mail:* info@lernerbooks.com *Web Site:* www.lernerbooks.com, pg 54

Schwarz, Tim, First Avenue Editions, 241 First Ave N, Minneapolis, MN 55401 *Tel:* 612-332-3344 *Toll Free Tel:* 800-328-4929 *Fax:* 612-332-7615 *Toll Free Fax:* 800-332-1132 *E-mail:* info@lernerbooks.com *Web Site:* www.lernerbooks.com, pg 97

Schwarz, Tim, Lerner Publications, 241 First Ave N, Minneapolis, MN 55401 *Tel:* 612-332-3344 *Toll Free Tel:* 800-328-4929 *Fax:* 612-332-7615 *Toll Free Fax:* 800-332-1132 *E-mail:* info@lernerbooks.com *Web Site:* www.lernerbooks.com, pg 152

Schwarz, Tim, Lerner Publishing Group, 241 First Ave N, Minneapolis, MN 55401 *Tel:* 612-332-3344 *Toll Free Tel:* 800-328-4929 *Fax:* 612-332-7615 *Toll Free Fax:* 800-332-1132 *E-mail:* info@lernerbooks.com *Web Site:* www.lernerbooks.com, pg 152

Schwarz, Tim, LernerSports, 241 First Ave N, Minneapolis, MN 55401 *Tel:* 612-332-3344 *Toll Free Tel:* 800-328-4929 *Fax:* 612-332-7615 *Toll Free Fax:* 800-332-1132 *E-mail:* info@lernerbooks.com *Web Site:* www.lernerbooks.com, pg 153

Schwarz, Tim, Runestone Press, 241 First Ave N, Minneapolis, MN 55401 *Tel:* 612-332-3344 *Toll Free Tel:* 800-328-4929; 800-332-1132 *Fax:* 612-332-7615 *E-mail:* info@lernerbooks.com *Web Site:* www. lernerbooks.com, pg 236

Schweizer, Karen, Theosophical Publishing House/Quest Books, 306 W Geneva Rd, Wheaton, IL 60187 *Tel:* 630-665-0130 *Toll Free Tel:* 800-669-9425 *Fax:* 630-665-8791 *E-mail:* questbooks@theosmail.net *Web Site:* www.questbooks.net, pg 268

Scinta, Sam, Fulcrum Publishing Inc, 16100 Table Mountain Pkwy, Suite 300, Golden, CO 80403 *Tel:* 303-277-1623 *Toll Free Tel:* 800-992-2908 *Fax:* 303-279-7111 *Toll Free Fax:* 800-726-7112 *E-mail:* fulcrum@fulcrum-books.com *Web Site:* www. fulcrum-books.com, pg 101

Scisco, Pete, Center for Creative Leadership, One Leadership Place, Greensboro, NC 27438-6300 *Tel:* 336-288-7210 *Fax:* 336-288-3999 *Web Site:* www. ccl.org/publications, pg 56

Scoggan, Nita L, Royalty Publishing Co, 1440 Church Camp Rd, Bedford, IN 47421 *Tel:* 812-278-8785 *Fax:* 812-278-8785 *E-mail:* neeto@admete.net *Web Site:* www.v-maximum-zone.com, pg 235

Scognamiglio, John, Kensington Publishing Corp, 850 Third Ave, New York, NY 10022 *Tel:* 212-407-1500 *Toll Free Tel:* 800-221-2647 *Fax:* 212-935-0699 *Web Site:* www.kensingtonbooks.com, pg 145

Scordato, Ellen, American Book Producers Association (ABPA), 160 Fifth Ave, Suite 622, New York, NY 10010 *Tel:* 212-645-2368 *Toll Free Tel:* 800-209-4575 *Fax:* 212-242-6499 *E-mail:* office@abpaonline.org *Web Site:* www.abpaonline.org, pg 676

Scordato, Ellen, Book Producing: Making Books Happen, 160 Fifth Ave, New York, NY 10010-7003 *Tel:* 212-645-2368 *Toll Free Tel:* 800-209-4575 *Fax:* 212-242-6799 *E-mail:* office@abpaonline.org *Web Site:* www.abpaonline.org, pg 742

Scorziello, Vincent, The MIT Press, 5 Cambridge Ctr, Cambridge, MA 02142 *Tel:* 617-253-5646 *Toll Free Tel:* 800-405-1619 (orders only) *Fax:* 617-258-6779 *Web Site:* mitpress.mit.edu, pg 175

Scott, Ardy M, Twilight Times Books, PO Box 3340, Kingsport, TN 37664-0340 Tel: 423-323-0183 Fax: 423-323-0183 E-mail: publisher@twilighttimes. com Web Site: www.twilighttimesbooks.com, pg 277

Scott, Barbara, Books for Everybody, 70 The Esplanade, Suite 210, Toronto, ON M5E 1R2, Canada Tel: 416-360-0044 Fax: 416-955-0794 E-mail: mail@booksforeverybody.com Web Site: www. booksforeverybody.com, pg 682

Scott, Cheri, Human Kinetics Inc, PO Box 5076, Champaign, IL 61825-5076 Tel: 217-351-5076 Toll Free Tel: 800-747-4457 Fax: 217-351-1549 (orders/ cust serv) E-mail: info@hkusa.com Web Site: www. humankinetics.com, pg 128

Scott, Clifford, Blue Mountain Arts Inc, PO Box 4549, Boulder, CO 80306 Tel: 303-449-0536 Toll Free Tel: 800-473-2082 Fax: 303-417-6496 Toll Free Fax: 800-256-1213 E-mail: booksbma@mindspring. com; ordersbma@mindspring.com Web Site: www.sps. com, pg 41

Scott, Craig R, Heritage Books Inc, 65 E Main St, Westminster, MD 21157 Tel: 410-876-0371 Toll Free Tel: 866-282-2689 Fax: 410-871-2674 E-mail: info@ heritagebooks.com Web Site: www.heritagebooks.com, pg 121

Scott, Eugene L, The Annual Great American Tennis Writing Awards, 15 Elm Place, Rye, NY 10580 Tel: 914-967-4890 Fax: 914-967-8178 E-mail: tennisweek@tennisweek.com Web Site: www. tennisweek.com, pg 777

Scott, Freda, Freda Scott Inc, 383 Missouri St, San Francisco, CA 94107-2819 Tel: 415-398-9121 Fax: 415-550-9120 E-mail: info@fredascott.com, pg 667

Scott, Giancarlo Ryan Tafari, Cornerstone Productions Inc, PO Box 3232, Wilmington, NC 28406 Tel: 910-523-7326 Fax: 404-288-8937, pg 69

Scott, Herbert, The Green Rose Prize in Poetry, Western Michigan University, Dept of English, 1903 W Michigan Ave, Kalamazoo, MI 49008-5331 Tel: 269-387-8185 Fax: 269-387-2562 Web Site: www.wmich. edu/newissues/greenroseprize.html, pg 777

Scott, Herbert, New Issues Poetry & Prose, Western Michigan University, Dept of English, 1903 W Michigan Ave, Kalamazoo, MI 49008-5331 Tel: 269-387-8185 Fax: 269-387-2562 Web Site: www.wmich. edu/newissues, pg 188

Scott, Herbert, New Issues Poetry Prize, Western Michigan University, Dept of English, 1903 W Michigan Ave, Kalamazoo, MI 49008-5331 Tel: 269-387-8185 Fax: 269-387-2562 Web Site: www.wmich. edu/newissues, pg 793

Scott, Jason, Prestwick House Inc, PO Box 246, Cheswold, DE 19936-0246 Tel: 302-736-2665 Fax: 302-734-0549 E-mail: info@prestwickhouse.com Web Site: www.prestwickhouse.com, pg 218

Scott, Joseph, Trident Media Inc, 801 N Pitt St, Suite 123, Alexandria, VA 22314 Tel: 703-684-6895 Fax: 703-684-0639 E-mail: info@samhost.net Web Site: www.edenplaza.com, pg 275

Scott, Kenneth J, University Press of Florida, 15 NW 15 St, Gainesville, FL 32611-2079 Tel: 352-392-1351 Toll Free Tel: 800-226-3822 (orders only) Fax: 352-392-7302 Toll Free Fax: 800-680-1955 (orders only) E-mail: info@upf.com Web Site: www.upf.com, pg 287

Scott, Kimberly M, The Periodical Publications Assn Inc (PPA), PO Box 10669, Rockville, MD 20849-0669 Tel: 301-260-1646 Fax: 301-260-1647 E-mail: periodicalpubs@yahoo.com, pg 697

Scott, Lesa, Heinemann, 361 Hanover St, Portsmouth, NH 03801-3912 Tel: 603-431-7894 Toll Free Tel: 800-225-5800 Fax: 603-431-4971; 603-431-7840 E-mail: info@heinemann.com Web Site: www. heinemann.com, pg 120

Scott, Lesa, Heinemann/Boynton Cook Publishers Inc, 361 Hanover St, Portsmouth, NH 03801-3912 Tel: 603-431-7894 Toll Free Tel: 800-541-2086 Fax: 603-431-7840 E-mail: custserv@heinemann.com Web Site: www.boyntoncook.com, pg 120

Scott, Linda, Doubleday Canada, One Toronto St, Suite 300, Toronto, ON M5C 2V6, Canada Tel: 416-364-4449 Fax: 416-957-1587 Web Site: www. randomhouse.ca, pg 542

Scott, Linda, Knopf Canada, One Toronto St, Suite 300, Toronto, ON M5C 2V6, Canada Tel: 416-364-4449 Toll Free Tel: 800-668-4247 (order desk) Fax: 416-364-0462 Web Site: www.randomhouse.ca, pg 552

Scott, Linda, Random House of Canada Ltd, One Toronto St, Unit 300, Toronto, ON M5C 2V6, Canada Tel: 416-364-4449 Fax: 416-364-6863 (edit & publicity); 416-364-6653 (subs rts) Web Site: www. randomhouse.ca, pg 559

Scott, Linda, Seal Books, One Toronto St, Suite 300, Toronto, ON M5C 2V6, Canada Tel: 416-364-4449 Toll Free Tel: 888-523-9292 (order desk) Fax: 416-957-1587 Web Site: www.randomhouse.ca, pg 560

Scott, Lisa, Periodical & Book Association of America Inc, 481 Eighth Ave, Suite 826, New York, NY 10001 Tel: 212-563-6502 Fax: 212-563-4098 Web Site: www. pbaa.net, pg 697

Scott, Megan, University of Iowa Press, University of Iowa, 100 Kuhl House, Iowa City, IA 52242-1000 Tel: 319-335-2000 Toll Free Tel: 800-621-2736 (orders only) Fax: 319-335-2055 Toll Free Fax: 800-621-8476 (orders only) E-mail: uipress@uiowa.edu Web Site: www.uiowapress.org, pg 282

Scott, Randy, Cook Communications Ministries, 4050 Lee Vance View, Colorado Springs, CO 80918 Tel: 719-536-3271 Toll Free Tel: 800-437-4337 Fax: 719-536-3269 E-mail: chariotpub@aol.com Web Site: www.cookministries.com, pg 68

Scott, Randy, Standard Publishing Co, 8121 Hamilton Ave, Cincinnati, OH 45231 Tel: 513-931-4050 Toll Free Tel: 800-543-1301 Fax: 513-931-0950 Toll Free Fax: 877-867-5751 E-mail: customerservice@ standardpub.com Web Site: www.standardpub.com, pg 257

Scott, Ricardo A, Cornerstone Productions Inc, PO Box 3232, Wilmington, NC 28406 Tel: 910-523-7326 Fax: 404-288-8937, pg 69

Scott, Sara, Hendrickson Publishers Inc, PO Box 3473, Peabody, MA 01961-3473 Tel: 978-532-6546 Toll Free Tel: 800-358-3111 Fax: 978-531-8146 E-mail: orders@hendrickson.com Web Site: www. hendrickson.com, pg 121

Scott, William, ASM International, 9639 Kinsman Rd, Materials Park, OH 44073-0002 Tel: 440-338-5151 Toll Free Tel: 800-336-5152; 800-368-9800 (Europe) Fax: 440-338-4634 E-mail: cust-srv@asminternational. org Web Site: www.asminternational.org, pg 25

Scovil, Jack, Scovil Chichak Galen Literary Agency Inc, 381 Park Ave S, Suite 1020, New York, NY 10016 Tel: 212-679-8686 Fax: 212-679-6710 E-mail: mailroom@scglit.com Web Site: www.scglit. com, pg 654

Scrivener, Martin, William Andrew Publishing, 13 Eaton Ave, Norwich, NY 13815 Tel: 607-337-5000 Toll Free Tel: 800-932-7045 Fax: 607-337-5090 E-mail: publishing@williamandrew.com Web Site: www.williamandrew.com, pg 300

Scriver, Julie, Goose Lane Editions, 469 King St, Fredericton, NB E3B 1E5, Canada Tel: 506-450-4251 Toll Free Tel: 888-926-8377 Fax: 506-459-4991 E-mail: gooselane@gooselane.com Web Site: www. gooselane.com, pg 548

Scudder, Dean, Sinauer Associates Inc, 23 Plumtree Rd, Sunderland, MA 01375-0407 Tel: 413-549-4300 Fax: 413-549-1118 E-mail: publish@sinauer.com Web Site: www.sinauer.com, pg 249

Scully, Kate, Northeastern Graphic Inc, 5 Emeline Dr, Hawthorne, NJ 07506 Tel: 973-221-0109 Fax: 973-221-0076 Web Site: www.northeasterngraphic.com, pg 607

Scurlock, Bill, Scurlock Publishing Co Inc, 1293 Myrtle Springs Rd, Texarkana, TX 75503 Tel: 903-832-4726 Toll Free Tel: 800-228-6389 Fax: 903-831-3177 E-mail: scurlockpubl@txk.net Web Site: www. muzzmag.com; muzzleloadermag.com, pg 244

Scurlock, Linda, Scurlock Publishing Co Inc, 1293 Myrtle Springs Rd, Texarkana, TX 75503 Tel: 903-832-4726 Toll Free Tel: 800-228-6389 Fax: 903-831-3177 E-mail: scurlockpubl@txk.net Web Site: www. muzzmag.com; muzzleloadermag.com, pg 244

Seabaugh, Karen S, American Association for Vocational Instructional Materials, 220 Smithonia Rd, Winterville, GA 30683-9527 Tel: 706-742-5355 Toll Free Tel: 800-228-4689 Fax: 706-742-7005 E-mail: sales@aavim. com Web Site: www.aavim.com, pg 11

Seagrave, Pia S PhD, Kirkland's Press, 101 Mount Rock Rd, Newville, PA 17241 Tel: 717-776-4232 Web Site: www.kirklandspress.com, pg 146

Seagrave, Ronald R, Kirkland's Press, 101 Mount Rock Rd, Newville, PA 17241 Tel: 717-776-4232 Web Site: www.kirklandspress.com, pg 146

Seamans, Robert, Educators Publishing Service Inc, 625 Mount Auburn St, Cambridge, MA 02139-9031 Tel: 617-547-6706 Toll Free Tel: 800-225-5750 Fax: 617-547-0412 Toll Free Tel: 888-440-2665 E-mail: epsbooks@epsbooks.com Web Site: www. epsbooks.com, pg 88

Searby, Ellen, Windham Bay Press, PO Box 1198, Occidental, CA 95465 Tel: 707-823-7150 Fax: 707-823-7150, pg 301

Searls, Hank, Devonshire House Books, 4435 Holly Lane NW, Gig Harbor, WA 98335 Tel: 253-851-9896 Fax: 253-851-9897 Web Site: critiquemaster.com, pg 596

Searls, Hank, Hank Searls Authors Workshop, 4435 Holly Lane NW, Gig Harbor, WA 98335 Tel: 253-851-9897 Fax: 253-851-9897 E-mail: hanksearls@ harbornet.com Web Site: critiquemaster.com, pg 747

Sears, Steven, The Monacelli Press, 902 Broadway, 18th fl, New York, NY 10010 Tel: 212-777-0504 Toll Free Tel: 800-631-8571 (cust serv) Fax: 212-777-0514; 201-256-0000 (cust serv) E-mail: info@ monacellipress.com; production@monacellipress.com; customerservice@penguinputnam.com Web Site: www. monacellipress.com, pg 177

Seastrand, Mark, Creating Keepsakes Books, 14901 S Heritagecrest Way, Bluffdale, UT 84065 Tel: 801-984-2070 Toll Free Tel: 800-815-3538 Fax: 801-984-2080 Web Site: www.creatingkeepsakes.com, pg 72

Seaton, Sharon, University of Missouri-Kansas City, New Letters Weekend Writers Conference, College of Arts & Sciences, Continuing Education Div, 5300 Rockhill Rd, Kansas City, MO 64110 Tel: 816-235-2736 Fax: 816-235-5279 Web Site: www.umkc.edu, pg 755

Seaver, Jeannette M, Arcade Publishing Inc, 141 Fifth Ave, New York, NY 10010 Tel: 212-475-2633 Fax: 212-353-8148 E-mail: arcadeinfo@arcadepub. com Web Site: www.arcadepub.com, pg 22

Seaver, Kate, Dorchester Publishing Co Inc, 200 Madison Ave, Suite 2000, New York, NY 10016 Tel: 212-725-8811 Toll Free Tel: 800-481-9191 (order dept) Fax: 212-532-1054 E-mail: dorchedits@ dorchesterpub.com Web Site: www.dorchesterpub.com, pg 82

Seaver, Richard, Arcade Publishing Inc, 141 Fifth Ave, New York, NY 10010 Tel: 212-475-2633 Fax: 212-353-8148 E-mail: arcadeinfo@arcadepub.com Web Site: www.arcadepub.com, pg 22

Seavey, Tom, Stenhouse Publishers, 477 Congress St, Suite 4B, Portland, ME 04101-3451 Tel: 207-253-1600 Toll Free Tel: 888-363-0566 Fax: 207-253-5121 Toll Free Fax: 800-833-9164 E-mail: info@stenhouse. com Web Site: www.stenhouse.com, pg 259

Seawall, Margaret, Sage Publications, 2455 Teller Rd, Thousand Oaks, CA 91320 Tel: 805-499-0721 Fax: 805-499-0871 E-mail: info@sagepub.com Web Site: www.sagepub.com, pg 237

Senk, John, Veterans of Foreign Wars of the US, 406 W 34 St, Kansas City, MO 64111 *Tel:* 816-756-3390 *Fax:* 816-968-1169 *E-mail:* info@vfw.org *Web Site:* www.vfw.org, pg 702

Senkus, Roman, Canadian Institute of Ukrainian Studies Press, University of Toronto, One Spadina Crescent, Rm 109, Toronto, ON M5S 2J5, Canada *Tel:* 416-978-6934 *Fax:* 416-978-2672 *E-mail:* cius@chass.utoronto.ca (edit off) *Web Site:* www.utoronto.ca/cius, pg 538

Sennholz, Lyn M, Center for Futures Education Inc, 345 Erie St, Grove City, PA 16127 *Tel:* 724-458-5860 *Toll Free Tel:* 800-966-2554 *Fax:* 724-458-5962 *E-mail:* info@thectr.com *Web Site:* www.thectr.com, pg 56

Senz, Lisa, St Martin's Press Paperback and Reference Group, 175 Fifth Ave, New York, NY 10010 *Fax:* 212-995-2488 *E-mail:* firstname.lastname@stmartins.com, pg 239

Seo, Ginee, Simon & Schuster Children's Publishing, 1230 Avenue of the Americas, New York, NY 10020 *Tel:* 212-698-7000 *Web Site:* www.simonsayskids.com, pg 248

Seow, Jackie, Simon & Schuster, 1230 Avenue of the Americas, New York, NY 10020 *Tel:* 212-698-7000 *Toll Free Tel:* 800-223-2348 (cust serv); 800-223-2336 (orders) *Toll Free Fax:* 800-943-9831 (orders) *Web Site:* www.simonsays.com, pg 248

Sepehri, Amin, Mage Publishers Inc, 1032 29 St NW, Washington, DC 20007 *Tel:* 202-342-1642 *Toll Free Tel:* 800-962-0922 *Fax:* 202-342-9269 *E-mail:* info@mage.com *Web Site:* www.mage.com, pg 161

Sequeira, Lee Romano, American Diabetes Association, 1701 N Beauregard St, Alexandria, VA 22311 *Tel:* 703-299-2046 *Toll Free Tel:* 800-232-6733 *Fax:* 908-806-2301 *Web Site:* www.diabetes.org, pg 13

Serafimidis, Sarah, Frog Ltd, 1435 Fourth St, Berkeley, CA 94710 *Tel:* 510-559-8277 *Toll Free Tel:* 800-337-2665 (book orders only) *Fax:* 510-559-8279 *E-mail:* orders@northatlanticbooks.com *Web Site:* www.northatlanticbooks.com, pg 101

Serafimidis, Sarah, North Atlantic Books, 1435 Fourth St, Berkeley, CA 94710 *Tel:* 510-559-8277 *Toll Free Tel:* 800-337-2665 (book orders only) *Fax:* 510-559-8279 *E-mail:* orders@northatlanticbooks.com *Web Site:* www.northatlanticbooks.com, pg 192

Serbun, David, Houghton Mifflin College Division, 222 Berkeley St, Boston, MA 02116-3764 *Tel:* 617-351-5000 *Toll Free Tel:* 800-225-1464 (orders) *Web Site:* www.college.hmco.com, pg 126

Serdinsky, Melissa, The Perseus Books Group, 387 Park Ave S, 12th fl, New York, NY 10016 *Tel:* 212-340-8100 *Toll Free Tel:* 800-386-5656 (cust serv) *Fax:* 212-340-8115 *Web Site:* www.perseusbooksgroup.com, pg 210

Serena, Jeff, The Globe Pequot Press, 246 Goose Lane, Guilford, CT 06437 *Tel:* 203-458-4500 *Toll Free Tel:* 800-243-0495 (cust serv) *Fax:* 203-458-4601 *Toll Free Fax:* 800-820-2329 (orders & cust serv) *E-mail:* info@globepequot.com *Web Site:* www.globepequot.com, pg 105

Sergel, Christopher III, Dramatic Publishing Co, 311 Washington St, Woodstock, IL 60098 *Tel:* 815-338-7170 *Toll Free Tel:* 800-448-7469 *Fax:* 815-338-8981 *Toll Free Fax:* 800-334-5302 *E-mail:* plays@dramaticpublishing.com *Web Site:* www.dramaticpublishing.com, pg 83

Sergel, Christopher, Dramatic Publishing Co, 311 Washington St, Woodstock, IL 60098 *Tel:* 815-338-7170 *Toll Free Tel:* 800-448-7469 *Fax:* 815-338-8981 *Toll Free Fax:* 800-334-5302 *E-mail:* plays@dramaticpublishing.com *Web Site:* www.dramaticpublishing.com, pg 83

Sergel, Gayle, Dramatic Publishing Co, 311 Washington St, Woodstock, IL 60098 *Tel:* 815-338-7170 *Toll Free Tel:* 800-448-7469 *Fax:* 815-338-8981 *Toll Free Fax:* 800-334-5302 *E-mail:* plays@dramaticpublishing.com *Web Site:* www.dramaticpublishing.com, pg 83

Sergel, Susan, Dramatic Publishing Co, 311 Washington St, Woodstock, IL 60098 *Tel:* 815-338-7170 *Toll Free Tel:* 800-448-7469 *Fax:* 815-338-8981 *Toll Free Fax:* 800-334-5302 *E-mail:* plays@dramaticpublishing.com *Web Site:* www.dramaticpublishing.com, pg 83

Serlin, Andra, Running Press Book Publishers, 125 S 22 St, Philadelphia, PA 19103-4399 *Tel:* 215-567-5080 *Toll Free Tel:* 800-345-5359 (cust serv & orders) *Fax:* 215-568-2919 *Toll Free Fax:* 800-453-2884 *Web Site:* www.runningpress.com, pg 236

Seroy, Jeff, Faber & Faber Inc, 19 Union Sq W, New York, NY 10003 *Tel:* 212-741-6900 *Toll Free Tel:* 888-330-8477 *Fax:* 212-633-9385 *Web Site:* www.fsgbooks.com/faberandfaber.htm, pg 93

Seroy, Jeff, Farrar, Straus & Giroux, LLC, 19 Union Sq W, New York, NY 10003 *Tel:* 212-741-6900 *Fax:* 212-741-6973 *Web Site:* www.fsgbooks.com, pg 95

Seroy, Jeff, Hill & Wang, 19 Union Sq W, New York, NY 10003 *Tel:* 212-741-6900 *Fax:* 212-206-5340 *E-mail:* fsg.publicity@fsgbooks.com *Web Site:* www.fsgbooks.com, pg 122

Seroy, Jeff, North Point Press, 19 Union Sq W, New York, NY 10003 *Tel:* 212-741-6900 *Toll Free Tel:* 888-330-8477 *Fax:* 212-741-6973 *Web Site:* www.fsgbooks.com, pg 192

Sery, Douglas, The MIT Press, 5 Cambridge Ctr, Cambridge, MA 02142 *Tel:* 617-253-5646 *Toll Free Tel:* 800-405-1619 (orders only) *Fax:* 617-258-6779 *Web Site:* mitpress.mit.edu, pg 175

Settevendemie, Lindy, Audio Renaissance, 175 Fifth Ave, New York, NY 10010 *Tel:* 212-674-5151 *Toll Free Tel:* 888-330-8477 (cust serv) *Fax:* 917-534-0980 *E-mail:* firstname.lastname@hbpub.com *Web Site:* www.audiorenaissance.com, pg 27

Settle, Alicia B, Per Annum Inc, 48 W 25 St, 10th fl, New York, NY 10010 *Tel:* 212-647-8700 *Toll Free Tel:* 800-548-1108 *Fax:* 212-647-8716 *E-mail:* info@perannum.com *Web Site:* www.perannum.com, pg 210

Settle, Alixandre M, Per Annum Inc, 48 W 25 St, 10th fl, New York, NY 10010 *Tel:* 212-647-8700 *Toll Free Tel:* 800-548-1108 *Fax:* 212-647-8716 *E-mail:* info@perannum.com *Web Site:* www.perannum.com, pg 210

Seward, Melea, W W Norton & Company Inc, 500 Fifth Ave, New York, NY 10110-0017 *Tel:* 212-354-5500 *Toll Free Tel:* 800-233-4830 (orders & cust serv) *Fax:* 212-869-0856 *Toll Free Fax:* 800-458-6515 *Web Site:* www.wwnorton.com, pg 193

Sewell, Vicki, University of South Carolina Press, 1600 Hampton St, 5th fl, Columbia, SC 29208 *Tel:* 803-777-5243 *Toll Free Tel:* 800-768-2500 (orders) *Fax:* 803-777-0160 *Toll Free Fax:* 800-868-0740 (orders) *Web Site:* www.sc.edu/uscpress/, pg 285

Sexton, Jane, North Books, PO Box 1277, Wickford, RI 02852 *Tel:* 401-294-3682 *Fax:* 401-294-9491, pg 192

Sexton, Jim, North Books, PO Box 1277, Wickford, RI 02852 *Tel:* 401-294-3682 *Fax:* 401-294-9491, pg 192

Sexton, Phil, Krause Publications, 700 E State St, Iola, WI 54990 *Tel:* 715-445-4612 ext 365 *Toll Free Tel:* 800-258-0929; 888-457-2873 *Fax:* 715-445-4087 *Web Site:* www.krause.com, pg 147

Seyer, David, Dayton Playhouse FutureFest Inc, 1301 E Siebenthaler Ave, Dayton, OH 45414 *Tel:* 937-333-7469 *Fax:* 937-333-2827 *E-mail:* futurefest@daytonplayhouse.com *Web Site:* www.daytonplayhouse.com, pg 769

Seymour, Antonia, Blackwell Publishing Professional, 2121 State Ave, Ames, IA 50014 *Tel:* 515-292-0140 *Toll Free Tel:* 800-862-6657 (orders only) *Fax:* 515-292-3348 *Web Site:* www.blackwellprofessional.com, pg 40

Seymour, Richard M, Iconografix Inc, 1830-A Hanley Rd, Hudson, WI 54016 *Tel:* 715-381-9755 *Toll Free Tel:* 800-289-3504 (orders only) *Fax:* 715-381-9756 *E-mail:* iconogfx@spacestar.net, pg 130

Seymour, Susan J, Harvard University Press, 79 Garden St, Cambridge, MA 02138-1499 *Tel:* 617-495-2600; 401-531-2800 (international orders) *Toll Free Tel:* 800-405-1619 (orders) *Fax:* 617-495-5898 (general); 617-496-4677 (edit & rts); 401-531-2801 (international orders) *Toll Free Tel:* 800-406-9145 (orders) *E-mail:* firstname_lastname@harvard.edu *Web Site:* www.hup.harvard.edu, pg 117

Shabelman, Doug, Burns Sports & Celebrities Inc, 820 Davis St, Evanston, IL 60201 *Tel:* 847-866-9400 *Fax:* 847-491-9778 *Web Site:* www.burnssports.com, pg 669

Shadid, Dina, North-South Institute/Institut Nord-Sud, 55 Murray St, Suite 200, Ottawa, ON K1N 5M3, Canada *Tel:* 613-241-3535 *Fax:* 613-241-7435 *E-mail:* nsi@nsi-ins.ca *Web Site:* www.nsi-ins.ca, pg 556

Shafer, Ardene, MENC - The National Association for Music Education, 1806 Robert Fulton Dr, Reston, VA 20191 *Tel:* 703-860-4000 *Fax:* 703-860-9443 *E-mail:* franp@menc.org *Web Site:* www.menc.org, pg 171

Shafeyeva, Yelena, Begell House Inc Publishers, 145 Madison Ave, Suite 601, New York, NY 10016 *Tel:* 212-725-1999 *Fax:* 212-213-8368 *E-mail:* orders@begellhouse.com *Web Site:* www.begellhouse.com, pg 35

Shaffer, Bryan, Purdue University Press, S Campus Courts-E, 509 Harrison St, West Lafayette, IN 47907-2025 *Tel:* 765-494-2038 *Toll Free Tel:* 800-247-6553 (orders) *Fax:* 765-496-2442 *E-mail:* pupress@purdue.edu *Web Site:* www.thepress.purdue.edu, pg 222

Shaffer, Mike, New Readers Press, 1320 Jamesville Ave, Syracuse, NY 13210 *Tel:* 315-422-9121 *Toll Free Tel:* 800-448-8878 *Fax:* 315-422-5561 *E-mail:* nrp@proliteracy.org *Web Site:* www.newreaderspress.com, pg 189

Shaffron, Nancy, Black Diamond Book Publishing, PO Box 492299, Los Angeles, CA 90049-8299 *Tel:* 310-472-9833 *Toll Free Tel:* 800-962-7622 *Fax:* 310-472-9833 *Toll Free Fax:* 800-962-7622, pg 39

Shafran, Andy, Muska & Lipman Publishing, 25 Thomson Place, Boston, MA 02210 *Tel:* 617-757-7900 *Fax:* 513-924-9333 *Web Site:* www.muskalipman.com, pg 181

Shafranski-Campabello, Nancy, Printing Industries of America Premier Print Award, 200 Deer Run Rd, Sewickley, PA 15143 *Tel:* 412-741-6860 *Fax:* 412-741-2311 *Web Site:* www.gain.net, pg 800

Shagat, Sandra, Zachary Shuster Harmsworth Agency, 1776 Broadway, New York, NY 10019 *Tel:* 212-765-6900 *Fax:* 212-765-6490 *Web Site:* www.zshliterary.com, pg 662

Shah, Jay, Triumph Learning, 333 E 38 St, 8th fl, New York, NY 10016 *Tel:* 212-652-0200 *Fax:* 212-652-0203 *Web Site:* www.triumphlearning.com, pg 276

Shakely, Lauren, Clarkson Potter Publishers, 1745 Broadway, New York, NY 10019 *Tel:* 212-782-9000 *Toll Free Tel:* 888-264-1745 *Fax:* 212-572-6181 *Web Site:* www.clarksonpotter.com; www.randomhouse.com/crown/clarksonpotter, pg 63

Shaker, Anthony F PhD, AFS Wordstead, 27 Belvedere St, St Julie, PQ J3E 3M4, Canada *Tel:* 450-922-0172 *Toll Free Tel:* 866-864-5448 *Web Site:* www.wordstead.com, pg 589

Shallcross, Andrea, Time Warner Book Group, 1271 Avenue of the Americas, New York, NY 10020 *Tel:* 212-522-7200 *Fax:* 212-522-7991 *Web Site:* www.twbookmark.com, pg 272

Shaloo, Sharon, Massachusetts Book Awards, Hampshire College MCB, 893 West St, Amherst, MA 01002 *Tel:* 413-559-5678 *Fax:* 413-559-5629 *E-mail:* massbook@hampshire.edu *Web Site:* www.massbook.org, pg 788

Shams, Shaadi, Bristol Publishing Enterprises, 2714 McCone Ave, Hayward, CA 94545 *Tel:* 510-783-5472 *Toll Free Tel:* 800-346-4889 *Fax:* 510-783-5492 *Web Site:* www.bristolpublishing.com, pg

Shanahan, Denise, Albert Whitman & Co, 6340 Oakton St, Morton Grove, IL 60053-2723 *Tel:* 847-581-0033 *Toll Free Tel:* 800-255-7675 *Fax:* 847-581-0039 *E-mail:* mail@awhitmanco.com *Web Site:* www.albertwhitman.com, pg 298

Shear, Donna, Northwestern University Press, 625 Colfax St, Evanston, IL 60208 *Tel:* 847-491-2046 *Toll Free Tel:* 800-621-2736 (orders only) *Fax:* 847-491-8150 *E-mail:* nupress@northwestern.edu *Web Site:* www.nupress.northwestern.edu, pg 193

Shear, Matthew, St Martin's Press Paperback and Reference Group, 175 Fifth Ave, New York, NY 10010 *Fax:* 212-995-2488 *E-mail:* firstname.lastname@stmartins.com, pg 239

Shearer, Deborah, Braille Co Inc, 65-B Town Hall Sq, Falmouth, MA 02540-2754 *Tel:* 508-540-0800 *Fax:* 508-548-6116 *E-mail:* braillinc@capecod.net *Web Site:* home.capecod.net/~braillinc, pg 45

Shearer, Robert G, Greenleaf Press, 3761 Hwy 109 N, Unit D, Lebanon, TN 37087 *Tel:* 615-449-1617 *Fax:* 615-449-4018 *E-mail:* info@greenleafpress.com *Web Site:* www.greenleafpress.com, pg 109

Sheats, Diane, The Westchester Literary Agency, 2533 Egret Lake Dr, West Palm Beach, FL 33413 *Tel:* 561-642-2908 *Fax:* 561-439-2228, pg 661

Sheedy, Charlotte, Charlotte Sheedy Literary Agency Inc, 65 Bleecker St, 12th fl, New York, NY 10012 *Tel:* 212-780-9800 *Fax:* 212-780-0308 *E-mail:* sheedy@sll.com, pg 655

Sheedy, Charlotte, Sterling Lord Literistic Inc, 65 Bleecker St, New York, NY 10012 *Tel:* 212-780-6050 *Fax:* 212-780-6095, pg 657

Sheehan, Donald, Festival of Poetry, Ridge Rd, Franconia, NH 03580 *Tel:* 603-823-5510 *E-mail:* rfrost@nci.net *Web Site:* www.frostplace.org, pg 743

Sheehan, Elizabeth, Routledge, 29 W 35 St, New York, NY 10001-2299 *Tel:* 212-216-7800 *Fax:* 212-564-7854 (main) *E-mail:* info@taylorandfrancis.com *Web Site:* www.routledge-ny.com, pg 235

Sheidlower, Jesse, Oxford University Press, Inc, 198 Madison Ave, New York, NY 10016-4314 *Tel:* 212-726-6000 *Toll Free Tel:* 800-451-7556 (orders) *Web Site:* www.oup.com/us, pg 200

Shein, Lori, Lucent Books Inc, 15822 Bernardo Center Dr, Suite C, San Diego, CA 92127 *Tel:* 858-485-7424 *Fax:* 858-485-9549 *E-mail:* info@gale.com *Web Site:* www.gale.com/lucent, pg 159

Sheinkman, Elizabeth, Elaine Markson Literary Agency Inc, 44 Greenwich Ave, New York, NY 10011 *Tel:* 212-243-8480 *Fax:* 212-691-9014, pg 642

Sheinkopf, Barry, The Writing Center, 601 Palisade Ave, Englewood Cliffs, NJ 07632 *Tel:* 201-567-4017 *Fax:* 201-567-7202 *E-mail:* 102100.1065@compuserve.com, pg 749

Shelander, Anne, Harbor House, 111 Tenth St, Augusta, GA 30901 *Tel:* 706-738-0354 *Fax:* 706-738-0354 *E-mail:* harborbook@knology.net *Web Site:* harborhousebooks.com, pg 114

Shelby, Tom, Hohm Press, PO Box 2501, Prescott, AZ 86302 *Tel:* 928-778-9189 *Toll Free Tel:* 800-381-2700 *Fax:* 928-717-1779 *E-mail:* hppublisher@cableone.net *Web Site:* www.hohmpress.com, pg 123

Sheldon, Robert, Johnson Books, 1880 S 57 Ct, Boulder, CO 80301 *Tel:* 303-443-9766 *Toll Free Tel:* 800-258-5830 *Fax:* 303-998-7594 *E-mail:* books@jpcolorado.com *Web Site:* www.jpcolorado.com; www.johnsonbooks.com, pg 142

Sheldrick, Grace, Wordsworth Associates Editorial Services, 9 Tappan Rd, Wellesley, MA 02482 *Tel:* 781-237-4761 *Fax:* 781-237-4758, pg 614

Sheldrick, Joseph E, Battelle Press, 505 King Ave, Columbus, OH 43201-2693 *Tel:* 614-424-6393 *Toll Free Tel:* 800-451-3543 *Fax:* 614-424-3819 *E-mail:* press@battelle.org *Web Site:* www.battelle.org/bookstore, pg 33

Shelton, Ken, Executive Excellence Publishing, 1366 E 1120 S, Provo, UT 84606 *Tel:* 801-375-4060 *Toll Free Tel:* 800-304-9782 *Fax:* 801-377-5960 *Web Site:* www.eep.com, pg 629

Shenk, Jay, Newbridge Educational Publishing, One Beeman Rd, Northborough, MA 01532 *Tel:* 508-571-6500 *Toll Free Tel:* 800-867-0307 *Fax:* 508-571-6502 *Toll Free Fax:* 800-456-2419 *E-mail:* info@newbridgeonline.com *Web Site:* www.newbridgeonline.com; www.newbridgepub.com, pg 190

Shenk, Jay, Sundance Publishing, One Beeman Rd, Northborough, MA 01532 *Tel:* 508-571-6500 *Toll Free Tel:* 800-343-8204 *Fax:* 508-571-6510 *Toll Free Fax:* 800-456-2419 *E-mail:* info@sundancepub.com *Web Site:* www.sundancepub.com, pg 262

Shenk, Timothy, Rod & Staff Publishers Inc, Hwy 172, Crockett, KY 41413-0003 *Tel:* 606-522-4348 *Toll Free Tel:* 800-643-1244 *Fax:* 606-522-4896 *Toll Free Fax:* 800-643-1244 (ordering in US) *Web Site:* www.anabaptistis.org, pg 233

Shepard, Christopher, The Pimlico Agency Inc, PO Box 20447, Cherokee Sta, New York, NY 10021 *Tel:* 212-628-9729 *Fax:* 212-535-7861, pg 648

Shepard, Jean H, The Shepard Agency, 73 Kingswood Dr, Bethel, CT 06801 *Tel:* 203-790-4230; 203-790-1780 *Fax:* 203-798-2924 *E-mail:* shepardagcy@mindspring.com *Web Site:* home.mindspring.com/~shepardagcy, pg 655

Shepard, Judith, The Permanent Press, 4170 Noyac Rd, Sag Harbor, NY 11963 *Tel:* 631-725-1101 *Fax:* 631-725-8215 *Web Site:* www.thepermanentpress.com, pg 210

Shepard, Judith, Second Chance Press, 4170 Noyac Rd, Sag Harbor, NY 11963 *Tel:* 631-725-1101 *Fax:* 631-725-8215 *E-mail:* info@thepermanentpress.com *Web Site:* www.thepermanentpress.com, pg 244

Shepard, Lance Hastings, The Shepard Agency, 73 Kingswood Dr, Bethel, CT 06801 *Tel:* 203-790-4230; 203-790-1780 *Fax:* 203-798-2924 *E-mail:* shepardagcy@mindspring.com *Web Site:* home.mindspring.com/~shepardagcy, pg 655

Shepard, Martin, The Permanent Press, 4170 Noyac Rd, Sag Harbor, NY 11963 *Tel:* 631-725-1101 *Fax:* 631-725-8215 *Web Site:* www.thepermanentpress.com, pg 210

Shepard, Martin, Second Chance Press, 4170 Noyac Rd, Sag Harbor, NY 11963 *Tel:* 631-725-1101 *Fax:* 631-725-8215 *E-mail:* info@thepermanentpress.com *Web Site:* www.thepermanentpress.com, pg 244

Shepard, Robert E, The Robert E Shepard Agency, 1608 Dwight Way, Berkeley, CA 94703-1804 *Tel:* 510-849-3999 *E-mail:* query@shepardagency.com *Web Site:* www.shepardagency.com, pg 655

Shepardson, Mark, Fraser Publishing Co, PO Box 217, Flint Hill, VA 22627 *Tel:* 540-675-9976 *Toll Free Tel:* 877-996-3336 *Fax:* 786-513-2807 *E-mail:* info@fraserpublishing.com *Web Site:* www.fraserpublishing.com, pg 100

Shepherd, Bernice H, Saint Louis Literary Award, 40 N Kingshighway Blvd, 10-J, St Louis, MO 63108 *Tel:* 314-361-1616 *Fax:* 314-361-0812, pg 803

Shepherd, David, Broadman & Holman Publishers, 127 Ninth Ave N, Nashville, TN 37234-0114 *Tel:* 615-251-2520 *Fax:* 615-251-5004 *Web Site:* www.broadmanholman.com, pg 48

Shepherd, Hans B Jr, Ravenhawk™ Books, 7739 E Broadway Blvd, No 95, Tucson, AZ 85710 *Tel:* 520-296-4491 *Fax:* 520-296-4491 *E-mail:* ravenhawk6dof@yahoo.com *Web Site:* ravenhawk.biz, pg 228

Shepherd, Jennifer, Doubleday Canada, One Toronto St, Suite 300, Toronto, ON M5C 2V6, Canada *Tel:* 416-364-4449 *Fax:* 416-957-1587 *Web Site:* www.randomhouse.ca, pg 542

Shepherd, Jennifer, Knopf Canada, One Toronto St, Suite 300, Toronto, ON M5C 2V6, Canada *Tel:* 416-364-4449 *Toll Free Tel:* 800-668-4247 (order desk) *Fax:* 416-364-0462 *Web Site:* www.randomhouse.ca, pg 552

Shepherd, Jennifer, Random House of Canada Ltd, One Toronto St, Unit 300, Toronto, ON M5C 2V6, Canada *Tel:* 416-364-4449 *Fax:* 416-364-6863 (edit & publicity); 416-364-6653 (subs rts) *Web Site:* www.randomhouse.ca, pg 559

Shepherd, Jennifer, Seal Books, One Toronto St, Suite 300, Toronto, ON M5C 2V6, Canada *Tel:* 416-364-4449 *Toll Free Tel:* 888-523-9292 (order desk) *Fax:* 416-957-1587 *Web Site:* www.randomhouse.ca, pg 560

Shepherd, Richard, The Artists Agency, 1180 S Beverly Dr, Suite 400, Los Angeles, CA 90035 *Tel:* 310-277-7779 *Fax:* 310-785-9338, pg 619

Sheppard, Christine, Library Association of Alberta, 80 Baker Crescent NW, Calgary, AB T2L 1R4, Canada *Tel:* 403-284-5818 *Toll Free Tel:* 877-522-5550 *Fax:* 403-282-6646 *Web Site:* www.laa.ab.ca, pg 690

Sheppard, Laura, Prentice Hall Press, 375 Hudson St, New York, NY 10014 *Tel:* 212-366-2000, pg 217

Sheppard, Nancy, Viking, 375 Hudson St, New York, NY 10014 *Tel:* 212-366-2000 *E-mail:* online@penguinputnam.com *Web Site:* www.penguin.com, pg 290

Sheppard, Nancy, Viking Studio, 375 Hudson St, New York, NY 10014 *Tel:* 212-366-2000 *E-mail:* online@penguinputnam.com *Web Site:* www.penguin.com, pg 290

Sher, Danis, Mary Jack Wald Associates Inc, 111 E 14 St, New York, NY 10003 *Tel:* 212-254-7842 *Fax:* 212-254-7842, pg 659

Sherer, Betsy, Cambridge Educational, 2572 Brunswick Ave, Lawrenceville, NJ 08648-4128 *Toll Free Tel:* 800-468-4227 *Toll Free Fax:* 800-329-6687 *E-mail:* custserve@cambridgeeducational.com *Web Site:* www.cambridgeeducational.com, pg 51

Sherer, John, The Brookings Institution Press, 1775 Massachusetts Ave NW, Washington, DC 20036-2188 *Tel:* 202-797-6000 *Toll Free Tel:* 800-275-1447 *Fax:* 202-797-6195 *E-mail:* bibooks@brook.edu *Web Site:* www.brookings.edu, pg 48

Sherer, Val, Jack Mason Award, Baipa, PO Box E, Corte Madera, CA 94976 *Toll Free Tel:* 866-622-1325 *E-mail:* info@baipa.net *Web Site:* www.baipa.net, pg 788

Sherick, Michael, Times Change Press, 8453 Blackney Rd, Sebastopol, CA 95472 *Tel:* 707-824-9456, pg 272

Sheridan, Carmel, Elder Books, PO Box 490, Forest Knolls, CA 94933 *Tel:* 415-488-9002 *Toll Free Tel:* 800-909-2673 (orders) *Fax:* 415-354-3306 *E-mail:* info@elderbooks.com *Web Site:* www.elderbooks.com, pg 88

Sheridan, Mary, Clarion Workshop in Science Fiction & Fantasy Writing, Michigan State University, 112 Olds Hall, East Lansing, MI 48824-1047 *Tel:* 517-355-9598 *Fax:* 517-353-4765 *Web Site:* www.msu.edu/~clarion, pg 743

Sherman, Alana, Alms House Press, PO Box 218, Woodbourne, NY 12788-0218 *Tel:* 845-436-0070 *Fax:* 845-436-0099, pg 9

Sherman, Ken, Ken Sherman & Associates, 9507 Santa Monica Blvd, Suite 211, Beverly Hills, CA 90210 *Tel:* 310-273-8840 *Fax:* 310-271-2875 *E-mail:* ksassociates@earthlink.net, pg 655

Sherman, Rebecca, Writers House LLC, 21 W 26 St, New York, NY 10010 *Tel:* 212-685-2400 *Fax:* 212-685-1781, pg 662

Sherman, Stephen, Radix Press, 2314 Cheshire Lane, Houston, TX 77018-4023 *Tel:* 713-683-9076, pg 224

Sherman, Susan, Charlesbridge Publishing Inc, 85 Main St, Watertown, MA 02472 *Tel:* 617-926-0329 *Toll Free Tel:* 800-225-3214 *Fax:* 617-926-5720 *E-mail:* books@charlesbridge.com *Web Site:* www.charlesbridge.com, pg 59

Sherman, Virginia, Pacific Press Publishing Association, 1350 N Kings Rd, Nampa, ID 83687-3193 *Tel:* 208-465-2500 *Toll Free Tel:* 800-447-7377 *Fax:* 208-465-2531 *Web Site:* www.pacificpress.com, pg 202

Sherman, Wendy, Wendy Sherman Associates Inc, 450 Seventh Ave, Suite 3004, New York, NY 10123 *Tel:* 212-279-9027 *Fax:* 212-279-8863, pg 655

Sherr, Roger, Genealogical Publishing Co Inc, 1001 N Calvert St, Baltimore, MD 21202 *Tel:* 410-837-8271 *Toll Free Tel:* 800-296-6687 *Fax:* 410-752-8492 *E-mail:* orders@genealogical.com *Web Site:* www.genealogical.com, pg 103

Sherrard, Katy, Christian Literature Crusade Inc, 701 Pennsylvania Ave, Fort Washington, PA 19034-8449 *Tel:* 215-542-1242 *Toll Free Tel:* 800-659-1240 (orders) *Fax:* 215-542-7580 *E-mail:* clcbooks@safeplace.net *Web Site:* www.clcpublications.com, pg 61

Sherry, Cynthia, Chicago Review Press, 814 N Franklin St, Chicago, IL 60610 *Tel:* 312-337-0747 *Toll Free Tel:* 800-888-4741 *Fax:* 312-337-5110 *E-mail:* editorial@ipgbook.com, pg 60

Shevin, David, Bottom Dog Press, c/o Firelands College of Bowling Green State University, PO Box 425, Huron, OH 44839-0425 *Tel:* 419-433-5560 *Fax:* 419-433-9696 *Web Site:* members.aol.com/lsmithdog/bottomdog, pg 44

Shia, Lilian, Advantage Publishers Group, 5880 Oberlin Dr, San Diego, CA 92121 *Tel:* 858-457-2500 *Toll Free Tel:* 800-284-3580 *Fax:* 858-812-6476 *Toll Free Fax:* 800-499-3822 *E-mail:* apgcuserv@advmkt.com *Web Site:* www.advantagebooksonline.com, pg 6

Shiebler, Hugh, Barron's Educational Series Inc, 250 Wireless Blvd, Hauppauge, NY 11788 *Tel:* 631-434-3311 *Toll Free Tel:* 800-645-3476 *Fax:* 631-434-3723 *E-mail:* info@barronseduc.com *Web Site:* www.barronseduc.com (Books can be purchased online), pg 32

Shields, Brenda, Canadian Library Association (CLA), 328 Frank St, Ottawa, ON K2P 0X8, Canada *Tel:* 613-232-9625 *Fax:* 613-563-9895 *E-mail:* info@cla.ca *Web Site:* www.cla.ca/, pg 683

Shields, Brenda, CLA Book of the Year for Children Award, 328 Frank St, Ottawa, ON K2P 0X8, Canada *Tel:* 613-232-9625 *Fax:* 613-563-9895 *Web Site:* www.cla.ca/, pg 767

Shields, Brenda, CLTA/Stan Heath Achievement in Literacy Award, 328 Frank St, Ottawa, ON K2P 0X8, Canada *Tel:* 613-232-9625 *Fax:* 613-563-9895 *Web Site:* www.cla.ca/, pg 767

Shields, Brenda, Amelia Frances Howard-Gibbon Illustrator's Award, 328 Frank St, Ottawa, ON K2P 0X8, Canada *Tel:* 613-232-9625 *Fax:* 613-563-9895 *Web Site:* www.cla.ca/, pg 779

Shields, Brenda, The Young Adult Canadian Book Award, 328 Frank St, Ottawa, ON K2P 0X8, Canada *Tel:* 613-232-9625 *Fax:* 613-563-9895 *Web Site:* www.cla.ca, pg 814

Shields, Drew, Tyndale House Publishers Inc, 351 Executive Dr, Carol Stream, IL 60188 *Tel:* 630-668-8303 *Toll Free Tel:* 800-323-9400 *Web Site:* www.tyndale.com, pg 277

Shields, Duncan, Doubleday Canada, One Toronto St, Suite 300, Toronto, ON M5C 2V6, Canada *Tel:* 416-364-4449 *Fax:* 416-957-1587 *Web Site:* www.randomhouse.ca, pg 542

Shields, Duncan, Knopf Canada, One Toronto St, Suite 300, Toronto, ON M5C 2V6, Canada *Tel:* 416-364-4449 *Toll Free Tel:* 800-668-4247 (order desk) *Fax:* 416-364-0462 *Web Site:* www.randomhouse.ca, pg 552

Shields, Duncan, Random House of Canada Ltd, One Toronto St, Unit 300, Toronto, ON M5C 2V6, Canada *Tel:* 416-364-4449 *Fax:* 416-364-6863 (edit & publicity); 416-364-6653 (subs rts) *Web Site:* www.randomhouse.ca, pg 559

Shields, Duncan, Seal Books, One Toronto St, Suite 300, Toronto, ON M5C 2V6, Canada *Tel:* 416-364-4449 *Toll Free Tel:* 888-523-9292 (order desk) *Fax:* 416-957-1587 *Web Site:* www.randomhouse.ca, pg 560

Shields, Patrick, Shields Publications, PO Box 669, Eagle River, WI 54521-0669 *Tel:* 715-479-4810 *Fax:* 715-479-3905 *E-mail:* shields@nnex.net *Web Site:* www.wormbooks.com, pg 246

Shih, Santos, Prentice Hall Career, Health, Education & Technology, One Lake St, Upper Saddle River, NJ 07458 *Tel:* 201-236-7000 *Fax:* 201-236-7755, pg 217

Shilling, Julie, University of Oklahoma Press, 4100 28 Ave NW, Norman, OK 73069-8218 *Tel:* 405-325-2000 *Toll Free Tel:* 800-627-7377 (orders) *Fax:* 405-364-5798 (orders) *Toll Free Fax:* 800-735-0476 (orders) *E-mail:* oupress@ou.edu *Web Site:* www.oupress.com, pg 284

Shillingford, Gordon, J Gordon Shillingford Publishing, RPO Corydon Ave, Winnipeg, MB R3M 3S3, Canada *Tel:* 204-779-6967 *Fax:* 204-779-6970 *Web Site:* www.jgshillingford.com, pg 561

Shimabukuro, Jill, Association of American University Presses, 1427 E 60 St, Chicago, IL 60637 *Tel:* 773-702-7700; 773-702-7600 *Toll Free Tel:* 800-621-2736 (orders) *Fax:* 773-702-9756 (sales); 773-660-2235 (orders); 773-702-2708 *E-mail:* general@press.uchicago.edu *Web Site:* www.press.uchicago.edu, pg 26

Shimp, Betty, Theosophical Publishing House/Quest Books, 306 W Geneva Rd, Wheaton, IL 60187 *Tel:* 630-665-0130 *Toll Free Tel:* 800-669-9425 *Fax:* 630-665-8791 *E-mail:* questbooks@theosmail.net *Web Site:* www.questbooks.net, pg 268

Shinder, Jason, The National Writer's Voice Project, 101 N Wacker Dr, Suite 1400, Chicago, IL 60606 *Tel:* 312-419-8658 *Toll Free Tel:* 800-USA-YMCA (800-872-9622) *Fax:* 312-977-4801 *Web Site:* www.ymca.net, pg 745

Shinder, Jason, The Writers Community, 101 N Wacker Dr, Chicago, IL 60606 *Toll Free Tel:* 800-USA-YMCA, Ext 6830 *Fax:* 312-977-1729 *E-mail:* jason.shinder@ymca.net *Web Site:* www.ymca.net, pg 812

Shine, Deborah, Star Bright Books, The Star Bldg, Suite 2B, 42-26 28 St, Long Island City, NY 11101 *Tel:* 718-784-9112 *Toll Free Tel:* 800-788-4439 *Fax:* 718-784-9012 *E-mail:* info@starbrightbooks.com; orders@starbrightbooks.com *Web Site:* www.starbrightbooks.com, pg 258

Shiner, Roger, Academic Printing & Publishing, 9-3151 Lakeshore Rd, Suite 403, Kelowna, BC V1W 3S9, Canada *Tel:* 250-764-6427 *Fax:* 250-464-6428 *E-mail:* app@silk.net *Web Site:* www.academicprintingandpublishing.com, pg 535

Shinker, William, Penguin Group (USA) Inc, 375 Hudson St, New York, NY 10014 *Tel:* 212-366-2000 *Fax:* 212-366-2666 *E-mail:* online@uspenguingroup.com *Web Site:* www.penguin.com, pg 208

Shinn, Heidi, Center for Strategic & International Studies, 1800 "K" St NW, Washington, DC 20006 *Tel:* 202-775-3119 *Fax:* 202-775-3199 *E-mail:* books@csis.org *Web Site:* www.csis.org, pg 57

Shipton, Susan, Annick Press Ltd, 15 Patricia Ave, Toronto, ON M2M 1H9, Canada *Tel:* 416-221-4802 *Fax:* 416-221-8400 *E-mail:* annick@annickpress.com *Web Site:* www.annickpress.com, pg 535

Shirey, Sally, Ligonier Valley Writers Conference, PO Box B, Ligonier, PA 15658-1602 *Tel:* 724-537-3341 *Fax:* 724-537-0482 *E-mail:* sarshi@wpa.net, pg 744

Shiroish, Julie, Penguin Books, 375 Hudson St, New York, NY 10014 *Tel:* 212-366-2000 *E-mail:* online@penguinputnam.com *Web Site:* www.penguin.com; www.penguinclassics.com, pg 207

Shiroishi, Julie, Viking, 375 Hudson St, New York, NY 10014 *Tel:* 212-366-2000 *E-mail:* online@penguinputnam.com *Web Site:* www.penguin.com, pg 290

Shirrell, Robert, Association of American University Presses, 1427 E 60 St, Chicago, IL 60637 *Tel:* 773-702-7700; 773-702-7600 *Toll Free Tel:* 800-621-2736 (orders) *Fax:* 773-702-9756 (sales); 773-660-2235 (orders); 773-702-2708 *E-mail:* general@press.uchicago.edu *Web Site:* www.press.uchicago.edu, pg 26

Shirzad, Farhad, Ibex Publishers, 8014 Old Georgetown Rd, Bethesda, MD 20814 *Tel:* 301-718-8188 *Toll Free Tel:* 888-718-8188 *Fax:* 301-907-8707 *E-mail:* info@ibexpub.com *Web Site:* www.ibexpub.com, pg 129

Shivel, Gail, Wolf Den Books, 5783 SW 40 St, Suite 221, Miami, FL 33155 *Toll Free Tel:* 877-667-9737 *Fax:* 305-667-7751 *E-mail:* info@wolfdenbooks.com *Web Site:* www.wolfdenbooks.com, pg 302

Shively, Art, CTB/McGraw-Hill, 20 Ryan Ranch Rd, Monterey, CA 93940-5703 *Tel:* 831-393-0700 *Toll Free Tel:* 800-538-9547 *Fax:* 831-393-7825 *Web Site:* www.ctb.com, pg 74

Shoemaker, David, Counterpoint Press, 387 Park Ave S, New York, NY 10016 *Tel:* 212-340-8100 *Fax:* 212-340-8135 (edit); 212-340-8115 *E-mail:* counterpointpress@perseusbooks.com *Web Site:* www.counterpointpress.com, pg 70

Shoemaker, Jack, Shoemaker & Hoard, Publishers, 3704 Macomb St NW, Suite 4, Washington, DC 20016 *Tel:* 202-364-4464 *Fax:* 202-364-4484 *Web Site:* www.shoemakerhoard.com, pg 246

Shoemaker, Victoria, The Spieler Agency, 154 W 57 St, 13th fl, Rm 135, New York, NY 10019 *Tel:* 212-757-4439 *E-mail:* spieleragency.com, pg 656

Sholevar, Bahman, Concourse Press, PO Box 8265, Philadelphia, PA 19101-8265 *Tel:* 610-325-0313 *Fax:* 610-359-1953, pg 66

Sholzberg-Gray, Sharon, CHA (Canadian Healthcare Association) Press, 17 York St, Suite 100, Ottawa, ON K1N 9J6, Canada *Tel:* 613-241-8005 (ext 264) *Fax:* 613-241-5055 *E-mail:* chapress@cha.ca *Web Site:* www.cha.ca, pg 540

Shooter, James C, Phobos Books, 200 Park Ave S, Suite 1109, New York, NY 10003 *Tel:* 212-477-3225 *Fax:* 212-529-4223 *E-mail:* info@phobosweb.com *Web Site:* phobosweb.com, pg 211

Shore Sterling, C L, The Lee Shore Co Ltd, 7436 Washington Ave, Suite 100, Pittsburgh, PA 15218 *Tel:* 412-271-1100 *Toll Free Tel:* 800-898-7886 *Fax:* 412-271-1900 *E-mail:* info@leeshoreagency.com *Web Site:* www.leeshoreagency.com, pg 640

Shorney, John, Hope Publishing Co, 380 S Main Place, Carol Stream, IL 60188 *Tel:* 630-665-3200 *Toll Free Tel:* 800-323-1049 *Fax:* 630-665-2552 *E-mail:* hope@hopepublishing.com *Web Site:* www.hopepublishing.com, pg 125

Shorney, Scott, Hope Publishing Co, 380 S Main Place, Carol Stream, IL 60188 *Tel:* 630-665-3200 *Toll Free Tel:* 800-323-1049 *Fax:* 630-665-2552 *E-mail:* hope@hopepublishing.com *Web Site:* www.hopepublishing.com, pg 125

Shorney, Steve, Hope Publishing Co, 380 S Main Place, Carol Stream, IL 60188 *Tel:* 630-665-3200 *Toll Free Tel:* 800-323-1049 *Fax:* 630-665-2552 *E-mail:* hope@hopepublishing.com *Web Site:* www.hopepublishing.com, pg 125

Shotts, Jeffrey, Graywolf Press, 2402 University Ave, Suite 203, St Paul, MN 55114 *Tel:* 651-641-0077 *Fax:* 651-641-0036 *E-mail:* wolves@graywolfpress.org *Web Site:* www.graywolfpress.org, pg 108

Shoults, Randy, Alabama Artists Fellowship Awards, 201 Monroe St, Suite 110, Montgomery, AL 36130-1800 *Tel:* 334-242-4076 *Fax:* 334-240-3269, pg 758

Shoup, William, Society for Protective Coating, 40 24 St, 6th fl, Pittsburgh, PA 15222-4656 *Tel:* 412-281-2331 *Fax:* 412-281-9992 *E-mail:* books@sspc.org *Web Site:* www.sspc.org, pg 251

Shrestha, Heather H, Paul H Brookes Publishing Co, PO Box 10624, Baltimore, MD 21285-0624 *Tel:* 410-337-9580 *Toll Free Tel:* 800-638-3775 *Fax:* 410-337-8539 *E-mail:* custserv@brookespublishing.com *Web Site:* www.brookespublishing.com, pg 48

Shreve, Elizabeth, Henry Holt and Company, LLC, 115 W 18 St, New York, NY 10011 *Tel:* 212-886-9200 *Toll Free Tel:* 888-330-8477 (orders) *Fax:* 212-633-0748 *E-mail:* publicity@hholt.com *Web Site:* www.henryholt.com, pg 124

Shriner, Ellen, The Gislason Agency, 219 SE Main St, Suite 506, Minneapolis, MN 55414 *Tel:* 612-331-8033 *Fax:* 612-331-8115 *E-mail:* gislasonbj@aol.com *Web Site:* www.TheGislasonAgency.com, pg 632

Shuchman, Ryan, Clock Tower Press, 3622 W Liberty Rd, Ann Arbor, MI 48103 *Tel:* 734-769-5600 *Toll Free Tel:* 800-956-8999 *Fax:* 734-769-5607 *Web Site:* www.clocktowerpress.com; huronriverpress.com, pg 63

Shulman, Joel J, Jelmar Publishing Co Inc, PO Box 488, Plainview, NY 11803-0488 *Tel:* 516-822-6861 *Fax:* 516-822-6861, pg 140

Shults, Marina, Reader's Digest Trade Books, Reader's Digest Rd, Pleasantville, NY 10570-7000 *Tel:* 914-244-7445 *Fax:* 914-244-7605, pg 229

Shultz, Ellen, The Metropolitan Museum of Art, 1000 Fifth Ave, New York, NY 10028 *Tel:* 212-879-5500; 212-535-7710 *Fax:* 212-396-5062 *E-mail:* info@metmuseum.org *Web Site:* www.metmuseum.org, pg 173

Shultz, Jerome S, American Institute of Chemical Engineers (AICHE), 3 Park Ave, New York, NY 10016-5991 *Tel:* 212-591-7338 *Toll Free Tel:* 800-242-4363 *Fax:* 212-591-8888 *E-mail:* xpress@aiche.org *Web Site:* www.aiche.org, pg 15

Shultz, Sheldon, Trident Media Group LLC, 41 Madison Ave, 36th fl, New York, NY 10010 *Tel:* 212-262-4810 *Fax:* 212-725-4501 *Web Site:* www.tridentmediagroup.com, pg 659

Shuman, Eric, Thomson Learning Inc, 200 First Stamford Place, Suite 400, Stamford, CT 06902 *Tel:* 203-539-8000 *Fax:* 203-539-7581 *E-mail:* communications@thomsonlearning.com *Web Site:* www.thomson.com/learning, pg 270

Shumate, Kimberly, Harvest House Publishers Inc, 990 Owen Loop N, Eugene, OR 97402 *Tel:* 541-343-0123 *Toll Free Tel:* 800-547-8979 *Fax:* 541-342-6410 *E-mail:* admin@harvesthousepublishers.com *Web Site:* www.harvesthousepublishers.com, pg 117

Shumate, Thomas, St Anthony Messenger Press, 28 W Liberty St, Cincinnati, OH 45202 *Tel:* 513-241-5615 *Toll Free Tel:* 800-488-0488 *Fax:* 513-241-0399 *E-mail:* books@americancatholic.org *Web Site:* www.AmericanCatholic.org, pg 237

Shur, Rudy, Square One Publishers, 115 Herricks Rd, Garden City Park, NY 11040 *Tel:* 516-535-2010 *Fax:* 516-535-2014 *E-mail:* sq1info@aol.com *Web Site:* squareonepublishers.com, pg 256

Shurtleff, William, Soyfoods Center, PO Box 234, Lafayette, CA 94549-0234 *Tel:* 925-283-2991, pg 255

Shuster, Todd, Zachary Shuster Harmsworth Agency, 1776 Broadway, New York, NY 10019 *Tel:* 212-765-6900 *Fax:* 212-765-6490 *Web Site:* www.zshliterary.com, pg 662

Shute, Katherine, Alberta Book Awards, 10523-100 Ave, Edmonton, AB T5J 0A8, Canada *Tel:* 780-424-5060 *Fax:* 780-424-7943 *E-mail:* info@bookpublishers.ab.ca *Web Site:* www.bookpublishers.ab.ca, pg 758

Shute, Katherine, The Book Publisher's Association of Alberta, 10523 100 Ave, Edmonton, AB T5J 0A8, Canada *Tel:* 780-424-5060 *Fax:* 780-424-7943 *E-mail:* info@bookpublishers.ab.ca *Web Site:* www.bookpublishers.ab.ca, pg 682

Sibbald, Anne, Janklow & Nesbit Associates, 445 Park Ave, New York, NY 10022 *Tel:* 212-421-1700 *Fax:* 212-980-3671 *E-mail:* postmaster@janklow.com, pg 636

Siberell, Brian, Creative Artists Agency, 9830 Wilshire Blvd, Beverly Hills, CA 90212-1825 *Tel:* 310-288-4545 *Fax:* 310-288-4800 *Web Site:* www.caa.com, pg 626

Sibley, Ellen, Barron's Educational Series Inc, 250 Wireless Blvd, Hauppauge, NY 11788 *Tel:* 631-434-3311 *Toll Free Tel:* 800-645-3476 *Fax:* 631-434-3723 *E-mail:* info@barronseduc.com *Web Site:* www.barronseduc.com (Books can be purchased online), pg 32

Sickels, Sandra Jones, The Haworth Press Inc, 10 Alice St, Binghamton, NY 13904-1580 *Tel:* 607-722-5857 *Toll Free Tel:* 800-429-6784 *Fax:* 607-722-

1424 *Toll Free Fax:* 800-895-0582 *E-mail:* getinfo@haworthpressinc.com *Web Site:* www.haworthpress.com, pg 118

Sickles, Robert, Eye On Education, 6 Depot Way W, Larchmont, NY 10538 *Tel:* 914-833-0551 *Fax:* 914-833-0761 *Web Site:* www.eyeoneducation.com, pg 93

Sickman-Garner, Peter, University of Michigan Press, 839 Greene St, Ann Arbor, MI 48104-3209 *Tel:* 734-764-4388 *Fax:* 734-615-1540 *E-mail:* um.press@umich.edu *Web Site:* www.press.umich.edu, pg 282

Siconolfi, Marcie, Cold Spring Harbor Laboratory Press, 500 Sunnyside Blvd, Woodbury, NY 11797-2924 *Tel:* 516-422-4100 *Toll Free Tel:* 800-843-4388 *Fax:* 516-422-4097 *E-mail:* cshpress@cshl.edu *Web Site:* www.cshlpress.com, pg 64

Siddique, Ms Reshmi M PhD, QualHealth Inc, PO Box 6539, Lawrenceville, NJ 08648-0539, pg 223

Sidman, Murray, Authors Cooperative, 1700 Ben Franklin Dr, Suite 9E, Sarasota, FL 34236-2374 *Tel:* 941-388-5009 *E-mail:* authcoop@comcast.net *Web Site:* www.authorscooperative.com, pg 28

Sieferman, Valentine, Western States Arts Federation, 1743 Wazee St, Suite 300, Denver, CO 80202 *Tel:* 303-629-1166 *Fax:* 303-629-9717 *E-mail:* staff@westaf.org *Web Site:* www.westaf.org, pg 705

Sieff, Ben, Centering Corp, 7230 Maple St, Omaha, NE 68134 *Tel:* 402-553-1200 *Fax:* 402-553-0507 *E-mail:* j1200@aol.com *Web Site:* www.centering.org, pg 57

Sieff, Janet, Centering Corp, 7230 Maple St, Omaha, NE 68134 *Tel:* 402-553-1200 *Fax:* 402-553-0507 *E-mail:* j1200@aol.com *Web Site:* www.centering.org, pg 57

Sieff, Nick, Centering Corp, 7230 Maple St, Omaha, NE 68134 *Tel:* 402-553-1200 *Fax:* 402-553-0507 *E-mail:* j1200@aol.com *Web Site:* www.centering.org, pg 57

Siegel, Bobbe, Creative Arts Book Co, 833 Bancroft Way, Berkeley, CA 94710 *Tel:* 510-848-4777 *Fax:* 510-848-4844 *E-mail:* staff@creativeartsbooks.com; capublisher@yahoo.com *Web Site:* www.creativeartsbooks.com, pg 72

Siegel, Bobbe, Bobbe Siegel Literary Agency, 41 W 83 St, New York, NY 10024 *Tel:* 212-877-4985 *Fax:* 212-877-4985 *E-mail:* bobbesiegelagency@yahoo.com, pg 655

Siegel, Charles, Thomson Learning Inc, 200 First Stamford Place, Suite 400, Stamford, CT 06902 *Tel:* 203-539-8000 *Fax:* 203-539-7581 *E-mail:* communications@thomsonlearning.com *Web Site:* www.thomson.com/learning, pg 270

Siegel, Martha, The Mathematical Association of America, 1529 18 St NW, Washington, DC 20036 *Tel:* 202-387-5200 *Toll Free Tel:* 800-331-1622 (orders) *Fax:* 202-265-2384 *E-mail:* ldouglas@pmds.com *Web Site:* www.maa.org, pg 165

Siegel, Maury, Associated Editors, 27 W 96 St, New York, NY 10025 *Tel:* 212-662-9703 *Fax:* 212-662-0549, pg 590

Siegel, Peter, Bobbe Siegel Literary Agency, 41 W 83 St, New York, NY 10024 *Tel:* 212-877-4985 *Fax:* 212-877-4985 *E-mail:* bobbesiegelagency@yahoo.com, pg 655

Siegel, Rosalie, Rosalie Siegel, International Literary Agent Inc, One Abey Dr, Pennington, NJ 08534 *Tel:* 609-737-1007 *Fax:* 609-737-3708 *E-mail:* rsiegel@ix.netcom.com, pg 655

Siegel, Roslyn, Fine Communications, 322 Eighth Ave, 15th fl, New York, NY 10001 *Tel:* 212-595-3500 *Fax:* 212-595-3779, pg 96

Siegel, Tema, Craven Design Studios Inc, 234 Fifth Ave, 4th fl, New York, NY 10001 *Tel:* 212-696-4680 *Fax:* 212-532-2626 *Web Site:* www.cravendesignstudios.com, pg 665

Sieger, Peter, Teachers College Press, 1234 Amsterdam Ave, New York, NY 10027 *Tel:* 212-678-3929 *Fax:* 212-678-4149 *E-mail:* tcpress@tc.columbia.edu *Web Site:* www.teacherscollegepress.com, pg 265

Siembieda, Kevin, Palladium Books Inc, 12455 Universal Dr, Taylor, MI 48180-4077 *Tel:* 734-946-2900 *Fax:* 734-946-1238 *Web Site:* www.palladiumbooks.com, pg 202

Siemens, John, Crabtree Publishing Co, 350 Fifth Ave, Suite 3308, PMB 16-A, New York, NY 10118 *Tel:* 212-496-5040 *Toll Free Tel:* 800-387-7650 *Toll Free Fax:* 800-355-7166 *E-mail:* letters@crabtreebooks.com *Web Site:* www.crabtreebooks.com, pg 71

Siemens, John, Crabtree Publishing Co Ltd, 612 Welland Ave, St Catharines, ON L2M 5V6, Canada *Tel:* 905-682-5221 *Toll Free Tel:* 800-387-7650 *Fax:* 905-682-7166 *Toll Free Fax:* 800-355-7166 *E-mail:* custserv@crabtreebooks.com; sales@crabtreebooks.com; orders@crabtreebooks.com *Web Site:* www.crabtreebooks.com, pg 541

Sieper, Susannah, A K Peters Ltd, 888 Worcester St, Suite 230, Wellesley, MA 02482 *Tel:* 781-416-2888 *Fax:* 781-416-2889 *E-mail:* service@akpeters.com *Web Site:* www.akpeters.com, pg 1

Sierra, Hector, National Geographic Books, 1145 17 St NW, Washington, DC 20036 *Tel:* 202-857-7000 *Fax:* 202-857-7670 *Web Site:* www.nationalgeographics.com, pg 183

Sifton, Elisabeth, Hill & Wang, 19 Union Sq W, New York, NY 10003 *Tel:* 212-741-6900 *Fax:* 212-206-5340 *E-mail:* fsg.publicity@fsgbooks.com *Web Site:* www.fsgbooks.com, pg 122

Sigier, Jacques, Editions Anne Sigier Inc, 1073 Blvd of Rene Levesque W, Sillery, PQ G1S 4R5, Canada *Tel:* 418-687-6086 *Toll Free Tel:* 800-463-6846 (Canada only) *Fax:* 418-687-3565 *E-mail:* sigier@annesigier.qc.ca *Web Site:* www.annesigier.qc.ca, pg 543

Sikes, Toni Fountain, Guild Publishing, 931 E Main St, Madison, WI 53703-2955 *Tel:* 608-257-2590 *Toll Free Tel:* 800-930-1856 *Fax:* 608-257-2690 *E-mail:* artinfo@guild.com *Web Site:* www.guild.com, pg 111

Silber, Blake, Bridge Publications Inc, 4751 Fountain Ave, Los Angeles, CA 90029 *Tel:* 323-953-3320 *Toll Free Tel:* 800-722-1733; 800-843-7389 (CA) *Fax:* 323-953-3328 *E-mail:* info@bridgepub.com *Web Site:* www.bridgepub.com, pg 47

Silberfeld, Heath Lynn, Enough Said, 414 NW 36 Ave, Gainesville, FL 32607 *Tel:* 352-371-2935; 352-262-2971 *Web Site:* www.navi.net/~heathlynn, pg 598

Silbersack, John, Trident Media Group LLC, 41 Madison Ave, 36th fl, New York, NY 10010 *Tel:* 212-262-4810 *Fax:* 212-725-4501 *Web Site:* www.tridentmediagroup.com, pg 659

Silbert, Doug, Stephen Pevner Inc, 382 Lafayette St, Suite 8, New York, NY 10003 *Tel:* 212-674-8403 *Fax:* 212-529-3692, pg 648

Silbert, Wendy, Harvey Klinger Inc, 301 W 53 St, New York, NY 10019 *Tel:* 212-581-7068 *Fax:* 212-315-3823 *E-mail:* queries@harveyklinger.com, pg 637

Siler, Jennifer, University of Tennessee Press, 110 Conference Center Bldg, Knoxville, TN 37996-4108 *Tel:* 865-974-3321 *Toll Free Tel:* 800-621-2736 (ordering) *Fax:* 865-974-3724 *E-mail:* custserv@utpress.org *Web Site:* www.utpress.org, pg 285

Silk, Courtney Devon, Random House Children's Books, 1745 Broadway, New York, NY 10019 *Tel:* 212-782-9000 *Toll Free Tel:* 800-200-3552 *Fax:* 212-782-9452 *Web Site:* www.randomhouse.com/kids, pg 226

Silva, Jane, Twenty-Third Publications, 185 Willow St, Mystic, CT 06355 *Tel:* 860-536-2611 *Toll Free Tel:* 800-321-0411 (orders) *Fax:* 860-536-5674 (edit) *Toll Free Fax:* 800-572-0788, pg 277

Silvas, Sharon, Spinsters Ink, 191 University Blvd, Suite 300, Denver, CO 80206 *Tel:* 303-761-5552 *Toll Free Tel:* 800-301-6860; 800-729-6423 (orders) *E-mail:* spinster@spinstersink.com *Web Site:* www.spinsters-ink.com, pg 255

Singleton, Susanne, Scott Foresman, 1900 E Lake Ave, Glenview, IL 60025 *Tel:* 847-729-3000 *Toll Free Tel:* 800-535-4391 (Midwest) *Fax:* 847-729-8910 *E-mail:* firstname.lastname@scottforesman.com *Web Site:* www.scottforesman.com, pg 243

Sinocchi, Michael, Productivity Press, 444 Park Ave S, Suite 604, New York, NY 10016 *Tel:* 212-686-5900 *Toll Free Tel:* 888-319-5852 *Fax:* 212-686-5411 *Toll Free Fax:* 800-394-6286 *E-mail:* info@productivitypress.com *Web Site:* www.productivitypress.com, pg 219

Sioles, Lee Campbell, Louisiana State University Press, PO Box 25053, Baton Rouge, LA 70894-5053 *Tel:* 225-578-6294 *Toll Free Tel:* 800-861-3477 *Fax:* 225-578-6461 *Toll Free Fax:* 800-305-4416 *E-mail:* lsupress@lsu.edu *Web Site:* www.lsu.edu/guests/lsupress, pg 159

Sipe, Keith R, Carolina Academic Press, 700 Kent St, Durham, NC 27701 *Tel:* 919-489-7486 *Toll Free Tel:* 800-489-7486 *Fax:* 919-493-5668 *E-mail:* cap@cap-press.com *Web Site:* www.cap-press.com; www.caplaw.com, pg 54

Sippell, Kelly, University of Michigan Press, 839 Greene St, Ann Arbor, MI 48104-3209 *Tel:* 734-764-4388 *Fax:* 734-615-1540 *E-mail:* um.press@umich.edu *Web Site:* www.press.umich.edu, pg 282

Sippola, Carlene, Whole Person Associates Inc, 210 W Michigan St, Duluth, MN 55802-1908 *Tel:* 218-727-0500 *Toll Free Tel:* 800-247-6789 *Fax:* 218-727-0505 *E-mail:* books@wholeperson.com *Web Site:* www.wholeperson.com, pg 298

Sirvet, Ene, James Fenimore Cooper Prize, Columbia University, 603 Fayerweather Hall, MC 2538, New York, NY 10027, pg 768

Sirvet, Ene, Allan Nevins Prize, Columbia University, 603 Fayerweather Hall, MC 2538, New York, NY 10027, pg 793

Sirvet, Ene, Francis Parkman Prize, Columbia University, 603 Fayerweather Hall, MC 2538, New York, NY 10027, pg 797

Siscoe, Nancy, Random House Children's Books, 1745 Broadway, New York, NY 10019 *Tel:* 212-782-9000 *Toll Free Tel:* 800-200-3552 *Fax:* 212-782-9452 *Web Site:* www.randomhouse.com/kids, pg 226

Sisk, Jonathan, Rowman & Littlefield Publishers Inc, 4501 Forbes Blvd, Lanham, MD 20706 *Tel:* 301-459-3366 *Toll Free Tel:* 800-462-6420 *Fax:* 301-429-5748 *Web Site:* www.rowmanlittlefield.com, pg 235

Sisko, Judith, Henry Holt and Company, LLC, 115 W 18 St, New York, NY 10011 *Tel:* 212-886-9200 *Toll Free Tel:* 888-330-8477 *Fax:* 212-633-0748 *E-mail:* publicity@hholt.com *Web Site:* www.henryholt.com, pg 124

Sisko, Judy, St Martin's Press LLC, 175 Fifth Ave, New York, NY 10010 *Tel:* 212-674-5151 *Fax:* 212-420-9314 *E-mail:* firstname.lastname@stmartins.com *Web Site:* www.stmartins.com, pg 238

Sisler, William P, Harvard University Press, 79 Garden St, Cambridge, MA 02138-1499 *Tel:* 617-495-2600; 401-531-2800 (international orders) *Toll Free Tel:* 800-405-1619 (orders) *Fax:* 617-495-5898 (general); 617-496-4677 (edit & rts); 401-531-2801 (international orders) *Toll Free Fax:* 800-406-9145 (orders) *E-mail:* firstname_lastname@harvard.edu *Web Site:* www.hup.harvard.edu, pg 117

Sitarz, Dan, Nova Publishing Co, 1103 W College St, Carbondale, IL 62901 *Tel:* 618-457-3521 *Toll Free Tel:* 800-748-1175 *Fax:* 618-457-2541 *E-mail:* info@novapublishing.com *Web Site:* www.novapublishing.com, pg 194

Sitarz, Janet, Nova Publishing Co, 1103 W College St, Carbondale, IL 62901 *Tel:* 618-457-3521 *Toll Free Tel:* 800-748-1175 *Fax:* 618-457-2541 *E-mail:* info@novapublishing.com *Web Site:* www.novapublishing.com, pg 194

Sitjar, Lisa, St Martin's Press LLC, 175 Fifth Ave, New York, NY 10010 *Tel:* 212-674-5151 *Fax:* 212-420-9314 *E-mail:* firstname.lastname@stmartins.com *Web Site:* www.stmartins.com, pg 239

Sitzes, Jason, Writers Retreat Workshop (WRW), 5721 Magazine St, Suite 161, New Orleans, LA 70115 *Toll Free Tel:* 800-642-2494 *E-mail:* wrw04@netscape.net *Web Site:* www.writersretreatworkshop.com, pg 749

Sivry, Jean-Michel, Flammarion Quebec, 375 Ave Laurier ouest, Montreal, PQ H2V 2K3, Canada *Tel:* 514-277-8807 *Fax:* 514-278-2085 *E-mail:* info@flammarion.qc.ca *Web Site:* www.flammarion.qc.ca, pg 547

Skag, Paul, Capstone Press, 151 Good Counsel Dr, Mankato, MN 56002 *Toll Free Tel:* 800-747-4992 *Toll Free Fax:* 888-262-0705 *Web Site:* www.capstonepress.com, pg 53

Skaggs, Steve, Bob Jones University Press, 1700 Wade Hampton Blvd, Greenville, SC 29614 *Tel:* 864-242-5100 *Toll Free Tel:* 800-845-5731 (orders only) *Fax:* 864-298-0268 *E-mail:* asmith@bju.edu *Web Site:* www.bjup.com, pg 142

Skavlem, Melissa Kline, Hanser Gardner Publications, 6915 Valley Ave, Cincinnati, OH 45244-3029 *Tel:* 513-527-8977 *Toll Free Tel:* 800-950-8977 *Fax:* 513-527-8801 *Toll Free Fax:* 800-527-8801 *E-mail:* hgfeedback@gardnerweb.com *Web Site:* www.hansergardner.com, pg 113

Skender, Edward, Stackpole Books, 5067 Ritter Rd, Mechanicsburg, PA 17055 *Tel:* 717-796-0411 *Toll Free Tel:* 800-732-3669 *Fax:* 717-796-0412 *Web Site:* www.stackpolebooks.com, pg 257

Skidmore, Ken, ARE Press, 215 67 St, Virginia Beach, VA 23451 *Tel:* 757-428-3588 *Toll Free Tel:* 800-333-4499 *Fax:* 757-491-0689 *E-mail:* are@edgarcayce.org *Web Site:* www.edgarcayce.org, pg 23

Skinner, Catherine, Connecticut Academy of Arts & Sciences, PO Box 208211, New Haven, CT 06520-8211 *Tel:* 203-432-3113 *Fax:* 203-432-5712 *E-mail:* caas@yale.edu *Web Site:* www.yale.edu/caas, pg 67

Skinner, Knute, 49th Parallel Poetry Award, Mail Stop 9053, Western Washington University, Bellingham, WA 98225 *Tel:* 360-650-4863 *E-mail:* bhreview@cc.wwu.edu *Web Site:* www.wwu.edu/~bhreview, pg 774

Skinner, Sharon, Impact Publishers Inc, PO Box 6016, Atascadero, CA 93423-6016 *Tel:* 805-466-5917 (opers & admin); 805-461-5911 (edit) *Toll Free Tel:* 800-246-7228 (orders) *Fax:* 805-466-5919 (opers & admin offices); 805-461-0554 (edit offices) *E-mail:* info@impactpublishers.com *Web Site:* www.impactpublishers.com; www.bibliotherapy.com, pg 131

Skipwith, Jo, St Martin's Press LLC, 175 Fifth Ave, New York, NY 10010 *Tel:* 212-674-5151 *Fax:* 212-420-9314 *E-mail:* firstname.lastname@stmartins.com *Web Site:* www.stmartins.com, pg 238

Sklare, Rose, Textbook Writers Associates Inc, 12 Nathan Rd, Newton Centre, MA 02459 *Tel:* 617-630-8500 *Fax:* 617-630-8502 *E-mail:* info@textbookwriters.com *Web Site:* www.textbookwriters.com, pg 612

Sklyar, Dimitri, American Marketing Association, 311 S Wacker Dr, Suite 5800, Chicago, IL 60606-2266 *Tel:* 312-542-9000 *Toll Free Tel:* 800-262-1150 *Fax:* 312-542-9001 *E-mail:* info@ama.org *Web Site:* www.marketingpower.com, pg 15

Skolkin, David, Museum of New Mexico Press, 725 Camino Lejo, Santa Fe, NM 87501 *Tel:* 505-476-1158 *Toll Free Tel:* 800-249-7737 (orders) *Fax:* 505-476-1156 *Toll Free Fax:* 800-622-8667 (orders) *E-mail:* mnmpress@aol.com *Web Site:* www.mnmpress.org, pg 180

Skolnick, Irene, Irene Skolnick Literary Agency, 22 W 23 St, 5th fl, New York, NY 10010 *Tel:* 212-727-3648 *Fax:* 212-727-1024 *E-mail:* sirene35@aol.com, pg 656

Skomal, Susi, American Anthropological Association, Publications Dept, 2200 Wilson Blvd, Suite 600, Arlington, VA 22201 *Tel:* 703-528-1902 ext 3014 *Fax:* 703-528-3546 *Web Site:* www.aaanet.org, pg 11

Skutley, Mary Lynn, American Psychological Association, 750 First St NE, Washington, DC 20002-4242 *Tel:* 202-336-5500 *Toll Free Tel:* 800-374-2721 *Fax:* 202-336-5620 *E-mail:* order@apa.org *Web Site:* www.apa.org/books, pg 17

Skutt, Alexander, McBooks Press Inc, 520 N Meadow St, Ithaca, NY 14850 *Tel:* 607-272-2114 *Toll Free Tel:* 888-266-5711 *Fax:* 607-273-6068 *E-mail:* mcbooks@mcbooks.com *Web Site:* www.mcbooks.com, pg 166

Skydell, Ceil, United Synagogue Book Service, 155 Fifth Ave, New York, NY 10010 *Tel:* 212-533-7800 (ext 2003) *Toll Free Tel:* 800-594-5617 (warehouse only) *Fax:* 212-253-5422 *E-mail:* booksvc@uscj.org *Web Site:* www.uscj.org/booksvc, pg 279

Skyhorse, Brando, Grove/Atlantic Inc, 841 Broadway, 4th fl, New York, NY 10003-4793 *Tel:* 212-614-7850 *Toll Free Tel:* 800-521-0178 *Fax:* 212-614-7886 *Web Site:* www.groveatlantic.com, pg 110

Slabaugh, Gerri, Adventure Publications, 820 Cleveland St, Cambridge, MN 55008 *Tel:* 763-689-9800 *Toll Free Tel:* 800-678-7006 *Fax:* 763-689-9039, pg 6

Slabaugh, Gordon, Adventure Publications, 820 Cleveland St, Cambridge, MN 55008 *Tel:* 763-689-9800 *Toll Free Tel:* 800-678-7006 *Fax:* 763-689-9039, pg 6

Slabaugh, Marlene, Evangel Publishing House, 2000 Evangel Way, Nappanee, IN 46550 *Tel:* 574-773-3164 *Toll Free Tel:* 800-253-9315 (orders) *Fax:* 574-773-5934 *E-mail:* sales@evangelpublishing.com *Web Site:* www.evangelpublishing.com, pg 92

Slagle, Claire, Charles C Thomas Publisher Ltd, 2600 S First St, Springfield, IL 62704 *Tel:* 217-789-8980 *Toll Free Tel:* 800-258-8980 *Fax:* 217-789-9130 *E-mail:* books@ccthomas.com *Web Site:* www.ccthomas.com, pg 269

Slaney, Karen, Rational Island Publishers, 719 Second Ave N, Seattle, WA 98109 *Tel:* 206-284-0311 *Fax:* 206-284-8429 *E-mail:* ircc@rc.org *Web Site:* www.rc.org, pg 228

Slarrow, Kathy, Park Place Publications, 591 Lighthouse Ave, No 22, Pacific Grove, CA 93950 *Tel:* 831-649-6640 *Toll Free Tel:* 888-702-4500 *Fax:* 831-649-6649 *E-mail:* publisher@parkplace-publications.com; info@parkplace-publications.com *Web Site:* www.parkplace-publications.com, pg 204

Slate, Audrey, Dobie-Paisano Fellowship Project, 702 E Dean Keeton St, Austin, TX 78705 *Tel:* 512-471-8542 *Fax:* 512-471-9997 *Web Site:* www.utexas.edu/ogs/Paisano, pg 770

Slater, Charles, Music Publishers' Association of the United States, 2435 Fifth Ave, Suite 236, New York, NY 10016 *Tel:* 212-327-4044 *Fax:* 212-327-4044 *Web Site:* host.mpa.org; www.mpa.org, pg 691

Slater, Daniel, NAL, 375 Hudson St, New York, NY 10014 *Tel:* 212-366-2000 *E-mail:* online@penguinputnam.com *Web Site:* www.penguin.com, pg 181

Slattery, Joan, Random House Children's Books, 1745 Broadway, New York, NY 10019 *Tel:* 212-782-9000 *Toll Free Tel:* 800-200-3552 *Fax:* 212-782-9452 *Web Site:* www.randomhouse.com/kids, pg 226

Slattery, Kathie, BBC Audiobooks America, One Lafayette Rd, Hampton, NH 03842 *Tel:* 603-926-8744 *Toll Free Tel:* 800-621-0182 *Fax:* 603-929-3890 *E-mail:* info@bbcaudiobooksamerica.com, pg 34

Slattery, Kathryn, Guideposts Young Writers Contest, 16 E 34 St, New York, NY 10016 *Tel:* 212-251-8100 *Toll Free Tel:* 800-932-2145 *Fax:* 212-684-0679 *Web Site:* www.guidepostsbooks.com, pg 777

Slawsky, Donna, Information Diva, 31 Jane St, New York, NY 10014 *Tel:* 212-229-1591 *Fax:* 413-778-3815 *Web Site:* www.informationdiva.com, pg 602

Sleigh, Eric, Carswell, One Corporate Plaza, 2075 Kennedy Rd, Toronto, ON M1T 3V4, Canada *Tel:* 416-609-8000 *Toll Free Tel:* 800-387-5164 (Canada & US) *Fax:* 416-298-5094 (Toronto); 403-233-8159 (Calgary); 604-685-5343 (Vancouver); 514-985-6605 *Toll Free Fax:* 877-750-9041 *E-mail:* comments@carswell.com *Web Site:* www.carswell.com, pg 539

Smith, George D, Signature Books Publishing LLC, 564 W 400 N, Salt Lake City, UT 84116-3411 *Tel:* 801-531-1483 *Toll Free Tel:* 800-356-5687 (orders) *Fax:* 801-531-1488 *E-mail:* people@signaturebooks. com *Web Site:* www.signaturebooks.com, pg 247

Smith, Ginger B, Success Advertising & Publishing, 3419 Dunham Rd, Warsaw, NY 14569 *Tel:* 585-786-5663, pg 261

Smith, Greg, Krause Publications, 700 E State St, Iola, WI 54990 *Tel:* 715-445-4612 ext 365 *Toll Free Tel:* 800-258-0929; 888-457-2873 *Fax:* 715-445-4087 *Web Site:* www.krause.com, pg 147

Smith, Gretchen E, Jane Chambers Playwriting Award, Southern Methodist University, PO Box 750356, Dallas, TX 75275-0356 *Tel:* 214-768-2937 *Fax:* 214-768-1136 *Web Site:* www.smu.edu, pg 781

Smith, H, M S G-Haskell House Publishers Ltd, PO Box 190420, Brooklyn, NY 11219-0420 *Tel:* 718-435-7878 *Fax:* 718-633-7050, pg 160

Smith, Harry, International Titles, 931 E 56 St, Austin, TX 78751-1724 *Tel:* 512-451-2221 *Fax:* 512-467-1330, pg 635

Smith, Harry, The Smith Publishers, 69 Joralemon St, Brooklyn, NY 11201-4003 *Tel:* 718-834-1212 *Fax:* 718-834-1212 *E-mail:* thesmith1@aol.com; artsend@ma.ultranet.com *Web Site:* members.aol. com/thesmith1, pg 250

Smith, Ileene, Random House Publishing Group, 1745 Broadway, New York, NY 10019 *Toll Free Tel:* 800-200-3552 *Toll Free Fax:* 800-200-3552 *Web Site:* www.randomhouse.com, pg 227

Smith, J Reynolds, Duke University Press, 905 W Main St, Suite 18-B, Durham, NC 27701 *Tel:* 919-687-3600 *Toll Free Tel:* 888-651-0122 (orders only) *Fax:* 919-688-4574 *Toll Free Fax:* 888-651-0124 *Web Site:* www.dukeupress.edu, pg 84

Smith, Jack, Banner of Truth, PO Box 621, Carlisle, PA 17013 *Tel:* 717-249-5747 *Toll Free Tel:* 800-263-8085 (orders) *Fax:* 717-249-0604 *E-mail:* info@ banneroftruth.org *Web Site:* www.banneroftruth.co.uk, pg 31

Smith, James Clois Jr, Sunstone Press, PO Box 2321, Santa Fe, NM 87504-2321 *Tel:* 505-988-4418 *Fax:* 505-988-1025 (orders only) *Web Site:* www. sunstonepress.com, pg 262

Smith, Janet Byrne, e-Scholastic, 568 Broadway, 9th fl, New York, NY 10012 *Tel:* 212-343-7100 *Fax:* 212-343-4949, pg 85

Smith, Jeanmarie, Aspen Publishers, A Wolters Kluwer Company, 1185 Avenue of the Americas, New York, NY 10036 *Tel:* 212-597-0200 *Toll Free Tel:* 800-234-1660 (cust serv); 800-447-1717 (orders); 800-950-5259 (legal educ); 800-LAW-PLGL (paralegal textbook); 800-317-3113 (bookstore sales); 800-364-2512 (Loislaw) *Web Site:* www.aspenpublishers.com, pg 26

Smith, Jeffrey, Bridge to Asia, 665 Grant Ave, San Francisco, CA 94108 *Tel:* 415-678-2990 *Fax:* 415-678-2996 *E-mail:* asianet@bridge.org *Web Site:* www. bridge.org, pg 705

Smith, Jerome K, Gollehon Press Inc, 6157 28 St SE, Grand Rapids, MI 49546 *Tel:* 616-949-3515 *Fax:* 619-949-8674, pg 106

Smith, Jill N, University of Denver Publishing Institute, 2075 S University Blvd, D-114, Denver, CO 80210 *Tel:* 303-871-2570 *Fax:* 303-871-2501 *Web Site:* www. du.edu/pi, pg 755

Smith, Joan, Concourse Press, PO Box 8265, Philadelphia, PA 19101-8265 *Tel:* 610-325-0313 *Fax:* 610-359-1953, pg 66

Smith, Jody, Concourse Press, PO Box 8265, Philadelphia, PA 19101-8265 *Tel:* 610-325-0313 *Fax:* 610-359-1953, pg 66

Smith, Julie, Holt, Rinehart and Winston, 10801 N MoPac Expy, Bldg 3, Austin, TX 78759 *Tel:* 512-721-7000 *Toll Free Tel:* 800-225-5425 (cust serv) *Fax:* 512-721-7833 (mktg); 512-721-7898 (edit) *Web Site:* www.hrw.com, pg 124

Smith, June, Houghton Mifflin College Division, 222 Berkeley St, Boston, MA 02116-3764 *Tel:* 617-351-5000 *Toll Free Tel:* 800-225-1464 (orders) *Web Site:* www.college.hmco.com, pg 126

Smith, June, Houghton Mifflin Co, 222 Berkeley St, Boston, MA 02116-3764 *Tel:* 617-351-5000 *Toll Free Tel:* 800-225-3362 (trade books); 800-733-2828 (text books); 800-225-1464 (college texts) *Fax:* 617-351-1125 *Web Site:* www.hmco.com, pg 126

Smith, Kerry, Rolling Stone's Annual College Journalism Competition, 1290 Avenue of the Americas, 2nd fl, New York, NY 10104 *Tel:* 212-484-1616; 212-484-1636 *Fax:* 212-484-3434 *Web Site:* www.rollingstone. com, pg 803

Smith, Kevin, Pocket Books, 1230 Avenue of the Americas, New York, NY 10020 *Toll Free Tel:* 800-456-6798 *Fax:* 212-698-7284 *E-mail:* consumer. customerservice@simonandschuster.com *Web Site:* www.simonsays.com, pg 215

Smith, Larry, Bottom Dog Press, c/o Firelands College of Bowling Green State University, PO Box 425, Huron, OH 44839-0425 *Tel:* 419-433-5560 *Fax:* 419-433-9696 *Web Site:* members.aol.com/lsmithdog/ bottomdog, pg 44

Smith, Laura, Adams Media, An F+W Publications Co, 57 Littlefield St, 2nd fl, Avon, MA 02322 *Tel:* 508-427-7100 *Fax:* 508-427-6790 *Toll Free Fax:* 800-872-5628 *E-mail:* authors@adamsmedia.com; orders@ adamsmedia.com *Web Site:* www.adamsmedia.com, pg 5

Smith, Laura, Bottom Dog Press, c/o Firelands College of Bowling Green State University, PO Box 425, Huron, OH 44839-0425 *Tel:* 419-433-5560 *Fax:* 419-433-9696 *Web Site:* members.aol.com/lsmithdog/ bottomdog, pg 44

Smith, Laura, Krause Publications, 700 E State St, Iola, WI 54990 *Tel:* 715-445-4612 ext 365 *Toll Free Tel:* 800-258-0929; 888-457-2873 *Fax:* 715-445-4087 *Web Site:* www.krause.com, pg 147

Smith, Laura, Writer's Digest Books, 4700 E Galbraith Rd, Cincinnati, OH 45236 *Tel:* 513-531-2690 *Toll Free Tel:* 800-289-0963 *Fax:* 513-891-7185 *Web Site:* www. writersdigest.com, pg 305

Smith, Laurie, Altitude Publishing Canada Ltd, 1500 Railway Ave, Canmore, AB T1W 1P6, Canada *Tel:* 403-678-6888 *Toll Free Tel:* 800-957-6888 *Fax:* 403-678-6951 *Toll Free Fax:* 800-957-1477 *E-mail:* orderdesk@altitudepublishing.com; sales@ altitudepublishing.com (ordering) *Web Site:* www. altitudepublishing.com, pg 535

Smith, Lisa Garrett, Reader's Digest General Books, Reader's Digest Rd, Pleasantville, NY 10570-7000 *Tel:* 914-238-1000 *Toll Free Tel:* 800-431-1726 *Fax:* 914-244-7436, pg 229

Smith, Lisa Garrett, Reader's Digest Trade Books, Reader's Digest Rd, Pleasantville, NY 10570-7000 *Tel:* 914-244-7445 *Fax:* 914-244-7605, pg 229

Smith, Lois, BNA Books, 1231 25 St NW, Washington, DC 20037 *Tel:* 202-452-4343 *Toll Free Tel:* 800-960-1220 *Fax:* 202-452-4997 (editorial off); 732-346-1624 (cust serv) *E-mail:* books@bna.com *Web Site:* www. bnabooks.com, pg 42

Smith, Lynn K, SLA Annual Conference, 313 S Patrick St, Alexandria, VA 22314 *Tel:* 202-234-4700 *Fax:* 703-647-4901 *E-mail:* sla@sla.org *Web Site:* www.sla.org, pg 747

Smith, Lynn K, SLA Workshops, 313 S Patrick St, Alexandria, VA 22314 *Tel:* 703-647-4900 *Fax:* 703-647-4901 *E-mail:* sla@sla.org *Web Site:* www.sla.org, pg 747

Smith, Lynn K, Special Libraries Association (SLA), 313 S Patrick St, Alexandria, VA 22314 *Tel:* 703-647-4900 *Fax:* 703-647-4901 *E-mail:* sla@sla.org *Web Site:* www.sla.org, pg 701

Smith, M Lee, M Lee Smith Publishers LLC, 5201 Virginia Way, Brentwood, TN 37027 *Tel:* 615-373-7517 *Toll Free Tel:* 800-274-6774 *Fax:* 615-373-5183 *Web Site:* www.mleesmith.com, pg 250

Smith, Martha, Pearson Education - Elementary Group, 299 Jefferson Rd, Parsippany, NJ 07054-0480 *Tel:* 973-735-8000, pg 206

Smith, Mary Dupuy, Teacher Created Materials Inc, 6421 Industry Way, Westminster, CA 92683 *Tel:* 714-891-7895 *Toll Free Tel:* 800-662-4321 *Fax:* 714-892-0283 *Toll Free Fax:* 800-525-1254 *E-mail:* tcminfo@ teachercreated.com *Web Site:* www.teachercreated.com, pg 265

Smith, Mary P, Thorndike Press, 295 Kennedy Memorial Dr, Waterville, ME 04901-4517 *Tel:* 207-859-1026 *Toll Free Tel:* 800-233-1244 *Fax:* 207-859-1009 *Toll Free Fax:* 800-558-4676 (orders) *E-mail:* printorders@ thomson.com; international@thomson.com (orders for customers outside US & CA) *Web Site:* www.gale. com/thorndike, pg 270

Smith, Michael E, Peter Smith Publisher Inc, 5 Lexington Ave, Magnolia, MA 01930 *Tel:* 978-525-3562 *Fax:* 978-525-3674, pg 250

Smith, Monte, Eagle's View Publishing, 168W 12 St, Ogden, UT 84404 *Tel:* 801-393-4555; 801-745-0905 (edit) *Toll Free Tel:* 800-547-3364 (orders over $100) *Fax:* 801-745-0903 *E-mail:* eglcrafts@aol.com *Web Site:* eaglefeathertradingpost.com, pg 85

Smith, Nicholas, Altair Literary Agency LLC, PO Box 11656, Washington, DC 20008-0856 *Tel:* 202-237-8282 *Web Site:* www.altairliteraryagency.com, pg 619

Smith, Nikki, Smith/Skolnik Literary Management, 963 Belvidere, Plainfield, NJ 07060 *Tel:* 908-822-1870 *Fax:* 908-822-1871, pg 656

Smith, P David, Western Reflections Publishing Co, 219 Main St, Montrose, CO 81401 *Tel:* 970-249-7180 *Toll Free Tel:* 800-993-4490 *Fax:* 970-249-7181 *E-mail:* westref@montrose.net *Web Site:* www. westernreflectionspub.com, pg 297

Smith, Paige, Vintage & Anchor Books, 1745 Broadway, New York, NY 10019 *Tel:* 212-751-2600 *Fax:* 212-572-6043, pg 291

Smith, Patience, Harlequin Enterprises Ltd, 233 Broadway, Suite 1001, New York, NY 10279 *Tel:* 212-553-4200 *Fax:* 212-227-8969 *E-mail:* customer. ecare@harlequin.ca *Web Site:* www.eharlequin.com; www.luna-books.com; www.mirabooks.com; www. reddressink.com; www.steeplehill.com, pg 115

Smith, Patricia, Michael Snell Literary Agency, PO Box 1206, Truro, MA 02666-1206 *Tel:* 508-349-3718, pg 656

Smith, R Bob III, Psychological Assessment Resources Inc (PAR), 16204 N Florida Ave, Lutz, FL 33549 *Tel:* 813-968-3003 *Toll Free Tel:* 800-331-8378 *Fax:* 813-968-2598 *Toll Free Fax:* 800-727-9329 *Web Site:* www.parinc.com, pg 221

Smith, Robert S, Review & Herald Publishing Association, 55 W Oak Ridge Dr, Hagerstown, MD 21740 *Tel:* 301-393-3000 *Toll Free Tel:* 800-234-7630 *Fax:* 301-393-4055 (periodicals); 301-393-3222 *E-mail:* editorial@rhpa.org *Web Site:* www. reviewandherald.com, pg 232

Smith, Robin C, Columbia University Press, 61 W 62 St, New York, NY 10023 *Tel:* 212-459-0600 *Toll Free Tel:* 800-944-8648 *Fax:* 212-459-3678 *Web Site:* www. columbia.edu/cu/cup, pg 65

Smith, Ronald, Oolichan Books, Box 10, Lantzville, BC V0R 2H0, Canada *Tel:* 250-390-4839 *Fax:* 250-390-4839 *E-mail:* oolichan@island.net *Web Site:* www. oolichan.com, pg 556

Smith, Ronnie L, Writer's Relief, Inc, 245 Teaneck Rd, Ridgefield Park, NJ 07660 *Tel:* 201-641-3003 *Fax:* 201-641-1253 *Web Site:* www.wrelief.com, pg 615

Smith, Rose Mary, Allen A Knoll Publishers, 200 W Victoria St, 2nd fl, Suite A, Santa Barbara, CA 93101-3627 *Tel:* 805-564-3377 *Toll Free Tel:* 800-777-7623 *Fax:* 805-966-6657 *E-mail:* bookinfo@knollpublishers. com *Web Site:* www.knollpublishers.com, pg 146

Smith, Sandy, Best Publishing Co, PO Box 30100, Flagstaff, AZ 86003-0100 *Tel:* 928-527-1055 *Toll Free Tel:* 800-468-1055 *Fax:* 928-526-0370 *E-mail:* divebooks@bestpub.com *Web Site:* www. bestpub.com, pg 37

Smith, Shelagh, Canadian Bookbinders & Book Artists Guild (CBBAG), 60 Atlantic Ave, Suite 112, Toronto, ON M6K 1X9, Canada *Tel:* 416-581-1071 *Fax:* 416-581-1053 *E-mail:* cbbag@web.net *Web Site:* www. cbbag.ca, pg 683

Smith, Stephen R, American Institute of Chemical Engineers (AICHE), 3 Park Ave, New York, NY 10016-5991 *Tel:* 212-591-7338 *Toll Free Tel:* 800-242-4363 *Fax:* 212-591-8888 *E-mail:* xpress@aiche.org *Web Site:* www.aiche.org, pg 15

Smith, Steve, Blackwell Publishers, 350 Main St, Malden, MA 02148 *Tel:* 781-388-8200 *Fax:* 781-388-8210 *E-mail:* books@blackwellpublishing.com *Web Site:* www.blackwellpublishing.com, pg 40

Smith, Steve, DBI Books, 700 E State St, Iola, WI 54990-0001 *Tel:* 715-445-2214 *Toll Free Tel:* 888-457-2873 *Fax:* 715-445-4087 *Web Site:* www.krause.com, pg 77

Smith, Steve, Steve Smith Autosports, PO Box 11631, Santa Ana, CA 92711-1631 *Tel:* 714-639-7681 *Fax:* 714-639-9741 *E-mail:* sales@ssapubl.com *Web Site:* www.ssapubl.com, pg 250

Smith, Sue, Eagle's View Publishing, 168W 12 St, Ogden, UT 84404 *Tel:* 801-393-4555; 801-745-0905 (edit) *Toll Free Tel:* 800-547-3364 (orders over $100) *Fax:* 801-745-0903 *E-mail:* eglcrafts@aol.com *Web Site:* eaglefeathertradingpost.com, pg 85

Smith, Suzanne, Alfred A Knopf, 1745 Broadway, New York, NY 10019 *Tel:* 212-751-2600 *Toll Free Tel:* 800-638-6460 *Fax:* 212-572-2593 *Web Site:* www. randomhouse.com/knopf, pg 146

Smith, Suzanne, Pantheon Books/Schocken Books, 1745 Broadway, New York, NY 10019 *Tel:* 212-751-2600 *Toll Free Tel:* 800-638-6460 *Fax:* 212-572-6030, pg 203

Smith, Trisha, State University of New York Press, 90 State St, Suite 700, Albany, NY 12207-1707 *Tel:* 518-472-5000 *Toll Free Tel:* 800-666-2211 (orders) *Fax:* 518-472-5038 *Toll Free Fax:* 800-688-2877 (orders) *E-mail:* orderbook@cupserv.org; info@ sunypress.edu *Web Site:* www.sunypress.edu, pg 258

Smith, Valerie, Penmarin Books Inc, 1044 Magnolia Way, Roseville, CA 95661 *Tel:* 916-771-5869 *Fax:* 916-771-5879 *E-mail:* penmarin@penmarin.com *Web Site:* www.penmarin.com, pg 208

Smith, Valerie, Valerie Smith, Literary Agent, 1746 Rte 44-55, Modena, NY 12548 *Tel:* 845-883-5848, pg 656

Smith, Viveca, Viveca Smith Publishing, PMB 131, 3001 S Hardin Blvd, Suite 110, McKinney, TX 75070-9028 *Tel:* 214-793-0089 *Fax:* 972-562-7559 *E-mail:* vsmithpublishing@aol.com *Web Site:* www. vivecasmithpublishing.com, pg 574

Smith, Wayne, Greenwood Publishing Group Inc, 88 Post Rd W, Westport, CT 06880-4208 *Tel:* 203-226-3571 *Toll Free Tel:* 800-225-5800 *Fax:* 203-222-1502 *E-mail:* bookinfo@greenwood.com (general); firstintial&fulllastname@greenwood.com (individuals) *Web Site:* www.greenwood.com, pg 109

Smith, Wayne, Teacher Ideas Press, 361 Hanover St, Portsmouth, NH 03801-3912 *Tel:* 603-431-3912 *Fax:* 800-225-5800 *Fax:* 603-431-2214 *Toll Free Fax:* 800-354-2004 (perms & foreign rts) *E-mail:* custserv@ teacherideaspress.com; permissions@teacherideaspress. com; foreignrights@teacherideaspress.com *Web Site:* www.teacherideaspress.com, pg 265

Smith, William, Barnard Co, 2402 Third St, Suite 206, Santa Monica, CA 90405 *Tel:* 310-314-7727 *E-mail:* seyahllib@aol.com, pg 570

Smith-Toomey, Mary Beth, National One-Act Playwriting Competition, 600 Wolfe St, Alexandria, VA 22314 *Tel:* 703-683-5778 *Fax:* 703-683-1378 *E-mail:* asklta@thelittletheatre.com *Web Site:* www. thelittletheatre.com, pg 792

Smithline, Alex, Harold Ober Associates Inc, 425 Madison Ave, New York, NY 10017 *Tel:* 212-759-8600 *Fax:* 212-759-9428, pg 647

Smithyman, Kathryn, Crabtree Publishing Co, 350 Fifth Ave, Suite 3308, PMB 16-A, New York, NY 10118 *Tel:* 212-496-5040 *Toll Free Tel:* 800-387-7650 *Toll Free Fax:* 800-355-7166 *E-mail:* letters@ crabtreebooks.com *Web Site:* www.crabtreebooks.com, pg 71

Smolin, Ronald, Trans-Atlantic Publications Inc, 311 Bainbridge St, Philadelphia, PA 19147 *Tel:* 215-925-5083 *Fax:* 215-925-1912 *E-mail:* order@ transatlanticpub.com *Web Site:* www.transatlanticpub. com; www.businesstitles.com, pg 274

Smyk, Dorothy, New Harbinger Publications Inc, 5674 Shattuck Ave, Oakland, CA 94609 *Tel:* 510-652-0215 *Toll Free Tel:* 800-748-6273 (orders only) *Fax:* 510-652-5472 *E-mail:* nhhelp@newharbinger.com *Web Site:* www.newharbinger.com, pg 188

Smyth, A Y, Safe Harbor Books, 504 Main St, New London, NH 03527 *Fax:* 603-526-3500 *E-mail:* safeharborbooks@aol.com, pg 573

Snell, H Michael, Michael Snell Literary Agency, PO Box 1206, Truro, MA 02666-1206 *Tel:* 508-349-3718, pg 656

Sneller, Mark MD, The Society of Southwestern Authors (SSA), PO Box 30355, Tucson, AZ 85751-0355 *Tel:* 520-546-9382 *Fax:* 520-296-0409 *E-mail:* wporter202@aol.com *Web Site:* www. azstarnet.com/nonprofit/ssa, pg 700

Snelling, Sarah, NavPress Publishing Group, 3820 N 30 St, Colorado Springs, CO 80904 *Tel:* 719-548-9222 *Toll Free Tel:* 800-366-7788 *Fax:* 719-260-7223 *Toll Free Fax:* 800-343-3902 *Web Site:* www.navpress.com, pg 185

Snider, Steve, St Martin's Press Trade Division, 175 Fifth Ave, New York, NY 10010 *E-mail:* firstname. lastname@stmartins.com *Web Site:* www.stmartins. com; www.minotaurbooks.com, pg 239

Snodgrass, Prof Kate, Boston University, 236 Bay State Rd, Boston, MA 02215 *Tel:* 617-353-2510 *Fax:* 617-353-3653 *Web Site:* www.bu.edu/writing/, pg 751

Snodgrass, R Michael, Brilliance Audio, 1704 Eaton Dr, Grand Haven, MI 49417 *Tel:* 616-846-5256 *Toll Free Tel:* 800-648-2312 (orders only) *Fax:* 616-846-0630 *Web Site:* www.brillianceaudio.com, pg 48

Snouck-Hurgronje, Jan W, The Nautical & Aviation Publishing Co of America Inc, 2055 Middleburg Lane, Mount Pleasant, SC 29464 *Tel:* 843-856-0561 *Fax:* 843-856-3164 *E-mail:* nauticalaviationpublishing@att.net *Web Site:* www.nauticalaviation.com, pg 185

Snowden, Elizabeth Regina, Alan Wofsy Fine Arts, 1109 Geary Blvd, San Francisco, CA 94109 *Tel:* 415-292-6500 *Fax:* 415-512-0130 (acctg); 415-292-6594 (off & cust serv) *E-mail:* beauxarts@earthlink.net (cust serv); editeur@earthlink.net (edit); order@art-books.com (orders) *Web Site:* art-books.com, pg 302

Snyder, A, A M Best Co, Ambest Rd, Oldwick, NJ 08858 *Tel:* 908-439-2200 *Fax:* 908-439-3385 *E-mail:* customerservice@ambest.com; sales@ambest. com *Web Site:* www.ambest.com, pg 37

Snyder, Becky, ABC-CLIO, 130 Cremona Dr, Santa Barbara, CA 93117 *Tel:* 805-968-1911 *Toll Free Tel:* 800-368-6868 *Fax:* 805-685-9685 *E-mail:* sales@ abc-clio.com *Web Site:* www.abc-clio.com, pg 3

Snyder, Eleanor, Faith & Life Resources, 616 Walnut Ave, Scottdale, PA 15683-1999 *Tel:* 724-887-8500 *Toll Free Tel:* 800-245-7894 *Fax:* 724-887-3111 *E-mail:* info@mph.org *Web Site:* www.mph.org, pg 94

Snyder, Elizabeth, Haystack Writing Program, PO Box 1491, Portland, OR 97207-1491 *Tel:* 503-725-3276; 503-725-4186 *Fax:* 503-725-4840 *Web Site:* www. haystack.pdx.edu, pg 744

Snyder, Elizabeth, Pacific Northwest Children's Book Conference, 1633 SW Park Ave, Portland, OR 97207 *Tel:* 503-725-4186 *Toll Free Tel:* 800-547-8887 (ext 4186) *Fax:* 503-725-4840 *E-mail:* snydere@pdx.edu *Web Site:* www.haystack.pdx.edu/children, pg 745

Snyder, Frank, Developmental Studies Center, 2000 Embarcadero, Suite 305, Oakland, CA 94606-5300 *Tel:* 510-533-0213 *Toll Free Tel:* 800-666-7270 *Fax:* 510-842-0348 *E-mail:* pubs@devstu.org *Web Site:* www.devstu.org, pg 79

Snyder, Matthew, Creative Artists Agency, 9830 Wilshire Blvd, Beverly Hills, CA 90212-1825 *Tel:* 310-288-4545 *Fax:* 310-288-4800 *Web Site:* www.caa.com, pg 626

Sobel, Nat, Sobel Weber Associates Inc, 146 E 19 St, New York, NY 10003 *Tel:* 212-420-8585 *Fax:* 212-505-1017 *E-mail:* info@sobelweber.com *Web Site:* www.sobelweber.com, pg 656

Soden, Pat, University of Washington Press, 1326 Fifth Ave, Suite 555, Seattle, WA 98101-2604 *Tel:* 206-543-4050; 206-543-8870 *Toll Free Tel:* 800-441-4115 (orders) *Fax:* 206-543-3932 *Toll Free Fax:* 800-669-7993 (orders) *E-mail:* uwpord@u.washington.edu *Web Site:* www.washington.edu/uwpress/, pg 286

Soehner, Kenneth, The Metropolitan Museum of Art, 1000 Fifth Ave, New York, NY 10028 *Tel:* 212-879-5500; 212-535-7710 *Fax:* 212-396-5062 *E-mail:* info@metmuseum.org *Web Site:* www. metmuseum.org, pg 173

Sofranko, John A, American Institute of Chemical Engineers (AICHE), 3 Park Ave, New York, NY 10016-5991 *Tel:* 212-591-7338 *Toll Free Tel:* 800-242-4363 *Fax:* 212-591-8888 *E-mail:* xpress@aiche.org *Web Site:* www.aiche.org, pg 15

Sokol, Dr Mick, Drury University One Act Play Competition, 900 N Benton Ave, Springfield, MO 65802-3344 *Tel:* 417-873-7430, pg 771

Sokoloff, Michele, Media & Methods, 1429 Walnut St, 10th fl, Philadelphia, PA 19102 *Tel:* 215-563-6005 *Toll Free Tel:* 800-555-5657 *Fax:* 215-587-9706 *Web Site:* www.media-methods.com, pg 170

Solcova, Eva, Trails Books, PO Box 317, Black Earth, WI 53515-0317 *Tel:* 608-767-8000 *Toll Free Tel:* 800-236-8088 *Fax:* 608-767-5444 *E-mail:* books@ wistrails.com *Web Site:* www.trailsbooks.com, pg 273

Soldevilla, Jeremy, Paul & Company, 140 Union St, Marshfield, MA 02050-6273 *Tel:* 781-834-9830 *Toll Free Tel:* 800-888-4741 (orders) *Fax:* 781-837-9996 *Web Site:* www.ipgbook.com, pg 205

Solis, Alicia, The Lyons Press, 246 Goose Lane, Guilford, CT 06437 *Tel:* 203-458-4500 *Toll Free Tel:* 800-243-0495 *Fax:* 203-458-4668 *Web Site:* www. lyonspress.com; www.globepequot.com, pg 160

Sollod, Celeste, Random House Value Publishing, 1745 Broadway, New York, NY 10019 *Tel:* 212-940-7422 *Fax:* 212-572-2114, pg 227

Solomita, David, Parsons School of Design, 66 Fifth Ave, New York, NY 10011 *Tel:* 212-229-8933 *Fax:* 212-229-5970 *Web Site:* www.parsons.edu/ce, pg 754

Solomon, Francis, American Public Human Services Association, 810 First St NE, Suite 500, Washington, DC 20002 *Tel:* 202-682-0100 *Fax:* 202-289-6555 *E-mail:* pubs@aphsa.org *Web Site:* www.aphsa.org, pg 677

Solomon, Jeremy, Rainmaker Literary Agency, 25 NW 23 Place, Suite 6, PMB 460, Portland, OR 97210-5599 *Tel:* 503-222-2249 *E-mail:* info@rainmakerliterary.com *Web Site:* www.rainmakerliterary.com, pg 650

Somers, Adam, PEN Center USA, 672 S Lafayette Park Place, Suite 42, Los Angeles, CA 90057 *Tel:* 213-365-8500 *Fax:* 213-365-9616 *E-mail:* pen@penusa.org *Web Site:* www.penusa.org, pg 697

Somers, Evelyn, Editors' Prize, 1507 Hillcrest Hall, Columbia, MO 65211 *Tel:* 573-882-4474 *Toll Free Tel:* 800-949-2505 *Fax:* 573-884-4671 *E-mail:* mr@ missouri.org *Web Site:* www.missourireview.org, pg 771

Somers, Evelyn, William Peden Prize in Fiction, 1507 Hillcrest Hall, Columbia, MO 65211 *Tel:* 573-882-4474 *Toll Free Tel:* 800-949-2505 *Fax:* 573-884-4671 *E-mail:* tmr@moreview.com *Web Site:* www.missourireview.com, pg 797

Somers, John, Reference Publications Inc, 218 Saint Clair River Dr, Algonac, MI 48001 *Tel:* 810-794-5722 *Fax:* 810-794-7463 *E-mail:* referencepub@sbcglobal.com, pg 230

Sommer, John, Advance Publishing Inc, 6950 Fulton St, Houston, TX 77022 *Tel:* 713-695-0600 *Fax:* 713-695-8585 *E-mail:* ap@advancepublishing.com *Web Site:* www.advancepublishing.com, pg 6

Sommers, Pam, Rizzoli International Publications Inc, 300 Park Ave S, 3rd fl, New York, NY 10010-5399 *Tel:* 212-387-3400 *Toll Free Tel:* 800-522-6657 (orders only) *Fax:* 212-387-3535, pg 233

Sommers, Pam, Universe Publishing, 300 Park Ave S, 3rd fl, New York, NY 10010 *Tel:* 212-387-3400 *Fax:* 212-387-3535, pg 280

Sonder, Mark, Mark Sonder Productions, 250 W 57 St, Suite 1830, New York, NY 10107 *Tel:* 212-262-4600 *Fax:* 212-246-0197 *E-mail:* msonder@marksonderproductions.com *Web Site:* www.marksonderproductions.com, pg 670

Sondhi, Krishna, Kumarian Press Inc, 1294 Blue Hills Ave, Bloomfield, CT 06002 *Tel:* 860-243-2098 *Toll Free Tel:* 800-289-2664 (orders only) *Fax:* 860-243-2867 *E-mail:* kpbooks@kpbooks.com *Web Site:* www.kpbooks.com, pg 147

Song, Helen, The Continuum International Publishing Group, 15 E 26 St, Suite 1703, New York, NY 10010 *Tel:* 212-953-5858 *Toll Free Tel:* 800-561-7704 *Fax:* 212-953-5944 *E-mail:* info@continuum-books.com *Web Site:* www.continuumbooks.com, pg 67

Sonnenfeld, Mark, Mark Sonnenfeld, 45-08 Old Millstone Dr, East Windsor, NJ 08520 *Tel:* 609-443-0646 *Web Site:* experimentalpoet.com, pg 253

Sorce, Pat, Rochester Institute of Technology, School of Print Media, 69 Lomb Memorial Dr, Rochester, NY 14623-5603 *Tel:* 585-475-2727; 585-475-7223 *Fax:* 585-475-5336 *E-mail:* spmofc@rit.edu *Web Site:* www.rit.edu/~spms, pg 754

Sorensen, Robbin, National Coalition for Literacy, 50 E Huron St, Chicago, IL 60611 *Tel:* 312-280-3275 *Toll Free Tel:* 800-228-8813 *Fax:* 312-280-3256 *E-mail:* ncl@ala.org *Web Site:* www.ala.org, pg 693

Soroka, Cynthia, Ariel Starr Productions Ltd, PO Box 17, Demarest, NJ 07627-0017 *Tel:* 201-784-9148 *Fax:* 201-541-8796 *E-mail:* darkbird@aol.com, pg 23

Sorsky, Richard, Linden Publishing Company Inc, 2006 S Mary, Fresno, CA 93721 *Tel:* 559-233-6633 *Toll Free Tel:* 800-345-4447 (orders only) *Fax:* 559-233-6933 *Web Site:* lindenpub.com, pg 155

Sosson, George, Dorchester Publishing Co Inc, 200 Madison Ave, Suite 2000, New York, NY 10016 *Tel:* 212-725-8811 *Toll Free Tel:* 800-481-9191 (order dept) *Fax:* 212-532-1054 *E-mail:* dorchedits@dorchesterpub.com *Web Site:* www.dorchesterpub.com, pg 82

Sotir, Mark, Sunburst Technology, 400 Columbus Ave, Suite 160E, Valhalla, NY 10595 *Tel:* 914-747-3310 *Toll Free Tel:* 800-338-3457 *Fax:* 914-747-4109 *Web Site:* www.sunburst.com, pg 262

Soto-Galicia, Silvia, Chemical Publishing Co Inc, 527 Third Ave, Suite 427, New York, NY 10016 *Tel:* 212-779-0090 *Toll Free Tel:* 800-786-3659 *Fax:* 212-889-1537 *E-mail:* chempub@aol.com *Web Site:* www.chemicalpublishing.com, pg 59

Soucoup, Dan, Nimbus Publishing Ltd, 3731 Mackintosh St, Halifax, NS B3K 5A5, Canada *Tel:* 902-455-5304 *Toll Free Tel:* 800-646-2879 *Fax:* 902-455-5440 *E-mail:* customerservice@nimbus.ns.ca *Web Site:* www.nimbus.ns.ca, pg 556

Soucy, Jean Yves, Editions de l'Hexagone, 1010, rue de la Gauchetiere Est, Montreal, PQ H2L 2N5, Canada *Tel:* 514-523-1182 *Fax:* 514-282-7530 *E-mail:* vml@sogides.com *Web Site:* www.edhexagone.com, pg 544

Soucy, Jean-Yves, VLB Editeur Inc, 955 Amherst St, Montreal, PQ H2L 3K4, Canada *Tel:* 514-523-1182 *Fax:* 514-282-7530 *E-mail:* vml@sogides.com *Web Site:* www.edvlb.com, pg 566

Soule, Susan, Cambridge University Press, 40 W 20 St, New York, NY 10011-4211 *Tel:* 212-924-3900 *Toll Free Tel:* 800-899-5222 *Fax:* 212-691-3239 *Web Site:* www.cambridge.org, pg 52

Soules, Gordon, Gordon Soules Book Publishers Ltd, 1359 Ambleside Lane, West Vancouver, BC V7T 2Y9, Canada *Tel:* 604-922-6588; 604-688-5466 *Fax:* 604-688-5442 *E-mail:* books@gordonsoules.com *Web Site:* www.gordonsoules.com, pg 561

Sounders, Margaret, Royalton Press, 362 N Bedford St, East Bridgewater, MA 02333 *Tel:* 508-378-1110 *Fax:* 508-378-1105 *Web Site:* www.drummondpub.com, pg 235

Sousa, Peg, Writer's Digest Books, 4700 E Galbraith Rd, Cincinnati, OH 45236 *Tel:* 513-531-2690 *Toll Free Tel:* 800-289-0963 *Fax:* 513-891-7185 *Web Site:* www.writersdigest.com, pg 305

Soussan, Lionel, Les Editions Phidal Inc, 5740 rue Ferrier, Montreal, PQ H4P 1M7, Canada *Tel:* 514-738-0202 *Toll Free Tel:* 800-738-7349 *Fax:* 514-738-5102 *E-mail:* info@phidal.com *Web Site:* www.phidal.com, pg 545

Southard, Greta, Advancement of Literacy Award, 50 E Huron St, Chicago, IL 60611 *Toll Free Tel:* 800-545-2433 (ext 5026) *E-mail:* pla@ala.org *Web Site:* www.pla.org, pg 757

Southworth, Donna K, Graphic Arts Publishing Inc, 3100 Bronson Hill Rd, Livonia, NY 14487-9716 *Tel:* 716-346-6978 *Toll Free Tel:* 800-724-9476 *Fax:* 716-346-2276, pg 108

Southworth, Miles F, Graphic Arts Publishing Inc, 3100 Bronson Hill Rd, Livonia, NY 14487-9716 *Tel:* 716-346-6978 *Toll Free Tel:* 800-724-9476 *Fax:* 716-346-2276, pg 108

Sova, Kathy, Theatre Communications Group Inc, 520 Eighth Ave, New York, NY 10018 *Tel:* 212-609-5900 *Fax:* 212-609-5901 *E-mail:* tcg@tcg.org *Web Site:* www.tcg.org, pg 268

Sowienski, Richard, William Peden Prize in Fiction, 1507 Hillcrest Hall, Columbia, MO 65211 *Tel:* 573-882-4474 *Toll Free Tel:* 800-949-2505 *Fax:* 573-884-4671 *E-mail:* tmr@moreview.com *Web Site:* www.missourireview.com, pg 797

Sox, A, Pacific Press Publishing Association, 1350 N Kings Rd, Nampa, ID 83687-3193 *Tel:* 208-465-2500 *Toll Free Tel:* 800-447-7377 *Fax:* 208-465-2531 *Web Site:* www.pacificpress.com, pg 202

Soye, Brian, Madison Press Books, 1000 Yonge St, Toronto, ON M4W 2K2, Canada *Tel:* 416-923-5027 *Fax:* 416-923-9708 *E-mail:* info@madisonpressbooks.com *Web Site:* www.madisonpressbooks.com, pg 553

Spadaccini, Vic, Blue Sky Marketing Inc, PO Box 21583, St Paul, MN 55121-0583 *Tel:* 651-687-9835 *Fax:* 651-687-9836, pg 42

Spagnuolo, Mary, Amy Writing Awards, PO Box 16091, Lansing, MI 48901-6091 *Tel:* 517-323-6233 *Fax:* 517-321-2572 *E-mail:* amyfoundtn@aol.com *Web Site:* www.amyfound.org, pg 759

Spahr, Dianne L, Forest House Publishing Co Inc & HTS Books, PO Box 13350, Chandler, AZ 85248 *Tel:* 480-802-1955 *Toll Free Tel:* 800-394-READ (394-7323) *Fax:* 480-802-1957 *E-mail:* info@forest-house.com *Web Site:* www.forest-house.com, pg 98

Spahr, Roy, Forest House Publishing Co Inc & HTS Books, PO Box 13350, Chandler, AZ 85248 *Tel:* 480-802-1955 *Toll Free Tel:* 800-394-READ (394-7323) *Fax:* 480-802-1957 *E-mail:* info@forest-house.com *Web Site:* www.forest-house.com, pg 98

Spain, Cathy, National League of Cities, 1301 Pennsylvania Ave NW, Washington, DC 20004-1763 *Tel:* 202-626-3000 *Fax:* 202-626-3043 *Web Site:* www.nlc.org, pg 184

Spalding, Jan, Harcourt School Publishers, 6277 Sea Harbor Dr, Orlando, FL 32887 *Tel:* 407-345-2000 *Toll Free Tel:* 800-225-5425 (cust serv) *Fax:* 407-352-3445 *Toll Free Fax:* 800-874-6418 *E-mail:* hbspcs@hbschool.com *Web Site:* www.harcourtschool.com, pg 114

Sparacio, Theresa, Paulist Press, 997 Macarthur Blvd, Mahwah, NJ 07430 *Tel:* 201-825-7300 *Toll Free Tel:* 800-218-1903 *Fax:* 201-825-8345 *Toll Free Fax:* 800-836-3161 (orders) *E-mail:* info@paulistpress.com *Web Site:* www.paulistpress.com, pg 206

Sparr, Babette, Sandra Dijkstra Literary Agency, 1155 Camino del Mar, PMB 515, Del Mar, CA 92014-2605 *Tel:* 858-755-3115 *Fax:* 858-794-2822 *E-mail:* sdla@dijkstraagency.com, pg 627

Spatt, Hartley, William Morris Society in the United States Fellowships, PO Box 53263, Washington, DC 20009 *Web Site:* www.morrissociety.org, pg 790

Spatz, Bruce, John Wiley & Sons Inc Education Publishing Group, 111 River St, Hoboken, NJ 07030 *Tel:* 201-748-6000 *Fax:* 201-748-6088 *E-mail:* info@wiley.com *Web Site:* www.wiley.com, pg 300

Spaulding, Richard M, Scholastic Inc, 557 Broadway, New York, NY 10012 *Tel:* 212-343-4469 *Toll Free Tel:* 800-scholastic *Fax:* 212-343-6930 *Web Site:* www.scholastic.com, pg 241

Spear, Cindy, Church Growth Institute, PO Box 7, Elkton, MD 21922-0007 *Tel:* 434-525-0022 *Toll Free Tel:* 800-553-4769 (orders only) *Fax:* 434-525-0608 *Toll Free Fax:* 800-644-4729 (orders only) *E-mail:* cgimail@churchgrowth.org *Web Site:* www.churchgrowth.org, pg 62

Spear, Garry, Consumer Press, 13326 SW 28 St, Suite 102, Fort Lauderdale, FL 33330-1102 *Tel:* 954-370-9153 *Fax:* 954-472-1008 *E-mail:* bookguest@aol.com *Web Site:* consumerpress.com, pg 67

Spear, Jody, Aaron-Spear, PO Box 42, Harborside, ME 04642 *Tel:* 207-326-8764, pg 589

Speck, Vicky, ABC-CLIO, 130 Cremona Dr, Santa Barbara, CA 93117 *Tel:* 805-968-1911 *Toll Free Tel:* 800-368-6868 *Fax:* 805-685-9685 *E-mail:* sales@abc-clio.com *Web Site:* www.abc-clio.com, pg 3

Spector, Robert Donald, The George Polk Awards, The Brooklyn Campus, University Plaza, Brooklyn, NY 11201 *Tel:* 718-488-1115 *Fax:* 718-246-6302, pg 799

Speirs, Lynn, Ingenix Inc, 2525 Lake Park Blvd, Salt Lake City, UT 84120 *Tel:* 801-982-3000 *Toll Free Tel:* 800-765-6014 *Web Site:* www.ingenix.com, pg 133

Speller, Robert E B Jr, Robert Speller & Sons, Publishers Inc, Times Sq Sta, New York, NY 10108-0461 *Tel:* 212-473-0333, pg 255

Speller, Robert E B Sr, Robert Speller & Sons, Publishers Inc, Times Sq Sta, New York, NY 10108-0461 *Tel:* 212-473-0333, pg 255

Spence, Thomas, Spence Publishing Co, 111 Cole St, Dallas, TX 75207 *Tel:* 214-939-1700 *Fax:* 214-939-1800 *Web Site:* www.spencepublishing.com, pg 255

Spencer, Darrell, Ohio University, English Dept, Creative Writing Program, Ohio University, English Dept, Ellis Hall, Athens, OH 45701 *Tel:* 740-593-2838 *Fax:* 740-593-2818 *Web Site:* www.english.ohio.edu/index.html, pg 753

Spencer, Melanie, Phaidon Press Inc, 180 Varick St, 14th fl, New York, NY 10014 *Tel:* 212-652-5400 *Toll Free Tel:* 800-759-0190 (cust serv) *Fax:* 212-652-5410 *Toll Free Fax:* 800-286-9471 (cust serv) *E-mail:* ussales@phaidon.com *Web Site:* www.phaidon.com, pg 211

Sperling, Ehud C, Bear & Co Inc, One Park St, Rochester, VT 05767 *Tel:* 802-767-3174 *Toll Free Tel:* 800-932-3277 *Fax:* 802-767-3726 *E-mail:* orders@InnerTraditions.com *Web Site:* InnerTraditions.com, pg 34

Sperling, Ehud C, Inner Traditions International Ltd, One Park St, Rochester, VT 05767 *Tel:* 802-767-3174 *Toll Free Tel:* 800-246-8648 *Fax:* 802-767-3726 *E-mail:* orders@InnerTraditions.com *Web Site:* www.InnerTraditions.com, pg 134

Sperry, Rod Meade, Wisdom Publications Inc, 199 Elm St, Somerville, MA 02144 Tel: 617-776-7416 Fax: 617-776-7841 E-mail: info@wisdompubs.org Web Site: www.wisdompubs.org, pg 301

Spicciati, Kathy, Insurance Institute of America Inc, 720 Providence Rd, Malvern, PA 19355 Tel: 610-644-2100 Toll Free Tel: 800-644-2101 Fax: 610-640-9576 E-mail: cserv@cpcuiia.org Web Site: www.aicpcu.org, pg 135

Spicer, Charles, St Martin's Press Trade Division, 175 Fifth Ave, New York, NY 10010 E-mail: firstname. lastname@stmartins.com Web Site: www.stmartins. com; www.minotaurbooks.com, pg 239

Spicer, Ed, The Pennsylvania State University Press, 820 N University Dr, University Support Bldg 1, Suite C, University Park, PA 16802-1003 Tel: 814-865-1327 Toll Free Tel: 800-326-9180 Fax: 814-863-1408 Toll Free Fax: 877 7782665 Web Site: www.psupress.org, pg 209

Spiegel, Cindy, Riverhead Books (Hardcover), 375 Hudson St, New York, NY 10014 Tel: 212-366-2000 E-mail: online@penguinputnam.com Web Site: www. penguin.com, pg 233

Spiegel, Robert, SouthWest Writers Conference Series, 3721 Morris St NE, Suite A, Albuquerque, NM 87111-3611 Tel: 505-265-9485 Fax: 505-265-9483 E-mail: swriters@aol.com Web Site: www. southwestwriters.org, pg 747

Spiegelman, Willard, John H McGinnis Memorial Award, 307 Fondren Library W, 6404 Hilltop Lane, Dallas, TX 75275-0374 Tel: 214-768-1037 Fax: 214-768-1408 E-mail: swr@mail.smu.edu Web Site: www. southwestreview.org, pg 788

Spiegelman, Willard, Elizabeth Matchett Stover Memorial Award, 307 Fondren Library W, 6404 Hilltop Lane, Dallas, TX 75275-0374 Tel: 214-768-1037 Fax: 214-768-1408 E-mail: swr@mail.smu.edu Web Site: www.southwestreview.org, pg 807

Spieler, F Joseph, The Spieler Agency, 154 W 57 St, 13th fl, Rm 135, New York, NY 10019 Tel: 212-757-4439 Web Site: spieleragency.com, pg 656

Spiers, Herb, SI International, 43 E 19 St, New York, NY 10003 Tel: 212-254-4996 Fax: 212-995-0911 E-mail: info@si-i.com Web Site: www.si-i.com, pg 667

Spike, John T, Abaris Books, 64 Wall St, Norwalk, CT 06850 Tel: 203-838-8402 Fax: 203-849-9181 E-mail: abarisbooks@abarisbooks.com Web Site: abarisbooks.com, pg 2

Spilhaus, A F Jr, American Geophysical Union (AGU), 2000 Florida Ave NW, Washington, DC 20009 Tel: 202-462-6900 Toll Free Tel: 800-966-2481 (North America) Fax: 202-328-0566 E-mail: service@agu.org Web Site: www.agu.org, pg 14

Spinelli, Kathleen, Brands-to-Books Inc, 155 W 72 St, Suite 302, New York, NY 10023 Tel: 212-362-6957 Fax: 212-874-2892 E-mail: agents@brandstobooks. com Web Site: www.brandstobooks.com, pg 622

Spinelli, Richard J, William S Hein & Co Inc, 1285 Main St, Buffalo, NY 14209-1987 Tel: 716-882-2600 Toll Free Tel: 800-828-7571 Fax: 716-883-8100 E-mail: mail@wshein.com Web Site: www.wshein. com, pg 120

Spinner, Dianna, The PRS Group Inc, 6320 Fly Rd, East Syracuse, NY 13057 Tel: 315-431-0511 Fax: 315-431-0200 E-mail: custserv@prsgroup.com Web Site: www. prsgroup.com, pg 220

Spiselman, David, CyclopsMedia.com, 1076 Eagle Dr, Salinas, CA 93905 Tel: 831-776-9500 Fax: 831-422-5915 E-mail: custserv@cyclopsmedia.com Web Site: www.cyclopsmedia.com, pg 75

Spitler, Curtis, Hampton-Brown Co Inc, 26385 Carmel Rancho Blvd, Carmel, CA 93923 Tel: 831-625-3666 Toll Free Tel: 800-933-3510 Fax: 831-625-8619 E-mail: customerservice@hampton-brown.com Web Site: www.hampton-brown.com, pg 113

Spitler, Donna, Center for Strategic & International Studies, 1800 "K" St NW, Washington, DC 20006 Tel: 202-775-3119 Fax: 202-775-3199 E-mail: books@csis.org Web Site: www.csis.org, pg 57

Spitzer, Anne Lise, Alfred A Knopf, 1745 Broadway, New York, NY 10019 Tel: 212-751-2600 Toll Free Tel: 800-638-6460 Fax: 212-572-2593 Web Site: www. randomhouse.com/knopf, pg 146

Spitzer, Philip, Philip G Spitzer Literary Agency, 50 Talmage Farm Lane, East Hampton, NY 11937 Tel: 631-329-3650 Fax: 631-329-3651 E-mail: spitzer516@aol.com, pg 657

Spizzirri, Linda, Spizzirri Press Inc, PO Box 9397, Rapid City, SD 57709-9397 Tel: 605-348-2749 Toll Free Tel: 800-325-9819 Fax: 605-348-6251 Toll Free Fax: 800-322-9819 E-mail: spizzpub@aol.com Web Site: www.spizzirri.com, pg 256

Spooner, Michael, May Swenson Poetry Award, 7800 Old Main Hill, Logan, UT 84322-7800 Tel: 435-797-1362 Fax: 435-797-0313 Web Site: www.usu. edu/usupress, pg 807

Spooner, Michael, Utah State University Press, 7800 Old Main Hill, Logan, UT 84322-7800 Tel: 435-797-1362 Toll Free Tel: 800-239-9974 Fax: 435-797-0313 Web Site: www.usu.edu/usupress, pg 289

Sprague, Lori, American Mathematical Society, 201 Charles St, Providence, RI 02904-2294 Tel: 401-455-4000 Toll Free Tel: 800-321-4267 Fax: 401-331-3842; 401-455-4046 (cust serv) E-mail: ams@ams.org Web Site: www.ams.org, pg 16

Sprague, Peter, Piano Press, 1425 Ocean Ave, Suite 6, Del Mar, CA 92014 Tel: 619-884-1401 Fax: 858-459-3376 E-mail: pianopress@aol.com Web Site: www. pianopress.com, pg 212

Sprague, Sydney, My Chaotic Life™, 23062 La Cadena Dr, Laguna Hills, CA 92653 Tel: 949-380-7510 Toll Free Tel: 800-426-0099 Fax: 949-380-7575 Web Site: www.mychaoticlife.com, pg 181

Sprague, Sydney Jae, Walter Foster Publishing Inc, 23062 La Cadena Dr, Laguna Hills, CA 92653 Tel: 949-380-7510 Toll Free Tel: 800-426-0099 Fax: 949-380-7575 Web Site: www.walterfoster.com, pg 99

Sprance, Elaine, LDA Publishers, 42-46 209 St, Bayside, NY 11361-2747 Tel: 718-224-9484 Toll Free Tel: 888-388-9887 Fax: 718-224-9487 Web Site: www. ldapublishers.com, pg 150

Springer, P G, P Gregory Springer, 206 Wood St, Urbana, IL 61801 Tel: 217-239-4800 Fax: 775-459-4675 Web Site: 8am.com, pg 611

Springer, Dr Ursula, Springer Publishing Co Inc, 11 W 42 St, New York, NY 10036 Tel: 212-431-4370 Toll Free Tel: 877-687-7476 Fax: 212-941-7842 E-mail: springer@springerpub.com Web Site: www. springerpub.com, pg 256

Springstead, Phil, Triumph Books, 601 S LaSalle St, Suite 500, Chicago, IL 60605 Tel: 312-939-3330 Toll Free Tel: 800-335-5323 Fax: 312-663-3557 E-mail: orders@triumphbooks.com Web Site: www. triumphbooks.com, pg 276

Sprinkel, Elizabeth A, American Institute for CPCU & Insurance Institute of America, 720 Providence Rd, Malvern, PA 19355-0716 Tel: 610-644-2100 Toll Free Tel: 800-644-2101 Fax: 610-640-9576; 610-644-7629 E-mail: cserv@cpcuiia.org Web Site: www.aicpcu.org, pg 14

Srinivasan, Seetha, University Press of Mississippi, 3825 Ridgewood Rd, Jackson, MS 39211-6492 Tel: 601-432-6205 Toll Free Tel: 800-737-7788 Fax: 601-432-6217 E-mail: press@ihl.state.ms.us Web Site: www. upress.state.ms.us, pg 287

Sroka, Marge, Society for Protective Coating, 40 24 St, 6th fl, Pittsburgh, PA 15222-4656 Tel: 412-281-2331 Fax: 412-281-9992 E-mail: books@sspc.org Web Site: www.sspc.org, pg 251

St John, David W, Elderberry Press LLC, 1393 Old Homestead Dr, 2nd fl, Oakland, OR 97462-9506 Tel: 541-459-6043 Fax: 541-459-6043 Web Site: www. elderberrypress.com, pg 88

St John, Mary Colman, The New Press, 38 Greene St, 4th fl, New York, NY 10013 Tel: 212-629-8802 Toll Free Tel: 800-233-4830 (orders) Fax: 212-629-8617 Toll Free Fax: 800-458-6515 E-mail: newpress@ thenewpress.com Web Site: www.thenewpress.com, pg 188

St Paul, Helen, Resource Publications Inc, 160 E Virginia St, Suite 290, San Jose, CA 95112-5876 Tel: 408-286-8505 Fax: 408-287-8748 E-mail: orders@rpinet.com Web Site: www.rpinet.com, pg 231

St Thomasino, Carol, Palgrave Macmillan, 175 Fifth Ave, New York, NY 10010 Tel: 212-982-3900 Fax: 212-777-6359 E-mail: firstname.lastname@ palgrave-usa.com Web Site: www.palgrave.com, pg 202

Stackler, Ed, Stackler Editorial Agency, 555 Lincoln Ave, Alameda, CA 94501 Tel: 510-814-9694 Fax: 510-814-9694 E-mail: stackler@aol.com Web Site: www.fictioneditor.com, pg 612

Stacy, Connie, Abingdon Press, 201 Eighth Ave S, Nashville, TN 37203-3919 Tel: 615-749-6290 (publicist); 615-749-6000; 615-749-6451 (sales) Toll Free Tel: 800-251-3320 Fax: 615-749-6056 Web Site: www.abingdonpress.com, pg 3

Stade, George, Fine Communications, 322 Eighth Ave, 15th fl, New York, NY 10001 Tel: 212-595-3500 Fax: 212-595-3779, pg 96

Stafford, John, Writers' Haven Writers (WHW), 2244 Fourth Ave, San Diego, CA 92101 Tel: 619-696-0569, pg 703

Stahl, Jeanine, Colorado Railroad Museum, 17155 W 44 Ave, Golden, CO 80402 Tel: 303-279-4591 Toll Free Tel: 800-365-6263 Fax: 303-279-4229 E-mail: library@crrm.org Web Site: crrm.org, pg 65

Stahl, Levi, Association of American University Presses, 1427 E 60 St, Chicago, IL 60637 Tel: 773-702-7700; 773-702-7600 Toll Free Tel: 800-621-2736 (orders) Fax: 773-702-9756 (sales); 773-660-2235 (orders); 773-702-2708 E-mail: general@press.uchicago.edu Web Site: www.press.uchicago.edu, pg 26

Stahl, Nikki, Jenkins Group Inc, 400 W Front St, Suite 4-A, Traverse City, MI 49684 Tel: 231-933-0445 Toll Free Tel: 800-706-4636 Fax: 231-933-0448 E-mail: info@bookpublishing.com Web Site: www. bookpublishing.com, pg 602

Stainton, Elaine, Harry N Abrams Inc, 100 Fifth Ave, New York, NY 10011 Tel: 212-206-7715 Toll Free Tel: 800-345-1359 Fax: 212-645-8437 E-mail: webmaster@abramsbooks.com Web Site: www.abramsbooks.com, pg 3

Stair, Lynne, Sopris West Educational Services, 4093 Specialty Place, Longmont, CO 80504 Tel: 303-651-2829 Toll Free Tel: 800-547-6747 Fax: 303-776-5934 E-mail: customerservice@sopriswest.com Web Site: www.sopriswest.com, pg 253

Staley, Larry, Foster City Writers Contest, 650 Shell Blvd, Foster City, CA 94404 Tel: 650-286-3380 Web Site: www.fostercity.org, pg 774

Staley, Shane Ryan, Delirium Books, PO Box 338, North Webster, IN 46555 Tel: 574-594-3200 Web Site: www. deliriumbooks.com, pg 78

Stalmaster, Hal, The Artists Group Ltd, 10100 Santa Monica, Suite 2490, Los Angeles, CA 90067 Tel: 310-552-1100 Fax: 310-277-9513, pg 619

Stamets, Lisa, Book Sales Inc, 114 Northfield Ave, Edison, NJ 08837 Tel: 732-225-0530 Toll Free Tel: 800-526-7257 Fax: 732-225-2257 E-mail: sales@ booksalesusa.com; customerservice@booksalesusa.com Web Site: www.booksalesusa.com, pg 43

Stamm, Courtney, Robert F Kennedy Book Awards, 1367 Connecticut Ave NW, Suite 200, Washington, DC 20036-1859 Tel: 202-463-7575 E-mail: info@ rfkmemorial.org Web Site: www.rfkmemorial.org, pg 782

Stampfel, Peter, DAW Books Inc, 375 Hudson St, 3rd fl, New York, NY 10014 *Tel:* 212-366-2096 *Fax:* 212-366-2090 *E-mail:* daw@us.penguingroup. com *Web Site:* www.dawbooks.com, pg 77

Stamps, Shelly, Conciliar Press, 10090 "A" Hwy 9, Ben Lomond, CA 95005 *Tel:* 831-336-5118 *Toll Free Tel:* 800-967-7377 *Fax:* 831-336-8882 *E-mail:* marketing@conciliarpress.com *Web Site:* www.conciliarpress.com, pg 66

Standley, Will, Wescott Cove Publishing Co, PO Box 560989, Rockledge, FL 32956 *Tel:* 321-690-2224 *Fax:* 321-690-0853 *E-mail:* customerservice@ wescottcovepublishing.com *Web Site:* www. wescottcovepublishing.com, pg 296

Stane, Kate, Avery, 375 Hudson St, New York, NY 10014 *Tel:* 212-366-2000 *Fax:* 212-366-2643 *E-mail:* online@penguinputnam.com *Web Site:* www. penguinputnam.com, pg 29

Stanek, Ruth, Binghamton University Writing Program, c/o Dept of English, PO Box 6000, Binghamton, NY 13902-6000 *Tel:* 607-777-2168 *Fax:* 607-777-2408, pg 751

Stanford, Edward, McGraw-Hill Higher Education, 1333 Burr Ridge Pkwy, Burr Ridge, IL 60527 *Tel:* 630-789-4000 *Toll Free Tel:* 800-338-3987 (cust serv) *Fax:* 614-755-5645 (cust serv) *Web Site:* www.mhhe. com, pg 167

Stanford, Eric, Stanford Creative Services, 7645 N Union Blvd, Suite 235, Colorado Springs, CO 80920 *Tel:* 719-599-7808 *Fax:* 719-590-7555 *Web Site:* www. stanfordcreative.com, pg 612

Stanhope, Faith, Open Road Publishing, PO Box 284, Cold Spring Harbor, NY 11724-0284 *Tel:* 631-692-7172 *Fax:* 631-692-7193 *E-mail:* jopenroad@aol.com, pg 198

Stanke, Gaila, Coffragants & Pocketaudio, 5400 rue Louis-Badaillac, Carignan, PQ J3L 4A7, Canada *Tel:* 450-447-6114 *Fax:* 450-658-1377 *E-mail:* coffragants@videotron.ca *Web Site:* www. coffragants.com, pg 540

Stanley, Andrew, Random House Inc, 1745 Broadway, New York, NY 10019 *Tel:* 212-782-9000 *Toll Free Tel:* 800-726-0600 *Web Site:* www.randomhouse, pg 226

Stanley, Andrew, Random House Sales & Marketing, 1745 Broadway, New York, NY 10019 *Fax:* 212-782-9000, pg 227

Stanley, Autumn, Procrustes/Sophia Editorial Services, 241 Bonita Los Trancos Woods, Portola Valley, CA 94028-8103 *Tel:* 650-851-1847 *Fax:* 650-210-9832, pg 608

Stanley, Cullen, Janklow & Nesbit Associates, 445 Park Ave, New York, NY 10022 *Tel:* 212-421-1700 *Fax:* 212-980-3671 *E-mail:* postmaster@janklow.com, pg 636

Stanley, George, John Wiley & Sons Inc Professional & Trade Group, 111 River St, Hoboken, NJ 07030 *Tel:* 201-748-6000 *Toll Free Tel:* 800-225-5945 (cust serv) *Fax:* 201-748-6088 *E-mail:* info@wiley.com *Web Site:* www.wiley.com, pg 300

Stanley, Robin, Standard Publishing Co, 8121 Hamilton Ave, Cincinnati, OH 45231 *Tel:* 513-931-4050 *Toll Free Tel:* 800-543-1301 *Fax:* 513-931-0950 *Toll Free Tel:* 877-867-5751 *E-mail:* customerservice@ standardpub.com *Web Site:* www.standardpub.com, pg 257

Stanley, Sydney, Advantage Publishers Group, 5880 Oberlin Dr, San Diego, CA 92121 *Tel:* 858-457-2500 *Toll Free Tel:* 800-284-3580 *Fax:* 858-812-6476 *Toll Free Fax:* 800-499-3822 *E-mail:* apgcuserv@advmkt. com *Web Site:* www.advantagebooksonline.com, pg 6

Stanton, Alice, University of Oklahoma Press, 4100 28 Ave NW, Norman, OK 73069-8218 *Tel:* 405-325-2000 *Toll Free Tel:* 800-627-7377 (orders) *Fax:* 405-364-5798 (orders) *Toll Free Fax:* 800-735-0476 (orders) *E-mail:* oupress@ou.edu *Web Site:* www.oupress.com, pg 284

Stanton, Claire, Kluwer Academic Publishers, 101 Philip Dr, Assinippi Park, Norwell, MA 02061 *Tel:* 781-871-6600 *Fax:* 781-871-6528; 781-681-9045 (cust serv) *E-mail:* kluwer@wkap.com *Web Site:* www.wkap.nl, pg 146

Stanton, Joyce, Marshall Cavendish Corp, 99 White Plains Rd, Tarrytown, NY 10591-9001 *Tel:* 914-332-8888 *Fax:* 914-332-1888 *E-mail:* mcc@ marshallcavendish.com *Web Site:* www. marshallcavendish.com, pg 164

Stanton, Steve, Skysong Press, 35 Peter St S, Orillia, ON L3V 5A8, Canada *E-mail:* skysong@bconnex. net *Web Site:* www.bconnex.net/~skysong/index.html, pg 561

Stanton, William, H W Wilson Foundation, 950 University Ave, Bronx, NY 10452-4224 *Tel:* 718-588-8400 *Toll Free Tel:* 800-367-6770 *Fax:* 718-538-2716 *Toll Free Fax:* 800-367-6770 *E-mail:* custserv@ hwwilson.com *Web Site:* www.hwwilson.com, pg 705

Staples, Debra, SynergEbooks, 1235 Flat Shoals Rd, King, NC 27021 *Tel:* 336-994-2405 *Toll Free Tel:* 888-812-2533 *Fax:* 336-994-2405 *E-mail:* inquiries@synergebooks.com; synergebooks@ aol.com *Web Site:* www.synergebooks.com, pg 263

Stapleton, Janet, Beacon Hill Press of Kansas City, PO Box 419527, Kansas City, MO 64141-6527 *Tel:* 816-931-1900 *Toll Free Tel:* 800-877-0700 (retail order) *Fax:* 816-753-4071 *Toll Free Fax:* 800-849-9827 (order) *Web Site:* www.beaconhillbooks.com, pg 34

Stark, Jeffrey, North-South Center Press at the University of Miami, 1500 Monza Ave, Coral Gables, FL 33146 *Tel:* 305-284-6868 *Fax:* 305-284-6370 *Web Site:* www. miami.edu/nsc, pg 192

Stark, Linda, Interweave Press, 201 E Fourth St, Loveland, CO 80537 *Tel:* 970-669-7672 *Toll Free Tel:* 800-272-2193 *Fax:* 970-667-8317 *E-mail:* customerservice@interweave.com *Web Site:* www.interweave.com, pg 138

Stark, Patty, John Wiley & Sons Inc Education Publishing Group, 111 River St, Hoboken, NJ 07030 *Tel:* 201-748-6000 *Fax:* 201-748-6088 *E-mail:* info@ wiley.com *Web Site:* www.wiley.com, pg 300

Stark, Sheldon, Institute of Continuing Legal Education, 1020 Greene St, Ann Arbor, MI 48109-1444 *Tel:* 734-764-0533 *Toll Free Tel:* 877-229-4350 *Fax:* 734-763-2412 *Toll Free Fax:* 877-229-4351 *E-mail:* icle@ umich.edu *Web Site:* www.icle.org/, pg 135

Starkey, Vickie F, W D Farmer Residence Designer Inc, 2007 Montreal Rd, Tucker, GA 30084 *Tel:* 770-934-7380 *Toll Free Tel:* 800-225-7526; 800-221-7526 (GA) *Fax:* 770-934-1700 *E-mail:* wdfarmer@ wdfarmerplans.com *Web Site:* www.wdfarmerplans. com; www.homeplansbyfarmer.com, pg 95

Starman Hessel, Carolyn, Jewish Book Council, 15 E 26 St, 10th fl, New York, NY 10010-1579 *Tel:* 212-532-4949 (ext 297) *Fax:* 212-481-4174 *E-mail:* jbc@ jewishbooks.org *Web Site:* www.jewishbookcouncil. org, pg 689

Starnino, Carmine, Vehicule Press, 125 Place du Parc Sta, Montreal, PQ H2X 4A3, Canada *Tel:* 514-844-6073 *Fax:* 514-844-7543 *E-mail:* vp@vehiculepress. com *Web Site:* www.vehiculepress.com, pg 566

Starr, Leslie, Wesleyan University Press, 215 Long Lane, Middletown, CT 06459-0433 *Tel:* 860-685-7711 *Fax:* 860-685-7712 *Web Site:* www.wesleyan. edu/wespress, pg 296

Staten, Jay, American Quilter's Society, 5801 Kentucky Dam Rd, Paducah, KY 42002 *Tel:* 270-898-7903 *Toll Free Tel:* 800-626-5420 (orders) *Fax:* 270-898-8890 *E-mail:* info@aqsquilt.com *Web Site:* www.aqsquilt. com, pg 17

States, Barbara, Rockport Publishers, 33 Commercial St, Gloucester, MA 01930 *Tel:* 978-282-9590 *Fax:* 978-283-2742 *Web Site:* www.rockpub.com, pg 233

Staveteig, Timothy G, The Pilgrim Press/United Church Press, 700 Prospect Ave, Cleveland, OH 44115-1100 *Tel:* 216-736-3761 *Toll Free Tel:* 800-537-3394 (cust

serv) *Fax:* 216-736-2207 *E-mail:* thepilgrimpress@ thepilgrimpress.com *Web Site:* www.thepilgrimpress. com; www.theunitedchurchpress.com, pg 213

Stay, Chuck, Printing Industries of America Premier Print Award, 200 Deer Run Rd, Sewickley, PA 15143 *Tel:* 412-741-6860 *Fax:* 412-741-2311 *Web Site:* www. gain.net, pg 800

Stead, Tonya, Canadian Magazine Publishers Association, 425 Adelaide St W, Suite 700, Toronto, ON M5V 3C1, Canada *Tel:* 416-504-0274 *Fax:* 416-504-0437 *E-mail:* cmpainfo@cmpa.ca *Web Site:* www. cmpa.ca/; www.magomania.com, pg 683

Steadman, Karen, Coteau Books, 401-2206 Dewdney Ave, Regina, SK S4R 1H3, Canada *Tel:* 306-777-0170 *Toll Free Tel:* 800-440-4471 (Canada Only) *Fax:* 306-522-5152 *E-mail:* coteau@coteaubooks.com *Web Site:* www.coteaubooks.com, pg 541

Stearns, Neil, Don Buchwald & Associates Inc, 6500 Wilshire Blvd, Suite 2200, Los Angeles, CA 90048 *Tel:* 323-655-7400 *Fax:* 323-655-7470 *Web Site:* www. donbuchwald.com, pg 623

Stebbins, Dr Chad, International Society of Weekly Newspaper Editors, Missouri Southern State College, 3950 E Newman Rd, Joplin, MO 64501-1595 *Tel:* 417-625-9736 *Fax:* 417-659-4445 *Web Site:* www. mssc.edu/iswne, pg 689

Stebbins, Sheryl, Random House Reference, 1745 Broadway, New York, NY 10019 *Toll Free Tel:* 800-733-3000 *E-mail:* words@random.com; puzzles@ random.com, pg 227

Stebbins, Sheryl, Random House Value Publishing, 1745 Broadway, New York, NY 10019 *Tel:* 212-940-7422 *Fax:* 212-572-2114, pg 227

Stech, Marko R, Canadian Institute of Ukrainian Studies Press, University of Toronto, One Spadina Crescent, Rm 109, Toronto, ON M5S 2J5, Canada *Tel:* 416-978-6934 *Fax:* 416-978-2672 *E-mail:* cius@chass.utoronto. ca (edit off) *Web Site:* www.utoronto.ca/cius, pg 538

Steel, John W, Harbor Lights Press (HLP), PO Box 505, Gloucester City, NJ 08030-0505 *Tel:* 856-742-5810 *E-mail:* harborlightspress@yahoo.com *Web Site:* www. harborlightspress.com, pg 114

Steele, Jennifer, Backbeat Books, 600 Harrison St, San Francisco, CA 94107 *Tel:* 415-947-6615 *Toll Free Tel:* 866-222-5232 (orders only) *Fax:* 415-947-6015; 408-848-8294 (orders only) *E-mail:* books@ musicplayer.com; books@cmp.com *Web Site:* www. backbeatbooks.com, pg 30

Steele, Jennifer, CMP Books, 600 Harrison St, San Francisco, CA 94107 *Tel:* 415-947-6615; 408-848-3854 (orders) *Toll Free Tel:* 800-500-6875 (orders) *Fax:* 415-947-6015; 408-848-5784 (orders) *E-mail:* books@cmp.com *Web Site:* www.cmpbooks. com, pg 63

Steele, Lyle, Lyle Steele & Co Ltd Literary Agents, 511 E 73 St, Suite 6, New York, NY 10021 *Tel:* 212-288-2981, pg 657

Steele, Summer, Beyond Words Publishing Inc, 20827 NW Cornell Rd, Suite 500, Hillsboro, OR 97124-9808 *Tel:* 503-531-8700 *Fax:* 503-531-8773 *Web Site:* www. beyondword.com, pg 38

Steere, Michael, Down East Books, PO Box 679, Camden, ME 04843 *Tel:* 207-594-9544 *Toll Free Tel:* 800-766-1670 (ME only) *Fax:* 207-594-7215 *Web Site:* www.downeastbooks.com, pg 83

Steffen, Julia, Association of American University Presses, 1427 E 60 St, Chicago, IL 60637 *Tel:* 773-702-7700; 773-702-7600 *Toll Free Tel:* 800-621-2736 (orders) *Fax:* 773-702-9756 (sales); 773-660-2235 (orders); 773-702-2708 *E-mail:* general@press. uchicago.edu *Web Site:* www.press.uchicago.edu, pg 26

Steffens, Brian, National Newspaper Association, University of Missouri, 127-129 Neff Annex, Columbia, MO 65211-1200 *Tel:* 573-882-5800 *Toll Free Tel:* 800-829-4662 *Fax:* 703-884-5490 *E-mail:* info@nna.org *Web Site:* www.nna.org, pg 694

Steger, Damian, Saint Mary's Press, 702 Terrace Heights, Winona, MN 55987-1318 *Tel:* 507-457-7900 *Toll Free:* 800-533-8095 *Toll Free Fax:* 800-344-9225 *E-mail:* smpress@smp.org *Web Site:* www.smp.org, pg 239

Stehlik, Liate, Pocket Books, 1230 Avenue of the Americas, New York, NY 10020 *Toll Free Tel:* 800-456-6798 *Fax:* 212-698-7284 *E-mail:* consumer.customerservice@simonandschuster.com *Web Site:* www.simonsays.com, pg 215

Steidel, Lauren, Society for Industrial & Applied Mathematics, 3600 University City Science Ctr, Philadelphia, PA 19104-2688 *Tel:* 215-382-9800 *Toll Free Tel:* 800-447-7426 *Fax:* 215-386-7999 *E-mail:* siam@siam.org *Web Site:* www.siam.org, pg 251

Steiger, Bill, American College of Physician Executives, 4890 W Kennedy Blvd, Suite 200, Tampa, FL 33609 *Tel:* 813-287-2000 *Toll Free Tel:* 800-562-8088 *Fax:* 813-287-8993 *E-mail:* acpe@acpe.org *Web Site:* www.acpe.org, pg 12

Stein, Constance, Mystic Seaport, PO Box 6000, Mystic, CT 06355-0990 *Tel:* 860-572-0711 *Fax:* 860-572-5321 *Web Site:* www.mysticseaport.org, pg 181

Stein, Elizabeth, Free Press, 1230 Avenue of the Americas, New York, NY 10020 *Tel:* 212-698-7000 *Toll Free Tel:* 800-223-2345 (cust serv); 800-223-2336 (orders); 888-866-6631 (fulfillment), pg 100

Stein, George, Yucca Tree Press, 270 Avenida de Mesilla, Las Cruces, NM 88005 *Tel:* 505-525-9707 *Toll Free Tel:* 888-817-1990 *Fax:* 505-525-9711 *E-mail:* thefolks@barbed-wire.net *Web Site:* www.barbed-wire.net, pg 306

Stein, Jonathan, Open Road Publishing, PO Box 284, Cold Spring Harbor, NY 11724-0284 *Tel:* 631-692-7172 *Fax:* 631-692-7193 *E-mail:* jopenroad@aol.com, pg 198

Stein, Judith, The Author's Friend, 548 Ocean Blvd, No 12, Long Branch, NJ 07740 *Tel:* 732-571-8051 *Toll Free Tel:* 877-485-7689 *Toll Free Fax:* 877-485-7689 *E-mail:* authfriend@yahoo.com, pg 591

Stein, Karen, Phaidon Press Inc, 180 Varick St, 14th fl, New York, NY 10014 *Tel:* 212-652-5400 *Toll Free Tel:* 800-759-0190 (cust serv) *Fax:* 212-652-5410 *Toll Free Fax:* 800-286-9471 (cust serv) *E-mail:* ussales@phaidon.com *Web Site:* www.phaidon.com, pg 211

Stein, Kathy, American Psychiatric Publishing Inc, 1000 Wilson Blvd, Suite 1825, Arlington, VA 22209 *Tel:* 703-907-7322 *Toll Free Tel:* 800-368-5777 *Fax:* 703-907-1091 *E-mail:* appi@psych.org *Web Site:* www.appi.org, pg 16

Stein, Lonny R, Barron's Educational Series Inc, 250 Wireless Blvd, Hauppauge, NY 11788 *Tel:* 631-434-3311 *Toll Free Tel:* 800-645-3476 *Fax:* 631-434-3723 *E-mail:* info@barronseduc.com *Web Site:* www.barronseduc.com (Books can be purchased online), pg 32

Stein, Sherry, The Fraser Institute, 1770 Burrard St, 4th fl, Vancouver, BC V6J 3G7, Canada *Tel:* 604-688-0221 *Toll Free Tel:* 800-665-3558 *Fax:* 604-688-8539 *E-mail:* sales@fraserinstitute.ca *Web Site:* www.fraserinstitute.ca, pg 547

Steinberg, Eden, Shambhala Publications Inc, Horticultural Hall, 300 Massachusetts Ave, Boston, MA 02115 *Tel:* 617-424-0030 *Toll Free Tel:* 888-424-2329 (orders only) *Fax:* 617-236-1563; 303-665-5292 (orders only) *E-mail:* editors@shambhala.com *Web Site:* www.shambhala.com, pg 245

Steinberg, Lawrence, Modern Publishing, 155 E 55 St, New York, NY 10022 *Tel:* 212-826-0850 *Fax:* 212-759-9069 *Web Site:* www.modernpublishing.com, pg 176

Steinberg, Michael, Michael Steinberg Literary Agent, PO Box 274, Glencoe, IL 60022-0274 *Tel:* 847-835-4000 *Fax:* 847-835-8881 *E-mail:* michael14steinberg@comcast.net, pg 657

Steinberg, Shelli, Mark Sonder Productions, 250 W 57 St, Suite 1830, New York, NY 10107 *Tel:* 212-262-4600 *Fax:* 212-246-0197 *E-mail:* msonder@marksonderproductions.com *Web Site:* www.marksonderproductions.com, pg 670

Steinberger, David, Counterpoint Press, 387 Park Ave S, New York, NY 10016 *Tel:* 212-340-8100 *Fax:* 212-340-8135 (edit); 212-340-8115 *E-mail:* counterpointpress@perseusbooks.com *Web Site:* www.counterpointpress.com, pg 70

Steinberger, David, Da Capo Press Inc, 11 Cambridge Center, Cambridge, MA 02142 *Tel:* 617-252-5200 *Toll Free Tel:* 800-242-7737 (orders) *Fax:* 617-252-5285 *E-mail:* custserve@lrp.com *Web Site:* www.dacapopress.com, pg 75

Steinberger, David, The Perseus Books Group, 387 Park Ave S, 12th fl, New York, NY 10016 *Tel:* 212-340-8100 *Toll Free Tel:* 800-386-5656 (cust serv) *Fax:* 212-340-8115 *Web Site:* www.perseusbooksgroup.com, pg 210

Steinbicker, Earl, Hastings House/Daytrips Publishers, 2601 Wells Ave, Suite 161, Fern Park, FL 32730 *Tel:* 407-339-3600 *Toll Free Tel:* 800-206-7822 *Fax:* 407-339-5900 *E-mail:* hastings_daytrips@earthlink.net *Web Site:* www.hastingshousebooks.com; www.daytripsbooks.com, pg 117

Steinbuck, Helene, Blue Mountain Arts Inc, PO Box 4549, Boulder, CO 80306 *Tel:* 303-449-0536 *Toll Free Tel:* 800-473-2082 *Fax:* 303-417-6496 *Toll Free Fax:* 800-256-1213 *E-mail:* booksbma@mindspring.com; ordersbma@mindspring.com *Web Site:* www.sps.com, pg 41

Steiner, Karen, Research Press, 2612 N Mattis Ave, Champaign, IL 61822 *Tel:* 217-352-3273 *Toll Free Tel:* 800-519-2707 *Fax:* 217-352-1221 *E-mail:* rp@researchpress.com *Web Site:* www.researchpress.com, pg 231

Steiner, Mark, Through the Bible Publishers, 2643 Midpoint Dr, Fort Collins, CO 80524-3216 *Tel:* 970-484-8483 *Toll Free Tel:* 800-284-0158 *Fax:* 970-495-6700 *E-mail:* discipleland@throughthebible.com *Web Site:* www.throughthebible.com, pg 271

Steinhardt, David J, IDEAlliance, 100 Daingerfield Rd, Alexandria, VA 22314 *Tel:* 703-837-1070 *Fax:* 703-837-1072 *E-mail:* info@gca.org *Web Site:* www.idealliance.org, pg 688

Steinhilber, Katy, Dorchester Publishing Co Inc, 200 Madison Ave, Suite 2000, New York, NY 10016 *Tel:* 212-725-8811 *Toll Free Tel:* 800-481-9191 (order dept) *Fax:* 212-532-1054 *E-mail:* dorchedits@dorchesterpub.com *Web Site:* www.dorchesterpub.com, pg 82

Stelzig, Christopher, Entomological Society of America, 9301 Annapolis Rd, Lanham, MD 20706-3115 *Tel:* 301-731-4535 *Fax:* 301-731-4538 *E-mail:* pubs@entsoc.org *Web Site:* www.entsoc.org, pg 91

Stensvaag, Christina, Codie Awards, 1090 Vermont Ave NW, 6th fl, Washington, DC 20005 *Tel:* 202-289-7442 *Fax:* 202-289-7097 *E-mail:* codieawards@siia.net *Web Site:* www.siia.net, pg 768

Stensvaag, Christina, Software & Information Industry Association (SIIA), 1090 Vermont Ave NW, 6th fl, Washington, DC 20005 *Tel:* 202-289-7442 *Fax:* 202-289-7097 *E-mail:* info@siia.net *Web Site:* www.siia.net, pg 700

Stepaniak, Dennis, Thomson Gale, 27500 Drake Rd, Farmington Hills, MI 48331-3535 *Tel:* 248-699-4253 *Toll Free Tel:* 800-347-4253 *Fax:* 248-699-8070 *Toll Free Fax:* 800-414-5043 *E-mail:* galeord@gale.com *Web Site:* www.gale.com, pg 270

Stepansky, Paul, The Analytic Press, 101 West St, Hillsdale, NJ 07642 *Tel:* 201-358-9477; 201-236-9500 *Toll Free Tel:* 800-926-6579 (orders only); 800-627-0629 (journal orders) *Fax:* 201-358-4700 (edit); 201-760-3735 (orders only) *E-mail:* tap@analyticpress.com *Web Site:* www.analyticpress.com, pg 19

Stephens, Christopher P, Ultramarine Publishing Co Inc, 12 Washington Ave, Hastings-on-Hudson, NY 10706 *Tel:* 914-478-1339 *E-mail:* washbook@sprynet.com, pg 278

Stephens, Edna C, EDCO Publishing Inc, 2648 Lapeer Rd, Auburn Hills, MI 48326 *Tel:* 248-475-4678 *Toll Free Tel:* 888-510-3326 *Fax:* 248-475-9122 *E-mail:* info@edcopublishing.com *Web Site:* www.edcopublishing.com, pg 87

Stephens, Ken, Broadman & Holman Publishers, 127 Ninth Ave N, Nashville, TN 37234-0114 *Tel:* 615-251-2520 *Fax:* 615-251-5004 *Web Site:* www.broadmanholman.com, pg 48

Stephens, Marvin, Editorial Bautista Independiente, 3417 Kenilworth Blvd, Sebring, FL 33870 *Tel:* 863-382-6350 *Toll Free Tel:* 800-398-7187 *Fax:* 863-382-8650 *E-mail:* info@ebi-bmm.org *Web Site:* www.ebi-bmm.org, pg 87

Stephens, Michael R, Kalmbach Publishing Co, 21027 Crossroads Circle, Waukesha, WI 53187 *Tel:* 262-796-8776 *Toll Free Tel:* 800-533-6644 *Fax:* 262-796-1615 (sales & cust serv) *Web Site:* www.kalmbach.com, pg 143

Stephensen, Don, Bethany House Publishers/Baker Bookhouse, PO Box 6287, Grand Rapids, MI 49516-6287 *Tel:* 616-676-9185 *Toll Free Tel:* 800-877-2665 *Web Site:* www.bethanyhouse.com; www.bakerpublishinggroup.com, pg 37

Stephenson, Don, Baker Books, PO Box 6287, Grand Rapids, MI 49516-6287 *Tel:* 616-676-9185 *Toll Free Tel:* 800-877-2665; 800-679-1957 *Fax:* 616-676-9573 *Toll Free Fax:* 800-398-3110 *Web Site:* www.bakerpublishinggroup.com, pg 30

Sterling, Anne, Sundance Publishing, One Beeman Rd, Northborough, MA 01532 *Tel:* 508-571-6500 *Toll Free Tel:* 800-343-8204 *Fax:* 508-571-6510 *Toll Free Fax:* 800-456-2419 *E-mail:* info@sundancepub.com *Web Site:* www.sundancepub.com, pg 262

Sterling, Cynthia, SterlingHouse Publisher Inc, 7436 Washington Ave, Suite 200, Pittsburgh, PA 15218 *Tel:* 412-271-8800 *Toll Free Tel:* 888-542-2665 *Fax:* 412-271-8600 *E-mail:* info@sterlinghousepublisher.com *Web Site:* www.sterlinghousepublisher.com, pg 259

Sterling, John, Henry Holt and Company, LLC, 115 W 18 St, New York, NY 10011 *Tel:* 212-886-9200 *Toll Free Tel:* 888-330-8477 (orders) *Fax:* 212-633-0748 *E-mail:* publicity@hholt.com *Web Site:* www.henryholt.com, pg 124

Stern, Debbie, AJL Scholarship, 15 E 26 St, New York, NY 10010-1579 *Tel:* 212-725-5359 *Fax:* 212-481-4174 *E-mail:* ajl@jewishbooks.org *Web Site:* www.jewishlibraries.org, pg 758

Stern, Gloria, Gloria Stern Agency, 2929 Buffalo Speedway, Suite 2111, Houston, TX 77098 *Tel:* 713-963-8360 *Fax:* 713-963-8460 *E-mail:* dstern1391@earthlink.net, pg 657

Stern, Ina, Algonquin Books of Chapel Hill, 127 Kingston Dr, Suite 105, Chapel Hill, NC 27514 *Tel:* 919-967-0108 *Fax:* 919-933-0272 *E-mail:* dialogue@algonquin.com *Web Site:* www.algonquin.com, pg 8

Stern, Jeffrey, Bonus Books Inc, 1452 Second St, Santa Monica, CA 90403 *Tel:* 310-260-9400 *Toll Free Tel:* 800-225-3775 *E-mail:* webmaster@bonusbooks.com *Web Site:* www.bonusbooks.com, pg 43

Stern, Jeffrey, Precept Press, 1452 Second St, Santa Monica, CA 90401 *Tel:* 310-260-9400 *Fax:* 310-260-9494 *E-mail:* webmaster@bonusbooks.com *Web Site:* www.bonusbooks.com, pg 217

Stern, Molly, Viking, 375 Hudson St, New York, NY 10014 *Tel:* 212-366-2000 *E-mail:* online@penguinputnam.com *Web Site:* www.penguin.com, pg 290

Stern, Walter B, Hartmore House Inc, 304 E 49 St, New York, NY 10017 *Tel:* 203-384-2284; 212-319-6666 *Fax:* 203-579-9109, pg 116

Stern, Walter B, Prayer Book Press Inc, 1363 Fairfield Ave, Bridgeport, CT 06605 *Tel:* 203-384-2284 *Fax:* 203-579-9109, pg 217

Sternlicht, Moshe, Moznaim Publishing Corp, 4304 12 Ave, Brooklyn, NY 11219 *Tel:* 718-438-7680 *Toll Free Tel:* 800-364-5118 *Fax:* 718-438-1305, pg 180

Sternlight, Judith, Random House Publishing Group, 1745 Broadway, New York, NY 10019 *Toll Free Tel:* 800-200-3552 *Toll Free Fax:* 800-200-3552 *Web Site:* www.randomhouse.com, pg 227

Stero, Paul, Hippocrene Books Inc, 171 Madison Ave, New York, NY 10016 *Tel:* 212-685-4371 (edit); 718-454-2366 (sales & cust serv) *Fax:* 718-454-1391 (cust serv); 212-779-9338 (edit) *Toll Free Fax:* 800-809-3855 (sales) *E-mail:* orders@hippocrenebooks.com *Web Site:* www.hippocrenebooks.com, pg 123

Stetter, John F, Southern Illinois University Press, PO Box 3697, Carbondale, IL 62902-3697 *Tel:* 618-453-2281 *Toll Free Tel:* 800-346-2680 *Fax:* 618-453-1221 *Toll Free Fax:* 800-346-2681 *E-mail:* jstetter@siu.edu *Web Site:* www.siu.edu/~siupress, pg 254

Stetzinger, Nancy, Lucent Books Inc, 15822 Bernardo Center Dr, Suite C, San Diego, CA 92127 *Tel:* 858-485-7424 *Fax:* 858-485-9549 *E-mail:* info@gale.com *Web Site:* www.gale.com/lucent, pg 159

Steven, Peter, Between the Lines, 720 Bathurst St, No 404, Toronto, ON M5S 2R4, Canada *Tel:* 416-535-9914 *Toll Free Tel:* 800-718-7201 *Fax:* 416-535-1484 *E-mail:* btlbooks@web.ca *Web Site:* www.btlbooks.com, pg 536

Stevens, Annabelle, Domhan Books, 9511 Shore Rd, Suite 514, Brooklyn, NY 11209 *Tel:* 718-680-4362 *Toll Free Fax:* 888-823-4770 *E-mail:* domhan@att.net *Web Site:* www.domhanbooks.com, pg 82

Stevens, Elliot L, Central Conference of American Rabbis/CCAR Press, 355 Lexington Ave, 18th fl, New York, NY 10017 *Tel:* 212-972-3636 *Toll Free Tel:* 800-935-2227 *Fax:* 212-692-0819 *E-mail:* ccarpress@ccarnet.org *Web Site:* www.ccarpress.org, pg 57

Stevens, Josh, Missouri Historical Society Press, PO Box 11940, St Louis, MO 63112-0040 *Tel:* 314-454-3150 *Fax:* 314-454-3162 *E-mail:* dtz@mohistory.org *Web Site:* www.mohistory.org, pg 175

Stevens, Marilyn R, Houghton Mifflin School Division, 222 Berkeley St, Boston, MA 02116-3764, pg 126

Stevens, Martin, Forum Publishing Co, 383 E Main St, Centerport, NY 11721 *Tel:* 631-754-5000 *Fax:* 631-754-0630 *Web Site:* www.forumbooks.com, pg 99

Stevens, R Blake, Collector Grade Publications Inc, PO Box 1046, Cobourg, ON K9A 4W5, Canada *Tel:* 905-342-3434 *Fax:* 905-342-3688 *E-mail:* info@collectorgrade.com *Web Site:* www.collectorgrade.com, pg 541

Stevenson, Dinah, Clarion Books, 215 Park Ave S, New York, NY 10003 *Tel:* 212-420-5800 *Toll Free Tel:* 800-225-3362 (orders) *Fax:* 212-420-5855 *Web Site:* www.clarion.com, pg 62

Stevenson, Dinah, Houghton Mifflin Trade & Reference Division, 222 Berkeley St, Boston, MA 02116-3764 *Tel:* 617-351-5000 *Toll Free Tel:* 800-225-3362 *Web Site:* www.houghtonmifflinbooks.com, pg 126

Stevenson, John, University of Washington Press, 1326 Fifth Ave, Suite 555, Seattle, WA 98101-2604 *Tel:* 206-543-4050; 206-543-8870 *Toll Free Tel:* 800-441-4115 (orders) *Fax:* 206-543-3932 *Toll Free Fax:* 800-669-7993 (orders) *E-mail:* uwpord@u.washington.edu *Web Site:* www.washington.edu/uwpress/, pg 286

Steward, Paul J, Cave Books, 277 Clamer Rd, Trenton, NJ 08628 *Tel:* 609-490-6359 (ed); 937-233-3561 (publr); 937-233-3561 (edit) *Web Site:* www.cavebooks.com, pg 55

Stewart, Amanda, Severn House Publishers Inc, 595 Madison Ave, 15th fl, New York, NY 10022 *Tel:* 212-888-4042 *Fax:* 212-759-5422 *E-mail:* editorial@severnhouse.com; sales@severnhouse.com *Web Site:* www.severnhouse.com, pg 245

Stewart, Jeff, Jeff Stewart's Teaching Tools, PO Box 15308, Seattle, WA 98115 *Tel:* 425-486-4510 *Fax:* 425-486-4510, pg 260

Stewart, Jill, Fitzhenry & Whiteside Limited, 195 Allstate Pkwy, Markham, ON L3R 4T8, Canada *Tel:* 905-477-9700 *Toll Free Tel:* 800-387-9776

Fax: 905-477-9179 *Toll Free Fax:* 800-260-9777 *E-mail:* godwit@fitzhenry.ca *Web Site:* www.fitzhenry.ca, pg 547

Stewart, Joan, The Joan Stewart Agency, 800 Third Ave, 34th fl, New York, NY 10022 *Tel:* 212-418-7255 *Fax:* 212-486-6518, pg 657

Stewart, Kerri, Focus Publishing/R Pullins Co Inc, 311 Merrimac St, Newburyport, MA 01950 *Tel:* 978-462-7288 (edit) *Toll Free Tel:* 800-848-7236 (orders) *Fax:* 978-462-9035 (orders) *E-mail:* pullins@pullins.com *Web Site:* www.pullins.com, pg 98

Stewart, Kimberly, Christian Living Books Inc, 12103 Woodwind Lane, Mitchellville, MD 20721 *Tel:* 301-218-9092 *Toll Free Tel:* 800-727-3218 (ordering) *Fax:* 301-218-4943 *E-mail:* info@christianlivingbooks.com *Web Site:* www.christianlivingbooks.com, pg 61

Stewart, MacDuff, University Press of America Inc, 4501 Forbes Blvd, Suite 200, Lanham, MD 20706 *Tel:* 301-459-3366 *Toll Free Tel:* 800-462-6420 *Fax:* 301-429-5748 *Toll Free Fax:* 800-338-4550 *Web Site:* www.univpress.com, pg 286

Stewart, Marian, University of Oklahoma Press, 4100 28 Ave NW, Norman, OK 73069-8218 *Tel:* 405-325-2000 *Toll Free Tel:* 800-627-7377 (orders) *Fax:* 405-364-5798 (orders) *Toll Free Fax:* 800-735-0476 (orders) *E-mail:* oupress@ou.edu *Web Site:* www.oupress.com, pg 284

Stewart, Michael, The Perseus Books Group, 387 Park Ave S, 12th fl, New York, NY 10016 *Tel:* 212-340-8100 *Toll Free Tel:* 800-386-5656 (cust serv) *Fax:* 212-340-8115 *Web Site:* www.perseusbooksgroup.com, pg 210

Stewart, Robert, BKMK Press of the University of Missouri-Kansas City, 5101 Rockhill Rd, Kansas City, MO 64110-2499 *Tel:* 816-235-2558 *Fax:* 816-235-2611 *E-mail:* bkmk@umkc.edu *Web Site:* www.umkc.edu/bkmk, pg 39

Stewart, Robert, G S Sharat Chandra Prize for Short Fiction, 5101 Rockhill Rd, Kansas City, MO 64110 *Tel:* 816-235-2558 *Fax:* 816-235-2611 *E-mail:* bkmk@umkc.edu *Web Site:* www.umkc.edu/bkmk/, pg 766

Stewart, Robert, John Ciardi Prize for Poetry, 5101 Rockhill Rd, Kansas City, MO 64110 *Tel:* 816-235-2558 *Fax:* 816-235-2611 *E-mail:* bkmk@umkc.edu *Web Site:* www.umkc.edu/bkmk/, pg 767

Stewart, Scott, Saunders College Publishing, The Public Ledger Bldg, 150 S Independence Mall W, Suite 1250, Philadelphia, PA 19106-3412 *Tel:* 215-238-5500 *Fax:* 215-238-5660 *Web Site:* www.hbcollege.com, pg 240

Stewart, Shirley, University of Texas Press, PO Box 7819, Austin, TX 78713-7819 *Tel:* 512-471-7233 *Fax:* 512-232-7178 *E-mail:* utpress@uts.cc.utexas.edu *Web Site:* www.utexas.edu/utpress, pg 267

Stewart, Skye, The Harvard Common Press, 535 Albany St, Boston, MA 02118 *Tel:* 617-423-5803 *Toll Free Tel:* 888-657-3755 *Fax:* 617-695-9794 *E-mail:* orders@harvardcommonpress.com *Web Site:* www.harvardcommonpress.com, pg 117

Stifora, Kelly, Turnstone Press, 607-100 Arthur St, Winnipeg, MB R3B 1H3, Canada *Tel:* 204-947-1555 *Toll Free Tel:* 800-982-6472 *Fax:* 204-942-1555 *E-mail:* editor@turnstonepress.com; mktg@turnstonepress.com *Web Site:* www.turnstonepress.com, pg 564

Stiles, Lane, Fairview Press, 2450 Riverside Ave, Minneapolis, MN 55454 *Tel:* 612-672-4180 *Toll Free Tel:* 800-544-8207 *Fax:* 612-672-4980 *Web Site:* www.fairviewpress.org, pg 94

Stiles, Lane, Mid-List Press, 4324 12 Ave S, Minneapolis, MN 55407-3218 *Tel:* 612-822-3733 *Fax:* 612-823-8387 *E-mail:* guide@midlist.org *Web Site:* www.midlist.org, pg 174

Stiles, Lane, Mid-List Press First Series Award for Creative Nonfiction, 4324 12 Ave S, Minneapolis, MN 55407-3218 *Tel:* 612-822-3733 *Fax:* 612-823-8387 *E-mail:* guide@midlist.org *Web Site:* www.midlist.org, pg 789

Stiles, Lane, Mid-List Press First Series Award for Poetry, 4324 12 Ave S, Minneapolis, MN 55407-3218 *Tel:* 612-822-3733 *Fax:* 612-823-8387 *E-mail:* guide@midlist.org *Web Site:* www.midlist.org, pg 789

Stiles, Lane, Mid-List Press First Series Award for Short Fiction, 4324 12 Ave S, Minneapolis, MN 55407-3218 *Tel:* 612-822-3733 *Fax:* 612-823-8387 *E-mail:* guide@midlist.org *Web Site:* www.midlist.org, pg 789

Stiles, Lane, Mid-List Press First Series Award for the Novel, 4324 12 Ave S, Minneapolis, MN 55407-3218 *Tel:* 612-822-3733 *Fax:* 612-823-8387 *E-mail:* guide@midlist.org *Web Site:* www.midlist.org, pg 789

Stillman, Herbert, H Stillman Publishers Inc, 21405 Woodchuck Lane, Boca Raton, FL 33428 *Tel:* 561-482-6343, pg 260

Stillo, Frank, Metropolitan Lithographers Association Inc, 950 Third Ave, 14th fl, New York, NY 10022 *Tel:* 212-644-1010 *Fax:* 212-644-1936, pg 691

Stillo, Sarah, Design Image Group, 231 S Frontage Rd, Suite 17, Burr Ridge, IL 60527 *Tel:* 630-789-8991 *Toll Free Tel:* 800-563-5455 *Fax:* 630-789-9013 *E-mail:* dig@designimagegroup.com *Web Site:* www.designimagegroup.com, pg 79

Stilson, Joyce, Maxim Mazumdar New Play Competition, One Curtain Up Alley, Buffalo, NY 14202-1911 *Tel:* 716-852-2600 *Fax:* 716-852-2266 *E-mail:* email@alleyway.com *Web Site:* alleyway.com, pg 788

Stimely, Sarah, Cottonwood Press Inc, 109-B Cameron Dr, Fort Collins, CO 80525 *Tel:* 970-204-0715 *Toll Free Tel:* 800-864-4297 *Fax:* 970-204-0761 *E-mail:* cottonwood@cottonwoodpress.com *Web Site:* www.cottonwoodpress.com, pg 69

Stimola, Rosemary B, Stimola Literary Studio, 308 Chase Ct, Edgewater, NJ 07020 *Tel:* 201-945-9353 *Fax:* 201-945-9353 *E-mail:* LtryStudio@aol.com, pg 657

Stine, Jane, Parachute Entertainment LLC, 156 Fifth Ave, Suite 302, New York, NY 10010 *Tel:* 212-691-1422 *Fax:* 212-645-8769 *Web Site:* www.parachutepublishing.com, pg 203

Stine, Jane, Parachute Publishing LLC, 156 Fifth Ave, Suite 302, New York, NY 10010 *Tel:* 212-691-1422 *Fax:* 212-645-8769 *Web Site:* www.parachutepublishing.com, pg 203

Stinson, Denise, Warner Books, 1271 Avenue of the Americas, New York, NY 10020 *Tel:* 212-522-7200 *Fax:* 212-522-7991 *Web Site:* www.twbookmark.com, pg 293

Stinson, Tammy, Waterloo Music Co Ltd, 3 Regina St N, Waterloo, ON N2J 4A5, Canada *Tel:* 519-886-4990 *Toll Free Tel:* 800-563-9683 (Canada & US) *Fax:* 519-886-4999 *E-mail:* info@waterloomusic.com *Web Site:* www.waterloomusic.com, pg 566

Stock, Tom, Blue Book Publications Inc, 8009 34 Ave S, Suite 175, Minneapolis, MN 55425 *Tel:* 952-854-5229 *Toll Free Tel:* 800-877-4867 *Fax:* 952-853-1486 *E-mail:* bluebook@bluebookinc.com *Web Site:* www.bluebookinc.com, pg 570

Stocke, Todd, Sourcebooks Inc, 1935 Brookdale Rd, Suite 139, Naperville, IL 60563 *Tel:* 630-961-3900 *Toll Free Tel:* 800-432-7444 *Fax:* 630-961-2168 *E-mail:* info@sourcebooks.com *Web Site:* www.sourcebooks.com, pg 253

Stocke, Todd, Sphinx Publishing, 1935 Brookdale Rd, Suite 139, Naperville, IL 60563 *Tel:* 630-961-3900 *Toll Free Tel:* 800-43-bright *Fax:* 630-961-2168 *E-mail:* info@sourcebooks.com *Web Site:* www.sourcebooks.com, pg 255

Stoiciu, Constantin, Humanitas, 990 Picard, Ville de Brossard, PQ J4W 1S5, Canada *Tel:* 450-466-9737 *Fax:* 450-466-9737 *E-mail:* humanitas@cyberglobe.net, pg 550

Stokaluk, David, Emond Montgomery Publications Ltd, 60 Shaftesbury Ave, Toronto, ON M4T 1A3, Canada *Tel:* 416-975-3925 *Toll Free Tel:* 888-837-0815 *Fax:* 416-975-3924 *E-mail:* info@emp.ca; orders@emp.ca *Web Site:* www.emp.ca, pg 546

Stoker, Bruce, Standard Publishing Co, 8121 Hamilton Ave, Cincinnati, OH 45231 Tel: 513-931-4050 Toll Free Tel: 800-543-1301 Fax: 513-931-0950 Toll Free Fax: 877-867-5751 E-mail: customerservice@ standardpub.com Web Site: www.standardpub.com, pg 257

Stoker, Leslie, Stewart, Tabori & Chang, 115 W 18 St, 5th fl, New York, NY 10011 Tel: 212-519-1200 Fax: 212-519-1210 Web Site: www.abramsbooks.com, pg 259

Stokes, Elena, Tom Doherty Associates, LLC, 175 Fifth Ave, 14th fl, New York, NY 10010 Tel: 212-388-0100 Toll Free Tel: 800-455-0340 Fax: 212-388-0191 E-mail: firstname.lastname@tor.com Web Site: www. tor.com, pg 81

Stokes, Susan S, Woodbine House, 6510 Bells Mill Rd, Bethesda, MD 20817 Tel: 301-897-3570 Toll Free Tel: 800-843-7323 Fax: 301-897-5838 E-mail: info@ woodbinehouse.com Web Site: www.woodbinehouse. com, pg 302

Stolen, Dr Joanne, SOS Publications, 43 De Normandie Ave, Fair Haven, NJ 07704-3303 Tel: 732-530-5896; 732-530-3199 Fax: 732-530-5896 Web Site: www. netlabs.net/hp/sosjs, pg 253

Stolley, Lisa, University of Illinois at Chicago, Program for Writers, 601 S Morgan St, Chicago, IL 60607-7120 Tel: 312-413-2229; 312-413-2200 (English Dept) Fax: 312-413-1005, pg 755

Stoloff, Sam, Frances Goldin Literary Agency, Inc, 57 E 11 St, Suite 5B, New York, NY 10003 Tel: 212-777-0047 Fax: 212-228-1660 E-mail: agency@goldinlit. com Web Site: www.goldinlit.com, pg 632

Stolper, Jonathan, Harry N Abrams Inc, 100 Fifth Ave, New York, NY 10011 Tel: 212-206-7715 Toll Free Tel: 800-345-1359 Fax: 212-645-8437 E-mail: webmaster@abramsbooks.com Web Site: www.abramsbooks.com, pg 3

Stolzenberg, Ronni, Lark Books, 67 Broadway, Asheville, NC 28801 Tel: 828-253-0467 Toll Free Tel: 800-284-3388 (cust serv) Fax: 828-253-7952 E-mail: info@larkbooks.com Web Site: www. larkbooks.com, pg 149

Stolzenberg, Ronni, Sterling Publishing Co Inc, 387 Park Ave S, 5th fl, New York, NY 10016-8810 Tel: 212-532-7160 Toll Free Tel: 800-367-9692 Fax: 212-213-2495 Web Site: www.sterlingpub.com, pg 259

Stone, Barbara, Sandlapper Publishing Inc, PO Drawer 730, Orangeburg, SC 29116-0730 Tel: 803-531-1658 Toll Free Tel: 800-849-7263 (orders only) Fax: 803-534-5223 Web Site: www.sandlapperpublishing.com, pg 239

Stone, Georgiana, Domhan Books, 9511 Shore Rd, Suite 514, Brooklyn, NY 11209 Tel: 718-680-4362 Toll Free Fax: 888-823-4770 E-mail: domhan@att.net Web Site: www.domhanbooks.com, pg 82

Stone, Ivy Fischer, Fifi Oscard Agency Inc, 110 W 40 St, New York, NY 10018 Tel: 212-764-1100 Fax: 212-840-5019 E-mail: agency@fifioscard.com Web Site: www.fifioscard.com, pg 647

Stone, John W, Artech House Inc, 685 Canton St, Norwood, MA 02062 Tel: 781-769-9750 Toll Free Tel: 800-225-9977 Fax: 781-769-6334 E-mail: artech@artechhouse.com Web Site: www. artechhouse.com, pg 24

Stone, Judi, Artech House Inc, 685 Canton St, Norwood, MA 02062 Tel: 781-769-9750 Toll Free Tel: 800-225-9977 Fax: 781-769-6334 E-mail: artech@artechhouse. com Web Site: www.artechhouse.com, pg 24

Stone, Kris, Piano Press, 1425 Ocean Ave, Suite 6, Del Mar, CA 92014 Tel: 619-884-1401 Fax: 858-459-3376 E-mail: pianopress@aol.com Web Site: www. pianopress.com, pg 212

Stone, Michelle, McClanahan Publishing House Inc, PO Box 100, Kuttawa, KY 42055-0100 Tel: 270-388-9388 Toll Free Tel: 800-544-6959 Fax: 270-388-6186 E-mail: books@kybooks.com Web Site: www.kybooks. com, pg 166

Stone, Ralph, Harlequin Enterprises Ltd, 225 Duncan Mill Rd, Don Mills, ON M3B 3K9, Canada Tel: 416-445-5860 Fax: 416-445-8655 Web Site: www. eharlequin.com; www.luna-books.com; www. mirabooks.com; www.reddressink.com; www. steeplehill.com, pg 549

Stone, Ruth, Binghamton University Writing Program, c/o Dept of English, PO Box 6000, Binghamton, NY 13902-6000 Tel: 607-777-2168 Fax: 607-777-2408, pg 751

Stone, Tom, The MIT Press, 5 Cambridge Ctr, Cambridge, MA 02142 Tel: 617-253-5646 Toll Free Tel: 800-405-1619 (orders only) Fax: 617-258-6779 Web Site: mitpress.mit.edu, pg 175

Stoner, Philip, Thomas Nelson Inc, 501 Nelson Place, Nashville, TN 37214 Tel: 615-889-9000 Toll Free Tel: 800-251-4000 Fax: 615-902-1610 E-mail: publicity@thomasnelson.com Web Site: www. thomasnelson.com, pg 269

Stoney, Cherea, American Public Human Services Association, 810 First St NE, Suite 500, Washington, DC 20002 Tel: 202-682-0100 Fax: 202-289-6555 E-mail: pubs@aphsa.org Web Site: www.aphsa.org, pg 677

Stookesberry, Tim, Allyn & Bacon, 75 Arlington St, Suite 300, Boston, MA 02116 Tel: 617-848-6000 Fax: 617-848-6016 E-mail: AandBpub@aol.com Web Site: www.ablongman.com, pg 9

Storch, Maury, Gefen Books, 600 Broadway, Lynbrook, NY 11563 Tel: 516-593-1234 Toll Free Tel: 800-477-5257 Fax: 516-295-2739 E-mail: gefenny@ gefenpublishing.com Web Site: www.israelbooks.com, pg 103

Storey, Douglas, The Catalog™ Literary Agency, PO Box 2964, Vancouver, WA 98668-2964 Tel: 360-694-8531 Fax: 360-694-8531, pg 624

Storrings, Michael, St Martin's Press Trade Division, 175 Fifth Ave, New York, NY 10010 E-mail: firstname. lastname@stmartins.com Web Site: www.stmartins. com; www.minotaurbooks.com, pg 239

Stortz, Diane, Standard Publishing Co, 8121 Hamilton Ave, Cincinnati, OH 45231 Tel: 513-931-4050 Toll Free Tel: 800-543-1301 Fax: 513-931-0950 Toll Free Fax: 877-867-5751 E-mail: customerservice@ standardpub.com Web Site: www.standardpub.com, pg 257

Story, Karin, Amber Quill Press LLC, PO Box 265, Indian Hills, CO 80454 E-mail: customer_service@ amberquillpress.com Web Site: amberquill.com, pg 10

Stouras, Tom, St Martin's Press LLC, 175 Fifth Ave, New York, NY 10010 Tel: 212-674-5151 Fax: 212-420-9314 E-mail: firstname.lastname@stmartins.com Web Site: www.stmartins.com, pg 238

Stovall, Scott, National State Publishing Association (NSPA), 207 Third Ave, Hattiesburg, MS 39401 Tel: 601-582-3330 Fax: 601-582-3354 E-mail: info@ govpublishing.org Web Site: www.govpublishing.org, pg 694

Stover, Jennifer, American Institute of Aeronautics & Astronautics, 1801 Alexander Bell Dr, Suite 500, Reston, VA 20191 Tel: 703-264-7500 Toll Free Tel: 800-639-2422 Fax: 703-264-7551 E-mail: custserv@aiaa.org Web Site: www.aiaa.org, pg 14

Stover, Joanna, Northeast Midwest Institute, 218 "D" St SE, Washington, DC 20003 Tel: 202-544-5200 Fax: 202-544-0043 Web Site: www.nemw.org, pg 193

Stowe, Arthur R, Printing Industries of Maryland, 2045 York Rd, 2nd fl, Timonium, MD 21093 Tel: 410-560-3300 Toll Free Tel: 800-560-3306 Fax: 410-560-3306 E-mail: pim@printmd.com Web Site: www.printmd. com, pg 698

Stowe, Jon, John Wiley & Sons Inc Education Publishing Group, 111 River St, Hoboken, NJ 07030 Tel: 201-748-6000 Fax: 201-748-6088 E-mail: info@ wiley.com Web Site: www.wiley.com, pg 300

Strachan, Bill, Hyperion, 77 W 66 St, 11th fl, New York, NY 10023-6298 Tel: 212-456-0100 Toll Free Tel: 800-759-0190 (cust serv) Fax: 212-456-0157 Web Site: hyperionbooks.com, pg 129

Strads, Gundars, American Book Award, The Raymond House, 655 13 St, Suite 302, Oakland, CA 94612 Tel: 510-268-9775, pg 759

Strads, Gundars, Before Columbus Foundation, The Raymond House, 655 13 St, Suite 302, Oakland, CA 94612 Tel: 510-268-9775, pg 681

Straley, Tina H, The Mathematical Association of America, 1529 18 St NW, Washington, DC 20036 Tel: 202-387-5200 Toll Free Tel: 800-331-1622 (orders) Fax: 202-265-2384 E-mail: ldouglas@pmds. com Web Site: www.maa.org, pg 165

Strand, Kurt, McGraw-Hill Higher Education, 1333 Burr Ridge Pkwy, Burr Ridge, IL 60527 Tel: 630-789-4000 Toll Free Tel: 800-338-3987 (cust serv) Fax: 614-755-5645 (cust serv) Web Site: www.mhhe.com, pg 167

strand, Kurt, McGraw-Hill Science, Engineering, Mathematics, 2460 Kerper Blvd, Dubuque, IA 52001 Tel: 563-588-1451 Toll Free Tel: 800-338-3987 (cust serv) Fax: 563-589-4700; 614-755-5645 (cust serv) E-mail: firstname_lastname@mcgraw-hill.com Web Site: www.mhhe.com, pg 169

Strand, Lisa K, Banta Literary Award, 5250 E Terrace Dr, Suite A-1, Madison, WI 53718-8345 Tel: 608-245-3640 Fax: 608-245-3646 Web Site: www.wla.lib.wi.us, pg 761

Strand, Lisa K, Notable Wisconsin Authors, 5250 E Terrace Dr, Suite A-1, Madison, WI 53718-8345 Tel: 608-245-3640 Fax: 608-245-3646 Web Site: www. wla.lib.wi.us, pg 795

Stranding, Suzette, The National Society of Newspaper Columnists (NSNC), Fillmore St, Suite 507, San Francisco, CA 94115 Tel: 415-541-5636 Web Site: www.columnists.com, pg 694

Strang, Stephen, Charisma House, 600 Rinehart Rd, Lake Mary, FL 32746 Tel: 407-333-0600 (all imprints) Toll Free Tel: 800-283-8494 (Charisma House, Siloam Press, Creation House Press); 800-665-1468 Fax: 407-333-7100 (all imprints) E-mail: webmaster@ charismahouse.com; webmaster@creationhouse.com Web Site: www.charismamag.com; www.strang.com (all imprints), pg 58

Strang, Stephen, CharismaLife Publishers, 600 Rinehart Rd, Lake Mary, FL 32746 Tel: 407-333-0600 Toll Free Tel: 800-451-4598 Fax: 407-333-7100 E-mail: charismalife@strang.com Web Site: www. charismamag.com, pg 58

Stranges, Dr Frank E, International Evangelism Crusades Inc, 21601 Devonshire St, Suite 217, Chatsworth, CA 91311-8415 Tel: 818-882-0039 Fax: 818-989-2165, pg 137

Stransky, L E, Blue Unicorn Press Inc, 4153 SE 39 Ave, Suite 35, Portland, OR 97202-3176 Tel: 503-775-9322 E-mail: unicornpress404@aol.com, pg 42

Stratton, Philippa, Stenhouse Publishers, 477 Congress St, Suite 4B, Portland, ME 04101-3451 Tel: 207-253-1600 Toll Free Tel: 888-363-0566 Fax: 207-253-5121 Toll Free Fax: 800-833-9164 E-mail: info@stenhouse. com Web Site: www.stenhouse.com, pg 259

Strauch, Thomas, Design Image Group, 231 S Frontage Rd, Suite 17, Burr Ridge, IL 60527 Tel: 630-789-8991 Toll Free Tel: 800-563-5455 Fax: 630-789-9013 E-mail: dig@designimagegroup.com Web Site: www. designimagegroup.com, pg 79

Straus, Robin, Robin Straus Agency Inc, 229 E 79 St, New York, NY 10021 Tel: 212-472-3282 Fax: 212-472-3833 E-mail: springbird@aol.com, pg 657

Strauss, Leslie R, Housing Assistance Council, 1025 Vermont Ave NW, Suite 606, Washington, DC 20005 Tel: 202-842-8600 Fax: 202-347-3441 E-mail: hac@ ruralhome.org Web Site: www.ruralhome.org, pg 127

Strauss-Gabel, Julie, Dutton Children's Books, 345 Hudson St, New York, NY 10014 Tel: 212-366-2000 E-mail: online@penguinputnam.com Web Site: www. penguin.com, pg 85

Strazzabosco-Hayn, Gina, The Rosen Publishing Group Inc, 29 E 21 St, New York, NY 10010 *Tel:* 212-777-3017 *Toll Free Tel:* 800-237-9932 *Fax:* 212-777-0277 *E-mail:* info@rosenpub.com *Web Site:* www.rosenpublishing.com, pg 234

Streibig, Michael H, Printing Association of Florida Inc, 6275 Hazeltine National Dr, Orlando, FL 32822 *Tel:* 407-240-8009 *Fax:* 407-240-8333 *Web Site:* www.pafgraf.org, pg 697

Streitfeld, Anika, MacAdam/Cage Publishing Inc, 155 Sansome St, Suite 550, San Francisco, CA 94104 *Tel:* 415-986-7502 *Toll Free Tel:* 866-986-7470 *Fax:* 415-986-7414 *E-mail:* info@macadamcage.com *Web Site:* www.macadamcage.com, pg 161

Strekofsky, Janice, Vision Works Publishing, 47 Sheffield Rd, Suite A, Boxford, MA 01921 *Tel:* 978-887-3125 *Toll Free Tel:* 888-821-3135 *Fax:* 630-982-2134 *E-mail:* visionworksbooks@email.com, pg 291

Strick, Louis, Taplinger Publishing Co Inc, PO Box 175, Marlboro, NJ 07746-0175 *Tel:* 646-215-9003 *Fax:* 646-215-9560, pg 264

Strickland, Albert Lee, Pacific Publishing Services, PO Box 1150, Capitola, CA 95010-1150 *Tel:* 831-476-8284 *Fax:* 831-476-8294 *E-mail:* pacpub@attglobal.net, pg 607

Strickland, Sherri, University Press of New England, One Court St, Lebanon, NH 03766 *Tel:* 603-448-1533 *Toll Free Tel:* 800-421-1561 (orders only) *Fax:* 603-448-7006; 603-643-1540 *E-mail:* university.press@dartmouth.edu *Web Site:* www.upne.com, pg 287

Strickland, Tessa, Barefoot Books, 2067 Massachusetts Ave, 5th fl, Cambridge, MA 02140 *Tel:* 617-576-0660 *Fax:* 617-576-0049 *E-mail:* ussales@barefootbooks.com; help@barefootbooks.com *Web Site:* www.barefootbooks.com, pg 32

Strickler, Sarah A, Woodbine House, 6510 Bells Mill Rd, Bethesda, MD 20817 *Tel:* 301-897-3570 *Toll Free Tel:* 800-843-7323 *Fax:* 301-897-5838 *E-mail:* info@woodbinehouse.com *Web Site:* www.woodbinehouse.com, pg 302

Stringer, Marlene, The Barbara Bova Literary Agency, 3951 Gulfshore Blvd, Suite PH1-B, Naples, FL 34103 *Tel:* 239-649-7237 *Fax:* 239-649-7263 *E-mail:* bovab4@aol.com *Web Site:* barbarabovaliteraryagency.com, pg 622

Stringfellow, James, Utah Geological Survey, 1594 W North Temple, Suite 3110, Salt Lake City, UT 84116 *Tel:* 801-537-3300 *Toll Free Tel:* 888-UTAH-MAP (882-4627 bookstore) *Fax:* 801-537-3400 *E-mail:* geostore@utah.gov *Web Site:* geology.utah.gov, pg 289

Striplin, Deborah, Oxbridge Communications Inc, 186 Fifth Ave, 6th fl, New York, NY 10010 *Tel:* 212-741-0231 *Toll Free Tel:* 800-955-0231 *Fax:* 212-633-2938 *E-mail:* info@oxbridge.com; custserv@oxbridge.com *Web Site:* www.mediafinder.com, pg 200

Strock, Eva, Pomegranate Communications, 775-A Southpoint Blvd, Petaluma, CA 94954-1495 *Tel:* 707-782-9000 *Toll Free Tel:* 800-227-1428 *Toll Free Fax:* 800-848-4376 *Web Site:* www.pomegranate.com, pg 216

Strode, Brinton, Oxford University Press, Inc, 198 Madison Ave, New York, NY 10016-4314 *Tel:* 212-726-6000 *Toll Free Tel:* 800-451-7556 (orders) *Web Site:* www.oup.com/us, pg 200

Strode, William, Harmony House Publishers - Louisville, 1008 Kent Rd, Goshen, KY 40026 *Tel:* 502-228-2010; 502-228-4446 *Fax:* 502-228-2010 *E-mail:* harmonypub@aol.com, pg 115

Strohlein, Marc, Classroom Connect, 8000 Marina Blvd, Suite 400, Brisbane, CA 94005 *Tel:* 650-351-5100 *Toll Free Tel:* 800-638-1639 (cust support) *Fax:* 650-351-5300 *E-mail:* connect@classroom.com *Web Site:* www.classroom.com, pg 63

Strohm, Christine, Hanser Gardner Publications, 6915 Valley Ave, Cincinnati, OH 45244-3029 *Tel:* 513-527-8977 *Toll Free Tel:* 800-950-8977 *Fax:* 513-527-8801 *Toll Free Fax:* 800-527-8801 *E-mail:* hgfeedback@gardnerweb.com *Web Site:* www.hansergardner.com, pg 113

Strohmeier, John, North Bay Books, 3110 Whitecliff Ct, Richmond, CA 94803 *Tel:* 510-758-4276 *Toll Free Tel:* 800-870-3194 *Fax:* 510-758-4659 *Web Site:* www.northbaybooks.com, pg 192

Strom, Laura, The Globe Pequot Press, 246 Goose Lane, Guilford, CT 06437 *Tel:* 203-458-4500 *Toll Free Tel:* 800-243-0495 (cust serv) *Fax:* 203-458-4601 *Toll Free Fax:* 800-820-2329 (orders & cust serv) *E-mail:* info@globepequot.com *Web Site:* www.globepequot.com, pg 105

Stromburg, Mike, Basic Health Publications Inc, 8200 Boulevard E, Suite 25-G, North Bergen, NJ 07047 *Tel:* 201-868-8336 *Toll Free Tel:* 800-575-8890 *Fax:* 201-868-8335, pg 33

Strone, Daniel, Trident Media Group LLC, 41 Madison Ave, 36th fl, New York, NY 10010 *Tel:* 212-262-4810 *Fax:* 212-725-4501 *Web Site:* www.tridentmediagroup.com, pg 659

Strong, Howard, The Boswell Institute, PO Box 7100, Beverly Hills, CA 90212-7100 *Tel:* 818-343-4434, pg 44

Strong, Marianne, Marianne Strong Literary Agency, 65 E 96 St, New York, NY 10128 *Tel:* 212-249-1000 *Fax:* 212-831-3241 *E-mail:* stronglit@aol.com, pg 657

Strossen, Nadine, American Civil Liberties Union, 125 Broad St, 18th fl, New York, NY 10004 *Tel:* 212-549-2500 *Toll Free Tel:* 800-775-ACLU (orders) *E-mail:* info@aclu.org *Web Site:* www.aclu.org, pg 676

Stroud, Susie, Greenwood Publishing Group Inc, 88 Post Rd W, Westport, CT 06880-4208 *Tel:* 203-226-3571 *Toll Free Tel:* 800-225-5800 *Fax:* 203-222-1502 *E-mail:* bookinfo@greenwood.com (general); firstintial&fulllastname@greenwood.com (individuals) *Web Site:* www.greenwood.com, pg 109

Stroud, Ward J, National Book Co, PO Box 8795, Portland, OR 97207-8795 *Tel:* 503-228-6345 *Fax:* 810-885-5811 *E-mail:* info@eralearning.com *Web Site:* www.eralearning.com, pg 182

Stroup, Rodger E, South Carolina Dept of Archives & History, 8301 Parklane Rd, Columbia, SC 29223 *Tel:* 803-896-6100 *Fax:* 803-896-6198 *Web Site:* www.state.sc.us/scdah/, pg 254

Stroup, Sheila, The National Society of Newspaper Columnists (NSNC), Fillmore St, Suite 507, San Francisco, CA 94115 *Tel:* 415-541-5636 *Web Site:* www.columnists.com, pg 694

Strowbridge, Clarence C, Dover Publications Inc, 31 E Second St, Mineola, NY 11501 *Tel:* 516-294-7000 *Toll Free Tel:* 800-223-3130 (orders) *Fax:* 516-742-6953; 516-742-5049 (orders) *Web Site:* www.doverpublications.com; www.doverdirect.com, pg 83

Struck, Kathryn D, Awe-Struck E-Books Inc, 2458 Cherry St, Dubuque, IA 52001-5749 *E-mail:* editor@awe-struckebooks.net; tech@awestruckebooks.net *Web Site:* www.awe-struck.net (ordering), pg 30

Struckmann, Dianne, Krieger Publishing Co, PO Box 9542, Melbourne, FL 32902-9542 *Tel:* 321-724-9542 *Toll Free Tel:* 800-724-0025 *Fax:* 321-951-3671 *E-mail:* info@krieger-publishing.com *Web Site:* www.krieger-publishing.com, pg 147

Strug, Richard, American Map Corp, 46-35 54 Rd, Maspeth, NY 11378 *Tel:* 718-784-0055 *Toll Free Tel:* 800-432-MAPS *Fax:* 718-784-0640 (admin); 718-784-1216 (sales & orders), pg 15

Strug, Richard, Hagstrom Map Co Inc, 46-35 54 Rd, Maspeth, NY 11378 *Tel:* 718-784-0055 *Toll Free Tel:* 800-432-MAPS (432-6277) *Fax:* 718-784-0640 (admin); 718-784-1216 (sales & orders) *Web Site:* www.americanmap.com, pg 111

Strug, Richard, Hammond World Atlas Corp, 95 Progress St, Union, NJ 07083 *Tel:* 908-206-1300 *Toll Free Tel:* 800-526-4953 *Fax:* 908-206-1104 *E-mail:* customerservice@hammondmap.com; feedback@hammondmap.com *Web Site:* www.hammondmap.com, pg 112

Strug, Richard, Langenscheidt Publishers Inc, 46-35 54 Rd, Maspeth, NY 11378 *Tel:* 718-784-0055 *Toll Free Tel:* 800-432-MAPS (732-6277) *Fax:* 718-784-0640 *Toll Free Fax:* 888-773-7979 *E-mail:* sales@langenscheidt.com *Web Site:* www.langenscheidt.com, pg 149

Strunk, Frank, Writers Retreat Workshop (WRW), 5721 Magazine St, Suite 161, New Orleans, LA 70115 *Toll Free Tel:* 800-642-2494 *E-mail:* wrw04@netscape.net *Web Site:* www.writersretreatworkshop.com, pg 749

Struzinski, Al, Running Press Book Publishers, 125 S 22 St, Philadelphia, PA 19103-4399 *Tel:* 215-567-5080 *Toll Free Tel:* 800-345-5359 (cust serv & orders) *Fax:* 215-568-2919 *Toll Free Fax:* 800-453-2884 *Web Site:* www.runningpress.com, pg 236

Stuart, Airie, Palgrave Macmillan, 175 Fifth Ave, New York, NY 10010 *Tel:* 212-982-3900 *Fax:* 212-777-6359 *E-mail:* firstname.lastname@palgrave-usa.com *Web Site:* www.palgrave.com, pg 202

Stuart, Carole, Barricade Books Inc, 185 Bridge Plaza N, Suite 308A, Fort Lee, NJ 07024 *Tel:* 201-944-7600 *Fax:* 201-944-6363 *E-mail:* customerservice@barricadebooks.com *Web Site:* www.barricadebooks.com, pg 32

Stuart, Lyle, Barricade Books Inc, 185 Bridge Plaza N, Suite 308A, Fort Lee, NJ 07024 *Tel:* 201-944-7600 *Fax:* 201-944-6363 *E-mail:* customerservice@barricadebooks.com *Web Site:* www.barricadebooks.com, pg 32

Stuart, Rob, HCPro, 200 Hoods Lane, Marblehead, MA 01945 *Tel:* 781-639-1872 *Toll Free Tel:* 800-650-6787 *Fax:* 781-639-2982 *Toll Free Fax:* 800-639-8511 *E-mail:* customer_service@hcpro.com *Web Site:* www.hcpro.com, pg 119

Stuart, Sally, Oregon Christian Writers, 1647 SW Pheasant Dr, Aloha, OR 97006 *Tel:* 503-642-9844 *Fax:* 503-848-3658 *E-mail:* miholer@viser.net *Web Site:* www.oregonchristianwriters.org, pg 696

Stuart, Sally, Oregon Christian Writers Coaching Conference, 1647 SW Pheasant Dr, Aloha, OR 97006 *Tel:* 503-642-9844 *Fax:* 503-848-3658 *E-mail:* miholer@viser.net *Web Site:* www.oregonchristianwriters.org, pg 745

Stubblefield, Max, Don Buchwald & Associates Inc, 6500 Wilshire Blvd, Suite 2200, Los Angeles, CA 90048 *Tel:* 323-655-7400 *Fax:* 323-655-7470 *Web Site:* www.donbuchwald.com, pg 623

Stubbs, Peter, Fitzhenry & Whiteside Limited, 195 Allstate Pkwy, Markham, ON L3R 4T8, Canada *Tel:* 905-477-9700 *Toll Free Tel:* 800-387-9776 *Fax:* 905-477-9179 *Toll Free Fax:* 800-260-9777 *E-mail:* godwit@fitzhenry.ca *Web Site:* www.fitzhenry.ca, pg 547

Stubits, Lorraine, McIntosh & Otis Inc, 353 Lexington Ave, Suite 1500, New York, NY 10016-0900 *Tel:* 212-687-7400 *Fax:* 212-687-6894 *E-mail:* info@mcintoshandotis.com, pg 643

Stueve, Sharon, Brighton Publications, PO Box 120706, New Brighton, MN 55112-0022 *Tel:* 651-636-2220 *Toll Free Tel:* 800-536-2665 *Fax:* 651-636-2220, pg 47

Stuhlmann, Barbara Ward, Barbara Ward Stuhlmann, Author's Representative, PO Box 276, Becket, MA 01223-0276 *Tel:* 413-623-5170, pg 658

Stultz, Russell A, Wordware Publishing Inc, 2320 Los Rios Blvd, Suite 200, Plano, TX 75074 *Tel:* 972-423-0090 *Toll Free Tel:* 800-229-4949 *Fax:* 972-881-9147 *E-mail:* info@wordware.com *Web Site:* www.wordware.com, pg 303

Stump, Sarah, The National Museum of Women in the Arts, 1250 New York Ave NW, Washington, DC 20005 *Tel:* 202-783-5000 *Toll Free Tel:* 800-222-7270 *Fax:* 202-393-3234 *Web Site:* www.nmwa.org, pg 184

Sturdevant, Erica, American Showcase Inc, 915 Broadway, New York, NY 10010 *Tel:* 212-673-6600 *Toll Free Tel:* 800-894-7469 *Fax:* 212-673-9795 *E-mail:* info@amshow.com *Web Site:* www.amshow.com, pg 17

Sturgis, Kent, Epicenter Press Inc, PO Box 82368, Kenmore, WA 98028 *Tel:* 425-485-6822 *Fax:* 425-481-8253 *E-mail:* info@epicenterpress.com *Web Site:* www.epicenterpress.com, pg 91

Sturm, John F, Newspaper Association of America (NAA), 1921 Gallows Rd, Suite 600, Vienna, VA 22182 *Tel:* 703-902-1600 *Fax:* 703-917-0636 *Web Site:* www.naa.org, pg 695

Sturrock, Philip, The Continuum International Publishing Group, 15 E 26 St, Suite 1703, New York, NY 10010 *Tel:* 212-953-5858 *Toll Free Tel:* 800-561-7704 *Fax:* 212-953-5944 *E-mail:* info@continuum-books.com *Web Site:* www.continuumbooks.com, pg 67

Stvan, Beck, Random House Publishing Group, 1745 Broadway, New York, NY 10019 *Toll Free Tel:* 800-200-3552 *Toll Free Fax:* 800-200-3552 *Web Site:* www.randomhouse.com, pg 227

Styles, Bonnie, Illinois State Museum Society, 502 S Spring St, Springfield, IL 62706-5000 *Tel:* 217-782-7387 *Fax:* 217-782-1254 *E-mail:* editor@museum.state.il.us *Web Site:* www.museum.state.il.us, pg 131

Suazez, Kathryn C, Congressional Quarterly Press, 1255 22 St NW, Washington, DC 20037 *Tel:* 202-729-1800 *Toll Free Tel:* 866-427-7737 *Fax:* 202-729-1809 *Toll Free Fax:* 800-380-3810 *E-mail:* customerservice@cqpress.com *Web Site:* www.cq.com, pg 66

Subers, Mark, Grade Finders Inc, 662 Exton Commons, Exton, PA 19341 *Tel:* 610-524-7070 *Fax:* 610-524-8912 *E-mail:* info@gradefinders.com *Web Site:* www.gradefinders.com, pg 107

Subers, William A, Grade Finders Inc, 662 Exton Commons, Exton, PA 19341 *Tel:* 610-524-7070 *Fax:* 610-524-8912 *E-mail:* info@gradefinders.com *Web Site:* www.gradefinders.com, pg 107

Subrizi, Mike, Market Data Retrieval, One Forest Pkwy, Shelton, CT 06484 *Tel:* 203-926-4800 *Toll Free Tel:* 800-333-8802 *Fax:* 203-926-0784 *E-mail:* mdrinfo@dnb.com *Web Site:* www.schooldata.com, pg 163

Suek, Ringo, Great Quotations Inc, 8102 Lemont Rd, Suite 300, Woodridge, IL 60517 *Tel:* 630-390-3580 *Toll Free Tel:* 800-830-3020 *Fax:* 630-390-3585 *E-mail:* greatquotations@yahoo.com, pg 108

Sugarman, Jeff, Inscape Publishing, 6465 Wayzata Blvd, Suite 800, St Louis Park, MN 55426 *Tel:* 763-765-2222 *Fax:* 763-765-2277 *Web Site:* www.inscapepublishing.com, pg 134

Sugden, Sherwood, Sherwood Sugden & Co, 315 Fifth St, Peru, IL 61354 *Tel:* 815-224-6651 *Fax:* 815-223-4486 *E-mail:* philomon1@netscape.net *Web Site:* monist.buffalo.edu, pg 261

Suggs, Shelba, SLA Workshops, 313 S Patrick St, Alexandria, VA 22314 *Tel:* 703-647-4900 *Fax:* 703-647-4901 *E-mail:* sla@sla.org *Web Site:* www.sla.org, pg 747

Suid, Roberta, Monday Morning Books Inc, PO Box 1134, Inverness, CA 94937-0034 *Tel:* 650-327-3374 *Toll Free Tel:* 800-255-6049 *Toll Free Fax:* 800-255-6048 *E-mail:* MMBooks@aol.com *Web Site:* www.mondaymorningbooks.com, pg 177

Sukenick, Ronald, Fiction Collective Two Inc, Florida State University, FC2, Dept of English, Tallahassee, FL 32306-1580 *Tel:* 850-644-2260 *Fax:* 850-644-6808 *E-mail:* fc2@english.fsu.edu *Web Site:* fc2.org, pg 96

Sullivan, Cayenne, Black Warrior Review Literary Awards, University of Alabama, Tuscaloosa, AL 35486-0027 *Tel:* 205-348-4518 *E-mail:* bwr@ua.edu *Web Site:* www.webdelsol.com/bwr, pg 763

Sullivan, Ellen, Crane Hill Publishers, 3608 Clairmont Ave, Birmingham, AL 35222 *Tel:* 205-714-3007 *Toll Free Tel:* 800-247-8850 *Fax:* 205-714-3008 *E-mail:* cranies@cranehill.com *Web Site:* www.cranehill.com, pg 71

Sullivan, Jerry, American Association of Collegiate Registrars & Admissions Officers, One Dupont Circle NW, Suite 520, Washington, DC 20036-1135 *Tel:* 202-

293-9161 *Toll Free Tel:* 877-338-3733 *Fax:* 202-872-8857 *E-mail:* info@aacrao.org *Web Site:* www.aacrao.org, pg 11

Sullivan, John, Soundprints, 353 Main Ave, Norwalk, CT 06851 *Tel:* 203-846-2274 *Toll Free Tel:* 800-228-7839; 800-577-2413, ext 118 (orders) *Fax:* 203-846-1776 *E-mail:* Soundprints@soundprints.com *Web Site:* www.soundprints.com, pg 253

Sullivan, Lisa, Harry S Truman Book Award, 500 W US Hwy 24, Independence, MO 64050-1798 *Tel:* 816-268-8248 *Fax:* 816-268-8295 *E-mail:* truman.library@nara.gov *Web Site:* www.trumanlibrary.org, pg 809

Sullivan, Mark A, Robert Schalkenbach Foundation, 149 Madison Ave, Suite 601, New York, NY 10016-6713 *Tel:* 212-683-6424 *Toll Free Tel:* 800-269-9555 *Fax:* 212-683-6454 *E-mail:* staff@schalkenbach.org *Web Site:* www.schalkenbach.org, pg 241

Sullivan, Mary, Cedco Publishing Co, 100 Pelican Way, San Rafael, CA 94901 *Tel:* 415-451-3000 *Toll Free Tel:* 800-227-6162 *Fax:* 415-457-4839 *E-mail:* sales@cedco.com *Web Site:* www.cedco.com, pg 56

Sullivan, Maureen, Dutton Children's Books, 345 Hudson St, New York, NY 10014 *Tel:* 212-366-2000 *E-mail:* online@penguinputnam.com *Web Site:* www.penguin.com, pg 85

Sullivan, Maurice, The Wine Appreciation Guild Ltd, 360 Swift Ave, Unit 30-40, South San Francisco, CA 94080 *Tel:* 650-866-3020 *Toll Free Tel:* 800-231-9463 *Fax:* 650-866-3513 *E-mail:* shannon@wineappreciation.com; info@wineappreciation.com *Web Site:* www.wineappreciation.com, pg 301

Sullivan, Moira, Maria Carvainis Agency Inc, 1350 Avenue of the Americas, Suite 2905, New York, NY 10019 *Tel:* 212-245-6365 *Fax:* 212-245-7196 *E-mail:* mca@mariacarvainisagency.com, pg 624

Sullivan, Monica, The Amwell Press, Ridge Plaza, 2004 Rte 31 & Cregar Rd, Clinton, NJ 08809 *Tel:* 908-638-9033 *Fax:* 908-638-4728, pg 19

Sullivan, Ruth, Workman Publishing Co Inc, 708 Broadway, New York, NY 10003-9555 *Tel:* 212-254-5900 *Toll Free Tel:* 800-722-7202 *Fax:* 212-254-8098 *E-mail:* info@workman.com *Web Site:* www.workman.com, pg 303

Sullivan, Susan, Elder Books, PO Box 490, Forest Knolls, CA 94933 *Tel:* 415-488-9002 *Toll Free Tel:* 800-909-2673 (orders) *Fax:* 415-354-3306 *E-mail:* info@elderbooks.com *Web Site:* www.elderbooks.com, pg 88

Sullo, Alice, Houghton Mifflin School Division, 222 Berkeley St, Boston, MA 02116-3764, pg 126

Sultan, Stephen, Dramatists Play Service Inc, 440 Park Ave S, New York, NY 10016 *Tel:* 212-683-8960 *Fax:* 212-213-1539 *E-mail:* postmaster@dramatists.com *Web Site:* www.dramatists.com, pg 84

Sultanik, Kalman, Herzl Press, 633 Third Ave, 21st fl, New York, NY 10017 *Tel:* 212-339-6020 *Fax:* 212-318-6176 *E-mail:* midstreamthf@aol.com *Web Site:* www.midstreamthf.com, pg 121

Summerfield, Mary, Association of American University Presses, 1427 E 60 St, Chicago, IL 60637 *Tel:* 773-702-7700; 773-702-7600 *Toll Free Tel:* 800-621-2736 (orders) *Fax:* 773-702-9756 (sales); 773-660-2235 (orders); 773-702-2708 *E-mail:* general@press.uchicago.edu *Web Site:* www.press.uchicago.edu, pg 26

Summers, Vic, Current Clinical Strategies Publishing, 27071 Cabot Rd, Suite 126, Laguna Hills, CA 92653-7011 *Tel:* 949-348-8404 *Toll Free Tel:* 800-331-8227 *Fax:* 949-348-8404 *Toll Free Fax:* 800-965-9420 *E-mail:* info@ccspublishing.com *Web Site:* www.ccspublishing.com, pg 75

Sumner, Tom, Franklin, Beedle & Associates Inc, 8536 SW St Helens Dr, Suite D, Wilsonville, OR 97070 *Tel:* 503-682-7668 *Toll Free Tel:* 800-322-2665 *Fax:* 503-682-7638 *Web Site:* www.fbeedle.com, pg 100

Sundem, Greg, Llewellyn Publications, PO Box 64383, St Paul, MN 55164-0383 *Tel:* 651-291-1970 *Toll Free Tel:* 800-843-6666 *Fax:* 651-291-1908 *E-mail:* lwlpc@llewellyn.com *Web Site:* www.llewellyn.com, pg 157

Supovitz, Elise, Candlewick Press, 2067 Massachusetts Ave, Cambridge, MA 02140 *Tel:* 617-661-3330 *Fax:* 617-661-0565 *E-mail:* bigbear@candlewick.com *Web Site:* www.candlewick.com, pg 52

Surman, Rita, Garamond Press Ltd, 63 Mahogany Ct, Aurora, ON L4G 6M8, Canada *Tel:* 905-841-1460 *Toll Free Tel:* 800-898-9535 *Fax:* 905-841-3031 *E-mail:* garamond@web.ca *Web Site:* www.garamond.ca, pg 547

Sussman, Harvey, Northeastern Graphic Inc, 5 Emeline Dr, Hawthorne, NJ 07506 *Tel:* 973-221-0109 *Fax:* 973-221-0076 *Web Site:* www.northeasterngraphic.com, pg 607

Sussman, Sheri, Springer Publishing Co Inc, 11 W 42 St, New York, NY 10036 *Tel:* 212-431-4370 *Toll Free Tel:* 877-687-7476 *Fax:* 212-941-7842 *E-mail:* springer@springerpub.com *Web Site:* www.springerpub.com, pg 256

Sussman, Susan, Diverse Talent Group, 1875 Century Park E, Suite 2250, Los Angeles, CA 90067 *Tel:* 310-201-6565 *Fax:* 310-201-6572, pg 628

Suter, Joe, Hendrickson Publishers Inc, PO Box 3473, Peabody, MA 01961-3473 *Tel:* 978-532-6546 *Toll Free Tel:* 800-358-3111 *Fax:* 978-531-8146 *E-mail:* orders@hendrickson.com *Web Site:* www.hendrickson.com, pg 121

Sutker, Catherine, New Harbinger Publications Inc, 5674 Shattuck Ave, Oakland, CA 94609 *Tel:* 510-652-0215 *Toll Free Tel:* 800-748-6273 (orders only) *Fax:* 510-652-5472 *E-mail:* nhhelp@newharbinger.com *Web Site:* www.newharbinger.com, pg 188

Sutton, Caroline, Random House Publishing Group, 1745 Broadway, New York, NY 10019 *Toll Free Tel:* 800-200-3552 *Toll Free Fax:* 800-200-3552 *Web Site:* www.randomhouse.com, pg 227

Sutton, Heather, Saint Mary's Press, 702 Terrace Heights, Winona, MN 55987-1318 *Tel:* 507-457-7900 *Toll Free Tel:* 800-533-8095 *Toll Free Fax:* 800-344-9225 *E-mail:* smpress@smp.org *Web Site:* www.smp.org, pg 239

Sutton, Jayne, EEI Communications, 66 Canal Center Plaza, Suite 200, Alexandria, VA 22314-5507 *Tel:* 703-683-0683 *Fax:* 703-683-4915 *E-mail:* info@eeicommunications.com *Web Site:* www.eeicommunications.com, pg 598

Sutton, Roger, Boston Globe-Horn Book Award, 56 Roland St, Suite 200, Boston, MA 02129 *Tel:* 617-628-0225 *Toll Free Tel:* 800-325-1170 *Fax:* 617-628-0882 *E-mail:* info@hbook.com *Web Site:* www.hbook.com, pg 763

Suzanne, Claudia, Wambtac Communications, 17300 17 St, Suite J-276, Tustin, CA 92780 *Tel:* 714-954-0580 *Toll Free Tel:* 800-641-3936 *Fax:* 714-954-0793 *E-mail:* wambtac@wambtac.com *Web Site:* www.wambtac.com, pg 613

Svehla, Gary, Midnight Marquee Press Inc, 9721 Britinay Lane, Baltimore, MD 21234 *Tel:* 410-665-1198 *Fax:* 410-665-9207 *E-mail:* mmarquee@aol.com *Web Site:* www.midmar.com, pg 174

Svehla, Susan, Midnight Marquee Press Inc, 9721 Britinay Lane, Baltimore, MD 21234 *Tel:* 410-665-1198 *Fax:* 410-665-9207 *E-mail:* mmarquee@aol.com *Web Site:* www.midmar.com, pg 174

Svendsen, Sharon, National Federation of State Poetry Societies Annual Poetry Contest, 13211 NW Holly Rd, Bremerton, WA 98312 *Web Site:* www.NFSPS.com, pg 791

Svensson, Tony, Trimarket Co, 2264 Bowdoin St, Palo Alto, CA 94306 *Tel:* 650-494-1406 *Fax:* 650-494-1413 *E-mail:* info@trimarket.com *Web Site:* www.trimarket.com, pg 275

Sverdrup, Christina, Hunter House Publishers, 1515 1/2 Park St, Alameda, CA 94501 *Tel:* 510-865-5282 *Toll Free Tel:* 800-266-5592 *Fax:* 510-865-4295 *E-mail:* acquisitions@hunterhouse.com *Web Site:* www.hunterhouse.com/, pg 129

Swados, Sharon, Bantam Dell Publishing Group, 1745 Broadway, New York, NY 10019 *Tel:* 212-782-9000 *Toll Free Tel:* 800-223-6834 *Fax:* 212-302-7985 *Web Site:* www.randomhouse.com/bantamdell, pg 31

Swain, Elizabeth, The University of Arizona Press, 355 S Euclid Ave, Suite 103, Tucson, AZ 85719-6654 *Tel:* 520-621-1441 *Toll Free Tel:* 800-426-3797 (orders) *Fax:* 520-621-8899 *Toll Free Fax:* 800-426-3797 *E-mail:* uapress@uapress.arizona.edu *Web Site:* www.uapress.arizona.edu, pg 280

Swain, Martha, McLemore Prize, PO Box 571, Jackson, MS 39205-0571 *Tel:* 601-576-6850 *Fax:* 601-576-6975 *E-mail:* mhs@mdah.state.ms.us *Web Site:* www.mdah.state.ms.us, pg 789

Swan, David, Sleeping Bear Press™, 310 N Main St, Suite 300, Chelsea, MI 48118 *Tel:* 734-475-4411 *Toll Free Tel:* 800-487-2323 *Fax:* 734-475-0787 *E-mail:* sleepingbear@thomson.com *Web Site:* www.sleepingbearpress.com, pg 250

Swanberg, Ron, Graphic World Publishing Services, 11687 Adie Rd, Maryland Heights, MO 63043 *Tel:* 314-567-9854 *Fax:* 314-567-0360, pg 600

Swann, Sy, National Federation of State Poetry Societies Annual Poetry Contest, 13211 NW Holly Rd, Bremerton, WA 98312 *Web Site:* www.NFSPS.com, pg 791

Swanson, Bill, Triumph Books, 601 S LaSalle St, Suite 500, Chicago, IL 60605 *Tel:* 312-939-3330 *Toll Free Tel:* 800-335-5323 *Fax:* 312-663-3557 *E-mail:* orders@triumphbooks.com *Web Site:* www.triumphbooks.com, pg 276

Swanson, Eric, John Wiley & Sons Inc Scientific/Technical/Medical Publishing, 111 River St, Hoboken, NJ 07030 *Tel:* 201-748-6000 *Toll Free Tel:* 800-225-5945 (cust serv) *Fax:* 201-748-8728 *E-mail:* info@wiley.com *Web Site:* www.wiley.com, pg 300

Swanson, Eric A, John Wiley & Sons Inc, 111 River St, Hoboken, NJ 07030 *Tel:* 201-748-6000 *Toll Free Tel:* 800-225-5945 (cust serv) *Fax:* 201-748-6088 *E-mail:* info@wiley.com *Web Site:* www.wiley.com, pg 299

Swanson-Davies, Linda, Glimmer Train Press Inc, 1211 NW Glisan St, No 207, Portland, OR 97209 *Tel:* 503-221-0836 *Fax:* 503-221-0837 *E-mail:* info@glimmertrain.com *Web Site:* www.glimmertrain.com, pg 105

Swart, Ed, Scholastic Trade Division, 557 Broadway, New York, NY 10012 *Tel:* 212-343-6100; 212-343-4685 (export sales) *Fax:* 212-343-4714 (export sales) *Web Site:* www.scholastic.com, pg 242

Swartzlander, Emily, Thurber Prize for American Humor, 77 Jefferson Ave, Columbus, OH 43215 *Tel:* 614-464-1032 *Fax:* 614-280-3645 *E-mail:* thurberhouse@thurberhouse.org *Web Site:* www.thurberhouse.org, pg 808

Sweeney, Deborah, The Gislason Agency, 219 SE Main St, Suite 506, Minneapolis, MN 55414 *Tel:* 612-331-8033 *Fax:* 612-331-8115 *E-mail:* gislasonbj@aol.com *Web Site:* www.TheGislasonAgency.com, pg 632

Sweeney, Emma, Harold Ober Associates Inc, 425 Madison Ave, New York, NY 10017 *Tel:* 212-759-8600 *Fax:* 212-759-9428, pg 647

Sweeney, Frances, PREP Publishing, 1110 1/2 Hay St, Fayetteville, NC 28305 *Tel:* 910-483-6611 *Toll Free Tel:* 800-533-2814 *Fax:* 910-483-2439 *E-mail:* preppub@aol.com *Web Site:* www.prep-pub.com, pg 217

Sweeney, Jon, GemStone Press, Sunset Farm Offices, Rte 4, Woodstock, VT 05091 *Tel:* 802-457-4000 *Toll Free Tel:* 800-962-4544 *Fax:* 802-457-4004 *E-mail:* sales@gemstonepress.com *Web Site:* www.gemstonepress.com, pg 103

Sweeney, Jon M, Jewish Lights Publishing, Sunset Farm Offices, Rte 4, Woodstock, VT 05091 *Tel:* 802-457-4000 *Toll Free Tel:* 800-962-4544 *Fax:* 802-457-4004 *E-mail:* sales@jewishlights.com *Web Site:* www.jewishlights.com, pg 140

Sweeney, Jon M, SkyLight Paths Publishing, Sunset Farm Offices, Rte 4, Woodstock, VT 05091 *Tel:* 802-457-4000 *Toll Free Tel:* 800-962-4544 *Fax:* 802-457-4004 *E-mail:* editorial@skylightpaths.com *Web Site:* www.skylightpaths.com, pg 250

Sweet, Christopher, Harry N Abrams Inc, 100 Fifth Ave, New York, NY 10011 *Tel:* 212-206-7715 *Toll Free Tel:* 800-345-1359 *Fax:* 212-645-8437 *E-mail:* webmaster@abramsbooks.com *Web Site:* www.abramsbooks.com, pg 3

Sweet, Neil, Down East Books, PO Box 679, Camden, ME 04843 *Tel:* 207-594-9544 *Toll Free Tel:* 800-766-1670 (ME only) *Fax:* 207-594-7215 *Web Site:* www.downeastbooks.com, pg 83

Sweetland, Helen, Sierra Club Books, 85 Second St, 2nd fl, San Francisco, CA 94105 *Tel:* 415-977-5500 *Fax:* 415-977-5792 *E-mail:* books.publishing@sierraclub.org *Web Site:* www.sierraclub.org/books, pg 247

Sweetland, Helen, Sierra Club Books Adult Trade Division, 85 Second St, 2nd fl, San Francisco, CA 94105 *Tel:* 415-977-5500 *Fax:* 415-977-5792 *E-mail:* books.publishing@sierraclub.org *Web Site:* ww.sierraclub.org/books, pg 247

Swenson, Troy, Academy of American Poets Fellowship, 588 Broadway, Suite 604, New York, NY 10012 *Tel:* 212-274-0343 *Fax:* 212-274-9427 *E-mail:* academy@poets.org *Web Site:* www.poets.org, pg 757

Swenson, Troy, The Academy of American Poets Inc, 588 Broadway, Suite 604, New York, NY 10012 *Tel:* 212-274-0343 *Fax:* 212-274-9427 *E-mail:* academy@poets.org *Web Site:* www.poets.org, pg 675

Swerdzewski, Joe, FPMI Solutions Inc, 4901 University Sq, Suite 3, Huntsville, AL 35816 *Tel:* 256-539-1850 *Fax:* 256-539-0911 *E-mail:* books@fpmi.com *Web Site:* www.fpmisolutions.com, pg 100

Swets, Gary, Reformation Heritage Books, 2919 Leonard St NE, Grand Rapids, MI 49525 *Tel:* 616-977-0599 *Fax:* 616-285-3246 *E-mail:* orders@heritagebooks.org *Web Site:* www.heritagebooks.org, pg 230

Swiac, Chris, Fodor's Travel Publications, 1745 Broadway, New York, NY 10019 *Tel:* 212-572-8784 *Toll Free Tel:* 800-733-3000 *Fax:* 212-572-2248 *Web Site:* www.fodors.com, pg 98

Swiatek, Rob, Donald Keyhoe Journalism Award, PO Box 277, Mount Rainier, MD 20712 *Tel:* 703-684-6032 *Fax:* 703-684-6032 *Web Site:* www.fufor.com, pg 782

Swift, Isabel, Harlequin Enterprises Ltd, 233 Broadway, Suite 1001, New York, NY 10279 *Tel:* 212-553-4200 *Fax:* 212-227-8969 *E-mail:* customer.ecare@harlequin.ca *Web Site:* www.eharlequin.com; www.luna-books.com; www.mirabooks.com; www.reddressink.com; www.steeplehill.com, pg 115

Swift, Isabel, Harlequin Enterprises Ltd, 225 Duncan Mill Rd, Don Mills, ON M3B 3K9, Canada *Tel:* 416-445-5860 *Fax:* 416-445-8655 *Web Site:* www.eharlequin.com; www.luna-books.com; www.mirabooks.com; www.reddressink.com; www.steeplehill.com, pg 549

Swift, Isabel, Worldwide Library, 225 Duncan Mill Rd, Don Mills, ON M3B 3K9, Canada *Tel:* 416-445-5860 *Fax:* 416-445-8655; 416-445-8736 *Web Site:* www.eharlequin.com, pg 567

Swift, Jackie, McBooks Press Inc, 520 N Meadow St, Ithaca, NY 14850 *Tel:* 607-272-2114 *Toll Free Tel:* 888-266-5711 *Fax:* 607-273-6068 *E-mail:* mcbooks@mcbooks.com *Web Site:* www.mcbooks.com, pg 166

Swift, Kent, Arrow Map Inc, 58 Norfolk Ave, Unit 4, South Easton, MA 02375 *Tel:* 508-230-2112 *Toll Free Tel:* 800-343-7500 *Fax:* 508-230-8186 *E-mail:* amisales@arrowmap.com *Web Site:* www.arrowmap.com, pg 24

Swinwood, Craig, Harlequin Enterprises Ltd, 225 Duncan Mill Rd, Don Mills, ON M3B 3K9, Canada *Tel:* 416-445-5860 *Fax:* 416-445-8655 *Web Site:* www.

eharlequin.com; www.luna-books.com; www.mirabooks.com; www.reddressink.com; www.steeplehill.com, pg 549

Switzer, David M, Crystalline Sphere Publishing, 47 Bridgeport Rd E, Waterloo, ON N2J 2J4, Canada *E-mail:* csp@golden.net *Web Site:* crystallinesphere.com, pg 595

Swope, Pamela K, Philosophy Documentation Center, PO Box 7147, Charlottesville, VA 22906-7147 *Toll Free Tel:* 800-444-2419 *E-mail:* order@pdcnet.org *Web Site:* www.pdcnet.org, pg 211

Syens, Gladys, Educators Progress Service Inc, 214 Center St, Randolph, WI 53956 *Tel:* 920-326-3126 *Toll Free Tel:* 888-951-4469 *Fax:* 920-326-3127 *E-mail:* epsinc@centurytel.net, pg 88

Sygall, Susan, Mobility International USA, 45 W Broadway, Eugene, OR 97401 *Tel:* 541-343-1284 *Fax:* 541-343-6812 *E-mail:* info@miusa.org *Web Site:* www.miusa.org, pg 176

Sylvan-Kim, Emily, Writers House LLC, 21 W 26 St, New York, NY 10010 *Tel:* 212-685-2400 *Fax:* 212-685-1781, pg 662

Sylve, Elvira C, Elvira C Sylve—Editorial & Secretarial Services, PO Box 870602, New Orleans, LA 70187 *Tel:* 504-244-8357 *Fax:* 504-244-8357 (call first) *E-mail:* elcsy58@aol.com, pg 612

Symon, Traci, Landmark Editions Inc, 1402 Kansas Ave, Kansas City, MO 64127 *Tel:* 816-241-4919 *Fax:* 816-483-3755 *E-mail:* l_m_e@swbell.net *Web Site:* www.landmarkeditions.com, pg 148

Symonds, Genevieve, The Amwell Press, Ridge Plaza, 2004 Rte 31 & Cregar Rd, Clinton, NJ 08809 *Tel:* 908-638-9033 *Fax:* 908-638-4728, pg 19

Szabla, Liz, Scholastic Trade Division, 557 Broadway, New York, NY 10012 *Tel:* 212-343-6100; 212-343-4685 (export sales) *Fax:* 212-343-4714 (export sales) *Web Site:* www.scholastic.com, pg 242

Szost, Bernadette, Portfolio Solutions, 2419 Rte 82, Suite 208, Billings, NY 12510-0074 *Tel:* 845-226-8401 *Fax:* 845-226-8937 *E-mail:* PSJDC@frontiernet.net, pg 666

Szucs, Loretto, Ancestry Publishing, 360 W 4800 N, Provo, UT 84064 *Tel:* 801-705-7305 *Toll Free Tel:* 800-262-3787 *Fax:* 801-426-3501 *E-mail:* editor@ancestry.com; dealersales@ancestry-inc.com *Web Site:* www.ancestry.com, pg 19

Szumski, Bonnie, Greenhaven Press®, 15822 Bernardo Center Dr, Suite C, San Diego, CA 92127 *Tel:* 858-485-7424 *Toll Free Tel:* 800-877-4253 (cust serv & orders) *Fax:* 858-485-9549; 248-699-8051 (cust serv) *Toll Free Fax:* 800-414-5043 (orders only) *E-mail:* customerservice@gale.com; galeord@gale.com (orders) *Web Site:* www.gale.com/greenhaven, pg 109

Szumski, Bonnie, Lucent Books Inc, 15822 Bernardo Center Dr, Suite C, San Diego, CA 92127 *Tel:* 858-485-7424 *Fax:* 858-485-9549 *E-mail:* info@gale.com *Web Site:* www.gale.com/lucent, pg 159

Szuter, Christine, The University of Arizona Press, 355 S Euclid Ave, Suite 103, Tucson, AZ 85719-6654 *Tel:* 520-621-1441 *Toll Free Tel:* 800-426-3797 (orders) *Fax:* 520-621-8899 *Toll Free Fax:* 800-426-3797 *E-mail:* uapress@uapress.arizona.edu *Web Site:* www.uapress.arizona.edu, pg 280

Tabian, Robert E, Robert E Tabian/Literary Agent, 31 E 32 St, Suite 300, New York, NY 10016 *Tel:* 212-481-8484 (ext 330) *Fax:* 212-481-9582 *E-mail:* retlit@mindspring.com, pg 658

Tabin, Brett, Clear View Press, PO Box 11574, Marina del Rey, CA 90295 *Tel:* 310-902-0786 *Fax:* 310-821-9007 *E-mail:* editor@clearviewpress.com, pg 63

Tabor, Richard, CyclopsMedia.com, 1076 Eagle Dr, Salinas, CA 93905 *Tel:* 831-776-9500 *Fax:* 831-422-5915 *E-mail:* custserv@cyclopsmedia.com *Web Site:* www.cyclopsmedia.com, pg 75

Tabori, Lena, Welcome Books, 6 W 18 St, 3rd fl, New York, NY 10011 *Tel:* 212-989-3200 *Fax:* 212-989-3205 *E-mail:* info@welcomebooks.com *Web Site:* www.welcomebooks.com, pg 295

Tasker, Simon, Scholastic Trade Division, 557 Broadway, New York, NY 10012 *Tel:* 212-343-6100; 212-343-4685 (export sales) *Fax:* 212-343-4714 (export sales) *Web Site:* www.scholastic.com, pg 242

Tasman, Alice, Jean V Naggar Literary Agency, 216 E 75 St, Suite 1-E, New York, NY 10021 *Tel:* 212-794-1082, pg 645

Tate, Lori, Teachers College Press, 1234 Amsterdam Ave, New York, NY 10027 *Tel:* 212-678-3929 *Fax:* 212-678-4149 *E-mail:* tcpress@tc.columbia.edu *Web Site:* www.teacherscollegepress.com, pg 265

Tatich, Margaret, The Haworth Press Inc, 10 Alice St, Binghamton, NY 13904-1580 *Tel:* 607-722-5857 *Toll Free Tel:* 800-429-6784 *Fax:* 607-722-1424 *Toll Free Fax:* 800-895-0582 *E-mail:* getinfo@haworthpressinc.com *Web Site:* www.haworthpress.com, pg 118

Tattersall, James, The Mathematical Association of America, 1529 18 St NW, Washington, DC 20036 *Tel:* 202-387-5200 *Toll Free Tel:* 800-331-1622 (orders) *Fax:* 202-265-2384 *E-mail:* ldouglas@pmds.com *Web Site:* www.maa.org, pg 165

Taublib, Nita, Bantam Dell Publishing Group, 1745 Broadway, New York, NY 10019 *Tel:* 212-782-9000 *Toll Free Tel:* 800-223-6834 *Fax:* 212-302-7985 *Web Site:* www.randomhouse.com/bantamdell, pg 31

Tauches, Lorraine, Candlewick Press, 2067 Massachusetts Ave, Cambridge, MA 02140 *Tel:* 617-661-3330 *Fax:* 617-661-0565 *E-mail:* bigbear@candlewick.com *Web Site:* www.candlewick.com, pg 52

Taus, Ellen, Oxford University Press, Inc, 198 Madison Ave, New York, NY 10016-4314 *Tel:* 212-726-6000 *Toll Free Tel:* 800-451-7556 (orders) *Web Site:* www.oup.com/us, pg 200

Tautkus, William, Regatta Press Ltd, 750 Cascadilla St, Ithaca, NY 14851 *Tel:* 607-277-2211 *Fax:* 607-277-6292 *Toll Free Fax:* 800-688-2877 *E-mail:* info@regattapress.com *Web Site:* www.regattapress.com, pg 231

Tavani, Mark, Random House Publishing Group, 1745 Broadway, New York, NY 10019 *Toll Free Tel:* 800-200-3552 *Toll Free Fax:* 800-200-3552 *Web Site:* www.randomhouse.com, pg 227

Taveras, Mary, George Braziller Inc, 171 Madison Ave, Suite 1105, New York, NY 10016 *Tel:* 212-889-0909 *Fax:* 212-689-5405 *E-mail:* georgebraziller@earthlink.net *Web Site:* www.georgebraziller.com, pg 46

Tavitian, Jan, American Program Bureau Inc, 36 Crafts St, Newton, MA 02458 *Tel:* 617-965-6600 *Toll Free Tel:* 800-225-4575 *Fax:* 617-965-6610 *E-mail:* apb@apbspeakers.com *Web Site:* www.apbspeakers.com, pg 669

Taylor, Alexander, Curbstone Press, 321 Jackson St, Willimantic, CT 06226 *Tel:* 860-423-5110 *Fax:* 860-423-9242 *E-mail:* info@curbstone.org *Web Site:* www.curbstone.org, pg 74

Taylor, Barbara, American Industrial Hygiene Association, 2700 Prosperity Ave, Suite 250, Fairfax, VA 22031-4319 *Tel:* 703-849-8888 *Fax:* 703-207-3561 *E-mail:* infonet@aiha.org *Web Site:* www.aiha.org, pg 14

Taylor, Carli, Cottonwood Press Inc, 109-B Cameron Dr, Fort Collins, CO 80525 *Tel:* 970-204-0715 *Toll Free Tel:* 800-864-4297 *Fax:* 970-204-0761 *E-mail:* cottonwood@cottonwoodpress.com *Web Site:* www.cottonwoodpress.com, pg 69

Taylor, Carol, Lark Books, 67 Broadway, Asheville, NC 28801 *Tel:* 828-253-0467 *Toll Free Tel:* 800-284-3388 (cust serv) *Fax:* 828-253-7952 *E-mail:* info@larkbooks.com *Web Site:* www.larkbooks.com, pg 149

Taylor, Fred, Sentient Publications LLC, 1113 Spruce St, Boulder, CO 80302 *Tel:* 303-443-2188 *Fax:* 303-381-2538 *E-mail:* contact@sentientpublications.com; salesmanager@sentientpublications.com *Web Site:* www.sentientpublications.com, pg 245

Taylor, Jean, Washington State University Press, Cooper Publications Bldg, Grimes Way, Pullman, WA 99164-5910 *Tel:* 509-335-3518 *Toll Free Tel:* 800-354-7360 *Fax:* 509-335-8568 *E-mail:* wsupress@wsu.edu *Web Site:* wsupress.wsu.edu, pg 293

Taylor, Joe, Livingston Press, University of West Alabama, Sta 22, Livingston, AL 35470 *Tel:* 205-652-3470 *Fax:* 205-652-3717 *Web Site:* www.livingstonpress.uwa.edu, pg 157

Taylor, Karin, Poor Richards Award, 20 W 44 St, New York, NY 10036 *Tel:* 212-764-7021 *Fax:* 212-354-5365 *E-mail:* info@smallpress.org *Web Site:* www.smallpress.org, pg 799

Taylor, Karin, Small Press Center, 20 W 44 St, New York, NY 10036 *Tel:* 212-764-7021 *Fax:* 212-354-5365 *E-mail:* info@smallpress.org *Web Site:* www.smallpress.org, pg 699

Taylor, Katrina, Platinum One Publishing, 21W551 North Ave, Suite 132, Lombard, IL 60148 *Tel:* 630-935-7323 *Fax:* 203-651-1825 *E-mail:* customerservice@platinumonepublishing.com *Web Site:* www.platinumonepublishing.com, pg 573

Taylor, Kelli, Newmarket Publishing & Communications, 18 E 48 St, New York, NY 10017 *Tel:* 212-832-3575 *Toll Free Tel:* 800-669-3903 *Fax:* 212-832-3629 *E-mail:* mailbox@newmarketpress.com *Web Site:* www.newmarketpress.com, pg 190

Taylor, Lynn, M E Sharpe Inc, 80 Business Park Dr, Suite 202, Armonk, NY 10504 *Tel:* 914-273-1800 *Toll Free Tel:* 800-541-6563 *Fax:* 914-273-2106 *E-mail:* info@mesharpe.com *Web Site:* www.mesharpe.com, pg 246

Taylor, Marci, American Press, 28 State St, Suite 1100, Boston, MA 02109 *Tel:* 617-247-0022 *Fax:* 617-247-0022 *E-mail:* ampress@flash.net *Web Site:* www.americanpressboston.com, pg 16

Taylor, Mark, Standard Publishing Co, 8121 Hamilton Ave, Cincinnati, OH 45231 *Tel:* 513-931-4050 *Toll Free Tel:* 800-543-1301 *Fax:* 513-931-0950 *Toll Free Fax:* 877-867-5751 *E-mail:* customerservice@standardpub.com *Web Site:* www.standardpub.com, pg 257

Taylor, Mark, Tyndale House Publishers Inc, 351 Executive Dr, Carol Stream, IL 60188 *Tel:* 630-668-8303 *Toll Free Tel:* 800-323-9400 *Web Site:* www.tyndale.com, pg 277

Taylor, Mark A, Standard Publishing Co, 8121 Hamilton Ave, Cincinnati, OH 45231 *Tel:* 513-931-4050 *Toll Free Tel:* 800-543-1301 *Fax:* 513-931-0950 *Toll Free Fax:* 877-867-5751 *E-mail:* customerservice@standardpub.com *Web Site:* www.standardpub.com, pg 257

Taylor, Nick, Authors Guild, 31 E 28 St, New York, NY 10016 *Tel:* 212-563-5904 *Fax:* 212-564-8363; 212-564-5363 *E-mail:* staff@authorsguild.org *Web Site:* www.authorsguild.org, pg 680

Taylor, Nick, The Authors League of America Inc, 31 E 28 St, New York, NY 10016 *Tel:* 212-564-8350 *Fax:* 212-564-8363 *E-mail:* staff@authorsguild.com *Web Site:* www.authorsguild.com, pg 681

Taylor, Peter, Dawbert Press Inc, PO Box 67, Duxbury, MA 02331 *Tel:* 781-934-7202 *Toll Free Tel:* 800-933-2923 *Fax:* 781-934-2945 *E-mail:* info@dawbert.com *Web Site:* www.dawbert.com; www.familiesonthego.com; www.petsonthego.com, pg 77

Taylor, Rich, Motion Picture Association of America Inc (MPAA), 1600 "I" St NW, Washington, DC 20006 *Tel:* 202-293-1966 *Fax:* 202-293-7674 *Web Site:* www.mpaa.org, pg 691

Taylor, Sydney, Sydney Taylor Book Awards, 15 E 26 St, New York, NY 10010-1579 *Tel:* 212-725-5359 *Fax:* 212-481-4174 *E-mail:* ajl@jewishbooks.org *Web Site:* www.jewishlibraries.org, pg 808

Taylor, Yuval, Chicago Review Press, 814 N Franklin St, Chicago, IL 60610 *Tel:* 312-337-0747 *Toll Free Tel:* 800-888-4741 *Fax:* 312-337-5110 *E-mail:* editorial@ipgbook.com, pg 60

Taylor-Conrey, John, Archer Books, PO Box 1254, Santa Maria, CA 93456-1254 *Tel:* 805-934-9977 *Fax:* 805-934-9977 *E-mail:* info@archer-books.com *Web Site:* www.archer-books.com, pg 23

Taylor-Sherman, Claire, Augsburg Fortress Publishers, Publishing House of the Evangelical Lutheran Church in America, 100 S Fifth St, Suite 700, Minneapolis, MN 55402 *Tel:* 612-330-3300 *Toll Free Tel:* 800-426-0115 (ext 639 subns); 800-328-4648 (orders); 800-421-0239 (perms) *Fax:* 612-330-3455 *Toll Free Fax:* 800-421-0239 (perms & copyrights) *E-mail:* customerservice@augsburgfortress.org; copyright@augsburgfortress.org (for reprint permission requests) *Web Site:* www.augsburgfortress.org, pg 28

Teague, Andrew, Council of State Governments, 2760 Research Park Dr, Lexington, KY 40511 *Tel:* 859-244-8000 *Toll Free Tel:* 800-800-1910 *Fax:* 859-244-8001 *Web Site:* www.csg.org, pg 70

Teague, Beverly, Book Builders LLC, 425 Madison Ave, 19th fl, New York, NY 10017 *Tel:* 212-371-1110 *Fax:* 212-893-8680 *E-mail:* mail@bookbuildersllc.com *Web Site:* www.bookbuildersllc.com, pg 592

Teal, Patricia, Patricia Teal Literary Agency, 2036 Vista del Rosa, Fullerton, CA 92831 *Tel:* 714-738-8333 *Fax:* 714-738-8333, pg 658

Teeple, Charlotte, The Canadian Children's Book Centre, 40 Orchard View Blvd, Suite 101, Lower Level, Toronto, ON M4R 1B9, Canada *Tel:* 416-975-0010 *Fax:* 416-975-8970 *E-mail:* ccbc@bookcentre.ca *Web Site:* www.bookcentre.ca, pg 683

Tegge, Jeff, Sphinx Publishing, 1935 Brookdale Rd, Suite 139, Naperville, IL 60563 *Tel:* 630-961-3900 *Toll Free Tel:* 800-43-bright *Fax:* 630-961-2168 *E-mail:* info@sourcebooks.com *Web Site:* www.sourcebooks.com, pg 255

Teich, Annie Galvin, Pflaum Publishing Group, 2621 Dryden Rd, Dayton, OH 45439 *Tel:* 937-293-1415 *Toll Free Tel:* 800-543-4383 *Fax:* 917-293-1310 *Toll Free Fax:* 800-370-4450 *Web Site:* www.pflaum.com, pg 211

Teitelbawn, Maura, Abrams Artists Agency, 275 Seventh Ave, 26th fl, New York, NY 10001 *Tel:* 646-486-4600 *Fax:* 646-486-2358, pg 617

Tel, Martijn, Harcourt Achieve, 10801 N MoPac Expressway, Austin, TX 78759 *Tel:* 512-343-8227 *Toll Free Tel:* 800-531-5015 *Toll Free Fax:* 800-699-9459 *E-mail:* ecare@harcourt.com *Web Site:* www.harcourtachieve.com, pg 114

Tel, Martijn, Rigby, 10801 N MoPac Expressway, Austin, TX 78759 *Tel:* 512-343-8227 *Toll Free Tel:* 800-531-5015 *Toll Free Fax:* 800-699-9459 *E-mail:* ecare@harcourt.com *Web Site:* www.harcourtachieve.com, pg 232

Tel, Martijn, Steck-Vaughn, 10801 N MoPac Expressway, Austin, TX 78759 *Tel:* 512-343-8227 *Toll Free Tel:* 800-531-5015 *Toll Free Fax:* 800-699-9459 *E-mail:* ecare@harcourt.com *Web Site:* www.harcourtachieve.com, pg 258

Telikicherla, Puja, The Brookings Institution Press, 1775 Massachusetts Ave NW, Washington, DC 20036-2188 *Tel:* 202-797-6000 *Toll Free Tel:* 800-275-1447 *Fax:* 202-797-6195 *E-mail:* bibooks@brook.edu *Web Site:* www.brookings.edu, pg 48

Temme, Paul, CMP Books, 600 Harrison St, San Francisco, CA 94107 *Tel:* 415-947-6615; 408-848-3854 (orders) *Toll Free Tel:* 800-500-6875 (orders) *Fax:* 415-947-6015; 408-848-5784 (orders) *E-mail:* books@cmp.com *Web Site:* www.cmpbooks.com, pg 63

Temple, Johnny, Akashic Books, PO Box 1456, New York, NY 10009 *Tel:* 212-433-1875 *Fax:* 212-414-3199 *E-mail:* akashic7@aol.com *Web Site:* www.akashicbooks.com, pg 7

Temple, Johnny, International Association of Crime Writers Inc, North American Branch, PO Box 8674, New York, NY 10116-8674 *Tel:* 212-243-8966 *Fax:* 815-361-1477, pg 688

Templeton, Joan, The Ibsen Society of America, Dept of English, Long Island University, Brooklyn, NY 11201 *Tel:* 718-488-1050 *Fax:* 718-246-6302 *Web Site:* www.ibsensociety.liu.edu, pg 688

Thomas, Hargis, Oxford University Press, Inc, 198 Madison Ave, New York, NY 10016-4314 *Tel:* 212-726-6000 *Toll Free Tel:* 800-451-7556 (orders) *Web Site:* www.oup.com/us, pg 200

Thomas, Harry, Other Press LLC, 307 Seventh Ave, Suite 1807, New York, NY 10001 *Tel:* 212-414-0054 *Toll Free Tel:* 877-843-6843 *Fax:* 212-414-0939 *E-mail:* editor@otherpress.com; orders@otherpress.com *Web Site:* www.otherpress.com, pg 199

Thomas, Harry, Other Press LLC, 307 Seventh Ave, Suite 1807, New York, NY 10001 *Tel:* 212-414-0054 *Toll Free Tel:* 877-THE-OTHER *Fax:* 212-414-0939 *E-mail:* orders@otherpress.com *Web Site:* www.otherpress.com, pg 573

Thomas, James A, ASTM International, 100 Barr Harbor Dr, West Conshohocken, PA 19428 *Tel:* 610-832-9500 *Fax:* 610-832-9555 *E-mail:* service@astm.org *Web Site:* www.astm.org, pg 27

Thomas, JoAnne, New Horizon Press, PO Box 669, Far Hills, NJ 07931-0669 *Tel:* 908-604-6311 *Toll Free Tel:* 800-533-7978 (orders only) *Fax:* 908-604-6330 *E-mail:* nhp@newhorizonpressbooks.com, pg 188

Thomas, John, Liturgy Training Publications, 1800 N Hermitage Ave, Chicago, IL 60622-1101 *Tel:* 773-486-8970 *Toll Free Tel:* 800-933-1800 (US & Canada only) *Fax:* 773-486-7094 *Toll Free Fax:* 800-933-7094 (US & Canada only) *E-mail:* orders@ltp.org *Web Site:* www.ltp.org, pg 156

Thomas, Karen, Kensington Publishing Corp, 850 Third Ave, New York, NY 10022 *Tel:* 212-407-1500 *Toll Free Tel:* 800-221-2647 *Fax:* 212-935-0699 *Web Site:* www.kensingtonbooks.com, pg 145

Thomas, Kelly, Society for Industrial & Applied Mathematics, 3600 University City Science Ctr, Philadelphia, PA 19104-2688 *Tel:* 215-382-9800 *Toll Free Tel:* 800-447-7426 *Fax:* 215-386-7999 *E-mail:* siam@siam.org *Web Site:* www.siam.org, pg 251

Thomas, Maja, Time Warner Audio Books, Sports Illustrated Bldg, 135 W 50 St, New York, NY 10020 *Tel:* 212-522-7334 *Fax:* 212-522-7994 *Web Site:* www.twbookmark.com/audiobooks, pg 271

Thomas, Mark B, Review & Herald Publishing Association, 55 W Oak Ridge Dr, Hagerstown, MD 21740 *Tel:* 301-393-3000 *Toll Free Tel:* 800-234-7630 *Fax:* 301-393-4055 (periodicals); 301-393-3222 *E-mail:* editorial@rhpa.org *Web Site:* www.reviewandherald.com, pg 232

Thomas, Michael Payne, Charles C Thomas Publisher Ltd, 2600 S First St, Springfield, IL 62704 *Tel:* 217-789-8980 *Toll Free Tel:* 800-258-8980 *Fax:* 217-789-9130 *E-mail:* books@ccthomas.com *Web Site:* www.ccthomas.com, pg 269

Thomas, Susan, Ludwig von Mises Institute, 518 W Magnolia Ave, Auburn, AL 36832 *Tel:* 334-321-2100 *Fax:* 334-321-2119 *Web Site:* www.mises.org, pg 160

Thomas, William, Abrams & Co Publishers Inc, 61 Mattatuck Heights Rd, Waterbury, CT 06705 *Tel:* 203-756-6562 *Toll Free Tel:* 800-227-9120 *Fax:* 203-756-2895 *Toll Free Fax:* 800-737-3322, pg 3

Thomas, William, Doubleday Broadway Publishing Group, 1745 Broadway, New York, NY 10019 *Tel:* 212-782-9000 *Toll Free Tel:* 800-223-6834; 800-223-5780 (sales) *Fax:* 212-302-7985 (correspondence); 212-492-9862 (orders), pg 82

Thomas, William, Graphic Learning, 61 Mattatuck Heights Rd, Waterbury, CT 06705 *Tel:* 203-756-6562 *Toll Free Tel:* 800-874-0029; 800-227-9120 *Fax:* 203-756-2895 *Toll Free Fax:* 800-737-3322, pg 108

Thomas, William D, The Letter People®, 61 Mattatuck Heights Rd, Waterbury, CT 06705 *Tel:* 203-756-6562 *Toll Free Tel:* 800-227-9120; 800-874-0029 *Fax:* 203-756-2895 *Toll Free Fax:* 800-737-3322 *Web Site:* letterpeople.com, pg 153

Thomas-Pittari, Diane, Harcourt School Publishers, 6277 Sea Harbor Dr, Orlando, FL 32887 *Tel:* 407-345-2000 *Toll Free Tel:* 800-225-5425 (cust serv) *Fax:* 407-352-

3445 *Toll Free Fax:* 800-874-6418 *E-mail:* hbspcs@hbschool.com *Web Site:* www.harcourtschool.com, pg 114

Thompson, A, Academic International Press, PO Box 1111, Gulf Breeze, FL 32562-1111 *Tel:* 850-932-5478 *Fax:* 850-934-0953 *E-mail:* info@ai-press.com *Web Site:* www.ai-press.com, pg 4

Thompson, Allister, Napoleon Publishing/Rendezvous Press, 178 Willowdale Ave, Suite 201, Toronto, ON M2N 4Y8, Canada *Tel:* 416-730-9052 *Toll Free Tel:* 877-730-9052 *Fax:* 416-730-8096 *E-mail:* napoleonpublishing@transmedia95.com *Web Site:* www.transmedia95.com, pg 555

Thompson, Hedy, English Literary Studies (Monograph Series), University of Victoria, Dept of English, Victoria, BC V8W 3W1, Canada *Tel:* 250-721-7237 *Fax:* 250-721-6498 *E-mail:* english@uvic.ca *Web Site:* www.engl.uvic.ca, pg 546

Thompson, Hugh, Association of College & Research Libraries, 50 E Huron St, Chicago, IL 60611 *Tel:* 312-280-2511 *Toll Free Tel:* 800-545-2433 (ext 2517) *Fax:* 312-280-2520 *E-mail:* acrl@ala.org *Web Site:* www.ala.org/acrl, pg 26

Thompson, Dr Jack, SAE (Society of Automotive Engineers International), 400 Commonwealth Dr, Warrendale, PA 15096-0001 *Tel:* 724-776-4841 *Toll Free Tel:* 877-606-7323 (cust serv) *Fax:* 724-776-0790 *E-mail:* publications@sae.org *Web Site:* www.sae.org, pg 237

Thompson, Jackie, Timber Press Inc, 133 SW Second Ave, Suite 450, Portland, OR 97204 *Tel:* 503-227-2878 *Toll Free Tel:* 800-327-5680 *Fax:* 503-227-3070 *E-mail:* mail@timberpress.com *Web Site:* www.timberpress.com, pg 271

Thompson, John, Broadman & Holman Publishers, 127 Ninth Ave N, Nashville, TN 37234-0114 *Tel:* 615-251-2520 *Fax:* 615-251-5004 *Web Site:* www.broadmanholman.com, pg 48

Thompson, John, Illumination Arts Publishing, 13256 Northup Way, Suite 9, Bellevue, WA 98005 *Tel:* 425-644-7185 *Toll Free Tel:* 888-210-8216 *Fax:* 425-644-9274 *E-mail:* liteinfo@illumin.com *Web Site:* www.illum.com, pg 131

Thompson, Keith, Thompson Educational Publishing Inc, 6 Ripley Ave, Suite 200, Toronto, ON M6S 3N9, Canada *Tel:* 416-766-2763 (admin & orders) *Fax:* 416-766-0398 (admin & orders) *E-mail:* publisher@thompsonbooks.com *Web Site:* www.thompsonbooks.com, pg 563

Thompson, Kim, Fantagraphics Books, 7563 Lake City Way NE, Seattle, WA 98115 *Tel:* 206-524-1967 *Toll Free Tel:* 800-657-1100 *Fax:* 206-524-2104 *E-mail:* ffbicomix@fantagraphics.com *Web Site:* www.fantagraphics.com, pg 95

Thompson, Liana, Texere, 55 E 52 St, New York, NY 10055 *Tel:* 212-317-5511 *Fax:* 212-317-5178 *E-mail:* Firstname_Lastname@etexere.com *Web Site:* www.etexere.com; www.etexere.co.uk, pg 267

Thompson, Margaret, The Federation of British Columbia Writers, PO Box 3887, Sta Terminal, Vancouver, BC V6B 2Z3, Canada *Tel:* 604-683-2057 *Fax:* 604-608-5522 *E-mail:* fedoffice@bcwriters.com *Web Site:* www.bcwriters.com, pg 687

Thompson, Myles C, Texere, 55 E 52 St, New York, NY 10055 *Tel:* 212-317-5511 *Fax:* 212-317-5178 *E-mail:* Firstname_Lastname@etexere.com *Web Site:* www.etexere.com; www.etexere.co.uk, pg 267

Thompson, Pam, Interlink Publishing Group Inc, 46 Crosby St, Northampton, MA 01060 *Tel:* 413-582-7054 *Toll Free Tel:* 800-238-LINK (238-5465) *Fax:* 413-582-7057 *E-mail:* info@interlinkbooks.com *Web Site:* www.interlinkbooks.com, pg 136

Thompson, Pat, American Catholic Press, 16565 S State St, South Holland, IL 60473 *Tel:* 708-331-5845 *Fax:* 708-331-5484 *E-mail:* acp@acpress.org *Web Site:* www.acpress.org, pg 12

Thompson, Robert, Music Publishers' Association of the United States, 2435 Fifth Ave, Suite 236, New York, NY 10016 *Tel:* 212-327-4044 *Fax:* 212-327-4044 *Web Site:* host.mpa.org; www.mpa.org, pg 691

Thomsom, Michael, Wm B Eerdmans Publishing Co, 255 Jefferson Ave SE, Grand Rapids, MI 49503 *Tel:* 616-459-4591 *Toll Free Tel:* 800-253-7521 *Fax:* 616-459-6540 *E-mail:* sales@eerdmans.com *Web Site:* www.eerdmans.com, pg 88

Thomson, Leah, Healthy Healing Publications, PO Box 436, Carmel Valley, CA 93924 *Tel:* 831-659-8324 *Fax:* 831-659-4044 *E-mail:* customerservice@healthyhealing.com *Web Site:* www.healthyhealing.com, pg 120

Thomson, Ron B, Pontifical Institute of Mediaeval Studies, Dept of Publications, 59 Queens Park Crescent E, Toronto, ON M5S 2C4, Canada *Tel:* 416-926-7142 *Fax:* 416-926-7292 *E-mail:* pontifex@chass.utoronto.ca *Web Site:* www.pims.ca, pg 558

Thomson, Ryan, Captain Fiddle Publications, 4 Elm Ct, Newmarket, NH 03857 *Tel:* 603-659-2658 *E-mail:* cfiddle@tiac.net *Web Site:* www.captainfiddle.com, pg 53

Thomson-Black, Jean E, Yale University Press, 302 Temple St, New Haven, CT 06511 *Tel:* 203-432-0960; 401-531-2800 (cust serv) *Toll Free Tel:* 800-405-1619 (cust serv) *Fax:* 203-432-0948; 401-531-2801 (cust serv) *Toll Free Fax:* 800-406-9145 (cust serv) *E-mail:* customer.care@trilateral.org (cust serv) *Web Site:* www.yale.edu/yup/, pg 305

Thoreson, John, J Weston Walch Publisher, 321 Valley St, Portland, ME 04104 *Tel:* 207-772-2846 *Toll Free Tel:* 800-341-6094 *Fax:* 207-772-3105 *Toll Free Fax:* 888-991-5755 *E-mail:* customerservice@mail.walch.com *Web Site:* www.walch.com, pg 292

Thornton, Allen, Susan Thornton, 5108 South St, Vermilion, OH 44089 *Tel:* 440-967-1757 *E-mail:* thornton@hbr.net, pg 612

Thornton, David, Group Publishing Inc, 1515 Cascade Ave, Loveland, CO 80538 *Tel:* 970-669-3836 *Toll Free Tel:* 800-447-1070 *Fax:* 970-678-4392 *E-mail:* innovatr@grouppublishing.com *Web Site:* www.grouppublishing.com, pg 110

Thornton, Greg, Moody Press, 820 N La Salle Blvd, Chicago, IL 60610 *Tel:* 312-329-2111 *Toll Free Tel:* 800-678-8812 *Fax:* 312-329-2019 *Web Site:* www.moodypress.org, pg 177

Thornton, John F, The Spieler Agency, 154 W 57 St, 13th fl, Rm 135, New York, NY 10019 *Tel:* 212-757-4439 *Web Site:* spieleragency.com, pg 656

Thornton, Susan, Susan Thornton, 5108 South St, Vermilion, OH 44089 *Tel:* 440-967-1757 *E-mail:* thornton@hbr.net, pg 612

Thornton, Thomas N, Andrews McMeel Publishing, 4520 Main St, Suite 700, Kansas City, MO 64111-7701 *Tel:* 816-932-6700 *Toll Free Tel:* 800-851-8923 *Web Site:* www.universal.com/amp, pg 169

Thorpe, Andrea, Sarah Josepha Hale Award, 58 N Main, Newport, NH 03773 *Tel:* 603-863-3430 *Fax:* 603-863-3022 *E-mail:* rfl@newport.lib.nh.us *Web Site:* www.newport.lib.nh.us, pg 777

Thorpe, Diantha C, The Shoe String Press Inc, 2 Linsley St, North Haven, CT 06473 *Tel:* 203-239-2702 *Fax:* 203-239-2568 *E-mail:* info@shoestringpress.com; books@shoestringpress.com *Web Site:* www.shoestringpress.com, pg 246

Thorpe, Megan, Silver Lake Publishing, 3501 W Sunset Blvd, Los Angeles, CA 90026 *Tel:* 323-663-3082 *Fax:* 323-663-3084 *E-mail:* theeditors@silverlakepub.com; results@silverlakepub.com *Web Site:* www.silverlakepub.com, pg 247

Thrasher, Belinda, Appalachian Mountain Club Books, 5 Joy St, Boston, MA 02108 *Tel:* 617-523-0655 *Fax:* 617-523-0722 *Web Site:* www.outdoors.org, pg 21

Thrasher, William, Moody Press, 820 N La Salle Blvd, Chicago, IL 60610 *Tel:* 312-329-2111 *Toll Free Tel:* 800-678-8812 *Fax:* 312-329-2019 *Web Site:* www.moodypress.org, pg 177

Threadgill, Carolyn, Parenting Press Inc, 11065 Fifth Ave NE, Suite F, Seattle, WA 98125 *Tel:* 206-364-2900 *Toll Free Tel:* 800-99-BOOKS (992-6657) *Fax:* 206-364-0702 *E-mail:* office@parentingpress.com *Web Site:* www.parentingpress.com, pg 204

Threndyle, Steven, North American Snowsports Journalists Association, 460 Sarsons Rd, Kelowna, BC V1W 1C2, Canada *Tel:* 250-764-2143 *Fax:* 250-764-2145 *E-mail:* nasja@shaw.ca *Web Site:* www.nasja.org, pg 695

Thrombly, J, Wittenborn Art Books, 1109 Geary Blvd, San Francisco, CA 94109 *Tel:* 415-292-6500 *Toll Free Tel:* 800-660-6403 *Fax:* 415-292-6594 *E-mail:* wittenborn@art-books.com *Web Site:* art-books.com, pg 302

Thuillot, Dominique, Editions Hurtubise HMH Ltee, 1815 De Lorimier, Montreal, PQ H2K 3W6, Canada *Tel:* 514-523-1523 *Toll Free Tel:* 800-361-1664 (Canada only) *Fax:* 514-523-9969; 514-523-5955 (edit) *E-mail:* hurtubisehmh@hurtubisehmh.com *Web Site:* www.hurtubisehmh.com, pg 545

Thumann, Brian, The Fairmont Press Inc, 700 Indian Trail, Lilburn, GA 30047 *Tel:* 770-925-9388 *Fax:* 770-381-9865 *Web Site:* www.fairmontpress.com, pg 94

Thurston, Cheryl, Cottonwood Press Inc, 109-B Cameron Dr, Fort Collins, CO 80525 *Tel:* 970-204-0715 *Toll Free Tel:* 800-864-4297 *Fax:* 970-204-0761 *E-mail:* cottonwood@cottonwoodpress.com *Web Site:* www.cottonwoodpress.com, pg 69

Thurston, Linda, Bilingual Press/Editorial Bilingue, Hispanic Research Ctr, Arizona State Univ, Tempe, AZ 85287-2702 *Tel:* 480-965-3867 *Fax:* 480-965-8309 *E-mail:* brp@asu.edu *Web Site:* www.asu.edu/brp/brp, pg 38

Tibbitts, Gordon, Blackwell Publishers, 350 Main St, Malden, MA 02148 *Tel:* 781-388-8200 *Fax:* 781-388-8210 *E-mail:* books@blackwellpublishing.com *Web Site:* www.blackwellpublishing.com, pg 40

Tichenor, Irene, Bibliographical Society of America, PO Box 1537, Lenox Hill Sta, New York, NY 10021-0043 *Tel:* 212-452-2710 *Fax:* 212-452-2710 *E-mail:* bsa@bibsocamer.org *Web Site:* www.bibsocamer.org, pg 681

Tierney, Frank, Borealis Press Ltd, 110 Bloomingdale St, Ottawa, ON K2C 4A4, Canada *Tel:* 613-798-9299 *Fax:* 613-798-9747 *E-mail:* borealis@istar.ca *Web Site:* www.borealispress.com, pg 537

Tierney, P J, Beacon Press, 41 Mount Vernon St, Boston, MA 02108 *Tel:* 617-742-2110 *Toll Free Tel:* 800-225-3362 (orders only) *Fax:* 617-723-3097; 617-742-2290 *Web Site:* www.beacon.org, pg 34

Tierney, Pat, Harcourt Inc, 6277 Sea Harbor Dr, Orlando, FL 32887 *Tel:* 407-345-2000 *Toll Free Tel:* 800-225-5425 (cust serv) *Fax:* 407-352-3445 (cust serv), pg 114

Tierney, William, Spence Publishing Co, 111 Cole St, Dallas, TX 75207 *Tel:* 214-939-1700 *Fax:* 214-939-1800 *Web Site:* www.spencepublishing.com, pg 255

Tietz, Angelika, University of Oklahoma Press, 4100 28 Ave NW, Norman, OK 73069-8218 *Tel:* 405-325-2000 *Toll Free Tel:* 800-627-7377 (orders) *Fax:* 405-364-5798 (orders) *Toll Free Fax:* 800-735-0476 (orders) *E-mail:* oupress@ou.edu *Web Site:* www.oupress.com, pg 284

Tietze, Anna, The Plough Publishing House, Spring Valley, Rte 381 N, Farmington, PA 15437 *Tel:* 724-329-1100 *E-mail:* contact@bruderhof.com *Web Site:* www.plough.com, pg 215

Tigay, Alan M, The Harold U Ribalow Prize, 50 W 58 St, New York, NY 10019 *Tel:* 212-451-6289 *Fax:* 212-451-6257 *E-mail:* imarks@hadassah.org *Web Site:* www.hadassah.org, pg 802

Tighe, Sharon, Editorial Consultants Inc (WA), 3639 36 Ave S, Seattle, WA 98118 *Tel:* 206-323-1039 *Fax:* 206-229-3448 *E-mail:* meowmixz@aol.com, pg 597

Tiley, Warren, W W Norton & Company Inc, 500 Fifth Ave, New York, NY 10110-0017 *Tel:* 212-354-5500 *Toll Free Tel:* 800-233-4830 (orders & cust serv) *Fax:* 212-869-0856 *Toll Free Fax:* 800-458-6515 *Web Site:* www.wwnorton.com, pg 193

Tilley, Kim, American Society for Photogrammetry & Remote Sensing, 5410 Grosvenor Lane, Suite 210, Bethesda, MD 20814-2160 *Tel:* 301-493-0290 *Fax:* 301-493-0208 *E-mail:* asprs@asprs.org *Web Site:* www.asprs.org, pg 17

Tillinghast, Ron, Hay House Inc, 2776 Loker Ave W, Carlsbad, CA 92008 *Tel:* 760-431-7695 *Toll Free Tel:* 800-650-5115; 800-654-5126 (orders) *Fax:* 760-431-6948 *E-mail:* www@hayhouse.com *Web Site:* www.hayhouse.com, pg 118

Tilton, Robert, The University of Connecticut, The Realities of Publishing, Dept of English, 337 Mansfield Rd, Rm 332, Storrs, CT 06269-1025 *Tel:* 860-486-2141 *Fax:* 203-486-1530 *E-mail:* halfyawk@aol.com (instructor) *Web Site:* www.uconn.edu (for university); www.sp.uconn.edu/~en291isi/wecometopublishing.html, pg 755

Timmons, Barbara K, Management Sciences for Health, 165 Allandale Rd, Boston, MA 02130-3400 *Tel:* 617-524-7799 *Fax:* 617-524-2825 *E-mail:* bookstore@msh.org *Web Site:* www.msh.org, pg 162

Timony, Glenn, Penguin Group (USA) Inc Sales, 375 Hudson St, New York, NY 10014 *Tel:* 212-366-2000 *E-mail:* online@penguinputnam.com *Web Site:* www.penguin.com, pg 208

Timson, Deborah, Ideals Publications Inc, 535 Metroplex Dr, Suite 250, Nashville, TN 37211 *Tel:* 615-781-1427 *Toll Free Tel:* 800-558-4343 (customer service) *Fax:* 615-781-1447 *Web Site:* www.idealsbooks.com, pg 130

Tingley, Megan, Little, Brown and Company Books for Young Readers, 1271 Avenue of the Americas, New York, NY 10020 *Tel:* 212-522-8700 *Toll Free Tel:* 800-759-0190 *Fax:* 212-522-7997 *Web Site:* www.twbookmark.com, pg 156

Tinney, Diane, Moo Press Inc, PO Box 54, Warwick, NY 10990-0054 *Tel:* 845-987-7750 *Fax:* 845-987-7845 *E-mail:* info@moopress.com *Web Site:* www.moopress.com, pg 177

Tinney, Gary, Carolrhoda Books Inc, 241 First Ave N, Minneapolis, MN 55401 *Tel:* 612-332-3344 *Toll Free Tel:* 800-328-4929 *Fax:* 612-332-7615 *Toll Free Fax:* 800-332-1132 *E-mail:* info@lernerbooks.com *Web Site:* www.lernerbooks.com, pg 54

Tinney, Gary, First Avenue Editions, 241 First Ave N, Minneapolis, MN 55401 *Tel:* 612-332-3344 *Toll Free Tel:* 800-328-4929 *Fax:* 612-332-7615 *Toll Free Fax:* 800-332-1132 *E-mail:* info@lernerbooks.com *Web Site:* www.lernerbooks.com, pg 97

Tinney, Gary, Lerner Publications, 241 First Ave N, Minneapolis, MN 55401 *Tel:* 612-332-3344 *Toll Free Tel:* 800-328-4929 *Fax:* 612-332-7615 *Toll Free Fax:* 800-332-1132 *E-mail:* info@lernerbooks.com *Web Site:* www.lernerbooks.com, pg 152

Tinney, Gary, Lerner Publishing Group, 241 First Ave N, Minneapolis, MN 55401 *Tel:* 612-332-3344 *Toll Free Tel:* 800-328-4929 *Fax:* 612-332-7615 *Toll Free Fax:* 800-332-1132 *E-mail:* info@lernerbooks.com *Web Site:* www.lernerbooks.com, pg 152

Tinney, Gary, LernerClassroom, 241 First Ave N, Minneapolis, MN 55401 *Tel:* 612-332-3344 *Toll Free Tel:* 800-328-4929 *Fax:* 612-332-7615 *Toll Free Fax:* 800-332-1132 *E-mail:* info@lernerbooks.com *Web Site:* www.lernerbooks.com, pg 153

Tinney, Gary, LernerSports, 241 First Ave N, Minneapolis, MN 55401 *Tel:* 612-332-3344 *Toll Free Tel:* 800-328-4929 *Fax:* 612-332-7615 *Toll Free Fax:* 800-332-1132 *E-mail:* info@lernerbooks.com *Web Site:* www.lernerbooks.com, pg 153

Tinney, Gary, Runestone Press, 241 First Ave N, Minneapolis, MN 55401 *Tel:* 612-332-3344 *Toll Free Tel:* 800-328-4929; 800-332-1132 *Fax:* 612-332-7615 *E-mail:* info@lernerbooks.com *Web Site:* www.lernerbooks.com, pg 236

Tinney, Michael, White Wolf Publishing Inc, 1554 Litton Dr, Stone Mountain, GA 30083 *Tel:* 404-292-1819 *Toll Free Tel:* 800-454-9653 *Fax:* 678-382-3883 *Web Site:* www.white-wolf.com, pg 298

Tinsley, Tuck III, American Printing House for the Blind Inc, 1839 Frankfort Ave, Louisville, KY 40206 *Tel:* 502-895-2405 *Toll Free Tel:* 800-223-1839 (cust serv) *Fax:* 502-899-2274 *E-mail:* info@aph.org *Web Site:* www.aph.org, pg 16

Tio, Teresa, Institute of Puerto Rican Culture, PO Box 9024184, San Juan, PR 00902-4184 *Tel:* 787-724-0700 *Fax:* 787-724-8393 *E-mail:* www@icp.gobierno.pr *Web Site:* www.icp.gobierno.pr, pg 780

Tisch, Victoria, Holiday House Inc, 425 Madison Ave, New York, NY 10017 *Tel:* 212-688-0085 *Fax:* 212-421-6134, pg 123

Tisne, Claire, Random House Publishing Group, 1745 Broadway, New York, NY 10019 *Toll Free Tel:* 800-200-3552 *Toll Free Fax:* 800-200-3552 *Web Site:* www.randomhouse.com, pg 227

Tisseyre, Charles, Editions Pierre Tisseyre, 5757 Cypihot, St-Laurent, PQ H4S 1R3, Canada *Tel:* 514-334-2690 *Toll Free Tel:* 800-263-3678 *Fax:* 514-334-8395 *Toll Free Fax:* 800-643-4720 (Canada only) *E-mail:* ed.tisseyre@erpi.com, pg 563

Titan, Keith, Random House New Media Division, 1745 Broadway, New York, NY 10019 *Tel:* 212-782-9000, pg 227

Tittle, Martin B, Barbara S Anderson, 706 W Davis, Ann Arbor, MI 48103-4855 *Tel:* 734-995-0125; 734-994-6182 *Fax:* 734-994-5207, pg 590

Titus, Dan, Juice Gallery Multimedia, Box 151, Chino Hills, CA 91709 *Tel:* 909-597-0791 *Fax:* 909-597-0791 *E-mail:* info@juicegallery.com *Web Site:* www.juicegallery.com, pg 143

Tobar, Ruth, Children's Book Press, 2211 Mission St, San Francisco, CA 94110 *Tel:* 415-821-3080 *Fax:* 415-821-3081 *E-mail:* info@childrensbookpress.org *Web Site:* www.cbookpress.org, pg 60

Tobias, Ann, Handprint Books Inc, 413 Sixth Ave, Brooklyn, NY 11215-3310 *Tel:* 718-768-3696 *Fax:* 718-369-0844 *E-mail:* publisher@handprintbooks.com *Web Site:* www.handprintbooks.com, pg 113

Tobias, Teri, Robbins Office Inc, 405 Park Ave, 9th fl, New York, NY 10022 *Tel:* 212-223-0720 *Fax:* 212-223-2535, pg 652

Tobiassen, Virginia, McFarland & Co Inc Publishers, 960 Hwy 88 W, Jefferson, NC 28640 *Tel:* 336-246-4460 *Toll Free Tel:* 800-253-2187 (orders only) *Fax:* 336-246-5018; 336-246-4403 (orders) *E-mail:* info@mcfarlandpub.com *Web Site:* www.mcfarlandpub.com, pg 166

Tobin, Daniel, Emerson College Publishing Seminars, 120 Boylston St, Boston, MA 02116-8750 *Tel:* 617-824-8280 *Fax:* 617-824-8158 *E-mail:* continuing@emerson.edu *Web Site:* www.emerson.edu/ce, pg 743

Tobin, Peter, National Publishing Co, 11311 Roosevelt Blvd, Philadelphia, PA 19154-2105 *Tel:* 215-676-1863 *Toll Free Tel:* 888-333-1863 *Fax:* 215-673-8069 *Web Site:* www.courier.com, pg 184

Tod, Robert, TODTRI Book Publishers, 4049 Broadway, Suite 153, New York, NY 10032 *Tel:* 212-695-6622 ext 10 *Toll Free Tel:* 800-696-7299 *Fax:* 212-695-6988 *Toll Free Fax:* 800-696-7482 *E-mail:* todtri@mindspring.com *Web Site:* TODTRI.com, pg 272

Todd, Anne, Prentice Hall Business Publishing, One Lake St, Upper Saddle River, NJ 07458 *Tel:* 201-236-7000, pg 217

Todd, Jerry, St Martin's Press Paperback and Reference Group, 175 Fifth Ave, New York, NY 10010 *Fax:* 212-995-2488 *E-mail:* firstname.lastname@stmartins.com, pg 239

Todd, Trish, Fireside & Touchstone, 1230 Avenue of the Americas, New York, NY 10020, pg 97

Toff, Nancy, Oxford University Press, Inc, 198 Madison Ave, New York, NY 10016-4314 *Tel:* 212-726-6000 *Toll Free Tel:* 800-451-7556 (orders) *Web Site:* www.oup.com/us, pg 200

Toke, Arun N, Skipping Stones Honor Awards, 1309 Lincoln St, Eugene, OR 97401 *Tel:* 541-342-4956 *E-mail:* info@skippingstones.org *Web Site:* www.skippingstones.org, pg 806

Tokerud, Bjarne, Antiquarian Booksellers Association of Canada (ABAC), 824 Fort St, Victoria, BC V8W 1H8, Canada *Tel:* 250-360-2929 *Fax:* 250-361-1812 *E-mail:* info@abac.org *Web Site:* www.abac.org, pg 678

Tolen, Rebecca, Indiana University Press, 601 N Morton St, Bloomington, IN 47404-3797 *Tel:* 812-855-8817 *Toll Free Tel:* 800-842-6796 (orders only) *Fax:* 812-855-7931 (orders only); 812-855-8507 *E-mail:* iupress@indiana.edu; iuorder@indiana.edu (orders) *Web Site:* www.iupress.indiana.edu, pg 132

Toler, Violet M, Wayside Publications, PO Box 318, Goreville, IL 62939 *Tel:* 618-995-1157 *Web Site:* www.waysidepublications.com, pg 295

Toll, Kate, University of California Press, 2120 Berkeley Way, Berkeley, CA 94720 *Tel:* 510-642-4247 *Toll Free Tel:* 800-777-4726 *Fax:* 510-643-7127 *Toll Free Fax:* 800-999-1958 *E-mail:* askucp@ucpress.edu *Web Site:* www.ucpress.edu, pg 281

Tolnay, Tom, Birch Brook Press, PO Box 81, Delhi, NY 13753 *Tel:* 607-746-7453 (book sales & prodn) *Fax:* 607-746-7453 *E-mail:* birchbrook@usadatanet.net; birchbrkpr@yahoo.com *Web Site:* www.birchbrookpress.info, pg 39

Tom, Henry, The Johns Hopkins University Press, 2715 N Charles St, Baltimore, MD 21218-4363 *Tel:* 410-516-6900 *Toll Free Tel:* 800-537-5487 *Fax:* 410-516-6968 *Web Site:* www.press.jhu.edu, pg 141

Tomaselli, Valerie, American Book Producers Association (ABPA), 160 Fifth Ave, Suite 622, New York, NY 10010 *Tel:* 212-645-2368 *Toll Free Tel:* 800-209-4575 *Fax:* 212-242-6499 *E-mail:* office@abpaonline.org *Web Site:* www.abpaonline.org, pg 676

Tomaselli, Valerie, Book Producing: Making Books Happen, 160 Fifth Ave, New York, NY 10010-7003 *Tel:* 212-645-2368 *Toll Free Tel:* 800-209-4575 *Fax:* 212-242-6799 *E-mail:* office@abpaonline.org *Web Site:* www.abpaonline.org, pg 742

Tomasino, Christine K, The Tomasino Agency Inc, 70 Chestnut St, Dobbs Ferry, NY 10522 *Tel:* 914-674-9659 *Fax:* 914-693-0381 *E-mail:* BookNView@aol.com, pg 658

Tomb, Lynn Stowe, Merriam-Webster Inc, 47 Federal St, Springfield, MA 01102 *Tel:* 413-734-3134 *Toll Free Tel:* 800-828-1880 (orders & cust serv) *Fax:* 413-731-5979 *E-mail:* merriam_webster@merriam-webster.com *Web Site:* www.merriam-webster.com, pg 172

Tombrello, Drew, Wichita State University Playwriting Contest, 1845 Fairmount St, Wichita, KS 67260-0153 *Tel:* 316-978-3368 *Fax:* 316-978-3202 *Web Site:* www.wichita.edu, pg 811

Tomfohrde, Dennis, Voyageur Press, 123 N Second St, Stillwater, MN 55082 *Tel:* 651-430-2210 *Toll Free Tel:* 800-888-9653 *Fax:* 651-430-2211 *E-mail:* books@voyageurpress.com *Web Site:* www.voyageurpress.com, pg 292

Tomita, Susan, ALI-ABA Committee on Continuing Professional Education, 4025 Chestnut St, Philadelphia, PA 19104 *Tel:* 215-243-1600 *Toll Free Tel:* 800-CLE-NEWS *Fax:* 215-243-1664; 215-243-1683 *Web Site:* www.ali-aba.org, pg 8

Tomlinson, Mark, Society of Manufacturing Engineers, One SME Dr, Dearborn, MI 48121 *Tel:* 313-271-1500 *Toll Free Tel:* 800-733-4763 (cust serv) *Fax:* 313-271-2861 *Web Site:* www.sme.org, pg 252

Tompkins, Kate, Andrew Mowbray Inc Publishers, PO Box 460, Lincoln, RI 02865-0460 *Tel:* 401-726-8011 *Toll Free Tel:* 800-999-4697 *Fax:* 401-726-8061 *E-mail:* service@manatarmbooks.com *Web Site:* www.manatarmbooks.com, pg 180

Tondorf-Dick, Mary, Little, Brown and Company Adult Trade Division, 1271 Avenue of the Americas, New York, NY 10020 *Tel:* 212-522-8700 *Fax:* 212-522-2067 *Web Site:* www.twbookmark.com, pg 156

Toohey, Cathy, Scholastic Paperbacks, Teaching Resources & Reading Counts, 557 Broadway, New York, NY 10012-3999 *Tel:* 212-965-7241 *Fax:* 212-965-7487 *Web Site:* www.scholastic.com, pg 242

Toolan, Brian, Creative Homeowner, 24 Park Way, Upper Saddle River, NJ 07458-9960 *Tel:* 201-934-7100 *Toll Free Tel:* 800-631-7795 *Fax:* 201-934-8971 *E-mail:* info@creativehomeowner.com *Web Site:* www.creativehomeowner.com, pg 72

Toolan, Henry, Creative Homeowner, 24 Park Way, Upper Saddle River, NJ 07458-9960 *Tel:* 201-934-7100 *Toll Free Tel:* 800-631-7795 *Fax:* 201-934-8971 *E-mail:* info@creativehomeowner.com *Web Site:* www.creativehomeowner.com, pg 72

Toomey, Jeanne, Jeanne Toomey Associates, 95 Belden St, Rte 126, Falls Village, CT 06031 *Tel:* 860-824-5469; 860-824-0831; 860-824-3020 *Fax:* 860-824-5460, pg 658

Topalian, Nadine, Grosset & Dunlap, 345 Hudson St, New York, NY 10014 *Tel:* 212-366-2000 *E-mail:* online@penguinputnam.com *Web Site:* www.penguin.com, pg 110

Topping, David, Dumbarton Oaks, 1703 32 St NW, Washington, DC 20007 *Tel:* 202-777-0091 *Fax:* 202-339-6419 *E-mail:* publications@doaks.org *Web Site:* www.doaks.org, pg 84

Topping, Stephen, Johnson Books, 1880 S 57 Ct, Boulder, CO 80301 *Tel:* 303-443-9766 *Toll Free Tel:* 800-258-5830 *Fax:* 303-998-7594 *E-mail:* books@jpcolorado.com *Web Site:* www.jpcolorado.com; www.johnsonbooks.com, pg 142

Torgus, Judy, La Leche League International Inc, 1400 N Meacham Rd, Schaumburg, IL 60173 *Tel:* 847-519-7730 *Fax:* 847-519-0035 *E-mail:* llli@llli.org *Web Site:* www.lalecheleague.org, pg 151

Tornetta, Phyllis R, Phyllis R Tornetta Literary Agency, 4 Kettle Lane, Mashpee, MA 02649 *Tel:* 508-539-8821 *E-mail:* phyl4@capecod.net, pg 659

Toro, Maria, The New York Botanical Garden Press, 200 St & Kazimiroff Blvd, Bronx, NY 10458-5126 *Tel:* 718-817-8721 *Fax:* 718-817-8842 *E-mail:* nybgpress@nybg.org *Web Site:* www.nybg.org, pg 189

Torres, Alicia, AIP Science Writing Award, One Physics Ellipse, College Park, MD 20740-3843 *Tel:* 301-209-3096 *Fax:* 301-209-0846 *Web Site:* www.aip.org/aip/awards, pg 758

Torres, Karen, Warner Books, 1271 Avenue of the Americas, New York, NY 10020 *Tel:* 212-522-7200 *Fax:* 212-522-7991 *Web Site:* www.twbookmark.com, pg 293

Torres, Luisa, Salem Press Inc, 2 University Plaza, Suite 121, Hackensack, NJ 07601 *Tel:* 201-968-9899 *Toll Free Tel:* 800-221-1592 *Fax:* 201-968-1411 *E-mail:* csr@salempress.com *Web Site:* www.salempress.com, pg 239

Torres, Steve, Harcourt Trade Publishers, 525 "B" St, Suite 1900, San Diego, CA 92101 *Tel:* 619-231-6616 *Toll Free Tel:* 800-543-1918 (cust serv) *Toll Free Fax:* 800-235-0256 (cust serv) *Web Site:* www.harcourtbooks.com, pg 115

Torrey, Kate D, The University of North Carolina Press, 116 S Boundary St, Chapel Hill, NC 27514-3808 *Tel:* 919-966-3561 *Toll Free Tel:* 800-848-6224 (orders only) *Fax:* 919-966-3829 *Toll Free Fax:* 800-272-6817 (orders) *E-mail:* uncpress@unc.edu *Web Site:* www.uncpress.unc.edu, pg 283

Tosco, Kathleen, Shenandoah International Playwrights Retreat, 717 Quick's Mill Rd, Staunton, VA 24401 *Tel:* 540-248-4113 *Fax:* 540-248-4113 (call first) *E-mail:* sip@ntelos.net, pg 805

Totaro, Frank, Simon & Schuster Children's Publishing, 1230 Avenue of the Americas, New York, NY 10020 *Tel:* 212-698-7000 *Web Site:* www.simonsayskids.com, pg 248

Touchie, Pat, Heritage House Publishing Co Ltd, 17665 66 "A" Ave, No 108, Surrey, BC V3S 2A7, Canada *Tel:* 604-574-7067 *Toll Free Tel:* 800-665-3302

Fax: 604-574-9942 *Toll Free Fax:* 800-566-3336 *E-mail:* publisher@heritagehouse.ca; editorial@heritagehouse.ca; distribution@heritagehouse.ca *Web Site:* www.heritagehouse.ca, pg 550

Touchie, Rodger, Heritage House Publishing Co Ltd, 17665 66 "A" Ave, No 108, Surrey, BC V3S 2A7, Canada *Tel:* 604-574-7067 *Toll Free Tel:* 800-665-3302 *Fax:* 604-574-9942 *Toll Free Fax:* 800-566-3336 *E-mail:* publisher@heritagehouse.ca; editorial@heritagehouse.ca; distribution@heritagehouse.ca *Web Site:* www.heritagehouse.ca, pg 550

Tourtlotte, Alan N, Optical Society of America, 2010 Massachusetts Ave NW, Washington, DC 20036-1023 *Tel:* 202-223-8130 *Fax:* 202-223-1096 *E-mail:* custserv@osa.org *Web Site:* www.osa.org, pg 198

Towers, Cheryl R, The Local History Co, 112 N Woodland Rd, Pittsburgh, PA 15232 *Tel:* 412-362-2294 *Toll Free Tel:* 866-362-0789 *Fax:* 412-362-8192 *E-mail:* info@thelocalhistorycompany.com *Web Site:* www.thelocalhistorycompany.com, pg 157

Towle, Holley, TowleHouse Publishing, 394 W Main St, Suite B-9, Hendersonville, TN 37075 *Tel:* 615-822-6405 *Fax:* 615-822-5535 *E-mail:* vermonte@aol.com *Web Site:* www.towlehouse.com, pg 273

Towle, Mike, TowleHouse Publishing, 394 W Main St, Suite B-9, Hendersonville, TN 37075 *Tel:* 615-822-6405 *Fax:* 615-822-5535 *E-mail:* vermonte@aol.com *Web Site:* www.towlehouse.com, pg 273

Towne, Susan, Marquis Who's Who, 562 Central Ave, New Providence, NJ 07974 *Tel:* 908-673-1001 *Toll Free Tel:* 800-473-7020 *Fax:* 908-673-1189 *Web Site:* www.marquiswhoswho.com, pg 164

Towne, Susan, National Register Publishing, 562 Central Ave, New Providence, NJ 07974 *Tel:* 908-673-1001 *Toll Free Tel:* 800-473-7020 *Fax:* 909-673-1189 *Web Site:* www.nationalregisterpub.com, pg 185

Townes, H A, Bawn Publishers Inc, 8877 Meadowview Dr, West Chester, OH 45069-3545 *Tel:* 513-759-6288 *Fax:* 513-759-6299 *E-mail:* bawn@one.net *Web Site:* www.bawnagency.com, pg 620

Townsend, Charles D, ACETO Bookmen, 5721 Antietam Dr, Sarasota, FL 34231-4903 *Tel:* 941-924-9170, pg 4

Townsend, Larry, Southern Illinois University Press, PO Box 3697, Carbondale, IL 62902-3697 *Tel:* 618-453-2281 *Toll Free Tel:* 800-346-2680 *Fax:* 618-453-1221 *Toll Free Fax:* 800-346-2681 *E-mail:* jstetter@siu.edu *Web Site:* www.siu.edu/~siupress, pg 254

Townsend, Markus, Hamilton Books, 4501 Forbes Blvd, Suite 200, Lanham, MD 20706 *Tel:* 301-459-3366, pg 112

Townsend, Robert, Fellowship In Aerospace History, 400 "A" St SE, Washington, DC 20003 *Tel:* 202-544-2422 *Fax:* 202-544-8307 *E-mail:* info@historians.org *Web Site:* www.historians.org, pg 773

Townsend, Robert B, American Historical Association, 400 "A" St SE, Washington, DC 20003 *Tel:* 202-544-2422 *Fax:* 202-544-8307 *E-mail:* aha@historians.org *Web Site:* www.historians.org, pg 14

Townson, Donald, Townson Publishing Co Ltd, PO Box 1404, Bentall Centre, Vancouver, BC V6C 2P7, Canada *Tel:* 604-263-0014 *Fax:* 604-263-0014 *E-mail:* info@townson.ca *Web Site:* www.townson.ca, pg 563

Toy, Linda, McGraw-Hill Humanities, Social Sciences, Languages, 2 Penn Plaza, 20th fl, New York, NY 10121 *Tel:* 212-904-2000 *Toll Free Tel:* 800-338-3987 (cust serv) *Fax:* 614-755-5645 (cust serv) *E-mail:* first name_last name@mcgraw-hill.com *Web Site:* www.mhhe.com, pg 168

Toye, Michael, International Universities Press Inc, 59 Boston Post Rd, Madison, CT 06443 *Tel:* 203-245-4000 *Toll Free Tel:* 800-835-3487 *Fax:* 203-245-0775 *E-mail:* orders@iup.com *Web Site:* www.iup.com, pg 138

Truncale, Joseph, NAPL, 75 W Century Rd, Paramus, NJ 07652 *Tel:* 201-634-9600 *Toll Free Tel:* 800-642-6275 *Fax:* 201-634-0324 *E-mail:* membership@napl.org; orders@napl.org *Web Site:* www.napl.org, pg 692

Trupin, Jim, JET Literary Associates Inc, 2570 Camino San Patricio, Santa Fe, NM 87505 *Tel:* 212-971-2494 (NY voice mail); 505-474-9139 *Fax:* 505-474-9139 *E-mail:* query@jetliterary.com *Web Site:* www. jetliterary.com, pg 636

Trupin-Pulli, Elizabeth, JET Literary Associates Inc, 2570 Camino San Patricio, Santa Fe, NM 87505 *Tel:* 212-971-2494 (NY voice mail); 505-474-9139 *Fax:* 505-474-9139 *E-mail:* query@jetliterary.com *Web Site:* www.jetliterary.com, pg 636

Trusky, Tom, Hemingway Western Studies Series, Boise State University, 1910 University Dr, Boise, ID 83725 *Tel:* 208-426-1999 *Toll Free Tel:* 800-992-TEXT (992-8398) *Fax:* 208-426-4373 *Web Site:* www.boisestate. edu/hemingway/series.htm, pg 121

Trusky, Tom, Idaho Center for the Book, 1910 University Dr, Boise, ID 83725 *Tel:* 208-426-1999 *Toll Free Tel:* 800-992-8398 *Fax:* 208-426-4373 *Web Site:* www.lili.org/icb, pg 130

Tryneski, John, Association of American University Presses, 1427 E 60 St, Chicago, IL 60637 *Tel:* 773-702-7700; 773-702-7600 *Toll Free Tel:* 800-621-2736 (orders) *Fax:* 773-702-9756 (sales); 773-660-2235 (orders); 773-702-2708 *E-mail:* general@press. uchicago.edu *Web Site:* www.press.uchicago.edu, pg 26

Trzaska, Jennifer, Penguin Group (USA) Inc Sales, 375 Hudson St, New York, NY 10014 *Tel:* 212-366-2000 *E-mail:* online@penguinputnam.com *Web Site:* www. penguin.com, pg 208

Tsai, Alan, Marshall Cavendish Corp, 99 White Plains Rd, Tarrytown, NY 10591-9001 *Tel:* 914-332-8888 *Fax:* 914-332-1888 *E-mail:* mcc@marshallcavendish. com *Web Site:* www.marshallcavendish.com, pg 164

Tsuchiya, Tomoko, Quintessence Publishing Co Inc, 551 Kimberly Dr, Carol Stream, IL 60188 *Tel:* 630-682-3223 *Toll Free Tel:* 800-621-0387 *Fax:* 630-682-3288 *E-mail:* contact@quintbook.com *Web Site:* www. quintpub.com, pg 224

Tubach, Lisa, Individual Artists Fellowships, 3838 Davenport St, Omaha, NE 68131-2329 *Tel:* 402-595-2122 *Fax:* 402-595-2334 *Web Site:* www. nebraskaartscouncil.org, pg 780

Tucker, Dale, The Metropolitan Museum of Art, 1000 Fifth Ave, New York, NY 10028 *Tel:* 212-879-5500; 212-535-7710 *Fax:* 212-396-5062 *E-mail:* info@ metmuseum.org *Web Site:* www.metmuseum.org, pg 173

Tucker, Dan, American Book Producers Association (ABPA), 160 Fifth Ave, Suite 622, New York, NY 10010 *Tel:* 212-645-2368 *Toll Free Tel:* 800-209-4575 *Fax:* 212-242-6499 *E-mail:* office@abpaonline.org *Web Site:* www.abpaonline.org, pg 676

Tucker, Dan, Book Producing: Making Books Happen, 160 Fifth Ave, New York, NY 10010-7003 *Tel:* 212-645-2368 *Toll Free Tel:* 800-209-4575 *Fax:* 212-242-6799 *E-mail:* office@abpaonline.org *Web Site:* www. abpaonline.org, pg 742

Tucker, Ginger, University Press of Mississippi, 3825 Ridgewood Rd, Jackson, MS 39211-6492 *Tel:* 601-432-6205 *Toll Free Tel:* 800-737-7788 *Fax:* 601-432-6217 *E-mail:* press@ihl.state.ms.us *Web Site:* www. upress.state.ms.us, pg 287

Tucker, Janet, Text & Academic Authors Association Inc, PO Box 76477, St Petersburg, FL 33734-6477 *Tel:* 727-821-7277 *Fax:* 727-821-7271 *E-mail:* text@ tampabay.rr.com *Web Site:* www.taaonline.net, pg 701

Tucker, Joe, National State Publishing Association (NSPA), 207 Third Ave, Hattiesburg, MS 39401 *Tel:* 601-582-3330 *Fax:* 601-582-3354 *E-mail:* info@ govpublishing.org *Web Site:* www.govpublishing.org, pg 694

Tucker, Kathleen, Albert Whitman & Co, 6340 Oakton St, Morton Grove, IL 60053-2723 *Tel:* 847-581-0033 *Toll Free Tel:* 800-255-7675 *Fax:* 847-581-0039 *E-mail:* mail@awhitmanco.com *Web Site:* www. albertwhitman.com, pg 298

Tucker, Suzi, Zeig, Tucker & Theisen Inc, 3614 N 24 St, Phoenix, AZ 85016 *Tel:* 602-957-1270 *Toll Free Fax:* 800-688-2877 *E-mail:* zttorders@mindspring.com *Web Site:* www.zeigtucker.com, pg 307

Tudoran, Dorin, International Foundation for Election Systems, 1101 15 St NW, 3rd fl, Washington, DC 20005 *Tel:* 202-828-8507 *Fax:* 202-822-9744 *Web Site:* www.ifes.org, pg 137

Tufariello, Frank, Data Trace Publishing Co, 110 West Rd, Suite 227, Towson, MD 21204-2316 *Tel:* 410-494-4994 *Toll Free Tel:* 800-342-0454 (orders only) *Fax:* 410-494-0515 *E-mail:* info@datatrace.com *Web Site:* www.datatrace.com, pg 76

Tugeau, Chris, Christina A Tugeau Artist Agent LLC, 3009 Margaret Jones Lane, Williamsburg, VA 23185 *Tel:* 757-221-0666 *E-mail:* chris@catugeau.com *Web Site:* www.CATugeau.com, pg 667

Tugeau, Jeremy, Tugeau 2 Inc, 2132-A Central SE, Suite 196, Albuquerque, NM 87106 *Tel:* 505-842-0922 *Web Site:* www.tugeau2.com, pg 667

Tugeau, Nicole, Tugeau 2 Inc, 2132-A Central SE, Suite 196, Albuquerque, NM 87106 *Tel:* 505-842-0922 *Web Site:* www.tugeau2.com, pg 667

Tulchin, Lisa, Lynne Rienner Publishers Inc, 1800 30 St, Suite 314, Boulder, CO 80301 *Tel:* 303-444-6684 *Fax:* 303-444-0824 *E-mail:* cservice@rienner.com *Web Site:* www.rienner.com, pg 232

Tulku, Tarthang, Dharma Publishing, 2910 San Pablo Ave, Berkeley, CA 94702 *Tel:* 510-548-5407 *Toll Free Tel:* 800-873-4276 *Fax:* 510-548-2230 *E-mail:* info@dharmapublishing.com *Web Site:* www. dharmapublishing.com, pg 79

Tungseth, Marlene, Walker & Co, 104 Fifth Ave, 7th fl, New York, NY 10011 *Tel:* 212-727-8300 *Toll Free Tel:* 800-289-2553 *Fax:* 212-727-0984 *Toll Free Fax:* 800-218-9367 *E-mail:* firstinitiallastname@ walkerbooks.com *Web Site:* www.walkerbooks.com, pg 292

Tunis, Harry B, National Council of Teachers of Mathematics, 1906 Association Dr, Reston, VA 20191-1502 *Tel:* 703-620-9840 *Toll Free Tel:* 800-235-7566 *Fax:* 703-476-2970 *E-mail:* orders@nctm.org *Web Site:* www.nctm.org, pg 183

Tunseth, Scott, Augsburg Fortress Publishers, Publishing House of the Evangelical Lutheran Church in America, 100 S Fifth St, Suite 700, Minneapolis, MN 55402 *Tel:* 612-330-3300 *Toll Free Tel:* 800-426-0115 (ext 639 subns); 800-328-4648 (orders); 800-421-0239 (perms) *Fax:* 612-330-3455 *Toll Free Fax:* 800-421-0239 (perms & copyrights) *E-mail:* customerservice@ augsburgfortress.org; copyright@augsburgfortress.org (for reprint permission requests) *Web Site:* www. augsburgfortress.org, pg 28

Tuohy, Peter, American Institute of Certified Public Accountants, Harborside Financial Ctr, 201 Plaza Three, Jersey City, NJ 07311-3881 *Tel:* 201-938-3000 *Toll Free Tel:* 888-777-7077 *Fax:* 201-938-3329 *Web Site:* www.aicpa.org, pg 15

Tupholme, Iris, HarperCollins Publishers Canada, 2 Bloor St E, 20th fl, Toronto, ON M4W 1A8, Canada *Tel:* 416-975-9334 *Fax:* 416-975-9884 (publishing); 416-975-5223 (sales) *E-mail:* hccanada@harpercollins. com *Web Site:* www.harpercanada.com, pg 549

Turan, Kenneth, Los Angeles Times Book Prizes, 202 W First St, 6th fl, Los Angeles, CA 90012 *Tel:* 213-237-5775 *Fax:* 213-346-3599 *Web Site:* www.latimes. com/bookprizes, pg 786

Turchi, Peter, Warren Wilson College, MFA Program for Writers, PO Box 9000, Asheville, NC 28815-9000 *Tel:* 828-771-3715 *Fax:* 828-771-7005 *E-mail:* mfa@ warren-wilson.edu *Web Site:* www.warren-wilson. edu/~mfa, pg 756

Turcotte, Denis, Quebec Dans Le Monde, CP 8503, Quebec, PQ G1V 4N5, Canada *Tel:* 418-659-5540 *Fax:* 418-659-4143 *E-mail:* info@quebecmonde.com *Web Site:* www.quebecmonde.com, pg 559

Turcotte, Roger, Modulo Editeur Inc, 233 Ave Dunbar, Rm 300, Mont Royal, PQ H3P 2H4, Canada *Tel:* 514-738-9818 *Toll Free Tel:* 888-738-9818 *Fax:* 514-738-5838 *Toll Free Fax:* 888-273-5247 *Web Site:* www. moduloediteur.com, pg 554

Turcotte, Roger, Modulo-Griffon Inc, 233 Dunbar Ave, Suite 300, Mont Royal, PQ H3P 2H4, Canada *Tel:* 514-738-9818 *Toll Free Tel:* 888-738-9818 *Fax:* 514-738-5838 *Toll Free Tel:* 888-273-5247 *Web Site:* www.moduloediteur.com, pg 554

Tureen, Ed, Institute for International Economics, 1750 Massachusetts Ave NW, Washington, DC 20036 *Tel:* 202-328-9000 *Toll Free Tel:* 800-522-9139 *Fax:* 202-328-5432 *E-mail:* orders@iie.com *Web Site:* www.iie.com, pg 134

Turnbull, Diane, Ayer Company, Publishers Inc, One Lower Mill Rd, North Stratford, NH 03590 *Tel:* 603-669-7032 *Fax:* 603-669-7945 *E-mail:* ayerpub@yahoo. com *Web Site:* www.ayerpub.com, pg 30

Turner, Debra, University of Nebraska Press, 233 N Eighth St, Lincoln, NE 68588-0255 *Tel:* 402-472-3581 *Toll Free Tel:* 800-755-1105 (orders) *Fax:* 402-472-0308 *Toll Free Fax:* 800-526-2617 *E-mail:* press@ un1.edu *Web Site:* www.nebraskapress.unl.edu; www. bisonbooks.com, pg 283

Turner, Duncan, Alberta Book Awards, 10523-100 Ave, Edmonton, AB T5J 0A8, Canada *Tel:* 780-424-5060 *Fax:* 780-424-7943 *E-mail:* info@bookpublishers.ab.ca *Web Site:* www.bookpublishers.ab.ca, pg 758

Turner, Duncan, The Book Publisher's Association of Alberta, 10523 100 Ave, Edmonton, AB T5J 0A8, Canada *Tel:* 780-424-5060 *Fax:* 780-424-7943 *E-mail:* info@bookpublishers.ab.ca *Web Site:* www. bookpublishers.ab.ca, pg 682

Turner, Erin, The Globe Pequot Press, 246 Goose Lane, Guilford, CT 06437 *Tel:* 203-458-4500 *Toll Free Tel:* 800-243-0495 (cust serv) *Fax:* 203-458-4601 *Toll Free Fax:* 800-820-2329 (orders & cust serv) *E-mail:* info@globepequot.com *Web Site:* www. globepequot.com, pg 105

Turner, Gary, Golden Gryphon Press, 3002 Perkins Rd, Urbana, IL 61802 *Tel:* 217-840-0672 *Fax:* 217-384-4205; 217-352-9748 *E-mail:* gryphon@goldengryphon. com, pg 106

Turner, Geraldine, IODE Book Award, 40 St Clair Ave E, Suite 205, Toronto, ON M4T 1M9, Canada *Tel:* 416-925-5078 *Fax:* 416-925-5127, pg 780

Turner, Jeffrey, US Government Printing Office, Superintendent of Documents, Washington, DC 20401 *Tel:* 202-512-1707 *Toll Free Tel:* 888-293-6498 (cust serv); 866-512-1800 (orders) *Fax:* 202-512-1655 (bibliographic info); 202-512-2250 (orders & pricing) *Toll Free Fax:* 866-512-1800 *E-mail:* orders@gpo.gov *Web Site:* bookstore.gpo.gov (sales); gpoaccess.gov, pg 289

Turner, John H, Elsa Peterson Ltd, 41 East Ave, Norwalk, CT 06851 *Tel:* 203-846-8331 *Fax:* 203-846-8049 *E-mail:* epltd@earthlink.net, pg 608

Turner, Laura, Violet Prose Publications, PO Box 245, Victor, NY 14654 *Tel:* 585-924-3063 *Fax:* 585-924-4118 *E-mail:* VioletProsePubs@aol.com *Web Site:* www.VioletProsePubs.com, pg 574

Turner, Laurie, Empire Press Media/Avant-Guide, 444 Madison Ave, 35th fl, New York, NY 10122 *Tel:* 212-563-1003 *Fax:* 212-536-2419 *E-mail:* info@avantguide.com; editor@avantguide.com *Web Site:* www.avantguide.com, pg 90

Turner, Peter, Shambhala Publications Inc, Horticultural Hall, 300 Massachusetts Ave, Boston, MA 02115 *Tel:* 617-424-0030 *Toll Free Tel:* 888-424-2329 (orders only) *Fax:* 617-236-1563; 303-665-5292 (orders only) *E-mail:* editors@shambhala.com *Web Site:* www. shambhala.com, pg 245

Turner, Philip, Carroll & Graf Publishers, 245 W 17 St, 11th fl, New York, NY 10011-5300 *Tel:* 646-375-2570 *Fax:* 646-375-2571 *Web Site:* www.carrollandgraf.com, pg 54

Turnmire, Margie, McFarland & Co Inc Publishers, 960 Hwy 88 W, Jefferson, NC 28640 *Tel:* 336-246-4460 *Toll Free Tel:* 800-253-2187 (orders only) *Fax:* 336-246-5018; 336-246-4403 (orders) *E-mail:* info@mcfarlandpub.com *Web Site:* www.mcfarlandpub.com, pg 166

Turok, Katharine, Words into Print, 200 W 86 St, Suite 14-1, New York, NY 10024 *Tel:* 212-877-3211 *Fax:* 212-873-3796 *E-mail:* sas22@ix.netcom.com *Web Site:* www.wordsintoprint.org, pg 614

Turriff, Tracey, Doubleday Canada, One Toronto St, Suite 300, Toronto, ON M5C 2V6, Canada *Tel:* 416-364-4449 *Fax:* 416-957-1587 *Web Site:* www.randomhouse.ca, pg 542

Turriff, Tracey, Knopf Canada, One Toronto St, Suite 300, Toronto, ON M5C 2V6, Canada *Tel:* 416-364-4449 *Toll Free Tel:* 800-668-4247 (order desk) *Fax:* 416-364-0462 *Web Site:* www.randomhouse.ca, pg 552

Turriff, Tracey, Random House of Canada Ltd, One Toronto St, Unit 300, Toronto, ON M5C 2V6, Canada *Tel:* 416-364-4449 *Fax:* 416-364-6863 (edit & publicity); 416-364-6653 (subs rts) *Web Site:* www.randomhouse.ca, pg 559

Turriff, Tracey, Seal Books, One Toronto St, Suite 300, Toronto, ON M5C 2V6, Canada *Tel:* 416-364-4449 *Toll Free Tel:* 888-523-9292 (order desk) *Fax:* 416-957-1587 *Web Site:* www.randomhouse.ca, pg 560

Tusken, Matt, PRIMEDIA Business Directories & Books, 9800 Metcalf Ave, Overland Park, KS 66212 *Tel:* 913-967-1719 *Toll Free Tel:* 800-453-9620; 800-262-1954 (cust serv) *Fax:* 913-967-1901 *Toll Free Fax:* 800-633-6219 *E-mail:* bookorders@primediabooks.com *Web Site:* www.primediabooks.com, pg 218

Tutela, Joy E, David Black Literary Agency, 156 Fifth Ave, Suite 608, New York, NY 10010 *Tel:* 212-242-5080 *Fax:* 212-924-6609, pg 621

Tutiah, Dr Marvis, Hyperion Press Ltd, 300 Wales Ave, Winnipeg, MB R2M 2S9, Canada *Tel:* 204-256-9204 *Fax:* 204-255-7845 *E-mail:* tamos@mts.ca, pg 550

Tutiah, Marvis, Tamos Books Inc, 300 Wales Ave, Winnipeg, MB R2M 2S9, Canada *Tel:* 204-256-9204 *Fax:* 204-255-7845 *E-mail:* tamos@mts.net *Web Site:* www.escape.ca/~tamos, pg 562

Tuttle, Jon, Trustus Playwrights' Festival, 520 Lady St, Columbia, SC 29201 *Tel:* 803-254-9732 *Fax:* 803-771-9153 *E-mail:* trustus@trustus.org *Web Site:* www.trustus.org, pg 809

Tuttle, Reiko Chiba, Tuttle Publishing, Airport Business Park, 364 Innovation Dr, North Clarendon, VT 05759-9436 *Tel:* 617-951-4080 (edit); 802-773-8930 *Toll Free Tel:* 800-526-2778 *Fax:* 617-951-4045 (edit); 802-773-6993 *Toll Free Fax:* 800-FAX-TUTL *E-mail:* info@tuttlepublishing.com *Web Site:* www.tuttlepublishing.com, pg 277

Tweed, Charles, Jewel Box Theatre Playwriting Competition, 3700 N Walker, Oklahoma City, OK 73118-7099 *Tel:* 405-521-1786, pg 781

Tweeddale, John, Prentice Hall Engineering/Science & Math, One Lake St, Upper Saddle River, NJ 07458 *Tel:* 201-236-7000, pg 217

Twitchell, Gary, Neo-Tech Publishing, PO Box 60906, Boulder City, NV 89006-0906 *Tel:* 702-293-5552 *Fax:* 702-293-4342 *Web Site:* www.neo-tech.com, pg 187

Twomey, Anne, Warner Books, 1271 Avenue of the Americas, New York, NY 10020 *Tel:* 212-522-7200 *Fax:* 212-522-7991 *Web Site:* www.twbookmark.com, pg 293

Twomey, Mark, Liturgical Press, St John's Abbey, Collegeville, MN 56321 *Tel:* 320-363-2213 *Toll Free Tel:* 800-858-5450 *Fax:* 320-363-3299 *Toll Free Fax:* 800-445-5899 *E-mail:* sales@litpress.org *Web Site:* www.litpress.org, pg 156

Tyler, Diane, Smithsonian Federal Series Section, 750 Ninth St NW, Suite 4300, Washington, DC 20560-0950 *Tel:* 202-275-2233 *Fax:* 202-275-2274, pg 251

Tyler, Diane, Smithsonian Institution Press, 750 Ninth St NW, Suite 4300, Washington, DC 20560-0950 *Tel:* 202-275-2300 *Fax:* 202-275-2274 *E-mail:* inquiries@sipress.si.edu *Web Site:* www.sipress.si.edu, pg 251

Tyler, Ron, Texas State Historical Association, University Sta, DO-901, Austin, TX 78712 *Tel:* 512-471-1525 *Fax:* 512-471-1551 *E-mail:* comments@tsha.utexas.edu *Web Site:* www.tsha.utexas.edu, pg 267

Tyler, Stephanie, FourWinds Press LLC, 4157 Crossgate Dr, Cincinnati, OH 47025 *Tel:* 513-891-0415 *Fax:* 513-891-1648 *Web Site:* www.fourwindspress.com, pg 571

Tyler, Tracy, Random House Children's Books, 1745 Broadway, New York, NY 10019 *Tel:* 212-782-9000 *Toll Free Tel:* 800-200-3552 *Fax:* 212-782-9452 *Web Site:* www.randomhouse.com/kids, pg 226

Tyler-Parker, Sydney, Thomas Geale Publications Inc, PO Box 370540, Montara, CA 94037-0540 *Tel:* 650-728-5219 *Toll Free Tel:* 800-554-5457 *Fax:* 650-728-0918, pg 269

Tyner, Kim, Stewart, Tabori & Chang, 115 W 18 St, 5th fl, New York, NY 10011 *Tel:* 212-519-1200 *Fax:* 212-519-1210 *Web Site:* www.abramsbooks.com, pg 260

Tynes, Emily, American Civil Liberties Union, 125 Broad St, 18th fl, New York, NY 10004 *Tel:* 212-549-2500 *Toll Free Tel:* 800-775-ACLU (orders) *E-mail:* info@aclu.org *Web Site:* www.aclu.org, pg 676

Tyrrell, Robert, Orca Book Publishers, PO Box 468, Custer, WA 98240-0468 *Tel:* 250-380-1229 *Toll Free Tel:* 800-210-5277 *Fax:* 250-380-1892 *E-mail:* orca@orcabook.com *Web Site:* www.orcabook.com, pg 198

Tyson, Janet, EcceNova Editions, 15-1594 Fairfield Rd, Victoria, BC V8S 1G1, Canada *Tel:* 250-595-8401 *Fax:* 250-595-8401 *E-mail:* info@eccenova.com *Web Site:* www.eccenova.com, pg 543

Tyson, Marie, The Pilgrim Press/United Church Press, 700 Prospect Ave, Cleveland, OH 44115-1100 *Tel:* 216-736-3761 *Toll Free Tel:* 800-537-3394 (cust serv) *Fax:* 216-736-2207 *E-mail:* thepilgrimpress@thepilgrimpress.com *Web Site:* www.thepilgrimpress.com; www.theunitedchurchpress.com, pg 213

Tyson-Flyn, Bonnie, Pacific Press Publishing Association, 1350 N Kings Rd, Nampa, ID 83687-3193 *Tel:* 208-465-2500 *Toll Free Tel:* 800-447-7377 *Fax:* 208-465-2531 *Web Site:* www.pacificpress.com, pg 202

Tytel, Tanni, Penguin Young Readers Group, 345 Hudson St, New York, NY 10014 *Tel:* 212-366-2000 *E-mail:* online@penguinputnam.com *Web Site:* www.penguin.com, pg 208

Tzetzo, Elizabeth, The Perseus Books Group, 387 Park Ave S, 12th fl, New York, NY 10016 *Tel:* 212-340-8100 *Toll Free Tel:* 800-386-5656 (cust serv) *Fax:* 212-340-8115 *Web Site:* www.perseusbooksgroup.com, pg 210

Tzougros, George, Artist Fellowship Awards Program, 101 E Wilson St, 1st fl, Madison, WI 53702 *Tel:* 608-266-0190 *Fax:* 608-267-0380 *E-mail:* artsboard@arts.state.wi.us *Web Site:* www.arts.state.wi.us, pg 760

Ucciardo, Frank, Deadline Club, 15 Gramercy Park S, New York, NY 10003 *Tel:* 212-353-9598 *Fax:* 212-468-6360 *E-mail:* deadline@spj.org *Web Site:* www.pipeline.com/~deadline, pg 686

Ude, Wayne, Blue & Ude Writers' Services, PO Box 145, Clinton, WA 98236 *Tel:* 360-341-1630 *E-mail:* blueyude@whidbey.com *Web Site:* www.blueudewritersservices.com, pg 592

Udow, Roz, National Coalition Against Censorship (NCAC), 275 Seventh Ave, 9th fl, New York, NY 10001 *Tel:* 212-807-6222 *Fax:* 212-807-6245 *E-mail:* ncac@ncac.org *Web Site:* www.ncac.org, pg 692

Udris, Roslyn A, Paul H Brookes Publishing Co, PO Box 10624, Baltimore, MD 21285-0624 *Tel:* 410-337-9580 *Toll Free Tel:* 800-638-3775 *Fax:* 410-337-8539 *E-mail:* custserv@brookespublishing.com *Web Site:* www.brookespublishing.com, pg 48

Uettwiller, Carole, Harcourt School Publishers, 6277 Sea Harbor Dr, Orlando, FL 32887 *Tel:* 407-345-2000 *Toll Free Tel:* 800-225-5425 (cust serv) *Fax:* 407-352-3445 *Toll Free Fax:* 800-874-6418 *E-mail:* hbspcs@hbschool.com *Web Site:* www.harcourtschool.com, pg 114

Uhl, Xina Marie, XC Publishing, 931 E Avenida de las Flores, Thousand Oaks, CA 91360 *Tel:* 805-495-7768 *Fax:* 413-431-5515 *E-mail:* xuhl@xcpublishing.com *Web Site:* www.xcpublishing.com, pg 305

Uhler, Tony, ABC-CLIO, 130 Cremona Dr, Santa Barbara, CA 93117 *Tel:* 805-968-1911 *Toll Free Tel:* 800-368-6868 *Fax:* 805-685-9685 *E-mail:* sales@abc-clio.com *Web Site:* www.abc-clio.com, pg 3

Uhlich, Keith, Oxford University Press, Inc, 198 Madison Ave, New York, NY 10016-4314 *Tel:* 212-726-6000 *Toll Free Tel:* 800-451-7556 (orders) *Web Site:* www.oup.com/us, pg 200

Ullerick, Carolyn, LexisNexis®, 701 E Water St, Charlottesville, VA 22902 *Tel:* 434-972-7600 *Toll Free Tel:* 800-446-3410; 800-828-8341 (orders) *E-mail:* customer.support@lexisnexis.com *Web Site:* www.lexisnexis.com, pg 153

Ullman, Leslie, University of Texas at El Paso, Dept Creative Writing, MFA with Bilingual Option, 500 W University Ave, PMB 670, El Paso, TX 79968-9991 *Tel:* 915-747-5713 *Fax:* 915-747-5523 *E-mail:* mfadirector@utep.edu *Web Site:* www.utep.edu/cw, pg 756

Ulman, Juliet, Bantam Dell Publishing Group, 1745 Broadway, New York, NY 10019 *Tel:* 212-782-9000 *Toll Free Tel:* 800-223-6834 *Fax:* 212-302-7985 *Web Site:* www.randomhouse.com/bantamdell, pg 31

Ulrich, Don, Creative Arts of Ventura, PO Box 684, Ventura, CA 93002-0684 *Tel:* 805-643-4160; 805-659-0237, pg 665

Ulrich, Joyce, Pomegranate Communications, 775-A Southpoint Blvd, Petaluma, CA 94954-1495 *Tel:* 707-782-9000 *Toll Free Tel:* 800-227-1428 *Toll Free Fax:* 800-848-4376 *Web Site:* www.pomegranate.com, pg 216

Ulrich, Lamia, Creative Arts of Ventura, PO Box 684, Ventura, CA 93002-0684 *Tel:* 805-643-4160; 805-659-0237, pg 665

Underwood, Joanna, INFORM Inc, 120 Wall St, 14th fl, New York, NY 10005-4001 *Tel:* 212-361-2400 *Fax:* 212-361-2412 *Web Site:* www.informinc.org, pg 133

Underwood, Jon, Standard Publishing Co, 8121 Hamilton Ave, Cincinnati, OH 45231 *Tel:* 513-931-4050 *Toll Free Tel:* 800-543-1301 *Fax:* 513-931-0950 *Toll Free Fax:* 877-867-5751 *E-mail:* customerservice@standardpub.com *Web Site:* www.standardpub.com, pg 257

Underwood, Tim, Underwood Books Inc, PO Box 1609, Grass Valley, CA 95945-1609 *Tel:* 530-274-7199 *Web Site:* www.underwoodbooks.com, pg 278

Underwood, Will, Kent State University Press, PO Box 5190, Kent, OH 44242-0001 *Tel:* 330-672-7913; 330-672-8097 (sales office) *Toll Free Tel:* 800-247-6553 (orders) *Fax:* 330-672-3104 *Web Site:* www.kentstateuniversitypress.com, pg 145

Unger, David, Publishing Certificate Program at City College, Division of Humanities NAC 5225, City College of New York, New York, NY 10031 *Tel:* 212-650-7925 *Fax:* 212-650-7912 *E-mail:* ccnypub@aol.com *Web Site:* www.ccny.cuny.edu/publishing_certificate/index.html, pg 754

Unter, Jennifer, RLR Associates Ltd, 7 W 51 St, New York, NY 10019 *Tel:* 212-541-8641 *Fax:* 212-541-6052 *Web Site:* www.rlrassociates.net, pg 652

Unterburger, Amy L, InfoWorks Development Group, 2801 Cook Creek Dr, Ann Arbor, MI 48103-8962 *Tel:* 734-327-9669 *Fax:* 734-327-9686, pg 602

Unwalla, Fred, Pontifical Institute of Mediaeval Studies, Dept of Publications, 59 Queens Park Crescent E, Toronto, ON M5S 2C4, Canada *Tel:* 416-926-7142 *Fax:* 416-926-7292 *E-mail:* pontifex@chass.utoronto. ca *Web Site:* www.pims.ca, pg 558

Upchurch, Dave, Simon & Schuster Inc, 1230 Avenue of the Americas, New York, NY 10020 *Tel:* 212-698-7000 *Fax:* 212-698-7007 *Web Site:* www.simonsays. com, pg 249

Updike, David, Philadelphia Museum of Art, 2525 Pennsylvania Ave, Philadelphia, PA 19130 *Tel:* 215-684-7250 *Fax:* 215-235-8715 *Web Site:* www. philamuseum.org, pg 211

Updike, Jaci, Random House Sales & Marketing, 1745 Broadway, New York, NY 10019 *Fax:* 212-782-9000, pg 227

Uphoff, Count Joseph Jr, Arjuna Library Press, 1025 Garner St D, Space 18, Colorado Springs, CO 80905-1774, pg 23

Upton, Heidi, International Association of Business Communicators (IABC), One Hallidie Plaza, Suite 600, San Francisco, CA 94102 *Tel:* 415-544-4700 *Toll Free Tel:* 800-776-4222 *Fax:* 415-544-4747 *E-mail:* service_centre@iabc.com *Web Site:* www.iabc. com, pg 688

Upton, Pat, Workman Publishing Co Inc, 708 Broadway, New York, NY 10003-9555 *Tel:* 212-254-5900 *Toll Free Tel:* 800-722-7202 *Fax:* 212-254-8098 *E-mail:* info@workman.com *Web Site:* www.workman. com, pg 303

Urban, Amanda, International Creative Management, 40 W 57 St, New York, NY 10019 *Tel:* 212-556-5600 *Fax:* 212-556-5665 *Web Site:* www.icmtalent.com, pg 635

Urban, Thomas, Oriental Institute Publications Sales, 1155 E 58 St, Chicago, IL 60637 *Tel:* 773-702-9514 *Fax:* 773-702-9853 *E-mail:* oi-publications@uchicago. edu; oi-museum@uchicago.edu; oi-administration@ uchicago.edu *Web Site:* oi.uchicago.edu, pg 199

Urbania, Carl, Thomson Learning Inc, 200 First Stamford Place, Suite 400, Stamford, CT 06902 *Tel:* 203-539-8000 *Fax:* 203-539-7581 *E-mail:* communications@thomsonlearning.com *Web Site:* www.thomson.com/learning, pg 270

Urda, Gary, Simon & Schuster Sales & Distribution, 1230 Avenue of the Americas, New York, NY 10020 *Tel:* 212-698-7000, pg 249

Urdang, Laurence, Verbatim Books, 4 Laurel Heights, Old Lyme, CT 06371 *Tel:* 860-434-2104 *Web Site:* www.verbatimbooks.com, pg 290

Urmston, Craig, Kaeden Corp, PO Box 16190, Rocky River, OH 44116-0190 *Tel:* 440-617-1400 *Toll Free Tel:* 800-890-7323 *Fax:* 440-617-1403 *E-mail:* info@ kaeden.com *Web Site:* www.kaeden.com, pg 143

Urschel, William, The Narrative Press, 319 Salida Del Sol, Santa Barbara, CA 93109 *Tel:* 805-966-2184 *Fax:* 805-456-3915 *E-mail:* admin@narrativepress.com *Web Site:* www.narrativepress.com, pg 181

Ursell, Geoffrey, Coteau Books, 401-2206 Dewdney Ave, Regina, SK S4R 1H3, Canada *Tel:* 306-777-0170 *Toll Free Tel:* 800-440-4471 (Canada Only) *Fax:* 306-522-5152 *E-mail:* coteau@coteaubooks.com *Web Site:* www.coteaubooks.com, pg 541

Ursone, Adele, Hudson Park Press, Johnny Cake Hollow Rd, Pine Plains, NY 12567 *Tel:* 212-929-8898 *Fax:* 212-242-6137 *E-mail:* hudpark@aol.com *Web Site:* www.hudsonpark.com, pg 128

Uruburu, Paula PhD, Hofstra University, English Dept, 204 Calkins, Hempstead, NY 11549 *Tel:* 516-463-5454 *Fax:* 516-463-6395 *E-mail:* engpmu@hofstra.edu *Web Site:* www.hofstra.edu, pg 752

Usui, Emiko, MFA Publications, 465 Huntington Ave, Boston, MA 02115 *Tel:* 617-369-3438 *Fax:* 617-369-3459 *Web Site:* www.mfa-publications.org, pg 173

Utgoff, Kathleen P, National Bureau of Economic Research Inc, 1050 Massachusetts Ave, Cambridge, MA 02138-5398 *Tel:* 617-868-3900 *Fax:* 617-868-2742 *E-mail:* op@nber.org *Web Site:* www.nber.org, pg 182

Utley, Jennifer, Ancestry Publishing, 360 W 4800 N, Provo, UT 84064 *Tel:* 801-705-7305 *Toll Free Tel:* 800-262-3787 *Fax:* 801-426-3501 *E-mail:* editor@ancestry.com; dealersales@ancestry-inc.com *Web Site:* www.ancestry.com, pg 19

Uttech, Sara, American Society of Agronomy, 677 S Segoe Rd, Madison, WI 53711-1086 *Tel:* 608-273-8080 *Fax:* 608-273-2021 *E-mail:* headquarters@ agronomy.org *Web Site:* www.agronomy.org, pg 18

Vacanti, Judy, Research Press, 2612 N Mattis Ave, Champaign, IL 61822 *Tel:* 217-352-3273 *Toll Free Tel:* 800-519-2707 *Fax:* 217-352-1221 *E-mail:* rp@ researchpress.com *Web Site:* www.researchpress.com, pg 231

Vaccaro, Claire, G P Putnam's Sons (Hardcover), 375 Hudson St, New York, NY 10014 *Tel:* 212-366-2000 *E-mail:* online@penguinputnam.com *Web Site:* www. penguin.com, pg 223

Vacha, Brigitte E, Banta Literary Award, 5250 E Terrace Dr, Suite A-1, Madison, WI 53718-8345 *Tel:* 608-245-3640 *Fax:* 608-245-3646 *Web Site:* www.wla.lib.wi.us, pg 761

Vacha, Brigitte E, Notable Wisconsin Authors, 5250 E Terrace Dr, Suite A-1, Madison, WI 53718-8345 *Tel:* 608-245-3640 *Fax:* 608-245-3646 *Web Site:* www. wla.lib.wi.us, pg 795

Valcourt, Deborah, Henry Holt and Company, LLC, 115 W 18 St, New York, NY 10011 *Tel:* 212-886-9200 *Toll Free Tel:* 888-330-8477 (orders) *Fax:* 212-633-0748 *E-mail:* publicity@hholt.com *Web Site:* www. henryholt.com, pg 124

Valdez, Edna, MARC Publications, 800 W Chestnut Ave, Monrovia, CA 91016-3198 *Tel:* 626-303-8811 *Toll Free Tel:* 800-777-7752 (US only) *Fax:* 626-301-7786 *E-mail:* marcpubs@wvi.org *Web Site:* www. worldvisionresources.com, pg 163

Valencia, Patricia, National Coalition Against Censorship (NCAC), 275 Seventh Ave, 9th fl, New York, NY 10001 *Tel:* 212-807-6222 *Fax:* 212-807-6245 *E-mail:* ncac@ncac.org *Web Site:* www.ncac.org, pg 692

Valenciaro, Lola, Scholastic Trade Division, 557 Broadway, New York, NY 10012 *Tel:* 212-343-6100; 212-343-4685 (export sales) *Fax:* 212-343-4714 (export sales) *Web Site:* www.scholastic.com, pg 242

Valenti, Jack, Motion Picture Association of America Inc (MPAA), 1600 "I" St NW, Washington, DC 20006 *Tel:* 202-293-1966 *Fax:* 202-293-7674 *Web Site:* www. mpaa.org, pg 691

Valentine, Christine, Gryphon Editions, 515 Madison Ave, Suite 3200, New York, NY 10022 *Tel:* 212-750-1048 *Toll Free Tel:* 800-633-8911 *Fax:* 212-644-6828 *E-mail:* gryphonnyc@aol.com *Web Site:* www. gryphoneditions.com, pg 110

Valentini, Kimberly, Waterside Productions Inc, 2187 Newcastle Ave, Suite 204, Cardiff, CA 92007 *Tel:* 760-632-9190 *Fax:* 760-632-9295 *Web Site:* www. waterside.com, pg 660

Valentino, Michael, Cambridge Literary Associates, 253 Low St, Newburyport, MA 01950 *Tel:* 978-499-0374 *Fax:* 978-499-9774 *Web Site:* cambridgeliterary.com, pg 623

Valentino, Ralph, Cambridge Literary Associates, 253 Low St, Newburyport, MA 01950 *Tel:* 978-499-0374 *Fax:* 978-499-9774 *Web Site:* cambridgeliterary.com, pg 623

Valera, Milton G, National Notary Association, 9350 De Soto Ave, Chatsworth, CA 91311 *Tel:* 818-739-4000 *Toll Free Tel:* 800-876-6827 *Fax:* 818-700-0920 *E-mail:* nna@nationalnotary.org *Web Site:* www. nationalnotary.org, pg 184

Vales, Ray, Saunders College Publishing, The Public Ledger Bldg, 150 S Independence Mall W, Suite 1250, Philadelphia, PA 19106-3412 *Tel:* 215-238-5500 *Fax:* 215-238-5660 *Web Site:* www.hbcollege.com, pg 240

Valin, Julie, Dawn Publications Inc, 12402 Bitney Springs Rd, Nevada City, CA 95959 *Tel:* 530-274-7775 *Toll Free Tel:* 800-545-7475 *Fax:* 530-274-7778 *E-mail:* nature@dawnpub.com *Web Site:* www. dawnpub.com, pg 77

Valko-Warner, Mary JoAnne, Scott Meredith Literary Agency LP, 200 W 57 St, Suite 904, New York, NY 10019 *Tel:* 646-274-1970 *Fax:* 212-977-5997 *Web Site:* www.writingtosell.com, pg 644

Vallee, Marie-Claude, Editions Yvon Blais, 137 John, CP 180, Cowansville, PQ J2K 1W9, Canada *Tel:* 450-266-1086 *Fax:* 450-263-9256 *E-mail:* commandes@editionsyvonblais.qc.ca *Web Site:* www.editionsyvonblais.qc.ca, pg 546

Vallejo, Melissa, Stanford Publishing Courses at Stanford University, Green Library, Rm 245-B, 557 Escondidio Mall, Stanford, CA 94305-6004 *Tel:* 650-725-5311 *Fax:* 650-736-1904 *E-mail:* publishing.courses@ stanford.edu *Web Site:* publishingcourses.stanford.edu, pg 754

Vallely, Janis C, Flaming Star Literary Enterprises, 320 Riverside Dr, Suite 12-D, New York, NY 10025 *E-mail:* flamingstarlit@aol.com, pg 630

Vallely, Joseph B, Flaming Star Literary Enterprises, 320 Riverside Dr, Suite 12-D, New York, NY 10025 *E-mail:* flamingstarlit@aol.com, pg 630

Vallone, Lynne, ChLA Beiter Scholarships for Graduate Students, PO Box 138, Battle Creek, MI 49016-0138 *Tel:* 269-965-8180 *Fax:* 269-965-3568 *Web Site:* www. childlitassn.org, pg 767

Valvano, Al, Microsoft Press, One Microsoft Way, Redmond, WA 98052-6399 *Tel:* 425-882-8080 *Toll Free Tel:* 800-677-7377 *Fax:* 425-936-7329 *Web Site:* www.microsoft.com/presspass/exec/default. asp#qt, pg 173

Valvo, Vince, Law Tribune Books, 201 Ann St, 4th fl, Hartford, CT 06103 *Tel:* 860-527-7900 *Fax:* 860-527-7815 *E-mail:* lawtribune@amlaw.com *Web Site:* www. law.com/ct, pg 150

Van Andel, Cheryl, Baker Books, PO Box 6287, Grand Rapids, MI 49516-6287 *Tel:* 616-676-9185 *Toll Free Tel:* 800-877-2665; 800-679-1957 *Fax:* 616-676-9573 *Toll Free Fax:* 800-398-3110 *Web Site:* www. bakerpublishinggroup.com, pg 30

van Arsdale, Peternelle, Hyperion, 77 W 66 St, 11th fl, New York, NY 10023-6298 *Tel:* 212-456-0100 *Toll Free Tel:* 800-759-0190 (cust serv) *Fax:* 212-456-0157 *Web Site:* hyperionbooks.com, pg 129

Van Auken, Lisa, Creative Media Agency Inc, 240 W 35 St, Suite 500, New York, NY 10001 *Tel:* 212-560-0909 *Fax:* 212-279-0927 *E-mail:* cmagency@ yahoo.com *Web Site:* www.paigewheeler.com; www. thecmagency.com, pg 626

van Beek, Emily, Pippin Properties Inc, 155 E 38 St, Suite 2H, New York, NY 10016 *Tel:* 212-338-9310 *Fax:* 212-338-9579 *E-mail:* info@pippinproperties.com *Web Site:* www.pippinproperties.com, pg 648

Van Cleave, Fran, Prometheus Awards, 26 Partridge Hill, Honeye Falls, NY 14472 *Tel:* 585-582-1068 *Web Site:* www.lfs.org, pg 800

Van Cleve, John V, Gallaudet University Press, 800 Florida Ave NE, Washington, DC 20002-3695 *Tel:* 202-651-5488 *Fax:* 202-651-5489 *E-mail:* gupress@gallaudet.edu *Web Site:* gupress. gallaudet.edu, pg 102

Van Der Beets, Richard, West Coast Literary Associates, 951 Old County Rd, No 140, Belmont, CA 94002 *Tel:* 650-557-0438 *E-mail:* wstlit@aol.com, pg 661

van der Plas, Rob, Cycle Publishing, 1282 Seventh Ave, San Francisco, CA 94122-2526 *Tel:* 415-665-8214 *Toll Free Tel:* 877-353-1207 *Fax:* 415-753-8572 *E-mail:* pubrel@cyclepublishing.com *Web Site:* www. cyclepublishing.com, pg 75

Van Deventer, M J, Western Heritage Awards (Wrangler Award), 1700 NE 63 St, Oklahoma City, OK 73111 *Tel:* 405-478-2250 *Fax:* 405-478-4714 *Web Site:* www. nationalcowboymuseum.org, pg 810

Van Doren, Liz, Harcourt Trade Publishers, 525 "B" St, Suite 1900, San Diego, CA 92101 *Tel:* 619-231-6616 *Toll Free Tel:* 800-543-1918 (cust serv) *Toll Free Fax:* 800-235-0256 (cust serv) *Web Site:* www.harcourtbooks.com, pg 115

Van Dyke, Craig, John Wiley & Sons Inc Scientific/Technical/Medical Publishing, 111 River St, Hoboken, NJ 07030 *Tel:* 201-748-6000 *Toll Free Tel:* 800-225-5945 (cust serv) *Fax:* 201-748-8728 *E-mail:* info@wiley.com *Web Site:* www.wiley.com, pg 300

van Gigch, John P PhD, PSD Associates, 7392 Palm Ave, Sebastopol, CA 95472-6705, pg 649

Van Hooft, Karen, Bilingual Press/Editorial Bilingue, Hispanic Research Ctr, Arizona State Univ, Tempe, AZ 85287-2702 *Tel:* 480-965-3867 *Fax:* 480-965-8309 *E-mail:* brp@asu.edu *Web Site:* www.asu.edu/brp/brp, pg 38

Van Hook, Michael, Providence Publishing Corp, 238 Seaboard Lane, Franklin, TN 37067 *Tel:* 615-771-2020 *Toll Free Tel:* 800-321-5692 *Fax:* 615-771-2002 *E-mail:* books@providencehouse.com *Web Site:* www.providencehouse.com, pg 220

Van Meeuwen, Frank, Diamond Farm Book Publishers, Bailey Settlement Rd, Alexandria Bay, NY 13607 *Tel:* 613-475-1771 *Toll Free Tel:* 800-481-1353 *Fax:* 613-475-3748 *Toll Free Fax:* 800-305-5138 *E-mail:* info@diamondfarm.com *Web Site:* www.diamondfarm.com, pg 80

Van Meeuwen, Shawn, Diamond Farm Book Publishers, Bailey Settlement Rd, Alexandria Bay, NY 13607 *Tel:* 613-475-1771 *Toll Free Tel:* 800-481-1353 *Fax:* 613-475-3748 *Toll Free Fax:* 800-305-5138 *E-mail:* info@diamondfarm.com *Web Site:* www.diamondfarm.com, pg 80

Van Meter, Joann, Standard Publishing Co, 8121 Hamilton Ave, Cincinnati, OH 45231 *Tel:* 513-931-4050 *Toll Free Tel:* 800-543-1301 *Fax:* 513-931-0950 *Toll Free Fax:* 877-867-5751 *E-mail:* customerservice@standardpub.com *Web Site:* www.standardpub.com, pg 257

Van Meter, Susan, Harry N Abrams Inc, 100 Fifth Ave, New York, NY 10011 *Tel:* 212-206-7715 *Toll Free Tel:* 800-345-1359 *Fax:* 212-645-8437 *E-mail:* webmaster@abramsbooks.com *Web Site:* www.abramsbooks.com, pg 3

Van Natta, Corrine, Penguin Group (USA) Inc Sales, 375 Hudson St, New York, NY 10014 *Tel:* 212-366-2000 *E-mail:* online@penguinputnam.com *Web Site:* www.penguin.com, pg 208

Van Ness, Dr Gordon, John Dos Passos Prize for Literature, Dept of English & Modern Languages, 201 High St, Farmville, VA 23909 *Tel:* 434-395-2155 *Fax:* 434-395-2145, pg 770

Van Noord, Kate, Baker Books, PO Box 6287, Grand Rapids, MI 49516-6287 *Tel:* 616-676-9185 *Toll Free Tel:* 800-877-2665; 800-679-1957 *Fax:* 616-676-9573 *Toll Free Fax:* 800-398-3110 *Web Site:* www.bakerpublishinggroup.com, pg 30

Van Nostrand, Charles R, Samuel French Inc, 45 W 25 St, New York, NY 10010-2751 *Tel:* 212-206-8990 *Fax:* 212-206-1429 *E-mail:* samuelfrench@earthlink.net *Web Site:* www.samuelfrench.com, pg 101, 631

Van Raalte, Peter, Scholastic Entertainment Inc, 524 Broadway, New York, NY 10012 *Tel:* 212-343-7500 *Fax:* 212-965-7448, pg 241

van Straalen, Alice, Vintage & Anchor Books, 1745 Broadway, New York, NY 10019 *Tel:* 212-751-2600 *Fax:* 212-572-6043, pg 291

van Straaten, Tracy, Simon & Schuster Children's Publishing, 1230 Avenue of the Americas, New York, NY 10020 *Tel:* 212-698-7000 *Web Site:* www.simonsayskids.com, pg 248

Van Westering, Karen, The New York Public Library Helen Bernstein Book Award for Excellence in Journalism, Publications Office, Fifth Ave & 42 St, New York, NY 10018 *Tel:* 212-512-0202 *Fax:* 212-704-8620 *E-mail:* kvanwestering@nypl.org *Web Site:* www.nypl.org, pg 794

Van Woerden, Peter, Thieme New York, 333 Seventh Ave, 5th fl, New York, NY 10001 *Tel:* 212-760-0888 *Toll Free Tel:* 800-782-3488 *Fax:* 212-947-1112 *E-mail:* customerservice@thieme.com *Web Site:* www.thieme.com, pg 268

Van Zanten, Jan, Siddha Yoga Publications, 371 Brickman Rd, South Fallsburg, NY 12747 *Tel:* 845-434-2000 *Toll Free Tel:* 888-422-3334 (bookstore) *Fax:* 845-436-2131 *Toll Free Fax:* 888-422-3339 *E-mail:* info@siddhayoga.org; ebookstoreorders@syda.org *Web Site:* www.siddhayoga.org, pg 247

Vanasse, Andre, XYZ Editeur, 1781 rue Saint-Hubert, Montreal, PQ H2L 3Z1, Canada *Tel:* 514-525-2170 *Fax:* 514-525-7537, pg 567

Vanasse, Andre, XYZ Publishing, 1781 Saint Hubert St, Montreal, PQ H2L 3Z1, Canada *Tel:* 514-252-2170 *Fax:* 514-525-7537 *E-mail:* info@xyzedit.qc.ca *Web Site:* www.xyzedit.qc.ca, pg 567

vanBreen, Leslie, Hudson Hills Press LLC, 74-2 Union St, Manchester, VT 05254 *Tel:* 802-362-6450 *Fax:* 802-362-6459 *E-mail:* artbooks@hudsonhills.com *Web Site:* www.hudsonhills.com, pg 128

Vance, Charles E, Naval Institute Press, 291 Wood Rd, Annapolis, MD 21402-5034 *Tel:* 410-268-6110 *Toll Free Tel:* 800-233-8764 *Fax:* 410-295-1084; 410-571-1703 (customer service) *E-mail:* webmaster@navalinstitute.org; customer@navalinstitute.org (cust serv) *Web Site:* www.navalinstitute.org, pg 185

Vance, Lisa Erbach, The Aaron M Priest Literary Agency Inc, 708 Third Ave, 23rd fl, New York, NY 10017 *Tel:* 212-818-0344 *Fax:* 212-573-9417, pg 649

VanDam, Stephan C, VanDam Inc, 11 W 20 St, 4th fl, New York, NY 10011-3704 *Tel:* 212-929-0416 *Toll Free Tel:* 800-UNFOLDS (863-6537) *Fax:* 212-929-0426 *E-mail:* info@vandam.com *Web Site:* www.vandam.com, pg 289

Vandenberg, Alison, Minnesota Historical Society Press, 345 Kellogg Blvd W, St Paul, MN 55102-1906 *Tel:* 651-296-2264 *Toll Free Tel:* 800-621-2736 *Fax:* 651-297-1345 *Toll Free Fax:* 800-621-8476 *Web Site:* www.mnhs.org/mhspress, pg 175

VandenBos, Gary R, American Psychological Association, 750 First St NE, Washington, DC 20002-4242 *Tel:* 202-336-5500 *Toll Free Tel:* 800-374-2721 *Fax:* 202-336-5620 *E-mail:* order@apa.org *Web Site:* www.apa.org/books, pg 17

VandenDolder, Linda, Sinauer Associates Inc, 23 Plumtree Rd, Sunderland, MA 01375-0407 *Tel:* 413-549-4300 *Fax:* 413-549-1118 *E-mail:* publish@sinauer.com *Web Site:* www.sinauer.com, pg 249

Vander Kam, Claire, Wm B Eerdmans Publishing Co, 255 Jefferson Ave SE, Grand Rapids, MI 49503 *Tel:* 616-459-4591 *Toll Free Tel:* 800-253-7521 *Fax:* 616-459-6540 *E-mail:* sales@eerdmans.com *Web Site:* www.eerdmans.com, pg 88

Vander Zanden, Karla, Desert Writers Workshop, PO Box 68, Moab, UT 84532 *Tel:* 435-259-7750 *Toll Free Tel:* 800-860-5262 *Fax:* 435-259-2335 *E-mail:* info@canyonlandsfields.com *Web Site:* www.canyonlandsfieldinst.com, pg 743

Vanderhoof, Albert, Naturegraph Publishers Inc, 3543 Indian Creek Rd, Happy Camp, CA 96039 *Tel:* 530-493-5353 *Toll Free Tel:* 800-390-5353 *Fax:* 530-493-5240 *E-mail:* nature@sisqtel.net *Web Site:* www.naturegraph.com, pg 185

Vanderkooy, Diane, Scholastic Canada Ltd, 175 Hillmount Rd, Markham, ON L6C 1Z7, Canada *Tel:* 905-887-7323 *Toll Free Tel:* 800-268-3848 (Canada) *Fax:* 905-887-1131 *Toll Free Fax:* 800-387-4944; 866-346-1288 *Web Site:* www.scholastic.ca, pg 560

Vandermolen, Katharyn, Wm B Eerdmans Publishing Co, 255 Jefferson Ave SE, Grand Rapids, MI 49503 *Tel:* 616-459-4591 *Toll Free Tel:* 800-253-7521 *Fax:* 616-459-6540 *E-mail:* sales@eerdmans.com *Web Site:* www.eerdmans.com, pg 88

Vandersnick, Leia, Picador, 175 Fifth Ave, New York, NY 10010 *Tel:* 212-674-5151 *Fax:* 212-253-9627 *E-mail:* firstname.lastname@picadorusa.com *Web Site:* www.picadorusa.com, pg 212

Vandertuin, Victoria E, New Age World Literary Services & Books, 6426 Valley View St, Space 49, Joshua Tree, CA 92252 *Tel:* 760-366-0117 *E-mail:* newagesphinx@yahoo.com *Web Site:* www.joshuatreevillage.com, pg 646

VanMeer, Don, Carswell, One Corporate Plaza, 2075 Kennedy Rd, Toronto, ON M1T 3V4, Canada *Tel:* 416-609-8000 *Toll Free Tel:* 800-387-5164 (Canada & US) *Fax:* 416-298-5094 (Toronto); 403-233-8159 (Calgary); 604-685-5343 (Vancouver); 514-985-6605 *Toll Free Fax:* 877-750-9041 *E-mail:* comments@carswell.com *Web Site:* www.carswell.com, pg 539

Vanook, Ellen, Other Press LLC, 307 Seventh Ave, Suite 1807, New York, NY 10001 *Tel:* 212-414-0054 *Toll Free Tel:* 877-843-6843 *Fax:* 212-414-0939 *E-mail:* editor@otherpress.com; orders@otherpress.com *Web Site:* www.otherpress.com, pg 199

Vanook, Ellen, Other Press LLC, 307 Seventh Ave, Suite 1807, New York, NY 10001 *Tel:* 212-414-0054 *Toll Free Tel:* 877-THE-OTHER *Fax:* 212-414-0939 *E-mail:* orders@otherpress.com *Web Site:* www.otherpress.com, pg 573

Vardigan, Mary, Inter-University Consortium for Political & Social Research, PO Box 1248, Ann Arbor, MI 48106-1248 *Tel:* 734-647-5000 *Fax:* 734-647-8200 *E-mail:* netmail@icpsr.umich.edu *Web Site:* www.icpsr.umich.edu, pg 136

Varga, Victoria, Prometheus Awards, 26 Partridge Hill, Honeye Falls, NY 14472 *Tel:* 585-582-1068 *Web Site:* www.lfs.org, pg 800

Vargas, Christina, PrintImage International, 70 E Lake St, Suite 333, Chicago, IL 60601 *Tel:* 312-726-8015 *Toll Free Tel:* 800-234-0040 *Fax:* 312-726-8113 *E-mail:* info@printimage.org *Web Site:* www.printimage.org, pg 697

Vargas, Max, Florida Academic Press, PO Box 540, Gainesville, FL 32602-0540 *Tel:* 352-332-5104 *Fax:* 352-331-6003 *E-mail:* fapress@worldnet.att.net, pg 97

Vargo, Linda, National Association of College Stores (NACS), 500 E Lorain St, Oberlin, OH 44074 *Tel:* 440-775-7777 *Toll Free Tel:* 800-622-7498 *Fax:* 440-775-4769 *Web Site:* www.nacs.org, pg 692

Varma, Sarita, North Point Press, 19 Union Sq W, New York, NY 10003 *Tel:* 212-741-6900 *Toll Free Tel:* 888-330-8477 *Fax:* 212-741-6973 *Web Site:* www.fsgbooks.com, pg 192

Varnum, Keith, New Dimensions Publishing, 11248 N 11 St, Phoenix, AZ 85020 *Tel:* 602-861-2631 *Toll Free Tel:* 800-736-7367 *Fax:* 602-944-1233 *E-mail:* info@thedream.com *Web Site:* www.thedream.com, pg 187

Varvaro, Michelle, Playhouse Publishing, 1566 Akron-Peninsula Rd, Akron, OH 44313 *Tel:* 330-926-1313 *Toll Free Tel:* 800-762-6775 *Fax:* 330-926-1315 *E-mail:* info@playhousepublishing.com *Web Site:* www.playhousepublishing.com, pg 214

Vasilaky, Milla, Paulist Press, 997 Macarthur Blvd, Mahwah, NJ 07430 *Tel:* 201-825-7300 *Toll Free Tel:* 800-218-1903 *Fax:* 201-825-8345 *Toll Free Fax:* 800-836-3161 (orders) *E-mail:* info@paulistpress.com *Web Site:* www.paulistpress.com, pg 206

Vassilian, Hamo, Armenian Reference Books Co, PO Box 231, Glendale, CA 91209 *Tel:* 818-504-2550 *Toll Free Tel:* 877-504-2550 *Fax:* 818-504-9283 *E-mail:* info@vassiliansdepot.com *Web Site:* www.vassiliansdepot.com/arb, pg 23

Vater, Rachel, Donald Maass Literary Agency, 160 W 95 St, Suite 1-B, New York, NY 10025 *Tel:* 212-866-8200 *Fax:* 212-866-8181 *E-mail:* dmla@mindspring.com, pg 641

Vater, Rachel, Writers Retreat Workshop (WRW), 5721 Magazine St, Suite 161, New Orleans, LA 70115 *Toll Free Tel:* 800-642-2494 *E-mail:* wrw04@netscape.net *Web Site:* www.writersretreatworkshop.com, pg 749

Vaughan, Neil, NACE International, 1440 S Creek Dr, Houston, TX 77084-4906 *Tel:* 281-228-6223 *Fax:* 281-228-6300 *E-mail:* pubs@mail.nace.org *Web Site:* www.nace.org, pg 181

Vaughan, Tina, DK Publishing Inc, 375 Hudson St, 2nd fl, New York, NY 10014-3672 *Tel:* 212-213-4800 *Toll Free Tel:* 877-342-5357 (cust serv) *Fax:* 212-213-5202 *Web Site:* www.dk.com, pg 81

Vaughn, Jeanne, Paladin Press, 7077 Winchester Circle, Boulder, CO 80301 *Tel:* 303-443-7250 *Toll Free Tel:* 800-392-2400 *Fax:* 303-442-8741 *E-mail:* service@paladin-press.com *Web Site:* www.paladin-press.com, pg 202

Vaughn, Mary, Cambridge University Press, 40 W 20 St, New York, NY 10011-4211 *Tel:* 212-924-3900 *Toll Free Tel:* 800-899-5222 *Fax:* 212-691-3239 *Web Site:* www.cambridge.org, pg 52

Vaught, Rachel, Indiana Historical Society Press, 450 W Ohio St, Indianapolis, IN 46202-3269 *Tel:* 317-233-9557 (sales); 317-234-2716 (editorial) *Toll Free Tel:* 800-447-1830 (orders only) *Fax:* 317-234-0562 (sales); 317-233-0857 (editorial) *E-mail:* ihspress@indianahistory.org; orders@indianahistory.org (orders) *Web Site:* www.indianahistory.org; shop.indianahistory.org (orders), pg 132

Vavra, Janet, Inter-University Consortium for Political & Social Research, PO Box 1248, Ann Arbor, MI 48106-1248 *Tel:* 734-647-5000 *Fax:* 734-647-8200 *E-mail:* netmail@icpsr.umich.edu *Web Site:* www.icpsr.umich.edu, pg 136

Vayna, L K, Transatlantic Arts Inc, PO Box 6086, Albuquerque, NM 87197-6086 *Tel:* 505-898-2289 *Fax:* 505-898-2289 *E-mail:* books@transatlantic.com *Web Site:* www.transatlantic.com/direct, pg 274

Vayna, S A, Transatlantic Arts Inc, PO Box 6086, Albuquerque, NM 87197-6086 *Tel:* 505-898-2289 *Fax:* 505-898-2289 *E-mail:* books@transatlantic.com *Web Site:* www.transatlantic.com/direct, pg 274

Vayo, Charlotte, The Drummond Publishing Group, 362 N Bedford St, East Bridgewater, MA 02333 *Tel:* 508-378-1110 *Fax:* 508-378-1105 *Web Site:* www.drummondpub.com, pg 84

Vayo, Charlotte, Royalton Press, 362 N Bedford St, East Bridgewater, MA 02333 *Tel:* 508-378-1110 *Fax:* 508-378-1105 *Web Site:* www.drummondpub.com, pg 235

Vayo, Charlotte W, Pre-Press Company Inc, 362 N Bedford St, East Bridgewater, MA 02333 *Tel:* 508-378-1100 (plant); 508-378-1101 (sales) *Fax:* 508-378-1105 *Web Site:* www.prepressco.com, pg 608

Vayo, Rick, The Drummond Publishing Group, 362 N Bedford St, East Bridgewater, MA 02333 *Tel:* 508-378-1110 *Fax:* 508-378-1105 *Web Site:* www.drummondpub.com, pg 84

Vayo, Rick, Royalton Press, 362 N Bedford St, East Bridgewater, MA 02333 *Tel:* 508-378-1110 *Fax:* 508-378-1105 *Web Site:* www.drummondpub.com, pg 235

Vayo, Rick A, Pre-Press Company Inc, 362 N Bedford St, East Bridgewater, MA 02333 *Tel:* 508-378-1100 (plant); 508-378-1101 (sales) *Fax:* 508-378-1105 *Web Site:* www.prepressco.com, pg 608

Vega, Rita, Holloway House Publishing Co, 8060 Melrose Ave, Los Angeles, CA 90046-7082 *Tel:* 323-653-8060 *Fax:* 323-655-9452 *E-mail:* info@hollowayhousebooks.com *Web Site:* www.hollowayhousebooks.com, pg 124

Vegso, Peter, Health Communications Inc, 3201 SW 15 St, Deerfield Beach, FL 33442-8190 *Tel:* 954-360-0909 *Toll Free Tel:* 800-851-9100 (cust serv); 800-441-5569 (order entry) *Fax:* 954-360-0034 *Web Site:* www.hcibooks.com, pg 119

Veillette, Nicole, Social Sciences & Humanities Research Council of Canada (SSHRC), 350 Albert St, Ottawa, ON K1P 6G4, Canada *Tel:* 613-992-0691 *Fax:* 613-992-1787 *E-mail:* z-info@sshrc.ca *Web Site:* www.sshrc.ca, pg 699

Veillon, Magali, Black Dog & Leventhal Publishers Inc, 151 W 19 St, 12th fl, New York, NY 10011 *Tel:* 212-647-9336 *Fax:* 212-647-9332 *E-mail:* information@bdlev.com *Web Site:* www.bdlev.com, pg 39

Velde, LeAnn, AGS Publishing, 4201 Woodland Rd, Circle Pines, MN 55014-1716 *Tel:* 651-287-7220 *Toll Free Tel:* 800-328-2560 *Toll Free Fax:* 800-471-8457 *E-mail:* agsmail@agsnet.com *Web Site:* www.agsnet.com, pg 7

Veldhuizen, Mark, Doubleday Canada, One Toronto St, Suite 300, Toronto, ON M5C 2V6, Canada *Tel:* 416-364-4449 *Fax:* 416-957-1587 *Web Site:* www.randomhouse.ca, pg 542

Veldhuizen, Mark, Knopf Canada, One Toronto St, Suite 300, Toronto, ON M5C 2V6, Canada *Tel:* 416-364-4449 *Toll Free Tel:* 800-668-4247 (order desk) *Fax:* 416-364-0462 *Web Site:* www.randomhouse.ca, pg 552

Veldhuizen, Mark, Random House of Canada Ltd, One Toronto St, Unit 300, Toronto, ON M5C 2V6, Canada *Tel:* 416-364-4449 *Fax:* 416-364-6863 (edit & publicity); 416-364-6653 (subs rts) *Web Site:* www.randomhouse.ca, pg 559

Veldhuizen, Mark, Seal Books, One Toronto St, Suite 300, Toronto, ON M5C 2V6, Canada *Tel:* 416-364-4449 *Toll Free Tel:* 888-523-9292 (order desk) *Fax:* 416-957-1587 *Web Site:* www.randomhouse.ca, pg 560

Venezia, Molly, Rutgers University Press, 100 Joyce Kilmer Ave, Piscataway, NJ 08854-8099 *Tel:* 732-445-7762 (edit); 732-445-7762 (ext 627, sales) *Toll Free Tel:* 800-446-9323 (orders only) *Fax:* 732-445-7039 (acqs, edit, mktg, perms, prodn); 732-445-1974 (fulfillment) *E-mail:* garyf@rci.rutgers.edu *Web Site:* rutgerspress.rutgers.edu, pg 236

Ventrone, Ted A, American Institute of Chemical Engineers (AICHE), 3 Park Ave, New York, NY 10016-5991 *Tel:* 212-591-7338 *Toll Free Tel:* 800-242-4363 *Fax:* 212-591-8888 *E-mail:* xpress@aiche.org *Web Site:* www.aiche.org, pg 15

Ventullo, Thomas, Vision Works Publishing, 47 Sheffield Rd, Suite A, Boxford, MA 01921 *Tel:* 978-887-3125 *Toll Free Tel:* 888-821-3135 *Fax:* 630-982-2134 *E-mail:* visionworksbooks@email.com, pg 291

Verbit, Dolores, Jewish Publication Society, 2100 Arch St, 2nd fl, Philadelphia, PA 19103 *Tel:* 215-832-0600 *Toll Free Tel:* 800-234-3151 *Fax:* 215-568-2017 *E-mail:* jewishbook@jewishpub.org *Web Site:* www.jewishpub.org, pg 141

Verburg, Bonnie, Scholastic Trade Division, 557 Broadway, New York, NY 10012 *Tel:* 212-343-6100; 212-343-4685 (export sales) *Fax:* 212-343-4714 (export sales) *Web Site:* www.scholastic.com, pg 242

Vergin, Roger, American College, 270 S Bryn Mawr Ave, Bryn Mawr, PA 19010 *Tel:* 610-526-1000 *Fax:* 610-526-1310 *Web Site:* www.amercoll.edu, pg 12

Verhagen, Frank, Elsevier, 11830 Westline Industrial Dr, St Louis, MO 63146 *Tel:* 314-872-8370 *Toll Free Tel:* 800-325-4177 *Fax:* 314-432-1380 *Web Site:* www.elsevier.com; www.elsevierhealth.com, pg 89

Verkuilen, Michelle, Liturgical Press, St John's Abbey, Collegeville, MN 56321 *Tel:* 320-363-2213 *Toll Free Tel:* 800-858-5450 *Fax:* 320-363-3299 *Toll Free Fax:* 800-445-5899 *E-mail:* sales@litpress.org *Web Site:* www.litpress.org, pg 156

Vernac, Francine, Le Loup de Gouttiere Inc, 347 rue Sainte Paul, Quebec City, PQ G1K 3X1, Canada *Tel:* 418-694-2224 *Fax:* 418-694-2225 *E-mail:* loupgout@videotron.ca, pg 553

Vernon, John, Binghamton University Writing Program, c/o Dept of English, PO Box 6000, Binghamton, NY 13902-6000 *Tel:* 607-777-2168 *Fax:* 607-777-2408, pg 751

Verrill, Charles, Darhansoff, Verrill, Feldman Literary Agents, 236 W 26 St, Suite 802, New York, NY 10001-6736 *Tel:* 917-305-1300 *Fax:* 917-305-1400 *Web Site:* www.dvagency.com, pg 626

Verrill, Holly, Cambridge University Press, 40 W 20 St, New York, NY 10011-4211 *Tel:* 212-924-3900 *Toll Free Tel:* 800-899-5222 *Fax:* 212-691-3239 *Web Site:* www.cambridge.org, pg 52

Verschuuren, Gerard M, Genesis Publishing Co Inc, 36 Steeple View Dr, Atkinson, NH 03811 *Tel:* 603-362-4121 *Fax:* 603-362-4121 *E-mail:* genesis@genesisbook.com *Web Site:* genesispc.com, pg 104

Verstraete, Mark, FaithWalk Publishing, 333 Jackson St, Grand Haven, MI 49417 *Tel:* 616-846-9360 *Toll Free Tel:* 800-335-7177 *Fax:* 616-846-0072 *E-mail:* customerservice@faithwalkpub.com *Web Site:* www.faithwalkpub.com, pg 94

Vess, Gavin, CyclopsMedia, 1076 Eagle Dr, Salinas, CA 93905 *Tel:* 831-776-9500 *Fax:* 831-422-5915 *E-mail:* custserv@cyclopsmedia.com *Web Site:* www.cyclopsmedia.com, pg 75

Vetter, Bernadette, The Center for Learning, 24600 Detroit Rd, Suite 201, Westlake, OH 44145 *Tel:* 440-250-9341 *Fax:* 440-250-9715 *Web Site:* www.centerforlearning.org, pg 56

Vezina, Richard, Editions Saint-Martin, 5000, rue Iberville, bureau 203, Montreal, PQ H2H 2M2, Canada *Tel:* 514-529-0920 *Fax:* 514-529-8384 *E-mail:* st-martin@gc.airle.com, pg 545

Viberti, Victor L, Alba House, 2187 Victory Blvd, Staten Island, NY 10314 *Tel:* 718-761-0047 (edit & prodn); 718-698-2759 (mktg & billing) *Toll Free Tel:* 800-343-2522 *Fax:* 718-761-0057 *E-mail:* albabooks@aol.com *Web Site:* www.albahouse.org, pg 7

Vicinanza, Ralph M, Ralph M Vicinanza Ltd, 303 W 18 St, New York, NY 10011 *Tel:* 212-924-7090 *Fax:* 212-691-9644 *E-mail:* ralphvic@aol.com, pg 659

Vick, Fran, Brazo Bookstore (Houston Award), 3700 Mockingbird Lane, Dallas, TX 75205 *Tel:* 214-528-2655 *Web Site:* www.stedwards.edu/newc/marks/til/awards_and_rules.htm, pg 764

Vick, Fran, Carr P Collins Award, Center for the Study of the Southwest, Southwest Texas State University, San Marcos, TX 78666 *Tel:* 512-245-2232 *Fax:* 512-245-7462 *Web Site:* www.stedwards.edu/newc/marks/til/awards_and_rules.htm, pg 768

Vick, Fran, Soeurette Diehl Fraser Award, 3700 Mockingbird Lane, Dallas, TX 75205 *Tel:* 512-245-2232 *Fax:* 512-245-7462 *Web Site:* www.stedwards.edu/newc/marks/til/awards_and_rules.htm, pg 775

Vick, Fran, Friends of the Dallas Public Library Award, Center for the Study of the Southwest, Southwest Texas State University, San Marcos, TX 78666 *Tel:* 512-245-2232 *Fax:* 512-245-7462 *Web Site:* www.stedwards.edu/newc/marks/til/awards_and_rules.htm, pg 775

Vick, Fran, Jesse H Jones Award, 3700 Mockingbird Lane, Dallas, TX 75205 *Tel:* 214-528-2655 *Fax:* 512-245-7462 *Web Site:* www.stedwards.edu/newc/marks/til/awards_and_rules.htm, pg 781

Vick, Fran, O Henry Award, 3700 Mockingbird Lane, Dallas, TX 75205 *Tel:* 512-245-2232 *Fax:* 512-245-7462 *Web Site:* www.stedwards.edu/newc/marks/til/awards_and_rules.htm, pg 795

Vick, Fran, Natalie Ornish Poetry Award, 3700 Mockingbird Lane, Dallas, TX 75205 *Tel:* 512-245-2232 *Fax:* 512-245-7462 *Web Site:* www.stedwards.edu/newc/marks/til/awards_and_rules.htm, pg 796

Vick, Fran, Texas Institute of Letters, 3700 Mockingbird Lane, Dallas, TX 75205 *Tel:* 214-528-2655, pg 701

Vick, Fran, Texas Institute of Letters Awards, 3700 Mockingbird Lane, Dallas, TX 75205 *Tel:* 512-245-2232 *Fax:* 512-245-7462 *Web Site:* www.stedwards.edu/newc/marks/til/awards_and_rules.htm; www.english.swt.edu/css/til/rules.htm, pg 808

Vick, Fran, Stanley Walker Journalism Award, 3700 Mockingbird Lane, Dallas, TX 75205 *Tel:* 512-245-2232 *Fax:* 512-245-7462, pg 810

Vickers, Amy, WaterPlow Press™, Amherst Office Park, 441 West Street, Suite G, Amherst, MA 01002 *Tel:* 413-253-1520 *Toll Free Tel:* 866-367-3300 (orders only) *Fax:* 413-253-1521 *E-mail:* sales@waterplowpress.com *Web Site:* www.waterplowpress.com, pg 294

(international orders) *Toll Free Fax:* 800-406-9145 (orders) *E-mail:* firstname_lastname@harvard.edu *Web Site:* www.hup.harvard.edu, pg 117

Wachs, Mary, Museum of New Mexico Press, 725 Camino Lejo, Santa Fe, NM 87501 *Tel:* 505-476-1158 *Toll Free Tel:* 800-249-7737 (orders) *Fax:* 505-476-1156 *Toll Free Fax:* 800-622-8667 (orders) *E-mail:* mnmpress@aol.com *Web Site:* www.mnmpress.org, pg 180

Wachs, Noreen, Association of Jewish Libraries (AJL), 15 E 26 St, New York, NY 10010-1579 *Tel:* 212-725-5359 *E-mail:* ajl@jewishbooks.org *Web Site:* www.jewishlibraries.org, pg 680

Wachtel, Gina, Bantam Dell Publishing Group, 1745 Broadway, New York, NY 10019 *Tel:* 212-782-9000 *Toll Free Tel:* 800-223-6834 *Fax:* 212-302-7985 *Web Site:* www.randomhouse.com/bantamdell, pg 31

Wachtell, Diane, The New Press, 38 Greene St, 4th fl, New York, NY 10013 *Tel:* 212-629-8802 *Toll Free Tel:* 800-233-4830 (orders) *Fax:* 212-629-8617 *Toll Free Tel:* 800-458-6515 *E-mail:* newpress@thenewpress.com *Web Site:* www.thenewpress.com, pg 188

Wackerow, Elaine, New Readers Press, 1320 Jamesville Ave, Syracuse, NY 13210 *Tel:* 315-422-9121 *Toll Free Tel:* 800-448-8878 *Fax:* 315-422-5561 *E-mail:* nrp@proliteracy.org *Web Site:* www.newreaderspress.com, pg 189

Waddell, Roberta, Basic Health Publications Inc, 8200 Boulevard E, Suite 25-G, North Bergen, NJ 07047 *Tel:* 201-868-8336 *Toll Free Tel:* 800-575-8890 *Fax:* 201-868-8335, pg 33

Waddington, Denise, Harvard University Press, 79 Garden St, Cambridge, MA 02138-1499 *Tel:* 617-495-2600; 401-531-2800 (international orders) *Toll Free Tel:* 800-405-1619 (orders) *Toll Free Tel:* 800-405-1619 (orders) *Toll Free Tel:* 800-495-5898 (general); 617-496-4677 (edit & rts); 401-531-2801 (international orders) *Toll Free Fax:* 800-406-9145 (orders) *E-mail:* firstname_lastname@harvard.edu *Web Site:* www.hup.harvard.edu, pg 117

Wade, Anthony, Papyrus & Letterbox of London Publishers, 10501 Broom Hill Dr, Las Vegas, NV 89134-7339 *Tel:* 702-256-3838 *E-mail:* LB27383@earthlink.net *Web Site:* booksbyletterbox.com, pg 203

Wade, Lee, Simon & Schuster Children's Publishing, 1230 Avenue of the Americas, New York, NY 10020 *Tel:* 212-698-7000 *Web Site:* www.simonsayskids.com, pg 248

Wade, Liane Thomas, Antiquarian Booksellers' Association of America, 20 W 44 St, 4th fl, New York, NY 10036 *Tel:* 212-944-8291 *Fax:* 212-944-8293 *E-mail:* hq@abaa.org *Web Site:* www.abaa.org, pg 678

Wade, Linda, Crabtree Publishing Co, 350 Fifth Ave, Suite 3308, PMB 16-A, New York, NY 10118 *Tel:* 212-496-5040 *Toll Free Tel:* 800-387-7650 *Toll Free Fax:* 800-355-7166 *E-mail:* letters@crabtreebooks.com *Web Site:* www.crabtreebooks.com, pg 71

Wadsworth-Booth, Susan, Duquesne University Press, 600 Forbes Ave, Pittsburgh, PA 15282 *Tel:* 412-396-6610 *Toll Free Tel:* 800-666-2211 *Fax:* 412-396-5984 *Web Site:* www.dupress.duq.edu, pg 84

Waggoner, Lynn, Disney Publishing Worldwide, 500 S Buena Vista, Burbank, CA 91521 *Tel:* 212-633-4400 *Fax:* 212-633-4833 *Web Site:* www.disney.go.com/disneybooks, pg 81

Waggoner, Robert, Burrelle's Information Services, 75 E Northfield Rd, Livingston, NJ 07039 *Tel:* 973-992-6600 *Toll Free Tel:* 800-631-1160 *Fax:* 973-992-7675 *Toll Free Fax:* 800-898-6677 *E-mail:* directory@burrelles.com; directorysales@burrelles.com *Web Site:* www.burrellesluce.com, pg 50

Wagner, Alan, ISA, 67 Alexander Dr, Research Triangle Park, NC 27709 *Tel:* 919-549-8411 *Fax:* 919-549-8288 *E-mail:* info@isa.org *Web Site:* www.isa.org, pg 139

Wagner, Amy, T & T Clark International, PO Box 1321, Harrisburg, PA 17105 *Tel:* 717-541-8130 *Toll Free Tel:* 800-877-0012 *Fax:* 717-541-8136 *Web Site:* www.tandtclarkinternational.com, pg 263

Wagner, Don, Accent Publications, 4050 Lee Vance View, Colorado Springs, CO 80918 *Tel:* 719-536-0100 *Toll Free Tel:* 800-708-5550; 800-535-2905 (cust serv) *Fax:* 719-535-2928 *Toll Free Fax:* 800-430-0726 *Web Site:* www.accentpublications.com, pg 4

Wagner, Elizabeth, G P Putnam's Sons (Hardcover), 375 Hudson St, New York, NY 10014 *Tel:* 212-366-2000 *E-mail:* online@penguinputnam.com *Web Site:* www.penguin.com, pg 223

Wagner, Janet, St Martin's Press LLC, 175 Fifth Ave, New York, NY 10010 *Tel:* 212-674-5151 *Fax:* 212-420-9314 *E-mail:* firstname.lastname@stmartins.com *Web Site:* www.stmartins.com, pg 238

Wagner, JoAnn, The Center for Learning, 24600 Detroit Rd, Suite 201, Westlake, OH 44145 *Tel:* 440-250-9341 *Fax:* 440-250-9715 *Web Site:* www.centerforlearning.org, pg 56

Wagner, Matt, Waterside Productions Inc, 2187 Newcastle Ave, Suite 204, Cardiff, CA 92007 *Tel:* 760-632-9190 *Fax:* 760-632-9295 *Web Site:* www.waterside.com, pg 660

Wagner, Melissa, Quirk Books, 215 Church St, Philadelphia, PA 19106 *Tel:* 215-627-3581 *Fax:* 215-627-5220 *E-mail:* general@quirkbooks.com *Web Site:* www.quirkbooks.com, pg 224

Wagner, Ruth, Kabbalah Publishing, 155 E 48 St, New York, NY 10017 *Tel:* 212-644-0025 *Toll Free Tel:* 866-524-8723 *Fax:* 212-317-1264 *E-mail:* ny@kabbalah.com *Web Site:* www.kabbalah.com, pg 143

Wagner, Tim, Scott Publishing Co, 911 Vandemark Rd, Sidney, OH 45365 *Tel:* 937-498-0802 *Toll Free Tel:* 800-572-6885 *Fax:* 937-498-0807 *E-mail:* ssm@amospress.com *Web Site:* www.amosadvantage.com, pg 244

Wagshal, Menachem, Moznaim Publishing Corp, 4304 12 Ave, Brooklyn, NY 11219 *Tel:* 718-438-7680 *Toll Free Tel:* 800-364-5118 *Fax:* 718-438-1305, pg 180

Wahl, Anthony, Palgrave Macmillan, 175 Fifth Ave, New York, NY 10010 *Tel:* 212-982-3900 *Fax:* 212-777-6359 *E-mail:* firstname.lastname@palgrave-usa.com *Web Site:* www.palgrave.com, pg 202

Wahl, Kate, Stanford University Press, 1450 Page Mill Rd, Palo Alto, CA 94304-1124 *Tel:* 650-723-9434 *Fax:* 650-725-3457 *Web Site:* www.sup.org, pg 257

Wai, Logan, Newbridge Educational Publishing, One Beeman Rd, Northborough, MA 01532 *Tel:* 508-571-6500 *Toll Free Tel:* 800-867-0307 *Fax:* 508-571-6502 *Toll Free Fax:* 800-456-2419 *E-mail:* info@newbridgeonline.com *Web Site:* www.newbridgeonline.com; www.newbridgepub.com, pg 190

Wai, Logan, Sundance Publishing, One Beeman Rd, Northborough, MA 01532 *Tel:* 508-571-6500 *Toll Free Tel:* 800-343-8204 *Fax:* 508-571-6510 *Toll Free Fax:* 800-456-2419 *E-mail:* info@sundancepub.com *Web Site:* www.sundancepub.com, pg 262

Wainger, Leslie, Harlequin Enterprises Ltd, 233 Broadway, Suite 1001, New York, NY 10279 *Tel:* 212-553-4200 *Fax:* 212-227-8969 *E-mail:* customer.ecare@harlequin.ca *Web Site:* www.eharlequin.com; www.lua-books.com; www.mirabooks.com; www.reddressink.com; www.steeplehill.com, pg 115

Wainright, David, Players Press Inc, PO Box 1132, Studio City, CA 91614-0132 *Tel:* 818-789-4980, pg 214

Waintrub, George, Maval Publishing Inc, 567 Harrison St, Denver, CO 80206-4534 *Tel:* 303-338-8725 *Fax:* 303-745-6215 *E-mail:* maval@maval.com *Web Site:* www.maval.com, pg 165

Wainwright, Katie, Hyperion, 77 W 66 St, 11th fl, New York, NY 10023-6298 *Tel:* 212-456-0100 *Toll Free Tel:* 800-759-0190 (cust serv) *Fax:* 212-456-0157 *Web Site:* hyperionbooks.com, pg 129

Wainwright, Kristen, The Boston Literary Group Inc, 156 Mount Auburn St, Cambridge, MA 02138 *Tel:* 617-547-0800 *Fax:* 617-876-8474, pg 622

Waite, Diana S, Mount Ida Press, 152 Washington Ave, Albany, NY 12210-2203 *Tel:* 518-426-5935 *Fax:* 518-426-4116 *E-mail:* info@mtidapress.com *Web Site:* www.mountidapress.com, pg 179

Wakabayashi, Greg, Welcome Books, 6 W 18 St, 3rd fl, New York, NY 10011 *Tel:* 212-989-3200 *Fax:* 212-989-3205 *E-mail:* info@welcomebooks.com *Web Site:* www.welcomebooks.com, pg 295

Wakabayashi, Hiro Clark, Welcome Books, 6 W 18 St, 3rd fl, New York, NY 10011 *Tel:* 212-989-3200 *Fax:* 212-989-3205 *E-mail:* info@welcomebooks.com *Web Site:* www.welcomebooks.com, pg 295

Wakely, Sean, Wadsworth Publishing, 10 Davis Dr, Belmont, CA 94002-3002 *Toll Free Tel:* 800-357-0092 *Fax:* 650-592-3342 *Toll Free Fax:* 800-522-4923 *Web Site:* www.wadsworth.com, pg 292

Wakeman, James, ICS Press, 3100 Harrison St, Oakland, CA 94611 *Tel:* 510-238-5010 *Toll Free Tel:* 800-326-0263 *Fax:* 510-238-8440 *E-mail:* mail@icspress.com *Web Site:* www.icspress.com, pg 130

Wakiyama, Katsuo, Book East, 2330 NE 61 Ave, Portland, OR 97213 *Tel:* 503-287-0974 *Fax:* 503-281-3693, pg 43

Walch, Peter S, J Weston Walch Publisher, 321 Valley St, Portland, ME 04104 *Tel:* 207-772-2846 *Toll Free Tel:* 800-341-6094 *Fax:* 207-772-3105 *Toll Free Fax:* 888-991-5755 *E-mail:* customerservice@mail.walch.com *Web Site:* www.walch.com, pg 292

Walcott, Prof Derek, Boston University, 236 Bay State Rd, Boston, MA 02215 *Tel:* 617-353-2510 *Fax:* 617-353-3653 *Web Site:* www.bu.edu/writing/, pg 751

Wald, Alvin, Mary Jack Wald Associates Inc, 111 E 14 St, New York, NY 10003 *Tel:* 212-254-7842 *Fax:* 212-254-7842, pg 659

Wald, Mary Jack, Mary Jack Wald Associates Inc, 111 E 14 St, New York, NY 10003 *Tel:* 212-254-7842 *Fax:* 212-254-7842, pg 659

Waldman, Brett, Tristan Publishing, 2300 Louisiana Ave, Suite B, Golden Valley, MN 55427 *Tel:* 763-545-1383 *Toll Free Tel:* 866-545-1383 *Fax:* 763-545-1387 *E-mail:* info@tristanpublishing.com *Web Site:* www.tristanpublishing.com, pg 276

Waldman, Harry, The Mathematical Association of America, 1529 18 St NW, Washington, DC 20036 *Tel:* 202-387-5200 *Toll Free Tel:* 800-331-1622 (orders) *Fax:* 202-265-2384 *E-mail:* ldouglas@pmds.com *Web Site:* www.maa.org, pg 165

Waldron, Laura, University of Pennsylvania Press, 4200 Pine St, Philadelphia, PA 19104-4011 *Tel:* 215-898-6261 *Toll Free Tel:* 800-445-9880 (orders & cust serv only) *Fax:* 215-898-0404; 410-516-6998 (orders) *E-mail:* custserv@pobox.upenn.edu *Web Site:* www.upenn.edu/pennpress, pg 284

Wales, Elizabeth, Wales Literary Agency Inc, PO Box 9428, Seattle, WA 98109-0428 *Tel:* 206-284-7114 *Fax:* 206-322-1033 *E-mail:* waleslit@waleslit.com *Web Site:* www.waleslit.com, pg 660

Wales, Maureen, William H Sadlier Inc, 9 Pine St, New York, NY 10005 *Tel:* 212-227-2120 *Toll Free Tel:* 800-221-5175 *Fax:* 212-312-6080 *Web Site:* www.sadlier.com; www.sadlier-oxford.com, pg 237

Walford, Lynn, Book Publicists of Southern California, 6464 Sunset Blvd, Rm 755, Hollywood, CA 90028 *Tel:* 323-461-3921 *Fax:* 323-461-0917, pg 682

Walgren, Frank, NAL, 375 Hudson St, New York, NY 10014 *Tel:* 212-366-2000 *E-mail:* online@penguinputnam.com *Web Site:* www.penguin.com, pg 181

Walker, Brian, Charlesbridge Publishing Inc, 85 Main St, Watertown, MA 02472 *Tel:* 617-926-0329 *Toll Free Tel:* 800-225-3214 *Fax:* 617-926-5720 *E-mail:* books@charlesbridge.com *Web Site:* www.charlesbridge.com, pg 58

Walker, Chris, Humanics Publishing Group, 12 S Dixie Hwy, Suite 203, Lake Worth, FL 33460 *Tel:* 561-533-6231 *Toll Free Tel:* 800-874-8844 *Toll Free*

Fax: 888-874-8844 E-mail: humanics@mindspring. com Web Site: humanicspub.com; humanicslearning. com; humanicsdealer.com, pg 128

Walker, Craig, Scholastic Trade Division, 557 Broadway, New York, NY 10012 Tel: 212-343-6100; 212-343-4685 (export sales) Fax: 212-343-4714 (export sales) Web Site: www.scholastic.com, pg 242

Walker, David, The Field Poetry Prize, 50 N Professor St, Oberlin, OH 44074-1095 Tel: 440-775-8408 Fax: 440-775-8124 E-mail: oc.press@oberlin.edu Web Site: www.oberlin.edu/ocpress, pg 773

Walker, David, Oberlin College Press, 50 N Professor St, Oberlin, OH 44074-1095 Tel: 440-775-8408 Fax: 440-775-8124 E-mail: oc.press@oberlin.edu Web Site: www.oberlin.edu/ocpress, pg 195

Walker, Jack D, Leadership Ministries Worldwide, 515 Airport Rd, Suite 111, Chattanooga, TN 37421 Tel: 423-855-2181 Toll Free Tel: 800-987-8790 Fax: 423-855-8616 Toll Free Fax: 800-987-8790 E-mail: info@outlinebible.org Web Site: www. outlinebible.org, pg 150

Walker, James, Camden House, 668 Mount Hope Ave, Rochester, NY 14620 Tel: 585-273-5709; 585-275-0419 Fax: 585-271-8778 E-mail: boydell@boydellusa. net Web Site: www.boydell.co.uk/camdenfr.htm; www. camden-house.com, pg 593

Walker, Janet, The Brookings Institution Press, 1775 Massachusetts Ave NW, Washington, DC 20036-2188 Tel: 202-797-6000 Toll Free Tel: 800-275-1447 Fax: 202-797-6195 E-mail: bibooks@brook.edu Web Site: www.brookings.edu, pg 48

Walker, Janice, SPIE, International Society for Optical Engineering, 1000 20 St, Bellingham, WA 98225 Tel: 360-676-3290 Fax: 360-647-1445 E-mail: spie@ spie.org Web Site: www.spie.org, pg 255

Walker, Jayne, Jayne Walker Literary Services, 1406 Euclid Ave, Suite 1, Berkeley, CA 94708 Tel: 510-843-8265, pg 613

Walker, Lisa J, Education Writers Association, 2122 "P" St NW, No 201, Washington, DC 20037 Tel: 202-452-9830 Fax: 202-452-9837 E-mail: ewa@ewa.org Web Site: www.ewa.org, pg 686

Walker, Lisa J, Education Writers Association Workshops, 2122 "P" St NW, No 201, Washington, DC 20037 Tel: 202-452-9830 Fax: 202-452-9837 E-mail: ewa@ewa.org Web Site: www.ewa.org, pg 743

Walker, Lisa J, National Awards for Education Reporting, 2122 "P" St NW, No 201, Washington, DC 20037 Tel: 202-452-9830 Fax: 202-452-9837 E-mail: ewa@ewa.org Web Site: www.ewa.org, pg 791

Walker, Michael C, SRA/McGraw-Hill, a Division of McGraw-Hill Learning Group, 8787 Orion Place, Columbus, OH 43240 Tel: 614-430-4000 Fax: 614-430-6621 E-mail: sra@mcgraw-hill.com Web Site: www.sra-4kids.com, pg 256

Walker, Nancy, W H Freeman and Co, 41 Madison Ave, 37th fl, New York, NY 10010 Tel: 212-576-9400 Fax: 212-689-2383 Web Site: www.whfreeman.com, pg 101

Walker, Priscilla Alden, Amrita Foundation Inc, PO Box 190978, Dallas, TX 75219-0978 Tel: 214-522-7533 Fax: 214-522-6184 E-mail: prisi@amrita.com Web Site: www.amrita.com, pg 569

Walker, Ramsey R, Walker & Co, 104 Fifth Ave, 7th fl, New York, NY 10011 Tel: 212-727-8300 Toll Free Tel: 800-289-2553 Fax: 212-727-0984 Toll Free Fax: 800-218-9367 E-mail: firstinitiallastname@ walkerbooks.com Web Site: www.walkerbooks.com, pg 292

Walker, Richard, Amboy Associates, 620 Venture St, Suite A, Escondido, CA 92029 Tel: 760-546-4023 Toll Free Tel: 800-448-4023 Fax: 760-546-0404 Web Site: www.oshastuff. com, pg 10

Walker, Rick, Kids Can Press Ltd, 2250 Military Rd, Tonawanda, NY 14150 Tel: 416-925-5437 (Toronto, ON, Canada) Toll Free Tel: 800-265-0884; 866-481-5827 (orders) Fax: 416-960-5437 (Toronto, ON, Canada) E-mail: info@kidscan.com; lfyman@kidscan. com (orders) Web Site: www.kidscanpress.com, pg 145

Walker, Rick, Kids Can Press Ltd, 29 Birch Ave, Toronto, ON M4V 1E2, Canada Tel: 416-925-5437 Toll Free Tel: 800-265-0884 Fax: 416-960-5437 E-mail: info@kidscan.com Web Site: kidscanpress. com, pg 552

Walker, Robert, Hendrickson Publishers Inc, PO Box 3473, Peabody, MA 01961-3473 Tel: 978-532-6546 Toll Free Tel: 800-358-3111 Fax: 978-531-8146 E-mail: orders@hendrickson.com Web Site: www. hendrickson.com, pg 121

Walker, Susan, Upper Midwest Booksellers Association (UMBA), 3407 W 44 St, Minneapolis, MN 55410 Tel: 612-926-5868 Toll Free Tel: 800-784-7522 Fax: 612-926-6657 E-mail: umbaoffice@aol.com Web Site: www.abookaday.com, pg 701

Walker, Wendy, Atria Books, 1230 Avenue of the Americas, New York, NY 10020 Tel: 212-698-7000 Fax: 212-698-7007 Web Site: www.simonsays.com, pg 27

Walkowicz, Chris, Dog Writers' Association of America Inc (DWAA), 173 Union Rd, Coatesville, PA 19320 Tel: 610-384-2436 Fax: 610-384-2471 E-mail: dwaa@ dwaa.org Web Site: www.dwaa.org, pg 686

Walkowicz, Chris, Dog Writers' Association of America Inc (DWAA) Annual Awards, 173 Union Rd, Coatesville, PA 19320 Tel: 610-384-2436 Fax: 610-384-2471 E-mail: dwaa@dwaa.org; rhydowen@aol. com Web Site: www.dwaa.org, pg 770

Walkus, Grace, McGraw-Hill Education, 2 Penn Plaza, New York, NY 10121 Tel: 212-904-2000 E-mail: customer.service@mcgraw-hill.com Web Site: www.mheducation.com; www.mheducation. com/custserv.html, pg 167

Wall, Byron E, Wall & Emerson Inc, 6 O'Connor Dr, Toronto, ON M4K 2K1, Canada Tel: 416-467-8685 Toll Free Tel: 877-409-4601 Fax: 416-352-5368 E-mail: wall@wallbooks.com Web Site: www. wallbooks.com, pg 566

Wall, Martha, Wall & Emerson Inc, 6 O'Connor Dr, Toronto, ON M4K 2K1, Canada Tel: 416-467-8685 Toll Free Tel: 877-409-4601 Fax: 416-352-5368 E-mail: wall@wallbooks.com Web Site: www. wallbooks.com, pg 566

Wall, Patrick, A-R Editions Inc, 8551 Research Way, Suite 180, Middleton, WI 53562 Tel: 608-836-9000 Toll Free Tel: 800-736-0070 (US book orders only) Fax: 608-831-8200 E-mail: info@areditions.com Web Site: www.areditions.com, pg 2

Wall, Richard, George Freedley Memorial Award, Queens College, CUNY, Flushing, NY 11367 Tel: 718-997-3672 Fax: 718-997-3753 Web Site: tla. library.unt.edu, pg 775

Wall, Richard, The Theatre Library Association Award, Queens College, CUNY, Flushing, NY 11367 Tel: 718-997-3762 Fax: 718-997-3753 Web Site: tla. library.unt.edu, pg 808

Wall, Stephanie, Peachpit Press, 1249 Eighth St, Berkeley, CA 94710 Tel: 510-524-2178 Fax: 510-524-2221 E-mail: firstname.lastname@peachpit.com Web Site: www.peachpit.com, pg 206

Wallace, Dan, Gallaudet University Press, 800 Florida Ave NE, Washington, DC 20002-3695 Tel: 202-651-5488 Fax: 202-651-5489 E-mail: gupress@gallaudet. edu Web Site: gupress.gallaudet.edu, pg 102

Wallace, George, BOA Editions Ltd, 260 East Ave, Rochester, NY 14604 Tel: 585-546-3410 Fax: 585-546-3913 Web Site: www.boaeditions.org, pg 42

Wallace, Ivey B, Gallaudet University Press, 800 Florida Ave NE, Washington, DC 20002-3695 Tel: 202-651-5488 Fax: 202-651-5489 E-mail: gupress@gallaudet. edu Web Site: gupress.gallaudet.edu, pg 102

Wallace, Larry L, Abingdon Press, 201 Eighth Ave S, Nashville, TN 37203-3919 Tel: 615-749-6290 (publicist); 615-749-6000; 615-749-6451 (sales) Toll Free Tel: 800-251-3320 Fax: 615-749-6056 Web Site: www.abingdonpress.com, pg 3

Wallace, Lois, Wallace Literary Agency Inc, 177 E 70 St, New York, NY 10021 Tel: 212-570-9090 Fax: 212-772-8979 E-mail: walliter@aol.com, pg 660

Wallace, Ronald, Brittingham & Felix Pollak Prizes in Poetry, c/o Ron Wallace, Series Editor, University of Wisconsin, Dept of English, 600 N Park St, Madison, WI 53706 Web Site: www.wisc.edu/wisconsinpress/, pg 764

Walling, Donovan R, Phi Delta Kappa International, 408 N Union, Bloomington, IN 47401 Tel: 812-339-1156 Toll Free Tel: 800-766-1156 Fax: 812-339-0018 E-mail: information@pdkintl.org Web Site: www. pdkintl.org, pg 211

Wallis, Budge, Betterway Books, 4700 E Galbraith Rd, Cincinnati, OH 45236 Tel: 513-531-2690 Toll Free Tel: 800-666-0963 Fax: 513-891-7185 Toll Free Fax: 888-590-4082 Web Site: www.fwpublications. com, pg 38

Wallis, Budge, North Light Books, 4700 E Galbraith Rd, Cincinnati, OH 45236 Tel: 513-531-2690 Toll Free Tel: 800-666-0963 Fax: 513-891-7185 Toll Free Fax: 888-590-4082 Web Site: www.fwpublications. com, pg 192

Wallis, William Budge Jr, Writer's Digest Books, 4700 E Galbraith Rd, Cincinnati, OH 45236 Tel: 513-531-2690 Toll Free Tel: 800-289-0963 Fax: 513-891-7185 Web Site: www.writersdigest.com, pg 305

Wallman, Keith, Carroll & Graf Publishers, 245 W 17 St, 11th fl, New York, NY 10011-5300 Tel: 646-375-2570 Fax: 646-375-2571 Web Site: www. carrollandgraf.com, pg 54

Walls, John, Altitude Publishing Canada Ltd, 1500 Railway Ave, Canmore, AB T1W 1P6, Canada Tel: 403-678-6888 Toll Free Tel: 800-957-6888 Fax: 403-678-6951 Toll Free Fax: 800-957-1477 E-mail: orderdesk@altitudepublishing.com; sales@ altitudepublishing.com (ordering) Web Site: www. altitudepublishing.com, pg 535

Walsh, Barbara A, Holiday House Inc, 425 Madison Ave, New York, NY 10017 Tel: 212-688-0085 Fax: 212-421-6134, pg 123

Walsh, Harold F, Christopher Publishing House, 24 Rockland St, Hanover, MA 02339 Tel: 781-826-7474; 781-826-5494 Fax: 781-826-5556 E-mail: cph@ atigroupinc.com, pg 61

Walsh, James, Silver Lake Publishing, 3501 W Sunset Blvd, Los Angeles, CA 90026 Tel: 323-663-3082 Fax: 323-663-3084 E-mail: theeditors@silverlakepub. com; results@silverlakepub.com Web Site: www. silverlakepub.com, pg 247

Walsh, Jennifer Rudolph, William Morris Agency, 1325 Avenue of the Americas, New York, NY 10019 Tel: 212-586-5100 Fax: 212-903-1418 E-mail: wma@ interport.net Web Site: www.wma.com, pg 645

Walsh, John, Harvard University Press, 79 Garden St, Cambridge, MA 02138-1499 Tel: 617-495-2600; 401-531-2800 (international orders) Toll Free Tel: 800-405-1619 (orders) Fax: 617-495-5898 (general); 617-496-4677 (edit & rts); 401-531-2801 (international orders) Toll Free Fax: 800-406-9145 (orders) E-mail: firstname_lastname@harvard.edu Web Site: www.hup.harvard.edu, pg 117

Walsh, Margaret A, University of Wisconsin Press, 1930 Monroe St, 3rd fl, Madison, WI 53711 Tel: 608-263-1110 Toll Free Tel: 800-621-2736 (Orders) Fax: 608-263-1120 Toll Free Fax: 800-621-8476 (Orders) E-mail: uwiscpress@uwpress.wisc.edu (Main Office) Web Site: www.wisc.edu/wisconsinpress/, pg 286

Walsh, Mark, Artech House Inc, 685 Canton St, Norwood, MA 02062 Tel: 781-769-9750 Toll Free Tel: 800-225-9977 Fax: 781-769-6334 E-mail: artech@artechhouse.com Web Site: www. artechhouse.com, pg 24

Walsh, Mary, Ernest Hemingway Foundation/PEN Award for First Fiction, PO Box 400725, North Cambridge, MA 02140 Tel: 617-499-9550 Fax: 617-353-7134 E-mail: hemingway@pen-ne.org Web Site: www.pen-ne.org, pg 778

Warinner, Judy, Professional Resource Exchange Inc, 1891 Apex Rd, Sarasota, FL 34240 *Tel:* 941-343-9601 *Toll Free Tel:* 800-443-3364 *Fax:* 941-343-9201 *Web Site:* www.prpress.com, pg 220

Wark, Lee, Mason Crest Publishers, 370 Reed Rd, Suite 302, Broomall, PA 19008 *Tel:* 610-543-6200 *Toll Free Tel:* 866-MCP-BOOK (627-2665) *Fax:* 610-543-3878 *Web Site:* www.masoncrest.com, pg 165

Warne, Tim, The Mountaineers Books, 1001 SW Klickitat Way, Suite 201, Seattle, WA 98134 *Tel:* 206-223-6303 *Toll Free Tel:* 800-553-4453 *Fax:* 206-223-6306 *Toll Free Fax:* 800-568-7604 *E-mail:* mbooks@mountaineers.org *Web Site:* www.mountaineersbooks.org, pg 179

Warner, Daryn J, Mill Mountain Theatre, Center in the Square, 2nd fl, One Market Sq, Roanoke, VA 24011-1437 *Tel:* 540-342-5771 *Fax:* 540-342-5745 *E-mail:* outreach@millmountain.org *Web Site:* www.millmountain.org, pg 789

Warner, Peter, Thames & Hudson, 500 Fifth Ave, New York, NY 10110 *Tel:* 212-354-3763 *Toll Free Tel:* 800-233-4830 *Fax:* 212-398-1252 *E-mail:* bookinfo@thames.wwnorton.com *Web Site:* www.thamesandhudsonusa.com, pg 268

Warner, Sarah, Westview Press, 5500 Central Ave, Boulder, CO 80301 *Tel:* 303-444-3541 *Toll Free Tel:* 800-386-5656 *Fax:* 720-406-7336 *E-mail:* westview.orders@perseusbooks.com *Web Site:* www.perseusbooksgroup.com; www.westviewpress.com, pg 297

Warner, Todd, Practising Law Institute, 810 Seventh Ave, New York, NY 10019 *Tel:* 212-824-5700 *Toll Free Tel:* 800-260-4PLI (260-4754 customer service) *Fax:* 212-265-4742 *Toll Free Fax:* 800-321-0093 *E-mail:* info@pli.edu *Web Site:* www.pli.edu, pg 217

Warner, W L, GLB Publishers, 1028 Howard St, No 503, San Francisco, CA 94103 *Tel:* 415-621-8307 *Toll Free Tel:* 800-452-6119 *E-mail:* glbpubs@mindspring.com *Web Site:* www.glbpubs.com, pg 105

Warren, Albert, Warren Communications News, 2115 Ward Ct NW, Washington, DC 20037-1209 *Tel:* 202-872-9200 *Fax:* 202-293-3435 *E-mail:* info@warren-news.com *Web Site:* www.warren-news.com, pg 293

Warren, Anthony, Alba House, 2187 Victory Blvd, Staten Island, NY 10314 *Tel:* 718-761-0047 (edit & prodn); 718-698-2759 (mktg & billing) *Toll Free Tel:* 800-343-2522 *Fax:* 718-761-0057 *E-mail:* albabooks@aol.com *Web Site:* www.albahouse.org, pg 7

Warren, Fr Anthony, Alba House, 2187 Victory Blvd, Staten Island, NY 10314 *Tel:* 718-761-0047 (edit & prodn); 718-698-2759 (mktg & billing) *Toll Free Tel:* 800-343-2522 *Fax:* 718-761-0057 *E-mail:* albabooks@aol.com *Web Site:* www.albahouse.org, pg 7

Warren, Daniel, Warren Communications News, 2115 Ward Ct NW, Washington, DC 20037-1209 *Tel:* 202-872-9200 *Fax:* 202-293-3435 *E-mail:* info@warren-news.com *Web Site:* www.warren-news.com, pg 293

Warren, James, Columbia University Press, 61 W 62 St, New York, NY 10023 *Tel:* 212-459-0600 *Toll Free Tel:* 800-944-8648 *Fax:* 212-459-3678 *Web Site:* www.columbia.edu/cu/cup, pg 65

Warren, John, RAND Corp, 1776 Main St, Santa Monica, CA 90407 *Tel:* 310-393-0411 *Fax:* 310-451-6996 *E-mail:* jane_ryan@rand.org *Web Site:* www.rand.org, pg 225

Warren, Joy, University of Oklahoma Press, 4100 28 Ave NW, Norman, OK 73069-8218 *Tel:* 405-325-2000 *Toll Free Tel:* 800-627-7377 (orders) *Fax:* 405-364-5798 (orders) *Toll Free Fax:* 800-735-0476 (orders) *E-mail:* oupress@ou.edu *Web Site:* www.oupress.com, pg 284

Warren, Judy, Graphic Arts Sales Foundation (GASF), 113 E Evans St, West Chester, PA 19380 *Tel:* 610-431-9780 *Fax:* 610-436-5238 *E-mail:* info@gasf.org *Web Site:* www.gasf.org, pg 688

Warren, Maggie, Spring Point Publishing Services, 4 The Ledges, Hallowell, ME 04347 *Tel:* 207-622-3973 *Fax:* 207-622-3973, pg 611

Warren, Paul, Warren Communications News, 2115 Ward Ct NW, Washington, DC 20037-1209 *Tel:* 202-872-9200 *Fax:* 202-293-3435 *E-mail:* info@warren-news.com *Web Site:* www.warren-news.com, pg 293

Warren, Prof Rosanna, Boston University, 236 Bay State Rd, Boston, MA 02215 *Tel:* 617-353-2510 *Fax:* 617-353-3653 *Web Site:* www.bu.edu/writing/, pg 751

Warren, Roseanna, New England Poetry Club, 2 Farrar St, Cambridge, MA 02138 *Tel:* 781-643-0029, pg 695

Warren, Sarah, Beach Holme Publishing, 409 Granville St, Suite 1010, Vancouver, BC V6C 1T2, Canada *Tel:* 604-733-4868 *Toll Free Tel:* 888-551-6655 (orders) *Fax:* 604-733-4860 *E-mail:* bhp@beachholme.bc.ca *Web Site:* www.beachholme.bc.ca, pg 536

Warren-Lynch, Isabel, Random House Children's Books, 1745 Broadway, New York, NY 10019 *Tel:* 212-782-9000 *Toll Free Tel:* 800-200-3552 *Fax:* 212-782-9452 *Web Site:* www.randomhouse.com/kids, pg 226

Warwick, Liz, Periodical Writers' Association of Canada, 215 Spadina Ave, Suite 123, Toronto, ON M5T 2C7, Canada *Tel:* 416-504-1645 *Fax:* 416-913-2327 *E-mail:* pwac@web.net; info@pwac.ca *Web Site:* www.pwac.ca; www.writers.ca, pg 697

Warwick, Tari, Westview Press, 5500 Central Ave, Boulder, CO 80301 *Tel:* 303-444-3541 *Toll Free Tel:* 800-386-5656 *Fax:* 720-406-7336 *E-mail:* westview.orders@perseusbooks.com *Web Site:* www.perseusbooksgroup.com; www.westviewpress.com, pg 297

Warwick-Smith, Simon, Dunhill Publishing, 18340 Sonoma Hwy, Sonoma, CA 95476 *Tel:* 707-939-0562 *Fax:* 707-938-3515 *E-mail:* dunhill@vom.com *Web Site:* www.dunhillpublishing.net, pg 84

Warwick-Smith, Simon, Warwick Associates, 18340 Sonoma Hwy, Sonoma, CA 95476 *Tel:* 707-939-9212 *Fax:* 707-938-3515 *E-mail:* warwick@vom.com *Web Site:* www.warwickassociates.net, pg 660

Wasch, Ken, Software & Information Industry Association (SIIA), 1090 Vermont Ave NW, 6th fl, Washington, DC 20005 *Tel:* 202-289-7442 *Fax:* 202-289-7097 *E-mail:* info@siia.net *Web Site:* www.siia.net, pg 700

Wasch, Kenneth, Codie Awards, 1090 Vermont Ave NW, 6th fl, Washington, DC 20005 *Tel:* 202-289-7442 *Fax:* 202-289-7097 *E-mail:* codieawards@siia.net *Web Site:* www.siia.net, pg 768

Washington, Ida, League of Vermont Writers, PO Box 172, Underhill Center, VT 05490 *Tel:* 802-253-9439 *Web Site:* www.leaguevtwriters.org, pg 690

Washington, Sandra, Fairchild Books, 7 W 34 St, New York, NY 10001 *Tel:* 212-630-3880 *Toll Free Tel:* 800-932-4724 *Fax:* 212-630-3868; 212-630-3898 *Web Site:* www.fairchildbooks.com, pg 94

Wasinger, Meredith (Peggy) Mundy, Dutton Children's Books, 345 Hudson St, New York, NY 10014 *Tel:* 212-366-2000 *E-mail:* online@penguinputnam.com *Web Site:* www.penguin.com, pg 85

Wason, Traci, Thomas T Beeler Publisher, 710 Main St, Suite 300, Rollinsford, NH 03869 *Tel:* 603-749-0392 *Toll Free Tel:* 800-818-7574 *Fax:* 603-749-0395 *Toll Free Fax:* 888-222-3396 *E-mail:* cservice@beelerpub.com *Web Site:* www.beelerpub.com, pg 35

Wasp, Daniel, Graphic Learning, 61 Mattatuck Heights Rd, Waterbury, CT 06705 *Tel:* 203-756-6562 *Toll Free Tel:* 800-874-0029; 800-227-9120 *Fax:* 203-756-2895 *Toll Free Fax:* 800-737-3322, pg 108

Wasp, Daniel C, Abrams & Co Publishers Inc, 61 Mattatuck Heights Rd, Waterbury, CT 06705 *Tel:* 203-756-6562 *Toll Free Tel:* 800-227-9120 *Fax:* 203-756-2895 *Toll Free Fax:* 800-737-3322, pg 3

Wasp, Daniel C, The Letter People®, 61 Mattatuck Heights Rd, Waterbury, CT 06705 *Tel:* 203-756-6562 *Toll Free Tel:* 800-227-9120; 800-874-0029 *Fax:* 203-756-2895 *Toll Free Fax:* 800-737-3322, pg 153

Wassell, Sarah, American Anthropological Association, Publications Dept, 2200 Wilson Blvd, Suite 600, Arlington, VA 22201 *Tel:* 703-528-1902 ext 3014 *Fax:* 703-528-3546 *Web Site:* www.aaanet.org, pg 11

Wasserman, Barbara, Oxford University Press, Inc, 198 Madison Ave, New York, NY 10016-4314 *Tel:* 212-726-6000 *Toll Free Tel:* 800-451-7556 (orders) *Web Site:* www.oup.com/us, pg 200

Wasserman, Harriet, Harriet Wasserman Literary Agency Inc, 137 E 36 St, New York, NY 10016 *Tel:* 212-689-3257 *Fax:* 212-689-3257 *E-mail:* hawlainc@aol.com, pg 660

Wasserman, Marlie, Rutgers University Press, 100 Joyce Kilmer Ave, Piscataway, NJ 08854-8099 *Tel:* 732-445-7762 (edit); 732-445-7762 (ext 627, sales) *Toll Free Tel:* 800-446-9323 (orders only) *Fax:* 732-445-7039 (acqs, edit, mktg, perms, prodn); 732-445-1974 (fulfillment) *E-mail:* garyf@rci.rutgers.edu *Web Site:* rutgerspress.rutgers.edu, pg 236

Wasserman, Renata, Wayne State University Press, Leonard N Simons Bldg, 4809 Woodward Ave, Detroit, MI 48201-1309 *Tel:* 313-577-4600 *Toll Free Tel:* 800-978-7323 *Fax:* 313-577-6131, pg 294

Waterbury, Whit, Simon & Schuster Audio, 1230 Avenue of the Americas, New York, NY 10020 *Tel:* 212-698-7664 *E-mail:* audiopub@simonandschuster.com *Web Site:* www.simonsaysaudio.com, pg 248

Waters, Anne, John F Blair Publisher, 1406 Plaza Dr, Winston-Salem, NC 27103 *Tel:* 336-768-1374 *Toll Free Tel:* 800-222-9796 *Fax:* 336-768-9194 *E-mail:* blairpub@blairpub.com *Web Site:* www.blairpub.com, pg 41

Waters, Christian, Random House Sales & Marketing, 1745 Broadway, New York, NY 10019 *Fax:* 212-782-9000, pg 227

Waters, Eric, National Press Photographers Association Inc (NPPA), 3200 Croasdaile Dr, Suite 306, Durham, NC 27705 *Tel:* 919-383-7246 *Fax:* 919-383-7261 *E-mail:* info@nppa.org *Web Site:* www.nppa.org, pg 694

Waters, Lindsay, Harvard University Press, 79 Garden St, Cambridge, MA 02138-1499 *Tel:* 617-495-2600; 401-531-2800 (international orders) *Toll Free Tel:* 800-405-1619 (orders) *Fax:* 617-495-5898 (general); 617-496-4677 (edit & rts); 401-531-2801 (international orders) *Toll Free Fax:* 800-406-9145 (orders) *E-mail:* firstname_lastname@harvard.edu *Web Site:* www.hup.harvard.edu, pg 117

Waters, Mitchell, Curtis Brown Ltd, 10 Astor Place, New York, NY 10003 *Tel:* 212-473-5400, pg 623

Watkins, Anne Dean, The University Press of Kentucky, 663 S Limestone St, Lexington, KY 40508-4008 *Tel:* 859-257-8761; 859-257-8442 (mktg) *Toll Free Tel:* 800-839-6855 (orders) *Fax:* 859-323-1873 *Web Site:* www.kentuckypress.com, pg 287

Watkins, Dawn L, Bob Jones University Press, 1700 Wade Hampton Blvd, Greenville, SC 29614 *Tel:* 864-242-5100 *Toll Free Tel:* 800-845-5731 (orders only) *Fax:* 864-298-0268 *E-mail:* asmith@bju.edu *Web Site:* www.bjup.com, pg 142

Watkins, Julia M, Council on Social Work Education, 1725 Duke St, Suite 500, Alexandria, VA 22314-3457 *Tel:* 703-683-8080 *Fax:* 703-683-8099 *E-mail:* webmaster@cswe.org *Web Site:* www.cswe.org, pg 70

Watkins, Laura, BenBella Books, 6440 N Central Expressway, Suite 617, Dallas, TX 75206 *Tel:* 214-750-3600 *Fax:* 214-750-3645 *E-mail:* editor@benbellabooks.com *Web Site:* www.benbellabooks.com, pg 35

Watman, Max, The Nebraska Review Awards, University of Nebraska-Omaha, WFAB 212, Omaha, NE 68182-0324 *Tel:* 402-554-3159 *Fax:* 402-614-2026 *Web Site:* www.zoopress.org/nebraskareview/, pg 793

Watrous, Scott, Adams Media, An F+W Publications Co, 57 Littlefield St, 2nd fl, Avon, MA 02322 *Tel:* 508-427-7100 *Fax:* 508-427-6790 *Toll Free Fax:* 800-872-

5628 *E-mail:* authors@adamsmedia.com; orders@ adamsmedia.com *Web Site:* www.adamsmedia.com, pg 5

Watson, Alex, Elsevier, 11830 Westline Industrial Dr, St Louis, MO 63146 *Tel:* 314-872-8370 *Toll Free Tel:* 800-325-4177 *Fax:* 314-432-1380 *Web Site:* www. elsevier.com; www.elsevierhealth.com, pg 89

Watson, Ben, Chelsea Green Publishing Co, PO Box 428, White River Junction, VT 05001-0428 *Tel:* 802-295-6300 *Toll Free Tel:* 800-639-4099 (cust serv & consumer orders); 800-807-6726 (trade & wholesale orders) *Fax:* 802-295-6444 *Web Site:* www. chelseagreen.com, pg 59

Watson, Elnora E, Wichita State University Playwriting Contest, 1845 Fairmount St, Wichita, KS 67260-0153 *Tel:* 316-978-3368 *Fax:* 316-978-3202 *Web Site:* www. wichita.edu, pg 811

Watson, James, Gordon W Dillon/Richard C Peterson Memorial Essay Prize, 16700 AOS Lane, Delray Beach, FL 33446 *Tel:* 561-404-2043 *Fax:* 561-404-2045 *E-mail:* theaos@aos.org *Web Site:* www. orchidweb.org, pg 770

Watson, Kathleen, Klutz, 455 Portage Ave, Palo Alto, CA 94306 *Tel:* 650-857-0888 *Fax:* 650-857-9110 *Web Site:* www.klutz.com, pg 146

Watson, Neale W, Watson Publishing International, PO Box 1240, Sagamore Beach, MA 02562-1240 *Tel:* 508-888-9113 *Fax:* 508-888-3733 *E-mail:* orders@watsonpublishing.com *Web Site:* www.watsonpublishing.com; www.shpusa. com, pg 294

Watson, Rebecca, University of Louisiana at Lafayette, Center for Louisiana Studies, PO Box 40831, UL, Lafayette, LA 70504-0831 *Tel:* 337-482-6027 *Fax:* 337-482-6028 *E-mail:* ann@louisiana.edu *Web Site:* www.cls.louisiana.edu, pg 282

Watson, Triona, Media Associates, PO Box 46, Wilton, CA 95693-0046 *Toll Free Tel:* 800-373-1897 (orders) *Fax:* 916-687-8711; 916-687-8711 *E-mail:* carlya777@hotmail.com *Web Site:* www. media-associates.co.nz, pg 170

Watt, Sandra, Sandra Watt & Associates, 1750 N Sierra Bonita St, Los Angeles, CA 90046 *Tel:* 323-874-0791, pg 660

Watters, Ron, National Outdoor Book Awards, 1065 S Eighth Ave, Pocatello, ID 83209 *Tel:* 208-236-3912 *Fax:* 208-236-4600 *Web Site:* www.isu.edu/outdoor/ books/, pg 792

Watts, Benjamin, Stipes Publishing LLC, 204 W University, Champaign, IL 61820 *Tel:* 217-356-8391 *Fax:* 217-356-5753 *E-mail:* stipes@soltec.net *Web Site:* www.stipes.com, pg 260

Watts, Robert A, Stipes Publishing LLC, 204 W University, Champaign, IL 61820 *Tel:* 217-356-8391 *Fax:* 217-356-5753 *E-mail:* stipes@soltec.net *Web Site:* www.stipes.com, pg 260

Waugh, Rebecca, Dial Books for Young Readers, 345 Hudson St, New York, NY 10014 *Tel:* 212-366-2000 *Fax:* 212-414-4396 *E-mail:* online@penguinputnam. com *Web Site:* www.penguinusa.com, pg 80

Wavrin, Kelly, Milkweed Editions, 1011 Washington Ave S, Suite 300, Minneapolis, MN 55415 *Tel:* 612-332-3192 *Toll Free Tel:* 800-520-6455 *Fax:* 612-215-2550 *E-mail:* editor@milkweed.org *Web Site:* www. milkweed.org; www.worldashome.org, pg 174

Wax, Eva, Janus Literary Agency, PO Box 766, Ipswich, MA 01938 *Tel:* 978-312-1372 *E-mail:* ubklene@aol. com, pg 636

Waxman, Scott, Waxman Literary Agency, 80 Fifth Ave, Suite 1101, New York, NY 10011 *Tel:* 212-675-5556 *Fax:* 212-675-1381 *E-mail:* submit@waxmanagency. com *Web Site:* www.waxmanagency.com, pg 660

Way, Clifford, The Pennsylvania State University Press, 820 N University Dr, University Support Bldg 1, Suite C, University Park, PA 16802-1003 *Tel:* 814-865-1327 *Toll Free Tel:* 800-326-9180 *Fax:* 814-863-1408 *Toll Free Fax:* 877 7782665 *Web Site:* www.psupress.org, pg 209

Wayant, Patricia, Blue Mountain Arts Inc, PO Box 4549, Boulder, CO 80306 *Tel:* 303-449-0536 *Toll Free Tel:* 800-473-2082 *Fax:* 303-417-6496 *Toll Free Fax:* 800-256-1213 *E-mail:* booksbma@mindspring. com; ordersbma@mindspring.com *Web Site:* www.sps. com, pg 41

Waybright, David, BradyGAMES Publishing, 800 E 96 St, 3rd fl, Indianapolis, IN 46240 *Tel:* 317-428-3000 *Toll Free Tel:* 800-545-5912; 800-571-5840 (cust serv) *E-mail:* bradyquestions@pearsoned.com *Web Site:* www.bradygames.com, pg 45

Wayne, Bob, DC Comics, 1700 Broadway, New York, NY 10019 *Tel:* 212-636-5400 *Toll Free Tel:* 800-759-0190 (distribution) *Fax:* 212-636-5481 *Web Site:* www. dccomics.com; www.madmag.com, pg 77

Wayne, Jack, Canadian Scholars' Press Inc, 180 Bloor St W, Suite 801, Toronto, ON M5S 2V6, Canada *Tel:* 416-929-2774 *Fax:* 416-929-1926 *E-mail:* info@ cspi.org *Web Site:* www.cspi.org; www.womenspress. ca, pg 539

Weakley, Jeff, C P A Book Publisher, 9205 SE Clackamas Rd, Clackamas, OR 97015 *Tel:* 503-668-4977 *Fax:* 503-668-8614 *E-mail:* cpabooks@hotmail. com, pg 51

Weaser, Angela, Dalkey Archive Press, Illinois State University 8905, Normal, IL 61790-8905 *Tel:* 309-438-7555 *Fax:* 309-438-7422 *E-mail:* contact@ dalkeyarchive.com *Web Site:* www.dalkeyarchive.com, pg 75

Weaver, Carole J, Howie Publishing Inc, 1695 Quigley Rd, Columbus, OH 43227 *Toll Free Tel:* 888-933-9314 *Fax:* 614-237-2157, pg 571

Weaver, Kyle, Stackpole Books, 5067 Ritter Rd, Mechanicsburg, PA 17055 *Tel:* 717-796-0411 *Toll Free Tel:* 800-732-3669 *Fax:* 717-796-0412 *Web Site:* www. stackpolebooks.com, pg 257

Weaver, Muffy, Dawn Publications Inc, 12402 Bitney Springs Rd, Nevada City, CA 95959 *Tel:* 530-274-7775 *Toll Free Tel:* 800-545-7475 *Fax:* 530-274-7778 *E-mail:* nature@dawnpub.com *Web Site:* www. dawnpub.com, pg 77

Weaver, Patricia, Herald Press, 616 Walnut Ave, Scottdale, PA 15683-1999 *Tel:* 724-887-8500 *Toll Free Tel:* 800-245-7894 *Fax:* 724-887-3111 *E-mail:* hp@ mph.org *Web Site:* www.heraldpress.com, pg 121

Weaver, Patricia, Herald Press, 490 Dutton Dr, Unit C-8, Waterloo, ON N2L 6H7, Canada *Tel:* 519-747-5722 *Toll Free Tel:* 800-245-7894 (Canada & US) *Fax:* 519-747-5721 *E-mail:* hp@mph.org *Web Site:* www. heraldpress.com, pg 550

Weaver, Paul D, Houghton Mifflin Co, 222 Berkeley St, Boston, MA 02116-3764 *Tel:* 617-351-5000 *Toll Free Tel:* 800-225-3362 (trade books); 800-733-2828 (text books); 800-225-1464 (college texts) *Fax:* 617-351-1125 *Web Site:* www.hmco.com, pg 126

Weaver, Reg, National Education Association (NEA), 1201 16 St NW, Washington, DC 20036 *Tel:* 202-822-7200 *Fax:* 202-822-7206; 202-822-7292 *Web Site:* www.nea.org, pg 693

Weaver-Neist, Jennifer, Collectors Press Inc, 15655 SW 74 Ave, Suite 200, Tigard, OR 97224 *Tel:* 503-684-3030 *Toll Free Tel:* 800-423-1848 *Fax:* 503-684-3777 *Web Site:* www.collectorspress.com, pg 64

Webb, Cynthia, Avocet Press Inc, 19 Paul Ct, Pearl River, NY 10965-1539 *Tel:* 845-735-6807 *Toll Free Tel:* 877-428-6238, pg 29

Webb, Prof Dorothy, Waldo M & Grace C Bonderman Prize, 140 W Washington St, Indianapolis, IN 46204 *Tel:* 317-635-5277 *Fax:* 317-236-0767 *E-mail:* bonderman@iupui.edu *Web Site:* www. indianarep.com/bonderman, pg 763

Webb, Irene, Jodie Rhodes Literary Agency, 8840 Villa La Jolla Dr, Suite 315, La Jolla, CA 92037, pg 651

Webb, James T, Great Potential Press, PO Box 5057, Scottsdale, AZ 85261 *Tel:* 602-954-4200 *Toll Free Tel:* 877-954-4200 *Fax:* 602-954-0185 *E-mail:* info@ giftedbooks.com *Web Site:* www.giftedbooks.com, pg 108

Webber, Bert, Webb Research Group, Publishers, PO Box 314, Medford, OR 97501-0021 *Tel:* 541-664-5205 *Fax:* 541-664-9131 *E-mail:* pnwbooks@pnwbooks. com *Web Site:* www.pnorthwestbooks.com, pg 295

Webber, M J, Webb Research Group, Publishers, PO Box 314, Medford, OR 97501-0021 *Tel:* 541-664-5205 *Fax:* 541-664-9131 *E-mail:* pnwbooks@pnwbooks. com *Web Site:* www.pnorthwestbooks.com, pg 295

Webber, Peter B, Syracuse University Press, 621 Skytop Rd, Syracuse, NY 13244-5290 *Tel:* 315-443-5534 *Toll Free Tel:* 800-365-8929 (orders only) *Fax:* 315-443-5545 *E-mail:* supress@syr.edu *Web Site:* syracuseuniversitypress.syr.edu, pg 263

Webber, Sydney, Kodansha America Inc, 575 Lexington Ave, 23rd fl, New York, NY 10022 *Tel:* 917-322-6200 *Fax:* 212-935-6929 *E-mail:* info@kodanshaamerica. com *Web Site:* www.kodansha-intl.com, pg 147

Weber, Andrew, Random House Inc, 1745 Broadway, New York, NY 10019 *Tel:* 212-782-9000 *Toll Free Tel:* 800-726-0600 *Web Site:* www.randomhouse.com, pg 226

Weber, Anne, Bernan, 4611-F Assembly Dr, Lanham, MD 20706-4391 *Tel:* 301-459-2255; 301-459-7666 (cust serv) *Toll Free Tel:* 800-274-4447; 800-274-4888 (cust serv) *Fax:* 301-459-9235; 301-459-0056 (cust serv) *Toll Free Fax:* 800-865-3450 *E-mail:* info@ bernan.com *Web Site:* www.bernan.com, pg 37

Weber, Johann, AIMS Education Foundation, 1595 S Chestnut Ave, Fresno, CA 93702-4706 *Tel:* 559-255-4094 *Toll Free Tel:* 888-733-2467 *Fax:* 559-255-6396 *E-mail:* aimsed@aimsedu.org *Web Site:* www.aimsedu. org/, pg 7

Weber, John, Welcome Rain Publishers LLC, 532 Laguardia Place, Suite 473, New York, NY 10012 *Tel:* 718-832-1607 *Fax:* 212-889-0869 *E-mail:* welcomrain@aol.com, pg 295

Weber, Judith, Sobel Weber Associates Inc, 146 E 19 St, New York, NY 10003 *Tel:* 212-420-8585 *Fax:* 212-505-1017 *E-mail:* info@sobelweber.com *Web Site:* www.sobelweber.com, pg 656

Weber, Mark, The Noontide Press, PO Box 2719, Newport Beach, CA 92659-1319 *Tel:* 949-631-1490 *Fax:* 949-631-0981 *E-mail:* orders@noontidepress.com *Web Site:* www.noontidepress.com, pg 191

Weberman, Alisa, Listen & Live Audio Inc, PO Box 817, Roseland, NJ 07068-0817 *Tel:* 973-781-1444 *Toll Free Tel:* 800-653-9400 *Fax:* 973-781-0333 *Web Site:* www.listenandlive.com, pg 156

Webster, Derek, QWF Prizes, 1200 Atwater Ave, Suite 3, Montreal, PQ H3Z 1X4, Canada *Tel:* 514-933-0878 *E-mail:* admin@qwf.org *Web Site:* www.qwf.org, pg 801

Webster, Robert, Flying Frog Publishing, 107 Nob Hill Park Dr, Reistertown, MD 21136 *Tel:* 410-833-6261 *Fax:* 410-833-6193 *E-mail:* allied@allpubmd.com, pg 97

Wechsler, Robert, Catbird Press, 16 Windsor Rd, North Haven, CT 06473-3015 *Tel:* 203-230-2391 *Fax:* 203-286-1091 *E-mail:* info@catbirdpress.com *Web Site:* www.catbirdpress.com, pg 55

Weckbaugh, Ernie, Book Publicists of Southern California, 6464 Sunset Blvd, Rm 755, Hollywood, CA 90028 *Tel:* 323-461-3921 *Fax:* 323-461-0917, pg 682

Weckbaugh, Patty, Book Publicists of Southern California, 6464 Sunset Blvd, Rm 755, Hollywood, CA 90028 *Tel:* 323-461-3921 *Fax:* 323-461-0917, pg 682

Wecksler, Sally, Wecksler-Incomco, 170 West End Ave, New York, NY 10023 *Tel:* 212-787-2239 *Fax:* 212-496-7035 *E-mail:* jacinny@aol.com, pg 660

Wedel, Michelle, Sweetgrass Press LLC, PO Box 1862, Merrimack, NH 03054-1862 *Tel:* 603-883-7001 *Fax:* 603-883-7001 *Toll Free Fax:* 866-727-7757 *E-mail:* info@sweetgrasspress.com *Web Site:* www. sweetgrasspress.com, pg 263

Weed, Elisabeth, Kneerim & Williams, c/o Fish & Richardson PC, 225 Franklin St, Boston, MA 02110 *Tel:* 617-542-5070 *Fax:* 617-542-8906 *Web Site:* www. fr.com, pg 638

Weeden, Larry, Focus on the Family, 8605 Explorer Dr, Colorado Springs, CO 80920 *Tel:* 719-531-3400 *Fax:* 719-531-3484 *Web Site:* www.family.org, pg 97

Weese, Brian, Society for Human Resource Management (SHRM), 1800 Duke St, Alexandria, VA 22314 *Tel:* 703-548-3440 *Toll Free Tel:* 800-444-5006 (orders) *Fax:* 703-836-0367; 770-442-9742 (orders) *E-mail:* shrm@shrm.org; shrmstore@shrm.org *Web Site:* www.shrm.org, pg 251

Wehmueller, Jacqueline C, The Johns Hopkins University Press, 2715 N Charles St, Baltimore, MD 21218-4363 *Tel:* 410-516-6900 *Toll Free Tel:* 800-537-5487 *Fax:* 410-516-6968 *Web Site:* www.press.jhu.edu, pg 141

Weidemann, Tina, Christian Publications Inc, 3825 Hartzdale Dr, Camp Hill, PA 17011 *Tel:* 717-761-7044 *Toll Free Tel:* 800-233-4443 *Fax:* 717-761-7273 *E-mail:* editorial@christianpublications.com *Web Site:* www.christianpublications.com, pg 61

Weidman, Anna, University of California Press, 2120 Berkeley Way, Berkeley, CA 94720 *Tel:* 510-642-4247 *Toll Free Tel:* 800-777-4726 *Fax:* 510-643-7127 *Toll Free Fax:* 800-999-1958 *E-mail:* askucp@ucpress.edu *Web Site:* www.ucpress.edu, pg 281

Weidman, John, The Authors League of America Inc, 31 E 28 St, New York, NY 10016 *Tel:* 212-564-8350 *Fax:* 212-564-8363 *E-mail:* staff@authorsguild.com *Web Site:* www.authorsguild.com, pg 681

Weidner, James H, Weidner & Sons Publishing, PO Box 2178 (Cinnaminson), Riverton, NJ 08077 *Tel:* 856-486-1755 *Fax:* 856-486-7583 *E-mail:* weidner@waterw.com *Web Site:* www.arlhs. com/weidnerpublishing, pg 295

Weidner, Stephanie, Silver Lake Publishing, 11 S Mansfield Rd, Lansdowne, PA 19050 *Tel:* 610-626-8446 *E-mail:* publisher@silverlakepublishing. com; slp@silverlakepublishing.com *Web Site:* www. silverlakepublishing.com, pg 247

Weigl, Linda, Weigl Educational Publishers Ltd, 6325 Tenth St SE, Calgary, AB T2H 2Z9, Canada *Tel:* 403-233-7747 *Toll Free Tel:* 800-668-0766 *Fax:* 403-233-7769 *E-mail:* info@weigl.com *Web Site:* www.weigl. com, pg 566

Weigman, Leo, W W Norton & Company Inc, 500 Fifth Ave, New York, NY 10110-0017 *Tel:* 212-354-5500 *Toll Free Tel:* 800-233-4830 (orders & cust serv) *Fax:* 212-869-0856 *Toll Free Fax:* 800-458-6515 *Web Site:* www.wwnorton.com, pg 193

Weikart, Jim, International Association of Crime Writers Inc, North American Branch, PO Box 8674, New York, NY 10116-8674 *Tel:* 212-243-8966 *Fax:* 815-361-1477, pg 688

Weikersheimer, Joshua R, ASCP Press, 2100 W Harrison St, Chicago, IL 60612 *Tel:* 312-738-4866; 312-738-1336 *Toll Free Tel:* 800-621-4142 *Fax:* 312-738-1619 *Web Site:* www.ascp.org, pg 25

Weil, Robert, W W Norton & Company Inc, 500 Fifth Ave, New York, NY 10110-0017 *Tel:* 212-354-5500 *Toll Free Tel:* 800-233-4830 (orders & cust serv) *Fax:* 212-869-0856 *Toll Free Fax:* 800-458-6515 *Web Site:* www.wwnorton.com, pg 193

Weil, Wendy, Association of Authors' Representatives Inc (AAR), PO Box 237201, Ansonia Sta, New York, NY 10023 *E-mail:* aarinc@mindspring.com *Web Site:* www.aar-online.org, pg 679

Weil, Wendy, The Wendy Weil Agency Inc, 232 Madison Ave, Suite 1300, New York, NY 10016 *Tel:* 212-685-0030 *Fax:* 212-685-0765, pg 660

Weimann, Frank J, The Literary Group International, 270 Lafayette St, Suite 1505, New York, NY 10012 *Tel:* 212-274-1616 *Fax:* 212-274-9876 *Web Site:* www. theliterarygroup.com, pg 641

Wein, Lauren, Grove/Atlantic Inc, 841 Broadway, 4th fl, New York, NY 10003-4793 *Tel:* 212-614-7850 *Toll Free Tel:* 800-521-0178 *Fax:* 212-614-7886 *Web Site:* www.groveatlantic.com, pg 110

Weinberg, Jeffrey H, Water Row Press, PO Box 438, Sudbury, MA 01776 *Tel:* 508-485-8515 *Fax:* 508-229-0885 *E-mail:* contact@waterrowbooks.com *Web Site:* www.waterrowbooks.com, pg 294

Weinberger, Caspar Jr, Windswept House Publishers, 584 Sound Dr, Mount Desert, ME 04660 *Tel:* 207-244-5027 *Fax:* 207-244-3369 *E-mail:* windswt@acadia.net *Web Site:* www.booknotes.com/windswept/, pg 301

Weinberger, Mavis, Windswept House Publishers, 584 Sound Dr, Mount Desert, ME 04660 *Tel:* 207-244-5027 *Fax:* 207-244-3369 *E-mail:* windswt@acadia.net *Web Site:* www.booknotes.com/windswept/, pg 301

Weinberger, Russell, Brockman Inc, 5 E 59 St, New York, NY 10022 *Tel:* 212-935-8900 *Fax:* 212-935-5535 *E-mail:* rights@brockman.com, pg 623

Weiner, Deborah, Georgetown University Press, 3240 Prospect St NW, Washington, DC 20007 *Tel:* 202-687-6251 (acq); 202-687-5889 (busn); 202-687-5641 (mktg); 410-516-6956 (orders) *Toll Free Tel:* 800-537-5487 *Fax:* 202-687-6340 (edit); 410-516-6998 (orders) *E-mail:* gupress@georgetown.edu *Web Site:* www. press.georgetown.edu, pg 104

Weiner, Eric, Information Publications, 3790 El Camino Real, PMB 162, Palo Alto, CA 94306 *Tel:* 650-851-4250 *Toll Free Tel:* 877-544-4636 *Fax:* 650-529-9980 *Toll Free Tel:* 877-544-4635 *E-mail:* info@ informationpublications.com *Web Site:* www. informationpublications.com, pg 133

Weiner, John, Energy Information Administration, EI-30 National Energy Information Center, Dept of Energy, 1000 Independence Ave SW, Washington, DC 20585 *Tel:* 202-586-8800 *Fax:* 202-586-0727 *E-mail:* infoctr@eia.doe.gov *Web Site:* www.eia.doe. gov, pg 91

Weiner, Ruth, Seven Stories Press, 140 Watts St, New York, NY 10013 *Tel:* 212-226-8760 *Toll Free Tel:* 800-283-3572 *Fax:* 212-226-1411 *E-mail:* info@ sevenstories.com *Web Site:* www.sevenstories.com, pg 245

Weiner, Tina C, Yale University Press, 302 Temple St, New Haven, CT 06511 *Tel:* 203-432-0960; 401-531-2800 (cust serv) *Toll Free Tel:* 800-405-1619 (cust serv) *Fax:* 203-432-0948; 401-531-2801 (cust serv) *Toll Free Fax:* 800-406-9145 (cust serv) *E-mail:* customer.care@trilateral.org (cust serv) *Web Site:* www.yale.edu/yup/, pg 305

Weingarten, Seymour, The Guilford Press, 72 Spring St, New York, NY 10012 *Tel:* 212-431-9800 *Toll Free Tel:* 800-365-7006 (orders) *Fax:* 212-966-6708 *E-mail:* orders@guilford.com *Web Site:* www.guilford. com, pg 111

Weingel-Fidel, Loretta, The Weingel-Fidel Agency, 310 E 46 St, Suite 21-E, New York, NY 10017 *Tel:* 212-599-2959 *Fax:* 212-286-1986 *E-mail:* wfagy@aol.com, pg 661

Weinstein, Ted, Ted Weinstein Literary Management, 35 Stillman St, Suite 203, San Francisco, CA 94107 *Web Site:* www.twliterary.com, pg 661

Weinstein, Virginia, Holiday House Inc, 425 Madison Ave, New York, NY 10017 *Tel:* 212-688-0085 *Fax:* 212-421-6134, pg 123

Weintraub, Dori, St Martin's Press Trade Division, 175 Fifth Ave, New York, NY 10010 *E-mail:* firstname. lastname@stmartins.com *Web Site:* www.stmartins. com; www.minotaurbooks.com, pg 239

Weintraub, Joe, Association of American University Presses, 1427 E 60 St, Chicago, IL 60637 *Tel:* 773-702-7700; 773-702-7600 *Toll Free Tel:* 800-621-2736 (orders) *Fax:* 773-702-9756 (sales); 773-660-2235 (orders); 773-702-2708 *E-mail:* general@press. uchicago.edu *Web Site:* www.press.uchicago.edu, pg 26

Weintraub, Steve, Lawyers & Judges Publishing Co Inc, 917 N Swan Rd, Tucson, AZ 85711-1213 *Tel:* 520-323-1500 *Fax:* 520-323-0055 *E-mail:* sales@lawyersandjudges.com *Web Site:* www. lawyersandjudges.com, pg 150

Weintz, Walter, Workman Publishing Co Inc, 708 Broadway, New York, NY 10003-9555 *Tel:* 212-254-5900 *Toll Free Tel:* 800-722-7202 *Fax:* 212-254-8098 *E-mail:* info@workman.com *Web Site:* www.workman. com, pg 303

Weinzimer, Andrea, Time Warner Book Group, 1271 Avenue of the Americas, New York, NY 10020 *Tel:* 212-522-7200 *Fax:* 212-522-7991 *Web Site:* www. twbookmark.com, pg 272

Weir, Daniel, Epimetheus Books Inc, 2711 Centerville Rd, Suite 120-5336, Wilmington, DE 19808-1643 *Tel:* 646-345-2030 *E-mail:* epimetheus@att.net *Web Site:* www.epimetheusbooks.com, pg 91

Weis, Jennifer, St Martin's Press Trade Division, 175 Fifth Ave, New York, NY 10010 *E-mail:* firstname. lastname@stmartins.com *Web Site:* www.stmartins. com; www.minotaurbooks.com, pg 239

Weisbach, Rob, Simon & Schuster, 1230 Avenue of the Americas, New York, NY 10020 *Tel:* 212-698-7000 *Toll Free Tel:* 800-223-2348 (cust serv); 800-223-2336 (orders) *Toll Free Fax:* 800-943-9831 (orders) *Web Site:* www.simonsays.com, pg 248

Weisbach, Shira, University of California Press, 2120 Berkeley Way, Berkeley, CA 94720 *Tel:* 510-642-4247 *Toll Free Tel:* 800-777-4726 *Fax:* 510-643-7127 *Toll Free Fax:* 800-999-1958 *E-mail:* askucp@ucpress.edu *Web Site:* www.ucpress.edu, pg 281

Weisberg, Don, Doubleday Broadway Publishing Group, 1745 Broadway, New York, NY 10019 *Tel:* 212-782-9000 *Toll Free Tel:* 800-223-6834; 800-223-5780 (sales) *Fax:* 212-302-7985 (correspondence); 212-492-9862 (orders), pg 82

Weisberg, Don, Random House Inc, 1745 Broadway, New York, NY 10019 *Tel:* 212-782-9000 *Toll Free Tel:* 800-726-0600 *Web Site:* www.randomhouse.com, pg 226

Weisberg, Don, Random House International, 1745 Broadway, New York, NY 10019 *Tel:* 212-572-6106 *Fax:* 212-572-6045, pg 226

Weisberg, Don, Random House Sales & Marketing, 1745 Broadway, New York, NY 10019 *Fax:* 212-782-9000, pg 227

Weisberg, Robin, Humana Press, 999 Riverview Dr, Suite 208, Totowa, NJ 07512 *Tel:* 973-256-1699 *Fax:* 973-256-8341 *E-mail:* humana@humanapr.com *Web Site:* humanapress.com, pg 128

Weise, Don, Carroll & Graf Publishers, 245 W 17 St, 11th fl, New York, NY 10011-5300 *Tel:* 646-375-2570 *Fax:* 646-375-2571 *Web Site:* www.carrollandgraf.com, pg 54

Weisel, Trudy, Loyola Press, 3441 N Ashland Ave, Chicago, IL 60657 *Tel:* 773-281-1818; 773-244-4429 *Toll Free Tel:* 800-621-1008 *Fax:* 773-281-0555; 773-281-0152 (trade) *E-mail:* editorial@loydapress.com *Web Site:* www.loyolapress.org, pg 159

Weisman, Richard, Creative Homeowner, 24 Park Way, Upper Saddle River, NJ 07458-9960 *Tel:* 201-934-7100 *Toll Free Tel:* 800-631-7795 *Fax:* 201-934-8971 *E-mail:* info@creativehomeowner.com *Web Site:* www. creativehomeowner.com, pg 72

Weiss, Denise, Cold Spring Harbor Laboratory Press, 500 Sunnyside Blvd, Woodbury, NY 11797-2924 *Tel:* 516-422-4100 *Toll Free Tel:* 800-843-4388 *Fax:* 516-422-4097 *E-mail:* cshpress@cshl.edu *Web Site:* www.cshlpress.com, pg 64

Weiss, Dennis, CRC Press LLC, 2000 NW Corporate Blvd, Boca Raton, FL 33431 *Tel:* 561-994-0555 *Toll Free Tel:* 800-272-7737 *Fax:* 561-997-7249 (edit); 561-998-8491 (mfg); 561-361-6057 (acctg); 561-994-0313 *Toll Free Tel:* 800-643-9428 (sales); 800-374-3401 (orders) *E-mail:* orders@crcpress.com *Web Site:* www.crcpress.com, pg 71

Weiss, Eben, Ralph M Vicinanza Ltd, 303 W 18 St, New York, NY 10011 *Tel:* 212-924-7090 *Fax:* 212-691-9644 *E-mail:* ralphvic@aol.com, pg 659

Weiss, Edmond H, Fordham University, Graduate School of Business Administration, Dept of Communications & Media Management, 113 W 60 St, New York, NY 10023 *Tel:* 212-636-6199 *Fax:* 212-765-5573, pg 752

Weiss, Kay, Catholic Book Publishers Association Inc, 8404 Jamesport Dr, Rockford, IL 61108 *Tel:* 815-332-3245 *Fax:* 815-332-3476 *E-mail:* cbpa3@aol.com *Web Site:* www.cbpa.org, pg 684

Weiss, Kim, Health Communications Inc, 3201 SW 15 St, Deerfield Beach, FL 33442-8190 *Tel:* 954-360-0909 *Toll Free Tel:* 800-851-9100 (cust serv); 800-441-5569 (order entry) *Fax:* 954-360-0034 *Web Site:* www.hcibooks.com, pg 119

Weiss, Kim, Simcha Press, 3201 SW 15 St, Deerfield Beach, FL 33442-8190 *Tel:* 954-360-0909 ext 212 *Toll Free Tel:* 800-851-9100 ext 212 *Toll Free Fax:* 800-424-7652 *E-mail:* simchapress@hcibooks.com *Web Site:* www.simchapress.com, pg 248

Weiss, Louise, Access Editorial Services, 1133 Broadway, Suite 528, New York, NY 10010 *Tel:* 212-255-7306 *Fax:* 212-255-7306 *E-mail:* wiseword@juno.com, pg 589

Weiss, Renee, Quarterly Review of Literature, 26 Haslet Ave, Princeton, NJ 08540 *Fax:* 609-258-2230 *E-mail:* qrl@princeton.edu *Web Site:* www.princeton.edu/~qrl, pg 223

Weiss, Renee, Quarterly Review of Literature International Poetry Book Competition, 26 Haslet Ave, Princeton, NJ 08540 *Fax:* 609-258-2230 *E-mail:* qrl@princeton.edu *Web Site:* www.princeton.edu/~qrl, pg 801

Weisskopf, Toni, Baen Publishing Enterprises, PO Box 1403, Riverdale, NY 10471-0605 *Tel:* 919-570-1640 *Fax:* 919-570-1644 *Web Site:* baen.com, pg 30

Weissner, Patrica, Women Who Write, PO Box 652, Madison, NJ 07940 *Tel:* 908-232-1640 *Fax:* 908-317-8105 *E-mail:* info@womenwhowrite.org *Web Site:* www.womenwhowrite.org, pg 702

Weistrop, Susan, University of Wisconsin-Milwaukee Center for Architecture & Urban Planning Research, PO Box 413, Milwaukee, WI 53201-0413 *Tel:* 414-229-2878 *Fax:* 414-229-6976 *E-mail:* caupr@uwm.edu *Web Site:* www.uwm.edu/SARUP, pg 286

Weixel, Dr Kirk, Ligonier Valley Writers Conference, PO Box B, Ligonier, PA 15658-1602 *Tel:* 724-537-3341 *Fax:* 724-537-0482 *E-mail:* sarshi@wpa.net, pg 744

Welborn, Aaron, Black Warrior Review Literary Awards, University of Alabama, Tuscaloosa, AL 35486-0027 *Tel:* 205-348-4518 *E-mail:* bwr@ua.edu *Web Site:* www.webdelsol.com/bwr, pg 763

Welch, Christine, American Diabetes Association, 1701 N Beauregard St, Alexandria, VA 22311 *Tel:* 703-299-2046 *Toll Free Tel:* 800-232-6733 *Fax:* 908-806-2301 *Web Site:* www.diabetes.org, pg 13

Welch, Jim, Thomas Brothers Maps, 17731 Cowan, Irvine, CA 92614 *Tel:* 949-852-9189 *Fax:* 949-757-1564 *E-mail:* webmaster@thomas.com *Web Site:* www.randmcnally.com, pg 269

Welch, Sherry, Chicago Spectrum Press, 4824 Brownsboro Center Arcade, Louisville, KY 40207 *Tel:* 502-899-1919 *Toll Free Tel:* 800-594-5190 *Fax:* 502-896-0246 *E-mail:* evanstonpublish@aol.com *Web Site:* www.evanstonpublishing.com, pg 60

Welch, Sherry, Evanston Publishing Inc, 4824 Brownsboro Ctr, Louisville, KY 40207 *Tel:* 502-899-1919 *Toll Free Tel:* 888BOOKS80 *Fax:* 502-896-0246 *E-mail:* evanstonpublish@aol.com *Web Site:* www.evanstonpublishing.com, pg 93

Welch, Terri Armstrong, Nicholas Brealey Publishing, 3704 Beard Ave N, Minneapolis, MN 55422 *Tel:* 763-208-3169 *Toll Free Tel:* 888-BREALEY (273-2539) *Fax:* 763-208-3170 *E-mail:* booksmatter@earthlink.net *Web Site:* www.nbrealey-books.com, pg 46

Welday, David, CharismaLife Publishers, 600 Rinehart Rd, Lake Mary, FL 32746 *Tel:* 407-333-0600 *Toll Free Tel:* 800-451-4598 *Fax:* 407-333-7100 *E-mail:* charismalife@strang.com *Web Site:* www.charismamag.com, pg 58

Welday, David W III, Charisma House, 600 Rinehart Rd, Lake Mary, FL 32746 *Tel:* 407-333-0600 (all imprints) *Toll Free Tel:* 800-283-8494 (Charisma House, Siloam Press, Creation House Press); 800-665-1468 *Fax:* 407-333-7100 (all imprints) *E-mail:* webmaster@charismahouse.com; webmaster@creationhouse.com *Web Site:* www.charismamag.com; www.strang.com (all imprints), pg 58

Wellnitz, Clare, Columbia University Press, 61 W 62 St, New York, NY 10023 *Tel:* 212-459-0600 *Toll Free Tel:* 800-944-8648 *Fax:* 212-459-3678 *Web Site:* www.columbia.edu/cu/cup, pg 65

Wells, Leslie, Hyperion, 77 W 66 St, 11th fl, New York, NY 10023-6298 *Tel:* 212-456-0100 *Toll Free Tel:* 800-759-0190 (cust serv) *Fax:* 212-456-0157 *Web Site:* hyperionbooks.com, pg 129

Wells, Phyllis, University of Georgia Press, 330 Research Dr, Athens, GA 30602-4901 *Tel:* 706-369-6130 *Toll Free Tel:* 800-266-5842 (orders only) *Fax:* 706-369-6131 *E-mail:* books@ugapress.uga.edu *Web Site:* www.ugapress.org, pg 281

Wells, Sherry A, Lawells Publishing, PO Box 1338, Royal Oak, MI 48068-1338 *Tel:* 248-543-5297 *Fax:* 248-543-5683 *Web Site:* www.lawells.net, pg 150

Wells, Vicky, The University of North Carolina Press, 116 S Boundary St, Chapel Hill, NC 27514-3808 *Tel:* 919-966-3561 *Toll Free Tel:* 800-848-6224 (orders only) *Fax:* 919-966-3829 *Toll Free Fax:* 800-272-6817 (orders) *E-mail:* uncpress@unc.edu *Web Site:* www.uncpress.unc.edu, pg 283

Welsch, Sarah L, University Press of New England, One Court St, Lebanon, NH 03766 *Tel:* 603-448-1533 *Toll Free Tel:* 800-421-1561 (orders only) *Fax:* 603-448-7006; 603-643-1540 *E-mail:* university.press@dartmouth.edu *Web Site:* www.upne.com, pg 287

Welsh, April, NovelBooks Inc, PO Box 661, Douglas, MA 01516-0661 *Tel:* 508-476-1611 *Fax:* 508-476-3866 *E-mail:* publisher@novelbooksinc *Web Site:* www.novelbooksinc.com, pg 194

Welsh, Kara, NAL, 375 Hudson St, New York, NY 10014 *Tel:* 212-366-2000 *E-mail:* online@penguinputnam.com *Web Site:* www.penguin.com, pg 181

Welshons, Marlo, University of Illinois Graduate School of Library & Information Science, 501 E Daniel St, Champaign, IL 61820-6211 *Tel:* 217-333-1359 *Fax:* 217-244-7329 *E-mail:* puboff@alexia.lis.uiuc.edu *Web Site:* www.lis.uiuc.edu/puboff/, pg 281

Weltman, Sally, Hot House Press, 760 Cushing Hwy, Cohasset, MA 02025 *Tel:* 781-383-8360 *Toll Free Tel:* 866-331-8360 *Fax:* 781-383-8346 *Web Site:* www.hothousepress.com, pg 126

Weltz, Jennifer, Jean V Naggar Literary Agency, 216 E 75 St, Suite 1-E, New York, NY 10021 *Tel:* 212-794-1082, pg 645

Wendel, Ann, Research Press, 2612 N Mattis Ave, Champaign, IL 61822 *Tel:* 217-352-3273 *Toll Free Tel:* 800-519-2707 *Fax:* 217-352-1221 *E-mail:* rp@researchpress.com *Web Site:* www.researchpress.com, pg 231

Wender, Phyllis, Rosenstone/Wender, 38 E 29 St, 10th fl, New York, NY 10016 *Tel:* 212-725-9445 *Fax:* 212-725-9447, pg 652

Wentworth, K D, L Ron Hubbard's Writers of the Future Contest, PO Box 1630, Los Angeles, CA 90078 *Tel:* 323-466-3310 *Fax:* 323-466-6474 *Web Site:* www.writersofthefuture.com, pg 779

Werden, Barbara, Texas Tech University Press, 2903 Fourth St, Lubbock, TX 79412 *Tel:* 806-742-2982 *Toll Free Tel:* 800-832-4042 *Fax:* 806-742-2979 *E-mail:* ttup@ttu.edu *Web Site:* www.ttup.ttu.edu, pg 267

Werksma, Louann, FaithWalk Publishing, 333 Jackson St, Grand Haven, MI 49417 *Tel:* 616-846-9360 *Toll Free Tel:* 800-335-7177 *Fax:* 616-846-0072 *E-mail:* customerservice@faithwalkpub.com *Web Site:* www.faithwalkpub.com, pg 94

Werksman, Deborah, Sourcebooks Inc, 1935 Brookdale Rd, Suite 139, Naperville, IL 60563 *Tel:* 630-961-3900 *Toll Free Tel:* 800-432-7444 *Fax:* 630-961-2168 *E-mail:* info@sourcebooks.com *Web Site:* www.sourcebooks.com, pg 253

Werner, George, Pearson Higher Education Division, One Lake St, Upper Saddle River, NJ 07458 *Tel:* 201-236-7000 *Fax:* 201-236-3381, pg 206

Wernick, Marcia, Sheldon Fogelman Agency Inc, 10 E 40 St, Suite 3800, New York, NY 10016 *Tel:* 212-532-7250 *Fax:* 212-685-8939 *E-mail:* fogelman@worldnet.att.net; agency@sheldonfogelmanagency.com, pg 630

Werthman, George, South-Western, A Thomson Business, 5191 Natorp Blvd, Mason, OH 45040 *Tel:* 513-229-1000 *Toll Free Tel:* 800-543-0487 *Fax:* 513-229-1025 *Web Site:* www.thomson.com, pg 254

Werts, Lynn, University Press of Florida, 15 NW 15 St, Gainesville, FL 32611-2079 *Tel:* 352-392-1351 *Toll Free Tel:* 800-226-3822 (orders only) *Fax:* 352-392-7302 *Toll Free Fax:* 800-680-1955 (orders only) *E-mail:* info@upf.com *Web Site:* www.upf.com, pg 287

Werz, Ed, Childswork/Childsplay LLC, 135 Dupont St, Plainview, NY 11803 *Tel:* 516-349-5520 *Toll Free Tel:* 800-962-1141 (cust serv) *Fax:* 516-349-5521 *Toll Free Fax:* 800-262-1886 (orders) *E-mail:* info@childswork.com *Web Site:* www.childswork.com, pg 60

Werz, Ed, JayJo Books, 135 Dupont St, Plainview, NY 11803 *Tel:* 516-349-5520 *Fax:* 516-349-5521 *E-mail:* jayjobooks@guidancechannel.com *Web Site:* www.guidancechannel.com, pg 140

Werz, Edward W, The Bureau For At-Risk Youth, 135 Dupont St, Plainview, NY 11803-0760 *Tel:* 516-349-5520 *Fax:* 516-349-5521 *E-mail:* info@at-risk.com *Web Site:* www.at-risk.com, pg 50

Werz, Janice, The Bureau For At-Risk Youth, 135 Dupont St, Plainview, NY 11803-0760 *Tel:* 516-349-5520 *Fax:* 516-349-5521 *E-mail:* info@at-risk.com *Web Site:* www.at-risk.com, pg 50

Werz, Janice, Childswork/Childsplay LLC, 135 Dupont St, Plainview, NY 11803 *Tel:* 516-349-5520 *Toll Free Tel:* 800-962-1141 (cust serv) *Fax:* 516-349-5521 *Toll Free Fax:* 800-262-1886 (orders) *E-mail:* info@childswork.com *Web Site:* www.childswork.com, pg 60

Werz, Janice, JayJo Books, 135 Dupont St, Plainview, NY 11803 *Tel:* 516-349-5520 *Fax:* 516-349-5521 *E-mail:* jayjobooks@guidancechannel.com *Web Site:* www.guidancechannel.com, pg 140

Weschcke, Carl L, Llewellyn Publications, PO Box 64383, St Paul, MN 55164-0383 *Tel:* 651-291-1970 *Toll Free Tel:* 800-843-6666 *Fax:* 651-291-1908 *E-mail:* lwlpc@llewellyn.com *Web Site:* www.llewellyn.com, pg 157

Wesler, Cathy, Oakstone Medical Publishing, 6801 Cahaba Valley Rd, Birmingham, AL 35242 *Tel:* 205-991-5188 *Toll Free Tel:* 800-952-0690 *Fax:* 205-995-4656 *E-mail:* service@oakstonemedical.com *Web Site:* www.oakstonemedical.com, pg 195

Wesley, Mark, me+mi publishing inc, 128 S County Farm Rd, Wheaton, IL 60187 *Tel:* 630-752-9951 *Toll Free Tel:* 888-251-1444 *Fax:* 630-588-9804 *E-mail:* rw@rosawesley.com *Web Site:* www.memima.com, pg 169

Wessel, Donna B, American Literary Press/Noble House, 8019 Belair Rd, Suite 10, Baltimore, MD 21236 *Tel:* 410-882-7700 *Fax:* 410-882-7703 *E-mail:* amerlit@americanliterarypress.com *Web Site:* www.americanliterarypress.com, pg 569

Wesselmann, Jenny, AMACOM Books, 1601 Broadway, New York, NY 10019-7406 *Tel:* 212-586-8100; 518-891-5510 (orders) *Toll Free Tel:* 800-262-9699 (cust serv) *Fax:* 212-903-8168; 518-891-2372 (orders) *Web Site:* www.amanet.org, pg 10

Wessels, Cindy, University of Pittsburgh Press, 3400 Forbes Ave, 5th fl, Pittsburgh, PA 15260 *Tel:* 412-383-2456 *Fax:* 412-383-2466 *E-mail:* press@pitt.edu *Web Site:* www.pitt.edu/~press, pg 284

Whelchel, Sandy, National Writers Association Novel Contest, 3140 S Peoria St, Suite 295, Aurora, CO 80014 *Tel:* 303-841-0246 *Fax:* 303-841-2607 *Web Site:* www.nationalwriters.com (magazine available on-line), pg 792

Whelchel, Sandy, NWAF Annual Conference, 3140 S Peoria St, PMB 295, Aurora, CO 80014 *Tel:* 303-841-0246 *Fax:* 303-841-2607 *Web Site:* www.nationalwriters.com, pg 745

Whitaker, Robert Jr, Whitaker House, 30 Hunt Valley Circle, New Kensington, PA 15068 *Tel:* 724-334-7000 *Toll Free Tel:* 877-793-9800 *Fax:* 724-334-1200 *Toll Free Fax:* 800-765-1960 *E-mail:* sales@whitakerhouse.com, pg 297

Whitbread, Thomas, University of Texas at Austin, Creative Writing Program, Dept of English, One University Sta, B5000, Austin, TX 78712-1164 *Tel:* 512-475-6356 *Fax:* 512-471-2898 *Web Site:* www.en.utexas.edu/grad/crwconc.html, pg 756

Whitburn, Joel, Record Research Inc, PO Box 200, Menomonee Falls, WI 53052 *Tel:* 262-251-5408 *Toll Free Tel:* 800-827-9810 *Fax:* 262-251-9452 *E-mail:* books@recordresearch.com *Web Site:* www.recordresearch.com, pg 229

Whitcomb, Cynthia, Willamette Writers' Conference, 9045 SW Barbur Blvd, Suite 5-A, Portland, OR 97219 *Tel:* 503-452-1592 *Fax:* 503-452-1592 *E-mail:* wilwrite@willamettewriters.com *Web Site:* www.willamettewriters.com, pg 749

White, Aaron, BuilderBooks.com, 1201 15 St NW, Washington, DC 20005-2800 *Tel:* 202-822-0200; 202-266-8200 *Toll Free Tel:* 800-223-2665 (orders); 800-368-5242 ext 8368 (editorial) *Fax:* 202-266-8096 (edit); 202-266-5889 (edit) *Web Site:* www.builderbooks.com, pg 49

White, Carol, The Helen Brann Agency Inc, 94 Curtis Rd, Bridgewater, CT 06752 *Tel:* 860-354-9580 *Fax:* 860-355-2572 *E-mail:* helenbrannagency@earthlink.net, pg 622

White, Caroline, Penguin Books, 375 Hudson St, New York, NY 10014 *Tel:* 212-366-2000 *E-mail:* online@penguinputnam.com *Web Site:* www.penguin.com; www.penguinclassics.com, pg 207

White, Cindy L, American Biographical Institute, 5126 Bur Oak Circle, Raleigh, NC 27612 *Tel:* 919-781-8710 *Fax:* 919-781-8712, pg 12

White, Darrin, Milton Acorn Poetry Award, 115 Richmond St, Charlottetown, PE C1A 1H7, Canada *Tel:* 902-368-4410 *Fax:* 902-368-4418 *E-mail:* peiarts@peiartscouncil.com *Web Site:* www.peiartscouncil.com, pg 757

White, Darrin, Cavendish Tourist Association Creative Writing Award for Young People, 115 Richmond St, Charlottetown, PE C1A 1H7, Canada *Tel:* 902-368-4410 *Fax:* 902-368-4418 *E-mail:* peiarts@peiartscouncil.com *Web Site:* www.peiartscouncil.com, pg 766

White, Darrin, Feature Article Award, 115 Richmond St, Charlottetown, PE C1A 1H7, Canada *Tel:* 902-368-4410 *Fax:* 902-368-4418 *E-mail:* peiarts@peiartscouncil.com *Web Site:* www.peiartscouncil.com, pg 773

White, Darrin, Island Literary Awards, 115 Richmond St, Charlottetown, PE C1A 1H7, Canada *Tel:* 902-368-4410 *Fax:* 902-368-4418 *E-mail:* peiarts@peiartscouncil.com *Web Site:* www.peiartscouncil.com, pg 780

White, Darrin, Lucy Maud Montgomery Literature for Children Prize, 115 Richmond St, Charlottetown, PE C1A 1H7, Canada *Tel:* 902-368-4410 *Fax:* 902-368-4418 *E-mail:* peiarts@peiartscouncil.com *Web Site:* www.peiartscouncil.com, pg 790

White, Darrin, Sentner Memorial Short Story Award, 115 Richmond St, Charlottetown, PE C1A 1H7, Canada *Tel:* 902-368-4410 *Fax:* 902-368-4418 *E-mail:* peiarts@peiartscouncil.com *Web Site:* www.peiartscouncil.com, pg 805

White, Garret J, Houghton Mifflin College Division, 222 Berkeley St, Boston, MA 02116-3764 *Tel:* 617-351-5000 *Fax:* 617-225-1464 (orders) *Web Site:* www.college.hmco.com, pg 126

White, H T, Rohn Engh, Pine Lake Farm, 1910 35 Rd, Osceola, WI 54020 *Tel:* 715-248-3800 (ext 21) *Toll Free Tel:* 800-624-0266 (ext 21) *Fax:* 715-248-7394 *Toll Free Fax:* 800-photofax *E-mail:* psi2@photosource.com *Web Site:* www.photosource.com, pg 598

White, Howard, Harbour Publishing Co Ltd, 4437 Rondeview Rd, Madeira Park, BC V0N 2H0, Canada *Tel:* 604-883-2730 *Toll Free Tel:* 800-667-2988; 800-667-2988 *Fax:* 604-883-9451 *Toll Free Fax:* 877-604-9449 *E-mail:* info@harbourpublishing.com *Web Site:* www.harbourpublishing.com, pg 549

White, Hudson, Ocean Tree Books, 1325 Cerro Gordo Rd, Santa Fe, NM 87501 *Tel:* 505-983-1412 *Fax:* 505-983-0899 *E-mail:* oceantree@earthlink.net *Web Site:* www.oceantree.com, pg 195

White, Lori, The MIT Press, 5 Cambridge Ctr, Cambridge, MA 02142 *Tel:* 617-253-5646 *Toll Free Tel:* 800-405-1619 (orders only) *Fax:* 617-258-6779 *Web Site:* mitpress.mit.edu, pg 175

White, Mary Lou, American Medical Association, 515 N State St, Chicago, IL 60610 *Tel:* 312-464-5000 *Toll Free Tel:* 800-621-8335 (cust serv) *Fax:* 312-464-4184 *Web Site:* www.ama-assn.org, pg 16

White, Meg, American Medical Publishers Association, 14 Fort Hill Rd, Huntington, NY 11743 *Tel:* 631-423-0075 *Fax:* 631-423-0075 *E-mail:* info@ampaonline.org *Web Site:* www.ampaonline.org, pg 677

White, Pam, Random House Children's Books, 1745 Broadway, New York, NY 10019 *Tel:* 212-782-9000 *Toll Free Tel:* 800-200-3552 *Fax:* 212-782-9452 *Web Site:* www.randomhouse.com/kids, pg 225

White, Patricia, Publicom Inc, 60 Aberdeen Ave, Cambridge, MA 02138 *Tel:* 617-714-0300 *Fax:* 617-714-0268 *E-mail:* info@publicom1.com *Web Site:* www.publicom1.com, pg 609

White, Patricia, The Systemsware Corp, 973 Russell Ave, Suite D, Gaithersburg, MD 20879 *Tel:* 301-948-4890 *Fax:* 301-926-4243 *Web Site:* www.systemswarecorp.com, pg 263

White, Randall, EDC Publishing, 10302 E 55 Place, Tulsa, OK 74146-6515 *Tel:* 918-622-4522 *Toll Free Tel:* 800-475-4522 *Fax:* 918-665-7919 *Toll Free Fax:* 800-747-4509 *E-mail:* edc@edcpub.com *Web Site:* www.edcpub.com, pg 86

White, Raymond M, National Institute for Trial Advocacy, University of Notre Dame, Notre Dame, IN 46556-6500 *Tel:* 574-271-8370 *Toll Free Tel:* 800-225-6482 *Fax:* 574-271-8375 *E-mail:* nita.1@nd.edu *Web Site:* www.nita.org, pg 184

White, Robert, Audit Bureau of Circulations (ABC), Canadian Office, 151 Bloor St W, Suite 850, Toronto, ON M5S 1S4, Canada *Tel:* 416-962-5840 *Fax:* 416-962-5844 *Web Site:* www.accessabc.com, pg 680

White, Stephanie, Johnson Books, 1880 S 57 Ct, Boulder, CO 80301 *Tel:* 303-443-9766 *Toll Free Tel:* 800-258-5830 *Fax:* 303-998-7594 *E-mail:* books@jpcolorado.com *Web Site:* www.jpcolorado.com; www.johnsonbooks.com, pg 142

White, Syrus, Chalice Press, 1221 Locust St, Suite 1200, St Louis, MO 63103 *Tel:* 314-231-8500 *Toll Free Tel:* 800-366-3383 *Fax:* 314-231-8524 *E-mail:* chalicepress@cbp21.com *Web Site:* www.cbp21.com; www.chalicepress.com, pg 58

White, Terry, Christian History Project, 10333 178 St, Edmonton, AB T5N 2H7, Canada *Tel:* 780-443-4775 *Toll Free Tel:* 800-853-5402 *Fax:* 780-454-9298 *E-mail:* orders@christianhistoryproject.com *Web Site:* www.christianhistoryproject.com, pg 540

White, Todd, EDC Publishing, 10302 E 55 Place, Tulsa, OK 74146-6515 *Tel:* 918-622-4522 *Toll Free Tel:* 800-475-4522 *Fax:* 918-665-7919 *Toll Free Fax:* 800-747-4509 *E-mail:* edc@edcpub.com *Web Site:* www.edcpub.com, pg 86

White, Travis, Psychological Assessment Resources Inc (PAR), 16204 N Florida Ave, Lutz, FL 33549 *Tel:* 813-968-3003 *Toll Free Tel:* 800-331-8378 *Fax:* 813-968-2598 *Toll Free Fax:* 800-727-9329 *Web Site:* www.parinc.com, pg 221

White, Vernon S, National Book Co, PO Box 8795, Portland, OR 97207-8795 *Tel:* 503-228-6345 *Fax:* 810-885-5811 *E-mail:* info@eralearning.com *Web Site:* www.eralearning.com, pg 182

Whitehead, Katherine H, The Colonial Williamsburg Foundation, PO Box 1776, Williamsburg, VA 23187-1776 *Tel:* 757-229-1000 *Toll Free Tel:* 800-HISTORY *Fax:* 757-220-7325 *Web Site:* www.colonialwilliamsburg.org/publications, pg 65

Whitehorn, Clark, Montana Historical Society Press, 225 N Roberts St, Helena, MT 59620 *Tel:* 406-444-4741 (editorial); 406-444-2890 (ordering/marketing) *Toll Free Tel:* 800-243-9900 *Fax:* 406-444-2696 (ordering/marketing) *Web Site:* www.montanahistoricalsociety.org, pg 177

Whiteman, Douglas, Penguin Group (USA) Inc, 375 Hudson St, New York, NY 10014 *Tel:* 212-366-2000 *Fax:* 212-366-2666 *E-mail:* online@uspenguingroup.com *Web Site:* www.penguin.com, pg 208

Whiteman, Douglas, Penguin Young Readers Group, 345 Hudson St, New York, NY 10014 *Tel:* 212-366-2000 *E-mail:* online@penguinputnam.com *Web Site:* www.penguin.com, pg 208

Whiteside, Kay, Venture Publishing Inc, 1999 Cato Ave, State College, PA 16801 *Tel:* 814-234-4561 *Fax:* 814-234-1651 *E-mail:* vpublish@venturepublish.com *Web Site:* www.venturepublish.com, pg 290

Whiting, David, McGraw-Hill Learning Group, 8787 Orion Place, Columbus, OH 43240 *Tel:* 614-430-4000 *Fax:* 614-430-6621, pg 168

Whitman, John R, Kirchoff/Wohlberg Inc, 866 United Nations Plaza, Suite 525, New York, NY 10017 *Tel:* 212-644-2020 *Fax:* 212-223-4387 *E-mail:* kirchwohl@aol.com *Web Site:* www.kirchoffwohlberg.com, pg 603, 637, 666

Whitman, John R, Turtle Books Inc, 866 United Nations Plaza, Suite 525, New York, NY 10017 *Tel:* 212-644-2020 *Fax:* 212-223-4387 *E-mail:* turtlebook@aol.com *Web Site:* www.turtlebooks.com, pg 276

Whitman, Katherine R, Institute for Language Study, 7 Hollyhock Rd, Wilton, CT 06897 *Tel:* 203-762-2510 *Toll Free Tel:* 800-245-2145 *Fax:* 203-762-2514 *E-mail:* cortinainc@aol.com *Web Site:* www.cortina-languages.com; members.aol.com/cortinainc, pg 134

Whitman, Mara, The Graduate Group/Booksellers, 86 Norwood Rd, West Hartford, CT 06117-2236 *Tel:* 860-233-2330 *Toll Free Tel:* 800-484-7280 ext 3579 *Fax:* 860-233-2330 *E-mail:* graduategroup@hotmail.com *Web Site:* www.graduategroup.com, pg 107

Whitman, Marina V N, National Bureau of Economic Research Inc, 1050 Massachusetts Ave, Cambridge, MA 02138-5398 *Tel:* 617-868-3900 *Fax:* 617-868-2742 *E-mail:* op@nber.org *Web Site:* www.nber.org, pg 182

Whitman, Robert, The Graduate Group/Booksellers, 86 Norwood Rd, West Hartford, CT 06117-2236 *Tel:* 860-233-2330 *Toll Free Tel:* 800-484-7280 ext 3579 *Fax:* 860-233-2330 *E-mail:* graduategroup@hotmail.com *Web Site:* www.graduategroup.com, pg 107

Whitney, Jim, Educational Insights Inc, 18730 S Wilmington Ave, Suite 100, Rancho Dominguez, CA 90220 *Tel:* 310-884-2000 *Toll Free Tel:* 800-933-3277 *Fax:* 310-884-2015 *E-mail:* service@edin.com *Web Site:* www.educationalinsights.com, pg 88

Whitsitt, Richard, TSI Graphics, 1300 S Raney, Effingham, IL 62401 *Tel:* 217-347-7733 *Fax:* 217-342-9611 *Web Site:* www.tsigraphics.com, pg 612

Whitson, Skip, Sun Books - Sun Publishing, PO Box 5588, Santa Fe, NM 87502-5588 *Tel:* 505-471-5177; 505-471-6151 *Fax:* 505-473-4458 *E-mail:* info@sunbooks.com *Web Site:* www.sunbooks.com, pg 261

Wilkie, Craig, The University Press of Kentucky, 663 S Limestone St, Lexington, KY 40508-4008 *Tel:* 859-257-8761; 859-257-8442 (mktg) *Toll Free Tel:* 800-839-6855 (orders) *Fax:* 859-323-1873 *Web Site:* www.kentuckypress.com, pg 287

Wilkin, Erna, Creative Writing Day & Workshops, PO Box 801, Abingdon, VA 24212-0801 *Tel:* 276-623-5266 *Fax:* 276-623-5266 *E-mail:* vhf@eva.org *Web Site:* www.vahighlandsfestival.org, pg 743

Wilkinson, Christine, Wilkinson Studios Inc, 901 W Jackson Blvd, Suite 201, Chicago, IL 60607 *Tel:* 312-226-0007 *Fax:* 312-226-0404 *Web Site:* www.wilkinsonstudios.com, pg 667

Wilkinson, Thomas, Maisonneuve Press, PO Box 2980, Washington, DC 20013-2980 *Tel:* 301-277-7505 *Fax:* 301-277-2467 *Web Site:* www.maisonneuvepress.com, pg 161

Wilkofsky, Roth, Longman Publishers, 1185 Avenue of the Americas, New York, NY 10036 *Tel:* 212-782-3300 *Fax:* 212-782-3311 *Web Site:* www.ablongman.com, pg 158

Wilks, Rick, Annick Press Ltd, 15 Patricia Ave, Toronto, ON M2M 1H9, Canada *Tel:* 416-221-4802 *Fax:* 416-221-8400 *E-mail:* annick@annickpress.com *Web Site:* www.annickpress.com, pg 535

Will, Corrine, Heritage Books Inc, 65 E Main St, Westminster, MD 21157 *Tel:* 410-876-0371 *Toll Free Tel:* 866-282-2689 *Fax:* 410-871-2674 *E-mail:* info@heritagebooks.com *Web Site:* www.heritagebooks.com, pg 121

Willcox, Patsy, University of Oklahoma Press, 4100 28 Ave NW, Norman, OK 73069-8218 *Tel:* 405-325-2000 *Toll Free Tel:* 800-627-7377 (orders) *Fax:* 405-364-5798 (orders) *Toll Free Tel:* 800-735-0476 (orders) *E-mail:* oupress@ou.edu *Web Site:* www.oupress.com, pg 284

Willcox, Sally, Creative Artists Agency, 9830 Wilshire Blvd, Beverly Hills, CA 90212-1825 *Tel:* 310-288-4545 *Fax:* 310-288-4800 *Web Site:* www.caa.com, pg 626

Wille, Stefan, AKTRIN Furniture Information Centre, 164 S Main St, Suite 307, High Point, NC 27260 *Tel:* 336-841-8535 *Fax:* 336-841-5435 *E-mail:* aktrin@aktrin.com (Canada); aktrinusa@northstate.net (US) *Web Site:* www.aktrin.com, pg 7

Willems, Antenor R, SAE (Society of Automotive Engineers International), 400 Commonwealth Dr, Warrendale, PA 15096-0001 *Tel:* 724-776-4841 *Toll Free Tel:* 877-606-7323 (cust serv) *Fax:* 724-776-0790 *E-mail:* publications@sae.org *Web Site:* www.sae.org, pg 237

Willett, Bryce, Ulysses Press, PO Box 3440, Berkeley, CA 94703-0440 *Tel:* 510-601-8301 *Toll Free Tel:* 800-377-2542 *Fax:* 510-601-8307 *E-mail:* ulysses@ulyssespress.com *Web Site:* www.ulyssespress.com, pg 278

Willett, Rick, Sterling Publishing Co Inc, 387 Park Ave S, 5th fl, New York, NY 10016-8810 *Tel:* 212-532-7160 *Toll Free Tel:* 800-367-9692 *Fax:* 212-213-2495 *Web Site:* www.sterlingpub.com, pg 259

Willey, Paul, The Book Tree, PO Box 16476, San Diego, CA 92176 *Tel:* 619-280-1263 *Fax:* 619-280-1285 *E-mail:* booktree1@cs.com *Web Site:* www.thebooktree.com, pg 44

Williams, Barbara, Harmonie Park Press, 23630 Pinewood, Warren, MI 48091 *Tel:* 586-755-3080 *Toll Free Tel:* 800-886-3080 *Fax:* 586-755-4213 *E-mail:* info@harmonieparkpress.com *Web Site:* harmonieparkpress.com, pg 115

Williams, Bob, Burns Sports & Celebrities Inc, 820 Davis St, Evanston, IL 60201 *Tel:* 847-866-9400 *Fax:* 847-491-9778 *Web Site:* www.burnssports.com, pg 669

Williams, Bryan C, Abingdon Press, 201 Eighth Ave S, Nashville, TN 37203-3919 *Tel:* 615-749-6290 (publicist); 615-749-6000; 615-749-6451 (sales) *Toll Free Tel:* 800-251-3320 *Fax:* 615-749-6056 *Web Site:* www.abingdonpress.com, pg 3

Williams, Carol C, Abingdon Press, 201 Eighth Ave S, Nashville, TN 37203-3919 *Tel:* 615-749-6290 (publicist); 615-749-6000; 615-749-6451 (sales) *Toll Free Tel:* 800-251-3320 *Fax:* 615-749-6056 *Web Site:* www.abingdonpress.com, pg 3

Williams, Demetrius, American Public Human Services Association, 810 First St NE, Suite 500, Washington, DC 20002 *Tel:* 202-682-0100 *Fax:* 202-289-6555 *E-mail:* pubs@aphsa.org *Web Site:* www.aphsa.org, pg 677

Williams, Don, New Millennium Writings, PO Box 2463, Knoxville, TN 37901 *Tel:* 865-428-0389 *Fax:* 865-428-0389 *Web Site:* www.mach2.com, pg 794

Williams, H Randall, NewSouth Books, 105 S Court St, Montgomery, AL 36104 *Tel:* 334-834-3556 *Fax:* 334-834-3557 *E-mail:* info@newsouthbooks.com *Web Site:* www.newsouthbooks.com, pg 190

Williams, Henry, McIntosh & Otis Inc, 353 Lexington Ave, Suite 1500, New York, NY 10016-0900 *Tel:* 212-687-7400 *Fax:* 212-687-6894 *E-mail:* info@mcintoshandotis.com, pg 643

Williams, Jan, Jan Williams, Indexing & Editorial Services, 300 Dartmouth College Hwy, Lyme, NH 03768 *Tel:* 603-795-4924 *Fax:* 603-795-9346 *E-mail:* jan.williams@valley.net, pg 613

Williams, Jane, Health Administration Press, One N Franklin St, Suite 1700, Chicago, IL 60606-3491 *Tel:* 312-424-2800 *Fax:* 312-424-0014 *E-mail:* hap@ache.org *Web Site:* www.ache.org, pg 119

Williams, Jane A, Bluestocking Press, 3333 Gold Country Dr, El Dorado, CA 95623 *Tel:* 530-621-1123 *Toll Free Tel:* 800-959-8586 *Fax:* 530-642-9222 *E-mail:* customerservice@bluestockingpress.com *Web Site:* www.bluestockingpress.com, pg 42

Williams, Jim, Associated Press Broadcasters, 1825 "K" St NW, Suite 800, Washington, DC 20006 *Tel:* 202-736-1100 *Fax:* 202-736-1199 *Web Site:* www.ap.org, pg 679

Williams, John J, Consumertronics, 8400 Menaul NE, Suite A-199, Albuquerque, NM 87112 *Tel:* 505-321-1034 *Fax:* 505-257-5637 (orders only) *E-mail:* wizguru@consumertronics.net *Web Site:* www.consumertronics.net, pg 67

Williams, John Taylor, Kneerim & Williams, c/o Fish & Richardson PC, 225 Franklin St, Boston, MA 02110 *Tel:* 617-542-5070 *Fax:* 617-542-8906 *Web Site:* www.fr.com, pg 638

Williams, Jon, Oxmoor House Inc, 2100 Lakeshore Dr, Birmingham, AL 35209 *Tel:* 205-445-6000; 205-445-6560 *Toll Free Tel:* 800-366-4712 *Fax:* 205-445-6078 *Web Site:* www.oxmoorhouse.com, pg 201

Williams, Kerri, Sky Publishing Corp, 49 Bay State Rd, Cambridge, MA 02138-1200 *Tel:* 617-864-7360 *Toll Free Tel:* 800-253-0245 *Fax:* 617-864-6117 *Web Site:* skyandtelescope.com, pg 250

Williams, Kevin, Polestar Book Publishers, 9050 Shaughnessy St, Vancouver, BC V6P 6E5, Canada *Tel:* 604-323-7100 *Toll Free Tel:* 800-663-5714 *Fax:* 604-323-2600 *Toll Free Tel:* 800-565-3770 *E-mail:* info@raincoast.com *Web Site:* www.raincoast.com, pg 558

Williams, Kevin, Raincoast Publishing, 9050 Shaughnessy St, Vancouver, BC V6P 6E5, Canada *Tel:* 604-323-7100 *Toll Free Tel:* 800-663-5714 (Canada only) *Fax:* 604-323-2600 *Toll Free Fax:* 800-565-3700 *E-mail:* info@raincoast.com *Web Site:* www.raincoast.com, pg 559

Williams, Laurencia, Consumertronics, 8400 Menaul NE, Suite A-199, Albuquerque, NM 87112 *Tel:* 505-321-1034 *Fax:* 505-257-5637 (orders only) *E-mail:* wizguru@consumertronics.net *Web Site:* www.consumertronics.net, pg 67

Williams, Lynn, BajonHouse Publishing, 609 Broad Ave, Belle Vernon, PA 15012 *Tel:* 724-929-5997 *Fax:* 724-929-5997, pg 30

Williams, Mark, Krause Publications, 700 E State St, Iola, WI 54990 *Tel:* 715-445-4612 ext 365 *Toll Free Tel:* 800-258-0929; 888-457-2873 *Fax:* 715-445-4087 *Web Site:* www.krause.com, pg 147

Williams, Maurvene D, The Center for the Book in the Library of Congress, The Library of Congress, 101 Independence Ave SE, Washington, DC 20540-4920 *Tel:* 202-707-5221 *Fax:* 202-707-0269 *E-mail:* cfbook@loc.gov *Web Site:* www.loc.gov/cfbook, pg 684

Williams, Paul, The Overlook Press, 141 Wooster St, New York, NY 10012 *Tel:* 212-965-8400 *Fax:* 212-965-9834 *Web Site:* www.overlookny.com, pg 200

Williams, Randall, NewSouth Inc, 105 S Court St, Montgomery, AL 36104 *Tel:* 334-834-3556 *Fax:* 334-834-3557 *E-mail:* info@newsouthbooks.com *Web Site:* www.newsouthbooks.com, pg 191

Williams, Rex J, Cariad Ltd, 180 Bloor St, Suite 801, Toronto, ON M5S 2V6, Canada *Tel:* 416-929-2774 *Fax:* 416-929-1926 *E-mail:* cariadreps@hotmail.com, pg 593

Williams, Richard T, Bonus Books Inc, 1452 Second St, Santa Monica, CA 90403 *Tel:* 310-260-9400 *Toll Free Tel:* 800-225-3775 *E-mail:* webmaster@bonusbooks.com *Web Site:* www.bonusbooks.com, pg 43

Williams, Rob, Mountain Press Publishing Co, 1301 S Third W, Missoula, MT 59801 *Tel:* 406-728-1900 *Toll Free Tel:* 800-234-5308 *Fax:* 406-728-1635 *E-mail:* info@mtnpress.com *Web Site:* www.mountain-press.com, pg 179

Williams, Robert, Optometric Extension Program Foundation, 1921 E Carnegie Ave, Suite 3-L, Santa Ana, CA 92705-5510 *Tel:* 949-250-8070 *Fax:* 949-250-8157 *E-mail:* oep1@oep.org *Web Site:* www.oep.org, pg 198

Williams, Rodger, American Institute of Aeronautics & Astronautics, 1801 Alexander Bell Dr, Suite 500, Reston, VA 20191 *Tel:* 703-264-7500 *Toll Free Tel:* 800-639-2422 *Fax:* 703-264-7551 *E-mail:* custserv@aiaa.org *Web Site:* www.aiaa.org, pg 14

Williams, Roger, Evangel Publishing House, 2000 Evangel Way, Nappanee, IN 46550 *Tel:* 574-773-3164 *Toll Free Tel:* 800-253-9315 (orders) *Fax:* 574-773-5934 *E-mail:* sales@evangelpublishing.com *Web Site:* www.evangelpublishing.com, pg 92

Williams, Dr Roger L, United States Pharmacopeia, 12601 Twinbrook Pkwy, Rockville, MD 20852 *Tel:* 301-881-0666 *Toll Free Tel:* 800-227-8772 *Fax:* 301-816-8148; 301-816-8236 (mktg) *E-mail:* marketing@usp.org *Web Site:* www.usp.org, pg 279

Williams, Sarah, Chronicle Books LLC, 85 Second St, 6th fl, San Francisco, CA 94105 *Tel:* 415-537-4200 *Toll Free Tel:* 800-722-6657 (cust serv) *Fax:* 415-537-4460 *Toll Free Tel:* 800-858-7787 (orders) *E-mail:* frontdesk@chroniclebooks.com *Web Site:* www.chroniclebooks.com, pg 61

Williams, Scott, Haights Cross Communications Inc, 10 New King St, White Plains, NY 10604 *Tel:* 914-289-9400 *Fax:* 914-289-9401 *E-mail:* info@haightscross.com *Web Site:* www.haightscross.com, pg 112

Williams, Scott, Recorded Books LLC, 270 Skipjack Rd, Prince Frederick, MD 20678 *Tel:* 410-535-5590 *Toll Free Tel:* 800-638-1304 *Fax:* 410-535-5499 *E-mail:* recordedbooks@recordedbooks.com *Web Site:* www.recordedbooks.com, pg 229

Williams, Suzanne, The Canadian Writers' Foundation Inc/La fondation des ecrivains canadiens, PO Box 13281, Kanata Sta, Ottawa, ON K2K 1X4, Canada *Tel:* 613-256-6937 *Fax:* 613-256-5457 *Web Site:* www.canauthors.org/cwf, pg 705

Williams, Suzanne, Pantheon Books/Schocken Books, 1745 Broadway, New York, NY 10019 *Tel:* 212-751-2600 *Toll Free Tel:* 800-638-6460 *Fax:* 212-572-6030, pg 202

Williams, Thomas A, Williams & Co Publishers, 1317 Pine Ridge Dr, Savannah, GA 31406 *Tel:* 912-352-0404 *E-mail:* bookpub@comcast.net *Web Site:* www.pubmart.com, pg 300

Wilson, Natashya, Harlequin Enterprises Ltd, 233 Broadway, Suite 1001, New York, NY 10279 *Tel:* 212-553-4200 *Fax:* 212-227-8969 *E-mail:* customer. ecare@harlequin.ca *Web Site:* www.eharlequin.com; www.luna-books.com; www.mirabooks.com; www. reddressink.com; www.steeplehill.com, pg 115

Wilson, Phyllis, Oxford University Press Canada, 70 Wynford Dr, Don Mills, ON M3C 1J9, Canada *Tel:* 416-441-2941 *Toll Free Tel:* 800-387-8020 *Fax:* 416-444-0427 *Toll Free Fax:* 800-665-1771 *E-mail:* custserv@oupcan.com *Web Site:* www.oup. com/ca, pg 557

Wilson, Rick, Berrett-Koehler Publishers Inc, 235 Montgomery St, Suite 650, San Francisco, CA 94104 *Tel:* 415-288-0260 *Fax:* 415-362-2512 *E-mail:* bkpub@bkpub.com *Web Site:* www. bkconnection.com, pg 37

Wilson, Stepani, Masters Literary Awards, PO Box 17897, Encino, CA 91416-7897 *Tel:* 818-377-4006 *E-mail:* titan.press@sbcglobal.net *Web Site:* www. titanpress.info, pg 788

Wilson, Steve, McFarland & Co Inc Publishers, 960 Hwy 88 W, Jefferson, NC 28640 *Tel:* 336-246-4460 *Toll Free Tel:* 800-253-2187 (orders only) *Fax:* 336-246-5018; 336-246-4403 (orders) *E-mail:* info@ mcfarlandpub.com *Web Site:* www.mcfarlandpub.com, pg 166

Wilson, Susan, Southern Illinois University Press, PO Box 3697, Carbondale, IL 62902-3697 *Tel:* 618-453-2281 *Toll Free Tel:* 800-346-2680 *Fax:* 618-453-1221 *Toll Free Fax:* 800-346-2681 *E-mail:* jstetter@siu.edu *Web Site:* www.siu.edu/~siupress, pg 254

Wilson, Victoria, Alfred A Knopf, 1745 Broadway, New York, NY 10019 *Tel:* 212-751-2600 *Toll Free Tel:* 800-638-6460 *Fax:* 212-572-2593 *Web Site:* www. randomhouse.com/knopf, pg 146

Wilsterman, Dale, Charisma House, 600 Rinehart Rd, Lake Mary, FL 32746 *Tel:* 407-333-0600 (all imprints) *Toll Free Tel:* 800-283-8494 (Charisma House, Siloam Press, Creation House Press); 800-665-1468 *Fax:* 407-333-7100 (all imprints) *E-mail:* webmaster@ charismahouse.com; webmaster@creationhouse.com *Web Site:* www.charismamag.com; www.strang.com (all imprints), pg 58

Wilsterman, Dale, CharismaLife Publishers, 600 Rinehart Rd, Lake Mary, FL 32746 *Tel:* 407-333-0600 *Toll Free Tel:* 800-451-4598 *Fax:* 407-333-7100 *E-mail:* charismalife@strang.com *Web Site:* www. charismamag.com, pg 58

Wilt, Michael, Cowley Publications, 4 Brattle St, Cambridge, MA 02138 *Tel:* 617-441-0300 *Toll Free Tel:* 800-225-1534 *Fax:* 617-441-0120 *Toll Free Fax:* 877-225-6675 *E-mail:* cowley@cowley.org *Web Site:* www.cowley.org, pg 71

Wilton, Terry, Houghton Mifflin College Division, 222 Berkeley St, Boston, MA 02116-3764 *Tel:* 617-351-5000 *Toll Free Tel:* 800-225-1464 (orders) *Web Site:* www.college.hmco.com, pg 126

Wiltshire, Betty C, Pioneer Publishing Co, Hwy 82 E, Carrolton, MS 38917 *Tel:* 662-237-6010 *E-mail:* pioneerse@tecinfo.com *Web Site:* www. pioneersoutheast.com, pg 213

Wiman, Christian, The Ruth Lilly Poetry Prize, 1030 N Clark St, Suite 420, Chicago, IL 60610 *Tel:* 312-787-7070 *Fax:* 312-787-6650 *E-mail:* poetry@ poetrymagazine.org *Web Site:* www.poetrymagazine. org, pg 784

Wimmer, Sandy, Standard Publishing Co, 8121 Hamilton Ave, Cincinnati, OH 45231 *Tel:* 513-931-4050 *Toll Free Tel:* 800-543-1301 *Fax:* 513-931-0950 *Toll Free Fax:* 877-867-5751 *E-mail:* customerservice@ standardpub.com *Web Site:* www.standardpub.com, pg 257

Wimmer, Stephanie, Scholastic Trade Division, 557 Broadway, New York, NY 10012 *Tel:* 212-343-6100; 212-343-4685 (export sales) *Fax:* 212-343-4714 (export sales) *Web Site:* www.scholastic.com, pg 242

Winch, Bradley L, Jalmar Press, 1050 Canyon Rd, Fawnskin, CA 92333 *Tel:* 909-866-2912 *Fax:* 909-866-2961 *E-mail:* jalmarpress@att.net *Web Site:* www. jalmarpress.com, pg 140

Winch, Cathy, Jalmar Press, 1050 Canyon Rd, Fawnskin, CA 92333 *Tel:* 909-866-2912 *Fax:* 909-866-2961 *E-mail:* jalmarpress@att.net *Web Site:* www. jalmarpress.com, pg 140

Winchell, Rhonda J, The Author's Agency, 3355 N Five Mile Rd, Suite 332, Boise, ID 83713 *Tel:* 208-322-7239 *E-mail:* authoragency@aol.com, pg 620

Windham, Darrell, University of Texas Press, PO Box 7819, Austin, TX 78713-7819 *Tel:* 512-471-7233 *Fax:* 512-232-7178 *E-mail:* utpress@uts.cc.utexas.edu *Web Site:* www.utexas.edu/utpress, pg 267

Windsor, Deborah, Writers' Union of Canada, 90 Richmond St E, Suite 200, Toronto, ON M5C 1P1, Canada *Tel:* 416-703-0826 *Fax:* 416-504-9090 *E-mail:* info@writersunion.ca *Web Site:* www. writersunion.ca, pg 703

Winebarger, Allan, Penguin Group (USA) Inc Sales, 375 Hudson St, New York, NY 10014 *Tel:* 212-366-2000 *E-mail:* online@penguinputnam.com *Web Site:* www. penguin.com, pg 208

Wingate, Lascelle, Matt Cohen Prize: In Celebration of a Writing Life, 90 Richmond St W, Suite 200, Toronto, ON M5C 1P1, Canada *Tel:* 416-504-8222 *Fax:* 416-504-9090 *E-mail:* info@writerstrust.com *Web Site:* www.writerstrust.com, pg 768

Wingate, Lascelle, Shaughnessy Cohen Award for Political Writing, 90 Richmond St W, Suite 200, Toronto, ON M5C 1P1, Canada *Tel:* 416-504-8222 *Fax:* 416-504-9090 *E-mail:* info@writerstrust.com *Web Site:* www.writerstrust.com, pg 768

Wingate, Lascelle, Drainie-Taylor Biography Prize, 90 Richmond St W, Suite 200, Toronto, ON M5C 1P1, Canada *Tel:* 416-504-8222 *Fax:* 416-504-9090 *E-mail:* info@writerstrust.com *Web Site:* www. writerstrust.com, pg 770

Wingate, Lascelle, Marian Engel Award, 90 Richmond St W, Suite 200, Toronto, ON M5C 1P1, Canada *Tel:* 416-504-8222 *Fax:* 416-504-9090 *E-mail:* info@ writerstrust.com *Web Site:* www.writerstrust.com, pg 772

Wingate, Lascelle, Timothy Findley Award, 90 Richmond St W, Suite 200, Toronto, ON M5C 1P1, Canada *Tel:* 416-504-8222 *Fax:* 416-504-9090 *E-mail:* info@writerstrust.com *Web Site:* www. writerstrust.com, pg 773

Wingate, Lascelle, McClelland & Stewart Journey Prize, 90 Richmond St W, Suite 200, Toronto, ON M5C 1P1, Canada *Tel:* 416-504-8222 *Fax:* 416-504-9090 *E-mail:* info@writerstrust.com *Web Site:* www. writerstrust.com, pg 788

Wingate, Lascelle, Vicky Metcalf Award for Children's Literature, 90 Richmond St W, Suite 200, Toronto, ON M5C 1P1, Canada *Tel:* 416-504-8222 *Fax:* 416-504-9090 *E-mail:* info@writerstrust.com *Web Site:* www.writerstrust.com, pg 789

Wingate, Lascelle, W O Mitchell Literary Prize, 90 Richmond St W, Suite 200, Toronto, ON M5C 1P1, Canada *Tel:* 416-504-8222 *Fax:* 416-504-9090 *E-mail:* info@writerstrust.com *Web Site:* www. writerstrust.com, pg 790

Wingate, Lascelle, Pearson Writers' Trust Non-Fiction Prize, 90 Richmond St W, Suite 200, Toronto, ON M5C 1P1, Canada *Tel:* 416-504-8222 *Fax:* 416-504-9090 *E-mail:* info@writerstrust.com *Web Site:* www. writerstrust.com, pg 797

Wingate, Lascelle, Rogers Writers' Trust Fiction Prize, 90 Richmond St W, Suite 200, Toronto, ON M5C 1P1, Canada *Tel:* 416-504-8222 *Fax:* 416-504-9090 *E-mail:* info@writerstrust.com *Web Site:* www. writerstrust.com, pg 802

Wingate, Lascelle, Bronwen Wallace Memorial Award, 90 Richmond St W, Suite 200, Toronto, ON M5C 1P1, Canada *Tel:* 416-504-8222 *Fax:* 416-504-9090 *E-mail:* info@writerstrust.com *Web Site:* www. writerstrust.com, pg 810

Winge, Sara, O'Reilly & Associates Inc, 1005 Gravenstein Hwy N, Sebastopol, CA 95472 *Tel:* 707-827-7000 *Toll Free Tel:* 800-998-9938 *Fax:* 707-829-0104 *E-mail:* info@oreilly.com *Web Site:* www.oreilly. com, pg 199

Winick, Elizabeth, McIntosh & Otis Inc, 353 Lexington Ave, Suite 1500, New York, NY 10016-0900 *Tel:* 212-687-7400 *Fax:* 212-687-6894 *E-mail:* info@ mcintoshandotis.com, pg 643

Winick, Eugene H, McIntosh & Otis Inc, 353 Lexington Ave, Suite 1500, New York, NY 10016-0900 *Tel:* 212-687-7400 *Fax:* 212-687-6894 *E-mail:* info@ mcintoshandotis.com, pg 643

Winkel, Brian J, Undergraduate Paper Competition in Cryptology, Dept Math Sciences, US Military Academy, West Point, NY 10996 *Tel:* 845-938-3200 *Web Site:* www.dean.usma.edu/math/pubs/cryptologia, pg 809

Winkelstein, Jill, Napa Writing Retreats, PO Box 3214, Napa, CA 94558 *Tel:* 707-252-1030 *Toll Free Tel:* 866-848-2961 *E-mail:* info@napawritingretreats. com *Web Site:* www.napawritingretreats.com, pg 745

Winkowski, LaVerne, SAE (Society of Automotive Engineers International), 400 Commonwealth Dr, Warrendale, PA 15096-0001 *Tel:* 724-776-4841 *Toll Free Tel:* 877-606-7323 (cust serv) *Fax:* 724-776-0790 *E-mail:* publications@sae.org *Web Site:* www.sae.org, pg 237

Winnan, Audur H, Audur H Winnan, 747 Tenth Ave, No 16-K, New York, NY 10019 *Tel:* 212-581-9766, pg 614

Winnett, Caroline, Wilderness Press, 1200 Fifth St, Berkeley, CA 94710 *Tel:* 510-558-1666 *Toll Free Tel:* 800-443-7227 *Fax:* 510-558-1696 *E-mail:* info@ wildernesspress.com *Web Site:* www.wildernesspress. com, pg 299

Winningham, Sharon, School Zone Publishing Co, 1819 Industrial Dr, Grand Haven, MI 49417 *Tel:* 616-846-5030 *Toll Free Tel:* 800-253-0564 *Fax:* 616-846-6181 *Web Site:* www.schoolzone.com, pg 243

Winns, Nadine, Abbeville Publishing Group, 116 W 23 St, Suite 500, New York, NY 10011 *Tel:* 646-375-2039 *Toll Free Tel:* 800-ART-BOOK (278-2665) *Fax:* 646-375-2040 *E-mail:* abbeville@abbeville.com *Web Site:* www.abbeville.com, pg 2

Winns, Nadine, Artabras Inc, 116 W 23 St, Suite 500, New York, NY 10011 *Tel:* 646-375-2039 *Toll Free Tel:* 800-ART-BOOK *Fax:* 646-375-2040 *E-mail:* abbeville@abbeville.com *Web Site:* www. abbeville.com, pg 24

Winskill, Gail, Fitzhenry & Whiteside Limited, 195 Allstate Pkwy, Markham, ON L3R 4T8, Canada *Tel:* 905-477-9700 *Toll Free Tel:* 800-387-9776 *Fax:* 905-477-9179 *Toll Free Fax:* 800-260-9777 *E-mail:* godwit@fitzhenry.ca *Web Site:* www.fitzhenry. ca, pg 547

Winslow, Anne, Algonquin Books of Chapel Hill, 127 Kingston Dr, Suite 105, Chapel Hill, NC 27514 *Tel:* 919-967-0108 *Fax:* 919-933-0272 *E-mail:* dialogue@algonquin.com *Web Site:* www. algonquin.com, pg 8

Winstanley, Nicole, Westwood Creative Artists Ltd, 94 Harbord St, Toronto, ON M5S 1G6, Canada *Tel:* 416-964-3302 *Fax:* 416-975-9209, pg 661

Winston, Mary, Scholastic Inc, 557 Broadway, New York, NY 10012 *Tel:* 212-343-4469 *Toll Free Tel:* 800-scholastic *Fax:* 212-343-6930 *Web Site:* www.scholastic.com, pg 241

Winter, Heidi, Fenn Publishing Co Ltd, 34 Nixon Rd, Bolton, ON L7E 1W2, Canada *Tel:* 905-951-6600 *Toll Free Tel:* 800-267-3366 (Canada only) *Fax:* 905-951-6601 *Toll Free Fax:* 800-465-3422 (Canada Only) *E-mail:* sales@hbfenn.com *Web Site:* www.hbfenn. com, pg 546

Winter, Paul, EMC/Paradigm Publishing, 875 Montreal Way, St Paul, MN 55102 *Tel:* 651-290-2800 (corp) *Toll Free Tel:* 800-328-1452 *Fax:* 651-290-2899 *Toll Free Fax:* 800-328-4564 *E-mail:* educate@emcp.com *Web Site:* www.emcp.com, pg 90

Winter, Ralph D, William Carey Library, PO Box 40129, Pasadena, CA 91114-7129 *Tel:* 626-798-0819 *Toll Free Tel:* 866-732-6657 *E-mail:* publishing@wclbooks. com *Web Site:* www.wclbooks.com, pg 53

Winter, Thomas S, Eagle Publishing Inc, One Massachusetts Ave NW, Washington, DC 20001 *Tel:* 202-216-0600 *Fax:* 202-216-0612 *Web Site:* www. regnery.com, pg 85

Winterberg, Jenna, Walter Foster Publishing Inc, 23062 La Cadena Dr, Laguna Hills, CA 92653 *Tel:* 949-380-7510 *Toll Free Tel:* 800-426-0099 *Fax:* 949-380-7575 *Web Site:* www.walterfoster.com, pg 99

Winters, Clay, Boyds Mills Press, 815 Church St, Honesdale, PA 18431 *Tel:* 570-253-1164 *Toll Free Tel:* 877-512-8366 *Fax:* 570-253-0179 *Web Site:* www. boydsmillspress.com, pg 45

Winters, Jody, Bear & Co Inc, One Park St, Rochester, VT 05767 *Tel:* 802-767-3174 *Toll Free Tel:* 800-932-3277 *Fax:* 802-767-3726 *E-mail:* orders@ InnerTraditions.com *Web Site:* InnerTraditions.com, pg 34

Winters, Jody, Inner Traditions International Ltd, One Park St, Rochester, VT 05767 *Tel:* 802-767-3174 *Toll Free Tel:* 800-246-8648 *Fax:* 802-767-3726 *E-mail:* orders@InnerTraditions.com *Web Site:* www. InnerTraditions.com, pg 134

Winters, Tracy, Winters Publishing, 705 E Washington St, Greensburg, IN 47240 *Tel:* 812-663-4948 *Toll Free Tel:* 800-457-3230 *Fax:* 812-663-4948 *Toll Free Fax:* 800-457-3230, pg 301

Winterton, Danielle, Barbara Braun Associates Inc, 104 Fifth Ave, 7th fl, New York, NY 10011 *Tel:* 212-604-9023 *Fax:* 212-604-9041 *E-mail:* bba230@earthlink. net *Web Site:* www.barbarabraunagency.com, pg 622

Wintle, Edwin John, Curtis Brown Ltd, 10 Astor Place, New York, NY 10003 *Tel:* 212-473-5400, pg 623

Winton, Charlie, Avalon Publishing Group Inc, 1400 65 St, Suite 250, Emeryville, CA 94608 *Tel:* 510-595-3664 *Fax:* 510-535-4228 *Web Site:* www.avalonpub. com, pg 28

Winton, Helen M, The Reading Component, 1827 Ximeno Ave, PMB 195, Long Beach, CA 90815-5801 *Tel:* 310-521-6457 *Fax:* 562-597-0462, pg 610

Wirkus, Lin, The University Press of Kentucky, 663 S Limestone St, Lexington, KY 40508-4008 *Tel:* 859-257-8761; 859-257-8442 (mktg) *Toll Free Tel:* 800-839-6855 (orders) *Fax:* 859-323-1873 *Web Site:* www. kentuckypress.com, pg 287

Wirtz, Polly, William Andrew Publishing, 13 Eaton Ave, Norwich, NY 13815 *Tel:* 607-337-5000 *Toll Free Tel:* 800-932-7045 *Fax:* 607-337-5090 *E-mail:* publishing@williamandrew.com *Web Site:* www.williamandrew.com, pg 300

Wise, Jay, Peace Hill Press, 18101 The Glebe Lane, Charles City, VA 23030 *Tel:* 804-829-5043 *Toll Free Tel:* 877-322-3445 (orders) *Fax:* 804-829-5704 *E-mail:* info@peacehillpress.net *Web Site:* www. peacehillpress.com, pg 206

Wiseman, Paula, Simon & Schuster Children's Publishing, 1230 Avenue of the Americas, New York, NY 10020 *Tel:* 212-698-7000 *Web Site:* www. simonsayskids.com, pg 248

Wisenthal, Paul, The Professional Writer, PO Box 1631, Old Chelsea Sta, New York, NY 10113 *Tel:* 212-983-1951; 212-414-0188 *E-mail:* aprowrite@aol.com *Web Site:* www.theprofessionalwriter.com, pg 608

Wisman, Amy, Amon Carter Museum, 3501 Camp Bowie Blvd, Fort Worth, TX 76107-2631 *Tel:* 817-738-1933 (ext 625) *Toll Free Tel:* 800-573-1933 *Fax:* 817-336-1123 *Web Site:* www.cartermuseum.org, pg 54

Wissoker, Ken, Duke University Press, 905 W Main St, Suite 18-B, Durham, NC 27701 *Tel:* 919-687-3600 *Toll Free Tel:* 888-651-0122 (orders only) *Fax:* 919-688-4574 *Toll Free Fax:* 888-651-0124 *Web Site:* www.dukepress.edu, pg 84

Wissoker, Peter, Temple University Press, 1601 N Broad St, 083-42, USB Room 306, Philadelphia, PA 19122-6099 *Tel:* 215-204-8787 *Toll Free Tel:* 800-447-1656 *Fax:* 215-204-4719 *E-mail:* tempress@temple.edu *Web Site:* www.temple.edu/tempress, pg 266

Witcraft, Stacey, Random House Publishing Group, 1745 Broadway, New York, NY 10019 *Toll Free Tel:* 800-200-3552 *Toll Free Fax:* 800-200-3552 *Web Site:* www.randomhouse.com, pg 227

Withers, Laurel, Playwrights Project, 450 "B" St, Suite 1020, San Diego, CA 92101-8093 *Tel:* 619-239-8222 *Fax:* 619-239-8225 *E-mail:* write@playwrightsproject. com *Web Site:* www.playwrightsproject.com, pg 799

Witherspoon, G, Tropical Press Inc, PO Box 161174, Miami, FL 33116-1174 *Tel:* 305-971-1887 *Fax:* 305-378-1595 *E-mail:* tropicbook@aol.com *Web Site:* www.tropicalpress.com, pg 276

Witherspoon, Kim, Inkwell Management, 521 Fifth Ave, 26th fl, New York, NY 10175 *Tel:* 212-922-3500 *Fax:* 212-922-0535 *E-mail:* contact@ inkwellmanagement.com *Web Site:* www. inkwellmanagement.com, pg 635

Withey, Lynne, University of California Press, 2120 Berkeley Way, Berkeley, CA 94720 *Tel:* 510-642-4247 *Toll Free Tel:* 800-777-4726 *Fax:* 510-643-7127 *Toll Free Fax:* 800-999-1958 *E-mail:* askucp@ucpress.edu *Web Site:* www.ucpress.edu, pg 281

Withgott, James W, Merriam-Webster Inc, 47 Federal St, Springfield, MA 01102 *Tel:* 413-734-3134 *Toll Free Tel:* 800-828-1880 (orders & cust serv) *Fax:* 413-731-5979 *E-mail:* merriam_webster@merriam-webster.com *Web Site:* www.merriam-webster.com, pg 172

Witke, Barbara, Peachtree Publishers Ltd, 1700 Chattahoochee Ave, Atlanta, GA 30318 *Tel:* 404-876-8761 *Toll Free Tel:* 800-241-0113 *Fax:* 404-875-2578 *Toll Free Fax:* 800-875-8909 *E-mail:* hello@peachtree-online.com *Web Site:* www.peachtree-online.com, pg 206

Witlox, Cathy, WordWitlox, 642 Chiron Crescent, Pickering, ON L1V 4T4, Canada *Tel:* 416-420-0669 *Web Site:* www.wordwitlox.com, pg 614

Witt, James L, International Code Council Inc, 5360 Workman Mill Rd, Whittier, CA 90601-2298 *Tel:* 562-699-0541 *Toll Free Tel:* 800-423-6587 *Web Site:* www. iccsafe.org, pg 137

Witt, Joseph W, Empire Publishing Service, PO Box 1344, Studio City, CA 91614-0344 *Tel:* 818-784-8918, pg 90

Witt, Stephen L, Royalty Publishing Co, 1440 Church Camp Rd, Bedford, IN 47421 *Tel:* 812-278-8785 *Fax:* 812-278-8785 *E-mail:* neeto@admete.net *Web Site:* www.v-maximum-zone.com, pg 235

Witte, George, St Martin's Press Trade Division, 175 Fifth Ave, New York, NY 10010 *E-mail:* firstname. lastname@stmartins.com *Web Site:* www.stmartins. com; www.minotaurbooks.com, pg 239

Witter, Bret, Health Communications Inc, 3201 SW 15 St, Deerfield Beach, FL 33442-8190 *Tel:* 954-360-0909 *Toll Free Tel:* 800-851-9100 (cust serv); 800-441-5569 (order entry) *Fax:* 954-360-0034 *Web Site:* www.hcibooks.com, pg 119

Witter, Karen, Illinois State Museum Society, 502 S Spring St, Springfield, IL 62706-5000 *Tel:* 217-782-7387 *Fax:* 217-782-1254 *E-mail:* editor@museum. state.il.us *Web Site:* www.museum.state.il.us, pg 131

Witzleben, Donna, Society for Industrial & Applied Mathematics, 3600 University City Science Ctr, Philadelphia, PA 19104-2688 *Tel:* 215-382-9800 *Toll Free Tel:* 800-447-7426 *Fax:* 215-386-7999 *E-mail:* siam@siam.org *Web Site:* www.siam.org, pg 251

Wodele, Trey, The Gislason Agency, 219 SE Main St, Suite 506, Minneapolis, MN 55414 *Tel:* 612-331-8033 *Fax:* 612-331-8115 *E-mail:* gislasonbj@aol.com *Web Site:* www.TheGislasonAgency.com, pg 632

Woehlbier, Fred, Trans Tech Publications, c/o Enfield Distribution Co, 234 May St, Enfield, NH 03748 *Tel:* 603-632-7377 *Fax:* 603-632-5611 *E-mail:* usa-ttp@ttp.net; info@enfiedbooks.com *Web Site:* www. ttp.net, pg 274

Woessner, Steve, Brilliance Audio, 1704 Eaton Dr, Grand Haven, MI 49417 *Tel:* 616-846-5256 *Toll Free Tel:* 800-648-2312 (orders only) *Fax:* 616-846-0630 *Web Site:* www.brillianceaudio.com, pg 48

Wofsy, Alan, Alan Wofsy Fine Arts, 1109 Geary Blvd, San Francisco, CA 94109 *Tel:* 415-292-6500 *Fax:* 415-512-0130 (acctg); 415-292-6594 (off & cust serv) *E-mail:* beauxarts@earthlink.net (cust serv); editeur@earthlink.net (edit); order@art-books.com (orders) *Web Site:* art-books.com, pg 302

Woidill, Ken, Phaidon Press Inc, 180 Varick St, 14th fl, New York, NY 10014 *Tel:* 212-652-5400 *Toll Free Tel:* 800-759-0190 (cust serv) *Fax:* 212-652-5410 *Toll Free Fax:* 800-286-9471 (cust serv) *E-mail:* ussales@ phaidon.com *Web Site:* www.phaidon.com, pg 211

Woishnis, William, William Andrew Publishing, 13 Eaton Ave, Norwich, NY 13815 *Tel:* 607-337-5000 *Toll Free Tel:* 800-932-7045 *Fax:* 607-337-5090 *E-mail:* publishing@williamandrew.com *Web Site:* www.williamandrew.com, pg 300

Wojcik, Paul, BNA Books, 1231 25 St NW, Washington, DC 20037 *Tel:* 202-452-4343 *Toll Free Tel:* 800-960-1220 *Fax:* 202-452-4997 (editorial off); 732-346-1624 (cust serv) *E-mail:* books@bna.com *Web Site:* www. bnabooks.com, pg 42

Wold, Amanda, LernerClassroom, 241 First Ave N, Minneapolis, MN 55401 *Tel:* 612-332-3344 *Toll Free Tel:* 800-328-4929 *Fax:* 612-332-7615 *Toll Free Fax:* 800-332-1132 *E-mail:* info@lernerbooks.com *Web Site:* www.lernerbooks.com, pg 153

Wolf, Audrey R, Audrey R Wolf Literary Agency, 2510 Virginia Ave NW, Washington, DC 20037 *Tel:* 202-965-0405 *Fax:* 202-298-6966 *E-mail:* bigbad@ earthlink.net, pg 661

Wolf, Carol, Harcourt Achieve, 10801 N MoPac Expressway, Austin, TX 78759 *Tel:* 512-343-8227 *Toll Free Tel:* 800-531-5015 *Toll Free Fax:* 800-699-9459 *E-mail:* ecare@harcourt.com *Web Site:* www. harcourtachieve.com, pg 114

Wolf, Carol, Rigby, 10801 N MoPac Expressway, Austin, TX 78759 *Tel:* 512-343-8227 *Toll Free Tel:* 800-531-5015 *Toll Free Fax:* 800-699-9459 *E-mail:* ecare@harcourt.com *Web Site:* www. harcourtachieve.com, pg 232

Wolf, Carol, Steck-Vaughn, 10801 N MoPac Expressway, Austin, TX 78759 *Tel:* 512-343-8227 *Toll Free Tel:* 800-531-5015 *Toll Free Fax:* 800-699-9459 *E-mail:* ecare@harcourt.com *Web Site:* www. harcourtachieve.com, pg 258

Wolf, Jackie, Playhouse Publishing, 1566 Akron-Peninsula Rd, Akron, OH 44313 *Tel:* 330-926-1313 *Toll Free Tel:* 800-762-6775 *Fax:* 330-926-1315 *E-mail:* info@playhousepublishing.com *Web Site:* www.playhousepublishing.com, pg 214

Wolf, Maria, Institute of Governmental Studies, 102 Moses Hall, Berkeley, CA 94720-2370 *Tel:* 510-642-1428 *Fax:* 510-642-5537 *E-mail:* igspress@uclink2. berkeley.edu *Web Site:* www.igs.berkeley.edu, pg 135

Wolf, Ralph C, ArcheBooks Publishing, 9101 W Sahara Ave, Suite 105-112, Las Vegas, NV 89117 *Tel:* 702-253-1338 *Toll Free Tel:* 800-358-8101 *Fax:* 561-868-2127 *E-mail:* publisher@archebooks. com *Web Site:* www.archebooks.com, pg 22

Wolf, Sarah, Running Press Book Publishers, 125 S 22 St, Philadelphia, PA 19103-4399 *Tel:* 215-567-5080 *Toll Free Tel:* 800-345-5359 (cust serv & orders) *Fax:* 215-568-2919 *Toll Free Fax:* 800-453-2884 *Web Site:* www.runningpress.com, pg 236

Wolf, Wendy, Viking, 375 Hudson St, New York, NY 10014 *Tel:* 212-366-2000 *E-mail:* online@ penguinputnam.com *Web Site:* www.penguin.com, pg 290

Wolfe, Audra, Rutgers University Press, 100 Joyce Kilmer Ave, Piscataway, NJ 08854-8099 *Tel:* 732-445-7762 (edit); 732-445-7762 (ext 627, sales) *Toll Free Tel:* 800-446-9323 (orders only) *Fax:* 732-445-

7039 (acqs, edit, mktg, perms, prodn); 732-445-1974 (fulfillment) *E-mail:* garyf@rci.rutgers.edu *Web Site:* rutgerspress.rutgers.edu, pg 236

Wolfe, Honora, Blue Poppy Press, 5441 Western Ave, No 2, Boulder, CO 80301 *Tel:* 303-447-8372 *Toll Free Tel:* 800-487-9296 *Fax:* 303-245-8362 *E-mail:* info@bluepoppy.com *Web Site:* www.bluepoppy.com, pg 42

Wolfe, Irwin, The Bookbinders' Guild of New York, Dunn & Co, 110 Grand Ave, Ridgefield Park, NJ 07660 *Tel:* 201-229-1888 *Fax:* 201-229-1755 *Web Site:* www.bookbindersguild.org, pg 682

Wolfe, Janet, Scarecrow Press/Government Institutes Div, 4501 Forbes Blvd, Suite 200, Lanham, MD 20706 *Tel:* 301-921-2300 *Fax:* 301-429-5747 *Web Site:* govinst.scarecrowpress.com, pg 240

Wolfe, Leslie R, Center for Women Policy Studies, 1211 Connecticut Ave NW, Suite 312, Washington, DC 20036 *Tel:* 202-872-1770 *Fax:* 202-296-8962 *E-mail:* cwps@centerwomenpolicy.org *Web Site:* www.centerwomenpolicy.org, pg 57

Wolfe, Margie, Second Story Feminist Press, 720 Bathurst St, Suite 301, Toronto, ON M5S 2R4, Canada *Tel:* 416-537-7850 *Fax:* 416-537-0588 *E-mail:* info@secondstorypress.ca *Web Site:* www.secondstorypress.on.ca, pg 561

Wolfe, Mary, University of Illinois Press, 1325 S Oak, Champaign, IL 61820-6903 *Tel:* 217-333-0950; 212-577-5487 *Fax:* 217-244-8082; 410-516-6969 (orders) *E-mail:* uipress@uillinois.edu; journals@uillinois.edu *Web Site:* www.press.uillinois.edu, pg 282

Wolfe, Michael P, Book-of-the-Year Award, 3707 Woodview Trace, Indianapolis, IN 46268-1158 *Tel:* 317-871-4900 *Toll Free Tel:* 800-284-3167 *Fax:* 317-704-2323 *Web Site:* www.kdp.org, pg 763

Wolfe-Stead, Nancy, League of Vermont Writers, PO Box 172, Underhill Center, VT 05490 *Tel:* 802-253-9439 *Web Site:* www.leaguevtwriters.org, pg 690

Wolff, David, Sunburst Technology, 400 Columbus Ave, Suite 160E, Valhalla, NY 10595 *Tel:* 914-747-3310 *Toll Free Tel:* 800-338-3457 *Fax:* 914-747-4109 *Web Site:* www.sunburst.com, pg 262

Wolford, Henry, Easy Money Press, 5419 87 St, Lubbock, TX 79424 *Tel:* 806-543-5215 *E-mail:* easymoneypress@yahoo.com, pg 86

Wolfson, Michelle, Ralph M Vicinanza Ltd, 303 W 18 St, New York, NY 10011 *Tel:* 212-924-7090 *Fax:* 212-691-9644 *E-mail:* ralphvic@aol.com, pg 659

Woll, Thomas, Mint Publishers Group, 62 June Rd, North Salem, NY 10560 *Tel:* 914-276-6576 *Fax:* 914-276-6579 *E-mail:* info@mintpub.com *Web Site:* www.mintpub.com, pg 175

Wollheim, Elizabeth R, DAW Books Inc, 375 Hudson St, 3rd fl, New York, NY 10014 *Tel:* 212-366-2096 *Fax:* 212-366-2090 *E-mail:* daw@us.penguingroup.com *Web Site:* www.dawbooks.com, pg 77

Wolman, Baron, Squarebooks Inc, PO Box 6699, Santa Rosa, CA 95406 *Tel:* 707-545-1221 *Toll Free Tel:* 800-345-6699 *Fax:* 707-545-0909 *E-mail:* sales@fotobaron.com *Web Site:* fotobaron.com/squarebooks, pg 256

Wolny, Karen A, Routledge, 29 W 35 St, New York, NY 10001-2299 *Tel:* 212-216-7800 *Fax:* 212-564-7854 (main) *E-mail:* info@taylorandfrancis.com *Web Site:* www.routledge-ny.com, pg 235

Wolpin, Isaac, Moznaim Publishing Corp, 4304 12 Ave, Brooklyn, NY 11219 *Tel:* 718-438-7680 *Toll Free Tel:* 800-364-5118 *Fax:* 718-438-1305, pg 180

Wolterstorff, Klaas, Wm B Eerdmans Publishing Co, 255 Jefferson Ave SE, Grand Rapids, MI 49503 *Tel:* 616-459-4591 *Toll Free Tel:* 800-253-7521 *Fax:* 616-459-6540 *E-mail:* sales@eerdmans.com *Web Site:* www.eerdmans.com, pg 88

Wolverton, Peter, St Martin's Press Trade Division, 175 Fifth Ave, New York, NY 10010 *E-mail:* firstname.lastname@stmartins.com *Web Site:* www.stmartins.com; www.minotaurbooks.com, pg 239

Wolverton, Susan, Coe College Playwriting Festival, 1220 First Ave NE, Cedar Rapids, IA 52402 *Tel:* 319-399-8624 *Fax:* 319-399-8557 *Web Site:* www.coe.edu, pg 768

Womack, Randy L, Golden Educational Center, 857 Lake Blvd, Redding, CA 96003 *Tel:* 530-244-0101 *Toll Free Tel:* 800-800-1791 *Fax:* 530-244-5939 *E-mail:* info@goldened.com *Web Site:* goldened.com, pg 106

Womack, Theresa J, Golden Educational Center, 857 Lake Blvd, Redding, CA 96003 *Tel:* 530-244-0101 *Toll Free Tel:* 800-800-1791 *Fax:* 530-244-5939 *E-mail:* info@goldened.com *Web Site:* goldened.com, pg 106

Womer, Karin L, Down East Books, PO Box 679, Camden, ME 04843 *Tel:* 207-594-9544 *Toll Free Tel:* 800-766-1670 (ME only) *Fax:* 207-594-7215 *Web Site:* www.downeastbooks.com, pg 83

Wong, Beatrice, Unique Publications Books & Videos, 4201 W Vanowen Place, Burbank, CA 91505 *Tel:* 818-845-2656 *Toll Free Tel:* 800-332-3330 *Fax:* 818-845-7761 *E-mail:* info@cfwenterprises.com *Web Site:* www.cfwenterprises.com, pg 279

Wong, Chi-Li, AEI (Atchity Editorial/Entertainment International Inc), 9601 Wilshire Blvd, No 1202, Beverly Hills, CA 90210 *Tel:* 323-932-0407 *Fax:* 323-932-0321 *E-mail:* submissions@aeionline.com *Web Site:* www.aeionline.com, pg 618

Wong, Curtis F, Unique Publications Books & Videos, 4201 W Vanowen Place, Burbank, CA 91505 *Tel:* 818-845-2656 *Toll Free Tel:* 800-332-3330 *Fax:* 818-845-7761 *E-mail:* info@cfwenterprises.com *Web Site:* www.cfwenterprises.com, pg 279

Wong, Deborah, Duke University Press, 905 W Main St, Suite 18-B, Durham, NC 27701 *Tel:* 919-687-3600 *Toll Free Tel:* 888-651-0122 (orders only) *Fax:* 919-688-4574 *Toll Free Fax:* 888-651-0124 *Web Site:* www.dukeupress.edu, pg 84

Wong, Harry III, Kumu Kahua/UHM Theatre Dept Playwriting Contest, 46 Merchant St, Honolulu, HI 96813 *Tel:* 808-536-4222 *Fax:* 808-536-4226 *E-mail:* info@kumakahua.org *Web Site:* www.kumukahua.org, pg 783

Wong, Lane, Tortuga Press, 3919 Mayette Ave, Santa Rosa, CA 95405 *Tel:* 707-544-4720 *Fax:* 707-544-5609 *E-mail:* info@tortugapress.com *Web Site:* www.tortugapress.com, pg 272

Wong, May, NBM Publishing Inc, 555 Eighth Ave, Suite 1202, New York, NY 10018 *Tel:* 212-643-5407 *Toll Free Tel:* 800-886-1223 *Fax:* 212-643-1545 *E-mail:* admin@nbmpub.com *Web Site:* www.nbmpub.com, pg 185

Woo-Lun, Marlene, Linworth Publishing Inc, 480 E Wilson Bridge Rd, Suite L, Worthington, OH 43085-2372 *Tel:* 614-436-7107 *Toll Free Tel:* 800-786-5017 *Fax:* 614-436-9490 *E-mail:* linworth@linworthpublishing.com *Web Site:* www.linworth.com, pg 155

Wood, Ann, Penguin Group (Canada), 10 Alcorn Ave, Suite 300, Toronto, ON M4V 3B2, Canada *Tel:* 416-925-2249 *Fax:* 416-925-0068 *Web Site:* www.penguin.ca, pg 557

Wood, Beatrice, Family Process Institute Inc, c/o Eldredge, Fox & Porretti, 180 Canal View Blvd, Suite 100, Rochester, NY 14623 *Tel:* 716-879-4900 (ext 153) *Fax:* 212-744-0206 *E-mail:* info@familyprocess.org *Web Site:* www.familyprocess.org, pg 95

Wood, Deborah, Westwood Creative Artists Ltd, 94 Harbord St, Toronto, ON M5S 1G6, Canada *Tel:* 416-964-3302 *Fax:* 416-975-9209, pg 661

Wood, E Ann, Hoover Institution Press, 424 Galvez Mall, Stanford, CA 94305-6010 *Tel:* 650-723-3373 *Toll Free Tel:* 800-935-2882 *Fax:* 650-723-8626 *E-mail:* digest@hoover.stanford.edu; hooverpress@hoover.stanford.edu *Web Site:* www.hoover.org, pg 125

Wood, Eleanor, Spectrum Literary Agency, 320 Central Park W, Suite 1-D, New York, NY 10025 *Tel:* 212-362-4323 *Fax:* 212-362-4562 *Web Site:* www.spectrumliteraryagency.com, pg 656

Wood, Ira, Leapfrog Press, 95 Commercial St, Wellfleet, MA 02667-1495 *Tel:* 508-349-1925 *Fax:* 508-349-1180 *E-mail:* info@leapfrogpress.com *Web Site:* www.leapfrogpress.com, pg 151

Wood, James N, Art Institute of Chicago, 111 S Michigan Ave, Chicago, IL 60603-6110 *Tel:* 312-443-3600; 312-443-3540 (pubns); 312-443-3533 (sales & orders) *Fax:* 312-443-0849; 312-443-1334 (pubns) *E-mail:* webmaster@artic.edu *Web Site:* www.artic.edu, pg 24

Wood, John, McNeese State University, Writing Program, PO Box 92655, Lake Charles, LA 70609-0001 *Tel:* 337-475-5000; 337-475-5326 *Web Site:* www.mcneese.mfa.com, pg 753

Wood, Josh, Walker & Co, 104 Fifth Ave, 7th fl, New York, NY 10011 *Tel:* 212-727-8300 *Toll Free Tel:* 800-289-2553 *Fax:* 212-727-0984 *Toll Free Fax:* 800-218-9367 *E-mail:* firstinitiallastname@walkerbooks.com *Web Site:* www.walkerbooks.com, pg 292

Wood, Marian, G P Putnam's Sons (Hardcover), 375 Hudson St, New York, NY 10014 *Tel:* 212-366-2000 *E-mail:* online@penguinputnam.com *Web Site:* www.penguin.com, pg 223

Wood, Marian, Wood & Wood Book Services, 62 Great Ring Rd, Sandy Hook, CT 06482 *Tel:* 203-270-8206 *Fax:* 203-270-8362, pg 614

Wood, Michael, Anna Zornio Memorial Children's Theatre Playwriting Award, Paul Creative Arts, 30 College Rd, D-22, Durham, NH 03824-3538 *Tel:* 603-862-3038 *Fax:* 603-862-0298, pg 814

Wood, Philip, Ten Speed Press, PO Box 7123, Berkeley, CA 94707 *Tel:* 510-559-1600 *Toll Free Tel:* 800-841-Book *Fax:* 510-559-1629; 510-524-1052 (general) *E-mail:* order@tenspeed.com *Web Site:* www.tenspeed.com, pg 266

Wood, Dr Richard J, Infosential Press, 1162 Dominion Dr W, Mobile, AL 36695 *Tel:* 251-776-5656 *Fax:* 251-460-7181 *Web Site:* www.infosentialpress.com, pg 133

Wood, Wally, Wood & Wood Book Services, 62 Great Ring Rd, Sandy Hook, CT 06482 *Tel:* 203-270-8206 *Fax:* 203-270-8362, pg 614

Woodall, Amy H, PIA/GATF (Graphic Arts Technical Foundation), 200 Deer Run Rd, Sewickley, PA 15143-2600 *Tel:* 412-741-6860 *Toll Free Tel:* 800-910-4283 *Fax:* 412-741-2311 *E-mail:* info@gain.net *Web Site:* www.gain.net, pg 212

Woodford, Charles, Princeton Book Co Publishers, PO Box 831, Hightstown, NJ 08520-0831 *Tel:* 609-426-0602 *Toll Free Tel:* 800-220-7149 *Fax:* 609-426-1344 *E-mail:* pbc@dancehorizons.com; elysian@aosi.com *Web Site:* www.dancehorizons.com, pg 218

Woodford, Connie, Princeton Book Co Publishers, PO Box 831, Hightstown, NJ 08520-0831 *Tel:* 609-426-0602 *Toll Free Tel:* 800-220-7149 *Fax:* 609-426-1344 *E-mail:* pbc@dancehorizons.com; elysian@aosi.com *Web Site:* www.dancehorizons.com, pg 218

Woodhouse, Sharon, Lake Claremont Press, 4650 N Rockwell St, Chicago, IL 60625 *Tel:* 773-583-7800 *Fax:* 773-583-7877 *E-mail:* lcp@lakeclaremont.com *Web Site:* www.lakeclarmont.com, pg 148

Woodrow, Ralph, Ralph Woodrow Evangelistic Association Inc, PO Box 21, Palm Springs, CA 92263-0021 *Tel:* 760-323-9882 *Toll Free Tel:* 877-664-1549 *Fax:* 760-323-3982 *E-mail:* ralphwoodrow@earthlink.net *Web Site:* www.ralphwoodrow.com, pg 302

Woods, Charles, Grove/Atlantic Inc, 841 Broadway, 4th fl, New York, NY 10003-4793 *Tel:* 212-614-7850 *Toll Free Tel:* 800-521-0178 *Fax:* 212-614-7886 *Web Site:* www.groveatlantic.com, pg 110

Woods, Deb, Simon & Schuster Inc, 1230 Avenue of the Americas, New York, NY 10020 *Tel:* 212-698-7000 *Fax:* 212-698-7007 *Web Site:* www.simonsays.com, pg 249

Woods, Edward F, Kluwer Academic Publishers, 101 Philip Dr, Assinippi Park, Norwell, MA 02061 *Tel:* 781-871-6600 *Fax:* 781-871-6528; 781-681-9045 (cust serv) *E-mail:* kluwer@wkap.com *Web Site:* www.wkap.nl, pg 146

Woods, Julia, McGraw-Hill Ryerson Ltd, 300 Water St, Whitby, ON L1N 9B6, Canada *Tel:* 905-430-5000 *Toll Free Tel:* 800-565-5758 (cust serv) *Fax:* 905-430-5020 *E-mail:* johnd@mcgrawhill.ca *Web Site:* www.mcgrawhill.ca, pg 554

Woods, Paul, Meadowbrook Press, 5451 Smetana Dr, Minnetonka, MN 55343 *Tel:* 952-930-1100 *Toll Free Tel:* 800-338-2232 *Fax:* 952-930-1940 *Web Site:* www.meadowbrookpress.com, pg 169

Woodside, John, Sterling Publishing Co Inc, 387 Park Ave S, 5th fl, New York, NY 10016-8810 *Tel:* 212-532-7160 *Toll Free Tel:* 800-367-9692 *Fax:* 212-213-2495 *Web Site:* www.sterlingpub.com, pg 259

Woodsmall, John, Chelsea House Publishers LLC, 2080 Cabot Blvd W, Suite 201, Langhorne, PA 19047-1813 *Tel:* 610-353-5166 *Toll Free Tel:* 800-848-BOOK (848-2665) *Fax:* 610-359-1439 *Toll Free Fax:* 877-780-7300 *E-mail:* sales@chelseahouse.com *Web Site:* www.chelseahouse.com, pg 59

Woodsmall, John, Sundance Publishing, One Beeman Rd, Northborough, MA 01532 *Tel:* 508-571-6500 *Toll Free Tel:* 800-343-8204 *Fax:* 508-571-6510 *Toll Free Fax:* 800-456-2419 *E-mail:* info@sundancepub.com *Web Site:* www.sundancepub.com, pg 262

Woodson, Regina, Newspaper Association of America (NAA), 1921 Gallows Rd, Suite 600, Vienna, VA 22182 *Tel:* 703-902-1600 *Fax:* 703-917-0636 *Web Site:* www.naa.org, pg 695

Woodthorpe, Christopher, United Nations Publications, 2 United Nations Plaza, Rm DC2-0853, New York, NY 10017 *Tel:* 212-963-8302 *Toll Free Tel:* 800-253-9646 *Fax:* 212-963-3489 *E-mail:* publications@un.org *Web Site:* www.un.org/publications, pg 279

Woodward, Fred M, University Press of Kansas, 2501 W 15 St, Lawrence, KS 66049-3905 *Tel:* 785-864-4154; 785-864-4155 (orders) *Fax:* 785-864-4586 *E-mail:* upress@ku.edu *Web Site:* www.kansaspress.ku.edu, pg 287

Woodward, Karen, Westcliffe Publishers Inc, 2650 S Zuni St, Englewood, CO 80110-1145 *Tel:* 303-935-0900 *Toll Free Tel:* 800-523-3692 *Fax:* 303-935-0903 *E-mail:* sales@westcliffepublishers.com *Web Site:* www.westcliffepublishers.com, pg 296

Woodworth, Amy L, Crystal Productions, 1812 Johns Dr, Glenview, IL 60025 *Tel:* 847-657-8144 *Toll Free Tel:* 800-255-8629 *Fax:* 847-657-8149 *Toll Free Fax:* 800-657-8149 *E-mail:* custserv@crystalproductions.com *Web Site:* www.crystalproductions.com, pg 74

Wooldridge, Andrew, Orca Book Publishers, PO Box 468, Custer, WA 98240-0468 *Tel:* 250-380-1229 *Toll Free Tel:* 800-210-5277 *Fax:* 250-380-1892 *E-mail:* orca@orcabook.com *Web Site:* www.orcabook.com, pg 198

Wooldridge, Peggy, Naval Institute Press, 291 Wood Rd, Annapolis, MD 21402-5034 *Tel:* 410-268-6110 *Toll Free Tel:* 800-233-8764 *Fax:* 410-295-1084; 410-571-1703 (customer service) *E-mail:* webmaster@navalinstitute.org; customer@navalinstitute.org (cust serv) *Web Site:* www.navalinstitute.org, pg 185

Worcester, Anastasia, Paul H Brookes Publishing Co, PO Box 10624, Baltimore, MD 21285-0624 *Tel:* 410-337-9580 *Toll Free Tel:* 800-638-3775 *Fax:* 410-337-8539 *E-mail:* custserv@brookespublishing.com *Web Site:* www.brookespublishing.com, pg 48

Worcester, Anastasia, Health Professions Press, PO Box 10624, Baltimore, MD 21285-0624 *Tel:* 410-337-9585 *Toll Free Tel:* 888-337-8808 *Fax:* 410-337-8539 *E-mail:* custserv@healthpropress.com *Web Site:* www.healthpropress.com, pg 119

Wordsworth, Franklin, Wordsworth Communication, PO Box 9781, Alexandria, VA 22304-0468 *Tel:* 703-642-8775 *Fax:* 703-642-8775, pg 614

Workman, Carolan R, Algonquin Books of Chapel Hill, 127 Kingston Dr, Suite 105, Chapel Hill, NC 27514 *Tel:* 919-967-0108 *Fax:* 919-933-0272 *E-mail:* dialogue@algonquin.com *Web Site:* www.algonquin.com, pg 8

Workman, Carolan R, Artisan, 708 Broadway, New York, NY 10003-9555 *Tel:* 212-254-5900 *Fax:* 212-254-8098 *E-mail:* artisaninfo@workman.com *Web Site:* www.artisanbooks.com, pg 25

Workman, Carolan R, Workman Publishing Co Inc, 708 Broadway, New York, NY 10003-9555 *Tel:* 212-254-5900 *Toll Free Tel:* 800-722-7202 *Fax:* 212-254-8098 *E-mail:* info@workman.com *Web Site:* www.workman.com, pg 303

Workman, Katie, Workman Publishing Co Inc, 708 Broadway, New York, NY 10003-9555 *Tel:* 212-254-5900 *Toll Free Tel:* 800-722-7202 *Fax:* 212-254-8098 *E-mail:* info@workman.com *Web Site:* www.workman.com, pg 303

Workman, Peter, Workman Publishing Co Inc, 708 Broadway, New York, NY 10003-9555 *Tel:* 212-254-5900 *Toll Free Tel:* 800-722-7202 *Fax:* 212-254-8098 *E-mail:* info@workman.com *Web Site:* www.workman.com, pg 303

Workman, Peter, Yale University Press, 302 Temple St, New Haven, CT 06511 *Tel:* 203-432-0960; 401-531-2800 (cust serv) *Toll Free Tel:* 800-405-1619 (cust serv) *Fax:* 203-432-0948; 401-531-2801 (cust serv) *Toll Free Fax:* 800-406-9145 (cust serv) *E-mail:* customer.care@trilateral.org (cust serv) *Web Site:* www.yale.edu/yup/, pg 305

Worrell, Greg, Scholastic Education, 524 Broadway, New York, NY 10012 *Tel:* 212-343-6100 *Fax:* 212-343-6189 *Web Site:* www.scholastic.com, pg 241

Worrell, Greg, Scholastic Inc, 557 Broadway, New York, NY 10012 *Tel:* 212-343-4469 *Toll Free Tel:* 800-scholastic *Fax:* 212-343-6930 *Web Site:* www.scholastic.com, pg 242

Worrell, Greg, Scholastic Library Publishing, 90 Old Sherman Tpke, Danbury, CT 06816 *Tel:* 203-797-3500 *Toll Free Tel:* 800-621-1115 *Fax:* 203-797-3657 *Web Site:* www.scholasticlibrary.com, pg 242

Worrell, Ray, W W Norton & Company Inc, 500 Fifth Ave, New York, NY 10110-0017 *Tel:* 212-354-5500 *Toll Free Tel:* 800-233-4830 (orders & cust serv) *Fax:* 212-869-0856 *Toll Free Fax:* 800-458-6515 *Web Site:* www.wwnorton.com, pg 194

Worthington, Pepper, Mount Olive College Press, 634 Henderson St, Mount Olive, NC 28365 *Tel:* 919-658-2502 *Toll Free Tel:* 800-653-0854 *Fax:* 919-658-7180 *Web Site:* www.mountolivecollege.edu, pg 179

Wowk, Mary, Black Dog & Leventhal Publishers Inc, 151 W 19 St, 12th fl, New York, NY 10011 *Tel:* 212-647-9336 *Fax:* 212-647-9332 *E-mail:* information@bdlev.com *Web Site:* www.bdlev.com, pg 39

Wright, Beth, Publishers Association of the South (PAS), 4412 Fletcher St, Panama City, FL 32405-1017 *Tel:* 850-914-0766 *Fax:* 850-769-4348 *E-mail:* executive@pubsouth.org *Web Site:* www.pubsouth.org, pg 698

Wright, Betty, Rainbow Books Inc, PO Box 430, Highland City, FL 33846-0430 *Tel:* 863-648-4420 *Toll Free Tel:* 800-431-1579 (orders only); 888-613-2665 *Fax:* 863-647-5951 *E-mail:* rbibooks@aol.com *Web Site:* www.rainbowbooksinc.com, pg 225

Wright, Dan, Ann Wright Representatives, 165 W 46 St, Suite 1105, New York, NY 10036-2501 *Tel:* 212-764-6770 *Fax:* 212-764-5125, pg 661

Wright, Elena Dworkin, Charlesbridge Publishing Inc, 85 Main St, Watertown, MA 02472 *Tel:* 617-926-0329 *Toll Free Tel:* 800-225-3214 *Fax:* 617-926-5720 *E-mail:* books@charlesbridge.com *Web Site:* www.charlesbridge.com, pg 58

Wright, Elizabeth, The Overmountain Press, PO Box 1261, Johnson City, TN 37605-1261 *Tel:* 423-926-2691 *Toll Free Tel:* 800-992-2691 *Fax:* 423-929-2464 *Web Site:* www.overmountainpress.com, pg 200

Wright, Eve, Morning Glory Press Inc, 6595 San Haroldo Way, Buena Park, CA 90620-3748 *Tel:* 714-828-1998 *Toll Free Tel:* 888-612-8254 *Fax:* 714-828-2049 *Toll Free Tel:* 888-327-4362 *E-mail:* info@morningglorypress.com *Web Site:* www.morningglorypress.com, pg 178

Wright, G Patton, Harvard Ukrainian Research Institute, 1583 Massachusetts Ave, Cambridge, MA 02138 *Tel:* 617-496-8768 *Fax:* 617-495-8097 *E-mail:* huri@fas.harvard.edu *Web Site:* www.huri.harvard.edu, pg 117

Wright, Gary, Oxmoor House Inc, 2100 Lakeshore Dr, Birmingham, AL 35209 *Tel:* 205-445-6000; 205-445-6560 *Toll Free Tel:* 800-366-4712 *Fax:* 205-445-6078 *Web Site:* www.oxmoorhouse.com, pg 201

Wright, John D, Catholic Book Publishers Association Inc, 8404 Jamesport Dr, Rockford, IL 61108 *Tel:* 815-332-3245 *Fax:* 815-332-3476 *E-mail:* cbpa3@aol.com *Web Site:* www.cbpa.org, pg 684

Wright, Josh, Random House Inc, 1745 Broadway, New York, NY 10019 *Tel:* 212-782-9000 *Toll Free Tel:* 800-726-0600 *Web Site:* www.randomhouse.com, pg 226

Wright, Ken, Scholastic Trade Division, 557 Broadway, New York, NY 10012 *Tel:* 212-343-6100; 212-343-4685 (export sales) *Fax:* 212-343-4714 (export sales) *Web Site:* www.scholastic.com, pg 242

Wright, Martha, CEF Press, PO Box 348, Warrenton, MO 63383-0348 *Tel:* 636-456-4380 *Toll Free Tel:* 800-748-7710 *Fax:* 636-456-4321 *Web Site:* www.cefonline.com, pg 56

Wright, Matt, Ancestry Publishing, 360 W 4800 N, Provo, UT 84064 *Tel:* 801-705-7305 *Toll Free Tel:* 800-262-3787 *Fax:* 801-426-3501 *E-mail:* editor@ancestry.com; dealersales@ancestry-inc.com *Web Site:* www.ancestry.com, pg 19

Wright, Paul, University of Massachusetts Press, PO Box 429, Amherst, MA 01004-0429 *Tel:* 413-545-2217 *Toll Free Tel:* 800-537-5487 *Fax:* 413-545-1226; 410-516-6998 (fulfillment) *E-mail:* info@umpress.umass.edu; hfcustserv@mail.press.jhu.edu *Web Site:* www.umass.edu/umpress, pg 282

Wright, Tom, St Johann Press, 315 Schraalenburgh Rd, Haworth, NJ 07641 *Tel:* 201-387-1529 *Fax:* 201-501-0698, pg 238

Wright-Lampe, Betsy, The Florida Publishers Association Inc, PO Box 430, Highland City, FL 33846-0430 *Tel:* 863-647-5951 *Fax:* 863-647-5951 *E-mail:* fpabooks@aol.com *Web Site:* www.flbookpub.org, pg 687

Wrinn, Stephen M, The University Press of Kentucky, 663 S Limestone St, Lexington, KY 40508-4008 *Tel:* 859-257-8761; 859-257-8442 (mktg) *Toll Free Tel:* 800-839-6855 (orders) *Fax:* 859-323-1873 *Web Site:* www.kentuckypress.com, pg 287

Wry, Brigid, Alfred A Knopf, 1745 Broadway, New York, NY 10019 *Tel:* 212-751-2600 *Toll Free Tel:* 800-638-6460 *Fax:* 212-572-2593 *Web Site:* www.randomhouse.com/knopf, pg 146

Wu, Chih-Yu T, East Asian Legal Studies Program, 500 W Baltimore St, Baltimore, MD 21201-1786 *Tel:* 410-706-3870 *Fax:* 410-706-1516 *E-mail:* eastasia@law.umaryland.edu, pg 85

Wuenschel, Dan, Harvard University Art Museums, 32 Quincy St, Cambridge, MA 02138 *Tel:* 617-495-8286 *Fax:* 617-495-9985 *Web Site:* www.artmuseums.harvard.edu, pg 117

Wulker, Clare, The Editorial Bag, 3635 Pamela Dr, Columbus, OH 43230-1829 *Tel:* 614-939-9707 *Fax:* 614-939-9707, pg 597

Wunderlich, Margaret, Carolrhoda Books Inc, 241 First Ave N, Minneapolis, MN 55401 *Tel:* 612-332-3344 *Toll Free Tel:* 800-328-4929 *Fax:* 612-332-7615 *Toll Free Fax:* 800-332-1132 *E-mail:* info@lernerbooks.com *Web Site:* www.lernerbooks.com, pg 54

Wunderlich, Margaret, First Avenue Editions, 241 First Ave N, Minneapolis, MN 55401 *Tel:* 612-332-3344 *Toll Free Tel:* 800-328-4929 *Fax:* 612-332-7615 *Toll Free Fax:* 800-332-1132 *E-mail:* info@lernerbooks.com *Web Site:* www.lernerbooks.com, pg 97

Wunderlich, Margaret, Lerner Publications, 241 First Ave N, Minneapolis, MN 55401 *Tel:* 612-332-3344 *Toll Free Tel:* 800-328-4929 *Fax:* 612-332-7615 *Toll Free Fax:* 800-332-1132 *E-mail:* info@lernerbooks.com *Web Site:* www.lernerbooks.com, pg 152

Wunderlich, Margaret, Lerner Publishing Group, 241 First Ave N, Minneapolis, MN 55401 *Tel:* 612-332-3344 *Toll Free Tel:* 800-328-4929 *Fax:* 612-332-7615 *Toll Free Fax:* 800-332-1132 *E-mail:* info@lernerbooks.com *Web Site:* www.lernerbooks.com, pg 152

Wunderlich, Margaret, LernerClassroom, 241 First Ave N, Minneapolis, MN 55401 *Tel:* 612-332-3344 *Toll Free Tel:* 800-328-4929 *Fax:* 612-332-7615 *Toll Free Fax:* 800-332-1132 *E-mail:* info@lernerbooks.com *Web Site:* www.lernerbooks.com, pg 153

Wunderlich, Margaret, LernerSports, 241 First Ave N, Minneapolis, MN 55401 *Tel:* 612-332-3344 *Toll Free Tel:* 800-328-4929 *Fax:* 612-332-7615 *Toll Free Fax:* 800-332-1132 *E-mail:* info@lernerbooks.com *Web Site:* www.lernerbooks.com, pg 153

Wunderlich, Margaret, Runestone Press, 241 First Ave N, Minneapolis, MN 55401 *Tel:* 612-332-3344 *Toll Free Tel:* 800-328-4929; 800-332-1132 *Fax:* 612-332-7615 *E-mail:* info@lernerbooks.com *Web Site:* www.lernerbooks.com, pg 236

Wunderlich, Mark, The Nebraska Review Awards, University of Nebraska-Omaha, WFAB 212, Omaha, NE 68182-0324 *Tel:* 402-554-3159 *Fax:* 402-614-2026 *Web Site:* www.zoopress.org/nebraskareview/, pg 793

Wurfbain, Ludo J, Safari Press, 15621 Chemical Lane, Bldg B, Huntington Beach, CA 92649 *Tel:* 714-894-9080 *Toll Free Tel:* 800-451-4788 *Fax:* 714-894-4949 *E-mail:* info@safaripress.com *Web Site:* www.safaripress.com, pg 237

Wurzbacher, Eric, nursesbooks.org, The Publishing Program of ANA, 600 Maryland Ave SW, Suite 100-W, Washington, DC 20024-2571 *Tel:* 202-651-7000 *Toll Free Tel:* 800-637-0323 *Fax:* 202-651-7001 *E-mail:* anp@ana.org *Web Site:* www.nursesbooks.org, pg 194

Wyatt, Matthew, McGraw-Hill International Publishing Group, 2 Penn Plaza, New York, NY 10121 *Tel:* 212-904-2000 *Web Site:* www.mcgrawhill.com, pg 168

Wyatt, Nancy, Oxmoor House Inc, 2100 Lakeshore Dr, Birmingham, AL 35209 *Tel:* 205-445-6000; 205-445-6560 *Toll Free Tel:* 800-366-4712 *Fax:* 205-445-6078 *Web Site:* www.oxmoorhouse.com, pg 201

Wyatt-Kelsey, Nancy, Metamorphous Press, 265 N Hancock St, Portland, OR 97227 *Tel:* 503-228-4972 *Toll Free Tel:* 800-937-7771 (orders only) *Fax:* 503-223-9117 *E-mail:* metabooks@metamodels.com *Web Site:* www.metamodels.com, pg 172

Wyckoff, Joanne, Beacon Press, 41 Mount Vernon St, Boston, MA 02108 *Tel:* 617-742-2110 *Toll Free Tel:* 800-225-3362 (orders only) *Fax:* 617-723-3097; 617-742-2290 *Web Site:* www.beacon.org, pg 34

Wydra, Denise, Bedford/St Martin's, 75 Arlington St, Boston, MA 02116 *Tel:* 617-399-4000 *Fax:* 617-426-8582 *Web Site:* www.bedfordstmartins.com, pg 35

Wylde, Aidan, Bristol Publishing Enterprises, 2714 McCone Ave, Hayward, CA 94545 *Tel:* 510-783-5472 *Toll Free Tel:* 800-346-4889 *Fax:* 510-783-5492 *Web Site:* www.bristolpublishing.com, pg 48

Wylie, Andrew, The Wylie Agency Inc, 250 W 57 St, Suite 2114, New York, NY 10107 *Tel:* 212-246-0069 *Fax:* 212-586-8953 *E-mail:* mail@wylieagency.com, pg 662

Wynn, Art, Burrelle's Information Services, 75 E Northfield Rd, Livingston, NJ 07039 *Tel:* 973-992-6600 *Toll Free Tel:* 800-631-1160 *Fax:* 973-992-7675 *Toll Free Fax:* 800-898-6677 *E-mail:* directory@burrelles.com; directorysales@burrelles.com *Web Site:* www.burrellesluce.com, pg 50

Wynn, Mychal, Rising Sun Publishing, PO Box 70906, Marietta, GA 30007-0906 *Tel:* 770-518-0369 *Toll Free Tel:* 800-524-2813 *Fax:* 770-587-0862 *E-mail:* info@rspublishing.com *Web Site:* www.rspublishing.com, pg 232

Wypych, Anna, ChemTec Publishing, 38 Earswick Dr, Scarborough, ON M1E 1C6, Canada *Tel:* 416-265-2603 *Fax:* 416-265-1399 *E-mail:* info@chemtec.org; orderdesk@chemtec.org *Web Site:* www.chemtec.org, pg 540

Wyrick, Charles L Jr, Wyrick & Co, 284-A Meeting St, Charleston, SC 29401 *Tel:* 843-722-0881 *Toll Free Tel:* 800-227-5898 *Fax:* 843-722-6771 *E-mail:* wyrickco@bellsouth.net, pg 305

Wyrick, Connie H, Wyrick & Co, 284-A Meeting St, Charleston, SC 29401 *Tel:* 843-722-0881 *Toll Free Tel:* 800-227-5898 *Fax:* 843-722-6771 *E-mail:* wyrickco@bellsouth.net, pg 305

Wyrwa, Richard, W E Upjohn Institute for Employment Research, 300 S Westnedge Ave, Kalamazoo, MI 49007-4686 *Tel:* 269-343-5541; 269-343-4330 (pubns) *Toll Free Tel:* 888-227-8569 *Fax:* 269-343-7310 *E-mail:* publications@upjohninstitute.org *Web Site:* www.upjohninstitute.org, pg 288

Wysocki, Patricia, Newsletter & Electronic Publishers Association, 1501 Wilson Blvd, Suite 509, Arlington, VA 22209 *Tel:* 703-527-2333 *Toll Free Tel:* 800-356-9302 *Fax:* 703-841-0629 *Web Site:* www.newsletters.org, pg 695

Wysong, Joe, Gestalt Journal Press, PO Box 278, Gouldsboro, ME 04607-0278 *Tel:* 845-691-7192 *Fax:* 775-254-1855 *E-mail:* tgjournal@gestalt.org *Web Site:* www.gestalt.org, pg 104

Yager, Dr Jan, Hannacroix Creek Books Inc, 1127 High Ridge Rd, PMB 110, Stamford, CT 06905-1203 *Tel:* 203-321-8674 *Fax:* 203-968-0193 *E-mail:* hannacroix@aol.com *Web Site:* www.hannacroixcreekbooks.com, pg 113

Yamate, Sandra S, Polychrome Publishing Corp, 4509 N Francisco Ave, Chicago, IL 60625 *Tel:* 773-478-4455 *Fax:* 773-478-0786 *E-mail:* info@polychromebooks.com *Web Site:* www.polychromebooks.com, pg 216

Yambert, Karl, Westview Press, 5500 Central Ave, Boulder, CO 80301 *Tel:* 303-444-3541 *Toll Free Tel:* 800-386-5656 *Fax:* 720-406-7336 *E-mail:* westview.orders@perseusbooks.com *Web Site:* www.perseusbooksgroup.com; www.westviewpress.com, pg 297

Yammer, Channi, Simon & Schuster Children's Publishing, 1230 Avenue of the Americas, New York, NY 10020 *Tel:* 212-698-7000 *Web Site:* www.simonsayskids.com, pg 248

Yang, Caren, Saint Mary's Press, 702 Terrace Heights, Winona, MN 55987-1318 *Tel:* 507-457-7900 *Toll Free Tel:* 800-533-8095 *Toll Free Fax:* 800-344-9225 *E-mail:* smpress@smp.org *Web Site:* www.smp.org, pg 239

Yankelevich, Matvei, Ugly Duckling Presse, 106 Ferris St, 2nd fl, Brooklyn, NY 11231 *Tel:* 718-852-5529 *E-mail:* udp_mailbox@yahoo.com *Web Site:* www.uglyducklingpresse.org, pg 278

Yanosey, Robert J, Morning Sun Books Inc, 9 Pheasant Lane, Scotch Plains, NJ 07076 *Tel:* 908-755-5454 *Fax:* 908-755-5455 *Web Site:* www.morningsunbooks.com, pg 178

Yanulavich, Dana, State University of New York Press, 90 State St, Suite 700, Albany, NY 12207-1707 *Tel:* 518-472-5000 *Toll Free Tel:* 800-666-2211 (orders) *Fax:* 518-472-5038 *Toll Free Fax:* 800-688-2877 (orders) *E-mail:* orderbook@cupserv.org; info@sunypress.edu *Web Site:* www.sunypress.edu, pg 258

Yao, Mei C, Chinese Connection Agency, 67 Banksville Rd, Armonk, NY 10504 *Tel:* 914-765-0296 *Fax:* 914-765-0297 *E-mail:* chinese@attglobal.net, pg 624

Yarshater, Prof, Bibliotheca Persica Press, 450 Riverside Dr, Suite 4, New York, NY 10027 *Tel:* 212-851-5723 *Fax:* 212-749-9524, pg 38

Yassky, Ellin, Hugh Lauter Levin Associates Inc, 9 Burr Rd, Westport, CT 06880 *Tel:* 203-227-6422 *Fax:* 203-227-6717 *E-mail:* inquiries@hlla.com *Web Site:* www.hlla.com, pg 128

Yates, Gary, The Alexander Graham Bell Association for the Deaf & Hard of Hearing, 3417 Volta Place NW, Washington, DC 20007-2778 *Tel:* 202-337-5220 *Fax:* 202-337-8314 *Web Site:* www.agbell.org, pg 8

Yates, John, University of Toronto Press Inc, 10 St Mary St, Suite 700, Toronto, ON M4Y 2W8, Canada *Tel:* 416-978-2239 (admin) *Fax:* 416-978-4738 (admin) *Web Site:* www.utpress.utoronto.ca, pg 565

Yates, Steve, University Press of Mississippi, 3825 Ridgewood Rd, Jackson, MS 39211-6492 *Tel:* 601-432-6205 *Toll Free Tel:* 800-737-7788 *Fax:* 601-432-6217 *E-mail:* press@ihl.state.ms.us *Web Site:* www.upress.state.ms.us, pg 287

Yearout, Floyd, Bay/SOMA Publishing Inc, 444 De Haro, Suite 130, San Francisco, CA 94107 *Tel:* 415-252-4350 *Fax:* 415-252-4352 *E-mail:* info@baybooks.com *Web Site:* www.baybooks.com, pg 33

Yearwood, Gabriel, M S G-Haskell House Publishers Ltd, PO Box 190420, Brooklyn, NY 11219-0420 *Tel:* 718-435-7878 *Fax:* 718-633-7050, pg 160

Yee, Henry, St Martin's Press Trade Division, 175 Fifth Ave, New York, NY 10010 *E-mail:* firstname.lastname@stmartins.com *Web Site:* www.stmartins.com; www.minotaurbooks.com, pg 239

Yeffeth, Glenn, BenBella Books, 6440 N Central Expressway, Suite 617, Dallas, TX 75206 *Tel:* 214-750-3600 *Fax:* 214-750-3645 *E-mail:* editor@benbellabooks.com *Web Site:* www.benbellabooks.com, pg 35

Yefimov, Igor, Hermitage Publishers, PO Box 310, Tenafly, NJ 07670-0310 *Tel:* 201-894-8247 *Fax:* 201-894-5591 *Web Site:* www.hermitagepublishers.com, pg 121

Yellin, Herb, Lord John Press, 19073 Los Alimos St, Northridge, CA 91326 *Tel:* 818-363-6621 *Fax:* 818-366-6674 *Web Site:* lordjohnpress.com; lordjohnpress.net, pg 158

Yeping, Hu, Council for Research in Values & Philosophy (RVP), Catholic University, Washington, DC 20064 *Tel:* 202-319-6089 *Fax:* 202-319-6089 *Toll Free Fax:* 800-659-9962 *E-mail:* cua-rvp@cua.edu *Web Site:* www.crvp.org, pg 70

Yersak, John, Information Today, Inc, 143 Old Marlton Pike, Medford, NJ 08055-8750 *Tel:* 609-654-6266 *Toll Free Tel:* 800-300-9868 (cust serv) *Fax:* 609-654-4309 *E-mail:* custserv@infotoday.com *Web Site:* www.infotoday.com, pg 133

Yess, Mary E, The Electrochemical Society Inc, 65 S Main St, Pennington, NJ 08534-2839 *Tel:* 609-737-1902 *Fax:* 609-737-2743 *E-mail:* ecs@electrochem.org *Web Site:* www.electrochem.org, pg 88

Yezzi, David, Discovery/The Nation Poetry Contest, 92 St YM-YWHA, 1395 Lexington Ave, New York, NY 10128 *Tel:* 212-415-5759 *Web Site:* www.92y.org, pg 770

Yocum, Richard, Venture Publishing Inc, 1999 Cato Ave, State College, PA 16801 *Tel:* 814-234-4561 *Fax:* 814-234-1651 *E-mail:* vpublish@venturepublish.com *Web Site:* www.venturepublish.com, pg 290

Yodanis, Amy, Blackwell Publishers, 350 Main St, Malden, MA 02148 *Tel:* 781-388-8200 *Fax:* 781-388-8210 *E-mail:* books@blackwellpublishing.com *Web Site:* www.blackwellpublishing.com, pg 40

Yoder, Denny, International Students Inc, 7222 Commerce Center Dr, Suite 200, Colorado Springs, CO 80919 *Tel:* 719-576-2700 *Toll Free Tel:* 800-474-4147 ext 111 (orders) *Fax:* 719-576-5363 *E-mail:* information@isionline.org *Web Site:* www.isionline.org, pg 138

Yoffie, Eric H, URJ Press, 633 Third Ave, New York, NY 10017-6778 *Tel:* 212-650-4100 *Toll Free Tel:* 888-489-UAHC (489-8242) *Fax:* 212-650-4119 *E-mail:* press@urj.org *Web Site:* www.urjpress.com, pg 289

Yokitis, Phoung, Motion Picture Association of America Inc (MPAA), 1600 "I" St NW, Washington, DC 20006 *Tel:* 202-293-1966 *Fax:* 202-293-7674 *Web Site:* www.mpaa.org, pg 691

Yokoi, Rosemary, Paragon House, 2285 University Ave W, Suite 200, St Paul, MN 55114-1635 *Tel:* 651-644-3087 *Toll Free Tel:* 800-447-3709 *Fax:* 651-644-0997 *Toll Free Fax:* 800-494-0997 *E-mail:* paragon@paragonhouse.com *Web Site:* www.paragonhouse.com, pg 204

Yonce, John, Porter Sargent Publishers Inc, 11 Beacon St, Suite 1400, Boston, MA 02108 *Tel:* 617-523-1670 *Toll Free Tel:* 800-342-7470 *Fax:* 617-523-1021 *E-mail:* info@portersargent.com *Web Site:* www.portersargent.com, pg 216

York, Dolores, Reader's Digest Trade Books, Reader's Digest Rd, Pleasantville, NY 10570-7000 *Tel:* 914-244-7445 *Fax:* 914-244-7605, pg 229

Yoseloff, Julien, Associated University Presses, 2010 Eastpark Blvd, Cranbury, NJ 08512 *Tel:* 609-655-4770 *Fax:* 609-655-8366 *E-mail:* AUP440@aol.com, pg 26

Yoseloff, Julien, Bucknell University Press, c/o Associated University Presses, 2010 Eastpark Blvd, Cranbury, NJ 08512 *Tel:* 609-655-4770 *Fax:* 609-655-8366 *E-mail:* aup440@aol.com, pg 49

Yoseloff, Julien, Fairleigh Dickinson University Press, c/o Associated University Presses, 2010 Eastpark Blvd, Cranbury, NJ 08512 *Tel:* 609-655-4770 *Fax:* 609-655-8366 *E-mail:* aup440@aol.com, pg 94

Yoseloff, Julien, Susquehanna University Press, Associated University Presses, 2010 Eastpark Blvd, Cranbury, NJ 08512 *Tel:* 609-655-4770 *Fax:* 609-655-8366 *E-mail:* aup440@aol.com, pg 262

Yoseloff, Julien, University of Delaware Press, Associated University Presses, 2010 Eastpark Blvd, Cranbury, NJ 08512 *Tel:* 609-655-4770 *Fax:* 609-655-8366 *E-mail:* aup440@aol.com, pg 281

Yost, Nancy K, Lowenstein-Yost Associates Inc, 121 W 27 St, Suite 601, New York, NY 10001 *Tel:* 212-206-1630 *Fax:* 212-727-0280 *Web Site:* www.lowensteinyost.com, pg 641

Yother, Michele, Gallopade International Inc, 665 Hwy 74 S, Suite 600, Peachtree City, GA 30269 *Tel:* 770-631-4222 *Toll Free Tel:* 800-536-2GET (536-2438) *Fax:* 770-631-4810 *Toll Free Fax:* 800-871-2979 *E-mail:* info@gallopade.com *Web Site:* www.gallopade.com, pg 102

Young, Amy, Robert Miller Gallery, 524 W 26 St, New York, NY 10001 *Tel:* 212-366-4774 *Fax:* 212-366-4454 *E-mail:* rmg@robertmillergallery.com *Web Site:* www.robertmillergallery.com, pg 175

Young, Cheryl, The MacDowell Colony, 100 High St, Peterborough, NH 03458 *Tel:* 603-924-3886 *Fax:* 603-924-9142 *E-mail:* info@macdowellcolony.org *Web Site:* www.macdowellcolony.org, pg 787

Young, David, The Field Poetry Prize, 50 N Professor St, Oberlin, OH 44074-1095 *Tel:* 440-775-8408 *Fax:* 440-775-8124 *E-mail:* oc.press@oberlin.edu *Web Site:* www.oberlin.edu/ocpress, pg 773

Young, David, Oberlin College Press, 50 N Professor St, Oberlin, OH 44074-1095 *Tel:* 440-775-8408 *Fax:* 440-775-8124 *E-mail:* oc.press@oberlin.edu *Web Site:* www.oberlin.edu/ocpress, pg 195

Young, Debby, Harbor Press Inc, 5713 Wollochet Dr NW, PO Box 1656, Gig Harbor, WA 98335 *Tel:* 253-851-5190 *Fax:* 253-851-5191 *E-mail:* info@harborpress.com *Web Site:* harborpress.com, pg 114

Young, Denise, The RGU Group, 560 W Southern Ave, Tempe, AZ 85282 *Tel:* 480-736-9862 *Toll Free Tel:* 800-266-5265 *Fax:* 480-736-9863 *Toll Free Fax:* 800-973-6694 *E-mail:* info@thergugroup.com *Web Site:* www.thergugroup.com, pg 232

Young, Emily, Duke University Press, 905 W Main St, Suite 18-B, Durham, NC 27701 *Tel:* 919-687-3600 *Toll Free Tel:* 888-651-0122 (orders only) *Fax:* 919-688-4574 *Toll Free Fax:* 888-651-0124 *Web Site:* www.dukeupress.edu, pg 84

Young, Geoffrey, The Figures, 5 Castle Hill, Great Barrington, MA 01230 *Tel:* 413-528-2552 *Web Site:* www.geoffreyyoung.com, pg 96

Young, Glenn, Applause Theatre & Cinema Books, 151 W 46 St, New York, NY 10036 *Tel:* 212-575-9265 *Fax:* 646-562-5852 *E-mail:* info@applausepub.com *Web Site:* www.applausepub.com, pg 21

Young, Gretchen, Hyperion, 77 W 66 St, 11th fl, New York, NY 10023-6298 *Tel:* 212-456-0100 *Toll Free Tel:* 800-759-0190 (cust serv) *Fax:* 212-456-0157 *Web Site:* hyperionbooks.com, pg 129

Young, Hilary, Regal Books, 1957 Eastman Ave, Ventura, CA 93003 *Tel:* 805-644-9721 *Toll Free Tel:* 800-446-7735 (orders) *Fax:* 805-644-9728 (editorial); 805-644-4729 (purchasing); 805-650-8713 (sales & corp serv); 805-658-3388 (orders) *Toll Free Fax:* 800-860-3109 (orders) *E-mail:* info@regalbooks.com *Web Site:* www.gospellight.com, pg 230

Young, Jeffrey R, Dissertation.com, 23331 Water Circle, Boca Raton, FL 33486-8540 *Tel:* 561-750-4344 *Toll Free Tel:* 800-636-8329 *Fax:* 561-750-6797 *E-mail:* publisher4@dissertation.com; orders4@dissertation.com *Web Site:* www.dissertation.com, pg 81

Young, Jenna, Limelight Editions, 512 Newark Pompton Tpke, Pompton Plains, NJ 07444 *Tel:* 973-835-6375; 908-788-5753 (orders only) *Fax:* 973-835-6504; 908-237-2407 (orders only) *E-mail:* info@limelighteditions.com *Web Site:* www.limelighteditions.com, pg 155

Young, Lawrence, Higginson Book Co, 148 Washington St, Salem, MA 01970 *Tel:* 978-745-7170 *Fax:* 978-745-8025 *E-mail:* orders@higginsonbooks.com; higginson@cove.com *Web Site:* www.higginsonbooks.com, pg 122

Young, Marian, The Young Agency, 156 Fifth Ave, Suite 617, New York, NY 10010 *Tel:* 212-229-2612 *Fax:* 212-924-6609, pg 662

Young, Michelle D, University Council for Educational Administration, Univ of Missouri, 205 Hill Hall, Columbia, MO 65211-2185 *Tel:* 573-884-8300 *Fax:* 573-884-8302 *E-mail:* ucea@missouri.edu *Web Site:* www.ucea.org, pg 280

Young, Sherrie, National Book Awards, 95 Madison Ave, Suite 709, New York, NY 10016 *Tel:* 212-685-0261 *Fax:* 212-213-6570 *E-mail:* nationalbook@national.org *Web Site:* www.nationalbook.org, pg 791

Young, Tita, International Research Center for Energy & Economic Development, 850 Willowbrook Rd, Boulder, CO 80302 *Tel:* 303-442-4014 *Fax:* 303-442-5042 *E-mail:* iceed@colorado.edu *Web Site:* www.iceed.org, pg 138

Young, Woody, Joy Publishing, PO Box 9901, Fountain Valley, CA 92708 *Tel:* 714-545-4321 *Toll Free Tel:* 800-454-8228 *Fax:* 714-708-2099 *Web Site:* www.joypublishing.com; www.kit-cat.com, pg 142

Youngdahl, Jon, Vincent Astor Memorial Leadership Essay Contest, 291 Wood Rd, Annapolis, MD 21402-5034 *Tel:* 410-268-6110 *Toll Free Tel:* 800-233-8764 *Fax:* 410-295-1049 *E-mail:* articlesubmission@navalinstitute.org *Web Site:* www.navalinstitute.org, pg 760

Youngdahl, Jon, Arleigh Burke Essay Contest, 291 Wood Rd, Annapolis, MD 21402-5034 *Tel:* 410-268-6110 *Toll Free Tel:* 800-233-8764 *Fax:* 410-295-1049 *E-mail:* essays@navalinstitute.org *Web Site:* www.navalinstitute.org, pg 764

Younger, Bob, Morningside Bookshop, 260 Oak St, Dayton, OH 45410 *Tel:* 937-461-6736 *Toll Free Tel:* 800-648-9710 *Fax:* 937-461-4260 *E-mail:* msbooks@erinet.com *Web Site:* www.morningsidebooks.com, pg 178

Younger, Mary E, Morningside Bookshop, 260 Oak St, Dayton, OH 45410 *Tel:* 937-461-6736 *Toll Free Tel:* 800-648-9710 *Fax:* 937-461-4260 *E-mail:* msbooks@erinet.com *Web Site:* www.morningsidebooks.com, pg 178

Yowell, J B, Public Utilities Reports Inc, 8229 Boone Blvd, Suite 400, Vienna, VA 22182 *Tel:* 703-847-7720 *Toll Free Tel:* 800-368-5001 *Fax:* 703-847-0683 *E-mail:* pur@pur.com *Web Site:* www.pur.com, pg 221

Yranski, Joseph M, George Freedley Memorial Award, Queens College, CUNY, Flushing, NY 11367 *Tel:* 718-997-3672 *Fax:* 718-997-3753 *Web Site:* tla.library.unt.edu, pg 775

Yranski, Joseph M, The Theatre Library Association Award, Queens College, CUNY, Flushing, NY 11367 *Tel:* 718-997-3762 *Fax:* 718-997-3753 *Web Site:* tla.library.unt.edu, pg 808

Ytreberg, Martin, Pacific Press Publishing Association, 1350 N Kings Rd, Nampa, ID 83687-3193 *Tel:* 208-465-2500 *Toll Free Tel:* 800-447-7377 *Fax:* 208-465-2531 *Web Site:* www.pacificpress.com, pg 202

Yu, C Dick, Canadian Scholars' Press Inc, 180 Bloor St W, Suite 801, Toronto, ON M5S 2V6, Canada *Tel:* 416-929-2774 *Fax:* 416-929-1926 *E-mail:* info@cspi.org *Web Site:* www.cspi.org; www.womenspress.ca, pg 539

Yubasz, Wayne, Birkhauser Boston, 675 Massachusetts Ave, Cambridge, MA 02139 *Tel:* 617-876-2333 *Toll Free Tel:* 800-777-4643 (cust serv) *Fax:* 617-876-1272 *E-mail:* service@birkhauser.com *Web Site:* www.birkhauser.com, pg 39

Yudell, Deenie, Getty Publications, 1200 Getty Center Dr, Suite 500, Los Angeles, CA 90049-1682 *Tel:* 310-440-7365 *Fax:* 310-440-7758 *E-mail:* pubsinfo@getty.edu *Web Site:* www.getty.edu/bookstore, pg 104

Yuen, Christine, Dominie Press Inc, 1949 Kellogg Ave, Carlsbad, CA 92008 *Tel:* 760-431-8000 *Toll Free Tel:* 800-232-4570 *Fax:* 760-431-8777 *E-mail:* info@dominie.com *Web Site:* www.dominie.com, pg 82

Yuen, Raymond, Dominie Press Inc, 1949 Kellogg Ave, Carlsbad, CA 92008 *Tel:* 760-431-8000 *Toll Free Tel:* 800-232-4570 *Fax:* 760-431-8777 *E-mail:* info@dominie.com *Web Site:* www.dominie.com, pg 82

Yukawa, Ted, Heian International Inc, 20655 S Western Ave, Suite 105, Torrance, CA 90501 *Tel:* 310-328-7200 *Fax:* 310-328-7676 *E-mail:* heianemail@earthlink.net *Web Site:* heian.com, pg 120

Yule, Sean, Alfred A Knopf, 1745 Broadway, New York, NY 10019 *Tel:* 212-751-2600 *Toll Free Tel:* 800-638-6460 *Fax:* 212-572-2593 *Web Site:* www.randomhouse.com/knopf, pg 146

Yule, Sean, Pantheon Books/Schocken Books, 1745 Broadway, New York, NY 10019 *Tel:* 212-751-2600 *Toll Free Tel:* 800-638-6460 *Fax:* 212-572-6030, pg 203

Yun, Lisa, Binghamton University Writing Program, c/o Dept of English, PO Box 6000, Binghamton, NY 13902-6000 *Tel:* 607-777-2168 *Fax:* 607-777-2408, pg 751

Yun, Oliver, Theta Reports, 1775 Broadway, Suite 511, New York, NY 10019 *Tel:* 212-262-8230 *Fax:* 212-262-8234 *Web Site:* www.thetareports.com, pg 268

Yung, Cecilia, G P Putnam's Sons (Children's), 345 Hudson St, New York, NY 10014 *Tel:* 212-366-2000 *E-mail:* online@penguinputnam.com *Web Site:* www.penguin.com, pg 223

Yurwit, Lisa M, Paul H Brookes Publishing Co, PO Box 10624, Baltimore, MD 21285-0624 *Tel:* 410-337-9580 *Toll Free Tel:* 800-638-3775 *Fax:* 410-337-8539 *E-mail:* custserv@brookespublishing.com *Web Site:* www.brookespublishing.com, pg 48

Yurwit, Lisa M, Health Professions Press, PO Box 10624, Baltimore, MD 21285-0624 *Tel:* 410-337-9585 *Toll Free Tel:* 888-337-8808 *Fax:* 410-337-8539 *E-mail:* custserv@healthpropress.com *Web Site:* www.healthpropress.com, pg 119

Zabel, Bryce, Academy of Television Arts & Sciences (ATAS), 5220 Lankershim Blvd, North Hollywood, CA 91601-3109 *Tel:* 818-754-2800 *Fax:* 818-761-2827 *Web Site:* www.emmys.tv, pg 675

Zaber, Trace Edward, Amber Quill Press LLC, PO Box 265, Indian Hills, CO 80454 *E-mail:* customer_service@amberquillpress.com *Web Site:* amberquill.com, pg 10

Zaccaria, Jim, Shambhala Publications Inc, Horticultural Hall, 300 Massachusetts Ave, Boston, MA 02115 *Tel:* 617-424-0030 *Toll Free Tel:* 888-424-2329 (orders only) *Fax:* 617-236-1563; 303-665-5292 (orders only) *E-mail:* editors@shambhala.com *Web Site:* www. shambhala.com, pg 245

Zacharius, Steven, Kensington Publishing Corp, 850 Third Ave, New York, NY 10022 *Tel:* 212-407-1500 *Toll Free Tel:* 800-221-2647 *Fax:* 212-935-0699 *Web Site:* www.kensingtonbooks.com, pg 145

Zacharius, Walter, Kensington Publishing Corp, 850 Third Ave, New York, NY 10022 *Tel:* 212-407-1500 *Toll Free Tel:* 800-221-2647 *Fax:* 212-935-0699 *Web Site:* www.kensingtonbooks.com, pg 145

Zachary, Lane, Zachary Shuster Harmsworth Agency, 1776 Broadway, New York, NY 10019 *Tel:* 212-765-6900 *Fax:* 212-765-6490 *Web Site:* www.zshliterary. com, pg 662

Zachry-Reynolds, Lauren, University of Texas Press, PO Box 7819, Austin, TX 78713-7819 *Tel:* 512-471-7233 *Fax:* 512-232-7178 *E-mail:* utpress@uts.cc.utexas.edu *Web Site:* www.utexas.edu/utpress, pg 267

Zack, Andrew, The Zack Company Inc, 243 W 70 St, Suite 8-D, New York, NY 10023-4366 *Tel:* 212-712-2400 *Fax:* 212-712-9110 *Web Site:* www. zackcompany.com, pg 662

Zack, Elizabeth, BookCrafters LLC, Box C, Convent Station, NJ 07961 *Tel:* 973-984-7880 *Web Site:* bookcraftersllc.com, pg 592

Zackheim, Adrian, Prentice Hall Press, 375 Hudson St, New York, NY 10014 *Tel:* 212-366-2000, pg 217

Zadrozny, Mark, Cambridge University Press, 40 W 20 St, New York, NY 10011-4211 *Tel:* 212-924-3900 *Toll Free Tel:* 800-899-5222 *Fax:* 212-691-3239 *Web Site:* www.cambridge.org, pg 52

Zafian, Anne, Time Warner Book Group, 1271 Avenue of the Americas, New York, NY 10020 *Tel:* 212-522-7200 *Fax:* 212-522-7991 *Web Site:* www.twbookmark. com, pg 272

Zafran, Enid, American Society of Indexers Inc (ASI), 10200 W 44 Ave, Suite 304, Wheat Ridge, CO 80033 *Tel:* 303-463-2887 *Fax:* 303-422-8894 *E-mail:* info@ asindexing.org *Web Site:* www.asindexing.org, pg 678

Zafran, Enid, H W Wilson Co Indexing Award, 10200 W 44 Ave, Suite 304, Wheat Ridge, CO 80033 *Tel:* 303-463-2887 *Fax:* 303-422-8894 *E-mail:* info@ asindexing.org *Web Site:* www.asindexing.org, pg 811

Zagat, Eugene H, Zagat Survey, 4 Columbus Circle, New York, NY 10019 *Tel:* 212-977-6000 *Toll Free Tel:* 800-333-3421 (gen inquiries); 888-371-5440 (orders); 800-540-9609 (corp sales) *Fax:* 212-977-9760; 802-864-9846 (order related) *E-mail:* corpsales@zagat.com; shop@zagat.com *Web Site:* www.zagat.com, pg 306

Zagat, Nina S, Zagat Survey, 4 Columbus Circle, New York, NY 10019 *Tel:* 212-977-6000 *Toll Free Tel:* 800-333-3421 (gen inquiries); 888-371-5440 (orders); 800-540-9609 (corp sales) *Fax:* 212-977-9760; 802-864-9846 (order related) *E-mail:* corpsales@zagat.com; shop@zagat.com *Web Site:* www.zagat.com, pg 306

Zagury, Carolyn, Vista Publishing Inc, 151 Delaware Ave, Oakhurst, NJ 07755 *E-mail:* info@vistapubl.com; sales@vistapubl.com *Web Site:* www.vistapubl.com, pg 291

Zagury, David, Vista Publishing Inc, 151 Delaware Ave, Oakhurst, NJ 07755 *E-mail:* info@vistapubl.com; sales@vistapubl.com *Web Site:* www.vistapubl.com, pg 291

Zajdel, George, ASTM International, 100 Barr Harbor Dr, West Conshohocken, PA 19428 *Tel:* 610-832-9500 *Fax:* 610-832-9555 *E-mail:* service@astm.org *Web Site:* www.astm.org, pg 27

Zaks, Rodnay, SYBEX Inc, 1151 Marina Village Pkwy, Alameda, CA 94501 *Tel:* 510-523-8233 *Toll Free Tel:* 800-227-2346 *Fax:* 510-523-2373 *E-mail:* pressinfo@sybex.com *Web Site:* www.sybex. com, pg 263

Zapel, A Mark, Meriwether Publishing Ltd/ Contemporary Drama Service, 885 Elkton Dr, Colorado Springs, CO 80907-3557 *Tel:* 719-594-4422

Toll Free Tel: 800-937-5297 *Fax:* 719-594-9916 *Toll Free Tel:* 888-594-4436 *E-mail:* merpcds@aol.com *Web Site:* www.meriwether.com, pg 171

Zapel, Arthur L, Meriwether Publishing Ltd/ Contemporary Drama Service, 885 Elkton Dr, Colorado Springs, CO 80907-3557 *Tel:* 719-594-4422 *Toll Free Tel:* 800-937-5297 *Fax:* 719-594-9916 *Toll Free Tel:* 888-594-4436 *E-mail:* merpcds@aol.com *Web Site:* www.meriwether.com, pg 171

Zapel, Ted, Meriwether Publishing Ltd/Contemporary Drama Service, 885 Elkton Dr, Colorado Springs, CO 80907-3557 *Tel:* 719-594-4422 *Toll Free Tel:* 800-937-5297 *Fax:* 719-594-9916 *Toll Free Fax:* 888-594-4436 *E-mail:* merpcds@aol.com *Web Site:* www.meriwether. com, pg 171

Zappala, Hank, Emerson College Publishing Seminars, 120 Boylston St, Boston, MA 02116-8750 *Tel:* 617-824-8280 *Fax:* 617-824-8158 *E-mail:* continuing@ emerson.edu *Web Site:* www.emerson.edu/ce, pg 743

Zappala, Jenny, Pacific Northwest Writers Conference, 23607 Hwy 99, Suite 2C, Edmonds, WA 98026 *Tel:* 425-673-2665 *E-mail:* staff@pnwa.org *Web Site:* www.pnwa.org, pg 746

Zarrello, Michael, Information Today, Inc, 143 Old Marlton Pike, Medford, NJ 08055-8750 *Tel:* 609-654-6266 *Toll Free Tel:* 800-300-9868 (cust serv) *Fax:* 609-654-4309 *E-mail:* custserv@infotoday.com *Web Site:* www.infotoday.com, pg 133

Zeckendorf, Susan, Susan Zeckendorf Associates Inc, 171 W 57 St, Suite 11-B, New York, NY 10019 *Tel:* 212-245-2928, pg 663

Zeda, Reina, Demos Medical Publishing LLC, 386 Park Ave S, Suite 201, New York, NY 10016 *Tel:* 212-683-0072 *Toll Free Tel:* 800-532-8663 *Fax:* 212-683-0118 *E-mail:* info@demospub.com *Web Site:* www. demosmedpub.com, pg 79

Zeiders, Barbara, Zeiders & Associates, PO Box 670, Lewisburg, PA 17837 *Tel:* 570-524-4315 *Fax:* 570-524-4315, pg 615

Zeig, Jeffrey K, Zeig, Tucker & Theisen Inc, 3614 N 24 St, Phoenix, AZ 85016 *Tel:* 602-957-1270 *Toll Free Fax:* 800-688-2877 *E-mail:* zttorders@mindspring.com *Web Site:* www.zeigtucker.com, pg 307

Zeitlin, Randy, Cambridge University Press, 40 W 20 St, New York, NY 10011-4211 *Tel:* 212-924-3900 *Toll Free Tel:* 800-899-5222 *Fax:* 212-691-3239 *Web Site:* www.cambridge.org, pg 52

Zeligman, Peter, Empire Press Media/Avant-Guide, 444 Madison Ave, 35th fl, New York, NY 10122 *Tel:* 212-563-1003 *Fax:* 212-536-2419 *E-mail:* info@avantguide.com; editor@avantguide.com *Web Site:* www.avantguide.com, pg 90

Zell, Carla, Conciliar Press, 10090 "A" Hwy 9, Ben Lomond, CA 95005 *Tel:* 831-336-5118 *Toll Free Tel:* 800-967-7377 *Fax:* 831-336-8882 *E-mail:* marketing@conciliarpress.com *Web Site:* www.conciliarpress.com, pg 66

Zell, Thomas, Conciliar Press, 10090 "A" Hwy 9, Ben Lomond, CA 95005 *Tel:* 831-336-5118 *Toll Free Tel:* 800-967-7377 *Fax:* 831-336-8882 *E-mail:* marketing@conciliarpress.com *Web Site:* www.conciliarpress.com, pg 66

Zeller, Ann E, The Direct Marketing Association Inc (The DMA), 1120 Avenue of the Americas, New York, NY 10036-6700 *Tel:* 212-768-7277 *Fax:* 212-768-4547 *E-mail:* dma@the-dma.org; customerservice@the-dma.org *Web Site:* www.the-dma.org, pg 80

Zellmann, Stacy, University of Minnesota Press, 111 Third Ave S, Suite 290, Minneapolis, MN 55401-2520 *Tel:* 612-627-1970 *Fax:* 612-627-1980 *E-mail:* ump@ tc.umn.edu *Web Site:* www.upress.umn.edu, pg 282

Zelman, Bert N, Publishers Workshop, 63 Montague St, Brooklyn Heights, NY 11201-3350 *Tel:* 718-797-1157 *Fax:* 718-797-1157, pg 609

Zenner, Boyd, The University of Virginia Press, PO Box 400318, Charlottesville, VA 22904-4318 *Tel:* 434-924-3468 (cust serv); 434-924-3469 (cust serv) *Toll*

Free Tel: 800-831-3406 (cust serv) *Fax:* 434-982-2655 *Toll Free Fax:* 877-288-6400 *E-mail:* upressvirginia@ virginia.edu *Web Site:* www.upressvirginia.edu, pg 285

Zeoli, Stephen, Safer Society Foundation Inc, 8-10 Conant Sq, Brandon, VT 05733 *Tel:* 802-247-3132 *Fax:* 802-247-4233 *E-mail:* ssfi@sover.net *Web Site:* www.safersociety.org, pg 237

Zerla, Aimee F, The American Ceramic Society, 735 Ceramic Place, Westerville, OH 43081-8720 *Tel:* 614-794-5890 *Fax:* 614-794-5892 *E-mail:* info@ceramics. org *Web Site:* www.ceramics.org, pg 12

Zerman, Melvyn B, Limelight Editions, 512 Newark Pompton Tpke, Pompton Plains, NJ 07444 *Tel:* 973-835-6375; 908-788-5753 (orders only) *Fax:* 973-835-6504; 908-237-2407 (orders only) *E-mail:* info@limelighteditions.com *Web Site:* www. limelighteditions.com, pg 155

Zerter, Bill, John Wiley & Sons Canada Ltd, 6045 Fremont Blvd, Mississauga, ON L5R 4J3, Canada *Tel:* 416-236-4433 *Toll Free Tel:* 800-467-4797 (orders only) *Fax:* 416-236-4447; 416-236-8743 (cust serv) *Toll Free Fax:* 800-565-6802 (orders) *E-mail:* canada@wiley.com *Web Site:* www.wiley.ca, pg 567

Zerter, William, Canadian Publishers' Council (CPC), 250 Merton St, Suite 203, Toronto, ON M4S 1B1, Canada *Tel:* 416-322-7011 *Fax:* 416-322-6999 *E-mail:* pubadmin@pubcouncil.ca *Web Site:* www. pubcouncil.ca, pg 683

Zettersten, Rolf, Warner Faith (Christian Book Division of Time Warner Book Group), 2 Creekside Crossing, 10 Cadillac Dr, Suite 220, Brentwood, TN 37027 *Tel:* 615-221-0996 *Fax:* 615-221-0962 *Web Site:* www. twbookmark.com, pg 293

Zevnik, Brian L P, Alexander Hamilton Institute, 70 Hilltop Rd, Ramsey, NJ 07446-1119 *Tel:* 201-825-3377 *Toll Free Tel:* 800-879-2441 *Fax:* 201-825-8696 *E-mail:* editorial@ahipubs.com *Web Site:* www. ahipubs.com, pg 112

Zhang, Kathi, John Wiley & Sons Inc Education Publishing Group, 111 River St, Hoboken, NJ 07030 *Tel:* 201-748-6000 *Fax:* 201-748-6088 *E-mail:* info@ wiley.com *Web Site:* www.wiley.com, pg 300

Zheutlin, Leslie, Harvard Business School Press, 300 N Beacon St, Watertown, MA 02472 *Tel:* 617-783-7400 *Toll Free Tel:* 888-500-1016 *Fax:* 617-783-7664 *E-mail:* bookpublisher@mail1.hbsp.harvard.edu *Web Site:* www.hbsp.harvard.edu, pg 116

Zhivago, Kristin, Smokin' Donut Books, 381 Seaside Dr, Jamestown, RI 02835 *Tel:* 401-423-2400 *Toll Free Tel:* 877-474-8738 *Fax:* 401-423-2700 *E-mail:* info@ smokindonut.com *Web Site:* www.smokindonut.com, pg 574

Ziccardi, Anthony, Random House Publishing Group, 1745 Broadway, New York, NY 10019 *Toll Free Tel:* 800-200-3552 *Toll Free Fax:* 800-200-3552 *Web Site:* www.randomhouse.com, pg 227

Zickgraf, Ralph, F A Davis Co, 1915 Arch St, Philadelphia, PA 19103 *Tel:* 215-568-2270 *Toll Free Tel:* 800-523-4049 *Fax:* 215-568-5065 *E-mail:* info@ fadavis.com *Web Site:* www.fadavis.com, pg 76

Ziegler, Alan, Columbia University School of the Arts, Writing Division, 415 Dodge Hall, School of the Arts, Columbia University, 2960 Broadway, New York, NY 10027 *Tel:* 212-854-4391 *Fax:* 212-854-7704 *E-mail:* writing@columbia.edu *Web Site:* www. columbia.edu/cu/arts/writing, pg 752

Zielinski, Mark, Facts on File Inc, 132 W 31 St, 17th fl, New York, NY 10001 *Tel:* 212-967-8800 *Toll Free Tel:* 800-322-8755 *Fax:* 212-967-9196 *Toll Free Fax:* 800-678-3633 *E-mail:* custserv@factsonfile.com *Web Site:* www.factsonfile.com, pg 93

Ziemacki, Richard, Cambridge University Press, 40 W 20 St, New York, NY 10011-4211 *Tel:* 212-924-3900 *Toll Free Tel:* 800-899-5222 *Fax:* 212-691-3239 *Web Site:* www.cambridge.org, pg 52

Zwettler, Rob, McGraw-Hill/Irwin, 1333 Burr Ridge Pkwy, Burr Ridge, IL 60527 *Tel:* 630-789-4000 *Toll Free Tel:* 800-338-3987 (cust serv) *Fax:* 630-789-6942; 614-755-5645 (cust serv) *Web Site:* www.mhhe.com, pg 168

Zychowicz, James L, A-R Editions Inc, 8551 Research Way, Suite 180, Middleton, WI 53562 *Tel:* 608-836-9000 *Toll Free Tel:* 800-736-0070 (US book orders only) *Fax:* 608-831-8200 *E-mail:* info@areditions.com *Web Site:* www.areditions.com, pg 2

Zylstra, Judy, Wm B Eerdmans Publishing Co, 255 Jefferson Ave SE, Grand Rapids, MI 49503 *Tel:* 616-459-4591 *Toll Free Tel:* 800-253-7521 *Fax:* 616-459-6540 *E-mail:* sales@eerdmans.com *Web Site:* www.eerdmans.com, pg 88

Publishers Toll Free Directory

A & M Books, Rehoboth Beach, DE *Toll Free Tel:* 800-489-7662, pg 569

A D D Warehouse, Plantation, FL *Toll Free Tel:* 800-233-9273, pg 1

A-R Editions Inc, Middleton, WI *Toll Free Tel:* 800-736-0070 (US book orders only), pg 2

AAPG (American Association of Petroleum Geologists), Tulsa, OK *Toll Free Tel:* 800-364-AAPG (364-2274) *Toll Free Fax:* 800-898-2274, pg 2

Abacus, Grand Rapids, MI *Toll Free Tel:* 800-451-4319, pg 2

Abbeville Publishing Group, New York, NY *Toll Free Tel:* 800-ART-BOOK (278-2665), pg 2

Abbey Press, St Meinrad, IN *Toll Free Tel:* 800-962-4760, pg 2

ABC-CLIO, Santa Barbara, CA *Toll Free Tel:* 800-368-6868, pg 2

Abdo Publishing, Edina, MN *Toll Free Tel:* 800-800-1312, pg 3

ABELexpress, Carnegie, PA *Toll Free Tel:* 800-542-9001, pg 3

ABI Professional Publications, Saint Petersburg, FL *Toll Free Tel:* 800-551-7776, pg 3

Abingdon Press, Nashville, TN *Toll Free Tel:* 800-251-3320, pg 3

Abrams & Co Publishers Inc, Waterbury, CT *Toll Free Tel:* 800-227-9120 *Toll Free Fax:* 800-737-3322, pg 3

Harry N Abrams Inc, New York, NY *Toll Free Tel:* 800-345-1359, pg 3

Absey & Co Inc, Spring, TX *Toll Free Tel:* 888-412-2739, pg 4

Academic Press, San Diego, CA *Toll Free Tel:* 800-321-5068 (cust serv), pg 4

Academy Chicago Publishers, Chicago, IL *Toll Free Tel:* 800-248-7323, pg 4

The Academy of Producer Insurance Studies Inc, Austin, TX *Toll Free Tel:* 800-526-2777, pg 4

Accent Publications, Colorado Springs, CO *Toll Free Tel:* 800-708-5550; 800-535-2905 (cust serv) *Toll Free Fax:* 800-430-0726, pg 4

Acres USA, Austin, TX *Toll Free Tel:* 800-355-5313, pg 4

Acropolis Books Inc, Atlanta, GA *Toll Free Tel:* 800-773-9923, pg 569

ACS Publications, San Diego, CA *Toll Free Tel:* 800-888-9983 (orders only), pg 4

ACTA Publications, Chicago, IL *Toll Free Tel:* 800-397-2282 *Toll Free Fax:* 800-397-0079, pg 4

Action Publishing LLC, Glendale, CA *Toll Free Tel:* 800-705-7482, pg 5

ACU Press, Abilene, TX *Toll Free Tel:* 800-444-4228, pg 5

Adams Media, An F+W Publications Co, Avon, MA *Toll Free Fax:* 800-872-5628, pg 5

ADC The Map People, Alexandria, VA *Toll Free Tel:* 800-232-6277, pg 5

Addicus Books Inc, Omaha, NE *Toll Free Tel:* 800-352-2873 (orders), pg 5

Adirondack Mountain Club, Lake George, NY *Toll Free Tel:* 800-395-8080, pg 5

Advantage Publishers Group, San Diego, CA *Toll Free Tel:* 800-284-3580 *Toll Free Fax:* 800-499-3822, pg 6

Adventure Publications, Cambridge, MN *Toll Free Tel:* 800-678-7006, pg 6

Aegean Park Press, Walnut Creek, CA *Toll Free Tel:* 800-736-3587 (orders only), pg 6

Aerial Photography Services Inc, Charlotte, NC *Toll Free Fax:* 800-204-4910, pg 6

African American Images, Chicago, IL *Toll Free Tel:* 800-552-1991, pg 6

Agathon Press, Bronx, NY *Toll Free Tel:* 800-488-8040 (orders only), pg 6

AGS Publishing, Circle Pines, MN *Toll Free Tel:* 800-328-2560 *Toll Free Fax:* 800-471-8457, pg 7

AIMS Education Foundation, Fresno, CA *Toll Free Tel:* 888-733-2467, pg 7

Aio Publishing Co LLC, Charleston, SC *Toll Free Tel:* 888-287-9888, pg 7

Alba House, Staten Island, NY *Toll Free Tel:* 800-343-2522, pg 7

The Alban Institute Inc, Herndon, VA *Toll Free Tel:* 800-486-1318, pg 7

Alexander Street Press LLC, Alexandria, VA *Toll Free Tel:* 800-889-5937, pg 8

Alfred Publishing Company Inc, Van Nuys, CA *Toll Free Tel:* 800-292-6122 (dealer sales) *Toll Free Fax:* 800-632-1928 (dealer sales), pg 8

Algora Publishing, New York, NY *Toll Free Tel:* 888-405-0689, pg 8

ALI-ABA Committee on Continuing Professional Education, Philadelphia, PA *Toll Free Tel:* 800-CLE-NEWS, pg 8

Allen D Bragdon Publishers Inc, South Yarmouth, MA *Toll Free Tel:* 877-8-SMARTS (876-2787), pg 9

Allied Health Publications, Salt Lake City, UT *Toll Free Tel:* 800-221-7374 (enrollment); 800-497-7157, pg 9

Allworth Press, New York, NY *Toll Free Tel:* 800-491-2808, pg 9

ALPHA Publications of America Inc, Tucson, AZ *Toll Free Tel:* 800-528-3494 *Toll Free Fax:* 800-770-4329, pg 9

Alpine Publications Inc, Loveland, CO *Toll Free Tel:* 800-777-7257 (orders only), pg 9

Althos Publishing, Fuquay-Varina, NC *Toll Free Tel:* 800-227-9681, pg 10

Altitude Publishing Canada Ltd, Canmore, AB Canada *Toll Free Tel:* 800-957-6888 *Toll Free Fax:* 800-957-1477, pg 535

AMACOM Books, New York, NY *Toll Free Tel:* 800-262-9699 (cust serv), pg 10

Frank Amato Publications Inc, Portland, OR *Toll Free Tel:* 800-541-9498, pg 10

Ambassador Books Inc, Worcester, MA *Toll Free Tel:* 800-577-0909, pg 10

Amber Lotus, Berkeley, CA *Toll Free Tel:* 800-625-8378 (orders only), pg 10

Amboy Associates, Escondido, CA *Toll Free Tel:* 800-448-4023, pg 10

America West Publishers, Carson City, NV *Toll Free Tel:* 800-729-4131 *Toll Free Fax:* 877-726-2632, pg 10

American Academy of Orthopaedic Surgeons, Rosemont, IL *Toll Free Tel:* 800-346-2267 *Toll Free Fax:* 800-999-2939, pg 11

American Academy of Pediatrics, Elk Grove Village, IL *Toll Free Tel:* 888-227-1770, pg 11

American Association for Vocational Instructional Materials, Winterville, GA *Toll Free Tel:* 800-228-4689, pg 11

American Association of Blood Banks, Bethesda, MD *Toll Free Tel:* 866-222-2498 (sales), pg 11

American Association of Cereal Chemists, St Paul, MN *Toll Free Tel:* 800-328-7560, pg 11

American Association of Collegiate Registrars & Admissions Officers, Washington, DC *Toll Free Tel:* 877-338-3733, pg 11

American Association of Community Colleges (AACC), Washington, DC *Toll Free Tel:* 800-250-6557, pg 11

American Bankers Association, Washington, DC *Toll Free Tel:* 800-BANKERS (226-5377), pg 12

American Bar Association, Chicago, IL *Toll Free Tel:* 800-285-2221 (orders), pg 12

American Bible Society, New York, NY *Toll Free Tel:* 800-322-4253 (orders only), pg 12

The American Chemical Society, Washington, DC *Toll Free Tel:* 800-227-5558, pg 12

American College of Physician Executives, Tampa, FL *Toll Free Tel:* 800-562-8088, pg 12

American College of Surgeons, Chicago, IL *Toll Free Tel:* 800-621-4111, pg 13

American Correctional Association, Lanham, MD *Toll Free Tel:* 800-222-5646, pg 13

American Counseling Association, Alexandria, VA *Toll Free Tel:* 800-422-2648 (ext 222 - book orders only) *Toll Free Fax:* 800-473-2329, pg 13

American Diabetes Association, Alexandria, VA *Toll Free Tel:* 800-232-6733, pg 13

American Eagle Publications Inc, Show Low, AZ *Toll Free Tel:* 866-764-2925, pg 13

American Federation of Arts, New York, NY *Toll Free Tel:* 800-232-0270, pg 13

American Federation of Astrologers Inc, Tempe, AZ *Toll Free Tel:* 888-301-7630, pg 13

American Foundation for the Blind (AFB Press), New York, NY *Toll Free Tel:* 800-232-3044 (orders), pg 13

American Geophysical Union (AGU), Washington, DC *Toll Free Tel:* 800-966-2481 (North America), pg 14

American Health Publishing Co, Euless, TX *Toll Free Tel:* 800-LEARN41, pg 14

American Historical Press, Sun Valley, CA *Toll Free Tel:* 800-550-5750, pg 14

American Institute for CPCU & Insurance Institute of America, Malvern, PA *Toll Free Tel:* 800-644-2101, pg 14

American Institute of Aeronautics & Astronautics, Reston, VA *Toll Free Tel:* 800-639-2422, pg 14

American Institute of Certified Public Accountants, Jersey City, NJ *Toll Free Tel:* 888-777-7077, pg 15

American Institute of Chemical Engineers (AICHE), New York, NY *Toll Free Tel:* 800-242-4363, pg 15

American Institute of Ultrasound in Medicine, Laurel, MD *Toll Free Tel:* 800-638-5352, pg 15

American Law Institute, Philadelphia, PA *Toll Free Tel:* 800-253-6397, pg 15

American Library Association (ALA), Chicago, IL *Toll Free Tel:* 800-545-2433, pg 15

American Map Corp, Maspeth, NY *Toll Free Tel:* 800-432-MAPS, pg 15

American Marketing Association, Chicago, IL *Toll Free Tel:* 800-262-1150, pg 15

American Mathematical Society, Providence, RI *Toll Free Tel:* 800-321-4267, pg 16

American Medical Association, Chicago, IL *Toll Free Tel:* 800-621-8335 (cust serv), pg 16

American Phytopathological Society, St Paul, MN *Toll Free Tel:* 800-328-7560, pg 16

American Printing House for the Blind Inc, Louisville, KY *Toll Free Tel:* 800-223-1839 (cust serv), pg 16

American Products Publishing Co, Beaverton, OR *Toll Free Tel:* 800-668-8181, pg 16

American Psychiatric Publishing Inc, Arlington, VA *Toll Free Tel:* 800-368-5777, pg 16

American Psychological Association, Washington, DC *Toll Free Tel:* 800-374-2721, pg 17

American Quilter's Society, Paducah, KY *Toll Free Tel:* 800-626-5420 (orders), pg 17

American Showcase Inc, New York, NY *Toll Free Tel:* 800-894-7469, pg 17

American Society for Nondestructive Testing, Columbus, OH *Toll Free Tel:* 800-222-2768, pg 17

American Society for Quality, Milwaukee, WI *Toll Free Tel:* 800-248-1946, pg 17

American Society for Training & Development (ASTD), Alexandria, VA *Toll Free Tel:* 800-628-2783, pg 17

American Society of Civil Engineers (ASCE), Reston, VA *Toll Free Tel:* 800-548-2723, pg 18

American Society of Health-System Pharmacists, Bethesda, MD *Toll Free Tel:* 866-279-0681 (orders), pg 18

American Society of Mechanical Engineers (ASME), New York, NY *Toll Free Tel:* 800-843-2763 (cust serv), pg 18

American Technical Publishers Inc, Homewood, IL *Toll Free Tel:* 800-323-3471, pg 18

American Trust Publications, Burr Ridge, IL *Toll Free Tel:* 888-319-5858, pg 18

American Water Works Association, Denver, CO *Toll Free Tel:* 800-926-7337, pg 18

Amirah Publishing, Long Island City, NY *Toll Free Tel:* 800-337-4287 (IBTS), pg 19

Amsco School Publications Inc, New York, NY *Toll Free Tel:* 800-969-8398, pg 19

Anacus Press, Minneapolis, MN *Toll Free Tel:* 800-846-7027, pg 19

The Analytic Press, Hillsdale, NJ *Toll Free Tel:* 800-926-6579 (orders only); 800-627-0629 (journal orders), pg 19

Ancestry Publishing, Provo, UT *Toll Free Tel:* 800-262-3787, pg 19

Andrews University Press, Berrien Springs, MI *Toll Free Tel:* 800-467-6369 (Visa & MC orders only), pg 19

Angel City Press, Santa Monica, CA *Toll Free Tel:* 800-949-8039, pg 20

Angelus Press, Kansas City, MO *Toll Free Tel:* 800-966-7337 *Toll Free Fax:* 888-855-9022, pg 20

The Anglican Book Centre, Toronto, ON Canada *Toll Free Tel:* 800-268-1168 (Canada only), pg 535

Annual Reviews, Palo Alto, CA *Toll Free Tel:* 800-523-8635, pg 20

ANR Publications University of California, Oakland, CA *Toll Free Tel:* 800-994-8849, pg 20

Anti-Aging Press, Miami, FL *Toll Free Tel:* 800-SO-YOUNG, pg 569

Antique Collectors Club Ltd, East Hampton, MA *Toll Free Tel:* 800-252-5231, pg 20

Antique Trader Books, Iola, WI *Toll Free Tel:* 888-457-2873, pg 20

Anvilpress Inc, Vancouver, BC Canada *Toll Free Tel:* 800-565-9523 (ordering), pg 535

AOCS Press, Champaign, IL *Toll Free Tel:* 800-336-AOCS (336-2627), pg 20

Aperture Books, New York, NY *Toll Free Tel:* 800-929-2323, pg 20

The Apex Press, New York, NY *Toll Free Tel:* 800-316-2739 *Toll Free Fax:* 800-316-2739, pg 21

Appalachian Trail Conference, Harpers Ferry, WV *Toll Free Tel:* 888-287-8673 (for orders only), pg 21

APS Press, St Paul, MN *Toll Free Tel:* 800-328-7560, pg 22

Aqua Quest Publications Inc, Glen Cove, NY *Toll Free Tel:* 800-933-8989, pg 22

Aquila Communications Inc, St Laurent, PQ Canada *Toll Free Tel:* 800-667-7071 *Toll Free Fax:* 866-338-1948, pg 536

Arbutus Press, Traverse City, MI *Toll Free Tel:* 866-794-8793, pg 22

Arcadia Enterprises Inc, Fruitland, MD *Toll Free Tel:* 877-742-2682, pg 22

Arcadia Publishing, Mount Pleasant, SC *Toll Free Tel:* 888-313-2665 (orders only), pg 22

ArcheBooks Publishing, Las Vegas, NV *Toll Free Tel:* 800-358-8101, pg 22

ARE Press, Virginia Beach, VA *Toll Free Tel:* 800-333-4499, pg 23

Armenian Reference Books Co, Glendale, CA *Toll Free Tel:* 877-504-2550, pg 23

Jason Aronson Inc, Lanham, MD *Toll Free Tel:* 800-462-6420 (orders), pg 23

Arrow Map Inc, South Easton, MA *Toll Free Tel:* 800-343-7500, pg 24

Arsenal Pulp Press Book Publishers Ltd, Vancouver, BC Canada *Toll Free Tel:* 888-600-PULP (600-7857), pg 536

Art Image Publications, Derby Line, VT *Toll Free Tel:* 800-361-2598 *Toll Free Fax:* 800-559-2598, pg 24

Artabras Inc, New York, NY *Toll Free Tel:* 800-ART-BOOK, pg 24

Arte Publico Press, Houston, TX *Toll Free Tel:* 800-633-2783, pg 24

Artech House Inc, Norwood, MA *Toll Free Tel:* 800-225-9977, pg 24

Ascension Press, West Chester, PA *Toll Free Tel:* 800-376-0520 (sales off), pg 25

ASCP Press, Chicago, IL *Toll Free Tel:* 800-621-4142, pg 25

Aslan Publishing, Fairfield, CT *Toll Free Tel:* 800-786-5427, pg 25

ASM International, Materials Park, OH *Toll Free Tel:* 800-336-5152; 800-368-9800 (Europe), pg 25

ASM Press, Washington, DC *Toll Free Tel:* 800-546-2416, pg 25

Aspen Publishers, A Wolters Kluwer Company, New York, NY *Toll Free Tel:* 800-234-1660 (cust serv); 800-447-1717 (orders); 800-950-5259 (legal educ); 800-LAW-PLGL (paralegal textbook); 800-317-3113 (bookstore sales); 800-364-2512 (Loislaw), pg 26

Association for Computing Machinery, New York, NY *Toll Free Tel:* 800-342-6626, pg 26

Association for Supervision & Curriculum Development (ASCD), Alexandria, VA *Toll Free Tel:* 800-933-2723, pg 26

Association of American University Presses, Chicago, IL *Toll Free Tel:* 800-621-2736 (orders), pg 26

Association of College & Research Libraries, Chicago, IL *Toll Free Tel:* 800-545-2433 (ext 2517), pg 26

The Astronomical Society of the Pacific, San Francisco, CA *Toll Free Tel:* 800-335-2624 (Cust Serv), pg 27

Athletic Guide Publishing, Flagler Beach, FL *Toll Free Tel:* 800-255-1050, pg 27

Atlantic Publishing Inc, Ocala, FL *Toll Free Tel:* 800-555-4037, pg 27

Atwood Publishing, Madison, WI *Toll Free Tel:* 888-242-7101, pg 27

Audio Renaissance, New York, NY *Toll Free Tel:* 888-330-8477 (cust serv), pg 27

Augsburg Fortress Publishers, Publishing House of the Evangelical Lutheran Church in America, Minneapolis, MN *Toll Free Tel:* 800-426-0115 (ext 639 subns); 800-328-4648 (orders); 800-421-0239 (perms) *Toll Free Fax:* 800-421-0239 (perms & copyrights), pg 28

August House Publishers Inc, Little Rock, AR *Toll Free Tel:* 800-284-8784 *Toll Free Fax:* 800-284-8784 (orders), pg 28

Ave Maria Press, Notre Dame, IN *Toll Free Tel:* 800-282-1865 *Toll Free Fax:* 800-282-5681, pg 29

Avery Color Studios, Gwinn, MI *Toll Free Tel:* 800-722-9925, pg 29

AVKO Dyslexia & Spelling Research Foundation Inc, Clio, MI *Toll Free Tel:* 866-285-6612, pg 29

Avocet Press Inc, Pearl River, NY *Toll Free Tel:* 877-428-6238, pg 29

Avotaynu Inc, Bergenfield, NJ *Toll Free Tel:* 800-286-8296, pg 29

Backbeat Books, San Francisco, CA *Toll Free Tel:* 866-222-5232 (orders only), pg 30

Baker Books, Grand Rapids, MI *Toll Free Tel:* 800-877-2665; 800-679-1957 *Toll Free Fax:* 800-398-3110, pg 30

The Baltimore Sun, Baltimore, MD *Toll Free Tel:* 800-829-8000, pg 31

Bancroft-Sage Publishing, Minneapolis, MN *Toll Free Tel:* 800-846-7027, pg 31

Bandido Books, Orlando, FL *Toll Free Tel:* 877-814-6824 (pin 1174), pg 31

Banner of Truth, Carlisle, PA *Toll Free Tel:* 800-263-8085 (orders), pg 31

Bantam Dell Publishing Group, New York, NY *Toll Free Tel:* 800-223-6834, pg 31

Baptist Spanish Publishing House (d/b/a Casa Bautista de Publicaciones), El Paso, TX *Toll Free Tel:* 800-755-5958 (cust serv & orders); 800-985-9971 (Casa Bautista Miami), pg 31

Barbed Wire Publishing, Las Cruces, NM *Toll Free Tel:* 888-817-1990, pg 32

BAR/BRI Group, Chicago, IL *Toll Free Tel:* 800-328-9352 *Toll Free Fax:* 800-430-9378 (orders), pg 32

Barcelona Publishers, Gilsum, NH *Toll Free Tel:* 800-345-6665, pg 32

Barnes & Noble Books (Imports & Reprints), Lanham, MD *Toll Free Tel:* 800-462-6420 (orders only) *Toll Free Fax:* 800-338-4550 (orders only), pg 32

Barron's Educational Series Inc, Hauppauge, NY *Toll Free Tel:* 800-645-3476, pg 32

Basic Books, New York, NY *Toll Free Tel:* 800-242-7737 (orders), pg 33

Basic Health Publications Inc, North Bergen, NJ *Toll Free Tel:* 800-575-8890, pg 33

Battelle Press, Columbus, OH *Toll Free Tel:* 800-451-3543, pg 33

Baylor University Press, Waco, TX *Toll Free Tel:* 800-710-3217, pg 33

Baywood Publishing Co Inc, Amityville, NY *Toll Free Tel:* 800-638-7819, pg 33

BBC Audiobooks America, Hampton, NH *Toll Free Tel:* 800-621-0182, pg 34

Be Puzzled, San Francisco, CA *Toll Free Tel:* 800-347-4818, pg 34

Beach Holme Publishing, Vancouver, BC Canada *Toll Free Tel:* 888-551-6655 (orders), pg 536

Beacham Publishing Corp, Nokomis, FL *Toll Free Tel:* 800-466-9644, pg 34

Beacon Hill Press of Kansas City, Kansas City, MO *Toll Free Tel:* 800-877-0700 (retail order) *Toll Free Fax:* 800-849-9827 (order), pg 34

Beacon Press, Boston, MA *Toll Free Tel:* 800-225-3362 (orders only), pg 34

Bear & Co Inc, Rochester, VT *Toll Free Tel:* 800-932-3277, pg 34

Beard Books Inc, Frederick, MD *Toll Free Tel:* 888-563-4573 (book orders), pg 34

Groupe Beauchemin, Editeur Ltee, Laval, PQ Canada *Toll Free Tel:* 800-361-2598 (US & Canada); 800-361-4504 (Canada Only), pg 536

Beautiful America Publishing Co, Woodburn, OR *Toll Free Tel:* 800-874-1233, pg 34

Beekman Publishers Inc, Woodstock, NY *Toll Free Tel:* 888-BEEKMAN (orders), pg 35

Thomas T Beeler Publisher, Rollinsford, NH *Toll Free Tel:* 800-818-7574 *Toll Free Fax:* 888-222-3396, pg 35

Bell Springs Publishing, Willits, CA *Toll Free Tel:* 800-515-8050, pg 35

Bellerophon Books, Santa Barbara, CA *Toll Free Tel:* 800-253-9943, pg 35

The Benefactory, Cohasset, MA *Toll Free Tel:* 800-729-7251, pg 36

Benjamin Scott Publishing, Pasadena, CA *Toll Free Tel:* 800-488-4959, pg 36

John Benjamins Publishing Co, Erdenheim, PA *Toll Free Tel:* 800-562-5666, pg 36

Bentley Publishers, Cambridge, MA *Toll Free Tel:* 800-423-4595, pg 36

R J Berg/Destinations Press Ltd, Indianapolis, IN *Toll Free Tel:* 800-638-3909, pg 36

Berkshire House, Woodstock, VT *Toll Free Tel:* 800-245-4151, pg 37

Bernan, Lanham, MD *Toll Free Tel:* 800-274-4447; 800-274-4888 (cust serv) *Toll Free Fax:* 800-865-3450, pg 37

Bess Press, Honolulu, HI *Toll Free Tel:* 800-910-2377, pg 37

Best Publishing Co, Flagstaff, AZ *Toll Free Tel:* 800-468-1055, pg 37

Bethany House Publishers/Baker Bookhouse, Grand Rapids, MI *Toll Free Tel:* 800-877-2665, pg 37

Bethlehem Books, Bathgate, ND *Toll Free Tel:* 800-757-6831, pg 37

Betterway Books, Cincinnati, OH *Toll Free Tel:* 800-666-0963 *Toll Free Fax:* 888-590-4082, pg 38

Between the Lines, Toronto, ON Canada *Toll Free Tel:* 800-718-7201, pg 536

Bhaktivedanta Book Publishing Inc, Los Angeles, CA *Toll Free Tel:* 800-927-4152, pg 38

Biblo & Tannen Booksellers & Publishers Inc, Cheshire, CT *Toll Free Tel:* 800-272-8778 *Toll Free Fax:* 800-272-8778, pg 38

Big Guy Books Inc, Carlsbad, CA *Toll Free Tel:* 866-210-5938 (Booksellers cust serv); 800-741-6493 (For parents, teachers, schools & libraries), pg 38

Binford & Mort Publishing Inc, Hillsboro, OR *Toll Free Tel:* 888-221-4514, pg 38

Birkhauser Boston, Cambridge, MA *Toll Free Tel:* 800-777-4643 (cust serv), pg 39

George T Bisel Co Inc, Philadelphia, PA *Toll Free Tel:* 800-247-3526, pg 39

Bisk Education, Tampa, FL *Toll Free Tel:* 800-874-7877 *Toll Free Fax:* 800-345-8273, pg 39

BizBest Media Corp, Pacific Palisades, CA *Toll Free Tel:* 800-873-5205; 877-424-9237, pg 39

Black Diamond Book Publishing, Los Angeles, CA *Toll Free Tel:* 800-962-7622 *Toll Free Fax:* 800-962-7622, pg 39

Black Rose Books Ltd, Montreal, PQ Canada *Toll Free Tel:* 800-565-9523 *Toll Free Fax:* 800-221-9985, pg 536

Blackbirch Press®, Farmington Hills, MI *Toll Free Tel:* 800-877-4253 *Toll Free Fax:* 800-414-5043 (orders), pg 40

Blacksmith Corp, North Hampton, OH *Toll Free Tel:* 800-531-2665, pg 40

Blackwell Publishing/Futura, Elmsford, NY *Toll Free Tel:* 800-759-6102, pg 40

Blackwell Publishing Professional, Ames, IA *Toll Free Tel:* 800-862-6657 (orders only), pg 40

John F Blair Publisher, Winston-Salem, NC *Toll Free Tel:* 800-222-9796, pg 41

Bloomsbury Publishing, New York, NY *Toll Free Tel:* 800-221-7945, pg 41

Blue Book Publications Inc, Minneapolis, MN *Toll Free Tel:* 800-877-4867, pg 570

Blue Dolphin Publishing Inc, Grass Valley, CA *Toll Free Tel:* 800-643-0765, pg 41

Blue Dove Press, San Diego, CA *Toll Free Tel:* 800-691-1008 (orders), pg 41

Blue Mountain Arts Inc, Boulder, CO *Toll Free Tel:* 800-473-2082 *Toll Free Fax:* 800-256-1213, pg 41

Blue Note Publications, Cocoa Beach, FL *Toll Free Tel:* 800-624-0401, pg 41

Blue Poppy Press, Boulder, CO *Toll Free Tel:* 800-487-9296, pg 42

Bluestocking Press, El Dorado, CA *Toll Free Tel:* 800-959-8586, pg 42

Blushing Rose Publishing, San Anselmo, CA *Toll Free Tel:* 800-898-2263, pg 42

BNA Books, Washington, DC *Toll Free Tel:* 800-960-1220, pg 42

BNI Publications Inc, Anaheim, CA *Toll Free Tel:* 800-873-6397, pg 42

BoardSource, Washington, DC *Toll Free Tel:* 800-883-6262, pg 42

Bonus Books Inc, Santa Monica, CA *Toll Free Tel:* 800-225-3775, pg 43

Book Marketing Works LLC, Avon, CT *Toll Free Tel:* 800-562-4357, pg 43

Book Peddlers, Minnetonka, MN *Toll Free Tel:* 800-255-3379, pg 43

Book Publishing Co, Summertown, TN *Toll Free Tel:* 888-260-8458, pg 43

Book Sales Inc, Edison, NJ *Toll Free Tel:* 800-526-7257, pg 43

Bookhaven Press LLC, McKees Rocks, PA *Toll Free Tel:* 800-782-7424 (orders only), pg 44

Books in Motion, Spokane, WA *Toll Free Tel:* 800-752-3199, pg 44

Books on Tape®, Westminster, MD *Toll Free Tel:* 800-733-3000 *Toll Free Fax:* 800-659-2436, pg 44

Eddie Bowers Publishing Inc, Peosta, IA *Toll Free Tel:* 800-747-2411, pg 44

R R Bowker LLC, New Providence, NJ *Toll Free Tel:* 888-269-5372; 888-269-5372 (cust serv - press 2 for returns), pg 44

BowTie Press, Irvine, CA *Toll Free Tel:* 800-426-2516, pg 45

Boyds Mills Press, Honesdale, PA *Toll Free Tel:* 877-512-8366, pg 45

Boys Town Press, Boys Town, NE *Toll Free Tel:* 800-282-6657, pg 45

Bradford Publishing Co, Denver, CO *Toll Free Tel:* 800-446-2831, pg 45

BradyGAMES Publishing, Indianapolis, IN *Toll Free Tel:* 800-545-5912; 800-571-5840 (cust serv), pg 45

Brandywine Press, Naugatuck, CT *Toll Free Tel:* 800-345-1776, pg 45

Brassey's Inc, Dulles, VA *Toll Free Tel:* 800-775-2518 (orders only), pg 45

Breakaway Books, Halcottsville, NY *Toll Free Tel:* 800-548-4348 (voicemail), pg 46

Breakthrough Publications Inc, Emmaus, PA *Toll Free Tel:* 800-824-5000, pg 46

Breakwater Books Ltd, St Johns, NF Canada *Toll Free Tel:* 800-563-3333, pg 537

Nicholas Brealey Publishing, Minneapolis, MN *Toll Free Tel:* 888-BREALEY (273-2539), pg 46

Brenner Information Group, San Diego, CA *Toll Free Tel:* 800-811-4337, pg 46

Brentwood Christian Press, Columbus, GA *Toll Free Tel:* 800-334-8861, pg 46

Brethren Press, Elgin, IL *Toll Free Tel:* 800-323-8039, pg 46

Brewers Publications, Boulder, CO *Toll Free Tel:* 888-822-6273 (Canada & US), pg 46

Brick Tower Press, New York, NY *Toll Free Tel:* 800-68-BRICK (682-7425), pg 47

Bridge Learning Systems Inc, American Canyon, CA *Toll Free Tel:* 800-487-9868, pg 47

Bridge-Logos Publishers, Newberry, FL *Toll Free Tel:* 800-631-5802 *Toll Free Fax:* 800-935-6467, pg 47

Bridge Publications Inc, Los Angeles, CA *Toll Free Tel:* 800-722-1733; 800-843-7389 (CA), pg 47

Briefings Publishing Group, Alexandria, VA *Toll Free Tel:* 800-888-2086, pg 47

Bright Mountain Books Inc, Fairview, NC *Toll Free Tel:* 800-437-3959, pg 47

Brighton Publications, New Brighton, MN *Toll Free Tel:* 800-536-2665, pg 47

Brill Academic Publishers Inc, Boston, MA *Toll Free Tel:* 800-962-4406, pg 47

Brilliance Audio, Grand Haven, MI *Toll Free Tel:* 800-648-2312 (orders only), pg 47

Bristol Fashion Publications Inc, Harrisburg, PA *Toll Free Tel:* 800-478-7147 *Toll Free Fax:* 800-543-9030, pg 48

Bristol Publishing Enterprises, Hayward, CA *Toll Free Tel:* 800-346-4889, pg 48

Paul H Brookes Publishing Co, Baltimore, MD *Toll Free Tel:* 800-638-3775, pg 48

Brookhaven Press, La Crosse, WI *Toll Free Tel:* 800-236-0850, pg 48

The Brookings Institution Press, Washington, DC *Toll Free Tel:* 800-275-1447, pg 48

Brookline Books, Brookline, MA *Toll Free Tel:* 800-666-2665; 800-345-6665 (orders), pg 49

Brooklyn Botanic Garden, Brooklyn, NY *Toll Free Tel:* 800-367-9692 (orders) *Toll Free Fax:* 800-542-7567 (orders), pg 49

Brown Barn Books, Weston, CT *Toll Free Tel:* 888-227-3308, pg 49

BrownTrout Publishers Inc, San Francisco, CA *Toll Free Tel:* 800-777-7812, pg 49

Brunner-Routledge, New York, NY *Toll Free Tel:* 800-634-7064 (orders); 800-797-3803, pg 49

BuilderBooks.com, Washington, DC *Toll Free Tel:* 800-223-2665 (orders); 800-368-5242 ext 8368 (editorial), pg 49

Building News, Vienna, VA *Toll Free Tel:* 888-264-2665, pg 49

Bulfinch Press, New York, NY *Toll Free Tel:* 800-759-0190, pg 50

Bull Publishing Co, Boulder, CO *Toll Free Tel:* 800-676-2855, pg 50

Bureau of Economic Geology, University of Texas at Austin, Austin, TX *Toll Free Tel:* 888-839-4365 *Toll Free Fax:* 888-839-6277, pg 50

Burrelle's Information Services, Livingston, NJ *Toll Free Tel:* 800-631-1160 *Toll Free Fax:* 800-898-6677, pg 50

Business & Legal Reports Inc, Old Saybrook, CT *Toll Free Tel:* 800-727-5257, pg 50

Business Research Services Inc, Bethesda, MD *Toll Free Tel:* 800-845-8420, pg 50

Doug Butler Enterprises Inc, LaPorte, CO *Toll Free Tel:* 800-728-3826 (press 1), pg 570

Butte Publications Inc, Hillsboro, OR *Toll Free Tel:* 866-312-8883, pg 50

C & T Publishing Inc, Concord, CA *Toll Free Tel:* 800-284-1114, pg 51

Cache River Press, St Louis, MO *Toll Free Tel:* 888-PUBLISH (782-5474), pg 51

Cambridge Educational, Lawrenceville, NJ *Toll Free Tel:* 800-468-4227 *Toll Free Fax:* 800-329-6687, pg 51

Cambridge University Press, New York, NY *Toll Free Tel:* 800-899-5222, pg 52

Cameron & Co, San Francisco, CA *Toll Free Tel:* 800-779-5582, pg 52

Canada Law Book Inc, Aurora, ON Canada *Toll Free Tel:* 800-263-2037, pg 538

Canadian Bible Society, Toronto, ON Canada *Toll Free Tel:* 800-465-2425, pg 538

Canadian Institute of Chartered Accountants, Toronto, ON Canada *Toll Free Tel:* 800-268-3793 (Canadian orders), pg 538

Canadian Museum of Civilization, Hull, PQ Canada *Toll Free Tel:* 800-555-5621 (North America only), pg 538

Capital Books Inc, Sterling, VA *Toll Free Tel:* 800-758-3756, pg 52

Capstone Press, Mankato, MN *Toll Free Tel:* 800-747-4992 *Toll Free Fax:* 888-262-0705, pg 53

Aristide D Caratzas, Publisher, Scarsdale, NY *Toll Free Tel:* 800-204-2665, pg 53

The Career Press Inc, Franklin Lakes, NJ *Toll Free Tel:* 800-CAREER-1 (227-3371), pg 53

William Carey Library, Pasadena, CA *Toll Free Tel:* 866-732-6657, pg 53

Caribe Betania Editores, Nashville, TN *Toll Free Tel:* 800-322-7426, pg 53

Carlisle Press - Walnut Creek, Sugarcreek, OH *Toll Free Tel:* 800-852-4482, pg 53

Carolina Academic Press, Durham, NC *Toll Free Tel:* 800-489-7486, pg 54

Carolrhoda Books Inc, Minneapolis, MN *Toll Free Tel:* 800-328-4929 *Toll Free Fax:* 800-332-1132, pg 54

Carroll Publishing, Bethesda, MD *Toll Free Tel:* 800-336-4240, pg 54

Carswell, Toronto, ON Canada *Toll Free Tel:* 800-387-5164 (Canada & US) *Toll Free Fax:* 877-750-9041, pg 539

CarTech Inc, North Branch, MN *Toll Free Tel:* 800-551-4754, pg 54

Amon Carter Museum, Fort Worth, TX *Toll Free Tel:* 800-573-1933, pg 54

Cascade Pass Inc, Marina Del Rey, CA *Toll Free Tel:* 888-837-0704, pg 54

Catholic News Publishing Co Inc, New Rochelle, NY *Toll Free Tel:* 800-433-7771, pg 55

Cato Institute, Washington, DC *Toll Free Tel:* 800-767-1241, pg 55

Caughman Associates, West Conshohocken, PA *Toll Free Tel:* 877-BUY BOOK, pg 570

Caxton Press, Caldwell, ID *Toll Free Tel:* 800-657-6465, pg 55

CCC Publications LLC, Chatsworth, CA *Toll Free Tel:* 800-248-LAFF (248-5233), pg 55

CCH Canadian Limited, A Wolters Kluwer Company, Toronto, ON Canada *Toll Free Tel:* 800-268-4522 (Canada & US cust serv) *Toll Free Fax:* 800-461-4131, pg 539

CCH Inc, Riverwoods, IL *Toll Free Tel:* 888-224-7377, pg 55

Cedar Fort Inc, Springville, UT *Toll Free Tel:* 800-759-2665, pg 56

Cedco Publishing Co, San Rafael, CA *Toll Free Tel:* 800-227-6162, pg 56

CEF Press, Warrenton, MO *Toll Free Tel:* 800-748-7710, pg 56

Celebrity Press, Nashville, TN *Toll Free Tel:* 800-327-5113, pg 56

Celestial Arts Publishing Co, Berkeley, CA *Toll Free Tel:* 800-841-BOOK, pg 56

Center for Futures Education Inc, Grove City, PA *Toll Free Tel:* 800-966-2554, pg 56

Centerstream Publishing LLC, Anaheim Hills, CA *Toll Free Tel:* 877-312-8687, pg 57

Central Conference of American Rabbis/CCAR Press, New York, NY *Toll Free Tel:* 800-935-2227, pg 57

Centre Franco-Ontarien de Ressources en Alphabetisation, Sudbury, ON Canada *Toll Free Tel:* 888-814-4422 (orders, Canada only), pg 540

Chain Store Guide, Tampa, FL *Toll Free Tel:* 800-927-9292, pg 58

Chalice Press, St Louis, MO *Toll Free Tel:* 800-366-3383, pg 58

Champion Press Ltd, Fredonia, WI *Toll Free Tel:* 877-250-3354, pg 58

Charisma House, Lake Mary, FL *Toll Free Tel:* 800-283-8494 (Charisma House, Siloam Press, Creation House Press); 800-665-1468, pg 58

CharismaLife Publishers, Lake Mary, FL *Toll Free Tel:* 800-451-4598, pg 58

Charles River Media, Hingham, MA *Toll Free Tel:* 800-382-8505 (orders), pg 58

Charles Scribner's Sons, Farmington Hills, MI *Toll Free Tel:* 800-877-4253 *Toll Free Fax:* 800-414-5043, pg 58

Charlesbridge Publishing Inc, Watertown, MA *Toll Free Tel:* 800-225-3214, pg 58

The Charlton Press, North York, ON Canada *Toll Free Tel:* 800-442-6042 *Toll Free Fax:* 800-442-1542, pg 540

Chatelaine Press, Burke, VA *Toll Free Tel:* 800-249-9527, pg 59

Chatsworth Press, Chatsworth, CA *Toll Free Tel:* 800-262-7367 (US); 800-272-7367 (CA), pg 59

Chelsea Green Publishing Co, White River Junction, VT *Toll Free Tel:* 800-639-4099 (cust serv & consumer orders); 800-807-6726 (trade & wholesale orders), pg 59

Chelsea House Publishers LLC, Langhorne, PA *Toll Free Tel:* 800-848-BOOK (848-2665) *Toll Free Fax:* 877-780-7300, pg 59

Chemical Education Resources Inc, Philadelphia, PA *Toll Free Tel:* 800-523-1850 ext 3781 *Toll Free Fax:* 800-451-3661, pg 59

Chemical Publishing Co Inc, New York, NY *Toll Free Tel:* 800-786-3659, pg 59

Cheng & Tsui Co Inc, Boston, MA *Toll Free Tel:* 800-554-1963, pg 59

Cherokee Publishing Co, Atlanta, GA *Toll Free Tel:* 800-653-3952, pg 59

Chess Combination Inc, Bridgeport, CT *Toll Free Tel:* 800-354-4083, pg 60

Chess Digest Inc, Ardmore, TN *Toll Free Tel:* 800-524-3527 (orders), pg 60

Chicago Review Press, Chicago, IL *Toll Free Tel:* 800-888-4741, pg 60

Chicago Spectrum Press, Louisville, KY *Toll Free Tel:* 800-594-5190, pg 60

Child's Play, Auburn, ME *Toll Free Tel:* 800-472-0099; 800-639-6404 *Toll Free Fax:* 800-854-6989, pg 60

The Child's World Inc, Chanhassen, MN *Toll Free Tel:* 800-599-READ (599-7323), pg 60

Childswork/Childsplay LLC, Plainview, NY *Toll Free Tel:* 800-962-1141 (cust serv) *Toll Free Fax:* 800-262-1886 (orders), pg 60

China Books & Periodicals Inc, San Francisco, CA *Toll Free Tel:* 800-818-2017, pg 60

Chitra Publications, Montrose, PA *Toll Free Tel:* 800-628-8244, pg 60

Chosen Books, Grand Rapids, MI *Toll Free Tel:* 800-877-2665, pg 61

Chouette Publishing, Montreal, PQ Canada *Toll Free Tel:* 877-926-3325, pg 540

Christian Fellowship Ministries, Phoenix, AZ *Toll Free Tel:* 888-678-1543, pg 61

Christian History Project, Edmonton, AB Canada *Toll Free Tel:* 800-853-5402, pg 540

Christian Literature Crusade Inc, Fort Washington, PA *Toll Free Tel:* 800-659-1240 (orders), pg 61

Christian Living Books Inc, Mitchellville, MD *Toll Free Tel:* 800-727-3218 (ordering), pg 61

Christian Publications Inc, Camp Hill, PA *Toll Free Tel:* 800-233-4443, pg 61

Christian Schools International, Grand Rapids, MI *Toll Free Tel:* 800-635-8288, pg 61

Christopher-Gordon Publishers Inc, Norwood, MA *Toll Free Tel:* 800-934-8322, pg 61

Chronicle Books LLC, San Francisco, CA *Toll Free Tel:* 800-722-6657 (cust serv) *Toll Free Fax:* 800-858-7787 (orders), pg 61

Chronicle Guidance Publications Inc, Moravia, NY *Toll Free Tel:* 800-622-7284, pg 62

Church Growth Institute, Elkton, MD *Toll Free Tel:* 800-553-4769 (orders only) *Toll Free Fax:* 800-644-4729 (orders only), pg 62

Cinco Puntos Press, El Paso, TX *Toll Free Tel:* 800-566-9072, pg 62

Circlet Press Inc, Cambridge, MA *Toll Free Tel:* 800-729-6423 (orders), pg 62

Clarion Books, New York, NY *Toll Free Tel:* 800-225-3362 (orders), pg 62

Clarity Press Inc, Atlanta, GA *Toll Free Tel:* 800-729-6423 (orders); 877-613-1495 *Toll Free Fax:* 877-613-7868, pg 62

Clark Publishing Inc, Logan, IA *Toll Free Tel:* 800-845-1916 *Toll Free Fax:* 800-543-2745, pg 63

Clarkson Potter Publishers, New York, NY *Toll Free Tel:* 888-264-1745, pg 63

Classic Books, Murrieta, CA *Toll Free Tel:* 888-265-3547 *Toll Free Fax:* 888-265-3550, pg 63

Classroom Connect, Brisbane, CA *Toll Free Tel:* 800-638-1639 (cust support), pg 63

Clear Light Publishers, Santa Fe, NM *Toll Free Tel:* 888-253-2747 (orders), pg 63

Cleis Press, San Francisco, CA *Toll Free Tel:* 800-780-2279 (US), pg 63

Clock Tower Press, Ann Arbor, MI *Toll Free Tel:* 800-956-8999, pg 63

Close Up Publishing, Alexandria, VA *Toll Free Tel:* 800-765-3131, pg 63

Clovernook Printing House for the Blind, Cincinnati, OH *Toll Free Tel:* 888-234-7156, pg 63

CMP Books, San Francisco, CA *Toll Free Tel:* 800-500-6875 (orders), pg 63

Coach House Books, Toronto, ON Canada *Toll Free Tel:* 800-367-6360, pg 540

Coaches Choice, Monterey, CA *Toll Free Tel:* 888-229-5745, pg 64

Cobblestone Publishing Co, Peterborough, NH *Toll Free Tel:* 800-821-0115, pg 64

Cold Spring Harbor Laboratory Press, Woodbury, NY *Toll Free Tel:* 800-843-4388, pg 64

Collectors Press Inc, Tigard, OR *Toll Free Tel:* 800-423-1848, pg 64

College Press Publishing Co, Joplin, MO *Toll Free Tel:* 800-289-3300, pg 64

The Colonial Williamsburg Foundation, Williamsburg, VA *Toll Free Tel:* 800-HISTORY, pg 65

Colorado Railroad Museum, Golden, CO *Toll Free Tel:* 800-365-6263, pg 65

Columba Publishing Co Inc, Akron, OH *Toll Free Tel:* 800-999-7491, pg 65

Columbia Books Inc, Washington, DC *Toll Free Tel:* 888-265-0600 (cust serv), pg 65

Columbia University Press, New York, NY *Toll Free Tel:* 800-944-8648, pg 65

Comex Systems Inc, Mendham, NJ *Toll Free Tel:* 800-543-6959, pg 65

Common Courage Press, Monroe, ME *Toll Free Tel:* 800-497-3207, pg 65

Commonwealth Business Media, East Windsor, NJ *Toll Free Tel:* 800-221-5488; 888-215-6084 (orders), pg 65

Communication Creativity, Buena Vista, CO *Toll Free Tel:* 800-331-8355, pg 66

Company's Coming Publishing Ltd, Edmonton, AB Canada *Toll Free Tel:* 800-875-7108 (US & Canada), pg 541

Comprehensive Health Education Foundation (CHEF), Seattle, WA *Toll Free Tel:* 800-323-2433, pg 66

Conciliar Press, Ben Lomond, CA *Toll Free Tel:* 800-967-7377, pg 66

Concordia Publishing House, St Louis, MO *Toll Free Tel:* 800-325-3040 *Toll Free Fax:* 800-490-9889, pg 66

Congressional Quarterly Press, Washington, DC *Toll Free Tel:* 866-427-7737 *Toll Free Fax:* 800-380-3810, pg 66

Continuing Education Press, Portland, OR *Toll Free Tel:* 866-647-7377, pg 67

The Continuing Legal Education Society of British Columbia, Vancouver, BC Canada *Toll Free Tel:* 800-663-0437, pg 541

The Continuum International Publishing Group, New York, NY *Toll Free Tel:* 800-561-7704, pg 67

Cook Communications Ministries, Colorado Springs, CO *Toll Free Tel:* 800-437-4337, pg 67

Copley Publishing Group, Acton, MA *Toll Free Tel:* 800-562-2147, pg 68

Cornell Maritime Press Inc, Centreville, MD *Toll Free Tel:* 800-638-7641, pg 68

Cortina Learning International Inc, Wilton, CT *Toll Free Tel:* 800-245-2145, pg 69

Corwin Press, Thousand Oaks, CA *Toll Free Fax:* 800-417-2466, pg 69

Coteau Books, Regina, SK Canada *Toll Free Tel:* 800-440-4471 (Canada Only), pg 541

Cottonwood Press Inc, Fort Collins, CO *Toll Free Tel:* 800-864-4297, pg 69

Council for Exceptional Children, Arlington, VA *Toll Free Tel:* 888-232-7733 (cust serv), pg 70

Council for Research in Values & Philosophy (RVP), Washington, DC *Toll Free Fax:* 800-659-9962, pg 70

Council Oak Books LLC, Tulsa, OK *Toll Free Tel:* 800-247-8850, pg 70

Council of State Governments, Lexington, KY *Toll Free Tel:* 800-800-1910, pg 70

The Countryman Press, Woodstock, VT *Toll Free Tel:* 800-245-4151, pg 70

Course Technology, Boston, MA *Toll Free Tel:* 800-881-8922, pg 71

La Courte Echelle, Montreal, PQ Canada *Toll Free Tel:* 800-387-6192 (orders only) *Toll Free Fax:* 800-450-0391 (orders only), pg 541

Covenant Communications Inc, American Fork, UT *Toll Free Tel:* 800-662-9545, pg 71

Cowley Publications, Cambridge, MA *Toll Free Tel:* 800-225-1534 *Toll Free Fax:* 877-225-6675, pg 71

CQ Press, Washington, DC *Toll Free Tel:* 866-427-7737 *Toll Free Fax:* 800-380-3810, pg 71

Crabtree Publishing Co, New York, NY *Toll Free Tel:* 800-387-7650 *Toll Free Fax:* 800-355-7166, pg 71

Crabtree Publishing Co Ltd, St Catharines, ON Canada *Toll Free Tel:* 800-387-7650 *Toll Free Fax:* 800-355-7166, pg 541

Craftsman Book Co, Carlsbad, CA *Toll Free Tel:* 800-829-8123, pg 71

Crane Hill Publishers, Birmingham, AL *Toll Free Tel:* 800-247-8850, pg 71

CRC Press LLC, Boca Raton, FL *Toll Free Tel:* 800-272-7737 *Toll Free Fax:* 800-643-9428 (sales); 800-374-3401 (orders), pg 71

CRC Publications, Grand Rapids, MI *Toll Free Tel:* 800-333-8300, pg 72

Creating Keepsakes Books, Bluffdale, UT *Toll Free Tel:* 800-815-3538, pg 72

Creative Book Publishing, St Johns, NF Canada *Toll Free Tel:* 877-722-1722 (Canada only), pg 541

Creative Bound International Inc, Carp, ON Canada *Toll Free Tel:* 800-287-8610 (N America), pg 541

The Creative Co, Mankato, MN *Toll Free Tel:* 800-445-6209, pg 72

Creative Homeowner, Upper Saddle River, NJ *Toll Free Tel:* 800-631-7795, pg 72

Creative Publishing International Inc, Chanhassen, MN *Toll Free Tel:* 800-328-0590 (sales), pg 72

Criminal Justice Press, Monsey, NY *Toll Free Tel:* 800-914-3379, pg 72

Cross Cultural Publications Inc, South Bend, IN *Toll Free Tel:* 800-273-6526, pg 73

The Crossing Press, Berkeley, CA *Toll Free Tel:* 800-841-2665 (orders & cust serv), pg 73

The Crossroad Publishing Company, New York, NY *Toll Free Tel:* 800-395-0690 (orders) *Toll Free Fax:* 800-462-6420 (orders), pg 73

Crown House Publishing, Norwalk, CT *Toll Free Tel:* 877-925-1213 (orders), pg 73

Crown Publishing Group, New York, NY *Toll Free Tel:* 888-264-1745, pg 73

Crystal Clarity Publishers, Nevada City, CA *Toll Free Tel:* 800-424-1055, pg 74

Crystal Productions, Glenview, IL *Toll Free Tel:* 800-255-8629 *Toll Free Fax:* 800-657-8149, pg 74

CTB/McGraw-Hill, Monterey, CA *Toll Free Tel:* 800-538-9547, pg 74

Cumberland House Publishing Inc, Nashville, TN *Toll Free Tel:* 888-439-2665, pg 74

Current Clinical Strategies Publishing, Laguna Hills, CA *Toll Free Tel:* 800-331-8227 *Toll Free Fax:* 800-965-9420, pg 75

Current Medicine, Philadelphia, PA *Toll Free Tel:* 800-427-1796, pg 75

Cycle Publishing, San Francisco, CA *Toll Free Tel:* 877-353-1207, pg 75

Da Capo Press Inc, Cambridge, MA *Toll Free Tel:* 800-242-7737 (orders), pg 75

Damron Co, San Francisco, CA *Toll Free Tel:* 800-462-6654, pg 75

Dandy Lion Publications, San Luis Obispo, CA *Toll Free Tel:* 800-776-8032, pg 75

John Daniel & Co, Publishers, McKinleyville, CA *Toll Free Tel:* 800-662-8351, pg 75

The Dartnell Corp, Palm Beach Gardens, FL *Toll Free Tel:* 800-621-5463, pg 76

Data Trace Publishing Co, Towson, MD *Toll Free Tel:* 800-342-0454 (orders only), pg 76

Davies-Black Publishing, Palo Alto, CA *Toll Free Tel:* 800-624-1765, pg 76

Davies Publishing Inc, Pasadena, CA *Toll Free Tel:* 877-792-0005, pg 76

F A Davis Co, Philadelphia, PA *Toll Free Tel:* 800-523-4049, pg 76

Dawbert Press Inc, Duxbury, MA *Toll Free Tel:* 800-933-2923, pg 77

The Dawn Horse Press, Middletown, CA *Toll Free Tel:* 877-770-0772, pg 77

Dawn Publications Inc, Nevada City, CA *Toll Free Tel:* 800-545-7475, pg 77

DawnSignPress, San Diego, CA *Toll Free Tel:* 800-549-5350, pg 77

DBI Books, Iola, WI *Toll Free Tel:* 888-457-2873, pg 77

dbS Productions, Charlottesville, VA *Toll Free Tel:* 800-745-1581, pg 77

DC Comics, New York, NY *Toll Free Tel:* 800-759-0190 (distribution), pg 77

DC Press, Sanford, FL *Toll Free Tel:* 866-602-1476, pg 77

De Vorss & Co, Camarillo, CA *Toll Free Tel:* 800-843-5743, pg 78

B C Decker Inc, Hamilton, ON Canada *Toll Free Tel:* 800-568-7281, pg 542

Ivan R Dee Publisher, Chicago, IL *Toll Free Tel:* 800-462-6420 (orders) *Toll Free Fax:* 800-338-4550 (orders), pg 78

Marcel Dekker Inc, New York, NY *Toll Free Tel:* 800-228-1160 (outside NY), pg 78

Delta Systems Co Inc, McHenry, IL *Toll Free Tel:* 800-323-8270 *Toll Free Fax:* 800-909-9901, pg 79

Demos Medical Publishing LLC, New York, NY *Toll Free Tel:* 800-532-8663, pg 79

Denlinger's Publishers Ltd, Edgewater, FL *Toll Free Tel:* 800-362-1810 *Toll Free Fax:* 800-589-1191, pg 79

Deseret Book Co, Salt Lake City, UT *Toll Free Tel:* 800-453-3876, pg 79

Design Image Group, Burr Ridge, IL *Toll Free Tel:* 800-563-5455, pg 79

Destiny Image, Shippensburg, PA *Toll Free Tel:* 800-722-6774 (orders only), pg 79

Developmental Studies Center, Oakland, CA *Toll Free Tel:* 800-666-7270, pg 79

Dharma Publishing, Berkeley, CA *Toll Free Tel:* 800-873-4276, pg 79

Diablo Press Inc, Pleasant Hill, CA *Toll Free Tel:* 800-488-2665 (orders only), pg 80

Diamond Farm Book Publishers, Alexandria Bay, NY *Toll Free Tel:* 800-481-1353 *Toll Free Fax:* 800-305-5138, pg 80

Diamond Publishers, Southfield, MI *Toll Free Tel:* 888-386-9688, pg 571

DIANE Publishing Co, Collingdale, PA *Toll Free Tel:* 800-782-3833, pg 80

Discipleship Publications International (DPI), Billerica, MA *Toll Free Tel:* 888-DPI-Book, pg 80

Discovery Enterprises Ltd, Carlisle, MA *Toll Free Tel:* 800-729-1720, pg 80

Discovery House Publishers, Grand Rapids, MI *Toll Free Tel:* 800-653-8333, pg 80

Dissertation.com, Boca Raton, FL *Toll Free Tel:* 800-636-8329, pg 81

DK Publishing Inc, New York, NY *Toll Free Tel:* 877-342-5357 (cust serv), pg 81

Dog-Eared Publications, Middleton, WI *Toll Free Tel:* 888-364-3277 *Toll Free Fax:* 888-364-3277, pg 81

Tom Doherty Associates, LLC, New York, NY *Toll Free Tel:* 800-455-0340, pg 81

Domhan Books, Brooklyn, NY *Toll Free Fax:* 888-823-4770, pg 82

Dominie Press Inc, Carlsbad, CA *Toll Free Tel:* 800-232-4570, pg 82

The Donning Co/Publishers, Virginia Beach, VA *Toll Free Tel:* 800-296-8572, pg 82

Dorchester Publishing Co Inc, New York, NY *Toll Free Tel:* 800-481-9191 (order dept), pg 82

Dorland Healthcare Information, Philadelphia, PA *Toll Free Tel:* 800-784-2332, pg 82

Dorset House Publishing Co Inc, New York, NY *Toll Free Tel:* 800-DHBOOKS (342-6657 orders only), pg 82

Doubleday Broadway Publishing Group, New York, NY *Toll Free Tel:* 800-223-6834; 800-223-5780 (sales), pg 82

Douglas & McIntyre Publishing Group, Vancouver, BC Canada *Toll Free Tel:* 800-565-9523 (orders in Canada) *Toll Free Fax:* 800-221-9985 (orders in Canada), pg 542

Douglas Publications Inc, Richmond, VA *Toll Free Tel:* 800-223-1797, pg 83

Dover Publications Inc, Mineola, NY *Toll Free Tel:* 800-223-3130 (orders), pg 83

Down East Books, Camden, ME *Toll Free Tel:* 800-766-1670 (ME only), pg 83

Dramatic Publishing Co, Woodstock, IL *Toll Free Tel:* 800-448-7469 *Toll Free Fax:* 800-334-5302, pg 83

Dufour Editions Inc, Chester Springs, PA *Toll Free Tel:* 800-869-5677, pg 84

Duke University Press, Durham, NC *Toll Free Tel:* 888-651-0122 (orders only) *Toll Free Fax:* 888-651-0124, pg 84

Dun & Bradstreet, Short Hills, NJ *Toll Free Tel:* 800-526-0651, pg 84

Duquesne University Press, Pittsburgh, PA *Toll Free Tel:* 800-666-2211, pg 84

Dustbooks, Paradise, CA *Toll Free Tel:* 800-477-6110, pg 85

Eagan Press, St Paul, MN *Toll Free Tel:* 800-328-7560, pg 85

Eagle's View Publishing, Ogden, UT *Toll Free Tel:* 800-547-3364 (orders over $100), pg 85

Eakin Press, Austin, TX *Toll Free Tel:* 800-880-8642, pg 85

Eastern Washington University Press, Spokane, WA *Toll Free Tel:* 800-508-9095, pg 86

Eastland Press, Seattle, WA *Toll Free Tel:* 800-453-3278 (orders only) *Toll Free Fax:* 800-241-3329 (orders), pg 86

Eckankar, Minneapolis, MN *Toll Free Tel:* 866-485-5556 (CN orders); 888-408-0301 (US orders) *Toll Free Fax:* 866-485-6665 (CN orders), pg 86

Eclipse Press, Lexington, KY *Toll Free Tel:* 800-866-2361, pg 86

ECS Publishing, Boston, MA *Toll Free Tel:* 800-777-1919, pg 86

EDC Publishing, Tulsa, OK *Toll Free Tel:* 800-475-4522 *Toll Free Fax:* 800-747-4509, pg 86

EDCO Publishing Inc, Auburn Hills, MI *Toll Free Tel:* 888-510-3326, pg 87

Nellie Edge Resources Inc, Salem, OR *Toll Free Tel:* 800-523-4594, pg 87

EDGE Science Fiction & Fantasy Publishing, Calgary, AB Canada *Toll Free Tel:* 877-254-0115, pg 543

Editions Anne Sigier Inc, Sillery, PQ Canada *Toll Free Tel:* 800-463-6846 (Canada only), pg 543

Les Editions Brault et Bouthillier, Westmount, PQ Canada *Toll Free Tel:* 800-668-1108, pg 543

Editions Marcel Didier Inc, Montreal, PQ Canada *Toll Free Tel:* 800-361-1664 (Canada), pg 544

Editions du Phare Inc, St Jerome, PQ Canada *Toll Free Tel:* 800-561-2371 (Canada), pg 544

Editions du renouveau Pedagogique Inc, St-Laurent, PQ Canada *Toll Free Tel:* 800-263-3678 *Toll Free Fax:* 800-643-4720, pg 544

Editions Fides, St-Laurent, PQ Canada *Toll Free Tel:* 800-363-1451, pg 545

Editions Hurtubise HMH Ltee, Montreal, PQ Canada *Toll Free Tel:* 800-361-1664 (Canada only), pg 545

Editions Marie-France, Montreal-Nord, PQ Canada *Toll Free Tel:* 800-563-6644, pg 545

Les Editions Phidal Inc, Montreal, PQ Canada *Toll Free Tel:* 800-738-7349, pg 545

Editorial Bautista Independiente, Sebring, FL *Toll Free Tel:* 800-398-7187, pg 87

Editorial Portavoz, Grand Rapids, MI *Toll Free Tel:* 800-733-2607, pg 87

Editorial Unilit, Miami, FL *Toll Free Tel:* 800-767-7726, pg 87

Educational Directories Inc, Schaumburg, IL *Toll Free Tel:* 800-357-6183, pg 87

Educational Impressions Inc, Hawthorne, NJ *Toll Free Tel:* 800-451-7450, pg 87

Educational Insights Inc, Rancho Dominguez, CA *Toll Free Tel:* 800-933-3277, pg 87

Educational Technology Publications, Englewood Cliffs, NJ *Toll Free Tel:* 800-952-2665, pg 88

Educators Progress Service Inc, Randolph, WI *Toll Free Tel:* 888-951-4469, pg 88

Educators Publishing Service Inc, Cambridge, MA *Toll Free Tel:* 800-225-5750 *Toll Free Fax:* 888-440-2665, pg 88

Edupress Inc, San Clemente, CA *Toll Free Tel:* 800-835-7978, pg 88

Wm B Eerdmans Publishing Co, Grand Rapids, MI *Toll Free Tel:* 800-253-7521, pg 88

Elder Books, Forest Knolls, CA *Toll Free Tel:* 800-909-2673 (orders), pg 88

Edward Elgar Publishing Inc, Northampton, MA *Toll Free Tel:* 800-390-3149 (orders), pg 89

Elsevier, Burlington, MA *Toll Free Tel:* 800-545-2522 (cust serv) *Toll Free Fax:* 800-535-9935 (cust serv), pg 89

Elsevier, St Louis, MO *Toll Free Tel:* 800-325-4177, pg 89

Elsevier Engineering Information Inc (Ei), Hoboken, NJ *Toll Free Tel:* 800-221-1044, pg 89

EMC/Paradigm Publishing, St Paul, MN *Toll Free Tel:* 800-328-1452 *Toll Free Fax:* 800-328-4564, pg 89

Emerald Books, Lynnwood, WA *Toll Free Tel:* 800-922-2143, pg 90

Emmaus Road Publishing Inc, Steubenville, OH *Toll Free Tel:* 800-398-5470, pg 90

Emmis Books, Cincinnati, OH *Toll Free Tel:* 800-913-9563, pg 90

Emond Montgomery Publications Ltd, Toronto, ON Canada *Toll Free Tel:* 888-837-0815, pg 546

Encounter Books, San Francisco, CA *Toll Free Tel:* 800-786-3839 *Toll Free Fax:* 877-811-1461, pg 90

Encyclopaedia Britannica Inc, Chicago, IL *Toll Free Tel:* 800-323-1229, pg 91

Enslow Publishers Inc, Berkeley Heights, NJ *Toll Free Tel:* 800-398-2504, pg 91

Environmental Ethics Books, Denton, TX *Toll Free Tel:* 800-264-9962 *Toll Free Fax:* 800-295-0536, pg 91

Lawrence Erlbaum Associates Inc, Mahwah, NJ *Toll Free Tel:* 800-9-BOOKS-9 (926-6579), pg 91

Ernst Publishing Company LLC, Clarksville, NY *Toll Free Tel:* 800-345-3822 *Toll Free Fax:* 800-252-0906, pg 92

eSchool News, Bethesda, MD *Toll Free Tel:* 800-394-0115, pg 92

Essence Publishing, Belleville, ON Canada *Toll Free Tel:* 800-238-6376, pg 546

ETC Publications, Palm Springs, CA *Toll Free Tel:* 800-382-7869, pg 92

Great Potential Press, Scottsdale, AZ *Toll Free Tel:* 877-954-4200, pg 108

Great Quotations Inc, Woodridge, IL *Toll Free Tel:* 800-830-3020, pg 108

Great Source Education Group, Wilmington, MA *Toll Free Tel:* 800-289-4490 (orders), pg 108

Warren H Green Inc, St Louis, MO *Toll Free Tel:* 800-537-0655, pg 108

Greenhaven Press®, San Diego, CA *Toll Free Tel:* 800-877-4253 (cust serv & orders) *Toll Free Fax:* 800-414-5043 (orders only), pg 108

Greenleaf Book Group LLC, Austin, TX *Toll Free Tel:* 800-932-5420, pg 109

Greenwood Publishing Group Inc, Westport, CT *Toll Free Tel:* 800-225-5800, pg 109

Grey House Publishing Inc, Millerton, NY *Toll Free Tel:* 800-562-2139, pg 109

Greystone Books, Vancouver, BC Canada *Toll Free Tel:* 800-667-6902, pg 548

Griffin Publishing Group, Irvine, CA *Toll Free Tel:* 800-472-9741, pg 109

Group Publishing Inc, Loveland, CO *Toll Free Tel:* 800-447-1070, pg 110

Groupe Educalivres Inc, Laval, PQ Canada *Toll Free Tel:* 800-567-3671 (Info Service), pg 548

Grove/Atlantic Inc, New York, NY *Toll Free Tel:* 800-521-0178, pg 110

Gryphon Editions, New York, NY *Toll Free Tel:* 800-633-8911, pg 110

Gryphon House Inc, Beltsville, MD *Toll Free Tel:* 800-638-0928, pg 110

Guerin Editeur Ltee, Montreal, PQ Canada *Toll Free Tel:* 800-398-8337, pg 549

Guernica Editions Inc, Tonawanda, NY *Toll Free Tel:* 800-565-9523 (orders) *Toll Free Fax:* 800-221-9985 (orders), pg 110

Guernica Editions Inc, Toronto, ON Canada *Toll Free Tel:* 800-565-9523 (orders) *Toll Free Fax:* 800-221-9985 (orders), pg 549

Guild Publishing, Madison, WI *Toll Free Tel:* 800-930-1856, pg 111

The Guilford Press, New York, NY *Toll Free Tel:* 800-365-7006 (orders), pg 111

H D I Publishers, Houston, TX *Toll Free Tel:* 800-321-7037, pg 111

Hachai Publications Inc, Brooklyn, NY *Toll Free Tel:* 800-50-HACHAI (504-2424), pg 111

Hackett Publishing Co Inc, Indianapolis, IN *Toll Free Fax:* 800-783-9213, pg 111

Hagstrom Map Co Inc, Maspeth, NY *Toll Free Tel:* 800-432-MAPS (432-6277), pg 111

Hal Leonard Corp, Milwaukee, WI *Toll Free Tel:* 800-524-4425, pg 112

Half Halt Press Inc, Boonsboro, MD *Toll Free Tel:* 800-822-9635 (orders only), pg 112

Alexander Hamilton Institute, Ramsey, NJ *Toll Free Tel:* 800-879-2441, pg 112

Hammond World Atlas Corp, Union, NJ *Toll Free Tel:* 800-526-4953, pg 112

Hampton-Brown Co Inc, Carmel, CA *Toll Free Tel:* 800-933-3510, pg 113

Hampton Press Inc, Cresskill, NJ *Toll Free Tel:* 800-894-8955, pg 113

Hampton Roads Publishing Co Inc, Charlottesville, VA *Toll Free Tel:* 800-766-8009 (orders) *Toll Free Fax:* 800-766-9042, pg 113

Hancock House Publishers, Blaine, WA *Toll Free Tel:* 800-938-1114 *Toll Free Fax:* 800-983-2262, pg 113

Hancock House Publishers Ltd, Surrey, BC Canada *Toll Free Tel:* 800-938-1114 *Toll Free Fax:* 800-983-2262, pg 549

Hanley & Belfus, Philadelphia, PA *Toll Free Tel:* 800-545-2522 (orders), pg 113

Hanley-Wood LLC, Addison, IL *Toll Free Tel:* 800-837-0870, pg 113

Hanser Gardner Publications, Cincinnati, OH *Toll Free Tel:* 800-950-8977 *Toll Free Fax:* 800-527-8801, pg 113

Harbour Publishing Co Ltd, Madeira Park, BC Canada *Toll Free Tel:* 800-667-2988; 800-667-2988 *Toll Free Fax:* 877-604-9449, pg 549

Harcourt Achieve, Austin, TX *Toll Free Tel:* 800-531-5015 *Toll Free Fax:* 800-699-9459, pg 114

Harcourt Assessment Inc, San Antonio, TX *Toll Free Tel:* 800-211-8378, pg 114

Harcourt Canada Ltd, Toronto, ON Canada *Toll Free Tel:* 800-387-7278 (North America); 800-387-7305 (North America) *Toll Free Fax:* 800-665-7307 (North America), pg 549

Harcourt Inc, Orlando, FL *Toll Free Tel:* 800-225-5425 (cust serv), pg 114

Harcourt Interactive Technology, Roslyn Heights, NY *Toll Free Tel:* 800-745-3276, pg 114

Harcourt School Publishers, Orlando, FL *Toll Free Tel:* 800-225-5425 (cust serv) *Toll Free Fax:* 800-874-6418, pg 114

Harcourt Trade Publishers, San Diego, CA *Toll Free Tel:* 800-543-1918 (cust serv) *Toll Free Fax:* 800-235-0256 (cust serv), pg 115

Harmonie Park Press, Warren, MI *Toll Free Tel:* 800-886-3080, pg 115

Harris InfoSource, Twinsburg, OH *Toll Free Tel:* 800-888-5900 *Toll Free Fax:* 800-643-5997, pg 116

Harrison House Publishers, Tulsa, OK *Toll Free Tel:* 800-888-4126 *Toll Free Fax:* 800-830-5688, pg 116

Hartley & Marks Publishers Ltd, Vancouver, BC Canada *Toll Free Tel:* 800-277-5887 *Toll Free Fax:* 800-707-5887, pg 549

Hartman Publishing Inc, Albuquerque, NM *Toll Free Tel:* 800-999-9534 *Toll Free Fax:* 800-474-6106, pg 116

Harvard Business School Press, Watertown, MA *Toll Free Tel:* 888-500-1016, pg 116

The Harvard Common Press, Boston, MA *Toll Free Tel:* 888-657-3755, pg 117

Harvard Education Publishing Group, Cambridge, MA *Toll Free Tel:* 800-513-0763, pg 117

Harvard University Press, Cambridge, MA *Toll Free Tel:* 800-405-1619 (orders) *Toll Free Fax:* 800-406-9145 (orders), pg 117

Harvest Hill Press, Salisbury Cove, ME *Toll Free Tel:* 888-288-8900, pg 117

Harvest House Publishers Inc, Eugene, OR *Toll Free Tel:* 800-547-8979, pg 117

Hastings House/Daytrips Publishers, Fern Park, FL *Toll Free Tel:* 800-206-7822, pg 117

Hatherleigh Press, Long Island City, NY *Toll Free Tel:* 800-528-2550, pg 117

The Haworth Press Inc, Binghamton, NY *Toll Free Tel:* 800-429-6784 *Toll Free Fax:* 800-895-0582, pg 118

Hay House Inc, Carlsbad, CA *Toll Free Tel:* 800-650-5115; 800-654-5126 (orders), pg 118

Haynes Manuals Inc, Newbury Park, CA *Toll Free Tel:* 800-442-9637, pg 118

Hazelden Publishing & Educational Services, Center City, MN *Toll Free Tel:* 800-328-9000, pg 118

HCPro, Marblehead, MA *Toll Free Tel:* 800-650-6787 *Toll Free Fax:* 800-639-8511, pg 118

Health Communications Inc, Deerfield Beach, FL *Toll Free Tel:* 800-851-9100 (cust serv); 800-441-5569 (order entry), pg 119

Health Forum Inc, Chicago, IL *Toll Free Tel:* 800-242-2626, pg 119

Health InfoNet Inc, San Ramon, CA *Toll Free Tel:* 800-446-1947, pg 119

Health Professions Press, Baltimore, MD *Toll Free Tel:* 888-337-8808, pg 119

Health Research, Pomeroy, WA *Toll Free Tel:* 888-844-2386, pg 119

Heart Math, Boulder Creek, CA *Toll Free Tel:* 800-450-9111, pg 120

Hearts & Tummies Cookbook Co, Wever, IA *Toll Free Tel:* 800-571-BOOK, pg 120

William S Hein & Co Inc, Buffalo, NY *Toll Free Tel:* 800-828-7571, pg 120

Heinemann, Portsmouth, NH *Toll Free Tel:* 800-225-5800, pg 120

Heinemann/Boynton Cook Publishers Inc, Portsmouth, NH *Toll Free Tel:* 800-541-2086, pg 120

Helgate Press, Central Point, OR *Toll Free Tel:* 800-795-4059, pg 120

Hellgate Press, Gold Hill, OR *Toll Free Tel:* 800-795-4059, pg 121

Hemingway Western Studies Series, Boise, ID *Toll Free Tel:* 800-992-TEXT (992-8398), pg 121

Hendrickson Publishers Inc, Peabody, MA *Toll Free Tel:* 800-358-3111, pg 121

Hensley Publishing, Tulsa, OK *Toll Free Tel:* 800-288-8520 (orders only), pg 121

Herald Press, Scottdale, PA *Toll Free Tel:* 800-245-7894, pg 121

Herald Press, Waterloo, ON Canada *Toll Free Tel:* 800-245-7894 (Canada & US), pg 550

Herald Publishing House, Independence, MO *Toll Free Tel:* 800-767-8181, pg 121

Heritage Books Inc, Westminster, MD *Toll Free Tel:* 866-282-2689, pg 121

The Heritage Foundation, Washington, DC *Toll Free Tel:* 800-544-4843, pg 121

Heritage House Publishing Co Ltd, Surrey, BC Canada *Toll Free Tel:* 800-665-3302 *Toll Free Fax:* 800-566-3336, pg 550

Heuer Publishing LLC, Cedar Rapids, IA *Toll Free Tel:* 800-950-7529, pg 122

Hewitt Homeschooling Resources, Washougal, WA *Toll Free Tel:* 800-348-1750, pg 122

Hi Willow Research & Publishing, Salt Lake City, UT *Toll Free Tel:* 800-873-3043, pg 122

High Plains Press, Glendo, WY *Toll Free Tel:* 800-552-7819, pg 122

Hillsdale College Press, Hillsdale, MI *Toll Free Tel:* 800-437-2268, pg 123

Himalayan Institute Press, Honesdale, PA *Toll Free Tel:* 800-822-4547, pg 123

Hippocrene Books Inc, New York, NY *Toll Free Fax:* 800-809-3855 (sales), pg 123

Hobby House Press Inc, Grantsville, MD *Toll Free Tel:* 800-554-1447, pg 123

Hogrefe & Huber Publishers, Cambridge, MA *Toll Free Tel:* 800-228-3749; 866-823-4726, pg 123

Hohm Press, Prescott, AZ *Toll Free Tel:* 800-381-2700, pg 123

Hollywood Creative Directory, Hollywood, CA *Toll Free Tel:* 800-815-0503, pg 124

Henry Holt and Company, LLC, New York, NY *Toll Free Tel:* 888-330-8477 (orders), pg 124

Holt, Rinehart and Winston, Austin, TX *Toll Free Tel:* 800-225-5425 (cust serv), pg 124

Home Planners LLC, Tucson, AZ *Toll Free Tel:* 800-322-6797 *Toll Free Fax:* 800-531-2555, pg 125

Homestore Plans & Publications, St Paul, MN *Toll Free Tel:* 888-626-2026, pg 125

Honor Books, Colorado Springs, CO *Toll Free Tel:* 800-708-5550, pg 125

Hoover Institution Press, Stanford, CA *Toll Free Tel:* 800-935-2882, pg 125

Hoover's, Inc, Austin, TX *Toll Free Tel:* 800-486-8666 (orders only), pg 125

Hope Publishing Co, Carol Stream, IL *Toll Free Tel:* 800-323-1049, pg 125

Horizon Publishers & Distributors Inc, Bountiful, UT *Toll Free Tel:* 800-759-2665, pg 125

Hot House Press, Cohasset, MA *Toll Free Tel:* 866-331-8360, pg 126

Houghton Mifflin College Division, Boston, MA *Toll Free Tel:* 800-225-1464 (orders), pg 126

Houghton Mifflin Co, Boston, MA *Toll Free Tel:* 800-225-3362 (trade books); 800-733-2828 (text books); 800-225-1464 (college texts), pg 126

Houghton Mifflin Trade & Reference Division, Boston, MA *Toll Free Tel:* 800-225-3362, pg 126

House to House Publications, Ephrata, PA *Toll Free Tel:* 800-848-5892, pg 127

Howard Publishing, West Monroe, LA *Toll Free Tel:* 800-858-4109, pg 127

Howell Press Inc, Charlottesville, VA *Toll Free Tel:* 800-868-4512 *Toll Free Fax:* 888-971-7204, pg 127

Howie Publishing Inc, Columbus, OH *Toll Free Tel:* 888-933-9314, pg 571

HRD Press, Amherst, MA *Toll Free Tel:* 800-822-2801, pg 127

Human Kinetics Inc, Champaign, IL *Toll Free Tel:* 800-747-4457, pg 128

Humanics Publishing Group, Lake Worth, FL *Toll Free Tel:* 800-874-8844 *Toll Free Fax:* 888-874-8844, pg 128

Hunter House Publishers, Alameda, CA *Toll Free Tel:* 800-266-5592, pg 128

Hunter Publishing Inc, Edison, NJ *Toll Free Tel:* 800-255-0343, pg 129

Huntington House Publishers, Lafayette, LA *Toll Free Tel:* 800-749-4009 (sales), pg 129

Huntington Press Publishing, Las Vegas, NV *Toll Free Tel:* 800-244-2224, pg 129

Hyperion, New York, NY *Toll Free Tel:* 800-759-0190 (cust serv), pg 129

Ibex Publishers, Bethesda, MD *Toll Free Tel:* 888-718-8188, pg 129

Iconografix Inc, Hudson, WI *Toll Free Tel:* 800-289-3504 (orders only), pg 130

ICS Press, Oakland, CA *Toll Free Tel:* 800-326-0263, pg 130

Idaho Center for the Book, Boise, ID *Toll Free Tel:* 800-992-8398, pg 130

Ideals Publications Inc, Nashville, TN *Toll Free Tel:* 800-558-4343 (customer service), pg 130

IEEE Computer Society, Los Alamitos, CA *Toll Free Tel:* 800-272-6657, pg 130

Ignatius Press, San Francisco, CA *Toll Free Tel:* 877-320-9276 (book orders), pg 131

Illumination Arts Publishing, Bellevue, WA *Toll Free Tel:* 888-210-8216, pg 131

Images from the Past Inc, Bennington, VT *Toll Free Tel:* 888-442-3204, pg 131

ImaJinn Books, Canon City, CO *Toll Free Tel:* 877-625-3592, pg 131

Impact Publishers Inc, Atascadero, CA *Toll Free Tel:* 800-246-7228 (orders), pg 131

In Audio, Falls Church, VA *Toll Free Tel:* 800-643-0295, pg 132

Incentive Publications Inc, Nashville, TN *Toll Free Tel:* 800-421-2830, pg 132

Indiana Historical Society Press, Indianapolis, IN *Toll Free Tel:* 800-447-1830 (orders only), pg 132

Indiana University Press, Bloomington, IN *Toll Free Tel:* 800-842-6796 (orders only), pg 132

Industrial Press Inc, New York, NY *Toll Free Tel:* 888-528-7852, pg 132

InfoBooks, Santa Monica, CA *Toll Free Tel:* 800-669-0409, pg 133

Information Gatekeepers Inc, Boston, MA *Toll Free Tel:* 800-323-1088, pg 133

Information Publications, Palo Alto, CA *Toll Free Tel:* 877-544-4636 *Toll Free Fax:* 877-544-4635, pg 133

Information Today, Inc, Medford, NJ *Toll Free Tel:* 800-300-9868 (cust serv), pg 133

Ingenix Inc, Salt Lake City, UT *Toll Free Tel:* 800-765-6014, pg 133

Inner Ocean Publishing Inc, Makawao, Maui, HI *Toll Free Tel:* 800-863-1449 *Toll Free Fax:* 800-755-4118, pg 134

Inner Traditions International Ltd, Rochester, VT *Toll Free Tel:* 800-246-8648, pg 134

Institute for International Economics, Washington, DC *Toll Free Tel:* 800-522-9139, pg 134

Institute for Language Study, Wilton, CT *Toll Free Tel:* 800-245-2145, pg 134

Institute of Continuing Legal Education, Ann Arbor, MI *Toll Free Tel:* 877-229-4350 *Toll Free Fax:* 877-229-4351, pg 135

Institute of Electrical & Electronics Engineers Inc, Piscataway, NJ *Toll Free Tel:* 800-678-4333, pg 135

Institute of Psychological Research, Inc., Montreal, PQ Canada *Toll Free Tel:* 800-363-7800 *Toll Free Fax:* 888-382-3007, pg 551

Instructional Fair Group, Grand Rapids, MI *Toll Free Tel:* 800-417-3261 *Toll Free Fax:* 888-203-9361, pg 135

Insurance Institute of America Inc, Malvern, PA *Toll Free Tel:* 800-644-2101, pg 135

Interchange Inc, Plymouth, MN *Toll Free Tel:* 800-669-6208 *Toll Free Fax:* 800-729-0395, pg 136

Intercultural Press Inc, Yarmouth, ME *Toll Free Tel:* 866-372-2665, pg 136

Interlink Publishing Group Inc, Northampton, MA *Toll Free Tel:* 800-238-LINK (238-5465), pg 136

International Code Council Inc, Whittier, CA *Toll Free Tel:* 800-423-6587, pg 137

International Foundation of Employee Benefit Plans, Brookfield, WI *Toll Free Tel:* 888-334-3327, pg 137

International Linguistics Corp, Grandview, MO *Toll Free Tel:* 800-237-1830, pg 137

International Medical Publishing Inc, McLean, VA *Toll Free Tel:* 800-530-3142, pg 137

International Risk Management Institute Inc, Dallas, TX *Toll Free Tel:* 800-827-4242, pg 138

International Society for Technology in Education, Eugene, OR *Toll Free Tel:* 800-336-5191 (orders only), pg 138

International Students Inc, Colorado Springs, CO *Toll Free Tel:* 800-474-4147 ext 111 (orders), pg 138

International Universities Press Inc, Madison, CT *Toll Free Tel:* 800-835-3487, pg 138

International Wealth Success Inc, Merrick, NY *Toll Free Tel:* 800-323-0548, pg 138

InterVarsity Press, Westmont, IL *Toll Free Tel:* 800-843-7225, pg 138

Interweave Press, Loveland, CO *Toll Free Tel:* 800-272-2193, pg 138

Irwin Law Inc, Toronto, ON Canada *Toll Free Tel:* 888-314-9014, pg 551

ISI Books, Wilmington, DE *Toll Free Tel:* 800-526-7022, pg 139

Island Press, Washington, DC *Toll Free Tel:* 800-828-1302, pg 139

iUniverse, Lincoln, NE *Toll Free Tel:* 877-288-4737, pg 139

Richard Ivey School of Business, London, ON Canada *Toll Free Tel:* 800-649-6355, pg 551

Ivy House Publishing Group, Raleigh, NC *Toll Free Tel:* 800-948-2786, pg 572

Jane's Information Group, Alexandria, VA *Toll Free Tel:* 800-824-0768 (sales) *Toll Free Fax:* 800-836-0297, pg 140

Jewish Lights Publishing, Woodstock, VT *Toll Free Tel:* 800-962-4544, pg 140

Jewish Publication Society, Philadelphia, PA *Toll Free Tel:* 800-234-3151, pg 141

JIST Publishing Inc, Indianapolis, IN *Toll Free Tel:* 800-648-5478 *Toll Free Fax:* 800-547-8329, pg 141

John Deere Publishing, Davenport, IA *Toll Free Tel:* 800-522-7448, pg 141

The Johns Hopkins University Press, Baltimore, MD *Toll Free Tel:* 800-537-5487, pg 141

Johnson Books, Boulder, CO *Toll Free Tel:* 800-258-5830, pg 141

Jones & Bartlett Publishers Inc, Sudbury, MA *Toll Free Tel:* 800-832-0034, pg 142

Bob Jones University Press, Greenville, SC *Toll Free Tel:* 800-845-5731 (orders only), pg 142

Jones McClure Publishing Inc, Houston, TX *Toll Free Tel:* 800-626-6667, pg 142

Jossey-Bass, San Francisco, CA *Toll Free Tel:* 800-956-7739, pg 142

Joy Publishing, Fountain Valley, CA *Toll Free Tel:* 800-454-8228, pg 142

Judaica Press Inc, Brooklyn, NY *Toll Free Tel:* 800-972-6201, pg 142

Judson Press, King of Prussia, PA *Toll Free Tel:* 800-458-3766, pg 142

Kabbalah Publishing, New York, NY *Toll Free Tel:* 866-524-8723, pg 143

Kabel Publishers, Rockville, MD *Toll Free Tel:* 800-543-3167, pg 143

Kaeden Corp, Rocky River, OH *Toll Free Tel:* 800-890-7323, pg 143

Kalmbach Publishing Co, Waukesha, WI *Toll Free Tel:* 800-533-6644, pg 143

Kane/Miller Book Publishers, La Jolla, CA *Toll Free Tel:* 800-968-1930, pg 144

Kar-Ben Publishing, Minneapolis, MN *Toll Free Tel:* 800-4-KARBEN (452-7236) *Toll Free Fax:* 800-332-1132, pg 144

KC Publications Inc, Las Vegas, NV *Toll Free Tel:* 800-626-9673, pg 144

J J Keller & Associates, Inc, Neenah, WI *Toll Free Tel:* 800-327-6868 *Toll Free Fax:* 800-727-7516, pg 144

Kendall/Hunt Publishing Co, Dubuque, IA *Toll Free Tel:* 800-228-0810 (orders only) *Toll Free Fax:* 800-772-9165, pg 144

Kennedy Information, Peterborough, NH *Toll Free Tel:* 800-531-0007, pg 145

Kensington Publishing Corp, New York, NY *Toll Free Tel:* 800-221-2647, pg 145

Kent State University Press, Kent, OH *Toll Free Tel:* 800-247-6553 (orders), pg 145

Key Curriculum Press, Emeryville, CA *Toll Free Tel:* 800-995-6284 *Toll Free Fax:* 800-541-2442, pg 145

Kids Can Press Ltd, Tonawanda, NY *Toll Free Tel:* 800-265-0884; 866-481-5827 (orders), pg 145

Kids Can Press Ltd, Toronto, ON Canada *Toll Free Tel:* 800-265-0884, pg 552

Kindred Productions, Winnipeg, MB Canada *Toll Free Tel:* 800-545-7322, pg 552

Kinship Books, Rhinebeck, NY *Toll Free Tel:* 800-249-1109 (orders), pg 145

Kirkbride Bible Co Inc, Indianapolis, IN *Toll Free Tel:* 800-428-4385, pg 146

Kiva Publishing Inc, Walnut, CA *Toll Free Tel:* 800-634-5482, pg 146

Allen A Knoll Publishers, Santa Barbara, CA *Toll Free Tel:* 800-777-7623, pg 146

Alfred A Knopf, New York, NY *Toll Free Tel:* 800-638-6460, pg 146

Knopf Canada, Toronto, ON Canada *Toll Free Tel:* 800-668-4247 (order desk), pg 552

Krause Publications, Iola, WI *Toll Free Tel:* 800-258-0929; 888-457-2873, pg 147

Kregel Publications, Grand Rapids, MI *Toll Free Tel:* 800-733-2607, pg 147

Krieger Publishing Co, Melbourne, FL *Toll Free Tel:* 800-724-0025, pg 147

Kumarian Press Inc, Bloomfield, CT *Toll Free Tel:* 800-289-2664 (orders only), pg 147

LadybugPress, Sonora, CA *Toll Free Tel:* 888-892-5000, pg 148

LAMA Books, Hayward, CA *Toll Free Tel:* 888-452-6244, pg 148

Lanahan Publishers Inc, Baltimore, MD *Toll Free Tel:* 866-354-1949 *Toll Free Fax:* 888-345-7257, pg 148

Landauer Books, Cumming, IA *Toll Free Tel:* 800-557-2144, pg 148

Landes Bioscience, Georgetown, TX *Toll Free Tel:* 800-736-9948, pg 148

Peter Lang Publishing Inc, New York, NY *Toll Free Tel:* 800-770-5264 (cust serv), pg 148

Langenscheidt Publishers Inc, Maspeth, NY *Toll Free Tel:* 800-432-MAPS (732-6277) *Toll Free Fax:* 888-773-7979, pg 149

LangMarc Publishing, Austin, TX *Toll Free Tel:* 800-864-1648, pg 149

Lantern Books, New York, NY *Toll Free Tel:* 800-856-8664, pg 149

Laredo Publishing Company Inc, Beverly Hills, CA *Toll Free Tel:* 800-547-5113, pg 149

Lark Books, Asheville, NC *Toll Free Tel:* 800-284-3388 (cust serv), pg 149

Larson Publications, Burdett, NY *Toll Free Tel:* 800-828-2197, pg 149

Laughing Elephant, Seattle, WA *Toll Free Tel:* 800-354-0400, pg 149

Laureate Press, Bangor, ME *Toll Free Tel:* 800-946-2727, pg 150

The Lawbook Exchange Ltd, Clark, NJ *Toll Free Tel:* 800-422-6686, pg 150

LDA Publishers, Bayside, NY *Toll Free Tel:* 888-388-9887, pg 150

Leadership Ministries Worldwide, Chattanooga, TN *Toll Free Tel:* 800-987-8790 *Toll Free Fax:* 800-987-8790, pg 150

Leadership Publishers Inc, Des Moines, IA *Toll Free Tel:* 800-814-3757, pg 150

Leading Edge Reports, Commack, NY *Toll Free Tel:* 800-866-4648, pg 151

Leaping Dog Press, San Jose, CA *Toll Free Tel:* 877-570-6873 *Toll Free Fax:* 877-570-6873, pg 151

The Learning Connection (TLC), Lake Wales, FL *Toll Free Tel:* 800-218-8489, pg 151

Learning Links Inc, New Hyde Park, NY *Toll Free Tel:* 800-724-2616, pg 151

Learning Resources Network (LERN), River Falls, WI *Toll Free Tel:* 800-678-5376 *Toll Free Fax:* 888-234-8633, pg 151

LearningExpress LLC, New York, NY *Toll Free Tel:* 800-295-9556, pg 151

Lectorum Publications Inc, New York, NY *Toll Free Tel:* 800-853-3291 (admin, mktg & sales); 800-345-5946 (orders) *Toll Free Fax:* 877-532-8676, pg 151

Lederer Books, Baltimore, MD *Toll Free Tel:* 800-773-6574, pg 151

Lee & Low Books Inc, New York, NY *Toll Free Tel:* 888-320-3190 ext 25 (orders only), pg 152

J & L Lee Co, Lincoln, NE *Toll Free Tel:* 888-665-0999, pg 152

Legal Education Publishing, Madison, WI *Toll Free Tel:* 800-957-4670, pg 152

Leisure Arts Inc, Little Rock, AR *Toll Free Tel:* 800-643-8030, pg 152

Lerner Publications, Minneapolis, MN *Toll Free Tel:* 800-328-4929 *Toll Free Fax:* 800-332-1132, pg 152

Lerner Publishing Group, Minneapolis, MN *Toll Free Tel:* 800-328-4929 *Toll Free Fax:* 800-332-1132, pg 152

LernerClassroom, Minneapolis, MN *Toll Free Tel:* 800-328-4929 *Toll Free Fax:* 800-332-1132, pg 153

LernerSports, Minneapolis, MN *Toll Free Tel:* 800-328-4929 *Toll Free Fax:* 800-332-1132, pg 153

The Letter People®, Waterbury, CT *Toll Free Tel:* 800-227-9120; 800-874-0029 *Toll Free Fax:* 800-737-3322, pg 153

LexisNexis®, Charlottesville, VA *Toll Free Tel:* 800-446-3410; 800-828-8341 (orders), pg 153

LexisNexis Academic & Library Solutions, Bethesda, MD *Toll Free Tel:* 800-638-8380, pg 153

LexisNexis Canada, Markham, ON Canada *Toll Free Tel:* 800-668-6481 *Toll Free Fax:* 800-461-3275, pg 552

Liberty Fund Inc, Indianapolis, IN *Toll Free Tel:* 800-955-8335, pg 153

Libraries Unlimited, Westport, CT *Toll Free Tel:* 800-225-5800, pg 154

Lidec Inc, Montreal, PQ Canada *Toll Free Tel:* 800-350-5991 (Canada Only), pg 552

Mary Ann Liebert Inc, Larchmont, NY *Toll Free Tel:* 800-654-3237, pg 154

Life Cycle Books, Niagara Falls, NY *Toll Free Tel:* 800-214-5849, pg 154

Life Cycle Books Ltd, Toronto, ON Canada *Toll Free Tel:* 866-880-5860 *Toll Free Fax:* 866-690-8532, pg 552

LifeQuest, Fort Wayne, IN *Toll Free Tel:* 800-774-3360, pg 154

Light-Beams Publishing, Lee, NH *Toll Free Tel:* 800-397-7641, pg 154

Light Technology Publishing, Flagstaff, AZ *Toll Free Tel:* 800-450-0985, pg 154

Liguori Publications, Liguori, MO *Toll Free Tel:* 800-464-2555, pg 154

Linden Publishing Company Inc, Fresno, CA *Toll Free Tel:* 800-345-4447 (orders only), pg 155

Lindisfarne Books, Hudson, NY *Toll Free Tel:* 800-856-8664 (orders), pg 155

LinguiSystems Inc, East Moline, IL *Toll Free Tel:* 800-776-4332, pg 155

Linns Stamp News-Ancillary Division, Sidney, OH *Toll Free Fax:* 800-488-5349, pg 155

Linworth Publishing Inc, Worthington, OH *Toll Free Tel:* 800-786-5017, pg 155

LionHearted Publishing Inc, Zephyr Cove, NV *Toll Free Tel:* 888-546-6478 *Toll Free Fax:* 888-546-6478, pg 155

Lippincott Williams & Wilkins, Philadelphia, PA *Toll Free Tel:* 800-638-3030 (cust serv), pg 156

Listen & Live Audio Inc, Roseland, NJ *Toll Free Tel:* 800-653-9400, pg 156

Little, Brown and Company Books for Young Readers, New York, NY *Toll Free Tel:* 800-759-0190, pg 156

Liturgical Press, Collegeville, MN *Toll Free Tel:* 800-858-5450 *Toll Free Fax:* 800-445-5899, pg 156

Liturgy Training Publications, Chicago, IL *Toll Free Tel:* 800-933-1800 (US & Canada only) *Toll Free Fax:* 800-933-7094 (US & Canada only), pg 156

Living Language, New York, NY *Toll Free Tel:* 800-726-0600 (orders) *Toll Free Fax:* 800-659-2436, pg 157

Llewellyn Publications, St Paul, MN *Toll Free Tel:* 800-843-6666, pg 157

The Local History Co, Pittsburgh, PA *Toll Free Tel:* 866-362-0789, pg 157

Logos Bible Software, Bellingham, WA *Toll Free Tel:* 800-875-6467, pg 157

Lone Eagle Publishing, Los Angeles, CA *Toll Free Tel:* 800-815-0503, pg 157

Lone Pine Publishing, Edmonton, AB Canada *Toll Free Tel:* 800-661-9017 *Toll Free Fax:* 800-424-7173, pg 552

Lonely Planet Publications, Oakland, CA *Toll Free Tel:* 800-275-8555 (orders), pg 157

Loompanics Unlimited, Port Townsend, WA *Toll Free Tel:* 800-380-2230 (orders only), pg 158

Looseleaf Law Publications Inc, Flushing, NY *Toll Free Tel:* 800-647-5547, pg 158

Lost Classics Book Co, Lake Wales, FL *Toll Free Tel:* 800-283-3572 (wholesale orders); 888-211-2665 (educational), pg 158

Lotus Press, Twin Lakes, WI *Toll Free Tel:* 800-824-6396 (orders only), pg 159

Louisiana State University Press, Baton Rouge, LA *Toll Free Tel:* 800-861-3477 *Toll Free Fax:* 800-305-4416, pg 159

Loyola Press, Chicago, IL *Toll Free Tel:* 800-621-1008, pg 159

LRP Publications, Palm Beach Gardens, FL *Toll Free Tel:* 800-341-7874, pg 159

LRS, Los Angeles, CA *Toll Free Tel:* 800-255-5002, pg 159

The Lyons Press, Guilford, CT *Toll Free Tel:* 800-243-0495, pg 160

M R T S, Tempe, AZ *Toll Free Tel:* 800-666-2211 *Toll Free Fax:* 800-688-2877, pg 160

MacAdam/Cage Publishing Inc, San Francisco, CA *Toll Free Tel:* 866-986-7470, pg 160

Macalester Park Publishing Co, Minneapolis, MN *Toll Free Tel:* 800-407-9078, pg 161

Macmillan Reference USA™, Woodbridge, CT *Toll Free Tel:* 800-444-0799, pg 161

Madison House Publishers, Lanham, MD *Toll Free Tel:* 800-462-6420, pg 161

Mage Publishers Inc, Washington, DC *Toll Free Tel:* 800-962-0922, pg 161

Magick Mirror Communications, New York, NY *Toll Free Tel:* 800-356-6796, pg 572

Maharishi University of Management Press, Fairfield, IA *Toll Free Tel:* 800-831-6523, pg 161

Mandala Publishing, San Rafael, CA *Toll Free Tel:* 800-688-2218 (orders only), pg 162

Manhattan Publishing Co, Croton-on-Hudson, NY *Toll Free Tel:* 888-686-7066, pg 162

MapEasy Inc, Wainscotte, NY *Toll Free Tel:* 888-627-3279, pg 162

Mapletree Publishing Co, Highlands Ranch, CO *Toll Free Tel:* 800-537-0414, pg 163

MAR*CO Products Inc, Warminster, PA *Toll Free Tel:* 800-448-2197, pg 163

Marathon Press, Norfolk, NE *Toll Free Tel:* 800-228-0629, pg 163

MARC Publications, Monrovia, CA *Toll Free Tel:* 800-777-7752 (US only), pg 163

Marion Street Press, Oak Park, IL *Toll Free Tel:* 866-443-7987, pg 163

Market Data Retrieval, Shelton, CT *Toll Free Tel:* 800-333-8802, pg 163

Markowski International Publishers, Humelstown, PA *Toll Free Tel:* 800-566-0534 (orders only), pg 164

Marlor Press Inc, St Paul, MN *Toll Free Tel:* 800-669-4908, pg 164

Marquette University Press, Milwaukee, WI *Toll Free Tel:* 800-247-6553, pg 164

Marquis Who's Who, New Providence, NJ *Toll Free Tel:* 800-473-7020, pg 164

Marshall & Swift, Los Angeles, CA *Toll Free Tel:* 800-544-2678, pg 164

Martindale-Hubbell, New Providence, NJ *Toll Free Tel:* 800-526-4902, pg 164

Martingale & Co, Woodinville, WA *Toll Free Tel:* 800-426-3126, pg 164

Mason Crest Publishers, Broomall, PA *Toll Free Tel:* 866-MCP-BOOK (627-2665), pg 165

Math Teachers Press Inc, Minneapolis, MN *Toll Free Tel:* 800-852-2435, pg 165

The Mathematical Association of America, Washington, DC *Toll Free Tel:* 800-331-1622 (orders), pg 165

Maupin House Publishing, Gainesville, FL *Toll Free Tel:* 800-524-0634 (orders only), pg 165

Maximum Press, Gulf Breeze, FL *Toll Free Tel:* 800-989-6733, pg 166

Maxit Publishing Inc, Lompoc, CA *Toll Free Tel:* 866-686-5100, pg 166

McBooks Press Inc, Ithaca, NY *Toll Free Tel:* 888-266-5711, pg 166

McClanahan Publishing House Inc, Kuttawa, KY *Toll Free Tel:* 800-544-6959, pg 166

McCormack's Guides Inc, Martinez, CA *Toll Free Tel:* 800-222-3602, pg 166

McCutchan Publishing Corp, Richmond, CA *Toll Free Tel:* 800-227-1540, pg 166

The McDonald & Woodward Publishing Co, Granville, OH *Toll Free Tel:* 800-233-8787, pg 166

McDougal Littell, Evanston, IL *Toll Free Tel:* 800-462-6595 (orders) *Toll Free Fax:* 888-872-8380, pg 166

McFarland & Co Inc Publishers, Jefferson, NC *Toll Free Tel:* 800-253-2187 (orders only), pg 166

McGraw-Hill/Dushkin, Dubuque, IA *Toll Free Tel:* 800-243-6532, pg 167

McGraw-Hill Higher Education, Burr Ridge, IL *Toll Free Tel:* 800-338-3987 (cust serv), pg 167

McGraw-Hill Humanities, Social Sciences, Languages, New York, NY *Toll Free Tel:* 800-338-3987 (cust serv), pg 168

McGraw-Hill/Irwin, Burr Ridge, IL *Toll Free Tel:* 800-338-3987 (cust serv), pg 168

McGraw-Hill/Osborne, Emeryville, CA *Toll Free Tel:* 800-227-0900, pg 168

McGraw-Hill Ryerson Ltd, Whitby, ON Canada *Toll Free Tel:* 800-565-5758 (cust serv), pg 554

McGraw-Hill Science, Engineering, Mathematics, Dubuque, IA *Toll Free Tel:* 800-338-3987 (cust serv), pg 169

Andrews McMeel Publishing, Kansas City, MO *Toll Free Tel:* 800-851-8923, pg 169

McPherson & Co, Kingston, NY *Toll Free Tel:* 800-613-8219 *Toll Free Fax:* 800-613-8219, pg 169

MDRT Center for Productivity, Park Ridge, IL *Toll Free Tel:* 800-879-6378, pg 169

me+mi publishing inc, Wheaton, IL *Toll Free Tel:* 888-251-1444, pg 169

Meadowbrook Press, Minnetonka, MN *Toll Free Tel:* 800-338-2232, pg 169

R S Means Co Inc, Kingston, MA *Toll Free Tel:* 800-448-8182 *Toll Free Fax:* 800-632-6732, pg 169

Medals of America Press, Fountain Inn, SC *Toll Free Tel:* 800-308-0849 *Toll Free Fax:* 800-407-8640, pg 170

MedBooks, Richardson, TX *Toll Free Tel:* 800-443-7397, pg 170

Media & Methods, Philadelphia, PA *Toll Free Tel:* 800-555-5657, pg 170

Media Associates, Wilton, CA *Toll Free Tel:* 800-373-1897 (orders), pg 170

Medical Group Management Association, Englewood, CO *Toll Free Tel:* 888-608-5601, pg 170

Medical Physics Publishing Corp, Madison, WI *Toll Free Tel:* 800-442-5778, pg 170

MedMaster Inc, Fort Lauderdale, FL *Toll Free Tel:* 800-335-3480, pg 170

The Russell Meerdink Co Ltd, Neenah, WI *Toll Free Tel:* 800-635-6499, pg 170

Mega Media Press, El Cajon, CA *Toll Free Tel:* 800-803-9416, pg 170

Mel Bay Publications Inc, Pacific, MO *Toll Free Tel:* 800-863-5229 *Toll Free Fax:* 800-660-9818, pg 171

Mercer University Press, Macon, GA *Toll Free Tel:* 800-637-2378 (ext 2880, outside GA); 800-342-0841 (ext 2880, GA), pg 171

Meriwether Publishing Ltd/Contemporary Drama Service, Colorado Springs, CO *Toll Free Tel:* 800-937-5297 *Toll Free Fax:* 888-594-4436, pg 171

Merriam-Webster Inc, Springfield, MA *Toll Free Tel:* 800-828-1880 (orders & cust serv), pg 172

Merryant Publishers Inc, Vashon, WA *Toll Free Tel:* 800-228-8958, pg 172

Mesorah Publications Ltd, Brooklyn, NY *Toll Free Tel:* 800-637-6724, pg 172

Messianic Jewish Publishers, Baltimore, MD *Toll Free Tel:* 800-773-6574, pg 172

Metal Bulletin Inc, New York, NY *Toll Free Tel:* 800-638-2525, pg 172

Metamorphous Press, Portland, OR *Toll Free Tel:* 800-937-7771 (orders only), pg 172

Metro Creative Graphics Inc, New York, NY *Toll Free Tel:* 800-223-1600, pg 173

MGI Management Institute Inc, White Plains, NY *Toll Free Tel:* 800-932-0191, pg 173

Michelin Travel Publications, Greenville, SC *Toll Free Tel:* 800-423-0485; 800-223-0987 *Toll Free Fax:* 866-297-0914, pg 173

Michelin Travel Publications, Laval, PQ Canada *Toll Free Tel:* 800-361-8236 (Canada) *Toll Free Fax:* 800-361-6937 (Canada), pg 554

Michigan Municipal League, Ann Arbor, MI *Toll Free Tel:* 800-653-2483, pg 173

Michigan State University Press (MSU Press), East Lansing, MI *Toll Free Fax:* 800-678-2120, pg 173

MicroMash, Englewood, CO *Toll Free Tel:* 800-823-6039, pg 173

Micromedia ProQuest, Toronto, ON Canada *Toll Free Tel:* 800-387-2689, pg 554

Microsoft Press, Redmond, WA *Toll Free Tel:* 800-677-7377, pg 173

MidWest Plan Service, Ames, IA *Toll Free Tel:* 800-562-3618, pg 174

Midwest Traditions Inc, Milwaukee, WI *Toll Free Tel:* 800-736-9189, pg 174

Mike Murach & Associates Inc, Fresno, CA *Toll Free Tel:* 800-221-5528, pg 174

Milady Publishing, Clifton Park, NY *Toll Free Tel:* 800-998-7498, pg 174

Milkweed Editions, Minneapolis, MN *Toll Free Tel:* 800-520-6455, pg 174

The Millbrook Press Inc, Brookfield, CT *Toll Free Tel:* 800-462-4703, pg 174

Milliken Publishing Co, St Louis, MO *Toll Free Tel:* 800-325-4136 *Toll Free Fax:* 800-538-1319, pg 175

The Minerals, Metals & Materials Society (TMS), Warrendale, PA *Toll Free Tel:* 800-759-4867, pg 175

Minnesota Historical Society Press, St Paul, MN *Toll Free Tel:* 800-621-2736 *Toll Free Fax:* 800-621-8476, pg 175

The MIT Press, Cambridge, MA *Toll Free Tel:* 800-405-1619 (orders only), pg 175

Mitchell Lane Publishers Inc, Newark, DE *Toll Free Tel:* 800-814-5484 *Toll Free Fax:* 866-834-4164, pg 176

MMB Music Inc, St Louis, MO *Toll Free Tel:* 800-543-3771, pg 176

Modulo Editeur Inc, Mont Royal, PQ Canada *Toll Free Tel:* 888-738-9818 *Toll Free Fax:* 888-273-5247, pg 554

Modulo-Griffon Inc, Mont Royal, PQ Canada *Toll Free Tel:* 888-738-9818 *Toll Free Fax:* 888-273-5247, pg 554

Moment Point Press Inc, Needham, MA *Toll Free Tel:* 800-423-7087 (orders), pg 176

The Monacelli Press, New York, NY *Toll Free Tel:* 800-631-8571 (cust serv), pg 177

Monday Morning Books Inc, Inverness, CA *Toll Free Tel:* 800-255-6049 *Toll Free Fax:* 800-255-6048, pg 177

Mondia Editeurs Inc, St-Jerome, PQ Canada *Toll Free Tel:* 800-561-2371 (Canada), pg 554

Mondo Publishing, New York, NY *Toll Free Tel:* 800-242-3650, pg 177

Money Market Directories, Charlottesville, VA *Toll Free Tel:* 800-446-2810, pg 177

Montana Historical Society Press, Helena, MT *Toll Free Tel:* 800-243-9900, pg 177

Monthly Review Press, New York, NY *Toll Free Tel:* 800-670-9499, pg 177

Moody Press, Chicago, IL *Toll Free Tel:* 800-678-8812, pg 177

Moon Lady Press, Marshfield Hills, MA *Toll Free Tel:* 800-840-0205, pg 178

Moon Mountain Publishing, North Kingstown, RI *Toll Free Tel:* 800-353-5877, pg 178

Morehouse Publishing Co, Harrisburg, PA *Toll Free Tel:* 800-877-0012 (orders only), pg 178

Morgan Quinto Corp, Lawrence, KS *Toll Free Tel:* 800-457-0742, pg 178

Morgan Reynolds Publishing, Greensboro, NC *Toll Free Tel:* 800-535-1504 *Toll Free Fax:* 800-535-5725, pg 178

Morning Glory Press Inc, Buena Park, CA *Toll Free Tel:* 888-612-8254 *Toll Free Fax:* 888-327-4362, pg 178

Morningside Bookshop, Dayton, OH *Toll Free Tel:* 800-648-9710, pg 178

Mosaic Press, Niagara Falls, NY *Toll Free Tel:* 800-387-8992, pg 179

Mosby Journal Division, St Louis, MO *Toll Free Tel:* 800-325-4177, pg 179

Mount Olive College Press, Mount Olive, NC *Toll Free Tel:* 800-653-0854, pg 179

Mountain n' Air Books, La Crescenta, CA *Toll Free Tel:* 800-446-9696 *Toll Free Fax:* 800-303-5578, pg 179

Mountain Press Publishing Co, Missoula, MT *Toll Free Tel:* 800-234-5308, pg 179

The Mountaineers Books, Seattle, WA *Toll Free Tel:* 800-553-4453 *Toll Free Fax:* 800-568-7604, pg 179

Andrew Mowbray Inc Publishers, Lincoln, RI *Toll Free Tel:* 800-999-4697, pg 180

Moznaim Publishing Corp, Brooklyn, NY *Toll Free Tel:* 800-364-5118, pg 180

Multicultural Publications, Akron, OH *Toll Free Tel:* 800-238-0297, pg 180

Editions Multimondes, Sainte-Foy, PQ Canada *Toll Free Tel:* 800-840-3029 *Toll Free Fax:* 888-303-5931, pg 555

Multnomah Publishers Inc, Sisters, OR *Toll Free Tel:* 800-929-0910, pg 180

Museum of New Mexico Press, Santa Fe, NM *Toll Free Tel:* 800-249-7737 (orders) *Toll Free Fax:* 800-622-8667 (orders), pg 180

Mustang Publishing Co Inc, Memphis, TN *Toll Free Tel:* 800-250-8713, pg 181

My Chaotic Life™, Laguna Hills, CA *Toll Free Tel:* 800-426-0099, pg 181

NAFSA: Association of International Educators, Washington, DC *Toll Free Tel:* 800-836-4994 (Book orders only), pg 181

Napoleon Publishing/Rendezvous Press, Toronto, ON Canada *Toll Free Tel:* 877-730-9052, pg 555

National Academies Press, Washington, DC *Toll Free Tel:* 800-624-6242, pg 182

National Association of Broadcasters (NAB), Washington, DC *Toll Free Tel:* 800-368-5644, pg 182

National Association of Secondary School Principals, Reston, VA *Toll Free Tel:* 800-253-7746, pg 182

National Association of Social Workers (NASW), Washington, DC *Toll Free Tel:* 800-227-3590, pg 182

National Braille Press, Boston, MA *Toll Free Tel:* 800-548-7323 (cust serv), pg 182

National Council of Teachers of English (NCTE), Urbana, IL *Toll Free Tel:* 800-369-6283; 877-369-6283 (cust serv), pg 183

National Council of Teachers of Mathematics, Reston, VA *Toll Free Tel:* 800-235-7566, pg 183

National Council on Radiation Protection & Measurements (NCRP), Bethesda, MD *Toll Free Tel:* 800-229-2652, pg 183

National Crime Prevention Council, Washington, DC *Toll Free Tel:* 800-627-2911 (orders only), pg 183

National Golf Foundation, Jupiter, FL *Toll Free Tel:* 800-733-6006, pg 184

National Institute for Trial Advocacy, Notre Dame, IN *Toll Free Tel:* 800-225-6482, pg 184

National Learning Corp, Syosset, NY *Toll Free Tel:* 800-645-6337, pg 184

The National Museum of Women in the Arts, Washington, DC *Toll Free Tel:* 800-222-7270, pg 184

National Notary Association, Chatsworth, CA *Toll Free Tel:* 800-876-6827, pg 184

National Publishing Co, Philadelphia, PA *Toll Free Tel:* 888-333-1863, pg 184

National Register Publishing, New Providence, NJ *Toll Free Tel:* 800-473-7020, pg 185

National Resource Center for Youth Services (NRCYS), Tulsa, OK *Toll Free Tel:* 800-274-2687, pg 185

National Science Teachers Association (NSTA), Arlington, VA *Toll Free Tel:* 800-722-NSTA (sales), pg 185

National Underwriter Co, Erlanger, KY *Toll Free Tel:* 800-543-0874, pg 185

Natural Heritage Books, Toronto, ON Canada *Toll Free Tel:* 800-725-9982 (orders only), pg 555

Naturegraph Publishers Inc, Happy Camp, CA *Toll Free Tel:* 800-390-5353, pg 185

Naval Institute Press, Annapolis, MD *Toll Free Tel:* 800-233-8764, pg 185

NavPress Publishing Group, Colorado Springs, CO *Toll Free Tel:* 800-366-7788 *Toll Free Fax:* 800-343-3902, pg 185

NBM Publishing Inc, New York, NY *Toll Free Tel:* 800-886-1223, pg 185

NDE Publishing, Richmond Hill, ON Canada *Toll Free Tel:* 800-675-1263, pg 555

Neal-Schuman Publishers Inc, New York, NY *Toll Free Tel:* 866-672-6657 *Toll Free Fax:* 866-209-7932, pg 186

E T Nedder Publishing, Tucson, AZ *Toll Free Tel:* 877-817-2742, pg 186

Neibauer Press, Warminster, PA *Toll Free Tel:* 800-322-6203, pg 186

Nelson, Scarborough, ON Canada *Toll Free Tel:* 800-268-2222 (cust serv); 800-430-4445, pg 555

Nelson Information, New York, NY *Toll Free Tel:* 888-371-4575; 888-280-4864 (orders), pg 186

New Age World Publishing, Miami, FL *Toll Free Fax:* 888-739-6129, pg 187

New City Press, Hyde Park, NY *Toll Free Tel:* 800-462-5980 (orders only), pg 187

New Dimensions Publishing, Phoenix, AZ *Toll Free Tel:* 800-736-7367, pg 187

New Directions Publishing Corp, New York, NY *Toll Free Tel:* 800-233-4830 (PA), pg 187

New Forums Press Inc, Stillwater, OK *Toll Free Tel:* 800-606-3766, pg 188

New Harbinger Publications Inc, Oakland, CA *Toll Free Tel:* 800-748-6273 (orders only), pg 188

New Horizon Press, Far Hills, NJ *Toll Free Tel:* 800-533-7978 (orders only), pg 188

New Leaf Press Inc, Green Forest, AR *Toll Free Tel:* 800-643-9535, pg 188

The New Press, New York, NY *Toll Free Tel:* 800-233-4830 (orders) *Toll Free Fax:* 800-458-6515, pg 188

New Readers Press, Syracuse, NY *Toll Free Tel:* 800-448-8878, pg 189

New Strategist Publications Inc, Ithaca, NY *Toll Free Tel:* 800-848-0842, pg 189

New Victoria Publishers, Norwich, VT *Toll Free Tel:* 800-326-5297 *Toll Free Fax:* 800-326-5297, pg 189

New World Library, Novato, CA *Toll Free Tel:* 800-227-3900 (ext 52, retail orders), pg 189

New World Publishing, Halifax, NS Canada *Toll Free Tel:* 877-211-3334, pg 555

New York Academy of Sciences, New York, NY *Toll Free Tel:* 800-843-6927, pg 189

New York State Bar Association, Albany, NY *Toll Free Tel:* 800-582-2452, pg 190

New York University Press, New York, NY *Toll Free Tel:* 800-996-6987 (orders), pg 190

Newbridge Educational Publishing, Northborough, MA *Toll Free Tel:* 800-867-0307 *Toll Free Fax:* 800-456-2419, pg 190

NeWest Press, Edmonton, AB Canada *Toll Free Tel:* 866-796-5433, pg 556

NewLife Publications, Peachtree City, GA *Toll Free Tel:* 800-235-7255 *Toll Free Fax:* 800-514-7072, pg 190

Newmarket Publishing & Communications, New York, NY *Toll Free Tel:* 800-669-3903, pg 190

Nightingale-Conant, Niles, IL *Toll Free Tel:* 800-572-2770, pg 191

Nilgiri Press, Tomales, CA *Toll Free Tel:* 800-475-2369, pg 191

Nimbus Publishing Ltd, Halifax, NS Canada *Toll Free Tel:* 800-646-2879, pg 556

No Starch Press Inc, San Francisco, CA *Toll Free Tel:* 800-420-7240, pg 191

Norman Publishing, Novato, CA *Toll Free Tel:* 800-544-9359, pg 191

North Atlantic Books, Berkeley, CA *Toll Free Tel:* 800-337-2665 (book orders only), pg 191

North Bay Books, Richmond, CA *Toll Free Tel:* 800-870-3194, pg 192

North Light Books, Cincinnati, OH *Toll Free Tel:* 800-666-0963 *Toll Free Fax:* 888-590-4082, pg 192

North Point Press, New York, NY *Toll Free Tel:* 888-330-8477, pg 192

North River Press Publishing Corp, Great Barrington, MA *Toll Free Tel:* 800-486-2665 *Toll Free Fax:* 800-BOOK-FAX (266-5329), pg 192

Northland Publishing Co, Flagstaff, AZ *Toll Free Tel:* 800-346-3257, pg 193

Northstone Publishing, Kelowna, BC Canada *Toll Free Tel:* 800-299-2926, pg 556

Northwestern University Press, Evanston, IL *Toll Free Tel:* 800-621-2736 (orders only), pg 193

Jeffrey Norton Publishers Inc, Madison, CT *Toll Free Tel:* 800-243-1234 *Toll Free Fax:* 888-453-4329, pg 193

W W Norton & Company Inc, New York, NY *Toll Free Tel:* 800-233-4830 (orders & cust serv) *Toll Free Fax:* 800-458-6515, pg 193

Nova Press, Los Angeles, CA *Toll Free Tel:* 800-949-6175, pg 194

Nova Publishing Co, Carbondale, IL *Toll Free Tel:* 800-748-1175, pg 194

Novalis Publishing, Toronto, ON Canada *Toll Free Tel:* 800-387-7164 *Toll Free Fax:* 800-204-4140, pg 556

nursesbooks.org, The Publishing Program of ANA, Washington, DC *Toll Free Tel:* 800-637-0323, pg 194

Nystrom, Chicago, IL *Toll Free Tel:* 800-621-8086, pg 194

Oak Knoll Press, New Castle, DE *Toll Free Tel:* 800-996-2556, pg 194

Oaklea Press, Richmond, VA *Toll Free Tel:* 800-295-4066, pg 195

Oakstone Medical Publishing, Birmingham, AL *Toll Free Tel:* 800-952-0690, pg 195

Ocean View Books, Denver, CO *Toll Free Tel:* 800-848-6222 (orders only), pg 195

Oceana Publications Inc, Dobbs Ferry, NY *Toll Free Tel:* 800-831-0758 (orders only), pg 195

Off the Page Press, Buena Vista, CO *Toll Free Tel:* 888-852-6402, pg 196

Ohio State University Foreign Language Publications, Columbus, OH *Toll Free Tel:* 800-678-6999, pg 196

Ohio State University Press, Columbus, OH *Toll Free Tel:* 800-621-2736 *Toll Free Fax:* 800-621-8476, pg 196

Ohio University Press, Athens, OH *Toll Free Tel:* 800-621-2736, pg 196

Omnibus Press, New York, NY *Toll Free Tel:* 800-431-7187 *Toll Free Fax:* 800-345-6842, pg 196

Omnidawn Publishing, Richmond, CA *Toll Free Tel:* 800-792-4957, pg 196

Omnigraphics Inc, Detroit, MI *Toll Free Tel:* 800-234-1340 (cust serv) *Toll Free Fax:* 800-875-1340 (cust serv), pg 197

One Planet Publishing House, Seattle, WA *Toll Free Tel:* 877-526-3814 (87-PLANET-14) *Toll Free Fax:* 877-526-3814 (87-PLANET-14), pg 197

OneOnOne Computer Training, Addison, IL *Toll Free Tel:* 800-424-8668, pg 197

OneSource, Concord, MA *Toll Free Tel:* 800-554-5501 (sales), pg 197

Online Training Solutions Inc, Redmond, WA *Toll Free Tel:* 800-854-3344, pg 197

Open Court, Chicago, IL *Toll Free Tel:* 800-815-2280 (orders only), pg 197

Open Horizons Publishing Co, Fairfield, IA *Toll Free Tel:* 800-796-6130, pg 197

OPIS/STALSBY Directories & Databases, Lakewood, NJ *Toll Free Tel:* 800-275-0950, pg 198

Orange Frazer Press Inc, Wilmington, OH *Toll Free Tel:* 800-852-9332, pg 198

Orbis Books, Ossining, NY *Toll Free Tel:* 800-258-5838 (orders), pg 198

Orca Book Publishers, Custer, WA *Toll Free Tel:* 800-210-5277, pg 198

Order of the Cross, La Grange, IL *Toll Free Tel:* 800-611-1361 *Toll Free Fax:* 800-611-1361, pg 198

Oregon Catholic Press, Portland, OR *Toll Free Tel:* 800-548-8749 *Toll Free Fax:* 800-843-8181, pg 198

Oregon State University Press, Corvallis, OR *Toll Free Tel:* 800-426-3797 (orders) *Toll Free Fax:* 800-426-3797 (orders), pg 199

O'Reilly & Associates Inc, Sebastopol, CA *Toll Free Tel:* 800-998-9938, pg 199

Organization for Economic Cooperation & Development, Washington, DC *Toll Free Tel:* 800-456-6323, pg 199

Other Press LLC, New York, NY *Toll Free Tel:* 877-843-6843, pg 199

Other Press LLC, New York, NY *Toll Free Tel:* 877-THE-OTHER, pg 573

Our Sunday Visitor Publishing, Huntington, IN *Toll Free Tel:* 800-348-2440 (orders) *Toll Free Fax:* 800-498-6709, pg 199

Outdoor Empire Publishing Inc, Seattle, WA *Toll Free Tel:* 800-645-5489, pg 200

The Overmountain Press, Johnson City, TN *Toll Free Tel:* 800-992-2691, pg 200

Richard C Owen Publishers Inc, Katonah, NY *Toll Free Tel:* 800-336-5588, pg 200

Oxbridge Communications Inc, New York, NY *Toll Free Tel:* 800-955-0231, pg 200

Oxford University Press Canada, Don Mills, ON Canada *Toll Free Tel:* 800-387-8020 *Toll Free Fax:* 800-665-1771, pg 557

Oxford University Press, Inc, New York, NY *Toll Free Tel:* 800-451-7556 (orders), pg 200

Oxmoor House Inc, Birmingham, AL *Toll Free Tel:* 800-366-4712, pg 201

Ozark Mountain Publishing Inc, Huntsville, AR *Toll Free Tel:* 800-935-0045; 800-230-0312 *Toll Free Fax:* 800-935-0045; 800-230-0312, pg 201

Ozark Publishing Inc, Prairie Grove, AR *Toll Free Tel:* 800-321-5671, pg 201

P & R Publishing Co, Phillipsburg, NJ *Toll Free Tel:* 800-631-0094, pg 201

P S M J Resources Inc, Newton, MA *Toll Free Tel:* 800-537-7765, pg 201

Pacific Press Publishing Association, Nampa, ID *Toll Free Tel:* 800-447-7377, pg 201

Pacifica Military History, Pacifica, CA *Toll Free Tel:* 800-453-3152 (orders & inquiries), pg 202

Paladin Press, Boulder, CO *Toll Free Tel:* 800-392-2400, pg 202

Panoptic Enterprises, Burke, VA *Toll Free Tel:* 800-594-4766, pg 202

Pantheon Books/Schocken Books, New York, NY *Toll Free Tel:* 800-638-6460, pg 202

Para Publishing, Santa Barbara, CA *Toll Free Tel:* 800-727-2782, pg 203

Parabola Books, New York, NY *Toll Free Tel:* 800-560-6984, pg 203

Paraclete Press, Orleans, MA *Toll Free Tel:* 800-451-5006, pg 203

Paradigm Publications, Taos, NM *Toll Free Tel:* 800-873-3946, pg 203

Paradise Cay Publications Inc, Arcata, CA *Toll Free Tel:* 800-736-4509, pg 203

Paragon House, St Paul, MN *Toll Free Tel:* 800-447-3709 *Toll Free Fax:* 800-494-0997, pg 204

Parenting Press Inc, Seattle, WA *Toll Free Tel:* 800-99-BOOKS (992-6657), pg 204

Park Place Publications, Pacific Grove, CA *Toll Free Tel:* 888-702-4500, pg 204

Parkway Publishers Inc, Blowing Rock, NC *Toll Free Tel:* 800-821-9155 *Toll Free Fax:* 800-821-9155, pg 204

Parlay International, Emeryville, CA *Toll Free Tel:* 800-457-2752, pg 204

Pastoral Press, Portland, OR *Toll Free Tel:* 800-548-8749 *Toll Free Fax:* 800-462-7329, pg 205

Pathfinder Publishing Inc, Oxnard, CA *Toll Free Tel:* 800-977-2282, pg 205

Pathways Publishing, Boxborough, MA *Toll Free Tel:* 888-333-7284, pg 205

Patient-Centered Guides, Sebastopol, CA *Toll Free Tel:* 800-998-9938, pg 205

Patrick's Press, Columbus, GA *Toll Free Tel:* 800-654-1052, pg 205

Paul & Company, Marshfield, MA *Toll Free Tel:* 800-888-4741 (orders), pg 205

Pauline Books & Media, Boston, MA *Toll Free Tel:* 800-876-4463 (orders only), pg 205

Paulist Press, Mahwah, NJ *Toll Free Tel:* 800-218-1903 *Toll Free Fax:* 800-836-3161 (orders), pg 206

Peace Hill Press, Charles City, VA *Toll Free Tel:* 877-322-3445 (orders), pg 206

Peachtree Publishers Ltd, Atlanta, GA *Toll Free Tel:* 800-241-0113 *Toll Free Fax:* 800-875-8909, pg 206

Pearson, Indianapolis, IN *Toll Free Tel:* 800-545-5914, pg 206

Pearson Custom Publishing, Boston, MA *Toll Free Tel:* 800-428-4466 (orders), pg 206

Pearson Education Canada Inc, Don Mills, ON Canada *Toll Free Tel:* 800-567-3800; 800-387-8028 *Toll Free Fax:* 800-263-7733; 888-465-0536, pg 557

Pearson Professional Development, Glenview, IL *Toll Free Tel:* 800-348-4474, pg 207

Pearson Technology Group (PTG), Indianapolis, IN *Toll Free Tel:* 800-545-5914, pg 207

T H Peek Publisher, Palo Alto, CA *Toll Free Tel:* 800-962-9245, pg 207

Peel Productions Inc, Columbus, NC *Toll Free Tel:* 800-345-6665, pg 207

Pelican Publishing Co Inc, Gretna, LA *Toll Free Tel:* 800-843-1724, pg 207

Pencil Point Press Inc, New Hope, PA *Toll Free Tel:* 800-356-1299, pg 207

Penfield Books, Iowa City, IA *Toll Free Tel:* 800-728-9998, pg 207

Pennsylvania Historical & Museum Commission, Harrisburg, PA *Toll Free Tel:* 800-747-7790, pg 209

The Pennsylvania State University Press, University Park, PA *Toll Free Tel:* 800-326-9180 *Toll Free Fax:* 877 7782665, pg 209

PennWell Books & More, Tulsa, OK *Toll Free Tel:* 800-752-9764, pg 209

Penton Overseas Inc, Carlsbad, CA *Toll Free Tel:* 800-748-5804, pg 209

Per Annum Inc, New York, NY *Toll Free Tel:* 800-548-1108, pg 210

Peradam Press, North San Juan, CA *Toll Free Tel:* 800-241-8689 *Toll Free Fax:* 800-241-8689, pg 210

Perfection Learning Corp, Des Moines, IA *Toll Free Tel:* 800-762-2999, pg 210

The Perseus Books Group, New York, NY *Toll Free Tel:* 800-386-5656 (cust serv), pg 210

Peter Pauper Press Inc, White Plains, NY *Toll Free Tel:* 800-833-2311, pg 210

Petroleum Extension Service (PETEX), Austin, TX *Toll Free Tel:* 800-687-4132 *Toll Free Fax:* 800-687-7839, pg 211

Peytral Publications Inc, Minnetonka, MN *Toll Free Tel:* 877-PEYTRAL (739-8725), pg 211

Pflaum Publishing Group, Dayton, OH *Toll Free Tel:* 800-543-4383 *Toll Free Fax:* 800-370-4450, pg 211

Phaidon Press Inc, New York, NY *Toll Free Tel:* 800-759-0190 (cust serv) *Toll Free Fax:* 800-286-9471 (cust serv), pg 211

Phi Delta Kappa International, Bloomington, IN *Toll Free Tel:* 800-766-1156, pg 211

Philosophy Documentation Center, Charlottesville, VA *Toll Free Tel:* 800-444-2419, pg 211

Phoenix Learning Resources, Stamford, CT *Toll Free Tel:* 800-526-6581, pg 212

Phoenix Society for Burn Survivors, E Grand Rapids, MI *Toll Free Tel:* 800-888-BURN (888-2876), pg 212

PIA/GATF (Graphic Arts Technical Foundation), Sewickley, PA *Toll Free Tel:* 800-910-4283, pg 212

Pictorial Histories Publishing Co, Missoula, MT *Toll Free Tel:* 888-763-8350, pg 212

Pieces of Learning, Marion, IL *Toll Free Tel:* 800-729-5137 *Toll Free Fax:* 800-844-0455, pg 212

The Pilgrim Press/United Church Press, Cleveland, OH *Toll Free Tel:* 800-537-3394 (cust serv), pg 213

Pineapple Press Inc, Sarasota, FL *Toll Free Tel:* 800-746-3275 (orders), pg 213

Pippin Publishing Corp, Toronto, ON Canada *Toll Free Tel:* 888-889-0001, pg 557

Pitspopany Press, New York, NY *Toll Free Tel:* 800-232-2931, pg 213

Planning/Communications, River Forest, IL *Toll Free Tel:* 888-366-5200, pg 214

Platypus Media LLC, Washington, DC *Toll Free Tel:* 877-872-8977, pg 214

Playhouse Publishing, Akron, OH *Toll Free Tel:* 800-762-6775, pg 214

Pleasure Boat Studio: A Literary Press, New York, NY *Toll Free Tel:* 888-810-5308 *Toll Free Fax:* 800-810-5308, pg 214

Pocket Books, New York, NY *Toll Free Tel:* 800-456-6798, pg 215

Pocket Press Inc, Portland, OR *Toll Free Tel:* 888-237-2110 *Toll Free Fax:* 877-643-3732, pg 215

Polestar Book Publishers, Vancouver, BC Canada *Toll Free Tel:* 800-663-5714 *Toll Free Fax:* 800-565-3770, pg 558

Police Executive Research Forum, Washington, DC *Toll Free Tel:* 888-202-4563 (cust serv), pg 216

Pomegranate Communications, Petaluma, CA *Toll Free Tel:* 800-227-1428 *Toll Free Fax:* 800-848-4376, pg 216

Popular Culture Inc, Harbor Springs, MI *Toll Free Tel:* 800-678-8828 *Toll Free Fax:* 800-678-8828, pg 216

Portage & Main Press, Winnipeg, MB Canada *Toll Free Tel:* 800-667-9673 *Toll Free Fax:* 866-734-8477, pg 558

Porter Sargent Publishers Inc, Boston, MA *Toll Free Tel:* 800-342-7470, pg 216

Possibility Press, Hummelstown, PA *Toll Free Tel:* 800-566-0534, pg 216

Pottersfield Press, East Lawrencetown, NS Canada *Toll Free Tel:* 800-NIMBUS9 (646-2879-orders only) *Toll Free Fax:* 888-253-3133, pg 558

Practising Law Institute, New York, NY *Toll Free Tel:* 800-260-4PLI (260-4754 customer service) *Toll Free Fax:* 800-321-0093, pg 216

Prairie View Press, Rosenort, MB Canada *Toll Free Tel:* 800-477-7377, pg 558

Prakken Publications Inc, Ann Arbor, MI *Toll Free Tel:* 800-530-9673 (orders only), pg 217

PREP Publishing, Fayetteville, NC *Toll Free Tel:* 800-533-2814, pg 217

Presbyterian Publishing Corp, Louisville, KY *Toll Free Tel:* 800-227-2872 (US only) *Toll Free Fax:* 800-541-5113 (US only), pg 217

Prestel Publishing, New York, NY *Toll Free Tel:* 888-463-6110 (cust serv), pg 217

Prima Games, Roseville, CA *Toll Free Tel:* 800-632-8676, pg 218

PRIMEDIA Business Directories & Books, Overland Park, KS *Toll Free Tel:* 800-453-9620; 800-262-1954 (cust serv) *Toll Free Fax:* 800-633-6219, pg 218

Primedia Business Magazine & Media, Overland Park, KS *Toll Free Tel:* 800-262-1954, pg 218

Primedia Consumer Magazine & Internet Group, New York, NY *Toll Free Tel:* 800-521-2885, pg 218

Princeton Architectural Press, New York, NY *Toll Free Tel:* 800-722-6657 (dist), pg 218

Princeton Book Co Publishers, Hightstown, NJ *Toll Free Tel:* 800-220-7149, pg 218

The Princeton Review, New York, NY *Toll Free Tel:* 800-733-3000, pg 218

Princeton University Press, Princeton, NJ *Toll Free Tel:* 800-777-4726 *Toll Free Fax:* 800-999-1958, pg 219

PRO-ED Inc, Austin, TX *Toll Free Tel:* 800-897-3202 *Toll Free Fax:* 800-397-7633, pg 219

Pro Lingua Associates Inc, Brattleboro, VT *Toll Free Tel:* 800-366-4775, pg 219

Pro Quest Information & Learning, Ann Arbor, MI *Toll Free Tel:* 800-521-0600 *Toll Free Fax:* 800-864-0019, pg 219

Productivity Press, New York, NY *Toll Free Tel:* 888-319-5852 *Toll Free Fax:* 800-394-6286, pg 219

Professional Communications Inc, Caddo, OK *Toll Free Tel:* 800-337-9838, pg 219

The Professional Education Group Inc, Minnetonka, MN *Toll Free Tel:* 800-229-2531, pg 219

Professional Publications Inc, Belmont, CA *Toll Free Tel:* 800-426-1178, pg 219

Professional Publishing, Burr Ridge, IL *Toll Free Tel:* 800-2McGraw (262-4729), pg 220

Professional Resource Exchange Inc, Sarasota, FL *Toll Free Tel:* 800-443-3364, pg 220

Prometheus Books, Amherst, NY *Toll Free Tel:* 800-421-0351, pg 220

Promissor Inc, Evanston, IL *Toll Free Tel:* 800-255-1312, pg 220

ProStar Publications Inc, Annapolis, MD *Toll Free Tel:* 800-481-6277 *Toll Free Fax:* 800-487-6277, pg 220

Providence Publishing Corp, Franklin, TN *Toll Free Tel:* 800-321-5692, pg 220

Pruett Publishing Co, Boulder, CO *Toll Free Tel:* 800-247-8224 *Toll Free Fax:* 800-527-9727, pg 220

Psychological Assessment Resources Inc (PAR), Lutz, FL *Toll Free Tel:* 800-331-8378 *Toll Free Fax:* 800-727-9329, pg 221

PTG Software, Indianapolis, IN *Toll Free Tel:* 800-858-7674, pg 221

Public Utilities Reports Inc, Vienna, VA *Toll Free Tel:* 800-368-5001, pg 221

PublicAffairs, New York, NY *Toll Free Tel:* 800-242-7737 (orders), pg 221

Les Publications du Quebec, Ste Foy, PQ Canada *Toll Free Tel:* 800-463-2100 (Quebec province only), pg 559

Les Publications Graficor 1989 Inc, Montreal, PQ Canada *Toll Free Tel:* 800-565-5531 *Toll Free Fax:* 800-814-0324, pg 559

Purdue University Press, West Lafayette, IN *Toll Free Tel:* 800-247-6553 (orders), pg 222

Pureplay Press, Los Angeles, CA *Toll Free Tel:* 800-247-6553 (orders only), pg 222

Purple Mountain Press Ltd, Fleischmanns, NY *Toll Free Tel:* 800-325-2665, pg 222

Purple People Inc, Sedona, AZ *Toll Free Tel:* 866-787-7535, pg 222

The Putnam Publishing Group, New York, NY *Toll Free Tel:* 800-631-8571, pg 222

Quail Ridge Press, Brandon, MS *Toll Free Tel:* 800-343-1583, pg 223

Quality Education Data, Inc, Denver, CO *Toll Free Tel:* 800-525-5811, pg 223

Quality Medical Publishing Inc, St Louis, MO *Toll Free Tel:* 800-423-6865, pg 223

Quantum Leap SLC Publications, Atlanta, GA *Toll Free Fax:* 877-571-9788, pg 223

Quick Publishing, St Louis, MO *Toll Free Tel:* 888-782-5474, pg 223

Quintessence Publishing Co Inc, Carol Stream, IL *Toll Free Tel:* 800-621-0387, pg 224

Quixote Press, Wever, IA *Toll Free Tel:* 800-571-BOOK, pg 224

Ragged Edge Press, Shippensburg, PA *Toll Free Tel:* 888-948-6263, pg 224

Rainbow Books Inc, Highland City, FL *Toll Free Tel:* 800-431-1579 (orders only); 888-613-2665, pg 225

Rainbow Studies International, El Reno, OK *Toll Free Tel:* 800-242-5348, pg 225

Raincoast Publishing, Vancouver, BC Canada *Toll Free Tel:* 800-663-5714 (Canada only) *Toll Free Fax:* 800-565-3700, pg 559

Rand McNally, Skokie, IL *Toll Free Tel:* 800-333-0136, pg 225

Random House Children's Books, New York, NY *Toll Free Tel:* 800-200-3552, pg 225

Random House Inc, New York, NY *Toll Free Tel:* 800-726-0600, pg 226

Random House Publishing Group, New York, NY *Toll Free Tel:* 800-200-3552 *Toll Free Fax:* 800-200-3552, pg 227

Random House Reference, New York, NY *Toll Free Tel:* 800-733-3000, pg 227

Raven Tree Press LLC, Green Bay, WI *Toll Free Tel:* 877-256-0579, pg 228

Rayve Productions Inc, Windsor, CA *Toll Free Tel:* 800-852-4890, pg 228

RCL Resources for Christian Living, Allen, TX *Toll Free Tel:* 800-527-5030 *Toll Free Fax:* 800-688-8356, pg 228

Reader's Digest Association (Canada) Ltd/Selection du Reader's Digest (Canada) Ltee, Montreal, PQ Canada *Toll Free Tel:* 800-465-0780, pg 559

Reader's Digest Association Inc, Pleasantville, NY *Toll Free Tel:* 800-431-1726, pg 228

Reader's Digest Children's Books, Pleasantville, NY *Toll Free Tel:* 800-934-0977, pg 228

Reader's Digest General Books, Pleasantville, NY *Toll Free Tel:* 800-431-1726, pg 228

Reader's Digest USA Select Editions, Pleasantville, NY *Toll Free Tel:* 800-310-6261, pg 229

Record Research Inc, Menomonee Falls, WI *Toll Free Tel:* 800-827-9810, pg 229

Recorded Books LLC, Prince Frederick, MD *Toll Free Tel:* 800-638-1304, pg 229

Red Wheel/Weiser/Conari, Boston, MA *Toll Free Tel:* 800-423-7087, pg 230

Redleaf Press, St Paul, MN *Toll Free Tel:* 800-423-8309 *Toll Free Fax:* 800-641-0115, pg 230

Thomas Reed Publications Inc, Boston, MA *Toll Free Tel:* 800-995-4995 (customer service), pg 230

Reedswain Inc, Spring City, PA *Toll Free Tel:* 800-331-5191, pg 230

Referee Books, Racine, WI *Toll Free Tel:* 800-733-6100, pg 230

Regal Books, Ventura, CA *Toll Free Tel:* 800-446-7735 (orders) *Toll Free Fax:* 800-860-3109 (orders), pg 230

Regatta Press Ltd, Ithaca, NY *Toll Free Fax:* 800-688-2877, pg 230

Regnery Publishing Inc, Washington, DC *Toll Free Tel:* 888-219-4747, pg 231

Regular Baptist Press, Schaumburg, IL *Toll Free Tel:* 800-727-4440 (orders only); 888-588-1600, pg 231

Rei America Inc, Miami, FL *Toll Free Tel:* 800-726-5337, pg 231

Renaissance House, Beverly Hills, CA *Toll Free Tel:* 800-547-5113, pg 231

Reprint Services Corp, Temecula, CA *Toll Free Tel:* 800-273-6635, pg 231

Research Press, Champaign, IL *Toll Free Tel:* 800-519-2707, pg 231

The Resource Centre, Waterloo, ON Canada *Toll Free Tel:* 800-923-0330, pg 559

Fleming H Revell, Grand Rapids, MI *Toll Free Tel:* 800-877-2665, pg 232

Review & Herald Publishing Association, Hagerstown, MD *Toll Free Tel:* 800-234-7630, pg 232

The RGU Group, Tempe, AZ *Toll Free Tel:* 800-266-5265 *Toll Free Fax:* 800-973-6694, pg 232

Rigby, Austin, TX *Toll Free Tel:* 800-531-5015 *Toll Free Fax:* 800-699-9459, pg 232

Rising Sun Publishing, Marietta, GA *Toll Free Tel:* 800-524-2813, pg 232

Rising Tide Press, Tucson, AZ *Toll Free Tel:* 800-311-3565, pg 232

River City Publishing, LLC, Montgomery, AL *Toll Free Tel:* 877-408-7078, pg 232

RiverOak Publishing, Colorado Springs, CO *Toll Free Tel:* 800-323-7543, pg 233

The Riverside Publishing Co, Itasca, IL *Toll Free Tel:* 800-323-9540, pg 233

Rizzoli International Publications Inc, New York, NY *Toll Free Tel:* 800-522-6657 (orders only), pg 233

James A Rock & Co Publishers, Rockville, MD *Toll Free Tel:* 800-411-2230, pg 233

Rocky River Publishers LLC, Shepherdstown, WV *Toll Free Tel:* 800-343-0686, pg 233

Rod & Staff Publishers Inc, Crockett, KY *Toll Free Tel:* 800-643-1244 *Toll Free Fax:* 800-643-1244 (ordering in US), pg 233

Rodopi, New York, NY *Toll Free Tel:* 800-225-3998 (US only), pg 234

Ronsdale Press, Vancouver, BC Canada *Toll Free Tel:* 888-879-0919, pg 560

The Rosen Publishing Group Inc, New York, NY *Toll Free Tel:* 800-237-9932, pg 234

Ross Books, Berkeley, CA *Toll Free Tel:* 800-367-0930, pg 234

Rothstein Associates Inc, Brookfield, CT *Toll Free Tel:* 888-768-4783, pg 234

The Rough Notes Co Inc, Carmel, IN *Toll Free Tel:* 800-428-4384 *Toll Free Fax:* 800-321-1909, pg 235

Rowman & Littlefield Publishers Inc, Lanham, MD *Toll Free Tel:* 800-462-6420, pg 235

Runestone Press, Minneapolis, MN *Toll Free Tel:* 800-328-4929; 800-332-1132, pg 236

Running Press Book Publishers, Philadelphia, PA *Toll Free Tel:* 800-345-5359 (cust serv & orders) *Toll Free Fax:* 800-453-2884, pg 236

Russell Sage Foundation, New York, NY *Toll Free Tel:* 800-524-6401, pg 236

Rutgers University Press, Piscataway, NJ *Toll Free Tel:* 800-446-9323 (orders only), pg 236

Rutledge Hill Press, Nashville, TN *Toll Free Tel:* 800-251-4000 (ext 2703), pg 236

William H Sadlier Inc, New York, NY *Toll Free Tel:* 800-221-5175, pg 237

SAE (Society of Automotive Engineers International), Warrendale, PA *Toll Free Tel:* 877-606-7323 (cust serv), pg 237

Safari Press, Huntington Beach, CA *Toll Free Tel:* 800-451-4788, pg 237

Sagamore Publishing LLC, Champaign, IL *Toll Free Tel:* 800-327-5557 (orders), pg 237

Saint Andrews College Press, Laurinburg, NC *Toll Free Tel:* 800-763-0198, pg 237

St Anthony Messenger Press, Cincinnati, OH *Toll Free Tel:* 800-488-0488, pg 237

St Augustine's Press Inc, South Bend, IN *Toll Free Tel:* 888-997-4994, pg 238

St James Press, Farmington Hills, MI *Toll Free Tel:* 800-877-4253 *Toll Free Fax:* 800-414-5043, pg 238

Saint Mary's Press, Winona, MN *Toll Free Tel:* 800-533-8095 *Toll Free Fax:* 800-344-9225, pg 239

Saint Nectarios Press, Seattle, WA *Toll Free Tel:* 800-643-4233, pg 239

Salem Press Inc, Hackensack, NJ *Toll Free Tel:* 800-221-1592, pg 239

Sandlapper Publishing Inc, Orangeburg, SC *Toll Free Tel:* 800-849-7263 (orders only), pg 239

Santa Monica Press LLC, Santa Monica, CA *Toll Free Tel:* 800-784-9553, pg 240

Santillana USA Publishing Co Inc, Miami, FL *Toll Free Tel:* 800-245-8584 *Toll Free Fax:* 888-248-9518, pg 240

Sara Jordan Publishing, Toronto, ON Canada *Toll Free Tel:* 800-567-7733 *Toll Free Fax:* 800-229-3855, pg 560

Sasquatch Books, Seattle, WA *Toll Free Tel:* 800-775-0817, pg 240

W B Saunders Ltd, Philadelphia, PA *Toll Free Tel:* 800-545-2522 (cust serv), pg 240

Savage Press, Superior, WI *Toll Free Tel:* 800-732-3867, pg 240

Saxon, Austin, TX *Toll Free Tel:* 800-531-5015 *Toll Free Fax:* 800-699-9459, pg 240

Scarecrow Press Inc, Lanham, MD *Toll Free Tel:* 800-462-6420 *Toll Free Fax:* 800-338-4550, pg 240

Scepter Publishers, New York, NY *Toll Free Tel:* 800-322-8773, pg 241

Robert Schalkenbach Foundation, New York, NY *Toll Free Tel:* 800-269-9555, pg 241

Schirmer Trade Books, New York, NY *Toll Free Tel:* 800-431-7187 *Toll Free Fax:* 800-345-6842, pg 241

Scholastic Canada Ltd, Markham, ON Canada *Toll Free Tel:* 800-268-3848 (Canada) *Toll Free Fax:* 800-387-4944; 866-346-1288, pg 560

Scholastic Inc, New York, NY *Toll Free Tel:* 800-scholastic, pg 241

Scholastic Library Publishing, Danbury, CT *Toll Free Tel:* 800-621-1115, pg 242

Schonfeld & Associates Inc, Riverwood, IL *Toll Free Tel:* 800-205-0030, pg 242

School of American Research Press, Santa Fe, NM *Toll Free Tel:* 800-390-6070, pg 243

School Zone Publishing Co, Grand Haven, MI *Toll Free Tel:* 800-253-0564, pg 243

Schreiber Publishing Inc, Rockville, MD *Toll Free Tel:* 800-822-3213 (sales), pg 243

Scott Foresman, Glenview, IL *Toll Free Tel:* 800-535-4391 (Midwest), pg 243

Scott Publications Inc, Muskegon, MI *Toll Free Tel:* 866-733-9382, pg 243

Scott Publishing Co, Sidney, OH *Toll Free Tel:* 800-572-6885, pg 244

Scurlock Publishing Co Inc, Texarkana, TX *Toll Free Tel:* 800-228-6389, pg 244

Seal Books, Toronto, ON Canada *Toll Free Tel:* 888-523-9292 (order desk), pg 560

Seascape Press Ltd, Santa Barbara, CA *Toll Free Tel:* 800-929-2906, pg 573

Seedling Publications Inc, Elizabethtown, PA *Toll Free Tel:* 800-233-0759 *Toll Free Fax:* 888-834-1303, pg 244

The SeedSowers, Jacksonville, FL *Toll Free Tel:* 800-228-2665, pg 244

SelectiveHouse Publishers Inc, Gaithersburg, MD *Toll Free Tel:* 888-256-6399 (orders only), pg 244

Self-Counsel Press Inc, Bellingham, WA *Toll Free Tel:* 877-877-6490, pg 245

Self-Counsel Press Inc, North Vancouver, BC Canada *Toll Free Tel:* 800-663-3007, pg 561

Seven Stories Press, New York, NY *Toll Free Tel:* 800-283-3572, pg 245

Shambhala Publications Inc, Boston, MA *Toll Free Tel:* 888-424-2329 (orders only), pg 245

M E Sharpe Inc, Armonk, NY *Toll Free Tel:* 800-541-6563, pg 246

Show What You Know® Publishing, Columbus, OH *Toll Free Tel:* 877-PASSING (727-7464), pg 246

Siddha Yoga Publications, South Fallsburg, NY *Toll Free Tel:* 888-422-3334 (bookstore) *Toll Free Fax:* 888-422-3339, pg 247

Sierra Press, Mariposa, CA *Toll Free Tel:* 800-745-2631, pg 247

Signature Books Publishing LLC, Salt Lake City, UT *Toll Free Tel:* 800-356-5687 (orders), pg 247

Silman-James Press, Los Angeles, CA *Toll Free Tel:* 877-SJP-BOOK (757-2665), pg 247

Silver Moon Press, New York, NY *Toll Free Tel:* 800-874-3320, pg 247

Silver Pixel Press, Hauppauge, NY *Toll Free Tel:* 800-645-2522, pg 248

Silverback Books Inc, San Francisco, CA *Toll Free Tel:* 866-348-8595, pg 248

Simcha Press, Deerfield Beach, FL *Toll Free Tel:* 800-851-9100 ext 212 *Toll Free Fax:* 800-424-7652, pg 248

Simon & Pierre Publishing Co Ltd, Toronto, ON Canada *Toll Free Tel:* 800-565-9523 (orders: Canada & US) *Toll Free Fax:* 800-221-9985 (orders), pg 561

Simon & Schuster, New York, NY *Toll Free Tel:* 800-223-2348 (cust serv); 800-223-2336 (orders) *Toll Free Fax:* 800-943-9831 (orders), pg 248

Simon & Schuster Adult Publishing Group, New York, NY *Toll Free Tel:* 800-223-2336 (orders); 800-223-2348 (cust serv), pg 248

Six Strings Music Publishing, Torrance, CA *Toll Free Tel:* 800-784-0203, pg 249

SkillPath Publications, Mission, KS *Toll Free Tel:* 800-873-7545, pg 249

Sky Publishing Corp, Cambridge, MA *Toll Free Tel:* 800-253-0245, pg 250

SkyLight Paths Publishing, Woodstock, VT *Toll Free Tel:* 800-962-4544, pg 250

Slack Incorporated, Thorofare, NJ *Toll Free Tel:* 800-257-8290, pg 250

Sleeping Bear Press™, Chelsea, MI *Toll Free Tel:* 800-487-2323, pg 250

Smart Luck Publishers, Las Vegas, NV *Toll Free Tel:* 800-945-4245 *Toll Free Fax:* 800-876-4245, pg 574

Smith & Kraus Inc Publishers, Hanover, NH *Toll Free Tel:* 800-288-2881 (orders only), pg 250

M Lee Smith Publishers LLC, Brentwood, TN *Toll Free Tel:* 800-274-6774, pg 250

Smokin' Donut Books, Jamestown, RI *Toll Free Tel:* 877-474-8738, pg 574

Smyth & Helwys Publishing Inc, Macon, GA *Toll Free Tel:* 800-747-3016; 800-568-1248, pg 251

Snow Lion Publications Inc, Ithaca, NY *Toll Free Tel:* 800-950-0313, pg 251

Tom Snyder Productions, Watertown, MA *Toll Free Tel:* 800-342-0236, pg 251

Society for Human Resource Management (SHRM), Alexandria, VA *Toll Free Tel:* 800-444-5006 (orders), pg 251

Society for Industrial & Applied Mathematics, Philadelphia, PA *Toll Free Tel:* 800-447-7426, pg 251

Society for Mining, Metallurgy & Exploration Inc, Littleton, CO *Toll Free Tel:* 800-763-3132, pg 251

Society of Manufacturing Engineers, Dearborn, MI *Toll Free Tel:* 800-733-4763 (cust serv), pg 252

The Society of Naval Architects & Marine Engineers, Jersey City, NJ *Toll Free Tel:* 800-798-2188, pg 252

Socrates Media, Chicago, IL *Toll Free Tel:* 800-822-4566, pg 252

Sogides Ltee, Montreal, PQ Canada *Toll Free Tel:* 800-361-4806, pg 561

Solano Press Books, Point Arena, CA *Toll Free Tel:* 800-931-9373, pg 252

Soli Deo Gloria Publications, Morgan, PA *Toll Free Tel:* 888-266-5734, pg 252

Solucient, Evanston, IL *Toll Free Tel:* 800-366-7526, pg 252

Soncino Press, Brooklyn, NY *Toll Free Tel:* 800-972-6201, pg 253

Sophia Institute Press, Manchester, NH *Toll Free Tel:* 800-888-9344 *Toll Free Fax:* 888-288-2259, pg 253

Sopris West Educational Services, Longmont, CO *Toll Free Tel:* 800-547-6747, pg 253

Sorin Books, Notre Dame, IN *Toll Free Tel:* 800-282-1865 *Toll Free Fax:* 800-282-5681, pg 253

Soundprints, Norwalk, CT *Toll Free Tel:* 800-228-7839; 800-577-2413, ext 118 (orders), pg 253

Sourcebooks Inc, Naperville, IL *Toll Free Tel:* 800-432-7444, pg 253

South Carolina Bar, Columbia, SC *Toll Free Tel:* 800-768-7787, pg 253

South-Western, A Thomson Business, Mason, OH *Toll Free Tel:* 800-543-0487, pg 254

Southern Illinois University Press, Carbondale, IL *Toll Free Tel:* 800-346-2680 *Toll Free Fax:* 800-346-2681, pg 254

Speck Press, Denver, CO *Toll Free Tel:* 800-996-9783, pg 255

The Speech Bin Inc, Vero Beach, FL *Toll Free Tel:* 800-4-SPEECH (477-3324) *Toll Free Fax:* 888-FAX-2-BIN (329-2246), pg 255

Sphinx Publishing, Naperville, IL *Toll Free Tel:* 800-43-bright, pg 255

Spinsters Ink, Denver, CO *Toll Free Tel:* 800-301-6860; 800-729-6423 (orders), pg 255

Spizzirri Press Inc, Rapid City, SD *Toll Free Tel:* 800-325-9819 *Toll Free Fax:* 800-322-9819, pg 256

Sports Publishing LLC, Champaign, IL *Toll Free Tel:* 877-424-BOOK (424-2665), pg 256

Springer Publishing Co Inc, New York, NY *Toll Free Tel:* 877-687-7476, pg 256

Springer-Verlag New York Inc, New York, NY *Toll Free Tel:* 800-777-4643, pg 256

Squarebooks Inc, Santa Rosa, CA *Toll Free Tel:* 800-345-6699, pg 256

ST Publications Book Division, Cincinnati, OH *Toll Free Tel:* 800-925-1110, pg 256

Stackpole Books, Mechanicsburg, PA *Toll Free Tel:* 800-732-3669, pg 257

Standard Publishing Co, Cincinnati, OH *Toll Free Tel:* 800-543-1301 *Toll Free Fax:* 877-867-5751, pg 257

Standard Publishing Corp, Boston, MA *Toll Free Tel:* 800-682-5759, pg 257

Star Bright Books, Long Island City, NY *Toll Free Tel:* 800-788-4439, pg 257

Starlite Inc, St Petersburg, FL *Toll Free Tel:* 800-577-2929, pg 258

State University of New York Press, Albany, NY *Toll Free Tel:* 800-666-2211 (orders) *Toll Free Fax:* 800-688-2877 (orders), pg 258

Statistics Canada, Ottawa, ON Canada *Toll Free Tel:* 800-700-1033 (Canada & US); 800-267-6677 (orders) *Toll Free Fax:* 800-889-9734; 877-287-4369 (orders), pg 562

Steck-Vaughn, Austin, TX *Toll Free Tel:* 800-531-5015 *Toll Free Fax:* 800-699-9459, pg 258

Stemmer House Publishers Inc, Gilsum, NH *Toll Free Tel:* 800-345-6665, pg 259

Stenhouse Publishers, Portland, ME *Toll Free Tel:* 888-363-0566 *Toll Free Fax:* 800-833-9164, pg 259

Sterling Publishing Co Inc, New York, NY *Toll Free Tel:* 800-367-9692, pg 259

SterlingHouse Publisher Inc, Pittsburgh, PA *Toll Free Tel:* 888-542-2665, pg 259

Stone Bridge Press LLC, Berkeley, CA *Toll Free Tel:* 800-947-7271, pg 260

Stoneydale Press Publishing Co, Stevensville, MT *Toll Free Tel:* 800-735-7006, pg 260

Storey Books, North Adams, MA *Toll Free Tel:* 800-793-9396, pg 260

Stylewriter Inc, Provo, UT *Toll Free Tel:* 866-997-9462, pg 260

Stylus Publishing LLC, Sterling, VA *Toll Free Tel:* 800-232-0223, pg 261

Summit Publications, Indianapolis, IN *Toll Free Tel:* 800-419-0200, pg 261

Summit University Press, Corwin Springs, MT *Toll Free Tel:* 800-245-5445, pg 261

Summy-Birchard Inc, Miami, FL *Toll Free Tel:* 800-327-7643, pg 261

Sunbelt Publications Inc, El Cajon, CA *Toll Free Tel:* 800-626-6579, pg 261

Sunburst Technology, Valhalla, NY *Toll Free Tel:* 800-338-3457, pg 262

Sundance Publishing, Northborough, MA *Toll Free Tel:* 800-343-8204 *Toll Free Fax:* 800-456-2419, pg 262

Sunset Books/Sunset Publishing Corp, Menlo Park, CA *Toll Free Tel:* 800-227-7346; 800-321-0372 (California only), pg 262

Surrey Books, Chicago, IL *Toll Free Tel:* 800-326-4430, pg 262

Swagman Publishing Inc, Castle Rock, CO *Toll Free Tel:* 800-660-5107, pg 262

Swallow Press, Athens, OH *Toll Free Tel:* 800-621-2736 (orders only) *Toll Free Fax:* 800-621-8476 (orders only), pg 262

Swan Isle Press, Chicago, IL *Toll Free Tel:* 800-621-2736 *Toll Free Fax:* 800-621-8476, pg 263

Swedenborg Foundation Publishers/Chrysalis Books, West Chester, PA *Toll Free Tel:* 800-355-3222 (cust serv), pg 263

Sweetgrass Press LLC, Merrimack, NH *Toll Free Fax:* 866-727-7757, pg 263

SYBEX Inc, Alameda, CA *Toll Free Tel:* 800-227-2346, pg 263

Synapse Information Resources Inc, Endicott, NY *Toll Free Tel:* 888-SYN-CHEM, pg 263

SynergEbooks, King, NC *Toll Free Tel:* 888-812-2533, pg 263

Syracuse University Press, Syracuse, NY *Toll Free Tel:* 800-365-8929 (orders only), pg 263

T & T Clark International, Harrisburg, PA *Toll Free Tel:* 800-877-0012, pg 263

T J Publishers Inc, Silver Spring, MD *Toll Free Tel:* 800-999-1168, pg 574

Tapestry Press Ltd, Littleton, MA *Toll Free Tel:* 800-535-2007, pg 264

Tarascon Publishing, Lompoc, CA *Toll Free Tel:* 800-929-9926 *Toll Free Fax:* 877-929-9926, pg 264

Taschen America, Los Angeles, CA *Toll Free Tel:* 888-TASCHEN (827-2436), pg 264

The Taunton Press Inc, Newtown, CT *Toll Free Tel:* 800-283-7252; 800-888-8286 (orders), pg 264

Taylor & Francis Editorial, Production & Manufacturing Division, Philadelphia, PA *Toll Free Tel:* 800-354-1420, pg 264

Taylor & Francis Inc, Philadelphia, PA *Toll Free Tel:* 800-354-1420, pg 264

TCP Press, Whitchurch-Stouffville, ON Canada *Toll Free Tel:* 800-772-7765, pg 562

Teach Me Tapes Inc, Minnetonka, MN *Toll Free Tel:* 800-456-4656, pg 265

Teacher Created Materials Inc, Westminster, CA *Toll Free Tel:* 800-662-4321 *Toll Free Fax:* 800-525-1254, pg 265

Teacher Ideas Press, Portsmouth, NH *Toll Free Tel:* 800-225-5800 *Toll Free Fax:* 800-354-2004 (perms & foreign rts), pg 265

Teachers & Writers Collaborative, New York, NY *Toll Free Tel:* 888-266-5789, pg 265

Teacher's Discovery, Auburn Hills, MI *Toll Free Tel:* 800-521-3897 *Toll Free Fax:* 888-987-2436, pg 265

Teaching Strategies, Washington, DC *Toll Free Tel:* 800-637-3652, pg 265

Technical Association of the Pulp & Paper Industry (TAPPI), Norcross, GA *Toll Free Tel:* 800-332-8686, pg 266

Technology Training Systems Inc (TTS), Aurora, CO *Toll Free Tel:* 800-676-8871, pg 266

Temple University Press, Philadelphia, PA *Toll Free Tel:* 800-447-1656, pg 266

Templegate Publishers, Springfield, IL *Toll Free Tel:* 800-367-4844 (orders only), pg 266

Templeton Foundation Press, Radnor, PA *Toll Free Tel:* 800-561-3367, pg 266

Ten Speed Press, Berkeley, CA *Toll Free Tel:* 800-841-Book, pg 266

Teora USA LLC, Chevy Chase, MD *Toll Free Tel:* 800-358-3754 *Toll Free Fax:* 800-358-3754, pg 266

Teton New Media, Jackson, WY *Toll Free Tel:* 877-306-9793, pg 267

Tetra Press, Blacksburg, VA *Toll Free Tel:* 800-526-0650, pg 267

Texas A&M University Press, College Station, TX *Toll Free Tel:* 800-826-8911 (orders) *Toll Free Fax:* 888-617-2421 (orders), pg 267

Texas Christian University Press, Fort Worth, TX *Toll Free Tel:* 800-826-8911 *Toll Free Fax:* 888-617-2421, pg 267

Texas Tech University Press, Lubbock, TX *Toll Free Tel:* 800-832-4042, pg 267

Texas Western Press, El Paso, TX *Toll Free Tel:* 800-488-3789, pg 267

TFH Publications Inc, Neptune City, NJ *Toll Free Tel:* 800-631-2188, pg 268

Thames & Hudson, New York, NY *Toll Free Tel:* 800-233-4830, pg 268

Theosophical Publishing House/Quest Books, Wheaton, IL *Toll Free Tel:* 800-669-9425, pg 268

Thieme New York, New York, NY *Toll Free Tel:* 800-782-3488, pg 268

Thinkers' Press Inc, Davenport, IA *Toll Free Tel:* 800-397-7117, pg 268

Thinking Publications, Eau Claire, WI *Toll Free Tel:* 800-225-4769 *Toll Free Fax:* 800-828-8885, pg 269

Charles C Thomas Publisher Ltd, Springfield, IL *Toll Free Tel:* 800-258-8980, pg 269

Thomas Geale Publications Inc, Montara, CA *Toll Free Tel:* 800-554-5457, pg 269

Thomas Nelson Inc, Nashville, TN *Toll Free Tel:* 800-251-4000, pg 269

Thomas Publications, Gettysburg, PA *Toll Free Tel:* 800-840-6782, pg 269

William A Thomas Braille Bookstore, Stuart, FL *Toll Free Tel:* 888-336-3142, pg 269

Thomson Delmar Learning, Clifton Park, NY *Toll Free Tel:* 800-347-7707 (cust serv); 800-998-7498 *Toll Free Fax:* 800-487-8488 (cust serv), pg 269

Thomson Financial Publishing, Skokie, IL *Toll Free Tel:* 800-321-3373, pg 270

Thomson Gale, Farmington Hills, MI *Toll Free Tel:* 800-347-4253 *Toll Free Fax:* 800-414-5043, pg 270

Thomson Peterson's, Lawrenceville, NJ *Toll Free Tel:* 800-338-3282 *Toll Free Fax:* 800-772-2465, pg 270

Thorndike Press, Waterville, ME *Toll Free Tel:* 800-233-1244 *Toll Free Fax:* 800-558-4676 (orders), pg 270

Through the Bible Publishers, Fort Collins, CO *Toll Free Tel:* 800-284-0158, pg 271

Tiare Publications, Lake Geneva, WI *Toll Free Tel:* 800-420-0579, pg 271

Tide-mark Press, Windsor, CT *Toll Free Tel:* 800-338-2508, pg 271

Tidewater Publishers, Centreville, MD *Toll Free Tel:* 800-638-7641, pg 271

Tilbury House Publishers, Gardiner, ME *Toll Free Tel:* 800-582-1899 (orders), pg 271

Timber Press Inc, Portland, OR *Toll Free Tel:* 800-327-5680, pg 271

Time Being Books, St Louis, MO *Toll Free Tel:* 866-840-4334 *Toll Free Fax:* 888-301-9121, pg 271

Editions Pierre Tisseyre, St-Laurent, PQ Canada *Toll Free Tel:* 800-263-3678 *Toll Free Fax:* 800-643-4720 (Canada only), pg 563

TODTRI Book Publishers, New York, NY *Toll Free Tel:* 800-696-7299 *Toll Free Fax:* 800-696-7482, pg 272

Tommy Nelson, Nashville, TN *Toll Free Tel:* 800-251-4000, pg 272

Torah Aura Productions, Los Angeles, CA *Toll Free Tel:* 800-238-6724, pg 272

Totline Publications, Grand Rapids, MI *Toll Free Tel:* 800-417-3261 *Toll Free Fax:* 888-203-9361, pg 273

Tower Publishing Co, Standish, ME *Toll Free Tel:* 800-969-8693, pg 273

Traders Press Inc, Greenville, SC *Toll Free Tel:* 800-927-8222, pg 273

Trafalgar Square, North Pomfret, VT *Toll Free Tel:* 800-423-4525, pg 273

Trails Books, Black Earth, WI *Toll Free Tel:* 800-236-8088, pg 273

Trails Illustrated, Division of National Geographic Maps, Evergreen, CO *Toll Free Tel:* 800-962-1643 *Toll Free Fax:* 800-626-8676, pg 273

Training Resource Network Inc (T R N), St Augustine, FL *Toll Free Tel:* 800-280-7010 (orders), pg 273

Trakker Maps Inc, Orlando, FL *Toll Free Tel:* 800-327-3108, pg 273

Tralco Lingo Fun, Hamilton, ON Canada *Toll Free Tel:* 888-487-2526 *Toll Free Fax:* 866-487-2527, pg 563

Transaction Publishers, Piscataway, NJ *Toll Free Tel:* 888-999-6778, pg 274

Transcontinental Music Publications, New York, NY *Toll Free Tel:* 800-455-5223, pg 274

Transnational Publishers Inc, Ardsley, NY *Toll Free Tel:* 800-914-8186 (orders only), pg 274

Transportation Technical Service Inc, Fredericksburg, VA *Toll Free Tel:* 888-ONLY-TTS (665-9887), pg 274

Treehaus Communications Inc, Loveland, OH *Toll Free Tel:* 800-638-4287 (orders), pg 275

Triad Publishing Co, Gainesville, FL *Toll Free Fax:* 800-854-4947, pg 275

Trident Press International, Naples, FL *Toll Free Tel:* 800-593-3662 *Toll Free Fax:* 800-494-4226, pg 275

TripBuilder Inc, Westport, CT *Toll Free Tel:* 800-525-9745, pg 275

TriQuarterly Books, Evanston, IL *Toll Free Tel:* 800-621-2736 (orders only), pg 275

Tristan Publishing, Golden Valley, MN *Toll Free Tel:* 866-545-1383, pg 276

Triumph Books, Chicago, IL *Toll Free Tel:* 800-335-5323, pg 276

Truman State University Press, Kirksville, MO *Toll Free Tel:* 800-916-6802, pg 276

Turnstone Press, Winnipeg, MB Canada *Toll Free Tel:* 800-982-6472, pg 564

Tuttle Publishing, North Clarendon, VT *Toll Free Tel:* 800-526-2778 *Toll Free Fax:* 800-FAX-TUTL, pg 277

Twayne Publishers, Famington Hills, MI *Toll Free Tel:* 800-877-4253, pg 277

Twenty-First Century King James Bible Publishers, Gary, SD *Toll Free Tel:* 800-225-5521, pg 277

Twenty-Third Publications, Mystic, CT *Toll Free Tel:* 800-321-0411 (orders) *Toll Free Fax:* 800-572-0788, pg 277

Tyndale House Publishers Inc, Carol Stream, IL *Toll Free Tel:* 800-323-9400, pg 277

Type & Archetype Press, Charleston, SC *Toll Free Tel:* 800-447-8973, pg 277

ULI-The Urban Land Institute, Washington, DC *Toll Free Tel:* 800-321-5011 *Toll Free Fax:* 800-248-4585, pg 278

Ulysses Press, Berkeley, CA *Toll Free Tel:* 800-377-2542, pg 278

Unarius Academy of Science Publications, El Cajon, CA *Toll Free Tel:* 800-475-7062, pg 278

Unicor Medical Inc, Montgomery, AL *Toll Free Tel:* 800-825-7421 *Toll Free Fax:* 800-305-8030, pg 278

Unique Publications Books & Videos, Burbank, CA *Toll Free Tel:* 800-332-3330, pg 279

United Nations Publications, New York, NY *Toll Free Tel:* 800-253-9646, pg 279

United States Holocaust Memorial Museum, Washington, DC *Toll Free Tel:* 800-259-9998 (orders), pg 279

United States Institute of Peace Press, Washington, DC *Toll Free Tel:* 800-868-8064 (cust serv), pg 279

United States Pharmacopeia, Rockville, MD *Toll Free Tel:* 800-227-8772, pg 279

United Synagogue Book Service, New York, NY *Toll Free Tel:* 800-594-5617 (warehouse only), pg 279

The University of Akron Press, Akron, OH *Toll Free Tel:* 877-827-7377, pg 280

University of Alaska Press, Fairbanks, AK *Toll Free Tel:* 888-252-6657 (US only), pg 280

The University of Arizona Press, Tucson, AZ *Toll Free Tel:* 800-426-3797 (orders) *Toll Free Fax:* 800-426-3797, pg 280

The University of Arkansas Press, Fayetteville, AR *Toll Free Tel:* 800-626-0090, pg 280

University of British Columbia Press, Vancouver, BC Canada *Toll Free Tel:* 877-377-9378 *Toll Free Fax:* 800-668-0821, pg 564

University of California Press, Berkeley, CA *Toll Free Tel:* 800-777-4726 *Toll Free Fax:* 800-999-1958, pg 281

University of Denver Center for Teaching International Relations Publications, Denver, CO *Toll Free Tel:* 800-967-2847, pg 281

University of Georgia Press, Athens, GA *Toll Free Tel:* 800-266-5842 (orders only), pg 281

University of Hawaii Press, Honolulu, HI *Toll Free Tel:* 888-847-7377 *Toll Free Tel:* 800-650-7811, pg 281

University of Healing Press, Campo, CA *Toll Free Tel:* 888-463-8654, pg 281

University of Iowa Press, Iowa City, IA *Toll Free Tel:* 800-621-2736 (orders only) *Toll Free Fax:* 800-621-8476 (orders only), pg 282

University of Massachusetts Press, Amherst, MA *Toll Free Tel:* 800-537-5487, pg 282

University of Missouri Press, Columbia, MO *Toll Free Tel:* 800-828-1894 (orders), pg 283

University of Nebraska Press, Lincoln, NE *Toll Free Tel:* 800-755-1105 (orders) *Toll Free Fax:* 800-526-2617, pg 283

University of Nevada Press, Reno, NV *Toll Free Tel:* 800-682-6657 *Toll Free Fax:* 877-682-6657, pg 283

University of New Mexico Press, Albuquerque, NM *Toll Free Tel:* 800-249-7737 (orders only) *Toll Free Fax:* 800-622-8667, pg 283

The University of North Carolina Press, Chapel Hill, NC *Toll Free Tel:* 800-848-6224 (orders only) *Toll Free Fax:* 800-272-6817 (orders), pg 283

University of Notre Dame Press, Notre Dame, IN *Toll Free Tel:* 800-621-2736 (orders) *Toll Free Fax:* 800-621-8476 (orders), pg 284

University of Oklahoma Press, Norman, OK *Toll Free Tel:* 800-627-7377 (orders) *Toll Free Fax:* 800-735-0476 (orders), pg 284

University of Pennsylvania Press, Philadelphia, PA *Toll Free Tel:* 800-445-9880 (orders & cust serv only), pg 284

University of Scranton Press, Scranton, PA *Toll Free Tel:* 800-941-3081 *Toll Free Fax:* 800-941-8804, pg 285

University of South Carolina Press, Columbia, SC *Toll Free Tel:* 800-768-2500 (orders) *Toll Free Fax:* 800-868-0740 (orders), pg 285

University of Tennessee Press, Knoxville, TN *Toll Free Tel:* 800-621-2736 (ordering), pg 285

The University of Utah Press, Salt Lake City, UT *Toll Free Tel:* 800-773-6672, pg 285

The University of Virginia Press, Charlottesville, VA *Toll Free Tel:* 800-831-3406 (cust serv) *Toll Free Fax:* 877-288-6400, pg 285

University of Washington Press, Seattle, WA *Toll Free Tel:* 800-441-4115 (orders) *Toll Free Fax:* 800-669-7993 (orders), pg 286

University of Wisconsin Press, Madison, WI *Toll Free Tel:* 800-621-2736 (Orders) *Toll Free Fax:* 800-621-8476 (Orders), pg 286

University Press of America Inc, Lanham, MD *Toll Free Tel:* 800-462-6420 *Toll Free Fax:* 800-338-4550, pg 286

University Press of Colorado, Boulder, CO *Toll Free Tel:* 800-627-7377, pg 286

University Press of Florida, Gainesville, FL *Toll Free Tel:* 800-226-3822 (orders only) *Toll Free Fax:* 800-680-1955 (orders only), pg 286

The University Press of Kentucky, Lexington, KY *Toll Free Tel:* 800-839-6855 (orders), pg 287

University Press of Mississippi, Jackson, MS *Toll Free Tel:* 800-737-7788, pg 287

University Press of New England, Lebanon, NH *Toll Free Tel:* 800-421-1561 (orders only), pg 287

University Publishing Group, Hagerstown, MD *Toll Free Tel:* 800-654-8188, pg 287

Unlimited Publishing LLC, Bloomington, IN *Toll Free Tel:* 800-218-8877, pg 288

W E Upjohn Institute for Employment Research, Kalamazoo, MI *Toll Free Tel:* 888-227-8569, pg 288

Upper Room Books, Nashville, TN *Toll Free Tel:* 800-972-0433, pg 288

Upstart Books™, Fort Atkinson, WI *Toll Free Tel:* 800-448-4887 *Toll Free Fax:* 800-448-5828, pg 288

Upublish.com, Boca Raton, FL *Toll Free Tel:* 800-636-8329, pg 288

The Urban Institute Press, Washington, DC *Toll Free Tel:* 877-UIPRESS (847-7377), pg 288

Urban Land Institute, Washington, DC *Toll Free Tel:* 800-321-5011, pg 288

URJ Press, New York, NY *Toll Free Tel:* 888-489-UAHC (489-8242), pg 289

US Conference of Catholic Bishops, Washington, DC *Toll Free Tel:* 800-235-8722 (orders only), pg 289

US Games Systems Inc, Stamford, CT *Toll Free Tel:* 800-544-2637 (800-54GAMES), pg 289

US Government Printing Office, Washington, DC *Toll Free Tel:* 888-293-6498 (cust serv); 866-512-1800 (orders) *Toll Free Fax:* 866-512-1800, pg 289

Utah Geological Survey, Salt Lake City, UT *Toll Free Tel:* 888-UTAH-MAP (882-4627 bookstore), pg 289

Utah State University Press, Logan, UT *Toll Free Tel:* 800-239-9974, pg 289

VanDam Inc, New York, NY *Toll Free Tel:* 800-UNFOLDS (863-6537), pg 289

Vandamere Press, Saint Petersburg, FL *Toll Free Tel:* 800-551-7776, pg 289

Vanderbilt University Press, Nashville, TN *Toll Free Tel:* 800-627-7377 (orders only) *Toll Free Fax:* 800-735-0476 (orders only), pg 289

Vanwell Publishing Ltd, St Catharines, ON Canada *Toll Free Tel:* 800-661-6136, pg 565

Victory in Grace Printing, Lake Zurich, IL *Toll Free Tel:* 800-784-7223, pg 290

Vision Works Publishing, Boxford, MA *Toll Free Tel:* 888-821-3135, pg 291

Visual Reference Publications Inc, New York, NY *Toll Free Tel:* 800-251-4545, pg 291

Vital Health Publishing, Ridgefield, CT *Toll Free Tel:* 877-848-2665 (orders), pg 291

Volcano Press Inc, Volcano, CA *Toll Free Tel:* 800-879-9636, pg 291

Voyageur Press, Stillwater, MN *Toll Free Tel:* 800-888-9653, pg 291

Wadsworth Publishing, Belmont, CA *Toll Free Tel:* 800-357-0092 *Toll Free Fax:* 800-522-4923, pg 292

J Weston Walch Publisher, Portland, ME *Toll Free Tel:* 800-341-6094 *Toll Free Fax:* 888-991-5755, pg 292

Walker & Co, New York, NY *Toll Free Tel:* 800-289-2553 *Toll Free Fax:* 800-218-9367, pg 292

Wall & Emerson Inc, Toronto, ON Canada *Toll Free Tel:* 877-409-4601, pg 566

Wm K Walthers Inc, Milwaukee, WI *Toll Free Tel:* 800-877-7171, pg 292

Warner Bros Publications Inc, Miami, FL *Toll Free Tel:* 800-327-7643, pg 293

Warren, Gorham & Lamont, New York, NY *Toll Free Tel:* 800-431-9025; 800-678-2185 (cust serv), pg 293

Washington State University Press, Pullman, WA *Toll Free Tel:* 800-354-7360, pg 293

Water Environment Federation, Alexandria, VA *Toll Free Tel:* 800-666-0206, pg 294

WaterBrook Press, Colorado Springs, CO *Toll Free Tel:* 800-603-7051 (orders) *Toll Free Fax:* 800-294-5686 (orders), pg 294

Waterfront Books, Burlington, VT *Toll Free Tel:* 800-639-6063 (orders), pg 294

Waterloo Music Co Ltd, Waterloo, ON Canada *Toll Free Tel:* 800-563-9683 (Canada & US), pg 566

WaterPlow Press™, Amherst, MA *Toll Free Tel:* 866-367-3300 (orders only), pg 294

Watson-Guptill Publications, New York, NY *Toll Free Tel:* 800-278-8477 (orders only), pg 294

Wayne State University Press, Detroit, MI *Toll Free Tel:* 800-978-7323, pg 294

Wayside Publishing, Sandwich, MA *Toll Free Tel:* 888-302-2519, pg 295

Weatherhill Inc, Trumbull, CT *Toll Free Tel:* 800-437-7840 *Toll Free Fax:* 800-557-5601, pg 295

Weigl Educational Publishers Ltd, Calgary, AB Canada *Toll Free Tel:* 800-668-0766, pg 566

Weil Publishing Co Inc, Augusta, ME *Toll Free Tel:* 800-877-9345, pg 295

Weiss Ratings Inc, Jupiter, FL *Toll Free Tel:* 800-289-9222, pg 295

Werbel Publishing Co Inc, Dix Hills, NY *Toll Free Tel:* 800-293-7235, pg 296

Wesleyan Publishing House, Noblesville, IN *Toll Free Tel:* 800-493-7539 *Toll Free Fax:* 800-788-3535, pg 296

West, A Thomson Business, Eagan, MN *Toll Free Tel:* 800-328-9352 (sales); 800-328-4880 (cust serv), pg 296

Westcliffe Publishers Inc, Englewood, CO *Toll Free Tel:* 800-523-3692, pg 296

Western National Parks Association, Tucson, AZ *Toll Free Tel:* 888-569-SPMA (orders only), pg 296

Western Reflections Publishing Co, Montrose, CO *Toll Free Tel:* 800-993-4490, pg 297

Westminster John Knox Press, Louisville, KY *Toll Free Tel:* 800-227-2872 (US only) *Toll Free Fax:* 800-541-5113 (US only), pg 297

Westview Press, Boulder, CO *Toll Free Tel:* 800-386-5656, pg 297

WH&O International, Wellesley, MA *Toll Free Tel:* 800-553-5678, pg 297

Wheatherstone Press, Portland, OR *Toll Free Tel:* 800-980-0077, pg 297

Whitaker House, New Kensington, PA *Toll Free Tel:* 877-793-9800 *Toll Free Fax:* 800-765-1960, pg 297

White Cliffs Media Inc, Incline Village, NV *Toll Free Tel:* 800-345-6665 (orders only), pg 298

White Cloud Press, Ashland, OR *Toll Free Tel:* 800-380-8286, pg 298

White Mane Kids, Shippensburg, PA *Toll Free Tel:* 888-WHT-MANE (948-6263), pg 298

White Mane Publishing Co Inc, Shippensburg, PA *Toll Free Tel:* 888-948-6263, pg 298

White Stone Books, Lakeland, FL *Toll Free Tel:* 866-253-8622 *Toll Free Fax:* 800-830-5688, pg 574

White Wolf Publishing Inc, Stone Mountain, GA *Toll Free Tel:* 800-454-9653, pg 298

Whitecap Books Ltd, North Vancouver, BC Canada *Toll Free Tel:* 888-870-3442 ext 239 & 241 (cust serv) *Toll Free Fax:* 888-661-6630 (orders only), pg 567

Whitehorse Press, Center Conway, NH *Toll Free Tel:* 800-531-1133, pg 298

Albert Whitman & Co, Morton Grove, IL *Toll Free Tel:* 800-255-7675, pg 298

Whitston Publishing Co Inc, Albany, NY *Toll Free Tel:* 877-571-1900, pg 298

Whittier Publications Inc, Island Park, NY *Toll Free Tel:* 800-897-TEXT (897-8398), pg 298

Whole Person Associates Inc, Duluth, MN *Toll Free Tel:* 800-247-6789, pg 298

Wide World of Maps Inc, Phoenix, AZ *Toll Free Tel:* 800-279-7654, pg 298

Michael Wiese Productions, Studio City, CA *Toll Free Tel:* 800-379-8808, pg 299

Wildcat Canyon Press, Tulsa, OK *Toll Free Tel:* 800-247-8850, pg 299

Wilderness Adventures Press Inc, Belgrade, MT *Toll Free Tel:* 800-925-3339 *Toll Free Fax:* 800-390-7558, pg 299

Wilderness Press, Berkeley, CA *Toll Free Tel:* 800-443-7227, pg 299

Wildlife Education Ltd, Poway, CA *Toll Free Tel:* 800-992-5034 (subns); 800-992-5034 (sales), pg 299

John Wiley & Sons Canada Ltd, Mississauga, ON Canada *Toll Free Tel:* 800-467-4797 (orders only) *Toll Free Fax:* 800-565-6802 (orders), pg 567

John Wiley & Sons Inc, Hoboken, NJ *Toll Free Tel:* 800-225-5945 (cust serv), pg 299

John Wiley & Sons Inc Professional & Trade Group, Hoboken, NJ *Toll Free Tel:* 800-225-5945 (cust serv), pg 300

John Wiley & Sons Inc Scientific/Technical/Medical Publishing, Hoboken, NJ *Toll Free Tel:* 800-225-5945 (cust serv), pg 300

William Andrew Publishing, Norwich, NY *Toll Free Tel:* 800-932-7045, pg 300

William K Bradford Publishing Co Inc, Concord, MA *Toll Free Tel:* 800-421-2009, pg 300

Williamson Books, Nashville, TN *Toll Free Tel:* 800-586-2572 (sales & orders), pg 300

Willow Creek Press, Minocqua, WI *Toll Free Tel:* 800-850-9453, pg 300

H W Wilson, Bronx, NY *Toll Free Tel:* 800-367-6770 *Toll Free Fax:* 800-590-1617, pg 300

Wimmer Cookbooks, Memphis, TN *Toll Free Tel:* 800-548-2537 *Toll Free Fax:* 800-794-9806, pg 301

Wind Canyon Books Inc, Brawley, CA *Toll Free Tel:* 800-952-7007, pg 301

Windsor Books, Babylon, NY *Toll Free Tel:* 800-321-5934, pg 301

The Wine Appreciation Guild Ltd, South San Francisco, CA *Toll Free Tel:* 800-231-9463, pg 301

Winters Publishing, Greensburg, IN *Toll Free Tel:* 800-457-3230 *Toll Free Fax:* 800-457-3230, pg 301

Winterthur Museum, Garden & Library, Winterthur, DE *Toll Free Tel:* 800-448-3883, pg 301

Wisconsin Dept of Public Instruction, Madison, WI *Toll Free Tel:* 800-243-8782, pg 301

Wittenborn Art Books, San Francisco, CA *Toll Free Tel:* 800-660-6403, pg 302

WJ Fantasy Inc, Bridgeport, CT *Toll Free Tel:* 800-222-7529 (orders) *Toll Free Fax:* 800-200-3000, pg 302

Wolf Den Books, Miami, FL *Toll Free Tel:* 877-667-9737, pg 302

Wood Lake Books Inc, Kelowna, BC Canada *Toll Free Tel:* 800-663-2775 (orders) *Toll Free Fax:* 888-841-9991 (orders), pg 567

Woodbine House, Bethesda, MD *Toll Free Tel:* 800-843-7323, pg 302

Woodland Publishing Inc, Orem, UT *Toll Free Tel:* 800-777-2665, pg 302

Ralph Woodrow Evangelistic Association Inc, Palm Springs, CA *Toll Free Tel:* 877-664-1549, pg 302

Word Wrangler Publishing Inc, Livingston, MT *Toll Free Tel:* 866-896-2897, pg 303

Wordware Publishing Inc, Plano, TX *Toll Free Tel:* 800-229-4949, pg 303

Workman Publishing Co Inc, New York, NY *Toll Free Tel:* 800-722-7202, pg 303

World Bank Publications, Washington, DC *Toll Free Tel:* 800-645-7247 (cust serv), pg 303

World Book Inc, Chicago, IL *Toll Free Tel:* 800-967-5325 (consumer sales, US); 800-463-8845 (consumer sales, Canada); 800-975-3250 (school & library sales, US); 800-837-5365 (school & library sales, Canada); 866-866-5200 (web sales) *Toll Free Fax:* 800-433-9330 (school & library sales, US); 888-690-4002 (school library sales, Canada), pg 303

World Citizens, Mill Valley, CA *Toll Free Tel:* 800-247-6553 (orders only), pg 303

World Eagle, Littleton, MA *Toll Free Tel:* 800-854-8273, pg 304

World Leisure Corp, Boston, MA *Toll Free Tel:* 877-863-1966, pg 304

World Publishing, Nashville, TN *Toll Free Tel:* 800-363-0308 *Toll Free Fax:* 800-822-4271 (orders), pg 304

World Resources Institute, Washington, DC *Toll Free Tel:* 800-822-0504, pg 304

World Scientific Publishing Co Inc, Hackensack, NJ *Toll Free Tel:* 800-227-7562 *Toll Free Fax:* 888-977-2665, pg 304

World Trade Press, Novato, CA *Toll Free Tel:* 800-833-8586, pg 304

The Wright Group/McGraw-Hill, a Division of McGraw-Hill Learning Group, Chicago, IL *Toll Free Tel:* 800-537-4740, pg 304

Write Stuff Enterprises Inc, Fort Lauderdale, FL *Toll Free Tel:* 800-900-2665, pg 304

Writer's AudioShop, Dripping Springs, TX *Toll Free Tel:* 800-88-WRITE (889-7483), pg 304

Writer's Digest Books, Cincinnati, OH *Toll Free Tel:* 800-289-0963, pg 305

The Writings of Mary Baker Eddy/Publisher, Boston, MA *Toll Free Tel:* 800-288-7090, pg 305

Wyndham Hall Press, Lima, OH *Toll Free Tel:* 866-895-0977, pg 305

Wyrick & Co, Charleston, SC *Toll Free Tel:* 800-227-5898, pg 305

Xlibris Corp, Philadelphia, PA *Toll Free Tel:* 888-795-4274, pg 305

Yale University Press, New Haven, CT *Toll Free Tel:* 800-405-1619 (cust serv) *Toll Free Fax:* 800-406-9145 (cust serv), pg 305

Yardbird Books, Airville, PA *Toll Free Tel:* 800-622-6044 (Sales), pg 306

Ye Galleon Press, Fairfield, WA *Toll Free Tel:* 800-829-5586 (orders only), pg 306

Ye Olde Genealogie Shoppe, Indianapolis, IN *Toll Free Tel:* 800-419-0200, pg 306

YMAA Publication Center, Roslindale, MA *Toll Free Tel:* 800-669-8892, pg 306

York Press Inc, Timonium, MD *Toll Free Tel:* 800-962-2763, pg 306

Young People's Press Inc (YPPI), San Diego, CA *Toll Free Tel:* 800-231-9774, pg 306

Yucca Tree Press, Las Cruces, NM *Toll Free Tel:* 888-817-1990, pg 306

YWAM Publishing, Seattle, WA *Toll Free Tel:* 800-922-2143, pg 306

Zagat Survey, New York, NY *Toll Free Tel:* 800-333-3421 (gen inquiries); 888-371-5440 (orders); 800-540-9609 (corp sales), pg 306

Zaner-Bloser Inc, Columbus, OH *Toll Free Tel:* 800-421-3018 *Toll Free Fax:* 800-992-6087, pg 306

Zeig, Tucker & Theisen Inc, Phoenix, AZ *Toll Free Fax:* 800-688-2877, pg 307

Zephyr Press Catalog, Chicago, IL *Toll Free Tel:* 800-232-2187, pg 307

Zondervan, Grand Rapids, MI *Toll Free Tel:* 800-727-1309 (cust serv), pg 307

Zone Books, Brooklyn, NY *Toll Free Tel:* 800-405-1619 (orders & cust serv) *Toll Free Fax:* 800-406-9145 (orders), pg 307

LiteraryMarketPlace.com

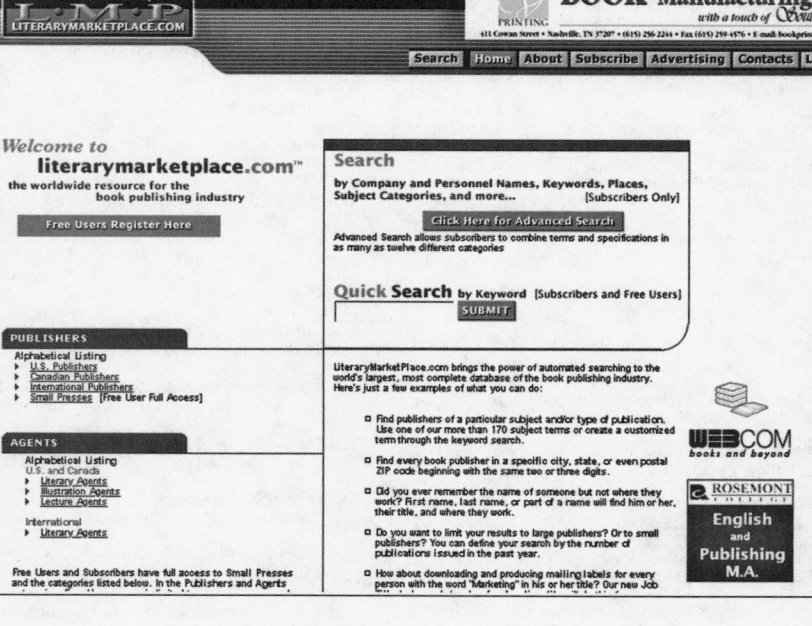

Literary Market Place (LMP) is the premier resource for people involved in the book publishing industry in both the U.S. and Canada. For those interested in book publishing on a global scale, International Literary Market Place (ILMP) provides industry data for more than 180 countries.

Now, you can get all the information listed in both *LMP* and *ILMP* online at
literarymarketplace.com!

Whether you're looking for a literary agent, or for information about summer writers' conferences, literarymarketplace.com can provide all the answers to your questions.

For More Information, Contact:

Information Today, Inc.

143 Old Marlton Pike Medford, NJ 08055
Phone: 800-300-9868 or 609-654-6266 www.infotoday.com

Index to Sections

Index to Advertisers